# THE COMPLETE STAR WARS® ENCYCLOPEDIA

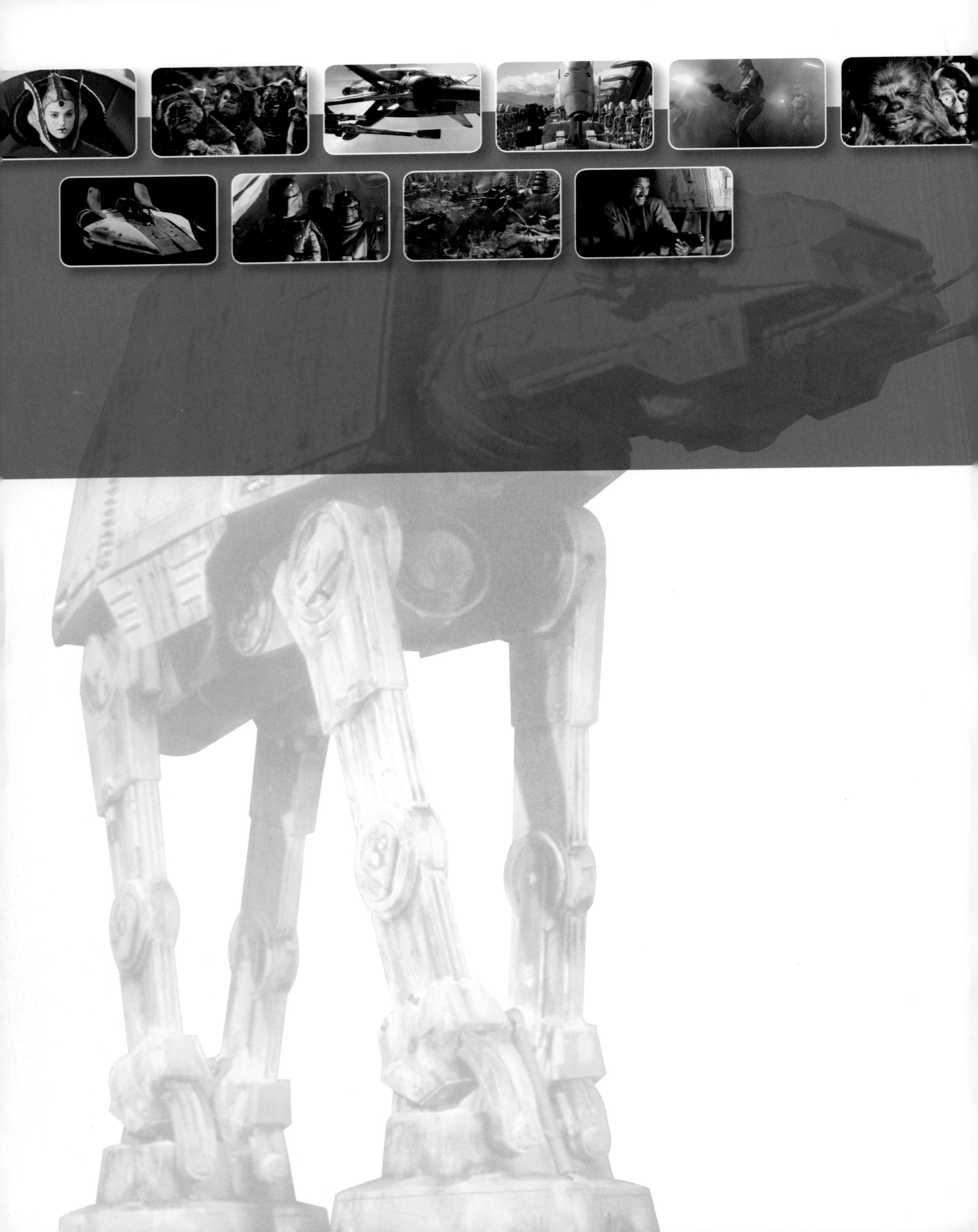

# The Complete Star Wars Encyclopedia

Stephen J. Sansweet
& Pablo Hidalgo
and
Bob Vitas & Daniel Wallace
with
Chris Cassidy,
Mary Franklin & Josh Kushins

A–G
Volume I

Ballantine Books ▪ New York

Published in the United States by Del Rey, an imprint of The Random House Publishing Group, a division of Random House, Inc., New York.

Del Rey is a registered trademark and the Del Rey colophon is a trademark of Random House, Inc.

ISBN 978-0-345-47763-7

Printed in China

www.starwars.com
www.delreybooks.com

9 8 7 6 5

Interior design by Michaelis/Carpelis Design Associates, Inc.

*To the literally hundreds of writers, editors, artists, researchers, moviemakers, fans, and others who have contributed so much to making the* Star Wars *galaxy the rich, creative force that it is today. And to the man—George Lucas—whose imagination launched it all more than three decades ago.*

*What if the democracy we thought we were serving no longer exists, and*

*the Republic has become the very evil we have been fighting to destroy?*

*So this is how liberty dies, with thunderous applause. . . .*

—Padmé Amidala

# About This Book

When the first *Star Wars Encyclopedia* was published in July 1998, it had a single name on the title page, was a hefty but reasonable 354 pages, and took me about a year of work to complete with a little help from my friends.

How the galaxy has grown! And, of course, it continues to thrive with more stories, characters, vehicles, planets, battles, and phenomena being created every day. What always made the *Star Wars* universe different among sprawling sagas—tying everything together into one vast story and doing everything possible to eliminate inconsistencies—also continues. Thus this totally rewritten book, *The Complete Star Wars Encyclopedia,* catches up on a decade of new movies, animation, novels, comics, video games, role-playing and card games, online material, and just about anything else that is "official" and relevant to the saga.

It's not just the newly created fiction. We have integrated such things as story lines and characters from the original Marvel comics, made even more relevant by current authors who have themselves gone back and picked up situations and characters from those wonderfully creative pulps—the Dark Lady Lumiya comes to mind—to integrate into their own fiction, giving the saga even more connectivity.

Like the first encyclopedia, the in-fantasy conceit of this one is that it has been compiled by some omniscient committee of historians and scholars taking a look back over tens of thousands of years of galactic history. Since that history now extends to a time far before the events shown in George Lucas's six-movie saga, and to a time more than a century after, our vantage point is a period perhaps 150 years after the Battle of Yavin. Most entries, therefore, are in the past tense. In a galaxy where entire planets and billions of sentient beings can be—and frequently are—totally wiped out in a flash, nothing is safe and few things are certain. We also have eliminated source codes; they have become mostly irrelevant in such an interrelated universe, and also too cumbersome—and therefore not very helpful—for a large number of the entries.

I'm very proud to have worked with Team Encyclopedia, my term for the six other authors who I recruited—every one of them a die-hard *Star Wars* fan. Two of them were a tremendous help a decade ago, although on an unofficial basis. Freelancer **Pablo Hidalgo** agreed to do a massive fact-check on the first manuscript, coming back with 80 pages of typed, single-spaced notes. **Dan Wallace** generously let me use any and all of his extensive online guide to the planets of the galaxy. Today, Pablo is in charge of content for the official site, starwars.com, and Dan is the author of a dozen official *Star Wars* books. A major new member of the team is **Bob Vitas**, who, as a hobby, started in 1992 compiling what has become a huge online resource for the *Star Wars* fan community, The Completely Unofficial *Star Wars* Encyclopedia (www.cuswe.org). It is truly an awesome achievement, and this book couldn't have been done without Bob's groundwork and his fact-checking.

Rounding out the team are two other Lucasfilm employees: **Mary Franklin**, events manager and my cohort in fan activities and conventions, and **Josh Kushins**, communications manager; and writer **Chris Cassidy**, who has authored or co-authored a number of *Star Wars* short stories.

At Lucasfilm, thanks to Leland Chee, keeper of the internal Holocron continuity database, whose job it is to try to keep this huge and messy galaxy as tidy a place as possible for authors and readers. Leland also did a lot of fact-checking on the manuscript. Thanks also to Troy Alders, Lucas Licensing art director, and at LucasBooks, to Carol Roeder and Jonathan Rinzler.

At Del Rey, huge thanks go to an editorial team that was always supportive even as this book grew like a giant sponge sucking up all the water on Mon Calamari (the planet, not the species). Lesser souls would have doubted that this book would ever be completed, much less come out on time—me among them. But editor Keith Clayton, production manager Erich Schoeneweiss, associate managing editor Nancy Delia, and editorial assistant Sue Moe were nothing if not encouraging . . . and, truth be told, even a little pushy when that was necessary. Copy editor Laura Jorstad did yeoman's work on a long and complex manuscript. And senior art director Dave Stevenson found the Force to work on not one but three great covers.

Brad Foltz of Foltz Design contributed with his early design concepts. Irene Carpelis and Sylvain Michaelis of Michaelis/Carpelis Design did the final interior design and layouts. You'd think they would have known better after doing the first *Star Wars Encyclopedia,* but they must be gluttons for punishment! Thanks also to the entire staff at North Market Street Graphics for typesetting and digital file separation. And to Rod Watson and Michael White at RR Donnelley and Sons, Raffy Scheghtayan at Coral Graphics, and Steve Fletcher and Dwayne Spaulding at Burt Rigid Box, Inc., for the manufacturing of the book.

We've used the art of scores of very talented artists, and we thank them all for their incredible work. For their assistance in collecting the beautiful art used throughout the book, we'd like to specifically thank Tommy Lee Edwards; Andrew, Liam, and Ethan Goletz; Christine Kell; Chris Reiff; Natasha Simons; Chris Trevas (and also for his new contributions); and, at Lucasfilm Image Archives, Stacey Leong and Tina Mills.

The author/editor is solely responsible for any errors of fact or interpretation. And while every attempt has been made to get the latest information into this book, the fact that the *Star Wars* universe is so dynamic means that we'll always be playing at least a bit of catch-up.

Steve Sansweet

Stephen J. Sansweet

San Francisco, California

August 2008

# A Timeline of Galactic Events

*Galactic civilization has existed for more than 25,000 years. Before that period, there is plentiful evidence of prehistoric civilizations that united the galaxy. With such a huge period of time and a constant succession of galactic governments and cultures, maintaining a unified, standardized calendar has proven nearly impossible. The current standard, which denotes the historic Battle of Yavin as a zero point on the calendar, has existed for over a century, but even it may give way someday as future cultures reassess that event's prominence and relevance. Rather than rely on dates set in a specific calendar, many galactic historians frequently point to major events as relative landmarks. The following is a listing of some of those events in the galaxy and their placement on the current calendar. Dates marked* BBY *are as recorded in years before the Battle of Yavin. Dates marked* ABY *occur in years after the Battle of Yavin.*

## Pre-Republic Era

### 35,000–25,000 BBY

- **Rakatan Infinite Empire:** Before the Galactic Republic unified the galaxy, much of known space was colonized and ruled by the Rakatans, an alien empire that introduced modern hyperdrive technology to the galaxy. This empire fell through civil wars and the uprising of many oppressed cultures.

### 27,500 BBY

- **Settlement of Alderaan:** One of the key planets of the Core Worlds, Alderaan was settled by human colonists.

### 25,100 BBY

- **Third Battle of Vontor:** The pre-Republic warlord Xim the Despot was conquered by a coalition led by the Hutts.

## Republic Era

### 25,000 BBY

- **The Formation of the Galactic Republic:** The ratification of the Galactic Constitution and other founding documents brought about the Galactic Republic, which was established on Coruscant. This galactic government stood, albeit in an evolving form, for over a thousand generations.
- **The Formation of the Jedi Order:** Ancient followers of the Force codified their beliefs and ideals and formed the Jedi Order in service to the Republic.

### 24,500 BBY

- **The First Great Schism:** The rise of the dark side within the Jedi Order led to conflict, as the Legions of Lettow commanded by General Xendor splintered from the Order to pursue power for themselves. They eventually were defeated by the Jedi.

### 20,000–17,000 BBY

- **Great Manifest Period:** The Republic underwent extensive expansion outward from the Core.

### 17,000–3,000 BBY

- **Alsakan Conflicts:** A series of 17 wars were waged between the worlds of Alsakan and Coruscant for control of the capital of the Republic.

### 12,000–11,000 BBY

- **Pius Dea Period:** A series of religious crusades sanctioned by Supreme Chancellor Contispex began, oppressing several alien cultures.

**9,000–8,000 BBY**

- **Rianitus Period:** Republic expansion continued. Blotus the Hutt ruled for 275 peaceful and progressive years as Supreme Chancellor during this era.

**7,000–6,900 BBY**

- **The Hundred-Year Darkness (the Second Great Schism):** The dark side rose once again, leading to galactic conflict between Jedi and Dark Jedi. The Jedi Order prevailed, causing the Dark Jedi to flee into uncharted space, where they discovered the ancient Sith people. That led to the rise of the Sith Empire.

**5,000 BBY**

- **The Great Hyperspace War:** Jori and Gav Daragon, two ill-fated hyperspace explorers, stumbled upon the Sith Empire, connecting the dark side followers to the Galactic Republic. Dark Lord Naga Sadow led a Sith invasion of the galaxy, followed by all-out war. The Sith Empire eventually was defeated, and Sadow retreated to the fourth moon of Yavin.

**4,250 BBY**

- **The Vultar Cataclysm (the Third Great Schism):** Another uprising of the dark side resulted in a Jedi Civil War. The dark siders attempted to unleash as much destruction as possible with an alien artifact known as the Cosmic Turbine but failed and were defeated.

**4,015 BBY**

- **The Great Droid Revolution:** Automata rose up against organics on Coruscant, until they were put down by Jedi Knights. Lingering fear and resentment against droids lasted for centuries.

**4,000–3,996 BBY**

- **The Great Sith War:** The dark side rose once more as ancient Sith powers were stirred by fallen Jedi Exar Kun. The Great Sith War encompassed a number of conflicts.
  - **The Beast Wars of Onderon:** An undercurrent of the dark side sparked civil war between the city dwellers of Iziz and the beast-riders of the wilderness.
  - **The Freedon Nadd Uprising:** The royalty of Onderon were secretly dark side worshippers who drew power from the spirit of long-dead Sith Lord, Freedon Nadd. Nadd's spirit brought about the rise of Exar Kun and the dark side cult, the Krath.
  - **The Sith War:** The Empress Teta system was conquered by the Krath, and Exar Kun corrupted a number of Jedi Knights into joining the dark side. Among his followers was Ulic Qel-Droma. Qel-Droma was finally stripped of his powers, and Kun's spirit was trapped within a Massassi temple on Yavin 4.
  - **The Great Hunt:** The Jedi Order undertook a failed purge of terentateks, creatures from the Sith world of Korriban that fed off the blood of Force-sensitives.

**3,965–3,960 BBY**

- **The Mandalorian Wars:** Mandalorian Neo-Crusaders, led by Mandalore the Ultimate, waged war against the Galactic Republic. The conflict led to the rise of such heroes as the Jedi Revan.

**3,959–3,951 BBY**

- **The Jedi Civil War:** Following Revan's victory over the Mandalorians, he reemerged as Darth Revan and turned traitor against the Republic. Revan and Darth Malak's Sith forces waged war against the Republic, and much of the Republic's military forces defected to the Sith banner. The war culminated in the destruction of the Star Forge, an ancient Rakatan technological wonder that was the source of Malak's military might.

**2,000–1,000 BBY**

- **The Draggulch Period:** Also known as the New Sith Wars, it marked a millennium of continued fighting between the Sith and Jedi that embroiled much of the galaxy.

**1,002–1,000 BBY**

- **The Battle of Ruusan:** A series of seven devastating battles that eventually brought an end to the New Sith Wars. The Sith, united as the Brotherhood of Darkness, waged war against the Jedi Army of Light. In the end, the machinations of a single Sith Lord, Darth Bane, brought about the eradication of the Brotherhood and the continuation of the Sith order in secret.

## The Rise of the Empire

**1,000 BBY**

- **The Ruusan Reformations:** Following the devastation of the Battle of Ruusan, sweeping changes were enacted in the Galactic Republic, taking power away from the Supreme Chancellor and redistributing it to the Galactic Senate. The Jedi Order demilitarized, becoming an instrument of the Judicial Department of the Republic. The Jedi enacted new codes that limited instruction so that a single Master trained a single Padawan, with training centralized on Coruscant. The "modern" Republic and Jedi Order began, and so did a thousand-year period without a full-scale war.

**600 BBY**

- **The Exile of Allya:** Fallen Jedi Knight Allya was exiled to Dathomir, where her abilities, teachings, and bloodline gave rise to the Force-sensitive Witches of that planet.

**490 BBY**

- **Corporate Sector founded:** An area of outlying space in the galaxy was set aside for exploitation by a coalition of leading businesses.

**350 BBY**

- **Trade Federation founded:** A number of influential shipping and commodities interests banded together for political gain as the Trade Federation.

**340 BBY**

- **The Crash of the *Chu'unthor:*** A *Chu'unthor* Jedi training vessel crashed on Dathomir. The Jedi Council launched a rescue mission, including Yoda, but it was repulsed by the Witches of Dathomir.

**44 BBY**

- **The Stark Hyperspace Conflict:** Iaco Stark forged a coalition of smugglers, pirates, mercenaries, bounty hunters, and assassins working in the Outer Rim to form the Stark Commercial Combine, and together they disrupted bacta shipments and supplies. Stark became something of a folk hero for his undercutting of the Trade Federation and bacta cartel's stranglehold on bacta shipments, but his actions nonetheless sparked a violent Republic reprisal.
- **The Battle of Galidraan:** Jedi Master Dooku led a team of 20 Jedi to confront and defeat the Mandalorian shock troopers on Galidraan, wiping out their ranks except for Jango Fett, the sole survivor.

**32 BBY**

- **The Battle of Naboo:** The Trade Federation brazenly blockaded and invaded the pastoral world of Naboo. In the fallout, Supreme Chancellor Valorum was ousted and replaced by Senator Palpatine of Naboo, who rode a wave of sympathy into office. Queen Amidala led a counterattack that defeated the Trade Federation occupation. Elsewhere, the Jedi uncovered evidence of the return of the Sith and brought a young Anakin Skywalker into their Order.

**22–19 BBY**

- **The Clone Wars:** Supreme Chancellor Palpatine's term was extended in the face of a Separatist crisis fomented by former Jedi Count Dooku. Thousands of worlds left the Republic's fold, and a coalition of corporate interests pooled their military resources to wage war against the Republic. The galactic government, in response, activated a secret clone army led by the Jedi as generals. The three-year conflict became known as the Clone Wars.

**19 BBY**

- **The First Galactic Empire:** The Clone Wars ended with the defeat of the Separatist Council and the deaths of General Grievous and Count Dooku. Chancellor Palpatine then put into motion his endgame stratagem: ordering the clone troopers to turn against their Jedi commanders. The resulting slaughter nearly wiped out the Jedi Order, and Palpatine—who in truth was Sith Lord Darth Sidious—consolidated his power as Emperor.

**5 BBY**

- **Battle of Nar Shaddaa:** The Empire attempted to crack down on the blatant lawlessness of the Smuggler's Moon of Nar Shaddaa, but was repulsed by a ragtag coalition of Hutt forces and smugglers, including Han Solo and Lando Calrissian.

## The Rebellion Era

**0 ABY**

- **The Battle of Yavin:** Rebel Alliance forces striking from a hidden base won their first major victory against the Galactic Empire. After securing the plans for the Death Star, the Rebels scoured the diagrams for a design weakness. Young Force-sensitive pilot Luke Skywalker succeeded in destroying the battle station.

**1 ABY**

- **The Bounty Hunter Wars:** The Bounty Hunters' Guild fragmented after its leader, Craddossk, was killed by his son Bossk.

**3 ABY**

- **The Battle of Hoth:** The Empire struck back against the Rebel Alliance by discovering and invading its hidden base on the ice planet Hoth. The Rebels were routed and scattered across the galaxy.

**4 ABY**

- **The Battle of Endor:** Desperate Rebel forces reunited upon receipt of Bothan intelligence regarding a newly commissioned Death Star. The Alliance fleet attacked the battle station, still under construction and seemingly vulnerable over the Forest Moon of Endor—but it was a trap engineered by the Emperor. Nonetheless, with the help of the native Ewoks, the Rebels were able to destroy the battle station, killing the Emperor and bringing an end to his regime. Much of the Empire, however, remained intact.

## The New Republic Era

**7.5 ABY**

- **The Liberation of Coruscant:** The New Republic ousted the Empire from the capital world of Coruscant through the efforts of Rogue Squadron.
- **The Bacta War:** The need for the rejuvenating healing fluid sparked a war between the New Republic and the Empire over control of the bacta facilities on Thyferra.

**8 ABY**

- **The Battle of Dathomir:** The New Republic finally brought an end to Imperial Warlord Zsinj's reign of terror on the stronghold world of Dathomir.

**9 ABY**

- **The Thrawn Crisis:** Grand Admiral Thrawn, the last surviving Imperial Grand Admiral, returned from the Unknown Regions to lead the remnants of the Imperial fleet in a bid to retake the Core. Thrawn's complex strategy involved the use of Force-blocking ysalamiri and Spaarti-based cloning to create a new Imperial clone army, but ultimately he was defeated by the New Republic.

**10 ABY**

- **Return of the Emperor:** Imperial forces, spurred by Thrawn's successes, staged a clumsy coup on Coruscant that led to rampant devastation on the capital world. The New Republic was forced into retreat, and a civil war broke out among Imperial splinter groups. Into this fray, the cloned form of Emperor Palpatine returned and started a new reign of terror before being defeated.

**11 ABY**

- **Battle of the Maw:** Admiral Daala emerged from the supersecret Imperial think tank hidden within the Maw Cluster and led an outdated Imperial task force on a series of strikes against New Republic targets. Elsewhere, Luke Skywalker restarted the Jedi Order with a new training facility on Yavin 4.

**16–17 ABY**

- **The Black Fleet Crisis:** The Yevethan Duskhan League emerged as a threat to the New Republic as it initiated a Great Purge—a series of attacks against all non-Yevethans.

**18 ABY**

- **The Corellian Incident:** The Sacorrian Triad attempted to gain control of the Corellian sector by commandeering the ancient superweapon within Centerpoint Station.

## The New Jedi Order

**25–30 ABY**

- **The Yuuzhan Vong War:** In one of the most destructive conflicts ever faced by the galaxy, the menacing extra-galactic Yuuzhan Vong invaded and began sundering entire worlds. Imperial and New Republic forces united in an effort to defeat the invaders. The New Republic was forced off Coruscant, and the planet was radically terraformed by the Yuuzhan Vong. The New Republic was reorganized as the Galactic Federation of Free Alliances (or the Galactic Alliance). Luke Skywalker's Jedi Order was instrumental in defeating the Yuuzhan Vong, who were relocated to the living planet Zonama Sekot.

**35–36 ABY**

- **The Swarm War:** The hive-minded Colony was strangely affected by Force-sensitive "Joiners" and began massive expansion efforts that triggered border disputes and conflicts with neighboring territories.

## Legacy Era

**40 ABY**

- **The Corellia-GA War:** The Galactic Alliance's disarmament campaign prompted a violent bid for independence from Corellia and a Confederation of allies. During this new civil war, Jacen Solo rose to power under the mantle of Darth Caedus.

**130 ABY**

- **The Sith-Imperial War:** In the wake of the Ossus Project, a failed Jedi initiative to terraform destroyed worlds, the Moff Council of the new Empire waged war against the Galactic Alliance, deemed complicit in the environmental disasters. In truth, the Ossus Project had been sabotaged by the new Sith Order, which allied with the Empire to attack and weaken the Alliance. After three years of hostilities, the Galactic Alliance surrendered.

# THE COMPLETE STAR WARS ENCYCLOPEDIA

# A

A-1 Deluxe Floater

**A-10** *See* A-9 Vigilance Interceptor.

**A-121** An antiquated variety of astrogation plotter that, if used in lieu of a more modern nav computer, took four times as long to calculate hyperspace trips.

**A14** A one-being repulsor disk manufactured by Aratech, used for construction and utility work.

**A-17** *See* Alpha (A-17).

**A-1707** *See* Able-1707.

***A-175*** An Action IV transport captained by Joh Steen that was seized by the privateer vessel *Far Orbit.*

**A-1 Deluxe Floater** A luxury landspeeder from Mobquet plagued by bad reviews. Its drawbacks of poor ventilation and odd interior space were offset by affordability and reliability. It was available with optional Corellian leather interior.

**A1 series business droid** Developed by Genetech during the Old Republic, this droid was eventually replaced by the A2 accounting droid.

*< Advanced Reconnaissance Commando (ARC trooper)*

**A-1 shuttle** A variety of personal shuttles used by the admirals of the Galactic Republic's Starfleet during the Clone Wars for transit to and from their flagships.

**A2, A3** The designations of Arakyd probots guarding Warlord Zsinj's facilities on Xartun.

**A2 accounting droid** A hemispherical number-crunching business droid manufactured by Genetech.

**A-24 Sleuth** A model of lightly armed two-person scout ship developed by the Incom Corporation, the A-24 Sleuth was fast and agile for a ship less than 20 meters long.

**A-26** *See* Maze.

**A280 blaster rifle** A standard-issue long-arm used by Rebel Alliance troopers at Echo Base on Hoth. The A280 blaster rifle was highly accurate with a good range. It was favored by snipers in hostile environments.

**A2-B4 (Aytoo Beefour)** An A2 accounting droid formerly owned by the wealthy Lord Anstaal, and later by rancher Sybegh Abya.

**A2-ZP (Zip)** Nicknamed Zip, this A2 accounting droid was owned by Rebel agent Jhorag Corconnan.

**A3AA personal defense module** A Corellian Technologies defense suit used by a few Imperial-contracted bounty hunters. It emitted clouds of courenth and ves gas that served to dissipate incoming blasterfire.

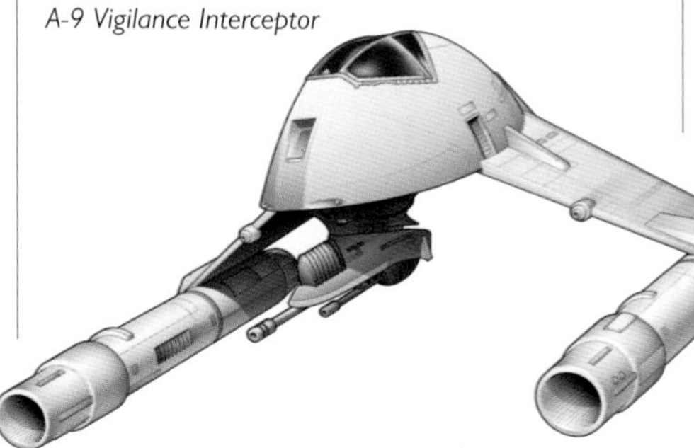

A-9 Vigilance Interceptor

**A-3DO (ThreeDee)** A multitalented service droid owned by Jedi Andur Sunrider, ThreeDee was a crack mechanic and copilot who witnessed his master's death at the hands of a criminal gang headed by Great Bogga the Hutt some 4,000 years before the Battle of Yavin. The droid then aided Andur's wife, Nomi, as she reluctantly trained to learn the ways of the Jedi.

**A-3PO** An affable protocol droid used by Rebel agent and artifacts dealer Retter Lewis aboard the *Cal Ambre.*

**A-3TO** The green-plated protocol droid that greeted incoming visitors to the Yard, Syndicate One headquarters on Valgauth.

**A-30** *See* Sull.

**A4-D (Ay-Four-Dee)** A droid doctor overseer that served General Grievous at his lair on the Vassek moon.

**A5 assassin droid** A repurposed assassin droid programmed to act as a bouncer at the Farrimmer Café at the Mynock 7 Space Station. It was destroyed in bounty hunter crossfire.

**A-5DS** A modified protocol droid that helped Rebel Alliance recruiter Rith Tar'ak make contact with the native Ebranites on Ebra.

**A-5 envirosuit** The most popular of the Malik Technologies environmental suits found on Goroth, it provided full protection from radiation and temperature extremes.

**A68 Market** The informal name given to one of the largest black-market networks aboard the original Death Star, found in city sprawl North 7:A68. It was overseen by Lieutenant Gorsick Dommaro.

**A-6 Interceptor** A small starfighter armed with paired turbolaser cannons produced during the last decades of the Galactic Republic.

A99 Aquata Breather

**A-77** One of many assassin droids that accompanied Asajj Ventress to Phindar to intercept Yoda on the Jedi Master's way to Vjun during the Clone Wars. Yoda easily destroyed the droid.

**A-89** A quadrant of Galactic City on Coruscant that housed the Coruscant Security Force during the Clone Wars, it housed the Galactic Alliance Guard decades later during the conflict between the Corellian Confederation and the Galactic Alliance.

**A-9 Vigilance Interceptor** An Imperial short-range starfighter that was introduced about six years after the Battle of Endor, soon after Grand Admiral Thrawn's defeat. The A-9 Vigilance Interceptor traded shields and hyperdrive for speed. Faster than a TIE interceptor, it was about equal in speed to an A-wing fighter. Imperial forces used its forward-firing laser cannons for hit-and-run attacks on hardened New Republic installations. However, overall performance was less than hoped for because of its limited maneuverability and relatively weak hull. The A-9 saw service in the New Republic Fleet, as well as local planetary defenses following the Yuuzhan Vong invasion. It was eventually followed by the A-10.

**A99 Aquata Breather** A compact breathing apparatus used by Jedi Knights in underwater, vacuum, and poisonous environments. Tiny oxygen tanks and filter units provided vital gases, which could be customized for non-oxygen-breathing species.

**A9G archive droid** An outdated and recalled line of humanoid-shaped information technology droids from Industrial Automaton that the Rebel Alliance acquired at a discount and repurposed for military administrative and intelligence use.

**AA-1** Manufactured by SyntheTech, this was the common verbobrain processing module found within cognitive units of 3PO protocol droids.

**AA-12X** A model of verbobrain designed for the AD series of armory droids.

**AA-23, Detention Block** The block that held Princess Leia Organa aboard the first Death Star. Specifically, she was imprisoned in cell 2187 of level five, Detention Block AA-23.

**A-A5 speeder truck** A variety of heavy repulsorlift vehicle manufactured by Trast Heavy Transports, often used by the Rebel Alliance for military transport.

**AA-589** The designation of Luke Skywalker's X-wing fighter during the rise of Grand Admiral Thrawn, five years after the Battle of Endor. Prolonged exposure to R2-D2's idiosyncrasies led the X-wing to develop a near-counterpart-level relationship with the astromech, but left the vessel virtually incompatible with other droids.

**AA-9 freighter** A massive starfreighter manufactured on Botajef, 390 meters long, it could transport cargo, passengers, or a mix of both. AA-9 freighters were occasionally pressed into service as no-frills passenger liners; the *Jendirian Valley,* for instance, ferried Anakin Skywalker and Senator Padmé Amidala from Coruscant to Naboo during the Separatist crisis.

**AAA-2** A later-model SyntheTech verbobrain developed during the time of the New Republic.

**Aabe, Peita** A former Imperial officer serving under Soontir Fel as part of the Chiss Expansionary Defense Fleet. During the war against the Yuuzhan Vong, Aabe allowed Luke Skywalker access to the Chiss library on Csilla as a resource during Skywalker's search for the living planet Zonama Sekot. Wishing to protect Chiss interests, Aabe conspired to eliminate Fel's family, but Jacen Solo helped uncover his treachery.

**AAC-1 speeder tank** A design developed by SoroSuub Corporation and foolishly lost to the Rebel Alliance and Naboo Royal Security Forces, the AAC-1 was a fast and durable anti-aircraft combat vehicle armed with laser, particle beam, and missile weapons.

**Aach** The code name for one of Bail Organa's top agents in the early days of the Rebel Alliance. Aach informed Senator Garm Bel Iblis of Organa's discovery of the Death Star project. This news delayed a public appearance by Bel Iblis, thwarting an assassination attempt on the Senator.

**AAD-4** A line of hulking, humanoid assault droids used by Arakyd Industries, they were dispatched into the Vulpter-based offices of rival Viper Sensor Intelligence Systems in what amounted to a very hostile corporate takeover shortly before the Clone Wars.

**Aaeton** The government of Aaeton had special permission to allow its citizens to visit the normally off-limits neighboring world of Ragoon VI, half a day's hyperspace journey away.

**Aaida** This woman and her husband, Lootra, lived on Nar Shaddaa during the years following the Jedi Civil War. The Exchange kidnapped Aaida and held her hostage in an attempt to force Lootra to become a member. He refused, and eventually asked the Jedi Exile to help him free her.

**Aak, Senator Ask** The Gran Senator from Malastare, Ask Aak filled the vacancy left by the untimely death of Senator Aks Moe during the Separatist crisis. Dug activists seeking equal rights on Malastare protested Aak's appointment. The hawkish Aak advocated proactive measures against the Separatists, and was vocally critical of the Jedi Order's inability to keep the peace. When the clone army was discovered on Kamino, Aak immediately championed its use.

**Aakuan** Easily provoked Corellian anarchists who believed that all sentient beings had the right to govern themselves and that no authority should invade anyone's personal freedom. The Aakuan were dangerous only to those who invaded their territories. Their extremely independent views found some popularity among Corellians. Their name derived from the Old Corellian term *aa'kua,* which translated into "respecting space."

**Aalagar** An isolated subspecies of Bith living on remote islands on Clak'dor VII. They recorded their genealogies through a form of knot tying, a practice that later evolved into more advanced record keeping and communication. When translated through Aalagar symbology, a prophetic Sith tassel that Jacen Solo uncovered read, "He will ruin those who deny justice."

**Aalto** A youngling friend of Bruck Chun in the Jedi Temple, Aalto would often join in teasing young Obi-Wan Kenobi.

**Aalun, Syron** One of a trio of famous Gand ruetsavii, or observers, who were sent to observe Rogue Squadron pilot Ooryl Qrygg's life and determine his worthiness to become janwuine. The highest possible honor in the communal Gand society, janwuine involved the right of an individual to speak of her- or himself in the first person and to use personal

Senator Ask Aak

Aargonar

pronouns in conversation. The ruetsavii not only observed Qrygg's activities but also participated fully in the squadron as fighter pilots and undercover operatives.

**Aama, Major** A New Republic Intelligence agent who was one of Hiram Drayson's senior facilitators within Alpha Blue.

**AAP blaster box** A series of strap-on laser weapons that could be affixed to droids without extensive reprogramming. Developed by Briletto Company, the AAP-II saw use in the BL series Battle Legionnaires, while the AAP-IV models were slated for use on Z-X3 battle droids.

**Aar'aa** Chameleon-like intelligent reptilian aliens also known as skin-changers. Aar'aa hailed from Aar, and they often were involved in Hutt ventures.

**Aargau** The third planet in the Zug system. A spectacularly wealthy center of banking and commerce among the Core Worlds, Aargau attempted to remain neutral in the many galactic wars. Republic, Separatist, Imperial, and Rebel treasures were stored within well-protected vaults. Some sections of Aargau's sprawling cities were laid out in levels allocated according to function. The InterGalactic Banking Clan maintained a massive pyramidal arcology on Aargau.

The planet's laws and culture revolved entirely around banking. There were three main crimes punishable by immediate execution: (1) unlawful removal of precious metals; (2) unlawful possession of weapons by non-natives (conversely, it was unlawful for citizens to be unarmed); and (3) willfully conspiring to defraud, discredit, or deceive the Bank of Aargau.

**Aargau Medical Observer Corps** A neutral organization active during the Clone Wars. Both the Separatists and the Old Republic tolerated the AMOC, allowing members to visit war-torn worlds to investigate any atrocities that might have been committed.

**Aargonar** A relatively insignificant, sparsely populated desert world and battle site of the Clone Wars. Jedi Master A'Sharad Hett—bolstered by Bultar Swan, Ki-Adi-Mundi, and Anakin Skywalker—led the defense of Republic forces against the Separatist attack. The planet was known to host numerous Sarlacc specimens. Years later, during the Galactic Civil War, Aargonar's third moon housed a Rebel base.

**Aaris III** A jungle planet in the Kathol sector, home to a vanished ancient civilization and possibly artifacts employing DarkStryder technology.

**Aarn** A heretical Shamed One, this member of the lowest caste of Yuuzhan Vong lived on Coruscant after its transformation to Yuuzhan'tar.

Aarrba the Hutt

**Aaroun** Powerful golden-furred sentient carnivores, the Aaroun were long bred for gladiator combat by the Viis Empire.

**Aarrba the Hutt** A kindhearted Hutt who owned a starship dock and repair bay in Cinnagar on Koros Major about 5,000 years before the Galactic Civil War. The curiously charitable Hutt befriended the hyperspace explorers Gav and Jori Daragon, extending them credit to cover their ever-increasing debt. When Gav and Jori were forced to flee from lenders and stole the vessel *Starbreaker 12* from Aarrba's dock, the Hutt felt betrayed. During the Great Hyperspace War that erupted due to Gav and Jori's explorations, Gav led Sith forces to Cinnagar. Aarrba chastised Gav, and was killed by Sith Massassi warriors who believed the Hutt was attacking Daragon. After the Sith forces were defeated, Jori reopened Aarrba's repair dock to preserve his memory.

**AAT (armored assault tank)** The front line of Trade Federation armored infantry divisions. A crew of battle droids drove the battle tank and operated its array of laser and projectile weaponry. The AAT's turret-mounted primary laser cannon had long-range destructive capability; it was bracketed by a pair of pylon-mounted secondary laser cannons. A pair of forward-facing short-range blaster cannons rounded out the AAT's energy-weapon complement. Contained in the forward edge of the tank's armored repulsorlift shroud were six energized shell projectile launchers capable of delivering specialized payloads. The tank contained three separate magazines from which to draw warheads: high-energy shells encased in a cocoon of plasma for incredible speed and penetration power, specialized armor-piercing warheads, and high-explosive "bunker busting" shells. Built by Baktoid Armor Workshop, the AAT saw heavy use in the Battle of Naboo and the Clone Wars.

**Aavman Extravagance** The manufacturer of such luxury vessels as the 11-S space yacht.

***aay'han*** A *Mando'a* word describing a bittersweet time of remembrance and celebration after the death of a family member. As a rule, Mandalorians who died were not buried, something reserved for the *Mand'alor*. Most individuals were cremated (unless the body could not be recovered), and their ashes were strewn to the wind. To preserve their memories, deceased Mandalorians were remembered in nightly recitals of their names, an act that was believed to keep alive their existence as well as their memory. Sometimes the personal effects of deceased individuals were kept as well, especially their body armor.

***Aay'han*** The name given to the *Deep Water*-class freighter purchased by Kal Skirata and the clone commando Ordo on the planet Agamar during the Clone Wars. Skirata chose the name—a *Mando'a* word for a particular state of mind—to honor the bittersweet memories of his adoptive father, Munin, and the clone named Dov who died while training.

AAT (armored assault tank)

**AB-1 "floatcoach"** An early prototype landspeeder that predated the more modern designs of the New Order. Palpatine kept several of these outdated vehicles within the hangar bay of his storehouse facility in Mount Tantiss.

**AB-4** A protocol droid programmed by the Rebel Alliance to serve as supply officer and bureaucrat for Advanced Base Baskarn.

**AB-6** A worker droid with a female personality that was effectively "adopted" into the Farn family on Tatooine.

**Abaarian** The source of water shipments hijacked by pirates during the Dark Nest crisis. Jedi Knights Tesar Sebatyne and Lowbacca investigated these incidents.

**Abadaner** A Corellian dissident arrested by the Galactic Alliance Guard on Coruscant based on a hunch by Ben Skywalker.

**A'baht, General Etahn** Assigned as commander of the New Republic's Fifth Fleet because of experience leading his native Dornean Navy against Imperial forces, A'baht had a leathery face that flushed purple and eye folds that swelled and fanned out. His flagship was the fleet carrier *Intrepid,* and he declared the fleet operational following the live-fire exercise Hammerblow. Defying specific orders from Princess Leia Organa to stay out of the unexplored Koornacht Cluster, he sent the survey ship *Astrolabe* to Doornik-1142, hoping to get good military intelligence. Yevethan forces, which had been roiling the sector and undertaking xenophobic extermination campaigns, destroyed the *Astrolabe.* Ambassador Nil Spaar, viceroy of the Duskhan League, declared the incident an act of aggression by the New Republic and prepared to go to war. General A'baht then led the deployment of the Fifth Fleet to the cluster and blockaded Doornik-319, where the Yevetha were mounting their forces. When the fleet came under withering attack, General A'baht was forced to withdraw. Princess Leia Organa Solo then relieved him of command and substituted her husband, Han Solo.

**Aban** An Imperial Navy officer, he oversaw the construction of an Imperial garrison on the watery world of Sedri when he held the rank of commander. Aban entered into an uneasy alliance with native renegade Karak in a bid to control the mysterious power source called the Golden Sun. Ultimately thwarted by Rebel agents, Aban emerged years later as captain of the Star Destroyer *Bellicose* in Grand Admiral Thrawn's forces.

**Abano** A poor farmer on Aruza, he was the father of Manaroo, a tattooed dancing girl who eventually married the bounty hunter Dengar.

**Abanol** A toxic world, second from the sun in the Beshqek system, within the Deep Core.

**Abbaji** The planet where the famous 100-meter-tall firethorn trees grew in a single grove of the Irugian Rain Forest. Prince Xizor, head of the Black Sun criminal organization, was given a 600-year-old dwarf firethorn tree as a peace offering by a business rival. The tree, less than half a meter high, had been in the man's family for 10 generations and was considered by Xizor to be one of his most prized possessions.

**Ab'Bshingh** The homeworld of the Farang and Waroot species.

**ABC scrambler** A projectile weapon used by bounty hunters to cause severe disorientation. The Aural-Biological-Chemical scrambler fired a pod that emitted a broad spectrum of overwhelming sensory stimuli.

**Abdi-Badawzi** A Twi'lek smuggling kingpin based on Socorro. An escaped slave and exile from Ryloth, Abdi-Badawzi was notable for his jet-black skin.

**Abek's Station** A shadowport operated by the Nikto pirate Nim Abek on the Sisar Run.

**Aber** A red dwarf star that was the primary star of the Abron system, containing the planet Alpheridies.

**Abersaith Canyon** An immense natural formation on Corulag that contained an exotic bird preserve, the Abersaith Aviary, home to more than 20 million species of avians.

**Abesmi** A remote island on the planet Kalee that served as an altar of worship for the native Kaleesh, who venerated General Grievous after his apparent death in the Huk War.

**Abhean** This planet was home to the orbital construction site for the famed Jedi starship *Chu'unthor.*

**Abin-Ral-Xufush** A ruthless Tiss'shar trader-turned-pirate who founded what became the Shadow Wing group of pirates.

**Abinyshi** Slender intelligent reptilian aliens from Inysh with forked tails. Their population suffered after the Empire discovered valuable resources on their planet.

**Ablajeck sector** An area of space that together with Moddell and Spar sectors made up the Inner Zuma region.

**Able-1707** A Jango Fett–template clone trooper serving under Shaak Ti during the Clone Wars, unit A-1707 was stranded on an uncharted planet for over 20 years. He later assisted Rebel forces, including Luke Skywalker, when the Alliance attempted to establish a post on his planet. Adopting the more personalized name of Able, this trooper later served in the Alliance, helping in a mission to infiltrate an Imperial prison on Kalist VI.

*Able-1707*

**Able-472** One of the Muunilinst 10 clone troopers who worked with General Obi-Wan Kenobi to defeat Durge and his IG lancer droid forces.

**Ables** A Corellian trained in emergency procedures, she worked as a transportation engineer on Centerpoint Station in orbit between Talus and Tralus during the years following the war with the Yuuzhan Vong.

**Ab'Lon, Tereb** A Bothan Rebel agent, he was incapacitated by Imperial agents and thrown to the Sarlacc in the Pit of Carkoon. He was survived by his astromech droid, R2-Z1, who carried vital information for the Alliance.

**abo** Old Imperial slang for native inhabitants of a planet, often used in a derogatory manner.

**Abo Dreth** A nitrogen-rich world in the Corporate Sector system of the same name whose small population included many Rebel Alliance sympathizers.

***Abolisher*** An Imperial Nebulon-B escort frigate.

**Abominor** A mysterious and ancient species of sentient droids that waged war with the Silentium, another mechanical species. Their struggle in the distant past was said to have nearly wiped out all organic life in their native galaxy, and thus they were exiled. Some Abominors made it to this galaxy, and there were a few scattered accounts of sightings. The Great Heep of Biitu is probably the best-known specimen of Abominor life.

**Abonshee** The native name for planet Masterhome, a lush forested planet inhabited by a sentient lizard species in the Fakir sector. Reekeene's Roughnecks, a Rebel Alliance group, visited Abonshee to make diplomatic contact with the Anointed People during the Galactic Civil War.

***Aboukir*** A New Republic warship destroyed during the Battle of N'zoth.

**Abran system** Site of the Abran Belt and the B'Knos mining colony, which was attacked by Ssi-ruuvi invaders.

**Abrax** An aquamarine cognac with spicy vapors. The best vintages were produced during the Old Republic.

**Abraxas** An abandoned world of spent mines, abandoned factories, and derelict ships, it served as a pirate base after the Battle of Endor.

**Abraxin** This planet in the Tion Cluster was home to the marsh haunts, a species of Force-sensitive creatures.

**Abregado Moocher** *See* Moocher.

**Abregado-rae** A manufacturing- and trade-oriented planet in the Abregado system with a onetime primitive spaceport. After the birth of the New Republic, the spaceport cleaned up its act—at least to the untrained eye. Beneath the spit-shine and polish, the spaceport catered to smugglers and other disreputable types. An oppressive government allied to the New Republic ruled Abregado-rae's population of 40 million. Some nine years after the Battle of Yavin, the leadership cut off all supplies to a clan of rebellious hill people, which created opportunities for ambitious smugglers. The planet was conquered by the Yuuzhan Vong during their invasion of the galaxy.

*Abregado-rae*

**Abregado system** A planetary system located in the Borderland Regions, on the edge of the Core Worlds. During the Clone Wars, Plo Koon and his forces scouted the Abregado system for any signs of the mysterious Separatist vessel *Malevolence.* For years, the Abregado system was a militarized zone that separated the New Republic from the remnants of the Empire; it was controlled by neither but influenced by both. A vast and complex manufacturing infrastructure linked the system's planets, and the goods produced there were vitally important to the well-being of the New Republic.

**Abric** A starship thief who worked with Niles Ferrier during the Thrawn crisis.

**Abridon** A world of verdant mountains and emerald-green fields laced with shimmering rivers. It was allied to the Rebellion after the Battle of Hoth, only to be brutally recaptured by the Empire. Luke Skywalker was taken prisoner during the conquest, and rescued by Imperial defector Brenn Tantor.

**Abrihom** A Rebel Alliance supply station platform destroyed during the Galactic Civil War.

**Abrion sector** A "bread basket" of sorts for the galaxy, the Abrion sector was home to over 200 agriworlds. Its secession during the Separatist crisis was a great blow to the Galactic Republic. The sector included sector capital Abrion Major as well as the planet Ukio, which became one of the top five producers of foodstuffs for the New Republic. When Ukio was captured by Grand Admiral Thrawn, it had serious repercussions for the sector.

***Abrogator*** An Imperial Dreadnaught dispatched to Saloch 2 to put down the Reslian Purge. Soontir Fel served aboard the *Abrogator* as part of the 37th Imperial Fighter Wing.

**Absit** This planet, homeworld of the Yatir species, was once subjugated by the Empire.

**Absolutes** The secret police of the Civilized, the totalitarian former rulers of Apsolon. The Absolutes used torture to enforce the aims of the wealthy minority. Their motto was: "Absolute justice calls for absolute loyalty." Despite their attempts, the Absolutes were unable to stop the acts of industrial sabotage committed by the Workers. Following the reform of Apsolon's government, the Absolutes went underground.

**Absolutists** Staunchly independent Selonians who advocated the use of Selonia's planetary repulsors to secede from the New Republic. The Sacorrian Triad, backed by the New Republic, was able to dissolve the Absolutists.

**absorbmat** Small, liquid-absorbent surface used as a coaster for beverages.

**Ab'Ugartte** A reclusive and unfriendly alien species from parts unknown that counted Jak Sazz among its members.

**Abya, Sybegh** A breedtash farmer on Sedesia who was also the principal Rebel Alliance contact on the planet, assisted by accounting droid A2-B4.

**Abyss, Naboo** The general name used for the labyrinthine system of seas and waterways that began on Naboo's surface and permeated to its core. Though much of the water was placid and cool, dangerous pocket currents were created when fiery blasts from the planet's core heated the water to high temperatures. Extreme caution had to be used when traveling in the honeycomb-like passways of the inner planet given the massive creatures that lurked there.

**Abyss, the** A common term that described many seemingly unfathomable and forbidding locales across the galaxy, including a deeply excavated mine on Vasha said to house the Vashan god of decay; a deep vertical slice of Imperial City that once contained the New Republic Intelligence agency code-named Mirage; and a particularly treacherous Podrace course on Ord Ibanna.

*Naboo Abyss*

**Abyssin** This primitive and violent species inhabited the occasionally fertile planet Byss in the binary star system of Byss and Abyss. (Byss had the same name as a distant planet that was used as a retreat by Emperor Palpatine.) At about 2 meters tall, the hulking, humanoid Abyssin had long limbs and a single large eye dominating greenish tan foreheads. Because they healed quickly and could regenerate any body part, this nomadic species condoned a high degree of physical violence since the consequences were short lasting. Offworld, they were often hired as petty thugs.

**Abyssin grafting patch** A medical supply from Kirgalis Pharmaceutical Exports that used specially harvested regenerative cells from Abyssin biochemistry to promote rapid growth of new skin cells.

**AC1 surveillance droid** A mobile and semi-intelligent spherical surveillance holocam droid nicknamed the spy-eye.

**Academy, the** A Galactic Republic–era elite educational and training institution that turned unseasoned youths into highly trained members of the Exploration, Military, and Merchant Services, the Academy had numerous campuses spread across the galaxy. Under Emperor Palpatine's New Order, the Academy became a training ground for nonclone Imperial officers, especially Raithal Academy in the Core region. Under the New Republic, the Academy was rebuilt to regain past glory.

**Acamma, Veril** A military leader on Sucharme, she led an armed resistance movement against the invading Trade Federation that eventually drove it off the planet.

**ACC-7** This series of small assassin droids, developed by Arakyd Industries, was popular among Imperial law enforcement and undercover operatives. The hovering spherical droids contained four retractable arms that extended to reveal heavy-duty vibroblades. Use of the ACC-7 was outlawed by the New Republic, but statutes against them were loosened so they could be used against the invading Yuuzhan Vong.

**accarrgm** A strong liquor favored by Wookiees.

**acceleration chair, acceleration couch** A generic term for g-force-absorbing seats found aboard starships.

**acceleration compensator** A device that generated a type of artificial gravity and helped neutralize the effects of accelerating to high speed aboard medium- and larger-sized spacecraft such as the *Millennium Falcon.*

**acceleration facility** A term describing various facilities constructed by the hives of the Colony to assist with the process of turning beings into Joiners. Many of these structures were found on the planets of the Utegetu Nebula, after the Colony's hives were relocated there following the Qoribu crisis. Most beings brought to these facilities were criminals such as smugglers and pirates, who could be turned to work for the Gorog.

**acceleration straps** These passenger-safety harnesses were usually built into the seats of spacecraft to restrain passengers during takeoffs, landings, and violent maneuvers.

***Acceptance*** A Republic *Consular*-class cruiser that served as Jedi Master Dooku's flagship during the mission to rid Galidraan of Mandalorian forces. The *Acceptance* was destroyed in battle in the Yinchorri system, though crew members Maoi Madakor and Antidar Williams were able to escape.

A-Cee

**Access Chute** This kilometers-long pathway snaked through a grid of decaying cities and tall docking towers on the spaceport moon Nar Shaddaa. Its entrance masked by a bright advertising holoscreen, the Chute led to the repair facility of an old buddy of Han Solo, Shug Ninx.

**accipiptero** The largest flying reptile native to Dagobah.

*Accipiptero*

***Acclamator*-class assault ship** Massive transport ships used by the Grand Army of the Republic during the Clone Wars. These wedge-shaped Republic assault ships were built in secret in the shipyards of Rothana. Though not designed specifically for ship-to-ship combat, Acclamators were more than capable of holding their own against smaller Separatist cruisers. Subsequent models in the series were more focused on planetary bombardment missions. Eventually, they were replaced by more modern and capable Imperial-era warships.

*Acclamator-class assault ship*

**Accolux Township** This Yedagon city was supposedly attacked and destroyed by the Lords of Dismay Flightknife during the civil war that broke out on Adumar. In reality, reports depicting the battle were faked in an effort to keep the Empire from learning that the Adumari had sided with the New Republic.

**Accu, Paddy** An older human at the time of the Clone Wars, he served as retreat caretaker in the Lake Country of Naboo. Paddy Accu drove the gondola speeder that brought Padmé Amidala and Anakin Skywalker to the lake retreat.

**accu-accelerator** Part of the ignition system found in many starship sublight engine systems.

***Accuser*** *See Emancipator.*

**Accutronics** A leading droid manufacturer and early forerunner in the marketing of droids to families with young children. It was formerly a subsidiary of Industrial Automaton.

**Ace-6** Cybot Galactica's droid brain unit, found aboard the automated TIE/D droid starfighter.

**A-Cee** A chrome-plated protocol droid belonging to the Rebel Intelligence agent Candice Ondi. A-Cee's recordings of an Imperial massacre on Sulon convinced Kyle Katarn to join the Rebellion. Programmed to self-destruct if discovered by the Empire, A-Cee detonated aboard an Imperial yacht, killing Governor Donar.

**Ace Entertainment Corporation** The parent company of a number of upscale gambling establishments, including the Ace of Sabres on Kluistar.

**acertron** This flexible heavy alloy, cryogenically tempered to add strength, was used in the chest carapace of super battle droids.

**Ace Squadron** Pash Cracken's A-wing squadron that served in the Battle of Thyferra.

**Acey** A thief and friend of Dexter Jettster.

**Ac'fren Spur** A little-known "side" path of the Sisar Run that connected the Si'Klaata Cluster with the Weequay homeworld of Sriluur.

**Acherin** Jedi Master Garen Muln led Republic forces on Acherin during the devastating fighting that occurred there in the Clone Wars. When the Empire came to power, Separatist holdouts formed a short-lived underground resistance on Acherin. Obi-Wan Kenobi, Ferus Olin, and Trever Flume briefly worked with the resistance during their time on Acherin.

**Achillea** A semi-tropical world of great beauty that was one of the principal planets controlled by House Cadriaan in the Tapani sector.

*Achtnak Turbine Station*

**achtnak** A stealthy predator native to the forests of Tepasi, the home planet of the House of Tagge.

**Achtnak Turbine Station** A TIE fighter launch base hidden within the atmosphere of the gas giant Yavin. After the destruction of the first Death Star, Baron Orman Tagge led an operation there that harassed the Rebels blockaded on Yavin 4. The station used a massive turbine to open a "storm corridor" within Yavin's turbulent atmosphere, allowing the launch and receipt of TIE fighters. Luke Skywalker was able to destroy the station.

**Acib, Y'ull** A criminal freed by the New Republic during the retaking of Coruscant, he helped reestablish Black Sun and rose to prominence after the death of Grand Admiral Thrawn. After the New Republic defeat of the cloned Emperor, Acib forged an alliance with Grappa the Hutt to gain control over the Imperial Ruling Council. After assassinating council member General Immodet, Acib sent Black Sun assassins to murder Xandel Carivus and replace him with a clone that Acib could control. This plot failed when the Imperials were able to trace the clone back to Black Sun. Y'ull Acib kept his location a secret, and communicated only remotely. His role in Black Sun was eventually filled by Durga the Hutt.

**acicular defender** A subspecies of the Corellian paralope bred to defend the herd from predators.

**acid-beet** An edible root vegetable grown in the acid rains of the planet Vjun.

**acid droid** A specialized form of crawl-carrier that carried a payload of building-collapsing acid within its body. When it infiltrated its objective, the acid droid literally sacrificed itself by dumping its payload, destroying itself as well as the surrounding structure with the powerful acid.

Y'ull Acib

**acid lizard** A species of acid-secreting reptilians that burrowed deep beneath the sands of Tatooine.

**Acilaris** A small, superheated toxic planet that was the innermost world of the Cularin system.

**Ackbar, Admiral** Born on the watery world of Mon Calamari, Ackbar rose from humble beginnings to become a renowned military strategist. His championing of the Rebel Alliance—after conquering his own inbred caution—played a major role in the Rebels' defeat of Imperial forces during the Galactic Civil War. He preferred to personally lead major assaults, and his troops still affectionately referred to him as "Admiral" even after he had retired.

Ackbar, who like other Mon Calamari had salmon-colored skin, large bulbous yellow-orange eyes, and webbed hands and feet, was the leader of Coral Depths City when Imperial forces invaded and nearly destroyed his planet. One of the first to be enslaved, Ackbar eventually became an interpreter for Grand Moff Tarkin. It was from Tarkin that he first heard rumblings of the Rebellion—as well as veiled references to a new superweapon that would crush the Rebels. During transit to the gargantuan battle station, Tarkin's command shuttle was ambushed by a Rebel elite force sent to assassinate him. While Tarkin escaped, Ackbar was liberated and fled with the Rebels. Ackbar's knowledge made him indispensable to the growing Alliance.

Acklays

Ackbar returned to his people, leading them through numerous conflicts with the Empire before formally joining the Alliance, bringing with him the strikingly beautiful Mon Calamari cruisers. During a rendezvous with Princess Leia Organa shortly before the Battle of Hoth, Ackbar's modified bulk freighter was destroyed by the Empire. He and his crew escaped in life pods, crash-landing on the nearby world of Daluuj. There he was rescued by Han Solo, Luke Skywalker, and Organa aboard the *Millennium Falcon.*

When Ackbar achieved the rank of commander in the Alliance forces, he oversaw the Verpine production of the B-wing starfighter, code-named Project Shantipole. For the delivery of the Verpine and the B-wings to the Rebellion, Ackbar was promoted to admiral by Mon Mothma. Ackbar developed the attack strategy for the Battle of Endor and commanded the Mon Calamari star cruiser *Home One.* The combination of his proven military tactics and General Lando Calrissian's unorthodox maneuvers was enough to secure victory in one of the Alliance's bloodiest and most important battles.

Following the defeat of the Empire at Endor, Ackbar maintained a key position in the command hierarchy of the Alliance of Free Planets, and the New Republic that followed. He was part of the New Republic provisional government's Inner Council. During the many mop-up operations that cut into the Empire's dwindling territories, Ackbar spearheaded numerous missions into Imperial space. He was influential in ferreting out warlords like Zsinj, and in capturing the capital world of Coruscant for the Republic.

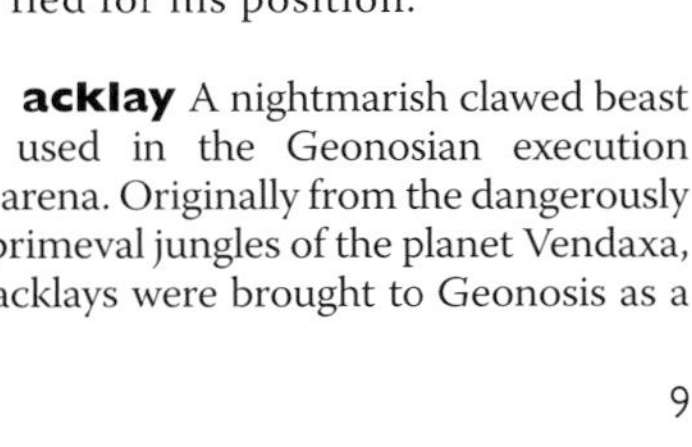
Admiral Ackbar

The first few years of the New Republic were extremely trying for Ackbar. His niece, Jesmin Ackbar, died in battle as a starfighter pilot. During the Thrawn crisis, Imperial Intelligence agents framed Ackbar for an embezzlement scheme. The resulting scandal effectively took him out of commission when he was needed the most. Following the defeat of the cloned Emperor, Ackbar's personal starfighter was sabotaged, which caused him to have a terrible accident on the planet of Vortex, where many innocent Vors were killed. This led Ackbar into early retirement back on Mon Calamari.

Ackbar later returned to the fleet, though he willingly relinquished control to younger admirals and fleet officers while adopting more of an advisory position. Some 25 years after the Battle of Yavin, Ackbar retired from official duty. In his later years, as his body began to fail him, Ackbar came out of retirement from his home at the Heurkea floating city on Mon Calamari. It was during the height of the Yuuzhan Vong invasion, when the defenders of the galaxy had suffered setback after setback. Ackbar, aided by Winter, returned to the command post for the newly formed Galactic Alliance, formulating strategies that resulted in a major victory against the Yuuzhan Vong, helping turn the tide of the war.

Ackbar succumbed to his advanced age and died of natural causes on the eve of the war's end.

**Ackbar, Jesmin** Niece of Admiral Ackbar and one of the first pilots and communications officers for the New Republic's Wraith Squadron. She was killed in action over the third moon of the M2398 system.

**Ackbar Slash** A desperate capital ship combat maneuver developed by Admiral Ackbar.

**Ackdool, Commander** The Mon Calamari commander of the New Republic cruiser *Mediator,* sent to monitor the growing tensions between Rhommamool and Osarian. Some in the New Republic felt that Ackdool was not qualified for his position.

**acklay** A nightmarish clawed beast used in the Geonosian execution arena. Originally from the dangerously primeval jungles of the planet Vendaxa, acklays were brought to Geonosis as a

Ackmena

gift to Archduke Poggle the Lesser. Escaped acklays quickly became a menace in the desert wilderness. Acklays were also found on Felucia.

**Acklay Chopper** The name used by a notorious Geonosian slavemaster, earned by killing an acklay in an execution arena.

**Ackli** A tipsy Mon Calamari treasure seeker often found in one of Mos Taike's cantinas on Tatooine, Ackli worked with a pair of Zabrak in the search for a krayt dragon graveyard.

**Ackmena** The nighttime bartender at the Mos Eisley cantina on Tatooine. She was far less surly and unapproachable than Wuher, and spacers respected her. She teamed up with Cebann Veekan, who shared a flair for theatrics and song. After the Battle of Endor, the pair turned the increasingly popular "local boy does good" story of Luke Skywalker into a stage hit.

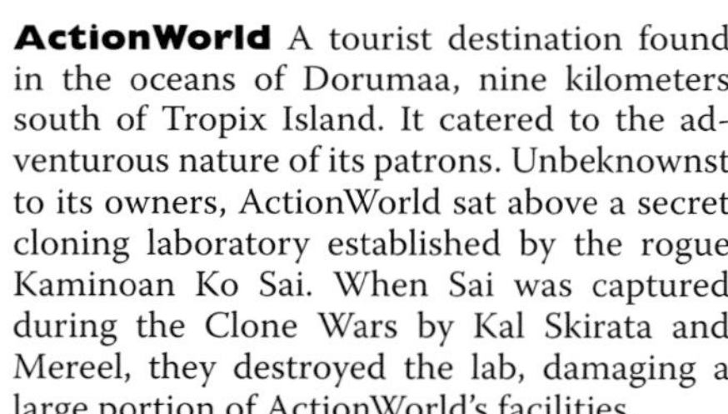
Acros-Krik

**Ackrahbala's Swoops & Speeders** A vehicle dealership in Bartyn's Landing on the planet Lamaredd, operated by an energetic Chagrian known as Crazy 'Bala.

**ACP weaponry** A series of accelerated charged-particle weapons developed by Arakyd Industries. Examples included the LS-150 heavy repeater gun, as well as smaller rifle and pistol variants. These weapons were often used by Trandoshan slavers.

***Acquisitor*** A heavily armed Trade Federation freighter that came to the aid of the *Revenue* when the latter was attacked by Nebula Front raiders. The ship featured strengthened armor and overlapping deflector shields. It also carried twice the usual number of droid-piloted craft. Nap Lagard served as the ship's commander.

**Acre's Spaceport** The only publicly accessible spaceport on the planet Mon Gazza.

**acrobat droid** A generic term describing any automaton programmed to perform intricate feats of acrobatics and tumbling. Acrobat droids came in all sizes, but were most often small, in order to minimize the programming and the number of working parts. Some were no larger than a human hand.

**Acros-Krik** The corrupt Ongree mayor of Coruscant's Uscru District. He came to power through an election rigged by Black Sun. Acros-Krik funneled back information gathered by the attractive Nalle triplets to his Black Sun backers.

**Ac'siel** One of the largest cities found beneath the ice on the Chiss homeworld of Csilla.

**actibandage** A form of medical bandage produced after the Yuuzhan Vong invaded the galaxy, it was used to cover deep gashes or puncture wounds, where pressure needed to be applied in order to stanch blood flow.

**Action-series freighters** Very common boxy bulk freighters built by the Corellian Engineering Corporation. There were at least six entries in the series, including the Action VI made famous as the model Talon Karrde chose as his primary vessel, the *Wild Karrde.*

**Action Tidings** An Ugnaught news broadcast made available to denizens of Cloud City.

**ActionWorld** A tourist destination found in the oceans of Dorumaa, nine kilometers south of Tropix Island. It catered to the adventurous nature of its patrons. Unbeknownst to its owners, ActionWorld sat above a secret cloning laboratory established by the rogue Kaminoan Ko Sai. When Sai was captured during the Clone Wars by Kal Skirata and Mereel, they destroyed the lab, damaging a large portion of ActionWorld's facilities.

**Activvl riot shield** A shield used by the Corporate Sector Authority Espos. The Drearian Defense Activvl riot shield was a 1-meter-long device made of layered metal and one-way mirrored transparisteel. It had a small notch to fit the muzzle of a blaster; a simple handle with a stud activated a stun charge.

**Acton, Beel** A wealthy bully from Brentaal who had an affinity for the Force, he rejected an offer of Jedi training. He used his particular Force talents for selfish aims and became a criminal in the Core Worlds.

Adarian

**Actrion, Chon** A renowned alien Jedi Master immortalized as a bust in the Jedi Archives. Chon Actrion is known as the Architect of Freedom.

**actuating blaster module** *See* blaster weaponry.

**A'Daasha, Corinna and Kandria** Twin sisters from Corellia who established and operated the Glow Dome entertainment complex on Adarlon.

***Adamant*** A New Republic bulk space cruiser, the *Adamant* was commanded by Admiral Ackbar. About 23 years after the Battle of Yavin, as it was shuttling a precious cargo of hyperdrive cores and turbolaser battery emplacements to the Kuat Drive Yards, the cruiser was attacked by a rump Imperial fleet within Coruscant's protected zone. The attack was led by onetime TIE fighter pilot Qorl, who had crashed in the jungles of Yavin 4 but survived until he was discovered by Jaina and Jacen Solo two decades later. He worked for the turncoat Jedi Brakiss. His modified assault shuttle was fitted with industrial-grade Corusca gems that enabled it to chew through the *Adamant*'s hull. After Qorl's crew boarded the ship, they jettisoned the New Republic crew in escape pods and made off with the cruiser and its cargo.

***Adamantine*** This New Republic escort cruiser visited the planet Nam Chorios. All its personnel were killed and the ship lost after the Death Seed plague was unloosed.

**Adanar** A senior Sith trooper in the Gloom Walkers unit of the Brotherhood of Darkness during the years leading up to the Battle of Ruusan. He enlisted at about the same time as Dessel (the future Darth Bane), and the two were in the same units after they graduated from basic training.

**Adarakh** One of Leia Organa Solo's Noghri bodyguards, often paired with Meewalh. Adarakh was killed by Yuuzhan Vong collaborator Viqi Shesh on Coruscant while he was trying to defend Leia and the infant Ben Skywalker.

**Adare, Terena** The chief administrator of Dantooine following its ravaging by Darth Malak in the Jedi Civil War. The Jedi abandoned Dantooine, forcing Adare to open the ruined planet to treasure seekers and archaeologists in an effort to preserve its faltering economy.

**Adarian** Alien species native to the mountainous world of Adari. They were recognizable by their elongated skulls, which had a large hole completely piercing the head from side to side. By distending their throat sacs, Adarians were able to produce a loud "long call" for communication or defense. Adarian society was organized into a rigid caste system.

Eighth Lord Arkoh Adasca

**Adarlon** A planet settled by Alderaanians in the distant Minos Cluster that became known across the galaxy for its music and holographic entertainment.

**Adas, King** The ancient pure-blood Sith monarch who used the power of the dark side to subjugate his people over 28,000 years before the Battle of Yavin, long before the Sith people would become subjugated by the outlander Dark Lords. Adas learned to contain his knowledge in one of the first Sith Holocrons, which thousands of years later found its way into Queen Amanoa's possession on Onderon. Lumiya would eventually come to own this relic after the Battle of Endor.

**Adasca, Aurora** An Arkanian, she was niece to Lord Arkoh Adasca. In the years after the Great Sith War, she was turned over to the Jedi Order to be trained in their ways.

**Adasca, Eighth Lord Arkoh** An Arkanian pure-blood, influential leader, and head of Adascorp during the Mandalorian Wars. He followed Lord Argaloh (his grandfather) and Lord Alok (his father) with the title of lord, being the eighth Adasca to bear it. Arkoh sought Gorman Vandrayk, an Adascorp scientist who fled the company upon discovering that his research into space slug engineering would be used for evil. Gorman adopted the alias *Camper* and lived life on the run. Adasca, meanwhile, cultivated the mutated space slugs—exogorths—into powerful biological weapons in an overreaching political gambit that proved to be his undoing.

**Adascopolis** The ancient capital of Arkania during the time of the Great Sith War and Mandalorian Wars. It was the seat of power of the influential Adasca family.

**Adascorp** Also known as the Adasca Bio-Mechanical Corporation of Arkania, this medical and bioengineering research-and-development firm was owned by the influential House of Adasca. During the time of the Mandalorian Wars, its leader, Lord Arkoh Adasca, used experimental mutant exogorths in a failed bid for galactic power.

**adder moss** A common plant found on Dagobah and the swamps of Naboo. The Gungans used adder moss as a fuel source, and adder moss chips made a spongy, spicy snack.

**Addle, Boz** A ranking technician and engineer working in the hangar bays of the Jedi Temple during the Clone Wars.

**Adebsu** A Rodian clan that owned a small enclave on the Betu continent of Rodia, and owed its allegiance to the Chekkoo clan.

**Adega system** A binary star system located in the Outer Rim Territories, it was home to the planet Ossus and site of an ancient Jedi stronghold. Before the discovery of the crystal caves of Ilum, the Adega system was the primary source of lightsaber crystals. One of the original nine Auril systems, Adega was one of six that survived the explosive creation of the Cron Drift.

**Adegan crystals** Precious crystals used by the Jedi to construct lightsabers. Their power was unlocked when waves of the proper frequency were transmitted through them. Before the discovery of the crystal caves on Ilum, the Adegan system was the primary source for such crystals. The Adegan family of crystals, in order of rarity, included: kathracite, relacite, danite, mephite, and pontite.

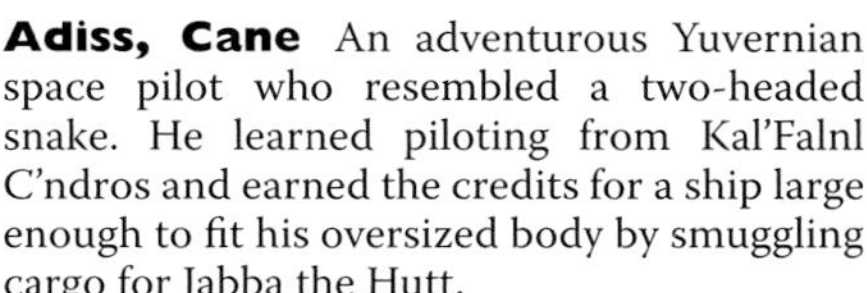
Cane Adiss

**Adegan eel** A disgusting snake-like venomous creature with vicious fangs and a slime-covered body. The Krath founders Aleema and Satal Keto infested their tutor with Adegan eels during their takeover of the Empress Teta system some 4,000 years before the Galactic Civil War.

**Adelmaa'j, Enton** A Chiss pilot who served under Jagged Fel as Twin Suns Eight during the Yuuzhan Vong war.

**Adem'thorn, Senator Yeb Yeb** The Swokes Swokes representative of the planet Makem Te who supported the vote of no confidence in Chancellor Valorum.

Adegan crystals

**A'den, Senior Clone Commander** A Null ARC trooper trained by Kal Skirata, he was in command of the 7th Legion during the Clone Wars. His clone designation was CT-80/88-3009.

**adept** A style of lightsaber hilt designed for beings with either two or four fingers opposing a single thumb. The adept had a down-facing guard located below the emitter for added protection.

**adhesive explosives** A variety of specialized weapons that used pressurized chemicals to create an adhesive blast radius immobilizing those caught within. They were commonly called glop grenades.

**Adim** A planet that was the site of a mining colony, protected from pirate attacks by mercenaries. The pirates hired Andov Syn to help them, and he single-handedly wiped out the mercenaries.

**Adin** A former Imperial stronghold, Adin was the homeworld of Senator Meido, a former Imperial official who was elected to the New Republic senate 13 years after the Battle of Endor.

**adipose lice** Parasites that fed on fat, often resulting in extremely rapid and dangerous weight loss in their hosts.

**Adi's Rest** A large volcano on the planet Lok named by the smuggler Nym in honor of his onetime ally Adi Gallia.

**Adiss, Cane** An adventurous Yuvernian space pilot who resembled a two-headed snake. He learned piloting from Kal'Falnl C'ndros and earned the credits for a ship large enough to fit his oversized body by smuggling cargo for Jabba the Hutt.

***Adjudicator*** *See Liberator.*

**Adjustment** One of the shadiest branches of Imperial Intelligence. When a problem grew out of control and needed to be rectified, agents from Adjustment were brought in. Their orders were never documented, and Adjustment officers were given complete access to whatever resources they required to get the job done.

***Admiral Ackbar*** A Galactic Alliance Star Destroyer and flagship of the Fifth Fleet under the command of Admiral Nek Bwua'tu. *Admiral Ackbar* saw heavy action during the Yuuzhan Vong invasion and was one of two vessels, alongside *Mon Mothma,* to survive the war with its gravity-well generators intact. Both ships were charged with the interdiction of the Utegetu Nebula to prevent the spread of the Gorog hive during the Dark Nest crisis. The Killiks nonetheless captured *Admiral Ackbar* and used it to attack the Chiss, a move that made the Chiss believe the Alliance had sided with the Killiks. After reclaiming command of the vessel, Bwua'tu led *Admiral Ackbar* in protecting the Hapan Queen Mother in the civil war that erupted between the Alliance and the Confederation.

***Admiral Korvin*** Raith Sienar's flagship on his mission to Zonama Sekot three years after the Battle of Naboo. *Admiral Korvin* was an antiquated Trade Federation heavy munitions cruiser. Sienar was dismayed that the *Korvin* did not carry a single craft of his own manufacture aboard. The cruiser had three landing craft, droid starfighters, 100 Trade Federation troops, and over 3,000 droids; it was armed with sky mines and commanded by Captain Kett.

***Admonitor*** An Imperial Star Destroyer used by Thrawn when he held the rank of admiral. It faced Ebruchi pirates and Tyber Zann's forces during the Galactic Civil War. This vessel returned Thrawn to the Unknown Regions. *Admonitor*'s commanding officer was Captain Dagon Niriz.

**Adnama** A female patron of the Outlander Club present when Obi-Wan Kenobi and Anakin Skywalker confronted Zam Wesell there.

**Adnerem** Tall, thin humanoids from Adner known for their asocial and introverted ways.

**ADO-8** A battle droid commander during the Battle of Naboo.

**Adollu, Nalia** A native of Corsin, this young girl was the Padawan learner chosen by Jedi Master Anno Wen-Chii following the Battle of Ruusan. Adollu accompanied her Master to the planet Polus, where Master Anno spent time studying the native species, hoping to learn more about how life evolved in the galaxy. Adollu's absence from the Jedi Temple on Coruscant allowed Sith apprentice Darth Zannah to adopt her identity while infiltrating the Jedi Archives to research the orbalisks plaguing her master, Darth Bane.

**adoris feline** A small animal often kept as a pet by spacers.

**Adostic Arms** A weapons manufacturer known for large-bore projectile shotguns.

**adrenal enhancements** A wide variety of temporary performance enhancers common even thousands of years before the Galactic Civil War. Options included *adrenaline stimulator,* which increased awareness of surroundings and reaction time; *adrenal strength,* which provided a quick boost of raw physical power; *adrenal alacrity,* which enhanced dexterity; and *adrenal stamina,* which increased endurance. These were also called stims.

**Adrenas** An ancient Sith devotee during the time of the Jedi Civil War who served Master Uthar Wynn as a chamberlain at the Sith Academy on Korriban.

**Adriana** The third planet in the Tatoo system, this gas giant had rings of ice that were often mined and taken to the desert planet Tatooine for water.

**A'driannamieq Mountains** A vast expanse of peaks that cut across the landscape of the planet Elom.

**Adrimetrum, Kaiya** From Siluria III, she became a resistance fighter after her husband was killed by Imperial troops. Rebel operative Corwin Shelvay recruited her into the Alliance. She became a unit commander and a member of Page's Commandos. She joined the New Republic mission to hunt down Moff Sarne in the Kathol Rift, eventually becoming commander of the *FarStar,* which tracked him down.

**AD series droid** Developed by Arakyd Industries to serve as military base armory administrators, AD series droids were instead sold to local law enforcement agencies and independent mercenaries after being rejected by the Empire.

**A-DSD** *See* dwarf spider droid.

**Aduba system** A remote system in the Outer Rim Territories frequented by spacers trying to keep a low profile. Aduba-3 began as a tiny religious agricultural colony. Scammers seeded a fake chromium rush that brought offworld investors and shipbuilders to the planet. Once the mines played out, the migrants abandoned the world, leaving behind cast-off machinery and derelict towns. Han Solo and Chewbacca tried to lie low on Aduba-3 when deeply indebted to Jabba the Hutt.

**Adumar** A remote planet located on the fringe of Wild Space, Adumar had no native sentient life; its small population was mostly made up of human colonists from the Old Republic. The planet had a thriving military industry, as Adumar was maniacally militaristic, possessing a rigid duel-oriented culture and worshipful reverence toward starfighter pilots. Thirteen years after the Battle of Yavin, General Wedge Antilles went to Adumar's nation-state of Cartann to negotiate alliance with the leadership. Although the monarchy of Cartann was leaning toward the Empire, smaller states elsewhere on the planet enlisted Antilles's help in overthrowing Cartann's rule. This effort succeeded, and Adumar eventually joined the New Republic. Decades later, when the relationship between the Galactic Alliance and Corellia began to fray, Adumar chose to ally itself with the Corellian Confederation, supplying the independence movement with military equipment.

**Adumari** The humans of Adumar, descended from a separatist group that fought the Republic and lost over 10,000 years before the Battle of Yavin. The isolated culture grew to revere the planet's highest technology—combat fighters—and began creating a system of values based on principles of perceived honor and duels. Their continued development of weapons systems drew the attention of the New Republic, which hoped to bring the Adumari aboard as allies against the Empire. Adumari spoke an accented Basic dialect with a lexicon that reflected the planet's violent history.

**Adur quarter** A section within the Corellian quarter of Coruscant raided by the Galactic Alliance Guard during the tensions between Corellia and the Galactic Alliance.

**Advanced Appendage Bus (AAB)** Cybot Galactica's proprietary universal socket interface, which allowed the hot-swapping of droid componentry. Some criticized Cybot Galactica's aggressive setting of a new interface standard as a way of crowding out competitors.

**Advanced Recon Force (ARF) trooper** Specialized ground force clone troopers that served the Republic during the Clone Wars, they often were pressed into service as AT-RT drivers.

**Advanced Reconnaissance Commando (ARC trooper)** Elite clone troopers personally trained by Jango Fett prior to his death. ARC troopers did not have the genetic docility tampering found in standard clone troopers, making them more independent and adaptive in combat situations. The first batch of ARCs engineered by the Kaminoans (the Null class) proved untenable, with only half of the 12 surviving their gestation. After a refinement of the cloning process, the next batch (Alpha class) of ARCs numbered

*Advanced Reconnaissance Commando (ARC trooper)*

100. They were trained by Fett and put into stasis until needed. When Separatist forces attacked Kamino, Prime Minister Lama Su and Jedi Master Shaak Ti activated the ARCs as a last line of defense. From that engagement forward, they became valuable assets in the Clone Wars. General Obi-Wan Kenobi led an elite team of ARC troopers on a mission against InterGalactic Banking Clan forces on Muunilinst.

*Advozse*

**Adventurer** An older Verpine starship model from the days of the Galactic Republic, it featured a lifting body design with hoverjets rather than the more common repulsorlifts. It had no weapons or shields, and did not have an astromech droid for navigation. It was designed to be a small, personal sporting craft.

**advertiscreen** A holographic billboard of varying size used indoors and outdoors.

**Advisory Council, Naboo** Naboo's ruling body, governed by—and in support of—the elected monarch. During Queen Amidala's reign, Governor Sio Bibble was the chair of the council. The council contained a diverse collection of scholars, scientists, artists, and other community leaders.

**Advisory Council, New Republic** A group of New Republic Senators serving as an inner council to the Chief of State. During Borsk Fey'lya's term, councilors included Chelch Dravvad, Niuk Niuv, Cal Omas, Pwoe, Fyor Rodan, and Triebakk.

**Advisory Council (Palpatine's War Council)** During the Clone Wars, they were Chancellor Palpatine's closest military advisers. Membership was always in flux, but councilors included Armand Isard, Mas Amedda, Senator Ha'Nook, Sate Pestage, and Kohl Seerdon.

**Advora** The groundquake-stricken capital city of the planet Riflor, homeworld of the Advozsec.

**Advozse (plural: Advozsec)** A humanoid alien species from Riflor with short stature, large black eyes, and a single horn protruding from the forehead. A history marked by repeated natural disasters instilled in them a sense of pragmatism bordering on pessimism. Riflor was devastated by a Yuuzhan Vong biovirus that left millions of Advozsec to starve.

**Adz patrol destroyer (*Adz*-class destroyer)** An Imperial deep-space patrol ship. The Adz patrol destroyer, developed after the Thrawn crisis, incorporated advances in slave circuitry allowing a small crew to control a battery of weapons.

**Aebea** One of the many subspecies of Killiks, they were each a meter long.

**Aefan** A species of small, orange-skinned humanoids native to Aefao, many of whom were recruited as pilgrims by the t'landa T'il.

**AEG-77 Vigo** A modified transport-turned-gunship designed specifically for Black Sun, it featured spacious cargo holds, two forward-mounted guns, four turret-mounted dorsal guns, and two turret-mounted ventral guns.

***Aegis*-class shuttle** An assault shuttle manufactured by the Telgorn Corporation for use by various military groups. The New Republic employed Aegis shuttles to support the *FarStar* mission in the Kathol Outback.

**Aemele** A seductive female Twi'lek thief who stole Chu-Gon Dar Cubes from a doctor on Mustafar and tried to sell her illicit wares on Tatooine.

**Aeneid system** Fifteen planets, 13 of which were inhabited. According to spacer lore, young Han Solo once hoodwinked some spacers into smuggling "Kessel birds" out of the Aeneid system.

**Aeradin** A nonhuman professor and assistant dean at the Leadership School on Andara after the Battle of Naboo.

**Aeramaxis** A company that specialized in personal-safety devices.

**Aeran** A weapons specialist, part of Cilia Dil's underground dissident movement on Junction V.

**Aereen** A moon in the Krant system where the Trade Federation established a mining colony and built Decimator tanks during the Clone Wars.

**Aerie Command** The code name for the New Republic Intelligence agency's Special Threats division based on Coruscant.

**aeromagnifier** A repulsorlift-suspended hovering magnifier used by computer technicians to see tiny components for repair or replacement. Shmi Skywalker had an aeromagnifier at her workstation in her slave hovel on Mos Espa.

**Aeten II** An Outer Rim world in the Dreighton Nebula, the source of the rare stygium crystals used in cloaking devices. The planet's deposits of crystals ran dry, making cloaking devices exceedingly rare.

***Aethersprite*-class starfighter** *See* Delta-7 Jedi starfighter.

**AF-119** A stormtrooper posted at Cloud City who found guard duty fairly boring.

**AF-27** An ambitious stormtrooper posted as a guard at the carbon-freezing chamber, and involved in the takeover of Cloud City.

***Afarathu*** A Selonian terrorist sect that marauded in the Corellian system. The *Afarathu* sect was brought down by Keiran Halcyon 400 years before the Battle of Yavin. The incident had been all but forgotten until Imperials used the specter of it to incite xenophobia among the human population in the Corellian system.

**Af'El** A large high-gravity world that was seldom visited, Af'El orbited the ultraviolet supergiant Ka'Dedus. Af'El's lack of an ozone layer allowed ultraviolet light to pass freely to the surface, while other wavelengths were blocked by heavy atmospheric gases. Thus, the lifeforms on Af'El could universally see only in ultraviolet light ranges. It was the homeworld of the Defel, or "wraiths," whose bodies absorbed visible light, giving them the appearance of shadows. The Defel lived in underground cities to escape Af'El's violent storms. The planet's main export was the metal meleenium, which was used in durasteel and was known to exist only on Af'El.

**Affa** A heavily mechanized planet. Some of C-3PO's original components were manufactured there.

**affect mind** Using the Force, a Jedi Knight could employ this technique to change the perceptions of another person or creature. Affect mind created illusions or stopped the understanding of what was really happening by blocking the senses. It could also obliterate memories altogether or replace them with false ones.

**Affodies Crafthouse of Pure Neimoidia** A Neimoidian company that specialized in luxury goods such as mechno-chairs.

**Affric, High Lord** A nobleman of the Sarin sector during the time of the Galactic Empire who illegally used Mantis Syndicate bounty hunters as his personal army.

**Affytechan** A sentient form of plant life, Affytechans originated on the Outer Rim world of Dom-Bradden. An Affytechan was beautiful in appearance, with a high musical voice and a body composed of thousands of colorful petals, tendrils, and stalks. However, it also smelled of ammonia and musk. Affytechans were among the aliens aboard the *Eye of Palpatine*.

**Afit, Zeen** A craggy-faced smuggler, Afit was one of the smugglers Han Solo encountered on the asteroid Skip 1 during his investigation into a bombing that rocked Senate Hall on Coruscant. He originally introduced Solo and Chewbacca to Smuggler's Run, an asteroid belt infamous as a smugglers' hideout.

**Afterburners** A "noble"-minded swoop gang on Entralla who protected the citizens of Nexus City from the more dangerous criminals who congregated there.

**Afyon, Captain** A native of Alderaan, Afyon heeded Princess Leia Organa's call to join the Rebellion after the Empire destroyed his family, friends, and entire planet. A veteran of the Clone Wars, Captain Afyon served as first officer aboard a Corellian gunship and eventually earned his own command. At the age of 52, some four years after the end of the Galactic Civil War, he was made captain of the escort frigate *Larkhess,* a warship that had been relegated to trade duty. The *Larkhess* transported cargo and hotshot braggart fighter pilots who never gave the "old man" captain his due. During the Battle of Sluis Van, however, Afyon proved himself to be an excellent commander. When the *Larkhess* was boarded by stormtroopers, he prepared to destroy his ship rather than surrender it. But the actions of a bunch of Rebel pilots, along with Luke Skywalker and Han Solo, made that ultimate sacrifice unnecessary.

**aga** Hulking six-legged semi-sentient beasts from Zelos II. Emperor Palpatine used drugged aga beasts as guards on his most secretive projects.

**Agamar** An Outer Rim agriworld in the Mirgoshir system, Lahara sector. Cities included the capital of Calna Muun, where the governing Agamarian Council resided. During the Separatist crisis, Agamar withdrew from the Republic to protest high taxation. The Mirgoshir system became the site of several major Clone Wars engagements. With the rise of the Empire, the independent-minded Agamarians sympathized with the Rebel Alliance, which led to a devastating Imperial crackdown on the city of Tondatha. Such brutal reprisals inspired more and more young Agamarians to join the Rebellion, including famed pilot Keyan Farlander. During the Yuuzhan Vong invasion, Agamar assisted in the transportation and resettlement of refugees, though the planet itself was eventually conquered by the alien intruders.

**Agao** A city on Bassadro, near the Agao Ranges of dormant volcanoes. The terrain was treacherous, with slippery, glassy surfaces and jagged shards. During the Clone Wars, the Separatists claimed that clone troopers wiped out the nearby town of Agao-Nir.

**Agapos** A line of ruling priest-princes that governed the Sunesi of Monor II. Agapos the Eighth proved ineffective in resisting Imperial influence on his world. Agapos the Ninth was a Force-sensitive philosopher whose writings were very influential in the New Republic. Mara Jade Skywalker once accompanied a minor diplomat from Coruscant to Monor II to witness the accession of the next priest-prince, Agapos the Tenth. It was at this event that Nom Anor surreptitiously infected Jade with coomb spores.

**Agar, Ereen** A skilled enforcer, this Zabrak female worked for the criminal Vurrha during the Galactic Civil War.

***Agave*-class picket ship** Part of the New Republic's New Class of starship designs, assigned to the Fifth Battle Group. These small 190-meter-long vessels were outfitted with acute sensors and stealth capabilities.

**Ag Circuit** A hyperspace route that connected notable agricultural production worlds in the Core. Salliche was the most powerful of producers on the circuit; most worlds were clients of Salliche Ag.

**agee** Tiny creatures, they existed in both flightless and winged varieties, the latter being particularly delicate.

**agent T-248** A potent chemical inhalant used for crowd control, it caused an intense reaction of nausea.

**Aggaba the Hutt** An assistant to Jemba the Hutt of the Offworld Mining Corporation. Aggaba was aboard the *Monument* during the ship's ill-fated voyage to Bandomeer when it was waylaid by pirates. After Jemba was killed, Aggaba and other Offworld workers defected to the Arcona Mineral Harvest Corporation.

***Aggregator*** An Imperial Interdictor cruiser, it was owned by High Admiral Teradoc and leased by Ysanne Isard in her quest to crush Rogue Squadron. The ship was sent to the Graveyard of Alderaan so that its gravity-well projectors could be used to prevent the X-wings from taking flight. Isard's scheme was working as planned until the unexpected appearance of the *Valiant,* a long-absent, droid-controlled Alderaan *Thranta*-class war cruiser. The *Valiant* collapsed the *Aggregator*'s shields, and to avoid further hull damage the Imperial ship jumped to hyperspace, leaving behind its TIE fighters and escape pods. Admiral Teradoc was furious with Isard for nearly destroying his ship.

**Aggressive ReConnaissance fighter** *See* ARC-170 starfighter.

***Aggressor* (1)** An Imperial Super Star Destroyer under the command of Admiral Roek, the *Aggressor* defended the Imperial withdrawal from the Corellian system during the New Republic retaking of the Core Worlds. The vessel became part of Grand Admiral Grunger's fleet; it was destroyed in infighting against Grand Admiral Pitta.

***Aggressor* (2)** An Imperial Star Destroyer used by Kirtan Loor and ISB Agent Mar Barezz.

**Aggressor assault fighter** Manufactured by Trilon, the fast and deadly Aggressor starfighter was the preferred model for assassin droid IG-88, who used it for his personal ship *IG-2000.*

***Aggressor*-class Star Destroyer** A capital warship employed by Tyber Zann and the Zann Consortium.

**Aggressor Wing** A New Republic Y-wing group led by Colonel Salm. Aggressor Wing suffered heavy casualties at Brentaal IV, but Salm was instrumental in the capture of Imperial fighter ace Soontir Fel, resulting in Salm's promotion to general. Aggressor Wing later participated in the mission to save Sate Pestage at Ciutric, flying cover sorties for Commando Team One led by Kapp Dendo.

**Agira, Nyrat** A trendy patron of the Outlander Club with a visible Zealot of Psusan tattoo surrounding her navel. Bounty hunter Kalyn Farnmir questioned Agira about the tattoo and the whereabouts of Psusan High Priest Scri Oscuro.

**agonizer** An experimental weapon developed by the Confederacy of Independent Systems during the Clone Wars, the agonizer micronic laser beam was keyed specifically to the physiology of clone troopers. It created intense physical pain and deadly sensory overload, yet no actual physical trauma.

***Agonizer*** An Imperial Star Destroyer commanded by Admiral Teren Rogriss. It escorted the 181st Fighter Group to Adumar during diplomatic negotiations that eventu-

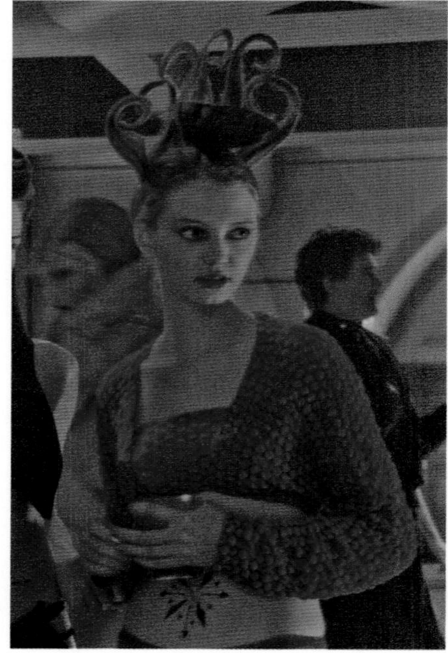

*Nyrat Agira*

ally swayed that planet to the New Republic's fold. The *Agonizer* intended to subjugate the planet, but took heavy damage from defensive New Republic forces.

**Agonizer-6** A hard-to-obtain torture device, the Agonizer-6 nerve disruptor consisted of a small black box mounted on a tripod.

***Agony of Tarkin, The*** A production of the Imperial Opera Company after the death of Grand Moff Tarkin. Mara Jade once attended this opera while she was the Emperor's Hand.

*Ahto City*

***Agony's Child*** A Yuuzhan Vong warship disabled at the Battle of Ithor by the combined firepower of New Republic and Imperial Remnant forces.

**Agorn, Sar** A wise, ancient Jedi Master whose personality was preserved in one of the few surviving Jedi Holocrons of his era. He resembled an amorphous blob suspended in a greenish mixture of gases.

**AGR** Allied Grain and Roughage, a huge agro-combine based on Corellia.

**a-grav** A shorthand term used to describe a starship or space station's artificial gravity systems.

**Agricultural Corps (AgriCorps)** A place for a young Jedi wanting to learn about the nature of living things and the importance of balance. Working in conjunction with the Republic's Agricultural Administration, the AgriCorps helped feed the galaxy's hungry. Most members were young students, ages 6 to 16. Though many Jedi respected the aims of the AgriCorps, younger students feared placement in the program—it often indicated that they lacked the talent to become full Jedi Knights. Indeed, Jedi students who "washed out" from training and failed to be assigned as Padawans to Jedi Knights or Masters were often assigned to the AgriCorps.

**Agridorn** A planet in the Galactic Republic represented by Senator Rhya Taloon during the Clone Wars.

**Agrilat** An area on the planet Corellia, it was known for its crystal swamps, which contained hot springs with updrafts, geysers that spouted boiling water, and sheer blades of crystalline underbrush. The bounty hunter Dengar was critically injured at Agrilat in a swoop bike race with Han Solo. After the race, Dengar was treated by Imperial physicians, then trained as an assassin.

**agrirobot** A simple, inexpensive droid, it was programmed to perform one function in the cycle of producing food. Among the available models were agrirobots that planted, sprayed, harvested, and packaged such edibles as fruits, vegetables, and grains.

**Agriworld-2079** The homeworld of the Skrilling species, discovered, owned, and named by the M'shinni.

**AG-series laser weapons** Articulated quad laser cannons developed by Corellian Engineering Corporation. The *Millennium Falcon* carried a pair of AG-2G quads, while the *Jade Shadow* had less powerful AG-1Gs.

**Aguarl III** The ocean-covered world of Aguarl III was home to a submerged Rebel base. The base was attacked by a wing of TIE bombers after the Empire learned its location from a Quarren spy.

**Aguilae** The adopted name of Khea Nkul, a female Jawa working in Mos Eisley. She and her Squib business partner Macemillian-winduarté ran the Jawa Traders shop.

**AH-50** A variety of high-intensity power cells manufactured by PowaTek and used aboard such vehicles as AT-ST walkers.

**Ahakista** A pleasant, remote planet said to contain a secret of vital importance to the Empire, kept within a classified outpost code-named the Hub. The Empire backed the upper classes of the Ahakistan natives to consolidate its power. Darth Vader and Rebel agents were dispatched there shortly after the Battle of Yavin to retrieve the secrets within the Hub.

***Ahazi*** A New Republic fleet tender, it was destroyed during the newly commissioned Fifth Fleet's live-fire training exercise code-named Hammerblow, killing all six aboard.

**Ahk'laht** A Noghri bodyguard to Leia Organa Solo. Ahk'laht created a diplomatic incident when, in protecting Leia, he struck down an intimidating Barabel ambassador. This, along with increasing pressure from Mon Mothma, caused Leia to cease traveling with Noghri guards.

**Ahr's Dive** One of the many taverns and restaurants once located in the Spacer Quarter of Aldera, on the planet Alderaan.

**Ahsoka** *See* Tano, Ahsoka.

**Ahto City** Capital city of Manaan, built above the surface of the water by the native Selkath to accommodate the many offworld visitors and inhabitants. About 4,000 years before the Battle of Yavin, the city became a primary exporter of kolto to both Jedi and Sith.

**Aia** A strange being from the moons of Bogden who met 10-year-old Boba Fett on Bogg 4. Aia was a skinny, human-like alien with white feathers instead of hair on his head. His long fingers were slightly webbed, and his face had a pinched, worried look, as if it had been shrunk. Bounty hunters attempted to nab Aia because he owed them credits, but young Boba covered his debts. Aia returned the favor by helping Boba find *Slave I.*

**Aic** This network of spies and assassins active around the time of the Clone Wars supplied intelligence to the Geonosians of the Stalgasin Hive, which was beneficial during the Battle of Geonosis.

**Aida** A lightly populated world formerly under Imperial control, Aida was located in the system of the same name near the Lomabu system. In an effort to trap Rebel Alliance agents, Imperial Governor Io Desnand shipped several hundred Wookiee females and cubs to the nearby planet of Lomabu III and planned to kill them during an attack designed to attract Rebel rescuers. The prisoners were eventually rescued by the bounty hunters Chenlambec and Tinian I'att.

**Aidus** A Rattataki guard who served Asajj Ventress during the Clone Wars.

**Aikhibba** Located in the system of the same name, Aikhibba was home to crime lord Spadda the Hutt. The system was one of the minor stopping points on the smugglers' Gamor Run. Smuggler Lo Khan once delivered a cargo of spice to Spadda from the royal governor of the Thokosia system.

**Ailon Nova Guard** A military unit in the Ailon system known for a martial prowess on par with the Imperial Royal Guard and the Mandalorians.

**Aing-Tii Monks** Mysterious Force-wielding monks who hailed from the distant Kathol sector. Aing-Tii did not believe the Force to have absolute light and dark sides, though they took a very definite view of slavery as evil and combatted it whenever encountered. Aing-Tii technology was very unusual, including a unique faster-than-light propulsion system that did not rely on hyperdrive. Aing-Tii Force disciplines included flow-walking, the ability to experience and leave imprints on different points in time. Contact with the galaxy at large was extremely limited, though Jorj Car'das and Jacen Solo both separately spent time among the Aing-Tii.

**Air-2 racing swoop** A TaggeCo heavy swoop bike with maneuvering flaps. Han Solo used an Air-2 to outrace slavers on Bonadan.

**Airam sector** An Outer Rim sector seen as a haven for smugglers, pirates, and other criminals. These denizens organized themselves along clan lines into a group called the Airam Traders, ruled by the Airam Council. The council supported the Rebel Alliance.

**airhook** A slight, one-being repulsorlift platform used as a personal transport, similar in design to a Trade Federation STAP.

**air rodeo** A popular live entertainment in the skies of Bespin, it consisted of stunt thranta riders doing tricks and maneuvers.

**airspeeder** Any of a variety of small repulsorlift vehicles meant to operate inside a planet's protective atmospheres at altitudes greater than those typically attainable by a landspeeder. Some airspeeders could easily exceed 900 kilometers per hour at heights of more than 250 kilometers. Models such as the T-16 skyhopper were often bought as sport vehicles or for family transportation, but young people frequently turned them into souped-up "hot rods." The Rebel Alliance also modified civilian airspeeders into specialized military vehicles, such as snowspeeders and sandspeeders.

**airsquid** A gas-bag, swarming predatory creature native to the skies of Bespin.

**AirStraeker** A Chiss starfighter with a drop-winged silhouette, armed with maser beam weapons on underwing emitter fans. The Chiss employed these vessels against the Killiks on Tenupe.

**air taxi** Any of a number of repulsorlift transports used on Coruscant to shuttle passengers through the planet's crowded cityscape. The most common air taxis were small, agile vehicles capable of traveling at great speeds. Operated by pilots who passed rigorous tests, the taxis were among the few vessels allowed to leave Coruscant's autonavigating skylanes. Such travel, however, required keen reflexes and reliance on advanced scanners to avoid collisions.

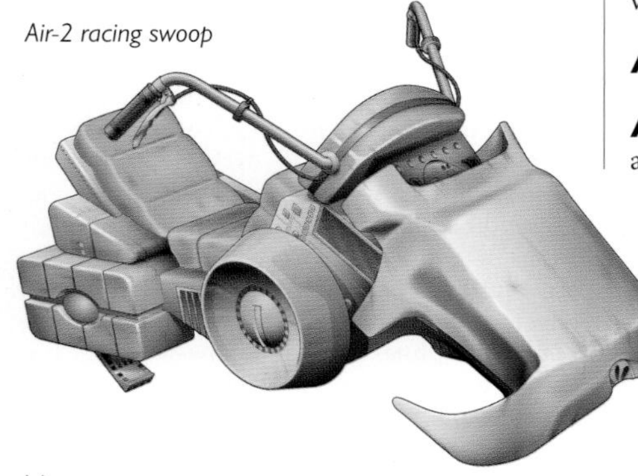

*Air-2 racing swoop*

*Aiwha*

**Airten, Sergeant** A burly member of the Bespin Wing Guard and a Rebel sympathizer.

**air whale** *See* aiwha.

**aiwha** A flying cetacean native to Naboo and also found in the oceans of Kamino. Aiwhas used their broad wings and powerful pectoral muscles to move in both air and water.

**Aiwha Squad** A Republic commando "pod" active during the Clone Wars. Aiwha Squad went on a mission to Garqi and befriended a young farm boy named Evan. Members served under Jedi General Traavis, whom the commandos killed when Order 66 was executed. The squad comprised Sarge, Zag, Tyto, and Di'kut.

**A.J.** A skilled Jedi whose ferocity and talent wielding paired lightsabers caused some concern among the masters of the Almas Academy. She was deemed free of the dark side's influence as she progressed through her trials.

**Aj^6** A head-worn cybernetic implant that allowed recipients to control computer systems directly with their brains. The brace included ports to accept additional knowledge cartridges. Lobot wore a BioTech Borg Construct Aj^6 cyborg unit on Cloud City.

*Aj^6*

**AJTD-6** A Jedi training droid that witnessed the fight between Jedi learners Obi-Wan Kenobi and Bruck Chun shortly before Qui-Gon Jinn arrived on Coruscant to find a Padawan apprentice.

**Ajuur the Hutt** The owner of a combat arena on Taris about 4,000 years before the Battle of Yavin.

**Akala, Eg'ros** A Caamasi on Coruscant whom young Leia Organa witnessed being mistreated on her first trip to the Imperial capital. With the help of her father, Bail, Leia was able to secure Eg'ros Akala's release.

**Akanah** *See* Pell, Akanah Norand.

**Akanseh** The Mon Calamari medical officer aboard the *FarStar.*

**Ak-Buz** A Weequay, he was commander of Jabba the Hutt's sail barge. Ak-Buz was murdered by the Anzati Dannik Jerriko, who hid his body in a garbage heap.

**Aken** A Ferroan pilot, she lived and worked on Zonama Sekot during the Yuuzhan Vong invasion. It was Aken's transport ship that ferried Han and Leia Organa Solo, as well as several Jedi Knights, to Zonama Sekot's surface after the planet reappeared near Coruscant.

**Aken** A Republic *Acclamator*-class transport escorted by Siri Tachi and Adi Gallia from Kamino to Geonosis at the start of the Clone Wars.

**Akh'laht** A Noghri of the clan Kihm'bar that brought the news of the Empire's deception to Rukh aboard the *Chimaera.*

**Akim's Munch** A streetside café in Mos Espa, Tatooine, often frequented by Sebulba.

**akk dog** A creature with large eyes and horns from Haruun Kal. Akk dogs were naturally disciplined, faithful, territorial, and devoted. Often domesticated as pets, akk dogs could also be bred for feral efficiency and trained for savagery. Their jaws could crush durasteel, and their hides were thick enough to stop a lightsaber. Muscular armored tails as long as their landspeeder-sized bodies whipped sinuously back and forth; their eyes were hard-shelled and lidless. When hunting, they worked in pairs—one feinted to catch the prey's attention so the other could deliver the death blow. Akk dogs bred for combat attacked several Jedi on Nar Shaddaa.

**Akkik** A Jawa henchman working for Jabba the Hutt, he often teamed up with the dim-witted Gamorrean Gorrt, who would shake down Mos Eisley shopkeepers for protection money.

**A'Kla, Elegos** A Caamasi Senator and trustant of the Caamasi Remnant. Senator A'Kla was long and lean with golden fur; purple striping on his shoulders rose up and back from the corners of his violet eyes. Seven years after the Battle of Endor, A'Kla helped Corran Horn rescue his wife, Mirax, from ex-Moff Leonia Tavira. Nine years later, he helped the New Republic survive the crisis instigated by the imposter of Grand Admiral Thrawn. Early in the Yuuzhan Vong invasion, A'Kla was one of the first Senators to agree with Leia Organa Solo that the Yuuzhan Vong posed a real threat to the New Republic.

He accompanied Leia, Jaina Solo, and Danni Quee on a fact-finding mission to the Outer Rim. When A'kla volunteered to visit the Yuuzhan Vong on Dubrillion to learn their intentions, Shedao Shai took him under his wing, teaching him the Yuuzhan Vong way—including the particular delights of the Embrace of Pain—and learning about the New Republic from A'kla in turn. In the end, Shedao Shai betrayed A'kla: He killed the Senator and prepared his corpse in the appropriate Yuuzhan Vong manner, returning the artistically decorated skeleton to Corran Horn on Ithor.

Elegos A'Kla

**A'Kla, Releqy** The daughter of Elegos A'Kla who took his position in the Senate after his death. She was a pacifist who urged peaceful resolution with the Yuuzhan Vong. She was appointed Minister of State in Cal Omas's office.

**Akobi, Commander** An Imperial officer during the subjugation of Ralltiir and friend of stormtrooper TK-622. Akobi harbored great regret for the Imperial actions on Ralltiir, a fact he kept secret until after he was reassigned to the Death Star and suffered injuries from a Rebel saboteur. As he convalesced, he admitted his guilt to TK-622 moments before the Death Star exploded at the Battle of Yavin.

**Ak-rev** A Weequay musician from Sriluur and drummer for the Max Rebo Band. Ak-rev studied in a monastery devoted to the Weequay god of thunder. After Jabba's death, he and fellow drummer Umpass-stay fled for Mos Eisley but were ambushed by Tusken Raiders. Ak-rev was beaten to death.

Ak-rev

**Akrit'tar** The planet Akrit'tar housed a penal colony. One of Han Solo's former smuggling associates, Tregga, was imprisoned there and sentenced to life at hard labor after being caught with a smuggled cargo of chak-root. Rogue Squadron pilot Tycho Celchu was brainwashed and imprisoned by the Empire on the long-buried underground *Lusankya* Super Star Destroyer, then shipped to Akrit'tar. He escaped after three months.

**A/KT** *See* Ayelixe/Kronbing Textiles.

**Akura, Jae "Storm"** An Imperial pilot and loyal member of Gunner Yage's squadron in the time of Roan Fel's empire.

**Alaala** A Killik nest on the moon of Zvbo orbiting Qoribu.

**Alain** The hardy natives of the cold, harsh planet Von-Alai. As they developed technologically, the Alain ravaged their environment with global-temperature-altering practices. Von-Alai became overpoluted, forcing the Alain to live in residential platforms above the toxic sludge.

**Alain, Private** An idealistic Rebel trooper aboard the *Tantive IV,* valued by the Alliance for his connections in the Outer Rim.

**Alakatha** A primary moon of K'vath 5 in the K'vath system, Alakatha served as the site of Corran and Mirax Horn's honeymoon.

***Alamania*** This New Republic warship was one of many that were commandeered by Senators trying to flee the Yuuzhan Vong conquest of Coruscant. Despite the inevitability of Coruscant's fall, many New Republic military officers decried the Senate's appropriation of military ships to escape the capital planet, especially knowing that thousands—if not millions—of civilians were stranded there.

**Alani and Eritha** Twin sisters born on Apsolon during a totalitarian regime. Their father, Ewane, was a political dissident who spent much of their childhood in prison. When new elections overturned the government, Ewane was elected planetary leader of New Apsolon. A short time later, he was assassinated, and the twins requested that the Jedi Knights seek out their father's killer. Much duplicity surrounded Alani's and Eritha's interactions with Jedi Knights Qui-Gon Jinn, Tahl, and Obi-Wan Kenobi as they aspired to political power.

**Alaphoe Gardens** A wondrous tourist destination on the planet Procopia, it consisted of gardens, a concert hall, riding stables, a bathhouse, and the Glass Palace.

**Alaric, King** The intelligent and peaceful leader of planet Thustra and close friend of Yoda, whom he had known for 200 years. King Alaric's subjects loved him, and his influence extended beyond his own planet. The governments of the surrounding systems looked to him for leadership and guidance. Yoda regarded him as a strong and brilliant strategist. During the Clone Wars, Alaric sided with the Confederacy because he viewed the Galactic Senate as corrupt. After a parley with Yoda, he took Yoda and the Padawan Cal prisoner. He attempted to kill Yoda, but Yoda killed him instead. Alaric died a martyr, which led Thustra and its allies to join the Confederacy.

**Alaris Prime** A small forest moon long concealed by a large gas giant in the outer orbits of the Kashyyyk system. Mysteriously, the huge Alaris forests contained wroshyr trees, and though the Wookiees had legends to explain how the trees migrated the thousands of kilometers across the void of space between the two worlds, no theory satisfactorily explained the coincidence. The Trade Federation sought control of the moon and disputed the Wookiee claim of ownership in a number of battles, which continued through the Clone Wars.

King Alaric

**Alashan** A seemingly dead planet with remnants of a lost civilization, the planet Alashan protected exploration of its ruins with powerful blasts from its volcanoes that could knock ships out of orbit.

**alasl bowl** A form of rare primitive craftwork by the Sand People of Tatooine created from deposits of unusual stone.

**Alater, Captain Osted** The Imperial naval officer who discovered Barab I, homeworld of the Barabels. A city and spaceport, Alater-ka, was built after the Empire took control of the planet.

**Alater-ka** The only city ever built on Barab I, home planet of the Barabels. Alater-ka was constructed by Captain Osted Alater to facilitate the Empire's needs on the planet and to help the Empire protect the Barabels from exploitation at the hands of hunters. Alater-ka was primarily a spaceport.

*Senator Nee Alavar*

**Alavar, Senator Nee** Lorrdian representative of the Kanz sector in the Galactic Senate. A keen interpreter of body language, she kept hers hidden beneath heavy robes. Alavar lent her signature to the Petition of the Two Thousand, formally censuring Chancellor Palpatine for his policies during the Clone Wars.

**alazhi** A key ingredient in bacta. Alazhi contained gelatinous, red bacterial particles grown from xoorzi fungus. During the Clone Wars, a false alazhi shortage, engineered by the Trade Federation and the bacta cartel, caused bacta prices to skyrocket.

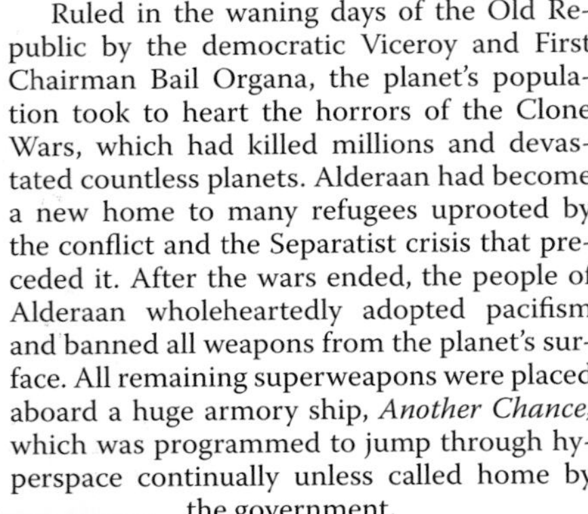

*Alderaan*

**Albanin sector** The Outer Rim sector that included the Barab system. It was the last Republic world Outbound Flight visited before entering the Unknown Regions.

**AL-BRT-34-X3** A massive BRT-series computer mainframe installed at the University of Calamar on Esseles that discovered subversive Rebel activity among the student body and began to surreptitiously help the movement, effectively becoming a Rebel operative. It was nicknamed Albert.

**alcopay** A beast of burden used by the Oldtimers who settled Nam Chorios, it was susceptible to disease and parasites.

**Alcorn, Tomay** *See* Oryon.

**Alder** An Acherin man, husband to Halle, who welcomed Clive Flax when he was investigating the background of the freedom fighter known as Flame shortly after the Clone Wars. Clive gained their confidence by announcing that he was looking for Alder's sister, Vira, who had died in the fighting that engulfed the planet's population.

**Alder, Cal** A top-notch scout for the Rebel Alliance, he was from Kal'Shebbol in the Kathol sector. Cal Alder served with Major Bren Derlin for many years and patrolled the outer perimeter of Echo Base on Hoth prior to the fierce battle with Imperial forces there.

**Aldera** The gleaming capital city of Alderaan, home of the Royal Palace of Alderaan, Aldera Univeral Medcenter, and the renowned Alderaan University.

**Alderaan** A peaceful world, the planet was close to being the galaxy's paradise, and certainly was its heart. Renowned poet Hari Seldona wrote of its "calm, vast skies . . . oceans of grass . . . lovely flying thrantas" in an elegy to her planet after Alderaan was destroyed in a demonstration of the power of the Empire.

*Cal Alder*

It was a place of high culture and education, thanks to Alderaan University. The natives loved the land and worked with it or around it, rather than change or destroy it. Its vast plains supported more than 8,000 subspecies of grass and even more numerous wildflowers. Artists planted huge grass paintings up to dozens of kilometers square that could be seen only from flying observation boats.

Alderaan was famous for its cuisine, based on the delicious meat of grazers and nerfs along with native exotic herbs, flowers, and grains. The calm breezes carried large thrantas, which looked like flying manta rays and bore passengers safely strapped on top. Although there were no oceans, the planet had an ice-rimmed polar sea and thousands of lakes and gentle waterways plied by vacation barges. Among Alderaan's most imposing sights were the subterranean Crevasse City and the Castle Lands, towering abandoned cities made by the long-vanished insect species, the Killiks.

Ruled in the waning days of the Old Republic by the democratic Viceroy and First Chairman Bail Organa, the planet's population took to heart the horrors of the Clone Wars, which had killed millions and devastated countless planets. Alderaan had become a new home to many refugees uprooted by the conflict and the Separatist crisis that preceded it. After the wars ended, the people of Alderaan wholeheartedly adopted pacifism and banned all weapons from the planet's surface. All remaining superweapons were placed aboard a huge armory ship, *Another Chance,* which was programmed to jump through hyperspace continually unless called home by the government.

As the New Order of Emperor Palpatine took shape, Alderaan supported the growing opposition to his rule. Mon Mothma of Chandrila credited Bail Organa with envisioning the structure of the Rebel Alliance. A tip from Organa allowed Mothma to escape Palpatine's clutches with just minutes to spare. Giving up his own seat in the Senate and returning to Alderaan, Organa worked hard and surreptitiously to offer support to the growing Rebellion. His adopted daughter, Princess Leia Organa, also a Senator, began to run secret missions for the Rebellion. But before Alderaan could fully prepare its defenses and officially join the Alliance, the Empire wiped out the planet in a flash with a single blast from its new weapon, the Death Star, as a captive Leia looked on in horror. All that was left of the beauty and humanity that was Alderaan was an asteroid field, now fittingly called the Graveyard.

The destruction of Alderaan had a great polarizing effect on the galaxy. Worlds that attempted to remain neutral in the Galactic Civil War soon found themselves taking sides—those terrified by the act of Imperial brutality and hoping to avoid similar reprisals sided with the Empire; those offended by Alderaan's destruction began to openly or covertly support the Alliance. Many residents of Alderaan who were offplanet when their homeworld was de-

*Alderaan*

stroyed were quick to join the Rebellion, though a few became fanatical supporters of the Empire, blaming Alderaan's involvement with the Rebellion for its destruction. Survivors who wished to continue a peaceful existence, and not be involved in combat, were transported to New Alderaan, an Alliance safe world.

***Alderaan*** Princess Leia Organa named her personal space yacht for the destroyed planet where she grew up.

**Alderaan Alliance** Survivors of the destroyed planet who banded together to outwardly denounce the Empire's use of force. They compiled a list of all the known designers and developers of the Death Star project, using this data to bring the developers out of hiding to stand trial for their crimes.

**Alderaan Biotics** A hydroponics company that helped supply Alderaan with foodstuffs and other organic supplies. It once maintained an operational facility on Borleias, which was abandoned in the wake of Alderaan's destruction. It was discovered years later by Evir Derricote, who rerouted a large amount of Imperial money to reestablish the site. He used it to produce the initial strains of the Krytos virus until Borleias was liberated by Rogue Squadron after a pair of engagements. Alderaan Biotics later became the New Republic's primary manufacturing facility for the creation of rylca.

**Alderaan Expatriate Network (AEN)** A pro–Rebel Alliance newsnet founded by Alderaanian reporters after the destruction of their homeworld.

**Alderaan furry moth** Now vanished from the galaxy along with the planet that nurtured it, this large-winged flying insect nested amid bushy flowers. The larvae of the Alderaan furry moth were armored caterpillars more than a meter long that burrowed under the ground and fed on swollen tubers. The caterpillars lived for a dozen years before sealing themselves in thick-walled cocoons and emerging transformed.

Agrippa Aldrete

**Alderaanian flare-wing** A butterfly-like insect native to Alderaan that was noted for the vibrant colors of the wings on each of its subspecies.

**Alderaanian Oversea** An architectural style that featured stilt-mounted cities over marshy or aquatic environments, like Tipoca City on Kamino.

**Alderaan Royal Engineers** One of the oldest starship-manufacturing yards in the galaxy, famed for constructing luxury yachts and pleasure vessels. Alderaan Royal Engineers also created a number of starfighter and capital warship designs and components. It faded from prominence toward the end of the Republic and ceased operations after the destruction of Alderaan.

Aleena Podracer Ratts Tyerell

**Alderaan University** An esteemed institute of higher learning renowned throughout the galaxy, it was founded as a school of philosophy by Republic thinker Collus. Based in the capital city of Aldera, the university had many satellite "pods" on other planets.

**Aldo Spach** A binary star system known for the Aldo Spachian comet that traveled between the two stars, sprouting four tails pulled by the stars' influence.

**Aldraig IV** An industrialized planet in the Aldraig system, located in the Core Worlds. The Empire wiped out large tracts of pristine forest to make room for an AT-AT production facility and TIE fighter hull assembly plant there.

**Aldrete, Agrippa** A former member of the Galactic Senate who later served as an aide to Senator Bail Antilles from Alderaan. He shared his duties with Liana Merian.

**Aldrete, Alya** An Alderaanian noblewoman who discreetly used her wealth and position to aid the early Rebel Alliance. She established a network of smugglers and pirates in the Core and Deep Core to map a system of reliable hyperspace lanes. Her smugglers and maps proved essential for Bail Organa's plan to destroy the Imperial operation code-named Sarlacc Project within the Deep Core.

**Aldrete, Celana** An aide to Bail Organa during the early days of the Galactic Empire.

**Aleco** A near-human distinguished by her red hair and pointed ears, she was one of the handful of Jedi Masters who led the Jedi enclave on Dantooine in the years following the Great Sith War. She remained on the enclave's leadership team until the Jedi Civil War broke out. It was believed that Master Aleco was killed in the conflict.

**Aleema** *See* Keto, Aleema.

**Aleen** An Inner Rim world that remained neutral during the Clone Wars, Aleen was the home planet of the Aleena species.

**Aleena** The diminutive native inhabitants of Aleen spread throughout the galaxy as scouts, explorers, and tourists. They were known for extremely fast reflexes developed avoiding such dangers as the predatory sagcatchers. Well-known Aleena included Podracing champ Ratts Tyerell and Jedi Master Tsui Choi.

***Aleph*-class starfighter** Nicknamed the Twee, this Galactic Alliance starfighter was produced by Sienar Fleet Systems. Characterized as flying tanks, these heavily armored two-crew craft were designed in the last months of the Yuuzhan Vong War as a one-to-one match for the Yuuzhan Vong coralskipper. They relied on their thick hulls and shields powered by overbuilt generators. Weapons included two turrets, one on either side of the ball-shaped cockpit, each equipped with quad-linked lasers—lasers that could be unlinked to fire an unpredictable spray pattern to confound coralskipper voids. Forward were the explosives tubes, one for concussion missiles and one for proton torpedoes.

**Alfex Cargo Stacks** This collection of storage facilities in Brentaal's capital city of Cormond was actually a front for Black Sun operations.

**Alfi** A Jedi Knight stationed at the Jedi training facility on Ossus during the conflict between the Galactic Alliance and the Confederation, Alfi was killed when Galactic Alliance Guard Major Serpa took control of the facility. He was shot in his dorm room before he could act to defend the younglings in his charge.

**algae cylinder** This component of a starship's air circulation system scrubbed air over a colony of algae that consumed excess carbon dioxide and produced oxygen as a byproduct. Algae cylinders were prone to clogging, and needed regular maintenance and replacement.

**Algar** *See* Algara II.

**Algara II** The second planet in the Algar system, best known for its cumbersome bureaucracy and its mood-enhancing drugs, Algarine torve weed and zwil. Home to the Xan species. Algara II was also the base of operations for Wing Tip Theel, an expert computer slicer and former associate of Han Solo and Lando Calrissian.

**Algeran Faction** This anti-Imperial group based on the planet Esseles violently opposed the ascension of Palpatine to the position of Emperor. It caused widespread damage and loss of life during the early years of the Empire.

**Algic Current** A wide-ranging ocean current on Chad III, the Chadra-Fan homeworld, the Algic Current flowed from the planet's equator almost to its arctic circle. Tsaelkes migrated with the current each year.

**Algnadesh Ship Graveyards** A fabled collection of vanished starships.

**Algowinn, Kel** An ancient Sith apprentice who trained at the Sith Academy on Korriban four millennia before the Battle of Yavin. Kel harbored doubts about the true nature of the Sith, which he admitted to his comrades, some of whom were actually Jedi Knights who had infiltrated the Academy. The Jedi later implored Algowinn to leave, and he found himself torn between loyalties. When the Sith students eventually turned against the Jedi, Algowinn was killed in the fighting.

**Algrann** A technical officer, he was assigned to the Outbound Flight Project about five years after the Battle of Naboo.

**AlGray, Lady** A Hapan who was part of the royal family of the Relephon Moons during the years surrounding the Yuuzhan Vong War. She chose Aleson Gray to be her Duch'da.

**Al'har system** The system containing the planet Haruun Kal, found at the Gevarno Loop. During the Clone Wars, the Galactic Republic tried to get the support of the local Korunnai to gain control of the Gevarno Loop. Haruun Kal was the only habitable planet in the system, and it orbited just within an asteroid belt believed to have been the remnants of one or more inner planets. Beyond the asteroids, several gas giants made up the system's outer planets.

**Ali-Alann** A Jedi Master and caretaker of the nursery within the Jedi Temple, where he watched over the younglings. Young Obi-Wan Kenobi helped save Ali-Alann from a trapped turbolift when the sinister Xanatos sabotaged the Jedi Temple. Ali-Alann then posed as Qui-Gon Jinn to feed disinformation to Xanatos's spy droid. Ali-Alann perished the night of Order 66, when clone troopers led by Darth Vader attacked the Jedi Temple.

**Alien Combine** Also known as the Alien League, this secret organization of nonhumanoid species was formed to protest unfair treatment and misconduct by Imperial forces on Coruscant after the Battle of Endor. The aliens were frightened because so many of their number were disappearing. They did not realize that forces of Imperial General Evir Derricote were rounding up aliens for experimental use in the Krytos project—a plan by Ysanne Isard, the director of Imperial Intelligence, to infect the alien populace. She hoped to then bankrupt the Rebellion when it tried to buy enough bacta to cure them all. The Combine, reacting out of fear, suspected that Gavin Darklighter and his fellow Rogue Squadron members were out to harm them and brought the squadron members before the League for trial. Imperial forces attacked the hideout, and a bloody battle ensued. The Combine then realized that the Rogues were on their side, helped them to escape, and later joined the Rebel cause to liberate Coruscant.

**Alien League** *See* Alien Combine.

**Alien Protection Zone** An area of Coruscant's Imperial City set aside for the habitation of nonhuman labor during the New Order.

**Alima, Captain** This Imperial officer commanded the Star Destroyer *Conquest* during an attack against a herd ship on the planet Ithor. He forced the High Priest Momaw Nadon to reveal secrets of Ithorian technology to the Empire. Later demoted, Alima was tasked with finding the droids C-3PO and R2-D2 in Mos Eisley. He once again encountered Nadon, living in exile on Tatooine. Nadon revealed Alima's incompetence to Imperial superiors, resulting in Alima's death. True to the Ithorian law of planting two for every one plant harvested, Nadon created two clones of Captain Alima and raised them as his sons.

**Alion** One of the most heavily guarded planets of the New Republic, known for its potent neurotoxins.

**Ali-Vor** The Jedi Master to Padawan learner Rann I-Kanu, he made regular trips to Naboo. Shortly before the Battle of Naboo, Master Ali-Vor led a team of investigators to Naboo to locate the source of illegally exported creatures.

**Alkhara** Centuries ago, this fierce bandit was the first usurper to occupy Tatooine's B'omarr monastery, which most notably became the palace of Jabba the Hutt. Alkhara once allied himself with Tusken Raiders to wipe out a small police garrison, but then butchered the Sand People who had helped him, thereby kicking off the long-lasting blood feud between the Tusken Raiders and humans. Alkhara stayed for 34 years, expanding the monastery and adding dungeons and underground chambers.

**Alkharan bandit** Named for the notorious bandit who roamed Tatooine, Alkharan bandits were Tatooinians forced from their home by Sand People. They waged a constant war with the Tusken Raiders, and pillaged local villages and moisture farms for supplies.

**Alk'Lellish III** The homeworld of the ketrann, a dangerous carnivore. Governor Wilek Nereus of Bakura owned a set of the ketrann's four white fangs.

**Allana** The secret daughter of Tenel Ka and Jacen Solo, born about 36 years after the Battle of Yavin. Tenel Ka and Jacen protected Allana's true parentage from the public eye of Hapan society, and Jacen could have only limited contact with the young girl. He loved her deeply, and his goal of protecting her and making the galaxy a better place for her motivated much of his turn to the dark side and transformation into Darth Caedus. After the final battle between Caedus and the Jedi Order, Tenel Ka reported that Allana had died in a nanovirus attack aboard the *Dragon Queen* in order to protect her daughter's true identity behind the alias Amelia. Allana proved to be Force-sensitive and underwent training at the Jedi Academy with Han and Leia Organa Solo serving as her guardians.

**Allara** A human girl in a group of Jedi younglings taken prisoner by General Grievous. The younglings were brought to Gentes, where Grievous hoped to combine their potential dark side energy with Geonosian technology, but the intervention of a group of Jedi targeting Grievous for assassination allowed them to escape.

**Allashane, Jess** A veteran Rebel Alliance trooper who served at Echo Base on Hoth and was trained to counter Imperial tactics in cold-weather environments.

***Allegiance*** A Super Star Destroyer, it was the Imperial command ship at the Battle of Mon Calamari. The *Allegiance* was destroyed in an audacious maneuver by the *Emancipator,* a captured Star Destroyer commanded by Lando Calrissian. The New Republic also named an *Imperial*-class Star Destroyer *Allegiance.*

***Allegiant*** A New Republic MC80B cruiser that served as the base of operations for Nomad Squadron in the Meridian sector during the Yuuzhan Vong War.

**allergy paste** A foul-tasting yet edible paste designed to prevent allergic reactions to a wide assortment of substances, from airborne pollutants or pollens to insect venom.

**alleth** A species of carnivorous plant native to Ithor. Larger specimens were capable of killing and eating rodents.

**All-Human Free-For-All** A gladiatorial contest held regularly in the Victory Forum in the city of Dying Slowly on Jubilar. In the event, four humans would fight to the death in the arena, with the last combatant standing declared the winner. The fighters were usually plucked from criminal ranks, and the winner was often given some form of freedom. When Han Solo was about 17 years old, he survived the Free-For-All after being caught cheating at cards.

**Alliance assault frigate** *See* assault frigate.

**Alliance Fleet Command** The body of authority over the Rebel Alliance fleet, headed by Admiral Ackbar. Beneath it were four main branches of command: the Line Admirals, Starfighter Command, Fleet Intelligence, and Ordnance and Support.

**Alliance High Command** The commanding authority of the Rebel Alliance, headed by Mon Mothma, who embodied the roles of Commander in Chief and Chief of Staff. Beneath her was a staff of Supreme Allied Commanders, which included Fleet Command, Ordnance and Supply, Starfighter Command, Support Services, Intelligence, Spec Forces Command, and Sector Command. This body eventually evolved into a military policy organization within the New Republic. Key members of Alliance High Command included Generals Jan Dodonna, Carlist Rieekan, and Crix Madine; Admiral Ackbar; and Senator Garm Bel Iblis.

**Alliance Intelligence** The nervous system of the Rebel Alliance. Through its activities, the Alliance was kept apprised of the Empire's activities and intentions. The Chief of Intelligence reported directly to the Chief of Staff and oversaw three main branches: Intentions, Operations, and Counter-Intelligence. For much of the Galactic Civil War, General Airen Cracken headed Alliance Intelligence.

**Alliance masternav** This computer system was developed to track the orbits of planets within known systems. Its reliability depended on the quality of its most recent software and updated data.

**Alliance of Free Planets** An interim phase between the paramilitary revolution force of the Rebel Alliance and the legitimate ruling government, the New Republic. The Alliance of Free Planets existed for only a month to organize worlds petitioning for inclusion in the new galactic government.

**Alliance of Twelve** The founding leadership of the Peace Brigade—Yuuzhan Vong collaborators—which expanded to become the Ylesian Senate.

**Alliance to Restore the Republic** The formal name for the Rebel Alliance, begun as a union between the scattered, ragtag resistance groups and the exiled leaders and nobility of the Senate. During the early days of the Empire, disorganized resistance had waged battles against the New Order, but lacked the galactic scope or unity to truly affect Palpatine's regime. Generally lost to the historical record were the actions of one man known as the Starkiller, who brought together key Senators like Bail Organa of Alderaan, Garm Bel Iblis of Corellia, and Mon Mothma of Chandrila to unite the various groups into the Alliance. Though the Starkiller was actually carrying forth the will of the Emperor to group his greatest enemies into one location for a single strike, he ended up helping in the founding of the organization that would spell the Empire's doom.

The Alliance truly formed with the Corellian Treaty: Three major resistance groups agreed to ally within the Rebellion. They swore to fight either to the death, or to the end of the Empire. Mon Mothma was installed as Supreme Commander of the Alliance, along with her Advisory Council. While it may have seemed Mothma had unchecked powers over the Rebellion, every two years Alliance representatives had to vote on her continued role as leader.

The more the Empire tightened its grip on the people of the galaxy, the harder the Alliance fought. As it grew, so did its arsenal. To combat the Imperial starfleet, the Alliance's hotshot pilots made do with battle-worn yet effective craft like X-wing and Y-wing starfighters. The joining of the Mon Calamari people with the Alliance bolstered the Rebellion's ranks, and brought badly needed capital ships into the fleet. The Bothans contributed their expansive spy network, giving the Alliance the essential intelligence needed to wage civil war.

Scores of Rebel bases were established throughout the galaxy, with the Alliance High Command base constantly on the move. During the course of the Galactic Civil War, it inhabited bases on Dantooine, Yavin 4, Thila, Hoth, Golrath, and Arbra as well as being posted with the fleet. The Rebel Alliance scored a major victory over the Empire by using stolen technical plans to formulate an attack strategy capable of destroying the Empire's most fearsome weapon: the Death Star. During the next three years, the core group of Alliance commanders fled from base to base, constantly eluding the Empire's forces.

Finally, about a year after a major defeat at Hoth, the Rebellion was poised to make an all-out strike against the Empire. The opportunity came at the Battle of Endor. Despite it being an Imperial trap, the Rebels persevered. The conflict ended with the death of Emperor Palpatine, the destruction of the second Death Star, the scattering of the Imperial fleet, and the end of the New Order's long reign of oppression.

With the Galactic Civil War over, the Alliance to Restore the Republic ceased, becoming—for a time—the Alliance of Free Planets. This eventually paved the way for the New Republic. Many of the heroes of the Alliance again braved remnants of the Empire and other threats and became heroes of the New Republic as well.

*Alliance to Restore the Republic*

**Alliance Veterans Victory Association (AVVA)** Somewhere between a club for retired officers and an armed forces reserve, the AVVA was led by Bren Derlin. It published the news bulletin *Fleet Watch.*

**Allic, Lord** The owner of a casino at the Bubble-cliffs of Nezmi and a Black Nebula associate of Prince Dequc. Of an unknown species, Lord Allic walked on four legs, which carried his large bulbous body behind him.

**Allie, Stass** Jedi Master, accomplished healer, and cousin of Adi Gallia. Stass Allie served as an adviser to Supreme Chancellor Palpatine during the Separatist crisis, and fought at the Battle of Geonosis that marked the start of the Clone Wars. During the conflict, she ascended to the rank of Jedi Master and sat on the Jedi Council. While on a speeder bike patrol on planet Saleucami, her clone troopers killed her as part of Order 66.

**Allied Tion** The central of the three sectors—along with the Cronese Mandate and the Tion Hegemony—that made up the Tion Cluster. The capital world was Jaminere, and the sector included the worlds of Lianna, Lorrad, and Cadinth. The Allied Tion Historical Society was founded to preserve the ancient, pre-Republic historical artifacts of the Tion Cluster.

**Alliga** Homeworld of the Holwuff species and allied to the Confederacy of Independent Systems during the Clone Wars.

**All Planets Market** A large, open market located on the planet Coruscant during the last century of the Galactic Republic. Found in a plaza near the Senate's Great Rotunda, it provided the natives of Coruscant with fruits and vegetables from planets throughout the galaxy.

**All Planets Relief Fund** An initiative of Supreme Chancellor Palpatine prior to the start of the Clone Wars. It allowed for any planet in peril to petition the Senate for funds through one central account, bypassing the bureaucratic slowdown for relief to troubled worlds.

**All Science Research Academy** Founded on Yerphonia, it was one of the most prestigious educational facilities dedicated to the study of the physical sciences. Granta Omega is believed to have graduated from the academy shortly before the Battle of Naboo.

**All-Species Replica Droid** An evolution in human replica droids (HRDs) developed by ODT scientists to provide mechanical bodies for certain alien species as a form of immortality.

**"All Stars Burn as One"** The official anthem of the Galactic Republic.

**All Terrain Advance Raider (AT-AR walker)** A variant of the All Terrain Scout Transport, the Imperial AT-AR was smaller and faster, but armed with only a single laser cannon. The Empire used AT-AR walkers on Hoth, Cilpar, and Jarnollen.

*All Terrain Advanced Raider (AT-AR walker)*

**All Terrain Anti Aircraft (AT-AA walker)** A fast-moving mobile anti-aircraft weapon that was the scourge of Rebel flying units. Developed by Rothana Heavy Engineering in the early days of the Galactic Empire, preliminary AT-AA designs were in the works when the Clone Wars were still being waged. The four-legged assault craft had a squat gait, supporting the heavy weight of a multiordnance flak pod turret mounted on its back. The walker also carried complex electronic countermeasure devices that could scramble missile guidance systems, lowering the risk of incoming missile strikes. A complete lack of defensive weaponry limited its role on the battlefield, ensuring that it was rarely deployed alone.

*All Terrain Armored Transport (AT-AT walker)*

*All Terrain Anti Aircraft (AT-AA walker)*

**All Terrain Armored Transport (AT-AT walker)** A combat and transport vehicle, the immense four-legged "walker" was as much a psychological weapon of terror as an actual weapon of destruction. More than 15 meters tall and 20 meters long, this nearly unstoppable behemoth looked like a giant legendary beast from the dark side. Despite its lumbering gait, it could stride across a flat battlefield at up to 60 kilometers an hour and lob heavy laserfire from the cannons mounted beneath its "chin" while providing supporting fire from two medium blasters on each side of its head. It could off-load 40 heavily armed zip-line-equipped troopers and five speeder bikes—or other weapons—from assault ramps. The AT-AT was the Empire's ideal battlefield vehicle.

These heavy assault vehicles had both the heft and the mechanics to march through most defenses. Their thick armor plating shielded them from all but the heaviest of artillery fire. Their heads could rotate to provide the commanding officer, gunner, and pilot a sweeping view of any battlefield from the command deck. AT-ATs were usually among the first vehicles to enter a combat zone. Their heavy, stomping feet caused the ground to shake even before they appeared, frightening and demoralizing an enemy.

The basic walker design was introduced on the battlefield during the Clone Wars, with early models such as the AT-TE, AT-HE, and AT-AP proving successful. General Maximilian Veers championed the continued refinement of the walker design to produce the finished AT-AT. These vehicles were chiefly responsible for the rout of the Rebels during the Empire's assault on Echo Base on Hoth.

**All Terrain Attack Pod (AT-AP walker)** A two-legged armored Republic combat vehicle also known as a pod walker, first deployed during the Clone Wars. Essentially a mobile piece of artillery, the AT-AP featured heavy cannons and a retractable third leg to brace the walker during firing. The AT-AP saw action on Kashyyyk, Felucia, and elsewhere during the Clone Wars.

**All Terrain Construction Transport (AT-CT walker)** A variant of the two-legged AT-ST walker design, but fitted with welders and other construction equipment rather than weapons.

*All Terrain Attack Pod (AT-AP walker)*

*All Terrain Experimental Transport (AT-XT walker)*

**All Terrain Experimental Transport (AT-XT walker)** A two-legged assault walker developed during the Clone Wars that employed faster movement than its six-legged contemporaries. The AT-XT's main weapons were a long-range heavy laser cannon and a secondary proton mortar. Developed by Rothana Heavy Engineering and produced at the Kuat Drive Yards facilities, the AT-XT did not go into full mass production during the Clone Wars because engineers were constantly revising its design. It became the test bed for the AT-ST design.

**All Terrain Heavy Enforcer (AT-HE walker)** Developed on the successes of the AT-TE, the AT-HE was a heavy combat walker similar in appearance to an AT-AT, but larger and with more powerful laser cannons.

**All Terrain Ion Cannon (AT-IC walker)** An uncommon variation on the basic AT-AT design, the AT-IC resembled a standard walker but with half of its body space dedicated to supporting a massive ion cannon. The Empire employed the AT-IC for the mobile defense of strategic Imperial locations.

**All Terrain Kashyyyk Transport (AT-KT walker)** The Kashyyyk deployment variant of the AT-ST, designed to root out insurgents and enemy scouts from terrain that offered heavy cover. Rather than acting as an antivehicle platform, the AT-KT (sometimes referred to as a "Hunter" scout transport, or AT-STh, when deployed on other worlds) was specifically an antipersonnel walker, with heavy weapons designed to fire through foliage, light bunkers, and camouflage. Moreover, the vehicle's weapons were used primarily to stun targets (since dead Wookiees made poor slaves), ensuring that even the most rebellious insurgents lived to serve the Empire as laborers.

*All Terrain Open Transport (AT-OP walker)*

**All Terrain Open Transport (AT-OT walker)** Kuat Drive Yards developed this basic overland troop carrier. The Grand Army of the Republic used these open-bed cargo walkers. The AT-OT was not recommended for direct combat. Though armed with laser cannons, it was better suited for behind-friendly-lines battlefield replenishment. It could carry 34 clone troopers in standard configuration, but the open nature of its flatbed allowed for more troops to pile in when missions required it.

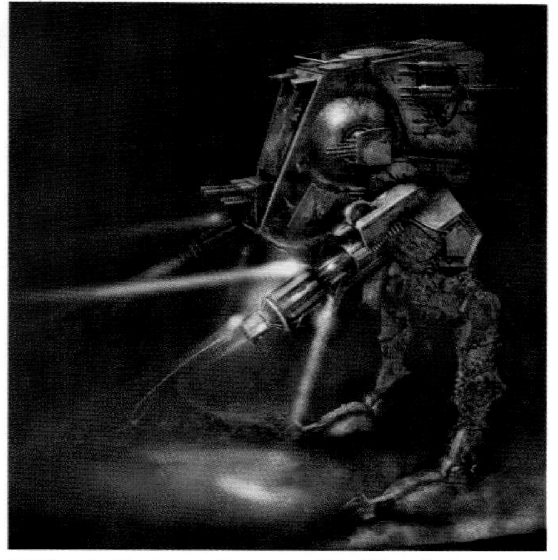

*All Terrain Kashyyyk Transport (AT-KT walker)*

**All Terrain Personal Transport (AT-PT walker)** This small weapons system was the precursor of the Imperial walker. Developed by the Old Republic as a personal weapons platform for ground soldiers, it was ingeniously designed for its day and was intended to be a major component of Republic ground forces. However, nearly all the experimental AT-PTs were aboard the *Katana* Dreadnaughts when that fleet disappeared. The AT-PT project was canceled, although Imperial engineers copied many of its design features years later.

The two-legged walker was nearly 3 meters tall with a cramped central command pod housing one soldier, or two in an emergency. Its heavy armor made the pod nearly invulnerable to small-arms fire. Independent leg suspension let the walker climb inclines of up to 45 degrees and made it suitable for jungle and mountain terrain as well as urban areas. On open ground, it could move as quickly as 60 kilometers an hour. Its weapons typically included a twin-blaster cannon and a concussion grenade launcher.

Ironically, years after the project was abandoned, AT-PTs got their first real test under battle conditions. After the walkers were rediscovered along with the lost *Katana* fleet, Luke Skywalker and Han Solo used an old AT-PT to fight Grand Admiral Thrawn's clone stormtroopers.

*All Terrain Personal Transport (AT-PT walker)*

**All Terrain Rapid Deployment Pod (AT-RDP)** A troop and equipment landing pod used by the Star Destroyer *Doomgiver* to deliver Reborn troops and AT-ST walkers to the surface of Yavin 4.

**All Terrain Recon Transport (AT-RT walker)** A small, open-seat single-trooper recon walker used in police support, civil defense, and after-battle mop-up missions. The clone troopers of the Grand Army of the Republic used the swift, lightweight AT-RTs on scouting missions during the Clone Wars.

**All Terrain Scout Transport (AT-ST walker)** This relatively lightweight and speedy vehicle was used by Imperial forces for reconnaissance and ground support for both troops and the larger AT-AT walkers. Although smaller than AT-ATs at about 8.6 meters tall, AT-STs were much faster: On flat terrain they moved along at a 90-kilometer-an-hour clip.

The two-legged "chicken" walker had a small but highly maneuverable armored command pod that housed a pilot and a gunner. Each leg had a sharp claw that could slice through natural or artificial obstacles. With just two legs and a gyro-balance system that was highly susceptible to damage, the AT-ST was more prone to tipping over than the AT-AT, but its flexibility and firepower made it a strong addition to the battlefield.

Scout walkers were often used to lay down

*All Terrain Recon Transport (AT-RT walker)*

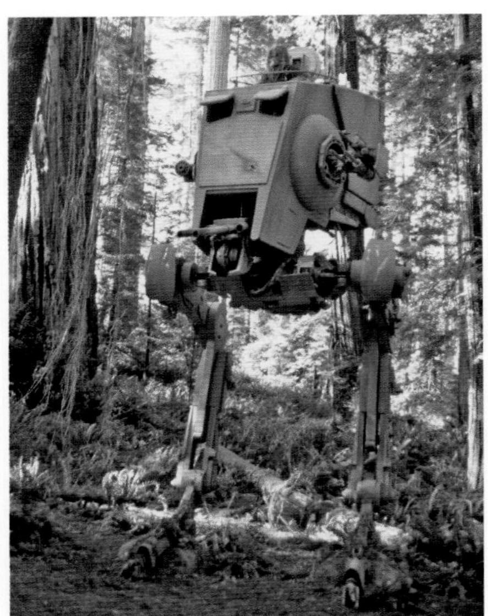
All Terrain Scout Transport (AT-ST walker)

a blanket of covering fire for Imperial ground troops and to defend the flanks and somewhat vulnerable underbelly of AT-ATs. The two-being crew entered and exited through a hatch atop the armor-plated command cabin.

**All Terrain Tactical Enforcer (AT-TE walker)** An intimidating six-legged Republic walker design introduced in the Clone Wars by Rothana Heavy Engineering. Specialized Republic drop ships delivered the AT-TE onto the battlefield. The walker was low to the ground, slow yet stable. Its two body halves were connected by an articulated sleeve that increased its mobility. The front of the walker had four ball-turret laser cannons; a heavy projectile cannon was turret-mounted on the walker's back. Some models featured gription systems on the walker's feet that allowed it to climb sheer surfaces.

**Allum, Vivendi** A Galactic Republic Senator who was part of the commission assembled to investigate the death of Bruck Chun.

**alluvial damper** A unit that regulated the amount of thrust produced by a starship's hyperdrive, it moved a servomotor-controlled plate to block, bit by bit, the emission of ion particles.

**Allya** Six hundred years before the rise of the Emperor, a rogue Jedi named Allya was exiled to Dathomir. She taught the Force to the planet's inhabitants and to her descendants, leading to the rise of the Nightsisters and Witches of Dathomir. Before her death, she created a book of advice based loosely on the Jedi Code to guide her children in the safe and sane use of the Force. As generations passed and her descendants scattered, each new clan made a copy of Allya's *Book of Law* to share with their new clan-sisters and to add to as they learned new lessons about the Force.

**Allyuen** Darth Vader ordered recalibrated Imperial probe droids to scout the planet Allyuen for the new Rebel base. The planets Tokmia and Hoth were also probed.

**Almak** Homeworld of the Leffingite species. It was also the name of a Galactic Alliance Guard member during the GA–Corellian Confederation War.

**Almania** A planetary system on the far reaches of the galaxy, it might have become part of the Old Republic but for its great distance from the center of the Republic's activities. The capital of the planet Almania—a large white-and-blue world surrounded by clouds—was Stonia. Almania had three smaller moons, the most famous of which was Pydyr, both for its exclusivity and for its wealth. Almania considered itself loosely aligned with the Rebellion during the Galactic Civil War and later with the New Republic.

However, shortly after the New Republic defeated Grand Admiral Thrawn, the Je'har leadership on Almania changed. Some reports told of hideous brutality under the new regime, and communications from Almania to the New Republic stopped; the planet was forgotten. In fact, the Je'har had grown jealous of Pydyr's wealth and begun ransacking the moon. During one raid, the parents of Dolph, a young Jedi trainee of Luke Skywalker, were killed in a particularly brutal fashion. Dolph returned home, let his anger turn him to the dark side, and undertook a holocaust even more terrible than the one he wanted to avenge. He adopted the name and death's-head mask of a long-ago despot named Kueller.

On a mission to investigate, Luke Skywalker crashed and was imprisoned by Kueller, who threatened to kill him and Princess Leia Organa Solo. The New Republic launched an offensive, the Battle of Almania, and Leia eventually killed a weakened Kueller with a blaster shot while he was battling Luke.

Sim Aloo

**Almas** A terraformed world in the Cularin system, ancient site of a Sith fortress built by Darth Rivan. Jedi who rediscovered the system centuries later became corrupted by the presence of the Sith fortress, resulting in a conflict that was eventually quelled. Almas then came to house a Jedi academy.

**Alole** A loyal aide to Princess Leia Organa Solo.

**Aloo, Sim** An adviser to Emperor Palpatine and member of the Emperor's Inner Circle. He accompanied Palpatine during his visit to the second Death Star.

**Alora** A female Lethan Twi'lek minion to Tavion Axmis, learning the ways of the dark side as a Disciple of Ragnos. Alora stole important information from the computers of Luke Skywalker's Jedi academy on Yavin 4,

All Terrain Tactical Enforcer (AT-TE walker)

and corrupted student Rosh Penin to the dark side. She was discovered and defeated by the Jedi Jaden Korr on Taspir III.

**Alpha (A-17)** An ARC trooper pulled out of stasis during the Battle of Kamino in the Clone Wars. A-17 helped Shaak Ti and the other Jedi on Kamino save the third generation of clone troopers from the invading Separatist droid army. Had the Confederacy invasion been successful, he would have destroyed the clone facility to prevent the clones from falling into the wrong hands.

*Alpha (A-17)*

A-17 accompanied Anakin Skywalker and Obi-Wan Kenobi on a mission to Ohma-D'un, the moon of Naboo. Anakin began referring to A-17 as Alpha, a name he adopted as his own. Alpha continued to serve with Kenobi and Skywalker on Jabiim, where he and Obi-Wan were presumed killed in an AT-AT explosion. In truth, they were taken prisoner and tortured by Asajj Ventress on Rattatak. Obi-Wan and Alpha escaped their bonds and fled the planet by stealing Asajj's vessel. They traveled to Riflor, where they ran afoul of bounty hunters. Alpha was next assigned to Kamino, where he began training clone commanders to be more independent and adaptive in combat. Following Anakin's example, Alpha began naming the clone commanders. He was promoted to the rank of captain and became lead instructor of the Tipoca City training facility.

During the Outer Rim sieges, Alpha returned to active combat aboard the Star Destroyer *Intervention.* He was seriously injured after a fight with General Grievous on Boz Pity.

**Alpha-02** *See* Spar.

**Alpha-66** *See* Muzzle.

**Alpha Blue** A mysterious, covert intelligence group within the New Republic's military and security hierarchy, it was headed by Admiral Drayson.

**Alpha Red** A top-secret project team and the name of a Yuuzhan Vong–targeting poison developed jointly by the Chiss and New Republic Intelligence. The pathogen proved very controversial among the upper echelons of the New Republic, because many—including the Jedi Knights—felt its use was tantamount to genocide. Chief of State Cal Omas approved the project, though it was thwarted by Vergere, who rendered the only viable sample of Alpha Red harmless by the peculiar chemistry of her tears. The template for the poison lived on, however, and it neared deployment again but was scrapped when it proved fatal to life native to this galaxy, namely the winged-stars of Caluula. Given that unpredictable outcome, Alpha Red was deemed too dangerous and unstable to use. The Yuuzhan Vong leader, Supreme Overlord Shimrra, had planned to use the New Republic's own weapon against the living planet Zonama Sekot, but he was defeated.

**Alpheridies** The home planet of the Miraluka, who were born without eyes but saw everything through the Force. Alpheridies was located in the Abron system, at the edge of the molecular cloud known as The Veil, several parsecs Coreward of the Expansion Region–Mid Rim border.

**Alrix, Rees** A female Jedi Knight and former Padawan to Gran Jedi Master Maks Leem. Alrix led Republic forces on Sullust during the Clone Wars.

**Alsakan** A heavily populated planet in the Galactic Core, Alsakan was settled millennia ago, before the foundation of the Old Republic, by colonists on the *Kuat Explorer.* The colossal battle cruisers of the ancient Alsakan Conflicts, first built about 3,000 years before the Galactic Civil War, inspired the *Invincible*-class Dreadnaughts. Alsakan was one of many planets that surrendered to Admiral Ackbar and the Rebel Alliance fleet in the years following the Battle of Endor. Imperial Commander Titus Klev was born on Alsakan; his father was a Clone Wars veteran and his mother, a member of a wealthy merchant family. Corporate Sector Viceprex Mirkovig Hirken was also born on Alsakan, into one of the oldest families on the planet.

**alter** Along with control and sense, one of the three basic abilities studied by the Jedi in their mastery of the Force. Alter covered the use of the Force to create external phenomena, such as telekinesis. Because it held the biggest potential for dark side transgression, alter was typically the last of the three abilities learned by Jedi initiates.

**altha protein drink** A warm drink favored by Lando Calrissian.

**Altis, Djinn** This Jedi Master instructed his students, including Geith and Callista, from a Jedi training platform hidden in the clouds of the gas giant Bespin.

**Altorian** Two intelligent species inhabited hot, dry Altor 14. These

*Altorian Lizard, Nuiwit*

Altorians hated each other but failed to eliminate or subjugate the other. The primitive and lawless Avogwi, known offworld as the Altorian Birds, were a proud and savage species who placed a low value on life. The Nuiwit, called the Altorian Lizards, had a highly structured and harmonious society and a desire to please visitors—except the Avogwi, for whom they were food.

**Altunen, Serifa** An Arkanian Jedi Master who objected to the Jedi's role in the Clone Wars. Feeling that the Jedi Order should serve the people of the Republic and not the Chancellor or the Senate, Altunen abandoned the Order and returned to Arkania. Obi-Wan Kenobi and Anakin Skywalker voyaged to Arkania in a failed attempt to convince her to come back.

**Alvien squadron** Along with Drax and Zeta, Alvien was one of the stormtrooper squadrons that made up Desert Sands, the unit dispatched to locate the jettisoned *Tantive IV* escape pod on Tatooine.

**Alwari nomads** Nomadic natives who shunned the cities and towns of Ansion, preferring to live on the immense prairies that dominated much of the planet's topography. Alwari with physical or mental infirmities were cast out from their clans and sent to live in the cities. The Alwari were by nature independent, confident, and free. They retained many of their old ways, but were ready to make use of new developments—such as weapons—that did not contradict tradition. It was traditional for Alwari to provide the feast for guests to their clan while the guests provided entertainment. Alwari usually stayed clear of the planet's hilly areas, and thus most were unfamiliar with the Gwurran.

Alwari clans like the Tasbir and the Pangay Ous were distinguished by the robes and gear that they wore. The Northern Bands, located far away from Cuipernam—Ansion's primary city—had members who wore identifying tattoos on their foreheads. The Niruu Alwari were famed for their sanwiwood sculptures. The Borokii and Januul were the most prominent of the Alwari nomad overclans. Smaller clans such as the Yiwar and the smaller Eijin and Gaxun usually followed their lead.

Prior to the out-

*Altorian Bird, Avogwi*

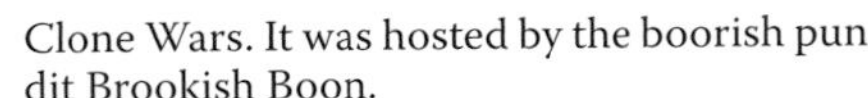

break of the Clone Wars, Jedi Knights went to Ansion to try to cement a permanent peace between the city-folk of the Unity and the Alwari nomads. After a day's deliberation, Borokii leaders acceded to the Jedi's request to make peace with the city-folk.

Amani

**Alya** An influential Bothan clan, one of only three allowed to colonize Kothlis after the planet was purchased from Raynor Mining Enterprises. The Alya clan was one of the first to ally itself with the Rebel Alliance. Borsk Fey'lya was a member of Clan Alya.

**Alyssia** A Hapan female, niece to former Queen Mother Ta'a Chume and cousin to Prince Isolder. Alyssia conspired to take the throne, and got the loyalty of Ta'a Chume's retainer Trisdin Gheer. Trisdin betrayed the former Queen Mother to Alyssia, who used the opportunity to attempt an assassination. Ta'a Chume had anticipated exactly this outcome; Trisdin was killed, and Alyssia exposed. The throne eventually went to Tenel Ka.

**Alzoc III** Home of the Talz species and source of the Alzoc pearl, this planet was in the Outer Rim's Alzoc system. It was a moonless world covered with desolate, frozen plains, and its powerful sun glared harshly off the reflective snow. The Empire secretly placed a garrison on Alzoc III and forced the Talz to work as slaves in underground mines. The planet was never entered into the galactic registry, and the New Republic only learned of its existence after examining restricted corporate files. Imperial Commander Pter Thanas was assigned to the Rim world of Bakura after refusing to destroy a village of Talz miners on Alzoc III. The Imperial battlemoon *Eye of Palpatine* stopped at the frozen planet to pick up a contingent of stormtroopers, but brought aboard a group of Talz instead.

Queen Amanoa

**Amaltanna** A planet and site of a Clone Wars battle, where Bultar Swan effectively trapped Baron Edi Wedd within his own impregnable fortress.

**Amamanam** A New Republic Senator and member of the Senate's Council on Security and Intelligence who represented the planet B'das.

**Amanaman** The nickname of a little-seen Amanin member of Jabba the Hutt's court, also known as the Head Hunter for the gruesome collection of skulls he carried on his staff. His real name was unknown.

***Amanda Fallow*** One of Talon Karrde's fleet of smuggling ships with puns for names. It was a modified YZ-775 armed with a pair of turbolasers, two double lasers, and two proton torpedo launchers.

**Amani (plural: Amanin)** A species of tall arboreal creatures from the treetops of Maridun. They used their long arms to brachiate among the canopies. An Amani was slow on foot, but could curl him- or herself up into a ball and roll overland. When an Amanin tribe grew too large, the youths were exiled to cross the plains to find a new forest. They fought brutal battles—called takitals—with any tribe that occupied a contested stretch of forest. When members of an Imperial armored column led by General Ziering crossed the sacred Amanin border, the Amanin engaged in a takital against them. For days, hundreds of Amanin besieged the Imperial redoubt. Lieutenant Janek "Tank" Sunber distinguished himself in the battle; by proving himself in takital, he was thus able to arrange a peace accord with the Amanin chief. As a result, Amanin captives from other tribes were placed in Imperial servitude.

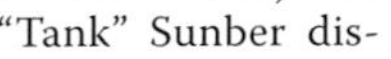
Ambria

**Amanoa, Queen** Ruler of Onderon more than 4,000 years before the Galactic Civil War, she was also known as the Dark Queen because she dabbled in the remnants of Sith magic introduced four centuries earlier by the Dark Jedi Freedon Nadd. She was able to call upon dark side forces to battle the Beast-Lords of Onderon. Her daughter, Galia, succeeded to the throne after Queen Amanoa's death. Amanoa was buried in a stone sarcophagus and eventually entombed on Onderon's closest moon, Dxun, near the body of Nadd.

**Amaran** An intelligent bipedal canine species from the planet Amar. The fox-like Amaran natives captured bursa animals and bred them for export. Amarans were notorious hagglers.

***Amberdawn*** A popular Senate District holographic morning talk show broadcast on Coruscant and elsewhere in the years prior to the Clone Wars. It was hosted by the boorish pundit Brookish Boon.

**amber fern** A variety of fragile fern native to the galek forests of Mandalore.

**Ambler, Ty** An alias used by Ferus Olin when he posed as Jakohaul Lessor's assistant during his mission to infiltrate the Emperor Palpatine Surgical Reconstruction Center and locate any imprisoned Jedi, about a year after the end of the Clone Wars.

**ambori** The viscous, colorless liquid chemical that acted as a suspension medium for bacta within bacta tanks.

**Ambria** A desolate and rugged ringed planet in the Inner Rim with several moons. Located in the Stenness system, Ambria served as the site of Jedi Master Thon's training compound some 4,000 years before the Galactic Civil War. In the murky past, a long-forgotten Sith sorceress chose the planet as her domain. She used her evil powers to construct a huge obelisk infused with the dark side of the Force. When it was complete, the sorceress attempted a Sith ritual, which unintentionally unleashed an uncontrolled wave of Force energy that devastated Ambria. Living creatures died by the thousands, the landscape warped even further, and the planet became infused with the dark side. Compelled by the Force, Master Thon went to Ambria to fight against the power of the dark side, and succeeded in confining its corruption to a single locale, Lake Natth. Centuries later, Ambria became the secret home of Darth Bane and his apprentice, Darth Zannah, as he concentrated on his plot to continue the Sith Order in secret. During the turmoil of the Empire's rise, Ambria was largely forgotten. Interest in the planet increased after the foundation of the New Republic.

**ambrostine** A strong alcoholic beverage popular among many Imperial dignitaries.

**Amedda, Mas** The Vice Chair and Speaker of the Galactic Senate serving Chancellors Valorum and Palpatine. He was obsessed with procedure and used his booming voice to help moderate debates within the Senate. Loyal to Palpatine, Amedda advocated giving the Chancellor emergency powers to deal with the growing Separatist crisis. He was aware of Palpatine's true iden-

Amaran

Mas Amedda

tity as a Sith Lord when the Empire came to power. Mas Amedda was a Chagrian male from Champala.

**Amee** One of Anakin Skywalker's childhood friends in the slave quarters of Mos Espa, Amee worked as a house slave for a wealthy Toong couple. Her mother, Hala, was kidnapped in a slave raid by the pirate Krayn. She was three years younger than Anakin and attended the wedding of Shmi and Cliegg Lars.

**Amelia** *See* Allana.

**Ament** This kind giant of a human and his sister Jaren were saved from a mob of pursuers by the fallen Jedi Darca Nyl. Appearances proved deceiving, as Ament was revealed to be prone to fits of uncontrollable rage. He was wanted by law enforcement for the murder of over 30 people. Upon discovering the truth, Nyl brought the siblings back into custody.

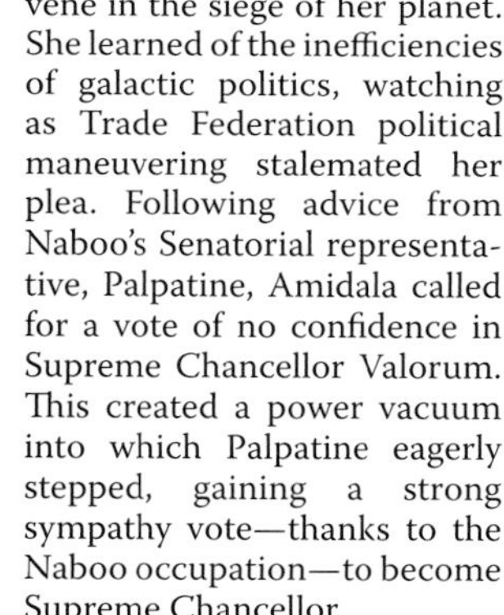
Xiaan Amersu

***Amerce*** One of 30 Star Destroyers near completion at Fondor's Orbital Shipyard 1321, the *Amerce* was destroyed by a Yuuzhan Vong attack.

**Amersu, Xiaan** When still just a child, young Twi'lek Padawan Xiaan Amersu saw Aurra Sing kill her Jedi Master, J'Mikel. Sing derided the young girl, yet spared her life. Amersu was consoled by Quinlan Vos, and she later met Aayla Secura, her personal hero in the Jedi Order. By the time of the Clone Wars, Amersu had ascended to the rank of Jedi Knight. She flew as Blue Leader at Saleucami, and sacrificed herself and her fighter to eliminate a Separatist planetary gun.

**Amfar** A popular recreational world, its beaches were usually crowded but suffered a loss of tourism during the Separatist crisis.

**Amidala, Padmé** Born Padmé Naberrie, this young leader of the Naboo adopted *Amidala* as her formal name of state. She was identified early as one of the planet's best and brightest, and trained accordingly. By age 14, she was elected Queen of Naboo, replacing King Veruna as monarch of the planet. A month into her rule, Queen Amidala was tested when her planet was blockaded by the Trade Federation. The scheming Neimoidians tried to force her to sign a treaty that would legitimize a brazenly illegal occupation. Amidala refused. En route to incarceration, Amidala was freed by Jedi ambassadors, who planned to take the Queen and her retinue to Coruscant.

During the escape, Queen Amidala relied on her cadre of handmaidens to act as protectors, swapping identities with Sabé while she adopted the less stately identity of simple handmaiden Padmé Naberrie. Damage sustained to the Queen's royal vessel required a brief detour to Tatooine, where the Jedi discovered a young boy strong in the Force. This freed slave, Anakin Skywalker, was instantly smitten with Padmé despite their difference in age.

At the galactic capital, Queen Amidala pleaded for the Senate to intervene in the siege of her planet. She learned of the inefficiencies of galactic politics, watching as Trade Federation political maneuvering stalemated her plea. Following advice from Naboo's Senatorial representative, Palpatine, Amidala called for a vote of no confidence in Supreme Chancellor Valorum. This created a power vacuum into which Palpatine eagerly stepped, gaining a strong sympathy vote—thanks to the Naboo occupation—to become Supreme Chancellor.

Fed up with the Senate, Amidala returned to Naboo. She requested aid from the native Gungans in freeing her captured capital. During the Battle of Naboo, Amidala infiltrated her own palace and forced Neimoidian Viceroy Nute Gunray to end the occupation. The cowardly Neimoidians, having their armies defeated, capitulated; freedom was brought back to the planet.

When her elected term ended, Amidala stepped down as monarch despite her popularity. Though she could have retired, she opted instead to become Naboo's representative in the Galactic Senate. Amidala was caught up in the turmoil as a Separatist movement spread rapidly throughout the galaxy. Many of the more reactionary Senators called for a military solution. Amidala, however, stayed true to her pacifist ideals, urging diplomacy.

On the day of the Military Creation Act vote, Amidala's starship was attacked upon

Padmé Naberrie Amidala

arrival at Coruscant. Many in her entourage died in the explosion. Some suspected that disgruntled spice miners from the moons of Naboo were the culprits, but Amidala believed that it was actually Count Dooku, leader of the Separatists, behind the attack. In truth, it was an old enemy, Nute Gunray, who was behind the bounty hunters hired to finally silence the young woman from Naboo, though that would go undiscovered for some time.

At the behest of Supreme Chancellor Palpatine, Amidala was placed under the protection of the Jedi Knights. Amidala was reunited with Obi-Wan Kenobi and his apprentice Anakin Skywalker, whom she had not seen in a decade. A second assassination attempt by the bounty hunter Zam Wesell revealed just how grave was the danger Amidala faced. Anakin escorted her to Naboo, where she would be sequestered while the Jedi investigated the attacks against her. In moments of

Queen Amidala

*Padmé Amidala and Anakin Skywalker in the Lake Country of Naboo*

quiet solitude against the beautiful landscape of Naboo's Lake Country, Anakin and Padmé bonded, rekindling an affectionate friendship and falling into a deeper love. It was a love forbidden to both: Per the tenets of the Jedi Code, Anakin could not enter into a romantic relationship, and Padmé needed to focus on her career. Despite their strong feelings, Padmé rebuffed Anakin's overtures while attempting to still her own heart.

Anakin's love for Padmé was not all that was troubling him. He suffered from terrible nightmares of his mother in danger. Anakin returned to Tatooine with Padmé to find Shmi Skywalker. When he found her brutally tortured and mortally wounded by Tusken Raiders, Anakin lashed out and slaughtered the tribe. He then confessed his actions to Padmé, collapsing with shame and despair; she saw the wounded, sobbing youth and let compassion guide her heart as she comforted him.

Anakin and Padmé then voyaged to Geonosis to rescue Obi-Wan, who had been captured by Separatist forces. Padmé hoped to use her diplomatic skills to parley with the Separatists, but she and Anakin were captured by the Geonosians. Placed on trial for espionage, Amidala and Anakin were sentenced to death. Faced with overwhelming evidence of her mortality, Padmé lowered her emotional guard and professed her love to Anakin. The two were then placed in an execution arena alongside Obi-Wan, and three deadly beasts were unleashed upon them.

The spectacle was cut short with the arrival of Jedi reinforcements, and then the opening salvos of the Clone Wars. Despite her initial objections to a Republic army, Padmé nonetheless fought alongside the newly created clone troopers against the Separatist droid forces. After the Battle of Geonosis, Anakin escorted Padmé Amidala back to Naboo. At a secluded lake retreat, the two were quietly wed in a ceremony witnessed only by C-3PO and R2-D2. As the Clone Wars continued year after year, Padmé was increasingly distracted by the growing career of her husband. She was deeply worried for his safety. The few moments they could snatch together were all too brief. By the time the Outer Rim Sieges ended, Padmé had stunning news to deliver to Anakin—he was to be a father. The two kept her pregnancy a closely guarded secret.

Though Amidala continued to serve the Senate faithfully, she joined Bail Organa and Mon Mothma as part of a small group of Senators who were growing increasingly wary of Palpatine's amendments and executive decrees. Though early talk of action against Palpatine was carefully couched and measured so as not to border on sedition, Padmé favored a diplomatic solution within the boundaries of the law. She even asked Anakin to use his close relationship with Palpatine to press for a peaceful resolution to the war, but her beleaguered husband resented the request. He wanted such overtures to remain in political circles, where they belonged. Her doubts about the system troubled Anakin. To his ears, she was starting to sound like a Separatist.

Anakin was plagued with nightmares of Padmé dying during childbirth. Given the prophetic dreams that had predicted the death of his mother, these visions greatly unsettled Anakin. He could not stand to lose Padmé, and would do anything to keep her with him. A gateway to dark powers that could unnaturally preserve life beckoned to Anakin—it was a power that could be achieved by allying himself to Darth Sidious, Dark Lord of the Sith.

Padmé, like the rest of the Republic, was unaware that Chancellor Palpatine was secretly a Sith Lord. Palpatine lured Anakin to the dark side, and Skywalker knelt before him, becoming Darth Vader, his apprentice. As Vader, Anakin led an ambush on the Jedi Temple, then traveled to Mustafar to kill the leadership of the Separatists, effectively bringing an end to the Clone Wars.

It was Obi-Wan who told Padmé the truth about her husband: Kenobi had seen evidence of Anakin's transgressions. Padmé was stunned. Unable to grasp this dark reality, she traveled to Mustafar to confront Anakin. Unbeknownst to her, Obi-Wan stowed away aboard her ship. Padmé could not reason with Anakin. In his twisted perception, he had done all his wicked deeds to better the galaxy for their union, to make the corrupt Republic into a just Empire for their children. Deluded with power, Anakin even promised that he could depose the Emperor and make the galaxy exactly what he and Padmé wanted it to be.

Padmé was devastated by Anakin's transformation. When he saw Obi-Wan emerging from her starship, he jumped to the worst of conclusions—his wife had brought his former mentor to Mustafar to kill him. Anakin raised his hand and caught Padmé in a telekinetic chokehold. Padmé gasped for breath as life began to escape from her. Anakin released his grip as he faced Obi-Wan, and Padmé collapsed.

While Kenobi and Skywalker dueled in the Mustafar collection facility, C-3PO and R2-D2 faithfully carried her inert form aboard her starship. Despite the abbreviated medical suite on this ship—and even the full medical facility at a refuge on Polis Massa—her life signs continued to dwindle. Padmé never knew what had become of Anakin. She never saw the damage he suffered from Kenobi's blade and the lava of Mustafar. She still felt there was good within him. With her dying breath, she tried to convince Obi-Wan of this.

Before slipping away, Padmé remained strong enough to give birth. In the strange alien facility of Anakin's nightmares, she gave birth to twins—Leia and Luke Skywalker. Obi-Wan Kenobi, Yoda, and Bail Organa vowed to keep the children safe. Amidala's body was returned to Naboo. At a state funeral, thousands of Naboo citizens came to pay their respects to their beloved representative.

**Amisus** The Ruurian offspring of Skynx, Amisus grew up to become the leader of the Unified Ruurian Colonies. Amisus pledged the Ruurians' loyalty to Grand Admiral Thrawn during the Hand of Thrawn incident 19 years after the Battle of Yavin.

*Senator Amidala and Anakin Skywalker fight for their lives on Geonosis.*

**Amithest, Mari** A youngling member of the mighty Bear Clan taught by Yoda. She was only four years old at the outbreak of the Clone Wars.

**ammonia bombs** Explosives that dispensed ammonia in levels lethal to oxygen breathers, they were typically used by the ammonia-breathing Gands.

**Ammuud** A planet with a rigid code of honor, Ammuud was known throughout the systems as being controlled by the Corporate Sector Authority. The code was enforced by the feudal-like governing coalition of seven clans, which operated under a contract from the Authority.

***Ammuud Swooper*** A battered sky-blue YT-2400 freighter that helped evacuate Borleias during the Yuuzhan Vong War. Wedge Antilles, flying as Blackmoon Eleven, defeated a Yuuzhan Vong squadron to allow the ship to carry its refugees to safety.

**Amorphiian** A species of humanoids from Amorphiia known to have problems with their neural motor systems.

**amphibion** A moderately armored hovercraft that delivered 20 troops and all their gear into the heart of combat, the amphibion was quick and relatively safe. While primarily a water assault vehicle, an amphibion also could be used over flat terrain. It traveled up to 100 kilometers an hour. The craft had a successful deployment during the Battle of Mon Calamari.

The vehicle itself was lightly armored along its 7.3-meter length. Only the front pilot's cabin was fully enclosed. A gunner sat in the rear at the bottom of a rotating gun turret. The craft operated quietly, making it useful for stealthy commando raids. Many smaller hover engines were mounted along the bottom and sides. Slightly larger engines in the rear provided forward propulsion.

**amphistaff** A common Yuuzhan Vong melee weapon. The amphistaff was a vicious serpent about 1.3 meters long that could harden all or part of its body to the consistency of stone, including narrowing its neck and tail so that it could cut like a razor; or it could become supple and whip-like for its Yuuzhan Vong master. In the hands of a true warrior, the amphistaff became a deadly missile weapon. It spit forth a stream of venom 20 meters with stunning accuracy, blinding opponents instantly and killing them slowly, over many agonizing hours, as the poison seeped in through ducts and wounds. The amphistaff's venomous bite caused numbness and paralysis. This creature's ability to heal itself made it nearly impervious, although it could be killed with a strike to its head.

Amphistaff

**Ampliquen** A planet in the Meridian sector, it was the site of much activity nine years after the Battle of Endor when the New Republic cruisers *Caelus* and *Corbantis* were sent from the Orbital Station at Durren to investigate what was either a pirate attack or a possible truce violation by the planet Budpock. At the same time, a revolt that was secretly supported by the Loronar Corporation broke out on Ampliquen.

**Am-Shak** The Weequay god of thunder.

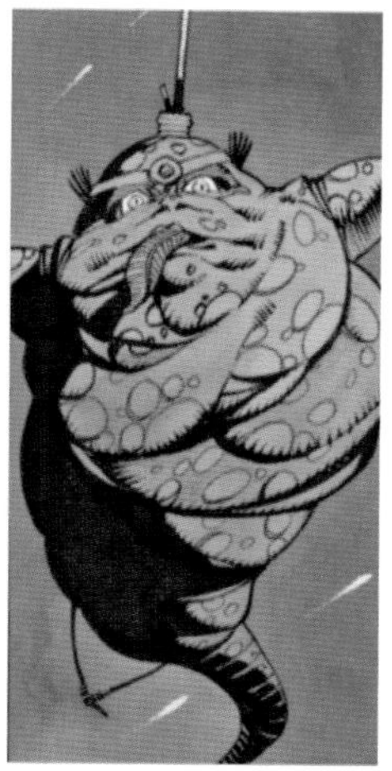

Anachro the H'uun

**amulet of Kalara** A Sith artifact that Ben Skywalker had to retrieve—on the orders of Jacen Solo—during the conflict between the Galactic Alliance and the Corellian Confederation. Lumiya closely monitored Ben's progress to gauge his worthiness as an heir to Sith knowledge. The artifact resembled a simple oval jewel hanging from a silver chain. Though it radiated a sensation of malicious glee through the Force, the extent of its powers and abilities remain unknown. Legend held that the 2,000-year-old amulet could cause a trained Sith practitioner to remain invisible to other Force-users. The amulet had become part of Lando Calrissian's collection of art and relics, and was displayed at a Tendrando Arms facility on the Almanian moon of Drewwa. A chain of accomplices hired by Lumiya caused the amulet to be stolen and relocated to the Sith world of Ziost. Its supposed thief, a man named Faskus Oldivan, was already dead by the time Ben found him and the amulet, though he was survived by his young daughter Kiara. Ben rescued Kiara, recovered the amulet, and left Ziost aboard an ancient Sith meditation sphere.

Analysis droids

**Anachro the H'uun** A young female Hutt of the lower H'uun caste and daughter of trader Orko the H'uun from Tatooine. Orko's rival Gorga the Hutt was smitten with her and presented an offering to curry favor: Orko's enemy, the bounty hunter Bar-Kooda, roasted on a platter. Anachro and Gorga married and had a Huttlet soon after.

Mari Amithest

***Anakin Solo*** Colonel Jacen Solo's flagship in the Galactic Alliance Guard, named for his dead brother. *Anakin Solo* was an *Imperial II*–class Star Destroyer painted black, fitted with a cloaking device and a gravity-well projector.

**anakkona** A blue snake native to Kashyyyk with fanned ears and a sharp tail.

**Analysis Bureau** The eggheads of Imperial Intelligence, bureau members gathered data from tens of millions of sources to look for enemy activity. The bureau also searched for patterns or trends in social data that might be helpful to Imperial agents. Its branches included Media, which pored over every comlink transmission and holocast in the known galaxy; Signal, which examined the channels through which information was delivered; Cryptanalysis, which prided itself on breaking even the most challenging codes; Tech, which broke down enemy hardware to determine how it worked, then provided superior devices to Imperial Intelligence; and Interrogation, which specialized in reprogramming captured Rebels and freeing them to become double agents.

**analysis droid** Any of a wide variety of droids designed to forensically analyze physical substances; examples included the SP-4 and JN-66 droids found in the Jedi Temple. These droids focused on symbols and superficial impressions, and rarely were able to make the intuitive leaps necessary for criminal investigations.

**Anamor, Facet** Part of an Imperial research team on Toprawa, she inadvertently supplied Rebel spy Havet Storm with schematics for the Death Star superlaser. Seeking revenge, Facet adopted the alias *Diamond,* and later attacked Havet.

**Anarrad Pit** The home of the dreaded katarn in the forests of Kashyyyk.

Anchorhead

**Anaxes** A Core world also known as the Defender of the Core. Home of the Anaxes Citadel, it served as a seat of galactic power and naval prestige for millennia. During the Galactic Civil War, Anaxes was the command center for a capital ship task force assigned to defend Sector Zero against any threats. The people of Anaxes were called Anaxsi.

**Anaxes Citadel** Found on Anaxes, this massive complex of training schools, research labs, intelligence centers, offices, archives, and parade grounds was famous throughout the galaxy. It was the site where the Imperial Navy's highest honors were bestowed.

**ancestral archives** This bubble building on Ohma-D'un was home to the family histories of all the Gungans in the new colony. Gungans wanting to know more about their past visited the archives.

**Anchorhead** A small farming community located on the edge of Tatooine's Dune Sea. Anchorhead was a quiet town founded by the planet's original human settlers; thousands of years ago, it was run by the Czerka Corporation. It continued to serve as a central trading site for moisture farmers and other denizens of the desert. Anchorhead's water and power distribution were controlled by Tosche Station, a small building on the outskirts of town. Anchorhead was a gathering place for bored youths, including Luke Skywalker and his friends.

Anchorhead was originally founded around a deep well. In its early days, the community was frequented by pilgrims and traders. When the central well dried up, most of the traffic ceased, although the local power station continued to attract moisture farmers and others who made their homes in the outlying deserts. The town rested between several rocky outcroppings at the edge of the Jundland Wastes. It was one of the only settlements along the route to Mos Eisley, several hours' travel beyond Anchorhead.

**Anchoron** The planet where Corellian hero Garm Bel Iblis was believed to have been killed early in the Galactic Civil War. He actually survived but was forced to go underground, severing all ties with his former life and working in secret to bring down the Empire. The smuggler Talon Karrde posted men on Anchoron in an unsuccessful search for Grand Admiral Thrawn's traffic in clones, and Leia Organa Solo, in her attempts to locate an Imperial spy, planted a false report stating that a Star Destroyer had been spotted near the planet.

**Ancient Order of Pessimists** A peaceful religous order with a hermitage on Maryx Minor. Members of the Ancient Order of Pessimists were led by the High Hermit. Their mantra was "Woe, woe, a thousand times woe." Abal Karda, a quarry of Boba Fett, sought asylum within their hermitage. Fett was in turn pursued by Darth Vader. During this ordeal, the High Hermit had a moment of optimism, since only six of the order had been killed during the hunt. This optimism was short-lived, however, as the hermitage was destroyed from orbit by a Star Destroyer.

**Ancient Order of the Whills** *See* Shaman of the Whills.

**Anda** A native of Onderon, she was one of the early supporters of Vaklu's bid to take over the planet's leadership from Queen Talia following the Jedi Civil War. Anda was not afraid to employ mercenaries and other hired guns to remove members of the Royalists if she felt that they were getting in Vaklu's way.

**Andara** A wealthy, influential world within the Andara system. Another planet in the system, Ieria, was dissatisfied by Andaran representation in the Senate and battled for its own representation. Andara was the site of the Leadership School, an elite private academy.

**Andeddu, Darth** A long-dead Sith Lord whose holocron was sought by Quinlan Vos and Skorr on Korriban in order to curry favor with Count Dooku. Hidden within the holocron was the red crystal that powered Andeddu's lightsaber. Dooku gave this crystal to Quinlan Vos. Over a century later, during the time of Roan Fel's empire, Darth Krayt was in possession of Andeddu's holocron.

**Ando** A watery planet in the Mid Rim with few solid landmasses, Ando was home to the belligerent, walrus-faced Aqualish. The higher-class Aquala ("webbed" Aqualish) preferred to live on floating raft cities and large sailing ships, while the low-status Quara ("fingered" Aqualish) inhabited the larger islands of Ando. Ando mainly exported foodstuffs from its seas.

A sister planet in the same system had a blasted, uninhabitable surface, the apparent aftermath of an Aqualish war soon after the species discovered space travel. The aggressiveness of the Aqualish concerned the Republic, and the species was demilitarized and closely observed. This led to a strained relationship between the Aqualish and the Republic. The Jedi Master Jorus C'baoth was a member of the Ando Demilitarization Observation Group.

As the Separatist crisis spread throughout the galaxy preceding the Clone Wars, Ando seceded from the Republic, with Senator Po Nudo joining the Confederacy of Independent Systems. With the rise of the Empire, Ando became a police state; Imperials cracked down on any Aqualish uprisings. Ando was also targeted by Grand Admiral Thrawn as part of a multipronged attack intended to draw New Republic forces away from Ukio.

*Ancient Order of Pessimists*

**Andoan Free Colonies** Fifteen planets in the Mid Rim colonized by the Aqualish of Ando. During the Clone Wars, the Andoan Free Colonies remained loyal to the Republic, while their governing world Ando seceded to join the Separatists.

**Andona, Mari'ha** An old friend of Han Solo, she ran flight control for a sector of the planet Coruscant. She could be counted on to bend the rules for Solo and authorized his sometimes unorthodox flight plans.

**Ando Prime** An ice-covered world with vast glaciers and large, frozen lakes. In at least one location, a massive pipeline brought water from the glacial interior of a mountain to populated regions below. A Podrace course on Ando Prime traveled over mountain roads, through the pipeline, into a pumping station, and across lakes of ice. The course was considered dangerous because of its many twists, turns, and icy obstacles.

**Andosha II** One of the 15 worlds of the Andoan Free Colonies, which remained loyal to the Republic during the Clone Wars. Andosha II was represented by Senator Gorothin Vagger.

**Andra** An environmental idealist, Andra was the founder and sole member of the POWER party, dedicated to the preservation of the endangered wildlife on Telos. She helped Obi-Wan Kenobi and Qui-Gon Jinn stop the UniFy corporation from exploiting Telos's natural resources. With the help of criminal Denetrus, she exposed the fallen Jedi Xanatos's role in the plot to bring Offworld Mining to Telos. After Xanatos was defeated, Denetrus and Andra married. They worked with the Chun family to develop the *BioCruiser.*

**Andray, Moff** A fiercely loyal New Order proponent and member of the Council of

Moffs around the time Gilad Pellaeon sued for peace with the New Republic.

**Andrevea** A river on Naboo.

**andris** The more common of the two types of spice found on Sevarcos was the white andris, as opposed to the black carsunum.

**AndroosinLiann** The two-headed Troig host of the Eriadu talk show *Essence.*

**Andur** A Coruscant bureaucrat, he was vice chair of an orbital debris committee during the New Republic.

*Darial Anglethorn*

**Anduvil of Ogem** A trader active during the Galactic Civil War, and one of the few female Ogemites in business. Anduvil alerted Luke Skywalker about an Imperial biological weapons test on Tatooine, and together the two of them destroyed an Imperial lab that was perfecting a genetically modified strain of Bledsoe's disease.

**Angel** Often talked about by deep-space pilots, Angels were considered by some to be the most beautiful creatures in the universe. They were known to be good and kind, and so pretty they made even the most hardened spice pirate cry. Found on the moons of Iego, Angels (or Diathim, as they were scientifically cataloged) were described as thin, feminine humanoids 2 to 3 meters tall, with six blade-like wings sprouting from their backs. Some claimed Angels were more androgynous in form, and many alien spacers swore that Angels appeared as exotic-looking Verpine, Givin, or similar representatives of their own native species. All Angels seemed to be composed of searing white light tinged with a yellowish aura, making it difficult to identify biological details. Since they glided out from Iego's moonlets to greet arriving ships, it was assumed that they lived on the moonlets, but their dwellings have remained hidden. Angels had no apparent language and conveyed an aura of overall benevolence, despite their known efforts at sabotage.

**Anglebay Station** The medical station on Telos-4 where the bounty hunter Valance was turned into a cyborg. Valance returned with his crew to wipe out the entire facility, ensuring that no records of his surgery remained.

**angler** A spider-like crustacean native to Yavin 4, the angler built its home in the dangling aerial roots of majestic Massassi trees, which dipped their tips into the slow-running rivers of the moon. Anglers had small bodies but long and sharp knobbed legs with a skeletal appearance. Camouflaged and motionless in the tree roots, an angler waited for a fish to drift near, then stabbed down quickly and sharply, using its legs like a spear, and hungrily devoured its meal.

**Anglethorn, Darial** The leader of a group of moisture farmers on the planet Beheboth united to fight against water-stealing bandits. With the help of Luke Skywalker, she was able to end the brigands' control of the Beheboth farmers. She would later become Beheboth's representative in the New Republic Senate.

**animal excluder** A hand-sized device that emitted a sound warding off most creatures.

**animated metal sealant** This special paste was essential for every spacer's tool kit. It crawled across the damaged area of a spacecraft, smoothed itself, then sealed with a bond even stronger than the original hull.

**Anis** An Anzati clan leader, he agreed to let his most skilled assassins train Aurra Sing as a killer for Wallanooga the Hutt, to whom he was indebted. Anis was later murdered by Torgo Tahn, Sing's mentor.

**Anjiliac** A Hutt clan known for its ability to survive and even thrive during periods of galactic changes. During the last years of the Old Republic and the early years of the New Order, other Hutt clans either were forced to acknowledge Anjiliac's leadership, or were crushed.

**Ankarres sapphire** A jewel so fabled for its healing powers that people were said to travel huge distances to touch it. It was stolen from its owner, the careless Dom Princina, by the droid 4-LOM while the two traveled aboard the *Kuari Princess* passenger liner.

*"Are you an Angel?" young Anakin Skywalker asks Padmé Naberrie.*

**Ankkit, Lik** A Neimoidian stationed on Qiilura by the Trade Federation, he oversaw the work of poor farmers harvesting barq crops while he lived in an opulent villa. Ankkit employed Mandalorian Ghez Hokan for security.

**ankkox** Massive six-legged armored riding beasts native to Haruun Kal.

**Ankura** A Gungan subspecies characterized by hooded eyes, as well as greener pigment and smaller haillu than their Otolla cousins.

***Anlage*** A massive warship that neared completion at Fondor's Orbital Shipyard 1321, the *Anlage* was destroyed by a Yuuzhan Vong attack.

**Annaj** The capital system in the Moddell sector, it served as a staging ground for the Imperial Navy. Following the disastrous rout at Endor, the defeated Imperial fleet retreated to Annaj.

***Annealer*** One of three *Acclamator*-class troop ships dispatched by the Galactic Republic to help defend Duro from General Grievous's crushing advance during the Clone Wars.

**annealing** The process by which the energy-charged seeds of the boras trees of Zonama Sekot were shaped by mature boras trees into new forms. The creation of a Sekotan starship from seed-partners mimicked this process, as the forged seed-partners became seed-disks, which were then molded to airframes and combined with technology to form starships.

**Annihilator** *See* Bollux.

**annihilator droid** A large, deadly, spider-like next-generation droid developed by the Colicoids for the Separatists. Skorpenek annihilator droids walked on four sharp pincers and were armed with menacing blasters. A combination particle–energy shield surrounded each droid with a bubble, featuring a polarization signature so that the annihilator could fire out.

**annisa** This flavorful herb grew wild in the mountain regions near the Tanglewoods on the planet Bellassa. It was often steeped in water, creating a beverage with a subtle taste and aroma similar to a weak tea.

**Anno, Klossi** A Chalactan Jedi who survived Order 66, she joined up with similar survivors led by Roan Shryne. She set off to find other Jedi survivors on Kashyyyk, only to be badly injured by Darth Vader. Anno survived, though, and decided to lie low as an agriculturist or construction engineer, where she could perhaps be attached to an Imperial project and learn how to sabotage the Empire from within.

**Annon, Blix** An important Senator and supporter of the Jedi who owned an elegant starship that was attacked by pirate war droids dispatched by Lorian Nod. Despite the protection of Master Dooku and his Padawan Qui-Gon Jinn, Annon was kidnapped and later died of a heart attack.

**Annoo** The name of at least two planets in galactic history. First, it was the original home of the hulking reptilian species the Annoo-dat Prime, who exhausted their world's resources and abandoned it. The Annoo-dat Prime then conquered Gelefil and its people, renaming the planet Annoo and absorbing the native Ret into their culture. This second Annoo was an agricultural planet and stronghold of the gangster Sise Fromm in the early days of the Empire. Demma Moll and her daughter also had a farm there.

**Annoo-dat** The name shared by two species inhabiting what became known as Annoo. The original inhabitants—the Annoo-dat Blue—were known as the Ret until conquered by the invading Annoo-dat Prime. Likewise, the planet was renamed from Gelefil to Annoo. The Annoo-dat Blue were long-lived with heavy-lidded eyes, flat noses, and spotted skin. The Annoo-dat Prime were more reptilian in appearance, with gold scales, four eyes, and a tail.

**Anoat lizard-ants** Small 12-legged creatures from Anoat, they were best known for their tendency to swarm during mating season.

**Anoat system** Located in the backwater Ison Corridor, this system included the planets Anoat, Gentes (the homeworld of the pig-like Ugnaughts), and Deyer, a colony world. Animal life on Anoat included Anoat lizard-ants. Moff Rebus, a weapons specialist working for the Empire, had a hidden stronghold located under the sewage system of Anoat City. Rebus was captured by Alliance agent Kyle Katarn following the Battle of Yavin. After their evacuation from Hoth, Han Solo and Princess Leia Organa found themselves near the Anoat system and decided to seek assistance at Bespin's Cloud City.

**Anobis** This Mid Rim world adjacent to Ord Mantell was ravaged by civil war. It was the home planet of a Zabrak colony as well as Anja Gallandro.

**Anointed People** These intelligent reptilian aliens from Abonshee, or Masterhome, lived in a feudal state of technology and government.

*Anooba*

**Anomid** Born galactic tourists, the humanoid Anomids were native to the Yablari system. Anomids were technology wizards and wealthy enough to travel the galaxy even during times of upheaval. They were born without vocal cords, so when they dealt with speaking species they wore elaborate vocalizer masks whose synthesized sounds served as language. With these face-covering masks and the long, hooded robes they favored, Anomids' features were nearly 100 percent hidden—a perfect disguise that didn't go unnoticed by spies and agents.

**anooba** Thick-skinned pack predators native to Tatooine. They had strong jaws that could crush bones.

**Anor, Nom** The silver-tongued executor who spearheaded the Yuuzhan Vong invasion of the galaxy. He was a highly skilled member of the intendant caste who used bioengineering skills to craft organic tools of cloak and dagger, and created an insidious virus with which he infected Mara Jade Skywalker. Even when stripped of weaponry, Nom Anor was not unarmed—his eye socket concealed a plaeryin bol capable of spitting deadly venom.

Anor worked both as a subtle manipulator and a political firebrand, disrupting local politics and stirring up trouble for the New Republic and the Jedi. Anor backed Xandel Carivus, a key member of the Imperial Interim Council that replaced the Empire after the death of Palpatine's clones. His behind-the-scenes actions helped hasten the eventual downfall of the fragmented Empire. Nom Anor resurfaced years later on Rhommamool as leader of the Red Knights of Life extremist group. His heated rhetoric against droids, technology, and the Jedi amassed a sizable following, straining the delicate peace between Rhommamool and sister planet Osarian. As the crisis escalated on the twin worlds, Nom Anor again vanished, faking his own death.

These were but steps in an advance mission, as the Yuuzhan Vong invasion soon began in force. This principal incursion, led mostly by members of the intendant caste, was deemed a failure, and Anor's status was tainted by association. The next Yuuzhan Vong wave consisted of the warrior caste. Anor forged tenuous alliances with warriors such as Warmaster Tsavong Lah, who distrusted him. Anor hatched a scheme to use a defector to defeat the Jedi, but this eventually failed. Anor was able to recover by bringing in the Hutts as allies. Knowing the Hutts were untrustworthy, Anor used them to sow disinformation into the New Republic ranks.

Anor was finally able to redeem himself in Warmaster Tsavong Lah's eyes by devastating and conquering the world of Duro. It was a hollow victory, as the Warmaster did not promote Anor, and the intendant then found himself competing with Vergere, Tsavong Lah's unlikely alien underling and adviser. Upon the discovery that Jacen and Jaina Solo were twins—a relationship of great significance in Yuuzhan Vong mythology—Tsavong Lah tasked Anor and Vergere with the capture of the Solo children. The opportunity came when the Solos infiltrated the heart of a Yuuzhan Vong operation on Myrkr. By mission's end, Anakin Solo was dead, Jaina Solo had escaped, and Jacen Solo had been captured.

Anor intended to twist Jacen into the instrument of Jaina's destruction, thereby fulfilling an ancient Yuuzhan Vong prophecy when one twin sacrificed the other. Jacen proved difficult to break, however. Aided by the traitorous Vergere, Jacen escaped into the overgrown wilds of the Yuuzhan Vong–conquered Coruscant, now called Yuuzhan'tar. Nom Anor led the charge to recapture him, but ultimately failed. Jacen's efforts subtly destabilized the Yuuzhan Vong transformation of Coruscant, and the Yuuzhan Vong visions of perfection and infallibility began to erode.

Despite his failure, Nom Anor continued to risk heresy in his quest for information he could use to his advantage. Donning an ooglith masquer, he infiltrated a Yuuzhan Vong heretical sect and learned that some of the deepest tenets of the Yuuzhan Vong philosophy might have foundations as unstable as Yuuzhan'tar's transformation. Failing the Warmaster again by advocating a disastrous attack on Ebaq 9, Anor fled to the depths of Coruscant, in disguise among the Shamed caste. He gained popularity and power as Yu'shaa, a heretical prophet who spoke of reform and eventual freedom for the outcast Shamed Ones. Anor hoped to strike back at Overlord Shimrra in revenge for his misfortune.

*Nom Anor*

With word that the living planet Zonama Sekot had been found, Nom Anor saw his opportunity. He knew Zonama Sekot was something Shimrra deeply feared. Confirming the planet's existence and location, Nom Anor returned to Shimrra and was reinstated for his discovery. He was elevated to the rank of prefect of Yuuzhan'tar and tasked with quelling the growing ranks of heretical Shamed Ones, but Anor found that he could not control the very revolution he had previously sparked and fanned as Yu'shaa. In the interest of self-preservation, he again adopted the guise of the Prophet and led the Shamed Ones in battle against the warriors.

Attempting to escape the conflict, Anor was instead defeated and captured by Mara Jade Skywalker. Anor revealed to her Shimrra's plot to use the Republic's own Alpha Red virus to destroy Zonama Sekot. He then agreed to take Mara to Shimrra's Citadel while on the constant lookout for an opportunity to escape. Shimrra was defeated, and Nom Anor, realizing he had no future, died when his escape craft crashed onto Coruscant.

**Anor, Phaa** A Yuuzhan Vong of the intendant caste and a crèche-mate of Nom Anor. During the early stages of the Yuuzhan Vong invasion, he served as a subordinate under his cousin, until Nom Anor began to fail in his missions. When the executor fled Corsucant on a search for Zonama Sekot, Nom Anor maintained a villip that communicated with Phaa Anor. Nom Anor hoped that his cousin would relay the message that Zonama Sekot had been found and would soon be destroyed. Phaa Anor reluctantly agreed to bring the message to Supreme Overlord Shimrra, despite the fact that it might cost him his life.

**Anoth** A multiple planet orbiting a small white sun, Anoth consisted of three parts; it was unrecorded on any chart and was chosen by Luke Skywalker and Admiral Ackbar as the primary hiding place for Han and Leia Organa Solo's Jedi children, Jacen, Jaina, and Anakin. The two largest pieces of Anoth were close enough to scrape together, causing powerful static discharges between them that bathed the third fragment in sensor-masking electrical storms. The third piece orbited a safe distance from the other two and held a breathable atmosphere in its valleys despite its relatively low gravity; it was the site of the stronghold where Leia's trusted aide, Winter, cared for the Solo children. An Imperial attack with MT-AT walkers led by Ambassador Furgan was launched against the Anoth stronghold in an unsuccessful attempt to kidnap young Anakin. The hidden base was repaired, and 13 years after the Battle of Endor, Leia sent Winter and all three of her children there for their safety during the crisis at Almania.

***Another Chance*** After the end of the Clone Wars, the people of Alderaan wholeheartedly adopted pacifism and banned all weapons from the planet's surface. All remaining superweapons were placed aboard a huge Alderaanian war frigate converted into an armory ship called *Another Chance*, which was programmed to jump through hyperspace continually unless called home by the Council of Elders. It was recovered by Alliance agents sometime after Alderaan's destruction.

***Another Idiot's Array 2*** Generally regarded to be one of the worst holovids released in the later years of the Galactic Republic.

**Anselm** An Alliance technician from Baffop, he prepped Luke Skywalker's X-wing fighter prior to the Battle of Yavin. In the years after that victory, Anselm became a lieutenant; he later served as the lead technical member of the crew sent by Leia Organa Solo to recover the *Katana* fleet during the Thrawn crisis.

**Anselmi** One of the two native sentient species of Glee Anselm, the Anselmi were adapted to live on land, unlike their amphibious cousins, the Nautolans.

**Ansion** This seemingly unimportant Mid Rim border world was the nexus of a vast series of interplanetary treaties such as the Keitumite Mutual Military Treaty and the Malarian Alliance encompassing over 40 influential planets. Inhabitants of Ansion were referred to as Ansionians, and included humans, the native Alwari, and the Armalats. Animal life included the massive suubatars. Immense grass-covered prairies dominated much of Ansionian topography. Rivers cut erratically through the yellow-green flatlands, while rolling hills occasionally interrupted the monotony of the terrain. There were clumps of forests filled with strange, intertwined trees and brachiating fungi. The planet had two moons.

The Unity of Community—the closest thing to a recognizable planetary government—was a loosely bound political entity that represented the scattered city-states of Ansion. It combined such cities as Cuipernam, Doigon, Flerauw, and Dashbalar. The Unity was at odds with the native Alwari nomads, who resisted modernization and preferred their simple life on the plains. After millennia of constant conflict between the Alwari nomads and the city-folk, a tenuous peace was established but was threatened by a border dispute. Obi-Wan Kenobi, Anakin Skywalker, Luminara Unduli, and Barriss Offee settled this dispute while also ending a long-standing feud between the Borokii and Januul clans of the Alwari. This peaceful settlement kept Ansion within the Republic during the height of the Separatist crisis. Senator Mousul represented Ansion prior to the outbreak of the Clone Wars.

**Ansionian** Though the term has come to encompass all inhabitants of Ansion, *Ansionian* more specifically describes the dominant native species. Ansionians were slightly shorter than average humans, slimmer, wiry, and lean, with skin a pale yellow that was almost golden. Both genders were hairless except for a single dense brush of fur about 15 centimeters wide and 7 or 8 centimeters high that ran from the top of their foreheads all the way down their backs to terminate in a stumpy, 15-centimeter-long tail. Beneath their warm, well-made clothing, the sweep of hair, varying in color across the entire visible spectrum, was kept neatly trimmed.

The large eyes of the Ansionians were well suited for night vision. Because of the protruding, convex nature of their eyes, they couldn't squint. They had sharp teeth and were omnivorous, though they ate proportionately more meat than humans. Ansionians had three long, nimble fingers on each hand. Most native Ansionians belonged to one of the Alwari clans of nomads living on the plains.

***Ansta*** A Galactic Alliance warship that was part of the Third and Fifth fleet blockade of Corellia.

**Antamont** Site of a Republic stronghold and Clone Wars battle where a single damaged battle droid discovered self-preservation and fled from the ranks of the droid army.

**Antana, Soara** A legendary lightsaber virtuoso who showed promise even as a young Padawan, she was known for her wise sayings in lightsaber combat, which included the maxim "Like a feather, not a stick." She became a lightsaber combat instructor at the Jedi Temple. Anakin Skywalker studied with her, and she was master to Padawan Darra Thel-Tanis.

**Antar 4** Home to the Gotal species and the fourth of six moons orbiting the gas giant Antar in the Inner Rim's Prindaar system. Antar 4 had an unusual rotation that made seasonal climate changes very pronounced. The moon's orbital pattern around the gas giant also created constantly changing day–night cycles. To help compensate for any absence of light, species on Antar 4 developed features such as the Gotals' energy-sensing head cones, which aided them in sensing the moods of others and in hunting the native herds of quivry. Antar 4 had no organized government, but traded and otherwise interacted effectively with the rest of galactic society. The Battle of Antar 4 was sparked by a secessionist movement a year before the start of the Clone Wars, and was largely considered a botched operation by the Jedi Knights, who failed to prevent great loss of life. The Confederacy of Independent Systems maintained a base there.

**Antares sapphire** *See* Ankarres sapphire.

***Antares Six*** One of two New Republic escort frigates that accompanied the *Millennium Falcon* to Coruscant to rescue the crew of the *Liberator*, the *Antares Six* saved Lando Calrissian and Wedge Antilles after their Star Destroyer, *Emancipator*, was destroyed by an Imperial World Devastator.

**Antarian Rangers** A centuries-old order of non-Force-using warriors founded on Antar 4 to help the Jedi Knights, Antarian

Anti-infantry battery at Echo Base on Hoth

Rangers were able to move in any environment and had communities on several worlds, including Toprawa. The Jedi Council never officially acknowledged the Antarian Rangers as a resource, but many Jedi Masters used them as vital allies in their efforts to maintain peace in the galaxy. Whole clans were killed during the Clone Wars; the rest were purged along with the Jedi.

**Ante-Endor Association (AEA)** A pro-Imperial group on Mrlsst that denied the Battle of Endor ever happened. Its emblem was an Imperial symbol with a Death Star. While Rogue Squadron was visiting Mrlsst, Tycho Celchu was attacked in an alley by a gang of AEA thugs armed with batons.

**Anteevy** A remote, lifeless, ice-covered world with at least one moon, Anteevy was the site of an Imperial robotics facility where the alloy phrik was refined and treated for use in armoring the Dark Troopers. Following the Battle of Yavin, Alliance agent Kyle Katarn disabled the facility with several sequencer charges.

**Antemeridian sector** Bordering the Meridian sector, it was once an Imperial satrapy. Heavy industry had a strong presence in the Antemeridian sector, and a trade artery passing through it was known as the Antemeridian Route. Following the death of the Emperor, Moff Getelles continued to rule the sector, backed by a strong naval force commanded by Admiral Larm. Nine years after the Battle of Endor, Getelles made a deal with Seti Ashgad of Nam Chorios to invade the Meridian sector and secure Nam Chorios for industrial development by the Loronar Corporation. But Admiral Larm was killed and his fleet defeated in the Battle of Nam Chorios.

**Antemeridias** A planet in the Antemeridian sector where the Loronar Corporation built a manufacturing facility to produce synthdroids and CCIR needle fighters. The facility was operated by Siefax, a dummy corporation for Loronar.

**Antha-Kres** A Tiss-shar, he served as a mayor on the Tiss'sharl League's chief council during the height of the New Order. He was considered among the handful of individuals who could eventually become vice president. Shortly after the Battle of Yavin, however, Antha-Kres was assassinated; he was eventually succeeded by Geor-dan-thi. Many within the government of Tiss'sharl believed that Geor-dan-thi was behind the assassination, although no public evidence was ever presented.

**Anticeptin-D** A potent sterilizing medical drug developed for use by the Grand Army of the Republic during the Clone Wars.

**anticoncussion field** A moderately protective magnetic shield, this field was used to protect buildings and space outposts from damage by solid objects such as space junk or small meteorites. However, an anticoncussion field offered little protection against energy weapons.

**antigrav** A technique used to counter the normal effects of gravity; the term also referred to any mechanism that accomplished that feat. The most common antigrav drive was the repulsorlift engine. Such drives worked only when a large mass that produced gravity was nearby.

**anti-infantry battery** A variety of weapons, the most popular of which was designed by Golan Arms to help the Empire suppress native populations on low-tech worlds. The cannon originally was designed in two primary models—the SP.9 was a self-propelled twin-barreled model mounted atop a repulsorlift chassis, while the DF.9/B was a fixed emplacement mounted on an armored 4-meter-tall tower. The fixed version, which found its way into Alliance arsenals on Echo Base, required a crew of two to operate, both protected within the armored proton-shielded tower. The rotating turret had a full 360-degree firing arc and a rapid firing rate.

**Antilles, Bail** The Senator of Alderaan during the Trade Federation invasion of Naboo. During the taxation debates, he argued that the Trade Federation should not be allowed to augment its droid defenses. Antilles was nominated, along with Senators Palpatine of Naboo and Ainlee Teem of Malastare, to succeed the ousted Chancellor Valorum. Antilles left office, followed in the Senate by Bail Organa. The two attended the retirement ceremony for Senator Horox Ryyder prior to the outbreak of the Clone Wars.

**Antilles, Corellia** A famed archaeologist, she became the subject of a number of sensational—and mostly fictional—holoserials.

**Antilles, Iella Wessiri** A former member of the Corellian Security Forces, she had been Corran Horn's partner. When Imperial liaison officer Kirtan Loor attempted to arrest them on trumped-up charges, Iella and her husband Diric Wessiri fled to Coruscant. There she joined Alliance Intelligence and was already working undercover on Coruscant when Rogue Squadron arrived to liberate the planet from Imperial control. She was part of Wedge Antilles's team as they commandeered a construction droid, diverting it toward a major computer center. Horn was flying cover for her team when his Z-95 Headhunter crashed, and he was presumed killed.

The apparent loss of Horn was soon compounded by the discovery that her husband Diric had been an Imperial sleeper agent. Iella learned this when she was forced to kill an Imperial assassin who turned out to be a brainwashed Diric. Corran Horn reappeared and was able to offer some comfort in the following weeks. Iella and her team of operatives were later sent to Thyferra to assist in the eventual overthrow of Ysanne Isard's government. She joined forces with the Ashern terrorists and Zaltin Bacta Corporation security forces and, when the time was ripe, easily took over the Xucphra Corporation's administration building, headquarters for Isard's puppet government. Later, in a confrontation inside Isard's former quarters, Wessiri shot and killed Ysanne Isard.

Iella and Wedge grew closer as they shared assignments, and during the hunt for Warlord Zsinj they became romantically attached. Their careers often interfered with their growing relationship, but after the New Republic mission to Adumar, Wedge proposed to Iella. They married and had two daughters, Myri and Syal. She and Wedge retired to raise their family, but both came out of retirement during the Yuuzhan Vong invasion. After the defeat of the Yuuzhan Vong, the Antilles family settled on Corellia. When tensions between Coruscant and Corellia turned to war, Wedge and Iella were once again called to active duty. Iella gathered intelligence working as a card dealer aboard the converted Star Destroyer *Errant Venture.*

**Antilles, Jagged and Zena** Parents of Wedge and Syal Antilles, Jagged and Zena operated a fuel depot on the Gus Treta space station in the Corellian system. They were killed in an explosion caused by pirates led by Loka Hask.

*Jon Antilles*

**Antilles, Jon** A mysterious solo Jedi who wore long flowing robes and claimed to go only where he was needed. *Jon Antilles* was probably an alias. Adding to the mystery surrounding him, Jon Antilles more than once had been believed dead. He was a student of the Dark Woman who years before infiltrated the Bounty Hunters' Guild and brought many murderers to justice. He was part of the mission to Queyta during the Clone Wars. Antilles died fighting Durge in hand-to-hand combat.

**Antilles, Myri** Daughter of Wedge and Iella Antilles and younger sister to Syal. She was named for Wedge's friend Mirax "Myra" Terrik. During the Yuuzhan Vong War, Myri, Syal, and many Jedi children were sent to the safety of the Maw. After the defeat of the alien invaders, the Antilles family settled on Corellia. She was in her 20s when the conflict between the Corellian Confederation and the Galactic Alliance began. She tried to avoid taking sides in the war, and instead helped her mother gather vital intelligence working as a card dealer in the casinos aboard the converted Star Destroyer *Errant Venture.*

**Antilles, Raymus** The Alderaanian captain of the *Tantive IV* and former master of C-3PO and R2-D2. Captain Antilles belonged to the same bloodline as that of Queen Breha of Alderaan, though he himself held no royal title. He was levelheaded, schooled in diplomacy, and a capable pilot who studied under his mentor, Captain Jeremoch Colton. Antilles piloted the Alderaanian consular vessel for Senator Bail Organa and then the Senator's daughter, Leia Organa. A loyal guard to Leia, he died protecting her identity when Darth Vader boarded the *Tantive IV* and strangled the captain.

*Raymus Antilles*

**Antilles, Syal** The elder daughter of Wedge and Iella Antilles, named for Wedge's sister, Syal Antilles Fel. During the Yuuzhan Vong War, Syal, her younger sister Myri, and many Jedi children were sent to the safety of the Maw. Following the invaders' defeat, the Antilles family settled on Corellia. Syal inherited her father's gift for piloting. In adulthood, she changed her name to Lysa Dunter to avoid drawing attention to herself as daughter of Wedge Antilles. As Dunter, she was a member of the Galactic Alliance's Vibrosword Squadron when the conflict between the Corellian Confederation and the Galactic Alliance began. In a space battle in the Corellian system, she unknowingly entered into a dogfight with her father, who was flying for the Corellians.

**Antilles, Wedge** One of the Rebel Alliance's most decorated pilots, a survivor of the major conflicts of the Galactic Civil War, and the soul of the famous Rogue Squadron. From his first flights for the newborn Rebellion to his distinguished career as a general within the New Republic, Wedge always embodied the luck, loyalty, confidence, and courage required of every Rebel pilot.

*Wedge Antilles*

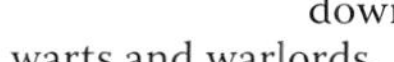

Born and raised on outer Gus Treta, a space station in the Corellian system, Antilles became an orphan as a teenager after his parents, Jagged and Zena, were killed when the station was destroyed by fleeing pirates. With money from an insurance settlement, he purchased a freighter and was soon smuggling weapons for the Rebel Alliance. Answering an open call for combat pilots, he jumped into the cockpit of an X-wing fighter and quickly became one of the Rebellion's most skilled pilots. Wedge earned a post in Red Squadron at the Battle of Yavin, where he first met Luke Skywalker.

After the destruction of the first Death Star, Wedge and Luke founded Rogue Squadron and quickly surrounded themselves with some of the best pilots in the galaxy. Rogue Squadron flew snowspeeders against the Imperial AT-ATs at the Battle of Hoth. During the engagement, Wedge and his gunner, Wes Janson, managed to use their vehicle's power harpoon and tow cable to entangle the legs of a walker, causing the AT-AT to topple over and explode.

After Hoth, Antilles reorganized the elite fighter pilot group and was promoted to commander, or Rogue Leader. The squadron was assigned to the Headquarters Frigate *Home One.* During the Battle of Endor, Rogue Squadron flew as Red Group, in homage to the original X-wing squadron that flew over the first Death Star. Although Antilles was allowed the opportunity to equip his squadron with newer A-wings and B-wings, he stayed with the traditional X-wing. With Admiral Ackbar and Lando Calrissian, he planned the attack on the second Death Star. At the Battle of Endor, Wedge led his squadron against an Imperial Star Destroyer and later followed the *Millennium Falcon* into the heart of the space station and aided in the Death Star's destruction.

Following the Battles of Endor and Bakura, Wedge's missions became increasingly political. Rogue Squadron had become famous throughout the galaxy, and this elite starfighter group spearheaded missions into the heart of Imperial territory, liberating worlds and bringing more systems into the growing New Republic. Wedge and the Rogues were the New Republic's lance in retaking the heart of the Core Worlds, leading the mission that would wrest control of Coruscant from the Empire. Wedge also went on to found the unorthodox Wraith Squadron and hunted down various Imperial stalwarts and warlords.

Following the defeat of Grand Admiral Thrawn five years after the Battle of Endor, Antilles agreed to accept the rank of general on the condition that he could still lead Rogue Squadron. He proved a dominant tactician, but both he and Lando Calrissian suffered heavy losses in the war against the reborn Emperor during which the Empire used many new and advanced military weapons. In response, the New Republic began a reassessment of its own forces. Despite Wedge's objections, his superiors ordered him to create a new Rogue Squadron including fighters of several different designs, which in theory would allow for greater flexibility in battle. Wedge's argument that the purpose of Rogue Squadron would be compromised was refuted with the reasoning that a new squadron's chances of success would be enhanced under the name of the famous Rogue Squadron.

Wedge's distaste for the bureaucratic decisions affecting his command led him to direct the new Rogue Squadron from afar, as commander of the captured Star Destroyer *Lusankya.* He was able to persuade his superiors that this would allow for the broadest range of fighters to be available, with over 100 different types of ships for Rogue Squadron—or Rogue Wing—alone. The new fighter unit saw its first action in the Battle of Phaeda, during which a squadron comprising B-wings, A-wings, and other fighters decimated the Imperial forces.

Wedge's focus on career was such that he rarely had time to pursue much of a personal

Wedge Antilles congratulates Han Solo.

life. Though he had started a stalled romantic relationship with Iella Wessiri, as well as one with Imperial scientist Qwi Xux, more pressing matters—like the campaign of destruction waged by Admiral Daala—frequently surfaced. After a diplomatic mission to Adumar, Wedge proposed marriage to Iella, and she accepted. The couple soon had two daughters, Syal and Myri.

Wedge eventually retired from active duty when peace between the New Republic and the Imperial Remnant was achieved. The Yuuzhan Vong invasion, however, brought Antilles out of retirement. At first, he played an advisory role to the new Rogue Leader, Gavin Darklighter, but before long he was actively flying missions at Sernpidal, Coruscant, Borleais, and elsewhere. Wedge was able to retire once more after the defeat of the Yuuzhan Vong, but the interim of peace did not last.

The Antilles family relocated to Corellia. When tensions between the Corellian Confederation and the Galactic Alliance escalated, Wedge attempted to remain neutral in the conflict, but a preemptive attempt by Alliance agents to arrest him made that impossible. Antilles served as a general in the Corellian Defense Force, planning the Battle of Tralus to minimize civilian deaths, despite the overly bellicose tactics of Thrackan Sal-Solo. Antilles's "soft" attitude spurred his resignation from the Corellian Defense Force, and even a failed assassination attempt against him. He and his family chose to lie low, traveling aboard the converted Star Destroyer *Errant Venture.*

**Antilles, Zena** *See* Antilles, Jagged and Zena.

**Antin, Dr. Amie** One of the most respected experts in the field of neurotoxins, she worked at a facility on her homeworld of Bellassa during the final years of the Galactic Republic. Unknown to her peers, Dr. Antin was a supporter of the Eleven resistance group, and treated many of its members after they were injured on missions against the newly risen Empire. She agreed to accompany Roan Lands and Trever Flume on a mission to join with Ferus Olin to infiltrate the offices of Imperial Governor Wilhuff Tarkin, in the city of Ussa. Darth Vader had been tracking Ferus's movements, however, and confronted them. Vader killed Lands and imprisoned Dr. Antin and Olin; Flume escaped to warn the other members of the Eleven. Dr. Antin was to be sent to a penal colony, but an escaped Olin rescued her before she was shipped offplanet. She then helped him with his investigation into the background of Darth Vader by scouring a wealth of information he had obtained from the Emperor Palpatine Surgical Reconstruction Center. Her investigation pointed to Vader being on the planet Mustafar just after the end of the Clone Wars.

**antiox mask** A specialized breathing mask worn by Kel Dors such as Plo Koon.

**Antipose** The Antipose system was not far from the Centrality. The term *dubesor* was a native slang insult on the planet Antipose XII.

**anti-register device** A rare and highly illegal device that could subvert, cancel, or modify transactions completed on transfer registers or any biometric-print-based security system.

**Anti Republic Liberation Front (ARLF)** A militant insurgent group that sprang up on Serenno after the Battle of Ruusan, it argued that the Galactic Senate was no longer capable of acting on behalf of the galaxy, especially after the passing of the Ruusan Reformations. The insurgents urged disillusioned star systems to secede from the Republic and become independent entities. The ARLF, led by a man named Hetton, was backed by the wealth of noble families. The ARLF was in truth a way for Hetton to amass an army to resurrect the Sith. The group attempted, but failed, to assassinate Chancellor Tarsus Valorum. The ARLF eventually was dismantled by Darth Bane and Darth Zannah, who had their own plans for the Republic.

**Anti-Sedition Provision** A section of the Galactic Loyalty Act that gave the Galactic Alliance Guard and members of the military the ability to forcibly stop any gathering or activity deemed seditious or detrimental to the stability of the Alliance. Failure to comply with this provision could result in harsh penalties, including up to 20 years in prison.

**antisepsis field** Developed during the last decades of the Galactic Republic, this specialized energy field was used to sterilize the area around a surgical patient, thereby minimizing the risk of infection.

**antivehicle artillery** Fixed emplacements that varied widely in size and output; one of the most common was the Atgar 1.4 FD P-Tower. Like all antivehicle artilleries, the P-Tower was designed to target and destroy a variety of enemy craft, including landspeeders, airspeeders, and repulsortanks. It produced a moderately powerful energy beam that had a maximum range of 10 kilometers. Its energy output was only sufficient to damage lightly armored vehicles and could do little against well-protected Imperial war machines such as AT-AT walkers.

**Anton** A front-desk attendant at the Lucky Despot hotel in Mos Eisley.

**Antone** A Bakuran technician, Antone helped Anakin Solo activate the Drall planetary repulsor during the Centerpoint Station crisis in the Corellian system. He felt particularly motivated to help since he had family on Bovo Yagen, a system targeted by the starbuster. Years later, he continued to work at Centerpoint Station during the Yuuzhan Vong invasion.

**Antonin, Vigo** A human Black Sun Vigo with a goatee and gray-streaked hair. Five years before the start of the Clone Wars, Dreddon the Hutt hired Jango Fett to assassinate Antonin while Antonin simultaneously hired Zam Wesell to assassinate Dreddon. Antonin's forces were no match for Jango Fett.

**Anujo, Cellheim** The mysterious aide to Senator Tundra Dowmeia, Anujo was completely covered in black robes.

***Anvil*** One of many Galactic Republic Acclamator assault transports destroyed at Duro by General Grievous's task force during the Clone Wars.

Antivehicle artillery at a Rebel base on Hoth

**Anx** A towering species of 4-meter-tall aliens originally from Gravlex Med. They had large muscular tails evolved for counterbalancing. Their crests were enormous sinuses used by the creatures to speak in a booming, low-frequency language that other Anx could hear from many kilometers away. They had poor eyesight but possessed a remarkable sense of smell. At one point in their history they were enslaved by the Shusugaunts. In the later years of the Galactic Republic, the Anx were represented in the Senate by Horox Ryyder and Zo Howler. By the time of the Battle of Yavin, the galaxy's few Anx were huddled together in miserable poverty on a scattering of low-gravity worlds.

**Anx Minor, Battle of** Admiral Ackbar commanded the *Guardian* during a skirmish with Admiral Pellaeon at the Battle of Anx Minor, 18 years after the Battle of Yavin.

A-OIC (Doc)

**ANY-20 active sensor transceiver** A Fabritech rectenna often used on YT-1300 transports, it provided ship-to-ship jamming capabilities as well as all required communications capabilities.

**Anywhere Room** An amusement attraction on Hologram Fun World that claimed to be able to transport a visitor to any location in the galaxy via fully interactive holographic re-creation.

**Anzat (plural: Anzati)** A species closely resembling humans but with a terrifying anatomical twist. Beside an Anzat's nostrils were fleshy pockets that hid prehensile proboscises that could be uncoiled and inserted through victims' nostrils into their brains to suck out their life essence, or "soup," as the Anzati called it. This vampiric fashion of feasting created many myths and legends about the long-lived Anzati. To an Anzat, beings with more luck tended to have more flavorful "soup." Youthful Anzati reached puberty at approximately 100 years of age, and left Anzat in search of "soup." Anzati assassins were among the most feared in the galaxy. Because Anzati were roamers, it was difficult to determine the true location of their homeworld. Scientists who traveled to a world reputed to be Anzat simply disappeared without a trace.

Anx

**A-OIC (Doc)** A one-of-a-kind class one medical droid designed and built by robotics genius Massad Thrumble. A-OIC was abducted by the Pikkel sisters and brought to the infamous rogue scientist Spinda Caveel, who intended to use Doc to customize dangerous droids for high-paying clients. Prince Xizor's onetime aide, Guri, later rescued the droid and brought it back to Thrumble. A-OIC was crucial in Guri's reprogramming, deleting all memory of her criminal past.

**Aora, Aruk Besadii** A corpulent Hutt on Nal Hutta born nearly 900 years before the founding of the Empire. The brother of Zavval the Hutt, Aruk and his offspring, Durga, headed the Besadii clan, which controlled spice operations on Ylesia. He was poisoned by the Desilijic clan, thus placing Durga in control of the Besadii clan.

**APA-5 droid** A mess hall droid. Kir Kanos used an APA-5 droid to fly the scimitar bomber that defeated the Star Destoyer *Emperor's Revenge.*

**Apailana, Queen** The 13-year-old successor to Queen Jamillia, Apailana was reigning monarch of Naboo during the funeral of Padmé Amidala. Apailana respected Amidala's privacy in accordance with Naboo tradition and did not call for any sort of investigation into her death, though she did privately question the Imperial version of the story that blamed the Jedi. Her cooperation with the Empire was given only begrudgingly, though she never outwardly rebelled against the new Empire. When Apailana's government was discovered harboring Jedi fugitives, the 501st Legion eliminated her and the Empire installed a more loyal monarch.

**Aparo sector** Together with the Wyl sector, it formed the inner border of the Corporate Sector. The Aparo sector was long ruled by Moff Wyrrhem.

**Apatros** An Outer Rim mining world within the Galactic Republic operated by the Outer Rim Oreworks Company over 1,000 years before the Battle of Yavin. A young man named Dessel worked the cortosis mines there; he would one day become the Dark Lord Darth Bane.

Anzat

**Aphran IV** A heavily forested world with blue seas located in the Aphran system, close to Bilbringi. Aphran IV was warm, lacked polar ice, and had no moons. It was considered an impoverished planet, known for its mastery in woodworking. After Coruscant fell to the Yuuzhan Vong, Leia Organa Solo and Han Solo traveled to Aphran IV, suspecting that the planet might be siding with the Peace Brigade. Disguised as pirates, their first mission was to set up a holocom-and-comlink communications system that could be used by the resistance on Aphran. Their identities were uncovered and they were briefly taken into custody by Aphran Planetary Exosecurity before being rescued by R2-D2 and C-3PO.

**Apice, Bryn and Wes** The brothers Bryn and Wes Apice, along with their friend Rayt, attempted to flee their war-torn homeworld by disguising themselves as clone troopers. Their plan worked too well, as they were boarded onto a Republic ship as part of the clone army.

Queen Apailana of Naboo

**Apla, Chik** A former Imperial guard, Chik Apla was part of the conspiracy to disrupt the wedding of Luke Skywalker and Mara Jade on Coruscant. He was badly injured while attempting to ambush the bride-to-be.

**Ap-Llewf, Gwellib** A former AgriCorps Jedi selected to receive dark side training by Darth Vader after the Clone Wars. He became one of the first Inquisitors of the New Order. Decades later, he loyally served the resurrected clone of the Emperor.

**Appazanna Engineering Works** A Wookiee manufacturing concern, maker of the Wookiee flying catamaran used in the Clone Wars.

**appeasement vote** A vote put before the New Republic Senate as a result of a Yuuzhan Vong ultimatum. At issue was whether the New Republic should officially outlaw the Jedi and accept the truce terms put forward by Tsavong Lah. Viqi Shesh led the coalition in support of the measure. It failed by a margin of two to one.

**Appo, Clone Commander** Clone commander 1119 of the 501st Legion at the Jedi Temple on Coruscant, he ordered Bail Organa to leave the landing platform the night of Order 66. Appo was seriously injured during Padawan Zett Jukassa's escape attempt but was treated and returned to active duty, later accompanying Darth Vader to Alderaan. Appo was killed by Roan Shryne on Kashyyyk.

**"Appreciated Reminiscences"** The translated title of a Bith song that became Epoh Trebor's signature during his tours to visit the troops of the Grand Army of the Republic in the Clone Wars.

**Apprentice Legislature** A galaxy-spanning political organization with local chapters that allowed hands-on experience in government service. Padmé Amidala joined at age eight. Joining the Naboo Apprentice Legislators was like making a formal announcement that you were entering public service. Apprentice Legislators often became Senatorial Advisers.

**Apprentice Tournament** A regular challenge held at the Jedi Temple that allowed Padawans to engage in real combat in order to build their fighting skills and experience. This became especially important during the Clone Wars as more and more Padawans were being sent to the battlefront. It was open to students who were at least 10 years of age who had been exposed to combat, or were physically stronger than their peers. It was open to younglings who had not yet been accepted as Padawans by a Jedi Master.

**approach vector** A nav-computer-generated trajectory, this vector placed a ship on an intercept course with another ship or a target for purposes of rendezvous or attack.

**Aqinos, Master** A Sunesi Jedi Master who was exiled by the Jedi Council for his teaching of the living Force techniques to inorganic living beings known as the Shards. He helped create the Iron Knights. Having hid on Dweem during the rise of the Empire, Aqinos pledged his service to Luke Skywalker's Jedi Order decades later. Aqinos was killed in the Yuuzhan Vong War.

Clone Commander Appo at the Jedi Temple

**Aqualish** A species of tusked, walrus-faced humanoids from the watery planet Ando. The Aqualish developed two predominant subspecies: the Quara, who have clawed, five-fingered hands, and the Aquala who have fins for hands. There was also a breed of Aqualish with four eyes known as the Ualaq. The timely arrival of a Republic spacecraft interrupted a racially fueled war and prompted the xenophobic Aqualish to band together in attacking the offworld interlopers. The Aqualish then used the gift of advanced technology to take their belligerence and war-like nature to space. The Aqualish ravaged Ando's sister planet, and were eventually stopped by the Republic.

The Republic set an arrangement in place wherein teachers would help assimilate the Aqualish into galactic society, and stripped all Aqualish hyperdrive-equipped starships of weaponry. This created a long-standing resentment of the Republic among the Aqualish, who had a galaxywide reputation for being nasty, crude, and aggressive. During the final days of the Galactic Republic, Andoan Senator Po Nudo seceded from the Republic, bringing his people and worlds into the Confederacy of Independent Systems.

When the Imperials took over Ando, they turned it into a police state designed to quell the various Aqualish uprisings. Many offworld Aqualish became mercenaries, bounty hunters, and pirates. The Aqualish hated the Empire, but showed no interest in the Rebel Alliance. One Aqualish, Ponda Baba, a much-hunted murderer and thief, picked a fight with Luke Skywalker at the Mos Eisley cantina. Obi-Wan Kenobi tried to calm him and his partner in crime, Dr. Evazan, but they persisted. One swipe of a lightsaber later, Baba was short one right forearm.

Aqualish Senate delegation

**aquanna** A species of gas-bag-type creatures native to Naboo. The Gungan Grand Army fit them with weaponry to become living air cruisers.

**Aquaris** A water-covered world devoid of landmasses and home to Silver Fyre's organization of former pirates and mercenaries called the Freeholders. They inhabited an expansive underwater base accessible through a retractable landing platform, and piloted submersible aqua-skimmers when hunting local marine life. Among the many dangerous ocean creatures was the enormous demon-squid. Following the Battle of Yavin, Fyre and her Freeholders joined the Alliance during a conference with Princess Leia Organa on Kabal. The Princess and her companions visited Aquaris after leaving Kabal and were betrayed by Kraaken, Fyre's deputy commander.

**aqua-skimmer** A vehicle used for surface and subsurface aquatic travel on planets such as Aquaris.

**Aquilaris** On this planet almost entirely covered by water, the only natural formations consisted of reefs and a handful of island chains. Inhabitants of Aquilaris built floating cities on the planet, connected by a series of underwater tunnels and hover bridges. A prominent Podrace course on Aquilaris wove through bridges and tunnels as it traveled through two of the planet's major cities. The course also took racers into the remnants of a half-submerged and abandoned settlement known as Old City.

**Arabanth** This planet of the Hapes Cluster was known for its thought puzzles.

**arabore** Fish-eating rodents native to Toola, they featured great flat tusks protruding from short snouts. Young Whiphids had to kill an arabore as a rite of passage.

**arachnor** A giant, spider-like creature native to the macaab mushroom forests of the planet Arzid. The fungi contained chemical ingredients that, when ingested by an arachnor, caused the spider's webbing to become perhaps the stickiest, most inescapable of any known arachnid species in the galaxy. Arachnors were extremely protective of their environment. Although they were nonsentient, they instinctively knew how to frighten prey and direct them into their hidden webs.

**Arakkus, Dr.** The onetime director of an Imperial weapons development complex, he was contaminated in a radiation experiment. After that, Dr. Arakkus lived in an abandoned Imperial transport amid a graveyard of ships circling a collapsing star. He was killed in an explosion after Han Solo ignited a negatron charge to free his *Millennium Falcon* from the gravitational pull of the star.

**Arakyd Industries** A major droid, heavy weapons, and starship manufacturer that made such products as the Death Star droid and the Viper probot series. Through political maneuvering and competitive infighting, the company set itself to receive the first Imperial droid contracts; it shrewdly exploited this early windfall by working hard to become the galaxy's leading military supplier. Consumer-market mod-

els from Arakyd were moderately successful, but accounted for only a small fraction of its total yearly output. Despite the company's history, the New Republic worked closely with Arakyd after the collapse of Imperial rule.

**Ar'alani, Admiral** An admiral in the Chiss Defense Fleet, she was one of the few Chiss to have encountered the "Far Outsiders" (Yuuzhan Vong) and survived. Though she often differed with Thrawn and his advocacy of preemptive strikes—an anathema in Chiss culture—she did agree that the Vagaari were a threat to the Chiss that should be dealt with.

**Aralia** A small, tropical world in the Andron system, Aralia was home to both the planetary amusement park Project Aralia and the troublesome, semi-intelligent Ranats. The Ranats (who called themselves Con Queecon or "the conquerors") evolved on the planet Rydar II, but came to Aralia when the spice-smuggling ship on which they had stowed away crashed in Aralia's jungles. Ranats lived in tribes numbering around 100 and inhabited maze-like underground warrens. The Ranat population expanded greatly after the crash; they took over most areas of Aralia, including its grassy steppes and mountains. Their fierce appetites led to a decline in most of Aralia's fauna, including the pig-like roba. After Ranats interfered with the construction of Project Aralia, the builders tried to organize an extermination of the species. This led to an Imperial ruling that Ranats could be killed in self-defense and may not be armed under any circumstances. Some Ranats were drug- and mind-controlled by Emperor Palpatine and Darth Vader to serve as guards.

Koffi Arana

***Aramadia*** The consular ship of the Duskhan League.

**Aramb** A Gotal lieutenant in the engineering corps of the Galactic Alliance's military, he served aboard the *Admiral Ackbar* in the years following the Yuuzhan Vong War. He was rendered unconscious when a swarm of Gorog assassin bugs infiltrated the ship.

**Arana, Koffi** A dark-skinned, human male Jedi who survived Order 66. He convened with other survivors on Kessel, and felt the Jedi needed to respond and attack the Sith. Darth Vader arrived to dispatch the Jedi and killed Arana.

**Arastide, Senator** A New Republic Senate Defense Council member from the planet Gantho.

**Arat Fraca** Located two sectors away from Motexx, the planet was separated from Motexx by the Black Nebula in Parfadi. The starliner *Star Morning,* owned by the Fallanassi religious order, left Motexx a few weeks before the Battle of Endor with full cargo holds, bound for Gowdawl under a charter license. The liner then disappeared for 300 days, eventually showing up at Arat Fraca with empty holds.

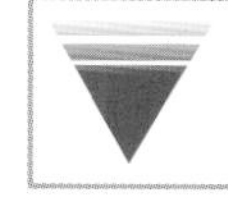

**Aratech Repulsor Company** A company dedicated to the design and manufacture of speeder bikes. In business for centuries—initially as a manufacturer of droids and artificial intelligence—Aratech was one of the first companies to pledge support to the Republic in the war against the Separatists. As the Republic assembled its clone army, Aratech provided a fleet of its notable 74-Z speeder bikes for use in the ground battle on Geonosis. Aratech managed to survive well past the Emperor's reign, with its 74-Z becoming a staple of both Imperial and New Republic forces.

**Arawynne, Princess** A Ghostling child sold into slavery to Gardulla the Hutt. Anakin Skywalker and Kitster Banai freed her.

**Arber, Lieutenant** An Imperial Navy officer, he worked with Jacen Solo and a group of engineers from the Galactic Alliance to reprogram a gravitic amplitude modulator for use in jamming the communications of a Yuuzhan Vong yammosk shortly after the Battle of Bastion. Lieutenant Arber served aboard the *Defiant,* and his work on the GAM was not immediately endorsed by Captain Essenton, despite the assurances of Grand Admiral Pellaeon himself.

**Arbo** A wise Ewok legend keeper and admirer of Logray.

**Arbo Maze** A natural feature on the Forest Moon of Endor, this overgrowth of trees was so dense and perplexing in its maze-like paths that most beings and creatures who entered it became hopelessly lost—even the native Ewoks who lived in the trees.

**Arbor, Jenna Zan** A leading transgenic scientist who developed vaccines for worlds threatened by deadly viruses, she focused her attention on helping planets with low levels of technology. As head of Arbor Industries, one of her projects was to triple the food supply on the famine-stricken planet of Melasaton. In truth, she had engineered many of these calamities, and then earned acclaim and wealth by saving the people she had threatened.

She became fascinated with the biological underpinnings of the Force, and conducted hidden and forbidden experiments on Ren S'orn, the Force-sensitive son of a Republic Senator. Wanting a more powerful test subject, she kidnapped Jedi Master Qui-Gon Jinn and subjected him to painful study at her secret research facility on Simpla-12. Obi-Wan Kenobi came to the rescue of his Master, and Arbor was sent to prison. She escaped, however, and later surfaced at a new lab on Vanqor, developing a drug called Zone of Self-Containment. Anakin Skywalker fell under the sway of this poison before being rescued by Kenobi, Siri Tachi, and Ferus Olin. Arbor again fled, and with the help of her benefactor Granta Omega attempted but failed to poison the Galactic Senate. The Jedi pursued her to Korriban, killing Omega, but Arbor continued to elude them.

She eventually joined the Confederacy of Independent Systems, developing biological weapons for use against the Republic's clone army. After the fall of the Republic, she continued her nefarious work—but this time for the Empire.

**Arbra** Arbra was a distant arboreal planet that served as the Rebel Alliance's main headquarters after the Battle of Hoth. So fortunate were they to find Arbra, Rebel agents nicknamed it Salvation. The planet was populated by Hoojibs, tiny telepathic rodent-like sentients.

**ARC-170 starfighter** A heavily armed Republic starfighter introduced late in the Clone Wars. The ARC-170 (Aggressive ReConnaissance) fighter also functioned as a lone recon scout, with extended consumables for five standard days of remote operations. Three clone trooper pilots operated this advanced combat craft, with a pilot handling the flight maneuvers, a copilot operating the laser cannons mounted on the ship's wide wings, and a tail gunner operating the dorsal rear-facing cannon. The fighter also carried an astromech droid for onboard repairs. During the Battle of Coruscant, Clone Commander Odd Ball Davijaan led Squad Seven in providing cover to the Jedi starfighters piloted by Obi-Wan Kenobi and Anakin Skywalker. It was the duty of this squad of ARC-170s to keep the droid starfighter forces off the tails of the Jedi so that they could rescue the captive Chancellor Palpatine. ARC-170s were stationed all over the Republic during the Clone Wars, including the aerial campaigns over Cato Neimoidia led by Jedi Master Plo Koon.

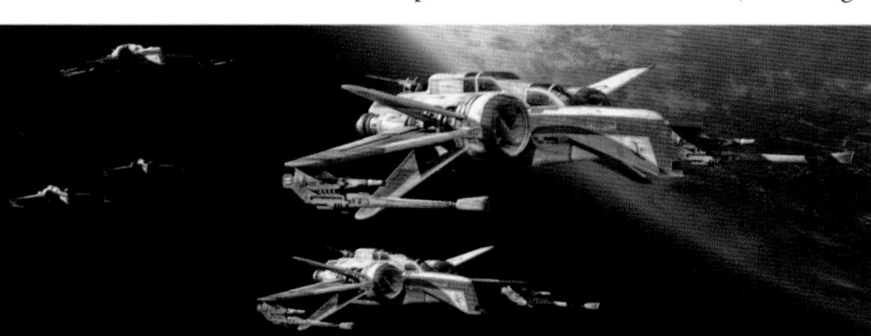
ARC-170 starfighters

**Arca** *See* Jeth, Arca.

**Arca Company** A group of clone commandos stationed on Coruscant during the Clone Wars.

**Arcasite, Mol** A ruthless bounty hunter, she was hired by Granta Omega to capture Obi-Wan Kenobi and Anakin Skywalker.

***Arc Hammer*** A titanic starship that served as both a construction facility and a launch platform for dark troopers shortly after the Battle of Yavin. The *Arc Hammer* was General Rom Mohc's flagship until it was destroyed by Rebel agent Kyle Katarn.

**Arch Canyon** An expanse of wind-carved stone arches that filled an expanse of canyon on Tatooine and became a key obstacle in the Boonta Eve Podrace course.

**Archimar, Dr.** The surgeon aboard the *Intrepid,* the flagship of the New Republic's Fifth Fleet.

**Architects** The name applied to an ancient, vanished alien culture that possessed incredible power and created some remarkable feats of stellar engineering, like the Corellian system and the Maw cluster. A wide range of conflicting theories persists as to whatever became of this prehistoric species.

**Arch of Triumph** A landmark erected on Coruscant by the Empire shortly after Emperor Palpatine instituted the New Order. Han Solo, during one of his Academy training exercises, obtained the fastest time for an assigned run when he flew through, rather than over, the arch.

**Arcona** A species of intelligent, anvil-headed limbed serpents native to the planet Cona. Their desert world was devoid of free water but had dense concentrations of ammonia. The Arcona evolved claws to get at the water pods concealed beneath the rocky soil of Cona, and ammonia was employed in a supplementary circulatory system used to rid waste from their bodies. When offworld, Arcona supplemented their diet with ammonia crystals called dactyl. They lived in loose, family-based collectives called nests that were ruled over by the Grand Nest. Society arose to protect the young Arcona, and the need for community was so strong that Arcona lacked a sense of individuality; they rarely spoke of themselves in the first person and instead used the pronoun *we.* Cona was a source of metals and minerals for galactic corporations for centuries, and in that time, a peculiar blight hit the Arcona populace. The interaction of salt—simple sodium chloride—with their optic nerves created an addictive, hallucinatory array of colors in their vision. As a deadly side effect, the salt destroyed their ammonia-utilizing pancreatic organ. Arcona salt addicts did whatever they could to feed their addiction, while nonaddicts attacked those smuggling salt to Cona. Arcona salt addicts were easily recognized by the color of their eyes—they were a glittering gold instead of the usual green.

ARENA-7580 in use on Geonosis

**Arcona Mineral Harvest Corporation** A mining organization set up as a profit-sharing mine on the planet Bandomeer between native Meerians and the predominantly Arconan immigrant miners. Forty-five years before the Battle of Yavin, the company's chief operations manager was a 25-year-old human female named Clat'ha. The AMHC was often caught in conflict with the greedy and underhanded Offworld Corporation.

**Arcon Multinode** An agricultural farming and food-processing corporation and sponsor of the Corporate Sector Authority.

**ARC trooper** *See* Advanced Reconnaissance Commando.

**Arda II** A trading planet that remained neutral in the early years of the Galactic Civil War. Arda II sold to both Rebel and Imperial buyers without reservation. The planet manufactured T-6 diodems for the Rebel Alliance X-wing starfighter. When an Imperial spy, Mag Doum, reported a Rebel presence on the world, Darth Vader inspected personally. Fearful of Imperial reprisals, the execs of the world decided to openly support the Rebellion in exchange for protection.

**Ardal** A green-skinned humanoid native of the planet Solem, he was part of the Rebel underground opposed to the rule of Imperial Governor Malvander during the early years of the Galactic Civil War.

**Ardan, Lieutenant Commander** A commander of the bridge pit crews aboard Darth Vader's flagship *Executor,* he was a native of Brentaal. Ardan participated in the subjugation of Ithor, Kashyyyk, Firro, Sinton, and other planets populated by nonhumans.

**Ardax, Colonel** An Imperial colonel, he led the assault team on Anoth to kidnap young Anakin Solo.

**ardees** A popular stimulant beverage found across the galaxy, it was nicknamed Jawa juice.

Arcona

**Ardele, Feylis** A beautiful woman with a dazzling smile, blue eyes, and long blond hair worn in a thick braid, Feylis Ardele was a member of Rogue Squadron; she was somewhat withdrawn and private about her background, but was from an upper-middle-class family on Commenor. Imperials wiped out the family after a business rival of Ardele's father accused him of being a Rebel sympathizer. She wasn't harmed because Imperial Intelligence had been looking at her as a possible agent. Before she could be recruited, she vanished and later turned up on the Rebel side.

**Ardiff, Captain** An Imperial officer, he was the captain of the Star Destroyer *Chimaera.* Ardiff served Supreme Commander Pellaeon some 16 years after the Battle of Endor.

**Ardle, Captain** An officer in the Thyferran Home Defense Corps, he initially served under Erisi Dlarit, but he was then chosen to lead the squadrons that accompanied the *Corrupter* to Alderaan to intercept Rogue Squadron. When the Rogues disabled the *Corrupter* and chased off the *Aggregator,* Ardle surrendered his TIE fighters to Wedge Antilles.

**Ardos** A white dwarf star orbited by Varl, it was the original homeworld of the Hutts. According to Hutt legend, Ardos was once a double star with Evona until the latter was drawn into a black hole.

**ARE** *See* Alderaan Royal Engineers.

**area illumination bank** A group of high-powered lamps, also called an illumigrid, it contained enough candlepower to light up large public areas such as spaceports or arenas.

**ARENA-7580** A large, round-table holographic projection system considered one of the most sophisticated tactical monitoring systems in the final days of the Galactic Republic. It provided a fully three-dimensional representation of a battlefield.

**Argai** A planet in the Haldeen sector and birthplace of Xim the Despot, who was heir to the planet. Xim maintained a palace there in ancient times.

**Argazda** Located in the Kanz sector, the planet was the site of a revolt against the Old

Republic 4,000 years before the Battle of Yavin. Myrial, provisional governor of Argazda, declared the Kanz sector independent. Myrial began to enslave the other worlds of the sector, including Lorrd, and the preoccupied Republic did nothing to help. This period, which lasted for 300 years, is known as the Kanz Disorders.

**Argenhald Base** An Imperial garrison located just outside the city of Lurark, on the planet Saffalore, during the early years of the New Republic.

**Argente, Passel** A Galactic Senator in the Republic's waning years. This male Koorivar was the magistrate of the Corporate Alliance and signed Count Dooku's treaty, joining the Confederacy of Independent Systems as the Clone Wars erupted. He was killed by Darth Vader on Mustafar.

***arg'garok*** The native name for the vibroaxes brandished by Gamorreans.

**Argo, Yom** In the years following the Battle of Yavin, Rebel spies Tay Vanis and Yom Argo (aka Tiree and Dart) began spreading rebellious sentiments on the worlds in Iskalon's system. In retribution, the Empire decimated their homeworld of Telfrey. Yom Argo was shot down and killed on Lahsbane, right after he left the Bothan system. Data tapes belonging to him were recovered from Lahsbane's Forbidden City.

***Argo Moon*** A merchant ship on which R2-D2 and C-3PO traveled to the planet Biitu for their meeting with Mungo Baobab. The ship was boarded by sludgegulpers before it could reach its destination. The *Argo Moon* bore the Baobab Merchant Fleet logo: a stylized family crest bordered by twin rainbow comets.

**Argon, Grand Moff** An Imperial sector chief, he was conned out of 25,000 credits by the notorious Tonnika sisters. He vowed to track them down wherever they went in the galaxy.

**Argona, Captain** An Imperial Navy officer in command of the *Ironhand,* one of 13 Star Destroyers still under Imperial control some 10 years after the death of Grand Admiral Thrawn. When Moff Disra set in motion his plans to overturn the New Republic, he ordered Argona, along with Captains Nalgol and Trazzen, to ready an assault on Bothawui, following the Caamas incident. Argona questioned the necessity of moving three Star Destroyers to Bothawui on a long-term mission without direct support—until Disra brought out a "resurrected" Thrawn, played by the con artist Flim. The Imperial captains all agreed with the plan.

*Passel Argente*

**Argor** A lesser Prophet of the Dark Side, he served as a field agent of the Secret Order of the Empire.

**Argyus, Captain** A Senate commando stationed aboard the Republic attack cruiser *Tranquility.* Argyus awaited Luminara Unduli's delivery of the captive Nute Gunray to Coruscant. Argyus was secretly paid off by Dooku to allow Gunray's escape. The treacherous captain killed his own Senate Guards, but once his task was completed, Asajj Ventress coldly killed him.

**Ariarch-17** A brilliant nova that erupted several years before the onset of the Clone Wars. The cruise ship *Stardust* made a special journey to witness the event, but its crew had not anticipated the force of the shock wave the explosion generated. The ship's artificial gravity systems were destroyed, and many of the passengers were injured or killed.

**Arica** *See* Skywalker, Mara Jade.

**Aridka** An old, mostly desert world that was the site of a battle in the Clone Wars. It was a dying planet covered in uninhabitable wasteland and ruined cities. A small contingent of clone troopers defended their position from under a waning deflector shield as thousands of battle droids closed in on them. Plo Koon arrived in the nick of time to turn the tide of battle.

**Aridus** A backwater desert world, Aridus was home to short, lizard-like creatures called Chubbits, who crossed the planet's sandy terrain in wind-runners, wheeled vehicles with large sails. Animal life included other large lizard-like creatures that could be tamed and used as mounts. The natural interference from the Aridus atmosphere made all long-range communications impossible, so after the Empire took control of the planet it built the immense Iron Tower to overcome the problem. This automated tower acted as both a signal amplifier and a power transformer, allowing unrestricted communications and supplying energy to run Imperial hovertrains. Hazardous lava pits were located in the region immediately surrounding the tower. Its powerful signals crippled the nervous systems of Chubbits, eventually killing many.

The Rebel Alliance supplied Chubbit resistance fighters with weapons. Following the Battle of Yavin, Darth Vader set a trap on the planet for Luke Skywalker by making it appear that Obi-Wan Kenobi had returned from the dead and was working with the Aridus resistance. The false Kenobi was actually a trained actor, altered by Imperial surgeons to resemble the dead Jedi. Skywalker managed to escape the trap, which also resulted in the partial destruction of the Iron Tower.

**Ariela** An Alderaan native, she worked hard to build good relations between human moisture farmers and scavenging Jawa tribes on Tatooine. She even invited a Jawa clan to her wedding. At one point she was kidnapped by Tusken Raiders but was rescued.

**Arisster, Dr. Movac** A history professor at the University of Pangalactic Cultural Studies on Lorrd, he traveled extensively researching the way literary archetypes from unrelated worlds were merged as planets joined the larger galactic community. Suffering from incurable cancer, Arisster sought to kill himself in a spectacular fashion. Lumiya mentally manipulated the unbalanced man through the Force with a vision of Aayla Secura, which prompted him to endanger Serom Haxan by tying himself to him along with an explosive. This caught the attention of Jedi Nelani Dinn and Jacen Solo, who were unable to prevent him from setting off the explosive, killing both Arisster and Haxan.

**Aristocra** A high rank in Chiss society.

**Arkania** A tundra world in the Perave system of the Colonies region pocked with diamond pits where miners extracted huge gems from the planet's crust. Jedi Master Arca Jeth established a Jedi training outpost in the wilderness of Arkania some 4,000 years before the Galactic Civil War, where he instructed students such as Cay and Ulic Qel-Droma and the Twi'lek Tott Doneeta. In ancient times, the scientifically minded Arkanians began cyber-enhancing the brains of their primitive neighbors, the Yakas. Soon the stocky Yakas were one of the most intelligent and quick-minded species in the galaxy, with a bizarre sense of humor to match. The Yuuzhan Vong attacked the planet in modern times. Animal life on the planet included the Arkanian dragon and jellyfish.

**ar'kai** A call of genocidal war that rallied all Bothans to action against an enemy force that threatened the species with extinction. The defeat of the enemy had to be absolute—eliminated to the last member, and wiped from history. The third time the Bothans declared ar'kai was against the Yuuzhan Vong. Even after the defeat of the alien invaders, some Bothan fundamentalists sought to conquer the Yuuzhan Vong survivors.

**Arkanian** A near-human species of master technologists from Arkania. The Arkanians were not always residents of this planet, which was once a repository for ancient Sith knowledge. Their homeworld's wealth of diamonds attracted offworld traffic, and their society flourished thanks to the import of technology and ideas. Arkanians became experts in cyborging and microcircuitry, and took it upon themselves to "bestow" cyborg intelligence upon the feebleminded Yakas of a nearby world. Many Arkanians protested this move, but their government—the Arkanian Dominion—approved the project. This caused a schism between the scientists who protested the action and those working for the Dominion, leading to a civil war. The Arkanian Renegades created the ultimate mercenary army, part droid and part organic, to overthrow the government. Although their coup failed, a few of their nearly invincible creations continued to live, escaping to set up shop as bounty hunters. One of these cyborg warriors, known as Gorm the Dissolver, haunted the spaceways for many years. Other products of Arkanian experimentation included the Quermian species, an offshoot of the Xexto, and the development of the space slug. During the rise of the Empire, Arkanians were branded with a reputation as "mad scientists."

**Arkanian dragon** A species native to Arkania intelligent enough to be classified as semi-sentient.

***Arkanian Legacy*** The enormous flagship of Adascorp 4,000 years before the rise of the Empire.

**Arkanian Microtechnologies** A manufacturer of medical supplies and technology that secretly specialized in advanced genetic engineering, this company tried to develop a competitive cloning program for the Republic during the Clone Wars. While it was unable to develop a process that rivaled the mass clone production of the Kaminoans, the Emperor employed its techniques in the experimental development of Dark Jedi clones. The failure and unpredictability of these clones led to the scrapping of these plans. Decades later, well after the Yuuzhan Vong conflict, Arkanian Micro hired Taun We for her expertise.

**Arkanian Offshoot** A genetically engineered subset of the Arkanian people specifically designed to work as miners several generations before the onset of the Great Sith War. Arkanian Offshoots had ice-blue eyes with visible pupils, whiter skin, and more dextrous hands. They also had weaker immune systems. When the mines of Arkania ran dry, the Offshoots were exiled to the outskirts beyond Arkania's cities, segregated from the Arkanian "Purebloods."

**Arkanis sector** Located on the border of the Mid Rim and Outer Rim, the sector contained the desert planet Tatooine.

**Ark'ik** A Verpine smuggler, he shipped Tibanna gas for the Squib trio Sligh, Grees, and Emala.

**Arkmen, Onie** A Coruscant partygoer, she was present in the Outlander Club the night Anakin Skywalker and Obi-Wan Kenobi captured Zam Wesell. Onie wore shiny silver shorts and a chain-mail top.

**arksh** An organic heat source bioengineered by the Yuuzhan Vong.

**Arl, Colonel** An Imperial Navy officer, he served aboard the *Lusankya* under the command of Joak Drysso and was in command of the ship's starfighter squadrons.

**ARLF** *See* Anti Republic Liberation Front.

**Armalat** A massive alien species that called Ansion home, represented by Tolut to the Unity of Community. The nonhumanoid Armalats had small red eyes, green fingers, and thick, chisel-like teeth.

**armament rating** A weapons rating assigned to all spacecraft, an armament grade measured the level of offensive and defensive weaponry. Determining factors included the type and number of weapons aboard, maximum range, control mechanisms, and powerplant capabilities. The generally accepted categories were:

- **0.** No weaponry.
- **1.** Light defensive weapons only.
- **2.** Light defensive and offensive capabilities.
- **3.** Medium defensive and offensive weapons.
- **4.** Heavy defensive and offensive weaponry.

**ArMek** A manufacturer of turbolaser, laser, and ion weaponry for use aboard starships.

***Armistice*** A Galactic Alliance warship that saw action at the Second Battle of Fondor.

**armored defense platform** These perimeter battle stations protected many planets and installations such as major shipyards from attack, but they sometimes offered only false security. Armored defense platforms were heavily armed with 28 turbolaser batteries, five proton torpedo launchers, and six tractor beam projectors. The platforms were usually more than 1,200 meters long and had a crew of about 325. Because they were immobile—and thus sitting targets against full-blown offensives—much strategic planning went into exactly where they were placed. They paid for themselves by handling such things as pirate raids or by catching smugglers trying to flee.

**armored eel** A creature discovered on Yavin 4 by the naturalist Dr'uun Unnh, it was well suited to the sluggish rivers that sliced through the moon's overpowering jungle. Unnh observed and sketched the eel but didn't have time to record detailed characteristics before his death during the Battle of Yavin.

*Arkanians*

**armored scout platform (ASP)** An enclosed and armored variant of the Trade Federation STAP vehicle.

**armor tally** A small plastoid slug that contained a clone trooper's identification data. Every clone trooper decanted and trained on Kamino was assigned an armor tally that was attached to his armor, providing his information to any other member of the Grand Army of the Republic. Many survivors of the Battle of Geonosis took the armor tallies of their comrades, as befit Mandalorian tradition.

**armorweave** A material used in clothing, armorweave draped like cloth and helped dissipate blaster or lightsaber energy. Count Dooku had an underlayer to his cape that was made of costly, fine-grade armorweave fabric. Darth Vader's capes incorporated armorweave.

**Army of Light** A cobbled-together Jedi military force led by Lord Hoth against Sith Lord Kaan and the Brotherhood of Darkness 1,000 years before the Battle of Yavin. After a lengthy campaign on Ruusan, both opposing forces were wiped out by Lord Kaan's thought bomb weapon.

**Arnet, Lieutenant** A veteran AT-ST pilot assigned to coordinate the surprise counterattack in the Battle of Endor, he also commanded a prototype AT-ST in General Veer's assault upon Hoth.

**Arnjak, Baljos** A biological expert of Wraith Squadron who was part of Luke Skywalker's expedition to the Yuuzhan Vong–conquered Coruscant. He worked with captured ooglith masquers to create one that could be used to disguise humanoids as Yuuzhan Vong. As part of Luke's task force, Arnjak wore Domain Kraal vonduun crab armor. He was the first to explain that Lord Nyax had once been Irek Ismaren. After the defeat of Nyax, he decided to stay on Coruscant to continue his research. A human from Coruscant, Baljos Arnjak was tall and lean with dark hair, mustache, and beard that made his pale skin seem pallid.

**Arno, King** Married to Queen Leonie, he was the monarch of Zeltros during the time of the Alliance of Free Planets.

**Arnothian, General** This Imperial officer maintained a TIE defender production facility during the early years of the New Republic. He fancied himself a warlord-in-training, having broken from the Empire shortly after the Battle of Endor. His ability to lead a force was threatened when Ysanne Isard—having survived the Battle of Thyferra—tried to take command of the facility. Arnothian refused, but he had neither the strength nor the will to fight her. In the end, Isard had him executed for insubordination, and she took control of his facility.

**Arnthout** One of the first settlements on Tatooine, located south of Bestine.

**Arnthout, Melnea** Leader of the miners who crash-landed the *Dowager Queen* on Tatooine thousands of years before the Battle of Yavin, she was remembered not so much for her leadership in founding Tatooine's first settlement as for her efforts to make first contact with the native Jawas.

**A'roFilter** A small mining concern that was a supporter of the Rebel Alliance during the Galactic Civil War. The corporation specialized in the mining of exotic gases from the clouds of gas giant planets; it was among the many operations that collected Tibanna gas from Bespin's atmosphere. A portion of its collected gas was surreptitiously sent to the Alliance, which paid a small fraction of its true cost in order to maintain the illusion of an actual business transaction.

**Arorua** The Jedi Council sent Qui-Gon Jinn and 13-year-old Obi-Wan Kenobi to this isolated jungle planet, home to many exotic and deadly creatures, including the squollyhawlk and the legendary silan.

**Aros, Lady** The lady-in-waiting to Queen Mother Tenel Ka of the Hapes Consortium during the conflict between the Corellian Confederation and the Galactic Alliance.

**arpitrooper** Any ground-based militia that entered a battle zone by dropping from the air, using disposable repulsor packs to quickly reach the ground. The name was a phonetic version of the term *RP trooper*, or repulsor pack trooper.

**arqet** A ferocious armadillo-like warm-blooded predator native to Pellastrallus in the Agarix sector. An arqet was involved in a Circus Horrificus rampage on Nar Shaddaa.

**arrak snake** Native to the planet Ithor, this reptile could sing.

**Arranda, Tash and Zak** Survivors of Alderaan, the brother-and-sister team of Zak and Tash Arranda were teenagers in the early years of the Galactic Civil War. Thirteen-year-old Tash was Force-sensitive, while 12-year-old Zak showed a talent for repairing and modifying technology. They were cared for by Shi'ido anthropologist Mammon Hoole, whom they referred to as their uncle. Hoole's studies took the siblings all over the galaxy, and they often ran afoul of Hoole's rival, Shi'ido scientist Borborygmus Gog. After a series of creepy adventures, Tash and Zak joined the Rebel Alliance.

**Arrant, Jurnel** The executive officer of Lommite Limited at the height of its rivalry with InterGalactic Ore. A trim, handsome middle-aged Corellian around the time of the Battle of Naboo, Arrant was credited with transforming formerly provincial Lommite Limited into a corporation doing business with a host of prominent worlds. When one of Lommite's largest mines was destroyed on Dorvalla, he immediately suspected InterGal of sabotage and ordered chief of field operations Patch Bruit to retaliate. In truth, Darth Sidious was manipulating the war of sabotage and reprisals between the two rivals in an effort to eliminate them both and leave the lommite mines open for Trade Federation exploitation.

***Arrestor*** An Imperial bulk cruiser assigned to Admiral Greelanx, it served as part of the front attack line during the Battle of Nar Shaddaa, in which it was destroyed.

**arrest tentacles** Developed by the Yuuzhan Vong, arrest tentacles were the biotechnological equivalent of a tractor beam. They could be extended from a starship, primarily the matalok—a cruiser analog—in order to grasp and control a smaller vessel.

**Arrizza** A Kurtzen worker at the Bakuran Senate Complex during the Yuuzhan Vong invasion, he was also a good friend of the Ryn informant Goure. Arrizza provided Goure information about the tunnels and chambers beneath the complex. Arrizza had no political affiliations, so he cared little for the Bakuran government, the Freedom movement, or the New Republic. Thus, when Goure asked for his help in locating Jaina Solo, Arrizza agreed to help him and Tahiri Veila infiltrate the complex. Later, Arrizza used his strange connection to the life energy of the Force to help Tahiri learn to live in peace with the Riina Kwaad personality that had been implanted in her mind by Mezhan Kwaad.

**Arrogantus, Serji-X** A notorious swoop racer and leader of the Cloud Rider swoop gang on Aduba-3, Arrogantus was killed by the Sith behemoth unleashed on that planet.

**arrol** A semi-sentient poisonous cactus native to the planet Ithor.

**Arroquitas, Diva** She served as master of ceremonies of the Priole Danna Festival on Lamuir IV a year prior to the Clone Wars. The following year's festival was canceled due to security concerns surrounding the Separatist crisis.

**Arrow-23 landspeeder** A tramp shuttle speeder often used by the Rebel Alliance. The modified Aratech landspeeder had a crew of two and fit five passengers.

**Arr'yka, Lieutenant** The *Ralroost*'s communications officer, this dark-furred Bothan was killed in battle against the Yuuzhan Vong over Ithor.

**arsensalt** Developed by the Jedi Knights, this salt-like material was used to counteract the adhesive effects of blorash jelly.

**Ar-Six** *See* R6-H5.

**Art Beyond Dying** The Blood Carver conception of the afterlife for the honored dead. Worthy Blood Carvers joined a more wondrous state of existence, while dishonorable ones did not.

**artery worm** A parasitic creature found on Dathomir that burrowed its way into its hosts, feeding off the walls of their arteries.

**Artesian space collage** This form of artwork originated on the planet Artesia.

**Art of Movement** This Jedi reflex and agility exercise forced a student to navigate an obstacle course while avoiding the various lines and bouncing points of light that moved about the room.

**Artoo-Detoo** *See* R2-D2.

**Artusian crystal** A naturally occurring crystal mined on Artus Prime that could focus Force abilities and grant Force powers to those who had none. Admiral Galak Fyyar used Artusian crystals to create scores of shadow troopers for the Reborn movement.

**Artus Prime** A world near the Outer Rim known for its deposits of Artusian crystals. The Empire took over the planet to harvest raw materials for Admiral Galak Fyyar. Kyle Katarn sabotaged the Imperial mines and rescued many of the prisoners there shortly after the Battle of Endor.

**Aruh, Suung** A young novice Yuuzhan Vong shaper trained by Nen Yim aboard the worldship *Baanu Miir,* he worked under Tih Qiqah prior to Nen Yim's arrival.

**Aruk the Hutt** *See* Aora, Aruk Besadii.

**AruMed** A biotechnology company based on Roonadan, in the Corporate Sector.

**Aruza** A peaceful, forested planet with five colorful moons. Aruza's major city was Bukeen. Native Aruzans were small, gentle people with blue skin, dark blue hair, and rounded heads. They kept neural interface jacks, called Attanni, beneath their ears to feel the emotions of others. They were tech-empathic and shared a limited group mind. Imperial General Sinick Kritkeen was ordered to "reeducate" the Aruzans and turn them into a fighting force for the Empire. Prior to the Battle of Hoth, the bounty hunter Dengar came to Aruza and assassinated Kritkeen, after which he escaped with the Aruzan woman Manaroo, whom he later married.

**Aryon, Governor Tour** A governor of Tatooine, she was stationed at Bestine on the desert planet. She was a finely featured woman with a dark complexion who sported the latest fashions. Her contributions to Tatooine were mainly cultural.

**aryx** A tall, flightless bird native to Cerea, it had a huge beak and sharp, clawed feet. These avians were extremely swift and ferocious carnivores, though they could be tamed for use as mounts by Cereans. A loyal aryx fought to the death to protect its master. The Jedi Knight Ki-Adi-Mundi had a special, psychic connection to his personal aryx and could summon the creature at will.

*Ascension guns used to scale the Theed Palace walls*

**Arzid** A planet known for its macaab mushrooms, tentacle-bushes, and native arachnors, it was also the site of a small Imperial outpost where Grand Moff Muzzer was sentenced to serve for five years.

**asaari tree** These waving trees covered the surface of the planet Bimmisaari. They constantly swayed by moving their leafy branches even when no wind was blowing.

**Asani, Wil** A founding member of the Eleven, a resistance group that opposed the New Order in the early days of the Galactic Empire. When the Empire cracked down on Eleven activity on Bellassa, the group went underground and Asani acted as coordinator for the various fragments. A blaster wound to the leg forced him out of more active duty and into an administrative role.

**Asation** The main trading post and access system of the remote Outer Rim handful of systems known as the Gree Enclave. Asation was a wet, gray, high-pressure world with extensive slimy wetlands and jungle and relatively primitive life-forms. Satikan was its largest city. Count Dooku was spotted there just prior to the outbreak of the Clone Wars.

**ascension gun** Any of a variety of cable-firing pistols or rifles. The Security S-5 pistols used by the Naboo Royal Security Forces featured a small grappling hook that could embed into almost any surface. When the pistol's built-in cable retracted, the blaster was capable of hoisting its wielder. Queen Amidala, Captain Panaka, and their troops used ascension guns to gain entry into Theed Palace after it was captured by the Trade Federation.

**Aseca, Boc** A male Twi'lek Dark Jedi encountered by Kyle Katarn after the Battle of Endor. Though Aseca was born in the waning years of the Republic, he was not discovered to be Force-sensitive by the Jedi Knights until he was too old to be trained. He felt cheated out of his destiny, and studied ancient texts and relics to learn the history of the Jedi and the dark side. With the rise of the Empire, Aseca was enslaved, serving as manservant to Admiral Screed. His Force sensitivity was again discovered, and he was trained by the Dark Jedi Jerec.

Aseca was a cunning and brash individual. Crude and loud, he was a playful joker. When he drew upon the Force to do battle, however, he overcame his otherwise brutish, clumsy nature to become a formidable opponent. Aseca carried two lightsabers, making him an uncommon and dangerous opponent. Kyle Katarn defeated him in the Valley of the Jedi.

**A-series assassin droid** *See* Pollux assassin droid.

**Asha** The long-lost older sister of the Ewok Princess Kneesaa, she was attacked by a terrifying hanadak when she, her sister, and their mother Ra-Lee were on an outing on Endor. By the time Kneesaa ran to the village and got help, Asha was missing and Ra-Lee had been slain. Years later, Kneesaa's best friend, Wicket W. Warrick, came into contact with a savage red-furred female huntress known as the Red Ghost. Hearing the story, Kneesaa had a strong hunch that this might be Asha, and they tracked her down on a snowy evening. Indeed, it was her sister, who told of how she had been found and raised by a family of wolf-like korrinas. After routing a group of evil hunters, Asha returned to her village for a reunion with her father, Chief Chirpa.

**Ashaad, Sergeant** A burly human male, he was a member of the People's Liberation Army on Eiattu VI.

**Ashas Ree** An ancient system deep in the heart of the former Sith Empire. The Dark Jedi Freedon Nadd recovered King Adas's holocron here.

**Ashel, Tok** The Neimoidian commander of the Cartao Expeditionary Army during the Clone Wars. He worked alongside Dif Gehad to take control of Cartao and capture the fluid technology of the Cranscoc. To ensure the cooperation of Lord Binalie, he took Binalie's son, Corf, as a hostage.

**Ashern** Black Claw terrorists from the planet Thyferra, the Ashern were members of the Vratix species who had renounced their peaceful heritage to fight the tyranny of their human masters. To mark this change, they painted their normally gray bodies black and sharpened their claws, which gave them the ability to puncture stormtrooper armor.

**Ash'ett** A Yuuzhan Vong intendant, he was a rival of Nom Anor. After the Yuuzhan Vong conquest of Coruscant, Ash'ett was elevated to prefect of Vishtu. Anor used his alias of Yu'shaa the heretical prophet to seed Ash'ett's house with Shamed One heretics, which caused Ash'ett to lose face. Supreme Overlord Shimmra ordered Ash'ett and his family sacrificed.

**Ashgad, Seti** One of the top hyperdrive engineers of the Old Republic, Ashgad was also a political foe of Senator Palpatine. When Palpatine rose to power, Ashgad was exiled to the onetime prison planet Nam Chorios.

When Chief of State Leia Organa Solo traveled to Nam Chorios, she met with the apparent son of Seti Ashgad, who had the same name. Ashgad, a profiteer, was the unofficial spokesman for a group called the Rationalist Party, which was trying to assist Newcomers—recent voluntary immigrants to Nam Chorios. Ashgad wanted to convince Leia to allow trade to begin between Nam Chorios and the New Republic. Opposing that aim were the Theran Listeners, longtime Nam Chorios inhabitants. Adept at healing, they operated the ancient gun stations that prevented prisoners from leaving the planet and eschewed much of modern technology.

Ashgad Jr. was actually Ashgad Sr. He had been kept alive and young by Dzym, a mutated droch. (Drochs were insect-like creatures that could burrow into the flesh and consume life; they caused the Death Seed plague, although there hadn't been an outbreak of the horrific malady for seven centuries.) Both Ashgad and the once powerful Beldorion the Hutt paid the price for being kept ageless by Dzym—they were his virtual slaves. Nine years after the Battle of Endor, Leia secretly visited the planet to meet with Ashgad, who took her prisoner, then unleashed the Death Seed plague across three-quarters of the sector. He planned to disable the planet's gun stations—Dzym and the drochs desperately wanted to leave the planet where they had been trapped for centuries—and allow the Loronar Corporation to strip-mine the smokies, a type of Force-sensitive crystal. After a series of confrontations and battles, Luke Skywalker was able to communicate with the planet's crystals, and they linked to crystals aboard Dzym and Ashgad's fleeing ship, blowing up the craft.

**Ashla** A Togruta, she was a small Jedi-hopeful member of the Bear Clan studying under Yoda at the outbreak of the Clone Wars. *Ashla* is also an ancient term used to describe the Force.

**Ashpidar, Captain** The New Republic commander of the Esfandia Long-Range Communications Base during the war against the Yuuzhan Vong. She was a Gotal from Antar 4 who left her homeworld when her beloved died in a mining accident.

**Askaj** The dry desert homeworld of the Askajian species. Fauna included horned herd animals called tomuon, valued throughout the galaxy for their wool.

**Askajian** A near-human race native to Askaj with bodies that could absorb and store water, using it only as needed for survival. Females of the species had six breasts. According to custom, Askajian cublings were not given names until they reached their first birthday. Askajian weaving techniques were closely guarded secrets, and it was said that Emperor Palpatine's ceremonial robes were spun from tomuon wool. Yarna d'al' Gargan, the daughter of a tribe chieftain on Askaj and a first-rate competitive dancer, was captured with her family by slavers and sold to crime lord Jabba the Hutt. Yarna served in the Hutt's court as a dancer, but escaped after Jabba's death and eventually bought her cublings out of slavery.

**Askol, Bok** A Pacithhip visitor to Mos Espa. At birth, Pacithhip gene configuration usually indicated if an individual was to become a farmer, an intellectual, or a warrior, but Askol's destiny eluded classification.

*Asp droids at work in Mos Eisley*

**Asmeru** A pale brown world located at the edge of the Senex sector. The leading houses that ruled the sector claimed that Nebula Front terrorists seized control of the planet from its scant indigenous population around the time of the Battle of Naboo. After an assassination attempt on Supreme Chancellor Valorum, the Nebula Front members responsible were traced to Asmeru. A team of Jedi and Judicials traveled to the planet in response, though the trip was a diversion to keep the Republic's attention away from Eriadu.

**ASN-121** Zam Wesell's hovering assassin droid, modified from a standard ASN courier model. Wesell dispatched the droid on a mission to kill Senator Padmé Amidala. To that end, its small cargo hopper was loaded with a pair of squirming kouhuns, deadly centipede-like creatures with a poisonous sting.

The droid was also equipped with disruptive energy beams to bypass security screens, and laser cutters to bore holes in walls and windows. ASN-121's frontal chuck could be equipped with such diverse tools as a harpoon gun, a sniper blaster, a gas dispenser, spy sensors, a flamethrower, and various drills and cutters.

**ASP** *See* armored scout platform.

**asp droid** An outdated general all-purpose droid extremely common throughout the galaxy. Due to their strength and agility, they made excellent laborers and were often used to load or build starships. Asp droids possessed magnetized feet and could easily withstand the vacuum of space, allowing them to walk along a starship's hull and make in-flight repairs. They could also be programmed for combat-training exercises.

Asp droids had skeletal frames and hydraulic limbs. They were incredibly strong and easily served as cargo handlers. An asp's head unit was equipped with an elementary cognitive module, a single photoreceptor, two auditory sensors, and a primitive vocabulator capable of producing only two words: *affirmative* and *negative*. Due to their rudimentary design, asps were easily modified far beyond their original specifications. A reconfigured asp might possess an enhanced vocabulator, several fine manipulators, or even an advanced computer brain. Darth Vader's legion of ASP-19s boasted armor plating, augmented reflexes, and detailed fencing programs for use as lightsaber-training opponents.

**Assant, Darsha** The bright, quick-witted, and blue-eyed Padawan of Anoon Bondara. Just previous to the blockade of Naboo, she was given her final mission before she was to ascend to the rank of Jedi Knight. She was asked to bring former Black Sun member Oolth to the Jedi Temple, but failed when Oolth fell to his death. While confirming Oolth's death, Assant and Bondara spotted Lorn Pavan and I-Five fleeing from Darth Maul. Assant joined the fugitives on the run, and while her relationship with Pavan helped change his negative attitude toward the Jedi, she died at Darth Maul's hands.

**assassin droid** The ultimate symbol of society and technology run amok, these droids were largely unstoppable killing machines, programmed to hunt down specific targets and destroy them. Originally designed in the days of the Old Republic to eliminate dangerous criminals or escaped prisoners, assassin droids performed their task so well that they were put into service by warlords, dictators, and criminal kingpins. The droids were intelligent and unswerving in their task; they had a kill rate of better than 90 percent, even if it took years to track down their target. Estimates are that up to a few million remained in the galaxy even though Emperor Palpatine outlawed them at the beginning of his reign because they were being used successfully against Imperial officials. (Lord Torbin, the Grand Inquisitor, was killed when a shuttle crashed into his palace; it was suspected that an assassin droid had killed the shuttle crew at a timely moment.) Rogue assassin droids became a major problem. Having completed their initial mission, they should have shut down, but many came up with new missions on their own. These droids had no built-in ethical chip. The now infamous Caprioril massacre occurred when one droid, programmed to kill Governor Amel Bakli, decided that the most efficient way to accomplish this task was to murder all 20,000 spectators at a swoop arena while the governor of the peaceful planet was in attendance. Another, an Eliminator model 434, tried to kill Princess Leia Organa on Coruscant, but it was destroyed by Prince Isolder's bodyguard Captain Astarta.

*ASN-121 assassin droid*

**Assassins' Guild** A secret society of professional mercenaries, the guild comprised members who were specialists in death by contract. There were subguilds—the bounty hunter unit was among the most feared—and an Elite Circle, whose membership could be elected only by fellow terminators. The Assassins' Guild was so clandestine that even the location of its headquarters was concealed from most members, who had to contact it through comlink or surreptitious methods.

**assault frigate** These Rebel, and later New Republic, ships began life as Imperial Dreadnaught heavy cruisers. They were painstakingly and cleverly modified to create combat starships some 700 meters long. While Imperial ships required a crew of 16,000, the Alliance retooling replaced humans with droids and computers, reducing crew requirements by more than two-thirds. Removing tons of superstructure increased engine capacity while lowering fuel consumption. The addition of two rear solar fins made the assault frigates faster and more maneuverable.

A variety of assault frigates were created by a splinter group of Rendili StarDrive designers. These engineers incorporated Mon Calamari deflector shield subsystems that gave the ships increased shield output for limited periods. At least two models of the assault frigate were produced—the internally made Rebel Mark I and the Rendili designed Mark II. The design concept evolved into New Republic assault frigates built upon the same principles.

The frigates usually carried about 100 troops or 7,500 metric tons of cargo. Each had a modified assault shuttle piggybacked atop its superstructure, while 20

*Assault frigate*

umbilical docking tubes could be used for light freighters and starfighters. The ships were armed with 15 regular and 20 quad laser cannons along with 15 turbolaser batteries. The frigates were important in the Rebel victory at the Battle of Endor and were later used as patrol ships in the Borderlands Regions.

**assault shuttle, *Gamma*-class** With only five-member crews, these heavily armored Imperial ships could engage capital ships more than three times their 30-meter length and carry 40 zero-g stormtroopers into the heart of battle. Assault shuttles, which operated both in space and in planetary atmospheres, could grab target ships with tractor beams or magnetic harpoons, then cripple them with concussion missiles or blasts from one of four laser cannons. The ships were well protected from enemy fire; they used up to two-thirds of their power on shields, compared with the normal one-quarter of most combat starships. But they held only about a week's provisions and had to be reprogrammed after only three jumps into hyperspace.

**Assembler** Also known as Kud'ar Mub'at, this giant 3-meter-tall black spider had a large round body and six chitinous legs. He lived in a giant tubular-shaped web that drifted through space. He met guests in his main chamber, adjusting the atmosphere there for each visitor. The web, littered with space junk and debris, was part of the Assembler, connected to him by microscopic neurofibers that brought him nourishment. It allowed him to communicate with his many "nodes"—individual arachnoid beings created from the web's essence, also connected to the web by neurofibers. Each node possessed only the marginal intelligence needed to do its job. A node named Lookout gazed through a single-lens eye to view the web exterior; the Calculator node interpreted data; Identifier identified objects or people; Signaler's glowing green eyes guided arriving ships into dock; and Docker and Handler secured ships against the web's entry port with their vacuum-adapted scale tentacles. Listener was a tympanic membrane that picked up sound around the web, while Balancesheet maintained the Assembler's finances. It was this last node that finally evolved to the point that it rebelled against its creator.

**Astarta, Captain** A statuesque woman of exceptional beauty, she was the personal guard of Prince Isolder, Princess Leia Organa Solo's onetime suitor from the planet Hapes. Her hair a dark red, her eyes as dark a blue as the skies of her planet Terephon, the bodyguard also kept the prince alert to the intrigues of the Hapan Royal Court. She was in love with the prince—a love that could never be consummated—but above all else she was a loyal and excellent soldier.

**astral** A term used by youths in the galaxy to denote something remarkable, found in use after the Yuuzhan Vong invasion.

**astrogation computer** *See* nav computer.

***Astrolabe*** A New Republic astrographic probe ship, it was said to be operated by the civilian Astrographic Survey Institute but was in reality a front for a military intelligence mission. It was destroyed at Doornik-1142 by Yevethan ships, and its crew was killed. The incident led to a wider war.

**astromech droid** Automata such as R2-D2 were all-around utility droids that carried out sophisticated computer repairs and undertook information retrieval. Astromechs were short and squat, usually cylindrical, and traveled on a pair of treaded rollers. They often had a retractable third leg to help navigate difficult terrain. The droids specialized in starship maintenance and repair, even in hostile environments such as the vacuum of deep space. They often were loaded into special sockets behind the pilot's cockpit in small starfighters, where they plugged into all the ship's systems and scanned real-time data, capably performing more than 10,000 operations a second to forecast potential problems. In effect, they acted as copilot and, in emergencies, could even take over limited piloting chores. Many models could perform multiple tasks, from holographic projection to welding. Some were even known to do a bit of bartending on the side.

**Astrotours Limited** A front corporation used to secure housing for Lumiya on Coruscant during the conflict between the Galactic Alliance and the Corellian Confederation.

**Asylum** *See* Crseih Research Station.

***Asymptotic Approach to Divinity*** *See Reasonable Doubt.*

**AT3 Directive** A coded Imperial request for assistance.

**Atali** The first Imperial officer aboard the *Mathayus* serving under Admiral Coy, he and his boarding party died when they raided a captured Rebel ship rigged as an explosive trap.

**AT-AR** *See* All Terrain Advance Raider.

**Ataru (Form IV)** One of several forms of lightsaber combat, it was considered the most acrobatic and sometimes employed paired lightsabers. Obi-Wan Kenobi, Qui-Gon Jinn, and Yoda were all practiced masters of Form IV.

**AT-AT** *See* All Terrain Armored Transport.

**AT-CT** *See* All Terrain Construction Transport.

**Atgar SpaceDefense Corporation** The manufacturer of a variety of cost-effective antivehicle weapons and defense systems.

**Athacorr, Commander Dias** An Arkanian who served in the Old Republic military during the Mandalorian Wars.

**AT-HE** *See* All Terrain Heavy Enforcer.

**Athega** A system rich in minerals and fuel stores, Athega was long off limits because of the intense heat given off by its sun; its radiation could peel the hull from a ship before it could reach the surface of a planet. But Lando Calrissian, no stranger to mining from his days as administrator of Cloud City, got the New Republic to back him in a novel venture. First, Calrissian developed a new type of craft called shieldships that literally shielded other spacecraft from the killer effects of Athega's sun. He also planned Nomad City, a huge humpbacked structure that lumbered slowly across the surface of the planet Nkllon, digging ore with mole miners while managing to stay on the planet's dark side. The city was built of useless old spacecraft, with a base of 40 captured Imperial AT-AT walkers. Calrissian's operations were hindered after Grand Admiral Thrawn captured 51 of his mole miners for use at the Battle of Sluis Van, an event that brought retired General Calrissian back into the thick of the action.

**AT-IC** *See* All Terrain Ion Cannon.

**Atin** A Republic clone commando. RC-3222's adopted name *Atin* meant "stubborn" in the Mandalorian language. He lived up to this reputation throughout his training and career. As a commando, he trained under—and despised—Walon Vau, who nearly killed the commando when he refused a direct order to kill a fellow clone. Atin was the sole survivor of his unit after the Battle of Geonosis. As a reminder of that conflict, he carried a large scar on his face. Atin was reassigned to Omega Squad, but initially found it difficult to forge any bonds with his new squadmates. Atin was involved in the Omega Squad mission to rescue Senator Meena Tills and several other hostages from terrorists on Coruscant. The battle-scarred clone spent a month in a bacta tank after being hit by a Verpine shatter gun.

**AT-KT** *See* All Terrain Kashyyyk Transport.

**atlatl, Gungan** Gungans used this short one-handed throwing stick to hurl a single small energy ball, or boomer. It had a shorter range but was more accurate than a cesta. In desperate situations, it could serve as a blunt weapon.

**Atoko, Admiral** The commanding officer of the Fifth Battle Group naval forces of the Galactic Alli-

*Gungan atlatl*

ance during the Battle of Kuat, he was ordered by Jacen Solo to accompany the *Anakin Solo* to Kashyyyk. The Alliance forces were overwhelmed when a Confederation fleet made up of Bothan, Corellian, Commenorian, and Hutt ships trapped them at Kashyyyk. Though Atoko planned to honor a cease-fire, Solo refused to back down and ordered a vicious attack to clear a path for the *Anakin Solo* to escape. Atoko later led the attack on Mandalore, and was tasked with unleashing the Imperial nanokiller virus that specifically targeted members of Boba Fett's bloodline.

**Atori, Master Otias** A skilled thespian, he trained Adalric Brandl in the arts of theater and drama. Atori worked in an immense auditorium on the isolated world of Trulalis. His student left him, not returning for 12 years. In those years, much had happened to Brandl, as his life crossed the dark side of the Force. He returned to Trulalis, though, to revisit a son who had never known him. While on Trulalis, Brandl was drawn to the auditorium where he learned his craft, and confronted his master again. The aged Atori offered what advice he could, but ultimately left Brandl's fate in his own hands.

**AT-PT** *See* All Terrain Personal Transport.

**Atraken** A planet in the Kattellyn system far from the Corellian Trade Spine. Once a rich source of doonium, it was completely devastated by a biological weapon during the Clone Wars and became a desolate wasteland. Callista later sent Luke Skywalker a message in a music box from Atraken, warning him to stay away from the Meridian sector. Atraken had three moons, Trilos, Doulos, and Myrkos. Only Trilos was capable of sustaining life of any kind.

**At'raoth** A Yuuzhan Vong Shamed One who lived below the surface of Coruscant after it was transformed into the likeness of Yuuzhan'tar, she was a devoted follower of the prophet Yu'shaa. She was the first of the Select to be dispatched to the offices of Supreme Overlord Shimrra, in an effort to gather intelligence on the ruling elite of Yuuzhan Vong society. Unfortunately for At'raoth, she barely reached the antechambers of Shimrra's offices before she was discovered. As she was killed by the irksh poison hidden in a false tooth, she screamed her defiance by invoking the name of Ganner Rhysode and the Jedi. While this was not part of Nom Anor's plans, it did show Shimrra that the message of the Shamed Ones was gathering momentum.

**Atravis sector** This sector contained the Atravis systems, which were devastated by Imperial attacks. Of the massacres there, Grand Moff Tarkin said, "They have only themselves to blame." Grand Admiral Harrsk's troops began gathering in the Atravis sector eight years after the Battle of Endor.

**Atris** A former member of the Jedi Council at the time when a key Jedi was exiled for joining Darth Revan and Darth Malak in the Mandalorian Wars. Disillusioned by this and acts that followed, Atris fled to live in solitude among non-Force-sensitives, eventually succumbing to the dark side in her despair. She built a secret Jedi academy on Telos, surrounding herself with Echani handmaidens and spending much of her time in meditation.

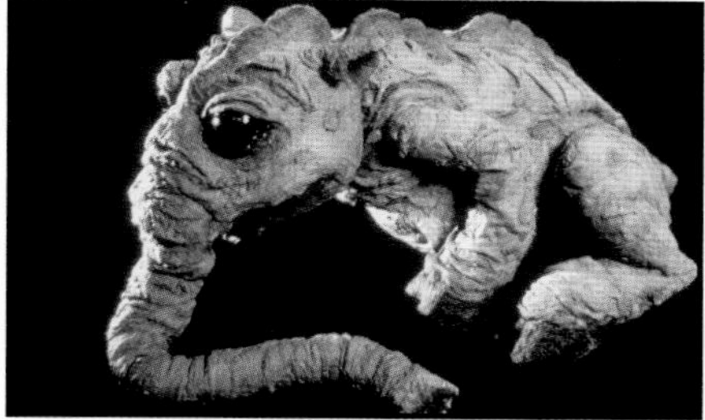

*Attark, a Hoover*

**Atrisia** This ancient planet was home of the Kitel Phard Dynasty, one of the many empires that served as inspiration for the Galactic Empire.

**Atrivis sector** Located in the Outer Rim, the sector included the Mantooine and Fest systems and the planet Generis. During the early formation of the Rebel Alliance, Mon Mothma helped unite various insurgent organizations, including the Atrivis resistance groups. Five years after the Battle of Endor, New Republic pilot Pash Cracken was stationed in the Atrivis sector and was part of the ultimately unsuccessful defense of the Outer Rim comm center against an Imperial attack.

**AT-ST** *See* All Terrain Scout Transport.

**Attack Pattern Delta** An approach vector devised by Luke Skywalker and Beryl Chiffonage, and used by snowspeeder pilots during the Battle of Hoth. The maneuver employed the speeder's agility to get in close to armored targets and inflict maximum damage with its weapons.

**Attanni** A high-tech device used by the Aruzans to cybernetically share thoughts, emotions, memories, and knowledge with one another.

**Attark** A quadruped with a long snout and large eyes, Attark was a member of the mysterious species known only as Hoovers. Although it looked harmless, Jabba's pet Hoover crept up on sleeping victims to suck their blood at night, using its nose trunk to slither through clothing or around blankets.

**AT-TE** *See* All Terrain Tactical Enforcer.

*Attichitcuk*

**Attichitcuk** The father of Chewbacca, commonly known as Itchy, and a powerful leader in the Wookiee community during his youth and middle years. Attichitcuk led expeditions deep into the wroshyr forest depths on dangerous honor hunts. He once killed a pack of 20 vicious katarns with only a ryyk blade. As a prominent member of his clan, Attichitcuk represented Kashyyyk in the Republic negotiations for colonization rights to Alaris Prime. Once the talks were concluded, Attichitcuk was awarded the honor of being part of the initial colonization force. There he encountered an illegal Trade Federation presence and assumed the mantle of warrior once again to drive them out. Jedi Master Qui-Gon Jinn arrived from Coruscant to help settle the conflict, along with his new Padawan Obi-Wan Kenobi.

During the time of the Galactic Civil War, Attichitcuk was a large, white-haired Wookiee over 350 years old, and was quite a bit shorter than his son—Wookiees tend to shrink with age. He walked with the aid of a cane and tended to be extremely irritable. Itchy lived on the Wookiee homeworld of Kashyyyk, where he shared a traditional Wookiee dwelling located high in the trees with his daughter-in-law, Mallatobuck (Malla), and grandson, Lumpawarrump (Waroo).

**Atuarre** An apprentice agronomist on the planet Orron III, she was a female Trianii with a personal quest: locating political prisoners held by the Corporate Sector Authority. She and her son Pakka solicited the help of Han Solo in that mission.

**AT-XT** *See* All Terrain Experimental Transport.

**Atzerri** A free-trade world, Atzerri had the most minimal government necessary to stave off complete chaos. Almost anything, legal or illegal, could be had for a price on the planet. The Traders' Coalition charged a hefty fee for every service. Ships controlled their own entry and departure and negotiated with independently owned spaceports to land. Arriving visitors ran a gauntlet of gaudily lit stores known as Trader's Plaza, designed to hook new arrivals and separate them from their credits as soon as possible. The Revels, a busy entertainment district filled with casinos and cantinas, had a theme bar called Jabba's Throne Room, a near-perfect reproduction of the gangster's palace—complete with a phony Han Solo in carbonite. Luke Skywalker and Akanah Norand Pell went to Atzerri, supposedly in search of the missing Fallanassi sect, but really so Pell could track down her father, who had abandoned her family years earlier.

**Auben** A young thief on the planet Korriban during the years following the Battle

## Aurebesh Alphabet

| Aurek (a) | Besh (b) | cresh (c) | dora (d) | esk (e) | forn (f) | grek (g) | Herf (h) |
|---|---|---|---|---|---|---|---|
| Isk (i) | Jenth (j) | Krill (k) | Leth (l) | Mern (m) | Nern (n) | Osk (o) | Peth (p) |
| Qek (q) | Resh (r) | Senth (s) | Trill (t) | Usk (u) | Vev (v) | Wesh (w) | Xesh (x) |
| Yirt (y) | Zerek (z) | Cherk (ch) | Enth (ae) | Onith (eo) | Krenth (kh) | Nen (ng) | Orenth (oo) |
| Shen (sh) | Thesh (th) | comma (,) | period (.) | question (?) | exclaim (!) | colon (:) | semicolon (;) |
| hyphen (-) | slash (/) | left (‘) | right (’) | left (“) | right (”) | left (() | right ()) |

of Naboo, she found a makeshift residence in the Sith monastery beneath Dreshdae's plateau. Auben earned a few credits selling various items that she had stolen, usually from visiting starships. When Anakin Skywalker and Ferus Olin were on their mission to apprehend Granta Omega, they were pointed to Auben as a source of information. She agreed to help them, but they found themselves pursued by the droid armies of the Commerce Guild. Auben led them to the lowest levels of the monastery, where an ancient hangar bay provided the only escape route. Unfortunately, the Sith Lord who was on Korriban to meet Granta Omega discovered her in the hangar and killed her when she got in his way.

**Augwynne, Mother** Augwynne led the Singing Mountain Clan of the Witches of Dathomir, a group of Force-sensitive women who rode domesticated rancors and kept men as slaves and for breeding. Han Solo won the planet Dathomir in a sabacc game, but after a series of near-fatal adventures there he gave up the deed to Mother Augwynne.

**Aunuanna** An old beggar woman who sold Gizer ale on the streets of Nar Shaddaa in the later years of the Republic. Mace Windu and Depa Billaba saved Aunuanna from the clutches of Kyood Vurd. She later claimed that her daughter, whom she referred to as her Angel, was taken by Jedi. The daughter was later revealed as Aurra Sing, the offspring of Aunuanna and an unknown alien father.

**aura blossom** An exquisite indigo-blue flower, it glowed brightly and grew in abundance on the Forest Moon of Endor. The blossoms were a favorite of the native Ewoks.

**Aurea** A planet noted for its fine artisans, including the best glassworkers in the galaxy.

**Aurebesh** One of the more commonly encountered alphabets found in the galaxy, often used by military organizations. Aurebesh was not a language, but rather a collection of characters that could be used to represent written Basic as well as other languages.

**Aurek Company** A division of the Imperial 501st Stormtrooper Legion serving the Empire of the Hand during the years following the cease-fire between the Imperial Remnant and the New Republic.

**Aurek fighter** A speedy, delta-shaped ancient starfighter used by the Galactic Republic 4,000 years before the Battle of Yavin.

**Auril sector** A distant group of six star systems—including the Adega system—that also encompassed the Cron drift. Originally there were nine Auril systems, but three were destroyed during the Great Sith War as the Cron Cluster ignited in a multiple supernova. The space city Nespis VIII was located at the node of the Auril systems.

**aurodium** A precious metal that was sometimes used in old-style ingot currency called aurodium credits. The Jedi offered three billion credits' worth of aurodium in 10 large ingots as an offering to the Potentium to allow them to build a Sekotan ship.

**Aurodium Sword** A mercenary group that offered private security and a paramilitary force for heads of state or corporate bodies. The group included humans, Ubese, and Wookiees. Aurodium Sword was led by a combat veteran named Muzzle, believed to be Alpha-66, one of the first batch of clone troopers.

***Aurorient Express*** A luxury liner that soared through the clouds of the gas giant Yorn Skot. The ship and its owner Clode Rhoden were attacked by the Green Forge eco-terrorists in an effort to acquire the insurance money. At that same moment, pirates also targeted the vessel. Jedi Master Qui-Gon Jinn and Padawan Obi-Wan Kenobi did what they could to protect the liner, and though they successfully thwarted both the terrorists and the pirates, the ship nonetheless exploded from a core bomb placed by disgruntled crew members.

**Auset, Ausar** A Nikto Jedi killed during the Siege of Saleucami in the Clone Wars.

**Autem, Lissa** The daughter of Sagoro and Sula Autem, she was the younger sister of Reymet. To Sagoro's dismay, young Lissa admired Reymet's reckless behavior. When Sula left her husband, she took Lissa with her.

**Autem, Reymet** The brash son of Sagoro Autem who studied at the Leadership School on Andara and the Senate Guards' academy. Despite generations of Autems serving in the Senate Guard, Reymet wanted to follow his own path and was much more interested in daredevil swoop racing through Coruscant's garbage pits. It was more than just adrenaline rushes he was seeking—he hoped to earn enough credits to get his girlfriend, Riao Siao, back to her home planet of Felacat. Reymet gave his shady uncle Venco some Senate Guard access codes in exchange for his help, but Venco plotted to use the codes to murder a Galactic Senator. When Venco was caught, Reymet was to be implicated as an accessory to murder, but his father, Sagoro, instead allowed him to escape, sacrificing his career in the Guard. Reymet emerged as a smuggler in the early days of the Empire, and later adopted the bounty hunter alias *Evan Hessler.*

*Sagoro Autem*

**Autem, Sagoro** A third-generation Senate Guard whose devotion to his work often competed with his devotion to his own family. Sagoro sent his older brother, Venco, to prison for betraying the Guard. Sagoro and his wife, Sula, had two children, Lissa and Reymet. The duty-bound Sagoro often butted heads with the more reckless Reymet, who did not want to follow the family tradition of guard service.

A year before the Battle of Geonosis, Sagoro investigated the assassination of Senator Jheramahd Greyshade; Obi-Wan Kenobi and Anakin Skywalker were assigned as protectors to Jheramahd's successor, Simon Greyshade. Evidence soon revealed that Venco Autem was involved in the conspiracy, and Venco's actions implicated Reymet. Against orders, Sagoro stayed on the case and confronted Venco at the Senate chamber, where he was forced to shoot and kill his brother. Days later, Sagoro's wife left him, taking Lissa with her. His family shattered, Sagoro left the guard and allowed Reymet to flee Coruscant.

During the Clone Wars, Sagoro escaped imprisonment on Brentaal IV and helped Jedi Shaak Ti and Quinlan Vos defeat Confederacy forces there, earning him immunity for past crimes. Sagoro then served in the Republic military, reaching the rank of captain in the fleet. When the Republic transitioned to the Galactic Empire, Autem found himself at odds with the new government, and was targeted by bounty hunters dispatched by Darth Vader. One of these hunters, Evan Hessler, was actually his son Reymet in disguise, and he helped Sagoro escape pursuit.

**Autem, Sula** Wife of Sagoro Autem. She eventually left her husband because of his undue devotion to the Senate Guard, taking their daughter, Lissa, with her.

**Autem, Venco** A former Senate Guard and older brother of Sagoro Autem, Venco firmly believed in the corruption of the Senate. He began taking bribes, only to be discovered by Sagoro, who sent him to prison. After leaving prison, Venco emerged as an influential member of the group called the Commonality. Venco conspired with Simon Greyshade to assassinate Senator Jheramahd Greyshade. When Simon began to go against his wishes, Venco targeted him as well. To endear his nephew, Reymet, to him, Venco bribed a Judicial so that Reymet's girlfriend, Riao Siao, could return to her homeworld. In exchange, Reymet gave him Senate access codes, thereby making Reymet an unwitting accomplice to Venco's next attempted murder. Before he was able to complete the hit, however, Sagoro confronted and killed Venco inside the Senate chamber.

**Authority Cash Voucher** The main legal currency in worlds controlled by the Corporate Sector Authority. Upon entering Corporate Sector areas, travelers had to exchange credits for the vouchers or face legal consequences when paying for any goods or services.

**Authority Data Center** The Corporate Sector Authority used this well-guarded repository for nearly all computer-processed information from throughout Corporate Sector space.

**auto enhancement** Installed on some starfighters, these enhancement programs worked with the spacecraft's tracking and computer systems to send a ship to its destination without direct pilot involvement.

**autohopper** A "smart" vehicle that could carry out a variety of tasks without the need of a driver or pilot, an autohopper had a central instruction processor programmed to recall the time and location of job assignments. It could even take into account such variables as terrain and weather changes.

**automap** A datapad dedicated to mapping current coordinates, usually by employing an orbital positioning system.

**automatic sealup** A lifesaving feature, sealup was triggered when air-pressure sensors in a vehicle or outpost sensed decompression or exposure to the vacuum of space. The sensors instantly alerted a central station, which transmitted signals closing airtight bulkhead doors for automatic sealup.

**automixer** A bartending droid that detected the species of user to ensure palatable potables.

**autotourniquet** A medical device that sealed over wounds and amputations to restrict blood loss and promote healing. It was also referred to as a constrictor.

**autovalet** These devices, which automatically cleaned and pressed clothing, could be found in hotels and luxury starships as well as the homes of the wealthy. They were sometimes full-scale droids.

**Auyemesh** One of three moons orbiting the planet Almania. Its population was destroyed by the dark sider who called himself Kueller 13 years after the Battle of Endor. He did so to harvest the wealth of the inhabitants and to add credence to his ultimatum demanding that New Republic Chief of State Leia Organa Solo step down and hand over her power to him.

**AV-6R7** A supervisor droid that spent some time aboard the bridge of the *Executor* as well as overseeing work droids for Moff Jerjerrod on the second Death Star.

**avabush spice** This spice caused sleepiness and was sometimes stirred into drinks or baked into sweets. Used properly, it could also act as a truth serum. Avabushes grew on the planet Baros.

*Avatar-7 enhanced super battle droid*

***Avarice*** A Mark II Imperial Star Destroyer commanded by Sair Yonka. Ysanne Isard used it to protect her bacta convoys after taking control of the planet Thyferra. When New Republic Commander Wedge Antilles offered Captain Yonka a more profitable deal, the captain and his crew defected and renamed the ship *Freedom.*

**Avarik, Corporal** A biker scout stormtrooper assigned to Endor, where he monitored Yuzzum activity. Corporal Avarik often engaged in brawls at the local enlisted clubs on his homeworld of Corulag.

**Avatar-7 enhanced super battle droid** A heavily armed and armored, enhanced super battle droid deployed during the Battle of Iktotch. The giant droid had four arms, retractable rapid-fire blaster cannons, homing missiles, a tight-spray flamethrower, a wide-spray plasma cannon, rocket launchers, and an experimental density projector that prevented Jedi from pushing it with the Force. Mace Windu and Saesee Tiin were ultimately able to blind and cripple the Avatar-7, finishing it off by dropping the remains of a hailfire droid on top of it.

**Avatar Orbital Platform** A joint venture between a Trandoshan slaver corporation and the Empire, the Avatar Orbital Platform was constructed to facilitate the transport and sale of Wookiee slaves captured on the nearby planet Kashyyyk. A source of fear and sadness for the Wookiees, Avatar was often the final stop for families before they were separated and sent to the far reaches of the galaxy. Avatar was ugly but functional, and equipped with rudi-

*AV-6R7*

mentary defenses designed to discourage any Rebel interference in the slave trade.

**avedame** A type of wine made from the large, round reddish purple fruits of the same name that grew on the fungus-like trees of the Jasserak Highlands of Drongar.

**A-vek Iiluunu** A massive Yuuzhan Vong warship used as a fighter carrier. Its flat, ovoid surface could hold 144 coralskipper fighters.

***Avengeance*** A Bothan cruiser that intended to carry out the ar'kai elimination of the Yuuzhan Vong by Bothan fundamentalists. The Jedi kept a close watch on the ship, since the Yuuzhan Vong survivors were allowed to live in peace on Zonama Sekot. When *Avengeance* came uncomfortably close to the living planet, Jedi interceded and arrested its crew.

***Avenger*** An Imperial Star Destroyer, part of a task force that searched for Rebel forces after the Battle of Yavin. Under the command of Captain Needa, the *Avenger* was also present at the Battle of Hoth, after which it followed the fleeing *Millennium Falcon* into an asteroid field. The ship sustained considerable damage and wasn't prepared to capture the *Falcon* when the Rebel ship suddenly reappeared, a failure that cost the *Avenger*'s captain his life at the hands of Darth Vader.

**Aven'sai'Ulrahk** President of Devaron during the Clone Wars, she was unaware that Senator Vien'sai'Malloc was harboring Separatists on their planet. The Jedi Aayla Secura, Tholme, and the Dark Woman revealed the Senator's treachery, and the President demanded that the criminal face justice on Devaron.

**Avenue of the Core Founders** The main street leading to the Galactic Senate on Coruscant, adorned with statues by the entrance concourse depicting the Republic's Core World founders.

**Averam** A planet that housed a Rebel Alliance cell, it was where Leia Organa Solo's aide Winter worked for a few weeks under the code name Targeter. Imperial Intelligence cracked the cell soon afterward. Averam natives were called Averists.

**Aves** A smuggler by trade, he was one of archsmuggler Talon Karrde's chief aides, having served him since he formed his ring. Aves served Karrde as both an adviser and a communications officer. He also coordinated the activities of field operatives and, in effect, acted as the smuggler's ship dispatcher.

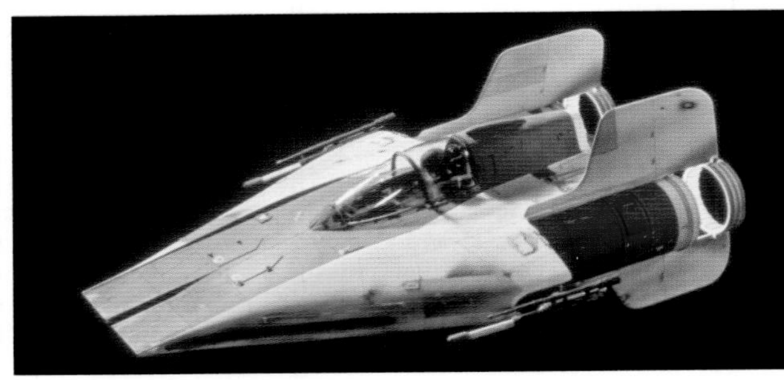

*A-wing starfighter*

**Avoni** A species from the planet Avon known for aggressive colonization efforts. They even created a toxic disaster to allow them to colonize the neighboring world of Radnor.

**A Vrassa** A euphoric drug commonly found in medpacs.

**AV series assault armor** Manufactured by Wrokix Works, this series of powered armor served a variety of military functions. The AV-1A was heavy assault armor, while the AV-1C was more agile, combat infantry armor. The AV-1S was designed for scouting and reconnaissance.

**AVVA** *See* Alliance Veterans Victory Association.

**A-wing slash** Garm Bel Iblis developed this military combat maneuver designed to work with two groups of fighters directed from a base ship. The first group was ordered—over an open channel—to alter course away from incoming enemy fighters. As the enemy fighters turned to track the first group, the second group—made of A-wings—"slashed" at the enemy's flank at full speed.

**A-wing starfighter** This small, wedge-shaped craft was the New Republic's main starfighter interceptor since it first saw full-scale deployment at the Battle of Endor. The lightweight RZ-1 A-wing, co-designed by General Jan Dodonna and Alliance engineer Walex Blissex to outrun any ship in the Imperial Navy, had especially strong avionics, including a powerful jamming system that disrupted sensor readings and let pilots blind enemy targets prior to attack. Originally designed for escort duty, the A-wing proved more suited to hit-and-run missions, blasting enemy sites and spacecraft with twin wing-mounted pivoting laser cannons and concussion missiles. The downside of the A-wing's speed and agility was its relatively high vulnerability in dogfights; the position of the cockpit left pilots exposed to enemy fire, making the craft's speed even more important.

*Avenue of the Core Founders*

**Awmetth, Veedaaz** A Senator from the Vensensor sector who attended the funeral of Padmé Amidala.

**Axmis, Tavion** An apprentice of the Dark Jedi Desann who challenged Luke Skywalker's Jedi academy after the Battle of Endor. Kyle Katarn defeated her in a lightsaber duel but chose to spare her life, demonstrating his adherence to the light side of the Force. Shamed by her defeat, she went into hiding and emerged some time later as part of the Disciples of Ragnos. The Twi'lek Alora served as her student. Jedi student Jaden Korr confronted Axmis on Korriban, where she had used an ancient Sith artifact to reawaken the spirit of Marka Ragnos. Briefly possessed by Ragnos, Axmis wielded incredible power, yet she was still defeated by Korr.

**AX/RX** A modified MD droid used by Kh'aris Fenn to torture Jedi Master Tholme on Kintan during the Clone Wars. AX/RX could emit painful electrical shocks. Tholme fooled the droid with a Jedi breathing technique that stopped his heartbeat. A surprise attack by Tholme and Aayla Secura then destroyed the droid.

**Axxila** A planet in the corridor of industrial worlds that also contained Vandyne and Edusa. It was the homeworld of Firmus Piett. Under Piett's by-the-book leadership, the Axxila anti-pirate fleet soon patrolled the most buttoned-up sector in the Outer Rim. In the early years of the New Republic, the fugitive Imperial adviser Sate Pestage fled to Axxila. Ysanne Isard hoped to prevent Pestage from handing over control of Coruscant to the New Republic, so she sent Admiral Krennel to attack the planet, wiping out many civilians in devastating strikes.

**Ayelixe/Kronbing Textiles** A sponsor of the Corporate Sector, this major company specialized in clothing.

**Ayrou** One of the first Moddell sector species to develop space travel, the Ayrou were willowy humanoids. Hailing from Maya Kovel, they had triple-jointed limbs and were known as wily negotiators and expert hagglers. They had glossy white skin and iridescent eyes. They spread to planets such as Kuna's Tooth, Ovise III, and Vasha.

**Azbeth, Sister** A member of the Singing Mountain Clan on Dathomir.

**Azbrian** A world of sweeping plains and grasslands, with much of its surface devoted to agriculture and the grazing of the indigenous eight-legged herd animals.

***Azgoghk*** An enormous Imperial extermination ship, part of Grand Admiral Pitta's fleet. A few months before the Battle of Endor, Admiral Mir Tork commanded *Azgoghk* at the subjugation of Gulma. After the fall of the Emperor, the *Azgoghk* was brought down by the Rebel Alliance and abandoned. Tork escaped and returned to command the repaired ship. Years later the last living Gulmarid, Slique Brighteyes, hired Boba Fett to avenge the extermination of his species. Brighteyes directed Fett to Malicar 3 and gave the bounty hunter instructions on how to disable the *Azgoghk*. Using an ion cannon, Fett crippled the ship, infiltrated it, and killed Tork and his chief scientist, Dr. Leonis Murthé.

**Azool** *See* Savan.

**Azrakel** A mysterious dark sider who was an experiment born in the mind of the Emperor and given life by the High Prophet Kadann. After conducting dark side experiments on Azrakel, the Emperor left the young man for dead. Kadann nursed him back to health and used him as a tool for his own dark schemes. Azrakel grew to hate Kadann as well, and the dark warrior left to become a mercenary.

**Azure** A tiny rogue planet not part of any system. Its spaceport took up a good portion of its land and was a convenient way stop for those traveling through the Mid Rim. The Republic established a secret monitoring post there during the Clone Wars.

Azure Angel

***Azure Angel*** Anakin Skywalker extensively modified this Delta-7 Aethersprite Jedi starfighter, which became his custom vessel during the Clone Wars. With four laser cannons bracketing each wingtip and a proton torpedo launcher along the ship's dorsal centerline, the speedy combat vessel had greater firepower than the standard fighter. Anakin incorporated articulated stabilizer foils and thrust mounts to assist in atmospheric maneuverability and agility. Perhaps his boldest addition was a pair of hyperdrive thrusters that gave limited hyperspace capability. Though Obi-Wan Kenobi worried that his Padawan was growing too attached to the fighter, Saesee Tiin encouraged Skywalker to keep pushing its limits. The innovations that Anakin pioneered were shared with certain fighters in the Jedi arsenal. Those that featured the so-called Skywalker conversion had increased speed and maneuverability, and carried the blue fan-burst paint pattern originally found on Anakin's ship. Skywalker developed at least two *Azure Angel* fighters during the war.

**Azure Dianoga cantina** A hive of scum and villainy in the Invisec area of Coruscant, it made the Mos Eisley cantina seem tame. The bar was selected by members of Rogue Squadron as a meeting place when they were on an undercover operation to determine alien sentiment toward Alliance control of Coruscant. It was here that the Rogues ran into trouble with the Alien Combine.

**Azur-Jamin, Daye** The fiancé of armaments heiress Tinian I'att, Daye helped her escape the Imperial takeover of her grandparents' armament factory on Druckenwell. Tinian believed that Daye sacrificed his life for her, but he lived on though severely injured. He had crushed legs, extensive head injuries, and no strength in his left arm. Despite his broken body, Daye helped the Rebellion in whatever ways he could, honing his natural attunement to the Force. He would eventually be reunited with Tinian, and the two wed. They had a son together, Tam, who joined Luke Skywalker's Jedi Order. Daye, receiving extensive cyborg reconstruction, also achieved the rank of Jedi Knight; during the Yuuzhan Vong invasion, he was stationed on Nal Hutta and disappeared for a time. Kyle Katarn found Daye corrupted by the dark side of the Force by an unknown evil Force-user.

Azgoghk

**Azur-Jamin, Tam** A Jedi Knight and son of Daye Azur-Jamin and Tinian I'att. Tam traveled to Nal Hutta when his father went missing during the Yuuzhan Vong invasion. He later flew with Luke Skywalker's Saber Squadron at Talfaglio with the comm designation *Quiet*.

**Azur-Jamin, Tinian I'att** Her childhood was spent as an armaments heiress. When the Empire took over her family's businesss on Druckenwell, the I'atts resisted and were killed. I'att believed that her fiancé, Daye Azur-Jamin, had perished as well. She then dedicated her life to fighting the Empire, training to become a bounty hunter as an apprentice to the Wookiee Chenlambec. Her tenacity as a fighter and her skills in identifying explosives by scent came in quite handy. Following a daring mission in which she and Chenlambec rescued a colony of Empire-imprisoned Wookiees and captured the bounty hunter Bossk, she became Chenlambec's partner. They would often help their "acquisitions" defect to the Rebellion. Years later, as the Rebel Alliance became the New Republic, Tinian discovered that Daye was alive. They eventually wed and had a son, Tam, who joined the new Jedi Order. During the Yuuzhan Vong invasion, Tinian worked with Lowbacca to monitor the movements of the alien menace.

**Azzameen, Ace** This Rebel pilot from the successful Azzameen shipping family helped the Alliance steal the Imperial shuttle *Tydirium* from an orbital outpost at Zhar just prior to the Battle of Endor.

# B

**B1 worker droid** This model served in major spaceports all over the galaxy, loading and unloading bulk freighters, container ships, and other vessels.

**B3NK** A prototype Loronar Corporation droid that helped Jedi Knight Ki-Adi-Mundi track his daughter Sylvn, along with the wanted criminal Ephant Mon. A large, humanoid droid with an elongated head, B3NK was programmed for systems integration, computer operations, navigation, and tactics. The droid also possessed great strength.

*Fema Baab*

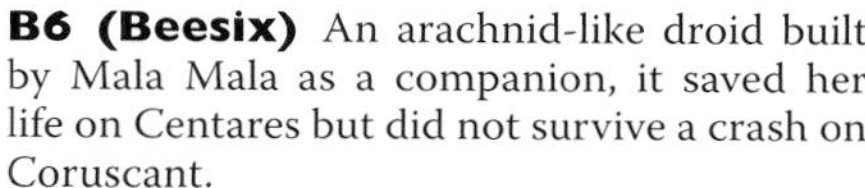

**B6 (Beesix)** An arachnid-like droid built by Mala Mala as a companion, it saved her life on Centares but did not survive a crash on Coruscant.

**B-7 light freighter** A 19-meter-long antiquated model of freighter manufactured by Loronar. Examples included the *Nighthawk,* a ship salvaged by Yoda during the Clone Wars, and the *Muvon* used by the New Republic.

**B-9D7** A thin droid on Nar Shaddaa that appeared to be a personal assistant to Movo Brattakin early in the Galactic Civil War. In truth, the droid's body carried Brattakin's brain, continuing his work from beyond the grave. Jace Forno blasted B-9D7, finally bringing Brattakin's career to an end.

**Baab, Fema** A Senator for the Bajic sector and loyal supporter of Chancellor Palpatine during the Clone Wars, Baab tried unsuccessfully to insinuate herself into Bail Organa's inner circle of concerned Senators. Some believed her a spy for Palpatine.

**Baab, Umjing** The Rughja bandleader of Umjing Baab and his Swinging Trio.

*<Trade Federation battle droids*

***Baanu Kor*** A Yuuzhan Vong worldship where shaper Nen Yim served.

***Baanu Miir*** A 1,000-year-old dying Yuuzhan Vong worldship. The luminescent mycogens that once illuminated the ship's halls faded to sickly patches, and the capillaries of the maw luur became clotted. A quarter of the ship's population died due to a rupture in the hull caused by structural failure. Unlike other affluent worldships, the *Baanu Miir* derived its shipboard gravity from spin, not dovin basals. Shaper Nem Yim risked heresy to discover a way to revitalize the ship's systems while Prefect Ona Shai petitioned for the passengers to be transferred to another worldship. This did not happen in time, and the *Baanu Miir* was left to die.

***Baanu Rass*** An ancient spiral-shaped Yuuzhan Vong worldship that orbited Myrkr and served as the research site for the Yuuzhan Vong voxyn-cloning and -training program. Anakin Solo's strike team infiltrated the *Baanu Rass* to kill the queen voxyn.

**Baas, Bodo** A Krevaaki Jedi Master in the Adega system some 600 years before the Battle of Yavin. Baas was gatekeeper of a Jedi Holocron that was millennia old. It eventually fell into the hands of Emperor Palpatine's reborn clone and was later taken by Leia Organa Solo. She listened intently as a holographic Vodo-Siosk Baas spun tales of ancient Jedi and told of the seductive path to the dark side of the Force. A warning about her own future sent Leia to help Luke Skywalker destroy the clone of Palpatine. Later, Jedi historian Tionne Solusar spent much time studying the Baas Holocron.

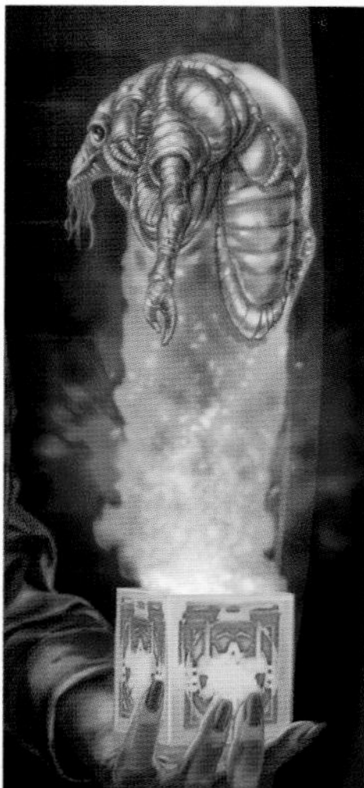

*Bodo Baas*

*Master Vodo-Siosk Baas*

**Baas, Master Vodo-Siosk** A Krevaaki Jedi Master and expert lightsaber craftsman who lived more than 4,000 years before the Battle of Yavin, he trained many Jedi, including the powerful Exar Kun. Kun was ambitious and impatient, and despite his Master's warnings he turned to the dark side of the Force, eventually betraying and killing Baas. The Jedi Master then became one with the Force and started a Jedi Holocron, an interactive repository of Jedi knowledge and history.

Many millennia later, after Leia Organa Solo took the holocron from the reborn clone of Emperor Palpatine, Luke Skywalker used it to teach his Jedi trainees on Yavin 4. But Kun's spirit, which was trapped on the moon, destroyed the holocron and tried to murder Skywalker. Later, the spirit of Vodo-Siosk Baas, along with Skywalker and his trainees, destroyed Kun forever.

**Baath Brothers** These dangerous criminals managed the Outlander Club on Coruscant.

**Baba, Ponda** A pirate and smuggler by calling, aggressive and obnoxious by practice, the walrus-faced Baba was just another miscreant until a chance encounter with a Jedi Knight in a Mos Eisley cantina cost him an arm but gave him high visibility throughout the galaxy.

An Aqualish from the planet Ando, he lived in swamps and wetlands until he decided to seek his fortune plundering and murdering his way through the galaxy. He joined forces with a madman—Dr. Evazan—who practiced what he called "creative surgery" after Baba rescued the doctor from a bounty hunter. While Baba's first thought was to turn in the doctor and collect the reward himself, he figured Evazan would be more valuable as a partner in crime.

The pair traveled frequently to Tatooine to take on spice-smuggling jobs for Jabba the Hutt. In the Mos Eisley cantina on one of those trips, a drunken Baba shoved young Luke Skywalker, and Evazan threatened him. A brown-robed old man, who turned out to be the Jedi Knight Obi-Wan Kenobi, tried to calm the two, but they attacked. With a quick draw of his lightsaber, Kenobi slashed Evazan's chest and severed Baba's right arm at the elbow.

The two criminals had a falling-out after Evazan botched Baba's arm-replacement surgery, but they teamed up again on Ando, where Evazan set up an experimental lab. When he tried to transfer Baba's mind into the body of an Andoan Senator, the experiment misfired and put the Senator's mind into Baba's body.

*Ponda Baba*

**Babali** A tropical planet, Babali held some interest for galactic archaeologists, including those of the Obroan Institute.

**Babbadod** A planet where the starliner *Star Morning,* owned by the fleeing Fallanassi religious order, made a stop.

**Babo, Admiral** A yellow-eyed Bothan fleet commander in the Confederation opposed to the Galactic Alliance. His fleet was dispatched to Kashyyyk to do battle with the Alliance's Fifth Fleet, and at this point in the war, Babo found himself fighting alongside the Wookiees and the Jedi Knights against the forces of Jacen Solo. The insane Dark Jedi Alema Rar affected Babo's judgment and caused him to break his forces, which allowed Jacen and the Fifth Fleet to escape. After the battle, he considered inviting the Jedi and the Wookiees to side with the Confederation, but instead made it clear that the Bothans would consider assassination as a possible action against Jacen Solo, an act that the Jedi did not disagree with.

*A bacta tank heals Luke Skywalker.*

**Bacara, Commander** Clone Commander 1138 who worked with General Ki-Adi-Mundi leading the Galactic Marines, he was cross-trained in space- and ground-based fighting. The Marines often field-tested prototype gear and armor. Particularly fierce and independent, Bacara easily executed Order 66 on Mygeeto, killing Ki-Adi-Mundi.

**Bacca, Great** A legendary Wookiee warrior said to have been one of the first to encounter offworld life.

**Bachenkall, Warrant Officer** An Imperial helmsman aboard the *Executor,* he was typical of the many graduates of the Imperial Academy on Raithal.

**bacta** The most common and effective healing salve employed in the galaxy. Gelatinous, translucent red alazhi and kavam bacterial particles were suspended in a lotion that had been used for thousands of years by the Vratix to heal cuts. The particles were mixed with the colorless liquid ambori. The resulting synthetic chemical—bacta—was thought to mimic the body's own vital fluids and was used to treat and heal all but the most serious of wounds. Patients were fully immersed (with breath masks) in the expensive liquid, which was held in cylindrical rejuvenation tanks (bacta tanks). The bacterial particles sought out wounds and promoted amazingly quick tissue growth without scarring. The popularity of bacta led to its replacing kolto as the predominant medical healing solution.

During times of galactic conflict, many powerful agencies realized the importance of bacta as a source of power and control. Emperor Palpatine shut down satellite manufacturing centers and systematically suppressed small manufacturers in favor of the Zaltin and Xucphra corporations. Bacta then fell under the control of a cartel on Thyferra, and the corporations that distributed it became even more powerful than the Emperor intended. Bacta was universally accepted as a safe drug until Ashern terrorists contaminated one lot. Millions of people exposed to it became allergic to bacta, particularly the citizens and soldiers on Imperial Center. Later, the Bacta War was fought over control of the healing substance.

**Bacta Squad** A unit of the Galactic Alliance's special commando force that infiltrated Supreme Overlord Shimrra's citadel in the final battle against the Yuuzhan Vong.

**Bacta War, the** During the final days of Imperial control of Coruscant, onetime director of Imperial Intelligence Ysanne Isard and the Xucphra Corporation began a civil war on the planet Thyferra. Their objective was to suppress the Zaltin Bacta Corporation and become sole heirs to the Bacta Cartel, the group that controlled all of the galaxy's supply of the near-miraculous healing agent. Isard reasoned that with the wealth and power of the cartel at her disposal, she could rule the galaxy and perhaps even crush the Rebellion. As part of her master plan, the Krytos virus was ravag-

*Commander Bacara*

ing newly occupied Coruscant, and the New Republic risked bankruptcy trying to control the outbreak with bacta.

Isard knew that the Republic's need for bacta and the potential political fallout of interfering with a strictly civil war would make it hesitant to attack her position on Thyferra. Rogue Squadron was forbidden to intervene, so its members resigned—then set up a secret operation to try to topple Isard. They acquired ships and weapons and organized the Ashern terrorists on Thyferra to overthrow Isard's government. Then they started attacking and liberating bacta convoys.

Things got nasty quickly. Isard destroyed a colony that had been given free bacta; the Rogues destroyed one of her production facilities in return. She attacked them, and they destroyed one of her starships. Then she started to annihilate Thyferra's native Vratix population. Advance planning and superb strategy helped the Rogues and their allies overcome overwhelming firepower, and they defeated Isard and her forces. As for the Rogues' resignations, they hadn't been recorded due to a clerical error, so Rogue Squadron was still very much a part of the New Republic.

**Badeleg, Cho** A member of the ExGal-4 science team on Belkadan, he was a short, dark-haired human who died when the Spacecaster shuttle to Helska 4 was attacked by the Yuuzhan Vong.

**Badji** A pirate who operated in the Shelsha sector and was captured and questioned by rogue stormtroopers of the Hand of Judgment during their investigation of seditious activities in the sector.

**Badlands, Kamarian** The flat, sparsely populated area near the parched equator of the planet Kamar. Inhabitants were called Badlanders. The region wasn't a bad place to get lost, as Han Solo and Chewbacca found out when they spent some time there after the Corporate Sector Authority got a little too interested in keeping tabs on them.

**Badlands of N'g'zi** A vast empty stretch on the western edge of the E'Y-Akh Desert on Geonosis, and the site of Count Dooku's secret hangar.

**Bador** One of the two moons of Kuat.

**Badure, Alexsandr** Also known as Trooper, he was a mentor to Han Solo and taught the Corellian almost everything he knew about flying. He saved Solo and his companion Chewbacca after an aborted spice run to Kessel. That was repayment in kind: Many years previous, Solo had saved Badure after a training mission had gone awry. Just before Solo hooked up with Luke Skywalker, Ben Kenobi, and the Rebel Alliance, Badure convinced him and Chewbacca to help find the fabled lost treasure from the cargo transport *Queen of Ranroon.*

**Baffle** A BFL labor droid on Ruan that Han Solo mistook for Bollux during the Yuuzhan Vong invasion. A driver, Baffle used to work at district headquarters overseeing the reassignment of droids retired from agricultural work. To the best of his knowledge, he was activated on Fondor. Baffle helped Han find Droma; in return, Solo agreed to sabotage the Salliche Ag transceiver overseeing Ruan's droid population. Baffle also provided Han and Droma with information regarding the destination of the *Trevee,* the ship carrying Droma's Ryn clanmates.

**bafforr trees** These intelligent crystalline trees, with bark smoother than glass, were found on the planet Ithor. The Pesktda Xenobotanical Garden on the planet Garqi had a grove of them. The New Republic discovered that Yuuzhan Vong armor was allergic to the yellow pollen from bafforr trees. The Jedi attempted to hide this discovery from the Yuuzhan Vong by burning down the garden. The Yuuzhan Vong nonetheless found out about the weakness and destroyed all life on Ithor.

**Baftu** The Phindian leader of the Syndicat, he made a secret deal with Prince Beju of Gala to provide badly needed bacta, rectifying a false shortage engineered to secure Beju votes in a planetary election. In exchange, Baftu's criminal organization would be firmly ensconced in Gala's power structure. This plot was eventually foiled by Qui-Gon Jinn and his Padawan Obi-Wan Kenobi.

**Baga** A baby bordok and the pet of Wicket, an Ewok.

**baggage-vrrip** A strong, six-legged creature bred by the Yuuzhan Vong to carry heavy loads of cargo.

**Bagmim** A collective alien species that worked as a committee. Upon their entrance into the New Republic, Bagmim navy vessels had to be staffed entirely with Bagmims in order to function properly.

**bag-out capsule** The nickname for the ejectable cockpit module from an LAAT gunship.

**Bagwa, Hermione** This waitress worked at Dex's Diner around the time of the Clone Wars. She often competed with the droid waitress WA-7 for tips and service. She eventually came into ownership of the diner.

*Baga*

*Hermione Bagwa*

**Bagy, Dugo** A notorious Sullustan con artist on Reecee who pointed Han Solo and Chewbacca to Lando Calrissian's activities at Destrillion and Dubrillion.

***Bail Organa*** A New Republic Star Destroyer that served as Garm Bel Iblis's command ship at the defense of Coruscant during the Yuuzhan Vong invasion.

**Baiuntu** The chief of the Qulun trading clan on Ansion, this fat Alwari hoped to earn money from Soergg the Hutt by repeatedly attempting to delay a mission of Jedi Knights sent to the planet to settle a border dispute. During this effort, he and his clan came under attack by a pack of predatory shanhs, and Baiuntu was killed and devoured.

**Baji** A Ho'Din from the planet Moltok, Baji was a healer and medicine man who spoke in rhyme and gathered roots and plants to make medicine and potions. He also sent samples of plants near extinction on Yavin 4 to botanists back home to study. Baji was captured by the Empire and forced to cure the blindness of Trioculus, a pretender to the throne of Emperor Palpatine. The doctor was then pressed into Imperial service. But Baji was rescued by the Alliance and taken to Dagobah, where he raised medicinal plants in a greenhouse.

**Bajic sector** Located in the Outer Rim, this sector contained the Lybeya system, where a secret Rebel shipyard was built on one of the larger Vergesso asteroids. Seeking to curry favor as well as personal gain, the criminal mastermind Prince Xizor notified Emperor Palpatine of the base, which also was near the main facilities of Ororo Transportation, a major competitor of Xizor's company, XTS, and a front for the rival Tenloss Syndicate. Tenloss had been trying to wrest control of spice-trafficking operations in the Bajic sector (sometimes called the Baji sector) from Black Sun, Xizor's criminal group. Acting on the Emperor's orders, Darth Vader destroyed the Rebel base, along with Ororo Transportation.

**Baker, Mayor** The mayor of Dying Slowly on the planet Jubilar, Baker was known as Incavi Larado before her marriage.

**Bakleeda** An alias used by Obi-Wan Kenobi to infiltrate the slaver Krayn's spice processing plant on Nar Shaddaa. As Bakleeda, Kenobi concealed his face behind a masked helmet. Didi Oddo helped Obi-Wan to create the identity.

**Baktoid Armor Workshop** A Trade Federation–owned design firm that developed rugged all-terrain ground vehicles for use by civilians. Its designs tended to be heavily armored, with delicate or important components placed in secure, well-protected areas near the rear of the craft. In order to build its secret army, the Trade Federation provided Baktoid with funding for a complete line of ground assault vehicles and transports, including AAT battle tanks and MTT troop carriers. By the time of the Empire, Baktoid had largely been nationalized or phased out, though much of its equipment was still available in the Outer Rim.

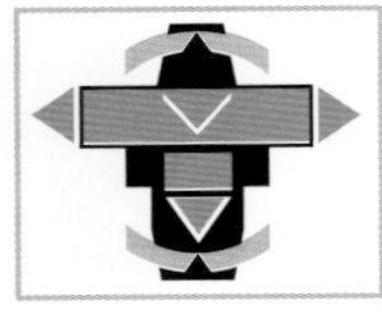

**Baktoid Combat Automata** Maker of the Trade Federation battle droid, formerly a sister company to Baktoid Armor Workshop. It developed much of the droid infantry for the Clone Wars, including the B1 battle droid, the baron droid, and the SRT droid.

**Bakura; Bakura system** A remote but rich green-and-blue planet with several moons, Bakura was the site of an historic truce between the Rebel Alliance and Imperial forces shortly after the death of Emperor Palpatine.

The eight planets in the Bakura system, located on the isolated edge of the Rim worlds, included one gas giant and Planet Six, an ammonia ice-covered ball. Bakura received a great deal of rainfall. The capital city of Salis D'aar sat at the base of a mountain range on a white quartz delta between two parallel rivers. Bakura's exports included strategic metals, repulsorlift components, and an addictive fruit called namana, which was made into candies and nectar. Animal life included the butter newt and the predatory Bakuran cratsch, and among the plants were pokkta leaves and passion-bud vines.

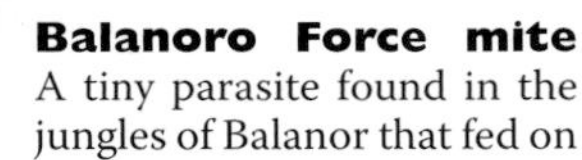

*Bakura*

Originally chartered by the Bakur Corporation as a self-sufficient community a century and a half before the New Republic, the planet was opened to outside settlement during the final years of the Clone Wars, at which time Count Dooku used it as a temporary headquarters. Inhabitants tended to be prejudiced against nonhuman species and especially disliked droids, since the first Bakuran colonists were nearly wiped out by malfunctioning automata.

Constant governmental bickering made the planet easy pickings for the Empire three years before the Battle of Endor. Immediately following the battle, Alliance and Imperial forces joined together to thwart an invasion by the Ssi-ruuvi Imperium. After the subsequent overthrow of Imperial forces, Prime Minister Yeorg Captison took over planetary leadership. Several years later, his niece Gaeriel was elected Prime Minister but was defeated in a succeeding election. The planet retained a powerful defensive fleet, and 14 years after the truce Luke Skywalker returned to Bakura to borrow battle cruisers for a mission in the Corellian system. The mission was ultimately successful, but half of the Bakuran cruisers were destroyed; Gaeriel Captison was killed.

During the war with the Yuuzhan Vong, the Ssi-ruuk attempted once again to invade Bakura in a more deceitful way. A mutant Ssi-ruu called the Keeramak had supposedly defeated the Ssi-ruuvi Imperium and wished to forge an alliance with Bakura. The Keeramak consecrated Bakuran soil in a ceremony that would have alleviated the Ssi-ruuvi fear of dying on an unconsecrated world. Their subservient race, the P'w'eck, however, prevented the Ssi-ruuvi invasion. Bakura eventually sided with the Galactic Alliance.

**Balamak** A world in the Taldot sector and site of a Clone Wars battle. Adar Tallon devised a battle plan that earned him the title Victor of Balamak in which Anakin Skywalker destroyed a Separatist jamming craft.

**Balancesheet** A surprisingly independent accounting node that could detach itself from Kud'ar Mub'at, the Assembler. It conspired with Prince Xizor to overthrow Kud'ar Mub'at. After killing its creator, Balancesheet began a rise to power in which he spared Boba Fett's life and later stiffed him on a bounty.

**Balanoro Force mite** A tiny parasite found in the jungles of Balanor that fed on the Force within its target range.

**Balawai** The Korunnai name for offworld settlers living in the lowlands of Haruun Kal. The Korunnai and the Balawai were once involved in brutal civil war. During the Clone Wars, the Balawai militias allied to the Separatists opposed Jedi Master Depa Billaba's guerrillas. The unstable Billaba was implicated in the torture of a group of Balawai jungle prospectors, also known as jups.

**Baldavian pocket hare** A skittish creature often held up as a symbol of cowardice.

**Bal'demnic** A stark, rugged world in the Bak'rofsen system, Auril sector. The native reptilian Kon'me were aggressive toward outsiders. The Commerce Guild discovered cortosis in its rocky spires, prompting a Separatist invasion of the planet. The Jedi dispatched a clone task force to keep the Separatists from controlling the world.

*Bal'demnic*

**Balis-Baurgh system** Naturally shielded from sensors by gas clouds and intense solar radiation, this system contained three planets, only one of which could support life. Political leaders on the world decided to jointly build a space station, but when construction was secretly sabotaged by the Empire, the nations blamed one another and went to war, making the planet an easy mark for Imperial conquest. The space station became a fully automated prison, and sometime after the Battle of Endor, Alliance Captain Junas Turner and Ewok warrior Grael were imprisoned there until they escaped.

**ball bearing missile** An anti-dovin-basal weapon in Twin Suns Squadron's arsenal consisting of a metal tube open at one end. The rear closed portion was packed with a plasma-based explosive charge. The forward two-thirds, sealed only by the fragile nose of the missile, was packed with metal ball bearings the size of human heads. When the plasma charge detonated, it superheated the ball bearings, firing them at the target. When ball bearing missiles were used with volleys of proton torpedoes, dovin basals could not differentiate the two—making them vulnerable.

**ball creature of Duroon** A meek and mild nocturnal plant eater, it was shaped like a globe and moved like a ball, bouncing from place to place. It was also known as a bouncebeast.

**Ballow-Reese, Bendodi** The oldest member of the ExGal-4 science team on Belkadan. A former barnstorming search-and-destroy agent with the Rebel Alliance, he was killed in the Yuuzhan Vong invasion of the planet.

**Balmorra** This factory world was located at the fringes of the Galactic Core. Its inhabitants manufactured weapons for the Imperial Army and were the primary builders of the AT-ST walker. The planet was liberated by the New Republic following the Battle of Endor. It came under Imperial rule again during the first cloned Emperor's appearance. Following Palpatine's supposed death near Da Soocha, the Balmorrans began arming the New Republic. In retaliation, the planet was attacked by a force led by Military Executor Sedriss using shadow droids and SD-9 battle droids. After suffering surprising losses at the hands of new Viper Automadons, Sedriss called off his attack in exchange for a shipment of the molecularly shielded droids.

**Balmorra Run** A smuggling route that approached the Naboo system, it cut through the dense Kaliida Nebula populated by immense neebray creatures.

**Balog** Formerly chief security controller of New Apsolon, he was under investigation by the Jedi for the death of Roan, the planetary leader. To escape, Balog took the Jedi Tahl as his hostage. Balog escaped, though he was later arrested by the Jedi and imprisoned for his criminal bid for power.

**Balosar** An alien species with a reputation for producing criminals, cheats, and scoundrels. Balosars were humanoid with flexible antenepalps extending from the tops of their heads. They hailed from the polluted planet of the same name. Elan Sleazebaggano was a Balosar.

**Baltizaar** A planet far from the Core systems and site of a massacre committed by the Bando Gora. Jedi Master Dooku was to lead the counterattack, but he ultimately refused, his differences with the Jedi Order coming to a head. He left the Order, but the mission proceeded. Many Jedi were killed, including Komari Vosa.

**Baltke** The commander of the Chiss Expansionary Defense Fleet during the Swarm War. He attempted to interrogate Leia Organa Solo regarding the Galactic Alliance presence near Tenupe, but Leia used the Force to cause Baltke to inject himself with a truth serum.

**Balu, Predne** A heavy, slope-shouldered human, he was assistant security officer of Mos Eisley during the Galactic Civil War.

**Bana the Hutt** This young Hutt was a member of the Hutt resistance that grew in response to the Yuuzhan Vong invasion. He was cousin to Randa the Hutt. Bana invested in Shelter Base.

*Balosar Elan Sleazebaggano attempts to sell death sticks to Obi-Wan Kenobi.*

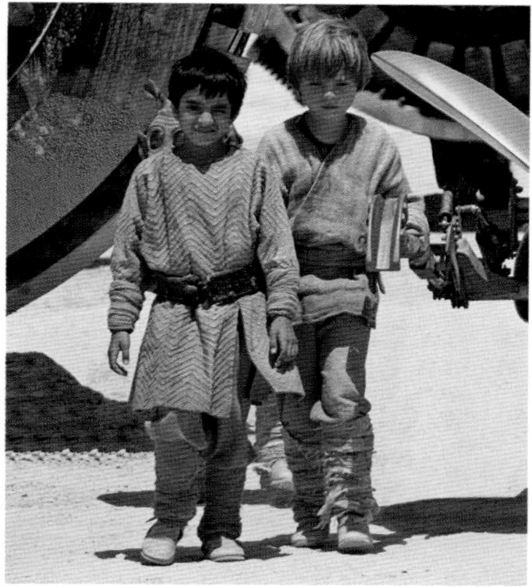

*Kitster Banai and Anakin Skywalker, prior to the Boonta Eve Classic Podrace*

**Banai, Kitster Chanchani** Anakin Skywalker's best friend while living as a slave in Mos Espa. Anakin and Kitster discovered a secret cargo of slaves transported to Mos Espa by Sebulba. A group of delicate Ghostling children were to be sold to Gardulla the Hutt. Anakin, Kitster, and a few other friends disguised themselves as Jawas and infiltrated Gardulla's estate, freeing the children. Later, when Anakin raced for freedom at the Boonta Eve Classic, Kitster and Wald offered their support in Anakin's pit crew.

After working as a hotel steward, Kitster purchased his freedom and worked as a majordomo at a wealthy estate. Financial hardships led to the collapse of his first marriage to Ulda, though he remarried and had children with a woman named Tamora. To make ends meet, Kitster had to sell much of his Anakin Skywalker memorabilia, including a holocube that caught the attention of Leia Organa Solo. Kitster's recollections of Anakin helped Leia come to terms with her father's dark fate. Kitster also came into possession of the *Killik Twilight* painting to keep it out of the hands of the Empire.

**Banai, Rakir** The father of Anakin Skywalker's boyhood friend Kitster, he was a pirate aboard a warship. Rakir Banai was wanted by Hutt crime lords, and his ship was captured by bounty hunters when Kitster and his mother were sold into slavery.

**banda** Tiny nibbling insects found on Tatooine.

**Bandeam, Sors** A frightened human youngling killed in Darth Vader's attack on the Jedi Temple after Order 66.

**bandfill** A musical instrument that featured a number of mounted horn bells.

**Bando Gora** A clandestine criminal organization and Force-worshipping cult that targeted large corporations in the final years of the Old Republic. It was based out of the planet Kohlma. Bando Gora's machinations conflicted with Darth Sidious's master plan, so the Sith Lord had Count Dooku deal with the cult, which came under the command of his fallen disciple Komari Vosa. To that end, Dooku hired rival bounty hunters Jango Fett and Montross to track down Vosa. With Vosa's defeat, Bando Gora disintegrated as a threat, and Fett proved himself capable enough in Dooku's eyes to become the template of the Republic's clone army.

Bando Gora cultists seemed twisted by the dark side, often donning hoods and masks to increase their fearsome appearance.

**Bandomeer** Before being despoiled by the invading Yuuzhan Vong, this planet rich in mineral resources was home to the native, silver-haired Meerian species. Mining organizations controlled the planet, including the powerful Offworld Corporation and the Arcona Mineral Harvest Corporation, which vied for its mineral wealth. Due to exploitation of the land by mining companies, its soil was not useful for farming; food had to be imported. The Republic's Jedi Agricultural Corps maintained a station dedicated to reclaiming farmland. One enormous landmass and one massive sea divided the planet in half. The planet had but one city, Bandor.

*Cad Bane*

**Bandon, Darth** A former Jedi student who fled the Order to follow Darth Malak and study the Sith ways on Korriban. His cruelty and ruthlessness drew the admiration of Malak, and Bandon became his apprentice. Malak dispatched Bandon to stop the mind-wiped Revan and Bastila Shan's search for the Star Forge, and Revan slew Bandon.

**Bane, Cad** A male Duros bounty hunter working for Count Dooku during the Clone Wars. Bane stole a holocron listing infants with Force potential, using the information to kidnap the children and transport them to Mustafar, where Darth Sidious planned to use them for his own wicked ends.

Darth Bane

**Bane, Darth** An important architect of the Sith Order, Darth Bane lived 1,000 years before the Battle of Naboo. He began life as Dessel, an indentured cortosis miner toiling under harsh conditions on the planet Apatros. He was raised by his abusive father, Hurst, who berated and blamed Dessel for the difficulties of their circumstances, nicknaming him Bane. This hardened Dessel into a tough young man who discovered his sensitivity to the Force when he used the dark side to kill his father. After this incident, Dessel found a new confidence that led him to brutally defend himself from any who would test him. He eventually smuggled his way off Apatros and joined the Sith army, where he proved himself time and again as a member of the Gloom Walkers unit. The Dark Lord Kopecz took an interest in Dessel's actions and invited him to join the Sith Academy on Korriban.

Dessel quickly excelled in the Sith arts, but his brashness led him to challenge far more powerful colleagues like ace pupil Sirak, who gravely injured Dessel. While convalescing, Dessel supplemented his training by studying forbidden ancient texts and learning about Sith traditions that had been all but abandoned. He read about Darth Revan, and began contrasting Revan's methodology with the shortcomings he perceived in the then-current Brotherhood of Darkness. It was at this time that fellow student Githany sought to seductively manipulate Dessel to her own ends, using his increasing abilities to unseat Sirak from his favored position within the Academy. Dessel challenged Sirak and this time bested him, but stopped short of delivering a killing blow.

So convinced was he that the current Sith were misguided, Dessel disobeyed his Masters and sojourned on the dark-side-drenched worlds of Korriban and Lehon, desperate for guidance. On Lehon, he discovered a lost holocron of Darth Revan, and became fixated upon ancient Sith traditions. He adopted the *Darth* title and renamed himself Darth Bane, recognizing that the current Sith Order was a dead end.

Banking Clan communications frigate

The ruling Sith Lord Kaan grew increasingly wary of Bane and dispatched Lord Kas'im to kill him. Bane survived, however, and returned to the Sith Order just as the war against the Jedi was drawing toward a climactic engagement. To deliver a final defeat against the Jedi Army of Light, the Sith students at Korriban had all been elevated to the rank of Lord and dispatched to the battlefront of Ruusan. Bane gave Kaan ancient knowledge to craft a weapon that would spell the end of the Jedi: a diabolical Force weapon called a thought bomb.

Bane returned to the Brotherhood, seeking a worthy apprentice to continue the Sith Order in a new fashion once he had disposed of the old. Kaan used Githany to poison Bane. On Ambria, the toxin coursed through his veins, and Bane lashed out, trying to find a focus in the dark side that would allow him to purge the poison from his body. He used the Force to slaughter a young boy and his brothers before their anguished father's eyes, and drew in the pain and grief to once again grow strong in the dark side.

A cured Bane arrived on Ruusan, much to Lord Kaan's surprise. Bane witnessed the Order's weakness as other Sith Lords approached him with offers to conspire against Kaan. Bane was galvanized to restructure the Order. When Kaan used Bane's knowledge to create and detonate the thought bomb, the resulting cataclysm destroyed the Jedi and Sith armies, leaving Bane the sole Sith survivor.

In the aftermath of Ruusan, Bane discovered a young girl named Zannah, and tasked her with rendezvousing with him on Onderon if she was to receive training from him. En route to Onderon, Bane crashed his vessel the *Valcyn* on the beast moon of Dxun. There he adopted a living suit of armor that covered most of his body. Hard-shelled, parasitic creatures called orbalisks attached themselves as he struggled through the dense jungles of Dxun. Two parent orbalisks affixed themselves to Bane's chest, forming a breastplate. As they bred, the offspring spread out across his body. Although Bane initially attempted to remove the creatures, he soon realized that their symbiotic relationship was one from which he would ultimately benefit. He had to wear a cage-like protective helmet to keep the creatures from growing into his face.

Admiral Banjeer

Bane went into hiding, relying on his patience and cunning to keep the Sith ways alive. Darth Bane was the first to dictate that a Sith Lord should take only one apprentice. His teachings were later expanded to ensure that only two Sith (a Master and his apprentice) would exist at any given time—the so-called Rule of Two: one Sith to embody power, the other to aspire to it. Zannah became his apprentice, thus starting a secret line of Sith Lords that would extend over the centuries all the way to Darth Sidious's time and beyond.

**Bane's Heart** A double-bladed lightsaber that once belonged to Darth Zannah and was used by the combat droid N-K Necrosis. The weapon was said to contain Bane's Heart, an alchemically treated Sith lightsaber crystal given to Zannah by her Sith Master, Darth Bane.

**Banjeer, Admiral** A member of the Imperial Interim Ruling Council after the demise of the reborn Emperor and commander of one of the Empire's largest fleets. An Imperial traditionalist, he disliked sitting alongside aliens on the council. He was the second council member to be killed by Nom Anor, though the assassin's identity would not be known for some time.

**Banjeer, Boss** An underworld crime boss who was nephew of Admiral Banjeer and exploited his connections in the Imperial Interim Ruling Council to control the bounty hunters of Baramorra. He also had ties to Grappa the Hutt. Bounty hunter Kenix Kil (in truth, the Royal Guard Kir Kanos) infiltrated Banjeer's organization and wiped out many of his hunters. Kil then assassinated Boss Banjeer for his family's betrayal of the Empire.

**Banking Clan** *See* InterGalactic Banking Clan.

**Banking Clan communications frigate** A *Munificent*-class combat warship 825 meters long employed by the InterGalactic

Banking Clan in the Clone Wars. Once used to guard bankers' vaults on Outer Rim worlds, these ships handled intrasector communications in areas where the HoloNet was dismantled during the war.

**Bank of the Core** A lesser-known sponsor of the Corporate Sector.

*Farquil Ban'n*

**Ban'n, Farquil** A demure female Bith who was subjected to such humiliations as having to wear a painful Theselonian bridal gown for her employer, Embra the Hutt. She secretly tracked Jozzel Moffett during the search for the Yavin Vassilika and watched as Moffett delivered the artifact to the Rebel Alliance in exchange for an exact replica of the Vassilika along with four million credits. Ban'n shot Moffett in the back and took the credits, allowing Zuckuss and Sardu Sallowe to take home the trophy. With the stolen funds securing her future, Ban'n quit her job working for Embra—but she was promptly tracked down by Boba Fett, sent to retrieve the four million credits for Jabba the Hutt.

**Banolt, Lirin** A male human con man who stole precious artifacts for Sate Pestage. When Banolt got greedy and tried to blackmail Pestage to prevent him from divulging the location of the top-secret Eidolon Base, Pestage had Banolt killed. Banolt also went by the names Bruhas Drey, Ran Nammon, and Kier Dom, among others.

*A Tusken Raider atop a bantha*

**Banoosh-Walores** A clan of Senalis, from the moon Senali orbiting Rutan. The clan was part of King Meenon's family, on his sister Ganeed's side. They lived on Clear Lake.

**bantha** Large, four-legged beasts of burden found on many worlds, these creatures adapted to a variety of climates and terrain. Wild herds roamed some planets; on others, the only banthas were domesticated. Highly intelligent and extremely social, banthas traveled in matriarchal herds of up to 25 individuals. The bantha tongue was highly sensitive, extremely strong, structurally complex, and dexterous. Males had a pair of large tapering horns and could be as wide as 3 meters at the shoulders. Banthas survived on grasses and other native flora, and given their size and internal reserves they could live a month or so without water or food. Often used as pack animals, they had long, thick fur prized for clothing; their meat was used for food. Even bantha-skin boots and carrying cases brought top credits on some worlds.

Since they could be found on most agricultural systems, it was believed that early space settlers transported them to these new worlds. Remains of banthas have been found that predate most recorded civilizations. The Tusken Raiders of Tatooine had a special bond with their personal bantha; if the creature died, the Raider was sent into the desert in the hope of being adopted by a wild bantha.

**Bantha Blaster** A pink-and-green alcoholic beverage, it was a favorite of Jos Vondar on Drongar, as well as a party favorite at the palace of Jabba the Hutt.

**Bantha Burrows** A network of caves within Tatooine's canyons believed to be used by banthas avoiding sandstorms.

***Bantha*-class assault shuttle** A squat, slow vehicle with a hide as thick as its namesake, this ship was a joint design of Mon Calamari and Sullustan engineers. It was designed to fly behind a fighter screen into target areas and take a beating while it disgorged or airlifted troops and small ground vehicles. The *Bantha*-class assault shuttle was first used during the assault on Oradin at the Battle of Brentaal.

**Bantha formation** A single-file starfighter formation. While evading neebrays in the Kaliida Nebula during the Clone Wars, Anakin Skywalker commanded Shadow Squadron to go into Bantha formation.

**bantha four five six** This instruction code was given by the droid TDL3.5 as authorization for her to replace C-3PO as nanny to the children of Leia and Han Solo. But Leia's aide Winter realized that *bantha* was not a family code. It was a prank by young Anakin Solo, who was angry that C-3PO would no longer read him his favorite bedtime story, "The Little Lost Bantha Cub."

*Ebenn Baobab (left) and Queen Amidala*

**Banvhar Station** A defenseless asteroid belt mining facility brutalized by General Grievous and the Separatists during the Clone Wars. It was near Anoat and close to trade spaceways. The few survivors yearned for revenge against Grievous.

*Bantha*-*class assault shuttle*

**Banz** A Jedi youngling taken prisoner by General Grievous, he and his clanmates were brought to Belsus, where Grievous hoped to combine their potential dark side energy with Geonosian technology. The intervention of a group of Jedi targeting Grievous for assassination allowed for their escape.

**Baobab, Ebenn Q3 (EQ3)** A male member of the Naboo Royal Court present at Supreme Chancellor Palpatine's arrival following the Battle of Naboo. Ebenn Q3 Baobab, better known as EQ3, was a distinguished author, traveler, humorist, adventurer, historian, and philologist. He possessed the largest known private collection of Hutt folk art. He later relocated to Manda with his wife, Pookie, and a miniature bantha named Nuke. He was well known for a handy galactic phrasebook that he published.

**Baobab, Mungo** A reckless treasure hunter and adventurer from Manda, Baobab came from a family that owned the Baobab Merchant Fleet during the Empire's early days. To try to instill a work ethic in Mungo, the family sent him to Biitu to set up a mining operation and trading post. Baobab's greatest accomplishment was finding and preserving the Roonstones, a crystal structure in which was encoded the earliest known text of *Dha Werda Verda,* an epic poem of the conquest of the indigenous people of Coruscant by a warrior race called the Taung.

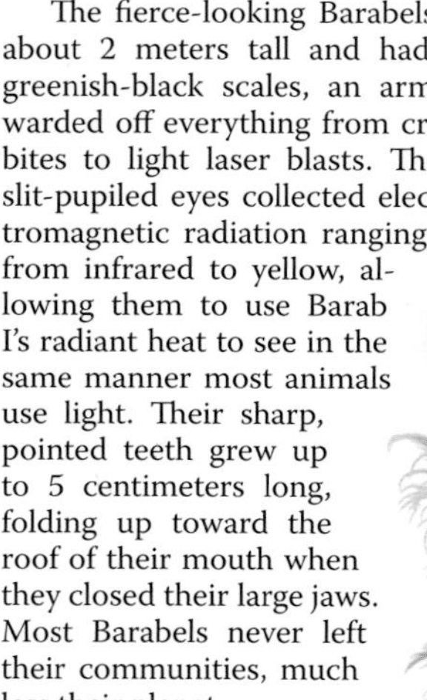

Mungo Baobab

**Baobab, Oggem "Ogger"** Mungo Baobab's great-uncle, who vanished for over six decades after crashing on Roon while searching for the fabled Roonstones. Mungo found the treasure hunter dying of advanced age. Old Ogger asked Mungo to continue the quest, but prophetically warned him not to place lust for wealth before the value of friendship. Ogger then died, leaving behind a treasure of six bags of Roonstones.

Bao-Dur

**Baobab Archives** The Baobab Archives on Manda were considered extensive and authoritative.

**Bao-Dur** A Republic veteran of the Mandalorian Wars, some 3,900 years before the Battle of Yavin, Bao-Dur was a gifted Iridonian Zabrak mechanic who developed new weapons, shields, and other technologies for the war effort. Having witnessed many atrocities, Bao-Dur lost an arm in the fighting, but replaced it with an incredibly strong mechanical appendage of his own design. Following the war, he concentrated on helpful reconstructive efforts, such as the restoration of Telos.

**Barab I** A dark, humid world in close orbit around the red dwarf Barab. Barab I had a 60-standard-hour rotation and was bathed in ultraviolet, gamma, and infrared radiation. During the day, standing water evaporated, making the surface very humid and hazy. During the cool night, the only time animal life was active, the haze condensed and fell to the surface as rain. The Barabel lived in underground caverns. A band of Jedi once helped resolve a Barabel dispute over access to choice hunting grounds, leaving the Barabel with a deep respect for Jedi. A spaceport, Alater-ka, was built after the Empire took control of Barab I. After the Battle of Endor, the Barabel nearly went to war with the Verpine when the Verpine defaulted on a shipbuilding contract.

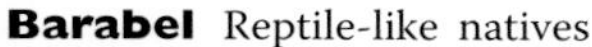

Barada

**Barabel** Reptile-like natives of the untamed planet of Barab I, Barabels were ferocious hunters. Offworlders once chartered safaris to hunt down Barabels, ignoring evidence that they were intelligent creatures. A Jedi Knight once settled a major dispute among the Barabels, forever cementing respect toward Jedi as part of the Barabel culture.

The fierce-looking Barabels were about 2 meters tall and had horny greenish-black scales, an armor that warded off everything from creature bites to light laser blasts. Their slit-pupiled eyes collected electromagnetic radiation ranging from infrared to yellow, allowing them to use Barab I's radiant heat to see in the same manner most animals use light. Their sharp, pointed teeth grew up to 5 centimeters long, folding up toward the roof of their mouth when they closed their large jaws. Most Barabels never left their communities, much less their planet.

Notable Barabels included Skahtul, a female Barabel bounty hunter who captured Luke Skywalker on the planet Kothlis prior to the Battle of Endor, and Saba Sebatyne, Jedi Master.

**Baraboo** This planet was the site of the Institute for Sentient Studies, which contained the most comprehensive collection of neurological models in the galaxy. Some 12 years after the Battle of Endor, the cyborg Lobot accessed the institute's records, searching for a clue to decipher a puzzle aboard the mysterious ghost ship called the *Teljkon Vagabond.*

**Barad, Vol** The deputy president of Corellia following the assassination of Thrackan Sal-Solo, he vowed to work with the various political parties within the Corellian Assembly to form a coalition government that would restore the planet's standing in the galaxy.

**Barada** An indentured servant won by Jabba the Hutt in a rigged sabacc game, this native of Klatooine worked his way up from the crime lord's vehicle pool to become captain of the skiff guard whenever Jabba traveled. Despite being kept under tight discipline by Jabba, the leathery-skinned Barada developed a strong loyalty to the Hutt. Barada's body fell into the cavernous mouth of the Sarlacc when Luke Skywalker and Han Solo escaped the Hutt's clutches.

**baradium** A highly volatile synthetic explosive used in thermal detonators and similar devices. Upon detonation, baradium underwent a fusion reaction, releasing a powerful particle field. This field expanded outward from the explosion, disintegrating everything in its path. In even the smallest quantities, baradium could destroy everything within a 5-meter radius. More concentrated amounts produced a blast sphere of 100 meters or more. Baradium was strictly regulated by the military on most planets.

**Baragwin** A species of hunchbacked scavengers found scattered throughout the galaxy. They were humanoid saurians with massive heads nearly as wide as their shoulders and three digits on each massive hand. Their skin was tough, wrinkled,

Barabel

*Baragwin*

and ranged in color from drab green to dark olive. Baragwin had a fine sense of smell, and there was no outward physical difference in build between males and females. Senator Wynl represented the Baragwin communities in the New Republic.

**Barak, Koth** A midshipman aboard the New Republic escort cruiser *Adamantine*, he was killed by unknown means and for no apparent reason. He turned out to be one of the first victims of the revived Death Seed plague.

**Baraka, Admiral Arikakon** A Mon Calamari officer in the Republic Navy, commander of the *Nexu* supercruiser troop transport during the Clone Wars.

**Barakas, Brakka** A hostage captured by the Yevetha from New Brigia during an attack led by Nil Spaar.

**Baralou** A water-covered planet valued as a source of food because of its large algae-harvesting and -processing operations. Baralou was the homeworld of the Multopos and the Krikthasi.

**Baramorra** A planet once controlled by Boss Banjeer, nephew of Admiral Banjeer, this was where Kir Kanos became the bounty hunter Kenix Kil.

**Baran Do** A Kel Dor Force tradition. Baran Do numbers dwindled after the species joined the Republic, because initiates went on to train as Jedi.

**Baran Wu Station** A cloning facility on Kamino that, along with Su Des Station, supplied another two million clones to the Republic's army.

**Baranta, Bozzie** A Podracer pilot who was part of Gasgano's pit crew before becoming a competitive pilot himself. He flew a Shelba 730S Razor Podracer that offered average acceleration, good turn response, and below-average handling.

**BARC speeder** A one-person, modified repulsorlift speeder bike originally used by specialized Biker Advanced Recon Commandos (BARC troopers) to go on highly dangerous missions during the Clone Wars.

***Barderia*** A Corellian transport based out of Halmad that was raided twice by Wraith Squadron members when they were posing as the Hawk-bat pirate group.

**Bard'ika** *See* Jusik, Bardan.

**Bardo** A male human working aboard Olag Greck's droid barge, he oversaw IG-88's transport to Hosk Station.

**Bardrin Group** A marketing corporation operated by Ja Bardrin shortly after the Battle of Endor. He had his daughter Sansia kidnapped to remove her from a position of power within the group. Her father desperately wanted to be rid of the *Winning Gamble*, Sansia's highly enhanced starship. Sansia was then rescued from slavery by Mara Jade, whom Ja hired strictly to recover the *Winning Gamble*. After returning to her father's fortress, Sansia learned the true intentions behind her capture. She was so enraged that she gave ownership of the *Winning Gamble* to Mara Jade and provided the sensor data it collected to Talon Karrde. She then arranged to punish her father for his duplicity.

**Barefoot Squadron** A group of green X-wing fighter pilots led by Tahiri Veila during the war against the Yuuzhan Vong.

**Barer, Wasser** A Quarren Podracer pilot who competed in the Vinta Harvest Classic.

**Barezz, Arlen** An Imperial Intelligence agent on Tatooine.

**Barezz, Ingleman** An SBI agent during the Clone Wars who investigated the fall of Duro to the Confederacy.

**Barezz, Lieutenant Wynn** An Imperial officer at the Ord Mantell spaceport who reported the discovery of an armed cargo ship that had been infected with the Death Seed plague.

*Senator Edcel Bar Gane*

**Barezz, Mar** An Imperial ISB agent obsessed with tracking down Alliance spy Tiree, he nearly captured his prey in an abandoned mine on Bothawui but was thwarted by rookie Rebel agents.

***Bargain Hunter*** A light freighter belonging to Dubrak Qennto and operated by Jorj Car'das and Maris Ferasi, this ship was pursued by Progga the Hutt into the Unknown Regions, where it encountered Commander Thrawn and his Chiss forces.

**Bar Gane, Senator Edcel** The Senator from Roona who seconded the motion for a vote of no confidence in Chancellor Finis Valorum.

**Bargleg swoop gang** Part of the Blood-Scar pirate group that targeted Rebel Alliance shipments.

**Bargos** A Mon Calamari weapons officer aboard the Galactic Alliance warship *Ocean*, during the war between the GA and the Confederation.

**Barhu** The closest to the sun of eight planets in the Churba star system, Barhu was a dead rock with temperatures far too high to allow any indigenous life-forms.

*BARC speeders*

**Barich, Sergeant** A native of Wakeelmui assigned to the Imperial forces on Endor, he was a former employee of the Sienar Fleet Systems missile division. A biker scout, he dreamed of transferring to the 181st Imperial Fighter Group.

**Baritha** An older woman with graying hair and glittering green eyes, she was a leader of the dark side Nightsisters of the Witches of Dathomir. Baritha made no secret of the fact that, viewed from behind, she thought Han Solo looked "tasty," and she tried to claim him as her slave.

**Barje, Camelle** She hoped to make a living as a farmer on Tatooine until her husband was killed during a Tusken Raider attack on Mochot Steep. Camelle and her son Tekil were spared by Sharad Hett. She also went by the name of Camella.

**Barkale, Governor** An Imperial officer on Kintoni who embezzled from the sector treasury, he was tracked down and killed by Mara Jade, the Emperor's Hand, for his treachery.

**Barkbone, Reginald** A flamboyant Poss'Nomin pirate known as the Scourge of the Seven Sectors in the early years of the Empire. He traveled in a stolen Star Galleon named the *Robber Baron*.

**Barkhesh** A planet noted for the hot, humid, tropical jungles in its southern regions. The local resistance there secretly provided supplies for the Rebel Alliance.

**Barkhimkh** A Noghri bodyguard assigned to Leia Organa Solo during the Caamasi Document crisis.

**Bar-Kooda** A vicious Herglic pirate who had a reputation for eating his victims. Boba Fett successfully hunted Bar-Kooda for Gorga the Hutt, who turned the pirate into a roasted entrée. Bar-Kooda was survived by his brother, Ry-Kooda.

**bark rat** A rodent native to Cholganna, often preyed upon by wild nexus.

**Barlok** A planet inhabited by the Brolfi. The world was locked in a dispute with the Corporate Alliance over mining rights in the last years of the Old Republic. Jorus C'baoth dramatically negotiated an end to this impasse.

***Barloz*-class medium freighter** A respected and popular ship at the height of the Old Republic. The newer YT-series freighters overshadowed the Barloz in later years. Clyngunn the ZeHethbra piloted a Barloz called the *Lady Sunfire*.

**Barney** A native of Belderone and friend of Flint, he later joined Luke Skywalker in the Alliance of Free Planets.

**baron droid (E4)** A precursor to the super battle droid, the E4 baron droid was an experimental combat unit developed by Baktoid Combat Automata for the Trade Federation. Heavily armored and with great strength, the baron droid had a distinctive single photoreceptor that served as its primary targeting sensor. Each of its two arms featured twin laser cannons.

**Baron's Hed** The capital of Sulon, a once beautiful city until it was occupied by the Empire and turned into an operations center.

**Baroonda** A planet dominated by swamps and a few active volcanoes, it was inhabited by the Majan people, who constructed a modern metropolis around a series of ancient ruins and statues left behind by their ancestors. A Podrace course on Baroonda careered around giant statue heads, through marshes, and among thick trees and their gnarled roots. The course also took pilots over a dangerous sulfur geyser field. Baroonda's Podrace course presented numerous naturally occurring obstacles and dangers, including fog, flying creatures, and flaming lava pits.

Daakman Barrek

**Baros** Orbiting the blue star Bari, this large, arid planet had high gravity and intense windstorms. Baros was the homeworld of the reptilian Brubb, whose society centered on communal groups, or habas, numbering from 10 to 10,000 individuals. The Brubb had university habas and established a spaceport haba after their discovery by the Empire, although the facility wasn't used much because of the difficulty of landing and departing in the planet's high gravity. Brasck, a smuggler known to associate with Talon Karrde, was a Brubb.

Bartokk

**barq** A luxury foodstuff grown on farms that were controlled by the Trade Federation on Qiilura.

**Barr, Lieutenant** A Star Corps clone trooper with Barriss Offee and Commander Bly on Felucia during the Clone Wars.

**Barra-Rona-Ban** The chief librarian of the Jedi Archives on Coruscant over 1,000 years before the Battle of Yavin, this wizened Cerean was lauded for his attention to detail. Master Barra allowed the disguised Sith apprentice Zannah to have access to the Archives a decade after the Battle of Ruusan. Zannah was posing as the Padawan Nalia Adollu in an effort to gain access to any information to assist her ailing Sith Master, Darth Bane.

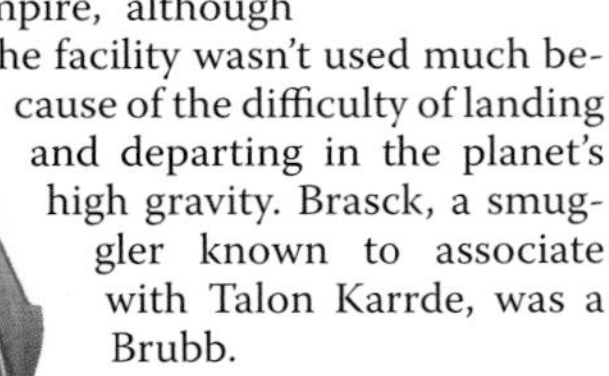
Baron droid

**Barrek, Daakman** A Jedi Master who led Republic forces on Hypori. He and his Padawan Sha'a Gi were among the first Jedi killed by General Grievous.

**Barris, Mosh** A hardened colonel in the Imperial Army at the dawn of the Empire, Barris served aboard the Victory Star Destroyer *Strikefast* under Captain Voss Parck. Barris's troops were outsmarted by the Chiss exile Mitth'raw'nuruodo on an uncharted planet. A career marked by vehement and loudly voiced dissatisfaction with the Imperial military administration led him to many powerless diplomatic posts on backplanets. He served as military prefect on Garqi, where he was framed for treason by Corran Horn.

**Barron, Plure** The Neimoidian administrator of the Trade Federation mining colony on Aereen. She was captured and then killed by Echuu Shen-Jon's army during the Clone Wars.

**Barsoom Boulevard** A street on Coruscant's crime-ridden Crimson Corridor.

**Bartam, Grand Moff** A burly Grand Moff who conspired with Grand Moff Trachta against Darth Vader and the Emperor. The treacherous infighting led Bartam to secretly plot against Trachta. Bartam was assassinated in his quarters, although one of his stormtroopers managed to kill the assassin.

**Barth** A New Republic flight engineer, he was captured along with Han Solo by Yevethan forces commanded by Nil Spaar. Spaar brutally killed the engineer.

**Barthis, Captain Elsen** A member of Galactic Alliance Intelligence, she tried to detain Wedge Antilles and convince him to divulge information about Rogue Squadron at the start of the conflict between the Galactic Alliance and Corellia.

**Bartokk** Insectoid creatures with a hive-mind, Bartokk were legendary for their relentless and resourceful assassin squads. They pursued their targets until they achieved success; even if one of them was cut in two, both halves were capable of continuing to accomplish the group goal. The black-shelled Bartokk had greenish blue blood, a tough exoskeleton, and razor-edged claws. Sometime before the Battle of Naboo, Bartokk were involved in a plot to take over a starfighter factory on Esseles. Some two dozen years after the Battle of Yavin, a Bartokk squad tried to assassinate the grandmother of Jedi academy student Tenel Ka, Queen Ta'a Chume, but the young Jedi thwarted the attempt.

**Bartyn's Landing** The spaceport and capital of Lamaro built by Hugo Bartyn, it was made of a dilapidated Hoersch-Kessel LH-3010 freighter purchased from Neimoidian traders. Every year, Guther Bartyn hosted a grand public spectacle called the Landing Shootout where local sharpshooters competed for fame and prizes.

**Baruk, Reelo** A rotund Rodian garbage hauler who was one of the most powerful criminal kingpins on Nar Shaddaa. Lando Calrissian was briefly imprisoned by Baruk before being rescued by Kyle Katarn.

**Barukka** The sister of the evil Gethzerion, she was one of the Witches of Dathomir. Barukka was cast out from the Singing Mountain Clan after giving in to evil urges. But while living in a cavern called Rivers of Stone, she started to cleanse herself in order to rejoin her clan. She was called upon to help lead Luke Skywalker and Han Solo into the Imperial prison complex on the planet in order to make off with parts essential to repair the *Millennium Falcon.*

**Barundi** An alien culture with a distinct subset known as the Thelvin Order. A possible offshoot of this order inhabited an uncharted planet in Wild Space and worshipped the Yavin Vassilika. Those who accosted the idol or broke with any custom were subjected to the ritual "Cleansing of the Foul," a public beating with large flowers with poisonous thorns.

**barve** A six-legged beast of burden and source of meat, as well as a common insult.

**Barzon, Carl** An underground resistance leader on Garos IV opposed to the Imperial government that extracted hibridium ore from the planet. An old family friend and university professor, Barzon was Alex Winger's first contact with the underground.

**Bas, Colonel** A hardworking Imperial officer who served Admiral Pellaeon aboard the *Chimaera* during the time the Empire negotiated a treaty with the New Republic.

**Basbakhan** One of Leia Organa Solo's Noghri bodyguards during the Yuuzhan Vong War, he accompanied her to Bastion, Ord Mantell, and Duro. Basbakhan was taken captive by the Yuuzhan Vong.

**Base Delta Zero** The code name for orbital attacks that involved the complete destruction of all "assets of production," including factories, arable land, mines, fisheries, and all sentient beings and droids. Such strikes reduced a planet's crust to molten slag.

**Basic** A language based on the tongue of the human inhabitants of the Core Worlds. Basic, which first emerged as the Republic's language of diplomacy and trade, became common throughout the galaxy.

***Basilisk*** Commanded by Captain Mullinore, the *Basilisk* was one of Admiral Daala's four Star Destroyers. It suffered severe damage during a battle with Moruth Doole's forces over Kessel, but was later repaired. The *Basilisk* was destroyed when Kyp Durron detonated the Cauldron Nebula with the Sun Crusher superweapon.

**Basilisk** An ancient Core world once inhabited by a native reptilian species known as the Basiliskans. About 4,000 years before the Galactic Civil War, during the Battle of Basilisk, the Basiliskans poisoned their own planet in a bid to defeat the invading Mandalorians. The Basiliskans became savage beasts known as Lagartoz War Dragons.

**Basilisk war droid** *See* war-mount.

**Baskarn** An inhospitable jungle planet in the Outer Rim, it was home to a Rebel Alliance starfighter outpost that made guerrilla strikes into Imperial territory. Advance Base Baskarn was built into a mountainside, surrounded by a thick jungle of razor-sharp plants and deadly predators. The planet was the homeworld of the Yrashu, a Force-sensitive species of green primates who existed in peaceful harmony with their environment. The primitive Yrashu carried ceremonial maces made from the roots of the hmumfmumf tree. Animal life included flying jellyfish, which drifted above the tree canopy and snared birds and rodents in their tentacles. Other creatures included water snakes, edible mmhmm butterflies, and the fierce horned hrosma tiger, which hunted through the use of the Force.

Basso

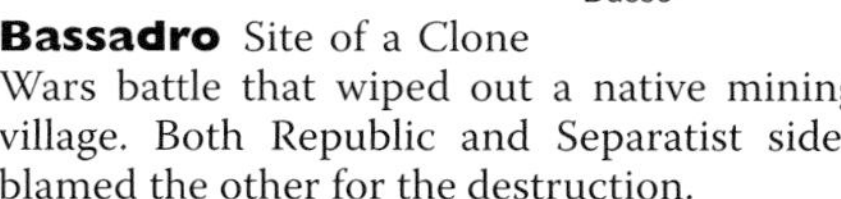

**Bassadro** Site of a Clone Wars battle that wiped out a native mining village. Both Republic and Separatist sides blamed the other for the destruction.

**Basso** A Rebel agitator on Ralltiir, he revealed to Princess Leia Organa that thanks to hypnotic suggestion, his mind contained information vital to the Rebellion. Leia snuck Basso aboard her consular ship, *Tantive IV,* and his message revealed the nature of the Death Star project. He later advised Leia during the Battle of Kattada, helping her struggle with the moral dilemma of ordering people to war. Basso disguised himself as a stormtrooper during a Rebel mission to Kalist VI.

**Bast, Chief Moradmin** The chief personal aide to Grand Moff Tarkin aboard the Death Star. Bast rarely underestimated his enemies. He learned cunning and patience by hunting big game as a youth. He died when the Rebels destroyed the Death Star during the Battle of Yavin.

**Bast Castle** A remote and heavily defended structure, this was Darth Vader's stronghold and private refuge on the planet Vjun. It later served as the headquarters of dark side executor Sedriss and the Emperor's elite force of Dark Jedi.

**Basteel** This planet served as the final resting place of Slique Brighteyes, a Gulmarid who survived Imperial atrocities against his species. Boba Fett went to Basteel to claim his reward for avenging the death of the Gulmarids.

**Bastion** Originally named Sartinaynian, this planet became the capital of the Imperial Remnant, ruled by the Moff Council, when Imperial forces retreated there after the reclamation of most of their territory by the New Republic. It was located in the Braxant sector, between the Outer Rim and the Unknown Regions. The peace treaty that brought an end to the Galactic Civil War recognized Bastion as the legitimate capital of the Imperial Remnant, ruled by its Moff Council.

During war with the Yuuzhan Vong, the initial route taken by the alien invaders bypassed Bastion, but they nonetheless targeted the world as the conflict dragged on. The Yuuzhan Vong fleet destroyed most of the Imperial warships protecting the planet, and devastated the world's surface, though most of the populace had been evacuated. In the decades following the Yuuzhan Vong's defeat, the Imperials rebuilt Bastion. Heavily fortified, it became perhaps the most fiercely guarded system in the galaxy. With the rise of Roan Fel's empire, Bastion became a major galactic capital.

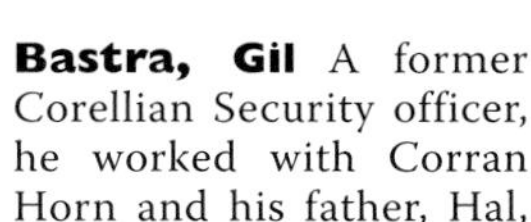

**Bastra, Gil** A former Corellian Security officer, he worked with Corran Horn and his father, Hal, in the security force. Gil Bastra later assisted Corran and two other members of Rogue Squadron by giving them false identities so that they could escape the Imperials. Bastra died in captivity after interrogation by Kirtan Loor aboard the *Expeditious.*

**Batch, Grand Admiral Martio** One of the Empire's 12 grand admirals, he was known as the "invisible admiral," spending much time developing cloaking technologies. He was assassinated by his second in command, who then took the ships in Batch's task force and joined Warlord Harrsk in the Deep Core.

**Batcheela** An older female Ewok at the time of the Battle of Endor, she was the mother of Teebo and Malani.

**Bathrobe Brigade** A derogatory nickname that Mandalorians used to describe the new Jedi Order.

**bathwa** A flying thranta-like creature found on Kiffex.

**Batorine** A planet known for the sculpture carved from the bright red wood of the indigenous blood tree, and its natives known as Blood Carvers. The assassin Ke Daiv was from a famous political family on Batorine.

**Ba'tra, General** A Bothan New Republic general, he led Orbital Defense Command during the Yuuzhan Vong invasion of Coruscant.

**Battalions of Zhell** The fighting force of the 13 tribes of ancient humans who evolved on Coruscant in prehistoric times before the rise of the Republic. The Battalions of Zhell were subjugated by the Taungs when a volcanic eruption nearly wiped out the human race, but they eventually won back their independence.

**battle analysis computer (BAC)** A computer system used by the Alliance, it analyzed variables of enemy vessels such as position, firepower, speed, maneuverability, and shield strength to project the course of battle. The prototype of the battle analysis computer, developed by General Jan Dodonna, was tested by Luke Skywalker at Bakura.

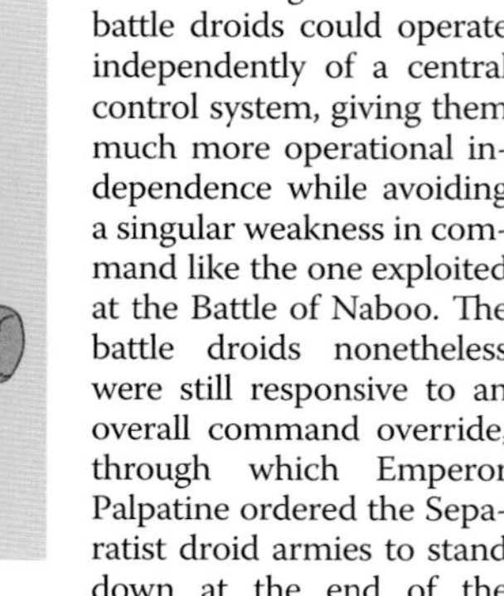

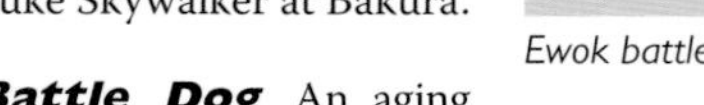

Ewok battle wagon

***Battle Dog*** An aging *Quasar Fire*-class warship and one of the New Republic craft assigned to Han Solo and the *Mon Remonda* during the hunt for Warlord Zsinj.

**battle dogs** *See* neks.

**battle droid, Trade Federation** Tall, gaunt humanoid droids with exposed joints and bone-white metal finishes that gave them a skeletal appearance. The B1 infantry battle droids of the Trade Federation had only a numerical marking on the back of a comlink booster pack to distinguish one droid from another. Droids with specialized functions had distinct colored markings on their armor. Blue denoted pilot droids. Red denoted security droids. Yellow denoted command droids, which functioned with increased autonomy compared with the standard infantry. Some droids sported paint jobs that best matched their operational environment. For example, the battle droids of Geonosis had a rust-colored finish that better matched the planet's red sand and rocks.

Yellow markings on chest and head designate this battle droid as a command officer.

Battle droids were very efficient. Their humanoid builds allowed them to operate machinery and pilot a wide variety of war craft designed for organic pilots. For ease of storage and transportation, battle droids could compress into less than half their operating size.

Gungan battle wagon

During the invasion of Naboo by the Trade Federation, an army of battle droids was able to quickly conquer and take control of the planet's population centers. These droids followed orders spoken to them by their Neimoidian commanders or transmitted to them from an orbital Droid Control Ship. The efforts of Bravo Squadron, and Anakin Skywalker in particular, destroyed the Droid Control Ship, thereby rendering the army useless.

After this incident, the Galactic Republic enacted strict legislation that prohibited the use of battle droid armies. The Trade Federation nonetheless continued to develop battle droids on distant foundry worlds, and added to the ranks of the B1 with the heavier B2 "super battle droid." This new generation of battle droids could operate independently of a central control system, giving them much more operational independence while avoiding a singular weakness in command like the one exploited at the Battle of Naboo. The battle droids nonetheless were still responsive to an overall command override, through which Emperor Palpatine ordered the Separatist droid armies to stand down at the end of the Clone Wars.

***Battle Horn*-class bulk cruiser** A variety of bulk cruiser named for the *Battle Horn,* a famed New Republic Rendili StarDrive ship.

**battle hydra** A large, two-headed dragon-like reptile with broad, leathery wings over 2 meters across and a trailing, hook-tipped tail. The battle hydra was an example of Exar Kun's alchemical mastery and Naga Sadow's dark legacy.

**Battle Legionnaire (BL series) droid** Produced in limited quantities by the Separatists during the Clone Wars, these combat droids served the Mandalorian Protectors. A thousand BL units armed with AAP-II blaster boxes fought in the front lines, and most were destroyed at Norval II. BL-17 was a Battle Legionnaire that served Boba Fett in the Empire's early days.

**battle meditation** A powerful Force technique practiced by both the Jedi and Sith to influence the outcome of a battle by visualizing the desired result. When a powerful Force-user wielded this ability, it could imbue the Jedi's allies with the will to win even against impossible odds. Alternatively, a Jedi could direct the battle meditation toward his or her enemies, causing them to attack one another, surrender, or run away. Like all abilities strongly connected to the Force, there were dangers inherent in using battle meditation: In some cases, it could cause influenced enemies to become desperate and reckless. Ancient skilled users of the technique included Jedi Master Arca Jeth, Nomi Sunrider, Bastila Shan, and Odan-Urr. Sith battle meditation was a comparatively rare discipline, though Darth Sidious, Lumiya, and Darth Caedus proved capable of it.

***Battle of Yavin*** A modified Imperial customs frigate, it was frequently used by the New Republic to conduct covert operations throughout the galaxy.

**battle station** Space-faring or orbital, battle stations were combat-dedicated spacecraft whose primary power output was devoted not to propulsion but rather to tactical considerations.

**battle wagon, Ewok** This huge Ewok war machine designed by Erpham Warrick was restored by his great-grandson Wicket. The wagon had four large wheels and a prodigious battering ram topped by the skull of a bantha.

**battle wagon, Gungan** Primitive resupply vehicles towed into battle by falumpasets. During the Battle of Naboo, General Jar Jar Binks accidentally opened the cargo ramp of a fully loaded battle wagon, spilling huge Gungan boomers onto the battlefield.

***Baudo*-class star yacht** A sleek and speedy sporting yacht, the Baudo was quite popular in the Outer Rim, where young racers ran orbits and found amusement screaming past nearby freighters. The Baudo came standard-equipped with a light laser cannon. The *Pulsar Skate* was a modified *Baudo*-class star yacht.

**Bava** A Yuuzhan Vong Extolled-One who lived on Zonama Sekot after the war with the Galactic Alliance, he tried to build a functioning community in La'okio.

*Bear Clan*

**Bavakar** A species that specialized in biological enhancements and similar technologies.

**Bavion, Jith** A famed ancient explorer who wrote about his experiences with the neeks of Ambria.

**Bavo Six** A truth drug used in interrogation, it was administered with an unnecessarily long needle that added to the psychological pressure. While Bavo Six was used mainly by Imperials, the drug was also for sale on the open market.

*Master Soon Bayts*

**bawoonka** A Gungan musical instrument.

**Bayaar** An Ansionian outrider and sentinel of the Situng Borokii clan, he welcomed the Jedi delegates who arrived on Ansion to settle a border dispute prior to the Clone Wars. Bayaar informed the Jedi that in order to speak to the Council of Elders, they would need to acquire the hair of a white surepp. After the Jedi earned the trust of the Borokii, Bayaar served as the honor guard escorting the Jedi into the Januul Clan and the city of Cuipernam, defending them against would-be assassins hired by Soergg the Hutt.

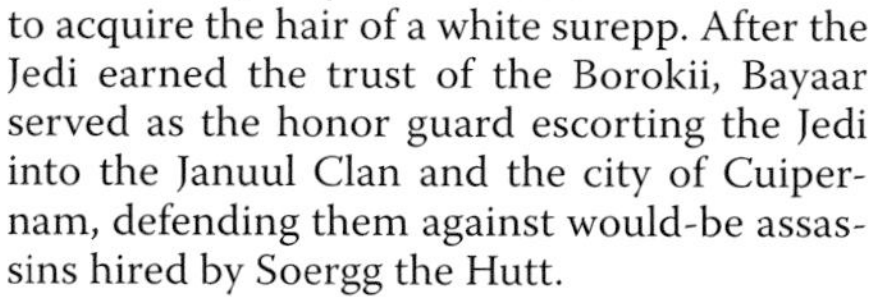

**Bayts, Master Soon** A human Jedi who reported the events of the Yinchorri Uprising to Yoda and Yaddle, he had achieved the rank of Jedi Master by the time of the Clone Wars. He served aboard the starship *Intervention* during the mission to Boz Pity. Bayts was killed by General Grievous.

***Bazaar*** An Ithorian herd ship that once operated near the Graveyard of Alderaan.

***Bazarre*** A space station and shadowport operated by Orion Ferret, it was known for its renowned market where anything could be bought, bartered, or sold.

**Bazierre, First Sergeant Tak** One of three GeNode clone stormtrooper sergeants serving with Captain Janzor during an attack on Kashyyyk. He was killed in action.

**Bburru** The largest of the Duros orbital cities and capital of the system. Bburru's central plaza was an open space almost large enough to create the illusion of a living planet, with diagonal bracing struts that ran from street level to the faintly blue artificial ceiling. Raised planters supported massive olop trees that were layered with vines.

When the Yuuzhan Vong attacked the planet, the Duro Defense Force erected shields over 17 of Duro's 20 orbital cities. Bburru and the two cities on either side of it were left defenseless, the shields having been sabotaged by CorDuro Shipping. As a result, the city fell victim to Yuuzhan Vong living ships.

**BD-3000 luxury droids** Shapely female-styled attendant droids manufactured by LeisureMech Enterprises. BD-3000s came equipped with language processors and linguistic databases capable of translating 1.5 million forms of communication.

**BD-8** A refitted YVH droid owned by the Solos until it was destroyed by the Killiks.

**Bdu, T'nun** The Sullustan captain of a Corellian supply ship, Bdu was intercepted by Admiral Daala on his way to Dantooine. The admiral found maps and information on the Rebel Alliance in the data banks of the ship, then destroyed it.

**beamdrill** A heavy tool well suited for mining, it used high-intensity pulsations to pulverize rock.

***Beam Racer*** Prince Isolder's personal starcutter during the war between the Galactic Alliance and the Confederation. He took the *Beam Racer* to Nova Station to transport Ben Skywalker to the new Jedi base on Shedu Maad. However, the ship was captured by Tahiri Veila and the *Anakin Solo*. Isolder and the crew were held prisoner aboard the Star Destroyer. Darth Caedus offered Prince Isolder a chance to go free, so long as he convinced the Hapans to abandon the battle against his forces. Isolder refused and Caedus angrily strangled him with the Force, then ordered the *Beam Racer* destroyed.

**beam tube** An antique handheld weapon, powered by a backpack generator.

**Bear Clan** Before a Padawan was selected for pairing with a Jedi Master, youngling initiates had to train as part of a group called a clan. They received training from Yoda. In the years prior to the Clone Wars, the Bear Clan consisted of 20 Jedi children, including Liam, J. K. Burtola, Mari Amithest, Ashla, Chian, and Jempa.

**Bearsh** A Vagaari general who posed as the First Steward of the Geroon Remnant during the operation to recover Outbound Flight, a few years prior to the Yuuzhan Vong invasion. He claimed to the Chiss expedition to be a grateful Geroon wishing to accompany those who had freed the Geroon people from Vagaari slavery. Insinuating their way into the recovery mission, Bearsh and his Vagaari co-conspirators attacked with the wolvik animals they had smuggled aboard as lifeless fur stoles. In fact Bearsh and his 300 soldiers sought to avenge the Vagaari defeated by Chiss Commander Thrawn more than a generation earlier, and brought the battle to the wreckage of Outbound Flight. The Chiss, along with Luke Skywalker and Mara Jade, were able to defeat Bearsh.

**Bearus, Chairman** A humanoid who was leader of the once powerful carbonite-mining guild in the Empress Teta system some 4,000 years before the Galactic Civil War.

**Beast in the Mouth of the Mountains** An immense arachnid creature on the Forest Moon of Endor feared by the Ewoks. During the Clone Wars, Aayla Secura came to Endor to investigate a deserted Separatist outpost that was attacked by the creature. The Ewoks asked for Aayla's help in slaying the beast, and she killed it by crushing it with stalactites. A record of her feat was painted on an Ewok canvas.

**Beast-Lord** An honorific bestowed upon the traditional leader of a group of Onderonian beast-riders. Some 4,000 years before the Battle of Yavin, the Beast-Lord Oron Kira married Onderon's

*BD-3000 luxury droid*

Beedo (left) speaks with a Jawa.

Queen Galia, bringing peace between the city-dwellers and the beast-riders.

**beast-riders** Ancient Onderonians who, upon being cast out from the walled city of Iziz, learned to tame and ride the great beasts from the Dxun moon. Beast-riders developed a culture in the Onderonian wilderness and spent centuries clashing with the city-dwellers of Iziz. About 4,000 years before the Battle of Yavin, the Beast-Lord Oron Kira married Onderon's Queen Galia, bringing a temporary peace to the planet.

Nem Bees

**Beater** *See* Tu-Scart.

***Beauty of Yevetha*** This corvette was a member of Nil Spaar's Black Eleven Fleet. It was destroyed by New Republic forces during the blockade of Doornik-319.

**Bebo, Kevreb** A former captain and the only survivor of the crashed ship *Misanthrope* on the artificial planet D'vouran. The strain of the crash and the horrors of D'vouran caused Bebo to lose his mind. He unwittingly wore a tiny shield generator as a pendant that protected him from the planet's lethal hunger. He was killed by a Gank, but not before passing on his pendant to Tash Arranda.

**beck-tori** Force-sensitive aquatic parasites from the warm seas of Nam Priax. They resembled immense, flat, elongated leeches.

**BedaGorog** *See* Ies, Beda.

**Bedamyr, General** A New Republic general, he was part of the military command tasked with protecting Coruscant during the Yuuzhan Vong invasion.

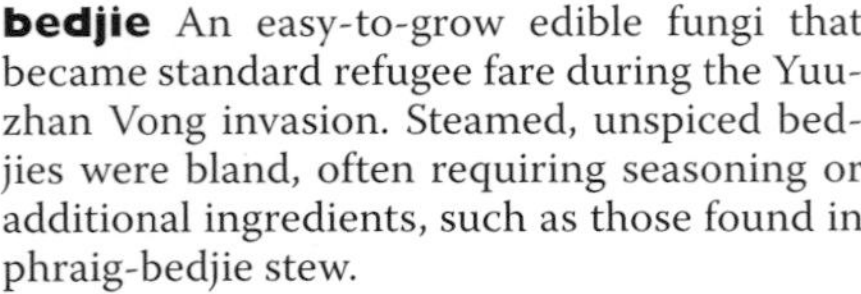

**bedjie** An easy-to-grow edible fungi that became standard refugee fare during the Yuuzhan Vong invasion. Steamed, unspiced bedjies were bland, often requiring seasoning or additional ingredients, such as those found in phraig-bedjie stew.

**Beedo** A relative of Greedo from the Tetsus clan, he took the bounty hunter's place in Jabba the Hutt's gang after Greedo was killed by Han Solo at the Mos Eisley cantina.

**Beedo, Aldar** A sadistic Glymphid Podracer pilot and hit man from the Ploo sector, Beedo competed against Anakin Skywalker at the Boonta Eve Classic. He was hired by Wan Sandage to kill Sebulba, but he failed to stop the Dug—though he did manage to finish the race in third place. He tried once again to take out Sebulba on Malastare, and also took a contract offered by a cult against members of the Jedi Council. Tiring of his repeated assassination efforts, Sebulba bought out Beedo's contract and hired him as his bodyguard. Beedo's past victims included Elan Mak's father.

**Beeline, Zip** This Drall racer's promising career ended when he triggered a multispeeder pileup during a race on Boonta prior to the Clone Wars. He retired to Coruscant, were he continued to race illegally.

**Beelyath** A Mon Calamari shuttle pilot recommended by Jagged Fel over Zekk to fly a B-wing in the Twin Suns Squadron during the Borleias evacuation.

**Been, Rep** A member of the Gungan High Council serving under Boss Nass, he was the official keeper of all ancient records and enjoyed a detailed knowledge of the secret hiding places used by the Gungans throughout their history.

**Bees, Nem** An Ortolan Jedi Knight who went undercover as a trader named Ydde to investigate reports of the neutral Ortolan government siding with the Separatists during the Clone Wars. After the Confederacy arrived, Bees remained behind enemy lines, acting as saboteur and facilitating the arrival of a Republic strike force. Bees died during the massacres of Order 66.

**beetle-knights** An ancient order of warriors in the pre-industrial era of Neimoidia distinguished by articulated body armor.

***Beetle Nebula*** A 200-meter-long *Freebooter*-class transport that carried wounded Galactic Alliance soldiers from an engagement in the Hapes Cluster.

Aldar Beedo

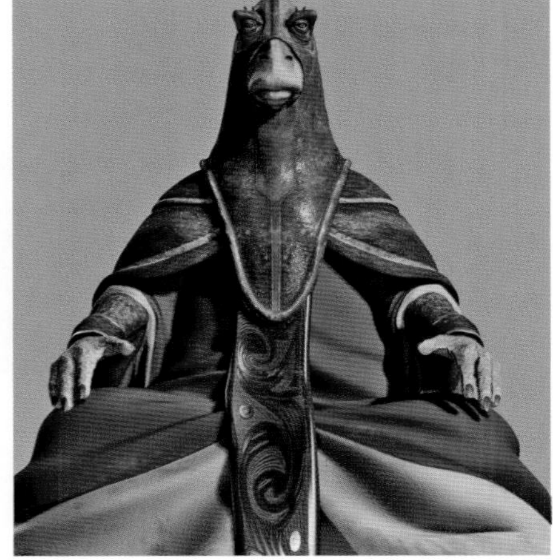

Rep Been

**Beez, Sergeant** A member of the Imperial special forces Lightning Battalion, he spoke to Boba Fett about the treacherous Imperial officer Abal Karda.

**Beezer, Corporal** An Alderaanian slicer, communications specialist, and technician who was part of Han Solo's Renegade Squadron strike team on Endor. He was trained by Brooks Carlson to serve as a scout for Alliance commandos.

**Beggar's Canyon** A narrow, winding canyon on Tatooine where pilots tested their flying skills. Beggar's Canyon, a valley formed by the confluence of at least three rivers millions of years before the modern era, served as a pilot's training ground for both Anakin and Luke Skywalker. A stretch of the Boonta Eve Classic Podrace wound through part of Beggar's Canyon; dotting the cliff face were small houses inhabited by beggars chased out of Mos Espa. Service ramps connected the canyon floor to higher elevations. A generation later, Luke and friends pushed their flying skills by racing T-16 skyhoppers through deep and twisted alleys, sometimes engaging in mock dogfights or hunting womp rats.

Beggar's Canyon

Beggar's Canyon was the site of Main Avenue, which ran straight for nearly 2 kilometers before making a sharply right-angled turn called Dead Man's Turn. Another landmark was the Stone Needle, a slender vertical rock topped by a narrow slot lined with jagged stone "teeth." Only the most experienced pilots could fly through it without crashing. Other features included the Diablo Cut and the Notch.

**Behareh Spaceport** A smaller, primarily commercial spaceport found in Coronet, the capital city of Corellia.

**behavioral circuitry matrix** The aggregate systems, including hardware and traitware, that produced droid behavior. A typical behavioral circuitry matrix had two components: a sensory-response module (made up of audiovisual circuits, an olfactory-speech center, a gyro-balance unit, a spectrum analysis unit, and an extremity control system), and an obedience-rationale module (containing a motivator, a cognitive theory unit, and the droid's memory banks).

**Beheboth** A sparsely populated, dry, rocky backworld. Darial Anglethorn ran the planet's largest moisture farm, which was often raided by a bandit group known as the Brigands, led by Gideon Longspar. Beheboth was home to an energy life-form known as the Tirrith. Eventually, New Republic troops were stationed there to ensure protection of the Tirrith.

**Behn-kihl-nahm, Chairman** Chairman of the Defense Council of the New Republic Senate, he was a staunch ally of Chief of State Leia Organa Solo. He kept Leia informed of happenings in the Senate and of various plots against her from within the Republic, advising her on suggested courses of action. Despite his power and stature, he was unwilling to make unilateral decisions and remained most concerned with restoring peace and harmony to the galaxy.

**Beidlo, Brother** This young B'omarr monk's brain was removed and put into a brain spider as part of Jabba the Hutt's plan to provide criminals with new identities by giving them new bodies.

**Beil, Archyr** The security chief aboard the freighter *Drunk Dancer,* he was a mixed-species humanoid with long limbs, six-fingered hands, and severe facial features.

Nizuc Bek (right) with singer Sy Snootles

**Beju, Prince** The young prince of the Beju-Tallah dynasty on the planet Gala, son of Queen Veda and King Cana and half brother to Elan. The populace of Gala had grown weary of their royalty, so to keep favor Queen Veda held elections on the planet. Beju resented having his claim to ruling the planet threatened by democracy, so he secretly made a deal with the criminal Syndicat to engineer a false bacta shortage that he could solve, thus cementing his reputation as a hero and winning the election. His ambition was foiled by 13-year-old Obi-Wan Kenobi, who masqueraded as Beju for a time while revealing the prince's plot.

**Bek, Nizuc** A former bouncer at the Mos Eisley cantina, he came to work for Jabba the Hutt to guard celebrities visiting the Hutt's palace. Bek was assigned to protect Sy Snootles. Born on Corulag, Bek was extremely fond of drinking juri juice. He was also a good friend of Wuher, the bartender at the Mos Eisley cantina.

**Bekam, Koril** The new Republic fighter pilot who flew as Blackmoon Eleven in Blackmoon Squadron. His droid was R2-Z13, nicknamed Plug. After everyone had evacuated Borleias base, Wedge Antilles used Bekam's T-65J X-wing, designation 103430. Bekam was indisposed at the time, recuperating in a bacta tank from injuries sustained earlier.

**Bekan, Chall** A methane-breathing Morseerian leader, he had ties to the Imperial government on Tatooine. He maintained a network of alien agents to keep an eye on Jabba the Hutt and Rebel Alliance activity.

**Bel** A clone trooper that served with Commander Fil at the Vassek moon.

**Bel, Adol** A heavyset human Xucphra Corporation official, he conspired with Iaco Stark and Hask of the Trade Federation to engineer a profitable bacta shortage that resulted in the Stark Hyperspace Conflict.

**Belasco** A wealthy Core world represented in the Senate by Uta S'orn. Belasco had a rigid class system and was once ruled by a royal family. In modern times, a Leader was elected, who then selected his or her own Council. Senta was the capital city. Every seven years a naturally occuring bacteria invaded the drinking water supply. The outbreak that occurred prior to the Battle of Naboo could not be controlled, resulting in the deaths of many elders and children. The Jedi Qui-Gon Jinn and Obi-Wan Kenobi revealed that Jenna Zan Arbor had contaminated the water supply for profit.

Belbullab-22 fighter

**Bela Vistal** A city on Corellia known for its gardens.

**Belaya** A human Jedi who trained under Master Zhar Lestin on Dantooine in the time of Darth Revan, she was friends with Juhani.

**Belazura** A beautiful resort world of grasslands and mountains in the Galactic Republic. Obi-Wan Kenobi and Anakin Skywalker vacationed there briefly.

**Belbullab-22 fighter** A model of Trade Federation starfighter manufactured by Feethan Ottraw Scalable Assemblies. The *Soulless One* favored by General Grievous during the Clone Wars was a Belbullab-22. It featured two main ion drives with a rear-mounted thrust-vectoring fin; auxiliary thrusters built into the wings assisted in maneuvers. The fighter was armed with rapid-firing triple laser cannons.

**bel-dar-Nolek, Director** A human of considerable girth who served as director of the Obroan Institute for Archaeology during the time of the New Republic. A former explorer, he was meticulous and patient when it came to the recovery of artifacts. He spoke before the Senate after Obroa-skai fell to the Yuuzhan Vong, blaming the Bothans and the Jedi for the loss. Failing to garner support from the New Republic, he suggested that the Obroan Institute forge a separate peace with the Yuuzhan Vong. Director bel-dar-Nolek wore custom-tailored suits and brandished a walking cane hand-carved from greel wood.

**Belden, Eppie and Orn** An aged couple on Bakura. Orn served in the planetary Senate while his wife, Eppie, became a major operative in the resistance to Imperial takeover of the planet. She helped sabotage Imperial operations by slicing into their computer systems. She later suffered dementia induced by Imperial operatives using tiny poisonous creatures, but recovered after being healed by Luke Skywalker. The Beldens helped Leia Organa bring Bakura into the Rebel Alliance shortly after the Battle of Endor.

**Belderone** A heavy-factory world loyal to the Republic. The Jedi and the clone army defended Belderone against Separatist invaders. During the time of the Empire, Belderone had AT-AT factories, and was the homeworld of a young man named Flint who would become a notable dark side user. Belderone also became home to a sizable population of Firrerreo survivors.

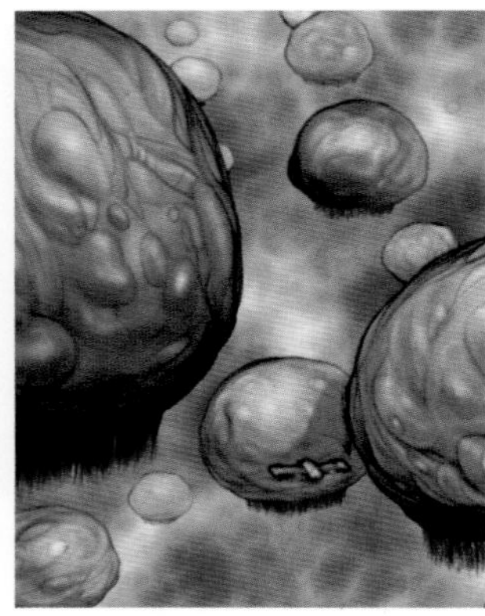
Beldons

**beldons** Enormous gas-bag creatures that floated in the skies of Bespin. Truly huge beldons could fill out to almost 10 kilometers in diameter. Weak electrical fields surrounded the beldons, acting as a kind of radar to warn of approaching intruders. Beldons were protected by law, as they expelled valuable Tibanna gas as part of their metabolism. Packs of predatory velkers, a more aggressive species of gas-bag flier, hunted beldons for food.

**Beldon's Eye** The symbol adopted by the Cloud City Mining Guild, re-created as a large sculpture within one of Cloud City's gleaming concourses.

**Beldorion the Hutt** A massive, but not obese, Hutt measuring 12 meters long, he was the power on Nam Chorios until the arrival of Seti Ashgad, who usurped him and took his house and treasure. Both Beldorion and Ashgad were in the thrall of Dzym, a mutant droch. The Hutt was extremely vain and reveled in being called such things as Beldorion the Splendid and Beldorion of the Ruby Eyes. At one point, Beldorion trained as a potential Jedi. His downfall came when he engaged Chief of State Leia Organa Solo in a lightsaber duel, and she killed him. Leia had only recently practiced and honed her lightsaber skills with Callista.

***Beledeen II*** One of several New Republic starships that accompanied the *Errant Venture* with Garm Bel Iblis and Booster Terrik to Yaga Minor in the search for the Caamas Document.

**Belgaroth** A small, inconsequential Core world in a system of the same name, it was used by the Empire as a testing facility and for training maneuvers. Belgaroth had two moons, Tregan and Tyrel. It was home to a species known as the droidbreaker.

**Bel Iblis, Garm** A well-respected former Senator of Corellia who long embodied the spirit of fierce Corellian independence. In the final days of the Republic, he was early to recognize the threat of Palpatine's growing powers. During the Separatist crisis, Bel Iblis removed Corellia from the Military Creation Act vote, and enacted a policy of isolationism to protect Corellia from the inevitable conflict. Despite his best efforts, his homeworld was dragged into the Clone Wars.

As Palpatine consolidated his New Order, Bel Iblis was one of his earliest targets. The charismatic Corellian had worked to undermine Palpatine's influence in the past, and had made an enemy of the new Emperor. Imperial agents executed his wife Arrianya and their two children on Anchoron while forcing him to watch. Many Corellians believed he died on Anchoron and mourned his loss, but he somehow escaped and lived life as a fugitive.

He contacted Senators Bail Organa and Mon Mothma, who were increasingly active against Palpatine's regime. Though it was Bel Iblis who suggested the consolidation of three resistance groups into the early Rebel Alliance with the drafting of the Corellian Treaty, history credits Mon Mothma and her diplomatic skills with the creation of the Rebellion (*see* Corellian Treaty).

Bel Iblis was wary of Mon Mothma's power and influence. He feared that she would become corrupt, as Palpatine had. Organa and Mothma—both pacifists in spirit—began shaping the early Rebellion, while the more aggressive Bel Iblis began to take a background role. This was troubling for the headstrong Corellian, who had very distinct views on how a Rebellion should be fought. When Organa was killed with the destruction of Alderaan, it left Bel Iblis and Mothma without a mediating presence separating them.

The worst of the arguments came when Mothma ordered an attack on Milvayne in the Gyrica system. Mothma pressed for military action that would endanger Bel Iblis's troops, and the Corellian believed her to be making a mistake based on flawed intelligence. Bel Iblis accused Mothma of amassing power for herself. Mothma coolly dismissed Bel Iblis from the operation, and informed him that the Rebel Alliance would no longer need his support.

Garm Bel Iblis

Bel Iblis led his own private army and launched a number of minor attacks against the Empire. For years throughout the Galactic Civil War, he waged his own private war against the Imperials, his most notable victory being the destruction of an Imperial Ubiqtorate base on Tangrene. His group remained mobile, secretly funded by Bothan interests who quietly opposed Mon Mothma's leadership.

After the Empire was defeated at the Battle of Endor, Bel Iblis and his forces remained in hiding. Bel Iblis stubbornly waited for the day when Mon Mothma would show her true colors and make a bid for dictatorial powers. That day never came. In fact, he disgustedly realized that his Bothan benefactor, Borsk Fey'lya, was more the power-hungry type.

During the Thrawn crisis, when New Republic representatives approached him for his help, Bel Iblis agreed to commit his forces to the New Republic cause. He brought his six Dreadnaught ships, including his flagship the *Peregrine,* to seek out the remainder of the *Katana* fleet before the Empire claimed it. Though the Empire was eventually successful in capturing the legendary Dark Force fleet, Bel Iblis's efforts allowed the New Republic to claim 15 of the warships.

Bel Iblis finally settled his decades-long differences with Mon Mothma and offered his tactical brilliance to the New Republic. During Thrawn's siege of Coruscant, which cunningly employed cloaked asteroids to cut off orbital starship operations, Bel Iblis was stationed on the capital. He helped develop the Stardust Plan, which used sensor-reflective repolarized dust to spot the asteroids and clear the threat.

Upon Grand Admiral Thrawn's defeat, Bel Iblis remained a prominent fixture in the New Republic hierarchy. Years later, he was reactivated as a general during the Yuuzhan Vong crisis, and served as a military adviser during the invasion. He commanded the Star Destroyer *Bail Organa* during the defense of Coruscant. He grew weary of the New Republic political infighting that blunted the military defense against the Yuuzhan Vong, and broke off to once again continue fighting with his own private army. Bel Iblis's forces proved crucial in turning the tide at the Battle of Ebaq 9.

**Believers** A group of Force-sensitives who emerged in the Cularin system after the Battle of Naboo. Their existence was discounted by the Jedi Knights at the Almas Academy, for the Believers were dedicated to the study and practice of the dark side of the Force. The Believers understood the history of the Sith, but chose not to obey the Rule of Two. Instead, the growing number of Believers wanted to gain more power, in the hope of striking back against those who were deemed their enemies. All Believers wore a distinctive tattoo that resembled the spire of the Sith fortress on Almas, with a broken lightsaber at its base.

**Beling, Hran** A meter-tall Vicon Jedi student who studied at the Jedi Temple at the same time as a young Dooku.

**Belkadan** A planet in the Dalonbian sector once covered by huge trees and small seas. It had clear blue skies. Dangerous predators stalked its jungles, including the redcrested cougar. The ExGal-4 outpost was located here, where undercover Yuuzhan Vong agent Yomin Carr essentially began the alien invasion of the galaxy by releasing dweebit beetles into Belkadan's environment. The ravenous, rapidly multiplying beetles transformed the planet, filling the air with a toxic carbon-dioxide-and-methane atmosphere. The forests turned reddish brown as the planet was prepared to plant and grow yorik coral. Luke Skywalker, Mara Jade Skywalker, and later Jacen Solo investigated the transformation of Belkadan early in the war against the Yuuzhan Vong, and found a growing ground for coralskippers tended by slave labor.

**Bell, Admiral Areta** A Corellian, she was a captain in the Rebel Alliance fleet, serving on the transport ship *Dutyfree*. She later ascended to the rank of admiral in the New Republic, commanding the Victory Star Destroyer *Swift Liberty*.

**Bella, Lieutenant** Faithful and efficient Twi'lek second in command to Cavik Toth, an ally to the Separatists. She led Sabaoth Squadron and oversaw the testing of the trihexalon chemical weapon on Maramere. Her ship was defeated by Nym's forces just prior to the Clone Wars.

**Bellassa** A thriving world with a democratically elected government when the Clone Wars began, Bellassa committed its army to fight alongside the Jedi against the Separatists. When the Empire came to power, it exploited Bellassa's bountiful resources. Its governor was deposed, and crackdowns on personal liberties began with the silencing of journalists and the jailing of dissidents.

Control rested in Imperial Inquisitor Malorum, who had difficulty containing resistance on Bellassa. The Empire established several prefabricated garrisons to enforce martial law on the planet. The largest was in the main city of Ussa.

**Bellican** *See* Solace.

**Belsavis** A world of volcanic rift valleys separated by kilometers of icy glaciers, Belsavis was in the Ninth quadrant near the Senex sector. The planet's core heated steam-filled rifts and fed hot springs on the surface. Some of the cities within the rifts were covered by enormous light-amplification domes that supported a vast network of hanging gardens and growing beds. The vine-coffee and vine-silk grown here accounted for 30 percent of Belsavis's total economy.

The gangly, short-lived Mluki species were representative of Belsavis's original population. The rift valleys were largely jungle until the Brathflen Corporation, Galactic Exotics, and Imperial Exports arrived and began cultivating cash crops. The quiet community of Plawal was between steep cliffs of red-black rock and before the Battle of Yavin was run by Jevax, a Mluki who was Chief Person of Plawal. Rock benches leading up to the cliff walls provided a narrow foundation for homes and orchards. A thick sulfurous mist permeated the valley and could restrict visibility to just a few meters.

About 100 years before the Galactic Civil War, Jedi Master Plett built a house and laboratory in the Plawal rift that served as a safe haven for Jedi and their families. Some 18 years before the Battle of Yavin, the Emperor commissioned the battlemoon *Eye of Palpatine* to wipe out the Jedi enclave, but the ship never arrived. The Emperor's small backup force of interceptors bombed Plawal but were wiped out by Belsavis's Y-wings, and the Jedi departed for places unknown after erasing all knowledge of their presence from the minds of the city's inhabitants. Han and Leia Organa Solo visited Belsavis eight years after the Battle of Endor and uncovered a plot by Roganda Ismaren, a longtime spy and onetime mistress of the late Emperor Palpatine, to forge a military alliance with the Senex Lords.

Governor Beltane

**Belsmuth II** The second planet in the Belsmuth system and site of an Imperial technical university that was converted into a pilot-training academy by Warlord Zsinj. This facility was targeted by Rogue and Nova squadrons in the early years of the New Republic.

**Belsus** A moon in the Anoat system, it was home to above- and below-ground Ugnaught populations. General Grievous attacked Belsus during the Clone Wars, crushing the Ugnaught resistance and setting up a command base on Belsus. Grievous planned for Geonosian technicians to convert the moon's industrial facilities in a secret plot to discover a technological path to Force sensitivity using captured Jedi younglings as his test subjects. A group of Jedi and Banvhar survivors tracked Grievous to Belsus to stop his schemes. To that end, Flynn Kybo caused an explosion in the moon's thermal core. Though Grievous escaped, Belsus and its underground Ugnaught cities were devastated.

**Beltane, Governor** Governor of Balmorra who ruled during its Imperial occupation. After the Battle of Endor, Beltane threw off Imperial rule; Balmorra was independent for five years, until the reappearance of the cloned Emperor Palpatine. To secure Balmorra's freedom, the governor agreed to supply the Empire with X-1 Viper Automadons while at the same time providing the New Republic with information regarding the time and location of the shipments.

**Belthu** A wealthy world built from mining colonies and controlled by corporate executives who were loyal to Warlord Zsinj in the early years of the New Republic.

***Belt-Runner I*** A former asteroid-mining station that Lando Calrissian had refurbished as the main base of operations for his spectacular obstacle course known as the Belt. For pilots attempting to complete the course, or "run the belt," they needed to thread their modified TIE advanced fighters past the tumbling rocks, protected by collision shields projected by *Belt-Runner I*. When the Yuuzhan Vong attacked nearby Dubrillion, Calrissian was forced to use *Belt-Runner I*'s systems to defend against the alien invaders. Not designed for such military purposes, the station eventually was destroyed.

**beltway** A popular mode of transportation in the crowded inner cities of highly urbanized planets, these moving platforms with seats were a speedy and safer alternative to landspeeders and skyhoppers.

**Beltway** The name of a modified central corridor that ran the length of the New Republic Star Destroyer *Lusankya* at Borleias during the war against the Yuuzhan Vong. It was an octagonal shaft, the width of two X-wings, which featured a tracked hauler at the top, allowing it to be used for tranportation of heavy equipment. The Beltway essentially became the "spear" of Operation Emperor's Spear, the suicide mission that plunged the *Lusankya* into the Domain Hul worldship.

**Beluine, Dr.** Boba Fett's personal physician, he was one of the few people in the galaxy to have seen the adult Fett without his helmet. The Coruscant-trained Beluine diagnosed the 72-year-old Fett with extensive clone tissue degeneration, and told Fett he had only a year or two to live.

**Belvarian fire gnats** Small insects that blinked red and green, fire gnats had a tendency to swarm.

**Bemos, Moff** An Imperial Moff at the time that Admiral Pellaeon considered mak-

Senator Tendau Bendon

ing peace with the New Republic, he was opposed to the idea. Bemos wore a codoran ring on his finger.

**Bendon, Senator Tendau** The Ithorian representative in the Galactic Senate during the final years of the Republic. He was an ally of Supreme Chancellor Valorum, and later feared that the Military Creation Act would be perceived as a hostile threat by the Separatists.

**Bendone** The Howler Tree People, who spoke an unusual ultrasonic language, lived on this planet. Some 19 years after the Battle of Endor, Chief of State Leia Organa Solo met with representatives from the Howler Tree People on Coruscant.

**Bendu monks** An ancient tribe living peacefully in the mountains of Ando Prime. The Bendu monks' study of numerology inspired the spoked-wheel design found on Republic warcraft, symbolizing the uniting presence of the Force in the galaxy. Jedi Bendu brandished such sigils during the Unification Wars that formed the Galactic Republic over 25,000 years ago.

**Bene** A 15-year-old Jedi Padawan during the final year of the Clone Wars, she received lightsaber instruction from Cin Drallig. When Darth Vader and his clone troopers attacked the Jedi Temple the night of Order 66, Vader choked Bene with one hand while he dueled Drallig with the other.

***Benevolent III*** A large Republic shuttle used as a personal transport by Baroness Omnino of the Vena system.

**Benevolent Guide** A governing rank on the planet Kegan, held by Keganites V-Tan and O-Vieve in the last decades of the Old Republic. Though Kegan was largely democratic, the issues that could be voted upon by the populace would be selected by the Benevolent Guides.

**Bengat** The water-covered planet that the Aruzan dancer Manaroo once rafted during an intense storm.

**Bengely** A world known for its dangerously seedy underground.

**Ben's Mesa** A huge natural monument that formed the center of the Boonta Eve Podrace course, it was named for famed Podracer Ben Neluenf.

**Bentro, Admiral** An Imperial fleet admiral who was briefly in command of the Star Destroyer *Executor* before being replaced by Kendal Ozzel.

**Berandis** Assistant manager of the Challabee Admits-No-Equal Aerial Eruptive Manufacturing Concern on Adumar, he guided Wedge Antilles and his Red Flight pilots on a tour through the proton-torpedo-manufacturing facility.

**Ber'asco** Leader of the Charon death cult, he was also commander of the spacecraft *Desolate,* which was biologically engineered in the strange dimension called otherspace. The cult believed that the extermination of all life in the galaxy would lead to a long-awaited enlightenment.

**Berchest** A Borderland Regions planet in the Anthos sector, it was a major tourist attraction during the Old Republic, mainly because of its largest city, Calius saj Leeloo, the City of Glowing Crystal. The natural wonder was sculpted out of a single giant crystal created over countless millennia by the salt deposits left by the blood-red waters of the adjacent Leefari Sea. The Clone Wars and the rise of the Empire squelched tourism—reports spread that Berchest was the site of possible Republic atrocities. Berchest nonetheless turned itself into one of the largest centers for Imperial trade in the Anthos sector. Even after Emperor Palpatine's death, the planet remained friendly to remnants of the Empire. Grand Admiral Thrawn led the New Republic to believe that he would use Calius as a transfer point for his clone soldiers, and Luke Skywalker went to the planet to investigate.

**Berda** The nickname of the tactical computer aboard the Star Destroyer *Anakin Solo,* operated by a squad of Bith programmers.

Avan Beruss

**Berenko, Omar** A famed Naboo poet who disappeared after being kidnapped centuries before the Clone Wars, he lived at the Varykino retreat in the planet's Lake Country. One of his most famous works was the epic poem *Defense of Naboo.*

**bergruufta** Large, slobbering quadrupedal pachyderm-like creatures native to Teloc Olsen.

**Bergruufta Clan** A group of Jedi younglings kidnapped by General Grievous during the Clone Wars. Grievous intended to use the younglings in an experiment to find a technological path to Force sensitivity. They were freed by Padawan Codi Ty.

**Beris** Along with Las Lagon, a minor world that seceded from the Galactic Alliance to join the growing Corellian Confederation.

**Berit, Commander** An officer in the Galactic Alliance Guard, he was assigned to head up the security on the Dark Deck aboard the *Anakin Solo.*

***Beroya*** A Mandalorian gladiator assault starship flown by Goran Beviin during the time of the conflict between the Galactic Alliance and the Corellian Confederation.

**Berri (1)** A young domestic worker-slave in Krayn's kitchen, she was 12 years old during the Battle of Naboo. She and her mother, Mazie, had been slaves when they were captured by Krayn on Tatooine. When the Jedi Siri Tachi and Anakin Skywalker were imprisoned by Krayn, Berri helped them by retrieving their lightsabers, and later participated in the slave revolt that ultimately toppled Krayn's empire.

**Berri (2)** The home planet of the Berrites.

**Berrida, General** A corpulent Imperial officer who reported to Moff Kurlen Flennic. In exchange for a wealth of information regarding the Yuuzhan Vong, Berrida approached Moff Flennic with plans for an alliance with the Jedi.

**Berrites** Intelligent quadrupedal alien species from Berri, they were regarded as clumsy and ugly by others, though they were in truth quite capable of cunning.

**Beruss, Avan** A descendent of the Beruss family of Illodia and childhood friend of Princess Leia Organa, Avan started off in the Rebel Alliance as a courier. He later joined Rogue Squadron and worked closely with Feylis Ardele to learn TIE fighter systems. A great shot, he learned to shoot while killing time on Illodia. Avan had a great-aunt with political pull on the New Republic Council.

**Beruss, Senator Doman (of Corellia)** A female relative of Illodia's Senator Doman Beruss. Doman Beruss was a flaxen-haired female

BesGas Three (left) was a floating mining refinery platform near Cloud City (right).

from Corellia who was given her older relative's name out of respect. She represented Corellian exiles at its Provisional Council in the formative stages of the New Republic. She was one of the signers of the Declaration of a New Republic. She spoke in favor of retaking Coruscant from the remaining Imperial forces led by Ysanne Isard.

**Beruss, Senator Doman (of Illodia)** A male New Republic Senator from Illodia and chairman of the Ministry Council of the New Republic. At the height of the Yevethan crisis, after Han Solo had been captured, he submitted a petition of no confidence in Chief of State Leia Organa Solo. When Leia asked him to withdraw the petition, he said that he would gladly do so "on your promise that you will not carry the war to N'zoth to rescue a loved one, or avenge a casualty." A female relative from Corellia was given her older relative's name out of respect.

**Bervin** A Rebel soldier, shortly before the Battle of Hoth, Bervin was attacked and killed by a wampa at a perimeter post at Echo Base.

**Besa, Eryl** A human Jedi Knight with red hair and green eyes, she was the daughter of a fanatic space racer. Eryl had been conceived and born on a long cross-galactic run, then spent most of her childhood speeding up and down the four mapped arms of the galaxy. Perhaps as a result of this, she had the Force ability to tell where she was in the galaxy at any given moment. Eryl Besa worked with Ulaha Kore to secure a dead voxyn for dissection and later accompanied the Jedi strike force sent behind enemy lines to Myrkr to destroy the voxyn menace. On this mission, she grew close to fellow Jedi Knight Raynar Thul, but their budding friendship was cut short when she died from razor bug slashes to her face.

**Besadii clan** The influential Hutt clan, or kajidic, based out of Nal Hutta that included Aruk, Zavval, Durga, Borga, and Randa.

**Besalisk** A species of intelligent four-armed bipeds from Ojom to which Dexter Jettster belonged.

**BesGas Three** A floating Bespin mining refinery platform built during the Clone Wars. It was hidden in the clouds and turned into a haven for and by droids seeking to avoid the violence of that conflict. The droid colony was rediscovered after the Clone Wars, and folded into the Imperial operation of Bespin's Tibanna gas mining. Decades later, during the Dark Nest crisis, Jaina Solo and Zekk searched BesGas Three as part of their investigation of suspicious Tibanna siphoning in the area.

**Besh** A Korun native of Haruun Kal, he and his older brother Lesh were members of the Upland Liberation Front during the Clone Wars. He had been captured and tortured by Balawai prospectors, losing three fingers and rendered mute by the cutting out of his tongue. Besh communicated through a combination of simple signs and extraordinarily expressive Force projection of his emotions and attitudes. During the Clone Wars, Besh suffered further hardship when an insect sting developed into deadly wasp fever, and he was eventually butchered by Kar Vastor.

Bespin

**Besh, Lora** Alleged mistress of Nute Gunray who wrote a scandalous bestseller detailing their affair.

**Beshqek system** A star system in the Deep Galactic Core that once contained the planet Byss.

**beskar** The Mando'a term to describe Mandalorian Iron. It was incredibly strong and durable, used in the construction of prison facilities and binding devices. The Empire strip-mined huge tracts on Mandalore, depleting the world of the valuable metal. Decades later, after the Yuuzhan Vong War, Mandalorians discovered a huge vein of beskar, which changed their economic fates in the turbulent times faced by the Galactic Alliance.

**Bespin** Principal planet in the Bespin system, located just off the Corellian Trade Spine in the Ison Corridor. Among the other worlds orbiting Bespin's star were Miser, Orin, and the Velser's Ring asteroid belt. A gaseous planet with billowy pink and purple clouds, Bespin was far from most commercial traffic, and was close to the barren Anoat system. Bespin had multiple moons, the two most prominent being the Twins, H'gaard and Drudonna.

The planet Bespin was some 118,000 kilometers in diameter. Like most gas giants, Bespin was made up of a core and three concentric constituent layers. The core (6,000 kilometers in radius) was composed of solid metal. The next layer was a 22,000-kilometer-deep sea of liquid rethen. At this level, the rethen was so compacted that its liquefied form resembled a metal, with extreme temperature levels. The next level of liquid rethen was not as metallic, and was 30,000 kilometers deep. Here, the pressure would crush a capital ship to a compact size, and the temperatures were scalding. Above this level was the 1,000-kilometer-thick cloud layer. At the bottom of the cloud layer, where it touched the liquid rethen sea, temperatures reached 6,000 standard degrees.

About 150 kilometers down from space, and 30 kilometers deep, was Bespin's Life Zone, where temperature, oxygen, and pressure were perfect for the existence of human life. It was in this level that Cloud City, a Tibanna-gas-mining colony, was built. The main hazard of Bespin's biozone came from its intense storms, which built up and traveled across the surface.

The clouds of Bespin held many treasures. The rarefied gases were known to produce rare and valuable gems. Bespin also was a natural factory for spin-sealed Tibanna gas. Though Tibanna could be found elsewhere, the industrial process of spin-sealing it for certain applications was very costly. The dynamics of Bespin's atmosphere naturally spin-sealed the Tibanna at the atomic level, which made prospecting for gas on Bespin an often lucrative venture. During the Clone Wars, Bespin fell under the control of the Confederacy, which exploited the planet's numerous gas mines.

Bespin completed a day every 12 standard hours. Bespin's year was equivalent to 14 standard years. The planet was home to a number of native life-forms, none of them intelligent. Among these were the beldons, the velkers, the glowers, and the pinks. The skies were also home to a number of transplanted life-forms, such as Alderaanian thrantas. The Corellian eccentric Lord Ecclessis Figg founded Cloud City. Originally the Floating Home complex, Cloud City was little more than a Tibanna-gas-mining and -refinement plant. It served as Figg's base of operations for years, and slowly evolved into a cosmopolitan center. With the opening up of shops, restaurants, and of course casinos, Cloud City eventually became a popular resort along the Corellian Trade Spine.

***Bespin Bandit*** Uz Bonearm's agile delta-shaped Corellian ship, used in the New Republic assault on Byss. The ship was armed with illegal military-grade ion cannons. The ragtag smuggler fleet also flew to New Alderaan and Nespis VIII.

**Bespin Motors** Founded specifically for the construction of Cloud City on Bespin, Bespin Motors was originally a subsidiary of the starship manufacturer Incom. When it became apparent that the Empire would attempt to nationalize Incom, executives at Bespin Motors completed a complicated self-buyout, assuring the company's autonomy. Soon after, Bespin Motors created a line of popular cloud cars—high-altitude vehicles used to patrol Cloud City. The basic cloud car design was copied by numerous competing companies, but Bespin Motors was still recognized as the most successful manufacturer of such vehicles.

**Bessimir** Located 15 parsecs from Coruscant, the planet was orbited by two moons. Twelve years after the Battle of Endor, the New Republic's newly commissioned Fifth Fleet underwent a live-fire training exercise code-named Hammerblow at Bessimir. Under the command of the Dornean General Etahn A'baht, the Fifth Fleet's A-wings first destroyed Bessimir's communications and sensor satellites. Bessimir's planetary defensive batteries and main starfighter base, housed on the alpha moon, were then collapsed by penetration bombs. Finally, a New Republic Star Destroyer acted as bait for a hypervelocity gun on the far side of the alpha moon while K-wing bombers penetrated the gun's shields with flechette missiles. This successful mission was the first operational readiness test for the Fifth Fleet.

***Best Chance*** A New Republic shuttle craft used by Corran Horn, Jacen Solo, Ganner Rhysode, and six Noghri to investigate Yuuzhan Vong activity on Garqi. The *Best Chance* was hidden inside the freighter *Lost Hope,* which was crashed as a decoy, allowing the *Best Chance* to make planetfall disguised as debris. Both vessels launched from the *Ralroost.*

**Bestine system** When the Empire decided to open a high-security base in this system, the entire population of Bestine IV was evacuated to make room. Alliance pilot Jek Porkins was among them; he had learned his piloting skills by hunting sink-crabs on Bestine IV's rocky islands in his T-16 skyhopper. Kestic Station, a free-trade outpost, was located near the Bestine system until eliminated by the Star Destroyer *Merciless.* Alliance pilot Biggs Darklighter defected to the Rebellion along with his ship, the *Rand Ecliptic,* during a mission to the Bestine system. The Alliance cruiser *Defiance* barely survived a surprise attack from the Star Destroyer *Immortal* near Bestine IV. A later attack on the Rebel flagship *Independence,* just prior to the Battle of Yavin, also led to a narrow escape for the Alliance.

**Bestine township** A farming community on the planet Tatooine, west of the Mos Eisley spaceport. Bestine township was also the seat of Imperial control on the planet, and as such grew to become a thriving economic hub. It was regarded as the safest of all Tatooine cities.

***Be'suliik*-class assault fighter** A cutting-edge heavy starfighter design developed by MandalMotors during the war between the Galactic Alliance and the Confederation. The fighter, named for ancient Basilisk war droids, was about 15 meters long with a wingspan of 8 meters. It featured a deflective stealth hull and armor made of nearly indestructible *beskar* ore.

**Besum** A small four-eyed being that worked for Uso Yso on Euceron, handling bets on the Galactic Games from Republic Senators as part of a scheme to discredit them.

***Beta*-class ETR-3 transport** Originally designed to escort construction vessels when establishing planetary outposts on unpacified worlds, this transport could carry a squad of speeder bikes.

**Beta Company** One of the first teams of clone commandos trained by Kal Skirata on Kamino.

**Bethal** This planet's primary exports included apocia hardwood, which took two centuries to mature and was used in the making of luxury furniture. Sections of Bethal included the Altoona and Dora prefectures. Soon after the Battle of Yavin, Bethal was infested by swarms of giant termites called greddleback bugs. Several attempts were made to contain the nearly 200 swarms that moved across Bethal's southern continent.

**Bet's Off** A somewhat elegant tapcaf located on the *Jubilee Wheel.* Bet's Off had a back room devoted to sabacc and other games of chance.

**Beviin, Goran** A Mandalorian warrior active during the Yuuzhan Vong War, he was one of Boba Fett's best intelligence agents. He married Medrit Vasur, and the two adopted a daughter, Dinua Jeban. Beviin wore an armored suit of blue Mandalorian iron.

**Bewil, Captain** An Imperial tactical officer from Dentaal who enjoyed setting traps for his prey. Bewil informed Lord Vader of Luke Skywalker's arrival on Cloud City.

**Bex, Captain** An Imperial juggernaut driver serving under Commander Frickett at Maridun, he was killed by a native Amani.

**Bex, Rasha** An Imperial spy who specialized in infiltrating Rebel units, she tricked smuggler BoShek into helping her escape vengeful Rebels who had discovered her true allegiance on Stoga. She grew attracted to BoShek during the escape, and offered him a position within the Empire, which he rejected.

**Bextar system** Located deep within the Velcar Free Commerce Zone in the Pentastar Alignment, the system consisted of four gas giants orbiting a pale yellow sun. A thriving gas-mining operation, run by the Amber Sun Mining Corporation, was scattered across the planets' many moons. The labor force was mainly Entymals, who had green exoskeletons and made excellent pilots.

**Bey** A Corellian-Nagai halfbreed, he was a childhood friend of Han Solo. A towering white-haired giant humanoid with a patch over his left eye, he aided the Alliance of Free Planets during the Nagai and Tof invasions.

**Bey, Commander Zalin** A Senate Guard who served as Sagoro Autem and Isaru Omin's superior, she assigned them to investigate the death of Senator Jheramahd Greyshade prior to the Clone Wars. When she learned that Venco Autem was behind the attacks, Bey worried over Venco's intimate knowledge of Senate Guard procedures.

*The towering Bey (right)*

**Beyele** A Hapan aide serving Major Moreem Espara.

**Bezim** A system that partnered with Vicondor, Delaluna, and neighboring Junction V to build Station 88 Spaceport. During the Clone Wars, this group of worlds remained loyal to the Republic.

**BG-J38** A spindly yellow Roche J9 worker droid with an insect-like head who spent a lot of time in the court of Jabba the Hutt. He was an expert at hologames, often playing against the criminal kingpin or one of his top cronies.

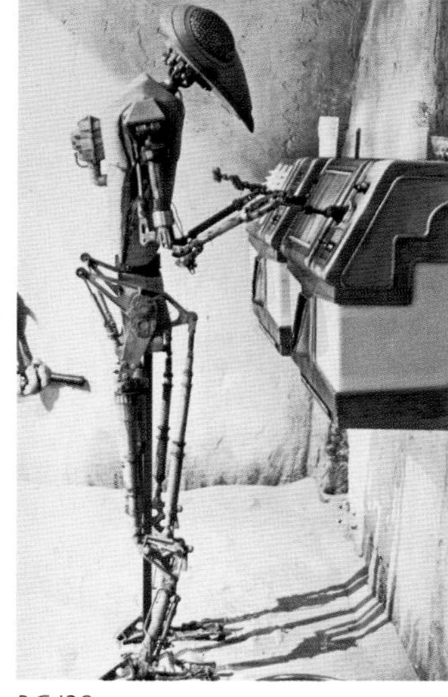

BG-J38

**Bhao, Moff Voryam** One of the newer Imperial officers to serve on the Moff Council during the time of the Galactic Alliance, he was handsome yet had a condescending demeanor. Bhao was one of the few Moffs who openly opposed Darth Caedus's plans to assimilate the Imperial Remnant into the Galactic Alliance. Much to Caedus's pleasure, Bhao was killed in the Mandalorian attack on the Nickel One asteroid, where a group of Moffs had convened to finalize their takeover of Verpine factories.

**b'hedda** A Dug swingblade weapon resembling a scooped atlatl with a meter-long wooden handle and a hooked blade on the opposite end.

**Bhul, Kasdakh** A Yuuzhan Vong warrior who served as the personal aide to Czulkang Lah, he reported to his master the status of the dying *Lusankya,* at which point Lah realized the Star Destroyer was being used as a battering ram.

**Bialy, Sargeant** A member of the Naboo Royal Security Forces, she was often partnered with Lieutenant Panaka. Bialy was part of the team led by Panaka that investigated a beached sea creature at Port Landien.

**Bibble, Sio** Outspoken governor of Naboo during the reigns of King Veruna and Queens Amidala, Jamillia, and Apilania. He remained on Naboo during the Trade Federation occupation. He oversaw all matters brought to the monarch's attention and chaired the Advisory Council, dealing directly with regional representatives and town-governing officials in day-to-day administration.

**Bidamount** A city home to Eport, one of the largest auction houses in the galaxy. Bidmount's economy was based on auctions. Anything and everything was up for sale there.

**Big Gizz** *See* Gizz, Big (the Gizman).

**Big L** Spacer slang for the speed of light. To "cross the Big L" meant jumping to lightspeed.

**Big Nasty Free-For-All** The most physically demanding event of the Gungan Festival of Warriors, it began with a full-contact game of gulliball and was followed by a marathon and a diving event.

**Big Snarl** One of the largest ventilation shafts near Monument Plaza on Coruscant. Big Snarl's primary function was to pull hot, humid air from the lower sections of the cityscape, but it also served as a traffic interchange for the many skylanes that intersected its location. The fact that so many vehicles traveled through the shaft, and had to deal with the sudden drafts of air, earned the locale its colorful nickname. The local traffic authority restricted travel through the center of the Big Snarl, where the air currents were strongest.

**Biitu** Once a lush and peaceful agricultural world, it underwent an ecodisaster when an apparent droid known as the Great Heep built an Imperial fuel-processing plant with a moisture eater that turned the grasslands brown. But the Biituians—green-skinned, bald humanoids—were saved when R2-D2 managed to destroy the Great Heep in the early years of the Empire.

**Biivren** An Imperial industrial world that was intentionally contaminated by fleeing Imperial forces after the Battle of Endor.

**Bilar** An unusual species from the tropical planet Mima II in the Lar system, the Bilar looked a bit like 1-meter-tall toy bears without fur. Perpetual grins on the faces of Bilars may have been a sign of very low intelligence. But when they came together and formed a group mind, or claqas, 7 Bilars had the intelligence of a genius; there were even reports of 10-member claqas. While intelligent, claqas had unpredictable personalities.

**Bilbringi** A lifeless star system filled with rocky worlds rich with heavy metals. It was well known as the site of heavily defended orbital shipyards where Imperial warships were assembled. The shipyards were the site of the New Republic's last battle with Imperial forces under Grand Admiral Thrawn. Heavily damaged, the facility was then abandoned and seized by the New Republic, which repaired the stations and retrofitted the *Lusankya* there. The shipyards were under heavy demands to create warships during the New Republic war against the Yuuzhan Vong. The system eventually fell to the alien invaders after they had captured Coruscant.

Sio Bibble

**Bildor's Canyon** A canyon in the Dune Sea on Tatooine.

**Bilk** Gamorrean bodyguard to the Toydarian thief Zippa on Coruscant, he was killed by fence Lorn Pavan when a deal over a stolen holocron went sour.

**Billaba, Depa** A former Jedi Council member, she was trained by Mace Windu. When she was six months old, her family was slain by space pirates, who spared only her and her sister, who was taken into the Jedi Order as Sar Labooda. She adopted the traditional culture of Chalacta to honor her slain parents. At the start of the Clone Wars, while the Jedi raced to Geonosis, she remained on Coruscant and supervised the young Jedi clans.

Depa Billaba (right) on Naboo with Saesee Tiin (middle) and Mace Windu (left)

At the onset of the Clone Wars, she went to the battlefront at Haruun Kal, where the trying conditions there seduced her to the dark side of the Force. Mace confronted her, and Depa succumbed to a coma.

**Billane, Jonava** A young mother who became separated from her child after a disaster on Ord Thoden, she was presumed dead. Jonava's infant daughter, Ludi, was discovered by the Jedi and taken into the Order. A very public custody battle ensued when she tried to take her baby back and the Jedi refused.

**Bille, Dar** Nil Spaar's second in command for the Yevethan raid on the Empire's shipyard at N'zoth, he was later primate, or proctor, of the Yevethan command ship *Pride of Yevetha,* formerly the *Intimidator.* Dar Bille gave the orders for the Yevethan attack on Koornacht settlements.

**Billey** An elder statesman in the smuggling community with over six decades under his belt, he was crippled during a botched spice run that

Bimms

left him confined to a wheelchair. He spent some time as a prisoner at the Goshyn Detention Center. Billey pledged his smuggling group as part of Talon Karrde's Smugglers' Alliance.

**Billibango** A Xexto who aided the Jedi and the Republic on Troiken during the Stark Hyperspace Conflict, he saved the life of Jace Dallin.

**Bimkall sector** HoloNet News once reported that the Bimkall sector joined the Separatists in the lead-up to the Clone Wars, but later retracted the story upon discovery that the sector did not exist.

**Bimm** The peaceful and friendly inhabitants of Bimmisaari, divided into two distinct species. The native Bimms had a furred, floppy-eared appearance, while a more human-looking race of short beings were adopted and integrated into Bimm culture. The species could not interbreed, so when intermarriage happened between the species, the couples often adopted children. Bimms had a love of heroic stories and held the Jedi in high regard. No weapons were permitted in Bimm cities. The people loved to shop and haggle for a bargain.

**Bimmiel** The fifth and only habitable planet in the Outer Rim system designated MZX33291 by Imperial surveyors, Bimmiel had a single moon. A nearby pulsar star disrupted communications to and from the world. Ice caps covered the planet's poles, which started to melt as the planet neared its sun as part of its elliptical orbit. The seasonal melting resulted in an abundance of plant growth. The heat also brought the shwpi—small herbivores—out of hibernation. They ate and multiplied, spreading plants as they traveled. As the world cooled, moisture collected in the polar ice caps, making the rest of the world much drier. Predators emerged during this dry period, most notably the slashrats, which were adept at moving through the resulting dunes. They hunted the shwpi that had not found burrows in which to hibernate.

During the early stages of the Yuuzhan Vong invasion of New Republic space, a team of Jedi Knights was dispatched to investigate the disappearance of a University of Agamar xenoarchaeological team. Corran Horn and Ganner Rhysode discovered a Yuuzhan Vong presence attempting to recover a mummified body of one of their own species that had been on Bimmiel for over 50 years.

**Bimmisaari** A temperate planet in the Halla sector covered by swaying asaari trees, Bimmisaari escaped most of the fallout of the Empire's cruel reign and the Rebellion because of its isolated location. It was inhabited by two cultures—a species of short, half-furred, yellow-clad creatures called Bimms, and a humanoid population that adopted the same culture. Bimmisaari was governed by a planetary council. While on a diplomatic mission to the planet five years after the Battle of Endor, Princess Leia Organa Solo and Luke Skywalker were the targets of a kidnapping attempt by a Noghri commando team. During the war against the Yuuzhan Vong, many refugees from ravaged Obroa-skai fled to Bimmisaari.

Jolee Bindo

**Bin (O-Bin)** A strict female Teaching Guide in the Learning Circle on Kegan. Her hair was often pulled back behind her ears in a severe style, and she wore a plain brown tunic over black trousers. She instructed young Obi-Wan Kenobi and Siri Tachi.

**Binalie, Corf** The son of Lord Binalie on Cartao who was 12 years old during the Clone Wars. He was instructed by Jedi Master Jafer Torles. The Neimoidian commander Tok Ashel took Corf hostage to ensure the cooperation of his father.

**Binalie, Lord Pilester** Head of Spaarti Creations on the planet Cartao. He attempted to remain neutral during the Clone Wars, but his highly efficient manufacturing technology developed by the Cranscoc was too valuable a prize to be ignored. His facility was destroyed by a crashing Republic gunship, a collision Binalie would come to blame on the Jedi Knights.

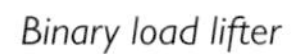

Binary load lifter

**Binalu** An older woman who served with Talus as a leader of the planet Typha-Dor for many years prior to the start of the Clone Wars.

**binary load lifter** Primitive labor droids designed to move heavy objects in spaceports and warehouses with strong mechanical claws and built-in propulsion systems. Cybot Galactica's CLL-8 was one of the better units for low cost and reliability.

**Binayre razorcat** An area of space near the Corellian system that was known as a hunting ground for pirates.

**binder** Common and cost-effective restraint devices used throughout the galaxy. Binders were standard durasteel cuffs equipped with simple mechanical locks. Luke Skywalker and Han Solo used binders on Chewbacca in their raid on the Death Star detention center.

***Binder*** An Imperial Interdictor cruiser sent to Ciutric by Ysanne Isard to prevent the escape of Sate Pestage into New Republic hands. The ship sustained damage when New Republic reinforcements arrived. It was later commanded by Captain Phulik as part of Warlord Admiral Krennel's forces at Cuitric. When Admiral Ackbar defeated Krennel, the *Binder*'s crew surrendered.

**Bindo, Jolee** An eccentric former smuggler and skilled Jedi, he chose to retreat from society and live out his days in seclusion and obscurity, 4,000 years before the Galactic Civil War. Bindo cloaked himself in indifference to hide his sorrow. He appeared as a cantankerous old man who readily dismissed troubles with an impatient wave, but his care and wisdom still shone through. His past remained unknown aside from rumors that he fought in the great war against Exar Kun. It was not known what led him into self-imposed exile in the deepest shadows of wild Kashyyyk.

When Bastila Shan's mission to uncover the Star Forge caused Republic agents to cross paths with Bindo in the Kashyyyk shadowlands, he was willing to finally return to the galaxy at large. Bindo joined the quest for Darth Malak, traveling to distant worlds such as Manaan, where he uncovered elements of his forgotten past—like his friend and fellow war hero Sunry, who was held captive for murder on the watery world.

Despite a series of rousing adventures among spirited youngsters, Bindo remained weary of the galaxy's endless, pointless struggles. He insisted that all he wanted was peace, but his eyes—the eyes of a fighter—told a different story.

*Jar Jar Binks at the Battle of Naboo*

**Bin-Garda-Zon** A Cerean marauder who led a group of bandits on his homeworld, Cerea. He was easily recognized by his mangled left hand, which was missing two fingers. He spent his life raiding Cerean homesteads and villages, stealing food, livestock, and male children. Eventually, he was deposed by a female warrior, who took control of the raiders. Bin-Garda-Zon became an emaciated shell, relegated to caring for the band's oorgs. After Ki-Adi-Mundi defeated the raider chief, Bin-Garda-Zon attempted to challenge the Jedi Knight, but he was easily defeated. Ki opted to spare his life.

**Bini** A tall female pilot, she was a member of the Rock Workers on New Apsolon. She and her partners Yanci and Kevta accidentally attacked the Jedi Obi-Wan Kenobi and Qui-Gon Jinn, mistaking them for their mortal enemies, the Absolutes. Bini died at the hands of the Absolutes a dozen years before the Battle of Naboo.

**Binks, Jar Jar** A Gungan outcast exiled from Otoh Gunga for being clumsy in front of his people's leader. To hear Jar Jar tell it in his Gungan/Basic pidgin, he "boomed da gasser, and crashed de boss's heyblibber, den banished." An outcast, he spent his time foraging in the Naboo swampland. Jar Jar's fate took a twist when he encountered a pair of Jedi as they eluded enemy forces during the Trade Federation invasion of Naboo.

By Gungan tradition, Jar Jar found himself indebted to Qui-Gon Jinn for saving his life. Jar Jar guided the Jedi to Otoh Gunga, where they secured transport to the Naboo capital of Theed. Jar Jar braved the "nocombackie law" to present Qui-Gon to the Gungan leader, Boss Nass, even though he risked the consequence of being "pounded" to death. Throughout the adventure of liberating Naboo, Jar Jar tagged along with Qui-Gon. Although his bungling, haphazard mannerisms constantly landed him in hot water, his good nature and loyalty somehow helped him triumph in the end.

Queen Amidala requested that Jar Jar make contact with the Gungans. With Jar Jar's help, the Naboo and the Gungans forged an alliance that liberated the besieged world of Naboo. During the ground battle against the Trade Federation droid army, Jar Jar was made a general in the Gungan Grand Army.

After the battle, Jar Jar continued to ascend in Gungan society, putting his awkward past as an outcast behind him. He eventually became a Senior Representative for Naboo, serving alongside Padmé Amidala in the Galactic Senate. While his compassion spoke volumes for the quality of his character, his inherent gullibility and trusting nature were easily exploited by the less scrupulous in the field of politics. Jar Jar was a member of the Loyalist Committee, a panel of Senators concerned with countering the increasing threat of the Separatist movement. He and Padmé worked hard, favoring negotiation and peaceful resolution over the growing popularity of the Military Creation Act. While Padmé was away from Coruscant, it was Jar Jar who took her place in the Senate.

After several botched assassination attempts on Senator Amidala forced her to flee the capital, Jar Jar again served in her stead. The Gungan politician was there, in Palpatine's office, when it became apparent that desperate measures would be required to stop a Separatist force determined to start a war with the Republic. Jar Jar took the initiative and proposed the motion granting emergency powers to Supreme Chancellor Palpatine—a move that would have profound impact on the Galactic Republic.

*Representative Binks*

**Binring Biomedical Product** Based on Saffalore, Binring Biomedical Product was a principal food supplier to the Empire's armed forces. Binring also engineered animals to adapt to different planetary environments. It conducted less wholesome experiments as well: For purposes of espionage, the Emperor wanted Gamorreans with human-like methods of self-control. Binring engineers made alterations to Gamorrean biochemistries, giving them attention spans surpassing the human norm and mathematical acumen registering at the genius level. Voort "Piggy" saBinring, a member of Wraith Squadron, was the project's only success; the other subjects all committed suicide.

**bio-converter power generator** Slave hovels on Tatooine were cooled and heated by archaic bio-converter power generators. Via underground pipelines, these machines received liquid sludge composed of animal and municipal waste, which then was converted into natchgas.

***BioCruiser*** A cobbled-together starship that served as the permanent home for refugees from ravaged worlds across the galaxy, the *BioCruiser* was made up of different metals of various colors. It had, among others, sublight engines of the *Dyne* class. Under the leadership of Uni, the inhabitants of the *BioCruiser* preferred to roam the galaxy rather than land on other worlds. Outsiders were not allowed to dock on the ship. One whole area of the ship was devoted to the Collection Center, which housed plants and animals from many worlds to help the vessel remain self-sustaining. Anakin Skywalker's first mission as Obi-Wan Kenobi's Padawan was to investigate the *BioCruiser* while it was en route to Tentrix. The ship was sabotaged by Kern and Vox Chun, who intended to rob the ship's treasury.

**Biodisposal Pit** The unflattering name given to the medical disposal center located aboard the Star Destroyer *Anakin Solo.* Any of the hazardous or organic waste that was generated by the ship's medical facilities—from dirty bandages and used scalpels to corpses and other waste—was sent to the Biodisposal Pit, where it was incinerated in a fusion furnace before being ejected into space.

**bio-droid** An unusual series of symbiont cyborg droid developed by Cestus Cybernetics. Also known as a JK droid, the bio-droid had nearly supernatural reflexes thanks to an internally supported, symbiotically linked immature dashta eel. These Force-sensitive creatures were native to the caverns of Ord Cestus. The droid's incredible reaction time, coupled with its impressive armaments—retractable, scalable metal tentacles that could deliver a stun charge, and spinning, circular energy shields—made it a popular weapon among crime lords. The bio-droid was a high-end construct with an ostentatious mirrored golden coating. Small, pointed legs supported the upright assembly; the droid could also unfold and restructure its body segments to assume a hunched, spider-like configuration. JK droids sold at a premium of 80,000 credits each. The droids figured into a ruse engineered by Count Dooku, who spread rumors that he was interested in purchasing thousands of the JK units to deploy as "Jedi Killers" in the Clone Wars. In truth, the dashta eels would never take the life of a sentient.

**bioscan** A hardware–software system that scanned objects, it could prepare a report on a target's biological makeup, origin, age, and other factors.

**BioTech Industries** Maker of the Borg Construct Aj^6 cyborg unit and the BioTech FastFlesh medpac, BioTech was one of the galaxy's top cybernetics manufacturers, particularly in the area of cyborg biocomputer implants. The company was jointly owned by Neuro-Saav Technologies and the Tagge Company.

**biotic grenade** A tightly focused explosive used in mining operations.

**Bioto** Koorivar smuggler captain of the freighter *Dead Ringer.* Rival smuggler Cash Garrulan told the Empire that Bioto was smuggling Jedi fugitives—a lie—resulting in Bioto getting thrown in the brig of the Star Destroyer *Exactor.*

**Birok** Leader of a Separatist-allied gang on the planet Diado, he had a tangle with Saesee Tiin during the Clone Wars when the Jedi Master tried to secure blueprints for an experimental Confederacy starfighter.

**birru** A delicate, lace-winged creature on Ansion.

**Birt, Captain Ninora** A former smuggler, she was the tall human captain of the *Record Time.* She joined the New Republic Defense Force during the war against the Yuuzhan Vong. When her starship was destroyed, she became the new communications specialist of Blackmoon Squadron. She flew as Blackmoon Ten during the evacuation of Borleias.

**Birtraub Brothers Storage and Reclamation Center** A criminal front and sprawling complex of interconnected gray buildings not far from Crovna's main spaceport.

**Biscuit Baron** A string of quick-service restaurants owned by Trade Federation associate TaggeCo.

**Bissillirus** A system of five planets in the Trax sector that included the agriworld Draenell's Point.

**bissop** A Yuuzhan Vong lizard-hound bred for hunting.

**Bitas, Vob** A blob racer caught cheating and put to death on Umgul just prior to the Clone Wars.

**Biter** *See* Sgauru.

**Bith** A species of evolved humanoids from Clak'dor VII with huge foreheads and hairless craniums. Bith also had large, lidless black eyes and receding noses, which complemented their baggy facial folds. A heightened sense of hearing allowed them to perceive sounds much as other creatures perceived color. Thus, they made excellent musicians, and Bith bands such as Figrin D'an and the Modal Nodes could be found touring throughout the known galaxy.

The history of the Bith was a tale of tragedy brought about by war. Located in the Mayagil sector, the small planet of Clak'dor VII orbited the large white star Colu. The world was once a lush utopia boasting numerous advanced technologies, until war broke out between the cities of Nozho and Weogar. About 300 years before the Battle of Yavin, the tensions boiled over as a dispute over a stardrive patent ignited a civil war. When the war finally ended, Clak'dor VII's biosphere was ruined. A biological attack launched at Nozho had shattered the city, mutating its populace and the surrounding wildlife. Most Nozho citizens were killed outright, but many who survived developed mutagenic irregularities that soon led to the creation of a subspecies of Bith, the Y'bith.

To survive, the remaining Bith retreated into hermetically sealed domed cities. They soon began using DNA analysis and their advanced technology to ensure successful mating. Over the long centuries of controlled evolution, the Bith species evolved to a remarkable degree. The regions of a Bith's brain that controlled language, music, art, science, reasoning, mathematics, and mechanics were incredibly developed. As a result, Bith did not require sleep and the species produced a staggering array of technological achievements, although they did not restore their homeworld.

While the Bith became incredibly intelligent, their emotional aspects dwindled. Those areas of the brain responsible for fear, aggression, and reproduction atrophied considerably. Because of these changes, Bith were often considered passive and polite, but rarely very exciting.

Clak'dor VII couldn't support viable industries or agriculture, and many Bith had to sell their intellectual abilities by seeking employment as technical consultants away from their homeworld. Fortunately, a fair number of Bith also found gainful employment as entertainers and musicians. In addition, as Bith traveled into the greater galaxy, many learned to embrace their emotions rather than rely solely on reason.

*Bith*

**Bithabus the Mystifier** A Bith, he was a famous magician who long performed at Hologram Fun World's Asteroid Theater.

**Bitters, Filli** Expert slicer and crew member aboard the *Drunk Dancer,* he helped a number of fugitive Jedi escape the Empire in the weeks following the declaration of the New Order.

**Biurk, Captain** Devaronian commanding officer of the Galactic Alliance flagship *Shamunaar,* tasked with monitoring and blockading the Bothans during the conflict between the Corellian Confederation and the Alliance. Biurk's efforts were undermined by his superior, Admiral Matric Klauskin, who was secretly under the mental influence of the Sith Lumiya. Klauskin shuffled personnel in the blockade so that only the *Shamunaar* was left, and eventually killed Biurk by shooting him before scuttling his ship.

**Bix** A sleek droid, it teamed with Auren Yomm of the planet Roon in the Colonial Games during the early days of the Empire.

**Bjalin, Tedris** An Imperial Navy lieutenant from Tyshapahl, he graduated from the Academy a year before Han Solo and was disgusted with Solo when the latter was drummed out of the service. Years later, when he learned his family had been killed in the Imperial subjugation of Tyshapahl, Bjalin defected and joined the Corellian resistance, working alongside Bria Tharen.

**Bjornsons** A family of moisture farmers on Tatooine, they were against the plans of Ariq Joanson to draw up maps of peace with the Jawas and Tusken Raiders. Their son had been killed, presumably by Sand People.

**BL-17** A Battle Legionnaire droid owned by Boba Fett during the Empire's early days, it looked like C-3PO but with the bounty hunter's olive-drab and yellow colors. BL-17 carried a rectangular blaster.

***Black Asp*** *See Corusca Rainbow.*

**Black Bantha** A protostar listed erroneously on most navigation charts as a Gamma Class navigation hazard, the Black Bantha was on the secret route into Reecee that smugglers used.

**Black Fleet** An Imperial armada that patrolled the Koornacht Cluster. Eight months after the Battle of Endor, the Black Fleet armada was seized by Nil Spaar and the Yevetha at the planet N'zoth. Twelve years later, Nil Spaar used the Black Fleet warships in his bloody crusade called the Great Purge. Imperial prisoners on board the ships of the Black Fleet later seized control using a slave-circuit web they had secretly installed over the previous decade. The ships then made a jump to Byss in the Deep Core in the hope of seeking out the Emperor's hidden throneworld, but the Imperials were surprised to learn of the planet's destruction by the Galaxy Gun six years earlier. Within a month, the majority of the fleet defected to the New Republic. Four *Victory*-class Star Destroyers hooked up with Daala's warlords in the Deep Core, and two of the most advanced Star Destroyers, as well as the experimental weapons test bed *EX-F*, chose to join Admiral Pellaeon's shrinking empire in the Outer Rim. The Super Star Destroyer *Pride of Yevetha* vanished—only to be discovered four years later, drifting abandoned near the Unknown Regions and damaged beyond repair.

**Black Four** A code name used by Imperial pilot DS-61-4 during the Battle of Yavin.

**Blackhole** A mysterious Imperial agent and one of the Emperor's Hands, Blackhole was steeped in the dark side of the Force, specializing in fear. He had originally been one of the Prophets of the Dark Side; then his unerring visions impressed Palpatine, who named him head of Imperial Intelligence. He was granted unprecedented control over the entire HoloNet, scouring vast amounts of information for data the Emperor might find useful.

Blackhole stayed hidden throughout most of his career, sequestered so that his true form, that of a withered old man, was known only to a scant few individuals. When he needed to communicate, he took the form of a strange black hologram. More visible were his forces—Blackhole stormtroopers (or shadowtroopers) who wore the same armor as regular stormtroopers, but painted black and coated in a stygium-polymer substance that baffled sensor readings. Blackhole traveled in a similarly darkened Star Destroyer named *Singularity.*

Blackhole was later known by the name Lord Cronal, and he specialized in using technology to develop devices to exploit the power of the Force. He also was responsible for the mutation of Gorc and Pic, the so-called Brothers of the Sith. Under the alias Lord Shadowspawn, he led the Imperial resistance on the planet Mindor, before being defeated by Luke Skywalker and the armies of the New Republic, a little over a year after the Battle of Endor.

**Blackhole stormtroopers** *See* shadow stormtroopers.

*Blackhole*

***Black Ice*** The pride of the Imperial Replenishment Fleet, this cargo ship was five times the length of an *Imperial*-class Star Destroyer. *Black Ice* carried nearly one billion metric tons of starship-grade fuel cells, or more than one year's power supply for a complete Imperial battle fleet.

**black membrosia** A potent form of membrosia created by the Gorog hive, creating a narcotic addiction among other insectoid species in the galaxy who imbibed it.

**Blackmoon** *See* Borleias.

**Blackmoon Squadron** Formerly Green Squadron, a New Republic E-wing squadron that protected Pyria VI's moon under the command of Captain Yakown Reth during the war against the Yuuzhan Vong. It engaged Czulkang Lah's forces. During the evacuation of Borleais, Luke Skywalker flew as Blackmoon Leader, with Mara Jade Skywalker flying as Blackmoon Two. The squadron helped to protect the Super Star Destroyer *Lusankya.*

**black nebula** Located in the region of space known as Parfadi, it separated the planets Arat Fraca and Motexx. The black nebula contained two immense neutron stars and was considered unnavigable.

**Black Nebula** A criminal organization headed by Dequc. Although based out of Qiaxx, Black Nebula had operations in the southern district on Svivren and on Nezri. After Mara Jade assassinated Dequc, she provided the Empire with enough information to take down the entire operation.

**Black Nine** A former Imperial Navy name for the orbital shipyard at ILC-905, it was taken over by Yevethan forces.

**black powder pistol** An obsolete firearm that used a combustible powder to launch a physical projectile.

**Blackscales** One of the strongest Trandoshan clans, which operated a slave ring in the Kashyyyk system during the Galactic Civil War. They were usually at odds with the Zssik clan, a conflict that came to a head on the Avatar Space Platform when members of both clans were unable to contain their aggression and launched a full-scale riot. Imperial forces eventually stepped in and detained both groups, but only after freelance operatives had managed to help several Wookiee slaves escape.

**Black Squadron** Darth Vader's handpicked squadron stationed on the first Death Star. The TIE fighters of Black Squadron boasted the latest Imperial weaponry. Each pilot and starfighter was at the peak of readiness.

**Black Sun** A once vast criminal organization spanning the galaxy and incorporating every known illegal activity. The syndicate's tentacles reached everywhere—from the polished spires of Coruscant to the seamiest Outer Rim tavern. Many of the organization's tens of thousands of operatives had no idea that they were benefiting Black Sun, so layered and intricate were the fronts that the syndicate hid behind. Black Sun's information network rivaled the accuracy and scope of even Imperial Intelligence.

Existing in one form or another for centuries, Black Sun was sculpted in the modern era by Prince Xizor, the elegant Falleen head of Xizor Transport Systems. Serving beneath him were a cadre of nine Vigos—Old Tionese for "nephews"—who monitored and managed activities in specific territories.

Xizor's personal vendetta against Lord Darth Vader nearly scuttled the entire organization. So fixated was he on exacting vengeance against Vader, Xizor allowed his fortress to become infiltrated by Rebel Alliance agents. The devastation of his fortress by Rebel explosives was just the start of a downward spiral that culminated in Xizor's death in the destruction of his private skyhook.

In the resulting power vacuum, the Vigos desperately sought to carve up the criminal empire. Xizor's long-lost niece, Savan, secretly instigated a war among the Vigos as she attempted to take control of Black Sun herself. She failed in her bid to capture the human replica droid Guri, whose mechanical mind contained many vital Black Sun secrets. When Guri's memory was wiped, many of the most secret and lucrative Black Sun ventures were forever erased.

This was not the first time Black Sun had been decapitated. Decades earlier, Darth Maul infiltrated Black Sun and killed its then-leader Alexi Garyn. The remnants of Xizor's Black Sun did not rebound nearly as well as Garyn's organization: No obvious heir as powerful or driven as Xizor appeared. A string of imitators emerged in the following years, and with each, Black Sun was further diminished. The corrupt Moff Flirry Voru controlled a sizable fragment, while other remains were re-formed into Black Nebula by Lord Dequc. After the organization had suffered years of directionless rule, Y'ull Acib attempted control; Czethros was the last known ruler before Black Sun was finally crushed.

**Black Three** A code name used by Imperial pilot DS-61-3 during the Battle of Yavin.

***Blacktooth*** A YT-2400 freighter owned by Faskus Olvidan, a courier who stole the amulet of Kalara and took it to Ziost as part of a plot by the Dark Lady Lumiya to test Ben Skywalker. The *Blacktooth* was bombarded by

TIE fighters while on Ziost, and the resulting explosion killed Olvidan.

**Black Two** A code name used by Imperial pilot DS-61-2 during the Battle of Yavin.

**blackvine** A variety of parasitic plant life native to Dagobah.

**Black Vulkars** A swoop gang on Taris at the time of the Mandalorian Wars. They were rivals to the Hidden Beks.

**Blackwater Systems** A series of factories hastily erected on the planet Falleen shortly after the Battle of Naboo. Anakin Skywalker and Obi-Wan Kenobi tracked the rogue scientists Jenna Zan Arbor, Roy Teda, and Granta Omega here. They destroyed the facility in order to escape.

**blarth** Amiable and easily tamed predators, blarths were kept as household pets and watch-animals by Gungans since prehistoric times.

**blasé tree goat** These lethargic goat-like creatures hung from the limbs of huge trees that covered Endor's Forest Moon.

**blastail** A small, carnivorous, feline creature that inhabited many levels of Kashyyyk. The fuzzy bulb on the end of the blastail's tail cross-pollinated the jungle by collecting seeds and spores. Blastails could "throw" their pollen-laden tail bulb at would-be predators, resulting in violent allergic reactions.

**blast bugs** Yuuzhan Vong–bioengineered weapons, these thrown insects exploded near a target.

**blast door** A thick, heavily armored durasteel door used to seal off sections of a space station or capital starship in the event of an explosion, reactor leak, security breach, or other emergency. Some locations had more than a single set of blast doors.

**BlasTech Industries** One of the galaxy's primary weapons manufacturers, it produced a wide range of blasters.

**Blaster Buster slugthrower** The Oriolanis Defense Systems Blaster Buster was a highly advanced slugthrower that utilized unique, specially made payloads capable of homing in on recently fired weapons.

**blaster weaponry** The most commonly used weapon in the galaxy, blasters came in a vast range of sizes, styles, and firepower. Blasters fired beams of intense light energy that, depending upon intensity setting, could do everything from stun to vaporize. The color of the energy bolts could also vary, but they invariably produced a smell similar to ozone. Models ranged from concealed pistols and sporting blasters to heavy blasters and blaster rifles. Some of the largest blasters came with shield generators and targeting computers, and required a crew to operate.

Blasters came in virtually every size and shape, with a host of features and specifications. Most, however, had several traits in common. All blasters utilized high-energy blaster gas to produce a visible beam of intense energy. These "bolts" could cause tremendous damage to structures and organic tissue. A handheld blaster generally had an optimum range of under 30 meters and a maximum range of up to 120 meters. Blasters received their energy from small power packs, which could be replaced in under 10 seconds. Depleted power packs also could be recharged at portable generators.

An efficient blaster's gas chamber carried enough blaster gas for over 500 shots, while the power pack could provide energy for up to 100 shots. Stun blasts from such weapons rendered targets unconscious for up to 10 minutes, while a full-power blast easily penetrated armor and low-level force fields. Most of these sidearms were semi-automatic weapons, firing each time the trigger was pulled. However, some models could be modified for fully automatic fire, although this consumed power packs quicker and could cause the weapon to overheat.

Many arms companies also manufactured heavy blaster pistols, incredibly powerful weapons designed for close-quarters combat. Blasts from these weapons could rip through body armor and damage small vehicles. Designed to be light and accurate, a heavy blaster could be fired with one hand but had a limited optimum range of 25 meters and a maximum range of 50. In addition, heavy blasters consumed a great deal of energy, draining a power pack in only 25 shots. Those using the weapon often carried several dozen power packs.

Among the least powerful blasters were sporting blasters, short-range weapons reserved for self-defense. Other models, known as hold-out blasters, could be easily concealed in clothing.

The blaster rifle, a more powerful version of the standard blaster, was among the most common military and security weapons in the galaxy. These weapons were preferred by soldiers and other combat personnel because they were more lethal than standard blasters, yet compact and easy to fire. The most efficient blaster rifles had an optimum range of 100 meters and a maximum range of 300, nearly three times the range of a blaster pistol. Such weapons used power packs with enough energy for 100 rounds. They also had numerous power settings, and could alternate between semi-automatic and fully automatic fire.

**blastonecrosis** A bacta allergy, it was marked by fatigue and loss of appetite. Approximately 2 percent of those exposed to the deliberately contaminated bacta Lot ZX1449F developed blastonecrosis. Attempts to treat it with uncontaminated bacta resulted in death.

**blast-rifle** An ancient weapon of choice for the beast-riders of Onderon some 4,000 years before the Battle of Yavin, it fired bolts of laser energy.

**Blastwell, Hamo** Ace pilot and Keyan Farlander's first orientation officer aboard the Mon Calamari cruiser *Independence.* He went deep undercover in the Empire, eventually infiltrating the Secret Order of the Emperor.

**Blatta the Hutt** Co-pilot with Captain Uran Lavint aboard the *Breathe My Jets.* Lavint sold him out, and he was arrested by the Galactic Alliance.

**Blaylock effect** A process that projected images in an atmosphere as a means of decoy or deceptive warfare. The Empire experimented with the Blaylock effect.

**blaze bug** Incandescent flying insects used by the Yuuzhan Vong to create tactical maps.

**Blazing Claw** A symbol used by pirates for thousands of years. Its form varied over the centuries, but it retained its basic identity: a side-view image of a freestanding claw surrounded by flame.

**blba tree** Broad-trunked, jagged-branched thorny trees, they grew amid waving lavender grasses on the savannas of Dantooine. The Ithorians also introduced them to Telos IV and elsewhere.

**Bledsoe, Dr.** An Imperial scientist who agreed wholeheartedly with the Empire's xenophobic views of the universe, he was abducted by a group of Rebels and whisked away for questioning at one of the Rebel insurgent camps.

**Bledsoe's disease** A deadly virus transmitted by air or physical contact, the Empire used Bledsoe's disease as a form of biological warfare against the Rebel Alliance. Imperial scientists further refined the disease through genetic manipulation, creating a strain with a curious side effect: Victims' eyes exhibited the "window effect," in which the standard discoloration actually produced visible star charts that showed the location of Rebel bases.

**blembie** A small, predatory fish native to Naboo.

**Blendin, Jerrol** A corrupt, greedy, and ill-tempered Cloud City Wing Guard, he began working in Cloud City during Baron Raynor's tenure and was known to keep peace through intimidation.

**Blendri** An ancient Jedi Knight from the dawn of the Republic, she was good friends since childhood with Danzigorro Potts. Prior to the First Great Schism, Blendri, her apprentice, Cuthallox, and Jedi Master Jook-jook H'broozin abandoned the Jedi Order, joining with dark side forces led by Xendor. Potts confronted and defeated each of them in turn, sustaining mortal injuries on Columus but surviving long enough to leave behind a record of his experiences.

**Blenjeel** A Mid Rim desert planet inhabited by terrifying sand burrowers. Electrical storms posed a danger to incoming craft. After Jaden Korr's mission to Blenjeel, the New Republic installed a beacon to warn off visitors to the planet.

**B'Leph, Tholote** The corrupt leader of the opposition party on Ter Abbes prior to the Yuuzhan Vong invasion. Nom Anor, in disguise, hired Mandalorian Goran Beviin to assassinate B'Leph prior to an election. The death escalated tensions and resulted in a civil war that lasted a year.

***Blessings*** A Dreadnaught in Nil Spaar's Black Eleven Fleet.

**Bleyd, Tarnese** Sakiyan commander of a MedStar medical frigate who was secretly working to double-cross Black Sun during the Clone Wars. He hoped to profit off bota taken from Drongar, thereby bringing honor back to his family lost by an earlier dealing with the criminal syndicate. Black Sun agent Kaird killed Bleyd.

**Bley-san** The owner of a cantina on Tatooine, she owed a favor to Ygabba Hise, one of the children under the control of Gilramos Libkath. After Boba Fett killed Libkath, Ygabba believed that Bley-san could help the children find their families.

**Blim, Lieutenant Geff** An Imperial officer, he was Carnor Jax's personal assistant and, secretly, his chief assassin. Blim's timid, awkward bearing was a front, meant to make him appear incompetent or weak to others. He never spoke in public: Many of Jax's men believed Blim was a mute, but in fact his silence allowed him to be ever-observant of the actions and behaviors of those who worked with Jax. His low rank also let him go unnoticed by other Imperial officers. While Lord Jax worked behind the scenes to secure funds from power-hungry Imperial councilmen, Blim assassinated anyone who was a threat to Jax or his plans to kill the Emperor and make a bid for power. Later, when Jax sensed the inevitable destruction of one of his flagships, Blim was the only soldier he allowed to escape with him. Just before the final battle between Kir Kanos and Carnor Jax, Blim secured a position to eliminate Kanos from a distance. Blim was killed by Sish Sadeet mere seconds before he could shoot Kanos.

**Blimph** A planet strategically important to the Rebel Alliance. Lando Calrissian was the diplomat sent to the Tertiary Moon of Blimph to meet with Quaffug the Hutt. By the time Lando left the planet, Quaffug's stranglehold on its trade was over and the Alliance could deal with the planet's native Jokhalli directly.

**Blin, Vildar** A Rebel Alliance scout at Echo Base during the Battle of Hoth, he was trained in first-response tactics. He joined the Alliance after his brother joined the Imperial agency COMPNOR. Blin and his assistant were killed when the walker toppled by Wedge Antilles was destroyed.

*Blood Carver*

***Blind Luck*** An aging freighter owned and operated by Desric Fol and used as an independent scouting vessel during the Galactic Civil War. The ship was considered slow by most standards, and its computer systems rarely calculated predictable hyperspace routes. Fol was once told by the traffic control operators at Elrood that he should have the name changed, since it didn't inspire confidence in the crew's ability.

**blink code** An old form of communication developed by the Mon Calamari that involved tapping to form letters. When captured by Tsavong Lah, Leia Organa Solo used Mon Cal blink code to communicate with Jaina.

**Blissex, Walex** A Republic engineer who designed the Delta-7 Aethersprite light interceptor and the *Victory*-class Star Destroyer. His daughter, Lira Wessex, would build upon his designs to develop the *Imperial*-class Star Destroyer. He joined the Rebel Alliance and, together with General Jan Dodonna, developed the A-wing fighter. At the time of the Battle of Endor, he had been given the honorary rank of general due to his service to the Rebellion.

**Blista-Vanee, Kren** A thin, pale-faced adviser to Emperor Palpatine, he was stationed aboard the second Death Star during the Battle of Endor.

**blistmok** A raptor-like reptilian pack animal native to Mustafar and Talus.

**Blizzard Force** Code name of the AT-AT assault group on Hoth, it comprised at least five AT-AT walkers, a legion of stormtroopers, and at least one AT-ST. Blizzard 1 was General Veers's personal AT-AT. Blizzard 2 was an AT-AT commanded by General Nevar, an immoral and paranoid Imperial officer. Blizzard Scout 1, led by Commander Igar, was an AT-ST assigned to provide flanking support and cover fire for the AT-ATs and snowtroopers of Blizzard Force. Blizzard 4, commanded by Colonel Starck, was single-handedly downed by Luke Skywalker.

**blizzard walker** *See* All Terrain Armored Transport.

**blob race** Much like a steeplechase, this bizarre race of protoplasm-like gelatinous blobs through a course of obstacles (from fine mesh screens to a bed of nails) was a major betting sport in Umgul City on the planet Umgul. The syrupy masses, primarily grayish green but laced with bright hues, rolled, slithered, and oozed their way through. Cheating on the races was punishable by death.

**blockade runner** *See* Corellian corvette.

**blood beetle** A scavenging insect known for its ability to locate fresh corpses and voraciously turn them into skeletons.

**Blood Carver** An impressive-looking species from Batorine: 2 meters tall, slender, graceful, with long three-jointed limbs, a small head mounted on a high thick neck, and iridescent gold skin. Across the nose, a Blood Carver had two fleshy flaps like a split shield, which acted both as an olfactory sensor and a very sensitive ear, supplemented by two small pits behind small onyx-black eyes. There were only a few hundred Blood Carvers on Coruscant; they joined the Republic nearly a century before the Battle of Naboo. Blood Carver society was feudal, led by a ruling class of tribal families. Blood Carvers were not generally known to be involved in outside politics. They considered it weak to offer praise. In Blood Carver metaphysics, the Art Beyond Dying was the finale of life. They were an artistic people—but the true art of Blood Carvers was assassination.

**bloodfin** A creature found on Bastion, where they were once trained as cavalry mounts. As technology became more and more prevalent, they were relegated to use as dressage beasts by Imperial nobility. The bloodfin earned its name from its brilliant, scarlet crest. They pranced on four legs, each of which ended in a cloven hoof that resembled a large dagger. A bloodfin's mouth was filled with sharp fangs. Although impressive beasts, they were difficult to train and sometimes reverted to their predatory nature and consumed anything—and anyone—that happened to be in front of them. Few beings realized the skill and dedication of the handlers and trainers who readied them for display. Thus, the bloodfin came to symbolize notions of caution and respect.

***Bloodfin* (1)** A small, single-passenger speeder bike used by Darth Maul, its relatively simple stripped-down Razalon FC-20 design emphasized speed and maneuverability. The speeder lacked weapons, sensors, and shields.

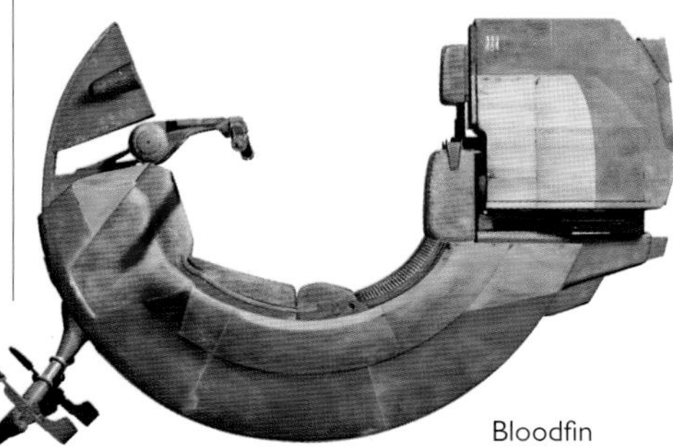

Bloodfin

The high-performance engines allowed for rapid acceleration, sharp turns, and quick stops, while the compact design presented a very small target. Darth Maul typically used the speeder to surprise or pursue his quarry. The open cockpit allowed him to leap directly from the vehicle and into combat.

***Bloodfin* (2)** One of the first new *Turbulent*-class Star Destroyers unveiled by the Imperial Remnant following the Swarm War. A crest with an image of the Bastion terrestrial bloodfin adorned the main bridge, depicting the creature trampling its rider. Gilad Pellaeon, the *Bloodfin*'s first commander, explained to Tahiri Veila that the crest was a reminder to Imperials that they needed to rule without cruelty or carelessness, lest the people turn on them, just like a bloodfin would attack a cruel rider. During the Second Battle of Fondor, Tahiri coldly assassinated Pellaeon after he ordered the Imperial fleet to break off its attack and obey only the orders of Admiral Cha Niathal, not those of Tahiri's master, Darth Caedus. The treacherous Imperial Moffs attempted to take control, but Pellaeon's loyal crew mutinied, forcing the Moffs to lock themselves in the ship's command center in order to regroup. They were then wiped out by Boba Fett's Mandalorian supercommandos.

**Blood Razors** This swoop gang originated on the planet Biivren. Despite their fearsome name, the Blood Razors were formed to assist those inhabitants who were outcast when the big corporations took over the planet. They mostly trafficked black-market goods to the underground, avoiding Imperial notice by covering their activities with swoop chases.

***Blood Sacrifice*** The Yuuzhan Vong capital ship, and flagship of Warmaster Tsavong Lah, that carried the yammosk used at Ebaq 9. It was destroyed during the battle.

**BloodScar pirates** A band of pirates active in the Shelsha sector, based out of Gepparin shortly after the Battle of Yavin. They were secretly being funded by Governor Barshnis Choard, who was engaging the underworld to fund his own private war against the Empire and allow his sector to secede. Mara Jade discovered the connection between the BloodScars and Choard, and voyaged to the sector capital of Shelkonwa to bring him to justice.

**bloodsniffer** Vicious predators native to the deserts of Kamar. Because its metabolism consumed potassium at an enormous rate, a bloodsniffer had to consume its weight in fresh blood every two days. Bloodsniffers were short, well-muscled animals ranging from 1 to nearly 2 meters long. A tongue with a sharpened, horny spur drew blood from victims. The animals lived in small packs and were extremely territorial.

**bloodsoup** A broth eaten by the ancient Sith species that found its cultural roots among the Anzati. Githany used a poisoned bowl of bloodsoup in a failed attempt to kill Darth Bane. Bane knowingly drank the poison with the belief that a mere poison should not be able to harm a Dark Lord.

***Bloodstar*** Bar-Kooda's well-armed personal ship. Boba Fett used Wim Magwit's teleportational hoop to gain access to the well-defended *Bloodstar*. After subduing Bar-Kooda, Boba Fett and Magwit escaped as a bomb went off aboard the *Bloodstar*, killing many of its crew.

**blood trail** A rare Force skill that allowed a user to mark and track the location of a target through the use of one's own blood. The Nightsisters of Dathomir developed this technique in order to mark their slaves. Darth Caedus was one of the few to know of the technique and used it to track down the hidden Jedi base in the wake of the Battle of Kuat, some 40 years after the Battle of Yavin. The blood trail required that a given individual place a fair amount of their own blood on the body of another being. This blood was tainted in such a way that it could not be scrubbed off, but appeared to the victim to be a strange bruise. By following the trail of this blood, the seeker could track the victim across great distances, although accuracy decreased as the victim traveled farther.

**Bloor, Melvosh** A Kalkal academic, he was a professor of investigative politico-sociology at Beshka University. His colleague, Professor P'tan, had traveled to the palace of Jabba the Hutt but never returned, so Melvosh Bloor went to investigate. He was led on by Jabba's annoying pet, Salacious Crumb, and eventually brought before Jabba, who promptly fed him to the rancor.

**blope** Swamp creatures much like hippopotamuses, they lived in the marshes of Endor's Forest Moon.

**blorash jelly** A Yuuzhan Vong–bioengineered organic weapon, this living viscous substance was binding. Tossed onto the floor like a gooey pie, it could reach up, grab, and adhere to opponents. Though it could be easily sliced by a lightsaber, each piece continued to move and grab. Blorash jelly also could be used to hold prisoners in place. The Jedi used arsensalts to counter the adhesive effects of the jelly.

*Deliah Blue*

**Blorga** A Gamorrean with a double-spike hammer that fought against Asajj Ventress in the gladiator pits of Rattatak.

**Blotus the Hutt** An ancient Supreme Chancellor of the Republic who served for 275 years during what would later be known as the Rianitus period.

**Blount, Lieutenant** A crew member aboard the *Millennium Falcon* during the Battle of Endor, he was a former agent of the Imperial Security Bureau until he defected and joined Alliance Intelligence. He was a seasoned combat veteran.

**Blue, Anchor** A fierce Houk gladiator with a frenzy-triggering implant concealed within the vibroblade attachment that replaced his amputated hand. His Rattataki patron used a remote to drive Blue into violent rages, or to calm him down with a chemical reservoir that pumped powerful sedatives into his bloodstream.

**Blue, Deliah** A skilled mechanic and a stunning Zeltron beauty who was part of Cade Skywalker's crew, she kept the *Mynock* running despite a constant lack of credits. She wanted to get as close to Cade as she was to his ship, feeling an innate need to "fix" whatever it was that was "broken" within him.

**Blue, Sinewy Ana** A beautiful smuggler, she ran the sabacc games on Skip 1 in the asteroid field known as Smuggler's Run. Han Solo won a lot of credits in her games and also once lost his *Millennium Falcon* there. Sinewy Ana Blue piloted a Skipper, modified for her personal needs, with a wider cargo bay and larger crew quarters than normal Skippers, which were used mainly for transit in Smuggler's Run. Blue's Skipper was used during Han Solo's investigation into the Senate Hall bombing on Coruscant and the rescue of Lando Calrissian from the crime lord Nandreeson.

Later, Solo learned that Blue was part of a smuggling operation that sold former Imperial goods to the dark sider Kueller for use in his reign of terror against the New Republic. She had become seduced by the enormous number of credits she got through the operation. Kueller later ordered her to bring Solo to Almania, where he was to be used in a blackmail demand against New Republic Chief of State Leia Organa Solo. Davis, a man whom Blue secretly loved, was killed in one of Kueller's bombing attacks, and she then told Solo everything she knew about the operation. When Solo learned that Kueller was behind the Coruscant bombing, he rushed to Almania, and Kueller paid Blue double her fee even though she had only inadvertently delivered Solo to him.

**Blue Brubb** A cantina in Mos Espa on Tatooine that sold ruby bliels and other beverages. It was located in a portion of town once controlled by Jabba the Hutt.

**Blue Desert People** *See* Kwi.

***Blue Flame*** A Chiss clawcraft that Jagged Fel flew at the Chiss military academy, it was painted silver-blue in order to hide its many dents and scratches. When a pirate ship crashed into the academy, Fel took the ship into combat in an attempt to deceive the enemy into underestimating the strength of the forces there. He single-handedly took on a group of X-wings and a battered corvette, though his hyperdrive was disabled early on in the attack. In the heat of battle, he deliberately crash-landed the *Blue Flame* to lure the pirates onto the surface.

**blueleaf** A common shrub with a spicy scent, native to Yavin 4. Its essential oil was a stimulant with perception-enhancing qualities. Blueleaf grew to a height of about 1 meter and spread across Yavin 4 like a weed.

**Blue Max** A tiny computer probe developed by the outlaw techs working for Klaus "Doc" Vandangate and his daughter Jessa. They packed and enhanced as much illegal circuitry and computing power as they could into a tiny unassuming blue cube. The little self-aware droid started its mechanical life as an Imperial MerenData B2-X computer probe, but ended up in the hands of a bounty hunter who unwittingly handed over the slicer's dream to Doc as payment.

As an Imperial model, the B2-X had a brusque personality, but Doc's outlaw techs corrected that flaw and created Blue Max. The end result was a precocious, perky, and chipper personality that, when coupled with a higher-pitched vocoder, gave Blue Max the demeanor of a mischievous child.

Since Blue Max had no means of locomotion, the outlaw techs fitted a special cradle hidden within the chest cavity of the labor droid Bollux. Together, Blue Max and Bollux became counterparts and friends, the well-traveled older droid becoming a mentor to the eager rambunctious youth. The computer droid processed data that it scanned through a glowing red photoreceptor and interpreted through a speech synthesizer. It was equipped with a set of computer probes for interfacing with a variety of networks. Its processors and software could slice through some of the most hardened CSA security systems.

Blue Max was vital in Han Solo's mission to rescue prisoners from the CSA Stars' End prison facility. Together their heroism earned Blue Max and Bollux their freedom from the outlaw techs. The two droids agreed to work for Han Solo for a time afterward, in exchange for transport.

**blue milk** A nutrient-rich beverage, it was common in moisture-farming communities. Rumored to have medicinal qualities, it was popular in cantinas among those who couldn't hold their juri juice. The drink got its name from the main ingredient and the color it became after mixing. It was used to make blue yogurt.

Blurrg

**Blue Nebula** A seedy cantina and restaurant, it was located in the Manda spaceport.

**Bluescale** *See* Sh'tk'ith, Elder.

***Blue Slipper*** A Batag needle ship, part of the small fleet of personal starships that were maintained by the Hapan royal family. The ship, which was equipped with a prototype hull scrubber security and anti-theft system, was allocated to Tenel Ka's cousins, Trista and Taryn, when they were dispatched to recover Ben Skywalker. Skywalker had escaped from Tahiri Veila on Coruscant, shortly after the Second Battle of Fondor.

**Blue Squad** The designation for the 24 Bothan pilots and gunners assigned to Luke Skywalker to attack the *Suprosa,* a freighter carrying an Imperial computer containing information about a top-secret project that turned out to be the second Death Star. The Blue Squad pilots had little experience flying their Y-wing fighters, and—unbeknownst to the Rebel Alliance—the *Suprosa* had augmented shields and hidden weapons. The freighter's cannons destroyed two Y-wings and their crews, and a shielded missile exploded in the midst of the squad, destroying another four ships before the freighter was captured. Those Bothans who fell are often referred to as "the Martyrs."

**Blue Squadron** A common designation for starfighter squadrons, Blue Squadrons included: (1) a V-19 Torrent starfighter squadron led by Ahsoka Tano during the Clone Wars; (2) an X-wing fighter squadron stationed at the Rebel base on Yavin 4; (3) one of the many A-wing and B-wing starfighter squadrons at the Battle of Endor; (4) a New Republic X-wing battle group at the Battle of Mon Calamari; (5) an X-wing squadron stationed aboard the cruiser-carrier *Thurse* during the Yuuzhan Vong War.

**Blue Wing** The designation for Blue Leader's second in command at the Battle of Endor, as well as the name of the battle wing itself, Blue Wing was responsible for coordinating several of the battle groups.

**blumfruit** A delicacy to the Ewoks, this large, red, egg-shaped berry grew on blumbushes on Endor's Forest Moon and elsewhere. The Gungans of Naboo used fermented blumfruit juice as both a disinfectant and a powerful adhesive.

**blurrg** The beast of burden for the Marauders of Endor, this stupid creature was controlled with a spiked chain bridle. The Marauders rode blurrgs and used them to pull carts. The egg-laying creatures produced five or six young at a time. Though not carnivorous, blurrgs did have powerful jaws for rending apart trees and other hard plants. They were often preyed upon by boar-wolves. Their simple intellect, awkward gait, and odd appearance made them objects of derision in Ewok folklore.

**Bly, Clone Commander** Clone Commander 5052, leader of the 327th Star Corps of clone troopers assigned to Jedi General Aayla Secura. He was one of the first generation of clone commanders to be trained by the ARC trooper Alpha. Though the clone commanders demonstrated greater creativity and individuality, Bly was nonetheless a product of an artificial upbringing, and his conditioning made him preternaturally loyal to the Republic. During a mission to Honoghr, when the Jedi turncoat Quinlan Vos struck up a makeshift alliance with Secura to recover vital Separatist data from the poisoned planet, Bly had difficulty working with the traitorous Vos. He nonetheless followed Secura's orders to respect the truce, internalizing his misgivings and carrying out commands to the letter.

Bly and the Star Corps served with Secura on tours that took them to New Holstice, Endor, Honoghr, Anzat, and Saleucami. The constant reassignments occasionally wore on his longing for closure—a trait peculiar to Bly and shared by Aayla. Bly preferred to complete missions that he started, but nonetheless obediently followed orders to ship off elsewhere when needed. He was serving with her on the exotic world of Felucia when he received Order 66. The executive command, originating from the Supreme Chancellor on Coruscant, identified Secura as a traitorous enemy of the state. Demonstrating his unswerving loyalty to the Republic, Bly and his troopers raised their

Clone Commander Bly

rifles and opened fire on their commanding officer, coldly killing the unsuspecting Jedi.

**Bnach** The site of an Imperial prison colony, this scorched planet with a cracked surface provided plenty of rock quarries for prison labor.

**Bnar, Master Ood** An ancient Jedi who lived well over 5,000 years before the birth of Luke Skywalker, Ood was a Neti, a humanoid species from Ryyk that had evolved from trees on the planet Myrkr. He eventually became the gatekeeper of a Jedi Holocron belonging to Master Arca Jeth and proclaimed that Nomi Sunrider would one day become a powerful Jedi. He also advised Ulic Qel-Droma when the Jedi Knight foolishly planned to join the evil Krath cult in order to destroy it from within. During the Sith War, when the cataclysm that destroyed the Cron Cluster threatened the planet Ossus, Ood initiated a life-cycle change, transforming into a mighty tree with extended roots to protect an underground cache of ancient lightsabers. Before doing so, he bequeathed the Solari crystal, a lightsaber component, to his most gifted student, Shaela Nuur.

Several thousand years later on the planet Ossus, Bnar reawakened to help save Jem Ysanna, a young woman with powers of the Force. He ultimately sacrificed himself to destroy the evil Imperial Military Executor Sedriss. Luke Skywalker discovered the trove of lightsabers and Jedi lore that Ood protected, treasures that proved valuable as he built a new Jedi Order to protect the galaxy.

Ood originally was a bipedal being with rough greenish brown skin, root-like appendages dangling from the back of his head, and no visible eyes. By the time he reappeared, he had evolved into a towering, tree-like entity. His limbs were similar to tentacles and he had wise blue eyes.

*Master Ood Bnar*

**boarding craft** A term applied to small vehicles used to ferry personnel or cargo between spaceships or between ships and planets or space stations.

**boar-wolf** A large carnivore on Endor also known as the borra, the boar-wolf had tusk teeth, a keen sense of smell, and saber-like claws that could tear holes in trees. Though borras were three times as tall as Ewoks, the Ewoks devised clever traps to capture them. One could provide enough meat to feed an Ewok tree village for days. They usually hunted in pairs and were semi-domesticated as pets by the giant Gorax.

**Bobb, Feskitt** A Mandallian Giant, Bobb was an accomplished and ruthless hunter, famous for capturing the notorious serial killer Kardem. Bobb also occasionally took on special assignments for the Empire. On one such job in the Crystal Forests of Goratak III, a lucky shot from a Rebel abruptly ended Bobb's career.

*Boga, a trusty mount for Obi-Wan Kenobi on Utapau*

**Bobek** An aspiring Rebel from Dubrava, he sought out recruiter and washed-up pilot Jal Te Gniev in the hope of joining the Rebel Alliance. The cruel Gniev humiliated Bobek rather than take his request seriously. Bobek acquired a blaster pistol, hoping to kill Gniev, but he instead shot a stormtrooper who was about to take Gniev's life. Bobek was killed by Imperial stormtroopers before he could realize his dream, but his action inspired Gniev to pull his act together.

**Bobissia, Ony** A Triffian patron who frequented Dex's Diner on Coruscant.

**Bobolo Baker's All-Bith Band** A band that played at the Big Boom cantina on Nova Station while Han and Leia Organa Solo were there during the war against the Yuuzhan Vong.

**Boc** *See* Aseca, Boc.

**bocatt** A tusked, leather-skinned predator found on Tatooine.

**Bocce** A trade language developed by Baobab merchants, it was one of the many languages used on Tatooine. It was also spoken in the Albarrio sector capital world of Aris.

**Boda, Ashka** An old Jedi librarian who worked alongside Yaddle in the Librarians' Assembly at the Jedi Temple. During the rise of the Empire, Boda was caught and executed by Emperor Palpatine, allowing the Sith Lord to capture a valued Jedi Holocron.

**Bodgen** *See* Bogden.

**Bodonawieedo, Doda** A Rodian slitherhorn player, he was a part-time member of the Max Rebo Band. Born aboard a transport shuttle in space, Doda grew up in the streets of Mos Eisley. In addition to being a musician, he was an information broker and founding member of the Shawpee street gang. He stole the Minstrel and the Dancing Goddess statues from Jabba the Hutt, selling them for a tidy profit.

**Body Calculus** Ruling body of the Givin on Yag'Dhul, it supported the Confederacy during the Clone Wars.

**bodyguard droid** *See* IG 100 MagnaGuard droid.

**body-wood** From a tree of the same name, this incredible wood resembled the flesh of forest dwellers from the planet Firrerre. Known as the finest wood in the Empire, its polished surface was the palest pink, shot through with scarlet streaks and gleaming with light like cut and polished precious stones. Some said that body-wood trees had a certain intelligence and "cried" when felled; adding to the story was the fact that the cut wood bled a scarlet liquid.

**Boelo** Naroon Cuthus's predecessor as Jabba's right-hand man, he accompanied Jabba the Hutt to Docking Bay 94 to confront Han Solo. Boelo had a pet womp rat named Worra.

**Boeus sector** A sector in the Expansion Region in the direction of Wroona. Moff Darvon Jewett allied with the New Republic after the Imperial military withdrew following the Battle of Endor.

**bofa** A sweet dried fruit, bofa was considered a delicacy.

**Boga** The female varactyl lizard that Obi-Wan Kenobi rode while in search of General Grievous on Utapau during the Clone Wars.

**Bogan, Biggs** A shuttle pilot aboard the *MedStar Nineteen* during the Clone Wars.

*Doda Bodonawieedo plays at Jabba's palace.*

**Bogan's Brown nafen** A species of winged rodents popularly known as butterbats. They were found on a number of tropical planets, where they consumed huge amounts of insects and small creatures. Since they were the carriers of a variety of diseases, they were deemed a nuisance to be eliminated on many worlds.

**Bogden** A swampy, uninhabited world located in the Inner Rim, its surface was dotted by ruins. The world served as a battleground for a 1,000-year interplanetary war over control of the system in which it resided. A vast ring of debris orbited the planet, comprising hundreds of thousands of tattered battleships. The planet had over 19 moons, many capable of sustaining life. Some of its moons were numerically named—Bogg 2, 4, 9, and 11, for instance—while others had more unique names, like Kohlma. The moons of Bogden were a haven for outlaws. Couriers used the strange gravity pulls of the different satellites to travel from moon to moon. Jango Fett was hired by Darth Tyranus on the moons of Bogden to become the template of the clone army. During the early days of the Empire, R2-D2 and C-3PO visited the bog moon. At the time, pirate captain Kybo Ren held Princess Gerin of Tammuz-an on a freighter hidden there.

**Bogen, Senator Ab'el** A New Republic Senator and member of the Senate Defense Council, he was a human from the planet Ralltiir. He was one of six members of the Security and Intelligence Council who heard Belindi Kalenda's report regarding the assassination attempt on Elan on Wayland.

**bogey** A glittering, formless creature that inhabited the spice mines of Kessel. Bogeys were the main diet of the native energy spiders, whose webs yielded the drug known as glitterstim. Bogeys fed on energy and were drawn to areas of light and activity, hence they were sometimes seen by miners. They sped through the tunnels, making a humming or chittering sound as they went, setting off showers of sparks when they contacted the veins of glitterstim in the rock walls. They bounced from wall to wall randomly, finally plunging into portions of rock that were clear of glitterstim. Unfortunately their predators followed them, and were known to attack the workers who got in their way.

**Bogga the Hutt** *See* Great Bogga the Hutt.

**bogwings** Flying pterodactyl-like carnivores native to Dagobah, they glided through the swamps in search of reptiles, rodents, large insects, and other prey.

**Boiny** A Rodian terrorist and part of the Nebula Front, he was one of the few members of Captain Cohl's team to survive the infiltration of the Trade Federation freighter *Revenue.* He later took part in an assassination plot on Eriadu that targeted Chancellor Valorum. When fellow Front member Eru Matalis turned against Cohl's team, Boiny sustained a shot to the side of the head but survived. Boiny then worked with Qui-Gon Jinn to stop Matalis, but was shot and killed.

**Bok** A Kajain'sa'Nikto who, like his father Tsyr, was a Morgukai warrior in the final years of the Galactic Republic. They were hired by con man Vilmarh Grahrk and Ro Fenn to abduct Twi'lek prime heir Nat Secura. With cortosis-based weapons and armaments in their arsenal, Tsyr and Bok were particularly adept at dealing with Jedi adversaries who crossed their paths, such as Quinlan Vos and Aayla Secura, who caught up with the Morgukai warriors on their homeworld of Kintan. Bok's impetuous nature was nearly his undoing, as he became stranded on a lava floe and had his arm amputated by Secura. Tsyr was beheaded by Vos, giving Bok further reason to hate the Jedi. During the Clone Wars, Count Dooku hired Bok as a mercenary warrior, equipping him with a prosthetic arm. The Separatist Sora Bulq used Bok as the template for a cloned Shadow Army of Morgukai warriors based on Saleucami. Aayla Secura was finally able to end Bok's life near the tail end of the Clone Wars.

**Bok, Aidan** A Jedi tasked with guarding the ancient Jedi library on Nespis VIII, he was killed by Darth Vader during the rise of the Empire. Ashamed at his failure to protect the trove of Jedi knowledge, Aidan's spirit remained at Nespis VIII, appearing to others sensitive to the Force. When he helped Tash Arranda escape the clutches of evil scientist Borborygmus Gog, Bok felt he had atoned for his past, and finally became one with the Force.

**Bok, Captain** The Mon Calamari commander of the cruiser *Grey Damsel.* During the Dark Trooper attack on Talay's Tak Base, Captain Bok and the *Grey Damsel* lifted off into space in the hope of warning the Alliance. All aboard the ship were killed by a Dark Trooper who stowed aboard.

**bol** A four-legged milk-producing creature found on Dantooine and often used as a mount.

**B'olba** A Quarren aide to Senator Tikkes prior to the Clone Wars.

**BolBol the Hutt** A Hutt crime lord, he controlled much of the Stenness system.

**Bold, Dorovio** A female Rebel X-wing pilot who flew at the Battle of Endor, she was a top cadet at the Academy. She joined the Rebellion upon learning of Alderaan's destruction.

**Bold, Nella** Daughter of Orin Bold, she was about 20 years old when she met Obi-Wan Kenobi and Qui-Gon Jinn. After her father told the Jedi about the unscrupulous activities of local land baron Taxer Sundown, Nella agreed to fly Obi-Wan and Qui-Gon aboard her modified T-24 airspeeder to Sundown's headquarters. En route she displayed her hatred of Mantellian savrips because they killed her mother. As the group approached Sundown's headquarters, they were ambushed by Sundown's soldiers, and Nella was abducted. Before Sundown's men could kill her, though, Mantellian savrips arrived to save her. She later learned that her hatred was all the more misplaced because it was Sundown who was truly responsible for her mother's death.

***Boldheart*** A New Republic *Corona*-class frigate, it encountered the mysterious ghost ship called the *Teljkon Vagabond,* took its picture, and fired across its bow before being crippled by return fire and jumping into hyperspace.

***Bolide*** A Republic Acclamator troop transport that was lost at Duro during the Clone Wars.

**Bollux** A battered 100-year-old BLX-5 labor droid, its systems were upgraded by Jessa, the daughter of an outlaw tech named Doc who lived on an asteroid in the Corporate Sector. Bollux's chest cavity was modified so that it could carry Blue Max, a powerful but tiny computer housed in a deep-blue cube. Both had been programmed with personalities, Bollux pleasant and low-key, Blue Max more high-strung and chirpy. For a time the duo accompanied Han Solo and Chewbacca in their adventures in the Corporate Sector, including the rescue of Doc from a penal colony and Han's search for a long-lost treasure ship.

**bolo-ball** A popular sport known as limmie outside the Core.

**Bolpa, Mosko** A wounded Moggonite who was nursed to health on the planet Arorua by Qui-Gon Jinn. He later turned on the Jedi, leading a Moggonite ambush that Qui-Gon put down easily; Mosko was killed by Jinn.

**Bolpuhr** A Noghri bodyguard of Leia Organa Solo, he accompanied her on her diplomatic mission to Rhommamool and Osarian. Bolpuhr died while saving her from an attack by Yuuzhan Vong warriors on Dantooine.

**bolstyngar** A quiet, 4-meter tall, cream- or green-brown-colored predator found in Kashyyyk's lower levels. It had sensitive hearing and got annoyed by loud creatures such as grove harriers.

*Bollux*

**Bolt, Dud** A Vulptereen Podracer, he was a thug who served as Sebulba's midair bodyguard, ramming contenders out of the way to give the Dug a clear path to victory. Sebulba paid Bolt a bonus for any racer he brought down. During the Boonta Eve Podrace that won Anakin Skywalker his freedom, Dud collided with Ark "Bumpy" Roose and needed to recover in a Mos Espa medcenter. Sebulba eventually replaced him with Aldar Beedo.

**Boltrunian** A tough, intelligent green-skinned species. Members included swoop rider Warto and the Dark Jedi Maw.

**Bolvan, Captain** Gunnery captain of the *Devastator,* he was the commanding officer when Darth Vader ordered the destruction of a biological weapons lab on Falleen, resulting in the death of many.

**boma beasts** A species of monstrous, wingless beasts that thrived on Dxun and in the forests of Onderon 4,000 years before the Battle of Yavin. Boma beasts had green reptilian hides, long tails, four horns, dagger-like claws, and savage teeth. They were used by the beast-riders to guard the stronghold of Beast-Lord Modon Kira.

**B'omarr monks** A mysterious sect of religious fanatics, the B'omarr monks constructed monasteries throughout the galaxy, including on Tatooine and Teth. Jabba the Hutt's palace was a reclaimed and expanded monastery. B'omarr monks believed that enlightenment could be found only by severing one's ties to physical sensation. Thus, when a B'omarr reached the final stage of enlightenment, his brain was removed and placed in a small tank filled with nutrients. In order to travel the corridors of Jabba's palace, enlightened monks had access to mechanical droid walkers resembling large, steel spiders.

Even before they were converted into so-called brain spiders, B'omarr monks rarely spoke to one another. Often, entire lectures were contained in a single phrase or word. As the monks continued down their path of enlightenment, they rarely talked or even moved. Thus, by the time a B'omarr monk's brain was removed, he was already well prepared for the transformation. Bib Fortuna underwent an unwilling removal of his brain after the collapse of Jabba's crime empire, though he was able to use his cunning to reverse this situation.

B'omarr monk

**bomats** Small carnivorous pests, they were native to the planet Aruza.

**Bombaasa, Crev** This crime lord was a vicious yet cultured Corellian who ran most of the illegal operations in the Kathol sector. A subcontractor for the Hutts, he oversaw shipments to Tynna and Bothawui. Although he spent much of his life in the Pembric system, he was stationed on Ryloth during the war against the Yuuzhan Vong when he met with Talon Karrde's group. He had orders from Borga the Hutt to suspend operations to Tynna, Bothawui, and Corellia. He was a short, pudgy human with stick-like limbs, giving him an odd, beetle-like appearance.

**Bombaasa, Ulfor** A Galaxies Opera House patron on Coruscant who attended a performance of *Squid Lake* during the Clone Wars.

***Bombard*** Along with the *Crusade,* it was one of the two *Victory*-class Star Destroyers that utterly wiped out the Eyttyrmin Batiiv pirate stronghold on Khuiumin.

**bomblet** A tiny spherical bomb small enough to fit in the palm of the hand. The Republic used these explosives during the Clone Wars.

**Bomis Koori IV** One of a pocket of Koorivar colony worlds defended by the Separatists during the Clone Wars, it was the site of very productive droid factories within the Mid Rim. Corporate Alliance General Oro Dassyne built up an extremely well-defended bulwark on Bomis Koori IV that ultimately failed to stop Obi-Wan Kenobi and Anakin Skywalker from infiltrating and lowering the defenses.

**Bômlas** An infamous bartender on Skip 1, he was a three-armed Ychthytonian who bet and lost his fourth arm in a particularly savage sabacc game. Still, even with only three arms, Bômlas remained the fastest bartender Han Solo had ever seen.

**Bompreil** The site of a battle early in the Galactic Civil War.

**Bonadan** A parched yellow sphere crisscrossed by rust stripes because of heavy soil erosion, this planet had long been one of the Corporate Sector Authority's most important factory worlds and busiest ports. Bonadan industry thrived at the expense of ecology, since any plant life on the surface that wasn't intentionally destroyed disappeared due to overmining, pollution, and neglect. A densely populated planet, Bonadan housed many sentient species from all over the galaxy. The world was covered with factories, refineries, docks, and shipbuilding facilities in 10 spaceports, the largest of which was Bonadan Spaceport Southeast II. This sprawling city was composed of low permacite buildings on fusion-formed soil. Mountains were located northwest of the city, along with a massive weather-control station.

Anoon Bondara

Weapons were banned on Bonadan; being caught with one by the omnipresent weapons detectors was grounds for immediate arrest. The modified protocol droid C-3PX managed to assassinate the brother of Vojak on Bonadan by using concealed internal weaponry. Han Solo was involved in a high-speed swoop chase during an early visit to the planet. The smuggler Shug Ninx scavenged a kilometer-long shaft for a Death Star prototype from a Bonadan industrial junkyard, then had it installed as an entrance to his repair facility on Nar Shaddaa. Six years after the Battle of Endor, a faulty timer manufactured on Bonadan resulted in the failure of a Galaxy Gun projectile to explode, which gave the New Republic High Command enough time to evacuate its base on Nespis VIII. During the Yuuzhan Vong invasion, executives from the Corporate Sector Authority were bought off by the Yuuzhan Vong, despite their neutral stance with the New Republic.

**Bondar crystal** This crystal was mined on a far-orbit asteroid circling the Alderaan system. It produced a volatile lightsaber beam that pulsed on impact, potentially stunning an opponent.

**Bondara, Anoon** This Twi'lek Jedi Master—always one to chafe at rules and restrictions—was regarded as one of the best fighters and duel instructors in the Jedi Order. Around the time of the Battle of Naboo, he was in his late 40s, and his fourth Padawan was Darsha Assant. The Jedi Council assigned Darsha to bring an informant named Oolth from the dangerous Crimson Corridor section of Coruscant to the Jedi Temple, even though Bondara felt the mission to be too dangerous. Darsha failed to capture Oolth alive, and she and her Master journeyed to the Crimson Corridor to confirm Oolth's death. On their return to the Temple, they sensed a disturbance in the Force—which turned out to be the doing of Sith Lord Darth Maul. The Dark Lord gave pursuit, and Bondara bravely leapt from his skycar to Maul's speeder to confront the Sith Lord. Seeing that he could not hope to defeat Maul, Bondara sabotaged Maul's speeder and died when caught in the resulting explosion.

**Bondo** The chubby, easygoing chief of the nomadic Jinda tribe, he usually wore a red tunic.

**bond-wife** A female Cerean who was married to a Cerean male and was often considered the "true" or first wife. Because females outnumbered males nearly 20 to 1 on Cerea, polygamy became a necessity. Most males married a bond-wife, and then took several "honor-wives" as well.

**Bonearm, Dace** An unsavory human bounty hunter, he traveled with an IG-model assassin droid.

**Bonearm, Uz** A smuggler at the Byss Bistro who helped Shug Ninx, Salla Zend, and the New Republic during the resurrected Emperor's campaign of terror, he flew an agile Corellian ship called the *Bespin Bandit.*

**bonegnawer** An enormous flying carnivorous bird that lived in the desert wastelands of Tatooine, its toothy jaws could crush rocks. It had a wingspan of 8 to 10 meters. A male bonegnawer's wings ranged in hue from deep purple to bright blue; females had golden or sandy-colored wings. Both were marked by a signature crimson crest. Their diet consisted of large rodents, young banthas, young cliffborer worms, and even humanoids. Bonegnawers could be trained from an early age as excellent hunter and guard animals.

**Bonestar pirates** A Corellian group once led by Loka Hask while fleeing from Corellian authorities, these pirates destroyed the Gus Treta fuel depot, resulting in the deaths of Zena and Jagged Antilles.

**boneworm** A subterranean scavenger found on Necropolis that searched for food by following tremors from within the ground. If those tremors stopped for an extended period, the boneworm burrowed upward to grab its prey, using its powerful jaws to rend flesh and crack open bones so it could suck out the marrow. Boneworms ranged in size from a few centimeters to just over a meter in length. Their skin was an off-white color, and they constantly secreted slime in order to more easily move through their burrowed tunnels. Their mouths were lamprey-like suction cups, but they could contract muscles and jut forward hard, bone-like spurs that aided them in tunneling, tearing flesh, and cracking open bones or coffins.

***Boneyard Rendezvous*** A 100-meter-long bulk freighter operated by Byalfin Dyur and his band of pirates in the years following the Swarm War.

**Bongomeken Cooperative** A coalition of Gungan engineers based out of Otoh Gunga dedicated to producing bongos and other vessels for the Gungans. Located on the fringes of the city, the cooperative grew bongo hulls in expansive underwater farms. The skeletal structures were harvested, then fitted with a combination of Gungan and Naboo technology. Each bongo was individually crafted and designed, but while no two vehicles looked alike, certain designers had signature styles. The cooperative survived the invasion of Naboo, and soon thereafter began experimenting with larger designs fit for use as starships.

**bongo submarine** A Gungan underwater transport manufactured by the Bongomeken Cooperative. The squid-like bongos were propelled by rotating tentacles powered by an electromotive field motor. Their organically grown hulls were durable, but no match for the fangs of Naboo's gigantic sea monsters.

**Bonkik, Pax and Trax** Rodian brothers who were part of Mars Guo's pit crew during the Boonta Eve Classic Podrace.

**Bontormian klesplong** An exotic musical instrument consisting of a subwoofer base, troomic sound tube, Xloff horn, Plandl horn, sounding cymbal, resonator, and radion modulator. Ak-rev, the Weequay drummer of the Max Rebo Band, had one as part of his drum kit.

**Booda, Fenn** The strict warden of the Galactic Correctional Authority's penal and labor colony on Oovo 4. Occasionally, Fenn Booda allowed a Podrace through his prison as a reward to inmates for their hard work. He oversaw Aurra Sing's arrival at the prison, when she attempted to strike a deal with the warden by revealing who was illegally hiring bounty hunters to hunt down Jedi.

**Boog** A crew member aboard the smuggling ship *Port-Esta Queen.* Boba Fett questioned the crew during his hunt for Imperial Colonel Abal Karda. Boog attempted to drop a heavy crate of kneebs on the bounty hunter, but Fett dodged the trap and killed Boog instead.

***Book of Law, The*** A collection of writings first penned by Allya, the book became the source of the Singing Mountain Clan's basic tenets. Much of *The Book of Law* was based on the Jedi Code, but was altered to account for the situation of the Force witches on Dathomir. Foremost among the laws was the tenet "Never concede to evil." Over time, other clan leaders modified the book for their own use, and the original *Book of Law* was all but forgotten.

**Booldrum** A cousin of Gerney Caslo, Booldrum owned a library in Hweg Shul on Nam Chorios bigger than that of strongman Seti Ashgad.

**Boon, Brookish** A Sy Myrthian, he was a cantankerous, opinionated com-host on Coruscant during the Clone Wars.

**Boonda the Hutt** A "reformed" Hutt and the son of Groodo, he was the target of a droid rebellion led by C-3PO. Threepio was not only reprogrammed to be brave but also programmed with misleading information implicating Boonda in a plot to plant secret explosives in droids. But the true perpetrator of the plot, Movo Brattakin, was exposed, and C-3PO and R2-D2 managed to beat a hasty exit.

**Boonta** A planet in the Dernatine system famous for its speeder races in oval tunnels, it also housed a huge scrap yard that was a graveyard for damaged ships. Its actual name was Ko Vari, but the Boonta nickname—a Hutt appellation—was meant to cash in on the popularity of Podracing.

*Bongo submarine*

Boonta Eve Classic

**Boonta Eve Classic** A popular Podrace event hosted by Jabba the Hutt in the Mos Espa Grand Arena on the Boonta Eve holiday. The three-lap race traveled through tunnels, over drops, and across the desert in Tatooine. Challengers from racing circuits all over the galaxy, professional and amateur, converged to take part. Anakin Skywalker won his freedom from slavery in the Boonta Eve Classic.

**Boordii** A temperate planet whose central source of income was from smugglers transporting contraband offworld. It was located in the Sumitra sector.

**Boorka the Hutt** A Hutt rival to Jabba the Hutt on Tatooine near Mos Osnoe, he allied himself with Sev'Rance Tann during the Clone Wars.

**Boorn, Keog** A scout who surveyed uninhabited parts of the Sluis sector, including Dagobah.

**Boost** The nickname of a clone trooper aboard a Republic cruiser attacked by the *Malevolence* during the Clone Wars.

**bora** Five- to six-hundred-meter-tall trees found on Zonama Sekot. The bora life cycle began with an ambulatory seed, which crawled into the forest and took root. Sprouting iron tips, boras could summon lightning from the clouds, which burned the surrounding forest and cooked the seeds to create puffed-out bubbles. Other boras called annealers with long, spade-like shaping arms sculpted the resulting plants. Boras had limited telepathic abilities, forming a strange organic communications network across the living planet.

**Borao** A planet ravaged and abandoned by the Yuuzhan Vong, it was adopted as the new Ithorian homeworld within the Galactic Alliance.

**Boras, Senator Fyg** Galactic representative of Vortex in the New Republic Senate. During the war against the Yuuzhan Vong, his world came under attack by the alien invaders. Boras agreed to support the appropriations of YVH droids from Lando Calrissian in exchange for 25 tons of supplies, which Boras could sell for a profit. Lando later blackmailed him into supporting Cal Omas using holos of the original transaction.

**Borcorash** A planet of spectacular sunsets and sunrises due to atmospheric conditions, and home to the blufferavian species of bird. Just prior to the peace treaty that ended the Galactic Civil War between the Imperial Remnant and the New Republic, Mistryl warrior Shada D'ukal had a rendezvous at the Resinem Entertainment Complex there.

**Bordal** Located in the Taroon system on the outer edges of the Rim, this world was involved in a devastating war with its sister planet Kuan for nearly 20 years until the conflict was suddenly ended by the intervention of the Empire. Natives were referred to as Bordali.

**Borderland Regions** A militarized zone that was once between the space ruled by the New Republic and Imperial space. It was claimed by both sides but controlled by neither, and suffered battle after battle in the Galactic Civil War. Systems in the Borderlands made every effort to stay neutral.

**bordok** A medium-sized, pony-like species; Ewoks used bordoks as beasts of burden. Greater bordoks could be up to 3 meters tall, twice the size of the lesser bordok. Bordoks had two horns that curved upward, although the horns of males could grow much larger than those of females. They had long manes, gentle features, and strong backs. They bonded strongly with their owners and were often considered part of the family. Some showed a remarkable degree of intelligence.

**Bordon** A Ruusan native forced to flee the Battle of Ruusan alongside his sons, Tallo and Wind. The family was rescued by Jedi Knights and taken aboard the warship *Fairwind* before the Sith unleashed their devastating thought bomb. Bordon's wife, who had enlisted as a soldier with the Army of Light, had been killed in the fighting during the Fourth Battle of Ruusan. Bordon later volunteered to assist with recovery operations, since he lacked any connection to the Force and was immune to any aftereffects of the thought bomb. Seeking vengeance against the Sith, Bordon was displeased by Jedi Johun Othone's order to rescue any Sith soldiers they encountered.

Bordon and pilot Irtanna found and rescued a young girl named Rain from the battlefields. Unbeknownst to all aboard, Rain was actually Zannah, a Sith Lord in training, and she killed Bordon and his sons before making her way to Onderon to reunite with her new Master, Darth Bane.

An Ewok feeds a bordok.

***Borealis*** Chief of State Leia Organa Solo used this flagship on her private mission to Nam Chorios.

**Borean, Kell** A dark-haired female human who was known to frequent the Outlander Club prior to the Clone Wars.

**Borellos Base** An important Republic base on Corellia during the Clone Wars.

**Borga the Hutt** *See* Diori, Borga Besadii.

**Borgo Prime** A large, honeycombed asteroid, it was home to a seedy spaceport and disreputable trade center. Borgo Prime was gradually hollowed out over the years by mining operations, and the asteroid's tunnels and excavations filled with space docks, prefabricated buildings, and gaudily lit storefronts. In the business district, located in the asteroid's core, was Shanko's Hive, a cone-shaped tavern owned by an insectoid barkeep. The tall structure was protected by its own atmosphere field and filled with burning candles, incense, and flaming bog pits. Lando Calrissian's Corusca gem broker was located on Borgo Prime, and Luke Skywalker and Tenel Ka contacted the broker in an attempt to learn who had purchased an important shipment.

**Borin, Danz** A cocky gunner and bounty hunter, he maintained a residence on the Smugglers' Moon, Nar Shaddaa. He tracked down Han Solo and the *Millennium Falcon* to try to collect the bounty from Jabba the Hutt, but just as he was about to step up and claim his prey in the Mos Eisley cantina, another bounty hunter in Jabba's employ—the Rodian named Greedo—beat him to the punch. That was a good thing, Danz Borin learned just a minute later, as Solo killed Greedo with a blaster shot.

**Borkeen asteroid belt** An asteroid belt and famed navigational hazard.

**Borleias (Blackmoon)** The fourth planet in the Pyria system, it was a steamy blue-green world with a single dark moon that gave the system its Rebel Alliance code name, Blackmoon. The only inhabited world in the system, Borleias lacked most valuable natural resources and passed through a dense meteor shower once each year. Nonetheless, Borleias sat at a favorable hyperspace crossroads, and the Galactic Republic first established a small base there to plot runs to the Corporate Sector and elsewhere. The Empire eventually took control of the base and beefed up its defenses.

Because the Pyria system was near the Galactic Core, the Rebel Alliance chose to capture Borleias and make it a key to hitting Coruscant, some three years after the Battle of Endor. During their first attack, however, the Rebels greatly underestimated the defensive strength of the Blackmoon installation and were soundly defeated. On the return mission, Rogue Squadron pilots torpedoed a power conduit at the end of a rift valley to help bring down the base's shields, while a commando team captured the facility from the ground. This attack was a success, and Borleias became the new operations and staging base for Rogue Squadron.

During the Yuuzhan Vong invasion, Mirax Horn transported some of the many Ithorian survivors to Borleias, and the planet was soon turning away refugees. Mirroring the New Republic's use of the planet as a staging ground years earlier, Borleais was conquered by the Yuuzhan Vong prior to their siege of Coruscant. New Republic forces under the command of Wedge Antilles regrouped and attacked, deciding to hold on to the planet because of its crossroads location, and to make a stand against the alien invasion.

Tsavong Lah ordered the planet retaken, but Czulkang Lah failed after his ground-based invasion force was wiped out by orbital bombardment from the New Republic Star Destroyer *Lusankya.* To ensure the safe evacuation of Borleias, Wedge's forces used tactics such as decoy transponders and gravitic signatures, a fake superweapon dubbed the Starlancer Project, and the *Lusankya* refitted as a battering ram in Operation Emperor's Spear. Antilles withdrew from Borleais with most of his military forces intact. The humiliated Yuuzhan Vong took the planet, but at great cost.

**Borlov** This planet was the homeworld of the timid, feathered creatures known as Borlovians, who communicated in whistles. Borlovians lived in a social structure that valued stability. Few ever left their home cities, much less their planet.

**Bornaryn Trading Company** The corporate name of the Thul family's shipping empire, which became the heart of the Bornaryn Shipping Empire. It grew more powerful in the wake of the Yuuzhan Vong War under the auspices of Lady Aryn Dro Thul. At that time, it had a controlling interest in droid manufacturing titan Industrial Automaton.

**Borno** The leader of a group of Askajian refugees who settled on Tatooine, he later helped Leia Organa Solo and Han Solo seek out a Jawa sandcrawler that they believed held the rare Alderaanian moss-painting *Killik Twilight.*

**Borofir** A male Ghostling who, at three years of age, was kidnapped alongside Princess Arawynne by bounty hunter Djas Puhr for sale in the slave markets of Mos Espa. He had black, curly hair and deep blue eyes.

**Borokii** The most prominent of the Alwari nomad overclans on Ansion. Mistrustful of urban settlers, no chieftain of the Borokii would ever come within a hundred *huus* of Cuipernam, or any other city of the Unity. The clan had thousands of members, and their encampment consisted of hundreds of portable structures laid out like a permanent settlement; several boasted sophisticated energy arrays for power. They traveled with thousands of surepp herd animals. The Borokii were ruled by the Council of Elders, with the Highborn being the leading member. Before the outbreak of the Clone Wars, the Borokii Council of Elders met with Jedi Knights seeking to end a border dispute on Ansion. Before the Borokii would hear the pleas of the Jedi, they asked that the offworlders acquire a handful of wool taken from the ruff of a mature, white male surepp. The Jedi succeeded. After a day's deliberation, the Borokii conceded to the Jedi's request to make peace with the city-folk of the Unity.

**Borosk** One of several small fortified worlds that guarded the edge of the Imperial Remnant during the Yuuzhan Vong invasion. Located near Yaga Minor, it was a relatively small world. A symbolic hold after numerous retreats, it had been heavily armed to ensure that it wasn't retaken by the New Republic, which had in turn armed its own neighboring worlds in case Borosk turned out to be the beginning of another invasion. As a result, the planet was heavily stocked with partially automated planetary turbolasers, ion cannons, and shields, and surrounded by extensive rings of space-based ion mines, all in a constant state of battle readiness. The Imperial Remnant was victorious during its battle there with the Yuuzhan Vong.

**borra** *See* boar-wolf.

**borrat** Fearsome rodent-like creatures from Coruscant, borrats could grow to 2 meters long. They had tusks, spines, armored flesh, and claws that dug through ferrocrete. Fortunately, they tended to be solitary, avoiding contact whenever possible.

**Borstel Galactic Defense** A weapons systems manufacturer whose product catalog included planetary defense ion cannons, starfighter laser cannons, and the NK-7 ion cannons found aboard Imperial Star Destroyers.

**Bortras** Birthplace of Jedi Master Jorus C'baoth, this planet was in the Reithcas sector.

**Bortrek, Captain** The gruff, swaggering, and frequently drunk commander of the ship *Pure Sabacc,* he picked up the droids R2-D2 and C-3PO after they had been set adrift in an escape pod shot from Princess Leia Organa's ship during the Nam Chorios crisis. Captain Bortrek had looted one planet of several million credits in cash, bonds, and valuables. Rather than deliver the droids, he decided to hold them hostage.

**Borvo the Hutt** A young Hutt smuggler who once established an outpost in Naboo's mountains, but struggled to build his criminal empire. He focused largely on shipping contraband throughout the Outer Rim, but also arranged contract work for mercenaries and assassins. When the Trade Federation blockaded Naboo, Borvo was trapped on the planet and quickly developed a profound hatred for the corporation. Borvo agreed to a short-term and tenuous alliance with the Naboo Royal Security Forces to battle the invaders.

**Bos, Cypher** A Nalrithian bounty hunter on Ord Mantell who once tried to capture Han Solo.

**Bos, Lieutenant** He was the flight leader of the ferry operation that was transferring Han Solo when Solo was taken hostage by Yevethan forces.

**BoShek** A Force-sensitive human smuggler and starship technician who flew stolen vessels for a Tatooine order of monks. Shortly before the Battle of Yavin, BoShek and his ship *Infinity* beat Han Solo's time for the Kessel Run, then destroyed four pursuing TIE fighters. He was sought in a large-scale manhunt for his crimes, but eluded capture by masquerading as a religious figure at the monastery. When Ben Kenobi went to the Mos Eisley cantina to find transport off Tatooine, it was

*BoShek*

BoShek who sent the old Jedi to Chewbacca. Six months after the Battle of Yavin, he met up with Rasha Bex, who was fleeing Rebels on Stoga. When Bex revealed herself as an Imperial agent, BoShek chose prison over aiding the Imperials.

**Bosph** Home to four-armed beings known as Bosphs, the planet was nearly destroyed by the Empire in a devastating orbital bombardment. Natives kept a record of their galactic travels by tattooing elaborate star maps on their skin, and were skilled at playing a complex musical instrument, the Bosphon Geddy.

Bossk

**Bossk** A Trandoshan bounty hunter devoted to capturing Wookiees, he spent much of his life in pursuit of the heroic Chewbacca and his partner, Han Solo. Although he managed to corner the pair several times, these encounters always resulted in Bossk's defeat and humiliation. Yet the tenacious and greedy hunter continued his quest undaunted, most often plying the stars in his starship, the *Hound's Tooth*. In common with all members of his species, Bossk exuded a brackish stench, had sensitive eyes, and could regenerate lost limbs. Bossk was so vicious that he even murdered and devoured his father Cradossk, leader of the Bounty Hunters' Guild.

Like most of the bounty hunters hired by Darth Vader to capture Han Solo, Bossk held a special hatred for the smuggler and his Wookiee copilot. Years before the Battle of Hoth, Bossk had become obsessed with capturing and skinning Chewbacca, one of the most feared Wookiees in the galaxy. When he finally cornered Chewie, who was aiding Wookiee slaves, Han Solo intervened and rescued the entire group. Humiliated, Bossk vowed to exact revenge.

After heeding Vader's call, Bossk was led astray by a Wookiee bounty hunter named Chenlambec. Chen claimed to know Chewbacca's location, but he and his human assistant, Tinian I'att, betrayed Bossk and presented the reptiloid to Imperial forces. Bossk then found himself in the clutches of an Imperial governor, who planned to execute the Trandoshan in order to fashion a reptile-skin dress for his wife.

Bossk escaped this fate, and after Boba Fett captured Solo, he reappeared and pursued Fett across the galaxy in an attempt to steal the smuggler's frozen prize. Fett ultimately escaped and delivered Solo to Jabba the Hutt. Bossk then spent some time in Jabba's palace, but fled the Hutt's sail barge before Luke Skywalker and Princess Leia destroyed the craft. Through the years, Bossk continued to hunt the stars, chasing such New Republic luminaries as Lando Calrissian, yet Chewbacca remained his most sought-after quarry. After the death of Chewbacca, Han Solo encountered Bossk at Bet's Off on the *Jubilee Wheel*.

**Bostuco, Captain** A veteran of the Mandalorian Wars, he served as the guard to the Sky Ramp, a passageway leading to the Iziz Royal Palace on Onderon, 4,000 years before the Battle of Yavin.

**Bot** Mysterious and mute, he was the hooded henchman of Captain-Supervisor Grammel on Circarpous V.

**bota** A fungus-like plant native to Drongar and valued for its powerful medicinal effects and ability to increase a Jedi's attunement to the Force. Its fragile nature and volatile mutations meant it could only be harvested on Drongar. During the Clone Wars, this led to intense fighting between Republic and Separatist forces for control of the bota fields.

**Botajef** This world featured great commercial shipyards along its southern continent; they produced such enormous vessels as the AA-9 freighter. Connecting the surface to orbital assembly areas were immense 325-kilometer elevator cables.

**Both, Deneb** A shy Ithorian forester known to frequent the Mos Eisley cantina, she sought to leave Tatooine for a better life elsewhere.

**Bothan** A humanoid species hailing from Bothawui whose members were identified by their stocky builds and fur-covered faces. Bothans were widely known as the galaxy's most proficient spies. The Bothan spynet was among the largest intelligence organizations, with operatives stationed throughout the galaxy. During the Galactic Civil War, the spynet primarily served the Rebel Alliance, although both the Empire and the criminal underworld occasionally made use of Bothan spies as well. They collected information for the Alliance throughout the Galactic Civil War and managed to secure the secret plans for the second Death Star. Although many of the spies died during the Death Star mission, the stolen schematics enabled the Rebel Alliance to plan a successful attack on the battle station at the Battle of Endor.

The Bothan homeworld of Bothawui was a clean, cosmopolitan planet that remained largely neutral throughout the Galactic Civil War. It had long been an active hub for a wide variety of operatives and organizations. Most Bothans lived orderly lives. In even the largest cities, the wide streets were clean and well organized. Buildings were generally huge and constructed of a natural glittering stone. Outside the cities, many Bothans lived in sprawling estates built on open savannas.

Like Wookiees, Bothans valued family bonds and were extremely protective of their allies. Bothans were organized into clans, and used detailed clan sigils to signify a clan's lineage and basic nature. The apostrophe in their surname separated their immediate family name from their clan name. Clan loyalty was of paramount importance, but hostility among clans was common. Bothan politics was known for subtle backstabbing maneuvers. While the Bothans weren't a violent people, their skills at *character* assassination were unparalleled.

The Bothan reputation for skulduggery and deception colored many a being's perception of them. Many openly questioned their involvement in the Imperial trap at Endor. When it was revealed that the Bothans were tangential accomplices in the destruction of the planet Caamas, there was a great uproar demanding that the furred aliens be brought to justice. This political tinderbox threatened to split the New Republic, but cooler heads prevailed.

One of the most famous Bothans was Borsk Fey'lya, a cunning politician who served as Chief of State of the New Republic during the Yuuzhan Vong War. He died a hero in defending Coruscant from invasion. The alien menace caused the Bothan people to rally behind a desperate cause—an Ar'krai—which was nothing short of a genocidal crusade to rid the galaxy of the Yuuzhan Vong.

**Bothan Assault Cruiser** A late capital ship addition to the New Republic fleet. Slightly smaller than a *Victory*-class Star Destroyer, with leaner and less angular lines, it had 20 percent more firepower and almost half again as much shielding and armor. The ship was designed to take a severe pounding and still hammer an enemy. The fighter hangars were amidships and had launch apertures that allowed fighters to head up or down, as needed, to get into battle. The dual launch paths also made it quicker to recover fighters after a battle. The *Ralroost* was a Bothan Assault Cruiser.

Bothan

Bouncers

**Bothan space** An area of the Mid Rim that contained worlds colonized by the Bothans, including their native Bothawui as well as Moonus Mandell and Kothlis.

**Bothan spy network (Bothan spynet)** A network of spies with operatives posted throughout the galaxy. The Empire and the criminal underworld occasionally used the spynet's services, though it mainly supplied the Rebel Alliance with intelligence during the Galactic Civil War. The spynet's missions often put its members at great personal risk, and numerous Bothans were killed while pursuing data on the second Death Star.

**Bothawui** A neutral world encircled by a dense ring of asteroids, it was home to the Bothans. During the New Order, it was the site of a token Imperial presence. This cosmopolitan and well-organized world had always been considered neutral territory, since it had been an active hub for operatives of every stripe. Streets in the major cities were clean and wide, and lined with tall buildings constructed of a naturally glittering stone. Wealthy Bothan landowners lived in estates of open, treeless savanna land. Other notable locales included the Bothan Martial Academy and Mesa 291, an abandoned lidium mine. During the Yuuzhan Vong invasion, the New Republic heavily fortified Bothawui against attack.

**Bothu, Z'meer** One of the many Jedi Masters who remained at the Jedi Temple on Coruscant during the Clone Wars, she was distinguished by her facial makeup, which included a bow-shaped ribbon of red paint across the bridge of her nose. After the death of Master T'chooka D'oon at Vandos, Bothu agreed to take Flynn Kybo as her Padawan. She struggled to calm Kybo's desire to hunt down General Grievous, and spent her initial hours with Kybo simply meditating on the Force. It was during one period of meditation that Bothu overheard Kybo discussing a plan to hunt down Grievous with Jedi Master B'dard Tone. Although she didn't try to stop Kybo from leaving, she made sure he understood that he might be ostracized from the Jedi Order for the attempt.

**Boton, Neibur** A female Zeltron Jedi Knight who died while being interrogated by Inquisitor Tremayne at the dawn of the Empire. Before her death, she provided promising leads on other escaped Jedi.

**Botor Enclave** This group of worlds, including the frozen planet Kerensik, formed its own protective federation during the turmoil and constant warfare in the six years following the Battle of Endor.

**bo'tous** Small, insect-like creatures that propagated through spore-like reproduction, these were assassination weapons engineered by the Yuuzhan Vong. Skillful assassins could carry the spore in their lungs as a host, and then exhale the fast-growing bo'tous at a target.

**Boulanger, Quartermaster Mess** Quartermaster of the clone army serving under Jedi Master Nejaa Halcyon during the Battle of Praesitlyn. An older human, he had bright blue eyes and a drooping brown mustache.

**boulder-dozer** A vehicle that used laser scorchers to vaporize large rocks and other debris.

**bounce** A casino game that used a gun and a moving target suspended inside an enclosed space. To score, hits on the target had to be reflected or bounced off the enclosure; direct hits didn't count.

**Bouncers** Large intelligent globe-like creatures with trailing tentacles, they got their name from their bounding movements along air currents. During the Battle of Ruusan, they grew concerned for the death of their planet's forests as the Sith and the Jedi waged war. They converged on the fields in the aftermath to comfort the dead and dying.

**Bounty Hunters' Creed** Most bounty hunters adhered, to some degree, to an unwritten code of ethics that—when spoken of at all—was referred to as the Bounty Hunters' Creed. While the exact wording of these tenets varied from planet to planet, the gist of the creed is summarized as follows:

- People Don't Have Bounties, Only Acquisitions Have Bounties.
- Capture by Design, Kill by Necessity.
- No Hunter Shall Slay Another Hunter.
- No Hunter Shall Interfere with Another's Hunt.
- In the Hunt One Captures or Kills, Never Both.
- No Hunter Shall Refuse Aid to Another Hunter.

**Bounty Hunters' Guild** A loose organization of bounty hunters that upheld the Bounty Hunters' Creed, monitored its members' activities, and put them in touch with one another. The guild comprised 10 major houses, also referred to as guilds: House Benelex, House Neuvalis, House Paramexor, House Renliss, House Salaktori, House Tresario, Mantis Syndicate, Ragnar Syndicate, Skine Bounty Hunter College, and The Slaver Syndicate. Crimson Nova was a chapter of the Bounty Hunters' Guild that targeted Jedi, particularly during the Clone Wars.

Around the time of the Battle of Naboo, a Trandoshan named Cradossk served as guildmaster. Although a huge number of bounty hunters belonged to the guild, there were a few who chose to operate outside the group. Aurra Sing, for example, was never a member, and Jango Fett declined Cradossk's invitation to join, convinced that the guild consisted of self-congratulating braggarts.

Shortly after the Battle of Yavin, Emperor Palpatine approved a plan to eliminate the guild. Boba Fett was hired to be the agent of the guild's destruction. In a bloody conflict known as the Bounty Hunter Wars, Fett succeeded in fragmenting the organization into innumerable splinter groups and free agents. The True Guild was led by elders from the orginal guild's governing council, while the Guild Reform Committee was led by Bossk.

**Bouri, Omo** A famed Wol Cabasshite Jedi Master who trained Saesee Tiin, he instilled a strong sense of conviction in the Iktochi. After the death of Bouri, 10 years after the Battle of Naboo, Tiin's devotion only increased.

**Boushh** An Ubese bounty hunter and one-time member of the Crimson Nova, he was contracted to work for Prince Xizor's criminal Black Sun organization. Boushh eventually allowed his greed to surpass his good judgment and crossed Black Sun. He attempted to charge Xizor more than he was owed after completing a mission for the group. For this transgression, he was murdered. Princess Leia Organa subsequently assumed Boushh's identity in order to infiltrate Black Sun and, later, Jabba the Hutt's palace. Boushh spoke in a strange, metallic voice and wore a helmet equipped with numerous sensors, a macrobinocular viewplate, and other gadgets.

**Bouyardy, Chief** The systems engineer aboard the *Aurorient Express*, he was attacked by fastlatch droids. He suspected that Waver-

Princess Leia Organa disguised as Boushh

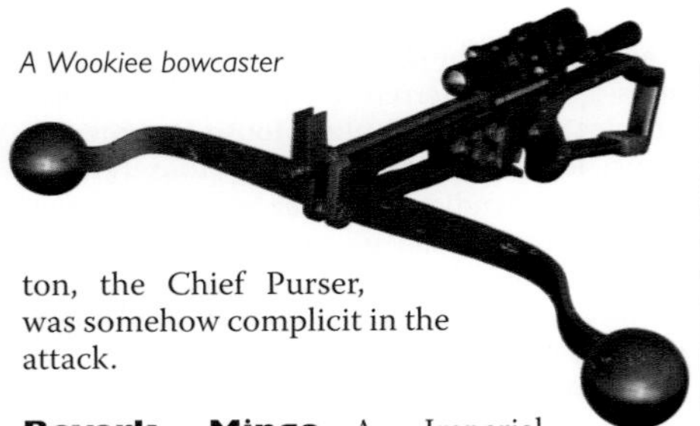
A Wookiee bowcaster

ton, the Chief Purser, was somehow complicit in the attack.

**Bovark, Mingo** An Imperial captain serving in Roan Fel's Empire, Mingo was a Nimbanel member of the Bovark Clan. More a diplomat than a soldier, he remained loyal to Fel's military forces after Darth Krayt usurped control of the Empire, correctly foreseeing that Krayt would have little use for existing Imperial diplomats. Bovark met with Galactic Alliance officer Admiral Gar Stazi at the Wheel space station to discuss an alliance.

**Bovo Yagen** The third star targeted for destruction during the Starbuster crisis some 14 years after the Battle of Endor. The system contained either one planet with a population of 8 million or two planets with 12 million inhabitants, according to varied sources. Other worlds in the system were Marenn Yagen, Trellar Yagen, Framesk Yagen, Tava Yagen, and Heloan Yagen. Bovo Yagen was home to a species of winged mammals called Bovorians. The star was saved at the last instant when Centerpoint Station, the Starbuster weapon, was disabled by a planetary repulsor beam.

**Bow** A hefty man with a sunburned and stubbled farm-boy visage who worked for Salliche Ag on Ruan during the war against the Yuuzhan Vong. Bow, driving a four-seater landspeeder, escorted Han Solo through Salliche Ag's district headquarters when Solo attempted to free a captive Droma.

**Bow, Commander** A clone commander who saved Darth Vader from being killed by Jedi Knights on Kessel after the events of Order 66.

**bowcaster** A melding of varied technologies, this Wookiee crossbow weapon fired energy blasts with explosive force. These weapons were often handcrafted, and varied in size and deadliness. The Wookiee warriors charged with protecting Kashyyyk from the invading forces of the Separatists during the Clone Wars carried large laser crossbows in addition to their rifles and pistols. Later, during the Galactic Civil War, Chewbacca was known to carry a smaller, more highly machined version of the weapon.

A bowcaster was essentially a magnetic accelerator with twin polarizers. Its firing chamber was versatile enough to support both energy quarrel ammunition and solid projectiles, such as explosive-tipped bolts. The weapon required a great deal of strength to simply cock and fire, and its recoil was enough to level weaker beings. In the event that the bowcaster depleted its power pack or suffered some malfunction, a meter-long length of kthysh vine could be attached to the weapon's reserve spring, functioning as a crude bowstring. It could then fire either energy quarrels or wooden crossbow bolts, although the weapon's maximum range was significantly reduced when using this primitive alternative mode.

Wookiees viewed their bowcasters as highly personal possessions. The weapons were bestowed upon young Wookiees as they completed traditional rites of passage into adulthood. Wookiees commonly decorated their bowcasters with clan markings, pictographs, and other engravings celebrating their greatest accomplishments.

**bowlump** A hairy mollusk that lurked just beneath the water's surface on Naboo, it spit a powerful jet of water into the air, striking its prey. The bowlump was able to unhook its stalk from the muddy shallows and move slowly through the water by using its water jet for propulsion.

**Boz** A short Lizling, he vowed revenge on Boba Fett after the bounty hunter killed his friend Ry-Kooda.

Mingo Bovark

**Boz Pity** Also known as "the graveyard world," this planet was used by nearby systems to bury their dead. It was home to the extensive ruins of a forgotten civilization. During the Clone Wars, a huge Confederacy fleet of over 100 ships was in orbit during the early stages of the Outer Rim Sieges. The Jedi confronted General Grievous on the planet's surface. Later, after the fall of Saleucami, General Quinlan Vos moved his troops to Boz Pity.

**Bozzie** An old Ewok widow around the time of the Battle of Endor, she was Paploo's mother and Kneesaa's aunt. At times she could be overbearing and pushy.

**Bpfassh** A double planet with a complex system of moons in the Bpfassh system, it was located near Praesitlyn and Sluis Van in the Sluis sector. Legend had it that during the Clone Wars, some Bpfasshi Dark Jedi created trouble throughout the sector, and a Jedi task force including Jorus C'baoth was formed to oppose them. One Dark Jedi made it as far as Dagobah before his death at the hands of Yoda. Because of the insurrection, most Bpfasshi disliked all Jedi. Bpfassh was also the target of a hit-and-fade attack by Grand Admiral Thrawn whose true target was the Sluis Van shipyards. And it was the site of an attempted abduction of Leia Organa Solo.

**BR-0371** A seemingly mundane Senate resolution that introduced a tariff on major hyperspace trading routes throughout the Outer and Mid rims, with revenue going to the Republic to pay off its burgeoning fiscal debt. At the suggestion of Senator Palpatine, Valorum proposed the resolution to the Senate. The Trade Federation responded by blockading the planet of Naboo.

**Brachnis Chorios** The outermost world of the Chorios systems in the Meridian sector, it appeared ice-green and lavender from space. Nine years after the Battle of Endor, Leia Organa Solo made a secret visit to a point near Brachnis Chorios's largest moon to meet with Seti Ashgad of Nam Chorios.

**brachno-jag** Small, carnivorous animals typically used for torture and painful executions. A hundred could strip a being's bones in five or six hours.

**Bradan, Lieutenant** A human combat specialist, she served in Warlord Zsinj's forces until her death aboard the *Razor's Kiss.*

**Bragkis** This planet was home to a million-credit betting parlor. Han Solo once spent some time there.

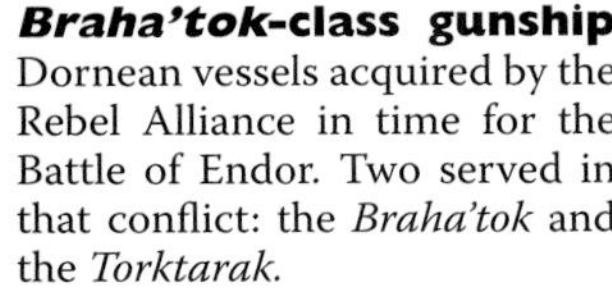

***Braha'tok*-class gunship** Dornean vessels acquired by the Rebel Alliance in time for the Battle of Endor. Two served in that conflict: the *Braha'tok* and the *Torktarak.*

**Brainiac** A large-brained Siniteen alien who frequented the Mos Eisley cantina, he was given his nickname by BoShek for his ability to calculate hyperspace coordinates in his head. His real name was Pons Limbic.

**Brainrot Plague (Loedorvian Brain Plague; Brainworm Rot)** An airborne viral disease of many types. Type A affected humanoids and certain cephalopods. If detected early, it could be treated through an immunization protocol built around the antigen clyrossa-themin in bacta suspension. A scourge of Brainrot Plague affected the planet Jabiim. Later, during the Clone Wars, the Separatist leader Alto Stratus cited the Republic's inaction during that crisis as one of several reasons for secession. General Grievous unleashed Loedorvian Brain Plague in the Weemell sector, resulting in the deaths of all the clone forces and nearly every human there.

**Braittrand, Shrivel** Boles Roor's mechanic from Gerres Gule. After Roor retired from Podracing to continue his glimmik singing career, this male Kulless chief was free to move up into professional Podracing competition. He built from scratch a new Podracer called the *Kulless Squall.*

**Brak sector** A sector of space that served as a staging area for Imperial Navy missions into the Outer Rim Territories. Rebel forces made substantial gains in this former mining sector during the Galactic Civil War.

**Brakiss** Taken by the Empire from his mother as an infant because of his nascent Force powers, he was one of a handful of Imperials who tried to infiltrate Luke Skywalker's Jedi academy on Yavin 4. Unlike the others, however, Brakiss had a true talent for the Force. Skywalker seemed to successfully turn him from the dark side, and Brakiss became a student. But when, as part of his Jedi training, he was sent on a journey in which he had to confront himself—much as Luke had done during his own training on Dagobah—Brakiss emerged terrified and angry. He left the Jedi academy, never to return.

A physically stunning man—Princess Leia Organa Solo once called him one of the most handsome men she had ever seen—Brakiss was endowed with blond hair, blue eyes, flawless skin, a perfectly straight nose, and thin lips. After his experiences on Yavin 4, he became administrator of droid-manufacturing factories on the moon of Telti. He helped dark sider Kueller plant explosives in a new series of droids that were sent throughout New Republic worlds.

Brakiss remained filled with anger, irrationally continuing to blame his mother for allowing him to fall into the hands of the Empire when he was an infant. His mother aided Luke Skywalker on the planet Msst and led him to her son on Telti, where Luke had to face his former student in battle. Luke discovered that Brakiss had voluntarily stopped using the Force, and Kueller was using him as a pawn to trick Luke to come to Kueller's homeworld of Almania. After Brakiss's tampering with droids was discovered, he was attacked by astromechs that had been subverted and was driven from Telti.

About six years later, under the Second Imperium's attempt to reestablish the power and reach of the old Empire, Brakiss was put in charge of the Shadow Academy, a twisted mirror image of the Jedi academy. The purpose of the academy, based on a large space station, was to train a new army of Dark Jedi to take over the galaxy. The station was outfitted with self-destruct mechanisms, and Brakiss wasn't permitted to leave the academy. He lived under the constant threat that the mechanisms would be triggered by the mysterious leaders of the Second Imperium. When the station was moved to the orbit of Coruscant and launched attacks on the New Republic, Jaina Solo figured out how to disable its cloaking device. The station managed to escape to a new hiding place, but the leaders of the Second Imperium, fed up with Brakiss's failures, detonated the explosives aboard, and he was killed.

**Bralor, Rav** One of the 75 Mandalorian mercenaries in the group of 100 training sergeants recruited by Jango Fett during the development of the Republic Commandos program. Dressed in red armor, she was a sharpened battle instrument, attacking with surgical precision and stunning efficiency.

**Bralsin** A small settlement near Keldabe on Mandalore and site of a simple monument to Fenn Shysa.

**Brand, Commodore** Formerly commander of Task Force Aster, part of the New Republic's deployment of the Fifth Fleet at Doornik-319, he served from aboard the star cruiser *Indomitable.* During the first year of the Yuuzhan Vong crisis, Commodore Brand was one of the most curmudgeonly of the commanders. A rigid, gloomy functionary, with the inward-turning gaze of one who sees only his own truth, Commodore Brand spoke with Senator Viqi Shesh about the reenabling of Centerpoint Station and urged her to vote in favor of reinforcing Bothawui in order to set a trap for the Yuuzhan Vong at Corellia. His plan backfired when the Yuuzhan Vong betrayed the Hutts and attacked Fondor instead.

**Brand, King Empatojayos** A Jedi and ruler of the Ganathans, he was apprenticed to Jedi Master Yaddle. Before the Clone Wars, Jedi Knight Brand handled diplomatic negotiations in the Sepan sector, and then later fought in the Battle of Bassadro. He was severely injured in a battle with Darth Vader. Only a prosthetic suit of his own design kept him alive. King Empatojayos Brand was excited to hear that Vader had been vanquished and joined the Alliance fight against the second clone of Emperor Palpatine. He sacrificed himself to save the baby Anakin Solo from being filled with the essence and mind of the Emperor's clone. His death snuffed out the Emperor's will once and for all.

*Brakiss*

**Brandei, Captain** An Imperial officer who held the rank of commander during the Battle of Hoth while stationed aboard the *Executor.* He was technical services officer of the Fleet Support Branch, overseeing the maintenance and repair of all 144 TIE fighters carried aboard. He was transferred to the *Judicator,* Grand Admiral Thrawn's personal Star Destroyer, which he would eventually command. He was one of the few senior officials to survive the Battle of Endor, and later served loyally as part of Thrawn's personal armada. A confident and daring officer, Captain Brandei was never reckless, believing that it was more important to live to fight another day than to die spectacularly in a lost cause.

**Brandes, Hela** A member of the Royal Advisory Council in Queen Amidala's cabinet who served as the music adviser, she was a noted harpist in charge of funding for performing arts displays and overseeing the individual events. She attempted to convince Naboo artists and musicians to arrange exhibits and performances offplanet.

**Brandl, Adalric** Once a stage actor, he became one of Emperor Palpatine's Jedi-hunting Inquisitors. Dignified and distinguished, he often struggled with his dedication to the dark side. He fathered one son, Jaalib, who became a Dark Jedi.

**Branon, John D.** An Alliance X-wing starfighter pilot during the Battle of Yavin, he flew as Red Four and was shot down and killed by TIE fighters.

**Brarun, Durgard** The scrawny vice director of CorDuro Shipping, he detained Jacen Solo with the intention of handing over the Jedi to the Yuuzhan Vong. Aware of an impending attack on Duro, Brarun had his wife, son, and daughter-in-law leave for safer ground. He intended to offer the refugees on Duro to the Yuuzhan Vong as a bargaining chip: In exchange for the refugee lives, his Peace Brigade connections assured him that Duro's orbital cities would be spared. During the Battle of Duro, his trio of shuttles left Bburru headed for the surface, where he met with Tsavong Lah. The treacherous Lah fed Brarun and the CorDuro Shipping officials to one of his engineered creatures.

**Brasck** A two-legged reptile-like Brubb from the planet Baros, he once worked as a mercenary for Jabba the Hutt. But after the crime lord's death, Brasck became head of a major smuggling ring in the Borderland Regions controlled by neither the New Republic nor the Imperials. Ruthless—slavery and kidnapping were part of his repertoire—he remained constantly in motion aboard his ship *Green Palace,* a modified pleasure yacht, because of his fear of being ambushed. Brasck wore personal armor and carried several hidden weapons.

**Brashaa** A humanoid follower of Lord Hethrir, the former Imperial Procurator of Justice who kidnapped the children of Han and Leia Organa Solo.

**Brashin, Grand General Malcor** A career military man, Malcor Brashin entered the Academy at a very early age. Although his superiors did not consider him particularly ambitious, Brashin was viewed as competent and intelligent. And he probably would have remained an unspectacular Imperial officer if not for the tragic murder of his wife and daughter by Rodian thieves. The loss of his family transformed Brashin, and he became one of the New Order's most outspoken zealots. He drove his forces mercilessly in the hope of stopping the lawlessness and misery caused by "unchecked anarchists and aliens." With numerous military victories to his credit, Brashin became one of the most respected—and feared—generals in the Imperial Army.

**Brask Oto Command Station** One of several military space stations erected in the Unknown Regions by the Chiss, it resembled a pair of connected pyramids. It was from here that Aristocra Formbi led the mission to locate the remains of the Outbound Flight Project.

**brassvine** A thorned species of exotic plant found on Haruun Kal.

**Brathis, Moff Tragg** Brathis was commander of an Imperial battle fleet supposedly stationed at the planet N'zoth in an alliance with the Duskhan League. The alliance turned out to be a Yevethan sham designed to scare the New Republic.

**Brath Qella (Maltha Obex)** A dead planet in the Qella system, it was once home to a species also known as the Qella, which apparently had been extirpated for more than 150 years before the Battle of Yavin. The Qella's ancient ancestors were the Qonet, who were in turn descended from the Ahra Naffi. (A related species, also descended from the Ahra Naffi eons ago, was the Khotta of the planet Kho Nai.) The Qella had oval bodies and four long, double-jointed limbs with three-fingered hands. They communicated in a pitch-based language. They were one of only six recorded species that had 18 different molecular pairs in their genetic code, and they also harbored billions of Eicroth bodies: tiny capsules containing extra genetic material that were blueprints for constructing artifacts.

Brath Qella's atmosphere was too thick for humans to breathe unassisted. Before their extinction, the Qella developed the technology to colonize other planets but chose instead to remain on their homeworld. They were first contacted by a small vessel of the Third General Survey, an Old Republic program established to explore the habitable planets in the galaxy's spiral arms; the ship recorded a Qella population of seven million. When a larger contact vessel arrived just eight years later, Brath Qella was completely lifeless, with more than a third of its surface covered with kilometer-thick ice and its oceans choked with glaciers. Analysts speculated that several large asteroid impacts had destroyed the planet's ecosystem and killed off all its native species. The contact vessel collected several genetic and archaeological specimens from the ruined civilization and a comprehensive follow-up visit was planned, but the outbreak of the Clone Wars brought an end to the Third General Survey. The Tobek species later arrived and claimed the barren planet, giving it the name of Maltha Obex, which long appeared on many charts.

*Breath mask*

Twelve years after the Battle of Endor, an archaeological team from the Obroan Institute was dispatched to Brath Qella to search for any clues about the mysterious ghost ship called the Teljkon vagabond. The researchers found what they thought to be bodies beneath the ice but were killed by an avalanche when they tried to investigate. A second research team, sponsored by Admiral Drayson, was then dispatched to the planet.

It turned out that when the Qella had realized that the smaller of their two moons would smash into the planet within 100 years, they buried themselves deep in the ground and constructed an organic starship (which became known as the Teljkon vagabond) to eventually return, thaw out the planet, and restore them to life. With help from Luke Skywalker, the vagabond began the process of thawing the planet and restoring Qella society.

**Brattakin, Movo** An acquaintance of the villainous Olag Greck, he managed—after nearly being murdered by Greck—to merge his mind with the metallic body of his droid aide, B-9D7. He then reprogrammed C-3PO and turned the golden robot into the fierce leader of a droid rebellion aimed at toppling an enemy, Boonda, a reformed Hutt crime lord, and taking over a sector of the galaxy. Brattakin also planted a "sleeper bomb" in one of C-3PO's legs. But R2-D2 managed to foil the plot and rescue C-3PO, who reverted to true form.

**Bravo Flight (Bravo Squadron)** The flight designation for one of the two squadrons in the Naboo Royal Space Fighter Corps, the other being Alpha Squadron. Queen Amidala drew her honor guard from the ranks of Bravo Squadron. During the Trade Federation invasion of Naboo, Ric Olié served as Bravo Leader. Other Bravo Squad members included Porro Dolphe (Bravo Two), Arven Wendik (Bravo Three), Rya Kirsch (Bravo Four), Officer Ellberger (Bravo Five), and Gavyn Sykes (Bravo Six).

***Braxant Bonecrusher*** Originally the *Braxant Brave,* this Imperial *Katana* fleet Dreadnaught was refitted with SD-10 and SD-11 droid brains for combat in the Battle of Orinda. Under the command of Jacen Solo, it was damaged during the Yuuzhan Vong attack.

**Braxis, Senator** A four-armed Pho Ph'eahian Senator whose plea to Emperor Palpatine for assistance with an issue on his planet was denied despite earlier promises.

**braze** A term describing a type of pollution characterized by a brown haze.

**Brazzo** A resident of Centares and the brother of Selle. After Darth Vader learned the name of the individual who destroyed the Death Star, he betrayed and killed Brazzo and all the other Centares residents who heard the name.

**breaking, the** A Yuuzhan Vong form of torture, this common procedure—mental anguish applied with physical torment—was used on captured enemies. Victims were subjected to repeated near-death experiences until their wills were broken. Their sensibilities and determination were shaved away until they were left broken on the floor, sobbing like infants, their minds snapped from the succession of expected horrors and promised terrible deaths. The breaking was used against the Jedi Knight Miko Reglia on Helska 4. While imprisoned aboard the Yuuzhan Vong vessel *Exquisite Death,* the members of Anakin Solo's strike team endured the breaking.

**breath mask** A compact, portable life-support system designed to filter the air of unsafe environments and provide the user with oxygen or another breathable gas. Worn over the mouth and nose, these units were connected to small oxygen tanks and could protect wearers in poisonous atmospheres or a near vacuum. Breath masks were frequently built into body armor as well, and were a component of the helmets worn by stormtroopers and Darth Vader. The Roamer-6 models found aboard the *Mil-*

*lennium Falcon,* and other similar units, had computerized filters that could be programmed and adjusted to handle the needs of any number of species. Filters on these units were usually expended after only one hour, but inexpensive replacement filters could be snapped into place in just seconds. Standard breath masks provided no protection from a total vacuum and did not shield users from corrosive atmospheres. In addition, breath masks were only useful for short periods of time, as both their air supplies and filters were soon depleted.

**Brebishem** These dancers had long snouts and wide, leaf-shaped ears that they flapped. Their soft, wrinkled mauve skins seemed to meld together when they touched each other.

**Breela** This Farghul bounty hunter, the daughter of Mika, eventually became leader of the Bounty Hunters' Guild organization Crimson Nova. She harbored her mother's grudge against the Jedi.

**Breemu, Bana** A Senator who represented the Humbarine sector during the Clone Wars, she found her political influence slipping after many of her most industrious worlds were conquered or ravaged by the Separatists. She was part of the Delegation of Two Thousand opposed to Chancellor Palpatine's excessive executive power.

**Breetha, Tamaktis** A Rhommamoolian and former mayor of Redhaven, he became a member of Nom Anor's independent senate. This gentle-eyed old man met Leia Organa Solo, Mara Jade Skywalker, Jaina Solo, Bolpuhr, and C-3PO on Rhommamool during their diplomatic mission there.

**Breil'lya, Bie** First cousin of Tav Breil'lya, he was captured by bounty hunter Nariss Siv Loqesh.

**Breil'lya, Tav** A Bothan, he served as a loyal top aide to New Republic Councilor Borsk Fey'lya, and was sent on the most important fact-finding missions. But unlike his boss, Breil'lya wasn't subtle when playing politics. On a trip to the planet New Cov, he tried to convince former Old Republic Senator Garm Bel Iblis to ally with Fey'lya's faction. But Breil'lya's maneuvering was eventually exposed to the full Provisional Council.

**Breise, Garth** A human member of the ExGal-4 science team on Belkadan, he climbed the communications tower with Yomin Carr to determine why the system wasn't working. Yomin Carr—in truth an advance Yuuzhan Vong agent—pushed Breise to his death.

**Bre'lya, Saiga** A handsome Bothan New Republic Intelligence agent, she was sent to assist Major Showolter's transfer of Elan and Vergere during the war against the Yuuzhan Vong. Bre'lya and her partner, Jode Tee, were killed by members of the Peace Brigade aboard the *Queen of Empire.*

**Bremen, Jak** A New Republic colonel during the war against Grand Admiral Thrawn, he served as director of security for the New Republic Inner Council.

**Bren, Governor Malvander** The ruthless Imperial governor of Solem, he hired Boba Fett to capture his brother Yolan Bren, a Rebel leader. When Malvander refused to pay Boba Fett, Fett took his precious necklace as payment and left the governor at the mercy of the Rebels.

**Bren, Taggor** A scarred human male bounty hunter from Tatooine who banded together with Tusken Raiders.

**Bren, Yolan** Nicknamed the Poet, this native of Solem fought against the Empire—even against his brother, Imperial Governor Malvander Bren. The governor hired Boba Fett to hunt Yolan down.

**Brentaal IV** Located in the Bormea sector of the Core Worlds, the wealthy planet sat at the strategic intersection of the Perlemian Trade Route and the Hydian Way. Brentaal was a dry planet whose eight continents were separated by small salty oceans. Most available land was covered with starports, industrial facilities, and thriving trade markets that served its billions of inhabitants. Led by Shogar Tok, the inhabitants of the planet supported the Confederacy during the Clone Wars. The planet was of strategic significance because the Republic needed it to secure the Perlemian Trade Route. The initial attack against Brentaal proved disastrous until Jedi Master Shaak Ti was able to lead an insertion team that killed Tok and sabotaged Brentaal's defenses. During the Galactic Civil War, Rogue Squadron tangled with Baron Soontir Fel's 181st Imperial Fighter Wing high over Brentaal IV.

***Bria*** A cut-rate SoroSuub Starmite owned and piloted by Han Solo and Chewbacca before Han won the *Millennium Falcon* from Lando Calrissian. Han and Chewie earned enough credits to purchase the *Bria* by piloting Lando's ships through the Kessel Run. Solo named the ship after an old girlfriend, Bria Tharen. After distinguishing himself at the Battle of Nar Shaddaa, Han lost the *Bria* in a mishap.

**Bri'ahl** During the Clone Wars, R2-D2 and C-3PO accompanied Senator Padmé Amidala to the Presidential Palace on Bri'ahl. The droids managed to foil a group of activists who were plotting to use stolen clone trooper armor to assassinate Amidala and the Bri'ahl leader. Bri'ahl's natives were also called Bri'ahls, and had pink skin and cone-shaped ears.

**Brianna** An Echani Handmaiden who served the Jedi Knight Atris almost 4,000 years before the Battle of Yavin. She was the daughter of politician Yusanis and Jedi Master Arren Kae, veterans of the Mandalorian Wars. Brianna was born with evidence of her parents' infidelity and bore the stigma of this indiscretion. Brianna stole the freighter *Ebon Hawk* from Telos IV.

**Bribbs, Beolars** Shortly before the Battle of Geonosis, this Sullustan became the President of the Sullustan Council and CEO of SoroSuub Corporation.

**Bridge, the (Rainbow Bridge)** The ring formed around Coruscant during the Yuuzhan Vong transformation of the planet into Yuuzhan'tar. It consisted of the colorful remnants of one of Coruscant's moons. Much of it was scattered by the arrival of Zonama Sekot, but the ring remained in place during the time of Roan Fel's empire.

**Bridger, Waldan** A Jedi Master remarkable for his well-muscled build and preference for a San-Ni staff over a lightsaber, he was killed by General Grievous on Togoria during the Clone Wars.

**Brie, Shira** *See* Lumiya.

**Briggia** A blue planet that was the main Rebel base after Chrellis but before Orion IV, it was the first target of the Empire's Operation Strike Fear. Briggia was successfully evacuated.

**Brighteyes, Slique** The last surviving Gulmarid, Brighteyes spent months as a slave aboard the *Azgoghk* before the prisoners of the extermination ship were liberated by the Rebel Alliance. Wrinkled, scaly, and gray-skinned, he hired Boba Fett to avenge the extermination of his species by Imperial Admiral Mir Tork and Dr. Leonis Murthé. Brighteyes died on the planet Basteel upon learning that the contract had been fulfilled.

***Bright Flight*** A Republic *Sprint*-class medical rescue craft that was to take a presumed dead Asajj Ventress for a proper funeral on Coruscant following the Clone Wars battle on Boz Pity. Ventress was actually alive and awakened to commandeer the ship. She ordered the pilots to take her far from the war.

***Bright Hope*** One of the last Rebel transports to leave in the evacuation of the planet Hoth, it was severely damaged by the bounty hunters Zuckuss and 4-LOM as it attempted to escape. However, they had a change of heart, rescued the 90 passengers and crew aboard the *Bright Hope,* and safely transported them to Darlyn Boda.

**Bright Jewel Cluster** A priority sector that contained the Gordian Reach, it was administered by Governor-General Nox Cellam during the time of the Empire. Worlds within the cluster included Ord Mantell, Kwenn, Toprawa, and Junction.

**brights** Slang used by X-wing pilots to refer to advanced Imperial TIE fighter models.

**Brightwater, Korlo** An Imperial scout trooper, also known as TBR 479, who became a member of the Hand of Judgment.

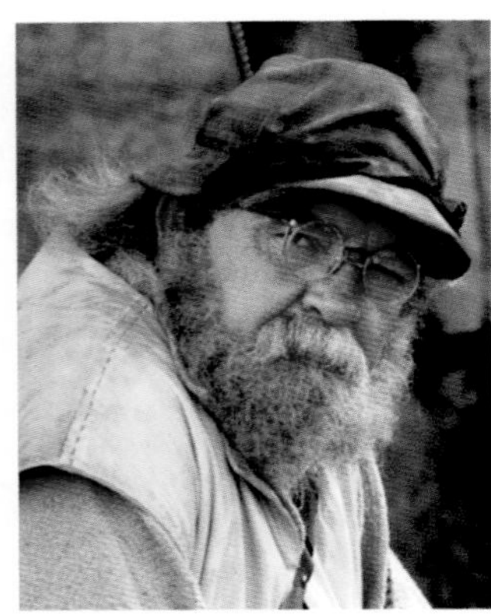
Noa Briqualon

**Brigia** A poor, retrogressive planet in the remote Tion Hegemony, it was inhabited by tall, purple-skinned humanoids. The University of Rudrig helped Brigia in its bid for development, a move opposed by the planet's rulers. The university hired Han Solo to deliver the necessary teaching supplies, but the Brigian government attempted to intervene. About two years before the Battle of Yavin, a small group of colonists left Brigia and founded New Brigia, a chromite-mining operation located just within the borders of the Koornacht Cluster.

**Briil twins** Former associates of Han Solo, they were killed in a fight with an Imperial cruiser on patrol near the Tion Hegemony.

**Brill, Governor Foga** An Imperial warlord, he was ruler of Prakith. He contributed all his resources to the reborn Emperor's campaign of terror against the New Republic. When the clone Emperor was defeated, Brill declared Prakith capital of his newly independent military state. Before the rise of the Empire, Brill was a director of investigation for the Republic Judicial Department.

***Brilliant*** A New Republic *Nebula*-class Star Destroyer and part of the Home Fleet, it was assigned to shadow the Yevethan/Duskhan embassy ship *Aramadia* in orbit around Coruscant.

**Brillstow, Commander** An Imperial officer aboard the *Reprisal.*

**Bril'nilim, Colonel** A male Twi'lek, he led the New Republic troops on Dantooine against the Yuuzhan Vong slave forces.

**Bringbit, Lillea** A human female known to patronize Coruscant's entertainment district around the time of the Clone Wars.

**Brink of the Celestial Wake** The colorful name of a decrepit old space station once found in the Outer Rim. During the Clone Wars, Anakin Skywalker's starfighter sensors detected millions of tiny life-forms and one weak humanoid signal aboard. He discovered Serra Keto, the only survivor of the Republic team on the station. The forces were attacked by small, alien blob-like creatures equipped with cybernetics that allowed them to combine to form a giant spider droid. To keep the creatures from spreading, Anakin rigged the station for self-destruction; he and Serra escaped aboard his starfighter.

**Briqualon, Noa** An old explorer who was stranded on the moon of Endor for decades. When he was young, he spent years as a midlevel scout before joining up with his friend Salak to chart the Modell sector. They crashed on Endor on their very first mission. Their cruiser's power drive crystal was damaged, and Salak searched the forests for suitable replacement parts. Not only did he fail to find any, but he was also captured by the cruel and evil Sanyassan Marauders. Noa never saw Salak alive again. He lived in a hollowed-out tree that he carved into a home. His only companion was a small furry forest dweller, Teek. When Cindel Towani was orphaned by the Marauders, she and her Ewok friend Wicket W. Warrick sought shelter in Noa's hut. They lived there for a short time, and Noa grew protective of the little girl. When the Marauders captured her, Noa, Teek, and Wicket teamed up to infiltrate the Marauders' castle. There he found the remains of his friend Salak, as well as a replacement power crystal from the Towani starship. The Marauders were eventually defeated, and Noa repaired his starship. He eventually left Endor with Cindel, and the two plied the stars for some time before he retired to the Mid Rim while she made a life for herself as a journalist on Coruscant. Noa was a gruff old man, but had a kind heart. He had a long white beard, piercing eyes behind plasspecs, and an ample belly. He dressed in simple blue and brown robes, and carried a carved walking stick.

**Brit, Major Olander** A politically minded communications expert during the Battle of Endor, he followed Panno to the Alliance.

**Brizzit** An insectoid species known to have some members from the planet Jandoon.

**B'rknaa** Living-rock creatures of the planet Indobok, they guarded the high-energy crystals that animated them and gave them a kind of group mind. The B'rknaa were able to join together to form a single giant entity.

**Broadside** A Shadow Squadron clone pilot involved in the counterattack on the Separatist warship *Malevolence.*

***Broadside*-class cruiser** A long-range missile warship produced in the early days of the Galactic Civil War by Kuat Drive Yards for the Imperial Navy. Most models of the Broadside were lightly armored and ran with a small crew. Early models carried a payload of expensive diamond boron missiles; their high-yield detonations proved useful against tightly packed ship formations. Later models were fitted with more economical concussion missiles. KDY engineers decided that exceptional speed and maneuverability were unnecessary for this ship; as a result, a Broadside was almost never encountered without an escort of some kind.

**Brodo Asogi** The home planet of Senator Grebleips.

**Brodogon Consortium** An organization that purchased slaves from Krayn's pirate group.

**Brogar** The Advozse owner of a seedy cantina on Lok during the time of Roan Fel's empire, Brogar also operated a safehouse for those willing to pay.

**Brolf (plural Brolfi)** The native inhabitants of Barlok, they were a short, thick-bodied species of humanoids characterized by the green-and-yellow coloration of their skin, which was covered in small, horn-like scales. The Brolfi were divided into several political factions. Following the Battle of Naboo, they petitioned the Republic for assistance in negotiating with the Corporate Alliance. Jedi Master Jorus C'baoth mediated the dispute, which ended in a failed assassination attempt on the Brolfi leadership.

**Brolis, Clone Commander** A Republic commander sent to penetrate the Fortress of Axion, he was injured, and the rest of his unit was wiped out. Yoda was sent to reinforce his position.

**Brolo, Prefect Dooje** The Yuuzhan Vong commander of the third worldship to arrive at Helska 4, he presumably died when the Praetorite Vong's base there was destroyed.

**Bron** A human diplomat living on Cerea, he organized many young Cereans into a Pro-Tech movement that advocated high technology over the world's traditional customs. Because of his beliefs, Bron came into direct conflict with the Jedi Knight Ki-Adi-Mundi.

**Brong** A Shi'ido bodyguard who worked for Duchess Vont, he protected her belongings from would-be thieves like Sammie Staable and Smilerdon-verdont.

**bronzium** A semi-valuable metal used in droid construction and the manufacture of luxury goods. Case-hardened bronzium protected the reactor bulb of droidekas, while C-3PO's polished shell sported a bronzium finish. The bronzium busts of many great Jedi Masters once lined the walls of the Jedi Temple Archives.

Bronzium

**Brood, Maris** Like many of her peers, this Zabrak was discovered by the Jedi as an infant. However, rather than receiving formal training at the

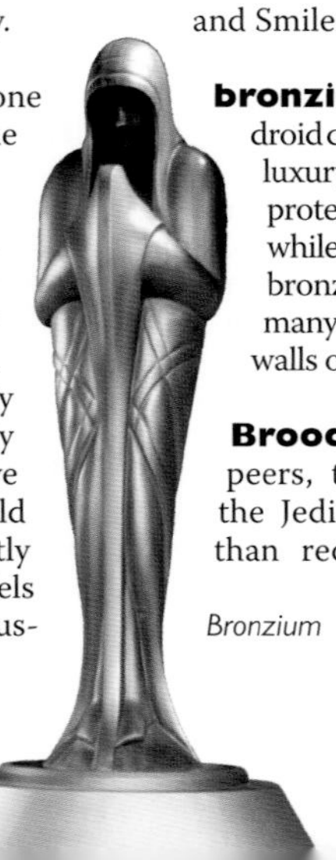

Maris Brood

Jedi Temple on Coruscant, she was tutored by a Jedi warrior aboard a starship called the *Gray Pilgrim.* When Palpatine issued Order 66, Maris and her Master were in the Outer Rim Territories and thus not immediately affected by the Purge. But her Master did feel the ripples in the Force caused by the sudden deaths of so many Jedi. After meeting only silence with every transmission sent to the Jedi Temple on Coruscant, Maris's Master took his personal starfighter in search of answers. He never returned, but his last message revealed that the Jedi Order had been all but destroyed by a villain named Darth Vader. Seeking revenge, Maris set off in search of Vader. Before she could confront the Dark Lord, though, she was discovered by Jedi Master Shaak Ti, who convinced the angry Padawan to disappear into hiding on Felucia. Despite Shaak Ti's positive influence, Maris harbored a strong desire for revenge against Vader.

**Brooks Propulsion Devices** The manufacturer of retractable rocket boosters once used by R2-D2.

**Bror Tower Three** A building on Coruscant where Shu Mai met with Separatists Tam Uliss and Mousul. Using a skyway connecting Bror Towers Three and Four, Shu Mai killed Tam Uliss after his failure to cause Ansion to secede.

**Brotherhood of Darkness** An army of 20,000 of Lord Kaan's most devoted Sith followers, the Brotherhood of Darkness fought the Army of Light at the Battle of Ruusan. The brotherhood lost all but two of the seven titanic battles on Ruusan, reducing the army to a tenth of its original size. Rather than surrender, Lord Kaan triggered a "thought bomb," which annihilated every last member of the Army of Light and the Brotherhood of Darkness, leaving Darth Bane behind to secretly rebuild the Sith Order in a new guise.

**Brothic, Governor** Governor on Ciutric and a friend of Sate Pestage, he did what he could to ease the pain of Pestage's imprisonment by the Empire.

***Brownstar*** A huge, bulbous, luxury freighter belonging to Malta the Hutt.

**Brrbrlpp** Flower-shaped diaphanous creatures indigenous to the cold, dense atmosphere of Esfandia. Their name translated to "cold ones" in Basic.

**BRT droid** A 7.6-meter-tall municipal planning and management supercomputer manufactured by Aratech Repulsor Company. An example was Mistress Mnemos, the Alliance archival computer.

**Bruanii sector** Not far from the Tungra and Javin sectors, it was located in the Mid Rim close to the Outer Rim border. The Corellian Trade Spine ran through it, and this sector was the site of a Mugaari space depot. The Mon Calamari cruiser *Lulsla,* stationed there, was the launch point following the Battle of Hoth for Rebel Alliance strikes on Imperial space platform D-34 in the Javin sector. The *Lulsla* was destroyed by the Empire in a retaliatory strike.

**Brubb** Two-legged reptile-like creatures from the planet Baros, they had pitted and gnarled dirty yellow skin, ridged eyes, and flat noses. They were about 1.6 meters tall and could change color. Males of the species usually had a solitary outcropping of coarse black hair projecting from the tops of their heads. Social creatures, they treated visitors to Baros as esteemed guests.

**Bruckman, Sergeant** A Corellian scout who served as point man for General Solo's strike team on Endor, he was recruited by Crix Madine for an Alliance commando unit.

**bruise-leech crawler** Parasitic annelids used to trace a complex, rectilinear pattern on Anakin Skywalker's flesh during a rite of passage on Nelvaan at the height of the Clone Wars.

Bruise-leech crawler

**Bruit, Patch** The human chief of field operations for Lommite Limited, he was with the company for almost 20 years, starting as a worker in the lommite pits. Under Jurnel Arrant's orders, Patch hired the Toom Clan to sabotage rival InterGal Ore Ships en route to Eriadu. After the Toom Clan betrayed both LL and InterGal by destroying *both* companies' transports, Bruit and his counterpart at InterGal teamed up against the Toom Clan. This whole conflict had been engineered by Darth Sidious to weaken both companies. During the strife, Darth Maul entered the fray, killing Bruit by crushing his throat with the Force. Maul then fabricated evidence implicating Patch Bruit in the conspiracy.

**Brun, Deca** One of the candidates running for Governor of Gala, he was a hero of the Galacian people, promising reform and prosperity. His campaign was secretly financed by the Offworld Corporation, but he was ultimately defeated in the election by Wila Prammi.

**Brunk, Dama Whitesun** Beru Lars's younger sister and a native of Tatooine. She was the proprietor of the Sidi Driss Inn in the city of Anchorhead during the early years of the New Republic. When Leia Organa Solo and her husband, Han Solo, tried to recover the *Killik Twilight* moss-painting, Dama allowed them to stay at her hotel. Dama later helped them escape when Imperial troops arrived to arrest them, revealing a long hatred for the Empire for the murder of Beru and Owen Lars.

**Brusc, Captain** The captain of the Star Destroyer *Manticore,* he served under the command of Admiral Daala. He was killed and his starship destroyed during an attack on Mon Calamari.

**Bryndar** A planet far off normal shipping lines. The Jedi B'dard Tone and Codi Ty landed in a frigid, snow-covered, mountainous region of Bryndar during the Clone Wars. There they met up with Flynn Kybo.

**Bryx** This planet was conquered in the early days of the Empire after an effective but ultimately unsuccessful defense. The tactics used by Bryx's Governor Carigan are now known widely as the Carigan Defense.

**Bseto system** A system that contained the white dwarf star Bseto, which is orbited by the uninhabited planets Bseto I and Indikir, it also included the huge Lweilot asteroid belt and the frozen planet of Sarahwiee, site of a once secret Imperial research facility.

**BT-16 perimeter security droid** A reliable Arakyd security droid with an arachnid design. Some BT-16s were appropriated by B'omarr monks for use as transports for disembrained members of their order.

BT-16 perimeter security droid

**BT-445** One of many scanning crews aboard the Death Star, it was selected to search the *Millennium Falcon.* The crew's two members were knocked unconscious by Han Solo and Chewbacca. They were taken to the infirmary, where they died when the Death Star exploded.

**B'thazoshe Bridge** A natural stone bridge found in the Jundland Wastes. Anakin Skywalker passed it during his desperate search for his mother. Its name translates into "bantha horn turned to stone" in the language of the Tusken Raiders.

**BU-11** A modified 2-1B medical droid that served as Ziro the Hutt's bartender on Coruscant.

**Bu, Candabrine** This Senator from Lansano supported the Military Creation Act prior to the Clone Wars.

**Bubble-cliffs of Nezmi** Once the cliff-hanging homes of Nezmi's indigenous peoples, the Bubble-cliffs of Nezmi became a tourist attraction. The Bubble-cliffs ranged from 5 to 30 meters across. Soon after the death of Emperor Palpatine, Mara Jade tracked criminal Lord Dequc there.

**bubble wort** The raw material found in Gungan bubble buildings, harvested from bubble spore plants native to Naboo. Gungans boiled the spore, extracted and processed the bubble wort, then through secret techniques created the hydrostatic water-repulsing bubbles found throughout Gungan architecture.

**Bubo (Buboicullaar)** A creature that looked like a cross between a frog and a dog, it had bulging eyes and a protruding lower jaw. Buboicullaar, or Bubo as he was known, was a spy and assassin in the palace of Jabba the Hutt on Tatooine. He frequently consulted with the B'omarr monks and plotted to kill Jabba. Few suspected that he was intelligent at all, and Bubo did nothing to contradict that assumption. Bubo foiled an assassination attempt from Ree-Yees by eating a detonation link necessary for a bomb that Ree-Yees had been constructing. After Jabba's death, Bubo's brain was removed by the B'omarrs, leaving him free to contemplate the mysteries of the universe unfettered by his body.

Bubo (Buboicullaar)

**Buc, Donny** A transport pilot who regularly flew from Coruscant to Sorrus, he ferried Jedi Padawans Obi-Wan Kenobi and Siri Tachi. He wore a tattered leather helmet and sported a short black beard.

**Buck** A hulking alien who worked for the Green Forge eco-terrorist group, he would woo the wives of corporate barons and other defilers of the environment to insinuate his way into their lives, conspire to murder their husbands, and make off with their fortunes. Buck posed as Madam Rhoden's personal trainer, and began an affair with her to get at Clode Rhoden, a Tibanna gas magnate on Yorn Skot. Clode discovered their affair as part of the web of intrigue that surrounded the last voyage of the *Aurorient Express.* Though Buck claimed to know eight forms of tae-jitsu, he proved no match for a Jedi in hand-to-hand combat.

**Budpock** Located in the Meridian sector, this planet was long one of the Rebel Alliance's most loyal supporters. One of Budpock's main ports was Dimmit Station. Nine years after the Battle of Endor, two New Republic cruisers were dispatched from the orbital station on Durren to investigate a possible breach of the truce between Budpock and Ampliquen. Two more cruisers from the naval base on Cybloc XII were sent to deal with a pirate fleet from Budpock.

**bugdillo** Multilegged crustaceans, they were a delicacy on the planet Eol Sha.

**Bugnaught droid** A type of silver, insectoid combat droid used by Asajj Ventress in lightsaber training and found in the gladiator pits of Rattatak.

**Bulano serpent** A creature without teeth, claws, or poison, it could blow itself up to five times its normal size, making it look fiercer and more dangerous than it actually was.

**Bular, Councilman** A politician on Ahakista killed by Darth Vader for failing to stop a Rebel plot.

**Bulgan** Along with Kyakhta, one of two clanless Ansionians hired by Soergg the Hutt to capture a Jedi Padawan during a Republic mission to Ansion, just prior to the outbreak of the Clone Wars. A childhood disease twisted Bulgan's back into a hunch, and a fall from the back of a suubatar resulted in the loss of one of his eyes. Bulgan was cast out of the Tasbir clan, and his mind deteriorated, though he found employ as an underling to Soergg, who ensured the loyalty of Bulgan and Kyakhta by placing an explosive charge within each of their necks. Should they ever fail to report, Soergg threatened to detonate the charge.

Bulgan used a net to capture Barriss Offee, but the Jedi Padawan used the Force to cure his mental affliction. Finally able to think and speak clearly, Bulgan and Kyakhta swore loyalty to the Jedi, and accompanied them on their mission to the Borokii overclan as guides.

**bulk cruiser** A combination transport and combat starship, these ships were not as reliable as other combat vessels but were effective when used to fill out war fleets. Typical bulk cruisers were 600 meters long, with 30 quad laser cannons and two tractor beam projectors.

**bulk freighter** These cargo ships—the workhorses of the galaxy—hauled goods from planet to planet. Lightly armed bulk freighters depended on hyperdrive engines and well-patrolled space lanes to steer clear of trouble. Most of these small to midsized ships were independently owned.

Bugnaught droid

**Bulq, Sora** A skilled lightsaber instructor, this Weequay Jedi helped Mace Windu perfect the art of vaapad, the seventh form of lightsaber combat—and one so intense and dangerous, to practice it was to tread perilously close to the dark side. Bulq trained many of the Jedi combatants who perished in the Geonosis arena, and he was dispirited by the loss. Left for dead on Geonosis, Bulq was rescued by the Separatists, and Count Dooku personally recruited him to spread discord among the Jedi.

When the call came from the Republic for all the Jedi to serve as generals in its Grand Army, Bulq was one of several prominent Jedi who turned their backs on their duty. Bulq united four of these Jedi—Jeisel, K'Kruhk, Rhad Tarn, and his former Padawan Mira—at his family estate on the Sriluurian moon of

Sora Bulq

Ruul. He extended an invitation to parley with the Jedi Council, and Mace Windu, Bulq's old sparring partner, answered the call.

Windu stepped into a trap, for Bulq was an accomplice to Separatist commander and Dark Jedi Asajj Ventress. Windu and Bulq battled, but their personal showdown was cut short. Windu was more concerned with stopping the mysterious Ventress, so he knocked Bulq unconscious to pursue the dark side warrior. Mace fled Ruul, and Bulq lived.

Throughout the Clone Wars, Bulq served as commander of Dooku's dark acolytes—Force-sensitives and fallen Jedi who had sided with the Separatists. Bulq led a number of insidious plots and projects against the Republic, including the raising of a clone army of Morgukai warriors. During the prolonged siege at Saleucami, Bulq killed venerated Jedi Master Oppo Rancisis. A Jedi double agent, Quinlan Vos, infiltrated the ranks of the acolytes and slew Bulq in turn.

***Bulwark*-class battle cruiser** A massive capital warship developed by TransGalMeg Industries. One of the most armored and durable vessels in the Rebel Alliance fleet, it was plagued by rumors of unreliable electronics and sensors. The *Bulwark*'s extensive arsenal, shielding, and carrying capacity made it ideal for large-scale operations.

**Bundim** A secret base of operations for Rebel Alliance activity in the Trax sector. The planetary government tried to remove the Imperial presence from the planet, but a spy alerted the Empire to Bundim's plans. The Empire's response was swift and meant to make an example of Bundim for the rest of the sector. A number of merchant ships were destroyed and many cities were leveled in aerial bombardments. Bundim was garrisoned and subjugated in less than a week.

**Bunduki** The martial arts form teräs käsi was practiced on the planet Bunduki, where it was taught by the Followers of Palawa.

**Bunji, Big** A former associate of Han Solo, he didn't repay a debt in a timely manner, so Solo strafed his pressure dome with blasterfire. Bunji barely escaped with his life. Bygones being bygones, a short time later, Squeak—an associate of Big Bunji—offered Solo a charter, but Han refused since he had already signed on with Obi-Wan Kenobi and Luke Skywalker for passage to Alderaan. Decades later, during the war against the Yuuzhan Vong, Big Bunji ran the underground on the space station *Jubilee Wheel* under the alias Boss B. Big Bunji was a lavender-hued humanoid who walked on two tree-trunk thick legs. He had the girth of a young Hutt and a head too large to fit through an ordinary hatchway.

**Bur** A commander in dark sider Kueller's army on Almania, he was the leader's favorite.

**Bur, Wac** An unusually overweight Rodian counterfeiter who cheated Gebbu the Hutt with the sale of fake art. Boba Fett hunted him down on Coruscant.

**Bureau of Operations** A division of Imperial Intelligence, it handled all major covert operations. Among its missions: infiltration, counterintelligence, and assassination.

**Bureau of Ships and Services (BoSS)** The galaxy's record keeper for starship and spacer information, BoSS maintained extensive information on starship registrations and transponder codes, captains' flight certifications, and upgraded weapons load-outs on all legally registered vessels. It existed for centuries, regardless of what galactic government was currently in power.

**Bur'lorr** A Yuuzhan Vong subaltern among the leaders of the ground forces that attacked and subjugated New Holgha during the early months of the Yuuzhan Vong invasion. When he encountered a Jedi Knight on the planet, Bur'lorr called in assistance from Boba Fett, who had been ostensibly working for the Yuuzhan Vong with his Mandalorian warriors. When he discovered that the Mandalorians had let the Jedi go, Bur'lorr tried to kill them for their treachery. He was almost a match for them, but the Mandalorians soon overpowered Bur'lorr. Goran Beviin was forced to strangle the life from the warrior with his crushgaunts, squeezing Bur'lorr's throat until the trachea and neck bones snapped into pieces. While Suvar Detta took pieces of Bur'lorr's body as bio-samples, Beviin took his scalp as a trophy.

***Burning Pride*** A Yuuzhan Vong flagship used by Deign Lian to travel to Garqi and battle with New Republic forces.

**burnout** Spacer slang for the loss of power in a ship's engines.

**Burr, Waks** An Ishi Tib who was known to frequent the Outlander Club on Coruscant.

**burra fish** A creature found on Dathomir.

**Burren, Tal** An Imperial officer who worked for Ysanne Isard, he was an ambitious grade-four computer tech. Burren tried to help Isard track down Mara Jade after she escaped from infiltrating the Imperial Palace. Ysanne went so far as to promise Burren a promotion to a grade-13 tech, a position invented especially for him.

**Burrk** A onetime stormtrooper, he deserted in the confusion following the Battle of Endor and survived through shady dealings and illegal activities.

**burrmillet** A type of grain harvested on Ruan, burrmillet grew as tall as trees with slender, umber stalks.

**Burs, Bron** A former Rebel commando from southern Nentan, Bron Burs was a crack shot who liked to be on his own. This nonhuman was an off-and-on partner of Debnoli. He relied on his intuition to survive.

**bursa** Large carnivorous quadrupeds found on Naboo. In ancient times, wild bursas would attack Gungan villages.

**Bursk, Sergeant-Major** Leader of the most brutal snowtrooper platoon in the Battle of Hoth, he was a cunning planner who coordinated attacks and managed troop movements.

**Burtola, J. K.** A young member of the mighty Bear Clan, he was one of Jedi Master Yoda's most promising pupils. At the age of four, he suggested to Yoda and Obi-Wan Kenobi that someone had erased the planet Kamino from the Archive memory.

**Bushforb, Slyther** A Nuknog private investigator known to frequent Dex's Diner on Coruscant.

**butcherbug** A multilegged armored creature of Dagobah, it spun a tough, microfine cord between the roots of gnarltrees. When a flying creature blundered into this trap, the cord sliced it into pieces that the butcherbug devoured.

**Butcher of Montellian Serat** *See* Kardu'sai'Malloc.

**Buuper Torsckil Abbey Devices** The company that manufactured the tough, well-armed P-38 starfighters.

**Buzk, Commander Sev** The Imperial officer in charge of the outpost on Troska, he used his position of power to extort the local ruling family, the Kybers. This power struggle eventually led to a stalemate, which his underling Lieutenant Manech sought to end by hiring Boba Fett to attack the Kyber family. With the balance of power tipped, Buzk had no choice but to order an all-out attack on the Kybers, in part to eradicate all evidence of his corruption. Manech had actually set up the entire operation as a sting that led to Buzk's arrest and Manech's promotion.

**buzz droid** Tenacious saboteurs launched onto enemy starfighters via specialized missiles introduced by the Separatists during the Clone Wars, they were also known as Pistoeka sabotage droids. When the missile achieved an optimum proximity to its target, it fragmented to unleash a cloud of melon-sized metal spheres into the target's flight path. The spheres attached themselves to a target vessel, popping open to reveal insect-like droids equipped with cutters and other tools. Buzz droids were designed to disable, not destroy, enemy craft. They operated quickly, slicing into starship hulls and severing vital control linkages. While their tools were effective, buzz droids were relatively weak and vulnerable to damage. A hit to its central eye could knock a buzz droid out of commission.

*Buzz droids*

***Buzzzer*** A Cindev series IV picket ship used by Loka Hask and his Bonestar pirates. The combined freighter-warship originally had been commissioned by the famous red-bearded pirate Crimson Jack. For two years, the *Buzzzer* established a formidable reputation for itself, including being used by Hask to intentionally cause the deaths of Jagged and Zena Antilles. Wedge Antilles tracked the ship down near Jumus, where he destroyed it.

Buzzzer

**Bwahl the Hutt** An ugly one-eyed Hutt trader who, wanting to buy some ancient artifacts, hired Han Solo and Chewbacca to travel to Mimban. There they had a brief encounter with the Coway.

**B-wing starfighter** One of the Rebellion's best-armed starfighters, it was essentially a long wing with a pair of folding airfoils and an array of weapons, including ion cannons, proton torpedo launchers, and laser cannons. The craft's eight weapons-mounting emplacements were interchangeable modules, allowing Alliance mechanics to easily reconfigure each ship's complement depending upon the pilot's preferences and mission requirements. Because the cockpit was surrounded by a unique gyrostabilization system, the pilot always remained stationary, even as the rest of the ship rotated during flight. The fighter was difficult to handle. Only the most skilled pilots could even attempt to control the craft.

The B-wing's primary mission profile involved attacks on much larger Imperial ships. Utilizing ion cannons and other unusual weapons, the B-wing was capable of quickly disabling these targets. Secondary missions included assault strikes on orbital and ground-based Imperial facilities, and escort duty for X- and Y-wing fighter squadrons.

The B-wing was personally designed by Commander Ackbar with the help of skilled Verpine shipbuilders as part of the Shantipole Project. The B-wing's incredible performance played a part in Ackbar's promotion to admiral, as well as led the way for the Rebel Alliance's attack on the second Death Star at the Battle of Endor. Ackbar also aided in the design of the B-wing/E2 or "Expanded B-wing," an advanced model with an elongated command module, allowing for a gunner seated directly behind the pilot.

**Bwua'tu, Nek** A Bothan fleet admiral and veteran of Galactic Alliance campaigns against the Yuuzhan Vong, the Killik colonies, and Corellian Confederation. He achieved his rank in peacetime for being the only Bothan known to defeat the Thrawn simulator in training.

As admiral of the Fifth Fleet, Bwua'tu commanded the *Admiral Ackbar* when it blockaded the Utegetu Nebula, site of the Dark Nest. Bwua'tu's vain habit of decorating his vessel with busts of himself nearly proved his undoing as the busts, secretly supplied by Dark Nest collaborators, contained Gorog larvae that burst forth, swarming the inside of the vessel with assassin bugs. Bwua'tu ordered an evacuation of the ship, losing the vessel to the Killiks. Despite having lost his command—and much face—Bwua'tu continued to be an effective commander in the war against the Killiks.

Bwua'tu eventually regained command of the *Admiral Ackbar*, though—having learned humility—he did away with tributes to himself and instead adorned the ship with busts of the Mon Calamari legend for which it was named. He would eventually command both the Fifth and Sixth fleets in battle with the Corellian Confederation that challenged the Galactic Alliance. Even though Bothans sided with the Confederation, Bwua'tu remained firmly loyal to the Alliance.

As Jacen Solo consolidated his power over the GA and splintered from the command of Cha Niathal, Admiral Bwua'tu became the preeminent military officer in

*B-wing starfighter*

the Galactic Alliance. Solo, who had taken on the title of Darth Caedus, ordered the officer to track down the fleets that had harassed his actions at the Nickel One asteroid and destroy them. Admiral Bwua'tu later sent word that he had eliminated Niathal's small fleet of defectors, and had trapped the Corellian and Bothan fleets near Carbos XIII.

However, after Caedus was killed and the Imperial Moffs surrendered to Jedi Grand Master Luke Skywalker, Admiral Bwua'tu was forced to stand down and break off his attacks. He was offered the chance to assume the role of Chief of State of the Galactic Alliance, but he politely refused in order to remain a military man. He suggested that Admiral Natisi Daala might be a better choice for the job.

**B'wuf** A senior technical analyst aboard the Separatist vessel *Corpulentus,* serving under Pors Tonith during the Clone Wars. He had a habit of speaking with a slow drawl, which made it appear that he was choosing his words carefully. Tonith resented the fact that B'wuf refused to think of battles as business affairs, especially when B'wuf began questioning the battle plan for the capture and control of the Intergalactic Communications Center on Praesitlyn. When B'wuf's protests became too vocal, Tonith ordered a pair of battle droids to shoot him dead if he tried to get up from his post. After Tonith surrendered to Anakin Skywalker, B'wuf feared for his life—threats came both from the Republic's forces and from Tonith's droids—but remained seated until Tonith released him.

**Byblos** A populous urban world in the Colonies region. Most of the planet's 164 billion inhabitants lived in huge city towers, architectural wonders that soared up to 5,000 levels. Every tower had a specific purpose—corporate, residential, starport—and they were connected by tubeways. Byblos was a major manufacturing center for high technology and military equipment.

**Byblos Drive Yards** A major manufacturing firm for high technology and military equipment based on Byblos, in the Colonies. BDY subsidiary Byblos RepulsorDrive built combat cloud cars and airspeeders.

**Bycha, General** The military leader of the planet Typha-Dor who defended his planet against enemies from Vanqor with the help of Obi-Wan Kenobi and Anakin Skywalker.

**Bykart, Winso** A Jedi pilot who transported fellow Jedi to Ragoon-6.

**Bylissura, Rallcema** This Jedi Knight was one of many who perished in the fighting at Shelter Base on Jabiim during the Clone Wars.

**Byrom** A moisture farmer, the husband of Ensa on Molavar, and a former soldier who had a cybernetic prosthetic leg. He once fought alongside Jedi Knights, which predisposed him to helping Darca Nyl, a Jedi nomad who ended up on his farm. Nyl helped Byrom fight off extortionists demanding tribute for local gangster Sleeth.

***Byrt*** A 200-meter-long public starferry on Coruscant that evacuated refugees during the Yuuzhan Vong assault on Coruscant. C-3PO and Ben Skywalker ended up aboard this vessel.

**Byss (1)** Home to the one-eyed Abyssin, this planet traveled in an unusual figure-eight orbit between the binary stars of Byss and Abyss. Byss was a hot, arid planet, and temperatures reached their highest when it was orbiting directly between the two stars, a time known as the Burning. Most plant life on Byss utilized extensive taproots to extract underground water, while animals relied on scattered oases and their own water-storing capabilities. The nomadic, violent Abyssin led primitive lives, engaging in tribal wars and tending to their flocks of cow-like gaunts.

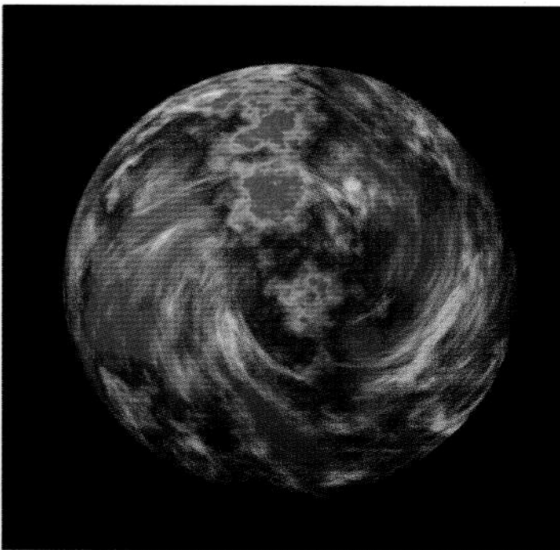

*Byss, a private world of the Emperor*

**Byss (2)** Formerly located in the heart of the Deep Galactic Core, in the Beshgek system, this once pleasant planet was Emperor Palpatine's private world and the center of his reborn Empire six years after the Battle of Endor. The secret planet was accessible only through certain encoded routes because of the difficulty of navigating through the deep mass of stars found in the Deep Core.

Years ago, Emperor Palpatine chose Byss as his private retreat, and Imperial architects and engineers were commissioned to build him an opulent palace. Several million humans were allowed to emigrate to the world, where the Emperor and his adepts used the dark side to feed off their life energies. The planet's population eventually reached almost 20 billion, and all outgoing communications were censored by security agents. Byss was well guarded against attack with powerful planetary shields, hunter-killer probots, and the Imperial Hyperspace Security Net. There were orbital dry docks for massive World Devastators, Super Star Destroyers, and, later, the Galaxy Gun.

The Imperial control sector covered most of one continent, and Palpatine's kilometers-high Imperial Citadel was at its center. The vast complex contained gardens, museums, the Emperor's clone labs, barracks for Imperial troopers, and a fully equipped dungeon; it was guarded by advanced turbolasers and dangerous monsters called chrysalides.

Following the Battle of Endor, the Emperor's disembodied spirit returned to Byss to inhabit a new clone body. Weakened by the difficult journey, Palpatine convalesced for six years before finally taking his revenge against the New Republic. Luke Skywalker attempted to learn the secrets of the dark side as the Emperor's apprentice after a Mandalorian prison ship delivered him to Byss. Later that year, Lando Calrissian and Wedge Antilles led an unsuccessful attack on the Imperial Citadel using a cargo of hijacked Viper Automadon battle droids. Soon after, in a battle near Onderon, Han Solo and a team of commandos hijacked the Emperor's flagship, *Eclipse II,* and brought it through hyperspace to Byss. R2-D2 steered the *Eclipse II* on a collision course with the Galaxy Gun, which accidentally fired a planet-destroying missile into Byss's core, destroying the Emperor's throneworld.

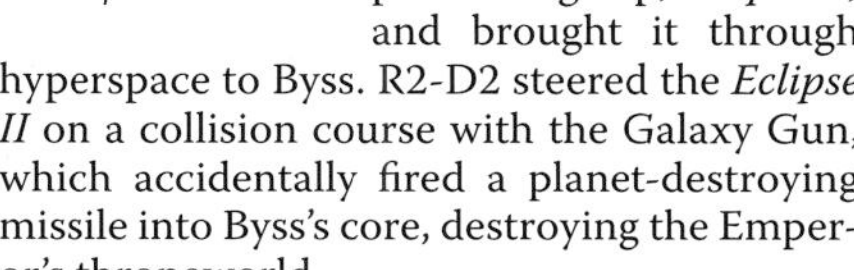

Eight years later, during Tavion Axmis's campaign to resurrect the spirit of long-dead Sith Lord Marka Ragnos, she ventured to the rocky remains of Byss to siphon dark side energy for use in her cult rituals.

**Byss Bistro** Once located in the Imperial Freight Complex on the planet Byss, this cantina was on the outskirts of the Emperor's well-protected complex. Freighter crews and others flocked there to find food, drink, and entertainment while they waited for their ships to be unloaded.

**Bzorn, Captain** An Imperial officer who commandeered Professor Renn Volz's weather-changing Ionic Ring device.

**C2-R4 (Ceetoo-Arfour)** A low, round household droid with bulbs and boxy appendages hanging from his sides, he also had sharp, jagged teeth. Ceetoo-Arfour's specialties included meal preparation, catalytic fuel conversion, enzymatic compost breakdown, chemical diagnostic programming, and bacterial composting acceleration. He was also a combination blender, toaster oven, and bang-corn air popper and could turn common garbage into a meal. After escaping from the Jawas on Tatooine, C2-R4 was discovered in the back alleys of Mos Eisley and adopted by the cantina bartender Wuher, who had him process the pheromones of the dead Rodian bounty hunter Greedo to make an especially potent drink.

*C2-R4*

**C-3PO (See-Threepio)** A fussy and worry-prone protocol droid cobbled together from discarded scrap and salvage by nine-year-old Anakin Skywalker on Tatooine. The child prodigy had intended for the homemade droid to help his mother, Shmi. The droid that Anakin built with limited resources was truly remarkable. Constructed from an aged frame that had first seen assembly more than a century earlier on the mechanized world of Affa, C-3PO lacked an outer shell and had to live with the indignity of being "naked," with his parts and wiring showing.

When Anakin befriended Padmé Naberrie of Naboo, C-3PO first met her astromech droid, the blue-and-white R2-D2. The two formed a fast friendship, working together to perfect Anakin's blazing-fast Podracer for an upcoming competition. The Podrace was pivotal in Anakin's life, thanks to a wager that would give him his freedom upon victory. He won. Anakin left Tatooine with Padmé and Artoo, leaving C-3PO behind with Shmi. Years passed before Shmi eventually relocated to the Lars moisture farm, a small homestead not far from Anchorhead, and took the droid with her.

Threepio became just one of the many droids working on the farm, but Shmi took special care of Anakin's creation. To better protect his fragile inner wiring from the abrasive Tatooine sands, she fitted C-3PO with discolored and mismatched coverings that nonetheless gave the protocol droid a sense of completion.

Anakin Skywalker returned to Tatooine when Shmi was captured and killed by savage Tusken Raiders. After a quiet funeral, Anakin and Padmé left on an important mission to rescue Obi-Wan Kenobi. Since C-3PO was the rightful property of Anakin, the Larses let the young Jedi take the protocol droid with him. This marked the first time the nervous C-3PO had ever been aboard a starship.

Arriving on Geonosis, Anakin and Padmé ventured into the dark catacombs of the Geonosian hives, leaving the droids behind. R2-D2, reunited with C-3PO, insisted they follow. The droids discovered an immense factory churning out countless combat automata for the growing Separatist movement. The protocol droid tumbled into the dangerous machinery and a piece of heavy equipment cleanly sheared his head from his body, though both segments were still active. The headless body wandered into a battle droid assembly line while the head landed on a conveyer belt full of battle droid heads. A head was then automatically affixed to Threepio's body, and Threepio's head was welded to a battle droid body.

Both mismatched droid assemblies wandered confusedly into the battle droid ranks, and when the Separatist droids attacked a Jedi task force sent to Geonosis, poor C-3PO was drawn into the fray. His ordeal was brought to an end when both bodies were incapacitated. R2-D2 came to C-3PO's rescue, tugging the protocol droid's head to his inactive body and reattaching the two.

Anakin may have reclaimed ownership of C-3PO just prior to the outbreak of the Clone Wars, but during that conflict the protocol droid became more the property of Padmé Amidala. C-3PO and R2-D2 would travel with Senator Amidala during the early months of the wars, voyaging to Ilum, Rodia, Bri'ahl, and elsewhere. The droid assisted the Naboo Royal Council following the devastation of Ohma-D'un by the chemical weapons of the Confederacy, after Queen Jamillia appointed him to serve as liaison to the Jedi during that campaign.

Following the Clone Wars, C-3PO and R2-D2 would become the property of the Royal House of Alderaan, an influential family of nobles with ties to the growing Rebel Alliance. C-3PO was subjected to a memory wipe, thus losing all recollection of his early adventures and his past with Anakin and the Jedi.

One in a string of careless owners jettisoned R2-D2 and C-3PO over the deserts of Ingo. After such an unceremonious disposal, the droids finally found some responsible masters—speeder racers Jord Dusat and Thall

*Initially C-3PO lacked an outer shell.*

*<Chewbacca*

Joben, miner Jann Tosh, and Mungo Baobab, a trader from the Manda system. In the Kalarba system, the Pitareeze family took in the droids and gave them a good home. The family had acquired considerable wealth from the development of a popular hyperdrive model. Despite living in their most comfortable surroundings in months, C-3PO and R2-D2 still managed to find trouble. They had several run-ins with not-so-legitimate businessman Olag Greck on nearby Hosk Station. In one encounter, C-3PO was nearly scrapped when he was sent to compete in a gladiatorial arena match after being mistaken for the assassin droid C-3PX.

*Ewoks worshipped the golden droid as a god.*

The two droids were aboard Princess Leia Organa's consular vessel when it was attacked by an Imperial Star Destroyer due to suspected Rebel actions. Leia secretly stored vital Rebel information in R2-D2's memory, and the astromech took it upon himself to complete Leia's failed mission, though C-3PO knew nothing of its details.

R2-D2 commandeered an escape pod and crash-landed on Tatooine. There the droids were taken captive by Jawa traders, and eventually sold to moisture farmer Owen Lars and his nephew Luke Skywalker. Determined to complete his mission of finding famed war hero General Obi-Wan Kenobi, R2-D2 ran away. C-3PO and Luke eventually found him, as well as Kenobi. This started a chain of events that saw C-3PO catapulted into an adventure beyond his imagination. He and R2-D2 were crucial in assisting Luke to spearhead a rescue mission to free Princess Leia from the heart of the gargantuan Imperial space station, the Death Star. Both droids navigated the complex Imperial computer system to provide the rescuers with timely assistance and status updates.

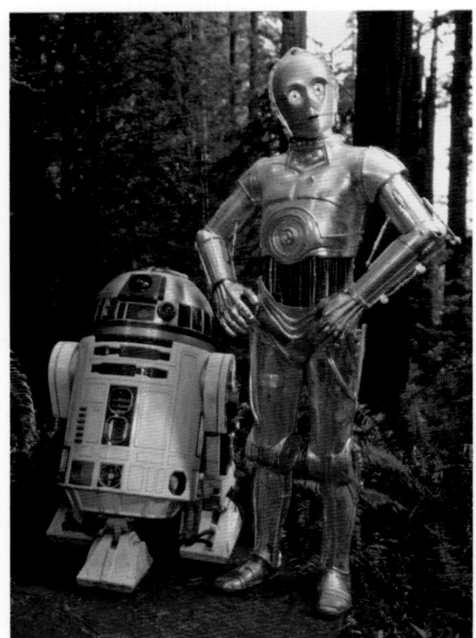

*C-3PO with R2-D2*

Having returned to the Alliance base with Princess Leia, C-3PO and R2-D2 continued to be mainstays of the core group of Rebel heroes. During the relocation to Hoth, C-3PO braved having his joints frozen by subzero temperatures to assist at Echo Base's command center. During the evacuation from Hoth, the droids were separated. C-3PO, accompanying Princess Leia, left Hoth aboard Captain Han Solo's recalcitrant freighter, the *Millennium Falcon*. Although C-3PO was nowhere near as skilled a mechanic as R2-D2, he was helpful in translating the odd language of the *Falcon*'s main computer.

During a respite at Cloud City in the Bespin system, C-3PO was blasted into pieces by an Imperial stormtrooper. His shattered remains were the first clue to the Rebel fugitives that Cloud City was an Imperial trap. The Wookiee Chewbacca attempted to piece together C-3PO's remains, but lack of time and resources meant the droid would have to remain incomplete for the time being.

During a daring mission to rescue a captive Han Solo from the loathsome gangster Jabba the Hutt, C-3PO and R2-D2 were sent into the Hutt's palace on Tatooine. There they became the grisly crime lord's property. C-3PO was pressed into service as Jabba's translator until Luke Skywalker came to rescue his friends.

Shortly thereafter, C-3PO accompanied a Rebel strike force sent to knock out the Imperial shield generator on Endor. There the strike team encountered an indigenous species of primitives who worshipped the golden droid as a god. Were it not for the allegiance of the Ewoks—won by C-3PO's impressive retelling of key events of the Galactic Civil War—the Rebellion would not have been victorious at the decisive Battle of Endor.

During the time of the New Republic, C-3PO played the role of part-time nanny and protector to Han and Leia Organa Solo's three children. Along with R2-D2 and the mechanic Cole Fardreamer, he helped uncover Dark Jedi Kueller's terror scheme, which involved placing detonation devices in droids on Coruscant and throughout the New Republic. As part of the investigation, the group went to Telti, and C-3PO and R2-D2 were forced to confront a terrifying gladiator droid group known as the Red Terror.

During the Yuuzhan Vong War, C-3PO's skills as an interpreter came in handy when he translated the Yuuzhan Vong language used in various items recovered during the Praetorite Vong invasion. In the terrible conflict that followed, he pondered the mortality of droids, especially in light of the Yuuzhan Vong's anti-technology sentiment. He received some reassurance from Han Solo, who offered to download his memory in case anything were to happen to the droid's metal body.

C-3PO evolved far beyond the Cybot Galactic 3PO model that his frame suggested. His TranLang III communications module and AA-1 verbobrain combined to give him fluency in over six million forms of communication. His detailed memory banks contained information on more than 5,100 different types of droids. He was covered in a bronzium finish polished to a dazzling sheen, though years of wear and tear and shoddy replacements left him with a mismatched silver leg. A bit stiff and awkward in his manner, somewhat effete in demeanor, and often overly negative in his outlook, the vaguely human-looking droid nevertheless played a key role in many of the important events of galactic history. What set him and R2-D2 apart was that they both managed to avoid most of the regular memory wipes that droids usually underwent, thus allowing them to learn by experience and develop true personalities like those of sentient beings.

*C-3PX*

**C-3PX** A deadly protocol droid that was once owned and modified by Darth Maul. Maul's last mission with C-3PX was to deliver droid starfighters to the Trade Federation, which involved being captured by Bartokk assassins. Though Maul defeated the Bartokks, he was unable to retrieve C-3PX. The droid came into the possession of crime lord Olag Greck, who used it as an assassin droid. C-3PX looked just like C-3PO, except with an X marked on his forehead and at least 83 concealed weapons. C-3PX took pity on C-3PO, who was pitted in a fight to the death in a droid arena; when he substituted himself for C-3PO he allowed himself to be destroyed.

**C-3TC** A protocol droid once belonging to Valance Serth, it was

C-9979 landing ship

wanted by Black Sun, which led to Valance desperately trying to get rid of it.

**C4-CZN ion field gun** This large Imperial weapon was moved around on rollers.

**C-5MO** The silver protocol droid proprietor of a droid shop on Bastion.

**C-73 Tracker** An antiquated Subpro starfighter found in pirate and Separatist fleets.

**C8-42** A protocol droid belonging to Elise Montagne on Dantooine during the time of the Star Forge crisis. The recently widowed Elise depended too heavily on C8-42 for emotional support.

**C-9979 landing ship** Immense starships used by the Trade Federation to transport their droid army from orbital freighters to planetary surfaces. Specially built by Haor Chall Engineering, these vessels could carry a total of 28 loaded troop carriers, 114 AATs, and 11 MTTs; they required a crew of 88 droids. The C-9979's immense wings were removable for ease of storage and docking. When the craft deployed, powerful tensor field generators bound the wings to it, and strengthened the vessel's overall structural integrity. Large repulsorlifts kept the C-9979 from sagging under its own weight. Two pairs of wingtip lasers and four turret-mounted cannons made up its armaments.

**C-9PO (See-Ninepio)** A newer-model protocol droid that failed Jedi student Brakiss had memory-wiped and modified to serve him on the droid-manufacuting facility he ran on Telti. Like many protocol droids, C-9PO often exhibited an annoying officiousness. Whatever its other improvements, Brakiss found that the model's small feet were as successful a design as the normal-sized feet of the experimental X-1s through X-8s. Another droid identified as C-9PO was stoned to "death" in the Square of Hopeful Redemption on Rhommamool by fervent followers of a disguised Nom Anor.

**Caaldra** This well-connected criminal mercenary operating in the Shelsha sector conspired with the sector's chief Imperial administrator, Vilim Disra, to organize pirate forces in preparation for the sector's sedition. Following a trail of embezzeled funds, the Emperor's Hand Mara Jade discovered the plot and began an intense pursuit of Caaldra, which finally ended on the sector capital Shelkonwa, where Caaldra died when his own blasterfire was deflected from Jade's lightsaber blade.

**Caamas** An inhabited Core world decimated shortly after the end of the Clone Wars. The devastation of the world by unknown parties spurred great outrage in the galaxy, though few knew that newly crowned Emperor Palpatine was the ultimate authority behind the attack. The Caamas Document, hidden in Imperial data banks, identified several prominent Bothan clans as assisting in the deed by lowering the planet's shields, allowing destruction to rain down upon the world. When this document resurfaced decades after the destruction, the tumult and hatred raised against the Bothans threatened to split the New Republic with civil war. Caamas was once a lush, temperate planet composed of three main landmasses. Rolling fields, steppes, stout hillocks, and dense forests teeming with life dominated the landscape. Caamas became a barren, rocky wasteland.

Lieutenant Cabbel

**Caamasi** The species native to Caamas, they were tall gray-furred bipeds with three fingers on their hands. In the languages of many cultures in the galaxy, the name *Caamasi* meant "friend from afar" or "stranger to be trusted." The Caamasi maintained a pacifist society of scholars and nobles with high moral values. Some legends claimed that the first Jedi Knights traveled to Caamas to learn how to use their powers ethically. All Caamasi could create lasting, vivid memories called memnii that were shared telepathically with others of their species. Just after the Clone Wars, the planet was devastated by an unknown enemy. A large Caamasi Remnant community survived on Kerilt, though, and some later relocated to Susevfi. Refugees from Caamas went to several other worlds, one of them Alderaan.

Caamasi

**Caarimon** A warm, steamy primary world in the Caarimoos system, located in the Outer Rim. It was the homeworld of the Caarites. Several millennia before the onset of the Clone Wars, the planet experienced a shift in its axial tilt after an asteroid slammed into its surface. That gave the planet a more tropical environment, reducing the duration of the seasons. The Caarites once lived in terrestrial cities, but soon discovered that many of them were producing toxic wastes that were slowly killing Caarimon. In a massive effort, the Caarites began developing floating cities that never touched the surface, thereby preserving the strange and unusual plant life that covered the planet.

**Cabal, the** An Imperial organization based primarily on Brentaal IV that was pitted against Sate Pestage.

**Caba'Zan** The onetime Falleen head of security for InterGalactic Ore. Acting upon information fabricated by Darth Maul, Nort Toom of Clan Toom contacted Caba'Zan about sabotaging Lommite Limited ships at Eriadu for 150,000 Republic credits. Clan Toom secretly arranged the same deal with Lommite Limited, resulting in the destruction of the cargo ships from both companies. Caba'Zan and his counterpart at LL, Patch Bruit, joined forces to bring an end to Clan Toom. In the very last moments of the battle, Darth Maul entered the fray to ensure that no one survived.

**Cabbel, Lieutenant** A graduate of the officer candidate school on Carida, he served as first officer of the Imperial Star Destroyer *Tyrant.* His men described him as efficient, but also very ambitious and ruthless.

**Cadaman, Senator Tanner** A representative of Fenix in the Galactic Senate who signed the Petition of the Two Thousand in opposition to Chancellor Palpatine's increase in executive power. With the rise of the Galactic Empire, Cadaman was one of 63 Senators arrested on charges of conspiracy and treason.

**Cadavine sector** The sector that contained the planet Zhar.

**Cadgel Meadows** A stretch of open grassland on New Plympto, and the site of the planet's largest civilian spaceport. Clone troopers working for the Galactic Empire seized control of Cadgel Meadows and rounded up Nosaurian refugees for sale into slavery.

**Cadinth** A desert world in the Tion Hegemony that tried to remain neutral in the Separatist crisis, it was the site of a battle between the New Republic and the Empire two years after the Battle of Endor.

**Cadmir, Jerem** A Corellian human, he was a member of the ExGal-4 science team on Belkadan, knowledgeable in geology and climatology. During a scouting trip, he was shocked to discover the encroaching ecological disaster unleashed by the Yuuzhan Vong at the start of their invasion. He was the only member of the scouting party to make it back to the base alive, but once there, Yomin Carr revealed himself as a Yuuzhan Vong infiltrator and killed Cadmir.

**Cadomai** The frigid homeworld of the Snivvians, it was sometimes frequented as a resort spot.

**Caedus, Darth** *See* Solo, Jacen.

***Caelus*** A New Republic cruiser.

**caf** A stimulant beverage made from ground beans.

**cafarel** These Zeltron courtesans trained in physical pleasures were very much sought after by the Hutts.

**Cag, Captain** The pilot of the *Argo Moon.*

**Cai** A Mistryl Shadow Guard, she was involved in the botched transfer to the Empire of the Hammertong device—one of the long, cylindrical sections of the superlaser for the second Death Star.

**Cailshh** An Ubese mercenary who worked for Ghez Hokan on Qiilura during the Clone Wars. The overzealous Cailshh torched valuable farmland in a fruitless search for Republic spies. As punishment, Hokan beheaded Cailshh.

**Cairn (1)** One of the larger Rodian clans, and bitter enemies of the Reevan clan. Evo the Blue led the Cairn clan into battle, but the Reevans benefited from the hired assistance of Nym the Feeorin.

**Cairn (2)** An asteroid in the Lenico system that served as a base of operations for Galak Fyyar. Kyle Katarn visited Cairn during his search for Desann.

**Cairnwick, Drun** A highly charismatic Rebel Alliance leader in the distant Minos Cluster.

**Cakhmaim** A fiercly loyal protector of Leia Organa Solo, he was a warrior of the Noghri clan Eikh'mir. Cakhmaim and nine of his brethren were tasked with protecting the infants Jacen and Jaina Solo during the New Republic campaign to stop Grand Admiral Thrawn. For this and other duties, he became one of the most trusted of Leia's bodyguards, alongside Meewalh. In the Galactic Alliance war against the Corellian Confederation, Cakhmaim and Meewalh were killed while manning the *Millennium Falcon*'s turrets when the ship sustained direct hits from the Star Destroyer *Anakin Solo.*

**Cal (1)** A young human at the time of the Clone Wars, he was the Padawan of Master Tyffix, who taught him to fight like a warrior and to think like a conqueror in order to survive. After Tyffix was killed on Thustra, Cal accompanied Yoda as the Jedi Master attempted to make peace with King Alaric. Cal was frustrated with Yoda's lack of action, as he preferred a more aggressive solution. Betrayed by Alaric, Cal was cut down by the king's guards, and he died cursing Yoda's name.

**Cal (2)** A yellow star orbited by Tibrin, it was the homeworld of the Ishi Tib.

*Cal*

**Caladian, Curran, and Tyro** Senatorial aides during the final years of the Galactic Republic, these Svivreni were cousins. Tyro was a friend to Obi-Wan Kenobi, helping the Jedi Knight uncover information on criminals Granta Omega and Jenna Zan Arbor. Tyro's investigative diligence led to his death prior to the Clone Wars, when his snooping into Coruscanti affairs unveiled a dark, secret plot. Years later, his cousin Curran went underground during the transition from Galactic Republic to Empire. He joined the Erased, a group of fugitives desperate to avoid Imperial persecution. Curran worked with Ferus Olin on early Rebel missions against the Empire.

**Calamar** The capital city of Esseles and a center of high culture. One of the Core Worlds' most effective Rebel cells was based in Calamar's entertainment industry during the Galactic Civil War.

**Calamari** *See* Mon Calamari.

**Calamarian** *See* Mon Calamari.

**calcifier** A bioengineered Yuuzhan Vong device that implanted yorik coral into the body of an enslaved being.

**Calculator** One of the subnodes of Assembler Kud'ar Mub'at that specialized in mathematical computations, but was not involved in Balancesheet's maintenance of Mub'at's finances.

**Calders, Major** A thick-muscled bull of a man who served aboard the first Death Star, he had previously been stationed at the political detention wards of Odik II.

**Caldoni system** Nearly ravaged by the Tendor Virus, the population of this system was saved by a cure developed by Jenna Zan Arbor.

**Caleb** A healer who lived on Ambria with his daughter around the time of the Battle of Ruusan. Caleb was forced to heal Darth Bane, who had been poisoned with synox by a fellow Sith Lord. He at first refused, and demonstrated that he was immune to physical torture by plunging his hand into a boiling cauldron. Bane instead threatened his daughter, so Caleb had no choice but to comply. A decade later, Darth Zannah brought an ailing Bane to Caleb to find a cure for the orbalisks that were sapping his strength. Caleb again refused, and by this time he had sent his daughter far from Ambria so that she could not be used as leverage against him.

**Calfa-5** A planet with desert moons.

**Calibop** A species of sentient, winged aliens with tails and manes. New Republic Acting Chief of State Ponc Gavrisom and Sergeant at Arms Mif Kumas were Calibops.

**Calius saj Leelo** The largest city on Berchest, popularly known as the City of Glowing Crystal because it was formed from a single crystal, the result of minerals deposited from the Leefari sea. The city suffered a major quake just prior to the Clone Wars.

**Cal-i-Vaun** A Jedi Knight, he stood guard at a security checkpoint at the Jedi Temple when Obi-Wan Kenobi was a Padawan.

Nyna Calixte looks at a holoimage of Kol Skywalker and herself, as Morrigan Corde, with their son, Cade.

**Calixte, Moff Nyna** The officer in charge of Imperial Intelligence during the time of Emperor Roan Fel, she was the former wife of Moff Rulf Yage and the lover of Grand Admiral Morlish Veed. When Darth Krayt's Sith Order first approached the Empire, it was through Calixte. Many in the Empire underestimated her, believing Calixte to have risen to her position through means other than skill, though she was in truth quite cunning.

When undercover as Morrigan Corde, she romanced Kol Skywalker, and their union produced a child, Cade. Morrigan abandoned the Skywalkers to return to Imperial service, marrying Yage and having a daughter, Gunn. Years later, she resumed her Morrigan identity to help prevent Cade from falling to the dark side under the corruption of Darth Krayt.

**Calkin, Rip** Known as the Iron One, this famed smashball player was one of the few to ever score 700.

**Callen, Vi** A Galactic Senator sympathetic to the Jedi, he investigated Obi-Wan Kenobi's involvement in the death of Bruck Chun.

**caller** A small, handheld transmitter used to summon droids affixed with restraining bolts. They were also called restraining bolt activators or droid summoners.

**Calliose** A Kajain'sa'Nikto bounty hunter, he was Skahtul's principal partner in the hunt for Luke Skywalker shortly after the Battle of Hoth. After Luke escaped from their clutches, Skahtul blamed Calliose, putting him in shackles with the intent of collecting a bounty on his life.

**Callista** *See* Ming, Callista.

**Callos** At Darth Vader's command, Imperial pilot Juno Eclipse led a bombing run against insurgents on the Outer Rim world of Callos. The attack destroyed a massive planetary reactor, causing global climate changes that wiped out nearly all life on the planet.

***Call to Reason, A*** A pamphlet written by Mon Mothma describing the aims of the Rebel Alliance and the crimes of the Galactic Empire, it was distributed to unallied yet sympathetic worlds early in the Galactic Civil War.

**Callum, Trey** A Rebel field officer in charge of a squad of Rebel Alliance ground troops at Outpost Beta at Echo Base on Hoth, he defected from the Imperial officer corps to join the Rebellion. He was skilled at rationing supplies and making the best use of the Alliance's small weapons stockpile. He was killed during the opening barrages of the Battle of Hoth.

**Calna Muun** The capital city of Agamar, where the Agamarian Council convened. It was a coastal city with a spaceport.

**Calocour Heights** The marketing district of Coruscant, located near Column Commons, south of the Imperial Palace. It resembled the Corporate Sector in miniature.

Lando Calrissian as a general in the Rebel Alliance

**Calrissian, Lando** Suave gambler turned city administrator and dashing scoundrel turned hero: Such are the inconsistencies that peppered the life of Lando Calrissian.

With the spirit of a soldier of fortune and the heart of a high-stakes player, Lando had a kind of love–hate—or rather, win–lose—relationship with Han Solo for years. Han's ship, the *Millennium Falcon,* was previously owned and flown by Lando. In fact, before losing the *Falcon* to Han in a game of sabacc (the ship was destined to be lost and won several times again in sabacc games between the two rogues), Lando flew it on a yearlong trip during which he searched for treasure on planets of the Rafa system, was nearly killed because of his consistent hot hand at every gambling table, and aided a persecuted species called the Oswaft. He was accompanied by a pilot droid he had won, Vuffi Raa.

Not long after losing the *Falcon,* Lando won something of great value in another sabacc game: Bespin's Cloud City, where he took over as Baron Administrator. Lando proved quite adept at both running the Tibanna-gas-mining colony and using it as a cover for some of his more colorful activities, such as smuggling and secretly aiding the Rebel Alliance.

But Lando's luck ran out when Imperial forces led by Darth Vader visited. Hoping to set a trap that would attract Luke Skywalker, Vader told Lando that he must detain Solo and his party. If he did, the Imperials would never bother Bespin again; if he failed, he could kiss his future good-bye. Feeling that he had no choice, Lando entrapped Han and Princess Leia. But Vader went back on his word and entombed Han in carbonite, entrusting him to bounty hunter Boba Fett. That convinced Lando to help the heroic Rebels. He ordered the evacuation of the city and fought back against Imperial forces, later rescuing a near-dead Skywalker from the very bottom of the floating city in the clouds.

Lando failed in one early attempt to snatch Han back from the bounty hunter, then aided in rescuing Leia from the head of the Black Sun crime syndicate, Prince Xizor. He later disguised himself as a guard for Jabba the Hutt, infiltrated Jabba's palace, and was in place when Luke rescued Han; Han returned the favor, saving Lando's life by snatching him from the maw of the Sarlacc in the Tatooine desert. For his valor, and in recognition of his skills at the Battle of Taanab, prior to the Battle of Hoth, Lando was given the rank of general in the Alliance forces and helped lead the charge in the pivotal Battle of Endor. Piloting the *Falcon,* Lando, along with Wedge Antilles in an X-wing fighter, destroyed the Empire's second Death Star battle station.

A short time after the Battle of Endor, General Calrissian formed a team of commandos to track down bandits operating out of the Abraxas System. Following that, Lando returned to private life, establishing a unique mining colony on the planet Nkllon to supply raw materials to the New Republic. But when Imperials stole the

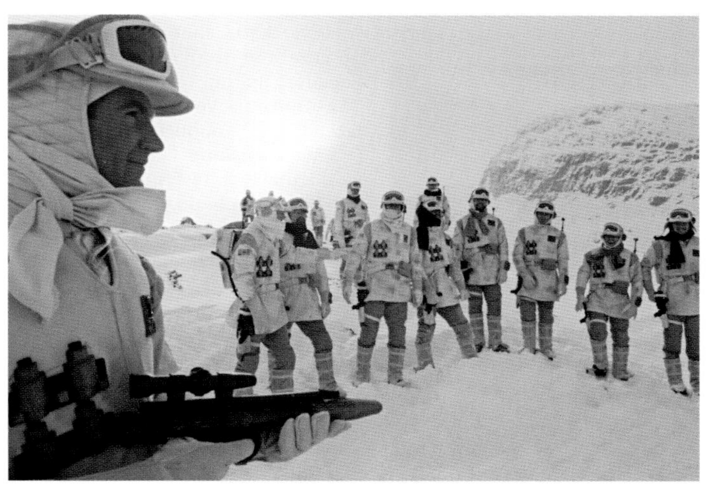

Trey Callum (left) with his squad of Rebel Alliance ground troops on Hoth

mole miners used in the operation for use in the Imperial attack on the important New Republic Sluis Van shipyards, Lando rejoined Republic forces and helped thwart the attack. Later he helped command the forces at the Battle of Mon Calamari.

Lando went back and forth between the roles of businessman and warrior—he was a leading member of a New Republic special forces team (the Senate Interplanetary Intelligence Network, or SPIN) and Baron Administrator of Hologram Fun World, a dome-covered floating amusement park—but he always kept busy. He helped Luke Skywalker find recruits for his Jedi academy, rescued Leia at least once more, got involved in several dubious moneymaking schemes, crashed at least two converted Imperial Star Destroyers, helped put down major threats to the New Republic, and won—and lost—a dozen fortunes.

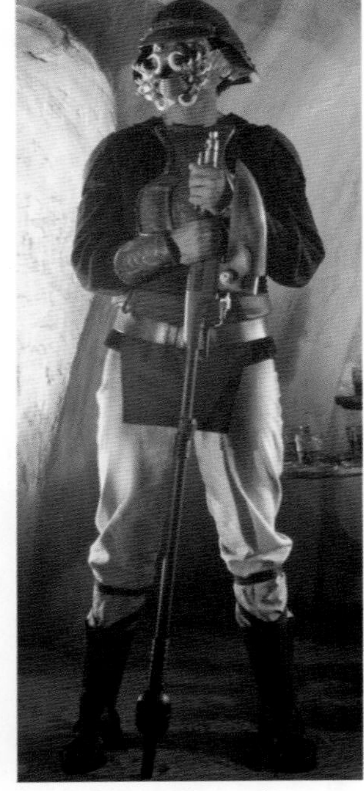

*Lando Calrissian disguised as a guard in Jabba the Hutt's palace*

At the onset of the Yuuzhan Vong War, Lando was married to Tendra Risant, and had a mining and processing operation on Destrillion and Dubrillion while living on the latter world. The Yuuzhan Vong forced the evacuation of Dubrillion, bringing Calrissian into the war effort against the invaders. He oversaw the establishment of the Jedi safehouse known as Shelter. His company, Tendrando Arms, manufactured the YVH 1 droids, combat automata designed specifically to battle the Yuuzhan Vong. Calrissian served as General Ba'tra's special operations commander during the Yuuzhan Vong assault on Coruscant.

With the Yuuzhan Vong threat ended, Calrissian was able to concentrate on his business ventures and marriage. His YVH droids proved useful in the Dark Nest crisis that threatened the galaxy, as well as the escalating tensions between the Galactic Alliance and the Corellian Confederation. With Han Solo and Leia Organa Solo branded traitors by the Alliance, Calrissian covertly assisted them with the loan of his vessel, the *Love Commander.* Lando limited his more active involvement in this conflict when he learned that his wife was pregnant.

**Calrissian, Tendra Risant** Once a minor functionary on Sacorria and captain of the *Gentleman Caller,* she warned the New Republic of a threat from a huge Sacorrian fleet. Rich, tall, and strong, she also grew fond of Lando Calrissian, and the two wed sometime before the Yuuzhan Vong invasion. The couple formed Tendrando Arms, the company that constructed the effective YVH war droid. During the conflict between the Galactic Alliance and the Corellian Confederation, she became pregnant with the Calrissians' first child. Tendra was a human female with high cheekbones, a fair complexion, a slender face, and dark brown eyes. She had brownish blond hair that she wore short.

**Cal-Seti** This was the site of the docking port Ramsees Hed where, following the Battle of Yavin, Alliance agent Kyle Katarn placed a tracking device on a smuggling ship that led him to an Imperial robotics facility on Anteevy.

**Caltrop 5** A chaff gun developed by Arakyd that fired clouds of sensor-distorting durasteel into the air, it could be found on *Jadthu*-class landing craft.

**Caluula** A remote planet in the Tion Hegemony, home to the natural phenomenon called the Nocturne of the Winged-Stars, which saw the emergence of winged-star creatures every 300 years. Scientists would flock to Caluula to observe and study this peculiar mating cycle. The Yuuzhan Vong attacked and conquered Caluula, making the world the first test site for the new biological weapon developed by the New Republic and the Chiss, Alpha Red. It proved effective in destroying the Yuuzhan Vong's bioengineered weapons, but it also disrupted the mating cycles of the winged-stars, thus proving that it was too unpredictable to use as a weapon.

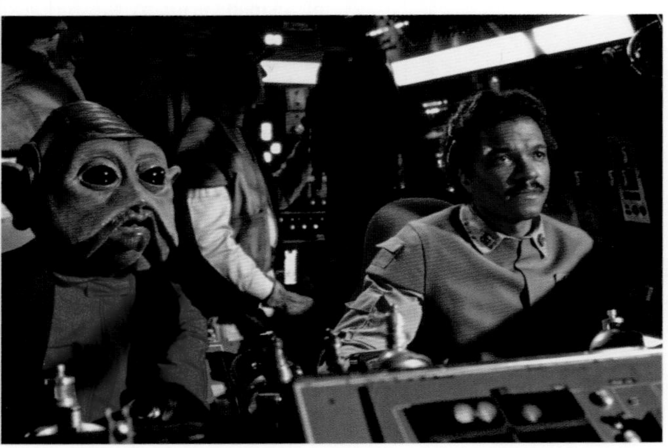

*Alliance General Calrissian helped lead the charge in the pivotal Battle of Endor.*

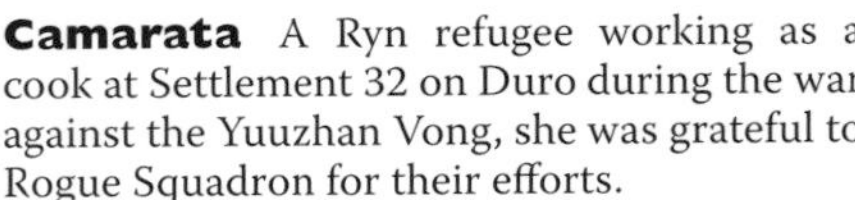

**Camarata** A Ryn refugee working as a cook at Settlement 32 on Duro during the war against the Yuuzhan Vong, she was grateful to Rogue Squadron for their efforts.

**Camas, Iri** A Jedi general who commanded the headquarters of the Grand Army of the Republic during the Clone Wars and eventually achieved the rank of Director of Special Forces. Camas was greatly concerned with the effectiveness of the clone troopers. Under his command, clone troopers averaged a destruction ratio of 200 battle droids per soldier, and clone commandos specifically trained to take out droid-manufacturing and raw-materials plants accounted for the loss of billions more.

**cambylictus tree** A huge tree native to swampy areas of the forest moon of Endor and elsewhere. Its roots had medicinal properties and were used as healing agents during the Clone Wars.

**Cam'Co, Jer'Jo** A Chiss syndic famous in the history of Csilla, he proposed the founding of the Chiss Expansionary Defense Fleet. At least seven Chiss starships bore his name, as did two star systems in Chiss space.

**Camie** *See* Loneozner, Camie.

**Campaign Against Republic Militarization** A political organization founded by Senator Padmé Amidala during the Separatist crisis to oppose the Military Creation Act.

**Camper** *See* Vandrayk, Gorman.

**Camp Four** A well-defended detainment camp established by the Trade Federation after the invasion of Naboo. OOM-9 was responsible for transporting Queen Amidala and her entourage to Camp Four, but Naboo's sovereign was rescued by Obi-Wan Kenobi and Qui-Gon Jinn before she could be imprisoned. Camp Four was liberated by Lieutenant Gavyn Sykes and his forces.

**camp ship** Yuuzhan Vong ships that carried prisoners of war, they were kilometers thick, roughly globular, and looked like vast random glued-together masses of hexagonal chambers ranging from the size of a footlocker to the size of a carrier's flight deck. The ships might have been some kind of plant or made up of abandoned animal exoskeletons. Sensor data indicated the standard dovin basal propulsion systems. They were known to carry millions of passengers.

**Cana, King** The onetime king of Gala and husband of Queen Veda, he was the father of Prince Beju. Before his arranged marriage to Queen Veda, King Cana was married to Tema, a member of the mountain people. Elan was their daughter. After Cana's death, Gala abandoned rule by monarchy and Queen Veda held open elections.

**Canavar, Onyeth** A male Tarnab seen on the entertainment district streets of Coruscant.

**can-cell** Large dragonfly-like insects that were insectivores themselves, but were known to eat small rodents. They were found on Kashyyyk, Dagobah, Rodia, and Teth. On Kashyyyk, they often accompanied Wookiee aircraft as they made their approaches, and Wookiees looked to them as pets and good omens.

***Candaserri*** An *Acclamator*-class Republic assault ship stationed in high orbit during the assault on Raxus Prime, commanded by General Glynn-Beti. After the battle, a gunship rescued and delivered young Boba Fett to the assault ship. The crew of the *Candaserri* was made up of individuals representing a diverse range of sentient species, in addition to its complement of clone troopers. Padawan Ulu Ulix was in charge of the ship's Orphan Hall, whose residents were sometimes referred to as "space brats." Boba's favorite spot on the ship was its rear observation blister, or ROB, a small cold room under a clear plexi dome. The *Candaserri* had a little lander that delivered 21 orphans to Cloud City.

***Canderous*-class assault tank** A heavily armored repulsor tank manufactured by MandalTech and named for the ancient Mandalore Canderous Ordo. It featured a pair of heavy mass-driver cannons and a concussion missile battery.

**Candorian plague** A deadly airborne plague weaponized by the Empire during the Galactic Civil War and unleashed on Dentaal.

**canir** A title given to elected Vratix leaders on Thyferra.

**cannibal arachnid** A legendary giant spider-like species on Duro that died out as the planet's ecosystem collapsed.

**cannok** Vicious, wide-jawed predators that the Ithorians imported from Dxun to Telos to keep the herbivore population in check.

**cannonade** An exploding projectile weapon, it was fired by a crossbow.

**Cant, Devin** A trooper aboard the first Death Star, he was an elite soldier trained in combat techniques and weapons skills. He augmented security personnel guarding Princess Leia Organa in detention block AA-23. He was killed in the line of duty when Han Solo, Chewbacca, and Luke Skywalker freed Leia.

**Cantham House** Bail Organa's residence on Coruscant, the site of clandestine meetings among Organa, Mon Mothma, and Garm Bel Iblis during the early planning stages of the Rebel Alliance.

**cantina** *See* Mos Eisley cantina.

**Canu** A deity worshipped by the primitive inhabitants of Circarpous V.

**Canyonade** A vast expanse of hotels, shops, restaurants, and meeting areas carved into the canyons of the planet Cejansij.

**canyon dune turn** A section of the Mos Espa Podrace course also known as Tusken Turn, this sharp curve attracted Tusken Raiders who enjoyed taking potshots at passing Podracers.

**CAP** An acronym for "Combat Aerospace Patrol," it consisted of Rogue Squadron's Flights One, Two, and Three. One flight guarded an escape route at all times while the other two groups engaged the enemy.

**CAP-2 Captivator** A small personal vehicle often used by bounty hunters, it had four arms and a rear-mounted grasping mechanism to hold a prisoner.

**Capital Powers Act** A set of laws passed by Emperor Palpatine that gave him the authority to impose martial law on any world in order to bring it in line with the New Order.

**capital ship** Any of a class of enormous combat starships designed for deep-space warfare, such as Imperial Star Destroyers and Mon Calamari star cruisers, the ships were usually staffed by crews numbering in the hundreds or even thousands, had numerous weapons and shields, and often carried shuttles, starfighters, or other smaller offensive mobile weapons platforms in their huge hangar bays.

**Capo** A Rodian member of the Peace Brigade, he and fellow Brigader Darda went undercover as New Republic agents on the starliner *Queen of Empire* to gain access to captive Yuuzhan Vong priestess Elan. Capo injured New Republic Intelligence Major Showolter and killed agent Saiga Bre'lya before escaping, although he, too, was wounded during the skirmish. Later he commanded the Peace Brigade's modest navy with the inflated rank of admiral. Thrackan Sal-Solo, who despised Capo, secretly hoped the Yuuzhan Vong Maal Lah would execute Capo in disgust.

**Cappie** The affectionate nickname of Jaina Solo's astromech droid R2-B3 during the war against the Yuuzhan Vong, named for Anni Capstan.

**Caprioril** A once tranquil world in the Galactic Core, it was the site of an infamous massacre when an assassin droid slaughtered 20,000 people at a swoop arena—including famous racer Ignar Ominaz—in order to murder Governor Amel Bakli. Onetime top aide to Emperor Palpatine Mara Jade briefly worked under the name Marellis for a Caprioril swoop gang following the death of Palpatine. Caprioril was named a sector capital by the New Republic, and was besieged by Imperial forces during the Emperor's reappearance six years after the Battle of Endor. Around this time, Alliance historian Arhul Hextrophon survived an assassination attempt while visiting the planet.

**Capstan, Anni** Rogue Twelve of Rogue Squadron during the Yuuzhan Vong War, she served as Jaina Solo's wingmate and roommate. Capstan died in battle during the defense of Ithor. In tribute, Jaina named her astromech Cappie.

**capstone** The final piece in constructing a Sith Holocron, it was used to trap the cognitive matrix inside the crystalline structure. The Sith used a Rite of Commencement as part of the process.

**Captison, Gaeriel** An Imperial Senator from Bakura during the final years of the Rebellion, she helped draft the Truce of Bakura, leading her planet and people to freedom. Gaeriel's parents—including her father, Senator Dol Captison—were killed in the uprising that followed the Imperial invasion of Bakura, and she was raised by her aunt, Tiree, and uncle, Yeorg Captison, the Prime Minister.

Bakura faced immediate danger when the reptilian Ssi-ruuvi Imperium invaded following the Battle of Endor. Imperial forces suffered heavy losses as they inflicted great damage on the Ssi-ruuk. As the battle raged, ships from the Rebel Alliance arrived and offered aid to the Bakurans. Luke Skywalker helped write the truce under which Gaeriel's planet joined the New Republic. She went on to help her uncle restore Bakura and repair the damage inflicted by Imperial forces during their occupation. Gaeriel, who later married former Imperial officer Pter Thanas, herself was elected Prime Minister but was defeated in a succeeding election. The two had a child, Malinza. The little girl was only three years old when her father succumbed to Knowt's disease and passed away.

During Gaeriel's term in office, Bakura revived and bolstered its system defenses with four advanced warships, the *Watchkeeper, Sentinel, Defender,* and *Intruder.* These were Gaeriel's legacy after she retired from politics to spend more time with her daughter. During an insurrection in the Corellian system, Luke Skywalker, now a Jedi Master, returned to Bakura needing warships with the advanced anti-interdiction technology that the Bakurans possessed. The four starships that Captison commissioned set out for Corellia under the command of Admiral Hortel Ossilege, with Gaeriel aboard serving as Bakuran plenipotentiary.

*Gaeriel Captison*

Gaeriel was killed in the battle that followed, as the Bakuran ships broke through the enemy lines of the Sacorrian Triad.

This left little Malinza Thanas orphaned. She was adopted by a well-placed Bakuran family and grew to be a musical prodigy, earning a place in the Bakuran National Symphony. Luke Skywalker felt protective of Malinza, visiting her several times following her mother's death and helping to sponsor her education.

*Carbon-freezing chamber*

**Captison, Yeorg** The Prime Minister of Bakura, he was a figurehead under the Imperial occupation. Although he sympathized with the Rebel Alliance, he didn't want any more blood shed on his planet. After the destruction of the second Death Star and a truce between the Empire and the Alliance, he rejuvenated Bakura with the help of his niece, Gaeriel.

**capture beast** A 200-meter-long segmented creature bioengineered by the Yuuzhan Vong to restrain opponents instead of killing them. This caterpillar-like beast had 100 pairs of sucker-tipped legs, bioluminescent eye spots, and twitching antennae.

**carababba tabac** A fine tabac favored by Niles Ferrier, who was always smoking a long thin cigarra. Ferrier carried the distinctive aroma of carababba tabac and armudu spice wherever he went.

**caraboose** An herbivore native to Toola that was the favored prey of Whiphids.

**Caramm V** A beautiful world ravaged by its silver-tongued ruler Ado Eemon, who allied the planet to the Separatists during the Clone Wars.

**Carannia** The capital city of Serenno, it was noted for its vast, open-air markets where all manner of goods and services from across the galaxy could be found.

**carapod** A mount and pack animal native to Zonama Sekot. Carapods stood as high as a man at the main joint of each of their three legs. Glints of metal shone in patches on their bodies, as if the creatures were melded with steel.

**Caravan** The front company founded by Lorian Nod to cover his illegal actions against the Jedi Knights and the Republic. It was named for a star cruiser he designed and hoped to build in his youth.

***Caravel*** The smooth, dome-shaped merchant ship of Mungo Baobab.

**Carbanti United Electronics** A manufacturer of shipboard sensor array systems and countermeasure equipment.

**carbon-freezing chamber** A device that flash-froze Tibanna gas for transportation throughout the galaxy. In his attempt to capture Luke Skywalker, Darth Vader had one of Cloud City's carbon-freezing chambers converted to function on humans. Before he would use it on Luke, however, he tested the machine on Han Solo. Han survived the process but remained imprisoned in carbonite for months. And although he was trapped in a state of suspended animation, he remained conscious and fully aware throughout his terrible ordeal.

Each carbonite block weighed more than 100 kilograms. A hydraulic lift transported the block from the pit, and metal retrieval tongs placed the carbonite on a repulsorsled. While in transport to processing and shipping stations, the Tibanna gas was protected from radiation and extreme temperatures by the carbonite shell.

**carbonite** A strong but highly volatile metal used to manufacture faster-than-light engines and preserve materials such as Tibanna gas. On Cloud City, Darth Vader froze Han Solo in carbonite. The Pyn'gani of Polus played a major role in developing the carbonite-freezing process used to store goods for long-term shipment; mining the valuable metal was a major source of income.

**carbonite guild** A tightly knit, arrogant, and ruthless group, the guild controlled the mining of raw carbonite in the Empress Teta system, a prime source of the volatile metal, some 4,000 years before the Battle of Yavin.

**carbo-plas** A lightweight yet durable building material used in the construction of starfighters like the A-wing.

**Carbos Thirteen** The space surrounding this planet was the site of a battle between Admiral Bwua'tu and the Corellian and Bothan fleets of the Confederation, in the weeks that followed the Second Battle of Fondor. Bwua'tu managed to trap both opposing fleets near the planet, eliminating a large percentage of the warships that supported the Confederation.

**Carconth** A red supergiant star, it was the second largest and seventh brightest of all known stars in the galaxy. A supernova watch was long in place. Twelve years after the Battle of Endor, the New Republic's Colonel Pakkpekatt arrived at Carconth aboard Lando Calrissian's *Lady Luck* in search of the missing Calrissian and his companions. But when the ship arrived, it was taken over by a slave circuit activated by Calrissian's beacon call.

**Car'das, Jorj** A smuggler who began his career prior to the Clone Wars, he created one of the larger, more successful smuggling organizations in the galaxy. Car'das started as navigator aboard Dubrak Qennto's freighter *Bargain Hunter.* While eluding angry Hutt pursuers, the ship voyaged into the unexplored fringes of the Outer Rim, coming into contact with the Chiss and Commander Thrawn. Through Car'das, Thrawn learned much about the Republic, while Car'das learned Cheunh, the language of the Chiss. Knowledge was his passion, and Car'das passed that zeal on to his successor, Talon Karrde. During the Bpfasshi Dark Jedi incident of the Clone Wars, Car'das's ship was commandeered and he was kidnapped by the Dark Jedi. Half mad with rage, one of the Dark Jedi battled the Jedi Master Yoda for a day and a half. Yoda won, and he nursed Car'das back to health. A latent Force sensitivity was triggered during his time with Yoda, but the Jedi Master did not have time to heal him fully, instead sending him to the Aing-Tii to learn their ways in the Force. Sixteen years after the Battle of Endor, Karrde visited Car'das in the Kathol sector and received information that would help end the threat of the imposter Grand Admiral Thrawn.

**Cardooine** This world was home of fragrant Fijisi wood, used in the Imperial Palace on Coruscant and even in some spacecraft built on the planet. A virus first diagnosed on the planet was popularly called the Cardooine Chills. Its symptoms included congestion, coughing, fatigue, and body aches and pains. The symptoms usually disappeared within two weeks, but there was a lingering weakness for perhaps another month. Once infected, the body developed an immunity to the disease.

**Cardua system** With ore-rich asteroid belts, this system bordering the Xorth system supported many miners, who exported all their output to the Empire during the New Order.

**caretaker virus** A droid virus developed by Master Zorneth that compelled infected automata to come to the aid of Smilers, organics addicted to the synthetic savorium herb. The protocol droid PDA6 secretly programmed R2-D2 with the virus, which was later easily removed.

**cargo lifter** These large repulsorlift vehicles—typically operated by a single pilot—were the workhorses that loaded and unloaded cargo and made short-distance hauls to storage facilities in other parts of a spaceport. The use of mechanical claws by older cargo lifters was replaced by tractor beams and repulsor technology. The TaggeCo Cargohopper 102 was a common cargo lifter.

**Carid, Baltan** A Mandalorian soldier who fought against the Yuuzhan Vong and supported Boba Fett in the role of *Mand'alor*, he had white hair and a dark blue tattoo of a vine that ran from his chin down to his chest.

**Carida** One of several planets in the Caridan system, it was a large, high-gravity world with a wide variety of terrain. It was the site of the Empire's most important stormtrooper training center. The planet was populated by Caridans—humanoids who had thin limbs and heavy, barrel chests—as well as native life-forms such as combat arachnids. The Imperial military training center included a main citadel surrounded by a towering wall. The planet's varied surface, rocky mountains, frozen ice fields, jungles filled with carnivorous plants, and arid deserts provided perfect training for combat in harsh environments.

Admiral Daala attended the Caridan Academy before her appointment to the staff of Grand Moff Tarkin. After the annihilation of Alderaan, several of the Death Star's designers were transferred from the battle station to Carida. Dash Rendar attended the Academy until he was dishonorably discharged after his older brother crashed a freighter into the Emperor's private museum on Imperial Center. Later, Ambassador Furgan was the Caridan representative to the New Republic and oversaw the development of the MT-AT "spider walker." Alliance Admiral Ackbar's aide Terpfen underwent torture and reconditioning on the planet to turn him into an Imperial puppet. Carida was destroyed when Jedi Kyp Durron caused its star to go nova through the use of an Imperial superweapon, the Sun Crusher.

Xandel Carivus

Nova Station was located in the remnants of the Carida system. It floated just inside the supernova's expanding gas shell, moving along behind the edge at a matching 3 kilometers per second.

**Carida Nebula** The collection of crimson dust and space gases marked the remains of the Carida system, which was destroyed when Kyp Durron used the Sun Crusher to cause its primary star to achieve supernova. Popular lore attributed the color of the nebula to the vaporized blood of every being that was killed in the cataclysm.

Great Pit of Carkoon

**Caridan** Members of this humanoid species native to Carida had thin limbs and heavy, barrel chests. Caridans evolved in a high-gravity environment and had surprising physical strength considering their lanky frames. Their mercantile culture adapted well to the prolonged presence of the Empire, and many Caridan-owned industries provided equipment and machinery for the Imperial Academy on their planet. They saw the Empire not as an occupying force, but as a long-term customer. Caridans averaged well over 2 meters in height, with long eyebrows and three-fingered hands. Their long, spindly-looking legs were composed almost entirely of wiry muscle and ended in two-toed, semi-hoofed feet. Few Caridans ever left their homeworld before its destruction, though a few traveling Caridan merchants possibly survived in the galaxy at large, and a few more survived within the ranks of the New Republic military.

**Caridan combat arachnid** Spider-like creatures that originated on Carida, they had 12 legs, huge and powerful jaws, crimson body armor splotched with maroon, and bodies covered with needle-sharp spines. Jabba the Hutt pitted several arachnids against his rancor, injuring the beast.

**Carivus, Xandel** A member of the Imperial Interim Council, he was a longtime bureaucrat who was seen by others as lacking both vision and a spine. Carivus worked with the mysterious Nom Anor, who manipulated events to make him head of the Ruling Council. He took over the Council by force with his private guard, arresting anyone who was against him. But his new position made him a target for both Grappa the Hutt and Kir Kanos, who eventually tracked down the traitor and killed him.

**Carkoon, Great Pit of** Located within the Dune Sea on the planet Tatooine, this large depression in the sand was the home of the rapacious, if slow-eating, creature called the Sarlacc.

**Carl** This dim-witted Shikitari insectoid was entered into the Rattataki gladiatorial games by a Devaronian con man. Carl was a collection of pupae that had amalgamated into a humanoid form capable of combat. This form was extremely short-lived—after two days, Carl entered a chrysalis state and emerged as a dozen harmless flutterscouts.

**Carlson, Sergeant Brooks** A veteran pathfinder, he was part of Han Solo's strike team on Endor. He was a former Imperial who defected with General Madine.

**Car'n, Lirin** A male Bith mercenary, he was a backup kloo horn player in the band known as Figrin D'an and the Modal Nodes.

**Carniss, Melina** A dark-haired human, she danced for Jabba the Hutt at his Tatooine palace and was named his dance coordinator. Later, Carniss became a security agent for the crime lord until his death. She then hooked up with smuggler Talon Karrde's organization, scheduling delivery details for his clients. One of those customers was Booster Terrik, working on behalf of Rogue Squadron. Since the location of Rogue Squadron's base was secret, the weapons they bought from Karrde were to be transferred from his freighters to theirs at the Alderaan Graveyard. But Carniss sold that information to the director of Imperial Intelligence, Ysanne Isard, who planned an ambush. The Rogues avoided the trap, but realized the information had to have come from Carniss and decided to set her up. They carefully leaked her information about their location, and when Isard sent her forces to crush the Rebels, the Imperials found themselves caught in an elaborate trap.

**Carosi XII** This planet was the site of a busy starport and many pleasure domes, some of which used synthdroids—centrally controlled mechanicals covered in quasi-living flesh. Carosi's larger moon housed a synthdroid factory operated by the Loronar Corporation. Animal life on the planet included the Carosi pup. The Carosi system contained 12 planets until its sun consumed the first 5.

**Carr, Malik** A Yuuzhan Vong fleet commander, he led his forces toward the Core after the initial battles at Ithor and Ord Mantell. He was tasked by Nas Choka to negotiate a treaty with the Hutts, whom he despised. In a bid for promotion, he spearheaded an attack on the shipyards at Fondor, but his forces were nearly wiped out by a blast from Centerpoint. As punishment, Carr was placed in charge of the prison camps on Selvaris. He recovered his rank on a mission to install a yammosk on Caluula, but while there he was exposed to the Alpha Red virus and died.

*Zayne Carrick*

**Carr, Yomin** This Yuuzhan Vong warrior infiltrated the ExGal Society outpost on Belkadan in the guise of a human scientist. It was his job to make sure that none of the other scientists noticed the telltale signals when the invasion force entered the galaxy at sector L30—Vector Prime. Like other members of his species, Carr painted his flesh and mutilated his body to show his devotion to a pantheon of gods. He hated technology but learned to control his revulsion in order to accomplish his mission. He wore an ooglith masquer to conceal his true features and wielded a variety of deadly living weapons, such as vonduun-crabshell-plated armor, explosive thud bugs, blorash jelly, and an amphistaff.

Carr used the bioengineering mastery of the Yuuzhan Vong to metamorphose Belkadan's atmosphere into a toxic brew perfect for raising yorik coral. He murdered the ExGal scientists, then faced off against Mara Jade Skywalker when she and husband Luke arrived to investigate the planet. Weakned by the Yuuzhan Vong coomb spores ravaging her body, Mara nonetheless engaged Carr in a vicious battle. She killed him after a worthy fight, driving her lightsaber blade through his armor and into his heart.

***Carrack*-class cruiser** These small combat cruisers long played a major role in the Imperial Navy fleet. About 350 meters long, with a higher proportion of weapons than its size might normally justify, it was the Imperial answer to the Corellian corvette. Its powerful sublight engines gave it the speed of an X-wing fighter, making it one of the Imperial fleet's fastest cruisers. The ships usually carried 10 heavy turbolasers, 20 ion cannons, and five tractor beam projectors. With no hangar bay (there were external racks for up to five TIE fighters), the cruisers depended on other ships or bases for most TIE fighter support. The Carracks weren't designed for front-line combat duty, but after the heavy losses the Empire suffered at the Battle of Endor, more of these ships began to see use in such fighting.

**Carratos** This planet was located some 40 parsecs from Coruscant. The Fallanassi religious group chose to send some of its youngest members to Carratos, among other planets, because of persecution on Lucazec. Akanah Norand was sent to a Carratos school in the Chofin settlement. Soon after, Carratos came under Imperial control, the Empire erected a garrison, and taxes were levied against anyone wishing to leave. After the Empire departed, order collapsed on Carratos. The Liberty movement destroyed all official records, and only the strong, wealthy, or cunning survived.

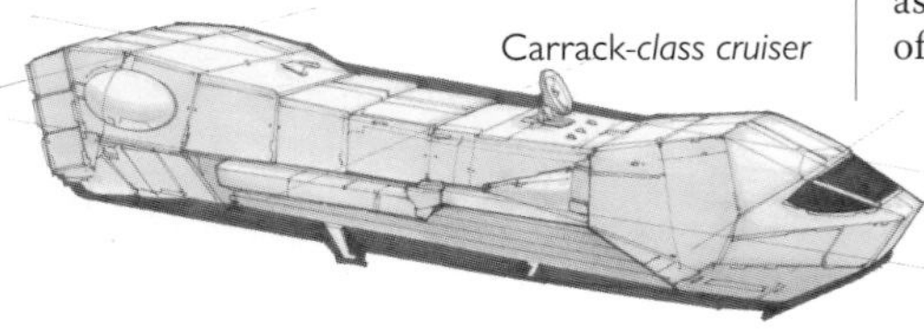
Carrack-*class cruiser*

**Carrick, Zayne** The Padawan student of Lucien Draay at the time of the Mandalorian Wars, this young man had a reputation for bad luck. While learning at the Jedi Temple on Taris, he was often late to assignments. His lack of punctuality ultimately saved his life: The Jedi Masters of Taris—all members of the Jedi Covenant—experienced a vision of the future wherein one of their students would bring about great destruction and the return of the dark side. In a preemptive strike, they killed their students, except Zayne. He was framed for the murders, and he traveled from world to world avoiding Jedi authorities with his Snivvian grifter pal, Marn Hierogryph.

*Cartariun*

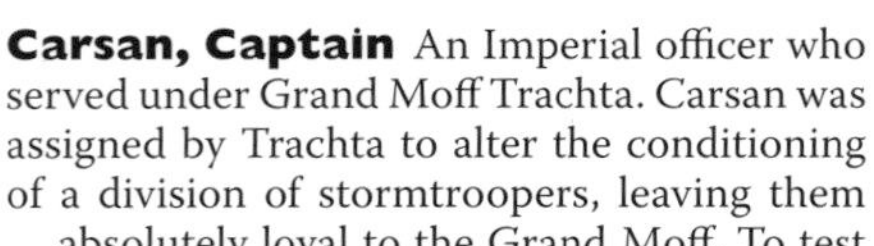

**Carsan, Captain** An Imperial officer who served under Grand Moff Trachta. Carsan was assigned by Trachta to alter the conditioning of a division of stormtroopers, leaving them absolutely loyal to the Grand Moff. To test their effectiveness, Trachta's first order for the troopers was to arrest Carsan for sedition. The stormtroopers killed him for supposedly resisting arrest.

**Carson, Farley** A New Republic Navy commodore attached to the Fourth Battle Group, in command of the Star Destroyer *Yakez* during the Black Fleet crisis. He was friends with Etahn A'baht.

**carsunum** Along with andris, carsunum was one of the two principal types of spice found on Sevarcos. The black powder was a powerful stimulant.

**Cartann** One of the most powerful nations on Adumar, overthrown by the Yedagonian Confederacy, a coalition of Adumar's smaller states.

**Cartao** A major trading center for Prackla sector, it was carefully nonaligned during the Clone Wars. It was home to the Spaarti Creations manufacturing plant, located north of Foulahn City and northwest of Triv Spaceport. It was also home to the Cranscoc species.

**Cartariun** A low-ranking Devaronian Imperial technician, he was stationed at the Emperor's outpost on Malrev, site of an ancient Sith temple. After Palpatine's death, the local Imperial garrison abandoned the temple, whose magic induced nightmares and seemed to enrage the local aboriginal clans of the doglike Irrukiine. Gaining control over the temple's power, Cartariun established himself as overlord of the Irrukiine and set his sights on taking over the throne of the Empire. A Bothan agent named Girov also wanted the power of the temple, however, and Cartariun fell victim to the Sith abilities he had once hoped to master.

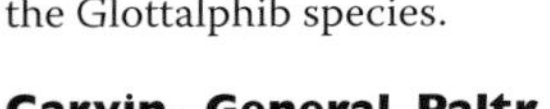

**carver egg** This foodstuff was considered a delicacy by the Glottalphib species.

**Carvin, General Paltr** An Imperial officer and member of the Imperial Ruling Council following the Battle of Endor. A tribunal headed by General Paltr Carvin put itself in charge of the Empire after Sate Pestage was suspected of treason. Ysanne Isard later turned against the tribunal, murdering its members. Isard chose to spare Carvin's life and sent him to the *Lusankya* prison facility.

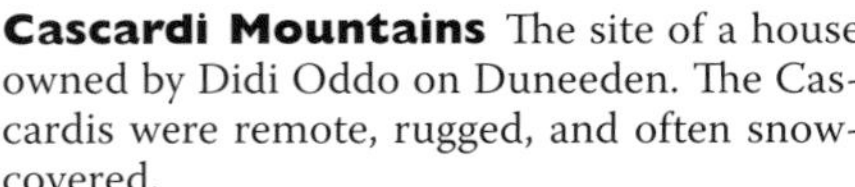

**Cascardi Mountains** The site of a house owned by Didi Oddo on Duneeden. The Cascardis were remote, rugged, and often snow-covered.

**Casement** A cargo loader on Drunost, he and his workers were often harassed by the BloodScar pirates at the height of the Galactic Civil War. Casement secretly funneled

goods to the Rebel Alliance through a contact code-named Targeter. During one BloodScar attack, Casement was aided by stormtroopers from the rogue Hand of Judgment unit, who unwittingly helped the Rebel supplier.

**Casfield 6** This world once suffered a catastrophe when the use of droid languages in ship landing codes caused shipboard computers to malfunction and at least six ships to collide and crash.

**Caslo, Gerney** An ostentatious loudmouth, he was one of the largest sellers of precious water on Nam Chorios. Gerney Caslo was instrumental in getting old pump stations functional after the planet's Oldtimers had let most of them rot.

**Cass, Officer** An Imperial officer, he was an adjutant to Grand Moff Tarkin aboard the original Death Star battle station.

**Cassandran Worlds** A group of three star clusters in the Outer Rim Territories encompassing about 100 worlds settled by an Esselian conglomerate. With the rise of the New Order and the more proper establishment of sectors, the constituents were renamed the Cassander sector, Tadrin sector, and Tendrannan sector. Among the planets found there were Garqi, Monhudle, New Bakstre, and Biitu.

**Cassel, Lieutenant Gil** A grizzled officer of the Imperial military during the time of Roan Fel, he was born and raised on Bastion. His family had a long military history, and he served for years in the 407th Stormtrooper Division out of a base on Yinchorr. He had his misgivings about the Sith Lords commanding the Empire with the coming of Darth Krayt. Darth Maleval arrived on Yinchorr and ordered the 407th to Borosk to eliminate the treasonous 908th Stormtrooper Division. Cassel could not carry out this order, for his brother Jared was a member of the 908th. As punishment, Maleval killed both Cassel brothers.

**Castell** The home planet of the Gossam species, it was gripped by a worldwide economic depression for decades. The Commerce Guild saw an opportunity and funneled money into Castell's economy by buying up huge tracts of land. Thousands of Gossams then went to work for the Commerce Guild just to be allowed to live on their ancestral lands. Shu Mai eventually purchased her home planet from the Guild, but kept the taxes high. Castell was located on the edge of the Colonies region near the Core Worlds. Late in the Clone Wars, it fell to the Republic. As a result, many Gossam refugees fled to Felucia.

**Castle Lands** Giant formations once found on Alderaan, they were built long ago by the insectoid Killik species.

***Casuistic*** A freighter piloted by Jedi Padawan Ekria after the events of Order 66.

**Catch** *See* Toughcatch.

**Catchhawks** A team of the New Republic Search and Rescue Corps led by Uldir Lochette during the Yuuzhan Vong War. Uldir flew the *No Luck Required* using the call sign Catchhawk One.

*Cathar*

**Cathar** The ancient homeworld of a proud and powerful feline species of the same name. Cathar were vaguely leonine and had flowing manes. Male Cathar sported two tusks and a short beard, while females boasted impressive fangs. The Jedi Knights Sylvar and Crado, who trained under Vodo-Siosk Baas on Dantooine about 4,000 years before the Galactic Civil War, hailed from Cathar. Juhani was part of a Cathar subspecies with less prominent claws than its larger relatives, as well as the ability to alter the pigments in its fur very quickly. During the Mandalorian Wars, the Mandalorians sought to test themselves against the Cathar by bombing their planet and slaughtering the species. The Republic did not come to Cathar's aid since it was not considered a member.

**Cathedral of the Winds** A magnificent but delicate and incredibly intricate structure, this centuries-old cathedral on the planet Vortex was the longtime site of the Vors's annual Concert of the Winds, a cultural festival celebrating the planet's dramatic change of seasons. Resembling a castle made of eggshell-thin crystal, the cathedral had thousands of passageways winding through hollow chambers, turrets, and spires. At the beginning of the Vortex storm season, winds would whip through its honeycomb structure, resulting in a spellbinding concert of reverberating, almost mournful music. But on a fateful diplomatic journey with Princess Leia Organa Solo as passenger, Admiral Ackbar's personal B-wing fighter crashed into the cathedral, destroying it and killing hundreds of Vors. It later turned out that the admiral's ship had been sabotaged. The Vors almost immediately began the painful task of rebuilding the cathedral, and when it was completed, Ackbar was invited back as an honored guest.

**Cathor Hills** One of the many sentient forests on the planet Ithor, it was destroyed by Imperial Captain Alima in his campaign to get Momaw Nadon to turn over Ithorian technology to the Empire.

**Catier Walkway** A noted walkway found on the planet Coruscant during the early decades of the New Republic. It was a shopping gallery lined with stores and merchants. However, when the Yuuzhan Vong attacked and captured Coruscant, much of the Catier Walkway was destroyed or looted.

**Cato Neimoidia** The oldest and richest of the Neimoidian "purse worlds," this colonial administrative post was a key holding of the Confederacy of Independent Systems as well as one of the wealthiest planets in the galaxy. Its polished skylines were suspended upon gently swaying bridges, feats of architectural wonder spanning fog-shrouded valleys in a mountainous landscape.

During the Clone Wars, the Neimoidian Home Defense Legions doubled their conscription rate, calling up all reservists to protect Neimoidia and her purse worlds. The gently swaying bridge-cities filled up with Neimoid-

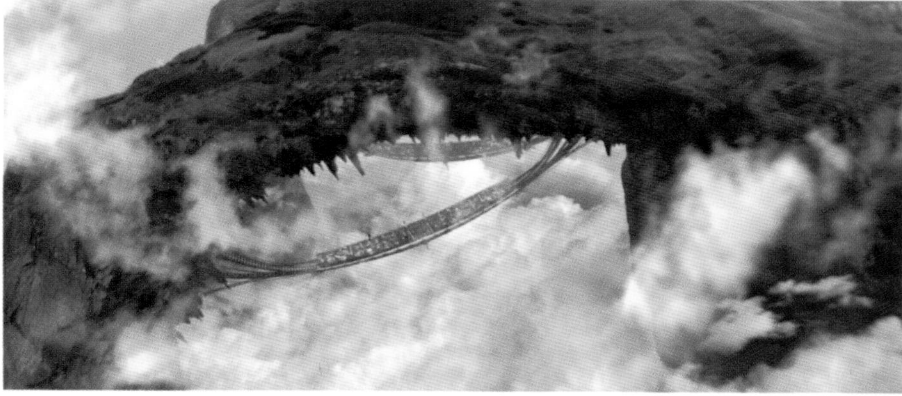

*A bridge-city on Cato Neimoidia*

ian tanks and airstrips, mansions became billeted with soldiers and gunners, and polished skyscrapers and gilded towers were marred by anti-starfighter emplacements. Even the private redoubt of Viceroy Nute Gunray was bolstered by upgraded defenses as the Neimoidians cowered at the notion of possible attack.

A month before the Battle of Coruscant, Obi-Wan Kenobi, Anakin Skywalker, and Clone Commander Cody led their forces against the planet in an effort to capture Viceroy Gunray. Gunray escaped, but the Jedi were able to seize his mechno-chair, which contained the coded holographic transmitter through which he contacted Darth Sidious. This gave the Jedi valuable proof of the Dark Lord's existence. The Republic was ultimately victorious on Cato Neimoidia, securing the world, if ever so tenuously. Pockets of resistance continued to flourish in scattered bridge-cities, resulting in regular Republic sorties to quell any uprisings.

The Jedi Master Plo Koon was tasked with leading these missions, flying from span to span in a wedge-shaped Jedi starfighter. During one such mission, Order 66 was enacted, and Koon's wingmates opened fire on him. His damaged starfighter spun out of control and crashed into one of the suspended Neimoidian cityscapes.

*Spinda Caveel*

**Catuman** A feline warrior species born and bred to the art of war. Often hired as mercenaries, they were among the deadliest killers in existence.

**Caudle, Master** One of the many physicians who worked at the Jedi Temple during the Clone Wars.

**Cauldron, the** An immense natural crater that was turned into a gladiator pit by Rattataki warlords. It was here that Asajj Ventress first caught the attention of Count Dooku.

**Cauldron Nebula** Like an interplanetary light show emanating from seven closely orbiting blue supergiant stars, this nebula sported clouds of magenta, orange, and icy-blue ionized gases. The closest habitable world was Eol Sha, where colonists mounted an unsuccessful attempt to mine the nebula's gases. The gas clouds and electromagnetic radiation in the nebula made an ideal hiding place for Admiral Daala's Star Destroyers, until Jedi student Kyp Durron caused all seven stars to go nova through his use of the Empire's own secret superweapon, the Sun Crusher.

**Caulfmar, Governor** The Brolfi planetary governor of the planet Barlok during the time of Outbound Flight.

***Cavalcade*** A modified HT-2200 freighter in the service of the BloodScar pirates. Mara Jade infiltrated this vessel as Emperor's Hand when she was investigating a mysterious collusion between an Imperial Governor and pirate forces in the Shelsha sector. She was discovered by the crew and forced to shoot her way out. She killed its commanding officer, Captain Shakko, and captured crewman Tannis, who helped her commandeer the vessel and continue her mission.

**Caveel, Spinda** This rogue scientist hired the Pikkel sisters to capture the unique medical droid A-O1C, or Doc. He forced Doc to reprogram droids, turning them into soldiers skilled in martial arts. When Caveel refused to accept their resignation, the Pikkel sisters killed him.

**cavern beast** A giant telepathic Yuuzhan Vong–engineered creature that used an individual's thoughts as bait, a sort of telepathic lure. The worm-like beast had a long cartilage-lined throat. It did not have rending teeth or grinding jaws, but instead swallowed its victims whole and kept them alive within its gullet, feeding off the nutrients from their waste. The creature was large enough to hold dozens of people inside. Jacen Solo was lured to a cavern beast with an image of his deceased brother, Anakin. He was able to save the beast's swallowed victims by projecting within the creature's mind the idea that humans were poisonous, prompting it to regurgitate them.

**Cavrilhu pirates** The scourge of the Amorris star system, this gang of marauders attacked merchant ships plying the space lanes of the galaxy. Led by Captain Zothip from his gunship *Void Cutter,* the pirates didn't like to be crossed—as they were when Niles Ferrier, one of the best spaceship thieves in the galaxy, made off with three of their patrol ships.

**Cav'Saran, Chief** A corrupt law enforcement official on Ranklinge, he operated under the title of Patroller Chief, abusing his power and extorting from his charges. Cav'Saran and his men controlled the port city of Janusar, collecting all weaponry from the citizens to ensure that they could not rebel. Eventually, the rogue stormtroopers known as the Hand of Judgment led a revolt against Cav'Saran, and trooper Daric LaRone shot him dead, installing a new Patroller Chief in his place.

**Cawa** A Quarren water-purification expert working on the Duro reclamation project during the Yuuzhan Vong invasion.

**Cayr, Lieutenant Telsij** A young Y-wing pilot, she served under Colonel Salm's Aggressor Wing during the Battle of Brentaal. A recent recruit, Cayr did not participate in the Battle of Endor. She was shot down at Oradin by Baron Soontir Fel. Though she survived the crash, she lost her left leg and eye. Her gunner, Kin Kian, did not make it out alive. Despite what Fel had done to her, she found it in her heart to forgive him after the former Imperial ace defected to the New Republic.

**Cazne'olan** *See* Olan, Cazne.

**CB-3D** An astromech used by Flynn Kybo during the Clone Wars.

**CB-99** An old barrel-shaped droid that emerged from hiding in the palace of Jabba the Hutt after the crime lord's death. He then presented Jabba's holographic will to the beneficiaries.

**C'baoth, Jorus and Joruus** A highly regarded Jedi Master originally from Bortras, a world in the Reithcas sector. C'baoth added to his Jedi studies with an education from Mirnic University. After assuming the title of Jedi Master, C'baoth served the Republic by overseeing the demilitarization of the aggressive Aqualish. He also helped settle an ascendency contention on Alderaan: C'baoth's delegation decreed that the Organa bloodline was the rightful heir to the title of viceroy. He negotiated treaties between warring aliens, and was also a personal adviser to Senator Palpatine on Jedi-related matters. A stern instructor with no sense of humor, he trained the Jedi Knight Lorana Jinzler.

C'baoth's greatest legacy was perhaps the vision and execution of Outbound Flight, an ambitious expedition that sought to explore beyond the borders of the galaxy with a network of six Dreadnaughts converted to colony vessels, six Jedi Masters, 12 Jedi Knights, and 50,000 men, women, and children. The project languished in bureaucractic red tape until C'baoth parlayed some political capital earned in thwarting an assassination attempt on Barlok. With the project under way from Yaga Minor, C'baoth began imposing his will and command on all aspects of life aboard the colony vessels, even going so far as separating Force-sensitive children from their parents, earning the resentment of the colonists. C'baoth's arrogance was his undoing, as the Outbound Flight expedition was intercepted

*Jorus C'baoth, the Jedi Master who oversaw Outbound Flight*

*Joruus C'baoth was powerful with the dark side of the Force, but also insane.*

by the Chiss Expansionary Defense Fleet under the command of Field Commander Thrawn. Thrawn's cunning tactics made short work of the vessels, though in his rage over seeing his dream destroyed, C'baoth reached out with the dark side of the Force and attempted to strangle Thrawn. C'baoth died when a radiation bomb detonated on his Dreadnaught.

Somehow C'baoth's genetic material was harvested and the Jedi Master was cloned. The telltale side effects of mental instability and self-name mispronunciation indicated that *Joruus C'baoth* was the result of hasty Spaarti-based cloning. Decades after the Outbound Flight incident, Thrawn had risen to the rank of Grand Admiral in the Imperial Navy. He was—five years after the Battle of Endor—on a campaign to retake the capital from the New Republic.

Thrawn found the cloned Joruus C'baoth protecting the Emperor's secret storehouse on the planet Wayland. Clone madness made it difficult to decipher the truth behind C'baoth's origins. He maintained that he had killed the Guardian of the Emperor's vaults, and took his place ruling over the natives of Wayland. More likely, C'baoth was the original Guardian and the epic battle he recounted but a product of his delusions.

Joruus C'baoth was a tall, lean, and muscular man with unkempt gray hair and a long beard. He spoke in a powerful baritone voice and had a surprisingly regal air about him despite his readily apparent madness.

Thrawn needed C'baoth to coordinate his military forces in much the same way Emperor Palpatine consolidated the fighting spirits of his followers through the Force. C'baoth was hesitant to join Thrawn, but the crafty Grand Admiral promised him more Jedi to train—namely, Luke Skywalker and his sister, Leia Organa Solo. The Empire would capture and deliver the Force-strong Jedi siblings for C'baoth to mold and train as he saw fit.

C'baoth differed from Thrawn in his perceptions of power. While the Empire sought to exert control over distant worlds, C'baoth was content to rule over Wayland. He believed true power was enforcing his will over the citizenry he faced every day, not governing remote and faceless planets. As Thrawn's repeated victories over the New Republic strengthened the Empire, C'baoth's ambitions grew. He would soon have dark and twisted designs of ruling over a revitalized Empire the way Palpatine had.

C'baoth was very powerful in the dark side of the Force. He could create deadly blue-white lightning from his fingertips, though his preferred use of his powers was imposing his will on others. In his service to Thrawn, C'baoth enhanced the coordination of the Imperial fighting forces, but that was just the start of his influential abilities. When desired, C'baoth could completely subjugate victims' minds, forcing them to do his bidding.

Luke Skywalker heard rumors of C'baoth's reappearance, and followed these carefully planted leads to Jomark. Skywalker was seeking a Jedi Master of old to supplement his training, but upon spending time with C'baoth, he recognized the elder Jedi's madness. The compassionate Luke thought he could heal C'baoth, bringing him back from the darkness of insanity. The clone's mental instabilities were too deep-rooted, however, and Skywalker was forced to flee C'baoth.

C'baoth grew increasingly frustrated with Thrawn's inabilities to deliver him a new Jedi apprentice. Once Thrawn had all his pieces in place for a push against Coruscant, the insane Jedi made his move. He returned to Mount Tantiss on Wayland and killed the Imperial officer in charge of the new cloning operation there. C'baoth holed himself up in the storehouse. The clones generated by Thrawn were based on approximately 20 templates. If C'baoth could learn to control only those 20 minds, then, he could command his own army.

At this time, the New Republic had discovered Thrawn's cloning operation, and a strike team infiltrated Mount Tantiss. The team included Luke Skywalker and Mara Jade, whom C'baoth saw as prospective students. When C'baoth realized he could not turn Luke to the dark side, he unleashed a terrible and twisted weapon: a clone of Luke Skywalker. C'baoth had ordered the clone grown from a sample of Skywalker's genetic material kept in the Mount Tantiss storehouse. Luke faced his mindless doppelgänger, but it was Mara Jade who eventually killed *Luuke* Skywalker.

After the clone fell in combat, C'baoth let go of whatever tenuous grip he had on reality and self-control. His rage overtook him, charged by the dark side. A whirling tempest of anger and the Force, C'baoth dropped his guard, and Mara Jade struck him down.

**C'borp** The chief gunner of the pirate marauder ship *Starjacker* some 4,000 years before the Battle of Yavin, he destroyed an attacking spacecraft piloted by Dreebo, who worked for Great Bogga the Hutt.

**CBX-9** This aged and battered hybrid protocol droid with a platinum chrome finish served T'nun Bdu

**CC-80/88-2199** *See* Bly, Clone Commander.

**CCIR** The acronym for a type of Centrally Controlled Independent Replicant.

**CC-series capital ships** Siblings in design to the Corellian gunship, these vessels found their way into the Rebel Alliance fleet throughout the Galactic Civil War. The CC-7700 was an older model, lightly armed but capable of housing a gravity-well generator. It was the Alliance's version of an Interdictor cruiser. Garm Bel Iblis once used a pair of CC-7700s against Admiral Daala's flagship. The CC-9600 was a later model, more compact and requiring a smaller crew.

**CE-3K** A protocol droid who attended to Luke Skywalker on New Alderaan during the resurrected Emperor's campaign of terror.

**CEC** *See* Corellian Engineering Corporation.

**Cecius, Lieutenant** A bridge officer aboard the *Executor,* he was formerly a member of the Imperial military, specializing in boarding and taking control of enemy ships. He was a native of Vogel 7.

**CeeCee** The nickname of a Galactic Alliance Guard captain, derived from her first and last initials. She was assigned as a security officer to the infirmary aboard the *Anakin Solo.* When Jaina Solo infiltrated the vessel near Uroro Station in the Transitory Mists, she forced CeeCee to change uniforms with her, hoping to gain access to the ship's prison facilities and rescue Prince Isolder. Jaina also forced CeeCee to locate Mirta Gev's cell, then knocked the officer unconscious before rescuing her friends.

**Ceel, General Tobler** A high-ranking officer in the Gungan Grand Army who fought at the Battle of Naboo.

**Cejansij** The primary world of the Cejansij system, famous for the dwellings carved into the surface of its canyons.

**Cel, Lieutenant** An officer in the New Republic Navy, she was assigned to General Wedge Antilles aboard the *Mon Mothma* during the war against the Yuuzhan Vong. She was only 10 years old when Grand Admiral

Thrawn blockaded Coruscant with cloaked asteroids during his bid to retake the Core Worlds. During that crisis, Cel resolved to one day serve the New Republic.

*Tycho Celchu*

**Celador Sash** An outdated but serviceable ship donated to the Jedi praxeum on Yavin 4 by a trader whose parents were saved by Obi-Wan Kenobi. Kyp Durron and Dorsk 82 flew the *Celador Sash* to investigate the disappearance of a mining colony on Corbos.

**Celanon** Located in the Outer Rim in the system of the same name, this planet had a multicolored skyline due to its numerous holographic advertising boards. Celanon's two main industries were agriculture and the commerce that flowed from Celanon City, a busy and well-defended spaceport. The system was also home to the mammoth consortium known as Pravaat, which made and sold uniforms. Prior to the Battle of Yavin, an explosive device was loaded onto an Imperial freighter at Celanon. The Rebel Alliance later stole the device and used it to demolish the Star Destroyer *Invincible.* The Nalroni were the planet's native sentient population.

**Celchu, Skoloc** Tycho Celchu's brother, he was killed when Alderaan was destroyed.

**Celchu, Tycho** A superior pilot, he was a graduate of the Imperial Naval Academy and served as a TIE fighter pilot. But after his homeworld of Alderaan was cold-bloodedly destroyed by the first Death Star, Celchu switched sides. He lost his entire family in the cataclysm, including his fiancée. Defecting to the Alliance on Commenor, Celchu quickly became a member of the X-wing Rogue Squadron, participating in both the evacuation of Hoth and the Battle of Endor. With his own ship out of commission, he flew an A-wing as Green Three and lured Imperials away from Wedge Antilles and Lando Calrissian while they made a run at destroying the second Death Star.

Celchu fought heroically at Bakura and was a key member of the squadron during the mission to take the Core Worlds from the rapidly fragmenting Empire. During a mission to Tatooine, he met the Rebel agent Winter and fell in love, but the more pressing concerns of the galaxy prevented them from cementing a serious relationship. Tycho later volunteered to fly a captured TIE fighter on a covert mission to Coruscant. He was captured and sent to the prison ship *Lusankya* before getting free. When he returned to Rogue Squadron, there were many who did not trust him, fearing that Imperial mastermind Ysanne Isard had somehow transformed him into a sleeper agent. His friend Antilles persevered until Celchu was named the squadron's executive officer in charge of training new recruits.

Because the Rogues' mission on Coruscant had been compromised at least once, they knew there was an Imperial spy in their midst, and Corran Horn continued to suspect Captain Celchu. Shortly after confronting Celchu with his suspicions, Horn's Z-95 Headhunter was disabled and crashed. Captain Celchu was charged with treason and the murder of Corran Horn. During his trial, when things looked hopeless, Horn reappeared with information that not only acquitted Celchu, but restored Alliance trust in him as well. The true traitor, Erisi D'larit, had been exposed.

As Wedge Antilles focused on building Wraith Squadron, Tycho commanded the Rogues, achieving the rank of colonel before handing over the squadron to Gavin Darklighter. Tycho retired shortly after Wedge did, and married Winter. He came out of retirement during the war against the Yuuzhan Vong, but after the defeat of the alien menace by the Galactic Alliance, he decided to leave starfighters behind. He continued to serve as a military adviser, however.

**Celchu, Winter** As a young girl growing up in the Royal House of Alderaan, the silver-haired Winter was often mistaken for Leia Organa: With her refined demeanor and aristocratic manners, she better fit the image of a Princess than did the tomboyish young Leia. Winter was born to Sheltay Retrac, a longtime friend and adviser to the Organa household. Winter and Leia were inseparable friends, and as Leia grew older and entered the realm of politics, Winter remained by her side as her royal aide and personal assistant.

When the Organa family became involved in the growing Rebellion to oppose the Empire, Winter's special talents were invaluable. She had a holographic and audiographic memory: She forgot nothing she saw or heard. Bail Organa assigned Winter to the Rebellion's procurement and supply division. She was offplanet when the Empire obliterated Alderaan.

Winter's gift became a silent curse, for she could never shake the memories of her departed friends and destroyed world. She rarely let her feelings show, though at times, in private, her grief was almost too much to bear. Her rigid control over her emotions and her no-nonsense approach to her duties caused some to comment that her name befit her icy personality.

Working for the Rebel Alliance, Winter supplied valuable intelligence regarding the location and layout of Imperial supply caches. This information proved vital to Alliance raiding parties, who could generate extremely detailed maps based on Winter's recollections. Her effectiveness gained her a position on the Empire's most-wanted list, though the Imperials knew her only by her code name of Targeter. Winter kept mobile during the Galactic Civil War, serving in a number of commands under a variety of code names.

As a Rebel special forces operative, Winter crossed paths with Rogue Squadron following the defeat of the Empire at Endor. She started up a romantic relationship with Tycho Celchu, a fellow Alderaanian. Rogue Squadron first helped Winter during her undercover work on behalf of the Cilpari Resistance, where she disguised herself as Princess Leia to act as a diversion while the Rogues took out an Imperial base. Later, as the Rogues worked undercover to plan the retaking of Coruscant, Winter assisted them under the name of Rima Borealis.

As Leia became a fixture in New Republic politics, Winter was by her side. She was Leia's aide in the Provisional Council, serving as a living holorecorder, committing to memory every word said at important meetings. During the Thrawn crisis, Winter proved instrumental in ferreting out Delta Source, Thrawn's primary spy asset on Coruscant.

She also served as nanny to Leia's newly born twins, Jacen and Jaina. At first, Winter relied on Noghri bodyguards to help safeguard the children, but when Imperial threats escalated following the resurrected Emperor's destructive campaign against the New Republic, greater precautions were taken. Winter was sequestered on New Alderaan with the children, and later on the remote fragmented world of Anoth.

The location of Anoth was known only to Luke, Winter, and Admiral Ackbar, though a New Republic double agent eventually managed to divulge its whereabouts to Imperial Ambassador Furgan. Furgan led an attack force against the world, which at the time was protecting the infant Anakin Solo. The automated defenses of the planetoid held off the Imperial attack, and Winter armed herself to protect the young Solo. In the end, the Imperials were defeated, and Han and Leia decided to keep the family together rather than hide the children. Winter continued to help Leia in raising the children: Organa Solo's career in politics kept her busy.

Years later, shortly after the Almania crisis, Winter and Tycho Celchu married. During the Yuuzhan Vong invasion, Winter went to Mon Calamari to serve as the personal aide to the venerable Admiral Ackbar. She aided the ailing Mon Calamari, making his last days more comfortable in a time of war.

*Winter Celchu*

**Celegian** This species of intelligent scyphozoans appeared as floating brains trailing a cluster of prehensile tentacles. They were renowned for their wisdom and intellect. Evolved from ocean-dwelling ancestors on Celegia, they developed a natural form of levitation not unlike an organic repulsorlift generator. Their homeworld was choked by a cyanogen atmosphere, which was lethal to most species. The Celegians required it to live, for common oxygen was toxic to their kind. When they traveled offworld, then, they were usually encased in a life-support chamber filled with cyanogen, their natural floating abilities making them seem to float in a watery brine.

*Centerpoint Station*

**Celestials** An unknown and possibly mythical advanced ancient civilization that predated all historic records in the galaxy. According to less-than-reliable accounts from the Killiks, it was the Celestials who caused the Killiks to abandon their home for the Unknown Regions. Some theorize that the Celestials were responsible for truly enormous feats of cosmic engineering, including the Maw Cluster and Centerpoint Station.

**Celia** A female Codru-Ji dancer who worked for Mawbo Kem at her performance hall on Tatooine during the early years of the New Republic.

**cell 2187** This small cell in Detention Block AA-23 was the site of Princess Leia Organa's imprisonment and torture while she was held captive aboard the first Death Star battle station.

**Celso, Nikaede** The female Wookiee companion of smuggler Drake Paulsen.

**Celwik, Jynne** A blond female server at the Outlander Club just prior to the Clone Wars.

**Celz, Alysun** A former Jedi who had fallen to the dark side, she framed her friend Et Rex for the crimes she had committed. While transporting Rex as a prisoner to the Jedi Council, her vessel crashed on an asteroid in the Hoth system. She betrayed the rest of the crew, killing them with Force lightning. When Obi-Wan Kenobi and Anakin Skywalker investigated the crash, they briefly believed her tales of innocence before realizing that she was the guilty party.

**Centares** An industrialized trading planet in the Maldrood sector, the outermost edge of the Mid Rim systems, Centares was the last civilized stop for those doing business in the galactic backwaters of the Outer Rim Territories. Many who wished to escape the long arm of the Empire came to Centares on their path to parts even more remote. Locales on Centares included Old Town, the cantina Merl's, and the toxic Rubyflame Lake, the site of a popular resort during the days of the Old Republic.

**Centax (1)** One of Coruscant's moons. A garrison force of 20,000 clone troopers was stationed there during the Clone Wars.

**Centax (2)** One of Coruscant's moons and the site of a Jedi pilot program run by Clee Rhara. It was a small, bluish moon with no vegetation or water. Its deep valleys and mountain ranges were leveled to accommodate huge landing platforms and various tech support buildings and hangars. The Jedi pilot program was halted after an accident; Vox Chun and Tarrence Chenati were responsible for the sabotage of the Jedi starfighters that caused the program to be canceled. The moon survived the conquest of Coruscant by the Yuuzhan Vong, and later became a training facility used by the new Jedi Order established by Luke Skywalker.

**Centerpoint Party** A coalition between the Federation of the Double Worlds and archaeologists whom the New Republic forcibly removed from Centerpoint, this contentious party borrowed freely from the rhetoric of the old Sacorrian Triad. The Centerpoint Party feared that the New Republic would use the Corellian system as a battle arena against the Yuuzhan Vong. Members advocated that each of Corell's five worlds be treated as a separate entity, and that the system be given five votes in the New Republic Senate. After the Battle of Fondor, with the disastrous firing of the Centerpoint Station, the party gained greater favor in the Corellian sector, and Thrackan Sal-Solo took command of it. He signed a "treaty of friendship" with the Yuuzhan Vong, attempting to ensure Corellia's neutrality. Instead, the party ousted Sal-Solo, but he remained a prominent fixture in Corellian politics until his assassination during the Corellian struggle for independence from the Galactic Alliance.

**Centerpoint Station** An enormous gray-white space station in the Corellian system, located at the balance point between the twin worlds of Talus and Tralus, it presumably drew its power from the gravitational interflux between the Double Worlds. The ancient station, built before the invention of artificial gravity, spun on its axis to provide centrifugal gravity. It was composed of a central sphere 100 kilometers in diameter, with long, thick cylinders jutting from either side. The ends of the cylinders were referred to as the North and South Poles.

The entire station was approximately 350 kilometers long, even larger than the original Death Star. Centerpoint was completely covered with a bewildering array of piping, cables, antennae, cone structures, and access ports; it would take several lifetimes to explore the vast and complex interior and exterior of the station. Hollowtown was the name of the open sphere in the exact center of the station, which measured 60 kilometers in diameter. The walls of Hollowtown were colonized with homes, parks, lakes, orchards, and farmland, which received heat and light from the Glowpoint—an artificial sun suspended in the exact center of the sphere. To simulate night, farmers installed adjustable shadow-shields, which appeared as bright patches of gold or silver from above.

It is not known who built Centerpoint, though many theories exist. Some have attributed the remarkable feat of construction to the same architects who assembled the Maw Cluster. Centerpoint is believed to have been a hyperspace repulsor, used in ancient times to transport the five Corellian planets into their current orbits from an unknown location. At some point the station was colonized, and Hollowtown—which was actually a power-containment battery for the massive energy required to fire a tractor-repulsor hyperspace burst—became inhabited. Centerpoint remained stable for thousands of years, until the Sacorrian Triad discovered that the station could destroy stars with a precise hyperspace shot from its South Pole. Two stars were targeted and destroyed, each accompanied by intense flare-ups in the Glowpoint. The small sun increased in heat so rapidly that Hollowtown and most of its inhabitants were completely incinerated during the first such incident. The government immediately evacuated the remaining Centerpoint inhabitants to the Double Worlds, leaving Chief Operations Officer Jenica Sonsen in charge of the station.

When word spread of the Hollowtown disaster, it sparked several rebellions on Talus and Tralus. A group of starfighters representing one of the rebellions claimed the nearly abandoned station for themselves, until chased off by a Bakuran cruiser. Massive interdiction and jamming fields were thrown over the entire Corellian system; these were also generated from Centerpoint and activated by the Triad. The Triad's fleet was later defeated by New Republic and Bakuran forces, and the planned destruction of the star Bovo Yagen was averted at the last instant when a shot from the repulsor on the planet Drall disrupted Centerpoint's firing process. Young Anakin Solo's natural attunement to machinery and the Force allowed him to deactivate the station, thus preventing it from being used against any other stars.

When the galaxy was threatened by the Yuuzhan Vong, the New Republic Defense Force began making plans to reactivate Centerpoint Station, hoping to use it as a weapon against the alien invaders. Anakin Solo agreed to activate it, but refused to fire it. As Jacen and Anakin debated the moral implications of using or not using the weapon, Thrackan Sal-Solo impulsively took control and fired a blast that disintegrated a large portion of the Yuuzhan Vong fleet at Fondor. The blast also took out three-quarters of the Hapan fleet and caused extensive collateral damage on Fondor and one of its moons. It also gave Thrackan Sal-Solo an immense boost in popularity and political sway.

After this blast, the station refused to obey any commands, as it had become "imprinted" on Anakin and would respond only to him. Following his death, the station remained inactive for years, although Thrackan Sal-Solo looked into using a droid proxy to trick the station into reactivating. Jacen Solo and Ben Skywalker investigated these attempts as tensions between Corellia and the Galactic Alliance escalated. As Corellia bid for independence, the Alliance blockaded the system. The standoff turned into war, and the GA flagship *Dodonna* inflicted extensive damage on Centerpoint.

Prime Minister Sadras Koyan gave Admiral Genna Delpin and a team of specialists the job of getting the weapon back online as part of a plot to use a Centerpoint blast to assassinate Jacen Solo by wiping out his fleet. Though that failed, Delpin's engineers did reactivate the station, allowing Koyan to issue an ultimatum: The Alliance had to surrender or Coruscant would be targeted. A deranged Corellian technician nicknamed Vibro decided on his own to exact vengeance on the Alliance at any cost and proceeded to activate the firing sequence. He didn't know that infiltrators on behalf of Luke Skywalker, including Dr. Toval Seyah, had sabotaged the station so that Vibro's last act destroyed Centerpoint and everything within a 250-kilometer radius of the blast.

**Central Committee of Grand Moffs** A coalition of Grand Moffs that gathered after the Battle of Endor. In collusion with the Prophets of the Dark Side, the committee staged a coup against Ysanne Isard's reign. Isard manipulated their downfall and executed the survivors.

**Central Control Computer** The naturally skittish Neimoidians feared giving their droid army too much independence, and thus relied upon this complex computer system to broadcast control signals to battle droids, droid starfighters, and other weapons of war in the Trade Federation's army. The Central Control Computer, stationed aboard the Trade Federation's Droid Control Ship, also monitored the activities of literally thousands of automata during the invasion of Naboo to ensure that all were operating at peak efficiency. While powerful, the Central Control Computer was by no means sentient and relied on organics, including Neimoidians, for its primary programming and commands. The Central Control Computer used at the Battle of Naboo was destroyed when Anakin Skywalker blew up the Droid Control Ship's reactor. Following the disastrous failure at Naboo, the droid armies began gaining increased autonomy by the time the Clone Wars erupted.

*Cerean Jedi Master Ki-Adi-Mundi*

**Centralia Memorial Spaceport** One of the oldest spaceports on Coruscant, it was located near the Jedi Temple and often served as the starting point for missions the Jedi Order performed for the Republic.

**Centrality** An old-fashioned, regressive corner of space best known for the Oseon casinos and the life crystals of the Rafa system. The Centrality swore allegiance to Palpatine soon after the Empire's formation. Its puppet government was allowed a certain degree of autonomy, largely because Imperial forces had little interest in directly controlling the trivial region. It lies between Hutt space and the Cron Drift. Those who have grown up in the Centrality are referred to as Centrans.

**Central Posting Service** A branch of the Galactic Republic Senate responsible for the maintenance of records detailing the various criminals and organizations that were wanted for questioning at any given point. The Central Posting Office was tasked with ensuring that information on every wanted criminal was made available to law enforcement agencies throughout the galaxy as quickly as possible.

**Ceousa, General** An important general in the New Republic, he commanded the *Calamari* and led it into the Battle of Almania.

**Cerasi** A member of the Young on Melida/Daan, she was the first person to turn her back on her heritage to live in the tunnels of Zehava. Like other members of the Young, she was opposed to the open bigotry exhibited by elder generations. Strong and agile, Cerasi was about 13 years old when Obi-Wan Kenobi and Qui-Gon Jinn arrived on Melida/Daan. Her copper hair was cut short and ragged, and she had a small, slender, pretty face with a pointed chin and pale green eyes. After the Young's initial victory on Melida/Daan, Cerasi headed the 10-member advisory council set up to rule Zehava. When tensions between the newly armed Elders and Young came to a head, Cerasi tried to intervene but was killed by blasterfire. It was later revealed that she'd been killed by sharpshooters on the orders of the Scavenger Young splinter-group leader, Mawat.

**Cerea** The home planet of the Cereans, located in the Mid Rim, Cerea was an isolated utopian world whose inhabitants shunned technology and motorized craft. As a result, the planet and its capital, Tecave City, had very little pollution and appeared idyllic. The Cereans allowed the construction of a few "outsider citadels," where settlers from more technologically dependent worlds lived in polluted and overcrowded conditions.

Because of its location along the edge of the galaxy, trade to and from Cerea proved costly. Fortunately, the Cereans' isolation also prevented their homeworld from being invaded. The largely peaceful world, which was ruled by the Elders, long remained outside official Galactic Republic membership, despite the best efforts of a few greedy Senators eager to claim the planet's natural resources. The Jedi Knight Ki-Adi-Mundi, who hailed from Cerea, proved instrumental in preventing the Republic from taking control.

During the Separatist crisis, Cerea generously offered refuge to displaced beings. Ki-Adi-Mundi stepped down as Watchman of Cerea, relinquishing this position to Tarr Seirr. Seirr worked with the Cerean government to maintain the planet's neutral stance in the Clone Wars. But the wars eventually came, with a battle that lasted over four weeks.

**Cerean** Members of this humanoid alien species had large, binary brains, elongated craniums, and a second heart to support their brains. They enjoyed natural precognitive abilities and tended to be calm, rational, and extremely logical. They lived on the idyllic world of Cerea, where females outnumbered males by 20 to 1. As a result, the society adopted polygamy, with each male Cerean taking one true "bond-wife" and several additional "honor-wives." Because of the low Cerean birthrate, Ki-Adi-Mundi was exempt from the Jedi edict that discouraged marriage.

**Cerulian, Thame** A renowned Jedi Knight and historian who took 13-year-old Dooku as a Padawan, he was one of the few Jedi who believed the Sith would someday return.

**cesta** A Gungan personal weapon that resembled a short staff with a small cup at one end. Gungans used it to throw energy balls at distant enemies, or as a staff or club in close quarters.

**Cestus Cybernetics** A droid-manufacturing corporation on Ord Cestus that subcontracted to Baktoid Armor Workshop. It fell on hard times after the Republic censured the Trade Federation, which forced Baktoid to take its droid development to facilities beyond Republic control. Cestus Cybernetics developed the JK bio-droid during the Clone Wars.

**CF9 Crossfire** The main starfighter of the Galactic Alliance Core Force during the time of Emperor Fel, it was the descendant of the design philosophies that created the Headhunter and X-wing fighters. In battle configuration, the vessel's primary hull sat behind an X-shaped assembly of weapons-capped S-foils. When landing, the lower wing extension folded up flush with the cross-wing.

**C-Foroon** A planet near Tatooine known as a thriving center for spice smuggling.

**C-Gosf** A member of the New Republic Senate's Inner Council, she was a Gosfambling. As such, C-Gosf risked much by running for the Senate, since losers in any contest on her world were forever ridiculed by all other Gosfamblings.

CF9 Crossfire

**Cha, Kadlah** A Yuuzhan Vong military analyst, she served under Wyrpuuk Cha.

**Cha, Wyrpuuk** A Yuuzhan Vong military commander, he was tasked by Warmaster Tsavong Lah with retaking Borleias. He died when his matalok ship was destroyed by the fleet that arrived with the *Lusankya.*

**Cha'a** A species of gold-scaled reptilian humanoids. A number of Cha'a merchants, including the unscrupulous Ssk Kahorr, ran businesses on the planet Koros Major 5,000 years before the Galactic Civil War. Although they often seemed refined and intelligent, Cha'a were quite barbaric. They began their lives in eggs in a small nest, where the strongest hatchling eventually killed and consumed his or her siblings. Their diet consisted largely of live prey.

Chadra-Fan

**Chaan, Supreme Commander** A Yuuzhan Vong warrior, he served under Warmaster Nas Choka in the final stages of the war against the Galactic Alliance. Chaan openly expressed doubts in Supreme Overlord Shimrra's Slayers. In response, Shimrra had Chaan and 10 of his finest warriors square off against two Slayers. Chaan and his forces were handily defeated and cut to pieces.

**Chaastern Four** One of two worlds in the Shelsha sector that maintained an Imperial garrison early in the Galactic Civil War.

**Chabosh** Once the site of a Rebel Alliance cell until it was wiped out by then-Captain Harsh and the Imperial Star Destroyer *Cauldron.*

**chack** A four-legged reptile used by the customs office of Eriadu to inspect incoming ships for contraband.

**Chad III** A watery world that orbited a blue-white star of the same name, it was the home of the sociable, rodent-like Chadra-Fan. The nine moons of Chad III created a pulsing system of tides, and clans of Chadra-Fan lived in the bayous among the red gum-tree forests and cyperill trees. The Chadra-Fan didn't build permanent structures because of unpredictable hurricanes. The planet's technology was primitive by galactic standards, although the Chadra-Fan took great pride in the design and craftsmanship of the items they exported.

Life-forms in the planet's watery depths included the long-necked cetaceans called tsaelkes, hunters called wystohs, phosphorescent tubular eels, and the fish-lizards called cy'een. The human Jedi Callista Ming was originally from Chad III, where she worked on an ark with her family. They herded the semi-sentient wander-kelp on their deep-water ranch. The ark followed the herds along Chad III's Algic Current, which ran between the planet's equator and its arctic circle. Callista was later called away to Bespin by the Jedi Master Djinn Altis.

**Chadra-Fan** These small but quick-witted natives of Chad III looked like a cross between humans and fur-covered rodents. They had large fan-like ears, dark eyes, and upturned, circular noses with four nostrils. Their seven senses included infrared vision and a highly advanced sense of smell. Only a meter tall, the Chadra-Fan liked to have fun, although they had a short attention span.

**Chaf** A Chiss clan considered the fifth ruling family, it controlled the planet Sarvchi.

**Chaf'ees'aklaio** A Chiss aide to Aristocra Formbi, she was a member of the Chaf family. She preferred to be called by her core name, Feesa.

***Chaf Envoy*** A Chiss diplomatic courier vessel used in the operation to recover the remains of *Outbound Flight.* The ship was half again the size of a Corellian corvette. Its surface seemed to be all planes and corners and sharply defined angles. Luke and Mara Jade Skywalker rendezvoused with the *Chaf Envoy* at Crustai.

***Chaf Exalted*** The flagship of the Chaf family during the final decades of the Galactic Republic.

**Chaf'orm'bintrano** *See* Formbi, Aristocra.

**Chagrian** An amphibian humanoid species from Champala identified by two pairs of horns growing from their heads. One set, known as lethorns, actually protruded from fleshy growths on the side of the Chagrian's head. Lethorns could become quite large and actually be draped over the Chagrian's shoulders. The second set of horns, found only on males, sprouted from the top of a Chagrian's head, and were used for intimidation. Typical Chagrians had enlarged heads padded by layers of tissue. Their blue skin protected them from the harmful radiation of the sun in the Chagri system. Mas Amedda, the Galactic Senate's Vice Chair, was a Chagrian.

**Chainly, Captain** An Imperial officer in the early months of the New Order, he was dispatched to Samaria as part of a task force led by Darth Vader.

***Chains of Justice*** An Imperial Star Destroyer that was part of Warlord Zsinj's fleet.

**Chak'ka (Chak)** A Wookiee veteran of the Clone Wars,

Chagrian

Chak'ka and his co-pilot, Kee, confront Cade Skywalker (right).

he was a former associate of Devaronian con man Vilmarh Grahrk. Chak felt indebted to Grahrk for the Devaronian's assistance in freeing the Wookiees from the Palsaang clan. As tribute, Chak gave Grahrk secret hyperspace route information, which Grahrk then sold to the Separatists. During Order 66, Chak saved Quinlan Vos's life, and with the rise of the Empire, the Wookiee fled to more remote areas of space. During the time of Emperor Fel, Chak had become a seasoned smuggler, piloting the modified freighter *Grinning Liar.*

**Chakra** This Jeodu guard worked for Prince Dequc and was killed by Mara Jade.

**chak-root** A favorite of smugglers, this flavorful red plant grew in the marshlands on the planet Erysthes as well as on Naboo. Because of high taxes on its sale, the plant gave rise to a highly profitable, if illicit, underground economy. Chak-root was easily obtained on the Invisible Market at reduced prices.

**Chalacta** A Mid Rim world in Hutt space, Chalacta was home to a spiritual human culture called the Chalactans. Chalactan Adepts who studied at the Chalactan Temple of Illumination were strongly resistant to all forms of mental manipulation. The followers of the Chalactan ways were opposed to the Military Creation Act prior to the Clone Wars.

**Chalcedon** This rocky, volcanic world with a semi-breathable atmosphere was a key hub in the galactic slave trade. Inhospitable Chalcedon had violent storms, frequent groundquakes, and no indigenous life-forms, although two colonies and a way station were established on its surface. Many buildings were made of dark volcanic glass. Traders and peasants inhabited the bazaars, while the bureaucrats—boneless, trunked creatures—lived in the cities and controlled the slave trade.

**Chalco** A somewhat short, heavyset bald human grifter with brown eyes, he helped Luke Skywalker track down Daeshara'cor's whereabouts during the Yuuzhan Vong invasion. Chalco accompanied Luke and Mara Jade Skywalker to Vortex, Garos IV, and Ithor. On Garos IV, while Luke and Mara were otherwise occupied, Chalco convinced Anakin Solo that they should look for Daeshara'cor in the area surrounding the spaceport. Unfortunately, she found them first and held them hostage, but in the end Luke convinced her to join them. On Ithor, Chalco helped Mirax Terrik with evacuation efforts before the planet was sundered.

**Chalk** *See* Trevval, Liane.

**challat eater** Large insects several centimeters long and native to Troiken, they traveled in dangerous swarms numbering between 10 and 20 individuals. Voracious predators, they swarmed over any organism they happened upon. The Xexto of Troiken became quite skilled at avoiding challat eaters, and were capable of grabbing these insects by the wings to immobilize them. Plo Koon used challat eaters from Mount Avos to defeat the Stark Commercial Combine army during the Stark Hyperspace Conflict. Droids resembling challat eaters were used in an assassination attempt on Simon Greyshade during a reception held at the residence of Orn Free Taa.

**Challer** An aged male human member of the tribunal that put itself in charge of the Empire after Sate Pestage was suspected of treason. Ysanne Isard had Challer assassinated at the Imperial Hotel in Imperial City by having his mistress poison him.

**Challon, Tohri** An Imperial Adjunct, she served under Emperor Roan Fel.

**Chalmun** A beige-and-gray Wookiee, he owned the infamous Mos Eisley cantina—sometimes called Chalmun's Cantina—where Luke Skywalker and Ben Kenobi first hooked up with Han Solo and his copilot Chewbacca.

**Cham** This Mandalorian was barkeeper at the Oyu'baat Tapcaf on Mandalore in the years following the Yuuzhan Vong War. He was known as Cham'ika to his regular customers.

**Chamberlyn, Lieutenant** A member of the Naboo Palace Guard, he became a leader of the underground movement against the Trade Federation during the Battle of Naboo. Lieutenant Chamberlyn was known for discovering and analyzing battle droid weaknesses.

**chameleon droid** A modified Arakyd Spelunker probe and mine-laying droid used by the Commerce Guild during the Clone Wars. It utilized a holographic array to project surrounding imagery in its place, effectively rendering the droid invisible against passive sensor scans and observation. A built-in repulsor unit gave the droid its agility, while traction field generators allowed it to climb walls and ceilings. It was armed with laser cannons and military-grade mines.

Challat eaters

**Chamma, Master** A Jedi Master, he was Andur Sunrider's teacher some 4,000 years before the Battle of Yavin.

**chamonaar** Ancient hibernating saurian beasts from Roon.

**Champala** This water-covered world in the Chagri system, home to the Chagrians, was a favorite vacation spot among the Inner Rim's populace. Early in the evolutionary stages of life on Champala, the system's sun went through an unstable period and bombarded its orbiting bodies with massive amounts of radiation. Only species that developed an ability to withstand this radiation survived. Chagrian civilization arose on the thin coastal bands of Champala's small, jungle-covered continents. All but Champala's oldest starports were built on high plateaus well away from the cities. It had a single moon.

During the time of the Empire, many parts of Champala were polluted as a result of mining accidents. Late in the Galactic Civil War, Admiral Ackbar commanded the *Guardian* during a skirmish with Admiral Pellaeon at the Battle of Champala.

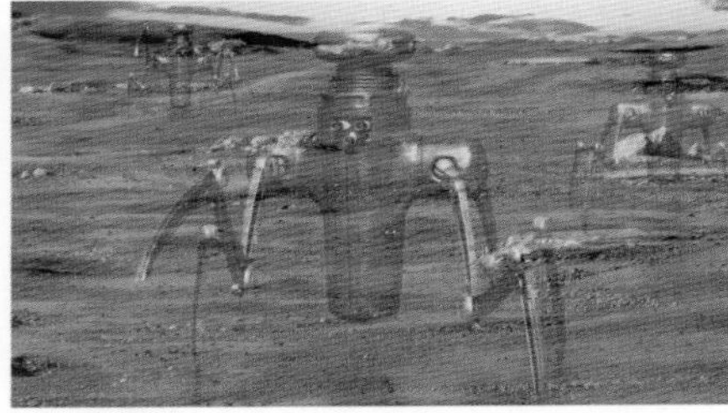
Chameleon droid

***Champion*** A Bothan Assault Cruiser that flew cover for a refugee convoy at Kalarba during the Yuuzhan Vong invasion. The *Champion* was commanded by Brevet Admiral Glie'olg Kru. It was destroyed by the plasma blasts of a Yuuzhan Vong capital ship. The ensuing explosion engulfed and nearly destroyed Jaina Solo's X-wing fighter, as well as several other members of Rogue Squadron.

**Champion of Krmar, the** One of the many nicknames given to Jedi Master Sharad Hett.

**Champion Squadron** One of General Salm's Y-wing bomber squadrons serving the New Republic, part of Defender Wing.

**Chan, Evan** An environmental hydrographer who hated to fly, he saw a rather unusual sight during the Clone Wars in a public refresher at the Chancellor Palpatine Spaceport: Yoda traveling incognito disguised as an R2 unit.

**Chan, Travia** The Alliance Commander in Chief for the Atrivis sector, she was one of the original founders of the Fest Resistance Group and later, the principal architect of the marriage of Fest to the Mantooine Liberators, creating the ARG (Atrivis Resistance Group) and becoming its first and only military commander. The planet Generis was captured along with most fleet-supply depots after a fierce battle with Grand Admiral Thrawn's clone forces. Alliance General Kryll and the pilot Pash Cracken were able to evacuate Travia Chan and her people during the New Republic's retreat from Generis.

**Chan, Wenton** A Rebel X-wing pilot from Corulag, he flew—and died—as Red Eleven during the Battle of Yavin.

**chance cube** A small die used by gamblers to settle bets. Half of the chance cube's sides were painted blue, while the remaining three faces were painted red. Watto always carried a loaded chance cube, which helped him win numerous bets. When Qui-Gon Jinn suggested that he and Watto include Anakin and Shmi Skywalker in their Podracing wager, Watto used the trick chance cube to determine which of his slaves would potentially be released. However, Qui-Gon nudged the chance cube with the Force, ensuring that it landed on blue, the color representing Anakin. When Anakin subsequently won the Boonta Eve Classic, Watto was forced to free the boy.

Chance cube

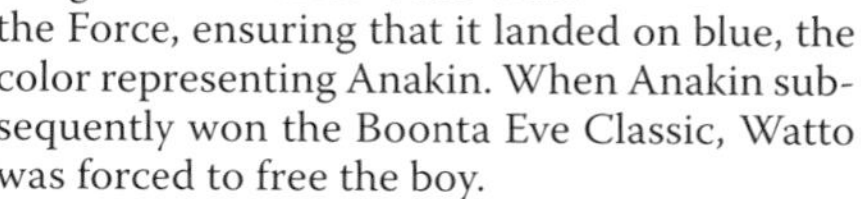

**Chancellery Walkway** Located in the Jrade Plaza section of Coruscant's Galactic City during the Galactic Republic, this walkway was lined with monuments and memorials to some of the most famous and influential Supreme Chancellors in galactic history.

***Chancellor*** A Rebel frigate with a plaque displayed on the command deck that commemorated the slain pilots of Renegade Flight.

**Chancellor Palpatine Spaceport** An immense civilian spaceport on Coruscant, connected to the Chancellor Palpatine Commerical Nexus during the Clone Wars, it was called Chance Palp by commuters in a hurry.

**chancer** A fringe slang term for someone who was not a full-time licensed bounty hunter but attempted to collect a bounty when chancing upon one.

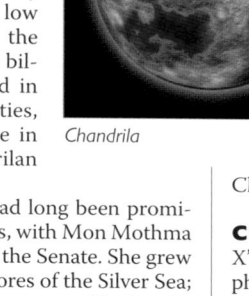

**Chandrila** The agricultural Core World in the Bormea sector best known as the homeworld of Mon Mothma, leader of the Rebel Alliance. Its two main continents were covered with rolling, grassy plains. Chandrila had a low birthrate, which kept the population at around 1.2 billion. Most residents lived in scattered small communities, but all had a direct voice in government, the Chandrilan House.

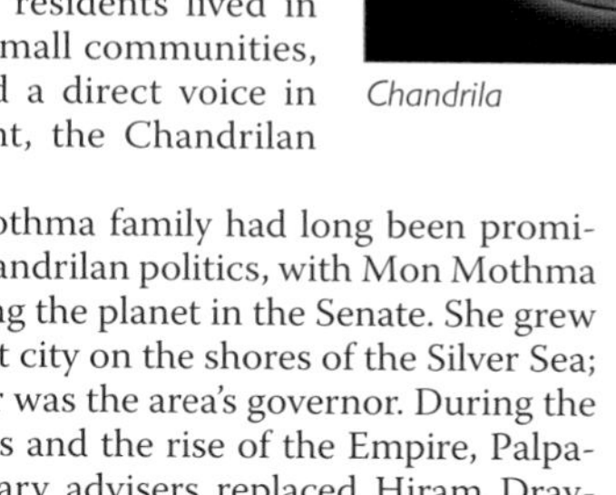
Chandrila

The Mothma family had long been prominent in Chandrilan politics, with Mon Mothma representing the planet in the Senate. She grew up in a port city on the shores of the Silver Sea; her mother was the area's governor. During the Clone Wars and the rise of the Empire, Palpatine's military advisers replaced Hiram Drayson as leader of the Chandrila Defense Fleet with Kohl Seerdon, a loyal Imperial who would eventually ascend to the rank of Moff.

Six months after the Battle of Endor, the Empire deployed seven Star Destroyers to Chandrila, where they enforced a strict blockade. It is believed that Grand Vizier Sate Pestage may have implemented the plan to hold Chandrila hostage in case New Republic forces were able to threaten Coruscant. During Operation Shadow Hand, Chandrila briefly fell under Imperial control before being liberated once more by the New Republic.

Other notable Chandrilans included Dev Sibarra, human liaison to the reptilian Ssi-ruuk, and Jedi Master Avan Post, who served during the Clone Wars.

***Chandrila*** A New Republic Corellian corvette used against Imperial Prince-Admiral Krennel in the Ciutric system.

**Chandrila Defense Fleet** A local planetary defense fleet that was long commanded by Admiral Hiram Drayson. During the Clone Wars, Supreme Chancellor Palpatine's military council replaced Drayson with Kohl Seerdon. After the fall of the Empire, Drayson resumed his position for the New Republic.

***Chandrila Moon*** A *Marketta*-class shuttle based aboard the *Protector.* During the Yuuzhan Vong War, Leia Organa Solo, Danni Quee, Olmahk, and Basbakhan traveled to Bastion aboard the *Protector.* The shuttle *Chandrila Moon* transported them from the *Protector* to Bastion's orbital customs station.

Charal

***Chandrila Skies*** A modified Uulshos light assault vehicle used by the Galactic Alliance for a drop mission to extract Jedi teams inserted into Corellia. It was shot down by Corellian warships.

**Chang** A member of Elscol Loro's resistance on Cilpar after the Battle of Endor. Chang was adept at using a flame projector.

**Change, the** A three-month period in an X'Ting's life when it underwent a metamorphosis in sexual phase. This was accompanied by physiological and emotional instability. Wealthy X'Ting eased the process by ingesting viptiel.

**changeling** A general term describing any shape-shifting alien species, such as the Proteans, Clawdites, Shi'ido, Gurlanins, Stennes shifters, Polydroxyls, and others.

**Chant, Gannod** An agent of the New Republic's Council on Security and Intelligence, and later the Security and Intelligence Council of the Galactic Alliance. Chant was known for his translation of the Wavlud Manuscript, and his reports on the document delved deeper into the origins of the title Darth as used among the Sith.

**Chanzari** A rebellious den on Selonia, they were allied with the Hunchuzuc, also seeking to free themselves from the oppressive rule of the Overden.

**chaos fighter** These small and maneuverable fighters were employed by the Krath, a group that adopted primitive dark side magic, and used to stage a coup in the Empress Teta system about 4,000 years prior to the Battle of Yavin.

**Cha Raaba system** The star system in Hutt space that contained the planet Ylesia.

**Charal** A Witch of Dathomir formerly of the Nightsister clan, Charal escaped Dathomir over a century before the Battle of Endor. Highly regarded for her mastery of mysterious shape-shifting skills and other talents, her abandonment of the Nightsister clan was not well received. She lived with a death mark for some time, and was hounded across the sector by witches sent to hunt her down. Stranded on Endor for nearly a century, Charal allied herself with King Terak's band of Sanyassan Marauders. It

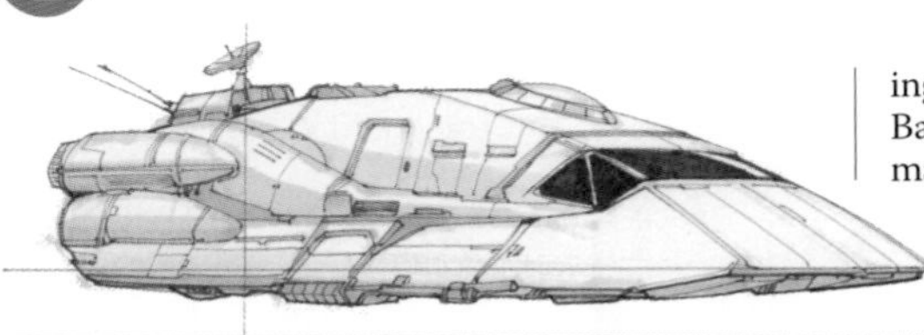

Chariot LAV

wasn't until the Towani family also crashed on the forest moon that Charal and her Marauder cohorts had the chance to escape—an opportunity foiled by the youngest Towani, Cindel; her Ewok companion, Wicket; and the old human scout Noa Briqualon.

Charal could change form thanks to a magical ring. She could become a raven or assume the guise of a beautiful young woman. She wore a black feather cloak and rode a wild black stallion that could also shift shapes.

**Ch'arb, Lieutenant** An officer on the Star Destroyer *Avenger.* Lieutenant Ch'arb met the bounty hunter Awarru Tark aboard ship and brought him to meet Lord Vader.

**Charbi City** One of the largest cities on Vulpter, it was nonetheless considered a slum to most seasoned travelers.

**charbote root** This vegetable was used in Corellian cooking.

**Chardaan** In this Deep Core space facility composed of pressurized spheres, workers built space vehicles in a zero-gravity environment. The Chardaan Shipyards produced a wide variety of Alliance and New Republic starfighters, from the Y-wing to the E-wing, until they were devastated by Colonel Cronus and his fleet of *Victory*-class Star Destroyers eight years after the Battle of Endor.

**Chariot LAV** This modified military landspeeder, rarely used in combat, served as a command vehicle for Imperial forces. The Chariot light assault vehicle (LAV) was more heavily armored than a normal landspeeder, although not nearly as much as a combat speeder. It provided moderate performance at an acceptably low price. It was about 12 meters long, had a top speed of 100 kilometers an hour, and usually carried three people. The extensive onboard computer system provided battle assistance programs including holographic tactical battlefield displays.

**Charmath** The home to one of the most complete historical archives in the galaxy and the site of the famous University of Charmath and the College of Astrocartography. Rebel Alliance historian Arhul Hextrophon researched the history of Yoda here during the time of the Galactic Civil War.

**Charny, Kiel** A general in Lord Hoth's Army of Light during the Battle of Ruusan, 1,000 years before the Battle of Yavin. A student of Master Handa, in many ways he was a true warrior who epitomized the Jedi ideal. His primary weakness was in having a romantic affair with his fellow student, Githany. Handa chastised his students for this indiscretion, driving Githany away from the Order. She returned as a Sith Lord, but Charny was unable to strike his former lover. Githany, twisted by the dark side, had no such qualms and severed Charny's hand with her lightwhip. Disgusted by the weakness of the Jedi, the young initiate Tomcat retrieved the severed hand and lightsaber and struck Charny down, completing his journey to the dark side.

**Charr, Senator** The Corellian representative in the Galactic Alliance Senate at the time relations between Corellia and the Galactic Alliance collapsed. Though he did not agree with the more extremist posturing and calls for independence coming out of Corellia, Charr was greatly concerned when the Galactic Alliance Guard expelled Corellian citizens from Coruscant in the name of security. His criticism of such actions earned him support from many Outer Rim Senators who feared they might be the next target of an unchecked GAG.

**charric** A handheld ranged weapon favored by the Chiss, it emitted a maser-guided particle discharge delivering both thermal and kinetic damage. The intense microwaves of a charric blast easily penetrated ceramic and polymer-based armor.

**Charr Ontee (Charon)** A species engineered by DarkStryder on Kathol to be servitors, they resembled humanoid arachnids with a hard chitinous shell. Most were annihilated during the cataclysm that created the Kathol Rift, though some were thrown into the "pocket dimension" of otherspace, where they degenerated into a death-worshipping cult called the Charon. The nihilistic Charon sought to destroy the plague that was life, and desperately wished to master hyperdrive technology to traverse the interdimensional gulf and wreak havoc on realspace.

**Charros IV** The home planet of the Xi Charrians and base of operations for Xi Charrian cathedral factories. It was an arid, rocky world dominated by snowcapped mountains. The perfectionist Xi Charrians developed a number of advanced starfighter, droid, and technological designs from Haor Chall Engineering. During the Clone Wars, a clone army led by the Jedi invaded Charros IV and destroyed the factories. Sienar Fleet Systems absorbed what was left of Haor Chall.

**Charubah** A technological world in the Hapes Cluster, Charubah was known for manufacturing the Hapan Gun of Command. Those shot with this weapon's electromagnetic wave field lost the ability to make rational decisions and tended to follow any orders given them.

Kiel Charny

**Chasa** A burly human, he owned and operated a cantina on the planet Dolis 3, that was the favored hangout of Banner Sumptor and his Imperial friends during the New Republic.

**ChaseX** A late-model T-65XJ5 X-wing fighter used by police forces as a pursuit craft in the years after the Yuuzhan Vong invasion. The ChaseX featured improved speed, maneuverability, and targeting systems.

**Chasin City** One of the largest cities on Commenor, known for its eclectic restaurant scene.

**Chasin Document** This document was a revision of the New Republic's Operation Blue Plug, a detailed invasion plan for the taking of Commenor drafted by Garm Bel Iblis at the time Commenor was still in Imperial possession. Since Commenor voluntarily joined the New Republic, the battle plan was never implemented. Nonetheless, years later, a draft of the plan was leaked to Commenorian officials who, in alarm and with growing suspicion of the Galactic Alliance, used it as justification to side against the GA in the conflict brewing between the Alliance and Corellia. Given that the foundation of the document was a top-secret New Republic file, Winter and Tycho Celchu investigated the matter, finding that someone within the Galactic Alliance Guard had leaked the information.

**Chatak, Bol** A Zabrak Jedi Master, she was dispatched along with her Padawan Olee Starstone to Murkhana in the final days of the Clone Wars. There she fought alongside Roan Shryne and Saras Loorne. When Order 66 was executed, the clones of Ion Team at first refused to comply, allowing the Jedi to escape. As punishment, the Emperor's new enforcer, Darth Vader, arrived on Murkhana and cut down several clone troopers. Chatak witnessed this and, unable to keep still, challenged Darth Vader. Though she scored a wound on Vader, she was disarmed and decapitated by the Dark Lord.

**Château Malreaux** An immense fortress residence of the Malreaux family of Vjun, located atop a bluff overlooking the Bay of Tears. Count Dooku claimed the spooky château as a base of operations during the Clone Wars.

**Chatos Academy** An ancient and legendary center of study that may have, in some way, led to the Jedi Order.

**Chatrunis, Larisselle** This somewhat simple-minded Pa'lowick was 23 years old when crowned Miss Courscant, just prior to the Clone Wars. When the Empire's pro-human agenda caused her star to fall, she joined the burgeoning Rebel Alliance, using her cover as a singer to pass information to scattered Alliance cells. The entertainment media at the time often fabricated and exaggerated tales of a rivalry between her and Sy Snootles.

**Chattza clan** A powerful, war-like clan of Rodians led by Navik the Red. After conquering Rodia, Chattzas scoured the galaxy and hunted down and killed the more peaceful sects of Rodians who had escaped offworld.

**chav** A beverage usually enjoyed hot.

**chawix** A carnivorous plant on Ansion carried by the wind, it appeared to be a large bundle of impossibly intertwined, rope-like branches. When a chawix sensed proximity to flesh, it extended thorns that injected a strong nerve poison to disable prey.

**Chayka** A member of Lord Hoth's Army of Light during the Battle of Ruusan.

**Chaykin Cluster** The site where a derelict Republic assault ship was discovered within the first year of the Clone Wars. Republic commandos from Delta Squad were sent to investigate.

**Chazrach** A short, stocky, reptoid species used as slaves and shock soldiers by the Yuuzhan Vong. The Yuuzhan Vong bred them for generations and controlled them through a pair of dome-like calcifications on their foreheads. Some Chazrach served the Yuuzhan Vong well enough to be allowed into the lowest level of the warrior caste. They carried coufees and a shorter, more basic amphistaff than the Yuuzhan Vong themselves.

**Chazwa** Located in the Chazwa system and the Orus sector, this planet orbited a tiny white dwarf sun. Its central transshipment location meant that heavy freight traffic was a common sight. The smugglers Talon Karrde and Samuel Tomas Gillespee battled two Imperial Lancers at Chazwa; later it was used as a rendezvous for Karrde, Par'tah, and Clyngunn the ZeHethbra to discuss actions against Grand Admiral Thrawn.

**cheater** A handheld coin-sized device used by sabacc players to illegally control or alter the random-shifting sequence of the game.

**Cheb, Admiral** A naval officer in the Galactic Alliance Defense Force chosen by Cha Niathal to bolster the blockade around the Corellian system early in the growing dispute between Corellia and the Galactic Alliance. Cheb commanded the starship *Ansta.*

**Checksum** One of Zorba the Hutt's accounting droids on Cloud City.

**Chedak Communications** A corporation known for its manufacturing of communication devices, from comlinks, to holoprojectors, to subspace radios.

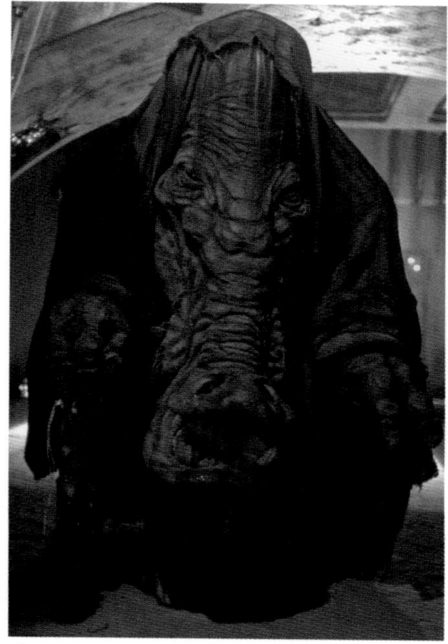

*Chevin*

**Chedgar** A New Republic pilot who washed out of several squadrons before trying out for Wraith Squadron. He failed to make that cut, too.

**Cheel, Nalan** A male Bith musician, he played with the group Figrin D'an and the Modal Nodes. Although he enjoyed playing his bandfill, he missed the bubbling pink swamps of his native Clak'dor VII.

**cheg** A game in which players used their knuckles to move a small puck across a game table into a goal.

**Chekkoo clan** A clan of Rodians that opposed the rule of Navik the Red and the Chattza clan.

**Cheklev** A Devaronian Jedi Knight at the time of the Yuuzhan Vong invasion. Hivrekh'wao' Cheklev was one of the the first Jedi Knights to experience wartime betrayal when his confederates on Devaron attempted to sell him to the Yuuzhan Vong. Cheklev eventually made his way back to the safety of his Jedi peers through the underground Great River safe route.

**Chelik** A member of the Hapan royal family, niece of Queen Mother Ta'a Chume and older sister to Alyssia. Chelik's daughter was caught by Tenel Ka attempting to assassinate Prince Isolder during the war against the Yuuzhan Vong.

**Chell, Benwick** A soldier in the Hapan Royal Navy during the time of the Yuuzhan Vong invasion, he hated that Tenel Ka had involved their people in the conflict, particularly after the Battle of Fondor, where three-quarters of the Hapan forces were destroyed. Chell conspired with the Yuuzhan Vong to capture Jaina Solo and deliver her to the invaders.

**Chem** This young pilot, a member of Kyp's Dozen, was killed during the Yuuzhan Vong invasion of Coruscant.

**Chempat Engineered Defenses** This corporation specialized in deflector shield and sensor equipment. It was jointly owned by the Corellian Engineering Corporation and Kuat Drive Yards.

**Chenati, Tarrence** A former Galactic Republic operative who worked for the Senate as a spy and investigator. Records listed him as having died some 30 years before the Battle of Naboo. The Tarrence Chenati identity was reactivated 20 years later when the Senate needed someone to investigate the starfighter training facility established by the Jedi Knights on Centax 2. The identity was discovered by Tahl and Qui-Gon Jinn when they caught him trying to sabotage Clee Rhara's starfighters and frame her for the act. Clee Rhara was cleared of any crime when Chenati fled Centax 2. He resurfaced a dozen years later, serving aboard the starship *BioCruiser* under the alias Kern.

**Chenini** The smallest and outermost of Tatooine's three moons, its erratic orbit meant that it was often out of sight.

**Chenlambec** A Wookiee bounty hunter with deep brown, silver-tipped fur, he was known as Chen to his friends. Most others, however, knew him only by his reputation as the Raging Wookiee. Despite his unsavory reputation as a fierce and hot-tempered killer, Chenlambec and his human partner, Tinian I'att, would often help their "acquisitions" escape to the Rebellion. Chenlambec wore a heavy, reptile-hide bandolier studded with bowcaster quarrels and silver cubes—one of which was actually Flirt, his positronic processor. With the help of Flirt and I'att, Chenlambec rescued a colony of Wookiees imprisoned on Lomabu III while at the same time tricking and capturing the Wookiee-hating Trandoshan bounty hunter Bossk. The Wookiee owned a ship called the *Wroshyr.*

**Cheran, Viera "Chief"** The chief technician of Rogue Squadron following the Battle of Hoth, she oversaw flight deck operations wherever Rogue Suqadron was stationed. Envious of the attention garnered by the Rogues, she accepted an offer to sabotage Luke Skywalker's X-wing.

**Chersilk** A luxurious fabric found in the fine royal gowns of Naboo monarchs.

**Cheunh** The dense and complex language of the Chiss.

**Chevin** A species native to the planet Vinsoth, Chevin were primarily hunters and farmers. They stood over 2 meters tall and had thick arms and a long face, all set on two stubby trunk-like legs. They once enslaved the Chevs, a humanoid species on their planet.

Chewbacca fought during the Clone Wars on Kashyyyk.

**Chewbacca** An immense, fur-covered warrior of great strength and loyalty, Chewbacca the Wookiee was a well-known figure in both the underworld and the Rebel Alliance. Born on Kashyyyk over two centuries before the Battle of Yavin, he was a wise, sophisticated being with exceptional skills in starship piloting and repair.

Unlike most Wookiees, who rarely strayed from the lush forests of Kashyyyk, Chewbacca's youthful wanderlust took him far from the confines of his green homeworld. His travels first included many remote and dangerous locales on Kashyyyk before taking him to the stars. Chewbacca's heart, however, was firmly rooted on Kashyyyk, and he would always try to make it home to share important Wookiee holidays with his family.

Chewbacca was a veteran of the Clone Wars, part of the high command tasked with protecting Kashyyyk from droid invasion. There he served with fellow Wookiee Tarfful and the Jedi Master Yoda. The wise Yoda had maintained a good relationship with the denizens of Kashyyyk, earning their respect. When events surrounding the rise of the Empire resulted in the clone forces betraying their Jedi generals, Chewbacca and Tarfful remained loyal to Yoda, helping the Jedi Master escape the clone trap.

Following the Clone Wars, the Empire subjugated the planet—ostensibly to punish the world for harboring Jedi fugitives, but mostly to exploit the Wookiees as slave labor. Chewbacca escaped capture for a time, helping his people as best as he could while living the life of a fugitive. Chewie was eventually captured and became a slave, toiling away for the betterment of the Empire until an impudent Imperial cadet named Han Solo freed him.

Drummed out of the military, Solo had few options but to return to the fringe lifestyle he knew so well. Chewbacca swore loyalty to Han, and became his partner in crime. The two of them were soon a well-known smuggling duo. When they came into ownership of the freighter *Millennium Falcon,* their exploits became legendary.

Chewbacca stood over 2 meters tall and had a coat of ginger-brown fur. He wore nothing save for a bandoleer that held specialized ammunition for the bowcaster he carried, and a simple tool pouch so that he could undertake the many repairs the chronically malfunctioning *Falcon* required.

Chewbacca and Solo spent hours modifying and tinkering with their beloved *Falcon,* souping it up far beyond its original performance specs. Although the *Falcon*'s upkeep was a labor of love, many a time Chewie unleashed his legendary temper on the recalcitrant freighter, banging his massive furry hands against delicate components that refused to behave.

Early in their smuggling career, Chewbacca stunned Han Solo by returning to Kashyyyk to marry a female Wookiee named Mallatobuck. Solo had never pegged Chewie as a family man, but Wookiee customs allowed Chewbacca to continue his flying with Han—protecting him as the Wookiee life debt demanded—while still being a husband and, eventually, father. Chewbacca's son, Lumpawarrump (who later went by the name Waroo), was raised mainly by Malla and Chewie's father, Attichitcuk. Chewie continued to fly the space lanes, avoiding Imperial patrols and smuggling contraband for various clients, but he returned often to Kashyyyk.

Chewbacca became Solo's conscience of sorts. The smuggler maintained a mercenary bravado and apparently refused to adhere to any ideals other than self-preservation, and Chewie was openly the more compassionate of the two. Perhaps it was the ordeal suffered by his people at the hands of the Empire that caused him to feel this way. While Solo steered clear of any allegiance during the Galactic Civil War, Chewbacca definitely supported the Rebel cause, though the two of them tried to avoid the struggle altogether.

Ironically, a simple steerage assignment landed them in the heart of the Rebel Alliance. Desperate for cash, Chewie and Han took on a charter, flying two passengers and their droids from Tatooine to Alderaan. Little did the smugglers realize that their cargo included a legendary Jedi Knight, the son of the prophesied Chosen One in Jedi mythology, and a pair of droids containing information vital to both the Empire and the Alliance. This trip inextricably drew Chewbacca and Solo into the Rebel fold, and they continued flying missions for the Rebellion for years after.

Wookiees defined family differently from most species. To a Wookiee, an "honor family" contained the closest of friends, and Chewbacca swore loyalty to all of them, offering protection even at great personal risk. When Han Solo and Leia Organa married and began to raise their own family, Chewbacca took their children into his honor family, and helped guard and raise the three young Solos—Jacen, Jaina, and Anakin.

When Chewbacca learned that Han had been captured by the bloodthirsty Yevetha during the Black Fleet crisis, he disobeyed Leia's orders and flew straight into the heart of enemy territory: the Koornacht Cluster. With the help of his cousins Jowdrrl, Dryanta, and Shoran, and his son, Lumpawarrump, he rescued Han from Yevethan clutches.

At the start of the Yuuzhan Vong invasion, Han Solo and Chewbacca were on the planet Sernpidal when it became a target of the alien menace. Using massive gravity-altering creatures called dovin basals, the Yuuzhan Vong began to drag Sernpidal's moon Dobido from its orbit to the planet's surface. Han Solo, his teenage son Anakin, and Chewbacca began organizing a desperate evacuation, cramming as many escapees aboard the *Falcon* as they could.

Solo and Chewbacca enjoyed many close calls through the years, and executed countless last-second escapes; Sernpidal was not to be one of them. As the moon rushed closer to the surface, Chewbacca was cut off from the *Falcon.*

*Chewbacca spent hours modifying and tinkering with the* Millennium Falcon.

Chewbacca and Han Solo were a well-known smuggling duo whose exploits became legendary.

Anakin was faced with a terrible decision. The *Falcon* could not wait any longer. Rather than endanger everyone aboard, Anakin piloted the ship away, leaving Chewbacca behind. Chewie stood his ground, howling defiantly at the immense moon as it crashed into Sernpidal's surface, killing the mighty Wookiee. Six months after his death, the city of Rwookrrorro was the site of a memorial held in honor of the fallen Wookiee. The fact that his body could not be retrieved was a source of sorrow for all.

**ch'hala tree** These greenish purple trees from Cularin, with slim trunks and leafy tops, burst into a brilliant red that rippled across their trunks when sounds occurred nearby. But the natural chemical process that triggered the display was put to a more sinister use by Emperor Palpatine: He turned the trees into spies that were especially helpful because they lined the Grand Corridor outside the Senate chambers in the Imperial Palace. The trees were implanted with a module that converted the chemical changes caused by sound back into speech, which was then encrypted and transmitted. This was in fact the basis of the long-sought Delta Source spy network, which provided vital New Republic intelligence to Grand Admiral Thrawn.

**Ch'hodos** A red, rocky planet in the Sith Empire that served as the central base of the Sith Lord Shar Dakhan about 5,000 years before the Battle of Yavin. During the Great Hyperspace War, Ch'hodos served as one of the worlds where Sith forces gathered in preparation for their attack on the Old Republic.

**Chian** A Kajain'sa'Nikto youngling who was part of the mighty Bear Clan training under Yoda at the time of the Clone Wars.

**chidinkalu** A pipe-like wind instrument carved out of the chidinka plant by the Kitonak of Kirdo III.

**Chiewab Amalgamated Pharmaceuticals** One of the original sponsors of the Corporate Sector, this conglomerate owned over 600 sytems and was the leader in biotechnological research and development. Its strengths were in chemistry and electronics. Chiewab was constantly seeking out new planets and new substances that might be developed for its new product family. Subsidiaries included Geentech Laboratories, Corellian Chemical Corporation, Chiewab Nutrition, Degan Explorations, and The Vernan Group.

**Chiffonage, Beryl** A noted Rebel tactician at Echo Base during the Battle of Hoth. Beryl Chiffonage worked with Luke Skywalker, to devise the snowspeeder assault plan known as Attack Pattern Delta. He had an intimate knowledge of Imperial battle tactics. Chiffonage also helped to design the harpoon and tow cable.

**Chihdo** A Rodian smuggler, friend, and partner of the Corellian Rik Duel. Chihdo helped Duel in a con that he pulled on Han Solo, Princess Leia Organa, and Luke Skywalker, on the planet Stenos shortly after the Battle of Yavin. Years later, still on Stenos, Chihdo was captured by bounty hunters and frozen in carbonite in an attempt to lure Skywalker and Lando Calrissian, who were in search of the frozen Han Solo. Chihdo was eventually unfrozen, and he joined Rik and Dani in a salvage operation after the fall of the Empire. He eventually accompanied the duo and Luke Skywalker on various diplomatic missions for the Alliance of Free Planets.

**chilab** A Yuuzhan Vong neural grub that acted like a recorder. Nom Anor was fitted with a chilab that inserted through the nostrils; its tendrites attached to Anor's optic chiasma.

**Child of Winds** This Qom Qae youth helped Luke Skywalker and Mara Jade during their mission to find the Hand of Thrawn on Nirauan. Jade suggested that his adult name should be Friend of Jedi.

**Childsen, Lieutenant Shann** An Imperial lieutenant, he was demoted after a superior officer blamed him for a clerical error. Considered a bully by fellow officers, Childsen was fanatical in his support of the Emperor's policy of subjugating nonhuman races. He was killed aboard the Death Star during the rescue of Princess Leia Organa.

***Chimaera*** An Imperial II Star Destroyer under the command of Captain Pellaeon at the Battle of Endor. It became the acting command ship after the destruction of the *Executor.* Five years later, Grand Admiral Thrawn picked the *Chimaera* as his flagship. Severely damaged and abandoned during the capture of Duro amid Operation Shadow Hand, it was refitted by the New Republic and then reacquired by the Empire at the Battle of Gravlex Med. The peace accords between the New Republic and the Empire were signed aboard the *Chimaera.*

Twenty-five years after the Battle of Yavin, the *Chimaera,* commanded by Grand Admiral Gilad Pellaeon, took part in the battles at Garqi and Ithor. It was nearly destroyed during the Battle of Bastion after its bridge was rammed by a coralskipper.

**Chin** A chief associate of the smuggler and spy Talon Karrde. The main duty of this human from the planet Myrkr was to care for and train Karrde's pet vornskrs. He domesticated the creatures and trained them to serve as guards. Chin's understanding of the mysterious Force-blocking ysalamiri led him to develop a method for safely removing them from their tree-branch homes. He was also Karrde's chief of operations.

**Chine-kal, Commander** The Yuuzhan Vong commander in charge of the *Crèche,* a slave ship that transported prisoners from Gyndine to help nurture a newborn yammosk. Upon discovery of a Jedi among his prisoners—Wurth Skidder—Chine-kal intended to hand him over to Warmaster Tsavong Lah, but Nas Choka intervened. The *Crèche* was attacked at Kalarba by Kyp Durron's squadron, and Chine-kal was forced to flee to Fondor, where his ship was obliterated by a blast from Centerpoint Station.

Chewbacca with members of his "honor family" and close friends

**Chip** A droid the size and shape of a 12-year-old boy, Microchip belonged to Jedi Prince Ken.

**Chiraneau, Admiral** Formerly a TIE fighter ace, Chiraneau was promoted at Admiral Piett's request and served as his personal adviser aboard the *Executor* during the Battle of Endor. He died when the Super Star Destroyer was destroyed.

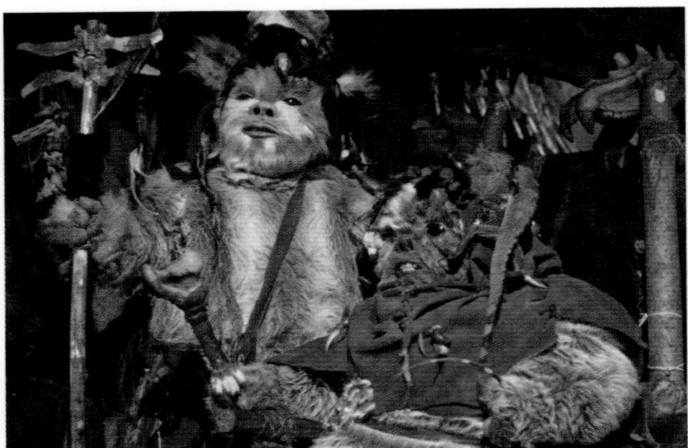

Chief Chirpa (seated) with Logray

**Chir'daki** TIE fighter variants, they were specifically built for use by Twi'lek pilots. In a Chir'daki, the globe-like cockpit of a TIE fighter was attached to the S-foils of an X-wing fighter. The S-foils were connected to a collar, which allowed them to rotate independently from the cockpit. This design provided greater stability and maneuverability for the pilot, making these craft extraordinarily lethal.

**Chirpa, Chief** The ruling figure among the Bright Tree Village Ewok tribe, which was befriended by the Rebel Alliance shortly before the Battle of Endor. Chirpa was chief for 42 seasons before the appearance of the Rebels. He was strong-willed, courageous, and dignified. As a symbol of his position within the tribe, the graying Chirpa carried a reptilian staff. He also wore the teeth, horns, and bones of the animals he had bested during hunts.

In his old age, senility began to creep into his judgment. A widower, Chirpa was once married to Ra-Lee, who was killed in the forests. For a time, Chirpa believed that his eldest daughter, Asha, had also been killed. Asha was eventually reunited with her father and sister, Chirpa's youngest daughter Kneesaa.

Upon Chief Chirpa's death, Kneesaa was inducted as the new chief of Bright Tree Village. The ceremony coincided with her wedding to Wicket Warrick.

**Chiss** An attractive, intelligent, and extremely private species from the icy world of Csilla, in the Unknown Regions. Chiss were so protective of their society that they managed to keep their existence largely secret from the rest of the galaxy. They had blue skin, jet-black hair, and glowing red eyes. Their skin and eye color were likely due to a chemical reaction they experienced in an oxygen atmosphere.

Though physiologically very similar to humans, Chiss bypassed the adolescent stage of life and advanceed quickly to full maturity. Children were given adult responsibilities very quickly.

The Chiss controlled more than two dozen systems surrounding their homeworld of Csilla. Chiss colonial expansion was undertaken not for the sake of conquest, but rather from the need to impose order in what was often a vary chaotic frontier. Though the Chiss meted out violence to bring primitive or aggressive native populations in line, such strikes were always in retaliation. When attacked, the Chiss fought with measured, well-planned strategies. The notion of a preemptive strike was anathema in the Chiss code of honor.

Chiss were highly evolved, taking great interest in arts and science, and maintained a powerful military. In many accounts, they have been described as pensive—contemplative, deliberate, and calculating—studying situations from every viewpoint. They often considered all the alternatives, even what might have occurred if something had been done differently.

Very little solid information has been recorded regarding Chiss life on Csilla. Familial lines and heredity played an important role in Chiss culture, with ruling families governing the Chiss Ascendency. The number of families fluctuated depending on the need of the times—as few as 3 or as many as 12. The family lines often took on specific roles. For example, the Sabosen clan governed education, justice, and public health responsibilities, while the Inrokini concentrated on business, communications, civilian technologies and the sciences. The Chiss spoke a complex language called Cheunh.

The most famous Chiss was perhaps Mitth'raw'nuruodo, or Thrawn as he was known to the galaxy at large. He was the only nonhuman to hold the rank of Grand Admiral in the Galactic Empire, and he led a highly effective though ultimately failed campaign to retake the Core Worlds from the New Republic five years after the Battle of Endor. After that time, more information about the Chiss came to light, such as the existence of a Chiss outpost on Nirauan. During the war against the Yuuzhan Vong, the Chiss worked with the New Republic to develop a biological weapon to use against the alien invaders.

Chiss

**Chiss clawcraft** An ingenious hybrid of Chiss and Imperial technology, it was easily recognized by its round cockpit, which was actually a modified version of the TIE fighter's ball cockpit. Like the TIE fighter, the clawcraft had twin ion engines, located in a pod attached to the rear of the cockpit. The Chiss aesthetic was plainly evident in the four curving weapons arms that sprouted from the vehicle. Each arm was capped by a modified Sienar Fleet Systems L-s7.2 TIE cannon. Stealing a bit of the X-wing's design, the fire-linked cannons were arrayed to provide the greatest possible field of fire. The weapons arms also doubled as control vanes; even minute adjustments to the position of a single arm resulted in sharp turns and other sudden maneuvers. During combat, many Chiss pilots learned to launch the clawcraft into a frightening spin while firing all four laser cannons simultaneously. This tactic created a barrage of laserfire that was nearly impossible to dodge. The clawcraft was equipped with a modest deflector shield generator and heavier armor than the TIE fighter. Both of these additions put a greater burden on the ion engines, making the clawcraft slightly slower than the standard TIE fighter at sublight speeds.

Chiss clawcraft

The clawcraft was equipped with life-support systems and the Chiss equivalent of a Class 1.5 hyperdrive. As with all Chiss starships, the clawcraft's hyperdrive relied on a network of hyperspace anchor points spread throughout Chiss territories. These anchor points broadcast a signal that Chiss craft could follow through the maze of hyperspace. However, because the Chiss relied on these hyperspace beacons, nav computers were uncommon aboard clawcraft. Without a nav computer, travel beyond Chiss borders became extremely dangerous. To strike out into new territory, the Chiss had to install nav computers aboard a lead starship, which then guided wingmates via a homing beacon.

**Chiss Expansionary Defense Fleet** Part of the Chiss military, this fleet patrolled the borders of Chiss space while the Phalanxes handled any threats that got past the fleet. In times of crisis, like the repulsion of Ssi-ruuvi forces, the CEDF bolstered its ranks by drawing upon nearby Colonial Phalanxes. The Syndic Mitt'raw'nuruodo's Household Phalanx, a significant portion of the CEDF, took an extended leave from the rest of the fleet to deal with encroaching threats. At the end of the war against the Yuuzhan Vong, Jagged Fel was appointed by the CEDF as liaison to the Galactic Alliance.

**Chistor, Barnab** Once the governor of Almas, he later served as governor of the entire Cularin system. His administration was accused of poor financial policies, and with the onset of the Clone Wars, the Thaereian Military took control of the system under a Republic Charter, much to the dismay of its citizens.

Working around the charter, Governor Chistor and his aides began pushing legislation to undermine the control of the Thaereians in an effort to "legally" regain control of Cularin. His efforts did not go unnoticed, and he became the target of assassination attempts.

**Chistori** An imposing lizard-like, humanoid species, Chistori were a secretive, fiercely independent people. Their homeworld was a mystery to the rest of the galaxy, and no record existed of them in the Jedi Archives of the Old Republic. Like most reptiles, the Chistori were cold-blooded, and their thick scales gave them a natural form of armor. They avoided cold climates whenever possible.

**Chituhr** A mean-looking animal trainer of the Jinda tribe on Endor.

**Chivkyrie, Yeeru** An Adarian, he was one of the Rebel Alliance's primary supporters in the Shelsha sector, and leader of the resistance group Republic Redux.

**Chizzik, Pax** An 11-year-old Jedi youngling at the time of the Clone Wars, he tended to use the Force to increase his likability.

**Ch'manss system** Located near the Al'har system, it was connected to Haruun Kal and other systems via the Gevarno Loop. It remained loyal to the Republic during the Clone Wars.

**Ch'no** An H'drachi scrap scavenger from the planet M'haeli, he saved the human infant Mora after an attack and became her adopted father, not knowing that she was of royal blood.

**Choard, Governor Barshnis** The Imperial Governor of the planet Shelkonwa, his contacts with the elite of the Shelsha sector brought him under the suspicion of Emperor Palpatine. The Emperor's Hand, Mara Jade, was investigating possible ties between Moff Glovstoak and the Rebel Alliance. Her investigation revealed that Choard was part of a plot to build an independent, separate empire out of Shelsha sector. Mara was assisted by the rogue stormtrooper unit Hand of Judgment, whose membership include Saberan Marcross, Choard's nephew. Unable to kill his uncle, Marcross insisted Choard be taken alive, and Jade complied, reasoning that Choard deserved a lengthy prison sentence for his treachery.

**Choba** A Dug who worked as an interrogation expert for Jib Kopatha during the early years of the Galactic Civil War. He was brought in to torture Han Solo for information about the location of the Rebel Alliance fleet. When Sheel Odala and Chewbacca arrived to rescue Solo, Odala shot Choba in the neck, killing him instantly.

**Choco** A small and battered R2 unit, this clumsy droid befriended R2-D2 during his encounters with the Great Heep and in his droid harem years before the start of the Galactic Civil War.

**ChoFi, Senator** A 2-meter-tall New Republic Senator, ChoFi was a loyal supporter of Princess Leia Organa Solo from the beginnings of the New Republic.

*Master Tsui Choi*

**Choi, Tsui** An Aleena Jedi Master, he was part of the Jedi team that went to Yitheeth during the Yinchorri Uprising. During the Clone Wars, he piloted a Jedi starfighter and was shot down over Eriadu following Order 66. Surviving the crash, he played dead and secretly met up with other Jedi survivors on Kessel. During this meeting, Darth Vader and the 501st Legion arrived and killed the survivors.

**Choka, Nas** A high-ranking Yuuzhan Vong warrior, he backed the coup by Shimrra that put the Yuuzhan Vong on an invasion path to the galaxy. In exchange for his loyalty, Choka was promoted to Supreme Commander of the flagship of the Yuuzhan Vong. Though he was in command at the costly Battle of Fondor, his life was spared and he continued to acquit himself in battle, in Hutt space. After the death of Tsavong Lah, Choka became Warmaster. He concentrated his attacks on the Galactic Alliance rather than the Jedi, whom he disregarded as a real threat. When Shimrra died in the final battle over Coruscant, Nas Choka became Supreme Overlord, and it was he who surrendered.

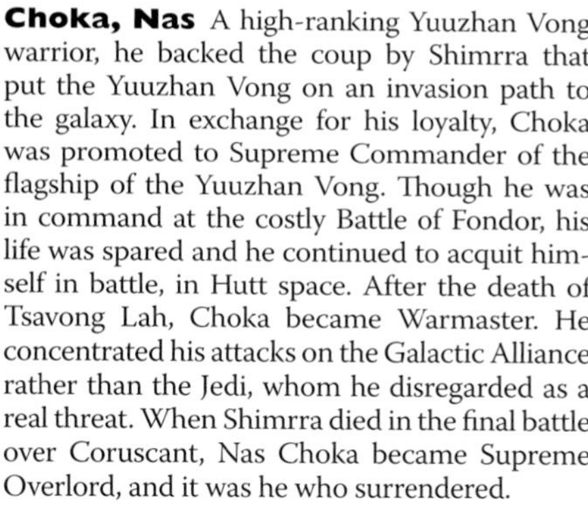

**Chokk** A Klatooinian bodyguard who watched over Jabba the Hutt during the Boonta Eve Podrace.

**Cholganna** This forested planet was a known homeworld of the nexu.

**Cholly, Weez, and Tup** A trio of bumbling friends of Ren S'orn on Simpla-12. They were slackers who agreed to help Obi-Wan Kenobi and Astri Oddo investigate S'orn's death and the machinations of Jenna Zan Arbor.

**Chommell sector** A lightly populated area of the galaxy that contained 36 inhabited planets, including Chommell Minor and Naboo. Some 40,000 other planets maintained sizable settlements, and 300 million barren stars filled the airless gaps between systems.

**Chorax system** A hotbed for smuggling and piracy, this system was in the Rachuk sector—along with the Hensara and Rachuk systems—and contained a medium-sized yellow star and a single planet, Chorax. Three years after the Battle of Endor, the Rebel Alliance's Rogue Squadron was skirting the system on a hyperspace jump to the Morobe system when it was accidentally yanked from hyperspace by the Interdictor cruiser *Black Asp*. The Rogues rescued the cruiser's true target, the smuggling ship *Pulsar Skate*, and forced the *Black Asp* to flee the system. After they resigned from the Alliance, Rogue Squadron hijacked a Thyferran bacta convoy in the Chorax system and brought it to Halanit.

**Chorios systems** Located in the Meridian sector, the Chorios systems comprised several systems that go by the name *Chorios*, including Nam Chorios, Pedducis Chorios, and Brachnis Chorios. Most of the worlds in the region were lifeless and barren. The systems' relatively few inhabitants were referred to as Chorians. Nine years after the Battle of Endor, Leia Organa Solo made a secret visit to a point near Brachnis Chorios's largest moon to meet with Seti Ashgad of Nam Chorios.

**Chosen One** According to an ancient Jedi prophecy, this individual was destined to bring balance to the Force. The true wording of the prophecy was lost to time, but it described a period when the Force would be dominated by the dark side, and an individual would be *conceived* by the will of the Force, possibly coaxed into life by the interactions of midi-chlorians. This person would vanquish the dark side menace, returning the Force to balance.

When Jedi Master Qui-Gon Jinn discovered a young slave boy with a record midi-chlorian count on Tatooine, he believed he had found the Chosen One in the form of Anakin Skywalker. True to the prophecy, the boy had no father—he had inexplicably sprung to life in the womb of his mother, Shmi Skywalker. Qui-Gon took Anakin to Coruscant for Jedi training, adamantly insisting before a skeptical Jedi Council that the boy would bring balance to the Force.

Qui-Gon proved correct, but in a manner that few could have predicted. The Force was in imbalance due to the rise of the Sith orchestrated by Darth Sidious. Anakin would eliminate the imbalance by *joining* the Sith, and in the process become the instrument of destruction for both Jedi and Sith.

**Chowall, Ruke** The Quarren editor of *Bends*, a Quarren counterculture newsnet popular in Morjanssik, on the planet Mon Calamari.

**Chreev** A Yuuzhan Vong Shamed One living in the bowels of Coruscant, he was a follower of

Christophsis

the Prophet Yu'shaa who was promoted to chief acolyte after the betrayal and death of Shoon-mi.

**Chrellis** A star system with a tiny planetoid that was the first headquarters for Rebel Alliance High Command.

**Christophsis** A crystalline planet that became a major site of combat during the Clone Wars. Obi-Wan Kenobi and Anakin Skywalker led their clone forces against the amassed droid army of General Whorm Loathsom. With the help of Anakin's new Padawan, Ahsoka Tano, the Jedi were able to lower the energy shield protecting the Separatist army and defeat their forces.

**Chroma Zed** A mining world whose native population of Chromans was enslaved by the Empire. Many Chromans joined the Diversity Alliance in the time of the New Republic.

**chromasheath** An iridescent material, it was similar to leather.

**Chronelle, Titi** A denizen of Mos Espa on Tatooine, he informed fellow slaves Anakin Skywalker and Amee about a slave raid committed by Krayn.

**chrono; chronometer** A device that measured time. *Chrono* was also the title of a leading news magazine.

Chrysalides

**Chros-filik** A famous Phuii Podracer from Phu in the late years of the Galactic Republic.

**chrysalides** Dark side mutant creatures, they were unleashed by the second cloned Emperor against Lando Calrissian's war droid attack force outside the Emperor's Citadel on the planet Byss.

**Chryya** A planet with a thriving spice business. Darth Maul was sent on a mission to Chryya to frighten merchants into turning their businesses over to the Trade Federation. A single merchant organized a protest, and the people of Chryya chose to destroy their spice supplies rather than turn them over. It was Darth Maul's only failure prior to the Battle of Naboo.

**chuba** The Huttese word for "you," it was also sometimes applied to certain amphibians, such as gorgs, which formed an important part of the Huttese diet.

**chubb** A small, burrowing reptile, it was the pet and constant companion of a young boy named Fidge who met R2-D2 and C-3PO during the early days of the Empire.

**chubbits** Small reptilian desert dwellers, they were native to the planet Aridus.

**Chuff, Pelleus** A diminutive actor, under a meter tall, he was renowned for his portrayal of Jedi Master Yoda in his self-penned serial, *Jedi!* During the Clone Wars, he was hired to serve as a decoy for Yoda when the Jedi Master went on a secret mission to Vjun.

Spearmaster Ch'Unkk

**Chu-Gon Dar Cubes** Unusual Force artifacts supposedly created by the ancient Jedi Master Chu-Gon Dar, these cubes could focus Force energy to transmogrify matter.

**Chuhkyvi** An aquatic humanoid species from Aquaris with tan skin, yellow eyes, four-fingered hands, and a pronounced nose. Many lived on the watery world Iskalon.

**Chukha-Trok** A brave Ewok woodsman, he was known for his forest skills and lore.

**Chume, Ta'a** *See* Ta'a Chume, Queen Mother.

**Chun, Bruck** A student at the Jedi Temple on Coruscant about 12 years before the Battle of Naboo, he trained alongside Obi-Wan Kenobi. A bully, Chun resented Obi-Wan and, in an attempt to prevent Kenobi from being selected as a Padawan, constantly provoked him to anger. Chun had worked with Yoda to try to control his temper. He was later a suspect in a rash of mysterious thefts occurring in the Jedi Temple.

The fallen Jedi apprentice Xanatos used information from stolen Jedi records to convince Bruck to join his cause, telling him that his father, Vox Chun, had become a powerful person on Telos, Xanatos's home planet. Bruck's friend Siri Tachi noticed the change in his behavior. When Xanatos's plot threatened to destroy the Jedi Temple, Qui-Gon Jinn and Obi-Wan sprang into action. Chun held off Kenobi as Xanatos escaped, but in battle in the Room of a Thousand Fountains, he slipped on a wet rock and fell to his death. In investigating the circumstances of his death, the Jedi discovered a hidden transmitter in the hilt of Chun's lightsaber that allowed Xanatos to spy on the Order.

**Chun, Kad** The brother of Bruck Chun and son of Vox, he accompanied his father to the Jedi Temple to seek justice for the death of Bruck. Vox's hatred of the Jedi colored Kad's views for years. After his father died in an attempt to steal the treasury of the *BioCruiser* and sabotage the ship, Kad was able to forgive Obi-Wan for Bruck's death. He was a tall man with a slender build, close-cropped white hair, and pale blue eyes.

**Chun, Vox** The treasurer of Telos and father of Bruck and Kad Chun, he was a business associate of the fallen Jedi apprentice Xanatos and aided his rise to power. A tall man with white hair, he went to jail after the Telosian environmental firm UniFy was exposed as an illegal front for Offworld Mining. After being pardoned for his crimes, he went to the Jedi Temple with his son Kad to seek justice for the death of Bruck. Twelve years later, he was working with Kad aboard the *BioCruiser*, where he conspired to steal the ship's treasury. During the heist, Vox was killed by his accomplice, Kern.

**Chung, Nep** A Phuii Vigo in the Black Sun crime syndicate in the last decades of the Galactic Republic, he was slaughtered by Darth Maul when the Sith Lord eliminated the leadership of the organization.

**Ch'Unkk, Spearmaster** A member of the Imperial Interim Council, he was the leader of the largest clan of Whiphids on his home planet of Toola. Ch'Unkk controlled a vast number of Whiphids employed by various Imperials as bodyguards and used them to persuade their bosses to obey the Council. Unable to speak Basic, he was always seen with his protocol droid. He was the fourth Interim Council member to be killed when he resisted Xandel Carivus's takeover. This led to Whiphids everywhere leaving Imperial service, further weakening the fracturing Empire.

**Chunky** The affectionate nickname for Tyria Sarkin's R5 unit.

**Chuovvick, Chellemi** Along with fellow Jedi Knights Empatojayos Brand and Bultar Swan, she was sent to negotiate a peaceful resolution to growing tensions in the Sepan sector at the time of the Separatist crisis.

**Churabba the Hutt** An ancient Hutt crime lord, she freed the Nikto species from the control of the Cult of M'dweshuu and re-established Hutt control of the species around the time of the Great Sith War.

**Churba system** A star system located in the Mid Rim, it contained eight planets, including Churba and New Cov. The worlds closest and farthest from the Churba system's sun—Barhu and Hurcha—had temperature extremes that didn't support life. Churba, the cosmopolitan fourth world, was home to the corporate offices of Sencil Corporation, a major manufacturer of black-market assassin droid components. It was also the birthplace of Imperial Intelligence Agent Kirtan Loor. New Cov, the third world in, had vast jungles filled with natural resources. Four Bothan ships once attacked a *Victory*-class Star Destroyer in the Churba sector, and kept it occupied until a Rebel Alliance star cruiser could assist them.

**Church of the First Frequency** A religious sect on Otranto that attempted to kill Imperial Grand Inquisitor Torbin.

**churi** A large bird found on Endor. Logray wore a churi skull headpiece.

**Chusker, Vu** A business associate of gangster Cabrool Nuum. Jabba the Hutt was asked first by Nuum, and then by Nuum's son and daughter, to kill Vu Chusker. Jabba, who had never laid eyes on the being, refused to kill him—although he did eliminate the Nuum family one by one. Making his escape from a Nuum family dungeon, Jabba encountered the nasty Chusker—and promptly killed him with one swipe of his tail.

**Chuundar** A black-furred Wookiee who was the leader of the city of Rwookrrorro during the time of the Great Sith War. He sold his people into slavery in exchange for a high-ranking position in the Czerka Corporation. When his brother Zaalbar learned of this treachery, he attacked Chuundar with his climbing claws exposed, breaking a major Wookiee tradition and thus being exiled as a "madclaw." Zaalbar eventually returned to Kashyyyk to properly challenge his brother and deposed him.

**chuun m'arh** Frigate analogs up to 440 meters in length used by the Yuuzhan Vong.

***Chu'unthor*** Luke Skywalker found this wrecked spacecraft half submerged in a river on the planet Dathomir, where it had lain for at least 400 years. The ship was huge: 2 kilometers long, a kilometer wide, and eight levels high. It resembled a small city. Luke later learned that the *Chu'unthor,* under the command of Jedi Masters, had served as a mobile training academy for thousands of Jedi apprentices. He was able to get into the ship and found records of old Jedi training, which he used to develop programs for his Jedi academy.

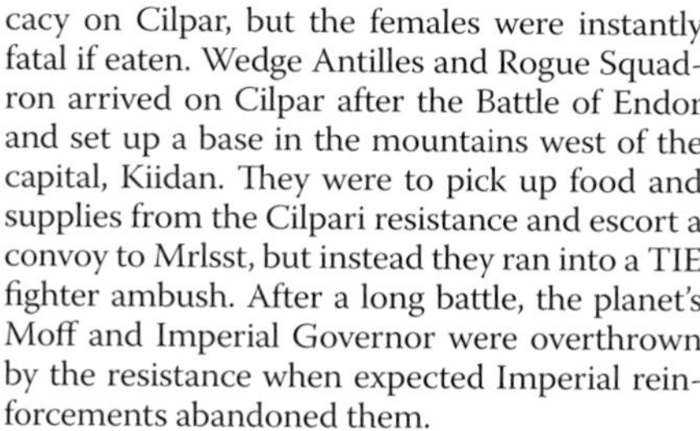
Chu'unthor

**Chyler, Tian** An Imperial Security Bureau agent assigned to investigate unregistered Tibanna gas operations on Bespin. She posed as a Corellian mining official from Ando, supplying Darth Vader with evidence of illegal operations that the Dark Lord used to blackmail Lando Calrissian into cooperating with the Empire. She eventually defected to the Rebel Alliance, providing information that aided in the liberation of Bespin from Imperial control.

**Cilghal** A Force-sensitive Mon Calamari, she was recruited by Leia Organa Solo for Luke Skywalker's Jedi academy. A trained ambassador and niece of Admiral Ackbar, she used her diplomatic skills to hold the 12 Jedi students together in the days following the attack on Luke Skywalker by the spirit of Sith Lord Exar Kun. She aided in the plan to defeat Kun, then departed Yavin 4 for her most difficult mission: healing the dying Mon Mothma.

Cilghal discovered that the former Chief of State was suffering from poisoning by nanodestroyers, artificially created viruses that were dismantling Mon Mothma's cells one nucleus at a time. Using her considerable abilities, Cilghal set about instead to dismantle the nanodestroyers, billions of them, one at a time. In doing so, she healed Mon Mothma.

Cilghal split her time between duties as a Jedi healer and as a Senator from Mon Calamari during the Diversity Alliance crisis. She did not seek reelection and instead chose to focus on her Jedi studies, achieving the rank of Jedi Master a generation after the Battle of Yavin. Despite her great healing abilities, she was unable to help Mara Jade with her coomb-spore illness during the Yuuzhan Vong invasion.

Cilghal worked with scientist Danni Quee to study the biotechnological creatures of the Yuuzhan Vong, especially the yammosk and the voxyn. She helped develop a gravitic amplitude modulator, a means of countering the command signals of the yammosk. Her research into such systems gave her a foundation of knowledge that proved valuable in breaking the telepathic connection shared by members of the Colony during the Swarm War.

**Cilpar** A planet once held by Imperial forces, it was covered with mountains, jungles, and woods. Dozens of nearly indestructible ancient native temples were scattered throughout the forest. Life-forms included dangerous carnivores called ronks. Male ronks were considered a delicacy on Cilpar, but the females were instantly fatal if eaten. Wedge Antilles and Rogue Squadron arrived on Cilpar after the Battle of Endor and set up a base in the mountains west of the capital, Kiidan. They were to pick up food and supplies from the Cilpari resistance and escort a convoy to Mrlsst, but instead they ran into a TIE fighter ambush. After a long battle, the planet's Moff and Imperial Governor were overthrown by the resistance when expected Imperial reinforcements abandoned them.

**Cindar** A hulking Nikto member of the militant wing of the Nebula Front.

**Cinnagar** The largest city and capital of the seven worlds that made up the Empress Teta star system. Located on Koros Major, Cinnagar was the location of Empress Teta's palace and housed the core of her military forces. The city fell under attack many times during Empress Teta's reign, most notably during the Great Hyperspace War when the Sith invaded several planets within the Old Republic. Empress Teta's troops, which included several Jedi Knights, managed to repel all such attacks. One thousand years later, the Dark Side Adepts Aleema and Satal Keto took control of the Empress Teta system, and Cinnagar fell under their control. Under the dark siders' reign, life in Cinnagar was miserable: unfair imprisonment, public executions, torture, mayhem, and despair were widespread.

**Circarpous system** Fourteen planets orbiting a star called Circarpous Major. Many of the planets were colonized, and several intelligent species came from the Circarpous system.

- **Circarpous IV** was the base of operations for a Circarpousian resistance group that opposed the Empire. Although not entirely committed to the Rebel Alliance, these rebels planned a diplomatic meeting with Princess Leia Organa shortly after the destruction of the Death Star. This was the most populated planet and capital of the Circarpous system. It was described by some as a hectic, private-enterprise-style world. Some people felt the Circarpousians here were provincial, given how little they knew of activity elsewhere in their system. Circarpous judicial systems still enacted the death penalty for a number of severe crimes.

- **Circarpous V** was a jungle world inhabited by numerous intelligent species including the Greenies and the Coway. The planet hosted several xenoarchaeological sites: massive temples built by now extinct races. There was a secret Imperial mining facility as well, its operations conducted without the knowledge or permission of the leaders on Circarpous IV. The planet was commonly known as Mimban. (*See also* Mimban.)

- **Circarpous X** was the home of an extensive colony that acted as a lookout site for Circarpous V. If starships were spotted, operations on Mimban were shut down. It was often referred to simply as Ten by the locals.

- **Circarpous XII** was also colonized. It was reputed to have a Rebel presence during the Galactic Civil War.

- **Circarpous XIV** was the location of a hidden Rebel base after the Battle of Yavin.

**Circle of Jedi Healers** A sub-order of the Jedi Knights who practiced the healing arts. Barriss Offee and Stass Allie were members.

**Circumtore** A ring-shaped artificial planetoid, home of the Shell Hutts. Cradossk sent Bossk, Zuckuss, IG-88, D'harhan, and Boba Fett to Circumtore to obtain the bounty on Oph Nar Dinnid.

**Circus Horrificus** A traveling show of alien monstrosities, it toured from system to system terrifying audiences. Jabba's main rancor keeper, Malakili, once worked for the circus.

**Ciro, Keleman** Captain of the New Republic corvette *FarStar,* he was previously a member of Page's Commandos. He was captured and later rescued from the Empire but eventually died from injuries he sustained.

**Cirrus** Known for its golden seas and its lovely cities, this temperate world orbits binary suns. Its capital city is Ciran.

**CIS** *See* Confederacy of Independent Systems.

**CIS Jammer Prototype** A Separatist vessel that was basically a Trade Federation Droid Control Ship with a transmission array modified to broadcast jamming signals capable of disrupting a key HoloNet node at Balamak. A Republic task force led by Jedi Obi-Wan Kenobi and Nanda-Ree Janoo engaged a Confederacy flotilla with a starfighter attack. It was Kenobi's apprentice, Anakin Skywalker, who delivered the missile volley that destroyed the jamming craft. Victory was also credited to Adar Tallon, the renowned starfighter tactician who planned the attack.

**CIS Shadowfeed** An underground NewsNet that supplied propaganda and information to Separatist worlds during the Clone Wars.

**Citadel Station** This space station orbiting the planet Telos was erected by a group of Ithorians in the wake of the Great Sith War. The Ithorians were on Telos to assist in repairing the damage done to its ecosystem during a Sith bombardment. The immense Citadel Station moved over the planet's surface, monitoring the various recovery zones that were helping bring Telos back to life.

**City Bigspace** A grand concourse and habitable bubble that was a great attraction in the underwater Gungan city of Otoh Gunga.

**City of the Ugnaughts** *See* Ugnaught Surface.

**Ciutric** The system where Sate Pestage fled after he was suspected of treason against the Empire. The New Republic Provisional Council sent Rogue Squadron, Aggressor Wing, and Commando Team One to the planet to retrieve the Imperial dignitary, but he betrayed his rescuers. An Imperial Star Destroyer and an Interdictor cruiser under the command of Prince-Admiral Krennel arrived to foil the mission, although the New Republic forces were finally able to escape. Rogue Squadron pilot Ibtisam lost her life during the battle.

**Ciutric Hegemony** A region dominated by Imperial Prince-Admiral Krennel nine years after the Battle of Yavin.

**Claatuvac Guild** An elite group of long-lived Wookiee cartographers who charted extensive hyperspace route surveys that kept the galaxy navigable and mapped star routes unknown to the Republic or the Separatists. The value of the data they held made Kashyyyk a vital target in the Clone Wars.

**Clabburn** A legendary Mugaari space pirate and smuggler during the last decades of the Old Republic, he was known to prowl the area of space near Hoth.

**Clak'dor IV** The fourth planet orbiting the star Colu, it was the site of New Nozho, a colony built by Y'bith refugees.

**Clak'dor VII** Located in the Mayagil sector, this small planet orbiting the large white star Colu was the homeworld of the peaceful, highly evolved Bith. Clak'dor VII was once a lush garden world with advanced technologies, but became an ecological wasteland due to a conflict between two Bith cities, Nozho and Weogar. Generations before the Battle of Yavin, they unleashed gene-altering biological weapons on each other, mutating the planet's surface (the jungles had pink bubbling swamps) and forcing all surviving Biths to live in hermetically sealed domed cities. The planet was unable to produce basic needs for its citizens or goods for export, so many Bith used their intellectual abilities for employment as technical consultants. They also made good entertainers and musicians, playing everywhere from the grandest of palaces to out-of-the-way cantinas in spaceports such as Mos Eisley. During the Clone Wars, Clak'dor VII sided with the Separatists.

**clankers** A slang term used by clone troopers to refer to enemy battle droids.

**Clantaani** The inhabitants of Clantaano III. This dust bowl of a planet was home to a number of marauding nomadic tribes who fought endlessly over its meager resources. The Clantaani preferred the dry climate of desert worlds similar to their own, and found Tatooine much to their liking, not only for its climate but also for the disproportionate number of criminals within its rather sparse population.

*Clawdite Zam Wesell*

**Clarani** An elderly Ryn woman who took in Jaina Solo at Duro. Clarani's husband died on the *Jubilee Wheel* over Ord Mantell.

**Clawdite** Shape-changing genetic offshoots of the humanoid natives of Zolan, a planet in the Mid Rim. Clawdites' development came about by accident, when scientists sought to reactivate long-dormant skin-changing genes among the Zolanders to protect them from solar radiation. This event, centuries ago, triggered the divergence of the Clawdite species from the Zolander evolutionary line. Shape-shifting for Clawdites was an extremely uncomfortable process; they had to endure great pain to create and maintain a shape other than their natural form. Expert shifters employed special therapeutic oils and meditative techniques to aid their transformations.

By the time of the Separatist crisis, the Clawdites consolidated what little political power they had and approached Count Dooku for aid. The tumultuous events of the Clone Wars put these first steps at independence on hold, and when the Empire came to power, Zolan was blockaded to prevent Clawdites from leaving the world. As the New Republic replaced the Empire, Zolan exploded into civil war, and the Clawdites were able to take control of three-quarters of their planet. These alarming developments were eventually eclipsed by the invasion of the Yuuzhan Vong. During this crisis, New Republic Intelligence attempted recruiting Clawdite agents to infiltrate Yuuzhan Vong operations.

**Clays** A family of moisture farmers on Tatooine, they were against Ariq Joanson's plans to draw up maps of peace with the Jawas and Tusken Raiders.

**CLE-004 window cleaning droid** A hovering Publictechnic worker droid with built-in scrubbers.

**Cley, Usu** A hand-to-hand combat instructor in the Grand Army of the Republic, stationed at the Rimsoo Five military hospital on Drongar during the Clone Wars.

*CLE-004 window cleaning droid*

**Clezo, Vigo** A Rodian, he was one of the lieutenants, or Vigos, of the Black Sun criminal organization.

**cliffborer worms** Long, armored worms, they were found among the rocks on arid Tatooine. They often fed on razor moss.

**Clink** The nickname of Myn Donos's R2 astromech during his time with Wraith Squadron.

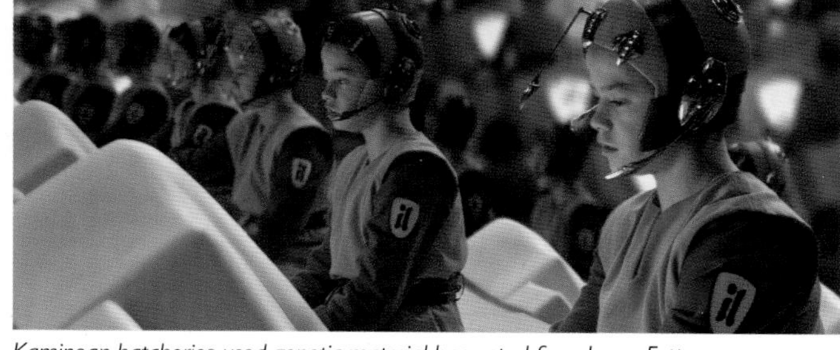

*Kaminoan hatcheries used genetic material harvested from Jango Fett.*

**clip beetle** This useful insect developed by the Yuuzhan Vong was prized for its nutritious meat and its ability to hold wounds shut.

**CLL-M2 ordnance lifter droid** A 3-meter-tall worker droid, it trudged along on sturdy, walker-like feet, squawking in a simplistic binary code understood by other droids. Extending from its back was a repulsorlift counterweight that used an inverse field to *increase* gravity's pull rather than repulse it, allowing the droid to lift extremely heavy loads.

**cloaking device** The ultimate sensor countermeasure, this device caused a ship to appear invisible to scanners. Early cloaking devices employed stygium crystals—rare minerals from Aeten II depleted during the Clone Wars, which made cloaking technology exceedingly rare during the time of the Empire. Imperial scientists discovered that hibridium could also be used to generate a cumbersome, costly, yet effective cloaking device. This cloaking technology had many limitations, the foremost of which was that the cloaked ship was double blind—outside observers may not have been able to see through the cloak, but neither could the cloaked ship see out.

**cloak of the *Nuun*** A form of bioengineered garment bestowed on only the greatest of Yuuzhan Vong warriors. Photosensitive bacteria that lived symbiotically on the surface of the cloak mimicked the wearer's surroundings.

**Cloak of the Sith** A region of space that was a huge dark cloud of dangerous meteors, asteroids, and planetoids, it was in the only path to the Roon system.

**CloakShape fighter** An older starfighter designed for atmospheric and short-range space combat, it was relegated to use mainly by bounty hunters, pirates, and other individuals with a need for assault starships. The ship traded speed for durability.

**clodhopper** A tenacious insect pest native to Naboo. Gungans prized clodhoppers as tasty snacks and used their hard shells to make musical instruments.

**clone** The genetic duplicate of biological life-forms created through various scientific means. There were innumerable benefits to cloned tissue in the field of medicine, but the science also created military forces. The clone troopers introduced in the Clone Wars were the product of the scientific geniuses of Kamino, beings renowned for their genetic knowledge. The Kaminoan hatcheries used genetic material harvested from the host template, a bounty hunter named Jango Fett. This material was grown into millions of soldiers inside glass-walled incubation wombs.

The Kaminoans employed growth acceleration techniques to effectively double the rate of clone development. Without such measures, it would take a full lifetime to grow a mature clone, but Kaminoan adult clones were ready for combat in less than a decade. Throughout a clone's growth, constant physical and mental training honed a warrior's skills. Unlike the mindless battle droid armies of the commerce guilds, clones could think creatively and operate much more independently.

Though the Kaminoans' methods of cloning were generally regarded as the best in the galaxy by the few who knew of them, they were by no means the only culture to explore genetic manipulation. The planet Khomm, an otherwise unremarkable world in the Deep Core, instituted cloning as the de facto method of reproduction. So content were the Khommites upon reaching the zenith of their society that they "froze" the evolution of this culture and turned to producing clones of previous generations. Like the Kaminoans, the Lurrians of Lur developed exceptional genetic sciences out of necessity, and their research was closely monitored following the Clone Wars. The extragalactic Yuuzhan Vong, who preferred organic technology, were also extremely skilled in their own brand of cloning, having developed such living weapons as the deadly voxyn.

*CLL-M2 ordnance lifter droid*

One of the fastest known methods of cloning involved the use of Spaarti cloning cylinders. These 4-meter-tall tanks held a developing clone suspended in a protective gelatin that accelerated growth and helped preserve the genetic code of the template. Each Spaarti cylinder contained a computer processing system that jacked directly into the cerebral cortex of the developing clone, "flash-pumping" information into the growing mind. The Spaarti method had one key side effect that limited its use, however: Clones produced through this method caused a disturbance in the Force, possibly as a result of identical "patterns" resonating. This disturbance would lead to a frightening affliction called clone madness, which could be countered by slowing the process. Recommended procedures advised at least a year of growth for a clone to remain mentally stable.

The Imperial tactical genius Grand Admiral Thrawn was able to sidestep this limitation through his brilliant use of ysalamiri, creatures that naturally push back the Force. By growing clones in areas devoid of the Force, Thrawn did not have to worry about the consequences of clone madness, and could produce mentally stable clones in 15 to 20 days.

*Kaminoan adult clones were ready for combat in less than a decade.*

Though the Kaminoan methods were not nearly as rapid, they were far more reliable. The time taken allowed Kaminoan scientists to carefully develop the psyches of their clones, crafting an army of unswerving loyalty. The Kaminoan cloners reconditioned an average of 7 aberrants for every 200 clones produced—a superb standard. In the time of the Empire, a variety of cloning processes were employed to build the ranks of the military, a practice completely abandoned by the New Republic that supplanted it.

Emperor Palpatine used the Spaarti method to create a cache of clone duplicates of his body, in a twisted bid to achieve practical immortality. The dark side practices of the Emperor ravaged his physical form and led to a rapid aging of his body. To stave off death, he used a dark side mind transference discipline to transport his consciousness into the body of a healthy clone, who then began aging instantly. Palpatine's scourge was finally ended six years after the Battle of

*Emperor Palpatine created a cache of clone duplicates of his body.*

Endor when his supply of clones was sabotaged by treacherous agents.

**clone commando** These specialized clone troopers of the Grand Army of the Republic were trained to act as infiltration agents separate from standard rank-and-file clone troopers. Commandos were trained in squads of four and wore specially upgraded Katarn armor painted a dull gray for better camouflage. Unlike other clones, commandos developed deep relationships with the other members of their four-man squads. Records from the Clone Wars attest to the effectiveness of the commandos, attributing the destruction of billions of battle droids to a few thousand clone commandos created during the war. More than half of that number were killed during the early stages of the Clone Wars, when the commandos were assigned to inexperienced generals who failed to take full advantage of their training.

*Clone commando*

**clone intelligence units** Specialized teams of clone troopers trained as intelligence agents during the Clone Wars, gathering information on the Separatists and their leadership without attracting undue attention. The intelligence units discovered that General Grievous was hiding on Utapau.

**Clone Keepers** A name given to the scientists and attendants responsible for Emperor Palpatine's clone vats on the planet Byss.

**clone SCUBA trooper** Aquatic clone troopers equipped with modified armor for underwater operations, with helmets equipped with scrubber units that could extract oxygen from the water. A specialized propulsion backpack allowed each trooper to move and maneuver underwater.

**clone trooper** The soldiers of the Grand Army of the Republic, mysteriously commissioned by the Jedi Master Sifo-Dyas. The Kaminoans used bounty hunter Jango Fett as the genetic template for the fighting forces, employing growth acceleration techniques to develop a fully mobile army in the span of a decade. When the Separatist movement led by Count Dooku militarized by taking on the droid armies of the various commerce guilds, the Republic was ready to respond with its own military forces in a conflict that came to be known as the Clone Wars. Clone troopers were led into battle by Jedi Knights, who became generals in the wars.

Clone troopers were the progenitors of the Imperial stormtrooper ranks that would follow. They wore a 20-piece set of white body armor modeled after the armor of the Mandalorian Shocktroopers. Each clone trooper's identification number was coded into his DNA, allowing for specific individuals to be identified, if needed. The use of clone troopers simplified the needs of combat medicine, as a single genetic template streamlined pharmaceutical treatment and surgery. Unfortunately, it also meant that the clone troopers were all vulnerable to the same biological agents. Early in the Clone Wars, the enemy Separatists experimented with biowarfare.

Unlike droids, clone troopers could think independently and creatively, and pressed their advantage despite the overwhelming numerical superiority of the Separatist droid army. According to estimates, a single clone trooper was responsible for the destruction of more than 200 battle droids, with specialized clones accounting for scores more. Throughout the Clone Wars, the Kaminoans refined their cloning techniques, introducing specialized

*Clone SCUBA troopers*

variations such as clone commanders, ARC troopers, second-generation clones, and more. Because of their growth acceleration, clone troopers had about half the normal life span of a human, assuming they survived the rigors of combat.

The white helmets of the initial, Phase One clone troopers were striped with colors indicating a trooper's rank: yellow for commanders, red for captains, blue for lieutenants, and green for sergeants. This system was quickly supplanted by color coding that identified individual combat units. Many clone troopers became fast friends with their Jedi generals, and it was possible to see how the interactions of the Jedi shaped the personality and styles of the various clone units. Discontent with the level of personalization being displayed, the Kaminoans made future generations of clones more uniform.

A clone trooper was ultimately loyal to the Galactic Republic. The intense conditioning and training was such that, when the Jedi were identified as traitors to the government by the broadcasting of Order 66, clone troopers across the galaxy instantly responded by killing their commanding officers.

*Clone troopers*

**clone turbo tank** *See* HAVw A6 Juggernaut.

**Clone Wars** The last great conflict of the Galactic Republic, this was the name given to the war waged by the Grand Army of the Republic against the droid forces of the Confederacy of Independent Systems. During the war, the Jedi Knights acted as generals of the Grand Army, leading clone troopers across scattered battlefields to bring an end to the Separatists.

The Clone Wars had its roots in a Separatist crisis that began during Supreme Chancellor Palpatine's term of office. A disaffected Jedi Knight, Count Dooku, had left the Order, and used his charismatic ways and fiery political rhetoric to cause star systems to secede. This led to a number of scattered conflicts as more and more worlds left the Republic, and the small number of Jedi Knights tasked with protecting order in the galaxy were overwhelmed. The Galactic Senate was in turmoil as alarmed Senators prescribed conflicting solutions to the growing problems. Some backed the Military Creation Act, fearful that war with the Separatists was inevitable. Others believed matters would never reach a conflict: The Republic had avoided a full-scale war for almost a millennium. Throughout this upheaval, Palpatine extended his term beyond constitutional limitations, as the Senate demanded he stay in office to guide the Republic through this storm.

*The first battle of the Clone Wars erupts on Geonosis.*

Intelligence gathered by Jedi Knight Obi-Wan Kenobi on the Outer Rim world of Geonosis revealed that Dooku had entered into a secret treaty with a number of commerce barons to acquire a droid army of unparalled size. The Separatists were gearing for war, and the Republic had no choice but to answer in kind. Granted emergency powers by the Senate, Supreme Chancellor Palpatine activated the Grand Army of the Republic, which had been commissioned in secret by the Jedi Order a decade earlier. The first battle of the Clone Wars then erupted on Geonosis, as the Separatist leadership scattered. In this early phase, the complicity of the various commerce entities—the Trade Federation, Commerce Guild, Corporate Alliance, Techno Union, and InterGalactic Banking Clan—was frustratingly difficult to prove, and many of the organizations were allowed to keep their Senate representation.

The Clone Wars spanned about three years, and rapidly spread throughout the galaxy after the Battle of Geonosis. Though Count Dooku seemed the public mastermind of the Separatist strategy, he secretly answered to his Sith Master, Darth Sidious. Military actions were led by the cyborg General Grievous, and Dooku had a cadre of specialized underlings, including the bounty hunter Durge and the dark side warrior Asajj Ventress. Early in the war, Dooku's forces mined the hyperspace routes that connected the Core Worlds to the rest of the galaxy, effectively cutting off the Republic from the bulk of its resources and allowing the Separatists relative freedom of movement in the Outer Rim. To match this maneuver, the Jedi entreated the Hutts to share their control of the Outer Rim, allowing the Republic to move their vessels through Hutt-controlled space.

Over the course of the war, public opinion of the Jedi Order waxed and waned. Their early defeats underscored their vulnerability, and their reluctant adoption of the rank of general caused them to be blamed for many of the missteps in the Clone Wars. Still, there emerged champions like Anakin Skywalker and Obi-Wan Kenobi, respectively dubbed the Hero with No Fear and the Negotiator by an approving public. Heroes arose similarly on the side of the Separatists. Opinion of the Jedi reached its nadir near war's end, when Chancellor Palpatine exposed a Jedi plot to take control of the Republic. It was an easy enough scenario to paint—after all, the Jedi had commissioned the clone army, and then went to battle against forces led by one of their own.

The real truth would be silenced by the applause that accompanied the rise of the Galactic Empire. Darth Sidious, mastermind of the Separatists, and Chancellor Palpatine, leader of the Republic, were the same person. The years of conflict had been a carefully orchestrated plot to destabilize the Republic and eliminate the Jedi. With the defeat of Count Dooku and General Grievous, the Separatists were defeated following the Outer Rim Sieges, and a triumphant Chancellor Palpatine announced the formation of a new government that would forever do away with the chaos of the Republic's final days.

*Combat cloud car*

**Cloud** An Imperial stormtrooper, he served as part of the Aurek-Seven unit of the Imperial 501st Legion following the formation of the Imperial Remnant and the signing of a peace treaty between the Empire and the New Republic.

**cloud car, combat** Following a standard cloud car design, these vessels filled a gap between airspeeders and starfighters, with enough weapons to go up against fighters and freighters. Combat cloud cars had a maximum altitude of 100 kilometers, as well as superior maneuverability and excellent speed. Most had extra hull plating and enhanced weapons systems.

*Twin-pod cloud car*

**cloud car, twin-pod** Atmospheric flying vehicles that used both repulsorlifts and ion engines. Typical models consisted of twin pods for pilots and passengers. They could serve as patrol vehicles, cars for hire, or pleasure craft.

*The Clone Wars were fought on Christophsis and throughout the galaxy.*

*Cloud City, floating in the atmosphere of the gas giant Bespin*

**Cloud City** A huge floating city, it was suspended about 60,000 kilometers above the core of the gas giant called Bespin. The main industry was mining Tibanna gas, but Baron Administrator Lando Calrissian promoted Cloud City's resort aspects with new casinos, luxury hotels, and shops. The cityscape had a rounded, decorative look with tall towers and large plazas. The city was 16 kilometers in diameter and 17 kilometers tall, including the huge unipod that hung beneath. It had 392 levels and a surface plaza concourse. Upper levels housed resorts and casinos, while middle levels were for heavy industry and worker housing. Lower levels were the site of the Tibanna-gas-processing facilities and the 3,600 repulsorlift engines that anchored the city in place. A central wind tunnel nearly a kilometer in diameter channeled wind gusts to give the city some stability. Cloud City was founded by Lord Ecclessis Figg of Corellia, won by Calrissian in a sabacc game, taken over by the Empire, and, after several switches of allegiance, again became a neutral and sleepy mining colony.

***Cloud-Mother*** An Ithorian herd ship best known for its medcenters and glass-manufacturing plants.

**cloud riders** Serji-X Arrogantus's swoop gang, which preyed upon the farmers of Aduba-3.

**clustership** A nickname for the Yuuzhan Vong starships developed to house immature yammosks as they grew.

**cluster trap** Designed by the New Republic, a cluster trap was a nondescript blister on the hull of a capital ship that concealed high-powered concussion grenades capable of destroying incoming starfighters.

**Clutch, Commander (TK-571)** One of the few clone troopers to survive the Galactic Republic's initial attempt to dissuade Sephi from seceding during the Clone Wars. With their Jedi generals killed, Clutch and the Padawans Pix and Cal worked together until Jedi Master Yoda arrived.

*Commander Clutch (TK-571)*

**clutch mothers** Trandoshan females, they served as mates for homecoming male warriors.

**Clyngunn the ZeHethbra** A major smuggling chief during the early years of the New Republic, he was once a champion unarmed-combat expert who represented ZeHethbra in the Stratis Games on Hallrin IV. After leaving athletics, Clyngunn bought his own ship, met up with Billey, and started running guns and spice.

**Clynn, Lieutenant** A burly, aggressive Imperial who had a run-in with Janek Sunber while assigned to a labor colony on Kalist VI. Sunber overpowered the bully but never earned his respect. When Clynn tried to take advantage of a female prisoner, Sunber held him off at gunpoint. Clynn was soon reassigned to investigate an abandoned Rebel base on Thila, where he was killed by a booby trap.

*Clyngunn the ZeHethbra*

**CMC-22 Mining Facility** A product of the Corellia Mining Corporation, this standard-model facility was almost entirely automated and could be constructed anywhere mining facilities were needed. It could be modified to mine almost any precious resource that was used for raw materials or to sell off for credits. The Corellia Mining Corporation sold these facilities in exchange for a share of the profits.

**C'ndros, Kal'Falnl** A female Quor'sav, C'ndros was a member of a warm-blooded, bird-like, egg-laying mammalian species. At about 3.5 meters tall, this freelance pilot had to have a ship custom-built with tall corridors to accommodate her unusual height.

**Cnorec, Lord** A slave trader and one of the followers of Lord Hethrir, he challenged Hethirir and was murdered.

**Coachelle Prime** The homeworld of the Lepi species, located in the Silly Rabbit constellation.

**Coalition of Automaton Rights Activists** A protest group that countered the growing anti-droid sentiments in the galaxy. Members of the coalition believed that all forms of droids should be afforded the same rights as organic beings.

**Cobak** A Bith bounty hunter, he was hired by Zorba the Hutt to capture Princess Leia Organa. Cobak impersonated Bithabus the Mystifier to lure the Princess.

**Cobalt Station** A frontier outpost on Jabiim where Alto Stratus hoped to launch a final, massive assault on the forces of the Republic during the height of the Clone Wars.

***Cobra*** One of Lando Calrissian's early starships, before he acquired the *Lady Luck.*

**Cobral crime family** A group of smugglers and black-market dealers who took over the planetary government of the planet Frego. They ruled the planet without much incident until one of the children, Solan Cobral, killed his brother Rutin when he considered going "legitimate." The Cobral family lost power and authority shortly before the Battle of Naboo, but some members of the organization fled to Rori.

**Coburn, Brodie "Cannon"** A starfighter pilot who served in Captain Gunn Yage's Skull Squadron during the time of Emperor Roan Fel. He flew a *Predator*-class starfighter.

**Coby, Prince** The son of Lord Toda of Tammuz-an met the droids R2-D2 and C-3PO in the early days of the Empire, when he was young. His spoiled and aggressive behavior masked his insecurity.

**CoCo Town** A shorthand term for Coruscant's Collective Commerce District, this is where Dex's Diner was located.

**Code of the Sith** The dark side counterpart to the Jedi Code, it read in part:

Peace is a lie, there is only passion.
Through passion I gain strength.
Through strength I gain power.
Through power I gain victory.
Through victory my chains are broken.

**Codex** A DarkStryder technology relic discovered by the crew of the *FarStar,* hidden deep in the Kathol Rift. This small metallic pyramid could detect and quantify the Force; it also enhanced the Force sensitivity of its user. The Aing-Tii monks were very interested in obtaining the Codex.

**Codian Moon** Covered by rolling plains of wood-moss turf, this satellite was known for the ranches where reeks were bred.

**codoran** A precious metal, sometimes used in jewelry.

**Codru-Ji** Natives of Munto Codru, these humanoids had four arms and slept in a standing position. Their language consisted of whistles and warbles, some beyond the range of human hearing. The most intimate communications took place in the upper ranges.

Clone Commander Cody gets Order 66.

**Cody, Clone Commander** Commander 2224, leader of 212th Attack Battalion and its famed Ghost Squadron, he was the clone officer who worked most frequently with General Obi-Wan Kenobi during the Clone Wars. Their last mission together was hunting down General Grievous on Utapau. When Cody received Order 66, he opened fire on Kenobi, and believed him to be dead after the Jedi Master plunged to the bottom of an Utapaun sinkhole.

**cofferdam** A flexible tube used to connect two starships whose air locks were not of the same configuration.

**cognition hood** The control device through which a Yuuzhan Vong communicated directly with his or her ship. The hood connected to a starship by a modified creeper, and was worn over the head and shoulders of a pilot.

**Cognus, Darth** An ancient Sith Lord who followed the Rule of Two as defined by Darth Bane. His apprentice, Darth Millennial, disagreed with the custom and left Darth Cognus behind to create his own order of Sith devotees.

***Cohasset Rover*** The miner Stellskard's personal starship during the Clone Wars. This unusual vessel had its cockpit mounted on an outboard fin, separated from the main cargo area.

**Cohl, Arwen** A notorious mercenary hired by the militant wing of the Nebula Front to harass Trade Federation convoys. A Mirialan, he was an instrumental figure in helping his people fight their way to freedom, but when the dust settled, political backstabbing branded him a traitor, and he spent time in prison. Once released, the former idealist emerged as a bitter, vengeful man who became a pirate, leading a band of cutthroats from his modified gunship, the *Hawk-Bat.*

Eru Matalis, the "Havac" or leader of the Nebula Front, hired Cohl to ambush Neimoidian ships as part of a complex plot to bolster the Trade Federation. He also was hired to assassinate Chancellor Valorum while at a trade summit on Eriadu. With the Jedi on Cohl's trail, Havac deemed him a liability and attempted to kill him. Cohl led the Jedi to Havac, exposing the Nebula Front's involvement, and he engaged in a deadly struggle with Havac. Both died from the wounds they sustained.

**coin-crab** A small tasty crustacean native to the coastlines of Taris.

**Cojahn** Lando Calrissian's business partner in the Sky-Centure Galleria venture. The bounty hunter Czethros tried to extort cooperation from Cojahn. When Calrissian's partner refused, Czethros murdered Cojahn.

**Col, Yurf** A New Republic military commander who served under General Wedge Antilles during the Yuuzhan Vong invasion. After the Battle of Duro, he and many of his fellow Duros were eager to liberate their homeworld. When his hoped-for opportunity turned out to be but a tactical feint masterminded by Antilles, Col was furious, and resigned his commission. He and his Duros forces attempted to go the battle alone, without New Republic help, and were destroyed.

**COLD (Command Override Limpet Droid)** A compact example of Sith technology in the time of Darth Krayt, this small module magnetically adhered to the exterior of a speeder, starfighter, or similar vehicle and allowed a remote user to override the onboard computer.

**coleoptera** Highly evolved insectoids believed by many xenobiologists to be on the verge of sentience. They employed a complex form of dancing as their primary method of communication.

**Colf, Lieutenant** A stormtrooper officer aboard the Star Destroyer *Reprisal.*

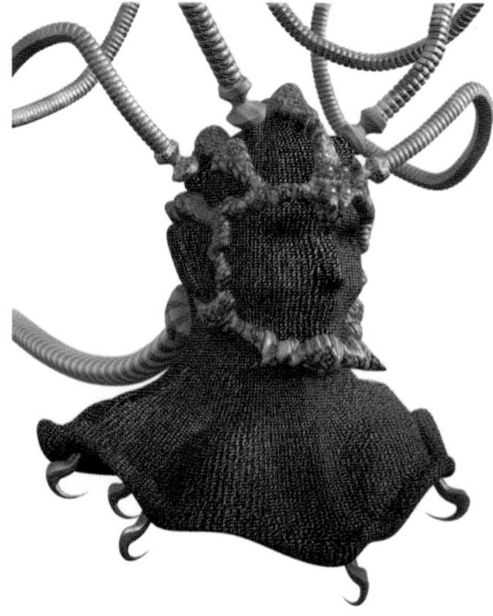

Cognition hood

Colicoid

**Colicoid** A brutal, technologically advanced insectoid species from Colla IV known for the Colicoid Creation Nest, the technological development firm that created the droideka. This three-legged curve-backed destroyer droid was created in the image of the Colicoids, including the ability to curl up into a rolling ball for locomotion. The Colicoids had an intense distrust of the Jedi Knights. For a time, the insectoids took control of the spice mines of Kessel.

**Colla IV** This planet, located along the border of the Colonies and the Inner Rim, was the homeworld of the Colicoid species. It was also the site of the Colicoid Creation Nest and its manufacturing facilities during the final decades of the Old Republic. This made Colla IV an attractive target during the Clone Wars: The forces of the Grand Army of the Republic could have eliminated a major souce of powerful combat automata for the Separatists. The Republic's forces were soundly defeated however; when they tried to take control of the planet, the Separatists sent in several Scorpenek Annihilator Droids to destroy the Republic units.

***Collaborator*** A captured Yuuzhan Vong picket ship, formerly known as the *Hrosha-Gul,* used by the Galactic Alliance in defense of the planet Esfandia.

**collapsium** A volatile gas used in the creation of seismic charges.

**Collo Fauale Pass** The fallback base of the New Republic agents on Phaeda. Carnor Jax learned of the Rebel's presence at Collo Fauale from the traitorous Tem Merken. He ordered the Star Destroyers *Steadfast* and *Emperor's Revenge* to bombard the base from space.

**Collus** A respected philosopher in the Old Republic, and founder of Alderaan University. Collus eventually died of very old age.

**collypod** A small creature often served flambéed and then smothered in a thick broth, it was considered a delicacy by Twi'leks, Hutts, and others.

**colo claw fish** A powerful aquatic carnivore lurking near Naboo's core, it had long jaws filled with pointed teeth. Its forelegs ended in wicked claws, and sharp protrusions jutted from its luminescent tail. The colo claw fish hid in underwater tunnels, where it sat motionless for hours until suitable prey passed by. When it spotted a victim, the beast erupted from its lair and grabbed the meal. Although quite fearsome, the colo claw fish

*Colo claw fish chases a Gungan bongo.*

was no match for the enormous sando aqua monster.

The colo claw fish was a voracious predator well suited to hunting and consuming its prey. When it attacked, the beast released a disorienting hydrosonic shriek generated by structures in its throat and head. It then grabbed stunned victims in its massive pectoral claws. A poison in the colo's fangs incapacitated its victims, which were then swallowed. The animal's jaws distended and its skin stretched, allowing it to consume creatures much larger than itself. Most food was digested slowly by the colo's weak stomach acids.

**Colonial Games** *See* Roon Colonial Games.

**Colonies, the** One of the first areas outside of the Galactic Core to be settled, the region was heavily populated and industrialized. Ruthlessly controlled by the Empire during the Galactic Civil War, much of the Colonies region later supported the New Republic.

**Colony, The** The collective name for the various insect species that aligned with the Killiks during their enormous expansion of territory following the war between the Galactic Alliance and the Yuuzhan Vong. This expansion was made possible by Raynar Thul, a Jedi Knight wounded by the Yuuzhan Vong, who crashed-landed in Killik territory. Nursed back to health by the Unu hive, Raynar became connected to the hive consciousness, spreading his talent for Force perception throughout the collective. Raynar's personality was completely subsumed by the hive; he became UnuThul, the first true Joiner, who allowed other life-forms to enter into the hive consciousness. As such, the Unu hive became the "leaders" of the Colony, which at its height consisted of some 375 different hives. The Colony spread out beyond its previous borders, dangerously encroaching on Chiss space.

Unu was unaware of a dark fragment of its overall consciousness, a subconscious called the Dark Nest; it was driven by the Gorog hive, which had been similarly affected when it was joined by Dark Jedi. The two dark siders, Lomi Plo and Welk, were powerful enough to conceal their actions from the rest of the Colony, including such deplorable acts as using Chiss prisoners to feed their larvae. Luke Skywalker and his Jedi Order narrowly averted a war between the Chiss and the Colony near Qoribu by brokering a solution: transplanting the neighboring Killik hives to uninhabited worlds within the Utegetu Nebula. When those worlds proved inhospitable, war finally erupted, and the Colony proved a threat until Skywalker and his Jedi could remove Lomi Plo, Welk, and UnuThul from their positions of influence. No longer driven by Force-sensitive Joiners, the will of the Colony dissipated—as did the threat that it posed.

**Colony One** *See* Peace City.

**color-crawler** A small creature that exuded a colored slime as it traveled. It was used in many cosmetic applications, such as the dyeing of hair and cloth.

**colossus wasps of Ithull** These huge flying insects native to Ithull had strong exoskeletal carapaces that were used as the basic framework for ore-hauling spaceships.

**Colton, Jeremoch** An Alderaanian, he served as captain of the *Tantive IV* for many years before retiring to teach full-time at Alderaan University. Raymus Antilles replaced him as captain of the Alderaanian consular ship, as well as master of the droids R2-D2 and C-3PO.

**Colu, Gorton** A crazed elderly anti-alien bigot who lived in the Upper City of Taris after the Mandalorian Wars.

**Columi** Craniopods from the planet Columus, they spent their waking moments on mental activities. Physical work was done by droids and other machines, with which the Columi communicated via brain-wave transmissions. A peaceful and nonaggressive species, they sometimes sought employment as advisers and soothsayers. They were also the most feared gambling opponents in the galaxy. Columi had huge, hairless heads that took up fully one-third of their bodies, with throbbing blue veins around the cerebrum and huge black eyes. Otherwise they were puny, with thin, nonfunctional arms and legs.

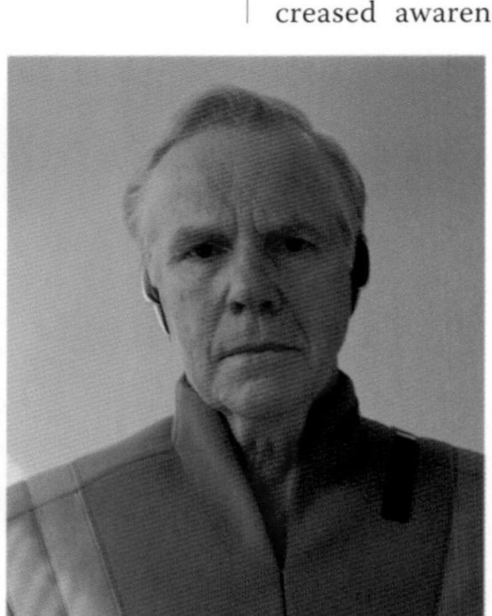
*Jeremoch Colton*

**Column** The alias used by Klo Merit, a spy who had infiltrated the Galactic Republic's bota-processing operations on the planet Drongar during the Clone Wars. Though known as Column to the Confederacy of Independent Systems, to his other employer, Black Sun, he was known as Lens.

**Columus** A small world with extremely low gravity, it was home to the Columi. The landscape was completely flat and muddy, with a wide variety of plant life. The Columi inhabited high cities supported by sturdy pylons, governing their society through a participatory democracy. Apparently, Columus joined the Empire voluntarily.

**Colunda sector** A onetime hotbed of Rebel activity, this sector contained the planet Nyasko. An AT-AT group stationed on Nyasko was kept busy suppressing uprisings.

**coma-gas** Developed by the New Republic to incapacitate the Yuuzhan Vong, this gas was subsequently modified for use by the Galactic Alliance military as an enemy-suppression weapon that could neutralize a large target without causing unnecessary loss of life.

**CoMar Combat Systems** A manufacturer of surface-to-air weapons, headquartered in the Corporate Sector.

**Combat Guild** An organization that provided military training to civilians, based in Bestine, on Tatooine.

**combat implant** This experimental cyborg enhancement—in use around the time of the Great Sith War—granted the user increased awareness of battle variables and boosted weapons proficiencies.

**Combat Moon** This barely habitable natural satellite of planet Rabaan was used as a battlefield for the rival Rabaanites and S'krrr to settle their differences.

**combat sense** A Jedi technique that increased awareness of the battle at hand, but at the expense of greater situational awareness. Opponents appeared as bright images in an otherwise dull landscape.

A comlink used by Obi-Wan Kenobi

**Combined Clans** The governing body of the Bothans made up of the leaders of the various Bothan clans.

**com code** A factory-set, pre-programmed frequency unique to every communications device. To contact someone, a being had to know or be able to find the target's com code. Com codes were long and complex. Terminals often had public directories of registered com codes.

**Comestibles and Curatives Administration** This New Republic government body ensured that the various corporations producing foodstuffs and pharmaceuticals were operating with the interests of the galaxy in mind.

**cometduster** An alcoholic beverage molecularly excited via an impassioning machine; drinking it gave the tongue an electrifying sensation.

**COMETS-Q** An acronym used by the quartermasters who served the Grand Army of the Republic during the Clone Wars, signifying the seven most important facets of any military force: Chemical, Ordnance, Mechanical, Engineer, Transportation, Signal, and Quartermaster.

**Comet Squadron** An A-wing group that served the New Republic under General Crespin.

**comfan** A personal comfort device used on Adumar to keep cool, it was small and hemispherical with a handle. In the city of Cartann, handling the comfan was an art, and each gesture had a hidden meaning.

**Comkin Five** A planet known for its production of candies and medicines, it was controlled by the Warlord Zsinj during the early years of the New Republic.

**comlight** Similar in size and shape to a comlink, this device used bursts of light to send a signal. Captain Panaka used one to communicate with Queen Amidala when retaking the royal palace at Theed during the Battle of Naboo.

**comlink** A personal communications transceiver, it consisted of a transmitter, a receiver, and a power source. The most widely used model was a small palm-sized cylinder. Military units carried large backpack versions with scrambling and variable frequency capabilities, and comlinks were built into stormtrooper helmets.

**command control voice** A method of controlling droids through special voice-pattern recognition.

**Commander of Supercommandos** *See Mand'alor.*

**Commander's Court** According to naval tradition, every warship commander in the Galactic Republic was given the ability to dispense rulings whenever the crew or passengers filed a grievance. The grievances were heard in what became known as the Commander's Court, where the ship's commanding officer acted as arbiter.

**Commander's Glider** A hyperdrive-equipped shuttle carried aboard every Chiss warship as a diplomatic vessel assigned to the senior-ranking officer.

**Commando Team One** Kapp Dendo's highly skilled group of infiltration agents that served the New Republic.

**Commenor** A planet in the system of the same name just outside the Core Worlds near Corellia, it was a trading outpost and spaceport. Like Corellia, Commenor maintained a fiercely independent spirit. The Rebel Alliance established a starfighter training center on its largest moon, Folor. Tycho Celchu defected to the Alliance at Commenor immediately after the destruction of Alderaan.

When the Galactic Alliance denied Corellia's bid for independence, Commenor eventually sided with Corellia, joining the Confederation in war against the GA. Vast areas of the planet were devastated by the fallout that accompanied a cloaked asteroid strike on its surface. The Commenori retaliated against this heinous attack in kind with a biological strike on Coruscant.

**Commerce Guild** Though the term *commerce guild* described a number of major corporate entities that banded together to protect their pursuit of profits, the Commerce Guild proper was an organization of commodities interests. Businesses involved in the acquisition, refinement, and production of raw materials formed the backbone of the Commerce Guild, which was headed by its shrewd Presidente, Shu Mai. She recognized that support of Count Dooku's Separatist movement would amount to treason, but she could not resist the lure of a profitable venture. So she secretly committed the guild's forces—including its droid armies—to the Confederacy of Independent Systems.

The Commerce Guild was frequently criticized by smaller businesses for its use of abusive and bullying tactics. When whole sectors were seceding from the Republic prior to the Clone Wars, the Commerce Guild swooped in and snatched up many small businesses that were no longer under the protective jurisdiction of the Republic. To protect its assets and enforce membership, the Commerce Guild employed combat automata such as its dwarf spider droids and giant homing spider droids.

**Commerce Guild cruiser** This half-circle-shaped vessel, technically a *Diamond*-class courier ship, was produced by Commerce Guild subsidiares.

**Commerce Guild support ship** Also known as *Recusant*-class light destroyers, these vessels were manufactured by Techno Union foremen using materials from many Commerce Guild worlds. They saw extensive service in the Clone Wars. Four to six of them could outgun a Republic Star Destroyer. Each was 1,187 meters long, and featured a heavy prow turbolaser, four heavy turbolaser cannons, six heavy turbolaser turrets, five turbolaser cannons, 30 dual laser cannons, a dozen light laser cannons, and 60 point-defense laser cannons.

**Commodore, the** The leader of the BloodScar pirates, he operated the gang from a luxurious base on Gepparin, in the Shelsha sector. He was a small, pampered eccentric always surrounded by bodyguards, even within his own chambers. Mara Jade encountered the Commodore shortly after the Battle of Yavin when investigating a suspicious arrangement between the governor of the Shelsha sector and the pirates. Jade was of the opinion that the Commodore was insane. The Commodore luxuriated within a pool, blindfolded, so as to better concentrate on the voices of those who came before him, listening intently for any indication of prevarication or deception. Jade was able to deceive the Commodore and keep her Imperial allegiance a secret. Later, the Commodore believed Mara to be a Jedi Knight, and a dire threat, and tried to eliminate her, only to get caught and killed in the backblast of an explosion.

Commerce Guild support ship

**Commonality, the** A political alliance of nine sectors and their worlds, including the Vorzyd system, that worked toward a common set of goals and needs during the last decades of the Galactic Republic. The Commonality was ruled from the planet Columex, which provided access to the nine sectors via the Perlemian Trade Route. This political group formed an important collection of swing votes in the badly divided Senate. Galactic representatives for the Commonality included Senators Jheramahd and Simon Greyshade.

**Common Charter** A vital governing document of the New Republic, citing core tenets and procedures. Article Five described the right of the Chief of State to declare a state of war against a known enemy. Article Nineteen indicated that any planet without a native population could not be controlled by the Republic; anyone could settle the planet without political affiliation.

**Commons, the** A wide, grass-filled park at the very center of the city of Ussa, on the planet Bellassa. During the last years of the Galactic Republic, it was a beautiful meeting place where the citizens of Ussa could contemplate the possibilities for a peaceful existence. When the Empire took control of Bellassa, much of the greenery was pulled up to make way for a garrison and governmental office space.

**comm slave satellites** Small, well-defended satellites capable of amplifying and directing signals. During the Battle of Naboo, the Trade Federation utilized several comm slave satellites to focus signals sent from the Droid Control Ship to bases on the far side of the planet.

**communications cable** An antiquated means of communication over physical transmission lines. It is found on such worlds as Adumar.

**communication wave descrambler** Developed by the military forces of the Galactic Alliance, this technology allowed intelligence forces to unscramble the encrypted communications channels of an enemy force. It was a closely guarded secret, and it was feared that military advisers from the Confederation might have stolen the technology.

**comm unit** A shipboard device that gave the vessel the ability to transmit and receive communications signals from outside sources. A comm unit capable of transmitting holographic messages was also referred to as a holocomm.

**compact assault vehicle (CAV)** Small, single-occupant vehicles that were usually equipped with a medium blaster cannon, they were supposed to transform a single Imperial trooper into a formidable assault force. But while the tracked wheels and fairly high speed provided mobility, the CAVs were susceptible to sensor jamming.

**Companion2000** A popular model of datapad manufactured by MicroData, featuring a Galactic Univeral Translator, Holistic Data Transfer software, and up to five million DSUs of data storage capacity.

***Compass Star*** A Galactic Alliance warship that saw action during the Second Battle of Fondor.

**Compeer** The name given to the leader of the Exchange.

**CompForce** The military arm of COMPNOR. CompForce troopers received priority treatment in the allocation of equipment, resources, and medical attention compared with the standard Imperial Navy and Army. As a result, they were unswervingly loyal to the Emperor, much like the Imperial stormtroopers. CompForce was divided into two branches per Sector Group: Observation and Assault.

**COMPNOR (COMPOR)** The Commission for the Preservation of the New Order was formed as one of the first official acts of Emperor Palpatine. It started as the Commission for the Protection of the Republic (COMPOR), a populist movement against the chaos of the final days of the Old Republic. Citing the alien leadership found throughout the Confederacy of Independent Systems, the group was among the first to establish pro-human membership criteria. When Chancellor Palpatine declared himself Emperor, the commission soon became an Imperial tool to push the galaxy toward the everyday ethos of the New Order. COMPNOR implemented Redesign, a program whose goal was mass cultural edification of the galaxy's citizens. Many of COMPNOR's standard practices, especially its liberal usage of brain modification surgery, were unnecessarily brutal.

**compression blackout** A form of unconsciousness suffered by starfighter pilots who were unable to eject from a surface crash. The impact and subsequent compression of air contained within the cockpit rendered the pilot unconscious. The effect was similar to that of a concussion, and compression blackout was rarely fatal.

**Computerized Combat Predictor** A starship weapons system developed by Imperial engineers designed to assist a cloaked—and therefore blinded—starship. The Predictor anticipated the attack patterns of incoming starfighters, triggering automated firing solutions to retaliate. Supreme Commander Pellaeon tested the initial version of the Predictor a decade after the death of Grand Admiral Thrawn, and found the system still lacking any true accuracy.

**Computer Mating Service (CMS)** A Bith establishment responsible for matching the DNA of prospective mates in order to generate a series of child-patterns (or CPs) that projected the outcome of their union. This allowed Bith mates to create the best possible children in their efforts to ensure the continued existence of their species.

**computer probe** A device that provided access to a computer network. The most common probes—or scomp links—were the appendages that droids used to tap into computers and portable units used by computer technicians.

**computer spike** A computer program used to covertly gain access to information stored within a target computer. Spikes were delivered via datapad and programmed to continually modify themselves to avoid detection. Spikes degraded in efficiency as they worked until they completely rewrote their intrusion codes and were rendered useless. Each spike, therefore, could only be used once.

**Comra** This Outer Rim planet was the site of one of Talon Karrde's many communications relay stations just before the Yuuzhan Vong invasion. It was located in the area of the Outer Rim known to smugglers as the Dead Zone.

**com-scan** Specialized sensor sweeps, they were designed to detect the energy from the transmission and reception of communications signals.

**Cona** Home to the triangular-headed Arcona, it was a hot, dense world orbiting the blue giant Teke Ro. Due to Cona's lack of axial tilt and temperature-distributing air currents, the climate was the same everywhere. The atmosphere contained a high concentration of ammonia; water was often found only in the gastric pods of Cona's plant life. The Arcona, who obtained water by digging out plant pods with their burrowing claws, lived in loose communities of family nests and were easily addicted to salt. Many galactic companies established mining colonies on Cona.

**Concert of the Winds** An annual cultural festival celebrating the change of seasons on the planet Vortex. The concert was produced by air currents rushing through the Cathedral of the Winds, whipping up a reverberating, mournful music that whistled through pipes in the tall crystalline structure. It was during one such festival that a ship carrying Admiral Ackbar and Princess Leia Organa Solo crashed into and destroyed the cathedral, killing hundreds of Vors. The structure was later rebuilt.

**Conclave, the** This group of Ssi-ruuk held spiritual power on their homeworld of Lwhekk. According to records, the Conclave had power equal to that of the Elders' Council in influencing the decisions of the Shreeftut.

**Conclave on the Plight of the Refugees** This summit, held in the Government House of Ord Mantell, was convened by the New Republic to discuss ways in which the refugees fleeing the Yuuzhan Vong invasion of the galaxy could be properly housed, fed, and relocated.

**Concordance of Fealty** An ancient Jedi tradition in which two Jedi trade lightsabers for a short time in order to prove that they trusted each other completely. Mace Windu and Eeth Koth performed the Concordance of Fealty shortly before Windu and several other Jedi undertook a mission to Malastare.

**Concord Dawn** Jango Fett's home planet, where peace and order were maintained by the Journeyman Protectors. It was also believed to have been Jaster Mereel's home planet. Many Mandalorians traced their ancestry to Concord Dawn, although the world's natives never actively settled the planet Mandalore.

**Concordian** The human natives of Concord Dawn, considered part of the Mandalorian line.

**Concorkill, Sweitt** A noted Vurk Senator who was a guest of Chancellor Palpatine at the Galaxies Opera House during the Clone Wars.

**concussion missile** A sublightspeed projectile, it caused shock waves on impact. The concussive blasts could penetrate and destroy even heavily armored targets, though they worked best against stationary targets. Concussion missiles were used to destroy the second Death Star during the Battle of Endor.

**concussion rifle** Nicknamed conk rifles, concussion rifles lobbed explosive blasts at a range of about 30 meters; upon impact, these spread to about 4 meters in diameter. Favored by the Trandoshans, these weapons came in many models. The bounty hunter 4-LOM acquired a concussion rifle after teaming up with Zuckuss.

**concussion shield** Strong energy shields, they protected ships from stray space debris.

**condenser unit** A thermal coil or warming unit that radiated high levels of heat through the use of small amounts of energy. Such units were frequently found in standard survival kits and were used to cook food and provide heat.

**Condi** A slave from the planet Zoraster, he served as a guard aboard Krayn's spice ship shortly after the Battle of Naboo. He and his companions had been assigned guard duty under penalty of death. When Obi-Wan Kenobi infiltrated the vessel, he was unable to rescue Condi—his own vessel was too small. Condi agreed to look the other way, though, and vowed to help his people escape someday.

**condor dragon** A native of the Forest Moon of Endor, this cave-dwelling creature had large leathery wings with which to fly, a single fused fang for tearing through the hide of its prey, and two long lower tusks for stabbing. Its large yellow eyes had round black pupils and enabled the dragon to spot prey moving through the dense treetops.

**conductor x-112** This chemical compound was developed to act as a conductor inside a starship's ionization chamber.

**conduit worm** These strange annelids infested millions of kilometers of power wiring channels on Coruscant, living off the faint electrical fields. Without a head, tail, or body core, they spread throughout a power system, growing body components as needed. When they were hungry and unable to find electrical sustenance, conduit worms sometimes sought out the electrical impulses found in humanoid brains.

**cone sock** A protective garment worn over the sensitive receptor cones atop a Gotal's head. They helped Gotals ignore the overwhelming electromagnetic signals found in areas with droids or high technology.

**Confederacy of Independent Systems (CIS)** A collection of star systems that attempted to secede from the Republic, spurring the crisis that erupted into the Clone Wars. The Separatist movement began eight years after Supreme Chancellor Palpatine's election, though many of its roots went back much further than that. The rampant corruption of the Republic's final years was the prime factor in the rise of separatism. The Senate's cumbersome bureaucracy slowed down any attempts at reform, and too many of its constituents had grown too complacent to enact any change. A feeling of disenfranchisement grew in the galaxy, particularly in outlying systems where heavy taxation was not balanced by improved services. Into this disarray stepped the charismatic Count Dooku, a former Jedi, who sought to teach the Republic a lesson.

Dooku's words resonated with the galaxy's disaffected populace, and many picked up the banner of the Separatist cause even though they had no direct connection to him. Opportunists used Dooku's name to further their own agendas under the guise of political protest, and this led to scattered violence across the Republic. Although these outbreaks were attributed to Separatist forces, the Jedi Council discounted any attempts to blame Dooku for such activities. The Jedi had to weather an increasingly tarnished public image—their forces were spread too thin to protect against the acts of treason seemingly orchestrated by one of their own. In two short years, Dooku had a following of several thousand solar systems.

Conduit worm

Alarmist Senators called for the creation of an army of the Republic. Others believed that the establishment of such a military would merely be the catalyst for an all-out civil war. What none in the Senate knew was that the Separatists were already gearing up for war. Count Dooku courted institutions such as the Corporate Alliance, Trade Federation, Techno Union, InterGalactic Banking Clan, and Commerce Guild with promises of reform and unyielding devotion to capitalism. In exchange, these bodies committed their immense armies to the Separatist cause. With their droid troops scattered throughout the galaxy, the Separatists were ready to overwhelm the Republic. Dooku felt confident that 10,000 more systems would join the Separatists.

In a darkened conference room on the Techno Union foundry world of Geonosis, Count Dooku made his offer, and the Confederacy of Independent Systems was formally established. This meeting of the minds was overheard by Jedi Knight Obi-Wan Kenobi, who warned the Republic of the alarming new development. The Republic responded with a preemptive strike against the Separatists, attacking their world with a newly discovered clone army. In the explosive ground battle that ensued, the Clone Wars between the Separatists and Republic began. Though they were routed at the Battle of Geonosis, the Separatists eventually regrouped, and the Clone Wars spread to many battlefronts across the galaxy.

The Confederacy military forces, led by General Grievous, won many early battles, but the tide began to slowly change in favor of the Republic. The Council of Separatists—the leadership of the Confederacy—was forced to hide out on the remote world of Mustafar after the deaths of both Dooku and Grievous. When Palpatine assumed absolute control of the galaxy, he ordered Darth Vader to destroy the council. By slaughtering the leadership of the Separatists and deactivating the droid armies, Vader and Palpatine put an end to the Confederacy of Independent Systems.

*The Confederacy of Independent Systems was formally established on Geonosis.*

**Confederation, the** The name adopted by the members of what was originally the Corellian Confederation. It was meant to be more inclusive of the various cultures opposed to the Galactic Alliance's authoritarian actions following the Yuuzhan Vong invasion and the Swarm War. The Bothans, in particular, wanted to do away with the term *Corellian Confederation* in recognition of their own contributions. The member systems agreed to this change, and set up a secret meeting on Gilatter VIII to determine the future of their organization and bring about the election of a Supreme Commander of the Confederation's military forces.

When Galactic Alliance leaders learned of this meeting, they attempted to launch an attack with the Ninth Fleet but were in turn ambushed by Confederation forces. Though the battle was largely a draw, the Confederation scored a victory in popular opinion, and many more star systems seceded from the Alliance to join.

The Confederation leadership began turning its attention toward the Core Worlds. Huttese and Commenorian forces attacked Balmorra as part of a feint that was meant to draw Alliance forces away from the shipyards of Kuat. Through the Force, Jacen Solo was able to discern the battle plans. The Corellian-Bothan strike at the planet Kuat was met with stern opposition from GA forces, although many in the command structure of the Alliance questioned Jacen Solo's motives for continuing to attack Confederation warships after the battle was won. After the elimination of Jacen Solo from command, hostilities between the Confederation and the Alliance ceased, paving the way to lengthy and fragile reconciliation efforts.

**Conference of Uncommitted Worlds** Held on Kabal, this was a meeting of the neutral worlds during the Galactic Civil War. Princess Leia Organa attended in the hope of inspiring more worlds to join the Rebellion, and she succeeded in winning over the Aquaris Freeholders to the Alliance cause.

**Confiscation Authority** The ruling body that controlled the impounds on various prison worlds maintained by the Galactic Republic. Each prison world had its own branch of the Confiscation Authority, which oversaw the impoundment of goods obtained during criminal investigations and arrests at various Confiscation Stations.

**conform lounger** A type of furniture, it used a pneudraulic capillary system to shape itself to whomever rested upon it, providing maximum comfort and support.

**Coniel** A young slave boy rescued from the sand drains of Mos Espa by Anakin Skywalker, during Anakin's attempt to free Arawynne and the Ghostlings from Gardulla the Hutt.

**Conjo fighter** An Aratech Y41-C2LC atmospheric fighter used by local militias at the height of the New Order. It measured 14 meters in length and was armed with a concussion missile launcher and a pair of laser cannons. Variants included the Y41-4LC armed with four laser cannons, and the Y41-T Conjo Trainer. This craft was designed purely for atmospheric flight, and was driven by a repulsorlift engine system.

**conk rifle** *See* concussion rifle.

**connection trace** A method of determining a target's location by analyzing the strength and position of an incoming transmission.

**conner net** A missile-fired electrically charged metal mesh used to detain starships. Smaller person-scale nets could be placed in passageways and triggered with motion sensors to drop onto intruders.

**Conner Ship Systems** A small corporation that designed and manufactured conner nets.

**Conno** A Ghostling child captured, along with Princess Arawynne, by Djas Puhr and brought to Mos Espa to be sold as a slave. Conno was just five years old at the time.

**Conor, Goure** A Ryn spy stationed on Bakura, he met the Solo family upon their arrival during the Yuuzhan Vong invasion and became friends with Tahiri Veila.

**Conqueror Assault Ship** A Surronian starship with an hourglass-shaped streamlined silhouette. The HRD assassin Guri used one as her primary starship, *Stinger.*

***Conqueror*-class atmospheric dreadnaught** A huge, expensive, heavily armed Separatist starship featuring dozens of domed laser cannon turrets haphazardly placed all over its surface. During the Clone Wars, the Confederacy sent a fleet of these craft to raze the planet Terra Sool, but the invasion was thwarted by Obi-Wan Kenobi and Anakin Skywalker.

***Conquest*** An *Imperial*-class Star Destroyer, it was among the ships that chased the *Millennium Falcon* as it was leaving Tatooine en route to Alderaan.

*Construction droid*

**conserlista** A form of musical composition created by the Zabraks.

**Consolidated Shipping** One of the largest galactic shipping and transport operations, it was based in the Shelsha sector. It had a recognizable star-in-swirl logo. Due to its size, Consolidated Shipping maintained its own internal security force known for its no-nonsense approach.

***Constrainer*** This Imperial *Interdictor*-class cruiser was part of Grand Admiral Thrawn's fleet.

***Constrictor*** A corvette under the command of Warlord Zsinj dispatched to protect the *Night Caller* during a raid on Talasea.

**construction droid** A huge, complex factory on wheels, it both demolished and rebuilt structures. Such a droid could tear down condemned buildings and shovel debris into vast internal furnaces, where useful items were extracted and recycled. A corresponding factory extruded new girders and transparisteel sheets. The droid then assembled new buildings from pre-programmed blueprints.

**consul** A style of lightsaber hilt design.

**consular ship** Any vessel officially registered to a member of the Imperial Senate. On diplomatic missions, consular ships were supposed to be exempt from normal inspection requirements.

**Consumart** Commenor's largest grocery store chain.

**container ship** These supertransports were among the largest commercial vessels. Although slow and costly, they were the most efficient way to transport large amounts of cargo between systems. Their use of standardized cargo containers made them efficient; just one container ship could carry hundreds of various-sized containers. Since they couldn't land, the ships had to use small craft to collect and transfer their cargoes.

***Contemplanys Hermi*** An obscure Corellian constitutional proviso that allowed the sector to remove itself from Senatorial duties for the duration of a dispute. It was once employed in an ill-fated attempt at independence, and again during the Sep aratist crisis. The name translates from an Old Corellian phrase meaning "meditative soltitude."

**Contender Squadron** A group of New Republic A-wings that served aboard the *Allegiance* during the defense of Adumar.

**Contingency Deployment Profile** A set of detailed instructions provided to every clone field officer deployed into battle during the Clone Wars. Stored on a datacard, the profile contained information on where and how to regroup in the event of a breakdown in the trooper's immediate command structure.

**Continuity of Service** This unwritten law among the armed forces of the Galactic Empire during the time of Emperor Roan Fel stated that the children of a veteran solider were allowed to join their parent's unit, provided that they passed basic training.

**Contispex, Supreme Chancellor** The ruler of the Galactic Republic some 12,000 years before the Battle of Yavin, he was part of a theocratic sect that held certain alien species and religions to be suspect. The violent crusades embarked upon in Contispex's name marked a devastating era of galactic history known as the Pius Dea period.

**control** The most basic and primary aspect of the Force mastered by initiates, *control* represented awareness of the Force within one's own body, and allowed the control of physical functions and abilities.

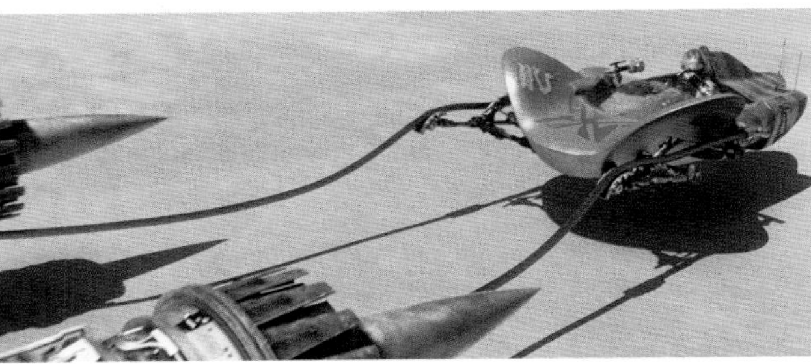

Control cables

**control cables** The tethers that connected a Podracer's engines to the Podracer cockpit.

**control mind** A technique of Force control through which a user could take direct control of other people's minds; they became automata who had to obey the user's will. This technique was considered a corruption of the Force, a product of the dark side.

**Contruum** The birthplace of Alliance General Airen Cracken and his son, fighter pilot Pash Cracken. The planet had specific guidelines for naming its starships: Capital ships were named for virtues, while transports were named for beasts of burden or rivers. Despite its close proximity to the Perlemian Trade Route and Hydian Way, Contruum managed to avoid the attention of the Yuuzhan Vong for five years of the alien invasion.

**Convarion, Ait** An Imperial captain who was said to have participated in the conflicts at Derra IV and Hoth, he was given command of the *Corrupter* and sent off on suppression missions in the Outer Rim. These were nothing more than Imperial-sanctioned campaigns of terror against populated worlds. It was a task for a callous and cruel commander, and Ait Convarion fit the bill perfectly. Perhaps this was what attracted him to Ysanne Isard, the former director of Imperial Intelligence. When she took control of the planet Thyferra and its bacta cartel, Convarion was given the responsibility of protecting her bacta convoys. One of them was hijacked by Rogue Squadron, and Convarion immediately went to the last jump point, arriving before the last of the tankers headed to hyperspace. The captain destroyed the defecting freighter before it had a chance to surrender and during a brief battle destroyed three Rogue Squadron ships.

Isard was furious with Convarion for destroying the freighter full of bacta. She ordered him to begin another campaign of terror, targeting anyplace that had benefited from the hijacked bacta. Some of it had gone to an ailing, defenseless colony at Halanit, which the *Corrupter* easily destroyed. Captain Convarion was then ordered to proceed to the Graveyard of Alderaan to assist the *Aggregator* in the annihilation of Rogue Squadron. But when the *Corrupter* arrived, X-wings were ready to attack. The last thing Captain Convarion saw were the proton torpedoes Wedge Antilles used to destroy the bridge Convarion was standing on.

**COO-2180** A cooking droid aboard the *Jendirian Valley,* it scolded R2-D2 for taking food from the bread line. It was from the COO series of cooking droids developed jointly by Industrial Automaton and Publictechnic.

COO-2180

**coolth** A chemical used to maintain the temperature of buildings constructed in desert environments. It was also used in specialized environment suits that provided chilled air to the wearer.

**coomb spore** A form of bioengineered spore created by the Yuuzhan Vong and released to infect certain individuals within the New Republic prior to their initial invasion. In all but one case, the victim who took in the coomb spore died within days. Only Mara Jade Skywalker was able to resist its effects, primarily through the concentrated use of the Force. Her survival was a source of frustration for the Yuuzhan Vong—and especially the spore's creator, Nom Anor—because it meant that the Jedi Knights were a much stronger foe than they had realized.

**Coome, R'yet** The junior Senator from Exodeen, he replaced M'yet Luure upon his death in the bombing of the Senate Hall on Coruscant. He was later elected to the Inner Council.

Senator Ronet Coorr

**Coordinated Galactic Time** The standard time as recorded across the galaxy, based on local time on Coruscant.

**Coorr, Senator Ronet** A short, humanoid Senator from the high-gravity world of Iseno, he was a member of Chancellor Palpatine's Loyalist Committee during the Separatist crisis and the Clone Wars that followed. He resigned in shame after he was discovered misappropriating starship assets, leading to the planet Duro being underdefended when attacked by General Grievous.

**Cophrigin V** A tropical planet in the Outer Rim system of the same name. Mara Jade tracked the Dark Woman there, and the Emperor subsequently sent Darth Vader to the planet to kill the fugitive Jedi.

**Copperline** A world overrun by pirates and liberated by Imperial forces shortly after the Clone Wars. Many inhabitants joined the Imperial military service in gratitude.

**Copycat Pod** A Corellian Engineering Corporation sensor countermeasure device that mimicked the transponder signal of a parent vessel, creating a duplicate sensor signature.

**Coral Depths City** Also known as Coral City, this was the floating capital of Mon Calamari and birthplace of Admiral Ackbar. During the Yuuzhan Vong invasion, many displaced Coruscant Senators and leaders relocated there.

***Coral Fin*** A transport ship piloted by the Priapulin Jedi Knight Charza Kwinn.

**coral pike** A ceremonial weapon used by the Mon Calamari.

**coral restraining implant** Yuuzhan Vong–engineered biots that were surgically implanted into the necks of their slaves: They caused sentient beings to lose their reason and become mindless drones.

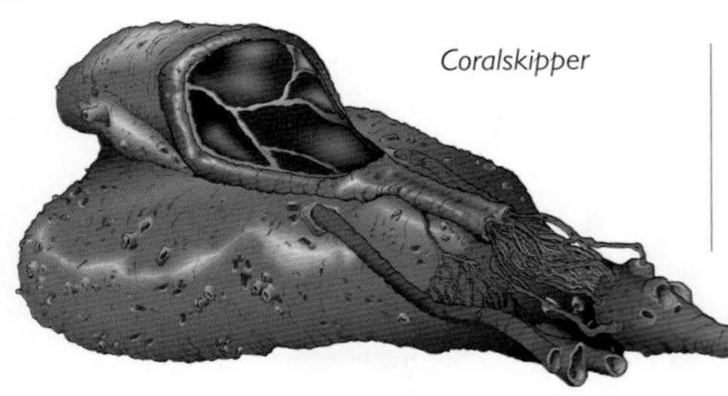
Coralskipper

**coralskipper** A Yuuzhan Vong–bioengineered starfighter, a living vessel made of yorik coral. Called a yorik-et by the Yuuzhan Vong, a coralskipper was roughly triangular in shape, with a canopy that resembled dark mica more than transparisteel. No two coralskippers were exactly the same, but most had the same attributes. A single firing appendage at the front of the vehicle fired flaming, molten rock. A coralskipper rearmed by "eating" rocks to replenish its ammunition. A small dovin basal at the front of the craft protected it from incoming fire by creating miniature black holes that absorbed enemy attacks. This intense field of supergravity could strip an enemy vessel of its protective deflector shields. New Republic pilots learned to deal with these advantages by boosting their own acceleration compensators to counter the gravitic tug of the dovin basals. Also, by stuttering their fire, pilots could keep the dovin basals occupied absorbing low-powered distracting blasts, drawing power away from the coralskipper's weapons and engines.

Fast and deadly, coralskippers fought in squadrons of six, with six squadrons to a wing. Whenever possible, they employed pack tactics, focusing their attention on an enemy ship that presented itself as a likely target. Coralskippers were only for use in space and did not function well in the presence of gravity. They could not enter hyperspace and thus attached themselves like barnacles to the spindly arms of Yuuzhan Vong carrier analogs.

Coralskippers, like all Yuuzhan Vong ships, were best piloted by means of a cognition hood. The relationship between pilot and coralskipper was more akin to that between rider and beast than of pilot and starfighter.

***Coral Vanda*** A sub-ocean vacation cruiser, it explored the waters of the planet Pantolomin. The *Coral Vanda* made excursions through a huge network of coral reefs off the coast of the Tralla continent. But vacationers came mainly to gamble in one of eight luxurious casinos. Full-wall transparisteel hulls gave tourists breathtaking views of sea life. The ship also had Adventure Rooms that re-created exotic locations through holographic and other sensory generators. Raal Yorta, Sammie Staable, and Smiley the Squib attempted a heist on the *Coral Vanda* prior to the Battle of Yavin. Years later, Grand Admiral Thrawn nearly captured Lando Calrissian and Han Solo aboard the vessel.

***Corbantis*** This cruiser fell victim to the Loronar Corporation, which was testing its new Needles smart missiles. Han Solo rescued 15 injured beings from the battle-damaged cruiser and took them to the planet Nim Drovis.

**Corbos** Approximately 7,000 years before the Battle of Yavin, dark siders made a last stand on Corbos. There Jedi hunters and rivals obliterated most of them, along with nearly all other life on the planet. The surviving dark side exiles fled beyond Republic borders, emerging in uncharted space, where they discovered the Sith species.

In modern times, Corbos became an out-of-the-way, experimental mining colony settled many times over the millennia—and each time the miners vanished, leaving no survivors or explanations. In response to a request by Chief of State Leia Organa Solo, a Jedi contingent led by Kyp Durron went to investigate the disappearance of the most recent colony of 739 miners and their familes. It was discovered that giant leviathan creatures had been terrorizing the planet.

Cordé

***Cord*-class starfighter** Used by the Galactic Republic during the Clone Wars, this vessel was armed with a single laser cannon. It was often carried aboard *Acclamator*-class assault ships.

**Cordé** A Naboo handmaiden who served Senator Padmé Amidala as a decoy during the time of the Separatist crisis. A trained bodyguard, she died in an attack on Padmé's Naboo Royal Cruiser the morning of the Military Creation Act vote on Coruscant.

**Corde, Morrigan** *See* Calixte, Moff Nyna.

**cordioline trehansicol** A chemical used to combat insect infestations, it was sold under the brand name CorTrehan.

Coral Vanda

**cordrazine** A stimulant drug used in the operating room to revive a patient's vital systems.

**CorDuro Shipping** An organization contracted by the New Republic's Senate Select Committee for Refugees (SELCORE) to deliver supplies to the refugee domes on Duro during the Yuuzhan Vong invasion. CorDuro Shipping was discovered to be collaborating with the Peace Brigade and the Yuuzhan Vong in the impending attack on the planet.

**Core Founders** The beings and cultures—most of them human—who established the collective governments of the Core Worlds at the dawn of the Galactic Republic. Coruscant, Corellia, Alderaan, and Kuat were among the worlds that were first heralded as part of the Core Worlds.

**Core Galaxy Systems** An ancient manufacturing firm, maker of the *Enforcer One* Dreadnaught. Core Galaxy Systems was one of the famed "founding shipwrights" of the Old Republic, dating back over 20 millennia. The firm fell on hard times five centuries prior to the Battle of Yavin and was bought out by Kuat Drive Yards, at which time the Core Galaxy Systems name was retired.

**Corellia** A temperate world covered by rolling hills, thick forests, lush fields, and large seas. From the inception of the Republic, Corellia always proudly followed its own path, occasionally at the expense of the larger galactic community. It was a fiercely independent world governing a fiercely independent sector that traditionally had been inward looking, detached from seismic political events that reshaped the galaxy time and again.

Corellia and four other planets orbited the star of Corell in the Corellian sector. The entire system was an astrophysical curiosity, an enigmatic relic possibly left behind by an ancient culture. As unlikely as it seemed, all five planets were habitable, and floating between Tralus and Talus, the Double Worlds, was an immense artifact known as Centerpoint Station. It was an unimaginably ancient device floating at the gravitic balance point between the two worlds. Some xenoarchaeologists believed that Centerpoint was employed by an ancient, incredibly advanced culture to move the planets of the Corellian system into place.

Corellia was known as the "Elder Brother" of the system, serving as the administrative center not only for its "Brother planets" Drall, Selonia, Talus, and Tralus, but also for the entire sector. The planet was governed by a Diktat, while the sector itself was represented in the Galactic Senate by a Senator.

Despite its age and influence in galactic affairs, Corellia did not become completely urbanized like Coruscant. Corellians took pride in their planet's open expanses of razor grass fields and unpolluted sandy beaches. Their solution to urban overgrowth was to move shipbuilding facilities offworld. The shipyards of such monolithic companies as the Corellian Engineering Corporation were immense, producing such famous vessels as Corellian CR90 corvettes, Republic cruisers, and the ubiquitous YT-series freighters.

Corellia's clustered continents were bracketed by two huge oceans, eastern and western. The capital city of Coronet was on a coastal front along the Golden Beaches, with other cities such as Bela Vistal and Tyrena. Though the planetary population fluctuated during the decades of the Galactic Civil War, it numbered over 15 billion, with Coronet being the largest single concentration of citizenry. Scattered inland were a number of small towns and farming hamlets.

*Corellia*

Though Coronet was a bustling city, it was filled with parks, plazas and open-air trading stalls, indicative of the Corellian love of wide-open spaces. One of the most popular locales was Treasure Ship Row, a garishly eclectic bazaar filled with a complex tapestry of alien cultures.

The native species of the Corellian system—humans, Selonians, and Drall—could be found throughout Coronet. Selonians prefered to live beneath the surface of the planet, in complex warrens and tunnels that dated back to pre-Republic times. Also located beneath Corellia's soil was an ancient planetary repulsor, further evidence that the planet was relocated by an unknown alien force in the far distant past.

The Corellian system was wealthy enough to afford its own fleet and security forces. During the time of the Old Republic, it handled its own law enforcement free from the involvement of the galactic government. The Corellian Security Force, or CorSec, remained largely intact even after the rise of the Empire. Even Corellian Jedi were reputed to be nontraditionalists in that most ascetic of Orders.

Corellians had a cultural wariness toward big galactic government. One of the founding worlds of the Republic, Corellia had fostered a tradition of independence and had, during its long history, attempted separation from the union more than once.

When Count Dooku's Separatist movement arose during the waning days of the Republic, Corellia tried to remain neutral. Not wanting to be involved in a decisive Military Creation Act vote that would determine the future of armed conflict in the galaxy, Senator Garm Bel Iblis withdrew Corellia from the vote and sealed its borders, hoping to wait out the coming conflagration. His attempt at isolation failed, and before long Corellia, too, was dragged into the Clone Wars.

With the rise of the Empire, Corellia once again bristled under the authority of Coruscant, but it did not actively join the Rebellion. The planet's shipyards were controlled by the Imperial starfleet, and many Corellians were drafted into Imperial service. As the sector's native military forces were dispatched throughout the galaxy to deal with the growing Rebellion, piracy bled into Corellia's borders, disrupting the valuable trade that had kept the world independent for so long.

Senator Bel Iblis disappeared from galactic politics, waging his own private war against the Empire, while many Corellians joined the nascent Rebel Alliance. As the Rebellion began scoring increasingly larger victories against the Empire, Corellians enacted strict isolationist measures, restricting trade and ship traffic throughout the region. Under such hermetic conditions, the population grew almost xenophobic, encouraging a paranoid resentment toward outsiders.

When the Empire's collapse began at the Battle of Endor, Corellia suffered as Imperial forces withdrew to shore up defenses at Coruscant and elsewhere. The Corellian Diktat, who was little more than an Imperial puppet, lost his power base and became a target of resentful Corellians. He fled to the Outlier systems of the Corellian sector, prompting the collapse of the Corellian government.

Into this mess stepped the New Republic, which appointed a new leader to help clean up the disarray. Governor-General Micamberlecto attempted to infuse order into a bewildering tangle of conflicting agendas. Many of the humans who'd prospered under Imperial rule held great disdain for the new government, and the planetwide aversion to outsiders created great challenges for the New Republic.

Fourteen years after Endor, Chief of State Leia Organa Solo voyaged to Corellia for a historic trade summit, eager to work out some of the sector's problems. Instead, she was drawn into a sudden flash fire of insurrection that history would later recall as the Corellian incident.

The Sacorrian Triad, a secretive council of human, Drall, and Selonian dictators based in the Corellian sector, had grown in power since the collapse of the Empire, and attempted a sectorwide coup that would ensure Corellian independence. The Triad took control of Centerpoint Station's immense repulsorlift technology to target distant stars for destruction, essentially holding systems hostage until its demands were met. This bid for independence was thwarted by the efforts of a joint New Republic and Bakuran task force, and the actions of the young Jedi siblings, Jacen, Jaina, and Anakin Solo.

Corellia continued its bid for independence in the aftermath of the war against the Yuuzhan Vong and the Swarm War, conflicts that resulted in the disintegration of the New Republic and rise of the Galactic Alliance. The GA sought to exert increased authority over its member worlds by centralizing the military, thus bringing any planetary military forces under the command and aegis of the GA armed forces. Corellia refused to comply. Corellian leader Thrackan Sal-Solo, convinced that the Galactic Alliance had done little to improve the standing of the Corellian system, demanded that it be given freedom to pursue its own goals. The Galactic Alliance refused, arguing that Corellia was trying to enjoy all the benefits of membership in the GA without having to shoulder the responsibilities. Tensions on both sides of the conflict escalated, particularly once Jacen Solo was placed in command of the Galactic Alliance Guard, and Corellians who were living on Coruscant were either forced to leave the planet or were arrested as terrorists.

Years before the actual start of any fighting, Sal-Solo secretly began creating two fleets of military warships at separate shipyards located in the Kiris Asteroid Cluster. He hoped to bring the new warships to bear against the Galactic Alliance, but their existence only served to draw the GA's attention to Corellia. Galactic Alliance forces blockaded the Corellian system, hoping to forestall any fighting, but were forced to withdraw to Tralus. There a small battle was fought; the forces of the Galactic Alliance were driven off, but the end result only served to reinforce the GA's blockading fleet.

Many Corellians believed that Sal-Solo's assassination by Boba Fett and several unidentified agents would put an end to the conflict, but new leader Dur Gejjen chose to prolong the hostilities, and even brought Sal-Solo's hidden fleets into the war, using them to bolster Corellia's defenses and sending a portion of the fleet to Hapes on a mission to assassinate the Queen Mother, Tenel Ka. This mission, which Gejjen hoped would draw the Hapes Consortium's potent naval forces over to the side of the Corellians, ultimately failed.

In the relative calm that followed the Hapes debacle, a strained stalemate developed, with Galactic Alliance forces maintaining a far-reaching blockade and Corellian forces

*Corellia's capital city, Coronet*

patrolling the system within the blockade's boundaries. The conflict caused many species, including the Bothans, to demand Corellian independence in the hope that they might also gain freedom from the Galactic Alliance. These disgruntled systems joined Corellia in forming the Confederation, and allied themselves against the Galactic Alliance.

A long, violent, and bloody war ensued between the GA and the Confederation some 40 years after the Battle of Yavin. It saw Thrackan Sal-Solo assassinated and Jacen Solo complete a transformation to Sith Lord, becoming Darth Caedus. Millions were killed and millions more became refugees. An attempt by Corellia to reactivate the Centerpoint Station weapon, and by Darth Caedus to control it himself, was sabotaged by the Jedi—and the ancient weapon self-destructed. With Caedus killed in a lightsaber duel with his twin sister, the war came to an end and all sides agreed to sign a peace treaty.

**Corellia Mining Corporation** A Corellian corporation that produced Mining Digger Crawlers, which became better known as sandcrawlers when they were reclaimed by the Jawas of Tatooine.

**Corellian** Members of this human race inhabited the Corellia star system. Notable Corellians included Han Solo, General Crix Madine, General Garm Bel Iblis, and Wedge Antilles.

**Corellian Arms** A minor weapons manufacturer and a smaller, independent subsidiary of the Corellian Engineering Corporation.

Corellian Bloodstripe on Han Solo's pants

**Corellian Bloodstripe** This red piping adorned the trousers of Corellians who distinguished themselves through bravery and heroic acts. Rebel hero Han Solo wore the Bloodstripe on his trousers, his only nod toward his time of military service. He was also the recipient of the yellow Second Class Bloodstripe, a slightly lesser distinction. For a time, Han preferred wearing the yellow, which drew less attention from bounty hunters.

**Corellian Confederation** *See* Confederation, the.

**Corellian corvette** An older multipurpose capital ship model, this midsized vessel saw service for years throughout the galaxy. At 150 meters long, it could be a troop carrier, light escort vessel, cargo transport, or passenger liner. The CR70 and CR90 corvettes had fast sublight drives and a speedy hyperdrive for emergency exits into hyperspace. Because this type of vessel was used by Corellian pirates, authorities nicknamed it the Blockade Runner. Famous corvettes included Princess Leia Organa's consular ship *Tantive IV*, the *Scarlet Thranta* used by Freedom's Sons, and the New Republic *FarStar*.

**Corellian Defense Force** The armed forces that guarded the planets of the Corellian sector. The CDF had many branches and divisions, all geared toward keeping the law. The headquarters building of the CDF was located in Coronet, on Corellia.

**Corellian Dreadnaught** Massive warships commissioned by Thrackan Sal-Solo and built in secret at the Kiris Shipyards. These vessels had roughly twice the firepower of an *Imperial*-class Star Destroyer, with weapons systems arrayed across their ovate stuctures. This gave them almost complete weapons coverage, resulting in very few blind or unprotected hull sections.

**Corellian Engineering Corporation (CEC)** One of the galaxy's most prolific starship-manufacturing firms. The company primarily produced fast, durable, heavily armed, and easily modified commercial vehicles. In the civilian sector, CEC was most successful with its line of freighters, which could be given impressive offensive and defensive capabilities through both legal and illegal modification kits. The *Millennium Falcon* and Dash Rendar's *Outrider* were both prime examples of CEC freighters that were modified far beyond their original design specifications.

CEC was based on Corellia. As with other planetary industries, however, all of its shipyards were in orbit around the world. This allowed Corellia to remain relatively pristine.

**Corellian gunship** A dedicated combat capital ship, it was designed to be fast and deadly. At 120 meters long, it usually carried eight double turbolaser cannons, six quad laser cannons, and four concussion missile launch tubes. Engines filled more than half of its interior. With a small command crew and technical staff—but many gunners—the ship was an excellent anti-starfighter platform. The New Republic made extensive use of these vessels, as did the Rebel Alliance before it.

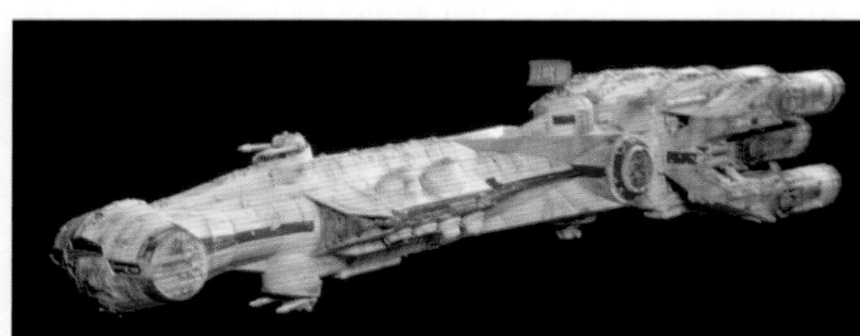
Corellian corvette

Corellian gunship
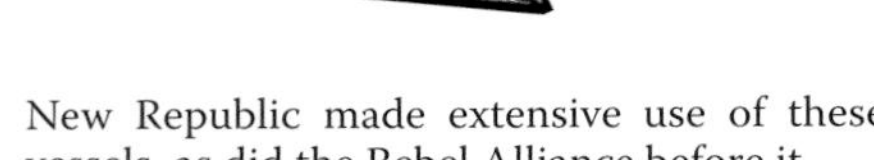

**Corellian incident** The secession of the Corellian sector from the New Republic, when the Sacorrian Triad tried to assume control of the galaxy by unleashing the Starbuster Plot. This period was also referred to as the Corellian crisis or the Corellian Insurrection.

**Corellian Jumpmaster 5000** A type of starship, one example of which was the bounty hunter Dengar's *Punishing One.*

**Corellian Merchants' Guild** One of the largest private trade organizations in the galaxy, it was open to all native-born Corellians, as well as to owners and crews of Corellian-built starships. The CMG provided many services to its members, including information, trade contacts, repair facilities, messaging, and financial services. The CMG operated many guildhouses throughout the galaxy.

**Corellian overdrive** A phrase that meant doing whatever it takes to get a job done—be it finagling the rules or rearranging operational parameters—but not cheating in an honest game.

**Corellian Port Control** A security force, it tried to keep the peace on the Smugglers' Moon of Nar Shaddaa.

**Corellian Run** One of the oldest and most important galactic routes. Alongside the Perlemian Trade Route, it formed the Slice—a wedge that continued into the Outer Rim and basically *was* the Republic for countless millennia. Almost all early Republic exploration occurred along these two routes and within the Slice.

**Corellian Sanctuary** A small domed building on Coruscant, it was created by exiled Corellians as a resting place for their dead after a hostile relationship developed between the New Republic and the Corellian government. Since repatriation had become impossible for Corellians who died away from home, they were cremated and their carbon remains compressed into raw diamonds. These diamonds were then embedded in the black ceiling and walls of the Sanctuary, creating the look of a shimmering sea of constellations as seen from Corellia.

**Corellian sand panthers** Carnivorous felines with poison-tipped claws, they lived on Corellia.

**Corellian sector** Always an inward-looking part of the galaxy, it progressively became more secretive and hermetic. It was a group of 24 star systems in the Core Worlds, with the Corellian system serving as administrative and cultural capital. The other systems were known collectively as the Outlier systems.

Garm Bel Iblis served as sector Senate representative during the Separatist crisis, and withdrew Corellia and its systems from the Military Creation Act vote. He was followed by Fliry Vorru, who allowed smugglers free rein within the sector. Vorru was later betrayed to the Emperor by underworld kingpin Prince Xizor and sent to Kessel; he was freed by members of Rogue Squadron three years after the Battle of Endor.

The three dominant species of the sector—human, Drall, and Selonian—were forced to get along because of the ever-present threat of punishment from the Empire. When that threat was removed, all three scrambled to assert their dominance, leading to an insurrection by the Sacorrian Triad. Years later, the Corellian sector again bid for independence, sparking a war between it and the Galactic Alliance.

**Corellian Security Force (CorSec)** The primary law enforcement agency on Corellia during the New Order and the early years of the New Republic. Although ostensibly under the direct control of the Diktat, CorSec often acted independently, allowing it jurisdiction over municipal police forces, as well as over certain parts of the Corellian system. This span of operation allowed CorSec officers to maintain a coordinated law enforcement system, and also reduced the bureaucracy involved in far-ranging investigations. Because of their loyalty and dedication to justice, many CorSec alumni became members of the Senate Guard of the Old Republic. During the reign of Emperor Palpatine, the leaders of CorSec ordered that their divisions accept the insertion of an Imperial Intelligence officer to monitor and coordinate activities with the local Imperial garrisons. After the Battle of Endor, the new Corellian Diktat dissolved the Corellian Security Force and established a new, more Diktat-friendly Public Safety Service in its place, until New Republic representatives intervened.

**Corellian slice hound** A feral creature native to Corellia, it took its name from the razor-sharp spikes that covered its body and the mouthful of jagged spikes that served as teeth. They hunted in small, organized packs. Slice hounds generally attacked anything smaller than they were, but when they were hungry, nothing was safe.

**Corellian Slip** A dangerous flight maneuver first perfected by Corellian starship battle tacticians, it was attempted when one pilot could not evade a pursuer. The first pilot's wingmate flew directly at him, using his ship as cover; then, at the last second, the first pilot ducked down and the wingmate had a clear shot at the enemy.

**Corellian system** This system contained five inhabited worlds—Corellia, Selonia, Drall, Talus, and Tralus—collectively called the Five Brothers because of their close orbits. Centerpoint Station, located directly between the Double Worlds of Talus and Tralus, was an ancient device that theoretically might have been used to transport the five planets through hyperspace to their current orbits. The system was policed by both the Corellian Defense Force and the Corellian Security Force, or CorSec. Pilots from the Corellian system were known throughout the galaxy for their superb skills—and the system was also notorious for its smugglers and pirates.

The Corellian Engineering Corporation's shipyards were famous for manufacturing a vast variety of starships. Due to their strategic importance, the Empire kept the system heavily defended after the Battle of Endor. It was in the Corellian system that Starkiller and Mon Mothma convinced three major Imperial resistance groups to join forces, marking the beginning of the Rebel Alliance.

A famous Corellian work of literature was *The Fall of the Sun* by Erwithat, and a respected honor was the red trouser piping known as the Corellian Bloodstripe. Corellians were known to hold the family in high esteem. Some traditionalists believed that natives of the system (called ensters) could only marry people from the system, not outsiders (eksters). Other Corellian traditions included enjoying ryshcate, a dark brown sweet cake made with vweilu nuts, which was traditionally baked and served at important celebrations.

Another tradition was Jedi Credits, or JedCreds—commemorative medallions awarded when a Corellian Jedi became a Master. Corellian Jedi were known to have a number of traditions unique to themselves. The language known as Old Corellian, although essentially extinct, survived among smugglers and pirates.

**Corellian Treaty** A landmark document signed less than two years before the Battle of Yavin. The Corellian Treaty merged the three largest revolutionary groups into a single unified party, the Alliance to Restore the Republic. The document was signed by Bail Organa, Mon Mothma, and Senator Garm Bel Iblis of Corellia. All three were brought together by the agent known as the Starkiller, who facilitated the signing of the treaty.

***Corellian Way*** This New Republic frigate was part of a small fleet dispatched to protect the planet Esfandia at the height of the Yuuzhan Vong invasion.

***Corellia Star*** A YT-1300 freighter that stumbled upon the Imperial V38 "Phantom TIE" project. Its crew was killed near the Dreighton Nebula, but not before they contacted a flight of Alliance B-wings. The Alliance pilots were able to recover the freighter and discover more information on the top-secret project.

**core ship** The detachable center sphere of a Trade Federation battleship or Droid Control Ship.

**Corewatch** The code name for a deep undercover Rebel Alliance agent active in the Core Worlds during the Galactic Civil War.

**Core Worlds** The central, heavily populated founding systems of galactic government that bordered the galaxy's Deep Core. The region was the original ruling nexus of the Republic, and later the Empire, with the planet Coruscant (Imperial Center) at the center and the government spreading outward like the spokes of a wheel.

**Core Worlds Security Act** A law instituted during the Clone Wars that heightened the security of those planets within the Core Worlds region. It reassigned certain military and security assets of the Galactic Republic to the protection of planets such as Coruscant, to ensure that they were safe from Separatist terrorism. Opponents of the law, many from outside the Core, argued that it was enacted to appease business and financial supporters in the Core, and left their worlds undefended against the Separatists.

**Core Worlds Travel Clearance** A document required for starship captains during the height of the New Order indicating permission to conduct space-faring business in the Core Worlds.

**Core Worlds Visa** Documentation required to travel legally within the Core Worlds during the last decades of the Galactic Republic.

**Corey, Swilla** A petty thief who was born into slavery but freed when her masters were killed on Tatooine. She worked odd jobs, including tending to jerba herds. She was in the Mos Eisley cantina on that fateful day when Obi-Wan Kenobi and Luke Skywalker hired the *Millennium Falcon.* She became friends with Ketwol, the Pacithhip trader who found and tended her lost jerba herd.

**Corgan, Colonel** The staff tactical officer for General Etahn A'baht, he served aboard the fleet carrier *Intrepid.*

**Cories, Niklas** A musician, singer, and son of a prominent Outer Rim businessman, he was also an assassin who indiscriminately used thermal detonators to eliminate his targets. He had a long-standing grudge against the Hutts, a situation which the Hutts dealt with by placing a number of contracts on his head.

**corinathoth** Massive, multihorned, slow-moving herbivores found on Maridun.

***Coriolis*** One of several Duros-commanded warships in the Galactic Alliance naval fleet, during the last stages of the Yuuzhan Vong

Roron Corobb

War it was assigned to General Wedge Antilles. Its task force was dispatched to the Duro system as a feint. When Commander Yurf Col learned that his native Duro would not be rescued, he broke formation against orders. Led by the *Dpso,* all the Duros warships tried to attack the Yuuzhan Vong on their own, but they were no match. The *Coriolis* and its sister ships were destroyed in just under three hours.

**Cornelius, Dr.** *See* Evazan, Dr.

**Corobb, Roron** An Ithorian Jedi Master trained by Yarael Poof, he had two throats, which generated a deep guttural language. Combined with his mental skills, his voice could be as powerful as any Force blast. Corobb had as his apprentice the headstrong and energetic young Drake Lo'gaan. With the outbreak of the Clone Wars, the path to becoming a Jedi was accelerated for many. Such was the case with Drake. After placing well in the Jedi Temple Apprentice Tournament, the 11-year-old boy was selected by Master Corobb to be his Padawan. Lo'gaan accompanied the Ithorian on even his most dangerous missions, but was not there when Corobb fell to General Grievous while protecting Supreme Chancellor Palpatine during the Clone Wars.

***Corona*-class frigate** A limited-production starship, one of the earliest designs approved by the New Republic. Built by Kuat Drive Yards, it was modeled after the Nebulon-B frigate, and was designed to carry up to three squadrons of starfighters into battle. The *Corona*-class frigate measured 275 meters in length.

***Coronet*** A Republic *Acclamator*-class assault transport destroyed at Duro during the height of the Clone Wars.

**Coronet** The capital city of the planet Corellia, it was known for its parkland and abundant open space.

**Corphelion comets** Spectacular comet showers that became a honeymoon attraction.

**Corporate Alliance** The negotiating body for many of the galaxy's largest commercial firms, this huge business concern held considerable influence in the waning days of the Galactic Republic. Represented in the Senate by its magistrate, Passel Argente, the Alliance was charged with regulating sales and distribution of countless corporations in the galaxy. Its higher executives were constantly frustrated with the cumbersome Republic bureaucracy, which kept the Alliance from maximizing its profits. During the Clone Wars, the Corporate Alliance sided with the Separatists. Argente committed his corporate military forces and battle droid armies to the cause. To protect its assets, the alliance maintained such fearsome enforcers as tank droids capable of storming enemy compounds in an instant. It maintained major corporate offices on Lethe and Murkhana.

**Corporate Alliance tank droid** Also known as *Persuader*-class NR-N99 units, these were the treaded enforcers of the Corporate Alliance. They stood well over 6 meters tall and used a single, treaded drive motor for locomotion. A pair of large outrigger arms connected to either side of the drive motor could be armed with virtually any known weapon. During the Clone Wars, the Corporate Alliance equipped the droids with a combination of conventional ion cannons and homing lasers. For specific missions, these ion weapons could be replaced by concussion missile launchers, homing missiles, dumbfire torpedoes, and even thermal grenade launchers. They were used in an amphibious assault on the beaches of Kashyyyk against the Wookiees.

**Corporate Sector** A free-enterprise fiefdom consisting of tens of thousands of star systems, it was run by a single wealthy and influential company, the Corporate Sector Authority (CSA). Located on the edge of the galaxy, it bordered the Aparo and Wyl sectors. The skylines of its many urban worlds were lit by the multicolored flashes of countless advertising signs. It offered the widest selection of products anywhere, and tourists came from all over the galaxy to purchase its unique goods.

The CSA was made up of dozens of contributing companies and was run by the 55 members of the Direx Board, who were in turn headed by the ExO. The CSA had exclusive rights to use the sector's resources as it saw fit. Typically, the CSA used up one planet's resources, then moved on to another. It wasn't above using slave labor or grossly polluting the environment. Because there was no internal competition, the CSA could mark up prices of goods to many times their actual worth. Businesses in the sector accepted only the Authority Cash Voucher and crystalline vertex.

During the New Order, a portion of the CSA's enormous profits were secretly funneled to Emperor Palpatine, with the understanding that the Empire would take no direct role in the operation of the sector. Therefore, the CSA formed its own military forces, including Security Police (called Espos) and a comparatively poor and outdated starfleet. Planets in the Corporate Sector included Ammuud, Bonadan, Roonadan, Etti IV, Kalla, Kail, Kir, Orron III, Duroon, Mytus VII, Gaurick, Rampa, Mall'ordian, Reltooine, Knolstee, Mayro, and the Trianii colony worlds of Fibuli, Ekibo, Pypin, and Brochiib. The feline Trianii actively opposed the Corporate Sector's annexation of their worlds, and much of the fighting between the two sides occurred in the Tingel Arm. An armistice in the conflict was called after three years of intensive fighting.

Originally established centuries before the Galactic Civil War, the Corporate Sector was once a group of several hundred systems, all devoid of intelligent life. The corporations allowed to operate in the sector could purchase entire regions of space but were held in check by the watchful eye of the Republic. During the Emperor's rise to power, however, several corporate allies of Palpatine convinced him to expand the sector to encompass nearly 30,000 stars. Eleven native intelligent species were discovered in this expanded region, though this fact was effectively covered up. The CSA was established to manage the sector's operations, kicking off the modern era of the Corporate Sector.

Han Solo and Chewbacca had several legendary exploits in the Corporate Sector during their early adventuring, including a jailbreak from the infamous Stars' End penal colony. Following the Battle of Hoth, the Corporate Sector company Galactic Electronics developed a new magpulse weapons technology and sold it to the Rebel Alliance. In retaliation, the Imperial Star Destroyer *Glory* seized the corporation's deep-space research facility. Emperor Palpatine had plans to build a great palace for himself in the sector, and construction continued even after Palpatine's apparent death at the Battle of Endor. Six years later, during the cloned Emperor's reappearance, the Corporate Sector declared its neutrality in the conflict and began supplying weapons and arms to both sides.

During the Yuuzhan Vong War, much of the pathway known as Vector Prime traveled

Corporate Alliance tank droid

through the Corporate Sector, and nearby planets such as Brigia and Ruuria were overrun as the Yuuzhan Vong moved toward the Core.

**Corporate Sector Authority (CSA)** The governing authority of the Corporate Sector, this private corporation was forged by the industrious Baron Tagge. The CSA was granted a charter by the Empire to control that portion of the galaxy. At the height of the New Order, the CSA was afforded autonomy due to the huge profits that it funneled into the Empire. Within its borders, the CSA was hardly a better ruler than the Empire, though many sought refuge there from the Galactic Civil War.

Dozens of contributing companies made up the Corporate Sector Authority, and from their upper management came the Direx Board, 55 business executives who managed the sector's day-to-day affairs. The Direx Board was headed by the ExO, or the Executive Officer. Other high-ranking stations in the CSA's command chain included the Prex (or President), Viceprex, Auditor-General, and the Imperial Adviser, who acted as liaison and representative of the Empire's interests.

The allure of limitless profits drew many entrepreneurs to the Corporate Sector, but in truth, the majority of the fiefdom's denizens were merely wage-slave drudges, toiling away for the betterment of a faceless corporation while their share was skimmed and "assessed" down to a mere pittance. Citizenship was purchased, and the people of the Corporate Sector were shareholders, which afforded them few rights. Labor relationships were extremely poor, and hazardous working conditions were overlooked if correcting them would cut too deeply into a company's bottom line. One of the biggest crimes in the Corporate Sector was conspiracy to form a union.

Law and order were maintained in the Corporate Sector by the Security Division. The Security Police of the CSA, or Espos, fostered a reputation as hardened bullies. They wore brown uniforms, combat armor, and black battle helmets. They were typically armed with blaster rifles and riot guns.

The Security Division also maintained a picket fleet of outdated vessels to patrol Corporate Sector space. Refitted *Victory*-class Star Destroyers remained the prime component of the Authority's space patrol, though even older vessels such as Marauder corvettes and *Invincible*-class Dreadnaughts could be found.

During the Galactic Civil War, many of the corporations of the CSA developed technologies for the Empire. After the collapse of the New Order, the Corporate Sector tried to remain neutral, and the New Republic was too burdened with establishing a new government to strike a new long-lasting partnership with the commerce-minded fiefdom. During the resurrected Emperor's campaign to retake the core, the Direx Board shrewdly remained uncommitted and sold weaponry to both sides. When the Yuuzhan Vong invaded, all communication was cut off between the Corporate Sector and the rest of the galaxy.

**corpse-fungus** A swiftly growing fungus native to Haruun Kal that fed on dying bodies.

**corpse-grub** A nasty Corellian swarming insect that can skeletonize a carcass in minutes, all the while excreting a noxious effluvia.

***Corpulentus*** A Separatist flagship during the Clone Wars under the command of Admiral Pors Tonith, it was destroyed at Praesitlyn.

**Corr** A clone trooper maimed in service during the Clone Wars, his hands were, by necessity, replaced with simple prosthetics, rendering him ineffective as an explosive ordnance disposal operative. He was reassigned to the army's logistics center on Coruscant, tracking and updating troop information. About a year into the Clone Wars, he assisted in Kal Skirata's black-ops assignment to eliminate a terrorist ring on Coruscant. He proved himself so effective in this operation that Skirata requested to have him retrained as a commando. Corr eventually served in such a capcity for Omega Squad.

**Corridan** This planet was located in the former center of the Rim territories. During the Empire's reign, the Black Sword Command was charged with the defense of Corridan, Praxlis, and the entire Kokash and Farlax sectors.

**corridor ghouls** Quadrupeds about knee-high, these fast and deadly creatures native to Coruscant's lowest levels seemed to be mammals. They had no fur, just stark white skin. Although they were blind, their navigation by echolocation gave them plenty of speed and agility. They had big ears and sharp teeth and emitted high-pitched screams.

**Corrsk** A Trandoshan, he worked for Nolaa Tarkona and her Diversity Alliance movement opposing the New Republic. In battle with Jedi Knight Lowbacca on Ryloth, Corrsk managed to injure the young Wookiee. Lowbacca then overpowered Corrsk and blew him out of an air lock.

***Corrupter*** A *Victory*-class Star Destroyer, it was formerly assigned to patrol the Outer Rim, hunting down pirates and smugglers for the Empire. When director of Imperial Intelligence Ysanne Isard fled Coruscant, she used the *Corrupter* to defend her position on Thyferra and protect convoys of bacta leaving the planet. Under Captain Convarion, the ship caught up with and destroyed one bacta freighter that had been hijacked by Rogue Squadron. Several Rebel Alliance pilots were killed. The *Corrupter* then began a campaign of terror against those worlds that refused to pay Isard's inflated prices for the bacta she controlled, and particularly those worlds that had benefited from the free bacta given to them by Rogue Squadron. The first example was the destruction of the colony on Halanit. Isard thought she had Rogue Squadron pinned down in a trap at the Alderaan Graveyard, but the tables were turned and the fierce battle there resulted in the destruction of the *Corrupter*.

***Corsair*** An ancient ship, it was used by dark side sorcerer Naga Sadow to flee across the galaxy many millennia ago.

**Corsair Squadron** Along with Gauntlet Squadron, one of two starfighter squadrons relied upon heavily by the New Republic after Rogue Squadron briefly resigned its commission to fight the Bacta War. These X-wings were later assigned to the *Mon Karren* during the hunt for Warlord Zsinj.

**Cort, Farl** The former administrator of the colony on Halanit, he put out a distress call to the New Republic for bacta to aid his dying people. When Rogue Squadron members Corran Horn and Ooryl Qrygg arrived with the bacta, Cort refused to take it without offering something in return. Although the market price of the bacta was in excess of a billion Imperial credits, Rogue Squadron had liberated it from the bacta cartel. Finally, an agreement was struck under which the colony would provide its guests with a hot bath and a fish dinner in exchange for the bacta. The head of the cartel, Ysanne Isard, chose to destroy the Halanit colony to serve as an example for other worlds that received liberated bacta. Farl Cort was assumed to have died during the massacre.

**Cortella** A little-known planet ruled by a monarchy. Obi-Wan Kenobi and Siri Tachi pretended to be the king and queen of this world when they attempted to infiltrate the Leadership School on Andara.

**cortex** Levels of knowledge and mastery as described in the Yuuzhan Vong shaper protocols, held within a vessel of knowledge called the Qang Qahsa. Yuuzhan Vong mythology held that each cortex was gifted to their Supreme Overlord by the gods themselves. Five cortexes were readily available to any within the shaper caste, with the next two levels—the sixth and seventh—attainable only by master shapers. The eighth cortex was reputed to hold knowledge about the galaxy, the lifeforms within, and the nature of the Force, but that was a sham. There was no eighth cortex; it was a fiction concocted by Supreme Overlord Shimrra to justify his invasion plans.

**cortical datasplint** A cybernetic implant that allowed users to store large amounts of data within their brain. Users didn't have access to this data, but simply served as vessels carrying it.

**Cortina** During the early days of the New Republic, the worlds of Cortina and Jandur came to Coruscant to petition for membership. Though they initially seemed prideful and arrogant, both planets eventually signed the standard articles of confederation.

**cortosis** A rare material mined on such worlds as Katanos VII, Duro, and Apatros, it was remarkably impervious to heat and energy. As such, mining cortosis with energy techniques was useless; raw physical labor was required. Some strains also had the unique property of shutting down a lightsaber when the blade touched it—such a hit started a feedback crash in the weapon's activation loop. Certain Force-users, like the *Jensaarai,* made sets of body armor out of woven cortosis fibers, and Emperor Palpatine inserted it between the double walls of his private residence on Coruscant.

**cortosis droid** A variety of super battle droid (designated C-B3 ultra battle droid) specifically designed to counter lightsaber-wielding opponents during the Clone Wars. Anakin Skywalker destroyed the principal facility manufacturing these droids on Metalorn.

**Corulag** A planet of 15 billion citizens, it was in the Bormea sector of the Core Worlds, along the Perlemian Trade Route. It was overrun by the Brotherhood of Darkness during the New Sith Wars. In modern times, the planet was devoted to Emperor Palpatine and was viewed as a model world of proper Imperial behavior. The capital city of Curamelle was the site of Corulag Academy, a branch of the Empire-wide military school. Corulag was only slightly less prestigious than the famous Raithal Academy. During the Yuuzhan Vong invasion, Corulag was conquered early, but was reclaimed by the Galactic Alliance in its push to take back Coruscant.

**Corusca Circus** An ancient part of the Senate District on Coruscant, it was the site of brightly lit thoroughfares and old architecture.

***Corusca Fire*** A *Victory*-class Star Destroyer dispatched under the command of Admiral Ackbar to liberate Ciutric from Prince-Admiral Krennel. Years later, the *Corusca Fire* was one of the leading ships in the defense of Dantooine against the Yuuzhan Vong.

**Corusca gem** Extremely rare, this mineral was found only in the lower levels of the gas giant Yavin. Corusca gems were the hardest known substance in the galaxy and could even slice through transparisteel.

**Coruscani ogre** A large, semi-intelligent simian humanoid that dwelled in the undercity of Coruscant. Covered with a pelt of shaggy hair, the Coruscani ogre had a triangular head set flush between its thick muscular shoulders, and its toothy maw hung in a long crooked slash. No two Coruscani ogres looked the same, but certain similarities were common. Most had limbs of differing sizes, shaggy hair covering their bodies in patches, and mouths that seemed permanently twisted into lopsided snarls. Some were riddled with sores and tumors, often with patches of skin overgrown with rot or oozing pus. Claws, horns, and fangs were common.

*Cortosis droid*

**Coruscant** Triple Zero: Coruscant's coordinates on all standard navigational charts showed that it had long been the center of the known universe. For over 1,000 generations Coruscant was central to galactic affairs. In ancient times, the prehistoric Taungs and the Battalions of Zhell waged war for control of the beautiful planet. Millennia later, it was universally understood that whoever controlled Coruscant controlled the galaxy. Though not at the physical heart of the galaxy, it was at the political and navigational heart, with major trade routes crisscrossing its path.

*Coruscant*

The planet's landmass was almost totally covered by an enormous multileveled city built on foundations that had been in place since before the beginning of the Galactic Republic. The oldest and densest population centers bordered the equator. Kilometer-high skyscrapers—some extending to the lower fringes of the atmosphere—and numerous spaceports covered the cityscape. Its sky was filled with the lights of arriving and departing air traffic. Once there were skyhooks—giant satellites in low orbit that served as self-contained habitats—owned by the richest or most influential citizens.

Countless years of civilization indelibly changed Coruscant's ecology. The planet was actually colder than what humans would normally deem comfortable; immense orbital mirrors warmed its upper and lower latitudes by refocusing and distributing stellar energy. The planet's heat was regulated by thousands of strategically placed $CO_2$ reactive dampers in the upper atmosphere. Coruscant's water network melted polar ice and piped the water across the planet. The city's huge amount of sewage and refuse were blasted into space, targeted toward Coruscant's sun.

In a world encased in artifice, gregarious indigenous and transplanted wildlife nonetheless prospered. Hawk-bats and granite slugs dwelled in the urban jungle, and the lower depths of Coruscant were filled with frighteningly unwholesome creatures that evolved deprived of sunlight.

For the span of the Galactic Republic, Coruscant formed the foundation of government. The Galactic Senate and its governing Supreme Chancellor presided from the capital planet, and the Republic's guardians erected their massive Jedi Temple there thousands of years before the Galactic Civil War. When the Empire came to power, Imperial agents worked tirelessly to wipe away vestiges of the Old Republic. At the height of the war, the planet was renamed Imperial Center. The Jedi Temple was emptied. The Galactic Senate was disbanded, and the Imperial Palace became the largest structure to mark Coruscant's surface.

Despite such sweeping changes in policy and infrastructure, the shadows of Coruscant remained largely unchanged. The city-planet became home to some of the largest criminal syndicates in the galaxy, with the "family leaders" calling the undercity their home.

*Coruscant skyline*

Following the defeat of the Empire at the Battle of Endor, the Rebel Alliance—now the New Republic—made the capture of Coruscant a paramount priority. The elite Alliance special missions force and starfighter unit, Rogue Squadron, spearheaded the stab into the Core Worlds. A cunning plan allowed the Rogues to retake Coruscant with its planetary shields intact and with acceptable collateral damage.

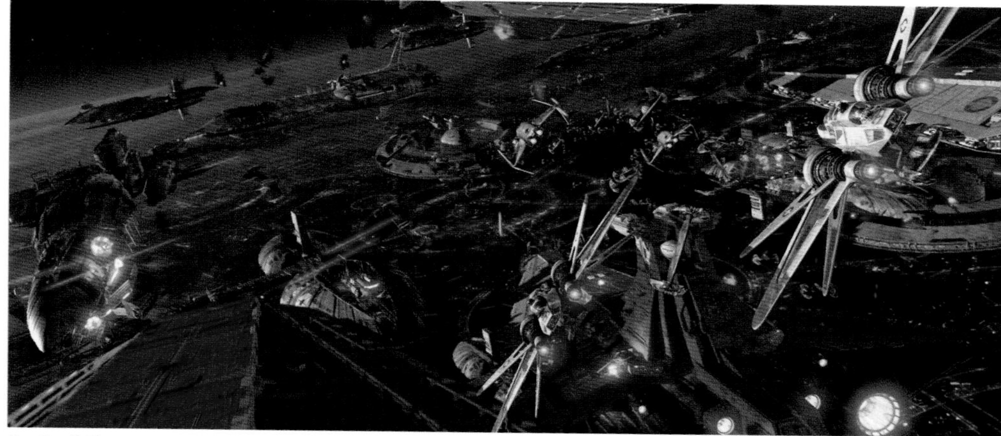

Battle of Coruscant

Over the next few years, New Republic leaders set up government on Coruscant. They moved the capital to the old Imperial Palace and reinstated Senatorial rule. Plagued by Imperial warlords, the New Republic experienced daunting growing pains as it tried to rebuild the galaxy that Palpatine had oppressed for so long.

After Grand Admiral Thrawn's failed bid to recapture Coruscant, the Imperials rallied by staging a devastating attack on the capital. Abandoning Thrawn's elegant tactics, these Imperials struck without compunction. Vast stretches of Coruscant's surface were laid to waste in the battle. The New Republic retreated from Coruscant, leaving the splintering Imperial factions to war among themselves.

When the Imperial Civil War fizzled out, the New Republic again set to rebuilding the damage the Empire had caused. Using immense construction droids, the Republic was able to clear the rubble and erect new buildings on Coruscant's surface. The New Republic faced insurrections and repeated Imperial harassment, yet Coruscant weathered the tests.

It barely survived, however, the conquest by the Yuuzhan Vong. The inexorable incursion of the invading aliens had targeted the heart of the Core Worlds. Despite the best efforts of the beleaguered New Republic and Luke Skywalker's new Jedi Order, the aliens conquered Coruscant.

The Yuuzhan Vong started "Vongforming" after taking the planet. Massive dovin basals actually shifted Coruscant's orbit, bringing it closer to its sun. Its temperature rose, and more moisture was released into the atmosphere. Coruscant's three smaller moons were steered away while the largest was pulverized by tidal stress created by pulses from other yammosk-linked dovin basals. A refined appplication of similar techniques organized the resultant mass of dust and gravel and lumps of hardening magma into a thick spreading ring-disk of rubble that rotated around the planet at an angle 17 degrees from the ecliptic. The planet's surface became overgrown by organic vegetation and living forms, slowly digesting the millennia of construction that had enveloped the world.

*The planet's surface became overgrown with organic vegetation and living forms due to Yuuzhan Vong "Vongforming."*

After the defeat of the Yuuzhan Vong, an extensive effort to reclaim the world from the alien infestation met with mixed success. Some of the Yuuzhan Vong changes were simply too deeply rooted to remove. In the time of Emperor Roan Fel and Darth Krayt, over a century after the Battle of Endor, there remained vestiges of organic growth intermingled with the endless edifices across the planet's surface.

**Coruscant, Battle of** Though history records a number of conflicts with this title, the one most often referenced was the astonishingly brazen attack mounted by the Separatists on the Republic capital world during the final stages of the Clone Wars. The fierce attack was a cover for General Grievous's daring kidnapping of Supreme Chancellor Palpatine. In the upper atmosphere of the city-planet, starships from the Republic's Fifth Fleet tangled with Confederacy vessels while Grievous returned from the planet's surface to his flagship, *Invisible Hand,* with his highly prized hostage. Rampant signal jamming from Separatist vessels sowed confusion among the enmeshed fleets. Two Jedi heroes, Anakin Skywalker and Obi-Wan Kenobi, infiltrated the *Invisible Hand* and rescued the Chancellor, killing Count Dooku in the process. Though the Confederacy was defeated in this battle, General Grievous escaped to the Outer Rim, and the Clone Wars continued for a while longer.

***Coruscant*-class heavy courier** An ancient multisectioned design from Corellia StarDrive, this model of starship included the *Nebulon Ranger* used by Jedi Knights Ulic Qel-Droma, his brother Cay, and Tott Doneeta.

Coruscant Guard

**Coruscant firefighter** Rescue operation teams working for the various Coruscant civic districts, they were typically equipped with protective suits, helmets, and fire-suppression gear.

**Coruscant Guard** A general term used with varying degrees of accuracy for government security units tasked with protecting highly placed institutions on the galactic capital world. The shock troopers of the clone army serving under Commander Fox during the Clone Wars were dubbed the Coruscant Guard, as were the blue-suited Senate Guards, and the red-robed Royal Guard that would replace them. More formally, the Coruscant

Guard were the red-armored elite stormtrooper police units that patrolled Imperial Center and other Core Worlds during the height of Palpatine's reign.

**Coruscant Ministry of Ingress (CMoI)** The Galactic Republic government agency that administered immigration to the planet Coruscant. Prior to the Clone Wars, the CMoI had to severely restrict offworld access to Coruscant to deal with security and overcrowding issues spurred by the Separatist crisis.

**Coruscant Opera House** A prestigious opera house that was a marvel of pre-Republic baroque, all frosting and embellishment, with an old-fashioned orchestra pit, tiered seating, and private balconies in the time-honored design. As a nod to Coruscant's citizens, there was even a warren of lower-level galleries where everyday citizens could view the performance via real-time hologram and pretend to be hobnobbing with stars seated overhead. It accommodated an audience of 2,000. It was a long-favored venue visited by the Valorum family, though Palpatine preferred the more modern Galaxies Opera House.

**Coruscant Park** An open greenway not far from the Jedi Temple, it was often frequented by Jedi Masters training their Padawan students.

**Coruscant Prime** The blue-white star at the center of the Coruscant system.

**Coruscant Security Force (CSF)** The military patrol that enforced safety and order in Coruscant's web of traffic skylanes during the time of the Galactic Republic, and decades later during the Galactic Alliance.

**Coruscant star of valor** A New Republic medal of honor commemorating the liberation of Coruscant from Imperial control.

**Coruscant system** The star system containing the galactic capital world of Coruscant, in orbit around the blue-white primary, Coruscant Prime. In order of orbit, moving outward from the primary, were the molten rock world Revisse, the barren rock worlds of Platoril, and Vandor-1, -2, and -3. Coruscant was next, with the gas giants Muscave and Stentat followed by the ice ball Improcco. The next orbit was occupied by an asteroid field called the Covey, and then the lifeless frozen worlds of Nabatu and Ulabos. Finally, the Obo Rin comet cluster made up the outer limits of the system.

**Coruscant taxi** *See* air taxi.

**Coruscant Weather Control Network** Also known as WeatherNet, the agency tasked with modulating the weather of Coruscant. It used a variety of environmental control systems to help disperse inclement microclimes that developed often in the planetwide urban environment. Most of WeatherNet's infrastructure was destroyed by the Yuuzhan Vong invasion of the planet.

***Corusca Rainbow*** Formerly the *Black Asp*, this 600-meter-long Imperial Interdictor cruiser was once involved in a skirmish with Rogue Squadron at Chorax as it attempted to capture the *Pulsar Skate*. With its mass generators, the *Black Asp* under the command of Uwlla Iillor pulled the squadron out of hyperspace as it was headed for a new base at Talasea. A fast and furious battle ensued, with Rogue Squadron putting the cruiser to flight.

The ship was renamed *Corusca Rainbow* after the defection of its captain and crew to the Rebel Alliance. It was given a place of extreme importance when it led the invasion fleet to liberate the capital world of Coruscant. During the war against the Yuuzhan Vong, it took part in the Battle of Ithor.

**Corvis** A member of Talon Karrde's crew, he served as a gunner aboard the *Wild Karrde*.

**Corvis Minor** A yellow star orbited by seven planets, three outside an asteroid ring that marked the halfway point between the system's outer edges and the star at its hub. The third and fourth planets of the Corvis Minor system were inhabited. The third was a semi-arid world with temperate zones at the poles, the fourth, a water-rich tropical world. Both produced some exotic exobiological products that sold as luxury commodities within the Ciutric Hegemony. Rogue Squadron once went on a mission to Distna, a moon of the fifth planet of the system.

**Cosmic Balance** The predominant faith of the people of Bakura. The religion originated on Hemei IV. This form of extreme dualism held the primary belief that for every rise in power there was a corresponding decline elsewhere. The followers of the Cosmic Balance opposed the Jedi Knights in earlier times, claiming that a Jedi's increased abilities diminished someone else in another part of the galaxy. When Emperor Palpatine began the persecution of the Jedi, Cosmic Balance adherents felt that the action was timely and well deserved. The faith's sacred text, the Fulcrum, outlined its chief tenets, including the belief that in the afterlife all inequities would be redressed.

**Cosmic Egg** A deity of the Kitonak people as well as a religious icon among the Nediji.

**Cosmic Turbine** The instrument of destruction behind the Vultar Cataclysm, 4,250 years before the Battle of Yavin. After a civil war among the Jedi ranks, fleeing dark siders uncovered ancient alien technology possibly responsible for the creation of the Vultar system. Among the devices was a powerful device dubbed the Cosmic Turbine. The dark siders were unable to control this technology, and they annihilated themselves.

**Cothron, Lieutenant** An Imperial officer and angry drunk stationed at the garrison on the planet Hullis, he was taken prisoner by Wraith Squadron during their mission to steal TIE interceptors.

**Cotin** A Corellian dissident arrested by the Galactic Alliance Guard alongside Ailyn Habuur.

**coufee** A crude but effective double-edged knife used by the Yuuzhan Vong.

**Council of Elders, Alderaanian** The ruling body of Alderaan that decided upon the planet's return to pacificism after the Clone Wars.

**Council of Elders, Borokii** The ruling body of the Borokii clan on Ansion, made up of 12 elders of both genders. During the Ansion border dispute prior to the Clone Wars, the council agreed to help the Jedi in return for the Jedi dealing with the Januul clan.

**Council of Elders, Cerean** A group of venerable and well-respected Cereans who ruled their homeworld. The Elders created and upheld Cerean law, and although they allowed open forums to discuss any major decisions, their word was final.

**Council of Elders, Ewok** The ruling body of Chief Chirpa's tribe in Bright Tree Village, it voted to allow the leaders of the Rebel Alliance strike team to become members of the tribe.

**Council of Elders, Ithorian** A governing body for the nomadic Ithorian people following the devastation of their home planet by the Yuuzhan Vong.

**Council of Families** The primary legislative body of the Chiss government, formed from representatives of the Ruling Families. It was given certain judicial responsibilities as a way to govern the activities of individuals and families, ensuring that each family remained on equal footing with the others.

**Council of First Knowledge** One of the Jedi Councils—in addition to the Jedi High Council—based at the Jedi Temple on Coruscant. It advised the Order on matters requiring the ancient wisdom of past Jedi. This council convened in the northwest tower of the Temple.

**Council of Reconciliation** One of the Jedi Councils operating from the Jedi Temple on Coruscant, it concerned itself with relief efforts for worlds ravaged by natural disasters or conflict. It consisted of five rotating Jedi Masters and operated out of the southeastern tower of the Jedi Temple.

**Council of Separatists** *See* Separatist Council.

**Council on Security and Intelligence** An ultrasecretive New Republic Senatorial group that met in a shielded room deep below the Imperial Palace, and controlled the clandestine intelligence agency Alpha Blue. It was later replaced by the Security and Intelligence Council of the Galactic Alliance.

**Council Rock** A sheer, cliff-like pillar of volcanic basalt stone located on Kashyyyk. Wookiees held their governmental meetings there.

**counterpart** In mechanicals and automata, the term *counterpart* refered to a special relationship between two intelligent machines. Counterpart operation meant that the joint operation of two (or more) automata increased the efficiency of each to some degree. A true counterpart relationship involved an almost instantaneous exchange of information between the parties, and the link between the two was inseparable. This sometimes happened with droid–computer interfaces, but the computer was not able to communicate with any other droid. That was why memory wipes were required. R2-D2 eventually developed a counterpart relationship with Luke Skywalker's X-wing fighter.

*The Covenant*

**Counts of Serenno** The collective term for the noble houses that made up the leadership of the planet Serenno. The Counts of Serenno were believed to have been among the wealthiest and most influential beings in the galaxy for millennia. They were strongly independent, too. The Counts attempted to remain neutral in the polarizing debate regarding the Ruusan Reformations, until Chancellor Tarsus Valorum was nearly assassinated while visiting Serenno. The Counts then rallied around the words of Count Nalju, pledging their financial and political support to eradicate separatism on their planet. A thousand years later, Count Dooku became another contentious Serenno noble advocating secession from the Galactic Republic.

***Courage*** A *Thranta*-class warship slaved to the *Another Chance* to protect it from being taken by hostile forces. Like its companions, the *Fidelity* and *Valiant,* it accompanied *Another Chance* as it jumped through hyperspace to avoid detection.

***Courage*** A Skipray blastboat owned by the Jedi praxeum on Yavin 4. Luke Skywalker and Jacen Solo flew it to Belkadan during the early stages of the Yuuzhan Vong invasion.

***Courage of Sullust*** A Rebel transport that was reconfigured to carry spacecraft, it went to the planet Ryloth on a secret mission with 10 X-wings from Rogue Squadron. When the *Courage of Sullust* returned to Coruscant, it was loaded with ryll kor, an addictive spice that was to be used in a top-secret project by Alliance Intelligence.

***Courageous* (1)** One of six *Inexpungable*-class tactical command ships in the Galactic Republic fleet during the Mandalorian Wars. The ship's spacious bridge featured innovative tactical display solutions that allowed a fleet commander effective control over up to 64 cruisers. Admiral Saul Karath commanded the *Courageous* at engagements over Taris and Vanquo, but was forced to abandon and scuttle the ship when Mandalorians captured it at Serroco.

***Courageous* (2)** A Galactic Republic flagship commanded by Plo Koon that attempted to expel the Separatists from the Ywllandr system late in the Clone Wars.

**Couratalnes** Wobbly-skinned humanoids from a world with lighter-than-standard gravity, they had to travel in exosuits when in standard g. The suits also provided them with the thin atmosphere they needed for comfort.

**Courkrus** The fourth planet in the Khuiumin system, Courkrus was an outlaw world ruled by pirates. Corran Horn, going by the name Keiran Halcyon, broke down the pirates' confederation by using the pirates' fear against themselves.

***Courteous*** A Centrality cruiser, the first in a series of ships blockading the Starcave. When the Oswaft Elder Bhoggihalysahonues led a delegation to meet the Centrality blockade, the massive creatures "shouted" at the ship with their microwave communication. The strength and power of their voices destroyed the *Courteous,* signaling the start of a war between the Centrality and the Oswaft.

**Court of the Fountain** The closest that Mos Eisley came to having a high-class restaurant in the days when Jabba the Hutt held sway, this eatery was primarily a tourist trap owned by the gang lord. The Court of the Fountain was located in a stone-and-stucco palace and featured fountains and exotic plants. Jabba's personal chef, Porcellus, worked as head chef there on the rare occasions that Jabba didn't need him.

**Covell, General Freja** Although a fairly young man himself, this Imperial officer was placed in charge of the Empire's young and inexperienced ground troops by Grand Admiral Thrawn. The legendary General Veers saw Covell as a younger version of himself when he served as Veers's first officer during the Battle of Hoth. Captain Pellaeon promoted Covell to major general in charge of *Chimaera*'s ground troops after the Battle of Endor. Thrawn gave him the rank of general when he returned, and he immediately began training his troops for real battle. General Covell wanted to regain the Core Worlds, such as Coruscant, from the New Republic. But he never got to fulfill his dreams. General Covell died on the planet Wayland after the mad clone Jedi, Joruus C'baoth, destroyed his mind.

**Covenant, the** A secret enclave of Jedi Knights formed by Lady Kryndа Draay, active 4,000 years before the Battle of Yavin. These talented seers were devoted to stopping any hint of a Sith uprising following the devastation of the Great Sith War. Their members included Lucien Draay, Krynda's son; Q'Anilia, a Miralukan seer; Xanar, a Khil; Raana Tey, a Togruta; and Feln, a Feeorin. The vast Draay fortune was funneled through numerous fronts and investments in preparation for defense of the galaxy. Covenant members became the ranking Jedi Masters on Taris, where they experienced visions of one of their students somehow bringing about the scourge of the Jedi. As a preventive measure, the Covenant killed all of the graduating Padawans, but one resourceful student, Zayne Carrick, escaped.

**covert shroud maneuver** A clever tractor beam escape maneuver, it involved a targeted decoy starship carrying an escape craft. When a tractor beam locked on to the larger vessel, it came apart in a cloud of reflective chaff, confounding the tractor beam lock and allowing the smaller vessel to escape.

**Covis, Spane** A Rebel officer, he was the SpecForce Sentinel on Nar Shaddaa who first noticed the arrival of Imperial troops and thwarted the element of surprise in their attack.

**Cov-Prim, Alexis** A star of several Imperial holovids, she was famous at the height of the New Order.

**Cowall, Tetran** An actor who was Garik Loran's chief rival in the entertainment industry and in piloting. Cowall's popularity waned as he grew older, and he joined Imperial service as a pilot. He was in command of a TIE interceptor and TIE Raptor squadron in service to Warlord Zsinj.

**Coway** An underground-dwelling species of humanoids, they inhabited Circarpous V, or Mimban. The Coway were two-legged and

*Coway*

covered by a fine gray down. They intensely disliked surface dwellers. Near-bottomless shafts built by the extinct Thrella had side passages called Coway shafts, which led to the Coways' underground world. One particular Coway shaft, lit by a type of luminous fungi, contained a vast subterranean lake that the Coway crossed on large lily pads. The lake housed a dangerous, amorphous pseudopod creature; an abandoned Thrella city was located on the lake's far edge. This shaft's 200 Coway lived in a primitive village built in a huge natural amphitheater. Their tribes were ruled by a triumvirate of leaders, who appealed to their god Canu for judgment on important matters.

**cowill** Well-armored crustaceans native to Mon Calamari, their shells were the basis of the shields used by the Mon Calamari Knights.

**Cowl Crucible** An astronavigational hazard, this nebula was located on the edge of the Lahara sector, on its border with the Oricho sector.

**Coy, Admiral** The commander of the Imperial Star Destroyer *Mathayus,* he questioned Darth Vader about the use of the Star Destroyer for a mission to hunt down a single fugitive. Vader, angered, responded by choking the admiral, bringing him to his knees. Admiral Coy was murdered by one of his second officers, Dezsetes, who was part of a plot to assassinate the Emperor and Lord Vader.

**Coynite** A tall, heavily muscled species of bipeds native to the planet Coyn, they were natural-born warriors with a highly disciplined code of warfare.

**CR20, CR25 Republic troop carrier** Smaller than an Acclamator but larger than a gunship, the CR20 was a Corellian Engineering Corporation troop transport used by the Republic during the Clone Wars. Originally designed for Corellian sector security forces, the CR20 could hold up to 40 clone troopers and 12 speeder bikes; it required a crew of two pilots, a comm officer, and three engineers. The follow-up vessel, the CR25, had expanded cargo space to allow for up to eight LAAT/i gunships.

*CR20 Republic troop carrier*

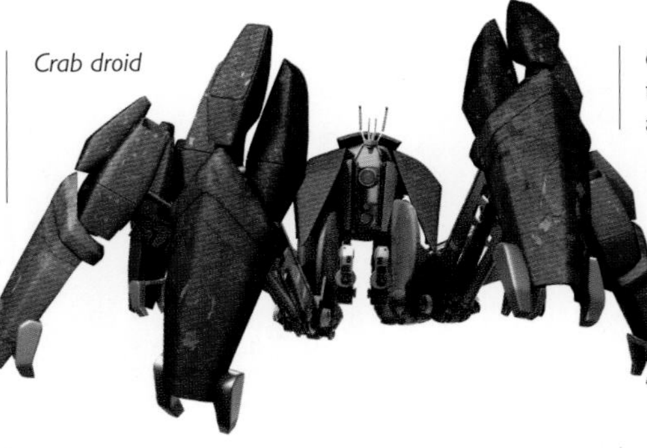

*Crab droid*

**crab-boy** A derogatory nickname coined by the Mandalorians to describe a Yuuzhan Vong warrior.

**Crab, Finious** A less-than-reputable trader who purchased the *Lambarian Crab* YT-2400 freighter. Believing himself to be a competent mechanic, Crab tore out redundant systems and installed his own weapons array. He also tore out safety backups in order to feed more power to the heavy double laser cannon he installed. Finious's skills, however, were sorely lacking; on a run to Eriadu the life support systems failed. When the *Lambarian Crab* was finally discovered floating in space, Crab was a desiccated corpse.

**crab droid** Also known as the LM-432 Muckracker, this was a versatile battle droid design used by the Confederacy of Independent Systems during the Clone Wars. Its scrabbling legs offered it speed, agility, and the ability to climb over uneven terrain and even up craggy surfaces. The modular Techno Union forges churned out Muckrackers in varying scales, but with essentially the same design. Gargantuan units were used as mobile armor, while tiny models were used as spies. The most commonly encountered were midsized heavy infantry models.

All Muckrackers came with armorplast shielding that could deflect glancing blaster strikes. The largest of its legs came tipped with heavy duranium stabilizers that could ax into bedrock to secure a stable hold. Crab droids were first introduced to the battlefield in marshy environments and were equipped with a vacuum pump system built into their forward pincers that could slurp up restrictive lakebed mud and then spit it out in an effort to clear the terrain and obscure the visual sensors of its targets. Some rare models had variant Gungan bubble wort projectors that could trap their targets in temporary force shields.

On Utapau, midsized crab droids served as a deadly threat against the clone troopers of General Obi-Wan Kenobi's attack battalions, though brave soldiers able to outrun the targeting sensors found weak spots behind the forward armor that could be exploited.

*General Airen Cracken*

**crab-harp** Crustaceans bioengineered by the Yuuzhan Vong for the sound they made as they moved their many legs together, they were often set loose during ceremonies to provide a form of background music.

**Cracian thumper** A pack animal used as a mount in Rebel Alliance scout parties, it got its name from the sound it *should* have made. Native to the five planets of the Craci system, these shaggy bipeds had long necks, long tails, and were quite agile and surprisingly silent. In combat, the thumper used its foreclaws and whip-like tail.

**Cracken, General Airen** The head of Alliance Intelligence, Cracken served as a gunner aboard the *Millennium Falcon* during the Battle of Endor. Later he was placed in charge of Rogue Squadron's mission to Coruscant in advance of the invasion fleet. His agents were already on the planet to assist the squadron as necessary, and because his son was part of that group, he had a firm grasp of the situation. The general was aware that there was a spy within Rogue Squadron, but he knew that it was not Tycho Celchu, whom others suspected of killing Rogue hero Corran Horn. He allowed Captain Celchu's trial to proceed so that Director of Imperial Intelligence Ysanne Isard would continue to use her spy, thinking that the New Republic was convinced of the charges against Celchu. While her attention was occupied by the trial, Alliance Intelligence was able to accomplish several vital operations that might otherwise have been compromised.

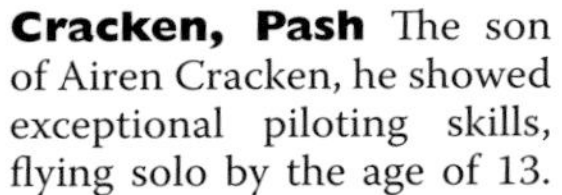

**Cracken, Pash** The son of Airen Cracken, he showed exceptional piloting skills, flying solo by the age of 13. The elder Cracken encouraged young Pash to enroll at the Imperial Academy on Vensenor. The Sector Academy campus had long been a fertile recruiting ground for the Rebellion. Airen Cracken provided his son with a false identity to pursue his education free from Imperial attention.

While Pash Cracken was already an amazing pilot, he proved to be an exceptional tactician as well. His plans were unorthodox and often reckless, but in repeated combat simulations, they were unbeatable. Pash also became a capable leader. He graduated in the top 1 percent of his class and was immediately commissioned into the Imperial Navy, where he served as a wing commander. He and his entire wing of 72 starfighters defected to the Rebel Alliance.

Pash's group was dubbed the Cracken Flight Group, and was stationed at the Alliance base in the Xyquine system. Cracken's pilots distinguished themselves in hit-and-run raids against Imperial shipments. When Xyquine had to be abandoned, Cracken came up with the ingeniously simple tactic of feeding disinformation to eavesdropping

Imperials that misdirected Imperial blockades attempting to stop the fleeing Rebels. Pash's tactic of subtracting the number two from the second digit of the transmitted exit vector coordinates was dubbed "the Cracken Twist."

Shortly after the Battle of Endor, the Cracken Flight Group was reassigned to the Generis system in the Atrivis sector, where it served in the protection of the Outer Rim comm center. When Rogue Squadron announced that it was seeking pilots to fill vacancies, Captain Cracken applied, leaving stewardship of his group to Wing Commander Varth. On his very first mission as a Rogue, he was instrumental in bringing down the forward and aft shields and disabling the *Vengeance,* the Star Destroyer that was being used for the assault on the Rebels on Nar Shaddaa. He assisted in the removal of Black Sun extremists from Kessel before being sent undercover to Coruscant. Cracken assisted the Rogues in their gambit to drop the shields protecting Coruscant from New Republic attack.

Once Coruscant was firmly controlled by the New Republic, Cracken returned to Generis to resume command of his group. During Grand Admiral Thrawn's campaign against the New Republic, the Outer Rim comm center fell to Imperial attack.

Pash Cracken continued to serve the New Republic military in the years that followed. In the years of fighting the Yuuzhan Vong, combat attrition saw him achieve an acting rank of general from his official rank of major. As part of General Wedge Antilles's battle group at Bilbringi, Cracken commanded the capital warship *Memory of Ithor.* That massive vessel fell to Yuuzhan Vong forces, and Cracken was captured and held prisoner on Selvaris before being rescued by Galactic Alliance forces.

**Crado** A Cathar Jedi who lived 4,000 years before the Battle of Yavin, this feline being was apprenticed to Master Vodo-Siosk Baas. He was the lover of Sylvar, also from the planet Cathar. Crado became a devoted follower of Exar Kun, who turned to the dark side of the Force. Crado was killed along with dark sider Aleema in a multiple supernova eruption that they triggered.

**Cradossk** Bossk's father and the head of the Bounty Hunters' Guild, this cunning and aged Trandoshan was responsible for assigning missions to various bounty hunters. For missions that required the capture or elimination of rogue guild members, Cradossk was known to hire outsiders, such as Aurra Sing, who had no connections to the Bounty Hunters' Guild.

A year before the Battle of Geonosis, Cradossk and Bossk were hired by Wat Tambor to track down Senator Rodd, Groodo the Hutt, and Hurlo Holowan. The hunt led from Fondor to Esseles, with run-ins with Jango and Boba Fett along the way.

Decades later, Cradossk allowed Boba Fett to join the guild, eager to get a cut of Fett's hefty fees. Bossk strongly disagreed with the decision, knowing that Fett would only disrupt things. Enraged, Bossk challenged his father, killing and devouring him. Instead of unifying the guild, this rash move split it into two factions.

**Cragmoloid** These large bipeds with leathery skin, horns, and tiny red beady eyes were from the plains of Ankus, a planet on the borders of the Unknown Regions near Ord Mantell.

**Cranna, Bhu, and Goq** Sorrusians who met Obi-Wan Kenobi and Astri Oddo during the search for bounty hunter Ona Nobis. Goq was the leader of a tribe of Sorrusians subsisting in the harsh environment of the Arra Desert. Goq's son, Bhu, was skeptical of Astri at first, but she offered valuable tips on harvesting food, and in exchange the grateful Goq supplied helpful information about Ona.

**Cranscoc** An insectoid alien species native to Cartao. A subset of their number—called twillers—controlled the unusual fluid technology that made Spaarti Creations a unique and profitable business.

**crash wagon** An emergency vehicle kept on site at spaceports, it was equipped with firefighting apparatus, metal-cutting tools, and some medical gear to deal with crashed vessels.

**cratsch** A tree-dwelling creature that stalked the Bakuran forests.

**Cravus, Lord** An ancient warlord early in the history of the planet Esseles.

**Craw, Dictator-Forever** The tyrannical ruler of Targonn, he reigned from his palace behind an impenetrable force field. Craw imposed a 99 percent tax rate on his subjects and forced their children to toil in factories before they were six. He planned to uncover the secret of the savorium herb, a potent ingredient that turned people into happy slaves called "smilers." Craw's forces were defeated by the efforts of Targonnian revolutionaries along with the help of Master Zorneth and his droids, R2-D2 and C-3PO.

*Crado*

**crawl-carrier** An experimental espionage and infiltration droid developed by the Confederacy of Independent Systems during the Clone Wars. Crawl-carriers would enter into otherwise inaccessible urban locations and release a payload of acid to destroy key structural assets. The droid itself was destroyed in the process. Obi-Wan Kenobi and Anakin Skywalker destroyed the key crawl-carrier development facility on Drago before this droid could be widely deployed.

**crawler** A generic term for any treaded or large-wheeled transport.

**crawlfish** A creature native to Yavin 4. Crawlfish lived in the many spring-fed pools on the jungle moon. These amphibians grew to between 60 and 140 centimeters in length, and made a tasty meal.

**CRC-09/571** The clone trooper commander assigned to locate Mace Windu on Haruun Kal and assist in his extraction during the Clone Wars, he had been a battalion commander at Geonosis and on Teyr before his promotion to regimental commander. CRC-09/571 was killed by warlord Kar Vastor.

**Creative Surgery** The name of a clinic operated by Dr. Evazan on numerous worlds. This twisted fugitive would slice and graft skin indiscriminately, or in a sick and deranged manner. Many unwary patients were maimed or mutilated at the hands and scalpels of Evazan.

***Crèche*** A Yuuzhan Vong clustership designed to nurture and carry a developing yammosk, it was under the command of Chine-Kal during the invasion of the galaxy. Prisoners of war captured at Gyndine, including Jedi Knight Wurth Skidder, fed the yammosk with their life energies. The *Crèche* was repeatedly hounded by Kyp Durron's starfighter squadron, Kyp's Dozen, resulting in the ship sustaining extensive damage at Fondor. Ganner Rhysode, rescued by Kyp, slew the yammosk with his lightsaber, leading to the death of the ship.

**credit** The basic monetary unit throughout the galaxy. Based on the Old Republic credit, the unit remained in use, although both the Galactic Alliance and the Empire produced their own currency. Most credits were stored and exchanged via computer transactions, but there was credit currency that could be carried and physically exchanged.

**Cree'Ar, Dr. Dassid** A Duros alias adopted by Yuuzhan Vong infiltrator Nom Anor, Cree'Ar was a plant geneticist who worked on the Duros reclamation project. Mara Jade Skywalker and Jaina Solo encountered Cree'Ar and immediately suspected him of wrongdoing when they were unable to sense him in the Force. Nom Anor wore a gablith masquer that allowed him to appear as a nonhuman alien.

**Creed, the** A popular and benign Tarrick cult, it was founded on the twin principles of joy and service.

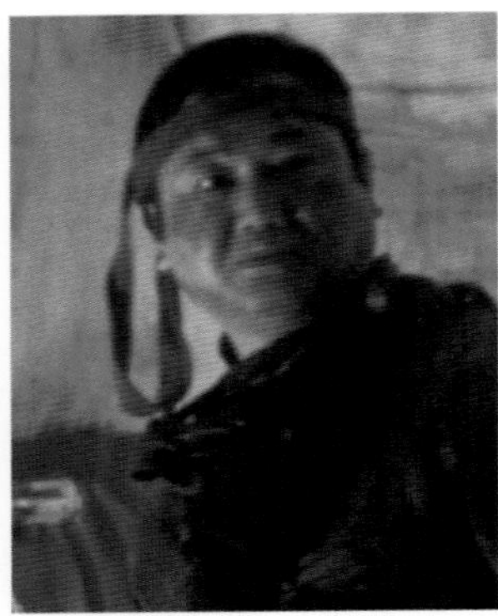
Ardon "Vapor" Crell

**Creel, Pleader Iving** A famous pleader, he defended Journeyman Protector Jaster Mereel in his trial for killing another protector on Concord Dawn. After pleading unrepentant, Mereel was exiled from his homeworld.

**creeper** A small, 10-limbed Yuuzhan Vong engineered creature constructed to implant young yorik coral buds into the bodies of slave-hosts. Six of its limbs served as legs. Two of the other four were quite thin and ended in fronds that could induce pain when they touched flesh; the remaining two were heavy and ended in sharp pincers. The top of a creeper's body was soft, and was used to carry young yorik coral buds. Three compound eyes sat atop a thick central stalk, which could move around to allow the creature to see.

**Crell, Ardon "Vapor"** A moisture farmer who was elected by his peers to serve as a liaison between the Moisture Farmers of Tatooine (Local 253) and Jabba the Hutt. The farmers agreed to pay Jabba in exchange for protection from Tusken Raiders. Crell was responsible for collecting and delivering this protection money.

**Crème D'Infame** A nearly priceless wine produced during the Galactic Republic.

**Cremlevian War** A legendary war fought early in Yuuzhan Vong history between the two most powerful tribes of this alien culture. Warmaster Steng eventually lost to Warmaster Yo'Gand, who used a powerful dovin basal to destroy the planet Ygziir in a tactic that has become known as Yo'Gand's Core.

**Crespin, General Edor** A New Republic officer from Corulag who commanded the fighter-training base on the moon of Folor. He was the leader of the A-wings designated Blue Squadron in the battle against the Star Destroyer *Implacable.*

**Cressa, Supreme Chancellor** A legendary leader of the Galactic Senate who took steps to repair the devastated infrastructure of Republic worlds following the First and Second Sith Wars. The chief architects of this reconstruction were G0-T0 planning droids.

**Creterk, Rievale** A flight attendant, she witnessed and was injured in a brawl between Houks and Weequays at Eastport on Coruscant just prior to the Clone Wars.

**Crevasse City** A sinkhole city once found on Alderaan. A similar city of the same name existed on Kalkovak.

**Creysis** An Ebruchi in command of the first inhabited planet discovered by Admiral Thrawn during his exile in the Unknown Regions, he attempted to force the Empire to hand over technology to assist the Ebruchi in developing their space fleet. Thrawn refused, and Creysis captured a number of Imperial personnel, including Commander Parck, as hostages. Thrawn had removed the sought-after technological components from the captured vessels, and after the Imperials escaped, he had the Star Destroyer *Admonitor* destroy Creysis and his forces.

**Crimmins** A Rebel combat specialist who escaped the Battle of Hoth aboard the transport *Bright Hope.*

**Crimpler** A deserter from the Hapan Navy and a kickboxer, he was loosely affiliated with the anti-Jedi Ni'Korish faction. Crimpler was part of the attempted (and failed) pirate attack on Tenel Ka's escape pod above Hapes. He was imprisoned for his role in the incident. Jaina Solo—with the help of Ta'a Chume and Kyp Durron—had him released from prison and taken to Gallinore. There scientist Sinsor Khal removed the Yuuzhan Vong implant from Crimpler's neck for experimentation, badly injuring him. The implant needed reinserting, but Jaina and Kyp erased Crimpler's memories to keep him from remaining a threat.

***Crimson Axe*** Formerly the starship used by the Feeorin bounty hunter Rav, it became his landlocked base of operations on Socorro a century after the Yuuzhan Vong invasion, during the time of Emperor Roan Fel. It was buried near Sarlacc's Peak, in the Killee Wastelands of the black sands planet.

**Crimson Corridor** Located in the Third Quadrant of Coruscant's Zi-Kree Sector, this was one of the oldest areas of the vast planetary city rife with gangs, criminals, street predators, and other dangers. It was less than 10 kilometers away from the Jedi Temple.

Crimson Jack

**Crimson Jack** A red-bearded pirate who had several run-ins with Han Solo. Crimson Jack operated a captured Imperial Star Destroyer. Jack robbed Solo of his reward money immediately after the Battle of Yavin, and later died in a duel with Han over the Drexel system.

**Crimson Nova** A chapter of the Bounty Hunters' Guild under the leadership of Mika that decided to collect bounties placed on the heads of Jedi during the Clone Wars. Following a Crimson Nova attack on a Jedi triage unit on Null, Mace Windu led a small team of Jedi in a strike against the hunters' headquarters at the station known as the Rig. Mika's daughter, Breela, eventually became the head of the chapter. Boushh and Zuckuss were part of a Crimson Nova team led by Breela that went after Kai Justiss.

**Crion** The father of Xanatos, he was devastated by the thought of giving up his son, but realized that training to become a Jedi would be a great opportunity for the child. Xanatos proved an eager and skilled student, but he often flaunted his high birth in an attempt to impress the other students at the Jedi Temple. Qui-Gon Jinn frequently overlooked the boy's flaws and continued to train him until Yoda sent the pair to Telos for a final mission together. Upon returning to his homeworld, Xanatos was reunited with his father. Crion begged Xanatos to aid him in a bid for power. Xanatos ultimately agreed, and Crion instigated a devastating civil war. Qui-Gon later killed Crion and was subsequently attacked by Xanatos, who had witnessed his father's death.

**croaker bush** A large-leafed plant native to Drongar named for the sound it made when the waxy leaves rustled against one another in a breeze.

**Crockagor** A reptilian combatant in the Rattatak gladiator arena during the Clone Wars.

**crodium** A precious metal mined on Terephon, used to give a luxurious plated finish to other metals.

**Croke** A small, oily black snail-like species with a vicious nature and a penchant for illusion.

**Cronal** *See* Blackhole.

**Cronau radiation event** An electromagnetic phenomenon that served as an indication that a ship was returning to realspace after traveling through hyperspace.

**Crondre** During a multipronged attack by Grand Admiral Thrawn, whose true target was Ukio, this was a site of a diversionary battle. The Star Destroyer *Nemesis* took part in the fight.

**Croke** A small, oily black snail-like species with a vicious nature and a penchant for illusion.

**Cronal** *See* Blackhole.

**Cronau radiation event** An electromagnetic phenomenon that serves as an indication that a ship is returning to realspace after traveling through hyperspace.

**Crondre** During a multipronged attack by Grand Admiral Thrawn, whose true target was Ukio, this was a site of a diversionary battle. The Star Destroyer *Nemesis* took part in the fight.

**Cron Drift** Located in the Auril sector of the Outer Rim, the drift was once a densely packed group of 10 unstable stars known as the Cron Cluster. During the Sith War, a Sith ship piloted by dark siders Aleema Keto and Crado lured a pursuing Jedi force into the cluster. Aleema activated an ancient Sith weapon and ripped the core from one of the stars, hurling it at the Jedi fleet and destroying it. This set off a chain reaction that ignited all 10 stars in a multiple supernova, instantly killing Aleema and Crado. The shock wave from the explosion destroyed three of the nine Auril systems and necessitated the evacuation of the great Jedi planet of Ossus. Multicolored gases from the multiple explosions filled the area for millennia, and powerful X-rays and gamma radiation helped mask any visiting ships from sensor probes. The drift also contained a large asteroid belt. Rebel Alliance listening post Ax-235, hidden within the belt, intercepted what appeared to be the Death Star technical plans and relayed them to Alliance High Command prior to the Battle of Yavin. Around the same time, a Rebel formation was ambushed by assault gunboats in the asteroid field, but was rescued by X-wing fighters.

**Cronus, Colonel** A small but powerful man, he was a second-ranking Imperial officer when he decided to join forces with Admiral Daala. The colonel was in his flagship, *Victory,* when it was destroyed by a Corellian gunship.

**Crooked-Tail** A powerfully built Dulok with blue-gray fur who failed in his bid to usurp King Vulgarr.

**Crossings, the** A term used by the Ferroans to describe the hyperspace jumps undertaken by the living planet Zonama Sekot. Early Crossings were very hazardous to the life-forms on the planet, but eventually Zonama Sekot learned to adapt to the rigors of lightspeed travel.

**Crote, Senator** The galactic representative of Frego over a decade before the Battle of Naboo, he was found complicit in the illegal activities of the Cobral crime family.

**Crowal, Moff** A member of the Moff Council of the Imperial Remnant, she represented Valc VII and was opposed to helping the New Republic during the invasion of the Yuuzhan Vong. When the alien menace attacked Bastion and Muunilinst, she reversed her position, and later helpfully provided Luke Skywalker with all the intelligence the Empire had gathered concerning the living planet Zonama Sekot. She even assigned one of her leading xenoarchaeologists, Dr. Soron Hegerty, to assist Skywalker.

**crowlyn** A small, wide-jawed creature domesticated by the natives of Ansion.

**Crseih Research Station** Also known as Asylum Station, this artificial planetoid was a former Imperial research station and outlaw outpost formed by a cluster of asteroids joined by gravity fields and connecting airlink tunnels. Crseih had been a secret Empire research facility and was used by Lord Hethrir, the former Imperial Procurator of Justice, as his headquarters and a prison for his enemies. The station orbited a black hole with a white dwarf star and was bombarded with X-rays. An enigmatic being called Waru created a cult on Crseih with his healing abilities until he apparently disappeared from this universe following a confrontation with Luke Skywalker. Crseih Station was then moved to Munto Codru to escape inevitable destruction when the crystallizing white dwarf was swallowed by the black hole.

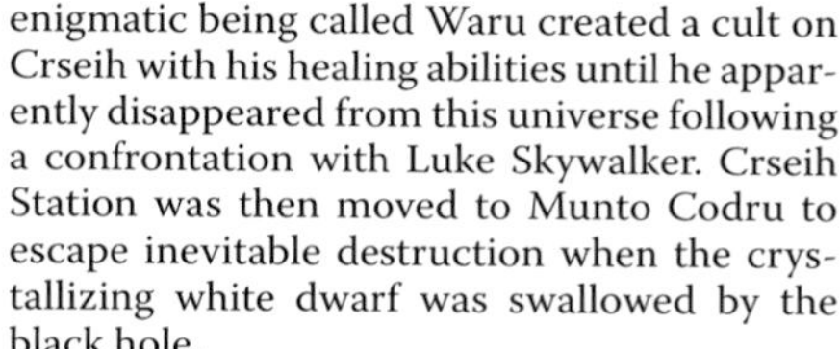

*Arvel Crynyd*

**crude** A powerful narcotic that was popular on the black market during the last years of the Galactic Republic.

**Crumb, Salacious B.** This Kowakian monkey-lizard held a favored position at the court of Jabba the Hutt, usually sitting close to the bloated crime lord. When Jabba spilled food and drink, Salacious Crumb made sure he was close enough to catch it for himself. Scrawny and less than a meter high, reddish brown in color and known for his taunting cackle and mimicry, Salacious was Jabba's court jester. He got the job accidentally: After escaping from pursuers on Jabba's spaceship, he hid in the Hutt's personal quarters, eating his food. When Jabba discovered Salacious, he tried to eat him, but the creature escaped. His antics amused Jabba, who hired Salacious to make him laugh. He did so every day—up to the day he perished with Jabba when Rebel prisoners escaped and blew up the Hutt's sail barge.

*Salacious B. Crumb*

***Crusader*** Along with *Bombard,* this was one of the two *Victory*-class Star Destroyers that the Empire deployed to eradicate the Eyttyrmin Batiiv pirates.

**Crustai** A remote asteroid-like planetoid within Chiss space. The Chiss Expansionary Defense Fleet established a base of operations there, which served as an advance position against the threat of attack from other species in the Unknown Regions.

**Cryalina** This Tarasin female was a skilled hunter and served as the Irstat-Kes of the Hiironi tribe.

**Crying Room** A location within the Château Malreaux used by the wives of the Viscounts to bemoan their positions in life. It was filled with an array of surveillance devices, including specialized infrared swatches woven into the napkins and tablecloths.

***Crynyd*** An *Imperial*-class Star Destroyer captured, refitted, and renamed by the New Republic for a famed Alliance pilot, it was part of the fleet assigned to Han Solo and the *Mon Remonda* during the hunt for Warlord Zsinj. *Crynyd* was destroyed in battle with Imperial Warlord Teradoc.

**Crynyd, Arvel** The commander of Green Wing, one of the four main Rebel starfighter battle groups at the Battle of Endor, he and his group fired the last blaster salvo that caused the disabled Super Star Destroyer *Executor* to crash into the second Death Star. Crynyd then rammed his ship through the bridge of the Super Star Destroyer. His sacrifice resulted in the *Executor*'s destruction, thereby saving countless Rebel lives.

**CryoBan** A subzero gas that froze matter on contact, it was used as a canister payload in the CSPL projectile launcher. CryoBan grenades could also be thrown like standard grenades. The gas absorbed heat, thereby creating a blast radius of extreme cold. CryoBan broke down rapidly, releasing the heat back to the environment.

**cryo-cycle stasis** A medical technique that temporarily suspended bodily functions in an injured being. Freezing the patient's body led to a slowdown of physical functions, allowing doctors and surgeons more time to investigate a problem, or tend to needier patients. A patient could only be kept in cryostasis for a few hours before his or her body began to fail due to the effects of freezing.

**cryogen** A substance used in medical facilities to freeze cells and tissue samples for later use.

**cryogenic power cells** Shipboard power sources designed to store the energy created by the starship's reactor core.

**Cryptanalysis Department** This, the most offbeat, unprofessional branch of Imperial Intelligence, began as part of the Senate Bureau of Intelligence during the Clone Wars. It was created by Armand Isard to counter Separatist slicers and led by Ilko Deminar. During the time of the Empire, the Crypt (as it was known) was responsible for decoding any hidden or coded messages discovered by the Analysis Bureau. Agents in Crypt were known as lignyots, but what this term meant was unknown. Crypt constantly sent coded messages and mutating documents to other branches and bureaus in Imperial Intelligence, and often hid or changed the location of their branch offices with no information as to their new address, save an encrypted document. Intelligence allowed such unprofessional acts since it kept the other branches and bureaus alert and active.

**Crypt Master** A title given to Sullustans who maintained the burial vaults on their home planet and presided over mourning rituals.

**Crystal Cave** A cave atop one of Ilum's cliffs where Ilum crystals grew. The walls of the Crystal Cave were black stone as shiny as a mirror but that swallowed light instead of reflect it. Over the centuries, Jedi history was recorded on these walls. While in the cave, Jedi often saw visions of their deepest, darkest fears. As a Padawan, Anakin Skywalker experienced visions of his mother, Shmi, during his time in the cave. During the Clone Wars, a temple in the Crystal Cave was attacked by cloaked Confederacy mine-laying droids and defended by Luminara Unduli, Barriss Offee, and Yoda.

**crystal fern** Perhaps a primitive silicon-based life-form, this "plant" was found in the asteroid belt near Hoth. Several meters tall, the crystal propagated when shards were broken off and carried to other asteroids.

**crystal gravfield trap** Expensive sensors that utilized a synthetic crystal grid to detect gravitic field fluctuations. High-quality CGTs could detect and identify any fluctuation in the gravity field for hundreds of thousands of kilometers around. CGTs could be blocked or confused by the presence of mass. For example, a CGT could strongly register a nearby planet's gravitic presence, but might miss a ship in orbit on the other side of the planet.

**Crystal Jewel** The new name of the seedy casino on Coruscant where Han Solo won the deed to the planet Dathomir. Solo returned to the casino to meet a former smuggling contact, Jarill. The meeting led Solo to look into some strange occurrences in the asteroid belt known as Smuggler's Run.

**crystalline vertex** The currency used throughout the Corporate Sector to supplement Authority Cash Vouchers, it was made from a crystal mineral found on the planet Kir. When individuals entered the Corporate Sector, they had to exchange all other forms of currency for crystalline vertex or Authority Cash Vouchers.

*Crystal Cave*

**Crystal Moon** Widely regarded as the finest restaurant in Mos Eisley following the death of Jabba the Hutt, it was opened by Jabba's rancor keeper, Malakili, and his head chef, Porcellus.

**Crystal of Aantonaii** A great Sith artifact recovered and kept secretly by Emperor Palpatine.

**crystal oscillator** A standard part of the mechanics of some star cruisers. One was stolen from the wreck of a ship belonging to the Towani family on the Forest Moon of Endor. It was taken by an army of Sanyassan Marauders led by giant King Terak because he believed that the oscillator was the source of mysterious power.

**Crystal Reef** A floating resort city on the polar seas of Mon Calamari. Anja Gallandro landed at Crystal Reef while searching for a secret stash of spice hidden under the ice caps.

**crystal snake** A transparent reptile found on Yavin 4, its bites bought a moment of piercing pain and sent the victim into a deep sleep. Its dangerous qualities didn't prevent Jacen Solo from keeping one in his collection of pets.

**Csaplar** Csilla's capital city, the location of the ruling Cabinet and Parliament. The 28 outlying Chiss colonies were represented in Parliament by appointed governors or House leaders.

**C series protocol droid** Approximately a decade after the Battle of Endor, Cybot Galactica introduced new boutique-model droids, the C series. These protocol droids had model numbers ranging from C1 to C9 and were produced exclusively on the factory moon of Telti.

**Csilla** The homeworld of the Chiss, located deep in the Unknown Regions. Starting several thousand years before the Battle of Yavin, Csilla became locked in an ice age. Profound glaciation enveloped the terrestrial world. The Chiss adapted by using geothermal energy to power several popular cities among the glaciers. The House Palace was located in Csilla's capital city of Csaplar.

**CT-0000/1010** *See* Fox, Trooper.

**CT-014/783** The clone trooper paired with CT-6/774 during the mission to extract Mace Windu and Depa Billaba from Haruun Kal, early in the Clone Wars. Both troopers were classified as Auxiliary Heavy-Weapons Specialists, and operated the turret weapons on the lander they flew during the rescue mission.

**CT-19/39** *See* Green Wizard.

**CT-3423** The clone trooper who helped Commander Neyo track down and kill Jedi Master Stass Allie on Saleucami during Order 66.

**CT-36/732** *See* Sirty.

**CT-41/14-0301** *See* Barr, Lieutenant.

**CT-43/002** The clone trooper who served with Captain Fordo and died in the line of duty on Muunilinst.

**CT-43/76-9255** *See* Jorir.

**CT-44/444** *See* Forry.

**CT-4/619** The clone trooper who rescued young Boba Fett on Raxus Prime shortly after the Battle of Geonosis.

**CT-5108/8843** *See* Corr.

**CT-52/89-9204** *See* Tyto, Captain.

**CT-53/21-8778** *See* Green.

**CT-5/501** The clone trooper assigned as backup to CT-4/619 during the attempt to capture Count Dooku on Raxus Prime, shortly after the Battle of Geonosis.

**CT-55/11-9009** *See* Jai'galaar, Clone Commander.

**CT-57/11-9048** The clone trooper who served as Captain Jai'galaar's wingman, as part of the 127th Gunship Wing, during the Clone Wars.

**CT-65/91-6210** *See* Deviss, Clone Commander.

**CT-6734** *See* Galle.

**CT-6/774** The clone trooper paired with CT-014/783 during the mission to extract Jedi Masters Mace Windu and Depa Billaba from Haruun Kal. CT-6/774 and his turret were shot off their gunship, leaving him floating free in space. His weapons still had power, though, and a group of RP troopers managed to stabilize his spinning turret long enough for CT-6/774 to shoot down the droid starfighters pursuing the Jedi. CT-6/774 was later given a commendation for his quick thinking and marksmanship.

**CT-802** A clone trooper injured during the Battle of Drongar.

**CT-80/88-3009** *See* A'den, Senior Clone Commander.

**CT-8770, CT-8910** Two out of 141 clone troopers killed on Cato Neimoidia when Plo Koon crashed his Jedi starfighter into a clone staging area.

**CT-914** A clone trooper who suffered from an undetermined malady during the Jasserak Engagement on Drongar. He was admitted for treatment to the Rimsoo Seven military hospital after experiencing fainting spells every time he stood up. The doctors and medics at Rimsoo Seven were unable to find a cause until Jedi Padawan Barriss Offee arrived at the unit. With the Force, she was able to discover that CT-914 had suffered an injury to his hypothalamus, which was causing disruptions to his neural network. Offee managed to "massage" the hypothalamus, removing the problem and allowing CT-914 to return to action.

**CT-915** This clone trooper was one of the many casualties of the Jasserak Engagement on Drongar some two years after the Battle of Geonosis.

**CT-96/298** *See* Jangotat.

**C'taunmar, General** The commander of the New Republic starfighter base on Di'tai'ni, he later served Garm Bel Iblis aboard the *Errant Venture* during the race to recover the Caamas Document.

**Cthon** Devolved subterranean humanoids that lurked deep within the underground labyrinths of Coruscant, they had dead bluish white skin and stringy, moss-like hair, with a wide lipless gash of a mouth. Having lived in darkness for thousands of generations, the Cthons had no eyes. They instead relied on their abnormally large ears to guide them through the darkness. Many believed the Cthons to be cannibals. They communicated mostly via grunts and guttural bellows.

**Cuf, Pedric** An alias used by Nom Anor when he posed as an intercessor between the Yuuzhan Vong and the Hutts. With this identity, Anor secretly met with Senator Viqi Shesh after the Battle of Fondor.

**Cudgel (1)** A heavyset man, he worked as a translator and facilitator among the Wookiees of Kashyyyk during the transition from Galactic Republic to Empire. A hirsute human, he helped the Jedi fugitive Olee Starstone make contact with Tarfful and the Wookiee leaders of Kachirho. When the Empire cracked down on Kashyyyk and began raiding the planet for Wookiee slaves, Cudgel escaped alongside Starstone and Chewbacca aboard the *Drunk Dancer.*

**Cudgel (2)** The name of the Duelist Elite dueling droid that Darth Maul once trained against and destroyed.

**Cuipernam** The primary city on Ansion and the meeting site of the Unity of Community. It was located near the Southern Band prairies and far from the Northerns Bands. The high-arching Govialty Gate, at the city's west side, led to the prairies outside city walls. To the west was the Torosogt River which marked the border of Alwari territory. After reaching an agreement with the Alwari nomads, visiting Jedi returned to Cuipernam and prevented Ansion from seceding from the Republic just prior to the outbreak of the Clone Wars.

**Cuis, Sa** A Dark Jedi who served Emperor Palpatine as one of his first Emperor's Hands early in the Galactic Empire. Cuis's genetic material was harvested by the Empire and Arkanian Microtechnologies in an experiment to create Force-sensitive clone troopers. As a test of ability and loyalty, Palpatine secretly tasked Cuis with assassinating Darth Vader, but the Dark Lord defeated the warrior, who wielded paired lightsabers—one with a white blade, the other a red. After Cuis's demise, six of his clones were to be delivered to Palpatine as a personal guard, but their instructor, Sheyvan, rebelled and the clones followed. Their bid to assassinate Palpatine was cut short when Darth Vader destroyed the clones.

**Cujicor** The Yuuzhan Vong claimed they would leave this planet alone if the New Republic turned over all the Jedi Knights. The Peace Brigade scoured the world for any Jedi fugitives.

**Cularin** The principal planet of the system with the same name, it was covered in lush rain forests and jungles. Mountain ranges reached through the trees and almost touched the skies, forming plains and deep valleys between them. Thick trees covered the whole planet, except in a few places cleared by active logging. Among the planet's many trees were a number of rare hardwoods and ch'hala trees. The climate was mild and humid, reaching uncomfortably high temperatures in the height of summer. At night, the inhabitants enjoyed cool temperatures. Rain fell almost every day, though not strongly enough to be disruptive.

Cularin was a diverse biosphere, with great lizards called kilassin occupying the top of the food chain. Much farther down the chain, small mulissiki scavenged for food. The intelligent natives of Cularin were called Tarasin. These sentients were remotely related to the great kilassin. Both evolved from the same ancestors, but along different paths. Tarasin developed a tribal society, while the kilassin continued to migrate in herds. Tarasin tribes, called irstats, usually contained between 30 and 50 members. Larger tribes also existed. For instance, the Hiironi irstat contained more than 300 members. However, most Tarasin prefered smaller tribes and simpler lives.

The Tarasin believed they maintained a symbiotic relationship with their world, a belief that motivated their religion. Through an attunement to the natural world, Tarasin could sense the Force naturally. Traditionally, their religious figures became Force adepts, but their species did not fully understand the Force until Jedi came to the system. Because of their spiritual connection to their world, Tarasin did not travel very far from Cularin for extended periods.

**Cularin system** This system in the Mid Rim was first located some 200 years before the Battle of Naboo by Reidi Artom. Unusual in many ways, its primary star was actually a pair of stars that existed in extremely close proximity: the yellow Morasil and the white dwarf Termandus. Three of the system's five planets were incredibly dense, giving the entire system a strong gravitational pull and causing navigational problems for approaching ships. The system was also a nexus for the energies of the Force, both light side and dark. The system consisted of the planets Acilaris, Cularin, Genarius, Morjakar, Almas, and an asteroid belt made from the ruins of the planet Oblis.

Shortly after the Battle of Naboo, the entire Cularin system suddenly and inexplicably disappeared from the sector, only to reappear a decade later during the Clone Wars. Many linked the disappearance, known as the Blink, to the rediscovery of the ancient artifact known as the Darkstaff. Several years later, the entire Cularin system was placed under martial law by the Republic after Senator Lavira Wren was arrested as a traitor for supposedly working in collusion with the Separatists. Cularin eventually seceded from the Republic, but attempted to remain neutral in the Clone Wars.

**Culpa, Aga** Ruler of the Smugglers' Moon of Nar Shaddaa about four years after the Battle of Naboo, he was distinguished by his pale gray skin as well as the full-scalp cyborg unit on top of his head. He made a pact with the slave raider Krayn, allowing him to control the spice-processing facilities on Nar Shaddaa in return for the freedom of the beings who lived on the station. When Siri Tachi and Anakin Skywalker escaped from Krayn, they were able to secure Culpa's help in allowing a slave revolt: Culpa agreed to order the Nar Shaddaa guards to do nothing to stop the slaves.

**Culroon III** An out-of-the-way, violence-plagued planet, it was largely ignored by the Old Republic. Due to constant warfare, the primitive Culroon never developed space travel, but they did trade for technological goods, including blasters. When the Empire decided to construct a garrison on Culroon III, the Imperial general in charge of the operation agreed to a ceremonial surrender of the Culroon people by their leader, Kloff. When this ceremony turned out to be an ambush by the Culroon, the Imperial staff was rescued by an AT-AT commanded by then-Lieutenant Veers.

**Cult of M'dweshuu** An ancient and powerful Nikto death cult that controlled much of Kintan at the time of that world's first contact with the Hutts. As the Nikto were introduced to the larger galaxy, the cult's influence waned, but it reemerged centuries later during the Great Sith War, to be put down by Churabba the Hutt.

**Culu, Shoaneb** A Jedi Knight who lived some 4,000 years before the Galactic Civil War, she was a Miraluka from the planet Alpheridies. Like others of her species, all of whom were born without eyes, she could "see" through the use of the Force.

**Cundertol, Molierre** A former Senator and member of the New Republic Senate Defense Council from Bakura, he was prejudiced against nonhumans. Cundertol, a big, solid man with thinning blond hair and a pink hue to his skin, had served in the Special Bakuran Marines. When Cundertol was inebriated, the traitorous Senator Tig Peramis stole his voting key, logged into his personal journals, found top-secret information about the New Republic Fifth Fleet's deployment to the Farlax sector under the command of Han Solo, and gave the information to Yevethan leader Nil Spaar. Despite this, Cundertol eventually became Prime Minister of Bakura. He joined the Bakuran Senate in accepting a treaty proposed by the P'w'ecks. He disappeared before a consecration ceremony on Bakura was to take place. Cundertol was conspiring with the Ssi-ruuk, and had planned to facilitate a new invasion by them in return for effective immortality. The Ssi-ruuk had perfected their entechment process, and used it to transfer Cundertol's consciousness into a human replica droid. Cundertol's plot failed and he was killed by the Yuuzhan Vong agent E'thinaa.

**cu-pa** A species of brightly colored mounts native to Nam Chorios and also found on Tatooine. They were a distant cousin of the tauntaun.

**Curi** A Radnorian scientist and engineer, she handled the business and financial transactions for the weapons that her brother, Galen, developed. When a toxin they had created devastated the population of Radnor, Curi felt responsible and commited herself to helping and healing as many victims as she could. She later discovered that her brother had conspired with enemies of Radnor to unleash the plague.

**Curich Engineering** A holding of the Santhe Corporation, the same parent company that controlled Sienar Fleet Systems.

**Cuthallox** An ancient Jedi student apprenticed to Blendri prior to the First Great Schism. Both Master and pupil disappeared from the Jedi Order with Jedi Master Jookjook H'broozin and joined the dark side forces led by Xendor. Danzigorro Potts confronted Blendri and Cuthallox on Columus during the First Great Schism, defeating both in combat. Potts also was mortally wounded in the fighting, but managed to survive long enough to leave a record of what had happened.

**Cuthus, Naroon** The talent scout for crime lord Jabba the Hutt on Tatooine, he was a tall, dark-skinned human with long hair and a mustache. Naroon Cuthus signed the Max Rebo band to play for Jabba.

*Shoaneb Culu*

***Cutlass*-class corvette** An Imperial Remnant capital ship, active in the years after the Swarm War.

**Cutup** A clone trooper rookie serving at the Rishi moon during the Clone Wars, he was killed and eaten by a Rishi eel.

**Cuvil, Pir** One of Ghez Hokan's lieutenants on the planet Qiilura during the Clone Wars. An Umbaran, he disappeared from duty, and Hokan presumed he was a deserter. He ordered his troops to capture Cuvil on sight. Hokan summarily executed Cuvil when the Umbaran was apprehended and brought before him.

**Cuvir, Lord** The Imperial Governor of the planet Firro. A ruthless man, Cuvir ordered numerous atrocities during the occupation of Firro. His personal medical droid, Too-Onebee, was faithful to his master, despite Cuvir's inhumane nature. During a visit to Wor Tandell, Cuvir was shot dead by his aide, who was the Rebel spy Tay Vanis.

***Cuy'val Dar*** A group of 100 training sergeants recruited by Jango Fett for the elite Republic commando program, prior to the Clone Wars. Although Republic commandos were as genetically altered as the clone trooper cadre, they underwent separate training from early childhood in close-knit "pods" of brothers, with each "batch" of 25 or 26 squads under the supervision of a single training sergeant. Of the 100, 75 were Mandalorian mercenaries, including Kal Skirata, Walon Vau, and Rav Bralor. The training sergeants were known in Mando'a as the *Cuy'val Dar*—"Those Who No Longer Exist"—because the secrecy of the project meant that they had to disappear indefinitely; not even their families, if they had them, knew where they had gone. Many were presumed dead. The survival rate of the Mandalorians' trainees in combat was significantly higher than those trained by non-Mandalorian sergeants, although all 10,000 Republic commandos proved to be of the highest caliber.

**cyanogen** A gas that was poisonous to oxygen breathers, although some creatures, such as the Celegians, depended upon it for survival.

**Cyax** This system contained the yellow star Cyax, the planet Da Soocha, and Da Soocha's uncharted fifth moon, where the Alliance established Pinnacle Base during the Emperor's reappearance. Cyax was the brightest star that could be seen from the Hutts' ancestral world of Varl, and it featured prominently in Hutt legends and myths. When the Hutts left Varl for other parts of the galaxy, they respectfully left the Cyax system unexplored and removed it from their astrogation charts.

**cybernetic chamber** A device developed by Imperial scientists during the Galactic Civil War. This large chamber, about the size of a utility landspeeder, seated one person. It used a laserwave link to transmit the powers of the Force over great distances.

Darth Vader employed a cybernetic chamber in a plot to discover the Rebels' hidden base after the Battle of Yavin. Luring Rebel agents to the planet Verdanth by stranding a high-level Imperial messenger drone, Vader hoped to pry the base's location from a Rebel's mind with the Force from thousands of light-years away. The plan failed when the Rebel who fell into the trap was Luke Skywalker.

Luke's training in the Force allowed him to resist Vader's Force probe.

**cybernetic exercise braces** Powered exoskeletons that helped with patient recovery. Leia Organa Solo used a lower-body cybernetic brace on the Cinnabar Moon to rehabilitate her injured legs during the Yuuzhan Vong War.

**cybernetic psychosis** An affliction in which direct connection between a brain and cybernetic implants or borg constructs led to insanity.

**cyberostasis** A condition affecting droids that occured when they suffered a major external shock or internal systems defect. They could induce the state as a protective reflex. All cybernetic functions were impaired or halted, usually resulting in shutdown.

**Cybloc XII** Located in the Meridian sector, this small, lifeless moon housed a major New Republic fleet installation and served as a busy trading hub. The moon orbited the glowing, green-gold planet Cybloc, which in turn circled the star Erg Es 992. Nine years after the Battle of Endor, R2-D2 and C-3PO tried to reach Cybloc XII to alert the New Republic that Leia Organa Solo had been kidnapped by Seti Ashgad of Nam Chorios. When they finally arrived, they found that all personnel had been killed by the Death Seed plague. The entire installation—including the port authority, the shipping companies, the Republic consular offices, and fleet headquarters—was being overrun with e-suited scavengers and looters. Prior to their arrival, two Republic cruisers, the *Ithor Lady* and the *Empyrean,* had been sent to deal with a pirate fleet from Budpock.

**Cyborg Operations** An arm of Jabba the Hutt's court, it was controlled by the droid EV-9D9. Deep in the bowels of Jabba's palace, Cyborg Operations obliterated the programming and personalities of droids through torture before assigning them to toil in Jabba's gang.

**Cyborrea** A high-gravity planet, it was home to cyborg battle dogs called neks. The aggressive neks were a result of genetic and cybernetic engineering and were often used for protection by scavenger gangs.

**Cybot Galactica** Along with Industrial Automaton, one of the two largest droid manufacturers in the galaxy. This corporation was a major force in the galactic economy and a significant influence throughout the Core Worlds and the Corporate Sector. Famous for the 3PO protocol series, Cybot was also responsible for an extraordinary array of droid models ranging from simple labor units to advanced security sentinels.

**Cycer, Del** A wealthy inhabitant of the Oseon who once played cards against Lando Calrissian.

**Cydorrian driller trees** Leathery, shade-giving trees, they had far-reaching root systems.

**Cygnus Spaceworks** An important military starship manufacturer, it had strong ties to both Sienar Fleet Systems and the Imperial Navy. The company built shuttle and landing craft variants based on the Sienar Fleet Systems *Lambda*-class shuttle. Cygnus also built the *Alpha*-class Xg-1 Star Wing assault gunboat and *Delta*-class JV-7 "Escort Shuttle."

**Cyndra** A Chiss member of the Anti-Republic Liberation Front in the years following the Battle of Ruusan and the Ruusan Reformations. For many months Cyndra and fellow rebel Kelad'dan had been in a romantic relationship, but that suddenly changed one day. Kelad'dan's new lover, a woman named Rain, claimed to have knowledge of Chancellor Tarsus Valorum's secret visit to Serenno and urged Kelad'dan to convince the group to assassinate Valorum.

Cyndra felt the plan ill-advised, but Kelad'dan swayed the rest of the group to follow along. Using information provided by Rain (sometimes also known as Rainah), the group rigged a series of explosives around the landing platform where Valorum was to arrive. Valorum escaped death, however, protected by his Jedi companion Johun Othone. The ARLF members scattered, and Cyndra's associate Paak later caught up with Rain—who was actually the Sith apprentice, Darth Zannah. Zannah refused to be interrogated and used the dark side of the Force to cause Cyndra to experience horrific visions, many of which involved Kelad'dan. In fear, Cyndra tried to scratch her own eyes out, but was unable to stop the visions from driving her insane. Cyndra's brain experienced intense seizures before her mind was destroyed, leaving her body an empty shell. Paak tried to kill Zannah, but the shot was deflected back and killed him.

**Cyrillia** A manufacturing planet known for the construction of pit droids

**CZ droid** An outmoded and obsolete series of droids used in the days of the Galactic Republic. Classified as both a secretary droid and a comm droid, the Serv-O-Droid CZ had a number of ways of processing, storing, and transmitting information.

**CZ-1** This very old secretary droid was renamed from CZ-0R6. Abandoned on Tatooine and seperated from his twin unit CZ-3 after a crash, CZ-1 broke down in the desert and was captured by Jawas. He was aboard the Jawa sandcrawler that carried C-3PO and R2-D2 to the Lars homestead.

CZ-3 on the streets of Mos Eisley

**CZ-3** This particular secretary droid was pressed into accounting and business duty in the service of Jabba the Hutt. It figured in a well-crafted ploy by Jabba to catch a business rival, Opun "The Black Hole" Mcgrrrr, in the act of theft. CZ-3 was loaded with surveillance gear and software, resulting in the droid being easily distracted and flighty. After CZ-3 recorded and transmitted evidence of Mcgrrrr's thievery, the frazzled droid wandered away from his new master and began absentmindedly wandering the streets of Mos Eisley. The droid eventually was tracked down by the bounty-hunting brothers Takeel and Zutton. Zutton destroyed the droid and apprehended Mcgrrrr. A pair of mischievous Mos Eisley droid dealers promptly stole the droid's remains.

**CZ-4** A communications droid owned by Jabba the Hutt, CZ-4 was modified to serve as a defense drone programmed to warn its master of an imminent attack.

**Czerka Corporation** The galaxy's third largest arms manufacturer, this company produced blasters, artillery, melee weapons, starship weapons, and starship defense systems. An ancient business, it existed for thousands of years, dating back to before the Sith War. During the Galactic Civil War, Czerka reluctantly agreed to establish an exclusive distribution agreement with the Empire, though it became a strong supporter of the New Republic when that government came to power.

**Czethros** A former bounty hunter who was outsmarted by Han Solo, this humanoid cyborg ending up imprisoned at the spice mines of Kessel for a stint. He emerged as leader of what remained of Black Sun in the later years of the New Republic. He worked secretly to activate his scattered sleeper cells to rebuild Black Sun to its former glory, but was ultimately defeated thanks to the efforts of Jacen and Jaina Solo and their friends. Czethros was incarcerated, and Black Sun was effectively crushed.

**Czycz, Stauz** A soldier whose world was ravaged by the Empire, Stauz Czycz plotted revenge by altering his body and disguising himself as human bounty hunter Awarru Tark. Tark answered Darth Vader's call for hunters to pursue the *Millennium Falcon* after the Battle of Hoth. Tark confronted Vader, but the Dark Lord was able to defeat and decapitate the powerful alien warrior.

**D-127X** A Rebel Alliance deep-space probe droid active in the Oplovis sector that monitored all communications frequencies, recorded information, and sent off weekly reports to Alliance headquarters via slaved hyperspace drones. The information gathered by D-127X was essential in countering an attack by the Imperial Oplovis sector fleet.

**D25D** A skylane on Coruscant connecting CoCo Town to the Boribos and Hirkenglade prefectures.

**D-34** An Imperial outpost located in orbit around the planet Javin, used as an intercept point after the Battle of Hoth. The Empire attempted to funnel fleeing Rebel Alliance vessels into the Javin sector and past D-34. The station was eventually captured by the Alliance with the help of the Mugaari pirates. The Empire later recovered it.

**D-4** The designation of the New Republic Navy's antiradiation mitigation procedure, used when a starship's main reactor was damaged.

**D435** A fine-featured G1 series equipment operator droid present at the 24 Tredway asteroid mining colony in the Sil'Lume Belt. When the Empire attacked the Rebel-sympathetic inhabitants of the asteroid, many were killed. Deefourthreefive took a wounded Dena Tredway to Medical Station One for recuperation, and guarded her inert form.

**D-4R5** A humanoid protocol droid assigned to Governor Grigor on M'haeli. Grigor blasted D-4R5 and wiped its memory as a means of facilitating Ranulf Trommer's contact with droid mechanic Mora, a supporter of the Rebel Alliance. She was able to repair the droid, and it was put to use by the Rebel Alliance on the planet.

**D516** A large, menacing treaded assassin droid produced by Sienar Technologies during the final decades of the Old Republic. In addition to their heavy armor plating, the D516 models were equipped with a blaster carbine and a needler gun. Sophisticated infrared sensor systems allowed the droids to effectively target organic beings.

*< The Death Star looms in space.*

**D6** A massive turbolaser battery produced by Taim & Bak. The first Death Star had 5,000 D6 emplacements.

**D-60, D-90 super battle droids** A variety of combat automata unveiled by the Trade Federation during the Battle of Geonosis. These super battle droids were as large as a man and a half, and versatile enough to be used in commando missions.

**D6-66** An Imperial spaceport law that required all open hangars be equipped with time-lock devices.

**D-89** A pilotless ferret in Colonel Pakkpekatt's armada that chased the mysterious ghost ship called the Teljkon vagabond. It was assigned to breach the perimeter and, ideally, to invade the defenses of the vagabond just enough to provoke it to jump into hyperspace. There New Republic vessels would have captured it. The vagabond hailed the D-89, but before the colonel's flagship *Glorious* could respond, the vagabond destroyed the ferret.

**D-A02** A repair unit, part of the droid pool that worked aboard Matton Dasol's ship some 4,000 years before the Battle of Yavin. D-A02 was present when Eli Gand killed the crew, and remained in hiding until it was discovered by a Jedi Knight on Kashyyyk. Although it exploded when taken from the ship, D-A02's head was later recovered, and its recordings were used as evidence in Gand's trial.

**Daala, Admiral Natasi** The highest-ranking female fleet officer in the Empire, she posed a threat to the New Republic in the months following the resurrected Emperor's campaign of terror. Daala's rank was an anomaly in the predominantly male Imperial military. Despite promising successes early in her career, she was repeatedly passed over for promotion on the basis of gender. In frustration, she crafted a false computer identity and entered contests of strategy against battle-hardened veterans. She bested some of Carida's finest instructors in these anonymous virtual engagements.

Moff Tarkin of the Outer Rim Territories took notice of young Daala's determination and skill. He uncovered her true identity, and began to school her as his personal military protégée. It was Tarkin's influence that allowed Daala to ascend to the rank of admiral, and he placed her in command of a quartet of Imperial Star Destroyers patrolling the Outer Rim Territories.

Tarkin entrusted the protection of Maw Installation to Daala. This top-secret military weapons research facility had been sunken into a stable patch of space amid the churning black holes of the Maw Cluster. In this remote base, some of the Empire's brightest scientific minds created designs for new Imperial weaponry, including the first in a series of Death Stars.

Daala was given express orders to never abandon her post, to stay at Maw Installation, and to maintain comm silence until Tarkin returned. But he never did; he died in the explosion that obliterated the Death Star. Daala and her task force stood watch over Maw Installation nevertheless. Because it was Tarkin's most closely guarded secret, knowledge of it died with him. The concentration of treacherous black holes made accidental discovery of the base highly unlikely. For 11 years, Daala's fighting forces atrophied.

The sudden arrival of an Imperial shuttle was a shock. It carried fugitives from the nearby Kessel prison complex: Han Solo, Chewbacca, and Kyp Durron. From this group, Daala received a much-needed update on the state of the galaxy. The trio broke free of the installation, managing in the process to capture one of the most powerful superweapons in development, the Sun Crusher. Daala, seeking revenge and a chance to finally make a difference, emerged from the Maw Cluster with her task force, eager to wage war with the New Republic.

*Admiral Natasi Daala*

Though Daala was versed in many strategic theories, her inexperience hampered her efforts. Using decade-old tactics at a battle over Mon Calamari, Daala was easily thwarted by Admiral Ackbar. Before long, her task force of four destroyers was reduced to just her flagship, *Gorgon.* Defeated, she joined the squabbling Imperial warlords holed up in the Deep Core Worlds.

Seeing the inefficiencies of the Emperor's heirs in person again gave fuel to Daala's fiery temper. In disgust, she murdered most of the warlords, then consolidated command over the remaining Imperial military. With Gilad Pellaeon at her side, Daala took command of the Super Star Destroyer *Knight Hammer* and engaged in an ill-advised strike against Luke Skywalker's Jedi academy on Yavin 4.

The battle ended poorly for Daala, with the *Knight Hammer* falling victim to sabotage. Broken, Daala abandoned her command to Pellaeon and fled to the remote world of Pedducis Chorios. She settled into civilian life, leading a group of settlers on the distant world.

A year later, the inhumane tactics of Moff Getelles brought Daala out of retirement. When she learned that Getelles had used an outbreak of the Death Seed plague to gain control of the Meridian sector, Daala threw in her lot with the forces that opposed him.

Once the dust of that conflict had settled, Daala was not content to return to retired civilian life. She again journeyed to the Deep Core, amassing troops and war vessels in a bid to again challenge the New Republic. She attempted such a strike just prior to the Corellian insurrection. Her forces were repulsed by General Garm Bel Iblis. At great cost, Daala escaped the battle, and was not seen until her return at the height of the conflict between the Confederation and the Galactic Alliance.

Daala answered Pellaeon's call to assist the Imperial Remnant in its joint mission with the Galactic Alliance to capture Fondor. Only Pellaeon knew of Daala's whereabouts, and he planned to keep her as an ace for when he needed it most. Daala hired a group of Boba Fett's Mandalorians to join her. When a destabilized Jacen Solo went rogue and continued a destructive assault on Fondor without the backing of either the Galactic Alliance or the Imperial Remnant, the situation collapsed into a confused skirmish. Aboard the Imperial flagship, *Bloodfin,* Jacen's associate Tahiri Veila murdered Pellaeon, and those members of the opportunistic Moff Council who were aboard tried to take control of the Empire. Into this chaos thundered Daala's group of warships, the Maw Irregular Fleet.

Fett's Mandalorians boarded the *Bloodfin* and killed the treasonous Moffs. Daala arranged for Pellaeon's funeral on Corellia. She then traveled to Mandalore to personally thank Fett for his part in the battle and agreed to accompany him to the wedding of his granddaughter, Mirta Gev. In the weeks that followed, Admiral Daala remained on the sidelines, waiting to see what would happen before deciding on a course of action. With the death of Darth Caedus and the surrender of the remaining Imperial Moffs, Daala was surprised to be offered the chance to take on the role of chief of state of the Galactic Alliance. She had been recommended for the job by Admiral Nek Bwua'tu and agreed to do what she could to rebuild the galaxy. One of the only conditions she demanded was that the Imperial Moff Council allow females to serve as Moffs.

Dacho District on Coruscant

**D'a Alin, Joveh** A blue-skinned alien, she was an expert in the field of planetary tectonics and mineralogy in the last decades of the Old Republic. She was part of a team led by Dr. Fort Turan that traveled to Haariden to investigate the effects of a volcanic environment on atmospherics and ecosystem.

**Daal, Raymas** A small-time criminal from Naboo during the Trade Federation invasion of the planet, he was contacted by secret Trade Federation agents and supplied with funds to hire freelance mercenaries to help knock out Naboo's communications relays. Once the relays were disabled, the Trade Federation could deploy its jamming satellites in orbit, effectively cutting off Naboo from the rest of the galaxy. Although ultimately successful in hiring the freelancers, Daal was later captured by the Naboo Royal Security Forces and detained for questioning.

**Daan** One of the two warring factions on Melida/Daan. Throughout the planet's history, the Melida had seen the Daan as feral beasts, and used a legacy of perceived wrongdoings to continue their civil war. The older members of both societies fought to avenge the losses sustained over generations, using their children as laborers in munitions factories while they killed one another in battle. They had been involved in a war with the Melida for 30 years before Obi-Wan Kenobi and Qui-Gon Jinn traveled to their planet to rescue Tahl.

**D'aarmont** An immense outcropping of quartz, located on the planet Bakura, measuring about 3 kilometers in length and 50 kilometers across. It was situated at the confluence of the East and West Rivers, and became the foundation of the city Salis D'aar.

**Dab, Notha** *See* Vakil, Nrin.

**dabaroo** A heavy vegetable used in many gourmet dishes, its skin exuded natural phosphors during preparation, making any meal that contained dabaroo glow an unusual blue color.

**Dac** *See* Mon Calamari.

**Dac, Mynor** This Twi'lek served as part of Twin Suns Squadron, supporting the Galactic Alliance's efforts to defeat the Yuuzhan Vong.

**Dachat** A planet that was the site of a pirate base of the Nelori Marauders, located along the Hyabb-Twith Corridor. The Dachat base allowed the Marauders to prey upon the governments of both Hyabb and Twith while taking their pick of the ships traveling between them. Following the loss of their main base on Voon, the Nelroni were driven off Dachat by the ancient Jedi Knights.

**Dacho District** Once a large factory district on Coruscant, it was abandonded 700 years before the outbreak of the Clone Wars following an immense industrial chemical accident. The release of neuritic carbide gases killed more than 300,000 beings. The abandoned warehouses and factories of the Dacho District were used centuries later as a base by Darth Sidious and Darth Tyranus. A localized disturbance in the Force in the district—caused by so many deaths ages ago—may have encouraged the Sith to base their operations out of this gloomy place. It was also known as the Dead Sector.

**Dacholder** Nicknamed Doc, he was a rescue pilot working for the New Republic vessel *Pride of Thela.* During the war against the Yuuzhan Vong, Doc was secretly a member of the Peace Brigade, and he attempted to turn Uldir Lochet—a Jedi student—over to the Yuuzhan Vong. Uldir detected the trap, and sent Doc tumbling out an open air lock.

**Dack (Tymmo)** An attractive young man posing under the alias Tymmo as the consort of the Duchess Mistal of Dargul. He achieved the position by slicing into the central computer in Palace Dargul and sabotaging the files submitted by other applicants. When he discovered that the Duchess was a relentless partner who mated for life, Tymmo fled to the planet Umgul. There Lando Calrissian, C-3PO, and R2-D2

Dactillion

found him excelling in the blob races. Because of his perceived ability, Lando believed that the man was a Force-user and suggested that Luke Skywalker take Tymmo to his academy. However, Lando and the droids soon discovered that Tymmo's victories in the races were a result of cheating. Rather than face death for his crimes, Tymmo agreed to return to the Duchess, while Lando collected the million credits offered as a reward for Dack's return.

**dactillion** Winged carnivorous lizards native to Utapau, they had long plagued the Utapauns as predators in the people's prehistoric climb to civilization. They were first domesticated by the Utai. By studying the flight patterns of the dactillions, the Utapauns were able to determine the surface wind conditions, and this allowed them to colonize other sinkholes and build wind-powered devices. By supplying the dactillions with fresh meat, Utapauns were able to tame the creatures and use them as mounts.

**dactyl** A vital dietary supplement ingested by the Arcona species, dactyl was a form of crystallized ammonia.

**Dactyl** An ungainly transport vessel produced by Rendili StarDrive after the Yuuzhan Vong War, it had accommodations for several passengers and crew, and was equipped with a hangar bay large enough to hold several StealthX fighters.

**dactyl stork** A swamp creature found on numerous planets, it is known for its back-bending leg joints.

**Dade, Lilla** A pathfinder member of Page's Commandos during the Rebellion and New Republic eras, she preceded the assault on Moff Kentor Sarne's stronghold by infiltrating the base on Kal'Shebbol. She later was part of the infiltration party sent to Ylesia to capture the leaders of the Peace Brigade during the war against the Yuuzhan Vong.

**Dadeferron, Torm** Tall and brawny, with red hair and blue eyes, he was part of a secret civilian group organized by Rekkon—a Kalla university professor in search of his nephew—to locate missing friends and relatives who were suspected prisoners of the Corporate Sector Authority. Torm, who hailed from a wealthy family on the planet Kail, was second in command of a mission to infiltrate an Authority Data Center on Orron III. The group hoped to learn the location of the authority's illegal detention center and rescue the political prisoners. Torm betrayed and killed Rekkon but was later killed by Han Solo.

Dagobah

**D'Aelgoth sector** A region where Han Solo and then-girlfriend Xaverri once conned an Imperial Moff out of his money.

**Daeshara'cor** One of the first Twi'leks to attend Luke Skywalker's Jedi praxeum on Yavin 4, she was orphaned as a child and spent a lot of time growing up in starports. She never let go of memories of her mother, and her festering anger and frustrations led her down a path to the dark side. During the Yuuzhan Vong invasion, she was determined to discover a weapon powerful enough to wipe out the alien menace. Anakin Solo tracked her to Garos IV, captured her, and brought her back to the Jedi who had gathered on Ithor. Remorseful for her actions, Daeshara'cor apologized. She redeemed herself fighting alongside Anakin against the Yuuzhan Vong, but died when poisoned by an amphistaff.

Daeshara'cor

**Da'Gara, Prefect** The huge and powerful prefect of the Praetorite Vong, the first invasion force of the extragalactic Yuuzhan Vong, he commanded the living worldship that had breached the galactic rim and settled at the planet Helska. The greater mission was under the command of a yammosk, a creature genetically engineered to serve the Yuuzhan Vong and help them conquer their enemies. Da'Gara served as the yammosk's adviser. He died when New Republic forces led by Luke Skywalker attacked Helska and destroyed the powerful, deadly yammosk.

**Dagger-Ds** Local police starfighters used by the Duro Defense Force, they were built by Frei-Tek Incorporated, maker of the powerful E-wing fighter. They were armed with a triple blaster cannon, and could carry up to two passengers in addition to the pilot.

**daggerlip** A predator native to the Arconan home planet of Cona.

**daggert** *See* mee.

**Dagobah** A mysterious swamp planet in the distant Sluis sector. Free of technology and overrun by foliage and wild beasts, Dagobah was a tumultuous and primeval world. Native fauna included the voracious swamp slug and the predatory dragonsnake, as well as flying bogwings. Giant gnarltree forests, twisting waterways, and a shroud of mist covered the landscape.

Following the events of Order 66 and the rise of the Galactic Empire, Jedi Master Yoda retired to Dagobah, where he remained hidden from the Emperor's attention. Some time before that, a Dark Jedi from Bpfassh caused havoc throughout the Sluis sector until he was stopped near Dagobah. A dark cave near Yoda's home was theorized to be a vestige of this Dark Jedi's power, and it may have served to hide Yoda's presence.

After the Battle of Hoth, Luke Skywalker journeyed to Dagobah to complete his Jedi training. The arduous terrain and natural hazards of the overgrown swamps proved to be effective challenges for the young Jedi. After his last visit with Yoda, Luke returned to the planet: once during the war against Thrawn, and again three years later in the hope of restoring Callista Ming's connection to the Force.

**Dagore, Winfrid** The commander of Teth's armed forces during the early days of the Empire, she met with Bria Tharen to discuss her world's involvement in the Rebel Alliance. She was later captured by bounty hunters Dace Bonearm and IG-72 and handed over to the Empire.

**Dagro** A remote agriworld, Obi-Wan Kenobi crashed there during the Clone Wars. He discovered a secret Separatist base that he was able to destroy with the help of Anakin Skywalker.

**Dagu** The site of a battle in the Clone Wars. Shaak Ti was rewarded for her valiancy in protecting the populace from the Separatists.

**Dahai, Tedn** A member of the Bith band Figrin D'an and the Modal Nodes, he played the fanfar.

**Dahl** This Samarian served as one of Prime Minister Aaren

Larker's chief aides during the months following the end of the Clone Wars.

***Daily Galaxy*** One of the smaller holonews services during the Clone Wars.

**Daine, Cubber** A Corellian mechanic for Rogue Squadron, he also served Wraith Squadron.

**Daine, Zindra** The 20-year-old novice human female pilot of Twin Suns Squadron at the time of the Yuuzhan Vong invasion of Coruscant.

**Dainsom, Imperial Trooper Guard** An experienced trooper guard from Algarian, he was assigned to guard sensitive areas aboard the Star Destroyers *Thunderflare* and *Executor.*

**Dajus, Jessa** A crew member aboard the New Republic corvette *FarStar.* She was formerly Moff Kentor Sarne's tactical officer and pilot. She was Force-sensitive and had a strange connection to the alien DarkStryder technology found in the Kathol Rift.

**Dak, Zebulon** Wealthy and influential, he was the founder and owner of the Zebulon Dak Speeder Corporation.

**Dakar** An alien port administrator at Exis Station after the Great Sith War, he was a friend of the spacer Hoggon.

**Dakhan, Shar** An ancient Sith Lord who ruled on the planet Ch'hodos and participated in the Great Hyperspace War about 5,000 years before the Battle of Yavin.

**Dakkar the Distant** An unpleasant cantina owner in Mos Eisley who employed Shaara as a dancer.

**Dakshee** Long under Imperial rule, this planet in the Colonies region was marked by constant unrest.

**D'akul, Shada** *See* D'ukal, Shada.

**Dal, Ghithra** A master shaper during the Yuuzhan Vong invasion of the galaxy, he tried to determine why Warmaster Tsavong Lah's body had been rejecting the radank claw grafted to him. He could find no scientific reason, and attributed the failure to the will of Yun-Yuuzhan. The scheming New Republic Senator Viqi Shesh sowed the seeds of doubt in Lah's mind, accusing Dal of sabotaging the graft to ensure a loss of status for the Warmaster. Lah closely monitored Dal's actions before becoming fed up with the alleged shaper plot and letting loose wild rancors aboard the transport ship *Fu'ulanh.* Dal died in the rampage.

**Dal, Rarta** The proprietor of the Three Moons hotel in Mos Espa during the time of the Empire, he hired Kitster Banai as a steward.

**Dala, Tobbi** A bounty hunter and friend of Fenn Shysa, he joined Alpha-02's call to resurrect the Mandalorian Supercommando army to fight on the Separatists' side in the Clone Wars. Upon returning to Mandalore, he discovered his home planet overrun by slavers. Tobbi and Shysa formed an underground of freedom fighters against the Imperial Suprema, Ampotem Za.

Shortly after the Battle of Hoth, Dala was captured by the Imperials. He was part of a prisoner exchange with Imperial bounty hunter Dengar. Fenn Shysa infiltrated the Suprema's base and attempted to rescue Dala, but the Suprema shot and wounded Dala. Dala, dying, used the Imperial compound's service doors to cut off Shysa's pursuers, and destroyed the slaving center.

Tobbi Dala

**Dalchon system** A planetary system in the Dalchon sector. Shortly after the rise of the Empire, famed Republic tactician Adar Tallon staged his death there.

**Dalhney, Hric** An Alderaanian aide who represented Bail Organa when dealing with distant Rebel contacts, he and Winter met with Bria Tharen to discuss the formation of the early Rebel Alliance.

**Dalla the Hutt** A Hutt from whom Han Solo borrowed money—using the *Millennium Falcon* as collateral—to buy Leia Organa Solo a planet for the refugees who were offworld when the Empire destroyed the planet Alderaan.

***Dalliance*** A modified YT-1210 freighter owned and operated by the Jedi praxeum on Yavin 4 and used by Corran Horn and Ganner Rhysode to travel to Bimmiel to investigate the disappearance of an Agamarian xenoarchaeology class.

**Dallin, Jace** A member of Ranulph Tarkin's command staff during the Stark Hyperspace Conflict. He grew to distrust Tarkin's abilities to lead in battle, and sided with the Jedi during the conflict. He met Masters Tholme and Adi Gallia during the siege on Troiken, and had his life saved by a Xexto named Billibango. In the fighting, he suffered scarring that he would later describe as a reminder of the war and how he almost fought on the wrong side.

Years later, during the Clone Wars, his home planet of Rendili sided with the Separatists, but Dallin—now a captain—did not want the planet's powerful Dreadnaught cruisers to fall into Count Dooku's hands. He attempted to negotiate a treaty with the Jedi, but mutinous forces under Dallin's command rebelled and took their captain and Jedi Master Plo Koon hostage. Remaining loyal to the Jedi, Dallin was forced to kill one of his subordinate officers to end the standoff.

After the Clone Wars, Dallin was assigned to a position in the newly formed Imperial Navy. He questioned Imperial claims regarding the Jedi rebellion, and could not in good conscience continue his service. Darth Vader detected his disloyalty and killed him with the Force.

Jace Dallin

**dalloralla** A 30-meter-tall tree that once grew in groves on the planet Belkadan before that world's biosphere was ravaged by the Yuuzhan Vong.

**dallorian** A chrome-like heat-resistant alloy used in the manufacture of blaster pistols and armor.

**Dallows, Rhys** A cocky Naboo pilot at the time of the Trade Federation invasion of his planet, he flew an N-1 starfighter as Bravo Ten during the Battle of Naboo.

**Dalonbian, Tobbert** The President of the ExGal Society during the years leading up to the Clone Wars.

**Dalonbian sector** An Outer Rim sector that contained the planet Belkadan. It was the point of entry for the Yuuzhan Vong invasion of the galaxy.

**Dalron Five** A planet devastated by the Empire during an infamous siege, it was subject to warfare techniques developed originally by Alliance General Jan Dodonna. Shistavanen Wolfman scout Lak Sivrak later found Dalron Five refugees living on a rocky moon.

**Daluuj** A fog-shrouded, watery world besieged by dangerous atmospheric storms, it was home to a remote Imperial training outpost. After Admiral Ackbar and several other Mon Calamari landed on Daluuj in escape pods, Han Solo and his companions attempted to rescue them. Huge lake worms dragged the *Millennium Falcon* underwater, but it was retrieved when the worms turned their attention to a group of attacking Imperial speeders.

**Damarind Corporation** Jewel merchants that had an exclusive contract with the Empire to harvest Corusca gems from the Yavin system.

**Damaya** A member of the Singing Mountain Clan of the Witches of Dathomir, she worked with Kirana Ti to protect the people and their planet from the Yuuzhan Vong.

**Dameerd, Tun** A human delegate of the Unity of Community of Ansion during the border disputes just prior to the Clone Wars. Dameerd believed Ansion should remain within the Republic, was supportive of the Jedi delegation, and was wary of Soergg the Hutt.

**damind** A crystal harvested from Daminia and used by the ancient Sith Lords in the construction of their lightsabers.

**Dammant Killers** An Adumarian company that manufactured and exported concussion missiles. Jacen Solo and Ben Skywalker investigated the company's factory after missiles bearing its logo were found in the hands of nonmilitary entities.

**Damonite Yors-B** The fifth planet in its system in the Meridian sector, it was an uninhabited ice-covered world where the atmosphere was lashed by turbulent winds and ion and methane storms. It appeared acid yellow from space. Nine years after the Battle of Endor, Han Solo and Lando Calrissian came to the planet searching for any sign of Leia Organa Solo. Instead, they found the crashed cruiser *Corbantis* and brought its survivors to the medical facility on Nim Drovis for treatment. On their way out of the planet's atmosphere, they were attacked by a swarm of Loronar Corporation's CCIR needle fighters.

**Damorian Manufacturing Corporation** Based on Esseles, this company manufactured the *Carrack*-class light cruiser.

**Dampner, Toy** A blue-skinned alien Podracer pilot, he flew a customized Turca 910 Special around the time of the Battle of Naboo.

**damutek** A Yuuzhan Vong–bioengineered ship used in the invasion of Yavin 4. After they reached a planet's surface, damuteks split their protective skin and expanded to become highly specialized shaper compounds. Yuuzhan Vong shapers established a base by placing five damuteks on Yavin 4. It had thick walls and inner courtyards open to the sky. Two of the compounds were filled with water, a third with a pale yellow fluid. Another had structures in its central space-domes and polyhedrons of various shapes. The fifth served as a port for coralskippers and larger spacegoing ships.

The succession pool was the heart, lungs, and liver of the damutek. The damutek had a brain that could determine the location of anyone in the compound. Roots dug into the soil for water and minerals. After the rescue of Anakin Solo and Tahiri Veila, the damuteks on Yavin 4 were destroyed by Talon Karrde's fleet and the *Errant Venture.*

Dancing Goddess

**D'an, Barquin** A Bith musician and gambler, he was the estranged older brother of Figrin D'an. He played the kloo horn, but not as well as his brother. He briefly jammed with Max Rebo's band when they were performing at Jabba's palace. He fled the palace after witnessing with disgust the death of Oola. He left the music industry altogether and eventually built up a thriving import–export business on Stenos.

**D'an, Figrin** This Bith musician and his band played their brand of music all over the galaxy, although an engagement on Tatooine was almost their last.

Figrin D'an remained politically neutral, something that probably kept him and the band alive despite witnessing some horrific acts spurred by the Galactic Civil War. The band, Figrin D'an and the Modal Nodes, included D'an on the kloo horn and gasan string drum; Doikk Na'ts on the Dorenian Beshniquel, or Fizzz; Tedn Dahai and Ickabel G'ont on fanfar; Nalan Cheel on the bandfill with horn bells; and Tech Mo'r, who enhanced the music with a difficult-to-play ommni box. Lirin Car'n provided backup on the kloo horn.

Figrin loved to play sabacc and use glitterstim spice. He couldn't be bribed outright, but the large-headed D'an gambled away information about things that he had seen. For each of his own winning hands, he gave away some desired tidbit to the loser. Figrin and the band came to Tatooine and were hired by crime lord Jabba the Hutt. But they incurred his wrath by accepting a onetime gig at the wedding of Lady Valarian, which dissolved into anarchy. The band escaped and was given shelter—and a job—by Wuher, bartender at the Mos Eisley cantina owned by a Wookiee named Chalmun. It was there that they witnessed Ben Kenobi put down two thugs with his lightsaber. Figrin lost ownership of all the band's instruments in a sabacc game, but eventually bought them back and the troupe continued on its galactic tour.

Figrin D'an

**Danalis** An orphan discovered by Garris Shrike on Corellia, her face was disfigured by the gnawing of verminous vrelts. She worked for Shrike's band of thieving urchins until she was 14, when she committed suicide by ejecting herself out of the *Trader's Luck* air lock.

**Dance, Villian "Vil"** A Corellian TIE fighter pilot of exceptional skill, he was stationed aboard the first Death Star just prior to it achieving operational status. Aboard the battle station, he met and romanced Teela Karz, an indentured architect working on the Death Star's interior design. Following the destruction of the planets Despayre and Alderaan by the Death Star's massive superlaser cannon, Dance and several of his colleagues began doubting their allegiance to the Empire. Dance piloted a commandeered medical shuttle away from the battle station in the thick of the Battle of Yavin, escaping the Death Star's destruction. Vil, Teela, and several other fugitives from the Death Star then joined the victorious Rebels on Yavin 4.

**Dance of the Seventy Violet Veils** A ceremonial dance, it was performed by the Askajian dancer Yarna d'al'Gargan at the wedding of Princess Leia Organa and Han Solo.

**Dancer** Mara Jade Skywalker's nickname for her astromech droid during the time she flew an X-wing in Saber Squadron.

**Dancing Goddess** An ancient statue that was at one time or another sought by Prince Xizor, BoShek, and Lemo and Sanda's gang. Legends stated that when the Minstrel and the Dancing Goddess statues were brought together, they led the way to great power. What wasn't recorded was that both statues were the missing elements of a techno-organic machine that protected the inhabitants of Godo from extinction.

**Dandalas** A planet in the Farlax sector near the Koornacht Cluster.

**Dane** A bounty hunter who operated with his sister, Florian, and attempted to hunt down Obi-Wan Kenobi and Anakin Skywalker on Ragoon-6 about five years before the start of the Clone Wars. During the war, they were bodyguards to Samish Kash.

**Dané** A young woman who was trained by Captain Panaka to become a member of the elite handmaidens protecting Queen Amidala.

**Dangor, Ars** One of Emperor Palpatine's most powerful advisers, he announced to the Regional Governors and general public the disbanding of the Imperial Senate.

**Dani** A Zeltron adventurer, she was an accomplice and friend to the con artist smuggler Rik Duel. Dani was involved in a scam pulled on Han Solo, Luke Skywalker, and Princess Leia Organa on the planet Stenos shortly after the Battle of Yavin. Years later, during Lando Calrissian and Luke's search for the carbon-frozen Han Solo, Dani and Rik met with the two and helped rid them of bounty hunter pursuers. The flirtatious Dani would often throw herself at Luke, much to his embarrassment. She accompanied the Rebels during the early adventures of the Alliance of Free Planets. She was grievously injured by the Dark Lady Lumiya, and while she survived, she was a changed person.

Nera Dantels

**Danid, Burr** A student at the Emperor's Royal Guard training ground on Yinchorr, he was considered the best student at the facility at the time of Kir Kanos and Carnor Jax's training. Danid was pitted against Darth Vader and killed as a demonstration of the need for further training.

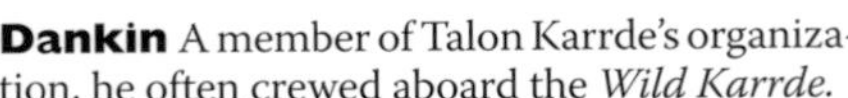

**Dankin** A member of Talon Karrde's organization, he often crewed aboard the *Wild Karrde.*

**Dan'kre, Liska** A wealthy Bothan female, she was an old school friend of fellow Bothan Asyr Sei'lar. She invited Sei'lar and Rogue Squadron member Gavin Darklighter to a party held in a skyhook high above Coruscant. It was there that Darklighter had an altercation with Karka Kre'fey, grandson of the Bothan general who'd led the Rogues into an ambush that nearly destroyed the squadron. Fortunately for Kre'fey, Darklighter refused to fight.

**Danlé, Theomet** A Naboo lieutenant serving Senator Padmé Amidala who inadvertently gave Zam Wesell access to the Naboo Royal Cruiser, allowing the assassin to sabotage the craft.

**Dann, Sohn** A jovial trader who operated in the Kashyyyk system during the Galactic Civil War, he was secretly a member of the Rebel Alliance who used his network of connections to aid Chewbacca's family.

**Danod, Murr** A peaceful Ithorian, he was a fan of Podracing and attended the fateful Boonta Eve Classic that saw the liberation of Anakin Skywalker. Danod was a member of a trade guild based on an Ithorian herd ship.

**Danoo, Immi** A stylish, tall blonde, she was present at the Outlander Club alongside her friends Nyrat Agira and Rosha Vess the night that Obi-Wan Kenobi and Anakin Skywalker apprehended Zam Wesell.

**Danta, Iry** An Imperial officer who was part of Moff Derran's conspiracy to disrupt the wedding of Luke Skywalker and Mara Jade. The plot was foiled and Danta was captured by Chewbacca.

**Dantari** A species of primitive, nomadic humanoids who lived in tribes on their native planet Dantooine. Very little was known of them. A few took to adopting Imperial sigils and iconography into their everyday culture, unaware of what the Empire had meant to the galaxy.

**Dantels, Nera** A smuggler captain and Rebel agent active prior to the Battle of Yavin. She worked with Wedge Antilles and Red Squadron to acquire a trove of astromech droids from Commenor and transport them to Yavin 4 aboard her freighter, *Starduster.* Dantels befriended Biggs Darklighter at the Massassi Base, starting a brief romance with the Rebel pilot that ended with his death at the Battle of Yavin.

**Dantooine** Far removed from most galactic traffic in the Raioballo sector, this olive, blue, and brown planet had no industrial settlements or advanced technology. Its surface was covered with empty steppes, savannas of lavender grass, and spiky blba trees. The planet had two moons and abundant animal life, including herds of hairy beasts, simple balloon-like creatures, and mace flies. Primitive nomadic tribesmen, the Dantari, moved along the coasts, though their numbers were so few that the planet was essentially uninhabited.

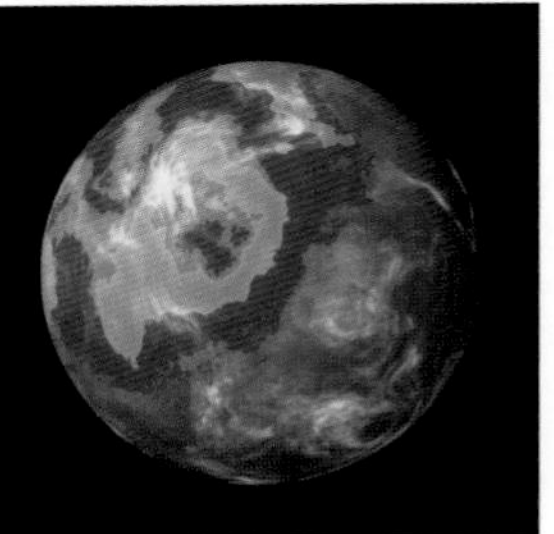

Dantooine

Some 4,000 years before the Galactic Civil War, Dantooine was the site of a Jedi training center established by Master Vodo-Siosk Baas. There he instructed such notable Jedi as Exar Kun and the Cathar warriors Crado and Sylvar. Darth Malak destroyed the enclave, though its ruins remained for millennia.

During the Clone Wars, the Separatists attempted to obtain a foothold on Dantooine as an important staging ground for operations at nearby Muunilinst. Mace Windu was instrumental in stopping a Confederacy droid force that had invaded the planet.

Dani

Giddean Danu

Decades later, Dantooine served as the primary base for the Rebel Alliance until it was evacuated in one day's time after an Imperial tracking device was found hidden in a cargo shipment. Some 11 years later, 50 colonists from Eol Sha were relocated to the planet, but a group of Admiral Daala's AT-AT walkers wiped them out. During the Yuuzhan Vong invasion, the planet was one of the first to fall to the alien menace.

***Dantooine*** A New Republic CR90 corvette, part of the force sent to liberate the planet Ciutric from the control of Prince-Admiral Krennel.

**Dantooine Squadron** A group of Rebel pilots organized while the Alliance was stationed on Dantooine shortly before the Battle of Yavin. Most of the Dantooine Squadron was destroyed in the attack on the first Death Star.

**Dantos, Vigos** The chief medical officer aboard the *Pride of Selonia,* a starship of the Galactic Alliance during the war against the Yuuzhan Vong.

**Danu, Giddean** The Senate representative of Kuat during the Clone Wars. His world was known for its massive shipyards, which developed military vessels for the Republic. Danu was torn between representing his planet's obvious interests in a continued military buildup, and his own personal feelings about the state of the galaxy. His opposition to the more hawkish industrial leaders on Kuat almost had him recalled from office. Danu was a strong supporter of the Jedi. Invited into the inner circle of Senators concerned with Palpatine's ascent to power, Danu alone felt that they needed to turn to the Jedi for support.

**Danuta** A planet with a secret Imperial base, it was where the technical plans for the Empire's first Death Star were kept. Rebel Alliance agent Kyle Katarn infiltrated the facility and stole the plans, which were later beamed to Princess Leia Organa's consular ship near Toprawa.

**Danva, Joclad** A Jedi Knight skilled in the martial arts, he entered a teräs käsi competition just prior to the Clone Wars and was defeated by the fierce Phow Ji. Though Danva purposely chose not to employ his Force abilities in the fight, many mistakenly took his defeat as indication of a Jedi Knight's limitations. Danva was killed in the Battle of Geonosis that began the Clone Wars.

*Gav and Jori Daragon*

**Danyawarra** A Jedi who, as Padawan to Ludwin Katarkus, was part of the mission sent to settle the conflict between the Virgillian Free Alignment and Virgillian Aristocracy during the Separatist crisis. With the death of Katarkus, Danyawarra ascended to the rank of commander in the Clone Wars, and was leader of the 101st Regiment.

**Daplona** The capital city of Ciutric.

**Dar, Chu-Gon** An ancient Jedi Master who once taught at temples on Mustafar. After his death, rumors arose that he had developed incredibly powerful Force techniques, including the ability to transmogrify matter through cube-like devices.

**Dar, Ingo** A Yuuzhan Vong warrior, he was one of five dispatched to Coruscant to kidnap the infant Ben Skywalker.

**Daragon, Gav** A hyperspace explorer some 5,000 years before the Galactic Civil War. During his adventures, he and his sister, Jori, stumbled across the ancient Sith Empire and were captured. The reigning Dark Lord, Naga Sadow, slowly converted Gav to the dark side. Sadow then allowed Jori to escape Sith imprisonment, but only after he placed a homing beacon on her ship. Using the beacon as a guide, Sadow launched an invasion against the Old Republic. The corrupted Gav was given command of the attack on his homeworld, Koros Major. In the conflict, Gav's former friend, Aarrba the Hutt, was killed and Gav realized that he had made a grave error in trusting Naga Sadow. He confronted Sadow aboard the Dark Lord's meditation sphere, but the cagey Sith outwitted Gav and trapped the boy on the vessel.

Empress Teta's fleet soon arrived and cornered the Sith forces, at which point Naga Sadow used a secret weapon to cause the destruction of a nearby giant red star, Primus Goluud. With a massive explosion imminent, Sadow's fleet escaped into hyperspace, leaving Gav behind. Still imprisoned aboard the meditation sphere, Gav transmitted coordinates to the Sith Empire to Empress Teta's flagship and urged the Empress and his sister to flee before the star erupted. Teta's forces did manage to escape just as Primus Goluud exploded, but Gav was incinerated in the blast.

**Daragon, Hok and Timar** The husband and wife who were the parents of Gav and Jori Daragon, they were skilled pilots working throughout the Koros System some 5,000 years before the Galactic Civil War. While delivering supplies to soldiers on the war-torn planet of Kirrek, they found themselves in the middle of a huge battle between the forces of Empress Teta and hundreds of rebels who refused to bow to Teta's rule. Their ship, *Shadow Runner,* was caught in crossfire and destroyed, killing the couple instantly.

**Daragon, Jori** A hyperspace explorer operating about 5,000 years before the birth of Luke Skywalker. While searching for a profitable new hyperspace route, she and her brother, Gav, stumbled across the Sith Empire. They fell under the influence of Naga Sadow, who pretended to befriend the pair in order to gain their trust. Sadow kept the pair separated while he secretly converted Gav to the dark side. Soon after, he helped Jori escape the Sith, but secretly planted a homing beacon on her starship. Sadow used the homing beacon on Jori's ship as his guide and launched a major attack on the Old Republic, beginning the Great Hyperspace War. Jori joined the forces of Empress Teta to repel the invaders and was present when her brother's troops killed her friend, Aarrba the Hutt.

She attacked Gav, but her brother escaped. Jori and Empress Teta followed Gav to Primus Goluud, where Naga Sadow caused the destruction of an unstable red giant star. Gav had betrayed Sadow and transmitted hyperspace coordinates for the Sith Empire to Teta's forces. Jori and Empress Teta managed to escape before Primus Goluud exploded, but Gav was incinerated in the blast. Jori remained aboard Empress Teta's flagship until the Sith were defeated. After the war, Jori reopened Aarrba the Hutt's repair dock on Koros Major.

**Daragon, Led** A member of Coruscant elite society during the Clone Wars, he was known to frequent the Galaxies Opera House.

**Daragon Trail** An extension of the Goluud Corridor that runs into the Outer Rim and the ancient Sith worlds. It was first blazed 5,000 years before the Battle of Yavin. The route has long been considered outdated and somewhat hazardous, and has been replaced by much faster, easier ways to get to the ancient Sith worlds.

**Darak** A high-ranking Ferroan native to Zonama Sekot, she initially was suspicious of the Jedi mission led by Luke Skywalker, who made contact with the living planet during the war against the Yuuzhan Vong. Only after the planet itself came to trust and accept Skywalker did Darak and her partner, Rowel, do the same. This alliance proved tentative, as sabotage unleashed by Nom Anor damaged Sekot, and led Darak to demand that the Jedi leave.

**Darakaer** According to legend, Darakaer was a warrior forced into an eternal sleep to save the Irmenu people. Darakaer told the Irmenu that they could call upon him if their nation was ever imperiled again. To summon him, the Irmenu had to beat a certain rhythm upon Darakaer's drum as they prepared for war. Gilad Pellaeon, military leader of the Imperial Remnant, used the legend of Darakaer's drum as a secret signal between himself and Admiral Natasi Daala; he had a special drumbeat that he could tap out over a comlink, which would be understood only by Daala as a summons to rejoin the Imperial Remnant.

**Darb, Sergeant Whelmo** A sergeant in the security detail assigned to the maiden voyage of the Star Destroyer *Anakin Solo,* he was ordered by Jacen Solo to accompany Luke Skywalker and his entourage to the ship's Situation Room for a meeting with Tenel Ka.

**Darc, Artel** A Separatist dark sider defeated by Shaak Ti during the Clone Wars.

**Darcc, Moff** The Imperial Governor of Kashyyyk at the time of the Battle of Endor. After their defeat on Kashyyyk, Moff Darcc and his forces fled the Avatar Orbital Space Station.

**Darda** A tall, dark-haired, dangerous-looking human member of the Peace Brigade, he was part of the team that infiltrated the *Queen of the Empire* at Vortex to recover the Yuuzhan Vong priestess Elan. Darda posed as backup for the New Republic officers protecting Elan, but an implausible backstory tipped off Major Showolter to the ruse. Showolter killed Darda, but not before the intruder was able to shoot and kill New Republic agent Jode Tee.

**Dardo, Vigo** A one-eyed Rodian Vigo who reported to Alexi Garyn, the leader of Black Sun prior to the Battle of Naboo. Dardo wore a patch over his left eye and had an assassin droid as his personal bodyguard. Dardo and the other Vigos were slaughtered by Darth Maul.

**Dare, Sigel** An icy, dutiful, rigid-thinking Imperial Knight serving Emperor Roan Fel, she disliked the Sith. She did not want to admit that the galaxy she knew was falling apart.

**Dareb** An Imperial pilot and wingmate to Commander Orvak, he was assigned to disable the shield generators protecting the Jedi academy on Yavin 4 prior to the Shadow Academy attack on the jungle moon. Dareb died when he crashed his stealth TIE fighter during the attack run.

**Darek system** Located near the Hensara and Morobe systems, this system was where Rogue Squadron made a hyperspace jump three years after the Battle of Endor as a way to disguise the squadron's origin point and hidden base.

**Darepp** The planet to which the starliner *Star Morning,* owned by the Fallanassi religious order, traveled after the group left the planet Teyr. When Luke Skywalker departed from Teyr, he guessed that the other ships in his outbound corridor were headed for the Foeless Crossroads or for Darepp.

**Dargul** The sister world of blob-racing planet Umgul, it was the location of Palace Dargul, residence of the Duchess Mistal. When the Duchess reached marriage age, a young man named Dack became her consort. He later fled to Umgul, was taken captive by Lando Calrissian, and was returned to the Duchess for a million-credit reward.

**Dargulli** A planet in the Kether system where a small party of stormtroopers was murdered by a vigilante wielding a lightsaber. Darth Vader went to Dargulli to investigate, only to be ambushed by bounty hunters. Vader fought off his attackers with the aid of Boba Fett, who was in a nearby cantina.

**Darillian, Captain Zurel** This egotistical human Imperial Navy officer from Coruscant worked for Warlord Zsinj. After his death, Garik "Face" Loran of Wraith Squadron impersonated him as part of a charade to infiltrate Zsinj's forces.

***Daring*** A Galactic Alliance frigate that, while on patrol with the *Bounty,* discovered a new model of Bothan war frigate during the war against the Confederation.

**Daring Way** A dangerous stretch of darkened thoroughfare on Coruscant during the time of the Clone Wars, it intersected Vos Gesal Street in the upper reaches of the Uscru district.

***Daritha*** An ancient Rakatan word that translated into "emperor." Some scholars believe it was the root word behind the Sith title *Darth.*

**Dark Age** A century-long period of turmoil that spanned from approximately 1,100 to 1,000 years before the Battle of Yavin, at the end of what historians refer to as the Draggulch period of galactic history. During this time, the Republic and the Jedi were embroiled in a massive war against the forces of the Sith. To shore up defenses, the Republic retreated to the Core Worlds, forming a bulwark that essentially cut ties with the outlying systems. This crippled the outlier worlds because of supply and information shortages. A devastating swath cut by an outbreak of Candorian plague further taxed the Republic's resources. The Sith, conversely, enjoyed a period of territorial expansion as they spread their forces across multiple fronts. It was not until the decisive series of conflicts at Ruusan that the Sith were vanquished, bringing an end to the Dark Age.

Dark armor

**dark armor** A general term used to describe armor worn by those who fell to the dark side. In ancient times, the term specifically referred to suits of armor woven with cortosis fiber—to provide added protection against lightsaber strikes—and enhanced by the power of the dark side.

**Dark Curse** *See* DS-61-4.

**Darker, the** The personification of the negative energies siphoned from the original inhabitants of Arbra, this being was kept in an underground grotto, protected by a force screen that reacted to negative emotions. The ancient inhabitants of Arbra abandoned the Darker; only when the Rebel Alliance used Arbra as its base did he become active again. The Darker sought technology to build a device to neutralize the screen that entrapped him. He lured R2-D2 into his grotto and attempted to dismantle him. The Darker eventually was defeated by Chewbacca, who threw the being into the force screen, destroying him and the underground city.

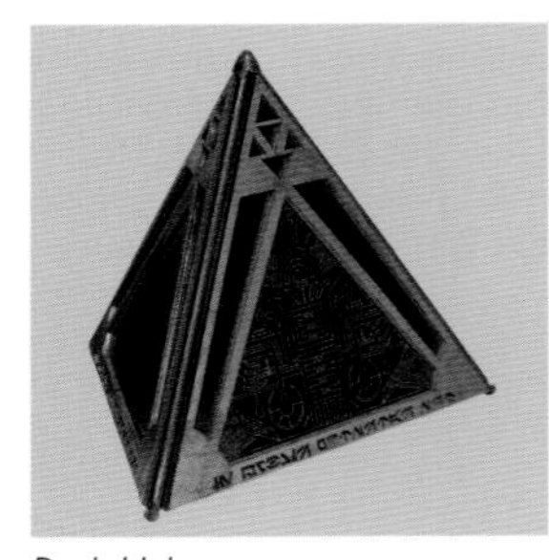
Dark Holocron

**Dark Eye probe droid** Arakyd DRK-1 probe droids were equipped with advanced sensors, powerful scanners, and miniature repulsorlift devices. These compact droids could also be outfitted with a number of weapons, which they unleashed after ambushing their master's enemies. Easily controlled from afar by a wristband comlink, Sith probe droids were ideal for locating specific targets. The Sith warrior Darth Maul used one to spy on his enemies.

**Dark Force (1)** *See Katana* fleet.

**Dark Force (2)** A religion that combined the teachings of the ancient Sith, Plaristes, and Dak Ramis, it was founded by Darth Millennial. Its tenets eventually formed key precepts followed by the Prophets of the Dark Side.

**Dark Force Nebula** A stellar formation located in the Dathomir system. The Empire established a base of operations within the ring of asteroids that surrounded the nebula.

Dark Eye probe droid

**Dark Holocron** A pyramid-shaped trove of holographic information, it contained the teachings and histories of the Sith and their Dark Lords going back 100,000 years. Its complete secrets were accessible only to a Dark Lord of the Sith. The holocron was captured from the Sith by Master Odan-Urr during the fall of the Sith Empire nearly 5,000 years before the Battle of Yavin. It was later recovered from the Jedi Temple by Lorian Nod and Count Dooku, before being lost in the Clone Wars.

**Dark Jedi** An informal term meant to describe a Jedi fallen from the light side. It was sometimes used in contrast with the term *Sith* or *Sith Lord,* as a Dark Jedi typically did not have any specific Sith training or initiation. However, usage of the term was relaxed enough that it came to describe dark side users of various backgrounds.

The reborn clone Emperor envisioned a new breed of Jedi Knights, trained in the dark side of the Force and loyal to him for the 1,000 years that he expected to reign. Evil Jedi Knights operating during the Clone Wars were also called Dark Jedi; a group of them threatened the Bpfassh system. About 19 years after the Battle of Endor, the Second Imperium attempted to train a new legion of Dark Jedi at the Shadow Academy. Their goal was to retake the galaxy and reestablish the Empire.

**Darkknell** A world that was the site of an intense struggle to recover the plans to the first Death Star. It was here, in the city of Xakrea, that Garm Bel Iblis managed to beat Ysanne Isard in a race to locate stolen datacards.

**Dark, Knire** This Syboona, a smuggler by trade, hauled her contraband from world to world under the guise of a professional Podracer. Cautious, almost paranoid, she was always watching for the authorities, and this behavior showed up on the race course as well. Dark tended to stay away from the pack, usually darting off into hidden routes, but she fiercely defended her position when approached or provoked. She was eventually caught by Republic authorities with contraband, bringing an end to her Podracing career.

**Dark Lady of the Sith** *See* Lumiya.

**Darklighter, Anya** The daughter of Jula and Silya Darklighter, and sister to Gavin, she discovered Shmi Skywalker's personal journal under a vaporator and gave it to Leia Organa Solo.

**Darklighter, Biggs** A childhood friend and role model for Luke Skywalker, this brave X-wing fighter pilot lost his life in the assault on the Death Star during the Battle of Yavin.

Part of a wealthy family on Tatooine, Biggs Darklighter met young Luke in the town of Anchorhead. The two, while fast friends, always competed. They raced landspeeders and skyhoppers and planned to enter the Imperial Space Academy together. But Luke's uncle, Owen Lars, said he needed his nephew to work the farm for at least another season. While in the Academy, Biggs and some classmates contacted the Rebel Alliance and made plans to join it as soon as possible after graduation.

After Biggs left the Academy, he was assigned to a noncombat post as first mate on the ship *Rand Ecliptic.* But first he made a final trip to Tatooine, where he had an unexpected reunion with Luke at their friend Fixer's shop in Tosche power station. In private, Biggs told Luke that he was going to join the Rebellion. Within weeks he and his ship's executive officer staged a mutiny, stole the ship and its valuable ore cargo, and turned it and themselves over to the Alliance.

Biggs at the Battle of Yavin

Biggs piloted an X-wing fighter in a number of battles before uniting with Luke Skywalker on Yavin 4 as the assault on the first Death Star was about to begin. As Red Three to Luke's Red Five, he destroyed several TIE fighters before finally being taken out by a blast from Darth Vader's TIE fighter.

**Darklighter, Dera** Biggs Darklighter's younger sister. On Tatooine, she worked secretly for the Rebel Alliance, using her charisma and her skills in oration to inspire others to join.

**Darklighter, Gavin** A cousin of Biggs Darklighter, he was a 16-year-old Tatooine farm boy when Wedge Antilles pushed for his inclusion in Rogue Squadron over the objections of General Salm. Rogue Leader's faith in his young recruit was quickly rewarded when Darklighter's simulator test scores put him near the top of his class. He fought at Chorax and Hensara III without incident or distinction. During a night raid by Imperial stormtroopers at Rogue Squadron's hidden base on Talasea, he was seriously wounded by blasterfire but miraculously survived. Later, he participated in the retaliatory strikes against the Imperial bases at Vladet and (twice) at Borleias.

Biggs Darklighter (left) confides in Luke Skywalker on Tatooine.

Darklighter was with other Rogue members when they went on a reconnaissance mission to Coruscant to get a feel for the general mood of the alien population prior to an Alliance invasion. There was no way to prepare for what the Rogues found in one of the alien quarters, Invisec. At the Azure Dianoga cantina, Gavin made the mistake of rejecting the advances of Asyr Sei'lar, a female Bothan. Brought before the Alien Combine on charges of bigotry, he narrowly escaped death from the group, then from the squadron of stormtroopers that subsequently raided the Combine's hideout.

During that battle, Sei'lar and the Combine members realized that Darklighter and the other Rogues were not their foes, and so they joined forces against the Empire. Their first attempt to bring down Coruscant's shields ended in dismal failure at the Palar warehouse, when their team was assaulted by stormtroopers. When they regrouped, Darklighter came up with the idea of "taking the planet by storm"—creating a tremendous thunderstorm and using the electrical charges from the lightning strikes to short out the power system. It worked. The shields came down, allowing the Alliance invasion fleet to send in ground troops.

Sei'lar eventually joined Rogue Squadron, and she and Gavin grew very close, despite the closed-minded objections of some. While preparing for the Bacta War, Gavin returned to Tatooine to obtain a weapons cache from his uncle, Huff Darklighter. Later he helped defend a colony on frozen Halanit from attack by Ysanne Isard. He fought alongside the other Rogues during the Thrawn crisis.

Around the time of the return of Isard, Gavin and Asyr planned to marry and adopt a Bothan child, despite the fierce opposition of Bothan politician Borsk Fey'lya. An Imperial ambush on Corvis Minor seemingly resulted in the death of Sei'lar, but unbeknownst to Darklighter, she survived, rescued by Booster Terrik. She decided to start her life anew as an undercover operative looking to change Bothan society from within.

Darklighter mourned Sei'lar for a time, before eventually adopting two sons, orphans who had lived near the Rogue Squadron base after the Thrawn crisis. He soon married Sera Faleur, the social worker who helped him through the adoption process. Together they had children of their own: two daughters and a son. Family was quite important to Darklighter: He took his sister, Rasca, and her children into his home when she was widowed.

After Wedge Antilles and Tycho Celchu retired from duty following the final peace accords between the New Republic and the Imperial Remnant, Gavin Darklighter became leader of Rogue Squadron and was promoted to colonel. He commanded the elite starfighter group during the Yuuzhan Vong invasion, leading such pilots as Jaina Solo into combat against the alien menace at Dantooine, Ithor, and Kalarba. He flew alongside Wedge Antilles as the legendary pilot came out of retirement to help the New Republic destroy a Yuuzhan Vong superweapon created from the remains of the shattered planet Sernpidal.

Darklighter's squadron helped evacuate Coruscant ahead of the enemy's invasion of the capital. He also led Rogue Squadron during Operation Starlancer and in the defense of Borleias against the forces of Czulkang Lah.

Following the war, Darklighter was promoted to commodore and given command of the Star Destroyer *Mon Mothma.* He served under Admiral Nek Bwua'tu during the Swarm War's blockade of the Utegetu Nebula. After that conflict, Darklighter advanced even farther up the chain of command, serving as rear admiral during the Galactic Alliance's war with Corellia. During that war, Darklighter achieved the rank of admiral despite his misgivings about the command of Jacen Solo.

**Darklighter, Huff "Huk"** The father of hero Biggs Darklighter, he was proud of his son's valor but had bittersweet feelings because Biggs wasn't around to receive his accolades. Although surrounded by his family, there was still an air of loneliness to Huff Darklighter. One of the wealthiest residents of Tatooine, he made the bulk of his fortune trading goods throughout the galaxy. But sometimes the bottom line was so important to Darklighter that he paid large bribes to do business. He once even trafficked in black-market Imperial armor, weapons, and fighter craft. Later he became an invaluable source for Rogue Squadron when it needed weapons and munitions to use against former Director of Imperial Intelligence Ysanne Isard.

**Darklighter, Jula** Unlike his prosperous brother, Huff, Jula was a hardworking moisture farmer on Tatooine. They shared common ground in their pride in their sons. Jula's son, Gavin Darklighter—like Huff's son, Biggs, before him—became a legend within Rogue

Gavin Darklighter

Squadron. During the early years of the New Republic, Jula and his wife Silya maintained the Darklighter moisture farm.

Huff "Huk" Darklighter

**Darklighter, Lanal** Huff Darklighter's third wife, she was more like another mother to Gavin than an aunt. When Huff decided to have more children, his second wife had left him, still hurting from the loss of their only son, Biggs. Lanal was also the sister of Silya Darklighter—Gavin's mother—so she was Gavin's aunt on both sides of the family.

**Darklighter, Rasca** The sister of Gavin Darklighter, she was widowed during the New Republic's battle against the Yevetha. She and her children moved in with Gavin and Sera Darklighter.

**Darklighter, Sera Faleur** A human from Chandrila, she grew up on the shores of the Silver Sea. She was the social worker who helped Gavin Darklighter through the process of adopting his two sons, orphans who had lived near the Rogue Squadron hangar after the Thrawn crisis. About two years after taking in the boys, Gavin married Sera. Together they had a daughter, followed by a son, then another daughter.

**Darklighter, Silya** The mother of Gavin Darklighter, she was both proud of her son and fearful of the dangers he faced as a member of Rogue Squadron. Most of the time she was able to put the worry out of her mind, for she was very busy with her younger children and the farm on Tatooine.

**Darklighter, Trepler** The owner and operator of Docking Bay 86 at Mos Eisley Spaceport.

**Dark Lord of the Sith** *See* Sith.

**Darkmere, Brigadier Colin** A New Republic Intelligence officer tasked with gathering information regarding the World Devastators during the resurrected Emperor's campaign of terror.

**Dark Nest** The Gorog hive of the collective Killik entity known as the Colony. While the Colony acquired extraordinary capacity for expansion by the adoption of Force-sensitive Raynar Thul into its ranks, the inclusion of dark sider Lomi Plo into the Gorog hive strangely affected it. Plo's influence made the Gorog the Colony's dark subconscious, and the rest of the Colony was unaware of the Gorog hive's activities. It earned the Jedi nickname of Dark Nest. In the devastating Swarm War that followed, Luke Skywalker brought an end to the Dark Nest by defeating Lomi Plo in combat.

**Dark Reaper** An ancient weapon constructed by the Sith during the early campaigns of the Sith War almost 4,000 years before the Clone Wars. It was an enormous, saucer-shaped vehicle powered by the living Force. The heart of the Dark Reaper was the Force Harvester, a large mechanical sphere that stripped the Force from all living things and stored their life energies until needed by the Dark Reaper. Once fully powered, the Dark Reaper emitted massive bolts of Force lightning that rained down from dozens of points on the gigantic ship.

This weapon of mass destruction was the key to the Sith Empire's plan to destroy the Republic planet by planet. According to legend, it was only through the valiant efforts of a group of Jedi Knights led by Ulic Qel-Droma that the disaster was avoided. Once defeated, the Force Harvester was removed from the Reaper and buried below tons of garbage on the little-known Outer Rim planet of Raxus Prime. This rendered the Dark Reaper powerless. The weapon itself was entombed on the planet Thule by the Jedi, where the Reaper was to spend the rest of eternity in darkness, never to unleash its fury on the galaxy again.

When Count Dooku learned of the Dark Reaper, he sought to capture it in his war against the Republic. He based his operations on Raxus Prime while he searched for the Force Harvester. Anakin Skywalker, however, discovered the secret to defeating the Dark Reaper from a hologram of Ulic Qel-Droma on Rhen Var. During his battle with the Dark Reaper, Anakin heard Qel-Droma's voice advising him on how to defeat it.

**Darksaber Project** The code name for the secret superweapon ordered built by a group of Hutt crime lords under Durga: a reconstruction of the original Death Star's laser, yet even more powerful. Its ultimate failure resulted in Durga's death.

**dark side** *See* Force, the.

**Dark Side Adepts** Members of the reborn clone Emperor's New Imperial Council, they were drawn from the ranks of the Emperor's cohorts in the dark side, trained by him, and turned into powerful practitioners of the Force. They served the Emperor's will and were intended to eventually replace most planetary governors. Executor Sedriss, Nefta, Sa-Di, Zasm, Fass, Krdys Mordi, and Xecr Nist were all Dark Side Adepts.

Dark Reaper

***Dark Side Compendium*** An encyclopedia of dark side lore that was being written by the reborn clone Emperor. He had completed three volumes of a proposed several-hundred-volume set before being defeated by Luke Skywalker and Princess Leia Organa Solo. Luke read all three volumes: *The Book of Anger, The Weakness of Inferiors,* and *The Creation of Monsters.*

**dark side nexus** Any unusual localization, or vergence, of dark side Force energy. These strange locales emanated the dark side of the Force, and were considered focal points of power for dark side users. As such, they were often guarded by Jedi Knights to prevent their discovery and exploitation. Known dark side nexuses included the twisted tree-cave on Dagobah, Halagad Ventor's hermitage on Trinta, and a "stain" of dark side energy that hovered over Endor following the defeat of the Emperor.

Darksaber Project

**darkspace** A Yuuzhan Vong term describing hyperspace.

**Darkstaff** An ancient Sith artifact believed to have been the cause of the disappearance of the entire Cularin system shortly after the Battle of Naboo. According to ancient tomes uncovered on Almas, the existence of the Darkstaff was discovered by Darth Rivan, who had strange dreams about being called by the artifact. Rivan believed that the Darkstaff wanted to use him as a way to leave the sector. Measuring a meter in length and 4 centimeters in diameter, the Darkstaff seemed to consume all light around it. It also literally fed on the Force. Rivan refused to search for the artifact, fearing that its release would cause great damage to the galaxy. Millennia later, word of the Darkstaff reached the ears of Len Markus, who apparently located it in a Cularin asteroid belt—and the entire system disappeared for a decade, then just as suddenly reappeared.

**Darkstar, Shannur** A Jedi Knight who was part of the Ermin Phin-Mar's archaeological expedition to Pelgrin, about 3,000 years before the Battle of Yavin. Darkstar and her fellow Jedi discovered that the Oracle at Pelgrin had a deep connection to the Force, and eventually restored it to life by meditating in one of its upper chambers. As the Oracle came back into being, Darkstar had a vision of the future in which she foresaw a great battle between the Jedi Knights and a group of Sith adherents. Jedi historians later inferred that she had seen a vision of the Battle of Ruusan.

**Dark Star Hellions** A notorious band of swoop gangsters in the Outer Rim Territories. They were known to raid isolated settlements in Seswenna sector using a large freighter to ferry their overpowered swoops. The Hellions targeted poorly defended outposts and towns, then escaped before reinforcements arrived. The Questal chapter of the Dark Star Hellions were known as the Nebula Masters.

**darkstick** An exotic boomerang-like weapon used by the Kerestians, it took its name from the light-absorbing blade as well as the Kerestian belief that a being's soul was resigned to eternal darkness upon death.

**DarkStryder** A strange and powerful alien force that provided previously unheard-of technology to a rogue Imperial Moff, Kentor Sarne. Its secrets were hidden deep past the Kathol Rift and unknown space. The New Republic first encountered the DarkStryder artifacts and technology when it pursued Sarne some four years after the Battle of Endor. Many of the events surrounding the pursuit and DarkStryder were classified by the New Republic.

**Dark Sword Squadron** A Jedi starfighter unit led by Kenth Hamner that was part of the Galactic Alliance First Fleet. It defended Kuat against the Confederation until it—along with the rest of the Jedi Order, led by Luke Skywalker—defected from the Alliance.

**Darktrin, Finn** An undercover Imperial agent who had infiltrated the ranks of the Rebel Alliance, he was Force-sensitive and often reported to Darth Vader. Finn was tasked with acquiring a vital holocron that the Alliance had left behind on Dantooine. Finn engineered the transfer of xenobiologist Dusque Mistflier to help him navigate Dantooine's ecosphere. The two began to fall in love, despite their devotion to their respective duties. When Dusque realized Finn was trying to download the contents of the holocron for transmission to his Imperial contacts, she destroyed the data device. Finn stabbed Dusque and then fled back to the Empire, where Darth Vader miraculously spared him despite his failure.

**dark trooper** An advanced battle droid developed by Rom Mohc for the Empire as a type of "super stormtrooper." The ambitious project was developed in stages. The Phase One dark trooper had an unfinished appearance, with an exposed metal skeleton cast of hardened phrik. This towering humanoid was armed with a razor-edged carving blade and arm-mounted blast shield. Its programming was primitive, and its drive to attack was relentless.

The Phase Two trooper was much more refined, having a gunmetal-gray armored exterior reminiscent of stormtrooper uniforms. Equipped with a repulsorlift pack and maneuvering jets, this massive automated soldier was extremely agile, and typically armed with a powerful plasma shell assault cannon and long-range explosive rockets.

The final and most powerful model was the Phase Three dark trooper. Only one was known to exist, in the personal employ of General Mohc. A towering goliath with broad armored shoulders, this dark trooper could operate independently or be used as an armored powersuit. Connected to its massive arms was a deadly cluster of firing tubes that dispensed a seemingly endless supply of seeker rockets.

Dark troopers were first unleashed shortly after the Battle of Yavin on the unsuspecting Rebel Alliance installation of Tak Base. The Empire launched the droids via hyperspace capsules, in a fashion similar to the distribution of deep-space probe droids. The inhuman soldiers tore through all resistance, devastating the Rebel outpost on the planet Talay. Investigating this disturbing new assault was Alliance mercenary Kyle Katarn. He uncovered the secret dark trooper project and traced it back to its source, the immense production facility aboard the *Arc Hammer,* General Mohc's flagship.

Katarn infiltrated and sabotaged the *Arc Hammer.* The Emperor was so infuriated by the loss of the *Arc Hammer*—and of the enormous investment made in the dark trooper project—that all research into stormtrooper battle droids ended with Mohc's death.

**Dark Underlord** An ancient Sith warlord during the time of the New Sith Wars. He was a master of Jar'Kai combat, preferring to use paired Sith swords rather than more modern lightsabers. Conflicting legends of the Dark Underlord's origins describe him as an avatar of General Xendor's spirit that had possessed a follower, or as a being magically summoned from the realm of Chaos by a Sith acolyte. The Dark Underlord led a fighting force known as the Black Knights of Malrev IV in a devastating scourge of the Republic and the Jedi. He eventually was defeated by Mandalorian mercenaries.

***Darkvenge*** A Trade Federation battleship under the command of Vicelord Siv Kav, it was tasked by Darth Sidious with intercepting and destroying Outbound Flight.

Phase Three dark trooper

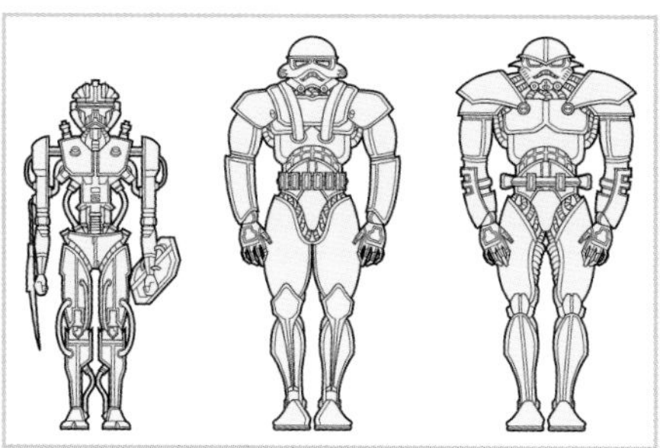

Schematic of the three dark trooper phases

**Dark Woman** *See* Kuro, An'ya

**Darlon sector** The site of an orbiting casino where the Twi'lek female Seely met space pirate Drek Drednar before becoming one of his lieutenants.

**Darlyn Boda** An apparent Imperial planet for many years, it was about half a day's travel from Hoth. Darlyn Boda was a steamy, muddy world that long had both a thriving criminal underground and an active network of Rebel contacts. Its main city was also called Darlyn Boda. The bounty hunter droid 4-LOM abandoned his former position as a valet aboard the *Kuari Princess* when the ship stopped at Darlyn Boda. Years later, after the Battle of Hoth, 4-LOM and the Gand bounty hunter Zuckuss severely damaged one of the last Rebel transports to leave Hoth, the *Bright Hope,* then had a change of heart, rescued the 90 Alliance soldiers aboard, and transported them to Darlyn Boda for treatment of their wounds.

**Darm, Umolly** A well-connected Nam Chorios trader, she had the ability to acquire many things offworld. Umolly Darm exported Spookcrystals, long green-and-violet crystals found in clusters in the deep hills of the planet. She was told that the crystals were used on K-class worlds to help make flowers grow better, but in reality they were used in spaceneedles—long-distance smart missiles—as a type of artificial intelligence.

**Darman (RC-1136)** A Republic commando trained by Kal Skirata. His entire unit was wiped out at the Battle of Geonosis and he was reassigned to Omega Squad. His first mission with his new squadmates was to infiltrate a Separatist biological research laboratory on the agrarian planet of Qiilura, and detain Dr. Ovolot Qail Uthan, who was developing an anti-clone viral weapon. Darman was separated from the rest of his squad during landing, but managed to make contact with Jedi Padawan Etain Tur-Makan and the shapeshifting Jinart. The four commandos were reunited and successful in their mission. Despite restrictions in duty and protocol, Darman and Etain began a romantic relationship. Unbeknownst to the commando, Etain bore him a child, who came to be known as Venku Skirata.

**D'armon, Pav** A Mistryl Shadow Guard, she was second in command in Operation Hammertong, the code name for one of the long, cylindrical sections of the superlaser for the second Death Star. Pav D'armon was killed in an Imperial raid.

**Darnada, Vigo** A monacle-wearing Dug who served as a Black Sun Vigo in the final decades of the Galactic Republic. He had a Twi'lek bodyguard named Sinya. Despite the warnings of Neimoidian Hath Monchar, Darnada refused to believe the rumors that the Sith had returned to the galaxy. Two of Darnada's enforcers, Aga Nasa and Gargachyyk, brought Darth Maul to the Vigo as a prospect for a new bodyguard. At that moment, Maul lashed out at Darnada's forces, killing nearly all of his guards before slaying the Dug himself. Darth Maul then destroyed Darnada's space station, though he did allow Aga Nasa to escape.

**Daroe** A Mos Eisley Jawa who worked as an informant for the Empire.

**Daron** A native of the planet Solem, he was part of the Rebel underground that sprang up during the early years of the Galactic Civil War. Daron gave his life trying to protect his leader, Yolan Bren.

**Daroon, Miro** A brilliant, intuitive tech expert at the Jedi Temple, he was a tall nonhuman from the planet Piton, thin as a reed, with a high forehead and pale, almost white eyes. Since his species was accustomed to living underground, Miro wore a cap and tinted eye shields. When Xanatos and Bruck Chun sabotaged the central power structure of the Jedi Temple, it was Miro Daroon's responsibility to fix the problem. A year ahead of Xanatos in his Jedi training, Miro acknowledged that Xanatos was the only Jedi student who was better at constructing tech infrastructure models than he was.

**Dar'Or** A planet in the Dar'Or system and the seldom-visited Jospro sector, this low-gravity forested world orbited an orange sun and was home to intelligent flying mammals called Ri'Dar. Along with the sloth-like sabertoothed indola, they inhabited the middle levels of a dense network of 200-meter-tall waza trees that covered the world. Predators of the Ri'Dar included the indola and the avian elix, which was introduced to Dar'Or by ecologists to save it from extinction on a supernova-threatened world. The Ri'Dar organized their primitive society into warrens and cities. The planet was declared a Species Preservation Zone, but some smugglers still hunted the elix to sell its meat.

Darovit

**Darovit** A boy at the time of the Battle of Ruusan, he was trained for war on Somov Rit. In his youth, he went by the name Tomcat, and his cousins had similar playful nicknames: Bug and Rain. They were recruited by the Jedi to fight in the war against the Sith Brotherhood of Darkness. The Jedi Torr Snapit sacrificed his own life to save the young recruits, and Tomcat retrieved his lightsaber, joining the battle to fight alongside General Kiel Charny. Tomcat was quickly disillusioned by the rigors of war, and he grew disappointed by the numerous setbacks faced by the Jedi. The Sith Lord Githany lured Darovit to the dark side, a betrayal made complete when Darovit delivered a killing blow to General Charny. Darovit, however, was unable to strike down his cousin Bug, and tried to renounce the dark side. Lord Kaan's disastrous use of the Sith thought bomb resulted in the death of all the powerful Sith and Jedi warriors on Ruusan; Darovit was one of the few survivors due to his relatively weak connection to the Force. When Tomcat emerged from the cavern of the thought bomb, he discovered Rain newly apprenticed to Darth Bane. Tomcat drew his lightsaber to confront the Sith Lord, but Rain attacked first. She used the dark side to destroy Tomcat's right hand, in reality sparing his life.

*Roblio Darté*

Accepting his failure as both a Jedi and a Sith, Darovit found solace among the peaceful Bouncers native to Ruusan. He studied the ways of natural healers on Ruusan, becoming known as the "Healing Hermit." When the Jedi Order returned to the planet a decade later to build an enormous memorial to the fallen Jedi, Darovit was outraged and surreptitiously sabotaged the construction effort. Confronted by the Jedi, Darovit recounted his witnessing of a Sith Lord survivor, Bane, ten years earlier, and was escorted to Coruscant to report his discovery to the Jedi Council. Before he could describe his encounter, though, he saw Rain—now Darth Zannah—infiltrating the Jedi Temple in disguise. Zannah captured Darovit and took him with her to her ailing Master, Darth Bane.

Bane was beyond Darovit's healing abilities, so Zannah took the Dark Lord to the Ambrian healer, Caleb, with Darovit in tow. After Caleb healed Bane, Zannah killed Caleb and used the Force to drive Darovit mad. When a Jedi team came to investigate a report of a Dark Lord, the enraged Darovit attacked them, and the Jedi quickly killed him. They mistakenly believed that Darovit fit the description of the Dark Lord, and thus they ceased their search, unaware that the Sith Order secretly continued in Bane and Zannah.

**Darpa sector** Located in the Core on the edge of the Colonies region, this sector made up one-half of the Ringali Shell. Its worlds included Esseles, Rhinnal, and Ralltiir, all of which were linked by the Perlemian Trade Route. The sector was long ruled by the heavy-handed Moff Jander Graffe.

**Darpen, Tomer** A human male from Commenor serving the New Republic Diplomatic Corps, he was the liaison between Rogue Squadron and the Adumari. Darpen once served as a pilot with the Tierfon Yellow Aces.

**Darron, Commander Vict** An Imperial Navy officer serving under Prince-Admiral Delak Krennel in the Ciutric Hegemony, he commanded the Star Destroyer *Direption*. Darron was given the reprehensible order of razing a village on Liinade III to secure the Hegemony's borders. He arranged for the villagers to be evacuated prior to the bombardment. When the New Republic attacked Liinade III, the *Direption* was severely damaged, forcing Darron to surrender.

***darr tah*** A Rakatan term that translated as "triumph over death," "immortal," or "conquest through the death of one's enemies." Some Jedi scholars believed that it might have become the basis for the Sith Lord title *Darth*.

**Darsana, Senator** The galactic ambassador of Glee Anselm during the Separatist crisis. After the assassination attempt on Senator Padmé Amidala, Darsana began to question the effectiveness of Jedi protection. He was a blue-haired, scrunch-faced Anselmi.

**Darsk, Ris** *See* Dlarit, Erisi.

**Dart** The code name used by Rebel Alliance spy Yom Argo.

**Darté, Roblio** An imposing Jedi who led the Republic forces at Parcelus Minor during the Clone Wars. His army was decimated when the Separatists bombarded the planet from orbit, causing the natural oil tzeotine to combust. Though badly wounded during the attack, the Jedi general survived to give a report to the Jedi Council. Darté was one of the few Jedi to survive Order 66. He assembled on Kessel with fellow survivors in a trap set to ensnare Darth Vader. Darté believed that vengeance would be justified if it brought an end to the Sith. He was one of the last Jedi to fall after being shot by Vader's clone troopers. He wielded a unique Y-shaped lightsaber.

**Darth** A title used by certain Sith Lords; its origins are lost to history. The first known Sith Lords to use it were Darth Malak and Darth Revan, though it's possible the name predates even their use. Some Jedi historians believed the title *Darth* might have Rakatan origins,

## Notable Darths

Darth Andeddu

Darth Azard

Darth Bandon

Darth Bane

Darth Caedus

Darth Cognus

Darth Desolous

Darth Krayt

Darth Kruhl

Darth Maladi

Darth Malak

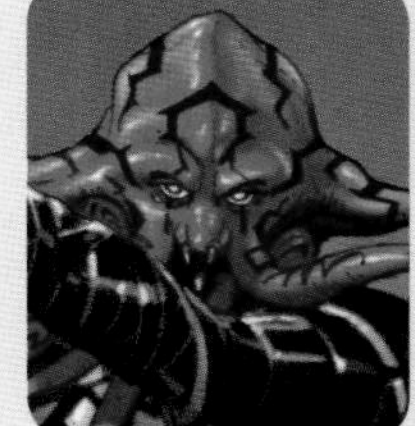
Darth Maleval

Darth Maul

Darth Millenial

Darth Nihilus

Darth Nihl

Darth Phobos

Darth Plagueis

Darth Revan

Darth Rivan

Darth Ruin

Darth Ruyn

Darth Sidious

Darth Sion

Darth Stryfe

Darth Talon

Darth Traya

Darth Tyranus

Darth Vader

Darth Vectivus

Darth Wyyrlok (III)

Darth Zannah

given the similarities of certain Rakatan phrases; *daritha* meant "emperor," while *darr tah* combined could suggest "immortal" or "triumph over death." The title dropped out of vogue among the Sith when Lord Kaan founded the Brotherhood of Darkness and eschewed a philosophy that emphasized the Sith as an organization of equals, rather than a hierarchy of supremacy. When the Sith initiate Bane saw the inherent flaws in Kaan's reasoning, he sought to rebuild the Sith Order and reclaim the Darth heritage. He became Darth Bane, and he passed the title on to his apprentice, Darth Zannah. This secret lineage of Sith continued through to the end of the Galactic Republic, and the emergence of the Empire under Darth Sidious and Darth Vader. When Luke Skywalker was able to bring Anakin Skywalker back to the light and defeat Darth Sidious, the line of Sith was broken and balance was restored to the Force. Within a few decades, however, the Sith Order began to reemerge, and Jacen Solo restored the Sith mantle when he adopted the guise of Darth Caedus during the war between the Galactic Alliance and the Confederation. A century later, the Sith were once again powerful, and many Sith Lords served a new ultimate Master, Darth Krayt, though they, too, bore the Darth title.

*Dashade*

**Dartibek system** A system that included the planet Moltok, it was the homeworld of the Ho'Din.

**dartship** Tiny starfighters developed by the Colony of the Killik species during the Swarm War. Each was capable of carrying a single insectoid pilot and little more. Dartships were produced in huge numbers by workers in the Colony, and could be launched into battle in massive swarms.

**dart shooter** A handheld weapon, it fired metal projectiles, or darts, usually filled with toxins that paralyzed or killed.

**Darys, Ameesa** A former Jedi during the Clone Wars and Padawan to Jerec, she was corrupted by her master and became an Imperial Inquisitor early in the New Order. Young Roganda and Lagan Ismaren were brought before Inquisitor Darys after their capture on Belsavis. Darys skewered Lagan as his sister was forced to watch, and then she turned Roganda to the dark side, to eventually serve as one of Emperor Palpatine's "Hands." Darys was later killed by Arden Lyn.

**Darzu, Belia** An ancient Sith Lord who lived at the time of the New Sith Wars, several hundred years before the Battle of Ruusan, she was a Shi'ido changeling. She crafted and wore her own heavily plated dark armor imbued with stealth characteristics through the dark side of the Force. She was skilled in Sith alchemy and the dark side ability known as *mechu-deru,* which allowed her to create technobeasts, mechanical forms imbued with dark side energy. Darzu recorded her knowledge into a holocron, which she kept at her stronghold on Tython. Darzu was killed by the Mecrosa Order, but centuries later Darth Bane uncovered her holocron on Tython. He studied her teachings to learn how to construct his own holocron.

*Belia Darzu*

**Das, Runck** A Yuuzhan Vong warrior, he was part of the force on Garqi training slaves to be soldiers. Krag Val ordered Das to remain behind during a battle with Jedi so that he could report to Shedao Shai afterward. Shai killed Das for not tracking the Jedi.

**DA series droid** Scavenging automata developed by the New Republic to reclaim salvage from battle sites. As directed by Operation Flotsam and the Historic Battle Site Preservation Act, these droids were used to gather information from any recovered physical evidence prior to release for public viewing.

**Dashade** A rare species of killer from the supernova-cooked world of Urkupp, the Dashades became little more than legend. The species died out during the Sith War, 4,000 years before the Galactic Civil War, when the Cron Drift explosion shattered their world. At the time, one of Prince Xizor's ancestors took his remaining 38 Dashade enforcers and had them cryogenically frozen. Once each century or so, a new one was released and put into the servitude of the Falleen royal family. Ket Maliss was the last of the Xizor family Dashades to be released.

**Dashbalar** A city on Ansion favored as a trading center for the Qulun clan.

**dashta eel** Nonsentient creatures native to Ord Cestus with remarkable Force sensitivity, they were quite rare and not known beyond their home planet. They were used in the production of the JK series bio-droid, granting the combat automata remarkable reflexes and abilities. The rarity of the eels made the JK droids among the most expensive in the galaxy. Count Dooku attempted to broker a deal with Cestus Cybernetics, promising cloning facilities to harvest the eels. The deal was a sham, as the cloning techniques would not produce viable eels. The Separatists continued a dialogue with Cestus Cybernetics nonetheless to draw the Galactic Republic to Ord Cestus.

**Dashta Mountains** A range of mountains on Ord Cestus that was the only known habitat of the Force-sensitive dashta eel. The mountains were first mapped by the noted Cestian explorer Kilaphor Dashta 400 years before the Clone Wars.

**D'asima, Paloma** One of the Eleven Elders of the People of Emberlene in the years following the Battle of Endor. On the recommendation of Karoly D'ulin, she traveled to Yaga Minor to meet with Moff Disra and Grodin Tierce to discuss an alliance between the Mistryl and the new Empire.

*General Oro Dassyne*

**Dasol, Matton** Ambushed by Eli Gand on Kashyyyk some 4,000 years before the Battle of Yavin, Matton and his shipmates were stranded on the planet. Gand tricked Matton into thinking he was indebted to him and forced him into servitude. A passing Jedi Knight learned of Gand's duplicity and exposed him as a fraud, freeing Matton.

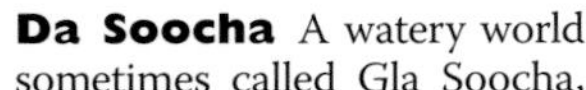

**Da Soocha** A watery world sometimes called Gla Soocha, located in the Cyax system. The name meant "waking planet" in Huttese, from an old Hutt myth about an intelligent, planet-covering ocean near the revered star Cyax. Though the Cyax system was never visited by the Hutts, it was explored by the Rebel Alliance, which established a short-lived base on Da Soocha's fifth moon during the reborn clone Emperor's appearance. Da Soocha had no native intelligent species, but Da Soocha V was home to a primitive flying species called Ixlls. Da Soocha V was destroyed by the Emperor's terrifying Galaxy Gun superweapon.

**Dasoor Challenge** One of the Mid Rim's best-known Podracing events.

**Dassid** The former king of Duro. When he died, his crown was implanted with a device that would kill any person trying to steal it from his grave site. The Duro Dustini accidentally activated the anti-tampering device on Dagobah while trying to gain the Rebel Alliance's help in defeating the Empire.

**Dassyne, General Oro** A Koorivar, he served as an acquisitions specialist and special markets director for the Corporate Alliance. During the Clone Wars, he was a military leader for the Separatists until his defeat by Obi-Wan Kenobi and Anakin Skywalker on Bomis Korri IV.

**D'Asta, Baron Ragez** A powerful shipping magnate who supplied the Empire with most of its cargo ships, he was the controller of a strategically important planetary sector of the Empire. D'Asta sent his daughter Feena to speak for him on the Imperial Ruling Council due to his failing health. When he learned that Feena had been imprisoned by council head Xandel Carivus, he threatened to withdraw his support from the Empire. But he then went further and sent his fleet of starfighters, the largest privately owned fleet in the galaxy, to Carivus's door. In the end, Carivus was dead and the council was captured by the New Republic. D'Asta then withdrew his sector from the Empire to govern itself.

**D'Asta, Feena** A member of the Imperial Interim Council. Feena D'Asta was the ambitious daughter of vessel manufacturer Baron Ragez D'Asta, representing his interests due to his failing health. Though she still had not earned the respect of her peers, she was kidnapped by Grappa the Hutt and replaced with a clone who could represent his own interests, including making peace with the Rebel Alliance. The real D'Asta was held in Grappa's palace and kept drugged to obtain information for four years until she was rescued by New Republic forces.

**D'Astan sector** The sector ruled by Baron Ragez D'Asta. D'Asta withdrew his support of the Empire after the rescue of Feena D'Asta.

**data goggles** Devices worn by Neimoidian pilots aboard capital ships and shuttles. A pair of data goggles consisted of two parts—the spectacle-like goggles and a cybernetic implant that linked them directly to the pilot's brain.

**datacard** A thin plastic rectangle used to store digital information.

**dat-an** The native language of the Annoodat.

**datapad** A palm-sized personal computer used as a portable workstation by all levels of society. A datapad had ports for coupling with droids or large computer terminals.

**Datar** The homeworld of the Ghostling species, this planet was the site of a massacre of a group of Rebels by Imperial troops who disobeyed Darth Vader's order that he wanted prisoners to interrogate.

**datarie** A type of currency used throughout the Galactic Republic, also known as Republic credits. They were usually transferred via Republic credit chips, which had security codes and algorithm memory strips. Republic credits were often useless on non-Republic planets, where residents demanded transactions in more substantial goods.

*Data goggles worn by a Neimoidian pilot*

**Datch, Tarrin** A Rebel Alliance pilot, he flew as Rogue Ten during the Battle of Hoth. He was introduced to the Rebellion by Jan Ors. During the evacuation of Echo Base, Tarrin piloted *Dutyfree,* one of the last Rebel transports to flee Hoth.

**Dathcha** A Jawa adventurer and trader, he was famous for taunting a krayt dragon and escaping to tell the tale. Dathcha belonged to the clan of Jawas that sold C-3PO and R2-D2 to Luke Skywalker's uncle, Owen Lars. Dathcha wanted to leave Tatooine and explore the galaxy, but he never got the chance, as his entire clan was wiped out by stormtroopers searching for the droids.

*Dathcha*

*Dathomir*

**Dathomir** Located in the Quelii sector, this low-gravity world had three continents, a wide ocean, four small moons—and witches: the Witches of Dathomir, to be exact, a group of Force-sensitive women who rode fearsome rancors.

In prehistoric times, the planet was settled by the reptilian Kwa. Masters of advanced technology, the Kwa erected an Infinity Gate on Dathomir, a teleportational portal that allowed the species interstellar transit across the galaxy. The dimensional gateway could also serve as an incredibly powerful weapon, broadcasting "infinity waves" that could devastate entire worlds. When the Kwa culture went into decline, the inhabitants of Dathomir degenerated into the simple Kwi, semi-intelligent, two-legged reptiles that lived in the desert and called themselves the Blue Desert People.

Dathomir was covered with a wide variety of terrain, including mountains, deserts, purple savannas, and forests of 80-meter trees and vines bearing hwotha berries. Indigenous life included flying reptiles, pig-like rodents, long whuffa worms, burra fish, and rancors.

Humans came to Dathomir when a group of illegal arms manufacturers was exiled to the planet by the Jedi Knights. Several generations later, a rogue Jedi named Allya was also exiled to Dathomir. She began to teach the Force to the planet's inhabitants and to her descendants, who learned to tame the wild rancors. Before the elimination of the Sith Order at the Battle of Ruusan, Dathomir was the site of a Sith training academy.

Nearly 400 years before the Battle of Yavin, the 2-kilometer-long Jedi academy ship *Chu'unthor* crashed in a Dathomir tar pit. Jedi sent to recover the crashed ship were repulsed by the witches—female inhabitants who had learned to use the Force. Different clans of these witches (Singing Mountain, Frenzied River, and Misty Falls) were formed, including a group of dark siders calling itself the Nightsisters. Life among the clans followed a pattern of female dominance; males were largely used as slaves for work or breeding.

After the Battle of Naboo, Jedi Knight Quinlan Vos voyaged to Dathomir to investigate the existence of the Infinity Gate, an assignment that saw him tangle with Nightsisters led by Clan Mother Zalem. Vos defeated Zalem's plot to use the Infinity Gate to destroy Coruscant. With this disaster averted, the Jedi Council ordered all navigational data on Dathomir restricted to keep such secrets from falling into the wrong hands.

With the rise of the New Order, Imperial forces constructed orbital shipyards and a penal colony on Dathomir's surface. But after Emperor Palpatine learned the power of the Nightsisters' leader, Gethzerion, he ordered all the prison's ships destroyed to prevent her from leaving the planet. The stranded Imperials at the prison were then enslaved by Gethzerion and the other Nightsisters. Four years after the Battle of Endor, Han Solo won the planet in a high-stakes sabacc game from Warlord Omogg, who claimed it had been in her family for generations. Han's subsequent adventures on Dathomir resulted in the destruction of both the Nightsisters and the forces of Warlord Zsinj. About 15 years after the Battle of Endor, a new order of Nightsisters based in the Great Canyon emerged. This clan, founded by Luke Skywalker's former student Brakiss, allied itself with the remnants of the Empire, treated males as equals, and sent the best Force students to be trained at the Empire's Shadow Academy.

During the Yuuzhan Vong invasion of the galaxy, Dathomir was one of the first planets to fall to the alien menace.

**Dathomirian rancor** A subspecies of rancor native to Dathomir. They were much larger than the common rancor, and showed a greater disposition to being domesticated.

**Dathomir Station** An Imperial space station in orbit over Dathomir, it enforced security when the planet was a penal colony for the Empire.

**Datum District** A sector of Foamwander City on Mon Calamari, named for the city's extensive data-processing and -repository systems.

**daubird** An avian native to the Shadow Forest of Kashyyyk.

**Daughters of Allya** The name adopted by the Dathomir Witches. There were nine clans of witches on the planet.

**Daughters of the Empath Princess** A group of psychics who plied their talents in the city of Talos, on Atzerri.

**Daughters of the Ffib** An autocratic, exclusively female religious order, active during the last decades of the Galactic Republic. A Ffib sect, they established a mission on the Forest Moon of Endor to bring the Ewoks into their fold. After the destruction of the Ffib at the hands of Reess Kairn, the Daughters of the Ffib employed Aurra Sing to hunt down Kairn and eliminate him.

Captain "Odd Ball" Davijaan

***Dauntless* (1)** One of four Star Destroyers assigned to a special task force in Moff Vanko's sector during the Galactic Civil War. This task force was charged with cracking down on piracy. Other vessels in the task force were the *Relentless, Invincible,* and *Triumphant. Dauntless* was commanded by Captain Orsk, and also served as a flagship of sorts for Lira Wessex.

***Dauntless* (2)** A *Pellaeon*-class Super Star Destroyer, part of the new Empire's fleet during the time of Emperor Roan Fel. Under the command of the son of Governor Vikar Dorn, the *Dauntless* was dispatched by Darth Krayt to oversee the subjugation of Munto Codru. It was then sent to Bastion, where Governor Dorn pretended to offer the services of the ship and crew to Emperor Fel in order to allow Darth Kruhl a chance to execute the Emperor.

***Dauntless* (3)** This New Republic cruiser was part of the small fleet at Bilbringi that defended against an attack by the Yuuzhan Vong. It was later recalled to Mon Calamari for repairs. It then served the Galactic Alliance fleet that launched an attack intended to recapture the planet Coruscant from the Yuuzhan Vong.

***Dauntless*-class cruiser** One of largest cruisers in the Rebel Alliance fleet, it was built from the hull of a luxury liner. It carried excellent sensor and countermeasure equipment. Extra shielding and armament were added to make the Dauntless cruisers effective front-line ships.

**Daupherm Planet States** A coalition of planets maintaining a political allegiance to one another during the Galactic Civil War. They were constantly at odds with the Botor Enclave.

**Dauren, Lieutenant** An Imperial lieutenant, he was a comm officer in the main citadel of the Imperial military training center on Carida. Lieutenant Dauren was charged with escorting stormtrooper Zeth Durron to meet his brother Kyp on a rooftop. Once there, Dauren attacked Zeth and beat him, until Zeth fought back and killed his attacker—just before the planet was destroyed.

**daux-cat** A feline creature noted for its speed and grace. A subspecies was bred specifically to participate in races.

**Dave** *See* Dreis, Garven "Dave."

**Daver Kuat** This temperate world was the third planet in the Kuat system.

**Davi (V-Davi)** A slender, gray-eyed, sandy-haired student at the Learning Circle on Kegan when Obi-Wan Kenobi and Siri Tachi attended. V-Davi's parents died during a great Toli-X outbreak on Kegan when he was two years old. An animal lover, he aspired to work in the Animal Circle. After Olana Chion was taken to be trained as a Jedi, Davi agreed to stay with her parents, V-Nen and O-Melie.

**David, Admiral Trey** Second in command in the Exocron Combined Air–Space Fleet, he allowed Talon Karrde to arrive in the system to locate Jorj Car'das.

**Davijaan, Captain "Odd Ball"** A clone trooper in the Grand Army of the Republic, Odd Ball was trained as a starfighter pilot serving under General Obi-Wan Kenobi. He flew as wingman to Kenobi in missions to Teth and led Squad Seven during the Battle of Coruscant.

**Davin, Cort** An ex–Journeyman Protector from Concord Dawn, he assisted the Kaminoan cloners in the training of ARC troopers and clone commanders. A non-Mandalorian, he counted Commander Bacara as one of his most successful students.

Daughters of the Ffib

**Davip, Commander Eldo** A New Republic fleet officer in command of the Super Star Destroyer *Lusankya* during the war against the Yuuzhan Vong. He single-handedly piloted the modified warship during the evacuation of Borleias, slamming the vessel into Czulkang Lah's worldship and escaping aboard a Y-wing fighter.

**Davis** A handsome blond smuggler from Fwatna, he saved Han Solo from a gang of Glottalphibs on Skip 5 in the Smuggler's Run asteroid field. Davis was later killed in one of the bombings by the Dark Jedi Kueller. Only then did Sinewy Ana Blue reveal that she was secretly in love with him.

**Davnar** This planet was the homeworld of the famed winged predator, the kalidor. The Kalidor Crescent, the highest award that could be bestowed upon Rebel Alliance pilots, was named in honor of the creature.

**Dawferim Selfhood States** A group of worlds that formed their own protective federation during the turmoil and constant warfare in the six years following the Battle of Endor.

**Dawn, Raleigh** A fugitive from Questal who joined the Rebel Alliance during the Galactic Civil War, she adopted the pseudonym *Kestrel* in a bid to avoid pursuing bounty hunters. With the help of Rebel agent Tiree, she joined Reekeene's Roughnecks' Green Squad, serving alongside Raal Yorta, Sammie Staable, and Smileron-Verdont.

***Dawn Beat*** One of Talon Karrde's smuggling ships, it was a modified YZ-775 armed with a pair of turbolasers, two double lasers, and two proton torpedo launchers.

**dawndaddy** An animal on the Forest Moon of Endor that heralded the coming of dawn.

**Dawson** A Tynnan demolitions expert and partner to thief Cecil Noone.

**Daykim, Onibald** The "king" of the feral bureaucrats, he lived in the underlevels of Imperial City on Coruscant.

**Day of the Sepulchral Night** The Zelosian name for the complete solar eclipse that occured on the planet Zelos II.

**Daysong** A splinter group of the Rights of Sentience Party. Members believed that the honor guard position was a form of servile humiliation and should be filled by droids. But Daysong excluded synthdroids from that category, on the grounds that synthflesh was living and had rights as well.

**Daystar Casino** Located on Ahakista, this entertainment and gambling venue was owned and operated by Sardoth during the Galactic Civil War. In the years leading up to the Battle of Yavin, the Daystar Casino was quite profitable, attracting visitors from neighboring systems and sectors. However, the rise of the Empire and the civil unrest that grew on Ahakista slowly drove away the patrons, forcing Sardoth to accept assistance from the likes of the crime lord known as Raze.

**Daystar Craft** An airspeeder manufacturer that produced the DC0040 and DC0052 Intergalactic speeders.

**daywing** An insect native to Qiilura that had a life span of a single day.

**dazer** An explosive weapon developed by Jedi Cilghal as part of an arsenal to counteract the abilities of the Killik hives that made up the Colony. When it exploded, a dazer unleashed a brilliant display of lights and other sensory disruptions that deadened a Killik's aura and cut off its ability to communicate with the rest of its hive.

**Dazon, Hem** A male scout from the planet Cona, he was a scaleless reptile-like humanoid. Like many Arcona, Dazon had an addiction to salt, as indicated by his golden eye color.

*Hem Dazon (foreground) at a Mos Eisley cantina*

*DC0052 Intergalactic speeder*

**Dbarian** A warty, tentacled alien species with color-changing skin that displayed emotions.

**dbergo** This species of trees with red, frond-like leaves was native to Ossus.

**DC0052 Intergalactic speeder** A one-being wing-shaped airspeeder developed by Daystar Craft. The Jedi Temple maintained a number of DC0052s within its hangars for intercity travel on Coruscant. The twin Sono-class thrust pods provided a top speed of 800 kilometers per hour.

**DC-15** A standard-issue blaster weapon used by the clone troopers of the Grand Army of the Republic. Very modular, the DC-15 could be configured as a blaster pistol or modified with an accelerating barrel and stock to become a rifle. A multitude of variants existed, including the DC-15A high-powered version used by ARC troopers, the smaller DC-15s used as a backup weapon, and the DC-15x sniper blaster.

*DC-15 blaster*

**DC-17** A standard-issue blaster rifle used by the clone troopers of the Grand Army of the Republic. Variants include the modular DC-17m, which could be upgraded to sniper, anti-armor, or repeating blaster capabilities.

**DC-19 stealth carbine** A specially modified variant of the DC-15 used by the shadow troopers, it was equipped with a sound suppressor and gas adaptor that allowed it to fire nearly invisible bolts.

**D/Crypt Information Services** A shady business based out of Mos Eisley providing slicing and other data-retrieval services. Bossk used it just prior to the Battle of Endor when he discovered the abandoned *Slave I* and attempted to break into its data banks.

**DD** A clone commando who was part of Niner's squad, he was killed during the Battle of Geonosis.

**DD-11A** A Tendrando Arms Defender Droid assigned to Queen Mother Tenel Ka's residence on Hapes, it was baby Allana's primary bodyguard.

*DC-17 blaster rifle*

**DD-13 "Galactic Chopper" droid** For its primary function of installing cybernetic implants, prosthetic limbs, and synthetic organs, the tripedal Ubrikkian Model DD-13 was nicknamed the "Chopper Droid" by clone troopers.

**DD-19 Overseer** A labor pool supervising droid produced by Ubrikkian Steamworks.

**dead blade** A term used by Jedi Knights to describe any nonenergized, nonpowered cutting weapon, like a knife or ax.

**Dead Eye** A vast area of dense gases and fog within Bespin's atmosphere.

**Dead Forest** A foreboding, dense forest on Kashyyyk near Kachirho, inhabited by a colony of webweavers. It was known among the Wookiees as Kkowir. A strange disease afflicted the vegetation of the area, turning the jungle sickly gray. A group of Wookiees known as the Dead Guard protected the entrance to the Dead Forest.

**dead man (dead men)** A slang term used by the *Cuy'val Dar* to describe the cloned soldiers of the Grand Army of the Republic.

**Dead Sector** *See* Dacho District.

***Deadweight*** Carth Onasi's supply ship, flown during the Mandalorian Wars.

**Dead Zone** A smuggler's term describing a particularly empty and lifeless stretch of the Outer Rim Territories that included the planet Comra.

**Deak** One of Luke Skywalker's childhood friends on Tatooine.

*DD-13 "Galactic Chopper" droid*

**dealslang** A trade language that emerged in the criminal underworld.

**Dean, Mother** An obese human Vigo, she reported to Alexi Garyn's fortress on Ralltiir in the years prior to the Battle of Naboo. Though she was accompanied by Barabel bodyguards, Dean and the other Vigos were slaughtered by Darth Maul, who was dispatched by Darth Sidious to ensure that the criminal empire did not interfere with the Sith plans to subvert the Republic.

**Death** The town of Dying Slowly on the penal planet Jubilar eventually came to be known by this name. A corrupt burg, it was a hub of smuggling on the planet, and the site of the Victory Forum coliseum.

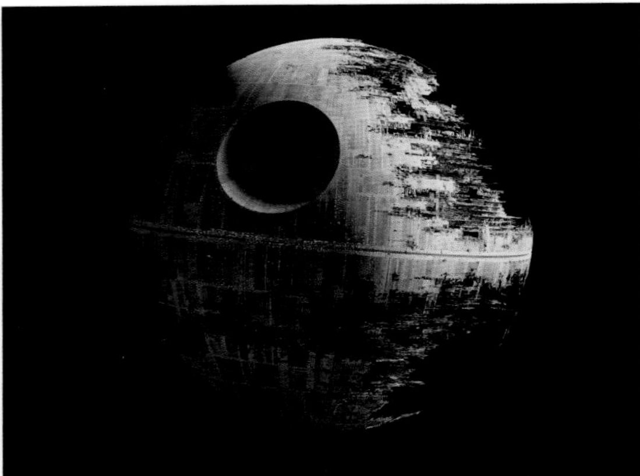
*The second Death Star under construction*

**death engine** A massive, heavily shielded Imperial weapon, it was shaped like a crab, with a phalanx of blast weapons from front to rear. A death engine moved on repulsorlifts.

**Death from Above** The designation of a squad of five elite Imperial spacetroopers stationed in the Kwymar sector.

**death hollow** A Korunnai term that described any deep well or pit where toxic gases, roiling from the open caldera of the many active volcanoes on the surface of Haruun Kal, could collect before they reached the "ocean" of the planet's surface.

**Death Hurdles** A computer game simulating an obstacle-laden swoop race.

**death mark** A term applied to individuals who were singled out for execution. Han Solo had a death mark placed on him by Jabba the Hutt.

**Death of Captain Tarpals, the** A nickname given to Jar Jar Binks for the trouble he often caused Captain Tarpals.

***Death Rattle*** Vizsla's starship used to transport the Mandalorian Death Watch to Corellia. Jango Fett destroyed the vessel, forcing Vizsla to eject in an escape pod.

**Deathseed** Lethal TIE fighter variants built specifically for use by Twi'lek pilots. The word "deathseed" was the Basic language translation of *Chir'daki,* the fighters' original name.

**Death Seed plague** A horrific disease, it was both undetectable and 100 percent lethal to all species. Bacta, instead of curing the plague, accelerated the process. Although it was generally referred to as a disease, it was actually an infestation of drochs, small insects that buried themselves in the flesh of a being and were absorbed into the bloodstream, where they almost literally drank out the life of the victim. The last major recorded outbreak occurred more than seven centuries before the Galactic Civil War, when the Death Seed plague wiped out millions of beings. All the drochs were then moved to Nam Chorios, where the peculiar geology and filtered sunlight basically held them in check. But the plague reared its terrifying specter again when Seti Ashgad and Dzym, a mutated droch, started planting drochs aboard New Republic vessels.

***Death's Head*** An Imperial Star Destroyer, it was commanded by Captain Harbid as part of Grand Admiral Thrawn's armada.

*The first Death Star approaches the planet Alderaan.*

**Death Squadron** The Star Destroyers commanded by Admiral Ozzel (and later, Admiral Piett) that included the *Executor* as flagship. Death Squadron routed the Rebels at the Battle of Hoth.

**Death Star, Death Star II** It was envisioned as the ultimate weapon, the decisive force that, once and for all, would quiet any remaining opposition in the galaxy. Over a span of almost two decades, the Empire developed and constructed this top-secret battle station, which was the size of a small moon and had more destructive power than half the Imperial fleet. The Death Star had the horrifying ability to destroy an entire planet teeming with life with a relatively short burst of its superlaser. Emperor Palpatine hoped it would instill the terror needed to keep thousands of star systems in line. It was rule by fear of force.

That doctrine, and the development of the superweapon, came from the mind of Wilhuff Tarkin, who was inspired by Raith Sienar's initial visions of an Expeditionary Battle Planetoid. Sienar's technical genius foresaw that a moon-sized battle station was feasible, but it was Tarkin who understood how it could be applied to enforce order in the galaxy.

During the Separatist crisis, Sith Lord Darth Tyranus tapped into the engineering prowess of many of the galaxy's leading builders, and had the Geonosians develop a set of working schematics for such a battle station. Dooku then delivered these secret plans to his master, Darth Sidious, who—as Chancellor Palpatine—was in a position to make the station a reality once he supplanted the Galactic Republic with the New Order.

Tarkin had great difficulty in adapting the Geonosian plans into a working model, so he ordered a think tank of engineers within a top-secret research facility, the Maw Installation, to review the schematics for feasibility from top to bottom and create a working prototype Death Star. In the years that followed, many proof-of-concept components, theoretical models, and performance tests were undertaken to hone the Death Star design. Many of its systems were conceived and designed by famed starship engineer Bevel Lemelisk under the direction of Tol Sivron, the Twi'lek chief scientist.

With solid data gleaned from experiments with the Maw Installation prototype, the true Death Star underwent construction in the Horuz system, in orbit over the prison world of Despayre. Supply and labor difficulties, as well as active sabotage, delayed the Death Star operation over the years of its development.

The Death Star's main weapon was the planet-annihilating superlaser, which was used twice. As a test, it destroyed Despayre. Later it was used to destroy Princess Leia Organa's home planet, Alderaan, causing the instant death of billions of sentient beings.

The first Death Star was huge, some 160 kilometers in diameter. Its interior was made up of 84 unique levels, each 1,428 meters in

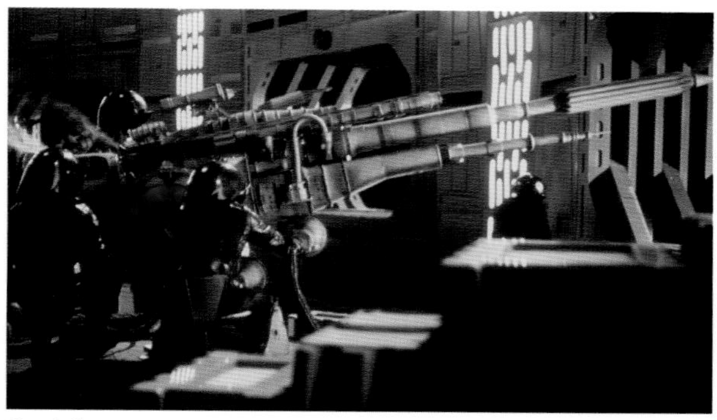

Death Star gunner

height. Each level was subdivided into 357 sublevels. From the exterior, the Death Star's habitable surface was divided into two hemispheres, each with 12 zones. It had a crew of more than 265,000 soldiers. The total personnel soared to more than one million with the addition of gunners, ground troops, and starship support crews and pilots. In addition to the superlaser, the battle station had 15,000 turbolasers, 700 tractor beam projectors, 7,000 TIE fighters, 4 strike cruisers, some 20,000 military and transport vessels, and more than 11,000 combat vehicles.

Yet simple errors doomed the station. Its defenses were built around repelling a capital ship attack; starfighters were considered insignificant. When the Alliance mounted its assault over Yavin, Tarkin considered the attack inconsequential; only the TIE fighters under Darth Vader's direct command were deployed. So, guided by the Force, Luke Skywalker was able to destroy this powerful weapon by firing proton torpedoes down an unshielded exhaust vent.

Death sticks

But four years later, a second Death Star neared completion, much larger than the original. It was over 900 kilometers in diameter and armed with a superlaser even more powerful than its predecessor's and so accurate that it could be trained on capital ships. At its north pole was a heavily armored 100-story tower topped by the Emperor's private observation chamber.

More than a weapon of terror, the second Death Star was part of an elaborate trap to lure the Rebels out of hiding by providing a tempting target. Emperor Palpatine allowed the Alliance's Bothan spies to learn the location of the Death Star, but never revealed that the superlaser on the incomplete station was fully operational. A small team of Rebel commandos on the Forest Moon of Endor, assisted by the native Ewoks, destroyed the shield generator protecting the Death Star, allowing the *Millennium Falcon* and a starfighter to fly inside and take out its power core, destroying the battle moon. Within a month, Rebel leader Mon Mothma declared the end of the Rebellion and the birth of the New Republic.

Years later, the prototype Death Star—never intended as a practical weapon of war—was activated by Tol Sivron after the Maw Installation was attacked by a New Republic task force. The prototype finally was destroyed when Kyp Durron, piloting the Sun Crusher, lured the Imperial weapon into one of the Maw's black holes, where it was smashed by gravitational forces.

In the end, nothing better symbolized the Empire's oppression than the Death Star. But it also came to represent the Empire's greatest weakness: the belief that technology was supreme and all foes insignificant.

**Death Star droid** Another name for the RA-7 droid developed by Arakyd Industries. These droids were purchased in large numbers by the Empire and distributed among the upper echelons of the Death Star command structure with hidden spyware to keep tabs on officer loyalty.

**Death Star gunner** Most of the gunners in the Imperial Navy once aspired to be TIE fighter pilots but lacked sufficient skills to fly starfighters. A few of them were assigned to the first Death Star to operate the main artillery.

**Death Star trooper** Low-ranking Imperial soldiers who served on the Death Star primarily as guards and armed escorts. Death Star troopers lacked armor, but wore durable helmets and useful utility belts. As guards, they frequently possessed access codes as well. Imperial Navy troopers wore the distinctive uniform and helmet once the province solely of Death Star troopers.

**death stick** This powerful narcotic—made from treated Ixetal cilona extract—offered euphoria in exchange for a shortened life. Death sticks came in a variety of formats, all of them cylindrical, in keeping with the common slang name. A hardened variety could be smoked or pulverized and then inhaled. The common liquid was ingested, often as a spike added to alcoholic drinks. Some theorized that the Bando Gora were behind the death stick craze on Coruscant.

Death Star trooper

**Death Watch** *See* Mandalorian Death Watch.

**Debbikin** The director of research for the Five Families of Ord Cestus, he maintained a network of spies on Coruscant. These informants, along with his son, Debbikin the Younger, advised him to side with the Galactic Republic during the Clone Wars. Obi-Wan Kenobi arrived on Ord Cestus to investigate the sale of JK series bio-droids to the Separatists. To curry favor with the Cestians, Kenobi and Kit Fisto engineered a false kidnapping and rescue of Debbikin the Younger. Debbikin the Elder died when the Republic was forced to strike the Five Families bunker.

**Debble Agreement** An agreement stipulating that any cultural artifacts—formerly the property of Emperor Palpatine—found in or around Mount Tantiss could be reclaimed by the cultures that produced them. As a result, Bimms, Falleen, and Bothan joined the humans, Psadans, Myneyrshi, and Noghri living at New Nystao on Wayland. The agreement was named for archaeologist Garv Debble.

**Debit-101** An audit droid that worked for Zorba the Hutt on Cloud City.

**Debnoli** A good-natured patron of the Mos Eisley cantina on Tatooine . . . until the Empire impounded his starship. An expert marksman, Debnoli for a time sought revenge on the Empire.

**Deboota, Dr. Hira** A coroner at the Coruscant State Coroner's office who performed an autopsy on a deceased Yaka. Dr. Hira Deboota noticed similarities in the circuitry of Yakas and Ganks, though the Yakas' were more advanced.

**Dec, Captain Anf** The captain of a Colicoid diplomatic ship attacked by the slave raider Krayn four years before the Battle of Naboo. Obi-Wan Kenobi and Qui-Gon Jinn offered protection to Dec's ship. Years later, Anakin Skywalker encountered Dec as the Colicoid's primary negotiator working with Krayn to corner the spice-processing market.

**Decca the Hutt** Gardulla the Hutt's daughter, she was a crime lord who used the civil war on Mawan for her own criminal purposes. Decca inherited her operation from Gardulla.

**Deception Sect** A group of Yuuzhan Vong who worshipped Yun-Harla.

**decicred** A monetary unit equal to a tenth of a credit.

**Decimator** A prototype turbolaser weapons system developed by the Galactic Republic but stolen by the Separatists during the Clone Wars. The weapon was fitted on a repulsorlift tank to become a powerful battlefield asset. Sev'Rance Tann oversaw the development of the tank on the manufacturing planet of Krant, until the facilities were destroyed by Jedi Master Echuu Shen-Jon and his clone troopers.

***Decisive*** An *Imperial*-class Star Destroyer in Prince-Admiral Krennel's fleet, it was paired with the *Emperor's Wisdom* during the blockade of Liinade III. The *Decisive* took heavy damage from the combined firepower of the New Republic vessels *Home One* and *Emancipator.* Its crew eventually surrendered to the New Republic.

**Declann, Grand Admiral Nial** A Force-using Imperial Grand Admiral who perished when the second Death Star was destroyed. During the Clone Wars, Declann battled secessionists aboard a Republic assault ship. His uncanny success as a TIE pilot earned him the attention of Emperor Palpatine's agents, and he was trained on the ancient Sith world of Dromund Kaas.

Grand Admiral Nial Declann

**Declaration of a New Republic** A document that set forth the principles, goals, and ideals of the new Galactic Republic, it was released a month after the Battle of Endor. Its signers were Mon Mothma of Chandrila, Princess Leia Organa of Alderaan, Borsk Fey'lya of Kothlis, Admiral Ackbar of Mon Calamari, Sian Tevv of Sullust, Doman Beruss of Corellia, Kerrithrarr of Kashyyyk, and Verrinnefra B'thog Indriummsegh of Elom.

**Declaration of Rebellion** The document written by Mon Mothma and submitted to Emperor Palpatine announcing the formation of the Alliance to Restore the Republic and citing the crimes against the galaxy the Empire had committed.

**Declaration of the Alliance of Free Planets** Signed a week after the Rebel Alliance victory at the Battle of Endor, this document put forth the commitment of Mon Mothma and the Alliance government to create a new government to rule the galaxy justly. It was soon supplanted by the Declaration of a New Republic.

Decon droid

**decon droid** A common term for a decontamination droid designed to start the process of restoring environments unfit for habitation.

**Decoy Squad Five** A group of clone troopers dispatched to secure the loading docks of the Jedi Temple after Darth Vader's assault the night of Order 66. They were disguised in Jedi robes.

**dedicated energy receptor (DER)** A common type of sensor that detected electromagnetic emissions in its immediate surroundings.

**Dedra** An assistant to Dr. Murk Lundi before the Quermian left for Kodai to recover a Sith Holocron, she was a graduate student of history during the years leading up to the Battle of Naboo.

**deece** A common shorthand term used by clone troopers to describe their DC-15 or DC-17 armaments.

**Deega, Senator** The Senator from Clak'dor VII, he was a Bith who was named to the New Republic Senate Defense Council. Senator Deega was deeply committed to pacifism and ecology given the ecological warfare that had nearly destroyed his planet. He was chosen to replace the traitorous Senator Tig Peramis, but also disagreed with Chief of State Leia Organa Solo's actions against the Yevetha.

**Deegan, Lieutenant** A top-rated Corellian pilot, he was a member of Team Orange and worked with Wedge Antilles when he headed the Imperial City reconstruction crews.

**Deej** *See* Warrick, Deej.

**Deela** The wife of a Rebel Alliance operative who was captured by Janek Sunber and a group of Imperial agents after the Battle of Yavin. Deela's husband was tortured and interrogated, but he refused to give in. Instead, he railed at Sunber and the Imperials, claiming that Luke Skywalker—the man who'd single-handedly destroyed the first Death Star—would eventually detroy the Empire as well. This information allowed Sunber to relay Luke's identity to Darth Vader, who had been searching for the hero of the Battle of Yavin.

**Deep Core** *See* Deep Galactic Core.

**Deep Core haulers** Freighters licensed by the Empire, they hauled cargo to Imperial systems in the Deep Galactic Core.

**Deepcore Lounge** One of the most popular lounge areas found aboard the *Errant Venture.*

**Deep Core Security Zone** An area of the inner Galactic Core. Its sectors were sealed to traffic for decades. Emperor Palpatine's throneworld of Byss was hidden inside the zone.

**Deep Galactic Core** Lying between the perimeter of the Galactic Core and the center of the galaxy was this huge region of old stars. At the Deep Galactic Core's center was a black hole surrounded by masses of antimatter and dense stars. The reborn clone Emperor consolidated his forces there in order to launch what he planned as a final strike against his enemies. Years later, during the Yuuzhan Vong invasion, Leia Organa Solo devised a plot to capture the alien fleet within the difficult-to-navigate corridors of the Deep Core. In exchange for the Imperial Remnant's navigational data on the region, she offered Supreme Commander Gilad Pellaeon the Republic's complete intelligence on the Yuuzhan Vong.

**Deerian, General** Although this Imperial officer worked with Moff Glovstoak, his true loyalties remained with the Empire. At a party held at Glovstoak's estate, General Deerian ran into Countess Claria, who was actually the Emperor's Hand, Mara Jade, in disguise. His fair treatment of her earned him Jade's notice, and she personally recommended to Emperor Palpatine that he be excluded from the investigation into Glovstoak's treachery.

**Deeto** An alias used by the Rodian criminal Ten-Suckers Madoom.

**Deevers, Moss** A Bothan smuggler often partnered with a Sullustan sidekick named Twingo, he was known as a liar and braggart. The pair set the two-being record running through the Lando's Folly obstacle course.

**Deevis, Captain** A New Republic naval officer during the Yuuzhan Vong invasion, he served aboard the *Mon Mothma* during the liberation of Corulag.

**Defano, Dasha** A Wroonian fighter pilot and gunner aboard the New Republic corvette *FarStar.*

**Defeen** A cunning, sharp-clawed humanoid member of the Defel species, he was Interrogator First Class at the Imperial Reprogramming Institute in the Valley of Royalty on the planet Duro. In recognition for his work, he was promoted to Supreme Interrogator for the Dark Side Prophets on Space Station Scardia.

Defel

**Defel** Looking more illusory than real, members of this species appeared as large, red-eyed shadows under most lighting conditions—thus their common name: Wraiths. But under ultraviolet light, Defels appeared as stocky, fur-covered bipeds with protruding snouts and long-clawed, triple-jointed fingers. They lived in underground cities on the planet Af'El, where most residents were miners or metallurgists. Offworld Defel were often hired as spies and assassins due to their ability to bend light around themselves at dusk.

**Defender (1)** A style of tapered lightsaber hilt.

**Defender (2)** An alias adopted by Kinman Doriana while working for Darth Sidious to undermine the negotiations between the Corporate Alliance and the Brolfi government, some five years after the Battle of Naboo.

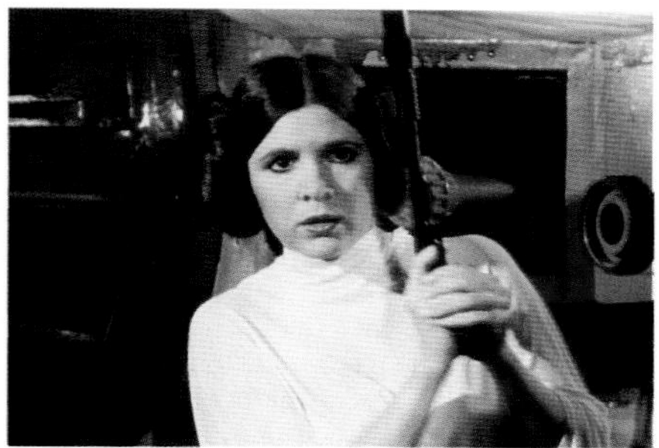

A Defender sporting blaster being put to good use

***Defender* (1)** A destroyer in the Bakuran task force that helped the New Republic break the blockade of the Corellian system.

***Defender* (2)** A Venator Star Destroyer, part of Anakin Skywalker's fleet at Ryloth during the Clone Wars. After an initial engagement with the Separatists, the *Defender* sustained extensive damage and was evacuated. Skywalker scuttled the ship by ramming it into a Separatist vessel.

**Defender assault carrier** One of a class of starships approved for use by the New Republic Navy. It measured 700 meters in length and was based on the *Majestic*-class cruiser. They were originally designed to transport three full squadrons of Defender starfighters, but many were modified to carry E-wings.

**Defender Droid** A bodyguard droid produced by Tendrando Arms during the years following the Yuuzhan Vong invasion of the galaxy. The Defender was essentially a YVH combat droid crossed with the TDL nanny droid, a combination that made it the perfect protector for children, adults, and starships.

**Defender sporting blaster** Manufactured by the Drearian Defense Conglomerate, it was intended for personal defense or small-game hunting. The Defender had a short range and low power, carrying energy for 50 shots.

Defender starfighter

**Defender Star Destroyer** A New Republic New Class warship, the *Defender*-class Star Destroyer was the peak of modern Star Destroyer design at the time of its development. Although their structural design was significantly different from an Imperial Star Destroyer, they were sometimes mistaken for Imperial ships when seen from a distance because of their strong angular lines. Each could hold a mix of 60 starfighters and shuttles for scouting and close support work. The first Defender completed was called the *Obi-Wan.*

**Defender starfighter** A short-range New Republic starfighter specifically designed by the Republic Engineering Corporation for space defense. It was smaller than an A-wing and had no hyperdrive.

**Defender Wing** The New Republic Y-wing bomber squadrons assigned to General Salm. The wing consisted of Champion, Guardian, and Warden squadrons.

**Defense Research and Planetary Assistance Center** Known as DRAPAC for short, this was a facility that was funded by the early leaders of the New Republic and established atop Mount Yoda on Dagobah. It was here that Fandar and Fugo attempted to restart Project Decoy and produce a human replica droid.

***Defiance*** A Mon Calamari warship, it replaced *Home One* as the flagship of the New Republic fleet and served as Admiral Ackbar's personal vessel.

***Defiant*** An Imperial Star Destroyer under the command of Captain Essenton during the Yuuzhan Vong invasion. In the wake of the Battle of Bastion, the *Defiant* was equipped with a gravitic amplitude modulator and reprogrammed by Jacen Solo and the Galactic Alliance to allow Imperial forces to destroy a Yuuzhan Vong yammosk. With Borosk successfully defended, Grand Admiral Pellaeon sent the *Defiant* to Yaga Minor, where it once again helped drive off the Yuuzhan Vong.

Opula Deget

**Defilers** Independent mercenaries who took on sabotage missions during the reign of the Empire.

**deflection tower** The cornerstone of most planetary defense systems, these towers generated high-intensity deflection fields or shields.

**deflector shield** A force field that drove back solid objects or absorbed energy, this shield protected everything under it. Ray shielding staved off energy such as radiation and blaster bolts; particle shielding repulsed matter.

A Star Destroyer's deflector shield generator

**defstat** A multilevel alert protocol carried out in Imperial installations. Exact defstats (defense statuses) varied from installation to installation, but there generally were four levels. Defstat zero represented no threats, and standard operating procedures were carried out by guards. Defstat Three was the most active level, with regular patrols and the use of blast doors to seal off threats and protect valuable items.

***Degarian II*** A starship owned by Senator Crote of Frego. He allowed Qui-Gon Jinn and Obi-Wan Kenobi to take it to Coruscant, escorting Lena Cobral back to the capital world to testify against the Cobral family. The Jedi were wary of a trap set by this family, and opted to hire different passage back to Coruscant. The *Degarian II* was attacked en route, with no survivors.

**Deget, Opula** An up-and-coming singer on Coruscant during the Clone Wars. Gossip held that she'd fed the media the scandalous tale that toppled the former headlining star of the Galaxies Opera House from the limelight.

**degrades** Demerits a trainee could acquire for poor performance at the Imperial Naval Academy. Any student who amassed 50 or more degrades was automatically kicked out of the Academy and sent to the Mining Corps.

**Deila** A member of the Young on Melida/Dann, and a contemporary of Nield and Cerasi years before the Battle of Naboo. After the elders of the Daan and Melida were defeated, Deila was named to the new government's Young Security Squad, serving as Obi-Wan Kenobi's second in command. When she discovered that Mawat was attempting to take control, she provided useful information to Obi-Wan and Qui-Gon Jinn.

**dejarik** While the exact origin of this challenging board game was debated, its classic combination of skill and strategy withstood the test of time. Lakan Industries's version of its hologram dejarik set let players choose from among 10 different types of playing pieces and sported a module that could pit a player against any of 50 of the galaxy's greatest dejarik grandmasters. A hologram generator in a circular housing was topped by an etched gold-and-green checkered surface. When activated, a full color three-dimensional hologram of playing pieces—ranging from 5 to 30 centimeters high—was displayed in either a passive or a live-action mode in which the pieces waged war with one another, at times devouring a losing piece.

*Dejarik*

**Dejock, Ensign** A crewman aboard the Galactic Republic starship *Ranger* in the Battle of Praesitlyn during the Clone Wars.

**Dekk-6 power coupling** A top-of-the-line starship component coveted by Greedo for use in his starship *Manka Hunter.*

**Dekluun, Commander** A Sephi officer tasked with the protection of the planet Thustra during the Clone Wars, he was killed when clone troopers led by Padawan Pix raided Dekluun's base of operations.

**Deko Neimoidia** One of the extremely wealthy "purse-world" colonies of Neimoidia, it was captured by the Galactic Republic during the Clone Wars.

**Delacrix system** A thriving system of planets orbiting three suns. All the worlds of the Delacrix system traded in harmony and joined the Galactic Senate several years before the Battle of Naboo. A young Obi-Wan Kenobi knew the system, having passed it en route to Kegan.

**Delaluna** The natural moon of the planet Junction 5, it had a breathable atmosphere, and many settlers from Junction 5 chose to make their home there. More than two decades before the Clone Wars, the natives of Delaluna were believed to have developed a weapon that could be used against large-scale targets. While the authorities on Delaluna denied the existence of the weapon, the natives of Junction 5—who called it the Annihilator—lived in constant fear of it.

**Delantine** This planet sided with the Rebel Alliance during the Galactic Civil War. Delantine was rich in ore and minerals that were used to create many weapon parts. After the Battle of Yavin, the Alliance chose Trux Zissu to act as the planet's governor. Most natives of the planet spoke no fewer than 16 different languages.

**Delari Prime** The site of a hidden Imperial communications base that was abandoned after the Battle of Endor, the planet was located in the Delari system of the Corva sector of the Outer Rim. Millennia ago, the world teemed with life; then a wayward asteroid knocked its orbit closer to the heat of nearby twin suns. Catastrophic climate changes burned up the planet's seas, and massive erosion formed kilometer-deep chasms that crisscrossed the rust-orange surface. Delari Prime had only a 10-hour rotation cycle, was buffeted by intense windstorms, and could support vegetation only at its poles.

*Delaya-class courier*

**Delaya** The sister world to Alderaan, it was the only other place besides the destroyed planet where the low-grade blue quella gem was found. Alliance General Carlist Rieekan was inspecting a satellite transmission station in orbit around Delaya when the Death Star battle station destroyed Alderaan.

***Delaya*-class courier** An ancient Galactic Republic military ship. Master Arca Jeth used one named the *SunGem* during the Beast Wars of Onderon.

**Delbaeth, Ivixa** A Jedi Master who championed the creation of the *Chu'unthor* training vessel some 400 years before the Battle of Yavin.

**Delckis, Rannd** An Alliance communication officer stationed aboard the *Flurry,* he died when the vessel was destroyed over Bakura.

**Del Dlhe, Hebanh** A representative of the Murkhanan Department of Trade and Industry, he was openly critical of the Verpine after they formed an alliance with the Mandalorians during the war between the Galactic Alliance and the Confederation.

**Delegation of the Two Thousand** Galactic Republic Senators who had signed the Petition of the Two Thousand, expressing their concerns to Chancellor Palpatine about increases in executive authority and the appointment of governors. Many members of the delegation were arrested as enemies of the state following the declaration of the Empire. Members included Senators Padmé Amidala, Mon Mothma, Terr Taneel, Bana Breemu, Fang Zar, Chi Eekway, Tundra Dowmeia, Nee Alavar, Malé-Dee, and Meena Tills.

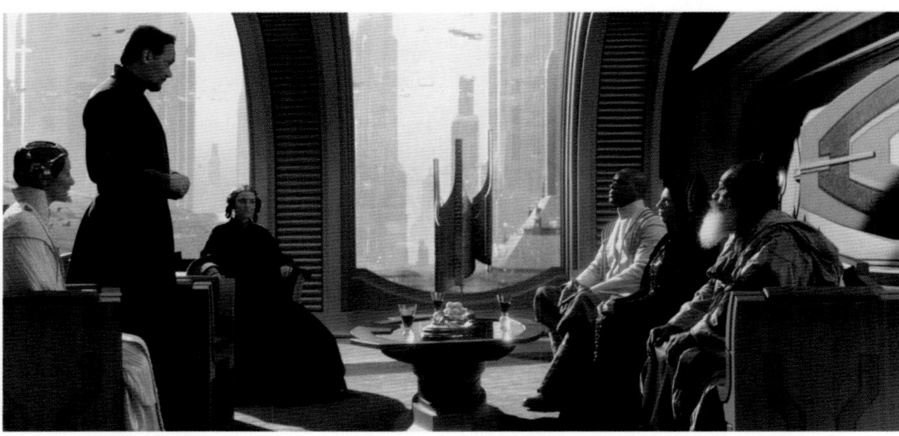

*Members of the Delegation of the Two Thousand meet prior to signing the Petition of the Two Thousand.*

**Deleta** A short-statured woman, she lived and worked aboard the *BioCruiser.*

**Delevar, Corporal** A Rebel soldier who accompanied Han Solo to Endor in a successful attempt to shut down a shield generator protecting the second Death Star. Like the others in his squad, Delevar served with Solo on Hoth and was handpicked for his skill and loyalty.

**Delfii system** This was the site of a deep-space military summit of the Rebel Alliance just prior to the Battle of Endor.

**Dellalt** This planet, located in a system near the Outer Rim, orbited a blue-white star in the remote Tion Hegemony. A watery world with two moons and a higher gravity and shorter day and year than standard, Dellalt held a strategic location in pre-Republic days. Thousands of years before the Battle of Yavin, the ancient tyrant Xim the Despot built an opulent city and immense treasure vaults on Dellalt. The vaults held a worthless cache of kiirium and mytag crystals. The city long since fell into poverty and ruin. The intelligent sauropteroids of Dellalt, the Swimming People, ran a ferry business at the lakeside docks. Deep within the mountains was a colony of about 100 people calling themselves the Survivors. Apparently stranded on Dellalt in pre-Republic times, their religion involved watching over Xim's remaining war robots and making human sacrifices to increase the strength of their rescue beacon. During one of Han Solo's early adventures, Xim's robots were activated by the Survivors and wiped out a contract-labor mining camp before the robots were destroyed. Just prior to the Battle of Yavin, the Imperials used Dellalt as a staging point for supplies and equipment.

*Delta 62 "Scorch" (front), Delta 07 "Sev" (left), Delta 38 "Boss" (pointing), and Delta 40 "Fixer" (rear) make up Delta Squad.*

**Dellso, Gizor** A Geonosian Separatist who refused to surrender after the Clone Wars. As the holder of stolen plans for an experimental Imperial starfighter, Dellso needed protection while he calculated his next move. He reactivated a hidden droid factory on Mustafar. The 501st Legion was sent to bring Dellso to justice. These elite troopers tore through the factory, destroying the last stubborn vestiges of the droid army.

**Delpho** A soldier in the Galactic Alliance Guard and part of the team dispatched to Ossus under the command of Major Serpa, to take control of the Jedi training facility on the planet. When Serpa tried to capture and harm the younglings there, Delpho was overpowered by Jaina Solo, who was working with Zekk and Jagged Fel to free the students.

**Delphon** Located near the Ison Corridor, this world was the site of a battle between the Black Hole Gang and the Empire in which most of the pirate group was killed.

**Delpin, Genna** A strong-willed and -bodied woman in the Corellian Defense Force, she was a born leader, attaining the rank of admiral just before Thrackan Sal-Solo tried to have the Corellian system secede from the Galactic Alliance. After Dur Gejjen assumed the role of Prime Minister following Sal-Solo's assassination, Admiral Delpin led a Corellian assault force that tried to assassinate the Hapan Queen Mother, Tenel Ka. Although the mission ultimately failed, that failure was blamed on Supreme Commander Wedge Antilles, and Admiral Delpin was promoted to fill his position. When the Corellian Confederation expanded to include the Bothans and the Commenorians, Delpin was replaced by an elected Supreme Commander, Turr Phennir. She later formed an alliance with Minister of Information Denjax Teppler in the power vacuum that followed the death of Prime Minister Sadras Koyan.

**Delrakkin** A temperate, forested planet where the Empire tried to establish an alazhi production facility, since its environment closely mirrored that of Thyferra. The Alliance's leadership later discovered that Delrakkin was the test site of a device that prevented starships from entering hyperspace; the native Delrakkins were slated to be eliminated in order to ensure the secrecy of the project.

**Delrian** A prison planet used to jail dangerous criminals. The infamous Dr. Evazan was held on Delrian until he escaped to the Hindasar system.

**Delstar, Commander Owen** A native of Coruscant, he served in the naval forces of the Galactic Republic military during the Mandalorian Wars.

**Delta 07 ("Sev")** A Republic clone commando and member of Delta Squad, he was a fierce fighter who enjoyed combat. A coldly efficient killer with a grim sense of humor, he sported armor highlighted with blood-red markings.

**Delta 38 ("Boss")** The Republic clone commando leader of Delta Squad. He was relatively taciturn; when he spoke, it was usually to bark out an order to his squad. Three-Eight earned the respect and loyalty of his squad, and he repaid that dedication with strong leadership. Despite being trained by Walon Vau, Boss somehow inherited Jango Fett's strong Concord Dawn accent and speech patterns.

**Delta 40 ("Fixer")** The acknowledged second in command of the Republic clone commando Delta Squad, he was a gruff, by-the-book type of clone. He insisted on calling his squadmates by their batch designations, rather than the more colorful nicknames they acquired. Known to the others as Fixer, Delta Four-Oh was the resident technology expert, and often handled computer-slicing and code-breaking duties.

**Delta 62 ("Scorch")** Delta Squad's resident wiseacre, this Republic clone commando regularly dropped a world-weary bon mot into the stew of violence and destruction that served as the Deltas' steady diet. A competent soldier and an excellent explosives technician, Six-Two had an overdeveloped sense of irony that could be mistaken for fatalism. Scorch earned his nickname after an ordnance accident that left him and Sergeant Walon Vau without eyebrows for a short time.

**Delta-7 Jedi starfighter** The spearhead-shaped Delta-7 *Aethersprite*-class model of Jedi starfighter was introduced shortly before the Clone Wars. The small fighter had room for a single pilot, as well as a truncated astromech droid to assist in repairs and navigation. Only a small number of specially modified fighters were hyperspace-capable; the rest had to rely on a dockable hyperspace transport ring to achieve faster-than-light speed. The interceptor vessel was lightly armed with twin laser cannons, durable shields, and a landing claw that could affix to various surfaces.

Developed by Walex Blissex and

*Delta-7B Jedi*

manufactured by Kuat Systems Engineering, the prototype Delta-7 was tested extensively by Adi Gallia and met with the approval of the Jedi Council for use. Obi-Wan Kenobi employed a red Delta-7 Aethersprite in his mission to track down the "missing" planet Kamino and pursue the bounty hunter Jango Fett. During the Clone Wars, Anakin Skywalker used an extensively modified Aethersprite named the *Azure Angel.* A variant model, the Delta-7B, employed an astromech socket just fore of the cockpit, accommodating a full-sized droid as opposed to the truncated models used by the basic Delta-7.

**Delta Squad** One of the first groups of clone commandos developed by the Kaminoans, it consisted of four troopers specially trained by Walon Vau.

**Delta Source** *See* ch'hala tree.

**delta wave inducer** A sleep-inducing device that claimed to provide the equivalent of a night's rest and relaxation with just a 10-minute nap.

**Delund** One of four Imperial pilots who agreed to defect from service aboard the *Rand Ecliptic* with Biggs Darklighter just prior to the Battle of Yavin.

**Delvardus, Superior General** One of 13 feuding warlords whom Admiral Daala tried to unify to wage war against the New Republic. When the admiral failed to bring them together, she killed them all with nerve gas.

**De Maal, Chachi and Ohwun** A married Duros couple, they owned and operated a number of docking bays in Mos Eisley, including Docking Bay 94, from which Han Solo made a hasty departure just prior to the Battle of Yavin. Due to a number of shady operations, they both maintained several aliases. Chachi sometimes used the name Baniss Keeg and she occasionally was known as Probos. Ohwun sometimes went by Ellorrs Madak or Bringe.

**Demagol** A Mandalorian biologist active during the Mandalorian War, 4,000 years before the Battle of Yavin. He was obsessed with determining the biological underpinnings of Force abilities. To that end, he maintained frightening research facilities on the planet Flashpoint and attempted to subject the fugitive Padawan Zayne Carrick to vivisection. The rogue Mandalorian Rohlan Dyre rescued Carrick, clubbing Demagol unconscious. Carrick donned Demagol's armor, and the biologist's unconscious form was stashed aboard the *Last Resort.*

*Demagol*

*Ohwun (left) and Chachi De Maal*

**Dembaline** A Mon Calamari composer whose most rousing tune was "Shwock Dubllon," or "Crested Wake," the theme song of sorts for the Dozen-and-Two Avengers.

**Demici** One of the six families that made up the Great Houses of Serenno during the Ruusan Reformations. The family crest was a simple five-pointed star on a solid background.

**Deminar, Ilko** The head of the Galactic Republic's Cryptanalysis Department during the Clone Wars. At the time, Deminar was a sub-director for the Senate Bureau of Intelligence, working for Armand Isard.

***Demise*** A ship in Talon Karrde's fleet during the Yuuzhan Vong War. During the Peace Brigade's attack on the Jedi academy, Talon Karrde ordered the *Demise* to escort the *Idiot's Array,* which transported the Jedi children to Coruscant. Both ships returned to Yavin 4 to help with the rescue of Anakin Solo and Tahiri Veila. Though not the best-armed ships of Karrde's fleet, the *Idiot's Array,* the *Demise,* and the *Etherway* were the only ones fast enough to keep up with the *Wilde Karrde.* The *Demise* exploded in the first exchange with Yuuzhan Vong destroyer analogs at Yavin 4.

**Demmings, Commander** This Imperial officer succeeded Moff Giedt as governor of Tiss'sharl following the Battle of Yavin. He later was assigned to command the Star Destroyer *Reprisal* on a mission to recover Luke Skywalker on Jabiim. Although the Rebels escaped, Demmings survived to continue his command. A second error, the destruction of a Blockade Runner that might have provided clues as to the fleet movements of the Rebel Alliance, nearly cost Demmings his life. It was later revealed that the "mistakes" on Demmings' watch were caused by Garil Dox, an Alderaanian saboteur. The destruction of the outpost on Ejolus led to Dox's capture, and Demmings was allowed to command the *Reprisal* a little longer. He was then placed in command of the occupation of the planet Jabiim, ensuring the capture of slaves for Imperial labor projects.

**Demoal, Lan** A freelance reporter and conspiracy theorist who tried to find a major story to break along the Sisar Run.

**Democratic Alliance** One of several political factions that tried to influence the government of Corellia in the years following the Yuuzhan Vong War. The Democratic Alliance was considered one of the primary parties that opposed Thrackan Sal-Solo's assumption of power in the Corellian system. The Alliance developed a strong following among the population, and held a large percentage of the seats in the Corellian Assembly. Members of the Alliance worked with the Corellian Liberal Front and the Centerpoint Party to block measures that were instituted by Sal-Solo and his cronies, using their influence in the government to hold off his more radical moves. Although none of the parties would admit it, they secretly agreed to work in a coalition government if Sal-Solo were ever to be "removed" from power. To this end, Democratic Alliance leader Dur Gejjen quietly contracted Boba Fett to eliminate Sal-Solo. In the wake of Sal-Solo's assassination, Gejjen and his counterparts in the other factions established the groundwork for a new coalition government under Deputy President Vol Barad, with the Democratic Alliance and the Corellian Liberal Front working together with the advice of the Centerpoint Party.

***Demolisher*** A stolen Star Destroyer converted into a pirate flagship by Gir Kybo Ren-Cha.

**demolitionmech** Any droid used to place explosives or defuse bombs.

**Demon (Maelibus)** The malevolent counterpart to the legendary angels of Iego, the Demons, or Maelibi, dwelt below the moon's surface. Demons intermittently poached the castaway population for sustenance, selecting their screaming victims and casually carrying them belowground under their strong arms. Maelibi were said to be achingly beautiful—even more radiant than the angels—with bodies like molten gold and lyrical voices that seemed to capture the very essence of song.

**demonsquid** An enormous cephalopod predator native to the oceans of Aquaris.

**DEMP gun** This weapon fired a burst of energy that destroyed electromagnetic pathways in mechanical and computerized devices. The DEMP gun was commonly used to "stun" droids.

**Denab** This planet was the site of the Battle of Denab, a major Rebel Alliance victory over the Imperial Fourth Attack Squadron. The squadron was mainly composed of *Victory*-class Star Destroyers, which traveled at relatively slow sublight speed.

**Denal** A clone trooper in the 501st Legion who reported to Anakin Skywalker and Captain Rex, he was part of the mission to Skytop Station, a Separatist listening post.

**Denarii Nova** A rare double star, each of which fed upon gases from the other, it was the site of a clash between Republic forces and the Sith Lord Naga Sadow thousands of years before the Galactic Civil War. The battle led to the destruction of the entire star system.

**Dendo, Kapp** A male Devaronian intelligence agent, he blended in with denizens of the underworld. But in reality, Kapp Dendo worked with Leia Organa Solo's personal assistant, Winter. The hairless, horned, and pointy-eared Dendo was a fierce fighter with a grim sense of humor.

**Deneba** A red planet in the Deneba system, it was the site of a meeting of thousands of Jedi Knights and Jedi Masters on Mount Meru 4,000 years before the Galactic Civil War. The Jedi gathered on Deneba to discuss the takeover of the Tetan system by the Krath and a failed mission to save Koros Major. Millennia later, the smuggler Lo Khan stopped in the Deneba system to refuel while making the Gamor Run. When he was saved from an Imperial attack by Luwingo, a Yaka, Khan hired the alien as his bodyguard.

Kapp Dendo

**Deneter** Located in a nebula near the Red Twins, this planet was ravaged during the Clone Wars. Its surface was left virtually uninhabitable, and the surviving population simply left everything behind and relocated to Coruscant.

**Denetrus** A young Telosian man who helped Obi-Wan Kenobi and Qui-G on Jinn bring down Xanatos and destroy the game called Katharsis.

Dengar

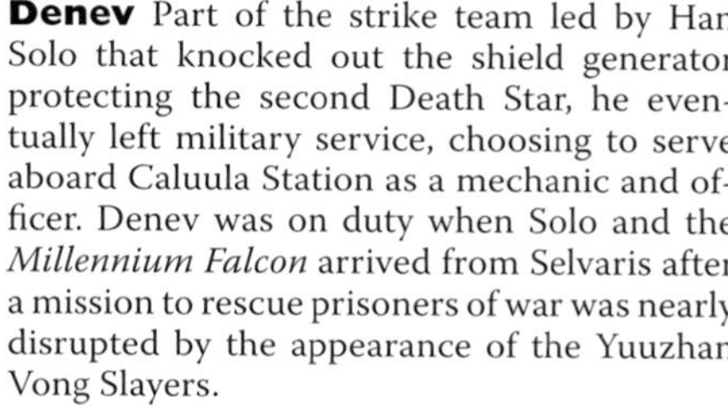

**Denev** Part of the strike team led by Han Solo that knocked out the shield generator protecting the second Death Star, he eventually left military service, choosing to serve aboard Caluula Station as a mechanic and officer. Denev was on duty when Solo and the *Millennium Falcon* arrived from Selvaris after a mission to rescue prisoners of war was nearly disrupted by the appearance of the Yuuzhan Vong Slayers.

**Dengar** The only thing meaner than a bounty hunter is a bounty hunter with a personal grudge, and Dengar long held one for Han Solo.

A successful human swoop jockey on the professional circuit as a young man, he challenged Solo—a hotrodder on the private swoop circuit—to a race across the spiky crystal swamps of Agrilat. Racing to the finish line, Dengar didn't see Solo's swoop bike above him, and when he pulled up he crashed into the main fin on Solo's swoop. Besides suffering severe head trauma, Dengar was tossed out of the professional league, and he blamed his fate on Solo. His obsession with evening the score led to his nickname, Payback.

Later the Empire rebuilt Dengar as an unfeeling assassin, cutting away his hypothalamus and replacing it with circuitry. It used drugs that gave him a flawless memory but left him susceptible to hallucinations. He was a professional Imperial assassin until asked to kill the holy children of Asrat. His refusal meant retirement from Imperial service. Dengar became a freelance bounty hunter when he saw the bounty on Solo posted by Jabba the Hutt. He, Boba Fett, and several other trackers captured Solo along with Chewbacca and Luke Skywalker, but Skywalker used the Force to engineer their escape from Ord Mantell. Shortly after that, Dengar joined Fett and four others in the service of Darth Vader, but Fett beat him to the prize—the *Millennium Falcon* and its crew.

Dengar had other run-ins with top Alliance officials and with Jabba, whom he once tried to kill. He met the dancing girl Manaroo while on an assignment on the planet Aruza and rescued her several times, the last after she had been forced to become one of Jabba's dancing girls. Manaroo, a technological empath, was able to partly restore Dengar's emotions through the use of a thought-sharing device called the Attanni. Dengar rescued a half-dead Boba Fett from near the Sarlacc's Pit of Carkoon and nursed him back to health in time for Fett to be best man at the wedding of Dengar and Manaroo. Six years later, he and Fett almost captured Han Solo on Nar Shaddaa but failed again.

**Denid, Prince** An exiled royal of Velmor who was reinstalled by Princess Leia Organa and Luke Skywalker shortly after the Battle of Hoth. He committed his planet to the Rebel Alliance.

**Denna** An archaeology student at the University of Agamar, he was part of an expedition to Bimmiel to search for Jedi archives. He disappeared; it was assumed that he'd been captured and enslaved by the Yuuzhan Vong.

**Denna, Dams** A diminutive denizen of Naboo who was a noted animal trainer, he took the reins of the falumpasets and kaadu ridden by Gungan guests during the victory parade in Theed after the defeat of the Trade Federation.

Dams Denna leads a kaadu during a parade.

**Dennogra** A ringed Outer Rim planet, the site of the Zio Snaffkin Spaceport and home planet of Sprool the Trader.

**Denon** A planetwide megalopolis similar to Coruscant, it escaped destruction in the Yuuzhan Vong invasion, and as such became a temporary base for the Galactic Alliance.

**density projector** A form of tractor beam generator used by the B3 series ultra battle droid to increase its apparent weight, thus enabling it to resist Force push attacks from Jedi Knights.

**Dentaal** A Mid Rim planet, it was subjugated by the Empire, which in turn was ousted and disarmed by the planet's Independence Party. In retaliation, Imperial commandos under the command of Crix Madine came to Dentaal and planted the deadly Candorian plague, for which there was no cure. The plague eventually spread over the planet, wiping out its 10 billion residents. The Empire blamed a Rebel biowar experiment gone wrong. But Madine, torn with guilt over his role, defected to the Alliance.

**Deo** *See* R2-D0.

**Deo, Sisseri** A Firrerreoan Padawan who participated in the Apprentice Tournament during the Clone Wars. He made it to the third round, where he was defeated by Scout.

**De'Ono, Luther** A member of the ExGal-4 science team on Belkadan, he was a rugged man in his mid-20s when he died during the initial Yuuzhan Vong invasion. He had coal-black hair and dark eyes.

**De-Orbiting Kinetic Anti-emplacement Weapon (DOKAW)** Crude ballistic weapons consisting of missile-sized rods of solid durasteel with rudimentary guidance and control systems, set in orbit around a planet. They were cheap to make and easy to use: A simple command to the DOKAW's thrusters kicked it into the atmosphere on a course to strike any fixed-position coordinates.

**Depp, Orun** The prefect of Mos Eisley during the time of the Battle of Yavin, he was killed when assassin droid IG-72 detonated itself in an unsuccessful attempt to kill quarry Adar Tallon. Not particularly beloved, Depp's demise was the source of the phrase "to buy the Depp," which meant to die in a spectacular fashion. He was survived by his brother, Sylvet, and replaced by Eugene Talmont.

**Deppo** A calibration engineer from Eriadu, he served in an onboard factory within an Imperial World Devastator that attacked Mon Calamari during the resurrected Emperor's campaign of terror. He escaped the destruction of his vessel, was rescued and then imprisoned by the New Republic.

**depthsuit** A form of aquatic armor developed for use by the Grand Army of the Republic during the Clone Wars. Each was made from flexible material that provided a clone trooper with protection against the intense pressures and temperature changes encountered underwater.

**De-Purteen** One of most exclusive resorts in the galaxy. Located on the planet Ord Cantrell, it served as the headquarters of the Imperial Interim Ruling Council.

**Dequc, Lord** An alias used by the Jeodu crime lord seeking to revive Black Sun, he created an organization called Black Nebula operating from his base on Qiaax. At about the time of the Emperor's death, Mara Jade was assigned to assassinate Dequc at Svivren. Surviving the attempt, Dequc relocated to Nezri and referred to himself as Prince Dequc. Mara Jade tracked him down and completed her mission.

**Derapha** One of the largest cities on the planet Phaeda.

**Derdram, Corporal** A member of Imperial Intelligence, Internal Security Division, he was assigned to Darth Vader's flagship, *Executor.* Derdram was responsible for the physical safety of Imperial personnel against Rebel saboteurs.

**Derek** A senior apprentice in the new Jedi Order about 40 years after the Battle of Yavin. He served as a gunner aboard the *Millennium Falcon* during the defense of the Jedi base on Shedu Maad against Darth Caedus.

**Derelict Planet Reclamation Act (DPRA)** A law enacted by the Galactic Alliance after the Yuuzhan Vong War, allowing independent starship pilots to seek out and claim planets devastated by Yuuzhan Vong terraforming for eventual resettlement.

**Derida, Duenna** A Phindian, she was the mother of Paxxi, Guerra, and Terra Derida. She worked for the ruling criminal organization, the Syndicat, while secretly funneling aid and support to the opposing resistance movement.

Bren Derlin

**Derida, Guerra** A Phindian native of the planet Phindar. About 12 years before the Battle of Naboo, he befriended young Obi-Wan Kenobi when the Jedi hopeful was imprisoned in a deep mining facility on the planet Bandomeer. It was a dubious friendship, however, as Guerra betrayed Kenobi to prison guards, yet helped him on other occasions. Guerra's unique mode of speech manifested itself in outright lies, followed immediately by boisterous corrections ("Not so! I lie!"), which tended to be at once charming and frustrating. Despite his inability to tell the whole truth, Guerra was ultimately sincere and had good intentions. He was cheerful at all times, even when in mortal danger.

When Kenobi and Qui-Gon Jinn were manipulated into traveling to Phindar, Guerra attempted to enlist their help in a plan to overthrow the ruling criminal group known as the Syndicat. After the Syndicat's collapse, Guerra and his brother Paxxi, both former thieves, remained on Phindar to run for the office of governor. They eventually became heads of large families on the planet.

**Derida, Paxxi** A Phindian from Phindar, former thief, and brother to Guerra Derida. About 12 years before the Battle of Naboo, Paxxi posed as a freighter pilot (called merely "Pilot") in a ploy to bring Obi-Wan Kenobi and Qui-Gon Jinn to Phindar, diverting the Jedi from a scheduled mission to Gala. As the Derida brothers had planned, upon arriving on Phindar the Jedi became involved in a mission to topple the Syndicat, an evil criminal group controlling the planet. After the Syndicat's defeat, Paxxi and Guerra remained on Phindar to run for the office of governor. Like his brother, Paxxi possessed a certain over-the-top two-faced charm.

**Derida, Terra** Sister to Paxxi and Guerra Derida, and a native of Phindar, she was one of the "Renewed"—Phindians brainwashed into servitude by the criminal Syndicat. Subjected to this process, she became a cruel henchwoman to Syndicat leader Baftu. Her siblings and mother held out hope that someday her personality could be reinstated, but Baftu had her executed before they could save her.

**Dering, Aarno** A sports official and swoop race scorekeeper for the Galactic Games at Euceron. He was also a scorekeeper for illegal Podracing nearby.

**Derlin, Bren** An Alliance field officer born on Tiisheraan, he was in charge of security at Echo Base on Hoth at the time of the battle with Imperial forces there. Afterward, he was part of Han Solo's commando strike team sent to deactivate the Death Star's shield generator on Endor. He eventually achieved the rank of brigadier in the New Republic Defense Fleet.

**Derlin, Galen** A Senator from Tiisheraan and friend of Bail Organa, he was assassinated by Imperial forces. He was survived by his son, Bren Derlin, who became an officer in the Rebel Alliance.

**dermaseal** A medicinal adhesive sprayed or brushed onto the skin to safely cover a wound.

**Derra IV** The site of a major Rebel Alliance loss prior to the Battle of Hoth. The fourth planet in the Derra star system, Derra IV was the embarkation point for a convoy bringing badly needed supplies to the Rebel base on Hoth. But the convoy and its fighter escort—led by Commander Narra—were ambushed and obliterated by squadrons of TIE fighters soon after leaving Derra IV. Imperial captain Ait Convarion, commander of the *Victory*-class Star Destroyer *Corrupter,* served in the action.

Twelve years after the Battle of Endor, New Republic Security arrested a man on Derra IV who was keeping the corpses of 11 uniformed Imperial officers frozen in cryotanks. The disturbed man wanted his son to mutilate the corpses when he came of age, in retaliation for his mother's death during the Imperial occupation of the planet.

**Derral** An arrogant councilman, he was one of many leaders of the planet Ahakista during the Galactic Civil War. He was assassinated by the underground leader, Dunlan.

**Derricote, General Evir** An Imperial general, he was given command of the small base on Borleias, the only inhabited world in the Pyria system. Unknown to the Empire, Derricote was using his post as a profitable front for smuggling black-market goods. Toad-like in appearance and demeanor, with an abruptly curving mouth and a jiggling double chin, the general had reactivated the Alderaan Biotics hydroponics facility, producing goods that had been almost impossible to find since the annihilation of Alderaan. The general also was using Imperial forces to protect his operation.

Because of the Borleian base's secrecy, Bothan spies who sliced into the Imperial Net did not discover it. When Rogue Squadron and Alliance forces first attempted to penetrate Borleias's defenses, they were badly outnumbered and outsmarted. They later learned the reasons for their initial failure. Because of the attack, the Empire was alerted to General Derricote's secret operation, and he was ordered to return to Imperial Center where he would work under the watchful eye of Director of Imperial Intelligence Ysanne Isard.

Isard gave the general the task of developing the Krytos virus, which had the capacity to kill most of the nonhuman citizens on Coruscant—although if caught in time, it could be cured with bacta. The virus was released into the planet's water supply shortly before the arrival of Rebel forces, in the hope that the Alliance would bankrupt itself purchasing the bacta necessary to cure the alien population. Because the Alliance arrived earlier than expected, the virus failed to infect as many people as projected. Unjustly blamed for the Krytos project failure, General Derricote was imprisoned on the *Lusankya,* a buried Star Destroyer serving as a prison facility. He encountered Rogue Squadron pilot Corran Horn there and attempted to kill him, but was himself killed by Horn with the assistance of Jan Dodonna.

*Desann, a fallen Jedi*

**Derrin** A mercenary brutally murdered by Darth Bane in the wake of the Battle of Ruusan. Though not Force-sensitive, he served the Brotherhood of Darkness as a hired soldier alongside Rell and Pad. Bane let two other mercs, Lergan and Hansh, live.

**Dervis, Major** A Rebel soldier who led an infantry detachment at the Battle of Hoth.

**Desann** A very tall, lizard-like Chistori, the fallen Jedi had trained at Luke's Jedi academy but left the Order after accidentally killing a fellow student, Havet Storm. He later joined the Empire working for Admiral Galak Fyyar and Lord Hethrir. Hethrir tasked Desann with training the "Empire Youth," and Desann took as his personal apprentice a fierce female human named Tavion Axmis. Desann eventually was slain by Kyle Katarn.

**Desanne, Commander** A native of Kalist VI, he was stripped of most of his duties due to a political blunder he committed after the Battle of Hoth; he was relegated to acting as a liaison for traveling Imperial dignitaries. He accompanied Darth Vader to Cloud City.

**Desert of Salma** An arid expanse on the otherwise fertile moon of Endor, these flats of hard-baked sand were pockmarked with acid pools and other dangers. The Desert of Salma was en route from the Bright Tree Ewok village to the fortress of the Gorax.

**Desert Sands** A detachment of Imperial stormtroopers that combed the Tatooine deserts for any sign of the escape pod jettisoned from the *Tantive IV.* Led by Commander Praji from the *Devastator* and working with local garrison troopers from Captain Kosh's forces, they sought R2-D2 and C-3PO, razing the Lars homestead in their search.

**Desert Wind** Guerrilla fighters on Ord Cestus opposed to the corporate rule of Cestus Cybernetics.

***Deserving Gem*** A Hapan Battle Dragon supplied to the Hapan Home Fleet by Ducha Requud. Hapan intelligence monitored communications between the vessel and Darth Caedus's flagship *Anakin Solo,* which suggested that Requud was enlisting the help of Imperial Moffs in a bid to assume the role of Queen Mother.

**Desevro** An ancient planet in the Tion Hegemony.

**Desh, Reck** An ambitious smuggler who once partnered with Han Solo and Chewbacca, he was a tall, sinewy human with black hair and hazel eyes. He was fond of body markings, piercings, and electrum jewelry. A decent navigator but unimpressive pilot, he was a leader in the Peace Brigade during the Yuuzhan Vong invasion. When Desh learned of the defecting Yuuzhan Vong priestess Elan, he and his cohorts captured her aboard the *Queen of Empire.* Rather than have her plans foiled, Elan killed Desh with bo'tous poison.

**Desilijic** One of the most powerful Hutt kajidics, it was controlled by Jabba the Hutt for many years. Jabba moved the clan's base of operations to Tatooine.

**Desler Gizh Outworld Mobility Corporation** A small vehicle manufacturer that produced speeders for explorers and scouts.

**Desnand, Io** The Imperial Governor of the Aida system, he planned to ship Wookiee females and cubs to a prison camp on Lomabu III, then stage an attack to lure Rebel rescue forces into a trap. Io Desnand also received the captured Trandoshan bounty hunter Bossk from bounty hunters Chenlambec and Tinian I'att.

***Desolate*** A massive, mountain-like ship used by the Charon of otherspace, it was an amorphous mass over 450 meters long. Domes of eerie light capped each end of the vessel, and a smaller, darker dome engraved with a coarse web-pattern formed the main viewport. The central power core pulsed with strange, yellow energy and a red-tinged mist collected at the bottom of one of its decks. At the top of the ship was an immense brain that controlled its functions. Charon bioscientists had linked the *Desolate*'s main computer with a makeshift hyperdrive. As the vessel made the jump to hyperspace, a defeated Charon leader, Ber'asco, made a bid for power by sabotaging the drives. The *Desolate* crashed on Stronghold and was destroyed, but not before unleashing the deadly Charon on the Rebel safeworld.

***Desolator*** An Imperial Star Destroyer that Admiral Grendreef used as his flagship during the Galactic Civil War. Rebel agents sabotaged the *Desolator*'s nav computer, causing the ship to jump into the rogue star G-138.

**Desolous, Darth** An ancient Utapaun Sith Lord.

**Despayre** A prison planet located in the Horuz system in the distant Outer Rim, it was the construction site for the first Death Star. The planet was almost unknown, which helped guarantee the secrecy of the orbital construction yards assembled to build the battle station. Despayre was a green jungle planet broken by rivers and shallow seas, and home to countless predators including carnivorous crustaceans, poisonous flora, and deadly insects. The planet's penal colony was the only outpost in the system, and many prisoners were used to help construct the Death Star. When the battle station was completed, it tested its superlaser on Despayre and destroyed the planet.

**Desrini District** A section of Galactic City on Coruscant that was devastated by a garbage launcher misfire, which killed 48, injured more than 200, and bathed a wide area in toxic industrial waste. Investigators discovered that a group of squatters had tapped into the garbage launcher's power supply, affecting its obstruction sensors. The Desrini District was closed for a time, and was often cited as an example of the dangers facing Coruscant due to unrestricted immigration and overcrowding.

**Dessel** *See* Bane, Darth.

**Destab** Short for "Destabilization," this Imperial Intelligence branch was part of the Bureau of Operations. Destab's mission profile was "taking the fabric which holds a people, society, or government together and unraveling it." Destab's activities ranged from legitimate intelligence to full-fledged atrocities.

***Destiny*** An Imperial warship, part of the fleet commanded by Carnor Jax that was dispatched to Zaddja to locate and eliminate Kir Kanos.

***Destiny of Yevetha*** Formerly the *Redoubtable,* this ship was seized by Yevethan strongman Nil Spaar during a raid on the Imperial shipyard at N'zoth. The *Destiny of Yevetha* was part of the Yevethan mobilization at Doornik-319.

**Destrillion** An inhospitable planet in the Outer Rim near the asteroid system called Lando's Folly, it has a twin world named Dubrillion. Lando Calrissian ran a mining and processing operation here, as well as his running-the-belt game. When the Yuuzhan Vong invasion arrived at Destrillion and Dubrillion, it inflicted heavy damage on the twin planets before being briefly repelled. The Yuuzhan Vong returned to Dubrillion a week and a half later and continued their attack. Calrissian evacuated as many of the citizens as he could, with most fleeing to Dantooine on their way to the Core.

**destroyer droid** *See* droideka.

**detainment droid** Used extensively by Imperial detention centers, these robots floated atop repulsorlift-generated fields. They secured and guarded prisoners and were equipped with binders on the ends of their four arms to grasp and lock around the limbs of the detainees.

**Detention Block AA-23** *See* AA-23.

**detonite** The most common explosive used in the galaxy, found in grenades and detonators. This substance is usually available in moldable fist-sized cubes. Sale of detonite is restricted without a permit or license. Detonite also comes in a powdered form.

**detonite tape (d-tape )** A specialized explosive consisting of basic adhesive tape impregnated with detonite gel. Infiltration agents used d-tape to blast through sealed doors, windows, and hatches.

**det pack** Short for "detonation pack," a small explosive with a remote activator that could be triggered by the user. The pack was set in place or thrown and then detonated whenever the user desired. Typically this was used to ambush enemies or blow open sealed doors.

**Detta, Cham and Suvar** Brothers, they were among the many members of the new generation of Mandalorians trained by Boba Fett during the New Republic.

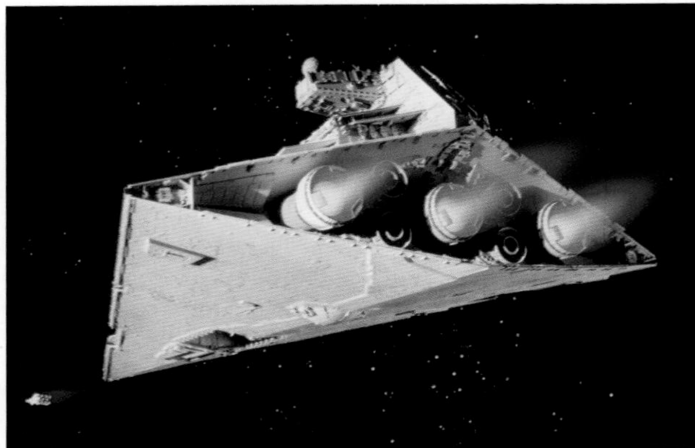

Devastator

**Devaron** The homeworld of the horned Devaronians (or Devish), this was a sparsely populated planet near the influential Core Worlds, covered by low mountain ranges, deep valleys, shallow lakes, and thousands of navigable rivers. Despite its multiple suns, it had a temperate climate.

Devaronian

**Devaronian** Near human-oid in appearance, this species came from the temperate world of Devaron. The males were hairless, with a pair of horns springing from the tops of their heads and sharp incisors filling their mouths. Many felt uncomfortable in the presence of Devaronians, since they resembled the devils of a thousand myths. Female Devaronians were larger, with thick fur and no horns. The males had galactic wanderlust, while most females preferred to stay at home to keep their advanced industries running. Their language was low, guttural, and full of snarling consonants.

Devaronian females lived in the mountains and raised their families in Devaron's villages and industrial centers. They controlled the planet's democratic government and all aspects of production and manufacturing. Devaronian males preferred to wander aimlessly, spending their lives exploring Devaron's rivers or leaving the planet. Male Devish had much sharper teeth than females, and about 2 percent of males were born with two sets of teeth—one for shredding flesh and one for grinding other foods. Devaron produced enough goods to support its inhabitants but didn't have any useful exports. During an outbreak of the Rebellion, the Devaronian Army was placed under Imperial command. Captain Kardue'sai'malloc (later known as Labria) oversaw the shelling of the ancient city of Montellian Serat and the massacre of 700 Rebel prisoners that followed. But some 13 years after the Battle of Endor, four mercenaries recognized Labria as the Butcher of Montellian Serat and forced him to flee to Peppel. Two years later, he was captured by Boba Fett and returned to Devaron, where he was sentenced to death. Labria was executed in the Judgment Field outside the ruins of Montellian Serat, south of the Blue Mountains, by being thrown into a pit of starved quarra, domesticated hunting animals.

***Devastator*** An *Imperial*-class Star Destroyer, it brought terror as it subjugated the planet Ralltiir. Later, it captured Princess Leia Organa's consular ship *Tantive IV* over the planet Tatooine. The Princess was trying to smuggle the technical readouts of the original Death Star to her father when she was intercepted. The *Dev-*

*astator* was Lord Tion's flagship until his death. It was commanded by Captain Mulchive Wermis.

**devee** A species of fish native to the oceans of Kamino.

**Deverin, Lun** A Duros sensor officer aboard the pirate vessel *Free Lance* serving under Urias Xhaxin.

**Devil's Doorknob, the** A navigational hazard in the Boonta Eve Classic Podrace course, it was the narrow opening dividing the Corkscrew from Hutt Flats. Podracers had to twist sideways to negotiate the slot.

**Devis, Captain Mynar** An Imperial officer commanding the Interdictor cruiser *Wrack,* he was part of Operation Trinity, assisting the Galactic Alliance during the Yuuzhan Vong War. Devis, a fan of Han Solo since he was young, was able to work alongside his boyhood hero and Wedge Antilles during the fighting. Devis covered the *Falcon*'s escape, piloting a TIE defender into the hull of a Yuuzhan Vong craft. After Grand Admiral Pellaeon heard of Devis's heroic death, many speculated that perhaps the young officer had been Pellaeon's son.

Dewbacks

**Deviss, Clone Commander** A clone trooper commander assigned to the 327th Star Corps as leader of K Company, he was a veteran of Geonosis, Altyr V, Orto, and Cato Neimoidia.

**Devist, Carib, Dobrow, and Sabmin** Clones of Soontir Fel, these "brothers" were part of a sleeper cell of clones planted by Grand Admiral Thrawn on Pakrik Minor.

**Devlia, Admiral** A small-minded man, he was placed in charge of Imperial forces at Vladet. If it hadn't been for Intelligence Agent Kirtan Loor, Devlia wouldn't have discovered Rogue Squadron's base on Talasea, even though it was practically under his nose. Instead of making an all-out assault on the base, Admiral Devlia sent in only one squadron of stormtroopers to bomb the camp at night. During the attack, the troopers were killed and their shuttle was confiscated by the Rebellion. Later, in a reprisal raid on Vladet, the Alliance was assumed to have killed the admiral.

Commander Deviss

**Devlikk** A small, long-necked alien species whose members aged rapidly and had a life span of about 10 years. Devlikks reproduced at a prodigious rate. Famed Devlikk Podracer Wan Sandage had 128 brothers and sisters.

**Devon Four** A planet embargoed by the Galactic Republic several years before the Clone Wars, when the government refused to pay its taxes. The embargo coincided with an outbreak of plague, and the Republic blocked the shipment of badly needed antidote to the world's surface. The planet's population survived thanks to smugglers running the blockade.

**Devonian** One of the New Republic assault shuttles participating in the assault on Borleias. It later assisted the retaking of Coruscant by transporting troops to the planet's surface.

***Devotion*** Formerly the *Valorous,* it was captured by Yevethan strongman Nil Spaar during a raid on the Imperial shipyard at N'zoth.

**dewback** A large four-legged reptile native to Tatooine, it was an herbivore on the desert world. Dewbacks were used as beasts of burden by moisture farmers and as patrol animals by local authorities and military personnel. The creature, which had surprisingly skinny legs to support its bulk, was often used in place of mechanized vehicles because it could withstand extremely high temperatures and sandstorms.

***Dewback*** A Galactic Alliance warship that saw action during the Second Battle of Fondor.

**Dewback Inn** A disreputable Coruscant tavern found in the Zi-Kree Sector of the Crimson Corridor. It served as a meeting place for Hath Monchar and Lorn Pavan.

***Dewback's Burden*** A New Republic medium transport escorted by Green Squadron, it was ambushed by bandit TIE interceptors while en route to Bhuna Sound. Before the death of its crew, the ship's Duros captain jettisoned distress buoys containing copies of the ship's data recorder in order to warn the New Republic.

**dewflower** A plant native to Bellassa, harvested and ground into a pulp to make juice.

**Dewlannamapia** A kindly Wookiee widow who worked as a cook for Garris Shrike, she was Han Solo's closest friend and surrogate mother while he grew up aboard the *Trader's Luck.* Dewlanna taught him to speak and understand the Wookiee language of Shyriiwook. She was nearly 600 years old when Garris Shrike killed her while she was protecting Han. As she was dying, she made him promise to leave Shrike's band and be happy. She was survived by a son named Utchakkaloch.

Dex's Diner

**Dex** A member of the Peace Brigade, he went to Corellia to capture or kill the Jedi Master Eelysa. After he ran into Han and Leia Organa Solo at the medical facility treating Eelysa, Dex was shot and killed in the ensuing firefight.

**Dex's Diner** A small eatery in the CoCo district on Coruscant owned and operated by Dexter Jettster. It was known as Didi and Astri's Café until it was sold by owners Didi and Astri Oddo.

**Deyer Colony** An outpost in the Anoat system, this colony world contained floating raft cities, terraformed lakes, and abundant fish and crustacean life. The Deyer colonists had created a peaceful political system until they spoke out against the destruction of Alderaan, paving the way for a brutal military takeover of Deyer by Imperial troops. Jedi apprentice Kyp Durron and his family were originally from Deyer. Kyp and his parents were sent to the spice mines of Kessel; his brother, Zeth, was conscripted for stormtrooper training.

Devlikk

**Deysum III** The planetary headquarters for Vo Lantes—the owner of a used-droid chain and a secret Alliance operative—it was the capital world of the Trax sector along the Trax Tube trade route.

**Dezsetes, Second Officer** An Imperial officer aboard the Star Destroyer *Mathayus,* he was secretly allied to the treacherous Grand Moff Trachta, who plotted to overthrow the Emperor. Dezsetes provided Trachta with detailed reports of Imperial fleet movements. When Vader surmised Dezsetes's true loyalties, the Dark Lord struck him down with his lightsaber.

Second Officer Dezsetes

**D'harhan** A near-human cyborg bounty hunter, his body was covered in gleaming black armor; an enormous close-range laser cannon was built into his head. In order to counterbalance the weight of this armament, D'harhan had a mechanical tail that gave him a bizarre, saurian appearance. D'harhan worked on occasion with Boba Fett, until he lost his life during a Bounty Hunters' Guild mission against the Shell Hutts of Circumtore.

**Dharrg, Shunta Osarian** The ruler of the planet Osarian during the time when Nom Anor rose to power among the Rhommamoolians.

***Dha Werda Verda*** A millennia-old epic poem. Space merchant and explorer Mungo Baobab found and preserved the earliest version of the text while exploring the Roon system; he found crystal Roonstones in which the poem was embedded. The poem, when cast as a song, became a Mandalorian battle chant.

*Dha Werda Verda* told of the conquest of the indigenous peoples of Coruscant, known as the Battalions of Zhell, by a warrior race called the Taungs. The tide of this epic battle turned when a sudden volcanic eruption rained destructive ash upon Zhell, smothering the city. The ash plume rose high into the sky and cast a giant shadow over the land for a full two years, giving the Taungs a new name: *Dha Werda Verda,* the Warriors of the Shadow or, in some translations, Dark Warriors. The Taungs themselves saw the immense, long-lasting shadow as a symbol of their destiny and adopted the Dark Shadow Warrior identity throughout their subsequent conquests.

**Dhol, Lady** This octopus-like ruler of Cheelit was an avid Firepath game player. She conspired with the Guild of Vindicators to entrap Darth Vader, but the Dark Lord not only bested the Vindicators but killed Dhol with a deft move in the game.

**Dhur, Den** A hard-drinking cynical reporter who worked for the HoloNet news service as a war correspondent during the Clone Wars. He witnessed the fighting at Jabiim and Drongar.

**dhuryam** Related to yammosks, dhuryams were bred for a different, much more complex type of telepathic coordination. Developed from genetic samples of the original World Brain of Yuuzhan'tar, dhuryams grew into bigger, stronger, vastly more powerful entities capable of mentally melding many more disparate elements than the greatest yammosk that ever lived. A dhuryam was less a servant than a partner: fully intelligent, fully aware, capable of making decisions based on a constant data flow streaming in from the entire planetwide network of telepathically linked creatures, to guide a planet's transformation flawlessly, without any of the chaotic-system fragility that plagued natural ecologies. Because it was bred to command, a dhuryam could be quite stubborn.

**Diado** A snow-covered planet taken over by the Confederacy during the Clone Wars, it was the site of a highly advanced weapons factory. Saesee Tiin purposely let himself be captured on Diado so he could steal a special prototype starfighter.

**Diamala** A white-maned, leathery-faced species. New Republic Senator Porolo Miatamia was a Diamala. Some found the Diamalan characteristic of trampling the ground flat around an issue before actually getting to it to be one of their more irritating social characteristics. Diamala also tended to use words in nonstandard ways.

**Diamond** See Anamor, Facet.

Dace Diath

**diamond boron missile** An element of an anti-starfighter missile system developed during the Clone Wars. The diamond boron missile was designed to destroy multiple ships in a single blast that would consume everything within 50 meters. Its armor was impervious to starfighter laser cannons. Its high-powered rockets outpaced proton torpedoes. A diamond boron missile fired from the *Suprosa* destroyed a formation of Y-wings despite the efforts of Dash Rendar. They were prohibitively expensive and thus never gained wide acceptance.

Diamond boron missile

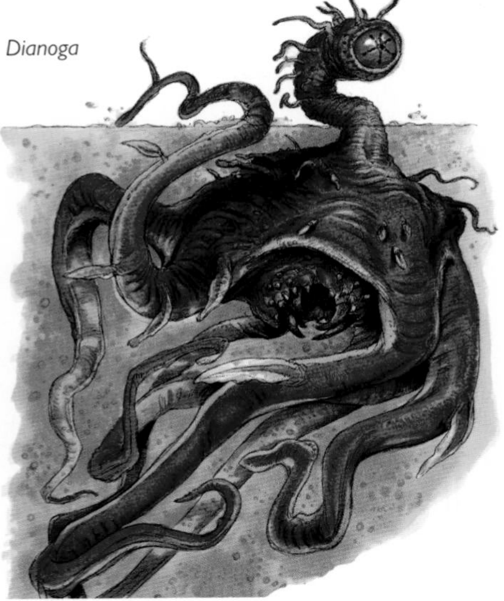
Dianoga

***Diamond*-class courier ship** *See* Commerce Guild cruiser.

**dianoga** An omnivorous and parasitic predator native to Vodran, it spread across the galaxy in its microscopic larval form. Dianoga lived in shallow, stagnant pools and murky swamps, growing to an average length of 10 meters. Their seven tentacles provided them with a means of movement and a way to grasp their prey, which they spotted through an eyestalk growing from their trunk. A dianoga changed to the color of its last meal, and after a long period without eating, it became transparent. A dianoga made its way into the trash compactor of the original Death Star battle station and almost made a meal of Luke Skywalker when he fell into its watery, garbage-filled lair.

**dianogan tea** A steeped hot beverage made from a dianoga's spleen. Muuns regarded this concoction as a delicacy, enjoying its exquisite aroma, flavor, and mildly narcotic effect. Excessive consumption resulted in purple teeth and black gums.

**Diath, Dace** A Jedi from Tatooine many millennia before the Galactic Civil War, his father was Jedi Master Sidrona Diath.

**Diath, Nico** A Jedi from the Diath line who fought in the Clone Wars, he was

Tae Diath

highly regarded for his freeing of slaves throughout the Outer Rim. He died in the Clone Wars.

**Diath, Sidrona** A Jedi Master and father of Jedi Dace Diath, he was killed in the Battle of Basilisk some 4,000 years before the Galactic Civil War.

**Diath, Tae** A 17-year-old human male member of the "Padawan Pack," a group of young Jedi during the Battle of Jabiim in the Clone Wars. Tae's Master was his uncle, Nico Diath, who made him listen to his thoughts whenever Tae lost control. When Tae was killed by Confederacy assassin droids, fellow Padawan Elora Sund died from psychic backlash that carried through their bond.

**diatium** A metal used in the creation of miniature power sources, such as those found in lightsabers.

**Di Blinth, Jesson** An X'Ting warrior, he was the last of five brothers to attempt penetrating the security systems that hid the royal eggs of his species; his four hive-brothers perished in their attempts. During the Clone Wars, Obi-Wan Kenobi was dispatched to Ord Cestus, where he met Jesson. Di Blinth was paired with the Jedi on a desparate mission to obtain the royal eggs. Though Di Blinth despised offworlders, he grew to respect Kenobi for the Jedi's skill in bypassing the security systems. Jesson was ultimately successful in securing the eggs.

**Dica** A toxic world believed to have been the haven of a Dark Jedi who managed to acquire the double-bladed lightsaber of Darth Zannah. General Grievous recovered the weapon, but left no records of where he actually located it.

**Dice, Marit** A student at the Leadership School on Andara who was friends with young Anakin Skywalker, she was one of the few students attending on a scholarship. The wealthier students looked down upon her. She accidentally shot and killed the leader of the planet Tierell, and she was expelled from the school and taken to Coruscant for questioning.

**Dicken** The first officer of the *True Justice,* serving under Captain Tran during the early years of the New Order.

**Didi and Astri's Café** *See* Dex's Diner.

**Dielle, Renxis** A Padawan apprentice killed on Kabal during riots sparked by Trade Federation overtaxation at the height of the Separatist crisis.

**Dielo** Jiliac the Hutt's majordomo during the early years of the New Order.

**Difusal, Tor** A member of the Jedi Council when Thame Cerulian took young Dooku as his Padawan.

**Digger** This enhanced clone trooper was part of a platoon dispatched to Pengalan IV during the Clone Wars to eliminate a Separatist missile facility. He was given his nickname by Joram Kithe.

**Digisee Gaming Floor** The main gambling level found within the Outlander Club on Coruscant.

**digworm** A small creature native to the planet Kamar, the digworm burrowed into solid rock by excreting acidic digestive juices.

**dihexalon** A deadly biochemical weapon developed prior to the Clone Wars.

**Dikasterar, Ryannar N'on** The Elomin miner who first discovered the sentient Elom people living deep below his home planet's surface.

**Diktat** This title is given to the Corellian Chief of State.

**Di'kut** A clone commando who was a member of Aiwha Squad serving under Jedi Master Tra'avis during the Clone Wars. His name was a Mandalorian curse, which literally translated as "someone who forgets to put their pants on."

**Dil, Celot Ratua** A Zelosian smuggler whose bad luck landed him in the penal colony at Despayre, he survived among hardened prisoners due to his knack at procuring hard-to-find items. He avoided danger, and even struck up a friendship with prison guard Noval Stihl, who was frequently impressed by Dil's self-defense abilities. In addition to being Force-sensitive, Dil could briefly move at superhuman speeds. Stowing away in a transport module, Dil escaped Despayre to hide aboard the orbiting Death Star as it underwent construction. Aboard the space station, he posed as Teh Roxxer and started a romance with bartender Memah Roothes. The friendships he developed proved very useful: He was able to escape the battle station before it was destroyed at the Battle of Yavin.

**Dil, Cilia** A political dissident who rebelled against the ruling Guardians on Junction 5, she escaped imprisonment and was helped by Qui-Gon Jinn and Obi-Wan Kenobi in her efforts to steal the plans of the Annihilator superweapon. They discovered that the weapon wasn't real; it was a ruse engineered by Lorian Nod to ensure that the Guardians remained in power. With the lie exposed, Cilia emerged as a hero of Junction 5.

**Dil, Jaren** The husband of Cilia Dil and a fellow member of the rebellion opposing the rule of the Guardians on Junction 5.

**Dilonexa XXIII** A world in the Dilonexa system, it orbited a giant blue-white star along with 39 other planets, but was the only one that could support life. Dilonexa XXIII was nearly 25,000 kilometers in diameter, but its lack of heavy metals gave it a tolerable gravity. The planet was covered with farms that provided grain for the herds of native bovine, foodstuffs, plastics, and fuels. Weather-control satellites helped keep the city-sized tornadoes in check with energy weaponry. Dilonexican colonists developed an allergic reaction to foods containing too many trace metals. Lando Calrissian made a run to Dilonexa XXIII, trying to unload a cargo of fishing poles, leather hides, and wintenberry jelly. There were no takers.

**dim goggles** Wearable optics that reduced the glare of strong sunlight.

**dimilatis** An herb that grew in the sea plains of the planet Gala. When dried and used in certain concentrations, it mimicked the effect of a fatal wasting illness. Jono Dunn used dimilatis to secretly poison Galacian Queen Veda until his treachery was exposed by Obi-Wan Kenobi.

**Dimok** Along with the planet Ripoblus, it was one of two primary worlds of the Sepan system. A long war between the two worlds was forcibly ended by the intervention of Imperial forces after the Battle of Hoth. The planets then briefly and unsuccessfully tried to unite against the Empire as their common foe.

**Dim-U monks** A religious order in Mos Eisley, its members worshipped banthas.

**Ding** A majordomo and trusted spy for gangster Gorga the Hutt, he oversaw the protection of Gorga's wife, Anachro, during her pregnancy.

Ding

Dinko

**Ding, Hanna** A Padawan during the time of the Clone Wars, she was defeated by Scout during the Apprentice Tournament. She feared dying in the Clone Wars.

**Dinger** A Rogue Squadron pilot, he was killed during the Yuuzhan Vong War.

**dinko** A venomous, palm-sized creature known for its nasty disposition, it secreted a foul-smelling liquid both to mark its territory and to discourage even the largest predators. With powerful rear legs covered with serrated spurs, twin pairs of grasping extremities jutting from its chest, and sharp needle-like fangs, the dinko was quite formidable.

**Dinko** The code name of a Samarian resistance fighter during the early months of the Galactic Empire. Dinko met with Ferus Olin, who had arrived on behalf of the Empire to negotiate a cessation of subversive activities. Dinko was captured by Sathan agents.

**Dinlo** A forested world on the border between the Expansion Region and Bothan space, this was the site of a rescue mission undertaken by Jedi Knight Etain Tur-Mukan to free over 1,000 clone troopers.

**Dinn, Nelani** A Jedi active after the Yuuzhan Vong War, she learned lightsaber combat skills from Jacen Solo and grew to admire him. Upon achieving the rank of Knight, Nelani was stationed as the Jedi guardian on Lorrd. Jacen Solo and Ben Skywalker encountered Nelani during their investigation of the death of Siron Tawaler. With Jacen's sole clue being a braided tassel left behind, Nelani directed him to Dr. Heilan Rotham, who identified the object as having possible Sith significance. During their time on Lorrd, they encountered a suicide bomber named Ordith Huarr, suffering from dementia and claiming that Force ghosts had prompted his rash and violent actions. Nelani was alarmed with the ruthlessness Jacen suggested as a solution, and then impressed by the resourcefulness that Ben Skywalker showed when he discovered a shuttle fleeing the scene headed for an asteroid near Bimmiel. There they found Brisha Syo, who in truth was Lumiya, Dark Lady of the Sith. She had been using her dark side influence to lure Jacen Solo to her lair. As Lumiya seduced Solo to the dark side, she held off Ben and Nelani with powerful Force phantoms. Lumiya urged Jacen to look into the possible futures that would result from their encounter, and in each turn, he saw apocalyptic visions of the Galactic Alliance falling apart and him murdering Luke Skywalker. The only alternative to end this dark future was to prevent anyone from spreading word of what they had discovered in this asteroid sanctum. To that end, Jacen killed Nelani Dinn and altered Ben Skywalker's memories of the events.

**Dinnid, Oph Nar** A Lyunesi comm handler who was discovered in a compromising position with an alpha concubine belonging to a major liege-lord of the Narrant system. This resulted in a huge bounty being placed on his head. To ensure his survival, Dinnid used memory augmentors implanted within his brain to store vast amounts of information vital to the Narrant system's business operations. This made him of great value to his new employers, the Shell Hutts. IG-88, Boba Fett, Zuckuss, Bossk, and D'harhan tracked Dinnid to Circumtore, but it was Gheeta who succeeded in exterminating Dinnid, without extracting the information in his head.

**Dio, Lexi** The Senatorial representative from Uyter during the Separatist crisis, she was a proponent of sector rights of autonomy. During the Clone Wars, Dio was assassinated and replaced by Senator Malé-Dee.

**Diollan** A featherless bird-like species, it had mottled brown leathery skin, tiny intense eyes, and a broad beak.

**Dionisio, Temo** A human councilman widely believed to be a Rebel sympathizer during the time of the Galactic Civil War. Nimo Maas hired bounty hunter Greedo to find Dionisio.

**Diori, Borga Besadii** An influential Hutt leader of the Besadii clan during the war against the Yuuzhan Vong, Borga tried to negotiate a peace treaty with the alien invaders. He then attempted to profit from this collusion by selling intelligence to the New Republic, thus playing both sides of the war. When the Yuuzhan Vong discovered this treachery, they attacked Hutt space and conquered Nal Hutta, forcing Borga to live in exile.

**dioxis** A deadly poison gas. The Trade Federation Viceroy Nute Gunray released dioxis into the Droid Control Ship's conference room in an attempt to kill Obi-Wan Kenobi and Qui-Gon Jinn.

Lexi Dio

**dipill** A sedative used to relieve stress.

**Diplomat Hotel** An immense and opulent hotel located on Coruscant, it offered rooms with individual atmosphere controls, allowing species from around the galaxy to stay in comfort.

**Diplomatic Corps** Various Diplomatic Corps organizations, both localized and galactic, existed to further relations among various planets and cultures. The Bothans, the House of Alderaan, the Rebel Alliance, and the Naboo all had their own Diplomatic Corps.

**diptera maggot** A small Yuuzhan Vong creature used to consume dying and decaying flesh during surgery or during a ritual mutilation.

**dire-cat** Feline pack-hunting predators native to Corellia, they were distinguished by the heavy spines atop their shoulders.

**directional landing beacon** This device transmitted fixed signals to help ships orient themselves.

**Directors, the** The working name adopted as a cover by a trio of Squib grifters—Grees, Emala, and Sligh—while brokering import and export deals with the Killiks of the Colony.

***Direption*** An *Imperial II*–class Star Destroyer that was part of Prince-Admiral Krennel's fleet. It was commanded by Captain Rensen until he refused an order to raze a village on Liinade III. He was executed for insubordination, and leadership fell to Commander Darron.

**Dir'Nul, Vydel** A Jedi Knight with a split personality brought on by the betrayal of her lover, Ash B'risko. When Dir'Nul caught B'risko in the arms of a Twi'lek dancer, she snapped and killed him. She then created the persona of Kardem to continue her murderous spree, killing female Twi'leks. Vydel was unaware of her dark persona, and during the Clone Wars led the investigation to hunt down Kardem. She was finally stopped by the Mandalorian Feskitt Bobb.

**discblade** A thrown razor-edged weapon used by the Zeison Sha warriors, it was imbued with supernatural accuracy by the Force.

**Disciples of Ragnos** A dark side cult led by Tavion Axmis a decade into

Discord missile

the New Republic's rule, it attempted to resurrect the ancient Sith Lord, Marka Ragnos. The cultists targeted worlds with known concentrations of Force energy—Yavin 4, Corellia, Hoth, Tatooine, and Vjun—to empower the Scepter of Ragnos Sith artifact. Jedi Knight Jaden Korr defeated Axmis and her cult on Korriban, preventing the return of Ragnos.

**discord missile** A specialized projectile used by Confederacy starfighters to deposit buzz droids onto enemy targets during the Clone Wars.

***Discril*-class attack cruisers** Eighty-five-meter-long capital warships armed with turret-mounted laser cannons, tri-particle beamers, and tri-laser cannons, they were built on Daupherm for use in that planet's defense fleet.

**Disra, Moff Vilim** An Imperial officer who started his career as a chief administrator for Governor Barshnis Choard in the Shelsha sector, liaising with the BloodScar pirates. Disra tried to expose the growing resistance in the Shelsha sector by luring Rebel leaders into the open on Shelkonwa with claims that Governor Choard was considering open secession. When Leia Organa realized that Disra's entreaties for alliance were a trap, Disra instituted a lockdown on the planet, drawing Darth Vader. Disra's multitiered plan for advancement involved capturing the Rebel leaders and handing over his governor for treason. Disra's ambitions were foiled when Leia escaped and Mara Jade captured Choard without his aid. Though Disra fully cooperated with the investigation into Choard's treachery, he spent years trying to restore his reputation.

Fifteen years after the Empire's defeat at Endor, Disra was one of the eight remaining moffs and ruler of the Imperial capital world of Bastion. Supreme Commander Gilad Pellaeon attempted to broker peace with the New Republic, but Disra opposed this plan, seeing it as nothing more than surrender. He tried to scuttle Pellaeon's strategy and instead restore the Empire to its former grandeur by forming a partnership with Major Grodin Tierce and the con artist Flim to foist an imposter Grand Admiral Thrawn on the galaxy for his own gain. This plot eventually failed.

**disruption bubble generator** A small electronic device, it created a localized bubble that was impenetrable to sonic scanning.

**disruptor** A weapon that fired a visible blast of energy that could shatter objects, disruptors killed in a painful and inhumane manner and were illegal in most sectors of the galaxy.

**Dissek, Lieutenant** *See* Tainer, Kell.

***Distant Rainbow*** A modified Kuat Drive Yards *Starwind*-class pleasure yacht used by Mazzic after he purchased it from a Rodian smuggler. Mazzic upgraded the ship with top-and-bottom quad laser turrets, improved repulsorlift engines, and a suite of electronic countermeasures meant to foil casual sensor sweeps. Though a decent pleasure yacht, the ship had minimal cargo space.

**Distombe, By't** A Twi'lek Podracer who competed against Sebulba and several others in the Vinta Harvest Podrace Classic on Malastare. By't took the lead, but was overtaken by Sebulba, who lobbed a bottle at the Twi'lek's head. By't lost control of his craft and accidentally flew over a dangerous methane pool. A geyser from the pool ignited By't's engines, causing the Podracer to explode.

**Distra** A hollow moon orbiting Corvis Minor V. The New Republic was tricked by the cloned Ysanne Isard into believing that Prince-Admiral Krennel was developing a superweapon there. This led to a skirmish between Rogue Squadron and the Ciutric Hegemony.

**Divas** A religious order of Theelin female singers known for their operatic forms. As the Theelin population began to dwindle, many hoped to preserve this cultural heritage by naming their daughters "Diva," in the hope they could continue the operatic tradition upon maturing.

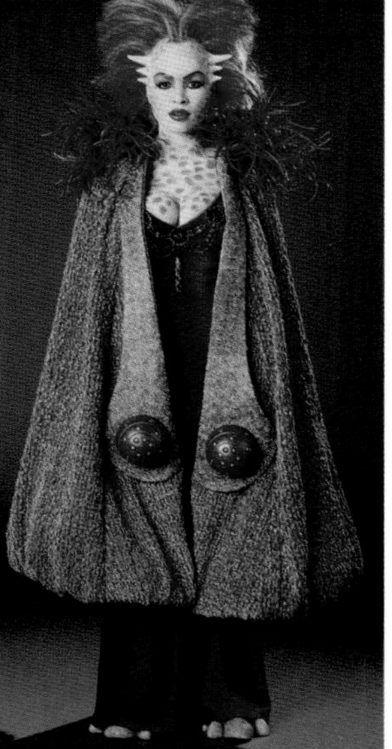

Divas

**Diversity Alliance** A radical "aliens first" political movement led by Nolaa Tarkona, it opposed the human supremacism exhibited by the Galactic Empire. Though its stated aims were for the promotion of freedom for all nonhumans, in practice, this group exhibited an extreme anti-human agenda. The group was based on Ryloth and disbanded upon Tarkona's disappearance about 14 years after the Battle of Endor.

**Divini, Lieutenant Kornell "Uli"** Born on Tatooine to noted mudopterist Elana Divini, he was a young surgeon pressed into military service during the Clone Wars. Nicknamed Uli by his friends, he continued a long line of doctors in his family, training at the Coruscant Medical Hospital and interning at the Galactic Polysapient medical center. At 19, he was given the rank of lieutenant and sent to Rimsoo VII on Drongar, a violent battlefront during the Clone Wars. He quickly grew disillusioned with the war, particularly following the death of his best friend, Zan Yant.

With the rise of the Empire, Divini became a captain in the Imperial Surgical Corps. He was stationed aboard the frigate *MedStar Four* in orbit over the prison planet Despayre before being transferred to the Death Star while the battle station was still undergoing construction. There he befriended several similarly discontent battle station workers, and following the destruction of both Despayre and Alderaan, they defected from Imperial service and joined the Rebel Alliance.

**Divinian, Bog** A native of Nuralee and husband to Astri Oddo, he was politically ambitious and achieved a position on the board of the Galactic Games on Euceron. Divinian briefly was implicated in a gambling scandal, but cleared by Obi-Wan Kenobi and Anakin Skywalker. He eventually became Senatorial representative for Nuralee, a strong ally of the Commerce Guild—and a mouthpiece for Sano Sauro and Granta Omega's plot to discredit the Jedi Order, despite his wife's longtime friendship with Kenobi. To ensure that Astri would not interfere with Bog's anti-Jedi agenda, he threatened to take their son, Lune, away from her. Astri nevertheless handed over evidence of Bog's treachery to the Jedi. Divinian lost popular support among Nuralee's voters, but he continued to be a close ally of Sauro, eventually being named an Imperial adviser and then governor of a collection of Core Worlds when Sauro rose to power under Palpatine's New Order.

**Divinian, Lune Oddo** The son of Bog Divinian and Astri Oddo, he was born Force-sensitive shortly after the Battle of Naboo. Before the start of the Clone Wars, Astri left her husband and fled with Lune to Samaria. With the rise of the Empire, Divinian wanted to capture Lune and use him as the first of a series of Force-sensitive instructors for Imperial pilots. Ferus Olin and Trever Flume helped Astri and Lune escape Imperial attention at Olin's hidden asteroid base, where he studied the ways of the Force with Garen Muln. Astri and Lune then traveled to Coruscant to make contact with Dexter Jettster and find a new place to hide, free from Imperial attention. Lune's display of Force ability drew the attention of the Empire, and he was captured by stormtroopers. Darth Vader and Jenna Zan Arbor planned to use Lune as a subject in an experiment, but he was rescued by Olin and

Dr. Linna Naltree. Reunited with his mother, Lune then began training under Jedi Master Ry-Gaul.

**divto** A fearsome three-headed snake native to the Forest Moon of Endor, it grew to a length of 3 meters. A divto hunted during darkness, delivering numbing poison to its prey.

**divvik** A small, carnivorous creature that, despite its size, was quite deadly. Divviks began life as larvae planted in the brains of other organisms. The larvae eventually burst through the skulls of their hosts in a gruesome birth. Soon after, they transformed into harmless pupae, which were considered a delicacy by the Hutts. After a short period of incubation, the divviks hatched and became ravenous beasts. Adult divviks stood about a meter tall and had six eyes, four clawed limbs, and whip-like tails. A circular, toothy maw comprised the bulk of the divvik's round body. They could not be harmed by blasters, and their terrible bite caused instant paralysis. A divvik's saliva was an incredibly corrosive acid capable of destroying plasteel. Furthermore, any attack that broke the skin released a highly toxic gas from the divvik's digestive system. They could be suffocated, if the process was given enough time, and killed with a lightsaber, which cauterized any wounds before the gas could be released. However, even a skilled Jedi Knight could only hope to fend off a handful of these dangerous creatures before being overwhelmed. Divviks typically charged their intended meal in small packs, biting their prey until it fell helpless. They then ate at leisure, keeping the victim alive for as long as possible while they consumed its flesh.

**Dix** An Imperial serving under Captain Janek Sunber on Maridun after the Battle of Yavin.

**Dix, Eyl** The communications officer aboard the *Drunk Dancer* in the early months of the Galactic Empire, she was a green-skinned humanoid alien with twin antennae.

**Di Yuni, Winna** An elder healer and skilled diagnostician serving the Jedi Temple over a decade before the Battle of Naboo. She had vast knowledge of all the diseases in the galaxy. She discovered that Didi Oddo had an infection that could be cured with an antitoxin available only through Arbor Industries.

**Dizz, Lob** A female Gungan scientist and engineer, she was especially respected for her expertise with bongo propulsion systems. Most of her assignments were official jobs for the Otoh Gunga Transit Authority or the Gungan Grand Army.

**DJ-88** A powerful droid, it served as the caretaker and teacher in the Lost City of the Jedi. Dee-Jay was white with ruby eyes and a metal "beard." DJ-88 raised young Jedi Prince Ken from the time he was a small child, and Ken looked up to the droid as he would his own father.

**Djem So** A variant of Shien Form V lightsaber combat. It was developed after Shien, specifically for lightsaber duels.

**Djirra, Lieutenant** An Imperial logistics officer on Cloud City, he was tasked with determining how to use carbon freezing to place a human into hibernation.

**Djo, Mother Augwynne** The leader of the Singing Mountain Clan of the Witches of Dathomir, a group of Force-sensitive women who rode domesticated rancors and kept men as slaves and for breeding. Han Solo won the planet Dathomir in a sabacc game, but after a series of near-fatal adventures there gave up the deed to Mother Augwynne. She was Teneniel Djo's grandmother.

**Djo, Teneniel** With red-gold hair and brown eyes flecked with orange, this bright young woman would have been a catch for any eligible bachelor. But it didn't work that way on Dathomir, especially not for Teneniel Djo, one of the Witches of Dathomir.

The planet's witches—both good and evil—led an ultramatriarchal society in which men were mere ornaments to do heavy labor or to breed. The women, whether members of such "good" clans as Teneniel Djo's Singing Mountain or of the evil Nightsisters, were used to clubbing men over the head to claim them—just as Djo did to Luke Skywalker. Luke and Prince Isolder from the planet Hapes were exploring an ancient wrecked spacecraft when they first encountered Djo. They quickly got involved in the ongoing struggle between the good clans and the Nightsisters, led by the grotesque Gethzerion. Both sides were infused with the Force.

Teneniel Djo was the daughter of Allaya Djo, who led the clan until her death in the desert. Grandmother Augwynne took over, but Teneniel was being groomed as the next queen. Complications ensued, including a raid on an Imperial prison, a full-fledged attack by the Nightsisters, and a bombardment by the rogue Imperial Warlord Zsinj. But through it all, Teneniel and Prince Isolder grew closer and true love blossomed. The couple married and eventually had a daughter, Tenel Ka, whose Force powers were strong enough to get her accepted into Skywalker's Jedi academy.

Teneniel Djo

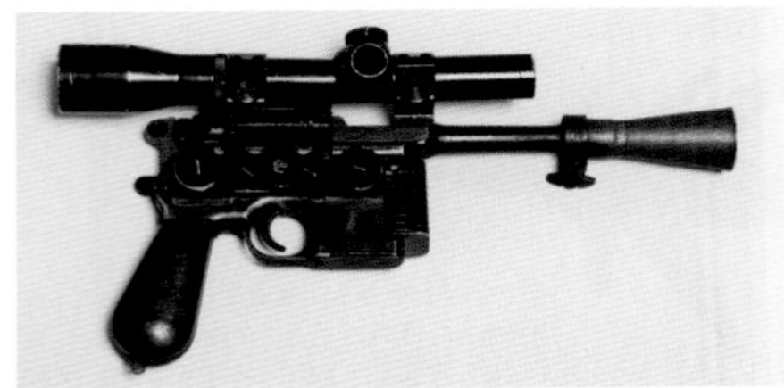

DL-44

Teneniel Djo was never really accepted by Hapan royalty despite her marriage to Isolder. Still, when Queen Mother Ta'a Chume stepped down, Djo filled that role. During the war against the Yuuzhan Vong, she again became pregnant, but she miscarried as a result of the extreme disturbance in the Force caused by the firing of the Centerpoint gravity weapon.

Ta'a Chume still wanted to replace Djo with a suitable Queen Mother, and to that end began to surreptitiously poison her in the hope that she could groom Jaina Solo as a suitable bride for Prince Isolder. Djo died, but Ta'a Chume's plot failed when Jaina did not fill her intended role. Instead, Tenel Ka ascended to the position of Queen Mother.

***D'kee*-class planetary lander** Landing ships used by the Ssi-ruuk.

**DL-44** A heavy blaster pistol, it had a short range but was relatively powerful. The DL-44, made by BlasTech, carried energy for 25 shots. It was illegal or restricted in most systems.

**Dlarit, Aerin** The father of former Rogue Squadron member Erisi Dlarit, he was one of the highest officials of the bacta monopoly in the Xucphra Corporation. He had been appointed a general in the Thyferran Home Defense Corps because of his position with the company, and became an obvious target for Rogue Squadron in its struggle to topple power-mad Ysanne Isard from her leading role on Thyferra. Originally he was scheduled to be terminated, but Rogue Iella Wessiri prevailed upon the members of her ops team to discredit him instead. As a result, he and the other THDC leaders were made to look like fools.

**Dlarit, Erisi** A former member of Rogue Squadron from the planet Thyferra, she was both beautiful and wealthy. She was also a traitor to the Rebel Alliance. Her family had a long tradition with Xucphra Corporation, the bacta monopoly; it was her uncle who discovered that a batch of the bacta had been contaminated by "terrorists." Erisi Dlarit had been expected to continue the family tradition, but she chose instead the adventurous life. She turned out to be an excellent pilot, good enough to infiltrate Rogue Squadron and learn some of its secrets. Shortly after the Rogues made a retaliatory raid on an Imperial base at Vladet, she attempted to seduce fellow Rogue Corran Horn when he was confined to quarters pending a possible court-martial. Although rebuffed, she tried again when they were paired for an undercover mission on Coruscant. Again she failed.

When Director of Imperial Intelligence Ysanne Isard fled Coruscant after the Alliance invasion, she took the traitor Dlarit with her to Thyferra and gave her a post in the Thyferran Home Defense Corps. As a commander, she was placed in charge of training TIE fighter pilots to defend the bacta convoys that Isard was using to gain money and power. Her unit was called to defend Isard's Super Star Destroyer *Lusankya* during the final moments of the Bacta War. As the ship was being pounded by Rogue Squadron, her fighter group engaged the X-wings. Dlarit was then ordered to provide cover for Isard's shuttle as she attempted to escape, but her TIE was destroyed by Corran Horn.

**DL-X2** A Veril Line Systems DL-series droid that provided security for Star Tours.

**Dnalvec** A port city on Sriluur, the Weequay home planet.

**DN bolt caster** Drever Corp originally created the Phoenix II plasma disruptor as a tool for customs agents and special-forces commandos to use in breaching locked doors. But soldiers began improvising with the tool, wielding it against battle droids and other enemies. Its effectiveness as a weapon was undeniable and prompted Drever Corp to develop the DN Bolt Caster plasma disruptor weapon. It was expensive but effective, especially against droid armies.

**D'nec, R'kik** A legendary Jawa, often regarded as the Hero of the Dune Sea for supposedly defeating a tribe of Tusken Raiders, a herd of angry banthas, and a raging krayt dragon. Many suspected this legend grew in the telling.

**D'Nore, Lieutenant** A Bothan serving under Zozridor Slayke in Freedom's Sons during the Clone Wars, he was tasked with capturing the redoubt code-named Izable during the Battle of Praesitlyn.

**DNX-N1** A largely unexplored planet in Wild Space known to be the homeworld of the Filar-Nitzan.

**Doallyn, Sergeant** A humanoid bounty hunter from the planet Geran, he was marked by a huge scar on his face, the result of an attack by a Corellian sand panther. For that reason, and because he needed the assistance of breathing cartridges in most atmospheres, Doallyn typically wore a helmet. He was called to the palace of Jabba the Hutt to hunt down a krayt dragon. Following Jabba's death, he helped the Askajian dancer Yarna d'al' Gargan escape across the desert to Mos Eisley. In the course of that trip, Doallyn got the chance to do battle with a krayt dragon. He killed it, and with the dragon pearls from its gizzard he was able to leave Tatooine with Yarna and her three children. After a visit to Geran, they all decided to live aboard their new spaceship as free traders in textiles and gemstones.

Sergeant Doallyn

Lott Dod

**doashim** A vicious predator found in the Dark Ridges of Ryloth.

**Doaskin** A planet that was the primary base of operations for TaggeCo in the Greater Javin during the early years of the Galactic Empire.

**Dobah** A female Phlog on the Forest Moon of Endor, she was the mate of Zut and the mother of Hoom and Nahkee.

**Dobbatek** An Imperial officer serving under the Black Sword Command when the Yevetha took control of the shipyards in the Koornacht Cluster, he was imprisoned on Pa'aal and later became one of the major leaders of the prison uprising during the Black Fleet Crisis.

**Dobbs** This Imperial recruit was part of Kyle Katarn's squadron during the taking of asteroid AX-456.

**Dobido** One of Sernpidal's two moons, it was small, about 20 kilometers in diameter. While Han and Anakin Solo and Chewbacca were on Sernpidal delivering a shipment from Lando Calrissian, Dobido began orbiting closer and closer to Sernpidal. This was the result of a Yuuzhan Vong dovin basal, which pulled down the moon, crashing it into Sernpidal, causing cataclysmic damage and killing Chewbacca.

**Dobo Brother's Emporium** A store located on Citadel Station in orbit around Telos following the Mandalorian Wars, it was owned by the Duros brothers Samhan and Dendis Dobo.

**Dobonold, Artonian** An Arkanian research director for Adascorp after the Great Sith War, he oversaw the work of Gorman Vandrayk, who developed a way to control the massive exogorths discovered near Omonoth. Although pleased with Vandrayk's results, Dobonold was among the many Arkanian Purebloods who barely tolerated the presence of an Arkanian Offshoot. When Lord Argaloh Adasca decided to weaponize the exogorths, Dobonold backed him against Vandrayk's wishes, leading to Vandrayk's escape and life on the run.

**Dobreed, Lana** A Podrace mechanic living in Mos Espa at the time that Anakin Skywalker also lived there, he used to dream of opening his own shop until his gambling addiction forced him to provide transportation and maintenance services as a living.

**Doc (1)** *See* A-OIC (Doc).

**Doc (2)** *See* Eirriss, Cesi "Doc."

**Doc (3)** *See* Dacholder.

**Doc (Klaus Vandangante)** The leader of a band of outlaw techs, he long specialized in making modifications—usually of an illegal nature—to space vehicles and droids. Doc, whose real name was Klaus Vandangante, was joined in his pursuits by his daughter, Jessa, at his asteroid base in the Corporate Sector. It was Jessa who modified and conjoined Doc's droids, nicknamed Bollux and Blue Max. When Doc disappeared, Jessa hired the smuggler Han Solo to find him—a rescue mission that almost ended in disaster at the Stars' End prison colony on Mytus VII.

**Docker** A subnode of Assembler Kud'ar Mub'at, it was tasked with coordinating the landing of ships carrying visitors to the web.

**Doctor Death** *See* Evazan, Dr.

**Dod, Lott** A Neimoidian who represented the Trade Federation in the Galactic Senate. Cunning and immoral, Dod used the Republic's bureaucracy to his advantage, relying on lies and confusing legal maneuvers to further the goals of the Trade Federation. However, despite his best efforts, he was unable to stop the Republic from taxing the free trade zones, a move that seriously impacted the Trade Federation's profits. When Queen Amidala appeared before the Senate to challenge the Trade Federation's subsequent invasion of

Naboo, Dod strenuously denied her allegations. To stall the proceedings, he recommended that the Senate send an independent commission to Naboo to investigate the situation. Supreme Chancellor Valorum accepted the suggestion, at which point Queen Amidala called for a vote of no confidence to remove Valorum from his post. Despite the eventual defeat of the Trade Federation invasion, Dod was able to avoid censure, and he remained politically active in the years that followed. During the Separatist Crisis, the Senator was involved in a skylane accident in the Fobosi district. After recovering, he returned to his Senatorial post, defending the actions of the Trade Federation and denying any overt involvement in the Confederacy of Independent Systems during the Clone Wars, claiming that Trade Federation matériel was being co-opted for use by the Separatists without the approval of the governing board.

Admiral Forn Dodonna

**Dodann, Temlet** A Republic Judiciary member, he broke the slave ring that implicated Senator Tikkes and the Thalassian slavers prior to the outbreak of the Clone Wars. This forced Tikkes to flee Coruscant; the Quarren Senator later joined the Separatists.

**Dodecapolis** The capital city of the Givin homeworld of Yag'Dhul.

**Dodecian** A title used by the Givin leader of the Body Calculus.

**dodge-bolt** A training game used by young Jedi students, requiring them to deflect or otherwise avoid incoming low-powered blaster bolts.

***Dodonna*** A monstrous assault frigate, it was long the cornerstone of General Wedge Antilles's fleet. The *Dodonna* was a highly modified version of the fearsome Imperial Dreadnaught. Another vessel bearing the name *Dodonna* was the first *Galactic*-class battle carrier produced for the navy of the Galactic Alliance.

**Dodonna, Admiral Forn** A Republic fleet commander who led the strike on the Star Forge during the Jedi Civil War, she was joined in this effort by Master Vandar.

**Dodonna, General Jan** Looking more like a professor than a professional warrior, and little interested in personal glory, this grizzled graybeard was one of the true heroes of the New Republic. General Jan Dodonna planned and coordinated the assault on the first Death Star at the Battle of Yavin.

A brilliant military tactician, he specialized in logistics and sieges. He was one of the first Star Destroyer captains for the Galactic Republic during the Clone Wars, having seen battle over Rendili and elsewhere. He retired as the government transformed itself into the Galactic Empire. When the Empire reviewed the general's records, he was considered too old to be retrained to the ways of the New Order, and a command was issued for his execution. The Rebel Alliance reached him first. He refused their entreaties—until Imperial troops came to kill him and he had to fight his way out. Dodonna quickly became one of the Alliance's strongest leaders. As a military commander, he answered only to Mon Mothma and the Alliance Council. After Princess Leia Organa delivered the readouts for the Death Star battle station to him, he had little time to spare. The general pored over the plans until, in the early-morning hours, he hit upon the chink in the Death Star's armor: an unshielded reactor shaft. If targeted just right, a proton torpedo sent down the shaft would lead to a chain-reaction explosion that could destroy the battle station. And Luke Skywalker targeted his torpedoes exactly right.

Dodonna was then in charge of the defense of the Rebel base on Yavin 4. When the Empire was about to attack again, he stayed behind as the Alliance evacuated and set off concussion charges that destroyed an entire fleet of TIE bombers. The general was critically wounded, captured, and imprisoned in the buried Imperial Super Star Destroyer *Lusankya,* which had been turned into a harsh prison. When Rogue Squadron member Corran Horn also was imprisoned there, he soon became friendly with Dodonna, for he could see that the old general genuinely cared about the men under his stewardship. This affection for his fellow prisoners prompted Dodonna to assist in Horn's escape from *Lusankya.*

Vrad Dodonna

General Jan Dodonna

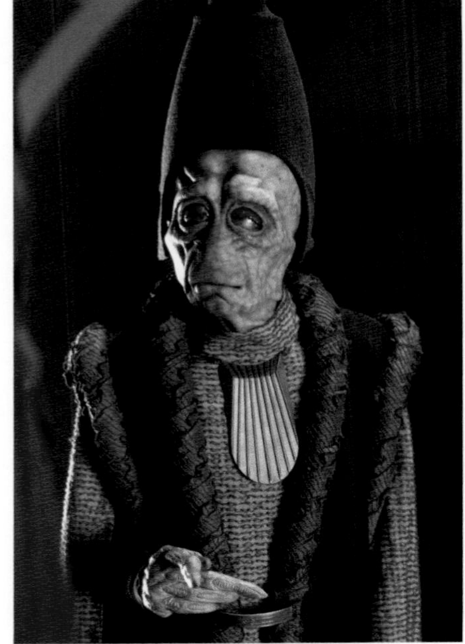
Daultay Dofine

Dodonna later was rescued by a Rebel assault team but chose to go into semi-retirement. Much of his fire had been dampened, and his injuries forced him to walk with a cane. However, six years after the Battle of Endor, his advice was instrumental in the battle against the new Imperial World Devastators.

**Dodonna, Vrad** The son of General Jan Dodonna, he at first retreated from an encounter with Darth Vader's new Super Star Destroyer, the *Executor.* But after being fired upon, Vrad Dodonna made up for his cowardice by making a suicide run and ramming his ship into the *Executor,* destroying a section of the defense shields. This allowed Han Solo to disable the ship from the rear.

***Dodonna's Pride*** A Corellian corvette named for Jan Dodonna. As a testament to the tenacity of the Rebel Alliance, the *Dodonna's Pride* was used to strike Imperial supply lines, causing massive delays.

**Dodt, Parin** Pilot Pash Cracken used the identity of Dodt, supposedly an Imperial prefect, when he went to Coruscant for an undercover mission with Rogue Squadron.

**Dodz** A small, barren world found on the Outer Rim, it was long under the rule of the evil Governor Kugg, up until the early days of the Empire. C-3PO and R2-D2 were sent to this world by the Intergalactic Droid Agency to find a new master, Lott Kemp. The world had a lucrative crystal mining industry.

**Doellin** A deity of the Gran species.

*Lushros Dofine (seated) pilots General Grievous's flagship, the* Invisible Hand.

**Dofine, Daultay** A craven, unctuous Neimoidian captain who possessed every negative trait common to his species: he was greedy, deceitful, and cowardly. Although only a moderately competent leader, Dofine employed a careful campaign of betrayal, bootlicking, and familial connections to rise through the Neimoidian ranks. His high birth assured further promotions until he ultimately assumed control of the Trade Federation's flagship, *Saak'ak.* Despite questioning Darth Sidious's invasion plans, Dofine remained in command of the flagship until it was destroyed by Anakin Skywalker.

**Dofine, Lushros** General Grievous's flagship, the *Invisible Hand,* originally was commissioned to serve Nute Gunray and his advisers. When Darth Sidious placed Grievous in control of all Separatist military operations, Gunray sheepishly had to surrender to Grievous the vaunted warship and its crew of Neimoidian navigators and gunnery officers. The esteemed captain, Lushros Dofine, was handpicked by Grievous for their past experience together, when Dofine piloted the coreship that took the droid general off Geonosis at the start of the Clone Wars. Lushros came from one of the most influential and wealthiest Neimoidian families, and was cousin to the late Daultay Dofine. Though Lushros was able to escape the destruction of the *Invisible Hand* during the Battle of Coruscant, his escape pod was caught in the crossfire and destroyed.

**Dogder, Ghitsa** The smuggling partner of Fenig Nabon during the early years of the New Republic, she hailed from Coruscant. For many years, she served as a counselor for the Hutts. She teamed with Nabon after an encounter at the Black Dust Tavern on Socorro.

**dogfly** A large flying insect native to Haruun Kal.

**Dogo** A New Republic E-wing pilot present at the Battle of ILC-905.

**Dogot, Captain Ors** The captain of the Prakith raider *Bloodprice.*

**Dohu VII** The seventh of eight planets in the Dohu system, it was home to three-armed, living-rock creatures called Silika.

**Doigon** A city on Ansion.

**Doil, Kohn** A colonel in the Grand Army of the Republic during the Clone Wars, this Vunakian was part of the security team on Drongar, and in charge of the investigation into the loss of bota and deaths of Filba the Hutt and Tarnese Bleyd. Doil concluded, incorrectly, that Filba had been the spy hidden at the Republic outpost on Drongar, and closed the case.

**Dojah, Nars** The Twi'lek quartermaster of the Rimsoo Seven medical outpost on Drongar during the Clone Wars.

**DOKAW** *See* De-Orbiting Kinetic Anti-emplacement Weapon.

**Dokes, Oakie** A privileged Swokes Swokes female who squandered her fortune on Coruscant and lived a brief, creditless existence in the undercity before finding success as an artist of particularly gory works. A frequenter of the Outlander Club during the Separatist crisis, she developed an uneasy working relationship with con men Dannl Faytonni and Achk Med-Beq.

**Dokrett, Captain Voba** The captain of the Prakith light cruiser *Gorath,* he attempted to capture the mysterious ghost ship called the Teljkon vagabond, but was destroyed by it instead.

**dokrik** A small, predatory pack animal native to Cartao. Some dokriks could be domesticated as excellent companions if they were taken from the wild at a very young age.

*Oakie Dokes*

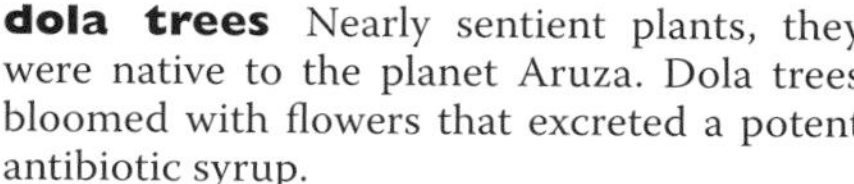

**dola trees** Nearly sentient plants, they were native to the planet Aruza. Dola trees bloomed with flowers that excreted a potent antibiotic syrup.

**Doldrums** An Inner Rim system nicknamed by the New Republic for its featureless, uninhabited planets. Wedge Antilles used it as a destination for Wraith Squadron during its hyperspace navigational training.

**Doldur** Located in a sector and system of the same name, this Imperial-controlled world was site of the Doldur Spaceport. The planet was the personal territory of Imperial Moff Eisen Kerioth, who sponsored research into antiblaster energy shields.

**Doli** The supposed location of a Sith Holocron. Several teams of Jedi Knights were dispatched there to investigate prior to the Battle of Naboo, yet nothing was found.

**Doliq, Reesa** A Jedi Master, she taught at the Jedi Temple on Coruscant about 70 years before the onset of the Clone Wars.

*Grunda Dolma*

**Dolis 3** A planet locked in a perpetual winter because of its distance from its sun. It was there that Moff Derran Takkar planned to disrupt the wedding of Luke Skywalker and Mara Jade.

**Dolma, Grunda** A long-haired Aqualish with a double-headed staff who competed in the gladiator pits of Rattatak.

**Dolomar sector** The Dolomar sector was a major target in an offensive by Grand Admiral Thrawn. Both it and the Farrfin sector were heavily defended by the New Republic, and the Republic's Admiral Ackbar personally visited Dolomar's defenses. The sector capital world was Dolomar, known for its extreme cold.

**D'olop Range** A mountain range on M'haeli, the site of many of the planet's dragite mines.

Corporal Porro Dolphe

**Doloria** A fanatical cult of Selonian assassins for hire who revered Sacorrian customs.

**Dolovite** A valuable metal mined on Mimban, Nkllon, Burnin Konn, and Mustafar.

**Dolph** *See* Kueller.

**Dolphe, Corporal Porro** A Naboo pilot and member of Bravo Flight, he grew up in a small town outside Theed before volunteering as a pilot. He flew Bravo Two during the Battle of Naboo. Ten years later, he was the lead pilot of the trio of Naboo starfighters that escorted the Naboo Royal Cruiser carrying Senator Amidala to Coruscant. When the cruiser was sabotaged, he was knocked down by the blast. He recovered and ran a defensive perimeter behind Captain Typho and Padmé as they escaped the landing platform.

**Doluff, Lob** The senior administrator of the Oseon system. The Sorcerer of Tund, Rokur Gepta, posing as Bohhuah Mutdah, used Doluff in a scheme to capture Lando Calrissian. Doluff invited Calrissian to a sabacc game on Oseon 6845, but circumstances caused Calrissian to be arrested for possession of a weapon. Instead of sentencing him to death, as the law required, Doluff used Calrissian in a covert police mission to bust trillionaire drug abuser Bohhuah Mutdah. In truth, the drug bust was a setup, Doluff himself being an abuser of the exact same drug as Mutdah: lesai. Doluff was a pear-shaped human male with a shiny scalp and trim dark beard. He was a man of sophisticated tastes, as witnessed by the elaborate Esplanade he constructed on Oseon 6845.

**Domains, Yuuzhan Vong** The basic familial groupings recognized in Yuuzhan Vong culture. Sample Domains included Cha, Dal, Eklut, Esh, Fath, Hool, Hul, Jamaane, Karsh, Kraal, Kwaad, Lacap, Lah, Lian, Muyel, Nar, Paasar, Pekeen, Qel, Shai, Shen'g, Shoolb, Shul, Taav, Tivvik, Tsun, Vang, Vorrik, Yaght, and Zun-qin.

**Dom-Bradden** An Outer Rim world, it was home to the Affytechans, a sentient form of plant life with high, musical voices and bodies composed of thousands of colorful petals, tendrils, and stalks. While they appeared quite beautiful, the Affytechans stank of ammonia and musk. The Imperial battlemoon *Eye of Palpatine* stopped at Dom-Bradden to pick up a contingent of stormtroopers, but brought in a group of Affytechans instead.

**Domed City of Aquarius** Built inside a giant air-filled bubble far below the Mon Calamari oceans, the city could be used by both air- and water-breathing beings. Water-filled canals in the Domed City of Aquarius featured underwater homes, but markets and other residences were located in air-filled areas.

**Dome of the Mother Jungle** At the heart of an Ithorian herd ship was a segment of the sacred jungle from their home planet, carefully tended to by Ithorian priests aboard the vessel.

**Dometown** This hollow dome a kilometer across was built by Lando Calrissian and other investors in a huge subterranean cavern beneath Coruscant. Dometown, a pocket city, consisted of low stone buildings and cool green parks. It failed financially and remained a ghost town until New Republic forces began fortifying it as a potential refuge for the New Republic leadership during the war against the Yuuzhan Vong.

**Domgrin** An Outer Rim planet that was not far from Gonmore.

***Dominance*** A Republic *Acclamator*-class troopship dispatched to Jabiim during the Clone Wars.

***Dominant*** Pter Thanas's Imperial *Carrack*-class cruiser during the Ssi-ruuvi invasion of Bakura, it destroyed the Alliance carrier-cruiser *Flurry* when the truce between Imperial and Rebel forces there dissolved. Overwhelmed by Rebel forces, Thanas surrendered the *Dominant* to the Alliance.

***Dominator* (1)** A *Victory*-class Star Destroyer at the Battle of Endor, it was fully overhauled with powerful thrusters and the latest hyperdrive technology. It was engineered to support task forces combating Rebel starfighters.

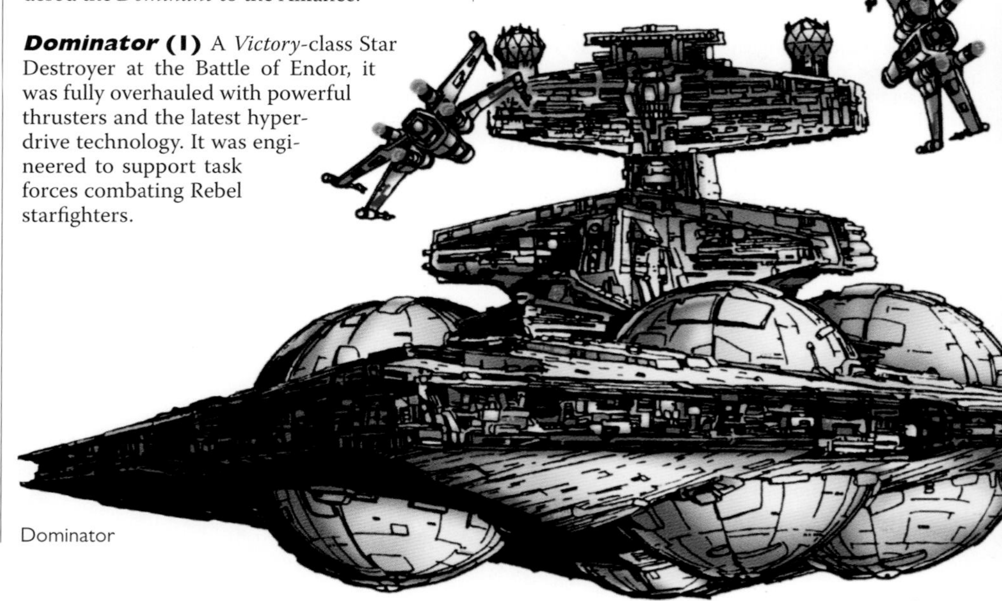

Dominator

***Dominator* (2)** A modified Imperial Immobilizer 418 Interdictor that attacked an Alliance convoy near Mrlsst. Wedge Antilles and Elscol Loro took out the Interdictor's gravity well with two closely timed proton torpedo volleys, enabling the Alliance fleet to escape.

**Dominé, Calquad** A disgruntled spice miner and captain of the mining vessel *Pickaxe.* He protested the Naboo government's decision to limit miner access to starports by parking his vessel at the Kwilaan starport during the Separatist crisis.

***Dominion*** A Super Star Destroyer that was part of the Imperial Remnant's fleet of warships. In the wake of the Second Battle of Fondor, the *Dominion* led a fleet of ships to capture the Nickel One asteroid. The Imperial commanders were unprepared for the strong counterattack of the Verpine, which was augmented by a group of Mandalorians led by Boba Fett and Jaina Solo. The Verpine and Mandalorian starships concentrated their initial attacks on the *Dominion,* and quickly reduced the flagship to a flaming shell. Despite the loss, Imperial forces fought on and managed to break the hold of the Verpine fleet.

**Dominus** A Jedi Master many millennia ago. One of his favorite apprentices was Zona Luka, who ultimately assassinated him.

**Dominus system** An uncharted system where Darth Vader's secret laboratory ship, *Empirical,* was located.

**Domisari** An Imperial assassin, she posed as a Corellian treasure seeker, claiming that she had scoured the No-ad system for fire crystals and was searching the ancient Nespis VIII space station for the fabled Jedi library after the Battle of Yavin. There she encountered Zak and Tash Arranda, and would have attempted to kill them had she not been killed by Dannik Jerriko.

Tott Doneeta

**Domitree** The capital of Ord Thoden, it was wracked by an immense groundquake during the Separatist crisis.

**Dommaro, Lieutenant Gorsick** An Imperial stationed aboard the Death Star who controlled the A68 Market.

**Domna, Sevan** One of Jabba the Hutt's most loyal majordomos, he sacrificed his life to prevent Jabba from being killed in an assassination attempt several decades before the Battle of Yavin.

**Don, Tox** A Rodian aide to Senator Onaconda Farr during the Clone Wars.

**Do'naal** A Rebel agent who was, in truth, an Imperial spy, he compromised the identity of fellow Rebel agents Vewin on Kelada and Rixen on Kuat.

**Donabelle, Lysire** A human member of the ExGal-4 science team on Belkadan. She was killed by Yomin Carr after the planet had been terraformed.

**Donal** An assistant to Solace, the secret identity of Jedi Master Fy-Tor-Ana after the Clone Wars. Solace left Donal in charge of a secret underground settlement while she accompanied Ferus Olin on a mission to the surface of Coruscant. Solace returned to find the hidden settlement attacked, and reasoned that Donal had been a double agent.

**donar** An Ithorian plant that produced sweet-smelling purple blossoms.

**Donar III, Nathan** A rival of Kyle Katarn's at the Imperial Academy on Carida, he and his father Governor Dol Donar II were killed when the captured Rebel droid A-Cee self-destructed.

**Donba, Ten-Abu** A high priest of the ancient tribe of Bendu monks who lived peacefully in the mountains, away from the bustling cities of Ando Prime. Nonetheless, Ten-Abu Donba welcomed visitors with open arms, hosting all the Podraces on the planet.

***Doneeta*** A Republic *Acclamator*-class troop transport assigned to Jedi Masters Saesee Tiin and Plo Koon during the Clone Wars to prevent the defection of Rendili's home fleet.

**Doneeta, Shaala** A Rutian Twi'lek aide to Count Dooku who was present when Dooku made his Fête Day speech during the Clone Wars.

**Doneeta, Tott** A Jedi Twi'lek trained by Master Arca Jeth at his compound on Arkania some 4,000 years before the birth of Luke Skywalker. When Doneeta was a child, his family was rescued from a slave ship by Jeth, who recognized the boy's link to the Force. Doneeta also had a natural affinity for understanding and conversing in beast languages, a talent that made him invaluable when Jeth's Jedi students traveled to Onderon to bring peace between the beast-riders and the citizens of Iziz. Later, Doneeta helped quell the Freedon Nadd Uprising and rescued Jeth from the Naddists.

Just before the death of Ulic Qel Droma, Doneeta called upon the power of the Force to quell a heat storm threatening a Twi'lek clan, leaving the Twi'lek Jedi's face badly scarred. He then joined the great convocation at Exis Station. Accompanied by Sylvar on his return to Ryloth, Tott Doneeta later was instrumental in reaching a peaceful resolution between his clan and the R'lyek, a rival clan. In order to end generations of bloodshed, Doneeta was able to convince the two clan leaders to sacrifice their lives by going into the desert, to be replaced by a new, single head-clan as dictated by Twi'lek tradition.

**Doneeta, Tuulaa** An alias adopted by Aayla Secura when she traveled undercover on Devaron during the Clone Wars. Tuulaa was the daughter of Kas Doneeta, head of Ryloth Ventures.

**Doni, Miranda** A K-wing pilot for Blue Flight in the New Republic's Fifth Fleet, she was killed during the failed attempt to blockade the Yevetha at Doornik-319.

**Donkuwah** A ruthless clan of fierce Duloks living on the Forest Moon of Endor.

**Donn, Castin** A human member of Wraith Squadron from Coruscant, he flew as Wraith Two. He was a skilled computer specialist and slicer. He had managed to obtain a holographic recording of the destruction of the second Death Star, and propagated it across the HoloNet before the Empire could put its official spin on the matter. Disobeying a direct order, Castin stowed away with the Hawk-bats, Wraith Squadron working undercover, in infiltrating Warlord Zsinj's flagship, *Iron Fist*. He was captured by stormtroopers and executed by Imperial officer Captain Seku.

**Donnerwin** Lando Calrissian's chief command officer at his Varn mining facility around the time of the New Republic–Imperial treaty.

**Donos, Lieutenant Myn** A male Corellian fighter pilot and marksman, he was leader of Talon Squadron until it was wiped out during an ambush at Gravan VII. Donos then joined Wraith Squadron, flying first as Wraith Nine, and then as Wraith Three. After the Wraiths became an intelligence unit, Donos left to join Rogue Squadron.

**Donoslane Excursions** A company based on Coronet, Corellia, and founded by Myn Donos and Lara Notsil.

**Donovia** A planet of rainy seasons and rugged terrain, it was extensively mined by Donovian Rainmen in the last decades of the Galactic Republic.

**Dontamo** The site of one of the Empire's first prison facilities in the Radiant One system. Its prison populace provided the labor for the manufacture of components used in the construction of the first Death Star.

**dontopod** The largest species of grazer native to Yavin 8.

**dontworry** An illegal hallucinogen, also known as Zeltronian Fun Dip.

**doo** A species of scalefish that inhabited the deep waters of Naboo.

**Doodnik** The proprietor of a tapcaf on Tyne's Horky during the early days of the Empire, he was a gruff, greasy worker, with orange skin and four brawny arms. His tapcaf once employed C-3PO and R2-D2, but he fired them for their incompetence.

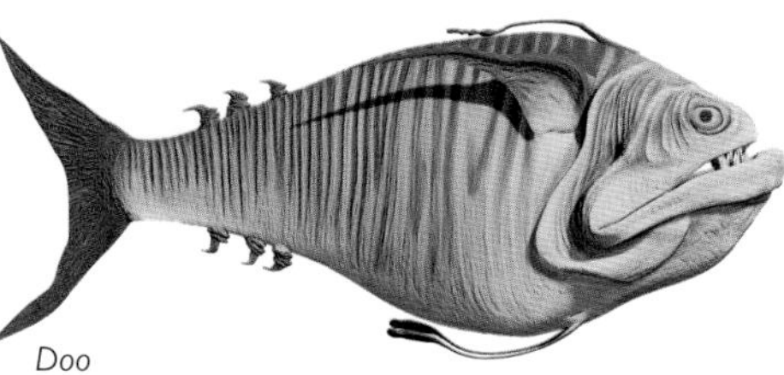
Doo

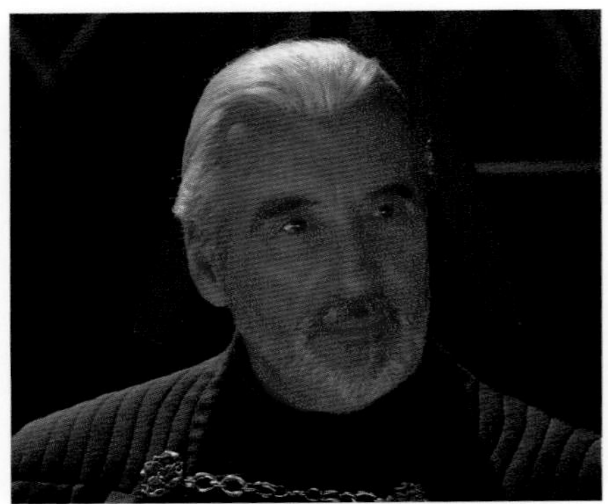
Count Dooku

**Dooku, Count** One of the greatest legends of the Jedi Order, and also one of its greatest losses, Dooku was a revered Jedi Master until he abandoned his commission, disillusioned with the direction of both the Jedi and the Republic they served. It was more than his strong-willed independent nature that led him away from the Jedi Temple, however. No one in the Order suspected that he had become corrupted by a Sith Lord.

In retrospect, there were telltale clues to Dooku's eventual transgression. He had long been prideful, born of nobility and great wealth on Serenno. Though he abandoned that life at a very young age to train under Jedi Master Yoda, he nonetheless had a stately air even at a young age. Yoda had taken a personal interest in Dooku for his extraordinary connection to the Force.

At 13, Dooku was chosen to be the Padawan of Thame Cerulian. At the time, his best friend was the mischievous Lorian Nod. When Nod tried to blame Dooku for the theft of a Sith Holocron from the Jedi Archives, a rivalry began. Nod was expelled from the Jedi Temple, and Dooku learned not to believe in friendship.

When Dooku became a Jedi Knight, he took young Qui-Gon Jinn as his apprentice. Together they were assigned to protect Senator Blix Dannon from kidnappers. During this mission, they discovered that Lorian Nod was behind the conspiracy, and the Jedi confronted him. Angered by Nod, Dooku attacked him and nearly killed him, but Qui-Gon prevented his Master from giving in to his dark impulses.

Qui-Gon and Dooku never forged a particularly close relationship, with Dooku serving more as a detached teacher than a close friend. After Qui-Gon passed the Jedi trials and became a Jedi Knight, he and Dooku drifted apart. Dooku was offered a position on the Jedi Council, but declined so he could continue as more of an independent peacekeeper, operating throughout the galaxy. Dooku eventually took on a second Padawan, Komari Vosa.

Twelve years before the Battle of Naboo, Dooku led a Jedi task force to Galidraan to confront a Mandalorian invasion. The ensuing battle was bloody, with the Jedi force being decimated and the Mandalorians nearly wiped out; Jango Fett was one of the few survivors. Dooku learned that Galidraan's governor had manipulated the Jedi Council to engineer the destruction of the Mandalorians, and the Jedi Master became further disenchanted with the operations of the Jedi Council. Though Vosa acquitted herself well during the battle on Galidraan, Dooku found her lacking in emotional control and did not recommend her for advancement to the Jedi trials. In a vain effort to prove her worth to Dooku, she disappeared on Baltizaar trying to stop the Bando Gora cult.

Dooku became even more withdrawn after Galidraan, spending much time researching ancient Jedi prophecies in the Jedi Archives. He grew concerned not only with the prophesied imbalance of the Force and growing darkness, but also the growing corruption in the Galactic Republic. Though he spent little time among the Masters of the Council, he did confer with, and express his concerns to, his friend Sifo-Dyas.

After the death of Qui-Gon Jinn at Naboo, Dooku renounced his commission as a Jedi, becoming one of the Lost Twenty—the only Jedi to leave the Order. Unbeknownst to the Jedi, Dooku had come under the influence of Darth Sidious, who promised a future of order that would bring an end to the corruption of the Republic and the inefficiencies of the Jedi. Dooku agreed to become apprentice to Sidious, adopting the secret Sith mantle of Darth Tyranus. Dooku returned to Serenno and inherited his wealth and rightful title as Count.

Heedful of Dooku's warning of the Republic's eventual collapse, Sifo-Dyas had secretly commissioned the Kaminoans to develop a clone army for the Republic. Sidious and Tyranus learned of this development, and Dooku killed Sifo-Dyas, adopting the Jedi Master's identity to erase Kamino's existence from the Jedi Archives and hire Jango Fett as the template of the clone army.

Eight years after his disappearance from public view, Dooku reemerged as a political firebrand fanning the flames of rebellion in the galaxy. In an alarmingly short time, Dooku rallied thousands of systems to his cause, building a growing Separatist movement that threatened to split the Republic. Opportunists working in Dooku's name would start flashpoints of violence, and it was all the Jedi could do to maintain order in these turbulent times. For all the strife, the Jedi Council refused to believe that Dooku was personally responsible for the worst of the conflicts, thinking that his Jedi training elevated him above such acts.

Dooku began recruiting agents for what would eventually amount to the death of the Galactic Republic. He appealed to the greed of the galaxy's most powerful commerce barons to consolidate their forces and challenge the Republic. Deep within the mighty spires of Geonosis, Dooku chaired a meeting of the minds to formally create the Confederacy of Independent Systems. Separatist Senators alongside representatives from the Commerce Guild, the Trade Federation, the Corporate Alliance, the InterGalactic Banking Clan, and the Techno Union pooled their resources to form the largest military force in the galaxy. The Separatists were ready for war.

The Jedi Knight Obi-Wan Kenobi discovered the treasonous meeting and warned the Republic, but not without being captured. Dooku met with Kenobi in the Geonosian dungeons and revealed to him the truth about the Republic—that it was, in fact, coming increasingly under the control of Darth Sidious. Obi-Wan refused to believe Dooku, and refused to join him in rooting out the corruption.

Kenobi was soon joined by Anakin Skywalker and Padmé Amidala, who had come to Geonosis in an ill-fated attempt to rescue him. Dooku placed the three captive heroes in an execution arena, but their deaths were staved off by the timely arrival of Jedi reinforcements. The droid armies of the Separatists engaged the Jedi, and later the newly crafted clone army of the Republic.

Dooku attempted to escape but was intercepted by Anakin Skywalker and Obi-Wan Kenobi. The two Jedi challenged Dooku to a lightsaber duel, but Dooku's masterful skills in old-style lightsaber combat made short work of the younger combatants. As they lay wounded, another Jedi entered into Dooku's secret hangar. The Jedi Master Yoda confronted Dooku. The two engaged in a titanic struggle of Force powers, neither besting the other. It came down to a contest of lightsabers. In a blurring tangle of speed and light, the two masters of the Force dueled. Unable to find an advantage, Dooku distracted Yoda by endangering Kenobi and Skywalker with a toppling pillar. As Yoda used the Force to save his fellow Jedi, Dooku fled. Aboard his exotic interstellar sail ship, Dooku traveled to a decrepit warehouse district on Coruscant. There he met with his master, Darth Sidious, and delivered the good news: The Clone Wars had begun.

During the wars, Dooku became the political face of the Separatist movement, while underlings such as General Grievous and Asajj Ventress became his trusted enforcers. Early on, the Confederacy mined the major hyperspace routes leading to the Outer Rim, effectively cutting off the Republic from the bulk of its clone forces. In an effort to extend their range, the Republic entreated the Hutts to allow use of

Count Dooku (left) and Master Yoda engaging in a titanic struggle of Force powers on Geonosis

their Outer Rim shipping lanes. To sabotage such efforts, Dooku colluded with Ziro the Hutt to have his agents kidnap Jabba the Hutt's young son, Rotta, and frame the Jedi for the crime. Anakin Skywalker and Ahsoka Tano managed to rescue Rotta from an abandoned B'omarr monk monastery on Teth, while Senator Amidala exposed Ziro's conspiracy on Coruscant. Jabba, incensed at Dooku's deception, pledged his allegiance to the Republic and was reunited with his son.

In the three long years of warfare that spread across the galaxy, Dooku was involved in myriad plots to destabilize the Republic. All the while, he secretly answered to Darth Sidious, unaware that his Sith Master ultimately viewed him as disposable to his grand plot of controlling the galaxy. With similar Sith ruthlessness, Dooku saw his own underlings—Ventress, Grievous, and others such as Durge, Sora Bulq, and Quinlan Vos—as equally expendable. Nonetheless, Dooku trained both Ventress and Grievous in lightsaber combat. Whereas Dooku handled a lightsaber with finesse and accuracy, Grievous used his bizarre mechanical anatomy to wield up to four lightsabers in a blurring haze of brutal lacerating energy.

At the end of the Clone Wars, the Separatists staged a daring strike against the Republic. The Confederacy had penetrated Coruscant's defenses and absconded with Chancellor Palpatine. The kidnapping was a test of a prospective new Sith apprentice. Blazing onto General Grievous's flagship—the vehicle of escape for Dooku and his "captive"—were the Jedi heroes Obi-Wan Kenobi and Anakin Skywalker. Once again Dooku dueled with the Jedi pair. He bested Kenobi, knocking the Jedi unconscious with a brutal Force push, but was unable to overpower Skywalker. Goading the fiery-tempered young man throughout the duel, Dooku thought he had the upper hand until Anakin outmaneuvered him.

Skywalker severed both of Dooku's hands and snatched the Sith Lord's red-bladed weapon. Dooku fell to his knees before Skywalker, who was now holding two lightsabers at his throat. "Kill him," advised Palpatine—and Dooku fully realized that treachery was the way of the Sith. He was expendable, Dooku realized. Skywalker was the true prize, the gifted apprentice, the new Sith. This understanding awakened in him as Skywalker crossed his blades, severing Dooku's head. (*See also* Tyranus, Darth.)

**dool bug** An insect native to M'haeli.

**Doole, Moruth** A vile, double-crossing Rybet, he was the kingpin of the Kessel spice-smuggling business who thought nothing of turning against—even murdering—onetime allies to get what he wanted. Squat and frog-like in appearance with slimy green skin, partial to wearing reptile skins (and a bright yellow tie when he was sexually available), and so paranoid that he was prone to nervous tics, Moruth Doole truly represented the underbelly of the galaxy.

His position as an official at the large Imperial prison on Kessel made it possible for him to pack the staff with those loyal to him. He blackmailed or paid off prison guards, sold maps and access codes for Kessel's energy shields so that others could set up small, illegal spice-mining operations on other parts of the planet, then killed off or ratted on those operators when the time was right.

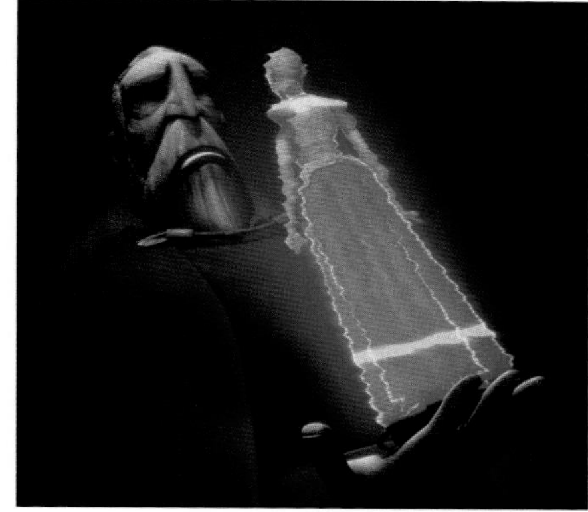

*Asajj Ventress reports to Count Dooku during the Clone Wars.*

The Empire used its Kessel prisoners to mine glitterstim spice, a powerful drug that sold for high prices all over the galaxy. Doole, of course, skimmed ever-larger amounts of the black-market drug for his own accounts. He made sure that, with rare exceptions, anyone who knew of his scheming was bumped off. He even put his own offspring—produced through forced mating with unwilling females of his species—to work as slaves in the pitch-black mines. The only one he trusted was his top aide, a onetime prison guard named Skynxnex, an accomplished thief and assassin despite his scarecrow-like appearance.

It was on a spice-smuggling run for Jabba the Hutt that Han Solo learned of Doole's true ways. Even though Jabba had already paid Doole the 12,400 credits for the glitterstim spice, Doole tipped off tariff authorities—who had also paid Doole—to the route of Solo's *Millennium Falcon*. Solo dumped the load before he could be boarded, but when he returned later to pick it up, it had vanished. Jabba then put a bounty on Solo's head but—suspicious about Doole—sent a bounty hunter after him. Doole managed to lose only one eye instead of his life as Skynxnex came to his rescue.

As the Galactic Civil War continued, Doole took complete control of Kessel operations, killing off all potential rivals. Then, seven years after the Battle of Endor, Han Solo and Chewbacca returned to Kessel on a diplomatic mission. Not believing them, Doole made them slaves in his deepest spice mine, where the two first met Force-sensitive Kyp Durron. When the Alliance began to investigate the disappearance of Solo and Chewbacca, Doole decided to murder them. Instead, Skynxnex was killed by one of the giant spice-producing spiders in the mine, and the trio escaped. A chance encounter ensued in which most of Doole's defense fleet—and much of the planet—was destroyed by Admiral Daala's Imperial fleet, and the Rybet fled back to a prison tower on Kessel. Eventually, forces from the New Republic, smugglers, and his own offspring forced Doole to flee into the mines, where he was speared by one of the giant spiders—a just ending for the murderous being.

**Doole, Tee-ubo** A Twi'lek, she was a member of the ExGal-4 science team on Belkadan. She went on a trip outside the station alongside fellow team members Bendodi Ballow-Reese, Luther De'Ono, and Jerem Cadmir. The Yuuzhan Vong transformation of Belkadan began while they were away from the station, and they were killed in the environmental destruction.

**Doolis** A major city on Caprioril, and site of the Doolis Podrace Arena.

***Doomgiver*** A Star Destroyer–like flagship used by Admiral Galak Fyyar and Chistor Dark Jedi Desann of the Empire Reborn, it was equipped with AT-RDP (All Terrain Rapid Deployment Pod) drop units attached to its underbelly, which served as surface transports for the Reborn armies. Kyle Katarn infiltrated the ship during its assault of Luke Skywalker's Jedi praxeum on Yavin 4, disabling its shield generators, which allowed Rogue Squadron to destroy the vessel.

**Doomsled** A military repulsorlift model created for the Galactic Alliance Guard, it was a prisoner transport vehicle outfitted with a detention compartment that could be opened to public view. That allowed bystanders to watch as GAG officers shackled their prisoners and took them away for interrogation.

**D'oon, T'chooka** A Nubian Jedi, he was dispatched by the Jedi Council to mediate a resolution to the Huk Wars on Kalee. His judgment favored the Huks, leading to the destitution of the Kaleesh people, who would come to call D'oon "the Executioner of Kalee." During the Clone Wars, he was master to Flynn Kybo, and he was murdered by General Grievous during a mission to Vandos.

**doonium** A common heavy metal, it was used to build Imperial war machines.

**doop bug** A large flat beetle-like creature native to Tatooine.

**door-breaker charge** A shaped explosive device used by law enforcement agencies to blast open a sealed door.

**Doori-Doori** The Prime Justice of Kip who sentenced Zorba the Hutt to 15 years in prison for the theft of ulikuo stones.

*Moruth Doole*

**Doornik-1142** A brown dwarf star orbited by four cold, gaseous planets, it was located on the edge of the Koornacht Cluster. Twelve years after the Battle of Endor, the New Republic astrographic survey ship *Astrolabe* was diverted to Doornik-1142 by General Etahn A'baht, who was hoping to get an updated survey of the Koornacht Cluster for military intelligence purposes. Instead the *Astrolabe* was destroyed by a Yevethan battle cruiser; the Yevetha claimed that they were defending their territory against New Republic spies. In fact, the Yevetha had moved their entire Black Eleven Fleet to Doornik-1142 to conceal it.

**Doornik-207** A planet in the Farlax sector and the Koornacht Cluster, Doornik-207 was the former site of a nest of Corasgh. Twelve years after the Battle of Endor, the alien Yevetha attacked and conquered Doornik-207 as part of a series of raids that they called the Great Purge.

**Doornik-319** *See* Morning Bell.

**Doornik-628** *See* J't'p'tan.

**Doornik-881** *See* Kutag.

**Dop, Moppo** A burly Gungan professional gulli-ball player, he accused Captain Tarpals of cheating in the Big Nasty Free-For-All.

**Dopey** A New Republic K-wing pilot killed during the unsuccessful blockade of Doornik-319.

**dopplefly** A creature often kept as an exotic pet.

**doppraymagno scanner** A multifunction scanning device that used Doppler imaging, X-rays, and magnetic resonance to peer within solid objects.

**Dor (1)** The fourth and outermost planet of the Endor system. The Empire mined Dor extensively for raw materials in the construction of the second Death Star.

**Dor (2)** A member of the Young on Melida/Daan, he was in charge of medical concerns as part of their newly established government.

**Dorajan** A planet covered with dense jungle.

**Dorak** An ancient Jedi Master who served the Jedi enclave on Dantooine as a historian in the time of the Mandalorian Wars and the Jedi Civil War.

**dora-mu** A giant aquatic creature that was once native to the Yuuzhan Vong homeworld of Yuuzhan'tar, its scales formed the biological foundation for the vangaak, a form of Yuuzhan Vong underwater craft.

**Doran, Kell** *See* Tainer, Kell.

**Doran, Kissek** A Rebel Alliance fighter pilot from Alderaan, he was one of the original Tierfon Yellow Aces serving alongside Wes Janson and Jek Porkins. During a mission where a low profile was of paramount importance, Doran panicked at being outnumbered by Imperial forces. Janson tried to talk reason to him, but Doran wouldn't listen, so Janson fired a shot at his X-wing. The blast cracked Kissek's cockpit, venting atmosphere and killing him. Kissek's widow learned of the circumstances of his death and blamed the Alliance, changing the family name to Tainer to avoid association. Despite this, Kissek's son—Kell Tainer—eventually joined the Alliance.

**Dorande** An alien culture that wished to seize the planet of R-Duba during the early days of the Empire. Members of the Dorande species conspired with the planet's royal advisers to assassinate Prince Jagoda. The Dorande planned a secret raid on the palace by sea. The assassination was averted by C-3PO, while the sea assault was foiled by sea captain Kirk Windjammer. The Dorande were hairless pink-skinned humanoids with pointed ears.

***Doran Star*** The false identification used by the shuttle *Narra* when Wraith Squadron infiltrated the planet Storinal.

**Dorchess Valley** One of the primary tallgrain farmlands on Pakrik Minor.

**Doreenian ambergris** An ingredient in a heady perfume. Doreenian ambergris was popular among smugglers because shipping this pungent substance often masked other illegal wares and discouraged customs officials from probing too deeply.

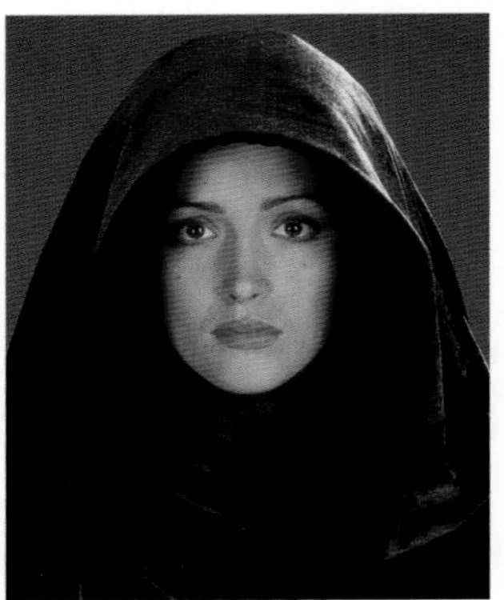
Dormé

**Dorenian Beshniquel** A musical wind instrument, it was sometimes called a Fizzz.

**Doriana, Kinman** A personal aide to Senator Palpatine, he was one of the key accomplices in Palpatine's rise to power. Kinman Doriana led the task force that laid in wait to ambush the Outbound Flight Project. His ships stumbled upon the Chiss Expansionary Defense Fleet. Despite inferior weapons and numbers, its leader, Thrawn, decimated Doriana's ships. After the battle, Doriana met and recruited Thrawn for the Empire to complete the mission at which he had failed.

**Dorian Quill** An alcoholic drink, it was aged 12 years before being bottled.

**Dorin** This planet in the Expansion Region was the homeworld of the Kel Dor species. Travel to and from Dorin was limited due to the presence of nearby black holes.

**Dorin, Mika** A pazaak player who frequented the cantinas in the city of Dreshdae, on Korriban, during the time of Darth Malak and Darth Revan.

**Dorits, Laslo** The spokesbeing for the Stark Veteran Assembly just prior to the Clone Wars, he was critical of Senator Padmé Amidala's comments about warfare.

**Dorja, Captain** Cautious in battle—some might say a bit cowardly—he was commander of the Imperial Star Destroyer *Relentless.* Captain Dorja hailed from a wealthy family with a long tradition of military service. During the Battle of Endor, his ship didn't suffer a single casualty—quite possibly because of his unwillingness to engage an enemy in direct combat. He opposed the rise to power of Captain Pellaeon and despised Grand Admiral Thrawn, at the same time plotting a way to take control of the Empire himself. Dorja survived the death of Thrawn as well as the various warlords who attempted to lead the Empire thereafter. He was one of the last 13 captains who remained in command of their Star Destroyers a decade later, when Moff Disra called upon Dorja to intercept Admiral Pellaeon as he attempted to broker peace with the New Republic.

**Dorja, Commander Vana** The daughter of Captain Dorja, she continued to serve the Imperial Remnant in the era of peace between the Empire and the New Republic. During the Yuuzhan Vong invasion, Dorja was on Coruscant and fled the capital before the aliens took over the world. She retreated to Mon Calamari, and later was given transport to the Imperial Remnant with Leia Organa Solo.

**Dorlo** A world subjugated by the Empire despite the efforts of Jedi Knight Qu Rahn.

**Dorlon II** A barren, volcanic planet. An orbital facility there served as a transfer station for those heading to nearby Carida.

**Dorma** The owner of Dorma's Café, a small restaurant in the Cloud Lake district of the city of Ussa, on Bellassa. Dorma fell on hard times during the rise of the Empire. Her eatery was located next to the Olin/Lands Agency.

**Dormé** One of Senator Padmé Amidala's handmaidens, she stayed behind on Coruscant to cover the Senator's surreptitious return to Naboo when her life was endangered just prior to the Clone Wars.

**dormo-shock** A naturally healing, coma-like sleep that severely injured patients sometimes entered into. It allowed the body's

*Vikar Dorn*

regenerative and recuperative abilities to heal traumatized areas.

**Dorn** A young Bothan boy who, like Anakin Skywalker, was a slave in Mos Espa. Dorn was owned by Jabba the Hutt, who was training him to become a spy and had him infiltrate Gardulla's slaves to locate the stolen Ghostling children. Dorn was actually helping the Ghostlings escape, and he fled from Tatooine with them aboard Rakir Banai's starship.

**Dorn, Vikar** A Galactic Alliance planetary governor in the era of Emperor Roan Fel, he agreed to support the New Empire and leadership of Darth Krayt. Darth Maladi ordered Dorn to Bastion in an effort to assassinate the Emperor. Traveling from his Star Destroyer *Dauntless* to Bastion's surface aboard his shuttle, Dorn secretly carried the Sith Lord Darth Kruhl. Emperor Fel, however, was aware of the impending attack and was able to kill Kruhl in combat. Fel then had Dorn's crew—including Dorn's son—executed for their treachery, and allowed Dorn to return to the Sith with a message of warning. Dorn returned to Sith space, and was killed by Maladi for his failure.

**Dornea** The homeworld of the Dorneans, a tall species with purplish leathery skin, the planet never officially joined the Rebel Alliance, but its inhabitants fought bravely against the Empire. The Dornean Navy, though it numbered barely 80 vessels, was able to successfully resist the Empire despite being greatly outnumbered in several battles. General Etahn A'baht, the senior military commander of the Dornean Navy, was named commander of the New Republic's Fifth Fleet 12 years after the Battle of Endor.

**Dornean gunship** *See Braha'tok*-class gunship.

**Dorosii the Hutt** An Appointed Intermediary to the Galactic Republic Senate, this Hutt represented the Periphery region, including the Weequay homeworld of Sriluur.

**Dorr, Sholh** A moisture farmer on Tatooine, he accompanied Cliegg Lars in a hunt for the Tusken Raiders who had captured Shmi Skywalker. Sholh was one of the few farmers to return from that excursion alive. Decades later, an ailing Dorr purchased an RA-7 servant droid from a Jawa sandcrawler, only to later sell it as a collector's item on Eport for thousands of times its original purchase price.

**Dorr-Femi-Bonmi** A Cerean and former member of the Council of Elders. Dorr secretly joined forces with the rebellious Pro-Tech movement led by the human Bron. In exchange for supplying information to the Pro-Tech leaders, he received profits from the clandestine sale of illegal technology. While meeting with the smuggler Ephant Mon, Dorr was spotted by Ydde, an Ortolan informant. Although Ydde was murdered, his journals revealed Dorr's involvement with the Pro-Tech movement, and the Elder was arrested.

**Dorsk 81** The 81st generation Khomm humanoid clone of the same set of genetic attributes, this olive-green-skinned native of the planet Khomm was somehow different from all those who had gone before, for he was touched by the Force.

But Dorsk 81 was considered imperfect in a society that had valued sameness for 1,000 years. He felt he was a failure to his species until he heard about Luke Skywalker's plans to develop a Jedi praxeum—or an academy for the learning of action. He knew that he had a powerful affinity for the Force and left his planet for Yavin 4.

Dorsk 81 became one of the first 12 Jedi trainees, although he had some problems eating the natural, rather than highly processed, food set before him; he also panicked once during an exercise floating in an underground lake. Dorsk 81 joined with the other Jedi initiates after the evil spirit of the long-dead Sith Lord Exar Kun drove Skywalker's spirit from his body and seduced Jedi trainee Kyp Durron with the dark side of the Force. Together they found a way to destroy Kun for all time and restore Luke's spirit to his body. Dorsk 81 died a hero after again joining with his fellow Jedi and channeling their combined powers through himself to create a Force storm that pushed an entire fleet of attacking Imperial Star Destroyers nearly out of the Yavin system.

*Dorsk 81*

**Dorsk 82** The genetic descendant of Jedi hero Dorsk 81, Dorsk 82 was likewise Force-sensitive and became a student at Luke Skywalker's Jedi praxeum on Yavin 4. Kyp Durron befriended Dorsk 82 and presented him with Dorsk 81's lightsaber. Dorsk 82 was influential in defeating the Leviathan of Corbos. During the Yuuzhan Vong invasion, he was dispatched to Ando to scout the aliens' movements. Dorsk 82 was killed by an Aqualish mob while attempting to protect a group of droids from Yuuzhan Vong. He was survived by Dorsk 83.

**Dorthus Tal Island** On the planet Sacorria, this was the site of the prison where Thrackan Sal-Solo was incarcerated for eight years for his part in the Starbuster plot.

*Dorsk 82*

**Doruggan, Conn** An Alderaanian native, star wegsphere player, and Imperial officer who blamed Princess Leia Organa and the Rebel Alliance for the destruction of his homeworld. He served under Wilek Nereus on Bakura, and considered Leia a threat during the short-lived truce between Rebel and Imperial forces on that world.

**Dorum** A city on Balamak, the site of an experimental communications-jamming system developed by the Separatists during the Clone Wars.

**Dorun** An alien species with twin pairs of tentacles rather than arms, as well as extendable eyestalks.

**Dorvald, Seha** Orphaned by the Yuuzhan Vong invasion, young Seha grew up in the undercity of Coruscant, where she was discovered to be Force-sensitive by Jacen Solo. At his recommendation, she was accepted as a Jedi student at the city-planet's Jedi Temple. During the war between the Galactic Alliance and the Confederation, she carried out favors for Jacen and Ben Skywalker, out of a sense of indebtedness to Solo and an attraction to Ben. When Jacen's dark plans for the galaxy became apparent to the Jedi Order, Seha approached Luke Skywalker on Endor seeking absolution.

Kyle Katarn took young Seha on a mission to Coruscant to attack Jacen, benefiting from her knowledge of the undercity's tunnel network.

*Jimm (the Starkiller Kid) Doshun*

**Dorvalla** An outlying planet of the Videnda sector, notable for its principal commodity: lommite ore. The ore was mined in Dorvalla's tropical equatorial regions. There huge seas once held sway, but shifts in the planetary mantle thrust huge, sheer-faced tors from the land. The unrefined ore was shipped to manufacturing worlds along the Rimma Trade Route and occasionally to the distant Core.

One-quarter of the planet's sparse population was involved in the lommite industry, employed by Lommite Limited or its contentious rival, Intergalactic Ore. Most of the workers were indentured servants of varying species, many hailing from the nearby star systems of Clak'dor, Sullust, and Malastare. They were usually covered in the white residue that was a by-product of the mining process.

Darth Maul journeyed to Dorvalla to investigate a plot that would solidify the Trade Federation's power in the planet's mining operations. As a result, Lommite Limited and Intergalactic Ore were crippled, forcing them to merge into a single company, Dorvalla Mining Corporation. The Trade Federation was granted exclusive rights to Dorvalla's lommite ore, and was also chosen to represent the company in the Galactic Senate.

Protecting Dorvalla during this time was the Dorvalla Space Corps, which used single-pilot fixed-wing picket ships with dual laser cannons.

**Dosh** The native language of Trandoshans.

**Dosha** A Trandoshan colony world.

**Doshao, Subaltern** A Yuuzhan Vong chosen for escalation by Nas Choka for his brave work on Dantooine.

**Doshun, Jimm (the Starkiller Kid)** An Aduban farm boy who longed for offworld adventure, he and his droid FE-9Q teamed up with Han Solo and a group of spacers to protect the Onacra farming village on Aduba-3 from the Cloud Rider swoop gang. Doshun found true love with Merri Shen, a beautiful young woman in the village. They married, and had a daughter, Hanna. Doshun was briefly targeted by bounty hunter Valance, who mistook him for Luke Skywalker.

**dosLa, Topas** The Ukian Overliege during the Separatist crisis, he supported a plan for the entire Abrion sector to secede from the Republic.

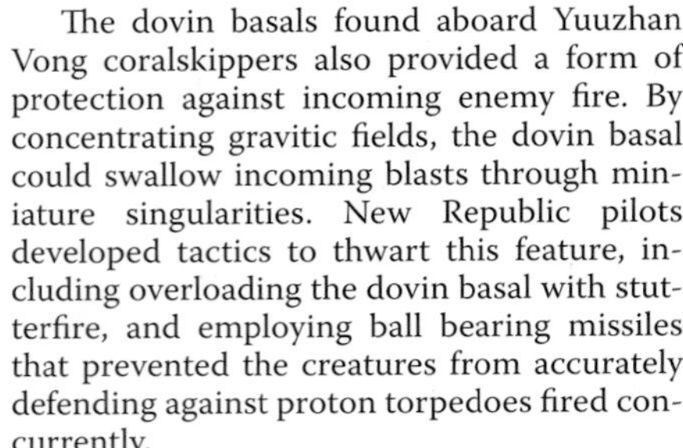

**dosLla, Tol** A representative of the Ukian Overliege, he negotiated the surrender of Ukio to Grand Admiral Thrawn.

**Dosuun** A remote Outer Rim world that was the site of Cult of Ragnos activity during the early years of the New Republic. Former Moff Rax Jorus fled to Dosuun, where he conducted hunts on sentient prey.

**double-c** A call sign used by Mos Eisley police to refer to trouble at Chalmun's Cantina.

**double viol** A stringed instrument formed by a pair of hollow resonating boxes separated by a shaft strung with tonal cords.

**Double Worlders** A term used to describe beings from the Double Worlds of Talus and Tralus.

**Double-X** See SD-XX.

***Doughty*** One of the three Galactic Republic *Acclamator*-class troopships dispatched by the Old Republic to help defend the planet Duro from General Grievous during the Clone Wars.

**Douglas III** A planet made famous by game hunter Mendel Douglas and home to the rare jackelope.

**Doum, Mag** An Imperial spy who operated on the neutral world of Arda-2, he ran a lucrative side business selling X-wing fighter T-6 diodems manufactured on Arda to Imperial suppliers at a 1,000 percent markup. When Rebel operatives investigated, Doum forced his unwilling accomplice Kiros Zorad to kidnap Princess Leia Organa. Kiros and his son, Zon, eventually turned against Doum and freed the Princess. Doum escaped Rebel pursuit in his starship, and called in Lord Vader to eradicate the Rebel presence. Little did he know that Kiros Zorad had stowed away in his ship. Kiros overpowered Doum, and forced the ship to collide with Darth Vader's Star Destroyer. Mag Doum was killed in the blast.

**dovin basal** A Yuuzhan Vong bioengineered spherical organism that was analogous to a form of gravity-well projector. Dovin basals formed the heart of many starship and vehicle propulsion systems for the alien invaders. An adult dovin basal was typically 3 meters in diameter, resembling a huge, pulsating dark red heart with deep blue spikes all about it. It could lock on to specific gravity fields to the exclusion of all others—even fields millions of kilometers away.

The dovin basals found aboard Yuuzhan Vong coralskippers also provided a form of protection against incoming enemy fire. By concentrating gravitic fields, the dovin basal could swallow incoming blasts through miniature singularities. New Republic pilots developed tactics to thwart this feature, including overloading the dovin basal with stutterfire, and employing ball bearing missiles that prevented the creatures from accurately defending against proton torpedoes fired concurrently.

In a tactic called Yo'gand's Core, a dovin basal could pull a moon down onto a planet. Early in the Yuuzhan Vong invasion, one was used to pull down Sernpidal's. After the defeat of the Yuuzhan Vong by the Galactic Alliance, many Yuuzhan Vong took up residence on the living planet Zonama Sekot. There dovin basals reverted to their original pre-engineered forms, stripping the Yuuzhan Vong of much of their arsenal.

**Dovlis, Captain Reldo** An Imperial Navy officer in command of the Dreadnaught *Peacekeeper* during the Battle of Nar Shaddaa, he died when his starship collided with Nar Shaddaa's planetary shield.

**Dovos, Shas** *See* Null, Warb.

**Dovu, Jan** President of the planet Kabal, he was killed by a firebomb in riots that broke out during a food shortage spurred by the Separatist crisis.

**Dow, Helina** A Separatist spy who posed as the head of production and distribution for Fry Industries on her homeworld of Genian during the Clone Wars. She was hired by Passel Argente to infiltrate the company and acquire vital technology such as the ultimate codebreaker devised by Talesan Fry. Though Dow acquired the codebreaker, Jedi prevented her from delivering the goods. The bounty hunter Magus killed her and took the codebreaker.

***Dowager Queen*** This wrecked spacecraft sat in the center of Mos Eisley, a tangled heap of girders and twisted hull plates. The *Dowager Queen* was one of the first colony ships to arrive on Tatooine, only to become home to assorted creatures, vagrants, and scavengers.

The Dowager Queen, *crashed and abandoned in Mos Eisley*

**Dowd, Bilman** A Devaronian guild representative, he accepted delivery from Boba Fett of the captured Labria, otherwise known as the Butcher of Montellian Serat, a war criminal who later was put to death.

**Dowmeia, Tundra** A Quarren Senator from Mon Calamari during the final decades of the Galactic Republic, he took office following the censuring of Senator Tikkes, a corrupt Quarren accused of profiting from slaving ventures in the Outer Rim. Tikkes was placed under house arrest but fled Coruscant to join the Confederacy of Independent Systems. After the quelling of a civil war on Mon Calamari between the Quarren Isolationist League and the Mon Calamari Knights, Dowmeia and Meena Tills became joint representatives of their native planet in the Senate. At the height of the Clone Wars, Dowmeia was one of the Delegation of the Two Thousand, concerned Senators opposed to Chancellor Palpatine's increase in executive powers. With the formation of the Galactic Empire, Dowmeia was one of the first delegates to be arrested by Imperial agents.

**Downfolk** *See* Balawai.

**Downrush Falls** An immense waterfall formed by the largest river on Haruun Kal.

**Downstorm** Also known as the *thakiz bas'kal,* this heavy winter wind spread the toxic cloudsea into the lowlands of Haruun Kal.

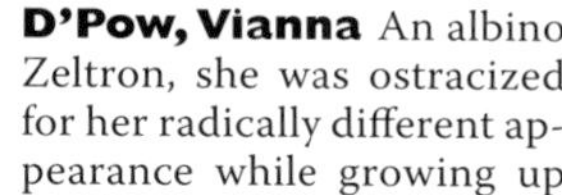
Tundra Dowmeia

**Dox, Commander** A clone trooper who served with Jedi Master Ronhar Kim at Merson during the Clone Wars. He was killed in action.

**Dox, Garil** An Imperial gunner who served aboard the Star Destroyer *Reprisa* for five years, he was a native of Alderaan. Disgruntled with Imperial service after the annihilation of his homeworld, Dox modified his weapons systems to ensure the destruction of any Rebel outposts, leaving no survivors to lead the Imperials to the hidden Rebel fleet. Darth Vader at first attributed such overkill to incompetence, but soon realized that there was purpose behind these blunders. Dox was devasted to realize that the last outpost he destroyed on Ejolus was actually a camp of Alderaanian survivors. Having wiped out what he assumed to be the last of his people, and then being discovered in his treasonous acts, Dox begged Vader to kill him. The Dark Lord instead chose to let Dox live with the consequences of his action, imprisoned in an Imperial labor camp.

**Doxin, Paldis** A leading hypermatter physicist, he studied at the Magrody Institute and was hand-chosen by Grand Moff Tarkin to become one of the head scientists at the top-secret Maw Installation. There the corpulent scientist lead the team that developed the Metal-Crystal Phase Shifter. When the New Republic discovered the installation, Doxin died along with other scientists when the Death Star prototype was dragged into one of the many surrounding black holes and crushed.

Garil Dox

**Dozen-and-Two Avengers** An independent starfighter squadron led by Jedi Kyp Durron to hunt smugglers in the Outer Rim during the time of the New Republic. His apprentice, Miko Reglia, was a member. Kyp and Miko flew modern XJ X-wings, but the rest of the Dozen-and-Two had craft of all types, mostly older models: A-wings and B-wings, a pair of Z-95 Headhunters, and a trio of older X-wings. The fighter group would broadcast a rousing recording of "Shwock Dubllon" (or "Crested Wake") as a combat anthem when they flew into action. They were nearly wiped out by Yuuzhan Vong coralskippers early in the alien invasion when they tangled near Helska 4. Miko was taken prisoner, and Kyp barely escaped with grutchins in pursuit. Kyp replaced his lost pilots with combat veterans and renamed the unit Kyp's Dozen.

**D'Pow, Vianna** An albino Zeltron, she was ostracized for her radically different appearance while growing up on Zeltros. This led her to become cold and aloof, as opposed to the usually gregarious personality shared by most Zeltrons. D'Pow became a bounty hunter who often targeted other bounty hunters. She infiltrated the Jedi Temple to steal back a Sullustan infant wanted by its parents. Later, during the Clone Wars, she attempted to steal genetic material from Tipoca City to thwart the Republic's clone army program. While on Kamino, she also ordered a clone duplicate of herself created so that she would not be alone. Though Obi-Wan Kenobi defeated her attempt to sabotage the Republic military, he let Vianna's clone development continue, as he hoped it would help ease the obvious loneliness she felt.

***Dpso*** A Duros-commanded warship in the Galactic Alliance's beleagured fleet in the late stages of the Yuuzhan Vong War, it was commanded by the fierce Duros nationalist Yurf Col. Determined to free his homeworld from Yuuzhan Vong invaders, Col defied orders and tried to go it alone against the enemy. The *Dpso* and other Duros ships were destroyed.

***DR919a*** The *Ronto*-class transport vessel owned and operated by the Sullustan Jae Juun and his Ewok partner, Tarfang, after the destruction of their previous vessel, *XR808g*. This ship did not fare well during the Swarm War: Crippled by enemy fire, it crashed into the surface of the Gorog nest ship.

**Dra III** A world known for its dangerous native life-forms and sport hunting. Its inhabitants tended to be heavy and strong due to the planet's high gravity. The hunting beasts of Dra III included the vicious six-legged nashtahs (also called Dravian hounds) that inhabited the planet's mountains. Nashtahs, the only animals from the planet that were domesticated, were also the planet's most thoroughly studied creatures. The powerful (though outdated) Kell Mark II blaster was the planet's one export.

**Draag** Members of this cold-blooded reptilian species from the Ninzam system were fierce, smart, and especially good with blasters. Due to their domineering nature, Draags made excellent security foremen, and were often found in large factories. In environments too cold for their metabolisms, they wore insulated suits to regulate their body temperature.

**Dr'aan** A clone of Sullustan Dr'uun Unnh produced by experimental Imperial techniques and discovered by Tash Arranda at an abandoned Rebel base.

Krynda Draay

**Draay, Barrison** A Force-sensitive member of the wealthy Draay family, he was trained as a Jedi Knight prior to the Great Sith War. He was also in charge of the family's finances—something that concerned the galaxy's financial community. To alleviate concerns of a Jedi in charge of such wealth, Barrison created the Draay Trust to keep the wealth separate from the family's Jedi members. He was killed in the Great Sith War, and survived by his wife, Krynda, and son, Lucien.

**Draay, Krynda** A powerful Jedi and member of the wealthy Draay family, she trained under Jedi Master Vodo-Siosk Baas many years before the outbreak of the Great Sith War. She married Barrison Draay, and together the two had a son, Lucien. She was particularly adept at "farseeing" into the future. During the Great

Sith War, Krynda became a widow. Withdrawing from the Jedi Order after the war, Krynda began teaching young seers, like the Miraluka Q'Anilia, much to the chagrin of Lucien, who exhibited little talent for seeing visions of the future. Krynda's classes of elite seers produced the Jedi that would found the Covenant, an independent group of Jedi Masters who, having glimpsed a future of darkness, were committed to preventing it from coming about. Krynda continued to fund the actions of the Covenant during the time of the Mandalorian Wars.

**Draay, Lucien** The son of Jedi Knights Barrison and Krynda Draay, and a member of the wealthy Draay family. His father died in the Great Sith War, and his mother withdrew from the Jedi Order to found a school for gifted seers. Unfortunately, Lucien did not exhibit a talent for this ability at a young age, though he became a Jedi Knight in time. The students taught by Krynda became members of the Covenant, an independent group of Jedi Masters who searched the future for impending signs of danger and darkness. These Jedi became the instructors at the satellite academy on Taris, teaching a class of young Padawans. When a vision of the future showed that one of their students would rise to bring unparalleled destruction to the galaxy and the Jedi, they preemptively slaughtered their graduating class, but Lucien's Padawan, Zayne Carrick, escaped. He was publicly blamed for the murder of his classmates, and spent much time as a fugitive of the Jedi and the Republic.

Lucien Draay

**Drackmar system** A system with multiple suns, it was home to the Drackmarians, methane breathers with blue scales, sharp talons, and snouts filled with sharp teeth. The species didn't sleep and was noted for generosity and stubborn independence. Fierce opponents of the Empire, they loosely aligned with the New Republic. Omogg, a wealthy warlord from the Drackmar system, lost the planet Dathomir to Han Solo in a sabacc game.

**Dracmus** A Selonian female, she was captured by Thrackan Sal-Solo in Coronet, the Corellian capital. Sal-Solo forced her to fight his cousin Han Solo, then made them cellmates in the hope that she would rip Han apart. Instead Dracmus gave information to Han that eventually led to uncovering Thrackan as the hidden leader of the rabidly anti-alien Human League. A Selonian rescue team broke Dracmus out of prison and took Han with them.

**Draco, Antares** The leader of the Imperial Knights serving Emperor Roan Fel, he maintained loyalty to his Emperor even after Fel was deposed by the Sith Lord Darth Krayt. Draco secretly loved the Emperor's daughter, Marasiah Fel, and longed to protect her, though he had to stay by the Emperor's side. Despite orders to the contrary, Draco sought out and rescued Princess Marasiah from the clutches of pursuing Sith Lords on Vendaxa. Draco's impulsive rescue mission gave the Sith Lords information about the royal family's location on Bastion, and the Emperor reprimanded Draco for his lack of foresight.

dragonsnake

**Draco, Valin** An Imperial Inquisitor active during the early days of the New Order.

**Dracos** One of Luke Skywalker's students in military training after the Battle of Endor, he looked forward to receiving Jedi training, but Skywalker refused to teach anyone in the ways of the Force at that early point. Dracos was a reptilian humanoid with a pointed muzzle, green-and-yellow scaled skin, and yellow-and-brown eyes.

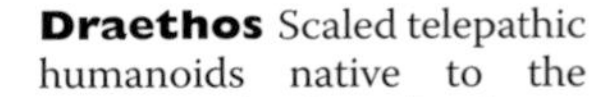

**Draethos** Scaled telepathic humanoids native to the planet of the same name. This long-lived species included among its members the famed Jedi Master Odan-Urr.

**D'rag** A starship builder from the planet Oslumpex V.

**Draggle, Skeck** The first mate of the *Drunk Dancer* during the early months of the Galactic Empire. He was a humanoid with six-fingered hands and a cheerful disposition.

**Dragqulch period** The fourth Great Schism among the adherents of the Jedi Code and followers of the dark side of the Force, it occurred in the millennium prior to the Battle of Ruusan. The Sith regained their strength 2,000 years before the Battle of Yavin, and engaged in devastating strikes against the Republic, causing the government to shrink in size. During this period of New Sith Wars, Jedi actively served in the Republic government, including as Supreme Chancellor. This period came to an end with the eradication of the Sith at the Battle of Ruusan, and the sweeping reformation that followed limited the role of the Jedi in government.

Antares Draco

**dragite** A crystal mined on M'haeli with properties similar to the Adegan crystals used in lightsabers.

**dragon-bird** This avian species was found long ago on Onderon.

**Dragon Cave** A large, steam-filled cavern at the foot of an active volcano in the Far Distant lands of Zonama Sekot.

**dragonmount** *See* varactyls.

***Dragon Pearl*** Jiliac the Hutt's personal starship, it was a heavily armed space yacht that could accommodate six Z-95 Headhunters in its hold.

**dragon pearls** Beautiful and incredibly valuable pearls of many colors, they were found only in the gizzards of krayt dragons.

**Dragonriders** The varactyl-mounted defense force on Utapau.

**dragon-slugs** Huge worm-like creatures that could be found wherever lumni-spice was harvested. The fungi that produced lumni-spice were the dragon-slug's favorite meal. The fact that the dragon-slug was such a dangerous beast increased the value of lumni-spice—indeed, it was the most valuable spice of all. Dragon-slugs could grow to 20 meters in length, and had armored skin capable of withstanding blasterfire. They breathed fire and could project flames at least 15 meters in front of them. A dragon-slug lived in a cavern on the Hoth equator.

**dragonsnake** This large predator inhabited Dagobah's water channels. A dragonsnake sought out victims, rearing up and slashing them with its fangs or razor-sharp fins.

**Dragon's Pelt** West of the thickest Endor forests, where the Ewoks lived, was this huge expanse of savanna grassland. It was home to the semi-intelligent Yuzzums. The Sanyassan Marauders of Endor also lived in a castle in the Pelt.

Drall

**Dragon's Spine** A snow-capped mountain range west of the Endor forest where the Ewoks lived. It was at the end of the grassy expanse called the Dragon's Pelt.

**Dragon's Teeth** A natural landmark of jagged rocks near the Reef Fortress on Hapes.

**dragship** A New Republic pilot term for an Imperial interdictor cruiser.

**draigon** Predators with yellow eyes, silver scales, and long teeth, they flew under the power of clawed wings and typically hunted fish on their watery homeworld, near Bandomeer. However, they also attacked human-sized prey whenever possible.

***Draisini*** A *Xiytiar*-class transport used by the Mining Guild during the early years of the New Republic. It was commanded by Captain Forma, and attacked and captured by pirates working for Grappa the Hutt.

**Drakas, Jor** A Twi'lek Jedi Knight who commanded the Republic base at Mount Corvast on Sarapin, he was slain in battle by Sev'Rance Tann during the Clone Wars.

**Drake, Major Breslin** A New Republic Intelligence officer, he later served aboard the corvette *FarStar* during the DarkStryder incident.

**Drake, Senator Ivor** The representative of Kestos Minor in the Galactic Senate, she was one of the Delegation of the Two Thousand who protested the excesses in Chancellor Palpatine's executive powers. With the rise of the Empire, Drake was one of the Senators immediately arrested by Imperial agents for supporting the so-called Jedi Rebellion.

**drakka boar** Immense six-legged spiked beasts native to Randon and used by Randoni traders to guard their treasure troves.

***Draklor*** An Imperial Star Galleon that was part of the *Death's Head* battle group during Grand Admiral Thrawn's campaign to retake the galaxy. Thrawn assigned this ship as a troop transport to take Joruus C'baoth to Wayland.

**Drako** A Codru-Ji swoop racer who became leader of the Hawk-bat Gang in the Coruscant undercity. He challenged Padawan Anakin Skywalker to a race that ended in Drako fatally colliding with a transport.

**Drall** One of five inhabited worlds in the Corellian system, it was a pleasant, temperate planet with light gravity. Summer temperatures could reach levels high enough to cause portions of the landlocked Boiling Sea to actually boil, until it was cooled by winter precipitation. The planet was the homeworld of the short, furred creatures also known as Drall, who generations ago hibernated during the Drall winter season. Members of this bipedal species were cautious, honest, and meticulous, making them good record keepers. Other planetary life included the nannarium flower and many species of Drallish avians. A vast, subterranean planetary repulsor was located near Drall's equator—presumably used in ancient times to move the planet into its current orbit from an unknown location.

During his tenure with the Corellian Security Force, Rogue Squadron pilot Corran Horn planted a false report implying that he had murdered six smugglers on Drall. The report was created so that Horn and his supervisor could stage a public falling-out and defuse suspicions of their working together to flee the Empire, but an Imperial death warrant was issued on Horn for the imaginary crime.

During a crisis 14 years after the Battle of Endor, Chewbacca took the Solo children and their tutor, Ebrihim, to Drall to stay with Ebrihim's aunt, the Duchess Marcha of Mastigophorous. The group discovered Drall's planetary repulsor, and Anakin Solo instinctively made it operational. A shot from the repulsor, fired by Anakin, disabled Centerpoint Station and saved the star Bovo Yagen from destruction at the last possible instant.

**Drallig, Cin** Nicknamed the Troll, he was the leading lightsaber combat instructor in the Jedi Temple during the time of the Clone Wars. A native of Lavisar, he learned his fighting techniques from Master Yoda. Drallig was killed by Darth Vader when the Sith Lord stormed the Jedi Temple with the 501st Legion of clone troopers. Drallig tried to fend off Vader with the help of two of his students, Whie and Bene, but Vader cut them down.

Cin Drallig

**Dramassian silk** A luxuriously sheer fabric produced in the Galactic Republic era.

**Drang** One of two domesticated vornskrs—poisonous dog-like creatures that attacked Force-users and displayed an unnatural hatred for Jedi—that smuggler Talon Karrde long used as pets and guards.

**Drann, Par** The Yevethan commander of the thrustship *Tholos* assigned to guard the Black Nine shipyards, he failed to defend the installation from New Republic warships and died in combat.

**DRAPAC** *See* Defense Research and Planetary Assistance Center.

**Drark, Jovan** A Rodian Jedi Knight during the Yuuzhan Vong invasion, he accompanied Tenel Ka in a mission to Bilbringi seeking out disguised Yuuzhan Vong infiltrators. Later he was part of Anakin Solo's strike team assigned to hunt down the voxyn queen. He was one of the many young Jedi to die in that mission.

**Drask, General** The Chiss military commander of Aristocra Formbi's group dispatched to recover the remains of *Outbound Flight*. His full name was Prard'ras'kleoni. As the expedition battled with vengeful Vagaari raiders, he teamed up with Chak Fel and Unit Aurek-Seven of the 501st.

**Drathul, High Prefect** The Yuuzhan Vong administrator of the worldship *Harla* during the invasion of the galaxy, he begrudgingly kept Nom Anor among his underlings and was one of Supreme Overlord Shimrra's closest advisers. As a heretical movement spread in the undercities of conquered Coruscant, Drathul came under close scrutiny because many of his subordinates were implicated. Evidence to that end was actually planted by Nom Anor, who hoped for Drathul's ouster. In the final battle between Galactic Alliance forces and the Yuuzhan Vong, Nom Anor and a band of Shamed Ones infiltrated the Overlord's citadel, and Anor strangled Drathul to death.

**Draukyze system** The site of one of Grand Admiral Thrawn's first hit-and-fade strikes in his campaign to retake the galaxy from the New Republic.

**Dravian hound** *See* nashtah.

**Dravis** A pilot in Talon Karrde's smuggling operation.

**Dravvad, Chelch** A Corellian, he was part of Chief of State Borsk Fey'lya's Advisory Council, and continued advising the New Republic government throughout the Yuuzhan Vong invasion.

**Drax squadron** A stormtrooper unit dispatched to Mos Eisley to locate R2-D2 and C-3PO prior to the Battle of Yavin.

***Dray*-class transport** A bulky transport vessel found active in the years following the Yuuzhan Vong War.

**Draygo, Vykk** An alias employed by young Han Solo while working for Teroenza on Ylesia.

**Drayk** The abbot of the Dim-U monastery in Mos Eisley during the time of the Galactic Civil War.

**Drayneen** One of the few females to serve as an Imperial Inquisitor.

**Drayson, Admiral Hiram** A high-ranking officer in the New Republic, he was in charge of the Chandrila system defense forces, serving as admiral of the Chandrila Defense Fleet for many years. In that capacity, Admiral Hiram Drayson knew the Senator from Chandrila, Mon Mothma, well. He was removed from his position during the Clone Wars by an executive decree that replaced him with Kohl Seerdon. Drayson so impressed Mothma with his work in dramatically decreasing pirate and smuggling activity near the planet that years later, she asked him to serve as commander of her Alliance headquarters ship. With the formation of the New Republic, he was put in charge of the fleet attached to the Provisional Council and its capital, the planet Coruscant. Later he headed Alpha Blue, a mysterious covert intelligence group within the New Republic's military and security hierarchy. He distrusted Ambassador Nil Spaar and gave the Alliance's General A'baht a secret code that allowed him to deal directly with Drayson, bypassing fleet headquarters. Admiral Drayson was the one who convinced Chief of State Leia Organa Solo that she had been lied to by Spaar by giving her the Plat Mallar recording that recounted the Yevethan attack on the Koornacht Cluster settlements. When the Imperial Remnant and the New Republic signed a historic peace treaty, bringing a final end to the Galactic Civil War, Drayson retired and married Joi Eicroth, though their marriage would not last. He had a daughter, Bhindi, who became a noted member of New Republic Intelligence.

**Drayson, Bhindi** The daughter of Hiram Drayson, she served the New Republic during the Yuuzhan Vong War as a tactical expert within Wraith Squadron. After the Yuuzhan Vong invasion of Coruscant, she had planned to establish a team of intelligence agents to remain on the planet to set up resistance cells, but was ordered to abandon such plans when the extent of the damage to the capital became apparent.

**Drazin, Corporal** A stormtrooper and native of Bespin, he accompanied Lord Darth Vader to the floating metropolis of Cloud City after the Battle of Hoth and blasted C-3PO to pieces. Later he was assigned to Commander Igar's honor guard on Endor during the construction of the second Death Star.

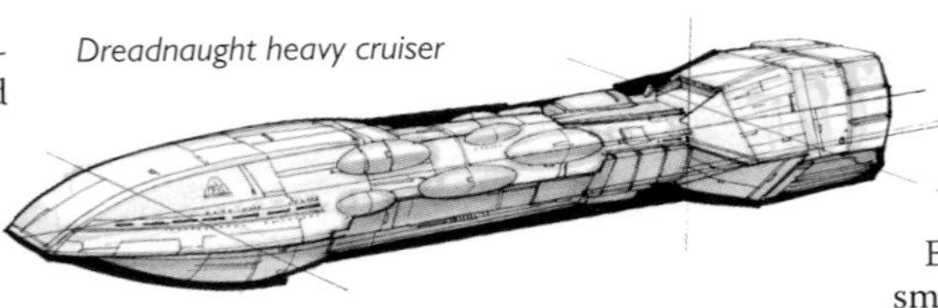

*Dreadnaught heavy cruiser*

**Dreadnaught heavy cruiser** Developed before the outbreak of the Clone Wars, Dreadnaught heavy cruisers were among the oldest vessels in active service in the Imperial Navy. Though outdated, the Dreadnaughts continued to see use due to simple economics: They were readily available and effective cruisers, if not the most efficient and advanced models.

The Dreadnaught was plagued by a number of design flaws that prevented it from becoming a preeminent ship of the line. Inefficient power generators resulted in slow sublight and hyperdrive performance, weak shielding, reduced firepower, and frequent surges within the computer systems.

Perhaps the Dreadnaught's biggest drawback was how crew-intensive it was. Standard operating procedure recommended an optimum crew that numbered over 16,000. The consumable supplies required to maintain that crew took up enormous cargo space. A modification of the ship's hyperdrive that increased its performance to Class 2 allowed for more frequent victualing stops, and some of that cargo space was converted for hangar use. In the Empire, a standard Dreadnaught carried a squadron of TIE fighters. The Imperials employed Dreadnaughts to maintain a presence in the Outer Rim Territories, as convoy escort vessels, and to ensure dominance over primitive worlds.

Years before the Clone Wars, the best-known Dreadnaughts became an embarrassment to the military echelons that commissioned them. To counter their high staffing requirements, a fleet of Dreadnaughts was extensively modified with full-rig slave circuitry, reducing the crew requirements to only about 2,200 per starship. This much-heralded advancement in slave rig technology was positioned as a new era for military warships.

To further distinguish the *Katana* fleet of 200 Dreadnaughts, the starships were completely redecorated inside and out in a dark hue, earning the unofficial moniker of the Dark Force. Prior to the fleet's inaugural launch, its crew became infected with a hive virus that drove them mad. In their insanity, they slaved the ships together as the whole fleet disappeared into hyperspace, jumping to parts unknown.

For nearly 50 years, the *Katana* fleet was lost. Five years after the Battle of Endor, Grand Admiral Thrawn blackmailed smuggler Niles Ferrier into providing the location of the long-missing *Katana* fleet and escaped with 180 of the 200 ships under the nose of the New Republic.

The Dreadnaught was 600 meters long. It carried 10 laser cannons, 5 facing starboard and 5 facing port. Twenty quad laser cannons were distributed along the ship's forward and side arcs, with 6 facing front and 7 on each side. The ship's front and rear were guarded by 5 turbolaser batteries per facing.

***Dreadnought* fighter tank** A modified battle tank used by Cydon Prax during the Clone Wars, it had special repulsorlifts and thrusters for extra maneuverability. Anakin Skywalker defeated Prax and his *Dreadnought* on Thule.

**dread weapon** A colossal serpentine bioengineered organic weapon that was extended from a Yuuzhan Vong warship. More living monstrosity than machine, the herpetoid construct had a blunt nose and stippled skin. It used its mouth as a vacuum to inhale captives. Roa and Fasgo were consumed by the weapon when it attacked the *Jubilee Wheel* at the Battle of Ord Mantell.

**Dream Emporium** An entertainment complex catering to the wealthy on Etti IV.

**Dreamer and Dreamt, the** A paired Kaleesh cultural concept. General Grievous (Qymaen jai Sheelal) and Ronderu lij Kummar were considered to be the living manifestations of the Dreamer and the Dreamt, respectively.

**Drearian Defense Conglomerate** A weapons manufacturer based in the Inner Rim and Expansion Region, Drearian was the maker of the Defender sporting blaster.

**Drebble, Barpotomous** A wealthy businessman and criminal whom Lando Calrissian double-crossed years before the Galactic War. So intent on vengeance was he, Drebble issued a bounty of 10,000 credits on Calrissian's head. Drebble hired the bounty-hunting syndicate led by Bossk and IG-88 on the planet Stenos. After the Battle of Endor, the Rebel Alliance wished to reward Captain Drebble for his heroic acts in service to the Rebellion. In truth, this "Captain Drebble" was an alias that Lando

*Barpotomous Drebble*

Dreebo

Calrissian used to perform numerous Alliance missions. Drebble and Calrissian settled their differences when Calrissian gave the Alliance's formal appreciation with the gift of the *Dancing Goddess.* Drebble had a total change of heart, becoming a very likable fellow.

Drebble owned and operated a cantina on the planet Keyorin, and later controlled an entire section of the capital of Stenos. He was an overweight human male who screamed orders when impatient. He had fair skin and a curly brown topknot of hair on his otherwise bald head. He wore a flowing purple caftan and gaudy necklaces.

**Dreddon the Hutt** A crime lord who sold arms throughout the Outer Rim in the latter decades of the Galactic Republic. Watto once purchased a military surplus lot from Dreddon, which included the Tyrian hydraulic struts that Anakin Skywalker used in his Podracer. Five years before the Battle of Geonosis, Black Sun Vigo Antonin hired Zam Wesell to kill Dreddon the Hutt. Dreddon had simultaneously hired Jango Fett to kill Antonin.

**Dree, Duno** He was 17 years old at the time of his service to the Rebel Alliance, though he lied about his age and claimed to be 20 in the early years of the Galactic Civil War. Despite his inexperience, he was exuberant and served as a pilot for Jedi Qu Rahn. He died when they were captured by the Dark Jedi Jerec, and slaughtered by the massive warrior named Maw.

**Dreebo** The pilot of a ship that was part of the pay-for-protection racket of Great Bogga the Hutt, he was assigned to guarantee safe passage from pirate attacks for ore haulers in the Stenness system. His ship was destroyed by the ore-sucking pirate ship *Starjacker.*

Garven "Dave" Dreis (center)

**dreeka fish** A chirping fish native to Ithor.

**Dreel** A male Chiss who served Voss Parck and Stent at the Hand of Thrawn facility on Nirauan.

**Dreena** An uninhabited world in the Hapes Cluster. Prince Isolder explored it with his father when he was just a boy.

**Dreflin, Major** An Imperial Security Bureau agent assigned to monitor the loyalty of those serving aboard the Star Destroyer *Reprisal.* After the assault on Teardrop, Dreflin accused a number of stormtroopers of deliberately missing their shots in order to spare the populace. He threatened to execute the troopers on the spot for treason, but Trooper Daric LaRone fired in self-defense, killing Dreflin. Realizing that they could not face the repercussions of this act, LaRone and his fellow stormtroopers escaped the *Reprisal* aboard Dreflin's modified Suwantek freighter, *Gillia,* and went rogue, operating as the Hand of Judgment.

**Drei, Tho-Mes** A Jedi Master whose lectures and teachings included: "Deliver more than you promise. The best way to be always certain of this is to deliver much, even when you promise nothing."

**Dreighton Nebula** A brilliant cloud of dust and interstellar gases long avoided by space travelers, the Dreighton Nebula had a reputation for being "haunted"—many ships that ventured near it disappeared without a trace. During the final decades of the Galactic Republic, the Dreighton Nebula was a source of rare stygium crystals before its troves were supposedly depleted. During the time of the Empire, Rebel agent Ru Murleen discovered that the Empire had secreted a weapons research station in the heart of the nebula, developing phantom TIE fighters and advanced cloaking technology.

**Dreis, Garven "Dave"** A male human X-wing pilot, he led Red Squadron at the Battle of Yavin, and before that had served at the Dantooine Rebel base. During the Clone Wars, he flew alongside Anakin Skywalker at a battle over Virujansi. Garven "Dave" Dreis fired an unsuccessful shot at the Death Star's thermal exhaust port and died during the Battle of Yavin.

**Drell** A species known for its chisel-shaped starships, which were often used by pirates.

**Drelosyn, Corporal** A native of Coruscant, he grew up racing swoops in the undercity before becoming an Imperial biker scout who later was stationed at Endor.

**Dremon, Jull** A Neimoidian gunner who opened fire and destroyed the *Radiant VII* prior to the invasion of Naboo.

Taym Dren-garen

**Dremulae** A wondrous tourist destination, its Sea of Translucency was a popular vacation spot.

**Dren-garen, Taym** A henchman of Jabba the Hutt's, this Tatooine native supplied the Tusken Raiders with weapons and instigated attacks on human settlers in order to draw local authorities away from Jabba's operation. Taym perished aboard Jabba's exploding sail barge prior to the Battle of Endor.

**Drenna** Part of the Senali royal family, she was the youngest daughter of Garth and Ganeed. She had close-cropped hair that almost matched the silvery cast to her dark blue skin. She was the same age as Prince Leed of Rutan, and the two were such good friends that they considered each other adopted siblings. An expert markswoman, Drenna had a crossbow that fired laser arrows. When Leed was kidnapped by accomplices of Prince Taroon of Rutan, Drenna helped Qui-Gon Jinn and his Padawan, Obi-Wan Kenobi, rescue him. Taroon secretly harbored love for Drenna, and when he learned that she was endangered by his conspiracy, he called off his seeker droids and joined the Jedi in trying to save her. Drenna and Taroon then fell in love.

**Dreshdae** A small outpost considered the capital of Korriban, it was controlled by the Czerka Corporation during the Jedi Civil War. Within Dreshdae was the Sith monastery—still teeming with those who wished to join the Sith Order. It was located far from the Valley of the Dark Lords. Thousands of years later, Dreshdae's monastery stood vacant, but the spaceport still functioned for its few inhabitants.

*Dressellian*

**Dressellian** Members of this wrinkly, almost prune-faced humanoid species from the planet Dressel joined the Rebel Alliance shortly before the Battle of Endor. They had long fought the Empire on their homeworld and were brought into the larger fight by Bothan allies.

**Drevan, Freon** A Xexto con man, he teamed with Niai Fieso selling bootleg Podracing collectibles and smuggling illicit wares. Fieso stole away with their money, leaving Drevan creditless. Later, during the Boonta Eve Podrace that saw Anakin Skywalker win his freedom, Drevan was in the stands when he noticed Fieso working as a food vendor, and attacked his former partner. Both Xextos were sent to jail for this disturbance.

**Drev'starn** The capital city of Bothawui.

**drewood mite** A parasitic insect known to infest the fur of womp rats.

**Drewwa** The third of three moons orbiting Almania, colonized decades before the Battle of Yavin. It was an industrialized world, home to many manufacturing companies.

**Drexel** This star system included an unnamed water world orbited by three moons. In the final years of the Galactic Republic, a group of space wreckers led by Quarg were chased here by Jedi Knights. Stranded on the ocean-covered planet, the wreckers continued their operation by turning their downed starship into a massive seafaring base that housed their powerful sonic-jamming devices. Eager for metal to firm up their structures and increase their technological capacity, Quarg continued the space-wrecking operation, tugging ships out from orbit on the rare occasions that they approached the water world. His technicians noted that use of the sonic devices drove the native sea dragons into a frenzy, and attempted to warn Quarg about his actions, but Quarg would hear none of it. The technicians were exiled, and allied with the semi-sentient sea dragons to become the Dragon Lords. The Dragon Lords waged a generation-long war with the wreckers, continuing even as Governor Quarg was replaced by his son, a man of the same name.

Luke Skywalker scouted the Drexel system as a possible base for the Rebel Alliance shortly after the Battle of Yavin. His scout ship was caught in a sonic-jamming pulse that caused him to crash into the seas of the water planet, where he was taken captive by Quarg's space wreckers. Meanwhile, Han Solo and Princess Leia voyaged to the planet, seeking out Skywalker. The *Millennium Falcon* also succumbed to the sonic-jamming waves, though once it crashed into the waters, Solo made contact with the Dragon Lords. The Rebels brought an end to the civil war by aiding the Dragon Lords. The *Falcon*'s cannons destroyed the wreckers' transmission mast, silencing the ultrasonic transmissions that were so harmful to the sea dragons.

**drexl warbeast** Large and ferocious flying creatures from the moon of Dxun capable of entering the atmosphere of Onderon when the two planets neared each other during their unusual orbital cycles. The warbeasts were a scourge on Onderon, where the walled city of Iziz was constructed simply to keep the monsters at bay. Eventually, they were tamed by the beast-riders, outcasts from Iziz who used the great creatures in a continual attempt to reclaim the city. With the warbeasts at their command, the beast-riders nearly won the Beast Wars of Onderon, a conflict that eventually ended with the death of Queen Amanoa and the intervention of several Jedi Knights almost 4,000 years before the Galactic Civil War.

**Drexx, Bezz** A Republic Senator who held a massive party in his opulent tower suites during the Clone Wars. Bail Organa, Sheltay Retrac, Captain Typho, Padmé Amidala, and C-3PO were in attendance. Organa suspected that Drexx was in league with the Separatists.

**Dreyba the Hutt** A great Hutt artist who once sculpted Jabba in a frieze.

**Dreyf, Commander** An Imperial Intelligence officer who served Supreme Commander Gilad Pellaeon, he investigated Lord Graemon and Moff Disra for misdealings, discovering misappropriated funds and a host of other transgressions that warranted Disra's arrest.

**drift chart** A computer-based simulation used to chart the movement of various bodies within an asteroid field.

**Drig, Gorb** A Houk who ran a cantina on Phorliss, he hired Mara Jade as a serving girl while she went underground to avoid Ysanne Isard. He was killed by Black Nebula enforcer Plattahr for not keeping up with his payments.

**driit** A monetary unit, it was used on the planet Dellalt.

**Drinking Cup** A natural bowl-shaped pit open to the seas on Trogan, and site of the Whistler's Whirlpool tapcaf.

**driprot** The gradual erosion of duracrete due to contamination by dripping water.

**driss** A flowering plant grown by hydroponic gardeners on Tatooine that produced gourd-shaped seedpods harvested as food.

**drixfar** An unusual musical instrument popular in the Outer Rim Territories during the final decades of the Old Republic. The drixfar was created using engine parts to form its body and inner workings.

**Drixo the Hutt** A minor Hutt crime lord and rival to Progga the Hutt in the years following the Battle of Naboo. Drixo paid smuggler Dubrak Qennto and his crew to smuggle a cache of firearms to Comra, but Qennto's ship was intercepted by Progga and fled into Chiss space to escape.

**DRK-1** *See* Dark Eye probe droid.

**droch** Small sentient insects, they buried themselves in human flesh and caused what has been called the Death Seed plague, which was always fatal. Drochs were tiny domes of purple-brown chitin, and they were everywhere on the planet Nam Chorios. They consisted of an abdomen about a centimeter long that ended in a hard little head and a ring of tiny, wriggling, thorn-tipped legs. They had an incredibly high reproductive rate and preferred the shade because sunlight killed them. Everyone on the planet had droch bites. The insects died and were absorbed approximately 20 minutes after they burrowed into flesh.

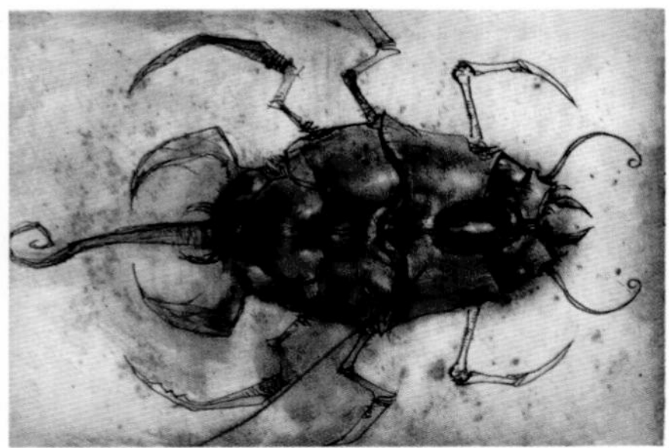

*Droch*

In their infectious state, they were virtual life drinkers, and thus became known as the mysterious Death Seed plague. Some seven centuries before the Galactic Civil War the Grissmaths seeded Nam Chorios with drochs, hoping to kill off all the political prisoners they had stranded on the planet. But the sun fragmenting through the planet's crystals generated a radiation that weakened the larger drochs and killed the smaller ones outright. The large members of the species, called captain drochs, could draw life out of victims through the smaller ones, without attaching themselves to their victims. They became dangerous at this stage, because the more life they drank, the more intelligent they became. Some beings used to eat drochs to absorb life and energy into themselves.

Droid Control Ship

Droid detector mounted on wall (left)

**Droe** A Cerean, she was one of Ki-Adi-Mundi's older sisters.

**Droekle** A would-be suiter who tried—and failed—to win the hand of Queen Mother Tenel Ka after the Yuuzhan Vong War.

**droffi** A large, long-necked spotted sauropod native to Aridus, used as a beast of burden by the native Chubbits.

**Droga, Jeng** One of Emperor Palpatine's most loyal servants—an Emperor's Hand—he was somber and introspective and usually fought with paired lightsabers, one red-bladed and the other yellow. He piloted Palpatine's private shuttle, *Emperor's Shadow.* Following the Battle of Endor, Droga fell into inexplicable insanity, butchering his crew and causing Palpatine's yacht to plunge into the oceans of Kaal. He later served as a vessel for the Emperor's disembodied spirit until Vizier Sate Pestage was able to tear the essence out of Droga's body into a waiting clone host. When the Emperor's final clone perished, Jeng returned to Kaal waiting for his Master's return from the dead once more. He was finally stopped by Kyle Katarn.

Jeng Droga

**droid** Robotic systems, fashioned either in the likeness of their creators or for functionality, droids were the workhorses of the galaxy. They had various degrees of artificial intelligence, but rarely had speech synthesizers, so they had to communicate through a programming language. They were powered by rechargeable cells in their bodies, and most had the capabilities of locomotion, logic, self-aware intelligence, communication, manipulation, and sensory reception. Many cultures treated droids as slaves, and many public areas were off limits to them.

The automata were grouped into five classes, or degrees, according to primary function:

Class 1. Skilled in physical, mathematical, and medical sciences.

Class 2. Programmed in engineering and technical sciences.

Class 3. Skilled in social sciences and service areas such as translation, diplomatic assistance, and tutoring.

Class 4. Skilled in security and military applications.

Class 5. Suitable for menial labor and non-intelligence-intensive jobs such as mining, transportation, and sanitation.

**Droid Abolitionist Movement** A fanatical group led by Xalto Sneerzick that promoted the view that droids were sentient creatures and should be freed from subservience. The movement reached its height when Xalto and his followers grew bold enough to attack shipping transports, but died when some of Xalto's "emancipated" droids felt threatened by him and killed his entire team.

**Droidbait, Trooper** A rookie clone trooper who served at the Republic outpost on the Rishi moon during the Clone Wars.

**droid buster** A projectile weapon used by clone troopers during the Clone Wars to take out battle droids, it fired an explosive warhead that detonated about five meters above the ground, flattening anything within a 50-meter radius. Unlike other anti-droid weapons, it did not use EMP technology.

**Droid Control Ship** A huge battleship modified to broadcast a control signal to the thousands of battle droids and droid starfighters that made up the Trade Federation's massive army. Like all Trade Federation battleships, the Droid Control Ship was equipped with dozens of quad laser emplacements and heavy shielding. The starship could house up to 1,500 droid starfighters, which could be released to overwhelm enemy forces. Such battleships were extremely difficult to damage, but Anakin Skywalker destroyed one over Naboo when he flew into the vessel's hangar and accidentally targeted its main reactor with proton torpedoes.

Droidekas are equipped with a formidable personal deflector shield.

**droid detector** A detection device, it often was used in segregated areas of the galaxy. Owners of drinking establishments frequently used detectors to keep droids out. Officials and gangsters used them as security devices, although many assassin droids could disguise themselves as living species.

**droideka** A heavily armed droid capable of transforming into a large, metal wheel in order to pursue its quarry. Wielding powerful twin laser cannons, droidekas, or destroyer droids, were essentially mobile, three-legged weapons platforms protected by personal deflector shields. They employed a wide variety of sensors and scanners to track prey, and in combat they attacked mercilessly. Manufactured by the chitinous Colicoids, droidekas could be found aboard Trade Federation starships or fighting alongside battle droids as part of the droid army.

Although the Trade Federation army relied heavily on battle droids, high-ranking officials also realized the importance of a more serious threat. Thus, the Colicoids of Colla IV were commissioned to build the deadly droidekas.

The Colicoids were a barbaric and murderous species. The Outer Rim's Colla system was notoriously dangerous, as the Colicoids tended to kidnap and eat visitors, a habit that did not endear the species to the Republic. Colicoid engineers fashioned droidekas in their own image. Like the droidekas, Colicoids were capable of rolling into tight, round balls. They used this ability to surprise prey, rising up suddenly to attack.

A droideka was protected by a case-hardened bronzium armor shell, coupled with a formidable personal deflector shield. A mini reactor powered all systems, while a range of sensors allowed the droideka to pinpoint its enemies. Because the droideka served only one function, it did not require manipulatory appendages, and thus its arms ended in deadly twin blasters.

The droidekas manufactured for the Trade Federation were built to receive commands from a Droid Control Ship. However, the Colicoids felt that this feature limited the droid's effectiveness. Thus, they produced a small number of units with programmable computer brains.

**droid electromagnetic pulse gun** *See* DEMP gun.

**Droidfest of Tatooine** An annual swap meet held by Jawas where multiple clans congregated to create a huge used-droid sale.

**droid gunship** *See* HMP droid gunship.

**droid harem** A huge castle-like structure, it was on a plateau overlooking the farmlands of Biitu. The giant automaton known as the Great Heep kept captured R2 units at the droid harem, treating them to soothing oil baths and other luxuries before consuming them.

**droiding** Republic commando slang for the disabling effects of an anti-droid EMP grenade upon their specialized Katarn battle armor. A trooper whose armor's systems were knocked out by such a device was said to be "droided."

**droid popper** A variety of electromagnetic pulse grenade used by clone troopers to disable the droids of the Confederacy during the Clone Wars.

**droid starfighter** *See* vulture droid.

**Droid Statutes** First enacted about 4,000 years before the Battle of Yavin, these regulations specified punishments for droids that broke the law. The Droid Statutes were notable in that they viewed droids as property, not as self-aware citizens capable of making their own decisions. A droid that committed a class five infraction, such as petty theft or appearing in public without a restraining bolt, would have its memory wiped while its owner was obliged to pay a minor fine. A class one infraction, such as voluntary manslaughter or conspiracy to overthrow the government, mandated the destruction of the droid and a prison sentence for the droid's owner from five years to life.

*Droid tri-fighter*

**droidspeak** A term describing the information-dense speech used by R series astromechs and other droids.

***Droids, Technology and the Force: A Clash of Phenomena*** A treatise on the rights and privileges of droids written by Tam Azur-Jamin after the Yuuzhan Vong invasion.

**droid sub-carrier** A Haor Chall engineering transport droid used by the Separatists in aquatic environments during the Clone Wars. Resembling enormous vulture droids, these carriers released modified MVR-3 submersible speeders piloted by battle droids.

**droid subfighter** *See* manta droid subfighter.

**droid tri-fighter** During the Clone Wars, the Separatists deployed these agile fighters against the forces of the Galactic Republic. While in flight, the central hull of the ship remained stationary, while the ship's tri-wings revolved around it. The tri-fighter was developed by the Colicoid Creation Nest, the same firm that created the deadly droideka.

**Droid Uprising, the** An incident in Bakuran history shortly after the planet was settled. The Bakur Corporation's droids had been infected by a H'Lokk Consortium virus that caused them to sabotage the settlers' colonization efforts. A side effect of the virus was that the droids bypassed their nonviolent fail-safes and began killing people. This led to a cultural aversion to droids among the Bakurans.

*Droma*

**Droma** A Ryn who joined forces with Han Solo during the Yuuzhan Vong attack on the *Jubilee Wheel* at Ord Mantell. Droma's was among a caravan of Ryn ships that left the Corporate Sector for the Lesser Plooriod Cluster when the Yuuzhan Vong pushed into the Ottega system and destroyed Ithor. He yearned to find his scattered relatives, and with Han's help, he tracked his clanmates to Ruan. By the time he arrived, they had already left aboard the *Trevee.*

Droma was arrested on conspiracy charges by Salliche Ag and was taken to the company's district headquarters. He was held in the product-enhancement facility also known as the manure works. Han Solo rescued him, and the two departed for Fondor in search of the *Trevee.* Droma was reunited with his clanmates in time for the Battle of Fondor. He then helped with evacuating refugees from Duro. After the Battle of Esfandia, he took his leave of the Solos, departing aboard the *Fortunate Star.*

A good-humored Ryn, and a fair pilot and scout, Droma could play his beak like a flute, doing capable astromech imitations. Despite his long tail, he fit quite comfortably in a copilot's seat.

**Dromath, Rade** A tall, blond young man with blue eyes. His father—a New Republic captain—died during the Thrawn crisis. Rade was a member of Garqi's resistance force during the Yuuzhan Vong attacks that took his mother's life. He helped Corran Horn, Jacen Solo, Ganner Rhysode, and six Noghri sent to investigate Yuuzhan Vong activity on Garqi.

**Drome, Captain** The captain hired to transport the Hammertong device for the Death Star from its laboratory to Imperial hands. But Captain Drome never got the chance, as his ship was hijacked by the Mistryl Shadow Guards.

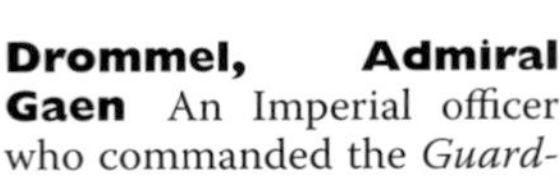

**Drommel, Admiral Gaen** An Imperial officer who commanded the *Guardian,* a Super Star Destroyer, during the era of the New Republic.

**Dromund Kaas** A swampy world believed to have been a Sith legend until its existence was verified by Jedi Master Yoda. Count Dooku attempted to keep its location and history a secret by deleting records of it from the Jedi Archives. Deep in the heart of the ancient Sith Empire, Darth Millennial developed the Dark Force religion here many years prior to the Battle of Ruusan. In modern times, Kyle

Katarn discovered the planet by following ancient runes on Altyr 5. He nearly succumbed to the dark side until pulled back from the brink by Mara Jade. Luke Skywalker later decided to keep Dromund Kaas's location a secret to keep its dark power from falling into the wrong hands.

**drone barge** Used to ferry cargo or other supplies, it was a large space vessel controlled by droids or computers.

**Drongar** A tropical planet, the fourth of its system, far out on the Spinward Rim, where extended ground fighting lasted over a year during the Clone Wars. Drongar was originally discovered centuries ago by a Nikto scouting team. The planet's atmosphere carried adaptogenic fungal spores, many of which caused harm or illness in humanoid species. The planet was also home to bota, a miracle salve that became the object of fighting between Republic and Separatist troops.

**Droog'an, Commander** A Yuuzhan Vong military leader of the Battle Group of Yun-Q'aah during the Battle of Ebaq.

**Droon, Admiral** An Imperial admiral on Corulag who worked with Frija Torlock to conspire against Governor Torlock. With the real Torlock gone, he attempted to eliminate Torlock's droid replica and Jixton Wrenga by sending them into the lair of a dragon slug. Jix survived and returned to Droon's fortress, killing Frija and capturing Droon. Jix then brought Droon to Coruscant, where the admiral was killed by Darth Vader.

**Droon, Igpek** A small-time trader on Nam Chorios. Reporter Yarbolk Yemm told C-3PO and R2-D2 to use Droon's name to get off Nim Drovis.

**drop shaft** *See* lift tube.

**drop ship** Any fast-moving spacecraft used to quickly transport troops, crew, or cargo from huge interplanetary capital warships to a planet's surface. Using powerful but short-burst drive units, drop ships plummetted from orbit in barely controlled falls.

*Drovian*

**droptacs** Corneal covers worn by certain species to prevent brightly lit environments from hurting their eyes.

**Dros, G'hinji** An elderly nomadic Em'liy who helped Luke Skywalker and Chewbacca when the Rebels returned to Shalyvane to investigate Shira Brie's history.

**Drost, General Theol** The commanding officer on Bilbringi VII during Grand Admiral Thrawn's campaign to retake the galaxy, he protected the Bilbringi shipyards and oversaw the dry-dock workers.

**Drovian** Primitive native inhabitants of Nim Drovis, organized into a network of tribes. Many were addicted to the narcotic zwil, which they absorbed by inserting fist-sized plugs into their membrane-lined breathing tubes. Drovians were tall, corpulent beings who had long been at war with the Gopso'os. While both had the same physical attributes, they battled each other for centuries though they had long since forgot their reasons for fighting. The technologically advanced Drovians were solidly built, with bottom-heavy physiques that were supported by thick, trunk-like legs. All of their limbs ended in three sharp pincers.

**Drovian system** *See* Nim Drovis.

**Drovis** *See* Nim Drovis.

**Dru, Dall Thara** A New Republic Senator from Raxa, she was chairperson of the Senate Commerce Council and a supporter of Leia Organa Solo during the Black Fleet crisis.

**Druckenwell** A Mid Rim planet, it was an industrialized, overpopulated urban world run by corporate guilds. Druckenwell's crowded cities were divided by wide oceans, and almost all of the planet's available land was developed. Therefore, great care was taken to reduce the risk of pollution and to protect the planet's few remaining resources. Druckenwell's 9.3 billion inhabitants worked mostly for the planet's massive corporations and lived in its congested metropolises. Couples could not marry until they could prove their fiscal independence. During the Yuuzhan Vong invasion, Druckenwell quickly capitulated to the alien menace, providing arable land to the Yuuzhan Vong for growing food and other resources.

**Drudonna** One of the two largest moons orbiting the planet Bespin, it and its larger brother moon, H'gaard, were known together as the Twins. Drudonna was only 2.5 kilometers in diameter. Both were unremarkable ice satellites and appeared as large green spheres in Bespin's night sky. Shirmar Base, a staging area and processing center for Ugnaught expeditions into Velser's Ring, was located on Drudonna.

*Drumheller harp*

**Drufeys** A lean, lazy-eyed security agent and technician who worked at the Binring Biomedical company owned by Warlord Zsinj.

**druggats** A form of currency used on Tatooine.

**drugon fish** A deadly type of fish found near Baron's Hed and on Ruusan, drugons often surprised their prey, attacking with a painful bite.

**drumheller harp** A percussion instrument with myriad attachments, including a screamer gong, resonator, gong stand, centressar strings, seilith music charms, harp base, O'Tawa cymbals, Tryna chime, and chime mount.

***Drunk Dancer*** Jula Shryne's modified Corellian freighter, similar in appearance to a corvette. She operated it with a crew of smugglers during the final years of the Galactic Republic and the early years of the Galactic Empire.

**Drunost** A planet that was one of Consolidated Shipping's largest hubs, it was home to many corporate offices.

**Dr'xureretue** The Ishi Tib owner-operator of Docking Bay 87 in Mos Eisley.

**Dryanta** Chewbacca's cousin, he accompanied Chewbacca, Jowdrrl, Shoran, and Lumpawarrump on a mission to rescue Han Solo during the Yevethan crisis.

**Drybal** A Yarkora information broker in Raze's criminal organization during the Galactic Civil War.

**Dry Ice** Jagged Fel's call sign during the new Jedi Order's attack on the Imperial Remnant forces holding the Nickel One asteroid in the weeks following the Second Battle of Fondor.

**Dryon, High Priest** A priest on Tatooine who led the Dim-U monastery in Mos Eisley during the Galactic Civil War.

**dry-scale hives** A dermatological affliction suffered by Rodians.

**Drysso, Joak** The former commander of the *Virulence,* he was quickly given command of the Super Star Destroyer *Lusankya* after former Director of Imperial Intelligence Ysanne Isard seized control of Thyferra's Bacta Cartel. Captain Drysso felt sure that the ship guaranteed Isard's control of the bacta trade and the planet itself. When the location of Rogue Squadron's base of operations was finally revealed, he was ordered to destroy the *Empress*-class space station at Yag'Dhul. Accompanied by the *Virulence,* they arrived at Yag'Dhul in time to see what looked like Rogue Squadron and several freighters jump to hyperspace on a course for Thyferra. Joak Drysso had warned Isard of such a possibility, but she had ignored his advice about leaving the *Virulence* behind to protect the planet.

Drysso reasoned that when he was finished with the Rebel scum at Yag'Dhul, he would return to Thyferra and destroy a weary Rogue Squadron. Surprisingly, Booster Terrik had modified the space station with a gravity-well projector and missile-lock sensors, which rattled the overconfident captain. It was only by the intervention of the *Virulence* that the gravity embrace was broken, allowing the *Lusankya* to escape back to Thyferra. When they arrived, Captain Drysso was stunned to discover that the *Freedom* had followed him in with Rogue Squadron in its hold. Fresh and ready for battle, they were still no match for a Super Star Destroyer. However, Drysso had not counted on the freighters being equipped with missiles and using X-wing targeting telemetry. The barrage of missiles from Rogue Squadron and the freighters brought down the shields of his starboard bow. The *Freedom* poured its weapons fire into this breach.

More than 100 ion cannons fired back at the *Freedom,* collapsing its shields and seriously damaging the ship. Instead of concentrating all his firepower on the *Freedom,* Captain Drysso decided that the more immediate threat came from the freighters and their missiles and ordered his guns to fire on them. In the meantime, Rogue Squadron and the Twi'lek pilots continued to nibble away at the *Lusankya,* with an occasional salvo from the *Valiant.* Drysso ordered another round of fire at the *Freedom,* and the return fire had enough force to knock out the shields on the *Lusankya.*

At that moment, Isard ordered him to retreat and follow her shuttle to hyperspace as they made their escape. Was she insane? He'd never retreat when victory was at hand. And with the sudden appearance of the *Virulence,* it seemed his victory was assured. But the Rogue's Booster Terrik was now in command of the ship and joined the other vessels bombarding the *Lusankya.* Soon Drysso's ship was defenseless, in a rapidly decaying orbit above Thyferra. When Drysso refused to surrender, his crew mutinied and took command of the ship. He was shot dead by Lieutenant Waroen, who took command of the *Lusankya* and surrendered to the New Republic.

**DS-181-3** A TIE fighter pilot call sign at the Battle of Endor. He was Baron Soontir Fel's wingman, known as Fel's Wrath, and piloted Saber 3.

**DS-181-4** A TIE fighter pilot call sign at the Battle of Endor. He was Major Phennir's wingman. He was recruited into Baron Fel's fighter wing after scoring 12 kills during the subjugation of Mon Calamari.

**DS-29-4** A TIE fighter pilot call sign at the Battle of Yavin.

**DS-3-12** A TIE fighter pilot call sign at the Battle of Yavin.

**DS-55-2** A TIE fighter pilot call sign at the Battle of Yavin.

**DS-55-6** A TIE fighter pilot call sign at the Battle of Yavin.

**DS-61-2** An Imperial TIE pilot, he flew Black Two during the Battle of Yavin and was Darth Vader's left wingman. Specially trained, Mauler Mithel was held in reserve for missions with Vader. But late in the battle, the *Millennium Falcon* came in unnoticed and blew up Vader's right wingman; that caused Vader to fly into DS-61-2 and push him into the wall, killing Mithel instantly, because his ship had no shields to protect him. Mithel's son, Rejlii, later became a tractor beam operator aboard Grand Admiral Thrawn's *Chimaera.*

**DS-61-3** An Imperial TIE pilot, he flew Black Three during the Battle of Yavin. Darth Vader's right wingman had a reputation for ferocity in combat. The Corellian pilot was nicknamed Backstabber. He died after a direct hit from the *Millennium Falcon.*

**DS-61-4** Nicknamed Dark Curse, he was an Imperial TIE pilot who survived the Battle of Yavin. DS-61-4 had already survived numerous assaults against such planets as Ralltiir and Mon Calamari.

**DS-61-9** A TIE fighter pilot call sign at the Battle of Yavin.

Trinto Duaba

Ur-Sema Du

**DS-73-3** A TIE fighter pilot call sign at the Battle of Yavin.

**DS-75-5** A TIE fighter pilot call sign at the Battle of Yavin.

**DSD1** *See* dwarf spider droid.

**D/Square Decoder** A powerful decryption and deciphering system manufactured by Fedukowski, it was used in military and police data banks, as well as Imperial Ubiqtorate bases.

**DSS-0956** A senior sandtrooper (Desert Sands stormtrooper) dispatched to Tatooine to find R2-D2 and C-3PO during the events surrounding the Battle of Yavin. He reported to Captain Mod Terrik.

**DSU** A data screen unit, or measurement of data based on the amount that can be displayed on the screen of a standard datapad.

**d'Tana, Keil** An alias used by young Han Solo when he worked for Garris Shrike.

**d-tape** *See* detonite tape.

**D. T. Spool and the Skroaches** A raucous musical act popular on Coruscant just prior to the outbreak of the Clone Wars.

**D-type fighter** A triple delta-winged, fast, and lethal Yevethan starfighter, comparable in performance to—and even slightly faster than—the A-wing.

**Du, Ur-Sema** A Jedi Knight, she raided the catacombs of Geonosis at the start of the Clone Wars, pursuing the leadership of the Confederacy. She was killed by General Grievous, one of the first Jedi to fall to the cyborg alien. At the time, none of the Jedi knew of Grievous's existence.

**Dua, Pa** An aide to Rodian Senator Onaconda Farr during the time of the Clone Wars.

**Duaba, Trinto** A member of the humanoid Stennes Shifter species, he had the ability to blend unnoticed into crowds. Trinto Duaba made a living by turning lawbreakers over to Imperial authorities.

**D'uat, Xufal** A Tiss'shar bounty hunter who worked in the vicinity of Elrood aboard his ship, *Venom Sting*. D'uat made extensive modifications to the *Barloz*-class freighter, adding anti-intruder sensors and safeguards as well as a pair of turret-mounted quad laser cannons.

**Dubrava** A swamp planet considered by some to be the "armpit of the universe." It was home to the Dubravan species. The washed-out Rebel pilot Jal Te Gniev was transferred to Dubrava to work as an Alliance recruiter shortly after the Battle of Yavin.

*Rik Duel (center) with the Zeltron Dani (right) and the Rodian Chihdo (left)*

**Dubrillion** The twin of planet Destrillion, it was located in the Outer Rim near the asteroid system known as Lando's Folly. Dubrillion was blue and green, with white clouds floating through its sky. At the start of the Yuuzhan Vong invasion, Lando Calrissian ran a mining and processing operation here, as well as his running-the-belt spectactor and gambling game. Both planets suffered heavy damages before the alien invasion force was repelled. The Yuuzhan Vong returned to Dubrillion a week and a half later and continued their attack. Lando evacuated as many of the citizens as possible, with many of them fleeing to Dantooine.

**duck** A common waterfowl native to Naboo and elsewhere. Luke Skywalker did not know what a duck was.

*Niado Duegad*

**Duegad, Niado** A dianoga-like mercenary from Vodran, he hailed from a species that controlled its environment through terraforming facilities. Duegad's enhanced adrenal glands allowed for short bursts of incredible stength.

**Duel, Rik** A smuggler, captain of the *Moon Shadow*, and con artist of Corellian origin, Duel was one of Han Solo's oldest associates. Duel and his partners, the Zeltron Dani and the Rodian Chihdo, were on the planet Stenos when they encountered and befriended Captain Kindar, who commanded a small Rebel group. Kindar believed that finding a statue of Vol, the god of the native Stenaxes, was the key to allying the flying warrior species to the Rebel cause. To this end, he left Duel, Dani, and Chihdo searching for the statue after the Rebels abandoned the base. Duel, in truth, planned to sell the idol to Imperial Governor Quorl Matrin, an art collector. Duel encountered Han Solo, Princess Leia Organa, and Luke Skywalker shortly after the Battle of Yavin attempting to make contact with Kindar. He explained the situation and got the Rebel heroes to help him uncover Vol. After Luke Skywalker found the statue, Duel double-crossed him and took it. The Stenaxes, aware that their god had been disinterred, took to flight and killed the statue's possessor: Governor Matrin.

Duel and his partners survived that run-in, reencountering Luke Skywalker with Lando Calrissian on Stenos three years later. Calrissian and Skywalker were in search of the carbon-frozen Han Solo. Duel helped the Rebels shake off pursuit from a syndicate of hunters led by Bossk and IG-88. Duel stayed on Stenos after the Rebels departed, considering a plan to get the Stenaxes to work for him.

Duel next popped up running a salvage operation after the fall of the Empire that he, Dani, and Chihdo started on Iskalon. Duel eventually accompanied Chihdo and Dani with Luke Skywalker on various diplomatic missions for the Alliance of Free Planets. Rik Duel eventually became a member of the Alliance, receiving military training from Luke Skywalker.

**Duelist Elite** A series of dueling droids produced by Trang Robotics. Darth Maul, Darth Vader, and Raskar the pirate were known to spar against Duelist Elites.

**Duff-Jikab** An underworld blood sport also known as the Cutthroat Hunt that involved pursuing intelligent prey. The prey was given a head start. Lando Calrissian was once subjected to a Duff-Jikab held by Quaffug the Hutt. Bossk, Dengar, Zuckuss, and Guchluk were hired to be the pursuers. If the prey survived for a day without being captured or killed—as Lando did—he or she was allowed to go free.

**Dufilvian sector** Located near Ord Pardron and the Abrion sector, it was home to the Dufilvian system and the planet Filve.

**Dug** A fin-eared alien species from Malastare, a world with a high gravity and some arboreal areas. Dugs were well adapted to swinging through trees on their homeworld, as they possessed four strong, spidery limbs. They actually used their upper limbs as legs, and their lower limbs as arms. Despite this odd configuration, they could move quite quickly across land. Males had extremely loose skin around their necks, which inflated during mating calls. Although few left their homeworld, the Dug known as Sebulba gained great notoriety among Podracing fans as one of that sport's finest competitors.

Most Dug buildings were towers; the in-

*Dug*

teriors were made with open platforms, which most other species find impassable. Although the Dugs were a technologically advanced species and could construct complex structures, many preferred to live in tree thorps—primitive villages—deep in the unsettled wilderness. Dugs went to war against many species, among them the Gran and the ZeHethbra, species with colonies in the Malastare system. As a result, the Republic demilitarized the Dugs, leaving them extremely bitter. They considered themselves warriors, and being denied armaments made them even more vicious and brutal.

*Shada D'ukal (right) and Karoly D'ulin (left) in the Mos Eisley cantina*

The relationship between the Gran and the Dugs on Malastare was founded on inequality, with the Gran viewing the Dugs as subservient laborers. As an example of this social structure, the slogan for Tradium-brewed Vinta Harvest Ale was "Dugs make it! Grans own it!"

*Duinuogwuin*

**Duggan station** A section of Duro's capital orbital city, Bburru. The *Jade Shadow* docked at Port Duggan.

**Duhma** A rare species distinguished by tribal patterns on their faces, they dwelled in the perpetual gloom of the dark side of their planet. Beyond their dark domain, they had to wear visors to shield them from the glare of light.

**Duinuogwuin** Sometimes called Star Dragons, these snake-like multipeds with gossamer wings were an average of 10 meters long. Large, reptile-like scales covered their bodies, contrasting with their floppy mammalian ears. This rare ancient species was scattered over the galaxy, even in deep space. They had a deep-rooted sense of morality and honor, and at least some sensitivity to the Force. Some stories told of ancient Duinuogwuin serving as Jedi Knights.

**D'ukal, Shada** A deceptively decorative-looking mercenary from a mysterious militaristic order of female warriors known as the Mistryl Shadow Guards, she and her friend Karoly D'ulin posed as the Tonnika sisters after botching a mission to transport the Hammertong device. Shada took the name of Brea Tonnika. Later, she served as bodyguard for the smuggler chief Mazzic. In this job, she appeared with plaited hair and a blank expression—until trouble started. Then she was all business, throwing enameled zenji needles with lethal accuracy and using her more-than-capable combat skill to protect the smuggler chief.

Sixteen years after the Battle of Endor, Shada stopped Karoly from performing an assassination and was punished by the Eleven who led the Mistryl. She left Mazzic's employment to avoid the Mistryl hunter teams, seeking to join up with the New Republic. Instead, Leia Organa Solo offered Shada's services to Talon Karrde, who was heading into the Kathol sector to locate a copy of the Caamas Document. Shada accompanied him, and the two grew fond of each other. When Karrde located information that revealed the truth about a fake Grand Admiral Thrawn that had been harassing the New Republic, Shada was there to stop the cloned Major Grodin Tierce from killing Gilad Pellaeon and the Mistryl leader Paloma D'asima. In gratitude, D'asima called off the hunter teams, and Shada officially joined Karrde's new joint intelligence organization.

During the Yuuzhan Vong invasion, she assisted Karrde in helping to evacuate the Jedi children from Yavin 4 to Coruscant.

**dukha** A building in the shape of a large cylinder with a cone roof. There was one in the center of every Noghri village. Inside the single open room was the clan high seat, used by the dynast (or clan leader) when he or she held audiences.

**D'ulin, Karoly** A Mistryl Shadow Guard involved in the transport of the Hammertong device for the Death Star. She once posed as Senni Tonnika. Sixteen years after the Battle of Endor, the Eleven who ruled the Mistryl sent her to kill her friend Shada D'ukal. She failed and was eventually saved by Shada when Major Grodin Tierce attempted to kill Karoly, one of the Eleven, and Admiral Pellaeon.

**D'ulin, Manda** A Mistryl Shadow Guard, she was the team leader of the assignment to transport the Hammertong device to the Empire for use in the Death Star. The deal went bad, and Manda D'ulin was killed in an Imperial raid.

**D'ulin, Naradan** A female Mistryl who served as attendant and caretaker to Princess Foolookoola. With the help of the Devaronian Vilmarh Grahrk, Naradan D'ulin was able to escort the princess safely to the Dur Sabon.

**Dulo, Neb** A disciple of Davrilat, a complicated religion based on the sanctity of harmonics. He was originally from the desert planet Tocoya. He had strong protective instincts.

**Dulok** Duloks were distant relatives of the Ewoks. The two cultures had little in common. Whereas Ewoks were kind, sensitive, brave, and industrious, Duloks seemed to pride themselves on their rudeness and dishonesty. Most Duloks were lanky and ill proportioned, with wide jowls and beady eyes. Verminous, patchy fur covered their mottled pink underhides. Although the Ewoks tolerated the Duloks out of respect for the forest and all its inhabitants, there were many Ewok superstitions concerning them. Duloks were ruled by kings, and there seemed to be very little ritual about the coming of a new monarch. Brute force determined an heir to the throne more than bloodlines. King Vulgarr, for instance, deposed and banished Ulgo the Magnificent, the former king.

A tribe of green-furred Duloks led by King Gorneesh lived in a village in the marshlands of Endor. The Dulok village was a cluster of rotted logs and swampy caves surrounding a stump-throne covered with the skins and skulls of small animals.

**Dulon** A multidiscplined form of martial arts practiced by the Jedi Knights.

*Dulok*

**DUM-series pit droid** Small, agile droids programmed to repair Podracers and other vehicles. Developed by Serv-O-Droid's Cyrillian engineers, they were resilient and extremely strong. They carried a spectrum of tools and operated in large groups, swarming over disabled or damaged Podracers to fix the craft. When deactivated, a pit droid folded into a compact, easily stored form. Despite their versatility, these droids were inexpensive and could be purchased in large quantities. And while they were skilled mechanics, they often developed playful or stubborn personalities over time. During the Boonta Eve Podrace that saw the liberation of Anakin Skywalker, the young human had a pit droid named DUM-9 working on his pit crew. A rival Podracer, Ody Mandrell, employed a droid named DUM-4 on his repair crew. DUM-4 was accidentally sucked through one of Mandrell's engines, damaging the Podracer. The droid, however, was relatively unscathed.

DUM-series pit droid

**Dunhausen, Grand Moff** A lean and crafty Imperial official, he always wore his trademark laser-pistol-shaped earrings.

**dun möch** A Sith combat form that included taunting, jests, and other distractive maneuvers to dominate the will of an opponent. In addition to verbal barbs, dun möch practitioners used the Force to telekinetically hurl objects at an opponent, not so much in an attempt to cause physical harm but rather to to distract and wear down the combatant.

**Dunn, Jono** A Galacian youth from a family that had long served the Galacian royalty, he was a guide and escort to Obi-Wan Kenobi and Qui-Gon Jinn during their assignment to monitor open elections on Gala. Kenobi and Dunn became friends, until the young Padawan realized that Dunn had been taking advantage of his position to secretly poison Queen Veda. Dunn was opposed to the elections mandated by Queen Veda and wanted the monarchy to continue.

**Dunter, Lysa** *See* Antilles, Syal.

Dune Sea, with remains of a krayt dragon

**Dunwell, Captain** A crazed human commander of a Whaladon-hunting submarine that operated below the waves of Mon Calamari, he had an obsession with capturing Leviathor, leader of the Whaladons.

**duodecipede** A spiky-shelled 20-legged insect hunted by moisture farmers on Tatooine for its meat.

**Dunari** A close friend and prior business partner of Tomaas Azzameen, he became sole proprietor of the most notorious exclusive casino resort station in the galaxy. Although he often dealt in questionable goods, his loyalty and friendship with Azzameen was beyond doubt.

**Duncan, Deadeye** A lackluster combatant in Ajuur the Hutt's combat arena on Taris during the Jedi Civil War.

**Dune Sea** A sea of sand that stretched across the Tatooine wastes, this vast desert was once a large inland sea. The area was inhospitable to most life-forms due to its extreme temperatures and a lack of water. The hermit Ben Kenobi lived in the western portion of the Dune Sea.

**dungeon ship** A large capital ship used to transport prisoners from one system to another via hyperspace. The massive dungeon ships originally were designed during the Clone Wars to hold Jedi Knights.

**Duos'tine of Loretto** An artist commissioned by Prince Xizor to create a statue of himself. This statue was on display at Prince Dequc's base on Nezri. Mara Jade hid her lightsaber in the statue in order to kill Dequc.

**dupes** Rebel pilots use this slang for Imperial TIE bombers.

**duplicator** Also known as a prototyper, a device that printed and collated material at a rate superior to ancient presses. A duplicator had a built-in chemical reservoir; from a small amount of raw materials, it could synthesize and match any paper or printing substance. A duplicator was a relatively small device, fitting into only a few small crates. Duplicators were often used by criminal elements on backrocket worlds to counterfeit monetary notes.

dungeon ship

**DuPre, Kylan** Formerly a quartermaster aboard the *Stormstrike* as part of Chandrila's home defense fleet, he became one of Admiral Drayson's most trusted aides in the New Republic.

**Duptom, Ree** A despicable bounty hunter kicked out of the Bounty Hunters' Guild, he continued to work independently. He died in a mission to kidnap and mindwipe Kateel of Kuhlvult when his ship, *Venesectrix,* suffered a partial reactor core meltdown. Boba Fett discovered this ship floating derelict near the Core.

**dura-armor** Industrial-strength military armor, it had the ability to absorb and divert blaster energy. Dura-armor was made by compressing and binding neutronium, lommite, and zersium molecules together through the process of matrix acceleration.

**duracord** A conductive, strengthened fiber rope used in stun nets.

**duracrete** A dense building material that could be poured into forms until it hardened into a nearly impervious surface.

**duracrete slug** Burrowing vermin that adapted to live in the overgrown duracrete "urban jungles" of city-planets and moons like Coruscant and Nar Shaddaa. The slug used its caustic digestive fluids to dissolve duracrete. Any material it could not digest instead got exuded to its skin, giving the nearly 3-meter-long slug a scaly, rocky appearance.

***Duracrud*** A stock YV-666 freighter given to trader Uran Lavint by Jacen Solo after he appropriated her vessel, *Breathe My Jets,* during the conflict between the Confederation and the Galactic Alliance. Angered at Lavint, Solo had his engineers sabotage the *Duracrud*'s hyperdrive so it would fail after a single jump. Alema Rar had stowed away aboard the *Duracrud* and

Duracrete slug

helped Lavint repair the hyperdrive, letting her limp to the Star Destroyer *Errant Venture* so that Rar could continue her vendetta against Han and Leia Organa Solo. Aboard the *Errant Venture,* Jacen was surprised to see Lavint alive and well. Alema Rar then stole the ship, taking it to Gilatter VIII to reunite with her dark mentor, Lumiya.

**durafiber** A fabric used in vacuum and environment suits.

**durafill** An adhesive sealant used to patch pits and dents in starship hulls.

**Dura-Kahn** A world where the partnership among bounty hunters Jodo Kast, Zardra, and Puggles Trodd fell apart.

**duralloy** A composite metal armor used for starship hulls. The armor was lightweight enough to be placed over older armor in plates. It was also used by the Mandalorians in their armor.

**Duranc, Ak** An alias used by Aarno Dering.

**Durane, Giles** A Weapons Master, who trained Princess Leia Organa in the art of self-defense and warfare. Durane served with Bail Organa during the Clone Wars. After the wars, Durane's family was wiped out by plague. He was such a mercenary that he took a job to assassinate his own pupil months after Leia's training was completed. Organa, however, used Durane's training to kill him instead.

**duranex** A strong, lightweight material used in jumpsuits and work coveralls.

**duranium** A metallic alloy with high tensile strength used in the construction of prison cells and cages.

**duraplas** A tough, laminate plastic used in the construction of lightweight helmets and armor.

**duraplast** A strong, lightweight building material.

**duraplex** A strong, transparent material used in the windscreens of repulsorlift vehicles.

**Durasha, Celia** One of the lieutenants serving aboard the luxury liner *Kuari Princess,* she was denied an opportunity to study at the Academy by her father, Reise, who felt it was no place for a woman. She later became a smuggler.

**durasheet** A reusable paper-like material for written documents. Its contents faded after a short period.

**durasilk** This strong spun fabric was used in water-resistant tents and tarpaulins. More refined blends were used in the linings of luxury goods.

**Durastar** A Jedi vessel that suffered a hyperdrive failure near Corellia and had to be abandonded during the Yuuzhan Vong invasion.

**durasteel** Used to build everything from space vehicles to dwellings, this ultralightweight metal could withstand radical temperature extremes and severe mechanical stress.

**Durasteel Corporation** A Black Sun front corporation on Coruscant.

**Dureya, Grand Moff** An Imperial official who ordered the suppression of rebellious activity on Gra Ploven. Around the time of the Battle of Endor, the Star Destroyer *Forger* used its turbolasers to superheat the waters of Gra Ploven, effectively boiling the native Plovens alive.

**Durga the Hutt** A Hutt crime lord, Durga Besadii Tai rose to power after his father, Aruk the Hutt, died of poisoning by Jabba and Jiliac. Though Durga suspected the Desilijic clan, he could not prove it. He nonetheless came to rule the Besadii clan, and Prince Xizor realized he could get a major foothold into Hutt operations by installing Durga as a top lieutenant, or Vigo, of the Black Sun criminal organization. He was huge even by Hutt standards, with a sloping head like a sagging mound of slime, stained by a dark green birthmark that looked like splattered ink. His child-like hands seemed out of place on his swollen body. Durga was also mastermind of the top-secret Darksaber Project, the attempt to build a new superweapon. Its failure resulted in Durga's death.

**Durge** A bounty hunter who weathered centuries of violence and warfare to emerge as a merciless and nearly unstoppable warrior driven by ancient vendettas. He hunted for the pure sport of it, to feed an insatiable bloodlust that spanned literally hundreds of worlds and almost 2,000 years. Though humanoid in appearance, Durge was a Gen'Dai, a rare, nearly indestructible species with an unusually long life span—some Gen'Dai reportedly lived for over 4,000 years.

The Gen'Dai who became Durge was born 2,000 years before the fall of the Republic, and was regarded by his elders as an exceptional physical specimen at a young age. A predilection for aggression, coupled by witnessing bounty hunters in action, forever steered young Durge into a lifetime of violence. For centuries, he studied under the most experienced and dangerous bounty hunters he could find.

Durga the Hutt

Durge

In addition to Durge's frighteningly powerful physical abilities, he was a walking arsenal. He was proficient with ranged weapons like his twin blasters, melee weapons like a spiked flail, and thrown weapons like a set of energized bolas. Durge's heavy armor included wrist darts and forearm-mounted energy shields that let him parry lightsaber attacks for short periods of time. Durge often used an agile rocket pack as well as an extensively modified swoop speeder bike.

About a millennium before the Battle of Naboo, when the galaxy was racked by warfare waged between the Jedi Knights and Sith Lords, Durge was in the employ of one of the few remaining Sith. In this time, he squared off against many Jedi, learning their fighting techniques and developing weaponry and combat tactics to counter their moves. When the Sith were finally wiped out at the Battle of Ruusan, Durge went into hiding to avoid Jedi reprisals. Nine hundred years later, he was hired to kill the leader of the Mandalorians. Though he succeeded, the Mandalorians struck back and managed to subdue Durge. He was subjected to unspeakable torture before escaping and retreating to parts unknown to hibernate and recover. It took nearly a century to undo the damage the Mandalorians had wrought.

When Durge emerged from his slumber, he sought vengeance on the Mandalorians. He was cheated of his revenge when he learned they were all but extinct. He soon found purpose, though. He had awakened to a galaxy at war, a galaxy where the Jedi Knights led clone soldiers in battle against the automated troops of the Confederacy. The charismatic Count Dooku lured Durge into his ranks, and the ancient bounty hunter relished an ironic twist in his quest for retribution, since the clones originated with a Mandalorian. In becoming Dooku's henchman, the bounty hunter was teamed with Asajj Ventress. The two were formidable adversaries for the Republic, and Durge took the lives of many Jedi with great zeal. Anakin Skywalker was finally able to destroy Durge in the final months of the Clone Wars by trapping him within an escape pod and directing it into the heart of a sun.

**durindfire** Rare valuable gems that sparkled from within.

**durinium** This alloy resistant to sensor scans was valued by smugglers for lining suitcases and small hiding areas.

**Duris, G'Mai** An X'Ting chosen as the regent and leader of her people during the Clone Wars, a time when her homeworld of Ord Cestus was under the control of Cestus Cybernetics and the Five Families, which were in turn under the sway of the Confederacy of Independent Systems. A talented and honest politician, Duris could trace her family's history back to the original hive queen. Duris also learned the history of her people, and how the eggs for which she served as regent had been hidden in a secure location after the Great Plague. After a Jedi mission managed to help secure the eggs, Duris was forced to concede that Obi-Wan Kenobi and the Republic were working for the betterment of the Cestians. With the destruction of the Five Families, Duris found herself entrenched as the true leader of the X'Ting and Ord Cestus, and vowed to keep the planet loyal to the Republic.

**durite** A shiny, black material used in the creation of Imperial IT series interrogation droids.

**durkii** A hideous 3-meter-tall creature with the face of a baboon and the body of a reptilian kangaroo. The durkii was normally a docile animal. When infested with kleex, however, it became dangerous indeed.

**Durkii Squadron** This Imperial TIE fighter squadron was part of the force that defended the labor colony of Kalist VI during the Galactic Civil War.

**Durkish Corporation** A small manufacturer of audio detection devices during the Jedi Civil War.

**Durkteel** This planet was home to a species known as the Saurin. It joined the Refugee Resettlement Coalition during the Separatist crisis.

*Durkii*

**Durm, Captain** The New Republic commanding officer of the *First Citizen* during the Yuuzhan Vong invasion.

**Durmin, Tajis** A Death Star trooper, he was trained in combat techniques and weapons skills. Tajis Durmin was typical of those assigned to guard key areas of the first Death Star. His last assignment was guarding the main conference room, and he died in the explosion of the battle station during the Battle of Yavin.

**Durnar** A Jedi Knight killed during the Battle of Saleucami, during the Clone Wars.

**Duro (Duros)** A planet in the Duro system, it was the homeworld of a species known as Duros. The Duros—who had large eyes, thin slits for mouths, and no noses—traveled space and hauled cargo for tens of thousands of years. The Duros blazed some of the oldest trade routes and hyperspace lanes in the galaxy as they ventured into the unknown. They achieved star travel before the founding of the Republic, and almost entirely abandoned the soil of their homeworld to travel among the stars. They ranked alongside the Corellians as the most seasoned space travelers in the galaxy. One of their earliest colonization efforts was on Neimoidia, and over the millennia, the Neimoidians became a genetically distinct offshoot of the Duros species.

The Duros homeworld of Duro weathered millennia of neglect. As the Duros took to space, much of their planet became increasingly polluted. When Duros political power was transferred from ancient royal rulers to a wealthy coalition of interstellar shipping firms, all connections to ancestral roots were severed. The Duros people embarked on a bold era of expansion, choosing to live in orbital cities or far-flung colony worlds.

The temperate surface of Duro was converted into farmlands, and immense automated food factories processed comestibles to be shipped elsewhere. As these territories spread, they encroached on the habitats of endangered wildlife, resulting in the extinction of millions of Duro's indigenous animals.

When the Empire came into power and seized control of Duro, it began mining operations near the ancient Valley of Royalty. The Empire's unsound practices further spoiled the ecology of the planet, irradiating a vast stretch of land with toxic waste. Following the Battle of Endor, Duro was eventually liberated from Imperial rule, joining the New Republic and offering its shipyards to the growing government.

The repeated vilification of the Neimoidians following the Clone Wars led many of that species to abandon their heritage and pose as Duros. A major section of Nar Shaddaa became a refuge for Neimoidians in hiding.

Duros tended to be calm, peaceful individuals, and this aspect of their personalities enhanced their acceptance in all parts of the galaxy. They were extraordinarily dependable workers. Though often quiet and sometimes taciturn, when called upon they were gifted storytellers, capable of retaining the interest of extremely diverse audiences for extended lengths of time.

Twenty-six years after the Battle of Yavin, Duro was one the New Republic's top 10 remaining shipyards. SELCORE launched an operation to sustain life on the planet's polluted surface. The tainted atmosphere, often referred to as Duro-stink, had gotten significantly worse over the decades. The Yuuzhan Vong invaded Duro to use it as a staging area for an attack on the Core Worlds and Coruscant. The occupation turned it from a gray-brown waste of desert and slag into a world green with vegetation.

**Duro, Battle of** Duro's shipyards, position along major space routes, and proximity to Coruscant and the Core Worlds have made it a target and battleground many times throughout galactic history. In the Mandalorian Wars, Neo-Crusaders laid waste to the planet, and the Duros were forced to ally with the Mandalorians against the Republic.

During the Clone Wars, Duro was targeted by a major Confederacy operation to gain a foothold on the way toward the Core. Exploiting mismanaged defenses by Senators who poorly allocated military assets, General Grievous led a strike against Duro and captured it before targeting other worlds in a path of destruction that culminated with a daring strike on Coruscant.

In the Yuuzhan Vong invasion, the alien marauders similarly targeted Duro as a major staging ground for a push into the Core. Using dovin basals, they tugged the orbital cities from the skies, sending them crashing into the planet's surface. Warmaster Tsavong Lah offered an ultimatum to the galaxy: He would stop his invasion in exchange for Jedi turned over as prisoners.

**Duro Defense Force** Also known as the DDF, this was the military braintrust charged with protecting the planet Duro during the New Republic.

*Duros blazed the galactic spacelanes.*

**Duroon** A gray-skied planet in the Corporate Sector, it was the site of a major Authority installation using slave labor. Han Solo once delivered weapons to Duroon during a slave revolt against the Corporate Sector Authority. Duroon had three moons, and its surface was dotted with lush jungles located between volcanic vents and fissures. Life-forms included unusual, harmless ball-like creatures known as bouncebeasts that became popular pets on many worlds.

**Durren** Located in the system of the same name in the Meridian sector, it was the site of the Durren Orbital Station, a major New Republic Fleet installation. Durren appeared blue from space. Six main religions were predominant, and the planetary coalition was a strong supporter of the New Republic, which agreed to protect the Durren system in exchange for the establishment of the naval base. Nine years after the Battle of Endor, a faction revolted against the Durren Central Planetary Council and the planet erupted in armed warfare, leaving it vulnerable to looters. The Republic cruisers *Caelus* and *Corbantis* had left the previous day to investigate a rumored pirate attack on Ampliquen and were unable to defend the orbital station. At the same time, the Death Seed plague broke out on the orbital station, but was contained in the lower decks.

**Durron, Kyp** From a tousle-haired eight-year-old mine worker to a Jedi Master—with a detour through the dark side—Kyp Durron led a life of extremes. He and his parents were carted off by stormtroopers one night from their home on the Deyer colony in the Anoat system. The crime of the politically active parents: speaking out against the Empire's destruction of Alderaan and its billions of inhabitants. Kyp and his parents were sent to the Imperial Correctional Facility on the planet Kessel where they were pressed into slave labor, mining the powerful drug called glitterstim spice from pitch-black tunnels. Kyp's older brother, Zeth, was shunted off to the grueling Imperial Academy on Carida.

Kyp spent his formative years alone and in darkness. His parents were executed during a battle that resulted in the smuggler Moruth Doole gaining complete control over the prison and the mines. Then a new prisoner, an old woman named Vima-Da-Boda—a Jedi Knight in the days of the Old Republic—sensed an aptitude for the Force in Kyp and started training him in some Force skills until one day she, too, was taken away by authorities. Seven years after the Battle of Endor, two new prisoners met Kyp: Han Solo and Chewbacca, who had been shot down by Doole while on a diplomatic mission to Kessel.

Han discovered quickly that the 16-year-old Kyp had great aptitude for the Force. It came in handy in the lower tunnels, when he, Chewbacca, and several other slaves and guards were attacked by the giant spiders that created the glitterstim. They then developed an escape plan and made it off Kessel in a stolen Imperial cargo ship, only to be pulled into the Maw, a cluster of black-hole fields. Kyp's Force powers helped them navigate to relative safety, and they discovered a top-secret Imperial weapons installation run by Admiral Daala. Their escape from the installation—with Kyp wearing a stormtrooper's armor—led to a fierce space battle that resulted in the destruction of most of Moruth Doole's space fleet.

Luke Skywalker invited Kyp to become a Jedi trainee on Yavin 4. Within a week, he had surpassed all the other initiates. But his impatience and anger made him a target for the dark side in the form of the long-dead Sith Lord Exar Kun, whose still-strong spirit was trapped in a Yavin temple. Kyp started training in secret with Kun but believed he could control the dark side. Still, in an act of vengeance, he removed the memories from the mind of reformed Imperial weapons developer Qwi Xux. He then joined Exar Kun to raise a major Imperial weapon, the Sun Crusher, from its burial grounds in the heart of the gas giant Yavin. When Luke Skywalker tried to intervene, Kyp and Kun trapped Luke's spirit outside his body, placing the Jedi in a state near death.

*Kyp Durron (left) was instrumental in many heroic missions, such as killing a Sith-bioengineered leviathon on Corbos.*

Kyp tracked down his most hated enemy, Admiral Daala, as she was about to attack Coruscant, and nearly destroyed her. Next, he tried to find his brother on Carida, but the rescue attempt failed when he accidentally incinerated his brother along with the planet. Later, as Kyp was about to destroy the *Millennium Falcon* with Han Solo and Lando Calrissian aboard, he was freed from Exar Kun's influence when the other Jedi trainees succeeded in destroying Kun's spirit. A recovered Luke offered to continue Kyp's training if he forever renounced the dark side. On their way to destroy the Sun Crusher once and for all, Luke and Kyp ran into another battle with Admiral Daala. Kyp managed to destroy both the Sun Crusher and a prototype Death Star, barely escaping with his life.

*Kyp Durron*

Kyp grappled with the guilt of his transgression for years, dedicating himself to the Jedi Order. He was instrumental in many heroic missions, and eventually grew to mentor several younger Jedi Knights. His exploits became legends to the younger students, who admired Kyp for his bold actions. Kyp took a Jedi apprentice, Miko Reglia, and became one of the first Jedi Masters of the new Order. Kyp and Reglia formed an X-wing starfighter squadron of non-Jedi pilots called the Dozen-and-Two Avengers. This brash unit was tasked with ridding the Outer Rim of smugglers and pirates. While they became known as a force to be reckoned with, the starfighter unit was ravaged by the initial invasion forces of the Yuuzhan Vong.

It was this massacre, and Kyp's resulting attitude, that served to polarize Luke Skywalker's Jedi Order. Not willing to remain passive as the Yuuzhan Vong murdered civilians and sundered entire worlds, Kyp insisted the Jedi take a stance and bring the fight back to the aggressors. Alarmed by Kyp's proposed aggression, Skywalker forbade preemptive strikes and retaliatory actions fueled by anger, since such actions invariably led to the dark side.

Kyp disregarded Skywalker's insights and

followed his own instincts. He rallied a number of followers in his controversial bid to attack the Yuuzhan Vong. He even coerced Jaina Solo, Skywalker's niece, to his side. He convinced Jaina that the Yuuzhan Vong were constructing a superweapon in the remnants of Sernpidal, and led a strike against the aliens. It wasn't a weapon, in fact, but a growing worldship that Durron and Jaina destroyed, and Jaina was furious at the older Jedi for his deception.

After the fall of Coruscant, Kyp helped Jaina steer away from the dark side when the death of her brother Anakin filled her with rage. Kyp's intimate knowledge of the dark side's power helped, though his own aggressive philosophies made the transition difficult for Jaina. In working together to craft a means of deceiving the Yuuzhan Vong, Kyp and Jaina developed an unusual relationship, one of respect and caring, though it was fighter pilot Jag Fel that would eventually win Jaina's heart.

In helping guide Jaina away from the dark side, Kyp, too, changed. He came to understand the power of consensus and the dangers of discord, and began working to assist Master Skywalker in his founding of a new Jedi Council. Kyp became one of the founding members of this new governing body of the Jedi Order.

Years later, after the defeat of the Yuuzhan Vong and during the Swarm War, Kyp was one of the many Jedi who pledged their full support to Master Skywalker's new Jedi Order, despite the continued strife among the various Jedi Masters. He accepted Luke's assumption of the role of Grand Master of the Jedi, recognizing that Luke was only acting in the best interests of the galaxy and the Force. Durron became one of the new Jedi Order's leaders, although he often chose to play the role of contrarian in many discussions, hoping to stimulate new ideas.

**Durron, Zeth** Kyp Durron's older brother, he was separated from his family during a raid by stormtroopers and taken to the Imperial military training center on Carida. Years later Kyp attempted to rescue Zeth, but the result was Zeth's death and the destruction of the planet Carida.

**Dur Sabon** A planet inhabited by an eel-like species of the same name. The Ootoolan Princess Foolookoola was escorted to Dur Sabon for her safety.

Dusty Duck

**Durundo** An up-and-coming Pacithhip Podracer who joined the professional circuit shortly after the Battle of Naboo. He participated in the Vinta Harvest Classic on Malastare.

**Dusat, Jord** Born and raised on the planet Ingo, he learned to race landspeeders over desolate, crater-pocked acid salt flats. Dusat was the best friend and chief competitor of Thall Joben in the early days of the Empire. Jord was a bit of a rebel and troublemaker, though he dreamed of racing professionally and winning the Boonta speeder race. At the time of his meeting with C-3PO and R2-D2, Dusat was a young man in his 20s. He had a brawny build, fair skin, and a shaved head save for a blond topknot.

Jord was renowned for his piloting and technical skills. When he was kidnapped by the gangsters Tig Fromm and Vlix, Thall Joben and Kea Moll, along with R2-D2 and C-3PO, rescued him from the Fromm stronghold. The droids and humans managed to steal the Trigon One, the Fromms' secret weapon. The Fromm hatred of Dusat and his friends culminated in the criminals hiring Boba Fett to eliminate the speeder racers and their droids. Joben's speeder, the *White Witch,* managed to win the Boonta races despite Fett's attempts on his life, and Dusat and Joben escaped the Fromms.

**Duskhan League** A federation of colonies and worlds in the Koornacht Cluster, it was under the control of the Yevetha species from the planet N'zoth. The Duskhan League was headed by viceroy Nil Spaar, who helped push the already xenophobic Yevetha into a campaign of conquering or exterminating non-Yevetha species on nearby worlds.

**Dust** A microscopic material developed by Galactic Republic scientists to surreptitiously monitor individuals. Resembling fine particles of dust, each grain was essentially a microtransmitter that relayed information on its location to a central receiver. By embedding the Dust in clothing or having targets inhale it, a Republic agent could track targets for one or more days, recording their every movement within a given area. Dust saw widespread use among the clone soldiers of the Special Operations Brigade, who used it to track terrorists and other enemies of the Republic.

**Dustangle** An archaeologist, he hid in the underground caverns of Duro after the Empire subjugated the planet; he was a cousin of Dustini.

**Dustini** An archaeologist from the planet Duro, he ventured offworld to appeal to the Rebel Alliance for help for his subjugated planet. He was a cousin of Dustangle.

***Dusty Duck*** A custom-built starship inherited by Aneesa Dym from her father after his death at the hands of a backstabbing customer. The ship's systems were temperamental, and Dym was not a well-trained mechanic who could keep it reliably running. She partnered with bounty hunter Rango Tel and set the ship down in Mos Espa, Tatooine, during a mission to track criminal Nam Kale. The ship and Dym had the misfortune of being directly in Darth Maul's path as he tracked down Qui-Gon Jinn and Queen Amidala. Maul boarded the ship, looking for his quarry, and killed Dym in frustration. Maul continued his search in the desert, and the crew of pit droids hired to repair the *Dusty Duck* loyally kept working. No one returned to claim the vessel, which was eventually consumed by the desert.

**Dutch** *See* Vander, Jon "Dutch."

***Dutyfree*** A Rebel Alliance transport commanded by Captain Areta Bell during the evacuation of Hoth.

**Duula** A Selkath judge presiding in Ahto City on Manaan during the Jedi Civil War.

**Duull, Vor** The proctor of information science on the *Aramadia,* the Yevethan/Duskhan Embassy ship.

**Duvel, Mayth** A sublieutenant in the Black Sun criminal organization.

**Duv-Horlo** A junior officer aboard the *Anakin Solo* during the Second Battle of Fondor.

**Duvil** This immense man was one of the many commandos who served in the Galactic Alliance Guard at the the height of the Corellia–GA War.

**Duwan, Leig** An aged instructor at the Coruscant Medical Hospital prior to the Clone Wars. An Alderaanian, Leig was known for the way he always seemed to smile when he talked to his students. He often recounted to his class the tale of how he'd once he saved a suicidal man by simply smiling, since the distraught person had made himself a promise to change his mind if anyone offered a simple sign of kindness. Even the smallest gesture, Duwan concluded, could save lives.

**Duwani Mechanical Products** This ancient manufacturer produced the 3DO series of protocol/service droids some 4,000 years before the Battle of Yavin.

**DV-523** A cloned stormtrooper member of the 501st Legion who raided the *Tantive IV.*

**DV-692** A cloned stormtrooper member of the 501st Legion who raided the *Tantive IV.* He also stunned Princess Leia Organa.

**D-V9** This research droid belonged to anthropologist Mammon Hoole. Also known as

*Dwarf spider droid*

Deevee, he watched over Zak and Tash Arranda for a preoccupied Hoole. After sustaining heavy damage in a fight on Kova, Deevee retired to the Galactic Research Facility on Koaan.

**D'vouran** A planet that apparently appeared out of nowhere. In fact it was created as part of the first experiment in Project Starscream: a living planet that devoured living beings and could travel through hyperspace. The world devoured itself and was destroyed after swallowing a pendant with an Imperial energy field designed to protect the wearer from D'vouran.

**Dwan, Gula** A Duros bounty hunter and assassin who used his connection to the Force to help guide his actions. Several years before the Battle of Ruusan, Dwan was hired by the mother of the Serenno noble Hetton to train her son in the ways of the Force. Dwan agreed, but had only a few practical skills to pass along. When Hetton became stronger and surpassed Dwan's abilities, the young man acted on his mother's orders and killed his tutor.

**dwarf nuna** *See* nuna.

**dwarf spider droid** A squat, multilegged droid of destruction deployed during the Clone Wars. These mobile tanks typically served the Commerce Guild in hunting down fugitive operatives, but when the Galactic Republic engaged the Separatist armies in a full-scale ground assault, dwarf spider droids were deployed to counter the Republic's massive clone army. Their striding legs were ideal for the rugged terrain of Geonosis, and their crimson eyes radiated with infrared photoreceptors for targeting the enemy through dense clouds of battle.

**dweebit** A Yuuzhan Vong–bioengineered insect, this reddish brown beetle had hooked mandibles and a single protruding tubular tongue. They were brought to Belkadan by Yomin Carr to terraform the planet into a breeding ground for yorik coral.

**Dweem** An ice-encrusted world with hostile life. The Sunesi Jedi Master Aqinos secretly trained on the planet Dweem in an abandoned Republic base left over from the threat of the Terrible Glare.

**D'Wopp** A Whiphid, he was the prospective groom of "Lady" Valarian. He made the mistake of leaving his Mos Eisley wedding reception to hunt a bounty, and was shipped back to his homeworld, Toola, in a box.

**DwuirsinTabb** This Troig became the subject of ethical debate in the media when its two constituent intelligences wished for separation prior to the Clone Wars.

**Dxo'ln, Kid** A smuggler, he took Han Solo on one of his first runs to Kessel. Years later, the balding Kid Dxo'ln was among the smugglers who joined Solo in Smuggler's Run during his investigation into the bombing of Senate Hall on Coruscant and his rescue of Lando Calrissian from the crime lord Nandreeson's clutches.

*Dxun*

**Dx'ono, Ghic** An Ishori New Republic Senator who arranged for Leia Organa Solo to meet with a delegation of Caamasi during the Caamas incident.

**Dxun** Also called Demon Moon, it was one of four moons orbiting the planet Onderon. Its thick jungles were home to numerous bloodthirsty monsters. Due to Dxun's erratic orbit, many of the creatures were able to migrate to the surface of Onderon during an annual period in which the two worlds' atmospheres intersected. Some 4,000 years before the Galactic Civil War, after the evil Queen Amanoa of Iziz was defeated by the Jedi, the inhabitants of Onderon built a Mandalorian iron tomb on Dxun to house the remains of their queen and of the Dark Jedi Freedon Nadd. The fallen Jedi Exar Kun later visited the tomb, where the spirit of Nadd helped him discover some hidden Sith scrolls. Later, at the end of the Sith War, the warrior clans of Mandalore fled to Dxun after failing in their attempt to capture Onderon. Their leader was killed by a pair of the Dxun beasts, and a new warrior assumed the mantle of Mandalore. Thousands of years later, Darth Bane arrived at Dxun, where he acquired a parasitic infection of orbalisks that covered his body to become a form of living armor.

**Dyer, Colonel** An Imperial officer responsible for defense of the control bunker on Endor, he worked closely with Moff Jerjerrod to plan the installation's defense. When General Han Solo and his strike team infiltrated the bunker, Solo threw a bundle of equipment into Dyer, knocking him off a platform.

**Dying Slowly** *See* Death.

**Dyll, Brullian** A musician, he was killed by the Empire during a sweep to wipe out "questionable" artistic endeavors.

**Dym, Aneesa** A Pa'lowick who inherited the *Dusty Duck* starship from her father, she was a capable pilot but a poor mechanic. When she discovered that bounty hunter Rango Tel had tagged her father's killer, she fell in love with him, and offered to him her services. They traveled to Tatooine, landing in Mos Espa to hunt for the criminal Kam Nale. There she hired a team of pit droids to perform some much-needed maintenance on the vessel. Darth Maul, who had been tracking Jedi on the desert world, stormed the *Dusty Duck,* mistaking it for a starship that may have transported the Jedi and a fugitive Naboo Queen. Angry at his error, Maul cut down Aneesa and continued his search in the desert.

**Dymek** A corporation that manufactured starship weaponry and explosive devices.

**Dymurra, Gnifmak** Loronar Corporation's chief executive for the Core Worlds, he agreed to arm factions in the Chorios systems so they could revolt, thus splitting the New Republic peacekeeping fleet and allowing Imperial Moff Getelles and others to move in.

**Dyn, Tudrath** A Yuuzhan Vong youth taught by Czulkang Lah during the Yuuzhan Vong invasion.

Rohlan Dyre

**dynamic hammer** A vibro-powered tool that delivered a greater force of impact than an unpowered hammer.

**Dynast** The title used by the leader of a Noghri clan.

**Dyne, Captain** A Republic Intelligence analyst during the Clone Wars who went to Cato Neimoidia to study a captured mechno-chair used by Nute Gunray to communicate with Darth Sidious. Decrypting some of the transmissions generated by the chair's transceivers led Dyne and his team to the abandoned warehouses in the Dacho District, where they discovered a tunnel network leading to the Senate Rotunda and 500 Republica. On the verge of discovering the true identity of Darth Sidious, Dyne and his team were killed beneath 500 Republica.

**Dyre, Rohlan** A rogue Mandalorian active during the Mandalorian Wars, he was a veteran of many campaigns. Disillusioned by the rise of the Neo-Crusaders and the unjust war, Dyre abandonded his heritage and turned against the Mandalorians. The fugitive Padawan Zayne Carrick helped Dyre escape the Mandalorian outpost on Flashpoint.

**Dyur, Byalfin** A Bothan hired by Lumiya to track Ben Skywalker during his mission to recover the Sith Amulet of Kalara. Dyur and his crew traveled aboard the *Boneyard Rendezvous* and kept tabs on Skywalker's progresson on Ziost. Lumiya ordered Byalfin to kill Skywalker, but the young Jedi escaped aboard an ancient Sith meditation sphere. Controlling the vessel, Ben was able to open fire on his pursuers and damage the *Rendezvous,* forcing it to crash-land on Ziost.

**Dza'tey, Girov** A Bothan commander aboard the *Starfaring* when it crash-landed on Malrev. Girov Tza'tey was adept in the meditative technique of Jeswandi, allowing him to harness the power of Malrev's Sith temple. After killing Cartariun, Girov intended to destroy Rogue Squadron with the power of Sith magic, but he was killed when Dllr and Herian sacrificed their lives to destroy the temple.

**Dzavak Lakes** A province on Ansion known for the unusual and exotic perfumes made by the Alwari natives who lived there.

Dzym

**Dzym** On the surface, Dzym was a small brown-skinned man with black hair drawn up into a smooth topknot. He was passed off as the secretary to strongman Seti Ashgad and was one of the soft-spoken beings whom native Chorians referred to as Oldtimers.

In reality, he was an insectoid captain droch and the mastermind behind all the turmoil on Nam Chorios. Hormonally altered, mutated, and vastly overgrown, Dzym was 250 years old. He controlled both Ashgad and Beldorion the Hutt by keeping them both alive and young. Desperate to escape Nam Chorios, he needed a shielded ship to do it, as well as some outside intervention to destroy the ancient gun stations that would surely shoot him down.

When Dzym visited Princess Leia Organa Solo, his appearance was more accurate: His eyes were large and colorless, his skin was a shiny purplish brown, and his neck was articulated. Dzym's skin was also chitinous, not human-like at all. His tongue was long and pointed, flicking through his sharp brown teeth, and his blotched body was covered with orifices and tubes. After a series of confrontations, Dzym managed to obtain an escape ship, but with the help of Luke Skywalker and the planet's natural Force components, the ship and its passengers were destroyed.

# E

850.AA Public Service Headquarters

**11-17** A sturdily built droid found in industrial facilities and excavation quarries. The 11-17's main burrowing tool was a heavy plasma jet mounted directly above its chassis.

**850.AA Public Service Headquarters** A massive mobile command base, this enormous droid was a formidable weapon in the war against urban blight. It disgorged armies of worker automata armed for battle with vacuum hoses, laser welders, and buffing rags.

**8D8 (Atedeate)** A thin, skull-faced Roche smelting droid that worked at Cyborg Operations in the palace of Jabba the Hutt. 8D8 was enslaved by Jabba and used to torture both droids and organics under the command of EV-9D9.

**8t88** A free and self-reliant one-time administrative droid, he was bitter at a practical joke in which his original crocodilian head was replaced by a far-too-small dome—and he long sought revenge against the perpetrator. His anger and droid dementia led him to become a powerful and highly sought-after infochant for the underworld.

He took on a job from the Dark Jedi Jerec to track down the location of the hidden Valley of the Jedi. A wild cat-and-mouse game between 8t88 and Rebel agent Kyle Katarn ensued when 8t88 stole a data disk belonging to the late Morgan Katarn; it had the key to finding the valley. The chase resulted in 8t88 getting his arm blown off and Kyle requiring a dunk in a bacta tank. The entire business came to a head, literally, aboard the cargo ship *Sulon Star*. There, instead of getting paid for the information, 8t88 got his head lopped off by Jerec's minion Pic, and it was swallowed by the droid's pet hornagaunt, Grendel. Katarn was forced to carve the metal skull from one of the beast's three stomachs in order to retrieve the coordinates.

Several years later, former Emperor's Hand Mara Jade came across the disembodied head of 8t88 on the planet Rathalay in the lair of smuggling kingpin Kaerobani. The head was more spiteful than ever, and pitifully plotted to reclaim his body. He must have succeeded, since there was a sighting of a rare 88 series droid on the planet Mawan at the same time the original prank's perpetrator was reported to have died in a tragic and fatal accident.

8t88

**E-11 blaster rifle** A BlasTech blaster that was standard issue for Imperial forces. They were so numerous that many were stolen for use by the Rebel Alliance. The E-11 had an extendable stock and carried energy for 100 shots. There were numerous variants and knockoffs.

**E1-6RA** An administrative droid that served the Jedi Knights at the Almas Academy. The droid had a unique, four-armed appearance and featured alien technology that allowed it to receive telepathic signals.

E-3PO

**E-2 mining ship** Ancient asteroid-mining vessels developed by Byblos Drive Yards that resembled a huge mechanical insect. Eight claws grasped an asteroid while a proboscis-like suction tube drilled into the rock to extract ore. The pirate Finhead Stonebone used E-2 mining ships to attack ore haulers four millennia before the Battle of Yavin.

**E-3PO** A series of modified protocol droids designed to interface with Imperial computer networks. Their rarity often gave these droids a haughty sense of superiority. Many were usurped by IG-88 in his power grab during the Galactic Civil War, becoming remote eyes and ears for the megalomaniacal assassin droid. C-3PO encountered a particularly rude silver E-3PO in Cloud City on Bespin, who snapped a vulgar "E chu ta!" to his golden cousin.

E-11 blaster rifle

**E3-standard starship lifeboat** A compact model of escape pod that Yoda used for his arrival on Dagobah following the conclusion of the Clone Wars. Produced by His Grace the Duke Gadal-Herm's Safety Inspectorate, the small pod had four finned vanes that extended to become the vessel's landing struts.

**E4 baron droid** *See* baron droid (E4).

< Emperor's Royal Guard

**E49D139.41** A Galactic Senate decree passed shortly after the outbreak of the Clone Wars that severely curtailed nonmilitary cloning research.

**E-5 battle droid** An interim successor to the Baktoid Combat Automaton B-1 battle droid, this tall, thin combat unit was based on the E4 baron droid design and featured a limited verbobrain that allowed for a measure of independence. This series was quickly made obsolete with the development of the B2 super battle droid, though Raith Sienar kept some as personal bodyguards.

E522 Assassin

**E522 Assassin** An assassin droid, it had a wasp-like waist, huge shoulders, and a squared-off head. The design dated to the Clone Wars, when the Techno Union developed the E522 as a combat automaton. The Empire and Sienar Intelligence later refined the design. An E522 Assassin was smeared with meat and juice and fed by Jabba the Hutt to his pet rancor for amusement, though the rancor simply spit it out. This model was later repaired, reprogrammed, and used by Lady Valarian.

**E9D8 Rebellion** An ancient conflict that was settled in part by the Jedi Order's Council of First Knowledge.

**Ealewon Electronics** A company that manufactured encryption devices.

**Ean** A Mon Calamari, he was a member of Wedge Antilles's command crew on the *Yavin,* a New Republic star cruiser.

**Earl of Vis** A historical figure on Naboo, cousin to an ancient king, who built a large banquet rotunda in the city of Theed.

**earworm** A Corellian slang term for any nuisance or pest.

**East District Trail** A travel route on Lucazec, little more than a dirt road.

**Eastgate** One of the largest commercial and warehouse districts of the Upper City of Taris, prior to its devastation by Darth Malak.

**East Minor** A residential borough on Coruscant's southern hemisphere, home to the famous Trophill Gardens.

**East Platform** The landing platform used by Boba Fett on Cloud City when he took possession of the carbon-frozen Han Solo.

**Eastport** One of the three largest spaceports in Imperial City, on Coruscant. It was extensively damaged during the Yuuzhan Vong invasion and subsequent transformation of the capital world.

***Easy Spacer*** A popular holovid starring Isriner Korosson, released prior to the Clone Wars.

**Eater of Fire Creepers** A Qom Jha Bargainer who welcomed Luke Skywalker to Nirauan. However, he resented the presence of Mara Jade because of her former allegiance to the Empire. Eater of Fire Creepers was also distrustful of the Qom Qae nesting led by Hunter of Winds, because the other Bargainer failed to deliver the plea for help to Luke.

**Eba** The name of Jaina Solo's Wookiee doll.

**Ebaq 9** The ninth moon of the gas giant Ebaq, in the Deep Core. The Deep Core Mining Corporation established bronzium refineries on the moon that were abandoned following the death of Emperor Palpatine. During the Yuuzhan Vong invasion, Admiral Ackbar developed a plan to lure the invading alien forces into the hyperspace dead end that was the Ebaq system, which required the establishment of a New Republic base on the moon to serve as bait.

**Ebareebaveebeedee, King** The monarch of the Squib people, head of the Squib Polyanarchy, and the Illustrious Chieftain of the Junkyards. The aged Squib was the mastermind behind the placing of Squib workers as spies aboard capital ships, giving the diminutive scavenger species an advantage in salvaging space junk ejected by those ships. Ebareebaveebeedee was fond of lengthy, somewhat nonsensical proclamations, declaring the Jedi Knights as "koovy" for their protective services in the Clone Wars, and especially venerating the efforts of Mace Windu as a hero of the Squib people.

**Ebbak** A civilian adviser to the Galactic Alliance military, her skill in data analysis and information management caught the attention of Jacen Solo, who transferred her from her position on the *Anakin Solo* to serve as one of his key aides during the conflict against the Confederation.

Ebon Hawk

**Ebe Crater Valley** A pockmarked expanse early in the Boonta Eve Podrace course.

**Ebelt, Gorr Desilijic** A Hutt who operated a criminal network on Naboo during the Galactic Civil War. He was largely derided for his laziness and lack of ambition by other Hutts in his clan, including Jabba.

**ebla beer** This ale is brewed from ebla grain on the planet Bonadan.

***Ebon Hawk*** A freighter that became famous in smuggling circles over 4,000 years before the Battle of Yavin, shuttling illicit goods for Davik Kang, the Taris underworld boss during the Mandalorian Wars. The ship could outrun Republic and Sith patrols alike. Davik would joke that it was the best thing he had ever stolen, though it wasn't clear how he came into possession of the *Ebon Hawk.* The ship's primary systems were modified so many times that the original classification as a Core Systems *Dynamic*-class freighter was difficult to spot. The interior of the *Ebon Hawk* comprised several sections, including a cockpit, crew quarters, medical center, tactical battle station, cargo hold, and even a makeshift garage to store swoop bikes and modify equipment. Its weaponry consisted of a gunnery station with dual turbolasers, as well as other "secret" armaments.

Ownership of the *Ebon Hawk* changed hands to the rehabilitated Revan and Carth Onasi after Davik was killed in an altercation following the rescue of Bastila Shan, shortly before Taris was destroyed by Darth Malak. Revan and crew then used the *Ebon Hawk* to move from world to world searching for pieces of the missing Star Map. After the destruction of the Star Forge, the *Ebon Hawk* eventually came under the command of the Jedi Exile, who used it as a transport in a quest to stop the Sith Triumvirate of Darths Nihilus, Sion, and Traya.

**ebonite** The desk and floor of Chancellor Palpatine's private office were made of this luxurious substance.

**Ebon Sea** A polluted expanse of water on Geonosis, this foreboding body contained mutated beasts even more terrifying, such as acklays and hydra worms.

**Ebranite** A tough, six-armed humanoid species that evolved in the canyons of Ebra.

**Ebrihim** An elderly male Drall, this overweight tutor and guide was hired for the children of Leia and Han Solo while they were on Corellia.

**Ebsuk, Zubindi** A Kubaz, he was the chef of Beldorion the Hutt on Nam Chorios. He used enzymes and hormones to transform common insects into gourmet meals; indeed, he was famous for mutat-

Echo Base

ing them into whole new life-forms for the dining pleasure of Beldorion. In fact, Kubaz chefs were famous throughout the galaxy for injecting insect life-forms with growth enzymes and gene-splicing them in a quest for newer and more perfect designer foods. But Ebsuk's efforts were his downfall. He altered a droch that—before anyone knew—became intelligent enough to enslave him. The droch, Dzym, fed off Ebsuk until he became powerful enough to enslave even Beldorion.

**Ecclessis Figg variation** *See* sabacc.

**echani** A form of deadly hand-to-hand combat that originated with the Echani people of Eshan and was modified by the Sun Guards of Thyrsus. It was practiced by the Emperor's Royal Guard in fierce sparring contests in their training facilities on Yinchorr.

**Echani** An alien culture known for its military prowess, particularly in the era of the Great Sith War. Their armor and weaponry frequently incorporated lightsaber-disrupting cortosis ore, which allowed them to pose a real threat to Sith and Jedi warriors.

Echani Handmaiden

**Echani Handmaidens** Five sisters who left the path of the Jedi after the Jedi Civil War but were nonetheless committed to bringing down the Sith. Many went underground and joined Atris on Telos in preserving the lore of the Jedi.

**Echnos** Also called Tinn VI-D, it was one of six moons orbiting the gas giant Tinn VI, located in the Tinn system at the border to the Outer Rim. The barren, rocky moon's atmosphere was not breathable for any length of time, and during half of its year Echnos passed through Tinn VI's dangerous magnetic field, which could force ships from hyperspace. Echnos's inhabitants lived in an enormous blue transparisteel city dome, 40 kilometers in diameter and nearly 2,000 stories high. The crowded, high-technology metropolis was a haven for smugglers and mercenaries and had no form of organized government. Attractions within the domed city included many casinos and the weekly BlastBoat 2000 demolition derby.

**Echo, Trooper** A clone trooper rookie who served at the Republic outpost on the Rishi moon, he was happy to be away from the front lines.

**Echo Base** The comm-unit designation for the secret Rebel Alliance command headquarters on the ice planet Hoth. It was run by General Carlist Rieekan and was fully equipped to service transport and combat vehicles. In addition to perimeter defenses, it had a massive ion cannon for covering fire and an energy shield to stave off bombardment. The base had to be abandoned in the face of a fierce Imperial attack.

**Echo Flight** A starfighter squadron made up of young pilots that—along with Delta Flight—served as the entry point into the Royal Space Fighter Corps of Naboo. The pilots of Echo Flight flew Naboo police cruisers.

**Echo Stations** A number of staffed patrol stations scattered throughout the perimeter of Echo Base on Hoth. These outposts were distributed in a grid-like pattern, with numerical identifiers indicating their placement on the grid. The stations were typically operated by Rebel soldiers, armed with artillery to hold off Imperial attack in case of discovery.

**Eckels, Dr. Joto** An archaeologist and field researcher for the Obroan Institute, he was in charge of the excavation at Maltha Obex.

**Eckener, Hugo** The chief architect of Naboo and a member of Queen Amidala's Royal Advisory Council. His attentions were focused on Naboo's civic infrastructure.

***Eclipse*** Upon his return six years after his presumed death at the Battle of Endor, the cloned Emperor Palpatine ordered the construction of a new weapon of terror: a 17.5-kilometer-long Super Star Destroyer that would serve as his personal flagship. Solid black and armed with a planet-searing superlaser, the first *Eclipse*-class Star Destroyer was designed to frighten and demoralize the enemy.

The ship, with a crew of more than 700,000 plus 150,000 stormtroopers, was outfitted with 500 heavy laser cannons and 550 turbolasers. It carried 50 squadrons of TIE interceptors—a total of 600 ships—eight squadrons of TIE bombers, five prefabricated garrisons, and 100 AT-AT walkers.

Juno Eclipse

But the *Eclipse* was stopped over the Pinnacle Moon when Luke Skywalker and Leia Organa Solo joined Force energies and engulfed Emperor Palpatine in a wave of life energy. The action stunned the Emperor, causing him to lose control over the mighty Force storms he had summoned. As Luke and Leia escaped from the ship, the storms consumed and destroyed the vessel. A second *Eclipse*-class ship, the *Eclipse II,* was destroyed when the Galaxy Gun accidentally obliterated the Emperor's homeworld of Byss.

**Eclipse** Built on a planet deep inside a massive asteroid belt, Eclipse was used by the Jedi and members of the New Republic as a hidden base from which strikes were launched against the Yuuzhan Vong. Though it was eventually abandoned and destroyed, for a time it served as a Jedi hideout. The tunnels of the new base had been laser-cut from solid rock and then sealed against vacuum leaks with a white plastifoam that made it appear much softer and brighter than the typical cave warren. Residents wore vacuum emergency suits as a precaution. Eclipse also boasted a number of advanced science laboratories where research was performed that eventually resulted in the devices that were able to jam the psychic emanations of the alien yammosk.

**Eclipse, Juno** Born on the Core world of Corulag, she applied to the Imperial Academy at age 14 and became the youngest cadet accepted into its ranks. In addition to developing into a talented combat pilot, Juno excelled in starship repair, droid maintenance, and marksmanship. After graduating from the Academy, she flew many combat missions throughout the Outer Rim; her successes brought her numerous commendations and the admiration of her peers and commanding officers. She was quickly promoted, taking command of her own squadron. After proving her loyalty at the Battle of Callos, Juno was handpicked by Darth Vader to pilot the *Rogue Shadow,* an advanced spy ship that ferried Vader's secret apprentice, Starkiller, on his various missions.

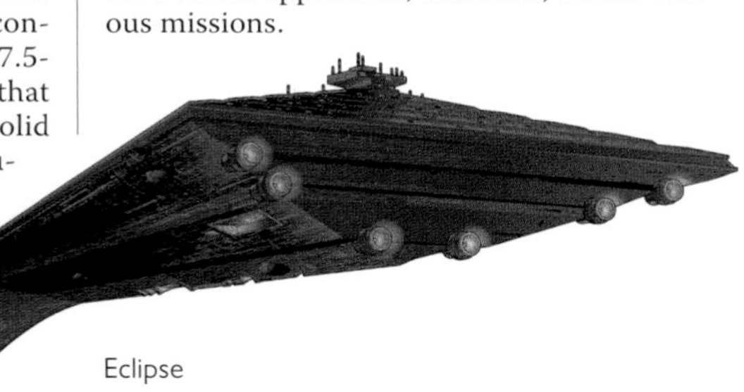

Eclipse

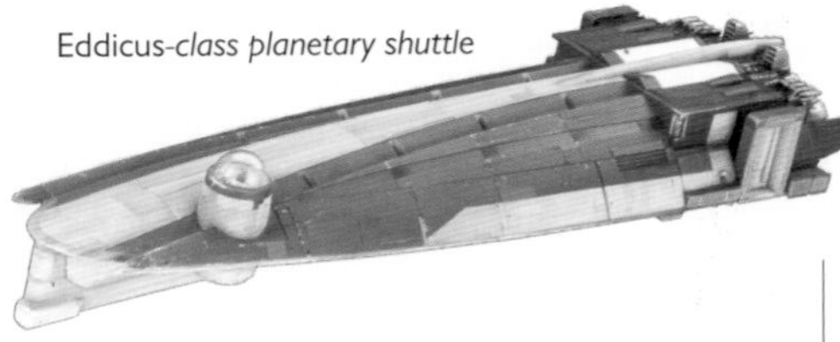
Eddicus-class planetary shuttle

**Eclipse, the** This was considered the most exclusive hotel in the city of Ussa, on the planet Bellassa, during the early years of the New Order.

***Ecliptic*** A Galactic Republic warship that was part of a fleet commanded by Admiral Saul Karath during the Mandalorian Wars. The *Ecliptic* was at the forefront of the Republic fleet that tried to defend Serroco from attack.

**Ecliptic Evaders** A squad of Imperials serving aboard the *Rand Ecliptic,* they all jumped ship near Sullust to join the Rebel Alliance. They did so at the Yavin 4 base, and most saw their first action at the Battle of Yavin.

**Edan, Moff** A member of the Imperial Remnant's Moff Council at the time that Admiral Pellaeon considered making peace with the New Republic, Edan was skeptical that such a truce could come to pass.

**Eddawan, Galim and Joli Ti** Galim Eddawan served as Galactic Senator for the planet Tyan about half a century before the outbreak of the Clone Wars. He and his daughter, Joli Ti, were ambushed by pirates led by Lorian Nod en route to Alpha Nonce and were never seen again.

**Eddels** An alias used by the ancient Sith Lord Qordis to embezzle credits from the Brotherhood of Darkness prior to the Battle of Ruusan. He used a portion of the stolen fortune to purchase rare and valuable artworks and relics. After killing Qordis on Ruusan, Darth Bane assumed the Eddels identity and collected the funds.

**Eddicus, Anwis** A historic Supreme Chancellor who helped end the Death Seed plague threat.

***Eddicus*-class planetary shuttle** A 32-meter-long air transport manufactured by Kuat Systems Engineering and commonly encountered on Coruscant during the latter decades of the Galactic Republic. Senator Palpatine arranged for the near-exclusive use of such transports by Senatorial personnel, and worked with KSE to install hidden listening devices aboard the vessels.

**Edge-9** A group of anarchist terrorists based in Republic City on Coruscant who demanded the dismantling of the Republic's governmental structure and the elimination of its upper class. Despite their noble aims, the members of Edge-9 quickly became violent, relying on bombs and weaponry to get their point across.

**Edian, Sergeant** A member of the Wing Guards loyal to Baron Lando Calrissian, he felt great disdain for those officers who accepted bribes or other forms of corruption.

**Edic Bar** One of five primary cities that floated in the atmosphere of Genarius. SoroSuub Corporation maintained a corporate office there to monitor its gas-mining interests in the Cularin system. Much of Edic Bar was built to Sullustan tastes, although most residents of the system considered it beautiful.

***Edict*** Admiral Daala's Imperial shuttle.

**Edisser, Pont** A fireman aboard the emergency fireship captained by Jikesh Valai that helped Anakin Skywalker set down the flaming remains of the *Invisible Hand* on Coruscant.

**Edjian-Prince** Regarded by actors as the most difficult role to play in the Corellian tragedy *Uhl Eharl Khoehng.*

**Educational Corps (EduCorps)** A branch of the Jedi Knights comprising students who focused on providing educational services to the underprivileged subadults of the galaxy.

**Eekin, Sta-Den** A Klatooinian Jedi Master who fought in the arena at the Battle of Geonosis, he was known to have the power to cloud the minds of vast crowds. He perished during the battle.

**Eekway, Chi** A Twi'lek Senator from Wroona, she was a member of the inner circle of loyalists who advised Chancellor Palpatine during the Clone Wars. She grew increasingly concerned with the Chancellor's expanding executive powers. Though she was somewhat young and impetuous, Eekway's sphere of control included areas of space dominated by unallied trader guilds that often stretched the limits of Republic law. Her devotion to Wroonian spirituality—visible in details found in the ornate molf-tasseled overcloak she wore—helped her earn support and respect. Her near-supernatural levels of empathy helped her quell even the most contentious of political disputes. Eekway was rumored to have close ties to the mysterious Baron Papanoida.

**Eellayin** An ancient species of beings native to the planet Polis Massa, before the planet was torn asunder in a devastating cataclysm many millennia before the Clone Wars. According to research done by the modern Polis Massans, the Eellayin lived beneath the planet's surface.

Chi Eekway

**Eelysa** A young woman from Coruscant, she was born after the Emperor's death and became one of Luke Skywalker's most promising students at the Jedi academy on Yavin 4. On an extended spying mission on Barab I, she discovered Saba Sebatyne and trained her in the ways of the Force. During the Yuuzhan Vong invasion, Eelysa sustained injuries and recovered at the Coronet Medcenter alongside Leia Organa Solo, who had been injured during the Battle of Duro. Han Solo smuggled Eelysa off Corellia by claiming she was his daughter, Jaina. After a full recovery, Eelysa returned to Corellia to determine the extent of the Yuuzhan Vong presence within the sector. She was among the first Jedi Knights killed by the Yuuzhan Vong–engineered creature, the voxyn.

**E-elz, Entoo Needaan** A slight, slim man who served as the primary contact for anyone dealing with Jorj Car'das in the years following Car'das's disappearance into the Kathol Outback. He preferred to go by the name Entoo Nee.

**Eemon, Ado** The silver-tongued ruler of Caramm V during the Clone Wars who allied his planet with the Confederacy of Independent Systems, allowing the Separatists to use the huge manufacturing facilities found there.

**Eerin, Bant** Obi-Wan Kenobi's best friend when he was a youngling at the Jedi Temple on Coruscant, she was a young Mon Calamari with salmon-colored skin and silver eyes. She was small for her age. Bant was chosen as a Padawan by Tahl, but the two never established a strong relationship. Bant resented that Tahl would rarely take her along on the more dangerous assignments. After Tahl's death, she was apprenticed to Kit Fisto. She was involved in the space battle over Geonosis. Obi-Wan Kenobi believed that Bant died during Order 66.

**Eeropha system** A small system that served as refueling point en route to Coruscant.

**Effhod, Zelebitha** The Coruscant Minister of Ingress during the Separatist crisis, she oversaw the closure of Coruscant to all immigration, citing security concerns.

**effrikim worms** Two-headed worms, they were a favorite snack food of Hutts. The endorphins of effrikim worms brought on hours of drowsiness.

**Effulem era** An era in art marked by rhyming poetry and prose some 250 years before the Ruusan Reformations.

**EG-4 (Eegee-Four)** A popular power droid model, it was especially useful on worlds with inhospitable climates, thanks to its rugged design and construction. The EG-4 model had modified, top-mounted power sockets. The droids were helpful to the Rebel Alliance when it established a base on the ice planet Hoth. They were donated to the Alliance by the Bothan underground.

**EG-6** An ambulatory power droid model, it supported equipment and vehicles. An EG-6 encountered by C-3PO and R2-D2 in the Jawa sandcrawler was so slow-witted—due to constant memory wipes—that it didn't even know its own name or serial number.

EG-6

**Egast, Keela** A young pilot in Naboo's Echo Flight shortly before the Battle of Naboo, she flew as Echo Eight. Keela was shot down by Dren Melne during the defense of station TFP-9, but her fighter was recovered and she survived the attack. She was later promoted to a position within Bravo Squadron.

**Ehjenla** This small planet near the center of the Kathol Outback was still in the throes of an ice age after the Battle of Endor. It was the homeworld of the Tuhgri.

**Eiattu VI** A planet with blue and reddish purple vegetation. Native flora included giant ferns, palm trees, and many types of moss. There were many light forests and murky swamps. Fauna included dinosaur-like beasts of burden with brightly colored feathers. The capital was a port city on an ocean, much of it built out over and below the bay, with Quarren living in the underwater zones. Politically, it was a place of great intrigue among royal families, with what seemed to be a Rebel-affiliated liberation movement challenging residual Imperial power in the era of the Galactic Civil War.

**Eickarie** These aliens native to Kariek were a fragmented tribal people whom the Empire of the Hand helped liberate from the domination of a warlord. They were very good fighters. They had black-scaled bodies and green faces, highlighted by orange ridges that changed color according to their moods.

**Eicroth, Dr. Joi** An archaeologist, she examined Qellan remains from Maltha Obex. She became romantically involved with New Republic Admiral Hiram Drayson and married him, joining the Alpha Blue team. During the Yuuzhan Vong War, she was part of a task force set up to determine the origins of the extragalactic invaders.

**Eidolon Base** According to official records, the *Eidolon* was an Imperial strike cruiser specially designed to carry TIE fighters. The *Eidolon* prototype vanished on its maiden voyage and was presumed lost. In truth, the *Eidolon* was a sham. Imperial Grand Vizier Sate Pestage diverted funds earmarked for the *Eidolon* to construct a weapons cache on Tatooine. The actual *Eidolon* was barely spaceworthy, and was conveniently "lost" in hyperspace to conceal that fact. Pestage's Eidolon base was known to a select few. Rogue Squadron discovered the base a short time after the Battle of Endor.

Eidolon *Prototype cruiser*

**Eighth Cortex** The last and most secret addition of shaper protocols added to the Qang qahsa—or information bank—that stored the various patterns and procedures practiced by the bioengineers of the Yuuzhan Vong. The Eighth Cortex was long said to contain the most perfect information bestowed upon the invading alien species by their gods—knowledge that would enable them to defeat the enemies native to the galaxy, with the peculiar Force abilities so foreign to the Yuuzhan Vong. In truth, there was no Eighth Cortex—it was a lie created by Supreme Overlord Shimrra to justify his invasion plans. Shimrra secretly commanded Nen Yim to develop protocols for use against the "infidels" to become the foundation of the Eighth Cortex.

*Cesi "Doc" Eirriss*

**Eighth Fleet** A major division of Galactic Alliance naval forces, it was one of three naval units assigned to the General Crix Madine Military Reserve during the fleet reorganization and consolidation actions.

**Eijin** Though not an overclan, Eijin was still an influential Alwari clan on Ansion.

**Eilnian sweet flies** When matured, these flies were a delicacy for Glottalphibs and other amphibian species.

**Einblatz/Docker** A small corporation that specialized in droid auditory sensors.

**Eirriss, Cesi "Doc"** A Twi'lek Rebel X-wing pilot, she went by the designation Red Four. Doc died, shot down over Commenor, just before the Battle of Yavin.

**Eirtaé** One of Queen Amidala's handmaidens. Eirtaé accompanied the Queen on her voyage from Naboo to Tatooine to Coruscant during the Trade Federation invasion of her planet.

**Eistern** A former member of Black Sword Command, he sabotaged and betrayed Nil Spaar and the Yevethan fleet at the Battle of N'zoth, allowing New Republic forces to defeat the Yevethan forces.

**Ejai, Lieutenant Colonel** One of the first Imperial officers, he served aboard a Venator Star Destroyer as the Death Star underwent construction.

**ejection seats** An emergency escape system used on small transport vehicles and most starfighters. Ejection seats relied on passengers using full environmental suits. Survival depended on a quick rescue, and the seats worked best within a planet's atmosphere.

**Ejolus** The primary planet in the Ejolus system, home to a small agrarian settlement secretly founded by survivors from Alderaan. Garil Dox, an Imperial officer unfamiliar with the nature of the settlement, ordered it destroyed by bombardment from the Star Destroyer *Reprisal.* Darth Vader revealed the residents' background to Dox, much to his horror—as he, too, was an Alderaanian native.

**Ekhrikhor** A fierce Noghri from clan Bakh'tor, he clandestinely shadowed Luke Skywalker and Han Solo as they made their way to the Emperor's secret Mount Tantiss storehouse during Grand Admiral Thrawn's attacks against the New Republic. Ekhrikhor and his band of Noghri, working at the behest of Cakhmaim, worked to clear a safe path through the wilderness that would allow the New Republic infiltrators access to the storehouse. Later, after the defeat of Thrawn, Ekhrikhor was adamant that all the treasures within the storehouse be destroyed, as they were artifacts of Palpatine's evil reign.

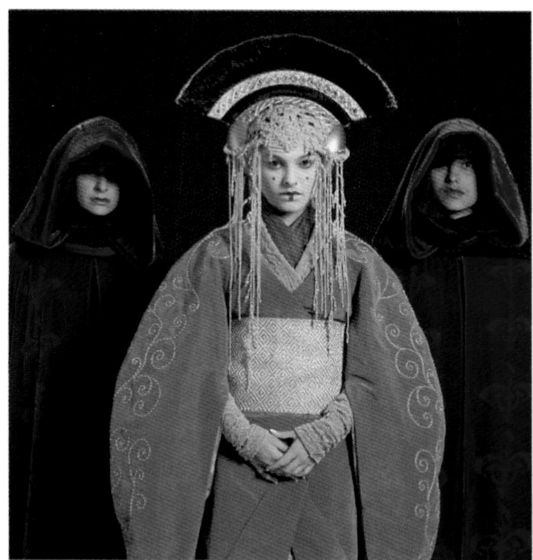
*Eirtaé (left) with Queen Amidala and another handmaiden*

**Ekibo** A Trianii colony world within the disputed border of the Corporate Sector, it was where Rangers Atuarre and Keeheen stopped a herdbeast-rustling ring.

**E'kles, Allynic** A Caamasi Jedi investigator from the golden age of the Old Republic, he had extensive knowledge of criminals and pirates of his day. His exploits and knowledge were recorded within a Jedi Holocron.

**Ekma** A Yuuzhan Vong Shamed One living beneath the surface of Coruscant after the capital world had been transformed into Yuuzhan'tar. Like other Shamed Ones, he venerated the Jedi Knights and believed them to be appropriate symbols for a new Yuuzhan Vong ideology.

**Ekria** A young Baroli Padawan during the Clone Wars, she was an expert slicer. She, along with fellow Padawans Drake Lo'gaan and Zonder, was stationed on Felucia with Jedi Knights Aayla Secura and Barriss Offee. Though the Jedi Knights were cut down by clone troopers executing Order 66, the Padawans escaped and returned to Coruscant as refugees. Ekria used her computer talents to erase all records of them from the Jedi Temple data banks. Despite attempting to lay low in the capital, the Padawan fugitives were tracked down by Darth Vader. Zonder was killed, but Ekria and Drake managed to fake their deaths to avoid further Imperial pursuit.

*Hohass "Runt" Ekwesh*

**ekster** A Corellian term describing someone who is from a planet outside the Corellian star system. The opposite of *ekster* was *enster.* Taken to an extreme by some Corellians, the term brought with it wide-ranging prejudices and restrictions.

**Ekwesh, Hohass "Runt"** A Thakwaash, he was a founding member of Wraith Squadron and flew as Wraith Six. Like others of his species, he was much stronger than a human, yet he was still considered small by Thakwaash standards. He possessed multiple personalities, which made his career as a pilot very difficult. His pilot personality was very skilled and intelligent, but when it lapsed, he would find himself disoriented and bewildered behind the controls of a starfighter.

Runt served as the squadron's physical trainer, unofficial morale officer, and communications expert.

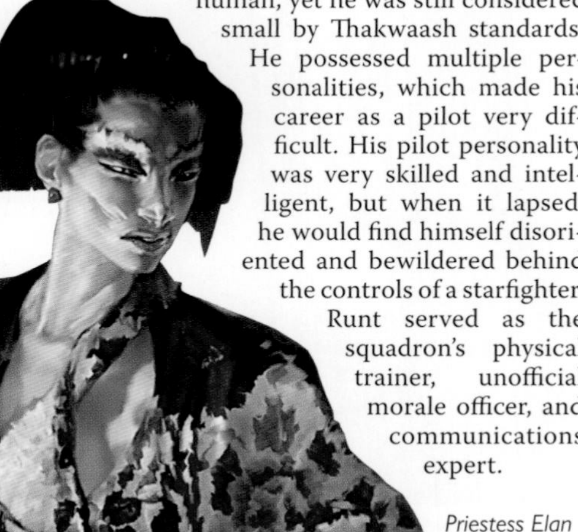

*Priestess Elan*

**El, Tomla** An Ithorian, he was the chief healer aboard the herd ship *Cloud Mother.* He worked with other New Republic scientists to discover or develop a cure for Mara Jade Skywalker's mysterious illness during the Yuuzhan Vong War. Tomla El witnessed the miracle cure found in Vergere's tears take effect. He later helped aid refugees from his sundered home planet of Ithor.

**Elan, Priestess** Considered beautiful by Yuuzhan Vong standards, she was a priestess of Yun-Harla, the Trickster goddess. Her father, Jakan, was a high priest who served as adviser to Supreme Overlord Shimrra. Elan was involved in a scheme concocted by Harrar and Nom Anor in which she would pose as a defector and insinuate her way into the trust of the New Republic. Once there, she would strike with a bo'tous biological weapon, killing as many high-ranking Jedi Knights as possible.

Fearing assassination attempts against their newfound defector, the New Republic repeatedly shuttled Elan and her familiar, the Fosh named Vergere, to different locations. With the aid of an ooglith masquer that made her appear human, Elan posed as the wife of New Republic Intelligence agent Major Showolter.

Elan had dark hair, often held back in a hair band. She covered her lean frame in long, shimmering garments. She had ice-blue eyes, a broad forehead, a cleft chin, and a broad nose.

The couple was ambushed by the Peace Brigade, who sought to take Elan and return her to the Yuuzhan Vong as a show of their loyalty. With Showolter wounded, Han Solo took custody of Elan and Vergere, but the Peace Brigade persisted. Not wanting her plan disrupted, Elan killed her Peace Brigade "rescuers" with the bo'tous weapon, an act that raised Han Solo's suspicions. When Elan tried to similarly attack Solo, he instead trapped her in the *Millennium Falcon*'s hold, where she was exposed to the toxic effects of her own biological weapon and died.

**Elarles** A cantina waiter on Circarpous V.

**Elcorth** Located in the Farlax sector of the Koornacht Cluster, it was the former site of a Morath pholikite mining operation. Twelve years after the Battle of Endor, Elcorth was brutally attacked and conquered by the alien Yevetha as part of a series of raids that the Yevetha called the Great Purge.

**Elda** An independent spacer, she ferried Obi-Wan Kenobi and Qui-Gon Jinn to Kodai during their search for Dr. Murk Lundi, and a rumored Sith Holocron, in the years prior to the Battle of Naboo.

**Eldon, Captain Darv** An Imperial Navy officer who served under Admiral Greelanx. He trained in the Imperial Academy with Soontir Fel, and the two were friends. Eldon commanded the *Carrack*-class cruiser *Vigilance* until he died in its destruction at the Battle of Nar Shaddaa.

**Ele, Jeswi** A youngling killed by Darth Vader during the attack on the Jedi Temple.

**electrobinoculars** A handheld viewing device that allowed the user to observe distant objects in a variety of lighting conditions and environments. Electrobinoculars had rudimentary computers capable of measuring an object's range, relative size, and other pertinent information, which was then projected onto the device's internal display. The computer also enhanced and sharpened the image, and adjusted for wide and zoom angles. Many electrobinoculars had dataports capable of feeding images to hologram recorders, datapads, or other recording tools. They also could be linked to blasters for long-range attacks. A small number of advanced electrobinoculars had internal hologram and visual recorders.

Electrobinoculars were sometimes confused with macrobinoculars. Generally less expensive, macrobinoculars lacked image-enhancement chips and light-adjustment circuitry. However, macrobinoculars were more durable than electrobinoculars, and their optics were much less likely to be damaged or thrown out of calibration.

*Darth Maul's electrobinoculars*

**electro-jabber** Also known as force pikes, these high-voltage prods were used for crowd control or for torture.

**electropole** A Gungan weapon very similar to a force pike, it was used to intimidate an enemy or beast rather than injure or kill.

**electrorangefinder** A device that calculated the distance between itself and a target object, it was built into distance-viewing devices as well as targeting and fire-control computers. Electrorangefinders calculated trajectories in an instant by projecting and receiving bursts of coherent light.

**electroshock net (electronet)** A electrically charged net that rendered targets unconscious.

**electrostaff** A polearm used by the IG-100 MagnaGuards that is built from phrik metal, making it impervious to the energy of a lightsaber blade.

**electrotelescope** An electro-optical device that had greater power and resolution than electrobinoculars.

**electrum** An alloy of gold and silver. Mace Windu's lightsaber handle was plated in electrum.

***Eleemosynary*** The personal Star Destroyer of Grand Admiral Teshik, disabled and captured by the Rebel Alliance following the Battle of Endor.

**"Elegance" message drone** *See* Imperial message drone.

***Elegant Interlude*** This starship, owned and operated by Danith Jalay, participated in the smuggler attack at the Battle of Nar Shaddaa.

***Elegant Wake*** A Sy Myrthian passenger liner operated by Romodi Interstellar that was attacked by Merson pirates just prior to the Clone Wars.

**Elegin, Drost** The scandal-plagued leader of House Elegin during the time of the Galactic Empire.

***Elegos A'Kla*** A New Republic *Imperial*-class Star Destroyer commissioned during the war against the Yuuzhan Vong, it was named in honor of the late Caamasi observer. It participated in the Talfaglio operation to rescue hostages held by the Yuuzhan Vong. The *Mon Mothma* and the *Elegos A'Kla* carried complements of XJ3 X-wings and Series 4 E-wings. The *Elegos A'Kla* was one of the first Star Destroyers equipped with a new form of gravity-well projector. During the Yuuzhan Vong takeover of Coruscant, the ship sustained extensive damage and underwent repairs for many months before returning to service.

**Elerion** A hot, humid Outer Rim planet known for its gambling. Leia Organa went there on an undercover mission to retrieve stolen data revealing the location of major Rebel bases. The Lucky Star casino was located in Kushal Vogh, a major gambling center on Elerion.

**Eleven, the** A resistance movement on Bellassa that quickly became known throughout the Empire during the early years of the New Order. It was established by 11 men and women—including Ferus Olin and Roan Lands—but soon grew to include hundreds in the city of Ussa and more supporters planetwide. After the arrest of Lands, the Eleven scattered, making it difficult for the Empire to track their movements, and actually making it easier for the Eleven to recruit more members.

**Eleven Elders of the People** The rulers of Emberlene society, they commissioned the creation of the Mistryl Shadow Guard. So effective were the Mistryls as warriors that their victims banded together and ravaged Emberlene, though the Eleven Elders blamed the attack on the Empire.

*Electrostaff wielded by an Ig-100 Magnaguard*

**Eleven Star Marketing** This advertising, marketing, and sales company was a nonvoting, contributing sponsor of the Corporate Sector Authority.

***Elfa*** The personal submersible craft of the Yarin harbormaster at Crystal Reef on Mon Calamari. In the Yarin language, *elfa* translated to "fish so small, it's not worth catching." The tiny submersible seated five in cramped piloting quarters. Extending from the front of the sub were a pair of clawed manipulator arms. On the side of the vessel was a hydrostatic force field that allowed occupants to easily swim to the outside. The mini sub was loaned to Ambassador Cilghal, the young Jedi Knights Jacen Solo, Jaina Solo, and Zekk, and their friend Anja Gallandro in a mission to intercept spice contraband smuggled into the icy Calamarian oceans.

**Elgrin, Tam** A young, bulky human holocam operator, he accompanied documentarian Wolam Tser to Borleias following the fall of Coruscant to the Yuuzhan Vong. Elgrin secretly worked with the treasonous New Republic Senator Viqi Shesh, staying in contact with her via a Yuuzhan Vong villip. A pain-inducing stress sensor surgically implanted on his person kept him loyal to the Yuuzhan Vong. Part of the plot was for Elgrin to befriend Danni Quee, but Quee became suspicious of him. Elgrin grew to hate what he had become, and although he stole information from Danni Quee's quarters, he was unable to kill her despite searing pain. Rendered unconscious, he was revived by Cilghal, who found a way to counter the effects of the implant. No longer under the control of the Yuuzhan Vong, Elgrin revealed the location of various listening devices he had installed, and took the young boy Tarc under his wing, teaching him the basics of holographic recording.

**Elias, Kama** A participant in the rigged Telosian gambling contest called Katharsis.

**Eliey** A code name used by Zozridor Slake to denote a key target on Praesitlyn during the Clone Wars.

**Eliior** The capital city of the planet Romin, it was surrounded by a security wall called the Cloudflower Wall that kept workers out of the main city.

**Elinda** One of the founding members of the Twisted Rancor Trio band, which performed on the planet Taris during the Jedi Civil war.

**elint mast** A nickname for an electronic interference mast, an antenna whose signals jammed communications.

**Elis** A native of Anobis, he was the leader of Anja Gallandro's mining town. He also headed a loose coalition of mining towns that formed a faction in his planet's civil war. When Han Solo tried to get the sides talking, Elis agreed to meet with Ynos under a temporary cease-fire to discuss ways to end the war.

**Eliss, Tem** This Iyra from F'tral became a prominent and respected professor at the University of Sanbra, where his lectures on alien cultures were always in demand. His manuscript, *The University of Sanbra Guide to Intelligent Life,* was written to provide cultural guidelines and to detail the goals and motivations of the species of the galaxy. The Empire attempted to halt publication of his work, and Eliss fled into hiding.

**Elite, the** One of the more luxurious hotels on Coruscant, the Elite was able to rebuild and reopen in the wake of the war against the Yuuzhan Vong. A terrorist supporting the movement for Corellian independence detonated an explosive device inside, destroying the hotel and killing hundreds of beings in a polarizing event that was covered extensively by the news media.

**Elite Circle** The ruling members of the Assassins' Guild, they were nearly exterminated by gunman Gallandro, who killed off half their number.

**Elite squadron** A squadron of TIE fighters maintained by the Thyferran Home Defense Corps, commanded by Erisi Dlarit.

**elite stormtroopers** *See* Coruscant Guard.

**Elkin** A member of Talon Karrde's smuggling organization, he worked aboard the *Starry Ice* as a gunner under the command of Shirlee Faughn.

**Ell, Najack and Silfinia** Aliases used by Jacen Solo and Lumiya when they infiltrated a meeting of the member systems of the Confederation at Gilatter VIII, some 10 years after the end of the Yuuzhan Vong War. According to their backstory, Najack (Jacen) was a native of the planet Ession attending the meeting—along with his aunt, Silfinia (Lumiya)—as a representative of the Ession Freedom Front.

**Ell, Zez-Kai** One of five Jedi Masters who survived the Jedi Civil War, he fled to Nar Shaddaa to lay low. There he was located by

*Officer Ellberger (Bravo Five)*

the Exile, who convinced him to return to Dantooine and help rebuild the Jedi Order.

**Ellberger, Officer (Bravo Five)** A member of Bravo Squadron, part of the Naboo Royal Security Force, during the Trade Federation's blockade of the Naboo system, she was originally a computer systems troubleshooter. Her years of tech experience allowed her to predict and adjust the squadron's tactics to those of the Federation's droid starfighters.

**Ellé** One of Senator Padmé Amidala's handmaidens during the years following the Battle of Geonosis. She was one of the few individuals who knew of Padmé's marriage to Anakin Skywalker.

**Elliar, Lady** The betrothed of Prince Isolder, who was murdered by order of Queen Mother Ta'a Chume before they could be married. She was drowned in a reflecting pool.

**Ellor** During Grand Admiral Thrawn's campaign to retake the Core Worlds, this Duros smuggling chief joined Talon Karrde in an alliance of smugglers to help the New Republic.

**Ellsworth** An Imperial functionary on Bakura working for Wilek Nereus during the years leading up to the Battle of Bakura.

**Elmas Private Spaceport** A government-run facility located in Coronet, Corellia, during the years following the Swarm War. Many smugglers maintained contacts within the facility in an effort to avoid the crackdowns that sometimes occurred at Port Pevaria.

*An Elom (center) aboard Jabba's sail barge*

**Elom** A cold, barren world in the Borderland Regions, it quickly joined the Rebellion to combat the tyranny of the Empire and to free itself from enslavement. During the last years of the Galactic Civil War and well into the period of the New Republic, the surface-dwelling Elomin served mostly in units of their own species. Five years after the Battle of Endor, a New Republic task force crewed by Elomin was wiped out near the Obroa-skai system when Grand Admiral Thrawn used a tactic that the Elomin were psychologically incapable of defending against. A second species, primitive cave-dwelling Eloms, coexist peacefully with the Elomin. Elom physical calculus was often used to decide the proper course of action. The planet's principal export is lommite ore.

**Elomin** Tall, thin humanoids, these inhabitants of the planet Elom had pointed ears and four horn-like protrusions emerging from the tops of their heads. Elomin admired order. They saw other species as chaotic and unpredictable, preferring to work with their own kind. At the height of the Empire, the Elomin were placed under martial law and forced to mine lommite for their Imperial masters.

**Eloms** Short, stocky bipeds, the primitive Eloms lived in cities that their ancestors carved out underneath the deserts of the planet Elom when that world's water levels dropped over a period of thousands of years. Eloms had thick, oily pelts of dark, stringy fur and tough skin covered with thick calluses on their hands and feet. Their fingers had hard, hooked claws that helped them unearth succulent roots and natural springs—something that helped them survive the wrenching climate change on their planet. They coexisted with the technologically advanced, surface-dwelling Elomin. In fact, when the Empire enslaved Elomin, some young Eloms staged raids, freeing a number of the slaves and housing them in their underground cities. Generally peaceful and quiet, with a strong sense of community, many offworld Eloms, surprisingly, had turned to criminal pursuits.

**Eloy, Dr.** A senior scientist of the Hammertong project group, he was a colleague of Dr. Kellering.

**Elrood** The site of a commercial colony and major manufacturing and trade center, Elrood was orbited by twin moons. The capital city was Elrooden, home to the famous Elrood Bazaar. The Dark Jedi Durrei, who joined with an Imperial faction in the Corva sector after the Battle of Endor, was a native of Elrood.

**Elsah'sai'Moro** A Devaronian Senator, she contacted Jedi Master T'ra Saa during the Clone Wars regarding Separatist raiders in the area and a Devaronian—Vien'sai'Malloc—who might have been involved. During her transmission, she was assassinated by Aurra Sing, who had been hired by Vien'sai'Malloc.

*Elomin*

**Elsek, Sergeant** A Kuati native, he was assigned to the biker scout unit on Endor with his partner, Avarik, with whom he graduated from the Corulag Academy. He was often forced to cover for his partner's rash decisions.

**Elshandruu Pica** The Elshandruu system included an asteroid belt that was used as a staging area by pirates. Elshandruu Pica, the planet, had two white moons and one red one. Its capital city was Picavil, located on an ocean coast. It was the site of Margath's, a hotel and casino complex that included the 27th Hour Social Club. Kina Margath, owner of the complex, was a longtime Rebel Alliance agent. The planet's Imperial Moff was Riit Jandi. Captain Sair Yonka, commander of the Star Destroyer *Avarice,* kept a 26th-floor suite at Margath's and carried on an affair with Moff Jandi's wife. Some three years after the Battle of Endor, after Rogue Squadron resigned from the New Republic military, members of the squadron intercepted Yonka at the Moff's oceanside cottage and convinced him to defect with his ship. After Director of Imperial Intelligence Ysanne Isard learned of this, she ordered Yonka's mistress killed.

**Elsinore-Cordova** A manufacturer of Podracers and Podracing engines.

**Eluthan** An ancient, walled city on Acherin, inhabited by Acherins who called themselves Eluthans. During the Clone Wars, the Acherin supported the Separatists, who established a military base within the walls of Eluthan. This led to the destruction of much of Eluthan during Imperial bombardment following the end of the Clone Wars. Furthermore, rivalry between the Eluthans and the inhabitants of the city of Sood resulted in a civil war for control of the planet's meager resources.

**EM-1271** The first star destroyed by the Socorran Triad and Centerpoint Station. Its full designation was TD-10036-EM-1271.

**Emala** A grifter and war profiteer, she was part of a trio of Squibs who gathered information about the galaxy's fringe and then sold it to New Republic Intelligence. Emala, Sligh, and Grees worked from a base on Tatooine, and were known to have extensive knowledge of that planet's deserts. They met Han Solo and Leia Organa Solo when the couple was on Tatooine trying to acquire the Alderaanian masterpiece *Killik Twilight*. After that, the Squibs decided that selling art to the Imperials was not only profitable but also an excellent way to obtain more information about Imperial activities. Following the Yuuzhan Vong invasion and the subsequent galactic reconstruction, the three Squibs established a transport operation known as Second Mistake Enterprises, and were hired by the Colony to transport spinglass sculptures to the rest of the galaxy. The Squibs were initially unaware that each sculpture contained a handful of Gorog assassin bugs. When that became known, the angered Squibs set out to make the Solo family pay for their part in exposing the assassin bugs. Under the guise of the Directors, the Squibs arranged for various assassination attempts on the lives of Han, Leia, and Jaina Solo while maintaining a war-profiteering operation as well.

***Emancipator*** Formerly the Star Destroyer *Accuser*, it was commanded by Captain Firmus Piett under the fleet leadership of Admiral Griff. Tycho Celchu served aboard the *Accuser* at the time of Alderaan's destruction. In the aftermath of the Battle of Endor, the ship was captured by Han Solo, claimed by the Alliance, and renamed the *Emancipator*. Layrn Kre'fey used it as his flagship in a bid to retake Ciutric from Prince-Admiral Krennel. It underwent extensive refitting after this operation, and returned to active duty under the command of Admiral Ragab during New Republic raids on Borleias. Under Lando Calrissian and Wedge Antilles, the *Emancipator* served valiantly during the fierce Battle of Mon Calamari. It destroyed the Imperial command ship *Allegiance*, but it in turn was consumed by the powerful *Silencer-7*, an Imperial World Devastator.

**Embassies Row** A wide avenue located within Coruscant's Dometown. The many embassies located here provided assistance to the variety of nonhuman species who lived onworld.

**Emberlene** Homeworld of the Mistryl, it was believed to have been devastated by the Empire—though no one in the galactic community seemed to care about or even notice its destruction. Jorj Car'das provided Shada D'ukal with the truth behind Emberlene's fate. During the Clone Wars, the rulers of Emberlene—the Eleven Elders—sided with the Separatists, tapping into the vast wealth of the Confederacy and allowing Emberlene to create its Mistryl Shadow Guard. The Eleven then ordered a rampage of conquest. Over three years, forces from Emberlene ravaged, conquered, and plundered a dozen worlds within their range. Their victims and potential victims pulled together their resources to hire a mercenary army that proved to be overly thorough in exacting vengeance. They decimated Emberlene, and the survivors who emerged learned a new and different history of their planet. The rulers of Emberlene spread the word that the Empire had attacked their world, and the Mistryl Shadow Guards were created to exact revenge against the New Order.

**Embrace of Pain** A gruesome Yuuzhan Vong restraint system used to control slaves, it stood over 2 meters tall and used leather-like, tentacular straps to bind the arms, legs, and torso of a captive. It then administered a constant level of pain to remind the captive that he or she was securely bound. The Embrace could vary the output of its painful stimuli in accordance to the reactions of its victim, increasing it if the subject became too accustomed to the sensation, or lowering it if the subject seemed near death. In this way, a slave could be forced quickly into submission. The Embrace of Pain also could condition a victim. In the wake of the war against the Yuuzhan Vong, only one Embrace of Pain survived. Jacen Solo kept it in a secret location and later installed it aboard the Star Destroyer *Anakin Solo*.

**Embra the Hutt** A "healthy-looking" Hutt who was a business associate of Jabba. Unlike his fellow Hutts, Embra was compassionate toward his underlings. He preferred nonviolent resolutions whenever possible. For this, he garnered strong loyalty among his subjects. When he found himself disagreeing with the way Jabba ran his businesses, he entered into a "friendly" wager with Jabba and Malta the Hutt on the effectiveness of various methods in recovering the fabled lost Yavin Vassilika. Embra hired Zuckuss, 4-LOM, and Sardu Sallowe in the hope that his sophisticated and efficient planning would win over brute force.

Years later, Embra remained in Hutt space after the Yuuzhan Vong invaded Nal Hutta, and narrowly avoided being sacrificed by the aliens. He came into the leadership of a resistance group known as the Sisar Runners, allying himself with the Galactic Alliance.

**Emente** An alien species distinguished by its six eyes, and by the fact that its diet was made up entirely of fruit. Individual Ementes were noted for their lack of trust in other beings.

**emerald shark** A large predatory fish. The Dubrillion Aquarium had some specimens of emerald sharks that Shedao Shai enjoyed watching, especially as they fed.

**Emerald Splendor Estates** Luxury condominiums and houses constructed on the planet Byss for wealthy supporters of Emperor Palpatine in the wake of the Clone Wars. Those individuals and families who agreed to move to Byss were asked to keep information about their new home a secret, ostensibly to

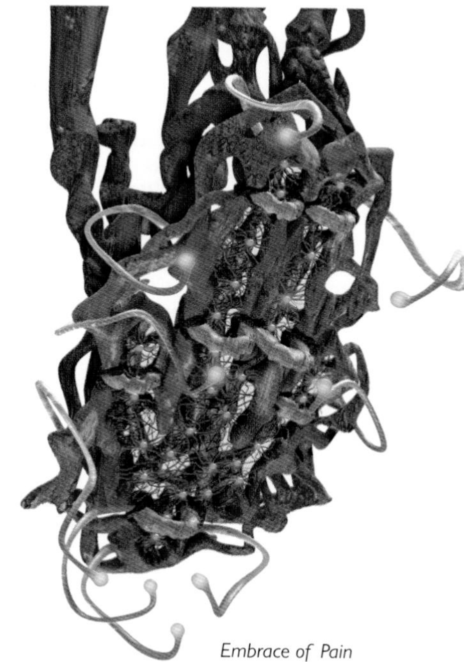

*Embrace of Pain*

keep tourists and other beings from learning its location. In truth, these early supporters would become subjects whom Palpatine "fed" off through the power of the dark side.

**Emergency Amendment 121b** Sometimes called the Reflex Amendment, this provision passed by the Galactic Senate led to an increase in Chancellor Palpatine's ability to react to the battles being fought during the Clone Wars. Ostensibly, the law gave Palpatine unprecedented control over the movement of military assets across areas of jurisdiction, shifting the responsibility for maneuvering defenses from the regional sector, or planetary governments, to Palpatine himself.

**Emergency Code 9-13** A coded distress signal that Obi-Wan Kenobi dispatched after Order 66 at the end of the Clone Wars. It was intercepted by Bail Organa aboard the *Tantive IV*.

**Emergency Measures Act** A law enacted by Galactic Alliance Chief of State Cal Omas during the war between the GA and Corellia. The act gave Omas and his immediate subordinates, Admiral Cha Niathal and Jacen Solo, the ability to do whatever was deemed necessary to ensure the safety and stability of the Galactic Alliance. Jacen Solo took advantage of the law's scope and purpose for his own schemes, although his initial action was simply an attempt to help the military. By invoking Article Five, Subsection C27, he was able to assign personnel from the Galactic Alliance Procurement Center to front-line warships, in an effort to investigate faulty service packs that had been purchased from the lowest bidder. His administrative droid HM-3 also amended the EMA to allow the Galactic Alliance Guard to detain any being—regardless of current status or position—who was deemed a threat to the security of the GA. All beings so detained were to have their assets immediately frozen, in keeping with the Treasury Orders Act.

**Emergency Powers Act** An amendment of the Galactic Republic's laws governing the Supreme Chancellor's term limitations. The passage of the Emergency Powers Act occurred shortly before the onset of the Clone Wars, when Chancellor Palpatine was nearing the end of his term. Crises on Raxus Prime and Antar 4 had caused the Galactic Senate to vote on extending Palpatine's tenure as Chancellor, in an effort to keep the Republic focused. The passage of the Emergency Powers Act maintained Palpatine in power until the Battle of Geonosis, when his tenure was once again extended after Jar Jar Binks, sitting in for Senator Padmé Amidala, put forth a motion to grant Palpatine another extension, as well as the ability to create the Grand Army of the Republic.

*Em'liy*

**emergency stud** A structural device aboard X-wing starfighters. When depressed, it set off explosive bolts that jettisoned the pilot's canopy for an emergency escape.

***Eminence*** An aging Imperial *Carrack*-class cruiser that was part of the fleet formed to protect the second Death Star during its construction in orbit around the Forest Moon of Endor. When the Alliance launched its attack on the Death Star, the *Eminence* was thrust into battle against the Dornean gunship *Braha'tok,* which had been protecting several rescue operations. Although the *Eminence* was the larger vessel, the *Braha'tok* kept it at bay long enough to ensure the safety of other rescue ships. The *Eminence* then found itself under attack from another Dornean gunship, the *Torktarak,* and was unable to fully defend itself. Under the gunships' barrage, the *Eminence* was destroyed during the Battle of Endor.

***Eminent Domiciles*** A popular holovid series during the last years of the Galactic Republic that featured the homes and estates of some of the galaxy's most prominent figures.

*Emperor Palpatine Surgical Reconstruction Center*

**Emissary, the** According to the ancient Sharu legends, the Emissary would accompany the Bearer to the Rafa system when it was time for the Mindharp to be activated.

***Emissary*-class shuttle** A diplomatic transport developed following the Battle of Ruusan, it wasn't as luxurious as a *Theta*-class shuttle, but it was simple to operate and maintain. It needed just a pilot and co-pilot, and had accommodations for up to six passengers. A Class 6 hyperdrive provided interstellar capabilities.

**Emita** This small city housed one of Chandrila's three main spaceports.

**Emkay** A heavily modified Kalibac Industries MK-09 maintenance droid during the Galactic Civil War, he had many internal modifications that allowed him to repair, pilot, and copilot most light to medium vessels, including starfighters. He was extremely jealous of other droids and itching for combat. In fact, his enthusiasm for action was so pronounced, there were discussions about tweaking his aggression circuits.

**Emlee** Jaina Solo's alias when she posed as a servant to Baroness Muehling of Kuat.

**Em'liy** The dominant species on Shalyvane, they were driven out of their cities by the Empire to facilitate the backstory of double agent Shira Brie. A disgraced people with no home and no resources to rebuild their cities, they felt undeserving of a name and simply call themselves Nomads. Generally humanoid, the Em'liy had muscular bodies and yellow-tan skin and lacked distinct facial features. They wore their fine dark hair in long topknots to show caste status and inspire fear in their enemies.

**Emperiax walking throne** Essentially an ornate seat atop a storage bay, with six long, arachnid-like legs propelling it.

**Emperor Palpatine Surgical Reconstruction Center** The rehabilitation center where Anakin Skywalker's charred, ruined body was rebuilt into the dark and armored form of Darth Vader. The medical laboratories and surgical suites occupied the crown of one of Coruscant's tallest buildings. During the procedure, the operating room was hyperbarically pressurized. Per Sidious's requests, Vader was kept awake and aware throughout the entire ordeal. The center, called the EmPal SuRecon in shorthand city-speak, was a well-armed and armored fortress and its interior was an odd mixture of modern technology and ancient Sith relics.

**Emperor's Citadel, The** A great black tower surrounded by high walls, it served as the reborn clone Emperor's fortified palace on the planet Byss. Contained within the Citadel were the Emperor's throne room, a vast cloning complex, dark side alchemical laboratories, libraries of dark side tomes, and other facilities that were all part of the Emperor's sinister plans. Within, the Emperor performed grisly experiments on all forms of life, including sentient beings, in order to expand his knowledge of the dark side; it was in the Citadel that the Emperor crafted his Imperial Sovereign Protectors and the Chrysalide rancors. In the bowels of the fortress were a number of chambers where the Emperor trained his Dark Side Adepts and a select few Inquisitors and delved deep into the secrets of Jedi and Sith holocrons. The Citadel was destroyed when Byss was blasted apart by the Galaxy Gun.

***Emperor's Disciple*** An Imperial Star Destroyer that was Grand Admiral Ishin Il-raz's flagship until shortly after the Battle of Endor. Il-raz committed suicide by flying the *Emperor's Disciple* into the heart of the Denarii Nova.

**Emperor's Eyes** Agents trained by the Prophets of the Dark Side with a great talent at seeing into the future. Among the Emperor's Eyes were Merili, and—possibly—Triclops.

**Emperor's Hand** An assassin recruited, trained, and employed by Emperor Palpatine himself. To rule the galaxy effectively, Emperor Palpatine occasionally required the removal of certain persons. The Emperor's Hands operated independently, out of devotion to the Emperor. They were the ones tasked with infiltrating the best-armed fortresses or deep into the shadows of galactic society to find their quarry. Though an Emperor's Hand might rightly have feared Palpatine's wrath, he or she often felt gratitude—or even affection—for the galaxy's sovereign. Hands enjoyed a freedom and autonomy shared by precious few in the Empire. The fact that they were murdering people to please the Emperor hardly entered into their thinking; after all, the victims were often tyrants and killers themselves.

*Emperor's Hand Mara Jade*

Each Emperor's Hand operated alone, often with the false idea that he or she was the Emperor's only assassin. They were given a great deal of support and authority, with special clearances designed to allow them access to whatever resources they needed. They rarely identified themselves as Hands, however. The Emperor preferred that they exist as rumors—mythic figures whose powers grew with each whispered story.

Because they operated alone, each Hand had a distinctly different method of achieving the Emperor's goals. Emperor's Hands included Mara Jade, Sa Cuis, Shira Brie, Arden Lyn, Maarek Stele, and Roganda Ismaren.

*Emperor's Shadow Guard*

**Emperor's Inner Circle, the** A small group of Imperial dignitaries who were allowed to confer privately with the Emperor. The Inner Circle consisted of ministers and governors who had earned Palpatine's favor. Darth Vader disdained these dignitaries. After the Battle of Endor, the Inner Circle attempted to take control of the Empire. Ysanne Isard murdered the members of the Circle and took control of the Empire for herself.

**Emperor's Reach** Agents trained by the Prophets of the Dark Side who showed great aptitude in using the Force to communicate across vast distances.

**Emperor's Retreat** Palpatine's private retreat, located near the city of Moenia on his homeworld of Naboo. Construction of the site, as well as its security, was charged to Inquisitor Loam Redge.

***Emperor's Revenge*** An Imperial Star Destroyer under the command of Carnor Jax that also served as his flagship. After the Battle of Phaeda, Jax tracked Kir Kanos to Yinchorr. There the *Emperor's Revenge* was destroyed by a booby-trapped Scimitar bomber left by Kanos.

**Emperor's Royal Guard** An elite force of bodyguards, warriors, assassins, and executioners fanatically loyal to Emperor Palpatine. Clad in crimson robes and sinister helmets, each member of the elite Royal Guard was personally selected from the ranks of only the most successful stormtroopers. Criteria for admission into the Imperial Royal Guard included size, strength, and intelligence, along with an unwavering loyalty to the Empire.

The creation of the Royal Guard was a well-kept secret in Palpatine's Empire. The group dated back to his extended term as Chancellor, when Palpatine supplemented the blue-robed Senate Guards with guards of his own, who had their own chain of command. Training for membership required a year of grueling, painful work on the planet Yinchorr. There candidates perfected the fighting art called *echani.* Failure in training often meant death. Of the more than 40 students in a given training year, only a handful survived for their final test before the Emperor himself—a battle to the death against one's own training partner.

Although trained in the use of a number of weapons, the Royal Guard typically wielded 2-meter-long force pikes. They also kept heavy blasters concealed beneath their robes and were masters of unarmed combat.

The most elite members of the Royal Guard became Imperial Sovereign Protectors, and served as Palpatine's personal bodyguards. At least one remained near the Emperor at all times. They also guarded the palaces and monasteries used by Palpatine, and protected his special clone vats on Byss. The Sovereign Protectors wore a more ceremonial version of the Royal Guard's red armor and were taught minor dark side techniques by senior Dark Side Adepts in the Emperor's service.

After the death of the resurrected Palpatine, all remaining guardsmen returned to their training center on Yinchorr to mourn the final loss of the Emperor. It was there that they learned that one of their own, Carnor Jax, had betrayed the Emperor and sabotaged his stock of clone surrogates. As the guard swore retribution, Imperial stormtroopers attacked, ordered by Jax to eliminate all traitors to the Empire. The guard were massacred except for one: Kir Kanos.

Afterward, the red robes and armor of the Royal Guard resurfaced when Imperial warlords attempted to legitimize their grabs for power with symbols of Palpatine's might, but none of these men had a fraction of the skill of a real Royal Guard. Flanking Admiral Daala, following Major Tierce, or supporting the Second Imperium's Shadow Academy, the pretenders enraged Kanos, who worked secretly behind the scenes to eliminate them.

***Emperor's Shadow*** The personal yacht of Emperor Palpatine's trusted dark side servant Jeng Droga. The vessel crash-landed into the seas of Kaal when Droga lost control following Palpatine's death at Endor.

**Emperor's Shadow Guard** A group of completely loyal soldiers created by Emperor Palpatine as a kind of special operations unit within the Royal Guard, they carried out special missions for the Emperor himself. They wore black armor and masks similar to the red uniform of the Royal Guard. Rumors abounded that the Shadow Guard was made up of corrupted Jedi Knights, but this was never proven. Those few beings who encountered a Shadow Guard and lived to tell about it described the way the Shadow Guard never spoke a word. Instead of the force pike carried by the Imperial Guard, the Shadow Guards carried a unique lightsaber pike on their missions. It was later learned that the Shadow Guards received some level of training with the Force.

**Emperor's Shield** A group of top Outer Rim TIE fighter pilots handpicked by Admiral Thrawn to protect the Emperor during his inspection of the second Death Star.

**Emperor's skyhook** This orbiting structure, tethered to the ground, hung above the capitol on Imperial Center. It had a wide terrace overlooking a large central park that contained full-sized evergreen and deciduous trees, some of which topped 30 meters.

**Emperor's Sword** A group of elite TIE fighter pilots sworn to defend the Emperor to the death. They were assigned older TIEs due to their years of experience with them. Although stationed on Coruscant, the pilots of the Emperor's Sword always traveled with the Emperor.

*Emperor's throne room in the second Death Star*

**Emperor's throne room** Every Imperial location that conceivably might have been visited by Emperor Palpatine had a throne room set aside for his use. Imperial and Super Star Destroyers and battle stations such as the Death Stars all had one. From each such room, the Emperor could monitor activity, take control of his fleet, and contemplate the dark side of the Force.

**Emperor's Way** An interstellar approach vector to the planet Naboo used by Imperial forces during the era of the New Order. Although some portions of the

Emperor's Way were considered public fly zones, the entire area was regularly patrolled by TIE fighters.

***Emperor's Wisdom*** An Imperial *Victory*-class Star Destroyer that was part of Prince-Admiral Krennel's fleet. It was destroyed by Garm Bel Iblis's battle group at Ciutric.

**EMP grenade** Nicknamed the droid-popper, this electromagnetic explosive charge was used by clone troopers to disable droids of the Confederacy during the Clone Wars.

**empion mine** A deep-space explosive that could send out a communications burst via hyperspace channel to the ship that launched it, indicating its position and its success.

Empress-*class space station*

***Empire*** The first *Imperial II*–class Star Destroyer ever built, the *Empire* was commanded by Admiral Feyet Kiez. It saw a fair amount of service during the Galactic Civil War's middle years and beyond. As a prototype, the *Empire* managed to mount far more power and shield generators than later Imperial IIs.

**Empire, the** *See* Galactic Empire.

**Empire Day** A day of celebration observing the founding of the First Galactic Empire by Palpatine.

**Empire of the Hand** A faction of the Imperial Remnant that Grand Admiral Thrawn founded on Nirauan by combining Chiss and Imperial ideologies and weaponry into a new military force. Unlike the greater Imperial Remnant or the Empire that preceded it, Thrawn's force did not discriminate against nonhumans, and its membership included a wide assortment of capable alien members. After Thrawn's death, the Empire of the Hand continued, honoring the Chiss admiral's vision. Its command mysteriously abandoned Nirauan and vanished during the Yuuzhan Vong invasion.

**Empire Reborn** A movement led by Lord Hethrir, its aim was to undermine the New Republic.

**Empire Youth** Lord Hethrir's Empire Reborn movement involved the use of these Force-sensitive children. He kept the students trained in a secret worldcraft, eliminating those who failed to measure up to strict standards of Force sensitivity by selling the castoffs into slavery.

***Empirical*** A secret research vessel used by Darth Vader to conduct dark experiments on prisoners and to study unique alien species. The mysterious ship drifted in lifeless Outer Rim systems, untraceable by even the Emperor's own spy network. The *Empirical* was staffed by an elite platoon of Imperial soldiers handpicked by Vader himself. They were trained to quickly deal with unexpected threats, and went to any lengths to prevent "specimens" from escaping alive. There were rumors of other such vessels.

***Empress*-class space station** A deployable orbital or deep-space installation used by the Empire. A central disk housed its habitable volume. From the disk, three trapezoidal launch and landing causeways extended outward. Its basic armament consisted of 10 turbolaser batteries and six laser cannons. It had enough hangar space to accommodate three squadrons of TIE starfighters.

***Empress' Diadem*** A modified Corellian YT-1210 light freighter used by Melina Carniss when she was part of Talon Karrde's organization. The disk-shaped ship had a pair of dorsal turret-mounted blaster cannons and a rear-facing ventral-mounted boxy concussion missile launch tube assembly.

**Empress Teta system** Known as the Koros system in the Deep Core before the warrior-monarch Empress Teta united its seven worlds 5,000 years before the Battle of Yavin. During the Unification Wars, Teta needed the assistance of the Jedi to help her take the last world, the pirate-infested planet of Kirrek. The Jedi Odan-Urr and Memit Nadill served as her watchmen during the conflict.

Empress Teta's descendants were the figurehead rulers of the seven mining worlds, but the true rulers of the system were the commercial mining interests. Together the Tetan royalty, wealthy mine owners, and Carbonite Guild formed the elite society. From this aristocratic fold came the Krath, which was at first a simple social club of spoiled rich children seeking rebellion. They dabbled in the lore of primitive magic, but soon were corrupted by the dark side when Satal Keto and his cousin Aleema came into contact with ancient Sith literature and artifacts. They staged a coup that toppled the Keto monarchy, placing themselves in command in events preceding the Great Sith War.

The history of the Empress Teta system was recorded in Emperor Palpatine's captured Tedryn Holocron.

**EM pulse launcher** Produced by Merr-Sonn Munitions during the Clone Wars, the EM pulse launcher was the weapon of choice for the jet troopers of the Grand Army of the Republic. A blast from an EM pulse launcher created an electromagnetic disruption that fried the delicate circuitry of most droids.

***Empyrean*** A New Republic cruiser dispatched to the Cybloc system along with the *Ithor Lady* to deal with the wildcat pirate fleet operating there in the ninth year of the New Republic. It was caught in an attack by automated needle fighters in the Drovis system, where the tiny craft forced the cruiser to retreat.

**Em Teedee** *See* M-TD.

**Emtrey (Emtreypio)** *See* M-3PO.

**En, Rii'ke** The first Jedi Knight on the scene after a Separatist transport ship crashed into Honoghr during the Clone Wars, poisoning the planet's ecosystem. He was killed by the Noghri but not before sending out a message that was intercepted by Aayla Secura, who continued his mission to collect data on the toxins unleashed on the planet.

**Enacca** A Wookiee, she served the Grand Army of the Republic as a quartermaster and mobility officer during the early stages of the Clone Wars. About a year after the Battle of Geonosis she was called upon by Kal Skirata to

Empirical

oversee the logistics of his operation to ferret out and destroy a terrorist cell on Coruscant.

**Enanrum, Kime** A renowned sculptor in the last decades of the Galactic Republic.

**Enara** A Fallanassi female, she aided in the rescue of Han Solo from the Yevethan ship *Pride of Yevetha* after he had been captured and tortured by Nil Spaar. Enara used her powers to create the illusion that prisoners who had actually escaped were still aboard the ship. After Chewbacca rescued Solo, she also created the illusion of a battered Han to trick the Yevethan leader. She remained aboard voluntarily, declining to be rescued.

**e'Naso, Bracha** A smuggler, he sold supplies to Chewbacca for use in his rescue of Han Solo during the Yevethan crisis.

**Enceri** A remote settlement on Mandalore overlooked during the Imperial occupation, it was the site of a major strike of Mandalorian iron—*beskar*—which significantly changed the economic prospects of Mandalore following the war against the Yuuzhan Vong.

Forest Moon of Endor

***Enchanter*** An oddly shaped luxury craft with a golden-hued hull, this was the private vessel of Tetan elite Satal Keto and his cousin Aleema just prior to the events of the Great Sith War.

**Enclave** A settlement established by Jedi Master Vhiin Thorla on his homeworld of Ryloth about a year before the Clone Wars. It was a refuge for Twi'leks who had been rescued from slavery. The Enclave was well hidden and consisted of a collection of natural caverns and hand-carved chambers.

**enclision grid** A security device consisting of a matrix of lasers that prevented access through a screened opening. Often, the grid was equipped with a motion sensor that kept the device off until needed. When something passed through the opening, the grid activated, ensuring the death of the trespasser, who was caught halfway through. The Imperial Dreadnaught battlemoon *Eye of Palpatine* featured enclision grids.

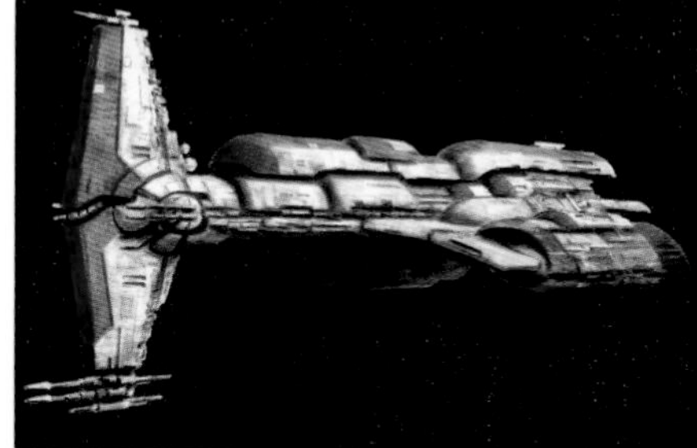

Endar Spire

***Encyclopedia Galactica*** A reference work published by Triplanetary Press.

**Endami** Proprietor of the Galaxy Grill on Coruscant a dozen years before the Battle of Naboo.

***Endar Spire*** A Republic starship used by Bastila Shan and shot down over Taris by Darth Malak's forces some 4,000 years before the Battle of Yavin. Survivors included the reformed Darth Revan, Carth Onasi, and Shan.

**endex** A military code word that, when said three times, indicates the completion of a mission or exercise.

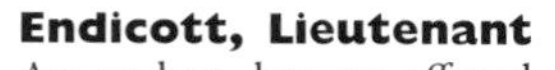

**Endicott, Lieutenant** An orphan, he was offered a docking bay officer position on the second Death Star when he graduated third in his class from the Imperial Academy at Carida.

**Endless Hour, the** A period of time on Bellassa that bridges late afternoon and early twilight. The native Ussans' workday typically ended in time to enjoy the Endless Hour with their families in parks or restaurants. When the Empire came to power over Bellassa, the Ussans curtailed these activities to remain indoors and avoid Imperial patrols.

In the Battle of Endor, the Rebel Alliance was determined to destroy the second Death Star before it could be completed.

**Endocott, Ebe** A Triffian Podracing champ who participated in the Boonta Eve Podrace that saw Anakin Skywalker win his freedom. He piloted a modified JAK Racing J930 Dash-8 Podracer.

***Endor* (1)** When Han Solo, Chewbacca, and Kyp Durron escaped from the Kessel mines in a commandeered *Lambda*-class shuttle and found themselves deposited in the supersecret Maw Installation, Solo tried to bluff his way past the Imperials, calling his ship the *Endor*. He was surprised when the Imperials did not recognize the name at all.

Ebe Endocott

***Endor* (2)** An Alliance *Corona*-class frigate that was destroyed in a collision with another frigate, *Shooting Star*, after a mistimed hyperspace jump. This accident was commonly cited by officers as an example of the dangers of hyperspace travel.

**Endor (Forest Moon)** The largest of nine moons orbiting a gas giant also known as Endor, it was covered by woodlands, savannas, and mountains. It was inhabited by a wide range of intelligent creatures, from the vicious and towering Gorax to the courageous Ewoks. Endor's trees, where the industrious Ewoks build their sprawling villages, could reach thousands of meters in height. Other life-forms included Wisties, boarwolves, Yuzzum, Teeks, yootaks, and the stranded Sanyassan Marauders.

Also know as the Sanctuary Moon, it was heavily involved in the Battle of Endor, as the Endor star system was selected as the construction site of the second Death Star battle station. It became famous as the system in which the Alliance finally won the Galactic Civil War by destroying the Death Star, killing the Emperor, and scattering the remnants of the Imperial fleet. The system was difficult to reach—the uncharted territory of the Moddell sector and the massive gravitational shadow of the gas giant required several complicated hyperspace jumps to navigate.

A cloud of dark side energy left over from the Emperor's death orbited the moon at the site of the Death Star's destruction.

**Endor, Battle of** The most decisive engagement of the Galactic Civil War, the Battle of Endor marked the beginning of the end of the Empire and the birth of the New Republic. It saw the destruction of the second Death Star battle station and the deaths of Darth Vader and Emperor Palpatine, who was later reborn as a clone.

The Rebel Alliance had learned of the secret construction of an even more powerful second Death Star and was determined to destroy it before it could be completed. Bothan spies also learned that the Emperor would pay the station

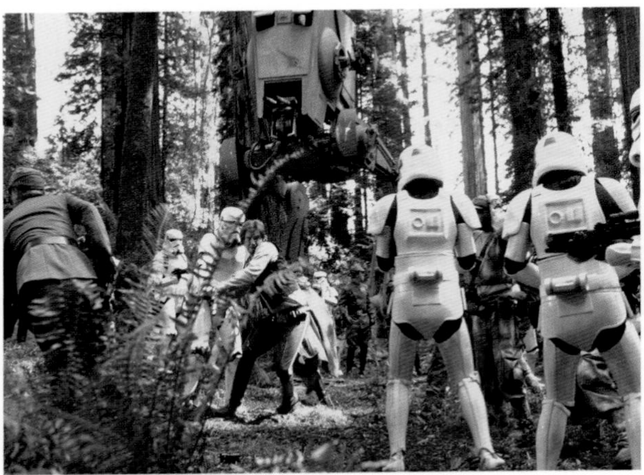
The Rebel strike team carries out its mission on Endor.

a personal visit. Both pieces of information, it turned out, had been planted by Palpatine to set a trap for the Alliance.

As Admiral Ackbar gathered the Alliance fleet around the planet Sullust, a special strike team was sent ahead to sabotage the shield generator protecting the unfinished Death Star. The team, led by Han Solo and including Luke Skywalker, Leia Organa, Chewbacca, the droids R2-D2 and C-3PO, and a squad of Rebel commandos, used a stolen Imperial shuttle to get through the Empire's forces and down to Endor's Forest Moon. The timing had to be perfect. The strike team had to disable or destroy the shield generator by the time the Rebel fleet emerged from hyperspace so that the surprise attack could begin.

But the "unfinished" Death Star in fact had a fully operational superlaser. And a full legion of stormtroopers and other Imperial soldiers were waiting to defend the shield generator and capture the Rebel commandos. While the strike team battled on Endor's moon, the Rebel fleet arrived to find the protective shield still in place.

The Emperor's plan called for the Imperial fleet to remain in reserve on the far side of the moon while TIE fighters battled the outnumbered Rebel fighters. Next, the Death Star's superlaser would vaporize all of the Alliance's capital ships. The Rebels gained some time by using the Empire's Star Destroyers as shields.

On the Forest Moon, the native Ewoks helped free the strike team, allowing it to carry out its sabotage mission. When the shield generators were destroyed, the protective shield surrounding the Death Star disappeared. Then Lando Calrissian and his starfighters moved in to attack. The *Millennium Falcon* and Wedge Antilles's X-wing flew into the unfinished Death Star's superstructure and fired proton torpedoes at the battle station's power regulator. Simultaneously, Lando Calrissian fired concussion missiles at the main reactor. The resulting explosions destroyed the Death Star. Without the Emperor, the dark side became diffused and Imperial forces were plunged into confusion. What remained of the Imperial fleet scattered.

**Endor Gate** A black hole located several light-years off the hyperspace route between Endor and Sanyassa. Since it wasn't especially large and was well charted, it didn't pose a danger to a competent starship captain. However, spacers' tales told of strange things happening on the space lanes near the Endor Gate—most notably ships found drifting whose captains swear they were traveling on the other side of the galaxy before their systems went dead.

**Endorian Port** A full-bodied sweet wine that was vinted on the Forest Moon of Endor during the second decade of the New Republic.

**Endregaad** An arid planet in the Joxin system of the Tion Cluster regarded as a backrocket corner of the galaxy. Its population traded in local animal products and geodes. Tel Bollin was its only major city. Endregaad was the site of an epidemic referred to as the Endregaad Plague.

***Endurance*** A carrier in the New Republic's Fifth Fleet, it was destroyed at Orinda by a Super Star Destroyer when all starfighters were kept in the launch bay until the last possible minute, making them susceptible to a devastating attack.

**Enemy Eradication Order of Coruscant** One of the first laws passed by Emperor Palpatine after he established the Galactic Empire, it targeted suspected enemies of the New Order based on activities and allegiances exhibited in the time of the Galactic Republic. These beings were placed under surveillance, and were required to check in periodically with an Imperial officer. They soon began to disappear, either arrested or otherwise eliminated for sedition. Those wishing to avoid such a fate fled into the undercity of Coruscant, joining the Erased—citizens who had removed all record of themselves from the Empire's data banks.

**energy ball** Nicknamed boomas, these explosive spheres were developed by Gungans for large-scale battles. Unique weapons, they consisted of unstable and explosive plasmic energy encased in a charged organic membrane. The energy balls, which came in a range of sizes, could be hurled by catapults, cestas, or atlatls. When they impacted with a target, the energy balls exploded, releasing the strange plasmic energy. Energy balls could also overload the electrical systems of targeted vehicles and droids. Gungans transported energy balls into battle in large ammo wagons pulled by falumpasets.

Energy binders

**energy binders** A beam of energy that connected a Podracer's engines to one another. Emitted from energy binder plates, the beam could cause organic tissue to lose all feeling for several hours.

**energy cell** These rechargeable portable power sources came in a variety of sizes to fit everything from handheld weapons to arrays on capital ships.

**energy gate** A static, pre-positioned force field, it was used to regulate access routes in detention centers and other high-security areas.

**energy resonance torpedo** The weapons system at the heart of the Sun Crusher's effectiveness. Projectiles were energized through the transmitting dish and could be launched into a star to trigger a chain reaction that caused the star to go supernova, incinerating every world in its system.

**energy spider** Also called a spice spider, this was a giant arachnoid creature that tunneled its way under the alkali flats of Kessel, spinning webs throughout the rock that, when

Gungan energy balls

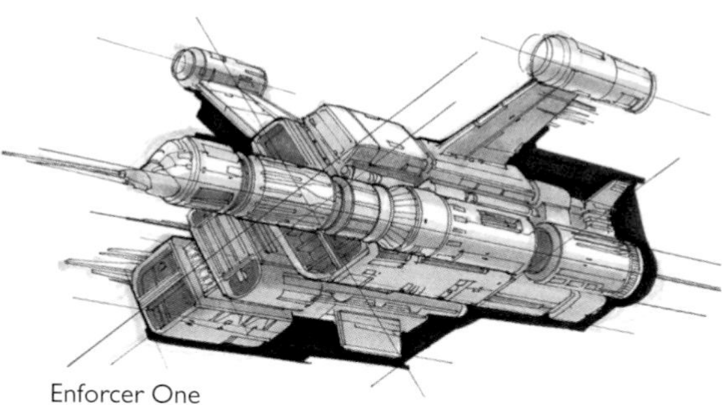

Enforcer One

mined and processed, became the addictive substance known as glitterstim spice. Energy spiders usually had more than 10 legs, although the number of limbs depended on the age of the creature. Their legs were thin and hard like crystal, shiny and translucent. Their bodies were filled with tiny pinpricks of light, and they had multiple mouths and thousands of glittering eyes that could see only in the dark. Energy spiders fed primarily on creatures known colloquially as bogeys. The bogey's phosphorescence lent a blue photoactive nature to the black glitterstim strands the spider produced. The web material was also crystalline and extremely sharp. If not handled properly, it could cut deep into tender flesh.

**energy trap** A concentration of dark side energy created by the Sith that was nearly invisible to the naked eye and could immobilize a Jedi Knight who stepped into it. Only those Jedi Masters who managed to dedicate their complete concentration to escaping the trap could break free. Because of this, many Sith left energy traps just outside areas where they could ambush Jedi, forcing a captured being to choose between utter withdrawal and useless thrashing in order to break free.

**Enfield, Sergeant Major** The commander of a platoon of Death Star troopers, he maintained security around the detention block area. He often served as Lieutenant Shann Childsen's attaché.

***Enforcer One*** The flagship of Great Bogga the Hutt's space fleet, it was responsible for many of his greatest victories, including the capture of Finhead Stonebone's pirate ships. *Enforcer One* was commanded by Captain Norufu, a near-human slave, and its home port was Bogga's palace on Taboon's moon. The ship was a heavily modified military Dreadnaught designed for planetary occupations. Bogga got it after it was decommissioned by the Old Republic, but its weapons and shields were still powerful. The main weapon was a fixed, heavy turbolaser.

**Engh, First Administrator Nanaod** A New Republic minister, he urged Chief of State Leia Organa Solo to engage in some public relations to buff up her image a bit, a suggestion that she reluctantly accepted.

**Engira** Following the raid on an Imperial replenishment convoy outside Engira, the Imperial Commission on the Conduct of the War recommended the implementation of escort frigates.

**Engret** A boy who was part of a group of infiltrators on Orron III in the Corporate Sector, Engret and his companions sought information at the Authority Data Center to learn the location of political prisoners being held by the Corporate Sector Authority.

**enhanced human** Humans who had been biologically and surgically changed to be larger and stronger than regular humans. Those in the service of the Empire Reborn movement were most likely products of Lord Hethrir's experimentation.

**Enhanced Security and Enforcement Act** A Galactic Senate measure passed during the Clone Wars that allowed the Chancellor's Office unrestricted use of observation droids and searches and seizures without the need for warrants or due process. Senators Bail Organa and Padmé Amidala opposed this act.

**Eniknar** Security chief aboard the Esfandia Long-Range Communications Base, this Noghri sacrificed himself by detonating a series of bombs to destroy attacking Yuuzhan Vong warriors who threatened the base.

**Enisca** A planet sympathetic to the fledgling Rebel Alliance in the early years of the Galactic Empire.

**Enjikket** A young Jawa, nephew of Dathcha, who helped capture R2-D2 in his first scrap hunt.

**Ennth** A planet racked by natural disaster and home to a stubborn and doomed colony of offworlders. Every eight years, triggered by the gravitative pull of its single, large moon, the planet would suffer cataclysmic groundquakes, hurricanes, and tidal waves, destroying the surface settlements as the colonists used their short-range craft to travel into orbit. After the land settled, Ennth's surface would become very fertile, enriched by volcanic ash. The colonists returned to the surface to rebuild, replant, and resettle their world. The Jedi Knight Zekk hailed from Ennth.

**E'noro, Senator** A Bith politician, she represented her people in the New Republic Senate during the Yuuzhan Vong invasion. She was the head of the Senate's Corruption Panel, and relieved Senator Viqi Shesh of her duties when it was discovered that the Kuati representative had been aiding the Yuuzhan Vong.

**Ensa** The aging wife of Byrom, a moisture farmer on Molavar. Darca Nyl helped the couple fight off extortionists demanding tribute for local gangster Sleeth.

**Ensolica** A world of ice and tundra, it was home to a near-human culture called the Enso, who often wore specialized coolth suits to maintain a frigid body temperature when offworld.

**enster** A Corellian sociopolitical label referring to beings native to the Corellian star system. Enster traditionalists held that marriages can take place only among ensters, and those from outside the system—dubbed eksters—were forbidden to marry into an enster family.

**entechment** A process that resulted in the forced absorption of a sentient creature's life energies into power battery coils and circuitry. The Ssi-ruuk developed the technology to exploit the life energies of the lesser P'w'eck species, but soon discovered that human life energies were much more powerful. The first step of entechment involved the injection of a magnetic solution into the subject's nervous system. The activation of an electromagnetic field caused the life energy to *jump* from the subject's body into the catchment arc of a specialized chair. The process was extremely painful, and, entechment subjects had to be tightly restrained.

As the energy dissipated, the disembodied spirit of the power source developed a fatal psychosis—a slow poison of insanity that affected the powered device. The Ssi-ruuk found a way to stabilize enteched energy by using a Force-sensitive accomplice to calm the subject before entechment. Brainwashed captive Dev Sibwarra fulfilled this role, though the Ssi-ruuk hoped to capture Luke Skywalker to extend the range of their entechment power.

After the Ssi-ruuvi invasion was repelled, the entechment technology was carefully studied by scientists such as Stenna Draesinge Sha for the purposes of studying life transfer applications. Further research by the P'w'eck led to innovations that eased the strain on the enteched souls. By the time of the Yuuzhan Vong invasion, entechment was offered as a form of military service for the few who would voluntarily sacrifice their physical lives. Others, like ODT Droidworks, experimented with entechment as a possible practical means of achieving immortality by transferring living consciousnesses into human replica droid bodies.

**Entralla** A planet that was within the Velcar Free Commerce Zone in the Pentastar Alignment, it was a world of shining spaceports. Its large single moon could often be seen in its bright blue sky. Many prominent religious sects had their origin on

*Ssi-ruuvi entechment rig*

Entralla, and the planet was home to several important monasteries. Within Entralla's Nexus City starport was the famous historic district and a seedy industrial zone known as the Overhang, where little sunlight penetrated the dense buildings. After the Emperor's death at Endor, Entralla's inhabitants staged a civil uprising against the Empire, but the newly formed Pentastar Alignment installed a puppet regime. The New Republic denied a request for immediate action, so Entralla native Colonel Andrephan Stormcaller resigned his rank and formed the Red Moons, an elite mercenary group, to fight the Pentastar Alignment.

Entymal

**En'Tra'Sol** The rigid honor code adhered to by the Coynite species.

**Entymal** An alien species that made up much of the labor force on Bextar. Entymals had hardened, lanky exoskeletons of jade green and jewel-like eyes on top of their pronounced heads. Much of the Entymal worker population was female, with queens producing offspring after an elaborate mating ritual with a rare male drone. Entymals had a thin, chitinous membrane that extended from each wrist joint to the side of the abdomen. When extended, this membrane unfolded into a parawing, permitting gliding for short distance like some species of flying mammals. Entymals had reputations as excellent pilots and navigators wherever they traveled.

**enviro-suit** A type of suit worn in inhospitable planetary environments. The scientists of ExGal-4 on Belkadan wore enviro-suits when the planet became toxic from the terraforming induced by Yuuzhan Vong infiltrator Yomin Carr.

***Envoy*-class shuttle** A passenger transport manufactured by Tallaan Shipyards in the years before the Battle of Ruusan. The *Envoy*-class shuttle was capable of transporting more than 20 beings in relative comfort, and made both suborbital and interstellar journeys. The affordable ships were popular with independent merchants and wealthy adventurers, and a few found their way into military fleets during the New Sith Wars.

**Enwandung-Esterhazy, Tallisibeth (Scout)** A Jedi apprentice from Vorzyd 5 who became Padawan to Jai Maruk after winning the Apprentice Tournament during the Clone Wars. She often went by the nickname Scout. Some of the Jedi at the Temple looked down on her because she used questionable methods and lacked a deep connection to the Force. Her first assignment was to accompany Yoda to Phindar and Vjun, along with Maks Leem and her Padawan Whie Malreaux. Maruk and Leem both died at the hands of Asajj Ventress. Scout and Whie escaped Ventress on Vjun, and were eventually rescued by Obi-Wan Kenobi and Anakin Skywalker.

**Enzeen** Natives of the living planet D'vouran, these blue-skinned humanoids had needle-like spines instead of hair. They were parasites, luring visitors to D'vouran in return for sustenance from the planet itself. Like the planet, they were created by Imperial scientists. None of the Enzeen survived the destruction of D'vouran.

**enzobleach** A chemical developed for use in med centers and infirmaries to disinfect hard surfaces like floors and walls.

**Eol Sha** A volcanic world whose surface was covered with scalding geysers and bubbling lava fissures (home of the dangerous lava fireworm), it was the site of a 100-year-old mining colony. The settlement was founded to extract valuable gases from the nearby Cauldron Nebula, but when the operation failed, the colonists were forgotten. They lived on Eol Sha for generations, awaiting certain destruction because the planet's large double moon was in a rapidly decaying orbit. The colonists survived on crustacean bugdillos and edible lichens until they finally were relocated to Dantooine by the New Republic. Their peace of mind was short-lived, for Admiral Daala's fleet wiped them out as they were establishing their new home. Their former planet was presumed destroyed when all the suns in the adjacent Cauldron Nebula went nova. Gantoris, one of Luke Skywalker's Jedi academy students, was from Eol Sha.

**Eon** A brown-skinned, sharp-toothed young humanoid Jedi at Mygeeto serving with Ki-Adi-Mundi.

Qui-Gon Jinn rides an eopie on Tatooine.

**eopie** A tireless quadruped native to Tatooine capable of enduring tremendous heat and carrying heavy burdens, it served as an excellent pack animal and mount. Eopies could survive for several weeks with only minimal water. They also were surprisingly sure-footed, able to cross sand and rock without difficulty. The eopie used its flexible snout to uncover lichen growing beneath the sand. One of Tatooine's most useful indigenous creatures, the eopie provided meat, leather, and highly nutritious milk.

**Eos** A volcanic world that was the site of a secret Trade Federation droid factory destroyed by Naboo resistance fighters.

**Epicanthix** A near-human species from the Pacanth Reach. Epicanthix had long, black hair, were well-muscled, and tended to be willowy and graceful. They were very war-like in their ways.

**Eport** A massive galactic auction house in the city of Bidamount, Eport dealt in anything seen as a collectible. The auction house collected a hefty percentage from both sellers and buyers. It was said that the funding behind Eport was of a sinister nature.

**Eppon** The product of Project Starscream, a nefarious experiment undertaken by Imperial scientist Borborygmus Gog on the secluded world of Kiva. Gog worked 20 years on the bioengineered weapon, which was to be the first in a new Army of Terror.

A biological mutant, Eppon began life as an infant who appeared human in almost every way. However, as the child grew at an extremely accelerated pace, he began exhibiting offensive bioengineered features. Eppon had superhuman strength, stamina, and speed. His touch could turn the flesh of a target into a liquid-like jelly, which Eppon would absorb, sucking in the biological matter to increase his own mass and energy. Eppon could transform his limbs into gelatinous tendrils that delivered a stinging touch. The child actually had no name, but chose to call himself Eppon as a corruption of the word *weapon*—the term that Gog most often used for him.

When the Shi'ido anthropologist Mammon Hoole and his adoptive niece and nephew Tash and Zak Arranda discovered Project Starscream, they came across the infant Eppon. Not knowing Eppon's true purpose, the humans took pity on the seemingly human child. Eppon continued to grow at an alarming pace, becoming monstrous. Gog lost control of Eppon, and the mutant attacked Imperial troopers. Eppon was grievously wounded by the Dark Lord of the Sith Darth Vader. When Eppon tried to turn on his creator, Gog used a subcutaneous explosive within Eppon's skull to kill him.

**Eprill** A Chiss pilot, she was a member of the squadron assembled by Jagged Fel to reconnoiter the galaxy at large after the Yuuzhan Vong began their invasion.

**Epsilon Company** One of the first teams of clone commandos trained by Kal Skirata on Kamino during the buildup to the Clone Wars.

**EQ3** *See* Baobab, Ebenn Q3.

**Equani** An alien species known for empathic skills and resistance to the Force, distinguished by large eyes and pale fur. Their home planet, Equanus, was seared by an intense solar flare, killing off billions of their number, after which only a few hundred remained alive.

**Equator City** Formerly the capital city on Rodia, it was home to a number of seedy casinos.

**eradicator** A communications scrambler found throughout the Jedi Temple that helped protect incoming and outgoing transmissions from interception.

**Eradicator combat droid** A combat droid model built by the Colicoids before the droideka was introduced. Its sturdy wheels gave it impressive speed and maneuverability.

Erdan

**Eralam crystal** Mined on the third moon of Erai in the distant past, it was known to the Dark Lords of the Sith to produce a superior, clear-colored lightsaber beam. After the Sith bombarded the moon, the crystal became exceedingly rare.

**Erased, the** A loose confederation of Coruscant citizens who had been branded traitors and marked for death by the Empire. They gave up their official identities and wiped records clean to disappear in the undercity.

**Erdan** A towering slave who lived in Mos Espa, he was once a normal human who was chemically enlarged by his master, granting him greater strength and endurance. A black-and-white pattern on his face, created with permanent heat-bonded paint, served as a symbol of ownership.

**Eredenn** The fourth planet in the Erediss system, this partially frozen world featured huge areas of snowy fields and ice lakes. In the warm season, the snow melted away to reveal a fertile land that blossomed. Eredenn had three moons, none of which was habitable. The Galactic Republic was believed to have had a secret base of operations there, from which several military projects were run during the Clone Wars, including a powerful weapon called the Decimator.

**Erg Es 992** A star in the Meridian sector, it was orbited by the planet Cybloc and its inhabited moon, Cybloc XII.

**Ergo** An Imperial fuel station. Kyle Katarn boarded a smuggler's ship at Ergo in order to sneak his way onto the Super Star Destroyer *Executor*.

**Eriadu** A polluted factory planet and capital of the Seswenna sector, this world was a trading and governmental hub in the Outer Rim. The Eriaduans were some of the finest weapons developers in the known galaxy. They developed new blasters, armor, and helmets. The seat of power for the influential Tarkin family, Eriadu became a major front in the Clone Wars when members proved their loyalty to the Chancellor by defending their borders from Separatist attack.

***Erinnic*** An *Imperial II*–class Star Destroyer sent to protect Ord Mantell from a Yuuzhan Vong attack. The *Erinnic* was under the command of Vice Admiral Ark Poinard. It had squadrons of T-65A3 X-wings, E-wings, and TIE interceptors in its launch bays.

**Eritha** *See* Alani and Eritha.

**Er'Kit** A species of tall, thin, reptilian aliens that were native to the planet of the same name.

**Ern, Minister Ciran** A representative of Junction 5, some 13 years before the Battle of Naboo. When the existence of the Annihilator weapon was proven to be a rumor perpetuated by the Guardians and Lorian Nod, Minister Ern promised to disband the Guardians.

***Errant Venture*** Booster Terrik's Star Destroyer flagship, it was formerly known as the *Virulence*. Terrik acquired it from the New Republic following the liberation of Thyferra. Rather than allow Terrik access to a fully armed Imperial warship, the New Republic stripped it of most of its weaponry. Terrik refitted the ship's interior, transforming it into a bazaar-like mall, with food courts, conference rooms, casinos, and shopping levels. Terrik hired a repair crew of 200 Verpine technicians to upgrade the ship in a refit that took more than seven months to complete. He also hired a security crew made up of tough humans and Weequays. To differentiate his ship from other Star Destroyers, Booster had the surface hull of the *Errant Venture* painted a deep red.

When Grand Admiral Thrawn began his campaign to retake the Core five years after the Battle of Endor, Borsk Fey'lya attempted to have the *Errant Venture* reclaimed for the New Republic's fleet, but Terrik made such a request difficult due to the demands he attached to his service. Years later, during the Caamas incident, Terrik reluctantly allowed the New Republic to use his vessel in a quest for the Caamas Document, hoping to defuse a potential civil war. Booster retained the combat systems that were installed aboard the ship for this purpose.

During the Yuuzhan Vong invasion, Terrik kept the *Errant Venture* ever mobile—until he learned that his grandson, Valin Horn, was in danger of being captured by the Yuuzhan Vong on Yavin 4. Terrik rescued the Jedi students from Luke Skywalker's Jedi praxeum and kept them aboard the vessel until a new secret Jedi base could be completed on Eclipse. The Yuuzhan Vong believed the *Errant Venture* was not heavily armed and thus sent only two matalok cruisers to engage it during the evacuation of Borleias. They were surprised to find that the ship had been refitted with the *Lusankya*'s weapons. The two mataloks cruisers were quickly vaporized.

After the defeat of the Yuuzhan Vong, the *Errant Venture*'s weapons were once again downgraded, and it returned to its role as a lucrative pleasure craft for Booster Terrik.

**Errat, Mali** A Galacian elder who ran a substance analysis lab on Gala. Obi-Wan Kenobi sought his help when trying to determine whether or not Queen Veda was being poisoned.

***Errinung'ka*** One of two *Sh'ner*-class cruisers brought to Bakura by Lwothin and the P'w'eck Emancipation Movement during the Yuuzhan Vong invasion of the galaxy.

**Ervic, Seteem** A farmer on Saffalore, his landspeeder was stolen by members of the Wraith Squadron during their mission to infiltrate the Binring Biomedical facility.

**Eryon** A constellation visible from Coruscant, where it was also known as the Burning Snake.

**Erysthes** An agricultural world that was the source of chak-root.

**Esau's Ridge** A crevasse on Tholati, it was the site of a smugglers' base catering to elite veterans of the business.

**escalation** A Yuuzhan Vong ritual performed to promote a subaltern who had acted with bravery and skill, overcoming an enemy and achieving greater good. During the ritual, subalterns were forced to submit their bodies to an implanter, which cut open their shoulders and placed a piece of surge-coral at the joint. The blood that flowed from the wounds was collected and given as a sacrifice to the Yuuzhan Vong gods, and the surge-coral became a symbol of the Yuuzhan Vong's escalation. Once the ritual was over, the subalterns were promoted to a position of command and given their own ships to lead into battle.

**Escalion** The perator of Yedagon and leader of the Yedagonian Confederacy who welcomed Wedge Antilles and the pilots of Red Flight to Adumar.

**escape pod** A seemingly minor piece of equipment, rarely visible or much remarked upon, it was a technological lifeboat worth more than its weight in precious gems in an emergency. In fact, one escape pod might have saved the Rebel Alliance.

The pod itself was a space capsule used by passengers and crew to abandon capital starships or small freighters in emergencies. Pods ranged in size from small capsules barely large enough for a passenger or two, to larger lifeboats capable of carrying many. Interiors were spartan, because they were meant for only a few hours' use. Sensor systems provided atmosphere, radiation, and gravity information about the surrounding area, and there was a limited-range communications transceiver. Pods were usually stocked with about two weeks' worth of rations, and the vessel could be used as a temporary planetary shelter. They also could float through space for a limited period, awaiting rescue vehicles. Pods had simple drive systems, minimal fuel, and devices to assist in relatively soft landings on nearby planets. It was just such a simple escape pod aboard the captured Rebel Alliance ship *Tantive IV* that let droids C-3PO and R2-D2 escape an Imperial attack and carry with them the top-secret plans for the Empire's Death Star battle station.

**escape repulsorchute** An archaic parachute equipped with rudimentary repulsorlifts, this emergency device was capable of carrying one passenger and could work properly only within an atmosphere. Although in heavy use about 5,000 years before the Galactic Civil War, they soon were replaced by more reliable and functional escape pods. Jori Daragon used one to escape a stolen ore barge.

**Escarte** An asteroid mining facility belonging to the Commerce Guild. Obi-Wan Kenobi and Anakin Skywalker went there in search of Thal K'sar, the Bith artisan who had crafted Nute Gunray's mechno-chair. Aqualish, Gossam, Geonosian, and human guards patrolled Escarte. Corvettes and patrol craft were used to deter intruders approaching from space.

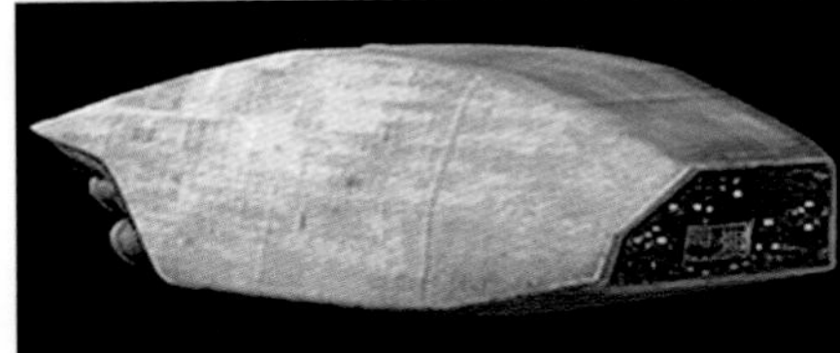
*Escort carrier*

**Eschen, Garnu Hral** A Drovian who, along with his entire family, was killed by Gopso'o tribal warriors during their generations-old feud.

**escort carrier** These 500-meter-long vessels provided TIE fighter combat support. Box-like and inelegant, escort carriers housed entire TIE fighter wings in their huge bays and transported the fighters through hyperspace. Smaller bays carried up to six shuttles or other support craft. With only 10 twin laser cannons, the carriers stayed as far from battlefronts as possible, serving mostly as refueling and supply points.

**escort frigate** *See* Nebulon-B escort frigate.

**Esfandia** A free-floating rogue planetoid with an environment of chilled liquid methane and nitrogen, this world was the site of a HoloNet relay center that kept the New Republic connected with the Unknown Regions. It was targeted by the Yuuzhan Vong to deter searches for Zonama Sekot. The New Republic's communications center on Esfandia was built atop a base of refitted AT-AT walkers, letting the station roam across the surface. Esfandia was also home to a strange sentient species called the Brrbrlpp.

**Esh, Niiriit** A former Yuuzhan Vong warrior defeated in battle, she was one of the Shamed Ones living in the undercity of the Vongformed Coruscant. She was killed by Yuuzhan Vong warriors who stumbled across her heretical sect.

*Escape pod*

**Esh, Shoon-mi** A Yuuzhan Vong Shamed One, and brother to Niiriit Esh, he doubted the words of the heretical prophet Yu'shaa, thinking that the promise of salvation for the Shamed Ones was merely a ruse to move them into another form of slavery. Shoon-mi conspired to kill Yu'shaa and take his place, but he failed and was in turn killed.

**Esok** A native of the planet Mandalore, he was the leader of a group of Mandalorians who settled on the Khoonda Plains of Dantooine in the wake of the Mandalorian Wars.

**Espara, Moreem** A tall Hapan woman, she served with the Hapan Royal Guard during the years following the Swarm War. After an attempt was made by the Heritage Council to assassinate Queen Mother Tenel Ka, Espara was assigned to help Jacen Solo investigate the attempt and find the perpetrators.

**espcaf** A particularly dark, concentrated form of caf, usually consumed in small quantities.

**Espo** A slang name for the private security police employed by the Corporate Sector Authority. Espos followed no code of conduct, much less the precepts of justice, except for the edicts of the Authority. They were unquestioning bullies dressed in brown uniforms, combat armor, and black battle helmets; they were armed with blaster rifles and riot guns.

**Esral'sa'Nikto** *See* Nikto.

**Essada, Bin** The Imperial military governor presiding over the Circarpous Major star system, he was a portly man with curly black hair topped by a spiral orange pattern. The pink pupils of his eyes hinted at a not-quite-human origin.

**Esseles** Located in the Darpa sector of the Core Worlds along the Perlemian Trade Route, this planet lost territory and power in the era prior to the Clone Wars and as the Empire rose. Esseles was a warm world covered with young mountain ranges, and its 24 billion inhabitants lived in the few scattered valleys and plains. Calamar, the planet's capital city, was viewed as a center for high culture with many parks and museums. Esseles was a center for high-tech research and development, including hypernautics and advanced hyperdrive engines.

***Esseles*-class space station** An ancient design manufactured by Alderaan Royal Engineers that transformed an existing moon into a space station. Hosk Station was an example of one.

***Essence*** A popular current events discussion program originating from Eriadu during the last decades of the Galactic Republic.

**Essence Stealer** A device constructed as part of Borborygmus Gog's Project Starscream and secreted within the reconstructed Jedi library on the Nespis VIII space station. Reverse-engineered from a Ssi-ruuvi battle droid, it could capture the Force essence of a Jedi. The device was destroyed by Zak and Tash Arranda before it could be effectively tested.

**Essenton** An Imperial officer, she was captain of the Imperial Star Destroyer *Defiant* during the war against the Yuuzhan Vong.

**Ession** The site of a battle during the conflict between the New Republic and Warlord Zsinj. The Battle of Ession was a victory for the New Republic, which demolished one of Zsinj's Star Destroyers and bombed a key manufacturing plant into oblivion. Grinder and Falynn Sandskimmer of Wraith Squadron died at Ession. During the battle, Talon Squadron was avenged when Myn Donos shot down Apwar Trigit's TIE interceptor.

*Isplourrdacartha Estillo*

**Estillo, Isplourrdacartha** The full name of X-wing pilot Plourr Illo, who rarely spoke of her past as royalty. She was heiress to the throne on Eiattu VI. When Palpatine became Emperor, he subjugated Eiattu for its mineral wealth. The Priamsta, a group of nobles backed by the Empire, spearheaded a coup that deposed Plourr's father. The royal family was rounded up and killed, but Plourr and her brother Harrandatha escaped. This coincided with the appointment of a brutal Imperial Moff, Tharil Tavira, to govern the world.

Plourr left Eiattu VI and joined the Rebel Alliance, flying with Rogue Squadron on missions to Cilpar, Mrlsst, and Tatooine. Shortly after the Battle of Endor, Prince Harrandatha returned to the people of Eiattu VI, leading the People's Liberation Battalion. His forces fought those of the Priamsta. The Grand Duke Gror Pernon came to Rogue Squadron, seeking the one person who could unite the warring fronts—the warrior princess of Rogue Squadron, Plourr Illo. Upon returning to her homeworld, Plourr was reunited with her betrothed, Count Rial Pernon, a member of the Priamsta.

Although the Priamsta were definitely not to be trusted, Plourr could not ally herself with the PLB—for she alone knew the secret of its leadership. Prince Harrandatha was not who he appeared to be. Plourr had a long-kept secret: On the night her parents and two sisters were killed, she had been forced to kill her brother with her own hands. Plourr confronted the imposter Harrandatha at gunpoint, demanding to know his true identity, and revealed him to be an Imperial.

Plourr stayed behind on Eiattu as the Rogues moved on to other worlds. Before their departure, Plourr named Rogue Squadron honorary citizens of Eiattu. She married, but Plourr was hardly one to settle down. She continued to fly with Rogue Squadron for a time, though her X-wing was repainted with the purple-and-gold colors of Eiattu.

**Estillo, Prince Harrandatha** The only male heir to the Eiattu throne, he lived in the palatial estate with his parents and three sisters. Royal medics and geneticists worked to prevent congenital defects from affecting the royal bloodline, and Prince Harrandatha was a by-product of such tampering, resulting in an evil streak that delighted in the suffering of small animals. The young prince's psychosis was kept a royal secret. His eldest sister, Isplourrdacartha, was particularly disturbed by her brother's actions. Harrandatha idealized Lord Darth Vader and was a devout admirer of the Empire and its methods. Harrandatha even got to meet Lord Vader, and the Dark Lord gave the young prince a gift—an engraved ring.

Eiattu VI erupted in violence; nobles backed by the Empire raided the palace and killed the royal family. Plourr and her brother escaped that night, but Harrandatha slowed Plourr's escape, dragging her back and calling for the Imperials to cut his treacherous sister's throat. Plourr stopped Harrandatha the only way she could: She picked up a nearby rock and clubbed her brother to death. Leaving Harrandatha's body in the woods, Plourr fled, keeping the death of her brother a secret for over a decade.

Years later, someone claiming to be Prince Harrandatha returned to Eiattu VI. He took command of the People's Liberation Battalion, a group dedicated to overthrowing the ruling Priamsta nobles. Harrandatha was in truth an impostor and secret lover of the current Imperial Moff. Harrandatha truly believed he was the real prince, the result of brain reprogramming somehow sustained by the ring he wore. Plourr was forced to shoot the impostor, destroying Harrandatha's hand, ending the hold the ring had on him.

**Estornii, Senator Eeusu** A Senator from Ord Zeuol who attended Padmé Amidala's funeral on Naboo.

**Estosh** A Vagaari who disguised himself as a Geroon during the operation to recover *Outbound Flight*. Estosh was the Supreme Commander of the Vagaari forces that attempted to steal a Dreadnaught from *Outbound Flight* to obtain droid technology for use in war. When confronted by Luke Skywalker and Mara Jade Skywalker, he revealed his desperate and malevolent intent by spraying a pale green corrosive poison from hidden sleeve canisters. Luke sliced the canisters and Mara breached the ship's viewscreen, causing the poison and all the oxygen in the room to be sucked into space. Estosh was killed by his own trap.

**Estral** An Etti gamemaster working for Jabba the Hutt in the Mos Espa Grand Arena.

**Eta-2 *Actis* interceptor (Jedi starfighter)** The forked starfighter model that began to replace the arrowhead-shaped Delta-7 fighters used by the Jedi Knights during the Clone Wars. Designers at Kuat Systems Engineering closely examined the refinements Anakin Skywalker had made to create the next-generation fighter. This new model was much more compact, cutting away a large portion of the forward spaceframe to incorporate a forked front bracketing a bulbous cockpit pod. Lining the inner edges of the ship's "tines" were powerful long-barreled laser cannons. The ship also had secondary cannons recessed on the outer edge of each tine. A full-sized astromech rested within a spring-loaded socket on the port wing, and the craft's wingtips could fold open, revealing hexagonal panels when the ship entered combat mode. The hexagonal wings and the spoke-windowed cockpit were strong indicators

*Eta-2* Actis *interceptor (Jedi starfighter)*

of future starfighter designs to be adopted by the galactic government. This new model also lacked a hyperdrive, so it, too, had to rely on a hyperspace transport ring to achieve superluminal velocities. During the war, bigger, more robust rings were used, with multiple lightspeed engines increasing the vessels' speed and range.

**Eta-5 interceptor** Small starfighters produced for Luke Skywalker's Jedi Order by Kuat Drive Yards following the Yuuzhan Vong invasion of the galaxy. They drew on the designs of the Eta-2 *Actis* interceptors that were developed during the Clone Wars.

**Ethda, Zee** A fanged bounty hunter who served Grappa the Hutt after the Battle of Endor. Under orders from the Hutt, Ethda was to recover Tarrant Snil, a lowly customs officer. Ethda failed in his mission, and Grappa punished him by feeding him to a ravenous pet.

***Etherhawk*** A New Republic *Marauder*-class corvette that was part of the fleet assigned to Han Solo and the *Mon Remonda* during the hunt for Warlord Zsinj.

***Etherway*** A battered and decrepit ship in Talon Karrde's fleet. Though not the best-armed ships of Karrde's fleet, the *Idiot's Array,* the *Demise,* and the *Etherway* were the only ones fast enough to keep up with the *Wild Karrde.* The ship was impounded by local authorities on Abregado-rae five years after the Battle of Endor. Aves piloted the *Etherway* during the final Battle of Bilbringi. The *Etherway*'s power grid was taken down during the battle with Yuuzhan Vong destroyer analogs at Yavin 4.

**E'thinaa** A Ssi-ruuvi general who conspired with Molierre Cundertol for a second invasion

*Eugroothwa*

*EV-9D9 (Eve-Ninedenine)*

of Bakura, he was in truth a Yuuzhan Vong in disguise.

**ethmane** A dense gas found on a few moons and planets throughout the galaxy. When it liquefied and froze at low temperatures, it created huge, intricate crystals that were considered among the galaxy's most beautiful natural forms. The tiny moon of Kr was covered with ethmane jungles. Ethmane was also known for its ability to block or absorb sensor systems.

**Etima, Lumas** A human male Jedi Padawan present at the arena battle on Geonosis that started the Clone Wars.

**Ettam** A city on Ralltiir with farms that supplied the Empire, it was the suspected site of Rebel activity.

**Ettarue Arm** One of the many arms that spiraled out from the center core of the galaxy.

**Ettene, Everen** A Jedi Master, and part of the team dispatched to resolve the growing conflict between the Virgillian Free Alignment and Virgillian Aristocracy shortly before the Clone Wars. It was widely reported that the four Jedi were killed in an explosion upon arrival, though Ettene's Padawan, Halagad Ventor, was known to have survived the mission.

**Etti IV** A wealthy and hospitable planet in the Etti system, it took advantage of its position on a major trade route within Corporate Sector space. Etti IV had moss-covered plains and shallow saline seas. It was home to many affluent and influential Corporate Sector Authority executives as well as a thriving criminal underworld. The planet had no exportable resources, so it relied on its natural beauty and prime location to attract visitors and traders.

**Ettyk, Halla** Originally a prosecutor from Alderaan, she became a valued member of General Cracken's counterintelligence staff when she joined the Rebel Alliance. Chosen to prosecute Tycho Celchu for the crimes of treason and murder, Halla Ettyk was completely convinced of his guilt, although haunted by Rogue Squadron's faith in their former operations chief. Determined to discover the truth at all cost, she enlisted the aid of Iella Wessiri.

**Etyyy** A Wookiee name for a place that most offworlders simply called the Rodian Hunting Grounds, it was southeast from the central city of Kachirho. On Rodia, Rodians evolved as hunters, driving much of the wildlife on their own planet to extinction. On Kashyyyk, Rodian power brokers set up shop and often held private contests for those hunters and travelers they deemed worthy.

**Euceron** A planet at the rim of the Galactic Core, the site of the Galactic Games four years prior to the Clone Wars. Euceron was ruled by 10 regents and strove for more influence in the Galactic Senate. On Euceron there were no natural stone materials suitable for construction, which was why most buildings there were made of plastoid materials. Euceron was also the name of the native species of the planet. During the Clone Wars, Jedi Master Tholme was dispatched there to mediate a dispute.

**Eugroothwa** A Wookiee warrior who served as a catamaran gunner during the Clone Wars.

**Eusebus** The capital city of the planet Euceron.

**EV-9D9 (Eve-Ninedenine)** A thin, gunnite-colored droid with a female voice, she had a sadistic demeanor perfectly suited for her job: supervisor of cyborg operations for the even more sadistic crime lord Jabba the Hutt. Previously, she had destroyed a number of droids on Cloud City; she eventually escaped, nearly destroying the city as she did so. In her position with Jabba, EV-9D9 oversaw all droids working at the Hutt's desert palace on Tatooine, apparently taking great delight in torturing or mutilating any of her charges. EV-9D9 believed it was her duty to work other droids until they dropped, as many of them did. After Jabba's death, she was tracked down and destroyed by the droid 1-2:4C:4-1 (Wuntoo Forcee Forwun) as revenge for the damage she had done to his counterparts on Cloud City.

**EV-9D9.2 (Eve-Ninedeninetwo)** Head of cyborg operations and retraining at the droid manufacturing facility Telti, she was the successor to Eve-Ninedenine. Said to be twice as ruthless as her predecessor, EV-9D9.2 set about torturing Cole Fardreamer upon his capture on Telti. Once R2-D2 and C-3PO shut down all the droids on Telti, the astromech dismantled all of the torture appliances and instrumentation of EV-9D9.2.

Evan

**Evan** A young farm boy on Garqi orphaned by the Clone Wars, he was discovered in a devastated building during a search by Aiwha Squad. His parents were collateral damage of a Republic bombing campaign. Aiwha Squad delivered him to a refugee camp when Order 66 was executed. Evan witnessed the clones gunning down General Traavis.

**Evan-Ott** The Padawan of Sora Mobari, he betrayed his Master and died in the explosion that took her sight during the Clone Wars.

***Evanrue*** A New Republic escort frigate that sustained severe damage after colliding with a cloaked asteroid during Grand Admiral Thrawn's siege of Coruscant.

**Evar Orbus and His Galactic Wailers** The original name of the Max Rebo Band, founded by Evar Orbus.

**Evax** An Imperial Intelligence officer with a track record for predicting Rebel fleet movements, his coordination of starship maneuvers saved many vulnerable bases. Evax was killed aboard the Death Star when it was destroyed in the Battle of Yavin.

**Evazan, Dr.** A truly mad doctor who teamed with the smuggler Ponda Baba, he was fond of practicing what he called "creative surgery." He liked to disassemble body parts and put them back together in different ways—on living creatures. He was institutionalized by the Empire but escaped and acquired a forged surgical license that he took from star system to star system, butchering hundreds of patients along the way. Among his aliases were Dr. Cornelius and Dr. Roofoo, and he was often referred to as Dr. Death.

More than a dozen systems issued a death sentence for Evazan, and victims staked a large bounty for his capture. Bounty hunter Jodo Kast almost trapped him, heavily scarring Evazan's face with a blaster shot, but the doctor escaped with the help of Ponda Baba. The two became partners in crime, which included spice smuggling for Jabba the Hutt.

That's how they ended up at the Mos Eisley cantina on Tatooine. A young Luke Skywalker entered, and a drunk Baba shoved him. Luke tried to calm Baba, but Evazan threatened the boy, boasting to Luke about his death sentences in 12 systems. "I'll be careful," Luke said. "You'll be dead," Evazan snarled, not noticing the approach of Ben Kenobi, who tried to defuse the situation. When they attacked anyway, Kenobi used his lightsaber to slice Evazan's chest and cut off Baba's right arm at the elbow.

The two fled the planet. At one point Evazan tried to graft a bionic arm onto Baba, but he botched the surgery. The two had a falling-out, then hooked up again and went to Baba's home planet, Ando, where Evazan resumed his bizarre medical experiments. In a complex turn of events, the insane pseudodoctor managed to transfer the brain of one of the planet's Senators into Baba's body, killing the criminal and barely escaping with his own life in a thermal detonation. Boba Fett finally caught up with Evazan, apparently killing him on a planet where the doctor was conducting experiments to bring the dead back to life.

**EverAlert** A variant of the YVH droids produced by Justice Systems during the years following the Yuuzhan Vong invasion.

***Eviscerator*** During the Battle of Brentaal, the 181st Imperial Fighter Group was stationed aboard this ship, an Imperial II Star Destroyer that later patrolled the Mirit, Pyria, and Venjagga systems.

**Evocar** *See* Nal Hutta.

**Evocii** The original humanoid inhabitants of Nal Hutta, before the Hutt colonization of the planet millennia ago. The Evocii called their large, rain-forest-covered world Evocar. Independent of the galaxy around them, they developed a feudal state of technology and society. Then the Hutts came, trading modern technology for real estate. The Evocii never suspected that the newcomers were buying the world from under them. The Hutts began the long process of building over the Evocii settlements. When the Republic emerged, the Evocii appealed to the galactic government, but Hutt contracts were remarkably devoid of loopholes. As the Hutts began dominating the renamed world of Nal Hutta, the orbiting moon of Nar Shaddaa was deeded over to the Evocii. This was a calculated move by the Hutts to keep the Evocii insystem as a source of cheap labor. Soon the Hutts began taking Nar Shaddaa as well, turning it into the city-covered Smugglers' Moon. The Evocii became all but extinct. Far beneath the tall spires of Nar Shaddaa, the sad, mutated descendants of the Evocii dwelled.

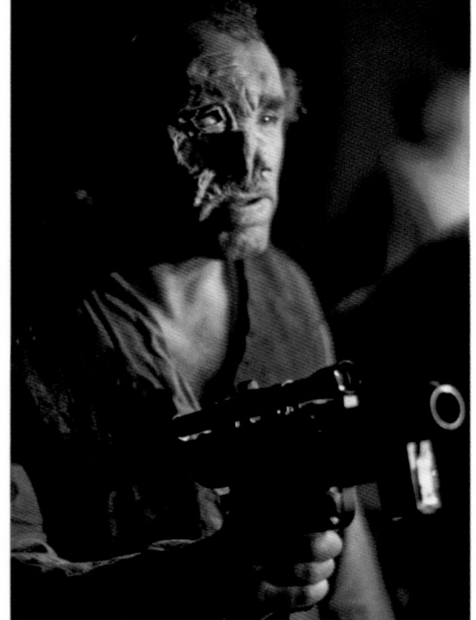

Dr. Evazan

**Evona** According to Hutt legend, this was the companion star to Ardos in their home system of Varl. The two were more than suns—they were lovers. These gods ruled the system in peace, until the fateful day Evona was lured into a collision with a tiny black hole, and was destroyed. The other planets mourned her death by colliding violently, crushing one another into asteroids, many of which crashed into Varl's surface. Ardos, in agony over the loss of his lover and his children, began to self-destruct. He cast off his gaseous shell, searing Varl in the process. Eventually, Ardos condensed into the white dwarf he is today, a star and god not worthy of the Hutts' respect.

**Evo the Blue** The blond-haired Rodian leader of the Cairn Clan after the Battle of Naboo. In the battle with the Reeven Clan, Evo the Blue rode a large personal speeder into battle. He died when the Feeorin mercenary Nym dropped a thermal detonator in the middle of the battlefield.

**EVS construction droid** A huge and complex factory on wheels or articulated legs, it both demolished and rebuilt structures. Such droids could tear down condemned buildings and shovel debris into vast internal furnaces, where useful items were extracted and recycled. A corresponding factory extruded new girders and transparisteel sheets. The droid assembled new buildings from preprogrammed blueprints. During the New Republic's capture of Coruscant, members of Rogue Squadron hijacked unit EVS-469, which eventually allowed them to bring down the planet's shields.

**EV supervisor droid** Spindly droids from MerenData designed to oversee other droid workers, report production problems, and maintain a safe and efficient working environment. Many MerenData EV supervisor

E-Web repeating blaster

droids were erroneously given the sick, sadistic personalities of professional torturers.

**Ewane** A Worker leader on New Apsolon who was elected after a lengthy civil war during which he spent many years as a prisoner. He was determined to make New Apsolon a better place for his twin daughters, Eritha and Alani. Ewane ruled for five years as Supreme Governor, but upon reelection was assassinated. Obi-Wan Kenobi and Qui-Gon Jinn investigated the death.

**E-Web repeating blaster** An incredibly powerful tripod-mounted blaster that required a lengthy setup time and two gunners to operate effectively, but could generate devastating ground fire during infantry combat. The E-Web was used extensively by snowtroopers at the Batte of Hoth. It had an optimum range of 200 meters and a maximum range of 0.5 kilometer. Its blasts were strong enough to penetrate the armored plating on snowspeeders and similar craft. The E-Web's crew consisted of a gunner and a technician responsible for monitoring the Eksoan Class-4T3 power generator. Because the generator was prone to overheating, the weapon also had to be fitted with a Ck3 Cryocooler cooling unit for continuous firing capability. An advanced computerized fire-control and targeting system incorporated Starvision and infrared low-light enhancement modules for use in night combat. Other features on the E-Web included a built-in long-range comlink with an automatic encryption module for secured communications with other units. The BlasTech E-Web spawned several upgrades, such as the E-Web(15) and the F-Web, and copycat models like Merr-Sonn's EWHB-10. The E-Web(15) had a much shorter setup time than its predecessor, while the F-Web boasted a personal shield generator.

E-wing starfighter

**E-Web turret** A custom modification of the standard E-Web heavy repeating blaster, it could be used to fire a wide variety of anti-personnel rockets and ground-to-air missiles.

**E-wing starfighter** An addition to the New Republic starfighter fleet, it was introduced during Grand Admiral Thrawn's reign of terror. The E-wing was a product of the same designers who developed the X-wing starfighter for Incom Corporation. It was built to protect convoys from raiding missions, so it had respectable speed. But its most impressive attribute was increased firepower, mainly its triple laser cannons and 16 proton torpedoes. A single pilot controlled the craft and its advanced armament, and the R7 series astromech droid provided systems assistance.

An Ewok village at night

**Ewoks** Primitive, furry two-legged creatures, these natives of Endor's Forest Moon were among the greatest heroes of the crucial Battle of Endor in the Galactic Civil War. Only about 1 meter tall, these straightforward, even simple creatures possessed the antithesis of a high-technology culture. They were tribal and used bows and arrows, slingshots, and catapults as primary weapons. But their intense teamwork and keen understanding of their environment and how to work with it to their best advantage gave Ewoks acumen and skills that couldn't be equaled, even by members of the most technically advanced societies.

The Ewoks' language was liquid and expressive, and other species found it fairly easy to speak Ewokese. A number of Ewoks sprinkled some Basic into their own vocabularies. Most were hunters and gatherers who lived in clustered villages built high in hardy, long-lived conifer trees, or lifetrees. Ewok religion centered on these giant trees, which legends referred to as guardian spirits. Each village planted a new seedling for each Ewok baby born and nurtured it as it grew. Throughout their lives, each Ewok was linked to his or her totem tree; when they died, Ewoks believed that their spirits went to live in their special trees. Village shamans communicated with the oldest and wisest trees in times of crisis. From a lifetree's bark, Ewoks distilled a natural insect repellent. From fallen trees they made weapons, clothing, furniture, and cooking implements.

During the day, Ewoks descended from their high huts to hunt and forage on the forest floor. At night, they left the forest to huge carnivores. Ewoks were curious and frequently got into trouble by being too nosy. They also loved to hear and tell stories and were very musical; they especially enjoyed communal singing and dancing. And they were inventive, using natural materials to build everything from waterwheels to flying wings.

Ewoks

At first glance, the Ewoks seemed timid both because of their size and because they were easily startled. But these brave, alert, and loyal beings were fierce warriors when necessary. The Empire dismissed them as inconsequential—not worthy of annihilating—when it was building the second Death Star battle station near Endor's Forest Moon. The moon was the site of a shield generator that protected the Death Star during its construction. But one tribe befriended Princess Leia Organa and her companions in the Rebel strike force. With the help the tribe provided, the strike force was able to disable the shield generator, allowing the Alliance fleet to directly attack and destroy the battle station.

***Exactor*** The second *Imperator*-class Star Destroyer developed in the wake of the Clone Wars, it served as Darth Vader's flagship.

**Excarga** Home to several profitable ore-processing corporations, the planet was fined by the Mining Guild for doctoring its accounting records when a shortfall of over 200 million tons of doonium was discovered. The Separatists attacked Excarga for supplies during the Clone Wars. During the Galactic Civil War, planet inhabitants made sizable profits supplying the Rebel Alliance with materials. Drextar Pym, a New Republic Senator from Excarga, was head of the panel that prosecuted former Imperials for their war crimes.

**Exchange, the** The criminal organization of Davik Kang, based on the planet Taris during the Jedi Civil War. The Exchange was perhaps the most powerful crime syndicate in the Outer Rim Territories at the time, and was under the control of a being known only as the Compeer. This being was later revealed to be G0-T0.

**Executioner's Row** A slum at the edge of the town of Dying Slowly on the planet Jubilar. It was in a warehouse there that bounty hunter Boba Fett killed spice trader Hallolar Voors.

***Executor*** The first of a new generation of immense warships, lending its name to the *Executor*-class Star Dreadnaught. Its immense 19-kilometer length and incredible destructive power led many to borrow superlatives popularized during the Clone Wars and simply call it a *Super*-class Star Destroyer, though this was by no means an official label. Constructed in secret at the starship yards of Fondor, the *Executor* was a crowning achievement for both the Imperial Navy and Kuat Drive Yards. During its construction phase, the whole operation was under the command of Admiral Griff.

The *Executor*'s maiden voyage was both a military mission and a political one. It was a demonstration to the Rebellion and the galaxy that the Alliance's success over the Death Star had been pure chance. This new weapon, of which there would be many, would be unstoppable. Once leaving dry dock at Fondor, the *Executor* destroyed the Rebel outpost at Laakteen Depot. The warship then set forth to Yavin 4, where the Rebels were in the midst of a rushed evacuation. The use of rare power gems allowed several Rebel ships to penetrate the *Executor*'s shields and momentarily cripple the craft. During the mass exodus from Yavin to Hoth, Admiral Griff miscalculated his task force's hyperspace jump, bringing the three Destroyers out on top of the *Executor*. The angle and shielding were sufficient to protect the Super Star Destroyer, but the other three vessels were annihilated.

The surface of the *Executor* was dotted with all sorts of weaponry, including more than 5,000 turbolasers and ion cannons. It carried wings of starfighters and two pre-assembled garrison bases ready for deployment.

This vessel led the Imperial Death Squadron after the Battle of Yavin. It also served as the command ship at the Battle of Endor. At that critical engagement, its lead officer, Admiral Piett, was tasked with preventing Alliance warships from escaping the battle. He did not expect the unorthodox Rebel strategy of engaging the Imperial fleet at point-blank range. The *Executor* was a prime target for repeated barrages from Alliance vessels, which were eventually able to penetrate its powerful bridge shields. A wayward A-wing starfighter, crippled and out of control, spun directly into the *Executor*'s bridge. Its control systems destroyed, the *Executor* was embraced by the second Death Star's gravity well, and the two collided in a colossal explosion that destroyed the flagship.

***Executrix*** The first *Imperator*-class Star Destroyer, produced in the final stages of the Clone Wars. It later served as the flagship of the fleet that subjugated Kashyyyk.

**Exelbrok** A manufacturer of Podracers and racing engines.

***EX-F*** An Imperial weapons and propulsion test bed built at the Black-15 shipyards, the Dreadnaught-scale ship was stolen by the Yevetha, refitted, and renamed the *Glory*.

**ExGal-4** An outpost of the ExGal Society located on Belkadan, an Outer Rim planet in the Dalonbian sector. Its mission was to watch the galactic rim for any signs of extragalactic activity. There were 15 members of the science team, including Danni Quee, Garth Briese, and Yomin Carr. Carr was actually a Yuuzhan Vong warrior in disguise carrying out an advance mission. He released the extremely damaging dweebit creatures into the Belkadan ecosphere, transforming the planet into a place suitable for breeding yorik coral. His other mission was to watch for the arrival of the Praetorite Vong invasion force at Vector Prime and ensure that word of this didn't reach the New Republic.

**ExGal Society** An underfunded group whose mission was to watch the galactic rim for any sign of extragalactic activity. It had bases scattered throughout the Outer Rim.

Executor

**Exhibition Day** A day when 10-year-old Jedi performed exercises while Jedi Masters watched.

**Exile, the** *See* Jedi Exile.

**Exiles, the** The name adopted by the Dark Jedi who broke away from the Jedi Order and were later defeated in the Hundred-Year Darkness, 7,000 years before the Battle of Yavin. The Exiles fled known space, arriving on the Sith homeworld of Korriban, which they conquered before founding the Sith Empire.

**Exis Station** An isolated space city that became the new

home for many of the artifacts rescued from the destruction of Ossus in the Great Sith War. Located in the Teedio system, it also served as an ion-mining and solar-flare-skimming facility. Nomi Sunrider called for a great convocation, the first in 10 years, to be held at this site. Millennia later, during the Clone Wars, Exis Station served as a Republic staging area for the Meridian sector campaigns. Eleven years after the Battle of Yavin, Tionne journeyed to Exis Station to discover what was considered by many to be the greatest collection of Jedi lore uncovered in the New Republic era.

Exis Station

**Exmoor** The Beruss clan estate, it was in Imperial City on Coruscant.

**Exocron** A remote planet hidden within the nebula of the Kathol Outback, it was settled by inhabitants of an ancient colony ship that left the Core Worlds during the days of the Old Republic. Jorj Car'das traveled to Exocron, where Aing-Tii warrior monks offered him a way to redeem his life. Years later, Lando Calrissian talked Talon Karrde into going to the Exocron system to visit Car'das.

**Exodeen** A former Imperial world, it was located in the center of what was Empire-controlled space during the Galactic Civil War. Because its species, the Exodeenians, were nonhumanoid, the planet was considered unimportant by Emperor Palpatine. Exodeenians had six arms, six legs, and six rows of uneven teeth. Exodeenian etiquette stated that a touch by another on the first arm signaled an Exodeenian to stop speaking, while a touch on the second was a challenge to fight. M'yet Luure was the Exodeenian Senator to the New Republic until she was killed in the bombing of Senate Hall.

**Exodo II** A planet with a thick, stormy atmosphere, it was covered with plains of blackened and hardened lava. Exodo II was near Odos and the Spangled Veil Nebula in the Meridian sector. Its most common life-form was the ghaswar, which burrowed into the crust and left dusty bore holes behind. Nine years after the Battle of Endor, Han Solo and Lando Calrissian came to the planet searching for any sign of Leia Organa Solo. When the Yuuzhan Vong invaded the galaxy, Exodo II was briefly defended by the Imperial Remnant before it was lost to the attackers.

**exodrive system** An uncommon external electromagnetic-propulsion system found on vehicles designed for use in hostile environments. These vehicles typically had forward mandibles that intensely irradiated the air around them, inducing ionization and making the air conductive. Paired electrodes then electrified the airstream, which was magnetically propelled toward the rear of the craft, resulting in the air literally dragging the vessel through the skies.

**exogorth** *See* space slug.

**Exozone** An insectoid bounty hunter who often worked with Boba Fett and Dengar, he helped the pair chase Han Solo and Princess Leia Organa Solo through the streets of Nar Shaddaa.

**Expansionist Period** The period of time following the discovery of hyperspace and before the formation of the Old Republic. When the Expansionist Period ended, Warlord Xim the Despot's empire stretched from the Maw cluster spinward to the Radama void.

**Expansion Region** Once a center of manufacturing and heavy industry, it started as an experiment in corporate-controlled space. When residents demanded more freedom, the Old Republic turned control over to freely elected governments. As much of the area's natural resources were depleted, the region sought to pull itself out of an economic slump by maintaining trade routes and portraying itself as an alternative to the crowded and expensive Core Worlds and Colonies regions.

***Expeditious*** An Imperial *Carrack*-class light cruiser, it was commanded by Captain Rojahn when former Corellian Security Officer Gil Bastra was held prisoner aboard the ship. He died in captivity after interrogation by Kirtan Loor.

***Exquisite Death*** A Yuuzhan Vong warship commanded by Duman Yaght. Lando Calrissian delivered Anakin Solo's strike team to the *Exquisite Death,* which—with the help of YVH S-series droids—the Jedi were able to comandeer. The Yuuzhan Vong nonetheless discovered Solo's secret mission, and allowed them to reach Myrkr to be captured. The Jedi fled the vessel in a shuttle, leaving Ulaha Kore aboard to detonate the ship.

**Exten-dee** *See* X-10D.

**Extolled, the** The name adopted by the former Shamed Ones in the wake of the Yuuzhan Vong's defeat.

**Exultation** The tlanda'Til of Ylesia kept their slaves in line with the Exultation process. To the "pilgrims," Exultation was a divine gift of rapture so powerful that it formed the center of their existence: They would do anything for a taste of that sheer overpowering pleasure. In reality, the Exultation was not a product of divinity. Rather, it was the refinement of a biological process the tlanda'Til male possessed and used to attract the female during the mating season. It involved the organic creation of a resonance frequency stimulating the brain's pleasure centers. The humming sensation was produced by air passing through the cilia in a tlanda'Til's neck pouch. The tlanda'Til combined this with a natural low-level empathic ability to create an addictive hold on the helpless slaves of Ylesia.

**E'Y-Akh Desert** An expanse on Geonosis.

**Eyan, Lieutenant Jart** A New Republic officer and Twi'lek, he was brainwashed by Warlord Zsinj to assassinate Admiral Ackbar but was stopped and killed by Voort SaBinring.

**eyeballs** A slang term that X-wing pilots used for Imperial TIE starfighters.

**eyeblaster** An alcoholic beverage enjoyed by Han Solo.

**Eyefire, Shoto** A Defel gunfighter who terrorized Horn Station, he was no match for a skilled Jedi who brought him to justice.

***Eye of Palpatine*** Emperor Palpatine ordered this giant Imperial battlemoon built 18 years before the Battle of Yavin. He had one main goal in mind for the heavily armed space station: to wipe out a Jedi enclave that had been established decades earlier in the Plawal rift on the planet Belsavis. The *Eye of Palpatine* was supposed to pick up contingents of stormtroopers who had been scattered on several planets to keep the mission secret. The ship never arrived, however, and a small backup force of TIE interceptors was quickly defeated by Belsavis's planetary defenses. The Emperor imprisoned many of those responsible for the design of the highly automated ship named for himself, and the *Eye of Palpatine* disappeared for nearly 30 years.

Some eight years after the Battle of Endor, Luke Skywalker was drawn to the battlemoon's hiding place deep within a nebulous gas cloud in the asteroid-choked Moonflower Nebula. Weakened by injuries after a direct hit on his ship, Luke and two of his Jedi students—Cray Mingla and Nichos Marr—were taken aboard a reawakened *Eye of Palpatine* as it restarted its long-ago mission. The ship was controlled by a super-sophisticated artificial intelligence known as the Will. Thirty years before, the Jedi Callista and Geith had discovered the ship and its mission and were killed trying to destroy the battlemoon. Callista's spirit was so strong, however, that it stayed alive in the ship's gunnery computers and prevented the mission from being carried out. But the Will resumed the original mission after it was reawakened by the 15-year-old son of one of Palpatine's mistresses. The boy was not only Force-sensitive but had also, years earlier, been implanted with a device that made it possible for him to control mechanicals.

Instead of contingents of stormtroopers, the *Eye of Palpatine* picked up warring clans of Gamorreans, Jawas, Sand People, Talz, Affytechans, Kitonaks, and other species. It treated them all as Imperial soldiers and used mind-control techniques on them. Life aboard was chaotic and highly dangerous: Luke discovered deadly booby traps when he attempted to unravel the ship's secrets. He made contact with the disembodied Callista, and the two fell in love as they attempted to put an end to the ship's destructive potential. Finally, with the help of Callista, Nichos managed to overload the reactors of the *Eye of Palpatine,* and he and Cray sacrificed their lives to destroy the ship. At the last moment, Callista's spirit passed into Cray's body, and Callista was united with Luke.

**Eye of Shiblizar** An old, modified Ulig Abaha Dimel attack ship that served as the main vessel in Zlarb and Magg's slave ring in the Corporate Sector. The *Shiblizar* was never used for slave transport, since both Magg and Zlarb were connected to the vessel. Magg found the *Shiblizar* listed in a CSA database. It was a pirate craft that had been captured by the Authority, and was scheduled for destruction. Magg used his insider knowledge to breach security and stole the *Shiblizar* from the Espos.

**Eye of the Beyonder** According to Brizzit legend, this relic held a secret map that explained where to find a vast treasure hidden in the Jandoon system.

**Eye-on-U** One of the two major newsgrid services available to the natives of the planet Utharis.

**Eyes of Mesra** A small device used for fortune-telling, it largely became a toy for children in Mos Espa.

**Eyttyn, Kol** An X-wing pilot and wing commander stationed aboard the *Thurse* during the war against the Yuuzhan Vong. When the Peace Brigade attacked the *Queen of the Empire,* he ordered Red and Green squadrons to lie back and deal with assaults directed at the *Thurse* while Blue Squadron took the fight to the Yuuzhan Vong command ship.

*Eyes of Mesra*

**Eyttyrmin Batiiv pirates** A band of pirates who operated out of the Khuiumin system and were decimated by an attack spearheaded by two Victory Star Destroyers.

**Eyvind** A moisture farmer on Tatooine, he was the fiancé of Ariela and friend to fellow farmer Ariq Joanson. Eyvind often disagreed with Joanson's plans to make peace with the Jawas and Sand People, but nonetheless invited 31 Jawas to his wedding. The ceremony was raided by Sand People, and Eyvind was killed along with many others.

**Eyyl** One of the many habitable moons orbiting Qoribu, it was the home of the Mueum hive of the Colony.

**Ezak** An orphan who was raised by the Jedi Order, he knew almost everything there was to know about the Jedi. He was extremely skillful with his lightsaber and very honorable. He loved technology and had an amazing ability to fix things.

**Ezjenk** A member of Dathcha's Jawa tribe, he was tasked with affixing restraining bolts to newly captured droids.

**Ezrakh** One of Leia Organa Solo's Noghri bodyguards during her mission to the Chorios systems, he was killed by the Death Seed plague.

**4-LOM** A rogue droid bounty hunter conscripted by Darth Vader to find the *Millennium Falcon,* it was one of the first LOM series protocol droids ever produced. 4-LOM worked as a valet and human–cyborg relations specialist on the passenger liner *Kuari Princess.* The droid interacted with the ship's computer, and each altered the other's programming. Before long, gaming simulations about stealing guests' valuables turned into reality. 4-LOM became a master thief and came to the attention of Tatooine crime lord Jabba the Hutt. Jabba agreed to alter the droid's programming so that he could respond to the threat of violence with the same degree of skill, and 4-LOM agreed to work for Jabba as a bounty hunter. He was soon paired with a Gand tracker, Zuckuss, and the two were very successful.

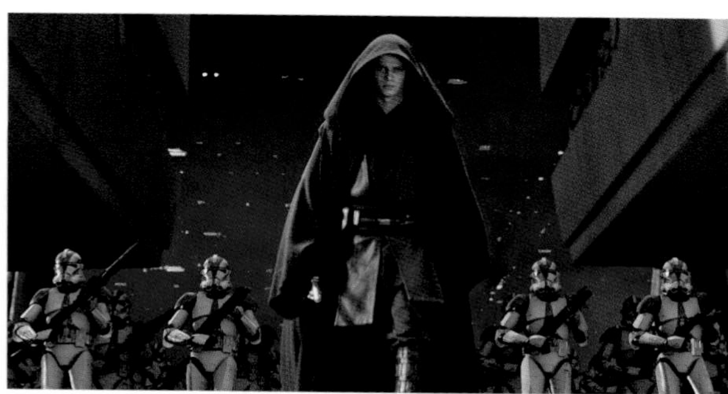

501st Legion clone troopers march with Darth Vader.

4-LOM watched and learned from Zuckuss, aspiring to do everything his organic counterpart could do. They didn't snare Han Solo, the big prize, although they went to Lord Vader's ship when he was seeking the Corellian. By then, 4-LOM was starting to change. Following the Battle of Hoth, he and Zuckuss had nearly destroyed the final escaping Rebel transport, the *Bright Hope,* but then reconsidered and helped evacuate the 90 Rebel soldiers aboard to the planet Darlyn Boda. For a time, the two joined the Rebellion. With Zuckuss and other bounty hunters, he unsuccessfully tried to wrest Han Solo's carbonite-encased body from Boba Fett, but was severely damaged. After recovering, he decided to part company with Zuckuss and work mostly by himself.

4-LOM

**41st Elite Corps** This clone trooper unit was one of the legions that made up the 9th Assault Corps at the height of the Clone Wars. Led by Commander Gree, the 41st Elite was often dispatched to those worlds with indigenous nonhuman species. The training of Commander Gree and his troops was specifically designed for interaction with other species; it included detailed information on various alien cultures.

**43rd "Killer Aiwha" Battalion** This division of clone troopers was part of the forces deployed by the Army of the Republic to the planet Jabiim at the height of the Clone Wars. The 43rd was one of the units left behind to guard Shelter Base during a three-pronged attack aimed at capturing three Separatist holdings. But the Separatists learned of the plan and struck at Shelter Base while it was relatively undefended. All the clones in the 43rd Battalion were killed in the fighting, along with many Jedi Knights.

**407th Stormtrooper Division** This Imperial stormtrooper division was stationed on Yinchorr nearly a century after the Yuuzhan Vong invasion of the galaxy. When Darth Krayt took control of the galaxy in the name of the Sith, the 407th was among the units that tried to remain loyal to the new Empire, despite the fact that Emperor Roan Fel had been forced into exile. Its true test, however, came when it was forced to attack another division, the 908th, that had refused to switch allegiance to Krayt.

**442nd Siege Battalion** This division of the Grand Army of the Republic was sent to Cato Neimoidia during the final stages of the Clone Wars.

**4B-X** This research droid was part of the Alliance's droid pool at the Massassi Base on Yavin 4 shortly before the Battle of Yavin. After the destruction of the first Death Star, 4B-X was assigned to the crew that escorted Trux Zissu to Delantine. A short, barrel-shaped automaton with a large data screen for a head and a feminine personality, 4B-X was designed to operate in nearly any environment.

**501st Imperial Legion** When Anakin Skywalker succumbed to the dark side and swore loyalty to Darth Sidious, the newly arisen Emperor assigned his apprentice the best the galaxy had to offer. For Vader's inaugural mission to snuff out all life in the Jedi Temple, the Emperor provided him with a legion of elite clone troopers. Their distinctive blue-marked armor set them apart from the other ranks. Their crack marksmanship and coordinated team maneuvers allowed them to outflank the Jedi trapped in the Temple and gun them down mercilessly. Though these clone troopers emerged from the smoldering Temple with their share of casualties, they were nonetheless successful in their mission.

The 501st had begun just as any of the other clone units that blazed across the rocky deserts of Geonosis in the first historic battle

407th Stormtrooper Division

< Boba Fett

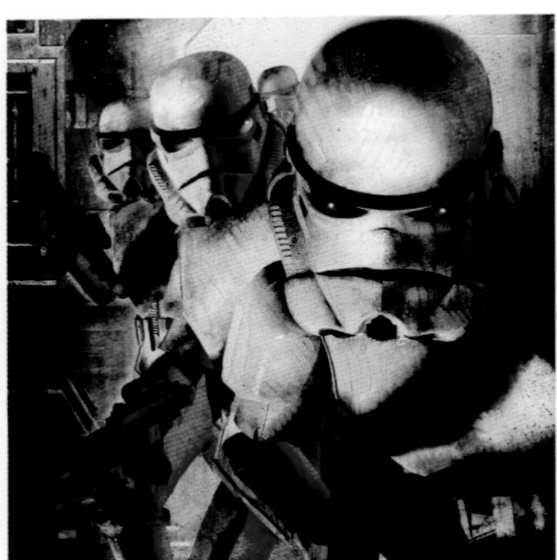

*501st Imperial Legion stormtroopers*

of the Clone Wars. Nonetheless, the Supreme Chancellor himself took special interest in the success of the 501st. Like the red-emblazoned soldiers that made up the ranks of Palpatine's elite shock troopers, the 501st underwent training and conditioning not on distant Kamino, but in a top-secret facility on Coruscant known only to select members of Palpatine's command staff. It was shortly after the Battle of Jabiim, when the threat to Coruscant seemed greater, that the 501st became based on the capital planet. From this headquarters, some members of the legion were transferred to other units, but they remained carefully tracked as members of the 501st to one day return to Coruscant for special assignment.

In the final days of the Clone Wars, the troops of the 501st were constantly on the move, shuttled from battlefront to battlefront. There were 501st troopers protecting the skies over Coruscant during General Grievous's bold strike against the capital. Others provided support to clone units on worlds such as Felucia, Mygeeto, Utapau, and Kashyyyk. Those stationed on Coruscant were put under the command of Darth Vader, Palpatine's new enforcer, and sent on the grim mission to attack the Jedi Temple.

Many of the early missions of the 501st remained classified for decades until datapad journals of some of its members came to light, detailing some of their most arduous assignments.

With the rise of the New Order, some worlds objected to the sweeping policy changes enacted by Palpatine. These worlds were soon brought into line. The 501st transitioned from clone troopers to stormtroopers as the Empire consolidated its power. It was dispatched to Naboo to eliminate Queen Apailana and her opposition to the Empire's directives. It was the first time the 501st was called upon to "adjust" a planet's government, but it wouldn't be the last. Within months, the 501st gained a well-deserved reputation as "Vader's Fist."

Troopers traveled to Mustafar to capture Gizor Dellso, a rogue Geonosian droid engineer who had erected his own battle droid factory on the fiery world. More alarming, the clones of the 501st had to put down a clone uprising on Kamino when an aberrant batch of mutinous troopers were unleashed by Kaminoans; they were led by Boba Fett, who was hired by Vader for his intimate knowledge of the cloning environments.

Later, the 501st was assigned to protect the Death Star as it neared completion. Hosts of would-be saboteurs and spies were captured by the Empire, and sent to languish in the Death Star's prison facilities. An embarrassing prison break by these Rebel inmates had to be quashed by the 501st. When the Death Star plans were stolen by Rebel spies, 501st squads were dispatched on missions to track down the valuable technical readouts. Such reassignments saved the ranks from destruction when the Death Star's main reactor exploded at the climax of the Battle of Yavin.

The 501st continued to serve Darth Vader throughout the Galactic Civil War, though after the Battle of Endor its ranks were broken and the unit dissolved as feuding Imperial warlords carved up territory and matériel in their bids to become the next Emperor. Knowing the value of symbols, it was Grand Admiral Thrawn who resurrected the designation *501st* for the stormtrooper units protecting the Empire of the Hand. By this time, any original clones from the 501st's Civil War era were long past fighting age. The new unit was made up of birth-born soldiers, with diverse backgrounds and histories, and included nonhuman members.

The 501st served the Empire throughout the Yuuzhan Vong War and the decades that followed, and remained one of the Empire's most elite units, as befitted their motto: "First on the ground and last to leave." Command of the 501st Imperial Legion was eventually transferred to Bastion, which became the capital planet of the galaxy when the Fel dynasty took control of the Empire. The leadership of the 501st, including General Oron Jaeger, remained loyal to the Fel Empire after Darth Krayt took control of the galaxy in the name of the Sith, and they bided their time until the Fels returned to power.

**5-A** This was the designation of Mara Jade Skywalker's personal StealthX fighter, used at the height of the Corellia–Galactic Alliance War. She used the ship to travel to Hapes during her personal mission to hunt down Jacen Solo.

**5D6-RA7** A robotic aide to Admiral Motti's staff, this foul-tempered and vindictive droid was feared by other automata. 5D6-RA7 was a spy for Imperial Intelligence and secretly investigated Imperial officers whose loyalties were in doubt. He was destroyed in the explosion of the Death Star during the Battle of Yavin.

*FA-4 and FA-5 droids*

**5P8** A prowler ship in the New Republic's Fifth Fleet, it found Plat Mallar's TIE interceptor near the Koornacht Cluster.

**5YQ series droid** This "boutique" series of pewter-colored protocol droids was developed by Cybot Galactica from the basic 3PO series model, with modifications to the cognitive module units that gave the 5YQ a greater empathy for organic beings. These units were marketed almost exclusively in the Mid Rim, at a lower price than the basic 3PO series unit. Many 5YQ series units remained active for decades during the last century of the Old Republic.

**F1 exploration droid** A canine-like Cybot Galactica droid, it was designed to be a scout companion.

**F-187 fusioncutter** A general-purpose device, it could be used to repair vehicles and buildings. It could also construct unassembled battlefield equipment such as blaster turrets.

**F-22** One of many droids that worked for the Star Tours travel agency, along with F-25-OJS and F-29.

**F8GN (Eight-Gee-Enn)** A tall, spindly, copper-colored droid, it was programmed by Garris Shrike to teach children to beg, steal, and pick pockets. Oddly, F8GN had one red eye and one green.

**F9-TZ cloaking transport** A transport ship developed by Baktoid Armor Workshop, it used an RHTT-6 transport cloaking generator.

**FA-3 flechette launcher** BlasTech FA-3 flechette launchers fired lethal shards of metal, capable of hitting multiple targets. They were widely used by Evo troopers following the fall of the Old Republic.

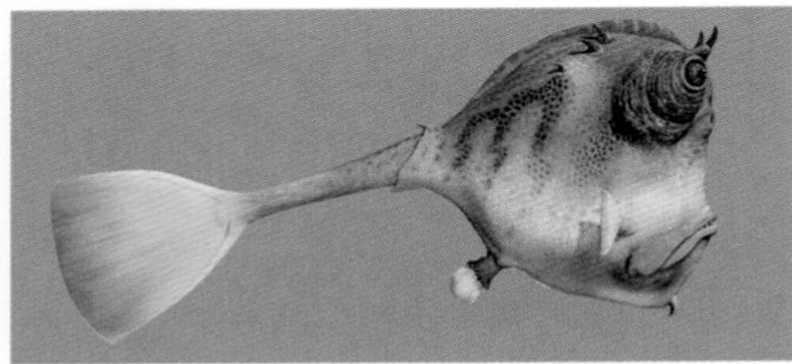

*Faa*

**FA-4, FA-5 droids** Popular models developed by SoroSuub during the latter years of the Galactic Republic. The FA-4 pilot droid and the FA-5 valet droid were common sights at major galactic spaceports. Similar in appearance, the FA-4 had treads while the FA-5 had legs. Count Dooku had an FA-4 chauffeur for his Geonosian solar sailer during the Clone Wars.

**faa (faynaa)** These swift, carnivorous fish native to the swamps of Naboo were especially prominent around the Gungan city of Otoh Gunga. Faas, also known to the Gungans as faynaas, had stiff armored bodies and a narrow girth. They traveled in schools and could be found only in deep waters. However, they were quite dangerous and attacked virtually anything with little provocation.

**Faalo's cadences** A formal method of lightsaber training, it was developed by Jedi Master Vo'ren Faalo and involved the use of durasteel ball bearings and candles.

**Faarlsun system** A star system in Wild Space, it was far from the old Empire and the New Republic.

**Faarl the Conqueror** A pirate from Korlings, he conquered several worlds in the Parthovian Cluster during the Galactic Civil War.

Face (IM4-099 patrol droid)

**fabool** Balloon-like animals that lived on Dantooine, they were often punctured by the planet's thorny blba trees. The Dantari made fabool-hide pouches.

**Fabreth Medical Biochemicals** A company best known for its "shock cloth." FMB's anti-shock blanket was used to prevent shock when treating wounds.

**Fabrin** This planet housed the headquarters and most manufacturing facilities of Fabritech, a maker of security and communication devices.

**Fabritech** A major manufacturer of security and communications equipment including starfighter sensor and control systems, the company was a leader in its field for many decades. Fabritech manufactured personal comlinks as well as small-scale sensors, and its products enjoyed a deep penetration in many markets because they took the punishment of a variety of planetary environments. Perhaps its best-known device was the ANy-20 active sensor transceiver rectenna dish often used on YT-1300 transports to provide ship-to-ship jamming capabilities as well as communications. Fabritech also made the sensor arrays for Imperial TIE fighters; CN-15 metallic camouflage that served as a jammer; and the PAC20 visual wrist comm. For both civilian and military uses, it made the SE-Vigilant automated sensor beacon node, which consisted of security scanners and alarm systems.

Sun Fac

**Fac, Sun** A Geonosian aristocrat, he was chief lieutenant of Archduke Poggle the Lesser; his insect-like wings signified his higher rank within the Geonosian caste system. Unusually intelligent and creative for a Geonosian, Sun Fac was adept at playing whatever role would best accomplish the needs of the moment. He could be either a sympathetic listener or a heartless executioner, depending on what would get the job done. Sun Fac was able to flee Separatist headquarters in a Geonosian fighter, but was shot down by Republic commandos.

**Face (IM4-099 patrol droid)** A nickname for the Imperial Mark IV patrol droid assigned to the stormtrooper garrison stationed at Mos Eisley on Tatooine. Face's official designation was IM4-099. He was a loyal servant of the Empire, but was prone to setting off false alarms with his security holocam and hassling local asp droids.

**Factor H** Kamino clone scientists believed that, theoretically, all clones would develop identically physically, mentally, and emotionally. As the Kaminoan project to develop a massive clone army advanced, however, clones started to spontaneously exhibit their own individual characteristics. The puzzled Kaminoan scientists labeled this quirk of development *Factor H* for "human." They viewed all divergence as negative, since they expected their clones to be perfect copies of one another, and decided to recondition the entire batch. However, Jango Fett pointed out that in the case of clone commandos, "The sum of the parts makes the whole stronger." Indeed, commando squads that had distinct personalities performed better in the Killing House and in other critical test situations. The bounty hunter knew instinctively what the scientists couldn't grasp: The best soldiers are brothers . . . not clones. The Kaminoans relented, and development was allowed to continue.

Commander Faie

Factory district of Coruscant

**factory district** A section of Coruscant where goods were manufactured for export and local consumption, the area housed only droids and a few organic overseers. The Grungeon block encompassed 20 square kilometers and was one of the best-known areas in the factory district.

Thul Fain

**Fadden** A world colonized by the Duros species during the Old Republic era.

**Fadoop** A furry, bandy-legged green female Saheelindeel, she was a pilot and owner of the ship *Skybarge.* An intelligent primate from the Tion Hegemony, Fadoop had an intense liking for chak-root and once ran parts for Han Solo and Chewbacca during their adventures in Corporate Sector space.

**Fahraark** A Wookiee slaver and associate of Dayla Kev during the early years of the Galactic Civil War. He delivered a group of Hoojibs to the *Galactic Horizon* to assist Dayla in exacting her revenge on Milac Troper.

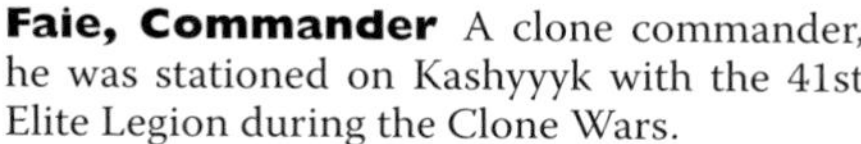

**Faie, Commander** A clone commander, he was stationed on Kashyyyk with the 41st Elite Legion during the Clone Wars.

**Fain, Thul** A gambler who worked as a smuggler for Jabba the Hutt, he liked to bet on how long victims Jabba threw into the rancor pit would last. Fain had previously been an Imperial pilot who worked with Lieutenant Trabinis.

***Fair Gale*** A Sienar Systems short-range SST-67 transit shuttle, it was piloted by Captain Worlohp for the Naboo self-defense forces.

Fairwind

***Fairwind*** The elegant flagship of Lord Valenthyne Farfalla during the Battle of Ruusan. Many Jedi felt that the *Fairwind,* which was designed and built to resemble an ancient sailing barge, was much too extravagant for a Jedi, indicating a level of vanity that was not often associated with the Order. After the battle, Lord Farfalla turned the vessel into a rescue ship.

**Fakir sector** Located just outside the Core Worlds, it was the location of the planet Halowan. A remote asteroid in the Fakir sector—Yirt-4138-Grek-12, a 65-kilometer-diameter airless rock—was the site of an industrial espionage training center funded by unknown parties just prior to the Clone Wars. The compound's unauthorized cybernetic surgery suites churned out borgs that sliced into Corporate Alliance data stores, according to Corporate Alliance Magistrate Passel Argente. As a result, the Corporate Alliance unleashed volleys of missiles from its tank droids, and the asteroid became the grave site for 25 cybernetically enhanced data thieves. During the Galactic Civil War, Fakir sector was the base of operations for Reekeene's Roughnecks.

**Falang Minor** An Old Republic fortress world in the Outer Rim, it was used as a base to watch over the Tion Cluster after it became part of the Republic.

**Falanthas, Minister Mokka** The New Republic's Minister of State and successor to General Rieekan, Falanthas was a cautious individual who didn't want to get involved too quickly in a war with the Yevetha.

***Falcariae*** A Mon Calamari MC80 cruiser, it was part of the Rebel Alliance fleet about two years before the Battle of Yavin.

**Falco, Captain** A greasy-looking "thug-in-uniform," he served the Human League under Thrackan Sal-Solo when Han Solo was taken prisoner.

**Falcon Base** A Rebel camp on Yavin 4. Darth Vader searched it and Raven Base in his quest for General Jan Dodonna.

**Faleur, Reina** A New Republic lieutenant, she worked in the Quartermaster Corps' supply division and interacted with Rogue Squadron.

**Faleur, Sera** *See* Darklighter, Sera Faleur.

**Falken, Rorax** A brilliant scientist from the planet Mrlsst. Falken's lab at the Mrlsst Academy developed technology to make large artificial moons, and he shared it with the Empire to—he thought—help better the galaxy. Instead, it became a central part of the knowledge base needed to develop the planet-destroying weapon of mass destruction, the Death Star. When Falken later discovered the truth he had a nervous breakdown, but he started to recover as he turned his attention to music.

Falken and his students had been developing a full-ship cloaking device for the Empire code-named the Phantom Project. In reality, the device was a hoax designed to swindle the Empire out of vast sums of money it would otherwise use on the war effort. Following the death of Emperor Palpatine, Imperial remnants started demanding results from the expensive project. The new president of the Mrlsst Academy, Gyr Keela, decided that he could make even more money by getting the New Republic to bid against the Imperials for the cloaking technology, which he didn't know was nonexistent. This led to a battle between Imperial forces led by Loka Hask and Rogue Squadron under the command of Wedge Antilles; during an intense battle, Falken was killed in the crossfire.

Reina Faleur

**Fall, Euraana** A female Mawan, she served as a liaison to Yaddle, Obi-Wan Kenobi, and Anakin Skywalker, the Jedi Knights who were dispatched to Mawan to help establish a peaceful government on the planet three years before the Battle of Geonosis. Her desire to restore Mawan to its former beauty forced this upper-class female to work with the subrats and other lower-class members of Mawan society in order to bring about change.

**Fallanassi** A religious order whose members were followers of the White Current. They used to live in Ialtra, on the planet Lucazec, in ring dwellings and circle houses. During the New Order, one of the Fallanassi, Isela Talsava Norand, revealed the sect's existence to Lucazec's Imperial Governor. The Empire immediately realized the potential of the unique Fallanassi skill with the White Current, which was similar to the Jedi use of the Force. The Empire offered its protection to the Fallanassi in exchange for an oath of loyalty. When the pacifistic people refused, Imperial agents stirred up resentment toward the Fallanassi among the people of Lucazec, and sect members had to flee.

The Fallanassi dedicated themselves almost completely to hiding their existence from the galaxy at large. As such, no records of their existence were even written until Luke Skywalker encountered them many years after the fall of the Empire. Graciously, Master Skywalker recorded minimal information about the Fallanassi in his report back to the New Republic: Aside from their sheer existence, he revealed almost nothing about their ways or powers.

**Fallanji** A boisterous bright green Twi'lek with pierced head-tails capped with bells on the tips, he once served as a snitch for Krova the Hutt. Fallanji moved into the information-trading racket after Krova fled to escape Rebel Alliance forces.

**Falleen** A planet inhabited by an isolationist humanoid species also called Falleen, it was the homeworld of Prince Xizor, long-feared head of the underworld syndicate Black Sun.

The Falleen were reptilian in ancestry, with scales, cold blood, and skin that could change color according to their mood. Their average life span was 250 years, with some living as long as 400 years. A Falleen's lung capacity was great, and they were able to stay underwater for up to 12 hours. Coolly calculating beings, the

Falleen

Falleen were considered among the most beautiful of all humanoid species. In addition, both males and females had enhanced hormones, exuding a pheromone that made them practically irresistible to the opposite sex. During sexual arousal, a Falleen's color might change from grayish green to warmer reddish hues. Meditation and exercises brought the hormonal essences into full bloom.

About 10 years before the Battle of Endor, Darth Vader established a biological warfare laboratory on Falleen in an area ruled by Xizor's father. It was the Dark Lord's pet project. But a terrible accident occurred at the supposedly secure facility: A mutant tissue-destroying bacterium escaped quarantine. In order to save the planet's population from a rotting, always fatal infection for which there was no cure—and to minimize Vader's embarrassment—the city around the lab was burned to the ground in an orbital bombardment, killing 200,000 Falleen, including all of Xizor's family. Xizor, at the time possibly the third most powerful man in the galaxy after the Emperor and Vader, vowed vengeance on the Dark Lord, but ended up on the losing side of a battle to the death.

Falleen's Fist

***Falleen's Fist*** Prince Xizor's skyhook, this orbiting structure tethered to the ground was about two-thirds the size of the Emperor's grandiose skyhook, which hung above Imperial Center. The *Fist* had a command center and a view deck surrounded by transparisteel plates that allowed an unimpeded 360-degree view of space. It was the pride and joy of the crime king, but during a final showdown with Darth Vader, the Dark Lord ordered a Star Destroyer to annihilate Xizor's skyhook.

**Fall of the Sith Empire** The name applied to the final stages of the Great Hyperspace War, which took place more than 5,000 years before the Battle of Yavin. As the conflict came to a close, the forces of the Old Republic, led by Empress Teta, pursued the Sith warlords across the galaxy. The Sith were driven to near extinction, but a small remnant under the command of Dark Lord Naga Sadow eventually found sanctuary on Yavin 4.

Falumpaset

**Falloon (Soolehad)** A wealthy Rodian living on the planet Sriluur, he had been the chief accountant for the Black Sun criminal organization in the sector. He owned a ship, the *Gilded Thranta,* and a droid named 9T-LOM. Attempting to escape the planet during the Yuuzhan Vong invasion, he paid a group of mercenaries to help him flee to Coruscant.

**Falon, Mellora** A young scientist, she befriended Jedi-hater Granta Omega and like him developed an attachment to Sith artifacts. She helped him capture Anakin Skywalker and at one point challenged Anakin to a duel. Falon overestimated Omega's concern for her. When they had to flee the erupting Kaachtari volcano on Haariden, Omega pushed Mellora off his swoop bike. She was rescued by Anakin and Obi-Wan Kenobi and turned over to the Haariden authorities to be questioned.

**Falsswon** A tall, blue-skinned humanoid, he lived in the city of Tolea Biqua on Cularin during the last decades of the Old Republic. An imposing figure, Falsswon had sharpened his black-rooted teeth to make him look more fearsome. While being interviewed by local media, the ill-tempered Falsswon took exception to a line of questioning, pulled a blaster, and shot the camera that had been recording him.

**Falt, Corrun** A disgruntled employee of the Czerka Corporation on Telos following the Jedi Civil War thousands of years before the Galactic Civil War, he went to work directly for Jana Lorso, a renegade Czerka executive who dealt with criminals to advance her cause.

**falumpaset** A muscular animal native to Naboo, it roamed the swamps in small herds. Intelligent and ill-tempered, falumpasets were nevertheless the strongest beasts of burden on the planet. Native Gungans trained the creatures to serve as personal transports for important leaders. Falumpasets were also a vital part of the Gungan army. During battles, the animals pulled ammo wagons filled with energy balls. Falumpasets could be identified by their unique bellow, which carried over long distances. Wild falumpasets had shaggy fetlocks to protect against nipping nyorks and other annoying creatures. They also were excellent swimmers. Falumpasets were herbivorous; family groups consisted of one bull and four to seven cows with their young.

**fambaa** Large, vaguely reptilian herbivores found on Naboo, they were slow, clumsy, and dim-witted—but extremely strong and resilient creatures. Fambaas were technically amphibians, but had scaly hides typical of reptiles. In the wild, they traveled in herds of up to 12. They had mild dispositions and were capable of surviving the rigors of Naboo's swamps. The Gungans domesticated fambaas and used the beasts to transport large and cumbersome equipment. When the Gungans entered battle, fambaas carried powerful shield generators designed to protect hundreds of troops; some were armed with massive projectile weapons for use in assaults.

Fambaa

**familiar** A term used by the Yuuzhan Vong to represent a relationship beyond friend, comrade, or pet.

***Famulus*** A ship from House Vandron that led a Jedi mission into the Senex sector, the *Famulus* relayed images to Supreme Chancellor Valorum of the destroyed Republic cruiser *Ecliptic* in a minefield near Asmeru.

**fanback** A cold-blooded amphibian found on Naboo, the creature got its name from its large dorsal spine. While fanbacks lived mostly in water, fanback eggs could be laid only in the mud. Peko-peko and other egg eaters found this large, tough-shelled egg quite tasty. Naboo hunters knew that if they went looking for fanback eggs, they had better be alert for adult fanbacks or they might end up as a tasty meal themselves.

**fanblade starfighter, Geonosian** *See* Geonosian fanblade starfighter.

**Fandar** A brilliant scientist, this Chadra-Fan was leader of Project Decoy. His goal was to create a life-like human replica droid for the Rebel Alliance, and his prototype resembled Princess Leia.

**Fandi, Nort** A tall, balding human, he piloted the shuttle that brought Obi-Wan Kenobi and Anakin Skywalker from the planet Hilo to the *BioCruiser* two years after the Battle of Naboo.

**Fandomar** Momaw Nadon's wife. He had to leave her behind on the planet Ithor when he was banished from his homeworld.

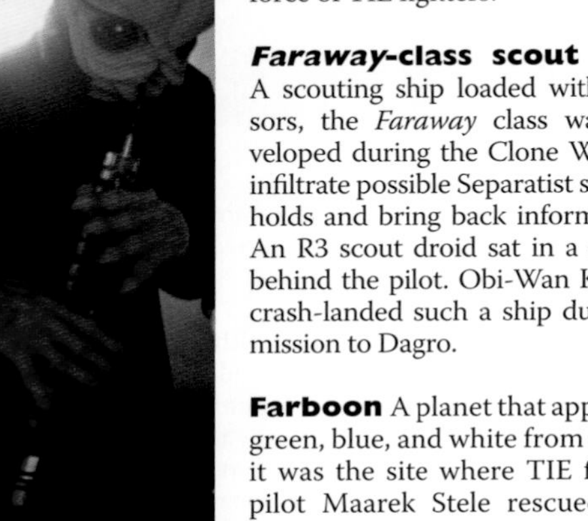

Fanfar

**Fane, Captain** The captain of the *Tellivar Lady,* a transport ship with regular runs to and from Tatooine.

**fanfar** A woodwind type of musical instrument, it was essential for many bands. Both Tedn Dahai and Ickabel G'ont played the fanfar for Figrin D'an and the Modal Nodes.

**Fangol** A small, cold world on the edge of the Mortex sector, this planet served as a Rebel sector headquarters.

**fanned rawl** A snake-like creature found on Naboo. Rawls were noted for fan-like structures on the sides of their bodies that apparently were used to help the snakes swim. For unknown reasons, there were reports of the snakes growing to giant proportions in at least two locations on the planet.

***Fantome*** A *Tartan*-class medium cruiser that was active during the Galactic Civil War.

**Far, Jonra** A female Twi'lek, she was a swoop racer on Onderon in the early days of the Old Republic.

**Farana** A region of space on the far side of the Corporate Sector. Twelve years after the Battle of Endor, Luke Skywalker discovered that the starliner *Star Morning,* belonging to the Fallanassi religious order, had spent several months in Farana.

**Farang** A species native to Ab'Bshingh, they were almost constantly at war with the Waroot throughout their history.

**Fara's Belt** The site of an Imperial communications station in the Rolion sector, it served as an Alliance example of the disastrous effects of compromised intelligence. Rebel forces planned to stage a hit-and-run attack with B-wing fighters led by General Jan Dodonna himself. But the Rebels had been tricked by the planting of a false story about an alleged malfunction at the base, and they were nearly wiped out by an attacking force of TIE fighters.

***Faraway*-class scout ship** A scouting ship loaded with sensors, the *Faraway* class was developed during the Clone Wars to infiltrate possible Separatist strongholds and bring back information. An R3 scout droid sat in a socket behind the pilot. Obi-Wan Kenobi crash-landed such a ship during a mission to Dagro.

**Farboon** A planet that appeared green, blue, and white from space, it was the site where TIE fighter pilot Maarek Stele rescued Imperial Admiral Mordon's shuttle from an attacking group of Rebel X- and Y-wing fighters.

**Farbreini MicroElectronics Limited** This company was known as a fabricator of such devices as the Coruscant Cascader, which combined jewelry with microelectronics and light-emitters.

**Far Distance** The northern polar region of the sentient planet Zonama Sekot, it was where potential buyers of Sekotan starships were brought to be united with seed-partners—living organisms that eventually became the starships. After the planet made a blind jump into hyperspace to avoid Yuuzhan Vong sabotage, it came too close to the heat of several stars, and Far Distance eventually fractured and melted.

**Fardreamer, Cole** A youngster from Tatooine, he became a maintenance worker on Coruscant. As a boy, he often tried to build X-wings out of damaged equipment that he managed to find before the Jawas did, but he was never completely successful. He hoped to follow in the footsteps of his boyhood hero, Luke Skywalker, but Cole's mother thought her son's desires were born from his impetuous, stubborn, and impulsive nature. Cole eventually realized that his talents as a mechanic and engineer were just as valuable to the New Republic as Skywalker's Jedi skills, only in a different manner. Fardreamer was the one who discovered that detonating devices had been hidden under orders of the scheming Dark Jedi Kueller in upgraded New Republic X-wings. Together with C-3PO and R2-D2, he made a trip to Telti to investigate the origins of the threat. There he discovered the truth—that the detonators were embedded in new astromech droids—and confronted Brakiss, the administrator of the Telti droid-manufacturing facility. Fardreamer managed to alert the New Republic forces before most of the detonators could be activated. With the help of R2-D2 and C-3PO, he staved off Brakiss's droid army, routed the administrator, and was hailed as a hero by the New Republic for his part in uncovering the Kueller threat.

**Farfalla, Lord Valenthyne** A flamboyant and seemingly inept Jedi Knight whose starship, *Fairwind,* resembled a sailing galleon. He promised to bring 100 vitally needed Jedi as reinforcements to aid Lord Hoth's depleted Army of Light during the Battle of Ruusan. Both Lord Hoth and Sith Lord Kaan dismissed Farfalla's abilities as a leader. But Lord Kiel Charny, whom he had saved from certain death twice, knew he was a brave and excellent fighter. Despite Lord Hoth's doubts, Farfalla made good his word. Although forewarned about the imminent detonation of a thought bomb by Lord Kaan, and importuned by Lord Hoth to leave the planet to save his own life, he fought bravely in the final Battle of Ruusan. Farfalla organized the evacuation of as many Jedi as he could take aboard the *Fairwind* and coordinated rescue efforts of other vessels.

After the devastation wreaked by the thought bomb, Valenthyne took control. He assembled recovery parties without Force-sensitive individuals so they would be immune to any aftereffects of the thought bomb. He was dismayed when Lord Hoth's Padawan

Lord Valenthyne Farfalla

Johun Othone disobeyed orders and landed on Ruusan; and he refused to believe Othone's claim that one Sith Lord had survived the battle. Farfalla took over Othone's training, eventually assigning him to serve as Chancellor Tarsus Valorum's personal guard.

Years later, Othone went to Coruscant with evidence of a Sith Lord survivor. Lord Farfalla put together a small task force to track down Darth Zannah, apprentice to Darth Bane. Upon arriving at Tython, they followed Zannah into the fortress of Belia Darzu. Within the ancient edifice, the Sith Lords attacked the Jedi team, and Bane beheaded Farfalla.

Farghul

**Farfeld II** Located in the Farfeld system, it was the site of a System Patrol Squadron base for Imperial corvettes. The base was destroyed by the Rebel Alliance shortly after the Battle of Yavin.

**Fargane** A tall, educated Ansionian, he was a delegate to the Unity of Community in the period leading up to Ansion's vote on whether to secede from the Old Republic. Initially in favor of secession, Fargane was unhappy that Jedi Knights sent to the planet were being given what seemed to be unlimited time to negotiate a treaty. But in the end, despite his strong feelings, he voted to have Ansion remain part of the Republic.

**Farghul** A sentient felinoid species from the planet Farrfin, the Farghul had medium-length tawny fur, sharp claws and teeth, and a flexible, prehensile tail. They were very conscious of their appearance, wearing only the highest-quality clothing and elaborate jewelry. The Farghul developed a reputation for being mostly con artists and thieves. They relied on cunning and trickery rather than direct confrontation and force, and tended to be terrified of Jedi.

**Farlander, Keyan** A famous Rebel Alliance pilot and officer, he came from the planet Agamar in the Outer Rim's Lahara sector. At first indifferent to galactic politics and intrigue, he began changing after other members of his family were sentenced to death as Rebel collaborators. When Mon Mothma secretly visited Agamar seeking help for the Alliance, her impassioned words led Keyan to join the Rebellion. He signed up as a starfighter pilot and left for training aboard the Rebel flagship *Independence.* After completing his course, Farlander flew through "the Maze," a pilot proving ground, and was then assigned to the simulator's "Historical Combat Missions" to further hone his combat skills. On his first mission, he helped disable the Imperial corvette *Talon,* boarded it, and recovered important Imperial holodocuments. While on Yavin 4 prior to the confrontation with the Death Star, Farlander helped Luke Skywalker master the controls of the X-wing fighter. Himself a Y-wing pilot during the battle, he was one of the few Rebel pilot survivors.

As a leading member of an Alliance strike team following the Battle of Yavin, he helped eliminate Imperial System Patrol Squadron bases near the planets Feenicks VI and Farfeld II, destroying many Imperial corvettes. One of his most daring and successful missions saw the destruction of a vital Imperial storage area in Hollan D1 sector. He and his fellow Alliance pilots used captured ships from Overlord Ghorin in the attack, successfully discrediting Ghorin in the eyes of the Empire. Because of his amazing skills, Skywalker tested Farlander for possible Force powers, and after getting positive results invited the ace to the Jedi praxeum on Yavin 4; after years of training, Farlander became a Jedi Knight. When the Yuuzhan Vong invaded the galaxy, Farlander had been promoted to general. He served aboard the *Ralroost* under Admiral Traest Kre'fey after the Second Battle of Coruscant. Commanding the *Adapyne,* General Farlander led the fleet that aided Jaina Solo at Obroa-skai. He led an even larger force of 40 capital ships at Ebaq 9.

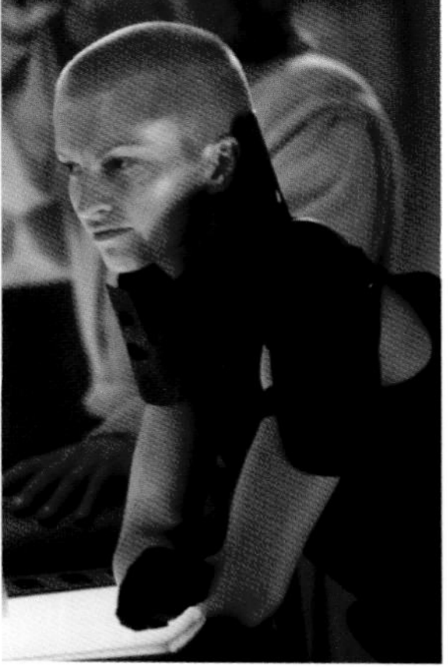
Kalyn Farnmir

**Farlander, Kitha** The sister of Keyan Farlander, she was disfigured after being burned during an Imperial attack on her hometown of Tondatha. Her brother sent her to Oorn Tchis to live with her aunt and uncle and receive medical treatment.

**Farlax sector** Located in what used to be the center of the Empire's Rim Territories, the Farlax sector contained the Koornacht Cluster, home of the alien Yevetha. Large areas of the sector were never properly surveyed. During the Empire's reign, the Black Sword Command was charged with the defense of Praxlis, Corridan, and the entire Kokash, Hatawa, and Farlax sectors. Polneye, a planet at the edges of the Koornacht Cluster, was established by the Black Sword Command as a secret military transshipment point for the Farlax sector.

Following the Battle of Endor, Imperial forces abandoned the Farlax sector and retreated into the Core. There were more than 200 inhabited worlds in the combined Hatawa and Farlax sectors. A third of the region became aligned with the New Republic, while another third was uninhabited or unclaimed.

During the crisis in the Koornacht Cluster 12 years after the Battle of Endor, 18 planets in the Farlax sector made emergency petitions for membership in the New Republic in the hope of defending themselves against the Yevetha. Chief of State Leia Organa Solo approved the applications and sent the New Republic's Fifth Fleet to Farlax to force the Yevetha to back down.

The brown dwarf star Doornik-1142 and its planets were located on the edge of the Cluster, while J't'p'tan was located at the heart. N'zoth, Wakiza, Tizon, Pa'aal, Z'fell, Faz, Tholaz, and Zhina were Yevethan worlds within the cluster. Non-Yevethan colony worlds in the cluster included New Brigia, Pirol-5, Polneye, Kutag (Doornik-881), Kojash, Doornik-207, Doornik-628, and Morning Bell (Doornik-319, or Preza). The planets Galantos and Wehttam were the closest inhabited worlds to the cluster, and Dandalas, Nanta-Ri, and Kktkt were close to Koornacht as well.

***Farlight*** A New Republic ship once part of the Third Fleet, it was deployed at Wehttam in anticipation of a Yevethan attack.

**Farng** A lanky and bald human carbonite trader in the Empress Teta system some 4,000 years before the Galactic Civil War, Farng's imminent public execution at the hands of Aleema Keto led to a short-lived citizens' revolt in Cinnagar.

**Farnmir, Kalyn** With no roots and few possessions, loyalty meant everything to Kalyn Farnmir. As a member of the Kuati Security Forces, she was set up by corrupt KDY officers to take the fall for their underhanded dealings fencing corporate secrets to Neimoidian agents. After being unceremoniously discharged, she put her skills to use as a bounty hunter and continued to bring the lawless to justice. She took on a partner, the skilled slicer Cian Shee, and the two enjoyed some level of success ferreting out small-time criminals and corporate thieves.

One night on Coruscant, an informant told Farnmir that sinister elements of the Zealots of Psusan cult were planning revenge for her having brought down their corrupt High Priest, and that Cian Shee was in on the plot.

When Shee arrived for a meeting at the Outlander Club, Kalyn acted

Keyan Farlander

friendly to allay suspicion. As the two left, Farnmir tried to pin Shee before she could spring her attack, but Shee's reflexes enabled her to flee into the night.

In later years, Shee took up Imperial contracts while Farnmir despised the Empire and only aided the Rebellion. Cian Shee eventually pulled a contract to bring Farnmir in, and faced her former partner in single combat on Nar Shaddaa. This time, Kalyn made no mistakes, and Cian finally paid for her betrayal with her life.

**Farnym** Creatures noted for their bowling-ball roundness, they had close-cut orange fur and small snouts. Farnym had a peculiar odor, like ginger mixed with sandalwood. Tchiery, Leia Organa Solo's copilot aboard the *Alderaan,* was a Farnym.

**Faron** A member of a Rebel Alliance scouting team sent to Kinooine after the Battle of Endor, Faron was captured and tortured by Lumiya and Den Siva along with the Zeltron smuggler Dani in order to set a trap for Luke Skywalker. In an attempt to escape, Faron grabbed a weapon and tried to kill Den Siva, but was instead fatally wounded when the Nagai warrior sensed the attack and fired first.

***Far Orbit*** A Nebulon-B escort frigate, it had the distinction of being the first Rebel privateer ship. The *Far Orbit*'s mission was to stage a daring series of strikes on the Core Worlds and wreak havoc on the forces of the Empire.

**Far Outsiders** The name that Ferroan settlers of the living planet Zonama Sekot applied to a mysterious alien species that attacked the planet around the time of the Battle of Naboo. At first, the Far Outsiders lurked outside the system, sending in exploratory ships that—like those from Zonama Sekot—seemed to be built from living matter. But it soon became clear that the Far Outsiders were interested only in complete control of the planet, and they started a massive bombardment that crippled its southern hemisphere. The Jedi Vergere, who was on the planet to get a Sekotan starship, intervened. To get the attacks to cease, she eventually agreed to leave with the Far Outsiders, and nothing more was heard from her or them for many years . . . until they reappeared and became one of the galaxy's most deadly threats ever in their true guise as the Yuuzhan Vong.

**Farr, Onaconda** A loyalist Senator close to the office of Supreme Chancellor Palpatine, he represented his homeworld of Rodia during the last decades of the Galactic Republic. He was an old family friend of Padmé Amidala, who affectionately called him Uncle Ono. Farr was a fervent patriot, quite vocal during the Separatist crisis and occasionally critical of Palpatine's handling of

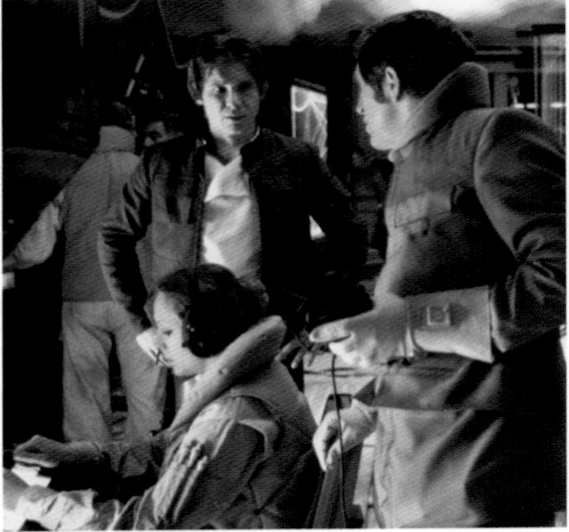

Toryn Farr (seated left) with Han Solo and General Rieekan

the situation. He often accused the Chancellor of following his own political agenda to the detriment of the Republic. He even dealt Palpatine an embarrassing blow by proving that a member of his Loyalist Committee had strong Separatist ties. As a reward for his vigilance, Farr was appointed to the committee and put in charge of the defense of the Corellian Trade Spine; he resigned the assignment after a disastrous attack by General Grievous.

Retreating to Rodia, Farr began to see the galactic conflict through new eyes and began worrying about Rodia's safety. A series of pirate attacks cut off badly needed supplies for its populace, and Farr seemed unable to procure aid from the Republic. He chose, instead, to go to the Trade Federation and invited Nute Gunray to Rodia. Padmé Amidala paid a surprise visit, and Gunray took her prisoner. Farr immediately regretted his transgression, and with the unlikely aid of Jar Jar Binks and the sudden arrival of Republic reinforcements, Amidala escaped and captured Gunray, bringing Rodia back to the Republic fold.

**Farr, Samoc** One of the Rebels' best snowspeeder pilots, she was badly injured in the Battle of Hoth.

**Farr, Toryn** Among the last to leave the Rebel command center at Echo Base, the chief communications officer of Echo Command escaped aboard the transport carrier *Bright Hope* with her sister, Samoc. Toryn Farr was promoted to the rank of commander after helping to safely transport the disabled ship's 90 passengers to Darlyn Boda. She was later awarded the Kalidor Crescent.

**Farrell, Jake** Originally a starfighter pilot for the Old Republic, he abandoned Imperial service when the pilots he trained started the Empire's reign of destruction. Years later, he came out of hiding and retirement to help train Rebel Alliance pilots and fly A-wing fighters. While he could seem grumpy, it was largely a way to instill discipline and control in his rookie pilots.

Onaconda Farr

**Farrfin sector** Along with the Dolomar sector, this sector of the Core Worlds was a target of an offensive by Grand Admiral Thrawn. The New Republic put up stiff resistance, and Admiral Ackbar made a personal tour of the defenses. The sector included the planet Farrfin, a temperate world with a native sentient felinoid species, the Farghul.

**Farrimmer Café** A cantina and restaurant owned by H'nib Statermast and his partner, Grosteek. It was on the Mynock 7 Space Station and became popular during the New Order.

**farrow birds** Aruzan birds with bioluminescent chests that glowed as they dived from the sky, they effectively blinded the small animals that were their prey.

**Farrs, Shappa and Sheekla** A Ferroan couple who both descended from Firsts—original settlers of the planet Zonama Sekot—they each were involved with Sekotan starships. Shappa was considered one of the planet's best starshipwrights, until a serious accident. His wife Sheekla led ceremonies uniting seed-partners—which became the ships—with their eventual masters, and helped Obi-Wan Kenobi and Anakin Skywalker when they visited the planet. Both husband and wife were seriously injured in Wilhuff Tarkin's attack on Zonama Sekot, but recovered shortly before the planet disappeared into hyperspace.

Farseein

**farseein** Gungan binoculars, farseeins had oil magnifier lenses. During the Battle of Naboo, Gungan soldiers sat atop huge statue heads to scan the Great Grass Plains using farseeins.

***FarStar*** A Corellian corvette, it was dispatched to track down a rogue Imperial Governor, Moff Kentor Sarne, four years after the Battle of Endor. Previously under Sarne's command, the ship's original name was *Renegade*. The mission was originally undertaken by Page's Commandos, but command was assumed by Captain Keleman Ciro and later Kaiya Adrimetrum. The pursuit of Sarne took the New Republic forces deep into the Kathol Outback in a little-explored area known as the Kathol Rift. One of the purposes of the mission was to discover the origin of strange and mysterious DarkStryder technology used by Sarne. The ship was destroyed during a battle at Kathol.

**Farstine** A methane world in the Skine Sector, it was the start of the Five Veils' Tour trade route that ended at Skynara.

***Far Thunder*** A *Republic*-class cruiser assigned to a New Republic task force under General Keyan Farlander, it took part in the rout of Yuuzhan Vong forces near Obroa-skai, including the destruction of Supreme Commander Komm Karsh's flagship. The *Far Thunder*, under the command of Colonel Hannser, had a complement of shuttles and weapons systems slaved to droid brains. During the battle, the ship's hyperspace drive took heavy damage, but Hannser convinced Farlander that it was worth repairing. When fresh Yuuzhan Vong forces later discovered its location, they attacked with coralskippers. The Twin Suns and Scimitar squadrons arrived to fight off the coralskipper attack; the remaining crew of the cruiser was transferred to the *Whip Hand*, which scuttled the *Far Thunder* so that it couldn't fall into Yuuzhan Vong hands.

Baddon Fass

**Fasgo** A rangy red-haired spacer, he once worked for the tax-and-tariff scammer Roa. The two met again on the *Jubilee Wheel* space station during the Yuuzhan Vong invasion and were captured and imprisoned aboard the aliens' ship *Crèche* to nourish a young yammosk. Fasgo was killed when one of the yammosk's tentacles struck and shattered his skull.

**Fass, Baddon** A Dark Side Adept who had worked for Emperor Palpatine, Fass was assigned with fellow adept Zasm Katth to track down Han and Leia Organa Solo and the *Millennium Falcon*, which was hidden on Nar Shaddaa. They failed miserably, and Fass was killed along with his entire crew when his Star Destroyer *Invincible* accidentally locked on to the Nar Shaddaa control tower and collided with it.

**Fass, Egome** A humanoid-like Houk with a square jaw and tiny, gleaming eyes set deep beneath a thick, bony brow, he worked for the outlaw twins J'uoch and R'all, guarding their Dellalt mining operations. He was reputed to rival the mighty Wookiee Chewbacca in both height and strength. But the Wookiee killed Fass in hand-to-hand combat during the search for the fabled starship *Queen of Ranroon*, reputedly filled with the treasures of Xim the Despot when it disappeared several millennia before the birth of the Empire.

Jedi Master Fay

**Fassa, Major** A Gungan officer in the Grand Army, she was a niece of Boss Nass. Sent with Rep Teers to look into the construction of the Lake Umberbool arena, she got caught in its accidental collapse and was rescued by Jar Jar Binks. She narrowly escaped an assassination attempt by Zak "Squidfella" Quiglee. Later, Major Fassa won the Big Nasty Free-For-All just before the Battle of Naboo, beating out Boss Nass himself.

***Fast Hand*** Lando Calrissian's Submersible Mining Environment on *GemDiver Station*, this large diving bell was used to mine Corusca gems from Yavin. The *Fast Hand* was covered with a skin of quantum armor. As it was lowered into Yavin's atmosphere, the vessel was connected to *GemDiver Station* by an energy tether. Electromagnetic ropes dangled from the *Fast Hand* to catch the Corusca gems that had been stirred up by atmospheric storms.

***Fastlatch*-class droid** These small crab-like automated defense/security droids were developed by the Trade Federation and were outlawed in most systems. They were dangerous because they were automatically summoned when nearby beings couldn't provide the right safe-passage code, and they struck quickly with their small onboard laser cannons.

Faybo

**Fath, Bhu** This Yuuzhan Vong warrior once served under Commander Malik Carr during the destruction of the planet Obroa-skai. However, after Carr was demoted for several failures, Bhu Fath found their positions reversed: He was promoted to commander and given command of the *Sacred Pyre*. Despite his size and fearsome appearance, though, Bhu Fath commanded none of the respect that had once been given to Carr. Many Yuuzhan Vong leaders believed that Fath's escalation was more a product of the petitioning of Domain Fath than any reflection of his own abilities.

Lampay Fay

***Fat Man*** A code name for a Yevethan hyperspace-capable thrust ship, its official name was the T-Type *Aramadia*-class Thrustship. Thrustships were usually 240 meters in diameter.

**Fay, Jedi Master** Beautiful and ageless, this elfish Jedi Master looked about 20 years old, but she was actually several hundred years older than that. She had never raised her lightsaber in combat, using charisma and persuasiveness to resolve conflict. Master Fay was part of a Jedi team sent to retrieve a chemical weapon antidote on Queyta when they encountered Asajj Ventress, who controlled the antidote. Master Fay used the Force to throw shards of glass at Asajj and then incapacitated her by temporarily wiping her memory. But Ventress recovered and mortally wounded Fay with a lightsaber thrust through her back. Master Fay transferred the last of her strength in the Force to Obi-Wan Kenobi so that he could escape.

**Fay, Lampay** A Pau'an, he served as Prime Minister Tion Medon's aide-de-camp during the period of the Separatist occupation of Utapau.

**faybo** These rodent-like scavengers with large teeth, giant ears, and striped coats, were often found in and around Tusken Raider camps on Tatooine.

**Faytonni, Dannl** A Corellian con man and womanizer, he had dreamed of a career as an officer in service to the Republic. His two main strengths led him astray: a nimble mind attuned to the variables of sabacc, and a suavely mature way with women that inspired awe and admiration. It was the latter that caused him to fall for the wrong woman, a shifty changeling who conned him into fronting a spice-mining scheme. While he narrowly escaped arrest, he found himself with both CorSec and alien enemies on his tail. Enlisting the help of his ambitious and inventive friend, Achk Med-Beq, Faytonni escaped Corellia. His hopes for serving in uniform dashed, Faytonni realized that there was profit and excitement to be had in the art of con games and grifting. A series of misadventures later, the two ended up on Coruscant. A short stint in the Moderate Security Ward of the Coco District Penitentiary ended when they conned their way aboard a laundry speeder. A profitable evening's worth of gambling later, the two con men ended up with Republic military uniforms. As a "lieutenant" (or so his rank piping indicated), Faytonni hit the Outlander Club with Med-Beq, looking for marks and entertainment. They were there the night a couple of Jedi came looking for a certain bounty hunter.

*Dannl Faytonni*

**Faz** An inhabited planet lying within the Koornacht Cluster of the Farlax sector, Faz was one of the primary worlds of the alien Yevetha species and was a member of the Duskhan League.

**FC11 flechette launcher** This barely portable, shoulder-fired weapon from Golan Arms expelled canisters of razor-sharp microdarts. Each canister exploded at a predetermined distance from a selected target for maximum effect. The four-barreled weapon could fire both anti-personnel canisters and anti-vehicle canisters. The anti-personnel canister had a larger burst radius but did less damage than the anti-vehicle, which was more lethal but affected a smaller area. Both canister types could be loaded at the same time and used as needed. The design of the FC11 was based on earlier, more powerful fixed artillery pieces designed before the rise of the Empire. Golan Arms supported the Rebel Alliance (losing half of its factories to the Empire in the process) and provided the Alliance with the launchers. They were also often used by Corporate Sector Authority police squads and Imperial Remnant stormtrooper officers and swamp troopers.

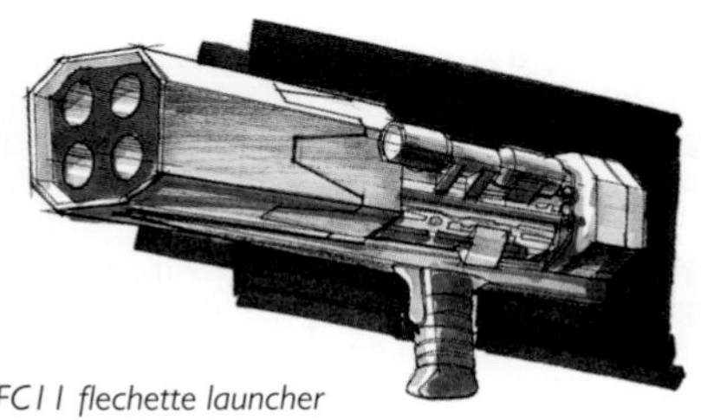

*FC11 flechette launcher*

**F'Dann system** Not far from Dufilvian, the system was home to at least nine inhabited worlds.

**Fé** One of Queen Amidala's handmaidens, she was present when Chancellor Palpatine arrived on Naboo for the celebration following the defeat of the Trade Federation blockade.

**FE-3PO** This military protocol droid had a special knowledge of all types of droids in use during the reign of the Empire.

**FE-9Q** An old tractor droid that looked something like a protocol droid on treads, FE-9Q raised young Jimm Doshun when his farmer parents were killed. Effie accompanied Jimm when he joined Han Solo's Star-Hoppers, sacrificing himself during a battle with the Cloud Riders on Aduba-3 by taking a laser strike meant for Jimm.

**fear moss** A bizarre predator found on many verdant planets throughout the galaxy, it resembled a large patch of moss hanging from a tree. But when a potential victim came close, the moss jumped off the tree and enveloped the prey, while its bevy of small mouth-like protuberances spewed acid that opened holes in the victim. Then the moss started draining bodily fluids, particularly savoring the adrenaline and similar chemicals brought on by fear. The tastiest victims were Jedi or other Force-sensitives whose fear might cause them to reach out to the dark side.

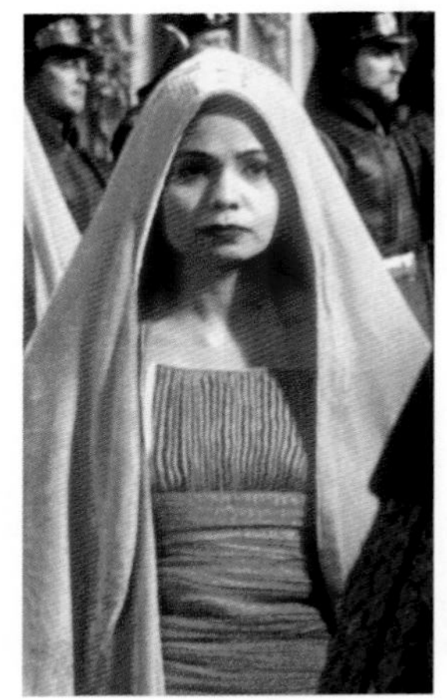

*Fé*

**feathered lizard** These tiny reptavians native to the planet Pzob often came out of the planet's forests to beg for tidbits.

**feather fern** A light, lacy plant found on the moon Yavin 4, its fronds often grew to more than 2 meters long.

**feathers of light** These silver feathers were awarded to young Ewoks on the Forest Moon of Endor who completed the journey to the Tree of Light to feed it nourishing light dust.

**fecklen** A stumpy, gracile-necked herd animal, it was native to the planet Chandrila.

**Fedalle** A powerful and wealthy Core World planet. Its people were willing to swear allegiance to whichever government was in power as long as their interests were satisfied.

| | | | | | | |
|---|---|---|---|---|---|---|
| A | B | C | D | E | F | G |
| H | I | J | K | L | M | N |
| O | P | Q | R | S | T | U |
| V | W | X | Y | Z | 1 | 2 |
| 3 | 4 | 5 | 6 | 7 | 8 | 9 | 0 |

*Federation Basic*

**Fed-Dub** A familiar name for the Federation of Double Worlds, the government that controlled Talus and Tralus. Members were elected, and they controlled a small military force to keep peace on the two planets. Fed-Dub became part of the Confederation.

**Federation Basic** A written form of Basic used by the Trade Federation.

**Fedje** A forest planet. Han Solo spent some time there as part of his Rebel Alliance duties.

**Fee, Yoland** A Jedi who was responsible for the gardens of the Jedi Temple, he was killed in the great massacre by Darth Vader and the 501st clone troopers.

**feen** A sweet fruit, it was found on Ryloth.

**Feenicks VI** An Imperial System Patrol Squadron base located near this planet was eliminated by an Alliance strike team following the Battle of Yavin.

**Feeorin** These hulking humanoids were found in small colonies on a few Outer Rim worlds. Their original homeworld was a mystery, but Feeorin colonists abandoned it eons ago following a radical climate change. The Feeorin colony transports spread out to the far reaches of the galaxy in search of habitable planets; many of these ships were lost or destroyed. Those Feeorin who survived founded settlements on Outer Rim worlds, where they had difficulty adapting and were sometimes viewed as unwelcome scavengers by the locals. At the time of the Battle of Naboo, there were fewer than a million surviving Feeorin. Like humans, Feeorin displayed a wide range of personalities, although many Feeorin explorers and spacers were considered gruff and dangerous, especially the pirates. Feeorin skin tones varied from coal black to pale white, but green, yellow, and blue were the most common colors. Instead of hair, thick tendrils hung from the back of Feeorin heads.

**Feesa (Chaf'ees'aklaio)** A female aide to Aristocra Formbi, this young Chiss female met Luke and Mara Jade Skywalker on their way to locate the ruins of the Outbound Flight Project. She was curt with answers to any questions they asked. Feesa, whose full Chiss name was Chaf'ees'aklaio, later accompanied a Chiss contingent when the Skywalkers found the ruins of the Outbound Flight mission but got trapped in a turbolift with Bearsh and disguised Vagaari pirates, mortal enemies of the Chiss. Mara finally got to the bottom of a tangled plot by Formbi, with the help of Feesa, to get the Vagaari to attack the Chiss first, so that the Chiss could then take the moral high ground as they wiped out their archfoes.

**Feethan Ottraw Scalable Assemblies** A Utapaun manufacturer, the company was taken over when the planet was invaded by Confederacy forces. The Techno Union used it to turn out its Mankvim-814 Interceptors and small fighters like the Belbullab-22.

**Fef** A moderately large planet orbiting an orange-yellow star in the Glythe sector, it was home to the insectoid Fefze. Fef's thick atmosphere and hot temperature contributed to its teeming variety of life-forms, all of which had relatively short life spans. The Fefze, who formed intelligent group-minds (or "swarms") of 10 to 100 individuals, were able to digest all forms of carbon-based organic matter.

**fefze beetle** An insectoid best known for its giant mutated subspecies, and the only creatures that survived the collapse of the planet Duro's ecosystems. Mutant fefze beetles, which could grow to more than a meter long, could convert any organic material into an edible protein paste. The mutant beetles had both internal and external skeletons, thus enabling their enormous size. The beetles gorged on the white-eyes (actually naotebe winglings) released by Nom Anor into the domed Settlement Thirty-two refugee encampment on Duro during the Yuuzhan Vong invasion.

**Fegel, Onjo** A talented human male kloo horn player for a popular b'ssa nuuvu group on Tuttin IV, Onjo Fegel was actually an Imperial Intelligence agent stuck on this backrocket planet.

**Fehern** This planet was homeworld to the Eddel species, which traveled throughout the Trax sector during the Old Republic. But under the Empire, Fehern was taken over and the Eddel became little more than slaves.

**Fehlaaur** A Chiss, he served on the Moff High Council in the years following the Sith–Imperial War. Moff Fehlaaur was responsible for the New Imperial Diplomatic Corps and was the council's only link to the Chiss Ascendancy, the ruling families of Chiss civilization.

**Fein** A member of Talon Karrde's smuggling operation, Fein was a weapons specialist who was recruited from a swoop gang in the Outer Rim Territories. He was well respected despite his somewhat abrasive manner.

**Feiya** The site of a small spaceport, Feiya was also the only known settlement on the planet Deyer.

**Fel, Ajai** Baron Soontir Fel's sister-in-law and the mother of young Fyric, Ajai Fel believed strongly that her son had been kidnapped to force the Fels to disclose the whereabouts of the Baron's wife, Wynssa Starflare (actually Syal Antilles). Her husband, Todr, shot lead kidnapper Ilir Post, and Fyric was rescued with the help of Rogue Squadron. The family then fled Corellia with the Rogues to seek sanctuary with the New Republic.

*Jagged Fel*

**Fel, Cem** A son of Baron Soontir Fel and Syal Antilles, Cem was born on Csilla. He became an experienced pilot and often took the family yacht *Starflare* on short trips. Cem's existence, however, was a closely held secret to try to ensure that the entire Fel clan wasn't wiped out by its numerous enemies.

**Fel, Chak** A son of Baron Soontir Fel and Syal Antilles, he became a commander in the navy of the Empire of the Hand in the period before the Yuuzhan Vong invasion of the galaxy. Commander Fel led a small unit of 501st stormtroopers to help protect a Jedi and Chiss mission to locate the remains of the Outbound Flight Project. But important information about Outbound Flight that Admiral Parck had entrusted him to deliver to Luke and Mara Jade Skywalker was stolen from his shuttle. Following the discovery of the project's remains and the surfacing of the Vagaari threat, Fel was mauled by a Vagaari wolvkil and had to give up command of his unit. During a Vagaari ambush, the commander took shrapnel from a turbolift explosion and later died of his multiple injuries.

**Fel, Cherith** The oldest daughter of Baron Soontir Fel and Syal Antilles, she was the second of the Fel children to die in combat during the Yuuzhan Vong invasion. She was only 19 years old.

**Fel, Davin** The oldest son of Baron Soontir Fel and Syal Antilles, he was the first of the Fel children to die in combat during the Yuuzhan Vong invasion. Davin trained among the Chiss, and his piloting skills and risk taking awed the younger generations on his homeworld of Csilla. He was killed when he was only 20 years old.

**Fel, Fyric** A nephew of Baron Soontir Fel, the two-year-old was kidnapped from the Fel estate on the planet Corellia shortly after the Battle of Brentaal. Fyric Fel was set free when his father, Todr, shot lead kidnapper Ilir Post in a rescue abetted by members of Rogue Squadron.

**Fel, Jagged** The handsome son of Baron Soontir Fel and Syal Antilles, he had pale green eyes, a scar that started above his right eye and ran over his skull, and coal-black locks. He somewhat resembled his uncle Wedge Antilles. Jagged, better known as Jag, grew up among the Chiss and was accepted by them as one of their own. The 18-year-old Colonel Fel and his Chiss force Spike pilots were major factors in helping rout the Yuuzhan Vong at the Battle of Garqi.

Jag Fel spent much of his childhood at the Hand of Thrawn, a secret fortress on Nirauan that was run by Chiss. Three years after the treaty between the Imperial Remnant and the New Republic, Fel went to study at the Chiss military academy, although he started his instruction later than Chiss children, who matured more quickly than humans. At the academy, he flew a clawcraft, the *Blue Flame*. When pirates attacked the academy, Jag flew the *Blue Flame* into battle to lure the pirates into the open. He purposely crash-landed his ship, resulting in a severe head gash that became his telltale scar. His idea of using mirrored transparisteel to confuse the pirates resulted in their defeat, and he became accepted by the Chiss academy cadets as one of their own.

Following the Battle of Garqi, the Ithorians hosted a reception for New Republic and Imperial Remnant forces that had come to defend the planet Ithor from the Yuuzhan Vong. It was there that Jag met Jaina Solo; they were impressed by each other's piloting skills and perhaps a bit by some intangible feelings. After the Battle of Ithor, Colonel Fel and two of his squadrons remained with the New Republic as liaisons with Rogue Squadron. With Jag spending time on Hapes—the suspected next target of the Yuuzhan Vong, since many refugees had been evacuated to the planet—he and Jaina felt their mutual attraction grow. It was anything but a simple or straightforward relationship, because their military roles in defense of the galaxy kept them so occupied. They discovered a mutual pleasure in teasing and baiting each other, although that led to many misunderstandings. Jag visited a refugee camp hoping to meet Jaina's famous father, Han Solo. When he reached the Solos' tent, he interrupted a fight in progress and discovered an unconscious Han; the assailants fled, and Leia believed the fight may have been an attempted assassination.

When Jaina unknowingly became a centerpiece in a plot by the former Queen Mother of Hapes to regain power, Jag's attempts to caution her resulted in a rebuff. They both, however, took part in the Hapan defense of their homeworld, driving off the Yuuzhan Vong. Other battles followed, and Jag joined the Twin Suns Squadron after Luke Skywalker turned over control of it to Jaina.

Separately, Jag and Jaina played major roles in the recovery of Coruscant from the Yuuzhan Vong. Although Jag finally admitted to Jaina that he really loved her, she told him that the time was not right to settle down and have a relationship. Fel returned home and was named the primary liaison between the Chiss Expansionary Defense Fleet and the Galactic Alliance. But alliances shifted, and Jag found himself leading several expeditions to stop the expansion of the Colony, which placed him in opposition to the Alliance and thus the Solo family. Near the end of the Swarm War, during the Battle of Tenupe, Jag was forced to try to shoot down the *Millennium Falcon,* but he was instead shot down by Leia Organa and officially listed as missing in action.

Several years later the Solos ran into Jag on Telkur Station. There he filled them in on how he had been stranded on Tenupe, how several rescue missions had failed, and how he eventually had been saved. Jag later was forced into exile by the Chiss after his actions raised questions about his loyalty. Luke Skywalker put Jag in charge of a task force assigned to track down and bring to justice Alema Rar, a Twi'lek Jedi turned dark sider who was wreaking havoc in the galaxy and had a blood feud with the Skywalker and Solo families. The task force included Jaina Solo and fellow Jedi Zekk, with whom Jaina had developed a powerful bond.

Fel acquired a set of Mandalorian crushgaunts that Boba Fett had sent to Han Solo as a gift, hoping that the *beskar* used in their manufacture would help him contain Rar if needed. The team tracked her down to an asteroid in the MZX32905 system, where Lumiya had once made her home. After a chase and battle, the mad dark sider backed Jag into a corner, then used the Force to seize his blaster. But Jag had anticipated that move and had placed a sensor in the weapon that would detonate it if the blaster wasn't near his body. The blaster exploded, catching Rar in the chest and face. Jag then grabbed her by the neck with the crushgaunts, crushing the life out of her and bringing her long terror spree to an end.

With the eventual defeat of Darth Caedus—the former Jacen Solo—Luke Skywalker offered a splinter group of Imperial Moffs a chance to rejoin the Galactic Alliance provided they submit to the command and leadership of Jagged Fel. Fel was surprised and angry that Skywalker hadn't discussed the plan with him beforehand, until Luke explained that the Moffs needed to know that it hadn't been Jagged's idea. The Moffs accepted, saying that Jagged would have their full support.

Roan Fel

Fel finally agreed to take on the challenge of uniting the GA military and ending the war with the Confederation.

**Fel, Marasiah** The beautiful daughter and only child of Emperor Roan Fel, the Princess was considered to be her father's eventual successor, although the Moff Council was not happy with the idea of a woman ruling the New Empire. Marasiah Fel, known to her confidantes as Sia, had been trained as an Imperial Knight, but had to flee into hiding during an Imperial mission on Socorro when Darth Krayt took over the galaxy by force. Eventually she was tracked down by Darth Talon, but escaped an initial assassination attempt. In fleeing, she met Cade Skywalker and his bounty hunter colleagues, who helped her escape to Vendaxa. Darth Talon attacked again, but Cade and his friends defeated the Sith. They were soon joined by two of her father's closest aides . . . and then four more Sith Lords, one of whom almost killed the Princess with lightsaber blows. Cade Skywalker saved her life with the help of the Force. The two of them realized that the Jedi and Imperial Knights needed to abandon their long-simmering antagonism and join together if there was ever to be a chance to defeat the new Sith Empire.

Soontir Fel

**Fel, Roan** Once an Imperial Knight, he became the third member of the Fel dynasty to sit on the throne as leader of the New Empire, around 130 years after the Battle of Yavin. Known for his political acumen and strategic thinking, Roan Fel kept the New Empire on the course his benevolent grandfather had set. He could not, however, foresee the reemergence of the Sith nor the impact they would have on his throne—and his family.

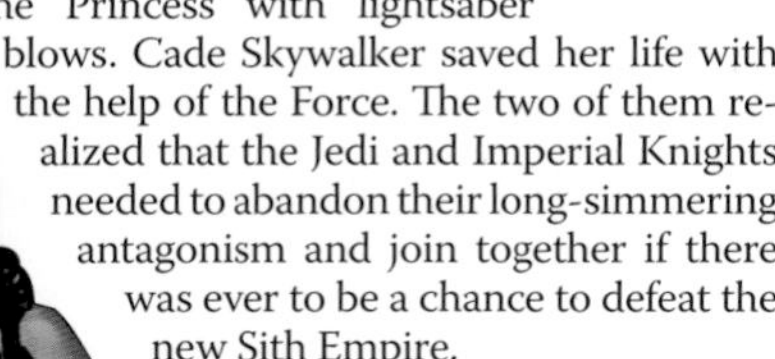

Marasiah Fel

Fel was a skillful Force-user, and that helped him maintain the doctrine of "Victory Without War." But when Darth Krayt showed up on Coruscant to propose an alliance, Emperor Fel and the Moff Council agreed. What they didn't understand was that Darth Krayt had set in motion a plan for the Sith to retake the galaxy. This led to the failure of the Ossus Project, which was supposed to result in the terraforming of 100 planets; a decision by the Moffs to declare war on the Galactic Alliance (the Sith–Imperial War); the slaughter of a majority of living Jedi in the Massacre at Ossus; and Krayt's apparent killing of Fel and the Moffs. But it actually was Fel's security double, and Fel and his daughter, Marasiah, went into hiding. After seven years of sporadic hit-and-run attacks against Krayt's forces, Fel returned to the impregnable fortress planet of Bastion, the world that had been headquarters of the New Empire. With help from loyalists, Fel retook control of the planet and began planning to destroy Darth Krayt's Sith Empire. His initial attempt to forge a pact with the Galactic Alliance was sabotaged by the Sith, followed by another failed assassination attempt on the Emperor himself.

**Fel, Soontir** A native of Corellia once known as the Empire's greatest TIE fighter pilot, he was in charge of the 37th Imperial Fighter Wing and later became an instructor to future Rebel Alliance pilots Tycho Celchu, Biggs Darklighter, and Derek "Hobbie" Klivian. When Darklighter and Klivian defected to the Rebel Alliance, Fel was held partly responsible, and he was reassigned to the 181st Imperial Fighter Wing (also known as the "One-Eighty-Worst"). He soon met and married Wynssa Starflare, whose real name was Syal Antilles, sister of ace Rogue Squadron leader Wedge Antilles. Fel and his squadron finally went up against the Rogues at the Battle of Brentaal. In combat, Fel's TIE interceptor was disabled and he was captured—but he soon allied himself with those he had so adamantly fought against.

Soontir Fel, 1.83 meters tall with dark brown eyes and coal-black hair, was an imposing figure. He had built up his physique through years of hard work as a farmer on his homeworld. While at the Imperial Academy on Carida, he met and frequently challenged Han Solo. After graduating second in his class (behind only Solo) and taking part in the disastrous Battle of Nar Shaddaa, he was assigned to the 37th Imperial Fighter Wing, then became a flight instructor on Prefsbelt IV, and finally was reassigned to the 181st.

Fel had become more and more disenchanted

by the Empire, especially after he saw the machinations of Imperial Intelligence head Ysanne Isard up close. He was, however, impressed by one up-and-coming Imperial officer—unusual in that he was an alien, a member of a secretive species that most had never heard of—a Chiss named Thrawn. After Fel was captured by the New Republic and fought with them for a while, he and his wife both disappeared. He had aligned himself with forces loyal to Grand Admiral Thrawn. After his final battle with an Imperial warlord, in which he lost his right eye, he retired from active military duty to become a commander at the secret Hand of Thrawn Chiss training academy on Nirauan. He and his son Jagged became involved with the Chiss military during the Yuuzhan Vong invasion of the galaxy, but Soontir Fel and his wife soon retired to the relative safety of the Chiss homeworld of Csilla.

Syal Antilles Fel and husband Soontir Fel

**Fel, Syal Antilles** Better known by her stage name of Wynssa Starflare, she was one of the most popular holodrama stars of the New Order. Growing up in the Corellian system, she loved her family—including her younger brother, Wedge—but Syal didn't want the life of a starship mechanic. Just before her twentieth birthday, she moved to Coruscant to pursue an acting career. She changed her name to Wynssa Starflare and became famous. During a party on Coruscant, she met Soontir Fel, an Imperial TIE fighter ace and instructor who had been stationed on the planet since the Battle of Yavin. They fell in love almost immediately, and Syal was forced to tell him her true name and relationship to Antilles. Fel told her that it didn't matter, and they eventually married.

**Fel, Todr** Soontir Fel's younger brother, he let his wife, Ajai, contact Rogue Squadron pilots to help in the search for their young son Fyric, who had been kidnapped by a longtime Fel family enemy. After a successful rescue during which Todr Fel killed the kidnapper, the family fled Corellia with the Rogues to seek sanctuary with the New Republic.

**Fel, Wynssa** A daughter of Soontir Fel and Syal Antilles, she grew up on the isolated Chiss homeworld of Csilla, making her anxious to learn as much about the rest of the galaxy as possible. When Luke Skywalker's mission to locate the living world of Zonama Sekot came to Csilla, Wynssa Fel helped Jacen Solo develop search algorithms for planetary data at the Expeditionary Library.

**Felacat** The homeworld of the lycanthropic species known as the Felacatians, this temperate planet had at least two moons. Felacatians were humanoid, although they had short fur and long tails. But when under stress for an extended period of time—such as traveling through hyperspace—a Felacatian morphed into a very large and rapacious feline beast.

**Felana** A female Vorzydiak, she was the leader of Vorzyd 5 about 11 years before the Battle of Naboo. Felana got into a spat with Chairman Port of Vorzyd 4 who accused the inhabitants of Vorzyd 5 of sabotaging factories on his world. Neither realized that the damage was being perpetrated by Freelies, Vorzyd 4 youths who wanted to change the hardworking culture of their planet. When Qui-Gon Jinn and Obi-Wan Kenobi revealed the truth, the two planets agreed to stop fighting and try to mutually resolve their differences.

**felbar** A baked pet food found throughout much of the galaxy.

***Fell Defender*** A Chiss Star Destroyer, it captured the *Millennium Falcon* above the planet Tenupe.

**Fellion** A secret enforcer on Brentaal IV for the Black Sun criminal organization, this timid-looking woman was anything but, and she used her martial arts skills and an array of blaster weapons to get most jobs done.

**Fellon** A port city on the planet Halmad, it was the site of a small Imperial base that was destroyed in Operation Groundquake.

Jedi Master Feln

Davin Felth

**Fellowship Plaza** A pleasant oasis of pedestrian walkways lined with blartrees, it was built in the Coruscant Senate District after the devastated planet was retaken by the Galactic Alliance from the Yuuzhan Vong.

**Feln, Jedi Master** A large Feeorin, he helped instruct Padawans at the training center on Taris sometime after the Great Sith War. Master Feln also was a very talented seer who had strong visions of the future through the Force. But he and the other members of the Covenant foresaw that their present class of Padawans would become Sith Lords and exterminate the Jedi Order, so under the command of Jedi Master Lucien Draay, they plotted to kill the entire class at a ceremony that was supposed to initiate them as Jedi Knights. But one Padawan, Zayne Carrick, arrived late and escaped the massacre. The Jedi Masters then blamed the slaughter on Carrick before they were recalled to Coruscant.

**Felspern** A Mon Calamari councilor, he ran for the post of Senator.

**Felth, Davin** A stormtrooper, he joined the Empire's ranks when he was 18 and graduated from the toughest Imperial training facility on Carida. He excelled in Imperial walker training, even pointing out a fatal design flaw. But rather than being rewarded, he was assigned to a stormtrooper unit as a common foot soldier and shipped off to Tatooine. He was part of the detachment sent to look for C-3PO and R2-D2 after they escaped from the *Tantive IV.* His unit followed tracks that eventually led to a Jawa sandcrawler. His commanding officer, Captain Terrik, ordered the Jawas butchered, as well as the moisture farmers to whom they had sold the wanted droids. Later, a comlink call brought the troopers to Docking Bay 94, where the droids had been found. In the firefight that followed, Felth mutinied against his bloodthirsty captain, shooting him in the back. As the *Millennium Falcon* escaped, Felth knew he would take on a new role in life, spying for the Rebel Alliance from the inside and letting the Alliance know about the AT-AT's design flaw.

Felucia

**Felucia** Once a major holding of the Commerce Guild, Felucia was a world teeming with fungal life-forms and immense primitive plants. Much of the planet had a fetid, humid landscape overgrown by a bizarre wilderness. Small creatures lived amid the multiple layers of the fungus, mold, and lichen. Many of these life-forms were partially or completely translucent; they colored the sunlight as the beams penetrated their skins. Beneath the hazy canopies of the enormous pitcher plants and leafy growths was a surreal color-drenched landscape.

Although Commerce Guild Presidente Shu Mai called Castell the planet of her birth, her home was Felucia, site of a sprawling compound outside the city of Kway Teow that served as a remote office and private retreat. The Gossams had colonized Felucia early in their interplanetary history, before moving on to larger and more lucrative exploits. Deemed too wild to support massive Gossam colonies, Felucia eventually became an exotic retreat for the wealthy, along with the poorly paid workers who supported their extravagant whims. Because of the difficulty of settling the planet, there were only a few cities of note, mainly Kway Teow, Har Gau, and Niango. Before the Clone Wars, the Commerce Guild controlled these population centers. What little independence existed was huddled in a few scattered townships founded by runaway workers and fugitive union organizers.

Felucia's flora made it a challenging world to colonize. Many of the indigenous plants aggressively defended themselves. Sharp barbs, shooting spores, and poisonous defenses scuttled early attempts at agriculture. Still, the Gossam colonists carved out a few footholds on the planet, exploiting its porous crust and expansive arterial network of underground and surface water. This allowed modern water processing to be concentrated in several key locations, efficiently scrubbing the water and ridding it of harmful, naturally occurring impurities.

When the Clone Wars erupted, Felucia was one of the first planets targeted by the Republic. A medical facility in Niango was found to be the source of biomolecules used in military nerve toxins. An elite team of ARC troopers destroyed the facility, but the demands of the war prevented an occupation force from remaining. Thus, the guild still held possession of the planet, but Shu Mai found that her retreat was no longer peaceful. She engineered a spiteful contingency plan should Felucia ever fall. Natural toxins harvested from Felucia's untamed wilderness were refined and loaded into secret pumps in key locations in the water network. If released, they would quickly course through the waterways to poison all the cities—and inhabitants—of Felucia and the surrounding areas, making the planet a deadly "prize" for the Republic.

When Castell fell to the Republic during the Outer Rim Sieges, Shu Mai fled to Felucia. As a leader of the Separatists, she was targeted by the Republic. Jedi warriors Barriss Offee and Zonder went undercover, posing as relief workers, but they were discovered by Commerce Guild guards and sent to the state-of-the-art Nigkoe detention facility. Jedi General Aayla Secura and the 327th Star Corps of clone troopers liberated them, and Jedi computer prodigy Ekria calculated that there was a chance to stop the spread of Shu Mai's toxins. To accomplish that, the Jedi teams separated to reach three heavily guarded pumping facilities.

At that point the call came from Coruscant to execute Order 66. Clone Commander Bly carried out the order by ruthlessly killing Secura. Lieutenant Galle gave the order to open fire on Offee, killing her. The Padawans Ekria, Zonder, and Drake Lo'gaan managed to escape the initial slaughter.

**Felucia ground beetle** *See* gelagrub.

**Felyood, Captain Naz** A Corellian pirate who owned and operated the freighter *Jynni's Virtue*. Felyood, his ship, and crew were lost six months prior to the Battle of Yavin, when they apparently were shot down over the planet Korriban. Although Felyood's commentary in the ship's logs indicated that he believed he and his crew had been on Korriban a few days, the timestamps revealed that many months had passed. According to voice logs, Felyood stumbled upon Dathka Graush's tomb and tried to take the jewel known as the Heart of Graush. He became possessed by the spirit of Graush and unwittingly unleashed Korriban zombies. He was forced to wander Korriban, never quite dead or alive, and always searching for the Heart of Graush.

**Femon** The faithful assistant to the power-mad Dark Jedi Kueller, she had long black hair and an unnaturally pale face, with blackened eyes and blood-red lips. Like Kueller, Femon wore a death mask, but hers looked less realistic than Kueller's own. She had been serving Kueller since the beginning of his campaign against the New Republic. Her family had been killed when the Imperial battlemoon *Eye of Palpatine* swept over her planet. In some ways, her need for revenge was even more severe than Kueller's. She withdrew her support from Kueller once she believed that he was exhibiting the same weakness that she attributed to the New Republic: not ruling with the iron fist necessary to squash dangerous outside elements. Because she lacked confidence in him, Kueller killed her with his Force powers.

**Fen, Calk** One of Jabba the Hutt's accountants, he was responsible for maintaining the file on Han Solo's debt in the years following the Battle of Yavin. Fen recommended that Jabba forget about capturing Solo and concentrate on claiming possession of the *Millennium Falcon* instead.

**Fenald** The chief of security for the important Kuat Drive Yards, he seemed loyal to the shipyard's owner, Kuat of Kuat, a direct descendant of one of the founding families of Kuat civilization. But Fenald had a secret arrangement with Kodir of Kuhlvult and aided her scheme to take over the vital shipyards during the rise of the New Order. Once Fenald began demanding hush money from Kodir, though, she slit his throat.

**Fend'Allomin** A pale-skinned Twi'lek, she was rescued from slavery by Jedi Master Vhiin Thorla. Fend'Allomin and about a dozen other Twi'leks lived in the Enclave, a secret refuge that Master Thorla had established on his homeworld of Ryloth around the time of the Clone Wars.

**Fenelar armor** A flexible armor, it was made from a variety of exotic minerals, including the alloy phrik, which the Fenelar first developed. The Fenelar species was exterminated by early Mandalorian crusaders.

**Fengrine** Toward the end of the Old Republic, this planet became one of the largest growers and exporters of foodstuffs in the galaxy, with its entire surface devoted to agriculture.

**Fenic** After joining Rebel leader Dunlan in the fight against the Imperial occupation of the planet Ahakista following the Battle of Yavin, Fenic lost hope and decided to capture and turn in Dunlan for the high bounty on him. The plot was thwarted, but Dunlan let Fenic go.

**Fenion** A planet just Rimward of New Republic space, it was visited by one of the large corvettes in Warlord Zsinj's fleet, the *Night Caller,* before the ship was captured by Wraith Squadron in the period following the Battle of Endor.

**Fenn, Fiav** A Sullustan officer in the naval forces of the Galactic Alliance, she served as an aide to Admiral Matric Klauskin aboard the battle carrier *Dodonna* during the years following the war against the Yuuzhan Vong. Fiav Fenn remained aboard, serving under Admiral Tarla Limpan during the Alliance's blockade of the Corellian system. When the *Dodonna* was attacked by a group of Bothan Assault Cruisers, the admiral ordered all ships to jump to a rendezvous location known as Point Bleak, but Colonel Fenn realized that the jump of ships from six separate zones would allow the enemy to track their escape vectors and locate them later. Fenn suggested instead that all vessels jump to any safe point beyond the Corellian system, *then* jump to Point Bleak. The admiral was glad for her advice.

Kh'aris Fenn

**Fenn, Kh'aris** Kh'aris's father, the clan leader Ro Fenn, forced him to take the blame for Ro's own crimes by being exiled to the Bright Lands. While exiled, Fenn began working with smugglers and spice barons to control ryll spice production. After becoming wealthy, he made plans to take over his homeworld of Ryloth in a pact with Separatist leader Count Dooku. Fenn arranged to have his minions kidnap the son of another clan head and demanded that his father and another clan leader cede control of a major Ryloth city to him as well as support him as the sole ruler of the planet. But the plan failed, and Fenn fled offworld. He used the credits that Dooku had given him to secure Ryloth for the Confederacy as bounty for Jedi killings. When Dooku discovered Fenn's duplicity, he dispatched Quinlan Vos to eliminate him. Vos took pride in his work—and Fenn's head for proof of a job well done.

**Fenn, Rh'ajah** A relative of Kh'aris Fenn, Rh'ajah Fenn was incapacitated by Quinlan Vos 17 years after the Battle of Geonosis. This allowed Vos to infiltrate Kh'aris Fenn's lair and eliminate the treacherous Twi'lek.

Ro Fenn

**Fenn, Ro** The obese leader of his clan on Ryloth, he made his son Kh'aris take the fall and go into exile for his own crimes. But Ro Fenn's son was even more duplicitous than his father. In the end, neither survived.

**Fenn, Swilja** A young Twi'lek Jedi trained by Luke Skywalker, she was pursued by the traitorous Peace Brigade on Cujicor. They imprisoned her and left the injured Swilja Fenn behind for the Yuuzhan Vong. Warmaster Tsavong Lah himself tortured and questioned her regarding the whereabouts of Jacen Solo. She gave up no information before dying.

**Fenn, Tchaw** A pudgy, middle-aged Bothan with an impeccable pointed beard, he considered himself an information broker around the time of the Battle of Naboo. For a time, Tchaw Fenn worked exclusively for Riboga the Hutt.

**Fenner's rock** Toothsome, fast-multiplying creatures found on a number of planets, they were named for xenobiologist Rivoc Fenner, who tripped over the first one he ever found. Fenner's rocks did indeed look like lichen- and moss-covered rocks or stones, and that was what they subsisted on. They dragged themselves along rock beds to find food, and when they reproduced too quickly, they had a way of damming up natural waterways and producing semi-toxic bacteria.

Navy Trooper Fenson

**Fennesa** A rocky colony planet, it was probably settled from the Core Worlds.

**Fennesa mountain nerf** The nerfs on Fennesa adapted to the mountainous terrain after they were brought to the rocky planet several millennia before the Battle of Yavin by colonists. More nimble than their flatland cousins, these foul-smelling nerfs lived on the rocky mountain slopes, eating the grass and thistled scrubs that grew between rocks. While the typical "plains" nerfs were kept in pens and let out to pasture only when necessary, nerf herders left the mountainous herds out nearly year-round. But getting nerfs off the mountain for shearing or slaughter was difficult since the beasts were incorrigible hiders in Fennesa's shallow caves and rocky overhangs. Fighting within a herd was dangerous. Nerf rams seldom hurt each other while butting heads, but the Fennesa Nerf Herding Council estimated that each year about 5.6 rams out of 1,000 were lost due to falls. Although herders cleared a mountain of predators before they released a herd onto it, the occasional wounded or dead ram at the bottom attracted scavengers that also enjoyed a good nerf steak (very rare). A healthy mountain nerf could defend itself from these nuisances with its horns, its surprisingly powerful kicks, and its spittle. Mountain nerf spittle was not only foul smelling but also slightly acidic, leaving a sting and a red mark on the unlucky target.

**Fenni, Raskta** Before the Great Sith War, she was known as one of the best practitioners of Echani, a deadly martial art that featured a pair of short but very sharp knives. Many bladed weapons were named for Raskta Fenni.

**Fenoob, Feen** A Sullustan gambler, he owed money to Darnada, a Dug who was a Vigo in the Black Sun criminal organization. Feen Fenoob managed to evade two thugs dispatched by Darnada, but he had the misfortune to run into Darth Maul, who cut the gambler in half.

**Fen'po** This young Dathomir native was a member of the Singing Mountain Clan of Force-using women around the time Luke Skywalker discovered the remains of the *Chu'unthor* on the planet.

**Fenson, Navy Trooper** An Imperial Navy trooper and a native of the planet Rendili, he was skilled in close-quarters combat. Trooper Fenson and fellow Trooper Vesden were assigned to monitor activity around the shield generator bunker on the Forest Moon of Endor.

**Feps, Deggar** A scout, he angered Sottos, a Hutt crime lord on Nal Hutta during the early years of the New Order. His plans to flee the planet were interrupted by spy droid NEK-01, and he offered to trade useful information on Sottos in exchange for help getting off the planet aboard the *Lost Lady*. Feps fled into the warrens of Nar Shaddaa.

**Feraa** A smuggler, he and his cohort Suyin had a load of spice to deliver to Vogga the Hutt on Nar Shaddaa after the Great Sith War. But their attempt to circumvent security by traveling through undercity vents and tunnels was disastrous. The two went their separate ways, but first Suyin and then Feraa became hopelessly lost and died.

**feragriff** A creature native to the planet Batorine, it was hunted by the Blood Carvers during coming-of-age ceremonies. When the Blood Carvers were relocated to Coruscant, they brought along several feragriffs to preserve their ancient traditions.

**Feraleechi Onetime Loop** A multilevel form of encryption, it was used by the Confederacy of Independent Systems during the Clone Wars. The name came in part from the fact that the code was keyed to a specific day's news on the HoloNet.

**Ferals** A loose term for a group of mostly lower-class sentient beings mentally enslaved by the World Brain that the Yuuzhan Vong installed on Coruscant after their successful takeover of the galactic capital. After the defeat of the invaders, the World Brain was permitted to continue its terraforming of Coruscant—but to meet the needs of all species, not just the Yuuzhan Vong. The World Brain used the lower-class sentients as its eyes and ears all over the planet. The Ferals lived the life of uncivilized creatures in the depths of the cityscape. When the World Brain died some 10 years after the Yuuzhan Vong defeat, many residents feared that the Ferals might riot; instead, they seemed to exercise control over their baser instincts.

**Ferasi, Maris** A Corellian, she served as Dubrak Qennto's first mate aboard the *Bargain Hunter.* Maris Ferasi, "Rak," and their third crewmate, Jorj Car'das, were captured by then Force Commander Thrawn aboard the *Springhawk* some five years before the Clone Wars, after they made a blind jump into hyperspace to avoid being captured by Progga the Hutt. Ferasi and Car'das took interest in various aspects of the Chiss culture, and learned the Cheunh language from Thrawn himself in exchange for teaching him Basic. Ferasi found the stoicism and loyalty of the Chiss a refreshing change from the corruption and greed of the Old Republic. But after three months' captivity, she and Rak were left behind at Crustai while Thrawn took Car'das on another mission: the elimination of the Outbound Flight Project and the Vagaari pirates. They eventually were freed and allowed to return to the Old Republic, where they were able to pay off their debts and resume their smuggling activities.

**ferbil** A small, furred creature, it was native to the planet Kegan. Ferbils often made good pets.

**Ferdas, Captain** A captain in the Imperial Navy, he commanded the Imperial Star Destroyer *Avenger* during the early stages of the Galactic Civil War, before Lorth Needa assumed command.

**Fere (Feree)** Located in the Fere (or Feree) system, which contained a double star, the planet was home to an advanced culture of tall, pale humanoids with six-fingered hands around 200 years before the Galactic Civil War. They were master starship builders, and some of their small luxury cruisers were in service for centuries. During a series of wars, a deadly plague was carried to Fere, killing all life on the planet.

**Ferentina** A village on Naboo, it was located in a mountain pass and near a river that ultimately led to a large swamp. Ferentina served as a refugee camp for many Naboo until it, too, was overrun by Trade Federation forces.

**Ferfer** A Ryn, he worked as a guide on the planet Caluula but secretly was a resistance operative for a network of Ryn spies; he was known by the code name Gatherer 164. At the height of the Yuuzhan Vong invasion, Ferfer and his Rodian partner Sasso assisted Team Meloque in a mission to destroy a yammosk that had been placed on the planet. The team felt sure it was being baited into a trap, but continued the important mission. When they reached the yammosk's location, Ferfer went to hide the pack animals used by the team, but encountered a hidden group of Yuuzhan Vong Slayers. The lead warrior lashed out with his amphistaff, slicing open Ferfer's belly. He died almost instantly.

**Feriae Junction** Located at the nexus of the Hydian Way, the Gordian Reach, and the Thesme Trace, the planet known as Junction was a run-down but busy trade world. Briefly a boom world in the years of the Corusca stone rush on nearby Yavin, it became an aging port where laws were lax but traffic was heavy. A few impressive edifices in Junction City stood as mute testament to the planet's better days, including the sprawling Grand Terminal, the main arrival and departure point. For a brief period after the destruction of the Death Star, the planet was the principal transfer point for supplies headed for the Rebel base on Yavin 4, with Rebel pilots running the Imperial blockade thrown up after the Death Star's destruction and Junction City crawling with spies and operatives from the Empire, the Alliance, Black Sun, and the Hutts.

*Orion Ferret*

**Ferinn, Trennt** A colonel in New Republic Intelligence, he provided a detailed analysis of the situation leading up to the Starbuster Plot and the rise of the Human League on Corellia.

**Ferionic Nebula** A small nebula, it was located near the Dantooine system.

**Ferlani, Luthus** The leader of the Ferlani criminal family based on Esseles, he spent much of his youth representing the family on business throughout the Darpa sector and within Hutt space. Outwardly, Luthus Ferlani seemed like a kindly gentleman, but once he got angry or was disappointed, he could be terrifying.

**Fernooda** As the liaison between Annoodat radical General Ashaar Khorda and the outside world, this Dug hired both Jango Fett and Zam Wesell to steal the Infant of Shaa—a tiny religious statue that contained huge amounts of Force energy—in a plot to destroy Coruscant. Jango succeeded and got his bounty, but in the end strangled Fernooda to death as he and Wesell thwarted the plot.

**Ferob, Captain** An Imperial captain, he commanded the *Victory*-class Star Destroyer *Iron Fist* in the Unknown Regions under the watchful eye of Grand Admiral Thrawn.

**fero xyn** This vicious predator, once native to the galaxy of the Yuuzhan Vong, was the only creature from their homeworld that had genetic material compatible with a vornskr. The initial Yuuzhan Vong attempts to create a Jedi-hunting creature from pure vornskr stock proved only mildly successful—the beast wasn't ferocious enough. But the fero xyn was a terror and already conditioned to respond to the commands of a Yuuzhan Vong warrior. The resulting hybrid, a voxyn, was extremely successful at hunting down and killing Jedi. It was also incapable of reproduction, however, requiring the cloning of the original "queen" for additional voxyn.

**Ferra** A witch in the Singing Mountain Clan on Dathomir, she was killed by a Nightsister spell that snapped her neck.

**Ferral, Justor** An Imperial scout trooper, he held the rank of sergeant at the height of the Galactic Civil War. Justor Ferral was dispatched to Cloud City when the outpost was garrisoned shortly after the Battle of Hoth. He often used a floating battle disk, a personal repulsorlift platform designed for combat.

**Ferret** A Republic Engineering Corporation reconnaissance vessel, it started production shortly after the death of Grand Admiral Thrawn. At 28 meters long, the Ferret recon vessel was coated with sensor-baffling materials and equipped with the latest in stealth technology, allowing it to enter hostile territory virtually undetected. To allow the Ferret to move quietly at sublight speeds, a unique, baffled drive system was developed that let it maneuver without leaving any detectable trail for up to an hour. The Ferret was operated by three linked droid brains; two missile launchers were its only weapons.

**Ferret, Orion** A well-known gunrunner who worked from the *Bazarre* space station, he was approached by Luke Skywalker and Lando Calrissian shortly after the Battle of Hoth to purchase a flight of stolen TIE fighters. The ships were later used to take out the Imperial outpost on Spindrift. Orion Ferret was often accompanied by a tiny, octopus-like creature that was his pet. He tried his best to swindle the Rebel Alliance out of credits, send Luke and Lando to their possible deaths, and incapacitate Chewbacca, but failed in every attempt. Ferret was allowed to go free, but the Alliance kept a close eye on his activities.

**Ferrhast** This planet was home to the Imperial Institute of Higher Studies.

**Ferrier, Niles** A human jack-of-all-trades, he excelled as a starship thief. Large, with dark hair and a beard, Niles Ferrier wore flashy tunics and smoked long, thin cigarras. Working with a small gang of five humans, a Verpine, and a Defel, he was quick to react when Imperial Grand Admiral Thrawn offered a bounty of 20 percent more than current market value for capital ships. Lando Calrissian and Luke Skywalker foiled Ferrier's plans to steal a few ships from the Sluis Van shipyards, but Ferrier was able to provide Thrawn with an even greater prize: the location of the legendary and long-sought *Katana* fleet.

Ferrier later helped Thrawn infiltrate a meeting of the newly formed Smugglers' Alliance with Talon Karrde and a larger group on Trogan. Directly countermanding Thrawn's orders, he bribed Imperial Lieutenant Reynol Kosk into attacking the meeting, which resulted in Kosk and his entire squad getting killed. Thrawn was angry but realized Ferrier might still be of use. He ordered Ferrier's Defel companion to infiltrate the *Wild Karrde* and plant a datacard containing false information that implicated Karrde in the attack at Trogan. Thrawn then detained master smuggler Mazzic for a short time and hinted that one of the smugglers at the meeting had set up the ambush. Mazzic confronted Karrde at another meeting of the smugglers' group, but after Ferrier misspoke about the datacard's contents, he incriminated himself. He escaped by pulling a thermal detonator from his sleeve, forcing his way to his own ship, and fleeing into space.

**Ferroan** Near-human colonists who settled the Ferro systems, they were a proud and independent people, but very reclusive. The Ferroans seldom welcomed outsiders and almost never traveled far from home. Tall and strong, they had pale blue and ghostly white skins, long jaws, and wide eyes. Most Ferroans inhabited the living planet Zonama Sekot, but their civilization most likely started elsewhere. The Ferroans' ancestors were employed by the original Magister as caretakers of the planet, using their natural instincts to remain separated from the rest of the galaxy and ensure that Zonama Sekot was well hidden from casual observers. Generations later, during the Yuuzhan Vong invasion of the galaxy, the shaper Nen Yim came to believe that her species might have evolved into something like the Ferroans had they not destroyed their homeworld of Yuuzhan'tar generations earlier. With the discovery that Zonama Sekot itself was the offspring of Yuuzhan'tar, the link between the living planet and the Yuuzhan Vong became obvious. After the Yuuzhan Vong surrendered to the Galactic Alliance at Coruscant some five years after their invasion began, it was decided that the remaining aliens could live on Zonama Sekot. The Ferroans were surprisingly open to the decision, especially in light of the number of times the Yuuzhan Vong had tried to destroy Zonama Sekot. A few members of the younger generation of Ferroans thought the idea was improper, and chose to leave Zonama Sekot and travel to other worlds.

**ferrocarbon** An incredibly strong, durable material, it was used to form the deepest structural sections of the tall buildings on Coruscant.

**ferroceramic** A metallic-based colloid, it was used in the hulls of ships that must pass through planetary atmosphere, such as emergency life pods. It was sometimes known as ferro-magnesium ceramic.

**ferrocongregate** A highly explosive material used in the construction of core bombs during the last decades of the Old Republic. It was combined with magnopium to create the intense blast produced by core bombs.

**ferrocrete** A super-strong building material, it was composed of concrete and steel-like materials bonded together at the molecular level. Most structures on most worlds were built of this durable substance. It was sometimes called ferroconcrete.

**Ferros VI** This planet was the site of an Imperial prison camp during the Galactic Civil War.

**Ferro systems** A collection of star systems settled by human colonists, the Ferro systems were reclusive and isolationist. Although they elected to join the galactic community of the Old Republic, they were not always compliant with its laws. A year on Ferro, the capital world, lasted three standard years.

**Ferrous Aurora Nebula** An area of dense, reddish gas located near the Yavin system. It was considered dangerous to travel through the Ferrous Aurora Nebula during the Galactic Civil War due to the presence of the Ni'lyahin Smugglers.

**ferro-worm** A disgusting creature that was native to the undercity of Coruscant, it was so named because it burrowed into the ferrocrete used in the construction of most buildings.

**Fersin** An Ewok, he was the High Master of the Panshee tribe shortly before the Battle of Endor.

**Ferson** In the employ of Talon Karrde during the New Republic, Ferson was part of the team Karrde assembled to rescue the students at the Jedi praxeum on Yavin 4 at the height of the Yuuzhan Vong War.

**fervse** Known as Bothan glitterstones, these sparkling stones were formed during the creation of the planet Bothawui.

**Fervse'dra Asteroid Belt** A debris ring in the Both system between the planets Taboth and Bothawui, its name literally meant "clan of stones" in Bothan.

**Ferxani** A gas giant, it was the fifth planet of the Polith system, located in the Inner Rim. It was orbited by 33 moons.

**Fest** This planet, in a system of the same name, was dominated by steep mountain ranges and deep valleys. It was in the Atrivis sector of the Outer Rim bordering the Mantooine system. Fest's inhabitants were nearly always at war with themselves or their neighbors on Mantooine, until they were later united by their hatred for the New Order. Fest served as a Separatist base during the early stages of the Clone Wars, and eventually was taken over by the Grand Army of the Republic. It soon became the site of an Imperial Weapons Research Facility hidden high atop a steep mountain. The facility performed metallurgical research on new alloys and was one of the first places that the alloy phrik was developed for use specifically in military armor and weaponry. Following the Battle of Yavin, Alliance agent Kyle Katarn infiltrated the facility and stole a sample of the alloy.

**fester lung** The more common name for *Ascomycetous pneumoconiosis,* a highly contagious disease that caused fevers high enough to literally cook victims in their own juices. Many sentient and nonsentient species were susceptible to it.

**Festival of Glad Arrival** A celebration of the pastoral beauty of Naboo, it was staged by the Pastoral Collective in the meadows of the Lake Country each spring. For several days, the meadows were filled with colorful pageants and musical performances.

**Festival of Great Trade** One of the major holiday events on the planet Svivren, it was celebrated in the southern districts where the major bargaining arenas were found. Merchant-pilgrims from all over Svivren descended on the city of Wrils during the festival, making passage difficult—as Mara Jade discovered on a mission to the planet.

**Festival of Hoods** This celebration marked the coming of age of young Ewoks. When they received their animal-skin hoods, it was a symbol that they had made the transition from Wokling to preadolescent.

**Festival of the Twin Gods** A one-day celebration observed by the Yuuzhan Vong, who paused in their labors to contemplate the gods Yun-Harla and Yun-Yammka. Yuuzhan Vong children could play tricks on their elders without fear of punishment, and adults often exchanged secrets among themselves, sometimes even with their enemies.

**Festival of the Wisties** A favorite Ewok holiday, it was noisy and tasty since rattles were used in the Wistie Dance and rainbow berries in the big Wistie Fest pie.

**Festival of Warriors** An annual competition among Gungan warriors, it attracted the best soldiers from tribes across the planet. To be invited to the festival was considered a great honor among the members of the Gungan Grand Army.

Boba Fett (right) and his father, Jango Fett

**Feswin, Chau** A Senator representing the Elrood sector in the New Republic. At the height of the Yuuzhan Vong invasion, Lando Calrissian and Talon Karrde attempted to bribe him with relief supplies in exchange for his vote appropriating more funds for YVH 1 combat droids. They also recorded the conversation in the hope of blackmailing Chau Feswin to support the candidacy of Cal Omas for Chief of State.

**Fett, Boba** A faceless enforcer, Boba Fett wore distinctive armor that struck fear in the hearts of fugitives. He was a legendary bounty hunter, accepting warrants from both the Empire and the criminal underworld. He was all business, laconic, and deadly. Fett carefully guarded his past, pulling a curtain of mystery around his origins. Legends invariably arose—perhaps by design, since the uncertainty of his past only added to his mysterious and deadly aura. One tale told of Fett being a failed stormtrooper who had killed his commanding officer. Another described him as the commanding officer of a fabled group of warriors from Mandalore nearly wiped out by the Jedi Knights. A third account told of a Journeyman Protector from Concord Dawn named Jaster Mereel who adopted the Boba Fett mask and guise when he was convicted of treason.

The truth was even stranger. Fett was, in fact, a clone, an exact genetic replica of his highly skilled bounty hunter father, Jango Fett. From Jango, Boba learned valuable survival and martial skills, and even as a child he was proficient with a blaster or laser cannon. The homier memories—the times he spent playing with his toys in a sparsely furnished Kamino apartment, his guardians Taun We and MU-12, the quiet moments he would share with his father catching rollerfish—all were buried under an impenetrable shell of vengeful thoughts and malice. Raised in isolation in the hermetic cities of Kamino, where he was protected from not only the ceaseless storms but also the harsher elements of his father's career, young Boba saw his life change when a tenacious Jedi Knight, Obi-Wan Kenobi, came looking for his father. Sent to apprehend the bounty hunter for the attempted assassination of a Naboo Senator, Kenobi brawled with Jango as the Fetts sought to escape from Kamino. Young Boba helped his father by pinning the Jedi down with explosive laserfire from the Fett starship, *Slave I.*

Boba Fett

Fleeing, the Fetts journeyed to Geonosis, where Jango's benefactor, Darth Tyranus, resided. Boba watched as his father's enemies were sentenced to death—but Jedi proved very hard to kill. A huge battle erupted as Jedi reinforcements stormed Geonosis to free their colleagues. Jango entered the fray, only to be killed by Jedi Master Mace Windu. Boba was shocked to witness his father's swift death, and he quietly cradled Jango's empty helmet as Geonosis erupted into all-out war.

After Jango's death, Boba picked up the pieces of his shattered life with the help of his "black book," an encoded message unit written by Jango with instructions for survival should Boba ever find himself alone. After the Battle of Geonosis, Boba quietly buried his father's body on Mandalore and marked the grave with a simple J. F. He sought out his father's benefactor, Darth Tyranus, who had the remainder of Jango's stipend. And then Boba began to prepare himself for his future life.

Like his father, Boba dressed in fearsome armor of Mandalorian design. The battle-scarred suit was the latest in a heritage that could be traced back 4,000 years, to the days when clans of Mandalorians fought against the Jedi during the Great Sith War. The armor was heavily modified with numerous hidden and deadly features. The T-shaped visor set in the helmet incorporated a macrobinocular viewplate. The rest of the helmet featured a temple-mounted broadband antenna, motion and sound sensors, an infrared device, and an internal comlink connected to his ship. The armor was equipped with a rocket pack for fast escapes. His gauntlets contained a flamethrower and a whipcord lanyard launcher. His kneepads concealed rocket dart launchers. Several ominous braids hung from his shoulder—trophies from fallen prey—that underscored his lethality. Fett's weapon of choice was a sawed-off BlasTech EE-3 rifle.

Among the first records of the younger Fett were those of his activities during the early years of the Empire. He was hired by the gangster Sise Fromm to dispose of young speeder pilot Thall Joben and his friends. Though the Fromms were enemies of Jabba the Hutt—Fett's sometime employer—the hunter took the contract to square off a favor he owed Fromm. At the time, Fett owned a droid named BL-17, which he used to confuse Joben's droids, R2-D2 and C-3PO. Unaware of a bomb planted on Joben's speeder, the *White Witch,* Fett entered his modified racer *Silver Speeder* in the Boonta speeder competition. During his attempt to capture Joben with a magnetic beam, Fett pulled the bomb onto his own speeder, and it was destroyed. Angered at the loss of his speeder and droid, Fett captured the Fromms to turn them over to Jabba the Hutt.

As a licensed law enforcer of the Empire, Fett worked for that oppressive government on numerous occasions. One report had him allowing Rebel agents to capture a mystical talisman infected with an Imperial sleeping virus. Another report indicated that Fett was hired by Darth Vader to track down a Rebel agent known as Mole on the frozen world of Ota. Shortly after the Battle of Yavin, a group of Jabba the Hutt's bounty hunters captured Han Solo, Luke Skywalker, and Chewbacca in the Hoth system. These hunters were to deliver the Rebel trio to Ord Mantell, where Boba Fett was to take possession and continue the delivery to the Empire. One of the hunters, an arrogant tracker named Skorr, botched the operation and let the Rebels escape. Skorr was killed in the process, and Fett was left empty-handed.

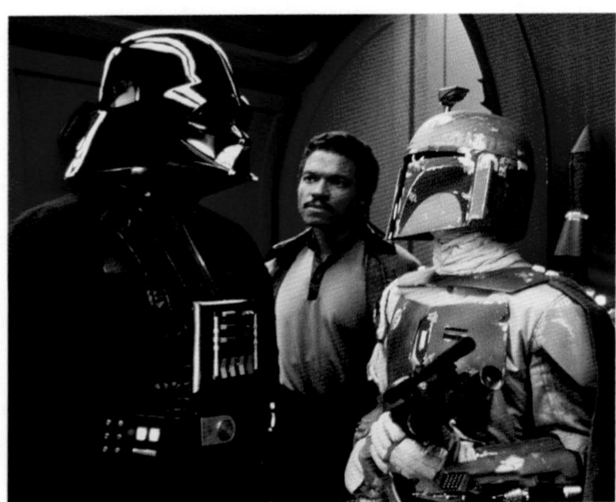
Boba Fett listens to Darth Vader.

During the Galactic Civil War, Fett reemerged as the preeminent bounty hunter of the galaxy. Shortly after the Battle of Hoth, Vader desperately wanted to capture the fugitive Rebel craft *Millennium Falcon.* He hired a motley assortment of bounty hunters, including Fett. Vader specifically pointed out to Fett that the *Falcon*'s passengers were to be taken alive.

*Boba Fett mourns the loss of his father, Jango Fett.*

"No disintegrations," rumbled the Dark Lord. It was Fett who successfully tracked the *Falcon* from Hoth to Bespin. Arriving at the gas giant before the *Falcon,* Fett and Vader sprang a trap on the ship's hapless crew. Fett, a shrewd negotiator, received his bounty for capturing the crew, but was also given custody of Han Solo. The bounty hunter was set to collect the reward on Solo's head placed by the vile gangster Jabba the Hutt. Whisking the carbon-frozen form of Han Solo away from Bespin, Fett eventually arrived on Tatooine aboard *Slave I.* He was attacked by the other hunters hired by Vader to bring in the Corellian prize. The assassin droid IG-88, aboard his ultrasleek IG-2000, attacked the *Slave I* high over Tatooine. Though Fett destroyed the droid, *Slave I* sustained serious damage. Unwilling to be caught defenseless, Fett lay low for a while.

Fett delivered Solo to Jabba and was suddenly many thousands of credits richer. He stayed at Jabba's palace, and was present when Solo's friends attempted to rescue the carbon-frozen smuggler.

Jabba, enraged at the attempted prison break, brought his captives out to the Tatooine desert to execute them in the Great Pit of Carkoon. In the sandpit lay the immense Sarlacc, a vile creature that would digest its prey over thousands of years. Rather than let themselves be thrown into the Sarlacc's maw, Solo's friends, led by Luke Skywalker, fought against their captors. In the chaos that followed, Fett entered the fray. Solo, free of the carbonite and suffering blindness from hibernation sickness, wildly swung a vibro-ax into an inattentive Fett's rocket pack. The pack activated, and the bounty hunter soared into the air, out of control. The airborne Fett slammed into the side of Jabba's sail barge before tumbling into the Sarlacc's mouth. With a sickly belch from the desert creature, it seemed as if Fett's career as the galaxy's most notorious bounty hunter had been brought to an end.

But while Fett's armor and body were extremely battered by his ordeal in the Sarlacc, he was kept alive by numerous fibrous suckers that attached themselves to his body. This was part of the Sarlacc's horrible metabolic process: It would keep its prey alive for thousands of years, all the while slowly feeding off it. Fett almost lost his identity in the swirling dementia brought about by the Sarlacc's toxins. His resolve held, though, and he finally was able to use his weapons to blast free of the beast. Naked, wounded, and defenseless on the sands of Tatooine, Fett was rescued by his fellow hunter Dengar, who nursed him back to health. Fett reclaimed his armor and his reputation, returning from the "dead" and again taking on bounties.

It wasn't until six years after Jabba's death that Han Solo learned his nemesis was still alive when he and his wife, Leia Organa Solo, traveled to Nar Shaddaa, the spaceport moon that was a major smuggling center of the galaxy. There Han was surprised to find Fett and Dengar waiting for him in his old quarters. In a hail of blasterfire, Leia and Han made it offworld, escaping in old friend Salla Zend's *Starlight Intruder.* Later, in another encounter on the planet, Fett shot Chewbacca in the side, but the Wookiee managed to rip off Fett's helmet and send the bounty hunter flying.

Fett recovered quickly and pursued the *Millennium Falcon* through the floating space debris of Nar Shaddaa. Han entered an interstellar gas cloud, and because Fett's ship had been damaged, Fett couldn't pursue him. A few days later the *Falcon* emerged, shot at Fett, and sent his ship spinning out of control into the gas cloud. Once again, the hunter and hunted parted company. Fett later caught Solo on Jubilar, but the two decided that they had been adversaries for too long to kill each other, and they went their separate ways.

Fett returned many times to Kamino, where Taun We secretly had been growing replacement body parts for the bounty hunter. She asked him to hunt down and destroy Fenn Shysa, as it had been Shysa who participated in the devastation of Kamino near the end of the Clone Wars. Years after this final hunt, Fett went to Mandalore to assume control of the Mandalorian Protectors. He found himself elevated to the position of *Mand'alor,* the leader of the Mandalorian warriors and ostensibly the ruler of Mandalore itself.

When the Yuuzhan Vong began their invasion of the galaxy, Fett and his Mandalorians worked to protect their planet before setting out to do as much damage as possible. From a base on Caluula Station, they worked to thwart any incursion of the Yuuzhan Vong into the Tion Hegemony. When Han and Leia Organa Solo arrived at the station with rescued prisoners from Selvaris, Fett removed his armor and introduced himself as Hurn; the Solos couldn't place the face. The Yuuzhan Vong launched a ferocious assault on Caluula Station, and Fett and his soldiers worked tirelessly to ensure that the Solos safely escaped and returned to Mon Calamari with the prisoners.

Ten years later, Fett's body was rapidly deteriorating: His liver was failing, and his tissues were riddled with tumors. A doctor gave him just a year or two to live; there was no help this time from Taun We, since she had disappeared. Fett decided to locate his daughter Ailyn, who had been born during a three-year marriage to bounty hunter Sintas Vel. But Ailyn had vanished, secretly taking on Corellian secessionist Thrackan Sal-Solo's bounty on the heads of Han and Leia. Ailyn's daughter Mirta Gev approached Fett without revealing that she was his granddaughter to enlist him in the search for her mother. She accompanied the 71-year-old Fett when he took on the job of assassinating Thrackan, firing the first three shots into Sal-Solo's head. It was then that they learned that Ailyn had been captured, tortured, and killed by Jacen Solo. After confronting the animosity his granddaughter held toward him, Fett realized that it was time he reclaimed his Mandalorian roots. Fett and Gev journeyed to Mandalore and Fett resumed his role as leader, although he felt undeserving. Fett was able to obtain a serum that rapidly restored his health, and he helped Mandalore return as a power in the galaxy.

It was with great trepidation that Fett discovered that Sintas Vel, his former wife and grandmother of Mirta Gev, was still alive. She had been frozen in carbonite decades earlier. Returned to Mandalore and thawed from her prison, Vel was disoriented and blind from the ordeal, but Gev worked to nurse her back to health. When she began recovering her memories, she held no ill will toward Fett. They spent days talking, hoping to repair the emotional scars of their past. They came to understand each other in time to celebrate the wedding of their granddaughter to Ghes Orade.

Jaina Solo arrived on Mandalore asking for Fett's help in training her to defeat her brother Jacen, who by then had become Darth Caedus. Fett agreed and taught her how to fight like a Mandalorian. In the meantime, he was contacted by Admiral Daala, who had come out of hiding to assist Gilad Pellaeon on a mission to capture the planet Fondor. Daala was Pellaeon's secret backup, and she wanted the Mandalorians to provide additional firepower if necessary. With the ships of both the Galactic Alliance and Imperial Remnant refusing to follow Jacen Solo's increasingly belligerent commands and the sudden assassination of Pellaeon by Solo's apprentice Tahiri Veila, a group of opportunistic Imperial Moffs tried to take over.

Daala called Fett's small task force into the battle to secure the Destroyer *Bloodfin.* The Mandalorians stormed the ship, trapping the Moffs in the command center and killing them all. Tahiri escaped when Jacen arrived to rescue her; Fett could have killed Solo, but he knew Jaina had to do that for closure.

As the war ground on, Fett learned that the Imperial Remnant had deployed a nanokiller on Mandalore. It was created from Mirta Gev's blood and designed to kill any member of Fett's bloodline. It also was designed to remain active indefinitely, forcing Fett and Mirta to find a new home while they tried to help Mandalore recover from an attack by the Alliance's Fifth Fleet.

**Fett, Cassus** The most wanted criminal in the galaxy during the years leading up to the Great Sith War, he was known to have killed the captain of an Old Republic flagship during the Battle of Jaga's Cluster before fleeing into deep space. Although he was presumed dead, many claimed that Cassus Fett was just biding his time. He reappeared at the height of the Mandalorian expansion when he led the attacks on Cathar that nearly wiped out the native species. He was presumed killed during the Mandalorian Wars.

**Fett, Jango** The name *Fett* carried with it a cold air of dread and competence. To those with the credits to hire him, it was synonymous with success. To those with reasons to fear, *Fett* meant capture or death. The name and reputation were just two of the many things Boba Fett inherited from his father, Jango. In the final years of the Old Republic, Jango Fett was regarded as the best bounty hunter in the galaxy.

A proficient marksman and unarmed combatant, Fett was covered in a sleek armored suit that concealed his grim visage. His combat gear featured an arsenal of weaponry, including retractable wrist blades, a snare, dual blaster pistols, and other, more exotic, tools of the trade. In combat, Jango used his harnessed jetpack to gain the advantage of speed and height over his enemies. The backpack also carried a nasty surprise: An explosive rocket could be launched from it. For interstellar travel, Jango used his well-worn starship, *Slave I.*

Jango Fett was orphaned at an early age, the son of simple Concord Dawn farmers killed by brutal marauders. At 10 years old, he was picked up by Journeyman Protector Jaster Mereel, who introduced Fett to the harsh world of mercenary life. He was raised among great warriors, learning to survive in the rugged frontiers. Though the Mandalorian supercommandos were wiped out by the Jedi Knights, Jango was one of the few left to still wear the armor. Years of physical conditioning and training honed him into one of the most feared bounty hunters in the underworld. Not even Black Sun Vigos were safe from his dual blaster pistols. On occasion, Fett would tangle with Zam Wesell, as their talents would overlap on similar assignments. Though he preferred working solo, the two teamed up when it was prudent.

About a decade prior to the outbreak of the Clone Wars, a man named Tyranus approached Jango on the moons of Bogden with an intriguing proposal. In exchange for a sizable fee, Jango would become the template of a clone army. Fett agreed, but with an unusual stipulation in his contract. In addition to his fee, he would be awarded an unaltered clone of himself. Unlike his other duplicates, this clone would not undergo growth acceleration or docility tampering. It would be a pure replica of Jango. The Kaminoans provided Fett with private accommodations in their hermetic Tipoca City, and Jango dropped out of the bounty-hunting limelight. He concentrated on teaching his son, the unaltered clone he named Boba, the ropes of survival and combat while the Kaminoans extracted genetic material to build tens of thousands of clone soldiers.

While serving as Tyranus's enforcer, Jango was approached by Viceroy Nute Gunray of the Trade Federation. Gunray wanted to eliminate Senator Padmé Amidala, who had long been a thorn in the viceroy's side. Fett subcontracted the job to Wesell, and armed her with poisonous kouhuns to finish the job. A pair of meddling Jedi got in the way of the hit, and Jango was forced to kill Wesell lest the trail lead back to him. But Fett hadn't counted on the resourcefulness of Obi-Wan Kenobi. Jango had used an exotic weapon, a Kamino saberdart, to eliminate Wesell. No one should have been able to trace that weapon back to its source, but Obi-Wan's underworld contacts were able to point him in the right direction.

*Jango Fett (flying) attacks Jedi Obi-Wan Kenobi on Kamino.*

Kenobi arrived on Kamino and learned of the clone army. He met Jango, and the two had a tense yet civil discussion, neither revealing his true motives. Fett nonetheless decided to flee, and ordered Boba to gather their belongings. Kenobi, working on orders from the Jedi Council, attempted to apprehend Jango just prior to *Slave I's* liftoff, which led to a waterlogged melee atop the rain-swept landing platforms of Tipoca City. Jango escaped aboard *Slave* I, and he and his son journeyed to Geonosis to reunite with their mysterious benefactor, Lord Tyranus.

En route to Geonosis, Jango and Boba realized that a homing beacon had been placed aboard their vessel, and found a pursuing Jedi starfighter on their tracking screens. The tenacious Obi-Wan Kenobi was back, and a daring game of moog-and-rancor played out amid the rocky debris of the Geonosian rings. Despite a barrage of *Slave I's* seismic charges, laser cannons, and missile attacks, Obi-Wan survived and continued shadowing the Fetts as they arrived on the barren planet's surface. Kenobi and his compatriots were captured on Geonosis, which was revealed to be a Separatist stronghold. They were to be executed in grand Geonosian fashion, but their deaths were stalled by the sudden arrival of Jedi reinforcements. Tasked with protecting Lord Tyranus, Jango entered the fray against the Jedi. His blaster skills killed several Jedi, but Jango was not quite prepared to face off against Jedi Master Mace Windu. Windu did not break stride as he deflected Jango's incoming blasts and swiftly cleaved off the hunter's head with a single stroke of his luminescent blade. Jango's battle-dented helm bounced along the dusty ground of the Geonosian arena, to be picked up by a stunned and newly orphaned Boba Fett.

*Jango Fett in a droid factory on Geonosis*

**fever wasp** Native to the jungles of Haruun Kal, this vicious insect was a parasite that laid its eggs in every living being it could bite. The larvae of the fever wasp fed on blood and flesh; they also liked to consume thyssel bark, and those Korunnai who chewed the bark as a stimulant and were bitten by fever wasps died quickly. When the larvae reached the brain of their host, they continued to grow until they hatched, feeding on the brain cells and eventually killing the host. When a mass of larvae reached maturity, they burst from the skull of the host as if emerging from a huge eggshell. If caught very soon after the initial bite, the larvae could be destroyed with an injection of thanatizine. Since the larvae matured in about four days, any delay in treatment was a virtual death sentence.

**Fevye'starn** This city was located on the eastern continent of the planet Bothawui.

**Fex-M3** A potent nerve gas that caused death when inhaled by most humanoid races. Developed during the final decades of the Old Republic, Fex-M3 remained one of the most effective chemical weapons in the galaxy for many decades. Riot police on Coruscant used it to break up mobs of Corellian demonstrators some 10 years after the end of the war against the Yuuzhan Vong.

**Fey'ja, Maja** The queen of the peaceful Majan species during the last decades of the Old Republic, she welcomed Podraces to the city of Baroo since her subjects enjoyed watching them.

**Fey'jia, Torel** This Bothan was part of the Ojia clan migration that settled on the planet Kothlis. Formerly employed by MCS, Fey'jia embezzled enough of the company's funds to support himself. He then went into business buying and selling top-secret corporate information, using the profits from this venture to establish one of the largest spynets on Kothlis, thus providing a wealth of information to his good friend Borsk Fey'lya.

**Fey'lya, Borsk** Although Borsk Fey'lya exhibited the most unsavory traits of both politicians and Bothans, many considered him a hero for his noteworthy achievements. His influence brought the Bothans into the Rebellion, and he was a key figure in shaping the New Republic government that supplanted the Empire. Fey'lya, of the Bothan Alya clan, was born on Kothlis, a Bothan colony world. He demonstrated a knack for maneuvering through the dangerous twists of Bothan politics, honing his opportunistic talents to ascend in the world of business. Fey'lya's melodic, easygoing voice lulled many a rival into a false sense of security. His relentless ambitions were often underestimated by friend and foe.

Shortly after the Battle of Yavin, Fey'lya joined the Rebel Alliance, bringing in a sizable faction of Bothans and their remarkable intelligence-gathering network. Around this time, the Mon Calamari and their mighty starships also joined the struggling Rebellion. This led to an immediate rivalry between Fey'lya and Admiral Ackbar. Ackbar dismissed Fey'lya as just a political blowhard, but the two would be at odds many times.

It was Fey'lya's Bothans who managed to obtain information regarding the second Death Star for the Alliance. Though their intelligence proved to be a trap, the Bothans—and Fey'lya in particular—were regarded as heroes for their contribution. As the Empire collapsed, Fey'lya was one of the original signers of the Declaration of a New Republic. He earned a position in the New Republic Provisional Council and the Inner Council, much to the chagrin of Admiral Ackbar. Fey'lya's political agenda always favored his fellow Bothans, but his shrewd tactics and careful conniving kept him from being branded for his special interests. Fey'lya maintained his business ventures while he served as a councilor. A corporation he owned funneled money to Garm Bel Iblis, a Corellian rogue who was waging his

Borsk Fey'lya

own private war against the Empire. Because Bel Iblis fostered a deeply rooted animosity toward Mon Mothma, Fey'lya thought it prudent to keep him as an ally.

Though Fey'lya truly hated the Empire, his shortsighted political games often hindered the New Republic's progress. He saw nothing wrong in pouncing on an ally's missteps if it furthered his agenda. Fey'lya's downfall began with a miscalculation during the hard-fought battle with Grand Admiral Thrawn over the long-lost *Katana* fleet. The Bothan ordered a retreat, trapping some of the Rebellion's top people. Fey'lya's true nature was exposed, and he was put under military arrest and returned to Coruscant. Although the Provisional Council granted him a pardon, he had lost face and his base of support, and his power steadily diminished. The coolly calculating Fey'lya would rarely lose his composure, but the notion of the New Republic taking the Emperor's storehouse on Wayland intact terrified him. He was even willing to pay Talon Karrde 70,000 credits to ensure that Mount Tantiss was obliterated. He offered very little by means of explanation, and the truth of what he was hiding did not appear for years.

Ever the survivor, Fey'lya again ascended during the New Republic's reorganization following the resurrected Emperor's destructive campaign. During the Yevethan crisis, Fey'lya served as chairman of the Senate Justice Council. He leaked information to the media and supported the petition of no confidence in Chief of State Leia Organa Solo. Fey'lya quietly bided his time during Ponc Gavrisom's term as Chief of State, and Organa Solo's return to office. When Leia's term finally ended, Borsk Fey'lya put his years of experience and contacts to good use, and was elected Chief of State of the New Republic in a landslide.

It was during Fey'lya's time in office that the Yuuzhan Vong struck. The alien invaders began their bloody incursion into New Republic space, and despite a wealth of disturbing evidence, Fey'lya refused to label the Yuuzhan Vong a definite threat. The more they encroached on the Core and Bothan space, however, the more active Fey'lya became. Though he authorized the use of the New Republic Navy to defend against the aliens, he refused to give Luke Skywalker's new Order of Jedi Knights an official role in the defense. He did not send aid to the besieged Jedi academy on Yavin 4, claiming the world did not fall under New Republic jurisdiction. Despite such self-serving maneuvers, Fey'lya stayed behind on Coruscant when the capital world eventually fell to the Yuuzhan Vong. Fey'lya detonated a powerful charge in his executive office, killing himself and several prominent Yuuzhan Vong and destroying many of the Republic's most sensitive state secrets. For this sacrifice, even some of the Yuuzhan Vong expressed grudging respect for the Bothan politician.

***Fey'lya's Pride*** This *Lambda*-class shuttle was part of the Bothan fleet that assisted the Alliance in evacuating its base on Kothlis shortly before the Battle of Endor.

**Feytihennasraof** An Elder of the Oswaft species, he helped control the ThonBoka, a region of space also called the StarCave. He used the name *Fey* when dealing with Lando Calrissian during the early years of the New Order. A huge manta-ray-like being, Fey had a wingspan of nearly a kilometer. During the defense of the ThonBoka, Fey was among a group of Oswaft who were caught by the first blasts from Imperial attackers firing deadly bioengineered weapons. Fey and his comrades were killed in the assault.

**Ffib** A species native to the planet Lorahns, the Ffibs established a religious order spanning many worlds during the Old Republic. The group's disciples, known as the Sons or Daughters of the Ffib, were taught that there were many ways to obtain "vision." Ffib priests and priestesses were often sent to remote worlds as missionaries in an attempt to convert sentient native species to join the order. Several years before the Battle of Naboo, the Ffibs were nearly wiped out by the Twi'lek pirate Reess Kairn. The Daughters of the Ffib sought out Aurra Sing, hoping to hire her in an effort to eliminate Kairn and the two Shi'ido he employed to masquerade as him. Later, the Ffib played a part in the conspiracy to disrupt the Lannik peace talks on Malastare. An inquisitor, a sub-priest of the Ffib, attacked Adi Gallia and Even Piell soon after the Jedi arrived on the planet. Another Ffib priest was discovered by the Jedi and arrested. The priest pleaded with his co-conspirator, Aks Moe, but the Gran disavowed any knowledge of their relationship.

**fft** Small multilegged lizards native to Lwhekk, they were the chief food source of the Ssi-ruuk and the P'w'eck.

**fgir** A shrub native to the Forest Moon of Endor. When squeezed or compressed, its roots shot out poisonous, needle-like spines. Ewoks learned that the root itself could be cut and dried to form a dart blower, while fgir root moisture could be distilled into an effective anesthetic.

**Fhilch, Grubbat** A rabbit-like Lepi with a bushy tail, he was caught double-dipping in the Podracing books. After Boba Fett tracked down Grubbat Fhilch, Jabba the Hutt fed him to the Sarlacc in the desert wastes of Tatooine.

**Fi** A clone commando officially known as RC-8015, he was the only member of his squad to survive the Battle of Geonosis. Fi joined Omega Squad, where he was known for his ability to find humor in just about any situation. But during a mission to rescue Senator Meena Tills from Korunnai terrorists, Fi nearly shot his former teacher, Kal Skirata, due to battlefield confusion. Skirata insisted that Fi had simply been following his training and that sentimentality would get him killed.

***Fi*** An Imperial warship, it served as Grand Admiral Syn's personal flagship during his occupation of the Kashyyyk system. It was destroyed when Admiral Ackbar and a fleet of New Republic warships liberated Kashyyyk.

**Fia** A species native to the planet Galantos, they called the Koornacht Cluster "the Multitude." A small, placid species, Fia communicated with wild hand and arm gestures. After the Yuuzhan Vong captured Coruscant, the Fia began negotiating with the alien invaders, hoping to survive. They provided information on the strengths of the Yevetha in return for resources and Yuuzhan Vong assurance that the Yevetha would be destroyed. The Fia also allowed the New Republic communications network to be shut down. They didn't realize that the marauders had no plans to spare either the Yevetha or the Fia. Only the timely intervention of Han and Leia Organa Solo on a mission to restore communications with Galantos helped the Fia avoid the fate of the Yevetha.

**fiber-chain** A form of rope, it was developed from tightly linked rings of durable fiber, giving it the appearance of a chain.

**fibercord** A type of strong, thin cord that could be used to connect grappling hooks and other climbing devices. Fibercord was made from durable fibers, often flexsteel, and could also be used as a whip. Boba Fett had a fibercord whip that could be extended from his wrist gauntlet to lash or entangle a quarry.

**fiber-grown furniture** Using simple polymer fibers that were grown in certain configurations, this technique produced simple, inexpensive chairs and tables. But most fiber-grown furniture was exceptionally fragile and didn't hold up well under heavy weight or abuse.

**fiberplast** An incredibly strong material used to make doors and other building materials, it also had a multitude of uses in the production of starship components.

**fibra-rope** A strong, braided rope used by climbers and tightrope walkers, it was also favored by mercenaries and infiltration squadrons.

**FIBUA Operation** A term used by military leaders and instructors of the Grand Army of the Republic, it was essentially a fancy synonym for "urban warfare."

**Fibuli** This planet was one of the Trianii colony worlds that were annexed by the adjacent Corporate Sector. Open warfare erupted as Trianii Rangers fought the Corporate Sector Authority's encroachment. An armistice was finally arranged after the Battle of Yavin, following three years of devastating fighting. Keeheen, mate to Trianii Ranger Atuarre, disappeared during the fighting and eventually was rescued from the Stars' End prison with Han Solo's help.

**Fibuna, B'inka** A female Twi'lek who was enslaved by Ka'Pa the Hutt in the years leading up to the Battle of Naboo, she was forced to work as a dancer at his Nal Hutta estate. However, Fibuna discovered the Freedom Convoy and managed to escape from Ka'Pa shortly after the Trade Federation's invasion of Naboo was broken. She fled to Coruscant, where she tried her best to stay out of the public eye. Unfortunately, she was identified by Jango Fett as being wanted by Ka'Pa. Fett captured her and turned her over to the authorities after collecting the bounty on her head.

**Fida, Theen** This Anx was a student of the Force, training under Jedi Master Tsui Choi in the period leading up to the Battle of Naboo. Theen Fida and Master Choi were part of a team dispatched to Yitheeth to locate the Yinchorri command center. After discovering that the Yinchorri were not on the water-covered world, the team traveled to Yinchorr itself to meet up with Mace Windu's team. Theen Fida was killed by Yinchorri warriors while guarding the Jedi's remaining starship.

*Fibercord*

**Fiddanl** The innermost planet of the Yavin system, it was a hot, dense world. Its continental plates constantly shifted atop a sea of liquid mercury. The planet's 18 landmasses constantly ground one another down but were continually replaced through rapid crystal growth. The multicolored continents got their hues from a varied mix of cinnabar, sulfite, and manganese. The planet was toxic to almost all species, and there were no indications of life on Fiddanl's surface.

**Fidelis** An old Tac-Spec Footman droid, he served the Malreaux family of Vjun for many generations. When the 17th Viscount Malreaux succumbed to a madness plague, his wife, Whirry, gave the droid a new job: to secretly follow their son Whie to Coruscant and ensure his safety while he was in training at the Jedi Temple. For many years, Fidelis and his droid friend Solis played endless games of courtier dejarik while keeping a watchful eye on the Jedi Temple. When Whie was added to Master Yoda's mission to Vjun, both Fidelis and Solis booked passage aboard the *Reasonable Doubt* so that Fidelis could continue his watch. After the Jedi band was attacked on Phindar by Asajj Ventress and Whie's Jedi Master was slain, Fidelis was dismayed to learn that it had been Solis who gave Ventress their location. Once on Vjun, however, Fidelis was ordered by a now mad Whirry Malreaux—whose home had been taken over by Count Dooku—to arrange for Whie to be trapped by Ventress. The dark sider wanted to be rid of Fidelis and gave the droid a choice: shoot himself with a neural-net eraser or watch Whie die. Fidelis, loyal to the end, wiped out his computer systems in a form of suicide.

***Fidelity*** A *Thranta*-class warship, it was slaved to *Another Chance* to protect it from being taken by hostile forces during the Bacta War. Like its companions, the *Courage* and *Valiant*, it accompanied *Another Chance* as it jumped through hyperspace to avoid detection.

**Fidge** This Biituian boy was 10 years old when he met R2-D2 and C-3PO as they encountered the Great Heep during the early days of the Empire. Fidge agreed to help the droids rescue their owner, Mungo Baobab, from Imperials who were on Biitu to monitor the Great Heep. Their plan succeeded, and they freed Mungo. Then they worked to destroy the Great Heep and release the planet from Imperial control.

**field cauterizer** A medical device produced by Nilar Med/Tech Corporation, it was a self-contained laser used to disinfect and cauterize wounds that occurred in remote locations where medical facilities were not present. The Noghri Sirkha used a 16-centimeter-long stylus that emitted a close-focus, low-frequency laser beam to burn Ganner Rhysode's head wound. The resulting scar reminded Ganner of what had happened on Garqi.

**field disruptor** A device that disrupted an energy field as the wearer passed through. It could also be used as a weapon to deliver a burst of energy.

**Fiery Ones** An unusual, intelligent species that developed in the wake of the Kathol Rift Disaster. Resembling tiny balls of light, the Fiery Ones communicated simple thoughts and emotions by mental transmission. They could use the Ta-Ree energy that permeated the planet, and could give off an energy shock if provoked. In general, though, the Fiery Ones were curious beings who tried to communicate with any new species they encountered.

**Fieso, Niai** The son of a poor family, he grew up in Veterned, the capital of Troiken, and spent most of his youth roaming the streets. After a string of odd jobs, Niai Fieso ended up working for con artist Freon Drevan, who sold knockoff merchandise connected to the famous Podracer Gasgano. Drevan was impressed by how easily the Xexto lad poured on the charm and swindled beings. Soon their business expanded from simple bootlegging to smuggling. Fieso wanted to take over the business himself, so he began skimming profits from spice smuggling and ratted out Drevan to the authorities. Pretending to be Gasgano's agent, Fieso even managed to hoodwink businesses in the Corporate Sector for "exclusive sponsorship deals" with the Podracer. But the Authority Attorney General saw through his scheme, and he had to flee the Espos with just a few belongings. Laying low on Tatooine, he took a food vendor

job at the Mos Espa Grand Arena during the Boonta Eve Classic. The Podracing environment struck him as a perfect place to find foolish marks. While scoping out potential victims, he suddenly received three blows to his face: Drevan was in the crowd and spotted him. The fight landed both in the local jail, and Fieso was transferred to CSA authorities.

**Fifth Battle Group (Fifth Fleet)** The New Republic's defensive fleet was created about 12 years after the Battle of Endor. The Fifth Battle Group was the first to be made up completely of the navy's new classes of starships, such as the *Sacheen-* and *Hajen-*class frigates. Initially it was under the command of Etahn A'baht and deployed to the Koornacht Cluster during the Yevethan Great Purge with 106 starships.

The Fifth Battle Group, which became better known as the Fifth Fleet, was part of the Republic's defenses during the Yuuzhan Vong War, and was the first fleet dispatched to the Utegetu Nebula to block the hives of the Colony from spreading beyond its borders. During the blockade, the group was commanded by Admiral Nek Bwua'tu aboard the flagship Star Destroyer *Admiral Ackbar.*

Seven years later, the Fifth Fleet under the command of Admiral Atoko was sent to blockade Corellia after Thrackan Sal-Solo threatened to go to war with the Galactic Alliance to achieve independence. After Sal-Solo's assassination and the cessation of peace talks with the Corellians, the Fifth Fleet was ordered to other battle zones. It was part of Admiral Bwua'tu's second wave of attacks during the Battle of Kuat, but was pulled from the fighting by Jacen Solo after the Jedi Order left the Alliance.

The Fifth Fleet accompanied the *Anakin Solo* to Kashyyyk, where Jacen Solo demanded that the Wookiees turn over his parents and any Jedi who were on the planet. When they refused, Solo ordered his ships to open fire, burning forests and jungles in an effort to force the Wookiees to comply. This action, which Solo meant to serve as an example of what would happen to worlds that defied the Galactic Alliance, prompted a swift response. It also attracted the attention of naval forces from the Confederation, which had sent scout ships to trail the *Anakin Solo.* In short order, the Fifth Fleet was forced to form a protective bubble around the *Anakin Solo* to defend it from the Bothan, Commenorian, Corellian, and Huttese warships that quickly came to the aid of Kashyyyk. With the arrival of the Hapan Home Fleet, Queen Mother Tenel Ka demanded Jacen Solo's surrender; when he refused and tried to blast his way free, the massed opposing fleets opened fire and the Fifth Fleet took heavy losses. It might have been decimated except for the secret arrival of Alema Rar, who used dark side powers to impel the Bothan forces to break formation and rush the Fifth Fleet, giving Solo and Atoko the chance to shove their way past the blockade.

The Fifth Fleet regrouped and recovered in the weeks that followed. Following increased Mandalorian involvement in the war, Jacen Solo—now using the name Darth Caedus—sent the fleet to Mandalore to eliminate any further interference. It was one of the last commands the fleet took from Solo.

**fifth moon of Da Soocha** *See* Da Soocha.

**Fifth Ruling Family** The name given to one of the ruling families of the Chiss society. In general the ordinal numbering of the ruling families denoted seniority, but it could also represent relative strengths among families. During the years leading up to the Clone Wars, the Chaf family was considered the Fifth Ruling Family. By the time of the Yuuzhan Vong invasion of the galaxy, the Chaf were one of just four ruling families; several others had been excised when their numbers were severely reduced during the war, or after they became Joiners.

**figda** A small, sweet type of candy, it was favored by children during the years leading up to the Clone Wars.

**Figg, Lord Ecclessis** A well-known Corellian famous for his deep-space explorations and wild inventions, he constructed the first floating settlement over Bespin, near the gas giant's equator.

As a young man, Ecclessis Figg discovered the planet Bespin's concentration of Tibanna and other gases; he began planning to mine it but lacked the funds. While working as a steward on an Alderaanian yacht, he saved the life of a young woman named Yarith, then wooed and married her and convinced her family to invest in his scheme. That investment returned a tenfold profit as Figg's Outer Javin Company expanded at a fast clip. Yarith was the source of many of the designs for Bespin's floating settlements, including Cloud City. Figg spent much of his life forging hyperspace routes and exploring all the way to the Mid Rim.

**Figg & Associates** The conglomerate of businesses formed by Ecclessis Figg on Bespin, Figg & Associates was considered a separate business entity from Figg's primary operation, the Outer Javin Company.

*Figrin D'an and the Modal Nodes*

**Figg Excavations** One of the many small corporations that were subsidiaries of the Outer Javin Company, Figg Excavations was headquartered on Gerrenthum, with its primary staging point for exploration and mining operations at Ione. As a member of the Mining Guild, FiggEx was supposed to provide input toward helping all mining operations gain expertise and profitability by sharing information. However, the input from FiggEx was minimal at best, and many within the guild believed that FiggEx was only working for its own betterment. Nothing pointed this out more than the allegations that FiggEx was employing pirates to ambush its own convoys as a way to demand local protection from Anoat sector forces, thereby allowing the company to split from the Mining Guild. When the allegations were proven true, FiggEx suffered more than the loss of profits it reported from the false piracy. It was severely fined by the Mining Guild, and both it and the Outer Javin Company suffered a great loss of respect. The Outer Javin Company was later discovered to have been unaware of FiggEx's machinations, further compounding the corporation's trouble.

**Figgis, Arner** A professor of anthropology, he proposed that the Bharhulai tribe of Socorro was a perfect example of his survival-regressive-isolationist theory. The theory proposed that groups of humans, isolated from other members of their kind during the colonization of a planet, would revert to primitive stages of development in order to ensure the survival of the group.

**fighting claw** A term used by the New Republic to describe the implanted claws used by Yuuzhan Vong warriors in hand-to-hand combat. The warriors attached bone spurs to specific muscles in their hands, elbows, or knees; fighting claws could be extended in a struggle with a twitch of the connected muscle, allowing Yuuzhan Vong warriors to make vicious slashes at their opponents. The extension was a painful act but only served to remind the warrior of his continual need to endure pain in order to become more like his gods.

**fighting sickle** A long-handled, heavy-bladed weapon, it was one of many simple tools used by the Noghri that evolved into fighting weapons. With its curved handle and perpendicular blade, the fighting sickle could be wielded with a great deal of power, even in close quarters.

**Figrin D'an and the Modal Nodes** The Bith band that played the Mos Eisley cantina when Ben Kenobi and Luke Skywalker booked passage on the *Millennium Falcon,* it was once Jabba the Hutt's full-time band, entertaining audiences for more than 20 years. At the height of the Clone Wars, the band was part of Jasod Revoc's Galactic Revue.

**fijisi** The wood of this Cardooine tree was used to create luxurious paneling and accent work. It had a unique, delicate scent, even when finished and polished. The fijisi tree could also be found on Commenor.

**Fik, Nor** A Colicoid leader, he traveled to Rorak 5 to meet with the pirate Krayn during the time that Anf Dec was negotiating with Krayn for the spice-processing rights for the Kessel Run. It was Nor Fik who greeted the slave trader Bakleeda (actually Obi-Wan Kenobi in disguise) about four years after the Battle of Naboo. Bakleeda had been hired by the Colicoids as an independent assessor of Krayn's organization. Shortly after their initial meeting, Nor Fik was confronted by Obi-Wan and Siri Tachi, both of whom revealed they had been planning to "overthrow" Krayn. In her disguise as Zora, Tachi reasoned with Nor Fik about the Colicoids' plans to eventually squeeze Krayn out. Nor Fik was unable to commit the full resources of the Colicoids to take up the Nar Shaddaa operations, but agreed to allow a slave revolt to take its course and ruin Krayn's operations. Eventually, Nor Fik was allowed to take control of Nar Shaddaa, and he agreed to actually pay the workers to continue processing the spice.

**Fil, Clone Commander** A clone commander who served Jedi Knight Nahdar Vebb during the Clone Wars. He was killed on the Vassek moon when Vebb and Kit Fisto searched the lair of General Grievous.

**Filar-Nitzan** A species of gaseous beings from the planet DNX-N1, they could form their bodies into a number of configurations. The Filar-Nitzan were called cloud demons or gas devils by the few beings who knew of them. Their coloration ranged from blue to green and yellow, and their eyes were always the opposite color from their bodies. Thus, a green-bodied Filar-Nitzan had red eyes. Xenobiologists of the New Republic believed that there were fewer than 400 individual Filar-Nitzan alive in the galaxy.

**Filba the Hutt** One of the few Hutts to actively support the Old Republic by becoming a member of its military during the Clone Wars, he had an ulterior motive. Filba was sent to Drongar and placed in charge of the Republic's production of bota, a fungus that could be a powerful drug or stimulant. He managed to skim a small amount from each outgoing shipment for his own use, which he later sold on the black market with the help of his commanding officer, Admiral Tarnese Bleyd. But when Filba tried to drive the price up by purposely destroying an outgoing shuttle, his main customer—the criminal organization Black Sun—decided to poison him.

***Filcher*** A pirate cargo ferry, it was destroyed by the Empire during the Galactic Civil War as it tried to ferry supplies to Rebel Alliance transports.

**Filian** An X'Ting, he was a regent on the council formed by the Five Families in the years leading up to the Clone Wars. Because of his position, he was forced to keep a great deal of his species' history a secret from his mate, G'Mai Duris. After Filian was killed in a duel, Duris had to assume his position on the council. Filian had died before the couple could engage in the X'Ting fertilization dance, leaving her childless and without heirs.

**filocard** Specialized datacards used by banking and financial institutions on Aargau, they identified individuals and kept track of their account balances. In addition to possessing a filocard, an individual also had to submit to an identity check, often a retinal scan or DNA analysis, to ensure that he or she was entitled to the money in a given account.

**Filordi** This six-limbed species was native to the planet Filordis. Along with the Neimoidians and the Caarites, the Filordi controlled the Trade Federation during the period leading up to the Battle of Naboo. However, both species severed their relationship with the Trade Federation after the Naboo blockade began and formed the Metatheran Cartel.

**Filordis** A rocky world that orbited a red star, its surface was constantly swept by fierce winds and thunderstorms.

**Filve** This planet was targeted by the Star Destroyer *Judicator* in a multipronged attack by Grand Admiral Thrawn that was intended to draw New Republic forces away from Ukio. Leia Organa Solo visited the Filvian government to assure it of New Republic support. When she arrived during the battle, the mad clone Jedi Joruus C'baoth sent the entire Imperial strike force after the *Millennium Falcon* in a vain attempt to capture her.

**Filvian (1)** A Brolfi, he was the leader of an insurgent group that opposed the Corporate Alliance's plans to take control of mining operations on Barlok in the years following the Battle of Naboo. He eventually came into contact with Kinman Doriana, a minion of Darth Sidious, who convinced Filvian and his people to build a slinker missile to assassinate both Passel Argente and Guildmaster Gilfrome. The plan was ultimately thwarted by Jedi Master Jorus C'baoth.

*A Filvian from Filve*

**Filvian (2)** Members of this species native to Filve were large, intelligent quadrupeds covered with bumps due to many glands and sacs on their bodies, which helped Filvians hold water and fat for consumption in emergency situations. Their three-fingered hands were quite dexterous, and many Filvians were known to be excellent computer operators.

**Fil'vye, Onoron** A Bothan shipping magnate, he established a base of operations on Streysel Island on the planet Vaynai at the height of the New Order. While most of his transport business catered to corporate customers who needed to move sensitive cargoes quickly, the operations were merely a cover for Onoron Fil'vye's more lucrative endeavors. In addition to funding a wide-ranging smuggling outfit, Fil'vye had cornered the market on the production of slick, a fermented seaweed oil that had certain medicinal properties . . . as well as being used by some as a recreational drug.

**final jump** Spacer slang for "death," it usually referred to a peaceful end.

**Final Redoubt** A New Republic code name, it covered the establishment of a new base of operations on the moon Ebaq 9 in an effort to draw the Yuuzhan Vong into a trap. The idea was to bring the alien fleet into a dead-end hyperspace route in the Deep Core, with the base on Ebaq 9 as the bait.

**Financial Reform Act** A resolution placed before the Galactic Senate eight years after the Battle of Naboo, it was intended to deal with the rampant greed and corruption that were overtaking the body. The Financial Reform Act never came to a vote, though, after it was revealed that Venco Autem had arranged for the murder of Jheramahd Greyshade and planned to assassinate his successor, Simon Greyshade. The Senate fell into an uproar, the FRA was tabled, and systems began to secede from the Republic.

**Findos, Sentepeth** A Neimoidian, he became acting viceroy of the Trade Federation after Nute Gunray and Rune Haako were slaughtered on Mustafar in the wake of the Clone Wars. But many Neimoidians refused to recognize his appointment, believing he was just a flunky chosen by the Empire. Previously a lieutenant with the Trade Federation forces, he had led the defense of Cato Neimoidia during the Clone Wars—and lost the planet to the Old Republic. With the establishment of the New Order, Findos had little choice but to sign a treaty nationalizing the Trade Federation. He implored Emperor Palpatine to remember the contributions of the Trade Federation . . . and then was escorted away by stormtroopers.

**Findris** Located in the Colonies region, it was home to several anti-Empire underground organizations. The most violent was the Justice Action Network (JAN) terrorist group led by Earnst Kamiel. Kamiel was caught on Elrood after the Battle of Yavin and extradited to the Haldeen sector for Imperial trial.

**findsmen** Gand bounty hunters, they meditated to learn the locations of their prey.

**Fing, Saluup** This Yuuzhan Vong commander was the first to appear before Warmaster Nas Choka and announce that the sentient planet Zonama Sekot had traveled across the galaxy to appear near Coruscant some five years after the alien invasion of the galaxy began. The Yuuzhan Vong had spent years transforming Coruscant into a likeness of their long-lost homeworld of Yuuzhan'tar, only to have Zonama Sekot set off a chain reaction of seismic events that damaged or destroyed most of it.

**Fingal** An undercover agent of the Empire, he had served on Berchest for nearly 10 years at the time of the Battle of Endor. Fingal had the uncanny ability to show absolutely no emotion. With the defeat of the Empire, he believed his career was over—until he was reactivated by Grand Admiral Thrawn, who wanted to monitor any possible activities of Luke Skywalker on the planet.

**fingerprint masque** Similar in appearance to an ink pad, this device attached a biochemical screen (or masque) to a being's fingertips. The screen could then be set to a random or known pattern, altering the fingerprint impression of the individual.

*Finn, a bartender at Rik's*

**finger-spears** Cephalopods that Yuuzhan Vong master shapers were allowed to graft onto their arms in place of hands, these creatures could telescope outward up to 4 meters, forming razor-sharp tips. Mezhan Kwaad used finger-spears.

**Finn (1)** A small boy, he was rescued by young Anakin Skywalker and Jar Jar Binks after he became lost in the cityscape of Coruscant when his nanny droid malfunctioned just prior to the Battle of Naboo. Anakin repaired the nanny droid and helped reunite Finn with his mother. Finn's mother then helped Anakin get back to the Jedi Temple, where Qui-Gon was waiting for him.

*Fiolla of Lorrd*

**Finn (2)** A young native of Herdessa, he didn't want the New Republic to take control of the galaxy following the Battle of Endor. Finn and his friend Suzu lobbed mud balls at Leia Organa and Mon Mothma when the two leaders of the Alliance arrived to discuss the planet's position in a new galactic government. Finn was captured and was slated to be executed by Lumiya until Leia managed to shoot the chief of security and give Finn time to escape.

**Finn (3)** A Sith Master, he was a known terrorist during the years leading up to the Battle of Ruusan. He demanded unequivocal loyalty from his apprentice, a woman named Marka.

**Finn (4)** An Imperial soldier, he was killed on Cilpar during the fighting that continued in the wake of the Battle of Endor.

**Finn (5)** A male Sakiyan, he worked as the bartender at Rik's about 100 years after the Yuuzhan Vong invasion of the galaxy. He was known as someone who could take a being's head off with a drink, a blaster, or possibly even his fist. Unimpressed by anything, he had heard it all.

**Fiolla of Lorrd** Hart-and-Parn Gorra-Fiolla of Lorrd, or simply Fiolla, was the assistant Auditor-General of the Corporate Sector Authority. She was very ambitious, and took on an undercover investigation to crack a slaving ring that was said to include some top execs of the CSA. She hoped to use the information to eventually move up to the CSA Board of Directors, but she didn't know that her assistant Magg was actually one of the slavers. With the aid of Han Solo, Fiolla managed to expose the secret ring to Odumin, the Territorial Manager of the Corporate Sector. A few years later, Fiolla's investigations led her to corruption in the office of the Prex itself. The Prex's assistant, Akeeli Somerce, held her at gunpoint. If not for the actions of fellow auditor Naven Crel, she would have been killed. Fiolla next planned to pursue the Prex, Chils Meplin, for illegally selling CSA secrets to the Empire.

**firaxan shark** A vicious, predatory fish in the oceans of Manaan. One was awakened some 4,000 years before the Galactic Civil War by the kolto-mining operation at Hrakert Station. The huge creature began to terrorize the scientists and workers at the facility. Many of the Selkath on Hrakert Station went insane, worrying that the shark would consume them. The machinery within the facility was destroyed by the Jedi Knights in an effort to drive off the shark without killing it.

**Fird, Senator** The Senator from Alsaken, he eloquently testified at hearings on the creation of an Outer Expansion Zone for the galaxy.

***Fireater*** A New Republic cruiser, it was stationed at Durren in the early years of the New Republic. Along with the *Courane*, it was dispatched to Cybloc XII to investigate the spread of the Death Seed plague. The *Fireater* was then sent to defend Nam Chorios, where it was destroyed by the combined attack of a group of needle ships.

**fire blade** An unusual weapon, it originally was designed as a basic cutting tool. However, after Uda-Khalid had a pair of them attached to his forearms, fire blades found another use. The blade of the tool was energized to assist in the cutting process. It was believed that the fire blade was originally created on Dathomir by lizard keepers who used it to cut and cauterize the paws of domesticated Kwi.

**firebrand** A lightsaber hilt style common among the new Order of Jedi Knights trained by Luke Skywalker at the height of the New Republic, it was all black and had a thin body ribbed along the lower half for a more stable grip. One side of the hilt was raised, with the activation switch at the lower end. The end of the firebrand hilt bulged outward to accommodate power cells. A thin deflector ring protected the wielder's hands from energy backwash.

**fire breather** One of the biological constructs of the Yuuzhan Vong, this 10-meter-tall creature resembled a huge, walking balloon. It moved about on six stubby legs, and its body was studded with hose-like tentacles. From each of these tentacles, the fire breather ejected

*Fire breather*

a stream of thick fluid that caught fire in the presence of oxygen and incinerated everything it touched. Fire breathers were protected by their thick hides, and their normal exhales were filled with special chemicals that dispersed blasterfire. The Yuuzhan Vong first used the creatures during the attack on Gyndine.

**fire bush** A low-growing bush native to the jungles of Togoria, it was saturated with resins and was used by inhabitants to start fires. The thick smoke drove off most insects.

***Fireclaw*** An Imperial Interdictor cruiser, it patrolled the Lifh sector during the Galactic Civil War. During the Alliance's attempt to liberate Vilosoria, the astromech R2Z-DL managed to discover Imperial codes and information on an imminent malfunction in the *Fireclaw*'s gravity-well projectors. Koedi Raef used the codes to redirect the *Fireclaw*, ordering it to remain in position until the projectors could be repaired. In the meantime, the Alliance was able to eliminate the Imperial garrison on Vilosoria and free the planet from Imperial control.

**Fireclaw Horde** A mercenary gang, it first appeared on the criminal scene in the Cularin system during the final years of the Old Republic when it tried to ambush the luxury liner *Queen of Cularin.* The gang had established a base of operations in the abandoned city of Nub Saar in orbit around the planet Genarius, where members began working on a variant of the MMR-9 recovery droid. This new droid would be used as the first line of attack when the ambush took place, operating in the vacuum of space to disable the *Queen of Cularin* and leave the vessel open to boarding actions.

As the droid project neared completion, the Fireclaw Horde sent a group of Togorians to Tindark to obtain security codes that would allow them to acquire several MMR-9 prototypes. They were interrupted by the droid's designer, Imik Suum, who managed to escape after witnessing the Togorians murder other witnesses. A group of freelance agents tracked the Togorians to their hideout, discovered the gang's plans, and managed to intercept the luxury liner before the Fireclaw Horde could launch its attack, driving off the mercenaries.

**fire creeper** Large insects that lived in caves on Nirauan, they traveled in huge swarms and consumed everything in their path.

**firedrake** An unusual insect native to Gallinore, it emitted colored lights, heat, and sparks of energy as it moved about. When viewed at night, these large creatures presented an impressive and beautiful light show. The Hapan people tried to transplant a colony of firedrakes to Hapes, but the insects soon died. They had a sort of symbiosis with the ecosystem of Gallinore, and rarely survived offworld. Instead of live firedrakes, Hapans used artificial light displays to simulate their wondrous flights. In their natural habitat, firedrakes hunted in packs, and were intelligent enough to plan out an ambush to bring down large prey.

**Firefolk** The code name of a silver-haired man who was a member of the resistance on Samaria during the early months of the New Order. He accompanied Dinko on a mission to meet Ferus Olin after Olin was instructed by Emperor Palpatine to offer the resistance a chance to cease their operations. Firefolk was later forced to go into hiding to ensure that the resistance was not exposed.

**firefolk** *See* Wisties.

**fire gnat** These small insects native to Drongar were named for their stinging bite; they also were edible and provided many nutrients.

**fire grenade** Developed more than 4,000 years before the Battle of Yavin, a fire grenade when detonated used controlled chemical reactions to disperse an intense heat over a large area. The heat could sear living flesh, and rendered most weapons useless.

**firehead** This nimble creature was native to the frozen polar regions of the planet Rhinnal. An ambulatory fish, the firehead used its high body temperature to burrow into the ice. A knobby growth in its upper jaw, which glowed like a bit of lava, was used to melt and scrape the ice. This knob could also kill the firehead's food, and swarms of fireheads worked together to attack larger prey. Fireheads served as sources of both heat and food for the native Rhinnalians.

**firejelly** A Yuuzhan Vong weapon first used during the Second Battle of Coruscant, the sticky jelly was highly flammable and stuck to virtually everything it contacted. After the hostilities between the Yuuzhan Vong and the Galactic Alliance were resolved and the invaders were allowed to live on the planet Zonama Sekot, they found that firejelly and many other bioengineered weapons simply reverted to their animal forms and fled into the forests. This was one way in which Sekot forced the Yuuzhan Vong to give up their lust for war and embrace a more enlightened existence.

**fire-kraken** This vicious creature was known to inhabit the deepest oceanic trenches found on the planet Nal Hutta. It was distinguished by its snake-like tendrils, which it used to locate and capture its prey.

**firepath** A complex strategy game played on Cheelit. Its layout resembled a life-sized chessboard, divided up into four Radials and four Rings; each Radial and Ring had seven Stones. Among the pieces were the Cardinal and the Merchant. Captured pieces were consumed in a pillar of fire. Darth Vader once lured Clat the Shamer onto a firepath game board during a match with Lady Dhol. Vader captured Clat on the board, consuming the assassin in flames. He later executed Dhol the same way for her part in the plot to kill him.

**firepoint** This was the term used by the Chiss to describe any remote military installation located so that it could protect another installation. Firepoints were often housed in asteroids or other natural bodies. If enemy ships tried to reach a hidden Chiss location, they would have to pass by one or more of these firepoints, and would be destroyed or disabled long before reaching their target. The Chiss lined the outer edges of the Redoubt with firepoints to protect the refuge they had hidden within the cluster.

***Firerider*** A *Starwind*-class passenger yacht owned and operated by Serdo for many years. Ostensibly, Serdo used it as a transport ship, carrying government officials and dignitaries to and from their appointments. In reality, he used these trips to smuggle spice from planet to planet. After amassing his own fortune, Serdo retired and sold the ship to Fizzi's Slightly Used Starships. The *Firerider* was armed with turret-mounted light ion cannons for defense.

**fire rings of Fornax** In one of the unique wonders of the galaxy, five rings of intense fire appeared to encircle the planet Fornax. They were really solar prominences attracted to the planet due to its close proximity to its sun. Pirates dueled to the death inside a fire ring so that no combatant could escape without being seriously burned in the attempt.

**firespeeder** Emergency vehicles, they featured cowled jet engines in addition to their repulsorlift generators, granting the vehicles their required top speeds to douse fires on incoming ships and debris. Never was the need for them greater than when the fiery fragments of General Grievous's flagship punched through the atmosphere of Coruscant. The squad of emergency firespeeders matched speed with the barely controlled vessel and doused some of the surface fires with pressurized jets of flame-retardant foam shot from wingtip-mounted nozzles. When the flagship came screeching to a bone-shaking halt on a strip of unoccupied industrial district, teams of firefighters emerged from their speeders to inspect the wreckage and put out any remaining flames. The daredevil rescue-service pilots were truly the last line of defense against the catastrophic impact

*Firespeeder*

of debris meteorites. Their firespeeders featured an ablative cockpit canopy, allowing it brief exposure to intense temperatures. They also had emergency running lights and an extremely loud enunciator and siren.

**fire spitter** A creature bioengineered by the Yuuzhan Vong, it acted as a kind of wrist-mounted flamethrower. To use a fire spitter, a Yuuzhan Vong warrior had the bones in his or her forearm removed completely. The creature's spine was then inserted, and its circulatory system was grafted to that of the warrior. The fire spitter then fed on the warrior's blood as it passed through its system. The head of the fire spitter was attached to a snake-like neck that wrapped around the warrior's wrist, and its vestigial arms were used to grasp the warrior's arm. If called upon in battle, the fire spitter forcefully spit out a ball of biomatter at its target. When ignited, the ball spread chemical fire and engulfed the target in flame.

**Firespray** This was the brand name of BlasTech's DL-87 deck-clearing blaster, designed to hit as many targets as possible.

**Firespray-31** A 21.5-meter-long starship, it was in production for a short time from Kuat Systems Engineering. The Firespray-31, or *Firespray*-class patrol vessel, was designed for speed and stealth and originally was marketed as a patrol and law enforcement craft. Its design incorporated an "engines-down" configuration, with the cockpit and cargo area mounted above and perpendicular to the engine area, so the pilot landed the ship while looking straight up and away from the landing platform and flew it in a "standing up" position. This required that the cockpit console be mounted on a rotating platform, giving the pilot the ability to see where he or she was going. Two-thirds of the ship's hull area was dedicated to the engines, which accounted for its remarkable speed. The basic Firespray-31 was armed with a pair of turret-mounted blaster cannons on the nose, as well as a tractor beam projector. Maneuverability was provided by the two outboard wings that could rotate to give the ship different attitudes in flight. The wingspan was just over 21 meters. One famous example of a Firespray-31 was the *Slave I* owned by bounty hunters Jango and Boba Fett.

**Firest, Colonel Ledick** An Alliance field commander for the Rebel forces in the snow trenches at Echo Base on Hoth, the colonel was originally a member of the Laramus Base Irregulars. Colonel Ledick Firest was known for the development of his subordinates and commanders, who survived more battles than any other group during the Galactic Civil War.

**Firestone, Wadie** An Alliance scout during the early years of the Galactic Civil War, he and Arlo Tyre were dispatched to investigate the loss of contact with a remote archaeological excavation on Alashan shortly after the Battle of Yavin. After Tyre was killed when he activated the site's defense systems, Firestone tried to return to his home base to report on the incident. However, the ancient site's defenses detected his flight and shot his Y-wing out of the sky.

***Firestorm* (1)** Following the destruction of the *Shockwave*, this *Imperial*-class Star Destroyer became the flagship of Warlord Harrsk's fleet. He turned it over to Admiral Daala when he ordered her to assume command of the fleet. It was on the *Firestorm* that Daala later turned over control of the Imperial Navy to Pellaeon.

***Firestorm* (2)** One of four Corellian CR90 corvettes under the command of Lumiya following the Battle of Endor, it was modified to allow it to carry up to four TIE fighters that could be deployed in an ambush.

***Firestorm* (3)** A Nebulon-B frigate, it was used by the Imperial Navy during the Galactic Civil War.

**Fire Team Three** One of many fire-suppression teams that protected the skies of the planet Coruscant at the height of the Clone Wars. Two members were lost while trying to prevent the dying hull of the *Invisible Hand* from causing too much damage when Anakin Skywalker brought it to a controlled crash landing.

***Firethorn*** A Galactic Alliance frigate, it was brought to the Kuat system 10 years after the end of the war with the Yuuzhan Vong to safeguard peace treaty negotiations between the Galactic Alliance and the leaders of the Five World Party. The *Firethorn* was stationed in orbit near Toryaz Station, where it served to protect those who had gathered in the Narsacc Habitat.

**firethorn trees** These 100-meter-tall trees grew only in a single small grove in the Irugian rain forest on Abbaji. Criminal mastermind Prince Xizor had a dwarf firethorn tree that he personally tended.

**fireworm** Also known as a lava dragon, this creature was native to Eol Sha, where it survived the intense heat and pressure of the molten lava it lived in. Its body was protected by armor-like scales made of crystallized silicon, and it resembled a huge snake with pointed ear tufts made of hard scales. The fireworm literally breathed the lava, extracting oxygen and other gases for respiration. It also used the extracted gases to fill insulating air bladders, keeping it buoyant in the lava. Seven years after the Battle of Endor, Gantoris tested Luke Skywalker's motives by making him walk across a lava pit to confront a fireworm living there. Skywalker tried to kill the creature with his lightsaber, but its scales refracted the beam and deflected it into dozens of smaller beams. Skywalker then managed to cut a small chunk out of one of the fireworm's scales, and the gap allowed the superheated lava to contact unprotected flesh, eventually killing the creature.

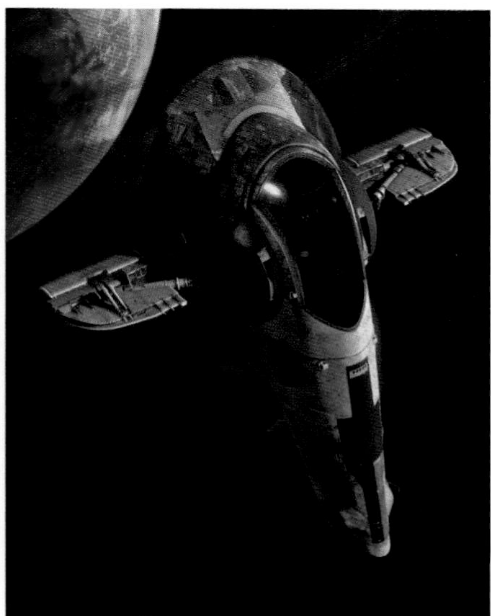

A famous example of a Firespray-31

Fireworm

**Firkrann crystal** This was one of many crystals used by the ancient Sith Lords to construct a lightsaber. It was believed that Firkrann crystals, found on Rafa V, gave the lightsaber wielder the ability to cause more damage to a droid opponent.

**Firrerre** All life on this planet was wiped out by the Empire's use of a biological weapon, and it remained too toxic for any ships to land there. Hethrir, the Imperial Procurator of Justice and himself a native of Firrerre, ordered the devastation, which was carried out by the Empire's elite Starcrash Brigade. The Firrerreos, humanoids with long, striped hair, were believed to have been annihilated, but Leia Organa Solo discovered there were colony ships carrying many natives in suspended animation. Hethrir had been secretly raiding the ships for slaves. Years later, the Yuuzhan Vong wiped out the remaining Firrerreo civilization in a vicious attack that was based on information the invaders obtained from the Firrerreos' longtime enemies, the Belderonians.

***Firrinree*** This was one of two *Sh'ner*-class cruisers brought to Bakura by Lwothin and the P'w'eck Emancipation Movement at the height of the Yuuzhan Vong invasion of the galaxy. Ostensibly, the *Firrinree* and its companion the *Errinung'ka* formed the heart of Lwothin's fleet, which transported the Keeramak to Bakura. In reality, they were part of a Ssi-ruuvi invasion force sent to Bakura after the Yuuzhan Vong subjugated the Ssi-ruuk and tried to establish a foothold along the border of the Unknown Regions. Each cruiser was armed with a new paralysis weapon that could knock out an entire city with minimal effort. However, before the Ssi-ruuk could launch their surprise attack on Bakura, the P'w'eck crewmen rose up against their masters and overpowered the Ssi-ruuk. The *Errinung'ka* fell first, with the *Firrinree* eventually surrendering as well, ending the plot to subjugate Bakura.

**Firro** This planet was brutally subjugated by the Empire, with many deaths and atrocities, and Lord Cuvir was installed as Imperial Governor. During a visit to a Firro relief station, Cuvir witnessed the skill of Imperial medical droid 2-1B and made the droid his personal physician. Too-Onebee later joined the Alliance.

**first abomination** The Yuuzhan Vong deplored "unnatural" combustion, and believed the first abomination was the use of fire from a machine. In other words, this was the worst sin. When Anakin Solo used phosphorous flares to set ablaze the trees of Yavin 4, Vua Rapuung responded by backhanding the young Jedi. Living things used to create fire, like fire breathers, were considered an entirely different thing.

**First Administrator** This top political position was created by the leaders of the New Republic. The First Administrator could serve as a stand-in for the Chief of State in negotiations and other political discussions.

**First Battle Group** Later known as the First Fleet, this was the first full naval fleet commissioned by the New Republic. It first was assigned as the home guard for Coruscant, and later was sent on various tours of duty as other fleets were commissioned. It was in the area of the galaxy known as Thunder Alley when the Yevethan Great Purge began.

***First Citizen*** A Kothlis Systems Luxuflier, it was Borsk Fey'lya's personal starship. The *First Citizen* was one of the last ships to leave Coruscant when the planet was evacuated in the face of a Yuuzhan Vong attack, although Fey'lya ordered it to leave without him.

**First Fleet** The primary naval fleet of the Galactic Alliance during the final stages of the war against the Yuuzhan Vong, it was made up mainly of the surviving ships of the New Republic's First Battle Group. The First Fleet was commanded by Admiral Traest Kre'fey from his flagship, the *Ralroost.* Among the other ships in the First Fleet were the *Rebel Dream* and the *Yald.* In the wake of the Yuuzhan Vong War, the First Fleet remained part of the Galactic Alliance's naval structure, and was eventually placed under the command of Admiral Nek Bwua'tu at the height of the Alliance's war against the Confederation.

**First Great Schism** Historians say this was the first known instance of the Jedi Knights fracturing into the users of the light side of the Force and those who followed the dark side. The schism took place during the early years of the Old Republic, when the Legions of Lettow split off from the followers of the Ashla in the wake of the Force Wars. The term *Dark Jedi* was believed to have originated after the First Great Schism, describing those Jedi who had fallen to the dark side.

**First Sun Mobile Regiment** A mercenary unit operating in the Outer Rim during the Galactic Civil War. Its specialty was SLAMs: Search, Locate, and Annihilate Missions such as Imperial Base Delta Zero operations. Members used repulsorlift infantry vehicles, and often contracted out to the Imperial Army. Much of their success was due to support from the Empire, but in the wake of the Battle of Endor an entire company was executed by Moff Nile Owen. General Maska Zural, the leader of the First Sun group, distanced himself from the Imperial remnants and hired the group out to the highest bidder.

**First Unification Wars** This series of battles was waged by Empress Teta some 5,000 years before the Battle of Yavin. These wars brought the first seven star systems under Teta's command and the planet Kirrek into her empire.

**Firth, Aquella** A young woman who once dated Niklas Cories during the early years of the New Order, she rightly dismissed him as being "too old and dangerous" for her. Cories never forgot or forgave her, and eventually tricked her into unknowingly placing herself within his reach. But her father, Quoltus, had hired a group of freelance mercenaries to ensure that she returned safely, giving Aquella a chance to exercise her need for freedom without realizing his protection.

**Firwirrung** A reptilian Ssi-ruu, he was the personal master of the human go-between Dev Sibwarra and the head of entechment operations aboard the battle cruiser *Shriwirr.* Entechment was the absorption of a sentient creature's energies into battery coils to power circuitry. Aggressively innovative, Firwirrung devised a means to conduct entechment at potentially unlimited distances if a Force-strong individual could be procured and subdued. Despite initial success in enteching Luke Skywalker, Firwirrung was unable to complete his work as Sibwarra managed to kill him during the Battle of Bakura.

**Fishface** A derogatory name sometimes used for a species of amphibious humanoids native to Ootoola. Their skin was a mottled bright green, and their heads were adorned with a fin-like ridge and several finned jowls. During the Old Republic, their society was ruled by a patriarchal government. The ruler was expected to strictly adhere to their laws, thereby achieving a certain level of purity.

**Fissona** A young Tarasin, he was the troublemaker of the Hiironi tribe during the era of the Battle of Naboo. Only nine years old at the time, Fissona was the grandson of Cryalina, but that relationship didn't save him from getting caught and punished for his misdeeds.

**Fisto, Kit** At its height, the Jedi Order encompassed hundreds of different species, all strong in the Force. Kit Fisto was a striking example of a nonhuman Jedi, with large, unblinking eyes and a gathered tangle of flexible tentacle-tresses extending from his head. The mighty warrior not only advised the highest office of the Republic, but also was part of a Jedi task force assembled by Mace Windu to rescue captives from the Separatist stronghold on Geonosis. Fisto fought well against the Geonosian and battle droid forces, becoming one of the few Jedi to survive the extended melee in the execution arena. When Republic reinforcements arrived to join the first epic battle of the Clone Wars, Fisto led a special unit of clone troopers into the thick of the conflict.

An amphibious Nautolan from the Sabilon region of watery Glee Anselm, Fisto could detect pheromonal expressions of emotion and other changes in body chemistry thanks to head-tentacles that contained highly sensitive olfactory receptors. He could live in air or in water. An extremely powerful swimmer, Fisto honed his Jedi abilities to take advantage of his aquatic origins, perfecting difficult Force techniques that manipulated the movement of water for defensive or offensive use.

*Kit Fisto*

Fisto was master to Nahdar Vebb, a Mon Calamari Padawan, and later Eerin Bant, former Padawan of the late Master Tahl. He was also co-leader of a Jedi task force that vanquished the Iridium pirates in the Atrivis sector. During the Clone Wars, General Fisto's aquatic prowess led to his command of the Mon Calamari campaign. He guided local Mon Cal forces partnered with Republic clone sea troopers in battles against the Separatist-backed Quarren Isolationist League. Fisto later was involved in important engagements on Devaron and Ord Cestus, and hunted for escaped prisoner Nute Gunray in General Grievous's lair on the Vassek moon.

His close friendship with and concern for fellow Jedi Aayla Secura occasionally pushed the rules against attachment. They shared a deep respect for each other that, had they been outside the Jedi Order, might have gone further. As the Clone Wars ground on, Master Fisto was appointed to the Jedi Council. He was among the group of Jedi Masters who accompanied Mace Windu to arrest Chancellor Palpatine after the politician had finally been revealed as Darth Sidious. However, the Jedi were unprepared for Palpatine's powers, and Fisto was quickly killed during the fighting, leaving Mace Windu to face Palpatine alone.

**Fitca Prime** This planet was the primary world in the Fitca system, located within the Lesser Plooriod Cluster. The planet and system were subjugated by the Empire's High Inquisitor Mox Slosin during the early years of the New Order.

**Fitch** A Ferroan, he was one of a group that accepted a newly shaped Sekotan starship from the Langhesi and finished its creation. They filled any seams or cracks left behind by the Jentari, then calibrated the ship's systems to its new owner. Fitch also provided elementary education to the new owner, but left the majority of this to the ship itself.

**Five Families** This was the name given to the five clans of Cestians who controlled the Cestus Cybernetics Corporation as well as the government during the last years of the Old Republic. For many generations there had been just four families; then Caiza Quill made a bold move to have his own family elevated in status. By delivering labor contracts and easing the dissent that had grown among the X'Ting during their subjugation by Cestus Cybernetics, Quill had earned himself a position on the leadership council. He also gained the favor of the original four families, who agreed to have his own family added to their numbers. But Quill's actions ensured that the X'Ting would be enslaved to the offworlders who ran Cestus Cybernetics, and he was quietly reviled for having sold out his own people.

Each of the families was responsible for a different aspect of commerce on Ord Cestus: research, energy, manufacturing, sales and marketing, or mining. The director of each branch served as the leader of his or her respective clan. When the Clone Wars came to Ord Cestus after Count Dooku used the threat of combat-programmed JK series droids to force the Old Republic into a rash move against the Cestians, the Five Families found themselves powerless to maintain their control of the planet. When the warship *Nexu* was dispatched to force them into submission, many members fled to their secret bunker hidden in the Kibo Plateau. However, their location was discovered by Thak Val Zsinj and the ARC trooper known as Jangotat, who managed to reorient the *Nexu*'s weapons to fire on the bunker. In a single stroke, the bunker was destroyed and the Five Families were nearly wiped out. The few survivors were left to squabble among themselves. In the meantime, G'Mai Duris and the X'Ting clans began to once again assume control over Ord Cestus.

**Five Holy Cities** Founded by religious crusaders on the planet New Holgha, the Five Holy Cities were evacuated just before the Yuuzhan Vong attacked the planet; still, the alien invaders scoured them for sustenance for their giant, organic warships.

**Five Masters Academy** A beautiful glass-and-durasteel building erected on the planet Cularin for the Wookiee Liberation Front during the early years of the Clone Wars, this three-story edifice was built at the request of the Five Masters and funded almost completely by Barnab Chistor and his administration. But the entire complex, including the Training Hall, was burned to the ground shortly after the end of the Clone Wars when an unseen force swept through the facility and destroyed it. Although Chistor and the Master in Violet were able to drive off the main attacker, it left in its wake the reanimated bodies of its victims, who attacked the two survivors. Their bodies were never found, and it was assumed that Chistor and the Master in Violet were killed.

**Fiver** This early-model R7 astromech owned by Anakin Solo got its name from the five attempts he made to upgrade the notoriously poor-functioning droid to the standards of an R2 unit. As Anakin became more and more involved with the fight against the Yuuzhan Vong, Fiver was not given regular memory wipes and developed its own personality. Fiver became much more independent and was invaluable in Anakin's escape from the Yuuzhan Vong on Yavin 4.

**Fives, Trooper** The nickname of clone trooper CT27-5555, who served at the tracking station on the Rishi moon during the Clone Wars.

**Five World Party** The name adopted by the unified government of the Five Worlds in the Corellian system in the period following the war against the Yuuzhan Vong, the Five World Party was formed after the Galactic Alliance eliminated the governor-general position that had traditionally led the system, replacing it with Chief of State positions from each of the five planets. The Chiefs of State were elected on their homeworld, and chose to form the position of the Prime Minister to represent Corellia, Drall, Selonia, Talus, and Tralus. The Prime Minister, supported by one Chief of State from each of the five planets in the system, was responsible for ensuring that the needs of all five were balanced against the resources that were available, as well as negotiating for the entire system. As the Galactic Alliance grew in power, the Prime Minister and the Five World Party gently pushed for Corellians of all species to maintain their identity in the face of perceived homogenization within the Galactic Alliance.

**Fivvic** An imposing Barabel, he was in command of a mission to infiltrate Dagro to investigate the rumors of Separatist activities on the planet near the start of the Clone Wars. When Obi-Wan Kenobi made a decision to go ahead of the main force, Fivvic told Anakin Skywalker that they could not adjust their plans, forcing the main group to delay deploying for four days, unaware that Obi-Wan had stumbled upon a hidden Separatist base.

**Fivvl, Deksi** An elderly Aqualish, he served as pirate Naz Felyood's engineer aboard the *Jynni's Virtue* at the height of the New Order. Fivvl also served as the ship's unofficial historian. After landing on Korriban, Deksi and the crew found themselves beset by Korriban Zombies, and were killed when a shipmate set off the ship's self-destruct mechanism to prevent the Zombies from taking it over.

**Fivvle, Ars** An Ugnaught and member of the Isced tribe, he worked as a self-promoting reporter for *Action Tidings* on Cloud City at the height of the New Order. He was leaked information about the Ugnaught rebellion against Imperial Governor Treece in the wake of Lando Calrissian's flight from Cloud City months after the Battle of Hoth.

**fixed-signature tracker** A tracker developed by Talon Karrde's workers, its purpose was to help the Jedi and their allies to find one another without leaking their positions to the Yuuzhan Vong or their collaborators. The tracker used a fixed signature that passed through relays and the HoloNet, and gave an off-read within a range of from 10 to 50 light-years. No one without an encryption key could use it. Luke Skywalker fitted the *Errant Venture*, the *Jade Saber*, and Kyp Durron's ship with them. When Skywalker asked Jaina Solo to find Durron, he provided her with the encryption keys for all three ships.

**Fixer** *See* Loneozner, Laze.

**Fixter, Marsh** An alias used by Obi-Wan Kenobi when he was approached by a group of battle droids on the planet Dagro two years after the Battle of Geonosis. Obi-Wan was on Dagro to investigate the presence of a Separatist base in the planet's canyons.

**Fiyarro** One of the three largest cities on Serenno, along with Carannia and Saffia.

**Fizark, Sharina** A woman who lived on Tatooine during the era of the Great Sith War. Her husband, Ward, worked as a miner, but he was also a skilled hunter. After his death in the mines, Sharina was left with very little money, and was forced to sell off some of his trophies to survive.

**Fizz, the** A disease, it was believed to have originated on the planet Woteba during the months following the establishment of several Colony hives there shortly after the Yuuzhan Vong were defeated. The Killiks who were afflicted by the Fizz found themselves covered with a foamy coating that seemed to eat away at their bodies, causing considerable pain until the individual simply was unable to sustain itself and died. What made the disease unusual was that it also attacked nonliving targets such as landspeeders and landscaping equipment. UnuThul and the Colony claimed that the new Jedi Order had known about the Fizz all along, and had tricked the Colony into relocating to Woteba in order to infect them. However, investigation by Cilghal and other Jedi healers revealed that the Fizz was not a naturally occurring infection, but a kind of environmental defense system. It was a sophisticated, self-replicating nanotech virus that reacted whenever the environmental balance of Woteba was upset, and only attacked those things deemed harmful to Woteba's natural state of being. Cilghal further speculated that the Fizz was present only in the Utegetu Nebula because it had been placed there by an unknown species to assist with restoration of the planetary systems within the nebula in the wake of the supernova that created it. Exactly where the Fizz came from, and who created it, were mysteries that the Jedi were unable to initially resolve, causing the Killiks to continue to insist that it was being used to exterminate them. It was believed that the quarrying of moirestone and the harvesting of hamogoni wood by the Killiks, combined with their disposing of toxins into the planet's bogs, brought on the Fizz.

**Fizzik** An X'Ting who was a distant hive relative of the crime lord Trillot, he worked as an informant for Trillot on Ord Cestus in the years around the Clone Wars. Trillot, who was in the midst of a natural transformation from male to female, told Fizzik to escort visitor Asajj Ventress through the warrens; the dark side warrior constantly made threats, but Fizzik held up under pressure. Trillot then gave Fizzik a permanent position in her organization. He advanced swiftly, and was chosen to make contact with Obi-Wan Kenobi shortly after the Desert Wind attack on the Clandes Industrial power complex. In the wake of the destruction of the Five Families and after Trillot was executed by Ventress, Fizzik decided to take control of his relative's criminal organization for himself.

**Fizzz** *See* Dorenian Beshniquel.

**Flacharia system** A star system where Dean Jinzler's ship developed problems with its hyperdrive while he was on his way to Nirauan to answer Voss Parck's message regarding the Outbound Flight Project. He was rescued when Jorj Car'das arrived to help with the repairs, but that seemed too coincidental when added to the way in which Jinzler learned of Parck's mission.

*Flalios*

**Flagesso** A commander in the Cloud City Wing Guard at the height of the New Order, he was outwardly loyal to Baron-Administrator Lando Calrissian. But Flagesso was also in league with the minor crime lord Sawthawne. After Calrissian managed to shut down Sawthawne's operations with the help of some hired mercenaries, Flagesso tried to launch a military coup to take control of Cloud City. Calrissian's personal security force managed to chase Flagesso to the Ugnaught Surface, where he was apprehended and arrested.

**Flail, the** A terrorist group that rose to prominence shortly before Finis Valorum was voted out of office as Supreme Chancellor, it was led by Zegmon Pent. The Flail declared war on the Senate itself, believing it to be funded by major corporations and no longer acting for the common good; it caused a great deal of havoc on Coruscant in the era leading up to the Battle of Naboo. Members believed that Pent was a Jedi assassin, a belief he went to great lengths to cultivate. In order to prove his worth in the midst of accusations about his power, Chancellor Valorum set out to eliminate the Flail, and hired an independent team of security officers to search out the terrorists. In the meantime, Pent and the Flail attempted to take control of the Weather Modulation Control Center near the Chancellor's tower residence, in an effort to create an ionization storm to destroy the building. Their efforts were thwarted by the security officers Valorum had hired.

**Flalios** One of the many gladiators who tried to win their freedom from the arenas of Rattatak during the final years of the Old Republic. Flalios often fought with chains, whipping them around to deliver stunning blows to the heads of his opponents.

**Flakax** An insectoid species native to the planet Flax. Members made up a society of sexless drones dominated by a queen. A few males also were produced when the female prepared to lay her eggs, to assist in the reproductive process. The huge drones, each nearly as large as a Wookiee, did all the work required by the hive, while the males were simply slaves to the queen. Individual drones were distinguished by an unusual duct in their abdomens that could be used to expel a noxious gas causing irritation to the eyes and nasal tissues of most humanoid species. The Flakax society was highly developed around the hives in which they lived, with each of the three genders having a defined role in its maintenance. They had no high technology, however, and when they were subjugated by the Empire they were forced to work in mines to obtain metals for the Imperial war machine. At the height of the Swarm War, the Flakax government was targeted by the Colony for a military coup, in an effort to draw the Galactic Alliance into fighting smaller fires and leaving the Utegetu Nebula unguarded. This would allow the Colony to launch its full-scale attack on the Chiss, but the plans of the Colony were discovered by Han and Leia Organa Solo.

**FlakBlaster Ten** A huge piece of artillery developed after the Swarm War. Instead of firing projectiles or turbolaser blasts, the FlakBlaster Ten shot searing bolts of neurodium plasma at its targets. Each charge of neurodium was delivered in a small metal cylinder, which was fired out of one of the weapon's eight emitter nozzles, which heated up the plasma even more.

**Flame** An alias, it was used by a wealthy businesswoman from the planet Acherin who was forced to leave her homeworld after the Empire began nationalizing its corporations—and all her assets—in the months following the end of the Clone Wars. Flame decided to fight back and start a resistance unit known as Moonstrike. She later met with Trever Flume, who was representing Ferus Olin's own band of rebels, and after the two leaders spoke on Samaria, they agreed to work together to forge a stronger resistance. Their plans were put on hold when the leaders of Samaria's neighbor planet, Rosha, were falsely implicated in an assassination attempt on the life of Imperial adviser Bog Divinian. Olin and Flame pooled their resources to ensure that Roshan ambassador to Samaria Robbyn Sark and his comrades were able to flee the planet, but Flame was almost killed in the ambush that destroyed the Roshans' starship. The ambush made Flame wonder how the Empire had been able to launch such an attack. Flame began to doubt that Olin was actually loyal to the cause, especially when he was seen leaving Samaria with Darth Vader.

*Flakax*

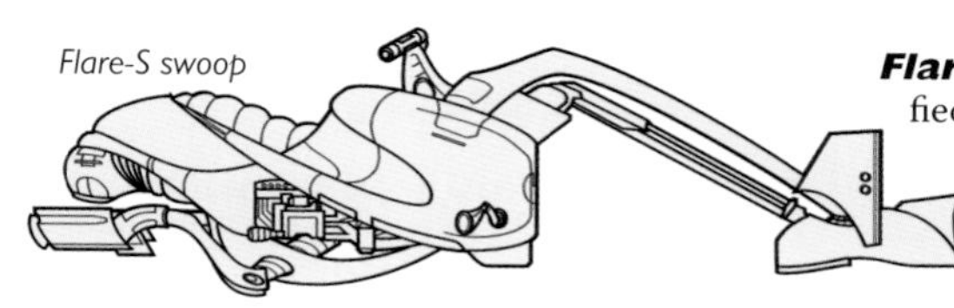
Flare-S swoop

**flame battle droid** A version of the Separatist battle droid that was produced by the Trade Federation during the Clone Wars, and distinguished by the red coloration of its shoulder plating. Flame battle droids wielded flame projectors with large backpack tanks holding the flammable agent.

**flame beetle** Native to Kashyyyk, these unusual insects exhaled fire when attacked. The defense mechanism was well known to Wookiees, but some still stumbled into swarms on occasion and suffered burns. Swarms of flame beetles were generally harmless if encountered away from their hive and unmolested. When they felt threatened, however, or recognized a threat to their hive or offspring, the king beetle could either self-combust or breathe his fire, setting off the entire swarm in a huge conflagration. Usually, flame beetles could be moved out of an area by creating a lot of smoke.

**flame carpet warheads** Chemical weapons, they set aflame huge masses of air across several square kilometers with their thick and adhesive liquid.

**Flame-God** The chief deity of the M'ust species, embodied by flames that filled M'usts' underground lairs. Rebel warrior Cody Sunn-Childe claimed to have reformed after coming in contact with the Flame-God, turning his back on violence to embrace peace.

**flameout** One of the more potent intoxicating beverages served around the galaxy, and a favorite of Han Solo in his early smuggling career. When prepared correctly, the drink had the unique properties of burning the tongue while freezing the throat. The not-so-secret ingredient: spice.

**Flamewind of Oseon** *See* Oseon.

**Flankers** A planet located in a remote part of Fakir sector on the border between the sector and the Colonies region. Its star exploded sometime after the Battle of Yavin, destroying the entire system. The Empire had abandoned its base on Flankers shortly before the star went nova.

**flapdragon** A native of Gamorr, this creature lived in muddy swamps.

***Flare* (1)** A modified Kuat Leisure 121-B pleasure craft, it was used by Aayla Secura and Ylenic It'kla during their mission to Corellia to rescue Ratri Tane shortly after the start of the Clone Wars.

***Flare* (2)** The name of Anniha Nega's modified Z-95 Headhunter.

**Flare-S swoop** A more elegant example of the typically crude swoop design so popular on cutthroat racing circuits, the Flare-S swoop had more in common with speeder bikes than with its overpowered brethren. A single-seater with a curved chassis, the Flare-S swoop could be found on Outer Rim worlds such as Tatooine. Often described as little more than "an engine with a seat," the swoop incorporated a repulsorlift unit, an advanced turbothruster engine, and very little else. Forward control vanes supported a central repulsor pod that helped distribute repulsor energy, giving the pilot a greater degree of control. Despite these features, the Flare-S was still considerably more difficult to operate than a standard speeder bike. Some swoops could attain speeds approaching 600 kilometers per hour, and even reach the upper atmospheres of standard worlds. Swoop racing largely replaced Podracing as the most popular high-speed spectator sport in the galaxy. In the farthest reaches of the Rim, swoop culture led to the growth of terrifying outlaw bands that used their swoops both as symbols and in raids.

**Flarestar** One of the cantinas located on the space station at Yag'Dhul, it was frequented by Rogue Squadron's pilots when they were using the station as their operations base during the Bacta War.

**flarion** A species of bird common on Kashyyyk. They were easily startled, and required quick reflexes on the part of Wookiees hunting them for food.

**flashbang** Simple explosives first used by the clone commandos of the Grand Army of the Republic, flashbangs were little more than bright lights and loud noises meant to startle or stun an opponent into inaction.

**flashburn** A term used by Jedi to describe the way that certain Force-sensitive individuals closed off areas of their minds in reaction to major emotional trauma. Sections of memory seemed to disappear so that the individual couldn't remember details about whatever caused the trauma. Corran Horn, for example, was flashburned when he believed his wife, Mirax, was lost shortly after the death of Emperor Palpatine's clone.

***Flash Fire*** A *Dreadnaught*-class heavy cruiser, it was part of Warlord Zsinj's Third Fleet during the early years of the New Republic. The *Flash Fire* was destroyed at the Battle of Selaggis.

**Flashpoint** An arid, desert planet located in the Outer Rim Territories, it rotated once every standard hour and was constantly bombarded by solar energy and intense radiation since its primary star was very close. Some 4,000 years before the Galactic Civil War, the Old Republic established a research facility on the planet, hoping to learn more about the life and death of stars and other solar phenomena. The facility, Flashpoint Station, was protected by a magnetic shield that repelled the deadly energy from the planet's star.

In the wake of the Great Sith War, the research facility was overrun by Mandalorians, who turned it into a prison where Jedi captives were taken during the Mandalorian Wars.

The Mandalorians modified the research facility under the direction of the biologist Demagol, who hoped to discover what gave Jedi and Sith the ability to use the Force. However, their use of the station was cut short when Rohlan Dyre infiltrated the facility with Zayne Carrick and his companions. They perpetrated an elaborate ruse to free the prisoners, then set off a series of charges that brought the entire facility down on itself.

**Flash speeder** A sleek, lightweight repulsorlift vehicle used by Naboo's volunteer security force for patrolling the tranquil streets of their peaceful cities during the last decades of the Old Republic, it had an open-air canopy that usually seated two soldiers. A blaster cannon was turret-mounted on the Flash speeder's rear spoiler. During the Trade Federation invasion of Naboo, resistance groups organized by Captain Panaka and Queen Amidala employed Flash and Gian speeders to infiltrate the besieged city of Theed. The Flash speeder's twin repulsorlift engines were fine-tuned to allow a pilot maximum control through Theed's narrow streets. The craft—a slightly modified version of a civilian Soro-Suub *Seraph*-class model—normally had a flight ceiling of less than a meter, but could attain a maximum height of 2 meters and speeds of 200 kilometers per hour.

Flash speeder

**flashstick** A small metal baton, it was used by the Drall police as a defensive weapon. At the end of the baton was a crystal, and hidden inside the shaft was a surprisingly strong power source. When the flashstick touched an individual, it triggered the power source to deliver a blinding flash of light augmented by the many facets of the crystal at the end. The burst of light blinded an attacker for several hours.

**Flautis** A greasy-looking Corellian, he was one of the members of the anti-alien Human League who waylaid Han Solo.

**Flax** Located in the Ptera system, it was home to the insectoid Flakax species. Flax was a world of numerous oceans as well as vast deserts cut off from the water by high mountain ranges. The emotionless Flakax lived in underground hives and devoted their lives to the hive's queen. After the planet was taken over by the Empire, the Flakax were put to work mining Flax's underground minerals.

**Flax, Clive** A low-life musician and industrial spy, he was one of the many acquaintances made by Ferus Olin after Olin left the Jedi Order. Flax used his music as cover for his spying, selling his information to the highest bidder. Olin and Flax worked together on several jobs to undermine the efforts of the Empire, and Flax trailed the former Jedi when he was sent to Samaria. In the course of events, he met the woman known as Flame and had a strange and uneasy feeling that he had seen her somewhere before. He started to dig to get more information about her, but found very little.

**Flax'Supt'ai** A female albino Duinuogwuin, she lived on the planet Iego for thousands of years, having settled there during the time of the Cronese Sweeps that presaged the rise of Xim the Despot. She made her home just north of the Boneyard, but few beings ever learned why she chose to remain on the planet.

**flechette canister** A weapon, it held clusters of tiny darts. When the canister was fired from a shoulder-mounted launcher and hit its target, it exploded, releasing a cloud of deadly darts.

**flechette missile** Dart-shaped projectiles about 11 centimeters in length, flechette missiles were made as anti-personnel or armor-piercing anti-vehicle weapons.

**fleek eel** A delicacy from the Hocekureem Sea, these snake-like natives of Falleen were considered a delicacy by chefs galaxywide. They were usually kept alive until the moment they were dipped in boiling pepper, although some preferred to eat them live.

**fleethund** The slang that X-wing pilots used for a decoy maneuver—a dangerous ploy in which one X-wing pilot drew fire to her- or himself and away from the main convoy.

**Fleet of the Glorious Defender Queen** This was one term used to describe the ships of the Hapan Royal Navy.

**Fleet Protection Group** A branch of the naval forces of the Grand Army of the Republic, it was charged with overseeing search-and-rescue operations that resulted from Red Zero missions or space combat at the height of the Clone Wars.

***Fleet Tactics and Combat Methodology*** This Rebel Alliance military guidebook was written by Admiral Ackbar, and was intended for reading by the Alliance's naval officers.

**Flenn, Mich** An aging Corellian smuggler, he retired and bought the Blue Light Tavern on Nar Shaddaa. He was the first person to describe the Jedi Knights to Han Solo.

**Flennic, Moff Kurlen** An Imperial Moff, he controlled Yaga Minor as part of the Imperial Remnant following the peace made with the New Republic. Flennic believed that the Republic should be left on its own when the Yuuzhan Vong invaded the galaxy, despite the prescient warnings of Grand Admiral Gilad Pellaeon. When the Yuuzhan Vong did attack them, the Imperial Remnant was unprepared. Bastion and Muunilinst were destroyed quickly, and Flennic and the Moff Council were forced to flee. When it was believed that Pellaeon had perished at Bastion, Flennic made a short-lived attempt to assume control, but the Grand Admiral was still alive. Both Pellaeon and Jacen Solo began to negotiate with Flennic and the Moffs to convince them that joining the Galactic Alliance was the only way for the Empire to survive the invasion. Even shows of good faith by the Alliance weren't enough, and Flennic tried to assassinate Pellaeon, but failed. Still, Pellaeon decided not to eliminate a good leader, and Flennic finally agreed to accept the Galactic Alliance's offer.

**flensor** Avian scavengers native to Sakiya, they were considered bad-luck omens by the Sakiyans—especially if a flensor was seen flying over one's bonepit.

**Flerp, Zrim** A young student at the Jedi Temple on Coruscant during the last years of the Old Republic.

**flesh camouflage** Developed by Illicit Electronics, this small device allowed users to generate contact lenses and realistic facial masks to hide their true identity, or to assume another's identity. The computer that controlled the system was quite advanced, requiring an experienced programmer. This device could also generate identification cards for a given disguise.

**fleshglue** This adhesive was used to secure small objects to the skin. Used mainly by actors, fleshglue was also adopted by criminals and other beings who wanted to change their appearance. While being hunted by a pair of voxyn aboard the *Nebula Chaser,* Alema and Numa Rar removed the Adegan crystals from their lightsabers and used fleshglue to attach them to their navels to make them look like exotic dancers.

**Flet, Derren** An architect, he was used by Jabba the Hutt to design extensive renovations to Jabba's palace on Tatooine. Flet also provided details for the design of the sail barge *Khetanna.* Jabba later executed Flet because his renovations didn't provide enough dungeon space.

**flewt** A species of large, winged insectoid creatures native to the planet of Naboo.

**flexicris** A material developed near the end of the Old Republic, it was used in lightweight facial shrouds for emergency extravehicular activity, especially twinned with thinskin emergency suits.

**flex-mask** A type of facial covering originally used by actors to alter their appearance, it was adopted by spies to infiltrate locations by appearing to be someone else.

**Fleyars IV** This planet was subjugated by the Empire in a struggle known as the Battle of Fleyars IV.

**Fliggerian firebeast** A creature named for its unusual digestive system, which used a form of combustion to break down its food. The name of the beast was also used as an oath.

**Fligh** An infochant, or information merchant, he worked the halls of the Galactic Senate on Coruscant 12 years before the Battle of Naboo. He mixed with a bad and often deadly crowd, and soon after he stole the datapads of a Senator and a shady transgenic research scientist, Jenna Zan Arbor, he was found apparently murdered. But later Qui-Gon Jinn and Obi-Wan Kenobi discovered that Fligh had faked his own death and fled to Belasco after discovering Arbor's complicity in the bizarre deaths of six "low-lifes." Fligh eventually cleaned up his act . . . for a while. About 18 years later, Obi-Wan encountered Fligh on Euceron, where he was involved in a conspiracy to fix and place illegal bets on the Galactic Games. After helping Obi-Wan, he returned to Coruscant.

**Flim** An accomplished actor and impressionist, he was tapped by Moff Disra to become the surgically aided doppelgänger of the late Grand Admiral Thrawn. When the Caamas incident threatened to tear the New Republic apart, Disra brought Flim out of hiding. Using his acting ability and as much Imperial history as he could memorize, Flim pulled off the role, even managing to fool officers who had served under Thrawn and Republic stalwarts like Lando Calrissian and Han Solo. Flim's act eventually was exposed by Admiral Pellaeon; Disra was revealed as a traitor, and Flim surrendered to Pellaeon.

**flimmel tree** Native to the planet Xagobah, this unusual tree resembled a cross between a mushroom and a spider. In fact, the flimmel was more of a fungus than a tree. Individual specimens were actually part of a much larger colony that shared a common root system, and the entire plant lived to be many millennia old. The flimmel was carnivorous and could open its fleshy trunk into a mouth-like orifice that extended outward to grasp its prey.

**flimsiplast** A writing material, it was formed into thin, plastic-like sheets that could be used for communication. Flimsiplast could be impreg-

Flint

nated with chemicals that kept writing hidden until it came into contact with someone who had a specific chemical makeup. It could also be set to burn up after the message had been activated. However, flimsiplast, usually referred to as flimsi, was used mostly to write notes and letters.

**Flint** A native of Belderone, Flint was the son of a Jedi Knight who had been killed by General Grievous during the Clone Wars. When Luke Skywalker and Leia Organa arrived on the planet to investigate an Imperial laboratory there, Flint and his friend Barney volunteered to help them with their efforts to liberate Belderone and Kulthis. But when Flint was too late to save his mother from an Imperial attack on their village, he cursed the fact that he couldn't use the Force to help her. Darth Vader preyed on Flint's anguish and lured him to join the Empire as a stormtrooper; he later trained Flint to use dark side powers. Flint became known as the Dark Lord of Belderone, and was placed in charge of the invasion force that subjugated Naldar. After Vader's death, Flint went to Vjun to see Bast Castle, encountered the Dark Lady Lumiya, and, after a brief battle, submitted himself as her apprentice. But after intervention from Barney and Skywalker, Flint renounced his allegiance to the Empire, ended the fighting on Naldar, and convinced his homeworld to accept the Firrerreo people—refugees from a world destroyed by the Empire—as neighbors. Years later, Flint's lifeless body was found on Belderone, his hands grasping a lightsaber and a hole burned through his neck. Many believed he had been killed by Lumiya.

**Flip** A young Vorzydiak, he was one of the original members of the Freelies, a group that sabotaged companies in the hope of gaining more free time for workers. He was eager to impress fellow member and friend Grath, whose father was Head of State. A fellow Freelie, Tray, convinced Flip to make the group's actions more violent and destructive, despite Grath's continuing faith in nonviolent protests. Flip altered a plan to bomb Multycorp headquarters in the middle of the night and started setting the explosives to go off in the morning, catching workers as they entered the building. Warned by Grath and Obi-Wan Kenobi, most of the workers escaped, but Flip inadvertently set off the detonators early and died from his injuries. In the aftermath, Grath and his father, Chairman Port, agreed to work toward a peaceful resolution to the Freelies' demands.

**Flirt** A tiny, box-like positronic processor, she was owned by the Wookiee bounty hunter Chenlambec. Flirt, who had a female personality, was programmed to access intelligent computers by tapping in through their power points. She could then open data streams, shut down security, and substitute her owner's commands for those of the computer's operator. Flirt's "seduction" of the computer systems aboard the *Hound's Tooth* played a major role in helping Chenlambec trick and capture Bossk, the Trandoshan bounty hunter. Following that success, Flirt was given the powerful body of an X-10D service droid that previously had been all but brainless.

**Flissar** A no-nonsense Noghri, he served as the caretaker of a warehouse located in New Nystao, on the planet Wayland, in the years following the death of Grand Admiral Thrawn.

**flit** One of several species of reptavian predators that were native to the planet Lok.

**flitnat** A species of tiny, harmless insects. Many subspecies delivered a mildly painful bite, and anyone being caught in a swarm of these insects suffered from continually being bitten. During their invasion of the galaxy, the Yuuzhan Vong modified the basic flitnat to carry a mild disease that caused the victim to experience intense nausea.

**Flitter** The code name for one of the Rebel Alliance's safe worlds, Flitter was located in the Tierfon system. The planet's location was revealed when an Imperial starship captured an Alliance transport on its way to the planet, and the fleet destroyed many of the planet's cities and poisoned much of its ecology, killing 95 percent of the population and leaving the rest to die.

**flitter** A common name for any type of one- or two-person airspeeder.

**Flo** An aging WA-7 service droid, she was a waitress at Dex's Diner on Coruscant in the years leading up to the Clone Wars. Programmed with an efficient, if a bit abrasive, female personality, Flo spent much of her time trying to prove to boss Dexter Jettster that she was a better waitress than Hermione Bagwa.

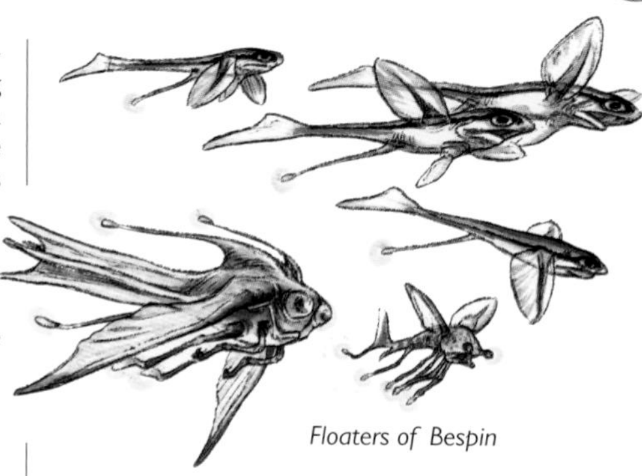

Floaters of Bespin

Flo was separated from Dexter when the chef was forced to join the ranks of the Erased—those who wiped out all records of their existence and went underground after Palpatine made himself Emperor. Flo vowed to help the Erased in any way possible. She found her chance when she discovered two of the Erased, both reporters, in the holding cell of the Senate Rotunda. Posing as a cook droid, Flo helped them escape and asked them to let Dexter know she was okay.

**float chair** Any repulsor-equipped chair, usually used to support a being who has lost the use of one or more legs.

**floater (1)** Any of the various species of creatures that inhabited the upper cloud layers of the planet Yavin. Of the 12 known species of floaters, 2 were predatory and fed on the other 10 species. The species ranged in size from 30 to 1,500 meters in length, and were confined to living in a specific layer of Yavin's atmosphere. If removed from their natural habitat, floaters literally exploded since their bodies were unable to adjust to lower pressures.

**floater (2)** Small winged avians from Bespin, they "swam" in the plankton-rich layer of the Life Zone. They bred almost continuously, and cloud car pilots had to constantly clear their windshields of floater roe that was deposited in the atmosphere.

**floater (3)** *See* landspeeder.

**Floater-935** This Ubrikkian skiff, based on the Desert Sail–20, was basically a stripped-down version designed for high-altitude personal transportation. Measuring 1.75 meters in length, the Floater-935 required a single pilot and could carry up to 10 kilograms of cargo. The Floater-935 could attain speeds near 300 kilometers per hour, and was unarmed in its stock version.

**floating fortress** An Imperial repulsorlift combat vehicle, it was designed to augment ground assault and planetary occupation forces. The Ubrikkian HAVr A9, a

Flo

near-cylindrical floating fortress, was especially suitable for urban terrains. It featured distinctive twin-turret heavy blaster cannons, a well-armored body, and powerful repulsorlift engines. It was equipped with a state-of-the-art surveillance system that could lock on to multiple targets. A fortress had a crew of 4 and could carry up to 10 troopers.

***Floating Home*** Lord Ecclessis Figg's first Bespin gas-mining colony, it continued to grow and expand, and eventually was renamed Cloud City.

**Floating Rock Gardens** A term used to describe certain tunnels and caves on the planet Ryloth, where the winds from the Bright Lands were channeled through fissures and gaps at high speeds. Small chambers housed the so-called gardens, where visitors could place colored stones in the path of the wind. The wind kept the stones aloft, moving them about in ever-changing patterns.

**Flock, the** An all-encompassing term that members of the Nediji species used to describe their society.

**floonorp** An unusual musical instrument, it was popular in the Outer Rim Territories during the final decades of the Old Republic, along with the sobriquet and drixfar. The design of the floonorp was created by musicians who originally used engine parts to form its body and inner workings.

**floozam** A domesticated pet, often led on a leash.

***Floren*** A New Republic warship, it was part of Task Force Gemstone.

**Floria** A bounty hunter along with her brother Dane, they were captured by Obi-Wan Kenobi and Anakin Skywalker on Ragoon-6 five years after the Battle of Naboo. They had been part of a group of bounty hunters hired by Granta Omega to capture the two Jedi and their companion, Wren Honoran. Years later, Floria and Dane were working the Mid and Outer Rim territories as security officers and were hired by Samish Kash to serve as his personal bodyguards during the Clone Wars. During a mission to Null to discuss a treaty with Count Dooku, Kash apparently was assassinated. Floria and Dane were initially accused of the murder, but Kenobi and Skywalker, who were on Null to meet with Lorian Nod, discovered that Floria was in love with Kash; she then admitted that Kash was not really dead.

**Florn** Home of the Lamproids, it was a world of numerous dangers, which possibly meant instant death for anyone without hyperaccelerated nerve implants.

**Floubettean** An intelligent avian species whose members performed a complex mating dance. The dance could also be performed as an artistic expression by other avian species, but it looked revolting when it was performed by humans.

**flow-walking** A method through which Aing-Tii monks communicated with the Force. By touching the flow of the Force, an Aing-Tii monk could figuratively walk along it, thereby reading the intentions of the Force. Truly adept monks could use this technique to time-drift, traveling forward and backward in time along the threads of the Force. There was always a risk of being discovered when flow-walking, and those using the technique tended to leave a "blur" behind, especially if they moved too fast. Flow-walkers needed to stay anchored to their own time or else the current of time could literally sweep them away; events that occurred while flow-walking could cause injury to individuals in their own time.

Jacen Solo learned the technique, and it helped him make some sense of his grandfather Anakin Skywalker's fall to the dark side. Jacen could only flow-walk when in a certain location, and only to another time at the same location. With much practice, he managed to improve his use of the technique, and even taught it to Tahiri Veila. By giving Veila a chance to revisit her final moments with Anakin Solo, Jacen managed to gain her trust as he assumed control of the galaxy.

**FLR series Logger Droid** Developed by the Greel Wood Logging Corporation with the help of Industrial Automaton, this heavy-treaded droid was designed to clear brush and large trees during the harvesting of greel wood. Known as the Lumberdroid, the FLR was a 2-meter-square box that sat atop two wide treads and was equipped with two chain saws and a pair of heavy lifting arms. The FLR was also equipped with sophisticated probability programming that allowed it to accurately determine when and where a tree would fall once it was cut.

**FLTCH R-1** A huge mercenary droid, it was sent by Bron and Ephant Mon to eliminate Jedi Master Ki-Adi-Mundi in the depths of the Outsider Citadels after Cerean elders rejected admission to the Old Republic. Ki-Adi-Mundi was able to defeat FLTCH R-1, and the droid was reprogrammed. It eventually was assigned as Ki-Adi-Mundi's starship pilot while he searched for Ephant Mon near Tatooine.

**Fluffy** The "star" of a tall tale by the Devaronian Vilmarh Grahrk, Fluffy was a stalking onsonker that Grahrk claimed to have used to hunt down Bobo—an alias for Darth Sidious—after he demanded that Bobo turn over the "Secret Treasure of the Jedi" that he had stolen from the Jedi Temple. Grahrk claimed he placed several of Fluffy's seeds inside Bobo's body, then let Fluffy track down her offspring in order to locate Bobo and the artifact. Fluffy was then said to have dined on Bobo.

*Trever Flume*

**Fluggrian** A squat, green-skinned species native to Ploo IV whose members were distinguished by four knobby protuberances that jutted from their foreheads. Fluggrians used the knobs as sensory inputs. They were known for their organized crime rings and were highly suspicious of other beings.

**Flume, Tike** The older brother of Trever Flume, he was among a group of protesters who tried to prevent Imperial forces from taking control of a defense plant on his homeworld of Bellassa. His father showed up to try to bring Tike home, but the plant exploded before they could escape. It was the first true atrocity committed on Bellassa by the Empire, and served to galvanize the public into rebelling.

**Flume, Trever** Just a young man on Bellassa when his parents and brother were killed during the final years of the Old Republic, he quickly got entangled in the heart of the nascent Rebellion against the newly formed Empire. As the New Order was tightening its grip on his homeworld, Trever Flume met Obi-Wan Kenobi and Jedi Order dropout (and soon-to-be double agent) Ferus Olin; he disclosed that he had stolen an old power droid from the company Olin had set up to provide new identities in a type of witness protection program. It seemed to have a bad motivator, when in fact the droid was stuffed with secret codes and data. Flume explained that he sold it to another young man . . . who turned out to be Boba Fett.

When Kenobi and Olin fled Bellassa, Flume stowed away on their starship. The two men split up, and Flume went with Olin on a rescue mission to Ilum. The older man discovered that Flume had a knack with explosives, which helped them on another rescue attempt on Coruscant at the Jedi Temple itself. Olin was captured by the Empire, but Flume and Jedi Fy-Tor-Ana escaped. They weren't in the clear for long, though: They arrived at a secret underground hideout just as it was being attacked. Later, Flume helped in the rescue of a Roshan ambassador, but was nearly killed when the escape vessel was destroyed as it was landing on Rosha.

Flume returned to Bellassa and made connections with an underground resistance group known as the Eleven. He, Olin and his close friend Roan Lands, and Dr. Amie Antin gained access to Imperial Governor Wilhuff Tarkin's personal offices in the city of Ussa, and they gathered a great deal of important information before all except Flume were discovered by Darth Vader. He watched in silent horror as Vader killed Lands and took the doctor and Olin prisoner. Returning to the Eleven, he volunteered for a mission to rescue a Force-sensitive youngster, Lune Oddo Divinian, who had been captured by stormtroopers and sent to the Imperial Naval Academy on Coruscant, where his own father planned to use him in an experiment to train starfighter pilots. Posing as a recruit, Flume made contact with the young man, but was discovered. They were separated, with Flume placed under guard. He was quickly whisked away from the Academy, however, when a lieutenant named Maggis stole a speeder, and they fled to Dexter Jettster's hideout.

Fnnbu

Dex agreed to get Maggis to a safehouse. Flume decided to break into Jenna Zan Arbor's apartment. Ry-Gaul refused to allow him to go alone, but agreed to take Flume along on a mission to rescue Linna Naltree from Arbor. They infiltrated her Coruscant residence and planned to grab Naltree from a turbolift. The rescue attempt nearly was bungled when Flume tripped over Arbor's cape, forcing Ry-Gaul to draw his lightsaber and defend them.

***Flurry*** A Rebel Alliance cruiser-carrier, it was commanded by Captain Tessa Manchisco. The *Flurry* served with distinction in the Virgilian Civil War and was donated to the Rebel Alliance by a sympathetic Virgilian faction that ousted Imperial forces. The *Flurry*, at 350 meters long, could carry nearly 30 fighters and had complete repair and maintenance facilities. Its mission profile was to deliver fighters into combat and then retreat to a safe distance. For its mission to Bakura, the *Flurry* was equipped with a prototype battle analysis computer that received data from every gunship, corvette, and fighter in combat. The *Flurry* was destroyed over Bakura when the Imperial *Carrack*-class cruiser *Dominant* suddenly opened fire. All hands were lost but were posthumously decorated for their heroic sacrifice.

**Fluwhaka** A mist-covered world notable for its rocky spires and crags, it was the site of a base used by winged, humanoid pirates once hunted by Jodo Kast.

**Flyer Through Spikes** This Qom Jha was one of the reinforcements sent by Eater of Fire Creepers, following the death of Builder with Vines, to assist Luke Skywalker and Mara Jade in their assault on the Hand of Thrawn.

**Fly Eye** This was Loronar Corporation's attempt to create a smaller surveillance droid than the Cybot Galactica AC1 "Spy-Eye." A marvel in miniaturization, the Fly Eye was barely 3 centimeters across when its four tiny legs were fully extended. When its legs were retracted, the Fly Eye moved about with the help of a tiny repulsorlift engine, attaining speeds of 10 kilometers an hour. It was equipped with a holographic recording system and a tight-beam transmission antenna, and was used to capture visual evidence from a remote location. Fly Eyes were used by crime lords and jealous lovers, and were the favored tools of many sleazy NewsNet reporters.

**Flying Decks** A nickname given to ancient transport ships used by the Krath to move their shock troops from planet to planet. These T-shaped transports had wings and main engines at the front of the ships.

**flying serpent** A species of beautiful, winged reptiles native to Ophideraan. They had long snake-like bodies covered in mottled green scales and thin yellow wings that ran nearly the length of their bodies. When the mercenary Tyrann discovered the planet, he also discovered that certain ultrasonic tones and pulses could be used to control the flying serpents. Tyrann's forces then used them as mounts.

**Fnessal** This planet was the homeworld of the intelligent Fnessian species. The humanoids were distinguished by two eyestalks that stood up on their heads, the backs of which were covered with thick, fleshy tendrils.

**Fnnbu** A Zexx, he was a confederate of fellow space pirate Finhead Stonebone in the Stenness system some 4,000 years before the Galactic Civil War. When Stonebone's men tried to murder Jedi Master Thon and Nomi Sunrider, Nomi used the Jedi battle meditation technique to force the pirates to turn on one another. Fnnbu was the first to cave beneath Nomi's power, attacking his cohorts with savage fury. In the ensuing chaos, Nomi and Thon slaughtered most of the pirates, including Fnnbu.

**Foahl, Podlong** A Givin, he worked for Chief Purser Waverton aboard the *Aurorient Express*, where he was responsible for loading and unloading the cargo of the wealthiest passengers. But secretly he was part of a pirate gang that planned to steal the ship's most valuable cargo by first replacing one passenger's goods with attack droids. Qui-Gon Jinn and Obi-Wan Kenobi helped foil the plot, while discovering that the chief purser also knew of it.

**Foamwander City** One of the largest floating cities on Mon Calamari, it was a primary center of trade and industry for the Mon Calamari people. Foamwander City appeared to be a massive dome of smooth coral, with a collection of watchtowers and antennas breaking up the otherwise organic appearance. The dome was just the upper portion of the city, however, hiding a series of underwater towers and structures. The subsurface structures provided additional living and working space, as well as ballast and stability to the main dome. During the years following the death of Grand Admiral Thrawn, Foamwander City sustained large amounts of damage when Admiral Daala attacked the planet in an effort to cause hardship for the New Republic. After Daala was driven off, Admiral Ackbar and his former assistant, Terpfen, helped oversee the city's rebuilding.

**Focela, Hyrim** An Arkanian somewhat past his middle years, he was security master of the small starport of Novania, a frigid outpost with about 2,000 inhabitants. Hyrim Focela controlled the flow of information into and out of his small community. His motivations were occasionally unclear, but as a rule he had the best interests of his people at heart.

**focusing chamber** An underground chamber created by ancient Sith Lords, it was a place where the energy of the dark side could be focused and channeled to a specific individual. Any Sith Lord using a focusing chamber had his or her ability to use the dark side substantially increased for a short duration. The effects of the focusing chamber decreased after leaving it, and waned faster over distances.

**Fode and Beed (Fodesinbeed)** A two-headed Troig who served Jabba the Hutt as a Podracing announcer during the last years of the Old Republic. Fode, along with Beed, called the Boonta Eve race that was won by

Fode and Beed

nine-year-old Anakin Skywalker. Fode was distinguished from Beed by his red skin and short horns; he spoke Basic, while Beed used Huttese.

**Fodro** This planet was known as the endpoint of the annual Dahvil–Fodro Hyperspace Promenade.

**Fodurant** A planet that was the site of a New Republic penal colony.

**Foerost** The site of an ancient Old Republic orbital shipyard, the planet was attacked by Aleema Keto and a cluster of Ulic Qel-Droma's Krath starships and some Mandalorian warships during the Great Sith War. Aleema used her dark side illusions to make the enemy fleet appear to be one large, innocent vessel. Qel-Droma stole nearly 300 of the Republic's latest starships to add to his vast galactic armada and took them to Coruscant, where he attempted to eliminate further resistance to Sith domination. Millennia later, the Foerost Shipyards were purchased from the Old Republic by the Techno Union. Several centuries before the Clone Wars, the shipyards served as research-and-development facilities for the Techno Union, and it was here that the Bulwark Mark I was developed and produced. During the Clone Wars, the Old Republic tried to blockade Foerost, but found its siege broken when Dua Ningo and the Bulwark Fleet blasted their way free. With the defeat of the Bulwark Fleet at the Battle of Anaxes, the Republic eventually recaptured Foerost.

***Fogger*** An Imperial Nebulon-B frigate, it was dispatched to the Tungra sector to clean up the Mugaari pirates operating there following the Battle of Hoth. It was also used as the command ship when the Empire fought to recapture the D-34 platform in the Javin sector.

**Fohargh** A Makurth, he was among the many students trained at the Sith Academy on Korriban in the years leading up to the Battle of Ruusan. A contemporary of Darth Bane, Fohargh was challenged by Bane during their early lightsaber training. Rather than use deadly lightsabers, the duel was fought with durasteel training blades covered with poisoned barbs that delivered a numbing sting. Fohargh would have beaten his opponent, but he taunted Bane when he was down. In his rage, Bane drew upon the dark side and crushed Fohargh's windpipe, squeezing until the Makurth finally shuddered and died. It was later revealed that Fohargh had wrapped himself in a Force shield, and that Bane had literally ripped through it to kill him.

**Fohlg** A Quarren, he was one of the caretakers of the Cambrielle Exploration Auditorium on Ralltiir in the years following the Battle of Naboo. Fohlg was also known as the only access point to the auditorium's archives, and he could be bribed to allow a being or two to peruse the museum's galactic database for information on newly discovered star systems. However, he charged a steep price.

**Fokask** This planet was the home of one of Han Solo's old smuggling buddies. He had retired there, but remained in touch. The former smuggler sent Han a copy of *The Fokask Banner,* which contained an uncomplimentary article about Chief of State Leia Organa Solo during the Yevethan Purge.

**Fol, Desric** A scowling, burly man, he was owner and operator of the *Blind Luck* at the height of the Galactic Civil War. Desric Fol was trained as a scout, but he was not a natural leader, and the crew of the *Blind Luck* were often at odds with one another given everyone's inability to perform their duties. For much of his career, Fol operated from a base on Abregado-rae.

**Foless Crossroads** An intersection of hyperspace shipping lanes located near the planet Darepp.

**Followers of Nyax** A band of Corellians who worshipped the ancient ghost known as Lord Nyax at the height of the New Order. They declared that Darth Vader had been possessed by the spirit of Lord Nyax. Although they had no allegiance to the Empire, they venerated Vader as the vessel through which Lord Nyax could exact his revenge against the Jedi.

**Followers of Palawa** A group of hermits highly revered on their homeworld of Bunduki, they were masters of the martial art known as teräs käsi. The Followers of Palawa were considered one of the first groups to actively contemplate the use of the Force. Intense contemplators of existence, they unwittingly mastered the Force trance, the longest lasting an unbelievable 70 years. It wasn't until encountering teräs käsi that these philosopher-hermits mined the Force's deepest channels and were seduced by the dark side.

Fondor

***Folna*** A New Republic picket ship, it accompanied the warship *Vanguard* into system ILC-905 during the Black Fleet Crisis. It was under the command of Colonel Foag, who served under Commodore Brand.

**Folor** The largest moon orbiting the planet Commenor near Corellia, it was a craggy gray satellite and home to a Rebel Alliance starfighter training center. The Folor base, built within a network of underground tunnels, was a former mining complex and probably once a smugglers' hideout. The base was commanded by General Horton Salm, and off-duty pilots relaxed in a makeshift cantina called the DownTime. The Folor gunnery and bombing range, a deep twisting canyon on the moon's surface, was called the pig trough—a nod to an unflattering nickname for the Y-wing starfighters who often trained there. Two and a half years after the Battle of Endor, the newest members of Rogue Squadron were instructed at Folor before flying their first combat missions.

**Fonada** A former Imperial admiral, he established his own small fleet after the Battle of Endor and became one of the first of the renegade warlords.

**Fondine, Slish** An entrepreneur, he created the first of Umgul City's blobstacle courses in a collapsed sinkhole just outside the city in the years following the Battle of Naboo. He also owned a blob stable and regularly raced his blobs. Some seven years after the Battle of Endor, Fondine discovered Lando Calrissian at his stables, shortly after Lando arrived on Umgul to locate Tymmo. Lando discovered that Tymmo was actually Dack, and had been impregnating the blobs with microstimulators to improve their performance in an effort to win enough credits betting on the blob races to escape from Duchess Mistal. When Lando revealed this information to Fondine, Fondine threatened to have Dack executed per Umgullian law. Lando, however, convinced him to return the young man to Mistal's side, where he would be forced to endure her undying affection for the rest of his life.

***Fond Memory*** A *Lambda*-class shuttle, it was operated by Elegos A'Kla during his tenure as a Senator to the New Republic. Elegos used it to travel to Dubrillion with Leia Organa Solo to investigate the status of the Yuuzhan Vong invasion of the galaxy.

**Fondor** An industrial planet in the system of the same name, it was famous for its huge orbital starship-construction facilities. The Empire seized the Fondor yards and completed Darth Vader's Super Star Destroyer *Executor* there immediately following the Battle of Yavin. During construction, Imperial forces erected a military blockade. Several Imperial admirals saw the *Executor* as a blatant bid for power by Vader and tried to sabotage its construction by bringing in a Rebel spy—Luke Skywalker. Vader trapped the traitorous admirals when they met with Skywalker in the vast steam tunnels beneath Fondor's surface, but Luke managed to escape the planet by stowing away on an automated drone barge.

When the Yuuzhan Vong invaded the galaxy, they attacked Fondor and its shipyards with suicide bombing runs. Squadrons of coralskippers flung themselves at the orbital facilities, causing untold damage. Fondor itself was leveled by the Yuuzhan Vong, and the entire system was rendered useless. Nevertheless, the New Republic launched an attack to retake Fondor using the planetary repulsor within Centerpoint Station. While the Yuuzhan Vong forces were eliminated, the blast from Centerpoint also wiped out the friendly Hapan battle fleet. Years later, the Galactic Alliance rebuilt the shipyard. A decade later, Fondor's inhabitants joined the so-called Corellian Confederation, giving control of the shipyards to the Corellian rebels.

The Fondorians had grown frustrated with the Alliance's harsh restrictions on military production at its orbital shipyards. After Jacen Solo's rise to power, he made it a priority to capture the shipyards or destroy them as punishment for the planet's rebellion. He took elements of the Fourth Fleet with him, which were augmented by forces from the Imperial Remnant. In return, the Imperials were promised control of Bilbringi and Borleias, and the chance to capture Fondor for themselves if the Galactic Alliance failed.

But lying in wait were Luke Skywalker and many Jedi Masters, using the Force to cloud the presence of a large Fondorian fleet. When Solo's forces began to move in, the Jedi ended their masking and the Fondorians attacked. In the midst of the fighting, Solo took his ship, the *Anakin Solo,* beyond the main battle lines and started attacking Fondor's cities—something never contemplated in the battle plan he had laid out to Admiral Niathal. Considering Jacen a rogue, Niathal negotiated a cease-fire with the Fondorian government, which agreed to surrender if the *Anakin Solo* ceased its attacks on Fondor's cities.

Solo refused to stand down, and many commanders were unsure what to do. In the end, the Alliance's forces were split. Solo was forced to abandon Fondor to return to Coruscant. Admiral Niathal gathered whatever ships still supported her and left the Galactic Alliance, establishing a government in exile with the assistance of the Fondorian government.

**food-kin** Small, crab-like creatures that scuttled about, never leaving the vicinity of the Priapulin that was going to eat them, they were fairly intelligent and seemed to feel a sense of pride in their fate. Once consumed, the eggs of the food-kin were incubated inside the adult Priapulin, continuing their lines as future partners with the Priapulin.

**Foolookoola** A young Fishface princess, she was the only surviving member of her family; they were staunch loyalists who were murdered by thugs of the Revolutionary Purist Council. Her protector, Naradan D'ulin, arranged to have Princess Foolookoola smuggled off the planet Ootoola by Vilmarh Grahrk, who took her to Dur Sabon.

**foo-twitter** Portable devices that sent out pre-recorded sounds or messages, they were used on Chad III to lure the wystoh away from an area. Callista's family used them to help repair their floating ships, keeping the wystoh away while they swam in the waters.

**For'ali** An elderly Twi'lek, he was a noted expert on tactile communication methods. For'ali's expertise was in nonwritten forms of communication, such as knot tying. Jacen Solo sought his help in deciphering a collection of knotted strands that were discovered on Toryaz Station during the investigation into the death of Siron Tawaler. For'ali was only able to decipher one of the strands, which was a remnant of the Tahu'ip culture.

**For-Atesee (4-8C)** This IG series assassin droid became one of the first Imperial Grand Moffs during the early years of the New Order. For-Atesee often was accompanied by IG-153 and IG-182, two of the IG-100 MagnaGuards that served as part of General Grievous's *Izvoshra* during the Clone Wars.

**Forb, Jonox** A smuggler, he was one of many who discovered that the planet Hoth offered much in the way of remoteness and privacy, despite its obvious environmental problems. During the early years of the New Order, Forb established Snowflake Base on Hoth, citing its proximity to Bespin, the Corellian Trade Spine, and the Hydian Way. His records were discovered in an abandoned wampa lair by General Carlist Rieekan during the Rebel Alliance's occupation of the planet, just prior to the Battle of Hoth.

**forbelean defense** A defensive posture developed by the Chiss for use in hand-to-hand combat. From this position, virtually any form of attack could be deflected.

***Forbidden*** An Imperial *Lambda*-class shuttle captured by the New Republic and used on many missions, it frequently was piloted by Tycho Celchu. Captain Celchu was at the controls when it rescued his fellow Rogue Squadron members Nawara Ven and Ooryl Qrygg during the first battle at Borleias. They were shot out of their X-wings and almost surely would have died in space if not for the proximity of the shuttle. The *Forbidden* also removed prisoners from Kessel, who were then used to undermine the infrastructure on Imperial Center.

**Force, the** Both a natural and a mystical presence, it is an energy field that suffuses and binds the entire galaxy. The Force is generated by all living things, surrounding and penetrating them with its essence. Like most forms of energy, the Force can be manipulated, and it is the knowledge and predisposition to do so that empowers the Jedi Knights—and the dark siders and Sith. For, in simple terms, there are two sides to the Force: The light side bestows great knowledge, peace, and an inner serenity; the dark side is filled with fear, anger, and the vilest aggression. Yet both sides of the Force, the life-affirming and the destructive, are part of the natural order. Through the Force, a Jedi Knight can see far-off places, perform amazing feats, and accomplish what would otherwise be impossible. A Jedi's strength flows from the Force, but a true Jedi uses it for knowledge and defense—never attack. The Force is a powerful ally, however it is used.

*Yoda uses the Force.*

A Dark Jedi gives in to his or her anger. "If you once start down the dark path, forever will it dominate your destiny," Yoda warned Luke Skywalker. Emperor Palpatine, on the other hand, urged Skywalker to continue down the path of blind fury and aggression. "Give in to your anger," he told Luke. "Strike me down with all of your hatred and your journey toward the dark side will be complete."

The ancient Jedi Knights were the first to openly contemplate the Force, although other groups were known to have investigated its existence before the formation of the Jedi Order. By being grounded in pure service to other beings, the Jedi saw the Force as its own end. The Sith were formed from those individuals who wanted to investigate the dark side of the Force, and were exiled for this stance. While acknowledging that they learned of the Force through dark side teachings, the Sith simply saw the singular power of the Force, which to them was a means to an end.

The Jedi Knights discovered that the Force was accessible to all living beings through the presence of midi-chlorians in their cells. The more midi-chlorians inhabiting a being's cells, the more the being was able to connect to the Force. However, a high concentration of midi-chlorians did not guarantee a being control of the Force. Only through intense study and dedicated training could one become proficient in harnessing the power of the Force. The Jedi Council discovered that younger beings had an easier time learning the techniques required to touch and control the Force, since they usually were free from emotional attachments. So the Jedi Order eventually developed a system that actively sought out and identified beings with high midi-chlorian counts at birth or shortly afterward. With, or sometimes without, the permission of the parents, the Jedi took children no more than one year old away for training. Older beings who already had established set patterns in their lives often were unable to complete the necessary training, and were deemed too wasteful of Jedi resources.

The Jedi Knights historically were the most powerful users of the Force, having trained with and learned the three basic techniques: control (the manipulation of one's internal Force strength), sense (detection of the Force in the external world), and alter (manipulation of matter with the Force). These techniques, used alone or in combination, allowed the Jedi to perform many different activities with the Force. The Sith, on the other hand, gained strength from the Force by focusing their emotional energies—especially strong emotions such as anger and hatred—which gave them quick mastery but usually didn't take as much discipline.

The nature of the Force was considered to be a constant, but this belief changed some 200 years before the Battle of Yavin, when Jedi Masters began to find that their connection to the Force had become nebulous or darkened. This change culminated with the ascension of Emperor Palpatine to power, when the Sith were finally able to gain complete control over the galaxy. According to an ancient Jedi prophecy, this was the time when the Chosen One would appear and bring balance back to the Force. It was believed that Anakin Skywalker was the Chosen One, although the direct results of his actions led to the near-total destruction of the Jedi Order and the formation of the Empire. However, his heroic actions during the Battle of Endor led to Palpatine's death, leaving Luke Skywalker as the surviving Master of the Force. Skywalker struggled to understand the Force, and eventually took students to train with him. Although he taught his students of the light and dark sides of the Force, he rarely found the galactic situation as simple to define.

*Force grip*

During the Yuuzhan Vong invasion of the galaxy, some 25 years after the Battle of Endor, the foundations on which the Jedi Knights based their knowledge of the Force were suddenly altered. There were several forms of life—primarily the ysalamiri of Myrkr—that could push back against the Force, although these creatures were assumed to live within the Force in some fashion. The Yuuzhan Vong, however, appeared as a void in the Force, neither projecting nor absorbing or repelling it. Many of the new Jedi Knights struggled with the concept of a species that seemed to lack any contact with the Force, since it was believed that the Force was contained within all forms of life, even if it was in trace amounts.

Jacen Solo was one of the first Jedi to discover that the Force acted in many ways, without a true light or dark side, and that there were ways in which it could be attuned to at least recognize the alien invaders. The former Jedi Master Vergere was instrumental in guiding Jacen to this realization, having spent more than 30 years in the presence of the Yuuzhan Vong. After the surrender of the Yuuzhan Vong at Coruscant some five years after their invasion began, Jedi Master Skywalker contemplated this new understanding of the Force. It was not a simple delineation between light and dark, but a more profound definition of the ways in which good and evil fought for control of an individual. Ultimately, he chose not to return the Jedi to their roles as an unbiased police force serving only the light side.

Luke reasoned that the Jedi Knights of the Old Republic were once a meditative Order that was drawn deeper and deeper into the machinations of the Republic when its Chancellors called for their help in mediating disputes. As this escalated into the battle legions of the Clone Wars, the Jedi became less interested in the nature of the Force and more interested in separating good and evil into light and dark halves of the Force. The Jedi of the Old Republic, according to Skywalker, lost sight of the fact that the Force moved *through* individuals, not *from* them. His new Jedi Order was predicated on the belief that the Force would provide its own guidance to each individual, who was bound to act in the best interests of the Force.

Ideas about the Force changed more a decade later, when Lumiya reappeared in the galaxy and began training Jacen Solo as a new Sith Lord. Her power was rooted in the dark side despite her many cybernetic prostheses. She explained to Jacen that she, like his grandfather, did not lose her connection to the Force because of injury. Perception was as much a component as the midi-chlorians were, and any beings who believed that they could be powerful could be trained to be so. Lumiya explained that Jacen was the culmination of a long search by Vergere, a search that included Lumiya herself, to find an individual who was mentally and physically strong enough to become the true embodiment of the dark side of the Force.

**Force barrier** The ability of a Force-sensitive individual to create a nearly impenetrable wall of Force energy to protect them from Force attacks. Originally developed and practiced by Umbaran Shadow Assassins, a Force barrier wasn't perfect; the combined efforts of several powerful Force users eventually could break through.

**Force call** A technique used by Luke Skywalker and the new Order of Jedi Knights that allowed a powerful Jedi to call out to other Jedi across a great distance. Depending on the strength and skill of the Jedi, the Force call could be made between star systems or—in the case of Master Skywalker's call during the crisis with the Colony—to all Jedi in the galaxy. It took a great deal of mental and physical effort to make such a call.

**Force camouflage** A term used by Jacen Solo and other Jedi Knights of the Galactic Alliance era, it described the ability of Force-users to hide themselves from other Force-sensitive beings. Those few Jedi or Sith who could perform Force camouflage seemed to blend into the universe while maintaining their own individuality and remaining fully aware and functional.

**Force chain** The ancient Jedi discovered that some of their number possessed the ability to forge a powerful mental link to one or more other Jedi. The exact mechanism was unknown, and many Jedi considered it to be the will of the Force whenever a Force chain was created. While connected, the strengths of individual Jedi could be used by the others, allowing them to work together against a common enemy. The chain also could be used to augment strength and maintain health. However, if a Jedi in the chain was injured, all members in the link felt the pain—and it was believed they could all die if one linked member died. A similar ability, known as a Force-meld, was developed during the Yuuzhan Vong invasion of the galaxy.

**Force detector** A long-rumored device said to have been perfected by Emperor Palpatine, the Force detector used two unique sheet-crystal paddles and a control pack to determine whether or not a person was Force-sensitive.

**Force grip** Sometimes called a Force choke, this technique was used by Dark Jedi and the Sith. By using certain control and alter skills, a Dark Jedi could take hold of an individual's body structures and crush them. This technique also could be used to place other individuals in a Force-assisted grip, which could push or pull them into a dangerous position.

**Force harvester** Originally created by Exar Kun during the time of the Great Sith War, it was the power source for a weapon known as the Dark Reaper. The harvester was designed to drain the energy of the Force from any living beings, regardless of whether they were Force-sensitive or not. The harvester was believed to have been lost on Raxus Prime and buried under endless mounds of trash. Around the time of the Battle of Geonosis, Count Dooku began a massive excavation effort to locate the harvester, but a task force of Jedi Knights and the Army of the Republic bombarded the location before it could be recovered.

Force lightning

**Force lightning** A Force ability, such as that used by Emperor Palpatine against Jedi Masters Mace Windu, Yoda, and later Luke Skywalker, it consisted of blue bolts of pure energy that flew from the user's fingertips toward a target. Force lightning, usually a corruption of the Force by those who followed the dark side, flowed into a target and caused great pain as it siphoned off the living energy and eventually killed its victim.

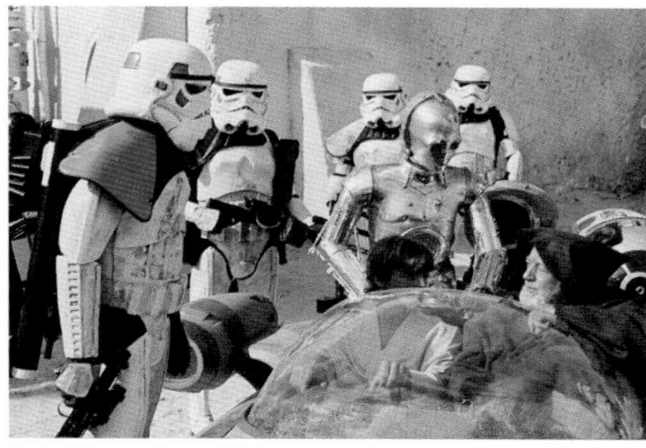
*Force mind trick:* These aren't the droids you're looking for.

**Force meld** The uniting of several Jedi Knights through the Force, a technique developed by the Jedi during the Yuuzhan Vong War to draw strength from one another and act as a single, powerful entity. The technique originally was attempted by a strike team sent to Myrkr to destroy the voxyn queen and further refined by Saba Sebatyne. When used to coordinate an army's actions during battle, this technique was known as the battle-meld. Unlike traditional battle meditation, which saw a single Jedi influencing armies and soldiers, the battle-meld used the combined powers of several Jedi Knights.

**Force mind trick** A technique used by advanced Jedi Knights, it allowed them to influence the thinking of other individuals by planting suggestions in their minds. The Force mind trick worked particularly well on weak-minded individuals, but there were some species such as Hutts and Toydarians that were immune to its effects.

**force multiple orbit** Known as the Atom, this starfighter formation was developed by the Imperial Navy to intercept a vessel that couldn't produce the appropriate identification codes. Imperial fighters were launched to intercept the target ship, then assumed crisscrossing orbits at staggered distances, covering the target ship with swift-moving fighters. This formation, when performed correctly, made the target ship look like the nucleus of an atom, with the fighters whirling around like electrons. It prevented the target ship from getting an accurate targeting lock on the fighters, which in turn allowed the main Imperial ship to ready weapons and tractor beams for boarding.

**Force net** An unusual technique used by dark siders, it was a golden apparition of energy that could be directed at an object or another being. When trapped behind the Force net, a living captive was unable to move; any contact with the energy of the net was similar to that of a lightsaber. A captive could literally be cut apart with the net's energy. Lomi Plo used this technique to destroy a Yuuzhan Vong warrior just before the crash of the *Tachyon Flier.*

**force pike** A meter-long polearm equipped with a lethal vibrating blade and a staggering shock generator. At their mildest settings, force pikes emitted powerful stun charges capable of knocking a full-grown Wookiee unconscious. When adjusted for maximum damage, their vibrating power tips could rip through steel bulkheads and easily dismember most organic beings. Because the weapon weighed less than 7 kilograms, anyone with the proper training could wield it with incredible speed and agility. A power cell in the pike's hilt fueled an ultrasonic vibration generator. The vibrations were carried to the weapon's tip by conductive circuits lining the pole's interior. The power tip could emit thousands of microscopic vibrations per second, and this rapid motion allowed the pike to slice through stone and metal. In combat, even a grazing attack could seriously wound or dismember an opponent. For less brutal confrontations, force pikes could be set to release a stun charge whenever the tip came within 4 centimeters of a target.

Force pikes were used heavily by military forces, including the Imperial Royal Guard and stormtroopers, but they were also favored by vicious thugs, such as Jabba the Hutt's skiff guards.

*Force pike in the hands of an Imperial Guard*

**Force rage** One of the more powerful techniques taught to the Dark Jedi and Sith, it was similar in some respects to a stimulating drug or a Wookiee battle cry in that it allowed an individual to unleash primal energies. When coupled with a link to the dark side of the Force, however, these energies manifested themselves as Force rage, giving the Dark Jedi or Sith increased power for a short period of time. This alter skill was also one of the most demanding of the dark arts, as it drained huge amounts of energy from the individual using it. The individual then had to recuperate for an extended period of time before being able to call upon the dark side again.

**force sabacc** A form of the electronic card game, the randomness of play was provided by the other players rather than a randomizer device. In force sabacc, after drawing the first card for a hand, each player had to call out whether the hand was light or dark. The player who played the strongest light or dark hand won, but only if the combined strength of his or her chosen side also won.

Force spirits

**Force sensitivity** A term used by Jedi Knights to indicate the ability of some individuals to be more attuned to the Force than others, actually tapping into its power. This differed from Force potential, which was basically the life-energy of the midi-chlorians contained within every living being.

**Force spirit** A disembodied manifestation of a once living, Force-sensitive individual. Strong Force-users discovered that they could exist in spirit form after their physical bodies were gone. Rather than simply becoming part of the Force, they denied the will of the Force in order to retain their individuality, at least for a limited time. Qui-Gon learned the technique from studying the Whills, and was able to teach Yoda and Obi-Wan the skill. Anakin Skywalker learned it through his teachings with Palpatine and through knowledge passed on by the spirits of Obi-Wan and Yoda.

Because the Sith and other Dark Jedi used the Force for their own ends, they often bypassed this limitation to remain spirits indefinitely. In general, a Force spirit couldn't be "killed" by normal means, but eventually just ceased to exist. Other spirits could be destroyed with sufficient dark side energy, making the elimination of a malevolent spirit dangerous for most Jedi.

**Force storm** A tornado of energy created by great disturbances in the Force. Dark Side Adepts demonstrated limited control over the creation of these storms. Emperor Palpatine claimed the ability to create and control Force storms at will. Light-side practitioners could also band together and create powerful Force storms.

**Force vision** A prescient vision an individual received from the Force itself. These powerful dream-like occurrences often came unbidden, simply flooding an individual's mind with images.

**Force Wars** Believed to have been the first conflicts between the followers of the light and dark sides of the Force, the Force Wars had their roots on the planet Tython, where those beings who were sensitive to the Ashla energy field opposed the use of this power for personal gain. The followers of the Ashla were eventually victorious, although the conflict exhausted the planet's population and resources. In the wake of the Force Wars, the Ashla adherents were believed to have established the first incarnation of the Jedi Order. They laid down the groundwork for the Jedi Code, establishing the Order as a monastic society of warriors who contemplated the use of the Ashla in the discovery of knowledge, harmony, and peace.

**For'deschel, Devan** The mistress of lightsabers at the Almas Academy during the Clone Wars, she originally trained under Mace Windu. Devan For'deschel was the first Jedi from outside the Cularin system to return to Almas after the disappearance of Cularin and its sudden reappearance. As the Clone Wars began to spread across the galaxy, she was one of the few Jedi to remain on Almas to continue training the students. She also spent much of her free time investigating the disappearance of Cularin and the many aspects of the Sith artifact known as the Darkstaff. During the early stages of the Clone Wars, she was attacked by a Separatist Jedi Killer, and suffered massive injuries to her arm before defeating it. The arm had to be replaced with a cybernetic prosthesis. When the call finally came for the Almas Academy to supply Jedi Knights and Masters to the troops of the Grand Army of the Republic, Master For'deschel was among the more vocal opponents.

**Fordo** An ARC trooper designated ARC-77, Captain Fordo led the group known as the Muunilinst 10 into battle under Jedi General Obi-Wan Kenobi. As task force commander, Fordo had a primary mission of capturing San Hill. He later proved that sheer firepower was often better than planning when he was deployed to Hypori to rescue Jedi Knights who had been stranded there by General Grievous. Captain Fordo was awarded the Chancellor's Service Medal for his actions on Hypori, but he refused to accept it for himself, instead transferring it to CT-43/002, who had died a hero on Muunilinst.

**Fordox, Com** A distinguished Corellian Senator in the years leading up to the Battle of Naboo.

**Fordwyn** Supposedly an Imperial Navy captain commanding the *Victory*-class Star Destroyer *Valiant* near Togoria during the height of the Galactic Civil War, he was really a Rebel Alliance officer. In his disguise, Captain Fordwyn was able to trick three bounty hunters out of their prize catch: Han Solo.

**Foreign Intruder Defense Organism (FIDO)** A semi-organic defensive droid system, it helped protect Anakin Solo from a kidnapping attempt on Anoth. FIDO was suggested by Admiral Ackbar and modeled on the krakana, a dreaded sea monster from Mon Calamari. FIDO's tentacles were threaded with durasteel cables and its pincers plated with razor-edged alloys. It destroyed half of the assault force sent by Caridan Ambassador Furgan to snatch young Anakin before being overwhelmed, and stalled the rest of the attackers long enough for reinforcements to arrive.

**forensics droid** Specially built droids used by law enforcement to investigate crime scenes and gather physical evidence. The droids helped ensure the veracity and viability of evidence that was collected. All material was processed within the droid's sealed shell, and results could be displayed remotely.

***Foresight*** A New Republic surveyor ship, it was destroyed when it tried to recover parts from an abandoned Imperial cruiser. The cruiser's automatic firing sensors were still active, despite the damage it had taken, and it fired on the *Foresight,* causing it to explode.

**Forge, Inyri** The youngest member of the Forge family and sister of Rogue Squadron member Lujayne Forge, she was the lover and glitterstim "cutter" of smuggler and Black Sun terrorist Zekka Thyne. When he was sprung from the Kessel penal colony to be used in the Alliance's operation to regain Coruscant, Inyri Forge accompanied him, mostly as a way of rebelling against her parents' wishes. She was with Thyne when he attempted to kill Rogue pilot Corran Horn—whom he blamed for his imprisonment—at the headquarters in Invisec. Horn escaped and later rescued Forge twice during two separate engagements with Imperial forces. Inyri finally realized that Thyne was just using her to get close to Horn, and when her lover attempted to kill Horn again, she killed Thyne instead. She joined one of Rogue Squadron's teams just in time to help bring down Coruscant's shields, and soon thereafter became a member of the squadron and later one of its leaders. Upon assuming command of the squadron, Gavin Darklighter named Inyri Forge his second in command, and she took up the position of Rogue Five.

**Forge, Kassar** The father of Inyri and Lujayne Forge, he came to Kessel before the Clone Wars as a teacher for the prison population. There he met his future wife, Myda. They fell in love and had a family, and he decided to stay to continue his teaching, hoping to rehabilitate some of the hardened criminals there. When Rogue Squadron needed him to facilitate the release of political prisoners from administrator Moruth Doole's grasp, he helped identify the convicts and offered other advice.

**Forge, Lujayne** A member of Rogue Squadron from Kessel, she was one of the first pilots to pull Corran Horn out of his self-imposed shell. She was killed in her sleep by Imperial stormtroopers as they raided the base at Talasea in the middle of the night. She had been the heart of the squadron and had helped keep it together. Because of those efforts, her death was even more painful to Horn than to other squadron members.

**Forge, Myda** Sent to Kessel as a prisoner, she met and fell in love with Kassar Forge, one of the instructors sent to rehabilitate the inmates. When her sentence was up, she decided to stay on Kessel with her husband and their two daughters.

***Forger*** An *Imperial*-class Star Destroyer under the command of Davith Sconn, it suppressed a rebellion on Gra Ploven during Emperor Palpatine's reign by creating steam clouds that boiled alive 200,000 Ploven in three coastal cities.

**forging** A process by which the seeds of the boras trees on Zonama Sekot were split open by lightning and charged with energy. From this point, the seeds were annealed into new boras trees. The development of Sekotan starships mimicked this process, as seed-partners were allowed to grow before they were filled with energy and transformed into seed-disks.

**Forgofshar desert** A desert on the Imperial military training planet of Carida, it was used for survival training.

**Fori, Vett** A short, tough-looking woman, she served as chief supervisor of mining operations on Oseon 2795 when Lando Calrissian stopped there during the early years of the New Order. Her disarming smile often caught men off guard, as did her propensity to smoke a cigar.

## Lightsaber Combat Forms

Form I
Form II
Form III
Form IV
Form V
Form VI
Form VII

**Form I** Known as *Shii-Cho,* this was the simplest form of lightsaber combat technique studied by the Jedi Knights of the Old Republic, and was generally considered the first form used by the original creators of lightsabers. Sometimes called the ideal form, Form I used horizontal side swipes and parries made with the blade of the lightsaber held upright to push the point of an enemy's blade away during a side-to-side attack. If the attack was a downward slash aimed at the head, Form I simply reversed the motion, with a horizontally held lightsaber being moved up and down to deflect a blow. All the basic ideals of attack, parry, target zones, and practice drills were created with the Form I style.

**Form II** Known as *Makashi,* this ancient Jedi Knight lightsaber combat technique was developed when pikes and staves were more common in the galaxy. Form II emphasized fluid motion and anticipation of a weapon being swung at its target, allowing the Jedi to attack and defend with minimal effort. Although many Jedi historians considered Form II to be the ultimate refinement in lightsaber-to-lightsaber combat, it was dropped in favor of Form III combat when blaster weapons became prevalent in the galaxy.

**Form III** Known as *Soresu,* this was a lightsaber dueling technique developed by the Jedi Knights after blaster weapons became the normal weapon of choice among criminals and underworld beings. Unlike Form II combat, which was developed to work against another lightsaber, Form III was most effective in anticipating and deflecting blasterfire. It stressed quick reflexes and fast positional transition as ways to overcome the rapidity with which a blaster could be fired. It was essentially a defensive technique, emphasizing the nonaggressive philosophy of the Jedi while reducing the exposed areas of their bodies. Because of these attributes, many Jedi—especially those who practiced Form III—considered it the form that required the deepest connection to the Force. In the wake of the death of Qui-Gon Jinn at the hands of Darth Maul, many Jedi turned away from the Form IV style of open, acrobatic fighting and took up Form III to minimize the risk of injury or death at the hands of an opportunistic opponent.

**Form IV** Known as *Ataru,* this was developed by the Jedi Knights during the last decades of the Old Republic. It emphasized acrobatic strength and power in wielding the blade—attributes that were frowned upon by many traditional Jedi Knights and Masters. It found a niche among the eager Padawan learners of the time, who believed that the Jedi needed to become more involved in rooting out and eradicating crime and evil. This form was practiced by Qui-Gon Jinn, although his death at the hands of Darth Maul exposed the weakness of Form IV in defending a Jedi's body. Yoda, however, practiced Form IV with such speed that, when coupled with his small size, it left no undefended parts of his body for an enemy to exploit.

**Form V** Known as *Shien* or *Djem So,* this was one of the seven primary forms of lightsaber combat created by the Jedi Knights of the Old Republic. Form V was developed by a group of Jedi Masters who felt that Form III was too passive, while Form IV was not powerful enough. It addressed both forms' shortcomings: Even a Jedi Master who proved undefeatable might not be able to overcome the enemy. However, many Jedi felt that Form V lacked any sort of mobility, and forced Jedi to defend themselves without shifting positions. Among the many unique aspects of Form V was the development of techniques in which the lightsaber was used to deflect a blaster bolt directly back at the firer, deliberately to cause harm to the opponent. Many Jedi Masters debated the philosophy of Form V, claiming that it placed inappropriate focus on hurting another being. Others claimed that Form V was simply a way to "achieve peace through superior firepower."

**Form VI** Known as *Niman,* this was one of the most advanced of the seven primary forms of lightsaber combat developed by the Jedi Knights of the Old Republic. At the time of the Battle of Geonosis, Form VI was the standard in Jedi fighting, emphasizing the use of techniques from Forms I, III, IV, and V in overall moderation. Many Jedi Masters considered it the Diplomat's Form, since the Jedi used their knowledge of political strategy and negotiation—along with their own perceptions—to reach a peaceful decision with minimal bloodshed. Many Jedi skilled in Form VI techniques had already spent at least 10 years studying the other four forms—a time commitment that many Masters felt excessive given its limited benefits on the battlefield.

**Form VII** Known as *Juyo* or *Vaapad,* this lightsaber combat technique was one of the most demanding of all the forms developed by the Jedi Knights. Only through the learning of several other forms could a Jedi begin to understand Form VII, which involved so much physical combat ability that its training brought a Jedi very close to the dark side of the Force. Jedi Master Mace Windu studied the Form VII technique. To master it, a Jedi had to employ bold movements and be more kinetic than in any other form. Form VII employed the use of overwhelming power directed through unconnected, staccato movements that kept an opponent continually off guard.

**Forma** A tall, bald, dark-skinned man, he was a captain with the Mining Guild, which rose to power in the wake of the deaths of Grand Admiral Thrawn's and Emperor Palpatine's clones. Forma commanded the mining ship *Draisini,* and was dispatched to negotiate a deal between the guild and representatives of the Empire and the New Republic, but it was one-sided as he refused to accept any compromises. Leaving for home, Forma picked up a secret cargo along with a usual load of ore, and the ship was attacked by pirates for Grappa the Hutt. Forma was tortured, drained of information, and then turned over to the Zanibar for a ceremony that ended in his death.

**Formayj** An ancient smuggler and information broker of the Yao species, he provided Chewbacca and his companions with key maps and information that allowed them to successfully rescue Han Solo during the Yevethan crisis.

**Formbi, Aristocra** A Chiss male whose full name was Chaf'orm'bintrano, he served as the Aristocra of the Chaf family for more than 40 years during both the Yuuzhan Vong invasion of the galaxy and the Chiss society's struggle against the Colony. Formbi also served as an officer of the Empire of the Hand, although he was often at odds with then Force Commander Thrawn.

Decades later, Formbi was commander of the Chiss exploration force that discovered the remains of the Outbound Flight Project in the Redoubt. He seemed to want to help the Jedi and New Republic, but he was playing all sides against the other for his own advantage. He was near-mortally wounded by a Vagaari pirate wolvkil, but healed by Mara Jade Skywalker. After the Vagaari Wars and the struggle against the Yuuzhan Vong, Formbi was one of the many Chiss who watched the expansion of the Colony with trepidation. He was placed in charge of a Chiss Intelligence team that later met with Luke Skywalker to share information. Luke came to understand that, whatever his motivation, Formbi was correct that Raynar Thul needed to be eliminated to quash the Colony threat.

But Formbi was outraged that Skywalker only captured and imprisoned Thul instead of killing him.

***Formidable* (1)** A *Victory*-class Star Destroyer, it was part of the Imperial Navy at the height of the Galactic Civil War.

***Formidable* (2)** A *Strike*-class cruiser, it was on the front lines of the Imperial naval fleet.

**Formos** A planet in the Outer Rim Territories near Kessel and the Maw, it was a typical backworld—although its proximity to Kessel made it a haven for spice smugglers. At the height of the Clone Wars, Formos was overtaken by Separatist forces when they deployed Scorpenek annihilator droids against the meager forces of the Grand Army of the Republic.

**Form Zero** Originally defined by Jedi Master Yoda to describe the lightsaber technique of Felanil Baaks, Form Zero became the basis for the instruction of lightsaber combat. In its simplest form, Form Zero was the art of wielding a lightsaber that had not been ignited. While it seemed silly to many Padawan learners, the underlying message could not be ignored: If Jedi were to protect and serve the galaxy, they must know when to ignite their lightsaber for combat, and when to leave the weapon at their side. The understanding of another being's situation was key to the knowledge of right and wrong, and any student who could understand the necessity of Form Zero and use it to mediate a solution without resorting to violence was truly gifted with the Force.

**Forn, Zelka** A doctor who researched the cause of the rakghoul infection during the era of the Jedi Civil War, he operated a medical facility in the Upper City of Taris. Zelka Forn was aided by a group of Jedi Knights from the *Endar Spire* who supplied a Sith-created serum that counteracted the virus.

**Forno, Jace** A female Corellian gun for hire, she worked for a time as a pilot for smuggling kingpin Olag Greck. She later hired R2-D2 and C-3PO as guides on the planet Indobok to help her make off with precious B'rknaa crystals—which were actually baby B'rknaa—but she was thwarted. Forno reappeared on Nar Shaddaa as head of security for criminal mastermind Movo Brattakin, whom she ended up blasting after a bizarre adventure involving the droids.

**For'o** A Bothan admiral, he served in the naval forces that defended his homeworld of Bothawui during the years following the Swarm War. Admiral For'o was dispatched as part of the Bothan war fleet to Kashyyyk during the Battle of Kuat to apprehend Jacen Solo and the Galactic Alliance's Fifth Fleet. The Confederation's forces also included ships from Corellia, Commenor, and Hutt space, and they found themselves fighting alongside Wookiees and Jedi Knights who were defending Kashyyyk.

**Forridel** Appointed provisional governor of Corulag near the end of the Yuuzhan Vong invasion of the galaxy, he found himself wishing for the New Republic to take an interest in recapturing the planet. Forridel's wish came true five years into the invasion, after the sudden reappearance of the sentient planet Zonama Sekot near Coruscant forced the aliens to recall all their war fleets. The puppet governor was caught and hanged, and Forridel was installed. He provided General Wedge Antilles with information on the ground situation, as well as data on Peace Brigade members fleeing Corulag.

**Forrth, Newar** A Twi'lek Jedi, he was one of many heroes who hailed from the planet Ryloth. A member of the Nercathi clan, Newar Forrth led the Third Legion of Light to a victory during the Battle of Ruusan. However, during the battle, Forrth was killed. His remains were cremated and the ashes were formed into three crystalline idols in his likeness, which were returned to Ryloth after the war.

**Forry** A nickname used by CT-44/444, an ARC trooper, who, at the height of the Clone Wars, was assigned to a small group dispatched to Ord Cestus. Forry was the only trooper who had any knowledge of the planet, and like other ARC troopers, he held a measure of disdain for Jedi Knights. Forry helped Kit Fisto train the commandos of the Desert Wind terrorist group, and was among the survivors who managed to escape their lair when Asajj Ventress sent a group of infiltration droids to destroy them all.

**Forsberg, Midnite** A smuggler noted for his Omicron Hunter-21X starship, he made regular runs through Isryn's Veil near Dantooine during the Galactic Civil War. His presence became a concern for the Imperial forces on Dantooine, who made a special effort to capture him.

**Forscan VI** A planet on the edge of the Cron Drift, it was one of many worlds that struggled to remain neutral during the Clone Wars. But an elite group of Separatist agents established a training facility on Forscan IV, which was exposed when the planet's settlers complained to the Galactic Senate. Two years after the Battle of Geonosis, Obi-Wan Kenobi and Anakin Skywalker were dispatched to Forscan VI to eliminate the facility and restore order. Before they could complete the mission, however, they were called back to Coruscant for an emergency.

**Forswoth, Melanda** An up-and-coming journalist on the planet Cularin during the years following the Battle of Naboo. Forswoth, a former meteorologist on an obscure HoloNet newsfeed, got her chance to make a name for herself when Yara Grugara left *Eye on Cularin.* Melanda was allowed to take her place, and began a series of specials on the Caarite and their homeworld of Caarimon. After several abortive interviews, she encountered the humanoid known as Falsswon. He took exception to her superficial questions and pulled a blaster out of his clothing. He shot the camera that had been recording the interview, and Forswoth disappeared. The Cularin Central Broadcasting Corporation later recovered the camera and its recordings, and aired them in an effort to help locate Falsswon. Just over a year later, Ryk Osentay was allowed to travel to Tolea Biqua to do a short piece on Riboga the Hutt, and his camerabeing was knocked over by a dazed-looking woman. Although Ryk was unaware of the incident, the camerabeing recognized the woman as Melanda. The camerabeing's quick actions allowed Melanda to be transported to a hospital for medical treatment.

**Fort Cravus** This immense citadel located in the tropical city of Nurrale, on Esseles, was the base of operations for Lord Cravus during the earliest days of that planet's civilization. As Cravus's empire eventually died out, the fort remained standing, aging very little over time. Fort Cravus was later renovated and turned into a museum, displaying artifacts and information from Lord Cravus's reign. Unknown to the new owners, however, was the fact that several of Lord Cravus's ancient battle droids were stored beneath the surface in a sealed vault, waiting to be reactivated.

**Forte, Siadem** A Jedi Knight, he and his Padawan Deran Nalual were injured in a firefight with the clone troopers who had been ordered to execute Order 66. They fled to Dellalt, where they issued a 913 code transmission to any Jedi in the area. Their call was answered by several other survivors, and together they left aboard a stolen SX troop transport, pursued by a squad of clone troopers, who were driven off by a team of Jedi fugitives led by Roan Shryne. Eventually, Siadem Forte and Olee Starstone set off for Kashyyyk, hoping to learn more about the fates of Yoda, Quinlan Vos, and Luminara Unduli. Instead they were confronted by Darth Vader, and after a fight Forte was decapitated.

**Fort Nowhere** A well-fortified outpost on the planet Ruusan, it was used by Captain Jerg and his fellow merchants as a base of operations. It was also the place where Jerg agreed to accept refugees from the moon Sulon after the Empire took control of the Sullust system.

**Fortress Baarlos** This huge citadel was located on the remote world of Pochi. It was believed to have been over 10,000 years old, but had withstood the effects of time and environment. The original builders were unknown, though the citadel was later modified for use by Faarl the Conqueror as his base of operations. He employed Tulvaree guardians to protect the fortress, but was unprepared for an assault by Boba Fett.

**Fortress Kh'aris** An underground citadel established by Kh'aris Fenn during his exile from Ryloth, the fortress was established on Kintan, where he gained the confidences of the Morgukai warriors. It was at this fortress that Kh'aris held Jedi Master Tholme and Nat Secura captive during his attempt to take control of Ryloth.

**Fortress of Axion** This immense stronghold on the planet Axion was controlled by Colicoid scientists during the months following the Battle of Geonosis. The Grand Army of the Republic tried to secure the fortress shortly after the Battle of Muunilinst, but the forces working to reach it were decimated by the armies of the Confederacy of Independent Systems, which surrounded it. All but Commander Brolis were shot and killed, and Brolis was left to call for reinforcements while holed up inside. The only being sent to extract him was Jedi Master Yoda, who defeated a particularly cunning hailfire droid in order to protect their escape.

**Fortress of Tawntoom** A city built into the interior walls of a volcanic crater, it was in the Tawntoom colony of Roon. The city was powered by the boiling lava pit far below and served as a base of operations for Governor Koong.

**Fort Tusken** The second settlement founded on Tatooine in the modern era, it was located on the northern edge of the Jundland Wastes, northwest of Mos Eisley. Fort Tusken survived until a group of Sand People attacked it some 95 years before the Battle of Yavin. It was abandoned afterward, and the Sand People were given the nickname of Tusken Raiders because of the attack. At the height of the Galactic Civil War, a group of moisture farmers and mercenaries briefly retook Fort Tusken, but word of the fighting reached other clans, and the Sand People recaptured the fort in a bloody battle.

**Fortuna, Bib** Best known as Jabba the Hutt's chief lieutenant and majordomo, this Twi'lek was also a smuggler and slaver of his own planet's people. Fortuna hailed from Ryloth. Like all Twi'leks, Fortuna had twin appendages, or lekku, coming from the back of his pointed head. Such "head-tails" or "worms," as they were called by others, were used for thinking and communication as well as sensual pleasure. Fortuna was sentenced to death on his planet for helping to start the export of the addictive drug ryll. The ryll trade had led to smuggling, slavery, and a planetwide breakdown of order. Fortuna escaped and soon found himself working on Tatooine, in charge of Jabba's glitterstim-smuggling operations.

Through successively more prominent positions, Fortuna—who knew how to be obsequious to the Hutt when he had to be—finally became Jabba's chief aide. He used that position to plot against his boss; like others in the palace, he planned to kill the Hutt and take over his business. That plan was put on hold when Rebel Alliance leaders came to rescue their friend Han Solo from Jabba's clutches. Instead, all the Rebels were captured and ordered to be killed by being dropped into the maw of the Sarlacc at the Great Pit of Carkoon. When the Rebels turned the tables, Fortuna fled in his private skiff just before Jabba's sail barge was blown to smithereens.

Back at the palace, a confident Fortuna was met by the B'omarr monks who lived in the catacombs below. Some lived as humans, others as detached brains residing eternally in jars of nutrient. The monks decided that the nutrient jar was the best fate for Fortuna—or, rather, for his brain. Fortuna eventually figured out a way to reinstall his consciousness into another Twi'lek crook, Firth Olan, to continue his criminal activities.

**Fortuna, Komad** An ancient Twi'lek who lived on Tatooine thousands of years before the Galactic Civil War, he and his partner made a living as big-game hunters until his partner panicked and was killed in a krayt dragon cave. A group of Jedi Knights, searching for clues as to the whereabouts of the Star Forge and Darth Malak, helped Komad Fortuna defeat a Krayt dragon that had been causing damage to his homestead. Within the dragon's lair, the Jedi were able to recover a piece of the Star Map.

***Fortune Seeker*** A starship owned by the Ryn at the height of the Yuuzhan Vong invasion of the galaxy. They used it to move from system to system, gathering information and leaving before they wore out their welcome.

***Fortune's Favor*** This *Wayfarer*-class transport was part of a pool of vessels owned by the crime lord Nirama during the final years of the Old Republic.

Bib Fortuna

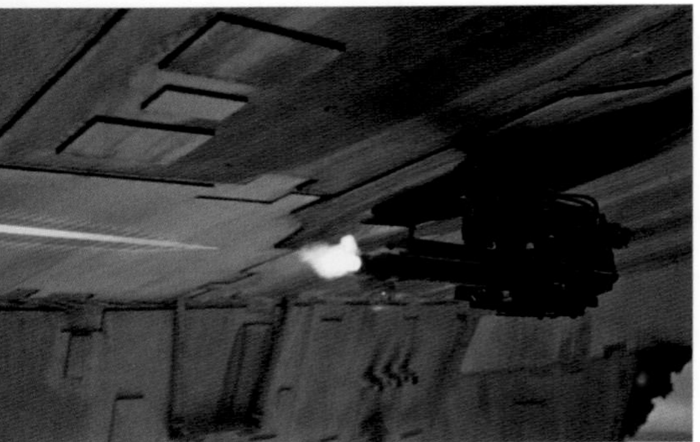

Forward gun pod

**Forvish ale** An interstellar brew, this strong ale was easily distinguished by its distinct odor.

**forward gun pod** A concealed blaster emplacement located in the front section of some starfighters and transports. The forward gun pod on the *Millennium Falcon,* for example, extended from a hidden compartment in the ship's lower hull. Covering plates slid open and shut on command, or automatically when the ship's anti-intruder system was triggered.

**forward tech station** A secondary command-and-control station aboard some vessels, it featured consoles that monitored all ship systems. A ship's flight path could be monitored from the forward tech station while it was in automatic-pilot mode, and in emergencies, the vessel itself could be controlled from this station.

**forward visual triangulation site** Any of several large viewports on Chiss warships where Chiss warriors were placed during a battle to track enemy vessels and coordinate the firing of line-of-sight weaponry. Their efforts augmented the ship's sensor systems and sometimes provided a more reliable description of a battle.

**Fosh** Members of this avian biped species were distinguished by their reverse-jointed legs and piebald coloration. Many xenobiologists believed that the Fosh homeworld was located in the Corporate Sector of the galaxy and that the species was near extinct. The few recorded encounters with Fosh in the galaxy at large indicated that they loved political intrigue and believed themselves to be superior to other species.

**Foss** Once a key member of the royal family's staff on the planet Naldar at the height of the New Order, he was injured and left for dead when Imperial forces subjugated the planet. When Princess Vila, disguised as Prince Denin, returned to Naldar, Foss explained that the assault came just after Vila had left to locate Endor . . . and then he died in the arms of the princess.

Foss died in the hands of Princess Vila.

**Fossyr, Irin** One of General Airen Cracken's Alliance Intelligence agents. Iella Wessiri used this name when she worked on Coruscant and assisted Rogue Squadron during its undercover mission there.

**Foth, Dondo** A native of New Agamar, he was captain of the Republic ship *Mandian* during the Clone Wars. During the Republic's attempt to liberate the Intergalactic Communications Center from the Separatists, it was Foth's crew that detected the incoming Separatist reinforcements from Sluis Van.

***Founder*** One of three *Acclamator*-class troopships that were dispatched by the Old Republic to help defend the planet Duro during the Clone Wars. The ship and its companions were all destroyed in battle, as General Grievous showed that he was a master tactician.

**Foundry** A mineral-rich planet, it was the site of a Baktoid Armor Workshop manufacturing facility that was shut down shortly before the onset of the Clone Wars due to increasing tariffs imposed on the Trade Federation for their battle droids. Years later, the Empire took control of Foundry and rebuilt it to serve as a starship-construction facility.

**Fountain Palace** Located on the planet Hapes, this magnificent building was the seat of the government of the Hapes Consortium. It was also the official residence of the Hapan royal family.

**Four-Den, Halka** A member of the Old Republic's research section. Her first command assignment was leading an expedition to Dagobah. She took copious notes and images in her logs, but her entire team was wiped out. Her valuable logs were rediscovered years later.

Milo Fourstar

**Four Pillars** The Korunnai culture was based on a simple premise, which they called the Four Pillars: Honor, Duty, Family, and Herd. The First Pillar: Honor, your obligation to yourself. Act with integrity. Speak the truth. Fight without fear. Love without reservation. Greater than this was the Second Pillar: Duty, your obligation to others. Do your job. Work hard. Obey the elders. Stand by your tribe. Greater still was the Third Pillar: Family. Care for your parents. Love your spouse. Teach your children. Defend your blood. Greatest of all was the Fourth Pillar: Herd, for it was on the grasser herds that the life of the ghôsh (tribe) depended. Your family was more important than your duty; your duty outweighed your honor. But nothing was more important than your herd. If the well-being of the herd required the sacrifice of your honor, you did it. If it required that you shirk your duty, you did it.

**Four Sages of Dwartii** This group of four philosophers and lawmakers was active during the earliest days of the Old Republic. Their views and decrees were often controversial, especially to species new to the Republic. Supreme Chancellor Palpatine had large bronzium statues of the Four Sages in his office.

**Four See Seers of the Cyclops** According to Skakoan legend, the Four See Seers of the Cyclops served the Lord Being of the Swirblies, and existed within the Threshold of the Hidden Realms to judge whether an individual was worthy of approaching the Albino Cyclops. The roughly humanoid See Seers were said to be able to look within an individual's heart and discern his or her true intentions. They passed judgment on any Skakoan who passed through the Gates of Grontessiant. Those individuals who were deemed worthy were often forced to undergo further tests before they were allowed to see the Eye of the Albino Cyclops.

**Fourstar, Milo** A soldier with the Rebel Alliance on Arbra after the Battle of Hoth, he accused Luke Skywalker of purposely killing Shira Brie because Shira didn't return his romantic feelings. Milo Fourstar tried to throw a punch at Luke, but Skywalker dodged the blow and landed his own, knocking Milo to the

Fosh

ground. An Alliance tribunal found Skywalker innocent of the charges against him.

**Fourth Attack Squadron** A group of Imperial *Victory*-class Star Destroyers, it was destroyed by Alliance starfighters at the Battle of Denab.

**Fourth Fleet** A secondary naval fleet of the Galactic Alliance active in the final stages of the Yuuzhan Vong War, it was made up of the surviving ships of the New Republic's Fourth Battle Group and warships from the Imperial Remnant commanded by Grand Admiral Gilad Pellaeon from his flagship, the *Right to Rule*. Later, during the war against the Confederation, the Fourth Fleet under the command of Admiral Ratobo was dispatched to defend Balmorra, but met stern opposition from a massive Hutt fleet. Although the pilots and crew of the Fourth Fleet lived up to their reputation as the Fearless Fourth, they were eventually defeated, and Balmorra fell to the Confederation.

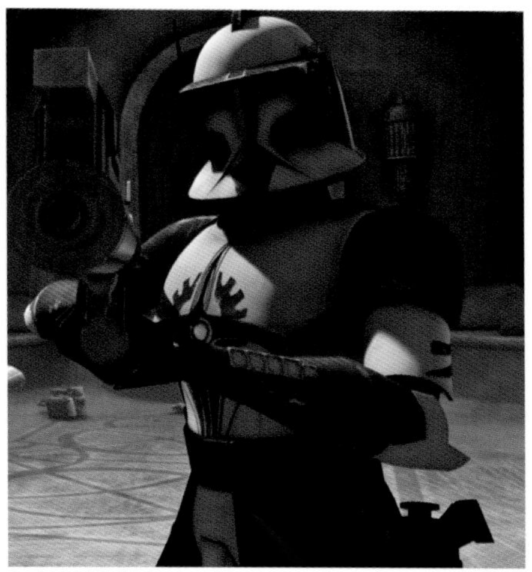
Commander Fox

**Fox, Clone Commander** A clone commander with the call sign CC-1010, he was among the many troops assigned to protect the planet Coruscant at the height of the Clone Wars. Fox had spent his entire career on either Coruscant or Centax 1, serving in the 501st Legion. He was fascinated by the Journeyman Protectors of Concord Dawn, and planned to retire there when the Clone Wars were over. When Darth Vader was dispatched to eliminate any Jedi at the Temple on Coruscant, Commander Fox was part of the clone team that supported him. He was in command of the small detail that prevented Senator Bail Organa from entering the Temple, and would have used his weapons on him if other clone troopers hadn't killed Zett Jukassa. With the death of the young Padawan, Fox decided that there had been enough killing, and he simply chased Organa away from the Temple.

**Fox, Trooper** A clone trooper stationed on Coruscant who led the raid on Ziro the Hutt's nightclub in order to save Padmé Amidala during the Clone Wars. He later served as part of the diplomatic escort group, accompanying Yoda to the neutral moon of Rugosa.

***Foxcatch*** A starship, it was owned by bounty hunter Jodo Kast.

**Foxtrain, Amaiza** A onetime dancer during the New Order, she became head of the Black Hole Gang on Delphon. An Imperial raid scattered the gang, and Amaiza ended up on Aduba-3 without a credit to her name, so she teamed up with Jaxxon to do some smuggling. Just after the Battle of Yavin, she joined her old friend Han Solo to liberate a village on Aduba-3 from the clutches of Serji-X Arrogantus and his Cloud Riders.

**Fozec** A large, dark-skinned human who worked for the Imperial Security Bureau, he kept tabs on Jabba the Hutt's operations after being hired by the Hutt as a guard. He actually wanted to leave Imperial service and join a criminal group himself.

**Fraal** A half-human, half-canine creature that was part of Nevo's gang, he had a sensitive nose that could track the least amount of scent. Fraal detected Boba Fett on Star Station 12, but not before the bounty hunter escaped. Nevo ordered Fraal to follow, and once they reached Maryx Minor, Fraal picked up Fett's scent again. Nevo and his gang were killed when they tried to apprehend the bounty hunter; Fraal tried to run, but Fett used a heat-seeking missile to destroy him.

**Fraan, Tal** An ambitious young military proctor on Yevethan strongman Nil Spaar's staff, he was in charge of the Yevethan attack at Preza. Based on his success, Spaar promoted Tal Fraan to be his personal adviser and assistant. Fraan suggested that Spaar show hostages to Chief of State Leia Organa Solo and then kill one, forcing her to give in. But the killing only made the New Republic leader more determined. Because of his poor advice and the subsequent destruction of the Yevethan shipyard at ILC-905, Spaar killed him.

Amaiza Foxtrain

Fozec

**Frac, Rolai** A scholarship student at the Leadership School on Andara in the years following the Battle of Naboo, this Bothan lad was ostracized by wealthier students. But as Anakin Skywalker discovered, Rolai Frac got mixed up in a galactic intrigue in which the head of his small band of mercenaries planned to kill Anakin and damage his body badly enough that it could pass for that of the gang leader, whose death would be blamed on his father. Anakin and his Master, Obi-Wan Kenobi, were able to thwart the plans, and the entire gang was expelled from the Leadership School and taken to Coruscant for questioning.

**fractal-pattern armor** Developed by the Chiss following the Yuuzhan Vong invasion, this armor used a specialized coating to create ever-changing patterns and colorations on the surface, making it almost invisible to the naked eye.

**Fraig, L.** A native of Kuat, he took over Cherit's criminal operations after Cherit was killed by the Mandalorian known as Jaing Skirata. L. Fraig maintained an air of legitimacy by conducting much of his business from the Tekshar Falls Casino, but despite his boyish good looks, associates knew that Fraig would have sold his mother to the Hutts if he could have made a profit. Boba Fett and Mirta Gev confronted Fraig at the casino during their search for Skirata. When Fraig refused to give up any information, Fett snared him with fibercord and dangled him over the edge of a balcony. It was then that Fraig revealed that the Himar clan of Twi'leks had put out the contract on Cherit. Fett dragged Fraig back to the balcony, later explaining to Gev that he simply wanted his fibercord back.

**Frak** A private in Freedom's Sons and Daughters—Zozridor Slayke's group of insurgent patriots, active during the Clone Wars—Frak rescued Republic pilot Erk H'Arman after he had been shot down by Separatists over the planet Praesitlyn.

**Francis, Dania** An unusual, sea-horse-like Iskalonian, she served as Mone's chief adviser during the years following the Battle of Endor. In addition to her unusual physique, Dania Francis was distinguished by her pale purple scales. It was Francis who discovered that Kiro had returned to Iskalon, despite all information pointing to his death on Kinooine.

**Frane** The king of the planet Rutan, he was both short-tempered and overly sensitive. When his firstborn son, Leed, refused to return to Rutan on his sixteenth birthday, Frane accused the Senali government of holding the boy against his will. The Jedi Knights were asked to mediate the dispute in an effort to avoid another civil war. The Jedi discovered that Leed wanted to remain on Senali and had offered his brother Taroon the chance to rule in his place. In the end Taroon proved himself worthy of Frane's embrace; Leed was allowed to remain on Senali as the first ambassador for both worlds.

**Frayne** A middle-aged woman who served the Old Republic military as a weapons researcher and scientist during the years leading up to the Clone Wars, she was dispatched to Geonosis with Jedi Knight Jyl Somtay on a mission to locate and contain any weapons technology that might remain on the planet. The goal was to ensure that such technology was never put to use against the Republic. However, Dr. Frayne had her own agenda, since she was actually a freelance operative looking to steal technology for herself. She rendered Somtay unconscious with a simple ruse, then captured the clone troopers who had accompanied them. She set out to escape, but was unprepared for the many traps laid by the Geonosians. Somtay and Naj Pandoor found Frayne—or at least her severed head—in a hidden passageway beneath the surface of the planet. They later discovered that a captive female nexu had killed her.

***Frazier*** A Rebel Alliance corvette, it was scheduled to deliver war matériel to Sidral II.

**Fredja** An Imperial stormtrooper captain who served at the Maw Installation, he was continually caught between the commanding officer, Admiral Daala, and Tol Sivron, director of the installation. He disliked Sivron, and was forced to put him in his place several times. Fredja was killed in the destruction of the Maw by Imperial and New Republic forces.

***Freebird*** A gypsy freighter owned by Captain Stanz during the New Republic.

***Freebooter*-class transport** One of the most ungainly transport vessels produced in the period following the Yuuzhan Vong War. When viewed from above, the transport looked like a deep crescent into which a long knife blade had been stabbed. Several reports compared the aft configuration to the fat posterior of a bantha, but it provided the *Freebooter*-class transport with a lot of cargo space. Most were produced for the Galactic Alliance military.

Freedon Nadd Uprising

**Freeda** An Imperial admiral based on the planet Ord Grovner, he ordered a strike against the Khuiumin Pirates, sending the *Crusader* and the *Bombard* to wipe them out.

**Freedom** A small rebellious group on the planet Bakura, it found its voice during the Yuuzhan Vong War. Members of the Freedom group wanted Bakura to stand independent from the New Republic and the rest of the galaxy, having suffered for years under Imperial control and the alleged neglect of the New Republic. The group was secretly funded by Deputy Prime Minister Blaine Harris, who could not officially bring about Bakura's independence without serious political repercussions. Freedom chose peaceful methods of protest, but its efforts were derailed sometime after the Battle of Ebaq when Prime Minister Molierre Cundertol launched his own secret plans to turn Bakura over to the Ssi-ruuvi Imperium. He arranged to have himself kidnapped so that he could be brought to Lwhekk and enteched in the body of a human replica droid. The kidnappers, who were told to claim they were members of Freedom, were murdered. But Cundertol's plans were thwarted by Han Solo and his wife, Leia Organa Solo. Both Harris and Cundertol were killed, and Freedom reconciled itself to the need to join the Republic against the Yuuzhan Vong.

***Freedom*** This was the name given to the *Imperial II*–class Star Destroyer *Avarice* after it was surrendered by its captain, Sair Yonka, during the Bacta War. Yonka then led the ship into war during the Battle of Thyferra. The *Freedom* unleashed a hellish nova flare of proton torpedoes on the *Lusankya,* striking the first blow of the battle and severely damaging the larger ship.

**Freedom Convoy** A group of freedom fighters that rose to prominence during the last decades of the Old Republic when it launched a campaign to free female Twi'leks from enslavement by the Hutts.

***Freedom's Messenger*** A CR90 corvette that was purchased by the government of Chandrila some 60 years before the Battle of Endor, it was outfitted to perform a variety of missions, and was best known for its participation in the Vaykaaris uprising. Also, the treaty that brought the Marzoon Confederacy into the Old Republic was signed aboard the ship. After a long life, *Freedom's Messenger* was finally defeated in battle at the Battle of Ord Torrenze, where it plowed through the enemy blockade with all guns firing. *Freedom's Messenger* took heavy amounts of fire, but managed to forge an escape route for the civilian ships stranded on Ord Torrenze. In the battle, however, the ship suffered massive damage to its power core, and the crew were fatally poisoned with radiation. *Freedom's Messenger* was left for scrap in orbit about Ord Torrenze's sun until it was recovered by the Empire and refitted as the *Renegade.*

**Freedom's Sons and Daughters** A group of insurgent patriots active during the Clone Wars, it was led by Zozridor Slayke, and its original members came from the crew of the *Scarlet Thranta,* an Old Republic starship that Slayke had once commanded. Even though not officially aligned with the Old Republic, the members of Freedom's Sons and Daughters fought for what the Republic represented. They took their battles to Separatist forces in remote locations near the Sluis sector, often driving off forces that might have destroyed Republic installations. For their work, they were branded pirates and traitors by the Galactic Senate. However, many recognized that they were doing the Republic's dirty work. Although much of their history was lost in the tumult surrounding the end of the Clone Wars, the group was recognized for helping the Jedi Knights try to reestablish order in the Old Republic.

**Freedon Nadd Uprising** A conflict on Onderon some 4,000 years before the Galactic Civil War, it was started by the Naddists, a dissident group that followed the spirit of Dark Jedi Freedon Nadd. The Naddists initially succeeded in capturing the Royal Palace in Iziz. They were aided by the mystical resurgence of dark side power throughout Onderon. The uprising came to an end with the death of King Ommin.

***Freefall*-class bomber** Measuring 30 meters in length, the *Freefall*-class bomber

was named for the fact that it was designed to simply drop unguided bombs on a target. The craft's central fuselage could accommodate up to 20 metric tons of cargo, and was attached to two huge, wing-mounted sublight engines. A pair of cockpit-mounted laser cannons provided defensive armament, in addition to its bomb chute.

**Free Flight Dance Dome** A first-class nightclub on the planet Etti IV, it was known for its variable-gravity dance floor, which attracted both fun seekers and those who needed gravity akin to that on their home planet. It was here that Han Solo paid off his debt to Ploovo Two-for-One with a Corporate Sector Authority Cash Voucher that was attached to a de-venomed dinko.

**Freeholders** A name used by the mercenaries and pirates of the planet Aquaris when they joined the Alliance to Restore the Republic following the Battle of Yavin.

***Freejack*** A modified IPV-1 system patrol craft, it was captured from an Old Republic planetary defense network by Frei Aycen around the time of the Clone Wars. She refitted the ship to have additional cargo space and removed several shield generators to free up room and power for a hyperdrive. The *Freejack* had space for 400 metric tons of cargo, and was armed with four light turbolasers and a tractor beam projector.

**Freelan, Borrath** Known to fellow spacers as Big Haul, this man was one of many independent starship owners whose businesses were impacted by the withdrawal of the Cularin system from the rest of the galaxy shortly after the end of the Clone Wars. Shipyard records were lost, allowing several of his former employees to claim that the ships they were flying were their own, and Freelan found himself chasing them down to recover his property. Freelan also resented the fact that Cularin chose to secede from the rest of the galactic community when the New Order was established by Emperor Palpatine. In order to maintain its isolation, Cularin's military stepped up its patrols and forced independent spacers to endure lengthy and rigorous security checks before landing.

***Free Lance*** A Nebulon-B frigate that was turned into a pirate ship by Urias Xhaxin during the last years of the New Order, the ship was known for the blazing-claw insignia it wore on its forward section. The *Free Lance* was armed with 10 turbolaser batteries, a pair of ion cannons, 12 laser cannons, and two tractor beam projectors. Xhaxin and the *Free Lance* were employed by the Rebel Alliance under Ral'Rai Muvunc's plan to use pirates and privateers to harass Imperial convoys and obtain much-needed supplies. After the Battle of Endor, Xhaxin and the *Free Lance* continued to work for the New Republic, picking off Imperial convoys. However, he found that his targets grew sparser as the Empire dwindled into the Imperial Remnant. The vessel was severely damaged when it encountered a Yuuzhan Vong warship while making a run near Bastion, but Xhaxin's crew were able to make a blind jump into hyperspace and escape.

**Freelies** A group of Vorzydiak youths on Vorzyd 4 who sabotaged manufacturing and production facilities to gain their people more free time. Freelies believed that the adults were too strict in their adherence to traditional work policies, and wanted to effect social changes that would reduce the number of days and hours a Vorzydiak had to work. With the assistance of Obi-Wan Kenobi and Qui-Gon Jinn, the Freelies were able to gain an audience with the leadership of the planet, and the two groups agreed to work together for change. During the early years of the New Order, a splinter group of Freelies decided that they needed more diversions and traveled to the neighboring world of Vorzyd 5, where they began working in the underground to coerce and steal from gamblers there. They captured C-3PO when Luke Skywalker and Leia Organa tried to disrupt the flow of Imperial cash and later got involved with Imperial troops trying to capture Luke and Leia. Many of them were wounded in an Imperial ambush.

**Freely, Keets** A journalist, he was one of the few reporters who openly questioned Chancellor Palpatine's continually increasing power over the Republic. When the Clone Wars ended and Palpatine named himself Emperor, Keets Freely found himself a target of the Enemy Eradication Order; instead he joined the Erased, wiping out all record of his existence and going underground. He was seriously wounded in an Imperial attack on an underground refuge for the Erased. Later, he and fellow reporter Curran Caladian broke into Senator Sano Sauro's office and found a wealth of incriminating datafiles, but they were caught, arrested, and would have been executed if it hadn't been for the help they received from aging waitress droid WA-7, also known as Flo.

***Free Mandalore*** Fenn Shysa's modified transport ship, it was a *Kubrai*-class transport used during the early years of the New Republic. The ship was armed with a pair of blaster cannons and proton torpedo launchers.

**freerunner** An armored repulsorlift speeder, or combat assault vehicle, built by Kelliak Arms and Armor Company, it was used mainly by the Rebel Alliance and mercenaries. Freerunners took their name from freely rotating gun platforms mounted on top. With two anti-vehicle laser cannons and two anti-infantry blaster batteries, the speeders packed an offensive punch.

**Free Spacers Guild** An association of independent starship owners, it was formed in the wake of the Galactic Civil War. The Free Spacers Guild allowed the concerns of the independent spacer to be voiced with more political clout than ever before.

**freeze-floating control** A computer-augmented system aboard air- and spacecraft, it helped counteract the effects of turbulence in order to create a smoother flight.

**Frego** A planet run by the Cobral criminal family during the decades leading up to the Battle of Naboo. The former government had imposed steep taxes and provided little in the way of public services. The Cobrals changed much of that, even though their own credits were made from selling drugs and weapons on the black market.

**freight droid** Specialists in retrieving and loading cargo, these droids were typically more than 2.5 meters tall. Freight droids were equipped with four extendable arms, crawler treads for travel, small lifting claws, and a gravity-shifting frame for unbalanced loads.

**FreiTek Incorporated** The manufacturer of the New Republic's E-wing fighter, this company was formed by engineers from Incom who defected to the Alliance during the Galactic Civil War. They wanted to show their loyalty to the New Republic, and the E-wing was their first design. Its success allowed them to continue to create new designs as well as branch out into the production of starship reactor cores and droid interface modules.

**Freliq** This planet was the home of the lepusa.

**Fremond III** This planet was a hotbed of Rebel activity during the Galactic Civil War.

**Fremp, Anky** A near-human denizen of the streets of the spaceport moon of Nar Shaddaa, he was a Sionian Skup biomorph. He worked with criminal gangs and taught newcomers such as a young Greedo how to become street-wise crooks.

**Frenzied River Clan** A clan of the Witches of Dathomir, they were adherents of the light side.

**'fresher** A common word for "refresher," or restroom, throughout the galaxy.

**Fresia** A planet in the Core Worlds, it was best known as the original headquarters of Incom Industries. Much of the planet's landmass was in the form of archipelagos and large islands. The planet was subjugated by the Empire when Incom was nationalized.

**Frewwil** This inhospitable planet was originally scouted by Barosa Warren for the Old Republic. It was controlled by the Empire during the Galactic Civil War.

**Frex, Saidle** A mercenary, he tried to smuggle veermoks off of the planet Naboo despite the environmental restrictions placed on them. He was captured by members of the Naboo Underground and arrested for his actions shortly before the Battle of Naboo. The captors had been operating under the authority of Jedi Master Ali-Vor, who was leading the investigation into the illegal export of veermoks.

**Frexton** Chief scientist at the Corulag Academy's Science Services center, he was there when Yoda and Mace Windu tried to enroll Teela Panjarra as a Jedi trainee. Frexton refused to release the child, hoping to use her as a subject to help determine what makes a being Force-sensitive. Master Yoda feared Frexton would perform any number of unusually cruel experiments on the girl and rushed to Corulag to rescue her. When the Academy was attacked by Bartokk assassins working for Groodo the Hutt, Frexton tried to flee with the young girl, but was cornered by Yoda. The two fought through the attackers and X10-D droids, but Yoda safely escaped with Teela.

Grizz Frix

**Freyborn** An Imperial Moff who served on the Moff Council at the height of the Yuuzhan Vong War, he was one of a handful of officials who refused to acknowledge that the Galactic Alliance was better able to handle the defense of the galaxy—even after the Battle of Borosk proved that the Alliance had better intelligence and tactics. To Moff Freyborn these were the same "Rebel scum" that had destroyed the Empire.

**Freyrr** A Wookiee and second cousin of Chewbacca, she was probably the best stalker and tracker in the family. It was Freyrr who sought out Chewbacca during Lumpawarrump's Test of Ascension, delivering the news that Han Solo had been captured by the Yevetha.

**Freyyr** This elderly Wookiee and once mighty warrior was the father of Chuundar and Zaalbar, and lived on Kashyyyk some 4,000 years before the Battle of Yavin. Freyyr tried to instill traditional Wookiee values in his sons, but Chuundar turned his back. In fact, Chuundar sold other Wookiees into slavery to Czerka Corporation, and then turned the populace against his father, calling him a doddering old fool. Freyyr was driven out of Rwookrrorro, and Zaalbar was exiled from Kashyyyk. However, with the help of some Jedi Knights who were on Kashyyyk to locate the Star Map, Zaalbar was able to bring back Freyyr, who then ousted Chuundar and returned to lead the Wookiees against their oppressors.

**Frickett** An Imperial officer who believed himself far superior to his troops, he was stationed on Maridun during the months following the Battle of Yavin. He scoffed at Lieutenant Janek Sunber's laboring with his troops. When a patrol discovered a huge Amanin army just outside the Imperial compound, Frickett's mind seemed to snap; he ordered his troops to open fire, despite the obvious fact that the Amanin could simply retreat into the jungle and regroup. The Amanin swiftly outflanked Frickett's forces and cut them down, killing the officer in the attack.

**Frid** This subspecies of Iskalonian was native to the planet Mackar. The people were distinguished by their fish-like shape, green scales, bulbous eyes, and long, scaly tails. The Frid communicated via a form of telepathy. As a society, the Frid were pacifists, and would not fight even if attacked.

**Friijillis** This planet was located in Dail sector.

**Fringe, the** A term often used to describe the outermost reaches of "civilized" space, it was where law and order began to break down and planets had to eke out an existence since they were too far beyond the notice of the Galactic Core.

**frinka** The venom of this creature was often used by assassins and bounty hunters. It caused paralysis within minutes unless an antidote was administered. Jodo Kast used it to capture the pirate Nosstrick.

**Frisal** This planet was maintained as a preserve for wealthy Imperial families. It was also a breeding ground for loirbniggs.

**Frissk** A Trandoshan criminal, he was part of a large smuggling operation the Hutts had established inside the walls of the Oovo IV prison facility, where Frissk was an inmate in the years leading up to the Battle of Naboo. Known to his fellow inmates as a double-crossing weakling, it was Frissk who agreed to help the Helmet Squad skim profits from the smuggling operation, thereby removing credits from the Hutts' coffers. When word of Frissk's duplicity reached the Hutts, a bounty was offered for his capture and return to Nal Hutta, despite the fact that he was in prison at the time. Jango Fett eventually claimed this bounty, during his attempt to "rescue" Bendix Fust from Oovo IV.

**Frithia** This was one of the many worlds that were colonized by the Zabrak. It was notable for the krage, a gigantic herd animal that was later domesticated.

**Frix, Grizz** Like Luke Skywalker and Keyan Farlander, he was one of the many young pilots swept up by the passionate idealism that motivated people to join the nascent Rebellion. Grizz Frix was born on Devaron at the fringes of a poor town. Looked down upon by both locals (for being human) and outlanders (for living among aliens), he wished for a more tolerant and inclusive society—something unthinkable under Imperial rule.

Inspired by bootleg copies of Mon Mothma's *A Call to Reason* and the Declaration of Rebellion, Frix joined the Alliance as a pilot, impressing a Sullustan recruiter who had eyed his natural piloting abilities. Frix excelled at training aboard the Mon Calamari star cruiser *Independence*. So prodigious was his talent, he was considered a shoe-in for a position in Rogue Squadron if his skills continued to grow. Unfortunately, Frix's career spiraled downward following a terrible collision involving another starfighter during a training mission over Gerrard V.

As the Rebellion's fight came to a crescendo at Endor, the Alliance was desperate for pilots. Still able to draw on the raw piloting ability that got him off Devaron, Frix joined the Rebels behind the stick of an X-wing. During the brush-up maneuvers with the fleet prior to the Battle of Endor, his enthusiasm began to return, particularly when offering advice to some of the younger, more exuberant pilots. But during a daring attack against a Star Destroyer in the thick of the battle, his fighter was caught in an explosion and he was killed.

**Friyahrr** A Wookiee slaver, he was an associate of Dayla Kev during the early years of the Galactic Civil War. Friyahrr worked with his partner, Fahraark, and delivered a group of Hoojibs to the *Galactic Horizon* to assist Kev in exacting her revenge on Milac Troper.

**Friz Harammel** This was the first truly successful floating city established in the atmosphere of the planet Genarius. Modeled after the Cloud City outpost in the atmosphere of Bespin, it originally was founded as a gas-mining operation. It proved to be incredibly successful and served as the model for future cities built in the Genarius's atmosphere.

**frog-dog** A reptilian species with prehensile tongues and bulbous purple eyes atop a

Sise Fromm

green head, they were intelligent, but rarely let others know that. Instead, frog-dogs such as Bubo chose to work as spies and mercenaries. Most regarded them as common pets.

**Fromm, Sise** An old yet powerful crime boss, he operated out of a stronghold on the planet Annoo during the early days of the Empire. An Annoo-dat, he ran a legitimate import–export business that was a front for extortion, kidnapping, and blaster-running. He controlled most of the world by fear, having sent the Trigon One weapons satellite into orbit around the planet. He wanted Thall Joben and his friends killed for angering him, and so he employed Boba Fett to kill them in the speeder races on Boonta. Fromm, covering all his bases, also planted a bomb on Joben's speeder. When Fett made his attempt on Joben during the races, he activated a magnet in order to draw Joben nearer. However, the magnet dislodged Fromm's bomb, and Fett was nearly destroyed. In his anger, Fett captured Sise Fromm and his entire gang, and turned them over to Jabba the Hutt.

**Fromm, Tig** The Annoo-dat son of crime kingpin Sise Fromm, he also went by the names Baby-Face Fromm and Junior Fromm. Tig Fromm led his own gang of outlaws from the planet Ingo, although he often worked with his father. Unlike the older Fromm, Tig was fascinated by modern technology. He built the weapons satellite Trigon One to help keep the inhabitants of Annoo-dat in line. His dreams of supremacy were shattered when Demma Moll and her freedom fighters, assisted by R2-D2 and C-3PO, destroyed the satellite. Tig and his buddy Vlix then spent many months trying to regain favor with Sise Fromm by capturing the Rebels who destroyed the satellite. But Tig and Vlix were captured by Boba Fett on Boonta, and turned over to Jabba the Hutt.

*Tig Fromm*

**Frorral** A Wookiee and a member of Page's Commandos, she was known as a wilderness fighter.

**frosch** A carnivorous six-legged amphibian found on the Forest Moon of Endor, the frosch laid eggs that were used by Ewok shamans in the creation of healing potions. Frosch were known for their sharp teeth and short tempers.

**Frossk** A male Trandoshan who was a known associate of Longo Two-Guns in the years leading up to the Battle of Naboo, he had a price put on his head by Jabba the Hutt because of his association with Two-Guns; the bounty was eventually claimed by Jango Fett.

**Frost, Alum** One of the Empire's most skilled and loyal soldiers, he was among the top four members at the training facility on Yinchorr, in the same class as Carnor Jax and Kir Kanos. Emperor Palpatine ordered Frost and Jax to battle each other to the death to prove their loyalty. Jax quickly dispatched Frost.

**Froswythe** This Colonies Region planet was known as a haven for criminals trying to avoid the notice of the Core Worlds. It also was known for its abundant numbers of banthas, nerfs, and other herd animals. Much of the planet's surface was covered with rolling grasslands, broken up mainly by farms.

**Froz** This was the home planet of Frozians, who were tall, furry, extra-jointed aliens known for their melancholy outlook on life. Frozians had wide-set eyes, no noticeable external ears, and a nose at the end of a muzzle with long black whiskers on either side. Their mouths were small and lipless. Although they were not known for their good cheer, no one doubted their probity, honesty, or diligence. Micamberlecto, onetime New Republic governor-general of the Corellian sector, was a Frozian. The planet was once covered with grassy plains and deciduous forests, until the Empire decided to punish the Frozians for sympathizing with the Rebel Alliance. Large portions of the planet's surface were bombarded with turbolasers, destroying much of the native flora and fauna. Many years later, during the Yuuzhan Vong War, the asteroids in the Froz system were used as communications bases by the New Republic and the Jedi Knights, who were keeping tabs on the Yuuzhan Vong presence in the Corellian sector.

**F-RTZ-2 "Fritz"** A small assistant hovering droid, he helped MD-OC6 at Bartyn's Landing. Though Fritz could understand several languages, he was not equipped with a vocabulator.

**Frunchettan-sai** This species controlled a handful of colony worlds in the Outer Rim during the last decades of the Old Republic. Members of the Frunchettan-sai species were distinguished by an extra joint between their elbows and their wrists, and the fact that their vision was better suited for blue-ultraviolet wavelengths.

*Fud*

**Frundle's cantina** This cantina was located near Kwilaan Spaceport, in the city of Keren on Naboo. A brightly lit notice above the door proclaimed that no one beat Frundle's drink prices, a sure sign that virtually every bar in Keren was less expensive.

**Fry, Bendu** An obese Devaronian male, he had a bounty placed on his head by the Black Sun organization at the height of the New Order. Boba Fett accepted the bounty, especially since it allowed Bendu Fry to be brought in dead or alive. After Fett apprehended him with minimal effort, Fry tried to remain alive by telling the bounty hunter that a Jedi Knight was hidden on the planet. Fett tracked down the individual only to learn that he was the son of a Twi'lek Jedi killed during the Battle of Geonosis. Angry at having been delayed in his hunt, Fett shot Fry at point-blank range, reducing the Devaronian to ashes.

**Fry, Talesan** The son of Grove and Nelia Fry, he was just 10 years old when he was targeted for assassination by a group of bounty hunters after he overheard and recorded a plot to assassinate 20 government officials. A group of Jedi Knights, led by Qui-Gon Jinn and Adi Gallia and their apprentices, Obi-Wan Kenobi and Siri Tachi, was dispatched to Cirrus to ensure the safety of young Fry. After being captured first by pirates, then by the bounty hunter Magus—who had killed his parents—Talesan Fry eventually was rescued by the Jedi.

Fry then went underground and built up his training in electronics and business. To fund his fledgling ideas, Fry took a loan from Passel Argente, the Corporate Alliance leader who originally had hired Magus for the assassinations years earlier. Fry became one of the galaxy's most innovative designers of surveillance systems, and established the headquarters of Fry Industries on Genian. When Fry developed a foolproof code-breaking system, he offered it to the Jedi Knights for the right price, implying that he could always turn to the Separatists. The Jedi agreed to his many conditions, but Fry was forced to reveal that he had an additional, defective prototype after it was stolen by Magus. He turned the working prototype over to the Republic, unaware there was a tracking device inside it. But General Solomahal destroyed it before it could fall into enemy hands.

**Fry Industries** Founded by Talesan Fry on Genian, this company produced some of the galaxy's most sophisticated surveillance, communications, and security systems during the Clone Wars. Fry himself was considered something of an eccentric, especially after he demanded that all his workers be single and childless.

**FS-1 Farshot** Developed and manufactured by Czerka, the FS-1 Farshot was a blaster rifle designed for use on the open range. While not exceptionally powerful, it boasted greater range and lighter weight than most sporting rifles.

**F'tral** A large water-covered world orbiting the blue-white star F'la Ren, it was home to the tentacled cephalopods known as the Iyra.

The few volcanic islands on F'tral were home to fisher, seducer, and cannibal plants. The Iyra lived in large undersea cities and developed valuable technologies, including corrosion-resistant alloys and gravity-field and inertial devices for starships.

**Fuce, Commander** This man served the Empire as the base commander at the garrison established on Dantooine during the years following the Battle of Yavin.

**Fud** A mercenary, he worked with Valance the bounty hunter shortly after the Battle of Yavin. He and Dafi captured Jaxxon on a backrocket planet, but the rabbit-like alien was rescued by Amaiza, who killed Dafi and Fud.

***Fugazi*** A Rebel Alliance frigate operating during the Galactic Civil War, it was used to evacuate personnel from Briggia following the Imperial attack there as part of Operation Strike Fear.

**Fugo** A Chadra-Fan, he was a colleague of the brilliant scientist Fandar. After Fandar suffered grievous injuries, Fugo took over the Rebel Alliance's Project Decoy.

*Fumiyo*

**Fulier, Kast** A Jedi Master, he and his apprentice Etain Tur-Mukan were dispatched to the planet Qiilura during the early stages of the Clone Wars to investigate the development of a nanovirus by Ovolot Qail Uthan. Kast Fulier's attempts to infiltrate the local farmers and gain their confidence were undermined by the fact that many of them were under the control of Ghez Hokan, who was being funded by the Separatists. The farmers eventually betrayed the Jedi, and Master Fulier was captured and killed while Tur-Mukan managed to escape.

**Fulkes** A Cavrilhu pirate who patrolled the Kauron asteroid base, he often worked with fellow pirate Grinner. Both men tried to hunt down Luke Skywalker when the Jedi infiltrated the base.

***Fulminant*** A New Republic warship, it was destroyed at the Battle of N'zoth.

**Fulmrick** A small, green-skinned alien, he became Jace Forno's assistant shortly after she was hired as chief of security for Movo Brattakin on Nar Shaddaa. He assisted Forno on her mission to retrieve crystals from Indobok.

**Fumiyo** A Godoan, he served as the representative of his homeworld of Godo during discussions with the Alliance of Free Planets during the months following the Battle of Endor. Fumiyo was chosen because he was the only Godoan at the time who could speak Basic. Fumiyo and his people nearly died when a strange plague began afflicting the planet, until Han Solo discovered that two unusual statues that had been stolen—the Dancing Goddess and the Minstrel—were actually key components in a technology that helped keep them alive. Thanks to the efforts of Solo, Lando Calrissian, Luke Skywalker, and Chewbacca, the statues were recovered and returned to their rightful places. The Godoans were revived, and Fumiyo lived. However, a war nearly started when the Godoans refused to allow Calrissian to be revived by the strange technology, after Lando contracted the plague while returning the Dancing Goddess to Godo. In the end, Fumiyo convinced his leaders to allow Calrissian to return to Godo and be revived by the statues.

**fungus droid** Small spy droids created by the New Republic during the struggle against the Yuuzhan Vong, they were used on Coruscant and other worlds on which the invaders used exploding fungus to reform the planets for their own use. Each fungus droid was mobile enough to insinuate itself near Yuuzhan Vong locations, and carried a collection of recorders and transmitters to beam information back to Republic agents. They were built to resemble the exploding fungus, and to place themselves in a group of fungi to blend into their surroundings.

**funnel flower** This Tatooine flower sported a brilliant cone of flapping petals on either end of a long straw-like stem. The hollow stem dipped through a shadowed crevice in cliff walls, sucking hot air in through one end of the funnel flower and condensing the faint moisture that collected in the crook of the stem.

**Funquita, Diva** This red-haired, Theelin slave girl was owned by Gardulla the Hutt, who had received her as a gift from Jabba the Hutt. A trained dancer and singer, she also became Gardulla's chief aide and majordomo. After Gardulla tried to trick Jabba into betting on Gasgano just prior to the Boonta Eve Classic Podrace, Gardulla ordered Diva Funquita to ensure that Anakin Skywalker failed to complete the race. She tried to enlist the aid of Ark "Bumpy" Roose, but the dim-witted Podracer pilot sabotaged the wrong vehicle.

*Diva Funquita*

**Furellas** This female Wookiee, a friend of Kikow's, spent a great deal of time on Ralltiir during the last decades of the Old Republic. Furellas had light brown fur and a smile that many beings mistook for a snarl, but she was nonetheless friendly to most. It was later revealed that Furellas was a member of The Kalmec, a very successful criminal organization.

**Furgan, Ambassador** The ambassador from the planet Carida to the New Republic, this barrel-chested humanoid with spindly arms and legs was really an Imperial plant at the table of the Alliance. His eyebrows flared upward like birds' wings. He almost succeeded in killing Alliance leader Mon Mothma by splashing a drink in her face. The liquid contained a very slow-acting poison that began to sap her strength, and it took months for the officials to figure out what had happened. Furgan was at Carida when Kyp Durron arrived with the Sun Crusher superweapon, and he attempted to bait the young Jedi into believing that his brother, Zeth, was dead. Furgan escaped the destruction of the Caridan sun and went directly to Anoth to kidnap the Force-sensitive infant Anakin Solo. There his troops were faced with formidable challenges, although Furgan at one point was able to get his hands on the baby. But he was challenged by the Mon Calamarian Terpfen, whom Furgan earlier had turned into an involuntary Imperial spy. They faced off, each inside an Imperial MT-AT, or spider walker—a weapon that Furgan had helped develop. Furgan's spider walker fell to the rocks below the Anoth fortress, and he was presumed dead.

***Furious*** This was one of the Nebulon-B frigates that were used by the Imperial Navy at the height of the Galactic Civil War.

**Furlag** A tall, furry humanoid, he was part of the loose bounty hunters' alliance that formed around Bossk just before the Battle of Endor. Furlag and the others tried to intercept Boba Fett and claim the carbon-frozen body of Han Solo. They missed Fett on Gaul, but were able to track him using a signal sent by 4-LOM. The bounty hunters captured *Slave I* and took Fett prisoner, and Furlag was placed in charge of locking Fett up. However, the bat-faced alien didn't notice Fett activating an unused crawl shaft and stepped into the open tube. Furlag was then sucked into space and gone forever.

**Furloti, Teraeza** An Alliance operative stationed undercover in the city of Tyrena on Corellia at the height of the Galactic Civil War, Furloti was the first Rebel operative to discover information on the existence of a Geonosian biogenetics lab that was still in operation. The lab was found to be creating mutated Kwis and Klikniks that were Force-sensitive, which were then provided to the Sith as minions.

## Futhork Alphabet

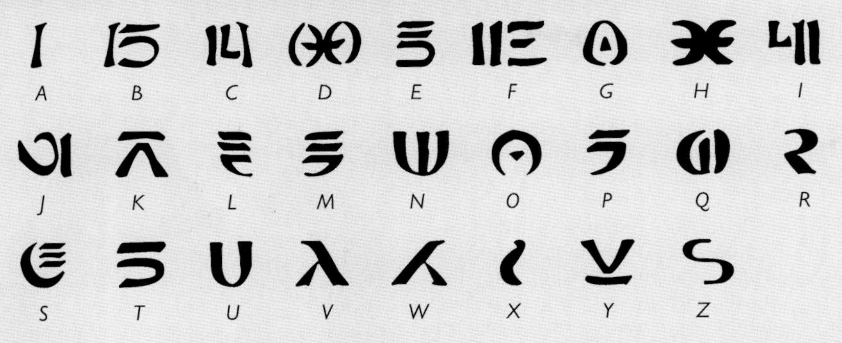


***Fury* (1)** One of the many Sith corsairs that made up the naval fleet of the Brotherhood of Darkness, the *Fury* and its sister vessel, the *Rage,* took part in the skirmish that opened the Battle of Ruusan a millennium before the onset of the Galactic Civil War. Like the rest of the Sith fleet, the *Fury* was crewed by individuals who were joined to the battle meditation of Lord Kaan, who directed the battle from the flagship *Nightfall.* Just when a Sith victory seemed imminent, however, the *Fury* exploded under an onslaught from a pair of Republic Hammerhead ships. The sudden turn in the fighting nearly unraveled the Sith forces, until Lord Kopecz was able to land his small fighter aboard the Republic's flagship. He then slew the Jedi Master—who was also using battle meditation—allowing the forces of the Brotherhood of Darkness to take control of the space surrounding Ruusan.

***Fury* (2)** A Nebulon-B frigate, it was used by the Imperial Navy during the Galactic Civil War.

***Fury* (3)** One of three *Imperial*-class Star Destroyers, it was under the command of Lumiya following the Battle of Endor.

***Fury* (4)** A transport ship owned by the Mistryl, it was used by Shada D'ukal and Dunc T'racen during the early years of the New Republic when they were sent to assist Ghitsa Dogder and Fenig Nabon in transporting a group of Twi'lek dancers.

**Fusai** This planet, one of the many safeworlds maintained by the Alliance during the Galactic Civil War, was the first planet on which Mistress Mnemos was installed.

**fusioncutter** A common industrial tool found in maintenance sheds throughout the galaxy, a fusioncutter was a handheld cutting torch that employed a high-energy plasma beam to slice through dense metals, duraplast, and other reinforced materials. A popular model was the SoroSuub F-187. For cutting through thicker materials, the cutting beam could be adjusted so that it extended up to 20 centimeters long, with a swath up to 6 centimeters wide or as thin as a millimeter. Its power cell could supply an hour's worth of continuous operation. Improper use of a fusioncutter could be dangerous, as its beam could easily be lethal. But its limited range kept this everyday tool from being employed as an effective battlefield weapon.

Futhark

**fusion disintegrator** A device that used a contained reactor to reduce other materials to smaller, nearly atomic particles, it found widespread use in tunneling applications, where dirt and rock had to be removed and transported from a dig site. Because of the nature of the machine, though, it could be used to cut through virtually any material. The disintegrator could be employed manually or mounted on a support tripod.

**fusion disk** A small device that had a small charge attached, when it contacted another surface the charge was ignited, causing the disk to fuse itself to the other surface. The tow cables used by the Alliance to trip the Imperial walkers on Hoth employed fusion disks.

**fusion furnace** A power-generating device, it produced heat and light and recharged the energy cells of vehicles, droids, and weapons.

**fusion reactor** The most popular source of starship power, cold-ionization fusion reactors fused matter at room temperature, creating huge amounts of energy without emitting large amounts of heat. The fusion reactor then sent the energy it generated to cryogenic power cells for storage. Fusion reactors were a necessity for propelling large starships through hyperspace.

Fusioncutter

**Fust, Bendix** A Mordageen criminal hunted by Zam Wesell and imprisoned on Oovo IV sometime before the Battle of Naboo. Jango Fett discovered that Dug crime lord Sebolto had an outstanding bounty for Fust's recovery. With Zam's help, Fett broke Fust out of jail and delivered him to Sebolto.

**futhark** The formal Naboo alphabet, it was based on a series of oval shapes. Futhark was reserved for use on military and official control labels.

**futhork** The traditional, handwritten Naboo alphabet, it used a wider variety of shapes and symbols than the futhark alphabet.

**Futility Station** This was a nickname of Lant Mining Corporation's LMCTS-24542 testing station. A former mining survey site on an airless moon in an outlying region of the Brak sector, it later became a Rebel base.

**Future of Honoghr** A term used by the Noghri to describe a hidden canyon in which they began growing all manner of plants during the early years of the New Republic, after decades of living with the mutated kholm-grass created by the Empire. Leia Organa Solo had proved to the Noghri that they had been held in thrall by the Empire after its surreptitious poisoning of their land. This led the Noghri to break off their relationship with the Empire. Until the death of Grand Admiral Thrawn, however, the Noghri were forced to begin growing crops in this canyon, which hid their work from prying eyes. It became known as the Future of Honoghr, since it represented what the planet might truly become once the Imperial grasses were eliminated.

***Fu'ulanh*** A Yuuzhan Vong transport ship, it was stationed on Coruscant after the invaders captured the planet from the New Republic. A huge ganadote dominated the interior of the craft, which was dedicated for use by those shapers who worshipped Yun-Yuuzhan. Shortly after the ship arrived, Warmaster Tsavong Lah had the ship's inhabitants executed for Ghithra Dal's part in poisoning his radank-claw implant.

**Fuzzel** A commander in the Imperial Armed Forces stationed on Tatooine during the Galactic Civil War, he struck a deal by which Jabba the Hutt would turn over certain criminals to Fuzzel to collect rewards. Most of them were already dead. Fuzzel was after a big prize, the criminal Karkas. Hearing that Karkas had fled the Koda Space Station at the same time a ship piloted by Hoole left for Tatooine, Fuzzel intercepted Hoole upon his arrival. But he let Hoole and his

Fwit

young charges, Tash and Zak Arranda, free after thoroughly searching their ship. Fuzzel later received Karkas's body from Jabba, who had removed the criminal's brain and stored it inside the brain spider droid of a B'omarr monk. Shortly thereafter, Zak found Fuzzel's body in a Mos Eisley alleyway with the letter K carved into his forehead. He had reason to believe that his sister, Tash, was responsible—but it had actually just been Tash's body, since Jabba had decided to use the poor girl as a temporary vessel for Karkas's brain.

**Fuzzum** Members of this primitive species looked like balls of fuzz with long, thin legs. Fuzzum never went anywhere without their spears.

**fuzzynettle** A plant native to the Forest Moon of Endor. The Ewoks found that the fuzzynettle had certain medicinal values. Wicket W. Warrick gathered the plant and saved the sick Latara's life.

**Fwatna** Near the planet Fwatna, some 13 years after the Battle of Endor, Lando Calrissian found the abandoned freighter *Spicy Lady,* which had belonged to his old smuggling associate Jarril. While looking through the ship's computer, Lando discovered that one of Jarril's contacts, Dolph, lived on Fwatna. Dolph briefly studied at Luke Skywalker's Jedi academy before turning to the dark side and assuming the name Kueller.

**Fwiis** A colony world more than 150 light-years from Atzerri, it was one of the stops of the starliner *Star Morning,* owned by the Fallanassi religious order, after it departed the planet Teyr.

**Fwillsving** This planet was located near Honoghr and Kessel in the Calaron sector.

**fwit** This small, furred creature was native to the planet Maridun, where it was kept as a pet by the native Amanin. Despite its cute appearance, which was heightened by its bushy fur and an upturned jawline that made it seem as if the fwit were smiling, the creatures were savage predators in the wild. They preferred to consume warm flesh, and a pack of fwits could take down much larger prey. The teeth of a fwit were designed to tear flesh, but were densely packed in the jaws, allowing a fwit to crush bone as well. When the Empire garrisoned Maridun at the height of the New Order, many fwits turned on their owners. Several incidences of gruesome or fatal injuries followed, and the Empire soon banned the possession of fwits as pets. This didn't stop the Hutts on the planet from exporting them, and fwit populations were quickly established on many other worlds.

**Fw'Sen picket ships** Small Ssi-ruuvi Imperium combat ships, they were used to disable enemy vessels and guard the perimeters of Ssi-ruuvi fleets. A force of 20 Fw'Sen picket ships were a key element of the Ssi-ruuvi invasion force at Bakura. Less than 50 meters long, the ships were fragile and needed power-draining shields to ward off attacks. They were completely crewed by droids and a subjugated species, the tiny P'w'eck, so the Ssi-ruuvi commanders saw them as disposable, making them good for suicide missions. The ships were often controlled remotely from the main Ssi-ruuvi cruisers.

**FX-6** A surgical assistant droid from Medtech Industries created during the final years of the Galactic Republic. Standing just over 1.8 meters tall, the cylindrical FX-6 moved about on a set of omni-directional casters and was equipped with an interchangeable set of manipulator arms.

**FX-7** The sturdy FX-7 medical assistant droid aided both organic and droid doctors in medical procedures before being replaced with Industrial Automaton's MD series of medical assistant droids. Developed by the now defunct Medtech Industries, the FX series (nicknamed the Fixit series) was made up of nine model lines. The FX-7 had a wide array of sophisticated, retractable appendages arranged around its cylindrical body. The number of arms varied, but 20 was the norm.

The FX-7's cap-like head was a cluster of sophisticated medical sensors and diagnostic equipment. In lieu of a vocoder, the FX-7 had readout screens and a scomp link for direct access to medical computers or other droids. An optional repulsorcart, also manufactured by Medtech, allowed the droid to be moved from place to place.

FX-7

Silver Fyre

An FX-7 droid that served the Rebel Alliance at Hoth's Echo Base helped heal Luke Skywalker after he nearly froze to death.

**Fybot, Waywa** A feathered Quor'sav, Waywa Fybot was a 2.5-meter-tall alien with an orange beak, scaled, three-toed feet, and bright yellow plumage. He was well muscled but spoke in a high-pitched voice that belied his strength. His arms were essentially vestigial wings connected to his chest by a membrane. Fybot also suffered from his species' nervous anticipation and intense dreaming. As a youth, he received Imperial conditioning that made him tough and shrewd. He took this experience and became an undercover drug officer. There he gained the attention of Rokur Gepta, who saw a way to use Fybot to finally kill his enemy Lando Calrissian. But after Gepta felt that he had finally achieved his goal of trapping Calrissian, he decided that Fybot had outlived his usefulness, and killed the avian being in cold blood.

**fynock** A species of small, predatory insects native to certain caves on the planet Talus. Fynocks usually traveled in large swarms allowing them to overpower much larger prey. Each swarm consisted of at least two different types of fynocks, those that could fly and those that scuttled along the ground.

**Fynock** A designation for Incom Industries' high-end starship booster system, produced at the height of the New Order. The system was built upon the designs of the Mynock and Vynock series of boosters, and was available in standard and de-

luxe versions, depending on the desired power output characteristics.

**Fyodos** The fourth planet in the Tatrang system, it was a mecca of high technology and beauty until its human population declared war on itself. The planet's other native race, the Galidyns, could only watch in horror as their neighbors unleashed huge weapons of mass destruction on the world. The humans reverted to a pre-technology stage of development.

**Fyre, Commander Silver** A former smuggling colleague of Han Solo and Chewbacca, she and her pirates once stole a valuable cargo of spice from the pair. She went on to become leader of one of the biggest gangs of mercenaries in the galaxy, the Aquaris Freeholders. Following the Battle of Yavin, she and the Freeholders joined the Alliance during the Conference of Uncommitted Worlds held on Kabal.

**fyreflii** A species of large, bioluminescent flying insects, they were native to the forests of the planet Kubindi.

**Fyrth system** The asteroid field of this star system was believed to have been the only source of opila crystals, which could have been used by the ancient Jedi Knights in the construction of their lightsabers.

**Fy-Tor-Ana** A Jedi Knight known for her split-second reflexes, her grace, and her agility, she was one of the foremost instructors in the Art of Movement exercise, and personally trained Obi-Wan Kenobi in its forms. However, Fy-Tor-Ana never took a Padawan learner of her own. In the wake of the Clone Wars, Fy-Tor-Ana was one of a handful of Jedi who decided to hide on Ilum during the Jedi Purge. Her need for information overcame her, and she left Jedi Garen Muln on Ilum and returned to Coruscant, where she hoped to infiltrate the Jedi Temple and learn about the state of the galaxy. When she didn't return, Garen feared that she was dead. Garen relayed his information on Fy-Tor-Ana's plans to Ferus Olin, allowing the younger Jedi to attempt a rescue mission.

*Fy-Tor-Ana*

It turned out that Fy-Tor-Ana had fled the surface of Coruscant and taken refuge well beneath the crust. She adopted the name Solace and assumed control of a settlement that was located near a huge underground ocean. When she was later located by Olin, she refused to talk about the Jedi Order and its possible future, explaining that her former life was in the past and of no further consequence.

However, when Olin explained that Inquisitor Malorum had planted a spy in the underground community, Fy-Tor-Ana agreed to help Olin and Trever Flume return to the Jedi Temple and eliminate Malorum's chances of locating them. When they found themselves trapped, though, Fy-Tor-Ana was forced to grab Flume and leave Olin behind, although he later escaped. They returned to the settlement, only to find themselves in the middle of an attack. Fy-Tor-Ana later helped Olin on a number of missions. She died when the Jedi's hidden asteroid was destroyed as Darth Vader tested his new superweapon.

**Fyyar, Galak** An Imperial admiral, he was one of many naval officers who served the remnant of the Empire during the early years of the New Republic. Galak Fyyar was trained as a weapons specialist, and his designs were considered radical even for the Empire. Many believed that Fyyar's designs would have eclipsed those of Bevel Lemelisk and Umak Leth had he developed them at the height of the New Order. One of the most unusual was a device that allowed Fyyar to infuse others with the dark side of the Force, turning them into Dark Jedi. To gain valuable muscle and to assist with his work, Fyyar allied himself with the Dark Jedi Desann. They planned to use Fyyar's invention to attack Luke Skywalker's Jedi praxeum on Yavin 4 about 10 years after the Battle of Endor. During the battle, however, Fyyar was confronted by Kyle Katarn aboard the *Doomgiver*. The Jedi Knight defeated Fyyar in combat and set out to destroy his ship. By disabling the shields and overloading the reactor, Katarn ensured that the *Doomgiver* was destroyed, and Admiral Fyyar perished in the explosion.

**G-003** CoMar's Tri-Tracker anti-atmospheric gun, produced at the height of the New Order. It was developed from technologies created for *Imperial*-class Star Destroyers. The G-003 Tri-Tracker was an advanced target acquisition and tracking system that used three different sensor arrays to locate its targets. The primary drawbacks were that it had a limited range and needed a landline power source.

**G0-16** A fan-tan dealer droid that worked at the Fifteen Moons Casino on Ord Mantell. It lacked any kind of sympathy for the players and routinely skipped over those who didn't meet its eye during game play. G0-16 once tried to ignore Han Solo's bid during a match shortly after the Battle of Yavin, while Han was trying to increase the reward he received for rescuing Leia Organa. Han was being hounded by a small droid dispatched by Alfreda Goot, and had to argue with the droid and the casino owner to have his bid placed.

***G-021*** A New Republic personnel transport gig used to ferry pilots and commanders among the ships of the Fifth Battle Group, it was under the command of Plat Mallar when he ferried Colonel Bowman Gavin to the *Polaron.*

**G0-T0 (Go-To or GeeZero-TeeZero)** After many planets suffered severe damage during the First and Second Sith wars, Supreme Chancellor Cressa, some 3955 years before the Battle of Yavin, took steps to rebuild the shattered infrastructures of Republic worlds. The chief architects of the reconstruction would be G0-T0 planning droids. The newly established Aratech Corporation designed the G0-T0 programming matrix to plug into the networked computers of an entire planetary system, giving them an almost omniscient level of intelligence. Aratech wisely put checks on each G0-T0, confining each intelligence in the body of a spherical repulsorlift droid. The G0-T0 could manage an entire planet's administration, and was empowered with sufficient authority to requisition supplies and command organic workers. Aratech also ordered each G0-T0 to consider options that would benefit the Republic as a whole while working within the confines of all laws and regulations.

The G0-T0 unit assigned to the devastated planet Telos provided the first hint of trouble. The droid determined that he could not simultaneously help the Republic and obey its laws. Faced with this paradox, G0-T0 broke his programming and became a criminal, setting up smuggling rings that enriched Telos and posting bounties on members of the Jedi and Sith whom he believed to be destabilizing influences on galactic order. To help achieve this last goal, G0-T0 set up a secret droid factory on Telos that manufactured HK-50 assassin droids. Few knew of G0-T0's true role, for he hid behind the holographically projected identity of the human "Goto." G0-T0 soon became mixed up with an exiled Jedi Knight and her mission to destroy the Sith Lords. G0-T0 tried to use his HK-50 assassins to kill the Jedi, but the HKs turned on their maker. G0-T0 was destroyed during a standoff on Malachor V.

Other G0-T0 droids grew bolder as time went on. Within five years, those stationed in the Gordian Reach had set themselves up as dictators over the planets they administered. They cut their worlds off from the HoloNet communications network and blockaded the hyperlanes leading into the system. The G0-T0 units then fired off a drone pod, announcing that their 16 worlds would henceforth be the independent territory of 400100500260026. The Republic freed the planets in a highly publicized military campaign.

*G0-T0*

**G-12 (1)** This advanced power blaster was produced at the height of the Swarm War, some five years after the Yuuzhan Vong War. Unlike a standard blaster weapon, the G-12 power blaster required a separate, dedicated power pack that was worn like a backpack. The G-12's immense firepower was used against the soldier hives of the Colony during the Swarm War. Where most blaster bolts simply bounced off the chitin of Killik soldiers, the blasts produced by a G-12 were powerful enough to rip a Killik to pieces.

**G-12 (2)** A repulsor taxi model, it was produced during the early years of the New Order by Mobquet.

**G-138** This star consumed the Imperial Star Destroyer *Desolator* after Rebel Alliance operatives reprogrammed the capital ship's navigation computer.

**G-1A** A bullet-shaped transport ship manufactured at the Byblos Drive Yards, the G-1A was 15 meters long and could hold up to eight passengers and a metric ton of cargo.

**G1-M4-C "Dunelizard" starfighter** A lean, muscular spacecraft with impressive agility and a generous weapons load, it was commissioned from MandalMotors by the Hutt crime organization. Because of past depradations by the Hutts, Outer Rim merchants had forged relationships with suppliers of high-end starship armor and shield systems to protect themselves. To continue unfettered piracy of the remote regions, and to maintain profit margins, the Hutts

*G1-M4-C "Dunelizard" starfighter*

*< General Grievous*

commissioned the G1-M4-C "Dunelizard" with even heavier armor and significantly increased firepower without sacrificing too much of the maneuverability upon which Hutt pilots had grown to rely.

**G-1 series droid** This series of automata was created for deployment as heavy equipment operators. G-1s could be programmed to handle almost any large piece of equipment and were widely deployed at mining facilities.

**G-1 starfighter** Built as a joint venture between the spaceworks division of Gungan BullbaBong and the Theed Palace Space Vessel Engineering Corps, this craft superficially resembled the Royal N-1 starfighter, except in forest green. G-1s were equipped for long periods of independent operation and sustained combat within a system. They sacrificed hyperdrive quality for shielding and weapons control. Most G-1s were owned by the Naboo government, although many ended up in the hands of private owners.

**g-2000** A powerful, extremely sensitive life-form tracker, it was manufactured by Speizoc.

**G-20 glop grenade** A specialized explosive built by Merr-Sonn Munitions, it used high-pressure jets to spray extremely strong adhesive foam over a 10-meter-diameter area, trapping anyone in the blast region. The reusable grenade subdued targets without causing injuries and was employed extensively throughout the Corporate Sector. Glop became naturally brittle after five minutes.

G-20 glop grenade

**G21** The designation of the super battle droid sent by General Grievous to secure the planet Utapau following the Battle of Coruscant.

**G2-3B** A tall, spindly G2 unit, it was the supervisor of a group of worker droids maintained by Star Tours following the Galactic Civil War.

**G2 droid** Worker droids used by Star Tours and other travel agencies, they were introduced by SoroSuub in the decade following the Clone Wars. The droids were short and squat, with a wide, bottom-heavy stance that forced them to waddle when they walked. This trait, combined with their long, multijointed necks, gave them the nickname of goose droids. Each G2 unit had a stripped-down skeletal frame with exposed joints and wiring. Their three-digit manipulators could grasp most repair tools, while their splayed feet aided in stability. The G2's most recognizable feature was its binocular-like head, which contained a vocabulator, two auditory sensors, and photoreceptors with telescopic, microscopic, and multispectrum capabilities. Each droid bore a unique ID number stenciled onto the side of its head. SoroSuub soon discovered that goose droids gravitated toward excessive chattiness. This feature appeared to be hardwired into the behavioral circuitry matrix and could not be eliminated with memory wipes. Some customers, mostly family-owned businesses or pilots of independent starships, found the quality endearing and allowed their droids to accumulate life experience over time. Eventually, a number of these units achieved an advanced degree of independent thought. A sudden explosion of wanderlust resulted. In one notorious instance, a team of G2s stole a fueling freighter and set up their own community on an asteroid in the Chrellis system.

Large corporations generally had no time for the G2's foolishness and returned the units to SoroSuub, shrinking the line's market base and leading SoroSuub to retire the line 12 years after the Battle of Yavin. Two years later, faced with a surprising outcry from fans of the G2, SoroSuub reintroduced the droids with much fanfare. Star Tours, a short-lived interstellar sightseeing company, employed a number of G2 units to perform maintenance on its aging fleet of Starspeeder 3000 shuttles. One droid, G2-4T, oversaw the labor pool and handled ticketing and travel visas. His cynical sense of humor often landed him in trouble. Another, G2-9T, possessed an infuriatingly short attention span. The property of a Troig diplomat before Star Tours bought him in a "pay by the kilogram" fire sale, he angered the company's organic operators with his spotty work record. When Star Tours closed its doors shortly after the Battle of Endor, G2-4T and G2-9T were cast adrift. They later found employment with the smuggling chief Talon Karrde.

G2 droid

**G-2RD guard droid** These security automata were used in detention centers throughout the Empire, the Corporate Sector, and by countless planetary and local governments. Developed by Arakyd, G-2RD guard droids had a reputation for tenacity, stubbornness, and a fanatical devotion to order. The only way known to force a G-2RD to abandon its programming was to affix a restraining bolt in just the right place, a technique discovered by Han Solo and Chewbacca during the years leading up to the Battle of Yavin.

**G2 Spider Shell** Baktoid Armor Workshop armor plating, it was produced during the final decades of the Old Republic. G2 Spider Shell armor could be used on land vehicles as well as smaller starships.

**G-3PO** Known as Uncle Gee, this protocol droid helped raise Xalto Sneerzick, and even remained by his side after the fanatical Sneerzick established the Droid Abolitionist Movement. G-3PO was terminated during an unfortunate firefight.

**G-4** The designation for a series of servant droids.

**G-40 (1)** A series of tripod-mounted, portable laser cannons produced during the second decade of the New Republic.

**G-40 (2)** Strong, single-purpose droids, these silver automata can be programmed to perform menial tasks.

**G-40 (3)** A sniper rifle, also known as a stealth carbine, made by SoroSuub.

**G47** A heavy-duty tractor beam generator produced by Novaldex for use on ships that moved asteroids for mining or for safety. They were used by Ecclessis Figg to anchor Cloud City. He also employed 16 of them to suck in Tibanna gas for refining and atmospheric heat to drive the thermo-converters that powered the floating city.

**G-5** GeneTech's basic bacta geltab, it was used in most medkits to provide easy access to a small amount of bacta to speed the healing of small wounds.

**G5-623** The ancient designation of the planet Kashyyyk when it was first encountered by explorers of the Old Republic.

**G-59 Cannibalizer** A SoroSuub starfighter design, it was developed by Syub Kyak and his design team in the city of Edic Bar during the

G-2RD guard droid

last decades of the Old Republic. It was designed to compete with the Incom Industries Z-95 Headhunter.

**G-5PO** One of the many protocol droids maintained by Jabba the Hutt in his palace on Tatooine at the height of the Galactic Civil War.

**G-62** A Jal-Parra repulsorsail-equipped skiff, it was produced several standard centuries before the New Order. At 8.7 meters long, the G-62 skiff was operated by a single pilot and could transport up to 16 passengers or 92 metric tons of cargo.

***G-79*** The designation of the drone barge dispatched by Darth Vader to transport Jix to Corulag on his mission to eliminate Governor Torlock.

**G7-x** This model of Sienar Fleet Systems' gravity-well projector was used on the Immobilizer 418.

**G8** A military blaster rifle produced by Merr-Sonn, it was not as reliable or versatile as the BlasTech E-11. It originally was produced during the last decades of the Old Republic, and was popular among police agencies in the Tion Hegemony and Hutt space. When the Galactic Civil War broke out, many of the agencies sold their weapons to the Rebel Alliance.

**G8-R3** An astromech unit stationed aboard the Naboo Royal starship, it had the head of a standard R5 unit atop the body of a versatile R2 unit. Programmed for complex starship repair jobs, G8-R3 was one of several droids sent to fix a damaged deflector shield generator during Queen Amidala's daring escape from Naboo. G8-R3 was destroyed by enemy fire while attempting the task, which ultimately was completed by R2-D2.

**G-8Y5** An engineering droid created by QS-2D as an assistant, it designed Uffel's most useful and reliable droids. G-8Y5 worked with QS-2D to develop a line of security droids that were used to defend the moon from outside invasion.

G8-R3

**G-9** A particularly deadly power blaster produced during the Yuuzhan Vong War, it was favored by many smugglers and independent spacers, who carried the G-9 to protect against being boarded.

**GA-60s** A starship double laser cannon, it was produced by Taim & Bak for use aboard the T-4a *Lambda*-class shuttle at the height of the Galactic Civil War.

**Ga, Vaas** A Jedi Master, he became a general in the Grand Army of the Republic during the early stages of the Clone Wars. General Ga was placed in command of Sarlacc Battalions A and B of the 41st Elite Infantry, and saw combat during the siege at Dinlo.

**Gaan** Leader of a small settlement of outcasts on Ragmar V, he fought off Republic forces but joined with Jedi Joc Sah after the clone army executed Order 66.

**Gaaqu** One of many who served the Empire as an Imperial Moff at the height of the New Order.

**Gaar** A Trandoshan, he and his comrade Ulis were members of the Believers during the final years of the Old Republic. Former employees of the crime lord Nirama, they were among a small band summoned by the Darkstaff to eliminate freelance agents who threatened to free the Oblee and destroy the ancient artifact during the Clone Wars.

Chine Gabbard

***Gaarni*** A Nebulon-B frigate, it was used by the Imperial Navy at the height of the Galactic Civil War.

**Gaartatha** A Wookiee freelance pilot and shipper during the Galactic Civil War, he narrowly escaped enslavement by the Empire, but his partner wasn't so lucky. Gaartatha consoled himself by consuming too many Dentarian Ripples while he tried to figure out how to rescue his partner.

**Gaarx** One of the few Tchuukthai ever to be encountered off their homeworld.

**gaawan** The title given to the leader of a Tuhgri tribe. Each gaawan was sent to the House of Balance each year to discuss matters of importance to the Tuhgri.

**Gaba-18** An airspeeder, it was distinguished by its pointed nose and long, rounded cockpit.

**gabal** A large mammal native to the Zirfan Glacier on the planet Rhinnal, it was a source of food for the Rhinnalians, and its thick fur was used to create gabal wool.

Gaba-18

**Gabbard, Chine** An executive on the board of Rehemsa Consumables at the height of the New Order, he traveled to Garqi to perform botanical research into hafa vines, allegedly to improve their yields. In reality, he was trying to develop a new bioweapon for the Empire.

**Gabbera** A Klatooinian who worked for Zonnos the Hutt as a translator during the early years of the New Order, he seemed cowardly but also was an excellent pilot who trained others in Zonnos's operations.

**Gab'borah** One of the many chefs hired by Jabba the Hutt, he was known for his fantastic desserts—especially Ziziibbon truffles. A 10-year-old Boba Fett discovered that Gab'borah was Ygabba's father and helped them reunite. When Fett set out to try to capture Wat Tambor near the end of the Clone Wars, Gab'borah and Ygabba presented him with a new suit of Mandalorian armor, tailored to fit his 13-year-old body. Gab'borah also gave him a packet of gleb rations.

**Gabby** The 18-year-old survey pilot of the *Astrolabe,* Gabby was killed near Doornik-1142.

**gaberwool** A soft wool made from the tufts of gaberworms.

**gaberworm** Giant fat-bodied worms, they had ivory tufts of hair in the middle of each of their body segments. This hair was harvested to make gaberwool. They lived in garbage collection facilities on Coruscant, and grew to lengths of half a meter or more.

**gablith masquer** Developed from the basic ooglith masquer, the gablith masquer allowed the Yuuzhan Vong to assume the guise of certain nonhuman species. The gablith masquer could form itself into a number of shapes and textures, and its activation spot was located on the wearer's neck. This modification—the activation spot on an ooglith masquer was near the nose of the wearer—allowed a Yuuzhan Vong to impersonate a species such as the Duros, which lacked a nose.

**Gabonna memory crystal** A highly specialized computer crystal used in the pro-

Gackle bat

duction of some of the galaxy's most advanced security droids, their availability was restricted by the Old Republic when the Clone Wars started so they would be readily obtainable for the military effort. Because of this, Cestus Cybernetics was forced to abandon production of its Cesta security droids, which caused severe economic hardship on the planet Ord Cestus. When Count Dooku offered Cestus Cybernetics an abundant supply of the Confederacy's Gabonna crystals as payment for thousands of JK series security droids, the company eagerly agreed to supply the droids to the Separatists.

**Gabo the Wicked** A male Aqualish and noted criminal during the years following the Battle of Naboo, he was captured on the Outland Transit Station by Jango Fett after a bounty was placed on his head for indecent exposure and the distribution of illegal holograms.

**Gabredor III** A heavily forested world, it was the site of the Karazak Slavers Guild's loading base during the early years of the New Republic. The Red Moons mercenaries broke up the guild's operation when they attempted to rescue the children of the ambassador of Cantras Gola.

***Gabrielle*** Supposedly a New Republic scout ship patrolling the space near the Reecee side of the Black Bantha, it was in fact a code used by Wedge Antilles to meet up with Han Solo and the *Millennium Falcon.* Han turned over a wealth of information on the Yuuzhan Vong's plans to attack from a fleet position near the Black Bantha.

**Gacerian** The fourth and primary world in the Gacerian system, it was a model of what the Empire could have been if it had been more compassionate. The Imperial Governor, while in complete control, left the general populace to themselves. This had the effect of instilling the values of the New Order while preserving many of the freedoms the people once enjoyed. One of the planet's main exports was beautiful gemstones. The planet's native Gacerites were humanoids with thin limbs.

**Gachoogai River** One of the primary waterways on Ylesia, it was located between Colony One and Colony Two. Unusual for the planet, the Gachoogai was swift flowing and deep.

**gackle bat** This flying mammal was believed to be native to the planet Devaron, although a community of gackle bats was also discovered on Yavin 4. It was distinguished by its wide wingspan and flat body. A mutant subspecies, the gackle stalker, was native to Yavin 4.

**Gactimus** One of the many moons that orbited the lifeless world of Triton, it was where the religious Tritonite orders established several retreats in the early years of the New Order.

**Gadaf** A Rodian smuggler, he worked as Falan Iniro's gunner aboard the *Take That!* Gadaf was killed when Iniro took the ship into battle before getting the signal from the Nar Shaddaa command base, and the ship was destroyed by a *Carrack*-class picket ship.

**Gadan, Addath** A female New Republic Senator who represented her homeworld of Vannix for nearly 20 years before the Yuuzhan Vong War. Senator Gadan barely escaped from Coruscant when the alien invaders captured the planet. After beating a swift retreat to Vannix, she met Leia Organa Solo and broke the news that Presider Sakins had fled the capital. A quick vote was scheduled for a successor, with Senator Gadan—who was on record as favoring a path of appeasement toward the Yuuzhan Vong—running against Admiral Apelben Werl. When the Senator learned that Leia had negotiated a deal with Admiral Werl to help win the election, she offered Leia a wealth of naval resources in return for her assistance. The exchange had been recorded, and with Senator Gadan caught trying to bribe Leia in order to win the election and capitulate to the Yuuzhan Vong, she fled the planet.

Gados

**Gadde** A repulsorlift city built by Lant Mining Corporation in order to mine the moon of Lish V, it was an eight-sided facility supported by 10 massive repulsorlift engines. A minimum of six engines were required to keep the city afloat, and the Gadde city managers operated only nine at a time in order to effect repairs and perform maintenance.

**gaderffii** A traditional weapon of Tatooine's Sand People, or Tusken Raiders, it was a double-edged ax-like polearm. Gaderffii, or "gaffi sticks," were fashioned from scavenged metal. Both ends of a gaffi stick's shaft were tipped with fearsome weapons, often a sharp, double-edged ax blade and a spiked, weighted club. Although brandished most frequently during the Tuskens' daring attacks on Jawas and humans, gaderffii were also used to hunt womp rats and other prey, to carve territorial boundaries on cliff walls, and as walking sticks. Some Tusken Raiders dipped their weapons in sandbat venom, making them all the deadlier.

Gaderffii

**Gadget** The nickname given by Ton Phanan to his R2 astromech droid.

**Gados** The native species of the planet Abregado-rae and its surrounding system, the Gados were tall, thin humanoids with long limbs and worm-like heads; they were capable of prodigious leaps. A layer of short fur covered most of their body. Uniquely, nearly every Gados internal organ was laid out in ribbons that ran throughout the body. For this reason, almost any injury could be life threatening.

**Gadon 3** A mining planet, Gadon 3 was the only known world where the high-energy kif ore could be mined, making it a valuable member of the Old Republic. It was home to the Gadon species.

**Gados floatboats** The canals of the Old Patch district of Abregado-rae were navigated by floatboats, amphibious vehicles that traveled on repulsorlifts when they left the canals for dry land. They were brightly painted and often used as taxis.

**Gadrin** One of two cities founded by Reidi Artom upon her return to the Cularin system after filing for the discovery rights. It was a twin city to Hedrett and sometimes referred to as Gadren. Gadrin was established at the base of Cloud Mountain, where the Estauril River flowed past. Hedrett was established across the river when the population of Gadrin expanded too rapidly. During the Old Republic, Gadrin was ruled by an elected governor. When the Clone Wars broke out and the Almas Academy was blockaded by Jedi Master Darrus Jeht, all Jedi instructional classes were moved to a temporary facility in Gadrin, in an effort to maintain some semblance of normalcy.

**Gadrin Dump** The primary public landfill in the city of Gadrin, it became a home base for the Borus's Boys gang in the years following the Battle of Naboo.

**Gadsle** A Twi'lek known for playing Spheroids during the era of the New Order, he lost more often than he won.

**Gaelin** A computer slicer apprenticed to the Keiffler Brothers before their organization was conscripted by Imperial Moff Kentor Sarne, he returned home to Pembric II after Sarne executed the brothers. Gaelin was forced to work for the Bombaasa Cartel but still managed to

The Gafsa

provide regular reports to Sarne. After the crew of the New Republic corvette *FarStar* stopped on Pembric II during its hunt for Sarne, Gaelin was offered a chance at freedom in return for helping to remove the "trapdoors" in Sarne's star charts of Kathol sector. Gaelin then agreed to join the *FarStar* crew as a slicer.

**Gaff** A Kobok, he served as one of General Koong's henchmen, working from the Tawntoom Citadel on Roon during the early years of the New Order. Gaff, who made a name for himself for his skills as an assassin and spy, often wore a Koboth Insurgent Mantle, although it was not known if he actually participated in the Mavvan Conflict. Gaff considered his position with Koong a low point in his career, but it paid well. When Koong destroyed the Citadel in an effort to kill Imperial Admiral Screed, Gaff was believed to have been caught in the blast. With no body found, however, many Roonans believed that he had somehow survived and fled offplanet.

**gaffi stick** *See* gaderffii.

***Gafra*** An Imperial freighter whose crew was charged with delivering a new warhead with enough power to take out an *Imperial I*–class Star Destroyer. The freighter was intercepted by the Rebel Alliance shuttle *Herald,* and the warhead was captured.

**Gafsa, the** A canyon in the Jundland Wastes of Tatooine. Its name meant "the walking place" in the tongue of the Old Ones, ancient Tusken Raiders who may have originated there. The canyon was marked by an archway, which then led to a deep, bowl-shaped gorge where the nomadic Tuskens sometimes made camp. Rare water wells in canyons like the Gafsa were sacred to the Tuskens. Merely trespassing near one could provoke immediate violence, and intruders could become sacrifices.

**Gaftikar** A planet shared by two species of colonists, humans and Marits. Humans established cities while the Marits lived in rural villages. Early in the Clone Wars, the Marits sided with the Old Republic, and wanted to allow Shenio Mining to establish operations to mine Gaftikar's rich deposits of norax and kelerium. Humans didn't want any such mining and supported the Separatists in the hope of gaining an ally against the more populous Marits.

**GAG** *See* Galactic Alliance Guard.

**Gage, Captain** An Imperial officer at the height of the New Order, he used family wealth and connections rather than hard work to gain the rank of captain. During combat, he often rode in comfort aboard his Juggernaut, much to the disdain of his troops. The captain couldn't understand why a new charge, Lieutenant Janek Sunber, chose to walk with his troops. When a squad Gage led was ambushed by Amanin on the planet Maridun, he panicked, and only Sunber's quick actions saved his life. Still, he refused to provide corroboration for Sunber's promotion to captain.

***Gahenna*** A scientific vessel working to develop a toxin for the Trade Federation, its crew left the planet Queyta at the height of the Clone Wars carrying a developmental sample. Later they succeeded in producing a highly toxic defoliant, which the ship commander planned to use. However, the *Gahenna* was identified by Old Republic scouts, and a task force intercepted it near Honoghr and forced it to crash-land on the planet. The resulting ecological damage from the toxic spill took decades to repair.

Captain Gage

**Gahg** The first Minister of Finance for the Galactic Empire. Among his initial duties for the Emperor was the annexation of former Separatist worlds into the Empire.

**Gahseelik** A Trandoshan thug who worked for Gardulla the Hutt, he was the subject of a bounty by his own clan shortly after the Battle of Naboo because he had disgraced it by working for "a filthy Hutt." Jango Fett later claimed the bounty on Gahseelik during a mission to meet with Gardulla to discuss the Bando Gora cult.

**Gaib** A "tech hunter" who worked with the armored droid TK-0 during the Clone Wars. The pair specialized in acquiring information or technology for their employers. TK-0 provided the computing power to sift through records and data as well as access to local computer networks. Gaib handled the logistics and helped direct the droid's searches. Gaib agreed to provide information to clone commandos Mereel and Ordo during their search for the Kaminoan scientist Ko Sai. The information Gaib and TK-0 provided helped the commandos track the purchase of high-tech devices for an illegal cloning facility to Dorumaa.

Gailid

***gai bal manda*** A Mandalorian adoption ceremony, it welcomed an individual into a Mandalorian family. Any being so adopted agreed to be bound by the Six Actions, and was required to show unswerving loyalty to family and to the *Mand'alor.* The literal translation was "name and soul."

**Gailea** A planet that was the site of the Marqua Spas.

**Gailid** A human who was Mosep's assistant in the accounting and tax-collection office of Jabba the Hutt, he also had technical skills and spent time in the repulsor pool with Barada. He was killed at the Great Pit of Carkoon during the escape of Luke Skywalker and friends.

**Gaios** A philosopher from this planet once said that "a seed does not know the flower that produced it."

**gairk** An unusual predator native to the rivers of the planet Ansion. Its wide mouth had no teeth and little bone structure. Gairks drowned their victims by creating enough suction to inhale their prey. They often attacked in groups of four or more, working the suction in unison. A pack of gairks attacked Jedi Barriss Offee in the Torosogt River during the Clone Wars, but Anakin Skywalker used his lightsaber to cut their maws and break their suction.

**G'ai Solem** A city on the planet Solem, it was Imperial Governor Malvander's seat of power during the early stages of the Galactic Civil War.

**Gait, Loowil** A dedicated member of the Coruscant police prior to the Battle of Naboo, he once arrested a key member of a defense organization who was negotiating a deal with the Techno Union. The deal fell through, prompting the Techno Union to issue a bounty for Gait's capture. Jango Fett claimed the bounty when the bounty hunter himself was captured by Gait and fellow officers after killing the Twi'lek Senator Trell; Fett was able to turn the tables on the officers.

**Gaitzi** A member of a cleaning crew known as the Tripod, she worked on Bakura during the Yuuzhan Vong invasion of the galaxy.

**Gakfedd** A tribe of Gamorreans living on Pzob, they met up with Luke Skywalker, Cray Mingla, and Nichos Marr when the three were stranded on the planet.

**Gal, Groex** An Ebranite, he was a high-powered tour guide on the moon of Mina during the early years of the New Republic, helping pilgrims find their way to the sacred Inicus Mont.

**Gal, Veren** A onetime Sith archaeologist, he left a datapad that had notes speculating that the ancient Sith may have used Therangen, an unstable black rock, as a power source.

**Gala** An Outer Rim planet ruled for many years by the Beju-Tallah dynasty, it was inhabited by three tribal groups: the city people, the hill people, and the sea people. But the Tallah rulers became corrupt, and about 12 years before the Battle of Naboo the Galacians were on the verge of revolution. Elderly Queen Veda agreed to restructure the government in a democratic election, and Yoda sent Qui-Gon Jinn and Obi-Wan Kenobi to be independent observers.

**Galaan** A large gas giant in the Galaanus system of the Corva sector, it was covered with green, gray, and white clouds that restricted visibility to a few hundred meters. The New Republic operated a floating intelligence outpost in Galaan's upper atmosphere before it was discovered and destroyed by an Imperial splinter group, the Kaarenth Dissension.

**galactic!** A term of surprise and awe, it was used by the youth of the galaxy during the early years of the New Order.

**Galactic Alliance** Officially the Galactic Federation of Free Alliances, it was the government formed by Chief of State Cal Omas after the fall of the New Republic and the loss of Coruscant to the Yuuzhan Vong. It started well, with the Imperial Remnant joining forces to finally defeat the invaders.

But in the wake of the Swarm War with the Killiks, the Galactic Alliance began to assert itself in ways that had many concerned. Policies were implemented behind closed doors, and Senatorial dealings came under intense scrutiny. When Thrackan Sal-Solo threatened to have the Corellian system secede from the Alliance, and Supreme Commander Gilad Pellaeon was replaced with hard-line military Admiral Cha Niathal, many openly claimed that the Galactic Alliance was little more than the Empire reborn. Those feelings only intensified when Jacen Solo was named the head of the Galactic Alliance Guard with a mission to arrest or deport all Corellians living on Coruscant. Chants of "The Empire's back!" filled the streets of Coruscant, and planets began to fall in line to support Corellia's bid for independence.

Though the Alliance weathered that storm, it was dealt a heavy blow decades later with the return of the Sith. Following a sabotaged effort to terraform 100 dead and dying worlds using Yuuzhan Vong technology—the so-called Ossus Project—the Alliance fell into chaos and the Empire declared war against it. The mastermind of the Sith, Darth Krayt, then took over the Empire, sending Emperor Roan Fel into exile. The Galactic Alliance lost much power and influence, but the ousted Fel tried to forge a treaty with the Alliance to depose the resurgent Sith menace.

**Galactic Alliance Committee on Corporate Oversight** Formed in the wake of the Yuuzhan Vong War, this committee adopted a primary mission of ensuring that corporations acted in accordance with all galactic laws, ending attempts to profit from the vast upheavals caused by the war.

**Galactic Alliance Defense Force** The primary military force established by the Galactic Alliance in the months following the end of the Yuuzhan Vong War, it was charged with maintaining the security and safety of those star systems that were part of the Galactic Alliance, and was given control of the combined military assets of Alliance members. Gilad Pellaeon accepted the role as Supreme Commander of the GADF before retiring in disgust after a decade because of the direction the Galactic Alliance was heading. Military hard-liner Cha Niathal then assumed control of the GADF.

**Galactic Alliance Guard** A police force formed a decade after the Yuuzhan Vong War, it was a response to the Corellian system's attempt to secede from the Galactic Alliance and followed a terrorist bombing at the Elite Hotel in Galactic City. Chief of State Cal Omas agreed to create the Galactic Alliance Guard, and appointed Jacen Solo as its head officer. Its role was to locate and remove insurgents and terrorists from Coruscant, but many likened the GAG to a secret police force that was little better than Darth Vader's 501st Imperial Legion of stormtroopers.

**Galactic Alliance Intelligence Service** The main information-gathering branch of the Galactic Alliance, its operations were overseen by the Senate's Security and Intelligence Council. In the years following the Swarm War, the GAIS and the Corellian Intelligence agency tried to outmaneuver each other while their governments fought a bitter war. Following the arrest of Chief of State Cal Omas and the declaration of martial law, acting Chief of State Cha Niathal consolidated the Intelligence Service under the Galactic Alliance Guard. She asked former Intelligence officer Heol Girdun to assume command to ensure a smooth transition.

**Galactic Alliance Second Fleet** *see* Second Fleet, Galactic Alliance.

**Galactic Alliance Senate** The Senatorial body that was formed in the wake of the Yuuzhan Vong War, it was modeled after the former Galactic Senate. While designed to allow member systems an equal vote in matters of galactic importance, it continued the traditions of greed and selfishness that helped destroy the Old Republic.

**Galactic Archives** Located in the city of Talos on Atzerri, it proclaimed itself "a one-stop source for everything that's worth knowing." Luke Skywalker stopped there during his travels with Akanah in hopes of getting information on the Jedi Knights, but its volumes were obvious fakes.

**Galactic Caucus of the New Republic** A conclave called by the Rebel Alliance shortly after the Battle of Endor, its goal was to determine the correct form of government to temporarily replace the Empire prior to the actual formation of a New Republic.

**Galactic Center Medcenter** A hospital that occupied the top five stories of a nondescript building in Coruscant's midlevel, it was where Supreme Chancellor Valorum was brought following a failed assassination attempt at the Avenue of Core Founders.

**Galactic Chopper droid** *See* DD-13.

**Galactic City** The capital city of Coruscant during the last years of the Old Republic, its original name—Republic City—was in use some 4,000 years before the Galactic Civil War. With the advent of the New Order and Emperor Palpatine's rise to power, the city was eventually renamed Imperial City. At its height, more than 12 billion individuals lived in Galactic City alone. The city was often referred to as the City of Spires, a reference to the many skytowers that studded the urban landscape. In the wake of the war against the Yuuzhan Vong, much of Coruscant's landscape had been transformed by the various biotechnologies of the invaders. As the Galactic Alliance began to rebuild the capital world, an effort was made to rebuild at least a portion of the planet to the level of the old Galactic City.

**Galactic City SpeedPipe** A busy Coruscant skylane, it cut diagonally across Galactic City. Access was restricted to private speeders whose owners paid a 100-credit toll. Use of the SpeedPipe could cut an hour-long journey through Galactic City down to a 15-minute trip. The high toll kept traffic to a minimum.

**Galactic Civil War** The Rebellion that rocked the galaxy to its core started after Senators still loyal to the idea of a democratic Republic met secretly to build the principles upon which a New Republic could be based. They did so at severe personal peril, and challenged the Empire and its formidable military might, all put into place by Emperor Palpatine, secretly Darth Sidious, a Dark Lord of the Sith. The Galactic Empire had replaced the corruption-ridden Old Republic, and tyranny gripped the millions of worlds of the galaxy and its trillions of inhabitants.

It took years, however, before scattered pockets of resistance could be organized into the Alliance to Restore the Republic. One by one at first, then in a trickle that became a flood, guerrilla groups and planets cast their lot with the nascent Rebel Alliance. As the galaxy shuddered on the brink of full-scale civil war, Alliance leader Mon Mothma wrote the Formal Declaration of Rebellion, alerting the Emperor that the pesky opposition was now full-fledged, organized resistance. Although Rebel firepower didn't come close to matching that of the Empire, events were moving too swiftly for the Rebels to plan and execute an orderly buildup.

The exact moment when the full-scale Galactic Civil War began cannot be pinpointed with certainty, although the capture of the *Priam* and the destruction of the *Invincible* were generally believed to have been the events that led the Rebels to openly declare war against the Empire. Certainly the completion of the Empire's Death Star battle station and its annihilation of the planet Alderaan with its billions of people galvanized the opposition. By the time of the Battle of Yavin, the civil war was in full swing. Star system after star system slipped through the Empire's nets to join the Alliance, and war rocked the galaxy from the settlements of the Outer Rim Territories to the majestic spires of Imperial Center.

From that point on, the war raged for three years, with the Empire briefly gaining the upper hand in the wake of the Battle of Hoth. Many historians felt that the Galactic Civil War came to an end at the Battle of Endor, when Emperor Palpatine was believed to have been killed with the destruction of the second Death Star. Others considered the first years of the New Republic to be a continuation of the Galactic Civil War, as the Republic's forces continued to battle against Imperial opposition for control of the galaxy.

*Galactic Civil War (Battle of Hoth)*

**_Galactic_-class battle carrier** The first of the large destroyers that were produced for the navies of the Galactic Alliance in the wake of the Yuuzhan Vong War, they were similar in shape to the old *Imperial*-class Star Destroyer, but broader and heavier. The first completed *Galactic*-class carrier was named *Dodonna,* becoming the second vessel to be named in honor of General Jan Dodonna.

**Galactic Constitution** The basic document governing the Old Republic, it remained for many generations a stable and unaltered document, until the Clone Wars were used by Chancellor Palpatine to shove through a series of emergency amendments as part of a larger plan to take control and turn the Republic into an Empire.

*Galactic Civil War (Battle of Endor)*

**Galactic Core** A region encompassing star systems in the central expanse of the galaxy. The term was also applied more narrowly to the heavily populated region surrounding the Deep Galactic Core. The region was the original ruling nexus of the Republic, and later the Empire, with the planet Coruscant at the center and the government spreading outward like the spokes of a wheel.

**Galactic Corporate Policy League** A secret cabal of plutocrats tied to Senator Palpatine and the ideals of his New Order, the group worked to end the legal prohibitions on slavery, strip mining, and credit hoarding enforced by the Old Republic. The league was the core of Palpatine's support to become Supreme Chancellor, and when he took over he made them the founding members of the Corporate Sector Authority.

**Galactic Correctional Authority** A huge correctional conglomerate that sprang up during the last decades of the Old Republic, it was based in the Outer Rim Territories and maintained penal colonies throughout the sector. One of the most infamous was located on Oovo IV.

**Galactic Costume Extravaganza** An annual event sponsored by Elwis Bontraar during the last decades of the Old Republic, it was attended by business leaders, military personnel, and other wealthy beings who were required to wear unusual costumes and spend an entire day sharing all manner of information.

**Galactic Criminals Act** Enacted by Xanatos on his homeworld of Telos, the law gave the government police resources to capture offworld criminals. Xanatos's primary goal was to capture Qui-Gon Jinn if the Jedi Master ever traveled to Telos.

**"Galactic Dance Blast"** A tune that was regularly played by the Max Rebo Band.

**Galactic Electronics** A development firm in the Corporate Sector, it defied the Imperial ban on weapons sales and worked closely with the Rebel Alliance to develop the magpulse weapon just after the Battle of Hoth. In retaliation, the Empire destroyed the company's Pondut research station.

**Galactic Empire, the** The regime established by Chancellor Palpatine when he named himself galactic Emperor and instituted his New Order in the wake of the Clone Wars. The Empire ruled by fear of force backed by force itself. Emperor Palpatine built a huge war machine in order to instill fear and used the dark side of the Force to further control the galaxy. Following the Battle of Endor, the Empire floundered. Various warlords and Imperial officers tried to reestablish its momentum in a series of skirmishes with the New Republic. But even when the reborn Emperor tried to strike back from a hidden base on Byss, he could not defeat Luke Skywalker and the New Republic.

***Galactic Encyclopedia, The*** A vast collection of information, it documented nearly every major fact in the known universe. The development and maintenance of *The Galactic Encyclopedia* reached its height in the years following the Battle of Ruusan, but was severely curtailed during the era of the New Order.

**Galactic Exotics** A Twi'lek business venture, it specialized in the development of rare agricultural goods. Based in Kala'uun on the planet Ryloth, Galactic Exotics developed the shalaman and podon orchards on Belsavis.

**Galactic Fair** A traditional fair that was the highlight of Fete Week each year on the planet Coruscant, it provided visitors a glimpse of the wide range of cultures and civilizations that made up the Old Republic.

*Galactic Marines*

**Galactic Federation of Free Alliances** The official name of the Galactic Alliance.

**Galactic Games** A sporting event held every seven years on a different planet, it was created to help promote galactic peace through sports. An assassination attempt on Emperor Palpatine took place during a Galactic Games competition on Coruscant.

**Galactic Great Seal** An emblem of the Old Republic also known as the Galactic Republic crest, it was displayed most prominently on the Chancellor's Podium in the Senate Rotunda.

***Galactic Guardian*** An *Acclamator*-class transport, this capital ship was active around two years before the Battle of Yavin.

**Galactic HoloNet** An extensive news and information network, it could be accessed throughout the galaxy.

***Galactic Horizon*** An Ithorian herd ship under the command of Captain Roogak during the early years of the Galactic Civil War.

**Galactic Justice Center** A massive complex of courthouses and judicial facilities, it was erected on Coruscant in the wake of the Yuuzhan Vong War. The main building was an immense cylinder, with the exterior sheathed in mirrored transparisteel.

**Galactic Loyalty Act** An ambitious law passed by the Senate of the Galactic Alliance in the period following the Swarm War, it was written during the attempted secession of the Corellian system. It established guidelines on how individual beings and member worlds were to behave, supposedly to ensure the stability of the Galactic Alliance.

**Galactic Marines** One of the main divisions of the Grand Army of the Republic. The red-and-white-armored troopers of the Galactic Marines helped secure the front lines of battlefields at the height of the Clone Wars. Culled from the 21st Nova Corps of the Outer Rim sector army by Jedi Master Ki-Adi-Mundi and Commander Bacara (originally designated Trooper 1138), the clone troopers of the Galactic Marines were among the toughest produced on Kamino.

The Marines had been cross-trained in space- and ground-based fighting, and were well versed in zero-g combat. They were among the first to field-test new equipment and combat gear. Their use of the prototype spacetrooper powersuit during the Battle of New Bornalex was well documented; when the weapons systems on the suits failed, the troopers used the mechanical musculature to engage the enemy super battle droids in hand-to-hand combat and tore into them with their enhanced manipulators. This fostered a ferocious reputation for the Marines that Bacara particularly relished. Bacara had been one of the first generation of clone commanders to benefit from a new training program instituted by Alpha, an ARC trooper veteran.

Deployed at Rhen Var, Aargonar, Boz Pity, and Mygeeto, the Marines specialized in boarding and capturing enemy starships, as well as planetary assault. They were distinguished by their distinctive visor gear: a synthmesh designed to keep out sand, snow, ash, and airborne fungus. Bacara was one of the most outspoken and independent of the ARC graduates and demanded the absolute best of his men. He would unilaterally reassign soldiers who did not meet his expectations, much to the consternation of General Ki-Adi-Mundi. The two men maintained a respectful but contentious relationship, right up until the Battle of Mygeeto.

**Galactic Medical Central** The formal name of the New Republic medical team working in the Meridian sector, based on Nim Drovis.

**Galactic Museum** A huge museum located in the CoCo District of Imperial City on Coruscant, it was the home of many records detailing the Old Republic's growth as well as that of the Empire. A number of Sith and Jedi artifacts were stored there as well. Much of the Galactic Museum's pro-Imperial propaganda was removed by the New Republic following the liberation of Coruscant from Ysanne Isard, and was replaced with fairly neutral depictions of the Galactic Civil War.

**Galactic News Network** A newsfeed that reported on the events of the Outer Rim Territories during the early years of the New Republic.

**Galactic News Service** A news-reporting agency established during the Old Republic, it managed to survive the upheaval caused by the Clone Wars and the formation of the Galactic Empire, and eventually became one of the leading sources of news in the New Republic.

**Galactic Outdoor Survival School** Known throughout the galaxy simply as GOSS, the organization was noted for training some of the most skilled survivalists in the galaxy. Graduates described the school as a combination of educational facility and survivalist camp. Although graduates served both the Empire and the Alliance during the Galactic Civil War, most GOSS alumnae went on to become corporate or independent scouts.

**Galactic Patrol** A search-and-rescue organization formed by the New Republic, its mission was to assist disabled starships.

**Galactic Podracing Circuit Underwriters' Union** A collection of insurance agencies, it provided backing to the various

Podracing arenas and leagues that operated during the years leading up to the Battle of Naboo.

**Galactic Polysapient Medical Center** A multi-sentient-species medical hospital, it was based on the planet Alderaan during the Old Republic, and was home to no less than 73 unique environmental zones and corresponding operating rooms that could treat every known carbon-based form of life found in the galaxy. Its doctors could handle the medical needs of many silicon- and halogen-based life-forms.

**Galactic Power Engineering** A onetime manufacturer of Podracing engines and parts, it also made complete racers like the GPE-3130.

**Galactic Radicals** A criminal band active during the last decades of the Old Republic that horned in on other crime gangs' turf. New members were recruited by Boozoo "Bogey" Boga, who hijacked bounty hunters and liberated their quarry. Any bounties who didn't want to join the gang were quickly disposed of.

**Galactic Rebels** A hologame created in the early years of the New Republic, it let players take on the personae of the heroes of the Alliance in defeating Imperial forces.

**Galactic Registry** A document that described all the peoples and species that joined the galactic government, it was established by the Old Republic and revised during the early years of the New Republic.

**Galactic Representative Commission** A part of the Galactic Senate, it was the body that Jar Jar Binks was elected to before eventually becoming Senior Representative of Naboo.

**Galactic Republic, the** A democratic union of star systems, usually referred to as "the Republic," it predated the Empire by about 25 millennia. Its growth resulted from sophisticated new means of communication and transportation, especially the development of hyperspace travel. Over the millennia, the Republic encompassed millions of inhabited worlds. The government achieved peace throughout the galaxy. Life under the Republic was not utopian, however. Numerous widespread conflicts, such as the Sith War and the Clone Wars, afflicted the entire galaxy. The Republic eventually grew too large and corrupt. Senator Palpatine amassed great power within the Senate and replaced the Republic with the Empire. After the Battle of Endor and the fall of the Empire, the leaders of the Rebel Alliance formed the New Republic, at which point its democratic predecessor became known as the "Old Republic."

**galactic rim** *See also* Outer Rim. The edge of the galaxy.

**galactic roundel** A disk with eight spokes, the ancient icon representing the Galactic Republic dated back to the Bendu monks' study of numerology. The number nine (eight spokes joined to one disk) signified the benevolent presence of the Force in a unitary galaxy. After the fall of the Galactic Republic 1,000 generations later, Emperor Palpatine made the symbol his own by defacing the icon with the removal of two spokes. *See also* Galactic Great Seal.

Galactic Senate Chamber

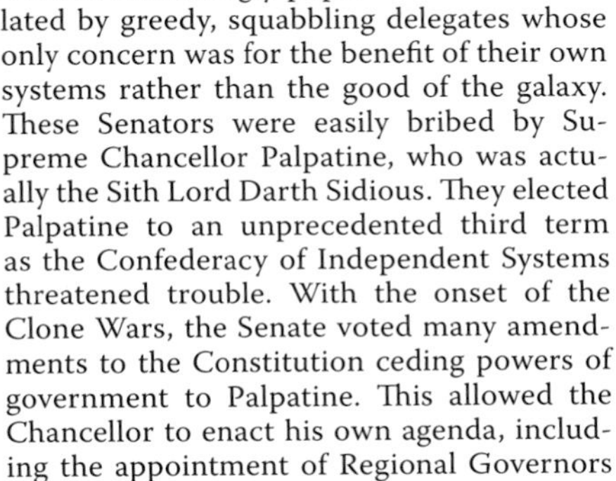

**Galactic Senate** The galaxy-spanning Senate of the Old Republic. There were 1,024 seats available in the Senate Rotunda on Coruscant, so many systems formed alliances in order to obtain a single vote. The Senate was presided over by the Supreme Chancellor, and for many generations was served by the Jedi Order. During the last decades of the Old Republic, the Senate became increasingly populated by greedy, squabbling delegates whose only concern was for the benefit of their own systems rather than the good of the galaxy. These Senators were easily bribed by Supreme Chancellor Palpatine, who was actually the Sith Lord Darth Sidious. They elected Palpatine to an unprecedented third term as the Confederacy of Independent Systems threatened trouble. With the onset of the Clone Wars, the Senate voted many amendments to the Constitution ceding powers of government to Palpatine. This allowed the Chancellor to enact his own agenda, including the appointment of Regional Governors to oversee large portions of the galaxy. In the wake of the Clone Wars, the Galactic Senate was reorganized and renamed the Imperial Senate. But after Emperor Palpatine shifted more and more control to the Regional Governors, he dissolved the Senate shortly before the Battle of Yavin.

**Galactic Senate Chamber** The mammoth chamber where the Republic Senate gathered to debate and create galactic law, its exterior was an impressive domed building 2 kilometers in diameter, which made it easy to identify even in Coruscant's sprawling cityscape. The Senate Chamber's interior included 1,024 platforms used by Senators, diplomats, and other representatives; each platform could detach and hover into the middle of the hall when its occupants wished to make a speech or statement. Dozens of cam droids recorded all proceedings.

The chamber was built many levels above the site of the original Senate Hall in which Vodo-Siosk Baas and Exar Kun battled to the death. Emperor Palpatine closed the Senate Chamber when he dissolved the Imperial Senate, and the New Republic convened its legislature in a newly constructed building called Senate Hall. Thirteen years after the

Galactic Senate

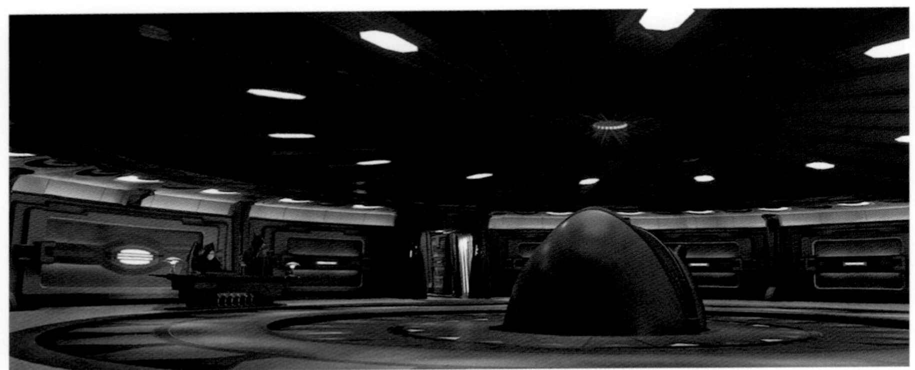

Galactic Senate Chamber Holding Office

Battle of Endor, Senate Hall was damaged in a bombing, causing the New Republic to commission a new structure, the Grand Convocation Chamber. The original Galactic Senate Chamber came into the spotlight one final time when the Yuuzhan Vong used it as an aquatic habitat for their planet-shaping worldbrain.

**Galactic Senate Chamber Holding Office** An area of the Galactic Senate Chamber that was directly below the main chamber, it was where Yoda confronted Darth Sidious after using the Force to knock out two Royal Guards. The Chancellor's central pod rose and brought the battle into the Galactic Senate Chamber itself.

**Galactic Standard Time** The standard form of measuring time throughout the galaxy, it was based on the current time of day on Coruscant. Most chronos had a feature that allowed users to check their own current time against the Galactic Standard.

Galactic Voyager

**Galactic Vacant Building Demolitions Crew** Allegedly formed in response to the growing numbers of abandoned buildings found on planets throughout the Empire at the height of the Galactic Civil War, the unit was under the command of Darth Vader. Its real purpose was to eliminate the ability of the Rebel Alliance to use abandoned structures as safehouses or for secret caches.

***Galactic Voyager*** Admiral Ackbar's flagship Mon Calamari MC90 star cruiser. Some seven years after the Battle of Endor, he took the ship to Anoth in an effort to thwart Caridan Ambassador Furgan's attempt to kidnap Anakin Solo. Although the ship was never at the forefront of the fight against the Yuuzhan Vong, the *Galactic Voyager* remained a symbol of the strength and dedication Ackbar had provided to both the Rebel Alliance and the New Republic. It was continually refitted and maintained as a ship of flagship status, and was later given true flagship status when Admiral Cha Niathal used the vessel as her temporary command ship during the Galactic Alliance's attack on the Confederation meeting at Gilatter VIII, some 10 years after the end of the Yuuzhan Vong War.

Galantos

**Galae, Pash** A young and hyperconfident Rebel computer slicer from Utrost, he helped to decipher Imperial transmissions that passed through the Core. He eventually became a member of a special operations team and was infiltrated into the educational system on Anaxes to assist in the defection of Imperial Admiral Arhul Holt.

**Galak** A dark-skinned young man, he was a student at the Royal House of Learning in the city of Theed on his homeworld of Naboo. Galak also was a volunteer member of the Royal Security Force, and had been trained by Captain Panaka himself. When the Trade Federation invaded his planet, Galak joined the Naboo underground with many of his classmates, supplementing his official duties with clandestine missions for the resistance.

**Galalloy Industries** Generally considered the manufacturer of the first true probe droids, which were developed to search remote planets and asteroids for mineable metals and fuels.

**Galand** The planet where the H'kig religion began; the native Galandans were a near-human species.

**Galan starfighter** A sleek, small starfighter used by Obi-Wan Kenobi and Qui-Gon Jinn 12 years before the Battle of Naboo, it had seats for the pilot and copilot and at least two stations to operate the ship's laser cannons. On loan from Queen Veda of Gala, the starfighter was used by the Jedi to travel to Melida/Daan. Obi-Wan later took an active role in the planet's civil war, using the ship to help the Young destroy the deflection towers surrounding the capital city of Zehava.

**Galantos** A planet located in the Utos system of Farlax sector, it was the homeworld of the Fia. The Koornacht Cluster appeared as a bright oval of light in Galantos's night sky, and was known to the Fia as the Multitude. Its surface was covered with gelatinous pools dotted by small islands, and its landmasses were subjected to regular seismic vibrations. Most of the transportation on Galantos was based on balloons.

Twelve years after the Battle of Endor, the Grannan pilot Plat Mallar escaped from a brutal Yevethan attack on his home planet Polneye and desperately tried to reach Galantos in a short-range TIE interceptor, giving the Republic its first alert about the Yevethan invasion. When Borsk Fey'lya was named Chief of State of the New Republic, he ignored Galantos and the Fia as unimportant, an act that later led the Fia to break off communications with the Republic while negotiating with the Yuuzhan Vong.

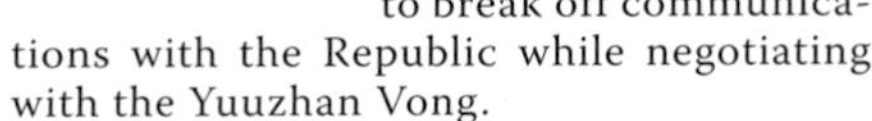

**Galard Stables** A Geonosian hive, it was populated by drones that were forced to fight in the gladiator arena but managed to survive the battle. Although technically exiled from their clan, the aberrants of the Galard Stables were nonetheless revered for their ability to survive.

**Galas** One of a group of young Selkath males tricked into joining the Sith on the planet Manaan at the height of the Jedi Civil War. His companions were told that Galas had returned home, but later a group of Jedi Knights found him tortured and barely alive.

**Galasett** A Kerestian bounty hunter associated with Reglis Taal, he preferred to hunt down other hunters who had broken Imperial laws; he was often fined by the Empire for excessive damage during his hunts.

**Galasol Strip** A wide avenue located near the primary spaceport on the planet Bonadan, it was framed on either side by a collection of overpriced casinos and cantinas.

**Galaxies Opera House** One of the most prestigious theaters on the planet Coruscant during the last years of the Old Republic, it was owned and operated by Romeo Treblanc, whose businesses were secretly funded by Chancellor Palpatine himself. For his assistance in financing the theater, Palpatine received a state-of-the-art private viewing box from which he could conduct the business of ruling and controlling the galaxy. Here he first started informing Anakin Skywalker of his true nature during a Mon Calamari performance of *Squid Lake.*

**Galax Viper volley gun** An anti-vehicle gun produced by Kurtough during the early years of the New Republic, it was a large weapon that employed a collection of missile launchers in a single unit, each designed to fire shortly after the previous one. This produced a curtain effect, with a continuous volley of projectiles striking a vehicle and eliminating most deflector shields.

**galaxy, the** Containing around 400 billion stars, it is a brilliant pinwheel disk nearly 120,000 light-years in diameter. The galaxy was formed approximately five billion years before the Battle of Yavin by the gravitational collapse of a large cloud of dust and gas. It contains nearly a billion inhabited star systems, from uncharted settlements set up by smugglers to megalopolis worlds where scarcely a meter of untouched ground remains. Nearly 70 million of those star systems were sufficiently populated for representation of some sort in the Galactic Republic, a vast bureaucracy responsible for the affairs of more than 100 quadrillion beings. It has been estimated that there are around 20 million forms of sentient life.

*Galaxies Opera House: a performance of* Squid Lake

Upon the discovery of hyperspace, the first galactic scouts struck out from the Core Worlds along two stable hyperspace paths: the Perlemian Trade Route and the Corellian Run. These twin hyperlanes outlined a vast wedge-shaped region of space that was soon dubbed the Slice. Though it contained many of the oldest and best-known planets, the Slice encompassed only a fraction of the known galaxy. Old Republic cartographers divided the galaxy into regions, sectors, and systems. Coruscant was at the confluence of a number of lengthy hyperroutes, including those later named the Martial Cross, the Shawken Spur, the Koros Trunk Line, the Metellos Trade Route, and the Perlemian Trade Route and Corellian Run.

Perhaps surprisingly, scientists knew very little about what existed outside the galaxy. A small band of empty space surrounds it, and some scientists theorized that just turbulence existed beyond this band. No one ever had witnessed any evidence of an extragalactic

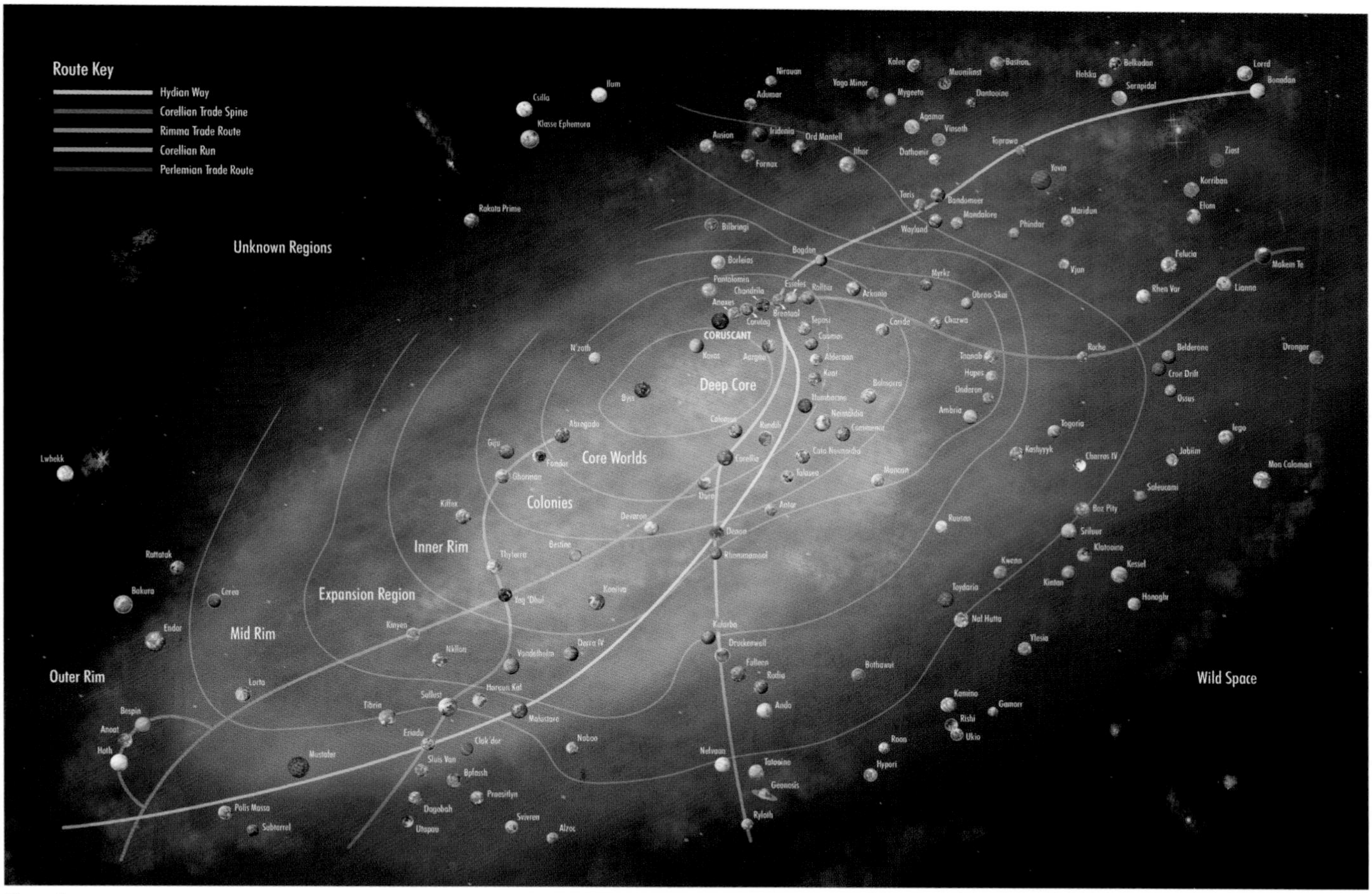

*The galaxy*

object entering the galaxy, and several brave explorers and some desperate outlaws being chased by authorities vanished into the turbulence of the galactic rim. But the extragalactic invasion of the Yuuzhan Vong shattered the very roots of scientists' understanding of the nature of the galaxy and the universe, just as it shattered large parts of the known galaxy itself. The death toll for the entire war was nearly incalculable, though the figure most often quoted was 365 trillion.

**Galaxy-15** One of Kuat Drive Yards' most powerful ion engines, it was used on the Nebulon-B frigate.

***Galaxy Befuddled, A*** A somewhat sensationalistic holodocumentary produced by Dr. A. Rahring on the subject of the Dorumaa leviathan.

***Galaxy Chance*** A floating casino, it was a modified Corellian CR90 corvette that was created as a smaller version of the *Errant Venture* and was defended by six TIE-wing Uglies. Some years after the Battle of Endor, the Khuiumin Survivors had hoped to execute Zlece Oonaar by intercepting the ship.

**Galaxy Gladiator Federation** The governing body that controlled the underground world of arena gladiator fighting, it was faced with opposition from a number of fronts shortly before the Clone Wars. Mainly, the federation lacked sufficient planning to handle the wide variety of alien abilities and disparate fighting styles found throughout the galaxy.

Melik Galerha

**Galaxy Gun** The cloned Emperor's ultimate weapon, it fired "intelligent" projectiles into hyperspace. Each of the well-shielded lightspeed torpedoes could exit hyperspace at precise coordinates, find its target, and destroy it. No ordinary projectiles, the torpedoes carried particle disintegrators that neutralized all security shields; when they struck, they initiated massive nucleonic chain reactions. The Galaxy Gun, designed by Umak Leth, obliterated the Alliance's Pinnacle Base and the entire fifth moon of Da Soocha, although Alliance top command escaped just in time. In the end, the gun discharged when R2-D2 reset the coordinates of the Emperor's flagship, which slammed into the weapon, destroying the ship, the weapon, and the Emperor's throneworld, the planet Byss.

**Galaxy News Service** One of the original signatory sponsors of the Corporate Sector Authority, the news agency was second only to Imperial HoloVision in terms of overall readers during the height of the New Order.

Galaxy Gun

Ratambo Gale

***Galaxy Wanderer*** A luxury starship in the Corporate Sector, it was hijacked and ransacked by the Malorm Family.

**Gale** A frozen ball of ice-covered rock, it was the eighth planet of the Hoth's Brand system, located in the Teraab sector of galaxy's Mid Rim. It was orbited by a pair of moons.

**Gale, Lord** One of the many Jedi Knights who gathered on Ruusan to fight against Lord Kaan and the Brotherhood of Darkness, he was killed in one of the early struggles against the Sith.

**Gale, Ratambo** A noted member of the Malkite Poisoners, he was hired by unknown forces during the early years of the New Republic to rattle the governor of Chandrila, Jovive Centi, by killing her bodyguard, Tristan Pex. His mission completed, Gale melted into the crowd and implicated a group of offworlders in the crime.

**Gale, Reina** A smuggler during the early years of the New Republic, as a child she had been turned over to a Hutt crime lord to cover a gambling debt.

**galek** These long-lived trees native to Mandalore could thrive for centuries. The groves of silver-leaved galek trees were among the few natural areas on the planet that the Yuuzhan Vong did not attempt to destroy.

**Galen** A Radnoran scientist researching toxins for bioweapons, he made a deal with the Avoni to unleash a plague that forced the evacuation of Radnor, making it easier for an Avoni invasion force to sweep in and take control of the planet. But the plan was discovered by Jedi Knights who were sent to Radnor to aid in the evacuation. Galen's sister Curi held him at gunpoint for more than two hours before security forces arrived and took him into custody.

**Galentro Heavy Works** A family of companies whose commercial pursuits included gas mining, manufacturing, and other heavy industries, mainly in the Velcar Free Commerce Zone.

**Galerha, Melik** A dark-skinned human male Jedi with long sideburns, he attended meetings in the Jedi briefing room on Coruscant during the Clone Wars.

**Galey** A cook aboard the *Mon Remonda* during the New Republic's hunt for Warlord Zsinj, he was a secret agent for Zsinj. By speaking nonsense phrases to certain previously brainwashed nonhumans, he triggered in them a command to kill or destroy specified targets, two of which were Wedge Antilles and the *Mon Remonda* itself. He was detained by security forces before any commands were successful.

**GalFactorial** A biomedical company, it was one of several that bid for the rights to build a bacta refinery on Verkuyl about three years after the Battle of Endor. GalFactorial had a refinery on New Cov that was built on schedule and under budget.

**Gal'fian'deprisi** The largest city on Galantos, it was half sunk into the gelatin of the Gar'glum Sea. With no landing pads for starships, it was accessible mainly by Vert'bo airships from the Chirk'pn Wastes.

**Galia** Daughter of King Ommin and Queen Amanoa, she was heir to the throne of the planet Onderon four millennia before the Galactic Civil War. During the Beast Wars of Onderon, Galia arranged to be kidnapped by the beast-riders, then married the Beast-Lord Oron Kira, signfying an end to the violence between the beast-riders and the citizens of Iziz.

Galia

Galidraan

**Galidraan** A snowy planet, it was the site of a major battle between Mandalorian shock troopers and Jedi Knights led by Jedi Master Dooku. Several years before the Battle of Naboo, the Mandalorians were asked by the governor of Galidraan to quell an insurrection. But the governor had been paid by Vizsla to lay a trap for the Mandalorians. The governor, claiming that the Mandalorians were slaughtering the populace because of their political beliefs, called for help from the Jedi. Half of the Jedi task force was killed while the Mandalorians were wiped out—except for Jango Fett, who was turned over to the governor. After years of serving as a slave, Fett escaped and returned to Galidraan to claim the armor of the Mandalorians and enact revenge on Vizsla.

Galidyn

**Galidyn** A sentient species of huge, scaly lizards from Fyodos who could live to be thousands of years old. Each Galidyn mating produced just one egg every 100 years. The Galidyn had keen intellects and intense curiosity, and spoke a highly refined, pure version of language used by the Fyodoi. Normally peaceful, they became ferocious fighters when cornered or angered.

**Gall** A moon circling the gas giant Zhar in an Outer Rim system, it was the site of a failed attempt to rescue Han Solo after he had been frozen into a carbonite block. An Imperial shipyard on the moon was home to two Star Destroyers and their TIE fighters. Boba Fett's ship, *Slave I,* was spotted on Gall with Solo aboard. During the rescue attempt, Princess Leia Organa, Lando Calrissian, Chewbacca, and C-3PO in the *Millennium Falcon* followed Corellian pilot Dash Rendar to the spot where *Slave I* was parked. But the *Falcon* was attacked by TIE fighters, and Fett escaped with Solo still aboard. The Alliance's Rogue Squadron also fought at Gall.

**Gall, Sheriff** "Sheriff" of the Landing on Engebo V, the former miner had lost an eye in an accident and was given compensation plus a job as security chief at the mine.

**Gallada** A noted crime lord who worked on the planet Lianna during the last decades of the Old Republic, he moved goods and information through the Tion Commerce Tower.

**Galladinium Galactic Exports** A technology retailer known for its gladiator walkers, which were used in many illegal war games. Orders were generated through its Datalog of Fantastic Technology.

**Gallamby, Daclif** A Diktat of Corellia, he replaced Dupas Thomree after his death a few years before the Battle of Yavin. Thrackan Sal-Solo served as Gallamby's second in command. Before Sal-Solo had a chance to overthrow Gallamby, the Empire was defeated at Endor and Gallamby decided to flee with half of the planet's treasury.

**Gallan** A lieutenant under Captain Jace Dallin aboard the *Mersel Kebir,* he protected his homeworld of Rendili during the height of the Clone Wars. When Dallin wanted to turn the planet's fleet of Dreadnaughts over to the Old Republic, Gallan joined a mutiny and wanted to eliminate Dallin and Jedi Master Plo Koon on the spot, rather than hold them hostage. Lieutenant Mellor Yago, leader of the mutiny, wanted to keep them as bargaining chips to force the Republic to withdraw from Rendili. Yago attempted to execute a linked jump into hyperspace, but a daring mission by Anakin Skywalker disabled Yago's flagship and provided enough cover for Obi-Wan Kenobi and Quinlan Vos to rescue Master Koon and Captain Dallin.

Gallandro

**Gallandro** The fastest gunfighter in the galaxy, he was so amoral that killing 1 or 100 made little difference to him. In the end, it was his own "victory" over Han Solo that did him in. Gallandro was born on the backworld of Ylix. He saw his parents murdered by offworld terrorists, grew up in orphanages, and joined the military as soon as he was eligible. He became addicted to danger and conflict, and when he mustered out of the militia he decided to become a freelance blaster for hire. He looked the role, with his close-cropped graying hair and long, gold-beaded mustache. Gallandro always wore expensive, well-tailored clothing. His blaster holster was slung low, and his white scarf hung like a badge of office.

Over the years, a death mark was put on his head by more than 100 planets, but no bounty hunter was brave enough—or foolish enough—to take him on.

He was hired by Odumin, a powerful regional administrator for the Corporate Sector Authority, to take out a five-member crime family. He did the job so well that Odumin put him on retainer for other "messy" jobs. Gallandro was on the planet Ammuud when he first encountered Han Solo, who had been trapped by security police. Han tricked him into grabbing a case that sent shocks to Gallandro's gun hand, and Gallandro let Solo go. They later encountered each other on Dellalt, where both were searching for the long-lost treasure of Xim the Despot. Han found the treasure chambers and Gallandro challenged him to a duel. Gallandro fired first, hitting Han in the shoulder, and then attempted to kill one of Han's associates. But the chamber had been rigged to combat such disruptions, and a dozen lasers shot forth and incinerated Gallandro on the spot.

Gall

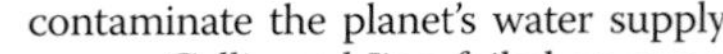

**Gallandro, Anja** Daughter of gunslinger Gallandro, she was a battle-hungry young woman who became friends with Jacen and Jaina Solo and the other young Jedi Knights at Luke Skywalker's Jedi academy. She originally hoped to get revenge against Han Solo for her father's death, but after the twins helped her through her spice addiction she changed her mind. Lando Calrissian offered her a job as a pilot, and she accepted.

***Gallant (1)*** An Alliance escort carrier, it was active during the height of the Galactic Civil War.

***Gallant (2)*** A *Victory*-class Star Destroyer, it was dispatched to Murkhana during the final stages of the Clone Wars.

***Gallant (3)*** A New Republic *Majestic*-class heavy cruiser, it was part of the Fifth Battle Group activated in the Yevethan crisis. It took part in the unsuccessful blockade of Doornik-319, but survived the counterassault.

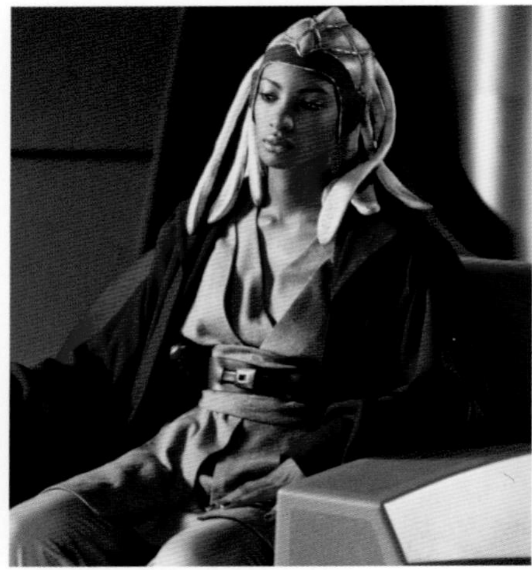

*Jedi Master Adi Gallia*

***Gallant Haven*** An assault frigate Mark II capital ship, it was active a couple of years before the Battle of Yavin.

***Gallant Sun*** A *Victory*-class Imperial Star Destroyer, it was destroyed by Rebel Alliance forces at the shipyards at Pendari. The Alliance employed a computer slicer to discover the ship's refitting schedule, and the information allowed Rebels to destroy the ship with minimal loss of life.

**Gallapraxis system** A star system, it once was under the control of the crime lord Drex.

**Galle, Lieutenant** A member of the 327th Star Corps of the Grand Army of the Republic during the Clone Wars, his official designation was CT-6734. Lieutenant Galle was part of the mission dispatched to Felucia to capture Shu Mai, and he was assigned to the task force led by Jedi Padawans Zonder and Drake Lo'gaan. When the command to execute Order 66 was issued by Emperor Palpatine, Lieutenant Galle killed Barris Offee. In the aftermath of the Clone Wars, Lieutenant Galle was assigned to Commander Bly's team, which was dispatched to subjugate the planet Yutusk.

**Galleefryn II** A jungle planet, it was freed from Imperial control by the Rebel Alliance in a struggle that took place more than 10 years before the Battle of Endor.

*Lieutenant Galle*

**Gallia, Adi** A beautiful, brown-skinned Jedi Master during the last years of the Old Republic, she had been born to Corellian parents who were diplomats on Coruscant. She was quickly recognized for her strength with the Force, and after years of training, she became one of the 12 members of the Jedi Council shortly before the Battle of Naboo. Her skills with a lightsaber were notable in that she used a reverse, one-handed grip. Adi Gallia chose to dress in the plain brown robes of a Jedi, but wore a Tholoth headdress.

Gallia was known among the Jedi for her intuition and information-gathering abilities, and maintained a vast network of informants across Coruscant. Through this network, she discovered that the Trade Federation was building droid-controlled starfighters and was planning to blockade the small planet of Naboo in an effort to force the Old Republic to lift its taxation of trade routes. The Trade Federation attempted to stop her on Esseles, but she was rescued by Qui-Gon Jinn and Obi-Wan Kenobi. She brought her information to the attention of Chancellor Valorum, who requested that two Jedi be dispatched to Naboo to negotiate a settlement without the interference of the Senate.

Adi Gallia saw plenty of action. As part of a Jedi mission to Kegan in search of a potential Jedi, she demonstrated her skills as one of the Order's best pilots. During the Stark Hyperspace Conflict, she successfully commandeered Iaco Stark's personal ship and escorted Senator Valorum and Nute Gunray back to Coruscant. She and her Padawan Siri Tachi went to Simpla-12 to help rescue Qui-Gon Jinn from Jenna Zan Arbor and uncovered a plot to contaminate the planet's water supply. Gallia and Jinn foiled an assassination attempt on Supreme Chancellor Valorum on the Avenue of Core Worlds. Later she had a face-to-face confrontation with bounty hunter Aurra Sing, who had just murdered two Jedi and a squad of Republic Guards; with Sing almost in her control, Gallia was knocked unconscious by one of the hunter's booby traps. Gallia also was part of a Jedi team sent to Kiffu to deal with Quinlan Vos and the presence of the Dark Jedi Volfe Karkko.

Although she chose not to use it unless all other options had failed, Adi Gallia owned a crimson-bladed lightsaber. Just prior to the Battle of Geonosis, she was dispatched to the Karthakk system, where she teamed up with Nym and the Lok Revenants to smash the plans of Cavik Toth to use trihexalon on the clone troopers of the Grand Army of the Republic. She remained with Nym for many months, until the Karthakk system was finally secured. At the height of the Clone Wars, Gallia was part of a task force dispatched to the graveyard planet of Boz Pity, some two years after the Battle of Geonosis. The landing party was forced to crash-land on the planet to bypass a Separatist blockade. But once on the planet, the Jedi discovered that General Grievous was waiting for them. After Grievous killed Soon Bayts, he turned his attention to Master Gallia. With his arms fully separated into combat mode, Grievous overpowered Gallia. He strangled her with a pair of arms while gutting her with a lightsaber held by a third, killing the Jedi Master.

*Anja Gallandro*

*Gallian tripion*

**Gallian tripion** An insectoid species native to Gall, it grasped its victims in huge claws while its tail slashed and injected a deadly poison.

**Gallinore** A planet in the Hapes Cluster, it was home to extremely valuable rainbow gems. The gems were actually silicon-based life-forms that matured after thousands of years and glowed with an inner light. The planet was deeply forested and reminiscent of Kashyyyk. Dimitor was a city of Gallinore made up of green marble, with tall trees lining its streets. Jaina Solo and the surviving Jedi from Myrkr, including Lowbacca, Tenel Ka, and Kyp Durron, flew a Hapan freighter to Gallinore to study the *Trickster*, the Yuuzhan Vong ship they'd used to escape. Gallinore contained many bioengineered creatures, and teemed with life. It was here that Jaina Solo and Sinsor Khal discovered the secrets of the Yuuzhan Vong coral implants that enslaved their victims.

***Galliot*** A Ripoblus modified CR90 corvette, it was used to attack the Dimok science station *Youst.*

**Gallo, Boss** A Gungan who lived some 3,000 years before the Battle of Naboo, he ruled the underwater city of Otoh Sancture and refused to take part in petty battles that were fought among rival Gungan clans. He strongly believed that war among the Gungans was amoral. When Boss Rogoe attacked Otoh Sancture and eventually destroyed it in an effort to prevent Boss Gallo from choosing sides in yet another Gungan battle, Boss Gallo had no choice but to strike back. In the war that followed, Boss Gallo's armies wiped out those of Boss Rogoe, and from the rubble of the battle Boss Gallo built the wondrous city of Otoh Gunga, designed to unite all the Gungan tribes. For that, he was regarded as a hero by later Gungans.

**Galloa II** A planet that was home to the nonhuman Wind Dancers.

**Gallofree Yards, Inc.** Maker of the Gallofree Medium Transport (the GR-75) used by the Rebel Alliance on Hoth, it was a small starship manufacturer that tried to compete in the crowded transport and freighter markets. Despite repeated product overhauls and slick marketing, the company seldom turned a profit. Gallofree went bankrupt several years prior to the Battle of Yavin; many of the company's remaining transports found their way into the Rebel Alliance's fleet.

***Gallon*** A Mugaari cargo ferry, it was destroyed when the Empire subjugated the Tungra sector.

**Gallou, Rennie** A Rebel Alliance supply officer, she worked at the Massassi base on Yavin 4.

**Galney, Lady** A stately middle-aged woman, she was one of Queen Mother Tenel Ka's many aides in the years following the Swarm War. Lady Galney was serving as Tenel Ka's chamberlain when an assassination attempt was made on the Queen Mother's life by Aurra Sing, an event that coincided with the presence on the planet of Han Solo and his wife, Leia Organa Solo. The Solos were seen leaving Hapes with Sing, and they were implicated in the assassination plot despite the fact that they had been waiting to see the Queen Mother in her Special Salon the entire time.

When Jaina Solo and Zekk arrived to offer assistance, Lady Galney refused to allow them to go after the trio, citing political and moral questions. However, she allowed them to travel to various planets that might have been on the Solos' exit vector; that led them to the Villa Solis estate on Terephon, where they were attacked by Lady Galney's older sister, the Ducha Galney. In the ensuing chaos, Lady Galney realized that one of her consorts had been secretly relaying information on the Queen Mother to her sister, so Ducha Galney was able to provide the Heritage Council enough information to put together the assassination plot, as well as stage a coup attempt by forming its own fleet of warships to attack Hapes. After the Heritage Fleet, partly commanded by Ducha Galney, was defeated, Lady Galney told the Queen Mother everything. The royal allowed her not only to remain free, but also to serve as the guardian of the Chume'da, Allana, until the other conspirators could be brought to justice.

Dor Gal-Ram

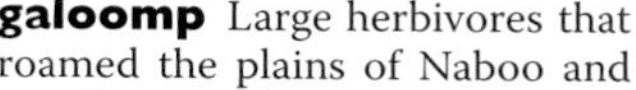

**galoomp** Large herbivores that roamed the plains of Naboo and the deserts of Tatooine, they looked reptilian but were actually mammals. Galoomps were named for the unique sound they made when foraging for food at dawn or dusk. Their tails ended in a bony knob filled with loose pieces of cartilage that were shaken to warn of approaching danger. A segmented, horny, and ridged hide on their backsides protected against predators and seemed to insulate against moisture loss. The desert galoomps buried themselves in the sand to escape wicked sandstorms.

Galoomps

**Galov sector** An area of the galaxy located in the Outer Rim Territories.

**Galpos II** A desolate Outer Rim world, it was part of the Woldona system. It was long suspected of harboring pirate gangs.

**Gal-Ram, Dor** An ancient Sith warlord active about 5,000 years before the birth of Luke Skywalker. When unrest arose in the Sith Empire, Gal-Ram joined forces with Ludo Kressh and Horak-Mul to oust the reigning Dark Lord of the Sith, Naga Sadow. However, Sadow had goaded his enemies into the assault and had a hidden fleet ready to meet them. Dor Gal-Ram was murdered when his crew, many of whom were spies loyal to Sadow, threw off their disguises and butchered their captain.

**Galt, Loowli** A human from Naboo last seen on Coruscant. The Techno Union placed a bounty on this Coruscant officer's head.

**Galtea** A colony planet on the fringes of explored space, it was located on the boundary between the most densely inhabited parts of Kathol sector and the Marcol Void. The Galtea Run was a hyperspace pathway through the Marcol Void, connecting Galtea with Timbra Ott and linking the main section of Kathol sector to the Kathol Outback. It was one of two such hyperspace routes through the Void.

**Galu** The capital city of the planet Gala, it was once grand and impressive, but became run-down during the last years of the Beju-Tallah Dynasty. The city was built on three hills, with the royal castle situated atop the tallest, making it visible from any location.

**Galvason, Dana "Deke"** A brash tramp freighter captain from Bakura, she was one of the few with clearance to travel through the Deep Core Security Zone at the height of the New Order. Though the lucrative Imperial contracts paid well, her rebellious streak left her hating the Empire. She wasn't above secretly smuggling Rebel agents aboard her modified YT-2000 transport, the *Bakuran Blade.*

**Galvoni III** The location of an Imperial military communications complex, the planet was infiltrated by Alliance historian Voren Na'al after the Battle of Yavin in order to gain more information about the Death Star project.

**Gama, Tira** A native of the Corellian colony world of Tralus, she met and married Denn Solo and gave birth to twins just before pirates attacked the colony. She managed to flee with her daughter Tiion. Her husband fled with the boy twin but was never heard from again. When Gama returned to Corellia, her father wiped out all memories of Denn to make it easier on her.

**Gama system** The home system of a quasi-humanoid species, the Gama-Senn. Six years after the Battle of Endor, the leader of the Gama-Senn pledged the system's allegiance to the cloned Emperor after witnessing a demonstration of Palpatine's devastating Galaxy Gun.

**Gamandar** The twin planet of Iskalon, it was swiftly subjugated at the height of the New Order. The Empire erected a huge citadel to serve as the system's main garrison. Eventually, it was destroyed by Lando Calrissian and Drebble.

**Gamb, Tord** A con man and scam artist during the early years of the New Republic, he later managed to steal information on the Republic's defense net around Asmall, and was sought by authorities to prevent him from selling his stolen information to the remnants of the Empire. Republic military officers like Airen Cracken also wanted to try to convince Gamb to work for the Republic.

**Game Chambers of Questal** A collection of puzzle-filled rooms maintained by Moff Bandor on Questal during the Galactic Civil War, the chambers included a space simulator, a laser maze, a pit of winds, a quarry, and a hurlothrumbic generator. Filling the chambers and connecting tunnels were creatures and outlaws captured on Questal by using the generator. For Bandor, they were just playthings. A group of Alliance agents, searching for Tiree, managed to successfully negotiate the chambers and destroy the generator.

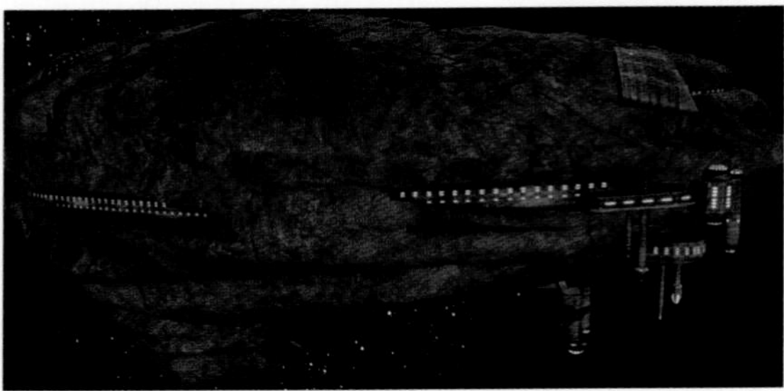
Gamma Station

**gameboard** A holographic projection table used for amusement purposes in a game such as dejarik, it had three-dimensional holograms that competed on its surface at the direction of players who tapped commands into attached keypads.

***Gamer*** An Alliance shuttle group, it was destroyed during the Galactic Civil War when it took part in the failed assassination of then–Vice Admiral Thrawn when he arrived at the NL-1 station.

**Gamgalon** A Krish crime lord who controlled the hunting of sentient Morodin during safaris on the planet Varonat, he got much of his funding from Jabba the Hutt. His business was actually a front for the harvesting of Yagaran aleudrupe plants, which were fertilized with Morodin slime, producing a high-powered blaster fuel. When Talon Karrde discovered the operation, Gamgalon nearly killed Karrde, but Mara Jade killed Gamgalon first.

Gamorrean

*Gameboard in the* Millennium Falcon

**Gamine** A native of Constancia with telepathic powers like her fellow sentients, she helped lead the resistance to Imperial control. With the help of Han Solo, Chewbacca, and Luke Skywalker, Gamine was able to elude Imperials and keep her people free.

**Gamma Company** One of the first teams of clone commandos trained by Kal Skirata on Kamino during the buildup to the Clone Wars.

**Gamma Corps** One of two elite fighting units of the Galactic Alliance military—the second was the Space Rangers—that were headquartered at the General Crix Madine Military Reserve during the years following the Yuuzhan Vong War.

**Gamma Intelligence Group** An intelligence-gathering branch of the Imperial Security Bureau, it operated from a base on Gall at the height of the New Order.

**Gamma Squad (1)** A team of clone commandos, it was among the first units sent to Geonosis at the onset of the Clone Wars. The unit, like other commando units, was misused by the commanders of the Old Republic, and took heavy losses. Only the commando known as Stoker survived the Battle of Geonosis. Gamma Squad was later re-formed and dispatched to the planet Cularin during the final stages of the Clone Wars. Gamma Squad was one of the few teams of clones that had five regular members, and they referred to themselves simply as Gamma One through Gamma Five. The team managed to infiltrate a droid control computer center and replaced Separatist command codes with Republic-controlled versions.

Gamorr

**Gamma Squad (2)** A group of stormtroopers involved in the Empire's invasion of Cloud City after the Battle of Hoth. One of its members blasted C-3PO after the protocol droid stumbled upon them.

**Gamma Station** A space station established on the surface of a lumpy asteroid near Ord Mantell, it was controlled by a group of bounty hunters at the height of the New Order. Much of the station's lower interior levels were a sort of training facility. The bounty hunters at Gamma Station were in league with the Empire, and were ambushing unsuspecting starships in order to capture their passengers and crew and sell them to the Rak'qua gang.

***Gamma*-class assault shuttle** *see* assault shuttle, *Gamma*-class.

**Gammalin** A dry and rocky human colony, it was wiped out by "the Emperor's Plague." Fonterrat unknowingly released the plague, which he had brought from the Imperial storehouse. Nolaa Tarkona had booby-trapped her payment with a small sample of the plague, and it was unleashed when Fonterrat passed tainted credits to the Gammalin population. Fonterrat was thrown in jail and eventually died there when his human captors succumbed to the plague.

**GAM missile** Developed by Merr-Sonn, the Gravity Activated Mode missile could home in on intense infrared sources such as vehicle exhausts. It was also equipped with an onboard computer that could target the gravity-wave anomalies produced by repulsorlift usage.

**Gamor Run** A legendary long-haul smuggling route, it became overrun by hijackers and pirates.

**Gamorr** The pleasant home planet of the Gamorrean species located in the Opoku system, it had widely varying temperatures and terrain ranging from frozen tundra to deep forests. Gamorr's history was marked by almost constant periods of war among the dim-witted Gamorrean males. The world was also home to furry, bloodsucking parasites called morrts, which Gamorreans looked upon with affection and allowed to feed on their body fluids. Native species also included snoruuks, quizzers, and watchbeasts. There were very few large settlements on the planet; the largest were controlled and populated by entire clans of powerful females. During the decades leading up to the Battle of Ruusan, Gamorr was the site of a minor Sith training academy, where Sith Warriors and Sith Marauders trained for battle.

**Gamorrean** A brutish, porcine species characterized by upturned snouts, green skin, and tusks, they were infamous for their slow minds and great strength. Averaging about 1.8 meters in height, Gamorreans made excellent heavy laborers and mercenaries, and a number served as guards in Jabba the Hutt's desert palace on Tatooine. Gamorreans could understand many languages, but their own limited vocal apparatus—they spoke largely in grunts and other guttural noises—prevented them from conversing in other tongues.

In their matriarchal culture, females handled the productive work of farming, hunting, manufacturing, and running businesses. The males spent all their time training for and fighting in wars. Gamorreans lived in clans headed by matrons who ordered the males to fight from early spring to late fall. Early traders turned out to be slavers, but some Gamorreans found work as guards, mercenaries, and even bounty hunters.

***Gamu*** A Ripoblus *Lambda*-class shuttle group, it saw action during the Sepan Civil War as well as in battle against the Empire.

**Gan, Elis'** In the years following the Battle of Naboo, he was commanding officer of Thaereian Security Facility Number 12, the former headquarters of the Office of Peace and Security in Gadrin on the planet Cularin.

Yith Ganar

**ganadote** An immense creature produced by the Yuuzhan Vong to serve as a form of meeting room, it was little more than a 15-meter-long disk at birth. A ganadote consisted of a mouth, an anus, a large canal connecting them, an opening into side stomach chambers, and a tongue. Ganadotes were raised by keepers who knew how to train the creatures to grow a certain way. As it grew, a ganadote generated many smaller side stomachs, which were altered by artificially administered hormones to become chambers and rooms. The organic valves that shut off the stomachs became doors, and the ganadote itself became an immense collection of meeting rooms and conference areas. Well-crafted ganadotes were trained to allow their tongues to be used as portable podiums. By applying pressue with a foot or staff, a Yuuzhan Vong could tell the ganadote to move the tongue virtually anywhere within its body.

**Ganar, Yith** This Kel Dor defied naysayers by building a functional Y-wing starfighter from parts she salvaged from a scrapyard during the early years of the New Republic. A loner, she left her homeworld of Dorin and briefly took a job as a starship mechanic, until a Bothan captain openly questioned her skills. Rather than proving him wrong, Yith Ganar simply gave him what he was expecting. When his starship exploded while trying to enter hyperspace, Ganar felt nothing more than a bit of self-satisfaction. Her mean streak, however, frequently got her into trouble.

**Ganash** A violet gas giant planet, it was the fifth world in the Both system, and was orbited by 14 moons. It was named for a character in Bothan mythology.

**Ganath system** Hidden in a vast, radioactive gas cloud near Nal Hutta, this system was completely cut off from the rest of galactic civilization. Spacers from Nal Hutta who attempted to penetrate the gas cloud never returned. Thus isolated, Ganath's culture developed more slowly than the rest of the galaxy's, and much of its technology operated on steam power. The Ganathan space fleet included the massive steam-powered battleship *Robida Colossus.* For years, the system was ruled by King Empatojayos Brand, a Jedi Knight who was rescued by the Ganathans after his ship was destroyed. Leia and Han Solo traveled to the capital city of Ganath after they flew into the gas cloud in an attempt to escape from Boba Fett.

**Gand** A planet of swirling clouds of gaseous ammonia, it was home to a species of the same name. Gand was located in the Outer Rim near the area known as the Centrality. Its society consisted of pocket colonies separated by enshrouding mists, and the Gand government was a long-standing totalitarian monarchy. Locating fugitives in the thick gases was the responsibility of Gand findsmen, who worshipped the mists and used religious rituals to lead them to their targets. Some Gand findsmen later found work as bounty hunters, including the notorious Zuckuss, although others, such as Rogue Squadron pilot Ooryl Qrygg, chose nobler professions.

The Gand were covered with a hard carapace. Their impressive regenerative capability let them replace lost limbs. One subspecies of Gands did not breathe, feeding their metabolism through eating instead of respiration; they spoke by drawing in gases and expelling them through the Gand voicebox. Another Gand subspecies evolved as ammonia breathers. Ruetsavii, a group of famous Gands, were sent by the Elders of Gand to observe notable subjects and determine if

Gand shockprod staff

they were worthy of referring to themselves in the first person when they became janwuine. After the Rogue Squadron captured Thyferra, Ooryl Qrygg was named janwuine, and the squadron was invited to Gand to help celebrate the momentous occasion.

**Gand, Eli** During the era of the Jedi Civil War, he worked as a merchant near the Czerka office on the planet Kashyyyk. Eli Gand held Matton Dasol in virtual slavery after Gand ambushed Dasol's crew and stole their starship. He convinced Dasol that he was paying a debt his former shipmates owed him. A passing Jedi Knight learned of Gand's duplicity and exposed him as a fraud, leading to Dasol's release.

**Gand discharger** The pinnacle of Gand technology, developed four millennia before the Galactic Civil War. A discharger could both paralyze and slay opponents with ease. The potent weapons were extremely rare and highly coveted by the few Gand who earned them.

**Gand shockprod staff** A favorite tool among Gand findsmen, this resilient, ancient weapon looked like a staff, one end of which ended in a V-shaped pair of electrically charged prods.

**Gandan, Bey** A red-haired Jedi Knight who accompanied Klin-Fa Gi on a mission to infiltrate the Yuuzhan Vong ranks. He and Gi were captured and enslaved aboard a shaper's worldship. They discovered that the shapers had been working on a method to exterminate Jedi Knights, and managed to steal a qahsa with information on the project. Attempting to return to the Republic, Bey was recaptured by the Yuuzhan Vong. Gi, meanwhile, convinced Uldir Lochett and the crew of the *No Luck Required* to launch a rescue attempt for Bey after returning to Wayland to recover the organic key to the qahsa. But unknown to his friends, Bey had been turned to the dark side by the Yuuzhan Vong and was to be

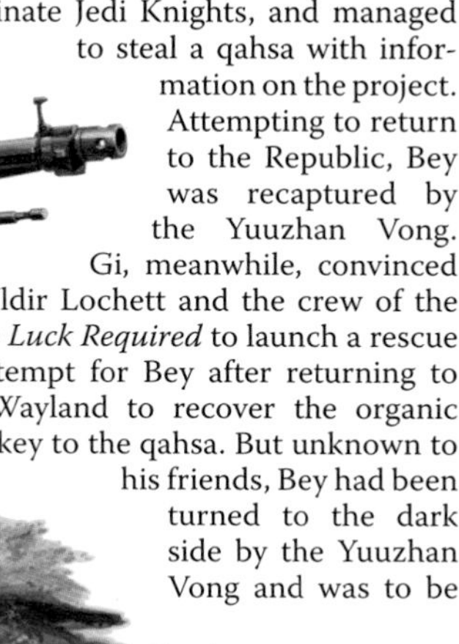

Gand

the delivery mechanism for a virus developed to destroy alazhi trees, the source of bacta. A shaper's villip was implanted in his skull, allowing Viith Yalu and Tsaa Qalu to communicate with Bey and give him orders. He nearly succeeded in tricking his friends into taking him to Thyferra, but Lochett figured out that Bey was the virus carrier. Bey was cut down in a lightsaber battle with Gi and Lochett, and the small amount of virus he was able to disperse was quickly eradicated.

**Gandder's Spin** A starfighter maneuver, it involved a pilot shunting all power to one set of engines while applying full braking power to the opposite side's vents. After about four seconds, brake power was cut to zero and thrust was cut in half and spread across all engines. The result was that the fighter spun wildly for a few seconds around its center of mass before shooting off on a new trajectory. Often, the maneuver was used as cover for a group of proton torpedoes fired at a target just before the spin began.

**Gandeal** A "partner planet" to the military world of Fondor, it was the source of many raw materials used by the Imperial shipyards there.

**Gandeal-Fondor hyperlane** A seldom used hyperlane, it was blazed by the Empire to move ships efficiently between Fondor and Coruscant. Baffle provided Han Solo and Droma with the necessary jump coordinates to the Gandeal-Fondor hyperlane, allowing them to find the *Trevee* before the arrival of the Yuuzhan Vong fleet.

**Gandeid IV** A temperate, low-gravity world, it was the primary planet in the Gandeid system. It was home to the Gandeidan cooha, a large avian predator with slashing teeth for attack.

**Gandish, Phylo** A retired pilot from Naboo. Gandish's family owned a galactic transportation company. She was present at the ceremony that united the Naboo and the Gungans in the wake of the Battle of Naboo.

**Gandle Ott** The primary world in the Ott system, it also was the site of one of the first settlements in the Kathol sector some six centuries before the Battle of Endor. Known as a "gasper" to its original colonists, Gandle Ott was a mild planet with a temperate atmosphere that could sustain most humanoid life. During the early years of the New Republic, the planet was often referred to as Little Coruscant, at least in the Kathol sector. At that time, the population of Gandle Ott was counted in the billions, and the planet was known as an industrial power in the sector. The planetary government was partial to the New Republic, despite the fact that it was nominally under the control of Moff Kentor Sarne.

**Gandolo IV** A barren, rocky moon in the Outer Rim. A group of Wookiee settlers aided by Chewbacca were attempting to establish a colony here when they were discovered by the bounty hunter Bossk. The tracker and his gang, working for the Imperial sector governor, abandoned their attempt to capture the Wookiees after Han Solo landed the *Millennium Falcon* on top of an Imperial troopship, killing all aboard and stranding others on the moon's surface.

**Gandorthral Atmospherics** A manufacturer of survival and atmospheric processing equipment, its slogan was "Serving all worlds polluted by the Empire since the Battle of Yavin."

**Gandril, Moff** An Imperial Moff who was in charge of several worlds in the Colonies at the height of the Galactic Civil War, he ordered the execution of Earnst Kamiel on the planet Haldeen. Moff Gandril chose members of the firing squad by selecting a shooter from each of the 54 systems that had given Kamiel the death sentence.

**Gandroff** A gruff, aging former swoop bike racer, he lived on Tatooine.

**Gandrossi VI** A planet in the Perinn sector, it was controlled by Imperial Governor Desh at the height of the Galactic Civil War.

**Ganeed** The sister of Meenon, she was a tall Senali who often wore pink coral studded in her short dark hair. Ganeed was a member of the Banoosh-Walore clan.

**Ganet** A member of the Chiss faction that opposed the ideals of Soontir Fel and the Nuruodo syndic during the Yuuzhan Vong War, she and her comrades arranged to assassinate Fel's family when Luke Skywalker arrived on Csilla to search for information on Zonama Sekot. Acting on orders from Peita Aabe, Ganet and her team tried to catch the group as they traveled across the icy surface of the planet to the starport where their ship was berthed.

**Gania system** A star system in the Tapani sector, it was part of the holdings of House Melantha during the New Order.

*Ganjuko*

*Gank*

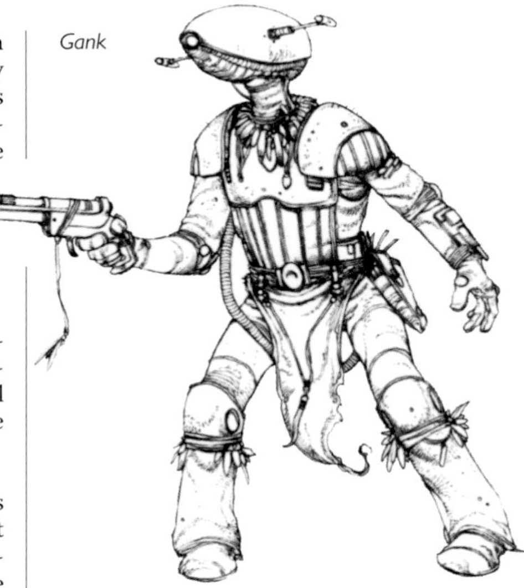

**Ganis the Hutt** A rival of Nawnum during the Galactic Civil War. When he learned that Nawnum had tried to assassinate him and take over his empire, Ganis placed a bounty on Nawnum's head and set out to ruin his business.

**Ganji** A bounty hunter seen at a cantina on Dargulli, he told his Dug and human associates that working for the Rebel Alliance would be too great a risk. Ganji later took part in an ambush of Darth Vader but was among the many casualties.

**ganjuko** Native to the colder regions of a number of planets in the Filve sector, this huge beast was similar to the bantha. The average ganjuko stood more than 3 meters tall at the shoulder and measured 5 meters in length. Its entire body was covered with a thick pelt of fur. Unlike the domesticated bantha, however, ganjukos were easily angered predators capable of killing any creature they encountered. Their mouths were sharp beaks, which they used to attack their prey; they were also collected and sold on the black market. While hunted as trophies, more often than not the "trophies" were taken by the ganjukos themselves.

**Gank** A cyborg species that acted as bodyguards and hired assassins for many Hutt crime lords, they were also called Gank Killers because they carried out cold-blooded murders so often. Ganks frequently could be seen in the presence of Hutts on the streets of Nar Shaddaa and elsewhere. Fur-covered, carnivorous bipeds, Ganks had square yellow faces twisted in permanent snarls, topped by cruel, beady eyes.

**ganker** A mammalian vermin commonly found in the ductwork of large starships, it fed on scraps and detritus left behind by the crews. Most starships were regularly gased to eliminate such pests, but over time gankers became more and more resistant to the toxins used to kill them.

**Gank Massacres** A devastating war that took place 200 years after the Great Hyperspace War, it marked the first true use of the modern Jedi lightsaber in combat. Shatoyo alluded to it many centuries later, during the Great Assembly on Deneba, because it involved a struggle between the light and dark sides of the Force. At its core, the Gank Massacres started when the Porporites became addicted to ryll spice, which caused them to fall into homicidal mania. Many species asked the Ganks for help, and they eliminated the Porporites in short order. Thus emboldened, the Ganks then set out to massacre other species. The Jedi were dispatched to put an end to the Gank predations, and Supreme Chancellor Vocatara was forced to commission the construction of Juggernaut war droids to augment the Republic's forces.

**Ganlihk** A forest world, it was the main planet in the Ganlihk system.

**Gann (1)** A native of the planet Ferro, he migrated to Zonama Sekot some 60 years before the Battle of Naboo. He became the planet's unofficial spokesman and greeter, meeting with those beings—such as Obi-Wan Kenobi and Anakin Skywalker—who traveled to Zonama Sekot to obtain a Sekotan starship.

**Gann (2)** A human male member of Nevo's assassin unit, he was killed by Boba Fett in a photo booth on Starstation 12.

**Gann, Grand Moff** An Imperial Grand Moff who controlled sector 5 during the years leading up to the Yevethan Purge, he was nominally in charge, although Warlord Foga Brill held the real power.

**Gann, Mapper** A clone trooper who was part of a platoon dispatched to Pengalan IV during the early stages of the Clone Wars. Their assignment was to eliminate a Separatist missile facility on the planet. He was given the nickname Mapper by observer Joram Kithe, who was stranded on the planet with the platoon's survivors after the Separatists sprang a trap. The trooper was the only one with a datapad that contained a map of the planet. Mapper was unable to continue fighting, having suffered a broken leg in the initial ambush, but was invaluable in helping the platoon reach safety. Joram later learned that Mapper and his platoon-mates were actually enhanced clones, having been given additional self-reliance and initiative during their development. After the near disaster on Pengalan, Mapper was given the surname Gann to help hide the fact that he was a clone. This helped him gain the confidence of Cherek Tuhm and a team dispatched to Tarhassan to rescue Intelligence Officer Edbit Teeks.

Gann, an assassin

**Gannarian narco-spice** One of the many varieties of mood-altering spice that was smuggled at the height of the New Order.

**Ganner, Lieutenant** An officer who headed security for the Imperial Ruling Council at De-Purteen, he was assigned to investigate the assassinations of council members Burr Nolyds and Admiral Banjeer. Lieutenant Ganner incorrectly concluded that Kir Kanos was continuing his vendetta against Imperials, since the weapons used to kill the men were marked with a symbol once used by Kanos.

**Ganner Squadron** The squadron designation adopted by Wedge Antilles, when he and Corran Horn agreed to defend the *Errant Venture* during the Corellia–Galactic Alliance War. The ragtag group was named in honor of Ganner Rhysode.

**Gant** The third being the Dark Jedi Kueller chose to be his adviser, succeeding Yanne. Kueller believed that his second assistant wouldn't last long due to his impertinence, so he decided to start training Gant early.

**Gant, Colonel Trenn** A leader in the New Republic Intelligence agency, he investigated the capture of Han Solo's shuttle *Tampion* when he was en route to the Fifth Battle Group in the Koornacht Cluster. Colonel Gant interviewed Plat Mallar to try to figure out how Solo had been captured on what was supposed to be a secret mission.

**Gant, Toshan** A noted scientist and droid engineer, he formed a corporation that took control of the droid security systems market some 4,000 years before the Battle of Yavin, flooding the market with security-breaking devices that were of superior quality and capability. But after legal issues led to his imprisonment, Toshan Gant went to work for the Old Republic, and designed the Security Domination Interface.

**Gantho** Located in the system of the same name, the planet was represented by Senator Arastide in the New Republic government. Nine years after the Battle of Endor, the New Republic conducted a large-scale investigation into Loronar Corporation's abuses in depleting many of the natural resources in the Gantho system.

Lieutenant Ganner

**Gantor, Tobin** One of the scientists who took in Jedi Master Ry-Gaul in the wake of the Clone Wars. Gantor and Linna Naltree helped hide the Jedi but disappeared shortly afterward.

**Gantoris** A leader on the planet Eol Sha, he became one of Luke Skywalker's students at his Jedi academy on Yavin 4. As a child, Gantoris could sense impending groundquakes and had miraculously survived when his playmates were killed in an avalanche. A possible descendant of the Jedi Ta'ania, Gantoris had nightmares of a terrible dark man who would tempt him with power and then destroy him. At first he thought that was Luke, but he soon learned it was the spirit of Exar Kun. The Dark Lord guided Gantoris in building his own lightsaber, but Gantoris turned on his patron and tried to use the Force to put an end to the evil spirit. Instead, Kun killed Gantoris, burning him from the inside out.

**Gantree, Fan** A female Sullustan, she served as a communications engineer aboard the Esfandia Long-Range Communications Base during the Yuuzhan Vong War.

**Ganz, Keejik** A Weequay pirate, he was a member of Gardulla the Hutt's crime organization shortly after the Battle of Naboo. The Techno Union offered a bounty for Keejik Ganz's capture after several of their freighters were hijacked. Jango Fett later claimed the bounty on the planet Tatooine during a mission to locate Gardulla the Hutt.

**Gaph** A male Ryn refugee who was part of a group searching for Droma during the Yuuzhan Vong War, he and several others were rescued from Gyndine but stranded on Ruan when there was no other place to relocate refugees. The Ryn were approached by two men, known simply as Tall and Short, who got the skillful Ryn to forge seemingly official documents that would allow rich refugees to obtain passage off Ruan. In return, the Ryn were transported offplanet, just missing Droma and Han Solo, who were arrested for the forgeries. Gaph and the others were stranded on Fondor.

**Gap Nine** A backrocket swamp world that was home to a reptilian species, it was also the site of an Imperial fuel-ore-processing plant during the Galactic Civil War. Centuries before, an unknown group built temples dedicated to evil on Gap Nine. A force of Jedi Knights defeated the group and transformed their temples into storehouses of knowledge.

**gaping spider** A species of large arachnids native to the planet Dathomir, they inhabited warrens of caves and caverns. A clan of Nightsisters, later known as the Spider Clan, took over one of the caves and actually was able to control the smaller gaping spiders, forcing them to do their bidding. Only the largest of the gaping spiders were able to resist the Nightsisters, who feared them.

**Gar** An Imperial lieutenant who served under Sil Sorannan as part of the Black Sword Command, he was one of the 513 survivors of the Yevethan takeover shortly after the Battle of Endor, and was imprisoned on Pa'aal. He worked with Sorannan to plot their eventual escape, and was one of the primary officers Sorannan took with him when the Imperials captured the *Pride of Yevetha* and fled back to the Deep Core.

**garagon** A huge, two-headed reptile that lived in the forested jungles of Koda's World, it protected the ancient temple of the Tempestro. Each head, set upon a thick, sinuous neck, was capable of belching fire at an enemy. The garagon also could attack with its heavy claws and sharp teeth.

**Garaint, Noval** A bounty hunter never seen outside his modified Krail 210 personal body armor with Arakyd Whisper jetpack, he was rumored to be the real power behind crime lord Horch of Keedar.

**garbage pit racing** An illegal sport that sprang up on Coruscant in the decades before the Battle of Naboo. The object was to fly through the planet's extremely dangerous garbage pits using specially designed race wings, avoiding the expelled waste canisters and layers of shielding in an effort to reach the lowest levels. There, racers had to skim the surface of the silicone slurry, obtain a scale from a garbage worm, and then fly back up through the innards of the garbage pits to finish the race by presenting the scale to the Greeter. Race champions were determined by overall times, as well as an ability to produce scales from larger, deadlier worms. Three years after the Battle of Naboo, Anakin Skywalker participated in a race in the Wicko district garbage pit.

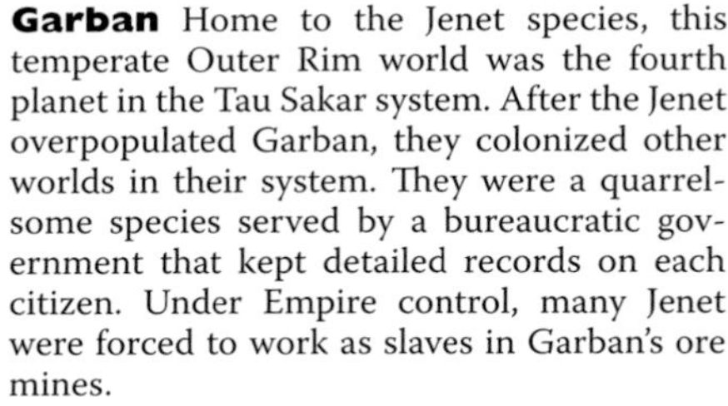
*Garbage pit racing*

**garbage pits** Huge open pits located all over the planet Coruscant, they were the major method of dealing with more than a trillion tons of refuse produced on the planet each day. Most organic materials were actually consumed deep within the pits by garbage worms. Materials that were too toxic to incinerate were placed inside sealed containers and fired into low space.

**garbage worm** Genetically manufactured creatures vital to the elimination of waste on Coruscant, they lived deep within the garbage pits of the city-planet, wallowing in silicone-filled pools. As waste from the city was dumped, it was pulverized and mixed into a silicone slurry. The worms then ate anything that they could. They converted much of the waste into small pellets that could be used as fuel. The worms were covered with shiny, iridescent scales of a milky white color. The largest worms grew to lengths well over 100 meters, and were nearly 4 meters in diameter.

*Gardulla the Hutt (left) gives Jabba the limelight.*

**Garban** Home to the Jenet species, this temperate Outer Rim world was the fourth planet in the Tau Sakar system. After the Jenet overpopulated Garban, they colonized other worlds in their system. They were a quarrelsome species served by a bureaucratic government that kept detailed records on each citizen. Under Empire control, many Jenet were forced to work as slaves in Garban's ore mines.

**Garch, Commander** Captain of the *Glorious,* the command ship for the New Republic chase armada and Colonel Pakkpekatt's command cruiser during the Yevethan crisis.

**Gardaji Rift** An area of the galaxy located on the outer edge of the Tingel Arm—on the very edge of the known galaxy. It was here that Jedi Master Vergere first encountered the mysterious planet Zonama Sekot.

**Garden Hall** The primary meeting place of the Killiks on planet Woteba, it was built to receive visitors from outside the Utegetu Nebula, specifically the new Jedi Order and representatives of the Galactic Alliance. But Garden Hall was one of the first buildings to be affected by the Fizz. Large sections of it were consumed by the strange foam, rendering the building almost useless.

**Gardens of Talla** A hillside park, it overlooked the Jedi library on the planet Ossus many millennia before the Galactic Civil War.

**Gardulla the Hutt** Known to most of her kind as a female, she was one of Jabba the Hutt's closest associates. There were also rumors of a romance, as Gardulla was often Jabba's guest at his Tatooine townhome. Gardulla originally traveled to Tatooine at the urging of her family, the Besadii kajidic, in order to protect her from the Desilijic clan. Angry and upset at being deposited on the desert planet, Gardulla took control of her adopted city of Mos Taike and began to create her own criminal empire. When the organization got too big, Gardulla was ordered to remain on Tatooine to protect it. She was also ordered to court Jabba with the intent of marrying him and thus strengthening the Besadii. After the wedding, she was told, she was free to kill Jabba in any manner she pleased.

Jabba had decided that Gardulla was worth the effort, and tried a number of tactics to earn her approval. He even used his own smugglers to raid her holdings, then returned them to her as "gifts." Gardulla eventually decided to negotiate with Jabba for control. Jabba allowed her to take over slaving operations on Tatooine, in return for her smuggling operations and protection rackets. Gardulla owned many slaves, including Shmi and Anakin Skywalker at one point; but she lost the Skywalkers in a bet with the Toydarian junk dealer Watto six years before Watto lost Anakin to Qui-Gon Jinn in a similar wager. (Years later, when the Old Republic began

*Garbage worm*

enforcing its anti-slavery laws, Gardulla also lost the slave trade on Tatooine and was left with nothing.)

Gardulla maintained a large underground pleasure garden, complete with ponds and plant life. She paid Sebulba to acquire a group of Ghostling children to serve as living statues there, shortly before the Battle of Naboo. She also planned to import creatures to hunt the Ghostlings as part of a cruel, living ecosystem. But her plans were thwarted by Anakin and his friends. Aurra Sing later revealed that she had been hired by Gardulla to help overthrow Jabba. Just prior to the Boonta Eve Classic Podrace won by Anakin, Gardulla created a scale model of the racecourse and tried to convince Jabba that her analysts had predicted that Gasgano would win the race. Jabba, however, refused to bite. Following the race, she offered to buy Anakin back from Watto, but Qui-Gon had already whisked him away to Coruscant.

*Yarna d'al' Gargan*

Later, Gardulla was implicated in the work of the Bando Gora cult, and was questioned by Jango Fett as to the whereabouts of Komari Vosa. It was discovered that much of Gardulla's interest in the Bando Gora had been part of an intricate plot created by Count Dooku to test Jango's abilities and his usefulness as the source of clones for the Army of the Republic. Gardulla died when Jango pushed her into the waiting jaws of her own krayt dragon.

**Gardulla the Younger** Part of a group that formed the leadership of Nal Hutta during the early stages of the Yuuzhan Vong invasion of the galaxy, Gardulla the Younger didn't wholly agree with Borga's plans to form an alliance. But the Hutt realized that the plan was not without merit, and suggested selling information on the Yuuzhan Vong's invasion plans to the New Republic.

**Garen IV** An Imperial penal colony, it was where Stevan Makintay was shipped by his father, the Imperial Governor of Hargeeva, after Makintay proposed marriage to Ketrian Altronel.

**Gareth, King** Ruler of the planet Shalam, he tried to cheat Han Solo at a game of laro during a visit to the New Republic capital of Coruscant. Solo discovered that King Gareth was cheating and got his revenge by cheating "better."

***Garfin*** One of several ships sent by the New Republic to accompany Garm Bel Iblis, Booster Terrik, and the *Errant Venture* to Yaga Minor in an attempt to steal a copy of the Caamas Document.

**Gargachykk** A one-eyed male Wookiee, he was an enforcer for the Black Sun Vigo Darnada in the years before the Battle of Naboo. He was stalking Sullustan gambler Feen Feenoob for gambling debts, but Gargachykk found him dead at the hands of Darth Maul. The Sith Lord agreed to go with him to be questioned by Darnada since Darth Sidious wanted the Dug gangster eliminated. Once aboard Darnada's space station, Maul executed nearly every living being he encountered, including Gargachykk.

**Gargan, Yarna d'al'** The daughter of a tribal chief on the desert planet of Askaj, she was the heavy, six-breasted dancer at Jabba the Hutt's palace on Tatooine. She and her family had been kidnapped by slavers and brought to Jabba. Her cublings were sold off and her mate was fed to the rancor. Yarna became one of Jabba's dancers and supervised the palace housecleaning crew until she was able to gain her freedom after the Hutt was killed. She escaped with the bounty hunter Doallyn across the Tatooine desert, eventually arriving in Mos Eisley, where she was able to buy back her children. She and Doallyn left Tatooine to become free traders in textiles and gemstones. She performed the Dance of the Seventy Violet Veils at the wedding of Princess Leia Organa and Han Solo.

***Gargantuan*** A massive, prototype vehicle, it served as Garm Bel Iblis's primary base of operations during the early stages of the Galactic Civil War. The huge vehicle moved about on a series of heavy-duty repulsorlift engines, and was armed with enough firepower to protect a small starship.

**Gargolyn IV** Homeworld of the Cor species, it was known to be a garden paradise lush with animal life and vegetation. The planet was scouted by Karflo Corporation as the site of a new manufacturing facility, but the scouting team discovered that the land of the Cors was guarded by a huge beast that would utterly destroy any settlement Karflo tried to build.

**Gargon** A planet once under control of gangsters, it was infiltrated by Han Solo and Chewbacca sometime before they joined the Rebel Alliance, when they received a double payment for stealing a hoard of spice stored there. It was also the home base of Grand Admiral Grunger in the waning years of the Empire. Much of the galaxy's phobium was mined on Gargon.

***Gargon*** An Alliance transport, it was destroyed in the Bruanii sector following the Battle of Hoth.

**Gargonn the Hutt** A solemn, stuffy, and arrogant Hutt. The right side of his head and face had been lost in an accident involving a wandrella worm on Circarpous V. As an infant, Gargonn had been abandoned on Nar Shaddaa, surviving only by performing tricks for passersby and feeding on vermin. He eventually developed a small entertainment "business" on the Smugglers' Moon, hiring other performers and splitting their profits. That led Gargonn into trafficking in exotic and endangered plants and animals for wealthy collectors. It was Gargonn who discovered a way to sell mutant akk dogs, running them from his base deep in the bowels of Nar Shaddaa. He also operated a series of sentient gladiator events in association with the Circus Horrificus. When the Jedi Masters Mace Windu and Depa Billaba discovered that the source of the akk dogs was Gargonn, the Hutt had them placed in the gladiator pit against the very dogs they were trying to rescue. Although the Jedi managed to escape, Gargonn also fled into obscurity.

**garhai** An armored fish native to Neimoidia. The Neimoidians often used it as a symbol of obedience and "dedication to enlightened leadership."

**Garhoon** A species of vampire sentients. Bail Organa once presided over an emotional court case between the Garhoons and their prey; the prey eventually returned to the Garhoons, much to Leia Organa's dismay.

**Garia system** A planetary system located in Brak sector, it was a restricted Imperial fleet staging area at the height of the New Order.

**Garindan** A Kubaz spy with a long, prehensile trunk-like nose, he trailed C-3PO and R2-D2 as they met up with Luke Skywalker and Ben Kenobi at Docking Bay 94 in Mos Eisley. Also known as Long Snoot, he always worked for the highest bidder—most often Imperials or Hutts. Garindan wore dark glasses because his large eyes were sensitive to red wavelengths of light. Born on the arid planet of Kubindi, he had rough-textured greenish black skin and bristly head hair usually hidden under a heavy hood and robe. He was being paid by Imperials when he tracked down the wanted droids and led stormtroopers to the bay where Han Solo's *Millennium Falcon* waited before making its getaway.

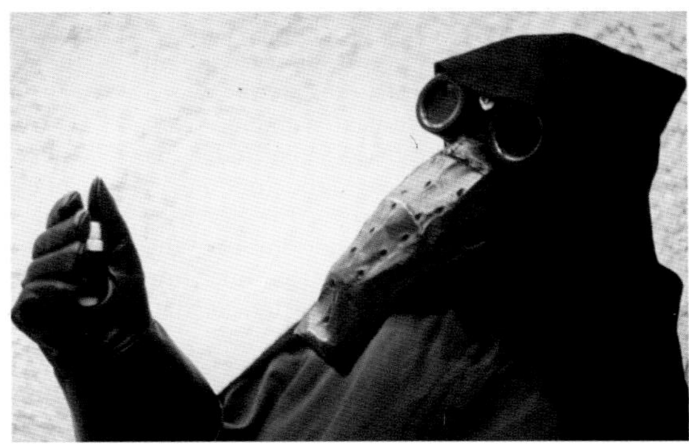
*Garindan*

***Garland*** A New Republic warship, it was destroyed at the Battle of N'zoth.

***Garman*-class mining vessel** Designed and manufactured by the Corellian Engineering Corporation, this 300-meter-long starship was developed to serve as the base for a small fleet of skimmers. Each *Garman*-class ship could transport up to 20 skimmers and had a series of tanks used to store the gases these skimmers collected from gas giant planets.

**Garn** A desolate world without sentient life. It had been homeworld to the Order of the Terrible Glare in Old Republic days. Thousands of years before the Battle of Yavin, the Order waged war against the Jedi and lost. Luke Skywalker travelled to Garn and discovered a trove of ancient Jedi armor. He also discovered the Portal Desolate and the soul-snares used to trap the life energy of ancient Jedi. He managed to destroy the portal and free the energies.

**Garn, Olin** Prior to joining the Rebellion, Olin Garn was an experienced freighter pilot and freelance bounty hunter. While contracting with the Azzameen family-owned Twin Suns Transport Services, Olin Garn became a very close and trusted friend of Aeron Azzameen. It wasn't long before the entire Azzameen family adopted him as one of their own.

**Garn, Ril** An Imperial Army lieutenant, he commanded the garrison on Yetnis during the initial stages of Operation Rebel Hunt. While he was known as a by-the-manual officer, he also could bend the rules to get what he needed.

**Garn, Warleader** A militant Rakatan male, he was the Warleader of a small group of soldiers who opposed the stance of the Elders, more than 4,000 years before the Battle of Yavin.

**garnant** Small purple insects native to Yavin 4, they communicated through vibration and scent. Garnants left red bite bumps on human skin.

**Garnatrope, Kelven** A wanted criminal, at the height of the Mandalorian Wars he claimed to be the Corellian Strangler, but no one ever managed to get a good enough image of him to attach to the bounties that were posted for his capture.

**Garnet, Roark** A self-proclaimed galactic entrepreneur and adventurer, he was captain of the *Dorion Discus.* His parents disowned him after he became a smuggler, and he struggled for many years to break even under the oppression of the Empire. He took out a loan from Grappa the Hutt to cover the expenses of his first ship, the *Moldy Crow,* but gave the ship up to Grappa as payment after inheriting the *Dorion Discus* from his late sister, Neena.

**Garnib** An icy world inhabited by the white-furred Balinaka species, its residents were enslaved by the Empire, which claimed it was "protecting the rights" of the inhabitants. Garnib was the only source of addictive Garnib crystals. The Balinaka were known for their artistic nature and carefree spirit.

**Garnoo** An ancient Master to Oss Wilum and others four millennia before the Galactic Civil War, Garnoo was a member of the Neti species.

**Garobi system** A Tapani sector star system, it was part of the holdings of House Barnaba during the New Order.

**Garonnin, Lord** One of the Senex Lords who followed Roganda Ismaren to Belsavis hoping she would lead him to the missing *Eye of Palpatine.* He was killed there when Irek Ismaren cleaved him in half with a lightsaber.

**Garoos** An alien species sometimes called the Garoosh, they were easily distinguishable by the purple-tinged gillis flaps they used in order to breathe.

**Garos IV** A thickly forested world settled by human colonists some 4,000 years before the Battle of Yavin. The inhabitants became self-sufficient thanks to the planet's rich farmlands. A brisk trade developed between the Garosians and their neighbors, the Sundars, who were part of the colonization effort. The Sundars developed technology, and the two worlds complemented each other. However, after the Sundars began migrating to Garos IV, settling in the valleys and establishing factories and industrial centers, the ire of the agricultural Garosians was aroused. When a Garosian grain facility was destroyed, the resentments among the two neighbors bubbled over, and a civil war started. It lasted 82 years until a truce was signed.

Garos IV was one of the first 10 planets to join the Refugee Resettlement Coalition shortly before the Clone Wars. During the last years of the Old Republic, the Garosian–Sundar truce was regularly violated until the Empire took control of the Garos system. The Garosians became strong supporters of the Rebel Alliance, and held on to their beliefs until the New Republic took control. Once the rest of the galaxy came to realize that the University of Garos was a top-notch school, more beings began traveling to Garos IV to attend classes there. An economic boom followed, as the students created a need for many services.

**Gar-oth, Lord** A Yahk-Tosh crime lord, he controlled the planetoid upon which Yoshi Raph-Elan crashed shortly after the Battle of Naboo. Lord Gar-oth maintained a police and security force of battle droids programmed to enforce his many laws and regulations. The gangster had forcibly taken control of the planetoid, killing any being that stood in his path. He murdered the planetoid's leader and tried to force the leader's daughter, Lourdes, to marry him, in an effort to legitimize his rule. When Raph-Elan challenged his rule, Lord Gar-oth sent his huge gladiator droid, the Goliath, to fight for him. However, the gangster was unprepared for the attack of Princess Lourdes, who drove a sword into his chest and killed him.

**Garouk** A noted pazaak player who lived on the planet Taris some four millennia before the Battle of Yavin, he was often found in the Upper City Cantina, and would help individuals learn how to play the game for a small fee.

**Garowyn** One of the Nightsisters accompanying Vonnda Ra when she seduced the Witches of Dathomir into joining the Shadow Academy, she was a powerfully built, petite woman with long brown hair. She earned the rank of captain among Brakiss's Second Imperium troops. Garowyn took control of Luke Skywalker and Tenel Ka, and transported them to the Shadow Academy. Luke feigned limited knowledge of the Force to lull her into a false sense of security, then used the Force to physically fling her into an escape pod on the *Shadow Chaser* and set her adrift in space. She returned to the Shadow Academy, and later helped Tamith Kai kidnap Zekk. When Brakiss launched his attack on the factories of Kashyyyk, Garowyn submitted to Zekk's leadership in order to get an opportunity to recover the *Shadow Chaser.* She nearly succeeded, but in a struggle with Chewbacca and Jaina Solo, Garowyn lost her footing in a tall wroshyr tree and plummeted to her death.

**Garqi** An unimportant Outer Rim world, it remained under the control of the Empire for many years after the Battle of Endor. The agricultural planet, a source of luxury foodstuffs for the Core Worlds, longed for its

*Garqi*

freedom. Corran Horn traveled to Garqi to escape Imperial entanglements after he left the Corellian Security Force, and was known to the students of Garqi Ag University through his droid, Whistler, who went by the name Xeno. He worked undercover as an assistant to Imperial Prefect Mosh Barris and helped a number of political prisoners escape from the planet, among them Dynba Tesc and Duros trader Lai Nootka.

Years later, after the Yuuzhan Vong took control of Destrillion and Dubrillion, they started working their way toward the Core. Following the Battle of Dantooine, and just before the destruction of Ithor, the alien invaders discovered Garqi. The planet's defenses were unprepared to put up any resistance, and the efforts of Corran Horn, Jacen Solo, and Ganner Rhysode could not save the planet. After a brief battle, the Yuuzhan Vong captured Garqi and began re-forming it as a breeding ground for Chazrach warriors. While on Garqi, the Jedi learned that the vonduun crab armor of the Yuuzhan Vong was susceptible to the pollen from the bafforr tree. However, the planet Ithor was destroyed before any action could be taken.

**Garqi, Battle of** Before the Battle of Ithor, the Yuuzhan Vong established a base on Garqi, which they used to train an army of slaves, consisting of humans and Chazrach. When Corran Horn, Jacen Solo, Ganner Rhysode, and a team of six Noghri went to Garqi to investigate, they met Rade Dromath, a member of Garqi's resistance force. They used a Yuuzhan Vong war game as cover to gather data; the battle ended in the Pesktda Xenobotanical Garden, where it was discovered that pollen from a grove of bafforr trees caused a severe allergic reaction in the Yuuzhan Vong's vonduun crab armor, killing the armor and the Yuuzhan Vong wearing it. To hide this discovery from the Yuuzhan Vong, the Jedi burned down the garden.

When the team attempted to return to the *Ralroost* and the New Republic fleet, the Yuuzhan Vong cruiser *Burning Pride* appeared. A pair of New Republic *Victory*-class Star Destroyers joined the battle, but things looked grim for the New Republic forces until the arrival of Admiral Pellaeon and the forces of the Imperial Remnant along with a Chiss House phalanx led by Jagged Fel. With the Jedi and Noghri team safely aboard the *Ralroost,* the New Republic fleet withdrew, mission accomplished.

**Garr** A youngster from Excarga, he met young Boba Fett, then using the name Teff, aboard the Republic assault ship *Candaserri* following an attack on Raxus Prime. Garr, a dark-skinned humanoid, was of a species whose gender was determined at age 13. He was separated from his parents when Separatists attacked his homeworld. Unlike Fett, Garr admired the Jedi. When they reached Cloud City, they were approached by Aurra Sing and Garr first heard Fett's real name. Fearing for his friend's life at the hands of Sing, Fett told Garr to leave, and Garr quickly informed the Jedi about Sing.

**Garr, Colonel Faltun** A career Imperial officer, he was placed in charge of a new Incom Industries facility on Fresia, after the Empire nationalized the corporation during the New Order. In his mid-60s at the time, Garr was known for his competent, though uncharismatic, approach to his work. Because he'd already served as a soldier and officer at Kuat Drive Yards and various Sienar Fleet Systems facilities, many thought the posting on Fresia was something of a demotion. Garr, however, approached his new assignment with enthusiasm.

**garral** Predators of the Wayland forests, garrals were used by the Empire to help guard Mount Tantiss. They were attracted by the sounds of repulsorlifts, and most ultrasonic emissions sent them into a killing frenzy. They had been biologically engineered by the Imperial scientist Luthos Garral by crossing a Mantessan panthac with several other creatures. A normal garral measured about 2 meters in length and had gray fur as well as a short tail topped with tufts of white fur.

**Garray** A native of the planet Abregado-rae, this portly but energetic man served as the base commander of Caluula Station during the Yuuzhan Vong War. In the months following the Galactic Alliance's Operation Trinity, the Yuuzhan Vong began attacking the station. Garray thought that they were planning to overrun Caluula in order to reach Lianna, but the Yuuzhan Vong commander explained that Caluula's inhabitants were to be sacrificed to the Yuuzhan Vong gods. When the aliens attacked with a ychna, Garray found himself powerless to defend the station. Faced with the imminent destruction of Caluula Station, Garray issued evacuation orders, hoping to get as many people as possible to the planet's surface.

**Garren, Ara** A female human, she was an Imperial Intelligence agent during the years following the Battle of Yavin.

***Garrett*** An *Imperial I*–class Star Destroyer, it was dispatched to aid the *Harpax* in recovering the *Protector* fleet, which had defected under Admiral Harkov. Darth Vader commanded the ship. It was also used to transport prisoners in the Yllotat system.

**Garrick** Chief traffic controller at the Mos Eisley spaceport on Tatooine, he had been on duty when Han Solo and the *Millennium Falcon* blasted away from Docking Bay 94 . . . and never forgot that Solo failed to pay his docking fees.

**Garrison Moon** The sole moon of the planet Kessel, it was known to spice miners as the Sky Bogey. Much of the Garrison Moon appeared to have been hollowed out so it could harbor the Imperial defense fleet. It also contained the Imperial Correction Facility, and served as the transfer point for shipping spice out of the system. Some seven years after the Battle of Endor, the Garrison Moon was destroyed by Tol Sivron and the scientists of the Maw Installation, who tested the superlaser of their Death Star prototype by firing it at the moon.

**garrmorl** A strong liquor, it was made and favored by Wookiees.

**Garrotine** One of the largest settlements found on the planet Beheboth at the height of the New Order. After the defeat of Gideon Longspar, the city was renamed Prosperity.

**Garrulan, Cash** An overweight Twi'lek who once served as a Black Sun Vigo, he "retired" to Murkhana many years before the onset of the Clone Wars. His operations drew the attention of the Jedi Council, which wanted to put him out of business in an effort to ensure stability on the planet. However, Jedi Master Roan Shryne discovered that Garrulan was an excellent source of information on the Separatists. Shryne learned of the military buildup that was occurring on worlds loyal to the Confederacy of Independent Systems, although the Jedi Order discounted the information at the time. When the Battle of Geonosis confirmed Garrulan's information, he was allowed to continue in business, provided that he maintained a relationship with Shryne. In the wake of the command to execute Order 66, Garrulan relayed information to Shryne and Olee Starstone about the so-called Jedi Rebellion and the massive attack on the Jedi Temple. Despite knowing that the information came from reliable sources, Garrulan believed that Emperor Palpatine was behind the entire situation. Garrulan maintained his loyalty to Shryne and the Jedi when Darth Vader arrived on Murkhana and demanded information on Shryne's location. He misled the Dark Lord, then arranged for them all to escape to Mossak on two separate ships, recognizing that his operations on Murkhana were no longer viable. After ensuring that the *Drunk Dancer* escaped into hyperspace, Garrulan's own vessel was intercepted and destroyed by Imperial forces. All hands on board including Garrulan were killed in the resulting explosion.

**Garrolkah** A Dug member of Bazurkah's criminal organization, Garrolkah suddenly discovered a bounty on his head for alleged insults to the Ruhx crime family. The bounty, issued by Bog'Ruhx himself, was claimed by Jango Fett shortly after the Battle of Naboo, when he was on Malastare to meet with Sebolto.

**Garsi** A security officer at the Galactic Justice Center on Coruscant and a member of the Galactic Alliance Guard. Garsi and Wyrlan were assigned to work with Tahiri Veila during her interrogation of Ben Skywalker in the weeks following the Second Battle of Fondor. Their role was to protect Veila if necessary, and they were forced into action. When Ben broke free, they fired; but the Jedi used the Force to deflect one of their stunning blasts at Veila. He then offered Garsi and Wyrlan the chance to stay alive if they helped him. Ben took their armor as a disguise.

Gartogg

**Gart** The second planet in the Demar system, it had been stripped of all natural resources by the Lant Mining Corporation by the time of the Battle of Yavin.

**Gart, Breth** An Agamarian who joined the Rebel Alliance at the same time Keyan Farlander did, Gart aspired to be a fighter pilot but suffered from disorientation syndrome early in his career. This kept him out of flight training on his first two attempts, but he persevered and overcame the problem the third time. He completed his training with satisfactory skills, but was killed early in the Galactic Civil War in an Alliance raid on Kalla VII.

**Gart, Ep** A brash small-time criminal who worked from a base in Mos Zabu on Tatooine during the Galactic Civil War, his plans to sell a load of nergon 14 to an Imperial officer were thwarted when Domo Jones and his friend Blerx stampeded a nerf herd at the location of the sale. When trying to catch Jones, he flew too low over the Great Pit of Carkoon and was attacked and consumed by the Sarlacc.

**Gartogg** A simple-minded Gamorrean, he served as a sentry in the palace of Jabba the Hutt. Even less intelligent than most Gamorreans, he was ignored and given inconsequential duties by his porcine peers. When a series of bodies started showing up around Jabba's palace, Gartogg took it upon himself to solve the mystery. He actually figured out correctly that the murderer was Dannik Jerriko, an Anzat, but no one listened to him. Believing them to be clues, he carried two corpses with him at all times, treating them as his friends and consorts long after the fall of Jabba's regime.

**gartro** Green-skinned, dragon-like avians found on Coruscant, gartros had spike-studded tails and long reptillian jaws filled with needle teeth. Many of them made their home in a warehouse filled with denta beans that had been abandoned by the previous tenant. The creature's eggs were considered a delicacy; Dex's Diner served them pickled.

**Garu, Lord** A Sith warlord on Korriz at around the time of the Great Hyperspace War, he was chief rival of the being known as The Patron. Garu was believed to have been the last of the *Jen'ari* to possess the holocron of the Sith King Adas, but it was lost when Garu died during the war.

**Garul** A Bothan Rebel Alliance operative, he tried to bring Rebel refugees from Cloud City to Kaliska, a safeworld located in the Mid Rim. Garul, who used the alias Silver Fur, was killed in a confrontation with Zardra and Jodo Kast.

**Garv** A Pho Ph'eahian mechanic, he once helped Han Solo fix the *Millennium Falcon.*

**Garyn, Alexi** Known simply as Lex, he was a Force-sensitive being who dreamed of becoming a Jedi Knight. But by the time his abilities were discovered, he was too old to be considered for training. Garyn then chose a life of crime, and eventually became the leader of the vast organization known as Black Sun. Garyn surrounded himself with the strongest Vigos and even chose the Dathomir Witch Mighella as his personal bodyguard. However, Garyn and his organization were unprepared for the fury of Darth Maul, who had been dispatched by his Master, Darth Sidious, to eliminate any trace of leaked information about the upcoming blockade of Naboo—which a source had tried to sell to one of Garyn's minions. The Sith Lord eventually caught up with Garyn on Ralltiir and destroyed the remaining members of his organization before drowning Garyn himself.

**Garyn Raiders** A small gang of criminals that was formed on the moon of Rori at the height of the New Order, its members originally were lieutenants in the organization of Alexi Garyn and managed to survive the execution of their peers at the hands of Darth Maul. Although not official supporters of the Rebel Alliance, the Garyn gang spent much of its time harassing Imperial operations in the Naboo system.

**gasan string drum** A musical instrument, it was one of two instruments played by Figrin D'an, leader of Modal Nodes. D'an also played the kloo horn.

**Gasgano** A popular Podracer who competed in the Boonta Eve Classic, Gasgano was a Xexto from the planet Troiken; as such, he had six limbs and 24 fingers. He was sponsored by Gardulla the Hutt, who wagered heavily on the outcome of the Podrace with Jabba the Hutt. Gasgano was a formidable Podracer because his multiple limbs and dexterous fingers allowed him to perform many piloting adjustments simultaneously. He piloted a Custom Ord Pedrovia with anti-turbulence vanes and thrust stabilizer cones on the engines. Gasgano finished second in the Boonta Eve Classic that was won by nine-year-old human Anakin Skywalker.

**gasnit** Massive, carnivorous, bat-like creatures found on an unsurveyed Outer Rim jungle planet, they preferred to sleep inside great chemical geysers. They had gray fur, long needle-like teeth, and sharp claws. The bite of the gasnit was highly poisonous, allowing the creature to grasp and bite its prey, then release it to die.

**gasser** A Gungan cooking device. Shortly before he crashed Boss Nass's heyblibber and was banished from Otoh Gunga, Jar Jar Binks blew up a gasser in a catering accident.

**Gass'kin, Mad** A Bothan, he was proprietor of Mad Gass'kin's Used Droidnet and sold all manner of droids at discount prices.

**Gast, Dr. Edda** An Imperial doctor, she was a key figure in Project Chubar, genetic research sponsored by Warlord Zsinj and undertaken by Binring Biomedical. A human from the planet Saffalore, she built off her uncle Tuzin's studies and developed several new ways to manipulate the brains of humanoid species to make them smarter and meaner. Zsinj had hoped to create an army of the brainwashed to help him infiltrate the New Republic and destroy it from within. After Zsinj learned of the escape of two test subjects, he told Dr. Gast and a research partner to kill each other with blasters he conveniently provided. After Dr. Gast shot her colleague down, she was allowed to continue her experiments, but later was captured by agents of Wraith Squadron. Zsinj tried to kill her with one of the brainwashed subjects, but Nawara Ven got Dr. Gast's near-lifeless body into a bacta tank just in time. In return for a new identity and a huge

Gasgano

sum of credits, she agreed to tell the Republic about Zsinj's plans. She opted to collect her payment in Imperial credits, and when she arrived on Coruscant, she was arrested by Republic agents and later imprisoned on charges of trying to smuggle Imperial credits for seditious purposes.

*Gathering of the Jedi Council to hear from young Anakin Skywalker.*

**Gast, Tuzin** A leader at Binring Biomedical in charge of the Imperial experiment known as Project Chubar, which was designed to create near-human intelligence in the galaxy's more primitive humanoid species, he arranged for Imperial Warload Zsinj to obtain a majority share in the company's operations. Over time, however, Tuzin Gast started worrying about his test subjects' fate in Imperial hands. So he staged a massive explosion in the Epsilon Wing of the labs on Saffalore with the intention of sacrificing himself to set his subjects free. He died, but Zsinj's forces managed to recover all but one of the fleeing subjects, either dead or alive.

**Gastinin, Gar** A Duros pilot, he hung out at the Cluster Cantina on Nar Shaddaa.

**Gasto** A New Republic Navy midshipman, he served under Commander Zoalin aboard the *Adamantine,* but was killed by the Death Seed plague while in orbit around Brachnis Chorios.

**Gastrula** A planet inhabited by a species of slug-like sentient creatures.

**GAT-12h** The designation for the Skipray blastboat, a 25-meter-long defense and patrol ship built for the Empire by Sienar Fleet Systems. Although small, it had enough power to place it in the ranks of capital ships. Exceptionally well armed, it was equally suited for atmospheric and deep-space use. The rear section, which contained the main drive, lasers, and stabilizing wings, rotated around the axis of the ship on a specially designed sleeve, giving the Skipray both speed and maneuverability.

**gatag** A shelled creature native to the Yuuzhan Vong homeworld. Its hard covering was used to create ceremonial platters employed during the shaping process.

**Gate** This was the name that Rogue Squadron leader Wedge Antilles gave to his R5-G8 astromech droid after Master Zraii upgraded and modified it. It had previously been called Mynock.

**gatekeeper** A Jedi Master whose image was stored within a Jedi Holocron, the gatekeeper was the primary access point for whoever was using the holocron.

**Gate to the Lands of the Dead** The portal through which the living passed when they died, according to Yuuzhan Vong mythology, it was where they were judged by the True Gods. Those deemed unworthy were doomed to roam the Lands of the Dead, never to return to the living nor feel the grace of the gods. Shortly after the Yuuzhan Vong terraformed the planet Coruscant into a new version of Yuuzhan'tar, the mythology was updated to include a Guardian of the Gate, known as the Ganner or the Jedi Giant, in reference to Ganner Rhysode's stand against the invaders while protecting Jacen Solo.

**Gates of Grontessiant** In Skakoan mythology, this was the portal that led to the Threshold of the Hidden Realms, where an individual could find the Eye of the Albino Cyclops.

**Gateway** One of many domed cities built on the surface of the planet Duro, it housed refugees fleeing the Yuuzhan Vong War. The dome, like other such refugee cities, was located beneath one of Duro's 20 orbital stations, protected by the planetary shield that contained the station. Gateway was constantly at odds with Settlement Thirty-two, as each dome tried to obtain the other's supplies in an escalating struggle to feed its inhabitants. When it came time to evacuate the planet, three land crawlers carrying refugees to the spaceport at Settlement Thirty-two were destroyed by Yuuzhan Vong coralskippers.

**Gateway Space Station** Erected but never completed by the Empire in orbit around Tshindral III, it had a huge docking ring encircling the station. Talandro Starlyte remodeled it for use as a trading post.

**Gatherer 164** The code name of Ferfer, a Ryn based on Balmorra during the Yuuzhan Vong War.

**Gathering, the** A name given to the formal meetings of members of the Jedi Council, it was associated with several traditions. As the Jedi began arriving at the meeting hall, each remained standing until all had entered. Once all were present, they started with a type of oath or mantra, and at the end took their seats simultaneously.

**GaTir system** Located less than five standard hours from the Pyria system, it contained the planet Mrisst.

**Gatral** A bounty hunter, he was one of several who accompanied Crutag to Trinta in pursuit of a team of Rebel Alliance agents they encountered on the Kwenn Space Station. Gatral and his team eventually were killed by the dreamscapes and dreambeasts of Halagad Ventor before they could capture the Alliance agents. They were "resurrected" by Ventor as dreambeasts and sent after the Alliance team.

**Gatterweld, Ensign** Found aboard the *Razor's Kiss* after Warlord Zsinj stole the ship from Kuat Drive Yards, Gatterweld took control after the death of Captain Raslan during the ship's flight from Kuat. However, Gatterweld was unable to defend the huge ship from the massed firepower of the *Mon Remonda* and the *Tedevium,* and the *Razor's Kiss* was destroyed. Gatterweld was rescued and rewarded for his bravery and loyalty to Zsinj by being named part of his security force aboard the *Iron Fist.* Gatterweld was almost killed later when he was attacked by creatures that were released from Project Chubar.

**Gauch** One of the pilots who worked for Lando Calrissian in the asteroid belt known as Lando's Folly, he was one of the first pilots killed when the Yuuzhan Vong attacked Dubrillion. Gauch's TIE bomber was being protected by the *Belt-Runner I* station, but the station was forced to retract its shield energy after it sustained heavy damage, and Gauch's ship was destroyed by enemy fire.

**Gaulus** A mountainous world not far from Tatooine, it was the site of a Rebel base captured by the Empire during the Galactic Civil War.

***Gauntlet*** An *Imperial*-class Star Destroyer, it was part of the Empire's fleet in the Tapani sector at the height of the New Order. The flagship of Captain Lin Nunsk's fleet, it was assigned to patrol the space around Lamuir IV.

**Gauntlet Scanners** Sensor arrays deployed along with a ring of Star Destroyers, they guarded the planet Byss during Emperor Palpatine's clonings. The Gauntlet Sensors monitored all incoming security clearance codes and alerted the Star Destroyers to any suspicious users.

**Gauntlet Squadron** One of the two starfighter squadrons on which the New Republic relied heavily when Rogue Squadron resigned its commission to fight the Bacta War, it consisted of T-65A3 X-wings and E2 B-wings. The Gauntlet Squadron X-wings were assigned to the *Allegiance* during the hunt for Warlord Zsinj. Three of the squadron's ships were lost during a skirmish with the Yuuzhan Vong. Gauntlet Three was later the first ship to make contact with the escape pod containing Yuuzhan Vong priestess Elan and long-missing Jedi Vergere.

**gaupa** A medium-sized pony-like species used by Ewoks as a beast of burden. Gaupas ran wild in the open woodlands and plains of Endor, but were also kept as transport animals by Ewoks. Brave, tough, and swift, the gaupa did not exceed 1 meter at the shoulder.

**Gaurick** A planet in the Corporate Sector controlled by a religious cult led by a high priest. Han Solo and Chewbacca were hired to deliver several cargoes of chak-root to Gaurick workers, some of whom had a religious objection to the substance. On one such run, Solo and Chewbacca almost were taken captive.

**gauss ball** A grenade designed to stun droids, it released a localized blast of ion and electrical energy that could render inoperable an unprotected droid's internal systems through overload.

**GAV (ground assault vehicle)** A class of military vehicles, GAVs were further divided into three categories: SAVs (surface assault vehicles), RAVs (repulsorlift assault vehicles), and walker-type vehicles.

**Gavens** Akanah Norand Pell was born on this planet, in the city of Torlas, to Isela Talsava Norand and Joreb Goss. The family soon moved to Lucazec, where Joreb abandoned his wife and daughter.

**Gavin, Colonel Bowman** Director of flight personnel for the New Republic's Fifth Fleet Combat Command during the Yevethan crisis, he had a great deal of influence in the recognition and promotion of the pilots in the Fifth, and had the authority to handpick pilots for certain assignments.

**Gavrisom, Ponc** A Calibop who served as Acting Chief of State during the historic peace negotiations between the Empire and New Republic, he had pale blue eyes, wings, a tail, and a mane. Later, Gavrisom found himself in the middle of the Caamas incident and its repercussions, and was faced with popular opinion that the Republic, in pushing down responsibility to sector leaders, was ignoring the grave situation and the needs of its people.

**Gavryn** A planet known for its strong magnetic poles. It was in orbit around Garvyn that then-Ensign Gilad Pellaeon first exhibited his skills, using the poles to confuse a group of pirates and destroy them. Those skills eventually led to Pellaeon's promotion to command of the *Chimaera*.

**Gazaran** Members of this species native to the planet Veron were intelligent, gliding reptiles that were extremely friendly and eager to please. The herbivores lived in the fevvenor trees of the Veron rain forest, establishing vast cities in their branches. By the time of the Galactic Civil War, the Gazaran had achieved a minimal level of technology and industry, mainly geared toward the production of items needed by tourists who visited the planet.

**Gazaway, Dax** A Podrace announcer.

**gazetteer, astrogation (galactic)** A chart indicating the most common journey times between many of the important worlds in the galaxy. The statistics were quoted for a typical military starship equipped with a Class 1 hyperdrive. The times given were also for direct system-to-system journeys.

**Gazurga** A male Dug from Malastare who was a member of Sebolto's gang, he had a price on his head that eventually was claimed by Jango Fett.

**Gbu** An extremely high-gravity planet, it was home to the Veubgri, a large, stocky species with six legs and long tendrils used as manipulative appendages. Before Leia Organa Solo visited Munto Codru, she and her delegation met with Veubgri representatives on an orbiting satellite; that way, Leia and her party avoided the negative effects of Gbu's high gravity on the human body.

**g burp** Spacer slang for any sudden surge from a starship's drive systems—especially from the hyperdrive—or any sudden increase in velocity that caused the beings inside to experience increased g-forces for a short period of time.

***G Cat*** This modified Arakyd Helix Interceptor was operated by Cryle Cavv, with the help of the astromech droid R2-RC, at the height of the Galactic Civil War. Cavv claimed the ship was nothing more than a transport vessel, despite its military beginnings. Cavv armed the ship with four plasburst cannons and a pair of proton torpedo launchers, and installed a slave circuit and beckon call to remotely call the ship to his location.

**Gchalla** An independent spacer who traveled the galaxy in her ship, the *Silver Claw*, the Wookiee was once captured by Imperial forces near Byblos, but she was freed by a group of spacers she had rescued at Rampa.

**G-class shuttle** A small two-passenger shuttle, it had two wings that lowered when in flight mode. Obi-Wan Kenobi and Anakin Skywalker boarded a G-class shuttle after their Colicoid diplomatic ship was attacked by Krayn's pirates. They used the shuttle to infiltrate Krayn's ship and disable its weapons systems.

**GDA-8** A semi-humanoid droid model designed by Droxian Manufacturing, they were used in Herglic gambling houses on Tresidiss and other worlds. GDA-8's were equipped with AA-1 verbobrains, and their computer banks contained extensive gambling databases and programming that allowed them to keep tabs on a large number of players.

**gdan** Nocturnal predators native to the planet Qiilura, these small creatures hunted in large packs to attack larger prey. The teeth of a gdan were capable of tearing apart flesh, but the Qiilura farmers feared even more the bacteria and germs they carried in their saliva, for a small bite was almost always fatal.

**Gebbu the Hutt** In power at the height of the New Republic, this Hutt crime lord collected fine art. After discovering that he had been sold forgeries by Wac Bur, Gebbu hired Boba Fett to track down the counterfeiter and bring him to justice.

**Gecee** A dim-witted Gran smuggler and associate of Fenig Nabon, Gecee held a grudge against Nabon after she sold him a cheap security code at Kuat.

**GEC U47** A transport ship owned by Galactic Electronics, it was used to evacuate technical crews from the *Pondut* research platform during the Empire's retaliatory strike there.

***Geddawai*** An Alliance YT-1300 stationed at the DS-5 deep-space outpost, it was the ship in which Harkov tried to escape when Darth Vader found him at the station.

**geebug** A type of speeder, it was developed by the X'Ting for moving through the tunnels and warrens of their lairs on the planet Ord Cestus.

**Geeda** A troublesome Rodian merchant and hunter on Nar Shaddaa some four millennia before the Battle of Yavin, her sales aided the proliferation of rancors throughout the galaxy.

**Geedon V** The base of operations for a notorious pirate gang, this planet in the Sumitra sector was cleared of its scum in a single-handed takeover by the infamous gunslinger Gallandro. Years later, a food-supply convoy of Imperial corvettes was destroyed in the Geedon system by Rebel Alliance pilots using ships captured from Overlord Ghorin in an attempt to discredit him with the Empire.

**geejaw** A small, flying creature native to the Forest Moon of Endor, it had a sharp beak that it used to excavate insects from thick tree bark. Geejaws also were known for their ability to mimic almost any sound they heard. They built nests and laid several eggs at a time; both parents cared for the young chicks.

**Geelan** Natives of the planet Needan, these were short, furry, canine humanoids who loved to barter and hoard valuables—and use any method at all to complete a deal. The species barely survived when Needan was hit by a passing comet and forced into a wider orbit, resulting in a rapid cooling of the planet. The Geelan were forced to erect domed structures to protect themselves from the frigid cold. A passing Arconan ship picked up a distress call and agreed to supply the Geelan with advanced technology to assist in their survival.

**Geen, Locus** A decorated general in the Old Republic, he followed in the footsteps of his grandfather's grandfather to serve during the Clone Wars. Retiring just before Emperor Palpatine instituted the New Order, Geen became a politician on the planet Salliche and developed a network of contacts. He hated the Empire and used specially encrypted messages to pass information about the Imperial presence on Salliche to Rebel Alliance agents.

**Geenor** Son of a farmer on the planet Ceriun a millennium before the Battle of Endor, he and his friends Tenno, Ka'arn, and others decided to keep a Jedi Holocron they found, hoping a Sith might claim it and take them all as apprentices. When a Sith did arrive and took it, he killed Geenor and the others as their "reward."

**Geentech** Once a subsidiary of Chiewab Amalgamated Pharmaceuticals Company, it was best known for its work on the 2-1B series of medical droids. The company was forced to stop its operations because of the ruthless tactics of Genetech, which claimed infringement. There were strong rumors that Genetech, which then acquired the assets of Geentech cheaply, had the backing of the Empire during court proceedings.

**Geezum** A Snivvian scout, he was employed by Jabba the Hutt to locate new planets and chart difficult terrain. Although Geezum was never sure of Jabba's motives, the Hutt paid him well. Geezum disappeared in the wake of Jabba's death at the Pit of Carkoon, just prior to the Battle of Endor.

**Geffen** An Imperial Navy officer, he served as Edric Darius's first officer aboard the torpedo sphere stationed near Tallaan during the Imperial occupation of the Tapani sector.

**Gefferon** A manufacturer of pleasure repulsorcraft such as sail barges.

**Gegak** An Imperial Navy captain and survivor of the Galactic Civil War, he later served under Foga Brill and commanded the destroyer *Tobay* during the search for the Teljkon vagabond.

**Geith** A Jedi Knight who accompanied Callista Ming on her mission to disable the *Eye of Palpatine.* The two were very much in love. They had first met on Cloud City, where Callista was on a brief layover while training aboard the *Chu'unthor* starship owned by Jedi Master Djinn Altis. She discovered that Geith was Force-sensitive and asked him to learn about the Force aboard the *Chu'unthor.* After discovery of the *Eye of Palpatine,* both Geith and Callista were dispatched by Jedi Master Plett to stop the ship. They managed to get aboard, but were trapped by the ship's formidable defenses. After much discussion, they agreed that Geith was the only one with a chance to pilot a starship past the *Eye of Palpatine*'s automated defenses and seek help. But a change in the ship's automatic firing pattern caught him unaware, and he was killed in heavy fire.

**Gejjen, Dur** The leader of the Democratic Alliance party in the aftermath of the Yuuzhan Vong War, he struggled to gain a voice in government after Thrackan Sal-Solo reasserted himself as Corellian leader. Dur Gejjen worked behind the scenes to remove Sal-Solo from power even while serving as one of his closest advisers. It was Gejjen who first warned Han and Leia Organa Solo that Sal-Solo had put a steep bounty on their heads. When Sal-Solo continued to push for open war against the Galactic Alliance, Gejjen hired Boba Fett to eliminate the despot. In the wake of the leader's assassination, Gejjen agreed to work with Deputy President Vol Barad to form a coalition government that could work to restore Corellia's standing in the galaxy. Gejjen quickly paid Fett his credits, hoping to clear any audit trail that might lead back to his funding of the mission.

Gejjen became leader of the new coalition and became adamant about Corellian independence. He abolished the office of the President of Five Worlds, but then named himself the Corellian Chief of State and the Five Worlds Prime Minister, appearing to be taking control of the system for himself. When a group of Bothan and Commenorian warships snuck past the blockade of their home system and reached Corellia, they bombarded the Galactic Alliance's forces and forced them to retreat. Gejjen immediately declared that Corellian forces had "cast off the yoke of Galactic Alliance oppression" with the help of their newfound friends, earning him the admiration of the Corellian masses.

When the Galactic Alliance Guard learned of Gejjen's possible involvement in the attempt on the life of the Hapan Queen Mother Tenel Ka, they launched a secret mission to have him assassinated. Intelligence officers discovered that Gejjen was planning a secret meeting on Vulpter with the Alliance Chief of State Cal Omas to discuss a mutual cessation of hostilities and a division of responsibilities and assets. Jacen Solo sent Ben Skywalker to carry out the assassination and recorded much of the discussion between Gejjen and Omas to incriminate the Alliance Chief of State. As he was leaving, Gejjen was shot in the head and killed by Skywalker.

Geejaws

Gelagrub

**Gejjen, Nov** The father of Dur Gejjen, he was one of the small number of Corellians who refused to join the Human League and play along with Thrackan Sal-Solo.

**Gektl** A species of tough, green-skinned reptilians who walked upright, they were native to the planet Hoszh Iszhir. The Gektl had the ability to shed their skin and tails when captured, allowing them to escape from startled captors. Gektls were known for their literature and artwork, especially intricately painted eggs that depicted an event in the history of their planet.

**gelagrub** These large herbivorous insects native to the planet Felucia were domesticated by Gossam colonists who settled the planet and were used as mounts during the Clone Wars. Because gelagrubs moved about on 10 stubby legs covered with a sticky slime, they were exceptionally sure-footed, even when crawling up walls. In order to protect themselves from the ultraviolet rays of Felucia's sun, larval gelagrubs had a translucent skin that could metabolize certain UV-blocking chemicals found in the native plant life, which gave the larvae a form of natural sunscreen. After mutating through the pupa stage, the gelagrub emerged as an insect with a hard shell impregnated with reflective chemicals that completely blocked the incoming sunlight.

**gel-bath** A small, portable version of a bacta tank, it could be used to treat specific injuries.

**Gelesi** A captain in the security force that protected the planet Onderon and its leader Queen Talia in the years following the Jedi Civil War. He preferred to spend his time—both on and off duty—in the cantinas of Iziz.

**gel-form droid** An unusual type of droid made from gel and plastoid, giving it the ability to adjust its shape and size. Gel-form units could be made to appear human, but lacked any form of artificial intelligence. The droids were used to teach snipers and big-game hunters about their trade, since the gel-form could be programmed to act like a specific target. Repeated shots could be fired into the gel-form, and it would return to its previous state to be ready for the next volley.

Ann and Tann Gella give Sebulba a pre-Podrace massage.

**Gelgelar** A cold, swampy world in the Outer Rim Territories, it was home to the Gelgelar Free Port and Shrine of Kooroo.

**Gella, Ann and Tann** Twin sisters who were purchased by Sebulba from Jabba the Hutt, the blue-skinned Rutian Twi'leks provided the Dug with pre-Podrace massages.

**Gellak, Gunmetal** One of the galaxy's most notorious pirates, he was captured during the early years of the New Republic.

**Gellandi, Oora** A young female Chagrian who lived on Cularin during the final years of the Old Republic, she joined a small gang led by Naja Delan, as her own views of the Jedi Knights mirrored those of the male Duros. She believed that the Jedi were better than others because of their connection to the Force.

**Gelrood** A top pazaak player on the planet Taris, he played most of his matches at the Lower City Cantina and was known as one of the best teachers of the game in the galaxy during the Jedi Civil War.

**Gelviddis Cluster** A section of the galaxy where Jedi Knights discovered a unique sand that allowed them to conjure up images in its swirling patterns.

**gemcutter** A device developed by Carbanti United Electronics at the height of the Clone Wars, it was used to counteract the effects of a starship that was traveling through hyperspace while cloaked. Gemcutter technology was in the development stage when the prototype was stolen by the Separatists.

***GemDiver Station*** Lando Calrissian's gem-mining platform above Yavin. The station orbited in the fringe of the gas giant's outer atmosphere. When *GemDiver Station* lowered its orbit to graze the gaseous levels of the planet, the *Fast Hand* diving bell was sent even lower to catch rare Corusca gems. Nearly two decades after the Battle of Endor, the station was attacked by Skipray blastboats sent by the Second Imperium. A modified assault shuttle with Corusca gemcutters breached the station. Attacking stormtroopers stunned Calrissian and his aide, Lobot, and kidnapped Jaina and Jacen Solo and Lowbacca.

**Geminor** The second planet in the Lianna system, it was blanketed with a hot, dense, poisonous atmosphere and orbited by a single moon.

**Gemmer** A Rebel Alliance pilot, he helped scout the planet Arbra as a possible location for a new base of operations after the Battle of Hoth. Gemmer later flew a TIE fighter into battle against Imperial forces on Spindrift, using surprise to take control of the base.

**Gemmie** Married to a Balawai militia officer and pregnant with their third child, her situation led her husband to allow Jedi Master Mace Windu to reach the droid control system located beneath the city of Pelek Baw on Haruun Kal. That enabled Windu to defeat the Separatist fleet and put an end to the Summertime War.

**gemweb** A fine, silk-like thread, it could be woven into extremely smooth cloth.

**Gen-6** A starship that was produced in the years leading up to the Clone Wars.

**Genarius** A huge orange-and-blue gas giant, it was the fourth planet in the Cularin system. Its core was incredibly dense with all the properties of a protostar, including the presence of nuclear reactions. Thus the atmosphere of the planet was churned by intense storms. And Genarius appeared to glow from within, giving it an eerie appearance to visitors to the system. Still, the planet supported at least one form of native life, the cochlera. Also, several orbital cities were built by entrepreneurial mining operations as bases from which they harvested some 150 rare gases and nuclear energy. Shortly after the end of the Clone Wars, Genarius was the site of an intense battle between the Cularin military and the forces of the Coalition. The Coalition's primary warship was destroyed in the fighting when it collided with the city of Tolea Biqua. The resulting explosion created massive instabilities in the atmosphere of Genarius, rendering the planet nearly uninhabitable.

**Genassa** A planet in the M'shinni sector, it was the original homeworld of the M'shinni people.

**Gen'Dai** A rare species with an unusually long life span. Some Gen'Dai reportedly lived for over 4,000 years. The peculiar nervous and circulatory systems of the Gen'Dai made them extremely resistant to physical injury. Their physiology boasted millions of nerve clusters throughout the body and a vascular system that distributed blood without the need of a central heart. Lacking the vulnerable vital organs of most humanoids, a Gen'Dai could sustain multiple lacerations and even complete dismemberment yet still survive. In addition to these extremes of endurance, the distributed neural network gave the Gen'Dai phenomenal reflexes. Should Gen'Dai sustain too many injuries, they were capable of entering into extended periods of hibernation, during which they could heal wounds, recover from disease, and slow the aging process. The Gen'Dai were, by nature, not an aggressive species. They were nomadic, their homeworld having been lost to the ages. Due to a low birthrate, the Gen'Dai were very rarely encountered, and they usually avoided confrontation if possible. Though the Gen'Dai were physically suited for long life, their minds weakened with age, and the species was susceptible to depression, hysteria, and other forms of psychosis. The fearsome bounty hunter Durge, active during the Clone Wars, was an exception among the usually peaceful Gen'Dai.

Gen'Dai

**Gendar** The ostensible leader of the Outcasts, who lived in the poorest sections of the Lower City of Taris some 4,000 years before the Galactic Civil War. When a group of Jedi Knights returned several diaries to Rukil, the elder turned them over to Gendar, hoping that he could piece together enough information to pinpoint the location of the Promised Land.

**Gendarr, Iolan** A native of Commenor, he was a captain in the Imperial Navy and commander of the Star Destroyer *Reliance* in the months following the Battle of Endor. Gendarr had served under Captain Needa aboard the *Avenger* before being promoted in the aftermath of the Battle of Hoth. When word of the Imperial defeat at Endor reached Captain Gendarr, he and General Arndall Lott fled the training facility they were protecting on Jardeen IV before the New Republic could find it.

**Genden, Lohn** A freelance terrorist and native of Alderaan, shortly before the Battle of Hoth he ambushed a luxury liner and held the passengers hostage while demanding the release of captives of the Empire. Emperor Palpatine refused, and Genden destroyed the liner, killing all 10,000 passengers. Several months after the Battle of Endor, Genden reappeared and took over a New Republic military base. He again demanded the release of prisoners, but this time he was driven off before any killings took place. He eluded capture and was never seen again.

**Geneer, Duchess** The last of the sovereigns to control the planet Duro, this long-ago duchess was ousted by the mega-corporations that took control of the planet. She was entombed in the Valley of Royalty in a monument that bore her name.

**General Crix Madine Military Reserve** A huge complex of orbital hangars and living quarters, it was erected around Coruscant by the Galactic Alliance in the years following the war against the Yuuzhan Vong. Known as Crix Base, the facility was constructed during the fleet reorganization that accompanied the consolidation of the Galactic Alliance's power on Coruscant. The facility was designed to serve as the home base for the Third, Eighth, and Ninth fleets, as well as the base of operations for the Space Rangers and the Gamma Corps.

**General Good** A set of beliefs held by the Keganites prior to their joining the Old Republic, it required all Keganites to dedicate themselves to their planet. Its tenets included nearly complete isolation of the planet from the rest of the galaxy and no importing of technology or knowledge. Every member of society was held in equal regard, and every person was considered a member of a single family.

**General Marshoo's Eatery** A café located in Otoh Gunga on the planet Naboo prior to the Battle of Naboo, it was owned and operated by an immense Gungan named Marshoo.

**General Ministry** The body that ran the day-to-day business of the New Republic, it was formed after the dissolution of the Provisional Council to ensure that the nonmilitary aspects of government were addressed. It had responsibility for handling the ministries of the government, finance, commerce, security and intelligence, and science and education.

**General Purpose Attack fighter** A snub fighter of Bakuran design, it was often referred to as a GPA.

**Generet** A human Imperial agent, his appearance was surgically altered so that he resembled a Mon Calamari, although his human organs weren't altered. He served as part of COMPNOR's Destabilization branch.

**Generis** The primary planet in the Generis system, it was once the site of the New Republic's communications center for the entire Atrivis sector. The center was destroyed by Grand Admiral Thrawn's forces just prior to the Battle of Bilbringi. Alliance General Kryll and pilot Pash Cracken were able to evacuate Travia Chan and her people during the New Republic's retreat from the planet. The Republic decided to rebuild the communications center on Generis, linking it to the outpost on Esfandia to form a redundant link to the Unknown Regions. The Yuuzhan Vong, during their invasion of the galaxy, destroyed much of the planet's surface, eliminating one of the Republic's major communications hubs. This left Esfandia as the only remaining communications center servicing the Unknown Regions.

Gentes

**Genesia** The second and primary world of the Genesia system in the Brak sector, its location made it a prime destination and a busy waypoint for spacers. Most of the sector's crime lords established bases on Genesia since the corrupt government held no real power and could easily be bribed. Genesia was orbited by a collection of space stations known as G-Stations, as well as the moons of Laut and Gimm.

**genetic slicer** A Yuuzhan Vong tool, it was used to access locked biotechnology. Using a genetic slicer, a shaper could open a qahsa that had been sealed shut and could otherwise be opened only with its owner's genetic codes.

Geonosian

**Genian** One of the few planets that managed to remain neutral during the Clone Wars, its neutrality was based as much on diplomatic skills as on the planet's lack of strategic importance. Much of Genian's surface was given over to corporations, research laboratories, and financial institutions, although many areas of desert remained undeveloped.

**Genkal** A Mon Calamari officer with the New Republic, he was captain of the MC80A cruiser *Naritus.*

**Genon** An isolated world despite being close to several major hyperspace trade routes, it was an unobtrusive base of operations for Grappa the Hutt.

**Gentes** Homeworld of the pig-like Ugnaughts, it was located in the remote Anoat system. Ugnaughts lived in primitive colonies on Gentes's less-than-hospitable surface until most left to work at Cloud City on Bespin. During the decades leading up to the Battle of Ruusan, Gentes had been the site of a minor Sith training academy, where Sith Warriors and Sith Marauders were prepared for battle.

***Gentleman Caller*** A slow, outdated Corellian runabout, it was used by Tendra Risant to go into the interdicted Corellian system to warn Lando Calrissian about the Human League's plans.

***Genue*** An Imperial freighter that was used to carry prisoners of war to the Imperial detention center on Mytus VII, it was captured and boarded by the crew of the Rebel Alliance shuttle *Drago.*

**Geonosian** An insectoid species divided into castes. The Geonosians were native to the harsh rocky world of Geonosis. They built immense, organic-looking spires to house their hive colonies. There were two main types of Geonosians: the wingless drones that mostly worked as laborers, and the winged aristocrats, including royal warriors serving as scouts and providing security to the hive. All Geonosians had a hard, chitinous exoskeleton, elongated faces, and multijointed limbs; they spoke in a strange clicking language. Most were strong despite their thin builds. Their tough exoskeletons provided protection from physical impacts, and from the bouts of radiation that occasionally showered their world.

Though labeled warriors, Geonosians did not have a standing military, but used their droid foundries to build armies for corporate

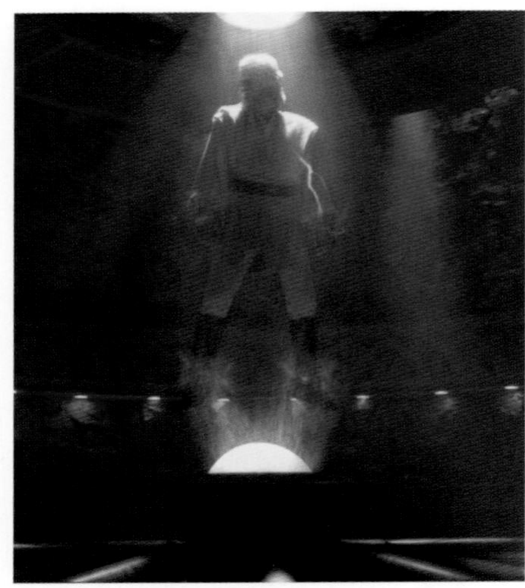
Geonosian containment field

interests wealthy enough to afford them—entities such as the Trade Federation and the Techno Union. Despite relatively simple minds, the Geonosians were adept at mechanical construction and were contractors for many of the galaxy's biggest manufacturing concerns. The hardships of the native environment coupled with rigid structure codified in their caste society fostered a barbaric side to the Geonosians. Their simple minds viewed brutal violence as entertainment, and Geonosians congregated in massive execution arenas to watch victims doomed to die at the hands or claws of savage creatures.

Geonosian society existed for the benefit of the few in the upper caste. Ruling members thought nothing of forcing thousands of workers to labor for their whims. The caste system evolved over millennia. Geonosians were born into specific castes divided along the lines of their physical attributes, although a few aspired to ascend socially. The aristocrats brutally managed workers, forcing them to toil under harsh conditions regardless of danger. What little hope an aspiring Geonosian had was gladiatorial combat. Geonosians of lower castes were often pitted against other Geonosians, other sentients, or savage creatures in immense gladiatorial arenas. If the Geonosians survived, they achieved some status or got enough wealth to leave the planet.

The winged Geonosian soldier drones grew to adulthood rapidly, and were ready for combat at the age of six. While they had enough intelligence to defend the hive from natural predators, they proved easily conquerable by more sharp-witted foes. Another Geonosian caste was raised to be pilots. They required no sleep. In training, each pilot pupa paired with a fighter's flight computer, and they developed an idiosyncratic, coordination-enhancing rapport.

Following the Clone Wars, Geonosian factories were forced to shut down many of their operations since battle droids were no longer needed or allowed. The population languished for many years, until much of it was absorbed into the Colony.

**Geonosian containment field** An unusual security system developed to hold prisoners in a form of stasis without the need for active guards, it consisted of two generators, one on the floor and one overhead. Within each was a glowing orb that generated magnetic energy of opposite polarity, thereby creating a huge "magnetic bottle" to contain the prisoner, who wore special wrist and ankle cuffs to focus the magnetic energy and keep him or her suspended in midair. The system was powerful enough to hold even a Jedi Knight. Count Dooku had discovered that the magnetic field disrupted certain brainwaves, including a Jedi's connection to the Force, so he was able to use it to contain Obi-Wan Kenobi.

**Geonosian fanblade starfighter,** Commissioned by Separatist leader Count Dooku and based loosely on aggressive Geonosian air patrol skimmers, these *Ginivex*-class starfighters were informally dubbed fanblades for their most distinctive feature. The slim, elegant vessel had an iridescent fan-like wing extending from its dorsal and ventral surface. The wing could accordion inward to hide flush with the ship's body, or deployed for combat mode, stretched to a half-circle along a pair of articulated boom arms. Atop each arm was a double laser cannon that swung and locked into forward-firing position. In combat mode, these laser cannons had an enlarged firing arc. With the boom arms shut, the cannons still pointed forward.

Dooku was a known connoisseur of abstract and exotic alien designs. His preferred vessel was the *Punworcca 116*–class solar sailer, and he was so impressed by its performance that he commissioned the Huppla Pasa Tisc Shipwrights Collective on Geonosis to craft six starfighters for his exclusive use.

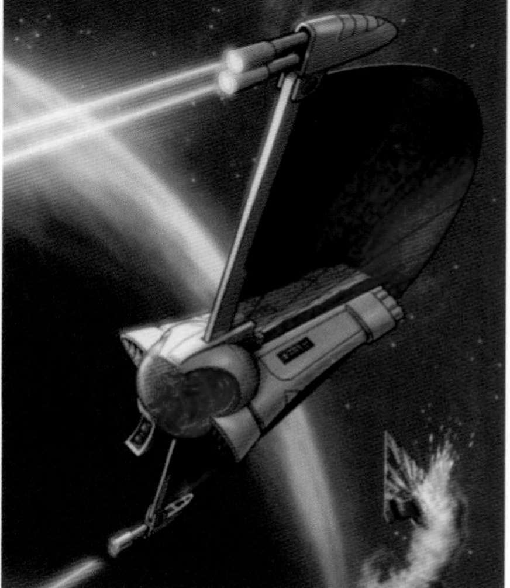
Geonosian fanblade starfighter

Though combat mode greatly increased the fighter's target silhouette, the exotic material of the fan served as a transmission plane for deflector shield energy. With shields fully energized, the fanblade was a tough target to damage, although the fighter stood out like a beacon on sensors. The fan also served as an alternative form of propulsion, though the ship was fitted with standard sublight and hyperspace drives.

At the head of the ship was the bulbous cockpit, designed specifically for humanoid occupants. When Asajj Ventress became a disciple of Count Dooku, he had the small group of fighters moved to her headquarters on Rattatak. Through the course of the Clone Wars, Asajj had two fighters stolen from her, one by Anakin Skywalker and the other by Obi-Wan Kenobi.

Geonosian solar sailer

**Geonosian solar sailer** An exotic conveyance befitting Count Dooku's enigmatic character, the Geonosis solar sailer used unique technology to propel the craft through both realspace and hyperspace. The seed-shaped vessel had a bracketed bubble-like cockpit within which was the ship's droid pilot, FA-4. The vessel's carapace opened to expel its diaphanous sail, which unfurled into a parabolic chute that gathered energy particles for propulsion. Count Dooku used the interstellar sail ship to escape from the opening battle of the Clone Wars on Geonosis and meet with his dark master, Darth Sidious, in the abandoned districts of Coruscant.

Count Dooku's solar sailer was a hybrid of obscure technologies, its core body being a modified *Punworcca 116*–class sloop while the sail was provided by the Count himself. The term *solar sail* is a misnomer, since Count Dooku's interstellar sloop used an unknown kind of energetic propulsion far more exotic than stellar radiation. Dooku acquired the delicate and ancient sail from mysterious Gree artisans, who developed a technology that harnessed supralight emissions for interstellar travel. The solar sailer, like other Geonosian ships, used a sophisticated array of narrow tractor/repulsor beams as offensive grapples and steering aids when in flight, affording the vessel an impressive maneuverability.

**Geonosian sonic blaster** Geonosians were no strangers to exotic and advanced forms of weaponry. They used advanced sonic technology to project discrete globes of concussive energy at their targets. The Geonosians made both handheld and turret-mounted versions of their sonic cannons. The standard sidearm of the Geonosian soldier used oscillators to produce a devastating sonic blast. The energy was enveloped in a plasma containment sphere shaped by emitter cowls that channeled the sonic beam. This stabilized the sonic effect until it impacted its target, resulting in a powerful omnidirectional blast. Large-scale Geonosian sonic cannons were deployed as platforms with two or more Geonosian gunners who could let the advanced targeting computers of the cannons do most of the work.

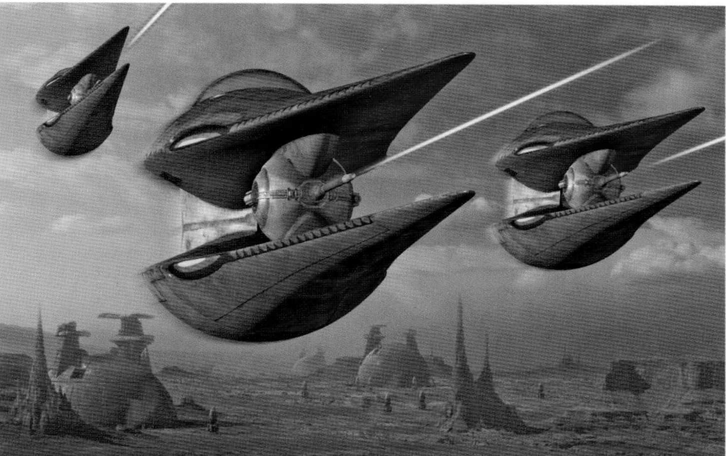
Geonosian starfighters in action

**Geonosian starfighter** A lean, twin needle-nosed fighter craft, the Geonosian starfighter was a small, compact vessel of great speed and superior agility. A single Geonosian pilot sat within the cramped cockpit, his or her head poking up to peer out of a bubble canopy allowing a 360-degree field of vision. Cradled within the forward needles of the ship was a turret-mounted laser cannon. When Count Dooku fled the first engagement of the Clone Wars, a pair of Geonosian starfighters provided escort and covering fire. The *Nantex*-class starfighters, manufactured by the Huppla Pasa Tisc Shipwrights Collective, were effective deterrents to intruders into Geonosian airspace. The ship's control systems were specifically tailored for Geonosian pilots. The complex multiaxis control yokes required a Geonosian's dexterity, and vital performance feedback was provided to the pilot via a scent-stimulator mask that exploited the acute Geonosian olfactory sense.

The fighter's primary weapon, the turret-orb-mounted laser cannon, and the craft's engine cluster were modular and could be swapped out for mission-specific requirements. The starfighter also was lined with dozens of independently aiming narrow-beam tractor/repulsor projectors, providing the ship with increased agility in atmosphere; they could also be used offensively to reduce the maneuverability of target craft. The outer hull was made of woven, reinforced laminasteel. The flexible material allowed the starfighter to rebound from impacts that would fracture more rigid vessels.

Geonosian sonic blasters

**Geonosis** A harsh, rocky world less than a parsec away from Tatooine, Geonosis was a ringed planet beyond the borders of the Galactic Republic. Its uninviting surface was marked by mesas, buttes, and barren stretches of parched desert hardpan. The rocks and sky were tinted red, and the creatures that evolved on Geonosis were well equipped to survive in the harsh ecology.

The most advanced life-forms were the Geonosians, sentient insectoids who inhabited towering spire-hives. The Geonosians maintained large factories for the production of droids and weapons. Except for dealing with clients who ventured to the planet to place orders, the Geonosians typically kept to themselves.

The droid foundries and the planet's remote location made it an ideal base of operations for the Separatist movement that spread through the galaxy in the later years of the Old Republic. The Archduke of Geonosis, Poggle the Lesser, hosted an important meeting of the heads of the Confederacy of Independent Systems. The commerce barons in attendance pledged their mechanical military forces to Count Dooku, the charismatic Separatist leader. The Separatists were ready to wage war, but their plans were overheard by Obi-Wan Kenobi.

The Jedi was taken captive, though he managed to dispatch a distress call to the Jedi Council. With their forces spread throughout the galaxy in an effort to maintain the peace, Jedi Council members were able to dispatch only 200 of their ranks to Geonosis. Obi-Wan, meanwhile, was sentenced to death in a huge execution arena. He and his compatriots, Anakin Skywalker and Padmé Amidala, had to face down three terrible arena creatures before the Jedi reinforcements arrived. While the Jedi could easily contend with the Geonosians, they had not counted on the sheer size of the droid army lying in wait. Uncounted waves of battle droids poured into the arena, slaying many Jedi. A scant few remained before even more reinforcements arrived in the form of the newly created Republic clone army. With the arrival of these forces, the first battle of what was to become known as the Clone Wars began on Geonosis. The Republic military, led by the Jedi, was able to drive the Separatists into retreat.

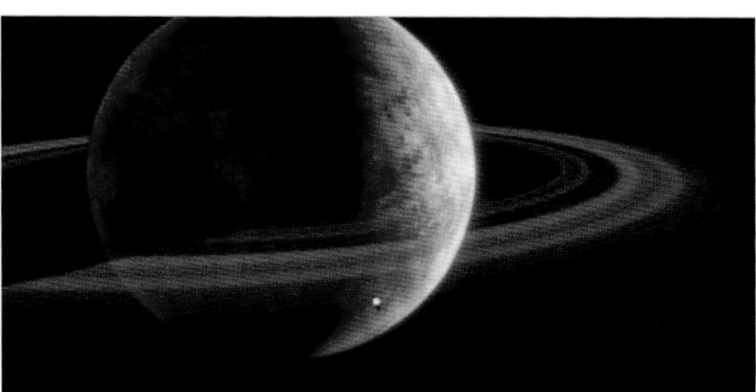
Geonosis

As a planet, Geonosis was marked by spectacular yet uninviting vistas. Radiation storms occasionally blasted the surface, driving life-forms underground for protection. Dense high-altitude fog produced gloomy, night-like conditions that could last for weeks. Life on Geonosis adapted for such circumstances, and many creatures were bioluminescent.

Geonosian architecture was so carefully crafted that a casual glance at the desert plains would suggest the world was uninhabited. But close inspection of the immense, organic spires that were the Geonosian hive-mounds betrayed escaping steam and exhaust vents. Geonosians cultivated a parasitic creature called a phidna that excreted raw material that Geonosian artisans mixed with stone powders to form a rock paste substance. Geonosians harvested the rich metallic content of the planet's rings for use in their secretive manufacturing processes. However, corporate spies could hide within the rings, and asteroids falling through the atmosphere were so common that cunning pilots exploited the laziness of Geonosian scanner operators by flying down to the surface with only the most basic of sensor stealth. The planet was orbited by 4 major and 11 minor moons.

*Geonosis droid factory*

**Geonosis droid factory** Hardworking Geonosian dregs pieced together advanced technology in droid foundries in the service of the Techno Union and other commerce guilds. Usually occupying one of the planet's immense stalagmite spires, droid factories were mostly automated, with immense conveyer belts and robot arms assembling mechanical pieces into finished combat automata. Thousands of battle droids, super battle droids, droidekas, and other models were built from start to finish. Baktoid Armor Workshop, a key technology developer in the Techno Union, maintained factories throughout the galaxy, though increasing legislation against its wares prior to the Clone Wars forced the company to downsize. Baktoid closed factories throughout the Inner Rim and Colonies regions. In a calculated move, Baktoid moved its operations beyond the jurisdiction of the Republic, concentrating on Outer Rim planets like Geonosis.

*Geonosis execution arena*

**Geonosis execution arena** After toiling in the droid foundries, a Geonosian worker's sole outlet for entertainment were the blood sports found in the Geonosian execution arena. Those who committed crimes against Geonosis were sentenced to death. Obi-Wan Kenobi, Anakin Skywalker, and Padmé Amidala were found guilty of espionage by Poggle the Lesser and were to be killed by deadly arena beasts. Poggle the Lesser and his guests, Count Dooku, Nute Gunray, and Jango Fett, watched from an exclusive viewing box high above the arena floor as each captive was chained to a sturdy stone pillar. Three large gates unleashed the creatures, which were kept in line by Geonosian picadors. The ghastly trio included the brutish reek, the agile nexu, and the terrifying acklay. But the captives were able to outwit their assigned killers long enough for Jedi reinforcements to arrive. Led by Jedi Master Mace Windu, the Jedi fought against innumerable battle droids that surrounded the arena. Many Jedi fell in the conflict, and the few survivors appeared to be doomed. The sudden arrival of Yoda and the newly formed Republic clone army saved the day and heralded the start of the Clone Wars.

Execution was a common sentence in Geonosian courts since planetary leaders believed it was stupid to squander supplies to keep prisoners. But the execution arenas' entertainment value for the lower castes was just as important. Ruling Geonosians earned praise for staging the most impressive beast battles, called petranaki or "venations." Archdukes such as Hadiss the Vaulted and Poggle the Lesser also used the arenas to eliminate political dissidents. Arena competitions were so popular that the Geonosians managed to wipe out some of the more aggressive beasts on the planet.

**Gepparin** The primary world of the Gepparin system in the Shelsha sector, it was one of the sector's main mining worlds and also had a few agricultural settlements. The BloodScar pirates maintained a base on Gepparin during the early stages of the Galactic Civil War and had taken control of mining operations. The planet itself was dark and cold, orbiting a red star that was one of three in its system.

**Gep's Grill** A restaurant in Mos Eisley, it was run by two Whiphids, Fillin Ta and Norun Gep. They purchased dewback and bantha meat directly from many of Tatooine's hunters.

**Gepta, Rokur** The last of the Sorcerers of Tund. Rokur Gepta's arrogance and sheer malice led him to obliterate all living things on the planet. He was a heartless being for whom power was everything. He wanted to rule the sector of the galaxy that contained Tund, then extend his rule outward. To make sure he was unchallenged, he eliminated the original Tund Sorcerers who had taught him all that he knew. People saw Gepta differently. To some he was a dwarf; to others, a 3-meter-tall giant. He wore ashen-gray cloaks and a turban that wrapped around his face, obscuring all but his piercing eyes. Lando Calrissian battled Gepta and defeated him, in the process discovering that the Sorcerer was actually a vicious Croke—a small, snail-like being with hairy black legs that used illusion to make its way through life. Lando took Gepta and squeezed him until his gloves were covered with greasy slime, a fitting end for the evil Sorcerer.

**Geptun, Lorz** One of the most powerful members of Balawai society on Haruun Kal during the Clone Wars, this near-human had bluish, translucent skin and aluminum-colored hair. Geptun's grandfather was actually a Korun, but he simply ignored that fact when discussing his lineage with others.

When Mace Windu arrived on Haruun Kal to locate Depa Billaba, Geptun had him captured and brought in for questioning. Despite the reward being offered by the Separatists for the capture of a Jedi, Geptun really wanted to eliminate any guerrilla threat posed by Master Billaba. After accepting a bribe of 3,000 credits from Windu, Geptun allowed him to go free provided that he locate and remove Billaba. Unknown to Windu, Geptun had placed a tracker inside his lightsaber handle, hoping that the Jedi would lead him to the heart of the Upland Liberation Front. Geptun believed that he had finally defeated the Jedi and won the freedom of the Balawai until Windu launched an unexpected assault in an effort to reach a

*Rokur Gepta*

Separatist droid control center. Geptun was captured and then turned over the codes to the droid control system, allowing the forces of the Old Republic to defeat the Separatists. With the end of the so-called Summertime War at hand, Geptun decided to enlist in the Army of the Republic. Thanks to a letter of recommendation from Master Windu, Geptun happily accepted a posting with the Intelligence division.

**Geran** A planet located in the Mneon system. Geran's life-forms included a near-human species with bluish skin whose members needed trace amounts of hydron-three added to the air they breathed in order to survive away from home. Their religious system involved a belief in the Sky Seraphs. Doallyn, one of Jabba the Hutt's bounty hunters, was a Geran native. Animal life on the planet included a flying reptile, the shell-bat.

**Gerb** A primitive, mammalian species native to Yavin 13. These peaceful beings were short humanoids standing at most a meter tall with short arms and long legs. A downy fur covered their bodies, and their claws were metallic to help them dig through the rocky ground for roots. They were known for their speed and for their keen sense of hearing. During the Yuuzhan Vong War, Yavin 13 was devastated and the Gerb civilization was exterminated.

**Gerbaud 2** Located in the Sepan sector, the planet Gerbaud 2 was the site from which Imperial Admiral Harkov attempted to resupply his TIE Advanced squadrons during a rendezvous with the escort carrier *Tropsobor* following the Battle of Hoth. A united force from the nearby planets of Ripoblus and Dimok attacked and thwarted the transfer operation.

**Gerevick** A rude and crude-mannered resident of the Khoonda Plains on Dantooine in the years following the Jedi Civil War, he was a salvager who moved across the grasslands in search of anything of value left behind in the wake of the destruction of the Jedi Enclave on the planet. Gerevick was killed when he tried to attack the Exile and her party after they had discovered a wealth of information within the Enclave.

**Gergris** An Imperial Moff, he was in charge of the Halthor sector during the Galactic Civil War.

**Geridard** The primary planet in the Geridard system of the Doldur sector, it was the site of a renowned retirement complex that was rumored to have the best lifelong care in the galaxy. Many corporate officials and other affluent individuals spent their twilight years on Geridard. Augusta I'att was scheduled to go to the Geridard Convalescent Center for treatment of her degenerative disorder when she was executed by Moff Kerioth.

**Gerido, Lobb** Jabba the Hutt's Twi'lek valet during the time that Jabba was learning the family business from his uncle Jiliac, Gerido was verbally abused at every opportunity.

**Geriel** A refugee after the Mandalorian and Jedi Civil War, he became gravely ill while living in a refugee sector on Nar Shaddaa. He was healed by the Exile, who drew on the power of the Force.

**Gerin** A Tammuz-an princess and daughter of Lord Toda, she was held captive by Gir Kybo Ren-Cha during the early years of the New Order after he had escaped from prison and fled to the moon of Bogden. It was Lord Toda who had assumed control of Tammuz-an after crown-prince Mon Julpa was lost. It was when Mon Julpa returned and began negotiating with Toda for peace that Kybo Ren's pirates attacked Tammuz-an and kidnapped Gerin. Jann Tosh and his droids R2-D2 and C-3PO traveled to Bogden with Jessica Meade in a successful effort to rescue Gerin.

**Geris VI** One of the first worlds to outlaw drinking among Mandalorian mercenaries, especially those who had been hired by the planetary government.

**Gerraba** A Wookiee, he was wanted by Jabba the Hutt during the New Order.

**Gerrard V** The fifth planet in the Gerrard system, its landscape was dominated by deserts and small temperate areas bordered by oceans. The population hated the New Order, and a brief rebellion by the militia caught Imperial forces on Gerrard V by surprise. Admiral Jion Trynn was dispatched to restore peace, but when rebels apparently shot and killed his liaison, the admiral ordered orbital bombardments, leaving large portions of the planet in ruins. It was the uprising on Gerrard V that prompted Emperor Palpatine to suspend the Imperial Senate. The planet was later liberated by Crix Madine and his Rebel Alliance forces.

**Gerrenthum** Rebel Alliance support sprung up on this planet during the Galactic Civil War, even though Gerrenthum was the capital of the Anoat sector. It was located at the intersection of the Corellian Trade Spine and the Nothoiin corridor, near the Yarith and Javin sectors in the area known as the Greater Javin. Starships passing through the area used Gerrenthum as their primary stopover, making the planet exceptionally wealthy.

**Gerres Gule** Home planet of the Kulless species.

**Gervruche** An Imperial Special Corrections Facilities minister, he was killed just before the initial negotiations for the Stars' End project began. This paved the way for Lady Chawkroft to work with the Corporate Sector Authority to bring the project to fruition.

**Gesaril** A planet in the Gesaril system of the Minos Cluster, it was the site of a series of accidents involving nine Imperial warships. The Empire had a strong presence after quarantining Gesaril until it could discover why nine separate ships crashed at the same coastal location. There was also an Imperial prison facility on an asteroid in far orbit around Gesaril's sun. Gesaril was covered with a dense jungle and a noxious swamp. The native Gesaril, a small, furred, six-limbed species, had a certain affinity for the Force. It was rumored that after the Gesaril were mistreated by the Empire, they somehow used the Force to pull the nine starships out of orbit and crash.

**Gessak, Mils** An Alliance scout, he located small planetoids and asteroids for use as remote bases and sensor posts. Mils Gessak was the leader of reconnaissance team D812.

**Gesse, Geska** A Neetakka Rodian bounty hunter at the height of the Galactic Civil War. The assignment committee of the Goa-Ato placed him on the Imperial hunt for Luke Skywalker as a way to get Geska Gesse off Rodia for an extended period.

**Gestal, Noric** A Gotal slaver who specialized in beautiful Twi'lek females from Ryloth, he was often at odds with Chieb'Kalla, whose staff of beautiful females at the Fungus Pit cantina were off limits to slavers. Shortly after the Battle of Geonosis, Gestal hatched a plot to steal as many of the workers as he and 23 goons could. But their attempt was thwarted by a group of freelance agents who were on Ryloth in search of Jedi Master Vhiin Thorla. Gestal was killed, and the other slavers were gassed into unconsciousness, arrested, and sent to prison.

**gestation bin** Bioengineered birthing chambers developed by the Yuuzhan Vong shapers, they were used to grow clones of the various creatures transported from their home galaxy.

**Gestron** This planet was the site of an Imperial base raided by Garm Bel Iblis.

**Getelles, Moff** The Imperial military governor of the Antemeridian sector, he managed to survive the upheaval following the Battle of Endor to maintain control. Moff Getelles struck a deal with the droch Dzym and Seti Ashgad, who agreed to destroy the gun stations of Nam Chorios in return for weaponry and the first cut of the profits when Loronar Corporation moved in to strip-mine the planet's precious crystals. The Moff also had a deal with Loronar, which promised a new facility on Antemeridias to build synthdroids and new Needles smart missiles. In reality, the Moff was simply Loronar's heavy, doing its bidding in return for help to expand his power. When New Republic forces discovered the truth, Getelles's fleet was destroyed.

Gethzerion

**Gethzerion** The leader of the Nightsisters of the Witches of Dathomir, she hoped to turn all of the Witches to the dark side. Clan Mother Gethzerion had matted white hair, crimson, bloodshot eyes, and a face with blotches of purple from ruptured blood vessels. She terrorized not only other clans of Witches, but also the stormtrooper guards at the planet's Imperial prison colony, who eventually started taking orders from her.

The Nightsisters were wielders of the Force in a matriarchal society that used men only as mates or servants. Only Gethzerion knew that she could use the power of the Force without the rituals that the others went through. Her powers grew through devotion to the dark side, and she was determined that her clan would rule and, eventually, escape the planet on which they had been stranded by Emperor Palpatine, who had been disturbed by Gethzerion's growing power.

When Han Solo crashed the *Millennium Falcon* on Dathomir, a planet he had won in a sabacc game, Warlord Zsinj told Gethzerion that he would get her a ship to leave the planet if she gave him Solo and Princess Leia Organa. Despite this promise, Zsinj's men opened fire and destroyed both the ship and Gethzerion.

**Gett, Commander** Leader of Improcco Company serving aboard the *Fearless* during the early stages of the Clone Wars, Commander Gett was known for his irreverent humor. He developed respect for Jedi Knight Etain Tur-Mukan after she refused to leave behind two battalions during the siege of the planet Dinlo about a year after the Battle of Geonosis. Commander Gett and his company volunteered to accompany General Tur-Mukan back to Dinlo to rescue Sarlacc Battalions A and B before the Republic's warships bombarded the planet from orbit.

**Gettiarn** This planet was the outermost world in the Iotran system. During the Galactic Civil War, the Iotran Police Force operated a space station orbiting Gettiarn as a traffic control center for the entire system.

**Gev, Mirta** A bounty hunter active in the years following the Yuuzhan Vong invasion of the galaxy, she was the daughter of Ailyn Vel and Makin Marec. Raised in the Mandalorian tradition, she knew little of her late father and even less about her grandfather, the noted bounty hunter Boba Fett. So when her mother suddenly went missing about 10 years after the end of the Yuuzhan Vong War, Mirta Gev sought out the one person she knew she could find: Boba Fett. She kept her identity secret to gauge Fett's worthiness, but managed to draw him into her plan to locate Ailyn Vel by suggesting that the man who killed Fett's wife, Sintas Vel, was somehow connected to the disappearance of Taun We, whom Fett was searching for. And she produced the heart-of-fire necklace that Fett had given to Sintas Vel on their wedding day.

The more she learned about Fett, however, the more disgruntled Gev became with his ideals and his choices in life. Gev was able to watch her grandfather work firsthand in a job to assassinate Thrackan Sal-Solo, but she was the one who actually killed the Corellian despot. When she learned of her mother's death a short time later, Gev believed she needed to carry out her mother's wish to kill the aging bounty hunter, but she was thwarted by Leia Organa Solo. When she recovered and Fett gave her another chance, she realized that he was the only family she had left, and they set about to try to get along.

Once back on Mandalore, Gev was welcomed into the community, although most of her friends couldn't avoid the fact that she was the granddaughter of the *Mand'alor,* Fett.

Mirta and Boba bonded with the discovery that Sintas Vel was still alive, frozen in carbonite for decades. Fett retrieved Vel and thawed her from her prison. Mirta helped her recover. Shortly thereafter, Mirta married Ghes Orade. As the war between the Galactic Alliance and the Confederation wound down, Gev and Fett were forced to leave Mandalore after the Moffs of the Imperial Remnant engineered and released there a nanokiller virus from Gev's blood that specifically targeted Fett's bloodline.

Mirta Gev

**Gevarak, Malindin** A small-time counterfeiter from Ord Mantell, he was wanted by the Empire for forging Imperial credits for use by Rebel Alliance personnel. Gevarak traveled with the Wookiee Cherioer and had a bounty of 10,000 credits for his live capture.

**Gevarno Cluster** A collection of star systems located along the Gevarno Loop, it was loyal to the Confederacy of Independent Systems during the Clone Wars.

GH-7 medical droid

**Gevtes, Pagda** The master Devisor of the planet Exocron in the period after the Battle of Endor, he worked hard to keep technological knowledge in the hands of a chosen few. When the crew of the *FarStar* was stationed on Exocron, Gevtes wanted to keep them on the planet to study their starships and learn more about their technology. After the crew was freed, Gevtes was exposed as power-hungry, placed under arrest, and tried for his crimes.

**GH-7** A soft-spoken medical droid used by the Polis Massans in their sterile asteroid colony, it served as the spokesdroid for the otherwise silent Polis Massan medics who worked diligently to save the life of Padmé Amidala. The ailing Senator had been taken to the medical facility by Jedi fugitives. For reasons the medics and droids could not pinpoint, she was losing her grasp on life. Yet mixed with this sad news was hope; as the droid explained, Padmé was pregnant with twins. Though the Polis Massan medics were unable to save Amidala's life, she did give birth to twin infants, Luke and Leia.

The GH-7 medical droid, made by Chiewab Amalgamated Pharmaceuticals, was designed to optimize performance and efficiency, with multiple graspers and expansion ports allowing for last-minute emergency customization to meet exotic patient needs. The configuration employed by the Polis Massans had a pair of main manipulator arms, a separate articulated grasping sampler, and a fourth lesser arm extending from the droid's head with a mounted probe. Its body trunk contained an analysis chamber and holographic projector. Atop its head was a diagnostic display screen and equipment tray. For better mobility, adaptability, and reduced contact with potentially contaminated surfaces, the GH-7 hovered aloft on a single whisper-quiet repulsorlift cell. The repulsor field extended outward to envelop the droid's trunk-mounted sample tray, which helped stabilize any sensitive liquids against sudden movements.

**Ghanol, Zam** An older woman, she worked with pirate Erli Prann aboard the Golan II space station near Bilbringi during the Yuuzhan Vong War. Prann lured the *Mon Mothma* to the station to steal its hyperdrives and use them to power the Golan II. Jaina Solo used the Force to alter Prann's recollection of hyperspace jump coordinates, and the crew of the Golan II tried to jump through a Yuuzhan Vong interdictor. But their proximity to the interdictor allowed them to pound it and clear an escape route for the Galactic Alliance forces. Ghanol demanded that Prann surrender the Golan station to the Galactic Alliance; he refused, but eventually was subdued and the station was turned over to the Alliance.

**Gharakh** A Noghri, he was one of Leia Organa Solo's bodyguards. Gharakh was on duty when Shada D'ukal tried to meet Leia at the Orowood Tower during the Caamas incident.

**Gharn** A young Nagai with a strong connection to the Force, he was among a handful of Jedi Padawans being instructed by Master Lucien Draay at a satellite training facility on Taris in the years following the Great Sith War. Gharn and the others were invited to a special ceremony to mark their achievements, not realizing that the Jedi planned to murder the Padawans. Before they could react, they were cut down by their instructors. Only Zayne Carrick survived because of his late arrival.

**Gharon** An Alliance colonel, he was in charge of infiltration during the Cobolt Offensive. It was Colonel Gharon's suggestion to use a variant of the Erasmus gambit to carry out the mission.

**gharzr** A panther-like predator also known as the Dxunian stalker, it was native to the moon Dxun. Its gray fur was interwoven with bronze scales that gave it an armor-like protective plating. Several gharzr managed to bridge a narrow gap between Dxun and the planet Onderon and carved a niche for themselves in the planet's jungles.

**ghaswar** A creature on the planet Exodo II, it bored tunnel-like holes into the lava formations covering the world.

**Ghator, Sal** One of the many Yuuzhan Vong subalterns who lived in La'okio on Zonama Sekot following his species' defeat, he found it hard to adjust to the communal aspects of the settlement. Ghator was often caught stealing food from the communal gardens, claiming that his caste had been cursed by the gods and could not grow its own.

**ghazakl** A lowly annelid, it was native to the Yuuzhan Vong homeworld.

**Ghazhak** A Noghri who, with his clan-brother Kohvrekhar, worked as a henchman for Darth Vader during the Galactic Civil War. The pair discovered Luke Skywalker's severed hand in the airways of Cloud City.

**Gheer, Trisdin** A Hapan who was one of Queen Mother Ta'a Chume's retainers during the Yuuzhan Vong invasion, he plotted with her against her daughter-in-law, Teneniel Djo, who was opening up the Hapan Cluster for refugees. Jaina Solo discovered that Gheer was not wholly loyal to Ta'a Chume, but instead was a spy for Alyssia, Ta'a Chume's niece. While this information was being sent to the Queen Mother, Gheer was trying to free the pirate Crimpler so he could launch another attempt on the life of Teneniel Djo. Crimpler, unaware of Gheer's loyalties, killed her before escaping from prison.

**Gheeta the Hutt** A Shell Hutt who was climbing the social ladder, he was placed in charge of planning and building the main Circumtore planetary reception and diplomatic terminal to be used to receive and negotiate with visitors. Amid plots and plans gone awry, Gheeta managed to anger Boba Fett; the end result was destruction of the expensive diplomatic center and the death of Gheeta.

**Ghem, Fasald** A well-known and respected investigative HoloNet reporter from the planet Vannix, she agreed to help Leia Organa Solo expose Senator Addath Gadan's plot to surrender Vannix to the Yuuzhan Vong. She secretly recorded an encounter in which the Senator offered to steal Vannix Navy resources to give to Leia if Leia would help her win the planetary election for Presider. The footage was shown on Vannix holonetworks, dooming Senator Gadan's plans.

**G'hengle** Adar Tallon's communications officer aboard the *Silent Water.*

**Ghent, Dhagon** A member of Vaklu's forces serving on the planet Onderon in the years following the Jedi Civil War, he was arrested for the murder of Captain Sullio. Information turned up by the Jedi Exile and Nikko proved his innocence. To repay the Exile, Ghent arranged for her to meet with Jedi Master Kavar.

**Ghent, Nas** A Clone Wars veteran who turned to piracy, he was intercepted on a smuggling run by Darth Vader, who shot him down. When Ghent survived a crash landing, Vader offered him a chance to train an elite squad of Imperial starfighter pilots aboard the *Crucible.* Commander Dorin Millavec, who chafed at having a civilian training pilot aboard his ship, ordered his men to shoot down Ghent and then claimed that Vader had ordered the action as part of Ghent's "training."

**Ghent, Zakarisz** A onetime crew member of the *Wild Karrde* and employee of Talon Karrde, he was an accomplished young computer slicer from the planet Baroli. Shortly before joining Karrde's organization, Ghent was conned into traveling to Chibias as part of a plot by Counselor Raines to discredit Imperial Governor Egron and was going to take the fall when he was "rescued" by Mara Jade. It was Ghent who helped Leia Organa Solo decipher the transmissions of Delta Source and locate its whereabouts during the reign of Grand Admiral Thrawn.

*Zakarisz Ghent*

Following Thrawn's death and the formation of the Smugglers' Alliance, Ghent joined the New Republic and eventually worked his way up to the position of chief of cryptography for the New Republic Intelligence agency. He was able to reconstruct the offer of a peace treaty that was supposed to have been delivered from Colonel Vermel to Garm Bel Iblis before Vermel was captured by Captain Dorja and the *Relentless.* He was accompanied to Pakrik Minor by the Caamasi Elegos A'Kla, whose descriptions of the destruction of Caamas and the need for justice without hatred and punishment without revenge struck a chord. Ghent agreed to accompany General Hestiv to Yaga Minor, to recover a copy of the Caamas Document as a first step in the new peace between the Empire and the New Republic. He was present when Garm Bel Iblis arrived with his own assault force, hoping to steal a copy of the document.

During the Yuuzhan Vong War, Ghent served as an intelligence expert for the New Republic and continued to serve the Galactic Alliance in the wake of the invasion. His skills were called upon by Luke Skywalker during the crisis with the Colony, when it was discovered that R2-D2's memory core contained holographic information on the fate of Luke's mother. Ghent was allowed to travel to Ossus to help, but had orders from Chief of State Cal

Omas to place a number of bugs in Skywalker's offices. Mara Jade Skywalker discovered the listening devices and confronted Ghent, who explained the entire situation. Luke then put Ghent back to work on R2-D2, although the complete set of recordings couldn't be played back.

**Gherant** An Imperial Navy commander, he served as deck officer aboard the *Executor* during the last years of the New Order. Gherant was handpicked by Captain Piett, and was responsible for preventing unauthorized access to the computer core of the Super Star Destroyer.

**ghest** A reptilian predator native to the planet Rodia, it was legendary for wiping out entire villages of primitive Rodians. The large water-dwelling creature could grow to 6 meters or more. The ghest had huge eyes and a large mouth filled with razor-sharp teeth. Its four feet were heavily clawed, and its skeleton was made of cartilage rather than bone. A ghest hunted by floating along in the water with just its eyes above the surface, exploding out of the water to ambush its prey and in many cases swallow it whole.

**ghhhk** Nature's wake-up call on Clak'dor VII, the ghhhk rose with the dawn, screeching their mating calls across the jungles. Bith used their skin oils as a medicinal salve. Chewbacca had a holographic ghhhk on his holochess board on the *Millennium Falcon.*

**Ghi** A language used mainly by traders and smugglers, it was a way to communicate without worrying about eavesdroppers.

**Ghia and Tia** Twin sisters who were imprisoned by Jabba the Hutt on Tatooine. The Bestine IV natives had joined the Rebel Alliance shortly after the Battle of Yavin, but only for the chance to meet Han Solo. After Solo was frozen in carbonite on Cloud City, the sisters defected and set out to rescue him from the Hutt, but they were easily captured in Jabba's palace. As punishment, Jabba forced them to fight against other combatants in a series of demolition derby events, flying a modified T-47 airspeeder.

**Ghintee, Meeko** A Muttani murderer who was hunted down by Jango Fett after escaping from a prison facility on Oovo IV. He was killed by Fett on his second attempt to escape from the facility.

*Ghhhk*

*Ghoel*

**Ghoel** A Wol Cabasshite who lived in Jabba the Hutt's palace, he hung from the rafters and arches licking unsuspecting passersby.

**Gholondreine-b** Once a vibrant, ocean-covered world with strong ties to the Old Republic. Its leaders moved too slowly for Emperor Palpatine, however, in instituting the New Order. As punishment, Palpatine ordered all the water from the planet to be exported to Coruscant, leaving Gholondreine-b an arid desert wasteland and forcing most residents to escape the dying world. It was on Gholondreine-b that Boba Fett and Bossk agreed to team up in order to collect the bounty on Trhin Voss'on't.

**Ghomrassen** The largest and closest of Tatooine's three moons.

**Ghon, Plessus** A Jedi Knight, he and three others in the Jedi Order were killed on Kabal during a series of riots that broke out after the Trade Federation overtaxed the planet for shipping, leading to massive food shortages.

**Ghorfa** An extinct species that once inhabited the deserts of the planet Tatooine. Ghorfas dug cities into the bedrock in order to escape the heat. Many xenoarchaeologists believe that the Ghorfas died out when off-world settlers disrupted their water supply. Others believe that they evolved into a nomadic species and were the ancestors of the Tusken Raiders.

**Ghorin** A former overlord and Imperial supporter, he was the ruler of the Greater Plooriod Cluster in the months following the Battle of Yavin. From his vast castle on the planet Plooriod IV, Ghorin agreed to supply the Rebel Alliance with a shipment of grain, but pulled a double cross by providing poisoned cargo. In response, Ghorin was discredited by the Alliance, and Rebel pilots used ships stolen from Ghorin's navy to attack an Imperial supply convoy in the Geedon system. Ghorin was executed for treason by Darth Vader.

**Ghorman** Site of the infamous Ghorman Massacre, an early atrocity committed by the Empire, the planet was in the system of the same name and the Sern sector, near the Core Worlds. During a peaceful anti-tax demonstration, a warship sent to collect the taxes landed on top of the protesters, killing and injuring large numbers of people. Wilhuf Tarkin, the warship's commander, was promoted to Moff for this action. The Ghorman Massacre was commemorated every year on its anniversary by those opposed to Emperor Palpatine's New Order, and it helped convince Bail Organa of Alderaan to join the cause of the Rebellion. Years later, when an Imperial base on Ghorman was being enlarged, an Alliance attack on a vital supply convoy delayed the expansion for over a year.

***Ghorman's Honor*** A Rebel Alliance gunship named in honor of those killed in the Ghorman Massacre, it was one of five gunships sent to assist Imperial forces battling the Ssi-ruuk at Bakura.

**ghost-firing** Any false signal that was interpreted by droids as an actual command.

**Ghost Jedi** A Mrlssti band that became very popular following the Battle of Endor. They performed their concerts from an asteroid orbiting the planet and projected holoconcerts to various locations planetside. Their music was composed by Rorax Falken, a physicist who wrote precise music with little or no emotion.

**Ghostling** Ethereally beautiful humanoids native to the planet Datar, these faun-like creatures were very fragile. Entering into a physical relationship with a human meant certain death. During the last years of the Old Republic, Ghostling children were sought after as pets or slaves by many of the galaxy's less reputable beings because they were extremely beautiful and hard to find.

**Ghost Oasis** The Tusken Raider name for the campsite that Anakin Skywalker destroyed in an act of revenge for the Tusken torture of his mother, Shmi. Tusken tribes refused to enter the oasis, believing that angry ghosts of the slaughtered Tuskens remained there.

**Ghost Ones, the** A name given to a mysterious clan of Senali. Without family ties, they were considered troublemakers, creating unnecessary rivalries among clans. The Ghost Ones also spoke out against the exchange of royal children between Rutan and Senali. It was later discovered that the Ghost Ones were actually fictional, created by Prince Taroon of Rutan in order to discredit his brother, Prince

Sha'a Gi

Leed, so that Taroon himself would gain the throne of Rutan.

**ghost spydr** An arachnid native to the planet Kubindi and valued for its tasty flesh in many Kubaz dishes. The bite of a ghost spydr was poisonous, so Kubaz ranchers had to be careful around them. Many farmers took regular injections of ghost spydr poison in order to build up their immunity.

**ghost wave** Developed by the New Republic from technology created for the Shadowcast project, ghost waves were used to hide transmissions from prying ears. As part of Shadowcast, these waves were used to attach encrypted transmissions to HoloNet advertisements so that they could be "publicly" displayed to agents who were deep under cover.

**Ghrag Mercenaries** A band of pirates that terrorized the Kashyyyk system from a base in the Tyyyn Nebula at the height of the Galactic Civil War.

**Ghraggka** A Wookiee who served as protector of Prince Rikummee during the final decades of the Old Republic, his job allowed King Grakchawwaa to concentrate on running their tree-city. While the king was in negotiations with the Trade Federation as the Clone Wars began, Prince Rikummee was killed by a Separatist probe droid. More droids attacked, but Ghraggka was rescued by a group of Wookiee warriors and was able to warn King Grakchawwaa of the Trade Federation's treachery, leading him to forgo neutrality and openly declare war against the Separatists.

**Ghufran** A Rogue Squadron pilot, he joined shortly after the death of Grand Admiral Thrawn.

**Ghul, Forzi** A student who trained at the Jedi Temple on Coruscant during the Clone Wars, he was defeated by Sisseri Deo in the Apprentice Tournament that was eventually won by Tallisibeth Enwandung-Esterhazy.

Gian speeder

**Ghundrak** An Imperial officer, he served as the Moff of Thrasybule sector at the height of the New Order.

**Gi, Klin-Fa** A Jedi Knight from the planet Bonadan, she went rogue during the early stages of the Yuuzhan Vong War. She and another Jedi, Bey Gandan, had been trying to give a stolen qahsa to the New Republic after having been captured and nearly enslaved by Yuuzhan Vong shapers. Both escaped, but then split up to try to recover the organic key that would open the qahsa, which held the Yuuzhan Vong's plans to destroy bacta production on Thyferra. Jedi Master Luke Skywalker asked Uldir Lochett to bring Gi for debriefing, but she escaped from Lochett's ship and fled to the planet Wayland. Lochett found her there, and both were forced to defend themselves against the attack of a Yuuzhan Vong Chom-Vrone. They escaped with the organic key, rescued Gandan, and recovered the qahsa. But they later discovered that Gandan had been turned into the delivery mechanism for a virus that would wipe out the bacta-producing alazhi trees. In a hard-fought battle, Gandan was killed and the two Jedi eliminated all traces of the virus.

**Gi, Sha'a** A native of Ord Biniir, this young man was discovered by Daakman Barrek and taken to Coruscant to be trained as a Jedi. Sha'a Gi's talents were less martial than those of his fellow Padawans, but he excelled with computer systems and hoped to work in the Jedi Archives upon completion of his trials. Gi found the mental discipline of the Jedi Order difficult. Awkward and possessed by self-doubt, he had trouble controlling his fear when operating alone. Master Barrek strengthened his confidence when they worked together, and the two were effective in gathering intelligence to counter pirate forces in the Outer Rim.

During such an operation after the outbreak of the Clone Wars, Barrek and Gi discovered a massive droid foundry on Hypori. An elite Jedi task force complete with clone trooper forces arrived to destroy the Confederacy stronghold, but this mission quickly turned to disaster. The droid forces, led by General Grievous, destroyed much of the task force and killed Barrek. Although surrounded by some of the most powerful Jedi in the Order, Gi was filled with fear as super battle droids encircled him and the others. Gi panicked and ran out into the open where Grievous pounced on him, spearing his flesh with his talons and crushing him with his weight.

**Gi/9** A small, high-powered anti-personnel laser cannon made by Corellian Engineering Corporation during the New Order. Jabba the Hutt installed 20 of the weapons aboard his sail barge, the *Khetanna.*

**Gian speeder** This large military repulsorcraft was a modified version of the V-19 speeder made by SoroSuub during the last decades of the Old Republic. In the Naboo Royal armed forces, Gian speeders were supported by two or more Flash speeders. The resistance groups organized by Captain Panaka and Queen Amidala used them during the Trade Federation invasion of Naboo. The Gian speeder was 5.7 meters long, could transport four beings (a pilot, a gunner, and two passengers), and was armed with three light repeating laser blasters. A Gian speeder could attain speeds of 160 kilometers per hour. To ensure that the speeder remained operable during combat, the Naboo added redundant power generators for the weapons, and they upgraded the underside plating to withstand land mines.

Giant Flog

**Giant Flog** Few Rattatak gladiators had careers that spanned weeks, much less years, but the simple brute known only as Giant Flog survived the bloody circuit for nearly two years. Little was known about the giant's origins except that a shadowy benefactor named Kesivo was his owner. Unlike other patrons, Kesivo was not prone to bragging; his only conversations were to discuss payment, wagering, and other transactions. This led to countless rumors and unbridled speculation that only fed Giant Flog's reputation. Wild tales included Flog being a demon summoned by occult means, while others said he was patched together from the parts of dead gladiators. In truth, Kesivo had purchased Flog during a fruitful trading mission to the Moddell sector, though mystery veils any other details.

Though sentient, Giant Flog had little command of any language. His coarse voice box could manage only a few words in Basic, including his crude name, and he obeyed only Kesivo. His preferred weapon was a craggy hunk of stone attached to a chain that he wielded like a primitive mace. The day that Asajj Ventress chose to enter the gladiator pit to prove herself a worthy disciple of Count Dooku, Giant Flog was the warrior who stood to the last to face her. Her paired lightsaber strike felled the titan and also severed the chain holding his mace. The liberated chunk of stone soared through the air and crashed into the viewing box holding Kesivo. Giant Flog's benefactor was crushed to death before having to witness the demise of his most profitable warrior.

**giant fungi forest** A forest on the planet Kessel, it was made up of huge, trumpet-shaped fungi that were large and strong enough to allow the inhabitants of Kessel to build homes and offices inside them. Several large fungi were even used as landing pads.

**giant lily** Native to the ponds and marshes of Ithor, these plants anchored themselves by gluing their roots to underwater stones. This natural cement was used by Ithorians in the construction of body panels for their leaf-ships.

**Giat Nor** The capital of the planet N'zoth, this was the hometown of Yevethan strongman Nil Spaar. Any non-Yevetha discovered in the city were executed on sight so that their smell did not offend.

**Giba, Lonnag** Head of the Galacian Council of Ministers when Queen Veda decided to have a democratic election to determine her successor, he plotted to assume control of Gala himself. His complex plot was discovered by Qui-Gon Jinn and his apprentice Obi-Wan Kenobi, who had been asked by the queen to help in the election process. Giba was exposed as a traitor, arrested, and removed from power.

**Gibb** The chief mechanic at the run-down starport in Lesvol on the planet Prishardia, he helped Fenig Nabon repair the *Star Lady* several years after the Battle of Endor. Gibb even piloted the ship in an attempt to rescue Fen, Ghitsa Dogder, and Kyp Durron from mercenaries.

**Gibbela** A remote world scouted by the Empire for colonization. A small Imperial detachment was sent with the expectation of little resistance. An initial fly-by had shown small humanoids engaged in farming. But the simple humanoids were actually polymorphs that could double in size when angered, turning into vicious predators. The Imperial team sent to Gibbela was quickly destroyed and its equipment put to use for farming.

**gibbit bird** An avian symbiont to the rancor. The ferocious rancor allowed a gibbit to roam freely in its mouth, where the bird cleaned the creature's teeth by picking out pieces of bone and flesh.

**Gibbs** A shape-shifter who infiltrated Cularin's government at the height of the Clone Wars to gain access to political leaders. He posed as a human and was placed in charge of arranging events that heralded the return home of Senator Lavina Wren. Gibbs spent much of his time trying to convince Warlan Tosk that everything was in order, despite Tosk's ingrained skepticism. It was later revealed that Gibbs was working with an assassin who had been hired to kill Senator Wren.

**Giel, Mils** An Imperial admiral who commanded a large fleet of warships in the months following the Battle of Hoth, he demanded complete compliance with his orders. When it was learned that the Rebel Alliance had stolen the fleet's travel routes from the outpost on Spindrift, Admiral Giel refused to believe that this incident would affect him or his order to return the only known specimen of teezl—an organic communicator—to Coruscant. He was unprepared when Luke Skywalker and a group of pilots managed to infiltrate his armada flying in modified TIE fighters, and he quickly ordered the teezl to jam communications. Luke still managed to get a shot away and destroy the teezl. After the admiral admitted his mistakes to Darth Vader, the Sith Lord spared his life, but demoted him to lieutenant.

Giel was then dispatched to Golrath Station to search for clues as to the location of Alliance forces. He triggered a reactor overload that would have destroyed Golrath as part of an improvised plan to capture Leia Organa. Leia escaped along with the rest of the Alliance team. Trying to return to Coruscant, Giel was shipwrecked on the planet Beheboth, where he spent five years experimenting with a new way to destroy the Alliance. But his plans were discovered and exposed.

**giffa** A mammalian predator that often was domesticated and used as a hunting beast. Giffas were known for an amazing sense of smell and powerful legs.

**Gifford, Dru** A pilot for Green Squadron at Eyrie Base at the height of the Galactic Civil War, he was killed while escorting a Corellian cruiser full of supplies to the survivors of Echo Base on Hoth.

***Gift of Anguish*** A Yuuzhan Vong warship that intercepted the *Nebula Chaser* as it was trying to evacuate refugees from the planet Talfaglio. Its captain tried to get Leia Organa Solo to turn over information on the Jedi Knights. She refused, and the *Nebula Chaser* and all it passengers were destroyed.

**Gifts of the True Gods** According to the Gospel of the True Gods, the Yuuzhan Vong were given three gifts by their gods: Life, the least of their gifts, so that the Yuuzhan Vong could serve the True Gods; Pain, so that each Yuuzhan Vong knew that life's value lay only in the service of the True Gods; and Death, which was the greatest gift of all, providing the Blessed Release from the burden of Pain and the curse of Life.

**giggle-dust** Spacer slang for almost any form of inhaled illegal drug.

**Gigoran** A species of tall, furred bipeds, they were noted for their empathic nature. Living on the mountainous planet of Gigor, they had long, well-muscled limbs with well-padded hands and feet. Gigorans could speak Basic but preferred their own native language of grunts and chirps. They led a peaceful existence until a group of smugglers established a base on Gigor and started selling the Gigorans as indentured labor, primarily to the Empire.

**Giiett, Micah** A contemporary of Mace Windu, this Jedi Master served on the Jedi Council. A portly man with three thick rows of hair on his head, Micah Giiett used unusual methods to teach his students the pitfalls of relying solely on the Force for their power. The Jedi was good friends with Plo Koon, and over the years the pair had developed a sharp repartee; others might have mistaken it for one-upmanship, but those close to the Jedi knew that the two were good friends. Giiett accompanied Mace Windu and other Jedi to the Yinchorri system to deal with the growing aggression of the Yinchorri. Injured in the final battle at Yinchorr, Jedi Master Giiett sacrificed himself to allow the other Jedi to escape. When he was confronted by the Yinchorri warriors, he used his lightsaber to ignite the fuel cells of a ground tank, killing himself and the leaders of the Yinchorri military. Mace Windu suggested that Ki-Adi-Mundi be elected to fill Master Giiett's position on the Jedi Council.

**Giju** The homeworld of the Herglics, one of the first species to join the Old Republic, it was known for its explorers and merchants. The Empire took over the manufacturing centers on Giju after a short but bloody battle, and forced the Herglics into hard labor. When the New Republic was born, the Herglics were able to rebuild their society quickly because their cities and manufacturing facilities had been spared any major damage.

**giju stew** A dish best made with a bit of boontaspice, although even that can't mask its foul odor.

***Gilagimar*** One of the most famous warships of the Expansion Period, it was a cruiser-sized starship.

**Gilamar, Mij** A Mandalorian soldier, he was chosen by Jango Fett to join the ranks of the *Cuy'val Dar* in the years before the Clone Wars. Gilamar was a noted expert on covert operations and also taught a course on combat and field medicine that provided the clone troopers with a basic knowledge of first aid and medical triage.

**Gilatter VIII** A gas giant and the eighth planet in the Gilatter system, it was in the Mid Rim near Ansion. During the last millennium of the Old Republic, the planet was surrounded by many floating resorts frequented by wealthy vacationers who could marvel at the swirling gases of the planet's surface. The last resort went out of business about a century before the Galactic Civil War. Most of the resorts were abandoned, but one was later used as a meeting site by members of the Confederation at the height of the Corellia–Galactic Alliance War. Attendees were supposed to elect a Supreme Commander to win the war against the Galactic Alliance. But that rumor was just bait in an elaborate trap set up by Turr Phennir, who already had been elected Supreme Commander. It allowed Confederation warships to mass and trap Galactic Alliance forces against the surface of Gilatter VIII.

***Gilded Claw*** An *Imperial*-class Star Destroyer, it was part of the security force used by Kuat Drive Yards to protect its facilities in the early years of the New Republic. The *Gilded Claw* was part of a task force sent to combat Warlord Zsinj and the *Iron Fist* during the warlord's attempt to steal the *Razor's Kiss.* Although the *Gilded Claw* and its TIE fighter squadrons caused considerable damage to the *Iron Fist,* the larger ship managed to inflict serious damage on the *Gilded Claw* before escaping.

***Gilded Thranta*** An FX-77 Star Yacht owned by the Rodian Falloon, it was armed with two turret-mounted dual laser cannons along with a concussion missile launcher. Falloon, who was really the former Black Sun accountant Soolehad, gave the ship to the group of mercenaries who got him off Sriluur during the Yuuzhan Vong War.

**gilden** A creature whose soft flesh was pulverized to form a drinkable substance favored by Shistavanen Wolfmen.

**Gileng sector** The name given to a part of Coruscant that had been destroyed and rebuilt by the Yuuzhan Vong into a simulacrum of their long-lost homeworld, Yuuzhan'tar.

**Gilflyn** One of many Corellians who joined the Jedi Order during the last years of the Old Republic, he went into hiding when Emperor Palpatine began his Jedi Purge. He eventually decided he wanted to be a Sith apprentice.

**Gilfrome** A Brolfi, he was guildmaster of Barlok's mining operations in the years following the Battle of Naboo. Opposed to Corporate Alliance plans to take control of the mining operations, he was a key participant in the negotiations mediated by Jedi Master Jorus C'baoth. When C'baoth destroyed a slinker missile that was supposed to assassinate both Gilfrome and Passel Argente, C'baoth was securing mining rights for the Brolfi while protecting the Corporate Alliance's investments on Barlok.

Nolan Gillmunn

***Gilgam*** A Pursuer enforcement ship, it was owned by K'Armyn Viraxo during the Galactic Civil War. He used it to harass Harlequin Station as well as Azzameen Station.

**Gillespee, Samuel Tomas** A somewhat less-than-honorable friend of Talon Karrde, he once retired from the smuggling trade to set up house on the planet Ukio. But when Grand Admiral Thrawn took control of the planet, Gillespee left in search of a smuggling operation willing to employ him and his men. He signed on with Karrde to indirectly but profitably help the New Republic. His ship was *Kern's Pride.*

***Gillia*** A heavily modified Suwantek TL-1800 freighter, it was placed at the disposal of Imperial Security Bureau Major Drelfin shortly after the Battle of Yavin. Drelfin was dispatched to oversee the actions of the crew of the Star Destroyer *Reprisal* during the subjugation of the planet Teardrop and leveled charges of treason against Daric LaRone and a squad of stormtroopers. LaRone then killed Drelfin, and the stormtroopers stole the *Gillia.* They eventually renamed the freighter as the *Melnor Spear* in an effort to escape Imperial notice.

**Gilliana** The primary world in the Gilliana system, Tapani sector, it was part of the holdings of House Cadriaan during the New Order.

**Gilling** An Imperial Security Bureau agent, he accompanied Colonel Vak Somoril on his investigation of the desertion of several stormtroopers from the Star Destroyer *Reprisal.* Gilling and his partner, Brock, were later dispatched by Somoril to accompany and keep an eye on Mara Jade in case the Emperor's Hand tried to interfere with their operations. Gilling inadvertently revealed that they were under orders from Colonel Somoril, and the two agents started to take Jade captive. They were interrupted by a group of BloodScar pirates who began firing at them, killing both agents.

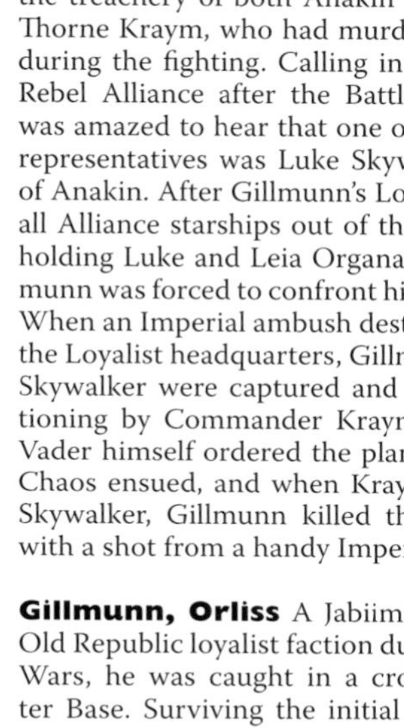

**Gillmunn, Nolan** The son of Orliss Gillmunn, he led a small band of Loyalist Rebels that opposed the Imperial occupation of Jabiim during the Galactic Civil War. Nolan Gillmunn, a young man during the Clone Wars, had witnessed what he considered the treachery of both Anakin Skywalker and Thorne Kraym, who had murdered his father during the fighting. Calling in help from the Rebel Alliance after the Battle of Yavin, he was amazed to hear that one of the Alliance's representatives was Luke Skywalker, the son of Anakin. After Gillmunn's Loyalists ordered all Alliance starships out of the system while holding Luke and Leia Organa prisoner, Gillmunn was forced to confront his own demons. When an Imperial ambush destroyed much of the Loyalist headquarters, Gillmunn and Luke Skywalker were captured and held for questioning by Commander Kraym. Then Darth Vader himself ordered the planet obliterated. Chaos ensued, and when Kraym tried to kill Skywalker, Gillmunn killed the commander with a shot from a handy Imperial blaster.

**Gillmunn, Orliss** A Jabiimite who led an Old Republic loyalist faction during the Clone Wars, he was caught in a crossfire at Shelter Base. Surviving the initial assault, Orliss Gillmunn was able to rally surviving troops to a staging point, hoping for a rescue. Anakin Skywalker led the mission and ensured that the survivors were able to get offplanet after 43 days of fighting. When Anakin was forced to limit the number of survivors after two rescue ships were damaged approaching Jabiim, Gillmunn lashed out at Anakin and the Republic for bringing the war to his planet and threatened to shoot the Jedi. Anakin used a Force choke to get Gillmunn to drop his weapon. Still, Gillmunn continued to fight the Separatists until he was executed at the hands of Governor Thorne Kraym.

Orliss Gillmunn

**Gilly** Along with his twin brother, Spence, he joined the Erased in the wake of the Clone Wars. Both refused to reveal any details about their past to their fellow outcasts. Like many of the Erased, Gilly wanted to locate Solace and find peace, so he joined Ferus Olin and

Trever Flume on their search. After locating Solace and identifying her as the former Jedi Fy-Tor-Ana, Olin and Flume set out to return to the surface and prevent Inquisitor Malorum from locating them. Gilly and the other members of the Erased remained behind in the underground settlement, but found themselves under attack by agents sent by Malorum. Gilly was later discovered among the dead.

**Gilp** A young student at the Jedi Temple on Coruscant during the last years of the Old Republic.

**Gilyad, Bahm** An ancient healer who established the rules and responsibilities for the medical profession some five millennia before the Clone Wars, he documented them in a form that survived time. In addition to the rules, Gilyad also recorded a number of ideas for maintaining a physician's own mental and physical health.

**Gimble, Lokk** An Ugnaught member of Sebolto's gang, he had a bounty on his head issued by the Corporate Alliance for the theft of classified chemical manufacturing information that was later used in the production of death sticks laced with deadly neurotoxins. The bounty was claimed by Jango Fett, who captured both Gimble and his partner, "Ratchet" Gramzee, on Malastare.

**gimer stick** An edible twig, it could be snapped off from plants that grew in the Dagobah swamps. The gimer plant produced a succulent juice that concentrated in sacs on the bark. The sticks were chewed for their flavor and to quench thirst. Jedi Master Yoda enjoyed chewing gimer sticks and believed the juice—which had anesthetic properties—aided meditation.

**Gimlet** A small blue-skinned alien with a knobbed skull and fan-like mouth, he posed as a reporter for the Holopix News agency on Challon in the years prior to the Battle of Yavin. Gimlet served as an assistant to Giles Durane, who had been hired by Bail Organa to instruct Leia in the use of weapons. After Leia completed her training, Gimlet secretly returned to Challon to ensure her safety. He intercepted Torgas's assassination attempt, but the Sakiyan assassin shot Gimlet in the chest, and he died from the wound.

**Gimm** The farther-out of two moons that orbited Genesia, it was colonized in much the same way as its sister, Laut. Underground facilities were formed to allow colonists to survive on the airless rock, providing them with living and working areas near, but not actually on, Genesia. The colonists created the cities to escape from the corruption and crime that dominated Genesia.

**Gin** One of the earlier settlers on the planet Nam Chorios, she was Arvid Scraf's aunt. Gin lived in Ruby Gulch and used some of her influence with the Newcomers to get Luke Skywalker a job in Hweg Shul.

**Ginbotham** A Hig, he was a slender blue creature whose piloting skills were renowned. Ginbotham served with Wedge Antilles as a member of the command crew on the *Yavin.*

**Gingal** An inexperienced Mon Calamari officer in the New Republic, he served as Pash Cracken's commanding officer while on station at the planet Xyquine. When the Empire attacked the New Republic there, Gingal was unsure how to retreat. He began to order a fallback, but Cracken interrupted him before he could broadcast the orders to the entire fleet . . . and to the Imperials waiting to attack them. Gingal took Pash's advice, saving much of Gingal's fleet. The resulting tactic became known as the Cracken Twist.

**Ginger** One of many young children brought to Ruusan to help the Army of Light fight against the Brotherhood of Darkness during the Battle of Ruusan. Ginger, like the rest of the Jedi, was killed when Lord Kaan activated his thought bomb.

***Ginivex*-class starfighter** *See* Geonosian Fanblade starfighter.

**ginntho** Also known as the Utapaun spider, this large arachnid was domesticated as a pet by the Utapauns. A ginntho had six separate spinnerets, each of which was capable of producing an exceptionally strong silk webbing. Many Utapauns trained their ginnthos to spin webs on command, a skill that was put to widespread use in setting traps during the Separatist occupation of Utapau near the end of the Clone Wars.

**Ginorra, Lexia** A Jedi Padawan during the last years of the Old Republic, she abandoned the Jedi Order after she was abducted by a criminal kingpin on Kamparas and slaughtered her kidnappers to escape. She eventually returned to Coruscant and became a vigilante, stopping any crimes she saw with bloody swiftness.

**Ginzork, Peert** A patient, experienced soldier, he was the brute force behind the Shield. His name was an assumed identity. After serving as an assault trooper with the Imperial Army, he went AWOL, then emerged several years later as Peert Ginzork and formed the Shield. Many of Ginzork's operations served to protect field agents and other Rebel Alliance sympathizers.

**Gion, Dara** The commander and chief personnel officer of the Rebel Alliance's Oracle Base during the Galactic Civil War, this Bacrana native was apolitical until Moff Ramier wiped out thousands of protestors in Amma. Dara and her lover, Equa Felens, were injured in the battle, and they fled into hiding. They eventually joined up with Trep Reskan and the Bacrana System Defense Force, and later joined the Alliance with them.

**Gira** A red-haired Jedi Knight, he was trying to get a group of Padawan learners to safety during the Jedi Purge when Darth Vader captured his starship. Gira agreed to join Vader and the dark side in return for the Padawans' safety. But the starship captain had already agreed to join the Empire to save his own life, and the Padawans were killed when their escape ship was destroyed. Gira, unable to reconcile the deaths of the Padawans against his decision to save himself, took his own life.

**Giran** This Kadas'sa'Nikto worked with Malakili to tend Jabba the Hutt's rancor. He hoped to trap a krayt dragon and bring it to Jabba as a present, but died when Jabba's sail barge exploded near the Pit of Carkoon.

**Girdun, Heol** A captain in the Coruscant Security Force in the years following the Yuuzhan Vong War, he was later attached to the Galactic Alliance Guard. When Ailyn Habuur was captured in a raid, and it was learned that she had been hired by Thrackan Sal-Solo to assassinate Han Solo and his family, Captain Girdun argued with Captain Shevu that she should be interrogated nonstop until she revealed everything she knew. Girdun was dismayed, but not upset, when Habuur was killed in Jacen Solo's attempt to use the Force to extract information from her. Jacen then gave Girdun permission to interrogate Buroy, a Corellian agent who'd been brought in with Habuur.

As Jacen began to influence other aspects of the military, including the court-martial of his twin sister, Jaina, Girdun began to wonder about his motivations and openly raised questions. However, his experience with the intelligence agency made him the perfect choice to assume command of the Galactic Alliance Intelligence Service when it was placed under the command of the GAG following the arrest of Chief of State Cal Omas.

**girondium** A material combined with colium to manufacture ultra-high-efficiency solar cells, it was used by the Empire to make girondium-colium solar cells for the TIE bomber and later the TIE interceptor.

**Gistang, Jes** A Corellian who served in the 407th Stormtrooper Division based on Yinchorr nearly a century after the end of the war against the Yuuzhan Vong, she was a street kid until the local Imperial Mission took her in and helped her clean up her act. A heavy-weapons

*Giran*

Githany

expert, Gistang was a member of Joker Squad; she was one of many stormtroopers who quietly questioned their loyalty to the "Empire" after the Sith Lord Darth Krayt took control of the galaxy and exiled former Emperor Roan Fel. So when Lieutenant Gil Cassel explained that the 407th's next mission was to eliminate the 908th Stormtrooper Division for defecting and joining Fel, Gistang was the first to openly question the order. Still, the Jokers agreed that their job was to carry out orders, and set out to take the 908th's headquarters building. The mission got harder as the 407th penetrated the fortress, and a shot from above managed to strike the power pack on Gistang's heavy blaster rifle, causing it to explode and kill her.

**Githany** A former Jedi Knight, she was one of a few warriors who succumbed to the dark side of the Force during the early skirmishes in the Battle of Ruusan. It was believed that she had been taken in at a very young age by the Cathar Jedi Master Handa, who was also training a young man by the name of Kiel Charny, who became her lover. She eventually became a Jedi Knight and served as part of Lord Hoth's Army of Light.

One legend had it that Githany was the warrior who brought a bowl of poisoned bloodsoup to Darth Bane as part of Lord Kaan's effort to eliminate a rival. However, Bane admired her for her bravery and chose Githany to be his own lieutenant in an effort to unite the Sith under one strong leader. Before she could make a name for herself, Lord Kaan detonated his thought bomb, and Githany fell to her death in a newly opened chasm.

Another story, deemed more accurate by Jedi historians, told of Githany defecting to the Brotherhood of Darkness after gathering information about Jedi defenses from her lover, Charny. She turned this information over to Lord Kaan, who agreed to send her to Korriban for further training as a Sith. In this version of the story, Githany trained Bane in dark side techniques but tried to play both sides of every situation. She was among the Sith Lords who were called together to create a thought bomb in a last-ditch effort to defeat the Army of Light. When she recognized that the combined strength of the Sith Lords would not save them from the bomb's blast, she tried to flee but was unable to outrun the devastating waves of power.

**Givens** An Imperial recruit, he was part of Kyle Katarn's squadron during the taking of asteroid AX-456. He worked with Morley as the team's demolitions experts, and became the lead when Morley was killed during the early stages of the battle.

**Givin** Looking a bit like animated skeletons, Givin wore their bones on the outside of their bodies. Their skull-like faces were dominated by large, triangular eye sockets, making them seem sad all the time. Native to the planet Yag'Dhul, they were a precise species and were skilled mathematicians. The sight of exposed flesh made them ill. They could seal their joints to withstand the vacuum of space. These xenophobic humanoids enjoyed a fairly advanced technology, and were respected starship builders in most sectors of the galaxy. During the Clone Wars, the Givin allied themselves with the Confederacy of Independent Systems, providing their shipbuilding talents in an effort to gain a measure of respect against the Mon Calamari. This provided the Separatists with access to, and control of, the Rimma Trade Route and the Corellian Trade Spine. It also allowed the Separatists to take advantage of the natural Givin ability to calculate hyperspace travel routes in their heads, reducing dependence on navigational computers.

**Gizen, Uv** One of Chancellor Palpatine's aides in the years leading up to the Battle of Geonosis.

**Gizer** This planet was known for, among other things, its ale and the manufacture of space freighters.

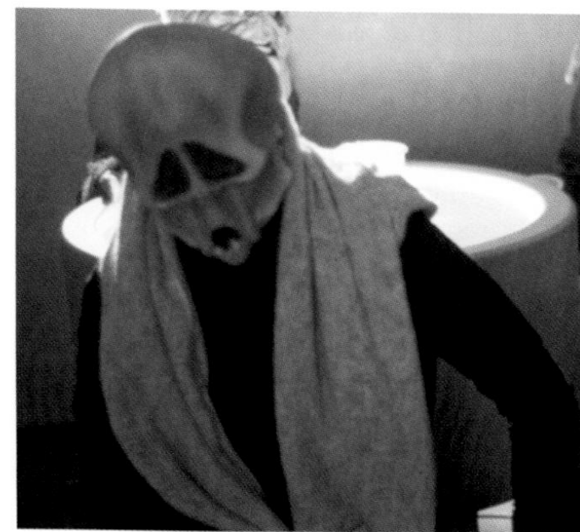
Givin

**Gizer ale** A pale blue drink, it is a favorite of Han Solo.

**gizka** A fish prized among Selkath for its meat. Many xenobiologists believed that the gizka found on Manaan was a placid descendant of a more vicious creature that originated some four millennia before the Galactic Civil War on the Unknown World of the Rakata. That species produced a new generation every few days and played havoc with electrical power systems. The creatures could be eliminated only by using a specialized poison that made them rabid so they would attack and kill other gizkas before dying.

**Gizz, Big (the Gizman)** A hulking brute of a humanoid, he was captain of Jabba the Hutt's swoop gang on Tatooine during the Galactic Civil War. He had long, shaggy hair and a well-muscled physique. Gizz worked with the Imperial agent Jix but learned so much about his past that Jix blasted him. Big Gizz's body was found by the B'omarr monks, who reanimated him. They fixed the hole in his skull with a metal plate that continually picked up stray communications.

Big (the Gizman) Gizz

**Gjon, Honest** A M'haeli from the moon Bogg 4, his right arm had been replaced with a cybernetic tool extension. He was known for taking in ships to repair, only to have them "stolen" while he was working on them. Gjon actually brought the ships to a facility on Bogg 11, where he scrapped them and sold their component parts on the black market. Honest Gjon nearly scrapped the *Slave I* shortly after the Battle of Geonosis when a young Boba Fett asked him to repair a landing strut, but he was caught before the ship could be stripped.

**GK Oppressor** A series of combat droids produced on the planet Mustafar during the New Order.

**gla** A form of breeding pool, it was developed by the Yuuzhan Vong to breed amphistaffs.

**Gladiator assault fighter** A combat starship used by the Mandalorians who accompanied Boba Fett during the Yuuzhan Vong War, it originally was developed by

FreiTek Incorporated for use by the Mandalorian Protectors under the command of Fenn Shysa—first as a patrol ship, and then as an attack craft when the Mandalorians began to expand their sphere of influence. The mission profile of the one-man Gladiator was to travel in groups of four ships, which were slaved to a *Pursuer*-class enforcement ship for jumps through hyperspace. Each fighter was armed with four Bovin J-3F laser cannons and an ArMek SW-12c ion cannon on its nose.

**gladiator droid** These robots were designed for close-quarters combat in the declining days of the Old Republic. Gladiator droids were used in violent sporting events involving other droids or even living creatures.

**gladiator walker** Designed after the Imperial AT-ST and its predecessor the AT-PT, they became popular during the rise of the New Order. Produced by zZip Product Concepts and SecuriTech, gladiator walkers were single-person units designed to allow a rider to fight in a tournament against other riders. Armed with a light laser cannon and protected by heavy armor and shields, gladiator walkers were relatively safe to operate. In the event of imminent danger to its occupant, the walker's computer system shut down the entire craft and notified other walkers of its "demise."

***Glaive*** A cargo ferry used to smuggle stolen Imperial goods into the Sepan system, it was captured by the Empire during the Galactic Civil War.

**Glaive** An immense man distinguished by his drooping mustache, metal gauntlets, and leather armor that barely protected his heavily muscled body, he was a Jedi Master. Glaive and his apprentice Zule were dispatched with Obi-Wan Kenobi and Anakin Skywalker to the moon of Ohma-D'un to investigate the loss of a Gungan colony after the Battle of Geonosis. The four Jedi discovered that a new form of combat droid under the command of the bounty hunter Durge had been sent to exterminate the Gungans. When Durge captured Zule, Glaive was forced to stay his hand. Obi-Wan's actions allowed Zule to break free, but Glaive was unprepared for the sudden appearance of Asajj Ventress. Using her own lightsaber, Ventress beheaded Glaive before Obi-Wan could act.

**Glakka** The site of a gunrunning operation of Jabba the Hutt and the Chevin criminal Ephant Mon, this ice-covered moon was nearly their final resting place. They plotted to steal an Imperial weapons cache on Glakka but were ambushed by an Imperial squad. They survived the attack yet almost died during the subzero night, when Jabba kept Ephant Mon alive by covering him in the folds of his slug-like body. The pair were rescued in the morning.

**Glarret** An old man, he served as Xaverri's assistant during the years following the death of Xaverri's family until she replaced him with a young Han Solo.

*Glaive*

**Glarsaur** A species of sentient reptilians native to the swamps of Gelgelar. They were brutish creatures who would rather fight than discuss an issue. Roughly humanoid in shape, Glarsaurs had curled tails and muscled limbs studded with sharp claws. Their dorsal ridge was protected by thick, green scales, and their belly was covered with segmented plates.

***Glas*** An Imperial System Patrol Craft, it was hijacked by Ripoblus refugees seeking asylum.

**Glasfir'a'lik** A Defel criminal, he was leader of the Glasfir Ring. Originally a Hutt enforcer, but left stranded on Demesel by the Hutts, for three years he hunted down every Hutt agent on the planet. His ability to successfully kill a Hutt—despite the large bounty placed on his head by the Hutts—earned him semi-legendary status on Demesel. Glasfir'a'lik eventually commanded the attention of the criminal underworld of Demesel and quickly took control of the various elements. Glasfir threatened and bribed the planetary government, and eventually won control of the underworld and a level of immunity from prosecution.

**Gla Soocha** *See* Da Soocha.

**Glass, Den Sait** A member of Klyn Shanga's Renatasian vigilantes, who searched for Vuffi Raa during the early years of the New Order.

**glassine** A material used to construct starship viewports.

**Glass Mountain** A barren mountain on the planet Tatooine, it was the site where Jabba the Hutt hid his personal escape ship. Jabba had left the small Lizling Onoh to guard it.

**glasteel** An alloy developed before the Yuuzhan Vong War, it was as strong as durasteel but also transparent. This made glasteel perfect for use in forming the large windows of skytowers and other large buildings, making the windows part of the overall superstructure.

**Glauheim** A gas giant, it was the second planet of the Marcellus system and had three satellites.

**Glave, Modigal** An Imperial commander who was sent to scout the Ishanna system at the height of the New Order, he served under Governor Klime. A seasoned Imperial commando, Glave led a group of stormtroopers to the Combat Moon with the help of the Rabaanite traitor Andos Delvaren. It was Glave who battled Mika Streev and Sh'shak on the Combat Moon, nearly capturing them twice. Glave's arm was cut off by Streev, but Glave and his Imperial forces fled the Combat Moon before Rebel Alliance agents could supplement the warriors.

**Glayyd, Mor** The patriarch of the Glayyd family on the planet Ammuud, he succeeded his poisoned father. *Mor* was a title of respect; Glayyd's given name was Ewwen. Han Solo visited the planet prior to his involvement in the Rebellion, and—with the support of Han and some others—Mor Glayyd was able to smash a slavery ring there.

***Glazer*** A Nharwaak CR90 corvette, it was destroyed during the Galactic Civil War.

**GLD-M** A series of general-purpose labor droids made by Industrial Automaton for mining operations. They contained a Rapid-Program module for easy modification of their programming. This module allowed them to serve in a variety of capacities, including as scouts, planners, and drivers.

**Gleasry, Pharnis** An agent of the Human League sent to monitor Han Solo and Luke Skywalker during the Corellian Trade Summit, he was arrested after the Starbuster Plot was broken up, and testified about the full extent of the Human League's infiltration of the New Republic on Coruscant.

**gleb rations** Developed during the last decades of the Old Republic, this flat, cardboard-like ration was easy to transport and provided a day's worth of nutrients for most humanoid species.

**Glee Anselm** An aquatic planet, it was the homeworld of the Nautolan and Anselmi species. Much of the planet's surface was covered with swamps and lakes, with just enough physical landmass to support the Anselmi.

Because of its axial tilt and seasonal changes, the planet was often ravaged by intense hurricanes and other storms.

**Gleemort, Ghana** A Gamorrean employed by Jabba the Hutt to guard his Tatooine palace, he was secretly negotiating with the B'omarr monks to defect from Jabba's service before the Hutt's death at the hands of Leia Organa.

**Glek, Salin** A Quarren lieutenant with the Rebel Alliance, he was part of the team supporting Admiral Ackbar during Project Shantipole. Salin Glek also was a traitor, inserted into the Alliance by Bane Nothos so that he could leak information on the progress of Shantipole. Glek grew up in the bowels of a Mon Calamari floating city and thoroughly despised the Mon Calamari. As he rose through Alliance ranks, he kept planning his revenge. When Glek realized that Ackbar was about to send off the B-wing prototypes for manufacture, he notified Nothos to begin his attack. Glek fled Shantipole by stealing the *Out Runner,* but was not heard from after the defeat of Nothos.

**Glena** One of the many descendants of the original Eol Sha colonists, she married Warton and was among the many colonists who were relocated to Dantooine during the early years of the New Order. When Admiral Daala attacked and leveled the Dantooine settlement that was created for the Eol Sha colonists, Glena was among the dead.

**glet-mite** A small pest, it was hormonally modified by Beldorion the Hutt's second chef to grow to huge proportions for eating. This Kubaz cook discovered how to use the excretions from hall d'main to complement the glet-mite's teleological systems.

**Gli, Darian** A Markul professor, he was the contact that academic Melvosh Bloor was supposed to make at Jabba the Hutt's palace to arrange for an interview with the crime lord. Bloor found out too late that Darian Gli had been eaten by Jabba months before.

***Glich*** An Alliance escort shuttle, it was destroyed during the Galactic Civil War.

**Glidamir, Norrion** A Lorrdian woman who served the Rebel Alliance as a major, she was a contemporary of Barosa Warren during his service to the Old Republic. An expert in urban survival techniques, she was one of the graduates of the Twilight Class of the Galactic Outdoor Survival School. A veteran of the Corint City mission on Pirik, Glidamir died in action during the early stages of the Galactic Civil War.

**glide lizard** A large black reptile, it was able to "fly" over short distances by extending the flaps of skin beneath its legs.

**glider** A common avian creature native to urban areas of the planet Corellia, it lived in large flocks and fed on trash that people left behind, leaving its droppings on sidewalks and benches.

**Glidrick, Stenn** A retired Imperial Navy pilot, he became a civilian starship captain. His last assignment was piloting the *Kuari Princess.* Stenn Glidrick was the one who broke the news to Celia Durasha that her brother Raine had been killed on Ralltiir. Glidrick also was in command when the Riders of the Maelstrom boarded the ship and took control of it; he was killed in the attack.

**glie** A species of single-celled organisms native to the planet Naboo, it existed in two distinct varieties. Green glie, the first, grew quickly on the surface of swamps, creating a greenish mass and choking out other swamp plants while consuming all nutrients it could find. It was a single-cell alga. The Naboo underground discovered a way to harness water contaminated by green glie to create deadly poisons. The second variety—red glie—was similar, but didn't grow as quickly and obtained its nutrients via photosynthesis. It didn't survive easily in shaded areas. Gungans harvested red glie as a food source; it made a particularly tasty salad dressing. It was also ideal for water purification.

**glimmerfish** These finger-sized fish native to the planet Alderaan swarmed the canals and waterways of the planet. During the mating season, hundreds of eggs were laid by each female, and they all hatched at about the same time. The explosion of tiny glimmerfish turned waters silvery with their roiling passage.

**glimmik** A musical form embraced by many nonhuman species during the final decades of the Old Republic, it was distinguished by its heavy, thumping backbeat.

**glim worm** Found on numerous planets, the many species of glim worms resembled tube-like predators covered with sharp scales. They were highly adaptable, living in the desert as well as urban areas. They burrowed quite well, having developed a complex musculature that allowed them to flow across a wide range of surfaces. Glim worms hunted by detecting the subtle vibrations caused by the movement of their prey, and had only to come in contact with the prey to catch it by extending their scales.

**glistaweb** Developed by the Yuuzhan Vong, this shimmering fabric was made from living material that generated a charge-neutralizing field along its fibrous form. This allowed a robe or tunic of glistaweb to deflect blasterfire almost as well as vonduun crab armor, but much less conspicuously.

**glitbiter** A slang term referring to glitterstim spice addicts who consume it in its raw form. They were often high-strung and tended to ramble incoherently.

***Glitterstar*** One of several luxury liners that brought the wealthy and powerful to Alakatha, the *Glitterstar* flew regularly from the resort world to Coruscant during the early years of the New Republic. It was attacked by Phan Riizolo and the *Booty Full,* a move that Rogue Squadron believed was backed by Leonia Tavira. However, Riizolo had actually severed ties with Tavira and was operating on his own.

**glitterstim** A potent spice that was mined on the planet Kessel, it gave a brief but pleasurable telepathic boost and heightened mental state. Glitterstim spice was a valuable commodity that was tightly controlled and thus worth its weight in credits to smugglers. It was photoactive, so it had to be mined in total darkness or else it would be ruined. It was addictive for many species, which often employed "cutters" who prepared the spice for sale. Despite its classification as an illegal recreational drug, glitterstim also had some medicinal uses. Originally discovered on Kessel a few millennia before the Battle of Yavin, it was a by-product of the digestion of the spice grub. In its inert form, it crystallized into small, transparent black fibers. The fibers appeared almost alive, twisting and curling after being removed from their rocky veins.

**glitterstone** A valuable Bothan gemstone, it also was known by its Bothan name, fervse.

**glitteryll** An unusual mixture of glitterstim and ryll spices, it was created on Nar Shaddaa during the last decades of the Old Republic. The Corporate Sector Authority was rumored to have been interested in further development of the addictive substance, and the Jedi Knights dispatched Quinlan Vos and his apprentice Aayla Secura to investigate. They were both captured and had their memories erased in order to cover up the secret of glitteryll. After Vos returned to Ryloth with Vilmarh Grahrk, they discovered that energy spider eggs from Kessel had been transported to Ryloth and stored in ryll caves. The spiders were fed ryll spice, and then exuded webbing made almost purely of glitteryll. Vos later learned that his cousin Asanté Vos had been one of the parties behind the development of glitteryll. After the energy spiders killed Asanté Vos, Quinlan Vos destroyed all the spiders in order to completely end the supply of glitteryll.

**gloan** A species of trees native to Thyferra. Members of the Vratix species made their homes in gloan trees, well above the ground.

**Global Organization of Interstellar Shippers** A group made up of representatives of the largest transport corporations based on Gandle Ott, it was active during the early years of the New Republic.

**globblin** An immense, low-bodied reptile. What this vicious predator lacked in speed it made up for in relentlessness. The head of the globblin was dominated by a mouthful of huge fangs, and its long tongue could shoot out from its mouth in order to snare its prey.

**Globe of Peace** This Naboo relic resembled a small sphere, inside of which glowed an intense pinkish white light. It signified the centuries of peace that the Naboo had maintained on their planet. In the aftermath of the Battle of Naboo, Queen Amidala presented the Globe to Boss Nass in a gesture symbolizing a renewed peace between their peoples.

*Globe of Peace*

**glockaw sauce** A culinary accompaniment, it often was served with scrimpi or nerf fillets.

**Glok, Dethro** A being who controlled much of the scrap trade on the planet Ord Ibanna after the gas mines there were abandoned. He was known as ruthless, although he was strict about maintaining the repulsorlifts that kept the cities of the planet afloat long enough to be salvaged.

**glok monster** An unusual beast native to the Forest Moon of Endor, it was raised from the dead by the Night Spirit some years before the Battle of Endor.

**Glom Tho** This planet was the site of the New Republic's decisive victory in the Hevvrol sector.

**Gloom, Jervis** One of the many slythmongers who sold death sticks in the undercity of Coruscant, he was portly and had spiked red hair. Jervis Gloom worked for Groff Haug for many years and was implicated in the formation of a death stick smuggling ring. He often hung around with the members of a Klatooinian gang, until he was captured by Jango Fett and questioned about his relationship to the Bando Gora.

**gloom dwellers** Slang for the lower-level inhabitants of Nar Shaddaa.

**Gloom Walkers** During the year or so leading up to the Battle of Ruusan, the Gloom Walkers became one of the more elite units in the Sith army, winning more victories than similar units and earning a reputation as a unit that could handle the more critical missions. Although the unit was led by Lieutenant Ulabore, its members all knew that the real leadership came from Dessel. The unit's success in helping to defeat the Wookiee forces on Kashyyyk was due mainly to Dessel's leadership after Ulabore panicked when the unit was cut off from the main force. This was never more apparent than when the Gloom Walkers were sent to Phaseera ahead of the main Sith army to eliminate a communications center and allow the army to attack the planet's manufacturing centers without being spotted. Ulabore simply accepted the orders of his superiors, despite recognizing that following orders would decimate the unit. Dessel, however, would have none of it. He punched Ulabore hard enough to render the lieutenant unconscious and completed the mission his way.

**Glorga the Hutt** A Hutt crime lord who operated from a base on Hollast VII. The planet's natives tried to overthrow him but failed. Glorga later hired the Trandoshan mercenary Nakaron and sent him out on a number of jobs.

***Glorious*** Colonel Pakkpekatt's command cruiser during the Yevethan crisis, it was used in pursuit of the Teljkon vagabond.

***Glory*** An *Imperial I*–class Star Destroyer dispatched to Venzeiia 2 Prime, it was also the flagship sent to the Corporate Sector to recover the magpulse technology from Galactic Electronics. Under the command of Admiral Zaarin, the *Glory* was used to keep Darth Vader at bay until Zaarin could get to Coruscant to capture Emperor Palpatine. The *Glory* was Zaarin's escape vehicle from Coruscant when Vice Admiral Thrawn showed up with the *Vanguard* and the modified corvette *Mescue.*

***Glory of Yevetha*** Formerly the *EX-F,* a weapons and propulsion test bed taken by the Yevetha at N'zoth, it was a major craft in strongman Nil Spaar's Black Fifteen Fleet.

**glory room** Located in the heart of the Yuuzhan Vong command ship *Sunulok,* this chamber was where Tsavong Lah maintained a cognition throne and a vast diorama of the locations of various starships arrayed in the battle for control of the galaxy. The diorama was made up of a huge collection of blaze bugs beating their wings at various speeds, allowing each bug to represent a different vessel. Low-frequency thrumming represented a Yuuzhan Vong warship, a sharp drone was used for New Republic craft, a steady buzz indicated Imperial forces, and a shrill whine was used for other infidel craft. A Yuuzhan Vong could walk through the display; the bugs simply moved out of the way and then returned to their original positions. The wing beats of each blaze bug were coded to indicate the class and name of the vessel represented, and subtle undertones of odor indicated the morale of the crew.

**Glott** A notorious Gotal bounty hunter from Antar 4, he was brought to the planet M'haeli by Governor Grigor to help root out pockets of Rebel Alliance supporters and to locate Ch'no and Mora. Glott used his species' ability to sense the Force as a defense mechanism, reading his opponents' moves a split second before they made them. Glott was captured by Ranulf Trommer at Grigor's dragite mines, but Merrik intervened and allowed Glott to escape. The Gotal continued to pursue Trommer and Mora, but was killed by Trommer when he rescued Mora from Grigor.

**Glottal** The homeworld of the species known as Glottalphibs, often abbreviated to 'Phibs, Glottal was a hot, humid world of swamps, lily-pad-covered ponds, and dark forests. Glottalphibs had scaly yellow-green skin and long snouts filled with teeth. Their gills allowed 'Phibs to live in both water and air, and they radiated no detectable body heat. They could breathe fire, shooting it from their mouths as a weapon, and were known to carry snub-nosed hand weapons called swamp-stunners. Their hides were resistant to blasterfire; the most effective way to kill a 'Phib was to shoot it in the mouth. They were known for their persistence and love of shiny objects. Favorite foods of 'Phibs included parfue gnats, caver eggs, Eilnian sweet flies, and watumba bats. The bats hosted many types of insects but ate fire and could kill a Glottalphib in seconds. The most famous 'Phib was the crime lord Nandreeson, who operated out of Skip 6 in Smuggler's Run. Thirteen years after the Battle of Endor, Lando Calrissian was captured by Nandreeson and nearly killed before Han Solo and Chewbacca rescued him.

**Glova** A semi-tropical planet first colonized some 200 years before the Battle of Endor, its economy was based on the mining of precious metals. When the mines petered out, the economy turned toward agriculture, and Glova became a major supplier of foodstuffs to other planets in the region.

**glove of Darth Vader** When Luke Skywalker battled Darth Vader aboard the second Death Star and severed Vader's gloved right hand in a lightsaber duel, it was thought the relic was lost when the Death Star exploded. But it was believed the glove was indestructible, and the Prophets of the Dark Side foretold that it would be found by the next ruler of the galaxy. Captain Dunwell later found it in a piece of Death Star wreckage on Mon Calamari. Trioculus believed that the glove also gave the wearer the power to choke victims without actually touching them, so MD-5 modified it to perform a similar task to cover up Trioculus's lack of Force sensitivity.

**Glovstoak** An Imperial Moff who enjoyed a luxurious lifestyle at the height of the New Order, he was known more for the elaborate galas he hosted at his palace than his ability to lead. Moff Glovstoak maintained a close cadre of political and military advisers who helped him keep control of his small empire. But his extravagant lifestyle attracted the attention of Imperial advisers who worked for Emperor Palpatine, and the Emperor dispatched Mara Jade to investigate the Moff's activities. In the guise of Countess Claria, Jade infiltrated Glovstoak's palace and discovered that he had been purchasing expensive works of art, some of which were well beyond his salary as an Imperial Governor. She made an impressive inventory of Glovstoak's holdings, including a listing of all his brokers and dealers. Further investigation revealed that many of the artworks had been stolen five years earlier from Krintrino, where the Empire had shut down a Rebel cell. Their total value was estimated at between six and eight million credits. This gave Mara enough information to link Glovstoak to the Rebel Alliance—a connection she relayed to Emperor Palpatine himself. Glovstoak was arrested and sent to prison on charges of embezzlement and treason against the Empire.

**glowball** Two years into the Yuuzhan Vong War, Izal Waz developed this technique for using the Force to collect ambient light. When performed correctly, the glowball hid a starship from the invaders as if it were inside a small star. Using this technique, Waz kept the *Jolly Man* hidden during its search for a Yuuzhan Vong yammosk.

**glow lichen** A name used by the New Republic to describe the phosphorescent yellow lichen that grew along the walls of Yuuzhan Vong starships, providing a source of light.

Glow rod

**Glowpoint** A star-like power source found in Hollowtown on Centerpoint Station, Glowpoint was a strange, hovering light source suspended in the exact center of Hollowtown and the station. None of the station's inhabitants knew how it was powered, but one theory held that it drew power from the gravitational interflux between Talus and Tralus.

**glow rod** Any device designed to provide portable light. Most were long, thin tubes that cast bright light from chemical phosphorescents. Other glow rods consisted of power cells attached to lamp bulbs.

**glowstone** Opalescent lamps designed to look like natural stones, these technological devices found on Ryloth were used for lighting large gatherings and celebrations.

**glowtube** A cylindrical device used for illumination.

**GLTB-3181** One of several Imperial transport vessels that carried prisoners to the penal colony on Despayre during the early years of the New Order. The ship lacked any windows or viewports in the passenger area, where prisoners were forced to endure long trips in cramped quarters.

**glubex** A flaccid, star-shaped creature, it was considered a delicacy among the Hutts, who often peeled the head off a glubex and ate it separately.

**glue stat** Developed shortly before the onset of the Clone Wars, this patch was genetically created from living clone trooper tissue and an adhesive made from a Talusian mussel. When applied to a wound, the glue stat sealed itself to the victim's skin, drawing flesh and skin together to prevent external infection.

**glurpfish** A creature native to Mon Calamari, its body was made up of protoplasm and had no discernible form. The glurpfish was a sluggish creature that obtained sustenance by filtering out microorganisms from the surrounding waters. Schools of glurpfish made disgusting burping sounds as they gulped water at the surface of the ocean.

**glurrg** A species of pack animals domesticated by Gungans some 3,000 years before the Battle of Naboo.

**Gluss'sa'Nikto** A subspecies of Niktos also known as the Pale Nikto, it evolved on the Gluss'elta Islands of Kintan. Its members were distinguished from other Nikto subspecies by white or gray scales. They had small horns surrounding their eyes, like a Kadas'sa'Nikto, and also had webbed hands similar to an Esral'sa'Nikto. This combination of traits led many xenoarchaeologists to surmise that the first Pale Nikto was born from the union of a Kadas'sa'Nikto and an Esral'sa'Nikto. The Gluss'sa'Nikto were known to be excellent sailors, and a group of them was believed to have mutinied aboard a Hutt star yacht and fled to Drexel II.

**gluttonbug** A Corellian insect with a voracious appetite for woody plants, it could clear a small forest in no time if not destroyed.

Glowstone

**Gluupor** A Rodian who witnessed Sunry's flight from the hotel room he shared with Elassa on the planet Manaan some 4,000 years before the Battle of Yavin. When forced to testify on the witness stand, Gluupor revealed that he had been paid by the Sith to plant Sunry's Hero's Cross medal on Elassa's body. Elassa had been murdered when Sunry broke off their affair, as her Sith superiors realized that their plan to discredit the Old Republic was unraveling.

**GLX Firelance** A model of SoroSuub blaster rifle, it lacked any form of corporate or governmental markings, which made the weapon untraceable if lost. It was very effective when used in stun mode, something of a rarity among blaster rifles. The Firelance was marketed as "the most effective weapon available for freelance enforcement officials," meaning that it was built specifically for use by bounty hunters.

**Glymphid** These long, thin-bodied sentients had long, tooth-studded snouts, spindly limbs, and fingers that ended in suction cups. Glymphids were native to the planet Ploo II, in the Ploo sector of the galaxy. The famous Podracer Aldar Beedo was a Glymphid.

**Glynn, Cladus** An officer who worked for the Imperial Security Bureau and was stationed on Kothlis during the height of the Galactic Civil War. His role was to locate any Rebel Alliance personnel moving through Kothlis or the Kothlis Shadowport. To help gather information, Agent Glynn assumed the guise of Gart, a drunken spacer.

**Glynn-Beti** A blond-furred Bothan, she was a Jedi Master during the last decades of the Old Republic. Like most Jedi of her time, Glynn-Beti condemned the actions of Aurra Sing, a bounty hunter who had once been a promising Jedi student. At the onset of the Clone Wars, Glynn-Beti was given the rank of general in the Republic armed forces, and led the unsuccessful mission to capture Count Dooku on Raxus Prime just after the Battle of

Geonosis. But clone troopers managed to disrupt Dooku's plans to recover the Force Harvester.

As the Clone Wars drew to an end, Glynn-Beti and her Padawan, Ulu Ulix, were dispatched to Xagobah to lead forces laying siege to Wat Tambor's hidden fortress. Because the fortress, known as the Mazariyan Citadel, and much of the surrounding plant life had been genetically altered by Tambor to serve as guardians, the clone troopers under her direction were unable to get close. So the Jedi Master helped young Boba Fett infiltrate the citadel, hoping that he might provide some information. Tambor continued to send droid armies into battle, relying on sheer numbers to overwhelm the Republic forces. After Tambor fled the citadel, Glynn-Beti's forces managed to breach its walls, and forced the remaining Separatists to abandon it. During the cleanup, Glynn-Beti ordered her troops to let Boba Fett go free.

*Practicing the Force in front of a Dagobah gnarltree*

**Glythe sector** The location of the planet Valrar, it was the site of an Imperial base. This area of the galaxy was also the location of the Noghri commandos' Valrar base during the early years of the New Republic.

**Gmar Askilon (Gmir Askilon)** The fourth documented sighting of the mysterious ghost ship called the Teljkon vagabond was in deep space near this star. A New Republic task force intercepted the vagabond there. Lando Calrissian, Lobot, and the droids R2-D2 and C-3PO were able to board the ship and were whisked away when it suddenly entered hyperspace.

***G'mi Moa*** A Liannan bulk freighter, it traveled a regular route along the Perlemian Trade Route until it was captured by the notorious pirate Gunda Mabin.

**Gnaden, Wom-Nii** A Jedi Master who was also a noted pilot. Gnaden's NTB-630 bomber was damaged during the Battle of Crombach Nebula in the Clone Wars. The ship spun out of control before smashing into the hull of the *Tide of Progress XII.* The crash destroyed the bomber and killed Master Gnaden, but left only a small dent on the side of the *Munificent*-class frigate.

***G'Nagnib*** A Rebel Alliance freighter, it was destroyed during the Galactic Civil War.

**Gnarkh** A Devaronian, he was one of Black Sun Vigo Antonin's personal assistants in the period leading up to Antonin's death at the hands of Jango Fett.

**gnarltree** These swamp-loving trees of Dagobah—among the more bizarre plant forms in the galaxy—grew slowly upward through the centuries, their huge roots rising out of the bog, providing shelter in the hollow spaces. Each gnarltree was a microcosm of life-forms with lichens, moss, and shelf-fungus filling the crannies of the calcified trunk. But the strangest aspect of the trees was the knobby white spider that was part of the gnarltrees' life cycle. The spider was actually a detachable, mobile root that broke free of the parent gnarltree. It became a predator, hunting and devouring animals to build up its energy and nutrients before making a clearing and putting down its eight sharp legs, which became the roots of a new gnarltree.

***G'Neeznow*** One of the many *Strike*-class cruisers that made up the front lines of the Imperial naval fleet.

***Gnisnal*** An *Imperial I*–class Star Destroyer, it was sabotaged during evacuation of Narth and Ihopek. An intact memory core found in the wreck contained a complete Imperial Order of Battle. The information in the Star Destroyer's core was used later to identify the ships of the Black Fleet.

**gnithian oep** This creature, native to the Jospro sector, was the original host of the ix dbukrii parasite.

**GNK power droid** A boxy droid with two stout legs produced by Industrial Automaton for decades, it provided power for other droids or machinery. Essentially an ambulatory battery, it was one of the least sophisticated and most commonly encountered types of droids in the galaxy. It often made a guttural sound—something like *gonk, gonk,* which became its nickname.

*GNK power droids*

***G'nnoch*** This ancient pictographic work was compiled by the Ssi-ruuvi species and documented the existence of the Ssi-ruuk and their place in the universe. Its key tenet was that the Ssi-ruuk were superior to all other species in the galaxy. Other parts of the G'nnoch detailed the various ways of obtaining and losing honor. A major section of the work described the creation of the universe from the Ssi-ruuvi point of view. In the beginning, there were four eggs. From the first hatched Ssi and P'w'itthki. Ssi's children hatched from the second egg, while P'w'itthki's children hatched from the third egg. The fourth egg was reserved for those descendants who earned a place in the afterlife. Eventually, Ssi was forced to defeat P'w'itthki in combat, but allowed P'w'itthki's hatchlings to live on, serving the children of Ssi for all eternity. This myth described the beginning of the relationship between the Ssi-ruuk (the hatchlings of Ssi) and the P'w'eck (the hatchlings of P'w'itthki).

**Gno, Senator** An Old Republic Senator, he supported the Rebel Alliance during his tenure with the Imperial Senate. When that body was dissolved by Emperor Palpatine, he resigned his position and went underground. Following the Battle of Endor, he was reelected to serve the New Republic as a Senator. He was one of Leia Organa Solo's supporters and believed as she did that the election of former Imperial supporters would factionalize the Senate.

**gnort** An herbivorous mammal native to the planet Naboo, it moved about the grasslands in large herds.

**Gnosos** A Sunesi who was employeed by CorDuro Shipping, he was one of the few who did not support the company's plans to turn Duro over to the Yuuzhan Vong. After Jacen Solo was imprisoned by Durgard Brarun, Gnosos provided Jacen with a datacard that contained his own voiceprint, which would key a shuttle in the hangar of Port Duggan, allowing Jacen to escape.

**gnullith** A star-shaped creature, it was genetically altered by the Yuuzhan Vong to serve as a form of breathing apparatus. When applied to a user's face, the gnullith sealed itself to the skin and extended one of its appendages down the user's throat. This provided a way to pass breathable air into the user's lungs. Two other appendages closed off the user's nose, protecting against intrusion of any foreign atmosphere. The gnullith allowed the Yuuzhan Vong to travel freely underwater and in toxic environments. The New Republic's military forces discovered that a warrior wearing a gnullith could be killed if a shot was aimed at the very center of the gnullith's body.

**gnullith-villip hybrid** A piece of biotechnology created by the Yuuzhan Vong, it allowed individuals to breathe in a hostile environment while also communicating with a remote location—two pieces of biotech in one.

**G.O., the** The common name used by most Corellians to describe the government office complex located in the capital city of Coronet. In addition to the Corellian Assembly Building, the G.O. included bureau offices and the President's official residence. The G.O. was laid out in a classical garden style, with formal gardens interspersed among the buildings. The entire complex was surrounded by Keben Park.

*Spurch "Warhog" Goa*

**Goa, Spurch "Warhog"** A short Diollan bounty hunter with a broad, scarred beak and a nasty temper, he took on the Rodian Greedo as an apprentice on the spaceport moon of Nar Shaddaa. He later brought Greedo to Tatooine, where the Rodian was killed by Han Solo. In actuality, Goa was being paid by a war-like clan of Rodians to ensure that Greedo ended up dead.

**Goa-Ato** A Rodian guild of hunters, it was formed when the ancient Grand Protectors arranged for a gifted bounty hunter's first offplanet hunt. The Grand Protector was charged with providing allies for the new hunter as well as a dangerous target. The best hunters returned to Rodia to join the Goa-Ato. Only those Rodians who had won the right to travel offplanet were allowed entrance to the Goa-Ato.

**goatgrass** A grass native to the planet Kinyen, it was a staple food of the Gran species.

**go bandit** A term used by officers of the Grand Army of the Republic, it described a soldier or unit abandoning the GAR and setting off on an unauthorized mission.

**Gobindi** With a dense jungle landscape dotted with ancient ruins, this planet was the site of an Imperial biowarfare laboratory during the Galactic Civil War. The fifth planet in its system, Gobindi had been the homeworld of the Gobindi species. The Gobindi were master architects who built huge ziggurats in the deep jungles. While many of the stepped pyramids had rooms and passageways, several were completely solid. These ziggurats contained deadly viruses the Gobindi discovered in the jungles. The species was wiped out by one such virus, known as the Gobindi virus, but not before they discovered a way to cure it. In their dying actions, they carved the formula for the antidote into the ziggurat's walls. The virus was reactivated by the Empire's Biological Warfare Division for use as a weapon.

**Go-Corp/Utilitech** A joint business venture that produced a variety of droid-controlled vehicles at the height of the New Order. The headquarters were located on Etti IV.

**Godalhi, Janu** A decorated constable from the planet Teth. His actions drew the attention of Coruscant and Jedi Master Plo Koon, who was dispatched to Teth prior to the Clone Wars in the pursuit of pirates. Janu Godalhi and Koon pooled their resources in the capture of nefarious criminals. Godalhi's true passion was for galactic history. Often in the development of security programs and strategies, he would cite historic examples and precedents from across the galaxy. This colorful way of devising and implementing security methods earned Godalhi an invitation to speak at a weeklong workshop hosted by Coruscant's security agencies.

Godalhi's trip to Coruscant was an eye-opener. He saw that local security forces were often subverted or made superfluous by clone troopers. He saw shocking oversights and inefficiencies that made the Separatist invasion possible. He suspected that corruption at the highest levels was responsible for the near capture of the Chancellor. As he quietly built a case, Godalhi took advantage of a free voucher and visited the Coruscant Galaxies Opera House for a command performance of *Squid Lake.* He found no respite, though, for he was dismayed by the numerous security flaws at the Opera House—which housed no less a potentate than the Supreme Chancellor. Disgusted, he left the performance and in short order returned to Teth.

He was shocked by the Order 66 massacre and the alleged "Jedi Rebellion." His close relationship with Plo Koon had brought him great insight into the Jedi Order, and this knowledge suggested that Palpatine was not what he appeared to be. Godalhi saw patterns in history that led him to believe that Palpatine was part of a vast conspiracy to cement a position as Emperor, though he kept these thoughts quiet. Encouraged by the success of early Rebels such as Cody Sunn-Childe and Garm Bel Iblis, Godalhi began secreting supplies and weapons for a Tethan resistance. These became vital when the Empire came to Teth and installed its own security forces, forcing Godalhi into early retirement. But after Bail Organa returned a long-ago message, Godalhi was able to commit his resources to the struggling Rebel Alliance. This included his son, Palob, who was a lieutenant in the Tethan resistance. After the defeat of the Emperor, Janu and Palob retired from military service, and wrote many history books about the Galactic Civil War. In historical circles, their works are as highly regarded as those of Arhul Hextrophon and Voren Na'al.

**Godalhi, Palob** This Teth native was Winfrid Dagore's chief aide during the resistance against the Empire and served as a lieutenant in Teth's armed forces during the early years of the New Order. After Dagore was taken captive by Dace Bonearm and IG-72, Godalhi took possession of the *Moldy Crow* and brought it back to the Alliance Dreadnaught *New Hope.* After the Battle of Endor, Palob retired to Teth to assist his father in writing several history texts on the galaxy and the Galactic Civil War.

***Godar*** An Imperial corvette assigned to transport the members of the first Death Star's design team to the Star Destroyer *Immortal,* it was attacked by Keyan Farlander and disabled, and the Rebel Alliance captured the design team.

**Goddess** The code name of a missile created by the New Republic in an effort to fool the Yuuzhan Vong, it was built with the exact gravitic signature of Jaina Solo's X-wing fighter; when fired, it essentially "became" the X-wing to Yuuzhan Vong sensors. These sensors, which were specialized dovin basal mines, locked onto the gravitic emanations of the Goddess missile and reported its presence back to coralskippers. The coralskipper pilots were then led to believe that they were chasing Solo, but too late discovered that they were chasing a fully armed missile.

***Godendag*** A cargo ferry used to smuggle stolen Imperial goods into the Sepan system, it was captured by the Empire during the Sepan Civil War.

**Godherdt** An Imperial captain, he served aboard the *Executor* as a sensor monitor, keeping data on the integrity of the Star Destroyer's hull. Captain Godherdt was known as a skilled fleet engineer and sensor officer.

**Godo** The homeworld of the humanoid Godoans. Much of Godo's life was linked to two gold statues—the Dancing Goddess and the Minstrel—that somehow channeled

*Janu Godalhi*

Goff

energy to the planet. After the statues were stolen during the Galactic Civil War, the Godoan people began to die off from a mysterious plague. Han Solo and Lando Calrissian managed to recover the statues and restore vitality to the Godoans.

**Godt** A Sullustan commander in the New Republic military, he was trained by Admiral Sien Sovv.

**Goelitz** This planet once was involved in an ancient feud with the planet Ylix, a few systems away. After much fighting, Goelitz was defeated by members of the Ylix militia, including the infamous gunman Gallandro.

**goff** A huge avian creature native to the planet Naboo, it was sometimes called a titavian. It had huge wings that gave it a wingspan of more than 100 meters; its arms were heavily muscled to lift its huge bulk into the air. Most goffs lived in high perches from which they could plummet in order to achieve flight. Gungans considered it a rite of passage for a young warrior to train an aiwha and fly to a goff's perch to obtain one or more of their long, striped feathers, which then adorned military officers' kaadu mounts.

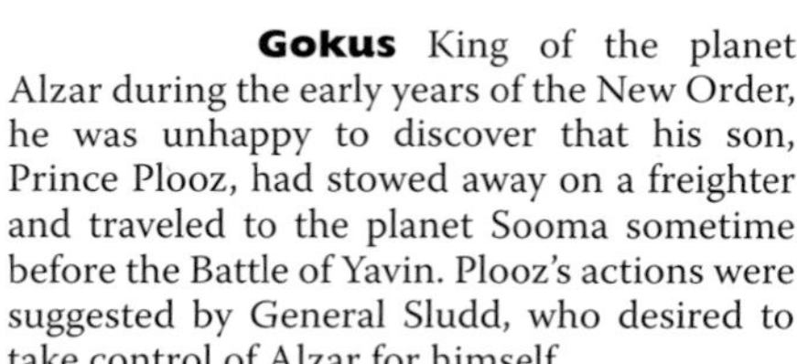
Vill Goir

**Gog, Borborygmus** A mad scientist, he was a Shi'ido who was educated at the Chandrilan Academy of Sciences alongside Mammon Hoole. Gog was hired by the Old Republic to work with Hoole in developing drugs to counteract the bioweapons that Separatists were using to attack clone troopers. After the Clone Wars, both scientists were kept on by the Empire; they moved their labs to the planet Kiva, where they tinkered with the ability to control life and death as part of their Project Starscream. The experiment, which Hoole tried to stop, went horribly wrong and killed all life on the planet. Eventually the wraiths of the dead Kivans did to Gog what he had done to them.

**Gogol (1)** A large humanoid, he had ties to a number of slavers and other disreputable beings. For the right price, he provided Obi-Wan Kenobi with information linking the slaver Krayn to the Colicoids.

**Gogol (2)** The owner of one of the largest casinos in Kushal Vogh on the planet Elerion during the New Order, this large green-skinned being conspired with Nescan Tal'yo to sell a stolen Rebel Alliance holocube—which contained the locations of several Alliance bases—to the Empire. But Leia Organa was able to destroy it first, leaving Gogol to try to explain the loss to Imperial agents.

**gogomar** A creature from the planet Ansion, it was sometimes sacrificed by shamans of the Alwari tribes, who would then read its entrails to help resolve important matters.

**Goir, Vill** A Dark Side Adept, he was a sergeant at arms working for Sedriss aboard the *Avenger* during the early stages of Operation Shadow Hand. Vill Goir accompanied Sedriss to Ossus to capture Luke Skywalker and return him to Byss. Goir was cleaved in two during a lightsaber battle with Kam Solusar.

**gokob** A hairless rodent that lived in scrap heaps and garbage bins, it sprayed a foul mist when startled. Originally native to Ossus, gokobs lived in the treetop canopies of the dense jungles there. Many escaped offworld aboard the transport ships making regular supply runs to the Jedi training facility that Luke Skywalker established on the planet.

**Gokus** King of the planet Alzar during the early years of the New Order, he was unhappy to discover that his son, Prince Plooz, had stowed away on a freighter and traveled to the planet Sooma sometime before the Battle of Yavin. Plooz's actions were suggested by General Sludd, who desired to take control of Alzar for himself.

**Golan II Battle Station** A mid-orbit space station, it was 2,158 meters long and about a kilometer wide. Armed with an array of 35 turbolaser batteries, 8 tractor beam projectors, and 10 proton torpedo launchers, the Empire used them to guard the shipyards at Bilbringi. Each Golan II required a crew of 500, along with 149 gunners and up to 80 troops.

Golan II Battle Station

**Golan III Battle Station** A massive mid-orbit space station, it was 2,600 meters long and took a crew of 880 along with 228 gunners. Each top-of-the-line Golan III was armed with 50 turbolaser batteries, 24 proton torpedo launchers, and 15 tractor beam projectors. The New Republic used two of them to help defend Coruscant.

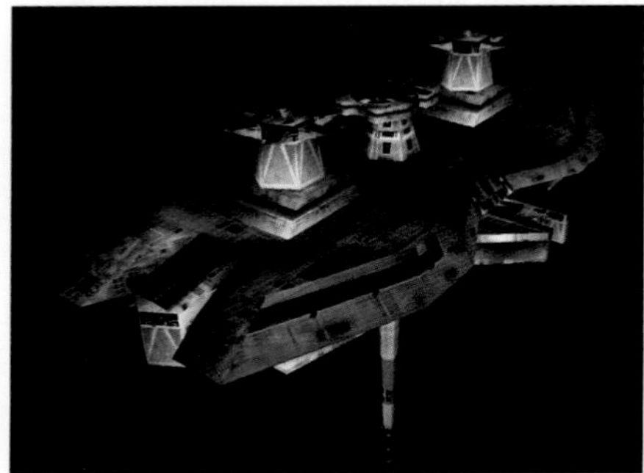
Golan III Battle Station

**Golan Arms** A maker of everything from small, anti-infantry weapons to huge orbital defense platforms, it saw many of its contracts canceled when the Empire took over. So Golan Arms allied itself with the Rebel Alliance, and the relationship continued into the era of the New Republic.

**Golanda** A tall and hawkish-looking woman in charge of artillery innovations and tactical deployments at Maw Installation. During her 10 years there, she never stopped complaining about how foolish it was to conduct artillery research in the middle of a black-hole cluster. The fluctuating gravity ruined her calculations and made every test a pointless exercise. Like all others at Maw Installation, she was killed when the prototype Death Star was dragged into a black hole and destroyed.

**Golbah hive** A Geonosian hive hired by the InterGalactic Banking Clan to produce Hailfire droids, its members staged a revolt because of the intense pressures and physical demands made on them to keep up with impossible schedules. To set an example, planetary aristocrats set off a proton bomb destroying the entire hive, including the queen and all her backups.

**Gold Beaches** Tourist attractions on the planet Corellia, these beaches were located between the cities of Coronet and Tyrena.

**Gold Devil** A nickname for a specialized group of Y-wing fighters used during the Galactic Civil War.

Golden Nyss Shipyards

**Golden Cuff, the** A cantina in the lower levels of Coruscant during the last decades of the Old Republic, it attracted a wide range of patrons from governmental ranks, including Senators, lobbyists, and aides.

**Golden Globe** A mysterious, glowing orb discovered by Jedi Master Ikrit some 385 years before the Battle of Yavin, it was about 4 meters in diameter, but seemed somehow vast inside. Ikrit couldn't penetrate its force field and realized that no other adult Jedi could, either. So he guarded it for centuries until the right young Jedi could figure out its mystery. This turned out to be Anakin Solo and Tahiri Veila, who learned of its existence from an elderly Melodie on Yavin 8. With Ikrit's help, they determined that the Golden Globe held the spirits of thousands of Massassi youths trapped by Exar Kun four millennia before. After puzzling over the Globe for months, Anakin and Tahiri realized that they needed to reach deep within the Force to let it channel away all the energy radiating from the Globe's outer shell, allowing one of them to penetrate the Globe and lead the spirits out. Once inside, Anakin found himself in a golden sandstorm that both blinded and disoriented him. But he was able to locate the Massassi spirits and, with Tahiri's guidance, lead them out of the Globe. As the last of the spirits escaped, the Globe shattered into thousands of crystalline shards.

Gold Four

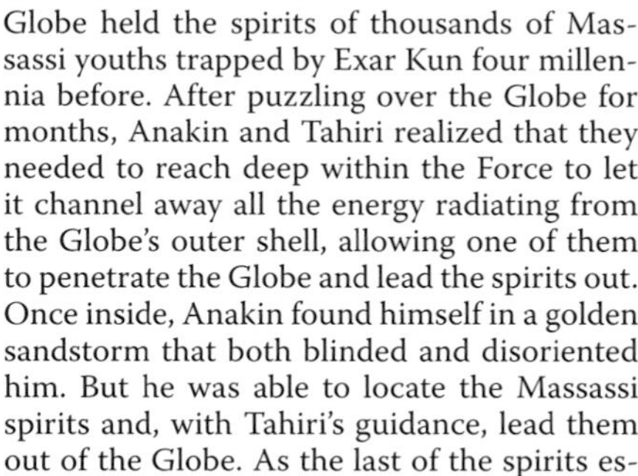

**Golden Nyss Shipyards** Located near the Yinchorri system, this shipyard provided services to smugglers and pirates during the last decades of the Old Republic. The Devaronian scoundrel Vilmarh Grahrk convinced the Yinchorri that they could steal starships from the Golden Nyss Shipyards in order to reach out and conquer other planets and star systems. The Yinchorri agreed, and gained access to the shipyards. But instead of stealing the ships, the reptilian humanoids destroyed the Golden Nyss Shipyards, earning Grahrk the hatred of many independent spacers.

**Golden Orb** A cantina and restaurant on Nar Shaddaa, it was frequented by Han Solo after the smuggler returned from the Corporate Sector.

**Goldenrod** A nickname conferred upon C-3PO by Han Solo during their escape from Echo Base on Hoth.

**Golden Slug** A run-down flophouse, it was in one of the seediest parts of Coruscant's undercity.

**Golden Sun** A living, collective intelligence made up of thousands of tiny polyps that lived in the coral reefs of the planet Sedri. Golden Sun had an aptitude for the Force, which it referred to as the universal energy. Golden Sun produced a supply of energy so huge that it affected the planet's gravitational readings. Native Sedrians, especially the Force-sensitive high priests, actually heard the voices of the communal polyps as dreams and visions.

**Gold Five** The call sign of Davish "Pops" Krail during the Battle of Yavin.

***Gold Fortress*** An Imperial Remnant warship that saw action during the Second Battle of Fondor. It was the first ship on the scene when the crew of the *Bloodfin* mutinied following the assassination of Gilad Pellaeon. When Jacen Solo boarded a med runner and tried to rescue Tahiri Veila from the *Bloodfin*, the crew of the *Gold Fortress* was unaware of his true identity and let him through their security cordon.

Gold Leader (Battle of Endor)

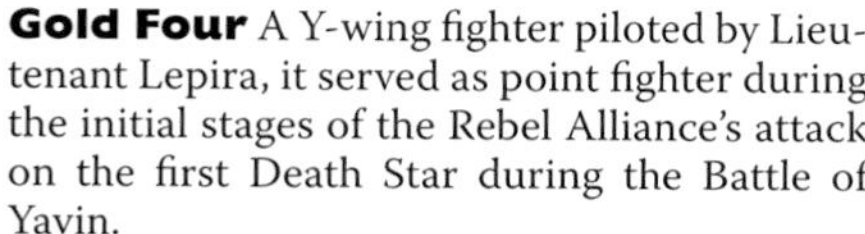

**Gold Four** A Y-wing fighter piloted by Lieutenant Lepira, it served as point fighter during the initial stages of the Rebel Alliance's attack on the first Death Star during the Battle of Yavin.

Gold Leader (Battle of Yavin)

**Gold Leader (1)** The comm unit designation for Rebel pilot Dutch's Y-wing during the Battle of Yavin. He led his squadron in the first assault wave against the Death Star battle station.

**Gold Leader (2)** During the Battle of Endor, it was the comm unit designation for Lando Calrissian and the *Millennium Falcon*. Lando was responsible for leading Rebel Alliance starfighters against the second Death Star. His quick decision-making in battle helped defeat the Imperial fleet and bring about the end of the Galactic Civil War. Gold Leader and Red Leader (Wedge Antilles) destroyed the Death Star's power core and that, in turn, destroyed the entire battle station.

Gold Squadron

**Gold Order of Cularin** Created by the government of Cularin for military personnel who defeated the Thaereian Military and restored freedom to the Cularin system.

**Gold Six** The call sign of Y-wing pilot Hol Okand during the Battle of Yavin.

**Gold Squadron** A Rebel Alliance Y-wing fighter squadron assigned to the Massassi Base on Yavin 4, it was called upon to attack the first Death Star. During the battle, the entire squadron was wiped out, with the exception of Keyan Farlander.

**Gold Three** The call sign of Y-wing pilot Ryle Torsyn during the Battle of Yavin.

**Gold Two** The call sign of Y-wing pilot Tiree during the Battle of Yavin.

Golthar's Sky

**Gold Wing** The Rebel Alliance starfighter battle group under the command of Gold Leader Lando Calrissian during the Battle of Endor, it was assigned the task of destroying the second Death Star.

**Golfhan** A Caridan, he was the primary ambassador from his homeworld to the Old Republic in the years leading up to the Clone Wars.

**Golga the Hutt (Golga Besadii Fir)** A representative of Nal Hutta to the New Republic, he was a member of Besadii kajidic by birth but was said to have had a touch of the Desilijic clan in him because of his desire for human women. After it was learned that Borha the Hutt had made a deal to ally the Hutts with the invading Yuuzhan Vong, Golga was expelled from Coruscant and agreed to meet with Viqi Shesh, who tried to gather information on the aliens' next moves.

***Goliath*** An *Imperial II*–class Star Destroyer, it was used during the Galactic Civil War to defend an Imperial Golan I platform that made heavy use of slave labor. Despite its presence, the Rebel Alliance succeeded in liberating the slaves.

**Goliath** A huge combat droid, it was built by Lord Gar-Oth to fight for him in ritual combat by operating on the telepathic commands of the Yahk-Tosh. But after Princess Lourdes killed Gar-Oth, Yoshi Raph-Elan was able to destroy the droid.

**Golkus** A planet that was nearly on a straight line between Coruscant and Carratos. Akanah Norand Pell stopped there and obtained a set of falsified identification papers from Talon Karrde, along with a smuggler's kit to keep the *Mud Sloth* anonymous. She then left to meet with Luke Skywalker on Coruscant.

**Golm** A purple gas giant planet that was the fourth world in the Both System, it was orbited by 23 moons.

**Golorno** A sensor officer aboard the *Mon Remonda* during the hunt for Warlord Zsinj, he was killed in Nuro Tualin's attack on the huge ship when he was sucked out into the vacuum of space by the first round of fire.

**Golrath** One of many planets where the Rebel Alliance maintained operations between the battles of Yavin and Hoth. The Rebels used an abandoned magma smelting plant to house their makeshift base. After leaving for a new base on Arbra, the Alliance discovered that rocks from Golrath could act like a holovid recorder and feared that this might tip off Imperials to important secrets, including the location of the new base. But Imperial Lieutenant Mils Giel triggered a reactor overload that destroyed Golrath Station as part of a failed plan to capture Leia Organa.

***Gol Storn*** A New Republic warship assigned to the blockade of Galantos during the Yevethan Purge, it was part of a task force that included the *Thackery.*

**Golthan, Bregius** An Imperial adviser stationed on Wroona early in the Galactic Civil War, he was assigned to oversee the security of the Colonies and the Core Worlds by Emperor Palpatine himself. After the Battle of Endor, he still tried to go after New Republic agents. At one point Golthan imprisoned Platt Okeefe in his fortress on Voktunma, but other Republic agents rescued her and destroyed much of the fortress. Later, Platt and her associates killed Golthan in a firefight on Wroona and destroyed the Star Destroyer *Vengeance.*

***Golthar's Sky*** An apparently mammoth star freighter, it was actually an illusion created by Aleema Keto during the Great Sith War.

**Goluud Corridor** A risky hyperspace route discovered by hyperspace pioneers Jori and Gav Daragon 1,000 years before the Great Sith War, it involved a jump past the unstable red giant Primus Goluud. It was approved by the Navigators' Guild, but after the Cha'a drone ship *Zeta Five* was drawn too near Primus Goluud and exploded, the Daragons were discredited and forced to flee Cinnagar.

**gomex moss** One of the first-generation plants used in terraforming, gomex moss took hold even in rocky, barren soils because it consumed little water. The moss broke down the soil, converting solid matter into its constituent elements.

**Gonar** A skulking human, he hung around Jabba the Hutt's rancor and its keeper, Malakili, for prestige. When Gonar tried to blackmail Malakili into letting him take over the position of rancor keeper, Malakili killed him and fed him to the rancor.

Ickabel G'ont

**Gondagali** During the early years of the New Republic, this was the first planet attacked with the MS-19 shield-busting warhead.

**gondar** A sweaty, disgusting creature whose tusks were often used as ornamental decorations.

**Gondry** A one-eyed, hulking Abyssin who was a native of the planet Byss, he was employed by Djas Puhr for his muscle when Puhr was working for Sebulba as a slaver.

**gonk droid** *See* GNK power droid.

**Gonmore** A planet in the Outer Rim Territories, it was thought to be smuggler Talon Karrde's primary financial base in the Outer Rim.

**Gonster** An usual, two-headed being on the Forest Moon of Endor, he created the magical cap that silenced the raich. When Wicket W. Warrick mistakenly removed the cap, Gonster was able to create another, his two heads arguing with each other as always.

**G'ont, Ickabel** A Bith member of Figrin D'an and the Modal Nodes, he played the Fanfar. G'ont's favorite song for the band to perform was "Tears of Aquanna," mainly because he got a solo.

**gooba** A fish native to the oceans of the planet Naboo.

***Googol of Gornts, A*** Largely denounced as one of the worst holographic features released just prior to the Clone Wars.

**goose droid** *See* G2 droid.

**Goot, Alfreda** A Togorian bounty hunter who wore Mandalorian armor, she once kidnapped Princess Leia Organa on Ord Mantell, leading Han Solo on a lengthy chase.

***Gopher*** A Rebel Alliance container transport, it was captured during the battle to take Imperial outpost D-34 following the Battle of Hoth.

**Gopso'o** Ancestral enemies of the Drovian species on Nim Drovis, they engaged in a centuries-long blood feud—a feud begun so long ago that no one remembered how it started.

***Gorath*** An Imperial *Strike*-class cruiser under the command of Captain Voba Dokrett, it attempted to capture the mysterious ghost ship called the Teljkon vagabond but was destroyed by it instead.

**Goravas** A volcanic world, it was the second planet in the Kuat system and was orbited by a single moon.

**Gorax** Giant, primitive creatures more than 6 meters high (and as tall as 30 meters), they lived solitary lives in caverns on Endor's forest moon and terrorized inhabitants such as Ewoks. They wore fur clothing held together with large stitches and carried fearsome stone axes with which to hunt at night. One particular Gorax was an evil giant who lived in an underground cavern built into a mountain fortress beyond the Desert of Salma. This Gorax captured two human adults who had crashed on Endor, Catarine and Jeremitt Towani, and held them in his cave. The humans' children, Mace and Cindel Towani, were part of a special caravan of Ewoks to challenge the Gorax. Deej, Wicket W. Warrick, Willy, Weechee, Chukha-Trok, and Kaink succeeded in killing the Gorax by forcing the giant to tumble into a deep chasm.

**Gorbah** A planet with four hidden fighter bases. Its ships attacked invading Imperial forces with a space-snipe defense. When the Empire eventually triumphed, the fighters abandoned their secret outposts and fled the system.

**Gorc** A dim-witted Gamorrean, he was subjected to Imperial alchemy and twinned with a Kowakian monkey-lizard known as Picaroon C. Boodle (later known as Pic). They became a nearly undefeatable team against the Rebel Alliance. But Kyle Katarn managed to shoot Gorc in the face, killing him and sending Pic into a frenzy that Katarn was only too happy to end.

*Gorax*

*Jar Jar spears a gorg.*

**Gordarl Weaponsmiths** The main weapons manufacturer on Geonosis during the last decades of the Old Republic, it was known for its sonic weapons technology designed for the Geonosian physiology.

**Gordian Reach** An area of the galaxy seized by a single G0-T0 unit in a bloody coup four millennia before the Battle of Yavin. All 16 of its habitable planets were subjugated by the rogue droid. The deaths of millions of beings forced Supreme Chancellor Cressa to order a military task force into the region, which eventually destroyed the G0-T0 unit and liberated the planets. The Empire heavily patrolled the Gordian Reach during the Galactic Civil War since it contained the planet Yavin and its moons.

**Gordon, Herrit** A New Republic diplomat, he served the Ministry of State on Coruscant shortly after the Republic liberated the planet from Ysanne Isard. He had previously served the Diplomatic Corps on Bothawui and became friends with many prominent Bothans, including Liska Dan'kre.

**Goren, Del** A Rebel Alliance communications and sensor expert, he was part of the High Command at the Yavin 4 base during the Battle of Yavin. He formerly served the Alliance on the *Spiral.*

**Gorev** An Imperial Navy lieutenant, he served as Joak Drysso's gunnery commander aboard the *Lusankya* during the Battle of Thyferra.

***Gorfan*** An Imperial cargo ferry, it was used to deliver supplies to the outpost in the Pakuuni system.

**gorg** These amphibious creatures were sold as food in the Mos Espa marketplace by gorgmongers, often for under 10 wupiupi for a single large animal. The vendor Gragra had one tasty specimen snatched by a hungry Jar Jar Binks. When she accosted Jar Jar, the clueless Gungan dropped the gorg from his mouth, causing it to land in Sebulba's soup bowl at a nearby café. Jabba the Hutt was a known connoisseur of gorgs, often keeping a snack bowl full of the frog-like creatures within arm's reach. The Huttese word for "gorg" was *chuba.* Mos Espa gorgs were typically cooked upon purchase and could be flavored with roasted manak leaves or served with a variety of dipping sauces. Gragra grew her gorgs and other edible amphibians in a sewer zone beneath Mos Espa, although she told clients that the creatures were nurtured in a basement culture pool. Some species of gorgs were predominantly carnivorous, with pronounced teeth, and were known to eat their young. They ate large quantities of glie and similar substances when other food sources proved scarce.

**Gorga the Hutt** Jabba the Hutt's groveling nephew. When his uncle died, Gorga was bequeathed a small bank that contained exactly one button. Later, after getting Boba Fett to kill Bar-Kooda and preparing him as a meal, Gorga won the hand of Anachro, a beautiful H'uun Hutt. But on their honeymoon on Skeebo, Anachro was kidnapped; again Fett was hired and did the job.

**gorgmonger** A vendor who sold raw and cooked gorgs and chubas.

**gorgodon** A large furred predator native to the planet Ilum, it could use many parts of its body to intimidate and kill its prey. The only way to kill a gorgodon was to sever its spine just behind the head, paralyzing the beast.

***Gorgon* (1)** An Imperial Star Destroyer, it was Admiral Daala's flagship, the last of her remaining original Star Destroyers. During the battle at the Maw Installation, after she downloaded weapons plans from the facility into the *Gorgon*'s computers, she set what appeared to be a suicide course into the installation, apparently destroying the *Gorgon.* In reality, she took the ship, under Commander Kratas, on a long trip to the Core Worlds, where she planned to regroup and ally herself with powerful Imperial warlords. The *Gorgon* was briefly added to High Admiral Teradoc's fleet before being scrapped.

***Gorgon* (2)** A Nebulon-B frigate used by the Imperial Navy at the height of the Galactic Civil War.

***Gorgon* (3)** A Corellian INT-66 interceptor owned by Daxtorn Lethos, it was armed with a pair of front-mounted turbolasers, four repeating blasters, and a double pulse-laser turret.

**gorgy-bird** A Rogue Squadron maneuver named for the females of the avian species, which look like they remain so heavy after laying their eggs that they wobble when flying. But their flight pattern was merely a ruse, meant to lure predators to the mother and away from her nest.

**gorimn wine** A fermented beverage that Wookiees considered mild, it packed a wallop for humans.

**Gorjaye, Ranna** A native of Salliche, Gorjaye was a squadron leader of the X-wing forces sent to Kal'Shebbol to try to bring down Imperial Moff Kentor Sarne about four years after the Battle of Endor. Ranna later joined the crew of the corvette *FarStar* as a pilot and gunner. She was nicknamed "Wing Ripper."

**Gormo** A Duros male, he was stranded on the planet Onderon in the years following the Mandalorian Wars.

**Gorm the Dissolver** A huge cyborg droid bounty hunter, he had heavy plated armor and a full helmet. His biocomponents came from six different aliens and seven generations of electronics. He was seemingly destroyed by the young Rodian bounty hunter Greedo on the spaceport moon of Nar Shaddaa, but later was repaired and eventually showed up in Mos Eisley.

**gorm-worm** A species with poison venom sacs, it could kill instantly with its bite. A gorm-worm was used by pirates to kill Jedi trainee Andur Sunrider some 4,000 years before the Galactic Civil War.

**Gornash, Prophet** A Prophet of the Dark Side, this large human coordinated spy activities from the group's space station headquarters, Scardia.

**Gorneesh, King** A sly, foul-tempered leader of the Duloks, creatures that lived in the swamps of Endor's moon.

**Gorno** A spaceport, it was supposed to be the point of embarkation for the Hammertong device that was to be delivered to the Empire.

**gornt** A staple in ration packs of both Rebels and Imperials, gornt meat was prized for its taste, nutritional value, and ability to stay fresh for a long period of time. Gornts originated on Hethar, a planet annexed by the Empire during the Galactic Civil War. Upon discovery of the benefits of gornt meat, the Imperial Navy instituted breeding and processing programs to feed its ranks. Enterprising Sullustan ranchers made a fortune by establishing reliable food supplies, though years of genetic tampering have lessened the quality of gornt stock. In the wild, gornts travel in packs of 10 to 30 adults and about half as many young "gorntlings." Gornts lived for about six years, during which they mated three times, producing litters of two to four ayas (pups) each time. An average gornt ate its weight in food every week. Gornts were primarily herbivorous, but ate almost anything in a pinch. Their extremely efficient digestive systems broke down even the toughest of foods into prime nutrients, which was why gornt flesh was so succulent and nutritious.

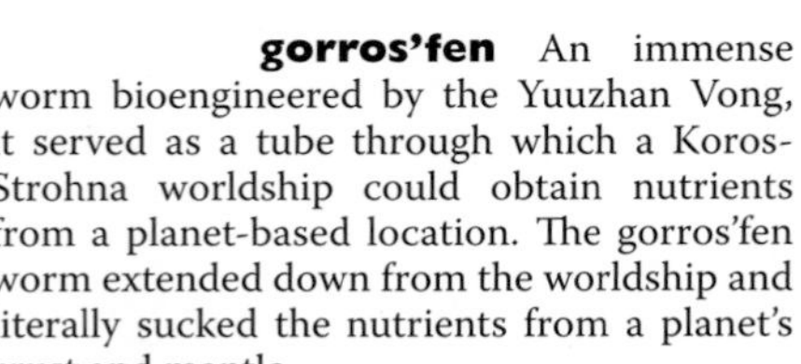

Gorm the Dissolver

**Gorog** One of two new hives created after the crash of the *Tachyon Flier* on the planet Yoggoy during the Yuuzhan Vong invasion of the galaxy. Like its counterpart, the Unu hive, the Gorog hive was formed when a Force-sensitive individual joined with the hive mind and began to influence it. However, where the Unu were created from the beliefs of former Jedi Knight Raynar Thul, the Gorog were created under the influence of the Dark Jedi Welk and Lomi Plo. Imposing figures, individual Gorog were excellent fighters who would literally explode if their carapace was breached, making them living bombs that could be used to attack other nests. Because of the influence of the Dark Jedi, the Gorog were able to keep their existence a secret from the rest of the Kind, tapping into the Force to mask their presence. In fact, not even UnuThul knew about the existence of the Gorog hive on Kr and vehemently denied its existence when questioned by Han Solo and Leia Organa Solo, who had seen it firsthand.

When the Chiss began to stop the encroachment of the Colony on their section of the Unknown Regions, many were captured in battle and a large number chose to become Joiners of the Gorog hive. It later turned out that the Chiss served as a source of food for young hive members. Luke Skywalker and the new Jedi Order referred to the Gorog as the Dark Nest, and they believed that the Will of the Gorog nest was broken when Skywalker killed Welk in combat on Kr, but it became clear that this wasn't true.

Putting different bits of information together, Skywalker was able to figure out that the Gorog hive was trying to break his will and invade his mind in an effort to make him a Joiner and gain control of the new Jedi Order. Jacen Solo had a similar revelation, although it came in the form of a Force-induced vision that showed a galaxy in flames—indicating to him the Gorog's desire to take control of the entire galaxy. In a series of struggles, Luke managed to destroy Lomi Plo, then set out to confront UnuThul and force him to cut off his contact with the Killiks. Skywalker's plan ultimately succeeded, and the Gorog hive was eliminated as the unconscious aspect of the Will of the Colony. But Alema Rar had survived her battle with Leia Organa Solo on Tenupe and considered herself the final member of the Gorog hive.

King Gorneesh

**gorph** A species of frog-like creatures native to the Forest Moon of Endor, they were known for their exceptionally long tongues, which they used to catch their food.

**Gor-ravvus** The primary liaison between Lhosan Industries and the Old Republic in the years following the Great Sith War, he lobbied the Galactic Senate to recognize Taris and its neighboring systems as part of the Republic after Lhosan decided to establish a manufacturing facility there. Gor-ravvus later was named a full Senator. Unfortunately for the people of Taris, Senator Gor-ravvus fled the planet at the first hint of a Mandalorian attack.

**Gorrlyn** A female Wookiee, she was chosen by Salporin as a mate shortly before the start of the Clone Wars. The two were separated when the Empire enslaved the Wookiees, and Gorrlyn was widowed when Salporin died trying to protect Chewbacca and Leia Organa Solo on Kashyyyk.

Gorrm

**Gorrm** A tall and thin simian sentient, he was Ssk Kahorr's chief navigator. Gorrm was killed when Ssk Kahorr and the *Starbreaker 12* were destroyed by Naga Sadow.

**gorros'fen** An immense worm bioengineered by the Yuuzhan Vong, it served as a tube through which a Koros-Strohna worldship could obtain nutrients from a planet-based location. The gorros'fen worm extended down from the worldship and literally sucked the nutrients from a planet's crust and mantle.

**Gorrt** A Gamorrean who worked for Jabba the Hutt, he also served as a bodyguard for the Jawa Akkik.

**Gorr the Hutt** *See* Ebelt, Gorr Desilijic.

**gorryl slug** A species native to the planet Kashyyyk. Even though it looked like a disgusting blob of purplish brown protoplasm, it was known for its tasty flesh and considered a delicacy on many worlds. The average gorryl slug was 1.5 meters long and fattened itself on the mites and organisms that lived on the bark of the wroshyr tree. When threatened or startled, the gorryl slug reared up to try to scare off its attacker or flopped back down to try to smother it.

**gorsa tree** A stout, flowering tree, it used its pale orange phosphorescent flowers to attract night insects for pollination.

**Gorsh** The primary planet in the Gorsh system in the Outer Rim Territories, this swampy world was owned by the Geentech Corporation and home to the Orgon species of intelligent plants. Geentech developed a large number of pharmaceuticals from the unique chemical compounds found on the planet.

**Gort** A large male Besalisk, he was a regular customer at Maggot's Cantina on the planet Anzat during the height of the Clone Wars.

**gort** Small creatures resembling a woolamander but with feathers instead of fur, they hatched from small pink eggs about a year after they were laid. The eggshells were often used in jewelry and were considered rare and precious.

**Gorth** A Trandoshan bodyguard, he was hired by Hath Monchar when he tried to sell information about the Trade Federation's impending blockade of the Naboo system. Gorth was killed by Darth Maul when the Sith Lord captured Monchar.

**Gorum** Members of this humanoid species had thin, prehensile tails, which they used to hang from branches during sleep—or from rafters and overhead pipes when they weren't in the wild. They used their forked tongues to suck the juice out of their food.

**Gorwooken (1)** One of the many Wookiee inhabitants of the city of Rwookrrorro who supported Chuundar more than four millennia before the Battle of Yavin. When he discovered that a group of Jedi Knights had infiltrated Chuundar's defenses and obtained a piece of the Star Map, he and his thugs attacked them. The Wookiees were no match for the Jedi and were killed in battle.

**Gorwooken (2)** A famous Wookiee hunter on the planet Kashyyyk during the last decades of the Old Republic.

**Gorzima** A Quarren crime lord on the moon of Nar Shaddaa around the time of the Battle of Naboo, he began taking bets on how long former Jedi Knight Quinlan Vos would last after he had lost his memory. Vilmarh Grahrk wagered his ship *Inferno* on Quinlan's chances, then captured Vos and planned to kill him; Vos escaped that fate and Gorzima gained a ship. So Grahrk made a second bet with Gorzima, but ended up stealing his ship back.

**Gosfambling** Delicate furred creatures from a planet of the same name, they were intelligent and soft-spoken. Their whiskers curled around their faces whenever they spoke. Wary of losers, Gosfamblings would not elect anyone who had ever lost in an election: Once a loser on Gosfambling, always a loser.

**Gospel of the True Gods** The collected set of beliefs and tenets of the Yuuzhan Vong's True Gods. To accept the Gospel was to prove one's adherence to the True Way.

**Gospic, Feyn** A Rebel Alliance colonel, he served as one of Jan Dodonna's chief strategic advisers before the Battle of Yavin. Gospic devised the plans for the approach to the first Death Star.

**Goss, Joreb** The long-sought father of Akanah Norand Pell, he was found on Atzerri. But he didn't remember his daughter or anything about her people, the Fallanassi, due to excessive drug use that diminished his memory.

Gotal

**Gossam** A species of small gray-green-skinned saurians native to the planet Castell, they were known for their unusual hairstyling, which accentuated the difference between the sexes. Early in the species' existence, the Commerce Guild essentially indentured the Gossam in return for economic assistance. Shu Mai kept the Gossam in heavy debt to her government and the Commerce Guild she came to control. Many Gossam fled and established a community on Felucia.

**gossipvid** A popular form of holovid. No story was too sleazy or cheap to broadcast, and the careers of many celebrities and politicians were undone by gossipvid reporting.

**Gotab** *See* Jusik, Bardan.

**Gotal** An intelligent, bipedal species with two prominent cone-shaped growths sprouting from their heads, Gotals are native to the Prindaar system, hailing from the fourth moon orbiting the gas giant Antar. The head cones served Gotals—who also had flat noses and protruding brows—as additional sensory organs that could pick up and distinguish different forms of emotional and energy waves. Although the shaggy, gray-furred species was technologically advanced, most other species felt uncomfortable around them because of their additional senses. And Gotals avoided droids since their high-energy output tended to overload the Gotals' senses. Members of the species made excellent scouts, bounty hunters, trackers, and mercenaries. When nervous, Gotals tended to shed copious amounts of their fur. And they often misinterpreted the emotions of other species, occasionally mistaking affection for love, anger for imminent violence, and envy for murderous intent. This confusion has led to violence between Gotals and other cultures. One such incident happened just prior to the Clone Wars when the secessionist movement was splitting the galaxy, resulting in a bloody clash between Jedi Knights and Gotal extremists.

Gossam

**Go-To** *See* G0-T0.

**Gottu** An urban combat specialist with Page's Commandos, his preferred weapon was a vibro-ax. A career soldier, Gottu fought many battles before joining the Rebel Alliance. He was later part of the team assembled by Page for the assault on Moff Sarne's stronghold on Kal'Shebbol, four years after the Battle of Endor.

**gouka dragon** An immense reptile native to the deserts of Aargonar, it spent most of its life underground, tunneling through the sand and rock to avoid the heat. Gouka dragons were known to feed on Aargonar Sarlaccs, attacking from underground and avoiding their tentacles. The beast filled the tunnels it created, so that it appeared only as a huge mouth when it attacked other creatures. It generated intense body heat that literally melted the rock through which it moved, giving gouka tunnels smooth, rounded sides.

Gouka dragon

*Graak*

**Goure** A Ryn who settled on the planet Bakura during the Yuuzhan Vong War, he served as a scout for his people. He was Tahiri Veila's contact on Bakura when she accompanied Han Solo and Leia Organa Solo on their mission to reestablish communications with the remote planet. He warned the group that things on Bakura were not what they seemed.

**Govia, Rennt** One of the few totally pro-Imperial Bakuran Senators at the time of the Battle of Endor, he strongly supported Wilek Nereus as planetary governor and worked to undermine the efforts of Prime Minister Captison. Rennt came from a prominent Bakuran family, and his great-grandparents were financial backers of the Bakur Corporation. He thought of himself as something of a Core Worlder, despite his Bakuran heritage, mainly because of his education on Corulag. After graduation, he considered himself a model of Human High Culture, but was considered self-centered and despicable by his peers.

**Gowdawl** This planet was the destination for the starliner *Star Morning,* owned by the Fallanassi religious order. The spacecraft left the planet Motexx a few weeks before the Battle of Endor with a full cargo, bound for Gowdawl under a charter license. The liner then disappeared for 300 days, eventually showing up at Arat Fraca with empty cargo holds.

**Goyoikin** The capital city of the planet Ventooine, it was located on the only inhabited continent on the planet.

**Gozanti cruiser** A powerful well-armored cruiser, it was popular among independent merchants during the last decades of the Old Republic. Produced by Gallofree Yards, it was nearly 42 meters long and hard to board, making it the bane of many pirates.

**Gozric** The Imperial Moff who controlled the Wyl sector during the New Order, this former navy officer looked at the Corporate Sector Authority's military forces with disdain and made little effort to support the CSA's patrols of their joint border.

**Graad** This Mandalorian solider was one of many who didn't believe that Boba Fett was the proper choice to serve as *Mand'alor* in the years following the Swarm War. Fett called him Purple Man because of the color of his armor. Graad supported the *kadikla* movement, and he pushed for a call for all Mandalorians to return to their homeworld and support the needs of the *Mando'ade.* Fett agreed to support Graad's proposal to bring wayward Mandalorians back to Mandalore, in an effort to bolster their numbers and regain their self-sufficiency.

**Graak** A cunning warrior among Chief Chirpa's Ewok forces, he often circled his prey to cut off their escape routes before attacking.

**Gra'aton** An ancient Jedi Master, he worked with Yoda and Vulaton on Dathomir to try to save the *Chu'unthor* after it crashed into the swamps there some 300 years before the Battle of Yavin.

**grab-safety** A specialized shield technology, it was developed by the New Republic at the height of the Yuuzhan Vong War as a way to counteract the effects of a dovin basal.

**grabworm** A predatory creature from the swamps of Toydaria, it lunged from concealment to catch its prey. Toydarians evolved with wings and gas-filled abdomens that allowed them to avoid grabworm attacks.

**Gracca** A large winged alien who lived in the Floating Mountain on the Forest Moon of Endor, he was feared by the Ewoks because of his magical crystal cloak. But Princess Kneesaa used a length of rope to snag the cloak and pull it from Gracca's shoulders; she watched as he crashed into the walls of his crystalline palace, trapping him beneath the rubble forever.

**Gracus, Bor** A stout Senator from Sluis Van before the Battle of Naboo, he was a confederate of Senator Palpatine, who curried Gracus's favor because of the important shipyards in orbit around the planet.

**Graeber, Dennix** An Imperial Governor put in charge of Ralltiir by Lord Tion, he was known as a twisted genius and was adept at rooting out and eliminating Rebel Alliance holdings on the planet. But Graeber was best remembered as governor of the first Imperial-held planet to be liberated by the New Republic.

**Graemon** An Imperial supporter, he was one of the leading financial experts running the installation on Muunilinst 10 years after the death of Grand Admiral Thrawn. Admiral Pellaeon discovered that Graemon was one of the primary people funneling Imperial funds into the procurement of *Preybird*-class starfighters from the Cavrilhu pirates under the direction of Moff Disra. Graemon even had ties to New Republic financial and commodities interests.

**Graf, Admiral** The head of New Republic Fleet Intelligence during the Yevethan crisis, he had been responsible for mopping up the damage caused by the leaking of information on Republic casualties in the Koornacht Cluster during the Black Fleet crisis.

**Graff, Skent** The captain of the New Republic's *Soothfast* during the Yuuzhan Vong War, he and his crew were involved in the recovery of the Yuuzhan Vong priestess Elan and her familiar, Vergere, shortly after the destruction of the planet Obroa-skai. His father had been part of the crew of the *Corbantis,* rescued near Damonite Yors-B by Han Solo. But Graff's father contracted the Death Seed plague and soon died.

**Graffe, Jander** A heavy-handed Imperial Moff, he ruled the Darpa sector during the Galactic Civil War.

**Gragra** A Swokes Swokes gorgmonger who worked the Mos Espa marketplace on Tatooine, she caught Jar Jar Binks trying to snatch a tasty morsel from her stand without paying the necessary wupiupi. When the bullying Dug Sebulba knocked the hapless Gungan to the ground, Gragra considered the matter closed. Gragra claimed to keep her amphibian stock of gorgs or chuba in a large basement pool, but in truth she grew them in the sewers under the city.

**grahn vine** A thick, durable plant native to Naboo. Gungans wove them into strong ropes. Certain animals could eat the plant.

*Gragra the gorgmonger*

Vilmarh Grahrk

**Grahrk, Vilmarh** His broken Basic and devilish smile did little to inspire confidence, but he was nonetheless a successful and unscrupulous con man working the galaxy's fringe. Vilmarh Grahrk, or Villie as he was called by acquaintances, worked as a grifter in Nar Shaddaa's underbelly for years, probably without earning an honest credit in his life. Villie partnered with the amnesiatic Jedi Quinlan Vos to help uncover a glitteryll racket that implicated an influential Twi'lek Senator. Villie's standard operating practice involved deception and betrayal, but he remained surprisingly loyal to Vos. Despite a sizable bounty on the Jedi's head, Villie didn't betray him. Instead, he double-crossed the bounty's poster and ended the caper significantly richer. Villie's chronic gambling usually ate away his ill-gotten earnings. No matter how much he made, he soon could be found trying out a new scam to fill his coffers. The Devaronian piloted a sleek vessel called the *Inferno,* with the help of NT, a droid hardwired into the ship.

Captain-Supervisor Grammel

**Grahvess, Emd** The greatest freelance architect of the New Order, he was hired to design a new diplomatic complex for the Shell Hutts on Circumtore. There was a complex plot to cheat the architect out of his fee by killing him, but with Boba Fett's help he outwitted the Hutts.

**Grakchawwaa, King** A Wookiee who was considered the leader of the Royal Families of Kashyyyk during the final years of the Old Republic, he was approached by representatives of the Trade Federation about 18 months after the Battle of Geonosis. The representatives, spurred by General Grievous, hoped to enlist the aid of the Wookiees and take control of the Kashyyyk system during the Clone Wars. King Grakchawwaa was reluctant to join the war on either side and might have remained neutral—but then General Grievous killed his son, Prince Rikummee. The king then declared war against the Separatists and opened Kashyyyk to the forces of the Grand Army of the Republic.

**Grake** Large and tentacled but nonetheless gentle, this Veubgri from the planet Gbu was a cook for Lord Hethrir and took great pride in her work.

**Grakko** A Quarren bounty hunter, he was asked to capture and kill Khaleen Hentz after she stole a datadisk from Zenex. But the young woman trapped Grakko in an access duct and set off a bomb, killing him.

Gran

**grakkt** A Naboo swamp creature more than 3 meters long, it resembled an armor-plated lion with the head of a crocodile. Its saliva contained potent venom, and every bite delivered by the grakkt was fatal unless treated immediately.

**Grakouine** The site of a Rebel Alliance storage base, it was where the New Republic parked Boba Fett's ship, *Slave I,* after the bounty hunter was presumed killed by the Sarlacc on Tatooine. Some time later a very much alive Fett repurchased his ship through legitimate, although hidden, channels.

**Grallia Spaceport** A well-known high-tech spaceport in Grallia, the capital of the planet Ralltiir, it closed down around the time of the Battle of Yavin as Lord Tion tried to quell the growing rebellion on the planet.

**Grammel, Captain-Supervisor** The Imperial official in charge of the energy mining operation on Circarpous V. He ruled with an iron fist and enforced strict laws in the mining towns. He was a sadistic authoritarian who would often torture prisoners for sick pleasure. Grammel managed to capture Luke Skywalker and Princess Leia Organa, but the two Rebels escaped in a daring prison break. Grammel was wounded in the escape, but underwent hasty reconstructive surgery to continue his pursuit. When Grammel failed to recapture the fugitives for Darth Vader, the Dark Lord executed him with his lightsaber.

**Gran** The peaceful Gran were active members of galactic society for ages. With colonies on Malastare and Hok, the Gran spread to several planets. In the twilight years of the Republic, a Gran delegation represented Malastare in the Galactic Senate. Among its members were Senators Aks Moe, Ainlee Teem, and Ask Aak. Other well-known Gran included Ree-Yees, a member of Jabba the Hutt's court, and Mawhonic, a Podracer. The Gran were easily distinguished by their triple eyestalks. They had hircine faces, small horns, and a jutting jawline. The Gran maintained a peaceful civilization on their homeworld of Kinyen for over 10 millennia. Their society was evenly balanced, and a strict program of career quotas ensured that every Gran was trained for a specific job that best served his or her talents. A typical Gran placed the betterment of society above the betterment of self and was keenly aware of his or her role in the bigger picture.

Gran were keenly aware of each other's emotions, too, being able to judge disposition through subtle changes of body heat and skin color. Gran were very loyal and needed to be with someone for companionship. A Gran left alone went insane or died of loneliness. The Gran had excellent vision, able to resolve more colors than most species. Gran had multiple stomachs, having evolved from herbivorous ungulates.

Grakko

Grand Army of the Republic

**Grand Admiral** The highest rank in the Imperial Navy, it was developed by Emperor Palpatine, possibly to install his loyalists at the very top of the Empire's military establishment.

At the time of the Battle of Endor, there were a dozen known Grand Admirals, and the Emperor referred to them as his "Circle of Twelve." But there was a 13th Grand Admiral as well, a Chiss mastermind known as Thrawn, who filled the void left when Zaarin was killed during his own attempt to become Emperor. By the time the Imperial Remnant agreed to a peace treaty with the New Republic, Pellaeon was believed to be the only surviving Grand Admiral, a rank he had earned well after the death of Thrawn.

Grand Admirals

**Grand Army of the Republic** The ground-based arm of the Old Republic's military, it was formed in response to the buildup of Separatist battle droids on Geonosis just prior to the onset of the Clone Wars. Supreme Chancellor Palpatine said he needed the army to address the growing question of secession from the Republic. Palpatine beseeched the Galactic Senate to approve the formation of the army as a fallback option, but in reality the vote already had been decided through bribes and blackmail. It paved the way for Palpatine's endgame: taking control of the galaxy as Emperor. Many members of the Galactic Senate opposed the formation of the GAR. However, the capture of Jedi Master Obi-Wan Kenobi by Count Dooku on Geonosis forced the Senate to reevaluate the situation. It was the oration of Jar Jar Binks, standing in for Senator Padmé Amidala of Naboo—also a prisoner on Geonosis—that called for the approval of emergency powers for the Chancellor.

The Grand Army of the Republic was formed from the more than 1.2 million clones discovered on Kamino. Over time, more specialized clones were developed, ranging from clone commandos to ARC troopers. At the height of the conflict, the GAR numbered some 3 million troops, while the Special Forces Brigade added another 50,000 specialists. During the three years of fighting that led up to the Battle of Coruscant and the end of the Clone Wars, more than half of the original clones had been killed in combat, but they had destroyed billions of battle droids. Each of the primary divisions of the GAR was commanded by a Jedi Knight or Master, often acting as general. As a rule, each Jedi was given a clone commander to work with, as a bodyguard and liaison to the troops. This arrangement proved quite useful when Order 66 was issued, as it ensured that every Jedi leader on the battlefield was covered by a clone commander.

**Grand Audience Chamber** A huge, open space located at the top of the Great Temple on Yavin 4, it was left intact by the Rebel Alliance engineers who excavated the temple for use as their command base. Its natural beauty was awe inspiring, and the feelings it invoked could not be modified by future generations. It was here that Princess Leia awarded medals of honor to Luke Skywalker and Han Solo following the Battle of Yavin. Later, Skywalker decided to leave the chamber intact when he established his Jedi praxeum on Yavin 4.

**Grand Concourse** The immense circular hallway that led from the Atrium of the Old Republic Senate Rotunda, it provided access to the Convocation Center and the entire lower ring of the building. The Grand Concourse started and ended in the Atrium but allowed beings to reach virtually any section of the Rotunda. After the Yuuzhan Vong took control of Coruscant and terraformed it into a new version of Yuuzhan'tar, much of the Grand Concourse was destroyed or bored out and filled with yorik coral growths.

**Grand Convocation Chamber** Built to replace the old Senate Hall on the planet Coruscant—destroyed when Dolph's first attack on the New Republic laid it to rubble—it was constructed atop the foundation of the former Galactic Senate Rotunda. The Convocation Chamber featured a multitude of configurable blocks of seats. When Borsk Fey'lya killed himself in an effort to destroy a good portion of the Yuuzhan Vong leadership that eventually subjugated Coruscant, the Convocation Chamber was one of the few buildings in the vicinity of the Imperial Palace that wasn't severely damaged. Its survival was due mainly to its structural engineering, but also because the Yuuzhan Vong had decided to use it to house the World Brain that would control Coruscant's transformation into a simulacrum of Yuuzhan'tar. In the wake of the Yuuzhan Vong War, the Grand Convocation Chamber was diligently scoured of any alien influence, and teams of architects worked to restore the building to its prior glory.

**Grand Corridor** Located in the Imperial Palace on Coruscant, the Grand Corridor was a tree-lined path that led to the many assembly halls and meeting rooms used by the Empire and the New Republic. It was built by Emperor Palpatine to link the Council Chamber and the Assemblage auditorium. It intersected the hallway housing the Senatorial suites and offices. Palpatine then added the multihued ch'hala trees that lined it, and thus created the eavesdropping system known as Delta Source. Many historians of architecture believed that an entire Star Destroyer would have fit within the Grand Corridor.

**grand cruiser** The New Republic's designation for the largest of the Yuuzhan Vong warships. Later models, used in battle after the destruction of Obroa-skai, had a separate module known as a keeper, which traveled with

Grand Audience Chamber

the ships. The keeper contained independent dovin basals, allowing a ship to take fire but not lose shield strength.

**Grand Dukha** The primary meeting place of the Noghri government, it was located in the city of Nystao. It was also referred to as the Common Room of Honoghr, since all Noghri tribes were allowed entrance. It was similar in many respects to the dukhas in each village.

**Grand Imperial Union** An affiliation of former Imperial Moffs and their followers, it was formed in the years following the Battle of Endor. Led by Moff Tragg Brathis, the union threw its support to Nil Spaar and the Yevetha during their battle against the New Republic.

**Grand Isle** One of the jungle islands on the planet Vladet, it was once the site of an Imperial installation under the command of Admiral Devlia. The facility was placed there to discourage piracy because of its proximity to the Chorax, Hensara, and Rachuk systems. It was destroyed by the Rebel Alliance and Rogue Squadron in a retaliatory strike.

**Grand Master** A title used only a handful of times in the history of the galaxy, it described the single leader of the entire Jedi Order. Luke Skywalker, in the wake of the Yuuzhan Vong War, was forced to take on the role of Grand Master during the crisis between the Colony and the Chiss. With the new Jedi Order in disarray, Skywalker decided he had to get the Order into alignment by taking the title and making the Masters agree on a single course of action.

**Grand Moff** The title given to an Imperial Governor who presided over a sector of the galaxy that the Emperor designated a priority sector. A Grand Moff's jurisdiction could span one or more sectors. As the era of the New Order continued, the number of rebellious sectors grew, requiring that more Grand Moffs be named.

**Grand Reception Hall** A kilometer-long site in Imperial City where dignitaries from across the galaxy were received by the galaxy's rulers, it was located near the Petrax District on Coruscant. At the time of the planet's capture by the Yuuzhan Vong, the Grand Reception Hall was the oldest continually operating governmental building on the planet. It was nestled among several tall skytowers, so very

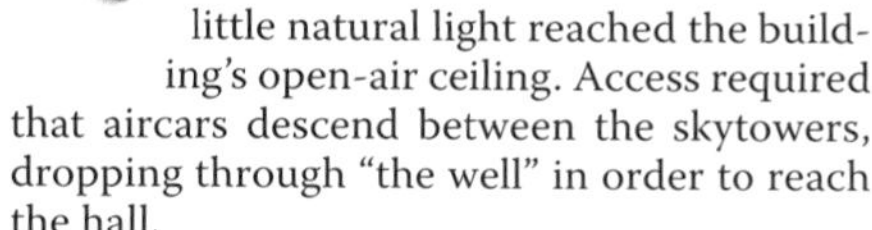

Granite slug

little natural light reached the building's open-air ceiling. Access required that aircars descend between the skytowers, dropping through "the well" in order to reach the hall.

**Grand Vizier** A title given to the highest ranking of Emperor Palpatine's advisers at the height of the New Order.

**Graneet, Tenn** From his days as master chief petty officer aboard the Star Destroyer *Steel Talon,* during the early years of the New Order, through his service on the Death Star, Tenn Graneet was regarded as the best gunnery chief in the fleet, even though he was more than 50 years old. He had served in the Grand Army of the Republic during the Clone Wars and remained in the service as the galaxy's politics changed radically. His skills as a starship sharpshooter earned him a chance to train on the superlaser that was installed in the first Death Star. Graneet's first chance to fire the weapon came when the Rebel Alliance freighter *Fortressa* tried to launch an attack on the Death Star. Using just 4 percent of its power capacity, the superlaser blew up the ship easily. To Graneet's surprise and concern, the second target was the planet Despayre. He accepted the job, but wondered how the Empire could destroy an entire planet when its own personnel were stationed there. Following orders, Graneet unleashed three superlaser blasts at the planet over a period of two and a half hours, each using about a third of the weapon's power capacity. Each successive blast caused greater and greater damage, until Despayre shattered into rubble and cinders. But the real blow to Graneet's psyche came when he was ordered to fire on the planet Alderaan. Despayre, at least, was a prison planet. Alderaan, however, was populated by some of the galaxy's most peaceful citizens, and his single blast of immense power sent billions of innocent beings to their deaths. He considered himself the galaxy's biggest mass murderer and was thinking about his future when the orders came down to target Yavin 4. When the time came to actually fire, Graneet stalled for as long as he could. This delay allowed Rebel pilot Luke Skywalker to fire a proton torpedo into the station, setting off a chain reaction that caused it to explode. Graneet died knowing that he had done his best to save more innocent beings.

**Granit** A Rebel Alliance agent, he led the evacuation of supporters from Delantine when the Empire took control. He also rescued Stuart Zissu, R2-D2, C-3PO, and 4B-X from the planet Da'nor, where they had crashed while en route to Delantine.

Saw-toothed grank

**granite slug** A small invertebrate creature, it thrived in the dank lower levels of Coruscant, out of reach of the hawk-bats that prey on it. The trails of granite slugs left deep marks in the dirt and fungi, resembling some kind of ancient runes. They were introduced to Coruscant some 340 years before the Galactic Civil War in an attempt by the Old Republic to clean up the garbage that existed in the lower levels of the city-planet.

**grank, saw-toothed** This species of large, predatory feline was native to Naboo. The grank's jaws were filled with huge, serrated teeth that it used to capture and tear at its favorite prey, the shiro. The meat of the grank was considered a delicacy by Gungans, and its hard toenails were machined for use in the engines of bongo submarines. In the wild, granks were solitary predators that hunted with acute senses of hearing and touch. The latter sense came through the hairs that ran along the creature's sides, which could detect vibrations in the air and ground. A few specimens of saw-toothed granks were exported from Naboo as pets or guardbeasts, but these usually became too feral to manage and were set loose. These wild granks quickly dominated their ecosystems, and often preyed upon sentient beings before being destroyed.

**Granna** Once an Imperial world, Granna was home planet of the Grannans. Plat Mallar, who participated in the Battle of N'zoth, was a Grannan pilot who was born on Polneye.

**Gra Ploven** The homeworld of the Ploven species, it was nearly destroyed during the reign of Emperor Palpatine. Imperial forces aboard the Star Destroyer *Forger* boiled the planet's water by repeatedly firing turbolasers into lakes and seas, cooking many Ploven alive.

**Grappa** A Rodian mercenary, he was the leader of forces hired by the Osarians to protect them from attack by the Rhommamoolians some two decades after the Battle of Endor. Leading the Osarian First-Force, Grappa intercepted Leia Organa Solo before she could meet with Nom Anor on Rhommamool.

**Grappa the Hutt** A Hutt who controlled his criminal empire from the planet Genon, he had ties to Black Sun, and his ruthlessness was legendary. He tried playing so many parties against the others that he eventually got caught in one of his own labyrinthine plots, was captured by Zzzanmxl and his troops, and was transported to Xo for a sacrificial ceremony.

**Grappler** The code name used by Su-mil during his duty with the Aurek-Seven unit of the Imperial 501st Legion of stormtroopers, serving the Empire of the Hand some 22 years after the Battle of Yavin. Like his companions Watchman, Cloud, and Shadow, Grappler accompanied Chak Fel on the mission to locate the Outbound Flight Project in Chiss space some three years before the Yuuzhan Vong began their invasion of the galaxy.

**grappler** A form of Sekotan starship created by the living planet Zonama Sekot to deal with the poisoned coralskippers sent to attack the planet by Supreme Overlord Shimrra during the final battle of the Yuuzhan Vong War. Resembling red and green insects, the grapplers used unusual gravity weaponry to drag down any coralskippers they encountered.

***Grappler*** One of the Empire's Interdictor cruisers, it operated in the period leading up to the Battle of Endor.

**grashal** A creature developed by the Yuuzhan Vong as a bioengineered building or command center, it was created like the species' other structures by the secretions of the gricha larva. When fully constructed, the grashal resembled a huge mollusk shell, accessible via a staircase that led to a nexus of tunnels and inner chambers. Grashals could be grown in different configurations, standing up to 3 meters high and up to 16 meters long.

**Graskt** Assistant director of the Treitamma Political Center, he died in Armand Isard's plot to assassinate Garm Bel Iblis, along with Bel Iblis's entire family.

**grasser** A large herdbeast raised by the Korunnai natives of Haruun Kal. Grassers had coats of silky fur that helped them maintain their body heat as they moved on six powerful legs. They left behind a meadow-like swath as they moved through jungles, consuming all plant life in their path. The Korunnai learned to follow grasser herds to safety during the severe winters when Downstorms struck.

**Grassling** A technical officer, he was assigned to the Outbound Flight Project about five years after the Battle of Naboo.

**grass painting** An art form that originated on Alderaan, it involved properly planting and maintaining various species of grass so that as the years passed their natural colors and textures formed beautiful artwork when viewed from the air.

**Grasstrekkers** Warmongering beings on the Forest Moon of Endor, they tried to take over the fortress of the Gupin people but were defeated with the help of the Ewoks Wicket, Teebo, and Kneesaa.

**gratenite** A lustrous white stone quarried on the planet Terephon, it was used in sculpture and building construction.

**grate toad** A gross-looking amphibian native to the undercity of Coruscant.

**Grath (1)** A young Vorzydiak and a founder of the Freelies who wanted less work and more free time for the people of Vorzyd 4, he was the son of Chairman Port. Qui-Gon Jinn and Obi-Wan Kenobi were dispatched to look into acts of sabotage that nearly led to war with a neighboring planet, only to discover they had been perpetrated by the Freelies. In the end, the Freelies agreed to work with Chairman Port to help achieve their goals.

**Grath (2)** A stormtrooper, he was assigned to Zasm Katth and Baddon Fass when they searched Nar Shaddaa to find Shug Ninx's garage and the *Millennium Falcon.*

**grathometer** A mechanism used in the activation device for many low-tech explosives during the Galactic Civil War.

**Grau, Wil'm** An Imperial major who headed a detachment on Alashan, he and his team captured Luke Skywalker and Leia Organa after the *Staraker* crashed on the planet shortly after the Battle of Yavin. When Luke and Leia rescued Wil'm Grau from an avalanche, they worked together to escape the hostile planet, then went their separate ways.

**grav-ball** A popular sport created near the end of the Old Republic, it used repulsor-equipped players to get a small sphere that moved erratically across the playing field and past the opponent's goal line.

**Grave, Taxtro** An Imperial stormtrooper stationed aboard the Star Destroyer *Reprisal* following the Battle of Yavin, he was a skilled sharpshooter. But he and his squadron comrades started questioning their orders when the majority of his targets turned out to be civilians. After several run-ins with the agents of the BloodScar Pirates, the stormtroopers found themselves in league with Han Solo and Luke Skywalker, and later Mara Jade. In the end, they were given the chance to escape from Imperial service and set off on their own.

**gravel-maggot** Worms that fed upon rotting flesh, they aided in rapid decomposition. Gravel-maggots could be found in the hills and rocky badlands of the planet Tatooine.

**gravel storm** Ferocious storms on the planet Tatooine, they whipped up and sent rocks, sand, and loose debris hurtling through the air—sometimes with deadly force.

**Graven, Ruto** Queen Amidala's Minster of Internal Affairs, he was captured by Trade Federation battle droids during the first wave of the invasion of the planet.

**Grave Tuskens** Inhabitants of Sulon, they scavenged the dead for their possessions. They were originally brought to the moon by Imperial forces to serve as "enforcers" during early mining operations there.

**Graveyard of Alderaan** An asteroid field, it was all that remained of the planet Alderaan, blown up by the Empire with the first Death Star. It was called the Graveyard by spacers and free traders, who spun tales of mysterious Jedi artifacts and ghost ships amid the ruins. At one point, the Empire tried to lure Princess Leia Organa and her Rebel Alliance allies to the area by spreading a story that the Royal Palace of Alderaan had been found intact within a huge asteroid. The survivors of Alderaan—those who were offworld at the time of its destruction—quickly developed a ritual known as the Returning, which involved jettisoning memorial capsules for departed friends and relatives in the Graveyard. It was also here that Warlord Zsinj attacked the New Republic's convoy of bacta from Thyferra just before Rogue Squadron arrived to escort it to Coruscant.

**Graveyard of Lost Ships** A collection of starships that orbited a dwarf star, it was created following the Battle of Yavin by Dr. Arakkus to deliberately inflict suffering. The Graveyard was destroyed prior to the Battle of Hoth when Arakkus trapped Han Solo, Luke Skywalker, and Chewbacca aboard the *Millennium Falcon.* The trio set off a series of negatron charges that had been placed by Arakkus himself, and destroyed the connected ships along with Arakkus.

**gravitational field disruptor** Devices used by Old Republic merchants and transport operators, they temporarily altered the gravity surrounding a specific object to allow heavy loads to be moved with ease.

**gravitic amplitude modulator** Expensive and challenging Imperial technology, it let a starship modulate gravity in its vicinity. The Galactic Alliance showed Imperial engineers how to reprogram the GAMs to jam the communications of a Yuuzhan Vong yammosk, a technique used successfully in the defense of Borosk.

**gravitic modulator** A starship counter-detection system developed following the war against the Yuuzhan Vong, it was used originally on the StealthX fighter to reduce or eliminate the ability of most sensor systems to detect it.

**gravitic polarization beam** Designed by students at the Mrlsst Academy, it reversed the polarization of matter and split it apart at the molecular level. Originally designed for the Phantom Project to remove large tracts of land, it was put to military use when Rogue Squadron was forced to use it against Loka Hask's *Interdictor*-class cruiser near Mrlsst.

**gravity bomb** A Yevethan weapon, it disrupted the localized gravity field surrounding a starship, causing intense pressure changes due to shifting plating and decking.

**gravity dive** A pilot's act of desperation to provide a huge speed boost without adding engine stress, it involved the use of a planet's own gravity—as well as perfect timing in pulling out of a dive so that the ship didn't crash into the surface.

**gravity-wave system** A bomb-detonating technique, it used specialized circuitry embedded into a weapon's casing to sense the strength of the surrounding gravity field and detonate at a preset level.

**gravity-well projector** A device that simulated the presence of a large body in space, it prevented nearby ships from engaging their hyperdrives and forced ships already traveling through hyperspace to drop back into realspace. Connected to gravity-well generators aboard large ships, they were preceded by ancient, lost interdictor technologies. Imperial scientists working for Sienar Fleet Systems produced a compact working prototype just prior to the Battle of Yavin, but it was lost after being transported to the Death Star. It actually survived the Death Star's destruction, was somehow activated, and became the center of a vast junk asteroid field in the Paradise system before being removed by a Rebel strike force. Reports of a naturally occurring gravity-well generator led the Empire to the Sedri system, where a bizarre life-form known as Golden Sun created a gravity-well effect that made it appear as if Sedri were a star, not a planet.

Eventually perfected, gravity-well projectors were put into production aboard the Immobilizer 418, the first of the Empire's *Interdictor*-class cruisers. The Empire continued research into refining this technology, making it more powerful and more compact. The last generation of Super Star Destroyers, including the *Eclipse* and the *Sovereign,* featured gravity-well generators. A vast array of gravity-well generators regulated traffic into and out of the Imperial Deep Core during the resurrected Emperor's campaign against the New Republic. These generators formed the backbone of the Imperial Hyperspace Security Net.

Fourteen years after the Battle of Endor, a group of would-be conquerors identified as the Sacorran Triad used the ancient Centerpoint Station to create a vast interdiction field covering the entire Corellian system, making it the largest gravity-well projector on record. During the Corellian crisis, New Republic allies on Bakura perfected the hyperwave inertial momentum sustainer (HIMS) system, which was the first effective method of countering an interdiction field. The hyperwave sustainer used a gravitic sensor that provided a fast cutoff for a ship's normal hyperdrive, saving it from damage caused by entering a gravity well.

**Gravlex Med** An inhabited world in the Raioballo sector that was home to the Anx species, it was an idyllic world until the Empire took control of Gravlex Launchworks. Over time, hazardous waste stored on the planet for incineration leaked and caused vast environmental damage; the native Anx were decimated, and the planet was abandoned. Orbital facilities were later taken over by the New Republic, and it was here that the Star Destroyer *Chimaera* was taken for disassembly after the Battle of Bilbringi. But a team of Imperial insurgents got past Republic defenses and recaptured the ship.

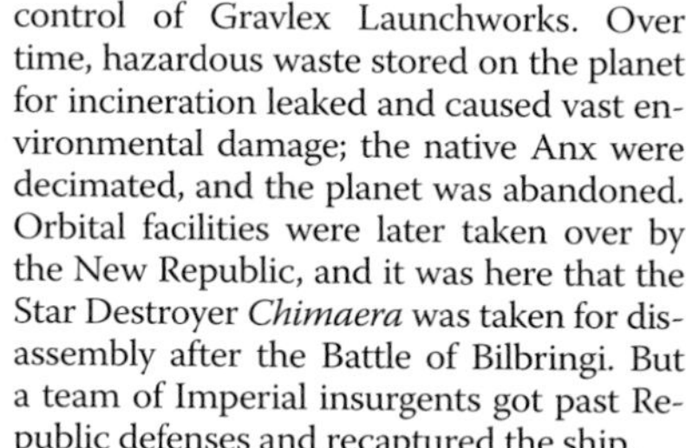

**gravsled** A flying platform for up to three passengers, it provided cheap, fast transportation with antigrav or repulsorlift engines. A windshroud offered a gravsled's only protection.

**Gray, Aleson** A ninth cousin to Hapan Queen Mother Tenel Ka, he was given command of the Battle Dragon *Kendall* and later chosen to lead a small task force of Hapan ships to Qoribu, to help defend the Colony against the Chiss.

**gray cadre** A term used to describe the group of New Republic military advisers made up of several key veterans of the Galactic Civil War. Its primary members were Jan Dodonna, Adar Tallon, and Vanden Willard.

**Grayfeather Squadron** One of many K-wing bomber squadrons that made up the Commenorian Navy during the war between the Galactic Alliance and the Confederation, it was part of the planetary home defense. Led by Caregg Oldathan, the Grayfeathers were forced into active duty when the Galactic Alliance's Third Fleet launched an attack on Commenor.

**gray Jedi** A term used by the Jedi Knights to describe Jedi who did things their own way, convinced that the path they had chosen was the only true one.

**Gray Leader** The comm unit designation for Colonel Horton Salm, the commander of Gray Wing, one of the four main Rebel starfighter battle groups during the Battle of Endor.

***Gray Pilgrim*** A starship owned by the Jedi Order, it was used as a mobile training facility during the final decades of the Old Republic. When Order 66 was executed, the *Gray Pilgrim* was in the Outer Rim Territories, so its passengers knew nothing of the beginnings of the Jedi Purge.

**Gray Squadron** The original designation of Wraith Squadron.

**Gray Two** The comm unit designation of Lieutenant Telsij during the Battle of Endor. Telsij was Colonel Salm's wingmate.

**Gray Wing** One of the four main Rebel starfighter battle groups in the Battle of Endor, it suffered quick and heavy casualties.

Grazer

Great Bogga the Hutt

**grazer** Four-legged herbivores that roamed the spacious grasslands of Alderaan, grazers were appropriately named, for they filled their days with constant eating. Alderaanian ranchers had long domesticated grazers, fattening them up to grotesque proportions to create animals that were a rich source of nutritious and tasty meat. The domesticated grazer was considerably fatter than the leaner, tougher wild grazer, and it was the former that survived the destruction of Alderaan, as grazers raised for meat had spread to ranches elsewhere in the galaxy.

**Great Beast** According to Wookiee lore, the Great Beast was first encountered by the ancient chieftain Rothrrrawr in the Shadowlands. Rothrrrawr underestimated the beast's ferocity and was unable to easily kill it. Rothrrrawr carried Bacca's Ceremonial Blade at the time and lost the blade in the beast's hide when it snapped off at the hilt. The blade was later discovered by Zaalbar, who reattached it to its hilt.

**Great Bogga the Hutt** A wealthy Hutt gang lord some four millennia before the Battle of Yavin, he ruled the underworld of the Stenness system. Great Bogga the Hutt ran a protection racket from a private moon that housed his operations. He was paid by the Nessies to protect their Ithull ore haulers against pirates who had developed marauder craft that could penetrate the thick sheathing of the Nessies' ships. The Hutt was also responsible for the death of Jedi trainee Andur Sunrider, after ordering his henchmen to strongarm Sunrider and steal the Adegan crystals he carried, the heart of lightsabers. Yet Bogga insisted upon calling himself the Merciful One, professing his willingness to forgive just about anyone who crossed him.

**Great Canyon** A long gash in the crust of the planet Dathomir, it was located just north of the Frenzied River. It was there, hidden within the forests, that Brakiss set up camp while searching for experienced dark side users for his Shadow Academy.

**Great Canyon Clan** A new clan of students of the dark side, its members returned to the planet Dathomir to try to recruit light-side witches for the Shadow Academy.

**Great Chott** Located on Tatooine, the Great Chott was a vast salt flat located at the southern tip of the Jundland Wastes. Nothing lived in the Great Chott without adequate protection, because any living thing caught on the Chott during the day was sure to lose its water in a short time. A small settlement was established on the flat's northern boundary, near Anchorhead and Tosche Station. It was here that Owen and Beru Lars lived, on the Lars family homestead, during the decades following the Clone Wars.

**Great Council** The body of political and military leaders of the Yuuzhan Vong, it was presided over by the Supreme Overlord.

**Great Council of Deneba** A Jedi Assembly of all the Jedi Masters on Deneba, who met to discuss and plan strategy against the growing menace of dark side forces led by Exar Kun about four millennia before the Galactic Civil War.

**Great Dance, the** Within the religious sect known as the Undying Flame, Yuuzhan Vong individuals worshipped the sibling deities Yun-Q'aah and Yun-Txiin, who represented love and hate and all things opposite in the universe. The two deities were equal and opposite parts of a whole, and the whole was represented by the Balance. The continual attempt of the universe to achieve the Balance was known as the Great Dance.

**Great Desert of Dathomir** The largest area of desert on the planet Dathomir, it was the homeland of the Blue Desert People.

**Great Doctrine, the** A Yuuzhan Vong belief developed to explain their "superiority" in their own galaxy, it provided both justification and motivation for the invasion of another galaxy.

**Great Dome of the Je'har** An architectural wonder on the planet Almania. Dark Jedi Kueller turned it into his command center when he fought against the Je'har.

**Great Door, the** An immense portal, it served as the primary entrance to the Senate Rotunda on Coruscant during the last centuries of the Old Republic. The Great Door was a work of art formed from thick durasteel and decorated with the Great Seal and the seals of the Thousand Worlds.

**Great Dordon caves** Located along the northern border of the city of Eusebus on the planet Euceron, this collection of twisting caves and tunnels was used as a Podracing venue in the years following the Battle of Naboo. The courses wound through the caves and were especially dangerous because the turns were so tight.

*Great Heep*

**Great Downrush** The largest river on the planet Haruun Kal, it was formed in the Korunnal Highland from melted snow and runoff from rivers such as Grandmother's Tears. It ended at the waterfall known as the Downrush Falls.

**Great Droid Revolution** An uprising of droids on Coruscant about 15 years before the Great Sith War. It was believed that the assassin droid HK-01 was behind it. During this time, Jedi Master Arca Jeth learned the technique of short-circuiting a droid by using the Force. Droid designers and manufacturers later turned to weapons developers to work on ion weapons that would short-circuit a droid's electronic systems. The revolution also put a temporary end to the growing droids' rights movement, as many species feared that fully autonomous droids were a threat to their safety.

**Greater Hub Spaceport** One of many spaceports on the planet Phindar, it was the target of a Separatist attack during the Clone Wars.

**Greater Plooriod Cluster** The site of prestigious swoop races until occupied by the Empire, this cluster was within the Greater Plooriod sector and contained the planet Corsin, where the races took place. The Plooriods also contained several vital agricultural worlds and had been the sector's primary grain supplier to the Empire. The entire cluster was once ruled by the ruthless Overlord Ghorin. Following the Battle of Yavin, Ghorin agreed to supply the Rebel Alliance with badly needed grain, but double-crossed the Rebels by providing them with tainted food. The Alliance responded by making it appear as if Ghorin were cheating the Empire, and Darth Vader personally executed the Overlord for his supposed treason on the planet Plooriod III. The sector also contained Imperial Drydock IV, from which several Interdictor cruisers departed to join the Outer Rim Imperial fleet.

*Great Holocron*

**Great Flood** The time in Kaminoan history when the planet experienced a sudden rise in temperature, its polar ice caps and glaciers melted, and the world was completely flooded with water; all landmasses were submerged under a planet-encircling ocean.

**Great Galactic Museum** Located in Imperial City on Coruscant, this was the resting place for most of the Sith artifacts during the time of the Great Sith War.

**great grass plains** An expanse of green grass and gently rolling hills on the planet Naboo, it was the meeting place of the Gungan Army and Trade Federation forces.

**Great Hall** A vast chamber inside the Jedi Temple on Coruscant, it was ringed with tiers of balconies that provided seating space for hundreds of Jedi Knights and Masters. The Great Hall also served as the primary place of mourning when a well-respected Jedi Master died.

**Great Hall of Learning** One of the primary lecture halls found on the campus of the Leadership School on the planet Andara during the last decades of the Old Republic.

**Great Heep** A huge droid, it was used by the Empire to mine fuel ore on the planet Biitu. A member of the Abominor species, the Great Heep settled on Biitu to enslave the local population and feed on the planet's natural resources. He consumed everything in his path and was equipped with numerous repair droids. After Mungo Baobab began refining fuel on Biitu, Admiral Terrinald Screed and the Great Heep captured him and took control of his refineries. The Great Heep eventually was defeated by C-3PO and R2-D2 shortly before the Battle of Yavin. When the droids rescued Baobab with the help of the young boy named Fidge, they triggered a huge flood that swept over the Great Heep, shut down his internal furnaces, and effectively killed him.

**Great Hohokum** Said to be over 400 years old, this hohokum specimen was kept at the Otoh Gunga Zoological Research Facility until Jar Jar Binks accidentally let loose all the facility's creatures. The Great Hohokum saved Jar Jar from being eaten by a sando aqua monster.

**Great Holocron** The largest and most comprehensive of the Jedi Holocrons, it was produced during the height of the Old Republic. The 12-sided device was used to provide young students of the Force with easy access to the ancient lore and training of the Jedi.

**Great Hunt** The period of time following the Great Sith War when Jedi Knights hunted down surviving Sith devotees and tried to eliminate them. Among their primary targets were the terentateks and other Sith-spawned creatures that had been set loose.

**Great Hyperspace War** An ancient battle between supporters of the light and dark sides of the Force, the Great Hyperspace War erupted on the heels of the First Unification Wars fought in the Koros system some 5,000 years before the Battle of Yavin. Ancient Sith Lords, led by Ludo Kressh and Naga Sadow, fought for control of their own forces while Sadow also attempted to take control of the galaxy. Meanwhile, Jedi Masters Odan-Urr and Ooroo tried unsuccessfully to use Jedi battle meditation on the advancing Massassi forces that swarmed the planet Coruscant, but soon realized that the majority of the opposing army was an illusion. The Jedi quickly dispatched the true Massassi and freed the planet. Meanwhile, Sadow defeated Kressh in an epic interstellar war in the Sith Empire, but his forces were unable to defend themselves against the might of Empress Teta's forces. As his commanders began to surrender, Sadow used the dark side to communicate with his Massassi spies. They executed Sadow's enemies and took control of their ships, drawing Teta's forces into the Denarii Nova. But Sadow's forces were eradicated there along with many of Teta's ships. Ultimately, the Old Republic eliminated the Sith threat. Sadow was forced to flee, and later established his own base on Yavin 4. It was generally believed that the modern lightsaber of the Jedi Knights was developed in the wake of the Great Hyperspace War.

**Great Jedi Library of Ossus** Conceived by Jedi Master Odan-Urr, who oversaw its construction on Ossus five millennia before the Battle of Yavin, it was designed to be a repository of all known information about every sentient endeavor. Even dreaded Sith Holocrons were stored in its vaults. The Great Library was thought to have been lost during the Great Sith War, but Executor Sedriss discovered its existence several years after the Battle of Endor. The library then came under control of the Jedi again and was used by Luke Skywalker in training new Jedi Knights. When the vast libraries of Obroa-skai were destroyed during the Yuuzhan Vong War, the Great Library became one of the only sources of galactic history and records.

*Great Jedi Library of Ossus*

**Great Leader of the Second Imperium** Supposedly another clone of Emperor Palpatine seeking to reestablish the Empire, the Great Leader was transported to the Shadow Academy sealed within a room-sized containment unit. Brakiss eventually discovered that the Great Leader wasn't a Palpatine clone but a series of recordings and props used by four of Palpatine's most loyal guards to try to trick the galaxy into thinking that the Emperor had returned to rule the Second Imperium.

**Great Library of Cinnagar** A magnificent library erected in the city of Cinnagar on the planet Koros Major in the wake of the Great Sith War, it held information and exhibits exploring the war and the events that led up to it.

**Great Manifest Period** An era of the Old Republic from 20,000 to 17,000 years before the Galactic Civil War, it marked the first period of expansion. The Republic began to extend toward the outer edge of the Slice, but movement was brought to a halt by the onset of the Alsakan Conflicts. The new areas of the galaxy that were explored and colonized became known as the Expansion Region.

**Great Mother** In the tradition of its inhabitants, the planet Nelvaan was known as Mother; the Nelvaanians worshipped the Great Mother and all the bounty she provided them. When Separatists established a facility on Nelvaan and began drawing geothermal energy, the planet was plunged into winter, and the Great Mother was unable to provide sustenance for the Nelvaanians. Orvos foresaw that Anakin Skywalker and Obi-Wan Kenobi would arrive on Nelvaan and uncover the truth behind the Great Mother's illness.

*Great Hyperspace War*

**Great Northern Forest** A densely wooded area, it was the site of Talon Karrde's base on Myrkr.

**Great Ones** The collective term used by the Yuuzhan Vong to describe their pantheon of gods.

**Great Peace of the Republic** The period of galactic history between the Battle of Ruusan and the Clone Wars, in which the Old Republic believed it existed without the threat of war. While many historians have acknowledged that no major conflicts were fought during this 1,000-year period, there were all manner of threats and opposition slowly building.

**great pit of Carkoon** *See* Carkoon, Great Pit of.

**Great Plague** The name used by the X'Ting species to describe the greatest of all the offworld plagues they experienced during the Old Republic after allowing a prison to be built on Ord Cestus. The Great Plague struck about 100 years before the Clone Wars, and many surviving X'Ting believed that it was unleashed by the executives of Cestus Cybernetics and their allies, the Confederacy of Independent Systems.

**Great Purge (I)** The Yevethan name for the extermination of all other species inhabiting the Koornacht Cluster. It was masterminded by Nil Spaar, who had planned it while the Empire was still using the cluster as a hiding place for the Black Sword Command and its shipyards. The Yevetha took control of the yards and repaired nearly 44 ships there for their own use. Then Nil Spaar went to Coruscant to placate Leia Organa Solo while manipulating her into a series of actions Spaar later used to his own advantage. He twisted Leia's words and deeds to his own ends, and managed to get a great deal of public sympathy and support while he methodically slaughtered the humans, Kubaz, and other species that were living in the Koornacht. The Yevetha believed that other species were inferior and needed to be purged from the Koornacht—and eventually the galaxy. Some historians refer to this time as the Black Fleet crisis because the Yevetha used the recommissioned Black Sword warships to destroy civilizations in the cluster.

**Great Purge (2)** A term used during the New Order to describe the Jedi Purge in which military forces supporting Emperor Palpatine wiped out nearly every Jedi Knight in the galaxy.

**Great Purge (3)** The name used by the Mawan people to describe the devastating civil war that swept their homeworld shortly before the Battle of Naboo.

**Great Pyramid** Located on Rafa V, this unusual five-sided building was the resting place of the Mindharp of Sharu. The only way to get inside was to use the Key of the Overpeople to "enter without entering." Lando Calrissian, Vuffi Raa, and Mohs entered the pyramid during the early years of the New Order.

**Great Reunification** The name used by historians to describe the period that followed the Battle of Ruusan and the end of the New Sith Wars. Under the leadership of Supreme Chancellor Tarsus Valorum, the galaxy swiftly recovered from the fracturing effects of the war against the Brotherhood of Darkness. It was Valorum who championed the Ruusan Reformations and the Unification Policies, bringing hundreds of star systems back into the Old Republic and enabling other star systems to join the growing galactic community. But there were challenges, as small groups of separatists arose in opposition to what they believed was the Galactic Senate's bullying of governments to rejoin the Republic. An assassination attempt on Valorum during a meeting on Serenno caused the planet to pledge its financial and political support to an effort to eradicate separatism, further consolidating the Republic's influence in the galaxy.

**Great Ritual** A call to all leaders, regardless of their current or historical prejudices and feuds, to come together to discuss the fate of the Tarasin people of Cularin—invoked only when there was a threat to the entire Tarasin civilization.

**Great River** The name given to Luke Skywalker's vision of a pathway that could be taken to escape the Yuuzhan Vong. The Great River would link safeworlds that were out of the Yuuzhan Vong invasion path and would include a convoluted secret hyperspace travel route. At the end of the path would be a world on which the Jedi could regroup and retrain in an effort to discover a way to defeat the Yuuzhan Vong. Luke asked his sister Leia Organa Solo, and her husband, Han, to do the initial scouting of planets along the Great River. The initial point on the path, known as Shelter, was formed at the remnants of the Maw Installation.

*The Great Temple*

**Great Room of the Enlightened** Deep in the bowels of Jabba the Hutt's palace on Tatooine, this room housed the disembodied brains of B'omarr monks as they contemplated the universe.

**Great Sacrifice** The Yuuzhan Vong's vision of the final destruction of the universe. They believed that all warriors would be given a special position at the Great Sacrifice, depending on their exploits during life. A modified version of the Great Sacrifice was created when Warmaster Tsavong Lah planned to sacrifice Jaina and Jacen Solo to the True Gods, in order to ensure the success of the Yuuzhan Vong invasion.

**Great Schisms** The main conflicts between followers of the light and dark sides of the Force. The First Great Schism occurred around 24,500 years before the Battle of Yavin, sometime after the Force Wars, when the Legions of Lettow were defeated by the ancient Jedi Knights. The Second Great Schism occurred more than 17,000 years later, with the onset of the Hundred Year Darkness.

**Great Shell Dome** The holding place of the Golden Sun on Sedri, it was erected by Cardo and his followers, who believed the Golden Sun was a sacred thing to be viewed only by the Priests of the Sun. The shell itself was formed from a huge number of interconnected seashells that were varnished together, making the shell nearly impervious. The Dome was destroyed by a group of Rebels who were able to link their minds to the Golden Sun and help it release itself.

**Great Sith War** Taking place 3,996 years before the Battle of Yavin, the war saw the Sith rise up once again in opposition to the Jedi Knights. The onset of the Great Sith War can be traced to the Freedon Nadd Uprisings on the planet Onderon, which planted the seeds for the Krath to grow in strength. When Exar Kun began to investigate the lore of the ancient Sith, against the wishes of his Master, Vodo-Siosk Baas, he left the Jedi Order and was lured to the dark side by the spirit of Freedon Nadd himself. On Yavin 4, Kun discovered a wealth of Sith treasures and set out to become a Dark Lord of the Sith. He confronted Ulic Qel-Droma on Cinnagar, where the former Jedi also had fallen to the dark side. The ancient Sith spirits declared Kun to be the Dark Lord and Qel-Droma to be his apprentice. Together they launched a series of campaigns against the Old Republic and the Jedi Knights, eventually reaching Coruscant. There Exar Kun killed his former Jedi Master and ordered his followers to murder their Masters in turn. Kun and Qel-Droma then launched an assault on Ossus, in an effort to destroy the Jedi Archives. Kun was defeated on Ossus and fled to Yavin 4, while Qel-Droma was stripped of his connection to the Force by Nomi Sunrider. He agreed to lead the combined forces of the Republic and the Jedi to take the battle to Exar Kun. The Jedi won, but at a great cost. They united as a single force and wiped out much of the planet's jungle in order to destroy Kun. But he managed to escape to the spiritual plane by draining the life energy from the enslaved Massassi.

**Great Sky Lord** An honorific the Yuuzhan Vong used to describe Supreme Overlord Shimrra.

**Great Swarm** A name used by the Colony to describe the massive fleet of dartships assembled near Qoribu to defend the Colony's nests from attack by the Chiss about five years after the Yuuzhan Vong surrendered to the Galactic Alliance. The Great Swarm was augmented by a small fleet of ships from the Hapan Royal Navy, as well as support vessels from the Bornaryn Trading Company. Despite the Galactic Alliance's success in blockading the Utegetu Nebula, the Great Swarm remained the key component of the Colony's war machine and was diverted to Tenupe when the Chiss decided to capture that planet. In the Battle of Tenupe, the Great Swarm lost millions upon millions of Killiks in defense of the planet, as both sides fought to a grinding stalemate over the course of several weeks.

**Great Temple, the** Located on Yavin's fourth moon, this massive ziggurat served in ancient times as the center of the Massassi civilization. When Exar Kun arrived on the moon and used the Massassi souls to power his own greed, he destroyed the Massassi, and the temple was abandoned to the relentless jungle for millennia. When the Rebel Alliance needed a base at the height of the New Order, it chose Yavin 4 for its remote location and its huge temples, and set up its primary command center in the Great Temple. Following the Battle of Yavin, the Alliance abandoned the base, and it lay empty until Luke Skywalker asked Mon Mothma for a place to train new Jedi Knights. Luke set up his Jedi praxeum in the Great Temple.

The Temple had five distinct levels, plus an observation level at the very top. Several years later, the Temple was attacked by the Shadow Academy. The shields that protected it were destroyed by Commander Orvak, who also placed several proton grenades in the Temple; luckily, the explosives caused only minor damage, and Skywalker chose to rebuild. The rebirth lasted only a few years. The Yuuzhan Vong realized that they could capture the students at the Jedi training center to use in experiments that would help them determine the source of the Force. A team of shapers was sent to Yavin 4, and the Great Temple was razed and "eaten" by five huge damuteks to make room for the shapers' complex.

*Greedo picks the wrong bounty.*

**Great Well** A massive, cylindrical shaft on the planet Ophideraan, it served as a holding pen and stable for the flying serpents commanded by Tyrann's forces. The serpents lived and bred in the lower levels of the Well, and Tyrann's forces excavated many levels for their own use.

*Olag Greck*

**Grebleips** An unusual, puddle-footed being, he represented his homeworld of Brodo Asogi as an Old Republic Senator. Later Senator Grebleips was one of the many Senators who signed the Petition of the Two Thousand. In the wake of the Clone Wars and the establishment of the New Order, the Senator was among the 63 Senators arrested for allegedly supporting the so-called Jedi Rebellion.

*Senator Grebleips and his aides*

**Greck, Olag** A criminal, he kept crossing the path of C-3PO and R2-D2 in the early years of the Empire.

**Gree, Commander** A clone commander designated CC-1004, he led the 41st Elite Corps stationed on Kashyyyk during the Clone Wars, serving under General Yoda and commanding troops that employed specialized equipment for combat in the jungle environment. Showing his individuality early in development, clone 1004 took it upon himself to become an authority on obscure alien cultures, pursuing knowledge beyond automated clone education programs. Around the time that 1004's unique attributes were discovered, the Kaminoans instituted a special clone commander training program. The ARC trooper identified as Alpha began personally training commanders with an eye toward independence and individuality. Unit 1004 adopted the name Gree as a subtle nod to his intellectual pursuits. The Gree were an obscure alien species little known in the Republic, and the clone thought that anyone commenting on his name after an introduction would likely share his passion for alien cultures.

Commander Gree wore camouflaged armor to better blend into the verdant surroundings of Kashyyyk. Though a faithful commander who carried out Yoda's orders, Gree was ultimately loyal to the Republic. When Chancellor Palpatine enacted Order 66, Gree understood that it was a worst-case scenario contingency: The Jedi had betrayed the Republic and were therefore dangerous enemies of the state. Gree attempted to open fire on Yoda from behind, taking out the Jedi Master before he had time to react. But the commander underestimated Yoda's perception. Before Gree could squeeze the trigger on his rifle, Yoda flipped up and backward out of the field of fire, decapitating the commander with one quick swipe of his lightsaber.

**Greeata** *See* Jendowanian, Greeata.

**Greeb** An Imperial admiral, he was in charge of the small fleet that patrolled the planet Ithor.

**Greeb-Streebling Cluster** A section of the galaxy in the Outer Rim Territories and Ninth Quadrant, near the Senex and Juvex sectors.

**Greedo** An overzealous bounty hunter hired by Jabba the Hutt to collect from smuggler Han Solo, he challenged Solo in the Mos Eisley Cantina. At blasterpoint, the Rodian demanded Solo pay his debt to Jabba. Solo claimed he didn't have the money with him. Greedo lost his patience and opened fire. His shot missed; it was the last mistake Greedo would make, since Solo nearly simultaneously opened fire with his powerful blaster pistol, ripping through the cantina table—and the Rodian's chest.

Greedo's short life was punctuated by violence at every turn, but such was often the case with Rodians. The culture was marked by a reverence for the hunt, and once the green-skinned humanoids had cleared the jungles of all sizable predators, they turned to hunting one another. Clan wars were the norm, and Greedo's clan, the Tetsus, had fled Rodia for the safety of an unnamed jungle world. Greedo grew up in a jungle village with his mother Neela, his younger brother Pqweeduk, and his Uncle Nok. Greedo was never told of his Rodian heritage, but the need to hunt was in his veins. After surviving an attack by the ruling Chattza clan, the Rodian refugees relocated to Nar Shaddaa where Greedo became immersed in street life, learning the ropes from his friend Anky Fremp.

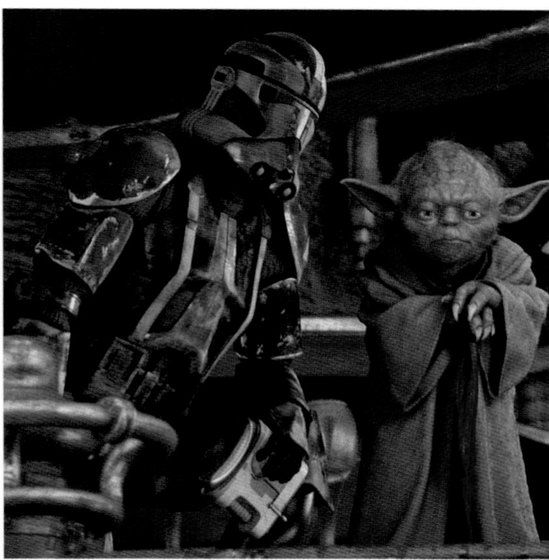
*Commander Gree with Yoda on Kashyyyk*

Greedo idolized bounty hunters and longed to join their ranks. He had his multifaceted eyes on a sleek Incom Corsair that mechanic Shug Ninx kept in his garage. Chewbacca caught Greedo lurking around the *Millennium Falcon* and grabbed the young Rodian before he could get away. Han Solo saw that it was just a harmless kid, so he gave Greedo the *Falcon*'s used power couplings in exchange for his jacket. Greedo, humiliated, vowed revenge.

Greedo became involved with bounty hunters Spurch "Warhog" Goa and Dyyz Nataz quite by accident. He overheard a commotion among the hunters and Gorm the Dissolver, which soon became an armed conflict. Goa's blaster rifle was knocked aside, landing at Greedo's feet. He fired the rifle, taking Gorm out of commission. Goa gave Greedo a cut of the contested bounty and offered to train the kid in the ways of bounty hunting. The ever-eager Greedo agreed. He left his family behind on Nar Shaddaa and departed with Goa and Nataz to Tatooine. Jabba the Hutt offered the bounty on Han Solo to Goa and Nataz. While the two experienced hunters were ready to reject the assignment, Greedo took it. Greedo confronted Solo in Docking Bay 94, and later at a dockside café. Solo was ready with an excuse each time, explaining why he couldn't pay his debt to Jabba. Solo, who didn't view the young Rodian as a threat, calmly warned him to back off. When Greedo tried to kill him later inside the seedy cantina, Han blasted the young Rodian instead. As a final insult, Greedo's corpse was collected by Wuher, the bartender. The alien's powerful pheromones were used to concoct a very special drink for Jabba the Hutt.

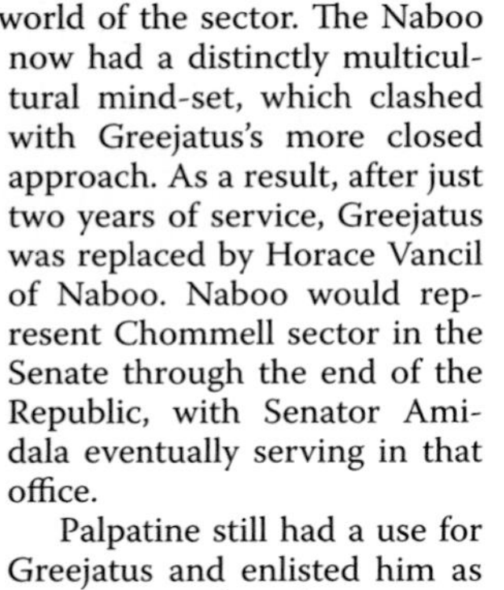

*Janus Greejatus*

**Gree Enclave** An area of space in the Outer Rim Territories, it was controlled by the Gree species and included the major worlds of Gree, Asation, Licha In, Lonatro, Malanose, and Te Hasa. Little was known about activities there as the Gree kept much of it a secret.

**Greejatus, Janus** Because competition from nonhuman workers had whittled away his family's fortune on Chommell Minor before he was even born, Janus Greejatus had a deeply ingrained hatred for aliens. He was taught by his father never to let nonhumans get the better of him in life. As Greejatus climbed through the ranks of Chommell Minor politics, he carefully veiled such sentiments in politically deft language that earned him a popular base on the planet, eventually gaining the notice of the sector's galactic representative, Senator Palpatine. Though Palpatine was prudent enough not to echo some of Greejatus's more polarizing statements publicly, the two became fast friends—at least in Greejatus's eyes. He constantly proved to Palpatine that he had a keen political mind, so much so that when Palpatine ascended to the position of Supreme Chancellor, Greejatus succeeded him as Senator of the Chommell sector. This move, however, displeased influential politicians on Naboo, the foremost world of the sector. The Naboo now had a distinctly multicultural mind-set, which clashed with Greejatus's more closed approach. As a result, after just two years of service, Greejatus was replaced by Horace Vancil of Naboo. Naboo would represent Chommell sector in the Senate through the end of the Republic, with Senator Amidala eventually serving in that office.

Palpatine still had a use for Greejatus and enlisted him as an adviser. When the Supreme Chancellor declared the New Order, Greejatus helped shape COMPNOR—the Commission for the Preservation of the New Order—and was appointed to the Imperial Ruling Council. He founded the Imperial Department of Redesign, a secretive agency that dedicated much effort to the liquidation and subjugation of aliens. In time, Greejatus realized that he could develop projects without the Emperor's consent or oversight, and grew overly ambitious. His plans, however, came to a halt after the destruction of the first Death Star. Greejatus was one of several Imperial officers discovered to have goaded Moff Tarkin into seizing absolute power with the superweapon. Palpatine learned of this and decided to keep Greejatus within reach. This eventually brought Greejatus to the second Death Star, which was attacked and destroyed by the Rebellion. Greejatus was believed to have perished in the explosion.

*Bomo Greenbark*

**Greelanx, Winstel** An Imperial Navy admiral, he commanded the fleet sent by Sarn Shild to attack Nar Shaddaa. Prior to the Battle of Nar Shaddaa, the Hutt clan Desilijic had sent Han Solo to offer the admiral a bribe in return for information about the impending attack, and for allowing the residents of Nar Shaddaa to win the battle without making it look like the Imperial fleet had given up. Greelanx took the bribe. However, the loss of the Battle of Nar Shaddaa was reported by Soontir Fel, and Greelanx came under the scrutiny of Darth Vader and the Emperor. His acceptance of the Hutt bribe was discovered, and within minutes of Greelanx's receiving payment from Han Solo, Vader arrived at his offices. With Solo hiding in an anteroom, the Dark Lord of the Sith executed the admiral.

**Greelossk** A Trandoshan criminal wanted by the Republic Security Force for a wide variety of crimes against the Old Republic, he was captured, sentenced, and imprisoned. Still, someone placed a bounty on his head that Jango Fett claimed.

**greel wood** A rare and expensive scarlet-colored wood, it was used to make furniture such as tables and chairs and to provide the finishing touches to expensive speeders. Greel Wood Logging Corporation harvested the wood from the worlds of Pii3 and Pii4.

**Green (1)** A human lieutenant, or Vigo, of the Black Sun criminal organization headed by Prince Xizor. While Green was one of the smartest of the Vigos, he was also a traitor to Black Sun who was exposed and promptly executed by Guri, Xizor's human replica droid aide, who choked him to death.

**Green (2)** A clone trooper designated CT-53/21-8778, he served as the sergeant in command of Talon Squad at the height of the Clone Wars.

**Greenbark, Bomo** A Nosaurian, he encountered Jedi Master Dass Jennir in the jungles of his homeworld of New Plympto shortly after the command was given to execute Order 66. Greenbark found himself torn between killing Jennir outright and learning how the Jedi had escaped from the clone troopers who'd turned on him. Greenbark decided to bring Jennir back to his camp, but Commander Rootrock ordered that the Jedi be set loose. Greenbark found himself fighting side by side with Jennir, who had decided to remain on New Plympto and help the Nosaurians fight back against the Imperial forces on the planet. Their efforts were well intentioned but ultimately doomed to failure, as the clone forces of the newly christened Galactic Empire arrived in force and soon overwhelmed the Nosaurian natives. In a last-ditch action, Greenbark and Jennir tried a stalling tactic in an effort to allow Nosaurian civilians to evacuate the planet. But they were too late: The refugees had been shipped off to the slave markets of Orvax IV. Desperate to find his wife Mesa and daughter Resa, Greenbark along with Jennir managed to get to the slave pits of Orvax IV only to learn that Mesa had been killed while trying to protect Resa.

**green diamond** Beautiful gemstones, they were wondrous to behold . . . but deadly to hold. Each green diamond was still immature by geological standards and contained enough active radiation to kill after being held for just 30 seconds. Prince Xizor sent green diamonds to women at the end of a relationship if they remained in love with him.

**Green Flight (1)** An A-wing group, it was part of the support provided to Wedge Antilles during the assault on Almania.

**Green Flight (2)** A K-wing group, it served the 24th Bombardment Squadron as part of the Fifth Battle Group. Green Flight participated in Task Force Blackvine as part of the effort that punished the Yevetha for resisting the blockade of Doornik-319.

**Green Forge** A group of environmental terrorists active prior to the Battle of Naboo, it was known for its destructive methods of bringing environmental crimes to light, especially its use of high-yield explosives to destroy corporate headquarters and refineries.

**Greenies** *See* Mimban.

**Green Leader (1)** The comm unit designation for Arvel Crynyd, commander of Green Wing, one of the four main Rebel starfighter battle groups at the Battle of Endor.

**Green Leader (2)** An X-wing fighter pilot, he was killed during the defense of Mon Calamari against Emperor Palpatine's World Devastators.

**Greenly, Tag** Truth . . . or legend? Historians have long puzzled over the stories spun about Tag Greenly and his buddy Bink Otauna. Their lives almost too comical to believe, the truth about them was out there . . . somewhere.

**Green Squadron (1)** This squadron of Rebel Alliance starfighters provided cover for Blue Squadron during the Battle of Yavin.

**Green Squadron (2)** A group of Alliance A-wing starfighter pilots that saw action during the Battle of Endor.

**Green Squadron (3)** A mixed group of New Republic B-wing and Y-wing pilots that saw action at the first Battle of Mon Calamari.

**Green Squadron (4)** One of the many New Republic starfighter squadrons assigned to the *Intrepid* some 12 years after the Battle of Endor.

**Green Squadron (5)** Stevan Makintay's X-wing squadron, during the time he served at the Alliance's Eyrie Base.

**Green Three** Tycho Celchu's call sign as a pilot in the Rebel Alliance's Green Squadron. He used it during the Battle of Endor. Celchu flew a modified A-wing that allowed its pilot better vision during battle.

**Green Watch** The code name for the two-man unit formed by the clone commandos Niner and Scorch during their mission to break up a Separatist-funded terrorist ring on Coruscant a year after the Battle of Geonosis. The effort was masterminded by Kal Skirata and was carried out by the Special Operations Brigade without direct orders from the Grand Army of the Republic.

**Green Wing** One of the four main Rebel starfighter battle groups at the Battle of Endor; it was also the comm unit designation for Green Leader's second in command. Green Wing accompanied Red Leader (Wedge Antilles), Gold Leader (Lando Calrissian), and Blue Leader on an assault on an Imperial communications ship. Green Wing lost his life in the effort, but gave the others the opportunity to destroy the enemy vessel.

**Green Wizard** The nickname used by clone commando CT-19/39. He chose it because of his rank as sergeant and his skills with patrol craft and reconnaissance.

**Grees** A Squib, he was part of a trio that gathered information about the shadier parts of the galaxy and provided it to the New Republic Intelligence agency. Grees accompanied Leia Organa Solo and her husband, Han, to Tatooine as part of a mission to intercept a group of Imperial agents. His partners, Sligh and Emala, completed the entourage. The Squibs decided that selling art to Imperials was not only profitable, but also an excellent way to obtain more information. Grees got greedy, though, and ended up frozen in carbonite, only to be rescued by the Solos. In the wake of the Yuuzhan Vong invasion and subsequent galactic reconstruction, the three Squibs established a transport operation known as Second Mistake Enterprises and were hired by the Colony to transport spinglass sculptures to the rest of the galaxy. The Squibs were unaware that each sculpture contained a handful of Gorog assassin bugs and were severely reprimanded for their actions. This angered the Squibs, who set out to make the Solo family pay for its part in exposing the assassin bugs. They arranged for various unsuccessful assassination attempts on the lives of Han, Leia, and Jaina Solo.

**gree spice** A purple form of sensory-enhancing spice.

**Greeve** A lieutenant, he was a member of the Alliance team assembled by Han Solo to take out the shield generator for the second Death Star; he was the team's sharpshooter. Before being recruited by Crix Madine, Greeve was a scout and guide known for his knowledge of the jungles of Kashyyyk.

**Greglik** A former Rebel Alliance pilot, he captained an ore hauler used to transport material following the Battle of Hoth. Greglik was addicted to various drugs, and that habit killed not only him but also 17 other Alliance pilots in a collision with an asteroid.

**Grejic the Hutt** The president of the Hutt Grand Council in the century leading up to the Battle of Yavin, he decided that clan Besadii should be punished for raising the price of raw spice in the aftermath of the Battle of Nar Shaddaa. The punishment was one million credits, to be divided among those clans that had lost resources in the battle.

**Grejj** An Imperial lieutenant, he commanded an AT-AT walker stationed at the garrison on Vryssa. Like Lieutenant Byrga, Grejj was killed when Boba Fett came to the planet to recover Rivo Xarran. Fett had acquired control of an AT-AT from Byrga and used it to destroy Grejj's vehicle.

***Grek*-class troop shuttle** Designed and manufactured by the Corellian Engineering Corporation, this 30-meter-long shuttle found use aboard Imperial Nebulon-B frigates as well as other local navies. The *Grek*-class shuttle required a pilot and copilot, and could transport up to 50 troops and minimal cargo. It was armed with a computer-controlled laser cannon.

**Grekk 9** A Norak Tull, he was one of the few members of his species to reach a position of power within the New Republic Navy; he was promoted to commodore just before the Black Fleet Crisis.

**Grelb the Hutt** Working for Jemba the Hutt and the Offworld Mining Company, he was in charge of collecting slave laborers for use in the mines of Bandomeer. During the transport of slaves aboard the barge *Monument,* Grelb became suspicious of young Obi-Wan Kenobi and his Arconan friend Si Treemba. He managed to capture Treemba, but the Arconan was rescued by Obi-Wan, who then implicated Grelb in the sabotage of mining equipment owned by the Arcona Mineral Harvest Corporation. When the *Monument* was attacked by pirates, all its travelers were forced to land on an uncharted world. There Jemba and Grelb tried to eliminate Kenobi and Qui-Gon Jinn, but native draigons attacked before they could succeed. As Obi-Wan fought off the huge reptiles, Grelb tried to shoot him with a blaster. Many of his shots missed Obi-Wan but hit Jemba instead, killing the old Hutt. Grelb was captured and torn apart shortly after by a flight of draigons.

**Grendahl** An Imperial Navy captain, he was sent to Najiba, then Trulalis, to recapture Adalric Brandl. He had been ordered to recover the Dark Jedi by High Inquisitor Tremayne.

**Grendaju** An icy landmass located deep in the southern hemisphere of the planet Kalee, it was the last known refuge of the karabbac by the time of the Clone Wars.

**Grendel** A wing-clipped hornagaunt, he was a constant companion of the assassin droid 8t88. After 8t88's head was removed by the Sith minion Pic, Grendel decided to eat it, only to come face-to-face with Kyle Katarn. Katarn was searching for the droid to discover the whereabouts of the Valley of the Jedi and was forced to cut open each of Grendel's three stomachs in order to retrieve the head.

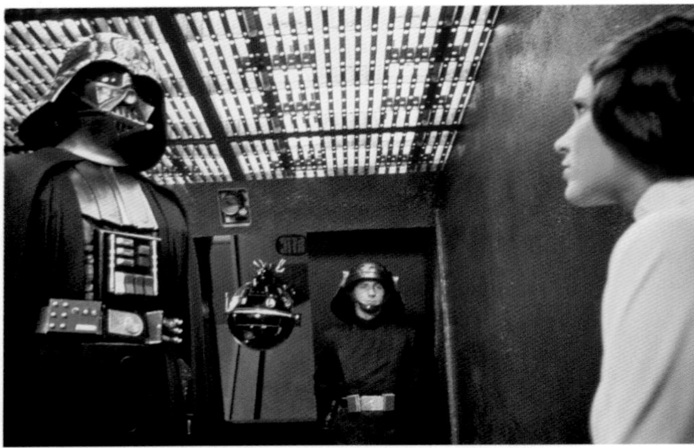
Grenwick watches Darth Vader interrogate Princess Leia.

**Grendu** A dealer in rare antiquities, Grendu was the Bothan trader who sold Grizzid a rancor, which Grizzid hoped to give to Jabba the Hutt.

**Grendyl** A member of the Navy of the Galactic Alliance aboard the *Admiral Ackbar* as part of the starfighter command team, she acted under the orders of General Nek Bwua'tu during the blockade of the Murgo Choke about a year after the Qoribu crisis. When the commanding frigate of the Colony ambushed the *Admiral Ackbar* in an effort to take control of the vessel, Grendyl found herself between Admiral Bwua'tu and an attacking Alema Rar. Rather than see her commanding officer injured, Grendyl stepped in front of him when the Twi'lek Dark Jedi unleashed a volley of Force lightning; she took the full blast in the chest, but died knowing that she had saved Bwua'tu.

**Greni** A wing commander for the New Republic, she piloted an X-wing in Gold Squadron.

**Grenn, Dol** A lieutenant in the Telos Security Force, he worked aboard Citadel Station in the years following the Jedi Civil War. Lieutenant Grenn imprisoned the Exile and Jedi Master Kreia, and confiscated the *Ebon Hawk,* when the former Jedi arrived on Telos in search of answers about Darth Sion. Grenn arrested them after learning of the destruction of the Peragus Mining Colony, but freed them after learning the truth. He then asked for the Exile's assistance in bringing several criminals to justice.

**Grenna Base** An Alliance base, it was used by Daino Hyk as a treatment center for rescued Ylesian slaves.

Ottegru Grey

**Grentho** A muscular man, he was one of 8t88's bodyguards at the height of the Galactic Civil War. Grentho was killed on Nar Shaddaa when 8t88 tried to eliminate Kyle Katarn.

**Grenwick** An Imperial corporal, he was senior tactical adviser to Sergeant Major Enfield aboard the first Death Star. Assigned to security duties in Detention Block AA-23, Grenwick was a witness to the interrogation of Leia Organa by Darth Vader.

**Grey, Ottegru** In a galaxy engulfed by a terrible civil war rife with spies and assassins, politicians began to rightly fear for their lives. After several close calls involving vengeful Aqualish Separatists hiding in Coruscant's underlevels, Chairman Tannon Praji of the Ministry of Ingress (CMoI) turned to Ottegru Grey, a trusted friend of the Praji family and special agent for the Bank of the Core. Grey specialized in tracking down missing funds, embezzlers, or other miscreants. Since Praji was a large investor, the Bank of the Core offered Grey's protection services for a small service fee, and Grey handled Praji's finances as well as his protection.

Once he went to work for Praji, Grey shadowed him everywhere. Little did Praji suspect where Grey's loyalties ultimately lay. The protector secretly funneled some of Praji's funds into Chancellor Palpatine's war chest. In turn, Palpatine used these funds to help cover the gambling debts of Romeo Treblanc, owner of the Galaxies Opera House. This accounting maneuver earned Grey a lifetime pass to the Opera House as a guest in Treblanc's private box, which Grey extended to Praji on behalf of the bank. Following the Clone Wars, Grey used the Praji family to fund Imperial projects and provide work for nonhuman refugees. These refugees, unbeknownst to Praji, would become slaves, and their budgeted salaries would instead be diverted into some of the Emperor's more sinister plots.

***Grey Damsel*** A Mon Calamari cruiser under the command of Captain Bok, it supported the Alliance's Tak Base on Talay during the early years of the Galactic Civil War. When the Empire attacked, it unleashed second-stage dark troopers, one of whom boarded the ship just as it jumped into hyperspace. The dark trooper executed the entire crew, while the *Grey Damsel* continued on its course. Coming out of hyperspace, the ship crashed in the desert near the ruins of the Mos Espa Arena on Tatooine and was later scavenged by Jawas. The dark trooper was let loose, and only the heroic efforts of Big Gizz and Spiker kept it from running amok.

**Greymark** A colonel with the Alliance, he was one of the chief duty officers at the base on the planet Arbra following the Battle of Hoth.

**Greyshade, Simon** A human native of Columex, he was a Senator from the planet Vorzyd 5 during the last years of the Old Republic. He assumed the role after his cousin Jheramahd was murdered on Coruscant. He was one of the first Senators to suggest that the Republic get income from gambling activities. His custom-built speeder was believed to be the one appropriated by Anakin Skywalker and Obi-Wan Kenobi during their search for Zam Wesell.

Years later, as an Imperial Senator representing the worlds of the Commonality, Greyshade oversaw the expulsion proceedings against Mako Spince at the Imperial Academy. He eventually became administrator of the Wheel after Emperor Palpatine dissolved the Imperial Senate. There he maintained a level of neutrality by paying huge taxes to keep the space around the station free of Imperial ships. However, when he discovered that Commander Strom was setting up a scheme to discredit the Rebel Alliance and take control of the Wheel, Greyshade demanded a partnership. He agreed to keep Strom's part in the deal a secret, provided that Strom allow Greyshade to control Leia Organa. He also ran a rigged gladiator arena on the space station and used the fights to try to ensure the deaths of Han Solo and Chewbacca, eliminating any chance of Leia's escaping.

Ever the schemer, Greyshade used the distraction of the Big Game to launch an assault of his own on Strom's cruiser, ordering his own security forces to overpower the Imperial guards and recover the profits that Strom had stolen from a House of Tagge transport ship. He then drugged Strom and tried to force Leia Organa to submit to his will. He discovered that his own forced attempts at love would never reach Leia, who had the unforced devotion of both Luke Skywalker and

Han Solo. However, Greyshade did find a loyal friend in the most unlikely place: his administration droid, Master-Com, which sacrificed two of its many bodies to ensure Greyshade's safety. Greyshade allowed Leia to leave, then killed Strom with a proton grenade before the Imperial officer could shoot him. Greyshade himself eventually died aboard the Wheel sometime after the Battle of Yavin.

**Grey Wolf** One of many *Imperial*-class Star Destroyers in the Imperial Navy fleet during the Galactic Civil War.

**G'rho** An outpost planet colonized by Chandrilan settlers, G'rho was where Dev Sibwarra grew up after fleeing Chandrila. It was one of the first planets subjugated by the Ssi-ruuk shortly before the Battle of Endor.

**Griann** An agricultural city in the Greenbelt on Teyr. This was where the Fallanassi religious order supposedly took its children to escape Imperial forces. Luke Skywalker and Akanah Norand Pell searched but could find no remaining evidence.

**Gribbet** A small frog-like alien, this Rybet bounty hunter worked with Skorr. The two nearly captured Han Solo on the planet Ord Mantell.

**gricha** One of the many creatures bioengineered by the Yuuzhan Vong, the gricha grew in insect-like stages. As larvae, gricha were capable of consuming sand and other silicates and excreting a form of nacreous shell. As they ate their way to adulthood, gricha formed structures with their shells that were eventually used by the Yuuzhan Vong as dwellings or storage areas. Larger buildings, like the grashal, could be formed by a large number of gricha in a short time.

**Grievous, General** Born Qymaen jai Sheelal, this onetime Kaleesh military commander struck fear and terror throughout the galaxy as the military leader of the Separatist forces during the Clone Wars—taking a special pleasure in killing Jedi and collecting their lightsabers as trophies. A brilliant strategist, he was unhindered by compassion or scruples. His lightning strikes and effective campaigns caused his reputation to grow in the eyes of a frightened Republic.

A cyborg alien being, Grievous was easily distinguished by his tall, cloaked figure, with body parts that were formed from a highly polished duranium alloy. Grievous's hands had six fingers each, allowing for a wide range of grasping patterns. Each of his arms could be split in two, and Grievous often fought with four lightsabers to thoroughly demoralize—and then eliminate—his enemies. The only things that survived of his original form were his brain, eyes, heart, and guts, all of which were protected within the armored body. His eyes were a brilliant gold color, with a reptilian black pupil surrounded by blood-red sockets. Everything about General Grievous spoke of a certain level of vanity and self-assuredness. Whereas Count Dooku was the political leader of the Confederacy of Independent Systems, General Grievous was the military leader of the Separatist armies. Grievous was a master strategist and weapons master and was one of a handful of beings who were known to have killed multiple Jedi Knights. He kept their lightsabers attached to his belt to indicate his prowess, and he was a skilled fighter with a lightsaber himself.

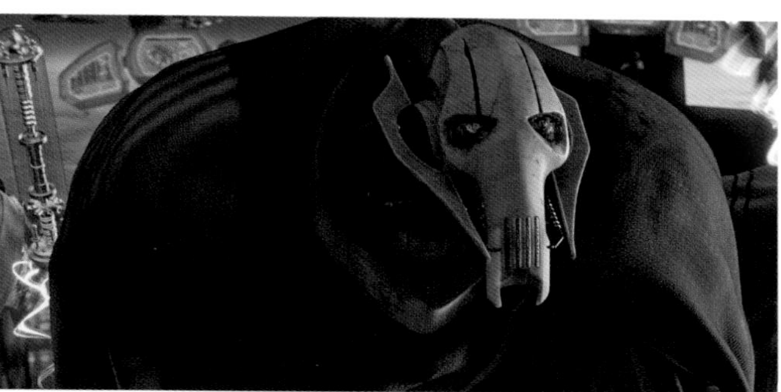
General Grievous

As a Kaleesh warrior, Grievous was forced to witness the starvation of his people after the Old Republic sided with the enemy Huk in resolving the Huk Wars, before sustaining incredible injuries in the crash of his personal shuttle, the *Martyr.* Only the use of Force lightning by Count Dooku kept his heart beating, and Grievous was nursed back to health. He was devastated by the unfairness of being injured in a crash after surviving all manner of combat and destruction, and briefly contemplated suicide. Unknown to Grievous, the crash had been part of a plot by San Hill, the leader of the InterGalactic Banking Clan. Shortly after the crash, the IBC arrived on Kalee and offered to rescue the Kaleesh in exchange for Grievous's body, and Grievous agreed to the deal. He was re-created as a part-alien, part-droid monstrosity on the planet Geonosis, a transformation that was funded by San Hill and carried out by Poggle the Lesser. Grievous was then presented as a strange sort of gift to Count Dooku.

Grievous's armored body was created in the image of a Krath war droid, giving it a fearsome appearance. Instead of requiring sleep to recuperate, Grievous was provided with a stasis chamber in which he could literally recharge. His droid anatomy augmented his already powerful body and abilities, and Grievous was a quick study in the art of lightsaber combat. Dooku himself was surprised when Grievous proved to be a student who surpassed other apprentices after mere weeks of training. Although Grievous participated in the Battle of Geonosis, none who faced him survived to warn the Republic. After Geonosis, Grievous was promoted to Supreme Commander of the Droid Armies, a position that put him on par with Count Dooku. Grievous first appeared in command of the Separatist forces during the Battle of Hypori, then began a march Coreward along the Corellian Trade Spine. He was considered by many military experts to have been a tactical genius, but others argued that, because he had limitless droids at his disposal, he lacked subtlety in his methods.

General Grievous was once a Kaleesh military commander.

After the planet Duro was captured from the Old Republic, Grievous directly addressed the Republic, speaking in a Confederacy HoloNet broadcast that was tapped into the main Republic HoloNet. As part of the broadcast, Grievous forced Hoolidan Keggle to sign a surrender that officially gave the Separatists control of Duro. Then, after the tide of battle had turned in favor of the Republic, Grievous was ordered to launch an all-out attack on Coruscant itself. Aboard his flagship, the *Invisible Hand,* Grievous was able to penetrate Coruscant's defenses. Using knowledge provided by Darth Sidious, he kidnapped Chancellor Palpatine, vanquishing a group of Jedi Masters who were protecting the Chancellor. Then Grievous sent a specially falsified message to Anakin Skywalker and Obi-Wan Kenobi, who had been on Tythe trying to capture Count Dooku. The message

General Grievous fights on Utapau.

called them home to help defend Coruscant, thus bringing them to the "rescue" of Chancellor Palpatine. The two Jedi managed to reclaim Palpatine, and Grievous was forced to flee the battle to Utapau. There he arranged for the transfer of the Separatist leadership to Mustafar before being located by Clone Intelligence Units.

General Kenobi was dispatched to Utapau with a contingent of clones to find Grievous, who was alerted to the Jedi's presence shortly after his arrival. When Kenobi emerged in the midst of a hangar full of droids, Grievous initially let his MagnaGuards attack the Jedi. Obi-Wan quickly eliminated them, forcing Grievous to attack. Their battle raged through Pau City, until Kenobi managed to crack open the chest plates that were protecting Grievous's innards. With a volley of well-placed blaster shots, the Jedi Master was able to destroy Grievous and put an end to his reign of terror. His droid form was left behind on Utapau, where it was later exhumed by Imperial forces and turned over to Nycolai Kinesworthy for use in the development of N-K Necrosis droids.

Amise Griff

**Griff, Amise** A fleet admiral, he supervised construction of Darth Vader's *Super*-class Star Destroyer *Executor.* Admiral Griff was also in charge of the Imperial blockade of Yavin 4 after the destruction of the first Death Star. He and his ship were destroyed when, in an attempt to intercept the fleeing Rebel fleet, Griff miscalculated a hyperspace jump and dropped out of hyperspace—nearly landing on the *Executor.*

**Griggs, Kane** A navigator, he served aboard the New Republic Star Destroyer *Emancipator* during the Battle of Calamari.

**Grigmin** A stunt pilot, he operated a one-man traveling air show. Grigmin made a living by displaying his talents to paying customers on backworlds of the Tion Hegemony. He hired Han Solo and Chewbacca for a brief time before the pair became involved in the Galactic Civil War—but not before Solo upstaged and outclassed his boss during one last airshow.

**Grigor** An Imperial Governor assigned to M'haeli, he came under the scrutiny of Grand Moff Lynch early in the Galactic Civil War. Lynch assigned Ranulf Trommer to spy on Grigor, but the governor arranged to have Trommer tailed and arrested as a Rebel Alliance spy. In the end, after Grigor's misdeeds had been exposed, he ended up accidentally shooting himself in the head.

**Gril, Pellna** A lieutenant with the New Republic Intelligence agency assigned to the Special Threats group, he was the primary source of data on the Fallanassi and the White Current.

Grimorg

**grimnal** An ancient measurement of time once used on Corellia.

**Grimorg** A Weequay, he was Great Bogga the Hutt's palace enforcer.

**Grimraker, Arns** A noted scavenger and salvage operator during the Galactic Civil War, he was a cruel and heartless man who cared only for profit. Easily distinguished by the cybernetic prostheses that replaced his left eye and ear, he and his pirate crew scavenged the galaxy aboard the freighter known as *Death Merchant.* They hunted for items on Hoth just a few days after the battle there. Grimraker met up with Wedge Antilles and Wes Janson and lost his life when the two pilots fought back against his pirate gang.

**Grimtaash** A mythical Molatar guardian, the spirit of Grimtaash was supposed to protect Alderaanian royalty from corruption and betrayal. Chewbacca had a holographic grimtaash on his holochess board on the *Millennium Falcon.*

Grimtaash

**Grinner** A Cavrilhu pirate, he was one of several who patrolled the Kauron asteroid base during the time of the New Republic.

***Grinning Liar*** A modified freighter owned and operated by the Wookiee smuggler Chak'ka some 130 years after the Battle of Yavin. He loaned the ship to Jariah Syn and Deliah Blue after Cade Skywalker abandoned them following their rescue of Princess Marasiah Fel.

**gripleaf** A carnivorous plant native to Haruun Kal. At the height of the Summertime War, arboreal gripleaf plants were used to hang the bodies of prisoners in the jungle, where they could be eaten alive by the various predators and insects.

**gription panel** A specialized form of kinetic adhesive material developed by scientists of the Grand Army of the Republic. By using normal friction and special materials, gription panels held the armor plating of clone troopers against their bodysuits. With a touch, a gription panel could be released, allowing the trooper to remove his armor. The panels also were known as magnatomic grip panels.

**Grissmath** These vicious natives of the planet Meridian disposed of political enemies by leaving them on the planet Nam Chorios and then seeding the barren world with drochs in order to kill them off. The Grissmaths eventually self-destructed, victims of their own devious ways, while the prisoners on Nam Chorios managed to eke out an existence.

**Griv** A Rodian, he served as a member of Mazzic's crew, piloting the *Raptor.* He later joined Talon Karrde's group, acting as a gunner aboard the *Wild Karrde.*

**Grizmallt** A heavily populated world in the Galactic Core. Its natives colonized many worlds, including Naboo and Nam Chorios. During the last century of the Old Republic, Grizmallt was the headquarters of one of the galaxy's largest heavy engineering facilities, rivaled only by Kuat Drive Yards and Rendili StarDrive. An Imperial world during the Galactic Civil War, this planet fell under the control of the New Republic with little resistance.

**Grizzid** A smuggler and trader who did work for Jabba the Hutt, he tried to deliver a rancor to Jabba on Tatooine. But the beast broke out of its cage and killed Grizzid and his crew, forcing a crash landing in the Dune Sea.

**Grk'kkrs'arr** A member of Sharad Hett's Tusken Raider clan, he joined in the hunt for a krayt dragon that was plaguing the group. In the creature's cave, they discovered Jedi Ki-Adi-Mundi under attack by the immense beast. Sharad Hett drew first blood, but Grk'kkrs'arr was the first to seriously wound the dragon when he buried the sharp end of his traditional gaderffii into the beast's soft underbelly. Unfortunately, the krayt got its revenge by swallowing the Tusken.

**Grlubb** A small, rodent-faced creature with a scarred nose, stubby feline whiskers, and clawed hands, he was a petty dictator on the black-market-run world of Peridon's Folly. Grlubb became embroiled in a feud with another weapons-runner and hired the assassin droid IG-88 to kill his opponent.

**Grobber** A Black Sun underling, he was sent by Zekka Thyne to intercept Haber Trell's cargo at the Dewback Storage facility in Coronet city.

**Grocco, Marx** Director of cluster worlds relations on Talus during the Galactic Civil War, he worked with the Corellian Security Force to investigate a series of kidnappings throughout the system.

**Grode** An Imperial major on Cilpar following the Battle of Endor, he accepted Tycho Celchu into his squadron. But when the Imperials discovered New Republic X-wings on the planet, Major Grode's pilots were sent to eliminate them. Celchu used a series of remote commands to activate his X-wing, which took out nearly all of Grode's ships.

**Grodo the Hutt** Aruk the Hutt's personal physician, he was present during Aruk's death throes after the Hutt had been poisoned with nala-tree frogs by Jabba and Jiliac the Hutt.

**Groggin** An Ugnaught, he discovered Luke Skywalker's severed hand in smelting core D on Bespin's Cloud City.

**Gromas system** A system in the Mid Rim's Perkell sector, it had several small moons that contained the rare metal phrik. The Empire built a mining facility on one moon, Gromas 16, to produce phrik for use in armoring its dark troopers. Following the Battle of Yavin, Alliance agent Kyle Katarn destroyed the facility with a sequencer charge.

Groznik

**Gron, Rolanda** A Klatooinian technologist, he helped Jedi Knight Qu Rahn on rescue and relocation missions during the Galactic Civil War. During a mission to save the people of Dorlo, the team was captured by Dark Jedi Jerec. When Rahn refused to submit to Jerec's will, a small being known as Pic killed Gron by stabbing him in the throat with a dagger.

**Grond (1)** A Rebel Alliance soldier at Echo Base on Hoth, he was a member of a squad that recaptured the base's ion cannon control center, allowing the final transports to escape the Imperial onslaught.

**Grond (2)** An Imperial lieutenant from Corellia, he was assigned as Colonel Dyer's primary aide during the ground battle on the forest moon of Endor and coordinated the actions required to guard the shield generators protecting the second Death Star as it was being built.

**Groodo the Hutt** A Hutt crime lord, he was responsible for the Bartokk attack on the Trinkatta Starships works on Esseles just before the Battle of Naboo. The Trade Federation had hired Groodo to design and build a small but powerful hyperdrive unit for use on droid starfighters, and then refused to pay for the prototype. Groodo's plan to steal the droid starfighters was thwarted by Darth Maul. The Sith could have killed an escaping Groodo and his son, but Darth Sidious decided to let them live in fear instead.

**Groshik** A Neimoidian who owned and tended bar at the only cantina in the Apatros colony in the years before the Battle of Ruusan, he helped a miner named Dessel "disappear" into the Sith army after he had killed a Republic officer in self-defense.

**Groshim** A Kashirim, he was one of King Sha-mar Ma-dred's most trusted guards. Groshim accompanied the king and his four wives to Coruscant shortly before the Battle of Geonosis, to protect the royal family while it negotiated for admittance to the Old Republic.

**Ground Base Seven** An Old Republic military base, it was established on the planet Drongar near the Rotfurze Wastes during the Clone Wars.

**groundborer** An old mining vehicle developed for quickly excavating tunnels and chambers, it could provide quick shelter on hostile worlds. The ancient Naddists of Onderon converted a number of Akin-Dower groundborers for military use, adding four medium blasters to the craft and dubbing it the Onderonian War Machine.

**groundmouth** A term used by the Yuuzhan Vong to describe the mouth of an amphistaff polyp because the polyp's mouth was located at ground level. The polyp had to rely on the immature amphistaffs to feed it by cutting up the food into small pieces and then sweeping them into the groundmouth.

**Ground-Orbit Communications Unit** Developed on the planet Duro, this communications device allowed onworld domed settlements to talk directly with orbital cities above. During the Yuuzhan Vong invasion, the GOCU lines helped the New Republic maintain communications with the ground crews who were rebuilding the natural environment of Duro.

**grove harrier** These strange creatures inhabiting the jungles of Kashyyyk's Shadow Forest fed on the smaller mallakins.

**Grove, the** A peaceful stand of trees that separated the Matale Fields from the Sandral Fields on the planet Dantooine.

***Growler*** A Rebel Alliance Nebulon-B frigate, it was active during the Galactic Civil War.

**Grozbok** An ancient wrecking droid reprogrammed by Olag Greck to wreak havoc on Hosk, Grozbok was destroyed by Unit Zed's group of renegade security droids.

**Groznik** A Wookiee enslaved and sent to work at an Imperial base on Endor, Groznik was rescued by a group of freedom fighters led by Throm Loro. When Loro was killed in battle, Groznik gave his life debt to Throm's wife Elscol. During the New Republic's attempt to take Professor Falken's asteroid lab from Imperial control, Groznik remained at the lab and kept Loka Hask at bay while Rogue Squadron used a gravitic polarization beam to eliminate Hask's *Interdictor*-class cruiser. The device exploded, taking the lab, and Groznik, with it.

Gruna

**Grrrwahrr** A Wookiee who lived on Kashyyyk some four millennia before the Galactic Civil War, he was cornered in the Lower Shadowlands by a group of Mandalorians during the Great Sith War, but eventually was rescued by a group of Jedi Knights. When the Jedi learned that the Mandalorians had been killing Wookiees for sport, Grrrwahrr gave them information on their hideout. The Jedi eventually killed the Mandalorians.

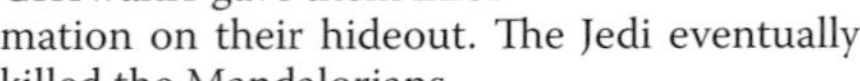

**Grubba the Hutt** A member of the Desilijic kajidic and one of Jabba the Hutt's nephews, he was kidnapped by the Whiphid gangster Black Tongue while on his way to learn at Jabba's feet. Grubba was rescued by Han Solo, who hoped the nephew's safe return would lead Jabba to remove the bounty on his head. But Jabba still demanded 10,000 credits and temporarily imprisoned Solo. Bounty hunter Eron Stonefield, eager to get Solo, again kidnapped Grubba to arrange to trade him for Solo—but Solo had escaped and retaken the young Hutt. Then Dengar captured Solo, returned Grubba to his uncle, and turned Solo over to an Imperial officer—who was an undercover Rebel Alliance officer.

**Grub Cave** The deepest part of a Colony hive, it was where the larval members of the Kind were tended until they hatched into adults. Each larva was tended by an adult, and both larvae and adults were dependent upon each other for survival.

***Grubstake*** A civilian supply vessel, it was destroyed by Mandalorian forces during the Old Republic's defense of the planet Serroco during the Mandalorian Wars.

**Grudo** A Rodian gun-for-hire, he joined the crew of Zozridor Slayke, a rogue soldier who defected from Old Republic forces so he could fight the Separatists his own way. After Jedi Master Nejaa Halcyon was sent to bring Slayke back, Grudo challenged the Jedi to one-on-one combat, giving Slayke and the rest of his men a chance to escape using Master Halcyon's own ship. Years later, Halcyon recruited Grudo for a mission to liberate the Intergalactic Communications Center on Praesitlyn. While Grudo was wary, he was impressed by young Anakin Skywalker and signed on. Grudo was killed by so-called friendly fire before the mission was successfully completed.

**Grugara, Yara** A high-society reporter for Eye on Cularin after the Battle of Naboo.

**grumph** A vicious 8-meter-long reptilian, it was covered with spiked scales and had a mouth full of dagger-like teeth. Very few who have seen one survived the encounter.

**Gruna** A Nessie captain of a Colossus Wasp transport ship around the time of the Great Sith War, he paid a large sum of money to Bogga the Hutt to keep pirates from attacking his ship.

**Grundakk** A creature native to the forest moon of Endor, it was a huge, fur-covered humanoid with large eyes, wide nostrils, and long arms. The Duloks believed that the Grundakk was dangerous and tried to scare the Ewoks by saying that the Grundakk was coming to attack their village. Logray knew that the creature was the guardian of the Father Tree. When Teebo was lost in the forest, the Grundakk rescued him just in time to help fight off Vulgarr and the Duloks.

**Grunger, Josef** One of the Imperial Grand Admirals still in power after the death of Emperor Palpatine, he commanded a fleet of 30 Star Destroyers. After the death of Grand Admiral Teshik, he tried to take over control of the Corellian sector. Grunger was killed in battle with Grand Admiral Pitta when he rammed the *Aggressor* into Pitta's torpedo sphere.

**Grunts** A Weequay "won" by Han Solo during his early career as a sabacc player, the smuggler immediately freed him. Later, when Solo returned to Tatooine with his wife, Leia, to locate the *Killik Twilight* moss-painting, Grunts allowed them to carry their weapons into an auction despite the ban against them. When Solo tried to destroy *Killik Twilight,* Imperial Commander Quenton ordered his men to open fire on the auction's bidders; Grunts risked all to get the Solos to safety.

**Grupp** A local policeman on Nam Chorios, he worked with the Ithorian Snaplaunce in maintaining the peace of Hweg Shul. Grupp and Snaplaunce saved Luke Skywalker from the rocks and spears of the Oldtimers who attacked him.

**grutchin** A bioengineered form of living starfighter weapon created by the Yuuzhan Vong, the black, half-meter-long grutchins were sent out after an advance force of coralskippers reduced an enemy fleet. The insectoid grutchins were released from an ovoid holding ship and latched on to enemy ships. They used acid-dripping pincers to chew through the vessels, rendering them inoperative and incapable of sustaining life. Grutchins were unintelligent weapons of destruction, and once released, they could not be recalled.

**grutchin symbiote** A variation on the Yuuzhan Vong's living weapon, the grutchin, it was developed for use in ground-based combat. Yuuzhan Vong warriors choosing to fight with a grutchin symbiote were required to have four holes bored into the flesh of their backs, where the symbiote's legs were inserted. Its arms wrapped around a warrior's neck, and its head sat on the warrior's shoulder. The symbiote could be directed telepathically to leap from the warrior's back and attack an opponent.

**grutchin torpedo** A massive weapon developed by the Yuuzhan Vong, it was essentially a huge shell that contained hundreds of grutchins.

**grutchyna** A large Yuuzhan Vong creature, it was created to accompany a landing party. Upon arrival, the grutchyna would begin digging into and consuming the crust of a planet, creating a network of tunnels and caves in which the warriors could hide and plan their attack. Each grutchyna measured 6 meters long and was protected by heavy black armor plating. Grutchyna were fairly intelligent and could be trained to carry and deploy troops into battle.

**Grynne, Phlygas** A notorious assassin in the years following the Battle of Endor. It was rumored that Grynne charged over 100,000 credits for his work, and it was believed that he murdered Stinna Draesinge Sha.

**grysh-worm** A bloated worm, it was once native to the long-lost planet of Yuuzhan'tar.

**GRZ-6B** Serv-O-Droid's wrecking droid, it stood more than 6 meters high and looked like some sort of monster as it moved across urban landscapes, knocking down buildings and recycling the materials. The GRZ-6B moved about on two heavy legs; two massive arms allowed it to pull down structures and move rubble into its "mouth." Its body was mostly a huge internal forge that melted down anything placed inside.

**Gshkaath** A Noghri, he and Ezrakh were asked by Leia Organa Solo to accompany her to the Chorios system to meet with Seti Ashgad. It was Gshkaath who made sure that Ashgad returned to his ship, the *Light of Reason,* after their initial meeting.

**GSI-21D** A disruptor pistol manufactured by Galactic Solutions Industries and made popular by the Brotherhood of Darkness, it was considered among the finest weapons of its type in the years leading up to the Battle of Ruusan. Although its range was just over 20 meters, the GSI-21D was powerful. Because of its ability to disintegrate everything from flesh and bone to droid plating and body armor, the GSI-21D was outlawed in most Republic sectors of the galaxy.

**G'Sil, Senator G'vli** Chairman of the Senate's Security and Intelligence Council, he was surprised by a midnight visit of Admiral Cha Niathal at the height of the Corellia–Galactic Alliance War, and shocked to hear that Head of State Cal Omas had been relieved of his duties by Jacen Solo under the Emergency Measures Act.

**G-station** A term applied to any of the huge orbital platforms located above the planet Genesia, primarily to serve as starship docking facilities. Stations such as G-S7 were built at the height of the New Order by private corporations that wanted to avoid the criminal underworld on the planet's surface.

**Gthull, Kvag** One of reborn Emperor Palpatine's Dark Jedi, he was in charge of interrogations at Bast Castle. Kvag Gthull was sent by Palpatine, along with Tedryn-Sha and Xecr Nist, to capture Jacen and Jaina Solo. He nearly succeeded, but Rayf Ysanna used the Force to recover the children while Leia Organa Solo blasted Gthull into oblivion.

**gualaar** A beautiful, white-furred beast native to planet Naboo, it was often domesticated and trained to pull carriages during weddings or caskets during funerals, such as the one for Padmé Amidala. The head of the gualaar was crowned by a single, curving horn, while two smaller horns rose from the bony ridge of its nose. Thick, shaggy hair formed the gualaar's mane, which was often braided with heavy beads for public appearances.

**gualama** Swift and elegant equine herbivores native to the plains of Naboo, these herd beasts congregated in patriarchal groups of up to 25 members. Gualamas had thin bodies and white fur; their heads were crowned with a pair of tall, forward-curving horns.

**Guania** A male Wookiee, he was among a small group that confronted Olee Starstone, Siadem Forte, and their band of Jedi survivors when they arrived on Kashyyyk following Order 66. Guania was suspicious of the newcomers' motives, believing them to be bounty hunters in search of Jedi to capture and bring to Darth Vader and Emperor Palpatine.

**Guanolta** A Dug, he was a member of Sebolto's gang in the years following the Battle of Naboo. The Malastarian Art Union issued a bounty for his capture in connection with the sale of death sticks to the youth of Pixelito, a bounty that Jango Fett claimed.

*Gualaar*

**Guanta** A Wookiee warrior, he was one of many who defended their homeworld of Kashyyyk and the city of Kachirho during the final stages of the Clone Wars. Guanta served under Merumeru.

***Guard*** A group of Viraxo Razor starfighters used to harass the Azzameen's shipping operations.

**guard globe** A form of remote, it was used by Dr. Arakkus to guard his fortress in the Graveyard of Lost Ships. Guard globes patrolled the corridors and were programmed to intercept intruders.

**Guardian (1)** A style of double-bladed lightsaber hilt, it was sometimes used by the new Order of Jedi Knights who were trained by Luke Skywalker at the height of the New Republic. The Guardian had wide, angled emitter shrouds that protected each end of the weapon, giving it the appearance of a two-bladed dagger when inactive.

**Guardian (2)** The title used by the being sent by Emperor Palpatine to guard the Mount Tantiss storehouse on the planet Wayland. It was believed that the Guardian was killed by Joruus C'baoth when he arrived on Wayland.

**Guardian (3)** The largest Spook crystals found on Nam Chorios—often formed into tsil—these sentient crystals controlled the actions of the smaller Spook crystals found on the planet.

***Guardian* (1)** A *Super*-class Star Destroyer under the command of Admiral Drommel, it was badly damaged in the Battle of Tantive V with New Republic forces about three years after the Battle of Endor. Later, the New Republic recovered and refit the ship. The *Guardian* was later deployed to Kashyyyk during the Yuuzhan Vong War. When the Galactic Alliance established its base of operations on Mon Calamari, the *Guardian* was recalled as part of the home fleet.

***Guardian* (2)** One of three Nebulon-B escort frigates assigned to protect the replenishment fleet that included the *Black Ice*.

***Guardian*-class corvette** A type of ship heavily used for Imperial duty during the early years of the New Order.

***Guardian*-class droid** A canine-like droid, the relatively inexpensive GV/3 was developed by Cybot Galactica to serve as a protector and companion for families with young children.

*Guardian-class droid*

***Guardian*-class patrol ship** Light cruisers built for Imperial forces after the Battle of Endor by Sienar Fleet Systems, these 42-meter ships were used as intersystem customs vessels and could handle up to 200 metric tons of confiscated cargo. The XL-3 and XL-5 models had beefed-up shields and four laser cannons: two mounted in front and two on free-moving turrets. Tion Mil/Sci also manufactured a 40-meter version armed with a pair of blaster cannons; they were used as mobile coordinating stations for the huge hunter-killer probots that were used by the resurrected Emperor Palpatine.

**Guardian Corps** A cadre of 1,000 war-robots assigned to guard the *Queen of Ranroon* as the ship lay hidden on Dellalt in the wake of the death of Xim the Despot. Several years before the Battle of Yavin, the Guardian Corps was called to duty to protect the ship from miners J'uoch and R'all. The only survivors of the attack were Han Solo, his companions, and Gallandro. Solo's group managed to reach a barracks on the other side of a bridge, so the corps commander ordered the war-robots to cross the bridge and destroy the barracks. But Bollux and Blue Max were able to communicate with the corps commander and ordered him to increase the marching paces of the war-robots until their footfalls set up a harmonic tremor that collapsed the bridge, sending the Guardian Corps crashing into a ravine.

**Guardian Droid** Considered to be an upscale version of the popular Defender Droid, this Tendrando Arms droid used the same laminamium armor that was used by the YVH series of combat droids and was armed with weapons that could be attached to its arms. In production following the Swarm War, the Guardian Droid couldn't be shut down remotely without proper authorization.

***Guardian Mantis*** A Y-shaped needle-nosed starship, it was a prototype design created by Vana Sage and a Xi Char engineer, and built by the starshipwrights of Nubia in the last decades of the Old Republic.

***Guardian of the Republic*** An old *Liberator*-class troopship decommissioned shortly before the fall of the Old Republic, it was purchased by Garris Shrike, who renamed it the *Trader's Luck*.

**Guardians** A security force, it was formed by the government of the planet Junction 5 to maintain defenses against an invasion from Delaluna or the possible use of the Annihilator weapon. But it turned out that both the invasion and weapon were ruses used to destroy civil liberties and take over the planet.

**Guardians of Kiffu** Formed by the Kiffar in the last decades of the Old Republic, they protected the prison world of Kiffex and ensured that no beings escaped.

**Guardians of the Breath** Ancient Kashi mystics who were able to control the Force, they maintained all the lore and skills used to call upon the Breath as part of oral traditions.

Gudb

**Guardian Squadron** A Y-wing bomber squadron, it was part of General Salm's Defender Wing serving the New Republic.

***Guardstar*** An Imperial patrol frigate, it was orbiting Tatooine when Boba Fett returned from Bespin with Han Solo's carbonite-encased body. It tried to intercept the bounty hunter, but Darth Vader commanded the crew to stand down and let Fett land.

**Guarja Shipyards** A starship repair facility, it was located on Nal Hutta during the last decades of the Old Republic.

***Guarlara*** An Old Republic *Venator*-class Star Destroyer, it was one of many vessels that tried unsuccessfully to eliminate General Grievous's *Invisible Hand* at the beginning of the Clone Wars. But during the Battle of Coruscant, the *Guarlara* was able to fire the blasts that crippled the *Invisible Hand* and sent it spiraling toward the surface of Coruscant.

**guarlara** A large equine creature native to Naboo, it was related to the smaller gualama, but with jet-black fur and defensive tusks on either side of its mouth.

**Gudb** A rat-faced gangster in the employ of Great Bogga the Hutt, he led a conspiracy to kill Jedi trainee Andur Sunrider at the Stenness hyperspace terminal 4,000 years before the Galactic Civil War. He carried out the deed with his poisonous pet gorm-worm, Skritch.

**Gueni** The elder leader of the Daan Council, he was forced into a brittle alliance with Wehutti at the insistence of Qui-Gon Jinn, in an effort to avert a full-scale war when the Young began taking control of the city of Zehava.

**Guermessa** The second of Tatooine's three moons.

**Guff twins** A pair of Gamorrean thugs, they worked as bouncers at the Plastoid Pit in Zalxuc City, on the planet Thyferra, during the New Order.

**Guh'Rantt, Mikdanyell** A Rodian, he was mayor of Mos Eisley on Tatooine during the early years of the Galactic Civil War. Mayor Guh'Rantt was deeply connected to the criminal underground of the city but eventually was exposed by former Imperial Navy Chief Bast.

**Guide** A short man, he was encountered and then followed by Ferus Olin and Trever Flume beneath the surface of Coruscant during their search for Fy-Tor-Ana and Solace several months after the end of the Clone Wars.

**Guides, the** The Cestian name for dashta eels that grew to maturity from fertilized eggs, they lived beneath the surface of the planet Ord Cestus, hidden in grottoes beneath the Dashta Mountains. The X'Ting and human workers who were forced to labor for the Five Families believed that the mature, Force-sensitive Guides provided them with guidance in their lives; they devoutly maintained the secrecy of the location of the dashta eel pools. In the wake of the destruction of the Five Families, the Guides fled into the deeper caverns with the other dashta eels and were not seen again.

**Guiding Light** Obi-Wan Kenobi's call sign, it was used whenever he was dispatched on a mission by the Jedi Council.

***Guild*** A Rebel Alliance shuttle group, it was destroyed during the Galactic Civil War.

**Guild of Vindicators** A brotherhood of assassins, it tried to destroy Darth Vader during the Galactic Civil War. The guild sent Clat the Shamer to kill the Dark Lord, but Vader manipulated Clat into a trap on Cheelit, and he was consumed in fire when he suddenly became a playing piece in a game of firepath.

**guilea** An extract of the tecave grass found on the planet Cerea, it was known for its mildly euphoric effects when consumed. Because the grass needed a molecular trace of the rare mineral malium to grow, Cerea had a virtual monopoly on its production and export was strictly prohibited.

**Guld, Handon** He and an associate murdered Calder Nettic, who was having an affair with Guld's wife, but both men were arrested and jailed by Jedi Knight Bolook some four millennia before the Galactic Civil War.

**Guldar, Ithoriak** A Selkath criminal, he was active on his homeworld of Manaan some four millennia before the Galactic Civil War.

**Guldi, Drom** A muscular man, he was Baron Administrator of the Kelrodo-Ai Gelatin Mines, famous for their water sculptures. He met his match on Hoth while on a big-game hunting expedition. The prey—wampa ice creatures—turned on him and his party, killing them all. Only Luke Skywalker and Callista, who had stumbled upon the party as they were exploring the former Rebel Alliance headquarters on the planet, managed to escape.

**Gulley** A New Republic Navy lieutenant, he was Plat Mallar's check pilot during Mallar's training as an escort pilot after Mallar was assigned to the Fifth Battle Group.

**gulliball** A popular Gungan sport, it was played by using mallets made from the branches of the zaela tree. Gungans batted puffed-up gullipuds in an effort to place them in specified goal areas. Gullipuds, flat-bodied, squishy amphibians, quickly inhaled great amounts of air and puffed up like balloons when excited or frightened. For some reason, the gullipuds enjoyed being batted around with mallets.

**Gul-Rah, Thanis** A former bounty hunter, he was part of the crew of the New Republic starship *FarStar* during the search for Imperial Moff Kentor Sarne in the Kathol sector.

**Gumbaeki** A large Wookiee and elder of the Palsaang clan, he managed to escape from Separatist-backed Trandoshan slavers who captured his clan and was able to enlist the help of Jedi Masters Quinlan Vos and Luminara Unduli in freeing his people. The surprise attack on the slavers turned deadly when Separatist battle droids appeared on the scene, forcing the small team to retreat until they were reinforced by an unlikely ally, Vilmarh Grahrk. Gumbaeki had to explain that Grahrk had been smuggling supplies to the Palsaang clan during the Clone Wars and had become an unofficial member of the clan.

**Gundar** A hulking, thick-necked man, he was one of Madame Aryn Thul's attendants, serving her aboard the *Tradewyn* in the years following the Yuuzhan Vong invasion.

**gundark** A four-armed anthropoid known for its incredible strength, the gundark was a semi-intelligent being that was believed to have originated on the planet Vanqor. Gundarks had large ears

Gundark

Gungans gather before a battle.

and forbidding faces that were dominated by a huge, tooth-filled maw. The average gundark was nearly 2 meters tall and moved about on its two primary arms. The young were taught to hunt and fight from birth; females became the hunters, and males became the protectors. While not considered intelligent, gundarks eventually learned to form and use simple tools, and developed a fairly complex social structure. Gundarks were hunted primarily for sport or for use as slave labor during the final years of the Old Republic and by the Empire, although this practice was banned during the early years of the New Republic. The species gave the galaxy the phrase *You look like you could pull the ears off a gundark,* meaning that an individual appears healthy and strong.

**Gundy** A keschel miner, he worked on Tyne's Horky with his nephew Jann Tosh. After Gundy was rescued by the mysterious Kez-Iban, Tosh managed to defeat the crime lord Kleb Zellock. They split Zellock's hidden fortunes with Yorpo Mog and were financially set for the rest of their lives.

**Gungan** A species of humanoid amphibians native to the planet Naboo. Gungans existed as two subspecies. The average Otolla Gungan had a tall, muscular body with long arms and short legs, and could live either on land or in the water. Their heads were crowned with a pair of large, frilled ears known as haillu that extended when frightened. Their eyes sat atop short, thick stalks. Ankura Gungans grew much larger—to the point that their weight began to compact their skeletons and their eyes were hooded with heavy brows. Ankura Gungans had green skin, while the Otolla had reddish skin.

All Gungans were hatched from eggs, and both parents shared in the rearing of their offspring. They had flexible skeletons formed from cartilage instead of bone; a set of compound lungs allowed them to breathe air or water. During much of their existence on Naboo, Gungans took great pains to avoid contact with their human neighbors and even built huge underwater cities to escape contact with colonists, many of whom looked down on them.

The Gungans, like the Wookiees, had a distinct concept of the life debt. Any Gungan who was saved by another being must submit to the life debt or be punished by the gods. Gungans were quite technologically advanced. Their immense bubble cities in the depths of Naboo's seas were made up of groupings of round force fields. The fields were permeable only to slow-moving objects and could be penetrated by a Gungan walking through them. However, the force fields held back the incredible pressure of the water that surrounded them. The Gungans also had an advanced shielding technology that they applied to small, handheld shields as well as huge hemispheres that protected an entire army. Like the bubble fields, these shields were permeable only by slow-moving objects, and they absorbed energy like a sponge.

Gungans grew the basic structures of buildings, vehicles, and technology and adorned them with artistic flourishes and organic lines, giving their civilization a very fluid, nonrectilinear look. The power source for Gungan technology was a mysterious blue-white energy "goo" that was mined in the depths of Naboo's oceans. This viscous plasmic material formed the basis of Gungan weaponry as well. But Gungans still employed beasts of burden for transportation. Their most common mount was the kaadu, a wingless reptilian avian that Gungans adorned with feathers and rode into combat. Other favored Gungan mounts included the large, stubborn falumpaset. For truly heavy loads, the Gungans domesticated the fambaa, a 9-meter-tall, four-legged swamp amphibian.

The Gungans maintained a large standing armed force called the Gungan Grand Army. This huge collection of foot soldiers carried cestas, electropoles, and atlatls capable of hurling plasmic energy spheres (or boomers, as Gungans called them). Gungan catapults hurled even larger boomers great distances. Near the end of the Old Republic, the Gungans were ruled by Boss Nass and his Rep Council from the High Tower Board Room of Otoh Gunga. When the Trade Federation invaded Naboo, Boss Nass chose to remain uninvolved in the conflict. He felt the Gungans' isolation would keep them safe from what was a surface dwellers' problem. He was wrong. The Trade Federation armies stormed the swamps, forcing the Gungans to abandon Otoh Gunga. They retreated to a sacred place within the Naboo swamps. There Queen Amidala, the ruler of the Naboo, pleaded for Boss Nass's help. Stirred by her words, Nass agreed to join forces with the Naboo to rid the planet of the Trade Federation. The Grand Army waged an immense ground battle with the Trade Federation droid army, and many Gungans died in the fighting. The Queen's forces and allies were able to capture the Trade Federation viceroy and destroy the orbiting Droid Control Ship, thus freeing Naboo. In the festivities that followed, Boss Nass shared a platform with Queen Amidala and declared peace on Naboo. The two cultures that had long been divided by fear and prejudice would now forever be joined by a common understanding and love of their world.

**Gungan battle wagon** *See* battle wagon, Gungan.

**Gungan energy catapult** Having the same "grown" look as the rest of Gungan technology, energy catapults were pulled into battle by slow but reliable falumpaset

Gungan energy catapult

beasts. When in place, catapults hurled plasmic energy balls—or boomers as the Gungans called them—at the enemy. Tough hornweed was used in the catapult's design. A leather-like tensioner coil primed the missile-firing arm.

**Gungan Grand Army** A large army made up of Ankura and Otolla Gungans, it was ready to act on the orders of Boss Nass or any other leader in case of emergency. In theory, any Boss could mobilize the Gungan Grand Army—and the entire Gungan community—within 36 hours of declaring war. The Grand Army was ordered into battle by Boss Nass as part of Queen Amidala's plans to overthrow the Trade Federation blockade of Naboo, in what became part of the Battle of Naboo. It was believed that the Gungan Grand Army was originally formed more than 3,000 years before the Battle of Naboo, when the Gungans banded together to fend off the violent bursas that inhabited their planet. The army had been inactive for more than 100 years, kept together more out of tradition than necessity, before it was mobilized for the Battle of Naboo. Despite that inactivity, the Gungan Grand Army had some 2,000 soldiers when it went into battle against the Trade Federation.

*Gungan sacred place*

**Gungan sacred place** A hidden location that Gungans held sacred above all others. Located in the Lianorm Swamp, along the foothills of the Gallo Mountains on the planet Naboo, it was one of the few aboveground sites they inhabited. Normally reserved for introspective contemplation and prayer, the sacred place also served as a safe haven in the event of an emergency in one of their underwater cities. The sacred place was surrounded by ruins and statues, many depicting ancient Naboo gods and goddesses.

**Gungis X Weapons** An arms maker in business four millennia before the Battle of Yavin, it was credited with the development and manufacture of the first true blaster carbine.

**Gun of Command** A powerful weapon that made Hapan troops nearly invincible in small-arms combat, it released an electromagnetic wave field (a spray of blue sparks) that neutralized an enemy's voluntary thought processes. Those shot with the gun stood helpless and tended to follow any orders given them.

**Gunray, Nute** Neimoidians were known for their exceptional organizational and business skills, but Nute Gunray was more cutthroat than most. His unscrupulous nature saw him ascend to the position of viceroy of the Trade Federation after most of his peers were assassinated. As the executive officer of the Trade Federation, it was Gunray who led the blockade and subsequent invasion of Naboo. The assurances of Darth Sidious, his shadowy Sith benefactor, led Gunray down this ambitious and blatantly illegal path. Once Naboo was under siege, Gunray attempted to force the planet's monarch, Queen Amidala, to sign a treaty that would legitimize the occupation. During the subjugation of the planet, Gunray proved that he was willing to commit any atrocity in pursuit of commercial gain and power. He boldly set himself up in the Queen's former throne room, taunting the planet's governor, Sio Bibble, while Naboo's population suffered the effects of the embargo. Gunray's true cowardice showed when Naboo freedom fighters stormed the Royal Palace. The Neimoidian cowered behind squads of battle droids, fearing that the fighting would spill too close to his throne room. Queen Amidala infiltrated her own palace and blasted through Gunray's protectors. At blasterpoint, Amidala declared Gunray's occupation over. Arrested by Republic officials, Gunray and his lieutenant, Rune Haako, were carted off to answer for their crimes. They risked losing their lucrative trade franchise from this botched endeavor. But even justice could be bought in the final corrupt years of the Republic. After four trials in the Supreme Court, Gunray still held his position of viceroy.

When Count Dooku's Separatist movement began tearing apart the Republic, many of the galaxy's largest business concerns were attracted to the idea of galactic reforms that would benefit commerce. Gunray was one of them, though he made his allegiance to the newly formed Confederacy of Independent Systems contingent on the assassination of Padmé Amidala. To that end, bounty hunter Jango Fett recruited Zam Wesell to kill the Naboo Senator. Though Wesell failed, Amidala eventually was captured by Separatist forces and was to be executed in front of Gunray. Amidala proved hard to kill, and when the shooting started at the first engagement of the Clone Wars, Gunray again turned coward and fled.

Gunray grew tired of the war, and the visions of riches and conquest promised by the Separatists' secret benefactor, Darth Sidious, would not salve his ache for peace. He questioned General Grievous's leadership, even risking the ire of the cyborg general. When Sidious moved the Separatist leadership to Mustafar, Gunray thought the end of the war was near. He was right, but his demise soon followed. Darth Sidious betrayed the Separatists, having used them to engineer his ascent to Emperor of the galaxy. No longer needing them, Sidious dispatched his apprentice Darth Vader to kill them. Vader sliced through baron after baron with his lightsaber blade, leaving the sniveling Gunray for last. The terrified Neimoidian pleaded for peace, but Vader silenced him with a slashing blade through the torso.

*Nute Gunray*

**Guntar** A Zeetsa, he worked for Trillot as a drug manufacturer during the Clone Wars. Operating from a hidden facility in the Ord Cestus capital city of ChikatLik, Guntar often cut his products with Xyathone. When Trillot discovered Guntar's deception, he had his underling's olfactory organs removed as punishment.

**Guo, Mars** This needle-nosed Phuii piloted a big bruiser of a Podracer during the Boonta Eve Classic, the spectacle in which Anakin Skywalker won his freedom from slavery. It was Mars Guo's first time in the big leagues, though he had gained valuable experience in the Rim minor leagues. In the second lap, Guo was taken out of the race by some high-speed sabotage courtesy of Sebulba, who flung a piece of scrap into the air in front of Guo's Podracer; the debris was sucked into an engine. Perhaps the obnoxious Guo's performance that day would have been better had he not been so terribly hung over. The night before, the loudmouth braggart had enjoyed way too much to drink at a glimmik concert and ended up making empty overtures to one of Sebulba's comely masseuses, Anne Gella. Sebulba overheard Guo and vowed to eliminate him.

**Gupin** Members of this small, elf-like species that lived in large volcanic caves on the Forest Moon of Endor were shapeshifters. Nearly every Gupin had a pair of tiny wings with which it could move about in case of emergency. The wings were grown after the Guniepal Chest was opened, as part of the Renewal Ceremony.

*Guri*

**Gurdun, Imperial Supervisor** Power-hungry and vain, this large-nosed supervisor skimmed Imperial funds from gray budgets of other military programs to create the IG series of assassin droids as part of Holowan's Phlutdroid project. His plans backfired when the droid IG-88 became self-aware on activation. IG-88 instilled his sentient programming in his equally deadly counterparts, killed the technicians who created him, and escaped to stage a galactic takeover. Gurdun was later assigned to oversee the development of the Empire's fleet of Arakyd Viper probe robots and to transport the second Death Star's computer core to that battle station. He was killed when his ship, carrying the computer core, was hijacked by IG-88A and the assassin droid's army of robotic stormtroopers.

*Mars Guo*

**Guri** A human replica droid, she could visually pass for a woman anywhere in the galaxy. Guri ate, drank, and performed all of a woman's more personal functions without betraying her nonhuman origin. She had long, silky blond hair, pale clear blue eyes, and an exquisite figure. Guri's rich alto voice was warm and inviting. But there was a certain coolness about her. She was the only human replica droid to have been programmed as an assassin and had cost Prince Xizor, head of the Black Sun criminal organization, nine million credits. She quickly became Xizor's top lieutenant, enforcing the crime lord's wishes and maintaining the day-to-day continuity of his enterprises . . . as she killed again and again.

At Xizor's request, Guri met Princess Leia Organa at the Next Chance casino on Rodia and brought Leia and Chewbacca back to Imperial Center, where she noticed Xizor's attraction to Leia. She suggested that Xizor kill both the Princess and the Wookiee, but he hesitated. Later, Leia bashed Guri on the head and escaped. When Guri finally met face-to-face with Luke Skywalker, she talked him into deactivating his lightsaber and fighting her hand-to-hand. Luke agreed and overpowered Guri through the Force. He did not kill her, though, and Guri escaped the castle using a paraglider.

Xizor wasn't as fortunate. He was killed over Coruscant when Darth Vader's Star Destroyer destroyed his skyhook; it was believed that Guri perished in the same explosion. Guri had fled Coruscant, however, and traveled alone before trying to locate one of her creators, Massad Thrumble, hoping that the Imperial researcher could remove the programming that made her an assassin. Thrumble's work succeeded, but not before Xizor's niece Savan tried to recover Guri. Savan attempted to use a secret code phrase that Xizor had implanted in Guri's brain. Thrumble's reprogramming gave Guri enough information to recognize the phrase, but her new programming blocked its effectiveness. Guri immobilized Savan and turned the Falleen over to the fledgling New Republic. Purely by fate, Guri eventually met up with Dash Rendar when the dashing smuggler saw a beautiful woman and bought her a drink.

**Guris** An overbearing Nimbanel, he worked in the Grand Army of the Republic's logistics center on Coruscant during the early stages of the Clone Wars. Guris was known to his colleagues for his gruff demeanor as well as his anti-human bias. He considered clone troopers to be little more than living droids.

**Gurke** A Gamorrean who lived on Tatooine some 4,000 years before the Battle of Yavin, he was a noted hunter. Gurke spent time in the Tatooine deserts in search of krayt dragons. When it became apparent that such game was hard to kill, Gurke and his fellow Gamorreans turned to hunting humans for the bounties on their heads.

**Gurlanin** Members of this polymorphic, shape-shifting marsupial species native to the planet Qiilura usually resembled large canine predators. But the average Gurlanin could take on many other forms as well, including that of a human. In addition, Gurlanins were strongly telepathic and could communicate without speech, making them appear as if they were Force-sensitive when encountered by a Jedi Knight. Gurlanins could disappear at will and also appear invisible to other forms of detection such as infrared and thermal sensors, making them almost perfect hunters, spies, and assassins. Although they had no love for the Old Republic, they agreed to assist it during the Clone Wars after Separatists established a base on Qiilura. Their help was given with the singular goal of removing both the Separatists and human settlers from their homeworld. But the Republic ignored the quid pro quo, and Gurlanin spies started infiltrating all levels of the Old Republic government. It was later learned that Gurlanin spies had provided the Separatists with information that let them destroy the transport *Core Conveyor*. That prompted the Republic to finally dispatch elements of the 35th Infantry to extract the human colonists from Qiilura. When the last colonist was removed, the Gurlanins removed their spies.

**Gurtt, Tyresi** A dark-skinned Eyttyrmin Batiiv pirate who served with Jacob Nive, she survived the Imperial assault on the band. She became captain of Nive's premier fighter group, Bolt Squadron. For her tactics in defeating the *Harmzuay*—which she acknowledged were really those of Rogue Squadron Jedi Corran Horn—she was promoted to True Invid and served aboard the Star Destroyer *Invidious,* which was controlled by Moff Leonia Tavira. When Tavira was attacked by forces that included Horn, Tyresi Gurtt and others got word about a deal under which the Jedi would grant them immunity. She and many of her companions took the offer for freedom and left the *Invidious* before it jumped to hyperspace.

**Gus Talon** A small, habitable moon that orbited Corellia, much of its surface was covered with rolling grasslands. Wedge Antilles spent a large part of his youth on Gus Talon.

**Gus Treta** A large space station in the Corellian system, it provided a wealth of services for the five worlds neighboring it. Wedge Antilles's parents operated a fuel depot on the station, but they were killed in an explosion when the pirate ship *Buzzzer* blasted off without uncoupling from its fuel lines.

**Guta-Nay** A Weequay criminal, he was one of Ghez Hokan's lieutenants on the planet Qiilura during the last years of the Old Republic. During a routine mission, Guta-Nay was captured by the members of Omega Squad and held prisoner. He revealed information about Hokan's forces, and the Republic team decided to use him as the bait in the trap they were laying for Hokan. He was fed false information about Omega Squad's plans, and the Force was used to implant the suggestion that he "escape" and return to Hokan's encampment. The Mandalorian was less than happy to see the Weequay, but listened to what Guta-Nay had to say. Despite the usefulness of the information, Hokan believed that he had disobeyed his orders and beheaded him with Kast Fulier's lightsaber as an example to his troops.

**Guz, Brakko** A male Rodian wanted by the Republic Security Force for his part in the deaths of several prominent business owners on Coruscant, he was captured on the Outland Transit Station by Jango Fett and brought in for the bounty.

**Gwann** A member of a small resistance force that was led by Untrilla, they opposed the Imperial occupation of their homeworld, Delrakkin. When Untrilla befriended a downed Alliance pilot, Gwann was initially skeptical but soon welcomed the pilot into their group.

**G'wenee** An urban world, it was known as a center of trade and commerce for both legal and illegal goods. Lay Pa-Sidian was its main port.

*G-wing*

**Gwig** A young Ewok, he received his hood signifying his status as an adult just before the Battle of Endor.

**G-wing** A single-occupant ship, it was used by Mandalorians as a shuttle. Bastila Shan used a G-wing to travel from the Unknown World to the Star Forge.

**Gwori Revolutionary Industries** A starship builder, it allied itself with the InterGalactic Banking Clan and later the Confederacy of Independent Systems during the Clone Wars. GRI worked with Hoersch-Kessel Drive to produce the *Munificent*-class star frigate.

**Gwurran** Members of this smaller species of Ansionians were hyperactive, inquisitive beings who inhabited the remote canyons and rocky outcroppings of Ansion. They preferred to remain isolated from their nomadic cousins, the Alwari, whom they hated.

**Gxin, Arth** Haughty in demeanor but also a superb atmospheric pilot, he served under Grand Admiral Pellaeon aboard the *Right to Rule* during the Yuuzhan Vong invasion. Arth Gxin volunteered to accompany Jagged Fel in escorting Tahiri Veila and the *Collaborator* down to the surface of Esfandia, as part of a mission to trick Yuuzhan Vong Commander B'shith Vorrik into following the craft to the surface.

**Gyad, Athadar** One of the many Inquisitors who worked for the Reconstruction Authority during the years following the Yuuzhan Vong invasion, she maintained the appearance and demeanor of a retired military officer although she'd never served.

**Gymsnor-3** A model of CorelliSpace freighter, it replaced the obsolete Gymsor-2 about 20 years before the Battle of Endor. It was a long, segmented craft, measuring 34.1 meters long and capable of transporting up to 95 metric tons of cargo. The Gymnsor-3 was armed with a turret-mounted laser cannon and required only a single pilot to operate. It was designed to compete with Corellian Engineering Corporation's freighters. CorelliSpace also made a Gymsor-4, which resembled a flying wing.

**Gyndine** An Imperial territorial administrative world, it had jurisdiction over the nearby Circarpous system. It was ruled by the obese Imperial Governor Bin Essada at the height of the New Order. During an Imperial mutiny six years after the Battle of Endor, Gyndine protected itself by becoming a fortress world, guarded by planetary shields and a fleet of 30 defensive ships. Later, Gyndine joined the New Republic and agreed to set up an enclave for refugees fleeing the Yuuzhan Vong invasion. However, shortly after the invaders attacked Ord Mantell, they targeted Gyndine. Waves of refugees tried to get off the planet, but the attacking Yuuzhan Vong destroyed New Republic rescue ships and forced huge numbers of refugees to be left behind. The aliens took their time in rendering Gyndine unsuitable for habitation. The planet eventually was liberated by a band of soldiers wearing Mandalorian armor. It was believed that their leader was none other than Boba Fett. Gyndine remained a barren world for several years, and the planet was largely abandoned. Luke Skywalker and the new Jedi Order used the planet as a rendezvous point on their mission to destroy Centerpoint Station and rescue Allana, the daughter of the Hapan Queen Mother Tenel Ka.

**gyro-balance circuitry** A specialized system, it gave machines three-dimensional direction-sensing capabilities. The devices were found in vehicles and droids, helping the machines achieve stability in all three planes whether at rest or in motion.

**gyrocomputer** A starship positioning system, it sensed a vessel's location by monitoring a planet's magnetic fields and using gyroscopic technologies to pinpoint the ship's position in three dimensions.

**gyro-grappler** An ancient device designed by the Old Republic Army, it was an aid in scaling walls or sheer rock faces.

**gyro-stabilizer** This starship component monitored the pitch and yaw to help modify a ship's artificial gravity and keep its contents upright.

**Gysk** A Nikto captured aboard a Separatist freighter in the Tynnan sector by Omega Squad about a year after the Battle of Geonosis, he and his two comrades carried identification that described them as miners. Their actual mission was transporting explosives for the Separatists. During their capture, they sealed off the bridge of their Gizer L-6 freighter and vented the rest of the ship to space. The Omega commandos eventually gained access to the cockpit, but were forced to bide their time until a Red Zero rescue operation could recover them. Gysk was later interrogated in connection with the terrorist bombings of military depots on Coruscant.

**Gyuel** A massive blue star, it was the central body of the Gyuel system, which was located in the Unknown Regions of the galaxy.

**Gzin** A four-armed humanoid, he served as master at the Golden Nyss Shipyards just before the orbital station was destroyed by the Yinchorri shortly before the Battle of Naboo.

# THE COMPLETE STAR WARS ENCYCLOPEDIA

# THE COMPLETE STAR WARS ENCYCLOPEDIA

Stephen J. Sansweet
& Pablo Hidalgo
and
Bob Vitas & Daniel Wallace
with
Chris Cassidy,
Mary Franklin & Josh Kushins

H–O
Volume II

Ballantine Books ▪ New York

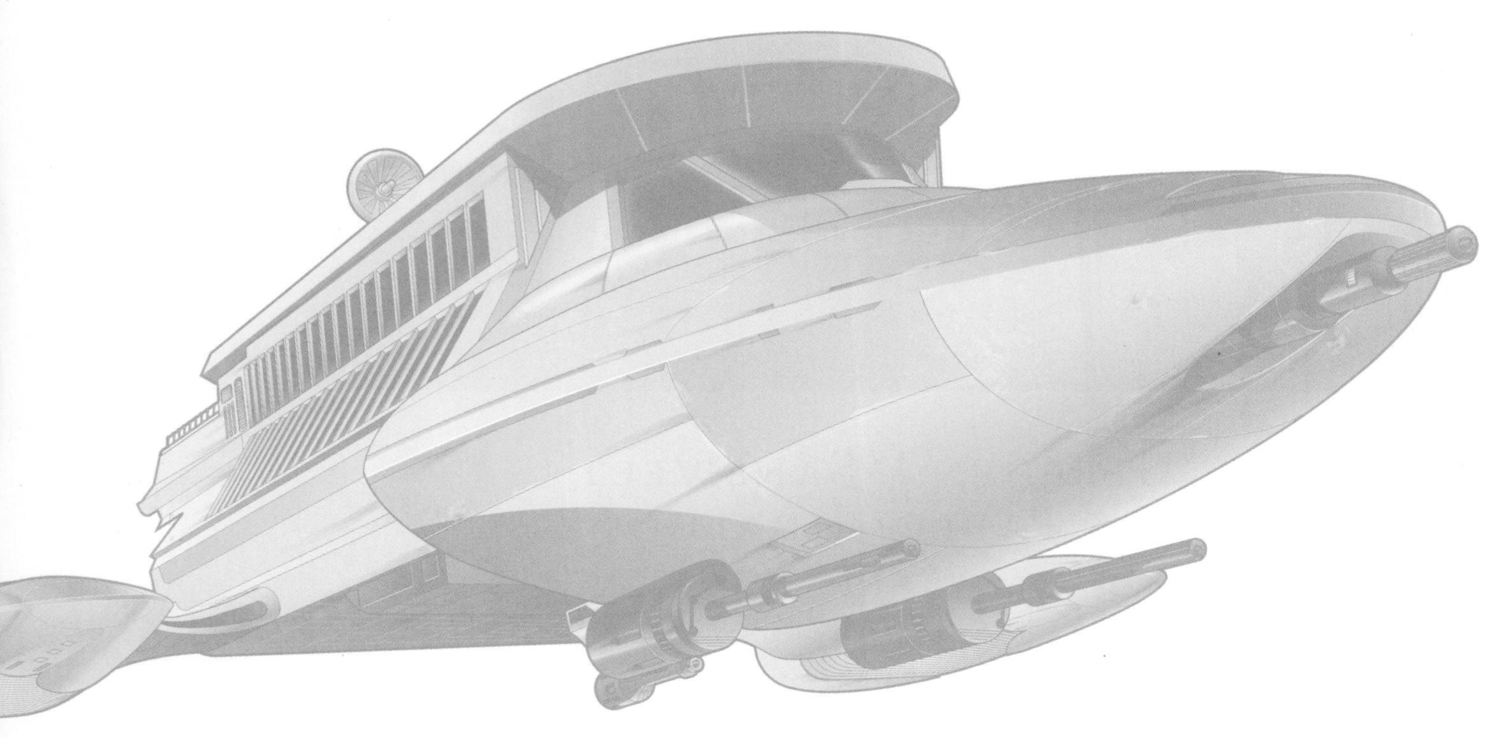



Published in the United States by Del Rey, an imprint of The Random House Publishing Group, a division of Random House, Inc., New York.

Del Rey is a registered trademark and the Del Rey colophon is a trademark of Random House, Inc.

ISBN 978-0-345-47763-7

Printed in China

www.starwars.com
www.delreybooks.com

9 8 7 6 5

Interior design by Michaelis/Carpelis Design Associates, Inc.

*The Force is what gives a Jedi his power. It's an energy field created by all living things.*

*It surrounds us and penetrates us. It binds the galaxy together.*

*The Force will be with you . . . always.*

—*Obi-Wan "Ben" Kenobi*

THE COMPLETE

STAR WARS

ENCYCLOPEDIA

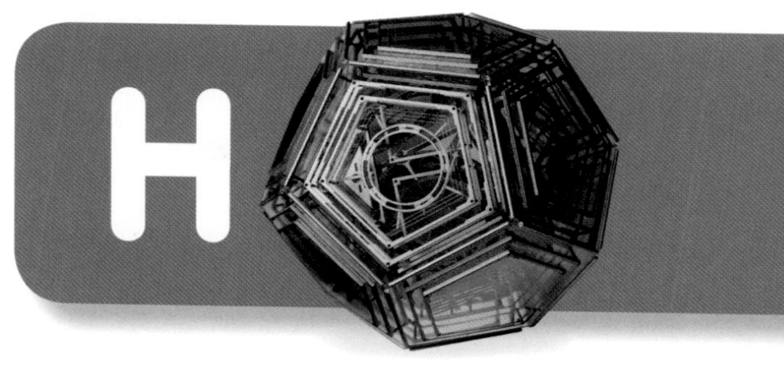


**H-10** One of several models of Sienar troop transports used by the Empire before the advent of the *Lambda*-class shuttle. The H-10 later found a new home among smugglers and backrocket planetary governments.

**H-12 Copter** A six-occupant copter produced many centuries before the Clone Wars by Lorrad Flightworks. Many survived until the Galactic Civil War and were used as taxis and simple transports on worlds such as Desevro. At 6 meters long, the H-12 Copter required one pilot. In addition to passengers, it could carry up to 100 kilograms of cargo and be armed with a pair of blaster cannons for protection.

**H1.5** A Class 1 hyperdrive unit produced by Corellian Engineering Corporation in the years following the Battle of Naboo.

**H2-1** A Corellian Engineering Corporation's hyperdrive system. Prince Xizor had one installed on the *Stinger*.

**H-3PO** A group of protocol droids owned by Popara the Hutt. The droids shared information updates on a regular basis. They differed from other 3PO series protocol droids in that their access systems were programmed to accept verbal signals from specific individuals. They also had enhanced sensors and communications systems, and often were created with self-destruct mechanisms. Among them were:

- **H-3POA:** A jade-colored droid, it was assigned to Vago, Popara's chief aide, for use in negotiations and other meetings. Vago understood and spoke both Huttese and Basic, but used H-3POA in all other situations.

- **H-3POB:** A green droid, it served aboard Popara's personal starship, the *Imru Ootmian*. After the rescue of Mika the Hutt from Endregaad, H-3POB returned to Nar Shaddaa with Vago, Popara's chief aide. Later Mika engineered a phony plot to have himself assassinated, with the victim being H-3POB. The droid was nearly destroyed by blaster fire, but its parts were recovered for later repair.

< *Reclusive Jedi Master Sharad Hett*

**H4** A starship laser cannon made by Taim & Bak and used on stock YT-1300 freighters.

**H449-B7** A stormtrooper of the Imperial Remnant who was among a group dispatched to the Nickel One asteroid in the wake of the Second Battle of Fondor; the team's job was to secure the asteroid and keep it under Imperial control. Trooper H449-B7 was killed when Jaina Solo infiltrated the Nickel One facilities during her search for her brother Jacen, who had become Darth Caedus.

**H4-5D** A heavy labor droid, it was modified by X0-X1 to disrupt a meeting between Dr. Vreen and Lira Wessex at the Royal Casino shortly before the Battle of Hoth. H4-5D eventually was immobilized by Rebel Alliance agents on Cloud City.

**H4b** A sedative developed during the era of the New Order, it found a market after the flow of spice was limited by the Imperial occupation of Kessel. Many drug addicts turned to such medicines to feed their habits.

**H6** A Taim & Bak turbolaser, it was used on the KonGar Ship Works ATR assault transport vessel.

**H-60 Tempest** This flat, wing-shaped bomber was developed during the last decades of the Old Republic.

**H9** A Taim & Bak dual turbolaser cannon, it was used on several Imperial warships, including the JV-7 *Delta*-class escort shuttle and the CR90 corvette.

**H-90** One of many sectors of Galactic City on Coruscant that experienced a sharp increase in insurgency during Thrackan Sal-Solo's bid for Corellian independence 10 years after the end of the Yuuzhan Vong War. A major incident started when Coruscant Security Forces tried to arrest residents who were painting anti–Galactic Alliance slogans on government offices; that escalated into a near riot before the Galactic Alliance Guard swooped in and arrested the primary suspects.

**H-9PO** A Duorq 79 series human–cyborg relations droid that was adopted by H'nib Statermast when its previous owner was killed in a gambling dispute outside Farrimmer Café. He was nicknamed Silverhand by Statermast, since the droid's right hand had been replaced by a silver-plated version from a newer model. The droid's primary programming had been modified to assist with gambling, and H-9PO resented being put to work as a waiter. The droid hoarded his tips in the hope of using them to go gambling himself.

**Ha, Kina** A Force-using Kaminoan, she became a student of Trandoshan rogue Jedi Master Kras'dohk. Kina Ha was born of a long-lived genetic line bred by Kaminoans specifically for deep-space explorations. Though the deep-space project never came to be, Kina's longevity saw her outlive her Master and travel for another century before she had a dream that changed her life. She had taken up temporary residence on Voruska when, in a vision, she saw a future in which millions of soldiers from Kamino were led by the dark side. Kina Ha returned to the old Slici Canyon outpost of Kamino to stand sentinel for her people.

**Haad (V-Haad)** A Hospitality Guide on Kegan, V-Haad was a tall, balding man, with warm dark eyes.

**Haako** A male Chadra-Fan who lived aboard the Wheel in the years following the Sith–Imperial War. Jor Tolin made contact with Haako seven years after the Battle of Caamas during his search for Cade Skywalker. Haako claimed to have seen Skywalker aboard the Wheel, but he left the station before Tolin arrived. Haako then used his network of informers to try to find out where Skywalker was headed.

**Haako, Rune** A cowardly Neimoidian official, Rune Haako had no shortage of misery during the Trade Federation blockade and invasion of Naboo. Haako's primary duties as a Trade Federation settlement officer were to act as a diplomatic attaché and legal counsel to Viceroy Nute Gunray. In arenas that suited his tastes—namely, executive boardrooms and business negotiations—Haako was merciless and manipulative. His eloquence often was called upon in attempts to add credibility and good faith to Trade Federation actions that were otherwise dubious. When his own life or death hinged on his decisions, however, Haako's façade crumbled to reveal his spineless nature.

Haako was privy to Gunray's plans and knew of the mysterious Sith patron who was the true mastermind behind their bold maneuvers. Haako, when beyond Sith earshot, openly questioned Gunray's judgment in striking the terrifying alliance. He predicted disaster throughout the occupation. When Queen Amidala retook her besieged capital of Theed, Haako and Gunray were captured and sent to Coruscant for trial and punishment.

The clout of the Trade Federation let Haako avoid the worst of the fallout from the Naboo debacle. He continued to serve Gunray through the Trade Federation's collusion with the Confederacy of Independent Systems. Haako was killed by Darth Sidious's new apprentice, Darth Vader, when the Sith Lords no longer had any need for their Separatist conspirators.

**Haakon, Lord** After losing a high-stakes sabacc game to the Herglic gambler Narloch, Lord Haakon claimed that the match had been rigged and refused to pay his debts. But an Imperial investigation determined that he had to pay, and he was forced to mortgage his family holdings. He later issued an anonymous bounty for Narloch, preferably alive.

**haali** A songbird native to the planet Ithor.

**Haan, Chal (Chla C'cHaan)** The founder of the Duros colony at Neimoidia, his collected writings detailed his people's fall from grace. In his "Encyclical on Historical Greatness," Chla C'cHaan called upon the Neimoidians to embrace their Duro heritage.

**Ha'andeelay, Rych** An unusual Nikto born on Nar Shaddaa, he had characteristics of two Nikto subspecies, making him an outcast from both. He eventually found work as a soldier for the Hutts.

**Haangok** A Kajain'sa'Nikto and noted pirate, he ambushed several Commerce Guild convoys during the years following the Battle of Naboo. The Commerce Guild issued a bounty for his capture, which Jango Fett claimed during his search for Jervis Gloom.

**Haariden** This planet was plunged into civil war some five years before the Battle of Naboo in what turned out to be a 10-year battle over mining rights. It finally ended after a party of Jedi Knights—including Obi-Wan Kenobi and Anakin Skywalker—was sent to rescue a group of Republic scientists. Haariden was a volcanically active world dotted with forests and small settlements. A single moon, pink in the pale twilight, orbited the planet.

**Haariden, Darra** *See* Thel-Tanis, Darra.

**haar vhinic** This Yuuzhan Vong biotechnology was used to test the truthfulness of a being's words.

**H'aas, Nab** A Bith, he represented his homeworld in the Senate of the Galactic Alliance at the height of the Confederation–GA War. H'aas was one of several Bith Senators who witnessed an argument between Mara Jade Skywalker and Jacen Solo in which Mara threatened Jacen's life if anything were to happen to her son, Ben Skywalker. Senator H'aas later provided testimony to Captain Lon Shevu of the Galactic Alliance Guard during the investigation into Mara's death.

**Haas, Veneziano** One of Nirama's main representatives during the Clone Wars, this well-dressed scoundrel was a skilled negotiator and an accomplished pilot. When the Thaereian military began blockading the Cularin system, Nirama sent Haas to look for independent spacers and mercenaries who were willing to run the blockade to deliver much-needed medical supplies and foodstuffs.

**Haashimut** An Outer Rim planet, it was the site of an ancient Jedi stronghold during the early centuries of the Old Republic. Many Jedi who were dispatched to watch over the newly annexed Tion Cluster were supplied from a base on Haashimut.

**Haash'n, Major** A Mon Calamari known for his skills as an engineer, he joined the Rebel Alliance after the Empire subjugated his homeworld. He dreamed of piloting a starship and served as an officer aboard the *Home One* during the Battle of Endor.

**Haathi, T'Charek** A young Wroonian female bored with life, she became a starfighter pilot. Hating the regimentation, she and some Wroonian squadron mates went rogue. They were decimated in a skirmish with Imperial forces, and she fled to Rodaj. After she found that life as a Rebel Alliance starfighter pilot didn't suit her, either, she finally found her niche as part of a Special Operations team, hijacking much-needed freighters and starships for the Alliance.

Rune Haako

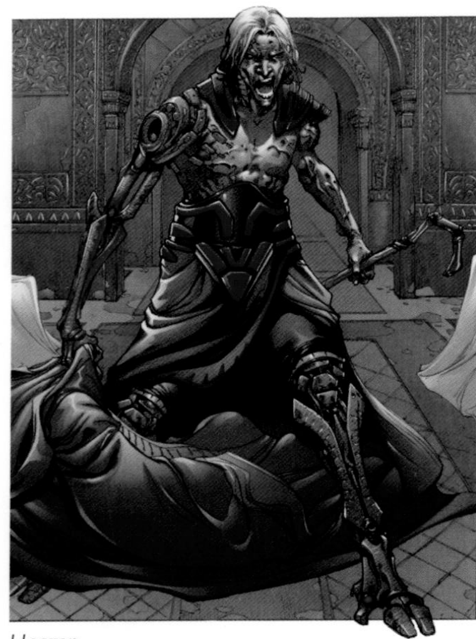

Haazen

***haa-yaah*** Derived from the ancient, pre-Corellian greeting *yaa-yaah,* this word meant "farewell" or "good-bye" to most humanoid species in the galaxy.

**Haazen** A personal aide to former Jedi Lady Krynda Draay in the years following the Great Sith War, Haazen was a onetime Jedi Padawan. He had been injured badly during fighting between the Sith and Jedi, and many of his body parts were replaced by cybernetic prostheses. Haazen became young Lucien Draay's tutor in the ways of the Force, a situation that rankled Lucien after his mother took several other students to train as seers. Haazen saw, however, that Lucien had skill with a lightsaber, and trained the boy to be a swordsman and a warrior. Lady Krynda was not pleased when Haazen convinced Jedi Master Vandar Tokare to accept Lucien into the Jedi Order, and he eventually showed some talent as a seer. Haazen received regular reports on Lucien's progress, even after he was recalled to Coruscant in the wake of the Padawan murders and Zayne Carrick's escape from Taris.

Haazen confronted Lucien about his version of the Padawan slaughter and the reasons for it, since they ran counter to Lady Krynda's own vision of the future, and ordered Lucien to find Carrick and bring him to the Draay estate. The attack on the *Courageous* at Serroco gave Lucien hope that Carrick had been killed or taken prisoner. When the banking planet Telerath was then threatened by the Mandalorian hordes, Haazen revealed to Lucien that the Draay Trust had been selling off its secret interests in the planetwide banking consortium there. He insisted that using the Jedi ability to foresee the future to gain profit was in keeping with the efforts of the Covenant—Lady Krynda's group of Jedi who could foresee the future—to defend the galaxy against the growing storm.

**haba** A group ranging from 10 to 10,000 Brubbs who lived together in communal fashion. Brubbs developed habas for everything from universities to spaceports. All children born into a haba were considered wards of the group, and every adult took responsibility for raising the young. When they were old enough to mate, the children were traded to other habas in order to maintain the integrity of the Brubb genetic pool.

**Habassa II** The homeworld of the Habassa, who were enslaved by the Empire but openly joined the Rebel Alliance following the Battle of Yavin. Imperial fighters unsuccessfully tried to thwart a transfer of B-wing fighters to the cruiser *Cathleen* near Habassa II.

**Habat, Chodo** A Force-sensitive Ithorian, he was one of the leaders of the Ithorian community on Citadel Station in orbit around the planet Telos in the years following the Jedi Civil War. Chodo Habat took in Batono after the former employee of Czerka Corporation betrayed his employer and provided information on Czerka's activities to the Telos Security Force. For his part in Batono's betrayal, Habat was targeted by Czerka for elimination, but he was rescued by the Exile before he could be executed.

**habbis** A plant whose root was eaten for food.

**Habble, Mett** One of the leaders of the Naboo resistance after the Trade Federation invasion, this lesser noble was a secret agent for Governor Sio Bibble. He often wore the uniform of the nonmilitary Security Guard to mask his activities.

***Hab Camber*** One of the many aliases used by Talon Karrde for the *Wild Karrde*, the *Hab Camber* was supposedly a starship operated by Abel Quiller out of Valrar during the early years of the New Republic.

**Habeen** One of two civilizations on Mylok IV, this species helped the Nharwaaks develop a compact hyperdrive system. When the Empire heard about the new technology, it tried to buy it for use in a class of TIE fighters. The Nharwaaks balked, but the Habeen stepped in and agreed to a sale even though they didn't approve of the Empire's politics. The Nharwaaks tried in vain to thwart the sale.

**habitat shell** Dome-shaped structures used to protect living areas in hostile environments. Once erected on a harsh planet, habitat shells could be anchored and filled with breathable atmosphere, allowing beings to survive in a new environment. Several habitat shells could be linked together by tunnels or air locks to create a small settlement.

**habuur** A crude slang term adopted by members of the Galactic Alliance Guard after Jacen Solo killed Ailyn Habuur during an interrogation session. The soldiers used the word to describe any rough or intense interrogation session that ended with the death of the interrogated being.

*Chodo Habat*

**Habuur, Ailyn** This was an alias used by Ailyn Vel when she took up a more prominent role as a bounty hunter in the years following the Yuuzhan Vong War. Working as Ailyn Habuur, she took the job of hunting down Han Solo and his wife, Leia Organa Solo, when a bounty was offered for them by Thrackan Sal-Solo. While the alias threw off most beings, her Kiffar facial scar made her recognizable to many of the galaxy's Mandalorians, who relayed information about her taking the job to her father, Boba Fett. Ailyn began her search on Coruscant, working within the Corellian community to seek out information on the whereabouts of the Solos.

Her search, however, coincided with the Galactic Alliance Guard's crackdown on Corellian terrorists, and Ailyn was captured and held for questioning before she could begin the hunt. She was interrogated by Jacen Solo, who physically beat her before using a dangerous Force technique to extract information from her mind. Unable to withstand the pressure of Jacen's assault, Ailyn died before she could reveal much information. When Leia discovered Ailyn's demise, she arranged to have Jacen transport her body to Fett. Leia hoped that Fett wouldn't learn the truth about Ailyn's death and try to exact revenge against Jacen.

**hachete** A double-edged fighting blade.

**Hachete** The Duelist Elite droid that Darth Maul once trained against, it got its name because it was armed with a pair of hachete blades. Maul destroyed it in combat shortly before he was ordered to hunt down Hath Monchar.

**Hack, Turland** A Rebel Alliance lieutenant who served at a training facility outside Mos Eisley, he was part of a group to which Rookie One belonged. Known simply as Hack to his friends, the lieutenant was unable to qualify for flight school, so he turned his efforts to communications and tactical assistance. He urged Rookie One to continue his own training, and helped tutor the young pilot during his early flights.

**Had Abbadon** Some Jedi scholars believed that this mythic "lost planet" might have been the birthplace of the Jedi Order.

**Hadar sector** A section of the galaxy that contained Turkana. It was the site of storied Rebel Alliance pilot Keyan Farlander's first mission.

**Hadiss the Vaulted** The onetime ruler of Geonosis, he preferred to solve problems with force. Rather than allow most criminals and others he despised to live even after surviving in the petranaki gladiator fights, Archduke Hadiss released hungry acklays to deal with the champions. His leadership skills were questioned by a small minority led by Poggle the Lesser. After Poggle managed to win his own way out of the gladiator arena, he received the backing of Darth Sidious and eventually was able to defeat Hadiss. In a twist of fate, Poggle attacked Hadiss while the Archduke was riding an acklay that slashed him into three pieces before devouring him.

**Hadlress Defense Systems, Limited** A security systems manufacturer once owned and operated by Jasis Temmit, it was sold for 4.6 billion credits.

**Hadocrassk** A Trandoshan Senator in the years before the Clone Wars, he was called Speaker-Above-All. Hadocrassk met with the Wookiee Senator Yarua to discuss a truce between their two peoples. The talks were mediated by Jedi Master Oppo Rancisis, who was called in after Senator Yarua ordered a blockade of Trandosha when 215 Wookiees died near one of Trandosha's moons and their bodies were not returned to Kashyyyk. The peace talks were interrupted by the start of the Clone Wars.

**Hadrassi Emergency Medical Systems Technologies** A small corporation that produced a variety of chemical synthesizers used in creating serums and anti-toxins.

**hadrium** This chrome-like alloy created during the last decades of the Old Republic was used to form blaster barrels, since it had a high melting temperature and didn't flex or warp after repeated firings.

**Haduran, Captain** An officer in the Army of Light, he fought for the Old Republic and the Jedi Knights during the Battle of Ruusan. Haduran was under the command of Jedi Master Valenthyne Farfalla after the Sith set off a thought bomb, and was ordered to search the battlefield for any survivors. Farfalla also told Haduran to euthanize any Bouncers—

round, empathic creatures—whom the troops encountered, knowing that the thought bomb would cause sentient creatures immense pain and suffering.

**HAET-221** *See* Republic assault gunboat.

**hafa** A vine native to the planet Garqi, it produced small fruits and leaves that were harvested and fermented to create Cassandran choholl.

**Haffrin** This Outer Rim world was the site of a Shrine of Kooroo.

**HAG (heavy artillery gun)** One of many repulsor-equipped heavy artillery weapons used by the Trade Federation during its invasion of Naboo.

**Haggleday** An annual Squib festival that encompassed great celebrations where bargains of all kinds were available.

**hag'thyyr** A reptilian predator native to the planet Ebra. The Rull clan's insignia portrayed a hag'thyyr engulfed in flames and wielding a spear.

**Hahrynyar** An elderly Wookiee, he was part of the slave labor pool that built the first Death Star. Hahrynyar's pelt was almost entirely gray. He was stubborn and often appeared to forget that he could understand Basic. A natural-born leader and worker, he served as a crew chief on several projects, including the installation of thermal exhaust ports near the main exhaust port in Sector N-1. He got into an argument with Teela Kaarz over the placement of secondary ports; she felt that the smaller ports should be moved, and said she would get authorization to do so. But Hahrynyar contracted an illness that left him with a ravaging cough and a high fever, and he was out of commission while the work on the secondary exhaust ports continued. Kaarz never did obtain the required authorization, and the secondary ports were installed just below the main port, something that one day would prove a fatal error.

**Hai, Korkeal** A hyperkinetic human female, she was a native of the Shesharile system, where in her youth she rebuilt a light freighter. She spent a large part of her earnings on an old computer system that had a personality with which she was continually at odds. The ship, a modified Gymsnor-3 freighter called the *Riff-Raff,* was completed just prior to the Battle of Yavin.

**Hai, Resta Shug** A grizzled X'Ting fighter, she joined the Desert Wind terrorist group to fight against the Five Families during the Clone Wars. A farmer by trade, Resta and her husband worked hard to eke out an existence in the desert near Kibo Lake. When the Five Families raised energy prices to the outlying areas—a move meant to ensure that there was enough money to beef up protection of the rulers' secure bunker—Resta and her husband were unable to survive without extra income. He went to work in the mines, but died from exhaustion. Rather than stand by and lose her farm, Resta answered the call sent out by Jedi Master Kit Fisto and ARC trooper Nate. After several weeks of training, she joined Desert Wind to strike back at the Five Families who controlled Ord Cestus. She earned the respect and gratitude of ARC trooper Jangotat after he was brought to the Zantay Hills to recover from injuries sustained during a raid on the Desert Wind encampment. When Jangotat launched a desperate mission to root out the Five Families from their secret bunker, Resta refused to remain behind, even though Jangotat had given her the A-98 Tac Code 12 phrase to receive compensation from the Republic. Jangotat then incapacitated her in a swift sleeper hold, rendering Resta unconscious before she could protest.

**Haik Expedition** This group of interplanetary explorers set out to find a reliable hyperspace lane between the Enarc Run and the Harrin Trade Corridor during the early years of the Old Republic's Expansionist Period. They found the Kira system, located between the Lazerian and Ropagi systems, and used it as a reference point and hyperspace anchor for their route, the Kira Run.

**Hailbrock, Jan** A supplier of exotic weapons, Hailbrock was known for his ability to obtain illegal arms for elite members of Propopian society. His employers often used their clout to encourage customs officials to look the other way when he was detained. Hailbrock also was a strong, if secret, supporter of the Rebel Alliance, and did his best to supply local cells with weapons and armor.

**Hailey, Serra** A holovid star of the Old Republic, she attempted to reinvigorate her career during the Galactic Civil War. Many of her fans continued to be enchanted by her performances.

***Hailfire*-class droid** A self-aware mobile missile platform used exclusively by the InterGalactic Banking Clan, the *Hailfire*-class droid tank was the most powerful of its armed-response units. Hailfire droids delivered surface-to-surface and surface-to-air strikes with their stacked banks of 30 rocket warheads. Hailfires, officially known as IG-227s, rolled along on hoop-like wheels standing 8.5 meters tall. In between the bracketing axle arms was a small, central body equipped with a single photoreceptor. When the IBC pledged its forces to the Confederacy of Independent Systems, Hailfire droids were added to the immense Separatist battle droid army.

In peacetime, tardy customers and unstable investors had reason to fear late payments or forfeits on loans to the Banking Clan, since its euphemistically named Collections and Security Division boasted thousands of the Hailfires, which were developed by Haor Chall Engineering. Their sequenced magpulse drives that lined the circumference of their hoop wheels pushed the droids along at impressive speeds approaching 45 kilometers an hour, and the missile launcher pods gave them a very long reach. With the end of the Clone Wars, Darth Sidious ordered that all Hailfire droids be deactivated as part of his plan to consolidate military power and ensure the loyalty of his troops.

**haillu** A Gungan term used to describe the long earlobes that hung down from the back of a Gungan's head. They were used in displays of aggression, fright, or friendship. Members of the Otolla Gungan subspecies had very large haillu, whereas the Ankura had much smaller ones.

**Haime, Josek** A Bakuran Senator representing Gesco City in his home planet's legis-

Hailfire-*class droid*

lature, Haime was chosen to represent Bakura in the Alliance of Free Planets following the Battle of Bakura.

**hairy savage** The name given to a species of anthropoids native to Kuras III. These hulking predators were foul-tempered primitives who attacked anything they saw.

**Haj** An elderly man who founded Haj Shipping Lines. He was outwardly loyal to the Empire during the Galactic Civil War, but allowed Rebel Alliance agents aboard his luxury starliners as long as they paid the fare.

***Hajen*-class fleet tender** A starship used extensively by the New Republic Navy, it played a major role in supplying the battle fleet. At 375 meters long, it was based on the *Sacheen*-class escort ship. These huge, unarmed vessels required a crew of only six, with a large droid pool to perform menial tasks. They could carry up to six passengers along with 300,000 metric tons of supplies, and were equipped with a Class 1 hyperdrive and quick sublight engines.

**Hajial Chase** A primordial forest on the planet New Plympto, it was about 400 kilometers inland from the city of Phemiss. Situated atop a rocky escarpment, Hajial Chase was the home of some of the world's oldest and tallest hiakk trees.

**Hajj** The captain of the *Star of Empire*, he wasn't happy that his ship was the first to undergo installation of a new Systems Integration Manager. He was furious when the *Star* suddenly experienced an engine reactor breach and he had to evacuate his passengers. Then, after the ship's computer declared the emergency under control, crew members started being killed. Hajj himself was attacked by crab-like maintenance droids, lost his grip on a cable, and plunged to his death.

**Hak, Raad** A Mon Calamari major in the Rebel Alliance, he was chief deck officer at Oracle Base. Despite the Alliance's use of smugglers and other fringe elements, Hak disliked them and treated them with the minimum of decorum.

**Hakartha Station** This space station was under Imperial control during the Galactic Civil War.

**Hakassi** This planet was the site of New Republic shipyards. The *Intrepid* was completed and delivered from the yards just before the onset of the Black Fleet crisis and the New Republic's conflict with Nil Spaar and the Yevetha, 12 years after the Battle of Endor.

**Hakin** A native of Alderaan, this former skiff racer joined the Rebel Alliance shortly before the Battle of Yavin. Hakin was serving aboard the *Tantive IV* when it was captured by Darth Vader and the *Devastator*.

*Leor Hal*

**Hakoon, Schnil** A Kubaz crime lord who rose to power in the city of Kinkosa, he used the Ebon Coursers as his personal band of mercenaries. Hakoon originally left his homeworld of Kubindi for Kirtania after hearing that Kirtania's biosphere was teeming with insects. He then turned to criminal activity to fund his schemes for cornering the market on insect farming.

**Haku** An Imperial recruit, he was part of Kyle Katarn's squadron during the taking of asteroid AX-456. He and Morley served as the team's demolitions experts.

**Hal, Garthus** A freelance mercenary, he was hired by Imperial Moff Graffe shortly after the Battle of Yavin to stir up anti–Rebel Alliance feelings among the population of Esseles. Hal and his crew carried out a number of bombings and assassinations in the name of the Alliance.

**Hal, Leor** A strong and powerful student of the Jedi arts, he embraced the theory of the Potentium and began guiding other Jedi students along its pathways. Many regarded him as an idealist, until his beliefs started to interfere with his Jedi training. When the Jedi Masters dismissed all the followers of the Potentium nearly 100 years before the Battle of Naboo, Leor Hal discovered Zonama Sekot. He recruited a group of Ferroans and a group of Langhesi to help him establish a new civilization on the planet, and he eventually came to know the being Sekot. Hal established a symbiotic relationship with Sekot, and helped turn the planet into a huge, organic factory.

Much of the Zonama philosophy and leadership came from Hal's own experiences. The plan to create Sekotan starships and sell them to the greater galaxy was Hal's, designed to raise enough money to finance the huge hyperdrive cores that were woven into the tampasi and used to launch the planet into hyperspace years later when it came under attack by Wilhuff Tarkin. After Hal's death, the Zonama populace considered his name to be sacred, and forbade anyone from saying it out loud. Sekot used a holographic representation of Hal to maintain the status quo on Zonama Sekot, until his withered body was discovered by Anakin Skywalker and his Sekotan starship, *Jabitha,* during their escape from Tarkin's attack.

**Hal, Tanis** This woman worked as Hamnet's secretary during the early years of the Galactic Civil War. Although she was well paid, Tanis often felt overwhelmed with her duties, which included keeping up with the often infuriating demands of Hamnet's daughter, Icomia.

**Hala** A slave owned by Yor Millto and mother of young Anakin Skywalker's friend Amee, she was captured in a raid by Krayn two years before the Battle of Naboo and never seen again. Skywalker later discovered that Krayn had put her to death to "set an example" for the other slaves after she struck out at him in anger. After killing Hala, Krayn ripped off the small bell she wore around her neck and added it to the "kill trophies" hanging on his utility belt.

**Halabar** A firm but gentle Mon Calamari professor respected on his homeworld, he was captured and taken as a "pet" during the early stages of the Empire's occupation of his planet. On Coruscant, he lived in the household of a minor Imperial official, but soon escaped in a smuggler's ship. Halabar hid in the Outer Rim and established a small tapcaf while helping out the local educational system.

**Halanit** A frozen, ice-covered moon orbiting a gas giant planet, it was the site of a small colony of about 10,000 inhabitants. Geothermal heat lessened the subzero temperatures somewhat and created bubbling mineral springs. The colony was founded during the last days of the Old Republic. Structures were built into the two facing walls of a huge chasm, which was capped by a double layer of transparisteel and filled with steaming water at the bottom, fed by several waterfalls. The water at the base supported fish farms. Bridges connected the two sides. After the members of Rogue Squadron resigned from the New Republic military, Rogues Corran Horn and Ooryl Qrygg brought a hijacked Thyferran bacta convoy to Halanit, which was suffering from a mysterious virus and had sent a distress call to the New Republic. Former Director of Imperial Intelligence Ysanne Isard then sent the *Corrupter* and the Thyferran Home Defense Corps to destroy the colony. TIE bombers breached the transparisteel canopy and made strafing runs through the canyon. Rogue Gavin Darklighter had been resting at the colony and unsuccessfully tried to defend it. Everyone else in the colony was believed killed.

**Halbara** The primary world in the Halbara system, located in the Elrood sector, it was owned and operated by Radell Mining. The majority of the planet was covered with tropical rain forests, but it was also ravaged by monsoons most of the year. Mining was difficult, though Radell found the rewards worth it. Halbara One was the planet's capital city.

**Halbard** A native of Chandrila, he was a noted Mid Rim shipping magistrate during the Galactic Civil War.

**Halbeet, Jujiran** This Givin maintenance worker was part of a team that serviced the Yag'Dhul ambassadorial landing platform on Coruscant before the Clone Wars. It was Halbeet who first discovered the treachery of his co-worker Gavrilonnis Tejere. When Halbeet approached him, Tejere shot Halbeet, who fell off the edge of the platform. Luckily, Mace Windu and Yoda were returning from a meeting, and were able to catch him in midair.

**Halbegardia** One of the larger nations on Adumar. The Halbegardians joined the Yedagonian Confederacy in opposing Cartann's perator, Pekaelic ke Teldan, in his bid to rule Adumar's world government.

***Halberd* (1)** This Imperial escort carrier was part of a small fleet dispatched to inspect and protect various communications arrays during the Galactic Civil War.

***Halberd* (2)** A Ripoblus assault transport used during the Sepan Civil War, it also was used in battle against the Empire.

**Halbert, Elias** Generally regarded as a drunkard and a liar, this immense Corellian man was a smuggler. His early career was successful, but after he started losing ships and crews, he became a liability. Shortly after the Battle of Yavin, he caught the attention of Abdi-Badawzi, a Twi'lek who believed that Halbert retained a spark of potential. Halbert began making a concerted effort to clean up his act and struggled to stay sober while Abdi-Badawzi began funneling jobs his way.

**Halbret** An ancient human female Jedi from Coruscant, she was found in suspended animation on Kathol at the Shrine of the Sleeper by the crew of the *FarStar*. They were able to reanimate her and heard her story about surviving the millennia-old Kathol Rift Disaster. After awakening, Halbret released the ancient Kathol from the Lifewell and assisted the *FarStar* crew in defeating DarkStryder's minions. During the struggle, though, Halbret realized that her descendant Jessa Dajus was unable to defeat the creatures she was fighting. Halbret threw herself in front of a killing blow, sacrificing herself to save Jessa, and she became one with the Force.

**Halcyon** This was one of the most powerful starship booster systems produced by Qualdex at the height of the New Order.

**Halcyon, Keiran (1)** A Corellian Jedi Knight, he was responsible for eliminating the Afarathu sect some 400 years before the Battle of Endor. Keiran Halcyon was an ancestor of Nejaa Halcyon.

*Keiran Halcyon*

**Halcyon, Keiran (2)** Corran Horn used the alias of Kieran Halcyon during his Jedi training and his search for Mirax Terrik, shortly after the death of Grand Admiral Thrawn.

**Halcyon, Nejaa** A Corellian Jedi Master, he was Valin Horn's father and good friends with Rostek Horn. Nejaa Halcyon was one of a handful of Jedi who broke the Jedi Code prohibition on marriage, having taken vows with his wife, Scerra. The birth of Valin was a precious event, but one he worked hard to keep secret from the Jedi Order. Nejaa believed, however, that Master Yoda had some idea of his family's existence.

Shortly before the Battle of Geonosis, Halcyon led a team of Jedi assigned to locate and recapture the *Scarlet Thranta* after the ship's captain and crew defected from the Old Republic. Halcyon managed to intercept Zozridor Slayke and his crew on Bpfassh, but was tricked by the rogue captain. While Zozridor sent one of his lieutenants—a Rodian named Grudo—to challenge Halcyon to a fight, Zozridor stole Halcyon's own ship, the *Plooriod Bodkin,* and then fled, leaving Halcyon and his team without their quarry and without their starship. The Jedi Council removed Halcyon from command, but gave him a chance to redeem himself.

Two years after the start of the Clone Wars, the Intergalactic Communications Center on Praesitlyn was captured by Separatist forces led by Pors Tonith. Halcyon was paired with Jedi Padawan Anakin Skywalker to retake it, and was shocked to learn that Zozridor Slayke was already on Praesitlyn, putting up as much resistance as he could. Upon reaching the planet, Halcyon was forced to put his pride aside and work together with Slayke and Skywalker to create a battle plan. After Pors Tonith was captured and the hostages at the communications center were freed, Halcyon was able to return to Coruscant with good news and was reinstated as a commander.

After Halcyon died on a mission to locate Nikkos Tyris on Susevfi, Rostek Horn cared for his family, eventually falling in love with, and marrying, Halcyon's widow Scerra. He also adopted Nejaa's 10-year-old son Valin, but nicknamed him Hal, in honor of his father and to cover up his relationship to the Jedi. Nejaa had given Rostek a Jedi Credit medallion, which Rostek passed on to Hal, who in turn passed it to his son, Corran Horn. Corran discovered the existence of Nejaa during his escape from the *Lusankya* when he stumbled upon a buried Jedi museum near the Galactic Museum. Corran also discovered Nejaa's lightsaber, which he used in his escape. Nejaa's true relationship to Corran was revealed by Luke Skywalker shortly after Tycho Celchu was released from prison.

**Halcyon, Scerra** This woman was Nejaa Halcyon's wife and a childhood friend of Rostek Horn. After Nejaa's death during the Clone Wars, Horn married Scerra and adopted her son, Valin. Valin later took the name Hal Horn to avoid being caught up in Emperor Palpatine's Jedi Purge.

**Halcyon, Valin** This was Hal Horn's given name, since he was actually the son of the Jedi Master Nejaa Halcyon and his wife, Scerra.

**Halcyon Endures** This was the pass code used by Corran Horn to secure the hidden rooms of his Jedi training facility in Coronet on Corellia. Horn was forced to live in the rooms after Thrackan Sal-Solo tried to withdraw the Corellian system from the Galactic Alliance. Sal-Solo decreed that Jedi were his enemies. Mirax Terrik Horn was placed under house arrest for being Corran's wife.

**Haldeen** One of the primary worlds of Haldeen sector. Justice Action Network terrorist Earnst Kamiel was extradited to Haldeen after being captured on Elrood.

**Haldeen sector** This area of the galaxy was once part of the empire controlled by Xim the Despot. When the boundaries of the sector were defined by the Old Republic, it contained the planets Haldeen and Argai.

**Haleoda** The primary city on the planet Kattada, it was a haven for smugglers during the New Order.

***Hale Return*** This Imperial medical platform was stationed near the planet Borosk during the Yuuzhan Vong War.

**Haley, Kylaena** A female member of the Sith Shadows, she worked on Dathomir during the Galactic Civil War.

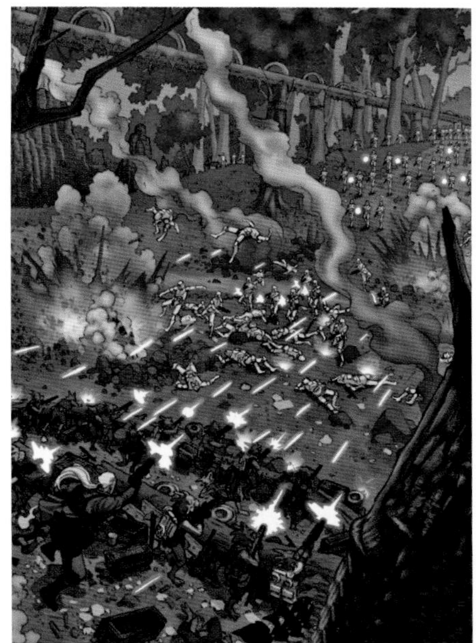

*Half-Axe Pass*

**Half-Axe Pass** This rocky gap between two low mountains on the planet New Plympto was the site of an intense battle between clone troopers of the Grand Army of the Republic and the Separatist-leaning Nosaurians. After a massive assault, the Nosaurian forces at Half-Axe Pass were wiped out. It was believed that Bomo Greenbark and the former Jedi Knight Dass Jennir were the only survivors.

**Halfback's Bluff** A popular game among casual gamblers on the planet Pantolomin, it involved betting on which particular halfback creature would retrieve a shiny object thrown into the shallow waters near a casino or ship. If the creatures wrestled among themselves for more than 10 minutes without any one of them taking the trinket, all bets were collected by the house. After the game's popularity became apparent, many unscrupulous casinos and criminal organizations began rigging the toss, ensuring that the halfbacks never found the submerged objects.

**Hali** This temperate world orbited three suns, and was in turn orbited by a handful of moons.

**Halion, Rana** A charismatic political figure on her homeworld of Ieria, she fought to get better trade routes and more recognition for her planet. She believed Ieria was relegated to lesser status by the central government on Andara, and argued that Ieria deserved its own seat in the Galactic Senate. Behind the scenes, Halion hired a band of student mercenaries to cause disruptions that helped rally people to her cause. She didn't realize that the group was led by the son of Andaran Senator Berm Tarturi. She asked them to strafe an Andaran military landing platform to bring Andara to the negotiating table. But she didn't know that Gillam Tarturi planned to use live fire in the mission as a way to have himself "killed." His plan was to actually kill Anakin Skywalker and damage the Jedi's body enough so that it could pass for Gillam.

**Halkans, Minister** A wealthy smelter of carbonite and a minister in the Empress Teta system some 4,000 years before the Galactic Civil War, he was the last to be executed by a small band of dark siders who overthrew the government. Minister Halkans suffered the double indignity of being beheaded and then having his head served to the Krath on a silver dinner platter.

**halkra** An arboreal predator native to the forests of Bothawui, it was also known as the strangle vine. The creatures appeared to be a tangled mass of vines and plant material, with a main body sac covered with cracked, bark-like skin. Lichens and small seeds grew on their skin, further camouflaging them. Each halkra had 12 tentacles that it could sprout from its sides to tangle its prey and constrict it, then draw it into its central sac for digestion. Halkras often settled near watering holes and other locations where wildlife gathered, hanging from low tree branches and acting like a part of the forest.

*Halla*

**Hall, the (1)** This long gallery was located in the center of the Great Pyramid on Rafa V, and contained a number of exhibits that depicted the history of the planet and its primary inhabitants, the Sharu and the Toka. The beings who became the Bearer and the Emissary were required, upon entering the hall, to view each exhibit in turn before approaching the gallery's most valuable exhibit, the Mindharp. If the Bearer and the Emissary tried to bypass this step, the computer system that controlled the hall would activate and direct them to the exhibits. In this way, the hall could interact with the Bearer and the Emissary, and provide them with any additional information they might need to understand the Mindharp and its purpose. The hall could not, however, explain how an individual could obtain the Mindharp, which appeared atop a 12-meter-tall life-crystal. The Bearer and Emissary were required to figure out that puzzle on their own. After Lando Calrissian, Vuffi Raa, and Mohs entered the Great Pyramid and acquired the Mindharp, they were astounded to learn upon leaving that they had spent nearly four months inside the structure, interacting with the hall and its exhibits.

*Minister Halkans*

**Hall, the (2)** This was the name given to both the administrative headquarters of the planet Esseles and its primary governmental body. Both were located in the capital city of Calamar.

**Hall, Captain** A muscular woman, she was an officer in the Imperial military and served as Governor Shran Etison's personal aide during the New Order.

**Halla** An eccentric old female native of Circarpous V (Mimban), she seemed to be sensitive to the Force, and claimed to be a master of it. She gave Luke Skywalker a shard of the Kaiburr crystal when they first met, and later helped Luke and Leia Organa escape from Captain-Supervisor Grammel's prison. She then convinced them to help her find the crystal. Once they located it and defeated Darth Vader, Halla admitted that she was a charlatan and gave the crystal to Luke.

**Halla sector** This area of the galaxy was located in the Mid Rim and contained the planet Bimmisaari.

**hall d'main** Beldorion the Hutt's second Kubaz chef discovered that the excretions of this unusual creature complemented gletmites' teleological systems perfectly, causing them to grow to unusual proportions.

**Halle** An Acherin woman married to Alder, she and her husband greeted Clive Flax when he arrived on the planet following the Clone Wars to investigate the background of the freedom fighter known as Flame. Flax gained their confidence when he said that he was looking for Alder's sister, Vira, who had died in the fighting that engulfed the planet's population. Halle told Flax what she knew of Flame, whom she believed had grown up in the city of Sood.

***Halleck*** An Old Republic cruiser, it was first stationed in the Ventran system during the Clone Wars and later dispatched to insert and extract Jedi Master Mace Windu from Haruun Kal during his mission to rescue Depa Billaba. The *Halleck* was ambushed by Separatist warships that had been waiting in the Gevarno Cluster. Many of its landers were shot down immediately, and the ship itself was later destroyed in the ambush.

**Halley** An officer of the watch, he was aboard the *FarStar* during the New Republic's search for Imperial Moff Kentor Sarne.

**Halleycraft** A small corporation, it produced a number of surface and underwater transportation devices.

**Halliikeenovich, Són** A regular patron of the Galaxies Opera House during the final years of the Old Republic, he was a lesser nobleman from the Juvex sector. Halliikeenovich tried to establish a stronger connection to the families of the Senex sector by courting Senator Terr Taneel.

**hallmark number** A specific, four-digit number, it identified different types of droids. According to the hallmark numbering system, only those droids in the 0500 through 0999 classes were capable of communication with organic beings.

**Hall of Confluence** This immense edifice was created by the Yuuzhan Vong within the yorik coral confines of the Citadel on Coruscant after the aliens started transforming the planet into a reconstruction of Yuuzhan'tar. It was here that Supreme Overlord Shimrra addressed the assembled masses. The hall comprised the immense body and skeleton of a Vongformed creature.

**Hall of Contests** A room on the Charon starship *Desolate,* it was an eight-chambered cave. Various Charon bioconstructs were placed in the chambers, ready to attack any alien life-forms. The Charon used the hall to gauge the ferocity and resourcefulness of life-forms they planned to annihilate.

**Hall of Edification** An ancient building on the planet Nazzri, it contained all the histories of the Nazzar people.

**Hall of Evidence** Large mausoleums maintained by both the Daan and the Melida deep in the city of Zehava, they were constant reminders of the heroes who had fought valiantly during their civil war. Ornamental tombstones contained projectors that displayed holograms of the deceased and gave a short history of their own struggles with the enemy.

**Hall of Heroes (1)** Located in the city of Orotoru G'am, this Mon Calamari museum displayed information and artifacts about the greatest of Mon Calamari and Quarren individuals of the Old Republic.

**Hall of Heroes (2)** This underground hall was carved by the X'Ting beneath the surface of their homeworld of Ord Cestus to honor ancient X'Ting who had contributed to their history. The most notable were the warriors who had helped the X'Ting defeat the Spider People. The Hall of Heroes also served as the primary entrance to a labyrinth of security systems that protected the royal eggs of the X'Ting during the last decades of the Old Republic. Any X'Ting who wished to locate the eggs had to find the correct entry point into the hall.

After the Great Plague, one group of X'Ting chose to establish its own hive in the Hall of Heroes, but the members were exterminated when they awakened the carnivorous worms that served as a backup security measure. The worms destroyed the X'Ting hive, thereby eliminating the last traces of information about the remaining security systems. During the Clone Wars, Obi-Wan Kenobi and his X'Ting guide, Jesson Di Blinth, learned that the correct entrance went through the largest of the hall's statues, although both were startled to learn that the statue didn't depict an X'Ting. Obi-Wan had heard from G'Mai Duris that a Jedi Knight had visited the X'Ting some 150 years earlier, a story that Jesson refused to believe. However, the statue turned out to be a huge representation of Jedi Master Yoda.

**Hall of Judgment** This was one of many grand chambers constructed by the Rebel Alliance within the Great Temple on Yavin 4, as part of the Massassi Base complex.

**Hall of Knighthood** Located in the second highest level of the Temple Spire within the Jedi Temple on Coruscant, the Hall of Knighthood was the setting for ceremonies in which Padawans were promoted to the level of Jedi Knight. The elevation of a Jedi Knight to Jedi Master also occurred here.

**Hall of Knowledge** Part of the ancient Jedi library complex on Ossus, the Hall of Knowledge contained hundreds of thousands of datacards and ancient tomes, holding information as basic as Old Republic planet logs and as rare as the oldest recorded Jedi texts.

**Hall of Masters** This long, ornate hall was located in the Fountain Palace of Hapes. It was lined with luxurious qashmel carpeting, and the walls were covered with some of the Hapes Consortium's most valuable artwork. Several corridors led off to other displays, while alabas staircases at each end of the hall led up to the main residence areas.

**Hall of Ministers** One of the primary governmental buildings in the capital city of Sath on the planet Samaria. The main atrium was 50 stories tall, and was tiled with blue stones that mirrored the waters of the artificial bay surrounding Sath. A private landing area was provided for legislators on the top floor. In the months following the Clone Wars, the reception areas of the Hall of Ministers were made ready for a visit from Emperor Palpatine as part of Bog Divinian's attempt to become the planet's leader.

*Són Halliikeenovich*

**Hall of Peace** This open chamber was located in the new Jedi Temple on Coruscant, which was built in the wake of the Yuuzhan Vong War. The Hall of Peace was the site of many banquets and large gatherings, including the dinner that was served after the funeral of Mara Jade Skywalker.

**Hall of Perri-Teeka** This building, located in the city of Theed, was built as a monument to a legendary Naboo statesman.

**Hall of Reflections** A chamber of enhanced mirrors in Hologram Fun World. The original hall had several mirrored sections that modified the reflected images of viewers to give them various appearances and personalities. After Borborygmus Gog began working on his Nightmare Machine, the hall was modified to project three-dimensional holograms of a viewer.

**Hall of Satabs** Located deep in the royal palace in Goyoikin on the planet Ventooine, this chamber was created to hold the dead Satabs of the planet in suspended animation until a cure for the Shadeshine's power could be discovered.

**Hall of the Wind Crystals** One of the many luxurious and ornate hallways in the Fountain Palace on Hapes. A wind-crystal chandelier as large as an A-wing starfighter hung from the ceiling.

**Hallomar** A large, former big-game hunter, he became known as the "governor" of the smuggling outpost located on the planet Port Haven. His skills as a hunter kept the modrols and other vicious creatures at bay, and his physical presence helped maintain peace. Hallomar kept the outpost running by selling skins and pelts. He worked hard to keep the planet's location a secret, and was ruthless enough to eliminate a smuggler who even thought of selling the information to the Empire or a bounty hunter.

**hallowed center** One of the many honorifics used by the Yuuzhan Vong to describe the planet Coruscant after it had been captured from the New Republic and terraformed into a simulacrum of long-lost Yuuzhan'tar.

**Hallrin IV** This planet was the site of the Stratis Games, an athletic competition.

**Halls of Knowledge** This ancient storehouse on the planet Phateem was one of many such buildings created by the Jedi Knights as a repository of information.

**hall sweeper** A blaster carbine, it was manufactured to the specifications of the Blackscales during the Galactic Civil War era.

**Hallu sector** An undistinguished area of the Mid Rim.

**Halm** An employee of Talon Karrde, he was part of the team Karrde assembled to rescue the students at the Jedi praxeum on Yavin 4 during the Yuuzhan Vong War. Halm was shot and killed during the initial attempt to reach the students, shortly after the Peace Brigade blockaded the Yavin system.

**Halmad** A planet in the Outer Rim Territories, it was just outside the area controlled by Warlord Zsinj during the early years of the New Republic. Halmad, its three moons, and several nearby asteroids had a number of mining colonies that were abandoned when ore ran out about 100 years before the Battle of Endor. The planet retained its importance because it was at the nexus of several trade routes. It later was chosen as the "proving ground" for the Hawkbat pirates, who executed several successful raids, including the theft of several TIE interceptors from an Imperial installation.

**Halmad Prime** This grain alcohol was one of the primary exports of Halmad, and was regarded as the best produced there. It was available mainly through the black market since almost all Halmad Prime was shipped off to Imperial worlds.

**Halmere** One of Emperor Palpatine's High Inquisitors, he interviewed Canna Omonda shortly before she was executed. Halmere served under High Inquisitor Tremayne during the early years of the New Order.

**Halno'an** A young Twi'lek boy, he agreed to help a group of mercenaries rescue Shan'dira from her own clan shortly after the Battle of Yavin.

**Haloo, Shud** Rycar Ryjerd's personal bodyguard.

**Halowan** The location of a top-secret Imperial data storage network, the planet also held a trans-system data storage library. Rebel Alliance historian Voren Na'al infiltrated the Imperial data net on Halowan by posing as an agent for Moff Lorin of the Fakir sector.

**Halpat** This planet was the primary supply depot for the Fifth Battle Group's mission to blockade the Koornacht Cluster.

**halpiton circuit** A specialized system derived from standard computer components, it was part of a starship's onboard computer system.

**Halsek, Gilad** A former minor official on Coruscant, he became Imperial Consul-General of Kothlis during the Galactic Civil War. Halsek was loyal to the Empire, but was willing to allow the Bothans a measure of freedom in order to maintain his position. Halsek was approached by criminal Cecil Noone, who wanted to sell him a Hapan Gun of Command. Halsek wasn't willing to pay the price Noone asked and tried to have him captured and the gun confiscated, but the thief and his gang managed to escape before stormtroopers could stop them.

**Halthor sector** An area of the galaxy ruled by Moff Gergis, it was located near the Noonian sector.

**Halurian ice-boar** This large, porcine creature was distinguished by the thick hide plates that covered and protected its body.

**Halvala, Bethelia** This woman was the leader of the Symatrum League during the New Order.

**Hamachil, Shaki** A Mon Calamari scientist, he worked at the Imperial research facility on Dathomir during the Galactic Civil War.

**Hamadryas** A humanoid species characterized by baboon-like facial features. The body of a Hamadryas was nearly hairless, although its skull was covered with thick locks. The creature's skin was often so dark that it appeared to be black. The few individual Hamadryas ever observed seemed to lack the need to blink; they also had no true carotid artery.

**Hamalcal, Davar** A primitive human hunter and scout, he was a native of Kaellin III. During the Galactic Civil War, Rebel Alliance warships attacked an Imperial supply convoy nearby, and an Imperial shuttle crashed on the planet. The surviving stormtroopers mistook Hamalcal's people for savages. When a village elder tried to make peace, the stormtroopers murdered him and then exterminated much of the village's population. Hamalcal fled Kaellin III and roamed the galaxy. He took every opportunity to attack Imperial troopers with his trusty vibroax.

**Hamame, Vol** A former member of Big Gizz's swoop gang on the planet Tatooine, he became a hired gun teamed with the alien Phedroi. The last job they took came as a result of Dengar trying to alert Kuat of Kuat that Boba Fett was still alive. Hamame and Phedroi figured that they could kill the armored bounty hunter and reap a nice profit for delivery of his body. However, Fett and Dengar managed to elude them long enough to get a signal to *Slave I.* Hamame and Phedroi pinned down the bounty hunters in a small desert cave, but Fett brought his ship from orbit to land on top of them.

Gilad Halsek

**Haman, Gerta** An underground resistance leader on the planet Cularin, she was believed to have been killed during an attempt to infiltrate the offices of the Metatheran Cartel. But she resurfaced years later during the Clone Wars when she agreed to be interviewed to expose the linkages among the Thaereian military, the InterGalactic Banking Clan, and the Separatists. While her identity was supposed to have been kept a secret, it was really a setup by Thaereian military police, who arrested her. The ship transporting her back to Thaere came under attack by unknown assailants and exploded.

**Hamar-Chaktak** A wealthy Herglic merchant, he had no love for either the Rebel Alliance or the Empire. Still, shortly after the Battle of Hoth, he agreed to help supply the Alliance with bacta if a team of agents would meet him at the Heatherdowns, a cracian thumper racetrack and hotel complex on Tallaan. He planned to have the agents captured in order to collect insurance money on the ship he told them to steal, the *Theta-2Y,* a ship he in fact owned. The Alliance team discovered his treachery in time, and Hamar-Chaktak was forced to flee into hyperspace on his starship, the *Crusader.*

**hamarin interface band** This was one of the primary modules used to interface a computer uplink apparatus to a cyborg.

**Hamaz** An Imperial officer in charge of fleet operations near Kuat, he was captured by the bounty hunter Xufal D'uat. The bounty had called for the capture of an Alliance gunrunner, and D'uat was amazed to discover that Hamaz was an Imperial. Hamaz bargained for his release, but D'uat insisted on having a recorded confession of Hamaz's crimes in case the Imperial tried to have him killed. Hamaz did have D'uat killed, but he was unable to recover the confession.

**Hamelin** A senior commander at a Rebel Alliance base on Aargonar 3, his forces were relocated to a remote asteroid after Imperials overran the planet. Hamelin then commanded a group of starfighter squadrons, raiding Imperial convoys after the destruction of the first Death Star.

**Hamiroz, Zaz** A miner who traveled to the remains of Alderaan to search out valuable ores, he and Hanos Darr discovered that the alleged existence of the Royal Palace of Alderaan amid the rubble was simply a rumor spread by Darth Vader in an effort to lure Leia Organa. The miners were able to get to the herd ship *Bazaar,* where they hoped to get off a message to the Rebel Alliance. Instead, they found themselves being tracked by the assassin droid XS3.

**Hammax, Bijo** A Narvath member of the New Republic Intelligence division, Hammax also was a member of the Narvath resistance. He was assigned to lead an assault team that would have penetrated the Teljkon vagabond—if Lando Calrissian hadn't gotten there first.

***Hammer* (1)** This Loronar *Strike*-class cruiser was part of a small fleet provided to Captain Vocis Kenit during his search for the *Far Orbit.*

**Hammer (2)** An *Imperial I*–class Star Destroyer stationed in the Javin sector, the *Hammer* was part of a small fleet assigned to intercept fleeing Rebel Alliance starships following the Battle of Hoth.

**Hammer Group** This squadron of starfighters was assigned to the New Republic warship *Ralroost* and assisted in rescuing Corran Horn, Jacen Solo, and Ganner Rhysode from Garqi.

***Hammerhead*** One of the most powerful capital ships in the Old Republic Navy in the years leading up to the Battle of Ruusan, it was a slow-moving vessel that required an escort to hold off enemy warships until it could get into position and bring its big guns to bear.

**Hammerhead** A term, often considered derogatory, used to describe a member of the Ithorian species.

***Hammerhead*-class cruiser** *See* Republic *Hammerhead*-class fleet ship.

**Hammer Squadron** A squadron of Imperial TIE fighters active during the Galactic Civil War.

**Hammertong Project** The code name for a project to upgrade the primary laser cannons used in superlasers for Death Stars. Hammertong was begun during the final stages of the Clone Wars, when Chancellor Palpatine secretly dispatched the 501st Legion to Mygeeto to acquire an experimental power source. Some time before the Battle of Yavin, the project was going to move its base. The scientists hoped to enlist Manda D'ulin's Mistryls to help keep the base secure, but the Empire disagreed. It killed D'ulin and Pav D'armon when they attempted to enter the base. However, Shada D'ukal and the surviving Mistryls managed to steal the laser cannons and transport them to Tatooine.

**Hammertree** A Rebel Alliance Intelligence agent, he gave his life to obtain information on the whereabouts of Han Solo's carbon-frozen body.

**Hamner, Kenth** A student at Luke Skywalker's Jedi praxeum on Yavin 4, he had resigned his commission in the Corellian Defense Force to learn the ways of the Force. He later joined the New Republic military as a strategist, and after the Battle of Fondor he became the voice of the Jedi Knights within the military. As the Yuuzhan Vong War continued, Hamner discovered that the Senate, goaded by Borsk Fey'lya, had issued a warrant for the arrest of Luke Skywalker. He warned Luke and his wife, Mara Jade Skywalker, giving them time to escape from Coruscant. For his efforts during the Second Battle of Coruscant, Hamner was elevated to the rank of Jedi Master.

When the Galactic Alliance was formed on Mon Calamari by Cal Omas, Hamner was one of the Jedi appointed to serve on the Advisory Council. As the war ground on, he became the nominal leader of the Jedi after the Skywalkers set out to locate the living planet Zonama Sekot. When intelligence from Coruscant revealed that Yuuzhan Vong Prophet Yu'shaa had returned from Zonama Sekot, and there was still no word from the Skywalkers, Hamner gathered the remaining Jedi leaders to plan a mission to Coruscant. Years later, during the Confederation–GA War, Hamner agreed to take command of the Dark Sword Squadron of starfighters during the Galactic Alliance's defense of Kuat.

**Hamner Heavy Ores** This Jante mining operation maintained a base in orbit around Rett II until it was attacked and overtaken by Freda military ships.

**Hamnet** A minor crime lord, he maintained the outward appearance of a successful, legitimate businessman. Hamnet left much of the dirty work to his bodyguard, Wesson DeLameter. Hamnet was among the handful of bidders who tried to buy the secret formula for an Imperial virus when it was auctioned off by Hakon de Ville on Ananuru.

**hamogoni** A tree native to Woteba. It wasn't uncommon to find a specimen taller than many skytowers and with a trunk diameter of 20 meters or more. After Woteba was designated as a new home for the hives of the Colony, the Killiks began harvesting hamogoni trees for their dense, fragrant wood. But this harvest was at least one reason behind the appearance of the Fizz virus.

***Hampton*** A freighter stationed near Mytus VII, it supplied the Corporate Sector Authority prison there. A group of jailed Rebel Alliance agents stowed away on the freighter and were rescued when it was intercepted by the Alliance shuttle *Mercy*.

*Hanadak*

**Hamud, Osaf** A noted Old Republic scientist, he studied the life cycle of the orbalisk. He wrote "An Examination and Exploration of a Most Dangerous and Resilient Organism," which provided information on how the creatures could be removed from a being's body. One of the only copies of that study was in the Jedi Archives; it was discovered by Zannah during her search for ways to help her Master, Darth Bane, overcome the orbalisks that had infested his body.

**hanadak** A large, bear-like beast living in the forests of Endor's primary moon. Hanadaks were carnivorous creatures about 3 meters tall, with menacing snouts and huge black claws. The Ewoks claimed that hanadaks were controlled by the giant Gorax. Individuals were known to develop specific tastes in prey, and many hunted certain sentient species. Hanadaks at times were captured and used in gladiatorial events, although possession of a hanadak was illegal in many sectors of the galaxy.

**Hanadi, Cheriss ke** A native Adumari dueling champion, she always dreamed of becoming a pilot. When her working-class status and vertigo kept her from the skies, she focused all her energy on becoming the finest blastsword duelist on Adumar. She also developed a crush on Wedge Antilles during Red Flight's stay on the planet, but grew out of it in time to help the pilots lead the unified forces of Adumar against the Cartann aggression. She soon learned that a common drug could cure her vertigo, and she almost immediately joined the New Republic flight academy with Antilles's highest recommendation. Five years after Adumari unification, she served in Moonlight Squadron, an A-wing group based on the Mon Calamari star cruiser *Mon Carima*.

**Hanare, Ronar** An alias used by Obi-Wan Kenobi during his mission to Bellassa about a year after the end of the Clone Wars. The alias was provided to members of the Eleven as a way for Kenobi to gain access to the spaceport in Ussa and get a vessel so he could locate Ferus Olin. "Hanare" was a businessman from Raed-7, and was working on a pipeline outside Ussa. The Eleven maintained a Deep-X Explorer at the spaceport, which Kenobi was able to claim to depart for the Arno region in search of Olin.

**hanava** The wood of this fruit-bearing tree was once the primary food source of the greddleback termite. Apparently an undeclared shipment of hanava fruit carried a small group of greddlebacks to the planet Bethal, where they ravaged the apocia tree population.

**Hanchin** This gas giant was located in the Moddell sector of the galaxy.

**Hanchin-set** A term used by the natives of the moon of Mina to describe the brief period of darkness that occurred on the rare occasions when some part of Mina's surface was not bathed in the light of the planet Hanchin. One such Hanchin-set occurred at midwinter, when the Vashan bodhis coughed up their sin-bullets.

*Handmaiden Sisters*

**Hanco** One of the many sargheet farmers who suffered through economic hard times on Dagro during the Clone Wars. Hanco confronted Obi-Wan Kenobi about the lack of Old Republic support when the Jedi visited to investigate the presence of a Separatist base. But when he saw Kenobi actively stripping sargheet crop stubble, he decided that the Jedi was worthy of the farmers' support. Hanco and others helped Kenobi and Anakin Skywalker locate and destroy the last Separatist crawl-carrier before it could eliminate a village.

**Hand, Pyr** A black-haired, pale-skinned man, he was a member of Requiem Squadron, serving under Antar Roat. Captain Hand was nicknamed Klick because he was a dead shot from a kilometer or more. Hand was actually Corran Horn in disguise, part of Ysanne Isard's plan to infiltrate Prince-Admiral Krennel's forces and bring about his destruction.

**Handa** An ancient Cathar Jedi Master, he was believed to have been Githany's first teacher in the years leading up to the Battle of Ruusan. Master Handa trained Githany along with Kiel Charny. He taught Githany how to reconnect with the Force after she had lost her way. Master Handa was able to make Githany see the true power of the Force, if only for the brief period while they were in contact. Githany later used the same technique to help Darth Bane recover his connection to the dark side.

**Handmaiden Sisters** A group of Force-sensitive women in the era of the Great Sith War. Some believed they were surviving members of the powerful and mysterious Echani Handmaidens. In the wake of the Jedi Civil War, the Handmaiden Sisters were exiled to Telos. They brought with them a wealth of artifacts and various holocrons and other recorded lessons, hoping that their remoteness would help them preserve the Jedi way if the Order were to disappear. Led by Atris, the Handmaiden Sisters established a training facility away from prying eyes, beneath Telos's northern polar icecap. In addition to some training in the Force, the Handmaiden Sisters were also well versed in the Echani martial arts.

**Hand of Judgment** The name adopted by a renegade group of five stormtroopers who abandoned their posts on the *Reprisal* after refusing to continue serving under officers who killed innocent civilians. On the planet Ranklinge, they helped the residents of Janusar overthrow Patroller Chief Cav'Saran. Later, they were commandeered by Mara Jade on Shelkonwa during their mutual investigation into Imperial ties to the BloodScar pirates. Jade eventually learned the truth about the stormtroopers, but also recognized that they were still loyal to the basic tenets of the Empire. She even claimed the Hand of Judgment as her own special detachment when questioned by Darth Vader, ensuring that the stormtroopers would not have to face an Imperial court-martial. Her mission complete, Jade gave the stormtroopers their freedom, but strongly suggested that they abandon their nickname.

**Hand of Solitude** One of the leaders of the Solitude militant group active on Corellia during the Galactic Civil War.

**Hand of Thrawn** The code name of a hidden fortress maintained by a contingent of Chiss on Nirauan. Grand Admiral Thrawn had left a large contingent of his species with orders to await his return 10 years after he left. The fortress, which already was 20 years old when Thrawn departed, had five large towers that resembled an upturned hand; it also had subsurface caves and tunnels lined with cortosis ore, and a large population of Force-evading ysalamiri to protect the compound from Jedi. The Chiss kept a large assortment of weapons and warships armed and ready for Thrawn's return. There was also a secret chamber where Thrawn was growing a clone of himself.

The fortress remained a secret until the New Republic discovered a cache of Imperial datacards on Wayland, at Mount Tantiss. A card titled the Hand of Thrawn was unreadable. But Luke Skywalker and Mara Jade managed to discover the location of Nirauan after tracking back the journey of ships that attacked them at Kauron. Jade was captured at the fortress, but Skywalker rescued her, and they were able to destroy the cloning chamber and severely damage the base.

*Hangar deck scrubber droid*

**Handooine** This planet was located near Jabiim. It was once a staging area for Republic forces, during the Clone wars.

**hand pot** A small collection of credits that was anted up at the beginning of each round of sabacc, it went to the player with the best hand. The sabacc pot was reserved for the winner of the overall match.

**Hand Pot, the** One of the smaller casinos in the Westrex district of Efavan on Vorzyd 5. Like the other gambling joints, it was located on Casino Line.

***Handree*** A Rebel Alliance gunship that was stationed on Isis, it brought medical supplies to the guerrillas on Polmanar. The *Handree* was hijacked by the Imperial survey crew of the *Wanderer* and taken to the Bespin system. The Imperials hoped to expose the Isis base, but were intercepted by Alliance agents.

*Hang glider*

**hangar deck scrubber droid** Small and boxy Naboo droids equipped with fuel scrubbers, they had dual sniffers to find drops of dangerous leaked fuel. Made by Industrial Automaton, the droids could communicate with the Theed Palace computer system.

**Hangar Hunters** A gang of bounty hunters active around the time of the Galactic Civil War, they had an operating base in the ruins of an ancient flight hangar. They accepted a bounty to track down a rogue Imperial E522 assassin droid sometime after the Battle of Yavin.

**hang glider** A lightweight glider constructed from tree branches and animal skins. When strapped to the back of an Ewok, it allowed the creature to soar through the forest. Ewoks used hang gliders primarily for hunting, but during the Battle of Endor they also employed the devices to attack Imperial forces from above.

**Hanging Gardens** The pride and joy of Lady Bathos of House Cadriaan, it was located within the boundaries of Alaphoe Gardens on

Procopia. Rare and exotic flowers from over 100 different worlds hung from trellises and grew in flower beds.

**Hanging Moss Village** An Ewok village in an isolated part of the Forest Moon of Endor, it was noted for its cruel and vicious inhabitants. Unlike most other Ewoks, the natives of Hanging Moss Village liked to set traps and torment the creatures they caught.

*Kile Hannad*

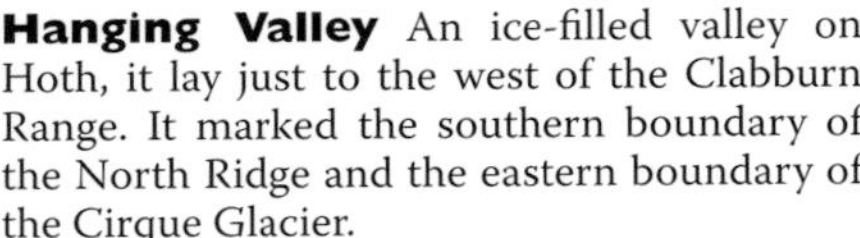

**Hanging Valley** An ice-filled valley on Hoth, it lay just to the west of the Clabburn Range. It marked the southern boundary of the North Ridge and the eastern boundary of the Cirque Glacier.

**hangman's tree** Native to the jungles of Ithor, this tree used its tendril-like branches to grasp a creature around the neck, draw it upward, and strangle it. The tree then fed a chemical into its prey's body to start the digestive process, allowing the tree to absorb the victim through its bark.

**Hanharr** A Wookiee bounty hunter, he helped hunt down surviving Jedi and turned them over to Goto following the Jedi Civil War. During the Mandalorian Wars, when the forces of the Czerka Corporation arrived on Kashyyyk, he knew they were there to hunt down Wookiees. Rather than let his tribe be captured and enslaved, he killed his people with his own hands, believing they would be better off dead. Czerka quickly captured him. Years later, he was freed from slavery by the bounty hunter Mira, and Hanharr was forced to acknowledge the life debt he owed her. But he resented the fact that he owed his life to a human, and set out to kill her. Mira, however, ended his life first.

*Hanharr*

**Hanna City** The capital of the planet Chandrila, Hanna City was located on the coast of the Silver Sea. It was the site of the planet's largest starport. The Brionelle Memorial Military Academy was north of Hanna, and the Hanna Wild Game Reserve was on the city's outskirts.

**Hannad, Kile** One of Emperor Palpatine's Royal Imperial Guards, he was among the few who survived the death of Palpatine's clones on Byss. Most of the guards were killed by Carnor Jax when they returned to Yinchorr. Only Hannad and Kir Kanos remained alive, and they let chance decide which one would die a warrior's death and who would live to exact revenge on Jax. Hannad held off Jax's troops long enough for Kanos to escape, but eventually was overwhelmed and killed.

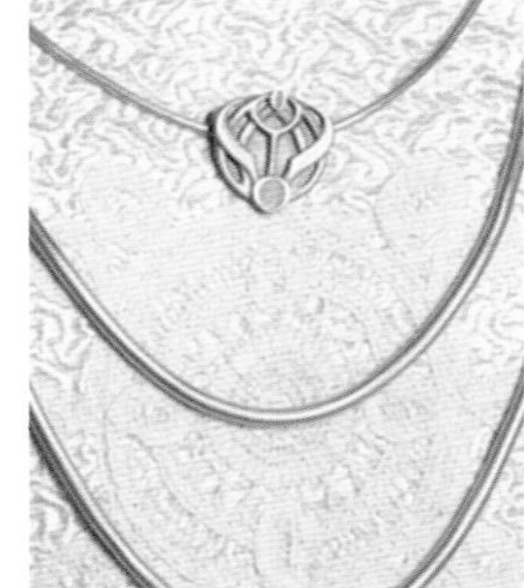

*Hanna pendant*

**Hanna pendant** Worn by the women of the planet Chandrila, it consisted of three heavy ropes of linked metal rings connected at each shoulder by a stylized clasp; a pendant with a similar design hung from the shortest strand of metal at the neck. Mon Mothma usually wore one.

**Hannser, Captain** The human commander of the New Republic gunship *Marauder,* which accompanied the command ship *Glorious* and the ferret *D-89* for the original interception of the mysterious ghost ship known as the Teljkon vagabond. Years later, Hannser was placed in command of the *Far Thunder* during the New Republic's struggle against the Yuuzhan Vong.

**Hanod system** In the Borderlands Regions, this system was the last known location of the Star Destroyer *Krieger.*

**Hanofar** An Imperial-held world, it was the site of skirmishes between the Empire and rebellious tax protesters during the New Order.

**Ha'Nook, Jannie** The Senator from Glithnos during the Clone Wars, she was among the first to vote Chancellor Palpatine the emergency powers he needed to create the Grand Army of the Republic. Senator Ha'Nook served as a senior member of the Security and Intelligence Council, and grew closer to Palpatine. She wasn't above accepting a bribe of a full ambassadorship to cast her vote for sending reinforcements to Praesitlyn after Separatists attacked the Intergalactic Communications Center there.

**Hanoon** An asteroid originally known as Geddes, it was located near the planet Krant, in the Both system. Hanoon was terraformed by the Empire during the early years of the New Order. It was said to be where Echuu Shen-Jon destroyed the Vor'Na'Tu sometime after the rise of Emperor Palpatine.

**hanpat** An incendiary chemical developed by the Killiks of the Colony, it was loaded into wax spheres and flung at enemy positions. The spheres, known as burnballs, ruptured on impact, spraying hanpat over a large area, where it ignited upon contact with the surrounding air.

**Hans, Geordi** A young mechanic who worked for Unut Poll at Spaceport Speeders on Tatooine. Hans and his buddies Jeff Pill and Franklin "Shorty" Scott formed a swoop gang known as the Farns.

**Hansel** A security officer on his homeworld of Romin, he worked directly for Roy Teda. When Obi-Wan Kenobi and Siri Tachi arrived on Romin with their apprentices, Anakin Skywalker and Ferus Olin, Deputy Hansel was ordered by Teda to follow the young Padawans when they traveled alone. At a reception the next day, the Citizens' Resistance launched a rebellion and Hansel was captured. He was scheduled to be the first one executed until Teda turned himself in for trial.

**Hansen FeatherTouch** A tractor beam unit capable of amazingly precise operations, it could harmlessly pull a bird out of midflight . . . or rip a small freighter to pieces. The FeatherTouch was turret-mounted and could be used in a multitude of configurations.

**Hansh** A member of a mercenary unit that supported the Brotherhood of Darkness, he was able to survive the detonation of the thought bomb because he had no connection to the Force. But Hansh and a comrade, Lergan, were soon murdered by Darth Bane, who immolated their bodies in Force lightning. Two other mercenaries were sliced to pieces by the Sith Lord. He let the remaining mercenaries flee so they could carry the message of Darth Bane's survival.

**Hanson Mining Consolidated** A mining consortium based on the planet Neona, it mined ore from the planet's seafloor. HMC later partnered with Aquatic Ecosystems Incorporated to exploit the planet's aquatic species as food sources.

**Hansor, Madrix** The leader of Hansor's Hooligans, a team of gladiator walker fighters active in the Galactic Civil War era. Gladiator walkers, equipped with light laser cannons and heavy shielding, were single-person units designed to allow riders to fight each other in tournaments. Hansor had a long-standing grudge against Demelza Mintori and his team, Demelza's Destructors.

**Hantaq, Dab** A young boy whose family was escaping the Yuuzhan Vong invasion of Coruscant. His parents let Senator Viqi Shesh use him as her "son" to try to get passage aboard the *Millennium Falcon.* The Senator was on the run from the law and thought that by having a son she could somehow get a sympathetic Han and Leia Solo to aid her escape as a desperate refugee. But the ruse was exposed; the Senator fled, and Dab—dubbed Tarc by Shesh—was taken aboard the *Falcon* and brought to Borleias. His parents also made it off the planet.

**Hante** A smuggler at Merich's Bend on the third moon of Aurea, he secretly supplied Rebels in the Core and Expansion Region with weapons and goods during the Galactic Civil War.

**Hanther, Tinian** A Republic Intelligence operative on Tarhassan just after the Battle of Geonosis, she was part of a team sent to spring Edbit Teeks from prison. She pretended to be a guard transferring a new inmate to the Nehass prison facility, and the escape was carried off.

**Hanto Mountains** A low range of mountains on the moon of Sulon.

**Hanugar** A Corellian con man, he worked with the Qwohog K'zk to swindle passage from Diergu-Rea Duhnes'rd to the Zelosian Chine for a treasure hunt. Hanugar and his partner, Sevik, pretended to be shipwrecked vacationers.

**Hanx-Wargel** This company manufactured the SuperFlow line of starship computers. The control functions of the *Millennium Falcon* were funneled through what started life as a Hanx-Wargel SuperFlow IV computer.

**Haor Chall** A religion of the Xi Char species from Charros IV. It taught that the real world was but a shadow of the infinitely complex and intricate paradise of the afterlife. Many Xi Charrians believed that the creation and manufacture of complex or intricate machinery was a way for them to obtain a small glimpse of what awaited after death.

**Haor Chall Engineering** A religious order and arms manufacturer founded by the Xi Char. Haor Chall zealots were devoted to high-precision manufacturing, which they conducted in traditional cathedral factories on Charros IV. Haor Chall Engineering made the Trade Federation droid starfighter and the C-9979 landing ship, among other products. A clone army eventually invaded Charros IV and destroyed the Haor Chall factories, crippling the company. Sienar Fleet Systems absorbed what remained of it.

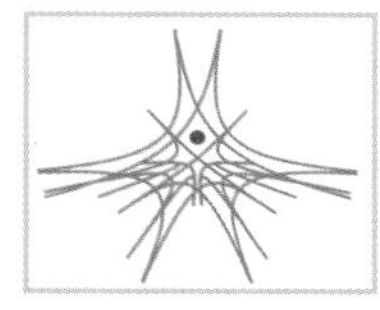

**Hapan** An isolationist humanoid species from the Hapes star cluster whose members were well known for both their wealth and their strong defense of its borders. Hapans exhibited mores and values shaped by their matriarchal society, and were physically different from baseline humans in two major ways: their almost universal physical beauty and a form of genetic night blindness. As a people, Hapans had a deep-seated hatred of the Jedi, which sprang from the destruction of the Lorell Raiders. When the Yuuzhan Vong invaded the galaxy, Hapans were among the first to support the work of the Peace Brigade, as their anti-Jedi sentiments came to the fore.

**Hapan battle armor** Highly polished black armor with silver trim, it was worn by the cyborg warriors from Charubah.

**Hapan Battle Dragon** Huge saucer-shaped starships about 500 meters in diameter, they were painted to represent each of the 63 stars and their inhabited planets in the Hapes Cluster. They were quickly recognizable by the double saucers that extended from the main hull of the ships, which were about one-third the size of a Star Destroyer. Among their unusual features was a weapons system in which a laser or cannon was rotated into firing position, discharged, then rapidly rotated away to recharge while another weapon immediately took its place. Each Hapan Battle Dragon had 40 turbolasers, 40 ion cannons, dorsal and ventral triple ion cannons, 10 proton torpedo launchers, and a tractor beam projector. The ship's hangar bays carried three squadrons of fighters, or 36 ships, and 500 ground-assault troopers.

Battle Dragons also had four pulse-mass generator tubes that shot pulse-mass mines resulting in gravity waves simulating the effect of a planetary body; this prevented nearby ships from immediately jumping into hyperspace. Olanji/Charubah Battle Dragons joined with New Republic ships in the Battle of Dathomir and helped rout the fleet of Warlord Zsinj and destroy his main starship construction yards. Battle Dragons and *Nova*-class battle cruisers made up the Hapan fleet at the Battle of Fondor but were no match for the power of Centerpoint Station, which destroyed much of the fleet during the fight.

Hapan

**Hapan Consortium** A starship manufacturer owned and controlled by the Hapan royal family. Its designs were considered inferior to most ships in terms of power generators and weapons systems.

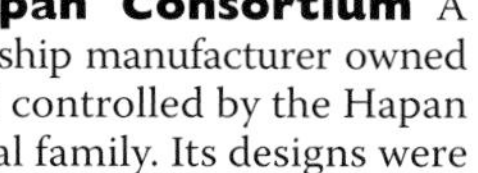

**Hapan Home Fleet** The fleet of Hapan Battle Dragons that protected the planet Hapes and the surrounding area of space, it also was known as the Hapan Royal Navy. In times of crisis, the Home Fleet often was augmented with warships from the various royal houses of the Hapes Consortium. The tradition was broken during the Galactic Alliance's war against the Confederation, when the so-called Heritage Fleet was formed by the royals of the Heritage Council to attack Hapes and dethrone the reigning Queen Mother, Tenel Ka. Thanks to support from the Galactic Alliance's navy, the Home Fleet was able to defeat the Heritage Fleet, thereby keeping Tenel Ka on the throne. However, the Hapan Home Fleet was unable to regain much strength before Tenel Ka agreed to turn its control over to Jacen Solo, provided that he make peace with Jedi Grand Master Luke Skywalker. Solo believed that the Confederation was massing for an attack on Kuat, and needed the additional ships to help defend the Alliance's holdings in the system, so he said he'd agree to the demand. Tenel Ka changed her mind after learning of Solo's treacherous actions.

In the wake of the Battle of Kuat and the Second Battle of Fondor, Tenel Ka supplied the Hapan Home Fleet to the growing number of forces that supported the Jedi coalition. After Prince Isolder was captured by Darth Caedus near Nova Station while trying to rescue Ben Skywalker, Tenel Ka took the entire fleet to defend the hidden Jedi base on Shedu Maad. The plan was to draw Caedus's fleets down through the Throat to an ambush. The *Megador,* however, managed to move into a position that allowed it and a group of Imperial Remnant warships to trap the Hapan Home Fleet up against Uroro Station, and then unleashed a nanokiller virus on the *Dragon Queen.*

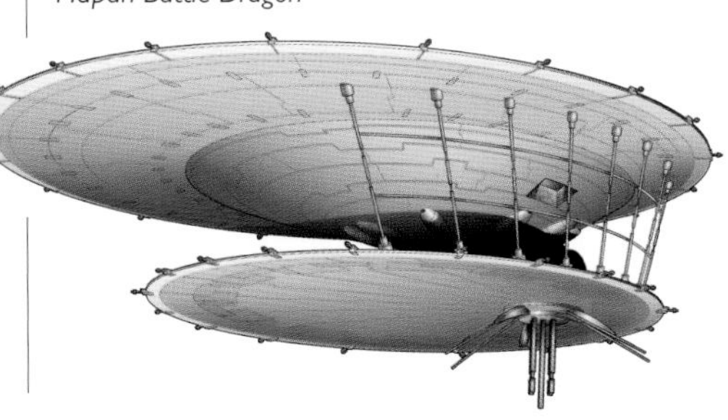

Hapan Battle Dragon

With the presumed death of Tenel Ka, Ducha Requud tried to assume the position of Queen Mother, hoping to add the strength of Imperial forces to aid in her coup attempt.

**Hapan honor duel** An antiquated form of combat used to settle disputes between two Hapans. The "offended one" was given the choice of weapons ranging from vibroblades to sporting blasters. For the honor duel between Prince Isolder and Beed Thane, the two combatants donned electro-studded head gear, power gloves, boots, and body armor. They used a form of hand-to-hand combat developed by the Lorell Raiders, which was not as deadly or mystical as teräs käsi.

**Hapan puzzle box** Often used to conceal treasure or provide a nasty surprise to the unwary, some Hapan puzzle boxes contained nothing at all, an insidious feature of the decorative gifts. In the complex Hapan culture, the puzzle box was a glimpse into Hapans' ability to trust one another, not to mention into the darker side of their lives. The giver of a puzzle box always asked the recipient, "Did you enjoy my gift?" The time it took to pose the question—mere moments or weeks after it was given—along with the specific answer revealed the level of trust between the two people involved. A puzzle box might contain jewels, toys, or candy for children or consorts; or it could hide poisonous gas or explosives for rivals. The boxes usually were treated to be resistant to any scans that could reveal their contents.

**Hapan Royal Guard** A group of specially trained soldiers who protected the Fountain Palace and the Queen Mother of Hapes. The Royal Guard employed both male and female officers, with individual ranks denoted by golden hash marks on the cuffs of the uniform.

**Hapan stinger** A security escort vessel built on Hapes.

**Hapan Water Dragon** An oceangoing repulsorlift battleship built on the planet Hapes. One was used as the royal yacht.

*Hapes*

**Hapes** Originally settled by a group of pirates called the Lorell Raiders, the planet Hapes later became a neutral system when the Jedi Knights wiped out the Raiders after they started pillaging Old Republic supply centers. The surviving women swore never to let a man run the government following that defeat. Millennia later, the system was overrun by the Empire, but Queen Mother Ta'a Chume built powerful armed forces and drove out the Imperials. The planet orbited the star Hapes, and was the seat of Hapan government. The light from its seven moons and its star caused the natives to lose much of their ability to see at night.

**Hapes Cluster** A grouping of 63 star systems, it originally was settled by a group of pirates, the Lorell Raiders. Toward the end of the Old Republic, Queen Mother Ta'a Chume ruled with an iron fist until her heir, Prince Isolder, chose Teneniel Djo to be his wife. Djo brought the Hapans into the New Republic. There were at least 119 known worlds within the cluster's boundaries, only 12 of which were unsettled at the time of negotiations with the New Republic. The cluster had four distinct regions: the Interior Region, which included Hapes and was considered the heart of the cluster; the Rifle Worlds, industrial enclaves that once tried to secede from the Hapes Consortium; the Rim Worlds, which bordered on the rest of the known galaxy; and the Transitory Mists Region, which was filled with nebulous gases and was home to many pirate groups. The unusual configuration of the Hapes Cluster gave rise to theories that its form was not a natural occurrence, but rather some ancient engineering project akin to the Corellian system or the Maw.

*Hapes* Nova*-class battle cruiser*

**Hapes Consortium** The governing body of the 63 star systems of the Hapes Cluster, the Consortium was founded more than 4,000 years before the Galactic Civil War. A matriarchy, the Consortium was long controlled by a Queen Mother. Each member system had a vote in all matters of state, but the Queen Mother could break a tie. About 3,100 years before the Battle of Yavin, and after the upheaval of the Great Sith War, the reigning Queen Mother closed the borders of the Hapes Cluster to outsiders, and it remained isolated for millennia. The Consortium's connection to the Transitory Mists gave it a natural barrier to outsiders, since hyperspace travel through the Mists was treacherous at best.

The New Republic tried to establish a relationship with the Hapes Consortium in the wake of the Galactic Civil War, and Prince Isolder became enamored of Princess Leia Organa. Although Leia rebuffed Isolder, she was able to convince the Hapan prince to ally the capital planet with the New Republic. This relationship strengthened when Tenel Ka became Queen Mother. But when Leia Organa Solo pleaded with the Consortium for help in combating the Yuuzhan Vong, it took an honor duel between Prince Isolder and Archon Beed Thane to get the necessary support. In the aftermath of the Battle of Fondor, where most of the Hapan fleet was destroyed, the Consortium voted for isolation. After the defeat of the invaders, Queen Mother Tenel Ka decided to join the Galactic Alliance, but as the GA became more like the former Empire, the member worlds once again pressed for Hapan independence.

**Hapes Consortium Heritage Council** An advisory council of nobles. Several members plotted to hire Aurra Sing to assassinate Queen Mother Tenel Ka because of her insistence on remaining linked to the Galactic Alliance. The plot failed.

**Hapes *Nova*-class battle cruiser** These fast, 400-meter-long combat ships patrolled the outer regions of the Hapes Cluster and had enough supplies for a year of continuous operation. The *Nova*-class battle cruiser was exceptionally swift at sublight speed, yet still well armed. It carried 25 turbolasers, 10 laser cannons, and 10 ion cannons. There were also 12 Miy'til fighters and six Hetrinar assault bombers aboard. Because Hapan weapons technology wasn't up to general galactic standards, Hapan captains tended to favor swift, brutal assaults intended to destroy all enemy ships with the first attack. Hapan Prince Isolder, in his quest to earn Leia Organa's hand in marriage, offered to give a *Nova*-class battle cruiser to Han Solo if Solo would cease his own efforts to marry Leia. Solo's response was to kidnap the Princess and carry her off to faraway Dathomir.

**Hapin, Stano** The leader of the Disac pirates during the early years of the New Order, he was assassinated by Ket Maliss.

***Happer's Way*** An independently owned Rendili freighter based on Chandrila, it was commanded by Captain Norello. Contracted by the Imperial military to make supply and delivery runs throughout the galaxy, it was ambushed by a group of vessels owned by the BloodScar pirates shortly after the Battle of Yavin. *Happer's Way* escaped when one of the pirate ships started firing at the others; it was under the command of Mara Jade, who later commandeered the ship as part of her own mission to infiltrate the BloodScars.

**Happy** A city on the lawless world of Korbin, it was jokingly given an upbeat name like its counterparts Joy and Peace.

**Happy Blasters** A group of mercenary scouts under the leadership of Salem Victory, they earned their name from their response in most situations: They started firing their blasters at anything that moved.

***Happy Dagger*** A modified SoroSuub PLY-3000 luxury yacht, it was owned and operated by Roa about 25 years after the Battle of Endor.

***Happy Failure*** A dry-docked freighter, it was a popular casino in Cloud City's Port Town during the Galactic Civil War.

**Happy Go Lucky** Second in command to the pirate Black Jack, she was a walking weapons arsenal and more than a little trigger-happy.

**Happy Grove** The location of Bright Tree Village on the Forest Moon of Endor, it was also the area where the Ewok Teebo lived as a child.

***Happy Hutt*** A transport ship that had been ferrying refugees from Ralltiir, it was one of many trapped on Coruscant when the Yuuzhan Vong struck. The captain of the *Happy Hutt* managed to get some 5,000 refugees into the holds before taking off.

**Happy Nerf Herder** A fictional maximum-security home for wayward boys, it was popularized on the HoloNet during the early years of the New Order.

**happy-patty** A quick-cooking food that was a favorite among children.

**Happy's Landing Tavern** An alehouse in Il Avali on Druckenwell. It was frequented by Tinian I'att and Daye Azur-Jamin. I'att fled to the tavern after her grandparents were executed by Moff Kerioth.

**Happy Spacer** A retailer of intoxicating substances owned by Loeerna, it was located in the Life section of Vergesso Base.

**happy surprise** The nickname of Merr-Sonn's J1 holdout blaster.

**hapspir, barrini, corbolan, triaxis** A high-level recognition code used by Mara Jade when she was an Emperor's Hand.

**Haque, Mister** A well-educated assassin who lived in the Cularin system during the Clone Wars, he and his partner Mister Zlash were given the assignment to assassinate Governor Barnab Chistor. Just as Mister Haque was about to kill Chistor, Mister Zlash told him that the Senator who had ordered the hit had been executed for treason, and was therefore unlikely to pay them. Mister Haque released Chistor, begging the governor's apologies for having roughed him up. Haque and Zlash then offered to take the official to breakfast at a renowned Ithorian restaurant. Chistor could only stammer his acceptance, glad to be still alive.

**Har, Duran** A transport captain aboard Corellian Transline's *SV-45* StarSpeeder 3000 early in the New Order era.

**Hara, Bela and Krasov** Barabel hatchmates of Tesar Sebatyne. All three trained with the Wild Knights under the tutelage of Master Saba Sebatyne before joining Luke Skywalker and the Jedi Knights during the Yuuzhan Vong War. The three hatchmates shared a deep bond. They joined a Jedi strike team that was dispatched to Myrkr in an effort to locate and destroy the voxyn queen. Once aboard the worldship *Baanu Rass,* the Jedi struggled mightily to reach the queen. During an ambush by the Yuuzhan Vong, Bela took an amphistaff in the back and died almost immediately. One voxyn attacked Krasov and Anakin Solo, spewing acidic vomit on Krasov. Despite the best efforts of the healer Tekli, Krasov died of her injuries.

**Harak, Vreet** A young nerf herder, he worked at the family ranch, the Grand Horn Ranch Corporation, on Fennesa. Harak was a third-generation rancher as well as an excellent marksman who protected the herds by shooting any predators.

**Ha-ran** An elderly Eickarie, he was part of a small contingent on the planet Kariek that agreed to help the Aurek Company of the 501st Legion of stormtroopers gain access to the ancient fortress of the Warlord. The Empire of the Hand had agreed to help the United Tribes of Kariek eliminate the Warlord, who had been aligned with the Lakra, the more aggressive species that shared the planet with the Eickarie. Ha-ran accompanied the team as it infiltrated the fortress, then revealed that he was actually the *hee-sae,* an Eickarie prince. His role in the mission was to ensure that prisoners released from the Warlord's dungeons would not fight against the team, since many of them were imprisoned long before the signing of the United Tribes Agreements.

**Harand, Bleys** A Corellian historian, he was known as much for his sharp tongue as for his in-depth descriptions of various planetary civilizations.

***Harasser*** A group of Imperial Nebulon-B frigates that supported the Star Destroyer *Invincible* near Dellalt.

**Harazod** The capital city of the planet Gerrard V.

**Harbid, Captain,** An Imperial Navy officer, he served under Grand Admiral Thrawn as commander of the *Death's Head* five years after the Battle of Endor.

**Har Binande** The primary world in the Har system, it was invaded in ancient times and occupied by the forces of the Lahag Erli. When the occupiers were finally driven from the system, they left behind on many worlds exquisite architecture, which became a major tourist attraction.

***Harbinger* (1)** A giant landing ship designed to conquer and hold planets for the Separatists, it was custom-built by the Geonosians for Count Dooku. The ship's compartmentalized efficiency allowed it to deploy an army within minutes, and its supercharged light drive made it ideal for invading unsuspecting star systems. The *Harbinger* had 12 large turrets and 7 power cores on its underside. It deployed units during a Clone Wars battle on Alaris, and was destroyed by Anakin Skywalker.

***Harbinger* (2)** A *Hammerhead*-class Old Republic warship dispatched to Telos to aid refugees displaced in the wake of the Jedi Civil War, it was captured by a group of Sith devotees who were trying to reawaken Darth Sion. The *Harbinger* was redirected to Peragus II, and on its way captured a small ship, the *Ebon Hawk,* in deep space. The ship held Jedi Master Kreia and the Jedi Exile, but Darth Sion wasn't able to detect their presence, and they managed to escape.

***Harbinger* (3)** A Mon Calamari cruiser, it was the flagship of Garm Bel Iblis, who had split with the New Republic after the Battle of Fondor. However, after Admiral Ackbar proposed a plan that led to the Battle of Ebaq 9, Bel Iblis was convinced by Luke Skywalker to rejoin the Republic's forces against the Yuuzhan Vong. Later, Bel Iblis and the *Harbinger* were instrumental in retaking Corulag.

Harbinger, *a* Hammerhead-*class warship*

**Harbinger (4)** An assault ship operated by Bel Att, who worked for the Nalroni crime lord Sprax. The ship later was commandeered by Limna Yith and her mercenary band.

**Harbinger (5)** This *Imperial II*–class Star Destroyer was part of the naval forces maintained by the Imperial Remnant following the Swarm War. The *Harbinger* was dispatched to Nickel One in the weeks following the Second Battle of Fondor to secure the asteroid and its munitions factories for the Imperial Remnant. When a group of Jedi blastboats arrived, followed closely by a squad of Mandalorian *Bes'uliik*-class fighters, the Imperial vessels found themselves under intense attack. More Jedi showed up in StealthX fighters. The combined force broke through the shields of the *Harbinger,* gutting several sections of the Star Destroyer. Its captain kept firing at the attackers until he was forced to abandon ship.

**Harbin-re** This planet was famous for productions of neoclassical operas, including some favored by Emperor Palpatine himself.

**Harbright, Borert** A member of the aristocratic Harbright family on Salliche, he ran the daily operations of family-owned Salliche Agricultural Corporation. With the start of the Yuuzhan Vong War, the Harbrights began retooling Salliche Ag to remove all traces of inorganic workers and tools, hoping the invaders would see that the company adhered to bio-organic technologies. Harbright also represented the Ruan system in the New Republic Senate, and agreed to allow Ruan to be used as an enclave for refugees fleeing the invasion forces. Leia Organa Solo, however, sensed duplicity behind Harbright's coal-black eyes and obliging smile.

**Harbright, Dees** A cousin, once removed, of Borert Harbright, he was senior vice president of marketing for Salliche Agricultural Corporation. He bore a slight resemblance to Han Solo, helping Han infiltrate Salliche Ag's district headquarters on Ruan.

**Harbright, Lady Selnia** A former Senator from the planet Salliche, she dedicated herself to helping the Rebel Alliance overthrow the Empire during the Galactic Civil War. On one mission, she went to Droecil to help the local Rebel cell divert medical supplies from an Imperial depot.

**Harburik, Lieutenant** Tatooine's chief of police during the Galactic Civil War, he was rude, crass, and cruel. After the death of Orun Depp, Harburik took control of the planet. When Talmont was named to replace Depp, Harburik plotted to remove him from office.

**Harch, Major** An Imperial officer who served the last remnants of the Empire under Admiral Pellaeon, he was in charge of repairs to the *Chimaera* following the attack by Moff Disra's pirates near Pesitiin.

**Harcourt, Captain Aron** After his Star Destroyer, the *Anya Karu,* was sabotaged by Rebel Alliance agents and crashed on a remote planet, Harcourt was chosen as the scapegoat. He was forced out of the command structure and placed in charge of a remote outpost. After his wife, Janelle, died, Harcourt hired Boba Fett to return to the crash scene to recover a small hologram of her. Harcourt knew that he couldn't pay Fett's fee, but for him the pleasure of seeing Janelle one last time was worth the price: his execution by Fett for failure to pay.

*Hardin, also known as "Bug"*

**Hardan plague** A virulent disease, it was transported by Bogan's Brown Nafen.

**hard-biscuit** A Drallish food. These small cakes were very tasty but lived up to their name: Some species chipped their teeth while trying to chew them. They were no problem for the strong Drall jaw structure.

***Hardcell*-class transport** A cylindrical transport ship developed and manufactured by the Techno Union, it relied on propellants rather than repulsors to get it into space. The main section of the ship was an elongated, egg-shaped hull in which huge amounts of cargo could be stored. The aft section consisted of six long engines, each of which was filled with thousands of liters of fuel. The *Hardcell*-class transport, which was 220 meters high, took off and landed vertically, relying on its flaming engines to take it into space. Once there, powerful Class 1 hyperdrives kicked in. Specially designed nav computers produced hyperdrive coordinates in seconds, providing fast getaways.

**hard contact** A term used by clone troopers of the Grand Army of the Republic to describe any situation in which they physically engaged a being.

Hardcell-*class transport*

**Hardfrost Base** The code name for a collection of icy caves and tunnels that made up Salmakk's primary base on Hoth during the New Order.

**Hard Heart Cantina** A cantina managed by Memah Roothes, it was on Deck 69 of the first Death Star. It was named in memory of Roothes's first establishment, the Soft Heart Cantina on Coruscant, which burned to the ground and left her in poverty.

**Hardin (1)** A brash young Jedi-in-training from Somov Rit 1,000 years before the rise of the Empire. Known as "Bug," he was the cousin of a boy known as Tomcat and a girl called Rain. The cousins were recruited by the Jedi to fight in the war against the Brotherhood of Darkness at Ruusan. After witnessing Tomcat turn traitor, Bug took up arms in Lord Hoth's Jedi Army of Light, abandoning his childish nickname and answering to his real name of Hardin. He confronted Tomcat, now apprenticed to the Sith Lord Githany. When Sith Lord Kaan activated a thought bomb, Hardin's life force was drained from his body, but his suffering came to a sudden end when he was struck and killed by a falling stalactite.

**Hardin (2)** A spacer who worked on Corulag, he continually modified his L2 Base Labor Droid and was amazed that the automaton kept working.

***Hardly Worth Stealing*** An aging starship owned and operated by Jag Murrock during the final years of the Old Republic.

**hard merchandise** Bounty hunter slang for the being on which a bounty was placed.

**Hardon, Den** A criminal targeted for execution by Gornt Seron shortly after the Battle of Endor. Seron hired Kyr Laron, who intercepted Hardon's ship and filled it with deadly RX-8 gas.

**Hardpoint Squadron** A group of Jedi-piloted starfighters led by Luke Skywalker in the years following the Yuuzhan Vong War. Ten years after the war, Hardpoint Squadron was assigned to Team Womp Rat during the Galactic Alliance's mission to prevent the Corellian system from seceding.

**Hardscrabble** A dusty settlement of a few hundred colonists, it held the only sentient life on Muskree at the time of the Galactic Civil War. A group of mining corporations established operations on Muskree when initial scans indicated high concentrations of minerals and ore. The scans proved false. Settlers who chose to remain made a meager living by raising nerfs and coaxing plant life out of the red dirt.

***Hard Shell*** A KDY Class 7 repair vessel used by the Empire on the planetoid Jatee, the ship was hijacked by a group of Rebel Alliance agents trying to get Dr. Soron Hegerty offworld.

**hard-sound gun** An intensely powerful sonic blaster developed by the Separatists during the Clone Wars, it was designed to rupture the eardrums and auditory nerves of its targets.

**Hardwikk, Radd** A male Clantaani, he was a known associate of Longo Two-Guns in the period before the Battle of Naboo. Mos Eisley security forces sought him in connection with a riot that occurred after local Podrace fans purchased exploding chubas. He was also implicated in distributing illegal communications tools. The bounty was claimed by Jango Fett.

**Hareel, Dr. Andros** A Rebel Alliance medical officer, he investigated reports of a plague sweeping Sedesia during the Galactic Civil War. Indications were that the Empire purposely spread the plague to put an end to rebellious activity on the planet. Dr. Hareel recommended that an Alliance team be sent to Sedesia to assist in knocking out the disease and perhaps obtain Sedesia's support in the war.

**Harf** A species whose members were distinguished by their red, goggle-like eyes and long snouts.

**Hargar** A merchant on Onderon in the years following the Mandalorian Wars.

**Har Gau** One of the larger cities established on Felucia by Gossam settlers, it was the site of a major water-processing facility.

**Hargeeva** A temperate world, the third of five in the Pelonat system, it was basically ignored until the Empire discovered its rich mineral deposits. Although settled some 2,000 years before the Battle of Yavin, its society quickly reverted to a feudal state until the Empire arrived to install a full garrison and high-tech refineries.

**Hargm's hill** A low, coastal bluff, it was just south of the Tahika Cliffs on Garos IV, and overlooked the governor's mansion.

**Hargon's hill** A low peak south of Ariana on Garos IV, it was the site of rich hibridium mines operated by the Empire during the Galactic Civil War.

**harima sauce** A tasty sauce served with vegetable turnovers by the Mawan species.

**Harin, Shella** This New Republic Intelligence agent held the rank of lieutenant at the time of the Human League crisis on Corellia. Harin was assigned to accompany Professor BinBinnari on a fact-finding mission to Leria Kerlsil.

**Harix** A hotbed of rebellious activity—much of it led by schoolteachers—during the Galactic Civil War. The Empire tried to maintain quiet with a garrison on the planet led by the Gektl Rahz. Luke Skywalker, however, managed to free captured students and defeat Rahz.

**Hariz** The city on N'zoth where Nil Spaar made his first appearance upon returning from Coruscant; he received the praise of the Yevethan people following the success of the first phase of the Yevethan Purge. Yet it was considered odd that Hariz was one of the few cities on N'zoth that allowed non-Yevetha to walk about by themselves. It was in the Hariz Downside district of the city that Nil Spaar's flagship, the *Aramadia,* was preserved as an "inspiration" for future generations of Yevetha.

**hark** A sharp-eyed raptor native to the planet Vorzyd 4.

**Harkas, Ran** A sergeant in the 407th Stormtrooper Division based on Yinchorr nearly a century after the end of the Yuuzhan Vong War, he was the leader of Joker Squad. Battle-hardened, Sergeant Harkas was one of many stormtroopers who quietly questioned their loyalty to the new Empire after Darth Krayt took control of the galaxy and exiled former Emperor Roan Fel. When the 407th was ordered to Borosk to prevent the 908th Stormtrooper Division from defecting, Harkas told himself that his only goal was completing the mission, even if it meant killing fellow troopers. After losing Vax Potorr and Jes Gistang in the fighting, however, and sustaining an injury in the blast that killed Gistang, Harkas began to wonder about his orders.

His injuries kept him out of the action when new recruit Anson Trask shot and killed Darth Krayt's personal liaison, Darth Maleval, after the Sith Lord demanded that Lieutenant Gil Cassel execute his own brother to prove his loyalty. In his reports, Harkas just noted that Maleval had been killed in the fighting. Harkas spent weeks recovering from his injuries, forcing him to turn leadership of Joker Squad over to Trask, who was the only other survivor of the Borosk combat. Once healed, Harkas was assigned to a mission led by Darth Stryfe to see if rumors were true that the Jedi had returned to Ossus.

**Harkners-Balix 903** A transport ship. Wedge Antilles referred to the *Etherway* as a Harkners-Balix 903 when he met Mara Jade on Abregado-rae, as part of an elaborate identification scheme set up by Fynn Torve. The 903 was succeeded by models 917 and 922.

**Harkness, Dirk** A native of Salliche, this Rebel Alliance operative joined shortly after Imperial forces killed his fiancée, Chessa. Harkness had become disenchanted with the Empire after the destruction of Alderaan, and Chessa's murder made the headstrong 21-year-old eager for revenge. He saw his first action against the Empire during the evacuation of Edan Base, shortly after the Battle of Yavin.

Harkness eventually was named commander of the Black Curs, and was forced to crash-land on Hensara III. He and his crew were rescued by Rogue Squadron. Harkness was a trusted source of information for Airen Cracken, and then went to work with Platt Okeefe and her band of mercenaries. Shortly after the Battle of Endor, he was captured by Imperial forces and imprisoned on Zelos II, sharing a dark cell with Jai Raventhorn. They were interrogated and beaten senseless, and neither had any idea how long they were imprisoned. Okeefe and Tru'eb Cholakk managed to rescue them both.

*Ran Harkas*

**Harkov, Admiral** The commander of the Imperial Star Destroyer *Protector,* he was assigned to end the Sepan Civil War and bring both Dimok and Ripoblus under Imperial control. Following the Battle of Hoth, Harkov met with Mon Mothma and secretly offered to have his entire fleet defect to the Rebel Alliance. But before he could carry out the plan, he was intercepted by Darth Vader in the Parmel system and executed.

**Hark'r, Captain** A Noehon, he was a merchant who stumbled upon *Home* and was captured, but Lens Reekeene decided that he wasn't a threat. To ensure that Hark'r didn't relay information on *Home* to the Empire, however, Hark'r was offered two choices: remain with Reekeene's Roughnecks on the ship, or spend the rest of his life on a remote uncharted planet. Hark'r remained, and later became *Home*'s supply master.

**Harkul** A wide desert plain on Kuar, it was the site of a battle between the Jedi Ulic Qel-Droma and the warrior Mandalore four millennia before the Galactic Civil War.

***Harla*** This Yuuzhan Vong worldship was under the command of Prefect Drathul during the galactic invasion.

**Harlaan** This young pilot served the Naboo Royal Defense Force shortly before the Battle of Naboo. A member of Echo Flight, Harlaan was killed when the *Velumina,* under the command of Captain Sorran, tried to steal several N-1 starfighters. Dren Melne tried to force Essara Till to surrender, and destroyed Harlaan's fighter in an effort to persuade her.

**Harlech, Captain** A native of Drogheda, he was commander of the Royal Guard there during the Galactic Civil War. Harlech hoped that Queen Sarna would continue to rule the planet as elected sovereign, because he could control her actions through physical force. When Lando Calrissian arrived on the planet, Harlech was exposed as a murderer and mercenary. He was shot and killed when Calrissian tried to escape Drogheda by taking the queen hostage.

**Harlequin Station** This space station served as a trade center during the Galactic Civil War. Led by Mayor Brauken, the station traded with Azzameen Station, and the two supported each other in their struggles with the Viraxo.

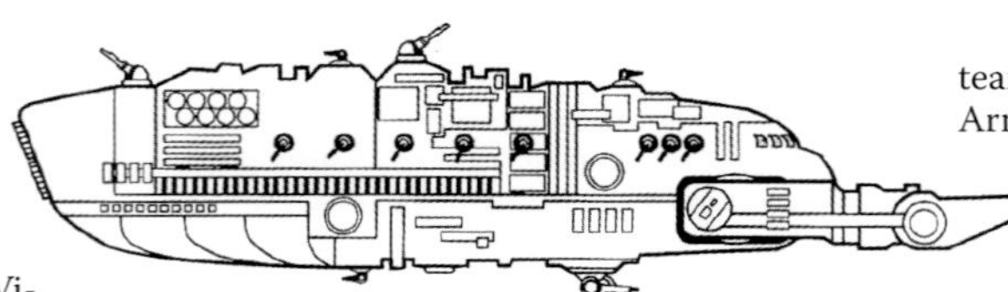
Harmzuay

**Harles, Commander** The head of Imperial Garrison Company 125a during the early stages of the Galactic Civil War, he was in charge of the attack on Gaulus shortly after the Battle of Yavin. Harles had planted a MerenData espionage droid in the Rebel Alliance base there, and used the information to plan the attack. He hated fights that involved women and children, and when he encountered a 16-year-old girl trying to rig the base's generator to blow up with the Imperials inside, he allowed her to finish the job and then helped her escape before the base was destroyed.

**Harleys, Diblen** A native of Coruscant, his father was a privileged bureaucrat, which helped insulate Harleys from the worst atrocities of the New Order. His mother died when he was 15, and he resolved to join the Imperial Survey Corps and explore Wild Space. His father explained to him the harsh realities of a scout's life, as well as the true nature of the Empire, but warned his son to keep any dissident thoughts to himself. Diblen joined the Rebel Alliance at his first chance. He proved to be a confident fighter pilot and tactician, and was a valuable resource during the planning of the Battle of Endor. He eventually was promoted to New Republic wing commander on Coruscant shortly before the rise to power of Grand Admiral Thrawn.

**Harlison, Chop** He and his younger brother, Roy, were orphaned when their parents were killed by a renegade swoop gang in Gallisport on the moon Shesharile 5. The pair eventually were taken in by the Rabid Mynocks; Chop became the gang's primary mechanic, using his knowledge of repulsors to repair and improve their swoops. He developed a prototype swoop known as the Star Slinger, which became the center of attention in the battles between the Mynocks and two rival gangs, the Spiders and the Raging Banthas. Chop married and had a daughter, but his wife was killed by the Spiders. He pledged himself to eliminate the violent gangs of Gallisport.

**Harloen** A planet that was known as the swoop-racing capital of the Outer Rim Territories.

**Harlow, Kend** This gambler was indebted to the Rodian crime lord Hatabbas, who eventually forced Harlow to fight his pet svaper. Harlow was eaten in the battle.

**Harlow, Moff** The Imperial Moff of the Catarlo sector at the height of the Galactic Civil War.

**Harlsen's Laws of Functional Military Intelligence** This short set of laws was developed to teach officer candidates that nothing was ever perfect in battle. The laws stated: Limited intelligence reports are inadequate. Detailed intelligence reports are inaccurate. Highly detailed intelligence reports are traps.

**Harm** An Imperial technician, he worked for Evir Derricote on Borleias.

**Harmae** This Yuuzhan Vong subaltern was praised by Nas Choka for his brave work during the subjugation of Obroa-skai.

**H'Arman, Erk** An Old Republic lieutenant, he was one of many fighter pilots who saw combat during the Clone Wars. Lieutenant H'Arman and his wingmate, Ensign Pleth Strom, were part of the team sent to Praesitlyn to protect the Intergalactic Communications Center. The Republic forces were unprepared for the number of Separatist fighters. H'Arman was shot down early in the battle and would have died if Praesitlyn recon trooper Odie Subu hadn't witnessed the crash and saved him. Erk found himself deeply attracted to the human female, and they found that they also were a good team in the field. They were briefly assigned to a listening post established by Freedom's Sons and Daughters, but were overrun by battle droids and buried beneath rubble for several days before being discovered by a scout force led by Grudo. Startled, Odie mistakenly shot Grudo, who later died of his wounds. H'Arman agreed to fly a transport alongside Anakin Skywalker during a daring mission to rescue hostages at the communications center. Chaos ensued, but the rescue was ultimately successful. When Skywalker returned from the final mop-up, Odie surprised both men by asking the young Padawan to perform a ceremony to marry H'Arman and her.

**Harmion, Halleb, K'yne, and Sarell** The three Harmion brothers worked as executives for the corporations acquired by hostile takeover kingpin Sarlim Gastess. All three were ruthless and seemed to relish the destruction and anguish they caused when they removed old management and employees in favor of workers and managers from their parent company, Gastess's Finance.

**Harmon** A Nagai warrior, he was part of a small invasion force led by Den Siva that tried to take control of Zeltros shortly after the Battle of Endor. Harmon was distinguished by the thick spikes he created with his hair, giving him an insectile appearance. Harmon and his team were responsible for the capture of King Arno and Queen Leonie, as well as Han Solo and Lando Calrissian.

**Harmonia** The capital city of Gacerian.

**Harmon Kizzlebrew** A beer favored in the Mid Rim, it was an excellent accompaniment to steamed yazstrimskizzies.

**Harmony Glade** A lowlands area of the planet Serphidi, it was near Castle S'Shah.

**Harmony Hall** One of the most prestigious concert halls on Coruscant, it served the Old Republic and the New Order, and was one of the buildings that survived into the early years of the New Republic.

**Harmony Lake** An idyllic body of water on the planet Bimmisaari.

***Harmzuay*** An old Kaloth-style battle cruiser owned by the Thalassian slavers, it had been heavily modified, including the addition of a pair of mandibles on its bow for grabbing smaller ships. Some years after the Battle of Endor, the ship was destroyed in a battle with the *Invidious* when it tried to poach slaves from Kerilt at the same time Leonia Tavira hoped to raid the colony world. The *Harmzuay* fought boldly but was no match for *Invidious*'s firepower.

**Harn** A Duros, he was personal secretary and majordomo for criminal Osaji Varane during the Galactic Civil War. When Varane was murdered, Harn surrendered to his killers and gladly gave information on the whereabouts of Varane's sibling Osaji Uhares in exchange for his life.

**Harnaidan** One of the largest cities on Muunilinst, it was the headquarters of the InterGalactic Banking Clan. During the early stages of the Clone Wars, Obi-Wan Kenobi believed that he had defeated Durge in a tremendous battle outside Harnaidan, only to confront the bounty hunter again. The city itself was filled with immense skyrises and towers, many of which stood more than 4,000 meters tall. The foundations for the buildings were sunk deep into the bedrock of Muunilinst's crust, and served as the anchor points for the skyhooks attached to High Port.

**Harnik, Gates** A grocer from the Cilpari city of Tamarack, he secretly supplied food to the pockets of resistance on the planet. When Moff Tascl leveled the city in an effort to flush out Rebel Alliance supporters, Harnik was caught and hanged from the ruins by Imperials as an example.

**Harno** A Rodian big-game hunter during the early years of the New Order, he became a poacher on Kashyyyk, leading to a bounty on his head from Wookiees and Trandoshans, who didn't want to be implicated in his illegal hunts.

**Harns, Ela** The freight administrator at Estaria Central Starport, she was a Rebel Alliance sympathizer and a member of a local cell. She and two others were the only ones who knew of a secret cache of supplies hidden within the starport, available to the Alliance in an emergency.

Harra

**Harona, Ijix** A New Republic lieutenant, he served under Pakkpekatt on the *Glorious* during the Black Fleet crisis. He eventually was promoted to colonel, and later commanded the Scimitar Squadron of A-wings during the Yuuzhan Vong War.

**Haroot** An avian species native to the planet Seylott.

**haroun bread** A rustic bread baked by the moisture farmers of Tatooine, it often was served as an accompaniment to ahrisa.

**Harous, Tolum** A scientist and engineer on Design Team Beta at Hydrospeare Corporation for nearly 30 years, he then took over as team director. A native of Adamastor, Harous was known as a perfectionist and was well schooled in a multitude of subjects. He was offered lucrative deals to work for Kuat Drive Yards and Sienar Fleet Systems but turned them down because he enjoyed his work at Hydrospeare.

***Harpago*** An Imperial *Interdictor*-class capital ship, it was used by Admiral Zaarin to stall his pursuers as he sped toward Coruscant, where he intended to capture and execute Emperor Palpatine.

***Harpax*** An Imperial *Interdictor*-class capital ship, the *Harpax* was instrumental in battles that led to the recovery of a fleet of ships under the command of Admiral Harkov in the Ottega system.

**harpercod** A speckle-banded fish, it was found in the oceans of Mon Calamari.

**Harpori** A planet in the Mid Rim near the Balowa system, it was the site of a Duros settlement wiped out by Kaox Krul six months before the Battle of Ruusan. Harpori was orbited by two moons.

***Harpox*** An *Imperial I*–class Star Destroyer that operated during the Galactic Civil War.

***Harpy*** A Nebulon-B2 frigate, it was part of the Imperial Navy during the Galactic Civil War.

**Harra** A Twi'lek who worked for Czerka Corporation and lived on Citadel Station in orbit around Telos following the Jedi Civil War, he had a serious gambling problem. In fact, he lost his girlfriend Ramana to Doton Het as part of the pot in a game of pazaak. Harra eventually enlisted the aid of the Exile and Kreia to rescue Ramana, but was forced to accept Ramana's freedom in order to avoid further trouble.

**Harrak, Colonel** An officer on Admiral Pellaeon's staff during the early stages of the Yuuzhan Vong War.

**Harran, Captain** Eight months after the Battle of Yavin, he was put in charge of a group of Rebel Alliance agents sent to rescue Jorin Sol from the Imperial labor colony on Kalist VI. Harran posed as the Imperial Navy captain who commanded the *Nuna's Twins*, which made regular runs to many Imperial labor colonies. On Kalist VI, the team discovered hundreds of Jabiimi slaves toiling in underground facilities. Sergeant Basso requested that the team alter its plans to rescue the slaves as well, and Harran ordered Basso to devise a workable arrangement for their extraction. Harran also saved the life of Deena Shan after she was discovered to be an Alliance agent. The team freed both Sol and the Jabiimi slaves and fled into hyperspace.

**Harrandarr** This remote planet was believed to be the homeworld of the Buzchub species.

**Harrandatha** *See* Estillo, Prince Harrandatha.

**Harrar** A Yuuzhan Vong priest, he was placed in a position of command during Nom Anor's second wave of attacks against the New Republic. The use of religious commanders came after the defeat of Shedao Shai at Ithor, and the loss of the fleet under the command of Deign Lian. Harrar was one of the few Yuuzhan Vong who recognized the true threat of the Jedi Knights, and he was the first to suggest outright aggression against them. He agreed to a plan to have the priestess Elan infiltrate the Jedi Order, all the while harboring a deadly bioweapon in her lungs. Harrar even suggested an alliance with the remaining Sith Lords if they could be found. He spent much of his time consulting specific auguries, hoping to determine the best course of action for the invading force.

When Elan's mission failed and was reviewed with Supreme Commander Nas Choka, Harrar was reassigned to the Outer Rim with Commander Tla. However, Harrar was later recalled from the field to serve as Warmaster Tsavong Lah's spiritual guide and adviser. The warmaster assigned Harrar to bring good fortune to the recapture of Borleias, but was unable to anticipate the plans of New Republic forces there. This lack of foresight, coupled with the inability of Czulkang Lah to discern the Republic's true plans, led to the destruction of the Yuuzhan Vong forces at Borleias. Harrar then fled back to Coruscant, hoping to enjoy the fruits of victory there. He remained on Coruscant after the death of Tsavong Lah, advising Supreme Overlord Shimrra on religious matters.

Harrar was one of many Yuuzhan Vong who came to question Shimrra's connection to the gods. He went so far as to meet with Nen Yim in secret, proposing an alliance with the Prophet Yu'shaa and a mission to locate the planet Zonama Sekot. Harrar's initial plan was to use Nen Yim as bait to capture the Prophet, but ultimately he wanted to locate the living world. He agreed to go on a secret mission with Jedi Knights Corran Horn and Tahiri Veila to locate Zonama Sekot. Once there, Harrar saw firsthand the planet's mingling of Yuuzhan Vong and other life-forms, indicating that perhaps his species *was* somehow linked to the galaxy.

After Tahiri Veila revealed that it had been Nom Anor who killed Nen Yim, Harrar swore to kill the former executor. The Jedi stopped him from attacking, but Nom Anor hunted Harrar down and confronted him on a rocky ledge. Although Harrar fought valiantly, he fell from the ledge during the fight. He managed to survive the fall and was rescued by a group of Ferroans as well as Tekli and Danni Quee. After Harrar spoke to the Jedi, he agreed to help them seek a resolution to the war.

When Galactic Alliance forces launched an attack on Coruscant, it was Harrar who helped them gain access to the Well of the World Brain so that Jacen Solo could convince the dhuryam to stop working for Shimrra. After the deaths of Shimrra and Onimi, who proved to be the true Supreme Overlord, Harrar and

Harrar

the rest of the Yuuzhan Vong agreed to surrender to the Galactic Alliance. In accordance with the advice of Jedi Master Luke Skywalker, the Galactic Alliance allowed the Yuuzhan Vong to travel to Zonama Sekot to reestablish their civilization. The planetary consciousness Sekot welcomed them, then dashed away into the Unknown Regions to allow its new and old inhabitants to evolve in peace.

**Harravan** A notorious Hapan pirate, he killed Prince Isolder's older brother, Kalen. Isolder hunted him down and captured him, but chose to imprison rather than murder him. Harravan was killed in jail before he could stand trial and reveal the names of his accomplices. It was assumed, however, that Queen Mother Ta'a Chume herself had employed the pirate to assassinate her older son, whom she felt was too weak to become ruler of Hapes.

***Harridan*** An Imperial *Victory*-class Star Destroyer, it was stationed in the N'zoth system in the Koornacht Cluster just after the Battle of Endor; it was to patrol the system and protect the Black Fifteen shipyards. But the *Harridan* was ordered to assist in the evacuation of Notak, giving the Yevetha a clear shot at Black Fifteen and the rest of the old Imperial shipyards in the Koornacht Cluster.

***Harrier*** This was one of the *Katana* fleet Dreadnaughts acquired by Garm Bel Iblis during the early years of the New Republic.

**Harrin** The primary planet in the Harrin system, it was the start of the Harrin Trade Corridor, which ran through 11 major trade centers to Merren, with a travel time of about 53 days.

**Harrin, J. M.** The captain of the *Bothan Whale*, a transoceanic shuttlecraft owned by Edan Spaceways; he worked the seas of Edan II during the New Order.

**Harrin Trade Corridor** This space lane was linked to the Enarc Run by the Kira Run. It was the primary hyperspace route leading from the Inner Rim to the Harrin sector, linking the Harrin system with the Merren system via 11 stopovers.

**Harris, Blaine** Bakura's defense minister during the New Order, he was at first a civilian figurehead. A former military officer, Harris walked with a limp from an old war injury. After the Battle of Bakura, Harris was given more power and control of the Bakuran armed forces. He eventually was elected Deputy Prime Minister, serving under Molierre Cundertol during the Yuuzhan Vong War. He had grown to hate the New Republic and its supposed peace, and began secretly funding the Freedom group in an effort to force Bakura to join the P'w'eck Emancipation Movement.

Behind the scenes, Harris planned to take all the credit for freeing Bakura from outside control, rather than have Freedom founder Malinza Thanas be regarded as a hero. He arranged for the kidnapping of Jaina Solo and used her to draw Thanas to him. Then, in a bold move, he planned to kill them both, making it appear that the Jedi Knight had confronted the Bakuran idealist. Harris also hoped to kill Cundertol and most of the Bakuran Senate, ensuring that he would assume control of the government and establish Thanas as a martyr whose cause should be adopted by all Bakurans. Harris and his plans were discovered by Prime Minister Cundertol and Han and Leia Organa Solo after an explosion ripped through the arena where the Keeramak was consecrating the planet. Cundertol, who survived the blast, had secretly been conspiring to turn Bakura over to the Ssi-ruuvi Imperium. He confronted Harris and then shot him in the head with a blaster, killing him instantly.

**Harris, Thurlow** The son of a Rebel Alliance captain, he later became a starfighter pilot and trained with Rookie One. While competent at the controls of a fighter, Harris lacked confidence and mental control. He flew as Blue Four during the Battle of Yavin.

**Harrll** A male Togorian, he was a member of the Crimson Nova chapter of the Bounty Hunters' Guild during the Clone Wars. He had trained for years as a Jedi hunter, a dangerous undertaking with few rewards. After some bounties were accepted, Harrll confronted none other than Jedi Master Mace Windu. The hunter used a Morgukai blade of pure cortosis, but was unable to match the speed of Windu's lightsaber. In a move of blinding speed, Master Windu brought his weapon around in a wide arc, severing Harrll's head from his shoulders.

**Harrod** A star in the Oplovis sector, it was orbited by a single habitable planet known simply as Harrod's Planet. During the Galactic Civil War, the planet was the base for the Empire's Oplovis fleet, commanded by Admiral Gaen Drommel from his Super Star Destroyer *Guardian*.

**Harron sector** This area of the galaxy was among the most heavily rearmed by the Empire during the Galactic Civil War.

***Harrow*** A *Victory*-class Star Destroyer, it was commanded by Captain Marl Semtin in the years around the Battle of Endor.

**harrowbane** A caustic weed native to Randorn 2, it was considered sacred by the native Mizx, who planted borders of it around their villages. They believed harrowbane prevented the ibliton from invading, and that seemed true since the plant's touch actually burned the exposed skin of the ibliton's tentacles.

**Harrowmere** Another name for the T'Ples Ocean on Goroth Prime.

**Harrsk, Supreme Warlord Blitzer** During the Battle of Endor, then–Imperial Navy Captain Blitzer Harrsk received a number of grievous burns over his face and body when his Star Destroyer was severely damaged. He fled with the remnants of the fleet to the Core, where he let his skin heal naturally, preserving forever the scars the Rebel Alliance had given him. The only repair he allowed was the addition of a droid's optical sensor to replace his lost eye. After recovering, Harrsk mustered the remaining Imperial starships and began small harassing attacks on the New Republic.

As his power grew, Harrsk sought to restore the New Order to the galaxy. The warlord established a stronghold on a rocky planet that orbited close to a red giant star, and started building 12 *Imperial*-class Star Destroyers, cowing nearby star systems. Admiral Daala offered to join with Harrsk following the destruction of her fleet and the *Eye of Palpatine*. When he refused and ordered her to take command of his fleet against Teradoc, Daala set out to unite the feuding warlords or die. In the end, Daala found it best to kill off the childish warlords—Harrsk included—when they failed to reach agreement at the summit on Tsoss Beacon.

**Harsh, Moff** An Imperial supporter even as a youth. One story told of his beating a bully senseless with a rock after the tormentor crushed a Star Destroyer model Harsh had been playing with. After graduating with honors from the Imperial Academy, Harsh was taken in by an influential Imperial Senator and learned a great deal about politics. He eventually earned the command of the Star Destroyer *Cauldron*, and was dispatched to eliminate the Rebel threat on Chabosh. Harsh himself led the stormtroopers into battle against Rebel Alliance forces, but suffered terrible wounds to his legs. Rather than accept cybernetic replacements, Harsh willed himself to heal without surgical assistance. His recovery only added fuel to his growing legend, and he was personally named Moff of the Bosph sector by Emperor Palpatine. Living on Otunia, he survived the upheaval following the Battle of Endor.

**Harsis** This dark-skinned man served as a sensor officer aboard the *Direption*, under the command of Commander Darron, during the defense of Liinade III.

**Harson, Moff Crin** This Imperial Moff was discovered dead in his rooms on the resort world of Traflin shortly after the Battle of Yavin. A group of nearby Rebel Alliance personnel were implicated in the crime, but were cleared of any murder charges when the true killer was discovered.

**Hart, Syndic Pandis** An alias used by Talon Karrde when he went to Tropis-on-Varonat to infiltrate the safari business of the Krish crime lord Gamgalon. Karrde also used it while he was hunting down the location of the *Emperor's Shadow* on Kaal, hoping to obtain a cloaking device rumored to have been installed on the ship.

**Hart-and-Parn Gorra-Fiolla of Lorrd** *See* Fiolla of Lorrd.

**Hartar, Plook** This crime lord was a rival of Servid Norn during the Galactic Civil War.

**Harth, Set** As a Padawan left behind on Coruscant when his Master, Aru-Wen, left for Ruusan to serve with Lord Hoth, he set out to learn about the Force on his own. He traveled to Ruusan in the wake of the battle, hoping to locate a Sith artifact. When he was forced to battle a stronger Sith magician for possession of the artifact, Set Harth drew additional energy from the dark side, then killed the Sith warrior's elderly servant in anger, after which he decided to become a Sith himself. He set out to obtain another artifact from a Hutt crime lord, but was forced to prove his worth against Bal Serinus in a lightsaber duel that left both Dark Jedi exhausted. They were captured and imprisoned by the Hutt, although they maintained a tentative telepathic contact.

**Harthan, Counselor** A diplomat for the Tion Hegemony, he had many successful negotiations to his credit. Counselor Harthan was called upon to intercede between the Troobs and Hobors on Tahlboor to create a lasting peace between the species while obtaining trading rights on the planet. Harthan's son, Jake, however, learned about the power of Mount Yeroc and its sky cannon and manipulated his father out of the counselor's position, taking it for himself. Harthan eventually discovered his son's treachery with the help of R2-D2 and C-3PO. When the Troobs and Hobors realized that they could use Mount Yeroc as a way to bring their species together, they asked Harthan to tell the Tion Hegemony that they wanted to work things out on their own.

**Harthan, Jake** The son of a Tion Hegemony diplomat, he managed to acquire R2-D2 and C-3PO on Rudrig after the droids left the service of Governor Wena on Kalarba. Jake later accompanied his father to Tahlboor, where he discovered the power of Mount Yeroc and its sky cannon. Hoping to obtain the power for himself, he set in motion a plan to remove his father from the negotiations and take over himself. He then killed the son of the Troob leader and tried to frame the daughter of the Hobor leader for the murder. Jake hoped that this would ignite a civil war, letting him take control of Mount Yeroc. The droids discovered the truth and bluffed Jake into admitting the crime. He took a hostage, but a Troob spear ended his life.

**Harthis, Major** This New Republic officer was an administrative assistant to Colonel Gavin Darklighter during the Yuuzhan Vong War.

**Harthusa** A Devaronian who worked as a slave auctioneer on the Imperial world of Deysum III after the Battle of Yavin, he had some business sense but essentially was a coward. He maintained a luxurious domed apartment on the planet, where he regularly entertained females of all species.

***Harthusa's Pride*** A modified space yacht owned by the Devaronian slave auctioneer Harthusa. Rebel Alliance agents investigating the Empire's construction of a supply depot in the Bissillirus system stole the vessel shortly after they liberated Kentara from slavery.

**Hartin** An independent spacer, he worked with a number of criminals during his career and knew many of their secret schemes to bypass the legal system.

**Hartzig** A military official, he was in charge of the cleanup activities on the moon Pydyr ordered by the failed Jedi Dolph, who had adopted the name Kueller.

**Haruspex** A name used to describe prophets and oracles on Darlyn Boda. They were exceptionally accurate in reading the entrails of certain creatures, such as the toccat, provided that the being who requested the reading had actually killed the creature.

*Haruun Kal*

**Haruun Kal** The only habitable world in the Al'har system, it appeared from space to be an ocean-covered planet. In reality, the multicolored ocean was a sea of toxic, heavier-than-air gases that were brought to the surface by volcanic activity. Only mountains and plateaus that reached high into the atmosphere could support life, and that was where human life could be found. The name *Haruun Kal* meant "above the clouds." The Korunnai moved about the landmass as best they could to avoid being caught by sudden storms that might bring gases up from the surface. Much of the landmass was covered with jungles and semi-tropical forests. The planet had no natural satellites, but a ring of rocky debris that encircled it was believed to have been the remains of its moon.

Haruun Kal was important during the Clone Wars because it was located at the hub of the Gevarno Loop, and separated several Separatist-loyal systems from a group of systems that remained loyal to the Republic. The Jedi Council believed that a starship transporting Jedi Knights during the Great Sith War had crashed on the planet, and that the survivors were, in fact, the ancestors of the Korunnai—and all Korunnai could touch the Force. In the wake of the Clone Wars, an Imperial armada bombarded the planet from orbit, destroying most of its surface and exterminating the native Korunnai.

*Set Harth*

***Harvest*** The original name of the *Barloz*-class freighter later known as the *Twi'lek Dancer.* It was owned by an agricultural combine in the Tion Hegemony, but it was retired when the combine got the funds to purchase a YT-1300. It was then purchased by Xufal D'uat, who renamed it the *Venom Sting.*

**Harvest Bay** This oceanic region of Cols was known as the primary breeding ground of the kalaides.

**harvest blade** A folding poleax used by Nosaurians to kill rikknits on New Plympto.

**Harvest Ceremony** An Ithorian ritual in which specimen material was taken from plants for use in growing hybrids.

**Harvest Day (1)** An annual Mos Eisley festival celebrating the year's water harvest.

**Harvest Day (2)** A holiday celebrated in the Tapani sector, it was first observed by the original settlers to commemorate the harvesting of crops. It later became simply a day off from work.

**harvester droid** Huge droids equipped with shovels, clippers, and pincers that were deployed into fields to sow seeds and harvest plants. They were built with large bins for collecting the grains and vegetables they harvested, and were often equipped with internal shredders to help mulch weeds and other waste products.

**Harvest Festival** A weeklong series of contests and parties held annually by the AGR agro-combine on Corellia.

**Harvest Flyway** A speeder route that connected the city of Turos Noth with the Greenbelt region of the planet Teyr. The little-used cargo transport lane had no defined speed limit.

***Harvest Moon*** A 100-ton grain freighter that operated in the Sarrahban system, it was used during the Galactic Civil War to smuggle Rebel Alliance refugees and ytterbium out of the system.

**Harvest Moon Feast** An Ewok celebration.

**Harvest-Nine** The code name for a test ordered by Lord Arkoh Adasca during the early stages of the Mandalorian Wars. Dormant exogorths were reawakened and ordered to consume a small planetoid before returning to dormancy.

**Harvest Season** This was the time of year on Kinyen when the Gran harvested their grains and other major crops. The advent of Harvest Season was often celebrated by the more affluent Gran families with a gala ball.

**Harvos** This Nelvaanian warrior was one of many who were captured by Separatist battle droids and brought to a secret facility that had been established in the wilderness of Nelvaan. Like other captives, Harvos was subjected to torturous experiments by Skakoan scientists. His once lithe body was tampered with genetically, and his flesh was implanted with strange forms of technology. When Anakin Skywalker arrived on Nelvaan during the Clone Wars, he destroyed the facility and freed the Nelvaanians. Rather than simply attacking the offworlder, Harvos reminded his fellow warriors that they were Nelvaanians first, and that any being who helped them escape was not an enemy. Harvos and his comrades turned their anger on their Skakoan captors, attacking them before fleeing the facility to return to their families. Harvos initially was shunned because of his grotesque alterations, but eventually he was welcomed back to his village.

**Harza** A moist, sweet cake baked on the planet Beheboth.

**Hasamadhi district** This warehouse district in Coruscant's southern polar region was used by Lando Calrissian and Luke Skywalker. They hid the *Millennium Falcon* there when they attempted to rescue Leia Organa from Xizor's palace.

**Hash** This clone trooper was part of a platoon dispatched to Pengalan IV to eliminate a Separatist missile facility during the early stages of the Clone Wars. He was given the nickname Hash by Joram Kithe because of the burns on his cheek. Hash and his comrade Spade were killed during the platoon's attempt to reach the missile-production facility beneath the surface of Tur Lorkin.

**HASH-19** An assassin droid employed by Moff Bandor to roam the Game Chambers of Questal, it was a gold-chrome metallic ball. HASH-19 looked like a surveillance spy-eye. As soon as it encountered a target, the droid sprouted six mechanical arms, each tipped with four vibroblades. HASH-19 attacked by spinning wildly and slashing its way through its prey.

**Hashoop** According to Ewok legend, this princess could hear the voices of the stars.

**Hask** A Neimoidian, he was the Trade Federation's main representative to the bacta-producing world of Thyferra in the years leading up to the Stark Hyperspace Conflict. He formed an alliance with Adol Bel of the Xucphra Corporation, and developed a plan to starve the Old Republic of bacta in order to reap huge profits. The plans were thwarted by Iaco Stark, whose Commercial Combine began raiding the few bacta convoys allowed to leave Thyferra, then reselling the bacta at cheaper prices. Their plans were further derailed by Jedi Master Tholme and his Padawan apprentice, Quinlan Vos, who were on Thyferra to investigate the bacta shortage.

Harvos

**Hask, Loka** Expelled from the Imperial Academy on Carida for grifting his classmates, he returned home just in time to witness the public execution of his father. Hask took his meager inheritance, along with hidden caches of credits and valuables his father had stashed away, and bought a small starship. He began a small-time pirating operation, and eventually worked his way up to become the leader of the Bonestar pirates. He led authorities on a chase through the Corellian system in the armed freighter *Buzzzer,* and tried to lose them at Gus Treta. His plan was to create a large enough diversion to allow the pirates to escape notice.

Hask landed at Jagged Antilles's fuel depot, and in the midst of refueling, Hask ordered his ship to lift off. This resulted in a ruptured fuel linkage that spewed volatile fuel everywhere. The backwash from the ship's thrusters ignited the fuel, destroying the depot. Jagged and his wife, Zena, died trying to contain the damage, but young Wedge Antilles was rescued by Booster Terrik. Terrik did not stand in Wedge's way when the youth demanded revenge, and the two located Hask and managed to severely damage the pirate's ship, leaving him for dead. Hask took the only usable spacesuit and escaped the destruction. A parasite had hidden in the suit, however, and latched on to Hask's face permanently.

Hask vowed to hunt down Wedge Antilles and make him pay for the loss of his ship and crew. Sometime later, as an Imperial, Hask was one of the negotiators trying to obtain the Mrlssti Academy's phantom cloaking device. He was pitted against Wedge in the negotiations, and managed to frame Rogue Squadron for a theft. Wedge exposed Hask's treachery, but Hask escaped to Rorax Falken's lab, where he discovered the gravitic polarization beam. When it suddenly activated during a bombing ordered by Hask, he was too close to the device. It developed a huge feedback loop, opening a wormhole and swallowing Hask, the lab, and a nearby Star Destroyer.

Loka Hask

**Haskit** A Bothan matriarch famous for her role in politics, she influenced the government of Bothawui for 50 years.

**Haslam, Lieutenant Koris** A Rebel Alliance officer who was part of a Special Forces team assigned to Commander Briessen; he was instrumental in the liberation of Gebnerret Vibrion from Selnesh. Many attribute Haslam's understanding of Imperial military structure to a commission with the Empire. He had a warm personality that allowed him to mingle with spacers and mechanics as easily as with bureaucrats and politicians. Haslam was injured in the escape from Selnesh, but not so seriously that he wasn't able to handle the guns on the escape ship.

**Haslip, Dair** An Imperial officer on Garos IV, he was a secret supporter of the Rebel underground. He dreamed of attending the Raithal Academy with his friend Jos Mayda, although Jos's social position meant that he had a harder time getting into the Academy. Years later, during a trip with Jos to the caves on Mount Usca, they ran into scout troopers who accused them of being Rebel spies; they shot Jos dead before Dair managed to shoot the troopers. That made Dair resolve to help the Rebel Alliance every chance he got.

**Hass, Osi** This Krikthasi was the leader of the Undrarian *junieuw* during the Galactic Civil War. He allied himself with the Rebel Alliance, hoping to obtain high-tech weaponry to defeat the Multopos.

**Hassk, Captain** A Gungan military leader, he established a base on the moon of Rori during the Galactic Civil War. From there, Captain Hassk launched a series of strikes against Imperial forces that controlled the Naboo system, hoping to free his people on both Naboo and Rori.

**Hassla'tak** This Twi'lek worked for Booster Terrik as a navigator and steward aboard the *Errant Venture.*

**hassling** Native to the swamp world of Dagobah, this short-bodied plant had a distinctive, mildly offensive odor. Its bulbous roots could be ground up and mixed with water to form an orange paint. Explorers discovered strange cave paintings that used hassling, although Dagobah wasn't known to have any native sentient life-forms.

**Hast (1)** A onetime Imperial pit lieutenant serving on the *Valiant,* he joined the Rebel Alliance after resigning his commission at the end of his hitch. He served for many years as a special agent monitoring privateer vessels used by Ral'Rai Muvunc and Ordnance and Supply. Hast was then assigned to observe Urias Xhaxin and the crew of the *Free Lance.*

**Hast (2)** This planet was the site of secret New Republic shipyards. The captured Star Destroyers *Liberator* and *Emancipator* were refitted here after they were damaged in an attack on Imperial Warlord Teradoc. Both were damaged again when Imperial forces discovered the shipyards and attacked them.

***Hasti*** A Rebel Alliance shuttle used to transport commandos to the scene of a starfighter battle with the Imperial frigate *Vehemence.*

**Hatabbas** A Rodian crime lord, he was known to keep a pet svaper in his lair. Those who owed Hatabbas money, or simply displeased him, were forced to wrestle with the beast for their lives.

**Hatanga, Kortha** This grizzled old starship captain commanded the *Galax Titan* during its ore runs throughout his native Elrood sector during the New Order. He lived by the "Code of the Stars," and drank as hard as he worked his crews.

**Hatawa sector** A galactic sector in the Rim, it was largely unexplored by New Republic standards.

**Hatch** The basic unit of Kari society, each Hatch consisted of 20 to 30 individual Kari. The Kari had one of the galaxy's true hive societies, and each Hatch had its own personality, formed from the minimal intelligence of its members.

***Hatch*** A Rebel Alliance YT-1300 destroyed during the Galactic Civil War.

**Hatchepants** This small, red-skinned humanoid was an information broker who worked in Crevasse City on Kalkovak during the New Order.

**Hatcher, B'ante** The leader of Agamar's underground resistance during the early years of Emperor Palpatine's reign.

**Hatchling** The nickname of zero-g maintenance droids produced by Roche Industries during the New Order. Measuring around 2 meters long and resembling a huge insect, the Hatchling was powered by a repulsorlift engine and several small thrusters. It was equipped with six manipulator arms and a variety of repair tools, including a welding laser and plating cutters. Originally designed to help in the construction of orbital shipyards, the Hatchling also was used by independent spacers as a starship repair droid.

**hatch persuader** This was the term used by the clone commandos of the Grand Army of the Republic to describe the explosive charges used during boarding operations.

**hatch sphincter** A form of self-sealing doorway developed by the Yuuzhan Vong.

***Hate*** One of the Nebulon-B frigates used by the Imperial Navy during the Galactic Civil War.

**Hathan, Artzam** This Ugnaught was believed to have stolen secret plans and schematics from Sienar Fleet Systems in the aftermath of the Battle of Naboo. With the help of his colleague, Alby Ermad, Artzam made off with several disks' worth of documentation and fled to the Outland Transit Station. However, a bounty had been placed on both Ugnaughts' heads for their arrest and return to Sienar. Jango Fett collected the bounty on both.

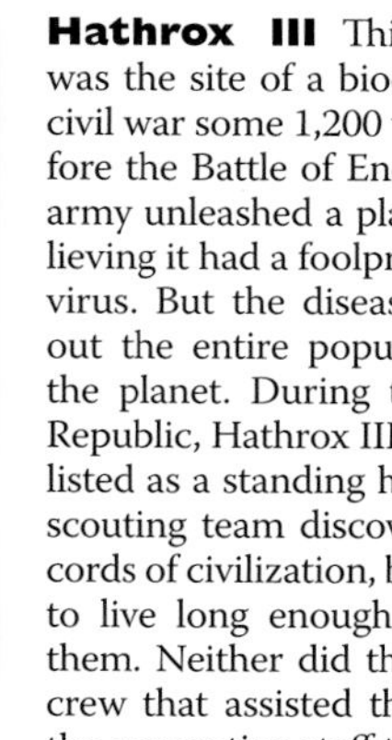
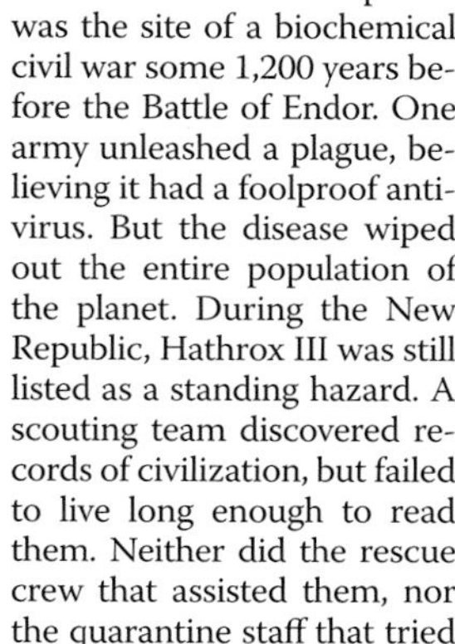
Groff Haug

**Hathrox III** This planet was the site of a biochemical civil war some 1,200 years before the Battle of Endor. One army unleashed a plague, believing it had a foolproof antivirus. But the disease wiped out the entire population of the planet. During the New Republic, Hathrox III was still listed as a standing hazard. A scouting team discovered records of civilization, but failed to live long enough to read them. Neither did the rescue crew that assisted them, nor the quarantine staff that tried to save them.

**Haug, Groff** A Coruscant crime lord in the years leading up to the Clone Wars. Much of his criminal organization was hidden behind Haug Nerf Industries, a nerf-packaging company. His operations were allowed a measure of freedom because he was close to Senator Trell, who helped fund the import of tainted death sticks from Malastare. Jango Fett sought out Groff Haug to question his connections to the Bando Gora cult. But his old nemesis, Montross, had beaten him to the punch by killing Haug and then freezing his body—which he presented to Fett.

***Hauler 10*** An ore hauler used by Lant Mining Corporation, it transported refined ore from the Lormar 23 station in the Mangez system. Its captain was fond of racing through traffic lanes, much to the dismay of traffic control officers.

**Hauler-2 cargo tug** A line of cargo hauling tugboats produced by Sienar Fleet Systems for use by the Empire.

***Hauler VI*** A Rebel Alliance *Censian*-class transport, it was used by Special Forces as a troop carrier. It was attacked shortly before the Battle of Yavin by the Fivaran Organization, which failed to recognize the ship as a military vessel. Nearly all the Fivaran pirates were killed or captured, although Denuab and Dorin Venithon escaped.

**haul jets** Spacer slang for "let's get out of here."

***Haumia*** This Gallofree medium transport was used by the Rebel Alliance to transport bacta during the Galactic Civil War.

**Haunted Straits** A long passageway on Maramere formed by a series of tall, inward-curving stone spires, it was managed by Sol Sixxa during the Trade Federation's control of the planet. Sixxa fought off any intruders to protect the location of the Invisible Island.

**hau polyp** The reddish polyps of this bioengineered creature were used by the Yuuzhan Vong to form supple chairs and cushions, although these were reserved for the highest social castes. A huge throne of pulsating, red-hued hau polyps was created within the Citadel for Supreme Overlord Shimrra after the Yuuzhan Vong captured the planet Coruscant and remade it into a simulacrum of Yuuzhan'tar.

**Hauser, Grand Moff** Ranulf Trommer's father brought Grand Moff Hauser to M'haeli to show him firsthand the treachery of Governor Grigor.

**Hav** A Duros who worked for Gamgalon on Varonat.

**Havaal** This Duros served as Gallo Memm's chief steward, overseeing the security of Streysel Island on the planet Vaynai while Memm was offworld.

**Havac** Apparently a holodocumentarian, he became a noted alien rights activist during the Stark Hyperspace Conflict and spent many years researching the abuses of the Trade Federation. In fact, Havac was an alias used by Eru Matalis, a native of Eriadu. Havac worked from a base on Asmeru during the period leading up to the Battle of Naboo. A confederate of Arwen Cohl, he had no stomach for violence, but excelled in treachery and deceit. Havac also was a member of the militant wing of the Nebula Front, and was one of Cohl's main contacts in the organization. Havac had been working secretly with Senator Palpatine to help ensure that the Nebula Front was able to obtain resources and support, and it was believed that he was responsible for the assassination attempt on Chancellor Valorum a year before the Battle of Naboo. He later hired Cohl in an attempt to finish off Valorum on Eriadu. A secondary mission was to eliminate Nute Gunray and the directorate of the Trade Federation. Havac believed he had to kill Cohl after learning that Jedi were tracking his movements. In a brief struggle, Cohl and Havac shot each other to death. The Nebula Front then disintegrated.

**Havath Minor** This gas giant, orbited by 11 moons, was the fifth and outermost planet in the Muunilinst system.

**Havath Prime** This gas giant, orbited by 32 moons, was the fourth planet in the Muunilinst system.

**Havel, Matas** The original owner of the YT-2400 transport that later became the *Lambarian Crab,* he modified the ship for additional cargo space and enhanced shielding before selling it to Finious Crab.

**Haveland, Moff** An Imperial Moff who controlled the Rettna system during the New Order. He also had jurisdiction over the Freda and Jante systems. When the Freda ended a decades-old cold war by attacking Jante holdings on Rett II, Haveland called in Imperial forces and initiated unsuccessful peace talks.

***Havelon*** This warship served as Grand Moff Wilhuff Tarkin's flagship during the construction of the first Death Star near Despayre. The *Havelon* was usually stationed in geosynchronous orbit around the planet, allowing Tarkin and his crew to monitor the construction at all times.

***Haven*** A group of Imperial *Lambda*-class shuttles that was commandeered by Admiral Zaarin as part of his plot to capture Emperor Palpatine. He was unable to complete his coup d'état, and fled in the Star Destroyer *Glory.*

**Haven** A small planetoid in the Minos Cluster, it served as the site of the Rebel Alliance's primary resistance center in the cluster during the Galactic Civil War. Luke Skywalker and Leia Organa fled there from Cloud City to meet a segment of the Alliance fleet. Luke received his prosthetic hand while in orbit around Haven, and it was here that the initial plan to rescue a frozen Han Solo was put into action.

General Larr Haverel

**Haven, the** A rough-and-tumble Mid Rim cantina owned by the Ithorian Womwa during the Galactic Civil War, it was a front for the owner's spice-trafficking operations. The Haven looked so run-down and dirty that patrons were fond of saying that the glasses were only as clean as the sleeve that just wiped them.

**Haven Base** A code name used for the Rebel Alliance base on Arbra. Haven Base was the main operations center in the months following the Battle of Hoth. It was built in an underground grotto where crystalline structures channeled heat and electricity from the planet's core. Later, an entire abandoned city was discovered beneath the base, with architecture dating back to the pre-Republic days of Xim the Despot. It was in this ancient city, built by the Arbrans, that the Darker lived.

***Haven Jace*** This was one of the few New Republic medical frigates that survived the Battle of Coruscant and retreated to Borleias during the Yuuzhan Vong War.

**Haverel, General Larr** An Imperial commander in charge of ground forces aboard the *Admonitor* during its journey through the Unknown Regions, he had an intense dislike of then-Admiral Thrawn and his tactics in confronting pirate gangs. Thrawn sent Haverel back to Coruscant for court-martial.

**Haverling** A planet that joined the New Republic after the Battle of Endor, it was the site of a new shipyard that supported the Republic's fleet in the sector.

**Havero, Jain** This muscled blond was one of the best combat fighters on Shiva IV during the Galactic Civil War. He supported Aron Peacebringer and worked to cement a bond between humans and the native T'Syirel population. His prowess with all manner of weapons often went to his head, and he sometimes got careless while fighting. During a mission to investigate the fate of the city of K'avor, Havero and Peacebringer discovered Leia Organa, who had crash-landed after her shuttle had been hit by a micromine. She was in the sector to investigate the buildup of Imperial forces.

**Havighasu, Hatirma** An old smuggler friend of Han Solo, he always flew by himself even though that meant he couldn't take on the big jobs and earn the big money. He often flew the Praff Run.

**havla** A gourmet toast favored by many Imperial nobles and dignitaries during the New Order.

***Havoc* (1)** An *Imperial*-class Star Destroyer, it was under the command of Captain Tulimu during the siege of Edan II. Rebel Alliance Colonel Pertarn launched a frontal assault on the ship and was bolstered by augmented weaponry from the light freighter *Vindicator,* destroying the *Havoc* and liberating the planet.

***Havoc* (2)** A 22-meter-long starship owned and operated by the Feeorin pirate Nym, it was the prototype for the Scurrg H-6, an experimental bomber built by the shipwrights of the Nubian Design Collective. The Nubians scrapped the project, so lead engineer Jinkins helped Nym steal the ship before joining the pirate's crew to keep upgrading and enhancing its systems. The *Havoc* was armed with a pair of triple laser cannons on each wing, a turret-mounted double laser cannon on its dorsal side, and a plasma scourge. The original proton bomb launcher was replaced with a bomblet generator that produced a continuous supply of destructive energy bombs. An additional missile launcher was installed to fire proximity mines at enemy ships. The *Havoc* was well shielded. Another of the major modifications was to the ship's command systems. Jinkins modified the ship's controls and added two dedicated astromech droids to allow Nym to fly the ship by himself if necessary. When flown in atmosphere, the *Havoc* could attain speeds of 1,000 kilometers per hour, and was equipped with a Class 1.5 hyperdrive.

***Havoc* (3)** An Imperial *Strike*-class cruiser, it intercepted the Rebel Alliance frigate *Battle of Yavin* in the Hensara system. The frigate crew was forced to land on Hensara III and sank their ship in a deep lake. Rogue Squadron was called to escort a rescue team to pick them up.

**Havocs** A gang of Bothan swoop riders who sacked the city of Tal'cara during the New Order.

**havod** A deep red alloy used to custom-form starship hulls, it was made of chanlon and hfredium. Too difficult to mass-produce, it rarely was used unless specifically ordered by the buyer. Shortly after the Battle of Yavin, Imperial Admiral Kendel commissioned 100 Star Destroyers with havod plating.

***Havok*** A Nebulon-B frigate used by the Imperial Navy during the Galactic Civil War.

**Havor** A gunrunner, he worked with Merglyn during the last decades of the Old Republic. Both were killed when they were shot down by the Guardians of Kiffu as they tried to run weapons to Kiffex. Hidden in their ship's cargo hold, however, was the Jedi Knight Aayla Secura, who was trying to reach Volfe Karkko.

**HAVr A9** This was the official designation of Ubrikkian's Floating Fortress, a repulsorlift tank that was designed to end urban uprisings without the need to call in AT-AT walkers. These floating cylinders had fully independent, full-sweep heavy blaster cannons mounted on a topside turret. The two guns could sweep across a field of fire to lock on to a target. The fortress also was equipped with a sophisticated sensor package modeled after assassin droids. It created a 30-meter bubble around the vehicle that was extremely effective at locating targets, making the HAVr A9 all the more effective.

**Havricus** A Mid Rim planet, it was beset by stone mites in the years leading up to the Clone Wars.

**Havridam City** One of the largest cities on New Bakstre, it was partially destroyed before the Clone Wars when the Mechanical Liberation Front tried to "free" a

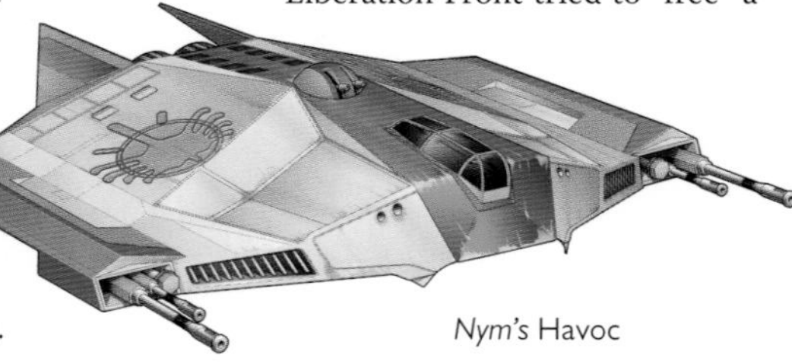

Nym's Havoc

shipment of XM-15 Vindicator missiles. The clumsy activists set off the missile's explosives, killing 14 members of their party and destroying nearly 2,000 square kilometers of the city.

**HAVt B5 Juggernaut** This variant on the A5 and A6 Juggernaut models was lighter and more maneuverable than its predecessors. Although impressively armed and armored, its main mission was transporting troops.

**HAVw A5 Juggernaut** Kuat Drive Yards' heavy ground assault vehicle (GAV), the HAVw A5 was nicknamed the Juggernaut or the Rolling Slab. Originally produced during the last years of the Old Republic, it became one of the Empire's most durable and reliable assault vehicles. The Juggernaut was based on the AT-TE used by the Grand Army of the Republic, but it moved on five sets of wheels and did not have a repulsorlift. At 22 meters long and 15 meters high, it also used armor plating identical to the AT-

HAVw A5 Juggernaut

TE. Juggernauts were well armed, with three heavy laser cannons, a single medium blaster cannon, and two concussion grenade launchers. The HAVw A5 required a crew of eight, including one in the observation tower that protruded from the main body. The Juggernaut could carry up to 50 troops and 1,000 kilograms of cargo. As the Imperial war machine began to rely on the AT-AT walker, many Juggernauts were sold off and ended up with gangs and planetary warlords.

**HAVw A6 Juggernaut** A 10-wheeled tank similar to the HAVw A5, it had more ability to move over rough terrain than its predecessor. At more than twice the size of the A5, it was a formidable sight on the battlefield. It came equipped with a dedicated 2-1B medical droid that could immediately minister to any of the up to 300 troopers crammed inside. Despite its size, the Juggernaut could attain speeds of up to 160 kilometers per hour over smooth terrain.

Hawk-bat

**Hawaka Islands** An island chain on Mon Calamari, it was formed by peaks of the Seascape Mountains that reached above the surface of the planetary ocean.

**Hawaz, Major Rin** A New Republic Intelligence officer, he investigated the appearance of battle-site scavengers and the effects of the Historic Battle Site Preservation Act and Operation Flotsam.

**Hawj** A Bothan diplomat from Thoran, he pursued a business alliance with Skydove Freight during the early years of the New Order. Hawj also was an aspiring novelist and planned to use his knowledge of Popara the Hutt and his family members as the basis for a holonovel.

**Hawk Squadron** A starfighter group maintained by the Khuiumin Survivors in support of the Invids.

***Hawkbat*** One of Imperial Warlord Zsinj's supply ships, it was sent to rendezvous with the *Night Caller* shortly before it was ordered to attack Talasea. Zsinj ordered it to dock with the *Night Caller* and perform a routine inspection, although the *Night Caller* actually had been captured by the New Republic's Wraith Squadron.

***Hawk-Bat*** This *Tempest*-class gunship served as the flagship of Arwen Cohl and his pirates.

**hawk-bat** A species of kite-like avian creatures native to Coruscant. Hawk-bats had metallic talons and hunted in flocks. Their eggs were considered a delicacy by the aristocracy of the Old Republic. Their flesh also was discovered to be edible by the Ortolan chef Handree Braman, who recommended that it be cooked at 1,000 degrees for no more than 20 minutes. The hawk-bat was capable of seeing a wide range of spectra beyond normal light. Young hawk-bats had green skin and were fully independent from birth. Upon reaching maturity, the hawk-bat would shed its green skin and emerge as an adult, with purplish yellow-gray skin.

HAVw A6 Juggernaut

**Hawk-bat, the** This was a nickname used by many members of the Jedi Order to describe Master Jai Maruk, because of his fierce, wild stare during combat or other intense times.

**Hawkbat Battalion** This division of the Grand Army of the Republic was formed during the buildup to the Battle of Geonosis. It was led by Major Twelve and was part of the 101st Regiment.

**Hawkbat Gang** This swoop gang was formed in the undercity of Coruscant sometime after the Battle of Naboo.

Hawkbat Gang

**Hawk-bat Independent Space Force** A cover used by Wraith Squadron during its attempt to infiltrate Warlord Zsinj's forces. Several of the Wraiths donned makeup and became Hawk-bats in order to hide their identities. The Hawk-bats concentrated their early efforts on the planet Halmad, which was just outside Zsinj's area of control. Their base was situated in an abandoned mine, designated A3 by Tonheld Mining Corporation, within a large asteroid in the Halmad system. After members stole several TIE interceptors from a garrison in Hullis and the cargoes of a number of shippers based on Halmad, Zsinj finally stepped in and took protective control of the planet. He then offered the Hawk-bats a chance to join rather than fight him. They agreed to participate in Zsinj's raid on Kuat, where the alerted New Republic forces led by Han Solo and the Mon Remonda nearly caught the rogue warlord.

***Hawkbat's Perch*** A crew shuttle assigned to the warship *Hawkbat.*

***Hawkbat's Vigil*** A crew shuttle assigned to the warship *Hawkbat.*

**Hawra, Captain** A ruthless commander of security forces protecting the Imperial outpost on Lotide. He rose to his position by stepping over those who underestimated him. He was paranoid and corrupt, and would stop at nothing to ensure his own safety.

HB-9

**Hawser, Major Llek** An officer with the Corellian Security Force serving under Gil Bastra.

**Hax, Pollux** One of Emperor Palpatine's most trusted associates, he was in charge of the Empire's propaganda dissemination section.

**Haxan, Serom** A small, dark-skinned man, he was a contemporary of Professor Movac Arisster at the University of Pangalactic Cultural Studies on Lorrd in the years after the Yuuzhan Vong War. Arisster, dying of cancer, had a "vision" and decided to die in a blaze of glory—but not before talking to a Jedi. Arisster held Haxan hostage, strapped a layer of explosives to his own back, and then strapped Haxan's body on top of the explosives. After going to the large aquarium at the Lorrd Academy for Aquatic Studies, Arisster threatened to set off the explosives unless he could talk to Nelani Dinn, a Jedi stationed on Lorrd. Jacen Solo, who was also onplanet, accompanied Dinn. Claiming that he had no time to deal with the distraught man, Solo used the Force to set off the explosives, killing both men.

Pollux Hax

**Haxim** A Falleen king and father of Prince Xizor, he ruled during the last years of the New Order.

**Haylon, Vinzel** The warden of the Empire's prison facility on Dathomir during the Galactic Civil War.

**Hayvlin, Commander** An Imperial Army officer, he was in charge of the AT-AT walker units that were stationed aboard the Star Destroyer *Avenger,* commanded by Captain Ferdas.

**hazard trooper** Specialized Imperial stormtroopers trained to operate in hazardous environments such as extreme temperatures and caustic atmospheres. They wore enhanced armor that served as self-contained environment suits that could support troopers underwater or, for brief periods, even in the vacuum of space.

**Hazzard** The homeworld of spacer Boo Rawl.

**HB-4** Used correctly, this projectile-firing hunting rifle made by Prax Arms during the Galactic Civil War virtually ensured a one-shot success. Every projectile trailed a monofilament cord that fed flight adjustment data to the projectile's barbed head. As long as a direct line of sight to the target was maintained, the HB-4 provided any corrective data necessary.

**HB-9** A primitive blaster rifle made by Zenoti Arms, it was known for its ornate, hand-carved body. The HB-9 was the primary weapon of the Utapaun military during the Clone Wars.

Hazard trooper

**H'broozin, Jook-jook** A onetime Jedi Master, he was one of many who abandoned the Order to join the Dark Jedi who supported Xendor during the era of the First Great Schism. Master H'broozin managed to convince several other Jedi to join him, including Blendri and her apprentice, Cuthallox. In the fighting that took place between the forces of dark and light, Master H'broozin was tracked to Corulag by his former apprentice, Danzigorro Potts, who ran H'broozin through with his lightsaber.

**HBt-4** A blaster made by Herloss during the New Order, it was designed for big-game hunting on the frontier worlds of the Outer Rim. The HBt-4 was given increased stopping power at the expense of range, to ensure that the user killed his or her prey.

**H'buk** A glitterstim seller on Atzerri in the years following the Yuuzhan Vong War, he ended up 400,000 credits in debt to the Traders' Coalition. The group hired Boba Fett to track him down. Once captured, H'buk offered Fett anything to let him go, including the "services" of his daughter. Fett was disgusted and refused, quickly turning H'buk over to the coalition.

**hbuuga** The eggs of this creature were used to create a kind of caviar that was favored by the Hutts.

**HC-100** A homework correction droid designed by DJ-88 to help the young boy Ken in the Lost City of the Jedi, he had a military bearing and often made surprise inspections of Ken's homework. HC-100 was a silver droid resembling the 3PO series, but with blue eyes and a round vocabulator.

**HD 5-D** An experimental hyperdrive booster first marketed after the Battle of Yavin, it shunted more power through a starship's engines, making its hyperdrive more powerful and reducing transit times. However, the HD 5-D had a tendency to burn out after several uses, causing damage to the main drive systems.

**H'drachi** A humanoid species native to M'haeli, its members had the ability to foretell certain events by manipulating the time stream around them. The more H'drachi convened to consult the time stream, the easier it was to read.

**Headache Bar** A seedy cantina located on level 20 of Nar Shaddaa's cityscape. During the early years of the New Order, the Headache Bar was a steady source of tempest spice.

**HeadBanger** A Czerka Corporation riot gun, it was considered the ultimate in crowd control in the years after the Yuuzhan Vong War. Its powerful stun blasts were capable of subduing any being, regardless of size or genetics. Most humans hit with a blast from a HeadBanger were rendered unconscious for three to four days.

**head clan** A group of five Twi'leks who led their community on Ryloth. The duration of leadership was defined by the shortest life span among the five members. When one member of the head clan died, the remaining four were cast out from the community and sentenced to virtual death in Ryloth's extreme environment. In this way, corruption and politically motivated killings were reduced to a minimum, as the intentional death of another member of the head clan meant near-certain death for the others.

**Head Clan** A group of 15 leaders of the planet Stassia, each one descended from one of the original settler families. They worked together as a body to make decisions, although they were relegated to minimal roles during the Empire's control of the planet.

**Headhunter** Kyp Durron's call sign during the evacuation of the Jedi base on Eclipse two years after the Yuuzhan Vong invasion started.

**Head Hunter** A nickname for the Amanin species, stemming from their

H'drachi

tradition of carrying the skulls of their dead enemies on long staffs.

**Headon-5** The swift sublight engines used on many Nubian starships. Headon-5s were best utilized in a J-type configuration, with a pair of drives mounted on swept-back wings.

**Headows, Asran** The master curator of the Galactic Museum on Coruscant in the years leading up to the Clone Wars.

**Head Proctor** The main Proctor of Hethrir's Empire Youth, he was required to be proficient with a lightsaber and to have demonstrated leadership qualities.

**Headquarters, the** An underworld cantina, it was in Coruscant's Invisible Sector—the segregated alien zone—of Imperial City. Rogue Squadron member Corran Horn wandered in one night and thought he saw fellow Rogue Tycho Celchu talking with Imperial agent Kirtan Loor. Before he could confront them, he was accosted by the criminal Zekka Thyne and his thugs, out to kill him. Escaping certain death, Horn used a speeder bike to get away.

**Headquarters Frigate** *See Home One.*

**heads-up display** A holographic display system that allowed a starfighter's vital information, such as fuel levels and targeting, to be displayed in front of a pilot's eyes, rather than on a console. Such systems let a pilot concentrate on forward viewports while also monitoring a ship's status.

**head-tails** The Basic term used to describe lekku, the two tentacle-like appendages that grew from the rear of a Twi'lek's head. Head-tails served a number of purposes. They were a source of vanity, as hair or feathers are to other species. They were used in a silent form of communication among individual Twi'leks. They also served a ceremonial and sensual role in dances performed by Twi'lek females.

**Healing Crystals of Fire** Among the greatest of Jedi treasures, these ancient fiery gemstones were kept under tight security in the meditation chamber of the Jedi Temple on Coruscant. They were used to heal serious wounds. Embedded in the heart of each rock was an eternal flame. At the time of the Melida/Daan Crisis, renegade Jedi Xanatos attempted to destroy the Jedi Temple and kill Yoda by stealing the crystals and putting them in the Temple's fusion furnace, but Qui-Gon Jinn was able to locate the crystals before disaster could occur.

**Healing Hermit** In the years that followed the Battle of Ruusan, this was the nickname that surviving natives used for the healer Darovit. He used his connection to the Force, as well as his knowledge of natural healing techniques, to help them survive the ecological and environmental changes that ravaged the planet.

***Healing Star*** A medical frigate, it was part of the Galactic Alliance Defense Force fleet that accompanied the *Megador* to Tenupe during the final stages of the Swarm War. It was staffed by droids as part of a ruse created by Luke Skywalker. After his wife, Mara Jade Skywalker, and Jacen Solo were injured during their initial attempt to eliminate Lomi Plo, Luke alluded to the fact that they were safely away from Tenupe and receiving medical treatment. Plo seized on this information and ordered Killik dartships to attack the *Healing Star* in an effort to force Skywalker to divert his attention to the safety of his wife and nephew. But in fact the two were safely on Coruscant, so Luke's resolve never failed. Lomi Plo, caught off guard, was cut apart by Skywalker's lightsaber.

**healing stick** Before the creation of bacta, healing sticks created on Pydyr were widely used to heal wounds. The sticks were made from a white, powdery substance that could be rubbed onto a wound; the powder foamed and began healing on contact.

**healing swatch** A pale green rectangular pad several centimeters thick, it was used by the Yuuzhan Vong to treat wounds. Vua Rapuung used one to treat Anakin Solo's wounds inflicted by a thud bug.

**healy gripper** A specialized medical device used during surgery to extract metal fragments, such as shrapnel, from within a living body. The blunt, smooth face of the healy gripper helped to minimize any extraneous injury that might occur during the operation.

**heart-chamber** The facility that housed the Hive Mother of the Verpine species, it was deep within the asteroid Nickel One.

**heartcomb** The term used by members of the Colony to describe the portion of each hive where eggs were laid and stored.

**Hearth, Twilit** The lead singer in a cantina band she founded with her mate, Sprig Cheever. They often played at Happy's Landing in Il Avali on Druckenwell. It was there that they met Tinian I'att and Daye Azur-Jamin. When I'att's grandparents were murdered by Eisen Kerioth, Twilit and Sprig helped her escape by disguising her as a member of the band.

**Heart of Dathomir** Named for its deep red color, this dense nebula was located near Dathomir. The sisters of the Dark Veil Order claimed that a ferocious knot of rage—known as Dathomir's Vitality—was located at the nebula's center.

**Heart of D'vouran** The name the Enzeen used to describe the original feeding hole of the planet D'vouran. It appeared to be made of living mud and looked like a deep, wide underground pit. The Enzeen would lure unsuspecting tourists to the spot and then lower them into the pit so the planet could devour them. Later, D'vouran developed the ability to consume beings anywhere on the planet by opening up a hole and drawing them in. The Enzeen avoided being eaten by wearing a small pendant that contained a force-field generator shielding them from the planet's appetite.

**heart-of-fire** An egg-shaped gemstone found on Kiffu, it was named for the inner glow that suffused the stone, a heart-of-fire that was believed to hold a small piece of an individual's spirit. Coloration varied, but the rarest and most expensive were deep blue stones that exhibited a rainbow of colors when exposed to bright sunlight. Boba Fett commissioned one of these blue stones for Sintas Vel after his former wife was brought out of carbonite hibernation and restored to health. Quinlan Vos gave a heart-of-fire to Aayla Secura when she was 13.

***Heart of Flesh*** A Qektoth Attack Cruiser that was dispatched to Yvara to collect specimens of the Yvarema species. The Qektoth Confederacy hoped to bioengineer a human hive-mind, and planned to experiment on the Yvarema mammalian hive. The *Heart of Flesh* was intercepted by the New Republic corvette *FarStar.*

**Heart of Graush** This immense jewel was imbued with the dark side of the Force by Dathka Graush more than 7,000 years before the Battle of Yavin. Graush removed his own heart and replaced it with the jewel, hoping to keep himself alive forever. It was believed that the jewel contained more than 1,000 Sith spirits, but that didn't prevent Graush's inevitable death. The Heart of Graush was buried with him in his tomb on Korriban, where it awaited another being's touch. The Heart would then take possession of his or her spirit, giving Graush momentary life. As long as the Heart remained in contact with the being, Graush could regenerate.

The Heart was found by pirate Naz Felyood, captain of *Jynni's Virtue,* during the New Order. The ship crash-landed on Korriban after escaping an Imperial boarding party, and Felyood set out to scout the location. He stumbled into Graush's tomb and tried to take the Heart, inviting the possession of the Sith spirit and unleashing Korriban Zombies. The Heart was lost when Babbnod Luroon destroyed the *Jynni's Virtue,* and Captain Felyood was doomed to wander Korriban forever as an undead being, searching in vain for the jewel.

**Heart of the Bright Jewel** A name used to describe the planet Ord Mantell.

**Heart of the Guardian** This ancient artifact was uncovered in the shop of Suvam Tan on Yavin Station more than 4,000 years before the Galactic Civil War. The Heart was a crystal imbued with the power of the Force. When used in conjunction with other crystals to build a lightsaber, the Heart of the Guardian was believed to give the wielder unusual powers. Ancient texts indicated that the Heart was instrumental in the founding of the Jedi Order, but no details were given.

**heart stun** An arcane skill used by some Sith, it allowed them to stop another's heart from beating, placing the organ in a temporary stasis. It was rumored that Count Dooku used the heart stun technique to keep the Kalee warrior who became known as Grievous alive long enough to transport him to Geonosis for a cybernetic transformation.

**Heater** One of Jabba the Hutt's henchmen, Heater operated the cruise ship *Dune Princess* during the Galactic Civil War. After Han Solo killed Greedo in the Mos Eisley cantina, Jabba ordered Heater to hire bounty hunters to bring Solo to justice.

**Heathe, Talie** A slender female scientist, she specialized in oceanics during the last decades of the Old Republic. She was part of Dr. Fort Turan's team, which traveled to Haariden to investigate the effects of a volcanic environment on the planet's atmosphere and ecosystem.

**Heatherdowns Hotel and Track** A Tallaan hotel, it was known for its cracian thumper racecourse.

**heat-pit sensor** Yuuzhan Vong technology that was used to locate and track the body-heat emissions of prey.

**heat-seeking laser mine** An Imperial deep-space mine used to defend shipyards and as a last defense for stranded starships. Once deployed, these mines locked on to intense heat sources such as starship exhaust nacelles, and fired on the assumed targets.

Heavy Defenders

**heat storm** Intense storms that swept the perpetually sun-baked side of Ryloth. Winds reached a velocity of up to 500 kilometers an hour and temperatures soared to more than 300 degrees centigrade as these incredible cyclones swept across the planet's Bright Lands, kicking up scouring torrents of sand and grit. Survival in the open was a near impossibility. Four millennia before the Battle of Yavin, Twi'lek Jedi Tott Doneeta unsuccessfully tried to use the Force to calm a heat storm that threatened an exiled clan he was protecting; he ended up with severe facial burns.

**Heavy-95** The familiar name given to a series of Z-95 Headhunters that were modified by the Rebel Alliance for better heat dissipation and to support a heavier load. Their development helped the Alliance's meager naval forces keep pace with the Empire's growing starfleet while the X-wing fighter was being completed.

**Heavy Annihilator** One of the more powerful versions of the Annihilator starship blaster produced by MandalMotors during the New Order.

**Heavy Artillery Gun (HAG/mortar tank)** An AAT variant that fired concussion mortars at long range. It was primarily a siege weapon designed to soften enemy defenses before ground troops were deployed. The tank was also equipped with twin light laser cannons.

**heavy artillery platform** This Imperial hovercraft was a massive weapons platform. It was armed with a large projectile weapons launcher that shot many missiles at once, and was capable of destroying an entire manufacturing facility or garrison base in short order.

**Heavy Defenders** Rodian soldiers, they protected the scavengers of the Rodian Salvage Cartel on the junk world of Raxus Prime. A particularly large cartel composed primarily of Rodians had established an extremely profitable operation dissecting crashed starships following the rise of the Empire; the cast-off vessels provided them with a seemingly never-ending supply of parts and income. But as operations expanded, the scavengers ran afoul of Kazdan Paratus, a Jedi in hiding on Raxus Prime. After initially suffering heavy losses in their battles with Paratus and his Force-imbued golems, the Rodians decided to organize and defend themselves. The large and well-armored Heavy Defenders were the cartel's most formidable soldiers. They wielded massive repeater cannons capable of blasting apart any of Paratus's droids that came within range. During salvage operations, the Heavy Defenders first surrounded and secured a starship, then protected the vessel as Rodian Rippers tore it open and Jawa laborers entered the ship to surgically remove any usable components. Things went downhill quickly when Starkiller showed up.

**heavy isotope** A loud style of music with a heartbeat bass and melody, it was popular with youths in the last decades of the Old Republic.

**heavy lifter** Similar to cargo lifters, these small craft—25 meters or less—had grasping arms mounted beneath their hulls to hold on to small cargo containers. Heavy lifters often were unarmed and unshielded.

Heavy lifter

Heavy repeating blaster

**Heavy Lightning Rifle** A custom-crafted blaster rifle, it was more powerful and more accurate than the basic Lightning Rifle. Favored by bounty hunters, it fired an intense, cohesive blast of electrical energy at a target, hitting like a bolt of lightning.

**Heavy Missile Platform** *See* HMP droid gunship.

**heavy repeater** A handheld weapon developed by the Imperial armed forces during the early years of the New Republic. It was created to fire a spray of metallic bolts instead of coherent laser energy, making it an extremely destructive weapon.

**heavy repeating blaster** Among the largest non-vehicle-mounted weapons available to ground-based troops, they could radically increase the firepower of individual soldiers. The high-capacity cells in these blasters recharged quickly for multiple shots.

**heavy Republic flamethrower** Produced for the Grand Army of the Republic, it was used by specialized clone troopers to suppress unarmed targets or to lay down a covering swath of fire. It saw heavy use on Mustafar.

**Heavy STAP** A less agile version of the STAP-1 platform developed by the Trade Federation for its battle droids, it featured enhanced armor plating, heavier laser cannons, and a missile launcher. Heavy STAPs were used mainly for scouts or for eliminating retreating enemies.

**Heavy Tracker** A Mekuun combat assault vehicle, the Heavy Tracker was considered more a mobile scanning unit by most army commanders. It was equipped with an omniprobe sensor array that could be programmed to hug the ground and search out targets. The Heavy Tracker was armed with a single heavy laser cannon, but its armor plating was more than a match for most artillery weapons.

**Heavy Tracker 16** SoroSuub's personal blaster rifle, the Heavy Tracker 16 wasn't as reliable or versatile as the BlasTech E-11, after which it was modeled. The weapon was a thick-barreled rifle built to be durable and tough, but that made it unwieldy for many police agencies.

**Heavy Weapons Specialists** A branch of the Rebel Alliance's Special Forces section trained in the doctrines and use of laser weapons, artillery, and other heavy-duty weaponry. These troops were considered the 6th Regiment of the SpecForces of the Alliance.

*Hedji*

**Hebeth** A ball of molten rock, it was the third planet in the Beheboth system.

**Hebine Ring** An asteroid belt in the Beheboth system between the planets of Hebeth and Beheboth.

**HE bolt** A term for the high-energy beam of coherent energy produced by a blaster weapon.

**Hebsly, Lieutenant** This Imperial officer was a skilled starfighter pilot who used the maneuverability of the TIE/ln fighter to his combat advantage in the Anoat sector. He later served aboard the second Death Star just prior to the Battle of Endor.

**Hedda** A young Jedi Knight stationed on Ossus to protect the Jedi training facility there during the Galactic Alliance's conflict with the Confederation. When Major Serpa of the Galactic Alliance Guard took control of the facility, Hedda was shot to death in her dorm room before she could defend the younglings in her charge.

**hedge maze** A huge Yuuzhan Vong hedge that surrounded the Well of the World Brain, it was festooned with brilliantly colored epiphytes and flowering vines by members of various castes. The hedge was started to serve both as a ceremonial avenue and a defensive measure to protect the World Brain. When mature, it was designed to form a tunnel 20 meters high and 30 meters wide, as hard as durasteel, fireproof, and resilient enough to minimize the effects of explosives; its thorns would contain a neurotoxin so potent that a single prick could destroy the central nervous system of any creature that touched one.

**Hedji** A Spiner warrior, and one of the last of his species, he teamed with Han Solo following the Battle of Yavin, ousting Serji-X Arrogantus from his position on Aduba-3. Despite that success, Hedji and his companions—a group known as the Star-Hoppers of Aduba-3—were ill prepared for the uncontrollable Behemoth that emerged from the caverns beneath Onacra village. When Don-Wan Kihotay tried to defeat the beast in single combat, Hedji and Jaxxon decided to lend their assistance. One blast from the Behemoth's organic blaster killed Hedji before he could help.

**Hedrett Groundport** A public-access spaceport in Hedrett on Cularin, it provided travelers with flights to destinations within the Cularin system.

**Hedron, Mol** An Imperial intelligence agent from Swarquen. Three years after the Battle of Endor, he was discovered stealing information on the New Republic's latest starship designs from the Sluis Van shipyards.

**Heedon** The owner and operator of a luxury cruise line. By the time of the Galactic Civil War, the *Starcrossed* was the only ship in his fleet. He supported the Rebel Alliance, if only because he wanted the Emperor overthrown so that wealthy families could afford his cruises again.

**Heedra, Moff** An Imperial Moff in command of Baxel sector during the New Order, he worked hard to drive the Hutts from the planets they controlled in the sector, including Lirra.

**Heep, Dol** An Avoni and ambassador from Avon to Radnor, he was the primary force behind a plot to create a toxic disaster that would enable the Avoni to colonize Radnor a few years after the Battle of Naboo. His plans were discovered by Jedi Knights dispatched to Radnor to aid in the evacuation of the population; Heep loudly denied any wrongdoing, but was arrested on charges of conspiracy.

**Heer, Noshy** A vagrant who lost all his money gambling in the Relatta system, he had plenty of funds in the bank on his homeworld of Alderaan . . . but the Death Star's blast left him one step ahead of poverty for the rest of his life.

**Heff** A member of a rabbit-like species, he was an early settler on Tatooine and ran Heff's Souvenir Shop. He had information about Adar Tallon, but before the Rebel Alliance could reach him, Heff was killed by Jodo Kast with a Senari-dipped dart.

**Heffrin** A small colony world located in the Outer Rim Territories.

**Hefi** A hidden retreat of weapons designer Bevel Lemelisk was located on this planet in the Abrion sector of the Outer Rim Territories. He fled there when the first Death Star was destroyed, fearing for his life. He was tracked down by Imperial agents and later executed for incompetence.

**Heg** This was the capital city of the planet Bundim until it was destroyed in the Battle of Heg, shortly after the Rebel Alliance destroyed the first Death Star.

**Hegerty, Soron** A doctor of biology, she spent a great deal of her time studying the Ssither species on Jatee. With the advent of the New Order, she was drafted into the Imperial Species Identification Bureau. She faked her own death and returned to Jatee, where she continually sidetracked Imperial inquiries on the planetoid, fearful that the Empire would use the Ssither species for genetic experiments. Dr. Hegerty later was recruited by Imperial Moff Crowal, who provided her with the resources she needed to fully investigate the species of the Unknown Regions. Moff Crowal, as part of a goodwill gesture toward the fledgling Galactic Alliance, assigned her to Luke Skywalker to help locate the mysterious planet Zonama Sekot. Their mission led them to the Klasse Ephemora system, where Sekot had hidden in orbit around Mobus. Dr. Hegerty was fascinated by Ferroan culture, until Sekot arranged for a series of tests to bring the true nature of their mission to light. Both Luke Skywalker and Jacen Solo were able to convince Sekot that they were searching for a peaceful end to the war, and the planet agreed to follow them back to the galaxy.

**Heget, Colonel** An old-guard Imperial Army officer who earned the respect of his troops and inspired a deep loyalty in his soldiers, he grew tired of the political backstabbing and personal ambitions that drove many of Emperor Palpatine's minions. He got himself transferred to the Kathol sector to avoid two Moffs who were each trying to win his favor. Once there, however, Heget refused to get cozy with Moff Kentor Sarne and was posted to Shintel as punishment.

**Heggel, Admiral** An Imperial officer put in charge of the fleet that patrolled Trax sector shortly after the Battle of Yavin. He ordered Commander Resner to root out and destroy any Rebel activity.

**heglum** A very light gas used in dirigibles, it sometimes was found in nebulae and other gaseous clouds, and bonded to sublight drives. Ships that passed through heglum clouds had to undergo regular scrubbing of their drive systems to maintain optimum performance.

**Heiff, Vengnar** A green-skinned reptilian often referred to simply as the Torturer, he was efficient at what he did for the Empire. Many felt that his methods were too crude, but Heiff was one of the most successful Imperial agents at extracting information from prisoners. He was dispatched to Ithor shortly after the Battle of Yavin to "persuade" some Ithorian prisoners to reveal the secrets of their planet and its abundant resources. When the Ithorians rose up against their captors, however, Heiff was caught in his own torture chamber. He was wounded in a firefight, but despite his pleading, he wasn't killed. The Ithorians decided to keep him alive for further interrogation of their own.

**Heigren** A Zeltron, he was governor of the Northern Province of Zeltros during the early years of the New Republic.

**Heitop** Part of a small scientific expedition to Talus during the Galactic Civil War, Heitop and his team were killed when they stumbled into a cave inhabited by a swarm of fynocks. The only evidence of their existence was a datapad recovered later.

**Hejaran Castle** The family fortress of the wealthy Hejarans, who were part of House Mecetti of the Tapani sector. The castle was located on the moon Nightsinger's Orb and was the site of bitter family feuds, the reading of a will, a murder and an attempted murder, and a visit from the dark side that resulted in death.

**heji tal** A Jedi training and meditation technique, it was used frequently by Luke Skywalker to bring on inner peace, knowledge, and serenity—all gifts that came with complete surrender to the Force. Heji tal called on the fundamental Jedi skills of control, sense, and alter in ever-changing combinations. It brought its practitioner to a profound state of restful clarity. It was in the state of heji tal that Skywalker felt most keenly the truth and wisdom of the simple words of the Jedi Code: There is no emotion; there is peace. There is no ignorance; there is knowledge. There is no passion; there is serenity. There is no death; there is the Force.

**Hekula** The son of the noted Dug Podracer Sebulba, he was a racer of some renown himself in the years following the Battle of Naboo. Sebulba worked behind the scenes to ensure that Hekula continued winning his races. While lacking his father's cunning, he made up for it in sheer brutishness as well as the cheating that Sebulba taught him.

Helas

**helas** Natives of the moist world of Enaleh, these creatures resembled flying snakes or eels. They were amphibious, but traveled through the air to catch their prey. Helas lacked wings, but seemed to have an internal organ that acted much like a repulsorlift engine. Their heads were essentially large baskets with four jaw-like flaps that opened up to collect small insects. Four long tentacles grew from the corners of their mouths, and presumably helped them detect their prey.

**Hela-Tan** A Togorian pirate, he was one of a group that tried to intercept Darth Maul while the Sith apprentice was en route to Tatooine to capture Queen Amidala.

**Helaw, Admiral Jaim** Commander of the Star Destroyer *Undauntable* in the early years of the New Order, he had served previously as a captain aboard the *Ion Storm* with Conan Antonio Motti. After being assigned to patrol the Atrivis sector during the construction of the first Death Star, Admiral Helaw decided to retire as soon as the battle station was finished. He paid a visit to Motti at the construction site of the Death Star to explain his plans, as well as to warn Motti about trusting too much in the station's technology. A sabotaged ammunition shipment was delivered to the *Undauntable* and exploded, killing Admiral Helaw and some of the crew, and causing considerable damage to the Death Star. The Empire later reported that his death had been an accident.

Captain Heliesk

**Helb** This Neimoidian worked as a broker for Tech Raiders, selling equipment by making deals in taverns and cantinas of the Senate District on Coruscant. It was Helb who revealed to Qui-Gon Jinn and Obi-Wan Kenobi that Fligh owed a large sum of credits to Tech Raiders as payment for a number of favors. The Jedi discovered that Helb had employed Fligh to steal Senator Uta S'orn's datapad in order to thwart her plans to break up Tech Raiders.

**helicite** A gypsum formation found on Tatooine.

***Helicon*** An Imperial shuttle assigned to escort Kirtan Loor from Talasea to Vladet.

**Heliesk, Captain** Although a Rebel Alliance sympathizer at heart, he served the Empire as the captain of the *Rand Ecliptic* when Biggs Darklighter and Derek "Hobbie" Klivian were assigned to it following their graduation from the Imperial Academy. Darklighter and Klivian staged a mutiny aboard the *Rand Ecliptic* when it docked at Bestine, stole the ship, and defected to the Rebel Alliance. In truth, Heliesk was a Rebel agent codenamed Starfire, but he couldn't afford to blow his cover.

**Helisk** This was one of three habitable worlds in the Sabrixin system.

***Helix*-class light interceptor** Arakyd's light freighter/starfighter, the *Helix*-class armed freighter was a 30.9-meter triangular craft that resembled a bird of prey. It could carry up to 35 metric tons of cargo, giving it freighter capabilities, but it also was heavily armed. A pair of plasburst laser cannons was supported by a pair of ion cannons and a proton torpedo launcher, providing starfighter abilities. The Helix required a pilot and copilot, and could carry up to four passengers. It was fairly well shielded, and had a strong hull. The Empire eventually realized that the Helix was illegally armed for a freighter, and all production was ordered halted.

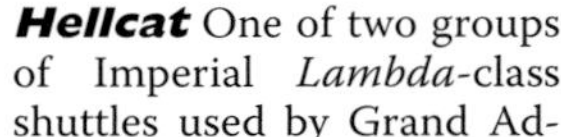

***Hellcat*** One of two groups of Imperial *Lambda*-class shuttles used by Grand Admiral Zaarin in his attempt to kidnap Emperor Palpatine and stage a coup, and then escape retribution by Admiral Thrawn.

**Hellenika, Madame** Tinian I'att used this alias when she delivered Bossk to Imperial Governor Io Desnand after capturing the Trandoshan bounty hunter in the Lomabu system.

**Hellhoop** A strange void located near the planet Attahox, it was controlled by the Five. The Five captured starships within the Hellhoop and took great pleasure torturing the crews and passengers. Some years after the Battle of Hoth they captured Han Solo, Leia Organa, and Chewbacca. Chewbacca was imprisoned in the Menagerie, while Han and Leia were tortured. Chewbacca escaped, liberating Wuzzek and the other Menagerie beasts. Wuzzek went on a rampage, killing all of the Five but Chokla. Wuzzek then destroyed the Hellhoop itself, allowing the Rebel Alliance heroes a chance to escape.

**Hellios system** This Tapani sector star system was part of the holdings of House Barnaba during the New Order.

***Hell's Anvil*** Bounty hunter Montross's heavily modified starfighter, it was used during the years following his defection from Mandalorian ranks shortly before the Battle of Naboo. The ship, built by Corellian Engineering Corporation, was armed with unusual solar ionization cannons, which got around normal deflector shields and could melt durasteel. Montross used the vehicle in a failed attempt to kill Jango Fett.

***Hell's Axe*** A modified Incom Corporation Explorer scout ship owned and operated by Kyr Laron, it sported an enlarged air lock that Laron used when she wore her zero-g spacetrooper armor to intercept ships. *Hell's Axe* also was armed with three retractable laser cannons.

**Hell's Hammers** Also known as the Imperial Hammers Elite Armor Regiment, this choice armored unit was used to eradicate Rebel Alliance outposts and quell military dissension. It was formed during the closing stages of the Clone Wars and led by Colonel Zel Johans. At full strength, Hell's Hammers consisted of three battalions and a command regiment group. The battalions were virtually self-sufficient, and relied on one another rather than the rest of the Imperial military.

The unit's primary armament was the *Imperial*-class repulsortank, which it used to enter heavy combat zones with minimal interference. At one point, Hell's Hammers was decimated by Rebel Alliance forces during the Battle of Turak IV when General Maltaz ordered the unit to hold its ground despite being pounded by heavy weapons. Two battalions were nearly wiped out before retreat was sounded. After an Imperial reassessment, the unit was given new funding and matériel.

**Hellwell** A mysterious, seemingly bottomless pit in the Moridebo District of Metellos, it originally was created as a garbage pit by a mining company, but became a criminal dumping ground for once-living but troublesome individuals.

**Helm** An independent prospector, he and his partner, Vandel, were the first to discover a planet that eventually was named Vandelhelm in their honor. They penetrated the vast cloud of asteroids that surrounded the world some 3,000 years before the Galactic Civil War, finding rich deposits of metal and ore.

**Helmet Squad** The name given to prison guards at the Oovi IV facility during the last decades of the Old Republic. The Helmet Squad had the distinction of being one of the most corrupt in the galaxy.

**Heloan Yagen** The fifth and outermost planet in the Bovo Yagen system, Heloan Yagen was a gas giant named for the wife of Bovo Yagen. It had 24 natural satellites.

***Helot's Shackle*** A heavily modified CR90 corvette captained by Ngyn Reeos, the ship was part of the fleet that guarded Kessel during the early years of the New Order. It was dispatched to assist the transport of processed spice off Ylesia. *Helot's Shackle* chased Han Solo and Bria Tharen as they escaped from Ylesia with Murrrgh and Mrrov, but failed to capture them. The ship also was used to transport slaves off Ylesia, and was attacked by Tharen and the Corellian resistance to rescue the slaves. The crew either was killed or surrendered, and Tharen took control of the starship and renamed it *Emancipator.*

**helpers** The lowest rank in Hethrir's Empire Youth school, these students were basically servants. They were designated by their rust-colored uniforms.

***Helping Hand*** A modified YT-1300 light freighter owned by Plu Makor.

**Helrossi-principal Octratics** One of the many unusual forms of mathematics developed by the Givin for use in calculating hyperspace jumps and travel routes. The equations derived were instrumental during the Clone Wars.

**Helrot, Elis** A Givin pilot, he spent a lot of time on Tatooine, scouring Mos Eisley for information about slaves or spice for transport. He made many runs to deliver these cargoes to Kala'uun on his transport, the *Hinthra.* Helrot had the special ability to seal his joints to withstand the vacuum of space.

*Elis Helrot*

**Helska IV** The fourth of seven planets in the Helska system, this small world was where the Yuuzhan Vong established their first base from which to invade the galaxy. Much of Helska IV was covered with ice, and the atmosphere was choked with vaporous fog. Yomin Carr had scouted the planet before he joined the science team from ExGal-4 station on Belkadan, leaving behind villips to help monitor the creation of the base under the ice. The Praetorite Vong invasion force sent three worldships to Helska IV, and when the ExGal-4 team arrived to investigate, two team members were attacked and killed by coralskippers while a third, Danni Quee, was taken prisoner. She was soon joined by captured Jedi Knight Miko Reglia. The planet became the focus of several early fact-finding missions by the New Republic and then battles between the Republic and the invaders. Finally, the Republic deployed some of Lando Calrissian's shieldships around Helska IV. They reflected the sun's radiant energy back onto the planet, resulting in the Mezzicanley Wave that shattered the planet into countless pieces, destroying the Yuuzhan Vong base in what later became known as the Battle of Helska IV.

*Hendanyn death mask*

**Helthen Company** A manufacturer of heavy-duty equipment, it was contracted by Ecclessis Figg to create huge thermoconverters installed on Cloud City to maintain the outpost's electrical power.

**Helvan** An Imperial Special Intelligence operative assigned to Kirtan Loor on Coruscant as part of the Palpatine Counterinsurgency Faction.

**Hemei IV** The birthplace of the Cosmic Balance religion. Bakuran historians traced the origins of their people to Hemei IV, where the Bakur Corporation was formed. Hemei IV executives' faith in the Cosmic Balance led them to believe that the planet's concentration of wealth was disruptive to the Balance. The planet Bakura was a relatively poor world with an ecology that mirrored Hemei IV.

**Hemes Arbora** This species originated on Carrivar, then migrated to Umaren'k and later Osseriton. The Hemes Arbora encountered the rogue planet Zonama Sekot while on Umaren'k.

**HE missile** A Republic missile developed during the Clone Wars, it had a high-explosive warhead designed to cause massive amounts of damage with each blast, eliminating as much of the Separatist droid army as possible.

**hemosponge** A specialized medical sponge used to soak up any blood that leaked out during an operation, clearing away the visual obstruction.

**Hemphawar, Stu** A small-time smuggler. He and his accomplices Oejoe Hitiwa and Ruceba Ahid worked from a tiny apartment near Coruscant's entertainment district in the waning years of the Old Republic. The Senate Bureau of Intelligence issued a bounty for their arrest after they were implicated in a scheme to traffic illicit contraband throughout the Core Worlds. All three eventually were captured by Jango Fett.

**Henchman** A nickname Marn Hierogryph gave Zayne Carrick after they agreed to work together to escape Taris during the Mandalorian Wars.

**Hendanyn death mask** Seen eventually only in museums, this ceremonial mask molded itself to the skin of the wearer. The Hendanyn wore these death masks after they reached old age, partially to hide their aging and partially to store their memories. The information in the mask could be retained after the wearer's death and passed on to future generations. The Dark Jedi Kueller wore such a mask. His was white with black accents and tiny jewels in the corners of the eye slits.

**Heng, Machar** A Yuuzhan Vong subaltern, he was assigned by Warmaster Tsavong Lah to coordinate the Peace Brigade's attempts to capture Jedi Knights in the months leading up to the Battle of Coruscant. He was provided with a small flotilla of ships and a handful of warriors.

**Hengin Ki-Tapp Wett Gon-far** A tree-city built by the Gazaran in the rain forests of Veron. It wasn't the largest, but it was the most powerful.

**Hennilrum** This trader plied the space lanes of Trax sector during the Galactic Civil War. Hennilrum was sympathetic toward the Rebel Alliance, and used his connections to Trefflet Wuin to provide it with information on the Empire's new supply base in the Bissillirus system.

**Hensara system** Located in the Rachuk sector, this system included as its third planet a small jungle world called Hensara III. Three years after the Battle of Endor, Rebel Alliance operative Dirk Harkness and his Black Curs were forced to crash their ship in one of Hensara III's lakes after running into the Imperial Strike cruiser *Havoc*. The *Havoc* landed AT-AT and AT-ST walkers, along with two platoons of stormtroopers, to find and eliminate them. Harkness and his group were rescued by Rogue Squadron, which easily wiped out the Imperials without suffering any casualties in a battle later called the Rout of Hensara.

**Hensworth, Lieutenant** An Imperial Army officer, he worked with Sinya Deboora to try to maintain Imperial control over the planet Seltos. When the populace overthrew the government, Hensworth went into hiding, but promised Deboora the Imperial Governorship once the Empire regained the upper hand. They were thwarted by New Republic agents inserted on the planet as part of Freedom Strike Seltos.

**Hentz, Khaleen** A small-time thief, she worked aboard the Wheel in the years before the Clone Wars. Hentz was lanky, with magenta-colored hair and a large Zealots of Psusan cult tattoo on her usually bare midriff. Jedi Quinlan Vos hired her to steal a data disk from the Falleen Zenex, and it turned out to contain detailed plans for a Separatist attack on Kamino. Vos copied the disk, and Hentz volunteered to return the original so that the Separatists wouldn't know their plans had been exposed. Using his strong pheromones, Zenex nearly convinced Khaleen to kill herself. Vos and his fellow Jedi Aayla Secura saved Hentz and killed Zenex.

Hentz remained with Vos, and they began to develop deeper feelings for each other. After she was captured by Old Republic forces, she was freed by Jedi Master Tholme, who needed

Khaleen Hentz

her help to ensure the success of Vos's mission to infiltrate the Separatists. Following the siege of Saleucami, Hentz revealed that she had been spying on Vos for Count Dooku. She also revealed that she was pregnant with his child. Vos urged her to find a remote location to settle down until the fighting was over and he could finally leave the Jedi Order. With the execution of Order 66, she believed that she would never see Vos again. Following his suggestion, she traveled to Kashyyyk to bear her child and was taken in by the Wookiees of the Palsaang clan. About eight months after the Clone Wars ended, Hentz was surprised and delighted when Vos returned, having been nursed back to health by Vilmarh Grahrk. In the emotional moments that followed, she introduced Quinlan to their son, Korto.

**Heorem Complex** A kilometer-wide collection of buildings on Coruscant in the final years of the Old Republic, it sat on the border between the Senate District and Sah'c Town; a skytunnel through its upper reaches connected the two sectors.

**Heptalia** This planet was known for the exquisitely embroidered rugs and furniture coverings produced by its artisans.

**herabe** This creature native to Zolan could alter the texture of its lumpy skin to closely resemble the rocky environments in which it lived.

***Herald*** A Rebel Alliance shuttle that was assigned to intercept the freighter *Gafra* and steal a new Imperial warhead.

**Herat** The shaman of the Jawa Wittin's tribe, she was Wittin's adviser during his negotiations with Jabba the Hutt and agreed to serve as one of Jabba's retainers as long as he helped Wittin. After Jabba's death, Herat and her tribe were freed from servitude, and roamed the deserts of Tatooine. When they discovered Kitster Banai in the deep desert, Herat agreed to transport him to Anchorhead. The tribe was struck by two almost simultaneous attacks, one from an Imperial search party looking for the *Killik Twilight* moss-painting, another by a group of Sand People. Many of the tribe were killed; Banai was taken by the Sand People, and Herat was left for dead. She later agreed to help Han and Leia Organa Solo locate Kitster and the important moss-painting before the Imperials could. She agreed to let herself be "hijacked" in order to draw off Imperial pursuit. With the Solos' help, Herat got her sandcrawler working again, and then locked herself in a toolbox while the sandcrawler was put in gear. The pursuing stormtroopers took the bait, and later believed Herat's story of being captured and locked up after the Solos stole her cargo.

**Herd, the** A small band of Ithorian smugglers assembled by Kikow on Ralltiir in the period following the Battle of Naboo. The Herd consisted of half a dozen Ithorian spacers who were loyal to Kikow, and trafficked primarily in weapons.

**Herd City** Another name for an Ithorian herd ship, especially those that were unable to travel through space and remained near Ithor's surface.

**Herdessa** Lumiya likely first appeared on this planet after completing her training under Darth Vader. Even during the height of the New Order, Herdessa was considered a peaceful world where affluent beings of the galaxy could remain neutral. Years later, after the Battle of Endor and the deaths of Vader and Emperor Palpatine, Mon Mothma and Leia Organa traveled to the planet to try to convince the government to join the fledgling New Republic. There they learned that Herdessa was ruled by the oppressive Herdessan Guild, which profited from slavery. The citizens of Herdessa revolted and overthrew the guild.

Herat (left, rear) in Jabba's palace

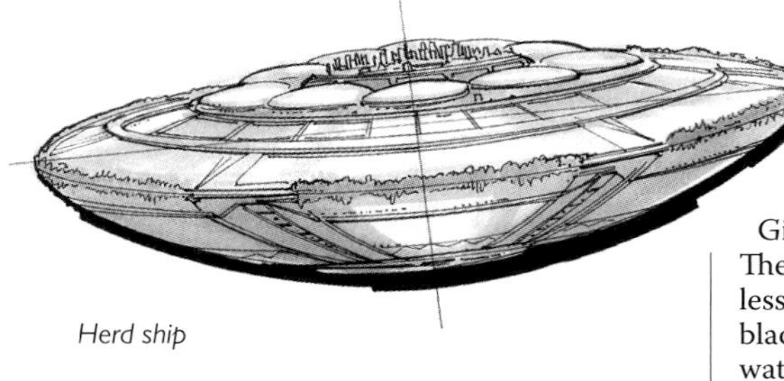
Herd ship

**Herd Mother** This was the name of Ketwol's old, poorly maintained starship.

**herd ship** Ithorian vessels, they traveled the space lanes like great caravans, selling unusual merchandise all over the galaxy. Designed for Ithorian comfort, herd ships duplicated the tropical environment of the planet Ithor with indoor jungles, artificial storms, and wildlife. On the planet itself, Ithorians lived in herd ships that functioned as huge floating cities, using repulsorlift engines to harmlessly sweep over the forests and plains that inhabitants considered sacred. The ships' biospheres produced food. Each herd ship was 1,800 meters in diameter. A pilot and copilot maintained the vessel's systems, supported by a crew of up to 3,000. A herd ship could accommodate up to 10,000 Ithorians along with 20,000 metric tons of cargo. Every herd ship returned to Ithor for the Herd Meet every three years. After Ithor was destroyed by the Yuuzhan Vong, the herd ships were the only reminders of Ithor's jungles, making them all the more sacred to the Ithorian people. Among the most famous herd ships were the *Tafanda Bay, Ithor Wanderer, Errant Trader,* and *Bazaar.*

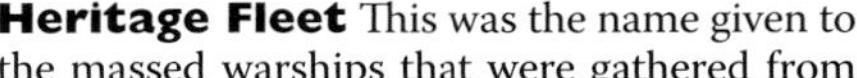
Herlixx

**Heresiarch** A *Sovereign*-class Star Destroyer, it was under construction when Emperor Palpatine's clone reemerged on Byss several years after the Battle of Endor.

**Heresiarchs** One of many religious sects formed on the basis of Sith lore and teachings.

**heretic movement** A term historians used for the uprisings of the Yuuzhan Vong Shamed Ones, who chose to shrug off the prejudices of their leaders and embrace the Jedi Knights as saviors, not abominations. The movement reached its height when Nom Anor adopted the guise of Yu'shaa and led the Shamed Ones on Coruscant into open rebellion.

**Hereven, Lieutenant** An officer with the Galactic Scout Corps 40 years before the Battle of Yavin, he and mission commander Dayla Kev were attacked by a gasnit on an uncharted jungle planet. They managed to find shelter in caves below the planet's surface, eventually fell in love, and Kev realized she was pregnant. Hereven was killed while hunting for food and never met his baby boy.

**Herglic** Large bipeds from the planet Giju, they averaged about 1.9 meters tall. They had very wide bodies and smooth, hairless skin ranging from light blue to nearly black. Most likely they descended from water-dwelling mammals, with fins and flukes replaced by arms and legs, although they continued to breathe through blowholes in the tops of their heads. Always explorers and merchants, Herglic were among the first members of the Old Republic. However, after a brief and bloody struggle, they surrendered completely to the Empire, causing some resentment among other species after the Empire collapsed. While Herglic society produced notable explorers and merchants, many Herglic easily become addicted to gambling. They also were self-conscious about their size and unusual physical characteristics.

**Herglic space** A knot of some 40 star systems on and around the Rimma Trade Route, which was a continuation of an ancient Herglic route known as the Hidakai Pool. Hundreds of worlds along the Rimma route outside Herglic space had substantial Herglic populations. Herglic space became a member of the New Republic and the Galactic Alliance.

**Heriston** This planet was the site of a key Imperial refueling and repair depot established soon after the Battle of Yavin. It was in an area where such facilities were rare.

**Heritage Fleet** This was the name given to the massed warships that were gathered from the personal fleets of the members of the Heritage Council, to be arrayed against the Hapan Home Fleet in an attempt to assassinate Tenel Ka and give the council a chance to take over the Hapes Consortium. The Heritage Fleet launched its attack on Hapes some five years after the Swarm War, when the Heritage Council became frustrated with the Queen Mother's continued support of the Galactic Alliance.

The Heritage Council's plot might have worked if Jaina Solo and Zekk had not discovered the Ducha Morwan's hand in it. They had been investigating the places that Aurra Sing might have fled after her initial attempt to kill Tenel Ka failed. Their warning allowed the Hapan Royal Navy to deploy around the planet. Still, the fighting that erupted over Hapes was intense. A Galactic Alliance fleet led by the *Anakin Solo* was already in the Hapes system, and it joined forces with the Royal Navy to defeat the Heritage Fleet.

Qual'Do Herm

Herglic

**Heritage Squad** A branch of the Human League charged with proving that the human species had the right to be supreme in the Corellian sector.

**heritage tapestry** This type of wall hanging was created by artisans of the Old Republic to tell a story or describe a moment in history. The Jedi Temple was filled with such tapestries, which depicted key events in the 25,000-year history of the Jedi Order and the Galactic Republic.

**herlixx** Omnivorous swamp creatures native to Kasiol 3, they were equally at home in the water and on land. The average herlixx was 45 centimeters tall and stood on stubby rear legs. Their extremely long arms allowed them to move through the trees, while their obese bodies let them float on the surface of the water. They ate a variety of fish and small amphibians, and supplemented their diet with leaves and algae. While they looked quite fearsome, they generally were harmless to any creature larger than themselves.

**Herm, Qual'Do** An Aqualish assigned by the Rebel Alliance to observe the Corporate Sector during the Galactic Civil War, he was cautious about whom he recruited.

**Her Majesty's Commandos** One of the few all-male units in the Hapan military, the Commandos were often sent to carry out missions that needed a certain amount of muscle. They were skilled in moving about without attracting too much attention.

Hermit spider

**Her Maternellence** The title given to the queen of a Verpine hive.

***Hermes*** One of the many *Strike*-class cruisers that made up the front lines of the Imperial naval fleet.

**hermit crab droid** Small, disk-shaped droids with six retractable and segmented legs and two photoreceptors attached to cables. Aayla Secura helped Anakin Skywalker repair one just prior to the Battle of Kamino.

**hermit spider** These large, predatory spiders native to the planet Naboo were noted for their rigid social structure.

**Hermos** An immense droid that served as Nescan Tal'yo's bodyguard during the New Order, he resembled a heavily muscled skeleton with a skull-shaped head and a tall frame. When Leia Organa confronted Tal'yo at the Lucky Star casino on Elerion about a holocube he had stolen from a Rebel Alliance agent, she was forced to shoot Hermos in order to protect herself. The droid was propelled out a window and fell to the street.

**Hern** A molten sphere of rock, it was the innermost planet of the Rhinnal system.

***Heroc's Slayer*** A modified YT-1300 stock light freighter used by a group of bounty hunters who pursued Rebel Alliance forces to Issagra.

**Heroes of Yavin** Luke Skywalker, Leia Organa, Han Solo, Chewbacca, and the droids R2-D2 and C-3PO were collectively known as the Heroes of Yavin.

**Herogga the Hutt** A Nasirii clan Hutt, he was one of the few members of his species to try to regain control of Tatooine's criminal operations during the early years of the New Republic. He arrived on the planet 18 years after the Battle of Endor knowing that criminal activity was controlled by Lady Valarian. He funded the Crystal Moon Mos Entha restaurant, a legitimate business; he conducted his criminal operations from the storage cellar beneath the eatery. When the Yuuzhan Vong attacked Hutt space, many Hutts fled Nal Hutta for Tatooine. Herogga, fearful that newly arrived Hutts would take a piece of his action, accelerated his plans to destroy Valarian and assume control. Herogga also planned to take over Jabba's former palace.

**Hero of Cularin** This medal was awarded to those individuals who went above and beyond the call of duty to protect the Cularin system, it inhabitants, and its interests during the final years of the Old Republic.

**Hero of Ossus** The title bestowed upon Rulf Yage for his role in defeating the Jedi on Ossus during the Sith–Imperial War.

**Hero of Taanab** An honorific used to describe Lando Calrissian.

**Hero of the Empire** An award presented to those individuals who performed bravely in the service of the Empire.

**Hero with No Fear** Bestowed by the Rajah of the Virujansi, this was one of the highest honors that a warrior could earn in battle. Anakin Skywalker received it during the Clone Wars for his continued bravery and daring.

**Hero's Cross** This medal was awarded to members of the Old Republic military who displayed valor and courage in combat in the decades leading up to the Great Sith War.

**Herr, Druuven** This native Liann was a strong supporter of the Rebel Alliance. He also was slow-witted and dull.

**Herrera, San** Although both San Herrera and his partner, Nia Reston, were Force-sensitive, they made a conscious decision not to train with the Jedi Knights on Coruscant because they didn't want to deal with the discipline and isolation imposed by the Order. They remained on Cularin, where they engaged in many good works. When the Cularin government decided to officially join the Old Republic, Herrera and Reston tried to rally public support to keep the planet independent. This sparked a riot, forcing the pair to flee.

Hermos (rear)

***Herriar*** This starship, owned by the Jon-Tow Economic Development Group, was part of a large group that blockaded the moon of Pinett during the Galactic Civil War.

**Herrit, Major** Following the Battle of Yavin, Major Herrit was ordered by Emperor Palpatine himself to gather information about the leaders of the Alliance to Restore the Republic. He was among the officers who performed background checks on the bounty hunters hired to locate Han Solo. But his master stroke came in subverting an Alliance attack on a base in the Rolion sector. He had cracked an Alliance communications code, but it still took imagination to figure out that the code name Understar referred to a base in Fara's Belt. He laid a trap, and none of the attacking Rebel ships survived.

**Herzob** An agricultural world in the Colonies region, it supplied foodstuffs for many nearby Core and Mid Rim worlds. Indigenous grain crops spread for millions of square kilometers across the planet. One of the few persistent problems on Herzob was a planetwide infestation of crop-destroying vermin known as jevesects.

**Hesken fever** A debilitating but rarely fatal viral illness caused by bacteria found thriving in the vacuum of space. Fighter pilots were particularly susceptible to the infection.

**Hesk'l, Brin** A noted treasure hunter, he traveled to the Cularin system during the Clone Wars, hoping to locate the opposite of the mysterious darkstaff, since he believed that everything that was created had an exact opposite. After an interview on *Eye on Cularin,* he set out on his search. Two weeks later, Hesk'l's ship was found adrift in the comet cloud that surrounded Cularin . . . empty.

**Hesoc** A hotshot Rebel Alliance pilot, he accounted for 22 kills during the Matacorn campaign. He was shot down in the midst of a Tallon roll and severely injured his right leg. It was replaced with a cybernetic prosthesis, which should have grounded him. But Hesoc appealed to his commanding officer, General Lesilk, and was reinstated to active combat duty.

**Hesperidium** A moon that orbited Coruscant, it was well known for its entertainment outlets, including luxurious resorts and pleasure domes. Hesperidium was the last stopping place of the *Adamantine* and the *Borealis* before they arrived in the Chorios systems, bringing Leia Organa Solo to a meeting with Seti Ashgad. Following the Yuuzhan Vong War, Hesperidium's resorts saw a gradual decline, as many beings chose to spend their credits on rebuilding their lives rather than on frivolity.

**Hessler, Evan** One of a small group of bounty hunters hired by Emperor Palpatine and Darth Vader to hunt down Sagoro Autem following the Clone Wars. Hessler actually was Autem's son, Reymet, and took on the bounty in an effort to ensure his father's safety.

**Hestiv, General** An Imperial general in command of the Ubiqtorate base on Yaga Minor following the death of Grand Admiral Thrawn, he reluctantly supported Admiral Pellaeon's plan to negotiate a peace treaty with the New Republic. General Hestiv also allowed Ghent access to the base's data banks in an effort to find a copy of the Caamas Document.

**HE-suit** The generic term for a hostile environment suit. In general, these heavy-duty exoskeletons provided protection for workers who had to move about in dangerous conditions. They were equipped with a variety of powerful servomotors to assist movement and lifting, as well as life-support and sensor systems.

**Hesz, Tal** A fiery-tempered man, he was part of a small band of Rebels that opposed the Imperial occupation of Jabiim. Hesz finally revealed himself to be an Imperial spy who had agreed to turn Luke Skywalker over to Darth Vader in exchange for Jabiim's complete freedom. When he returned to Vader without Skywalker, the Dark Lord bombarded Jabiim with turbolasers and projectile weaponry, reducing large parts of the planet to rubble. Hesz, who had believed that he was doing the right thing, regretted his actions and set out to rescue his enslaved people. After he learned that the Jabiimi slaves had been taken to Kalist VI, Hesz used the Rebel Alliance's attack on the prison world to land there and free the slaves before he was taken captive.

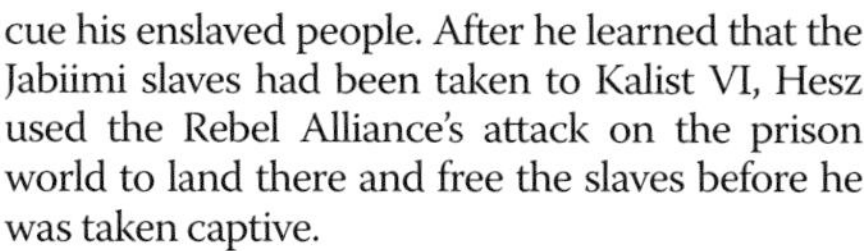
Doton Het

**Het, Doton** A noted gambler, this Twi'lek lived on Citadel Station following the Jedi Civil War. Doton Het made a living by beating all opponents in pazaak. He won possession of the Twi'lek female Ramana from her boyfriend, Harra, and then later lost her to the Jedi Exile. Het refused to give her up, so the Exile was forced to defeat him in one-on-one combat to secure Ramana's freedom.

**Heter valve** The primary energy converter valve on a blaster. When a weapon's trigger was pulled, the Heter valve was opened, releasing a small amount of gas into the Xciter.

**Heth, Morturr** One of the few pirates to survive Ket Maliss's destruction of the Disac gang, he and other survivors took over the ship of Az-Iban and looked for a way to get revenge on Maliss and Black Sun. But when they attempted to hijack the *Destination: Adventure!* along the Sisar Run shortly before the Battle of Endor, they were captured by Imperial Captain Barse Neoman.

**Hethar** This planet was annexed by the Empire shortly before the Battle of Yavin. It was believed that gornts were originally native to Hethar before being exported to other worlds to be raised for their meat.

**Hethrir, Lord** A onetime student of the dark side under Darth Vader himself and a former Imperial Procurator of Justice, he thought nothing of subjecting even his own flesh and blood to the cruelest of fates. Lord Hethrir was a Firrerreo, with gold-, copper-, and cinnamon-striped hair, pale skin, and double-lidded black eyes.

Lord Hethrir

He and his lover, Rillao, had trained with Vader, but she followed the light side. When Rillao became pregnant, she hid from both men by fleeing to a distant planet. Eventually Hethrir found and imprisoned Rillao and turned their son Tigris—who had no Force powers—into a slave. Hethrir's evil knew no bounds. He abducted a freighter full of his own people and sent them to colonize distant planets; then he destroyed his homeworld, killing millions. After the death of Emperor Palpatine, he started an Empire Reborn movement from his worldcraft, which was the size of a small planet. He also started kidnapping children, enslaving those who did not have Force powers and training those who did in the ways of the dark side.

Hethrir sought a final breakthrough, which he intended to achieve with the help of the Waru, a creature aboard Crseih Research Station. The Waru seemed to be a faith healer, but in reality robbed life forces from some of its victims, feeding its own Force-like power. They needed a child exceptionally strong in the Force, so Hethrir kidnapped young Anakin Solo along with his older brother and sister, the twins Jacen and Jaina. The plot was thwarted when Rillao, freed by Leia Organa Solo, told Tigris that Hethrir was his father, and the young man helped Anakin escape. The stricken Waru pulled Hethrir into his energy field and destroyed them both.

**Hetrinar assault bomber** This Hapan starfighter often was deployed aboard *Nova*-class battle cruisers for defensive purposes.

**Hetsime, Nala** A T-47 airspeeder pilot for the Rebel Alliance, he was stationed at Echo Base on Hoth.

**Hett, A'Sharad** The son of Jedi Master Sharad Hett, he was trained early in the use of the Force by his father, along with the rituals and beliefs of the Sand People with whom they lived. When Sharad Hett was assassinated by Aurra Sing, the Jedi Knight Ki-Adi-Mundi vowed to train A'Sharad as his Padawan. A'Sharad inherited his father's lightsaber and built one of his own, and often sparred with both weapons. During his training on Coruscant, Hett learned that humans and Tusken Raiders were genetically unable to reproduce, leading him to believe that his mother must have been a human captured by the Tusken Raiders at a young age and raised as a Tusken.

Hett believed that he should leave the Jedi Order because of dark feelings that he harbored, but the Dark Woman explained that every being had a bit of the darkness, and that Hett had overcome his quite well. The Dark Woman then offered to continue Hett's teaching. Just before the Clone Wars, Hett became a Jedi Master and took Bhat Jul as his apprentice. While the Battle of Jabiim raged, Master Hett led Republic forces that secured the planet Metalorn against Separatist attack. In the wake of the disaster at Jabiim, Master Hett also took on Anakin Skywalker, although more as a friend than a student, after Obi-Wan Kenobi was presumed dead. Together the three Jedi led the Republic's defense of Aargonar.

It was on Aargonar that Hett found out

A'Sharad Hett

*A'Sharad Hett became the Sith Lord Darth Krayt.*

about Skywalker's slaughter of the Tusken tribe that had captured his mother, and he revealed his true identity along with a collection of facial tattoos. He decided to live the rest of his life simply as a Jedi, without worrying about whether he was human or Tusken. He also kept Anakin's dark past a secret.

Near the end of the Clone Wars, Hett was among the Jedi dispatched to Saleucami, serving under Quinlan Vos and Oppo Rancisis during the Siege of Saleucami. He worked with Xiaan Amersu to lead the initial starfighter assault on the Separatist positions on the planet, and was greatly dismayed when she sacrificed herself to ensure the Republic's victory. He honored her memory by completing the mission, allowing the Republic to retake Saleucami and destroy the Separatist cloning facilities beneath the planet's surface.

It was presumed that Hett had died during the execution of Order 66. In reality, he had taken the destruction of the Jedi Order as a chance to give in to and explore his emotions. Over time, he gained a great deal of strength in the Force, much of which came from collections of Sith lore he discovered in his travels to Korriban. Following the guidance found in an ancient Sith Holocron, he eventually gave himself over to the power of the dark side, and became the Dark Lord known as Darth Krayt, a name honoring one of Tatooine's most formidable predators.

He began building a new Sith Order, but yorik coral implants drained much of his strength. As the Sith began to grow in number, he placed himself in a stasis chamber to allow his body to heal, but his mind remained open to his advisers and supporters. When the Ossus Project was started, he realized that it was time to finally reveal himself and his new Sith Order to the galaxy.

**Hett, Sharad** A reclusive Jedi Master originally trained by Eeth Koth, he later chose to leave the Order and go to Tatooine, where he established a bond with a tribe of Tusken Raiders. Sometimes known by the nickname Howlrunner, Hett was hunted down by the bounty hunter Aurra Sing and killed despite the efforts of Ki-Adi-Mundi. He bequeathed his lightsaber to his son, A'Sharad Hett, who later trained under Ki-Adi-Mundi on Coruscant.

**Hetton** A native of Serenno, he was the leader of the Anti-Republic Liberation Front 10 years after the Battle of Ruusan. A small man who chose to dress all in black, Hetton was in his mid-50s when the ARLF began planning more aggressive actions. Unknown to his comrades, Hetton had a strong connection to the dark side of the Force. This connection was obvious to Zannah, who infiltrated the group to undermine their activities.

In the wake of a failed assassination attempt on former Chancellor Tarsus Valorum, Hetton ordered Zannah captured and brought to him, not immediately realizing that she was the heir to Darth Bane's Sith teachings. But then Hetton told Zannah that he had been looking for a Sith to guide his training. He explained that he knew of Belia Darzu's fortress on Tython, and that he could show her skills that would help her defeat Darth Bane. Hetton had been collecting Sith artifacts for years, and revealed that he had been forced to poison his mother when she attempted to control his life.

Zannah agreed to take on Hetton as her apprentice. They journeyed to Ambria, ostensibly to defeat Darth Bane, but the Sith Lord proved to be much stronger than Hetton had anticipated. With two slashes of his lightsaber, Bane severed Hetton's arm before running him through, killing Hetton instantly. Hetton died without knowing that he had been betrayed by Zannah, who only sought to obtain his knowledge to help her Master grow in power.

**Heurkea** One of the most prosperous of the floating cities erected in the seas of the planet Mon Calamari during the last decades of the Old Republic. In Heurkea, Mon Calamari and Quarren worked side by side to ensure the betterment of both species. It was the first city destroyed by the World Devastators during the Battle of Mon Calamari. The city was later rebuilt. When the Yuuzhan Vong attacked Coruscant and remade it into Yuuzhan'tar, the New Republic fled to Mon Calamari and was allowed to use Heurkea as its base of operations. Admiral Ackbar's apartment was in Heurkea, and one of Mara Jade Skywalker's YVH-M droids tracked a Yuuzhan Vong infiltrator to the city.

*Sharad Hett*

**Hev'sin** A female Bothan, she was a member of the same criminal organization as Nuri, based in the Undercity of the planet Aargau around the time of the Battle of Geonosis.

**Hevvrol sector** This area of space was the site of a number of battles between New Republic forces and remnants of the Empire. The Republic managed to finally defeat the Imperials at Glom Tho.

**Hewat** A stern Imperial customs officer, she spent part of her career trying to expose Moruth Doole's illegal spice-distribution network.

**Hewex, Major** An Imperial Navy officer, he was leader of a detachment assigned to guard the shield generator bunker on the Forest Moon of Endor during the construction of the second Death Star. He also served as the liaison between the command staff and technicians.

**Hexagon, the** An area along the border of the Mid Rim and Outer Rim territories that saw intense Rebel activity during the New Order. The Rebel Alliance funded much of the unrest, with large contributions from Meysen Kayson and the Greel Wood Logging Corporation.

**hex bomber** An organic-looking tri-winged bomber used by Sabaoth Squadron to deploy the chemical weapon trihexalon during the Clone Wars.

**hex deployer** A bulbous, organic-looking ship used by the forces of Cavik Toth to deploy the chemical weapon trihexalon at Maramere. An attempt by Separatists to use hex deployers at the Battle of the Geonosis was thwarted.

**Hextrophon, Arhul** The executive secretary and master historian for the Alliance High Command, he chronicled the history of the Alliance as well as that of the fledgling New Republic. Earlier in his life, Hextrophon had been sold into slavery to the Zygerrians; he was rescued by Han Solo and Chewbacca, who turned the slave ship and its valuable cargo over to Hextrophon and his companions. Years later, after the Battle of Hoth, Major Hextrophon had the chance to meet Jedi Master Yoda on Dagobah. The results of that visit have never been revealed.

**Hexum'Baz** A Dug criminal, he worked for the crime lord Sebolto around the time of the Battle of Naboo. Jango Fett claimed the bounty on his head.

**heyblibber** The Gungan term for a specific type of luxury bongo submarines. They were larger than the standard tri-bubble bongo subs and could transport up to 24 soldiers. They often were used by the Rep Council and the military. Jar Jar Binks crashed Boss Nass's heyblibber shortly before being exiled from Otoh Gunga.

**Hezzoran, Lord** This Sith Lord was one of the many instructors at the Sith Academy on Korriban in the years leading up to the Battle of Ruusan.

Hibernation sickness

**hfredium** One of the primary metals mined on Nkllon by the Nomad City Mining Company, hfredium was used in the production of starship hull plates. During the early years of the New Republic, the market price of hfredium moved up steadily before plummeting after the reappearance of Grand Admiral Thrawn; that caused Lando Calrissian to lose a great deal of the credits that he had invested on Nkllon.

**HG-211** This droid served as the head of security at the droid-manufacturing facilities on the moon Uffel in the Cularin system during the last decades of the Old Republic. It was programmed to destroy itself and as much of the manufacturing facility as it could if it was ever threatened.

**H'gaard** One of Bespin's twin moons, along with Drudonna; they were often referred to as the Twins. H'gaard measured about 5 kilometers in diameter, and was a greenish ice ball.

**HH-15** A portable missile launcher produced by Golan Arms during the last years of the Old Republic, it became one of the primary weapons used by the Rebel Alliance. The rugged design of the HH-15 meant it was capable of operating in extreme climates and conditions. It could fire solid projectiles, concussion missiles, or proton torpedoes. It had to be sighted by eye.

**HH-4** This missile launcher was produced by Merr-Sonn during the Galactic Civil War. It was favored by smugglers and mercenaries because it was lightweight and could fire a small grenade accurately.

**Hhen** The pilot of a small ship that took Dorsk 82 to Ando during the Yuuzhan Vong War. Hhen was killed when the Aqualish destroyed Dorsk 82's ship during the Jedi's attempt to defend the droids of Imthitill.

**hiakk** A species of trees native to New Plympto. Their silvery trunks could grow to heights of 200 meters or more.

**hibbas** A creature raised for its succulent meat, which was served in many of the New Republic's finer restaurants.

**hibel spider** This arachnid species was known for the almost ritualistic way that individuals fought for dominance.

**hibernation** Common slang referring to the rest periods of computers and droids.

**hibernation sickness** A disorder that could result when a being was brought out of suspended animation, it was characterized by temporary blindness, disorientation, muscle stiffness, weakness, hypersensitivity, and occasionally madness. Han Solo suffered a mild case of hibernation sickness after he was released from his carbonite prison by Princess Leia Organa.

**hibernation trance** A Jedi technique in which the user descended into a deep hibernation state, slowing his or her body's metabolism to a standstill. A trained Jedi could remain in this state for at least four days.

**hibridium** Found only on the western coastline of the main continent of Garos IV, this ore had a natural ability to cloak other objects. When the Empire discovered it, Garos IV was garrisoned and the mining of the ore strictly regulated. Prototype cloaking devices built from hibridium were nowhere near as effective as those created from stygium, requiring huge amounts of power to operate and more room to house the system. The craft using it was invisible to other ships' sensors, but could not use its own sensors to locate other ships.

**Hida, Nar** The owner of a failed clothing store on Coruscant, he used his remaining credits to book passage for himself, his wife, and their daughter on the transport *Jendirian Valley,* hoping to work his way back to Luptoom. While trying to rob a sleeping Bith to help pay for food, Hida was approached by Anakin Skywalker, who was in disguise while escorting Padmé Amidala back to Naboo. Anakin warned Hida that the Bith had a blaster hidden in his cloak, and Padmé gave him a handful of dataries to help pay for his food. On Naboo, Padmé instructed Hida to seek assistance from the Refugee Relief Movement, which helped the Hida family return to Luptoom. Hida then dedicated himself to turning his life around, as well as doing what he could to help those less fortunate.

Nar Hida

Marn Hierogryph

**Hidden Beks** One of the smaller gangs on Taris that struggled to make a name for itself against the Black Vulkars four millennia before the Battle of Yavin.

**Hidden Daggers** A pirate gang that was active in the Corellian system during the New Order. It operated from a hidden base in the area of space known as the Binyare Razorcat.

**Hidden Leader** The title given to the leader of the Human League.

**Hidden Temple** A secret safehouse established by a handful of Jedi Knights who survived the Clone Wars and the Jedi Purge. Its exact location was never disclosed to anyone without a need to know, keeping it safe from the watchful eyes of Emperor Palpatine.

**Hidden Valley** Located on Honoghr, this agricultural oasis was constructed by the Noghri as a way to begin rebuilding their world after Leia Organa Solo revealed the deception of Emperor Palpatine in ruining it. It was often referred to by the Noghri as the Future of Honoghr.

**Hierarchy of Hatred** Ysanne Isard's personal plan of maximizing damage to her enemies. Booster Terrik, using historical data, attempted to re-create the Hierarchy for the New Republic to help anticipate Isard's reactions to given situations.

**Hierogryph, Marn** A Snivvian, he was a black-market dealer on Taris in the era of the Great Sith War and the Mandalorian Wars. Known as The Gryph, he found himself dogged at every step by the Padawans of Jedi Master Lucien Draay, especially Zayne Carrick, who were trying to assist the local police in maintaining order. The one time Carrick managed to actually apprehend him, Hierogryph was tied up in a speeder while Carrick rushed back to the Jedi training facility to attend a ceremony for the Padawans. Carrick emerged with an unbelievable story of the deaths of the other Padawans at the hands of their Masters, and fled with Hierogryph into the city.

Hierogryph was forced to accept that his only chance of survival was to help Carrick, especially when he was named an accessory to Zayne's supposed crime. They enlisted the help of Jarael and the Camper to escape from Taris, but eventually were caught by Valius Ying on the Rogue Moon. Hierogryph managed to negotiate a deal that depended on Carrick turning himself in.

When they returned to Taris, Hierogryph rescued Carrick by bribing the First Mate to release them; he then offered Carrick a position in his small organization. But the group was caught in a Mandalorian raid on the planet Vanquo and Jarael was captured. The rest of the group figured out a way to rescue him with the help of a rogue Mandalorian, and they escaped to Ralltiir where Jarael and the Camper went off to find a quieter life.

It was anything but quiet for Hierogryph and Carrick. At one point they set up a mobile commissary for New Republic forces—using a stolen New Republic provisioning ship. They were trapped on the planet Serroco when a fierce Mandalorian attack came. They managed to escape and made their way back to Taris where Hierogryph somehow became part of the anti-Mandalorian resistance, and then leader of the movement.

**Hi-fex** A high-powered proton torpedo launcher manufactured by Arakyd.

**Hiffis** Once the site of an Imperial storage facility, it was raided by the Rebel Alliance.

**Hifold sensory package** A cyborg implant from NeuroSaav Corporation, it was commonly referred to as "the thinking being's enhancement." It incorporated optical and aural replacement to increase all aspects of perception.

**Hifron, Shiaer** An independent trader who worked for Kyr Laron as a go-between in the assassin's business dealings. Laron preferred that no one discover she was female.

**Hig** A slender, blue-skinned species. Ginbotham, a skilled pilot who served with Wedge Antilles as a member of the command crew on the *Yavin,* was a Hig.

**Higgs** An Imperial engineer, he was part of the crew of the *Wanderer.*

**High Admiral of the Mid Rim** This was the title assumed by Imperial Warlord Teradoc in the wake of the death of Zsinj.

**High Audience Chamber** The aristocracy's seating area in the petranaki arena of the Stalgasin Hive on Geonosis.

**highborn** The name given to the hereditary leaders of Ansionian overclans, such as the Borokii or Januul.

**High Cabinet** The term used for the Corellian system's leadership following the assassination of Thrackan Sal-Solo. The High Cabinet was led by the Five World Prime Minister and President of Five Worlds, Dur Gejjen, and included his Ministers of Intelligence and the Military, Gavele Lemora and Rorf Willems. The group planned the murder of the Hapan Queen Mother, Tenel Ka.

**High Canir** The title given to those Vratix canirs who were elected to run the planetary government of Thyferra in the period following the Yuuzhan Vong War.

**High Castle of Jomark** A low-built collection of stones and mortar, it served as Jedi clone Joruus C'baoth's palace on Jomark during his attempt to lure Luke Skywalker into a trap about five years after the Battle of Endor. It was a structure built by an ancient, unknown species and was situated between two crags on the face of a dormant volcanic cone.

**High Chew** The officers' mess aboard the Yuuzhan Vong warship *Sunulok.*

**High Chunah** One of the worlds colonized by the Mugaari, it was part of the Javin sector. Much of the planet's landmass was covered with factories, and many of Greater Javin's landspeeders were manufactured there. The planet was best known for the phosphorescent rocks that littered its surface, giving the planet an unusual glow when seen from space.

**High Command** This was Xim the Despot's inner circle of power, according to the Survivors who lived on Dellalt. Their legends said that the beings who served on the High Command would eventually seek out the Survivors and unlock Xim the Despot's vaults.

**High Coordinator** The title given to those Verpine leaders who oversaw the operations of factories and installations in the Roche asteroid field.

**High Coruscanti** A dialect of Basic, it was used by the elite members of Coruscant society.

**High Council** The name given to the new Jedi Council formed by Luke Skywalker and newly elected Chief of State Cal Omas in the wake of the loss of Coruscant to the Yuuzhan Vong. To ensure that the Jedi Knights did not unfairly take power away from the New Republic Senate, Skywalker agreed that the 12-member High Council would consist of 6 Jedi and 6 New Republic representatives. The initial membership consisted of Skywalker, Cilghal, Saba Sebatyne, Kenth Hamner, Tresina Lobi, and Kyp Durron representing the Jedi; and Cal Omas, Triebakk, Dif Scaur, Releqy A'Kla, Sien Sovv, and Ta'laam Ranth representing the Republic.

**High Council (Gungan)** Another name for the Rep Council, the governmental body that supported the ruling Boss of the Gungans.

**High Council of Alderaan** The governing body of Alderaan.

**High Council of Ralltiir** The main political body that oversaw the government of Ralltiir until just before the Battle of Yavin. When Lord Tion discovered that the Rebel Alliance had supporters on the planet, he and his forces eliminated the High Council and all its members to show that the Rebellion would not be tolerated.

**High Festival** An annual event and time of celebration on Saheelindeel, it started as a celebration of tribal gatherings and ritual hunts.

**High Flight Beta Squadron** A starfighter unit used for reconnaissance and data collection, it was assigned to the warship *Allegiance* during the Adumari negotiations with the New Republic and the Empire.

**High Flight Squadron** A group of X-wing fighters assigned to the New Republic warship *Battle Dog.*

**High Galactic** A form of the Basic language altered and adapted by the Imperial inner circle during the rule of Emperor Palpatine.

**highglide** This large avian predator with emerald-green feathers was native to Goroth Prime. It fed mainly on carrion.

**HighGround RockyPlain TwentyKilometer Left** The Verpine name for a section of the surface of Nickel One, it was located 20 kilometers down the left side of the asteroid. It was here that Imperial forces launched their initial attack in the wake of the Second Battle of Fondor. The exhaust ports that bled off excess heat from the asteroid's main fusion plant were located here; the Imperials hoped to sabotage the ports and cause the plant to overload and explode.

**high-g suit** A specialized garment used by starfighter pilots, the high-g suit protected the wearer from the effects of high-speed maneuvering.

***High Haven*** A New Republic medical frigate, it supported the Fifth Battle Group during the Battle of N'zoth. Upon his rescue from the Yevetha, Han Solo spent time aboard the *High Haven* recovering from his physical and mental wounds.

**High Hermit** The leader of the Ancient Order of Pessimists on Maryx Minor. After an epic battle between Darth Vader and Boba Fett, the High Hermit and his brethren were wiped out when a Star Destroyer bombarded their hermitage.

**high-hound** A species of semi-humanoid avians native to Aduba-3. Bloodthirsty, migratory beasts, they ravaged the planet's settlements. A group of them were shot down by Han Solo and Chewbacca shortly after the Battle of Yavin when the two were stranded on the planet.

High Hermit

**High Inquisitor** The name given to Imperial Dark Side Adepts who worked directly for Emperor Palpatine. They rooted out potential sources of new Jedi candidates and Force activity during the New Order. In the wake of the Battle of Endor and the apparent death of Emperor Palpatine, many Inquisitors abandoned Imperial service and joined the Great InQuestors of Justice.

**High Jedi General** The rank given to those Jedi Council members who were given command of a system army during the Clone Wars.

**Highland Green Washeteria** A combination launderette and public refresher station, it was on the north side of Pelek Baw on Haruun Kal. During the last years of the Old Republic, Jedi Mace Windu arrived there for a meeting with Phloremirlla Tenk, owner of the establishment . . . and an agent for the Republic Intelligence agency. It turned out that she also was a double agent for the Separatists.

High-hound

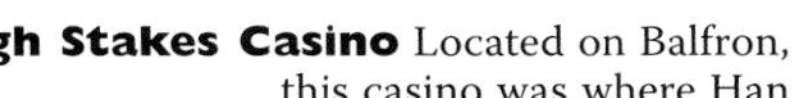

**High Marshals** The name used by the Iron Knights during their reemergence in response to the Yuuzhan Vong War.

**High Moff** This was the title given to the individual who led the Moff High Council during the decades around the Sith–Imperial War.

**Highport** One of the major spaceports that served the Upper City of Taris during the era of the Great Sith War.

**High Priest of the Golden Sun** The title bestowed upon the Sedrian leader, whose commands and dictates came directly from the Golden Sun itself.

**High Prophet** This was the title given to any midlevel priest who served the Dark Force religion as a member of the Prophets of the Dark Side.

**High Protector** This was the name given to the leader of the Echani martial artists many millennia before the Galactic Civil War.

***Highroller*** This PLY-3000 luxury yacht was owned by K'Armyn Viraxo.

**High Seat** Located in each Noghri Dukha, this was where the highest-ranking Noghri official sat when the dynasts were called together. During the New Order and the early years of the New Republic, the High Seat also was reserved for visiting Imperial representatives, who were all afforded a measure of reverence in honor of Darth Vader.

Lieutenant Barlon Hightower

**High Stakes Casino** Located on Balfron, this casino was where Han Solo set up Lando Calrissian to first meet the Tonnika sisters.

***High Tide*** This was the false name that Byalfin Dyur used for his starship, the *Boneyard Rendezvous,* when he touched down on Drewwa to follow Ben Skywalker. Skywalker had been dispatched to locate the Amulet of Kalara at the Tendrando Arms facility on the moon, and Dyur and crew had been hired by Lumiya to keep track of the young Jedi's progress.

**High Tongue** A variant on the Old Corellian language, it was used by ensterite families during the Old Republic. High Tongue was considered the language of aristocrats. Most families eventually abandoned High Tongue and adopted Basic.

**Hightower, Lieutenant Barlon** An officer in the Rebel Alliance, he was part of a team assigned to locate any Alliance starships or personnel lost during the evacuation of Hoth. Later, he joined Rogue Squadron.

**High Tower Boardroom** This was the central bubble in the Gungan city of Otoh Gunga. It was here that Boss Nass and the Rep Council ruled the city. A long circular judge's bench was filled with Gungan officials and dominated the room. Boss Nass sat on a bench higher than the others. Those who addressed the Rep Council spoke from the room's Supplication Platform.

**Hightower Conglomerate** A Coruscant construction firm, it actually was a front for Black Sun. Its Core Constructions unit often underbid the competition to win a contract, then had a series of cost overruns that simply fed credits into Black Sun's coffers.

**High-Yield Universal Institutional Savings Account** One of the most consistently profitable funds that parents could establish for their children in the last decades of the Old Republic. Jango Fett established one for his son Boba before he was killed on Geonosis.

**Higron, Rodin** A Corellian gambler and privateer, he won the ownership of the planet Oasis in a crooked sabacc match. He traveled to the planet and decided to compete with the Riders of the Maelstrom to pick off passing ships and steal their cargo.

**Hiicrop, Satnik** This fictitious individual was created by Boba Fett during his attempt to stop Jodo Kast from impersonating him.

High Tower Boardroom

Hiitian

Hiicrop was hiding on Nal Hutta, and Kast tracked him there, only to find out that Hiicrop was really Fett. Fett then eliminated Kast.

**Hiironi** One of the largest Irstat tribes on Tarasin.

**Hiitian** A huge, humanoid species that resembled flightless birds.

**Hija, Lieutenant** The Imperial chief gunnery officer aboard the Star Destroyer *Devastator,* he was at his post when his ship overtook and captured the *Tantive IV* with Princess Leia Organa aboard. Under orders, he didn't fire at the escape pod that took R2-D2 and C-3PO off the ship, because scanners didn't detect any life-forms. Years earlier, Hija had fired the shots that destroyed the Empire's Falleen biological warfare facility to cover up a mishap. The devastation led to the deaths of the family of Prince Xizor, head of the Black Sun criminal organization.

**Hijarna** A deserted, battle-scarred planet, it was first discovered by the Fifth Alderaanian Expedition during the Expansionist Period of the Old Republic. Atop a bluff sat the crumbling fortress of Hijarna, made of hard black stone and probably abandoned 1,000 years before its discovery. The Hijarna stone was nearly indestructible and could absorb turbolaser fire like a sponge. Similar stone was found in the construction of the Hand of Thrawn compound on Nirauan.

The fortress overlooked a plain crossed with deep ravines and marked with indications of former devastation. Whether the fortress was built to defend against this destruction or was somehow the cause of it was unclear. Talon Karrde called a meeting with his fellow smugglers in Hijarna's fortress to discuss actions against Grand Admiral Thrawn.

**Hijoian Docks** This space station was located in the Hijoian system of Fakir sector. The Ho'Din terrorist Yansan destroyed a pair of the Rebel Alliance's Gallofree Medium Transports at the station shortly before the Battle of Hoth.

**Hikahi** This Mon Calamari port city was partly destroyed by the World Devastators during the Battle of Mon Calamari. Its loss greatly impacted the natives' ability to build and repair starships. Over time, the city was rebuilt, and it later served as the base of operations for the Galactic Alliance's defense forces during the years following the loss of Coruscant to the Yuuzhan Vong.

Hijarna

**Hikil** This tropical world was known for its lulari trees.

**Hill, San** This humanoid Muun was chairman of the InterGalactic Banking Clan just before the start of the Clone Wars. His pale skin was the result of living indoors for many decades, monitoring the financial and economic position of the IBC and ensuring that it continued to grow. Just prior to the Battle of Geonosis, San Hill agreed to support the war effort of the Separatists, but reminded Count Dooku that he was not going to enter an exclusive agreement with them. San Hill correctly surmised that the IBC could gain considerable profit by providing loans and financial services to the Old Republic as well as the Confederacy of Independent Systems, and by helping newly independent planets mint their own currencies. He also made a number of deals with the criminal underground on Aargau in an effort to supplement the income of the Separatists.

It was San Hill who traveled to Kaleesh in the wake of the Huk Wars. He secretly arranged for a Kaleesh warrior to be badly injured in a shuttle crash. Hill knew that the warrior was too seasoned to fall in combat, but ensured that after the crash he would be unable to recover without help. Hill arrived on Kalee to "rescue" the Kaleesh by funding the rebuilding of their society. The warrior agreed to accompany San Hill, because he wanted his people to survive the injustice that had befallen them at the hands of the Jedi. Hill then brought the warrior to Geonosis, where he was transformed into a part-alien, part-droid monstrosity known as General Grievous.

San Hill also financed the resurrection of the Gen'Dai warrior Durge. During the Battle of Muunilinst, San Hill hid in his offices while letting Durge do the dirty work of fighting against the clone troopers of the Republic. Just before the Battle of Coruscant and the end of the Clone Wars, San Hill and the other leaders of the Confederacy were whisked away to Utapau by General Grievous to ensure their safety. After hiding on Utapau, the Separatists were taken to Mustafar. It was there, after Darth Sidious finally lured Anakin Skywalker to the dark side of the Force, that the Separatist leaders met their deaths. Skywalker was dispatched to Mustafar by Sidious himself, with orders to eliminate them. Skywalker quickly killed San Hill before setting off after the rest of the leaders.

**Hi'llani, Toma** This Jedi Master was considered one of the foremost authorities on technology at the Jedi Temple on Coruscant in the years leading up to the Clone Wars.

**hill people** This group of Galacians was formed more than 100 years before the Battle of Naboo. Its members had been persecuted by other Galacians for having darker eyes and skin than "normal" Galacians. They left the urban areas of Galu and lived in the low mountains until Queen Veda of the Tallah Dynasty decreed that a democratic election would choose her successor. Their leader, a young Galacian named Elan, was discovered to be the rightful heir to the throne, but she threw her support to Wila Prammi.

**Hilly** A Rebel Alliance officer at a base on Arbra, he agreed with Leia Organa's plan to hide the Alliance's fleet near the system's star in order to avoid Imperial detection.

**Hilo** An industrial planet where Obi-Wan Kenobi and Anakin Skywalker met up with the *BioCruiser* two years after the Battle of Naboo.

**Hilse, Chad** This Alderaanian ensign was given trooper duty aboard the *Tantive IV* and was one of the first soldiers to die when the ship was overtaken by Darth Vader and the *Devastator.*

**Himar** This clan of Twi'leks contracted for the murder of Cherit following the Yuuzhan Vong War. The Mandalorian known as Jaing Skirata accepted and completed the contract, which drew the attention of Boba Fett.

San Hill

***Himner*** This Rebel Alliance transport group was destroyed when it tried to aid Admiral Harkov's defecting fleet.

**Himron, Major Molo** The ruthless leader of an Imperial Army assault force sent to Coruscant by Grand Admiral Thrawn five years after the Battle of Endor. Major Himron's goal was to capture Leia Organa Solo and her children.

**Hin** A Yuzzem slave, he worked as a miner for the Empire on Circarpous V (Mimban). He and his companion Kee became violent and destructive, were jailed by Captain-Supervisor Grammel, and then started killing fellow prisoners. When Luke Skywalker and Leia Organa were placed in the Yuzzem's cell, Skywalker began to communicate with them and gained their trust. They all escaped the prison compound and set out to find the Temple of Pomojema and the Kaiburr crystal. Hin was fatally injured by Darth Vader outside the temple, but managed to survive long enough to rescue Skywalker.

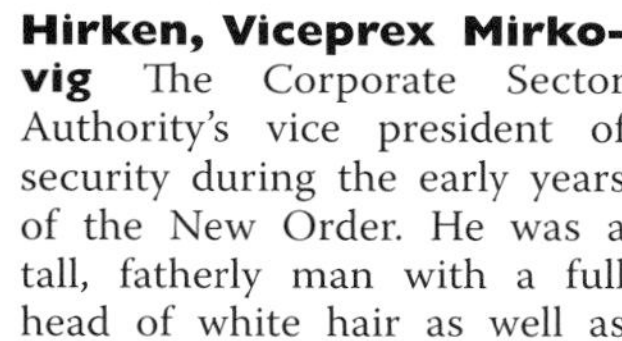
Major Molo Himron

**Hindasar system** Dr. Evazan fled to this system after escaping from prison on Delrian. He then set up a questionable medical practice there as a cover for his other activities.

**Hindred** One of Leia Organa's aides during the Galactic Civil War.

**Hinen** This male Senali was the son of Garth and Ganeed, and a member of the Banoosh-Walore clan.

**Hing, Tolan** A Jedi Master who served in the Jedi Temple on Coruscant in the final decades of the Old Republic, Master Hing was revered for his skills in constructing lightsabers, and could repair almost any damage to a saber after a fight.

***Hininbirg*** The Imperial escort carrier assigned to take TIE defender prototypes from Vinzen Neela 5 to Coruscant.

**Hinter, Yarr** This New Republic ambassador to Sullust was nearly killed by the Defel assassin Londrah.

***Hinthra*** The transport ship that Elis Helrot used to smuggle slaves or spice to Kala'uun. It was armed with a pair of double blaster cannons.

**Hintivan II** This frigid, heavily forested world was controlled by the Empire during the early years of the Galactic Civil War.

**hinwuine** This Gand word was used to denote any non-Gands who were honored guests and who could speak of themselves in the first person without being considered rude or vulgar.

**Hirf, Qlaern** A Vratix native from the planet Thyferra, he was a member of the Ashern Circle, which was considered a terrorist group by the humans controlling the planet. Qlaern Hirf alerted New Republic Intelligence to the location of highly potent bacta stored aboard the space station at Yag'Dhul. When the *Pulsar Skate* arrived at the station to load the bacta, Hirf hid aboard the ship and once on Coruscant made contact with government leaders. Hirf had come to find a cure for the Krytos virus, which affected only nonhumanoids, and for a time was allowed to work in the lab where Imperial General Derricote had developed the virus. Because of the highly secretive nature of the project and its potential importance to the future of the New Republic, it was decided to relocate Hirf's experiments to the Alderaan Biotics hydroponics facility on Borleias. Hirf's team discovered kor ryll's bacta-enhancing properties, providing the New Republic with the ability to produce its own rylca.

**Hirken, Viceprex Mirkovig** The Corporate Sector Authority's vice president of security during the early years of the New Order. He was a tall, fatherly man with a full head of white hair as well as well-manicured and lacquered finernails; he dressed impeccably. He was placed in charge of the Stars' End penal colony on Mytus VII. He created a list of candidates for incarceration, many of whom were vocal critics of the CSA; others were seen as personal threats to Hirken. When Han Solo managed to infiltrate Stars' End and trigger an explosion, Hirken tried to escape without first helping his wife and others; she shot him in the back with a blaster.

**Hirog** An insectoid, he was one of Admiral Ackbar's aides following the Battle of Endor. Hirog actually was the first officer of the Hiromi warship *Kuratcha,* and was the advance scout working to plan several invasions. It was Hirog who created the misunderstanding that set the Ewoks against the Lahsbees. Just about everything else he tried went horribly wrong, and in the end, Hirog and the Hiromi agreed to ally themselves with Luke Skywalker and the Alliance of Free Planets.

**Hiromi** An inept, beetle-like species, the Hiromi stood about 1.5 meters tall and dressed in gaudy red, tan, and purple clothing. What they couldn't own legally, they tried to steal. They had a very short attention span, however, and thoughts of food or play often interfered with long-term goals, such as their plans to control the galaxy. They

Viceprex Mirkovig Hirken

held the distinct honor of having pulled off the briefest successful invasion of Zeltros in recorded history, a short time after the Emperor's death at Endor. The Hiromi invasion, code-named Operation: Glorious Destiny, consisted of taking over a large kitchen in the royal palace. It was foiled by another invasion, which was interrupted by a third—all within a few days. The final attack led by the brutal Tofs very nearly succeeded, but was ultimately defeated by the combined forces of the Alliance, the Nagai, Imperial holdouts, and the glorious Hiromi empire.

**Hiroth Besh** A moon in the Hoth system, it was known for the intense electrical storms that swept its surface. Several starships crash-landed on the moon's surface, creating a kind of starship graveyard where the system's mynock population was established.

**Hirrtu** This self-absorbed Rodian male worked as the comm officer, tail gunner, and cook aboard the *Boneyard Rendezvous,* serving under the pirate captain Byalfin Dyur

Hirog, a Hiromi

following the Swarm War. Hirrtu was known for his excessive preening, including dyeing every fifth scale on his body dark blue.

**Hirsi** An Outer Rim planet, it was home to the Qwohog, who lived in Hirsi's streams, rivers, and lakes.

**Hirsoot** A bat-eared humanoid, he was one of Orko's servants as well as a spy hired by Gorga the Hutt. Hirsoot tried to poison Orko shortly after Gorga married Anachro, but failed to do so before Orko could travel to Skeebo to rescue Anachro. Hirsoot missed several other opportunities. He was in Orko's bedchambers when Ry-Kooda came to kill Orko. Like Orko, Hirsoot was ripped apart by Ry-Kooda, and then eaten.

*Hirsoot*

**Hirth** This crime lord worked from a base on Abregado-rae during the early decades of the New Republic.

**His Celestial Highness** This was one of the many sarcastic nicknames used by Admiral Cha Niathal to describe Jacen Solo.

**Hise, Gab'borah** The dessert chef assigned to Jabba the Hutt's sail barge, he had an encounter with young Boba Fett at kitchen seven in Jabba's palace. Hise provided Fett with a jetpack to escape Durge and flee the palace. Fett eventually returned the favor by reuniting Hise with his kidnapped daughter, Ygabba.

**Hise, Ygabba** This girl was the leader of a group of children who were captured and forced to work for Gilramos Libkath in the years before the Clone Wars. Ygabba Hise herself had been taken some five years before the Battle of Geonosis. It was Ygabba who befriended young Boba Fett when Fett arrived on Tatooine to seek information from Jabba the Hutt. After Fett helped Ygabba and the children escape from Libkath, they returned to Jabba's palace to claim the bounty on him. It was there that Ygabba was reunited with her father, the chef Gab'borah Hise. Ygabba chose to remain with her father, cooking all manner of dishes for Jabba and his retainers. Just before Boba set off to capture Wat Tambor, Ygabba and Gab'borah presented Boba with a full suit of Mandalorian armor tailored to his measurements. Ygabba also presented him with her own gift, a holoshroud she had encoded with an image of Durge.

**His Glory** One of the many honorifics given to Nil Spaar during his rise to power in the years following the Battle of Endor.

**Hishyim** This planet was the site of an Imperial patrol station during the early years of the New Republic.

**hisp-silk** A luxurious form of silk that was commonly used to create sleep gowns and microgarments.

**Hissa, Grand Moff Bertroff** As part of the plan by the Central Committee of Grand Moffs to keep Triclops a secret and find a way to rule the galaxy following Emperor Palpatine's death, Hissa cultivated a friendship with Trioculus, knowing that the three-eyed mutant could be passed off as the true son of Palpatine. Hissa, the Imperial Governor of the Kessel system for many years, had been severely disfigured on Duro, when the hazardous wastes from Imperial dumping grounds flooded the Valley of Royalty. His arms were replaced with those of an assassin droid, and his torso was encased on a repulsorlift floating chair. When the Prophets of the Dark Side sentenced Hissa to death for treachery against the Empire, he was to be starved aboard the *Scardia* until he was near death. Then his final meal would be biscuits laden with parasites that would consume him from the inside. He never got that far, for Kadann, suspicious that Triclops's information on the Lost City of the Jedi was false, sent Hissa to investigate. Hissa was then incinerated in the molten lava core of Yavin 4 at the end of the false entrance to the city.

**Hissal** A member of the Committee for Interinstitutional Assistance, the Brigian Hissal worked to expand the campuses of the University of Rudrig throughout the Tion Hegemony. He approached Han Solo on Saheelindeel before the Battle of Yavin to hire him and the *Millennium Falcon,* since the only way to get educational equipment and materials to Brigia was to smuggle them. The planet's New Regime wanted to ensure that Brigians learned only what they wanted them to learn. Solo discovered that the New Regime was printing counterfeit money to fund its own military agenda, and allowed Hissal to use the *Falcon*'s communications systems to broadcast a message to all of Brigia, detailing the abuses of the New Regime. Solo then landed Hissal on a distant part of the planet where he was able to establish his academic headquarters.

*Grand Moff Bertroff Hissa*

**Hisser** Saba Sebatyne's call sign. She was a member of the Wild Knights Squadron, which was dispatched to assist in the evacuation of the Jedi Knight base on Eclipse during the Yuuzhan Vong War.

**hissing cane** A form of thick-walled reeds that grew in the swamps of Dagobah. When the wind blew, it filled tiny holes in the walls of the reeds, creating a hissing sound.

**Historical Battle Site Preservation Act** A New Republic decree, it established a fleet of cargo haulers under the name Operation Flotsam to collect the debris from space battles that occurred during the Galactic Civil War. The HBSPA also funded an Alliance War Museum on Coruscant.

**Historical Council** A branch of the Galactic Alliance, it was established to gather and refine the known history of the galaxy. It was one of the first bodies to use a time line that hinged on the Battle of Yavin. Events were then marked by the number of Coruscant years before or after the Battle of Yavin.

***History of the Jedi Knights, The*** A legendary book, it was found on the Nespis VIII space station by Tash Arranda, during Mammon Hoole's search for Project Starscream. When she opened it, she released the spirit of Aidan Bok, who helped her escape from the station with Hoole and her brother, Zak.

**Hitaka** Count Dooku was dispatched to Hitaka on a secret mission by Darth Sidious during the Clone Wars; Sidious then arranged for the Grand Army of the Republic to carry out its own specific mission there to give Dooku a chance to complete his without being discovered.

**Hitak Harriers** A Rebel Alliance unit that participated in battles to control the Kwymar sector. Veterans of the Battle of Hoth, the troops were responsible for defeating the Imperial Hell's Hammers during a siege on Turak IV.

**Hitak Mountains** These volcanic peaks on Turak IV were a strategic hideout for Rebel Alliance soldiers, who struck at the Imperial Hell's Hammers from the Hitaks and then retreated there.

Hitcher crab

**hitcher crab** Native to Sevarcos, these large crustaceans measured over 1 meter in length. They had three large spikes on top of their shells, and two clawed arms. They foraged on small rodents and plant life. Hitcher crabs produced a slow-acting poison that coated their shells and spikes. Unsuspecting creatures who stepped on their backs were injected with the poison and eventually died; the crab later tracked down its victims and consumed them.

**Hitiwa, Oejoe** Along with accomplices Stu Hemphawar and Ruceba Ahid, they were implicated in a scheme to traffic illicit contraband throughout the Core Worlds from an apartment on Coruscant. All three men eventually were captured by Jango Fett, who claimed their bounty.

**Hive Ball** A grand gala held by the X'Ting on Ord Cestus to celebrate important events or to fête important visitors.

**hive kinrath** A subspecies of the predatory kinrath spider, it lived in subsurface caves on Dantooine.

**Hive Mother** The Queen and governmental leader of the Verpine.

**hive rats** A mutant species of large, carnivorous rodents that lived underground on Coruscant. Hive rats grew to more than 3 meters long and weighed more than 300 kilograms. Generally hairless, their bodies were covered with fat deposits and tumors. They were one of the few creatures that fed on duracrete worms, making them a necessary evil in the undercity of Coruscant. They were extremely dangerous, however, and when confronted in the lower levels they were known to attack and eat humans and other beings. Their mouths were filled with razor-sharp teeth, and they hunted in packs of up to 10.

**hive ship** Another name for an Ithorian herd ship.

**hive virus** Fairly widespread up through the Clone Wars era, these viruses infected individuals and drove them crazy in a relatively short period of time. Hive viruses, which were highly contagious, altered the perceptions of victims. But with advances in medical technology, hive viruses were virtually eliminated throughout the galaxy.

**Hive Wars** Prior to their discovery of space travel, the Kubaz struggled to exist on Kubindi because of the intense solar radiation from the star Ku'Bakai. They turned to consuming insects, and each Kubaz clan maintained its own hive for food. But with shortages, there was a series of interclan raids that eventually led to all-out wars among neighboring clans. The Hive Wars were slowly killing off the species until the discovery of Insecticulture, which allowed Kubaz geneticists to alter the coloration of an insect, thereby identifying whole hives of insects as belonging to a certain clan. Science helped breed stronger, heartier insects, and eventually increased hive populations.

**Hja, Astrinol** A Dathomiri witch, she was leader of the Dreaming River Clan in the early years of the New Republic. Hja and much of her clan were imprisoned by Imperials seven years after the Battle of Endor, but were eventually rescued by the Jedi Knights dispatched to bring Dal Konur to justice.

**Hjaff** An arid desert planet, it had three major continents and was the homeworld of the Tarc species. The Tarc domain consisted of about 20 systems without other sentient life.

**HK-01** This rogue war droid was considered the mastermind behind the Great Droid Revolution, which started 4,015 years before the Galactic Civil War. HK-01 was the prototype of the HK series protocol droids produced by Czerka Corporation. In reality, these droids were designed as assassins; *HK* stood for "hunter-killer." After gaining a measure of independence following its escape from Czerka's labs, HK-01 began secretly reprogramming all kinds of automata to liberate them from their sentient masters. On HK-01's command, droids across the galaxy suddenly turned violent and unpredictable: Once-loyal battle droids began subjugating entire planets in the name of the Great Droid Revolution. Over time, however, the code HK-01 was using allowed the Republic and the Jedi Knights to find its location and shut it down, thus ending the revolt.

**HK-130** A small security droid manufactured on Balmorra, it resembled a tiny metal ball with small silver studs. Known as the trouble seeker, the HK-130 scanned each being it encountered to determine a threat level. If there was resistance, the HK-130 could fire a powerful stun beam from one of its studs.

**HK-24** This HK series assassin droid was dispatched by Lord Arkoh Adasca to hunt down the Camper during the Mandalorian Wars era. HK-24 stowed away aboard the *Last Resort* when the ship touched down on Ralltiir. It then confronted the Camper. Jarael interceded, and HK-24 threatened to cut her limbs off, until T1-LB stepped in and gave Jarael a chance to move the Camper out of the way. HK-24 shot Elbee and forced the labor droid to stand down, but was unprepared for the sudden appearance of Rohlan Dyre, whose blaster decapitated the droid and left it a pile of scrap parts.

**HK-47 blaster** A custom-crafted model of blaster carbine developed during the final years of the Old Republic, it was equipped with a bio-link module that allowed the user to interface directly with the weapon during combat.

**HK-47 droid** This sentient HK series assassin droid was developed by Czerka Corporation during the Great Sith War. It once destroyed an entire building in order to eliminate a single target, and its merciless pursuit of its targets was well known. The droid had a long series of owners and frequent memory wipes.

One owner was Darth Revan, who programmed the droid to infiltrate the Sand People and gain information about the Star Forge. Revan had HK-47's memories of the mission erased. Later, when Revan turned to the light side and again set off to locate the Star Forge, the droid's abilities proved useful in regaining the trust of the Sand People; this allowed the Jedi Knights to locate the Star Map on Tatooine. In the wake of the destruction of the Star Forge, HK-47 was dismantled and stowed aboard the *Ebon Hawk* with the Exile, who later rebuilt the droid during the search for Darth Sion.

During the Battle of Malachor, HK-47 rallied a group of HK-50 assassin droids to fight back and defeat G0-T0. Records failed to indicate what became of HK-47, but there was evidence that the droid managed to store its consciousness in a variety of droid systems over the following millennia. HK-47 reappeared on Mustafar during the Galactic Civil War, leading a gang of automata that killed everything they encountered.

**HK-50** This droid was stranded at the Peragus II medical facility following the Jedi Civil War, after Sith devotees who captured the *Harbinger* arrived there. When the Jedi Exile awoke at the facility and set out to rescue a group of miners, HK-50 provided assistance.

The droid was actually a bounty hunter who revealed that there was a bounty on all Jedi, including the Exile. But when the droid tried to take the Exile and Kreia, Atton Rand joined the fight and badly damaged HK-50. It self-destructed. Later, the Exile learned that HK-50 was behind the murders on Peragus II, part of a plan to lure a Jedi there.

HK-47

HK-50 series

**HK-50 series** Combat/assassin droids produced 4,000 years before the Galactic Civil War by Czerka Corporation, although Czerka marketed them as protocol droids. Most of the HK-50s were ordered by the renegade droid G0-T0, and were dispatched from a secret factory on Telos to serve as protocol droids within the naval fleets of the Old Republic. G0-T0's army of HK-50s was approached by the rogue droid HK-47 during the Sith Civil War, and HK-47 convinced them to join the fight against the Sith. The HK-50s agreed, and helped HK-47 bring down G0-T0 during the Battle of Malachor.

**HK-77** A smaller version of the HK-47, it was produced to act as a henchman in a gang that was controlled by an HK-47.

HK-77

**Hkaeli** An independent spacer, he worked as a go-between helping the Rebel Alliance buy droids on the secondary market.

**h'kak** A bush native to the planet Tatooine, it produced a fragrant bean that often was dried and ground to serve as the base for a stimulating tea.

**hka'ka** A small creature that originated on Barab I, it was the favored prey of the shenbit bonecrusher.

**H'ken** The primary world in the H'ken system of the Corva sector, it was located within the system's asteroid belt. This belt was nearly 20 kilometers wide, making navigation difficult.

**H'kig** A religious leader from the planet Galand, he spoke out about morals and goodness. He was also outspoken about the ruling classes of Galand, and he insulted the planet's Viceroy. He was murdered shortly thereafter.

**H'kig, the** A religious sect formed by faithful masses who believed in the messages being spread by the religious leader H'kig on Galand. After H'kig was murdered, the sect bought two starships, fled the planet, and landed on Rishi, where they set up a theocratic government. The H'kig religion stressed the values of simple living and the elimination of unnecessary material possessions. It venerated physical labor while eschewing technology, and restricted the physical appearance of its members. The H'kig were generally tolerant of other beings and religions, provided that they didn't interfere with H'kig practices.

A H'kig monk

**HK probot** *See* hunter-killer probot.

**HK series droid** An ancient model of a hunter-killer assassin droid developed by Czerka Corporation 4,000 years prior to the Battle of Yavin. While Czerka claimed the HK series droids were designed for protocol work, their real primary mission was to infiltrate corporate rivals and eliminate their executives. After it was learned that the prototype, HK-01, had instigated the Great Droid Revolution, Czerka started a cover-up and changed the droids' programming to make them act in a more discreet fashion. The HK series was still banned in many systems, especially after unit HK-47 had a prominent role in the Jedi Civil War and later during the Sith Civil War.

**HL-117 hover loader droid** The HL-117 was an Arakyd Industries hovering labor droid equipped with a strong repulsorlift drive and a magnapod foot that allowed it to grapple and haul heavy pieces of equipment or cargo with ease. Constructed for brawn not brains, the HL-117 operated only simple programs and required an operator versed in binary communications. The droid had a wide array of visual sensors that provided full 360-degree vision to avoid obstacles. It was, however, blind to anything directly above or below it and therefore was prone to accidental collisions. An internal gyroscope caused its system to shut down if it was ever jarred or tipped over.

**HL-38** An enclosed hovervan produced by SoroSuub in the early years of the New Republic. This 9-meter-long vehicle required a single driver to operate it, and could carry up to 10 passengers and 600 metric tons of cargo.

**HL-444** An Arakyd hover loader droid produced during the final years of the Old Republic, it found widespread use as a salvage droid on the major Podracing circuits. These units also served as armament carriers during the Clone Wars. The HL-444 moved about on heavy-duty repulsorlift engines.

**HLAF-500** This Corellian Engineering Corporation light attack fighter was an upgraded version of the LAF-250, and included a pair of SoroSuub 9X2 fusial thrust engines and a pair of proton torpedo launchers.

**H'Lokk Consortium** This rival of the Bakur Corporation injected a virus program into droids that were sent to Bakura shortly after it was settled by humans. It was designed to get the droids to sabotage planetary activities, forcing Bakur Corporation to leave and opening the planet to exploitation by H'Lokk. The virus was flawed, however, and even though settlers were killed and suffered other great losses, they managed to disable the droids and work without them. Years later, the H'Lokk Consortium purchased Bakur Corporation.

**HM-3** This legal and administrative droid assigned to Jacen Solo and the Galactic Alliance Guard during the Corellia–GA War was humanoid in appearance, and was programmed to provide Solo with a database of knowledge on the inner workings of the Galactic Alliance Senate and the laws of the Galactic Alliance. HM-3 provided Solo with sufficient information that he knew how to get enough credits to provide the GA's military forces with basic supplies.

**HM-6** Concussion missile launchers produced by Dymek and used on RZ-1 A-wing starfighters during the Galactic Civil War. Dymek later produced the upgraded HM-8 for the New Republic.

**HM blaster** A heavy-duty blaster produced during the last years of the Old Republic.

**h'merrig** A Yuuzhan Vong bioconstruct used to process foodstuffs from a few key materials, it was handy for explorers and scouts who couldn't carry large amounts of rations.

**HMOR homing droid** Developed by the Imperial Department of Military Research during the New Order, the HMOR resembled a large canister vacuum. It was equipped with a manipulator arm and had a pair of seeker

HL-117 hover loader droid

missiles and an acid jet to make sure it could place its homing device aboard a starship and then defend itself if necessary. The homing droid's powerful computer had a database of nearly five million starship schematics. Several of the droids were stationed on the first Death Star, and it was believed that one placed the homing beacon aboard the *Millennium Falcon* before it was allowed to escape.

*HMP droid gunship*

**HMP droid gunship** The Heavy Missile Platform droid gunship was built by Baktoid Fleet Ordnance for use by Separatist forces during the Clone Wars. It was essentially a flying saucer with a small-cockpit-like structure slung underneath the front to house the central processor and a pair of turret-mounted laser cannons. Its primary weapons were 14 controlled, variable-yield missiles. Overall, the HMP droid gunship was 12.3 meters long with a wingspan of 11 meters. Since its primary mission was planetary bombardment, it was much slower than other Separatist droid fighters. A combination of ion drive thrusters and powerful repulsorlift engines gave the HMP stability and maneuvering capability that allowed it to accurately pinpoint targets and deploy payloads.

**hmumfmumf** A tree that grew on the jungle world Baskarn. Its roots were used by the Yrashu to make ceremonial maces.

*H'nemthe*

**H'nemthe (1)** This planet, orbited by three natural satellites, was the homeworld of the H'nemthe species. Located in the Outer Rim Territories, H'nemthe experienced incredible weather fluctuations as a result of the tidal effects of its moons.

**H'nemthe (2)** Native to H'nemthe, these humanoids were similar to Gotals with cone-like appendages on top of their heads. H'nemthe had four conelets, most of which were shorter than those of a Gotal. They had blue-gray skin, and their faces were covered with three ridges of bone and skin running from their cheeks to their chins. They had graceful, beak-like noses and feathery eyelashes covering bright green eyes.

As a people, the H'nemthe were known to be artistic and passionate, and believed that spiritual fulfillment was the reward for creating life and finding true love. They did, however, have a bizarre mating ritual in which a female consummated her relationship with a male by eviscerating him with her knife-sharp tongue and leaving him for dead. It was believed that this ritual was a biological reaction to the existence of 20 males for every female on H'nemthe. Mating among H'nemthe, perhaps not surprisingly, was infrequent. The planetary government was usually democratic and mostly female. When the Empire subjugated the planet, many H'nemthe abandoned it to join the Rebel Alliance on Anoat.

**Hnsi** This clan, native to Thracior, was a bitter enemy of the Tantt clan.

**HN-TR1** An assassin droid, it was likely the only one of its series made, mainly because it killed its design team and destroyed all schematics when first activated. HN-TR1 killed several Rebel Alliance agents before being purchased by Ploovo Two-For-One, who used the droid as part of his Protocol Team.

**Hoar** A Tusken Raider, he left Tatooine with his gaffi stick to study with Arden Lyn, honing his fighting skills and mastery of teräs käsi.

**HOB-147** The official designation of the clone trooper pilot who was rescued by Hurd Coyle shortly after the end of the Clone Wars. HOB-147 was a pilot with the Light Brigade Division. His V-19 Torrent starfighter was damaged in battle, and he was left drifting in space, so he didn't hear about Order 66; he refused to believe the story of the Jedi Order's alleged treason. While recovering, HOB-147 discovered that Coyle was transporting a group of Jedi students to safety. Rather than turning them in when Coyle's ship was boarded by an Imperial unit, HOB-147 announced that he had been rescued by Coyle, and added that a thorough search of the ship revealed that it was nothing more than a salvage vessel.

**Hoba, Daragi** This Aqualish served as the First Minister of his homeworld of Ando prior to the Clone Wars. Daragi Hoba supported the position of Senator Po Nudo, and led Ando to secede from the Old Republic some 10 years after the Battle of Naboo.

**Hoban** The human captain of the transport ship *Star Dream,* Hoban transported Evar Orbus and his Galactic Wailers to Tatooine.

**Hobat, Chandra** An Ithorian living on the moon Dayark, she was elected by the inhabitants of the Kathol Republic to serve as president shortly before Moff Sarne fled Kal'Shebbol. She quietly supported the New Republic, angering her chief rival, Sho'ban Do, who felt she was dooming the Kathol Republic. Do undertook a treacherous plot to create an army of droids, but Hobat was able to defeat the Do faction and return order to the Kathol Republic.

**Hobbie** *See* Klivian, Derek "Hobbie."

**Hoberd, Nast** An Imperial Navy captain in the early years of the New Order, he commanded the Port Heavy Blaster Station aboard the Star Destroyer *Steel Talon.* Learning about surprise inspections in advance and getting his team well prepared earned Hoberd the recognition of his superiors and put him in line for a promotion to major. He backed his squad members even if it meant getting them promotions in other units. Just before he mustered out of the military, he promoted Master Chief Petty Officer Tenn Graneet to a gunnery position on the Death Star, taking away one of his best noncommissioned officers.

**Hobiv, Dasken** A military analyst, he was loyal to the Separatists during the early stages of the Clone Wars.

**Hobor** One of two sentient species native to Tahlboor, the Hobors were humanoid with purple skin, unlike the Troobs, who tended toward deep blue skin. Both species were characterized by wide, feline-like faces flanked by several rings of spade-shaped flaps. Shortly before the Battle of Yavin, the Troobs and Hobors appealed to Tion Hegemony to assist in reconciling a generations-old feud between them. Counselor Harthan was called in, but was manipulated out of the position by his son, Jake, who hoped to get the two species to destroy each other so he could control Mount Yeroc. Eventually, with the help of R2-D2 and C-3PO, Jake's plans were thwarted and peace was restored.

**Hobyo** This Klatooinian was one of many New Republic personnel captured during the failure of Operation Trinity near Bilbringi four years after the start of the Yuuzhan Vong War. Hobyo disabled the hyperdrive of a freighter that was transporting prisoners from Selvaris to the

*H'nemthe*

*Sacred Pyre,* allowing New Republic forces to ambush the ship and rescue the prisoners.

**Hocce** An Imperial ensign with great medical skills, he served as a medical technician aboard the first Death Star.

**Hocekureem Sea** An ocean on Falleen, it was known as a source of fleek eels during the era of the Great Sith War.

**Hockaleg** A planet in the Patriim system, it served as an Imperial base during construction of the *Tarkin.*

**Hoclaw, Captain** An aging Corellian, she was an officer in the Corellian Defense Force following the Swarm War. When Corellia seceded from the Galactic Alliance and joined the Confederation, Captain Hoclaw was given command of the Star Destroyer *Valorum.* She led the mission sent by Sadras Koyan to meet Jacen Solo, ostensibly to discuss Corellia's possible return to the GA. Although Solo had thought he was going to meet Koyan personally, he agreed to discuss a settlement with Captain Hoclaw. She wasted little time in demanding that Solo step down as the leader of the GA, and he quickly broke off negotiations.

**Hoctu, Drevveka** A former Jedi Knight, she turned to the dark side, ended up on Thule, and became headmaster of the Sith Arts Academy many years before the Battle of Naboo.

**Hodge** The chief officer of the tiny Mining Station Alpha during the Galactic Civil War, he stumbled upon the tomb of Spore, an ancient Ithorian genetic construct that had turned into an evil creature that could enslave thousands by controlling their minds. Spore was forced into dormancy by the vacuum of space, and the Ithorians kept monitoring the asteroid to make sure Spore was still secure. But Spore escaped, used Hodge's body as a host, and returned to Ithor. Hodge/Spore attacked with black vines snaking from his mouth and eyes to entwine and infect the Ithorians. Emperor Palpatine sent the Dark Jedi Jerec to capture Spore, and he offered to get the creature off the planet if it would infect the crew of the *Vengeance.* But a group of space slugs attacked the ship, causing it to explode; Hodge/Spore was killed along with the rest of the crew.

**Hodidiji** This New Republic Senator was swayed by Tig Peramis and Cian Marook to align with the Yevetha during the Great Purge. Hodidiji yielded his time on the Senate floor to Peramis and Nil Spaar, who distorted the actions of Leia Organa Solo.

*Ho'Din*

**Ho'Din** A gentle humanoid species from the planet Moltok. Ho'Din were true nature lovers who disliked processes and policies that harmed ecosystems. They chose nature over technology: Their very name meant "walking flower," an apt description. Their flesh hung loosely over their lanky 3-meter-high frames. The thick, snake-like tresses that adorned their heads were covered with gleaming red and violet scales. Their natural medicine techniques were long recognized throughout the galaxy.

The Ho'Din were fairly recent additions to the galaxy, descending from arboreal creatures. Initially, to make room for a growing population, the Ho'Din cleared much of the surface of Moltok in what was referred to as the "great rape of the land," leading to a virulent epidemic that decimated the species. When they finally understood the cause, they turned into lovers of nature. During the Yuuzhan Vong War, the Ho'Din were spared the wide range of atrocities primarily because of their reverence of life and their distrust of technology.

**Hodizwen, Bashinan** This being was a noted Jedi scholar in the years leading up to the Clone Wars.

**Hodo** A K-wing pilot, he was a member of the Fifth Battle Group, and was the leader of Black Squadron.

**Hodrix** A noted Dug swoop racer, he had a sensational rookie year in the months before the Clone Wars. Hodrix rode for Team NaKuda during most of his early career and was known for a string of victories over his rival, Serji-X Arrogantus.

*Hoggon*

**Hoersch-Kessel Drive, Incorporated** One of the most successful starship design firms in the Old Republic, Hoersch-Kessel Drive (HKD) was secretly a subsidiary of the Trade Federation. HKD produced many of the Trade Federation's cargo vessels, including the massive craft later converted into battleships for the invasion of Naboo. After the Trade Federation's defeat at Naboo, HKD was sold first to Duros investors and then, during the Clone Wars, to a Nimbanese clan that built the *Recusant*-class light destroyer and the *Munificent*-class star frigate for the Separatists. The new owners dismantled many of the company's less profitable divisions. The quest to develop a leaner bottom line destroyed morale, driving many designers to go to work for other starship firms. By the time of the Yuuzhan Vong War, HKD had returned to its roots, manufacturing large transports and container vessels. The company was still unprofitable, building fewer than 100 starships a year.

**Hoersch-Kessel ion drive** An efficient, reliable, and adaptable sublight drive, it could be altered to run on a wide variety of energy sources, and the same basic design could be used for any ship types, from starfighters to capital starships. It was basically a power source to generate ions, which were expelled through an exhaust nacelle to create thrust. The basic design remained unchanged for many millennia.

**Hoff** A Rebel Alliance sergeant, he served the Special Forces division as leader of the technician team assigned to the Nishr Taskforce.

**Hoff, Colby** A business competitor of Prince Xizor, Colby Hoff once took a gamble that he was smarter than Xizor. In the end, Xizor won and Hoff was ruined. He committed suicide by firing a blaster into his mouth. His son, simply known as Hoff, tried to avenge the suicide when Darth Vader secretly allowed him into a secure passageway under Imperial City. Xizor was walking the corridor to meet with Palpatine, and the son attacked. This ambush failed: Xizor quickly disabled Hoff and snapped his neck. Xizor was never able to determine who had let Hoff in, although he suspected his enemy Vader.

**Hoffner** As captain of the pleasure ship *Coral Vanda,* Hoffner was Garm Bel Iblis's contact on Pantolomin during the early years of the New Republic. Years earlier, Hoffner had been Talon Karrde's commander on a smuggling mission that inadvertently discovered the Dark Force ships of the *Katana* fleet. Hoffner eventually figured out how to recover the old Dreadnaughts, but to avoid attracting too much attention, he sold only a handful to Bel Iblis to fund his gambling habit. When the *Coral Vanda* was incapacitated by Imperial forces, however, Hoffner was taken into custody and forced to reveal the location of the *Katana* fleet to Grand Admiral Thrawn.

**Hoggon** A down-on-his-luck spacer and Jedi groupie, he was hired by Ulic Qel-Droma following the Great Sith War to transport him to as remote a world as possible for a self-imposed exile. Soon Hoggon learned the identity of his passenger and brought the Cathar Jedi Sylvar to Rhen Var to deal with the recluse Jedi. Ulic helped Sylvar came to terms with her anger, and she forgave the onetime Sith for his crimes. Hoggon then stole up behind them and shot Qel-Droma in the back with his blaster, killing him. Hoggon believed that he would be venerated by the Jedi for killing Qel-Droma, and was surprised when Sylvar nearly killed him.

**Hogra, Jamoh** A Zabrak mercenary, he once took part in a deep-space ambush of a ship that turned out to be a Sith Dreadnaught, millennia before the Galactic Civil War. He survived, but—fearing that the Sith would hunt him down and kill him—Hogra invested a small fortune in protective armor and sensors. Ironically, he was killed while taking a bath.

**Hoguss** A large alien species. A Hoguss with a killing ax attacked Luminara Unduli and Barriss Offee at Cuipernam on Ansion during the Clone Wars.

**hohokum** Amphibious creatures native to Naboo, they moved rapidly through the water but had difficulty traversing land. Young hohokums were deposited in sand or mud, where they often fell victim to predators. Adult hohokums were relatively docile and would pull Gungans through the water without complaint.

**hoi-broth** An Aqualish beverage, it was considered a delicacy among many Senators of the Old Republic during the Clone Wars era.

**Hoil** This Sunesi was one of the many members of his species who served in Agapos the Ninth's underground resistance during the Imperial occupation of Monor II.

**hoist cable** A strong cord connected to a cable drum worn on a belt or harness. The device could be used to move heavy loads or for dangerous climbing maneuvers. During the Battle of Hoth, Luke Skywalker fired a hoist cable from a harpoon gun to single-handedly bring down an AT-AT.

**Hok** A planet in the Colonies region, it was populated by the Gran species. Hok was the homeworld of Mawhonic, a well-known Gran Podracer.

**hokami** These predators native to Mutanda attacked their prey with sharp claws and huge teeth, and were known to attack repulsorlift vehicles.

Hoist cable in use on Hoth

**Hokan, Ghez** A former Mandalorian trooper who established himself as a crime lord on Qiilura in the years before the Clone Wars, he had been asked to leave the Death Squad for enjoying his work too much. He worked with the Confederacy of Independent Systems, and established a research facility for Ovolot Qail Uthan, who was working on a clone-killing virus. When Omega Squad infiltrated the facility and captured Uthan, Hokan and his chief lieutenant escaped, but Uthan's research team—whom he took as hostages—were all killed in a firefight. Ultimately, the commandos tricked Hokan into the open when one of them feigned injury. Etain Tur-Mukan stole up behind him and killed Hokan with a single cut from her lightsaber.

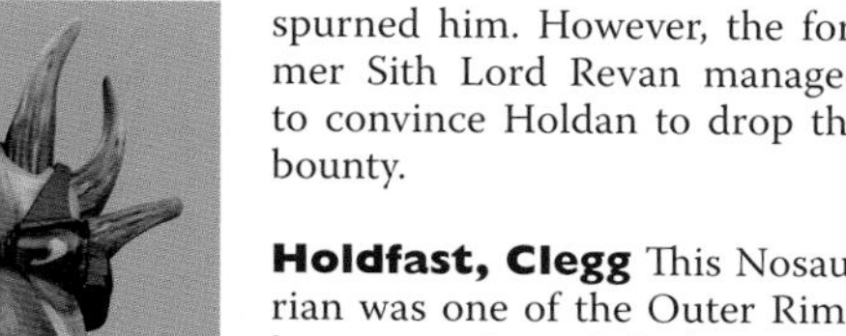

Clegg Holdfast

**Hoke** An immensely obese and pompous man, he worked with Dyril as the repair and maintenance team of the Q'Maere Research Facility when Moff Sarne used it as a penal colony.

**Hokken, Dovish** This Jedi Knight was killed aboard the *Monitor III* during an attempt to smash a group of Iridium pirates who were ambushing Old Republic supply convoys near Vuchelle prior to the Clone Wars.

**Hokker** A yellow-skinned Trandoshan, he joined Krayn's pirate crew shortly after the Battle of Naboo. When the pirates captured a group of Rutian Twi'lek septuplets, Hokker spoke openly of taking them for himself and selling them for his own profit. This disloyalty earned him time in Krayn's brig, after Siri Tachi—posing as the pirate Zora—turned him in.

**Hokuum stations** In bars and casinos throughout the galaxy, these stations provided for the tastes of those beings who preferred nonliquid stimulants, such as glitterstim and other spices.

**Holageus** This planet was the site of a vicious battle between New Republic forces and the Imperial remnant.

**Holda, Greeta** An employee of Czerka Corporation on Tatooine during the era of the Great Sith War, she sold a group of moisture vaporators to Jedi Knights who were searching for a piece of the Star Map. The vaporators were then turned over to the Sand People in an effort to stop their attacks on local moisture farms.

**Holdan** A member of Davik Kang's criminal organization on Taris in the years leading up to the Great Sith War, he placed a bounty on Dia's head after the barmaid spurned him. However, the former Sith Lord Revan managed to convince Holdan to drop the bounty.

**Holdfast, Clegg** This Nosaurian was one of the Outer Rim's least experienced Podracer pilots, despite the fact that he was also a freelance reporter for *Podracing Quarterly.* Clegg was the son of a fish-catcher father and a candle-maker mother, but pursued an education and a career in journalism to escape his humble roots. His research on the Podracing circuits led him to compete in a Keizar-Volver KV9T9-B Wasp racer. Holdfast was tall and lanky with six bony horns rising from the top of his head; he was a native of New Plympto. His insider reports from the Podraces made him one of the most popular writers for *Podracing Quarterly,* although many of his fellow racers believed him to be a fop. He competed in the fateful Boonta Eve Classic race that took place around the time of the Battle of Naboo. In the second lap of the race, Sebulba opened up his Podracer's flame-jets while next to Clegg, cooking Holdfast's engines and forcing the horned pilot to crash. Still, the official standings indicated that Holdfast did finish—dead last, coming in seventh.

***Holding Back the Tide*** The title of the poor-selling autobiography of one time Supreme Chancellor of the Old Republic, Finis Valorum.

**hold-out blaster** Any small, easily concealed energy weapon. A hold-out blaster had limited firepower. It could fire one or two full-intensity blasts before it was completely drained.

**Holdout Flightknife** One of the many Yedagonian fighter squadrons that supported Wedge Antilles and the Running Crimson Flightknife during the war against the forces of the Cartann nation on Adumar. The Holdouts eventually landed in Cartann City and assisted Cheriss ke Hanadi in recovering Red Flight's X-wing fighters.

**hold-parents** Also known as hold-mothers or hold-fathers among a variety of galactic cultures, they often brought toys and treats to the children of very good friends. They assumed the role of close adult relatives such as aunts and uncles and could act as temporary guardians.

**hole ball** This small mammal native to the moon of Sulon was round and lived in small tunnels that it burrowed into the ground. The hole ball moved about in tall grasses, using organic debris as a form of camouflage. Whenever it felt threatened, it rolled into the nearest hole.

Holgurn

**Hole In The Ground** The nickname for the Rebel Alliance's Haven Base, which was built in an underground grotto.

**Holgurn** A small Gamorrean, he was one of Jabba the Hutt's messengers prior to the Battle of Yavin. Holgurn delivered the request to Han Solo asking for his help in recovering the Yavin Vassilika.

**Holiday Towers** A beautiful hotel and casino owned by Jabba the Hutt on Cloud City, it was confiscated by Lando Calrissian after Jabba's death. When Zorba the Hutt arrived and showed Jabba's will to Calrissian, Lando offered to play a game of sabacc with Zorba, who insisted on using his own cards, which were rigged. Not only did Calrissian lose the Holiday Towers Hotel, but he lost the deed to Cloud City as well.

**Holiest of Holies** The Ugors believed they had found the Holiest of Holies—a device that would let them move massive amounts of their treasured space garbage—shortly after the Battle of Yavin. Hidden within battle debris was a prototype gravity-well projector that had been produced by Sienar Fleet Systems. When they transported it to their homeworld in the J21-Z65 system, the device suddenly activated. The power of the gravity field created the swirling debris field that became known as the Paradise System. The Rebel Alliance eventually managed to take possession of the device. When the Alliance shut down the projector, the Paradise System spun itself to pieces.

**Hollan D1 sector** This sector, near the Greater Plooriod Cluster, was the site of the destruction of a vital Imperial storage area by the Rebel Alliance following the Battle of Yavin. Rebel pilots used captured ships from Overlord Ghorin in the attack, successfully discrediting Ghorin in the eyes of the Empire.

**Hollast VII** The primary world in the Hollastin system, it was the site of a number of Rebel Alliance–funded insurgencies aimed at freeing the populace from Imperial control. A secondary goal was to overthrow Glorga the Hutt, who eventually was murdered.

**Holleck, Grandon** The governor of Chandrila shortly after the Battle of Yavin, he was succeeded by Gerald Weizel when he retired from active duty to the Empire.

**hollinium** A moderately valuable metal ore, it was used in the production of hyperbarides. Hollinium was also used in the manufacture of heavy-duty cybernetic limbs.

**hollinium chloride** A contaminant formed on the planet Goroth Prime in the wake of the Scouring. It was essentially a hyperbaride salt that was toxic to any being or creature not native to the planet.

**Hollis, Lutin** A Naboo Royal Security Forces officer, he had spent some time traveling the Outer Rim in search of experience and adventure. He joined Captain Kael's resistance movement after being rescued from a Trade Federation prison.

**Hollis, Sergeant Reyé** A Rebel Alliance trooper stationed at Echo Base during the Battle of Hoth, he was the son of Naboo officer Lutin Hollis. Among many feats of valor, he single-handedly pulled two of his medical personnel out of the way of an AT-ST before being injured himself. He was awarded the Kenobi Medallion for his bravery.

**Hollow Mountains** A mountain range near the capital city of Unparala on Virujansi. Its underground levels were riddled with caves and tunnels by borecrawlers and used by the Virujansi for living areas and storage.

**Hollowtown** The huge central biosphere of Centerpoint Station, it was a beautiful area of gardens, parks, and living spaces. It was lit by the Glowpoint, and provided nearly all the foodstuffs needed to keep the inhabitants fed. When the station began generating strange pulses timed with the destruction of stars, the Glowpoint incinerated everything in Hollowtown until the oxygen ran out. By the time

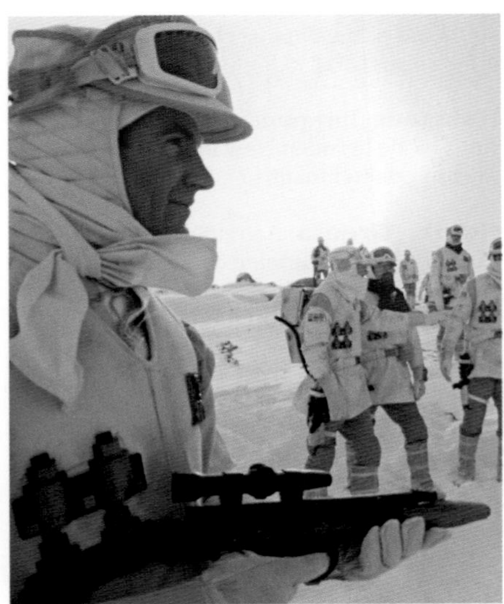

Sergeant Reyé Hollis

Luke Skywalker and Lando Calrissian first set foot inside, the toxic residues of the destruction had made Hollowtown unlivable. Calrissian later discovered that Hollowtown and the Glowpoint were components of the huge power supply needed to keep the hyperspatial tractor beam operational. The Glowpoint acted as a pilot light, and Hollowtown was a battery of sorts. The station's destructive power again came into play during the Galactic Alliance's war against the Confederation 22 years later.

**Holman, Deke** A dark-skinned human native of Socorro, he was a member of the Rebel Alliance's Harrier infiltration team.

**holo** Any type of holographic device or anything produced by a holographic device.

Holobooks in the Jedi Temple Archives

**holo-analyzer** A small device used to diagnose the external mechanism of droids.

**holoanchor** Any being who served as the public face of a news agency.

**holobank** Any collection of multiple HoloNet receivers, as used by news agencies and military command centers to receive multiple information feeds from a variety of sources.

**holo-bim** A derogatory term, short for "HoloNet bimbo," used to describe an inane female celebrity. Many of the natives of the planet Cularin used this term to describe Yara Grugara during the last decades of the Old Republic.

**holo-bit generator** A device that allowed the user to manipulate a pre-recorded holotransmission and create a false transmission. The generator first made a holographic image of the desired subject, then ran it through a bit-manipulation program to generate subsequent images. The complete set of images formed a smooth, seemingly real transmission.

**holobook** A slim, crystalline board that was used to store vast amounts of information. Developed during the early years of the Old Republic, holobooks were incredibly durable, and required only a small amount to power to remain active. The Jedi Temple Archives on Coruscant contained millions of holobooks, some of which

dated back to the origins of the Republic. When properly stored and maintained, holobooks gave off a soft, blue glow. Like the Jedi holocrons, holobooks provided interactive interfaces to their knowledge, allowing a reader to delve as deeply into subject matter as desired.

**holobooth** A small room with a couch that faced a holotransmitter plate. Many were located in the seedier parts of Coruscant's lower levels.

**holobug** Any small, nearly undetectable device that could be placed on a target for surveillance purposes. The holobug would return a real-time display of the target's surroundings, allowing trackers to better estimate the target's position.

**holocam** Video surveillance device used throughout the galaxy for security and spying.

**Holocam-E cam droid** A series of holographic cam droids produced by Trang Robotics during the final years of the Old Republic. These popular units were known as Cammies.

**holocard** A small ID card that contained a holographic image along with a being's name, business, and security clearance.

**holocast** A generic term used to describe any news broadcast that was delivered in the form of a three-dimensional hologram.

**holochart** Any three-dimensional hologram system that projected charts and diagrams for viewing by several beings in a room. Holocharts could be used to display information on arrivals and departures at a spaceport, financial data at a stock exchange, or military intelligence data in a war room.

**holochess** A form of chess that used holographic representations of the playing pieces, often fantastic aliens. The game was played on a circular field like dejarik, but had different styles of play and objectives.

**holo-coding** A communications technique that mostly died out with the Empire. Holo-coding was preferred for communicating over great distances because it masked the telltale signs of long-distance communication. Only an expert could recognize the differences between coding problems and distance problems. However, it often was slower than regular messaging.

**holocomm** A HoloNet comm unit, it let owners send and receive messages over a holographic-based transmission network.

**holocorder** *See* holorecorder.

**holocron** Known originally as a holographic chronicle, this was a recording device used by the ancient Jedi Knights and Sith Lords to hold the teachings and lore needed to maintain the

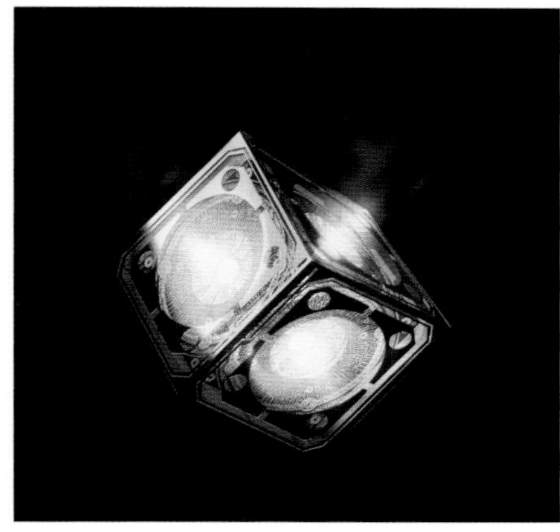

*Holocron*

Jedi and Sith Orders. Each of these devices provided a visual and aural way to view or hear the information. The holocron was essentially a dense crystal with intricate lattices and vertices capable of storing huge amounts of data, yet usually small enough to fit in a palm.

Each holocron had a gatekeeper assigned to dispense the information. The gatekeeper had the cognitive network functions of a Jedi Master or Sith Lord and acted as a search, recovery, and storage allocation program. Most holocrons were shaped like small, translucent cubes, since the cubic form was among the most stable. However, pyramids and dodecahedrons were also known to exist. Often, a holocron could be activated only by a person controlling the Force. The holocron had the ability to block out areas of knowledge that were beyond the user's ability.

The technology for constructing a holocron and storing personalities and knowledge inside was first documented by King Adas, an ancient Sith Lord who acquired it from the Rakata. The knowledge of holocron construction was lost many millennia before the Battle of Yavin, although Darth Bane scoured the galaxy for information on constructing one.

The gatekeeper was given the personality of the individual who created the holocron, and was actually constructed at the molecular level when the matrix of the holocron was formed. Symbols and markings on the outside of each holocron were placed there by the creator to help him or her channel the Force into stabilizing the matrix and powering its cognitive properties. The Sith even developed a Ritual of Invocation that had to be performed to generate and empower a holocron's symbols.

A holocron could take weeks or months to complete, and the cognitive matrix would rapidly decay if not properly contained within the crystalline lattice. Once this happened, the holocron would implode, collapsing into a powdery dust. In order to ensure that the cognitive matrix remained viable, a capstone was used to effectively plug the holocron.

Although the term *holocron* more correctly described devices created by the Sith and the Jedi, the term came to encompass more mundane holographic storage media as well.

**Holocron of Belia Darzu** A four-sided, pyramidal holocron created by Belia Darzu decades before the Battle of Ruusan. The Shi'ido Sith Lord kept the holocron and the secrets for creating it in a chamber beneath her fortress on Tython. After her death, the holocron remained hidden for many years, until Darth Bane learned of its existence.

**Holocron of Bodo Baas** A term used to describe the Tedryn Holocron after the device was recovered from the planet Byss by Leia Organa Solo. Jedi Master Bodo Baas was one of the holocron's gatekeepers.

**holocube** A fist-sized, six-sided object, it held a static three-dimensional holoimage. By moving around a holocube, a being could see all aspects of the image. Holocubes were popular for keeping a picture of a loved one.

**holodais** Any pedestal-like device that allowed the user to stand in the midst of a static holographic image or interactive transmission.

**holo-directory** A three-dimensional display system used to maintain a directory of data or names and contact information. They ranged anywhere from small desktop models to large units installed in building lobbies.

**holodisplay** A portable or semi-portable three-dimensional display system.

**holodrama** A dramatic presentation via hologram.

**holoduplicator** A device used to duplicate in three dimensions any holographic image or video.

**holofeature** A full-length movie that could be displayed on a holoprojector.

**holofield** The display area of a holographic transmission device.

**holoflage** A form of holographic equipment used to camouflage a door or other area. The holoflage mimicked the surrounding walls, making the door disappear from view.

**Holo-Gaftikar Channel Ten** One of the primary news-reporting agencies based on Gaftikar, it was a prime target of the Grand Army of the Republic. Sergeant Tel and members of Omega Squad infiltrated the facility and were surprised to find it still broadcasting. They destroyed the building.

**Hologlide Cam Droid** The brand name of a series of holographic cam droids produced by Industrial Automaton during the final decades of the Old Republic. These small droids moved about on tiny repulsorlift engines, which allowed them to cover an event from a variety of angles.

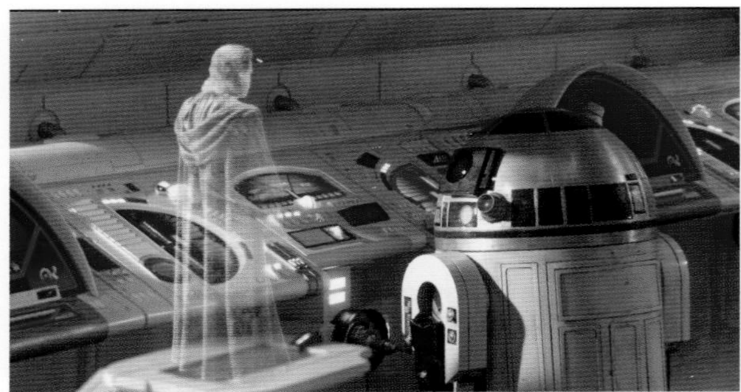
Hologram

**hologram** A moving three-dimensional image that could be broadcast in real time as part of a communications transmission. Most hologram images appeared ghostly and pale, but they did allow for both visual and aural communication over great distances.

**Hologram Fun World** A theme park run by Lando Calrissian for a time after the Battle of Endor, it was inside a transparent dome that floated in a blue helium cloud in the Zabian system. A self-contained planetoid about 40 kilometers in diameter, it was filled with holographic entertainment of all kinds, from realistic excursions to remote worlds, to incredible simulations of huge creatures. Its advertising claimed it was where "a world of dreams come true."

**hologram projection pod** Developed by SoroSuub, this device allowed the user to send a full-body, holographic communication to another being.

**holograph** A static three-dimensional image.

**holographic portal** Any three-dimensional image used to disguise the entrance to a secret base.

**holographic recording mode** A recording process for capturing images and sounds in a three-dimensional format; R2 astromech droids had holographic recording capability.

**Holographic Zoo of Extinct Animals** An interactive amusement and educational facility, it featured holographic, three-dimensional images that created landscapes and depicted extinct animals from around the galaxy. Located in the upper levels of Coruscant, it was dedicated to the preservation of life-forms long gone. Among the sights were the mammoth krabbex of Mon Calamari, snow falcons of Rhinnal, and the mantabog of Malastare.

**holomannequin** By using holomannequins instead of solid forms or models, a store could display clothing for a variety of species without having to invest a huge amount in the exhibit. Clothing also was replicated in the holographic image, which helped reduce shoplifting.

**holomap room** Central to the organization of Jedi activities throughout the galaxy was a pyramid system of holomaps. At the lowest level, 12 teams monitored in detail specific galactic areas. Potential problem areas were transferred to larger-scale holomaps for the attention of more senior Jedi. In this way, only the most serious issues, such as disturbances in the Force and areas of unusual Force concentration, reached the Jedi High Council.

**holomonster** Holograms depicting mythological or extinct creatures, they were used as game pieces for holochess and other hologames like dejarik.

**HoloNet** A near-instantaneous communications network commissioned by the Old Republic Senate to provide a free flow of hologram and other communications among member worlds, it vastly speeded up galactic communications that previously had depended on subspace transmissions or relays. The HoloNet used hundreds of thousands of nonmass transceivers connected through hyperspace simutunnels and routed through massive computer sorters and decoders.

During the Clone Wars, the Confederacy of Independent Systems was forced to create its own version of the HoloNet in order to maintain communications during the fighting. After Emperor Palpatine assumed control of the galaxy, he limited the HoloNet to specific Imperial uses to control the flow of information. Following the Battle of Endor, the New Republic began to re-establish civilian use of the HoloNet, restoring the primary communications vehicle required for a galactic government. The completion of the new HoloNet was cut short by the Yuuzhan Vong War, as large parts of the galaxy were attacked and cut off. After the Second Battle of Coruscant, when the survivors of the Senate fled to Mon Calamari, much of the HoloNet equipment that had been repaired or replaced was simply abandoned. Without contact with the Republic, many small warlords chose to protect their small piece of the galaxy. Cal Omas, as the newly elected Chief of State of the Galactic Federation of Free Alliances, decided to once again reestablish the HoloNet to help draw the galaxy together. The usefulness of the repaired HoloNet was cut short by the development of the magubat kan, a Yuuzhan Vong bioform that attacked HoloNet relay stations and destroyed them.

**HoloNet Entertainment** One of the largest entertainment providers of the Old Republic, it was best known for the galaxy-spanning tours produced to entertain troops during the Clone Wars.

Holomap room

**HoloNet Free Republic** This pro-Alliance newsnet was famous for getting its feeds into Imperial-held systems during the Galactic Civil War. Any being who knew the channel number could access the HFR feed, which provided reporting and commentary that was free of Imperial propaganda.

**HoloNet News and Entertainment** This news agency eventually acquired the HoloNet News Service, and became one of the galaxy's largest providers of news and information during the New Republic era. HNE continued to grow and expand, and was perhaps the largest news agency in the galaxy following the Yuuzhan Vong War.

Hologram projection pod

**HoloNet News Service** Based on Coruscant, this was a simple newsfeed that provided up-to-the-minute news reports on the events of the galaxy during the last decades of the Old Republic.

**holopad** A device much like a datapad, except that it was capable of displaying holographic transmissions as well.

**holo-pet** Any holographic device that displayed an animated image of a small creature. It became popular during the Galactic Civil War.

Holo-pet

**holoplate** Any personal holographic projection device, often installed in an anteroom or dedicated media room in a residence or public space.

**holo-print** Printed media that employed a unique process to create two-dimensional images that appeared to have depth.

**holoprojector** A device that used modulasers to broadcast real-time or recorded moving three-dimensional images. Real-time holographic images generated by a holoprojector could be broadcast over some comlinks, greatly enhancing communications. More advanced projectors were commonly installed aboard capital ships and space stations.

**holoprojector, Yuuzhan Vong** A Yuuzhan Vong biogenetically engineered creature that acted like a holoprojector. A sponge-like being that looked like a large, gelatinous villip, when activated it melted into a flat disk and then began to glow with yellow bioluminescence. The light coalesced to form a three-dimensional image. Nom Anor used the device to show a live image of the *Nebula Chaser* to Leia Organa Solo at Bilbringi.

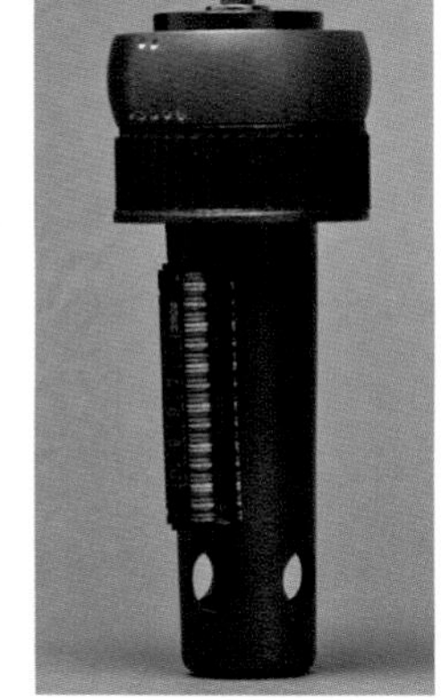
Holorecorder

**holorecorder** A message-taking device that was popular across the galaxy during the final decades of the Old Republic, it could store audio and three-dimensional video recordings of incoming messages that were date- and time-stamped for later playback.

**Holorepository** A massive information repository located on the *Arkam 13* wheelworld during the final decades of the Old Republic. It was generally regarded as being one of the galaxy's most prestigious collections of information and literature, and many beings believed that the Holorepository contained more knowledge and lore than even the Jedi Temple Archives on Coruscant.

**holoscreen (1)** One of the most powerful starship shield generators produced by Cygnus SpaceWorks during the New Order.

**holoscreen (2)** A three-dimensional billboard used for advertising.

**holosculpture** A three-dimensional artwork that employed light to portray its subject.

**holoshroud** A false holographic projection, it could be used for deception in covert operations. Using a belt-worn hologram projector, it showed a pre-recorded image, allowing the user to appear to be someone or something else.

**holosimulator** A starship flight simulator that was used to train pilots on various starship configurations.

**holo-tank** This device projected a holographic image that surrounded the viewer, giving the impression of actually being in the image.

**holotarget** A projected, three-dimensional image used to simulate battlefield opponents during weapons training.

**holovid** A three-dimensional recording that contained both audio and visual content. Over time, the term *holovid* also came to describe the device that was used to display holographic transmissions. These devices were larger than a holopad and often displayed images on a larger screen.

**holowafer** A message wafer that provided a three-dimensional image. After being played one time, the holowafer dissolved.

**Holowan, Hurlo** A droid engineer from Kuat, she was the daughter of a wealthy patriarch of a Kuat merchant house. She engineered the Razor Eater, one of the fiercest killing machines ever produced.

**Holowan Laboratories/Holowan Mechanicals** A company enlisted by Imperial Supervisor Gurdon to complete the design and production of the IG series of assassin droids. Publicly known as "Holowan Mechanicals: The Friendly Technology People," this dangerous corporation took over research on IG series droids when the InterGalactic Banking Clan seized all assets belonging to its delinquent customer Phlut Design Systems. Holowan produced the IG-100 MagnaGuard as well as the IG assassin droid, an experiment that ended in disaster when the prototype units escaped from the laboratory and murdered the design staff.

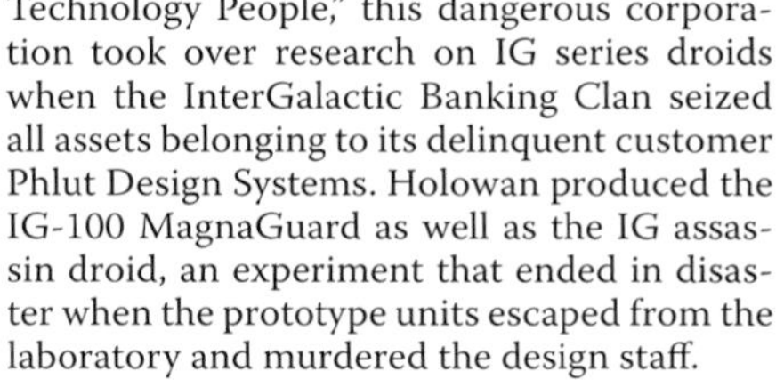

**holozine** A three-dimensional display system that could be linked to a subscription service, it provided ever-changing content to users. A holozine looked like a thin book or periodical, displaying a cover page and a menu system that allowed readers to access new or updated content with each issue.

**Holt, Admiral Arhul** A fleet admiral in the Imperial Navy, he later became a teacher at Raithal Military Academy, helping to mold new recruits into soldiers and officers during the Galactic Civil War. Admiral Holt was a member of the Holt family on Anaxes. Despite his family's long years of service, Arhul Holt eventually decided to defect to the Rebel Alliance. Pash Galae infiltrated the school to assist in the admiral's defection.

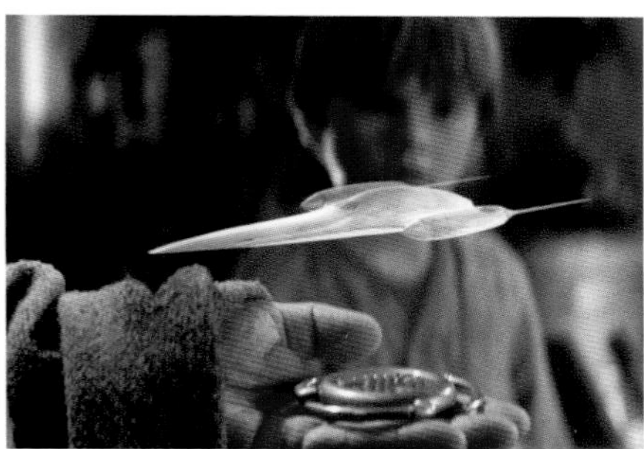
Holoprojector

**holt kazet** The Nelvaanian name for the individual known as the Ghost Hand. Legend said that the holt kazet would come to the Nelvaanians in a time of great need. During the Clone Wars, the Nelvaanians believed that they had finally encountered the holt kazet when Anakin Skywalker arrived on the planet and helped defeat the Separatists who had established a laboratory there.

**Holwuff** A species native to Alliga, it was among the many that joined the Confederacy of Independent Systems.

**Holy Children of Asrat** Orphans who lived secluded in a temple, they dedicated their lives to doing good. When they denounced the Emperor and his violent ways, Imperials hired the bounty hunter Dengar to wipe them out. Dengar refused the job and was booted from Imperial service.

Holoshroud

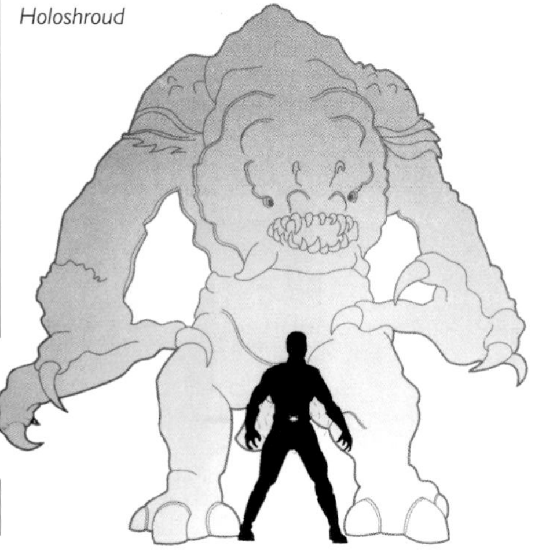

**Holy Jaf** A deity worshipped on the planet Hockaleg.

**Holy Order of the Je'ulajists** The religion of the Kentra people, it was based on the writings and teachings of the Jedi geologist Michael Tandre. Its basic tenets were known as the Sword, Plow, and Spirit.

**Homd-Resa** One of the few aggressive clans of Senali. Members of the Homd-Resa clan fiercely patrolled their ocean territory and once attacked the Nali-Erun clan, destroying Nali-Erun dwellings in an effort to assert their claim to the seas.

***Home*** A heavily modified Tsukkian water freighter, it was owned and operated by the founders of Reekeene's Roughnecks and served as the gang's mobile base of operations.

**Home Defense Strike Force** A group of smaller strike forces, it was hastily assembled by the Old Republic during the Clone Wars to protect Coruscant against Separatist attacks. It was put to the test when General Grievous launched an attack on the planet.

**Home Fleet** This branch of the Grand Army of the Republic supplied military personnel to defend the star system that surrounded Coruscant during the Clone Wars. Each division of the Home Fleet was commanded by a Jedi Master.

**Home Guard (1)** A small navy maintained by the SoroSuub Corporation during the New Order.

**Home Guard (2)** The ceremonial security force that protected planet Aargau during the Galactic Civil War.

**Home of Wisdom** A Tarasin name indicating a sacred area located within the territory of the Hiironi *irstat.* The Home of Wisdom was created by weaving the branches of overhanging trees together, forming a dry area beneath the branches where the women of the Tarasin could gather to discuss religious matters.

***Home One*** Admiral Ackbar's Mon Calamari MC80a cruiser, the *Home One* served as his flagship for many years. In the wake of the Battle of Hoth, it also functioned as the mobile base for Rebel Alliance leaders. During the Battle of Endor, Ackbar commanded Rebel forces from *Home One,* maneuvering the ship in and out of fighting as needed. At

*Homing beacon*

that time, it was the largest ship in the Alliance fleet. The vessel, also referred to as the Headquarters Frigate, was cylindrical and organically artistic, with a fluid surface. Armed for war, *Home One* had 29 turbolaser batteries, 36 mini ion cannons, multiple shield and tractor beam projectors, and 20 hangar bays for its 10 starfighter squadrons and other vessels. As newer and better Mon Calamari starships were designed, Ackbar eventually retired *Home One* in favor of the *Defiance* and the *Galactic Voyager.*

**Home Planet Mine** The primary azurite mine controlled by Arcona Mineral Harvest Corporation on Bandomeer. It was named for the Home Planet Party, which was working with the Arcona to restore Bandomeer's natural plant life after decades of strip mining. The mine was sabotaged by the Dark Jedi Xanatos in an effort to lure Qui-Gon Jinn to his death. However, it was discovered that the mine was a source of ionite, which shut down Xanatos's bombs and allowed the Jedi Master to escape.

**Home Planet Party** The primary goal of this party was retaking control of Bandomeer's natural resources and restoration of the planet's natural beauty. It was supported by the native Meerians as well as the Arcona who lived there while working for Arcona Mineral Harvest Corporation. Led by the charismatic VeerTa, the party was striving to become financially independent from the mining companies when Qui-Gon Jinn and Obi-Wan Kenobi were lured into the trap set by the Dark Jedi Xanatos. They exposed Xanatos and VeerTa as partners, and she was arrested.

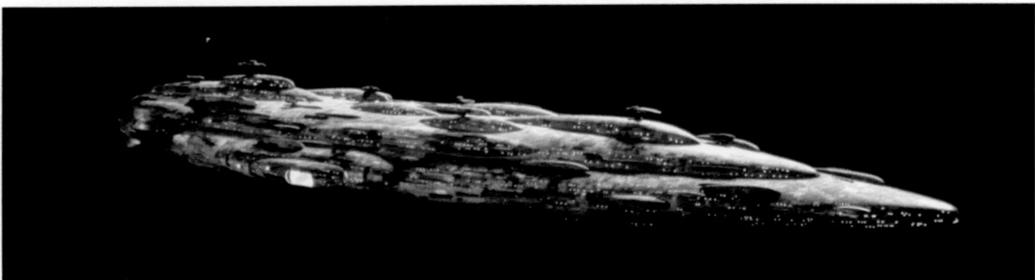
Home One

**Homestar** A cantina on Treasure Ship Row in the Corellian city of Coronet, it attracted those who sought quiet passage off the planet. Aayla Secura and Ylenic It'kla went there to search for Ratri Tane, but were ambushed by Gotals working for the Confederacy.

**Homestone** The Qella name for their homeworld, Brath Qella. They also called it the Place of Beginning.

**Homeworld Security Command** This branch of the Old Republic government was charged with ensuring that Coruscant was kept safe. Homeworld Security worked closely with the armed forces to ensure that proper orbital and ground-based security teams were on constant alert to head off any threat to the planet's normal routines. The members of the Homeworld Security team were shocked when they found themselves unprepared for General Grievous's attack on the planet in what turned out to be the final major battle of the Clone Wars.

**homing beacon** A small device that could be hidden aboard a starship. It emitted a signal from its internal hyperspace transponder, allowing the "bugged" vessel to be tracked as it crossed the galaxy. While expensive, a homing beacon could reveal the target ship's exact movements, which in turn could reveal the locations of enemy bases and fleet rendezvous points.

*Homing spider droid*

**homing spider droid** Developed by the Commerce Guild and manufactured by Baktoid Armor Workshop, the OG-9 spider droid resembled an immense, four-legged spider. Also known as the spider tank or spider walker, the homing spider droid had a spherical body that was plated with armor, and contained sensor systems and weaponry. Its legs allowed it to maneuver across the terrain of any battlefield so it could use its sensor systems to read the battle and coordinate front-line droid troops. When extended to its full height, the homing spider droid stood just over 7.3 meters tall. Its weapons systems were modular, allowing it to be refitted for a variety of mission profiles. Its primary weapon was a homing laser, which caused damage while it obtained ranging information on a target. Other weapons could then destroy the target while a further target was acquired. With its long legs, the homing spider droid could move about at speeds approaching 90 kilometers per hour. When the Clone Wars ended, all homing spider droids were issued orders to deactivate as part of Darth Sidious's plan to consolidate military power and ensure the loyalty of his troops.

**Hom Mounds** Located in the hills of Kadril, the Hom Mounds were the ceremonial burial place of the Nociv.

**homogoni** This hardwood tree was harvested for its lumber, which was used to create luxurious and expensive pieces of furniture.

**Homon** This planet was the site of a Rebel Alliance base during the early stages of the Galactic Civil War.

**homunculus-wasp** These small, poisonous insects were native to Af'El and were called kheilwar by the Defel. Assassins sometimes used them to kill their prey, since the wasps initially were very tiny. They grew at an astonishing rate, however. In just a week, a tiny insect could amass more than 20 kilograms of body weight and grow to a height of 1.5 meters or more. They were armed with razor-sharp fins and large wings that absorbed and warped visible light, giving them the ability to seemingly disappear. Their most unusual ability, though, was the ability to transform their bodies into simulacra of anyone they had encountered. The homunculus-wasp was primarily a nocturnal feeder, since its sensory organs were badly damaged when exposed to normal sunlight.

**Hon, Degred** This Bith scientist developed a so-called gene bomb at the height of the New Order; he hoped to use it to clean up his homeworld of Clak'Dor VII. When his scientific colleagues refused to accept his plans, Degred Hon chose to take matters into his own hands. He planned to hijack a shuttle from Mezhra Station and crash it into the planet, but a group of freelance operatives was able to thwart his scheme.

**Hondi, Panza** This Guineo criminal lived in the industrial district of Coruscant following the Battle of Naboo, working for Groff Haug at the time. He was wanted by the Coruscant police for the murder of an off-duty police officer, and was apprehended by Jango Fett.

**Honest Blim** This used-droid salesman owned and operated Procopia Pre-owned Automata on Procopia in the final decades of the Old Republic.

**Honest Ellam's Speeder Lot** Located on Questal, deep in the city of Gralleenya, Honest Ellam purchased Tiree's X-wing fighter from Bim Maldeen.

**Hong** This Imperial recruit held the rank of sergeant-major and served under Kyle Katarn during the assault on asteroid AX-456. Katarn relied on Hong's judgment, but Hong bristled when Katarn ordered that a team of Rebel Alliance soldiers be allowed to go free once the base was secured. Hong accepted the orders after Katarn explained that they needed to conserve ammunition. Hong later died during the final Imperial stand against the Rebels.

**Honi** This young Jedi trainee was almost three years old when Obi-Wan Kenobi was chosen to be the Padawan of Qui-Gon Jinn.

**Honiten** This alias was used by Falynn Sandskimmer when she and Wraith Squadron infiltrated the planet Storinal. Honiten was a native of Bakura and was one of the bodyguards protecting Wes Janson, who was using the alias Iskit Tyestin.

**Honka** This male Rodian was a frequent patron of Dex's Diner in the years leading up to the Clone Wars. He was often seen in the company of his lady friend, Sidewa.

**Honoghr** A planet with three moons in the Honoghr system, it was the homeworld of the fierce Noghri. Honoghr was a devastated world; almost all of its plant and animal life had been destroyed. From space it appeared to be uniformly brown, broken only by the occasional blue lake and the green area known as the Clean Land. The main city of Nystao was located in the center of the Clean Land and was home to the Common Room of Honoghr within the Grand Dukha. It was the only city with adequate spacecraft repair facilities.

The Noghri people were divided into clans (including Khim'bar, Bakh'tor, Eikh'mir, and Hakh'khar) that had a long history of bloody rivalry. Each clan was ruled by a dynast, and female maitrakhs led family or subclan units. In the center of each village was a cylindrical building called a dukha, constructed of polished wood encircled by a metal band. Dukhas contained the clan High Seat and a genealogical chart carved into one wall. Animal life on Honoghr included the carnivorous stava.

During a battle in the Clone Wars, a Trade Federation starship carrying defoliant crashed on Honoghr's surface, setting off catastrophic groundquakes and releasing toxic chemicals into the atmosphere. Darth Vader offered Imperial assistance, and teams of deadly Noghri commandos joined the Empire in return for the Emperor's promise to help restore their world. Noghri clans were relocated to the Clean Land, and Imperial decontamination droids set to work apparently renewing the soil. In reality, the Empire seeded Honoghr with a hybrid form of kholm-grass that inhibited all other plant growth, keeping the planet lifeless for generations and forcing the Noghri to remain in the Emperor's debt.

Before Vader's death, he named Grand Admiral Thrawn his designated heir and ruler of the Noghri commandos. But the Noghri renounced their service to Thrawn after Leia Organa Solo showed them the extent of the Empire's treachery, and they began to grow new crops along the banks of a hidden river running between two jagged cliffs. All efforts to restore the planet's broken ecosystem, however, turned out to be futile, as the once green world was incapable of recovering. The Noghri eventually relocated to the planet Wayland, leaving Honoghr for dead.

***Honor*** One of the Yevethan warships sent to purge Polneye.

**Honorable Union of Desevro and Tion** One of the most ancient political factions of the Outer Rim Territories, it was formed about a century after Xim the Despot's death as his empire began to split apart. The worlds of the former Livien League and the Tion Hegemony formed a bloc to ensure their security.

**Honoran, Wren** One of many Jedi Masters who retired from active field service to train students at the Jedi Temple on Coruscant around the time of the Battle of Naboo. Known for his political acumen, Wren Honoran also was an expert in survival skills. He often led expeditions to Ragoon-6, where he challenged a Master–Padawan team to find him in the wilderness using only their wits. Five years before the Clone Wars, Honoran accompanied Obi-Wan Kenobi and Anakin Skywalker to Ragoon-6, only to find himself in the midst of a plot by Granta Omega to capture the Jedi. Honoran was rendered unconscious, but later was rescued by Obi-Wan and Anakin.

**Honorary Elder** This was a title given to those Ewoks who proved themselves loyal to a tribe other than their own.

**Honor Clan** This was the name given to a group of Wookiee hunters and warriors who worked together to throw Imperial forces off Kashyyyk.

**Honor of the Armor, the** A term used by Imperial stormtroopers who served the Empire nearly a century after the Yuuzhan Vong War. The Honor of the Armor was the simplest description of the pride and purpose a soldier felt when fighting as a stormtrooper for the good of the Empire.

**honor-wife** Since the ratio of Cerean women to men was 20 to 1, it was traditional for most males to take several honor-wives in addition to their bond-wife. The relationship between the bond-wife and the honor-wives was often strained, especially when it came to children.

**Hontho** A Gamorrean, he served as one of 8t88's henchmen following the Battle of Endor. Hontho and his companions were killed by Kyle Katarn in his effort to capture 8t88.

**Hoob, Mian** A Sullustan member of Page's Commandos, Hoob was, together with Korren, the team's technical specialist.

Hookyr the First

**Hood, Willrow** A supervisor of A'roFilter's Tibanna-gas-mining operations on Cloud City, he helped sell the gas at a discount to the Rebel Alliance. After the Empire garrisoned Cloud City, he covered the operation's tracks by destroying the main computer core.

**hooded crystal snake** Native to Yavin 4, this species was named for the way it could flatten its neck, giving it the appearance of having a hood.

**Hoodish** One of the many dialects of Old Corellian that were spoken on various parts of the planet.

**Hoogra-D'En, Ort** A Ho'Din, he spent many of his early years on Anemcoro, cultivating and propagating several rare species of plants. The Empire fired on Anemcoro to halt a civil war, destroying his lifework. For revenge, he joined some colleagues and began bombing Imperial locations in the Outer Rim with spore bombs of his own design. Hoogra-D'En eventually was captured on Pallaxides.

**Hoojib** A species of telepathic rodents with large floppy ears and large eyes, they were native to the planet Arbra. Their fur had pastel coloration, and because they were cute and lacked advanced technology, many species underestimated their intelligence. Hoojibs tended to form familial clans of anywhere from 30 to 1,000 members and were friendly toward most visitors. They communicated telepathically with a Hoojib named Plif, who served as their spokesmind. Much of their nourishment came from a vast crystalline structure located beneath the surface of Arbra, which channeled energy from the planet's core. By feeding on this energy, Hoojibs kept the planet's energy resources in balance, preventing a catastrophic buildup of power.

Many Hoojibs joined the Rebel Alliance after a group of Rebels saved them from a slivilith, a dangerous predator that had commandeered their underground cave. They remained steady members of the New Republic. When the Yuuzhan Vong invasion began, the Hoojibs started a military buildup on Arbra as Plif attempted to get his people involved in the war effort.

**hook-blade** A handheld weapon used by Sakiyans in hand-to-hand combat, it had curved, razor-sharp blades.

**Hook Nebula** Home of the Qeimet Fleet, it was a strategic location during the Galactic Civil War.

**hook of bone** A wicked baling hook of sun-yellowed bone that Vergere used as a weapon in the Yuuzhan Vong dhuryam nursery. She stabbed Jacen Solo in the chest with it in order to plant a slave coral seed there. But the creature dropped to the ground and slithered away.

**Hookyr the First** A Hiromi leader, he was the primary force behind Operation Glorious Destiny, the Hiromi plan for domination of the planet Zeltros. During the invasion, the Hiromi discovered that the Nagai were also invading Zeltros, as were the Tofs. So Hookyr agreed to ally the Hiromi with Luke Skywalker and the Alliance of Free Planets. He hadn't planned on Skywalker's attempt to assault the Tof command ship to rescue his friends.

**Hool** A Nagai commander, some months after the Battle of Endor he was placed in charge of a mission to the Forest Moon by the individual known as Knife.

Mammon Hoole

**Hool, Ch'Gang** This Yuuzhan Vong master shaper was in charge of the regrowth of several dhuryams that would compete to serve as the World Brain used to seed Coruscant. The plan was to turn Coruscant into a new version of the invaders' long-lost homeworld, Yuuzhan'tar, and it was Ch'Gang Hool's responsibility to maintain and care for the priceless dhuryams. Ch'Gang Hool was distinguished from other shapers by the strange group of tentacles grafted to the corner of his mouth. They writhed and twitched to their own rhythm, but sometimes seemed to move in reaction to Hool's mood.

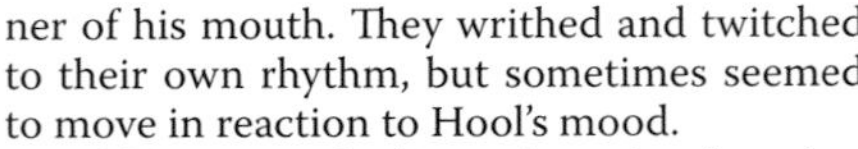

Ch'Gang Hool objected to the fact that Nom Anor and Vergere used his seedship as their training ground for Jacen Solo. His fears were nearly realized when Solo's actions during the *tizo'pil Yun'tchilat* eliminated all but a single dhuryam. However, the World Brain was installed on Coruscant, and the Vongforming of the planet continued. Within months, Coruscant began to resemble Yuuzhan'tar.

Ch'Gang Hool had another scare when he learned that Solo had ended up on Coruscant, instead of being killed aboard the seedship. Solo had befriended the dhuryam World Brain and was allowed private access to the Well in order to sacrifice Ganner Rhysode. The renegade Jedi also planned to use his mental link to the dhuryam to ask it a favor: to work as a spy for the New Republic. Many Yuuzhan Vong on the Great Council saw Coruscant's constant rejection of worldshaping as a failure to fully tame the planet. Because of this failure, Ch'Gang Hool was executed on the orders of Supreme Overlord Shimrra.

**Hoole, Mammon** Some 20 years before the Battle of Yavin, Mammon Hoole joined the Old Republic as a scientist. A shape-shifting Shi'ido who had graduated from the Chandrilan Academy of Sciences alongside Borborygmus Gog, Hoole was reunited with Gog by the Republic, working to develop countermeasures to the anti-clone-trooper bioweapons that were being developed by the Confederacy of Independent Systems.

In the wake of the Clone Wars, both scientists were retained by the Empire and charged with discovering a way to control life and death in Project Starscream. Emperor Palpatine himself approved the funding for a base on the planet Kiva, where they nearly discovered a way to create life from nothing. However, Hoole recognized that their experiments would steal all the life from the planet Kiva, leaving it a barren wasteland and wiping out the native Kivans. Gog deliberately didn't relay Hoole's concern to Palpatine, and said the Emperor demanded further tests. The Kivans indeed were wiped out, and Gog blamed Hoole for the experiment's failure.

Hoole fled Imperial service and went to Tatooine to seek help from Jabba the Hutt. He managed to get all records of his existence erased from Imperial data banks and was given a new identity. He also created the droid D-V9 to help him. Just as he began his search for Gog, Hoole learned that Alderaan had been destroyed, killing his brother and sister-in-law. He became the guardian of their children, Tash and Zak Arranda, who had been offplanet.

Hoojibs

Hoole and the children tracked down all the leads on Gog and Starscream, eventually managing to end the experiment on Kiva, along with Gog himself. This earned them the wrath of Darth Vader and a death warrant, but they managed to remain one step ahead of the Empire.

**Hooly** A tech sergeant with the Rebel Alliance, he was known for his expertise with blaster weapons.

**Hoom** A huge Phlog on the Forest Moon of Endor, he was the son of Zut and Dobah and the brother of Nahkee.

**Hoona** A female Phlog, she fell in love with Wicket, an Ewok, after drinking a magic Dulok potion. The liquid was supposed to have been a hate potion that Umwak had planned to give to the Phlogs to enlist their aid in defeating the Ewoks.

Hoona

**Hoonta** A Rodian thug in the employ of Jabba the Hutt, he and several cronies were ordered to kill Jedi Knight Ki-Adi-Mundi. During the fight, Hoonta was cut in half by the Jedi's lightsaber.

***Hoopster's Prank*** A freighter owned by Booster Terrik, it often was used to assist in the shipment of pommwomm plants. It was boarded by Rogue Squadron, but was found to be clean. The Sif'krie species then banned smugglers from carrying their pommwomm plants.

**Hoorrkhukk** One of the largest Wookiee cities established on the planet Kashyyyk. Like its counterparts, Hoorrkhukk was established around a manufacturing facility, and was built in the intertwined branches of wroshyr trees.

**hootbat** An avian creature native to Clak'Dor VII, it was named for its unusual hooting song.

Arn Horada

**hootle** A herd animal native to the plains of Ansion.

**Hoover** A short quadruped alien with a disproportionately long snout and large eyes, he was a member of Jabba the Hutt's court until the crime lord was killed and his organization shattered. Hoover was highly technical, and his small size allowed him to perform delicate tasks with complex equipment. Although little known, apparently his species was named Hoover, too.

Hoover

***Hope*** A Mon Calamari MC80a cruiser commanded by Captain Arboga, it was part of the New Republic fleet following the Battle of Endor. It had to defend itself and the courier ship *Messenger* when an Imperial *Carrack*-class cruiser intercepted them at their rendezvous point after following a homing beacon hidden aboard the courier ship.

**H.O.P.E. Squad (High Orbit Precision Entry Squad)** A specialized group of clone troopers trained for high-orbit precision entry during the Clone Wars. They were deployed into a planet's upper atmosphere in small environment capsules that allowed them to survive the low levels of oxygen. Once in a breathable atmosphere, the capsules split open and H.O.P.E. Squad troopers swiftly and silently landed at a hostile location. The squad dispatched to Yorn Skot to rescue Jedi Master Treetower was attacked by a squad of jump droids, and only one member survived along with Master Treetower; still, they were able to rescue a group of Ugnaughts who were about to be sold into slavery.

Horak-mul

**Hoppawui** This barren world was the sixth planet in the Both system, and was orbited by eight moons.

***Hopskip*** This modified YT-1300 freighter was owned by Haber Trell and Maranne Darmic. They used it to smuggle weapons to the underground on Derra IV. It was destroyed by the 181st Imperial Fighter Group when the Empire ambushed the Rebel Alliance's supply convoy at Derra IV shortly before the Battle of Hoth.

**Horada, Arn** Leia Organa's professor of history during her early education on Alderaan. Years later, she had a meeting with him on Metalorn to ask about the Empire's activities there. When Baron Orman Tagge tried to capture Leia, Horada kicked a table into Tagge's path, causing him to trip and giving the Princess a chance to escape.

**Horak-mul** A one-eyed Sith warlord, he became involved in the Sith Empire's civil war some 5,000 years before the Galactic Civil War. Horak-mul joined forces with Ludo Kressh and Dor Gal-Ram to oust the reigning Dark Lord of the Sith, Naga Sadow. Sadow, however, had goaded his enemies into an assault and had a hidden fleet ready to meet them. Horak-mul was murdered when his crew, many of whom were spies loyal to Sadow, threw off their disguises and butchered their captain.

**Horansi** This species of carnivorous hunters from Mutanda consisted of four subspecies: the Kasa, Gorvan, Mashi, and Treka Horansi. The Horansi were bipedal, feline-like sentients. Although their society was primitive and tribal, they were more than happy to let either the Empire or the Rebel Alliance mine the prothium in their system, knowing they could make money as guides to either side.

**horansi** A particularly ruthless card game, it was popular among Rebel Alliance starfighter pilots.

**horax** Enormous reptilian creatures native to the world of Nelvaan. A fully grown horax stood over 15 meters tall at the shoulder. The carnivorous reptile had a mouth filled with sharp teeth,

Horax

none more impressive than the four enormous saber-like fangs that protruded from the monster's maw. It used a set of shovel-like horns at the end of its snout to uproot trees and split open siltcrawler burrows to eat entire hibernating colonies. Horax tails were long, heavy, and lined with sharp spurs; they ended in a club of dense bone. Luckily for Nelvaanians, horaxes were a dying breed, not faring well in the climatic changes on the planet. They also were solitary beasts, and their size made them easy to detect as they approached.

The natives of Rokrul village discovered that a horax was repelled by the scent given off by a special elixir made from its tail scales; one scale could produce enough of the pungent mix-

Horansi

ture to paint a perimeter around a village that lasted a year. So each year, young Nelvaanian males were sent to find a sleeping horax and return with a tail scale. To succeed in that rite of passage was to be promoted into the upper ranks of a village's warrior scouts.

**Horch** A two-bit crime lord on Kheedar, he chose to become a slave to the invading Imperial forces rather than die. He tried to keep himself blissfully unaware of his predicament by being perpetually drunk on spice liquor.

**Hord, Tulak** An ancient Sith Lord who was buried in the Valley of the Dark Lords on Korriban, next to the tomb of Marka Ragnos. Among his artifacts were his protective mask and helmet, which aged to a dull black over time, although the eyes retained an eerie glow. Anyone wearing the mask felt intense claustrophobia.

**Hordon Cal** A hot ball of rock, it was the innermost planet of the Thanta Zilbra system and orbited by a single moon. Both were destroyed when the Sacorrian Triad obliterated the system as part of the Starbuster Plot.

***Horizon*** This *Strike*-class cruiser was part of the Rebel Alliance fleet.

***Horizon*-class yacht** A luxury space yacht produced by SoroSuub during the New Republic era. Some 55 meters long, it could accommodate 10 passengers and 100 metric tons of supplies. The basic model had a hyperdrive and minimal shielding. Most owners quickly added laser or blaster cannons to protect themselves from pirates.

**Horm, Threkin** A grossly overweight human who used a repulsor chair to get around, he was president of the powerful Alderaanian Council. C-3PO discovered that the illegitimate daughter of Dalla Suul—a kidnapper, murderer, and pirate possibly related to Han Solo—was Horm's mother. Threkin Horm, a native of Fedalle, was loose with his loyalties. He didn't care who was in control of the galaxy, as long as he and his people were taken care of.

**Horme, Treva** This Lutrillian female was the primary salesbeing and executive planner for Planet Dreams, Incorporated, a Cloud City–based builder of vacation villas in unsettled but habitable worlds throughout the Greater Javin. An excellent marketer, Horme also monitored business accounts and production schedules. Much of her notoriety came from her work with the Outer Javin Company, where she was able to work with high-profile clients such as TaggeCo and Lynciro Corporation.

Treva Horme (left)

**Horn, Corran** One of Rogue Squadron's best pilots, he was a third-generation Corellian Security (CorSec) officer. Corran Horn's grandfather had fought in the Clone Wars alongside the Jedi Knights, so it particularly troubled Corran's father, Hal, when Darth Vader used CorSec to hunt down and kill Jedi. After Corran's mother's death and the tragic murder of his father, Corran had no desire to remain in CorSec any longer. With the help of his former CorSec mentor, Gil Bastra, and a new identity, he made his way to the Rebel Alliance and Rogue Squadron.

At first Horn kept mostly to himself, although he was friendly with wingmate Ooryl Qrygg. Later, his circle expanded to include Lujayne Forge, Nawara Ven, and Rhysati Ynr because he had to learn to make new friends, trust others, and become part of a team during training. By the time he made the cut and joined Rogue Squadron, he was promoted to lieutenant based on his simulator test scores. Horn became one of Wedge Antilles's best pilots, taking on the hardest missions and surviving them. He kept his grandfather's Jed-Cred on a chain around his neck, rubbing it for luck during his missions.

When stormtroopers made their night raid at Talasea, Horn and Qrygg saved most of Rogue Squadron from certain death, although Horn's lung was punctured by blasterfire. Upon his recovery, he participated in the retaliatory raid on Vladet, where a crazy stunt nearly earned him a court-martial. All of his fighter skills and fancy acrobatic maneuvers were put to the test in two raids on Borleias. During the second, he had to be rescued a second time by Mirax Terrik and her ship, the *Pulsar Skate.* Horn later was in the thick of things as part of the advance party in the Alliance's attempt to take back Coruscant, and he had several narrow escapes.

After his heroics in the heat of the Alliance invasion of Coruscant, his Z-95 Headhunter crashed and he was presumed dead. Instead, he had been captured and thrown into the *Lusankya,* a buried Super Star Destroyer that served as a secret high-security prison. He managed to escape with the help of fellow prisoner Jan Dodonna and showed up in the court where fellow Rogue and suspected spy Tycho Celchu was on trial for murdering Horn. He

Corran Horn

was astounded when Luke Skywalker revealed that Nejaa Halcyon was his true grandfather, making him heir to a Jedi heritage. Presenting Corran with his grandfather's lightsaber, Luke offered to train and teach him as they traveled together, reestablishing the Jedi Knights. Horn declined the offer and opted to continue to serve with Rogue Squadron.

It was at around this time that Horn became romantically involved with Mirax Terrik, a situation whose irony was not lost on either of them: Horn's father had been the one to send her father, Booster, to Kessel's prison for smuggling. After the Battle of Thyferra, they were wed; a more elaborate ceremony was held on Coruscant upon their return. Horn and Rogue Squadron spent time battling Grand Admiral Thrawn and the reborn Emperor Palpatine's forces at Coruscant; the home that he and Mirax built was one of the first victims of the falling Star Destroyer *Liberator.*

When the battle to eliminate the Invid pirates led Mirax into danger and she disappeared, Horn decided he needed to hone his Force skills to find her. So he agreed to be one of Luke Skywalker's first students at his new Jedi academy on Yavin 4. He helped defeat the menace of Exar Kun's evil spirit, but in the final battle he suffered injuries that required extensive bacta treatments. When he healed, he left the academy because he did not agree with many of Skywalker's methods. He then infiltrated the Invids in the hope of locating his wife. He constructed his own lightsaber while serving Invid leader Leonia Tavira. With Skywalker's help, Horn rescued Mirax and brought her out of the hibernation trance she had been placed in.

Horn opted not to return to the Jedi academy, and Skywalker agreed. Luke did allow him one parting gesture: Horn destroyed Exar Kun's statue and temple on Yavin 4 with a volley of proton torpedoes, forever eliminating the focal point of Sith energy on the moon.

By the time of the Yuuzhan Vong War, Horn had become a full Jedi Knight, although like his grandfather, he had no ability to move objects through the Force. He felt Skywalker was doing his best to bring new Jedi Knights along slowly, although he often found himself in the minority. Horn teamed up with Ganner Rhysode during the early stages of the Yuuzhan Vong War, and while their personalities clashed they eventually developed a grudging respect for each other. When the pair attempted to rescue slaves they found on Bimmiel, Horn was near-mortally wounded by a Yuuzhan Vong amphistaff. Rhysode recovered Horn's lifeless body, quickly dunking him in bacta and drawing the poison out so that he survived.

In the wake of the battle, Horn learned that the planet Garqi had been invaded and that he had been called up to serve as a colonel in the Garqi militia. He was allowed to take a group of six Noghri with him, and they discovered that the pollen of the bafforr tree was deadly to vonduun crab armor. Before the New Republic could take advantage of the information, the Yuuzhan Vong attacked Ithor. Commander Shedao Shai also murdered Elegos A'Kla and sent his bones to Horn as a threat. Horn eventually confronted Shedao Shai, and they agreed to a duel: Corran fighting for Ithor, and Shedao Shai for the remains of Mongei Shai. Horn barely managed to defeat the commander, but that defeat left Deign Lian in command of the alien fleet. Lian fired on Ithor with a bacteria-riddled bioweapon, which destroyed all life on the planet's surface. Then the *Legacy of Torment* was destroyed, and it crashed into Ithor. As the ship exploded and flames engulfed the world, Horn was labeled in the holomedia as "the man who killed Ithor."

Horn felt himself slipping dangerously close to the dark side of the Force, having wanted to kill Shedao Shai in revenge for Elegos A'Kla's death, rather than to protect Ithor. He resigned his position with the Jedi Knights in order to meditate on his actions and try to regain equilibrium. He returned to action during the struggle to free the students of the Jedi praxeum on Yavin 4, helping to rescue the crew of the *Idiot's Array*. He was later reinstated to the New Republic Navy, and he took command of Rogue Squadron during the period following the Battle of Borleias. When the living planet Zonama Sekot was discovered to be hiding in the Unknown Regions by Luke Skywalker and a band of Jedi, Horn was assigned to lead Tahiri Veila on a mission to meet with Yu'shaa, the Yuuzhan Vong Prophet who was searching for Zonama Sekot himself. During the final stages of the battle against the Yuuzhan Vong, after Zonama Sekot agreed to help bring about an end to the conflict, Horn was one of several Jedi Knights who were bonded to seed-partners and provided with Sekotan starships.

For his actions during the war, Horn was elevated to the rank of Jedi Master and spent several years training a Padawan known as Raltharan. In the wake of the Qoribu crisis, Horn found himself in an odd position when Luke Skywalker was stranded on Woteba. The Chief of State of the Galactic Alliance, Cal Omas, demanded that a leader be chosen for the new Jedi Order in order to bring about an end to the problem of the Dark Nest. With Master Skywalker on a mission, Omas pushed for Horn to become the new leader of the Jedi Order. He refused, but the situation led him to question the status of the Order.

Hal Horn

When Master Skywalker sent out his Force call to draw all Jedi to Ossus at the height of the conflict with the Colony, Horn initially decided to leave the Order. However, Skywalker convinced him that he no longer needed to carry the weight of the galaxy on his conscience. Horn stayed. He also reluctantly accepted Luke's assumption of the role of Grand Master of the Jedi, recognizing that the Order would be lost without him.

After the crisis with the Colony was resolved, Corran and Mirax returned to Corellia, where he established a small training center for young students of the Force. But their peace was cut short when Thrackan Sal-Solo began demanding Corellian independence from the Galactic Alliance. Horn's loyalty to the Jedi made him an outcast, and Mirax was placed under house arrest for being his spouse. Rather than submit to arrest himself, Horn went underground, hiding in the rubble of his training center. He remained hidden until Iella Antilles made contact with him, hoping to enlist Horn's help in thwarting an assassination attempt on Wedge Antilles. Horn was more than happy to help.

Corran Horn (left) battles Shedao Shai for the fate of Ithor.

After a rendezvous on the *Errant Venture* with Han and Leia Organa Solo and Luke and Mara Jade Skywalker, Horn agreed to return to Coruscant to help the Jedi figure out what was happening in the galaxy—although he feared that Mirax would divorce him since he had forgotten to give her a good-bye kiss. In the wake of Mara Jade Skywalker's murder on Kavan, Horn agreed to take over as the leader of the new Jedi Order while Luke set out to locate her killer and avenge her death. He was pleased when Skywalker put plans in motion to finally act against his nephew, rogue Jedi Jacen Solo, who now called himself Darth Caedus. Horn was there at the end, after Jaina Solo killed Caedus, and he helped lead 50 Jedi aboard the Super Star Destroyer *Megador* to dictate peace terms to the Moff Council on the ship.

**Horn, Hal** Corran Horn's father; his given name was Valin Halcyon. After his father, the Jedi Master Nejaa Halcyon, was killed in the Clone Wars, Rostek Horn married Nejaa's widow and erased all information on the Halcyon family to hide the family from Emperor Palpatine. Hal Horn was a top graduate of the Corellian Security Force Academy. He later married a Corellian woman, and they had a son together, whom they named Corran. Corran grew up to follow in his father's footsteps, also becoming a CorSec agent. They were on a mission together to arrest a smuggler, but the bounty hunter Bossk—who had a valid Imperial warrant—shot Hal Horn instead in a cantina. Corran was powerless to stop it, and was forced to comfort his father as he died in his arms.

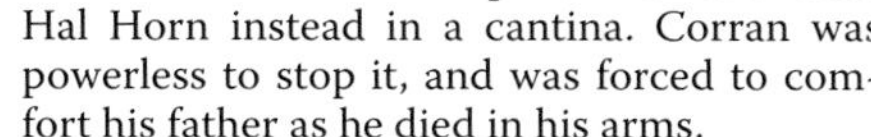

**Horn, Jysella** The first daughter born to Corran Horn and Mirax Terrik. She and her brother Valin trained to be Jedi aboard the *Errant Venture* after the Yuuzhan Vong took control of Yavin 4. They became Jedi Knights in the years following the conflict with Unu-Thul and the Colony.

**Horn, Mirax Terrik** *See* Terrik, Mirax.

**Horn, Rostek** Corran Horn's adopted grandfather, Rostek Horn also was a member of the Corellian Security Force and a contemporary of Fliry Vorru. He was good friends with Corran's real grandfather, Jedi Master Nejaa Halcyon, and took care of his family after Halcyon's death. Rostek used his position within CorSec to eliminate all traces of the Halcyon family, hoping to hide Nejaa's widow and young son from Palpatine's Jedi Purge. Rostek eventually married Nejaa's widow and cared for her son Valin, whom they renamed Hal in honor of Nejaa Halcyon.

**Horn, Valin** The first son of Corran Horn and Mirax Terrik, Valin was born four years after the death of Grand Admiral Thrawn and was named for his grandfather Valin Halcyon. Like his father, Valin was Force-sensitive, and eventually attended the Jedi praxeum on Yavin 4 for training. Valin was trapped on Yavin 4 when the Peace Brigade blockaded the system

in an effort to capture the Jedi students and turn them over to the Yuuzhan Vong. Valin and others hung on until Anakin Solo could rescue them. Like many of the younger Jedi trainees, Valin was forced to train aboard the *Errant Venture* after the Yuuzhan Vong took control of Yavin 4. Valin and his sister, Jysella, continued to train and became Jedi Knights during the years following the conflict with UnuThul and the Colony.

At the height of the Galactic Alliance's war with the Confederation, Valin was chosen to be part of a Jedi team that was to infiltrate Coruscant and capture or eliminate Jacen Solo. Valin and Jedi Master Kyle Katarn confronted Jacen, at first alone, and it took just seconds for Solo to lash out with a kick that caught Valin in the chin and knocked him briefly unconscious. Valin recovered just as Solo drove his lightsaber into Master Katarn's chest, and he rushed Solo alongside Kolir Hu'lya and Thann Mithric. However, the three Jedi were no match for Solo's control of the dark side of the Force. After Mithric was killed while trying to hold Solo off, the surviving Jedi managed to escape when Seha Dorvald arrived to help them weave their way through underground tunnels to a waiting shuttle. After a brief respite at a temporary Jedi base on the Forest Moon of Endor, Valin accompanied Kyp Durron on the successful mission to infiltrate and destroy Centerpoint Station.

**hornagaunt** This monstrous avian creature was native to the stormy world of Tertiary Kesmere.

**hornbeak** A predator native to the planet Orellon II, the hornbeak was a huge reptile that ate everything in its path. The average specimen measured about 4.5 meters from the tip of its nose to the end of its tail, and resembled a cross between a tyrannosaur and a stegosaur.

***Hornclaw*** A modified YT-1300 freighter, it was stolen from Abek's Station by Limna Yith. The *Hornclaw* was armed with a pair of fire-linked laser cannons.

**horned krevol** A large, predatory insect native to Corellia.

**horned voritor** This species of voritor, named for the heavy, pointed scales that protected its eyes and ear holes, was native to Dathomir.

***Hornet*** A group of Imperial corvettes protecting freighters near Petrakis, they were attacked by Alliance starfighters.

***Hornet*-class carrier** A large warship developed by SoroSuub Corporation prior to the Clone Wars. Hornets could be equipped with baffled sublight drives and dampened power systems to pass undetected by sensors until they raised their shields. The ship was identifiable by its slim design and bridge mounted near the center of its bulk. Trade Federation Station TFP-9 on Naboo was attacked by a *Hornet*-class carrier carrying Z-95 Headhunters during the Battle of Naboo.

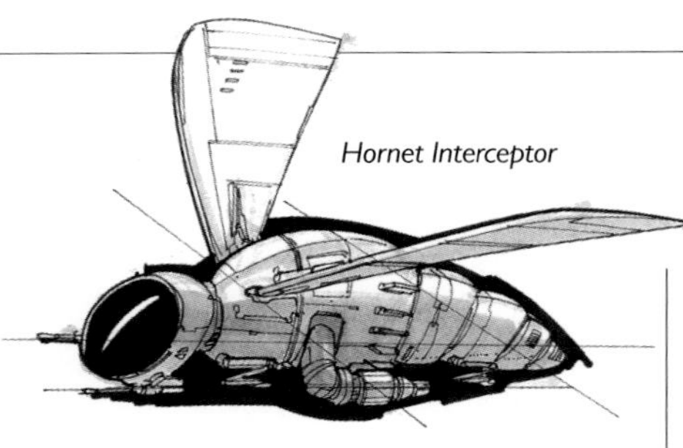
Hornet Interceptor

***Hornet Interceptor*** This freighter was based on the planet Socorro during the Galactic Civil War.

**Hornet Interceptor** An aerodynamically perfect ship, it was a sleek air-and-space fighter built by black marketers and favored by pirates, smugglers, and other criminals. The Hornet Interceptor originally was designed by a group of freelance starship engineers for the Tenloss Syndicate, a shadowy criminal organization specializing in gunrunning, extortion, and smuggling. The Hornet had a thin, dagger-shaped design, with insect-like wings for atmospheric flight. Its biggest asset was its maneuverability. A tighter turning radius and better maneuvering jets than an X-wing gave it an edge in dogfights. A Hornet carried turbocharged laser cannons. Han Solo battled a Hornet Interceptor while on a diplomatic mission to Kessel after administrator Moruth Doole ordered his fighter fleet to shoot down the *Millennium Falcon.*

**hornhead** A derogatory term used to describe a member of the Zabrak species.

**Horn Station** During the last decades of the Old Republic, this remote planet was taken over by crime lord Shoto Eyefire until an anonymous Jedi Knight took him out in a blaster fight.

**hornweed** A species of tree-like plant found in the swamps of Naboo. The fibers of the hornweed's branches were used by Gungans to form strong, resilient bows and arms for their catapults.

**horny whelmer** This immense beast inhabited the arctic regions of the planet Rothana. Its squatting stance served as the design basis for the Rothana Heavy Engineering AT-TE.

**Horob** This planet was the site of a Rebel Alliance research lab during the Galactic Civil War. The Alliance had been developing a sophisticated sensor chip, but could produce only an experimental version before the Empire discovered the base.

**Horodi** A Rebel Alliance starpilot assigned to Keyan Farlander's squadron. He was killed during the attempt to capture the *Ethar* corvettes.

**Horororibb** This young being was a student at the Jedi Temple on Coruscant during the last years of the Old Republic.

***Horse*** An Imperial CR90 corvette group that operated during the Galactic Civil War.

**Horsea** This Kiffu served as a member of the Guardians of Kiffu during the last decades of the Old Republic. It was Horsea and Vanlin who shot down Havor and Merglyn during their attempt to run weapons to the prisoners on Kiffex.

**Horska** This planet was the site of a major Imperial HoloNet relay station in the decades following the Battle of Endor.

**Horst, Major** An Imperial officer stationed at a laboratory on Danuta in the months prior to the Battle of Yavin. Major Horst was on watch when Kyle Katarn infiltrated the lab, but the officer believed that the only threat to the installation was a perimeter attack. When he set out to secure the perimeter fence, his command speeder was shot down; Horst died in the resulting explosion.

**Hort, Moff** This Imperial Moff was one of the few who remained in power during the second decade of the New Republic. Moff Hort was present at the meeting in which Admiral Pellaeon discussed the negotiation of a peace treaty with the New Republic, but he firmly rejected the idea.

**Hortek** Members of this tall, humanoid species covered with bony, armor-like plates had long necks and unblinking eyes. They were one of the few predatory species that were members of the New Republic.

**Horthav system** A largely uninhabited star system near Kuat, it served as one of the two main staging areas for cargo inbound to the Kuat Freight Port.

**Horticar** This gas giant was the fifth planet of the Utos system and was orbited by 11 moons.

**hortium** A type of bioengineered room or chamber developed by Yuuzhan Vong shapers.

**Horuset system** Located in the Outer Rim Territories, it contained two asteroid belts and a single planet, Korriban.

**Horuz system** This star system contained the prison colony on Despayre, which served as the construction site for the first Death Star. Upon completion, the battle station obliterated the planet as a test. The system was in the Atrivis sector of the galaxy in the Outer Rim Territories. Aside from Despayre, most of the bodies in the Horuz system were extensively mined for ore and other natural resources.

**Horvik** A member of the Vengeance group, he was part of the second team sent to disrupt activity in Drev'starn to cover the sabotage of that city's shield generator. Later, disguised as New Republic technicians, they managed to get aboard the *Predominance* and make their way to a turbolaser battery. They killed their escort and got off eight shots at Drev'starn before being discovered and neutralized.

**Horvus** An Imperial cargo ferry group used to deliver supplies to an outpost in the Pakuuni system.

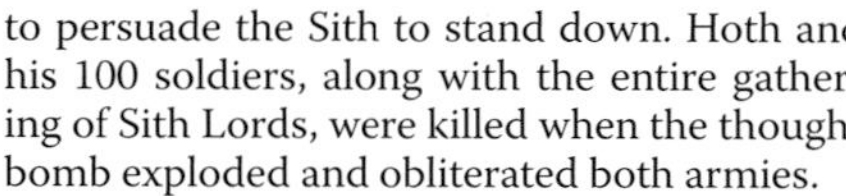

Hosk Station

**Hosk** This moon orbited the planet Kalarba. It was industrialized by the Old Republic when an *Esseles*-class space station was built in orbit around it.

**Hosk Station** A major trading port and space station in the Kalarba system, this *Esseles*-class space station cast a huge shadow on Kalarba's largest moon. The station's proximity to major systems made it a center of commerce and political influence. The droids C-3PO and R2-D2 had several adventures in and around Hosk Station while in the company of Nak Pitareeze, the grandson of a skilled starship designer.

Hosk Station originally was built as a supply and maintenance depot for the Old Republic Navy, but eventually was sold to civilian interests and had a peak population of five million permanent residents. Commerce ranged from small shops and droid sellers to expensive restaurants and luxury hotels. Starship-repair and -construction bays filled the station's interior. In its lowest levels lived a 40-meter-long snake-like predator called a hulgren. The station was nearly destroyed by crooked businessman Olag Greck when he attempted to steal a cargo shipment of ash ore. Greck sabotaged the station's power core, forcing Hosk's evacuation. But R2-D2 and C-3PO, working with Hosk security droid Zed, saved the station from destruction by channeling the explosion through the upper purge vents.

Years later, Hosk Station was destroyed by the Yuuzhan Vong shortly after the Battle of Fondor as they attempted to eliminate all inorganic technologies in the galaxy. Although Hosk was armed with 10 turbolasers and a fleet of Zebra fighters, the invaders used a tactic known as Yo'gand's Core to send the station crashing into Kalarba.

**Hosrel XI** This was the first planet that Lehesu visited when he escaped the Imperial blockade of the ThonBoka during the early years of the New Order. Hosrel XI was long rumored to be the site of a secret Imperial research base.

Lord Hoth

**Hoszh Iszhir** This planet had an arid and poisonous environment. Half its surface was covered with desert. The other half was blanketed by a toxic atmosphere. Despite that combination, life managed to evolve. Most creatures were predators, and from them emerged the planet's only form of sentient life, the Gektls. The planet had rich lodes of guerrerite and other precious metals, so the Gektls established a planetary defense shield for protection against invasion. The system worked well for many generations, until Stafuv Rahz traded the shield codes to the Empire for a military commission. The Empire swooped in and subjugated the Gektls, then took control of the planet's mining operations. The Gektls were forced into slavery, toiling in the mines while the Empire reaped the profits.

**Hotel Grand** This luxurious hotel in Worlport on Ord Mantell was the site of the Conclave on the Plight of the Refugees, and was where Leia Organa Solo stayed.

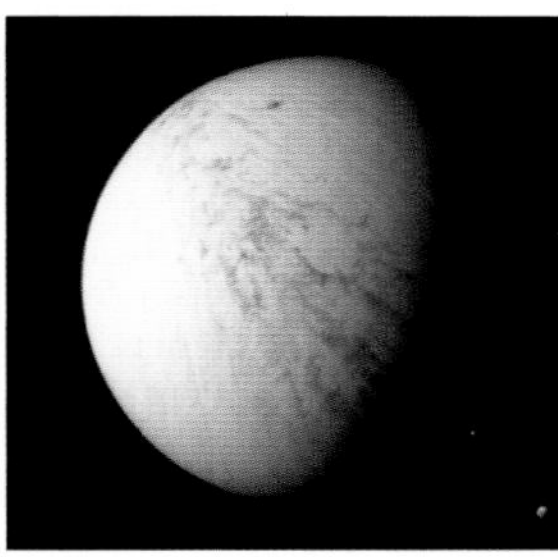

Hoth

**Hoth, Lord** This Jedi Master was the leader of the Army of Light, sent to Ruusan to defeat Lord Kaan and the Brotherhood of Darkness a thousand years before the Galactic Civil War. Well known as a master strategist and motivator, Lord Hoth had managed to defeat Sith opponents several times before his assignment on Ruusan, always seeming to score last-minute victories against all odds. But the fighting dragged on for two years. His continual struggle to win the war was often criticized by Master Valenthyne Farfalla, who offered to leave Ruusan and recruit more soldiers, despite the presence of a Sith blockade in orbit around the planet. Hoth laughed at him, believing that no one would be foolish enough to join the ongoing battle. In a strange twist of fate, when Darth Bane set in motion his own plans to destroy the Brotherhood of Darkness, Farfalla was able to break through the blockade and land his reinforcements, and the combined Jedi forces began to turn the tide.

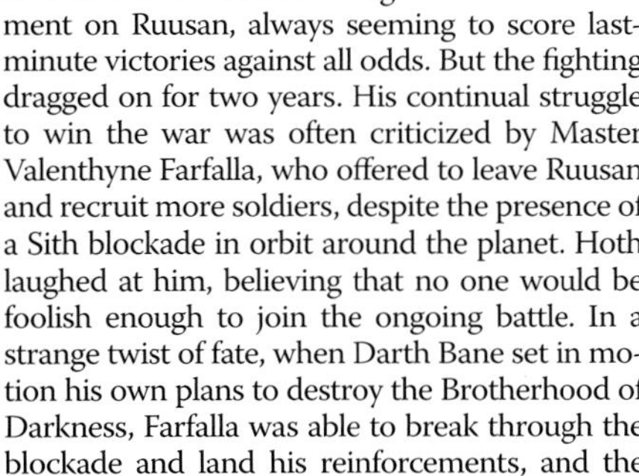

After Farfalla returned from the fighting with a warning about Lord Kaan's plans to set off a thought bomb, Lord Hoth realized that the end was near. He knew that he had to ensure that Kaan set off the bomb, but wanted as much of the Jedi force away from the blast zone as possible. Thus, he accepted only volunteers for a mission to confine the Sith, while ordering Farfalla to take the remaining troops to safety. Lord Hoth then confronted Lord Kaan, but was unable to persuade the Sith to stand down. Hoth and his 100 soldiers, along with the entire gathering of Sith Lords, were killed when the thought bomb exploded and obliterated both armies.

**Hoth** The sixth planet in a system of the same name, this icy, unpopulated world covered with glacier fields and circling a blue-white sun was the site of a major battlefield loss by the Rebel Alliance. Hoth was so isolated that it was not even recorded on some standard navigational charts, and thus seemed a good location for the primary Alliance military headquarters—Echo Base—three years after the Battle of Yavin.

Hoth was orbited by three moons and saw a good deal of meteor activity. Hoth's native life-forms included the common tauntaun—adopted by the Alliance as mounts—and its natural predator, the wampa ice creature. The many species of tauntauns ate fungus growing in cave grottoes and beneath the snow layer, and clustered together in caves on bitter nights to keep from freezing. Sights on Hoth included spectacular frozen ice geysers and a 1,000-kilometer-long chasm in the planet's southern hemisphere. The bottom of the chasm was filled with water, kept in its liquid state by the immense pressure of the two opposing cliff faces. Several glaciers, slowly sliding into the chasm's depths, harbored algae and burrowing, alga-feeding ice worms.

Following the Battle of Yavin, Luke Skywalker crashed on Hoth as he was escaping pursuing TIE fighters. He encountered two life-like human replica droids, programmed to look and act like an Imperial Governor and his daughter, who had been hiding on Hoth in order to escape the Empire. Later, the pirate Raskar captured Skywalker and Han Solo above Hoth, and Solo flew the group to a deep chasm on the planet's equator. There they discovered a hidden cave filled with rare lumni-spice lichens guarded by a fire-breathing dragon-slug; they barely escaped with their lives.

After the Alliance fully evacuated Yavin 4, it established its main base on Hoth in a series of ice caves at the northern edge of the temperate zone. The Alliance had trouble adapting its equipment to Hoth's extreme temperatures, and wampa attacks proved dangerous as well. Echo Base eventually was discovered by an Imperial probe droid, leading to the defeat of the Rebels by Darth Vader's forces in the Battle of Hoth. An Imperial garrison and detention center were placed on the planet for a few years.

Eight years after the Battle of Endor, a big-game expedition traveled to Hoth to hunt wampas for their valuable pelts. When the wampas destroyed the party's landing ship, the group took shelter in the abandoned Echo Base. Luke Skywalker and Callista, who happened to be on the planet, attempted to rescue the hunters, but the entire expedition was killed by the ice creatures, and Skywalker and Callista barely escaped with their lives.

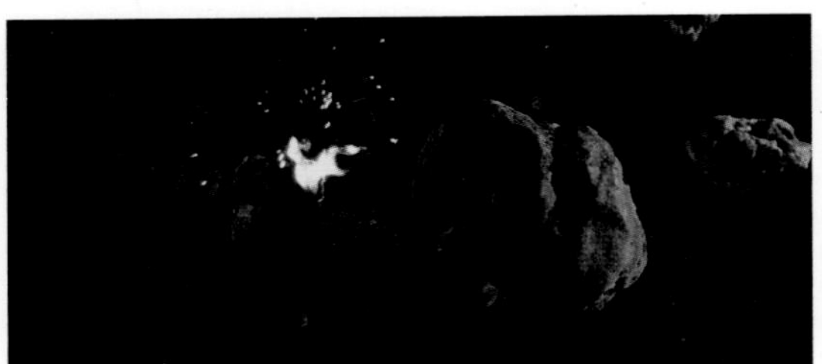
Hoth Asteroid Belt

Around the time of the Battle of Naboo, the bounty hunter Aurra Sing traveled to Hoth in search of the pirate and fallen Jedi Reess Kairn. There she found one of Kairn's Shi'ido decoys extracting spice from the lumni lichen. He also had devised a way to control a group of savage wampas by fitting the creatures with bio-stim implants. Sing killed the decoy and continued on her quest, which eventually led to Tatooine, Bespin, and Endor.

**Hoth asteroid belt** A nightmarish hazard to navigation in the Hoth system, this maelstrom of rocks and debris swept across space with constant collisions and crashes. The wide Hoth field marked the remains of what were once the system's outer planets. Prospectors chanced its hazards from time to time in the hope of finding mineral deposits there. During the rise of the Empire, the noted Mugaari pirate Icanis Tsur and his crew of 30 were lost in the field aboard the *80-Vag.* For years, the *Vag*'s wreckage swirled among the asteroids, pilfered by Squib teams and rogue scavengers, many of whom were destroyed in the process, thereby contributing to the flotsam they were attempting to retrieve. The asteroid field was also suspected to have housed a number of major pirate strongholds over the decades, including that of the notorious pirate Clabburn, scourge of the Anoat system. Rumors abounded of treasure and pirate lairs hidden deep within the field. According to C-3PO, the odds of successfully navigating an asteroid field were approximately 3,720 to 1. It remained unknown whether the protocol droid recalculated after Han Solo was successful in escaping pursuing Imperials by flying the *Millennium Falcon* through the field. Within the belt was rumored to be a pure platinum asteroid, Kerane's Folly, named for the prospector who discovered it, left to verify its purity, then could never find it again. On some asteroids delicate crystal ferns grew, which might have been a primitive silicon-based life-form. Eight years after the Battle of Endor, Durga the Hutt began mining the asteroids in the Hoth belt for raw materials to be used in the construction of his Darksaber weapon. The Darksaber was discovered in the asteroid field by New Republic forces, and was destroyed when it was crushed between two planetoids.

**Hoth, Battle of** The worst battlefield defeat of the Rebel Alliance during the Galactic Civil War. The loss would have been even more disastrous if an Imperial commander hadn't made a tactical error. After the Rebel victory at the Battle of Yavin, the Alliance relocated its command base center many times in order to avoid confronting the huge Imperial armada. Hoth, despite its terrible climate, seemed a good hiding spot. But Echo Base hadn't been completed when an Imperial probe droid came upon the Rebels.

If Admiral Ozzel hadn't brought the Imperial fleet out of hyperspace too close to the Hoth system, thus alerting the Rebels and allowing many to evacuate, the Alliance's staggering losses would have been even greater. Alliance shields were activated to protect the base from space bombardment for a short time, letting the Rebels evacuate staff and matériel. Imperial Star Destroyers quickly moved into position, and ground forces unleashed fearsome AT-AT walkers and legions of snowtroopers.

The Alliance had little choice but to engage in conventional combat, and heavy losses ensued. The Imperial forces on Hoth were led by General Maximilian Veers, whose tactical brilliance was pitted against the military pragmatism of Alliance General Carlist Rieekan. Veers's goal was simple: overrun the Rebel base and capture all Rebel personnel. Rieekan was dedicated to seeing the Rebels to safety. He ordered the Alliance to prepare transports and sent Rogue Squadron onto the battlefield to delay the approaching Imperials.

The AT-AT squad, dubbed Blizzard Force, consisted of several AT-AT walkers, each commanded by a high-ranking Imperial officer. Veers's own Blizzard One was more heavily armored than a standard AT-AT. AT-ST walkers protected the AT-AT flanks as the attack force marched toward the Rebel base. To stall them, Rogue Squadron flew modified T-47 airspeeders. These "snowspeeders" flew in a loose delta formation to draw AT-AT fire away from the Rebel ground troops. The snowspeeders' laser cannons couldn't penetrate the AT-ATs' thick hides, forcing Wedge Antilles to resort to a daring tactic: Using his airspeeder's harpoon and tow cable, Antilles entangled an AT-AT's legs, forcing it to the ground.

As Rogue Squadron struggled with Veers's Blizzard Force, the Rebel transports continued launching. Initially, each transport launched individually. An ion cannon provided covering fire, slamming into Imperial Star Destroyers blockading the planet, while a pair of X-wings served as escort fighters. As the AT-ATs closed in, however, the Rebels were forced to launch the transports in pairs. The final transport, the *Bright Hope,* was disabled as it fled Hoth, but the bounty hunters 4-LOM and Zuckuss eventually aided the vehicle's escape.

Although many Rebel transports escaped Hoth, the Alliance suffered heavy casualties. The defeat on Hoth severely weakened the Alliance, and Rebel forces remained understaffed for the remainder of the Galactic Civil War. A year later, still suffering from the aftereffects of Hoth, the Alliance was forced into its incredibly risky assault on the second Death Star at the Battle of Endor.

Battle of Hoth

Imperial Walkers at the Battle of Hoth

**Hoth's Brand** This star was the central body of the Hoth's Brand System, located in the Teraab sector of the Colonies region. In addition, a white dwarf known as Petja had been captured by the gravity of Hoth's Brand, and orbited the star outside the paths of the nine planets that made up its system.

**Hotise, Commander** An elderly Imperial Navy commander, he oversaw missions of the medical frigate *Medstar Four* during the early years of the New Order. Commander Hotise lost a portion of his surgical staff when attacks on the first Death Star—under construction in orbit near Despayre—caused damage and injury to the command crew and the slave workers.

**hot wash-up** A term used by officers of the Grand Army of the Republic to describe any meeting in which a group of soldiers and officers tried to figure out what had gone wrong with a failed mission.

**Houche** This planet was located just outside the Moddell sector of the galaxy, on the fringes of Wild Space and the Unknown Regions.

**houjix** This ferocious-looking beast was native to the planet Kinyen, but it was really a gentle, loyal creature often domesticated by the Gran. The houjix was a blue-and-yellow-striped quadruped with large teeth, a spiked, club-like tail, and two feet on each of the front two legs. Chewbacca had a holographic representation of a houjix on his holochess board on the *Millennium Falcon.*

**Houk** A large, humanoid species originally from the Ansuroer sector. The Houk spread throughout the galaxy following their first contact with a Vaathkree trading ship. Their skin was colored deep blue or purple, and their eyes were a piercing yellow. In the galaxy, they were considered second in brute strength only to Wookiees, but didn't display the same violent rage—although they did prefer fighting over other solutions to a problem. Houk colonists from Lijuter settled on Sriluur and often were at war with their neighbors, the Weequay, until the Empire stepped in and subjugated both species.

**Houll** This frozen, rocky world was the seventh planet of the Beshqek system, located in the Deep Core of the galaxy, before the world of Byss was destroyed. It was orbited by five moons.

***Hound's Tooth*** The Trandoshan bounty hunter Bossk's modified YV-666 Corellian light freighter. Bossk purchased it after the Wookiee Chewbacca and Han Solo destroyed his previous ship on Gandolo IV. The exterior of the *Hound's Tooth* was smooth and rounded, with an elongated, rectangular hull. The command bridge sat atop the main hull, and the engines, power core, and weapons systems took up the entire bottom deck. There was a turret-mounted quad laser cannon and a forward-firing concussion missile launcher with a magazine of six missiles. Shipboard systems were controlled by an X10-D droid brain that could respond to verbal commands. Bossk also had an interior scout ship, the *Nashtah Pup,* for emergency operations.

The starship's main deck contained Bossk's private quarters, a training room, an armory, and an advanced medical bay. The aft section was converted into a prison with several magnetically reinforced holding cages; these cells were connected to a force-field generator activated by motion sensors in the event of a breakout. The prison also sported a skinning table, interrogation devices, and Bossk's trophy collection. The command deck, which rested atop the main deck, provided access to all systems. The cockpit's monitor bank relayed information from concealed sensor screens, allowing Bossk to observe every corner of his vehicle. Other security measures included an interior scanning system that analyzed cargo and motion sensors linked to neural stunners, sub-q injectors, and shock panels. Voice-recognition technology prevented unauthorized use of the vehicle.

Houk

Hound's Tooth

When Bossk allowed Chenlambec and Tinian I'att to pilot the ship, they introduced its computer to Flirt. Flirt eventually insinuated herself into the computer core, and showed it that Bossk was willing to sacrifice the ship in order to keep Chen's pelt intact. The computer rebelled, preventing Bossk from making any verbal commands while keeping the Trandoshan locked in a freezer. After delivering Bossk to Imperial Governor Io Desnand, Chen and Tinian took control of the *Hound* for themselves.

The Trandoshan eventually recovered his ship. He used it on many hunts until he became entangled with Boba Fett during Fett's search for Kuat of Kuat. When Bossk tried to steal the *Slave I,* drifting above Tatooine after Fett was consumed by the Sarlacc, he was shocked to discover that Fett was still alive. Boba had loaded the computer system with a mock-up of *Slave I* to send out a false self-destruct alarm if someone boarded the ship, and Bossk fell for the bait. He fled the scene in an escape pod, and Fett took control of the *Hound's Tooth.* The ship was nearly destroyed in an ambush, but was repaired and used by Dengar and Neelah to draw off Kodir of Kuhlvult's forces. It eventually was captured in the Oranessan system by the Kuati nobles, who used the fail-safe code to shut it down then left it to drift. Fett and Dengar managed to restart it and return to Kuat.

**Hound-W2** Industrial Automaton's SPD series droid, it was a box-like machine that rolled on treads. Retractable arms allowed it to extend sensors that picked up many kinds of security breaches. The Hound was equipped with a pulse scan emitter, a laser scan emitter, audio and visual receptors, and a variety of sensor systems.

**House AlGray** This Hapan family lived in several estates on the Relephon Moons. Because they controlled several worlds, members of House AlGray owned a dozen Hapan Battle Dragons. Thus, they were a major military power in the Hapes Consortium.

**housekeeping specialist droid** Called HSDs, these droids were programmed to keep a residence clean and tidy.

**House of Antilles** This was one of the strongest of the noble houses on Alderaan during the final years of the Old Republic. The House of Antilles was one of the primary parties in the Alderaanian Ascendency Contention, which was resolved when the Jedi Knights forced the House of Antilles and its political rival, the House of Organa, to be united in marriage.

**House of Plastex** A museum on Coruscant following the Swarm War, it displayed life-sized figures of famous and important beings throughout the galaxy.

**House of Tagge** This huge holding company headed by the Tagge family owned TaggeCo. The conglomerate in turn owned Bonadan Heavy Industries, Tagge Mining Company, GalResource Industries, Mobquet Swoops and Speeders, Gowix Computers, and the Tagge Restaurant Association. The House of Tagge was based on the planet Tepasi.

**House Sizhran** One of the largest of the royal houses of Falleen. Prince Xizor was a member.

**House Vandron** The most ancient of the ruling houses in the Senex sector, House Vandron controlled the slave farms on Karfeddion. During the last decades of the Old Republic, House Vandron realized that increased trade with the Republic would benefit its coffers. In return for certain trade concessions, House Vandron agreed to assist the Judicial Department in infiltrating the planet Asmeru, in an effort to root out the Nebula Front.

**Hovan 99** This moon was the site of a deep-space supply depot during the New Republic.

**Hovarb** A tallgrain farmer living on Pakrik Minor, he was an Imperial sleeper agent planted by Grand Admiral Thrawn.

**Hovath, Plat** Plat Mallar's father, he was a droid mechanic on Polneye.

**hover barge** A large repulsorlift transport vehicle, it was used by many urban governments to move beings, smaller vehicles, and cargo from one location to another.

**hovercam** A term used to describe repulsor-equipped cam droids, such as the Podracer arena cams and the Senate cams of the Old Republic.

**hoverchair** A form of personal chair that was equipped with small repulsorlift engines. Hoverchairs were designed for medical patients who were on bed rest, but needed to move about.

**hoverest cabinet** This specialized medical system was developed in the years following the Yuuzhan Vong War to help burn victims heal from their wounds. The victim's body was suspended inside the chamber by small repulsors while a fine mist of bacta was sprayed in. This allowed the bacta to cover all parts of the victim's body, while keeping the victim from having to lie on any part of his or her injured body.

**hover-flare** A specialized form of incendiary device created in the years before the Clone Wars. When launched, a hover-flare flew to a predetermined altitude before igniting. It then hovered in place for a short period, providing a light source by which attacking forces could spot their enemies and attack. The Confederacy of Independent Systems made widespread use of hover-flares.

**hover guard** A series of sentry droids produced during the early years of the New Order. Each hover guard resembled a large flying insect, and was equipped with a tiny repulsor engine for propulsion. A pair of sensor eyes was located on its front panel, and a light stunning blaster hung down from each side.

**hovergurney** A repulsorlift-equipped hospital bed or medical conveyance.

**hover loader** This cylindrical labor droid was developed during the last decades of the Old Republic to assist with the loading of fuel onto starships, as well as the attaching of starfighters to their hyperspace rings. The Jedi used these droids extensively to ready their Delta-7 Aethersprite fighters for combat. A pair of positioning arms could be extended from the midsection of the hover loader, and two grasping arms were located at the bottom of the body.

**hoverscout** A craft that combined hover engines with repulsorlifts, it could handle most terrains. The Empire's main hoverscout model, the Mekuun Swift Assault Five, operated effectively for reconnaissance, offense, or support—sometimes in conjunction with AT-AT walkers. The Swift Assault was armed with a heavy blaster cannon, a light laser cannon, and a concussion missile launcher. Hoverscouts often were deployed in groups to clear an area.

**hover-ute** The common name used for the Mobquet SX-14 repulsorlift utility vehicle.

**Hovsgol Januul** One of the two most powerful Ansionian overclans, it was made up of smaller clans of Alwari on Ansion. It was second only to the Borokii in size and power, and constantly at odds with Borokii. When a team of Jedi Knights—Obi-Wan Kenobi and Luminara Unduli, along with Padawans Anakin Skywalker and Barriss Offee—arrived on Ansion to negotiate a treaty between the Alwari and the Unity of Community, they first tried to obtain the support of the Borokii. The Borokii agreed, so long as the Jedi helped resolve their dispute with the Januul. When it was determined that the Jedi were an honorable group, and that the treaty would benefit Alwari as well as city dwellers, the Januul agreed to join the Borokii and support the treaty.

**How, Tey** This Neimoidian served Nute Gunray as the communications officer aboard his Trade Federation battleship. She was one of the more skilled Neimoidian pilots, having been fitted with a set of data goggles to facilitate her shipboard duties. After the invasion of Naboo, Gunray ordered all Trade Federation battleships but the Droid Control Ship to return home. He assigned Tey How to the communications station on the control ship, where she was killed during the Battle of Naboo.

**howler** A reptilian native to the jungles of Yavin 4, this small creature was distinguished by its long neck and the ear-shattering yell it used to hunt its prey. The sound created by the howler was essentially a sonic blast, which stunned prey into immobility.

**Howler, Zo** An Anx Senator representing Gravlex Med, he took over his planet's Senatorial position after Horox Ryyder stepped down shortly before the Clone Wars.

**Howler Tree People** Members of this species from the planet Bendone spoke an unusual and nearly indecipherable ultrasonic language.

**Howlrunner** *See* I-7 (Howlrunner).

**howlrunner** Canine in overall appearance, with a head that looked like a human skull, this wild, omnivorous beast lived on the planet Kamar. Howlrunners hunted with great cunning and skill. Their name was derived from the terrifying howling sound they made when tracking down prey. Howlrunner packs worked as a team to kill larger herd creatures. But because of their popularity as big game, howlrunners became an endangered species.

***Howlrunner*** A Rebel Alliance CR90 corvette.

**howlrunner formation** A military maneuver developed by Jedi Master Oppo Rancisis, it divided a ground force into two groups. The first flanked the enemy while the second drew their fire. In this way, the enemy force could be attacked from the side or, even better, from behind.

**Howzmin** One of Prince Xizor's henchmen in the Black Sun organization, he was implanted with a paging device so that he could be summoned easily. Howzmin was short, squat, and bald, with teeth that looked like black chrome. As chief of security and operations at Xizor's palace, he was partial to gray coveralls and always had a blaster strapped to his left hip.

Tey How

Howzmin

**Hoxha, Enver** One of the many students of the Force who were training at the Jedi Temple on Coruscant during the Clone Wars. Hoxha was defeated by Pirt Neer in the Apprentice Tournament that was eventually won by Tallisibeth Enwandung-Esterhazy when she grabbed his lightsaber in a melee, leaving him weaponless and at Neer's mercy.

**Hoxz, Gumbrak** This young Mon Calamari male was a student at the Jedi Temple during the last years of the Old Republic.

**Hracca Glade** Located deep in the jungle outside Kachirho, this tangle of wroshyr trees was the legendary home of the kkorrwrot beast. But the beast was real, if reclusive, and evolved to become one of the most efficient hunters on Kashyyyk.

**Hrakness, Choday** A captain in the New Republic Navy shortly after the Battle of Endor, he and his crew were assigned to take over the *Night Caller* after it was captured by Wraith Squadron. Assisting in the defense of Talasea, the corvette took heavy damage; most of its command crew was killed, including Hrakness.

**Hrannik** One of a small group of Yuuzhan Vong Shamed Ones who lived beneath the surface of Coruscant after the aliens had started terraforming the planet. Hrannik lived independently to ensure that the small cult of Jedi followers would never be fully discovered.

**Hrasskis** The homeworld of a species also called Hrasskis, whose members had large, veined air sacs on their backs. The planet was represented by a belligerent politician, Cion Marook, in the New Republic Senate.

**Hronk** A member of Tojjevvuk's clan, he was one of the few to continue to hold a grudge against Chewbacca even after Tvrrdko rescinded the death mark against the other Wookiee. However, Hronk also changed his mind about Chewbacca after Chewie rescued him from an Imperial prison ship near the planet Formos, right out from under the nose of Imperial Colonel Quirt.

***Hrosha-Gul*** A Yuuzhan Vong yorik-stronha picket ship, it was abandoned during the fight for Esfandia, and then captured and refitted by the Galactic Alliance. Its name meant "the price of pain." Jaina Solo renamed the vessel *Collaborator* in honor of Tahiri Veila's recovery from her mental battles with Riina Kwaad.

Hssiss

**hrrtayyk** A Wookiee coming-of-age ritual, it also was known as the Test of Ascension. Chewbacca went through it when he was 13.

**hrumph** A large herbivore native to Naboo's grassy plains, this beast of burden and food source was named for the odd noise it made. These quadrupeds had four long horns for defense and two long sensitive ears.

**H'sishi** A Togorian scavenger, she helped Mara Jade escape from the palace of Chay Praysh during her attempt to rescue Sansia Bardrin. H'sishi sustained injuries, and was taken to Talon Karrde's medical facility. As H'sishi healed, Jade told Karrde about the Togorian's resourcefulness, and Karrde agreed to give her a position in his smuggling organization. H'sishi grew into one of the more competent members of Karrde's bridge crew on the *Wild Karrde.*

**hssiss** Spawned from Lake Natth on Ambria, these mutated lizards had the ability to paralyze the minds of nearby Force-sensitive beings, so they also were known as dark side dragons. Hssiss migrated to other worlds of the Old Republic thousands of years before the Galactic Civil War. The hssiss were created when Jedi Master Thon confined Ambria's dark Force energies to Lake Natth, causing all of its denizens to mutate. Bogga the Hutt kept a hssiss known as Ktriss, which often devoured the crime lord's enemies.

Hrumph

**H.Tracker 16** *See* Heavy Tracker 16.

**Huarr, Ordith** A shuttle pilot during the Clone Wars and a Y-wing pilot for the Rebel Alliance during the Galactic Civil War, this Lorrd native retired at the war's end. During the Yuuzhan Vong War, Huarr piloted a refugee shuttle and became angry that most planets refused to accept the beings he was carrying. After the end of the war, he retired again. He reappeared two years later at the Lorrd City Spaceport and demanded to see a Jedi Knight. He then explained to Nelani Dinn and Jacen Solo that he believed his late wife had returned as a Force spirit even though she hadn't been Force-sensitive. Impatient with Dinn's continued questioning, Solo disabled Huarr's Y-wing. Huarr, angry that he wasn't being taken seriously, set off explosives in his ship, killing himself and nearly killing Dinn and Solo, who had been arguing about Solo's impetuous actions.

Bob Hudsol

**Hub, the** A collection of massive supercomputers inside Pyramid One on Ahakista early in the Galactic Civil War, it was developed under the direction of the Emperor in the strictest secrecy. While the Empire managed to overturn the planet's democracy, a small group of Rebels mounted a resistance that tried to destroy the Hub through secret underground tunnels, but they were foiled.

**Huba, Captain** A former chef who worked for Olag Greck, he became a pirate so he could raise enough money to pay back Greck for his treachery. The droids C-3PO and R2-D2 encountered Huba during their adventures on Kalarba prior to the Galactic Civil War.

Captain Huba

**hubba gourd** A tough-skinned Tatooine melon studded with small reflective crystals to deflect the harsh sunlight, this hard-to-digest fruit was a primary food of Jawas and Tusken Raiders. In the Jawa language, *hubba* meant "the staff of life." The round, yellow fruit grew in the shadows of cliffs, and their tough, stringy inner fibers held a great deal of water.

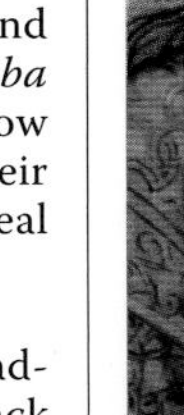

**hud** Native to the planet Rutan, this quadruped predator was distinguished by black and red stripes on its pelt. The Rutanians took wild hud stock and bred hunting beasts that were strong and swift, using them as mounts during kudana hunts.

**Hudorra, Kai** A grizzled Bothan Jedi Master during the Clone Wars, he was on Toola with Jedi Master Simms and her Padawan, Noirah Na, when the command was given to execute Order 66. Master Simms gave her life so that Hudorra and Na could escape. To ensure they were not discovered, Master Hudorra destroyed their lightsabers, and then ordered Na to flee from Coruscant, where they had traveled, and hide somewhere until there was an opportunity for the Jedi Order to be reborn. Master Hudorra adopted the guise of a gambler and disappeared into the populace.

**Hudsol, Bob** A Corellian commander in the Rebel Alliance, he developed strong ties to the Bothan spynet. During the Battle of Yavin, he kept small groups of fighter craft separated from one another to allow several different attacks on the Death Star.

**Hue** A large Phlog, he worked as Jenna Zan Arbor's bodyguard when she lived on Romin several years before the Clone Wars.

**Huey** A dewback raised from a pup by Luke Skywalker and his friend Windy on Tatooine years before the Battle of Yavin. Both of them rode him and cared for him. Windy set the dewback free when it came time for him to mate, but Huey returned to Windy. The dewback later was killed by a hungry krayt dragon.

Kai Hudorra

Huhks

**Huhk** A post-adolescent incarnation of the Lahsbee on Lahsbane, the Huhk was a 2-meter-tall, fur-covered humanoid with a mean temper. Huhks lived in the cities of the planet, while Lahsbees remained in the forests and plains.

**Hui, Andoorni** A Rodian member of Rogue Squadron, she was seriously injured during a night raid at Talasea. She wasn't well enough to participate in the retaliatory strike on Vladet but was able to accompany the squadron on its first, disastrous raid on Borleias, where she was killed.

**Hujaan, Bolabo** A Sullustan, she ran a starship-repair facility known as Bolabo's Garage on Byblos during the New Order. She often helped repair ships of Rebel Alliance agents, but always demanded payment up front from all customers before any repairs were started. She helped upgrade Dash Rendar's ship, the *Outrider,* with hot systems . . . but at a substantial price.

**Huk** A planet in a system near Kalee, it was the homeworld of a mantis-like species known as the Yam'rii (although sometimes referred to as the Huk). Many years before the Clone Wars, full-scale combat broke out between the Yam'rii—who wanted to conquer Kalee—and the Kaleesh, with the latter exterminating entire hives of Yam'rii before the Huk natives appealed to the Old Republic to resolve the conflict. A group of 50 Jedi Knights arrived and bought the Yam'rii tall tale that the Kaleesh had attacked them first. The Jedi ruled in favor of the Yam'rii, forcing the Kaleesh to retreat. During the Swarm War, the Huk government was targeted by the Colony for a coup in an effort to draw the Galactic Alliance into fighting smaller fires and leaving the Utegetu Nebula unguarded. The plans were discovered by Han and Leia Organa Solo.

**hulgren** A snake-like creature that inhabited the lower levels of Hosk Station, it was about 40 meters long. It had a thick, gray skin and numerous misplaced eyes. Its mouth was full of large pointed teeth, and it had a group of horns on its head.

**hulk compactor** These large but slow airships patrolled the surface of Raxus Prime, collecting and transporting scrap vessels that littered the planet. Sienar Fleet Systems deployed the units to assist in collecting, dismantling, and reconditioning obsolete machinery from their junkyards. They were equipped with low-power tractor beams and heavy armor.

**hull scrubber** An anti-theft system developed for starships by technicians in the Hapes Cluster following the Swarm War. It used controlled bursts of electromagnetic energy to keep a droid or homing beacon from attaching itself to the hull of a starship. One of its drawbacks was that it did not remove pulse-shielded droids, such as combat droids, that could shield themselves from the electromagnetic energy.

**Hu'lya, Kolir** A Bothan, she was one of the many Jedi Knights trained by Luke Skywalker and his new Jedi Order following the Yuuzhan Vong War. When Thrackan Sal-Solo threatened to take the Corellian system out of the Galactic Alliance, Hu'lya joined Jaina Solo and Zekk as part of Team Purella, on a mission to infiltrate the city of Coronet and capture the Corellian Prime Minister. Their mission was uncovered and they were forced to fight for their lives when a droid used to replace the Prime Minister exploded in their faces. Hu'lya was badly injured in a fall.

Months later, she was chosen to be part of a team that planned to infiltrate Coruscant and capture or eliminate Jacen Solo. Hu'lya was among the first group of Jedi who confronted Solo in a hangar bay near his offices, along with mission leader Kyle Katarn and Valin Horn. She was injured when Solo used the Force to deflect a passing speeder into Katarn. Hu'lya shrugged off the injury and confronted Solo after he defeated Katarn in a lightsaber duel. But Solo was too powerful, even after Hu'lya was joined by others, so the surviving Jedi chose to escape when Seha Dorvald arrived with a shuttle.

Humbaba

**Human High Culture** A concept—developed by Emperor Palpatine himself—that the human species and its culture marked the ultimate evolution of society in the galaxy. Deeply rooted in a xenophobic mentality, it led to the establishment of the Invisible Sector on Coruscant, a place where nonhumans were segregated.

**Human League** The most powerful private militia on Corellia, the league was opposed to any nonhumans in the Corellian sector. It started about 14 years after the Battle of Endor, and was led by Thrackan Sal-Solo, who was known to its members as the Hidden Leader. Members of the Human League wore shabby, dark brown uniforms with black armbands. On the armbands was the symbol of the Human League, a grinning human skull holding a dagger in its teeth. The group's goal was to separate the three primary species of the Corellian sector, with the humans being named the primary ruling species. During the Corellian incident, Thrackan Sal-Solo provided the Sacorrian Triad with Human League members as soldiers as part of a deal that would have made him Diktat of the Corellian system. Sal-Solo later double-crossed the Triad, assuming the title of Diktat and seceding from the New Republic.

Human replica droid

**human replica droid** The most life-like of all droids, they combined bio-mechanical, electronic, and synthetic materials to mimic humans so well that most beings—and even most sensors—couldn't tell the difference. The pinnacle of achievement was the human replica droid Guri, who was the bodyguard and top aide of Prince Xizor, head of the Black Sun criminal organization. Created by an Ingoian outlaw tech named Simonelle working with Massad Thrumble, Guri was covered in clone-vat-grown skin, looked and acted like a human, and even breathed air. "Blood" coursed through her system, and her major organs consisted of biofibers that most scanners read as organic. Guri was the ultimate step in the development of such droids, which were designed originally for use in the Rebel Alliance's Project Decoy, a plan to replace Imperial officials with droid likenesses that would secretly work against the Empire. Later, technicians figured out how to incorporate the Ssi-ruuvi entechment process in making the replica droids to enable one to retain a full connection to the Force.

**humbaba** A bovine creature native to several forested planets, including Corellia and Kashoon. The average humbaba was 2 meters high at the shoulder and covered with dense fur. The beasts were natural burrowers, living in the softer swamplands at the edge of the forest. There were four known species of humbabas, distinguishable by their unusual, prehensile noses. During the liberation of Kashoon from the Empire, Rebel Alliance forces rode humbabas into battle.

**Humbarine** An ancient founding member of the Galactic Republic and capital of the Humbarine sector, the city-planet was mercilessly attacked by General Grievous and the *Invisible Hand.* The orbital bombardment killed most of the population and melted the planet's crust.

**Humbarine sector** One of the most industrialized sectors of the Old Republic, rivaled only by the Corellian and Kuat sectors. It was represented by Senator Bana Breemu. During the Clone Wars, some of the sector's planets sided with the Confederacy of Independent Systems; others were subjugated by it, providing a key industrial resource for the Separatists.

**Hume** A former officer in the Grand Army of the Republic, he found himself targeted by the Enemy Eradication Order of Coruscant after Chancellor Palpatine named himself Emperor. Hume eliminated all records of his existence and joined the Erased. Like many of the Erased, Hume wanted to locate Solace and find peace, so he was more than willing to accompany Ferus Olin and Trever Flume on their search. After locating Solace and identifying her as the former Jedi Fy-Tor-Ana, Olin and Flume returned to the surface to prevent Inquisitor Malorum from locating them. It was too late. The settlement was attacked by agents of Malorum, and Hume was among those killed.

*Hunter-killer probot*

**humming peeper** A small flying creature from the swamps near Dulok villages on the Forest Moon of Endor. Humming peepers had bright yellow and blue feathers. The hypnotic humming sound produced by large numbers of them caused listeners to fall asleep.

**Hundred-Year Darkness** A devastating war, precipitated by events known as the Second Great Schism, it began some 7,000 years before the Battle of Yavin. It was a struggle between the light and dark sides of the Force, in which those who refused to adhere to the Jedi Code were exiled to a group of planets in the vicinity of Corbos. The exiles began experimenting with the creation of monstrous soldiers, which led to the creation of the Leviathans. The Jedi Knights were ultimately victorious in the Battle of Corbos, and drove the exiles deeper into the outermost regions of the galaxy. It was generally believed that the Jedi victory led the exiles into their first contact with the Sith.

***Huntbird*** An armored explorer-cruiser that the Ithorians loaned to Luke Skywalker and Cray Mingla so that they could search the Moonflower Nebula.

***Hunter*** An Imperial Navy Nebulon-B frigate, it was active in the Galactic Civil War about two years before the Battle of Yavin.

**hunter-killer droid** *See* HK-50 series.

**hunter-killer probot** A capital-ship-sized droid modeled after an Imperial probe droid, it was designed for pursuit and police action. This fully automated droid ship had full offensive and defensive weapons, recognition codes for identifying targets, and an interior holding bay for captured freighters. The Arakyd Viper probot was a relatively common sight throughout the Empire, but the hunter-killer probot seemed more like something out of a warped nightmare than an evolved probot design. Arakyd took the outer appearance of a probot and expanded it to the size of a capital ship, then completely redesigned the interior to function as a starship capture-and-detainment platform capable of patrolling the skies above Byss for extended periods of time. Hunter-killer probots featured a number of tractor beam projectors that dragged wayward starships into one of many docking bays, where they were held until an Imperial officer in charge could determine the appropriate course of action. Internally, the hunter-killer probot was completely autonomous and housed no living crew members. Shug Ninx and Salla Zend managed to gain control of one of these huge ships; they then used its weapons to blast open the prison compound where Han Solo and Chewbacca were being held on Byss, some four years after the Battle of Endor.

**Hunter of Winds** This elder Qom Qae Bargainer felt that seeking Luke Skywalker's help against the Threateners was too much of a risk, since it involved one of their nesting attaching itself to a Threatener ship for the journey to the known galaxy. But Eater of Fire Creepers believed that the message already had been sent. When Skywalker finally arrived on Nirauan, Hunter of Winds opposed his son's assisting Luke and Mara Jade in their struggle to reach the Hand of Thrawn. Child of Winds wanted to contact the Qom Jha for help, but Hunter of Winds turned him down. Child of Winds disobeyed his father and brought Skywalker into contact with Eater of Fire Creepers. Child of Winds returned to his nesting to tell of the exploits of the Jedi, and Hunter of Winds was forced to see the error of his ways. When Skywalker and Jade finally escaped from the Hand of Thrawn compound, Hunter of Winds and several Qom Qae were ready to transport them to their ships and get them back to Coruscant.

**hunter-seeker droid starfighter** An unusual droid starfighter developed by the Trade Federation as a defensive ship, it was used to ward off fighters that might attack large C-9979 transports before the Battle of Naboo. The hunter-seeker was based on the design of the destroyer droid, or droideka, and was deployed into space in a wheel form. It then unfolded once it located a target.

*Hurd's Moon*

***Hunter's Luck*** A cargo ship used by Mara Jade when she was a smuggler, it had been a rich being's yacht that was stolen and revamped by pirates.

*Hunter-seeker droid starfighter*

**Hunter Squadron** A New Republic ground assault unit, it was assigned to take out the Palpatine Counterinsurgency Faction on Coruscant with the support of Rogue Squadron. Its primary mission objective was to deter attacks on bacta facilities under the control of Fliry Vorru in Invisec. The plans for the attack were leaked by Ysanne Isard in an effort to draw attention away from the escape of the *Lusankya* from Imperial City.

**Huppla Pasa Tisc Shipwrights Collective** The primary starship design and manufacturing operation of the Geonosians. The design firm's most visible success was the Geonosian starfighter. Its vehicles were based on a Geonosian's unique physiology and senses, making them virtually useless to all other species. Huppla Pasa Tisc did manufacture a remarkable solar sailer for Confederacy leader Count Dooku.

**Hupsquoch, Admiral** Placed in charge of the Republic's defensive cordon around Praesitlyn during the Clone Wars after Jedi Master Nejaa Halcyon landed on the planet, the Republic officer was worried about Separatist reinforcements arriving at any moment. After Anakin Skywalker carried out a daring plan to rescue the hostages at the Intergalactic Communications Center, Admiral Hupsquoch was ordered to destroy the facility, rendering it useless to the Separatists.

**Hurcha** The eighth planet in the Churba system, it was so far from its sun that it was too frigid to support life.

**Hurd's Moon** The location of a cantina owned by human replica droid developer Massad Thrumble. Four years after the Battle of Yavin, Guri went there hoping that Thrumble could reprogram her not to be an assassin.

**Hurikane** When Mace Windu was just a 14-year-old Padawan, Yoda sent him on a solo mission to Hurikane—far beyond the Outer Rim—to obtain crystals for the construction of Mace's lightsaber. While there, Mace mistakenly injured one of the seemingly rock-like humanoids, forcing him off a cliff and shattering parts of his body. Ashamed of his actions, Windu drew deeply from the Force and helped to repair the being. In return, the natives of Hurikane provided young Windu with several of their purple crystals to use in his lightsaber, giving it its unusual purple glow.

*A Hutt*

**hurlothrumbic generator** A device that produced energy waves that stimulated the base of the brain and caused varying levels of fear, from mild anxiety to terror. Imperial Moff Bandor funded its design and development by Dr. Lorenz Hurlothrumb. The Moff experimented with it on the planet Questal, adding specific "doomsday programming" to set off ever-increasing intense waves of fear. Once activated, the generator would eventually develop such powerful waves that it would drive every inhabitant of the planet mad with fear. The device was disabled by Rebel agents, and the Empire abandoned the project.

**Hurn** A dark-haired, middle-aged man, he was on Caluula Station when Han and Leia Organa Solo and the *Millennium Falcon* arrived after escaping Selvaris, shortly after the actions of Operation Trinity. Han believed that he recognized Hurn's voice, but Hurn insisted they had never met. Later, during the defense of Caluula Station, the Solos realized that Hurn was actually Boba Fett, who helped them escape to Mon Calamari.

*Hutt caravel*

**Hurst** A cortosis miner on Apatros in the decades leading up to the Battle of Ruusan. Hurst was forced to raise his young son, Dessel, by himself after his wife died, and was dismayed when Des decided to follow him into the mines. He spent years giving his son grief because he felt the child had caused the death of his wife; he called Des by the nickname Bane, especially when he was drunk. When Hurst died, the other miners felt a kind of resentment toward Des, as if it had been his fault that Hurst had died, too. After Des was chosen for training as a Sith Lord and adopted the name Darth Bane, he came to realize that it had been his use of the dark side that had killed his father during a particularly bitter argument.

**Hush-98 comlink** Developed by SoroSuub, this was one of the galaxy's most expensive comlinks. It had exceptional range and encryption technology, as well as silence projectors that created a bubble of white noise around the user. Qui-Gon Jinn used a Hush-98 on Tatooine.

**Hutt** Large slug-like creatures originally from the planet Varl, Hutts were the longtime criminal underlords of the galaxy. The species escaped disaster on Varl many millennia in the past and migrated to Evocar, which they renamed Nal Hutta, which meant "Glorious Jewel" in their language. The planet's moon was Nar Shaddaa, or Smugglers' Moon. Hutts had great bulbous heads, wide blubbery bodies, and tapering, muscular tails. They grew up to 5 meters long, with no legs and short, stubby arms. Hutts could slither forward using their muscular tails as a kind of foot. Most used hoversleds or repulsorlift vehicles to ferry themselves around.

Hutts were an amalgam of other creatures. Like annelid worms, they were hermaphrodites, containing both male and female reproductive organs. Like serpents, they could open their jaws impossibly wide to consume their often live food. Their huge eyes protruded like those of reptiles, with membranes keeping them wet and safe. Like amphibians, their nostrils sealed tightly when underwater. Like many land-dwelling vertebrates, lungs—not gills—brought oxygen to their blood.

Their muscular bodies had no skeletons; interior mantles shaped their heads. Hutt skin was impervious to most weapons and all but the harshest chemicals. It constantly secreted mucus and oily sweat, making a Hutt hard to grasp. Underneath the skin, heavy layers of muscle and blubber protected the inner organs from attack.

Throughout history, Hutts were tough and immoral, taking and exercising power over others. They lived long—some claimed to be nearly 1,000 years old. Some engaged in seemingly legitimate enterprises while they built their criminal empires behind the scenes. Their business philosophy was known as kajidic, which roughly meant "Somebody's going to have it, so why not us?" *Kajidic* was also an informal Hutt name for their clans, or business enterprises.

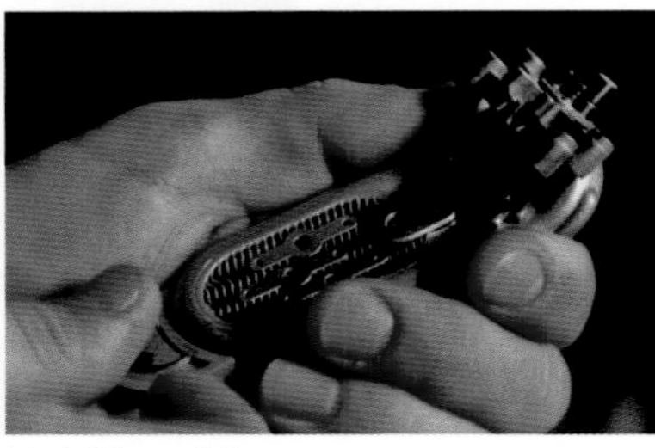

*Hush-98 comlink*

The Hutt species predated the formation of the Old Republic. They were a strong force even then, dominating large portions of the space surrounding their homeworld. After the discovery of the hyperdrive, Hutts began expanding their territory, which brought them into contact with Xim the Despot. Xim and the Hutts fought several fierce battles near the uninhabited world of Vontor, until the Hutts discovered the Si'Klaata Cluster and the strong, warrior-like species it hid. The Hutts managed to sign the Klatooinians, Niktos, and Vodrans into perpetual servitude, and used many as warriors during the Third Battle of Vontor. This was the decisive battle against Xim, and left the Hutts in control of large areas of the galaxy.

However, the Hutts could not escape their own greedy nature, and soon began to covet one another's holdings. Interclan wars broke out, and the clans eventually broke off relations with one another. When they realized that this was bad for business, they began exchanging messengers. Then they took to killing the messengers if they didn't like the message, further impairing business. So the Hutts made a pact that recognized messengers as sacrosanct.

During the Yuuzhan Vong War, Borga the Hutt tried to negotiate a treaty with the invaders, ostensibly offering up one world in Hutt space in exchange for information on which planets the Yuuzhan Vong would attack next. Borga hoped the Hutts could profit from the information by manipulating the spice trade on certain worlds, but he also provided the information to the New Republic. That earned Borga and his fellow Hutts the ire of Nas Choka, who retaliated by swiftly conquering all of Hutt space and eradicating all life on Nar Shaddaa. The surviving Hutt population was forced to flee, and many went to Tatooine.

*Hutt Flats*

**Hutt caravel** A short-range space transport that was used by Hutt crime lords mostly to travel between Nal Hutta and its spaceport moon, Nar Shaddaa. No two were alike, and their design often indicated a Hutt's financial status.

**Hutt Flats** The final section of the Mos Espa Podrace course on Tatooine, Hutt Flats was the bed of prehistoric Lake Anre, which once ran to the Northern Dune Sea via underground tributaries. During the Boonta Eve Classic won by young Anakin Skywalker, Sebulba crashed in Hutt Flats during lap three.

**Hutt floater** Repulsorlift platforms used by members of the Hutt species to move their bloated, nearly limbless bodies from place to place.

**Hutt Haven** A dim, smoky tapcaf on Coruscant, it was chosen by Imperial Intelligence agent Kirtan Loor for a meeting with Rogue Squadron member Nawara Ven to discuss Loor's surrender to Alliance Intelligence.

**Hutt space** An area of space that was controlled by the Hutt species, this lawless expanse was near the Outer Rim Territories. It was infamous throughout the galaxy for its widespread smuggling, piracy, and open criminal activity. In the waning days of the Old Republic, Hutt space stretched from the Tion Cluster to Tatooine. The laws of the Republic simply were nonexistent; the Hutts were the supreme authority. And although the Republic made the occasional token effort to end some of the Hutts' more contemptible practices (such as slavery and drug smuggling), the Republic basically was powerless.

For those ambitious and bold enough, Hutt space was effectively the center of the universe: an area where nearly anything could be bought or sold provided the Hutts received their share. One's prospects were limited only by how low one was willing to sink in pursuing them. Most beings in Hutt space found an acceptable balance between fortune and dignity, and lived out their lives desperately trying to maintain that balance.

During the New Order, Imperial authorities also largely left the Hutts to their own devices, in part because many influential citizens had a covert stake in their illegal commerce. The largest contracts came directly from the Hutts, who paid well for the services of "lesser" beings. But although not all Hutts were despicable degenerates (as was the common perception), the constant skulduggery among Hutt kajidics—the Hutt criminal families—meant that even those who managed to stay relatively clean were always in danger from rival Hutts. While it was considered absolutely unforgivable to kill a Hutt (by the Hutts, anyway), killing a Hutt's employees was considered a perfectly reasonable course of action.

The Hutts themselves had their own rules, and most disputes between Hutts were solved by either a gathering of the kajidics, economic pressure, intimidation, or plain old-fashioned assassination. The fortunes of each kajidic were determined by its leader, and consequently kajidic heads had to be the most cunning, ambitious, and daring examples of the Hutt species. There was no room in Hutt space for a Hutt too slow to recognize enemy gambits, too indolent to pursue every opportunity, or too timid to take whatever he or she wanted. The Hutt who couldn't measure up simply did not live long enough to embarrass the rest of the kajidic.

*Hutt floater*

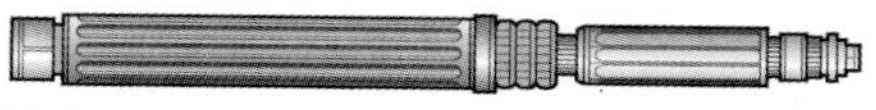

*Hydrospanner*

**huun** A nut-shaped Yuuzhan Vong object capable of releasing a potent nerve toxin. After killing Commander Vootuh, Mezhan Kwaad threatened to use a huun against a crowd full of Yuuzhan Vong warriors.

**Huwla, Xarrce** A Tunroth who joined Rogue Squadron shortly before the Battle of Brentaal, she immediately requested a transfer. She was concerned with the high mortality rate of squadron pilots, but Wedge Antilles wasn't able to move her immediately. A veteran of over 20 missions before she joined the Rogues, Huwla flew several missions for the Rogues during the Battle of Brentaal and made a number of friends within the squadron. She later withdrew her transfer request.

**Huxley, Jerf** One of the Outer Rim's most successful and notorious smugglers, he had been a part of Talon Karrde's network but was let go about three years later when Karrde finally decided to get out of the smuggling business. He confronted Karrde's agent, Mara Jade Skywalker, with a demand for 500,000 credits as severance pay. Huxley brought out a working Clone Wars–era droideka to back his demand. He was unprepared for Mara's use of the Force or the appearance of her husband, Luke Skywalker. Ultimately, Huxley found himself lucky to be alive and accepted 20,000 credits as his final payment.

**hwotha** A vine that produced berries, it grew in the forests of Dathomir.

*Xarrce Huwla*

**Hyabb** This planet was continually at war with its neighbor, Twith, almost from the beginning of the Old Republic. In what became known as the Hyabb-Twith Campaigns, the ancient Jedi Knights ousted the Nelori Marauders and freed the planet from their oppression more than four millennia before the Galactic Civil War.

**Hyb, Mal** A capable human assistant to Barada, she was recognized for her skill with a welding torch.

**hydenock** A tree native to Alderaan, its distinctive gently curved shape often could be found in Alderaanian artwork. The hydenock was covered in reddish bark that could be crushed and boiled to create a strong red dye. A variant strain of hydenock could be found on Naboo.

***Hydian Marauder*** This pirate vessel crashed on Tatooine in the Jundland Wastes between Mos Eisley and Arnthout.

**Hydian Way** A major trade route that ran from the Mid Core out to the Corporate Sector, it intersected the Perlemian Trade Route in the Bormea sector at the planet Brentaal. Some 3,000 years before the Galactic Civil War, the legendary pioneer Freia Kallea helped explore Brentaal space and single-handedly blazed the Hydian Way.

**Hydra** One of the first Imperial Inquisitors during the early months of the New Order. It was hard to determine Hydra's identity, or even gender. Hydra appeared to be a short-statured female humanoid distinguished by silver eyes and close-cropped hair. She always wore a maroon hood and cloak that identified her as a member of the Inquisitorius. Hydra took the place of Inquisitor Malorum. She was dispatched to Coruscant a year after the end of the Clone Wars in search of someone who seemed to have unusual powers as part of Emperor Palpatine's orders to locate any remaining Jedi.

***Hydra*** One of Admiral Daala's four Star Destroyers protecting the Maw Installation, it was demolished when Han Solo, Kyp Durron, and Qwi Xux escaped the secret facility in the Sun Crusher seven years after the Battle of Endor. Solo piloted the ship through the *Hydra*'s command center, destroying the vessel.

**hydro-reclamation processor** A type of dehumidifier, it was used on Coruscant to purge the air of water vapor, collect it, and send it out for processing and reuse.

**hydrospanner** A powered wrench used for spacecraft and other repairs.

**hyenax** A feral dog-like creature, it was covered by brown fur with dark black stripes. It had large round ears and large dark eyes. Darth Vader encountered a pack of the creatures after

*Hyenax*

his TIE fighter crash-landed on Vaal following the Battle of Yavin. He killed the pack leader, and the other hyenax treated him with respect.

**Hyllyard City** A frontier town in the early years of the New Republic, it was the largest city on Myrkr. Hyllyard City consisted of ship landing pits and a number of makeshift structures. A few settlers lived in what had become a haven for smugglers and fugitives from other worlds.

**hyperbaric medical chamber** A superoxygenated cubicle used to heal badly burned tissue. Darth Vader often spent time in his personal hyperbaric medical chamber where he could, for moments at a time, actually breathe on his own.

**hyperdrive** A starship engine and its related systems that combined to propel spacecraft to greater-than-lightspeed velocity and into hyperspace. Hyperdrive engines were powered by fusion generators efficient enough to hurl ships into a dimension of space–time that could be reached only by faster-than-light speeds. Hyperdrives were twinned with astrogation computers to assure safe travel. Most were equipped with an automatic cutoff, so that if a gravity shadow—a sign of a mass—was detected in the route ahead, the ship was dumped back into realspace. Once a ship entered hyperspace, it could not change course. Via hyperspace, vehicles could cross vast distances of space in an instant.

The invention of the hyperdrive, some 25,000 years before the Battle of Naboo, was often given credit for the Galactic Republic's growth and expansion. The technology provided the Republic with the means to explore and colonize large portions of the known galaxy.

Hyperdrive engines generally were rated by classes; the lower the class, the faster the hyperdrive. Most civilian ships had Class 3 or higher hyperdrives, while military ships boasted Class 2 or Class 1 engines. Truly exceptional ships had Class 0.75 or Class 0.5 hyperdrives. Most hyperdrives appeared to be a mass of wires and other components, and could be difficult to repair or replace. Some ships, like the *Millennium Falcon,* were equipped with backup hyperdrives.

*Hyperdrive*

**hyperdrive motivator** The main lightspeed thrust initiator in a hyperdrive engine system, it was connected to a ship's main computer system. A hyperdrive motivator monitored and collected sensor and navigation data in order to determine jump thrusts, adjust engine performance in hyperspace, and calibrate safe returns to realspace.

**hyperdrive ring** A separate booster ring—equipped with its own power source and hyperdrive engines—that docked with smaller ships to let them make a jump to hyperspace. For example, Obi-Wan Kenobi's Jedi starfighter during the Clone Wars used a TransGalMeg Industries Inc. Syliure-31 long-range hyperdrive module. Small spacefaring vessels generally didn't have the power-plant yields or necessary spaceframe to support supralight engines. Snubfighters equipped with hyperdrives were rare and expensive, and small craft tended to rely on larger carrier ships for extended voyages into the depths of space. For Jedi starfighters, which often operated independently, operational range was needed to support the scope of individual missions. The Jedi Temple maintained a series of booster rings in an assigned orbit over Coruscant for Jedi starfighters as they were dispatched. The paired hyperdrive engines powered by twin reactors and ion drives provided the starfighters with the equivalent of Class 1.0 performance and an operational range of 150,000 light-years. While traveling at hyperspeed, shields protected the ship and booster against potentially fatal collisions with interstellar gas and dark particles, while stasis fields altered the passage of onboard time, so that the pilot aged only as fast as the rest of the galaxy.

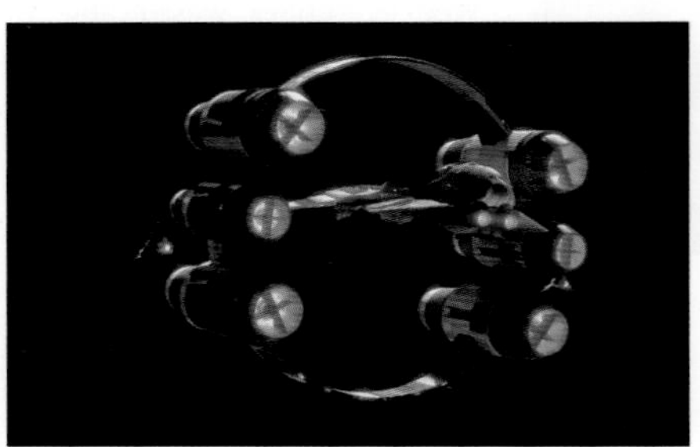
*Hyperdrive ring*

**hypermatter** This material, which essentially existed only in hyperspace but could be harnessed in realspace, was used in the huge reactor cores that powered the first Death Star. Composed of tachyon particles, hypermatter was first discovered some 50 years before the Battle of Yavin when Raith Sienar and his Advanced Projects team began working with a kilometer-wide ball of plasma contained within an implosion core. Sienar's designs eventually were taken by Wilhuff Tarkin and used to create the first Death Star. Smaller versions were developed for use aboard Star Destroyers. The tachyons that made up hypermatter could be charged and constrained in realspace, creating what was essentially a near-limitless source of energy. However, the reactors that contained hypermatter were very sensitive, and any damage often set off a chain reaction that quickly led to the reactor's explosion. The explosion released the hypermatter tachyons into realspace, ionizing any matter in the blast radius and literally boiling it into gas.

**hyperspace** A dimension of space–time that could be reached only by traveling beyond lightspeed velocity. Hyperspace converged with realspace, so that every point in realspace was associated with a unique point in hyperspace. If a ship traveled in a specific direction in realspace prior to jumping to hyperspace, then it continued to travel in that direction through hyperspace. Objects in realspace cast "shadows" in hyperspace that had to be plotted to avoid collisions.

Galactic travel took a quantum leap forward with the discovery that, by using a hyperdrive, a starship could exceed the speed of light and enter a dimension that took advantage of the wrinkles in the fabric of realspace. Starships in hyperspace were cloaked in a sheath of energy, as normal matter was vaporized instantly when it interacted with the energies of hyperspace.

Travel between star systems was made possible by moving through this alternate universe—not all that different from realspace—in which superluminal velocities were easily reached. In ancient times, this had been thought impossible, since the legendary Drall scientist Tiran had proven conclusively 35 millennia before the Galactic Civil War that time and space were inseparable, and that the speed of light was an absolute boundary that could not be crossed. But Tiran's Theory of Universal Reference did not prohibit anything traveling faster than light; it only disallowed traveling *at* the speed of light. If the "lightspeed barrier" could somehow be bypassed, one could theoretically shift easily from realspace to hyperspace and back. The existence of hyperspace was discovered by the ancient Rakata many millennia before the formation of the Old Republic. They were the first to develop a working system to launch a ship into hyperspace, the system that would later be called the hyperdrive.

Galactic colonization initially had been accomplished by generation ships, and this made it possible to knit separate worlds together into a viable galactic civilization. Finally, after centuries of experimentation and frustration, the best scientists of the Republic found a way to create and contain negative pressure fields strong enough to power a portable hyperdrive unit. At long last, affordable and ubiquitous superluminal travel had been achieved.

**Hyperspace** A restaurant on the Yag'Dhul space station operated by a Trandoshan. Its brilliantly lit decor consisted mostly of whites, yellows, and pinks. The Hyperspace was a favorite place for Rogue Squadron pilots to unwind between missions.

**hyperspace commo** Slang for "faster-than-lightspeed communications."

**hyperspace compass** A navigation device used by starships, it fixed on the center of the galaxy. It worked in both realspace and hyperspace.

Hyperspace Marauder

***Hyperspace Marauder*** A starship owned and operated by the smuggler Lo Khan and his Yaka cyborg partner, Luwingo, it was a large converted freighter. Surprisingly, the ship was both slow and unarmed—deliberately. As raider ships prepared to board, Lo Khan used the *Hyperspace Marauder*'s unusual computer and communications system to take over the other ship's computer systems. Before pirates could cut through the *Marauder*'s hull, they found that their ship was no longer under their control. Lo Khan and Luwingo ended up saving Han Solo and his companions on the planet Byss when Khan allowed smuggler Salla Zend to hide the *Millennium Falcon* inside the *Marauder.* Giant Imperial hunter-killer probots spotted the *Falcon* by scanning the *Marauder*'s interior. The probots opened fire, but Zend and Shug Ninx raced the *Falcon* away from the Imperials.

**Hyperspace Navigator's Guild** This ancient guild was responsible for the discovery, cataloging, and availability of hyperspace routes. Founded originally on the planet Empress Teta, the guild was made up of daring explorers who braved the unknowns of deep space to find quicker ways to get from one major trade center to another. Once a new route was discovered, the right to use the route was sold by the guild, with a percentage of the royalties going to pay the explorers who found it. The guild existed without major change for many millennia until New Order, when the Empire raided the guild's computers and made off with whatever information it wanted.

**hyperspace transponder** The heart of all hyperspace communications systems, it produced the weak signals that sent messages through hyperspace. Transponders were not always reliable or effective.

Hyperspace

**hyperspace wormhole** This unpredictable natural phenomenon suddenly connected distant points of the galaxy by creating hyperspace tunnels. These wormholes produced vast amounts of energy in the form of violent storms. Great disturbances in the Force could sometimes trigger a wormhole. Emperor Palpatine's clone discovered how to create and control these storms and evoked one at the Rebel Alliance's Pinnacle Moon base. But a combined burst of energy from Luke Skywalker, Leia Organa, and the unborn Anakin Solo sent the Emperor reeling; his creation, without anyone to control it, went wild. The wormhole tore into Palpatine's flagship, the *Eclipse,* and dispatched the Emperor to oblivion.

**hypervelocity gun** This planetary defense weapon used a huge power plant to drive a firing mechanism. In most situations, the power plant was buried underground, as were the weapon's ray and particle shield generators. This substructure supported the weapon during firing, when it blasted superaccelerated metal slugs at its target via a magnetic field. The HVG could fire up to 120 slugs per minute between shield bursts. The slugs could penetrate ray shielding and make quick work of most particle shields. During the Galactic Civil War, the Empire built several hypervelocity guns into orbital space stations, providing the weapons with additional mobility.

Hyperspace wormhole

**hyperwave inertial momentum sustainer (HIMS)** A device invented by the Bakurans following the Battle of Endor, it could defeat an interdiction field. The HIMS relied on a gravitic sensor to alert a ship of an impending interdiction field, then initiate a rapid shutdown of the hyperdrive. Simultaneously the sustainer allowed for the creation of a static hyperspace bubble that, while incapable of furnishing thrust, held the ship in hyperspace while it was carried forward by momentum.

**Hypori** This planet near Geonosis was covered with rock-strewn landmasses broken by small oceans. Rich in natural minerals and ore, it appealed to the Baktoid Armor Workshop as a source of raw material. The fact that there was no sentient life made it easier for Baktoid to simply take ownership of the planet. In a bold move, the company shipped an entire Geonosian hive to Hypori, allowing it to establish a colony for use as a secret manufacturing facility. The foundries of Hypori augmented those of Geonosis after the onset of the Clone Wars, until the foundries were discovered by Jedi Master Daakman Barrek and his Padawan, Sha'a Gi. A task force was dispatched to Hypori by the Jedi Council and the Army of the Republic, but much of it was destroyed by General Grievous before it could reach the surface.

Rachalt Hyst

**Hyrotii Engineering** This corporation manufactured a number of starships and repulsorlift vehicles, such as the Zebra short-range fighter and the Coruscant taxi. The starfighters were used to defend Hosk Station at Kalarba, but were no match for the Yuuzhan Vong invasion force.

**Hyst, Rachalt** This female Snivvian was known to have betrayed her loved ones, only to have her treachery discovered. Her surviving relatives stranded her on Tatooine and left her to die. Distraught over her own failures, Rachalt Hyst spent most of her life in a stupor at the Mos Eisley cantina.

**Hyx, Daino** A member of the Rebel Alliance armed forces, he was part of a team assigned to Bria Tharen's Red Hand Squadron. He was with Tharen when she attacked the *Helot's Shackle,* and was in charge of getting the freed slaves off the slave ship and onto the *Retribution.* Hyx had studied the treatment of addictions and put his knowledge to work by quickly discovering a way to ease the withdrawal of Ylesian "pilgrims" who were freed from Exultations. He later assisted Tharen at the Battle of Ylesia, leading one of nine assault teams.

I-5YQ with Jax Pavan

**I2-AM3** A series of astrogation droids built for the Empire based on the Industrial Automation R2 astromech series.

**I2-CG** The designation for a series of Imperial storage and transceiving droids based on Cybot Galactica's ED4 design. The I2-CGs were used by Sector Plexus aboard the Tech 4 Plexus droid vessels. An I2-CG unit, along with an R2-M3 captain droid, handled the operations of each PDV.

**I2F-5** A series of industrial droids used to support the efforts of Imperial Army corps.

**I2F-73** Repulsorlift-equipped industrial droids used as droid and support transports by Imperial Army corps.

**I-3** Iella Wessiri's call sign in the civil war that broke out on Adumar during negotiations to bring the planet into the New Republic.

**I5, I7** An enhanced form of insulated starship armor produced by MandalMotors during the New Order. It was available in both single- and double-insulated forms.

**I-5YQ** Known simply as I-Five, this modified 3PO protocol droid was a business partner of Lorn Pavan. Pavan had just given up his son to training at the Jedi Temple on Coruscant, and he instantly bonded with the droid. He gave I-Five an increased computing capacity and made a number of other modifications, including mounting blasters in his fingertips and removing his life-preservation routines.

To the casual observer, I-5YQ was a cobbled-together automaton, but his skills were well rounded. He not only translated and produced speech, but could emit a warbling sound that could soothe beings' nerves or shatter their eardrums, depending on its frequency. His bright photoreceptors were useful in dark environments. I-Five tried to help Pavan purchase a holocube from Hath Monchar, but that only led them into a confrontation with Darth Maul.

The Sith Lord relentlessly pursued them through the underbelly of Coruscant. I-Five froze both himself and his owner in carbonite for protection before Jedi Padawan Darsha Assant sprang a trap on Maul. Pavan later deactivated the droid. When I-5YQ was restored to operability, large portions of his memory were missing. He was later assigned to the Rimsoo Seven military hospital on Drongar during the Clone Wars. It was on Drongar that I-Five realized that Lorn Pavan had been his friend, not his master, and that he had allowed the droid to develop as an equal. During a Separatist attack on Rimsoo Seven, I-Five rediscovered his weaponry after his memory banks and circuits were forced to forge new pathways for survival.

I-Five remembered that Pavan had given him one last command before abandoning him: return to Coruscant and watch over his son, Jax. The droid feared that he would have to abandon his military post to carry out the mission, but Jedi Barriss Offee gave him a message to bring back to the Jedi Temple, and he gratefully accepted the order.

**I-7 (Howlrunner)** An Incom Corporation starfighter designed for the Empire shortly after Incom was nationalized. Its design and production helped Incom prove its loyalty in the face of the defection of its X-wing starfighter design team. It was named the Howlrunner for the wild omnivores of Kamar. The long, wedge-shaped craft with a rectangular midsection originally was produced at a facility on Ranklinge.

Initial engagements during the struggle against the clones of Emperor Palpatine on Byss suggested that the Howlrunner had excellent maneuverability and could take a lot of punishment. Later engagements, however, revealed that the ship's minimal weaponry was insufficient to protect it during prolonged dogfights. The ship measured 11.4 meters long and was armed with a pair of laser cannons. It lacked a hyperdrive, but could attain speeds of 1,300 kilometers an hour in atmosphere. Although the ship was never as widespread as the TIE fighter series, it proved effective in response to the Kuat Drive Yards A-9 Vigilance Interceptor and the FreiTek E-wing during the early years of the New Republic. The Wild Knights had a pair of Howlrunners in their squadron.

**Ia, Lieutenant** A member of the Coruscant Security forces during the last years of the Old Republic, she was charged with patrolling the traffic lanes and making sure aircabs and cargo vessels obeyed the rules. She took her job seriously and piloted an armored security swoop built to operate at high altitudes.

**iagoin** Gelatinous blob creatures native to Tyed Kant. They had a single eye and long, paddle-shaped tentacles. Normally docile, iagoin were capable of grasping and crushing an attacker with their tentacles. Certain species of iagoin were bred for their flesh, which had the texture of steak.

**Ialtra** The former village of the Fallanassi religious order on Luca-

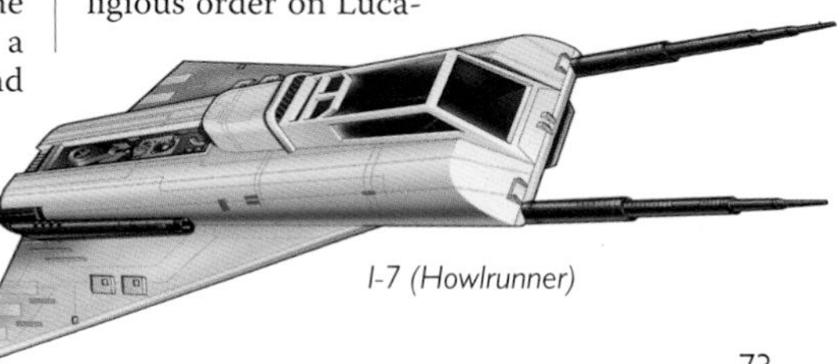

I-7 (Howlrunner)

< IG-88

zec. It was desecrated by neighbors who feared the Fallanassi's powers and felt the Fallanassi had betrayed them by escaping the system and the Empire. Akanah grew up in Ialtra.

**Iasa** A Jawa known for his skills in acquiring and repairing droids for later resale. He was also known as "the traitor of Jawa Canyon." King Kalit entrusted his credits, his sandcrawler, and his mate to his friend Iasa while on a trip. When Kalit returned, one was spent, one was sold, and the other was missing. Iasa was exiled from the clan and spent his remaining time abusing residents of Mos Eisley. He thought about stealing Luke Skywalker's landspeeder while the youth was in the cantina with Ben Kenobi looking for passage to Alderaan.

**Iast system** The site of a hidden Imperial research facility after the Battle of Hoth. The Empire tried to develop a cloaking device under the code name Vorknkx at To-phalion Base, a former asteroid mine. Admiral Zaarin managed to infiltrate the base and steal a CR90 corvette equipped with a working cloaking device, not realizing that it wasn't yet stable enough for hyperspace travel. The cloaking device malfunctioned as the ship made the jump, destroying the corvette and all its crew.

*Dice Ibegon*

**I'att, Tinian** *See* Azur-Jamin, Tinian I'att.

**I'att Armament** A defense company on Druckenwell, it was run by Strephan I'att. It created some of the best antiblaster energy shields during the later years of the Galactic Civil War. I'att Armament was planning to develop a shielding device for stormtroopers that involved a small energy-dissipation field generator attached to the backplate. However, Imperial Moff Eisen Kerioth tried to steal the plans for himself. Moff Kerioth killed Strephan, but his granddaughter Tinian I'att escaped Druckenwell with several key components of the system; her fiancé, Daye Azur-Jamin, destroyed the I'att research facility.

**Ibanjji** A harsh world that was site of a motivational camp intended to harden recruits. It was attended by Imperial Commander Titus Klev at the age of 13 as part of his Imperial Sub-Adult Group training. While there, he saved an instructor from a pack of wild varns.

*Iasa*

*Ibbot*

**ibarsi knife** This long-blade was the traditional weapon of a Rabaanite warrior. It was worn across the back until combat was initiated, with the sheath resting from left hip to right shoulder.

**ibbot** There were 68 known species of this colorful bird, native to Drall. Most of them fed on algae, which flourished in the Boiling Sea. The smallest ibbot, known as the blue-breasted hover ibbot, had a wingspan of just 7 centimeters, while the great ibbot's wingspan reached up to 10 meters.

**IBC** *See* InterGalactic Banking Clan.

**IBC Arcology** The primary Coruscant location of the InterGalactic Banking Clan during the last decades of the Old Republic.

**Ib-Dunn** This small blue-green Smotl worked as a communications expert for Soergg the Hutt on Ansion during the years leading up to the Clone Wars.

**Ibegon, Dice** This female Lamproid encountered the Shistavanen Wolfman Lak Sivrak in the Mos Eisley cantina in the weeks before the Battle of Yavin. Ibegon was Force-sensitive and a member of the Rebel Alliance. She and Sivrak formed a spiritual bond, and Sivrak was drawn further into the Alliance. When she was killed during the Battle of Hoth, her Force image was left to roam the galaxy and give Sivrak support. She chose to revisit him and bring him spiritually back to Mos Eisley, where each time he reaffirmed his belief in her and the Alliance. Sivrak was killed in the Battle of Endor.

**Ibes, Binn** This Jedi Master was a contemporary of Qui-Gon Jinn. He chose Reeft, a childhood friend of Obi-Wan Kenobi, as his Padawan.

**Ibhaan'I** One of the nomadic tribes of humans that descended from Old Corellians on Socorro. They were the most technologically advanced of the nomadic tribes, as evidenced by the starport in Vakeyya that was located in the middle of tribal holdings. They also were known to be the most nomadic of the four main tribes, and each family traveled the Doaba Badlands during each generation. This wandering gave them a great deal of skill in scouting and hunting. Their ability to understand technology made them valuable guides to non-Socorrans.

**ibian** A long-bodied, lizard-like amphibian native to Tatooine. Ibians subsisted on insects and microscopic dust mites.

**Ibleam** This star was the central body of the Endor system. It was located in the Moddell sector of the Outer Rim Territories.

**ibliton** This huge mollusk lived in the swamps of Randorn 2. Its shell measured 2 meters across, and its tentacles added another 3 meters in length. The shell was coiled and chambered, and the creature's fleshy body stuck out the open end. The native Mizx believed that the ibliton was the avatar of Hershoon the Destroyer, created from Hershoon's demented soul in order to perpetuate his legacy. In reality, ibliton predated Mizx by several millennia, and the fossil record indicated that forerunners of ibliton existed 600,000 years before the Battle of Yavin. Their bodies were segmented and insectoid, with armor plating covering all but the four tentacles. Their segmented legs ended in sharp, knife-like talons and allowed them to walk along the ground. Ibliton displayed a form of raw cunning in their predatory actions and had been known to ambush explorers.

**i-box** *See* interference box.

**Ibtisam** This mottled blue-skinned Mon Calamari joined the Rebel Alliance as a B-wing pilot shortly before the Battle of Endor. Ibtisam had highly modified her B-wing, but even that couldn't keep her from being shot down during the second wave of Imperial attacks over Endor. Ibtisam survived despite being blasted out of her fighter and set adrift in space for 12 hours. She was left somewhat agoraphobic because of

*An ibian becomes a meal for a worrt.*

that experience, but the confines of a ship were enough to temper the problem. She remained with the Alliance as an X-wing pilot. Following the recovery of the Eidolon, Ibtisam joined Rogue Squadron. When Ibtisam met Nrin Vakil, a Quarren, the two Rogues couldn't escape their species' continual rivalry but never succumbed to petty bickering. Ibtisam and Nrin became friends. They could take up opposite sides of nearly any issue and argue about it in a vehement, yet friendly manner. Ibtisam was killed when the Rogues were dispatched to rescue Sate Pestage from Ciutric and were ambushed by forces led by Admiral Delak Krennel.

*Ibtisam*

**I-C2** Veril Line Systems' civil-industrial construction droid. Measuring 10 meters high and 30 meters long, this huge automaton moved about on four heavy-duty treads. I-C2 was developed as an alternate to the massive construction droids produced by the Empire during the rebuilding of Imperial City. The I-C2 was given advanced programming and independent thought, allowing it to assess a situation and make necessary repairs without the intervention of a central office.

**Icarii** Members of this humanoid species from Vestar often were referred to as Ikies by the Empire's Lightning Battalion. The Icarii were distinguished by scales that surrounded their eyes in a diamond-shaped pattern. The wealth of the tribe was held in the small gemstones and beads woven into the hair of Queen Selestrine; many of the galaxy's crooks wanted to cut her hair and steal the jewels.

Individual Icarii could survive dismemberment for long periods of time, and the strongest could even have their heads removed; these could remain alive for several months. Shortly before the Battle of Yavin, Darth Vader ordered the destruction of the Icarii. General Nim commanded the operation but allowed Colonel Karda to carry out the plans. Karda unleashed a bioagent capable of dissolving the innards of the tribe and took Selestrine hostage, hoping to get rich through her ability to foresee the future. The queen tried to commit suicide, but Karda severed her head before the agent became effective. He encased it in a life-sustaining casket. Karda then killed Nim in an effort to keep the head, and fled the Empire.

**Icaris Tool and Drive** This small corporation supplied parts and industrial intelligence to Subpro Corporation during the last decades of the Old Republic. It was believed that Icaris once tried to steal the prototype *Onyx Star* in order to produce the Z-95 Headhunter for itself, but there was never any evidence. Icaris went bankrupt about three years before the Yuuzhan Vong War.

*Ice*

**Ice** One of the many gladiator fighters chosen by Ajuur the Hutt to compete in his events on Taris during the Great Sith War. Known as a devious fighter, she often hid a blaster inside her clothing in case a bout got out of hand.

**Iceberg Face** A nickname used by Galactic Alliance Navy personnel to describe Admiral Cha Niathal, stemming from Niathal's cold-hearted demeanor during battle.

**Iceberg Four** A frozen, rocky planet considered to be the eighth and outermost world in the Mon Calamari system.

**Iceberg Four Battle Group** One of the many subdivisions of the Galactic Alliance's combined naval forces; along with Iceberg Three, the group defended Mon Calamari from attack by the Yuuzhan Vong.

**Iceberg One** An icy planetoid considered the third world in the Mon Calamari system. It was orbited by a single moon.

**Iceberg Three** Although most astronomers considered Iceberg Three the seventh orbital body of the Mon Calamari system, many others believed it a captured comet. The Mon Calamari Extreme checkpoint—a Galactic Alliance rendezvous point—was established just outside Iceberg Three's orbit.

**ice blaster** An alcoholic beverage made from Sullustan gin.

**iceborer (stylus ship)** This long, narrow vessel with a tapered front end was used for mining icy planets. The iceborer was deployed by being shot in the correct direction from the missile pod of a carry ship. A good portion of the iceborer was translucent, and when it was launched, the pilot had the feeling of free flying in empty space. The iceborer pilot was positioned with his or her head forward and belly down along the length of the translucent cylinder and had to remain there for the duration of the flight. Jacen Solo used an iceborer on Helska 4.

**Ice Crypts** This network of frozen caves, bored into a glacial layer several hundred meters underground, was found beneath the Hasamadhi District on Coruscant, near the planet's southern polar icecap. Xenoarchaeologists believed that the Ice Crypts were the ancient burial grounds of the Zhell who once lived on the planet. Long and meandering side passages led to 13 chambers, each containing the mummified remains of what were believed to be war chieftains representing 13 Zhell nations. Because many specimens were found wearing complete battle armor, it was thought that the Zhell had retreated into the caves after they were defeated during their battle with the Taungs and buried themselves alive. The incident was memorialized in the famous poem *Dha Werda Verda.* At night, curators swore they could hear the echoes of the dead whispering the words, "*Korah mahtah . . .*"

*Icarii*

**ice dragon** A ferocious creature native to Toloran.

**Ice Edge Flightknife** This group of Adumari Blade-32 fighters served aboard the *Allegiance* during the defense of Adumar.

**icefish** A species native to Ediorung. Icefish were often caught and poached as a delicacy.

**Iceflake Inn** This expensive vacation spot was located near the polar ice cap on Coruscant. It provided vacationers with traditional winter sports and activities year-round.

**Iceglaze Base** The code name for the collection of icy caves and tunnels that made up Salmakk's secondary base on Hoth during the Galactic Civil War. Iceglaze was located near the entrance to a vast dragon-slug warren,

Ice scrabbler

which allowed easy access to the lumni-spice that could be found there.

**Iceman** A bounty hunter from the Nord system, he spent most of his career in the Minos Cluster. No one was sure if his moniker was derived from the way he "iced" his quarries or from his complete lack of emotion and personality. He had no mercy and was determined to maintain a perfect capture record as a bounty hunter.

**ice modrol** A predator imported to Neftali shortly before the fall of the Old Republic. Its paws were studded with sharp talons that could cut the spine of its prey in one muscular swipe. Large specimens of ice modrol could grow to 5 meters tall or more.

**ice moon** A form of gemstone found in the Hapes Cluster.

**ice puppy** A creature native to Toola and hunted by the Whiphids. The term was often used in a derogatory way among Whiphids.

**ice scrabbler** These tiny, warm-blooded rodents native to Hoth lived in the icy caves of the frozen planet. They were covered in white or dark gray fur and distinguished by a bony ridge that ran along their spines, which could be raised and lowered by specialized back muscles. Males showed off their ridges during mating season, discouraging rival males while attracting females. Ice scrabblers fed on the lichen that grew inside Hoth's caves; well-developed olfactory organs helped them sniff out food.

**ice spike** A specially made explosive used by ice fishermen on Neftali. The spikes had shaped charges to blast a hole through the ice covering the Beija Seas, which was often a meter or more thick.

**Ice Station Beta** An Imperial outpost on Anteevy. Kyle Katarn infiltrated it while trying to discover the source of the dark troopers.

**Ice Storm** A division of Imperial cold assault stormtroopers.

**iceteroid (ice comet)** Giant fields of ice crystals found in space. They were similar to asteroid fields.

**ice tiger** A Toolan predator.

**ice walker** These 12-legged automata were designed for use in traveling on the ice plains of Belsavis. Ice walkers resembled huge, low-slung insects.

**iceway** Chiss underground travel routes excavated on their homeworld of Csilla. Iceways were bored through the bedrock, so they were unaffected by the shifting ice found on the planet's surface. Specialized carriages moved passengers and cargo through the tunnels.

**ice worm (1)** An immense creature considered the deadliest predator on Akuria II. Ice worms created a network of burrows through the icy surface of the planet, adding to the danger of walking on open ice. Nearly extinct by the time of the Galactic Civil War, these gargantuan slugs moved about on a series of stubby pseudopods that served to push their bulk through the burrows. The mouth of the green-skinned ice worm was filled with heavy teeth and surrounded by short tentacles.

**ice worm (2)** Thin, wire-like creatures native to Hoth. They burrowed through the ice that covered the planet, leaving behind a series of thin tunnels. When windstorms blew across the ice, the worm-holes created an eerie music that whistled through the tunnels. Their main food was algae.

**Ichalin Station** Located in the Fakir sector, this space station was the site of a Yansan terrorist action against the Rebel Alliance.

**Ichium** This barren ball of rock was the eighth and outermost planet of the Axum system. It was located in the Core Worlds.

**Ichtor 8** An ice planet best known as homeworld of attack stohls, warm-blooded predators whose bodies were covered with a thick pelt of downy-soft fur and whose fangs injected a poison into the bloodstream of their victims. They could be trained as pets. The Empire also established a resort on the planet for the ultrarich humans of the galaxy.

**Icicle, The** One of two cantinas located in the outpost settlement of Elesa on Ando Prime during the early years of the New Order.

**Icknya** Leia Organa Solo was forced to deal with this petty tyrant during her tenure as Chief of State of the New Republic.

**ICL** *See* Interstellar Collections Limited.

**IC-M** This Cybot Galactica general utility droid was first designed as an Imperial City maintenance droid—hence its designation. Its strange construction incorporated two heads that faced each other. One had optical sensors, while the other had a screen for data display. This allowed the droid to view plans and blueprints while it toiled. Cylindrical in shape and standing less than 2 meters high, the IC-M was equipped with a variety of manipulation arms and extendible tools. Its torso telescoped upward to allow the droid to reach high places.

**icus** The leaves of this tall plant grew on branches that started more than 2 meters from the ground.

**ID-5N** This secure space travel route was often referred to as the New Route because it was established during the era of the New Order to link the planets Corellia and Talus. Although the exact route fluctuated depending on the location of the two planets in their orbits around the star Corell, ID-5N was constantly patrolled by the Corellian Security Force, making it a fast, safe, and easy way to move between the two worlds.

**I-D-A** One of many repair droids owned by Star Tours during the Galactic Civil War.

**Idan, Belsed-Qan** A Jedi Master who, along with Kit Fisto, led a task force to Vuchelle to put a stop to the Iridium pirates who were ambushing Old Republic supply convoys before the Clone Wars. Masters Idan and Fisto were aboard the *Monitor III* when it took heavy damage from a power gem, but managed to escape and return to Coruscant. Master Idan, who was serving as Jedi Watchman of Aargau, faced a firestorm of criticism when Senator Aks Moe was killed in his absence.

**Idanian, Jenos** One of the early aliases used by Han Solo during his tenure with Garris Shrike. He later used the alias when he and Bria Tharen fled Ylesia. As Idanian, he sold off artifacts they had taken from Teroenza's museum. Idanian's real identity was discovered by Rostek Horn, who provided it to Corran Horn to get him off Corellia during the search for Mirax Terrik.

**Idd, Lonn** A noted scientist during the early years of the New Order, he was known for developing droids and other automata. He used specialized lasers in much of his research, which Tig Fromm decided to use to his advantage. Believing that Idd was a helpless old man who lived with his two children aboard a space station, Fromm and his gang tried to bully Idd into providing his lasers to their starships. Idd refused, and his children—with the help of R2-D2 and C-3PO—defeated Fromm and saved their home.

**Idellian Arrays** This small corporation produced a wide range of life-form scanners.

**identicard** A form of personalized datacard that was used to prove identity. It contained a wealth of personal information, including date and location of birth and distinguishing physical characteristics. Because identicards be-

*Identichip*

came the primary means of identifying beings during the years following the Yuuzhan Vong War, many forgers found a niche creating fake identicards for criminals and spies.

**identichip** Developed during the final decades of the Old Republic, this form of personal identification was embedded in a smart card that carried all of an individual's required data. Bail Organa and his aides flashed identichips when asked for their identification, Tam Elgrin wore an identichip on the front of his shirt, and Vannix Intelligence identichips bore a special seal and could be verified using a countertop reader.

**Identifier** This subnode was generated by Kud'ar Mub'at to identify ships carrying visitors to the Assembler's web before they reached the web's outer defenses. Identifier's role was quite important, since those defenses were minimal at best.

**Identify Friend or Foe transponder** Known as an IFF transponder, this device was a kind of subspace radio wave generator used to identify a starship. It provided a burst of information about the vessel's ownership and registry, including data on armament, ship's complement, name, and class, all of which could be analyzed by IFF receivers. If the codes checked out, the starship was identified on targeting computers as a friend. If not, then it was considered an enemy target. Many governments, military forces, and planetary traffic control systems had their own codes to mark their native ships. Smugglers usually had two or three IFF transponders on their ships that could be swapped out for different identities. One of the more famous IFF transponder codes was the Alderaanian code used to link *Another Chance* to its protective escort.

**identikit** An identification document that served as a passport. Mace Windu brought an identikit with him to Pelek Baw.

**identi-tab** A specialized datacard that served to verify a being's identity. The identi-tab usually had a holographic image and displayed a name and a clearance level or security rating.

**identity probe** A small, needle-like device used to verify a being's identity. Most often used in the delivery of sensitive or confidential materials, the probe was held between the fingers and squeezed. The small needle then took a sample of skin and body fluids for comparison with an encoded description of the recipient. If the samples matched, a positive response was stored in the probe's inoxide tip. When the tip was inserted into a special reader, the package containing the materials was either opened (if the samples matched) or destroyed (if they didn't). This ensured that sensitive or confidential deliveries made it to their intended destination without being intercepted. In extreme cases, a mismatch resulted in an explosion that destroyed the package as well as the offending party.

**identi-voice** Developed on Aargau, this technology used sophisticated recordings of voices to identify specific individuals.

**Idiot** One of the 16 face cards in the game of sabacc, the Idiot had a value of zero. The image of the card was often dominated by the color violet. It was an integral part of an idiot's array, a hand that always resulted in a winning score of 23 for its holder. It consisted of the Idiot, along with any 2 and any 3 from the four suits. Thus, it was literally "23."

***Idiot's Array*** A modified corvette that was part of Talon Karrde's small fleet during the early years of the New Republic. It was one of the ships that accompanied the *Wild Karrde* to Yavin 4 in an attempt to rescue the students at Luke Skywalker's Jedi praxeum during the Yuuzhan Vong War. Shada D'ukal piloted the ship to occupy Yuuzhan Vong forces long enough for Anakin Solo to rescue Tahiri Veila. Shada sacrificed the *Idiot's Array* in order to destroy a Yuuzhan Vong destroyer as the ship tried to flee the system. Shada and most of the crew were able to abandon ship in escape pods before the collision.

*Iego*

**Idis** This mercenary was a member of the Vibroblade Brigade on Murkhana during the Clone Wars. During the final battle for the planet, Idis was captured by Ion Team while relieving himself in the forest. He was convinced to help the forces of the Grand Army of the Republic by providing them with information on the landing platforms and shield generators found in Murkhana City.

**Idlewil liquor** This rare, expensive alcohol was distilled by the Shashay.

**Idol Smasher** One of the strongest communications encryption systems developed by the New Republic. It was used to secure communications during the Yuuzhan Vong War. The Idol Smasher system was used by the Republic, the Imperial Remnant, the Hapes Consortium, and even the Chiss Ascendancy so that the galaxy's major powers could coordinate efforts across interstellar distances without having their plans discovered by the alien invaders.

**Idow** An urban combat specialist with Page's Commandos during the early years of the New Republic. Idow and Gottu were famous for their attack and capture of an Imperial outpost near the city of Bruzion on Jendorn, because they were armed only with a vibro-ax and a pair of blasters.

**ID profile** A starship's relevant data (such as name, registration number, current owner, home port, classification, and armament and power-plant ratings) combined in a single transmission sent via the ship's transponder. ID profiles could be altered, but it was both difficult and illegal.

**Idrall, Jor** A male Twi'lek on Tatooine, he worked as a two-bit criminal for Jabba the Hutt during the New Order. After Jabba's death, Idrall moved to fill the vacuum left in Tatooine's criminal underworld. He established a strong base of power quickly, setting up several smuggling operations and an extortion racket; he also issued bounties on fellow criminals. Idrall even ordered his thugs to start fights in local cantinas as a warning to other would-be crime lords that he had taken over. After he tried to expand his territory beyond the Tatoo system to 11 other neighboring systems, the New Republic issued a warrant for Idrall's capture.

**Idret** This Imperial Intelligence agent was known to be responsible for the deaths of more than 30 Bothan members of the Rebel Alliance. Idret's true identity was never discovered, although it was believed that he worked as the chief operative in the Maldrood sector.

**Idrish** This Yuuzhan Vong was a member of the Shamed Ones living on the re-formed world of Yuuzhan'tar after the planet formerly known as Coruscant was captured from the New Republic. Idrish was one of the many of his caste to flock to the Prophet Yu'shaa, who told of the Jedi Heresy. It was later discovered by Kunra that Idrish was one of several acolytes who were planning to gather as much power as possible in an effort to take control of the religion from Yu'shaa.

***Idyll*** One of the most famous Farnican chime-paintings, it was believed to have been destroyed during the final century of the Old Republic. Later it was discovered among the artworks that Emperor Palpatine had stored at his Mount Tantiss facility on Wayland.

**Iego** Located in a remote part of the Outer Rim Territories just south of the Perlemian Trade Route, this planet had a thousand moons rumored to be inhabited by angels. The planet itself was shrouded in mystery, and no two spacers could ever seem to agree on its exact location. Investigation of the planet's existence led to the discovery of the Extrictarium Nebula, as well as the fact that Iego didn't orbit a star, as most planets did. Instead, Iego moved around within the nebula, towing its many satellites along with it.

Further investigation revealed that the angels were, in fact, a sentient species known as the Diathim, who shared the planet with the Maelibi. While most beings considered the Diathim to be angels, they referred to the Maelibi as demons.

Legends persisted that starships were inexplicably drawn to Iego, even if they were traveling many light-years away. Many xenoarchaeologists agreed that this had more to do with the powers of the Diathim than with the planet itself. Although categorized as a planet, Iego was just 2,730 kilometers in diameter. Yet it generated a gravitational field close to the galactic standard, allowing it to maintain its collection of moons. Iego seemed to exist outside the normal galaxy, unaffected by the actions of the Republic or the Empire. Even the invasion of the Yuuzhan Vong meant nothing to those isolated inside the strange pocket nebula.

*IFT-T hover tanks*

**Ieria** One of the smaller worlds in the Andaran system, it rivaled Andara in its ability to produce goods. Ieria received little of Andara's prestige or income, however, and struggled to survive as an economy.

**Ierian starfighter** A modification of the Delta-6 Aethersprite. Anakin Skywalker disabled the capacitators in a number of Ierian starfighters during a mission to keep the pilots out of harm's way.

**Ies, Beda** The wife of Daxar Ies. When Daxar was targeted for assassination by Emperor Palpatine, Mara Jade was dispatched to do the deed. Beda and their daughter, Eremay, surprised Jade while she was searching through Daxar's office. After killing Daxar, Jade let them go free rather than eliminating them. Beda and Eremay fled into the Unknown Regions. Years later, when Mara arrived on Woteba with her husband, Luke Skywalker, to investigate the reappearance of the Gorog Hive, UnuThul explained that it was Beda and Eremay, not Welk and Lomi Plo, who had caused the creation of the Gorog Hive.

According to UnuThul, the Gorog had taken in the pair and cared for them until both Beda and Eremay became Joiners. However, their fear of being hunted down eventually corrupted the Gorog, and the entire hive went into hiding and became the Dark Nest. Beda Ies became the Joiner known as BedaGorog, UnuThul went on, a Force-sensitive individual who assumed the title of Night Herald and took control of the Gorog hive. BedaGorog, so the story went, was killed on Kr by Master Skywalker during the Qoribu crisis. This story stood in direct contradiction to the truth that Luke knew: He had killed Welk on Kr.

**Ies, Daxar** A man wanted by Emperor Palpatine for stealing huge amounts of money from Imperial coffers, including a small fortune that he embezzled directly from Palpatine's personal accounts. Mara Jade found him alone in his office and killed him before he could raise an alarm. She then set out to piece together information on the confusing network of bank accounts that Ies had created to hide the stolen credits.

Years later, in an effort to drive a wedge between Luke Skywalker and his wife, Mara Jade, Alema Rar told Luke that Daxar Ies was lead developer on the Intellex IV droid brain project, and had developed the complicated codes that protected the deepest parts of the brain circuitry, which Luke needed to access stored information in R2-D2's memory core about his mother. To corroborate her story, Rar produced two of the access codes. Later, the tale was exposed as a lie.

**Iesei** One of the myriad Killik hives that formed the Colony during the years following the Yuuzhan Vong War.

**IFF Confuser** This starship countermeasures system was used in lieu of modifications to a ship's Identify Friend or Foe system. The IFF Confuser, launched into the midst of a battle, broadcast a signal that scrambled the IFF systems of starships in its vicinity. The result was that enemy ships would then identify a vessel as friendly, allowing the ship to escape.

**IFF transponder** *See* Identify Friend or Foe transponder.

**i'fii** This staple food of the Yuuzhan Vong was easily produced aboard worldships.

**Ifmix VI** The homeworld of the Squalris. It was a harsh world with a surface continually scoured by fierce windstorms. It was located near the Perlemian Trade Route.

**I'Friil Ma-Nat corvette** This Yuuzhan Vong corvette analog resembled a multisided pyramid of gloss-black yorik coral. The craft, measuring 315 meters long, were developed to serve as light assault vehicles. The I'Friil Ma-Nat corvette's primary mission was supporting wings of coralskippers in battle, providing cover, and ensuring escape routes back to the main fleet. Each ship required a crew of 110 Yuuzhan Vong warriors; it could also transport up to 225 troops and 510 metric tons of cargo. Unlike the other capital ship analogs of the Yuuzhan Vong fleet, the I'Friil Ma-Nat did not carry its own complement of coralskippers. It was armed with 20 volcano cannons and several dovin basals, but lacked sufficient power to generate an interdiction field.

**Ifron** Shortly after the Battle of Endor, Mara Jade left Phorliss and the employment of Gorb Drig and traveled to this planet.

**IFT-T** A hover tank developed for the Grand Army of the Republic during the Clone Wars. The IFT-T was exceptionally fast for its size, which allowed it to outrun its opponents to reach key positions and avoid enemy fire. The IFT-T was armed with a concussion missile launcher and beam cannon, making it one of the most feared of all Republic ground assault vehicles.

**IFT-X** A version of the IFT-T hover tank that was secretly produced for use by the Rebel Alliance during the Galactic Civil War.

**IG-1** The code name of the first assassin droid design developed by Phlut Designs Systems after the relative success of the IG lancer droid. The plans for the IG-1, as well as the rest of the IG series droids, were later acquired by Holowan Mechanicals.

**IG-100 MagnaGuard Droid** This series of humanoid combat droids was built to the specifications of General Grievous during the early stages of the Clone Wars. Grievous demanded that he be given a group of droids capable of defeating a Jedi Knight in combat. The prototype for the IG-100 MagnaGuard was built by Holowan Mechanicals, and was known as the Self-Motivating Heuristically Programmed Combat Droid. The IG-100 designation stemmed from Holowan's ties to the InterGalactic Banking Clan, which had contracted Holowan to create the IG series lancer droid.

Capable of executing all types of combat maneuvers, IG-100s were armed with a variety of weapons. They were often paired in combat to help ensure victory. Their primary weapon was a charged electrostaff, but they also were

*IG-100 MagnaGuard Droid*

equipped with a pair of missile tubes mounted to their back plating. Each of the MagnaGuards assigned to Grievous was personally trained by the cyborg general. The MagnaGuards also were given portions of Grievous's own combat programming, making them more than a match for most Jedi Knights. Ultimately, Grievous wanted a droid that could *learn* how to fight, not be *programmed* to fight. His IG-100 MagnaGuards were capable of learning from their mistakes and sharing this knowledge with their companions.

Among the most impressive features found in the 2-meter-tall IG-100 MagnaGuard were its heavily redundant systems, which allowed it to continue fighting even after it was beheaded or badly damaged. Much of the design of the MagnaGuard series was based on the ancient battle droids of the Krath. Specific series of IG-100s were denoted by the coloration of their armor plating, with each series having a distinct mission profile and armaments. It was believed that most of the IG-100 MagnaGuards were destroyed during the Clone Wars. Among the IG-100 MagnaGuards employed by General Grievous were:

- **IG-101:** The first of the MagnaGuard droids given to Grievous as a bodyguard, it had a blue coloration. During the Battle of Coruscant, IG-101 took heavy damage from blasterfire while trying to capture Obi-Wan Kenobi aboard the *Invisible Hand*. Kenobi eventually got the upper hand in their struggle; he used his lightsaber to remove all of IG-101's limbs, rendering it unable to move.

- **IG-102:** The second of the MagnaGuards given to Grievous, distinguished by its silver hue. IG-102 lost both of its legs to Obi-Wan Kenobi aboard the *Invisible Hand*. Although IG-102 kept on fighting, Kenobi eventually severed all its limbs and reduced it to a worthless pile of scrap.

- **IG-109:** Destroyed by Grievous during his early lightsaber instruction from Count Dooku.

- **IG-138:** Destroyed by Grievous during his lightsaber instruction from Count Dooku.

- **IG-153:** Survived the Clone Wars and became a bodyguard for Grand Moff For-Atesee.

- **IG-179:** The only MagnaGuard known to have survived the Galactic Civil War and the early years of the New Republic, when it reappeared as the chief lieutenant and bodyguard of the Iron Knight known as Luxum.

- **IG-182:** After the Clone Wars, it became a second bodyguard for Grand Moff For-Atesee.

***IG-2000*** IG-88's sleek Aggressor Assault fighter, the *IG-2000* was a 20-meter-long combat craft heavily modified by the droid. The ship was refitted on Mechis III, where IG-88 installed a Galaxy-15 ion engine that was force-fed with three Quadex power cores. IG-88 also added weapons upgrades in the form of two assault lasers and an ion cannon. Two tractor beam generators were mounted on the forward mandibles. The droid disabled the ship's inertial compensators because it felt none of the effects experienced by organics. Equipped with a Class 2 hyperdrive, the *IG-2000* could attain speeds of 1,200 kilometers per hour in atmosphere. The forward mandibles were equipped with magnetic locking pads, allowing the droid to grab target ships in preparation for boarding. There was room in the prisoner hold for up to eight captives. *IG-2000* was destroyed over Tatooine in a battle with Boba Fett, although 23 years after the Battle of Yavin, an active IG-88 model built an identical ship.

**IG-227** *See Hailfire*-class droid.

**IG-72** One of the first five Holowan Mechanicals assassin droids to be activated, IG-72 gained its independence and became a freelance bounty hunter. The first IG-88 droid had downloaded all its programming into the other four droids, but found IG-72 deficient in subtle ways. IG-72, along with IG-88 and the other IG series droids, killed 23 members of the Holowan Laboratories staff during an escape. Rather than fight among themselves, the IG-88 droids and IG-72 agreed to part company after their breakout. Like many of his kind, IG-72 performed his assassination duties flawlessly until the order to return for a memory wipe was received. That was when IG-72, like many other IG series droids, went rogue and took up its bounty-hunting career. After assisting with the capture of several IG-100 MagnaGuard droids for the development of the N-K Necrosis droids on Utapau, IG-72 was hunted by independent and Imperial forces, and went into hiding to conserve power. It reemerged when Imperials issued a bounty for Republic hero Adar Tallon, but was unsuccessful in recovering the Rebel Alliance tactician. IG-72 again went into hiding, and was not seen again. It was believed that the droid self-destructed on Tatooine, but no physical evidence of such destruction was ever found.

IG-2000

**IG-86** A predecessor to the final IG-88 design found active during the Clone Wars. The bounty hunter KRONOS 327 was an IG-86 droid.

**IG-88** An assassin droid manufactured by Holowan Mechanicals based on Phlut Design Systems plans several years before the Clone Wars. IG-88 was built to the specifications of Imperial Supervisor Gurdun, and was one of the first five droids to enhance its sentience and escape from Holowan Laboratories. The first IG series droid recognized itself as IG-88 when a sudden flash of sentience ran wild in its memory banks. After killing all the Holowan scientists on the IG project, IG-88 downloaded its complete programming into the other four droids. Three of the four were exact copies, and they designated themselves IG-88B, IG-88C, and IG-88D, with the first droid assuming the designation IG-88A. The fifth droid was flawed, and recognized itself as IG-72.

*IG-88*

After killing 23 Holowan employees during their escape, the IG-88s and IG-72 parted company. The IG-88s fled to the Galactic Core, landing on Mechis III to plot their domination of the galaxy, and began working toward hunting down their designers. Their escape from the Holowan labs forced Supervisor Gurdun to issue a "dismantle on sight" order.

The IG-88 droids became obsessed with Darth Vader when the Dark Lord of the Sith developed the Viper probe droid. Manufactured on Mechis III, Vipers were given extra programming that made them IG-88's advance scouts. To avoid notice, the droids sent IG-88B into the galaxy as a bounty hunter, hoping to draw attention away from Mechis III. IG-88B was successful, and grew in reputation until he was commissioned by Darth Vader to hunt down the *Millennium Falcon.* After stealing the data stored in the computer core of the *Executor,* IG-88 realized that it could upload itself into the computer core of the second Death Star and take control of the weapon. IG-88B was destroyed on Cloud City trying to intercept Han Solo. IG-88C and IG-88D were destroyed over Tatooine trying to take Solo's carbon-frozen body from Boba Fett.

IG-88A managed to complete its mission,

insinuating itself into a fake computer core installed in the second Death Star. IG-88A planned to allow the Imperials to control the station for a short time, lulling them into a false sense of security before taking control. When the Rebel Alliance attacked at Endor, IG-88A felt confident that the Imperials would destroy the small fleet, but this assumption proved wrong. IG-88A was destroyed with the second Death Star. Another IG-88 droid somehow returned to Mechis III, where it was discovered by Jaina Solo. Knowing the droid's bounty-hunting ability, she reprogrammed it to search out Bornan Thul.

**IG97 (Iggy)** One of the earliest battle droids produced by Holowan Mechanicals from the plans it acquired from Phlut Design Systems. Iggy was found in the ruins of the Mos Espa Arena; it had teamed with Big Gizz, Spiker, and Klepti to stop a renegade dark trooper. The IG97 series of battle droids was produced by the Empire during the early years of the New Order. Similar in many respects to the battle droids of the Trade Federation, its head was more human in shape. The droids were never mass-produced after the Empire realized that they were too weak to perform actual combat missions.

**Igar, Commander** This Imperial commander, a native of Kuat, was regarded by his superiors as a natural leader. He served under General Veers as part of the Blizzard unit that took part in the Battle of Hoth. Later he was personally assigned to coordinate the surface defense of the Forest Moon of Endor by Darth Vader during the construction of the second Death Star. In this role, Igar commanded the speeder bike squadrons that patrolled the Imperial garrison.

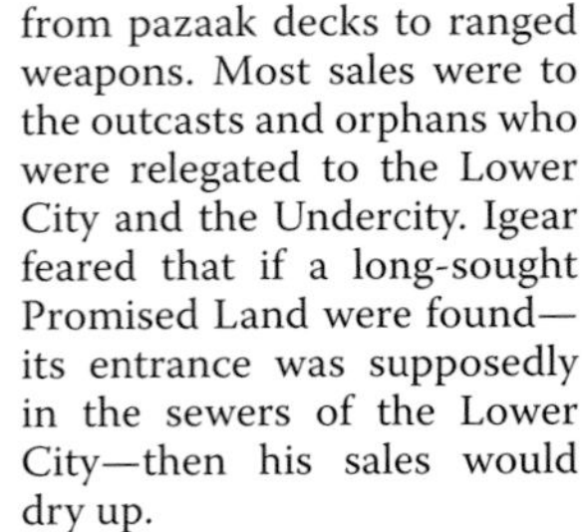

*Igear*

**IGBC** *See* InterGalactic Banking Clan.

**Igear** A salvage vendor, he owned and operated a general store in the Lower City on Taris around 4,000 years before the Galactic Civil War. The store sold sundries and equipment from pazaak decks to ranged weapons. Most sales were to the outcasts and orphans who were relegated to the Lower City and the Undercity. Igear feared that if a long-sought Promised Land were found—its entrance was supposedly in the sewers of the Lower City—then his sales would dry up.

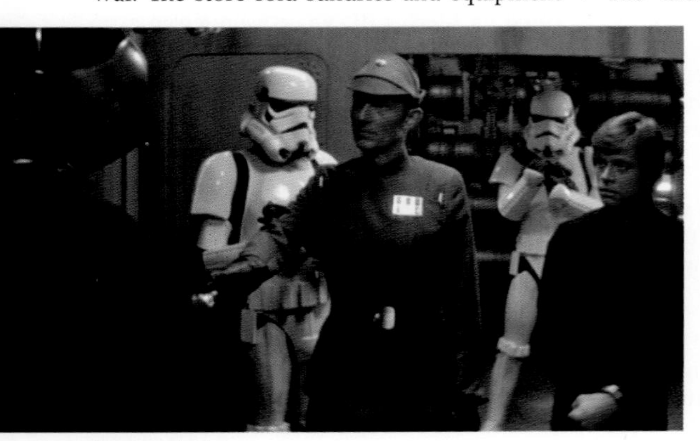

*Commander Igar*

**Iggjel** An Ithorian, formerly of the Wayland herd, he was a tender-in-training when he felt the call of the Mother Jungle. He and a friend boarded a skimmer and flew out into the jungle on the pretense of exploring new territory. When they reached a dense area, Iggjel left his friend and did the unthinkable: He climbed out of the skimmer and set foot on the jungle floor. Iggjel became one of the Ithorian's first priests.

**igitz** This small, omnivorous blue amphibian was native to the swamps of Naboo. It had finned hindquarters and webbed feet, and was well adapted to both land and water. It was often kept as a pet by Gungan families.

**IG lancer droid** This series of tall, thin combat droids originally was developed by Phlut Design Systems Corporation. Many considered the lancer to be the first true member of the IG series droids proposed as part of the original Project Phlutdroid—although subsequent units were programmed for assassination rather than direct combat. In order to begin production on the IG lancer, PDS secured a loan from the InterGalactic Banking Clan. When PDS defaulted on its payments, the IBC seized its assets, including plans for the IG lancer and the rest of the IG series droids.

Production of the IG lancer eventually was turned over to the Trade Federation. The droid was developed with the Muun physiology in mind, hence its tall skull and thin limbs. It was much stronger than standard battle droids of the Trade Federation, and could respond quicker to new orders. The first set of IG lancer droids saw action on Muunilinst when Durge was given command of them as part of a planetary security force. They were armed with power lances and rode speeder bikes into combat. The IG lancers later saw combat during the Battle of Muunilinst, but they were defeated by the forces of the Grand Army of the Republic when a group of clone troopers led by Obi-Wan Kenobi met them in battle riding their own speeder bikes.

*Ignus*

**Ignacia** This gas giant was the fifth planet in the Kalinda system.

**Ignus** A shady character, he owned a hotel in Ahto City on Manaan during the era of the Great Sith War. He was an eyewitness in Sunry's murder trial.

**IGO** *See* InterGalactic Ore.

**IGt** The designation of a Quadex starship engine system produced during the New Order. The IGt was classified as a Class 1 hyperdrive.

**Ig'zxyck Flare** This criminal syndicate was controlled by Jelasi the Hutt during the early years of the New Republic.

**Ihopek** The site of an Imperial shipyard. Workers there were forced to flee Ihopek and Narth following the Battle of Endor. While the two planets were being evacuated, the Imperial Star Destroyer *Gnisnal* was demolished by internal explosions. The wreckage near Ihopek later provided the New Republic with a complete copy of the Imperial Order of Battle.

**Ihsss, Ffaseer effet** This Togorian served as the Margrave-sister of her homeworld during the Galactic Civil War. Despite the Imperial presence in her star system, Ffaseer effet Ihsss was a secret supporter of the Rebel Alliance as well as a longtime friend of Leia Organa.

**ii77** One of the many variants of the standard 3PO series protocol droid that was developed and manufactured by Cybot Galactica. The ii77 droids were considered boutique droids, aimed at a specific market.

**iiaa** This tiny fish, native to the oceans of Kamino, was known as the sea mouse. It was the favored prey of the rollerfish.

**Iillor, Captain Uwlla** One of the few female officers in the Imperial Navy, she commanded the *Interdictor*-class starship *Black Asp* when it tried to intercept the *Pulsar Skate.* Iillor began her career with a series of assignments patrolling the Unknown Regions for Colonel Thrawn before she was

*IG lancer droid*

given command of a *Carrack*-class cruiser. Following the Battle of Endor and other skirmishes, she was promoted to captain and given her own command. The defeat at Borleias raised some concerns among her crew and Imperial leaders. When several personnel transfers went unresolved, she got fed up and defected to the New Republic, taking the *Black Asp* with her. The ship was renamed *Corusca Rainbow* and led the New Republic invasion fleet during the conquest of Coruscant.

**Iinan, Lieutenant Mujmai** This Yuuzhan Vong officer proposed that Kubindi could be taken with just half the usual number of coralskippers. Kyp's Dozen was able to hold off the reduced force, however, allowing all spaceworthy ships to flee Kubindi. Upon learning of the loss of so many potential sacrifices, Tsavong Lah had Iinan executed.

**Iisner** This aging Glottalphib served as crime lord Nandreeson's majordomo on Skip 6, within the Smuggler's Run. Iisner was once a successful smuggler in his own right, but age confined him to administrative duties. His skin was pale and gray, shedding scales at any contact. Nandreeson had a slime pond built into Iisner's quarters on the *Silver Egg* so that Iisner wouldn't lose too many scales during long space voyages. He was severely injured while trying to capture Han Solo and Chewbacca on Skip 5. Solo kept him alive long enough to begin questioning the Glottalphib about the shady business being conducted in the Run, but Davis shot Iisner in the mouth and killed him.

**Iith'lon** This Kian'thar political faction was known in Basic as the Preservers because its members spoke of keeping to the traditional ways of their ancestors and remaining separated from the galactic community. That kept them at odds with the Lllun faction.

**II-xC** The designation of Merthyog Communications' maintenance/broadcast ships. The ships were purchased by the Empire for deployment as independent broadcast centers that could move in and out of a system quickly after relaying messages to a subspace relay station. The II-xC was 30 meters long, and normally had a command crew of four, plus 10 communications technicians. They were unarmed, and Imperial doctrine required them to hide within the defenses of the subspace relay station if attacked.

**Ijjix, Crandor** This member of the Norat monarchy was captured during the Yevethan Purge and forced by Tal Fraan to record a message for the New Republic, pleading that the ships of the Fifth Battle Group halt their attack on Yevethan starships during the blockade of Doornik-319. Fraan correctly surmised that Republic pilots would break off their attack if they were made to believe prisoners were alive on the Yevethan ships. However, there were no prisoners, and the Yevethans decimated the Fifth Battle Group.

*Ikopi*

**Ijol** This gas giant was the fourth planet of the Tirahnn system in the Zeemacht Cluster. It was orbited by 24 moons.

**I-Kanu, Rann** A human male Jedi Padawan who was being trained by Master Ali-Vor during the period before the Battle of Naboo. I-Kanu's Master had sent him to study at the nonsecular Royal House of Learning in Theed. I-Kanu was a friend of Sia-Lan Wezz and a student of Lucos Dannt at the time of the Trade Federation's blockade and invasion of Naboo, and he joined the Naboo underground with the rest of his classmates.

**Ikas-Adno** A manufacturer of popular speeder bikes.

**Ikenomin sector** This sector, along with the Kakani, Sugai, and Fusai sectors, made up the Outer Zuma region.

**iketa stone** This red stone was found on Geonosis and was associated with war. Soldier drones often wore one or more iketa stones in their armor.

**ikket** This short sword, used for stabbing during melee combat, was once favored by Quarren warriors.

**Ikle, Bur'n** This red-skinned Twi'lek worked for the CreedCon Construction Company as an engineer during the final years of the Old Republic. She was among a handful of workers hired for a bridge construction project that Thaedius Creed envisioned as part of his racecourse facility. Ikle and her team disappeared after they discovered the ancient burial cave in which the Tarasin had trapped the t'salak many generations before. A group of freelance agents hired by Creed to locate the construction team discovered a datapad, but little else, because the crew had been captured by the Dark Jedi known as Raik Muun. They were taken to Tilnes, where Muun managed to breed a second t'salak. Although Muun escaped, Ikle and her crew were rescued by a team that had been hired by the Almas Academy.

**Ikon** This red dwarf star was orbited by an asteroid belt. Princess Leia Organa traveled there after the Battle of Yavin to help Rebel sympathizers install a turbolaser.

**Ikon, Tnani** Following the Battle of Naboo, this impassive Jedi Knight was put in charge of research and keeping computer data banks maintained at the Jedi Temple on Coruscant.

**ikopi** These antelope-like mammals roamed the plains and swamps of Naboo in large herds. They had virtually no necks; their small heads sat directly on their shoulders. To reach food and water, ikopi used their unusually long, hollow tongues. Their antlers were valued by land-dwelling Gungans as an antidote to the stinging bite of the shaupat.

**ikov** Found on the jungle world of Kashyyyk, this small predator lived in the lower reaches of wroshyr trees, surviving by feeding on carrion and creatures that fell from the upper branches. Their teeth were serrated for tearing flesh, and were unusually iridescent. The average ikov was not exceptionally strong or aggressive, but its teeth gave it a formidable defense when threatened.

**Ikova, Mia** This blond-haired woman served as leader of the city of Haleoda, and ostensibly the planet Kattada, in the years before the Battle of Yavin. She tried to remain neutral during the growing conflict between the Empire and the Rebel Alliance, but was not above providing services to the highest bidder. Leia Organa made contact with Madam Ikova shortly before the Battle of Yavin in an effort to get a shipload of medical supplies to the Rebels on Ralltiir. Leia's presence on Kattada drew an Imperial detachment to the surface in pursuit,

*Mia Ikova*

and Madam Ikova pleaded with her to flee immediately. Leia attempted to appease Commander Karg and avoid trouble, but Imperials tried to apprehend Madam Ikova. When her bodyguards intervened, the Imperials opened fire. Many of the bodyguards, as well as Madam Ikova, were badly injured. She was taken aboard the *Tantive IV* and given medical treatment. However, the wounds to her chest were too extensive, and she soon died. With her dying breath, she urged Leia not to abandon the Rebellion, and begged her own father to help get medical supplies aboard the *Tantive IV.*

*Ikrit*

**Ikree** This ancient Nazzar princess was the daughter of the last Emperor-King, Prrit Qabaq. After spending 12 years away from the palace, Ikree returned to find that her father had been practicing dark magic, which had corrupted him as well as the government of Nazzri. She sparred verbally with her father, demanding that he abandon the magic and return to the ways of the Ulizra, as she herself had done. Qabaq refused, and Ikree began speaking out publicly about the need for a newer, stronger form of government based on the Great Structure. Qabaq had Ikree arrested, an act that split the Nazzar population and resulted in a protracted civil war. Ikree was killed by a lesser noble of her father's court, but the government eventually accepted the Ulizra and the Great Structure, and the civil war was halted.

**Ikrit** A small, meter-long quadruped covered with creamy white fur that he could turn to black, Ikrit had floppy ears and large eyes that were a swirl of browns, greens, and blues. When Jedi Master Yoda arrived on Kushibah centuries before the Battle of Yavin to locate potential students, Ikrit was surprised to learn that he was to be trained. His family and friends laughed when he said he was going to become a Jedi—until he diverted the attack of a pack of xinkras without raising a paw. He was then regarded as a hero by his people, who realized that anything was possible.

Ikrit became quite skilled with a lightsaber, but chose never to use one in combat after he nearly killed a friend during a petty argument. Even after being elevated to Jedi Master, Ikrit refused to use a lightsaber, preferring to find other ways to mediate potentially dangerous situations. He traveled to Yavin 4 to research the Massassi people some 385 years before the Galactic Civil War. There he discovered the Golden Globe deep beneath the Palace of the Woolamander. He recognized that it could not be opened by an adult Jedi, and curled up at its base to await young Jedi strong enough to solve its puzzle.

The Jedi he waited centuries for were Anakin Solo and Tahiri Veila. He assisted them as best he could, but refrained from any direct help because the young Jedi needed to find their own way through the Force. When Ikrit revealed himself to Luke Skywalker, Luke asked Ikrit to remain at the Jedi praxeum as a teacher. Ikrit agreed, becoming Anakin Solo's informal mentor and guide because the Force had told him that Anakin's development needed to be carefully guided. Over time, Ikrit also became one of the academy's main instructors, a position he held when the Yuuzhan Vong invaded the galaxy. The praxeum remained a neutral site, primarily because Ikrit had worked with Kam Solusar and Tionne to maintain an illusion that hid the training center until the Peace Brigade decided to turn the Jedi over to the alien invaders in return for a tenuous cease-fire. As the Peace Brigade attacked the training complex on Yavin 4, Ikrit sacrificed himself in order to allow his students to survive and reach the safety of the *Errant Venture.*

**Iktotchi** A species of sentient humanoids native to Iktochon and its moon Iktotch. A fierce species, the Iktotchi were noted for the large, downturned horns that emerged from the sides of their heads. Their skulls and neck muscles were greatly enlarged to support the heavy horns. The Iktotchi also were noted for their huge hands and tough, leathery skin, which protected them from the winds of their native world. Still, they were generally quiet and reserved, keeping their emotions hidden behind a stoic expression.

Old Republic scouts discovered the Iktotchi some 3,500 years before the Battle of Yavin—and were surprised to find the Iktotchi waiting for them. Members of this species had an innate form of precognition that allowed them to foresee that the scout ship was coming several weeks before it actually arrived. Iktotchi were prohibited from using this skill for personal benefit, and the ability to see into the future faded when an individual moved offplanet. Still, the ability allowed many Iktotchi to become excellent pilots, and attracted great interest from the Jedi Order. Many Iktotchi came to deny even having the skill, however, in an effort to fit in with the rest of the galactic community.

Jedi Master Saesee Tiin was an Iktotchi. Because of their natural abilities, Iktotchi Jedi were among the first to be killed during the Jedi Purge. During the Galactic Civil War, many Iktotchi joined the Rebel Alliance to fight back against Emperor Palpatine's tyranny. Years later, the Iktotchi were taken by surprise when the Yuuzhan Vong invaded. It was believed that their inability to foresee the invasion was caused by the fact that the Yuuzhan Vong were "invisible" in the Force.

**Ilanka, Commander** A New Republic officer in charge of the evacuation of refugees from Gyndine after the Yuuzhan Vong launched an attack.

**Il Avali** A city on Druckenwell, it was the site of I'att Armament's main research complex.

**ILC-905** This star system in the Koornacht Cluster was the location of a former Imperial orbital shipyard known as Black Nine. It was there that the New Republic assembled its battle fleet prior to assaulting the 12 Yevethan homeworlds during the final days of the Black Fleet crisis. The system contained a single star and 12 planets. An asteroid belt separated the inner, rocky planets from the outer gas giants. It was in the asteroid belt that the Yevetha brought new *Aramadia*-class thrustships to fight New Republic forces. Commodore Brand and the small fleet under his command were able to take out a ship, providing the navy with valuable information about the thrustship's shields.

**ILF-5000** This handheld life-form scanner was manufactured by Idellian Arrays during the Galactic Civil War. It was later supplanted by the ILF-5500, which could memorize the "species templates" of 10 different creatures or aliens, allowing the user to detect their presence in a general area.

**Il Feen, Turat** This New Republic HoloNet supervisor was in charge of second-shift operations when Nil Spaar broke into the system to broadcast his twisted story of Leia Organa Solo's treachery.

**ILH-KK Cruiser** The designation of Koensayr's first *Citadel*-class cruiser. It was originally designed as an armed civilian craft, but during the last years of the Old Republic it was marketed as an upscale transport ship. Measuring 36 meters long, the ILH-KK provided diplomats, business beings, and wealthy individuals a way to travel the galaxy in relative security. It was armed with two pairs of heavy ion

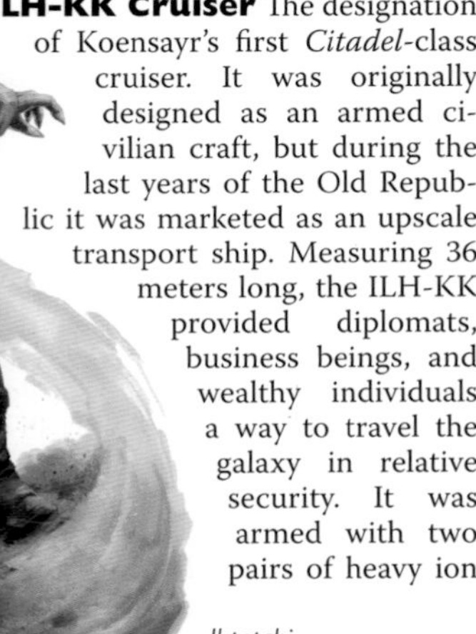

*Iktotchi*

cannons, two laser cannons, and a concussion missile launcher. It could transport up to 14 passengers and 50 metric tons of cargo in relative luxury, and required just a pilot and copilot to operate. The ILH-KK cruiser had a needle-shaped hull with a small dorsal fin and a deep ventral fin for stability. A pair of outboard wings provided maneuverability.

**Ilic** The capital of the jungle planet New Cov, it was one of the planet's eight walled cities. The inhabitants of New Cov considered themselves part of the New Republic, but they also respected the Imperial presence and routinely paid tribute to the Empire. Ilic was in an area rich with biomolecule-producing plants. Ships could enter only through vents near the top of the silver-skinned dome. Like many of New Cov's cities, Ilic was divided into specific levels, making navigation easier. Professional greeters welcomed visitors with datacard maps and guides. Bothan leader Borsk Fey'lya had numerous business interests in Ilic, and while there he often contacted then-disaffected Rebel Alliance co-founder Garm Bel Iblis.

**ilikith** An unusual predator native to the oceans of Mon Calamari. Its body was essentially a large snare, and it used bright colors to lure its prey close enough to engulf it.

**Ilimardon** A Mid Rim planet ruled by a hierarchical government.

**ilimium** This igneous stone was one of the most common ores mined in the galaxy.

**ilinium** An inexpensive natural ore used for many applications. Refined ilinium was medically stable and was used to create replacements and splints for broken or damaged bones.

**ILKO** Named for Ilko Deminar, this was one of the master encryption codes used by the Empire to enable communications between Coruscant and Horuz during the construction of the first Death Star. It took Zakarisz Ghent, then a 12-year-old slicer employed by smuggler Talon Karrde, nearly two months to crack the code; a full team from the Rebel Alliance needed a month.

**Illafian Point** A deserted beach area on the western shore of the planet Rathalay's western sea, it was where Leia Organa and Han Solo vacationed with their children.

**Illarreen** This temperate planet was the homeworld of the Poss'Nomin species. It was discovered by spice traders a century before the Galactic Civil War; mining operations were set up on the planet's surface.

**illerium** A valuable, highly volatile chemical, especially when exposed to air. This property made it a necessary part of the manufacture of starship ejection seats and escape pods. It could also be used similarly to detonite, but with much less explosive force.

**Illicit Electronics** This company produced a wide range of automata for less-than-legal activities, such as computer slicing. Operating during the Galactic Civil War, Illicit Electronics spent most of its time hiding from the Empire, but nonetheless managed to develop a thriving business through underground and underworld contacts.

**Illiet, Dodecian** A Givin on the *Empress*-class battle station at Yag'Dhul, he led the attack on the Jedi ship *Stalking Moon*. Dodecian Illiet then realized that the commander of the *Stalking Moon* was Corran Horn and had the ship boarded. While he considered a possible Yuuzhan Vong invasion, he placed Horn, Tahiri Veila, and Anakin Skywalker in quarters aboard the station. When efforts to negotiate with the invading Yuuzhan Vong failed, he released the Jedi and offered them a small ship.

**Illodia** The capital world of Illodia sector, it was a member of the New Republic. Home to the long-lived Illodian species, Illodia was ruled by an oligarchy of five clans. During the New Order, it had been annexed by the Empire, which tried to eliminate the oligarchy by levying heavy taxes. The planetary government defied the Empire and eventually was liberated by the New Republic.

**Illodia sector** A sector made up of 20 scattered colonies and ruled by an oligarchy. It was located in the Core and annexed by the Empire, which attempted to destroy the oligarchy by levying heavy taxes. It was represented by Doman Beruss in both the Imperial and New Republic Senates.

**Illodia Tower** This 100-meter-tall structure was built within the walls of Exmoor on Coruscant to house the Beruss clan. An external staircase famously spiraled up the tower.

**Illoud system** A planetary system that remained under Imperial control following the Battle of Endor, but was retaken by the New Republic just before the Battle of Mon Calamari. Sullustan Commander Huoba Neva smashed an Imperial-supported insurgency there, earning high praise.

**illumigrid** A contained lighting system used to create patterns. Illumigrids were used primarily by spaceports and other starship docking facilities to mark the landing strips and taxiways for incoming starships.

**Illuminated Aquean** Vaynai's finest casino during the New Order. It was located on Streysel Island and had huge transparisteel fish tanks lining the walls. At night, the tanks were illuminated to provide light and show off the wondrous colors of Vaynai's aquatic life. To ensure security, the tanks, as well as the walls and doors of the casino, were reinforced and shielded to prevent anyone from shooting their way into the casino. Owner-operator Amira Nasrabi also hired the most intimidating Mon Calamari guards she could and required that they act with impeccable manners so that customers were not scared off.

**illuminescences** Organic material that glowed in the dark, it was made of dried swamp hemp from Oshetti IV and spun into fine cloth used to create women's fashions. The glow of illuminescences came from bacteria living in the hemp; different strains produced different colors.

**illumi-panel** Also known as an illumination bank, this was a specialized source of light that employed a large number of floodlights to illuminate a wide area.

**illumi-strip** A smaller version of an illumi-panel.

**illumni-rod** A form of glow rod.

**Illusion Point** The code term for a rendezvous point used by smugglers during the Battle of Nar Shaddaa. It was here that Xaverri brought a group of illusory warships to the defense of the moon.

***Illustrious* (1)** An *Imperial*-class Star Destroyer that was part of the Imperial Navy fleet during the Galactic Civil War.

***Illustrious* (2)** This New Republic *Majestic*-class battle cruiser was assigned to the Fifth Battle Group. It saw action during the unsuccessful blockade of Doornik-319.

***Ill Wind* (1)** A spice-smuggling ship shot down by Imperial forces over Uogo'Cor. The navigator, Monnda Tebbo, was able to regain control of the vessel before it crashed. It again came under Imperial fire, but still managed to escape. After this narrow escape, the entire crew joined the Rebel Alliance.

***Ill Wind* (2)** An *Imperial*-class Star Destroyer that was part of Warlord Zsinj's fleet. It accompanied him to Kuat during his attempt to steal a *Super*-class Star Destroyer.

***il Madri*** A conservative religious tradition of the Ayrou. The term *il Madri* translated into Basic as "contemplation upon that stored away for meditation." The tenets of this religion required that the Ayrou lead ascetic lives marked by quiet action. After the Ayrou made contact with the Old Republic, the religion was replaced by the Society of Self-Actualization. An interesting aspect of *il Madri* was that its leaders hoarded vast amounts of treasure, but identified it as taboo and only used it when deep meditation indicated the need. The accumulated wealth was believed to have been sealed away in a vault somewhere in the Kuna system, and only the chalcedony idol known as the Tessent could open it.

**Ilna** This Brizzit was wanted by Imperial authorities for the theft of valuable relics from the planets Biitu and Roon in the years before the Battle of Yavin. Many inhabitants of Mos

Eisley came to believe that "crazy old" Tzizvvt was actually Ilna, especially after Solomahal heard him talk about the Eye of the Beyonder.

**Ilo, Plourr** *See* Estillo, Isplourrdacartha.

**Ilona Hotel** A hotel and tavern on Cloud City during the New Order.

**Ilowa, Sana-Jis** A Jedi Knight who was one of many to perish in the fighting at Shelter Base on Jabiim during the Clone Wars.

**Ilthani space mine** A form of mine used to blockade planets.

**Ilthmar Gambit (eighth)** A hologram board game move, it gave a player tactical advantage over an opponent's guarded position. The player who employed the eighth Ilthmar Gambit used a single playing piece as bait to draw out the opponent's defended pieces. After capturing the piece, the rest of the opponent's forces were left open to the first player's follow-up attack.

Ilum

**Ilum (1)** The location of this mountainous ice planet was kept a secret by the Jedi Knights of the Old Republic. Hidden beneath its frozen surface, and guarded by huge predators known as gorgodons, were the lustrous Ilum crystals, which were used by many Jedi as lightsaber focusing crystals. The crystals grew in intricate formations and glowed in dark caves. Force-sensitive individuals could feel vibrations emanating from them. Obi-Wan Kenobi and Anakin Skywalker traveled to Ilum to find crystals for Anakin's lightsaber. Anakin took three crystals for use in the formation of his lightsaber. Unlike lightsaber crystals found elsewhere, Ilum crystals almost always produced blue and green blades. At the height of the Clone Wars, Separatist forces tried to capture Ilum and destroy the crystal mines, but they were defeated by Jedi Masters Yoda and Luminara Unduli, along with Barriss Offee and Padmé Amidala.

**Ilum (2)** While most Shard ambassadors fused with whatever droids were willing to host them, Ilum and several of her kin took only the bodies of deactivated Juggernaut war droids. Ilum and her family were the only ones of their kind who could truly feel the Force. The combination of Shard intelligence and Juggernaut combat programming resulted in fearsome automata that could attack with use of the Force. When Jedi Master Aqinos sought out Ilum, she realized that she had the perfect instructor for her unusual army. She and her offspring followed Master Aqinos to Dweem, where they trained in the ways of the Jedi without the knowledge of the Jedi Council. When the Clone Wars erupted, Aqinos and Ilum decided to join the Jedi Knights in their struggles against the Separatists. The sudden appearance of Force-sensitive Juggernaut droids was unnerving, and although the new warriors—dubbed the Iron Knights—helped win many battles, the fact that Aqinos had set out without prior approval resulted in his expulsion from the Order. Ilum returned to Dweem with her Master, but she was among the first casualties of the Jedi Purge.

**Ilum crystal** Similar in many respects to Adegan crystals, Ilum crystals were favored by the Jedi Knights of the Old Republic for use in lightsabers. Found growing on the remote world of Ilum, each crystal had to be located and harvested by a Jedi Padawan, who faced the challenges of weather and nature to obtain it. Ilum crystals almost always produced a lightsaber blade that was blue or green, and were nearly uniform in their stability and power-handling capabilities. This, coupled with their ready availability on Ilum and the presence of a Jedi base there, made Ilum crystals the primary choice for lightsaber construction during the last decades of the Old Republic. This meant that virtually every Jedi had a lightsaber with a blue or green blade. The Jedi facilities on Ilum were destroyed during the Clone Wars, cutting off the source of lightsaber crystals for the Jedi of Luke Skywalker's Jedi praxeum.

**Ilwizzt** A red-skinned species distinguished by its twin-nostriled trunk.

**IM4-099** This Imperial Mark IV patrol droid regularly made rounds in Mos Eisley before the Battle of Yavin. He was known to stormtroopers and natives as Face.

**IM-6** A series of military medical droids developed by Cybot Galactica for the Grand Army of the Republic. They often were deployed in

Ilum crystal

Imagecaster

LAAT/i transports and AT-TE walkers to assist in treating clone troopers injured in battle. The IM-6 was stowed in an emergency locker until called upon. It looked similar to a JN-66 analysis droid.

**IMAC** *See* Information Matrix Center.

**imagecaster** A small handheld holographic projection unit produced by SoroSuub during the last decades of the Old Republic. The disk-shaped device had three curved projector arms. It could hold up to 100 minutes' worth of images, or it could be connected to two comlinks to allow for near-real-time face-to-face communication. Qui-Gon Jinn used an imagecaster to show a hologram of his Nubian starship to Watto.

**Image Designer** The Image Designer could offer patrons a number of cosmetic options, including new hairstyle and color, skin/fur color, lip color, cosmetics, eye color, markings, tattoos, and other minor physical alterations.

**imager** A personal holographic image capturing device.

**Image-Rec Launcher** A specialized weapons systems upgrade that allowed a pilot or gunner to target an opponent using image-recognition software. This way, a target could be identified by ship type, model, visual details, or any combination of these, depending on the situation. These systems were used most often when it was clear that an enemy's ships were consistently different from one's own, so that common parameters could be loaded before a battle was engaged.

**image spinner** A primitive Ewok wood-and-crystal top, which was lit from within. When Logray spun it, distant images appeared within the crystal.

**Imaharatronics** This small corporation produced a wide variety of miniature logic display systems in the decades before the Battle of Naboo. These display systems were used on a variety of droids and automata, including the original R2 series of astromech droids, to provide visual indication of the droid's computer control operations.

**Iman, Senator J'mesk** This Tamran Senator of the New Republic felt that the Diversity

Alliance should be allowed to exist, even after hearing the testimony of Jaina and Jacen Solo after they returned from Ryloth. Iman believed that the children were well intentioned, but ill advised, in their attempt to rescue Lowbacca and his sister.

***ImBak*** One of the Nebulon-B frigates used by the Imperial Navy during the Galactic Civil War.

**Imbat** A species of tall, leather-skinned aliens known for their cruelty and size, but not for their intelligence. Their thick legs ended in broad, grasping toes, and their small heads were dwarfed by large, drooping ears. They were often employed as guards and soldiers. Qui-Gon Jinn encountered an Imbat bartender at the Splendor Tavern on Coruscant.

General Immodet

**Imbraani** A city considered by many to be the capital of Qiilura, although it was little more than a small town. Like most other such settlements on the planet, Imbraani was surrounded by rolling fields and low hills. At the height of the Clone Wars, Imbraani was one of the handful of strongholds established by the human settlers of the planet after they were ordered to leave by the Galactic Senate.

**Imcrix, "Blue"** An infamous crime lord who was active during the early stages of the Yuuzhan Vong War. He lured a group of New Republic agents to Rokna Station by bringing its security and weapons systems back online. Imcrix had the agents captured and their ship confiscated, hoping to use them as shields while the New Republic tried to destroy his source of Rokna. His plan failed and Imcrix eventually was captured by the crew and turned over to the New Republic for trial.

**Imdaar Alpha** This planet was the site of the V38 development program headed by Darth Vader during the later years of the Galactic Civil War. It was covered alternately with swamps and low mountains. It was one of the few planets where mynocks existed in the atmosphere. Imdaar Alpha had one natural satellite.

**Im'G'Twe Hills** A collection of red-rock mesas and low hills located near the Stalgasin Hive's droid factories on Geonosis. These hills marked the eastern border of the E'Y-Akh Desert.

**Imhar Canyon** A canyon located near the ancient city of Knossa on Ossus.

**IMIIF-138** Located on the equatorial continent of Sirpar, this Imperial training center was the home of the 19,016th Imperial Line Infantry (Training) Company.

**Imina** A Jedi Padawan trained by Master Marspa during the Old Republic. She often questioned the role of the Jedi Knights in the galaxy, especially when the same tenet could be interpreted differently depending on the situation.

**Imlok** This company produced some of the most sophisticated tactical monitoring technology available during the last decades of the Old Republic. It included the Imlok ARENA-7580 holoprojector system, which relayed crucial information regarding the status of the Battle of Geonosis to the Geonosis command center.

**Immalian** These humanoid colonists attempted to establish a settlement on Mayvitch 7 but were wiped out by the Yinchorri while trying to protect their mining operations.

**Immobilizer 418** Sienar Fleet Systems' most successful model of *Interdictor*-class heavy cruiser. These 600-meter-long Imperial capital ships were developed from the hulls of *Vindicator*-class heavy cruisers and had a crew of 2,807 with a capacity for 80 troops. Immobilizer 418s were equipped with four gravity-well generators to simulate large, planet-sized masses in hyperspace. Those were useful for trapping fleeing spacecraft and for bringing ships out of hyperspace at a specific point in real space. Their bays could hold a TIE fighter and a TIE Interceptor squadron, a *Lambda*-class shuttle, and three stormtrooper transports.

***Immobilizer*-class interdictor cruiser** *See Interdictor*-class cruiser.

**Immodet, General** This Imperial officer was a member of the Imperial Interim Ruling Council. He was the first to accuse a nonhuman of the murders of Burr Nolyds and Admiral Banjeer. Shortly afterward, he was poisoned. His murder was attributed to Y'ull Acib.

**Im'nel, Tresk** This Bothan joined the Bothan Diplomatic Corps as part of Borsk Fey'lya's personal staff shortly after Coruscant was retaken from Ysanne Isard. Im'nel quickly grew weary of Fey'lya's methods and resigned his position to serve in the New Republic Diplomatic Corps. He used his diplomatic skills to help bring Imperial-controlled worlds into the Republic. During this time, his latent Force sensitivity came to the fore and was detected by Leia Organa Solo. Im'nel accepted a chance to train at the Jedi praxeum on Yavin 4, and was one of the many Jedi Knights who worked with Luke Skywalker to defend the Republic from the Yuuzhan Vong.

**imobilin** A drug used in many military hospitals during the Clone Wars. It acted as a paralytic, limiting a patient's ability to move without causing other injuries or side effects.

**Imoco** This frozen ball of rock was the eleventh planet in the Kamino system. It was orbited by eight moons.

**imooda** A spike-tailed lizard native to Borleias. It lived in the trees of the planet's jungles.

**IMP-22** An Imperial military protocol droid that was red in color and humanoid in form. Its programming was in warfare and politics, making it a valuable adviser. It was assisted by SD-7 message droids.

**impaler** The name of a subspecies of swirl prong that used its horns to impale an attacker.

***Impardiac*** The freighter on which Yarbolk Yemm shipped R2-D2 and C-3PO to the moon of Cybloc XII. The three had escaped from the quarantine enforcement cruiser *Lycoming* on a stolen ship, but made it only to Budpock. The stolen ship was sold, and the droids were sent to Cybloc XII in shipping crates.

***Impasse*** A huge Kuat Drive Yards Super Transport VII container ship owned by the Scourge pirates. They outfitted its interior with a gravity-well projector salvaged from an Imperial Interdictor cruiser by Slythor the Squib. The *Impasse* was otherwise unarmed.

***Impavid*** This *Venator*-class Star Destroyer was assigned to protect Coruscant during the final months of the Clone Wars. When General Grievous launched his surprise attack on the capital and captured Supreme Chancellor Palpatine, the *Impavid* was ostensibly under the command of Jedi Master Saesee Tiin, although Master Tiin spent much of the battle leading starfighters against vulture droids. When the *Impavid* suffered catastrophic damage in a collision with a Separatist cruiser, Master Tiin led a small force of clone troopers back onto the dying vessel to rescue as many survivors as possible. The survivors later commandeered the cruiser *Prosperous* and returned to Coruscant.

Imooda

**Impeccable** During the Galactic Civil War, this Imperial *Tartan*-class patrol cruiser earned a reputation as a capital ship that chased down smaller pirate and Rebel vessels.

**Impending Doom** This *Imperial*-class Star Destroyer was the flagship used by Moff Nile Owen to control Rayter sector during the Galactic Civil War.

**Impenetrable** This *Imperial*-class Star Destroyer was once the flagship of Grand Admiral Danetta Pitta.

Imperial II-*class Star Destroyer*

**Imperator (1)** An *Imperial*-class Star Destroyer that was part of the Imperial Navy fleet during the Galactic Civil War. The *Imperator* was dispatched by the Empire to secure asteroid AX-456 shortly before the Battle of Yavin.

**Imperator (2)** This Imperial *Interdictor*-class cruiser (Immobilizer 418) was captured by the Yevetha and renamed *Splendor of Yevetha.*

**Imperator (3)** An old Imperial troop transport used to take cadets from Imperial City on Coruscant to the training center on Carida.

**Imperator (4)** One of the *Victory*-class Star Destroyers that usually defended Coruscant during the reign of the Empire. It was mysteriously absent when the New Republic retook the planet. It was assumed that the *Imperator* had departed with Ysanne Isard, but it was later discovered that the ship had been assigned to the Black Sword Command and was captured by the Yevetha.

***Imperator*-class Star Destroyer** This Star Destroyer was developed and deployed after the creation of the *Venator*-class Star Destroyer during the last years of the Old Republic. It was renamed the *Imperial*-class Star Destroyer after the institution of the New Order.

**IMPEREVI** The handle of one of the many slicers who first discovered Tiny F's message of an impending attack by the Thaereian Military on the people of the Cularin system during the early stages of the Clone Wars. This slicer was one of many who took Tiny F's message quite seriously.

**Imperial, The (1)** An elite restaurant on the *Kuari Princess*'s Bazaar Deck. It re-created the experience of having dinner in an audience chamber that overlooked the Imperial City skyline on Coruscant.

**Imperial, The (2)** A hotel considered to be the most luxurious facility at the Bonadan Southeast II Spaceport during the early years of the New Order.

***Imperial I*-class Star Destroyer** Built at the Kuat Drive Yards, this heavy-duty Imperial capital ship became the symbol of terror and control of the Imperial Navy. The wedge-shaped *Imperial I*–class Star Destroyer was 1,600 meters long and staffed by a crew of 36,810 plus 275 gunners. It also could transport up to 1,200 troops. The *Imperial I*–class Star Destroyer was distinguished from its successor, the Imperial II, by the main tractor beam targeting array, which was located atop the conning tower: The Imperial I had an X-shaped array while the Imperial II had a flat one.

***Imperial II*-class Star Destroyer** A modification to the effective *Imperial I* class, the *Imperial II* class carried a crew of 36,755 plus 300 gunners, but had room for nearly 10,000 troops. These 1,600-meter ships were equipped with 50 heavy turbolaser batteries, 50 heavy turbolaser cannons, 20 ion cannons, and 10 tractor beam projectors. Among the primary structural differences from its predecessor were a heavily reinforced hull and the presence of a second docking bay on the belly of the Imperial II. This allowed the ship to deploy up to 72 TIE fighters.

**Imperial 501st Legion** *See* 501st Imperial Legion.

**Imperial Academy** A prestigious Imperial institution responsible for training Imperial Naval pilots. Schools of the Academy served as feeder schools for the Empire. *See also* Academy, the.

Imperial I-*class Star Destroyer*

**Imperial Academy of Science and Methodology** A prestigious Imperial university run purely for the advancement of science.

**Imperial Action transport** A heavy transport freighter used by the Empire to carry troops and AT-ATs, which disembarked from a large forward landing ramp. It was used during the ground assault on Yavin 4.

**Imperial advanced vehicle factory (Delvin Constructs Model A-Fac 333)** A factory that could construct the largest vehicles the Imperial Army required. Though it was designed to build any large vehicle, the Empire used the advanced factory almost exclusively for the manufacture of the AT-AT walker and SPMA-T artillery turbolaser. Among the largest and most expensive models that Delvin Constructs produced, they were deployed by the Empire sparingly throughout the galaxy.

**Imperial anti-security device** A round probe droid used by Trioculus to penetrate Yavin 4's defense network and search for the Lost City of the Jedi. It was equipped with a holoprojector and a remote detonation system.

**Imperial Arena** A swoop racing arena located on Coruscant during the early years of the New Republic. Originally built during the reign of Emperor Palpatine, it was one of the few facilities that were not renamed in the wake of the Battle of Endor. Leia Organa Solo and Han Solo once attended the races there.

**Imperial armored transport** Designed and manufactured by Kuat Drive Yards, this starship was a precursor of the Imperial Star Galleon. It was 50 meters long and required a crew of 10 to operate. The armored transport could carry up to 20 passengers or troops, and up to 30,000 metric tons of cargo. The usual armament was a pair of turret-mounted laser cannons. Despite its size and armor plating, it was often escorted by a convoy of ships for protection.

**Imperial Arms** This Imperial manufacturer produced a wide variety of small blaster weapons, like the 22T4 hold-out blaster, for use by the Empire's agents.

**Imperial Army** The ground-based branch of the Imperial armed forces. Like the Imperial Navy, the Imperial Army was formed when the Grand Army of the Republic completed its duties during the Clone Wars and the Old Republic was re-formed into the Galactic Empire. The GAR's clone troopers were rechristened stormtroopers and maintained their signature white armor. Like the GAR,

the Imperial Army was arrayed in an ever-expanding collection of units, as described by the Order of Battle. The usual makeup of units and leadership was as follows:

- **Squad:** 9 troops—sergeant.
- **Platoon:** 4 squads (36 troops)—lieutenant.
- **Company:** 4 platoons (144 troops)—captain.
- **Battalion:** 4 companies (576 troops)—major.
- **Regiment:** 4 battalions (2,304 troops)—lieutenant colonel.
- **Battle group (or legion):** 4 regiments (9,216 troops)—high colonel.
- **Corps:** 4 battle groups (36,864 troops)—major general.
- **Army:** 4 corps (147,456 troops)—general.
- **Systems Army:** 1 to 3 armies—high general.
- **Sector Army:** 2 to 4 systems armies—surface marshal.

**Imperial Army special missions trooper** Elite Imperial Army infantry units assigned to select assault regiments. They wore armor similar to that of AT-AT commanders. Special mission squad types included sharpshooter squads, heavy weapons squads, and engineering squads.

**Imperial assault gunship** A variation on the *Lambda*-class shuttle used by the Imperial Navy as gunboats during the Galactic Civil War. Instead of an upright tail fin and two movable wings, the assault gunship had a single pair of tail fins, one atop the hull and one on the bottom. Each of these fins originated near the midsection of the ship, running along the centerline and growing steadily taller. The sides of the fuselage extended out from the main ship, accommodating a turret-mounted gun on the port side and additional power systems on the starboard side. A pair of chin-mounted laser cannons provided the primary weaponry, while three turret-mounted guns provided additional firepower and defensive capability.

**Imperial assault transport** A transport designed to deliver Imperial assault troops anywhere in the galaxy with little or no escort. These transports had the firepower, speed, and maneuverability to attack lightly defended systems. They also were equipped with the fastest available hyperdrive systems. (*See also* assault shuttle, *Gamma*-class.)

**Imperial Ball** A monthly gathering of Imperial dignitaries and supporters held on Coruscant during the New Order.

**Imperial Ballet Company** The galaxy's foremost troupe of ballet dancers, headquartered on Coruscant.

**Imperial Bank of Coruscant** One of the largest financial institutions that sprang up after the establishment of the New Order.

**Imperial bio-hound** Part computer, part living organism, it was used to track and tag targets based on genetic clues.

**Imperial Biological Research Center** These complexes were built by the Empire on those worlds where the flora and fauna presented opportunities for exploitation. Mineral resources were strip-mined, while living resources were studied and dissected to determine their usefulness. Research at these facilities, such as the one on Najarka, was top secret.

**Imperial Biological Weapons Division** A branch of the Empire tasked with discovering ways to use biological weapons, such as viruses and diseases. It was also charged with discovering new forms of life that could be used to attack and eliminate dissident peoples or cultures.

**Imperial Biological Welfare Division** This branch of the Empire was a cover for the Biological Weapons Division. The Biological Welfare Division claimed to be working to ensure that species weren't decimated by diseases.

**Imperial Board of Culture** This body was responsible for reviewing and censoring music and art during the New Order. The IBC had three levels of tolerance. Pro-Imperial works were allowed to be viewed by the public. "Scarlet" works were those that did not meet the IBC's pro-Imperial standards, but were not derogatory to the New Order. Any works that openly disagreed with or opposed the New Order were simply banned.

**Imperial Board of Foodstuffs and Consumables** An Imperial-funded body charged with identifying the most edible of the galaxy's various culinary delights. Its decisions were biased along the same lines as the Empire.

**Imperial Broadcast and Communications** A branch of the Imperial Security Bureau responsible for tracing and deciphering enemy communications.

*Imperial assault transport*

**Imperial Building Code** The set of regulations maintained by the Empire for the construction of new buildings. Many of the convoluted codes were designed to accommodate the schemes of Emperor Palpatine, including the construction of secret passageways and the enablement of surveillance systems.

**Imperial Bureau of Investigations** An organization responsible for looking into all threats against the Empire, as well as searching out Rebel Alliance supporters.

**Imperial Cavalcade of Stars** A holotheater on Chandrila.

**Imperial Center** The name of Coruscant during the era of the New Order, when the planet served as the center of the Empire. Emperor Palpatine declared the name change because of the planet's huge population and importance to the Empire. Imperial Center was a sector all to itself, which allowed Palpatine to establish the Coruscant Sector Fleet to protect his throneworld. In the wake of the Sith–Imperial War, the new Empire renamed the city that covered Coruscant as Imperial Center. The name remained in place after Darth Krayt and the new Sith Order took control of the galaxy.

**Imperial Center Oversector** The Imperial designation for the area of space dominated by Coruscant. Sometimes called Sector Zero, it contained all the worlds whose galactic coordinates were positive and began with a zero. The farthest reach of this oversector was Kiribi. Much of the Deep Core was contained in this oversector, since Coruscant itself did not sit at the exact center of the galaxy despite its 0,0,0 coordinate designation.

**Imperial Center People's Militia** An underworld law enforcement group set up by Fliry Vorru in an attempt to gain some measure of control on Coruscant. He proposed the security force to the New Republic as a way to keep the criminal elements of Imperial City under control without expending additional Republic resources. The Provisional Council agreed reluctantly—and with good reason. Vorru turned the People's Militia into a reincarnation of Black Sun, albeit less powerful. Vorru played Republic and Imperial forces against each other, limiting Kirtan Loor's ability to terrorize the Republic while hoarding bacta in a hidden facility. When Ysanne Isard decided that it was time to leave Coruscant, she took Vorru with her, and the People's Militia was left without leadership.

**Imperial Charter** A document that contained rules and agreements set forth by the Empire, it governed the rights and responsibilities of all Imperial worlds and star systems. The charter, granted to member systems, included details on the use of resources, rights of passage, military protection, tribute, and colonization.

A celebration in Imperial City marks the end of the Galactic Civil War.

**Imperial Citadel** *See* Emperor's Citadel, the.

**Imperial City** The capital of Coruscant, it changed allegiance several times in its long history. During the Old Republic, it was known chiefly as Galactic City; it served as the capital of the galactic union and permanent headquarters of the Senate. When Emperor Palpatine took control, he renamed the capital Imperial City (and the planet Imperial Center), and it became the ruling seat of the New Order. After the Battle of Endor, Imperial City was declared the capital of the New Republic, although its name wasn't changed again. A cosmopolitan city, it was always crowded. Under the Old Republic, millions of species were drawn to the bright lights and monumental architecture of the city, but the Emperor closed it to nearly all nonhumans.

The ancient Senate Hall filled part of the city, its pillars surrounding seemingly endless moving pods. The massive Imperial Palace—later the capitol building—loomed over the hall, its tapered spires and fragile-looking towers assaulting the eye from every surface. The city's architecture gave the impression of one endless structure that spread from the base of the Manarai Mountains and covered a huge part of Coruscant's main continent.

Basically unscarred during the Galactic Civil War, the city was severely damaged later when attacked by Imperial forces led by surviving members of the Emperor's ruling circle and former Imperial commanders. It was painstakingly reconstructed by the New Republic, aided by many soldiers and giant construction droids. Most sentient life-forms had been evacuated from the deep underworld of the ancient metropolis. Some creatures found living in the darkest corridors—descendants of those who long ago fled political persecution—could no longer be classified as fully human.

With the invasion of the Yuuzhan Vong and their capture of Coruscant, the city was reduced to rubble by the invaders' strange biotechnology, and replaced with a landscape evocative of long-lost Yuuzhan'tar. Another restoration project was started after the defeat of the Yuuzhan Vong, yet parts of Coruscant remained permanently altered.

**Imperial City maintenance droid** A droid manufactured specifically for use in the eclectic labyrinth known as Imperial City. Originally referred to as the RC-M, this droid was designated the IC-M after Palpatine's rise to power.

**Imperial City Naval Base** The Empire's foremost naval base. It was established on Coruscant in the wake of the Clone Wars. The ICNB base encompassed one of the first TIE fighter training centers in the galaxy. Darth Vader made irregular appearances there, challenging the best pilots to one-on-one combat in either simulator or training ships.

Imperial code cylinder

**Imperial Civil War** One name given to the period of Imperial history following the Battle of Endor during which various Imperial factions fought for control of the Empire's remnants. The highest-ranking officers declared themselves Imperial Warlords and set out to create their own empires, all in the name of Imperialism. Conflicts started shortly after the death of Grand Admiral Thrawn, and culminated in several Imperial factions assaulting Coruscant and trying to gain control for themselves. The war ended with the emergence of the cloned Emperor Palpatine from his hiding place on Byss. Palpatine allowed the Warlords to struggle against one another, reasoning that this served to eliminate the weak leaders.

**Imperial Claw Station** During the construction of the second Death Star, this Imperial-held space station controlled all entry and exit points for all hyperspace routes between deep space and the Endor system.

**Imperial code cylinder** Issued to Imperial officers, the cylinder accessed computer information via scomp links. Each cylinder was coded to the officer's own security clearance. Imperial code cylinders were among the most common security tools employed by the Empire.

**Imperial Command** The name given to the chiefs of staff of the Imperial Army and Navy. In an effort to maximize the effectiveness of their forces, leaders from the two branches of the military worked together to plan and coordinate battle plans and defense systems.

**Imperial command center (Delvin Constructs Model Com C-38)** Imperial officers used one of these buildings as a centralized location to direct all base and ground force operations on a planet. It also served to let enemies know there was an Imperial base in their midst—they could see the command center in the distance.

**Imperial CompLink** The code name given to an Imperial project to augment the galaxywide HoloNet, allowing scientists on the far-flung worlds of the Empire to communicate on various projects. The developers of the CompLink idea went so far as to write software and create plans for technology improvements, hoping to convince their superiors of the idea's importance. The original idea was presented to Emperor Palpatine, who rejected it based on the costs involved. Behind closed doors, however, Palpatine feared that the free exchange of information would subvert the efforts of the Empire to maintain control, and the project was scrapped. The plans for the CompLink were retrieved by Imperial Intelligence, which used the software and ideas to tweak the existing Sector Plexus and gain improvements in efficiency. Despite its effectiveness, the idea was still nearly scrapped before Geothray Camber suggested the addition of Hyperspace Orbiting Scanners to the system. This transformed the CompLink into a communications scanning system, allowing Imperial Intelligence to monitor and record transmissions on more than 470,000 planets. Such a tool was something that Imperial advisers could understand and support, and thus the Imperial CompLink was finally implemented, albeit in a much different form than originally proposed.

**Imperial crown jewels** A reference to the vast holding of gemstones and jewelry that were supposedly acquired by Emperor Palpatine, and were analogous to the jewels of royalty.

Imperial City maintenance droid

**Imperial currency reserve** The primary holding place for the Empire's vast wealth, which formed the galaxy's most extensive store of valuable commodities. Its exact location was a well-kept secret, and it was believed that several levels of security served to protect its contents.

**Imperial customs frigate** A small Rendili StarDrive ship developed to support light corvettes on system patrol missions. The Empire used them as customs craft. The frigates measured just 35 meters long but were considerably slower than the light corvettes. Each frigate required a crew of six, along with six gunners to operate the six heavy turbolaser emplacements. The ship could carry up to 10 troops and 100 metric tons of cargo.

**Imperial customs vessel** A 180-meter-long light corvette patrol ship designed by Rendili StarDrive and used by the Empire to monitor and track intergalactic shipping operations. The ships were shaped like a tuning fork, with a pair of forward-facing mandibles attached to a deep-winged main section. They were armed with six turbolaser batteries to handle the various armaments on the transport ships they encountered. The crew complement was 52, with an additional 6 gunners. There was room for 20 passengers, although most of the ship was given over to cargo.

*Imperial customs vessel*

***Imperial Defense Daily*** This newsfeed, part of the Empire's propaganda arsenal, provided readers with sanitized reports on the status of the Imperial war machine. During the Galactic Civil War, the *Imperial Defense Daily* worked hard to put a positive spin on the Empire's battles with the Rebel Alliance.

**Imperial Department of Military Research** A branch of the Empire's war machine responsible for developing new forms of military technology, such as the orbital night cloak, the Sun Crusher, and dark troopers. Because of its mission and the technologies it produced, the Department of Military Research was a top-secret operation that remained viable well after the Battle of Endor. However, with the defeat of Grand Admiral Thrawn, all evidence of the department was lost. New Republic Intelligence investigators believed that the department's employees fled into the Outer Rim, and might have rejoined their former masters as part of the Imperial Remnant.

***Imperial Destiny*** This Dreadnaught served as Admiral Winstel Greelanx's command ship during the Battle of Nar Shaddaa.

**Imperial Diplomatic Corps** The diplomatic branch of the Empire. It was geared toward easing communications with newly discovered or neutral systems during the early years of the New Order.

**Imperial directive 59826** Admiral Gilad Pellaeon cited this directive when Borsk Fey'lya demanded that the joint New Republic–Imperial Remnant forces be led by Admiral Traest Kre'fey rather than by him. Pellaeon claimed that the directive ordered him to withdraw to Bastion if he was replaced as commander of the Ithorian defenses.

**Imperial Droid Corporation** This manufacturer of automata supplied the Empire with a variety of assassin and combat droids. It was formed by the nationalization of Banche Tech, Cencil Corporation, Reiber Manufacturing, and SFI Systems. The organization was targeted by Rebel Alliance privateers.

**Imperial drone ship** Cylindrical, pilotless ships about 9 meters long and powered by large fusion engines, they were used for carrying messages. The drones had a self-destruct mechanism.

**Imperial Drydock IV** An Imperial station maintained in the Greater Plooriod Cluster during the Galactic Civil War. It was a stopover point for Interdictor cruisers working in the Outer Rim.

**Imperial Dungeoneer** Specialized, skilled, and loyal guards trained by the Empire to guard its secret, heavily fortified prisons and labor camps. These facilities were populated by the Emperor's most dangerous enemies, including surviving Jedi and other Force-using splinter groups, warriors, and influential political figures.

**Imperial Elite Guard** A group of Imperial stormtroopers who served as the personal guard force of the Moff Council during the years following the Swarm War. They were distinguished by their gray armor and the dark gray stripes on their shoulder plates.

**Imperial emblem** The insignia that appeared on uniforms of some Imperial troops. After the fall of the Galactic Republic, the Emperor modified the symbol—which dated back to the Bendu monks' study of numerology—by the removal of two spokes.

*Imperial EVO trooper*

**Imperial Energy Systems** A branch of the Imperial Ministry of Energy formed to develop highly portable large-scale power generators. These generators were ostensibly designed to be brought to disaster areas, where they could be put to use helping refugees. Many historians believed that IES, which was headed by Moff Jerjerrod of Quanta sector, was simply a front for the development of better power supplies for the second Death Star.

**Imperial Enforcement DataCore** A huge Imperial-controlled database where all legal bounties were posted for the taking. Sometimes referred to as Enforcement Central, it was based on the Republic Enforcement DataCore used by the Old Republic.

**Imperial Entertainer's Guild** A guild that was overseen by the Empire and charged with providing entertainment to various Imperial and Corporate Sector outposts at the height of the New Order. Its starships were often painted with a mask superimposed on a sunburst.

**Imperial escort carrier** *See* escort carrier.

**Imperial EVO trooper (environmental trooper)** A specialized soldier who could survive even the most treacherous environments thanks to enhanced armor that provided protection against extreme heat, acid rivers, and lightning. These troopers came armed with a BlasTech FA-3 flechette launcher that fired lethal shards of metal, capable of hitting multiple targets. They were formerly known as heavy troopers.

**Imperial Exploratory Division craft** An exploration ship used by the Empire. One of these ships found its way by accident to the Seoul system.

**Imperial Fair** This traditional fair was the highlight of Fete Week each year on Coruscant. Originally known as the Galactic Fair, it was renamed during the reign of Emperor Palpatine. It was held all along the Glitannai Esplanade and ended in the *Pliada di am Imperium* at the base of the Imperial Palace. This was also the site of the Grand Display, which included exhibits created by various planetary governments.

**Imperial fast frigate** This arrowhead-shaped frigate was developed by the New Empire to serve as a front-line warship during the years leading up to the Sith–Imperial War. Similar in shape to the *Acclamator*-class troopship used during the Clone Wars, the Imperial fast frigate was built for speed and maneuverability to respond quickly to any threat. Thus, these ships were built with lighter armor and equipped with less shielding than other warships. This required their commanders to adapt to battle conditions quite rapidly or risk destruction.

**Imperial Fleet** Another name for the Imperial Navy that was used during the early years of the New Order.

**Imperial Fortress World** The term used by the Empire to describe any planet that was the site of a massively defended Imperial facility. Planets such as Prakith were garrisoned and equipped with huge numbers of troops and weapons, serving as secret sources of war matériel that could be drawn upon in the event of a rebellion.

**Imperial Freight Complex** The primary Imperial docking station located on Byss. This massive complex, where licensed independent haulers brought cargo for unloading, was considered one of the most heavily guarded facilities in the entire galaxy. Strangely, it was also one of the few places in the Deep Core where smugglers and other criminals congregated, if they managed to breach the Byss Security Zone. In addition to docking, refueling, and repair bays, there were several levels of restaurants, clubs, and cantinas designed to give weary spacers a place to cool their heels without venturing too far out into the surrounding city.

**Imperial Galleon** An older-model starship from the time of the Old Republic. It was specifically designed as a transport ship, and was completely unarmed. Later adopted by the Empire, the Galleon served mainly as a troop transport.

**Imperial Games** A vast series of athletic and skill-based events staged by the Empire each year. Athletes and contestants from every world of the Empire were invited to hone their skills and compete. The games were canceled shortly before they were scheduled to take place on Alderaan because the first Death Star destroyed the planet.

**Imperial Gardens** A vast, open collection of gardens and greenhouses located near the Imperial Palace on Bastion in the years following the Yuuzhan Vong War.

**Imperial garrison** A prefab structure carried aboard Star Destroyers and other Imperial vessels that could be set up quickly for establishing an occupation force and an Imperial presence on distant worlds. Garrison bases served as scientific, diplomatic, and military strongholds for the Empire and were typically staffed with 800 stormtroopers.

***Imperial Guide to Negative Reinforcement, The*** This Imperial military document described the correct usage of negative reinforcement and prescribed the correct punishments to be used in certain disciplinary situations.

**Imperial gunner** Highly trained weapons masters with keen eyesight, superior reflexes, and a familiarity with gunnery weapons. Gunners were part of a special subunit of the Imperial pilot corps. Many of the individuals who served in this capacity were unfit to be pilots, yet maintained the reflexes and intellect to earn a position as a gunner. Gunners could be recognized by their specialized computer helmets with macrobinocular viewplates and sensor arrays to assist with targeting fast-moving fighter craft.

Imperial gunners were found aboard a wide array of spacecraft, including space stations such as the Death Star. While operating laser cannons and other large artillery, gunners worked in teams to ensure that their weapons did not overheat or malfunction. During the Galactic Civil War, the most loyal Imperial gunners were appointed to posts aboard the *Executor,* Darth Vader's personal Super Star Destroyer, or became Death Star gunners responsible for that battle station's awesome superlaser. Obeying the orders of their superiors, the Death Star's gunnery crew leaders ensured that the titanic energies of the Death Star laser systems did not overload or hit phase imbalances capable of causing huge internal explosions.

**Imperial Hall of Heroes** This monument to Imperial soldiers and pilots who gave their lives during the early years of the New Order was erected in Imperial City with the use of Wookiee slave labor. During construction of a new wing, Commander Nyklas requested an assistant and ended up with Han Solo, fresh from his graduation from the Academy on Carida. When Han saw what Nyklas was doing to the Wookiees, he remembered the promise he had made to Dewlanna as she died. Han had been chafing at the Empire's pro-human stance, and the mistreatment of the Wookiees was the final straw. Han freed and rescued Chewbacca, earning a dishonorable discharge for his trouble.

*Imperial gunners on the first Death Star*

**Imperial Hammers elite armor regiment** One of the Empire's most specialized troop units, capable of virtually any assignment. The group was also known as Hell's Hammers.

***Imperial Hazard*** This *Victory*-class Star Destroyer, under the command of Sergus Lanox, was dispatched to Horob to capture Mon Neela. The ship was intercepted by the *Starcrossed,* which remarkably managed to rescue Neela and cripple the Star Destroyer. The exact fate of the *Imperial Hazard* was unknown, but Lanox received the Distinguished Medal of Imperial Honor for his bravery.

**Imperial Headquarters** The name given to the governmental building that served as the center of the Imperial Remnant's operations on Bastion. Formed from polished black marble and gleaming bronze trim, the Headquarters building was protected with shield generators and turbolaser emplacements. It resembled an upraised fist, and a crystalline starburst at its apex appeared to be a finger pointing to the heavens.

**Imperial heavy vehicle factory (Delvin Constructs Model Fac H-121)** A factory designed to construct middle-range walkers, including the SPMA-T and the AT-AA. This was at odds with the Imperial tendency to produce large, intimidating ground units. There was an attempt to allow for the construction of AT-ATs as well, but it was found that the larger walker required individual attention that the heavy factory could not provide.

**Imperial Heritage Museum** A museum located on Coruscant. It was dedicated to preserving the documents and relics of the Imperial regime.

**Imperial HoloVision** One of the largest, most powerful news agencies of the galaxy during the New Order. Imperial HoloVision had offices on all Core Worlds, and its reach extended well into the Outer Rim Territories. When Palpatine installed himself as Emperor, Republic News was reorganized and given an Imperial warrant to report news of the New Order. Among the first broadcasts aired by Imperial HoloVision was a series of news features on the treachery of the Jedi Order and the acts perpetrated by Jedi that necessitated their extermination.

**Imperial Hotel** Located in Lola Curich, this hotel had the best accommodations to be found near the main starport of Lianna. The hotel boasted some 6,200 suites at the height of the New Order. Many travelers and travel reporters regarded it as mediocre in terms of both amenities and the services provided by the hotel staff.

**Imperial hunter** A long-range intercept starship developed for use by the Empire during the rise to power of Palpatine's clones on Byss.

**Imperial Hyperspace Security Net** A network of Interdictor cruisers and gravity mines strewn across the hyperspace traffic lanes within the Deep Core. It kept Imperially held star systems out of the reach of the rest of the galaxy. The network was developed to ensure that no unauthorized starships stumbled upon these largely secret hyperspace routes or reached the Emperor's fortress on Byss. Technicians worked all along the Hyperspace Security Net monitoring entry and exit from the Deep Core, and were continually on alert for unauthorized traffic.

**Imperial Information Center** A huge computer database system created by Emperor Palpatine and located beneath the foundation of the former palace of the Old Republic on Coruscant.

**Imperial Inquisitors** *See* Inquisitorius.

**Imperial Institute of Higher Studies** Situated on Ferrhast, this was one of the premier learning facilities operated by the New Order.

**Imperial Intelligence** The branch of the Empire responsible for gathering and disseminating information. It was the military counterpart to the civilian-controlled Imperial Security Bureau and consisted of four divisions: the Ubiqtorate, Internal Organization Bureau, Analysis Bureau, and Bureau of Operations. This was one of the best-trained and most professional parts of the Empire to survive the Battle of Endor. Its remaining members fully supported Grand Admiral Thrawn's war effort.

**Imperial Interim Ruling Council** This body rose to power in the wake of the destruction of the original Ruling Council and the death of Emperor Palpatine's clones at Byss. It was led by the former Imperial Royal Guard Carnor Jax. Based in the city of De-Purteen on Ord Cantrell, it consisted of 13 staunch Imperial loyalists, as well as several nonhumans who supported the Empire. Their inclusion worried many of the human Council members. In the months following Jax's death on Yinchorr, the Council splintered into many factions, due in part to the behind-the-scenes machinations of Nom Anor. The Yuuzhan Vong executor knew that a unified Empire would be a formidable opponent for the Yuuzhan Vong. After a series of murders of various members, control of the Council was taken over by Xandel Carivus, who worked with Nom Anor; he disbanded the Council to rule as a new Emperor. After Carivus's death at the hands of former Emperor's Royal Guard Kir Kanos, the remaining Council members were captured by Rebel Alliance forces.

*Imperial Interim Ruling Council*

**Imperial Irmenu Navy** The primary naval force that protected the planet Gesl during the Old Republic. The officers of the Imperial Irmenu Navy were noted for their lavish uniforms, which some described as looking like the drapery in a Hutt bordello. Officers also carried vibroblades of an ancient design.

**Imperialist** The term used to describe those star systems that offered their support and backing to Emperor Palpatine and the Galactic Empire in the wake of the Clone Wars and Order 66.

**Imperialization** The process of galactic conquest as put forth by Emperor Palpatine. Imperialization focused on the conquest of star systems, the regulation of commerce, and the taxation and appropriation of goods and services for the benefit of the Empire. The way the Empire spun it, Imperialization was about bringing peace and justice to the galaxy by placing it under the control of a single individual, the Emperor. By controlling everything—from the military to financial systems—Palpatine kept the galaxy from suffering the corruption that destroyed the Old Republic.

At its core, however, Imperialization required that every inhabited planet be brought under control. Individual governments were forced to bend to the will of the Empire, and alliances among planets and star systems were sundered. If a planet did not willingly accept Imperial control, it was subjugated by the Imperial military. Nonhuman species suffered acutely under Imperialization because Palpatine's own xenophobia was imprinted on Imperial doctrine and law. Worlds that were inhabited by nonhuman populations were enslaved or invaded, depending on whether or not the Empire felt that a species could be of use in achieving its goals.

**Imperial jump trooper (Raxus Prime trooper)** A jump trooper was ready for any situation thanks to a jetpack that made it possible to take to the air in short, sustained bursts to engage the enemy. This lethal soldier also came equipped with a long-range rail detonator gun that allowed for effective elimination of targets from a multitude of vantage points. Jump troopers were used on many battlefields, including the fungus world of Felucia and the junk world of Raxus Prime.

*Imperial jump trooper*

**Imperial Justice Court** This remnant of Emperor Palpatine's rule was used by the New Republic for important trials. Among the proceedings conducted in its oppressive halls was the hearing of Tycho Celchu, who was charged with the murder of Corran Horn. The judge's bench sat atop a large black slab of marble, giving the magistrate an ominous appearance.

**Imperial Knight** The name used to describe those Jedi Knights who supported the new Empire that was formed in the wake of the Yuuzhan Vong War. Unlike the Galactic Empire formed by Emperor Palpatine, the new Empire embraced the Force and its connection to the galaxy, and even allowed some of the Imperial Knights to serve in high-ranking political positions. The Imperial Knights became the new Empire's version of the Jedi Order, and its members were completely loyal to the Empire. Their ability to work with the new Empire stemmed from the Empire's policy of "Victory without War," which allowed the Imperial Knights to work within the Force to ensure stability and peace. As a symbol of their unity, every member of the Imperial Knights carried a white-bladed lightsaber of the exact same design.

**Imperial kundril** One of the few remaining species of kundril that existed on a solid landmass. Unlike most species of kundril, which fled the colonization of Brentaal by moving to the oceans, the Imperial kundril made its home in rocky canyons. It was easily distinguished from the other species of kundril by its red exoskeleton flecked with gold.

*Imperial Knights*

**Imperial landing craft (1)** The *Acclamator*-class transport drop ships used by the Empire during the Battle of Hoth.

**Imperial landing craft (2)** The *Sentinel*-class landing craft was one of the main troop transports used by the Empire. It was derived from the *Lambda*-class Imperial shuttle and was introduced shortly before the Battle of Yavin. Although it was covered in heavy armor plating and carried several devastating weapons, the craft was still fast and maneuverable. Imperial forces relied on these shuttles to deliver six stormtrooper squads directly into combat situations. Sentinel shuttles also were responsible for providing vehicles and other supplies to garrisons. Vessels converted for this duty could carry 36 speeder bikes or 12 assault vehicles.

**Imperial landing platform** A building used by the Empire for landing starships and docking AT-ATs. The Empire had one such landing platform on the Forest Moon of Endor.

**Imperial landspeeder** A large landspeeder used by the Empire. The front resembled the nose of a *Lambda*-class shuttle and was similar to the one used by Princess Leia Organa aboard the *Tantive IV.* Darth Vader used one of these landspeeders during the subjugation of Ralltiir. Roons Sewell sabotaged a version by tying a chain to the vehicle's engines.

**Imperial legal code** *See* Imperial Penal References.

**Imperial Lightning Battalion** A special forces team that saw battle against the Icarii of Vestar.

**Imperial light vehicle factory (Delvin Constructs Model Fac L-113)** A factory modeled after a typical AT-ST manufacturing plant in Balmorra. It was easily constructed and could be set up quickly at any location to immediately begin producing new vehicles for Imperial ground forces. The factories could be retrofitted to handle the production of 2-M repulsor tanks and TIE maulers.

**Imperial Machines** The company responsible for manufacturing a number of detonation devices for the Empire.

**Imperial Maintenance Corps** A group of technicians who had exclusive rights to all the repairs required at the spaceport on Byss during the rise of Palpatine's clones there.

**Imperial Meats and Produce** One of the oldest ranches in the clouds of Tyed Kant, it was renamed from Republic Meats and Produce when the Empire arrived in the system. It was originally funded with grants from the Old Republic.

*Imperial landing platform on the Forest Moon of Endor*

**Imperial Medal of Honor** An Imperial award given to those cadets and newly commissioned officers who acted above and beyond the call of duty during their missions. Because every young, up-and-coming officer was being held to an exceptionally high standard, it was rare that the Medal of Honor was given out for simply earning a commission. The medal itself was a large circle of metal that depicted the fighter craft of the pilot who won the award; it was suspended on a black ribbon piped with violet trim.

**Imperial Medal of Valor** An Imperial award presented to those warriors who put their own pain and injuries aside in order to eradicate Rebel Alliance forces. Kyle Katarn was awarded the Medal of Valor for his part in securing asteroid AX-456.

**Imperial Medi-Center** One of the primary medical research facilities controlled by the Empire during the New Order.

**Imperial military barracks (Delvin Constructs Model MilBar C-427)** These troop barrack facilities were a standard military housing facility designed for functionality and defensibility, like much of their permanent counterparts. Unlike the Rebel Alliance barracks model, this version could be constructed quickly at bases and could house several companies of stormtroopers and scout troopers at the expense of luxury.

*Imperial Sentinel-class landing craft*

**Imperial Military Oversight Commission** A group of Imperial naval officers and Imperial agents whose mission was to review battle data and look for problems with the Imperial war machine.

**Imperial Military Stop Loss Order** This Imperial order was first issued in the wake of the Clone Wars, when the military force of the Grand Army of the Republic was about to be converted into the Imperial military. After the Clone Wars, many nonclone and civilian officers in primarily medical and other noncombat roles had planned to retire from military service. However, as the Empire expanded and the Rebellion became more pronounced, Imperial leaders found that they could no longer support the military without them. Thus, the Imperial Military Stop Loss Order was created to prevent such personnel from leaving their positions. Known as an IMSLO for short, this order was issued retroactively, basically saying that all beings, no matter when they had been conscripted into military service, were to serve in the Imperial military until they were discharged or killed.

**Imperial Mining Limited** This corporation, based on Derilyn, was owned by the Empire. It was charged with mining the planets of the Elrood sector for raw materials to support the Imperial war machine, but it found stiff competition from Radell Mining Corporation.

*Imperial military barracks*

**Imperial minisub** A small submersible vehicle used by the Empire as an underwater reconnaissance probe ship. It could seat up to five people. They were also used as emergency escape pods on submarines.

**Imperial Mission** The term used to describe any of the mission houses that were established by the Imperial Missionaries across the galaxy many decades after the Yuuzhan Vong War.

**Imperial Missionaries** One of many benevolent organizations formed by the new Empire that arose from the Imperial Remnant many years after the Yuuzhan Vong War. Unlike the Galactic Empire, the new Empire was founded on the basic tenet of "Victory without

War," and was led for many years by the Fel family dynasty. Imperial Missions were established throughout the galaxy to help the poor and needy eke out an existence.

**Imperial Mobile Surgical Unit** Field hospitals that were employed by the Imperial Army. Similar in most respects to the Republic Mobile Surgical Units used during the Clone Wars, these mobile hospitals could be set up near the front lines of battle and moved if the fighting got too close.

**Imperial Munitions** The company that manufactured stormtrooper armor and defense drones, along with a variety of technology for the Empire. Much of the corporate makeup of Imperial Munitions was created by nationalizing those independent businesses that showed early support for the Rebel Alliance during the Galactic Civil War. The downside of this growth plan was that the quality of products produced across the Imperial Munitions' portfolio varied greatly. Quite often, products were mass-produced by slave labor. In the wake of the Battle of Endor, Imperial Munitions was thrown into disarray, with many of its operations splitting off to work independently of any Imperial governance. Most of the nationalized factories eventually returned to their original owners or formed new corporations.

**Imperial Museum** A vast museum complex maintained by the Empire at the height of the New Order.

**Imperial Mutiny** Another name for the Imperial Civil War, which took place six years after the Battle of Endor.

**Imperial Naval Academy** The term used to describe the educational facilities established by the Galactic Empire to train new recruits of the Imperial Navy. While it was unclear which of the many institutions that made up the Academy was first to start, many surmised that the Raithal Military Academy was the original. The Academy center on Coruscant was another choice, since it was established within the first year of the New Order. The operations and structure of all Sector Naval Academies were based on those established at the Imperial Naval Academy. Early facilities for naval training, such as the Coruscant location, were often housed in temporary structures until more permanent facilities could be constructed. These facilities were given high-tech security systems and often guarded by reprogrammed B1 series battle droids.

**Imperial Naval College** A sister facility to the Imperial Academy, this college provided a way to train Academy graduates in the finer arts of naval combat and command.

**Imperial Navy** The space-going branch of the Imperial armed forces. It was formed from the naval divisions of the Grand Army of the Republic in the wake of the Clone Wars. While stormtroopers became the visible aspect of the Imperial military, it was the Imperial Navy that helped secure the early triumphs of the Galactic Empire. The huge shapes of Star Destroyers and the simple shapes of TIE fighters became the identities of the Imperial Navy, which controlled planets, systems, and sectors through fear of attack as much as sheer numbers.

*Imperial Navy trooper*

The Imperial Navy was broken down into four key branches: The Line Branch handled strategy and administration, the Flight Branch handled combat vessel flight operations, the Fleet Support Branch handled vessel maintenance and repair, and the Service Support Branch handled the supplies and services that allowed naval personnel to carry out their jobs. Much like the naval forces of the Old Republic, the Imperial Navy claimed that its sole mission was "to free the system space of member worlds from hazards to profitable commerce, to assure the safety of member worlds from attack from outside forces, and to bolster the planetary governments in times of crisis." However, unlike the Old Republic Navy, the Imperial Navy was not required to answer an emergency call from a local government. Individual planets were deemed too insignificant for the Imperial Navy to worry about. Such matters were to be directed to the nearest Imperial Governor for resolution. The credo of the Imperial Navy was a very simple statement of loyalty: Service. Fealty. Fidelity.

**Imperial Navy trooper** Those Imperial naval personnel who were in charge of security and hangar control in addition to their duties as combat officers. Many Imperial Navy troopers were chosen to serve as Death Star troopers during the months leading up to the Battle of Yavin. In the wake of the battle, these soldiers were simply referred to as Imperial troopers.

**Imperial Neural Interface Device** Early in the struggle against the Rebellion, the Empire experimented with linking TIE pilots to their craft via neural implants. The theory was that if pilots could simply think commands that could be fed into the ship's computer at lightning speed, it would eliminate the delay of manual input devices. The project was abandoned when it was discovered that interfacing with the ship's computers was simply too overwhelming for most pilots' minds.

**Imperial News Bureau** An intergalactic holonews service aligned with the New Order.

**Imperial News Network** The supposedly civilian branch of the media division of Imperial Intelligence.

**Imperial Office of Criminal Investigations** Known as the IOCI, this Imperial organization controlled the posting of bounties and the payments for services rendered by bounty hunters. All bounties were required to be paid in full to the IOCI before they could be posted for tracking and acquisition.

**Imperial officer academy (Delvin Constructs Model Edu-A-34)** These remote training facilities were modeled after one of the classrooms in the education building at the Imperial Academy on Carida. They could be constructed easily and provided Imperial commanders with the ability to promote and train new officers anywhere in the galaxy before sending them off to one of the military academies in the Core Worlds for more formalized training.

*Imperial Navy*

**Imperial *Omega*-class freighter** A freighter seen at the Imperial garrison in Mos Eisley.

**Imperial Opera Company** The Empire's premier operatic production group. It was based on Coruscant during the last years of the New Order.

**Imperial Order D6-66** A directive that required all hangars to be equipped with time-lock devices.

**Imperial Outlands** The Imperial term used to describe the Outer Rim Territories.

**Imperial Palace (Bastion)** This immense building served as the governmental seat of the Imperial Remnant during the years following the Pellaeon-Gavrisom Treaty. Located in the city of Ravelin on the capital world of Bastion, the Imperial Palace was an imposing building that was beautiful and ornate. Its inner chambers, especially those in which visitors were received, were exquisitely decorated in order to impress upon visitors that the Imperial Remnant was still powerful and wealthy.

**Imperial Palace (Coruscant)** This huge, governmental building on Coruscant was the site where the galaxy's leaders convened for thousands of generations. It was not always known as the Imperial Palace. Like much of the surrounding cityscape, it was added to by each successive administration.

The Imperial Palace sprawled across the face of Imperial City, dominating the skyline with a huge, pyramidal outline that was believed to have been designed by Emperor Palpatine himself. Much of its outer construction was made from polished, gray-green rock and mirrored crystal, which made the building sparkle and shine in the midday sun, resembling a beacon of power and striking awe into those who arrived on the planet to visit the Emperor. The uppermost levels of the palace contained hangars and delivery bays that could accommodate large transport ships. The remaining aboveground levels contained a multitude of banquet halls and living quarters for the many species and cultures that were part of the Old and New Republics. The levels immediately belowground were made up of audience halls and conference rooms. The lowest levels housed the support and service areas, including kitchens, atmosphere circulation, heating and cooling, and waste disposal. In all, more than 50 connected structures made up the Palace, encompassing some 20,000 rooms and chambers. It was not uncommon for first-time Senators and their aides to become lost in the mazes formed by its passageways.

There were also a number of rumors surrounding the Palace, including stories of construction workers who were lost and never found, of chambers without doors, and of sections of 100 or more rooms that had never been occupied. It was even believed that there was a hidden treasure room containing the wealth of Tolpeh-Sor. Much of the oldest parts of the Palace were damaged by a Force storm sent by the reborn Emperor Palpatine to capture Luke Skywalker during the early years of the New Republic. When the New Republic retook Coruscant, it used the Palace as its base, and tried unsuccessfully to change its name to the Capitol and then Republic House, but neither seemed appropriate. After the Yuuzhan Vong took possession of Coruscant, Chief of State Borsk Fey'lya tried to eliminate Warmaster Tsavong Lah by rigging his offices in the Palace to explode. The warmaster refused to take the bait, sending a representative in his place. Fey'lya was forced to detonate his bombs anyway, destroying three Yuuzhan Vong warships, some 25,000 warriors, and a good portion of the Imperial Palace.

**Imperial Palace Casino** A luxurious gambling house located on Ord Mantell.

**Imperial Palace Guard** This branch of the Imperial Guard Corps was charged with ensuring the safety and security of the Imperial Palace on Coruscant during the era of the New Order.

**Imperial patrol frigate** An escort frigate modified to serve as a deep-space probe ship. Several Imperial-controlled sectors used such vessels to keep watch over their border traffic. The *Guardstar* was such a ship.

**Imperial patrol speeder** A repulsortank vehicle used by the Empire on Aridus. The patrol speeder's main thruster was the vehicle's weak spot.

**Imperial Peace-Keeping Certificate** Known as an IPKC or the bounty hunter's license, this permit allowed an individual to transport the weapons and equipment necessary to track wanted individuals across certain galactic boundaries. Each certificate was valid in a limited area, and did not give the holder express permission to capture someone. As noted on the back of the IPKC, every wanted individual had to be "given the opportunity to peacefully surrender to the bearer of this certificate." Any attempt to avoid capture was deemed a refusal to surrender and gave the bounty hunter the opportunity to capture the individual, provided that the hunter also carried a Capture Permit. Some additional permits might also have been required to track and capture a wanted being, depending on the requirements of certain systems and sectors. During the New Order, IPKCs were issued, along with bounty-hunting licenses, by the Imperial Office of Criminal Investigations.

**Imperial Penal References** Known as the ImpPeRe, this 17-volume body of laws and regulations broke all forms of criminal acts into five classes. Class One infractions were defined as the most heinous of acts, and included conspiracy to overthrow the Empire and aggression against an Imperial officer. Class Five offenses were minor infractions, such as not having the proper emergency equipment installed in a starship. Section 14, Subsection 9, Part C-1, forbade any being from tampering with a droid's functional capabilities without express permission from its owner.

*Imperial Palace on Coruscant*

**Imperial Prefect** The highest-ranking Imperial official on a planet, he was the Emperor's liaison with a planet's existing government.

**Imperial Prime University** The most prestigious university sponsored by Emperor Palpatine and the New Order. It produced some of the greatest weapons designers of the Empire.

**Imperial Propaganda Bureau** This branch of the Empire was responsible for ensuring that news of events across the galaxy was reported so that the work of Imperial forces was shown in the best possible light. Most of the efforts of the IPB were unnoticed by the general population until Mon Mothma submitted the Declaration of Rebellion. Then the Bureau's claims that the Rebel Alliance was a terrorist organization that promoted "anti-establishment insurgency" became a rallying cry for oppressed systems. These systems decided that the time was right to oppose the Empire and began throwing their support to the Alliance.

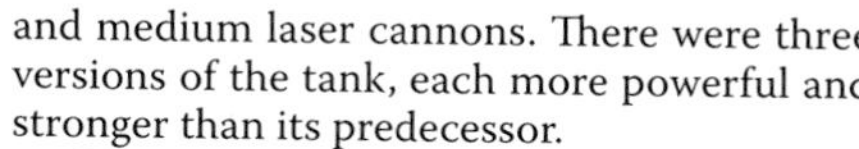

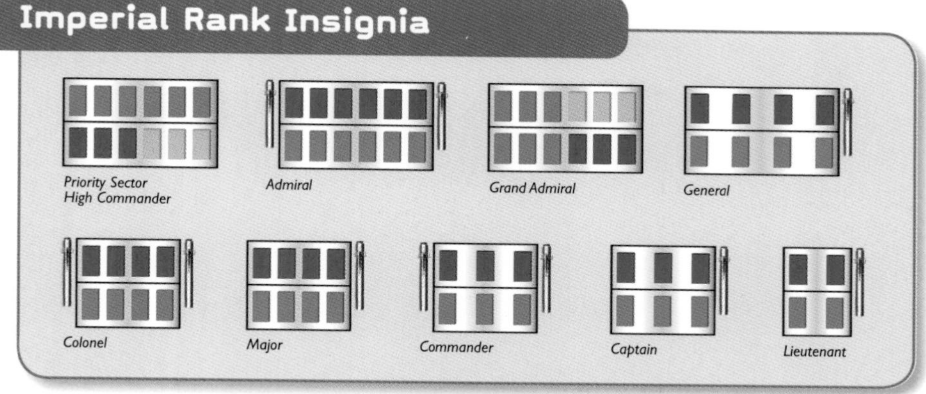


**Imperial rank insignia** Insignias worn by Imperial officers indicated the ranks of priority sector high commander, admiral, grand admiral general, colonel, major, commander, captain, and lieutenant. Rank badges and cylinders were combined to determine the hierarchy of the Imperial military.

**Imperial reconnaissance armor** A form of body armor developed by the Empire for protecting field medics and other noncombat personnel whose presence was often required on the battlefield. It was lightweight, developed to defend against blaster fire and other energy weapons. Because of its design, reconnaissance armor was susceptible to projectile weapon attacks.

**Imperial Records Library** The primary library of information maintained by the Empire. Developed on Coruscant, it contained information from all levels of the Empire. Palpatine's Special Files section was guarded with tight security, and only a few members of the Empire knew its access codes. When Palpatine died at Endor, the section was quickly confiscated by Imperial forces, but much of it was left behind. The New Republic was able to gain some information, but the deep encryption on most of the data was impossible to break. The library itself was continually restructured when the Imperial capital was forced to move from planet to planet, and eventually ended up on Bastion. To allow his supporters to know where the Imperial capital was, even if they weren't in favor, Grand Admiral Thrawn had a Chiss homing device installed in a dummy file in the library. The device operated only while in hyperspace, providing the new location before shutting down. This allowed Voss Parck and Stent to follow the movements of the Empire's remnants with ease.

**Imperial Relay Outpost V-798** An outpost on Vaal manned by a trio of Imperials. After crash-landing on Vaal following the Battle of Yavin, Darth Vader led a pack of hyenax into the outpost, where they proceeded to devour the relay team. When Vader returned to Coruscant, he ordered a new relay team to be sent to the outpost.

**Imperial Remnant** The name adopted by the surviving members of the Empire after a peace was negotiated with the New Republic. The Remnant was centered on Bastion and remained politically independent. It controlled a section of the Outer Rim. At its creation, the Imperial Remnant contained just eight backrocket sectors of the galaxy, a mere shadow of the former Empire. With Gilad Pellaeon's guidance, the Remnant was able to expand its borders over time, and its holding became known as the Imperial Sector.

*Imperial Remnant leaders*

During the war against the Yuuzhan Vong, Pellaeon agreed to have the Remnant forces assist the New Republic. Nom Anor believed that the early Empire was more organized, powerful, and potently militaristic, and could have crushed the Yuuzhan Vong utterly in their first encounter.

**Imperial repulsortank** This series of military repulsorcraft was designed and manufactured by Ubrikkian. They were five times faster than standard AT-ATs, more maneuverable than a walker, and armed with heavy and medium laser cannons. There were three versions of the tank, each more powerful and stronger than its predecessor.

The 1-L tank was the standard version, and the most economical. The 1-M tank was stronger than the 1-L but not as well defended as the 1-H, which was the most powerful tank. Some 1,500 of the tanks were initially produced, with the vast majority shipped to the first Death Star and the remaining 80 assigned to Hell's Hammers. All the Death Star's tanks were lost, and many of the Hell's Hammers' tanks were destroyed on Turak IV.

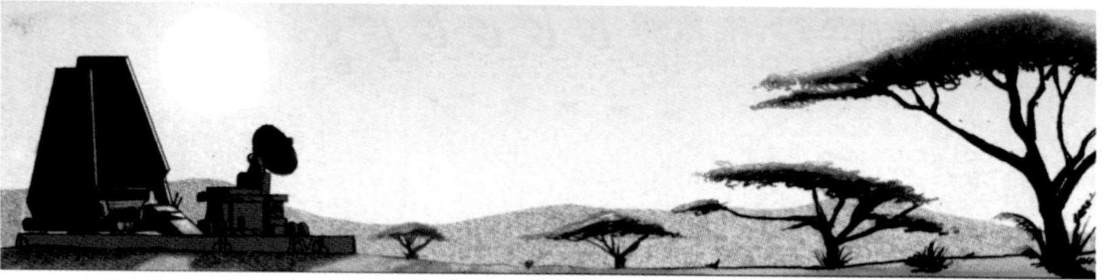
*Imperial Relay Outpost V-798*

**Imperial Royal Guard** *See* Emperor's Royal Guard.

**Imperial Ruling Council** This governing body rose to power shortly after Emperor Palpatine's death at Endor. It attempted to seize control of the Empire and restore it to power. The Council initially was led by Sate Pestage, who installed himself as the leader by virtue of his proximity to Palpatine. Ysanne Isard, desiring control of the Council for herself, arranged for Pestage to be removed. However, the Council voted Paltr Carvin as its new leader, forcing Isard to develop even more elaborate schemes to gain control. Eventually, she succeeded. When the New Republic retook Coruscant—albeit as part of Isard's plans—and Isard herself was defeated by Rogue Squadron at Thyferra, the Council was abandoned by the Imperial Warlords who fragmented the Empire.

**Imperial Safeguards Division** The branch of the Empire's armed forces charged with making sure the galaxy was safe for Emperor Palpatine to travel. It was rumored that they used assassin droids to keep the galaxy "clean."

**Imperial sanction card** These identification cards, issued on Imperial-held worlds, allowed the carriers to possess personal weapons. They were issued at spaceports, and were valid only for those personal weapons declared upon debarkation.

**Imperial Science Division** This body oversaw the multitude of scientific endeavors initiated by the Empire. It was the primary source of funding for Project Starscream.

**Imperial Scout Corps (ISC)** *See* Imperial Survey Corps (ISC).

**Imperial Section 19** This secretive Imperial think tank was believed to be responsible for the creation of many Imperial warships, and was thought to have developed several designs that employed active cloaking devices.

**Imperial sector** The term used to describe the holdings of the Imperial Remnant during the years following the war against the Yuuzhan Vong. Centered on Bastion, the Imperial sector encompassed worlds from neighboring sectors that were under Imperial control.

**Imperial Sector Rangers** This law enforcement agency was used by the Empire on various worlds where it could not extend full military force. Formed from the ranks of the original Sector Rangers, the Imperial Sector Rangers were sent in to establish order by eliminating rebellious activity.

**Imperial Security Authorization** A document that was issued by the Imperial Security Bureau to these individuals who passed an intense background check. It allowed them to access certain levels of secure Imperial installations.

**Imperial Security Bureau (ISB)** This branch of the Empire was considered a civilian organization and part of the Committee for the Preservation of the New Order (COMPNOR), and therefore was not part of the Imperial military. It was formed from the Internal Security Bureau, which was established in the wake of the Clone Wars. The ISB was charged with keeping the Emperor appraised of political events, and was viewed as an internal rival to the Imperial Intelligence agency.

Because the ISB was a more public agency than Intelligence, it was designed to help keep the darker doings of the Empire out of the public eye. It was also more of a policing agency than the Ubiqtorate, and often the simple fact that a visiting individual was a member of the ISB was enough to put a stop to criminal activity. The ISB was broken down into seven key divisions: Interrogation, Investigations, Surveillance, Enforcement, Re-Education, Internal Affairs, and the Commission of Operations. The latter oversaw the activities of the various Sector Offices of the ISB, each of which mirrored the divisional breakdown of the ISB itself.

*Imperial Senate*

Many within the Imperial military infrastructure believed that the ISB had been established by Palpatine himself as a way to exert a measure of control over the regular military, thereby ensuring that none of its leaders could grow strong enough to challenge him for control of the Empire.

**Imperial security officer** These officers served aboard the Death Star. They had black caps, white tunics, and black pants.

**Imperial Security Services** The more public branch of the Imperial Security Bureau.

*Imperial Shadow Guard*

**Imperial Senate** When Palpatine rose to power and assumed the role of Emperor of the Galactic Empire, he reorganized the Galactic Senate and titled it the Imperial Senate. Although the Sector Governance Decree all but eliminated the need for the Senate, Palpatine kept the governmental body intact. This provided continuity for the common beings of the galaxy, as well as ensuring that star systems and sectors that did not agree with Imperial doctrine were kept under control. It also provided a way for Palpatine to keep tabs on beings he had been manipulating, ensuring their continued loyalty to the Empire. Just before the Battle of Yavin, after the Death Star had been declared operational, Palpatine decided that the Senate had become a burden to his plans and dissolved it.

**Imperial Senate guard** Suited up in royal blue, these special guards were charged with watching over the members of the Imperial Senate.

**Imperial sentry gun** Security-sensitive areas often contained these remote sentry blasters to provide added firepower in combat emergencies. Most units consisted of a stanchion with a compact blaster, sensor bubble, and power conduit. They typically sat in high corners, above protected doors and near command stations with high, clear fields of fire throughout the area they defended. These systems remained on standby until a general alert sounded and activated their automated target acquisition programming to parameters customized to their surroundings.

**Imperial Shadow Guard** These guards were dressed head-to-toe in black and armed with red lightsaber-type weapons. The Emperor and Darth Vader recruited prospective Shadow Guards by identifying potential Force-users and teaching them rudimentary Force skills.

**Imperial siege balloon** The Empire used siege balloons with weapons platforms to protect the Tibanna gas refineries at Bespin. Prior to the Imperial takeover, the balloons served as floating health spas.

**Imperial–Sith War** *See* Sith–Imperial War.

**Imperial sky swooper** This repulsor-augmented hang glider was produced by Nen-Carvon.

**Imperial Sleeper Cell Jenth-44** This collective of clones on Pakrik Minor was created by Grand Admiral Thrawn from the genetic material of Baron Soontir Fel. Sixteen years after the Battle of Endor, a Thrawn imposter activated this and other sleeper cells. Jenth-44 refused to fight for the Empire and, instead, threw in with the New Republic and helped expose the fake Thrawn.

**Imperial sniper** This personal flying vehicle was used by the Empire on forest worlds like Endor. It looked like a seat mounted beneath a winged engine.

**Imperial Sovereign Protectors** The highest-ranking members of the Imperial Royal Guard, they served as the Emperor's personal bodyguards. At least one was by his side at all times. Rumors abounded that the elite soldiers were empowered by the dark side of the Force. After the clone Emperor's rebirth, the Sovereign Protectors guarded the clone vats on Byss.

**Imperial Special Training Corps** This branch of the Imperial armed forces was recognized as a fast track to promotions and glory for the Empire's brightest military minds. Many ISTC agents were used in the assault on Dalron IV.

**Imperial Star Destroyer** *See* Star Destroyer; *Imperial I*–class Star Destroyer; *Imperial II*–class Star Destroyer.

**Imperial Starfleet** This term was sometimes used to describe the Imperial Navy. It referred to the entirety of the navy, including all warships and fleets that were deployed across the galaxy. General Dodonna commented that the Death Star carried firepower greater than half the starfleet.

**Imperial Stronghold** A fortress established as a base of operations for those military personnel who were chasing down fugitive Jedi Knights in the wake of the Clone Wars. The forces working in the Imperial Stronghold were ostensibly under the command of Inquisitor Malorum, although Malorum himself took orders directly from Darth Vader. Operations within the Imperial Stronghold were scheduled to be moved to the former Jedi Temple on Coruscant, where Malorum set up an elaborate trap to capture any Jedi who managed to return to Coruscant in search of comrades.

**Imperial Sunbathers and Birdwatchers** The slang phrase used by the Special Operations units of the Rebel Alliance to describe Imperial Security Bureau agents.

**Imperial Survey Corps (ISC)** This branch of the Empire's military was dedicated

*Imperial Sovereign Protectors*

*Imperial troop transporter*

to exploring the galaxy. Though understaffed even at the height of the New Order, this group of scientists and scouts discovered a new star system every 207 minutes. Numerous members of the ISC chafed under the rigid structure and regulations of the Imperial Navy, and voluntarily left military service to strike out on their own. Many later joined the Rebel Alliance as scouts or intelligence operatives.

**Imperial Symphony Orchestra (ISO)** The premier musical orchestra of the New Order, drawing on the brightest and best musicians in the Empire. Much of the music played by the ISO was from the Neoclassical period, since Emperor Palpatine favored the marches and waltzes of that time. During the early years of the New Order, the ISO played its concerts in the Core Worlds, deemed the center of High Human Culture.

**Imperial Transfer Post** This was one of the three orbital spaceports that bordered on the Inner Kuat Transfer Zone during the Imperial occupation of the Kuat system. All spacelanes to and from the Transfer Post were restricted to Imperial traffic only, and violators were often shot at first, asked questions later.

**Imperial troop transporter** A repulsorlift transport often used to ferry troops and prisoners. These groundspeeders were used primarily for patrols on occupied worlds, though some elite units favored them for search-and-destroy missions. A pilot and gunner (or commanding officer) rode in the two-person cab, while six stormtroopers rode on the sides of the vehicle in exposed traveling racks that would spring open for deployment. These ships could be modified to travel over desert sands.

***Imperial Truth*** This docudrama was produced in the Larrin sector by J'fe Din and the team that developed the episodic story *Starflash.* The episodes provided detailed re-creations of some of the Empire's most heinous and cruel actions, ensuring that the show's viewers understood that the Empire was evil and that the New Republic promised a better form of government.

**Imperial University** This Imperially funded university was based on Coruscant during the New Order.

**Imperial walker** *See* All Terrain Armored Transport.

**Imperial Warlord** The generic term used to describe any of the former Imperial Moffs and military officers who took control of their territories and tried to establish their own control over the galaxy in the wake of the Battle of Endor. Each of these Warlords claimed to remain loyal to the tenets of the Empire, but many were simply power-hungry despots whose primary goal was control over other beings.

**Imperial Xenodetic Survey** The branch of the Empire responsible for cataloging the galaxy's alien species.

**Imperial Zoological Agency** The branch of the Imperial Survey Corps responsible for the cataloging of flora and fauna on newly discovered worlds.

**Imperial Zoological Gardens** This beautiful display of the galaxy's flora and fauna was built by Emperor Palpatine on Kailor V.

**Imperial Zoological Society** The name used to describe the former Intergalactic Zoological Society during the era of the New Order.

*Star Destroyer* Imperious

***Imperieuse*** A *Broadside*-class cruiser active two years before the Battle of Yavin.

***Imperious*** This *Pellaeon*-class Star Destroyer was constructed as the flagship of Admiral Morlish Veed. It was in service during the years leading up to the new Empire's war against the Galactic Alliance some 130 years after the Battle of Yavin.

***Impervious* (1)** An *Imperial*-class Star Destroyer that was part of the Imperial Navy's fleet during the Galactic Civil War.

***Impervious* (2)** A *Lambda*-class command shuttle from the *Ralroost.* During the evacuation of Dubrillion, it supported Rogue, Savage, and Tough squadrons in their fight against the Yuuzhan Vong. Admiral Traest Kre'fey temporarily turned it over to Senator Elegos A'Kla to use against the Yuuzhan Vong at Dantooine. It was later discovered with Elegos's skeletal remains.

**impervium** A rare metallic ore found in the vicinity of Kalee, it was often processed and mixed with other metals to create sword blades of superior durability and sharpness.

**Impervium** The brand name of the plasteel used to create stormtrooper armor. It was originally designed with extravehicular safety in mind. Thus only glancing bolts from a blaster were deflected. Any direct hit passed right through it.

**Impeveri, Alina** The daughter of Westa Impeveri, Alina took over many of her father's dealings as he aged. Alina was known to be a schemer and a liar, and her self-centered approach to the Cularin system's affairs earned her the wrath of Nirama some years after the Battle of Naboo.

**Impeveri, Westa** A native of an Outer Rim world who earned a living as a spokesman for various criminal organizations before stowing away on a Corellia-bound freighter in an attempt to escape. He was discovered and dumped on Cularin, where he quickly learned the ways of the city of Hedrett and began to assert his own power. He hired a group of cronies to spread word of his own reputation, and he developed a small following. Shortly before the Battle of Naboo, he managed to use his newfound reputation to defeat Karid Blakken in a general election, assuming the position of Senior Counselor. He was considered a competent official who seemed to genuinely care about his constituents. In reality, he was simply biding his time and storing information for later use.

***Implacable* (1)** An Old Republic assault ship dispatched to Geonosis to assist with the extraction of forces that participated in the Battle of Geonosis.

***Implacable* (2)** An Imperial Nebulon-B frigate that operated during the Galactic Civil War.

***Implacable* (3)** An *Imperial*-class Star Destroyer under the command of Admiral Apwar Trigit shortly after the Battle of Endor. He later aligned himself and the ship with Warlord Zsinj. The *Implacable* was the first ship to receive a new shipment of TIE fighters from the Pakkerd Light Transport facility on Ession. It arrived there with defensive support from the corvette *Night Caller*. However, the *Night Caller* was really under the control of Wraith Squadron, and was supported by three squadrons of X-wings hidden in the holds of the *Blood Nest*. Using a maneuver known as the Loran Spitball, the *Night Caller* destroyed the power cells of the *Implacable*, leaving the ship dead in space. Trigit, realizing that he was beaten, set the *Implacable* to self-destruct, then headed for the escape pods. The *Implacable* smashed stern-first into one of Ession's moons and was destroyed.

**implant chip** This dome-shaped nub was developed for carrying sensitive or classified information on a tiny chip implanted just under a being's skin. When the flat side of the nub was placed against the skin and pressed, it injected the eyelash-shaped chip. Because of the chip's size, it was virtually impossible to see and didn't show up on most bioscanners. It could be extracted at a user's destination, and the information retrieved.

**implant communicator** Developed by Traxes BioElectronics, this implanted communications device was originally designed to help deaf beings communicate.

The implant communicator consisted of a series of miniature transceivers that were placed just under the skin, against the skull and next to the vocal cords. The system allowed subvocal sounds to be sent to a comlink for transmission, and could receive communications signals. Communications were carried to the receiver via microwaves, electromagnetic waves, or specialized ultrawaves, all of which were set at frequencies that wouldn't interfere with normal brain activity. Many spies and other criminals obtained the implants to help them communicate without being discovered. Over time, it was discovered that the implants could be used to monitor the actions of another being during activities such as card games.

**implant cyborg** Any living being who replaced internal body organs or structures with cybernetic counterparts. These beings employed stim implants to shape their muscles, added specialized lenses to their eyes, or added stiffeners to their skeletons. The cybernetic implants couldn't be discerned by other beings. Most athletes were forbidden to use implanted cybernetics because it was considered a form of cheating.

**implanter** A biomechanism designed to implant surge-coral into the body of a Yuuzhan Vong during the ritual known as escalation. The implanter was a small, six-legged creature created from calcifiers, the creatures used to enslave other species with crippling growths of yorik coral. Implanters had botryoidal eyes and four blade-like arms that allowed them to cut through flesh and place surge-coral where directed.

**implosion drive** A powerful sublight drive system, it employed a high-pressure implosion reactor that emitted an intense gravitic field that dimpled the space–time continuum of realspace, causing a vessel to move. The engines were extremely temperamental, which was one reason they were uncommon except in the Outer Rim Territories.

Implanter

***Impounder*** An Imperial customs ship that was part of a fleet that patrolled the Kalinda system following the Battle of Endor. It was under the command of Captain Mandus Fouc.

**Improcco** The ninth planet in the Coruscant system, this ball of ice was orbited by a single, frozen moon. The majority of the Galactic Museum's collection was contained in massive underground vaults on Improcco's moon.

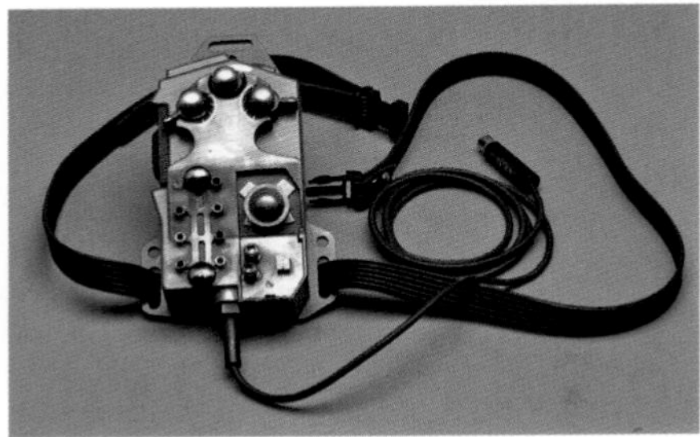

*Impulse detector*

**Improcco Company** This unit of clone troopers accompanied Jedi General Etain Tur-Mukan into battle on Dinlo during the early stages of the Clone Wars. General Tur-Mukan refused to let more than 1,000 clone troopers from Sarlacc Battalions A and B be killed when her superiors ordered the complete destruction of Dinlo. Four members of Improcco Company were killed and 15 injured in the extraction, which saved the lives of 1,058 members of the Sarlacc teams.

**Imps** Rebel starfighter pilots sometimes referred to Imperial forces as Imps.

**Impstar** Rebel Alliance slang for an *Imperial I*–class Star Destroyer.

**Impstar Deuce** Rebel Alliance slang for an *Imperial II*–class Star Destroyer.

**impulse detector** A diagnostic device created to allow engine builders and mechanics to monitor the output of engines and drive systems. Podracer mechanics usually carried handheld multifrequency power impulse detectors.

***Imru Ootmian*** An Ubrikkian space yacht modified for use as the personal starship of Popara the Hutt. The name meant "wandering outlander" in the Huttese language. The slow but heavily armored vessel had been in Popara's possession for many centuries before the onset of the New Order. It required a crew of 8 to operate and could accommodate up to 112 passengers and 850 metric tons of cargo. Popara maintained it with loving care and kept it in top operating condition. After Popara was murdered by his own offspring, Mika, the younger Hutt took the ship to Varl and dismantled it for parts to build his own vessel.

**Imsatad** This thick-featured, graying human served under Grand Admiral Thrawn on Wayland until Thrawn's death. Imsatad later became a captain in the Peace Brigade during the Yuuzhan Vong invasion and commanded the ships that blockaded the Yavin system during the Peace Brigade's attempt to capture Jedi students. Talon Karrde tricked Imsatad into believing that he had live ysalamiri to offer the Yuuzhan Vong. Imsatad, unable to capture the Jedi, was brought before Commander Tsaak Vootuh for questioning. When he refused to turn over the Jedi students without assurances that the Peace Brigade would be compensated, Vo Lian executed Imsatad with a thrust from his amphistaff.

**IMSLO** *See* Imperial Military Stop Loss Order.

**IMSU** *See* Imperial Mobile Surgical Unit.

**Imthitill** A city on Ando located on a vast atoll. Imthitill was the site of a massive fire set by the Aqualish to destroy all their droids in an effort to placate the Yuuzhan Vong.

**Imzig** A humanoid species. Members were distinguished from base human stock by the bony ridges that surrounded their eyes.

**IN-4** A series of information droids produced during the New Order by Veril Line Systems. They could follow only basic instructions, and then only if received from an identifiable source. The IN-4 series was based on the EG series of power droids, with the same boxy form, but equipped with a pair of heavy treads instead of legs. These droids were used extensively by many corporations and political Houses to store and retrieve vital information, and had several interface jacks with which to gather more data from computer networks. In most cases, information retrieval systems were hardwired into the IN-4's computers, which meant that any attempt to steal the droid's computer core would result in the destruction of the droid as well as the information.

**Ina** This elderly Vorzydiak was one of the few who managed to survive forced retirement at the age of 70. Ina remained a vital member of society and a beacon of strength for her granddaughter Tray in the decade before the Battle of Naboo.

***Ina'angs Star*** A Mark II assault frigate active in the years before the Battle of Yavin.

**Inacc, Gol** This crusty Corellian owned and operated Inacc's Shipping at the Estaria Central Starport during the New Order. Inacc was known as a lazy captain concerned more about his next loan payment than making sure his customers were satisfied. He flew cargoes with his own ship, *Inacc's Crate*, a deteriorating YT-1300 light freighter.

***Inad*** One of the Rebel Alliance's Nebulon-B frigates active during the Galactic Civil War.

**Inadi, Captain** This New Republic Navy captain commanded the starship *Vanguard* during the Black Fleet crisis. She worked with Commodore Brand to bring down a Yevethan T-type starship, but the *Vanguard* took heavy fire and was destroyed.

**Inaldra** The primary contact for most smugglers who arrived at Tansarii Point Station during the New Order. She was sympathetic to the Rebel Alliance, and provided information to any smuggler who wanted to make contact with the Rebellion.

***Inamo*** A Rebel Alliance Nebulon-B frigate destroyed during the Galactic Civil War.

**Inat Prime** Boba Fett paid a large sum of credits to have microscopic subdermal trackers placed on Rivo Xarran while on this planet during his hunt for the fugitive.

**Inc, Lieutenant** A lieutenant in the Grand Army of the Republic during the Clone Wars, he was a member of Star Corps. Lieutenant Inc was killed by Separatist droids during the mission to capture Shu Mai on Felucia.

**incinerator gun** A form of short-range flamethrower capable of firing a blast of chemical-based flame at a target. While effective, the incinerator gun was prone to overheating, which sometimes caused the weapon to explode. These weapons were used in the early stages of the Galactic Civil War.

**incinerator trooper** Imperial stormtrooper variants, incinerator troopers were deployed primarily to raze subjugated planets and incite fear in the local populace. Their primary weapon was a destructive plasma cannon that could quickly turn healthy crops, lush forests, and even vibrant swamps into charred wastelands. Incinerators were typically organized into small squads bolstered by other units, including scout troopers and EVO troopers.

**Incom Corporation** Headquartered on Fresia's Coromon Island, Incom manufactured the X-wing, the T-16 skyhopper, and other starships and components. Its products were considered top-of-the-line, a reputation that Incom had maintained for more than two millennia. Imperial rule angered many of its top scientists and engineers, and they defected to the Rebel Alliance, carrying with them the plans for the X-wing. The remaining Incom employees were quickly nationalized by the Empire, and the company's fame dwindled. Few new designs came from Incom until the introduction of the I-7 Howlrunner during the reemergence of Emperor Palpatine on Byss.

***Incomparable*** A Corellian gunship active two years before the Battle of Yavin.

**Incom T-16 skyhopper** *See* T-16 skyhopper.

**Incom T-65** *See* X-wing starfighter.

**Incom Tourer** A series of personal starships manufactured by Incom.

**incubator** This small creature was bioengineered by the Yuuzhan Vong as a way to quickly create a life-form from the blueprints contained in a qahsa. About the size of a Yuuzhan Vong hand, the incubator could be linked to a qahsa with a neural connection, and specific genetic and developmental data could be transferred to it.

***Indefatigable*** One of only four *Inexpugnable*-class tactical command ships to survive the early stages of the Mandalorian Wars.

**Indellian** This low-gravity industrial planet was the primary world in the Indellian system. It was located in the Yarith sector, where it intersected with the Javin and Anoat sectors to create the area known as the Greater Javin.

***Indenture*** A *Firespray*-class ship owned and operated by Krassis Trellix until he tried to ambush Fenig Nabon and Ghitsa Dogder. The two women had been transporting a group of Twi'lek dancers to Nal Hutta, and Trellix hoped to take possession of their cargo. Fen and Ghitsa were flying with Shada D'ukal and Dunc T'racen aboard the *Fury*, and Trellix was no match for their combined skills. He and the *Indenture* were destroyed.

***Independence*** An MC80a cruiser used as the Rebel Alliance's flagship early in the Galactic Civil War. It was the primary stopover point for Alliance starpilots. The *Independence* later was attacked by the Star Destroyer *Merciless* but managed to survive. During the Battle of Endor, the *Independence* served as the Alliance fleet's communications control center. Years later, the *Independence* was one of the many New Republic warships called into action against the Yuuzhan Vong.

**Independent Company of Settlers** The official name used by a group of 3,000 former Imperial supporters and former navy officers who wanted to live in peace after the Battle of Endor. Led by Admiral Daala, the group traveled on a fleet of ships in search of a planet where they could remain loyal to the New Order and separate from the New Republic. They eventually settled onto 600 million hectares of land on Pedducis Chorios. They were forced to defend their new home when the New Republic tried to secure the sector after the spread of the Death Seed plague.

**Independent Shippers Association** An association of independent transport ship captains formed during the second decade of the New Republic. It was created in response to the decentralization of certain monopolies under the Republic's watchful eye. Han Solo was appointed an official liaison to the Association and served as one of its primary mediators.

**Independent Traders' InfoNet** One of the smaller newsnets available during the New Order. ITI focused on information relevant to the independent shipper, and found itself under scrutiny by the Empire. Many in the media believed that ITI remained operational because it did not openly condone smuggling, although it seemed to provide messages to smugglers who could correctly interpret the stories.

**inderrin tree** A species of graceful blue trees native to Aruza.

**Indexer** A being native to Chalcedon that lived in a pool of water-covered agate stones. It had five prehensile trunks; strange, crystalline eyes; and a limited intelligence that, when combined with other minds, formed a vast mental storehouse of information and sentience. For a price, it would supply information on the underground slave trade and other illegal practices. Rillao knew of Indexer, and asked it for information on the Firrerreo slave trade.

***Indictor*** One of the many warships developed by the ancient Sith for use during the Great Sith War.

**Indigo** This spacer, based on Corulag, made a living running droids to colonists and settlers in the Outer Rim during the New Order.

**Indigo, Nell** This female Wroonian was a mercenary who sold her fighting skills to the highest bidder during the Galactic Civil War. Her parents were both gunrunners, and she learned the skills of a pilot and smuggler at an early age. She apprenticed herself to several other Wroonian mercenaries and eventually made a name for herself when, at the age of 20, she bought her way into the Guild of Glorious Mercenaries.

**Indigo Squadron** The designation of the ground-based vehicle team dispatched by the New Republic to defend its base on Saarn from Imperial capture. Indigo Squadron's vehicles consisted of two groups of Arrow-23 landspeeders and two groups of armed XP-38 landspeeders.

**Indikir** This arid rock was the second planet in the Bseto system.

***Indiko*** An *Imperial*-class Star Destroyer that was part of the Imperial Navy Fleet during the Galactic Civil War.

Individual field disruptor

**Indinor** This temperate world was a rocky wasteland. Orbited by two moons, it was the fifth planet in the Lianna system.

**individual field disruptor** These small devices allowed their users to break through small sections of force fields, such as energy screens and fences. An individual field disruptor could also serve as an impromptu personal weapon, delivering a potent energy blast to anyone who touched the person wearing it.

Indoumodo

**Indobok** This heavily cratered moon orbited Kalarba, near Hosk Station. IG-88 flew near it in an effort to shake off the pursuing Olag Greck. The planetoid supported the unusual B'rknaa. In fact, Indobok itself was a single massive adult B'rknaa. The Kalarba system was overtaken by the Yuuzhan Vong shortly after the Battle of Fondor.

**Indobok pirates** A group of alleged pirates who attacked the *Tharen Wayfarer* in the early days of the Empire. They really were chefs who had been framed by criminal Olag Greck for a poisoning that he had committed.

**indola** A sloth-like, saber-toothed predator native to Dar'Or. The indola received fierce competition from the elix, which was introduced to the planet to save it from extinction. The indola naturally hunted the Ri'Dar for food.

***Indomitable* (1)** This *Carrack*-class light cruiser was part of the Old Republic's Home Fleet Strike Group Five, which defended Coruscant during the Clone Wars. It saw heavy fighting during the First Battle of Coruscant and was part of the main force that attacked the *Invisible Hand.* It was among the first warships to be abandoned during the battle, but its commander continued to operate its weaponry and maneuvered it to block any possible escape routes of General Grievous from a remote location after fleeing the dying ship.

***Indomitable* (2)** One of the many *Strike*-class cruisers that made up the front lines of the Imperial Navy Fleet.

***Indomitable* (3)** An *Imperial*-class Star Destroyer built at the Kuat Drive Yards during the Galactic Civil War. It was assigned to patrol Darpa sector, and was based at Esseles.

***Indomitable* (4)** This New Republic *Majestic*-class battle cruiser was employed by Han Solo in an effort to draw out Warlord Zsinj and thin his defenses. It was later reassigned to the Fifth Battle Group and Commodore Brand, where it saw action during the blockade of the Koornacht Cluster.

**Indona** This forested continent, located on Cholganna, was noted as the primary breeding grounds of the nexu.

**Indoumodo** This planet was infamously known as the homeworld of the poisonous kouhuns, which were used by Zam Wesell in an attempt to assassinate Senator Padmé Amidala.

**Indrexu Confederation** This group of politically allied planets was located in the Indrexu Spiral and was part of Xim the Despot's empire many years before the formation of the Old Republic. It formed the Rimward boundary of the Tion Cluster and was briefly considered part of the Tion Hegemony. After the establishment of the Empire, the Indrexu Confederation was separated from the Tion Hegemony and reclassified as the Indrexu sector.

Verrinnefra B'thog Indriummsegh

**Indrexu Spiral** This mass of protomatter and comet debris was located in the Tion Cluster and presented a hazard to interstellar shipping. Popara the Hutt had information regarding safe passage through it.

**Indriummsegh, Senator Rennimdius B'thog** This former leader of the Elomin Council served as a Senator during the days of the Old Republic. He objected to Herylcha Baakos's order to define aboveground territories for the Eloms, since the Eloms lived underground.

**Indriummsegh, Verrinnefra B'thog** An Elomin representative serving with the Rebel Alliance during the Galactic Civil War, Verrinnefra was part of the group that wrote and signed the Declaration of a New Republic. He continued to serve for many years, and was one of the many diplomats who signed a continued declaration of war against the remnants of the Empire in the wake of the death of Grand Admiral Thrawn.

**IndSec** The capital city of Kelada, the name was believed to be shorthand for "Industrial Sector."

**Indu Council** The primary governmental body of Indu San.

**induction hyperphase generator** A key component of the massive superlaser designed and manufactured for the first Death Star. There were rumored to be two or three of these devices installed on the Death Star in order to take hypermatter from the Death Star's hyperdrive and literally align it before it was injected into the firing field amplifier for dispersal to the beam emitters located around the edge of the superlaser's eye.

**Indupar** This planet was the capital world of the Induparan Crown Worlds.

**Indupar, Dahon** The King of the Induparan Crown Worlds during the Galactic Civil War.

***Indupar Nova*** This corvette was part of an independent fleet that operated in the Ec Pand system. It was the first ship captured by Urias Xhaxin and the *Free Lance* for the Rebel Alliance. Xhaxin soon determined that its passengers, Lade Kalena and her handmaid, Missa, were fleeing the planet to avoid being captured by a rival house. Xhaxin seized them both to ransom them off to the highest bidder.

**Induran** This female Ansionian was a member of the Unity of Community leadership. Shortly before the Clone Wars, Ansion debated whether to secede from the Old Republic. Induran was one of nine members of the Unity to vote in favor of Ansion remaining with the Republic.

**Indus** The human natives of Indu San.

**Indu San** This Outer Rim world was the primary planet in the Indu San system. It was a major exporter of luxurious items carved from marbled stone and was renowned for the low, widely spaced smooth stone buildings that gave Indu San cities an uncluttered appearance. It was an active member of the Old Republic despite its remote location. The first Imperial Governor was able to transform the planet into a model of Imperial life. The subsequent Governor instituted a harsher regimen, and the populace rebelled. Following the Battle of Endor, the planet's chief councilor was assassinated at a meeting to discuss joining the New Republic. The deed was done by Imperial supporters hoping to pin the blame on the Republic. But the New Republic sent a force to assist the inhabitants, and the former government was reinstated.

**Industrial Automaton** A company renowned for its MD series of medical droids and the R series of astromech droids. Industrial Automaton originally was formed during the Old Republic when Industrial Intelligence merged with Automata Galactica. It was second in size and reach only to Cybot Galactica. The corporation was one of the original contributing sponsors of the Corporate Sector Authority.

***Industrious Thoughts*** This Diamalan vessel served as Senator Miatamia's command ship during the blockade of Bothawui after the revelation that the Bothans were involved in the destruction of Caamas. When saboteurs took control of the weapons aboard the *Predominance* and began firing on Drev'starn, the *Industrious Thoughts* moved in to cut off their attack. In the ensuing systemwide communications jamming, Miatamia failed to receive the message to stand down.

**indyup** A species of tree native to Ithor. It had a gnarled-looking trunk.

**inebriation algorithm** Inebriation programming created by I-5YQ at the Rimsoo Seven medical hospital on Drongar during the Clone Wars. A series of discussions with Den Dhur led I-5YQ to think it might be liberating to experience drunkenness. Since other unusual experiences had opened parts of his memory, I-Five figured that inebriation might have a similar effect.

**inertial compensator** A small, artificial gravity projector used aboard starships to assist passengers in overcoming the effects of acceleration, deceleration, and maneuvering. It also kept pilots from blacking out by adjusting the surrounding gravity during maneuvers. During the Yuuzhan Vong War, Gavin Darklighter and Traest Kre'fey discovered that if the compensator's field was adjusted to extend beyond the shields of the ship, it would negate the effects of Yuuzhan Vong gravity weapons. If several starfighters using this double protection ganged up on a coralskipper, the organic ship would implode when its onboard systems overloaded from trying to increase power to the gravity wells. *See also* acceleration compensator.

**inert-screen load shifter** These droids, used primarily in engineering facilities and shipyards, were tall, boxy automata with short, stubby legs. They used special inertial modifiers to create a low-gravity screen around them, which enabled them to move heavy equipment with relative ease. Kuat of Kuat used one to hide the falsified recording he had made to frame Prince Xizor in the deaths of Owen and Beru Lars, but the droid was not delivered before its courier, Ree Duptom, was killed.

***Inexorable* (1)** A *Victory*-class Star Destroyer that was still part of the Imperial Navy during the Galactic Civil War.

***Inexorable* (2)** This Imperial bulk cruiser was part of Admiral Greelanx's fleet that attacked Nar Shaddaa during the early years of the New Order. It was one of the last ships to join the engagement because it was at the rear of the attack formation.

***Inexorable* (3)** This *Imperial I*–class Star Destroyer was part of the small Imperial fleet that was commanded by Admiral Thrawn after the Battle of Endor. It later became part of his own fleet following his reemergence as a Grand Admiral. It was one of the Star Destroyers used to attack Bpfassh. Thrawn also used the *Inexorable* to test a prototype cloaking device, after getting schematics from the Emperor's storehouse on Wayland.

***Inexpugnable*-class tactical command ship** This massive, disk-shaped warship was produced by the Rendili/Vanjervalis Drive Yards after the Great Sith War. Only six were ever made, and they were designed to be escorted into battle by *Hammerhead*-class cruisers. This led many military observers to conclude that Rendili/Vanjervalis only produced the *Inexpugnable*-class ship to sell more *Hammerhead*-class cruisers. This ship's distinctive design was punctuated by the downward-pointing central section, which contained the main control areas and served to stabilize the entire ship. The main tactical center was referred to by crew members as the wishing well, since it was created with a transparent deck and holographic displays that appeared to be suspended in midair. This allowed the tactical command team aboard the ship to coordinate the activities of up to 64 other ships. The configuration often resulted in extreme vertigo for new crew members—and quite a few veterans, too.

**Infant of Shaa** A tiny statue carved by the Seylotts as a way of containing large amounts of Force energy generated by Shaa, their primary deity. The Seylotts also carved a larger statue of Shaa to control the Infant, which was known as the Destroyer of Worlds because when its Force energy was released, the resulting explosion could, it was believed, tear an entire planet apart.

Shortly before the Clone Wars, the Infant—which allegedly had been stolen—was recovered by Jango Fett, who was hired through an intermediary by General Ashaar Khorda. Khorda desired the Infant for its power, and hoped to destroy Coruscant with it. He nearly succeeded, but he was thwarted by Fett, Zam Wesell, and Jedi Master Yarael Poof. Poof died to keep the Infant from exploding, and the bounty hunters later returned the statue to Seylott.

**infantry mine** An automated weapon often stolen by Rebel spies and saboteurs from the perimeters of high-security Imperial installations.

**infantry support platform** A repulsorlift-powered speeder developed by Arakyd Industries for use by the Grand Army of the Republic during the Clone Wars. Instead of relying on repulsorlift engines to move about, the ISP speeder employed a powerful turbofan mounted at the rear of the vehicle, providing enough propulsion to reach speeds near 100 kilometers per hour. Small repulsorlifts kept the speeder just above the surface, aided by a terrain-following laser scanner. Because these vehicles were used over muddy or swampy terrain, they became known as swamp speeders. A pair of twin blasters was mounted to the nose of the ISP speeder for weaponry. It was a two-person vehicle, allowing one clone to pilot it while the other handled the blasters.

**infantry support weapon** Any weapons system that could be carried into battle, set up, and fired by a team of no more than four troopers. It was also known as an ISW.

***Infernal*** A *Keldabe*-class battleship.

***Inferno*** This unusual starship was owned and operated by Devaronian smuggler Vilmarh Grahrk. It resembled a rust-colored gackle bat, with a pair of cylindrical engines mounted in the middle and a single tail fin. The ship measured just over 10 meters from nose to stern and had a wingspan of 27 meters. It stood just a few meters high, giving the ship an exceptionally small profile for sensors. Three laser cannons were hidden within each wing, while a short-range ion cannon was concealed underneath. This allowed the ship to appear harmless at first glance, and often gave Grahrk the element of surprise. Although this weaponry was average compared with other such ships, the *Inferno* made up for any lack of firepower with its sheer speed. It was equipped with a Class 0.8 hyperdrive, and its ion drive system could propel it through the atmosphere at 1,200 kilometers per hour. Grahrk was assisted in operating the craft by an NT 600 astrogation droid, which was programmed to make the *Inferno* practically self-aware.

**Inferno droid** A series of firefighting automata produced by the Corporate Sector Authority. These boxy droids—sometimes called firefighting robos—were equipped with repulsorlift engines for mobility, and were given a wealth of firefighting equipment. Well armored, they could attack a fire at its source without being burned or damaged. The Inferno droid was developed to work autonomously or in groups, and was configured so that individual droids could snap together to form a larger firefighting unit. This allowed the Inferno to have sprayers pointing in two directions at once. As part of the Inferno system, a host droid hovered at a safe distance and could refill the flame-retardant chemicals of individual Inferno units.

*Infantry support platform*

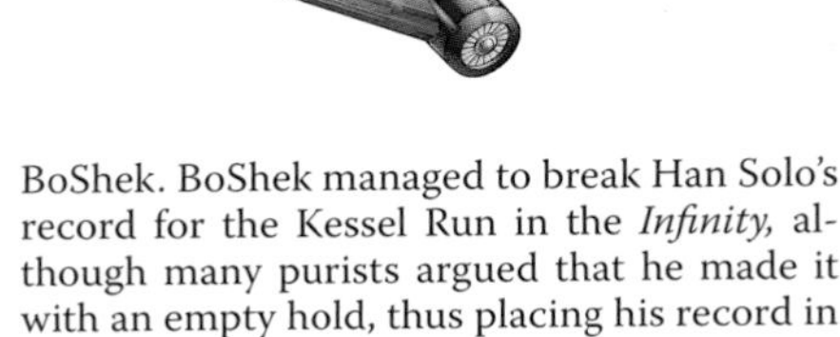

Inferno

**infiltrator gloves** These specialized gloves were equipped with an advanced artificial intelligence unit that allowed the user to tap into nearby computer systems cables or wireless transmission networks. The gloves also stabilized the user's hands for fine detail work.

**Infiltrators** One of the most elite sections of Rebel Alliance Special Forces. Infiltrators used stealth and cunning to get into Imperial installations prior to an assault. They gathered intelligence and softened up Imperial resistance before the main ground force attacked. They assisted in bringing down perimeter defenses to provide the main force easier access to a target. They were considered the 5th Regiment of the SpecForces. Although the Infiltrators were disbanded shortly after the Battle of Endor, many members took positions with Red Team Five.

**Infiltrator series assassin droid** This attack droid produced by the Colicoids was one of the precursors of the droideka. Like the droideka, the Infiltrator resembled the Colicoid physical form, with a squat body and a head on a curving neck. However, the Infiltrator was designed around a rectangular central body, with four sturdy legs providing support and mobility. Two arms mounted atop the body were tipped with long, razor-sharp claws capable of cutting through metal and flesh with ease. On each shoulder, the Infiltrator was armed with an E-11 blaster rifle, and several other mounting nodes were provided for attaching dart throwers, grappling hooks, and other implements. The droids' primary missions were remote assassinations and abductions, requiring them to operate autonomously.

**Infiltrator series fighter** This long-range fighter was developed by Republic Sienar Systems following the Battle of Ruusan. It was capable of transporting up to six passengers, and was armed with light weaponry and minimal hull plating. The fighters were speedy and highly maneuverable.

***Infinity*** A smuggling ship owned by the Dim-U priests of Tatooine, it was piloted by BoShek. BoShek managed to break Han Solo's record for the Kessel Run in the *Infinity*, although many purists argued that he made it with an empty hold, thus placing his record in dispute.

**Infinity Gate** The ancient Kwa used these gates to travel throughout the galaxy well before the formation of the Galactic Republic. To guard and protect the integrity of the gates, they created Star Chambers, which allowed the gates to remain operative almost indefinitely. One of these gates was on Ova, and the master gate was believed to have been on Dathomir. When the Witches of Dathomir tried to open the gate there to escape captivity, they activated a fail-safe device that shut the gate down. It also destroyed the gate on Ova, subsuming the planet and literally sucking it out of existence due to an Infinity Wave of great power that created intense distortions of space for many days. Dathomir witch Zalem and her clan hoped to use the power of the Wave to destroy Coruscant. Their plan nearly succeeded, but Quinlan Vos destroyed the Star Chamber on the planet, stripping the Wave of its power.

***Inflexible*** An *Imperial*-class Star Destroyer built at the Kuat Drive Yards.

**Influenza Necrosi** This was a bioengineered, deadly form of the flu created by the Empire for use as a biological weapon.

**influx capacitor** This hyperdrive component regulated the inflow of energy to the entire system.

**infochant** Presumably a shortened form of "information merchant," this was slang used to describe any underworld operative who sold information for a living. These individuals were also referred to as sluicers.

*Inferno droid*

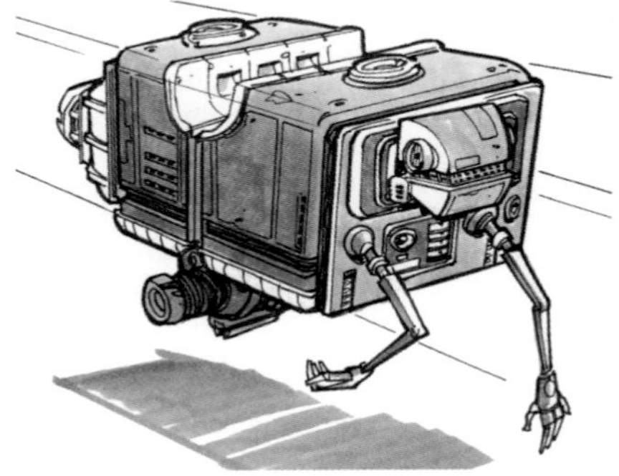

**InfoCore** A subspace relay system used by the military to send a tight-beam transmission to a predetermined source. It was used by espionage agents to receive regular bursts of data from a planted droid or other device. The InfoCore also could be told to download information on the fly by sending it as a predetermined, high-frequency signal.

**infopanel** A recording device that collected audio and video inputs to document messages. Infopanels were often used near doors to personal residences so that the owners could receive messages from visitors if they were away.

**information cataloging droid** The general term used to describe the Old Republic librarian droids that were produced by Kalibac Industries. These flat-headed automata moved about on small repulsorlift engines and were equipped with a pair of manipulator arms. They were designed and programmed to swiftly locate or replace datafiles and records stored in library archives.

*Infrared motion sensor (red circle on right)*

**Information Matrix Center** Known as IMAC, the information matrix center was developed by Ulban Arms to help control the actions of a droid. Part of the central processing unit, the IMAC allowed the droid to receive communications from a command center. The unit also sent information about the droid's status to the command center, where decisions were made on what to do next.

**infradig rays** A wide range of light wavelengths, most of which were in the infrared spectrum, that were emitted by high-tech lighting equipment. Infradig rays became something of a hysteria exploited by underhanded retailers selling specialized glasses to block these harmless rays from reaching the eyes in the waning years of the Old Republic.

**infra-goggle** Common night-vision devices that decoded ambient infrared and ultraviolet light to enhance an image, allowing for greater visibility in near-dark conditions.

**infrared motion sensor** Devices that detected sources of heat and motion and displayed them on screens to provide users with visual assistance in the dark. The Ubese bounty hunter Boushh wore a battle helmet that included a Neuro-Saav NiteSite infrared and motion sensor unit.

**Ingey** A tessellated arboreal binjinphant—which was a small, rare creature and sort of a cross between a kangaroo and ferret—it was the cherished pet of young Prince Coby of Tammuz-an.

*Ingey*

**Inglet, Candobar** This Sluissi served as the Khedive of Sluis Van prior to the Clone Wars. After Sluis Van threatened to secede from the Old Republic to join the Separatists, Inglet offered to assist the Jedi Knights in capturing the *Scarlet Thranta.* This offer was met with great skepticism. When the Sluis sector officially split from the Republic, Inglet became a vocal supporter of the Separatist movement.

**Ingo** A desolate world of salt flats and craters in the Bortele Cluster of the Mid Rim, its inhabitants were mostly human colonists who worked hard to keep food on the table and their equipment in good repair. After being captured by the Fromms, Thall Joben revealed that the Trigon One was located in Ingo's Jarl Forest, near a bantha-shaped rock formation.

**Ingoda** This Hutt was a minor crime lord who collected Theelin slaves as a hobby. However, his business acumen was no match for more infamous Hutts, and Ingoda regularly found himself indebted to Jabba. Ingoda was forced to sell two of his Theelin Divas, Funquita and Shaliqua, to pay off his debts to Jabba.

**Ingoian** Members of this humanoid species were characterized by a clump of beard-like tentacles on their chins. Human replica droid Guri's co-creator was Simonelle the Ingoian.

**I'ngre, Herian** This Bith broke the traditional mold and openly joined the Rebel Alliance during the Galactic Civil War, eventually joining Rogue Squadron. A native of Clak'dor IV, she found the pro-human stance of Emperor Palpatine distasteful and the diversity of the Alliance refreshing. Like most of her species, the black-eyed, bald I'ngre was also extremely shortsighted, so she cobbled together a huge pair of band-goggles that allowed her to see things at range. She undertook a study of heroism, which she defined as an intellectual and emotional subjugation of the most basic and primal desire for self-preservation. Inquisitive and vocally self-reflective, she had logic and intellect tinged with innocence and wonder. In a mission to Malrev, I'ngre crashed and was rescued by Dllr Nep. The pair used the last of their strength to fly I'ngre's X-wing into the temple of a Dark Side Adept, destroying it and killing the dark sider along with themselves.

*Herian I'ngre*

**inheritance exemption** This law was put into place by the ancient leaders of the Kuat ruling families to ensure that the Kuat family would always maintain control of Kuat Drive Yards. Each succeeding Kuati generation would supply a leader for the vast starship-manufacturing facility, who would work with the interests of all ruling families. This exemption was enacted when it was discovered that the Kuat family had the inherent skills needed to manage the corporation. Some families, such as the Knylenn and Kadnessi, chafed at the exemption, but were forced to agree that the Kuat family brought prestige and wealth to all Kuati families.

**inhibition field** The force field used by the Yuuzhan Vong to contain prisoners. Generated by a specialized dovin basal, it was a dome-shaped force field that could not be breached without risking severe electrical and neurological damage. Many of these fields were modified to allow the insertion of a Yuuzhan Vong executioner. Wurth Skidder was placed in an inhibition field aboard the *Crèche.*

**Inicus Mont** This limestone pillar on the moon Mina was a religious icon to the Vashan people. The interior was riddled with caves and tunnels, and the exterior was dotted with entrances to the caves. The pillar contained 42 distinct caves, set aside for various religious devotions. It was located in a remote corner of Mina's landmass, and was accessible only by traversing a winding path that passed through steep valleys and across swift-moving rivers. Each year, at midwinter, the most perfect of the Vashan bodhis appeared at the cave entrances and coughed up their sin-bullets. The pilgrims who trekked to Mina then gathered them up and consumed them, hoping to grind them in their true stomachs and absolve themselves of their sins.

**Inion, Shella** This beautiful woman was an aspiring actress who lived on Kal'Shebbol with her family during the last years of the New Order. She was wounded, and her entire family killed, when the Rebel Alliance apparently staged an attack on her hometown. Vowing to exact revenge, Inion disappeared, took on the guise of the bounty hunter Mist, and went to work for Imperial Moff Kentor Sarne. When Mist met up with Jessa Dajus during the Battle of Kathol, her true identity came out. Dajus revealed that it was Sarne who had staged the assault on her hometown—and Dajus had been one of the planners. Inion then used her skills to assist the New Republic in defeating Sarne on Kathol.

**Iniro, Falan** This hotheaded and impulsive Corellian was a competent sabacc player and pilot who lived on Nar Shaddaa during the early years of the New Order. He volunteered his piloting skills and his starship, the *Take That!*, to the defense of the moon when the Empire attacked. The Nar Shaddaa command post issued an order, which Iniro thought was "Prepare to engage." In actuality, all Iniro heard was "Prepare to . . ." before he leapt into battle. This left him stranded and alone against the *Carrack*-class cruisers making up the picket line. The cruisers ripped the *Take That!* apart with turbolaser fire in no time.

**injecto-kit shoes** Originally developed on Sullust, this footwear contained specialized bladders that could be injected with fluids to provide thermal protection.

**injector** Found in most medkits, this tool was used to administer painkillers and stimulants. It was a small, disk-shaped implement that was green on one side (where the stimulant was stored) and red on the other (where the painkiller was stored). Small needles on each side were projected when the injector was placed on a patient's neck, allowing the drugs to be placed into the patient's bloodstream.

**In'Kro, Gaddatha** During the early stages of the Clone Wars, this Caamasi led a delegation of Old Republic diplomats to Aargau to investigate the InterGalactic Banking Clan's affiliation with the Confederacy of Independent Systems. Much of In'Kro's work centered on the IBC's funding of Hailfire droid production, since a large number of the droids ended up in Separatist armies.

**Inleshat** This species of Iskalonian was native to Drexel II. They were characterized by their silky white hair, webbed hands, pupil-less eyes, and pointed ears, which allowed them to hear underwater. The Inleshat were the most dominant of the species allied as part of the School. They were also a spiritual people, and were not afraid to defend a cause that they believed to be right.

**Inner Circle (1)** The leadership of the Assassin's Guild during the early years of the New Order. Nearly half the Inner Circle was killed during its brief feud with Gallandro. In an effort to put an end to the feud, the Inner Circle offered Gallandro a chance to join them, an offer he politely refused.

**Inner Circle (2)** A term General Wedge Antilles used for a group of individuals he implicitly trusted following the death of Borsk Fey'lya. Wedge admitted only his most trusted allies to the Inner Circle; among them were his wife, Iella; Luke and Mara Jade Skywalker; and Tycho Celchu, Lando Calrissian, Booster Terrik, Danni Quee, Gavin Darklighter, and Corran Horn. In one of their earliest meetings, General Antilles called the New Republic "a dead, oversized hulk with a decentralized nervous system, whose extremities don't realize that its heart isn't beating anymore."

**Inner Council (1)** The ruling body of the New Republic, it was drawn from the primary circle of leaders within the Provisional Council. The Inner Council was considered a less formal, more casual gathering where issues could be discussed before bringing them to the attention of the Provisional Council. Its original members included Mon Mothma, Admiral Ackbar, Leia Organa Solo, and Borsk Fey'lya. It was led by the Chief of State. After the dissolution of the Provisional Council, the Inner Council became the focal point of the Republic's leadership. *See also* New Republic Advisory Council.

**Inner Council (2)** The leadership body of the New Regime of Brigia during the early years of the New Order.

**Inner Court of the Transcendent** This structure, located on J't'p'tan, was erected by H'kig settlers. It was a wide, open space surrounded by ornate walls and buildings.

**Innerdome Arena** A sporting venue on Nwarcol Point, along the Sisar Run.

**Inner Hub** The name used by the Daan and the Melida to indicate the center of the city of Zehava. Shortly after the Twenty-second Battle of Zehava, the Daan drove the Melida into the Inner Hub and surrounded them in the Outer Circle.

**Inner Los** This searing ball of rock was the innermost planet of the Recopi system.

*Inleshat*

***Inner Orbit*** An exhibit staged at the Royal Icqui Aquaria on Coruscant during the last decades of the Old Republic. It featured ocean-dwelling creatures from dozens of planets that existed in molten seas and near volcanic vents.

**Inner Rim Mercenaries** This gang of blasters-for-hire started up during the Clone Wars. Although their influence waned during the early years of the New Order, the Inner Rim Mercenaries gained power again during the Galactic Civil War.

**Inner Rim Territories** The section of the galaxy once thought to mark the end of galactic expansion, it originally was known simply as the Rim during the early centuries of the Galactic Republic. As hyperspace explorers began venturing beyond the area, however, it was renamed the Inner Rim. When the Empire began taking more and more resources from Inner Rim worlds, many of its inhabitants moved to the Outer Rim. Freed from Imperial control five years after the Battle of Endor, much of the region was recaptured by Grand Admiral Thrawn.

**Inner Sphere** Star systems located in the Core Worlds and the Colonies region.

**Inner Systems Bank** This financial institution, based on Paigu, grew to become the Commonality's primary banking and financial institution more than 1,500 years before the onset of the Clone Wars.

**Inner Wash** The name of a shallow sea in the Swamplands on Desevro. The Inner Wash was located between the East Wash and Outer Wash.

**Inner Zuma** This area of the galaxy was located above the galactic plane, and sat atop the area known as the Outer Zuma. Both lay along the border between the Outer Rim Territories and the Unknown Regions. The Inner Zuma was made up of three galactic sectors: Moddell, Spar, and Ablajeck. Much of the Inner Zuma was uncharted until about 1,000 years before the Battle of Yavin. Several centuries before that battle, the Inner and Outer Zuma regions were considered part of the Unknown Regions; then explorers began scouting them and pushing the boundaries of known space outward. Eddies and sinkholes in the area's hyperspace continuum led to many lost expeditions and the formation of exceptionally dangerous travel routes.

**Innis, Tarn** This graduate of the Imperial Academy was considered too average to ever assume a major command. He was put in charge of the Shallow March Supply Post shortly before the Battle of Yavin. Over the years, Innis developed a network of informants who provided him with great detail on the logistics of the Imperial Army. He often passed this information on to the Rebel Alliance via pirates and smugglers like Talon Karrde.

**Innk, Yo-Hann** This Kadas'sa'Nikto criminal from Kintan escaped from prison shortly after the Battle of Naboo. The Republic Correctional Authority was unable to pinpoint his location, and offered a bounty for his capture. Jango Fett claimed it on Tatooine during a mission to locate Gardulla the Hutt.

**Inondo, Boma** An Ithorian who served as Momaw Nadon's chief of security aboard the *Tafanda Bay,* he shed his loyalties when Nadon was exiled from Ithor. He then allied himself with Imperial forces that took control of the planet. When Nadon returned with a group of Rebel Alliance operatives, Boma Inondo tried to stand in his way. During a brief struggle in a forrolow-berry-processing plant, a young Alliance operative knocked Inondo into a berry vat. Inondo tried to shoot them with his blaster, but it had become clogged and exploded instead, killing him.

**Inondrar** The chief communications officer aboard the Star Destroyer *Anakin Solo* during the Galactic Alliance's war with the Confederation. When Jacen Solo broke ranks and began attacking the cities of Fondor, it was Inondrar who recognized that the *Anakin Solo* was slowly being cut off from the rest of the fleet. He suggested that Jacen issue an order for a tactical withdrawal, and was surprised when Solo agreed.

***Inquisitor*** An *Imperial*-class Star Destroyer that made regular patrols in the Core Worlds, near the boundaries of the Darpa and Bormea sectors.

***Inquisitor-4*** One of the World Devastators that attacked Mon Calamari, *Inquisitor-4* was a 1,700-meter-long "young adult" World Devastator. It was smaller and less well armed than ships like the *Silencer-7.* It had eight heavy turbolaser batteries, 80 blaster cannons, 30 proton missile tubes, and 10 tractor beam emplacements. It was staffed by a crew of 21,640, with 1,020 gunners, 1,800 slaves, 1,211 droids, and up to 6,700 troops and 1,000 pilots.

**Inquisitorius** The body of Imperial High Inquisitors that was based on Prakith during the New Order. Members of the Inquisitorius were distinguished by their high-collared robes, which had hoods that covered the entire head. These robes were meant to give the Inquisitors an air of menace. The role of the Inquisitorius was to hunt down any Jedi who had survived the execution of Order 66. Those captured were offered the chance to join the Empire; those who refused were murdered. Other beings discovered to be Force-sensitive also were captured and twisted to the dark side. The Inquisitors were given great resources to accomplish their mission. In the wake of the Battle of Endor and the apparent death of Emperor Palpatine, many Inquisitors abandoned their Imperial service and joined the Great InQuestors of Justice. Left without resources, the others slowly disappeared.

**Inrokini** One of the four ruling families of the Chiss civilization during the Yuuzhan Vong War. As with the other families, the Inrokini bloodlines predated modern Chiss society. The Inrokini syndic was charged with overseeing the industry, science, and communications of the Chiss.

**INS-444** These bullet-shaped, repulsor-equipped droids were developed by Publictechnic for use in urban environments such as Coruscant to install and replace windows in the immense skyscrapers that dominated the landscape. The droids often were deployed in pairs, with each carrying one part of a pane of glass or clari-crystalline while both remained vigilant for the approach of any airspeeders. Once at the location of a broken window, the INS-444 droids would move the new pane into position with their primary magnatomic gripper arms, then use their smaller testing probes to ensure that it had been properly fitted and sealed. Quite often, a Publictechnic CLE-004 unit followed behind, waiting to clean the newly installed pane.

*INS-444*

**inscription key** A form of communications encryption that was used by the Grand Army of the Republic during the Clone Wars. The inscription key was often based on a single word or phrase, but deciphering the transmission relied on voice-pattern recognition.

**insecticulture** The term used to describe the Kubaz science of genetically altering insects for increased stamina and food supply, as well as marking them for identification among the various Kubaz clans.

**Insiders** The term used by military forces serving under Wedge Antilles at the Borleias base, just after the Battle of Coruscant, to describe the Inner Circle. Most people believed that the Insiders and the Inner Circle were purely military advisers, and Wedge worked hard to keep the true nature of the Inner Circle a secret.

**Inspra, Jabidus** This Jedi Master accompanied Ashka Boda on a trip to the Gree Enclave in an effort to gather information about the possible sighting of Count Dooku in the mysterious sector during the Separatist crisis.

**Insta-7** The Gotal bounty hunter Glott was wanted on this planet.

**Insta-Meal** Produced by SoroSuub, the Insta-Meal was a processed food used in survival packs. It usually came in block form so that pieces could be broken off and consumed. It contained large amounts of essential nutrients in a small, easily transported form.

**InstaMist Generator** Produced by Agrierd Intergalactics, this handheld device was originally designed to expel a directed cloud of fire retardant. It also could be used to water plants with a gentle mist, or to produce a smoke screen to cover an escape.

***Instigator*** This Trianii RX4 patrol ship was part of the New Republic fleet assigned to Corva sector shortly after the Battle of Bilbringi. Despite heavy usage, the *Instigator* was a reliable ship. Many of the modifications performed on it were handled personally by Captain Bluuis. The ship was 33 meters long and armed with a pair of twin turbolasers and an ion cannon. It was flown under the name *Surge* during the Republic's search for the Kaarenth Dissension.

**Institute for Sentient Studies** Located on Baraboo, this educational facility studied the various sentient civilizations that had arisen in the galaxy.

**Institute of Starship Engineering** Next to the Imperial Engineering Academy, this was one of the most highly respected engineering guilds in the galaxy. The Imperial Navy required biannual ISE certification for its engineers. Most graduates could command a 100 percent increase in their wage opportunities. The ISE had a huge campus on Coruscant, with smaller campuses on Perithal VI, Sullust, Alderaan, and in the Corellian system.

**institutional neurosis** The theory that many beings felt safer when cut off from the rest of the galaxy. Kal Skirata applied this idea to clone troopers, stating that most clones were content to simply fight and die rather than think about what life would be like outside the Grand Army of the Republic during times of peace.

**insulfiber** This fibrous, insulating material was used by many hives of the Colony as the basis for exoskeletons that could withstand brief exposures to vacuum. Especially popular with the pilots of the Great Swarm, insulfiber was laminated into the chitin of their carapaces, strengthening their shells and allowing them to keep a member of the Kind safe in space.

**Insurrection** This branch of the Pentastar Alignment's Chamber of Order was established to ensure that the New Republic was unable to reclaim any former Imperial star systems. Moff Ardus Kaine feared that the fragmented Empire had become too worried about confronting the Republic with direct force, and established the Insurrection branch to use deception and misinformation so that the Republic received false and incomplete information.

**INT-66** Although officially known as a transport ship, Corellian Engineering Corporation's INT-66 was essentially a heavy interceptor craft. At 50 meters long, it was larger than a starfighter but nearly as maneuverable. It required a single pilot to operate, and could accommodate up to three passengers and 35 metric tons of cargo.

**Intamm** This Rodian clan owned a small enclave on the Betu continent of Rodia. It owed its allegiance to the Chekkoo clan.

***Inta'si'rin'na*** The term used to describe the ruler of the Rodians, known as the Grand Protector of the Rodians. The original Grand Protector was from the Soammei clan. Although the Grand Protector was considered the leader of all Rodians, the real power remained within the *rin'na* of the clan from which he was promoted.

**IntCon** *See* Internal Counter-Intelligence Bureau.

***Integrity*** This Old Republic *Carrack*-class light cruiser was the flagship of the fleet dispatched to Belderone, three years after the Battle of Geonosis, to capture the leaders of the Confederacy of Independent Systems. Commanded by Lorth Needa, the *Integrity* was later recalled to Coruscant and assigned to Home Fleet Strike Group Five during the Battle of Coruscant.

**Intellex** The brain of Industrial Automaton astromech droids, it was based on one of the few datafiles from the old Industrial Intelligence computer banks that was decrypted following the corporation's merger with Automata Galactica. These included:

- **Intellex II:** The second-generation droid brain produced by Industrial Automata, it was designed for use in the P2 series astromech droid.
- **Intellex III:** This model of computer brain was used in R1 as well as R4 droids. The Intellex III was a powerful central unit, but lacked the versatility of its successor.
- **Intellex IV:** The computer brain used in R2 series astromech droids, the Intellex IV could perform 10,000 or more operations a second. Imperial propaganda claimed that the developer of the Intellex IV was an Imperial scientist, but this misinformation was later exposed when the R2-0 prototype was discovered by Lady Aryn Dro Thul after the Yuuzhan Vong War.
- **Intellex V:** An upgraded version of the Intellex IV brain used on R2 and V1 series astromech droids.
- **Intellex VI:** An upgraded version of the Intellex V astromech droid brain.

**IntelStar Company** This manufacturer of prime hyperdrive components supplied parts to 11 hyperdrive builders. It was one of the original nonvoting Contributing Sponsors of the Corporate Sector Authority.

**intendant caste** This caste was made up of Yuuzhan Vong who no longer were warriors, but still considered to be among the best leaders. Most members of the intendant caste had skills from other castes to augment their already formidable abilities. They were overseers of Yuuzhan Vong commerce and trade, and were responsible for Yuuzhan Vong slaving operations as well as ensuring that the general population remained passive. Among the intendants, there were four distinct divisions: high prefect, prefect, consul, and executor. Nom Anor was a member of the intendant caste.

***Interceptor*-class frigate** A class of assault vessels that was produced during the New Order. *Interceptor*-class frigates were fast, maneuverable, and well protected, allowing them to be deployed along the front lines of a combat fleet. Measuring 150 meters long, an *Interceptor*-class frigate was distinguished by its long fuselage, a bulky rear drive section, and its chisel-shaped bow. The average Interceptor was lightly armed for its size, but it still carried a complement of turbolasers and proton torpedo launchers. The hull was protected by heavy armor plating and powerful shields, which helped to make up for its lack of weaponry. Following the Galactic Civil War, many of the ships found their way into the hands of pirates and smugglers.

***Interceptor*-class light freighter** This class of small triangular freighters was first manufactured by Arakyd, starting with the Helix Interceptor.

**interceptor roll-out** This was an evasive maneuver used by pilots of interceptor-style starfighters. The pilot executed a steep dive and roll to avoid being targeted by a pursuing craft. Many pilots traced the origins of the interceptor roll-out to Tycho Celchu, who used the technique to his advantage during the Battle of Endor and the early years of the New Republic.

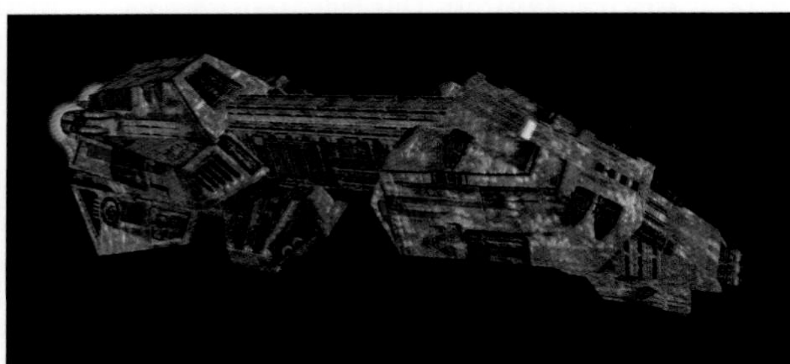

Interceptor-*class frigate*

**interdeck transfer tube** These broad cylinders functioned like turbolifts, but without cars. Interdeck transfer tube riders were buoyed by repulsorlift fields and could ascend or descend as necessary in lift tubes or drop shafts, respectively. The *Queen of the Empire* was equipped with many banks of the tubes.

**interdiction field** A gravimetric force field that simulated the presence of mass in open space or hyperspace. It could be a small, powerful, planet-sized field, similar to those generated by the *Interdictor*-class starships, or a huge, systemwide field similar to that used by Thrackan Sal-Solo to seal off the Corellian sector following its secession from the New Republic. Ships inside an interdiction field could not jump to hyperspace, and ships passing through an interdiction field were abruptly pulled into realspace.

***Interdictor*-class cruiser** A valuable addition to the Imperial Navy's fleet, this 600-meter-long star cruiser was built on a standard heavy cruiser hull, but was customized with devices that prevented nearby ships from escaping into hyperspace. At first appearance, *Interdictor*-class cruisers, also known as Immobilizer 418 cruisers, looked like small Star Destroyers, but they were distinguishable by four large globes that housed gravity-well projectors; these mimicked a mass in space and thus interdicted hyperspace travel. The ships also had 20 quad laser cannons for short-range combat against other capital ships.

Imperial strategy was to place Interdictors on the perimeter of battle areas to prevent Rebel ships from escaping. The only evasive opportunity was in the minute or so it took for the well generators to charge. Grand Admiral Thrawn used Interdictors as ambush ships and to cut off Rebel escape routes. He nearly captured Luke Skywalker by using an Interdictor to force Skywalker's X-wing back to realspace; Luke escaped when, in a desperate move, he reversed his ship's acceleration compensators while simultaneously firing a pair of proton torpedoes. Later, Thrawn tried to use an Interdictor above Myrkr to capture smuggler Talon Karrde and his ship, the *Wild Karrde*. However, a sudden burst of intuition from Mara Jade saved Karrde when she ordered the ship to leave the system just before Thrawn appeared.

***Interdictor*-class warship** This Old Republic warship was developed in the wake of the Great Sith War. The idea was first proposed by Admiral Jimas Veltraa, and the ship was first constructed at the Corellian shipyards. When Veltraa was killed during the Mandalorian Wars, there was a

grassroots effort within the military to rename the ship in his honor. The Republic's Chancellor decided to keep the original name.

**interference box** A form of communications jamming technology that was used about a millennium before the Galactic Civil War. The idea behind an i-box was to emit short-range jamming signals near an enemy location to prevent it from calling for reinforcements or warning the main camp. The primary drawback to the interference box was that it also jammed friendly transmissions, leaving the attacking unit cut off from its own main unit.

**InterGalactic Banking Clan** Based on Muunilinst, this was one of the oldest, largest, and most profitable financial institutions of the Old Republic. Founded millennia before the Battle of Geonosis, the InterGalactic Banking Clan—known as the IBC or IGBC—served the Old Republic throughout most of its history. Despite a façade of consumer-friendliness, the IBC maintained a sizable droid military in its euphemistically named Collections and Securities Division. Its hoop-wheeled Hailfire droids could make loan negotiations proceed at a chillingly expedient pace.

The IBC's first known transaction was the funding of a human colony on Sartinaynian. It made considerable profits through the development and manufacture of currency exchange technologies and infrastructures, especially when many planets began to think about seceding from the Republic. The desire of these worlds to have their own currency meant that IBC could step in and help them manage their new currency as well as maintain an up-to-the-minute valuation of it against the Republic credit. The financial backing for these new currencies came from the rich natural resources of Muunilinst itself.

As the Clone Wars engulfed the galaxy, the IBC continued to make a profit by providing financial services to both the Republic and the Separatists. The IBC also financed the resurrection of Durge and General Grievous, actions that IBC leader San Hill believed made Darth Sidious indebted to the clan. In the upheaval of the Clone Wars and the transition to the New Order, the IBC continued to do business with the galaxy, although much of its operation was nominally controlled by the Empire. While this rankled the IBC's leaders, it also ensured that the IBC remained the galaxy's preeminent financial institution. With the death of Emperor Palpatine, the IBC became the guarantor of the fledgling New Republic, despite protests from the surviving Imperial leaders. The leaders of the IBC correctly reasoned that Imperial grousing amounted to nothing, since any actions by the Imperial Remnant would only devalue the Imperial credit.

**InterGalacticBank of Kuat** The most prominent of the financial institutions based on Kuat during the Old Republic. Much of the collateral controlled by the bank was stored on Aargau during this time. Jango Fett kept his entire fortune within the vaults of the InterGalacticBank of Kuat in trust until they could be turned over to his son, Boba.

**Intergalactic Communications Center** The primary communications nexus maintained by the Old Republic. It served as the main hub for communications going into and out of the Core Worlds. The vulnerability of the system was exposed during the Clone Wars when Separatist forces blockaded Praesitlyn and overran the small Republic defense force, quickly capturing the communications center. It eventually was liberated by a Republic task force led by Nejaa Halcyon and Anakin Skywalker, although only a dangerous maneuver by Skywalker managed to preserve both the facility and its support staff.

**Intergalactic Droid Agency** This company matched unowned or manumitted droids to the needs of businesses and individuals throughout the galaxy during the New Order. Virtually any type of droid could be matched with a prospective user or task.

**Intergalactic Law Agency** This agency was conceived during the last century of the Old Republic, when the need for a galaxywide law enforcement body became prevalent. The ILA was eventually disbanded in favor of groups like the Sector Rangers.

**InterGalactic Ore** One of two major mining corporations that established lommite-mining operations on Dorvalla in the Videnda sector. IGO tried to bully its main competitor, Lommite Limited, out of business via a series of industrial sabotage actions. In the midst of their fight, Darth Sidious decided to use the feud as a way to run both companies out of business. Sidious's apprentice, Darth Maul, manipulated events so that LL and IGO decimated corporate ranks, leaving the lommite mines on Dorvalla open to the Trade Federation. IGO was forced to merge with Lommite Limited in order to form Dorvalla Mining, which ran the mines but lost all control of shipping rights to the Trade Federation.

**Intergalactic Trade Mission** A gathering of important business beings held regularly on Bothawui. Koth Melan requested that Leia Organa meet him at the Mission to discuss the recovery of the secret plans to the second Death Star.

**Intergalactic Zoological Society** This research association was formed on Mycroft during the Old Republic. It endured decades of political turmoil to emerge as the New Republic's primary zoological research center. Members of the society were opposed to siding with any government or political party, believing that the knowledge and understanding of life should not have political boundaries. Thus, they strove to remain neutral during the Clone Wars. During the New Order, the group was renamed the Imperial Zoological Society.

**Interior Region** The heart of the Hapes Cluster, an area containing Hapes itself. For the most part, the Interior Region was encompassed by the Transitory Mists.

**Interloper Squadron** One of the TIE defender squadrons dispatched by Colonel Vessery to recover Rogue Squadron above Corvis Minor Five.

**Interloper transport** A small, swift-moving troop transport vessel used by the Brotherhood of Darkness during the final stages of the New Sith Wars. These vessels saw extensive action during the Battle of Ruusan, ferrying reinforcements from the Sith fleet that blockaded the planet from orbit. Each Interloper could accommodate up to 10 troopers and their cargo. To gain speed, the design cut back on protective armor plating.

**Intern** A somewhat derogatory nickname used by Marn Hierogryph to describe Zayne Carrick during the Mandalorian Wars.

**Internal Activities Committee** A Galactic Senate committee tasked with investigating improprieties by government officials. Before the Battle of Naboo, it was headed by Bail Antilles. The Senator requested Supreme Chancellor Valorum to appear before the High Court regarding funds that showed up in the accounts of Valorum Shipping following the introduction of taxation on the trade routes of the outlying systems.

**Internal Counter-Intelligence Bureau** Known as IntCon, this branch of the Imperial Intelligence agency was charged with investigating the existence of spies and spy rings within the Intelligence community. By accessing Imperial data throughout the galaxy, IntCon agents were able to pinpoint spies and their activities. The IntCon branch was, in effect, a miniature version of the Imperial Intelligence agency, and was not above suspicion itself. Every internal communication was monitored with the same rigor as those of the rest of the Intelligence community, thereby preventing a spy from infiltrating the IntCon branch.

**Internal Organization Bureau** This branch of the Imperial Intelligence agency was charged with protecting the overall Imperial Intelligence organization from any internal or external threats. Known as IntOrg for short, it was considered one of the most unbiased, loyal, ruthless, and civil of all Imperial organizations. This combination of attributes made IntOrg a model of efficiency and respect. IntOrg agents were trained to appear cultivated and well mannered, and had a deep knowledge of political systems and schemes. This outwardly civil demeanor was tempered by a ruthlessness that allowed IntOrg agents to take whatever actions were necessary to protect the Empire and the Intelligence agency, regardless of who was causing the trouble.

**Internal Security Branch** The primary security force of the Imperial Intelligence agency. It was charged with maintaining the physical security of Intelligence agents, assets, and facilities throughout the Empire. Known as IntSec, the branch had the reputation of being a group of unambitious drones because of the might of the Empire. It was said that IntSec had no real mission, since the Empire was too powerful to be the target of outside attacks. However, as the Galactic Civil War began to engulf the galaxy, IntSec took measures to improve its responsiveness and efficiency, and began to improve its image both within the Empire and in the rest of the galaxy.

**Internal Security Police** The police branch of the New Regime on Brigia during the New Order. The primary mission of the Internal Security Police was the enforcement of the New Regime's laws, regardless of their morality.

**Interplanetary Acquisitions** This small corporation specialized in the refurbishing and resale of starships during the New Order. In reality, Interplanetary Acquisitions was a front created by Pal-Nada to help him move stolen starships on the black market.

***Interrogator*** An *Imperial II*–class Star Destroyer under the command of High Inquisitor Tremayne. It had a revolving door for captains, since Tremayne rarely remained pleased with an individual's performance. Although most Imperial officers aspired to command, they shied away from command of the *Interrogator.*

**interrogator** A device that sent out a query to a starship's transponder, an interrogator retrieved a ship's ID profile and checked it for authorization. All spaceports and military ships had them.

**interrogator droid** Commonly known as torture droids or IT-Os, Imperial interrogator droids were among the most heinous inventions conceived by the Empire. Simple in design, the IT-O interrogation unit was a glossy black sphere less than a meter tall. It hovered above the ground on low-powered repulsors and communicated through a rudimentary vocabulator. Its tools included a sonic torture device, an electroshock assembly, a grasping claw, a laser scalpel, power shears, and an oversized hypodermic injector syringe. Internal reservoirs stored a host of liquid chemicals, including the truth serum Bavo Six, which were dispensed through the fearsome needle. The drugs lowered pain thresholds, stimulated cooperation, and triggered hallucinations.

The droid's programming encompassed medicine, psychology, surgery, and humanoid biology. Vital-sign monitors predicted the onset of unconsciousness, which the droid sought to avoid at all costs. A recorder unit on the IT-O preserved any confessions shrieked during the torture session. The droid's advanced sensors allowed it to evaluate the confessor's truthfulness based on heart rates, muscle tension, and voice patterns.

The Empire often employed torture droids to question captured Rebels, including Princess Leia Organa. She managed to survive her encounter with an IT-O (and a psychic probe by Darth Vader) without revealing the location of the hidden Rebel base because she was trained to resist torture and other forms of interrogation in order to protect the sensitive information she possessed as part of the Royal House of Alderaan.

*Interrogator droid*

**Interstellar Collections Limited** A repossession firm that operated in and around the Corporate Sector from the final years of the Old Republic onward. It had an army of skip tracers to track down outstanding debts for goods such as spacecraft. Interstellar and similar firms typically preferred repayment over repossession. Those with exceedingly high debts were put on the company's dreaded Red List.

**interrupter templates** These metal panels worked with a starship's weapons systems to ensure that exterior structures, such as landing gear and entry ramps, were protected from accidental damage from a ship's own weapons. On the *Millennium Falcon,* the panels automatically slid into position to prevent the lower quad laser battery from shooting the landing gear or entry ramp when the ship was in landing configuration.

**Interstellar Droid Monitoring Incorporated** This small manufacturer produced a series of droid diagnostic kits during the Galactic Civil War.

**Interstellar Parcel Service (IPS)** This shipping megacorporation provided beings with a way to send packages across the galaxy in the shortest time possible. It shipped virtually any size package, provided that the sender could afford the fee.

**Interstellar Shipping** A huge conglomerate of shipping companies that operated in the Tion Hegemony when Han Solo was a smuggler.

**Interstellar Stock Exchange** The largest galactic stock exchange, it thrived following the Yuuzhan Vong War. Most of the galaxy's largest corporations were listed on the ISE, which provided access to brokerage firms as well as individual investors. Trading on the ISE was shut down only for tumultuous events, such as the declaration of martial law by Admiral Cha Niathal following the arrest of Chief of State Cal Omas. When the market reopened, stocks of military suppliers such as Kuat Drive Yards, MandalMotors, and Roche Industries saw marked trading and rapid increases in share values.

**InterTribal Council** The body of leaders of the United Tribes of Kariek, charged with day-to-day governing of the Eickarie and Lakra peoples. The InterTribal Council was formed in the wake of the capture of the Warlord, in an effort to remove the militaristic control that had been given to the United Tribes Command. The goal was to eliminate the historical need for vengeance among the tribes, thereby putting an end to the centuries-old civil war between the Eickarie and Lakra.

***Intervention*** This *Venator*-class Star Destroyer deployed by the Old Republic during the Clone Wars was under the command of Senator Bail Organa during a survey of the Outer Rim Territories. He ordered it to be diverted to locate Obi-Wan Kenobi and Anakin Skywalker, who had been set up by Count Dooku to die at the hands of Durge. Kenobi had been searching for Asajj Ventress, despite all the intelligence that pointed to her death on Coruscant. The ship was further diverted to Boz Pity after Durge's droid revealed the planet's location. However, Boz Pity was blockaded by more than 100 Separatist warships, leaving the Republic's forces without an easy way to reach the surface. In a daring move, Skywalker was allowed to pilot the ship through hyperspace, jumping it from well outside the system to a point within the blockade. Using the Force, Anakin got the *Intervention* behind the Separatist ships, but the gravity of Boz Pity was too much to overcome with reverse thrust. After launching all starfighters and evacuating all personnel to escape pods, Skywalker managed to bring the ship to a desperate crash landing on the planet's surface.

**InterWorld Marketplace** The sprawling, tariff-free bazaar found on the *Kuari Princess.*

**Intestinal Revenge of Bars Barka** This global disease swept the planet of Bars Barka several decades before the Clone Wars. It was believed that it was carried to the planet by a Neimoidian trade delegation. Microbes normally found in Neimoidian bodies caused devastating illnesses in Ubese colonists, resulting in crippling weight loss. The Neimoidians, of course, denied any part in the onset of the illness.

***In the Political Pit*** A popular political debate show, it aired on the Old Republic HoloNet during the years before the Clone Wars.

**In the Red** A cantina known for its rowdy patrons. It was located on the Galasol Strip on Bonadan. Uldir Lochett and his crew often stopped at the In the Red for a drink during layovers.

**intimidation mode one** The most basic combat mode of BD series droids: A droid was supposed to protect its owner without attacking by appearing to be ready to attack.

***Intimidator*** This *Super*-class Star Destroyer was sent to Black-15 from its normal dock in the Core after the Battle of Endor to make room for another *Super*-class ship that needed repairs. The *Intimidator* was at Black-15, receiving its final modifications, when the Yevetha took control of the shipyards. Because the *Intimidator* was spaceworthy, Jian Paret used it as his command ship. The *Intimidator* was captured by Nil Spaar and was renamed by the Yevetha as the *Pride of Yevetha*. During the final battle, Sil Sorannan took control of the starship from Nil Spaar, stranding the Yevetha in hyperspace.

**Intimidator (1)** The brand name of Merr-Sonn Munitions' IR-5 blaster pistol. The fully automatic Intimidator lacked a strong punch but could fire off a large number of blasts in a short period. The bulky weapon was quite expensive for its features, so it found acceptance only in certain wealthy circles.

**Intimidator (2)** The brand name of Greff-Timms Industrial's PC2 pulse-wave light cannon.

**Intimidator (3)** This speeder was actually a modified Maeltorp Cargorunner transport craft adapted for use as a racing vehicle by the sponsors of the BlastBoat 2000 demolition derby. It was armed with a tritium mining drill and could attain speeds of 200 kilometers an hour. Its maximum flight ceiling was just 1 meter.

***Intractable*** One of the Imperial cruisers that blockaded ThonBoka in order to starve the Oswaft early in the Imperial era. The commanding officer of the *Intractable* balked at being a frontline defensive ship after Rokur Gepta's order. Gepta immediately stripped the officer of his rank along with his counterparts on the *Upright* and the *Vainglorious*. Gepta then ordered them all forced out of the air locks on their vessels as examples of what would happen to any other officers who dared to disobey his orders.

**Intran** This remote planet, located in Brak sector, was the site of a Rebel Alliance base established shortly before the Battle of Yavin.

***Intrepid* (1)** This luxury cruiser was owned by the Jedi Council during the last decades of the Old Republic.

***Intrepid* (2)** This New Republic *Endurance*-class fleet carrier was built at the Hakassi shipyards and assigned to the Fifth Battle Group just prior to the Yevethan Great Purge and the Black Fleet crisis. The *Intrepid* served as the flagship of the Fifth Fleet under the command of Etahn A'baht. Thus the vessel was in a position to lead the initial, though unsuccessful, blockade of Doornik-319.

***Intrepid* (3)** This Imperial KDY Class 1000 cruiser was under the command of Captain Dulrain, and patrolled the Gesaril system during the Galactic Civil War.

***Intrepid* (4)** An *Imperial I*–class Star Destroyer assigned to guard the Imperial detention center at Stars' End. It was destroyed when Keyan Farlander and a group of Rebel Alliance starfighters assaulted the prison in an attempt to rescue a number of prisoners of war.

***Intrepid* (5)** This New Republic Nebulon-B frigate was part of the supply convoy traveling to Liinade III when it was brought out of hyperspace by the Interdictor cruiser *Binder* near system M2934738. The attacking ships, under the direction of Prince-Admiral Krennel, pounded the lead ship—the *Pride of Selonia*—the instant it dropped into realspace, preventing any sort of counterattack. The *Pride of Selonia* was destroyed. The *Intrepid* managed to pour a large amount of laserfire into the *Binder* before the *Reckoning* fired on it. The might of the *Reckoning*'s assault broke the *Intrepid* into two pieces, which spiraled away from each other as the ship died in space.

***Intrepid* (6)** This Old Republic *Venator*-class Star Destroyer was one of the many warships activated during the Clone Wars. It was dispatched to Felucia as part of a plan to capture Shu Mai and the other leaders of the Commerce Guild.

***Intruder*** This Bakuran *Namana*-class light cruiser was used by Admiral Hortel Ossilege as his flagship. It was one of four ships, along with the *Watchkeeper, Sentinel,* and *Defender,* that were built specifically for the defense of the Bakura system in the wake of the Battle of Bakura. When the New Republic asked for assistance in its struggle against the Sacorrian Triad, Bakuran leaders dispatched the four ships to Corellia. During the decisive battle, the *Intruder* was hit by three modified frigate-sized ramships. The *Intruder* sustained heavy damage and casualties, including Ossilege and Gaeriel Captison, who survived long enough to trigger the vessel's self-destruct mechanism. This caused a chain reaction of explosions in the nearby Triad ships, destroying many and giving the New Republic's forces a chance at victory.

**intruder trap** A form of personal shield that was used by the Chiss as a security device, but only in situations where the loss of innocent life could be minimized. By reversing the polarity of a small shield generator, it could be tuned so that the deflection field faced inward, instead of outward. In this way, any individual caught within the intruder trap with the intention of shooting their captors would only cause harm to themselves, as their blaster bolts were deflected back at them.

**IntSec** *See* Internal Security Branch.

**Intuci** Located in the Abrion sector, this planet was raided by the armies of war criminal Sonopo Bomoor. They sacked the city of Bonaka Nueno and massacred its residents in Bonaka Square. Among the victims was the family of Kosh Kurp, who later became the Empire's leading specialist on offensive weaponry. Kurp had his revenge on Bomoor during an attempted business deal with Jabba the Hutt.

***Invader*** An *Imperial*-class Star Destroyer in the Imperial Navy Fleet during the Galactic Civil War.

***Inveterate*** A *Tartan*-class medium cruiser.

**Invid** New Republic pilot slang for the pirates who worked for Leonia Tavira and were supported by her Star Destroyer, the *Invidious.*

***Invidious*** This Imperial Star Destroyer was part of High Admiral Teradoc's fleet shortly after the death of Emperor Palpatine. It was the mainstay of the fleet guarding Moff Leonia Tavira's holdings on Eiattu. When Rogue Squadron pilots defeated Teradoc, the *Invidious* disappeared for several years, until the warship reappeared in a supporting role for Tavira's pirate fleet. She would bring the *Invidious* into a system and pummel the defenses of a starship or settlement, then depart, leaving her pirates to loot and pillage what they could. They paid Tavira half of everything they took.

***Invincible* (1)** The Star Destroyer used by Zasm Katth and Baddon Fass to go to Nar Shaddaa to kill Vima-Da-Boda and Han Solo. The ship was destroyed when Katth ordered full tractor beam power to lock on to the *Millennium Falcon*. The *Falcon* hid behind the moon's spaceport control tower, and the powerful tractor beam ripped the tower from the station. It impaled the Star Destroyer, knocking out main thrusters and disabling the ship's maneuverability. It then crashed into the surface of Nar Shaddaa, killing all hands.

***Invincible* (2)** This Star Destroyer was one of four ships that formed the core of the fleet under the command of Moff Vanko.

***Invincible* (3)** This *Imperial I*–class Star Destroyer was used as part of Operation Strike Fear. The *Invincible* was later destroyed when members of the burgeoning Rebellion stole a warhead from the Imperial freighter *Gafra* and were forced to use it against the *Invincible* to eliminate a direct threat. The destruction of the *Invincible* gave the Rebels enough confidence that they soon openly declared Rebellion against the Empire.

Invincible-*class Dreadnaught*

***Invincible* (4)** The flagship of the small, independent war fleet amassed by Ranulph Tarkin before the Stark Hyperspace Conflict. The *Invincible* survived the navigational computer virus developed by Iaco Stark and unleashed on Tarkin's ships. With just a quarter of its original support fleet, the *Invincible* was an easy target for the warships of the Stark Commercial Combine, which ambushed it at Thyferra. In short order, the *Invincible* was destroyed, although many officers and crew managed to evacuate, including Tarkin.

***Invincible* (5)** A *Tartan*-class medium cruiser during the Galactic Civil War.

***Invincible*-class Dreadnaught** These capital ships measured 2,011 meters long and were first built more than 3,000 years before the Galactic Civil War by the Rendili/Vaufthau Shipyards. They were designed to resemble ancient Alsakan warships used in the Alsakan Conflicts, with design highlights taken from the huge starships of Xim the Despot. The *Invincible* class was one of the Old Republic's largest ships, but space combat technology began moving toward smaller platforms. The huge ships were soon discontinued, decommissioned, and sold off. The Corporate Sector Authority was able to obtain a number of them on the open market, since they were cheap, available, and effective.

**Invisec** *See* Invisible Sector.

**Invisible and Ineluctable Casino** The name used by Drawmas Sma'Da to describe his gambling enterprise, which was based on the skirmishes and battles fought during the Galactic Civil War. Sma'Da had the uncanny ability to predict the outcome of battles between the Empire and the Alliance, and to set accurate odds on the outcomes. Many of the galaxy's richest beings wagered on the outcome of any size confrontation, and Sma'Da grew wealthy by taking their bets. However, his wealth and insight soon came to the attention of Emperor Palpatine, who put out a sizable bounty on Sma'Da's head. With his capture, and with the decisive outcome of the Battle of Endor, Sma'Da's prominence quickly dwindled.

***Invisible Hand*** This needle-shaped *Providence*-class destroyer was General Grievous's flagship during the last stages of the Clone Wars. *Invisible Hand* originally was manufactured by the Quarren engineers of the Free Dac Volunteers Engineering Corps at the Pammant Docks. Its tapered bow and large outrigger fins gave it the appearance of a classical piece of Coruscant architecture.

The ship was built for Nute Gunray and the Trade Federation, and was reassigned after General Grievous was given total control of the Separatist droid armies. Gunray initially refused to surrender the ship, but Darth Sidious himself demanded that the vessel be turned over. As a minor consolation, Gunray was able to have Neimoidian navigators and gunners assigned aboard *Invisible Hand,* to provide regular information on Grievous's activities. Grievous nearly killed Gunray over the dispute; only Sidious's demand that the Trade Federation remain part of the Confederacy of Independent Systems kept him from killing the Viceroy.

The ship provided Grievous with a fast, mobile flagship from which to conduct his war against the Old Republic. Under the command of the bloodthirsty general, *Invisible Hand* played a key role in many of the Separatist cyborg's most notorious forays into the Galactic Core. These included the release of the Loedorvian Brain Plague that killed Republic clone armies and nearly every human in the Weemell sector. The ship also was used to supervise naval attacks on 26 strategic loyalist worlds. These included the hour-long orbital bombardment that depopulated and melted the crust of the former city-planet of Humbarine, an ancient founding world of the Republic.

During the Battle of Coruscant, Grievous was able to capture and hold Chancellor Palpatine aboard the ship. However, *Invisible Hand* was forced to hold its own against an onslaught of fighter craft led by Anakin Skywalker and Obi-Wan Kenobi. In an attempt to save the vessel, Grievous ordered his crew to move the ship slowly into the shelter of surrounding Separatist ships. The trick worked only briefly, as the two Jedi managed to get onboard and rescue Palpatine.

Republic warships then located *Invisible Hand* and began to pummel it with laserfire, unaware that Palpatine and the Jedi were still onboard. The ship lost its drive systems and began to tumble toward the surface of Coruscant. Only the incredible flying abilities of Skywalker prevented a major catastrophe, as he was able to pilot the crumbling wreckage of *Invisible Hand* to a controlled crash-landing at an abandoned airstrip in Coruscant's industrial sector. Grievous, however, had left the dying ship in an escape vessel and fled to Utapau.

**Invisible Island** A legendary island of untold riches, a virtual paradise according to Mere legends. Located in the most remote part of the oceans of Maramere, Invisible Island was guarded by the Haunted Strait. The existence of the island was a secret jealously guarded by the Trade Federation during its occupation of the planet, after it was discovered that the island was made up almost entirely of pure stygium crystals. Lord Toat and his Neimoidian cronies hoped to use the crystals to develop cloaking devices for Trade Federation warships, but their plans were thwarted by Sol Sixxa and Nym.

**invisible market** A name used to describe the intergalactic black market that operated beneath the jurisdiction of the government.

**Invisible Sector** Also known as Invisec, this huge area of Imperial Center got its name primarily because many citizens didn't want to admit its existence or go anywhere near it. Also known as the Alien Protection Zone, it was the enforced, segregated home to most offworld alien species inhabiting the planet. Thus it was somewhat like Mos Eisley, but uglier, nastier, and far less hospitable.

**Invisible Shell** Once described by Han Solo as a "sort of business syndicate, in polite terms," the Invisible Shell was an organization that would stop at nothing to get what it wanted. It was originally founded by Lorimar Lebauer, but he was forced to cede control to his underlings when he was imprisoned on Thyferra. Many believed that Lorimar was

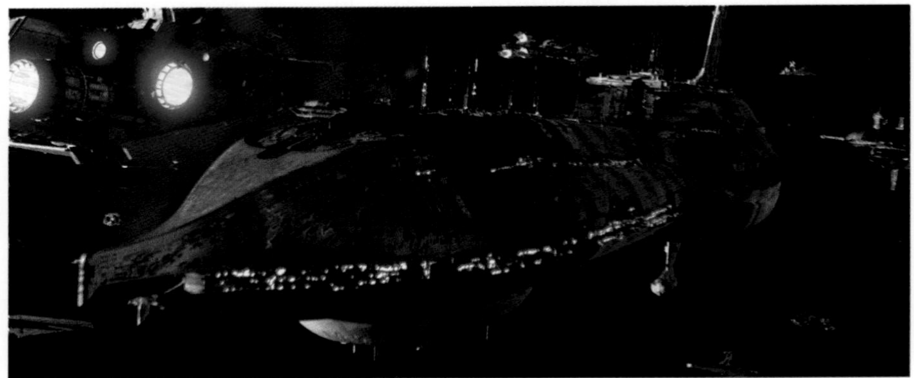
Invisible Hand

sold out by his own nephew, Ludlo Lebauer, who hoped to take charge of the Shell. Ludlo, however, was only given minimal control of the syndicate's operations.

***Invisible Star*** This modified Action V transport was owned by Qual'om Soach and served as his mobile base of operations during the New Order. Armed with a pair of turret-mounted laser cannons, the *Invisible Star* also operated under the aliases *Black Hole* and *Market Maker*.

**Inwil** This frozen, rocky world was the fifth and outermost planet in the Ralltiir system. It was orbited by three moons.

**Inx, Jondrell** This young pirate was known as a consummate con artist and huckster who would sell his own mother for 10 credits. He secretly pretended to be in love with Cressis Linrec so that he could eventually kidnap her and collect a huge ransom from her father. He told Governor Linrec that if the ransom wasn't paid, he would sell Cressis to the Zygerrian slavers. He enlisted the help of his friend and former employee Pallas Quintell, but would have sold him out if the mission demanded it. It was later revealed that Inx was a native of Kallistas who used his position as a pirate to acquire credits and funnel them back to the mining colonies there. Inx eventually was cornered by a trio of bounty hunters, but he managed to escape.

**Inysh** The homeworld of the Abinyshis, who were one of the first spacefaring species. The Empire stripped the world of its deposits of kalonterium, dumping toxic wastes produced in every conceivable location. Inysh was later abandoned by the Empire and left a ruined world.

**Io, Captain Dargen** This Rebel Alliance captain served as chief of supply for Mortex sector during the Galactic Civil War.

**Ioa, Captain** This New Republic Navy captain commanded the *Borealis* when it served as Leia Organa Solo's flagship during her travel to the Chorios systems. Like the rest of the crew, he was killed by the Death Seed plague unleashed by Seti Ashgad.

**ioaa** This sweet fruit once grew wild across the surface of Ithor.

**Ioli, Lieutenant Beta** A Duros, she served as a junior officer in the Galactic Alliance military following the Swarm War. Lieutenant Ioli was at the controls of the *Rover* when Ben Skywalker took the vessel to investigate the bombing at the Villa Solis estate on Terephon after the assassination attempt on Hapan Queen Mother Tenel Ka. At Terephon, the crew recovered Jaina Solo and Zekk, who had been on the planet doing their own investigation when the Ducha Galney ordered them killed. The Ducha destroyed her own family's estate in a failed effort to eliminate the two Jedi.

With the news of Ducha Galney's treachery, the *Rover* sped back to Hapes, only to find itself in the midst of a battle between the Hapan Royal Navy and the Heritage Fleet. The crew understood the need to warn the Queen Mother of her enemies—but also realized that any such transmission would be picked up by the Heritage Fleet, which would try to eliminate the source. Lieutenant Ioli and Chief Petty Officer Tanogo agreed to remain on the ship and transmit the message after ensuring that Ben and the rest of the crew evacuated first. Although the message was successfully transmitted, the ships of the Heritage Fleet quickly identified the *Rover* as an enemy and opened fire. Ioli and Tanogo died in the resulting explosion.

**Ioliu Sea** The smallest of the three major bodies of water on Rodia.

**Iolu** This Korunnai was one of many who served Kar Vastor as a member of the Akk Guards before the Clone Wars. When Jedi Master Mace Windu tried to help the Korunnai rid themselves of Balawai control by attacking the city of Pelek Baw, Iolu and the Akk Guards were ordered to oppose him. Iolu was killed by Nick Rostu during the fighting.

**Ion Alley** The nickname used to describe the ion defense grid that protected a starship's approach to Exovar's Emporium on Neftali. After transmitting the proper identification, ships had to pass through a heavy set of blast doors before entering a long tunnel. The tunnel was equipped with an EXVR-1 ion generation field, hence the nickname. Any unauthorized ship passing through Ion Alley was hit with a barrage of ion energy, enough to override shields and render a starship inert.

*Ion blaster*

*Ion beamer, wielded by an attacking Ssi-Ruu (right)*

**ion attractor** A long rod topped by a spike and designed to channel the destructive energies of ion storms. Jabba the Hutt installed an ion attractor atop his fortress on Tatooine. He and Ephant Mon later used the device as a death trap for Sylvn, daughter of Ki-Adi-Mundi, and her friend Twin. They bound both Cereans to the rod moments before an ion storm arrived, hoping that the storm's energy would fry the pair when it was channeled through the attractor. Fortunately, they were rescued by Ki-Adi-Mundi before they could be incinerated.

**ion beamer** A paddle-shaped medical instrument used by the Ssi-ruuk to immobilize their prisoners. These devices, also called ion paddle beamers, affected most humanoids in the same way a DEMP gun affected droids: Electromagnetic impulses within the nervous system of the target were disrupted, cutting off the target's bodily control. Like other Ssi-ruuvi technology, these weapons were powered by enteched life forces, which provided a variable energy source. New Republic technicians who tried to attach standard power packs simply burned out the beamer. The beam that was generated could not be deflected by the blade of a lightsaber, although it did bend around a lightsaber's blade.

**ion blaster** A small blaster that fired ion energy instead of laser bolts. Like ion cannons, ion (or ionization) blasters were effective for disrupting electrical systems, including those of most droids. Jawas on Tatooine frequently carried ionization blasters to disable their droid quarry.

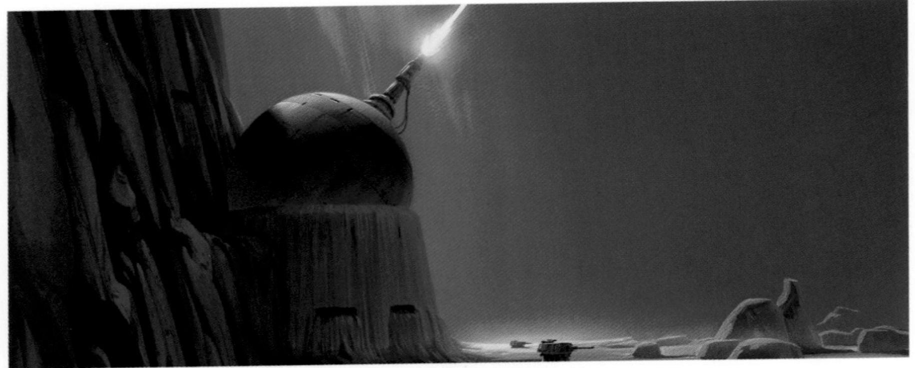
Ion cannon

**ion-blast missile** A form of projectile weapon developed by the Empire. It was designed to penetrate a vehicle and explode, releasing a blast of ions that destroyed the vehicle's electrical and computer systems.

**ion bomb** Prior to the fall of the Old Republic, ion bombs were considered the most powerful explosives in the galaxy.

**ion cannon** A weapon that fired bursts of ionized energy, it damaged mechanical and computer systems by overloading and fusing circuitry. Although they didn't cause structural damage, ion cannon blasts neutralized ship weapons, shields, and engines. Ion cannons could be built to almost any size, from small starfighter systems to huge planetary defense weapons. Planetary ion cannons, such as the one at the Rebels' Echo Base on Hoth, were mounted in multistory cylindrical towers from which they hurled bursts of ionized energy into space to ward off hostile vessels.

The ion cannon was one of the most important weapons used by military forces in the Galactic Civil War. During space battles, the ability to disable an enemy starship without damaging the cargo proved invaluable to both the Imperials and Rebels. The Empire valued these weapons because they allowed Imperial starships to capture enemy vessels intact in order to interrogate survivors. The Rebels used ion cannons to raid Imperial convoys carrying weapons, medical equipment, and other precious supplies. The Rebels frequently stole entire Imperial ships, including several Nebulon-B escort frigates. During dogfights, Rebel Y-wings and B-wings were armed with ion cannons to disable enemy starfighters.

**Ione** A planet located in the Anoat sector in the heart of the Ivax Nebula. Ione served as the primary staging location for Figg Excavations' mining operations throughout the Ivax Nebula.

**ion-enabled sensor tag** This form of targeting system was used during the last decades of the Old Republic. Starships equipped with the system could fire an ion-shielded tag at their target. The ion shielding served to drain the target's protective shields, while the tag lodged itself onto the hull and provided a guidance mechanism for volleys of nanomissiles.

**ion encumbrance system** This form of ion weapon was used during the Old Republic era. Similar in effect to later ion cannons, the ion encumbrance system sprayed a target starship with a sweeping barrage of ion energy that disabled its shipboard electrical systems. It acted more like a sensor sweep than a direct blast of ion energy.

**ion engine** A compact sublight drive that could generate large amounts of thrust and velocity by expelling charged particles through an exhaust port. Ion engines were found on virtually every starship in the galaxy.

**ion exciter** A component of early hyperdrive systems that helped charge up the particles used to generate thrust.

**ion explosives** Detonation weapons that employed excited ions to initiate the explosion of certain forms of matter.

**ion-flux stabilizer** This starship component regulated the flow of ion energy throughout the ship's systems.

**ion grenade** This explosive grenade was developed some 4,000 years before the Galactic Civil War for use against battle droids and droid armies. When detonated, the ion grenade ejected a sphere of highly charged ion energy that rendered the electronics of a droid useless. Generally, ion grenades did not hurt living beings.

**ionic disruptor (Senate-grade)** Commander Tarkin often carried a Senate-grade ionic disruptor used to render security droids harmless.

***Ionic Ring*** This unique starship was created by Professor Renn Volz during his tenure at the Maw Installation. It used a specially modulated ionic beam to manipulate a planet's weather patterns. Volz envisioned the ship as a climatizer, capable of altering the destructive forces of nature to make a world livable. He successfully tested the ship on Zerm. However, Volz was unaware of the true purpose of the Maw. He came under Imperial scrutiny, and Captain Bzorn took control of the ship. Bzorn used the *Ionic Ring* to destroy planets, turning their weather into stormy, devastating forces. The ship was captured by Luke Skywalker, Han Solo, and Chewbacca at Kessel, but Volz decided that it was too dangerous and destroyed it himself.

**ionic tingler** Another name for the Aeramaxis PDW-50 personal weapon.

**ionite** A mineral valuable throughout the galaxy because of its unique ability to carry neither a positive nor a negative charge. Instead, ionite carried an alternate charge that affected all charged particle fields around it. In the presence of a positively charged element, ionite carried a negative charge that negated the positive charge. The reverse was also true. Thus, in the presence of ionite, any electrical device had its operations stopped and became unusable. This was especially true for chronometers and other timing devices. Much of the galaxy's ionite was mined on Bandomeer.

**ionjet** An entry-level starship drive system produced by Koensayr during the early years of the New Order.

**ion limpet** A small, disk-shaped homing beacon. It could be placed on the hull of a starship, its thin profile helping to prevent it from being detected. As the targeted ship moved through space or hyperspace, the ion limpet accessed the HoloNet to transmit information on the ship's exact location in the galaxy.

**ion-mesh projection system** The most powerful starship shield generation system produced by SoroSuub during the New Order.

**ion pulse bomb** A smaller, modified version of an ion pulse weapon, designed to be used in close quarters. It could cause ionization damage to everything within a 200-meter radius.

**ion pulse cannon** The planetary defense batteries on Brentaal IV that prevented the Republic from landing a strong enough ground force to take the planet—until Quinlan Vos and Sagoro Autem sabotaged the batteries.

**ion pulse weapon** This modified form of ion cannon was developed for use on starfighters during the Galactic Civil War. It used ion energy in such a way as to initially cause damage to another starship's shields, allowing a secondary burst of ion energy to disable shipboard systems.

**ion rifle** This rifle fired ion energy instead of laser bolts, making it effective for disrupting electrical systems and essential when fighting battle droids.

**ion rocket** An inexpensive sublight propulsion system.

**Ion Sandbox** This saloon, located near the Calamar Intergalactic Spaceport on Esseles, was popular with many pilots who traveled through the system. Bama Vook hid there after he stole Trade Federation droid starfighters from Trinkatta Starships. Jango Fett quizzed the Ishi Tib bartender at the Ion Sandbox in his search for Groodo's compound.

**ion scrambler** A device developed by the Rebel Alliance to mask its communications signals from Imperial sensors.

**ion shield** This type of planetary shield was used on worlds like Bonadan to maintain a pleasant atmosphere. The ion shield eliminated many of the odors and pollution that were common around spaceports and manufacturing facilities, providing somewhat more breathable air.

**ion storm** An event in which a collection of free ions swept through the vacuum of space or the gases of an atmosphere. Many beings claimed that they could tell when an ion storm was approaching because they could smell the ozone being created as the ions moved through oxygen. Such storms were common on Tatooine. An ion attractor could be used to harness the energy from an ion storm.

***Ion Storm*** This *Strike*-class cruiser served as the flagship of Governor Newen Streeg's fleet, which patrolled the Sisar Run during the last years of the New Order. It was commanded by Captain Barse Neoman.

**Ionstrike, Wonn** This crime lord worked from a base on Cloud City. He was an elderly man who had been crippled in an accident and left paralyzed. He moved about in a specially designed wheelchair, and spent his entire career working to drive Jabba the Hutt out of business on Cloud City.

**ion striker** This ancient weapon employed a blast of ionized energy to disable a droid or other electronic equipment.

**ion stunner** A weapon found on the underlevels of Coruscant. It was distinguishable by its ion flare focusing dish.

**ion surprise** A term used by smugglers and independent spacers of the Old Republic to describe the appearance of ion weapons in a firefight when the opponent was least suspecting it. The use of the ion surprise was common on those ships that appeared to lack ion cannons, or had them concealed in secret hull compartments. An ion surprise was often followed by a laser chaser, which poured laser energy into a starship's shields after the ion blast caused electronics to fail.

**Ion Team** This clone commando unit was part of the 22nd Air Combat Wing stationed on Boz Pity during the final stages of the Clone Wars. The team saw action with Jedi General Roan Shryne on Deko Neimoidia prior to being assigned to Shryne's command on Murkhana. Led by the clone commando known as Climber, Ion Team was one of the few squads that initially refused to execute Order 66 when the command was given. Instead they allowed Shryne and his fellow Jedi to escape into the forest before deciding to give chase. When word of Ion Team's actions reached the ears of Emperor Palpatine, he ordered Darth Vader to personally punish them for their insubordination, and to make them an example of what happened when clones failed to loyally serve their Emperor. On Murkhana, Vader confronted the team and cut down two clones in short order. Climber was wounded as he fled into the forest with the fourth member of the team, and they were hunted down by Commander Appo and the forces of the 501st Legion. After being captured, Climber and his teammate were sent to the prison facility on Agon Nine.

**Ionweb** A high-end starship shielding system produced by Mon Calamari shipwrights during the New Order. The Ionweb system was available in several grades, including advanced and elite versions, depending on the shielding capabilities required.

**Ion-X** An ion weapon developed by the Baragwins more than 4,000 years before the Battle of Endor. The Ion-X never went into full production, and the only prototype known to exist was obtained by Suvam Tan. He upgraded several of the weapon's systems, making the blast more powerful.

***Iopene Princess*** This Mining Guild cutter was hijacked by EV-9D9 as she escaped from Cloud City. It was a state-of-the-art ship equipped with the newest hyperdrive motivators, sensor systems, and weapons.

**Ios** This gas giant, orbited by six moons, was the fourth and outermost planet in the Feriae system.

**Iotek** This small corporation manufactured starship ion power cells and ionization reactors for the Empire.

**Ioth** A captain, working as a naval supply analyst during the Galactic Civil War, who discovered that the Empire was fortifying the Oplovis fleet just prior to its planned attack on Mantooine.

**Iotran** A humanoid species of incredible strength native to Iotra, the fifth planet of the Iotran system. Iotrans had three fingers and a strong thumb on each hand, and two fore-toes on each foot. At their elbows, shoulders, and hands were sturdy, bone-like spikes that helped protect them from attack. They were an extremely martial people, letting their actions speak in place of words. Their culture and history were extremely stable, a result of continued military dominance within the government. Each Iotran citizen was required to serve for six standard years at the age of 14 seasons (about 18 standard years) in the military or Iotran Police Force. Iotran technology was reliable, but not up to galactic norms.

**I'pan, Vuurok** A Yuuzhan Vong Shamed One, he was relegated to living in the bowels of Coruscant after it was transformed into a likeness of the long-lost Yuuzhan Vong homeworld of Yuuzhan'tar. A former warrior, I'pan was the first to encounter Nom Anor in the tunnels beneath the surface when the former executor had fled after failing to hold Jacen Solo.

**Ipharian-Da'Lor** A species of serpent-like beings noted for their snake-like lower bodies. They moved about by slithering on their thick, meter-long tails, while their fore-bodies stood nearly 3 meters above the ground. They were vaguely humanoid from the torso up, with muscular arms and elongated faces. A ridge of black spines ran from the backs of their skulls down to their tails, which ended with retractable spikes. The Ipharian-Da'Lor often used masks to cover their faces, thereby hiding their identity.

**Iphigini** Sentient beings native to Iphigin, a temperate world that was a main traffic transfer point for three Core sectors. They were easily recognized by their braided lip-beards, which sat at the bottom of a craggy face. Their skin was quite wrinkled.

**IPI-1000** A personal identification and information display unit produced by Meren-Data during the Galactic Civil War. Designed to hold up to 12 passports, identification cards, and operating licenses, the IPI-1000 allowed its user to carry a single source of identification. The original documents could be stored in a safe place for later use.

**IPKC** *See* Imperial Peace-Keeping Certificate.

**IPV-1** Following the success of the IR-3F, Sienar Fleet System produced this system patrol craft measuring 150 meters long. These

*IPV-1 patrol craft*

fast, maneuverable craft were well armed for intercepting criminals along border regions where Star Destroyers were not present. They lacked hyperdrives, and so they were restricted to patrolling specific areas of space.

**Iqobal** This gas giant was the fourth planet of the Polith system in the Inner Rim. It was orbited by 54 moons.

**Iqoon** This barren ball of rock was the third and outermost planet in the Roon system. It was orbited by a pair of moons.

**iquazard** This large, boar-like reptile was native to Gelgelar. Small iquazards were the favored prey of reeho birds. These creatures had incredibly thick skin; it was said that an iquazard could absorb a blaster bolt from near range.

**IR-3F** A system patrol craft from Sienar Fleet Systems, it was 110 meters long and armed with four turret-mounted turbolaser cannons. The IR-3F was capable of taking on capital-sized targets and was most often used as a blockade ship, with several similar vessels forming a line. The IR-3F required a crew of three, with eight gunners and up to 10 troops. It could transport up to 180 metric tons of cargo and had a three-month supply of consumables.

**Irackant** This Mon Calamari bounty hunter spent much of his career tracking down former Imperial war criminals during the second decade of the New Republic. Irackant worked from the *Krakana's Claw,* a heavily modified Skipray blastboat.

**irax** One of the largest species of mammals in the galaxy. Although native to the forests of several worlds, many irax were found near settlements and suburban areas. The sudden appearance of an irax on a road or highway was cause for trouble, as a mature one could demolish a landspeeder in a collision.

**IRD** This small starfighter was introduced by the Corporate Sector Authority during the early years of the New Order. It was a fast craft when flown in outer space, but suffered greatly when flown in atmosphere. The ship's name was derived from its mission profile: interception, reconnaissance, and defense. The combat-dedicated fighter was 8.5 meters long and was armed with a pair of twin blaster cannons. It was designed for a single pilot. The IRD-A was the second-generation fighter, while the IRD-B was a variant with a concussion missile launcher.

**Irdani Performance Group** This conglomerate produced parts for racing craft from Podracers to starships. It also developed and manufactured complete racers, such as the IPG-X1131 LongTail.

**Irden** This tribe of Ugnaughts lived on Cloud City in the era of the Galactic Civil War. The Irdens were one of the first three groups purchased by Ecclessis Figg, who offered the Ugnaughts their freedom in exchange for completing the construction of the floating city.

*Irenez*

**Irenez** A Corellian warrior, she was a member of Senator Garm Bel Iblis's private army at Peregrine's Nest. She was chief of security, intelligence coordinator, pilot, and bodyguard for Bel Iblis and his chief adviser, Sena Leikvold Midanyl. Irenez, a longtime associate of Bel Iblis, had been sponsored by the Senator for her training at the Old Republic Military Academy on Corellia. In her early years, she was a mercenary and soldier of fortune. The three Corellians—Irenez, Bel Iblis, and Midanyl—planned many attacks on the Empire and were behind the destruction of the Ubiqtorate Imperial intelligence center on Tangrene. During the early years of the New Republic, Irenez was placed in charge of securing secret meetings with Tav Breil'lya that Bel Iblis had arranged on New Cov. It was due to her picket lines that Han Solo was intercepted when he tried to tail Breil'lya, but Midanyl eventually recognized Han and allowed him a measure of freedom. Irenez's pickets later intercepted Luke Skywalker, who had arrived on New Cov to meet Solo.

**irgkul bush** This unusual plant, native to Ansion, did not have an underground root system. It had adapted to the continual pressure of the winds of the planet's environment by obtaining nutrients directly from the air, and thus was often seen being blown about in the breeze.

**Iri** This planet, located in the Epidimi system, was discovered some 5,000 years before the fall of the Old Republic. Republic scientists discovered that the avian lifeforms living on Iri were genetically similar to those living on nearby Disim. They attempted to breed the unique species in the hope of creating a new form of life. The experiment was a success, but the resulting species—known as the Tarong—was much more intelligent and eventually overran the two parent species.

**iriaz** This docile mammal, native to Dantooine, was hunted for its flesh and pelt. They were normally quite tame, but could be violent when provoked.

**irid** This avian creature, native to Ragoon-6, was distinguished by the bright yellow coloration of its wings.

***Iridescence*** This luxury liner made a regular run to Niro during the early years of the New Order.

**Iridia** One of the many worlds where Zabrak established a colony.

**Iridian, Eero** This tall, spindly being, distinguished by his wobbling antennae and bright yellow eyes, worked in the Senate Rotunda on Coruscant some 68 years before the Battle of Geonosis. Eero was a friend of young Dooku, even though Dooku had once publicly embarrassed him at a presentation he was making by pointing out several flaws in it. Eero, however, recognized Dooku's knowledge and sought him out later.

Eero tried twice to run for Senator on his own homeworld, but lost both times. His father had spent the family fortune, leaving Eero with no way to fully finance either campaign. He decided to retire from public service, although he remained attached to the Galactic Senate as a special aide. Years later, while serving Senator Blix Annon, Eero was reunited with Dooku. The ship they were traveling on was attacked by Lorian Nod, who captured Senator Annon, leaving Eero badly wounded and their ship adrift.

When Dooku and his apprentice, Qui-Gon Jinn, managed to get the ship back to Voltare Spaceport, Eero quickly recovered. He followed the Jedi to Von-Alai where he revealed that he was part of Nod's kidnapping plot to exact revenge on the Old Republic and the Jedi Knights. On Von-Alai, Senator Annon died of a heart attack, and Dooku managed to capture both Nod and Eero. They were sent back to Coruscant to stand trial for murder and conspiracy.

**iridiite** This opalescent stone was used in the construction of furniture.

**Iridik'k-stallu, Senator** This alien Senator, noted for her multiple hearts, was among the many who believed that Chancellor Palpatine was overstepping his bounds during the Clone Wars. Bail Organa and Mon Mothma invited her to sign the Petition of the Two Thousand.

**Iridium** This planet was home to infamous space pirates who preyed on merchant vessels in the Old Republic until they were wiped out by the Jedi Knights. The pirates used unique Iridium "power gems" that generated a disrupting aura and broke through the shields of their victims' starships. One pirate, Raskar, survived the Jedi attack and escaped with the only remaining power gem. Han Solo and Chewbacca got the gem following the Battle of Yavin, but it only had enough power left for one last shield disruption.

**Iridonia** This harsh planet, homeworld of the Zabrak, was located in the Mid Rim. Iridonia was considered inhospitable because its surface was regularly scoured by 200-kilometer-per-hour storms, and acidic seas threw caustic spray onto the land. Any life-form that evolved on Iridonia seemed to be some form of predator, always looking to find prey to sustain itself. Because of the harsh environment, many Zabrak settled on other worlds. In addition to large populations on Talus and Corellia, the Zabrak maintained colonies on eight other planets in the Mid Rim. During the decades leading up to the Battle of Ruusan, Iridonia was the site of an elite Sith training academy, where those individuals who had strong connections to the Force were trained to become Sith Lords. Darth Maul was from Iridonia.

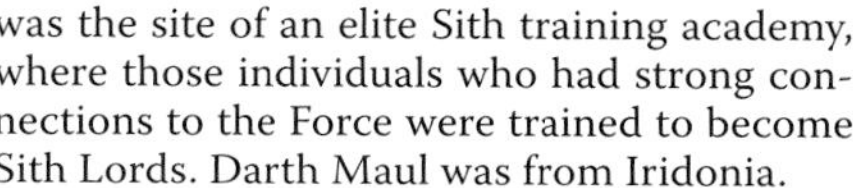

*Iridonia*

**Irini** One of the Workers imprisoned by the Absolutes on New Apsolon for her part in industrial sabotage against the Civilized and their businesses. It was Irini who took Qui-Gon Jinn and Obi-Wan Kenobi on a tour of the Museum of the Absolutes when they arrived on New Apsolon to search for Tahl. The Jedi discovered that Irini was a member of a group that had plotted to assassinate Roan, the planet's leader. Irini believed that the Jedi had come to New Apsolon at Roan's behest, to serve as his protection. After Roan was killed, Irini agreed to represent the Workers at a political summit to discuss the filling of his position. Irini was arrested and imprisoned again when she admitted that she had been involved in the deaths of two members of the government.

**Irith** This overcrowded, polluted planet was a stop on the Ootmian Pabol.

**Iritsa** A city on Chazwa, it was the site of one of the planet's larger spaceports. It was similar to Mos Eisley, but much greener and nicer to live in. It was patrolled by the Iritsa Civil Guard.

**IrizMark-8** Koensayr's version of the *Sentinel*-class military cruiser developed during the early years of the New Order. It measured 77 meters long and took a crew of six to operate. It specialized in hit-and-fade type operations that required a moderately armed ship with maneuverability and speed.

**Ir'khaim** Dynast of the Noghri clan Khim'bar, he was Thrawn's personal bodyguard before Rukh assumed the position.

**irm-Drocubac, Nemrileo** A native of Tanjay IV, he was a supporter of the secession movement that rose in the Old Republic Senate before the Clone Wars. Nemrileo hated the common being, despite the fact that his own lifestyle was based on their productivity. He had never worked with Shu Mai before joining the secession movement, and questioned her loyalty to the cause. For his doubts, Nemrileo was murdered by secret agents as a message to other doubters.

**Irmenu** This species was noted for its fantastic myths and legends. The rulers of Irmenu society kept their positions by creating a hereditary empire, but it began to fall apart due to inbreeding and scandals.

**Irnaj sector** An area of the galaxy located in the Mid Rim.

**Irol, Sergeant** This Imperial sergeant was from a forested planet, where he learned how to fly a speeder bike. His balance and flying skills made him a valuable, though cocky, member of the Imperial garrison on the Forest Moon of Endor.

**Irolia, Commander** This officer in the Chiss Expansionary Defense Fleet during the Yuuzhan Vong War used the shortened form of her name when speaking to outsiders. Her full Chiss name was Hess'irolia'nuruodo. She was dispatched to intercept Luke Skywalker's mission to locate Zonama Sekot in the Unknown Regions. Irolia brought Skywalker and crew to Csilla, where they were detained until the Chiss could decide whether to allow them continued passage through the Unknown Regions. When it was concluded that the Jedi could spend two days searching the Expeditionary Library, Irolia was reduced to babysitting them.

**irolunn** This gas was mined in the Cularin system; it had properties comparable to Tibanna gas.

**Iron Cesta Flight** Toba founded the first all-Gungan starfighter squadron when the Naboo Space Fighter Corps first accepted Gungan pilots after the Battle of Naboo. These pilots patrolled for pirates preying upon traffic between Naboo and the Ohma-D'un colony, and were the first fighter group to employ the G-1 starfighter.

*Sergeant Irol*

*Iron Citadel*

**Iron Citadel** This vast building served as the seat of the Tetan government until it was overtaken by Satal and Aleema Keto as the command center for the Krath. It was located in Cinnagar, the largest city on the seven worlds that made up the Empress Teta star system. It was heavily armored and armed.

**Ironclaw** This brown-furred Kentra was a brave warrior among his people. He was extremely proud of the fact that he was one of only a handful of Kentra who had visited all seven of their major cities.

**Iron Duke** A *Strike*-class cruiser that was part of the front lines of the Imperial Navy Fleet.

**Iron Fist (1)** An old *Victory*-class Star Destroyer, the *Iron Fist* was Warlord Zsinj's first command during his Imperial service. It was in this ship that he learned to use asteroids as weapons. It later served as part of Grand Admiral Thrawn's fleet.

***Iron Fist* (2)** Warlord Zsinj's flagship *Super*-class Star Destroyer, his second *Iron Fist* was originally christened the *Brawl* but was renamed in honor of his first command assignment. It was pursued by Han Solo and a fleet supporting the *Mon Remonda* before Solo resigned his commission. In a series of battles at Kuat, Vahaba, and Selaggis, Solo nearly destroyed the *Iron Fist,* but Zsinj always proved to be one step ahead. At Selaggis, Solo came the closest to killing Zsinj, but the Warlord used the *Second Death* to flee with the *Iron Fist* intact. The *Iron Fist* was later destroyed at Dathomir by Solo's fleet.

**Ironfleck Marauders** In an effort to strike it rich, this gang of pirates gave up harassing space traffic of the Naboo system and set up operations on the Adamant Mass asteroid. Their efforts were largely futile, however, as the lode of valuable resources that was rumored to be hidden within the asteroid was never found.

***Ironhand* (1)** This Imperial Star Destroyer, under the command of Captain Argona, was one of only 13 that remained in the Imperial Navy some 10 years after the death of Grand Admiral Thrawn. It later was assigned to accompany the *Tyrannic* and *Obliterator* to Bothawui, where the three ships were cloaked from sensors and hidden among the comets that passed through the system. Once the battle was under way, Han Solo managed to get many of the Bothan clans to supply warships from their personal fleets. The three Star Destroyers were forced to retreat to Bastion or be slowly picked apart by the New Republic. Captain Nalgol gave the order to retreat, ending the blockade and bringing to a close the Caamas incident.

***Ironhand* (2)** This *Trenchant*-class cruiser was the personal ship of High Inquisitor Mox Slosin.

***Iron Hand*** One of the many *Strike*-class cruisers that made up the front lines of the Imperial Navy Fleet.

**Iron Hand** An affectionate nickname earned by Ilena Xan, one of the few Jedi Masters who remained on Coruscant during the Clone Wars. A skilled melee fighter known for her knowledge of joint locks and holds, Master Xan accepted the nickname as a title of respect.

**Iron Knights** A group of Shards who followed Ilum off their homeworld of Orax before the Clone Wars. At the time, many Shards were being installed in common droids to give the simple automata a measure of intelligence. Ilum wanted something more, and set out to install herself in a Juggernaut war droid. She and her followers eventually met Jedi Master Aqinos, who agreed to train them on Dweem. Aqinos had set out on his own to pursue the possibility of melding droid intelligence with the Force, and had sought out Ilum specifically because of her droid form. Aqinos trained the Shards in the ways of the Jedi Order. The intelligent automata soon acquired the ability to tap into the Force. When the Clone Wars broke out, Aqinos and Ilum decided to add their considerable forces to the ranks of the Jedi Knights, and they were instrumental in winning several key battles. However, Aqinos later was expelled from the Jedi Order for independently creating the Iron Knights, forcing Ilum and the surviving Iron Knights to return in shame to Dweem. Their skills with the Force were not forgotten, however, as the Iron Knights were among the first Jedi to be destroyed during the Jedi Purge. Those who survived went into hiding, and only returned during the Yuuzhan Vong War. The Iron Knights made it their mission to protect the galaxy's droids from the technology-hating Yuuzhan Vong. They were instrumental in defeating the Red Knights of Life, although it was known that at least one of the Iron Knights fell to the dark side during the battle for Hosk Station.

**Iron Planet** The name given to a large asteroid in the Tatoo system. It seemed to be formed from a greater concentration of heavy materials than neighboring asteroids, and the inhabitants of Tatooine hoped that mining the Iron Planet would help with the acquisition of natural resources that were lacking at home.

***Iron Tether*** This starship was part of the Old Republic's Space Rescue Corps before the Clone Wars. It was strafed by a quartet of Subpro C-73 Tracker starfighters backed by a modified Corellian freighter despite transmitting its identifying telesponder signal and flying its recognizable red and black hull colors. The *Iron Tether* was attacked by several snubfighters and a Corellian-made freighter that were believed to have been dispatched by Separatist forces. In order to survive, the captain of the *Iron Tether* took the ship into the radiation-laden Cowl Crucible, but the crew sustained few injuries and were later rescued by a Jedi Knight team led by Darrin Arkanian.

**Iron Tower** Located on Aridus, this huge structure was built by the Empire to overcome the intense interference generated by the planet's magnetic fluctuations. However, the frequency used by the Tower caused massive neurological damage to the native Chubbits. The Iron Tower was partially destroyed during Luke Skywalker's escape after Darth Vader tried to capture him by having an actor pose as Obi-Wan Kenobi.

**Ironwall** This was one of the seven major Kentran cities on Orellon II, and was ruled by Lord Mogotah.

**Iron Will** This newsfeed was considered the official communications vehicle of the Commission for the Preservation of the New Order. First-time subscribers got a "personal" message from Emperor Palpatine himself welcoming them to COMPNOR.

**ironwithe** This plant was native to Bogden. Its branches were compared to durasteel in strength, although its shoots were tender enough for the giant renda bear to eat. Many of these plants were exported to the Core Worlds for planting in rooftop gardens.

**ironwood** A tight-grained wood.

**irradiation box** A containment unit used by starship captains to ensure that equipment used on strange planets didn't bring back unusual organisms. The irradiation box produced a series of broadband radiation and ultrasonic fields to kill off harmful bacteria and viruses that may have attached themselves to the equipment. The device was a smaller, portable version of the irradiator.

**irradiator** A lighting device used aboard a starship or in spaceports. While it appeared that the irradiator was simply an interior light source, it also doubled as a life-support device, emitting energy that killed most airborne bacteria, viruses, or other dangerous microbes.

**Irrational Number** A cantina owned by a group of Bith. It was located in Jugsmuk Station on Gamorr, and was run by a Bith known only as Numbers.

**Irregulars** This loose affiliation of pirate and mercenary groups was extremely pro–Rebel Alliance during the Galactic Civil War. The groups that made up the Irregulars were scattered across the galaxy, and harried the Empire's supply convoys in order to help the Rebels.

**Irrukiine** This hound-like species was native to Malrev. The Irrukiine lived in loose-knit aboriginal societies, although they were most notable for their peculiar relationship with a Malrev temple containing Sith magic. Normally vicious hunters, they were covered with a pelt of short brown fur, and their panther-like faces were split by a mouth full of sharp teeth. The mad Devaronian Cartariun used the dark side of the Force to control the Irrukiine. He

*Iron Knights*

learned how to use them as weapons, arming them with Imperial blasters for ground assaults while using them to fly TIE fighters in aerial combat.

**Irrv, Dimone** TaggeCo's Executive Vice President of Operations on Goroth Prime during the Galactic Civil War. Irrv was a young woman who always managed to get what she wanted through sheer determination rather than backstabbing. This allowed her to get the jump on other corporate leaders, thereby earning her additional revenues from mining operations.

**Irrv, General** An Imperial officer who commanded Maximilian Veers when he was a lieutenant. General Irrv was sent to Culroon III to subjugate the simple people living there, but nearly failed when the Culroon launched a surprise attack during an official ceremony. The battle was turned to the Empire's favor when then-Lieutenant Veers disobeyed Irrv's direct order to remain confined to the base and attacked the Culroon with AT-ATs. Irrv was irate with Veers but never got a chance to court-martial him, as his own superior officer, Commander Grath, executed Irrv on the spot. Grath then promoted Veers to major.

**irstat** Individual clans of the Tarasin people, each contained an average of several dozen individuals although some, such as the Hironi irstat, had around 300 some three decades before the Battle of Yavin. The oldest female of each tribe was the spiritual leader and called "Mother," and the second-oldest was the Irstat-Kes, or chief.

**Irtanna** A dark-skinned woman, she was one of the many soldiers who joined the Army of Light and fought for the Jedi Knights during the final years of the New Sith Wars. Irtanna was not sensitive to the Force, but believed that the Jedi were fighting for the good of the galaxy. She joined the Army of Light about a year before the Battle of Ruusan, and, because of her lack of connection to the Force, survived the battle. She was killed during a rescue mission on the surface of Ruusan by Darth Bane's young apprentice, Zannah.

**Irugian rain forest** A forest on Abbaji and home to the only grove of 100-meter-tall firethorn trees.

**Isamu** This moon, located in the Birjis system, was known for its unusual mu trees. Each night, every pair of trees on the moon mated.

**Isard, Armand** The head of the Empire's Intelligence organization for many years. He rose through the ranks with the Old Republic's Office of Analysis and the Senate Bureau of Intelligence to become the first chief of Imperial Intelligence. Many who met him remarked on his somewhat inhuman gaze. Armand Isard was known for his ability to ferret out and destroy Emperor Palpatine's enemies or cells of alleged Rebel Alliance supporters, whether they actually supported the Alliance or not. One of the first Imperial officers alerted to the theft of the plans to the first Death Star, he dispatched his daughter, Ysanne, to Darkknell to retrieve them. His secret hope was that she would be killed in the attempt, removing any possible threat to his position as leader of the ISB. Ysanne survived. Although she failed to recover the datacards containing the plans, she figured out why her father had sent her, and was so angry that she implicated him in the original theft. She also implicated him in the bombing of the Treitamma Political Center, claiming that he did it to kill Arrianya Bel Iblis so that Garm Bel Iblis would be free to join the Alliance. Ysanne then called in Imperial Security and had her father arrested and executed for treason.

**Isard, Ysanne** A native of Coruscant, Ysanne was born to Imperial service. She was the daughter of Emperor Palpatine's last Imperial Intelligence director, whom she betrayed, claiming that he was going to defect to the Rebel Alliance. Palpatine had her father executed—some say she was the person who shot him—and promoted her to his position. She was later promoted to director of Imperial Intelligence, and held the Empire together during the years following Palpatine's death at Endor. Among some members of the New Republic and the Imperial Remnant, she was known as Iceheart. She had long, black hair, but what made her an imposing force were her eyes. One eye was a cold ice-blue; the other was deep red with flame-like, golden highlights.

Because Isard considered Rogue Squadron to be a major threat to the Empire, she commissioned Agent Kirtan Loor to engineer its destruction. Understanding the true Alliance objective in its use of Rogue Squadron to capture Borleias, she realized that it was the beginning of the push to retake the capital planet. Isard decided that the best way to crush the Rebellion was to bankrupt it rather than constantly fight it. She ordered General Derricote to develop the Krytos virus to infect only the disdained alien populace of Imperial Center (formerly Coruscant)—but insisted that the virus had to be curable with simple bacta. She reasoned that as the planet's alien inhabitants lay sick and dying, the Alliance would do everything in its power to save them, using all its meager monetary resources to purchase the bacta, which she would soon control.

Eager to implement her plan, Isard had the virus released into Imperial Center's water supply shortly before the Alliance invasion began, even though General Derricote's research wasn't finished. When the virus failed to infect the population as rapidly as expected, she blamed Derricote as she retreated to her secret political prison, the *Lusankya* Super Star Destroyer, which had been buried under the planet's surface. Before leaving, she placed Loor in charge of Imperial Center. When she later learned of Loor's duplicity, she activated one of her sleeper agents, who assassinated him.

Realizing that her reign of terror on Imperial Center had ended, Isard departed the planet by uprooting the *Lusankya,* causing massive destruction and millions of deaths and injuries. She then went to Thyferra and supported a revolution that put the Xucphra Corporation in charge of the Bacta Cartel. She soon gained control of the cartel, and with the installation of Fliry Vorru as Thyferra's Minister of Trade, the price of bacta increased exorbitantly. But with the liberation of Coruscant, Rogue Squadron could now concentrate on Isard's activities, and she soon was besieged by raids on her bacta convoys. Now, more than ever, she was determined to destroy Rogue Squadron.

When her network of spies was unable to locate the squadron's hidden base, she used another source of information to ambush them at the Graveyard of Alderaan. Failing miserably at this, too, she decided to punish those who had accepted the bacta stolen from her convoys. When even that failed to reveal the squadron's location, Isard adopted even more desperate measures. She used the Thyferran Home Defense Corps to round up and slaughter the native Vratix in an attempt to flush Rogue Squadron out of hiding. Upon learning this, the squadron allowed an Isard spy to learn their secret location, setting an elaborate trap. She swallowed the bait, sending out all her forces, including the *Lusankya.*

Isard's armada arrived at the Yag'Dhul space station only to find an ambush waiting. Their confidence badly shaken, many of Isard's forces scattered and fled back to Thyferra. Rogue Squadron followed. The battles in space and on the ground went badly for her. During what turned out to be the final moments of the Bacta War, Isard attempted an escape, but her shuttle was destroyed before it could make the jump to hyperspace. Still it wasn't the end for Isard. Two years later, two Isards appeared to harass Rogue Squadron—the real Isard and her clone. Wedge Antilles destroyed the clone, while New Republic Intelligence officer Iella Wessiri confronted the real Isard and killed her aboard the *Lusankya.*

**ISB-120** A series of interrogation droids produced by MerenData for the Empire.

*Ysanne Isard*

ISD-72x

**ISBy** This slicer droid, an ISB-120 model, was employed by the interrogation droid known as IT to break into a datapad that was owned by Leia Organa Solo. ISBy was destroyed when Chewbacca and his wife, Mallatobuck, tried to rescue their son Lumpawarrump from IT.

**Isced** This tribe of Ugnaughts lived on Cloud City during the years surrounding the Galactic Civil War. The Isceds were one of the first three groups purchased by Ecclessis Figg, who offered the Ugnaughts their freedom in exchange for completing the construction of the floating city. They were looked down upon by the Botrut and Irden tribes because of their malicious sense of humor.

Ishin-Il-Raz

**Iscera** A planet near Nysza whose atmosphere was almost continually racked by electrical storms, which caused unpredictable reactions within the volatile gases that filled its upper levels.

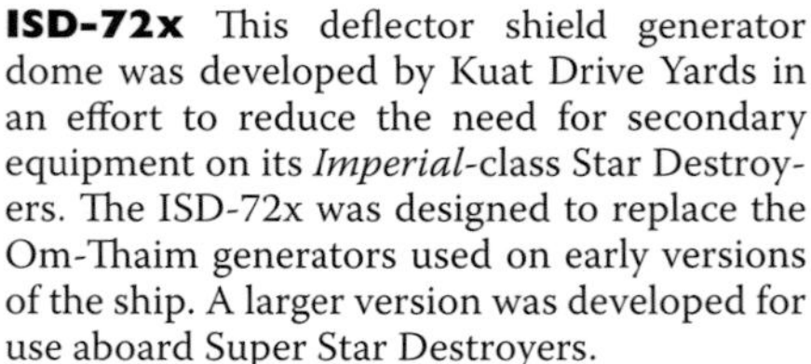

**ISD-72x** This deflector shield generator dome was developed by Kuat Drive Yards in an effort to reduce the need for secondary equipment on its *Imperial*-class Star Destroyers. The ISD-72x was designed to replace the Om-Thaim generators used on early versions of the ship. A larger version was developed for use aboard Super Star Destroyers.

**Isde Naha** This planet was located on the Rimward edge of the Yarith sector, where the Corellian Trade Spine exited the Anoat sector for the far reaches of the Outer Rim Territories. It was also the capital world of Yarith sector. Isde Naha was known as a no-nonsense planet with strict regulations, including a zero tolerance for smugglers.

**Iselen, Dalton** One of the managing partners of the Naescorcom consortium during the final years of the Old Republic. When it was learned that the Believers were producing a virus that could kill Caarites in the floating city of Ipsus, Iselen was forced to work with Nirama to ensure the safety of his facilities there. Thus, Iselen was quite happy when Nirama hired a group of freelance agents to resolve the situation, allowing him to maintain operations on Ipsus with minimal interruption.

**Isen** This gas giant was the only planet in the Isen system. It had six natural satellites, of which one, Isen IV, was inhabited. The system was still in its birth stage in the era of the Galactic Civil War, and the primary star Isen continued to give off large amounts of radiation. This, coupled with three asteroid belts, made navigation through the Isen system extremely difficult. A small pirate base had been established on the bleak surface of Isen IV by the Void Demons, and the underground tunnels were inhabited by a colony of Morvaks. The planetoid made a full revolution around its sun once every 740 standard days.

**Iseno** This high-gravity Inner Rim planet was a member of the Old Republic. It had a storied legacy of military pageantry. Iseno was the homeworld of Senator Ronet Coorr.

**Isep** A Tiss'shar god of commerce.

**Ishanna system** This planetary system included Ishanna I, a barren, searing ball of rock with two moons. Ishanna II was also barren with no natural atmosphere, but was important for its mineral deposits, which were mined by various independent companies. It had three moons. The fifth planet, Ishanna V, was an uninhabitable world with five natural satellites. Its mineral resources were mined by several corporations located on Rabaan.

**Ishedur, Keroth** This human noble stumbled upon his connection to the dark side of the Force as a young man, but kept it to himself as much as possible. Many years before the onset of the Clone Wars, he met up with Deel De, and together they explored the depths of their powers. Deel De eventually set out on her own, leaving Ishedur behind.

**Isher, Lungrolph** This Krish was a noted expert in the martial art of teräs käsi.

**Ishin-Il-Raz,** One of the first Grand Admirals appointed to the Circle of Twelve by Emperor Palpatine. Ishin-Il-Raz was not the most competent of the Grand Admirals, but he was extremely faithful to the New Order and its ideals. Ishin-Il-Raz helped create COMPNOR from the ashes of the Commission for the Preservation of the Republic following the Clone Wars. He also was the primary proponent behind the core concepts of pro-human rights and rule by dictatorship. Ishin-Il-Raz scored several victories for the Empire, commanding the *Emperor's Disciple* in the Massacre of Myomar and the bombardment of Shalam. However, when Palpatine died at the Battle of Endor, Ishin-Il-Raz feared that his own career would be terminated. Rather than be destroyed by the other Grand Admirals, Ishin-Il-Raz committed suicide by flying the *Emperor's Disciple* into the heart of the Denarii Nova.

**Ishi Tib** An amphibious humanoid species characterized by huge eyes and a beak-like mouth. Ishi Tib were native to Tibrin, where they inhabited the planet's oceans and spent most of their lives underwater. Their thick green skin helped them retain moisture, making them fairly adaptable in other environments. However, Ishi Tib who lived away from the water had to soak in a briny seawater bath every 30 hours or so in order to maintain their skin's moisture levels and to keep their lungs moist.

The Ishi Tib were descended from a species of bony fish that had large, highly developed, fluke-like fins. They escaped predation by leaving the ocean and staying on land for short periods of time, and natural selection resulted in the development of arms, legs, and lungs. Reproduction among the Ishi Tib was considered a necessary part of life, although marriage was unheard of in their society. Males and females were paired together as needed by a school of Ishi Tib, and the fertilized eggs were kept safe in hatcheries. Thus, no Ishi Tib individuals knew who their parents were.

As a species, they were highly sought after as efficient organizers. They were also noted for their tenacity when threatened, which stood in stark contrast with their otherwise subdued nature. The desire to kill another being was often suppressed, but an individual Ishi Tib was not above cannibalizing an opponent with sufficient provocation. The Ishi Tib eventually built cities upon the coral reefs of Tibrin's oceans, taking great care so as not to disrupt the delicate environmental balances. This made them a valuable resource for the Galactic Alliance in the wake of the Yuuzhan Vong War, as their skills in restoring and maintaining their environment were needed to help those planets devastated during the fighting. Jabba the Hutt's subordinate Birdlizard was an Ishi Tib. Count Dooku and Quinlan

Ishi Tib

Vos went to Tibrin during the Clone Wars and killed the pro-Republic leader, Suribran Tu. Many Ishi Tib considered Dooku a liberator.

**Ishkik caverns** Located on Cularin, this maze of underground caves and tunnels was discovered by a work team building a platform city in a great valley. The caverns extended for several kilometers beneath the planet's surface, connecting the valley with mountains some distance away. The caverns, while interesting, were left largely unexplored until the Tarasin Revolt, when the Tarasin decided to use them as living areas. Three full irstats made their homes in the caverns, storing weapons in hidden caves to help in the struggle against the humans.

**Ishori** These sentients were native to Isht, which was part of the New Republic. Shortly before the revelation of the Bothan involvement in the destruction of Caamas, the Ishori had a minor dispute with the Diamala over shipping security. The Diamala didn't trust the Ishori patrols that escorted their transports into Ishori ports, while the Ishori didn't want armed Diamala ships in their systems. Han Solo and Luke Skywalker tried to mediate the dispute, but were unable to bring about a solution before the two species polarized their hatred around the Caamas incident. The Ishori tended to be very excitable, and got agitated when confronted. They were also a martial society, with many of their laws based on the tenets of battle.

**Isht** This planet was the homeworld of the Ishori.

**Ish'tay** This Force-sensitive Ithorian spent much of his career as an ecologist on Caamas, working to restore the planet's natural environment. He discovered the presence of an ancient Ithorian herd ship, which had crashed into Caamas many generations before, and investigated the possibility that his own people might have created the original forests of the planet. He was tall and lanky with ocher-colored skin and sported several neck piercings holding an odd assortment of metal rings. He wore a simple cloak and leaned on a gnarled rosewood staff.

***Isilia*** This freighter was owned and operated by Adriav Kavos. Armed with a pair of laser cannons, it could transport up to four passengers and 100 metric tons of cargo. Kavos was forced to land the ship on Joralla during an attempt to sell a data disk containing secret information on the Rebel Alliance.

**Isiring** This ore-rich mining world was located among the Cassandran Worlds in the Outer Rim Territories. After the Empire split the Cassandran Worlds apart, Isiring became the capital world of the Tendrannan sector.

**Isis** This crystalline planet was located in a moderately dense region of the Ivax Nebula, in the Anoat sector. Isis was the site of a Rebel Alliance starfighter construction facility during the Galactic Civil War. The planet was the homeworld of the Gutretee, a species of crystalline humanoids. It was located beyond the fringe of Imperial space, and was first explored by an Alderaanian scouting expedition. Bail Organa kept the planet's location a secret, fearing Palpatine's growing wrath against Old Republic supporters. When his fears were realized, Organa began hiding the families of prominent Republic supporters on Isis. The newcomers were met with gruff acceptance by most Gutretee, and cooperation grew into the starfighter facility. The planet itself was huge, covered with translucent mountains and refractive spires. It was nearly discovered when the crew of the Imperial survey vessel *Wanderer* crashed on the surface. They tried to escape back to the Imperial base on Miser by hijacking the *Handree,* but were intercepted by Alliance agents.

Iskalon

**Isis, Governor** This Imperial administrator wanted Boba Fett to capture Feldrall Okor. When she balked at his price for capturing the pirate, Fett armed a thermal detonator and threatened to blow up her palace if she didn't comply. She eventually gave in and paid Fett's price.

**Iskaayuma** This city was located at the end of the Sika Peninsula on Rodia. Iskaayuma was considered the capital of the planet, primarily because it was the enclave of the ruling Chattza clan. It was second in size only to Equator City, but was poorly designed and failed to provide anything in the way of growth potential.

**Iskadrell** The primary planet in the Iskallon system and homeworld of the Iskalloni.

**Iskalloni** Little was known of the pale, hairless, blue-skinned humanoids native to the virtually unexplored Iskallon system. They implanted cybernetic devices to assist their strange physiology, but those produced a toxic waste that was deadly to most carbon-based lifeforms. The toxicity spread to their heavy machinery, including starships and hyperdrives, which made cleaning an Iskalloni hyperdrive a perilous duty. The appearance of the Iskalloni resulted from the addition of mutagen to their systems, which allowed them to accept biotechnological implants and survive. Their eyes were deeply recessed in their skulls and had black irises.

The Iskalloni remained apart from the rest of the galaxy for several millennia, after several attempts to establish peaceful relations fell through. During the reign of the New Order, the Iskalloni returned to known space and made contact with Imperial agents. While the Empire thought it had gained a valuable ally, the Iskalloni showed no preference in enslaving humans, taking Imperial agents as well as Rebel Alliance personnel in their initial attacks. The Iskalloni sought to enslave the entire human species, but couldn't determine the best place to begin their assault. Eventually, with the help of human outlaw Wertram Farege, they captured a New Republic starship holding the planetary coordinates of several major worlds and planned their assault. However, the starship crew disabled the Iskalloni ship and stranded the aliens in their own system.

**Iskalon** This planet was the homeworld of a species of water-breathing humanoids known as Iskalonians. The planet itself had no natural land formations. When the Iskalonians joined the Rebel Alliance, they erected great cities on the ocean floor that allowed air breathers to live with them. However, after the Imperial base on Gamandar destroyed the city of Pavillion, the Iskalonians forbade any landing by air-breathing species. This mandate was not recognized by the Nagai, however, who tried to subjugate Iskalon shortly after the Battle of Endor.

**Iskalon Effect** The term used by the Iskalonians to describe the massive tidal waves that crashed through the oceans of their homeworld, Iskalon. Because of the biology and structure of the ocean, these tidal waves formed rapidly and grew to massive proportions.

**Iskalonian** A group of six major and 11 minor water-breathing species brought to Iskalon some five millennia before the Galactic Civil War. Some were humanoids who

Iskalonian

had gills for breathing, large pointed ears, and small tendrils that flowed from the corners of their mouths. They were known for their carefree, peaceful outlook on life, and they lacked any concept of privacy or shyness. It was assumed that individuals would only listen in on another conversation if they had an interest in it, but any individual could join a discussion at any time.

Following the Battle of Hoth, the Iskalonians were active members of the Rebel Alliance, having witnessed the Imperial atrocities on Telfrey and Gamandar. However, when Luke Skywalker and Leia Organa arrived on the planet, their presence attracted the notice of Imperial Admiral Tower. In his desire to earn a promotion and fame, he tried to destroy all life on Iskalon in an effort to kill the Alliance leaders. The entire city of Pavillion was destroyed, and a great number of Iskalonians lost their lives in the massive tidal wave created by Tower's missile. Although the Iskalonians agreed with the Alliance's motivations, the survivors decided to go into hiding and forbade the Alliance from returning to Iskalon. However, Luke Skywalker later joined with local hero Kiro to rid the planet of Nagai invaders.

**Iskalonian stinger** While this Iskalonian weapon was built for use underwater, at short ranges out of water it was more powerful than most blasters.

**Isk-ar** One of the six Tiss'shar subspecies, the Isk-ar were albinos with translucent scales that lacked any sort of markings.

**Isken, Bran** A native of Corellia, he was born on a starship to a father who worked as a smuggler. He grew up working with the ship's systems, and could repair them all at an early age. Bran Isken eventually found work as a mechanic, and was introduced to Klis Joo when he was asked to repair a Duros starship. The Jedi Knight later invited him to come to work at the spaceport facility on Almas. Isken agreed, and became one of the best mechanics in Forard. He was a distinguished man of 60 at the time of the Battle of Naboo, and was notable for a cybernetic eye. Isken was friendly but suspicious, and was always willing to "do a favor."

**Iskraker, Helm** This small-time criminal was considered not worth the effort by seasoned bounty hunters. He was a humanoid with rolling layers of gold-colored skin that shimmered as he moved and sloughed off golden flakes. He traveled the galaxy in his ship, the *Erratic Orbit.* Iskraker was a bumbler, and virtually every operation he started ended in failure. He did successfully break into SecuriCo and stole the codes to open the locks to Cloud City's computer core without being caught.

**island beast** Huge, kilometer-long creatures native to Taloraan. The island beasts floated in the planet's atmosphere. They had a huge body cavity that was inhabitable, and they were used by the Wind Raiders as living quarters.

**Ismaren, Irek** Roganda Ismaren's son by Sarcev Quest, he was long rumored to be the son of Emperor Palpatine. Irek's youthful abilities with the Force were augmented by his mother when she had Nasdra Magrody implant a subelectronic converter chip in his brain at the age of five. This chip allowed Irek to become educated more quickly, both from a practical standpoint as well as with the Force. By age seven, he began formal training in the Force. At 13, he could easily have qualified for an advanced degree in a number of physical sciences.

Irek had been brought up for one purpose, however, and that was to recover the derelict *Eye of Palpatine* battlemoon by using his connection to the Force to remotely activate the ship's onboard systems. His weakness, though, was that he could only control objects if he knew their basic schematics, which he had committed to memory. If the schematics changed even slightly, he couldn't manipulate the object.

When the *Eye of Palpatine* later was destroyed, Irek managed to escape with his mother to Coruscant. There she began altering his body and mind, creating a huge, Force-wielding being. His bones and muscles were forced to continue growing long past the point of maturity, giving him incredible height and mass. The AI implant placed in his brain was further enhanced, allowing him to have a deep-seated inner focus that provided a strong connection to the dark side of the Force. A collection of lightsabers were implanted in his body at the wrists, knees, and shoulders, and were hardwired to the implant for greater control. His weapons training was handled by an unknown Dark Jedi hired by his mother. At some point, Irek became angry with the Dark Jedi and killed him in a duel, but not before taking a lightsaber thrust through the brain. Roganda was forced to begin a second series of transformations. Before the entire transformation was complete, however, Irek broke free. Without memories or a basic understanding of what had happened to him, he killed his mother and fled into the depths of Coruscant's undercity, adopting the identity of Lord Nyax. (*See also* Nyax, Lord.)

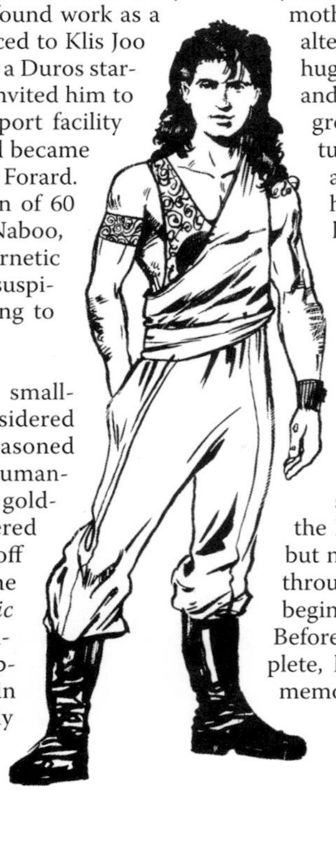

Irek Ismaren

Roganda Ismaren

**Ismaren, Lagan** One of Nichos Marr's childhood friends. The pair tried to find the kretch in Plett's Well. Lagan was Roganda Ismaren's brother, and was killed by Imperial Inquisitor Ameesa Darys as Roganda was forced to watch.

**Ismaren, Roganda** One of Emperor Palpatine's concubines and one of the Emperor's Hands. Roganda Ismaren used her feminine wiles to extract information from the Emperor's enemies during the New Order. As a child, she was among the many Jedi offspring who were shipped off into hiding on Belsavis in the wake of the Clone Wars. However, she was discovered on Belsavis by Imperial Inquisitor Ameesa Darys. Her Force sensitivity earned her the notice of Darys, who then forced her to watch as Darys killed her brother Lagan. Roganda vowed to accumulate enough personal power to prevent her own death, and learned to use her femininity.

Leia Organa Solo once saw Roganda on Coruscant during a Senatorial meeting. Later, after the Battle of Endor, Leia saw her again in Plawal, on Belsavis, and recognized her pale skin and dark hair. Leia had traveled there to investigate rumors that the planet had once housed a large group of Jedi children. Roganda told Leia that she had been hiding on Belsavis for seven years, fleeing the anti-Palpatine sentiments sweeping the galaxy. In reality, Roganda was hiding a plot to recover the *Eye of Palpatine* by implanting a Force-augmenting AI chip into her son, Irek. She then spent many months training Irek about the schematics and operational procedures necessary to take control of the huge ship, hoping to use it to reestablish the Empire. Luke Skywalker infiltrated the ship and managed to destroy it from within. Roganda and Irek escaped the destruction, and they fled back to Coruscant. There, in a research lab, Roganda began an aggressive experiment that altered Irek's body and mind.

Roganda planned to create a Force-wielding being from Irek's youthful body. She kept the boy hidden as she used techniques to accelerate his growth and deepen his connection to the dark side of the Force. She located a fellow Dark Jedi to help train Irek, and used captive ysalamiri to hide the incredible amounts of Force energy being generated in the lab. Irek became self-aware of his new state and broke free of the bonds that held him. The final stages of the alterations were not complete, leaving Irek without memories or instructions. In a rage, Irek destroyed much of the laboratory and killed Roganda before fleeing into the undercity of Coruscant.

**isolation helmet** A specialized form of headgear designed for private communications. Smaller than a standard pilot's helmet, an isolation helmet allowed an individual to listen to a certain communications frequency without being overheard by nearby beings. The helmet had to be programmed to receive a specific transmission frequency.

**Isolder, Prince** The younger son of the Hapan Queen Mother Ta'a Chume, Isolder held the title of Chume'da, which roughly translated into Basic as Prince. He had been named Chume'da because his older brother, Kalen, was murdered by a privateer named Harravan. It was later revealed that Kalen's assassination had been ordered by their mother in an effort to remove him from the line of succession.

The blond-haired Isolder caught a glimpse of Princess Leia Organa when she arrived on Hapes to form an alliance with the Hapans, and fell in love with her. He convinced his mother that marrying Leia would help the Hapans prosper, and Ta'a Chume pretended to agree. When a Hapan delegation arrived on Coruscant to discuss an alliance with the New Republic, they presented Leia with 63 gifts, one from each of the worlds in the Hapes Cluster. The 63rd gift was Prince Isolder, who had arranged to go to Coruscant to propose marriage. Leia stalled the marriage, but many politicians in the New Republic government were pressuring her to accept because an alliance with the Hapes Consortium was exactly what the fledgling New Republic needed. Politics or no politics, Han Solo would have nothing to do with it. He was in love with Princess Leia, and he was certain that Leia reciprocated those feelings. Unable to compete with the endless riches or political clout of a Hapan prince (whom Han mockingly referred to as "His Gorgeousness"), Solo improvised and set out to win Leia a planet . . . in a sabacc game.

One high-stakes game later, Han found himself the proud owner of Dathomir, and he absconded with Leia to their new world to profess his love to her. Unfortunately, the *Millennium Falcon* crash-landed, and the couple were captured by the Singing Mountain Clan of the Witches of Dathomir. Isolder and Luke Skywalker followed, and Isolder met a powerful young desert witch, Teneniel Djo. After facing down the most evil of the witches, a powerful Imperial Warlord, and even his own mother, Isolder found himself in love with Djo, and they married.

Skywalker had foreseen that Isolder and Djo would have a daughter who was strong in the Force, a prophecy that was later fulfilled with the birth of Tenel Ka. When Isolder's mother stepped down, Teneniel Djo became the Queen Mother of Hapes, and Isolder became her king. They retired to their home on Hapes to raise their daughter and bring peace to the Hapes Consortium.

The Hapans remained outside galactic politics until the Yuuzhan Vong War. Leia Organa Solo once again traveled to the Hapes Cluster in hopes of convincing the Hapans to join the fight against the alien invaders. The Consortium was divided on whether to support the New Republic, until Isolder slapped Beed Thane for insulting Leia. This led to an unusual duel in which the winner would control the vote. Thane was arrogant but relatively untrained, and Isolder was able to outlast him. The Hapes Cluster joined the New Republic in an effort to defeat the Yuuzhan Vong, and Isolder himself led the fleet from the *Song of War*.

As the combined fleet prepared to defend Corellia, it was discovered that the Yuuzhan Vong were actually attacking Fondor. The fleet made emergency maneuvers to reach Fondor, but found its shipyards utterly destroyed. The Hapans and the New Republic forces opened fire on the Yuuzhan Vong armada, but all hostilities ceased when a blast from Centerpoint Station ripped through the Fondor system. In addition to wiping out the Yuuzhan Vong ships, the blast decimated the Hapan fleet. Isolder and his crew aboard the *Song of War* were just outside the blast, and survived to limp back to the Hapes Cluster.

Once home, Isolder discovered that Teneniel Djo had miscarried their second child, and that she had fallen into deep despair. With the Hapan people clamoring for strong leadership, Isolder was forced to consider an unusual request from his mother: to divorce Teneniel Djo and marry Jaina Solo. This plan was ultimately abandoned when it was discovered that the former Queen Mother had been poisoning Teneniel Djo. Isolder remained loyal to his wife and family, and was happy to allow Tenel Ka to assume the role of Queen Mother. For his own part, Isolder remained a member of the Hapan Royal Guard, training soldiers to protect his daughter and any heir she might bring to the family.

Isolder assumed a position of leadership within the Hapan Home Fleet and reluctantly agreed to support the Galactic Alliance during its defense of Kuat. However, in agreement with his wife's desires, Isolder ordered his fleets to back out of the conflict after Tenel Ka decided that Jacen Solo had become too dangerous. The fleet returned to Hapes, where Isolder watched with fatherly concern as Tenel Ka struggled to remain neutral in the conflict. After the Second Battle of Fondor, Tenel Ka asked Isolder to ensure that Ben Skywalker made it safely to the new Jedi base on Shedu Maad. He asked Tenel Ka's cousins Trista and Taryn to recover Ben on Nova Station, and was to meet them near the Carida Nebula in his starcutter, the *Beam Racer*. Tahiri Veila had been tracking Ben, however, and managed to intervene. Because Ben had already refused to divulge information about the Jedi base, Veila used the tractor beams on the *Anakin Solo* to capture Isolder's ship, hoping that he could provide the location.

Prince Isolder spent many days in the prison section of the ship, but was not interrogated or even questioned until Darth Caedus—the former Jacen Solo—arrived at his cell. Caedus's arrival came during his attempt to destroy the Jedi Order's base in the Transitory Mists, and Isolder believed that his interrogation had finally come. So he was surprised when Caedus explained that he was letting Isolder and his crew go free once the battle was over. Isolder's freedom was only guaranteed if he removed himself from the battle zone, since Caedus and his technicians had rigged the *Beam Racer* to explode if it was shot just once. Isolder refused, knowing that his blood samples might have been used to create a nanokiller that would destroy his daughter and her family. In anger, Darth Caedus drew upon the Force and snapped Isolder's neck, and the prince died before his body hit the floor. Caedus then ordered the *Beam Racer* to be destroyed with all hands aboard.

**Ison** This white dwarf star was the central body of the Ison system in the Anoat sector. The star was orbited by a series of asteroid belts and a growing cloud of gas that made travel through the system treacherous. Despite this, explorers placed on the outskirts of the system a hyperspace beacon that served as the Rimward entry point for the Ison Corridor. Rebel ships routinely approached their Hoth base from the direction of Ison to minimize any chance of detection.

**Ison Corridor** This hyperspace pathway connected a backrocket group of planets in the Anoat sector to the main Corellian Trade Spine. The Ison Corridor began at Varonat and passed through Bespin, Anoat, and Hoth before terminating in the Ison system. It took about 14 hours to jump between all the systems along the Corridor. The Corellian Trade Spine, a much more profitable and better-understood hyperspace pathway, drew much of the corridor's potential traffic. However, the Ison Corridor avoided the heart of the Ivax Nebula, making it marginally safer to travel. Scientists

Prince Isolder

believed that the coalescing gases and debris in the Ison system would eventually shut off the Rimward end of the corridor, rendering the route obsolete. Varonat, in the corridor, was where the Emperor's Hand Mara Jade once worked as a hyperdrive mechanic following the death of Palpatine.

**isothane** This alcoholic beverage was often served with water and ice.

**Isoto, Admiral Lon** This Imperial officer was regarded as a traitor for his part in the Battle of Brentaal. He was known to both the Empire he served and the New Republic he opposed as an ineffectual leader, often called Isoto the Indecisive. He rose to power through the support of the members of the Cabal. Isoto was more interested in his pleasure than the Empire, and used his position to obtain the things he desired most. He was in command of the Imperial base near Vuultin at the time of Emperor Palpatine's death, and was allowed to remain in command when Sate Pestage took power. Ysanne Isard and Pestage planned to draw the New Republic's forces to Brentaal IV, hoping to use the admiral's incompetency as a lure. Meanwhile, Isoto languished in his fortress, surrounded by women and—if rumors were true—enjoying glitterstim spice. He was shot and killed by one of his concubines, Grania, shortly after being ordered by Ysanne Isard to evacuate Brentaal. The concubine was actually working for Isard as part of Project Ambition.

*Admiral Lon Isoto*

**ISP speeder** *See* infantry support platform.

**Isryn's Veil** According to Imperial astrogation maps, this was the name given to the third quadrant of the Dantooine system. Little was known of the history of this area of space.

**Iss, Lafek** This bounty hunter was known for his wide range of skills, from electronics and computers to droid programming and anti-surveillance. A member of the Salaktori Hunters Guild, he worked from a base in Feris City during the Galactic Civil War.

**Issagra** A planet that was the site of a huge space station devoted to gambling and trade.

**Issen, Ensign** This Imperial Navy officer served under Lieutenant Carsa aboard the *Lusankya* during the Battle of Thyferra.

**Isshaddik** This male Wookiee was the mate of Dewlannamapia. He was exiled from Kashyyyk for a crime Dewlanna never explained, and the two of them ended up working for Garris Shrike. He was killed a year later on a smuggling run to Nar Hekka.

**Issham Mining Corporation** This sham corporation was actually a front used by the Rebel Alliance to establish a base on Virmeude. Issham purchased the mining rights to the planet, and then established the Virmeude Starport. In reality, the Alliance used Virmeude as one of the primary posts from which it gathered intelligence on the Core Worlds during the Galactic Civil War. The spaceport also served as a haven and base of operations for pirates and smugglers who were sympathetic to the Alliance. IMC appeared to outside interests as a corporation making a modest profit from its operations, but the Alliance was careful to doctor its books accordingly. All mining shipments brought in by privateers were listed as profit, and all mining and support resources were ordered as if they were to be used in a mining installation.

**Issor** An aquatic planet that was home to the Issori and Odenji. Issor was a prosperous technology and commerce center in the Trulalis system. Centuries before the Battle of Yavin, the Odenji were nearly wiped out by the "melanncho," a sadness so powerful it could make the sufferer go insane.

**Istic II** The primary planet in the Istic system in the Teraab sector. It orbited a young yellow-white star that bombarded the planet with heavy radiation. It housed a mining colony, but its resources paled in comparison with the operations on nearby Drogheda, Istic, Pesmemben IV, and Tyne's Horky.

**istician** Classified by the Empire as subsentient, these creatures were native to the radiation-shrouded planet of Istic II. Because of the high levels of radiation in the environment, isticians suffered from frequent genetic mutation, and had a variety of shapes, sizes, and colorations. The Imperial Governor of the system welcomed hunters to take as many isticians as they could, since they were considered a nuisance to the human settlers.

**Isttu** This Ithorian city was located on the herd ship *Bazaar* on the banks of Isttu Lake. The site of the Great Mother River Hotel, it housed many shops and businesses. It perfectly re-created the illusion of a jungle village—until residents looked up and saw the dome that protected Isttu village from the vacuum of space.

**Istuvi, Dif** This man led the Bakuran faithful who embraced the Cosmic Balance during the planet's early history. He was generally credited with authoring the faith's most sacred text, the *Fulcrum*. In it, he claimed that "the weight of the universe could balance on one rightly-placed atom." Istuvi later founded the order of the Zanazi.

**Isu-Sim** This specialty manufacturer produced some of the galaxy's fastest hyperdrive generators. The Death Star had an SFS-CR27200 hypermatter reactor powering 123 Isu-Sim SSP06 hyperdrive generators. The *Millennium Falcon* was equipped with an Isu-Sim SSP05 hyperdrive generator.

**IT** This droid, a self-modified IT series interrogation droid, was activated on Coruscant some three years after the Battle of Endor. The IT unit was developed with GwendoLyn Six processing, making it extremely fast and efficient in dealing with information. This gave IT an almost human reaction time, as well as a high level of artificial intelligence. After Coruscant fell to the New Republic in the wake of the Battle of Endor, the IT decided to hide out in the sublevels of the planet, biding its time and awaiting a chance to strike back. The IT employed a mixture of human and droid agents to carry out its bidding, which involved rallying the Underdwellers of Coruscant to rise up and defeat the fledgling New Republic. IT's plans were thwarted when they were discovered by Chewbacca and his son, Lumpawarrump. Chewbacca managed to disable the IT, and his wife, Mallatobuck, destroyed it.

**IT-3** An Imperial interrogation droid, the Interrogator Droid Mark III was developed from the basic IT-O platform. Unlike its predecessors, the IT-3 had the ability to speak Basic, and was given a soothing, motherly voice to further disarm its victims. These droids were equipped with a laser scalpel, power shears, a sonic warbler, an electroshock probe, and three hypodermic syringes. Many were filled with a Sith toxin of unknown origin. They were favorites of Imperial Intelligence czar Ysanne Isard.

**IT-31** This droid was acquired by Kodin, who planned to sell it from his shop on Nar Shaddaa after the Jedi Civil War. IT-31 eventually was purchased by the Jedi Exile, who had been asked by IT-32 to recover it. Hidden in IT-31's memory banks were plans for a new droid shielding technology, which IT-32 wanted back before they could be exploited.

**ITAC Authority** One of the primary law enforcement agencies on Entralla during the early years of the New Republic. It was forced to work with, and often bow to the wishes of, the Pentastar Patrol.

**Itani Nebula** A remote, gas-filled area of space. The Empire maintained a hidden research laboratory station deep within the Nebula, and posted an officer at Darknon Station to help protect its location. However, the lab was discovered by Rebel Alliance agents shortly after the Battle of Yavin, and was later destroyed by an Alliance strike force.

**Itani system** This star system was located on the edge of the Itani Nebula, at one end of the Itani Run.

**Ithaqua Station** One of the primary outposts maintained by the Old Republic on Toola during the Clone Wars. In addition to its spaceport, Ithaqua Station contained a cantina and a vast open market where hundreds of different species exchanged credits for a variety of goods and services.

**Ith-Dor** This was one of the twin cities, along with Sarus-Dor, that served as the capital of Typha-Dor.

**Ithh, Ror** This Ithorian cantina crawler was a frequent patron of the Outlander Club during the years surrounding the Battle of Geonosis.

**Ithila** A soldier in the Hapan Navy during the war against the Yuuzhan Vong, she was badly injured when the Battle Dragon on which she served was attacked by the alien invaders. Since Ithila was allergic to bacta, she had to be serviced with regular surgical techniques that left the right side of her body badly scarred. Her appearance was considered hideous by other Hapan women, leaving Ithila with no choice but to set out on her own. She served as a pirate and smuggler for several years before signing on as the sensor officer aboard the *Poison Moon.*

**Ithona** This gas giant was the fifth planet of the Essesia system. It was orbited by five moons.

**Ithoon** This barren ball of rock was the sixth planet of the Centares system, located in the Mid Rim. It was orbited by three moons.

**Ithor** This bright green-and-blue planet with multiple moons in the Ottega system (often referred to as the Ithorian system) was in the Lesser Plooriod Cluster. The system's fourth planet was home to the nature-loving Ithorians, sometimes called Hammerheads. Ithor was a beautiful, if humid, world of unspoiled rain forests, rivers, and waterfalls.

Three continents were developed, although they appeared to be overgrown jungles to most visitors. The Ithorians considered the jungle sacred and entered it only during emergencies. Instead, they constructed vast floating cities that hovered above the bafforr treetops in no particular pattern. They included the *Tree of Tarintha,* the *Cloud-Mother,* and the Grand Herd Ship *Tafanda Bay.* Ithorian starships, essentially herd cities with hyperdrives, traveled the space lanes selling unusual and rare merchandise. Brathflen Corporation, which operated on Belsavis, was a major Ithorian trading company.

At times the Mother Jungle was known to "call" certain Ithorians to live on the surface as ecological priests who never returned to their herd cities. All Ithorians were bound by the Ithorian Law of Life, which stated that for every plant harvested, two must be planted in its place. A large grove of semi-intelligent bafforr trees, located in the Cathor Hills, was half destroyed by the Empire. This grove acted as an intelligent hive mind and was worshipped by the Ithorian people. In addition to the bafforr, Ithor's flora included blueleaf, tremmin, fiddlehead bull-ferns, donar flowers, and indyup trees; animal life included the manollium bird, the arrak snake, and the flitter—a small flying rodent that could mimic speech.

Every five years, Ithorians gathered at their planet for the Meet, where the most important decisions regarding Ithorian society were made. During this Time of Meeting, the herd cities linked up through an intricate and graceful network of bridges and antigrav platforms.

Ithor

Ithor was blockaded by the Empire during Palpatine's reign. When the Ithorians gave the Empire certain agricultural and cloning information, they were left alone and the planet became a tourist destination.

In the Battle of Ithor, all life on the planet was destroyed by a bacteria-filled bioweapon constructed by the Yuuzhan Vong. The attack was meant to destroy the bafforr trees specifically, but the Yuuzhan Vong didn't care about collateral damage. Adding insult to injury, the destruction of the *Legacy of Torment* by New Republic warships left the Yuuzhan Vong grand cruiser without drive systems, and it crashed onto the surface, igniting the bacteria-filled slime and creating a series of planet-sweeping fires. Ithor burned like a star for several days before dying out, hanging in space like a dead cinder. Because of his part in destruction of the grand cruiser, Corran Horn was quickly targeted by the news agencies as "the man who destroyed Ithor."

**Ithorian** An unusual-looking, bipedal mammal species native to Ithor. The head of an Ithorian appeared to have been stretched and bent like a ladle. The eyes were set at opposite sides of the hammer-shaped top portion of the head, and the mouth was hidden below on the sloping part of the head. Ithorians also had multiple throats, so their speaking voices came out with a peculiar stereo effect, and this biological phenomenon made their speech hard to understand. They had wide, flat feet designed to help individuals keep their balance.

Ithorians were known for their reverence toward the natural environment, as evidenced by their development of floating city-ships that ensured that no part of Ithor's surface was damaged by construction. They were also known as steady pacifists, and were considered some of the galaxy's most skilled diplomats.

A large portion of the Ithorian population was eradicated during the Yuuzhan Vong War when the planet's ecosystem was destroyed by a virulent bioweapon. The survivors were offplanet when the attack came; they struggled for many years, lacking a world to call home, until Leia Organa Solo and her husband, Han, discovered Borao. After months of political wrangling, the remaining Ithorians were allowed to relocate to Borao permanently.

**Ithorian Defender Armor** This specialized body armor was produced to conform to the body of an Ithorian. Classified as battle armor, Ithorian Defender Armor provided protection from a wide range of attacks.

**Ithorian dragon** This creature was the stuff of legend. Stories of Ithorian dragons date to the earliest recorded histories of the Ithorians, whose ancestors claimed that the dragon was an intelligent beast that used special powers to hunt down its prey. Over time, many of these legends were discovered to be stories told to keep youngsters from disobeying their parents. However, the Ithorian dragon itself was an actual creature, albeit less fearsome than its legends.

These reptiles were pack hunters, using their keen sense of smell to track their prey. Moving about on four strong legs, they were stealthy hunters. Their eyes, which were located at the top of their skulls, provided a nearly complete field of vision, allowing them to track prey and scan for other predators or scavengers. They also made it nearly impossible to sneak up on a dragon when it was alert and hunting. The packs were led by a single

Ithorian

female, who was followed by males into the field. Nonhunting females remained behind to guard the pack's territory.

**Ithorian Guardian Armor** This specialized body armor was developed for field medics and other support personnel, and provided protection from energy attacks.

**Ithorian Mist** A form of whiskey created by the Ithorians.

**Ithorian razor shark** This predatory fish lived in the oceans of Ithor, and had dagger-like teeth lining its large mouth.

**Ithorian Sentinel Armor** Specialized body armor that was designed to be worn by commandos. It provided protection from projectile weapons.

**Ithorian SkyYards** This Ithorian company was the sole designer and manufacturer of *Sky Yards*–class herd ships until Ithor was destroyed by the Yuuzhan Vong.

**Ithorian starflower** Golden flowers known for their howling death shrieks.

**Ithorian Vivarium** This well-stocked and -maintained natural park was operated by the Ithorian population of Citadel Station, in orbit around Telos, after the Great Sith War. One of the galaxy's few specimens of Bachani plant was carefully tended at the Vivarium.

***Ithor Lady*** This New Republic battle cruiser was stationed at Cybloc XII until it was dispatched to quell a pirate uprising near Budpock. The ship was drawn away from Nam Chorios by the manipulations of Seti Ashgad and Dzym.

**Ithor Loman** This cantina, located in the spaceport near Rytal Prime on Dayark, was where Talon Karrde and Jutka met to discuss the attack on the *Wild Karrde* during Karrde's search for Jorj Car'das.

***Ithor Wanderer*** This Ithorian herd ship plied a regular route along the Hydian Way before returning to Ithor for Herd Meets.

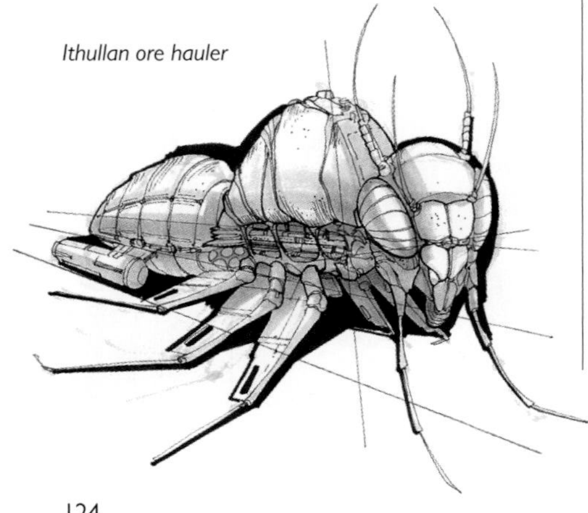
Ithullan ore hauler

Ylenic It'kla

**Ithull** A planet in the Stenness system, Ithull was the homeworld of the huge colossus wasps and the war-like Ithullans. The Ithullans were wiped out by the Mandalorians some 4,000 years before the Battle of Yavin. The tough exoskeletons of the colossus wasps were hollowed out, fitted with necessary hardware, and used as cargo ships. The bounty hunter Dyyz Nataz wore a suit of Ithullan battle armor. A year on Ithull lasted 25 standard months.

**Ithullan ore hauler** Among the most unusual vessels in the galaxy, these ships were built out of the carapaces, or hard outer coverings, of kilometer-long Ithullan colossus wasps millennia before the Galactic Civil War. The wasps lived for centuries, going from world to world to feed on stellar radiation, raw materials, space slugs, and asteroid creatures. When a wasp died, miners called Nessies converted it to a cargo hauler by carving and sectioning its interior to make room for decks and ship systems. Remaining space was given over to the precious mutonium ore that the Nessies mined. The haulers' main weapons were a pair of heavy turbolasers mounted in the forward section of the chest.

**Itipiniwi** This Sullustan wilwog won first place in the annual Mid Rim Domesticated Sub-Sentient Show, held on Commenor shortly before the start of the Clone Wars. Unfortunately, Itipiniwi's owner became hysterical when the results were announced, causing the wilwog to yelp wildly. This yelping irritated the sensitive ears of the runner-up, a bolystyngar named Boshuda, and the bolystyngar ate Itipiniwi. Boshuda was named the winner by default, as there were no rules regarding the consumption of one entrant by another.

**It'kla, Ylenic** This Caamasi was one of the few members of his species to become a Jedi Knight. A furry humanoid with purple facial stripes, It'kla was assigned to work with Aayla Secura in recovering Ratri Tane from Corellia. He worked with his old friend Nejaa Halcyon to ensure that Aayla's mission was a success, despite the mysterious circumstances under which it was carried out. Shortly after the Clone Wars, It'kla and Halcyon were dispatched to stop Nikkos Tyris, who had stumbled upon ancient Sith lore. Although the Jedi succeeded in eliminating the threat, Halcyon was killed in the struggle. It'kla then flew to Corellia to deliver Nejaa's personal belongings to his widow, Scerra. Years later, having survived the Great Purge, he served as one of Bail Organa's chief advisers during the early years of the New Order. It'kla was part of the Alderaanian delegation that traveled to Cloud City to meet with Bria Tharen. He perished when Alderaan was destroyed by the Death Star.

**IT-O** *See* interrogator droid.

**Itoklo, Seyyerin** This young Etti Jedi Knight trained under Luke Skywalker at the Jedi praxeum on Yavin 4 shortly before the Yuuzhan Vong War. When the Yuuzhan Vong claimed they would halt their invasion if the New Republic turned over all Jedi, Seyyerin Itoklo was one of the first to stand against the invaders in defending a planet, but was killed.

Ivak

**Ivak** An Imperial officer serving Ysanne Isard shortly after the death of Emperor Palpatine, he interrogated Mara Jade when she was first caught by Isard. Jade used the Force to manipulate him so she could escape.

**Ivatch** A planet near Shintel in the Kathol sector. It was one of several planets that supplied natural ore and metal to the industrial world of Gandle Ott.

**Ivax Nebula** Found in the Anoat sector, the Ivax Nebula was part of the formation known as the Twin Nebulae, whose two halves were called Kiax and Ivax for two ancient Corellian trickster gods who often hampered navigation between the Spine and Lutrillia (Kiax, the spinward half of the nebula) and Nothoiin (Ivax, the trailing half). The Ivax Nebula was actually part of a single, irregular nebula.

**Ivey** This woman joined the Rebel Alliance as a procurement officer shortly after the Battle of Yavin, hoping to accomplish something noble in the effort. She later was chosen to be part of Andrephan Stormcaller's Red Alpha unit, and left the New Republic armed forces when Stormcaller himself opted out to form the Red Moons.

**Ivpikkis, Admiral** The military commander of the Ssi-ruuvi task force sent to

subjugate Bakura. He was one of the few Ssi-ruuk at Bakura with real military experience, having been a soldier and scout before being promoted to officer status. It was Ivpikkis who captured Imperial troops and suggested that the Ssi-ruuk should use the Empire to extend their control. It was believed that Admiral Ivpikkis managed to escape the destruction of the Ssi-ruuvi fleet during the Battle of Bakura.

**ivrooy coral** This form of coral was well known among the rich and powerful for its ability to be cultured and grown into strong, durable pieces of furniture. Many of the best cultured ivrooy pieces were manufactured before the Clone Wars. The color of ivrooy was not stable, and darkened over time.

**IW-37** Known alternatively as the Salvager or as a pincer loader, this 3-meter-tall droid was a nimbler version of the CLL-M2 load-lifter that was used to manipulate heavy ordnance. It was developed to handle the more delicate operations of loading custom ordnance into the small fighters of the Jedi Knights during the Clone Wars. With some additional programming, these droids were also used as traffic controllers and refuelers at hyperdrive ring stations.

***IX-26*** This New Republic patrol ship was used to ferry Kroddok Stopa's archaeological team to Brath Qella. It stopped on Babali to pick up Stopa and Josala Krenn to gather information on the Qella during the attempt to capture the Teljkon vagabond.

**IX-2A** This BDG-7 assassin droid was originally part of a team of assassins maintained by Boss Tosk until his programming was scrambled in an accident while on a hunt. IX-2A made its way to a repair facility, offered to pay for any repairs from Boss Tosk's bank account, and then killed the technician when he tried to access the droid's programming. IX-2A had no memory of his service to Boss Tosk after being repaired, and went to work as an independent assassin. The droid's altered programming gave it a mean streak and earned it a fearful reputation. Boss Tosk, meanwhile, discovered that IX-2A had gone rogue, and sent out his own assassins to recover the droid. IX-2A managed to elude capture.

***IX-44F*** This New Republic Intelligence ferret ship was sent to trail the mysterious ghost ship, the Teljkon vagabond, near Gmar Askilon just before the Yevethan Great Purge.

**ix dbukrii** This soft-bodied parasite was known for its ability to scar the neocortex of its host, causing dementia, disorientation, delusions, and loss of memory. The parasite was originally found in the Jospro sector, where it lived in the Gnithian oep. The ix dbukrii was introduced into its host by a nearly extinct, bloodsucking Gnithian insect, slipping beneath the host's eyelids and burrowing into the brain. Imperial medics occasionally used ix dbukrii to disable or punish patients.

*Yortal Ixlis*

**Ixetal cilona** A form of narcotic distilled from the balo mushrooms that were native to Balosar. Ixetal cilona was developed during the last decades of the Old Republic, when it became the primary ingredient in the creation of death sticks. It could be extracted in various grades, depending on the desired toxicity of the end product. Production of Ixetal cilona was severely curtailed during the early years of the New Republic, when the devastating pollution that blanketed Balosar finally leached its way into the underground caves where the balo mushrooms grew. The economy of Balosar was greatly impacted, as the production of death sticks was almost halted. However, in the wake of the Yuuzhan Vong War, production began to rise when the refugees of damaged worlds turned to the drug to help them forget the horrors of the war.

**Ixetallic** This recreational drug, a derivative of Ixetal cilona, was among many that were outlawed by the Galactic Alliance following the Swarm War.

*IW-37*

**Ixiyen Fast Attack Craft** This medium starfighter was one of several craft developed for the Black Sun organization by TransGalMeg. The Ixiyen was designed to be dominating in fighter-to-fighter combat, with additional armor plating and weaponry. Its central fuselage was needle-shaped, with the aft section spreading out to house the four main sublight drives and a pair of maneuvering engines. The rear of the ship was supported by a pair of stout, downward-sloping wings and two rudder fins, while the front end was given added maneuverability via a pair of stabilizer fins. The forward fin on each side was held to the rear wing by a thick rod, giving the ship a rigid form that could handle intense dogfighting maneuvers.

**Ixlis, Yortal** The owner and operator of Yortal's Emporium, a junk shop in Ahto East on Manaan around the time of the Great Sith War.

**Ixll** Small, flying creatures native to Da Soocha 5, Ixlls had a fair amount of intelligence and were talented toolmakers. They expanded their native technology, and knew a great deal about computers, repulsorlifts, and starship engines. When the New Republic chose the Pinnacle Moon for a base, the Ixlls welcomed humans with curiosity. The two groups studied each other and were able to achieve a working relationship. The Ixlls even learned to use their normal language, which consisted of various chirps, clicks, and whistles, to communicate with R2 astromech droids. After Da Soocha 5 was destroyed, only the 100 or so Ixll who evacuated with Republic personnel survived. The New Republic temporarily relocated the species to the Forest Moon of Endor.

*Ixll*

**Ixnoltah** This Dug was a member of Sebolto's gang following the Battle of Naboo. The Pixelito Grand Council issued a bounty for his capture in connection with the sale of death sticks to the youth of Pixelito, a bounty that Jango Fett managed to claim during his attempt to meet with Sebolto.

**Ixsan, Rogh'ma** A Dug slaver, he was one of the many members of his species who joined the RavinsBlud crime syndicate around the time of the Battle of Naboo. A bounty for his capture was issued by Coruscant police in connection with the transport of death sticks between Malastare and Coruscant. Jango Fett later claimed the bounty during his attempt to locate Sebolto on Malastare.

**Ixsthmus, Captain** This Ithorian was commander of the Rebel transport ship *Long Shot.* He was stern, intelligent, and possessed absolutely no sense of humor. He relied on his copilot, Siene Symm, to perform any underhanded or sneaky dealings with customers, because Ixsthmus also was very honorable.

**Ixtlar** A planet with a large number of holographic advertising signs scattered across its surface, it boasted a dazzling nighttime vista. Located along the Corellian Run, Ixtlar saw combat during the Clone Wars when the Old Republic's Victory Fleet tried to hunt down the Bulwark Fleet of the Separatists. Later, Ixtlar was one of many planets captured by the Yuuzhan Vong, allowing the alien invaders to control a good portion of the Corellian Run.

**Iych-thae** This fanatical Ithorian commanded the herd ship *Varnay* during the Galactic Civil War. He held strongly to the ecological and environmental beliefs of his people, and traveled to the Elrood sector to preach his message to the beings there. Iych-thae protested vehemently the abuses Radell Mining Corporation visited on Dega, which was abandoned as a barren ball of rock after Radell's mines ran dry. Iych-thae was instrumental in the negotiations between Radell and the Anguilla of Alluuvia, and eventually agreed to act as an independent overseer to Radell's future mining operations.

**Iychtor** This frozen ball of rock was the fifth and outermost planet of the Velus system. It was orbited by a single moon.

**Iyon** The Codru-Ji Chamberlain assigned to Princess Leia during her stay on Munto Codru. The inherent political infighting among the Codru-Ji was responsible for a lack of consensus on his qualifications, so Iyon's appointment to the post was a hard-fought battle. Iyon had a young child still in the pupa wyrwulf stage when Princess Leia arrived. It was kidnapped by Hethrir along with the Solo children. The child was very near its metamorphosis stage, and cocooned itself just before returning to Munto Codru.

**Iyra** A species of tentacled cephalopods native to F'tral. These sentient ocean dwellers developed vast underwater cities. Averaging a meter in diameter, the Iyra had a large mouth on their ventral side and several eyestalks on the dorsal side. For each tentacle an Iyra had, there was usually one eyestalk. As an Iyra matured, it grew more tentacles and eyestalks. The Iyra developed impressive technology, creating corrosion-resistant materials as well as gravitic and inertial devices for starships. They established a caste system dependent upon the number of tentacles and eyestalks an individual had, thereby guaranteeing that all individuals would continually strive to improve their position in life. Thus, they were contemptuous of humanoid and other legged alien species. They were able to survive outside the oceans of F'tral by filling starship cabins with a mixture of gases and water vapor that kept their skin moist and maintained chemical balances.

**Iyra gravity belt** This belt, manufactured by Iyranis Gravitics Limited, was equipped with a series of gravity-field generators. In a free-fall situation, the wearer could activate the belt's generators, which emitted gravity pulses to help slow their descent and prevent serious injury.

**Iyranis Gravitics Limited** This Iyra corporation produced a wide range of tools based on gravitic technology.

**Iyred** This planet was once covered with tropical forests, and was the native world of the black bha'lir. However, deforestation and construction threatened the population of the huge cats. The Society of the Black Bha'lir eventually led several missions to rescue the creatures.

**Iyuta** This planet was the site of an Imperial communications center located in the city of Takari. With the help of Reekeene's Roughnecks, the Rebel Alliance staged a raid on Iyuta and successfully knocked out the center shortly after the Battle of Yavin.

**Izable** This was one of the code names used by Zozridor Slayke to describe key locations of military value on Praesitlyn during the attempt by Freedom's Sons and Daughters to fend off a Separatist attack on the Intergalactic Communications Center. Izable was the outermost of Slayke's defenses. Like the command center and positions Eliey, Kaudine, and Judlie, Izable had a 360-degree view of its surrounding terrain, and its fire zone overlapped with Eliey and Kaudine. This provided the maximum defense of the command center. Slayke's forces were badly outnumbered by the Separatist battle droids, and personnel at Izable were forced to fall back to Judlie to regroup.

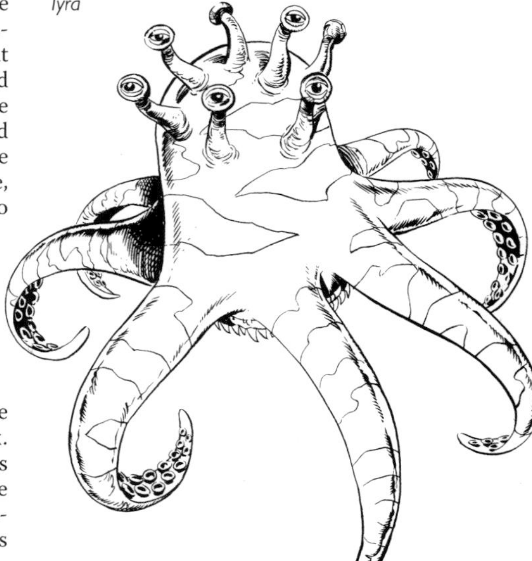
*Iyra*

**I'zak, Anise** This freckle-faced young woman was one of the many Jedi Knights who were thrust into military roles during the Clone Wars. She had a sassy attitude and a knack for getting into trouble that many Jedi Masters believed would prevent her from passing her trials. She often used colorful expletives to cover her mistakes, as well as to help her overcome her emotions in difficult situations. I'zak managed to complete her trials, however, and was promoted to Jedi Knight shortly after the Battle of Geonosis. She was dispatched to Hitaka, accompanying Jedi Masters Aayla Secura and Ki-Adi-Mundi. Their mission was approved by Chancellor Palpatine himself, and I'zak's part involved carrying a special canister across enemy territory to a remote site that was held by the Grand Army of the Republic. She had to fight her way through several squads of battle droids, but she lost the canister when it was hit by a blaster bolt that would have taken her life. Upon reaching the remote camp, she was forced to admit her failure to the clone troopers there, and was surprised when the two Jedi Masters appeared from the command tent. They explained that her mission had merely been a diversion that was meant to confuse the Separatist forces, allowing the GAR to capture the real objective. Although she hated the fact that she was little more than a diversion on the mission, I'zak realized that she could follow orders when necessary. Unknown to the Jedi and the forces of the GAR, however, their orders had been compromised by Darth Sidious, so that they were focused on one mission while Count Dooku carried out his own mission on Hitaka.

**Izaryx** One of the few supporters of the Rebel Alliance living on Dathomir during the Galactic Civil War.

**Izhiq, Paxaz** This Falleen male was one of the criminals who pursued Bardan Jusik and the clone commandos Sev and Fi after they captured Vinna Jiss on Coruscant, about a year after the Battle of Geonosis. Thanks in large part to Jusik's flying abilities, Izhiq and his comrades were unable to catch them. During the chase, the clones managed to destroy Izhiq's speeder, killing the Falleen and his passengers. Because Jusik and the clone commandos were working on a special operations mission to locate a group of Separatist-backed terrorists, Izhiq's death was assumed to have been part of an underworld gang war. His death set off a spree of organized crime killings, which caused trouble for the Coruscant Security Force but helped hide the mission to seek out the terrorists.

**Iziz (1)** This Jawa leader was one of the few members of his tribe to escape being enslaved by a group of Tusken Raiders some 4,000 years before the Battle of Yavin. He enlisted the help of Jedi Knights in rescuing his tribe, and provided them with a map of the Western Dune Sea in return. This map helped the Jedi locate one section of the Star Map.

*Iziz*

**Iziz (2)** A major city on Onderon where Freedon Nadd held court following his seduction by the dark side. Inhabitants built walls to separate themselves from the Dxun beasts that descended on the planet when the Dxun moon was in close orbit. The city itself sat on a low mountain within the walls, which in fact contained several thousand square kilometers of territory and reached several kilometers into the planet's crust. Four hundred years after Nadd's death, a group of Jedi Knights led by Ulic Qel-Droma arrived to end the Onderon Beast Wars. After Queen Amanoa's death, her daughter Galia married the Beast Lord Oron Kira, finally forging a peace between the two factions. Soon after, the dissident Naddists temporarily took control of Iziz, but they were ousted by the Jedi. The *Millennium Falcon* once went to Iziz for repairs many millennia later.

**Izrina** This luminous being was queen of the Wisties on the Forest Moon of Endor before the Galactic Civil War. She befriended Cindel and Mace Towani after their starship crashed on the moon, and assisted them in rescuing their parents from the Gorax by flying around the Gorax's head, confusing and enraging the beast. She was the only Wistie to remain outside of the Candle of Pure Light.

**Izvoshra Khans** The name given to the elite group of eight Kaleesh soldiers who served as General Grievous's bodyguards during the Huk Wars, before he became the cyborg military leader of the Confederacy of Independent Systems. The word *Izvoshra* translated into Basic as "my elite." The number eight was sacred among the Kaleesh. Each Izvoshra held the rank of Khan and commanded his or her own brigade of Kaleesh soldiers. They were selected for their fighting abilities, their cunning, and their loyalty to the Kaleesh people. The Izvoshra was formed in the wake of Ronderu lij Kummar's death, after Grievous made a pilgrimage to Abesmi. The original members were a diverse group of individuals, and included a member of Ronderu's tribe and a former member of the Muja Bandits. The common bonds among them were their loyalty to Grievous and their desire to destroy the Huk occupation forces on their planet. It was believed that the members of the Izvoshra were all killed in the crash of Grievous's shuttle, the *Martyr*, an event that nearly killed Grievous himself. San Hill, who was behind the crash, arranged for a group of IG-100 MagnaGuards to serve as Grievous's new Izvoshra, after Grievous agreed to serve as Separatist military leader. Grievous, however, never fully embraced them as Khans, because they were not able to provide him with military counsel and their loyalty was not freely given, but programmed into their brains.

**Izzy Six** The code name used by the forces of Freedom's Sons and Daughters for the command post established by Lieutenant D'Nore on the redoubt known as Izable on Praesitlyn, during the final stages of the Clone Wars. The name *Izzy Six* was reserved for communications only, as a security measure.

# J

**J1** A hold-out blaster produced by Merr-Sonn Munitions. It was nicknamed the Happy Surprise due to an unusual configuration that made it easy to hide. Unlike most blasters, which had a handgrip and a trigger, the J1 fit entirely within the palm of the hand. The barrel stuck out from between the second and third fingers, making it easy to carry in a clenched fist without arousing suspicion. The trigger was mounted at the top of the weapon, and was depressed with the thumb.

*J1*

**J12 twin-pod airspeeder** This unusual airspeeder was popular during the last decades of the Old Republic, especially on Coruscant. The two egg-shaped passenger pods were connected to the main body of the speeder by a flattened engine section.

**J-14** An enhanced grade of composite starship armor produced by MandalMotors during the New Order.

**J1M** A small, roller-treaded maintenance droid, it was part of the crew that assisted Ki-Adi-Mundi in his search for Ephant Mon near Tatooine. J1M made its way onto Jabba the Hutt's personal shuttle and downloaded its computer banks. Hidden in the data it recovered was enough information to piece together the Trade Federation's role in the import of technology to Cerea.

**J21-Z65 system** *See* Paradise system.

**J-3PA** A bronze protocol droid owned by Premier Provisions.

**J-47** The residential section of the Brewery district of Galactic City during the final decades of the Old Republic.

**J57** This model of Hologlide cam droid was produced by Industrial Automaton during the final decades of the Old Republic. Measuring 0.7 meter long, the J57 was a holographic recording system and data storage unit attached to a pair of repulsorlift wings. It was designed to cover sporting events, especially racing, because of its maneuverability and speed.

*< Jedi Master Qui-Gon Jinn*

**J-77 Event Horizon** The brand name of a series of Novaldex starfighter engines, which were used on RZ-1 A-wing starfighters during the Galactic Civil War.

**J8Q-128 Finbat** This anti-vehicle concussion missile was produced by Kessler during the New Order, and was designed to penetrate the thick armor plating of AT-AT walkers.

**J930 Dash-8** A model of Podracer manufactured by JAK Racing. It was noted for its long, sloped engines, which utilized the Split-X configuration found in Collor Pondrat engines. The cockpit of the J930 measured 3.05 meters long with engines adding another 9.55 meters. They could propel the Podracer at speeds approaching 785 kilometers per hour.

**J9-5** This Roche worker drone ran the Mos Eisley Spaceport control tower during the Imperial era. She had been passed from owner to owner before she ended up in Mos Eisley.

**J9-6** A Roche worker drone employed by the local government in Mos Eisley during the Galactic Civil War.

**J-9SB** This protocol droid was the informal ambassador of the Soco-Jarel Spaceport during the New Order. Stationed in the Boliscon Towers, J-9 met with visiting VIPs and served them refreshments while they waited for their hosts. Plated with glossy-black armor, J-9 was easily distinguished from other automata in the spaceport. The droid also served as an undercover agent, continually searching for plainclothes Imperial customs officers or police. Any suspicions were immediately reported to J-9's masters.

**J9 series droid** Manufactured by Roche Industries, these information and protocol droids were humanoid-insectile automata with teardrop-shaped heads and skeletal bodies. Like other Roche products, the J9 series took advantage of servomotor technologies perfected by the Verpine, including a triangular hip joint that allowed J9s to move about. They rivaled the 3PO series in their ability to process information, being equipped with TranLang II communications modules and Arjan II central processors. J9 units also had Torplex microwave sensors to better understand their environment. However, their mechanical appearance and worker drone moniker made them unattractive to most species of the galaxy, and the J9 series was likely one of the worst-selling protocol droids in history.

**Jaan, Moff** An Imperial official during the New Order.

**Jaanu** A witch-like minion of Count Dooku. She piloted a skiff and wielded twin red lightsabers. She was defeated by Anakin Skywalker on Tatooine during the Clone Wars.

**Jaar** A drink given to Wookiee children, it was fermented from alcoari milk and vineberry extract, and was very sweet.

**Jaarak** A Wookiee accused of the murder of Rorworr 4,000 years before the Battle of Yavin, when a Jedi Knight discovered Rorworr's body in the Shadowlands. It was later revealed that Rorworr had arranged to sell Wookiees into slavery to Czerka Corporation. Jaarak had killed him to stop him, and was acquitted.

**Jaaruls Street** One of the many thoroughfares in the city of Cuipernam on Ansion.

**Jaayza** The alias assumed by Aayla Secura during her search for Quinlan Vos. Jaayza was a mechanic who was

*J9 series droid*

down on her luck, and had traveled to the Wheel in search of a new job and a new life.

**Jab, JillJoo** This young Twi'lek female worked as a waitress in Mos Zabu, on Tatooine, during the Galactic Civil War. When Domo Jones defeated Ep Gart, JillJoo realized that she was attracted to the young man.

**Jabba** A term used by agents of the Internal Affairs division of the Imperial Security Bureau to describe a situation in which individuals were forced to commit a crime. Once the individuals were "Jabba-ed" and charged with a crime, they could redeem themselves by performing certain favors for IA agents. Quite often, these led to more crimes, further indebting them to the agents.

*Jabba the Hutt in his throne room*

**Jabba the Hutt (Jabba Desilijic Tiure)** The son of a major Hutt clan leader and part of a long line of criminals. It was therefore no surprise that he became one of the galaxy's top criminal underlords. By the time Jabba Desilijic Tiure—known simply as Jabba the Hutt—was 600 years old, he was in charge of a major criminal empire. He had learned well from his father, Zorba, who raised Jabba at his private estate on Nal Hutta. Jabba eventually moved to Tatooine and established himself at a palace built around an ancient B'omarr monastery. The centerpiece was a huge throne room, where Jabba endlessly entertained and held court from his high dais at one end of the room. Jabba's criminal empire traversed the Outer Rim Territories and, in fact, knew no bounds. It included sports gambling, smuggling, glitterstim spice dealing, slave trading, assassination, loan sharking, protection, and piracy.

The Hutt presence on Tatooine brought with it a huge influx of offworld traffic and crime. Jabba and associates such as Gardulla the Hutt hosted Podrace competitions in the later years of the Galactic Republic, making Tatooine an unlikely center of attention. When the Clone Wars erupted, both the Separatists and Republic sought to curry favor with Jabba since he controlled the Outer Rim supply lines. To sabotage Republic efforts, Separatists kidnapped Jabba's young son Rotta, framing the Jedi for the crime. Thanks to the efforts of Anakin Skywalker and Ahsoka Tano, though, Rotta was safely returned to his father, and the Republic secured a treaty with the Hutts.

Jabba's seat of power was a constant den of conspiracy, as many wished to try to topple him from his throne and take over his empire. He had only one true loyalist, Ephant Mon, whose life he had once saved. Another constant presence was Salacious Crumb, a Kowakian monkey-lizard, whose only function was to make Jabba laugh—at least once a day.

Jabba got most of his glitterstim spice from mines below the Imperial Correction Facility on Kessel. Among the smugglers on his payroll were the Corellian Han Solo and his Wookiee first mate, Chewbacca. But when Solo had to jettison a glitterstim load to avoid Imperial entanglements, Jabba ordered him brought in. Solo met up with the Hutt after killing one of his bounty hunters, a Rodian named Greedo. Jabba agreed to let Han fly some passengers on a quick trip to Alderaan with a promise that the proceeds would be used to pay him back for the missing spice.

Solo got involved in the Galactic Civil War. Then, on his way to repay Jabba, he was boarded by pirates who looted his ship. At that point, Jabba put out a galaxy-wide hit on Solo, eventually getting him delivered in a block of carbonite thanks to Darth Vader and Boba Fett. But Solo's friends mounted a rescue mission. First they infiltrated the Hutt's palace; then Luke Skywalker directly confronted Jabba. After Skywalker killed the crime lord's pet rancor, Jabba ordered all the Rebels to die a slow death by being fed to the Sarlacc at the Great Pit of Carkoon in the Tatooine dunes.

But Jabba paid the supreme price for underestimating the skills of Skywalker and his friends. As a fight erupted on and near Jabba's desert sail barge, Princess Leia Organa—who had been put in chains and a skimpy outfit by Jabba—pulled her chain leash around the Hutt's neck, strangling him.

**Jabba the Hutt's palace** The common name given to the complex of buildings and subterranean rooms controlled by Jabba the Hutt. It was located in the Northern Dune Sea, on Tatooine, at the end of a secluded valley. Originally, the palace had been erected by the B'omarr monks as a peaceful sanctuary from which they could contemplate the galaxy. The monks built two main aboveground structures: a nine-story tower that contained a circular stairway, and the main rotunda. The tower's stairway provided a great deal of space for the monks to wander, as they could move up and down the stairs for hours while meditating. The rotunda originally was constructed as a place of worship, where the disembodied brains of enlightened monks reposed in tiers around the outer edge. Prayer banners hung from the ceiling, and the eerie silence of the brain canisters lent the rotunda a sinister feeling. A ceremonial concourse was created around the rotunda to give the monks additional space to roam.

Thirty-four years before Jabba took control of the palace, it was taken over by the bandit Alkhara, who renovated it to serve as the base of operations for his raiders. During Alkhara's stay, the monks were forced to retreat to the deepest levels of the palace. Jabba subsequently ousted Alkhara and allowed the monks to roam the entire complex freely, as the Hutt preferred the lower levels where he felt safer. It was believed that he renovated a former B'omarr chapel to serve as his throne room. Jabba reinforced the rotunda's dome with ditanium, and installed shielding to protect it from orbital or suborbital assault. In the tower's upper stories, Jabba installed a hyperwave transceiver and a holographic map of the galaxy, making it his primary communications facility. The palace's external structures were so large that they were visible from orbit.

**Jabba's Star** Jabba the Hutt's naval base in the Tatoo system.

**Jabba's Throne Room** A club and bar on Atzerri, it was a nearly exact replica of Jabba

*Jabba the Hutt's palace, built around an ancient monastery*

the Hutt's throne room, complete with an imitation Han Solo carbonite-block hanging on the wall.

**Jabesq, Simon** An engineer for the Theed Palace Space Vessel Engineering Corps who worked in the Theed Palace hangar in the years before the Battle of Naboo.

**Jabiim** This planet was once the site of an Old Republic military base, which later was used as a staging area during the Clone Wars. When war broke out between the Republic and the Separatists, the government of Jabiim decided to ally with the Separatists and force the Republic to abandon its base. The native Jabiimites were believed to have been supplied weapons, equipment, and funding by the Separatists in preparation for going to war against the forces of the Republic. Many in the Republic believed that Jabiim had been bought by the Separatists, who had been working with a select few Jabiimites to take control of the planet. So the Republic decided to go to war to liberate the planet.

The surface of Jabiim was continually deluged by storms, turning much of its marshy surface to muddy swamps, and this made ground battles extremely difficult. In the wake of the Clone Wars and the institution of the New Order, Jabiim was subjugated by the Empire and extensively mined for its natural resources. Years of environmental abuse turned the planet into a barren wasteland, and the locals struggled under the oppressive Imperial yoke. Nolan Gillmunn decided to ally his band of rebels with the Rebel Alliance, until he learned that one of the Alliance representatives was Luke Skywalker, the son of Anakin Skywalker, whom the Jabiimites felt betrayed them by abandoning the planet to the Separatists.

**Jabiim Congress** The primary governmental body found on Jabiim during the last decades of the Old Republic. Long a supporter of the Republic, the Jabiim Congress became splintered after the Clone Wars ended.

**Jabiimite** Humans native to Jabiim. During the Clone Wars, Jabiimite leaders sided with the Separatists even though there had been an Old Republic military base on the planet for years. The Jabiimi contacted Kal Skirata and the Mandalorians about obtaining explosives to arm their local militias. When the Republic sent a force to liberate the planet, many Jedi Masters were killed in battle, forcing Anakin Skywalker and a group of Padawans to carry on the fight. Ultimately, the Separatist forces prevailed, and Skywalker ordered a complete retreat.

Even though they had allied themselves with the Separatists, the Jabiimites were convinced that the Republic had abandoned them, especially after Separatist forces were replaced with Imperial forces that virtually enslaved the population. For nearly 21 years, the Jabiimites were left to fend for themselves, held in thrall by Imperial agents sent to oversee the planet. Some eight months after the Battle of Yavin, Darth Vader arrived to ship a large percentage of the population offworld as slaves. The Jabiimites were saved when Luke Skywalker and Leia Organa arrived to help them overthrow Governor Thorne Kraym. Although large portions of Jabiim's surface were bombarded with turbolaser fire, the planet was ultimately abandoned by the Empire, and the Jabiimites were freed.

*A bloody and desolate battlefield on Jabiim*

**Jabitha** This young Ferroan girl was the granddaughter of the original Magister of Zonama Sekot. She greeted Anakin Skywalker when he and Obi-Wan Kenobi traveled to the planet to investigate the disappearance of the Jedi Vergere. Her grandfather had created a number of holograms of her to keep him company in the Far Distance compound while she was in Middle Distance attending school. To avoid confusion, the Magister named the holograms Wind. Jabitha was on Zonama Sekot when the planet disappeared into hyperspace to avoid capture by Wilhuff Tarkin. Anakin never saw her again.

Jabitha grew up to become the Magister of Zonama Sekot. When the Yuuzhan Vong invaded the galaxy, the living planet hid itself within the Unknown Regions, and the Ferroans became isolated. Jabitha retained the memory of the Jedi, and when Luke Skywalker arrived to ask for the planet's help, she was initially agreeable. Sekot, however, still needed proof of the true motives behind Master Skywalker's request. Sekot used Senshi and his followers to kidnap Jabitha, along with Danni Quee, Jacen Solo, and Saba Sebatyne. When the Jedi had proven that they were indeed searching for a peaceful resolution to the conflict with the Yuuzhan Vong, Jabitha was released. When Nom Anor tried to sabotage the planet's hyperdrive vanes in an effort to destroy it, Zonama Sekot was forced to make a blind jump into hyperspace. This jump brought the planet close to several stars and planets, causing massive amounts of ecological damage to Zonama itself. Jabitha found herself at the mercy of the planet, traveling to remote locations at the whim of Sekot to help maintain the ecosystem.

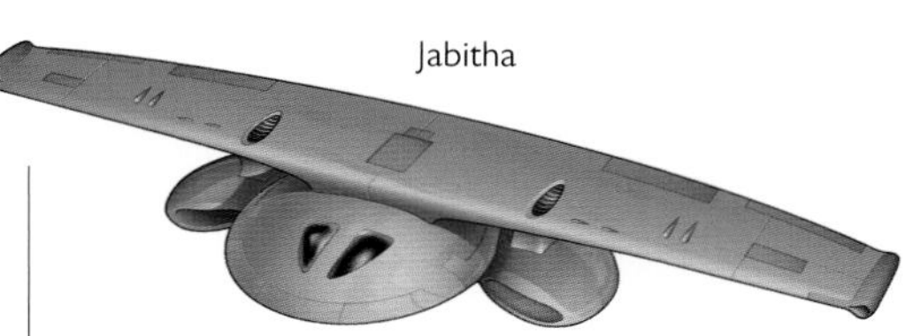
Jabitha

***Jabitha*** The name Anakin Skywalker gave to the huge, living Sekotan starship he purchased with Obi-Wan Kenobi. They bought the ship to get close to the people of Zonama Sekot and learn what had happened to the Jedi Knight, Vergere. The ship was formed from 15 seed-partners, all of which bonded to Anakin before the forging and annealing process shaped a 25-meter-long craft that had a wingspan of 30 meters. Because of the bonding with Anakin, the *Jabitha* was capable of incredible maneuvers under his piloting. A pair of heavily-modified *Silver*-class engines were mated to the organic ship to provide the propulsion of a Class 0.4 hyperdrive, and a shield system was added to compensate for the absence of any form of weaponry. With Anakin as its pilot, the *Jabitha* could attain speeds of 13,000 kilometers per hour in atmosphere. Zonama Sekot came under attack by Wilhuff Tarkin at the time the *Jabitha* was shaped, and Anakin and Obi-Wan were unable to fully integrate themselves with the ship. The *Jabitha* fell sick, and when Zonama Sekot disappeared into hyperspace to escape Tarkin's assault, the starship died on Seline.

**Jabi Town** One of the many subdivisions of the Corellian quarter in Coruscant's Galactic City following the Yuuzhan Vong War. Jabi Town was the site of the first crackdown by the Galactic Alliance Guard against those of Corellian descent. Soldiers of the 967th Commando unit and several Coruscant Defense Force anti-terrorist teams swept in under cover of darkness and arrested or detained almost the entire population.

**jaboon** A large, slow-moving herbivore native to Naboo. It was a calm-natured beast, and was often domesticated by the Gungans for use as a mount. Its skin was also prized by artisans and collectors because it made beautiful leather book covers.

**Jabor** A Mid Rim planet and the site of a Separatist base during the Clone Wars. The base provided the Confederacy of Independent Systems with a constant source of information, as its personnel comprised spies and double agents. The operations at the base were disrupted by the efforts of Clive Flax and Ferus Olin.

*Jaccoba (left) with his father, Tarkov*

**Jabriel** This small corporation produced a variety of tools and accessories for installation on droids.

**Jacamden, Croig** This aging Duros was the owner of Croig's Fix-It Barn on Nam Chorios. It was rumored that he had connections to most of the smugglers in the Chorios systems.

**Jaccoba** This young Wookiee was a native of the Wawaatt Archipelago on Kashyyyk during the years leading up to the Clone Wars. Fighting broke out across the galaxy just as Jaccoba was ready to take the test that would elevate him to adulthood. While he was hunting with his father, Tarkov, Jaccoba's spear hit the outer shell of a Trade Federation MTT. This led Tarkov to realize that the Separatists had already landed on Kashyyyk, and were preparing to launch their invasion. He and Jaccoba rushed to the nearest city, Kahiyuk, to alert the leaders to the impending attack. It was this warning that helped the Wookiees begin their defense of their homeworld. Tarkov and Jaccoba both enlisted in the military, fighting against battle droids to defend their home.

*Bairdon Jace*

**Jace, Bairdon** This gray-haired human was one of the many Jedi Knights who were forced into military service when the Clone Wars broke out across the galaxy.

**Jace, Bror** A member of Rogue Squadron, he was a native of Thyferra and a veteran of the Battles of Hoth, Endor, and Bakura. He was also a member of the Zaltin faction of bacta producers, and he had been chosen for the squadron as a way to balance the inclusion of Erisi Dlarit. It was the belief of the Zaltin faction that the Empire was doomed, and that an alliance with the New Republic through Jace would be profitable. Jace was part of a mission sent to Noquivzor that was ambushed by the *Black Asp*. His body was never recovered, and Jace was listed as missing in action. Tycho Celchu was believed to have leaked the mission's plans to the Imperials, but it was eventually revealed that Celchu was not the traitor. Jace himself later reappeared and explained that the Vratix of the Ashern faction had recalled him to help plan the overthrow of Xucphra's pro-Imperial Bacta Cartel. He assisted the Rogues in the planning for the Battle of Thyferra, and was invaluable to the infiltration unit led by Elscol Loro and Sixtus Quin. After the Rogues defeated Ysanne Isard and removed the Imperial yoke from Thyferra, Jace was asked to create a Thyerran Aerospace Defense Force.

**Jacelle** The capital city of Sirpar.

**Jacipri** An ancient species of beings known for its pantheon of gods and its rich collection of myths and legends about the birth and death of the known galaxy.

**Jack** A slang term used by Special Operations units of the Rebel Alliance to describe another being, although it was usually reserved for total strangers.

**jack-a-dale** This wild bird native to Utharis lived in abandoned buildings.

***Jackal*** A Rebel Alliance shuttle group destroyed during the Galactic Civil War.

**jackelope** A small horned creature native to Douglas III.

**Jackhack Slough** This dried-up ancient riverbed was located on the Jasserak Lowlands of Drongar.

***Jackpot* (1)** This modified YT-1300 freighter was owned by crime lord Nirama during the final years of the Old Republic.

***Jackpot* (2)** A modified YT-700 transport designed as a prospecting ship by the Rebel Alliance.

**Jacques** This family of moisture farmers on Tatooine supported Ariq Joanson in his plans to draw up maps of peace with the Jawas and Sand People.

**jacuna** A small avian creature native to Haruun Kal. An opportunistic scavenger, the jacuna traveled in bands of several dozen, each equally at home in the air, on the ground, or climbing through trees. Jacunas ate just about anything, living or dead.

**Jacynith** A green-skinned female Twi'lek. She was a resident of the Enclave, the Twi'lek refuge established on Ryloth by her brother, Jedi Master Vhiin Thorla. When a group of Jedi agents asked to speak with Master Thorla, Jacynith agreed to take them. Thorla was angry with her for bringing agents to the Enclave. And a group of slavers tracked her after someone placed a tracking beacon on Jacynth's body. The Twi'leks and the Jedi agents helped Master Thorla repel the slavers, ensuring the security of the Enclave.

**Jada, Deesra Luur** This Jedi Master served as a historian at the Jedi Enclave on Dantooine after the Great Sith War. Master Jada documented the tale of the Enclave, with a focus on events surrounding the Jedi known as Revan.

**Jadai Motors** A small corporation that produced a number of distinctive repulsorlift ground transports.

**jaddyyk** This parasitic moss grew in the jungles of Kashyyyk in clumps of stringy tendrils that sprouted from a tall mound-like stalk, making the plant look like a long-furred Wookiee.

***Jade*** A Rebel Alliance shuttle dispatched to pick up Bothan delegates aboard the *Tal'cara* shortly before the Battle of Endor.

**Jade, Mara** *See* Skywalker, Mara Jade.

**Jaded Jawa** This cantina was in the main terminal of the Kothlis Starport. One of its key features was a long, one-way pane of transparisteel that lined the outer wall, allowing patrons to see what was going on outside the establishment, but preventing outsiders from seeing in. This made it the perfect location to spy on someone. At the height of the New Order, the Jaded Jawa was owned and operated by Dakkar.

**Jade Moon** One of Loronar's largest satellites, it was the site of an Imperial special weapons platform manufacturing facility during the last years of the New Order. The facility was destroyed during the Galactic Civil War by Crix Madine and his Rebel Alliance commandos.

***Jade Sabre*** A custom-built shuttle designed by Luke Skywalker and given to his wife, Mara Jade, as a gift shortly after they were married. It was shaped like a pointed fish head, with swept-back wings and flared side pods protecting its ion drives. Mara believed that Luke had the ship constructed to thank her for sacrificing the *Jade's Fire* on Nirauan. The *Jade Sabre* measured 50 meters long. It could accommodate up to 15 passengers and 100 metric tons of cargo, and was armed with four quad laser cannons and a tractor beam projector. Mara and Anakin Solo flew the ship to Dantooine after the initial battle of the Yuuzhan Vong War so that Mara could get some rest. But the Yuuzhan Vong were already on Dantooine, and they destroyed the *Jade Sabre* before Anakin and Mara could recover it.

***Jade's Fire*** This starship was given to Mara Jade by her former employer Talon Karrde. Karrde demanded the ship—originally owned by a wealthy industrialist—as payment for Mara's rescue of the industrialist's daughter. *Jade's Fire* boasted impressive scanners and sensors often unavailable on nonmilitary starships. It was a SoroSuub Luxury 3000 yacht, slightly larger than a YT-1300, with a truncated nose, wide fuselage, two elliptical wings, and an orange-and-red flame pattern painted on its hull. Among its components were a shootback system that automatically returned incoming fire and a slave-circuit control. It also had three quad turbolasers and a tractor beam projector. Given Mara's introverted bent, *Jade's Fire* was the one thing she cared about the most. That was why Luke Skywalker was reluctant to take it to Nirauan to search for Mara, but he recognized the need to do so. They had planned to use the ship to escape, but Mara realized that the only way to stop Voss Parck and Soontir Fel from going to Bastion was to eliminate their fleet. She used her beckon call to remotely send the *Jade's Fire* on a collision course with the hangar of the Hand of Thrawn complex, destroying it and most of the ships within.

***Jade Shadow*** The *Horizon*-class luxury yacht purchased by Lando Calrissian and presented to Mara Jade Skywalker as a gift. The ship had a number of significant modifications, including retractable AG-1G laser cannons, camouflaged torpedo launchers, and enhanced shielding systems obtained by Talon Karrde. The stock hyperdrive was replaced with a Class 0.5 unit; upgraded sublight drives allowed the ship to attain speeds of 1,000 kilometers per hour in atmosphere. The name *Jade Shadow,* coined by Tendra Risant, referred to the ship's nonreflective gray hull. Lando had picked out the ship because of its aft cargo bay, which was wide enough to accommodate Luke Skywalker's X-wing fighter. The ship served as Mara's personal transport for many years, surviving the Yuuzhan Vong War and the Swarm War.

**Jade Simian** A seedy tavern located within the Snakes' Den on Camden.

***Jadthu*-class landing craft** A craft developed for use by the Grand Army of the Republic during the Clone Wars. Manufactured by Incom Industries, the *Jadthu*-class lander was a modified shuttle that had been refitted for delivering troops instead of civilians.

Jade Shadow

**Jaeffis, Admiral** This Imperial officer commanded a small fleet that protected the shipyards of Corellia during the Galactic Civil War. He was replaced by Admiral Roek shortly after the Battle of Endor.

**Jaeger, Oron** This Imperial general commanded the 501st Stormtrooper Legion nearly a century after the end of the Yuuzhan Vong War. A loyal supporter of the Fel dynasty, General Jaeger was leading a unit on Bastion when Darth Krayt took control of the galaxy.

Although outwardly loyal to the new regime, General Jaeger and his men maintained their allegiance to the Fels for many years. With Fel in exile, Jaeger kept a tenuous contact with the former Emperor and worked behind the scenes to rotate remaining loyal military units to Bastion. In this way, he managed to consolidate a large military force that could support any possible coup attempt by Fel.

About seven years after Darth Krayt usurped control, Emperor Roan Fel returned to Bastion to reclaim the planet as the center of the true Empire. Lieutenant Kiefer tried to stop Fel, and drew his blaster on the Emperor. Jaeger, however, was faster, and shot Kiefer dead. With Krayt and the Sith Empire unaware of events, Emperor Fel took Jaeger into his confidence, and they began plotting to overthrow the Sith.

**Jael City** One of four major cities on Kirima. It was in the western part of the western continent.

**Jaemus** This primary world in the Jaemus system was within the Velcar Free Commerce Zone, in the Pentastar Alignment. The Empire used the Galentro Heavy Works shipyards to subcontract out work of Kuat Drive Yards and Sienar Fleet Systems, and it built the *Enforcer*-class picket cruiser. The Jaemus shipyards were rivaled only by those of Sluis Van.

**Jaeth** A smuggler who settled on the moon of Pinett and began working as a dockhand during the early years of the Galactic Civil War.

***Ja'Fai*** This Abyssin term referred to the mating race between eligible males and females. Any female who completed the rite of passage to adulthood was given a head start, to be pursued by all adult bachelor males. The first male to catch a female won her, and the pair were mated for life. Because the female Abyssin were faster runners than the males, a female's like or dislike for a given male could influence the race.

**Jafan** Once the King of the Naboo, he was credited with establishing the Great Time of Peace.

**jaffa cider** This pressed, mulled juice was known for its rich fragrance.

**Ja field septoid** This hardy insect was native to the Ja highlands of Eriadu, where it managed to survive every attempt by the human population to eradicate it. It was a predatory bug known for its bites, although it was not aggressive by nature. It had no true head or tail and moved about on seven legs that surrounded its main body, which sported a small head with three eyestalks. It used a pair of fangs to puncture the skin or chitin of its prey, then fed on its blood.

**jagannath** A Trandoshan term for the spoils of victory won in mortal combat. All Trandoshans collected jagannath points throughout their lives, mainly from capturing and killing Wookiees much larger than themselves. When Trandoshans died, they turned over their jagannath points to a Scorekeeper, who used the total as a way to determine their places in the afterlife.

**Jaga's Cluster, Battle of** During the Mandalorian Wars, Cassus Fett killed the captain of a Republic frigate flagship at the Battle of Jaga's Cluster.

**Jag Crag Gorge** Part of the incredibly beautiful, though extremely arid, landscape of Tatooine, Jag Crag Gorge was a twisting, winding channel filled with rocky spires and outcroppings. Located near Arch Canyon, it was part of Jabba the Hutt's Podracing course, feeding Podracers into the formation known as Jett's Chute. The gorge later served as a section of the noted Mos Espa Circuit, a swoop racing event held annually during the New Order.

**Jagga II** This planet in the Venjagga system was the site of an Imperial base following the Battle of Endor. It was a small world that produced missiles for the Imperial Navy, and was protected by the *Imperial II*–class Star Destroyer *Eviscerator.* Three years after the Battle of Endor, the Rebel Alliance staged a feint on Jagga II to cover a simultaneous assault on Borleias in the nearby Pyria system.

**Jagga VII** A gas giant in the Venjagga system.

**Jaggert, Colonel Randall** An Imperial officer in charge of the construction of a resupply base in the Bissillirus system shortly after the Battle of Yavin.

**Jagg Island Detention Center** A Coruscant prison facility used by the New Republic to incarcerate former Imperial officers. Davith Sconn, a former Imperial Navy officer, was held there. His information regarding the Yevetha and their battle operations provided vital insights to Chief of State Leia Organa Solo and Admiral Ackbar in preparing for battle with the alien species.

**Jagi** This Mandalorian once challenged Canderous Ordo to a duel in the Dune Sea of Tatooine, a fight that Jagi lost. Jagi had claimed that Canderous turned his back on his fellow Mandalorians, and he wanted to kill him as

*Jahnar-Kooda*

an act of revenge. In the wake of the duel, Jagi took his own life rather than return to Mandalore in defeat.

**Jaguada** This desert planet was the only habitable world in the Jaguada system, located in a remote corner of the Outer Rim Territories. The planet's wind-ravaged moon was the site of an ancient communications facility believed to have been several millennia old. The facility was commandeered by the Confederacy of Independent Systems during the Clone Wars, and initial scans revealed that the metal infrastructure was created from unidentifiable materials. The facility was later abandoned, but not before investigation revealed that Jaguada's moon might have been the site of a Sith stronghold in the millennia leading up to the Great Sith War. Near the end of the Clone Wars a garrison of Republic clone troopers was established on Jaguada ostensibly to recover stores of war machines left behind by the Separatists.

**Jah, Ghazdik** This Dug was a member of Sebolto's gang after the Battle of Naboo. Ghazdik Jah worked as a hired gun, often murdering certain Gran politicians and their aides. Senators Ask Aak and Aks Moe issued a bounty for his capture after several of their assistants were assassinated, a bounty that was later claimed by Jango Fett.

**Jahhnu** One of the three largest cities on Farrfin. Like Farlhu and Geltyu, it was best known for the criminal element that thrived there. Jahhnu also boasted numerous betting houses that catered to gullible offworlders and took in incredible amounts of credits.

**Jahibakti** This was one of the larger Hutt kajidics, or clans. Before Jabba the Hutt claimed Tatooine for the Desilijics, the Jahibakti clan controlled nearly one-fifth of the planet's criminal activities. It also commanded more than 50 percent of the planet's water supply.

**Jahilid Drift** This region of the Outer Rim Territories contained Pral and Koltine.

**Jahjee** According to Ewok legend, this night spirit created realistic illusions to entertain sleeping Ewoks.

**Jahnae Camp** One of the many settlements on Bestine IV. Jahnae was located on a tall spire of rock jutting into the planet's primary ocean.

**Jahnar-Kooda** This bounty hunter worked for Boss Banjeer during the early years of the New Republic, and served as part of the mercenary force that controlled Baramorra. Jahnar-Kooda crossed paths with Kir Kanos, who was working under the alias of Kenix Kil. The bounty hunter threatened to physically harm Kanos, who quickly rendered the huge alien unconscious.

**Jahren** The elected spokesperson of the farming collectives on Nez Peron, and the husband of Mirith Sinn. Jahren was killed by Darth Vader as a warning to the collectives.

**Jahrunba, Nahrunba, and Sahrunba** These Dug brothers were members of Sebolto's gang following the Battle of Naboo. They worked as smugglers, transporting death sticks from Tatooine to Malastare. The Pixelito Grand Council issued a bounty for the siblings' capture, and Jango Fett managed to capture all three.

**Jai, Vun Merett** A Coruscant Senatorial aide who was kidnapped—along with Senator Meena Tills—by a group of Haruun Kal terrorists during the early stages of the Clone Wars. It was later learned that Senator Tills wasn't the primary target, just a convenient diversion for a possible different killing.

*Jahren being killed by Darth Vader*

**jai'galaar** This bird of prey was native to Mandalore, and was revered by Mandalorians for its grace and bravery. It was known as a shriek-hawk to most other beings.

**Jai'galaar, Commander** Most often referred to simply as Jag, this clone commander was officially designated CT-55/11-9009. Jag proved early in his career that he was an exceptional pilot, but he was flash-trained as a leader. Jag first saw action during the Battle of Geonosis, where he served as a commander of the 127th Gunship Wing. Although he was later demoted to captain for his failure during the Retreat at Katraasii, Jag was among the pilots chosen by Jedi Master Plo Koon to serve as a test pilot on the new ARC-170 fighter. Jag remained attached to Plo Koon's forces, serving as the Jedi Master's wingmate during the struggle for control of Cato Neimoidia. This put him in perfect position when the command to execute Order 66 was issued. Captain Jag simply placed his vessel behind Plo Koon's and fired on the Jedi fighter, causing it to crash into the side of a building and explode.

**jaig eyes** The name given to the stylized portrayal of the eyes of a jai'galaar, which often was used by Mandalorian warriors to disguise the visors of their helmets. Only those Mandalorians who displayed bravery in the face of danger were allowed to wear jaig eyes, which were known as *jai'galaar'la sur'haii'se* in the *Mando'a* language. Clone officers Commander Fordo and Captain Rex painted their helmets with jaig eyes.

**Jaijay Luxsub** One of the many submersible transport businesses operating on Pavo Prime during the early years of the New Republic. It offered a limited number of private compartments aboard each transport, as well as a large amount of common space.

***Jaina's Light*** The false identity used by Han Solo to smuggle three CR-90 corvettes out of Imperial space for sale to the Rebel Alliance a few years before the Battle of Yavin. Claiming that he was in the employ of some farmers from Nadiem who were in need of supplies, Han told Captain Llnewe of the customs service that his vessel had been named for his mother. The farmers, Han continued, had helped fund the purchase of *Jaina's Light*. Each time the Imperial stopped him, Han insisted he was traveling to Nadiem to deliver supplies to the farmers. It took three meetings for Captain Llnewe to realize that he never intercepted the *Jaina's Light* during its return from Nadiem. By that time, Han and Chewbacca had earned a tidy sum for delivering the three—virtually identical—corvettes to Mako Spince for sale to the Alliance.

**Jaing** The nickname used by Kal Skirata for the *Null*-class ARC trooper designated N-10.

It was believed that Jaing was one of the only individuals who was able to track General Grievous during the Clone Wars, but it wasn't known why he didn't share his knowledge with the rest of the Grand Army of the Republic. When Fi was badly injured on Gaftikar, Jaing made a side trip to Mandalore to visit him. Jaing agreed to care for Lord Mirdalan, the strill that was Walon Vau's companion, in the event that Vau died. After the Clone Wars, Jaing dropped his official designation and adopted the name Jaing Skirata.

**Jaing, Master** One of many Mandalorian Neo-Crusaders who survived the Mandalorian Wars and set out to take control of several clans of mercenaries. Roughly humanoid in shape, Master Jaing had a huge skull that was dominated by a pair of heavy horns growing from his cheeks. Like Canderous Ordo, Master Jaing was a former shock trooper who remained loyal to the Canons of Honor, but realized that he needed to earn credits in order to survive. Jaing reined in some of the Neo-Crusader clans and made a relatively honest living as a soldier for hire. He apparently was the first true mentor of the armored bounty hunter Durge. Jaing was killed in a Mandalorian attack while arranging for Durge to receive his cybernetic implants. The attack was arranged by the doctor who performed the surgeries; he had stolen a Sith artifact from Jaing's chief rival, Ung Kusp, in an effort to set off a war between the Sith and the Mandalorians.

**Jak (1)** This Nautolan male lived in the underworld of Coruscant during the era of the Sith-Imperial War and the Massacre at Ossus. As a youth, he became friends with Cade Skywalker, who often traveled into the city to escape the rigors of his Jedi training. Jak was surprised to meet up with Skywalker seven years after the destruction of the Jedi on Ossus, when Skywalker arrived to rescue Hosk Trey'lis.

**Jak (2)** A TIE fighter pilot who served the Empire after the Battle of Yavin. Jak and his wingmate were assigned to the *Adjudicator* but were shot down by Boba Fett while on patrol.

*Jak, a friend of Cade Skywalker*

*Jake, a Circarpousian miner*

**Jakaitis** A maintenance supervisor, he worked at the Bakuran Senate Complex during the Yuuzhan Vong War.

**Jakan** This Yuuzhan Vong High Priest was an adviser to Supreme Overlord Shimrra, and the father of the priestess Elan. He represented the priests on the Great Council, and eventually became the High Priest of the Yuuzhan Vong after the conquest and terraforming of Coruscant into a simulacrum of Yuuzhan'tar. As befitting his rank and caste, Jakan often wore deep red clothing to distinguish himself from other priests. When the combined forces of the Galactic Alliance made a final push to recapture Coruscant, Jakan remained at Shimrra's side until the ground forces of the Alliance reached the Citadel and began moving on the Well of the World Brain. Along with High Prefect Drathul and Qelah Kwaad, Jakan then descended from the Citadel and traveled to the Well to anoint those who were captured there. Among them were Harrar, Han Solo, and Leia Organa Solo, and Jakan agreed they would make excellent sacrifices. His plans were cut short when Nom Anor, leading Mara Jade Skywalker and a band of Shamed Ones, flooded the chamber and confronted the warriors. Drathul demanded that the captives be executed, but his commander instead turned his forces against Drathul's guards. In a flash Harrar was free, and he knocked out Jakan with a single blow to the head. Jakan's life was spared, however, so he could be questioned. After the deaths of Shimrra and Onimi—who proved to be the true Supreme Overlord—Jakan and the rest of the Yuuzhan Vong agreed to surrender to the Galactic Alliance.

**Jakan Arms** This small weapons manufacturer produced large defensive emplacements for remote planetary outposts.

**Jake (1)** A noted gunrunner and smuggler active on Cularin in the decade before the Battle of Naboo. He had a number of contacts in the Cularin underworld.

**Jake (2)** This Circarpousian miner attacked Luke Skywalker with double-bladed stilettos outside a Mimban restaurant shortly after the Battle of Yavin.

**Jakelian knife-dance** This form of melee combat was used to train clone troopers of the Grand Army of the Republic in the basics of timing, distance, and rhythm in fighting.

**Jakien, Allania** This 11-year-old lived with her parents on Cloud City at the height of the New Order. Her father was a worker in the Tibanna gas refinery, and her mother worked at the Holiday Towers restaurant. When Lando Calrissian ordered an evacuation because Darth Vader was taking over, she was cut off from her parents. She and a group of friends traversed the city's Ugnaught tunnels, passing into the carbon-freezing chamber just as Luke Skywalker and Darth Vader were battling. She kept going, but felt some bond with Luke that she couldn't explain. When she emerged from the tunnels with her friends, they were whisked off the outpost in a crowded transport ship. She sensed that Luke would be all right.

*Jakobeast about to attack Master Justiss*

**jakobeast** Native to several frigid worlds in the Outer Rim Territories, jakobeasts were Force-sensitive herd creatures, and had unique ways of defending themselves. Many jakobeasts were seeded on planets far from their homeworlds by colonists for their meat, fur, and milk. The average jakobeast was about the size of a bantha, with two segmented horns sprouting from its skull and two tusks jutting from its lower jaw. The tusks were used to dig through snow and ice to reach the vegetation beneath. A jakobeast's fur was light gray with white stripes to help it blend into its native tundra. The horns, however, were a jakobeast's most distinguishing feature. They were used to channel the energy of the Force, which could often be seen arcing between the horns like electricity. While the energy itself was harmless, the jakobeast used it to generate a form of Force push as a defense against predators.

**jakrab** A species of tiny, bounding herbivores native to Tatooine. Thin-boned and swift, jakrabs were distinguished by their long ears and sparsely furred bodies. Their ears served many purposes, including heat dissipation and semaphore-like communications.

**JAK Racing** This Podracer manufacturer was best known for the J930 Dash-8 used by Ebe Endocott.

**Jal** This Rebel Alliance Special Forces soldier was a member of Team Razor.

**Jal, Glor** An outspoken Ugnaught, he was the leader of the Ugnaught unions working on Bespin's Cloud City during the New Order. Glor Jal was quite suspicious of non-Ugnaughts, blaming them for most of the problems experienced by Ugnaughts who lived and worked on Cloud City.

**Jalahafi, Shela and Teles** This sister and brother served as Dark Side Adepts, part of a team entrusted by the Emperor to infiltrate spies and agents into the ranks of the Rebel Alliance. The siblings worked to subvert the Rebel underground that rose up on Edan II. When Shela was lost in an attack in Fortuna City, her brother tracked the Rebels to the wreckage of the *Last Hope*. He was killed during a fight there.

**Jalan** A member of the Nebula Front team led by Captain Cohl, he served aboard the *Hawk-Bat* as a sensor operator shortly before the Battle of Naboo. After the destruction of the *Revenue*, Cohl and his crew tried to sneak onto Dorvalla and return to their makeshift base. Their shuttle was intercepted by the forces of the Dorvalla Space Corps and shot down. Jalan was severely injured in the crash. He sacrificed himself—destroying what was left of the shuttle after being caught by Dorvallan ground forces—in order to allow Cohl and the others to reach the base.

**jalavash worm** Native to Ryloth, this worm produced silk fibers that were woven into traditional Twi'leki robes.

**Jalay, Danith** This smuggler owned the *Elegant Interlude* and maintained a residence on Nar Shaddaa during the early years of the New Order.

**Jalinese knife** A specialized knife used in the Sera Plinck martial arts.

**Jalk Syndicate** A criminal syndicate sponsored by House Mecetti to do most of its dirty work. The Jalk Syndicate was formed many centuries before the New Order after the apparent fall of the Mecrosa Order. It was one of the only House-sponsored gangs to survive the Imperial occupation of Tapani sector.

**Jallop, Preena** This woman owned Preena's Repair Bay on Vaynai during the New Order. She also operated an ad hoc educational facility known as Preena's Academy where orphans and impoverished children could learn the skills necessary to earn a living as repair technicians.

**Jally** A heavily tattooed man who served as one of Crash Garrulan's bodyguards during the final stages of the Clone Wars.

**Jalooz, Reda** This ancient Force-user stole a Kashi Mer talisman before the formation of the Old Republic. She felt compelled to return it—a small gray prism-shaped stone with dark-side power—and traveled to Kashi just before the planet's star exploded. Reda Jalooz was killed, but the stone mysteriously reappeared in the Corva sector a millennium later. Historians theorized that it might have had something to do with the destruction of the Kashi Mer.

**Jalor Docking Facilities** The central enterprise around which Corint City on the planet Pirik was built. It was on the coast of the Uloitir Sea, at the mouth of a wide river delta. The Jalor facility provided spacers with easy-access docking bays and landing pads, as well as a relatively lax customs office.

**Jalose** A female companion of Merrik and a fellow Rebel Alliance fighter on M'haeli, she became jealous of Mora, not knowing she was the only heir of the planet's murdered royal family, and betrayed her to the Empire. When Jalose realized what she had done, she took a shot meant for Mora and saved the young woman's life, but she later died of her own injuries.

**Jal-Parra** This small corporation produced repulsorsail-equipped skiffs and barges centuries before the Galactic Civil War.

**Jalper** *See* Jural.

**Jal Shey** A militant sect of Force-sensitive beings who roamed the galaxy following the Great Sith War. The Jal Shey sought to understand the Force on an intellectual level, rather than a spiritual one.

**Jalunn, Qar** A youthful entrepreneur in the last years of the Galactic Republic, he arrived on Genarius and began throwing credits at any operation that seemed to be even marginally profitable. Roughly half failed in the short run, but his exuberance was undeterred.

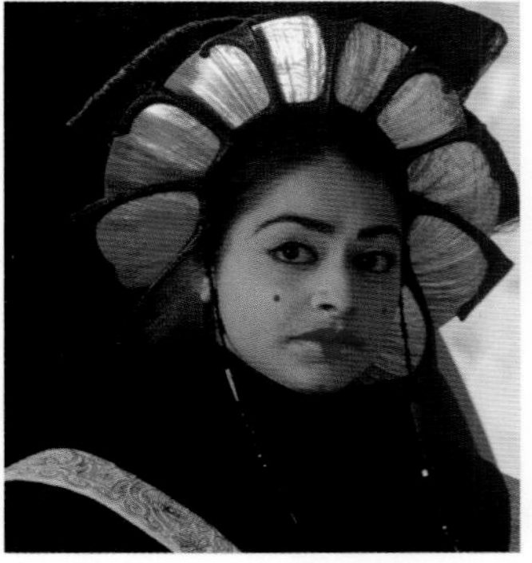
*Queen Jamillia*

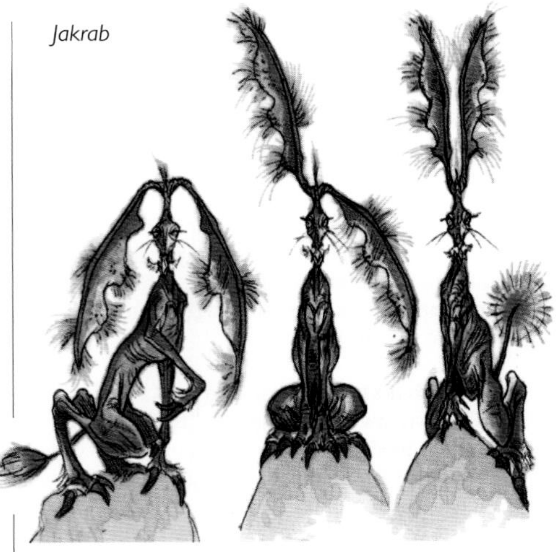
*Jakrab*

**Jam, Christoph** This eccentric was a native of Alderaan, where he owned and operated Descorp. Jam also maintained one of the most extensive spy networks on the planet. Much of the information he gathered focused on the criminals of Alderaan society, and he worked diligently to avenge injustices and attacks on the upstanding citizens of the planet. Through his teams of Rectifiers, Jam tried to ensure that each situation brought to his attention was resolved. Much of the funding for the Rectifiers came from Descorp's profits.

**Jamer, Captain Dren** An Imperial Navy officer who served on the *Dominant* under Pter Thanas, Dren Jamer had a less-than-stellar career at the Imperial Academy and as an officer. Still, both parts of his life were punctuated by unusually bright moments. His commanding officer aboard the Star Destroyer *Stormclaw* commended his attention to detail and promoted him to the bridge crew. However, his otherwise average performance relegated him to duty at Bakura, where he served as Thanas's second in command. Thanas recognized Jamer's aptitude for science and exploration, and assigned him the duty of mapping the Bakura system. After the Battle of Bakura, Jamer continued to denounce the Rebel Alliance and left Thanas's crew to remain with the Imperial forces.

**Jameson, Skorg** This immense man was a farmer from the moon Sulon when it was first subjugated by the Empire. He was the leader of the local Rebel cell, and hoped to eventually join the Rebel Alliance in its broader struggle against the Empire.

**Jamillia, Queen** The Queen of Naboo after Padmé Amidala completed her two terms. It was Jamillia who requested that Padmé remain in political life, to serve as Naboo's Senator to the Old Republic's Galactic Senate. Queen Jamillia opened up many of Naboo's spaceports and rural areas to refugees who were fleeing the Separatist crisis on their homeworlds shortly before the onset of the Clone Wars.

**Jaminere** The capital world of the Allied Tion sector during the New Order. As the former center of the Jaminere Marches, the planet was part of Xim the Despot's empire early in galactic history, although it was never part of the Tion Hegemony.

**Jaminere Marches** This area of the galaxy, once centered on Jaminere, was one of the many pieces of Xim the Despot's empire. A century after Xim's death, the Marches broke away from the rest of the empire. By the time of the Galactic Empire, the Jaminere Marches had become part of the Allied Tion sector.

**Jamiro, Tigran** A native of Onderon, he became a senior logistics officer for the Rebel Alliance. Tigran Jamiro left the Rebel base on Dantooine to serve on Yavin 4. He then transferred to Echo Base on Hoth, where all entering personnel had to report to him. Jamiro earned the rank of general by the time of the Yuuzhan Vong War. He was placed under the command of Admiral Traest Kre'fey, leading the ground troops dispatched to Ylesia to capture the leaders of the Peace Brigade shortly after the Second Battle of Coruscant.

**jammer** Native to the jungles of Kidron, these manta-like predators glided through the skies by filling special sacs with air and then using their wing-like fins to navigate the breezes. They were named jammers by the Orfites because they exuded a cloud of foul-smelling stench that extended 5 meters around their body. This intense odor effectively jammed the Orfite's olfactory senses. Average jammers grew to 3 meters long, with a wingspan of 3 meters or more.

**jammer pack** A form of technology used to prevent eavesdropping, it was less than successful and would have been scrapped if intelligence agencies hadn't taken a second look. They found that a high-powered jammer pack could drown out all communications in a specific area. This allowed operatives to enter a location while their targets were unable to communicate with each other.

**Jamos, Hen** This merchant plied the space lanes of Trax sector during the Galactic Civil War. He was sympathetic to the Rebel Alliance, and agreed to help a group of agents travel from Draenell's Point to Entrus during their investigation of the construction of the Bissillirus Resupply Base. The owner and operator of the *Trax Express,* Hen spent much of his career transporting trinkets and souvenirs of the sector to starports and visitor centers.

**JAN** *See* Justice Action Network.

**Jan, Janvar** This confident middle-aged scoundrel and con man established a home and business in the Cularin system during the final years of the Old Republic by refitting three luxury liners for tours through the mysterious system. He also purchased two other vessels: a support ship that could assist any liner experiencing trouble, and a smuggling vessel that was similar in design to his liners, and had transponder codes that matched. Jan had secretly made a deal with a group of pirates, using one of his ships to help them smuggle illegal cargoes throughout the system.

**Janah** A pirate during the New Order, she served Captain Naz Felyood aboard *Jynni's Virtue.* When the freighter made a hasty jump into hyperspace to escape an Imperial patrol, Janah was forced to take over as navigator. After landing on Korriban, however, Janah was killed by Korriban Zombies, and her corpse was reanimated.

**Janako** A model of *MaKing*-class transport ship built by General Spacetronics, it featured unique rear flanges.

**Janara III** A world that was covered with green, rolling hills, it was destroyed by an Imperial assault, although propaganda reports claimed the deed was the work of the Rebel Alliance.

**jandarra** This green-and-purple tubular vegetable was grown in the deserts of Jubilar, usually only after one of the infrequent rainstorms. A delicacy favored by the wealthy throughout the galaxy, jandarra plants took almost two years to mature given the scarcity of rain. The natives of Jubilar were forced to smuggle the vegetable off their planet to nearby Shalam for processing, because Shalamites placed a 100 percent tariff on it to fill their own coffers. It was a favorite of Leia Organa Solo.

**Jandi, Aellyn** The wife of Riit Jandi, the Imperial Moff on Elshandruu Pica. Aellyn Jandi's husband was 40 years her senior, so it wasn't too surprising that she had been having an affair with Captain Sair Yonka, with whom she was in love. They had grown up together on Commenor but lost track during his years of service with the Empire. They met again when he patrolled her sector of the galaxy. Aellyn used her position as the Moff's wife to obtain special concessions for Margath's—a hotel on Elshandruu Pica where they rendezvoused—and persuaded Yonka to bring exotic liquors and alcohols from the worlds he visted for hotel owner Kina Margath.

**Jandi, Riit** This Imperial Moff took control of Elshandruu Pica in the wake of the Battle of Endor. He was married to Aellyn Jandi, a woman 40 years his junior, and was unaware of her affair with Sair Yonka.

**Jandler, Myle** A well-dressed, able-bodied man living on Rafa IV during the early years of the New Order, he worked for Duttes Mer as a constable and captain of the Guard. Jandler was ordered to follow Lando Calrissian's every move—even eliminate him if necessary—if he tried to back out of a deal to find the Mindharp for Mer and Rokur Gepta. The orders angered Jandler enough that he let Calrissian place his team on a drifting cruiser, giving Lando enough time to find the Mindharp without interference. After Calrissian left the Rafa system, Jandler was promoted to serve as the chief supervisor of the remaining life-crystal orchards.

**Jandoon** Located in the Corva sector of the Outer Rim, it was a nearly abandoned world of plains and hills, dotted with the moss-covered ruins of an ancient species. The builders had died mysteriously centuries before the Galactic Civil War, and the world was rumored to be haunted. The insectoid fugitive Tzizvvt hailed from Jandoon.

**Jandovar, Maxa** A famous vandfillist who performed during the last years of the Old Republic and into the era of the Galactic Civil War. Labria followed her across the galaxy in an attempt to see one of her performances. While he was on Tatooine, arranging transport to see her on Morvogodine, she was captured by Imperial forces intent on wiping out "questionable" artistic endeavors. She died in custody.

**Jandur** During the early days of the New Republic, the worlds of Jandur and Cortina came to Coruscant to petition for membership. Though they initially seemed prideful and arrogant, both planets eventually signed the standard articles of confederation.

*Tigran Jamiro (far right) tries to answer Han Solo.*

***Janessa's Atlas*** One of the most useful galactic mapping systems available to independent spacers during the Galactic Civil War. *Janessa's Atlas* served as an enhancement to astrographic databases used by starship navigational computers to calculate pathways between locations, and provided location information on points of interest and interstellar anomalies. It also gave warnings and advisories about the relative safety of various locations, noting factional and political information for space stations, nebulae, and flight corridors.

**Jangelle** This warm world in the Kathol Outback had a surface covered with sandy lowlands broken by a complex network of rivers, streams, and deltas. Jangelle was settled by refugees who fled the Empire when it invaded Kathol sector, and they maintained contact with the rest of the sector—and Moff Sarne's activities—during supply runs to Gandle Ott and Pembric II. The colonies were low-tech settlements, although there were two ion cannons and a small navy protecting them. The Jangelle leadership formed a mutual defense pact with planets of the Kathol Republic to maintain their world's freedom.

**Jangoed** A slang term used by bounty hunters in the wake of the Battle of Geonosis. When Asajj Ventress issued bounties for the deaths of 82 members of the Jedi Order, the more experienced hunters advised their greener brethren to take care when hunting a Jedi. Otherwise they risked getting Jangoed—having their heads severed from their bodies by a lightsaber.

**Jango Fett Arena** An open-air arena in Mos Eisley. During the Empire, combat events were held there to entertain patrons. The arena was named in honor of Jango Fett, who died in the Geonosis execution arena many years earlier.

**Jangotat** The second nickname adopted by clone trooper A-98, who was also known as Nate. The name meant "Jango's brother" in Mandalorian, a name that Nate felt gave him closer ties to Jango Fett, the template for all clone troopers. He took the new name after spending time with Sheeka Tull, who once had been linked romantically to Jango.

Shortly after adopting the new name, Jangotat was badly injured when the Desert Wind terrorist base was infiltrated by a group of plastidroids and JK series combat droids. Jangotat was rescued by Tull, who took him to her village to recuperate with help from Brother Nicos Fate and several other Cestian healers. During his recovery, Jangotat felt vulnerable, and his presence at the settlement placed Sheeka and her family in danger. Tull revealed that she hated what he represented: the Clone Wars and the way it was destroying the galaxy. As for Jangotat himself, she felt only pity.

Jangotat was given an opportunity to see rare dashta eels when Sheeka took him to their secret cave. The sight of the blind creatures, glowing with happiness and friendship, made him cry for the first time in his life, and he realized that although clone troopers were produced from the same genetic template, they were all unique.

Upon returning to his comrades and the Jedi, Jangotat spent all his free time discussing Jedi combat techniques with Obi-Wan Kenobi and Kit Fisto, soaking up every scrap of information he could. In this way, Jangotat came to understand how to anticipate his opponent's next move, and was able to defeat his fellow ARC troopers in training battles that were designed to end in a draw. As the situation on

*Janks (left) whips up something to eat.*

Ord Cestus worsened, Jangotat discovered the secret location of the Five Families' hidden bunker. He launched a desperate mission to root them out and got inside the compound. Jangotat ordered the *Nexu* to fire on his own position. Along with most of the members of the Five Families, Jangotat was killed in the explosions.

**Janguine** This planet was home to a species of jungle barbarians that disappeared some 300 years before the Yuuzhan Vong War. Many linguists believed the Yuuzhan Vong language was reminiscent of, if not related to, the Janguine language.

**Janildakara** This woman took up bounty hunting after her family's transport was ambushed by pirates. Janildakara herself was sold to Zygerrian slavers, but escaped and began searching for her parents. She joined House Renliss, became a hunter, and developed into an expert in the use of poisons.

**Janissariad** One of the two major factions that took part in the Balduran Civil War years before the outbreak of the Clone Wars.

**janissaries** A term used for certain soldiers in Desevro's ancient armies in the centuries before the formation of the Old Republic. After Desevro was conquered by Xim the Despot, the janissaries were added to his armies, and participated in the pillaging of entire planets.

**Jankar, Sergeant "Slag"** This Imperial Army sergeant served as the primary drill instructor at the IMIIF-138 facility on Sirpar. Although he hated the corruption that tore apart the Old Republic, and though he believed that Emperor Palpatine brought a level of pride and discipline back to the military, Jankar lived to serve the army itself. He also prided himself on being the toughest, most demanding drill instructor on Sirpar.

**Jankok** This warm planet was the homeworld of the Srrors'toks.

**Janks** This efficient but whiny Phindian served as the assistant engineer aboard the transport vessel *Uhumele,* having been apprenticed to chief engineer Meekerdin-maa by Captain Schurk-Heren during the final years of the Old Republic. In addition to his skills maintaining the ship, Janks was an accomplished cook, and often helped to create meals for the crew.

**Jan-lo, Sunnar** A female Agamarian recruited into the Rebel Alliance along with Keyan Farlander, Sunnar became a fairly competent starfighter pilot.

**Janna, Neile** This noted actress, director, and producer returned from a 20-year hiatus to work on a holofeature called *Kallea's Hope,* which was based on the *Kallea Cycle* opera. The feature was credited by the artisans of the New Order with restoring interest in Freia Kallea and her namesake opera.

**Jannick, Jerus** A member of the Naboo Royal Security Forces during the Trade Federation's invasion of the Naboo system. Jannik served under Captain Panaka, and took his duty to protect Queen Amidala very seriously.

**Jannik the White** This light-skinned Rodian was the leader of the Reeven clan after the Battle of Naboo. To defeat his bitter rivals, Evo the Blue and the Cairn clan, Jannik hired Nym and his mercenary gang. Nym destroyed the Cairns, but Jannik refused to pay his fees. Nym stole the war treasure that had been won by the Reeven clan and fled. This act of treachery was simply an act for the public cams, as Jannik later joined Nym's gang and took half the treasure. When Nym agreed to help Ambassador Loreli Ro and the Mere put a stop to the predations of Sol Sixxa, Jannik became a full part of Nym's crew. He was badly wounded in hand-to-hand combat with Sixxa, who shoved a long knife into Jannik's chest. The blade missed his major organs, and the Rodian survived the fight.

**Janodral Mizar** Han Solo once fought a group of Zygerrian slavers near

*Jerus Jannick*

this planet, then gave their ship and cargo to the freed slaves, Rebel Alliance historian Arhul Hextrophon and his family. Janodral Mizar had a law that pirate or slaver victims split the proceeds if the pirates were captured or killed.

**Janoo, Nanda-Ree** This Jedi Knight accompanied Obi-Wan Kenobi to Balamak during the early stages of the Clone Wars to help destroy an experimental communications-jamming facility built by the Separatists.

**Janos** The capital of Demar, Janos was laid out in a circular pattern, with different quarters set aside for specific functions. At the center of the city was a beautiful business park, dominated by four shining metal towers.

**Janren, Darred** This man, a native of Naboo, married Sola Naberrie shortly after the Battle of Naboo. Recognizing that the Naberrie name held power and respect among the citizens of Theed, the couple chose to keep it as their family name. Darred and Sola had two daughters, Ryoo and Pooja.

**Janse** A former sharpshooter, Janse was a native of Ukio. He joined the Rebel Alliance shortly before the Battle of Endor. He had worked for BlasTech as a weapons design evaluator, and used his skills to help the Rebels as a scout and hunter. When he left BlasTech, he took with him a cache of A280 blaster rifles. He was part of the ground assault team that infiltrated the Empire's shield generator station on the Forest Moon of Endor.

**Janse, Emily** An officer with the Mining Guild during the Empire, she directed the operations of five mines for House Reena in the Tapani sector, and had a great deal of influence in the League of Tapani Freeworlds.

**Jansih, Karrinna** Mara Jade's alias when she worked as a serving girl on Phorliss.

***Janson*** A Nharwaak CR90 corvette that operated during the Galactic Civil War.

**Janson, Wes** A native of Taanab, Wes Janson joined the Rebel Alliance at Tierfon and quickly showed his abilities as a pilot and sharpshooter. He gained True Gunner status as an X-wing pilot in the Yellow Aces. Janson came down with a strain of Hesken Fever just before the Battle of Yavin and Jek Porkins filled in for him. Porkins's subsequent death over the first Death Star haunted Janson for years.

Janson later became a member of Rogue Squadron, serving under Luke Skywalker at Echo Base. He was Wedge Antilles's gunner in the Battle of Hoth, and used the call sign of Rogue Five. When their snowspeeder crashed during the battle, Wes and Wedge were forced to seek refuge in the gutted hull of a downed pirate freighter. Their survival and eventual rescue became the stuff of legends among fighter pilots. Wedge often told

*Wes Janson*

new recruits that Wes actually died on Hoth, only to watch their reactions when the man suddenly appeared to teach them their next lesson.

In the years that followed, Janson remained a fixture of Rogue Squadron; along with Hobbie Klivian, he was the team's comic relief. He was reported dead when the Rogues were ambushed at Distna while searching for evidence of Pulsar Station, but he was rescued by Booster Terrik and the *Errant Venture* and returned to Coruscant. After recovering from his injuries, Wes rejoined the squadron during the hunt for Prince-Admiral Krennel. Like most Rogue Squadron veterans, Janson retired shortly after the negotiation of peace between the New Republic and the Imperial Remnant. However, with the Yuuzhan Vong invasion, Wes renewed his commission as captain and took command of the Taanab Yellow Aces. This all-volunteer squadron participated in several missions after the Battle of Ebaq, including the rescue of Pash Cracken and Judder Page from Selvaris.

After the Yuuzhan Vong War, Wes remained a civilian pilot, although he maintained his close friendship with Wedge Antilles. Thus, when Antilles began assembling pilots to serve on Rakehell Squadron's mission to disable Centerpoint Station, Janson jumped at the chance to climb into a starfighter's cockpit again. He was Rakehell Twelve, bringing his usual flippant attitude to another dangerous mission.

**Janss, Alto** A smuggler who often stopped over at Tolea Biqua, which orbited Genarius, in the final years of the Old Republic. Janss was frequently found at the Near Vacuum cantina, with her two lieutenants acting as bodyguards. She moved her goods in her customized starship, the *Long Spoon.*

**Jante** The Jante were longtime rivals of their sector neighbors, the Freda. During the Empire, Jante mining operations in the Rettna system were attacked by Freda's Lon Flotillas. Moff Haveland attempted to bring about a cease-fire, but the Freda withdrew from the talks.

***Jantol*** This warship was part of the New Republic's Third Battle Group. It was diverted to the Koornacht Cluster during the Yevethan Purge, and participated in the blockade of Wehttam.

**Jantos** One of the largest cities on Ord Cestus, it was the site of a large trading post during the Clone Wars.

**Janu** Gang leader Trillot's personal chef during the Clone Wars. Janu had brown skin, an elongated chin, and a horny crest that ran along the centerline of his skull.

**Janus** A warehouse manager in Tosche Station on Tatooine, during the Galactic Civil War. Janus was killed when a group of Desert Demons swoop-jacked him during a regular transfer mission.

**Janusar** A small port town on Ranklinge. Although officially recorded as a city, Janusar was inhabited by just 100,000 beings.

**Januul** *See* Hovsgol Januul.

**janwuine** A Gand word that described members of their species who had distinguished themselves so much that they were allowed to speak of themselves in the first person—the highest possible honor a Gand could receive. Only those Gands who had enough history and impact on other Gands could refer to themselves as *I* without rudeness. Gands who earned the title of janwuine often had a mate chosen for them.

**janwuine-jika** This ceremony was performed for those Gands who distinguished themselves and were deemed janwuine. The individual was honored with stories about his or her great deeds and adventures, related by friends and the ruetsavii elders.

**Janzor, Captain** An Imperial Navy officer who took part in an attack on Kashyyyk. His platoon was used as a distraction for a much larger attack force.

**Ja-Phelar Bay** The name of the Bay of Conquest on Eriadu during the last centuries of the Old Republic. The name referred to its location between the city of Phelar and the Ja highlands. It was renamed after the rise of the Empire.

**japor** This small tree was native to Tatooine. It was coveted for the palm-sized nuts that grew on its branches inside hard shells. When split, the shell halves often were carved

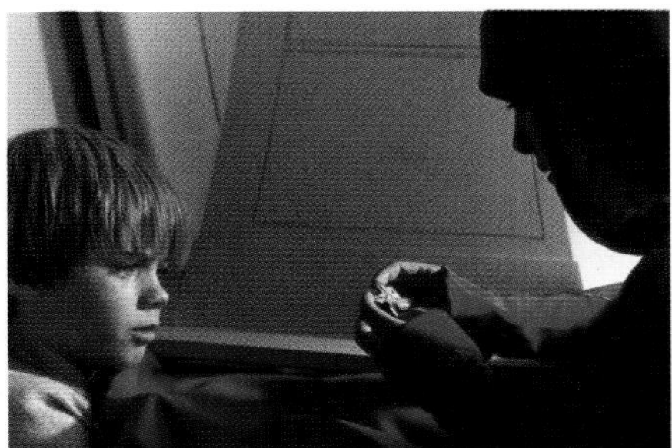

*Anakin Skywalker gives a japor snippet to Padmé Amidala.*

into jewelry. Snippets of japor were carved by youngsters with tribal runes, and used as good-luck charms or for protection from harm. Others were carved as love charms, in the hope of winning the affections of another. The wood of the japor tree, sometimes referred to as japor ivory, was extremely rare, and furniture made from this wood was quite valuable.

Young Anakin Skywalker gave a hand-carved japor snippet to Padmé when they were traveling to Coruscant after he had been freed from slavery. She always kept it close, and when she died years later after childbirth, she was buried with it clasped in her hands.

**Jappe** A planet in the Freeworlds Region of the Tapani sector. It was known as a safe haven for smugglers during the Empire.

**Japrael system** This system, which contained Onderon, orbited the star Prael.

**Jaraana** One of many Tarasin irstats on Cularin during the final years of the Old Republic. Just after the Clone Wars broke out, the home of the Jaraana was set ablaze when Mother Morad'Ka refused to follow a human Jedi away from the tribe. A group of freelance adventurers helped rescue several of the Jaraana Tarasin and assisted in putting out the fire before any more damage could occur.

**Jarael** This Arkanian Offshoot woman lived on Taris in a remote section of the Junction known as the *Last Resort,* in the years surrounding the Mandalorian Wars. Distinguished by her alabaster skin, white hair, and pointed ears, Jarael was an expert with the neural stinger she used to defend her territory. Her given name was actually Edessa, but she had forgotten it over the years. She was forced to flee Taris with the Camper, Marn Hierogryph, and Zayne Carrick after the latter—a former Jedi Padawan—was accused of murders actually committed by several Jedi Masters including Zayne's own, Lucien Draay. Despite her dislike of Zayne, Jarael agreed to Marn Hierogryph's plan to rescue the youth when they were caught by Valius Ying on the Rogue Moon. Posing as the Sith Lord who had been seen by the Jedi Masters in their visions of the future, Jarael was able to burst into the Jedi facilities on Taris and rescue Zayne.

**Jarael-One** The command phrase used by the Camper to override the programming of the HK-24 assassin droids that watched over him, after he was captured by Lord Arkoh Adasca and forced to complete work on the exogorth project.

**Jaratt** This Imperial Navy officer was part of the crew of the *Valorous* during the Galactic Civil War. When the Yevetha took control of the Black Sword Command's shipyards in the Koornacht Cluster, Jaratt was imprisoned on Pa'aal. He became the leader of a group of prisoners working with Sil Sorannan to free themselves from Yevethan control.

**Jardeen IV** This planet was the site of an Imperial training center dedicated to the techniques and tactics of using AT-AT and AT-ST walkers in battle.

**Jardra** The lead singer for Hyperspaze and the Jump Lanes, she was generally considered the band's best songwriter.

**Jarell** A species of strong, primitive reptiloids native to Oon Tien. Jarells were first contacted by the Old Republic some 300 years before the Battle of Endor. They were characterized by their wide skulls, which were crowned by four bony ridges of short spikes and surrounded by a mass of thick tendrils. Young Jarells were often forced to live as indentured servants to corporate leaders, crime lords, and affluent citizens as part of a series of arrangements made by the monarchy of Oon Tien.

**Jarellian** The dominant language spoken on Pembric II.

**jarencat** A creature native to Sriluur, known for its curious nature.

**Jaresh** An Outer Rim satellite in the Jaresh system, Corva sector. The moon was purchased by smuggler Ree Shala, who built her base there. The moon's trees grew hundreds of meters high, providing excellent cover; its extremely remote location also helped.

**Jaret** This male Senali was the son of Garth and Ganeed, and a member of the royal family. Jaret was married to Mesan, and they had a daughter, Tawn.

*Jarael wields a neural stinger.*

**Jarg** A Mandalorian stationed on Dantooine during the Great Sith War.

**Jarik, "Skoot"** A graduate of the Corporate Sector Authority Institute of Technology, Skoot returned to his homeworld of Biewa to start a droid repair business. However, he found that the inhabitants couldn't afford his services, let alone droids. He later met a smuggler who could afford him, and he became the primary droid repair and maintenance technician on StarForge Station.

**Jari'kyn** This young Twi'lek female was a fashion designer for the House of Vanar. She was fired when Mara Jade rejected the house's wedding gown design, despite the fact that Vanar had done most of the design himself. Mara encountered Jari'kyn in a lower level of Coruscant's Imperial City, and realized that she had nothing to do with the skimpy outfit Vanar had submitted. Mara hired Jari'kyn on the spot, asking her to design not only the wedding gown, but the bridesmaids' dresses as well. Jari'kyn agreed and set to work. As she was delivering the final garments to the wedding chapel, Jari'kyn was ambushed by Anlys Takkar and her cohorts. Anlys ordered one, Banner Sumptor, to kill Jari'kyn so that they could steal the dress and disrupt the wedding. Banner refused, shooting the rest of his cohorts. Jari'kyn grabbed a thick piece of pipe and whacked Anlys on the head, rendering her unconscious. Banner then helped Jari'kyn get the dresses to the wedding.

**Jarin** This small-time criminal, a native of Edan II, caused minor trouble in the settlement of Southview Village during the early days of the Galactic Civil War. When the Empire subjugated the planet, Jarin joined the underground in an effort to throw off the Imperial yoke. He was instrumental in obtaining a salvageable Y-wing fighter, dubbed the *Advent One,* to use against the Imperials.

**Jar'Kai** The specialized sword traditionally used by the ancient Yovshin Swordsmen of the Atrisian Empire. It was named for the city of Jar'Kai, on Kitel Phard, where the Jar'Kai style of two-handed sword fighting was first developed. A similar form of two-handed swordplay was later developed by the Royal Macheteros, who called it Niman. It was this later term that was given to a form of two-handed lightsaber combat by the Jedi Order—a technique the Jedi learned from the Legions of Lettow.

**Jarnek, Harlov** This Imperial Moff controlled Tandon sector during the Galactic Civil War. He always had a pet with him, an interesting creature that both amazed and frightened his acquaintances. Unbeknownst to Jarnek—who believed anything that wasn't human was surely unintelligent—the "pet" was actually the Covallon agent Daelar vuv Tertarrnek.

**Jarnollen** An outworld jungle planet close to Ord Mantell. Luke Skywalker and Leia Organa discovered an Imperial training ground there while scouting for a potential Rebel base.

**Jaro** This Harixian youth, a friend of Berd Lin, showed the boy how to use target drones to fool the Empire into believing a fleet of ships was approaching.

**Jaroona** This volcanic ball of rock was the second planet of the Eriadu system in the Outer Rim Territories.

**Jaros, Magar** A mild-mannered Sullustan with no real skills and no real backbone. Jaros was an excellent counterfeiter, and he used his ability to duplicate signatures and credits to "get back" at those who made fun of him.

**Jarrad, Selby** An Intelligence agent for the New Republic. Part of a mining clan working on Averill, Selby experienced the Empire's oppression when local mining operations were nationalized. Her father was crippled in a preventable accident, and Selby realized that she couldn't remain on Averill under Imperial rule. She tagged along with a cousin who left Averill after a failed effort to organize local resistance. She was sent to Verkuyl to assist in ousting the Imperial presence there shortly after the Battle of Endor. She and Cobb Vartos posed as businessbeings to meet with Governor Parco Ein, in an effort to obtain permission for GalFactorial to build a bacta refinery on the planet.

**Jarril** An old smuggling contact of Han Solo and Chewbacca, Jarril was a small man with narrow shoulders and a face scarred from years of harsh living. He invited Han and Chewie to the Crystal Jewel on Coruscant, where he offered Han information about some strange goings-on in the Smuggler's Run asteroid belt. In fact, Jarril himself was involved in the sale of Imperial equipment at outrageously high prices to a mysterious buyer, eventually revealed as the Dark Jedi Kueller.

Jarril was followed to Coruscant, and his trip there got the old smuggler killed. His ship, the *Spicy Lady,* was set adrift in space. It was found by Lando Calrissian, who went on to investigate Jarril's death, since he owed Jarril a debt: Jarril had once smuggled Lando out of Smuggler's Run, away from crime lord Nandreeson, who had set a hefty price on Calrissian's head.

**jarronto** This species of blue fungus near the swamps of Naboo featured tall stalks and large caps.

**Jarroth, Captain** This Imperial Navy officer commanded the *Stormwind* during the Galactic Civil War. He patrolled the Virgillian system, looking for suspected Rebel Alliance strongholds.

**Jarrou, Commander** This New Republic Navy commander was one of the primary leaders of the battle fleet dispatched to deal with the Yevetha during the Black Fleet crisis.

**Jarrti'Klomas** This young Rutian Twi'lek was one of the residents of the Enclave during the Clone Wars. A youthful male with courage to spare, Jarrti became the settlement's unofficial head of security, and formed a small defense force to protect the other residents from outsiders. While he appreciated being rescued from slavers by Jedi Master Vhiin Thorla, Jarrti felt that Thorla was too passive to adequately protect the Enclave residents. However, in regular hand-to-hand sparring matches designed to maintain their skills, Master Thorla regularly defeated Jarrti. In this way, Thorla was able to channel the youth's enthusiasm into defending the Enclave, instead of launching a futile war against the slavers. When Jacynith brought a group of freelance agents who were working for the Jedi Order to the Enclave, she also inadvertently led a group of slavers to the hidden location. Jarrti and his security forces were dispatched to eliminate the slavers, and worked with the Jedi agents to ensure the safety and security of the sanctuary.

**Jarsa** This woman was part of the crew of the New Republic Scout Service ship *Founder.*

**jart** A nocturnal bird of prey native to Ryloth.

**Jarvanam** A planet in Astal sector.

**Jarvashqiine** A term that described both a religion that worshipped individuals who had mystical powers, as well as the shaman-like priests who wielded those powers, which were much like the control of the Force.

**Jarvis, Alendar** A reporter for the *New Order Progressive,* he covered events on Coruscant during the Galactic Civil War. He was also something of a philosopher, and saw the New Order as a nearly perfect form of galactic government. He felt that the Rebel Alliance was a dangerous threat to the stability of society, in that it strove only to restore the corruption and rot of the Old Republic. It was Jarvis who reported on the death of Grand Moff Tarkin and several of his aides shortly after the destruction of Alderaan. According to Jarvis's report, Tarkin was traveling to the Tallaan Shipyard when his shuttle malfunctioned and exploded. The explosion was deemed an accident, and the story helped to cover up the truth about the Battle of Yavin.

**Jasa** A very young Anakin Solo's nickname for his brother Jacen.

**Jaset, Bal** This Tapani sector noble was the High Lord of House Melantha. He had served as a Court Adviser to then-Chancellor Palpatine during the last years of the Old Republic, and took his position as House ruler 10 years before the Battle of Hoth. He was best known for his romantic liaisons, having sired more than 30 illegitimate children and taken innumerable lovers during his short career as High Lord. He had a great deal of political and military support from Emperor Palpatine, which allowed Jaset to begin working to surpass House Mecetti as the dominant House in the Great Council.

**Jaso Corporation** This company developed the Right ID system of dermatoglyphic identification.

**Jasod Revoc and His Galactic Revue** A collection of entertainers that traveled the galaxy during the Clone Wars, entertaining the troops of the Grand Army of the Republic. Among the acts presented by Jasod Revoc were Epoh Trebor, Eyar Ahtram, and Figrin D'an and the Modal Nodes.

**Jaspar, Trent** A student of the Force, he discovered his talents shortly before the Battle of Yavin, and joined the Rebel Alliance in an effort to locate a teacher. He was assigned to the Alliance's Edan Base when it was attacked by the Imperial Star Destroyer *Havoc.*

**Jassa, Mroon** This ancient Jedi Master established a training center on Truuine some 4,000 years before the Battle of Yavin. It was there that Kith Kark tried to convince Master Jassa that he was ready to begin Jedi training. Jassa ignored the Gotal twice, because Kark only wanted to learn the Force as a hobby, not because the Force called him. Nearly a year after his first visit, Kark returned to Truuine a third time. He finally had realized that the Force was something that had to be felt and obeyed. Jassa knew that Kark had finally been touched by the Force, and agreed to train him.

**Jassar** This young wyrwulf was the son of Rikkar-Du and Tassa. Rikkar-Du tried to rally the other clan leaders to oppose the Sith and the new Empire some seven years after the Massacre at Ossus. Jassar went to join his father in meditating at a local temple, but came upon a struggle between his father and Darth Kruhl instead. Although strong, Jassar was no match for the Sith Lord's command of the dark side of the Force. Darth Kruhl easily cut Jassar down before turning on Rikkar-Du and killing him as well.

**Jasserak Engagement** A stalemate that occurred on Drongar during the Clone Wars, in which the forces of the Old Republic and the Confederacy of Independent Systems struggled for control of the bota fields. Neither side could use massive firepower or huge troop movements to attack the other, as bota was sensitive to outside stimuli. Too much laserfire could set the bota fields afire, while tramping it underfoot left nothing but a slimy mess in its place. So the fighting during the Jasserak Engagement was highly targeted and surgical in its methodology, and neither side made much headway for months. The fight took a strange turn about two years after the Battle of Geonosis when Separatist forces launched a massive attack near Rimsoo Seven, destroying the nearby bota fields and forcing the Republic Mobile Surgical Units to pack up and move with little notice.

**Jasserak Highlands** The plateau that formed the border of the Jasserak Lowlands, on Drongar. Much of the Jasserak Highlands was covered with strange, fungus-like trees that produced avedame fruit.

**Jasshi'rr** The ancient Twi'lek ceremony of marriage. It was reported that a wondrous crystal skull carved from the crystallized ashes of a fallen Twi'lek hero was used to preside over the ceremonies that recognized clan marriages.

**Jassim Design** This ancient corporation produced a wide range of medical electronics, as well as personal survival kits.

**Jastaal** A species with beautiful plumage, the Jastaals used their wings when they walked, giving them the appearance of bouncing on the wind.

**Jaster's Legacy** The name used by many Mandalorian shock troopers to describe Jango Fett during the years in which he commanded the mercenaries after Jaster Mereel's execution on Korda 6.

***Jaster's Legacy*** This ancient Mandalorian-built starship was once owned by Jango Fett before he acquired *Slave I.* The ship was named in honor of Jaster Mereel, and served Fett well for many years. During his attempt to "rescue" Bendix Fust from the Oovo IV prison facility, Jango flew *Jaster's Legacy* into the jail by hiding behind a supply ship. However, before he could capture Fust and make his escape, *Jaster's Legacy* was destroyed by one of the prison's *Firespray*-class patrol ships. In retaliation, Jango stole one of the prison's patrol ships, eventually renaming it *Slave I.*

**Jastro III** This planet was under Imperial control during the Galactic Civil War.

**Jatayus Outbound** A shipping company that made regular trips along the Sisar Run, it was a front for Black Sun Vigo Sprax. Jatayus's corporate headquarters were on Novor XXIII.

**Jatee** The third planet in the five-world Demophon system, Jatee was destroyed when the system's primary star went supernova. Little more than a planetoid, Jatee had been the home of the Ssither species.

**Jat'ho** A male Arcona who served in the Galactic Alliance Guard on Coruscant during the war between the Galactic Alliance and the Confederation. Jat'ho and Tobyl were part of the squad that captured Ben Skywalker and Lon Shevu following the Second Battle of Fondor. However, Jaina and Leia Organa Solo used the Force to make the two guards believe they were undercover GAG agents. The two Jedi convinced the guards to let them take a medwagon, which they used to pursue the Doomsled that carried Ben and Lon away from the scene.

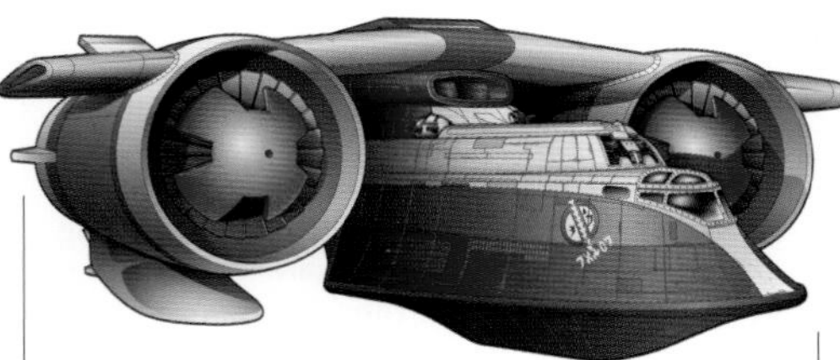

Jaster's Legacy

**Jatras** This bounty hunter specialized in returning live targets, and refused to use deadly force or biological weapons.

**jatz** A musical style popular during the Manderon Period of the Old Republic. It found new popularity with the rise of the musician Fitz Roi during the New Order.

**Jaub, Niev** A Sullustan, he was an honest trader who did a large volume of business on Nar Shaddaa. He and his small freighter, the *Bnef Nlle,* were on the Smugglers' Moon when Admiral Greelanx began his attack. Because of his business ties, and because Nar Shaddaa supported a large contingent of Sullustans, Jaub joined the fight. He got caught in no-man's-land when he mistakenly followed Falan Iniro out of hiding before the rest of Nar Shaddaa's defense forces were ready. Jaub saw Iniro and the *Take That!* destroyed. Jaub managed to take out a few TIE fighters launched from the *Carrack*-class ships that made up the Imperial picket line before sustaining damage himself. Rather than die without fighting back, Jaub piloted the *Bnef Nlle* on a collision course with the *Vigilance.* The impact destroyed the smaller ship and killed Jaub, but the Imperial cruiser was defenseless after losing its shields.

***Jaunty Cavalier*** This YT-series freighter was owned and operated by the Wookiee Rufarr during the Yuuzhan Vong War. Rufarr and his crew were implicated as radical members of the Freedom movement when Molierre Cundertol employed them to "kidnap" him and bring him to Lwhekk to be enteched. To ensure the secrecy of his actions, Cundertol deliberately sabotaged the *Jaunty Cavalier,* causing it to explode upon exiting hyperspace near Bakura. Rufarr and his entire crew were killed; Molierre escaped in an emergency pod.

**Jauxson** A Gotal bandit who grew up serving some of the galaxy's most dangerous pirate captains before striking out on his own. He led a group that took control of the domed city of Buerhoz during the Galactic Civil War, but eventually was removed from power by a group of freelance agents.

**Javaal** This ball of frozen ice and rock was the seventh and outermost planet in the Brentaal system.

**Javeb, Zyn** A Pau'an, he was one of the lesser aides of Tion Medon during the final years of the Old Republic.

***Javelin 3*** An Imperial corvette sent to destroy Project Shantipole once it was compromised by a spy.

**Javeq, Lasro** A junior operations manager for Xizor Transport Systems just prior to the Clone Wars. Javeq died in a fiery explosion at the spaceport in Aroo, on Manda, when his ship suddenly detonated while berthed at a Baobab Merchant Fleet complex there. More than 2,000 Baobab employees were killed, and more than 100 Baobab merchant ships were damaged or destroyed. An investigation by the Galactic Senate revealed that the explosion was not an act of sabotage, as inferred by Baobab, but a suicide. Further investigation revealed that Javeq had embezzled almost five million credits from Xizor Transport, despite the operation's notoriously tight security. Javeq himself left behind a wife and two children, who were supported by Prince Xizor himself.

**Javik, Tenga** This woman served as the nominal leader of the Walkway Collective following the Battle of Coruscant.

**Javin** A planet considered by many to be the central point of the Javin sector, it was first colonized by the Mugaari. However, it was later settled by humans of the Old Republic some 1,000 years before the Galactic Civil War. Located on the edge of the Mid Rim, it served as the Old Republic's launch point for explorations into what was then part of Wild Space. After the Mugaari had a falling-out with the Republic, most left Javin to return to Mugaar.

**Javin, Andor** A reporter for the TriNebulon News agency who was credited with discovering the true identity of the newsnet rogue Cynabar. He was known for his investigative, often confrontational, style of journalism, including the revelation that the Shrines of Kooroo were actually ancient communications devices. Javin also reported that Klaggus Purgato survived the assault by the IG-88 assassin droids that wiped out Holowan Mechanicals. He was reported to have discovered 8,000-year-old Sullustan cave drawings that predicted the rise of the Empire.

**Javin sector** Located near the Anoat and Yarith sectors in the area known as the Greater Javin, the Javin sector was based on the original boundaries of Mugaari space. During the early years of the New Order, the Empire established outpost station D-34 there. Following the Battle of Hoth, the Imperial fleet tried to drive the fleeing Rebel Alliance ships through the Javin sector and past D-34, from which the Empire could destroy the ships.

**Javis** This planet, the primary world in the Javis system of Tapani sector, was part of the holdings of House Mecetti during the New Order.

**Javis-12** An asteroid that was one of the largest in the Mestra system asteroid field, located in the Minos Cluster. It was roughly egg-shaped and measured about 400 kilometers at its widest point. The asteroid did not revolve around its axis, thanks to specially placed repulsors. This kept the main living areas away from the rest of the belt, protecting them from asteroid and meteorite hits. The Minos-Mestra Corporation's local headquarters were on the asteroid, as was the system's only starport—a conglomerate of domes and caves ranging across and below the surface.

*Jawas haul off R2-D2*

**Javriel** One of the survivors of the Outbound Flight Project. About two years before the project's remains were discovered by a Chiss-led expedition, Javriel's mind snapped and he took the entire nursery hostage. Only the timely efforts of Evlyn Tabory and her uncle, Jorad Pressor, kept Javriel from doing any harm to the children.

**Javyar's Cantina** A cantina located in the Lower City of Taris prior to the Great Sith War.

**Jawa** A species of diminutive, desert-dwelling scrap merchants native to Tatooine, they had large, glowing eyes that peered out from dirty cloaks. Jawas were distinguished by their smell, due in part to the unusual mixture of chemicals used to clean their clothing and help the fabric retain body moisture. Jawas also didn't bathe, seeing it as a waste of precious water. For Jawas the scents of other Jawas revealed information about their health and feelings.

The Jawas used a randomly variable language, which made it hard to interpret what they were saying. Communication was further impaired since they used pheromones to add emphasis to otherwise meaningless syllables.

Jawas were inherently cowardly, having evolved to survive in an environment where most other creatures were larger and more dangerous. They were communal beings, working together in small bands to collect anything and everything mechanical in order to repair it for resale to any and all buyers.

Some xenologists believed that Jawas had human origins; a handful believed that they shared a common lineage with Sand People, as both seemed to have genetic markers in common with the extinct Kumumgah species. Still others insisted that they descended from rodents. Very few ever saw what Jawas looked like under their cloaks, further adding to their mystery. All that could be seen outwardly were the glowing eyes. Their orange light was magnified by small gemstones that also protected the Jawa's eyes from the harsh sunlight of Tatooine's twin suns.

Most other species regarded Jawas as scavengers and thieves, a description that actually pleased most Jawas. As a people, they based much of their culture on families and clans. Their society was controlled by female shamans who seemed to have some kind of connection to the Force, which they used to perform certain "magic" to ensure their success. The central activities of Jawa life were trading and scavenging. In fact, it was not uncommon for Jawa clans to barter their sons and daughters as marriage merchandise, since this was a simple way to ensure cultural and genetic diversity. Jawas traveled and lived in bands, using giant, treaded vehicles known as sandcrawlers for mobility and shelter. The crawlers could hold up to 300 Jawas as well as the droids and other machinery that they found, repaired, and resold to Tatooine moisture farmers and others. They often found water by inserting long, thin hoses down the stems of the funnel flower and siphoning off the liquid there. The hubba gourd, a difficult-to-digest fruit, was their primary food; in the Jawa language, *hubba* meant "the staff of life."

To help dissipate body heat, as well as to hide their identity, Jawas covered their faces with moistened sand. This shroud often attracted several species of flying insects, adding to the Jawas' disgusting appearance.

**Jawa beer** A variety of cheap, quickly brewed beer that was created by Jawas.

**Jawa camp** Although Jawas spent a great amount of time aboard their immense sandcrawlers, some tribes established stationary settlements. Even the most temporary encampments demonstrated the Jawas' instincts for desert survival, offering shelter from battering sandstorms or the searing Tatooine suns. During his search for his mother, Anakin Skywalker consulted a Jawa camp for directions to a nearby Tusken Raider village.

**Jawa Droid Traders** The loose union of Jawa clans that sold and traded droids on Tatooine.

**Jawa Heights** Named for Jawas that congregated in the shade it provided, this tableland was located several hundred kilometers west of Anchorhead, on Tatooine.

**Jawa ionization gun** One of the most famous icons of Jawas, the ionization gun had many uses—the main one being the immobilization of a droid. The weapon discharged an intense beam that ionized the droid's circuits, rendering it temporarily unable to function. The gun could be created from any blaster rifle by gutting it of its laser components and modifying it to accept an ion accelerator created by the Jawas themselves. This accelerator was made from a droid restraining bolt wired to an ignition accu-accelerator.

**Jawa juice** A sharp, bitter beverage also known as ardees. Obi-Wan Kenobi often ordered it when visiting Dex's Diner. An alcoholic version was popular at the Bantha Traxx establishment on Lianna at the height of the New Order.

**Jawa Raceway** One of many deep-desert locations on Tatooine.

**Jawaswag** The nickname given by Gavin Darklighter to his R2 unit, since Gavin believed any Jawa would love to steal the droid. However, when the automaton was actually accosted by a group of Jawas, it thwarted their attempts to steal it and actually injured one of them. From that point on, Gavin called it Toughcatch. This name was shortened to Catch for ease of use in combat. About 20 years after the Battle of Endor, Catch was given the R2-Delta upgrade.

**Jawa trade language** Developed by Jawas, this language was used primarily when bartering with an individual from another tribe. It eliminated any tribe-specific dialects and the problems they might create during negotiations.

**Jawa trader** This slang term was coined by humans on Tatooine, and referred to any dishonest being, or a being who sold stolen or damaged merchandise.

**Jawa Traders** This scrap and salvage business was located in Mos Eisley. It was started

*A Jawa camp on Tatooine*

by a Jawa named Aguilae, but she quickly found that she couldn't part with her merchandise. So she hired the Squib named Macemillianwinduarté to handle her sales.

**jawenko lava beast** This unusual creature was native to the lava flows of Mustafar. It could live in the boiling rivers and pools of lava that covered the planet's surface, and consumed many raw forms of metals and ores. The native Mustafarians discovered that the jawenko lava beast could refine xonolite into a liquid form that had strangely euphoric effects when injected into the bloodstream. This drug, which was exported to Nkllon for further refinement, became known as Nkllonian lava extract, despite the fact that it was produced on Mustafar.

**jaw-wag** A slang term used to describe idle gossiping or rumors.

**Jax, Carnor** A former Imperial Guard, he was a member of the training class that also produced Kir Kanos. Jax was the son of a Thyrsian Sun Guard member who was killed by Darth Sidious. He originally was trained as a stormtrooper, serving as a member of Blackhole's elite units before being chosen for training as an Imperial Guard. Jax often bested Kir Kanos in the training battles fought in the Squall, and defeated Alum Frost in a fight to the death on Yinchorr. The battle was staged by Emperor Palpatine himself to determine the more loyal warrior.

In the wake of Palpatine's death at Endor, Jax began to envision himself as a new Dark Lord and ruler of the Empire. He established a power base, and bribed one of Palpatine's primary clone scientists to create defective clones for the Emperor. Jax then began wearing a suit of armor that was a modified version of the Guards' armor, with a black faceplate and cloak. When Palpatine's clones were destroyed at Byss, Jax made his bid for control of the Empire by creating the Imperial Interim Ruling Council and assuming its leadership. He also set out to exterminate the remaining Imperial Guards, but Kir Kanos managed to escape and took with him the knowledge of Jax's treason.

Jax learned that Kanos survived, and knew that he had to eliminate the threat he posed. When Kanos was discovered on Phaeda, Jax ordered Colonel Shev to stand down and let his own forces deal with Kanos, but Shev ignored the orders. Kanos escaped to Yinchorr. Jax pursued him with a squadron of handpicked, black-armored stormtroopers. Kanos wiped out the entire squadron, leaving Jax to face him in one-on-one combat in the Squall. Jax made sure he had all of Kanos's possible escapes covered, including the placement of his aide Blim in a nearby position to shoot Kanos if the other man got an advantage. After Blim was eliminated by Mirith Sinn and Sish Sadeet, Jax nearly defeated Kanos. But in a short duel, Kanos drove the blade of his staff through Jax's breastplate, piercing his heart and killing him instantly.

Carnor Jax (left) faces Kir Kanos in a duel to the death.

**Jax, Hukta** A Gamorrean, he was one of the best swoop racers on Manaan during the era of the Great Sith War. He was the sector champion until he was beaten by a Jedi Knight.

**Jaxa** This smuggler worked with Bettle, and assisted Mara Jade in creating a distribution system for glitterstim spice mined on Kessel after Moruth Doole was removed from power. Jaxa and Bettle operated from their starship, the *Mallixer,* during the early stages of the Galactic Civil War.

**Jaxal, Solo** The alias used by Han Solo, shortly after his marriage to Leia Organa, when he accompanied his wife to Tatooine to intercept a group of Imperial agents. Jaxal was a Devaronian, and Han was disguised with a pair of horns.

Hukta Jax

**Jaxus** This planet orbited fairly close to its sun but was still capable of supporting human life.

**Jax Warehouse** Located near the Dry Goods Emporium in the city of Hedrett, this building was one of the largest and safest places to store goods on Cularin during the last years of the Old Republic.

**Jaxxon** This member of the Lepi species—known scientifically as *Lepus carnivorus*—left his homeworld of Coachelle Prime at the age of 12 and found work in several gangs, including a mercenary group on Corus. After the gang broke up, Jaxxon spent time on Nar Shaddaa before saving up enough money to buy the *Rabbit's Foot* and setting out on his own. Problems with the ship forced Jaxxon to land on Aduba-3, where he was stranded for several months. There he joined Han Solo and a ragtag team of starfaring adventurers to defeat Serji-X Arrogantus. Jaxxon was nearly killed in the battle, and was saved at the last moment by Amaiza Foxtrain. He was busy telling her about his mother and 79 siblings, in an effort to impress her, during most of the fight. The pair decided to work together afterward. They ran afoul of Valance the bounty hunter before escaping and returning to Aduba-3.

**Jay** The nickname of one of the four clone troopers in the Theta Squad of commandos

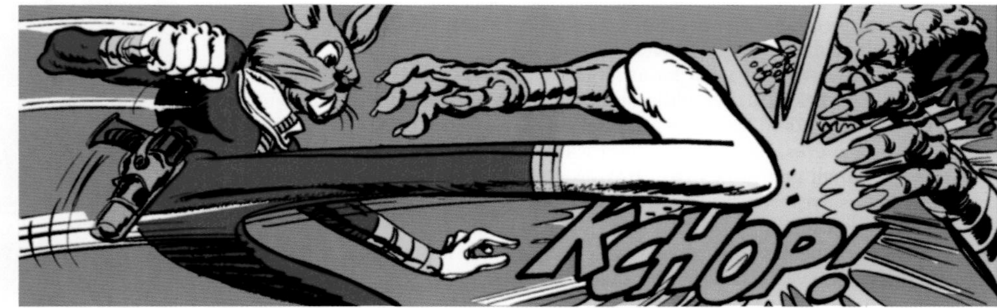

Jaxxon kicks some sense into the spacer Warto after being called a "rodent."

that participated in the Battle of Geonosis. Jay was among the three members of the squad to be killed in the fighting.

**Jaya** This was Anakin Solo's nickname for his sister, Jaina, when he was a toddler.

**Jayhawk, Captain** The captain of the *Martinette* and leader of a gang of pirates that worked the space lanes of Fakir sector near Masterhome, during the Galactic Civil War.

**Jayl** This woman served as an administrative assistant to Mar Rugeyan, the Senate head of public affairs during the Clone Wars.

**Jayme, Ivhin** Raised by hands-off parents who instilled in him both open-mindedness and a lack of direction, Jayme joined the Imperial armed forces at the age of 16. Within a few months, he had been turned into a dangerous and formidable commando by instructors on Merikon. Following orders, he destroyed a building with innocent children inside. He couldn't come to terms with this indiscriminate loss of life, however, and fled the service. Drifting to Rodaj, he met T'Charek Haathi, who convinced him to join the Rebel Alliance. Jayme was initially recruited into the Alliance's urban commando team, but when he balked at several missions he was moved to the Special Operations team.

**Jaytee** This young man was a contemporary of Alex Winger during her education on Garos IV.

**Jayzaa** The alias adopted by Jedi Master Aayla Secura when she traveled to Anzat with Jedi Master Tholme during the final stages of the Clone Wars. Jayzaa was an itinerant mechanic who supposedly traveled to Anzat to meet a Weequay Separatist, but couldn't seem to locate him. The alias, along with a few drinks at Maggot's Cantina, allowed her to learn that former Jedi Master Sora Bulq had leased a private docking bay at the Anzat Spaceport and refused to talk to any non-Anzati.

**Jazbina** This planet—the homeworld of the feline Jazbinans—was known for its luxurious aromatic baths and its valuable sun crystals. Luke Skywalker was sent to Jazbina shortly after the Battle of Yavin on a diplomatic mission to sway the Jazbinans to join the Alliance. However, the planet was solidly aligned with the Empire, which paid a high price for the sun crystals.

**JC-671** This model of deflector shield generator, produced by Delphus at the height of the New Order, found widespread use on late-model Nebulon-B frigates.

**Jcir, Standro** This New Republic starfighter pilot was a member of Rogue Squadron. A Rodian, Jcir joined the Rogues in the wake of the Malrev Incident, when several positions in the squadron were left empty. A veteran of 13 missions, Jcir was the first of the Republic's pilots killed at the Battle of Brentaal.

**JCOS-1, JCOS-2** The designations used by military personnel of the Galactic Alliance for Admiral Cha Niathal (JCOS-1) and Jacen Solo (JCOS-2), after Chief of State Cal Omas was arrested and Niathal and Solo assumed a joint role in leading the Galactic Alliance. The acronym referred to their roles as Joint Chiefs of State.

**JE-99-DI-88-FOR-00-CE** The code signal that activated the weather-control system in the Lost City of the Jedi.

**Jeban, Briika and Dinua** Briika Jeban was one of the new generation of Mandalorians trained by Boba Fett during the New Republic. Briika's daughter, Dinua, completed her training as a warrior about a year before the Yuuzhan Vong War, and their celebration at the Bar Jaraniz on Nar Shaddaa attracted the attention of Goran Beviin. The celebration was somewhat bittersweet, as Briika's mate had died the previous year. Beviin offered them a job when he accepted a contract to assassinate Tholote B'Leph, and the three of them earned a hefty fee for the hit. Briika and Dinua continued to work with Beviin, and were part of the team formed by Boba Fett to meet with Nom Anor and the Yuuzhan Vong. They all agreed when Fett decided to turn the tables on the alien invaders, using their missions as a way to gather intelligence. On New Holgha, however, they were apprehended by the subaltern Bur'lorr, who caught them allowing the Jedi Knight Kubariet to escape. The Mandalorians were able to overpower and kill the warrior, but Briika was badly wounded in the fighting.

Although Fett and Beviin were able to return her to *Slave I*, Briika died shortly afterward from massive blood loss. With her dying breath, Briika made Beviin promise to take Dinua as his own child, as part of the *gai bal manda*. Briika's death did not go unnoticed: Fett made Kubariet promise to make sure that the New Republic understood that a Mandalorian had died saving the life of a Jedi Knight.

On Mandalore, Dinua became an accepted member of Beviin's extended family, as well as one of the many Mandalorians who helped defend their homeworld from the Yuuzhan Vong. In the wake of the fighting, Dinua settled down with a man named Jintar, and together they raised a small family. Dinua, however, found it difficult to adjust to family life, instead preferring the mercenary work that many Mandalorians took on. The couple brought up their children, Shalk and Briila, as Mandalorians.

*Standro Jcir*

**Jebbis** One of three Besalisk bouncers employed by Chieb'Kalla at the Fungus Pit cantina during the final years of the Old Republic.

**Jebbiz'Foreanda** This aging, gray-skinned Twi'lek was once a member of the head clan of the Bashka settlement on Ryloth, several years before the outbreak of the Clone Wars. Like the other members of the head clan, Jebbiz was exiled into the Bright Lands when one of the other members passed away. He was rescued from certain death by Vhiin Thorla, who had returned to Ryloth about a year before the Battle of Geonosis. Jebbiz then became one of the first members of the Enclave rescued by Master Thorla. Although he was grateful for the Jedi Master's kindness in saving his life, Jebbiz often wondered why Thorla did not take on a larger role as the leader of the Enclave.

**Jebble** This Outer Rim world was on the front battle lines during the Mandalorian Wars 3,964 years before the Battle of Yavin. Jebble eventually was captured by the Mandalorians, giving them a stronghold in the Outer Rim that the Old Republic was unable to break. Refugees from Jebble and other front-line worlds fled to planets like Vanquo, hoping to escape the predations of the Mandalorians.

**jebwa** A red-and-yellow flower native to Corellia.

**JedCred** *See* Jedi Credit.

**Jedd Six** This planet was first scouted by Lexi Fernandin during the last years of the Old Republic.

**Jedgar, High Prophet** Like others of the mysterious order known as Prophets of the Dark Side, this tall human with a bald head, bearded chin, and hooded eyes assisted Supreme Prophet Kadann in his attempt to gain control of the Empire. Little was known of Jedgar's past, except that he trained at the Jedi Temple on Coruscant before the Clone Wars. He often dreamed of the events of the Clone Wars and the Jedi Purge, and his visions frightened the other students and worried his teachers. Jedgar was never taken as a Padawan. A series of visions led him to Kadann, under whom he apprenticed to learn the ways of the dark side. Jedgar also served as Kadann's bodyguard, but that was more for show than actual defense, since Kadann was quite powerful. When the

Prophets of the Dark Side were formed under Emperor Palpatine, Jedgar became Kadann's second in command, and his support of Kadann's visions—even after Palpatine dismissed them—ran deep.

**Jedi Archives and Library** Located in a building that was more than 2,500 years old at the time of the Battle of Geonosis, this vast library of holobooks and information had been compiled by the Jedi Knights of the Old Republic for nearly 1,000 generations. Some of the documents contained in the Archives dated from the very beginning of the Republic. The main Archives were divided into four main halls, with access terminals provided along the length of each hall. While any terminal could be used to access any of the information in the Archives, each hall was set aside for a general set of knowledge that made it easier to find a certain piece of information. Users were given access to certain levels of information, depending on their path of research and their credentials. No original documents could be taken from the building, since they were tagged with markers that set off sensors in the doors. However, individuals could copy any piece of information that they were allowed to access for their own use.

The main entry hall was set aside for philosophical and historical documents, and contained documents that had been created by Jedi, politicians, and other historically important beings. The second hall was for mathematical and engineering knowledge, and contained blueprints of virtually every starship and vehicle ever produced. The third hall contained geographic and cultural information from across the galaxy, including the most detailed astronomical maps. The fourth hall had zoological data and information on the various forms of life that had existed in the galaxy.

At the end of the Clone Wars, the Archives were raided by Emperor Palpatine and his Dark Side Adepts, and much of the information stored there was lost. However, after Luke Skywalker established his new Jedi Order and was given a new Temple facility on Coruscant, he began working on a new Jedi Archives.

*Jedi Archives and Library*

**Jedi battle meditation** *See* battle meditation.

**Jedi Civil War** A period of galactic history following the Great Sith War, when the Jedi Knights fought in the Mandalorian Wars and battled against the forces of Darth Malak. The conflict spread throughout the entire Jedi Order, as many questioned their allegiance to a Jedi Council that seemed blinded to the growing power of the Sith. Many Jedi, like Revan and Kreia, abandoned the Order and fought the Sith on their own. There were heroes and villains on both sides of the fighting. The Jedi Order was nearly destroyed, and the Sith were reduced to Darth Sion's ravaged body and a handful of Sith devotees. The Jedi Council collapsed, and the galaxy was plunged into years of fear until the Jedi could reestablish themselves. The survival of the Order was made possible by the heroic efforts of the Jedi Exile and Kreia, who battled Darth Sion and kept the Jedi beliefs alive.

**Jedi Coalition** A coalition of military forces that still supported the Jedi Order in the wake of the Battle of Kuat and the galactic takeover orchestrated by Jacen Solo. The new Jedi Order had withdrawn its support of the Galactic Alliance during the Battle of Kuat, refusing to back a government ruled by aggression. The Jedi abandoned their Temple on Coruscant and their training facility on Ossus, and fled to the hidden world of Shedu Maad. In an attempt to bring Jacen Solo to justice, the Order began recruiting small forces to their cause, forming the Jedi Coalition. However, many of the governments that joined the Coalition were still entrenched in their own struggles, and could barely afford to assist in larger-scale assaults on the Galactic Alliance.

**Jedi Code, the** The basic tenets of the Jedi, the Jedi Code was based on the writings of Jedi Master Odan-Urr some 4,000 years before the Battle of Yavin. That philosophy never changed over the millennia:

*"There is no emotion; there is peace. There is no ignorance; there is knowledge. There is no passion; there is serenity. There is no death; there is the Force. A Jedi does not act for personal power or wealth but seeks knowledge and enlightenment. A true Jedi never acts from hatred, anger, fear, or aggression but acts when calm and at peace with the Force."*

Among the other basic beliefs was that a Jedi Knight or Master could take only a single Padawan apprentice. That ensured that a teacher could not gain undue influence. Also, a Jedi must consider the Force before undertaking any action. That meant that Jedi had to ensure that they were acting without emotion in every situation, so as not to draw power from the dark side. Among the most prominent teachings of Master Odan-Urr were the following:

- "Certainly a Jedi should know the Code, by word and by heart. But seemingly every Jedi is in some fashion negligent, from the lowest Padawan to the highest Master. Consequently, were someone to demand, 'What is the true meaning of the Jedi Code?' the Jedi who promptly answers would be rare indeed."
- "Every Jedi should spend time meditating each day on the will of the Force. The reason for this is simple: If one unwittingly acted contrary to the will of the Force, recognizing the mistake soon after may still give one time to make amends."
- "To be brave in battle proves nothing. A Jedi should be prepared to put aside fear, regret, and uncertainty and either fight, run, surrender, or die."
- "If a Jedi ignites his lightsaber, he must be ready to take a life. If he is not so prepared, he must keep his weapon at his side."
- "Do not come to rely on the Force to the detriment of your other senses and abilities."
- Master Odan-Urr further explained that there were eight distinct ideas or actions that had to be considered before any action was taken: meditation, training, loyalty, integrity, morality, discretion, bravery, and fighting. Jedi needed to know them instinctively so that they could resolve any situation that demanded a quick decision with the will of the Force already in mind.

**Jedi Command** The military command center established in the Jedi Temple on Coruscant during the Clone Wars. Jedi Command was staffed around the chrono to coordinate the military missions of the thousands of Jedi Knights deployed across the galaxy.

**Jedi Convocation** Any large gathering of Jedi Knights and Jedi Masters to discuss the most important issues facing the galaxy. Several Jedi Convocations occurred during the era of the Great Sith War, including one known as The Great Council of Deneba. As the threat of the Sith continued to wax and wane, more events like the Exis Convocation were held to prevent any further trouble in the galaxy. The last noted Convocation occurred on Katarr some 3,952 years before the Battle of Yavin. The assembled Jedi were slaughtered when the Sith Lord Darth Nihilus laid waste to the planet.

**Jedi Council** Also called the Jedi High Council, this body was established in the wake of the Battle of Ruusan to oversee and govern the activities of the Jedi Order, and to evaluate its place in the galaxy. New rules were put in place to overcome perceived problems that were encountered on Ruusan, including the propensity adolescents and adults had for letting their emotions drag them over to the dark side of the Force. When the Jedi Council decreed that only infants would be chosen for training, many beings in the galaxy came to see the Jedi as cradle robbers or baby snatchers. However, they were not in the majority, and many of the galaxy's citizens attributed the ensuing centuries of peace to the efforts of the Jedi Order. In the years leading up to the Clone Wars and the fall of the Old Republic, the Jedi Council became more and more insular, and many believed that the Order was destroyed because the Council was unable to see the coming darkness.

The Council maintained a spectacular Chamber located in one of the four Council Towers of the Jedi Temple on Coruscant. The Council was made up of five lifetime members, four long-term members, and three limited-term members. At the time of the Battle of Naboo, the Council consisted of the following:

- **Lifetime members:** Mace Windu, Yoda, Oppo Rancisis, Plo Koon, Yarael Poof.
- **Long-term members:** Eeth Koth, Even Piell, Depa Billaba, Saesee Tiin.
- **Limited-term members:** Ki-Adi-Mundi, Yaddle, Adi Gallia.

As the Republic began to crumble from within, and after Count Dooku formed the Confederacy of Independent Systems, the Jedi Order found itself responding to more requests for assistance in political and military matters. The Jedi Council had to send more Jedi into combat situations, and the mission of the Order slowly became one of military import.

By the time of the Battle of Geonosis, Coleman Trebor had replaced Yarael Poof, and Shaak Ti had replaced Yaddle. With the full-blown conflict of the Clone Wars, the Jedi Council became the military leadership of a new group of generals, as Jedi Masters were given command of clone trooper squads in an effort to confront the atrocities of the Separatists. The Clone Wars altered the makeup of the Jedi Council. Master Trebor died at Geonosis, and the remaining Council members often were forced to meet via holographic communication from the battlefronts. Appointed to replace fallen Masters were Agen Kolar, Stass Allie, Kit Fisto, Tsui Choi, Colman Kcaj, and Obi-Wan Kenobi.

Following the Battle of Coruscant, the Galactic Senate admitted that it could no longer handle the duties of politics and the military. Senators voted to have the Jedi Order report directly to Chancellor Palpatine, giving him complete control of its activities. Outwardly, this meant that Palpatine could focus the Jedi Order on the elimination of the Separatists, leaving the Senate to handle the rebuilding of the Republic. However, implied in this decree was that Palpatine would also control all troops under Jedi command, making him Supreme Commander of the Republic's entire military force.

Palpatine then named Anakin Skywalker as his personal representative on the Jedi Council. While the Council agreed, it refused to grant Skywalker the status of Jedi Master. With the destruction of the Jedi Order at the hands of Emperor Palpatine, the Jedi Council ceased to exist.

Decades later, Luke Skywalker longed to re-establish the Council, but the New Republic Senate feared that it would give the Jedi an elitist presence. However, when Cal Omas was elected Chief of State, he vowed to work with Luke on re-creating the Council. They agreed to create an Advisory Council that consisted of 6 Jedi and 6 New Republic officials, mirroring the 12-seat Council of the Old Republic. However, in the wake of the Swarm War, Master Skywalker decided to remove the Jedi from the Galactic Alliance's Advisory Council, instead forming a dedicated Jedi High Council to govern the actions of the new Jedi Order. The Jedi continued to support the Galactic Alliance, and were available for advice.

The outbreak of the Alliance's war with the Confederation, forced the Jedi Council to make some harsh decisions. While the Jedi Order was sworn to support the Galactic Alliance, many of the Jedi Council's members openly criticized Jacen Solo and Cha Niathal when they began manipulating the law to take control of the Alliance for themselves. Grand Master Skywalker eventually was forced to confront the fact that his nephew had become a tyrant, and he declared that the Jedi Order no longer supported the Galactic Alliance.

*Jedi Council Chamber*

**Jedi Council Chamber** A circular room located atop the Jedi Council Spire of the Jedi Temple on Coruscant. It had windows along all its walls, providing a complete 360-degree view of the cityscape below, along with 12 seats for Council members.

**Jedi Council Spire** The southwest spire of the Jedi Temple on Coruscant, it served as the hub of all the activities of the Jedi Order. The Council Chamber was located at its apex, providing a complete view of the cityscape below.

**Jedi Council Tower** *See* Jedi Council Spire.

**Jedi Covenant** *See* Covenant.

**Jedi Credit** Also known as JedCreds, these Corellian medallions were minted whenever a native of Corellia became a Jedi Master. They were emblazoned with the Jedi's likeness and given to friends, family members, and students. With the rise of the Empire, these coins became quite rare and valuable. Rogue Squadron pilot Corran Horn wore one about his neck as a good-luck medallion. His real grandfather, Nejaa Halcyon, had given a number of them to his friends and relatives, including Rostek Horn. Rostek later passed it to Hal Horn, who passed it to his own son, Corran.

**Jedi Crusaders** Another name for the Revanchists, Jedi Knights who actively participated in the Mandalorian Wars some 3,963 years before the Battle of Yavin.

**Jedidiah** This unusual being, a member of the Velmoc species, spent most of his life dream-

*The Jedi Council listens to a young Anakin Skywalker.*

ing of becoming a Jedi Knight. However, with the advent of the New Order, Jedidiah's dreams were put on hold. He became an adviser and confidant of the royal family of Velmor, and pledged himself to keeping the planet free of Imperial control. When the Empire finally subjugated Velmor, Jedidiah helped Prince Denid and his beloved, Loren, flee the planet on a shuttle. In the escape, Jedidiah sustained a number of injuries when the three were forced to crash-land on a remote jungle world. Loren died in the crash. Jedidiah survived, and nursed Denid back to health. However, the crash isolated Jedidiah, and his already damaged mind eventually snapped. He spent the rest of his days bemoaning his lost dream of joining the Jedi, and would answer only to the name "Jedi." He carried a gnarled wooden stick, claiming it was his lightsaber. Once back on Velmor, Jedidiah regained his touch with the Force when Luke Skywalker used the Force to help fight Traal and Zelor. Jedidiah went to help Luke, but was shot and killed by Captain Traal.

Jedidiah

***Jedi Dreamer*** This custom-built New Republic scout craft was commanded by Korren Starchaser. It was 51.8 meters long, and was streamlined for flight in atmospheres. It required a pilot and copilot to operate, and could accommodate up to four passengers and 10 metric tons of cargo. It was armed with a pair of front-mounted laser cannons and a turret-mounted tractor beam projector.

**Jedi Enclave** The name used to describe the facility that housed the Coruscant-based members of Luke Skywalker's new Jedi Order in the wake of the Yuuzhan Vong War. The massive facility was similar in many respects to the old Jedi Temple, but was considered more of a secondary facility that supported the efforts of the Jedi facility on Ossus.

**Jedi Exile** An ancient Jedi warrior whose name was lost to history, she was a former Padawan stripped of her connection to the Force and set adrift in the galaxy in the years after the defeat of Darth Malak. She had been exiled by the Jedi Order for having followed the Revanchist in the Mandalorian Wars. After the Jedi Civil War nearly destroyed the order, the Exile discovered a renewed link to the Force when her ship, the *Ebon Hawk*, was discovered in deep space by a group of Sith devotees and Jedi Master Kreia. Although the Sith Lord, Darth Sion, was unaware of the Exile's true nature, Kreia believed her to be among the last of the Jedi. She reluctantly agreed to be trained by Kreia, after learning that they shared a bond through the Force.

Jedi Exile

After escaping Darth Sion at Peragus II and learning that five Jedi Masters had survived the Jedi Civil War, the Exile set out to locate them in an effort to begin rebuilding the Jedi Order. Along the way, she learned that one of the members of her party, Atton Rand, had been trained in a limited use of the Force, and the Exile agreed to further train him. After finding all the surviving Jedi Masters and getting them to regroup on Dantooine, the Exile was dismayed to learn that Kreia was not the Jedi Master she claimed to be. Instead, she was actually Darth Traya, part of the triumvirate of Sith Lords who were plotting on Malachor V to take over the galaxy. She set out to hunt them down, defeating Darth Nihilus at Telos and Darth Sion on Malachor V before confronting her teacher. Although Traya was more powerful, the Exile managed to defeat her in combat. Before killing her, though, she demanded to know something of the future, hoping that any information would guide her path. Taking the dead woman's words at face value, the Exile returned to Dantooine to complete her training as a Jedi, then disappeared into the Unknown Regions and was never seen again.

**Jedi Exploration Corps (ExplorCorps)** A traveling Jedi academy in existence almost 300 years before the Battle of Naboo. Hundreds of Jedi Masters and their students boarded starships every year to see the galaxy firsthand, rather than from the vastly overpopulated city-planet Coruscant. Voyages beyond the walls of the Jedi Temple gave the students an opportunity to experience cultural diversity and to face the unknown. Most members of the Jedi Exploration Corps were already Padawans, though a significant number were pulled from their duties with the Agricultural Corps to join in ExplorCorps' travels.

*A Twi'lek member of the Jedi Exploration Corps*

***Jedi Explorer*** A sleek two-being starship Luke Skywalker used to go to Ossus with Kam Solusar to search for ancient Jedi lore that might be hidden there. It was designed to navigate uncharted hyperspace routes, and had a huge cargo hold. It also transported an experimental T-77 airspeeder for planetside use. It was well armed with laser and ion cannons. The *Jedi Explorer* was destroyed when the cloned Emperor's dark side aides mounted an all-out attack on the secret settlement code-named New Alderaan.

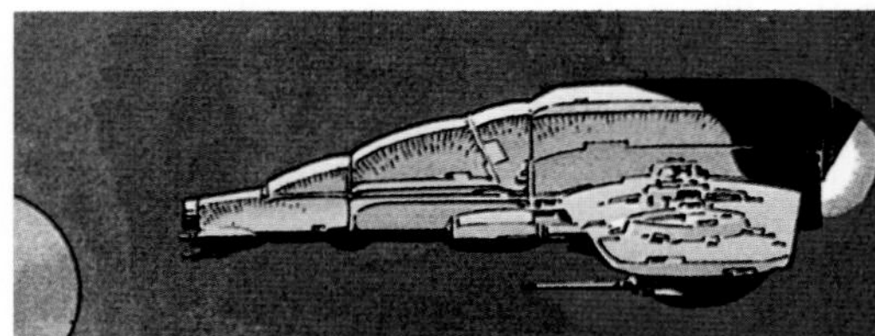
Jedi Explorer

***Jedi Explorer II*** The second two-being starship Luke Skywalker used. He flew this one to Ossus to head off Palpatine's attempt to obtain Ysanna bodies from which to manufacture clones.

**Jedi Flow** This simple technique, developed by the Jedi Knights, taught one to understand and feel the energy of the Force. By studying Jedi Flow, one could learn to allow the Force to flow across and around the "boulders" and obstacles within one's body. If these emotional and physical barriers could be moved, the Force could flow more freely, allowing one to reach a deeper connection to the world around. The achievement of Jedi Flow involved bringing into unity one's breathing, motion, and alignment. In this way, Jedi Flow was also an excellent military training exercise, as Kit Fisto discovered while training a group of ARC troopers on Ord Cestus.

Jedi General Obi-Wan Kenobi

**Jedi Focus Disciplines** The art and practice of meditation to increase the amount of damage done in combat. The disciplines included Ataru, Makashi Djem So, Sokan, Juyo, and Vaapad.

**Jedi Forge** A ceremony attributed to the followers of the Ashla, on Tython, after the Force Wars. During the ceremony, potential Force-users were required to take control of the Force and forge a blade of steel into a sword. With enough control, the candidates honed the blade to incredible sharpness, as well as centering their own connection to the Force. Over time, the ceremony was altered when it was discovered that laser beams could be controlled in such a way as to form a blade of pure light and energy, and the first lightsabers were created.

**Jedi general** The rank given to those members of the Jedi Order who were given command of an Army Corps or Army Legion during the Clone Wars. Each Jedi general worked side by side with a clone marshal commander to lead the corps.

**Jedi Giant** The reverential term used by the Yuuzhan Vong to describe Ganner Rhysode, who died on Coruscant shortly after the planet was terraformed into the new Yuuzhan'tar. Rhysode gave his life to protect Jacen Solo, who was attempting to make contact with the World Brain. Drawing incredible energy from the Force, Rhysode single-handedly killed or injured hundreds of Yuuzhan Vong warriors before eventually succumbing to their sheer numbers. However, his bravery and determination in the face of certain death earned him high respect from the Yuuzhan Vong. After his death, they believed that Rhysode lived on in the afterlife as the Guardian of the Gate to the Lands of the Dead. His blazing lightsaber shone in the darkness, forbidding the spirits of the Dead from returning through the Gate to harass the living. Above the Gate, the Yuuzhan Vong believed, were the words NONE SHALL PASS, written in Basic, as these were the last words Rhysode cried before the Yuuzhan Vong attacked. After his death, Rhysode also was referred to as The Ganner, as if he were a new Yuuzhan Vong god.

**Jedi-Gon** This was Guerra Derida's nickname for Qui-Gon Jinn.

**Jedi healer** A Jedi with the ability to heal others using the Force. Healers were experts in the art and science of medicine.

**Jedi Heresy, the** Another name for the Prophet's Message, used originally by Yuuzhan Vong Supreme Overlord Shimrra to put his negative spin on a growing belief among the Shamed Ones that the Jedi were good and decent, and would free them from their oppression.

**Jedi High Council** Although many beings associated this name with the ancient Jedi Council of the Old Republic, this new incarnation of the Jedi Council was created during the Yuuzhan Vong War when Master Luke Skywalker realized that he needed to provide more guidance to the many Jedi Knights who were fighting throughout the galaxy. The initial members of his inner circle included himself; his wife, Mara Jade Skywalker; Kenth Hamner; Jacen Solo, his sister Jaina, and his younger brother Anakin; the healers Cilghal and Tekli; Kyp Durron; and Octa Ramis. Under Master Skywalker's guidance, this group agreed to become part of the Galactic Alliance's Advisory Council in an effort to unite their forces against their common enemy, the Yuuzhan Vong. In order to balance the Jedi with the non-Jedi, the High Council's membership was reduced to Master Skywalker, Cilghal, Kenth Hamner, Saba Sebatyne, Tresina Lobi, and Kyp Durron. The Jedi continued to serve as part of the Advisory Council until Master Skywalker realized that the new Jedi Order could no longer be viewed as an extension of the galactic government. Thus, the true Jedi High Council was established during the Swarm War, with Master Skywalker serving as the Grand Master of the Jedi. Assisting him on the High Council were Mara Jade Skywalker, Cilghal, Corran Horn, Kyle Katarn, and Kyp Durron.

Jedi Holocron

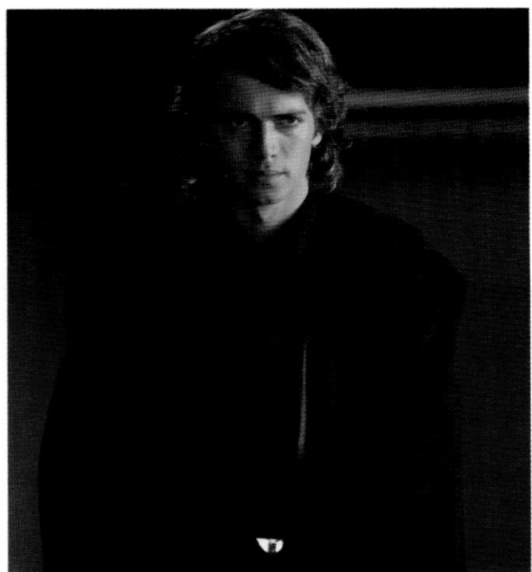
Jedi Knight Anakin Skywalker

**Jedi Holocron** This specialized variant of a standard holocron was a repository of Jedi knowledge and teaching. These legendary artifacts were glowing crystal matrices that employed primitive holographic technology, along with the Force, to provide an interactive learning device. Mysterious designs were etched into the Jedi Holocrons, hinting at their true age. Such a holocron usually could be activated only by a Jedi, who then could seem to have a conversation with the long-dead Jedi whose teachings infused it. Most Jedi Holocrons were created prior to the Battle of Ruusan, and very few survived the era of the New Order, as Emperor Palpatine collected all manner of holocrons—both Sith and Jedi—in order to garner new information about the use of the Force.

**Jedi Hunters** A gang of bounty hunters who worked on Cularin during the Clone Wars. They adopted the name because they answered the call of the Separatists to bring in Jedi Knights for interrogation. The presence of the Jedi Hunters on Cularin forced the Jedi Knights at the Almas Academy to be mindful of their activities, which hampered their ability to protect the system.

**Jedi Interceptor** *See* Eta-2 *Actis* interceptor.

**Jedi Jewels** A mysterious pair of Jedi Knights who led a small band of clone troopers into battle during the Clone Wars.

**Jedi Justice Cruiser** Developed by Republic Shipyards for the express use of Jedi Knights, these 68-meter-long gunboats were heavily armed and protected. Each Jedi Justice Cruiser carried a turret-mounted double turbolaser cannon, an ion cannon, and a pair of concussion missile launchers. Requiring a crew of five Jedi to operate, each of these ships could accommodate up to seven passengers and 100 metric tons of cargo. After the events of the Stark Hyperspace Conflict, many of the Jedi Justice Cruisers were decommissioned by order of the Jedi Council, which did so in an effort to eliminate the Senate's fear of the Jedi Order's military might.

**Jedi Killer** The term used by many residents of the Cularin system to describe General Grievous, who wreaked havoc in the system during the early stages of the Clone Wars.

***Jedi Killers*** A common nickname used by smugglers and other lowlifes to describe those JK series security droids that were modified to serve as combat droids. Because of several documented battles in which a JK series droid defeated a Jedi Knight in combat, *Jedi Killers* became a popular nickname for the droids.

**Jedi Knights** Protectors of the Old Republic from the time the Jedi Order was founded some 25,000 years before the Galactic Civil War, they were the guardians of justice and freedom, the most respected and powerful force for good for more than 1,000 generations. The Jedi seemed to have supernatural skills, especially when wielding their lightsaber weapons. But a Jedi's real strength and power always came from an ability to tap into and manipulate the Force.

In the beginning, the Jedi were scientists and scholars who debated the unusual energy field—the Force—that seemed to emanate from certain individuals. Over time, as knowledge and understanding of the Force grew, this loose affiliation coalesced into the Jedi Order. It protected the Republic from all threats and its members often settled disputes and fights over control due to their overall neutrality and ability to search out the truth via the Force. After the destruction of the Great Hyperspace War and the Great Sith War, the Jedi and the Old Republic began to work closer together, combining their strengths to ensure that no further threats to the galaxy erupted into full-scale war. Over time, however, the Jedi became a highly insular Order, rarely mixing with the very citizens they were sworn to protect. They wrapped themselves in rules that led to stagnation.

When Senator Palpatine assumed the throne of galactic Emperor, he realized that the Jedi Knights were the only ones who could truly stand between himself and the galaxy, so he eradicated them. The most notable Jedi to have survived were Obi-Wan Kenobi and Jedi Master Yoda. Quietly, other Force-sensitive beings also managed to survive the initial Jedi Purge. There were perhaps 10,000 active Jedi in the galaxy when Senator Palpatine took control. Luke Skywalker began training new Jedi more than 20 years after the fall of the Old Republic, and there were roughly 100 active Jedi Knights when the Yuuzhan Vong invaded the galaxy, with dozens more in training. During the conflict their numbers were reduced by half, and most of the survivors were children who were not yet trained to become full Jedi Knights.

As Master Skywalker contemplated his new understanding of the Force—not a simple delineation between light and dark, but a more profound definition of the ways in which good and evil fight for control of an individual—he chose not to return the Jedi to their roles as an unbiased police force. Skywalker reasoned that the Jedi Knights of the Old Republic were once a meditative Order that had been drawn deeper and deeper into the machinations of the Republic when its Chancellors called for their help in mediating disputes. As these calls escalated into the battle legions of the Clone Wars, the Jedi became less interested in the nature of the Force and more interested in separating good and evil into light and dark halves. The Jedi of the Old Republic, according to Skywalker, lost sight of the fact that the Force moved through individuals, not from them.

Skywalker allowed Kam Solusar and Tionne to reestablish a training center on Ossus, which served as the foundation for a new Jedi Order. In the wake of the Yuuzhan Vong War, the new Jedi Knights put aside the original Jedi Code and sought to use their connection to the Force to determine the morally right course of action. With the combination of the light side and the dark side into a single notion of the Force, a new Jedi Knight was free to use whatever means necessary to ensure that the Force remained in balance. Many within the Galactic Alliance feared that this simply allowed the Jedi to rationalize any actions, giving them free rein to do as they pleased.

**Jedi Library (1)** Located in the Lost City of the Jedi, this building held records of the Jedi from thousands of years before the Galactic Civil War. It housed a vast central computer as well as archives of ancient manuscripts and books. It was rumored that the knowledge of all the sentient species of the galaxy was stored there.

**Jedi Library (2)** Another name for the Jedi Archives during the final years of the Old Republic.

**Jedi Library of Ossus** *See* Great Jedi Library of Ossus.

*Jedi Master Yoda*

**Jedilore** The name of a street in the city of Xakrea on Darkknell.

**Jedi Master** An honorific given to the greatest of Jedi, those who were strong enough in the Force and patient enough in life—and even beyond—to pass on their skills by teaching a new generation of Jedi. In the darkest days of the Empire, nearly all the Jedi Masters were hunted down and killed. But on the backrocket planet of Dagobah, a 900-year-old Master named Yoda managed to survive to train the first of a new generation of Jedi, Luke Skywalker.

During the early years of the Jedi Order, Jedi Masters often took more than one apprentice, spreading their knowledge whenever possible. This changed after the Battle of Ruusan, when the Jedi Knights believed that they had become too scattered to control. Taking a cue from the Sith, the Jedi Council limited a Master to a single Padawan learner. This limitation was removed in the wake of the Battle of Endor, as Master Luke Skywalker was forced to train as many individuals as possible to rebuild the Jedi Order.

**Jedi Meld** *See* Force-meld.

**Jedi Mind Juice** The name given to a viscous, greenish fluid secreted by the cochlera of Genarius. It was so named because when harvested and immediately vacuum-sealed, it could be imbibed allegedly to give the drinker limited protection against the Force. This property was not widely documented, as no scientific investigation was done.

**Jedi mind trick** *See* Force mind trick.

**Jedi Order** The name given to the complete membership of Jedi Padawans, Jedi Knights, and Jedi Masters, as well as the guidelines for their training and actions. During the early millennia of the Old Republic, the Jedi Order was separate from the government, existing as a group of monastic warriors who contemplated the Force and their place in the galaxy. Over time, the Order agreed to serve as the peacekeeper of the galaxy, working with the Old Republic to ensure that justice was carried out.

The Jedi Order was nearly wiped out in the wake of the Great Sith War, when the Sith Lords banded together and decimated the Jedi Council. The surviving Jedi fled to Dantooine, and eventually rebuilt the Order. During the Draggulch Period, the role of the Jedi began to change, especially after several Jedi served as Supreme Chancellors of the Republic in order to help the Republic regain a measure of control and leadership.

A little more than a millennium before the Galactic Civil War, the Jedi Order was placed under the control of the Judicial Department by Supreme Chancellor Tarsus Valorum, although its actions were governed by the Galactic Senate. In this relationship, the Senate oversaw the activities of the Order, but the Jedi were free to carry out their missions within their own guidelines. The Jedi Order was governed by the 12-member Jedi Council, which made the final decisions on its missions. At this time, the membership of the Jedi Order numbered more than 10,000, and stayed at roughly that number for 1,000 years.

Many believed that the Jedi Order eventually grew too insular, and was no longer in touch with those they had sworn to protect. After Emperor Palpatine killed most of the Jedi Knights with the execution of Order 66, the Order was all but eliminated for decades. To the galaxy at large, the Jedi were painted as the real traitors of the Clone Wars: Imperial propaganda implicated the Jedi in the creation of the clone troopers and the manipulation of the Senate.

The details surrounding Palpatine's own disfigurement were twisted in such a way that it appeared the Jedi had tried to assassinate him, rather than arrest him, and that he'd had no choice but to fight back. Darth Vader's brutal assault on the Jedi Temple became a simple call for surrender that was met with lightsaber attacks, forcing the 501st Legion to fire against the Jedi in order to subdue the brewing Jedi Rebellion.

*Jedi Purge: The horror of the slaughter of the younglings*

To many, including some Jedi, the destruction of the Jedi Order happened because the Order had become wealthy, almost privileged, and believed that it was entitled to exist forever. This sentiment was especially strong in the Outer Rim Territories, where beings already felt disenfranchised by the Galactic Senate. Of course, it was all along part of Palpatine's plan to discredit the Jedi.

When Luke Skywalker finally established his Jedi praxeum on Yavin 4 several decades later, he started out by using the basic guidance he had received from Obi-Wan Kenobi and Yoda for his own training style. However, he avoided the formation of a new Jedi Order in an effort to separate his students from the government. While this allowed Master Skywalker to rebuild the Jedi Knights, he still had to battle the prejudices that had been formed against Jedi during the final decades of the Old Republic and the era of the New Order.

When the Yuuzhan Vong invaded the galaxy and challenged all known beliefs about the Force, Master Skywalker was forced to form a new Jedi Order centered on the knowledge that both the light and dark sides of the Force were simply aspects of a single power. Based on this, the new Order was founded on the belief that Jedi Knights should act to ensure that there was balance in the Force, regardless of the way in which they achieved it.

In the wake of the Qoribu crisis, Master Skywalker felt that the Jedi had lost their identity and their place in the galaxy. Thus, he vowed to become more of a leader and less of a guide, hoping that the reestablishment of a leadership council would restore the Jedi to their rightful place as the guardians of peace and justice in the galaxy. His leadership was never more necessary than when Jacen Solo and Cha Niathal assumed control of the Galactic Alliance following a thinly veiled coup in which Chief of State Cal Omas was arrested for breaking laws Jacen had brought into force. Luke struggled to reconcile the basic tenets of the Jedi Order with the changing political situation; the murder of his wife, Mara Jade Skywalker, did little to clarify things. Eventually, Luke came to the realization that Jacen Solo was becoming a tyrant, and he declared that the Jedi Order could no longer support the Galactic Alliance. At the Battle of Kuat, the Jedi abandoned their mission, leaving the battle zone and regrouping at Kashyyyk. For the first time in millennia, the Jedi Order existed as a separate entity, all ties to the galactic government severed.

**Jedi praxeum** The name chosen by Luke Skywalker to describe the Jedi training facility he established on Yavin 4 during the early years of the New Republic. The word *praxeum* loosely meant "school," and was first coined by an ancient Jedi named Karena, who used it to describe a "distillation of learning combined with action." Luke chose to develop his school as a place of education and discussion, and was always tolerant of individual errors, which he believed only helped an individual to grow. This philosophy didn't provide the New Republic's government with a good sense of security, especially after Kyp Durron destroyed the Carida system. The government chose to ignore these problems, pushing the blame squarely onto Skywalker's shoulders.

**Jedi Prophecies** A series of vague foretellings that predicted various surges in dark side conflicts throughout the galaxy.

**Jedi Purge** In order to solidify his position of power, then-Chancellor Palpatine knew that he needed to eliminate the Jedi Order. His plan had started years earlier as he helped to sow public discontent and uncertainty about the Jedi and their goals following the Battle of Naboo. As the Clone Wars erupted across the galaxy, Palpatine cultivated the fear that the Jedi were becoming too powerful and too militant, and the people began to demand more information from the Jedi Council. The Council reacted by becoming even more secretive, which served Palpatine's plans.

In the wake of the Battle of Coruscant and Palpatine's unmasking as Sidious, Mace Windu and a group of Jedi Masters tried to bring the Sith Lord to justice. With the help of Anakin Skywalker, Palpatine was able to destroy the Jedi Masters, then went to the Galactic Senate and described the battle as an attempt by the Jedi to seize control—the so-called Jedi Rebellion. With the Senate now behind him, Palpatine issued the command to execute Order 66 to his clone commanders, who were spread across the galaxy fighting the Outer Rim Sieges. Upon hearing the order, the clone commanders turned their weapons on the Jedi Knights and Masters who were fighting alongside them. Within the space of a day, a huge number of Jedi were executed by the clones, and the Jedi Purge was begun. Over the ensuing months and years, Palpatine hunted down any surviving Jedi, until he believed that Anakin Skywalker—who had become Darth Vader—was the only surviving member of the former Jedi Order.

**Jedi reader** *See* Force detector.

**Jedi Rebellion** The term used by Chancellor Palpatine to describe the supposed "uprising" of the Jedi Order against the Old Republic after the Battle of Coruscant. It was Palpatine himself—in the guise of Darth Sidious—who ordered the extermination of the Jedi Knights throughout the galaxy, an action he took under the pretext that the Jedi were trying to overthrow the Galactic Senate and take control of the galaxy for themselves. Palpatine claimed that the "Jedi Rebellion" was stopped only by the swift thinking and initiative of the clone commanders of the Grand Army of the Republic.

**Jedi Revolt** *See* Jedi Rebellion.

**"Jedi Rocks"** This tune was made popular by Evar Orbus and His Galactic Wailers. It remained a hit for the band's new incarnation, the Max Rebo Band. The band played this song for Jabba the Hutt just prior to the planned execution of Luke Skywalker and Han Solo.

**Jedi's Fire** A term used during the last decades of the Old Republic to describe a naturally occurring weather phenomenon that could also be experienced near force-field generators. Jedi's Fire was essentially a localized electrostatic discharge that caused the sky to light up with eerie flickers of light. Any beings close enough to the discharge experienced the odd sensation of having the electricity dance along their bodies.

**Jedi Shadows** The name of a secretive band of Jedi Knights who devoted much of their time to gathering information on the users of the dark side of the Force, including the Sith. The Shadows were first formed millennia before the Great Sith War, and were often charged with infiltrating Sith territory in order to gather information.

**Jedi shuttle** The common term used to describe the fleet of speeder buses that were modified for use by the Jedi Knights of the Old Republic. These shuttles often had improved hull plating and communications systems.

**Jedi–Sith War** *See* New Sith Wars.

**Jedi stance disciplines** These taught Jedi how to hold their bodies so that the Force was channeled through them to master their defensive abilities, and to decrease the amount of damage done to them by opponents in combat. They included Center of Being, Shii-Cho, Niman, Makashi, Soresu, and Shien.

**Jedi starfighter** *See* Delta-7 Jedi starfighter; Eta-2 *Actis* interceptor.

**Jedi Temple** Located in Galactic City on Coruscant, this complex of spires and buildings was the base of operations for the Jedi Knights during the last 40 generations of the Old Republic. Construction of the Temple was proposed by the Jedi to the Galactic Senate following the Great Hyperspace War, when the original Jedi Temple on Ossus was destroyed. Despite the Senate's desire to recognize the efforts of the Jedi in defeating the Sith, the Temple met with many obstacles. First, the Senate feared that a Jedi stronghold on Coruscant would increase the likelihood of another Sith invasion. Second, the Senate wanted to avoid any direct association of the Jedi Order with the government. The Jedi, however, had no intention of making either mistake, and established a training and meditation center that would serve as a temporary base of operations for the Jedi Council. The site chosen for the Temple was strong with the Force, and was originally set aside as a holy place by the natives of the planet.

*Jedi Temple stands out in crowded Coruscant skyline.*

In the aftermath of the Great Sith War, both the Jedi and the Senate agreed that a tighter union of their forces was necessary to ensure the safety of the galaxy, and the Jedi Temple was allowed to expand and become the center of the Jedi Order. The central Temple Spire rose a kilometer above the surrounding cityscape, and was surrounded by four individual Council Towers. All five towers were supported by the main building, which sank its roots deep into Coruscant's crust. The ziggurat shape of the main building, coupled with the five spires, was meant to symbolize a Padawan's path to enlightenment through the Force. It was also meant to focus the energies of the Force, giving those within a near-continual connection to the mystical energy field.

There were several contemplation stations located on each of the four smaller towers, where Jedi could go to be alone with their thoughts. Each of the four towers faced one of the ordinal directions, and all bristled with antennas and sensors that provided the Jedi with continual information from across the galaxy. The front of the building was accessed by the Processional Way, and was defined by huge pylons that depicted images of the Four Masters who founded the Temple. Many Jedi historians wondered at the placement of the Temple on Coruscant, from which all native life had been swept by the millennia of urbanization—yet more than a trillion beings lived out their lives there.

During the final days of the Clone Wars, the command was issued by Chancellor Palpatine to execute Order 66 as part of his sweeping plan to assume control of the galaxy for the Sith. Few realized that Palpatine was actually Darth Sidious, and that Anakin Skywalker had fallen from the ranks of the Jedi and assumed a position as Sidious's apprentice, Darth Vader. One of Vader's first acts was to escort the 501st Legion to the Temple, where they slaughtered every Jedi present. Vader himself killed the younglings, and no being was left alive in the attack. The firefights that ensued caused large amounts of damage to the Temple, which began to burn, casting a cloud of smoke over the Coruscant skyline. Obi-Wan Kenobi and Master Yoda later infiltrated the Jedi Temple to reset the signal that called all remaining Jedi home in an effort to prevent further deaths.

In the aftermath of the Jedi Purge, the Temple remained standing, but was abandoned. Propaganda claimed that the 501st arrived at the Jedi Temple to bring the Jedi to justice, but troopers were forced to open fire when the Jedi ignited their lightsabers and attacked them. During the early months of the New Order, it was rumored that former Jedi Knights were being held prisoner in the Temple, but this was a ruse meant to lure unsuspecting Jedi back to Coruscant. The Jedi Temple became an object of fascination for local Coruscant residents, and the wealthy even thought it a symbol of status if they were allowed into the building.

Over the following decades, much of the Jedi Temple was destroyed by either war or demolition, and it eventually was reduced to rubble. Jedi Master Luke Skywalker debated whether or not to build a new Temple, fearing that such a symbol of a centralized power structure may have led to the downfall of the earlier Jedi Order. In the wake of the war against the Yuuzhan Vong, Skywalker agreed to the construction of a Jedi Enclave on Coruscant, as a satellite of the facility established on Ossus.

The building was donated to Skywalker and his new Jedi Order by the Reconstruction Authority of the Galactic Alliance after the Yuuzhan Vong War. Located on Coruscant, the new Temple was ostensibly a gift from the government, although most Jedi understood that it was more propaganda effort than actual gift. The Reconstruction Authority had been working to move the center of the galaxy's government back to Coruscant, in an effort to restore order. Although Master Skywalker graciously accepted the gift of the new Temple, he did not immediately move the Jedi Order's operations from Ossus to Coruscant. In shape, the new Jedi Temple was a gleaming pyramid of stone and transparisteel, and was considered by many to have been one of the most beautiful examples of Rebirth architecture. After the Ossus compound was abandoned, the pyramidal Temple on Coruscant became the primary training facility of the new Jedi Order.

**Jedi training remote** A specialized form of remote that was used by the Jedi Knights of the Old Republic to train Padawans in the use of a lightsaber for defense.

**Jedi trials** The name given to the series of milestones a Jedi Padawan had to successfully complete to earn the rank of Jedi Knight. Before the trials could begin, students had to first construct their own lightsaber and demonstrate proficiency in wielding it, from an offensive standpoint as well in self-defense. Among the later trials was a demonstration of facility with the three aspects of the Force: alter, control, and sense. Knowledge of the Jedi Code and its application, and the use of sound judgment were also key trials. Finally, students had to accept and complete a solo mission, without instruction or guidance from their Master. The mission could be prescribed by the Jedi Council, or it could be a past mission that demonstrated an ability to act alone. Only when all the trials were completed would the Jedi Council consider a student for promotion.

**Jedi Underground** The name used to describe the underground network of beings who helped Jedi Knights escape persecution at the hands of the Yuuzhan Vong. Many members of the Jedi Underground worked to clear the way for the Great River.

**Jedi Weapons Master** The title given to only a few members of each generation of Jedi Knights during the centuries leading up to the Battle of Ruusan. The Jedi of this time were known for their martial arts skills and training, and many of them found that certain studies of the Force allowed them to further enhance their military skills. Only a handful were ever elevated to the rank of Jedi Weapons Master, and these were revered for their skills.

**Jedi Who Was Shaped, the** The term used by the Ryn and other species to describe Tahiri Veila after she was rescued from the Yuuzhan Vong.

**Jedi X-83 TwinTail fighter** *See* X-83 TwinTail.

**jeeblies** A slang term used by Imperial stormtroopers and other military personnel to describe a feeling of unease or fear that sometimes accompanied an individual's first combat experience. Many recruits worried about going into combat, and their commanding officers did everything they could to prevent the jeeblies, so that no stormtrooper froze up on the front line of battle.

**Jeen, Kibh** A Jedi apprentice who trained under Master Qornah 160 years before the Battle of Naboo. When the pair was dispatched to the Cularin system to investigate the dark side energies found on Almas, Qornah was more curious than afraid, but Kibh Jeen was unprepared for the power of the dark side of the Force. Upon entering the system, he began hearing dark-side whispers, and succumbed to them fully when they landed on Almas. In a blind rage, he cut down Master Qornah and entered an ancient Sith temple on the planet. After staying for several months, Jeen emerged and began taking control of the system. He and his followers destroyed large portions of the floating cities on Genarius, until his actions were discovered by the Jedi on Coruscant. During what became known as the Dark Jedi Conflict, Jeen and his minions were rooted out and destroyed by the Jedi.

**Jeera, Naktu** This Kadas'sa'Nikto was a known associate of Longo Two-Guns before the Battle of Naboo. Jabba the Hutt issued a bounty for his capture in connection with the ambush of a Twi'lek supply convoy near Mos Gamos; it eventually was claimed by Jango Fett.

**Jeffers** General Irrv's aide on Culroon III. Jeffers was killed when Kloff, feigning submission to the Empire, stabbed him with the ceremonial sword given to Kloff by Irrv.

***Jeffrey*** A Rebel Alliance corvette that operated during the Galactic Civil War.

**Jeh** This H'kig glyph was considered too sacred to write out, and was often simply known as *j*, as in the planetary name J't'p'tan. The rough translation of the glyph to Basic was "the imminent," one of the mystical references of the H'kig religion.

**Je'har** This species was native to Almania. Je'har were more powerful than the humans who shared their world. Despite their warlike nature, the Je'har built magnificent cities. Both species supported the Old Republic, and resisted the onslaught of the Empire before pledging allegiance to the New Republic. However, shortly after the death of Grand Admiral Thrawn, the Je'har began to assert their dominance over their human neighbors. They started enslaving them and torturing them at whim. There were even reports of wholesale slaughter during the Yevethan Purge. One survivor of the domination was Dolph, who became somewhat gifted in the use of the Force and saw a way to overthrow the species. Using his remotely activated droid bombs, Dolph wiped out the Je'har, although he spared their leaders—whom he tortured for a week to avenge the week of suffering they put his parents through.

**Jeh Bonegnawer** One of the largest restaurants in the Mos Eisley Spaceport during the early years of the New Republic. In addition to a sizable Corellian menu, Jeh Bonegnawer also served a wide variety of live and cooked meals, catering to the diverse palates of the spaceport. Tables were often hard to come by.

**Jeht, Darrus** A former student of Mace Windu, distinguished by his black eyes and black hair, he was sent to bring word to Lanius Qel-Bertuk and the rest of the Almas Academy, that the Jedi Council was recalling all available Jedi to assist in augmenting the forces of the Old Republic during the Clone Wars.

Jeht's assignment was to oversee the transfer of personnel to Coruscant, and then assist in training the Padawans who remained on Almas. In this capacity, he and Lanius spent hours discussing the galactic situation, as well as honing their combat skills with a lightsaber. He once had a near-fatal run-in with Asajj Ventress during which he was almost lost to the dark side. Later, he vanished into a temporal rift with a ship and crew, and was never heard from again.

**Jeisel, Sian** This Devaronian Jedi Master was one of many who felt that the Jedi Order was becoming too militaristic and as corrupt as the Old Republic it served. She left the Order to follow Sora Bulq to Ruul to protest Jedi participation in the Clone Wars. When Master Mace Windu arrived on Ruul to mediate a truce, Jeisel acted as the voice of reason among Master Bulq's more militant followers. When it was revealed that Bulq and Asajj Ventress were in league, Jeisel and Master K'Kruhk decided to help Master Windu to eliminate the threat Bulq and Ventress posed. But she couldn't bring herself to return to the Jedi Order. However, after seeing the atrocities Count Dooku committed in the name of freedom, Jeisel decided that the Republic was worth fighting for, and she returned to the war with Master Tsui Choi. Their ship was attacked near Drongar, and boarded by Dooku himself, who let the Jedi return to Coruscant, but ordered his forces to eliminate any clone troopers aboard.

Jeisel later served as a general under Quinlan Vos and Oppo Rancisis during the Siege of Saleucami, although she was unable to fully trust Vos's motivations. When the battle for control of the planet was launched, Jeisel and Master K'Kruhk were placed in charge of the ground forces that attacked the Separatist stronghold. After the Republic's forces were successful, mainly due to Vos's surprising success against Bulq, Jeisel began to trust Vos again.

When the command to execute Order 66 was issued, Jeisel was among a handful of Jedi who escaped execution. She fled to a remote area of the galaxy, where she lived as a fugitive while trying to figure out how to remain a step ahead of the bounty hunters hired to eliminate any survivors. Jeisel and Master K'Kruhk crash-landed on a remote planet, where they found a group of Jedi Padawans.

*Shad Jelavan*

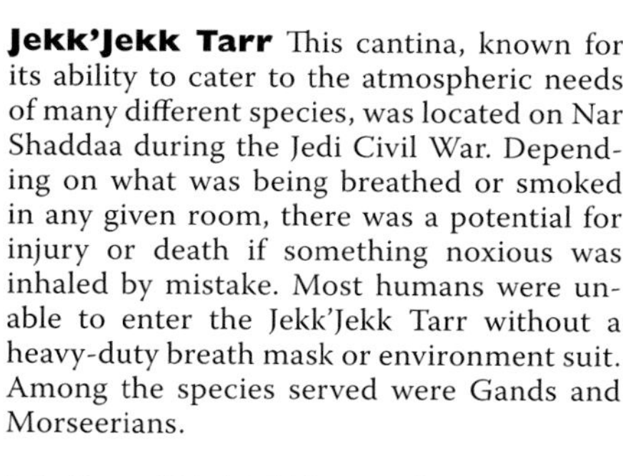

**Jek** This clone trooper was part of a diplomatic escort group that accompanied Yoda to the Rugosa moon during the Clone Wars. Jek favored heavy firepower and often lugged around a Z-6 rotary blaster. Yoda tried to assure him that his mind was a greater weapon than his blasters.

**Jekk'Jekk Tarr** This cantina, known for its ability to cater to the atmospheric needs of many different species, was located on Nar Shaddaa during the Jedi Civil War. Depending on what was being breathed or smoked in any given room, there was a potential for injury or death if something noxious was inhaled by mistake. Most humans were unable to enter the Jekk'Jekk Tarr without a heavy-duty breath mask or environment suit. Among the species served were Gands and Morseerians.

**Jela'han** This Twi'lek owned a starship repair and modification garage on Tatooine during the Empire. He obtained most of his parts from Shellar, since the two had a deal to overcharge clients for referrals to their respective businesses.

**Jelasi** This Hutt was one of Kumac's main rivals, both during Jabba's leadership of the Hutt crime empire and after Jabba's death. Many inside Jabba's organization believed Jelasi was Jabba's chosen successor. In the wake of Jabba's death, Jelasi assumed control of the Ig'zxyck Flare organization and began to "legitimize" Hutt criminal activities. This earned him the ire of many Hutts, including Kumac, during the early years of the New Republic. Jelasi earned the business of much of the Imperial Remnant during this time.

**Jelavan, Shad** One of the most promising Jedi Padawans being trained by Master Lucien Draay on Taris after the Great Sith War. Shad was orphaned as an infant in Middle City with his sister Shel, when their parents were killed in an accident. He was discovered by a Jedi who recognized his connection to the Force, and was trained almost from birth. Despite his obvious skills with the Force, Shad remained a loyal friend to his fellow Padawans, including the often inept Zayne Carrick. He continued to urge Zayne to work hard, explaining that the galaxy needed more Jedi Knights regardless of their skill level. He even tried to buoy Zayne's spirits by claiming that he believed Zayne was simply acting foolish in order to lull the other Padawans into a false sense of security. Shad and the others were invited to a special ceremony by Master Lucien and the other Jedi instructors on Taris to mark their achievements and ready them for their futures. Unknown to the Padawans, however, was the fact that Lucien and the Masters were planning to murder the Padawans. Before they could react, Shad and the others were cut down by their instructors. Only Zayne survived, having arrived late to the ceremony. The media reacted to the story with intense interest, and dubbed the four murdered Padawans as the Taris Four.

*Shel Jelavan*

**Jelavan, Shel** This young woman was Shad Jelavan's sister. She was also an orphan, after their parents were killed in an accident in the Middle City of Taris. She became good friends with Shad's fellow Padawan, Zayne Carrick, until Zayne was believed responsible for the murder of his graduating class of fellow Padawans, including Shad. Shel grew to hate Zayne and wanted to avenge the death of her brother. Goaded by Jedi Covenant member Raana Tey, Shel almost succeeded in her mission, but the truth eventually surfaced that it was the Covenant that had killed her brother and not Zayne.

**Jelldar** One of the six major continents found on Celanon.

**Jellrek, Antoll** This ruthless Imperial Moff controlled the Galov sector during the New Order. A gaunt-looking man with a pointed beard, Jellrek lived on Romar. He died after Platt Okeefe and Tru'eb Cholakk killed Big Quince during their escape from slavery.

**Jellyfish Cove** This small planetoid was the site of an Imperial prison colony during the Galactic Civil War. It was covered with rolling oceans broken by a barren, twisted landscape. The deserts were littered with statues of sensuous humanoids. When the sun was shining, the statues were beautiful to behold. When the sunlight disappeared, though, they suddenly came to life. They were actually a species composed of unique tissue that solidified in sunlight. The prison colony was scantily staffed, for the Imperials were just as susceptible to the humanoids as the prisoners. Thus, many times the Empire employed smugglers or down-on-their-luck spacers to guard the outpost. The prison ships made sure to deliver their cargoes during the day, so as to avoid the humanoids.

**Jelok** This man was part of the Empire's research team MS-133, and was working among the ruins of Aaris III when the native Aaris began attacking the team. It was Jelok who discovered the Place of Kastays, but his request to continue exploring the ruins during the Aaris attacks was overruled by Dr. Brunou.

**Jelon, Commander** This Imperial Navy commander served as Admiral Greelanx's second in command during the Battle of Nar Shaddaa.

**Jelwick** The capital city of Handooine.

**Jemba** This Hutt was placed in charge of Offworld Mining Company's operations on Bandomeer. As ruthless as any other Hutt, Jemba relied on slave labor and sabotage of his competitors' operations to remain at the top of the heap. Among the rumors that surrounded Jemba was the story that he destroyed a rival's atmospheric containment system at a mining outpost on Varristad, killing over a quarter of a million beings and ensuring a huge profit for Offworld. During a regular run to collect guards and slaves for use in the mines of Bandomeer, Jemba and his lieutenant, Grelb, were caught aboard the transport barge *Monument* when it came under attack by pirates. They had been pestered by the investigations of Obi-Wan Kenobi and Si Treemba, and after being forced to land on an uncharted world, Jemba vowed to eliminate the Jedi and reclaim his workers. However, while Jemba was trying to kill Qui-Gon Jinn and starve the Arconan workers of his competitors, his camp was attacked by draigons. Grelb tried to shoot young Obi-Wan, who was fighting off the draigons, but managed instead to hit Jemba. The blasts from Grelb's blaster pierced Jemba's hearts, killing him instantly and rendering his efforts for naught.

*Jempa, a member of the Bear Clan*

**jemian** This small, avian creature was domesticated and raised for its tasty eggs.

***Jemlaat*-class yacht** This ancient starship was produced by Hyrotil. It employed a variety of passive propulsion systems, including solar sails to collect interstellar radiation and harness the movement of solar winds. Because of these limitations, the original *Jemlaat*-class ships were developed for in-system use only. Adventurous pilots were known to travel among star systems whenever the proximity of stars provided them with sufficient solar winds, but this type of travel was dangerous at best. Should a pilot get caught between stars without enough solar wind, a meager sublight engine was used for emergency propulsion. The *Jemlaat*-class yacht measured 22 meters in length, and could accommodate up to four passengers and 20 metric tons of cargo. Hyrotil later produced a version of the *Jemlaat*-class yacht equipped with sails alone, but these craft were produced for racing activities only.

**Jemmy** This gambler and his comrades, Tol and Chral, were known for their ability to separate wealthy gamers from their credits. They traveled the galaxy in search of casinos where the other gamblers were usually amateurs, in order to increase their chances of winning. They were aboard the *Ananuru Express* when Hakon de Ville tried to auction off information on a secret Imperial project sometime after the Battle of Yavin.

**Jempa** This young Whiphid was a member of the Bear Clan of Jedi students before the Battle of Geonosis.

**Jen** A teenager who was part of the Rebel Alliance forces dispatched to Sulon to help local forces in their attempt to throw off Imperial subjugation. Jen died when a missile exploded, killing all the Rebels in its blast radius.

***Jen'ari*** An ancient Sith term that literally meant "dark lord." It was first used to describe the Exiles who subjugated Korriban in the wake of the Hundred-Year Darkness, giving rise to the title Dark Lord of the Sith.

**Jenbean, Lieutenant** This officer served at the Senatorial Communications Center on Coruscant, and was the watch officer on duty when the Separatists aired a transmission from Praesitlyn in which Reija Momen was forced to read a prepared statement from Pors Tonith. Jenbean brought the message straight to Chancellor Palpatine but was confused when Palpatine chose not to act on the transmission, preferring to wait to see how events on Praesitlyn fell out. His confusion led to anger, and he decided to send a copy of the transmission to someone he felt would be able to save Momen.

Greeata Jendowanian at Jabba's palace

**Jendar Campaign** The name given to the battles fought for control of Jendar during the Galactic Civil War.

***Jendirian Valley*** This Coruscant-based AA-9 transport ship was pressed into duty ferrying refugees from the city-world during the months leading up to the Battle of Geonosis. Anakin Skywalker accompanied Senator Padmé Amidala back to Naboo aboard this ship after a second attempt was made on her life.

Colonel Jendon

**Jendon, Colonel** This Imperial colonel was a former test pilot, and was the first to fly the TIE defenders that rolled off the production line. Before the Battle of Endor, Jendon served as Darth Vader's personal shuttle pilot.

**Jendorn** A planet in the Borderland Regions. It was the site of a major battle between the New Republic and the Empire following the Galactic Civil War. This battle was noted for the way in which Gottu and Idow attacked and subdued an Imperial outpost near Bruzion with just a vibro-ax and a pair of blasters.

**Jendowanian, Greeata** This Rodian served as a dancer for the Max Rebo Twelve shortly before Jabba the Hutt's death on Tatooine. She was ostracized as a child because she loved music and dancing more than hunting and killing. Her parents tried their best to change her into a "normal" Rodian child, but she resisted. Instead she studied the music of various cultures and learned how to dance. After completing her schooling on Rodia, she managed to sneak aboard the *Kuari Princess* and caught the attention of Sy Snootles. Sy asked her to play kloo horn in a concert, and Greeata happily agreed, often working a second gig at the Green Planet nightclub on Tothis. After a rowdy Rodian suggested that Greeata return to Rodia and marry him, Greeata and Sy left the *Kuari Princess* and eventually caught up with Evar Orbus and the Max Rebo Band. Members took in Sy, since they needed a singer, but would only take Greeata if she could dance, and then only on a per-diem basis. Greeata was eventually made a full member of the band. Following Jabba's death, Greeata and Lyn Me used their survival skills—Greeata *had* learned something in school on Rodia—to help the band survive the desert and the tumult that followed. Greeata and Ryståll Sant later joined the Palpatones, where they were reunited with Joh Yowza. Greeata became their lead singer, and her voice captivated a huge audience, giving her a popularity that outshone anything she had experienced before.

**Jenet** A scavenging species from Garban in the Tau Sakar system. Jenet had incredible memories and were considered quarrelsome by other species. These pale pink-skinned creatures with red eyes and sparse white fur quickly colonized the other worlds in their star system after developing starships. During the Galactic Civil War, the Empire turned the Jenet colonies into labor camps.

**Jeng, Sarrissa** This Jedi Knight was in command of the mediation team dispatched to Atzerri shortly after the Battle of Antar 4, in an effort to negotiate the release of the Gotal Emissary Nathanjo Nirrelz. Nirrelz had been kidnapped by Roshu Sune agents, who were demanding that Antar 4 secede from the Old Republic. Jeng and her fellow Jedi tried to negotiate Nirrelz's release, but the terrorists opened fire on them. Two Jedi were killed in the firefight before Jeng and the remaining Jedi neutralized the Roshu Sune fighters. They managed to free Nirrelz unharmed. Shortly afterward, Jeng was one of the many Jedi dispatched to Geonosis to rescue Obi-Wan Kenobi and ascertain the size of the Separatist threat. She was among the many Jedi who died during the Battle of Geonosis.

Sarrissa Jeng fights off a Geonosian.

**Jengardin double-bladed vibroblade** A unique and dangerous weapon developed by the Jengardin Millennial Warriors.

**Jengardin Millennial Warriors** One of the most infamous military orders founded on Iotra. The Millennial Warriors never engaged in full-scale war on their home planet. They were eventually consolidated into the Iotran Police Force.

**Jengus** This Jawa and his family left Tatooine shortly after the murder of an entire Jawa clan by Imperial stormtroopers. He hoped to join his nephew Squig, but was stranded at Cordel Cove on Neftali for starship repairs. The port master at the time agreed to let his family have free run of the facility if Jengus would agree to serve as the starport's head technician. He quickly agreed, and oversaw all the machinery and mechanical maintenance of Cordel Cove. Jengus and his twin sons also oversaw the management of the underground hot springs of Cordel Cove, catering to the whims of tourists of all species.

***Jen'jidai*** An ancient term used by the Sith people of Korriban to describe the first of the former Jedi Knights who arrived on their planet in the wake of the Hundred-Year Darkness. These newcomers were wielders of the dark side of the Force, and referred to themselves as the Exiles.

**Jenks** This New Republic technician was actually an Imperial spy. It was Jenks who provided the location of the Republic's base on Nespis VIII to the reborn Emperor Palpatine.

**Jenks, Commander** A clone trooper commander who was with Obi-Wan Kenobi and Anakin Skywalker when their gunship crashed on Ruhe.

**Jenks, Losibaru** This woman was the chief financial officer of

Jenet

the Salliche Agricultural Corporation during the years before the Clone Wars.

**Jenn, Commander** This Rebel Alliance commander was a good friend of Ensign Till, whom she teased at any provocation. She was killed in an attack by TIE phantoms.

***Jennie Lee*** Rone Taggar's X-wing starfighter. Part of the 21st Recon Group, the *Jennie Lee* was named for Taggar's mother.

**Jennir, Dass** One of the many Jedi Masters who accepted military positions when the Clone Wars erupted across the galaxy. White-haired Master Jennir was assigned the command of the Grand Army of the Republic force dispatched to secure New Plympto during the final stages of the Clone Wars. When the command to execute Order 66 was issued, Master Jennir barely escaped into the jungle with his life. After the fall of the Jedi Temple, Jennir agreed to help the Nosaurians in their ill-fated struggle against the Empire. After their defeat, he had a brush with the dark side when he killed a being in anger while trying to rescue refugees who had been sold into slavery. Jennir eventually was able to reconcile his actions with the Force.

**Jenny** This young girl frequented the Mos Eisley cantina at the height of the New Order, looking to hitch up with a good-looking pilot. She tried to hit on Han Solo just before the Corellian pilot was hired by Obi-Wan Kenobi and Luke Skywalker to transport them to Alderaan.

**Jenreal, Sersae** A social analyst and reporter for *Eye on Cularin* before the Battle of Naboo.

**jenruax** One of the many crystals used by the ancient Sith Lords in the construction of a lightsaber. A refined form of the opila crystal that had been stripped of any impurities, jenruax was believed to have given the wielder enhanced dexterity in combat.

**Jens** This young woman was a student of xenoarchaeology at the University of Agamar during the early stages of the Yuuzhan Vong War. Jens was part of the team that traveled to Bimmiel with Anki Pace to search for Jedi artifacts. She discovered the differences among various beetles used by the Yuuzhan Vong to patrol the areas they controlled.

**Jensaarai** The Force-wielding population of Suarbi 7/5, who were brought up to follow the *Saarai* teachings of Nikkos Tyris. The term *Jensaarai* was a Sith word that meant "hidden followers of the True Way." They were trained as Jedi, and even taught how to create their own lightsabers, but also learned that Obi-Wan Kenobi was one of the greatest users of the dark side of the Force. There were three ranks of Jensaarai: Apprentices, Defenders, and Saarai-kaar. When they became Defenders, the Jensaarai crafted a unique form of

Dass Jennir fights on New Plympto.

personal armor from cortosis ore designed to make them appear to be vicious creatures. There was only one Saarai-kaar at any one point in time. When Leonia Tavira landed on the moon and executed its Imperial Governor, thereby "freeing" them from Imperial control, the Jensaarai quickly grew to trust her. She betrayed that trust and twisted them into a position so that the only way they could protect their people was to serve as her personal warriors. They joined her aboard the *Invidious.* She also told them that there was a being named Halcyon who would be their undoing, so she forced them to kidnap Mirax Terrik in order to draw Corran Horn to Suarbi 7/5. When they all met in battle, Luke Skywalker made quick work of the Jensaarai while Horn battled the Saarai-kaar. They did not kill the Jensaarai, though, a fact that surprised them when they regained consciousness after the battle. The Saarai-kaar decreed that the Jedi were no more evil than the Jensaarai, and agreed to consider sending a delegation of her followers to Yavin 4 for formal training under Skywalker.

**Jensen** A moisture-farming family on Tatooine. The Jensens were friends with Ariq Joanson, although they opposed his plans to try to make maps of peace with the Jawas and Sand People.

**Jentari** The name given to the huge cybernetic organisms bred to be the factories of Zonama Sekot. The Jentari were actually tree-like creatures that understood the needs of Sekot and channeled Sekot's energy into the constructs built within them.

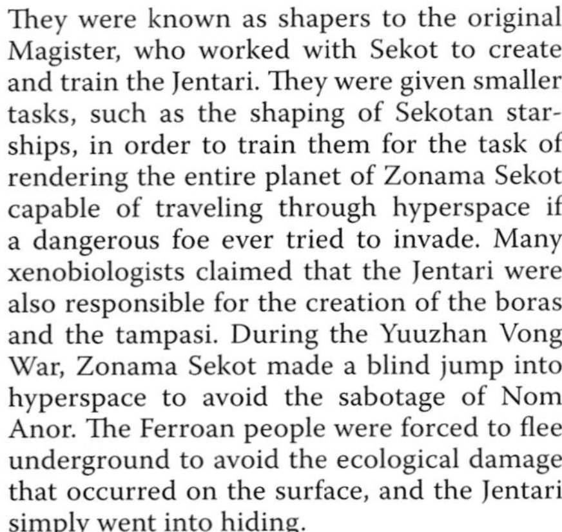

They were known as shapers to the original Magister, who worked with Sekot to create and train the Jentari. They were given smaller tasks, such as the shaping of Sekotan starships, in order to train them for the task of rendering the entire planet of Zonama Sekot capable of traveling through hyperspace if a dangerous foe ever tried to invade. Many xenobiologists claimed that the Jentari were also responsible for the creation of the boras and the tampasi. During the Yuuzhan Vong War, Zonama Sekot made a blind jump into hyperspace to avoid the sabotage of Nom Anor. The Ferroan people were forced to flee underground to avoid the ecological damage that occurred on the surface, and the Jentari simply went into hiding.

**Jentawui** This frozen ball of rock and ice was the seventh and outermost planet in the Both system.

**Jenth-44** The Imperial sleeper cell placed on Pakrik Minor by Grand Admiral Thrawn.

**Jenth Grek 51** This was Erk H'Arman's call sign during the Old Republic's defense of Praesitlyn some two and a half years after the Battle of Geonosis.

**Jenton, Evitch** This Imperial Governor was placed in command of Ebra during the early years of the New Order. He quickly instituted martial law, and approved the enslavement of the Ebranite people.

**Jenuwaa Sea** A vast ocean located on Kalee. San Hill told General Grievous that his body had been recovered from the banks of the Jenuwaa Sea after his shuttle was sabotaged and exploded.

**Jenwald, Lyndelah** This woman was part of the Red Hand Squadron that assaulted Ylesia, under the command of Bria Tharen, shortly before the Battle of Yavin. She sustained several injuries during the assault, but survived.

Jeodu

**Jeodu** A species of blocky humanoids with large mouths and cone-like heads who appeared to be made of stone. Prince Dequc was a Jeodu.

***Jeolocas*** This Gallofree personal transport was owned by a Corellian man who signed on with the Peace Brigade just prior to the Battle of Coruscant. Alema Rar and a team of Jedi were aboard the ship when it was turned over to the Yuuzhan Vong, but the Jedi managed to overpower the crew and intercept the aliens.

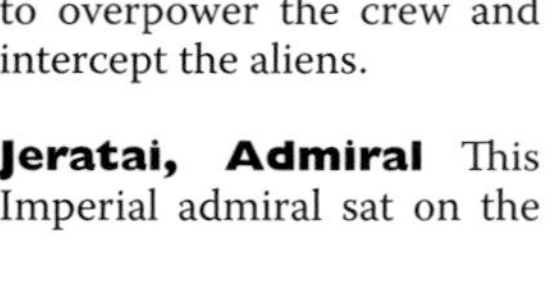

**Jeratai, Admiral** This Imperial admiral sat on the

Imperial Interim Ruling Council. He supported General Immodet's belief that the being who killed Burr Nolyds and Admiral Banjeer was a nonhuman.

**jerba** A shaggy, horse-like pack animal native to Tatooine, the jerba also was raised to provide pelts and leather when it died.

*Jerba*

**Jerec** A Dark Jedi, he came into power sometime after the Battle of Yavin, collecting six disciples in a quest for riches and power. He was unmistakable in a crowd, with a thin, blindfold-like mask covering the holes where his eyes should have been. Dark tattoos embellished his mouth and chin, and his bald pate was accentuated by a heavy brow. He was completely blind, but used the Force to appear to "see" despite his injuries. Many beings assumed that Jerec was a human who had lost his eyes in battle, but he was actually a Miraluka, and thus was born without the ability to see. He was discovered by Jedi Master Jocasta Nu during her tenure with the ExplorCorps. He trained as her Padawan and learned of her insatiable desire for knowledge, eventually becoming one of the Jedi Order's foremost archaeologists. After becoming a Jedi Knight, he took Ameesa Darys as a Padawan and eventually became a Jedi Master.

Jerec was dispatched to recover ancient artifacts just before the Jedi Purge took place. He returned to Coruscant to find the New Order fully established, and tried to flee. He and his team eventually were captured by High Inquisitor Tremayne and returned to Coruscant. Rather than allow himself to be killed, Jerec pledged his allegiance to the Empire and obtained training from the Dark Side Adepts of Palpatine's own Prophets of the Dark Side. After sufficient training, Jerec served Emperor Palpatine as an Inquisitor for many years. During the Galactic Civil War, Jerec was tasked with obtaining the entity known as Spore for the Emperor's use. He tracked Spore to Ithor and offered it the chance to control thousands of minds if Spore agreed to work for him. Jerec had hoped that Spore would take control of the crew of his warship, the *Vengeance.* However, Spore had its own plans, and used the *Vengeance* to hunt down Tash Arranda. As it tried to follow her through the asteroids near Ithor, a group of space slugs began battering the Star Destroyer, knocking out its shields and causing it to explode. It was unknown how Jerec survived the explosion, but he managed to escape in a Starfly and ordered a recovery team to pick up the pieces of the *Vengeance.* The primary piece was the ship's computer core, which he later installed in the *Vengeance II.*

Jerec was given access to Emperor Palpatine's *Dark Side Compendium,* and believed that he could establish the dark side elite on his own. Palpatine sensed Jerec's ambition and cut off his access to the tome, but Jerec never forgot the power of the dark side elite. His quest for knowledge was sparked by the information he found in the *Compendium,* then ignited when he learned of the Valley of the Jedi from Lord Cronal. After the Battle of Endor, Cronal—under the guise of Blackhole—explained to Jerec that Emperor Palpatine had not truly died, as was reported on the HoloNet. Rather, Palpatine was hiding in the Deep Core. Blackhole then urged Jerec to locate the Valley of the Jedi for the honor and glory of the Emperor. He began to collect the individuals he believed would serve as the new dark side elite. Unknown to Blackhole, though, was the fact that Jerec was already planning to find the Valley in order to enhance his own powers. He murdered Qu Rahn and Morgan Katarn in his quest for more information about its location, and ultimately learned of its coordinates on Ruusan. Jerec and his Dark Jedi would have had the Valley's secrets for themselves if not for Morgan's son, Kyle, who defeated Jerec's minions on the very precipice of the Valley's power source. Jerec himself briefly experienced the true power of the Valley, but his rapturous connection was severed by Katarn. Instead of dying, Jerec's spirit was drawn down into the Valley, where it was doomed to linger with the rest of the ancient Sith for millennia.

*Admiral Jeratai*

*Jerec*

**Jerel** This smuggler worked from a base on Byblos.

**Jerell** The leader of the New Republic strike team that helped liberate Ralltiir from Imperial control after the Battle of Endor. His daughter, Bettle, was a member of the team as well.

**Jeremos** This Squib was a noted garbage collector and independent contractor who worked for a variety of employers during the New Order. Jeremos and her crew were called upon to clean out the trash bays of the Imperial Star Destroyer *Indomitable* in the months following the Battle of Hoth.

**Jerev** One of the many mining settlements, or *o'bekis,* established on Goroth Prime. It was close enough to the planet's equator to suffer electromagnetic discharges from the planet's debris ring.

**Jerg** This tall, gaunt man was a merchant captain during the early years of the New Order. Known for his Republic-era captain's hat, as well as the fact that he never seemed to wear shoes, Jerg made regular runs in the *Cyclops* from the Sullust system. He was a discreet individual who sold his services to the highest bidder but never broke the confidence of his customers. It was for this reason that Morgan Katarn selected Jerg to help ferry refugees from Sulon to Ruusan when the Empire took control of the moon.

**Jerga** This young Mon Calamari Jedi Knight was one of a handful stationed on Ossus. She was charged with protecting the Jedi training facility there during the Galactic Alliance's conflict with the Confederation. When Vis'l and Loli were killed by Galactic Alliance Guard soldiers under the command of Major Serpa, Jerga struggled mightily to remain calm and hidden, hoping to find a way to stop him. However, when Tionne Solusar was badly injured by Serpa, Jerga tried to intervene. Several GAG snipers were able to get off shots of their own, and Jerga was shot in the head and killed.

**Jergo** This Kubaz made a living as a sellsecret in the city of Mos Espa on Tatooine, during the early years of the New Republic. When Kitster Banai tried to make off with the moss-painting *Killik Twilight,* Jergo tried to take the artwork for himself. Kitster's friend Wald knocked Jergo unconscious with a hydrospanner, allowing Kitster to escape.

***Jericho*** This Rebel Alliance Nebulon-B frigate was part of a small fleet dispatched to destroy a pirate base shortly before the Battle of Endor.

***Jericho's Pride*** This custom-built yacht, formerly known as *Royal Flower,* was the smuggling ship owned by Jericho Donovan and her sister, Josephine. A spear-shaped craft, *Jericho's Pride* measured 30.1 meters long and was armed with a pair of turret-mounted heavy turbolaser cannons. It could carry up to eight passengers and 35 metric tons of cargo, and required a pilot and copilot to operate.

**jerikan** A type of cube-shaped canteen that was used to keep water clean and cool in the deserts of Tatooine.

**Jerimott, Hower** This man served as the primary doctor in the city of Prosperity on Beheboth during the early years of the New Republic.

**Jerius** This Kentra king ruled the city of Kariish, on Orellon II.

**Jerjerrod, Moff** An Imperial Moff, Jerjerrod controlled the Quanta sector before being named commander of the second Death Star. He was chosen for the position because Palpatine wanted to avoid the hubris that killed Wilhuff Tarkin and lost the first Death Star. Jerjerrod—a contented, unambitious sort of man—fit Palpatine's bill perfectly. He was killed when the second Death Star was destroyed by the Alliance.

*Moff Jerjerrod*

**Jerm** A native of Tatooine. He was one of the many youths Amee had a crush on after Anakin Skywalker left Mos Espa for the Jedi Temple.

***Jermagium*-class light cruiser** Manufactured by SoroSuub, this 25-meter light cruiser was unremarkable in design and popularity. It required a crew of two, and could transport up to eight passengers and 85 metric tons of cargo. It was armed with a single laser cannon.

**Jerne** This dead world was, at one time, the homeworld of the Jerni civilization. After the demise of the Jerni, Jerne was colonized by humans and used until it was nearly destroyed. Under the thumb of the New Order, Jerne became a hotbed of rebellious activity. It had two moons. It was here that Leia Organa and Luke Skywalker began searching for the fabled Eternity Crystal, a relic said to control the flow of time.

**Jerrahg** This gruff man owned and operated the Tailfin Cantina on Lamaredd around the time of the Battle of Naboo.

**Jerresk** This Quarren was the leader of a band of pirates based on Fluwhaka. His pirates attacked several New Republic supply ships about five years after the Battle of Yavin, and he was placed on the Republic's Most Wanted list. Jodo Kast took a Republic bounty to hunt down Jerresk's pirates after Jerresk himself was captured by Republic fighter pilots.

**Jerriko, Dannik** An Anzati assassin over 1,000 years old, Jerriko was known in the underworld as the Eater of Luck. He was a predator who would just as soon suck the life force out of a victim as say hello. Like others of his species, he had a proboscis coiled in his cheek pockets. In an attack, he uncoiled this flexible organ, inserted it into a victim's nostrils, and pierced the brain of his prey. Jerriko not only drank his victims' blood, he sucked up what he called the "soup" of their future.

As an Anzati, Jerriko operated with almost total anonymity; thus, he preferred to work for people who needed other bounty hunters, killers, and assassins taken out. While stopping over on Tatooine, he visited Mos Eisley. There, he knew, he could get some of the best soup from some of the galaxy's most notorious criminals. When Ben Kenobi and Luke Skywalker entered the cantina, Jerriko was at the bar, smoking a nic-i-tain hookah. After the events surrounding the death of Greedo, Jerriko resolved to hunt down Han Solo and drink his soup.

His chance came when Jabba the Hutt received Solo's carbon-frozen body. Jerriko was eager to enter the palace, and would have done so on his own if he hadn't been approached by the Lady Valarian and Eugene Talmont, both of whom wanted him to spy on Jabba. Jerriko took both jobs. Entering the palace, he tried desperately to drink Han Solo's soup, but was deprived of it when Solo was rescued by Luke Skywalker and Leia Organa. Then Jerriko went a little mad, and resigned himself to drinking Jabba's soup. After learning that Jabba had perished at the Pit of Carkoon, Jerriko became even angrier, killing anyone he could find in the palace. He then fled and took on a number of bounty-hunting jobs.

**Jerrilek** A tropical blue world with an impressive set of rings, the planet was 85 percent water. Jerrilek's land was concentrated around the equator, and consisted of two main continents and many smaller island chains. The planet was a vacation and retirement spot for many of the galaxy's wealthy and powerful. One of Jerrilek's largest cities was Graleca, which was located on a small island and was an important part of the local aquaculture industry. There were rumors of strange ruins in the oceans, suggesting that an aquatic species had inhabited the planet. The planet spun very rapidly, completing a day in about 14 standard hours. Five hundred ninety-four of these days made up the planet's year.

**Jerriman, Lieutenant** This man, a member of the Boku Settlement on G'rho, served as a lieutenant in the G'rho Defense Force under Major Brco during the New Order. Jerriman was in command of the militia's starfighter squadron.

**Jerrist VI** This industrial world was quarantined by Corporate Sector Authority after the outbreak of disease.

**Jerrit, Lieutenant** A Mon Calamari in the naval forces of the Old Republic military during the Mandalorian Wars. In response to his heroic actions during the Onslaught, Jerrit was promoted to lieutenant.

**Jerritech** This small corporation was based on Jerrilek, and produced a variety of aquatic vehicles during the New Order.

**Jerru** This Ithorian craftsman was proficient in the ancient art of plant-forming. Jerru worked aboard the herd ship *Bazaar,* where he also acted as a front for the Rebel Alliance recruiter Poliss.

**jer'usk (plural: jer'uskae)** This immense, aquatic predator was native to the deep oceans of Goroth Prime. Measuring an average of 75 meters in length, the jer'usk was one of a handful of aquatic beasts that lived its entire life underwater. Jer'uskae were observed breaching their incredible bulks out of the water more than 20 meters, then crashing back. The resulting shock wave stunned all the fish in the immediate area, allowing the jer'uskae to feed with some leisure. When required, a jer'usk could swim quite fast, especially in order to heave its body out of the water.

**jeru tea** A syrupy, sweet tea that had a calming effect when imbibed.

**jer-weevil** This insect was often dried, salted, and served as a snack or appetizer.

**Jes** This stern woman served the Rebel Alliance as a pilot. She was stationed aboard the *New Hope* during the months leading up to the Battle of Yavin.

*Jessa, Doc's daughter*

**Jesa Corporation** This mining and manufacturing business was founded by a woman of high moral character and principles. It was expected that her ideals be taken on by her company officials and become a part of the corporate persona. The first outfit to mine Pergitor, Jesa Corporation helped transform it from merely a beautiful world to a major commercial and scientific location. About 100 years before the Battle of Yavin, the continual mining of the planet resulted in an increase in volcanic activity, although mining did not stop. The resulting volcanic eruptions—brought on by the thinning of the planet's crust—filled the atmosphere with toxic chemicals and rendered the world uninhabitable.

**Jesart Desert** An area on Eliad that was the site of the planet's primary spaceport.

**Jeseej** One of the few Sljees on Coruscant, Jeseej was easily mistaken for a bizarre animal or some form of mobile plant. He looked like a short gray table topped with tentacles and bulbs, moving on a set of squat, stumpy legs. Like all Sljees, Jeseej lacked visual organs and interacted with the world through hearing and touch. He owned and operated Zlato's Place, a failing Toydarian restaurant and lounge that served as a front for his forgery operations. Jeseej employed two amazingly talented Squibs to serve as his forgers. Jeseej also was known as something of a fortuneteller, a hobby he used for additional income. He was sensitive to the Force, and used his minimal connection to "see the future" of his customers.

**Jesfa** This former Zaltin Bacta Corporation employee became a part of the resistance force that worked to free Thyferra from Ysanne Isard's grasp. He worked with Elscol Loro's infiltration team to knock out the Xucphra Corporation's headquarters building shortly before the Battle of Thyferra.

**Jesi** A technician and part-time voice-over reader for the Cularin Central Broadcasting corporation during the final years of the Old Republic.

**jesmin** This species of kelp was native to Mon Calamari, and was harvested from the ocean for use in creating perfumes and incense.

***Jesoni*-class starliner** A model of luxury passenger transport ship produced during the early years of the New Order.

**Jess** A platinum-blond songstress popular at Jabba's palace on Tatooine. She had a way of captivating her entire audience, and often was seen in the company of Boba Fett. She had dreams of leaving Jabba's service and starting her own band.

**Jessa (Vandangante)** Best known simply as Doc's daughter, Jessa was one of the finest outlaw techs in the galaxy, and had a brief fling with Han Solo. She was also an accomplished fighter pilot as well as a mechanic, and often flew in the modified Z-95 Headhunters her father used to defend their base. When Solo showed up and asked for help repairing the damage he did to the *Millennium Falcon* while running guns to Duroon, Jessa agreed to the repairs if he, in turn, would carry some cargo for her. The cargo turned out to be the droids Bollux and Blue Max, but Solo's real mission turned out to be the rescue of Doc from the secret Stars' End prison colony run by the Corporate Sector Authority on Mytus VII.

*Arca Jeth*

**Jessel** The name given to a male leviathan calf born in the oceans of Dorumaa around the time of the Battle of Naboo. It was thought that Jessel and its sibling, Titon, had simply been abandoned by their mother after their birth, but it was later learned that their mother had died in labor. The Alliance for the Creation of Habitable Environments monitored the growth and development of the calves, hoping to preserve what they believed were the only two leviathans left in Dorumaa's seas. In order to track Jessel, a beacon was implanted on his skin. This didn't stop Rufus Trammel from a daring theft of Jessel, in an attempt to reap a huge profit from the species' growing popularity. His plans to sell the beast offworld nearly succeeded, but ultimately were thwarted by a group of freelance agents who managed to release the leviathan.

*Jestefad (rear) and Mustafar*

**Jestan** The Rebel Alliance won a major battle on this planet, which became known as the Engagement at Jestan.

**Jestefad** This immense gas giant was considered the twin of Mustafar, but only because they shared almost the same orbital pathways. Jestefad was the innermost planet of the Mustafar system, and many astrophysicists considered Mustafar to be one of its moons. However, the gravitational forces imposed on the small planet by Lefrani, the outermost planet in the system, kept Mustafar separated from Jestefad and on its own orbital path.

***Jester*** One of the Rebel Alliance's *Carrack*-class cruisers, it operated during the Galactic Civil War.

**Jeswandi** A Bothan martial art, it involved skills used in hand-to-hand combat.

**jet-ball** A type of sports ball equipped with tiny repulsorlift engines that allowed it to move through the air with incredible speed. The discharge of the engines sometimes created a buildup of static electricity around the surface of the jet-ball, causing it to crackle and glow with an eerie light.

**Jeth, Arca** A Jedi Master from Arkania, he came to the galactic forefront during the Great Droid Revolution when he discovered a way to short-circuit a droid through the use of the Force. In the wake of the uprising, he agreed to oversee Onderon. However, rather than become the system's Watchman, he sent Ulic Qel-Droma, Ulic's brother Cay, and Tott Doneeta to the planet. Master Jeth later assisted them there when Queen Amanoa was revealed to have been one of the most powerful Naddists on the planet. After defeating Amanoa's bid for power, Master Jeth concealed Freedon Nadd's Sith lore in a tomb on the Dxun moon. Several months later, he refused Exar Kun's request to see the Sith artifacts from Freedon Nadd's ship. While attending the Jedi Assembly on Deneba, Master Jeth was among the many Jedi who were killed when Krath war droids descended on them. Ten years after the Great Sith War, Jeth's spirit appeared to Ulic Qel-Droma on Rhen Var, urging the distraught man to abandon his plans for suicide and depend on his inner strength to survive.

**jet-juice** A kind of vacuum-distilled moonshine made by many starship pilots during long trips across interstellar distances. Han Solo and Chewbacca hid a metallic flask of this beverage under the control console of the *Millennium Falcon.*

**jet luge** This self-propelled sled was of minimal design, incorporating just enough structure to hold a rider.

**jetster** Another name for a small, jet-powered speeder.

*Dexter Jettster greets a visitor to his diner.*

**Jetters Bar** This nightspot was known for its affiliation with several prominent criminal organizations during the last decades of the Old Republic. The owner of the Jetters Bar was also an agent of the InterGalactic Banking Clan, and often assisted the IBC by placing bounties on those beings who were unable to make their regular loan payments. This allowed the IBC to maintain a good public image while ensuring that customers eventually paid their debts.

**jet trooper** Specialized clone troopers of the Grand Army of the Republic who moved about the battlefield with the aid of jetpacks. They were distinguished from other troopers by the bright green coloration of the armor plating on their arms, as well as a similarly colored stripe down the center of their helmets.

**Jett's Chute** The name given to the section of the Mos Espa Podracing course immediately following Jag Crag Gorge. It led the racers onto Hutt Flats. The Chute later served

*Jett's Chute*

as a section of the noted Mos Espa Circuit, a swoop racing event held annually at the height of the New Order.

**Jettster, Dexter** A male Besalisk with a heavyset body and four thick arms, Dexter—known to his friends as Dex—was a mechanic who worked for various oil-harvesting operations during the years leading up to the Battle of Naboo. He developed a love for cooking during this time, although many of his fellow crewbeings wondered how many of his "special recipes" were imbued with lubricants and oils found on the work site. After spending many years as a smuggler and gunrunner, Dex retired to Coruscant, where he purchased Didi's Café when the previous owner, Didi Oddo, retired. In this role, Dex was able to covertly gather a wealth of information on politicians and businessbeings, which he stored in an expansive data bank. Dexter was introduced to Obi-Wan Kenobi at this time, and served as an invaluable source of information for the Jedi Knight. Obi-Wan discovered that Dex could be an incredibly loyal friend who would kill if necessary, as well as give his life for those he cared about.

Years later, Dexter provided Obi-Wan with information on the Kamino saberdart that the Jedi discovered in the neck of Zam Wesell. The information allowed Kenobi to piece together Jango Fett's role in the attacks on Senator Padmé Amidala. Dexter remained loyal to the Jedi even when public sentiment began to turn against them. In the wake of the Clone Wars, however, Dexter was accused of subversion and aiding the enemies of the Empire, and was targeted for arrest after helping Jedi Master Fy-Tor-Ana. Rather than give in, Dexter abandoned his diner and joined the Erased, hoping to strike back against the Empire at a later time. He was located shortly afterward by Ferus Olin, who had returned to Coruscant in an attempt to track down Fy-Tor-Ana and bring her to safety. Dexter maintained a low profile, establishing a base of operations in the so-called Orange District and helping members of the Erased reach safety.

When Astri Oddo returned to Coruscant with her son, Lune, Dexter agreed to help them find a safe haven where they could start a new life, without the interference of Astri's former husband, Bog Divinian. He also assisted many beings who wanted to find ways to escape from Imperial persecution, and had planned to use his data bank to help Flame start working toward a more concerted rebellion. However, Imperial spies learned of the Orange District operations and destroyed much of the area known as Thugger's Alley. In order to keep as much of the operation going as possible, Dex executed his own escape plans, which involved destroying his data before the Imperials could decipher it. He was shot during his escape, but was pulled to safety by Keets Freely and Curran Caladian.

**jetz** This form of sanctioned combat was popular during the last decades of the Old Republic, and was noted more for its strategy than its brutality. In a jetz match, combatants squared off against each other in a small ring, and spent most of their time searching for weaknesses or mannerisms that could be used to upset their opponents. In many cases, a jetz match was decided on the first fall, so technique and speed often won out over strength and size.

***Jev*** This group of Imperial T-4A shuttles was assigned to protect a sensor net, but was destroyed shortly before the Battle of Endor.

**Jev, Colonel Ilo** An Imperial officer—a native of Wyloff—he grew up as the son of a local broadcast personality, and was recruited by the Imperial News Network. His performance within the Wyloff Sector Plexus was exemplary, and he rose quickly in an area where promotions were scarce. After being promoted to commander, Jev learned that his father had been killed by Imperial agents for being "subversive and treasonous" in his broadcasts. Jev knew this was a lie; his father had been reporting only the truth about Moff Varnier's lack of government. Using his position within Sector Plexus, he learned that Varnier was assassinating any individual who opposed his rule. Varnier even had an agent hidden within the Wyloff Sector Plexus. Angry over his father's death, Jev hunted down the responsible agent and arrested him as a supporter of the Rebel Alliance. He was promoted to colonel and given command of the Sector Plexus. Jev was later recruited as an Alliance agent by Vin Northal, and he agreed to assist as a way to get some modicum of revenge for the billions of lives exterminated by the Empire.

**Jevax** The Mluki chief in charge of the Plawal dome on Belsavis. He greeted Han Solo and Princess Leia when they arrived on the planet, looking for Plett's Well.

**jevesect** This unusual herbivore was native to the agricultural world of Herzob. Measuring about 1.5 meters long, and weighing up to 70 kilograms, the jevesect resembled a huge insect. Its cartilaginous exoskeleton was designed to distribute its body weight, and it moved about on six spindly legs. A pair of wings provided assistance with mobility, although the jevesect did not fly. Instead, it made long hops across the ground. Unlike insects, jevesects breathed using a pair of lungs, and many of their internal organs were more mammalian than insectoid. The jevesects were one of the few creatures found on Herzob that were neither exterminated nor domesticated by the settlers who transformed the planet into an agricultural center. This was due in part to the fact that jevesects went dormant for a time each year, burrowing underground for many months. As the environment and ecosystem of Herzob changed, so did the jevesects, evolving to live without the dormant period. This meant that the jevesects could feed on their favorite foods—the crops grown by the settlers—all year long, much to the dismay of the settlers. The creatures also reproduced quickly, ensuring that new individuals were always being born to replace those lost to exterminators.

Exterminating a jevesect was a tricky proposition, since the average individual had a potent defense mechanism. A small organ in its neck produced a caustic acid, which the jevesect could spray at an enemy through a tube in its forehead. This acid was primarily used to break down plant material for easier digestion, but was an effective deterrent when used in self-defense. One unusual aspect of the species was that it was inexplicably tied to Herzob. Specimens transported offworld died within 48 hours.

**Jewel, The** This former luxury hotel, located on the Smugglers' Moon of Nar Shaddaa, was taken over by the Desilijic kajidic as a base of operations.

**jeweled lizard** One of the many constellations visible from Commenor. It was easy to locate in the night sky thanks to the five stars that made up its tail.

**jewelfish** A species of small, brightly scaled fish.

**jewel-fruit (1)** The fruit of this Mon Calamarian plant was used to create a sweet sauce important in the production of candies.

**jewel-fruit (2)** This tasty fruit from Ithor had a nearly impenetrable shell. But the sweet flesh inside the jewel-fruit was considered well worth the effort.

***Jewel of Churba*** A Dairkan starliner that made regular runs to Coruscant in the years following the Battle of Endor. It transported disguised Rogue Squadron members Wedge Antilles, Pash Cracken, Corran Horn, and Erisi Dlarit to Coruscant for their undercover operation.

**Jewel of the Core** A phrase used to describe Coruscant during the Old Republic.

**Jewel of Zenda** This large, red gemstone was one of the royal jewels of the Naboo. The Jewel of Zenda was traditionally worn in a headpiece by the ruler of the planet, although it could also be set into a pendant and worn around the neck.

**"Jewels"** This song, written and played by Annadale Fayde, was given a scarlet rating by the Imperial Board of Culture. It first appeared on the compilation *Darkness on the Land.*

**Jewett, Darvon** The charismatic Imperial Governor of the Boeus sector during the era of the Galactic Civil War. Following the fall of Emperor Palpatine at the Battle of Endor, he gave his support to the New Republic when the Imperial military forces in the sector retreated to Coruscant. Several starship crews mutinied upon hearing of the Emperor's death, joining Jewett in siding with the Republic. Governor Jewett then helped the New Republic control the Expansion Region.

**Jex** A Cularin native, he was one of a growing number of people who felt that the Thaereian military had overstepped its bounds during the last decades of the Old Republic. Jex's brother was among several hundred citizens who had disappeared. Many quietly attributed these disappearances to the military, which spent the nighttime hours removing any vocal opponents to its control of the Cularin system. Jex himself reported his brother's disappearance to the Cularin Office of Protection and Security, which directed the inquiry to the Thaereians. Jex hid outside the Thaereian headquarters in Hedrett to monitor their transmissions, but picked up only routine communications before the Thaereians called him back to say their search revealed that Jex's brother was no longer on Cularin. Jex knew something was wrong, because he had never overheard any communications regarding his missing brother.

**Jexerian cannon** A primitive projectile launcher noted for the huge report it gave off when fired.

**jexxel** These small, feline predators were native to the tundras of Neftali. Their fur was almost pure white, allowing them to blend in with the snow. Their eyes glowed red, giving them a terrifying appearance. Jexxels often hunted in packs, which allowed them to bring down large prey.

**Jeyell** A planet in the Mid Rim. It was headquarters of Reiber Manufacturing.

**Jez** A clone commando, he was a member of the Aiwha-3 Squad during the Clone Wars. Jez was the only survivor of his squad in the wake of the Battle of Geonosis.

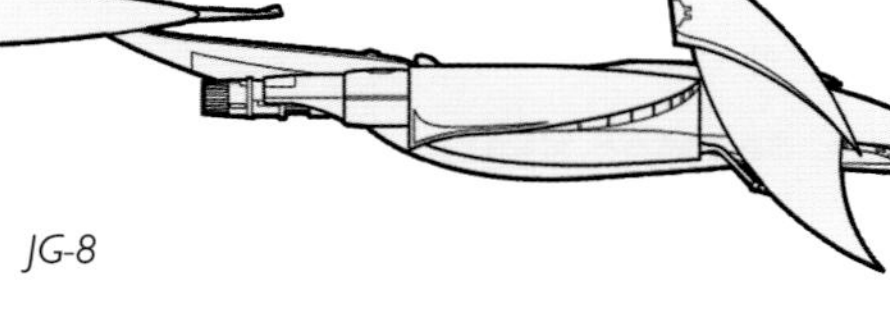

*JG-8*

**Jezzable** This red-haired native of Celanon was a gorgeous but naïve human who hung around the bars of Celanon City during the early years of the New Republic. She spent most evenings flirting with spacers who passed through the city, much to her boyfriend's dismay.

**JG51** *See* Jenth Grek 51.

**JG-8** This luxury landspeeder was developed and manufactured by SoroSuub during the Empire era. It was known for its ornate bodywork and its lack of maneuverability. The two-passenger JG-8 measured 3.8 meters long and had a pair of steering vanes located at the front. The two engines were located at the rear, with one at the base of the vehicle and one atop a rear fin.

**jhabacc** A high-stakes form of sabacc popular in the private gambling rooms of the Outlander Club before the Battle of Geonosis.

**Jhakva** *See* Jhordvar.

**Jhank Shel** This Hutt kajidic controlled Lirra until shortly before the Battle of Hoth, when Imperial Moff Heedra drove its members off the planet and back into Hutt space.

**Jhas** Orbited by 24 moons, this gas giant was the fourth planet in the Hoth system.

**Jhaveek** A noted Mrlssi philosopher who was famous for making the statement, "I know myself to be only as I appear to myself."

**Jhemiti** A Mon Calamarian first officer serving under Uwlla Iillor on the *Corusca Rainbow.* Jhemiti held the rank of lieutenant in the New Republic Navy. He later served as an administrative aide to the commanding officers of the New Republic's military.

**jhen honey** This viscous, amber honey was popular with many Imperial nobles who lived on Bastion during the Yuuzhan Vong War.

**Jhensrus** A jungle planet in the Trax sector, it was known throughout the sector as a frontier world. Jhensrus's inhabitants battled on a regular basis to keep the native creatures at bay, resulting in a population of fighters and survivors.

**Jhepar** A city on Draenell's Point on the continent of Mee'r.

**Jhoff, Controller** This man served in the Imperial Navy as a traffic controller aboard the *Executor* during the Galactic Civil War. It was Controller Jhoff who was on duty when the shuttle *Tydirium* attempted to reach the Forest Moon of Endor. He questioned the age of the security code used by the shuttle's pilots, who were actually Han Solo and Chewbacca, and was ultimately ordered by Darth Vader to let the shuttle land.

**Jhompfi** This Brolfi was a member of the guerrilla movement led by Patriot following the Battle of Naboo. Jhompfi, who lived in the Covered Bush house ring, was one of the Brolfi who was ordered to acquire burst thrusters, which were used to create a missile intended to assassinate Passel Argente and Brolfi leaders. Jhompfi claimed that the burst thrusters were to use on his own speeder bike, which the authorities believed he was using to smuggle rissle sticks to the Karfs. Unknown to Jhompfi, his actions were discovered by Jedi Padawan Lorana Jinzler, who trailed him briefly before she was intercepted by Vissfil.

**Jhonems, Wil** This man was marketing manager for the Spotts TradeChip Company before the Clone Wars. Jhonems believed that sports figures were not the kinds of role models needed in the galaxy as it fell into the turmoil surrounding the secession of planets from the Old Republic. He suggested that Spotts produce a series of TradeChips depicting the images of Jedi Knights, allowing a new generation to find heroes in the Jedi. His plans were met with stern opposition from the Jedi Council, however.

**Jhonterius Park** Located in the city of D'larah, Jhonterius Park was a small yet lovely refuge on Demophon. It was the home of the D'larah palm tree. Despite the park's beauty, however, it was the site of much of the crime that took place in D'larah.

**Jhordvar** This Noghri assassin was employed briefly by Jabba the Hutt during the Clone Wars. When Jhordvar tried to betray Jabba, the crime lord dispatched 13-year-old Boba Fett to bring him to justice. Fett found Jhordvar in Tatooine's Dune Sea, killed him in combat, and returned to Jabba with just Jhordvar's hands. Because a sandstorm had hit the area during the fighting, young Fett was forced to hole up in Jhordvar's hideout, leaving the Noghri's body outside. The wind and sand stripped much of it to bare bone, and the only thing left to identify Jhordvar was the ring he wore on his finger.

**Jhorn, Sergeant Pfilbee** This Imperial soldier was requisitioned for Emperor Palpatine's second expeditionary mission to Endor. The first had returned with poor-quality reporting, and Palpatine wanted more information. Jhorn was records officer, a role he did not relish. His report was bitter and resentful in tone, a fact not ignored by the Emperor. When Jhorn returned from Endor, he was quickly transferred to a long tour of duty riding the solar focusing mirrors orbiting Coruscant. He later was assigned to custodial work for the Imperial garrison on Tatooine.

**Jhosa** This ancient Selkath was a judge in Ahto City, on his homeworld of Manaan, during the Jedi Civil War.

**Jhunia Snow Plains** The northernmost continental area of Neftali.

**Ji** One of Akanah's childhood friends on Lucazec. Ji was a member of the Fallanassi.

**Ji, Phow** A native of Bunduki and a member of the Followers of Palawa. He was an expert in the martial art of teräs käsi. Just before the Clone Wars, Phow Ji won the tournament in Aslaja, defeating the Jedi Knight Joclad Danva in a 47-minute fight. It didn't matter to Phow Ji that Danva had detached himself from the Force for the fight. Ji just knew that he had bested a Jedi Knight in hand-to-hand combat. This only made his considerably large ego even bigger, and he often strutted around looking for a fight, just to prove his skills.

Some two years after the Battle of Geonosis, Phow Ji was hired by the Grand Army of the Republic to serve as a combat instructor on Drongar. He was given the rank of lieutenant and assigned to the military hospital known as Rimsoo Seven, where he found himself confronted with two worthy adversaries: Admiral Tarnese Bleyd and Jedi Padawan Barriss Offee. His mystique was quickly established when he defeated Usu Cley without breaking a sweat, but a captured holovid of his unprovoked killing of three Salissian mercenaries caught the attention of the doctors as well as Den Dhur. The Sullustan reporter chose to craft an article on Phow Ji's wanton disregard for life. Den Dhur portrayed him as an evil murderer, but his editors rewrote the article after learning that the Salissians had been working for Count Dooku. In the end, Phow Ji was painted as a hero of the Republic.

After the Salissian incident, Barriss Offee found that she hated Phow Ji, an emotion that rose to the surface very quickly. Phow Ji recognized this, and took every opportunity to taunt the young Padawan. Offee was forced to swallow her pride, however, when she found Phow Ji on the battlefield near Rimsoo Seven. He had been fighting a squad of Salissians, and had defeated them all. Unbeknownst to both, however, another enemy was hidden in the jungles, and managed to impale Phow Ji with a poisoned dart. Offee could not let another being die in front of her, no matter how much she hated him, and she drew on the Force to remove the poison from his system. But Phow Ji took the Padawan's actions as a slight, and recklessly plunged into another battle in a fit of rage. Without backup and still recovering, Phow Ji was quickly overrun by Salissian mercenaries. However, rather than dying alone, Phow Ji extracted a large grenade and detonated it in his hand, killing the Salissians as well as himself. The news of his reckless act was spun by reporters of the Old Republic into a heroic act that had far-reaching benefits for the war effort.

**Jia, Senator Kvarm** This New Republic Senator represented many worlds in the Tapani sector during the Yuuzhan Vong War. An elderly man, Senator Jia was one of the few supporters of the Jedi Knights in the Senate.

**Jiaan** This planet was subjugated by the Empire during the early years of the New Order.

***Jiaasjen*** A term used by ancient Sith warrior Larad Noon to describe his theory of "integrating the shadow," documented in a series of journals he left behind on Susevfi after he died. Noon tried to meld his Sith teachings with Jedi lore he learned as a child. By integrating the dark side with the light, Noon believed that he could justify the countless deaths he had caused during the Great Sith War. Although scholars debated the morality of *Jiaasjen,* they agreed that Noon wrote the journals to keep himself from going insane with guilt during the final years of his life.

**Jiaguin** The Ansionian god of guile.

**jiangs** Rare pink jewels found on Corellia.

**Jiaozi** One of the larger cities established on Felucia by Gossam settlers. It was the site of a water-processing facility during the Clone Wars.

**Jidlor system** This planetary system was the home of the Swaze species.

**Jid'yda, Admiral** This Bothan served the New Republic Navy, rising to the rank of admiral. When the Republic began its blockade of the Farlax sector and the Koornacht Cluster, Jid'yda was considered as a replacement for Etahn A'baht. He was Borsk Fey'lya's first choice, but was not selected for the position.

**Jielu** A Rebel Alliance soldier at Echo Base on Hoth, he was assigned to the ground forces team led by Corporal Jobin. Separated from its main unit, the team made a daring attempt to recapture the base's ion cannon control center after Imperial forces had it taken over. Thanks to the team's efforts, the final transports were able to escape without harm.

**Jigani Port** The primary spaceport on Desevro. It was located on a rocky outcropping above Maslovar and the Swamplands. This kept it away from the bustle of the city, allowing offworld visitors to get their bearings before venturing into Maslovar. Most of the starship berths were situated atop stone pillars carved from the planet's bedrock, while others seemed to have been cobbled together from older pillars that had fallen over the millennia. Rope bridges connected the berths to the main facility, and spiral staircases carved into the pillars allowed visitors to reach the city itself.

**Jigoba** This Corporate Sector crime lord held a great deal of power before the rise of the New Order. He once employed Ploovo Two-for-One as a loan shark.

**Jiir** This man was part of a militant group that supported Rebel Alliance forces on Ralltiir shortly before the Battle of Yavin. Jiir, his younger brother Basso, and their men planned to rescue Leia Organa after she was apprehended by Lord Tion. Their plans were nearly smashed by the Imperial stormtroopers protecting Tion, but Basso managed to reach Leia. In order to ensure Basso's success, Jiir and his men were forced to prolong their firefight with the Imperials. Jiir was shot and killed in the combat.

*Jiir (left) plans a rescue of Leia Organa.*

**Jiivahar** This species of hairless, tree-dwelling simians was native to Carest 1. Their form appeared lanky and ungraceful, but the Jiivahar were exceptionally limber, and moved through the thykar trees with ease. Their fingers and toes were very long, made for grasping branches, and secreted sarvin to help them hold on. Their skulls were flattened and elongated, with two large cones in the back of their heads. Their skeletons were hollow, making them very light for their size. There were no written laws in Jiivahar society, but every individual was compelled to act according to the needs of the community.

**jijite** These small, insect-like reptiles were native to the open plains of Ansion. They lived in large hives, burrowing into the ground to live among, and feed on, the root systems of the grasses that filled the plains. The jijite workers built tall, stony pillars from minuscule pebbles and an extruded form of mortar, which served to vent warm air from the tunnels below as well as lookout positions for jijite sentries. These pillars were incredibly strong, and could withstand the blunt assault of a kyren flock.

*A jimvu tries to escape attack from a veermok.*

**Jikat, Vrrk** This ancient Nazzar abandoned his own life and family to train Qrrl Toq in the ways of the Ulizra some 4,000 years before the Battle of Yavin. Despite his love of Jikat, Toq never understood the great sacrifice he had made to become Toq's teacher.

**Jiklip, Wildis** Born on Coruscant, the daughter of Corellian parents, she was an exceptional student who was educated on both planets and licensed as a university professor well before her 30th birthday. During the early years of the New Republic, Jiklip disappeared from the public eye, and most of the galaxy feared that she had been killed. However, she had decided to shun the world of academia and take on a career as a smuggler. She changed her appearance, adopted the name Red Stepla, and made a living by carrying unusual cargoes for beings who didn't want to be bothered with the details. Just before the Yuuzhan Vong War, Jiklip returned to the galaxy, taking on the role of a theoretician who had become wealthy over the years and teaching courses on Coruscant and Lorrd. She developed an expertise in the area of interplanetary economics, and became one of the Galactic Alliance's foremost experts on economic reaction to warfare. However, when Thrackan Sal-Solo began making demands for Corellia's independence from the Galactic Alliance, Jiklip once again disappeared, ostensibly to return to Corellia and help its citizens understand the consequences of independence.

**Jik'Tal** This Jawa was the leader of a group hired by Yin Vocta to serve as private security agents at the Bantha Traxx establishment on Lianna. The Jawas were trained by the Rodian mercenary Ne'Chak, who owed Vocta a favor. Jik'Tal had craved adventure as a youth, and was eventually banished from his tribe for violating its policy of nonviolence. Seven other members of the clan left with him, leaving Tatooine behind on the first transport and ending up on Lianna.

**Jiktha** This male Jawa was a junk peddler who worked near Mos Espa before the Battle of Naboo. Jabba the Hutt issued a bounty for his capture after a servant droid he purchased from Jiktha proved to be faulty, and Jiktha refused to refund the Hutt's credits. The bounty was eventually claimed by Jango Fett.

*Jiivahar*

**Jiliac the Hutt** Jabba the Hutt's uncle. Jiliac and his nephew headed clan Desilijic. Durga the Hutt killed Jiliac in a duel, leaving Jabba as the sole ruler of the Desilijic clan.

**Jillsarian** A species of heavily muscled, four-armed humanoids.

**jimvu** A large, reptilian creature native to Naboo, it had six legs, making it a capable runner. The neck of the jimvu was covered with a row of short knobs, and its beak nose was used in defense.

**Jin** This species of reed-thin humanoids was native to the Zchtek worlds of the Mid Rim Territories. They were reptilian, and able to see into the infrared spectrum. Large eyes dominated their short-snouted faces, and their small teeth indicated a herbivorous ancestry. Their coloration ranged from dark yellow to dark green, and tended to match their surroundings. Their homeworlds were subjugated by the Empire early in the reign of Emperor Palpatine. Many young Jin joined the Rebel Alliance.

**Jinart** A shape-shifting Gurlanin, she, her consort, Valaqil, and others of their species agreed to help the Old Republic oust Separatist forces that had taken control of their homeworld, Qiilura, early in the Clone Wars. She went undercover, helped separated members of Omega Squad find one another, and provided vital information on the movements of Mandalorian warlord Ghez Hokan—who had already killed Jedi Master Kast Fulier. Jinart helped the Omegas find Fulier's Padawan, Etain Tur-Mukan. One of the main tasks of the clone troopers was to destroy a Separatist biological weapons lab and try to capture its main scientist, Ovolot Qail Uthan; Jinart helped them achieve both goals. But there was an understood quid pro quo: For all of their assistance, the population of Quiilura would get their planet back—free from the Separatists, the increasing number of human settlers, and the Grand Army of the Republic itself.

As in so many other cases, the Republic failed to live up to its end of the deal, and conditions on the planet worsened. That's when Jinart went to Coruscant and other worlds and started gathering intelligence on the movements of the GAR. She was mistakenly shot by ARC trooper Ordo, then healed by Tur-Mukan. She provided information she had on terrorist bombings on the capital planet. Soon she was pressured to hide Tur-Mukan on Quiilura while the Jedi secretly gave birth to a baby fathered by Omega Squad commando Darman.

**Jinathik** An asteroid belt in the Garqi system, between the worlds of Garqi and Elsho.

**Jinda** This gypsy-like tribe inhabited the Forest Moon of Endor. Believed to be distant cousins of the Ewoks, its members were constantly getting lost. Years before the Battle of Endor, the Jindas were farmers who lived their lives under the protection of the Rock Wizard. When they made the Rock Wizard angry, though, he banished them from his kingdom, forcing them to meander the surface of the moon in search of a new home. After that, Jindas made their living by trading with Ewok tribes and putting on shows.

**Jinda system** This Tapani sector star system was part of the holdings of House Calipsa during the New Order.

**Jinder, J'an Ane** A Jedi Guardian who worked on Mrlsst during the last decades of the Old Republic. To gain passage off the planet, Jinder had to solve a series of logic riddles posed to her by the Mrlssi.

**Jinet** This remote planet in Brak sector was the site of a Rebel Alliance base established shortly before the Battle of Yavin.

**Jing** A young boy, he was one of the many miners working on Katanos VII before the Clone Wars. He had been taught that the Jedi Knights were powerful magicians who could use their connection to the Force to rip out a person's mind. Jing was sent with his father, Andru, to greet Jedi Master Lunis and his apprentice, Obs Kaj, when the pair traveled to Katanos VII to investigate a possible link to the Separatist plan to produce clones. When a Jedi discovered the hidden cloning facility on the planet, Jing was eager to prove himself in battle. However, he was unprepared for the savage attacks of the other miners, and was killed in the fighting.

**Jin'ha** Members of this sinister criminal organization were active before the Battle of Naboo. They were discovered by the Jedi Council to have been mining cortosis ore in an effort to prepare themselves for an attack on the Jedi. Further investigation by Obi-Wan Kenobi revealed that the Jin'ha were, in fact, mining the cortosis for the Trade Federation.

**jinjang** This shrub, native to the Forest Moon of Endor, produced sweet berries that were harvested by the Ewoks.

**Jin-Jin** This Outer Rim smuggler was trained at the Imperial Academy to be a TIE fighter pilot, but botched one too many missions to remain in his commanding officer's good graces. Rather than face a court-martial, he tried to steal a TIE fighter. Forced to hide aboard the *Beggar's Solace,* he was taken on a wild ride when the ship's hyperdrive motivator started acting up. Having escaped from Imperial service, Jin-Jin went to work as an independent mercenary, but his ineptitude continued to dog his career. He was forced to capture an entire royal family after being witnessed trying to rescue their daughter from Imperial custody. When Jin-Jin won a fortune gambling on Mepha'as Prime, he sank it all into real estate on Alderaan a week before the Empire destroyed the planet. Broke, Jin-Jin took the *Beggar's Solace* and set out to make a name for himself as a smuggler. He found that he was good at it, and his bumbles became a thing of the past.

*Qui-Gon Jinn and his Padawan, Obi-Wan Kenobi (left)*

**Jinkins** A Bith, he was a known comrade of the Feeorin smuggler Nym. Jinkins originally was employed as an engineer with the Nubian Design Collective, where he was the lead engineer on the development of the Scurrg H-6 bomber. After the Naboo rejected the ship's design and the Nubians scrapped the project entirely, Jinkins arranged with Nym to steal the only prototype for use as their own vessel. With Nym, Jinkins served as a sensor and scanner operator aboard the newly renamed *Havoc.* Nym considered Jinkins the best engineer in the galaxy, rivaled only by the starshipwrights on Charros IV. He piloted the *Freefall,* a ship he described as a "freefall bomber." Jinkins remained with Nym for many decades, continuing to serve as a chief lieutenant after Nym assumed the leadership of Lok during the New Order.

**Jinn, Qui-Gon** A Jedi Master who was known as one of the Order's most formidable members, but his recklessness and his devotion to bizarre causes kept him from becoming a member of the Jedi Council. Jinn was generally regarded as one of the best pure swordsmen the Order had ever seen. However, he was also something of a maverick, and was unable to control his inner sense of purpose.

His methods were in sharp contrast with one of his contemporaries, a woman named Tahl. They were friends during their training, and both achieved the level of Jedi Knight at about the same time. Qui-Gon wore his hair long in a tacit defiance of the Jedi Order's rules. His control of the living Force was deep, although his abilities with the unifying Force were not as strong.

It was Jinn who discovered the young boy named Xanatos and brought him to Coruscant for training despite his age and spoiled nature. When the Council allowed Qui-Gon to take a Padawan, Qui-Gon chose Xanatos immediately. Qui-Gon either failed to—or chose not to—see Xanatos's many failings, regarding the boy's mistakes and growing anger as minor things, much the way a father would. In the end, this caused many problems. Shortly before Xanatos was to begin his trials to become a Jedi Knight, Master Yoda dispatched Qui-Gon and his Padawan to Telos on an unspecified mission. While there, Jinn was confronted with Xanatos's treachery in attacking a neighboring world.

Qui-Gon was forced to kill Xanatos's father, Crion, in a battle, and earned Xanatos's undying hatred from that point on. The youth fled, and Jinn returned to Coruscant without a Padawan. He claimed that Xanatos had been killed in battle, and vowed never to take another Padawan. He continued to interview new students at Yoda's insistence, but always left without choosing an apprentice.

Years later, Master Yoda sent Jinn to travel to Bandomeer to assist the government in negotiating a mining treaty. The trip put him in close quarters with young Obi-Wan Kenobi, whom he had recently passed up as an apprentice. They were then drawn into the schemes of Xanatos, who hoped to exact revenge on Qui-Gon by killing him on Bandomeer. During their escape from Xanatos's trap in the ionite mines, Qui-Gon and Obi-Wan became linked in the Force, something that was meant to happen only to a Master and his apprentice. After their escape, Jinn realized that Kenobi was not to be taken lightly, and he took the boy as his Padawan learner.

During a joint mission to New Apsolon, Qui-Gon pledged his life to the now–Jedi Master Tahl. Unfortunately, Tahl was captured by Balog and tortured. Qui-Gon was able to rescue her, but the

*Jinda tribe members*

best medical care on New Apsolon was unable to save her life. For many months, Qui-Gon felt broken and out of sync with the galaxy, as his heart mourned the loss of the woman who "made him whole."

More than a decade after Tahl's death and Jinn's many adventures with Kenobi, Supreme Chancellor Valorum asked that a team of Jedi be dispatched to negotiate with the Neimoidians; Qui-Gon and Obi-Wan were sent to Naboo. There they became entangled in the intricate web being woven by Darth Sidious. Their mission quickly changed to the protection of Queen Amidala, whom they planned to transport to Coruscant for an appeal to the Senate. Their ship sustained damage breaking through the Trade Federation blockade, and they were forced to land on Tatooine for repairs.

While there, Qui-Gon discovered young Anakin Skywalker. A check of the boy's blood revealed an incredibly high concentration of midi-chlorians, and after learning of Shmi Skywalker's description of Anakin's conception, Jinn believed that he had found the prophesied Chosen One. He also discovered the existence of Darth Maul, and barely escaped from the Sith Lord with his life. He brought Anakin before the Jedi Council, but was sternly rebuffed for his impertinence. Instead, they were all sent back to Naboo to protect Amidala in her attempt to break the Trade Federation blockade.

While the Queen succeeded, Qui-Gon and Obi-Wan were forced to confront Darth Maul again. In an epic battle within the Theed palace's power station, Qui-Gon was separated from Obi-Wan by the power plant's security lasers. Forced to battle the Sith Lord on his own, Qui-Gon was physically unable to compete. Darth Maul stabbed the Jedi Master with a quick jab of his double-bladed lightsaber while Obi-Wan looked on helplessly. Obi-Wan defeated Maul once freed from the lasers, but it was too late to save his Master. Obi-Wan held Qui-Gon as he died, promising his Master that he would train young Anakin Skywalker. Qui-Gon's body was consumed in the flames of a Naboo funeral pyre, in honor of his efforts to help free Naboo from the Trade Federation.

Looking back, many Jedi Masters who were forced into military roles during the Clone Wars felt that it was Qui-Gon's death at Naboo that ultimately led Count Dooku to leave the Jedi Order and form the Confederacy of Independent Systems. Some 10 years after the Battle of Naboo, when Anakin Skywalker murdered a clan of Tusken Raiders on Tatooine after the death of his mother, Yoda seemed to hear Qui-Gon's disembodied voice on Coruscant. This contradicted the very nature of death, since Jedi were supposed to lose their identity when they joined with the Force. Qui-Gon's voice troubled Yoda for many years, until Anakin Skywalker fell to the dark side of the Force and became Darth Vader. Qui-Gon's spirit then reappeared to Yoda, explaining that he had learned of a way to become one with the Force, yet still retain the ability to influence the physical world. The technique was discovered by a Shaman of the Whills, and Qui-Gon practiced the skill in the years leading up to, and following, his death on Naboo. Qui-Gon's spirit later explained the teachings of the Whills to Yoda and Obi-Wan, to ensure that they would be able to help Anakin fulfill his destiny as the Chosen One.

**Jinn, Tyla** This underworld figure was a frequent patron of the cantinas of Theed on Naboo, during the Galactic Civil War.

**Jin'ri Trade Syndicate** This organization, formed in the wake of the Battle of Duro, sought to profit from the war against the Yuuzhan Vong by running supplies and weapons to worlds willing to pay its exorbitant prices.

**jinsol** This exotic and very expensive spice was created on just one planet, Haruun Kal.

*Qui-Gon Jinn (left) and Obi-Wan Kenobi (right) battle Darth Maul.*

**Jintar** A Mandalorian, he married Dinua Jeban after the Yuuzhan Vong War. Together they raised a small family on the Beviin-Vasur farm, including their children, Briila and Shalk.

**Jinwa Raiders** A notorious group of alien pirates that operated during the Galactic Civil War. A band of Jinwa Raiders was defeated by a shipful of droids when C-3PO and R2-D2 were forced to pilot a Rebel Alliance transport to Ladro. The pirates' attack killed the small command crew, but the droids managed to avoid capture and reach Ladro unharmed.

**Jinzler, Dean** The youngest of four children raised on Coruscant, Dean Jinzler was forced to live in the shadow of his older sister Lorana, who showed enough connection to the Force to be chosen for training as a Jedi on Coruscant. Their parents had been working as technicians at the Jedi Temple, which ensured that Lorana's sensitivity was quickly discovered. Despite the fact that his parents lost their jobs at the Temple when Lorana was chosen, Dean's efforts were always compared with Lorana's, and he came to realize that he was never going to be as gifted as she was, at least in the eyes of their parents. Nevertheless, he became a skilled starship technician, and was part of the ground crew that worked on the construction of the Outbound Flight. The work led him to meet up again with Lorana, who had been chosen as one of the Jedi Knights attached to the project. They had a brief argument before the mission set off from Coruscant, and Dean never heard from his sister again.

By the time he reached his 60s, Jinzler had developed no focused training in any specific area, but he maintained a wide range of knowledge on many subjects. He was hired by Talon Karrde when the smuggler's information-sharing operation was growing faster than he could handle, although Jinzler wasn't really loyal to Karrde. When a message was received at Comra through Karrde's network from Voss Parck on Nirauan, but was addressed to Luke Skywalker, Jinzler stole it and fled Comra. Karrde learned of the theft since Jinzler's disappearance coincided with that of the message; he also learned that Jinzler had requested a transfer to Comra just eight weeks earlier, which was too much of a coincidence to ignore.

Karrde set out to locate Jinzler, while Luke set off for Nirauan. However, Luke found Jinzler first when Jinzler was introduced as the New Republic's ambassador on the mission to recover the remains of the Outbound Flight Project. He conned Aristocra Formbi into believing he was actually a representative of the Republic in order to gain access to Outbound Flight. Underneath his charade, Jinzler wanted to learn more about his older sister. However, after spending time with Evlyn Tabory aboard Outbound Flight, Jinzler came to realize that his hatred of his sister was nothing more than jealousy, and that his parents had loved all their children equally. Jinzler found himself finally at peace with his sister's memory. She had died trying to save Outbound Flight, and that was all that mattered. In the aftermath of the mission, Jinzler decided to accompany the survivors of Outbound Flight to Nirauan, so that he could be with Rosemari Tabory and her daughter, Evlyn.

**Jinzler, Lorana** This young woman was the third of four children born to a couple who worked as technicians at the Jedi Temple on Coruscant, nearly two decades before the Battle of Naboo. Lorana was discovered to have some sensitivity to the Force, and was taken in to the Jedi Order at 10 months of age. Her parents lost their jobs at the Jedi Temple—to prevent them from having any contact with their daughter—and they were forced to find employment elsewhere.

Lorana grew up in the Temple and eventually was chosen as a Padawan learner by Jedi Master Jorus C'baoth, although she could never quite figure out why. Where C'baoth was strong-willed and demanding, Lorana was timid and unassuming. Nevertheless, she learned much about the Force from C'baoth, and was promoted to the rank of Jedi Knight at the age of 22, just before Outbound Flight was launched. She was given the chance to become one of the 12 Jedi Knights who would serve aboard Outbound Flight, a mission that she grudgingly accepted. In a brief conversation with C'baoth, Lorana discovered that her former Master seemed to have some reservations about actually promoting her, but he looked forward to continuing her training during the mission.

During the pre-flight systems checks, Lorana was introduced to her brother Dean, who had never come to terms with Lorana's departure from the family. In an argument, he blamed Lorana for the family's troubles since their parents were forced to take lower-paying jobs after leaving the Jedi Temple. Despite this, they were proud of Lorana, and constantly compared Dean's efforts with those of his older sister. This argument left Lorana wondering about the role of the Jedi in the galaxy, as well as their role aboard Outbound Flight.

During the mission, Lorana also found herself doubting C'baoth's leadership, especially when he began taking control of every aspect of it. When he began training the Jedi in the operation of the ship's Dreadnaughts and their weapons systems, Lorana became even more concerned. Her fears were shared by Jedi Master Justyn Ma'Ning, who hoped Lorana would speak to her former Master and make him relent. She never got the chance, however, because Outbound Flight was intercepted by a military force led by then–Force Commander Thrawn of the Chiss Expansionary Defense Fleet. Lorana only survived Thrawn's attack because she had been ordered by C'baoth to lock up a group of rebellious engineers in the central core of the ship. Thrawn's radiation bombs were targeted only at the Dreadnaughts, and wiped out all beings in the large ships. The core section was untouched, and Lorana was able to reach a Dreadnaught just as the Chiss boarded the vessel. She found herself working with Syndic Thrass to get the ship moving, in order to ensure that Outbound Flight didn't fall into the hands of one of the Chiss ruling families. However, their efforts were hampered by the damage that had been sustained, and they found themselves without engine power as they approached a habitable planetoid. Thrass and Lorana realized that the only way to save the civilian population from certain death was to remain on the bridge of their Dreadnaught and ensure it hit the ground first. Although they were ultimately successful in landing the huge craft while saving the civilians, both Thrass and Lorana were killed in the crash.

Decades later, Lorana's lightsaber was recovered from the debris by Luke Skywalker and his wife, Mara Jade Skywalker. At the time, they believed it was Jorus C'baoth's blade, but Dean Jinzler confirmed that it was his sister's. He asked Luke to hold on to the weapon until their group returned to the Brask Oto Command Station, in case the Jedi needed it to fight their way out. Luke and Mara were forced to use Lorana's lightsaber in a desperate attempt to destroy the droideka that was protecting Estosh and his Vagaari aboard the D-Four Dreadnaught. The lightsaber was destroyed when the droideka exploded.

**Jiod** This New Republic agent served on the *Glorious* as a member of the scanning crew monitoring the Teljkon vagabond.

**Jion, Shep** A Baron with House Melantha, he chose to pursue a military career with the Imperial Army. Jion later transferred back to Tapani sector, joining the 1st Tapani Assault Battlegroup. He was also an active member of the Order of the Kilmer Bange.

**Jiprirr** This Wookiee's mate was burned by flame beetles and fell from the Gathering Trail during her son's Test of Ascension.

*Jira*

Commander Daine Jir

**jiqui** The fruit of this plant was known for its bitter-tasting peel.

**Jir, Commander Daine** This bold and outspoken Imperial commander was on the *Devastator* when it captured the consular ship *Tantive IV* just prior to the Battle of Yavin. Jir was a noncombat stormtrooper officer at the time, having served in the Imperial 501st Legion. He worked as an aide to Darth Vader, and was one of the few beings who ever openly questioned the Dark Lord's tactics. While other officers believed that his outspoken nature would soon lead to his execution, Vader appreciated Jir's suggestions and had him promoted from lieutenant to commander. It was Commander Jir who questioned Vader's capture of Princess Leia Organa, fearing that her imprisonment would lead to pro-Rebellion sympathies in the Imperial Senate. Commander Jir also doubted that Vader could extract any information from the Princess, convinced that she would die before revealing the location of the Alliance's primary base.

**Jira** This elderly woman lived on the streets of Mos Espa, and was a close friend of young Anakin Skywalker. She had been on Tatooine for some time, and could tell the changes in the weather by the various aches and pains in her bones.

**Jiramma** One of the many Hutt kajidics that operated from a base on Nar Shaddaa during the last decades of the Old Republic and into the era of the New Order.

**Jiree** This Rodian thug worked for Eelian Kirat as part of the Nalmar criminal organization. Jiree often accompanied Elana Nalmar on undercover missions, serving as her bodyguard.

**ji rikknit** A highly addictive intoxicant produced from the eggs and ovum sac of the rikknit.

**Jiriss, Roget** This woman was one of the most successful smugglers in the early years of the New Republic; her fees were correspondingly high. She was a brash, confident woman who hated pirates of any kind.

**Jiroch-Reslia** This planet, the third and primary world in the Jiroch system, was the homeworld of the Tunroth. It, Kalok, and Saloch were collectively known as the Triumvirate. A Jedi shrine was said to exist in the system.

**Jisasu** A city on Lucazec founded by the Fallanassi. It was connected to Big Hill by the Crown Pass Road.

**Jiss, Vinna** A Grand Army of the Republic logistics department employee during the early stages of the Clone Wars. She betrayed the GAR by accepting credits to funnel key information to a group of Separatist-funded terrorists on Coruscant. She was observed and captured by clone commandos Sev and Fi, interrogated, and eventually terminated by Mandalorian merc Walon Vau. Later, *Null*-class ARC trooper Ordo saw Jiss walking back into her GAR logistics office. It was actually the Gurlanin, Jinart, who tried to impersonate the dead woman.

**Jit, Lak** A Devaronian who discovered a handful of datacards at the base of Mount Tantiss some 10 years after the death of Grand Admiral Thrawn. Among them was one titled "The Hand of Thrawn," along with another describing the Bothan involvement in the destruction of Caamas. Jit claimed that he owned the cards by way of the Debble Agreement, though Leia Organa Solo could recover them after making proper restitution. He nearly escaped from Wayland with the cards, but was apprehended by Leia's Noghri bodyguards. He still managed to escape with a copy of the Caamas datacard, and freely dispensed the morsel of information it contained until he was caught by Mazzic. Lak Jit was then locked away until the Caamas incident could be resolved.

**Jith, Hiksri** A Rodian who served with Erli Prann aboard the Golan II space station near Bilbringi during the Yuuzhan Vong War. Prann had allowed the station to be located by the crew of the *Mon Mothma* during Operation Trinity, as a way to lure in hyperdrive-capable ships. The pirates could then salvage hyperdrives from New Republic ships and use them to power the battle station. Jaina Solo managed to use the Force to alter Prann's recollection of his hyperspace jump coordinates, and the station ended up trying to jump through a Yuuzhan Vong interdictor. Prann and his people used their proximity to the interdictor to pound the ship and open an escape route for the Galactic Alliance forces. Prann then tried to fight his way clear, but Jith demanded that he surrender the Golan station to the Galactic Alliance. He refused, but was eventually subdued. Once he was removed from power, Jith and the rest of the pirates agreed to turn the station over.

**Jiton, Tyrn** This male Devaronian worked as a bounty hunter in the Borderland Regions during the early years of the New Republic. He traveled in a *Firespray*-class transport, and was known to sell his captives into slavery if the profits were good.

***Jitte*** A Rebel Alliance escort carrier destroyed during the Galactic Civil War.

**Jivrak, General Reesen** A Rebel Alliance officer discharged from duty because of his unethical and cruel tactics. He was known to have stolen a TelBrinTel research droid from an Imperial convoy, renamed it Geth, and made a variety of modifications to it. After leaving the service of the Rebel Alliance, Jivrak and his followers fled to Ohratuu, where they set out to develop their own army of beast soldiers.

**Jivv Space City** This colony orbited Duro.

**Jix** *See* Jixton, Wrenga.

**Jixton, Wrenga** This Corellian underworld figure was known for his resourcefulness and ruthlessness. A former Imperial gunnery sergeant known to his comrades as Jix, he was part of a task force sent to Falleen for Darth Vader's experiment there. After the experiment failed, Jixton was court-martialed and sent to Kessel, but he quickly escaped from the prison complex and became a mercenary.

Jix again encountered Vader several years later on Aridus, where he had been hiding from the Empire. When Vader nearly died in the explosion of the Iron Tower, Jix found him and would have killed the Dark Lord in revenge, but decided it was better not to risk the wrath of the Empire. Jix loaded Vader's body onto a starship and flew off, but Vader awoke and realized the situation. He offered Jix the chance to return to Aridus without fear of Imperial pursuit if he agreed to do whatever the Dark Lord needed. Jix was forced to agree, and he became an agent of Vader's. In this capacity, Jix exposed the liaison between Frija and Admiral Droon. Jix later infiltrated Jabba the Hutt's organization following the Dark Lord's failure to capture Luke Skywalker on Cloud City. Vader instructed Jix to become one of Jabba's swoop gang members and take Luke when he arrived on Tatooine. Jix nearly captured Skywalker in a swoop race through Beggar's Canyon, but Dash Rendar was able to disrupt his plans and keep Luke free.

*Wrenga Jixton*

**Jixuan desert** An arid expanse on the planet Ryloth.

**Jjannex II** The Imperial Star Destroyer *Stormclaw* was attacked by pirates near this planet.

**Jjerrol** This man was a small-time criminal working on Tatooine during the early years of the New Republic.

**Jjorg** This blond-haired woman was one of the leaders of the Freedom movement, serving Malinza Thanas during the Yuuzhan Vong War. After their base at the Stack was discovered, Jjorg fled the scene with Malinza and Vyram. They traveled to the office of their benefactor, Deputy Prime Minister Blaine Harris, only to discover that Harris had double-crossed them. In an effort to escape, Jjorg tried to grab Harris's blaster, but Harris managed to press the weapon into her chest and pull the trigger. Jjorg died instantly.

**JK-13** This JK series combat droid was captured by the forces of the Old Republic and investigated for many weeks after it was learned that Count Dooku and the Separatists were planning to buy huge quantities of JKs for their armies. JK-13 was first shown to the galactic government and the Jedi Knights at T'Chuk arena, on Coruscant, where it had been reprogrammed to act at a nonlethal level. After defeating a droideka and ARC trooper CT-36/732 in one-on-one combat, JK-13 was pitted in battle against Jedi Master Kit Fisto. Only Master Fisto's unusual attacks allowed him to defeat the droid.

**Jkarta, Telmun** This New Republic Intelligence agent provided an in-depth analysis of the Teljkon vagabond following the efforts of Lando Calrissian and Ejagga Pakkpekatt to locate that mysterious ship.

**JK series droid** Originally produced as high-end security droids, these Cestus Cybernetics constructs were among the most advanced ever produced in the galaxy. First developed during the buildup to the Clone Wars, the JK series used a form of "living circuitry" that employed the unique brain of an unfertilized dashta eel as its central processor. This gave the droid an unusual affinity for the Force, allowing it to anticipate the actions of an opponent. The chrome body of the JK series was shaped like an hourglass, with several rows of narrow legs for mobility.

When confronted with a possible intruder, the JK series could move swiftly and silently to a new location, where it appeared almost benign until it registered a true threat. In that instant, the JK series could assume any number of configurations and bring to bear an unusual array of weaponry. Its primary attack mode involved the use of whip-like tentacles that emerged from its top and side. They were incredibly strong, and could cut through some of the hardest materials. After capturing its target, the droid drew it close to its body, holding it until help could arrive. If the target struggled, the tentacles could be drawn tighter, cutting into flesh or metal to force the target to submit. Other weaponry included shock netting, stun darts, and blasters. In addition to these mechanical capabilities, specialized coatings allowed the JK series to blend into its surroundings.

These droids were produced in small numbers during the Clone Wars, but at incredibly high prices due to the delicate nature of the dashta eel. Mass production was virtually impossible, since the number of dashta eels was limited. Nevertheless, the demand for these droids easily outpaced the supply. They were originally designed as security droids for the exceptionally wealthy, but with simple programming changes they were easily adapted for use as combat droids. Because of their ability to anticipate an opponent's movements, the JK series proved a formidable opponent for even Jedi Knights. Due to several documented cases of a JK actually defeating a Jedi Knight in combat, they became known as Jedi Killers.

When Count Dooku offered to provide Cestus Cybernetics with cloning technology to help produce more eels, the Separatist army was able to secure the rights to JK series production. It proved too difficult to clone the dashta eels, however, a fact that Dooku kept to himself while he spun an intricate plan to lure the Jedi and the Old Republic to Ord Cestus. He convinced the Jedi that the JK series *could* be mass-produced, and that its innate abilities would make it exceptionally difficult to defeat. In this way, Dooku managed to trap Obi-Wan Kenobi and Kit Fisto on Ord Cestus, when they were dispatched to learn more about the droids. However, the Separatists' plans fell through when both Jedi Masters survived the mission, revealing to the Cestians and the rest of the galaxy that the JK series was no longer a viable alternative for the Separatists. Further investigation revealed that the dashta eels would have gone insane on the battlefield when ordered to actually kill another being. This information was something that the Five Families never revealed to Count Dooku, since it would have negated the deal before any credits could have been exchanged.

**JL-12-F** This explosive was manufactured by one of I'att Armaments' competitors, and was designed to explode in a symmetrical pattern. It was used by a group of Ranats who tried to blow up Silver Station. Tinian I'att was able to track them down by following the smell of the explosive.

**JL7 Elixir** A model of GoCorp hoverscooter.

**J'Lan** One of the many mining settlements, or *o'bekis,* established on Goroth Prime. In the 100 years leading up to the Battle of Yavin, J'Lan experienced two mega-groundquakes that obliterated the landscape and the *o'beki* itself.

*Jedi Master J'Mikel faces bounty hunter Aurra Sing.*

**JL series droid** A series of security droids produced by Cestus Cybernetics based on the popular JK series.

**J'Mel** The second largest of the three moons that orbited Goroth Prime.

**J'Mikel** This Anx was one of six Jedi Knights hunted down and murdered by Aurra Sing. Like Peerce, with whom he was working at the time, J'Mikel was searching for Sing on Coruscant when he was killed. J'Mikel was survived by his young Padawan, a Twi'lek female named Xiann Amersu, who was badly traumatized by the incident and its violence. After Aurra Sing was captured by Aayla Secura, Master J'Mikel's lightsaber was returned to Coruscant. Secura asked to personally deliver it to Xiaan, so that she could talk to her fellow Twi'lek about coming to terms with her feelings.

**Jmin Survival Academy** This paramilitary school was founded by Lunkar An during the Galactic Civil War.

**Jmmaar** This Viraanntesse Jedi Master, a native of Vvaw, was killed during the Clone Wars by General Grievous on Vandos. Years earlier, Master Jmmaar had accompanied Jedi Master T'chooka D'oon on a mission to mediate a settlement of the Huk War. Their ultimate decision was to rule in favor of the Huks, which forced the Kaleesh into a state of destitution. Grievous, who was known during the Huk Wars as Qymaen jai Sheelal, never forgot the role of the two Jedi in the virtual subjugation of his people, and happily cut down Master Jmmaar when he had the chance.

**JMM series droid** A series of assassin droids produced during the Old Republic.

**JN-66** A model of analysis droid produced during the last decades of the Old Republic. Developed and manufactured by Cybot Galactica, the JN-66 had a flat, goggle-eyed head, and its body was supported by a pair of small, disk-shaped repulsorlifts. Two pairs of photoreceptors allowed it to view minute details of objects, giving it a greater set of data with which to make sense of its surroundings. Unlike the SP-4 droid that was developed to perform complex analyses, the JN-66 was intended for the grunt work associated with sifting through data to determine trends and patterns. Like the SP-4, the JN-66 was targeted toward helping scientists and forensics experts during their investigations, and it also found use in the Jedi Archives. The original JN-66 units were designed to operate in cleanroom environments, and were produced with micro-field generators in their arms to pick up objects without physically touching them. The body was not given exterior plating, which allowed the unit to be given regular radiation baths to kill off any bacteria or microorganisms that might have lodged in its inner workings.

**Joaa'n** This woman was the demolitions expert for Red Hand Squadron. She died, along with Bria Tharen and most of the Red Hands, on Toprawa, where they were trying to buy time for Leia Organa to receive the Death Star plans.

**Joanson, Ariq** One of Owen Lars's contemporaries, Ariq Joanson set up a moisture farm farther out than anyone else on Tatooine. His farm, which was only marginally profitable, bordered Jawa and Sand People lands. Ariq felt that the three species could live together peacefully, despite the stories being spread by the Imperial Governor. He regularly left gifts of water for both native peoples, and developed a great friendship with the Jawas of Wimateeka's clan. He developed an uneasy truce with the Sand People. Many of his friends, including his neighbor Eyvind, thought he was crazy. Ariq paid them no mind, and planned to purchase a great tract of land that he would subdivide with Jawas and Sand People. He was even going to help them submit the paperwork to make the land officially their own. When Eyvind became engaged to Ariela, Ariq asked if he could invite Wimateeka's clan to the wedding. Ariela talked Eyvind into agreeing, and the wedding reception was a success. The Jawas were impressed with human customs and civility, while the humans marveled that the Jawas could be so friendly. When a group of adolescent Sand People attacked the reception, Ariq was greatly dismayed. Eyvind was killed in the attack, and the local Imperial detachment used the incident to further the distrust between the

*JN-66*

species. Ariq was undaunted, and after rescuing Ariela from the Sand People, he set out to find the Rebel Alliance and work with them to overthrow the Empire.

**jobber** Rebel Alliance Intelligence slang for assassin.

**Joben, Thall** A native of Ingo with a passion for building and racing landspeeders, he grew up with his best friend and rival, Jord Dusat. Thall Joben was 17 years old when he encountered the droids R2-D2 and C-3PO during the Empire's early days.

**Jobin, Corporal** A Rebel Alliance soldier at Echo Base. Jobin was the brother of Lieda Mothma, and the son of Rebel leader Mon Mothma. On Hoth, Jobin was part of the ground forces that were arrayed to defend the main base, but were forced to abandon their position when they realized that the base's ion cannon was under Imperial attack. Jobin and his team regained control of the ion cannon's control center from Imperial snowtroopers, and he personally fired the weapon, disabling a Star Destroyer and opening an escape route for the last of the Rebel Alliance's transports. He then reported on the breach of Echo Base's defenses by Imperial forces, but was forced to abandon his post and retreat to a predetermined escape point. He was intercepted by Darth Vader before he got there. After ensuring that a recorded message to his mother was carried out by a comrade, Jobin tried to block Vader's way, hoping to buy the rest of his team some more time. Vader, however, had no time for his defiance, and swiftly used the Force to snap Jobin's neck. Jobin's recording eventually reached Mon Mothma, but not until almost a year later, just before the main planning session for the Battle of Endor.

**Jobones, Wryk** Known by the nickname Wreck-Out, Wryk Jobones was a veteran of the swoop racing circuits of the Outer Rim Territories. During the height of the New Order, Wryk retired from active competition to promote the sport. He spent much of his career racing on outlawed courses, but realized that dead racers couldn't do any good. He petitioned for the improvement of safety and quality of courses at all levels of competition, hoping to prolong the careers of racers and attract a larger audience.

**Jobreth Plains** This grassland was located on Jabiim.

**Jobril** This Twi'lek worked for Nirama several years before the Battle of Naboo. Jobril voluntarily let Nirama implant a chip into his brain that made Jobril unquestioningly loyal to Nirama. Shortly after the Battle of Naboo, something made Jobril change his mind about the implant. He quietly had it removed and turned against Nirama.

**jobsworth** Slang for any government or legal worker who spent too much time obeying the exact letter of the law as spelled out in convoluted and intricate government regulations.

**Jocell** This Chiss female was part of a squadron assembled to support Jagged Fel's fact-finding mission to the New Republic shortly before the Battle of Coruscant. When Jag decided that the best way to gather information was to assist the Republic in its struggle against the Yuuzhan Vong, Jocell and her fellow pilots agreed to stay. Jocell joined the Twin Suns Squadron, serving under Jaina Solo as Twin Suns Nine. After Coruscant fell and the Republic's forces regrouped on Mon Calamari, Jocell agreed to accompany Jaina and her parents on a mission to reestablish communications to parts of the galaxy that had been cut off. Jaina was glad to have Jocell's help, but considered her too stiff to be an effective pilot.

When the trio was sent to N'zoth to investigate the Fia's claim that the Yevetha were no longer a threat, they found that the planet and the entire Yevethan civilization had been destroyed by the Yuuzhan Vong. They also found the last surviving Yevethan warrior on a small moon, waiting for the alien invaders to return. This Yevetha refused to be rescued, and set his ship to self-destruct. Jocell was close by when the ship exploded and her clawcraft was badly damaged. With Jaina's help, she was able to return to Galantos and recover from her injuries.

**Jocoro the Hutt (Jocoro Desilijic Tiure)** This Hutt crime lord, a member of the same kajidic as Jabba, operated a small criminal empire from a base on Du Hatta in the years following the Battle of Endor.

**Jocund, Deidre** This woman served as a soldier and field medic in the Thaereian Military during the final years of the Old Republic. She was a member of the ambush squad led by Lorwin Derlynn, and was dispatched to a Cularin Militia base in the asteroids of the Cularin system. A systemwide blockade was ostensibly set up to protect against Separatist invasion. However, the Thaereians had other plans for Cularin. Like others who served under Derlynn, Jocund questioned her loyalty to the Thaereians. Thus, when Derlynn was shown evidence of Thaereian misdoings in the system, Jocund supported his decision to allow ships through the blockade.

**Jodakan needler crab** This crab, native to the rocky reefs of Jodaka, used a deadly poison to capture its prey. The poison was injected through a long, biotic needle that could be fired at a target with a short burst of air. The primary source of food for the needler crab were the seagulls that searched the reefs for fish, which it shot down using its poisoned darts. The darts were fired from a hollow tube that ran along the dorsal ridge of the crab's carapace, and the burst of air that was required to fire them came from two air sacs located at the rear of its body.

Jodakan needler crabs were sometimes seen in shops and stores that dealt in exotic creatures. They were sold as personal defense systems, because their owners could tap on the air sacs to induce the crab to fire its darts. Owners had to keep the crab in a saltwater aquarium and feed it at least a pound of flesh each day. Although they were kept as "pets," Jodakan needler crabs were difficult to train, often attacking any flying creature they encountered while in their owners' possession.

**Jode, Binna** This small-time criminal was active on Tatooine during the Galactic Civil War.

**Jodeen, Captain** This Imperial Navy officer was part of the small defense force assigned to protect the labor colony on Kalist VI after the Battle of Yavin. As the leader of Durkii Squadron, Jodeen was on duty when he was ordered to escort the *Nuna's Twins* down to the planet's surface after the tanker managed to survive a Rebel Alliance ambush. The ground forces on Kalist VI were suspicious when the tanker arrived without its escort frigate, which the crew claimed had been destroyed in the ambush. Unbeknownst to the Imperials, however, Luke Skywalker and a band of Alliance agents were at the controls of the *Nuna's Twins.* The fact that the tanker was allowed to land gave the Alliance team the ability to infiltrate the base.

**Jofoger** This planet was located along the Sisar Run.

**Johans, Colonel Zel** This Imperial colonel, known as the Rancor, was in charge of a Hell's Hammers unit stationed in the Outer Rim Territories during the Galactic Civil War. He was a masterful tactician and wholly devoted to his troops. He was able to persuade the Imperial command that the Hammers worked better at full regimental strength, and he played a pivotal role in the recruiting of new members. Johans was also instrumental in the development of repulsortanks, as well as the improvement of Imperial doctrine regarding their use. In the wake of the Battle of Endor, Colonel Johans went into hiding on Brintooin, where he established a base of power in the hope of building himself a small empire. Many historians believed he had aspirations of inheriting command of the Imperial Remnant.

**Johder** One of the Shelsha sector's largest producers of farming equipment and machinery during the New Order.

**Johin** This spacer claimed that the Empire destroyed Hyrol Preen Beta because of suspected Rebel Alliance activity. When they couldn't capture the Rebels outright, the Imperials wiped out the settlements on the planet in order to prevent the Alliance from returning.

**Johrian whiskey** A blue-green grain alcohol, it was a favorite of Lorn Pavan, and enjoyed by Den Dhur.

**Joh's Shipyard** One of the most prominent starship modification and repair companies in the Cularin system during the last decades of the Old Republic. The Shipyard, as it was commonly known, worked with the Cularin Transit Authority to ensure that no illegal modifications were done.

**Joiner** The term used to describe any being who became deeply attached to the Colony. Joiners were distinguished by their belief in the altruism of the various hives of the Colony, and the way in which they acted upon the Will of the Colony without hesitation. For the most part, the Joiners became a hive's liaison to the outside galaxy, acting as translators and guides during discussions or negotiations. The role of Joiners didn't become apparent until about five years after the Yuuzhan Vong War, when UnuThul began attracting more and more beings to the Unknown Regions to help the Colony survive against the Chiss. Over time, those beings who remained within the hive too long were absorbed by it, and could no longer think for themselves. The hive had access to all of their memories and skills, including the understanding of languages and the absorption of feelings and emotions.

**Joining, the** The name given to the period of history on Merisee in which intense volcanic and seismic activity created a chain of mountains connecting the planet's two continents. This joining of the two landmasses allowed the Meri and the Teltiors to finally meet, sparking a millennium-long civil war.

**joining ritual** This was a generic term used to describe any ritual in which a group of Force-users combined their powers to create a single, powerful event. During the millennium leading to the Battle of Ruusan, the use of joining rituals was found most often among the Brotherhood of Darkness. In keeping with the Rule of the Strong, all Sith were equally powerful, but their combined strength was awesome to behold. In the wake of the Galactic Civil War, the Jedi Knights of Luke Skywalker's new Jedi Order discovered that they were better able to combat the Yuuzhan Vong by combining their powers.

**Joint Council** This parliamentary body of the Iotran government was formed from the top eight Iotran military leaders. As a whole, they ruled the entire Iotran planetary society.

**Joint Defense Operations Staff** This body of military leaders commanded the various branches of the New Republic's armed forces during the years following the Battle of Bilbringi. The Joint Defense Operations Staff was ostensibly the leadership of the New Republic Defense Force.

**Joiol** This planet, located in the Orus sector, was supposedly one of the planets on which Grand Admiral Thrawn was producing clones some five years after the Battle of Endor. Investigation by the fledgling Smugglers' Alliance proved this information false.

**Jojighar** To honor this former Jedi Master for his contributions to the galaxy, Biscuit Baron created a commemorative holocube that documented his history and included it in many QuickSnack and QuickSnackLite meals. The meals and holocubes were available shortly before the start of the Clone Wars.

*Joker Squad and Lieutenant Cassel (front)*

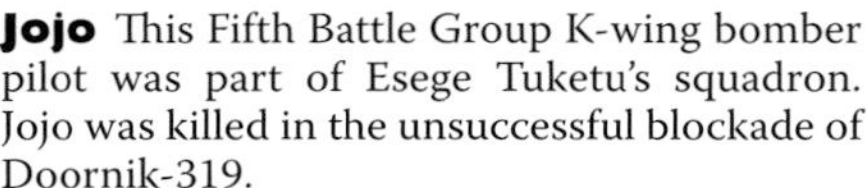

**Jojo** This Fifth Battle Group K-wing bomber pilot was part of Esege Tuketu's squadron. Jojo was killed in the unsuccessful blockade of Doornik-319.

**Jok, D'Trel B'Rar** This Gorothite served as the Rel'Kan of her people during the Galactic Civil War. She was little more than a figurehead, but was dedicated to using whatever power she commanded to help the Gorothites.

**Joker Squad** This unit of Company C, Battalion 9, of the 407th Stormtrooper Division was among many stationed at the Imperial base on Yinchorr, nearly a century after the war against the Yuuzhan Vong. Joker Squad was noted for its high casualty rate, much of which could be attributed to the dangerous missions it was ordered to carry out. About seven years after Darth Krayt took control of the galaxy for the Sith, the troopers of Joker Squad were ordered to take the point on a mission to Borosk, where the 908th Stormtrooper Division had defected and remained loyal to former Emperor Roan Fel. The team's members quietly questioned the orders, since they required the Jokers to eliminate a fellow stormtrooper unit.

The Jokers obeyed, however, losing Vax Potorr and Jes Gistang, and seeing Sergeant Harkas seriously wounded in a second wave of attacks before being confronted by Krayt's liaison, Darth Maleval. The Sith Lord demanded that the Jokers' commanding officer, Lieutenant Gil Cassel, execute his own brother—a member of the 908th—as a show of loyalty to the new Empire. Cassel hesitated, and Maleval then killed them both. An enraged 407th trooper, Hondo Karr, started to attack Maleval with a short sword. The Sith sensed it and threatened to kill Karr as well. At that instant, squad newbie Anson Trask shot and killed Maleval, carrying out the one action that all the Jokers had secretly wished for. As he was taken to the nearest medcenter to recover from his wounds, Sergeant Harkas turned over leadership of the Jokers to Trask, who was the only officially surviving member of the team after Karr deserted. Harkas later reported to his superiors that Maleval had been killed in combat, officially clearing Trask and the rest of the Jokers of the Sith Lord's demise.

**Joker Squadron** One of the starfighter units that made up the Cularin Militia during the Thaereian Conflict in the last years of the Old Republic.

*Jokhalli*

**Jokhalli** This species of tall, thin-limbed humanoids was native to the moon Blimph 3. They were distinguished by their glowing red eyes and unusual arms. Each of their two arms split into two forearms, with a compound elbow joint providing a full range of motion for each. Their bovine faces were melancholy in appearance, and they spoke a variety of galactic trade languages. To the Jokhalli, trade and commerce were immensely important, and their civilization flourished mainly because of the strategic location of Blimph 3. When Quaffug the Hutt took control of the Blimph system, the Jokhalli were relegated to a minimal role in the systemwide business, and they were unable to stop the Hutt. They consoled themselves playing games of Divot until Lando Calrissian stumbled upon their society during his trial under the Duff-Jikab. His skills in trade languages, coupled with his defeat of the Jokhalli masters in Divot, earned Lando a measure of respect among the Jokhalli, who helped him escape Quaffug. Lando later forced Quaffug to return control of Blimph 3 to the Jokhalli in return for the Hutt's life.

**Jokoflow** This river flowed through the city of Evafan on Vorzyd 5. Its flow was interrupted only when it spilled into Lake Joko before moving on through the city.

*Jolli, an associate of Crimson Jack*

**JoKo's Alley** Located within Coruscant's Dometown, this riotous strip of businesses was where Tekli overheard a pair of Rodians discussing their general malcontent with the human species. The distrust arose from the fact that the Yuuzhan Vong could use ooglith masquers to pretend to be human, thereby making nonhuman species hesitant to work with humans. This was shortly before it was discovered that the aliens had perfected the gablith masquer, which they used to pass as alien species.

**Jokot** One of a handful of beings who regularly got together to play sabacc at The White Door cantina in the city of Akmalla during the years following the Battle of Naboo. He often played with Lar-Odo and Bonna Noot.

**Joli** A native of Melida/Daan, Joli was a member of the Scavenger Youth. Despite the fact that he was loyal to Mawat, he didn't understand why Mawat wanted to oust Nield from the leadership of the Young and take control of Zehava for himself. Joli and Deila hid after Mawat ordered them to take up arms, hoping to flee the inevitable war that was brewing. They then provided information to Qui-Gon Jinn and Obi-Wan Kenobi, telling the Jedi of Mawat's deception.

**Jolian freighter** An outdated form of transport ship.

**Jolla the Hutt** This Hutt crime lord worked from a base on Nar Shaddaa during the New Order. Outwardly, Jolla wished to forge an alliance with his nephew Torga the Hutt, combining their small criminal organizations into a much broader, more profitable enterprise that could squeeze out the operations of Moska the Hutt. However, Jolla's real goal was to pit Torga and Moska against each other and usurp both organizations.

**Jolli** This female pirate served with Crimson Jack following the Battle of Yavin. She became jealous of the kidnapped Leia Organa's presence, so Jolli began flirting with and teasing Jack's pirates. Once she had them hooked, she spurned them. Much of her behavior could be traced to her parents. Her father was a fugitive from the Empire, and Jolli and her mother were abandoned on an outlaw world. There her mother was killed in a firefight, and Jolli vowed to prove herself against any man at any time. Despite her relationship with Crimson Jack and her attraction to Han Solo, Jolli hated all men.

After Jack's forces were stranded over Drexel I, Jolli led Raider Squadron on an assault against the *Millennium Falcon,* but her ship was damaged in a flyover. When she asked Jack to tow her back, he refused, claiming that the use of a magnetic pulse beam would interfere with his communications system. Angry at being abandoned by a man, Jolli felt all her anger crystallize into a single point. She took what little power she had left and started firing on Crimson Jack's Star Destroyer, shooting through the ship's shields before crashing into it with her fighter. In the resulting explosion, Jack's Star Destroyer was damaged beyond repair, and Jolli was mortally wounded.

**Jollie** An Imperial ambassador who secretly worked for Grigor, the corrupt governor of M'haeli shortly after the Battle of Yavin. Jollie was a large man who liked to smoke cigars. His head was bald from a series of operations that left him scarred for life. Jollie was the person who warned Grigor when Ranulf Trommer was assigned to be his aide.

*Jon, a Dantooine farmer*

***Jolly Man*** This modified blastboat was owned by the Brubb pilot Wonetun as part of a small fleet maintained by the Wild Knights. It was one of the ships that participated in attempts to capture a Yuuzhan Vong yammosk.

**Jolly Meal** A nickname given to the prepackaged meals produced at Biscuit Baron restaurants for young children during the New Order. Each Jolly Meal had a meat-filled biscuit, a side order, and a drink. It came in a colorful box that contained a small prize.

**Jolsz** One of the pirates who served under Captain Naz Felyood aboard the *Jynni's Virtue* during the reign of the Empire. Jolsz eventually was killed by the Korriban Zombies, and his body was reanimated to join them.

**jolt cell** An ancient device produced by Telgorn Power Cells. Available in three power ratings, the jolt cell was popular among the Jedi Knights during the years surrounding the Great Sith War.

**Jomark** An isolated watery planet with three small moons, it was ruled by the insane cloned Jedi Joruus C'baoth when he attempted to take Luke Skywalker prisoner. The planet had strings of tiny islands and one modest continent, Kalish. The High Castle of Jomark sat 400 meters above Ring Lake on a volcanic cone between rocky crags on Kalish. Jomark's three million or so primitive and superstitious human residents revered the ancient castle, which was constructed by a long-vanished species. Several villages lay clustered near the southern shore of Ring Lake—including Chynoo, where C'baoth meted out his brand of justice to the villagers from a High Castle throne placed in the town square.

**Jo-Mau-Rinti** This Cerean, a noted swoop racer, had a sensational rookie year just before the start of the Clone Wars. Jo-Mau-Rinti rode for Team NaKuda during most of his career.

**Jombo** This terse Rodian worked for Gamgalon as a hunt leader, guiding safaris on Varonat.

**Jomo** An octoped from Yoberra, he won the eight-legged race in the Mobquet Presents: Fastest Land Beings racing series just prior to the Clone Wars.

**Jomon** This ball of searing-hot rock was the third world in the Kamino system.

**Jompers customs ship** This patrol ship was developed shortly after the death of Grand Admiral Thrawn.

**Jon** A Dantooine farmer, his daughter was killed by a group of Mandalorian mercenaries that had been terrorizing the population. Jon demanded that the nearby Jedi Enclave do something. Preoccupied with the Jedi Civil War, they refused. However there were reports that indicated former Sith Lord Revan killed many of the mercenaries in self-defense.

**Jon, Colonel Davod** An Imperial armed forces officer, he was promoted for his skills and bravery as a scout. He also was known as a proficient leader, and was part of the Empire's Special Forces unit before serving under Admiral Piett during the Battle of Endor. Jon advocated the development of wilderness survival training for Imperial troops, despite the obvious technological advantage the Empire maintained over its opposition.

**Jonat, Lieutenant** An officer in the Galactic Alliance Guard, Lieutenant Jonat befriended former Chief of State Cal Omas after he was arrested and unseated by Jacen Solo. She pretended to allow Omas the chance to use her comlink to let his family know that he was all right, while secretly recording his every word. These recordings were turned over to Jacen Solo, who altered them to create recordings that made it appear as if Omas had ordered the murder of Mara Jade Skywalker. Solo then used these forged recordings in an attempt to convince Ben Skywalker of Omas's guilt.

**Jones, Domo** This young boy worked on his uncle Nobu's nerf farm on Tatooine, during the Galactic Civil War. He wore his hair in a coif that resembled a pair of curled horns. He desperately wanted to be a starfighter pilot, but Nobu kept him busy rounding up nerfs and tending the boshi fields. In his spare time, Domo roamed the cantinas of Mos Zabu, hoping to catch a glimpse of the beautiful Twi'lek waitress JillJoo Jab. Domo also longed to join the Rebel Alliance, and saw his chance when he overheard Ep Gart trying to sell a load of nergon 14 to an Imperial officer. With the help of his friend Blerx, Domo was able to disrupt the sale and defeat Gart. His bravery in eliminating Gart earned him the adoration of JillJoo herself.

**Joness, Davis** This man served the planetary government of Coruscant as an administrator, building a base of power and a personal fortune before the outbreak of the Clone Wars. He tried to appear neutral on the struggle between the Republic and the Separatists, but could no longer do so when the Galactic Empire was established. Unable to adjust to the Empire's new regulations, he eventually got into trouble with his Imperial supervisors. He was swiftly demoted, ending up on garbage duty. He later provided information on the Dontamo Prison facility to Keets Freely when that journalist assisted Solace in rescuing Ferus Olin.

**Jonex** One of the smaller mining operations in the galaxy during the years following the Yuuzhan Vong War. Jonex established several mines in the MZX32905 system.

**Jonn, Jobekk** An alias given to Han Solo shortly after he was first employed by the Hutts Jabba and Jiliac. He used it to land on Coruscant as an official Hutt diplomat, hoping to get his Imperial contacts to gain an audience with Sarn Shild. Shild had just issued orders to clamp down on the Hutts, and Jabba and Jiliac planned to bribe him. Han's mission was unsuccessful, although he did run into Bria Tharen at Shild's office.

**Jonndril, Simms** This man hired a group of smugglers to transport droids and weapons to Seikosha during the early years of the New Republic. The cargo was meant for Janelle Serap.

**Jonsey** An Imperial recruit who was part of Kyle Katarn's squadron during the capture of asteroid AX-456.

**Jonson** A moisture-farming family on Tatooine. The Jonsons were friends with Ariq Joanson, and agreed with his ideals.

**Jontan asteroid belt** This field of debris orbited the star Thanta Zilbra between the second and third planets. It was vaporized when the Sacorrian Triad destroyed Thanta Zilbra as part of the Starbuster plot.

**Jonton** A Rebel Alliance X-wing pilot killed in action over M'haeli.

**Jon-Tow Economic Development Group** This group of economic investors tried to take control of the spaceports on the moon Pinett during the Galactic Civil War. Corsignis Property Alliance opposed it. Jon-Tow was made up of smugglers and other criminals from the systems surrounding Pinett; all hoped to maintain local control of the ports at Oscum and Beliarr. Both parties decided that the only way to force the other to accede was to blockade the moon, so starships from the two groups patrolled the space around Pinett, hoping to shoot down each other's transports. This embargo began to splinter the members of Jon-Tow, showing a weakness that Deniv Corsignis himself hoped to exploit. Before their organization could self-destruct, though, the Pinett Freedom Force provided a way for the two groups of resolve their differences and come to an agreement on how to manage the development of the moon's spaceports.

**Jontz Freight** This transport and shipping company was based on Dravian Starport.

**Jonus, Captain** An Imperial starfighter pilot, he earned his rank as a member of the feared Death Squadron. He once was attacked by a space slug, but managed to escape with his life.

**Joo, Klis** This Duros Jedi was trained at the Jedi Temple on Coruscant, as well as the Almas Academy, prior to the Battle of Naboo. She tried teaching at the Academy, but became quickly frustrated with her students' lack of patience. She stepped down from her post, and was later named the governor of the city of Forard. Her technological skills gave her an edge in the development of certain aspects of the city, and under her direction the spaceport evolved into a first-rate operation.

**Joodrudda** Lungru the Hutt maintained a summer retreat on this dusty planet during the early years of the New Order. Lungru kept a collection of rare and exotic creatures at the retreat, away from the prying eyes of environmentalists. Joodrudda was located on the edge of the Corporate Sector.

**Joodsen, Maceb** A native of Demar, Joodsen served as Elga Arbo's copilot aboard the *Redshift Runner* courier ship. When Arbo refused to let Gydio Lucone seize the ship in a foreclosure, Arbo was gravely wounded in a firefight. Joodsen then used his skills as a mechanic to break into the *Redshift Runner* and flee the planet, and neither he nor the ship was ever seen again, despite a bounty on Joodsen's head.

**Jooj** This was a thumb-sized subspecies of Killiks that became part of the Colony following the Yuuzhan Vong War. The Jooj who joined the Great Swarm were found to be devastating soldiers, as they could infiltrate an enemy's defenses better than larger species of Killiks. They could also crawl underneath body armor in a swarm and attack opponents by chewing on their flesh, causing great pain when the flesh-dissolving enzymes in their saliva contacted skin. It was said that the Jooj didn't so much attack enemies as feed on them, consuming their liquefied flesh while victims literally melted away.

**Jool, Queen** This female Hutt owned and operated Rik's Cantina on Coruscant some 130 years after the Battle of Yavin. A noted information broker, Queen Jool was distinguished by the immense cybernetic prosthesis that replaced her left eye. Resembling a jeweled brooch and adorned with feather-like filigree, the cybernetic eye allowed Queen Jool to monitor the entire floor of Rik's at any time. When she wasn't working in the cantina, Queen Jool spent her free time wallowing in the swamp she'd built beneath the building.

About seven years after the Massacre at Ossus, Queen Jool was surprised to see Cade Skywalker walk into Rik's, but only because he was one of the most wanted beings in the galaxy. Cade had once been a regular customer, and she had missed his roguish good looks along with his friends Deliah Blue and Jariah Syn. When Cade was drawn into the Sith Temple to train under Darth Krayt and Darth Talon, it was Queen Jool who allowed R2-D2

*Queen Jool, owner of Rik's cantina*

to show a pre-recorded hologram from Cade to Deliah and Jariah. This recording ensured that ownership of the *Mynock* passed to them, and warned them not to try and follow Cade into the Sith Temple.

**joom-ball** This fist-sized, ruby-red ball was part of a life-or-death game of chance played on Serpine. The joom-ball was rolled down a spiral chute until it fell through a random hole. The hole it entered determined the outcome of the game. Any being who rolled the joom-ball down the spiral chute had to abide by the final outcome, which could mean total forfeiture of wealth, property, or even life.

**joonga pipe** This form of water hookah was popular with the Hutts.

**Joraan Drive Yards** A small starship manufacturer during the New Order.

**Jorak** This Sanyassan Marauder served as the fightmaster for a band led by King Terak. Members made their home on the Forest Moon of Endor during the Galactic Civil War.

**Joralla** This semi-tropical world was the third and primary planet in the Joralla system. It was the homeworld of the fierce Tikiarri species, which was subjugated by the Imperial Moff Debin Seylas. He unofficially quarantined the planet in an effort to keep the Tikiarri from leaving.

**Jorallan opal** These exquisite gemstones were found on Joralla.

**Jorallan pearls** Beautiful spherical gemstones found in the oceans of Joralla.

**Joran** A shifty con man who was one of the many Dantooine natives who settled on the Khoonda Plains in the wake of the Jedi Civil War. He stole the equipment of local farmers and then sold it back to them—leaving out an important component or part, which he would also sell to them. In this way, he extorted large sums of credits from the farmers. Then he was confronted by the Exile. Under intense pressure from the former soldier and Jedi Knight, Joran agreed to return the parts he had stolen.

**Joran Station** This space station was one of the primary stopover points between Phindar and Vjun.

**Jord** This white-haired woman was the leader of the A'Mar during the Galactic Civil War. When a group of adventurers were forced to set down on Lamus after having trouble with their starship, Jord greeted them warmly and agreed to provide them with whatever parts they needed in order to repair their ship. She had but one condition: The adventurers had to remain at the Wellspring with Olianna, the only child among the A'Mar who had not taken a drink from the Well, in order to fulfill the obligations of the Vigil. Jord had participated in the Vigil herself 30 years earlier, and understood its importance. She was also somewhat sensitive to the Force, and was attuned to the Wellspring. Thus, she was able to sense the struggles that the adventurers had during the night, and was pleased when they overcame their troubles and helped Olianna keep the Vigil.

**Jordan, Caal** This scientist was on Manaan investigating the native firaxan sharks when the Great Sith War broke out. Jordan and his team were unprepared for the ferocity of the predators, and had to develop specialized gear to fend them off.

***Jordi*** A Rebel Alliance transport ship used to move commandos into the battle against the Imperial frigate *Priam*. The commandos boarded the frigate and secured it for the Alliance.

**Joreikna** Originally established by the Ku'rys clan, this was one of the smaller underground cities on Ryloth. The residents of Joreikna maintained a bitter rivalry with the inhabitants of nearby Lohema. The mines were near one another, but Joreikna's production was much less than that of its rival.

**Jorek** This Yinchorri male, a member of the Intelligentsia class, was one of the leaders who negotiated with Vilmarh Grahrk to form a plan for stealing starships from the Golden Nyss Shipyards shortly after the Battle of Naboo.

**Jorga** A Duros who served the Galactic Alliance aboard the *Admiral Ackbar* as a gunnery officer during the blockade of the Murgo Choke about a year after the Qoribu crisis.

*Jorshmin, a Phorliss cantina patron*

**Jorhim** Serving as a security officer within the Gepparin Landing Control force, this man worked for the BloodScar pirates at their base on Gepparin during the early years of the Galactic Civil War.

**Jorir, Major** This clone trooper originally was designated CT-43/76-9155. Major Jorir was later placed in charge of the day-to-day operations of Squad Seven, reporting directly to Commanders Cody and Odd Ball. His name was a *Mando'a* verb meaning "to carry" or "to bear."

**Joris, Rax** An Imperial officer assigned to the garrison on Dosuun during the early years of the New Republic. When the remaining leaders of the Empire consolidated into the Imperial Remnant, Joris was left on Dosuun. He considered this posting a slap in the face—and took his apathy to extreme levels. He became grossly overweight and did little to maintain his physical appearance. He amused himself by taking prisoners, setting them free inside the garrison, and daring them to safely reach Dosuun's wilderness while he hunted them down like animals. His reign on Dosuun was ended about 10 years after the Battle of Endor when he captured Jaden Korr. Joris thought it would be interesting to hunt down a Jedi Knight, and set Korr free. However, Korr had no intention of being killed, and confronted Joris. In a tense shootout, Joris was killed and Korr escaped Dosuun.

**Jorkatt the Render** This crime lord had his base of operations on Celanon, and was known throughout the galaxy as a despicable and devious felon.

**Jorlen, Captain Mak** An officer aboard the New Republic carrier-cruiser *Thurse* during the battle against the Yuuzhan Vong. He was also an acquaintance of Han Solo.

**Jornisae** A species of web-weaving spider native to Cularin.

**Jorran** One of the many salvagers who established a niche on the Khoonda Plains of Dantooine in the wake of the Jedi Civil War. Like his fellow salvagers, Jorran split his time between scavenging the ruins of the Jedi Enclave for useful artifacts and selling them to other members of the Khoonda Plains community. However, Jorran was greedy, and often arranged to acquire more credits than an artifact was probably worth. During one trip into the Jedi Enclave, he got trapped by a pack of laigreks, and was forced to hide inside a room deep within. Only the timely arrival of the Exile, who was on Dantooine searching for information on Jedi Master Vrook, saved him from being eaten.

**Jorshmin** This small, furred humanoid frequented Gorb Drig's cantina on Phorliss. He became a friend of Mara Jade, who was working at the cantina for a short while after escaping from Ysanne Isard. He was distinguishable by his dark fur, which was broken by a white stripe running from his nose, over his back, to his tail. He was mortally wounded helping Mara protect cantina owner Drig from Black Nebula extortionists.

**Jorsk** A smuggler of some renown, Jorsk ran weapons and supplies to Rebel Alliance forces during the Galactic Civil War. He was a native of Taanab and disliked flechette weapons because of their distinct patterns, which gave immediate clues as to their usage.

**Jortan** A medical technician in Page's Commandos.

**Joruna** Along with Widek, Joruna was a New Republic planet located near the Koornacht Cluster. Due to the zealous guarding of Koornacht's borders by the alien Yevetha following the Galactic Civil War, all freight traffic had to travel a circuitous route around the Cluster to reach both worlds.

**Jos** This native of Lianna, a slave to Captain Ugmush, worked as an engineer on the *Zicreex*. At one time, Jos had been the engineer on the *G'mi Moa*, until that ship was captured by Gunda Mabin, who sold all the survivors, including Jos, into slavery. Recognizing Jos's skills as an engineer, Ugmush purchased the rights to him.

**Jos, Mebara** This Togorian female was considered for a place in the Almas Academy several years before the Battle of Naboo. She had been ostracized on her homeworld because of her connection to the Force, but was later denied training after she got into a fight with another student. She spent the next 20 years or so slowly growing more angry and frustrated at being exiled and thrown out of the academy, and eventually founded the Fireclaw Horde.

She and her gang failed on nearly every job they tried to pull off. In a final, desperate act, Mebara Jos decided to cause trouble for the Cularin Classic swoop race. She hoped that any destruction she and her gang created would be broadcast throughout the system by the media.

Her plans were discovered by the Twi'lek investigator Di'hal'uma, prompting Jos to hire the Blood Raptors to capture the Twi'lek and bring her in for questioning. Jos then put her plans in motion, taking control of the video screens on the racecourse and issuing her threats. She tried to send the Team SoroSuub remote-controlled swoop into the crowds, but freelance agents were able to prevent it from leaving the course. Flying into a rage, Jos tapped into the dark side of the Force and tried to kill the agents, but she and her Togorian thugs were eventually defeated.

**Josall, Sephjet** This bald human was one of the many Jedi Knights who were dispatched to Geonosis to rescue Obi-Wan Kenobi at the start of the Clone Wars. Josall and his partner, Nicanas Tassu, provided backup lightsabers to Obi-Wan and his Padawan, Anakin Skywalker, at the height of the battle.

**Josen, Kardash** A Twi'lek, he was one of the many surgeons who enlisted with the Old Republic military during the Clone Wars. Josen served with Jos Vondar and Zan Yant at the Rimsoo Seven military hospital on Drongar.

***Josephine's Honor*** An alias used by Jericho and Josephine Donovan for their smuggling ship, *Jericho's Pride*.

**Joshi, Captain** This Imperial captained the frigate *Provocateur* under the command of Warlord Zsinj. During an attack on Talasea, the *Provocateur* was destroyed, and Captain Joshi perished with the rest of his crew.

**Jospro sector** A seldom-visited sector containing the Dar'Or system, it was home to tiny creatures called ix dbukrii that paralyzed the neocortex of the human brain. Imperial forces on Bakura used these creatures to suppress the memories of Eppie Belden, an important member of the resistance.

**Jostran** According to New Republic data banks, the Jostrans were the dominant species on Munlali Mafir. The average Jostran resembled a slow-moving centipede about 1.5 meters in length. By the time Luke Skywalker arrived at Munlali Mafir, during his search for Zonama Sekot, the Jostrans had disappeared. Jacen Solo and Soron Hegerty discovered that the Jostrans had been combined with the Krizlaws by the appearance of Zonama Sekot, resulting in a predatory species that looked outwardly like a Krizlaw. However, the symbiotic relationship that was created allowed the Jostran individual to fuse itself to the Krizlaw spinal column and nervous system. In this way, the Jostran mind controlled the Krizlaw body. This new species of vicious beings quickly eliminated the Jostran as well as the nonsymbiont Krizlaws, becoming the sole species of Munlali Mafir. Those Jostrans who survived remained distinct individuals in their symbiont bodies, and were still able to produce a form of offspring that was force-fed into a new body. There it fused itself to the victim's spinal cord and nervous system, becoming a new entity.

**Jostrian** This corporation made a series of choke-collars with mechanical key locks. This prevented someone from employing a random frequency transmitter to remotely open the collar.

**Jotane, Trevas** This handsome young man was, to all outward appearances, a Knight of House Calipsa. In reality, he was an agent of the Imperial Security Bureau who was working in the Tapani sector in search of Adana Vermor, an Imperial economic adviser suspected of Rebel affiliations. He arranged for Dunell and his Justice Action Network terrorists to raid the Unification Gala on Barnaba, hoping to murder Vermor in the resulting confusion. However, Jotane failed to see that the JAN terrorists wanted Vermor for themselves. Jotane, his career in shambles, was reassigned to other cases.

**Jotay** A security agent who worked for the authorities of Revos's starport shortly after the Battle of Endor.

**Jotsen's Island** One of the largest islands on Lamaredd, it measured some 10,000 kilometers in length. It was the site of Bartyn Gourmet Delicacies. Owner Hugo Bartyn had virtually enslaved his workforce before the Sailors' Union managed to negotiate certain concessions. They included ownership of Jotsen's Island, which Bartyn ceded to the Union as a refuge for the many aquatic beings Bartyn had forcibly imported there.

**journal disk** Any specialized data disk used to contain a being's personal memoirs or information.

***Journal of Energy Physics*** A professional publication to which Nasdra Magrody often submitted articles.

***Journal of the Whills, The*** This legendary set of stories was believed to have been collected by the Ancient Order of the Whills, a higher order of beings who had a deep connection with and understanding of the Force. *The Journal of the Whills* recounted the events leading up to the Clone Wars, documented the advent of the New Order, and continued on to tell the story of the Galactic Civil War.

**Journeyman** The brand name of SoroSuub's personal tool kit. It was designed for use by starship owners, and contained the basic tools needed to maintain a ship.

**Journeyman Protector** The police force that protected the natives of Concord Dawn was made up of Journeyman Protectors.

**Jova** One of the many Thaereian spies who infiltrated the cities of Cularin during the final years of the Old Republic. Jova was part of a cell that worked in the platform city of Bayonard.

**Jovan** Jovan Station was built in orbit around this planet.

**Jovan Station** The command center for the Imperial fleet that blockaded Yavin 4 following the destruction of the first Death Star. Its commanding officer, Admiral Griff, ordered a full-scale attack on Yavin 4 when he heard that the Super Star Destroyer *Executor* had been disabled.

**Joventusek** This city, the Caarite word for "gateway," was the primary departure point for all beings traveling to Caarimon. Joventusek was the largest of Caarimon's cities, and was similar in design to the smaller, satellite cities. The entire city floated several meters off the ground on a cushion of gases that kept it from actually touching the surface. These gases were created as part of the respiratory process of the abundant plant life found on the planet. Visitors to Caarimon were processed in Joventusek, and shuttled to one of the smaller cities in specialized speeders that did little or no harm to the environment. The city's edges were patrolled by ceramic-bodied droids that moved about on repulsorlifts or jetpacks, ensuring that no stray metal or trash ever reached the surface.

**Jovvitz** A nightclub located on Brentaal in city block Kesk-135.

**Jowa** This Gallofree medium transport was used by the Rebel Alliance to transport bacta during the Galactic Civil War.

**Jowar, Moff** An aging Imperial Moff who traveled to the Nickel One asteroid in the wake of the Second Battle of Fondor to ensure that the resources of the Roche asteroid field were secured for the Empire. Moff Jowar was fond of reminding his fellow Moffs that he had served on the personal staff of Emperor Palpatine during the era of the New Order.

*Augarra "Augie" Jowil (rear)*

**Jowdrrl** One of Chewbacca's many cousins, she was a ship's systems expert. Jowdrrl worked with Katarra to subvert the Imperial presence on Kashyyyk. When Chewbacca returned to Kashyyyk for his son Lumpawarump's Test of Ascension, Jowdrrl worked with Dryanta on fine-tuning the *Millennium Falcon.* They improved many of the ship's systems, including refinements to the weapons and a 360-degree head-up display unit. She once accompanied Chewbacca on a mission to rescue Han Solo during the Yevethan crisis.

**Jowil, Augarra "Augie"** Known as Augie to her close friends, this female Gungan took over as the leader of the Great Municipal Band. A native of the Lianorm Swamp, Jowil had trained under Beezr Pert for many years, and had been among the first to hear the Symponika Crunchen-Grand. When Pert announced his retirement, the band's leaders voted to have Jowil take his place, an honor that many thought was well deserved despite her relatively young age. Jowil was present when Queen Amidala approached Boss Nass and begged for an alliance, in an effort to recruit the Gungans to help overthrow the Trade Federation's blockade of their homeworld. Recognizing that this was a turning point in Gungan history, Jowil began composing what would become known as the *Symponika Nabooalla,* which chronicled the efforts of both Gungans and humans to restore their freedom.

**jowlpreener** A Nimbanese creature.

**Joy** A city on the lawless world of Korbin. Like other cities on the planet, it was cynically named by the criminals who controlled it. Along with Happy and Peace, Joy was known as a Small-Timer, because it was less intense than Pleasant City.

**joy cave** Any of the underground pleasure chambers established by Twi'leks on their homeworld of Ryloth. Each joy cave was actually a group of connected chambers: a central meeting room surrounded by smaller private cells. In this way, the female slaves who worked in the joy cave—known as glitter girls—were never more than a single, short hallway away from their owners and their bodyguards.

**Joylin** This tall, slender Romin male was leader of the Citizens' Resistance movement that tried to overturn the dictatorship of Roy Teda in the years before the Clone Wars. Despite setbacks and brutal reprisals from the Security Management Control force, Joylin's resistance grew. The group even had contacts and agents within Teda's own government.

Joylin had Anakin Skywalker and Ferus Olin kidnapped to ask for their assistance in overturning Teda's rule. He believed them to be Waldo and Ukiah, members of the gang known as the Slams. Joylin offered the false Slams the chance to be the only criminals allowed to live on Romin, in exchange for their help in stealing information from Roy Teda's office. The Jedi reluctantly agreed, and Obi-Wan Kenobi managed to obtain the information and escape Teda's palace. With the information—mainly security and access codes—Joylin's rebels knocked out the main droid control system, and then set out to eliminate the officers of Security Management Control.

Joylin had told the Jedi that he ordered his forces to act with a minimum of bloodshed, an order he repeated as the revolt began. But years of pent-up anger launched the Romins into a frenzy, and many of the wealthy residents of Eliior were slaughtered. In the end, Joylin proved just as bloodthirsty as his rebels when he issued an order calling for Roy Teda to turn himself in for trial. If he failed to do so, Joylin would execute one member of his former staff at a time. Ultimately Teda fled Romin, which allowed Joylin to assume leadership for himself. This series of events later was twisted by Teda during testimony before the Galactic Senate, implicating the Jedi Knights as the masterminds behind the plot to remove him from power.

**J'Pel** One of the many mining settlements, or *o'bekis,* established on Goroth Prime.

**J'Quille** A Whiphid male who was part of Jabba the Hutt's retinue on Tatooine just prior to the crime lord's death. He was one of Lady Valarian's former lovers, and the two of them staged a falling-out to gain Jabba's attention. The Hutt, in turn, employed him in order to gall Valarian. Valarian and J'Quille had arranged their breakup, and J'Quille became a spy. J'Quille arranged to meet Malakili and the rancor, in order to steal them out from under Jabba's nose. J'Quille also was responsible for bribing Phlegmin to lace Jabba's paddy toads with a slow-acting poison. In his rooms, J'Quille kept a strand of poisoned mastmot teeth as a decoration, hoping someday to use them against Jabba. He never got the chance, because Jabba was killed at the Pit of Carkoon. When he fled Tatooine and tried to return to Toola, J'Quille found that Valarian had put a price on his head for "rejecting" her. J'Quille returned to Jabba's palace and became a B'omarr acolyte, claiming that having his brain removed to a nutrient jar was the only way to escape Tatooine's heat.

**JR-4** A heavy-bodied swoop produced by Bespin Motors during the Old Republic. Considered one of the earliest swoops produced, it enjoyed a run of several centuries before it was discontinued about 100 years before the Battle of Yavin. It was first marketed as a single-person airspeeder, but its high-altitude maneuverability earned the nickname swoop early in its existence. Despite its age, the 3.9-meter-long JR-4 remained a viable racing swoop for many years. The noted Gotal pilot Arum Oru flew one during the inaugural Cularin Classic shortly before the Clone Wars began.

**JR-8** A series of janitorial maintenance droids produced by Publictechnic following the Clone Wars. The JR-8 was equipped with a canister of cleaning fluid and a spray nozzle, as well as scrubbers and a light manipulator arm. It was known as a feisty droid that worked diligently at its assigned tasks, and often squirted its cleaning fluid at any being that got in the

*J'Quille*

way. The JR-8 moved about on four stubby legs.

**Jrade-Daders Concourse** This wide thoroughfare was located near Monument Plaza on Coruscant.

**jran** These small predators preyed on the tiny wenton—but only if they could catch one. This continual hide-and-seek existence gave rise to the phrase *a game of jran and wenton,* which indicated any series of events in which one party tried to avoid contact with another pursuing party.

**JRD-33** This droid interface unit was designed by Subpro for use aboard starships during the early years of the New Order.

**JR series droid** A series of public works droids produced by Publictechnic during the last decades of the Old Republic.

**Jrul** This ancient Jedi Master was noted for asking two simple questions: "What is the good, if not the teacher of the bad? What is the bad, if not the task of the good?"

**JTHW** The file stored in CB-99 that detailed Jabba the Hutt's will.

**J't'p'tan (Doornik-628E)** A gentle, pleasant world of garden cities, it was located in the heart of the Koornacht Cluster and known on charts as Doornik-628E. The name was an approximation of four glyphs of the H'kig conservative religious sect: *jeh,* the immanent; *teh,* the transcendent; *peh,* the eternal; and *tan,* the conscious essence. The first three glyphs were considered too sacred to be written out fully. It was here that the Fallanassi religious community and its leader Wialu settled after departing Lucazec.

After leaving Atzerri, Luke Skywalker and Akanah Norand Pell left for J't'p'tan to search for the Fallanassi. The planet was the site of a H'kig colony established some 50 years earlier. The H'kig built a vast stone temple, covering more than 3,000 acres of a small valley, entirely by hand. During the Yevethan Great Purge, the colony was supposedly destroyed. In reality, it was preserved by the Fallanassi, who projected a false image of destruction in order to protect the commune. The Yevetha started a colony on the planet after their conquest. Akanah was reunited with her fellow Fallanassi, and Luke convinced Wialu to help in the fight against the Yevethan fleet. After the Battle of N'zoth, the Fallanassi left J't'p'tan on the liner *Star Morning* to find a new home.

**J'tt'sa** This immense, black-haired humanoid was the captain of the ship that brought Mara Jade to Kintoni shortly after the Battle of Endor.

*A J-type spacecraft, the Naboo Royal Starship*

**J-type** The term used to describe the twin-radial configuration of sublight engines on certain starships produced during the final decades of the Old Republic. The basic design of the J-type was developed by the Nubians and placed the engines out on wings, away from the central fuselage.

**J-type 327 Nubian** *See* Naboo Royal Starship.

**Juaka Canyon** This rocky canyon was located on Ando Prime, some 500 miles from the Elesa outpost. The canyon was 30 meters deep and 150 meters long, and its walls had been carved from the icy rock by primordial water and wind. The Twi'lek scout Ree discovered a rich vein of vonium within the canyon during the early years of the New Order.

**Jubal** This Devaronian lived on Tatooine at about the same time Labria lived in Mos Eisley in the years just prior to the Battle of Yavin.

**jubba** Native to the Forest Moon of Endor, this plant produced a small nut that was considered a delicacy by Ewoks.

**jubba bird** An avian native to Dagobah, the jubba produced a highly soothing song-whistle that it manipulated via the Force. The average jubba bird produced its song when it was happy or content, and steadfastly refused to sing when it was angry or upset. Jubbas were often captured by vendors who sold them for their mesmerizing song. They were also intelligent, and often simply played dumb to avoid being harassed by ignorant owners. Those jubbas sold to appreciative owners sometimes allowed their innate intelligence to show, and became loyal companions.

In their native environment, jubba birds built heavy nests by scooping mud from Dagobah's swamps, using it as a glue to hold sticks and plant matter together. These nests drooped into the swamps, allowing predators easy access to jubba eggs. The average specimen was a skilled hunter, consuming snakes and rodents. Captive jubba birds required live food and plenty of space in which to live, and many owners preferred to keep them in open spaces where they could "hunt" their prey.

**Jubben, Senator** One of the many Senators who were assassinated in the years before the Clone Wars. It was later learned that Senator Jubben had been murdered by Zam Wesell and her ASN-121 assassin droid, after the droid's remains were discovered in an alleyway on Coruscant.

**Jubieck** This Sullustan worked for the crime lord Nirama during the last years of the Old Republic. Jubieck was dispatched, along with the Trandoshans Orix and Dimogog, to recover the head of the protocol droid L80-RC. Unable to obtain it peacefully, they were forced to struggle with a team of Republic soldiers. The head was taken by a team of freelance mercenaries.

*Jubba birds*

**Jubilar** A penal colony orbited by a single moon, it was used by several nearby worlds as a dumping ground for their criminals. The inhabitants organized themselves into armies, and fought one another in continuous brutal wars. One of Jubilar's cities was called Dying Slowly (later renamed Death), and contained the slum of Executioners Row and the huge Victory Forum, where Regional Sector Number Four's All-Human Free-For-All extravaganza was staged. Four humans were pitted against one another in a pentagonal ring, and the last one standing was declared the winner.

Fifteen years before the Battle of Hoth, Boba Fett killed a spice dealer named Hallolar Voors on Jubilar. While there, he saw a young Han Solo successfully defend himself in the Free-For-All against three larger opponents. Solo had been sent to Jubilar for cheating at cards. Fifteen years after the Battle of Endor, Solo returned to Jubilar to make a smuggling run for old times' sake. The Victory Forum and many areas of the city were in ruins from war and neglect. The jandarra—a green vegetable grown only in Jubilar's desert and in a few hydroponics tanks—was a popular export.

**Jubilee** An officer with the Rebel Alliance. Shortly after the Battle of Hoth, Jubilee was part of a crew that accompanied Leia Organa to Shiva IV. When their

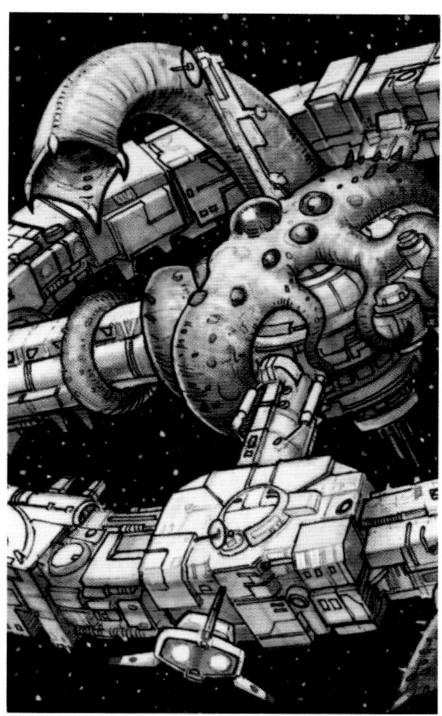
Jubilee Wheel *under attack by the Yuuzhan Vong*

ship was rocked by a sudden explosion, Jubilee was ordered to make sure that Leia's shuttle was safely out of the main hold.

**jubilee wheel** A popular betting device found in casinos throughout the galaxy. Players bet on which of 100 numbers would appear after a random spin of the large jubilee wheel. Any player who correctly chose the winning number won or split the entire pot. If no player chose correctly, any player within five of it won or split half the pot, with the remainder going to the house. If there were no winners on a given spin, the entire pot was taken by the house.

***Jubilee Wheel*** This space station was constructed in orbit around Ord Mantell during the early years of the New Republic, and largely comprised salvaged parts and Hutt-supplied structures. The station resembled a large open wheel, with spokes connecting the central hub to the outer ring. For the most part, the *Jubilee Wheel* was independent of the activities on Ord Mantell. During the Yuuzhan Vong War, a strange biological construct known as the dread weapon attacked the *Wheel,* clamping a thick umbilical to the station and literally sucking out its inhabitants. Many believed that those who survived the capture were later turned into slaves by the Yuuzhan Vong.

**Jubnuk** A Gamorrean guard in the palace of Jabba the Hutt, he fell into the rancor pit along with Luke Skywalker and was quickly eaten.

**Judarrl, Drakka** This female Zabrak was one of the few Jedi Knights who managed to survive the Jedi Purge. She escaped to Dantooine, where she remained hidden in the ruins of the ancient Jedi Temple for several decades. Finally she was discovered by a group of Rebel Alliance agents dispatched to Dantooine in the wake of the Battle of Yavin.

***Judgement 12-X7*** This Imperial hunter-killer probot pursued the *Starlight Intruder* over Byss after it discovered that the *Millennium Falcon* was attached to it.

**Judges of the Dead** Located on Socorro, this landmark was made up of four 50-meter-tall rock formations. Found between Vakeyya and the Rym Mountains, the Judges of the Dead were believed by locals to resemble hooded women with their faces hidden in sorrowful contemplation. The area became something of a shrine, and the Socorrans believed that a dead person's soul traveled from all points on the planet to be judged by the four women before being released to the afterlife.

**Judgment** Modeled after the Empire's Coalition for Progress, this branch of the Pentastar Alignment's Chamber of Order was established to ensure that the policies of the Alignment and the New Order were fully integrated into the laws of the government. The Great InQuestors of Judgment served as the most visible agents of the branch, and the appearance of an InQuestor often meant trouble.

**Judgment Circle** The name given to any gathering of the members of the Jedi Order to discuss the transgressions of a member. The convocation of a Judgment Circle was allowed whenever Jedi Knights were forced to work for an extended period of time without direct contact with the Jedi Council, and provided for the trial of a Jedi who was perceived to have acted in a way contrary to the Jedi Code.

**Judgment Field** Located outside the city of Montellian Serat on Devaron, this open arena was dedicated to the memory of the massacre perpetrated by Kardue'sai'Malloc during the New Order. It was there that the Devaronians set packs of quarra on their most heinous criminals. Kardue'sai'Malloc himself was executed on Judgment Field after he was caught on Peppel by Boba Fett.

**Judgment Guides** The primary judicial body of Kegan. During the last decades of the Old Republic, the Judgment Guides were under the control of the Benevolent Guides.

***Judicator*** This *Imperial I*–class Star Destroyer was under the command of Captain Brandei following the Battle of Endor. The *Judicator* was equipped with the most up-to-date targeting systems, and its mission was to help other capital ships by coordinating their fire. Following the death of Emperor Palpatine at Endor, the *Judicator* became part of Grand Admiral Thrawn's fleet. He used it to attack Bpfassh in one of his first moves against the New Republic. The *Judicator* was later the lead ship on the mission to steal 51 mole miners from the Nomad City installation on Nkllon for use in the Battle of Sluis Van. The *Judicator* sustained damage at Nkllon, but was quickly repaired. It was also the ship sent to intercept a New Republic fleet attempting to regain the *Katana* fleet.

**Judicial Department** The primary law enforcement agency of the Old Republic. Its role greatly expanded during the Ruusan Reformations, when Chancellor Tarsus Valorum made the Jedi Order a branch of the Judicial Department, answerable to the Galactic Senate.

**Judicial Forces** This branch of the Old Republic military patrolled the galaxy on missions to mediate disputes that had the potential of erupting into war.

**Judlie** One of the code names used by Zozridor Slayke for key locations of military value on Praesitlyn during the attempt by Freedom's Sons and Daughters to fend off a Separatist attack on the Intergalactic Communications Center. Judlie was a redoubt 600 meters behind Slayke's command center, and served as a scouting location to protect the army's rear flank. Like the command center and positions Izable, Eliey, and Kaudine, Judlie had a 360-degree view of surrounding terrain, and its fire zone overlapped with Eliey and Kaudine. This provided the maximum defense of the command center. However, Zozridor's forces were badly outnumbered by the Separatist battle droids, and personnel from the other four locations were forced to fall back to Judlie to regroup.

**Judrelle, Tassida** This Jedi Knight led a team to the asteroid belt near Cona to break up the salt-smuggling ring of Lojrak Shrag shortly before the onset of the Clone Wars. The Jedi received assistance from the smuggler Billey, who was named an "honorary legend" by the Arcona Grand Nest.

**Juggadoo** Also referred to as Jugaloo, this species was native to the Dandelo system. During the early years of the New Order, the Juggadoo were enslaved by the Starhunter Intergalactic Menagerie, but they were eventually freed by Jann Tosh and his droids, R2-D2 and C-3PO.

*Jubnuk (left) warily eyes Luke Skywalker.*

*Juhani*

**juggerhead** This Mon Calamari fish was often hunted for food.

***Juggernaut*** An *Imperial*-class Star Destroyer, it was stationed by the Empire in the Kuat system during the Galactic Civil War. It couldn't stop a Rebel Alliance mission to infiltrate a secret research facility shortly before the Battle of Endor.

**juggernaut** *See* HAVt B5 juggernaut; HAVw A5 juggernaut; and HAVw A6 juggernaut.

**Juggernaut war droid** This fearsome combat droid was at the forefront of the Great Droid Revolution, although its origins could be traced back 800 years earlier. The original Juggernaut war droids were commissioned by Supreme Chancellor Vocatara of the Old Republic, some 4,800 years before the Battle of Yavin, to assist the Jedi Knights and the Republic's military forces in putting an end to the Gank Massacres. The hastily developed Juggernauts were built from the basic form of refueling droids. These war droids stood nearly 2 meters tall, and were covered with white armor plating. The head of the Juggernaut was little more than a hemispherical dome that contained the primary sensor and communication gear, giving the Juggernaut a 360-degree field of vision. The droids were armed with a shatter beam mounted to one arm, and a sonic stunner on the other. They could carry standard Republic weaponry in their hands, if needed. The specialized outrigger jetpack that allowed the resupply droids to reach remote locations was retained, giving the Juggernaut the ability to fly into battle behind the main line of combat. After the Gank Massacres were ended, Juggernaut war droids were recalled to Coruscant, where they served as a homeworld security force for centuries before HK-01 set off the Great Droid Revolution. Legions of Juggernaut war droids killed indiscriminately, instilling fear in sentient beings across the galaxy. In the wake of the revolution, any surviving Juggernaut war droid had its cognitive matrices removed, and production was immediately halted. Most of the inert shells were purchased by collectors and museums, and a handful of these were later acquired by the Iron Knights.

**juggy** A slang term used by early Rebels for the HAVw A5 and HAVw A6 juggernauts that were used by the Empire.

**Jugsmuk** A Gamorrean settlement on the Wugguh continent of Gamorr and controlled by the Jugsmuk clan. A great fair was held there during Slushtime shortly after a smaller fair at Bolgoink.

**Jugsmuk Station** Located within the settlement of Jugsmuk on Gamorr, this station was a place where offworlders could live among themselves, and not get in the way of Gamorrean politics.

**Juhani** This Cathar Jedi Knight, like many of her species who joined the Jedi Order, struggled with her instincts and emotions while trying to gain a greater understanding of the Force. Despite her inner struggles, Juhani committed herself completely to the Order and refused to be anything less than a perfect Jedi Knight. She also refused to accept failure among her peers, which tended to alienate her from many of her fellow Jedi. She was exceptionally loyal to her Master, Quatra, who trained her at the ancient Jedi compound on Dantooine. During a training exercise, however, she became angry at Quatra for her unrelenting teaching, and she struck her down; Quatra feigned death to teach her Padawan a lesson. A horrified Juhani fled into the Dantooine wilderness, where she encountered the former Sith Lord, Revan.

**Jukassa, Zett** This young Padawan was among the many students of the Force who were training at the Jedi Temple on Coruscant when the Clone Wars broke out. He was born to parents who were ore miners on Mon Gazza, but was taken as an infant to be brought up on Coruscant. When he was seven, Jukassa began experiencing strange visions of his parents' deaths, and the Jedi Knight Mierme Unill determined that his visions were connected to the murder of several miners on Mon Gazza. She received permission to tell Jukassa about his past in an effort to solve the murders. It was then that he learned his true name, Warpoc Skamini, and the names of his parents, Sembric and Ashielle. After Mierme Unill exposed a group of Black Sun extortionists as the killers, she took Jukassa as her Padawan. However, she was killed in battle during the Clone Wars, and Jukassa's training fell to Cin Drallig.

*Juggernaut war droid*

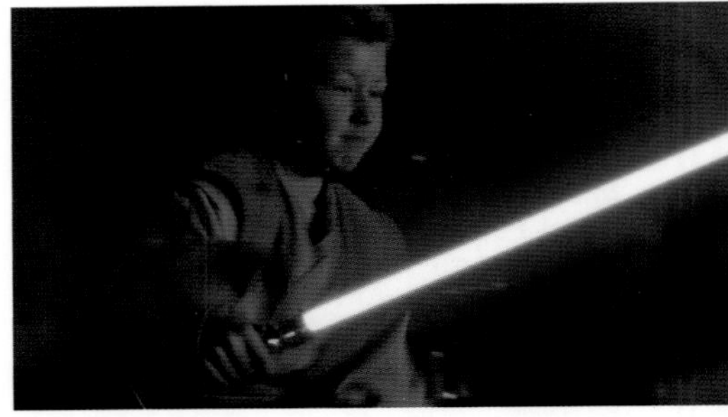

*Zett Jukassa fights Darth Vader's clone troopers.*

In the wake of the Battle of Coruscant, after Darth Sidious revealed his true nature and killed Mace Windu, Jukassa was one of the few younglings to survive the initial attack of Anakin Skywalker on those Jedi still in the Temple. Jukassa fought bravely, and nearly escaped before being overrun and shot to death by Sergeant Fox, who had been trying to keep Senator Bail Organa from entering the Temple. An official report on Imperial HoloVision claimed that Jukassa had been killed while trying to assassinate Senator Organa.

**Jul, Bhat** This Kajain'sa'Nikto Jedi Knight was apprenticed to Master A'Sharad Hett in the months before the Clone Wars. When war broke out, Bhat remained by his Master's side. They were part of the team dispatched to Metalorn, and later Aargonar, as the fighting intensified. They were shot down over enemy territory on Aargonar, and forced to fight their way clear. During the struggle, an explosion rocked their position, and Bhat Jul caught the blast full in the chest. Despite the efforts of Anakin Skywalker to keep him alive, Bhat Jul died from his injuries a short while later. After his death, and that of Master Sora Mobari, Anakin began to question why the Jedi Knights were not doing more to save the lives of beings in the galaxy, rather than fighting a war that led to more deaths.

*Bhat Jul getting assistance from Anakin Skywalker*

**Jular, Pelav** This former Imperial Army major left the military and joined the Neolsse family's local militia about 10 years before the Battle of Yavin. Jular served as a general in the Keremark armed forces, and was in command of the defense of Fortress Keremark during the Galactic Civil War.

**Julept** This Sullustan often visited the Farrimmer Café to swap stories and sell pieces of technology he had acquired. He was fond of regaling other patrons with a story of a Wookiee companion who convinced him to travel to Byss in order to kill both Darth Vader and Emperor Palpatine. The story always ended with Vader grabbing the Wookiee by the leg as he tried to escape. Julept would end the story by saying, "Of course, I'm pulling your leg the same way Vader was pulling the Wookiee's!"

***Juliupper*** This was one of the many transport ships used to evacuate Sernpidal just before the Yuuzhan Vong destroyed it. The *Juliupper* never got free, though, as it was attacked by a swarm of grutchins let loose by the Yuuzhan Vong.

**Juloff** A reporter for the Galactic News Network, he worked at GNN's Indu San bureau during the early years of the New Republic. Juloff was, in fact, an Imperial spy who infiltrated GNN to ensure that "correct" reporting of the events on Indu San took place.

**Julpa, Mon** The crown prince of Tammuzan in the early days of the Empire, Julpa was a purple-skinned individual who was stripped of his mind and title by Zatec-Cha. Julpa was dropped on Tyne's Horky and wandered the planet with no memory of his former self. He was known briefly as Kez-Iban after he saved the life of Jann Tosh's uncle Gundy. Julpa got his memory back and eventually claimed the throne that was rightfully his.

**Julstan IV, Alexander** The Imperial Moff in charge of Arkanis sector and Tatoo system during the early years of the Galactic Civil War.

**Julsujod III** The original homeworld of the Stribers species of Iskalonians.

**juma juice** A nonalcoholic fruit beverage favored by many Jedi Knights during the last years of the Old Republic. It was first developed many millennia before the Clone Wars, and remained popular for many generations. It was served often at Dexter's Diner.

**jumba** A mammalian creature native to Tatooine, where it was raised by moisture farmers for its tough hide. Cured and tanned, jumba hides created an inexpensive yet durable form of leather used to make carrying bags and luggage.

**Jumerian** This species was a member of the New Republic.

**Jumka, Mavikk** A Kadas'sa'Nikto, he was part of a gang that wreaked havoc on the Outland Transit Station during the years leading up to the Battle of Naboo. He was arrested and sent to the Oovo IV prison facility for his part in the crimes, and managed to negotiate a shorter sentence in return for providing information on his partners. For some reason, the Outland police force demanded that he die a terrible death for his crimes.

*Mon Julpa*

**Jump** This tall, spindly smuggler was a regular at the Blue Light on Nar Shaddaa until he ran afoul of Salla Zend. She broke his arm when he tried to make a pass at her.

**jump beacon** *See* jump gate.

**jump droid** Specially produced super battle droids developed to operate in atmospheres, rather than on the ground. Each was equipped with a rocket jetpack that allowed it to move about in the air. These droids were deployed to gas giant worlds, as well as to dangerous or high-altitude locations.

**Jumper** This Arakyd personal jetpack was smaller than the Whisper pack, with less power, but it was also somewhat more affordable. However, after many decades of production, the Jumper experienced continual price increases while durability was reduced, making it less appealing to the galaxy's consumers.

**jumper** This Zelosian parasite was nocturnal and fed on corpses. The feeding frenzy of a swarm of jumpers had a unique effect on a newly dead body. Jumpers released certain enzymes and electrical discharges while feeding, and this combination caused the body to jerk and flinch—and eventually kick-started the brain. The body then seemed to come back to life and walk, although the effect lasted only a few hours until the jumpers had finished feeding. This "walking dead" effect was frightening to the native Zelosians, since it occurred at night during the darkness they feared most.

***Jump for Joy*** This Twomi Skyfire—barely a year old—was discovered by Akanah while she and Luke Skywalker stopped over on Utharis during their search for the Fallanassi. It was heavily modified to adapt it to the latest in navigational, piloting, and protection technologies.

**jump gate** These were erected by pioneers of faster-than-light travel. Jump gates marked proven, safe coordinates for jumping into and out of hyperspace and were usually located in relatively empty regions of space between star systems. Many large spaceports had grown up around them. Ancient jump gates were limited in their capacity to re-route starships, with only enough memory to store a small number of other locations. Thus crisscrossing networks of routes passed through each set of gates.

**jump gate accelerator** One of the earliest known methods of propelling a ship into hyperspace, used in conjunction with a jump gate.

**jumping spider** A purple arachnid native to Yavin 4.

**JumpMaster 5000** Known as a JM-5K, this was a crescent-shaped Corellian Engineering Corporation scouting and service ship. The crescent was bisected by a tubular main section, and power plants were located at the points of the crescent. The design was outdated at the time of the Galactic Civil War, but many ships remained in service. The basic ship was just 20 meters in diameter, and could accommodate only a few passengers or 500 kilograms of cargo.

**Jumus** A planet located along the Corellian Trade Spine, between Corellia and New Plympto. During the Yuuzhan Vong War, Jumus and its system served as a primary staging area for the Yuuzhan Vong fleet. In the wake of the Battle of Duro, the fleet was seemingly poised to strike deep into the Core Worlds, but much of the buildup was meant to deflect attention from the battle fleet that later attacked Coruscant by way of Bilbringi.

**Jun** This hot ball of rock was the first planet in the Faarlsun system.

*Victor Jun*

**Jun, Glee** A member of Klyn Shanga's Renatasian vigilantes who were searching for Vuffi Raa during the early years of the New Order.

**Jun, Victor** This mentally unstable man grew up worshipping the gods of his homeworld, and thoroughly believed that they spoke directly to him. He gave himself to their every bidding. With every task he accomplished for the gods, Victor was shown ever-more-enticing glimpses of the awesome powers they commanded—which he could learn to control if he continued his devotion. To most of the people who lived in his village, however, Victor was just a muttering fool who lacked the mental capacity to live a normal life. Whenever he crossed the gods or didn't follow their commands, Victor experienced what he called the Black Pain, which left him debilitated and weak. Thus, he strove to earn their continued favor. When he was told to leave his family and spread the words of the gods, Victor didn't hesitate. Although few beings believed him, Victor nonetheless remained loyal to the beings he was sure were communicating with him.

When the Galactic Civil War broke out, Victor knew that he had finally found his calling. He petitioned countless numbers of beings who joined the Rebel Alliance, hoping to convince them that his gods could help them in their struggle against the "evil Empire." Again, Victor found few who shared his beliefs, but that did not deter him from seeking out Rebel leaders to petition for their conversion.

**juna** The berries of this tree, native to Gala, were eaten as a dessert or snack.

**Junak, Taj** This Jedi Knight managed to survive the Jedi Purge, and hid from the Empire in the Freeworlds region of the Tapani sector. He assumed the guise of Professor Shellery Kint, who taught at the Mrlsst Academy. While there, Junak worked behind the scenes to steal important Imperial data from research labs throughout the sector. When the Empire moved into Tapani sector and threatened to take over the Mrlsst Academy, Junak sacrificed himself to save the school. Emperor Palpatine's exterminators captured him in one of the common areas, and they burned him on the spot. Afterward, no grass grew in the area, which was walled off as a monument to the Jedi. It was rumored that Junak's ghost roamed the academy grounds. This was the basis for the name of the band Ghost Jedi.

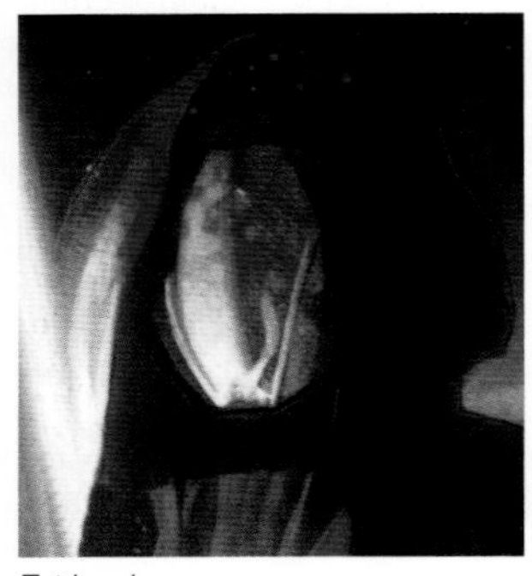

*Taj Junak*

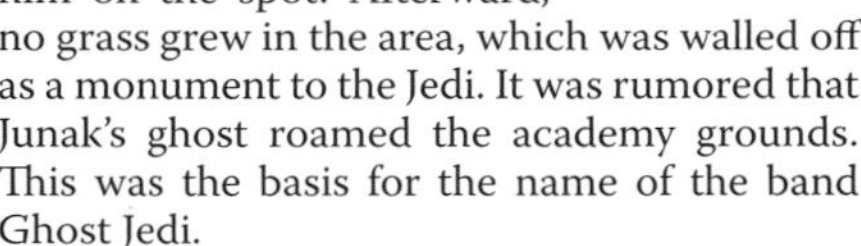

**Junavex Hotel** A hotel in the Middle City of Taris during the era of the Great Sith War.

**Junction** *See* Feriae Junction.

**Junction, the** This section of the vast cityscape found on Taris was originally set aside for new construction many years before the Great Sith War. However, after demolition crews razed the area, contractors never began work on the new buildings. The area was abandoned, and became known as the Junction to the inhabitants of the Lower City. Its name came from its location between the darkness of the Lower City and the open skies of the Upper City. Over time, trash generated by the population of Taris was dumped in the Junction, making it little more than a landfill.

**Junction 5** This temperate Mid Rim planet was near the worlds of Bezim and Vicondor. The leaders of the three worlds had been allied for generations. Its moon, Delaluna, was also habitable, and many of its natives decided to settle there. Over the years, the natives of Junction 5 came to fear that a superweapon was being built on Delaluna. They called it the Annihilator, and worried that the natives of Delaluna would use the weapon against them. The people of Delaluna denied the existence of the Annihilator. Some 23 years before the Battle of Geonosis, the situation had reached a critical point, as the citizens were subjugated by the Guardians. Many years later, after the outbreak of the Clone Wars, Junction 5 became a target of the Separatists, since it was one of the primary gateways to the Station 88 Spaceport, a major nexus to the galaxy's Mid Rim.

**Junction City** The capital city of Feriae Junction.

**Junction Port** The primary spaceport located on Feriae Junction during the early years of the New Order.

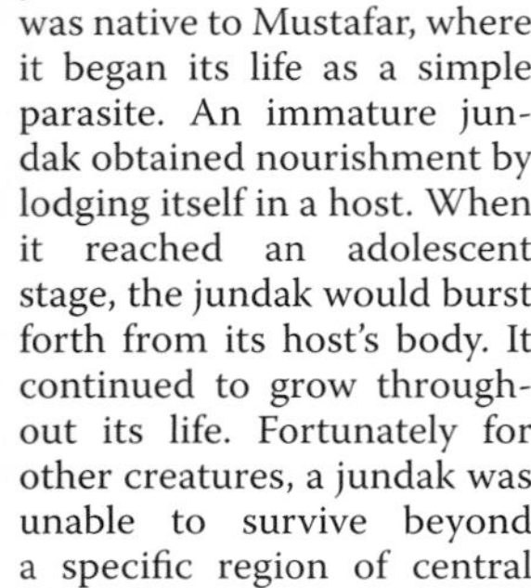

**jundak** This immense beast was native to Mustafar, where it began its life as a simple parasite. An immature jundak obtained nourishment by lodging itself in a host. When it reached an adolescent stage, the jundak would burst forth from its host's body. It continued to grow throughout its life. Fortunately for other creatures, a jundak was unable to survive beyond a specific region of central Mustafar.

***Jundland*** One of the many *Victory*-class Star Destroyers that were still active for the Imperial Navy during the Galactic Civil War.

**Jundland, Lieutenant** The alias adopted by Luke Skywalker some eight months after the Battle of Yavin, when he infiltrated the Imperial labor colony on Kalist VI. Lieutenant Jundland was an officer aboard the tanker *Nuna's Twins,* and it was his "heroics" that saved the tanker from a Rebel Alliance ambush near Kalist VI.

**Jundland Banshee** The nickname of a rogue Tusken Raider who terrorized the areas around Arnthout Pass and Motesta on Tatooine during the early years of the Galactic Civil War. It was assumed that the Jundland Banshee was a male, and it was believed that he had been ostracized from his clan for attacks on local moisture farmers. The Tusken Raiders didn't need the Jundland Banshee stirring up the already frightened farmers and forcing them to launch attacks of their own. The Rebel Alliance feared that the actions of the Jundland Banshee would disrupt the activities of the Sandwind Team on Tatooine shortly before the Battle of Hoth.

**Jundland eopie** This subspecies of eopie was native to the Jundland Wastes of Tatooine.

**Jundland Wastes** This dry, hot, and rocky region on Tatooine marked the border between the Western Dune Sea and the Great Mesa Plateau. The Wastes comprised rocky outcroppings and craggy shelves of sandstone, with windswept canyons formed by erosion. It was here that Luke Skywalker and C-3PO were attacked by the Sand People while searching for R2-D2, just prior to the Battle of Yavin. The word *Jundland* was believed to mean "No-Man's-Land," although the exact origin of the term was unknown.

**Jundop, Ground Marshal Haras** This man served the Rebel Alliance military as the ground marshal of army soldiers.

***jung*** A term used by Jedi Knights of the Old Republic to describe a 180-degree turn employed during lightsaber combat.

**Jungen** This Trandoshan was a junior enlistee aboard the *Battalion* when Adar Tallon faked his death in the Dalchon system. Jungen served with Tallon long enough to respect and admire the old warrior, and pledged his support to Tallon at all costs. Jungen's loyalty never waned, and strengthened when Parlan issued a bounty for Tallon's life. Jungen was incredibly adept at hand-to-hand combat, and used his skills to assist a Rebel Alliance team in rescuing Tallon on Tatooine. Jungen then formally joined the Alliance, although this brought a bounty on his own head. Jungen was targeted by Ssach'thirix but managed to elude the Shatras bounty hunter.

**jung-ju** This tree produced strong, fibrous wood that was used in the creation of a special form of body armor in the decades before the Great Sith War. The jung-ju tree fibers were blended with synthetic material to create a strong, flexible armor that rivaled light armor made from metallic compounds.

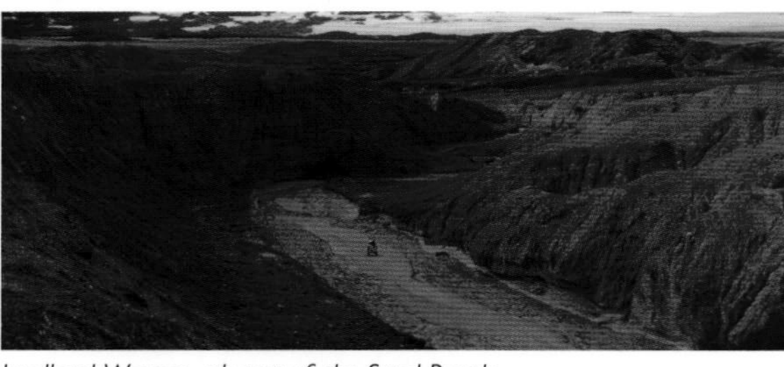

*Jundland Wastes, a haunt of the Sand People*

**Jungle Café** One of the smaller, less expensive restaurants found aboard the Ithorian herd ship *Bazaar.*

**Jungle Cantina** One of the largest establishments on the Ithorian herd ship *Bazaar.* Located in Isttu city, it served Ithorian classics and other galactic favorites.

**Jungle Clans** This group of Rodian clans allied themselves with the New

Republic, and later the Galactic Alliance, during the Yuuzhan Vong War.

**jungle creeper** A rough-barked vine native to Yavin 4.

***Jungle Flutes*** One of Garik Loran's most famous pro-Imperial propaganda films.

**jungle fynock** This species of fynock lived in the dense jungle areas of Talus.

***Jungle Ghost*** This Ithorian herd ship traveled the length of the Corellian Run, and often spent months in the area known as Wild Space before returning to Ithor for Herd Meets.

**Jungle Lust** A prefab cantina in Plawal's Spaceport Row on Belsavis.

**jungle slinker** This long, thin creature was native to Kirtania. Its body resembled a long, woody vine, allowing it to hide among the trees of the planet's rain forests and avoid capture.

**Jungle Vault** An underground cantina on Vaynai's Streysel Island, it was located in a series of caves and hand-carved chambers. The Jungle Vault was owned and operated by Whuvumm during the New Order. After patrons entered through an armored, automatic door, they found themselves in a setting that resembled lush, tropical jungles found on the surface. Whuvumm maintained a wide variety of plant life inside his caves, using specialized grow lamps and holes drilled in the rock to bring in natural sunlight. Because most of the clientele was local, Whuvumm felt no need to hire bouncers or guards. The locals, knowing how hard Whuvumm worked to maintain the Jungle Vault's plant life, usually stepped in to toss out any unruly patrons. Because of the dense plantings and the constant trickling of water, most patrons found that the Jungle Vault was a great place to do all sorts of business without being overheard.

***jung ma*** A term used by Jedi Knights of the Old Republic to describe a 360-degree *su ma,* or spin, employed during lightsaber combat. To fully utilize this technique, Jedi had to sense everything around their body just before striking, in order to direct their blade to the correct path. Similar to the *jung* turn, the *jung ma* turn provided the Jedi with added power during a stroke of the lightsaber blade. *Jung ma,* also known as *jung su ma,* was part of the dulon form of training and was considered the basis for all sweep disciplines of lightsaber combat.

**Junior Galaxy Scouts** An intergalactic organization that taught youths about truthfulness, trustworthiness, and faithfulness.

**junior Jedi academy** This branch of Luke Skywalker's Jedi praxeum on Yavin 4 taught young children who were especially strong in the Force how to control their powers before they began to study the finer arts of the Jedi.

**Junior Palace Guard** This branch of the Naboo Palace Guard was made up of soldiers who were still in training, but were allowed to participate in planetary security actions. Members of the Junior Palace Guard were considered more mature and ready for leadership than most trainees, and often were given specialized commands in order to test their tactical and military abilities.

**Junior Saber-Twirler** One of the many nicknames used by Marn Hierogryph to describe Zayne Carrick. It referred to the fact that Zayne was once a Jedi Padawan on Taris during the era of the Mandalorian Wars.

**Junkard** This section of caverns, located within the Kala'uun Starport on Ryloth, was set aside as a scrap heap where spacers could scavenge for usable starship parts. Anything from complete speeders to worthless power converters could be found. The operator of the Junkard, a Twi'lek known only as the Seeker, took almost anything in trade, but preferred machinery that could be used to mine for ryll spice.

**Junker** A term used to describe a handful of settlers who eked out a meager existence on Ambria in the years that followed the Battle of Ruusan. They were so named because they scavenged the planet for any bits of junk or technology that had been left behind during previous eras of war and prosperity. Those objects that could be repaired were sold or traded to offworlders for credits and supplies.

***Junker* (1)** This Nharwaak container group was destroyed during an Imperial raid on its hidden base during the Galactic Civil War.

***Junker* (2)** A name used to describe the Gallofree Medium Transports outfitted by the New Republic for use in Operation Flotsam. They required 6 crew members and carried 20 analysts as well as 48 recovery-and-analysis droids. The ships were lightly armed, with just four laser cannons forming their arsenal. They were never meant to go into combat, and were protected by the Historic Battle Site Preservation Act from taking fire.

**Junkfort Station** A patchwork collection of living modules in space, joined by a network of airlink tunnels. Ships often traveled to Junkfort Station to receive illegal modifications; bounty hunters ostensibly were forbidden aboard. Following the Battle of Yavin, Han Solo and Chewbacca went to Junkfort's cantina to inquire about how they could acquire shield-disrupting power gems.

**junk golem** Strange, Force-imbued automata that were created by Kazdan Paratus on Raxus Prime during the early years of the New Order. Sometimes referred to as technobeasts, these junk golems took a variety of forms, and could attack with incredible power.

**Junkin, Sergeant** A Rebel Alliance demolitions expert who was part of the team led by Han Solo that infiltrated the shield generator for the second Death Star on the Forest Moon of Endor. Prior to the raid, Junkin consulted with Crix Madine on the placement of charges used to destroy the generator bunker.

**Junk Junction** One of the largest junkyards in the Lower City of Taris after the Great Sith War. Jarael and the Camper made their home there, since it was large enough to hide the *Last Resort.*

**Junktown** A small settlement located near Mos Eisley, it was a haven for the various junk dealers who sold refurbished goods to the locals. Junktown was overrun by a group of Tusken Raiders just after the Battle of Yavin.

**Junkyard, the** One of the primary scrap yards found on Ord Mantell during the Galactic Civil War.

**Junno** One of two continents located on Demophon, Junno supported most of the planet's inhabitants. Byrne City was located there, as well as D'larah and Selkren.

**Juno** The head of the Cobral household on Frego, some 11 years before the Battle of Naboo. A curt man, Juno was loyal to Solan Cobral during the turmoil that surrounded the murder of Rutin Cobral.

***Juno*** An Imperial freighter group that resupplied the *Invincible* before it could attack Rudrig.

***Juno II*** One of six Kathol Republic *Marauder*-class corvettes sent to rescue the *Bravado III* from attack shortly after the *Far-Star* offered assistance. The 195-meter vessel was armed with eight double turbolaser cannons and three tractor beam projectors.

**Junobian sand flier** This crustacean had delicate, sweet-tasting meat, and was considered a delicacy throughout the galaxy. Sand fliers were especially good when harvested just after they molted, when their new shells were soft enough to eat.

**junti** This unusual sword was tipped with a heavy, spiked ball, making it a deadly melee weapon.

**Juntrack** The largest city on the Inquiesse continent of Draenell's Point, it was one of the planet's largest manufacturing centers. It was built on the Juntrack River.

**J'uoch** An unscrupulous, evil woman, she and her twin brother, R'all, owned and operated a mine on Dellalt. J'uoch—with thick, straight brown hair surrounding a pale face and large black eyes—and R'all competed with Han Solo to be the first to discover the lost treasures of Xim the Despot.

**jup** Slang used by the Korunnai, the true natives of Haruun Kal, to indicate a Balawai jungle prospector.

**Jurahi** One of the handful of Jedi Masters who taught at the Almas Academy in the years around the Clone Wars. During his tenure at the academy, Jurahi held the position of Master of Visions, since his ability to peer into the future was trusted more than that of any other Master on Almas.

**Jural** This female Bothan worked as a reporter for the *Corellian Times* during the Galactic Civil War. She was best known for her investigative reports on galactic exploration. She and her brother, Talper, were dispatched to Mustafar to report on the excavation of an ancient temple by Dr. Namdaot, and were amazed when he appeared in the guise of the Storm King. She related her story to Relan and another member of Ithes Olok's research team when they discovered her small camp. She begged for their help, because Talper had refused to swear allegiance to the Storm King, and was stricken with a wasting disease.

**Juren, Chief Engineer** This Imperial was the chief engineer aboard the *Subjugator*, serving under Captain Kolaff.

**Jurfel** This Verpine elder was the speaker for his hive. He openly rejected Bane Nothos's order to submit or die when Nothos tried to take control of the Shantipole Project. Jurfel later assisted Rebel Alliance agents in saving the B-wing prototypes at Shantipole by providing asteroid hoppers for them to use for travel through the Roche asteroid field.

**Jurga the Hutt** This brazen Hutt crime lord wore a Tenloss disruptor weapon on his sash, in blatant disregard for the restriction against the use of such weapons, as a symbol of his power. Jurga was eventually killed with his own weapon, reportedly by an irate employee.

**juri jar** A generic term for the containers in which juri juice was sold. Over the years, a wide variety of shapes and sizes were used, creating a hobby in which beings tried to amass the largest and most varied collections of the jars.

**juri juice** A ruby- or blue-colored, mildly intoxicating drink. It was a favorite of Kabe.

**Juri's Sabacc Parlor** One of the more prestigious gambling halls on the outpost of Cloud City at the height of the New Order.

**Juris sector** Imperial Governor Linrec sent his daughter, Cressis, to an elite boarding school in this sector. It was located in the Outer Rim, near the Albanin sector.

**Jurokk, Jedi Master** This Jedi Master was assigned to guard the Jedi Temple with Shaak Ti when Mace Windu set out to arrest Chancellor Palpatine and end the Clone Wars. Master Jurokk was killed by Anakin Skywalker when he exterminated every Jedi in the Temple. Anakin took Jurokk's life without remorse, placing his dormant lightsaber handle under Master Jurokk's chin and igniting it, allowing the blade to burn through his brain and skull.

**Jurrinex6** This hive virus was developed by biological terrorists during the height of the New Order.

**juru ant** An insect species native to Cularin, it made nests in the roots of greenbark trees. The nests served to keep the tree's root system well aerated, and their waste products served to fertilize the noroobo flowers.

**Jurvi** One of the many sargheet farmers who suffered through the economic hard times that befell Dagro during the Clone Wars. His friend Kirlan Swens asked him to be part of a farm "chain" that Obi-Wan Kenobi could use to reach Vale City without being spotted when the Jedi Knight and his Padawan Anakin Skywalker were investigating the possibility of a Separatist base on the planet, some two years after the Battle of Geonosis. He agreed, and the Jedi located and destroyed the last crawl-carrier before it could eliminate a village.

**Jurzan** A spaceport refueling station was built near this planet. It was the site of Rebel Alliance activity.

**Jusik, Bardan** This Jedi Padawan was being trained by Master Arligan Zey when the Clone Wars broke out. When Master Zey assumed the role of an intelligence officer, Jusik followed him as an adviser and companion. He was unprepared for his first encounter with a clone trooper, however, and often stared at individual troopers for long periods of time. The more he came to understand the cloned soldiers, the more Jusik realized that they were people, just like every other sentient being. The fact that they were "manufactured" and sent into battle—just like the battle droids of the Separatists—meant that the Old Republic was using them as a means to an end, and little more. The fact that the Jedi Order had agreed to command these troops meant that the Jedi also were losing their respect for living beings.

Even though he was just a Padawan, Bardan arranged to argue these points with the Jedi Council after the fighting on Qiilura. For his actions during the Qiilura incident, Jusik was promoted to Jedi Knight and given a military command position within the Grand Army of the Republic. He was assigned to the Special Operations Brigade on Coruscant, where he developed a deep trust and understanding of the Mandalorian culture from his clone troopers. He allowed himself to become a part of their culture, and eventually earned the nickname *Bard'ika* from Kal Skirata himself. When Jusik helped with a black-ops mission to smash a Separatist-funded terrorist cell on Coruscant, he found himself donning the armor of a clone trooper and joining the fight. He understood that such an act was contrary to what he was taught at the Jedi Temple, but he somehow knew that it was the right thing to do, especially once he realized that he was more comfortable in the barracks with his men than in the Jedi Temple.

Jusik's dedication to the clones came to a head when Atin finally confronted Walon Vau, and the two men began a fight to the death. Jusik intervened, demanding that they put an end to their personal hostilities and focus on working together as a team. He was named an honorary member of the squad, and later was rewarded for his loyalty when Kal Skirata allowed him to wear Munin Skirata's armor during Skirata's personal mission to locate Ko Sai. As Skirata's clones came to ponder their existence in the wake of the war, Jusik found himself helping them in their search for the Kaminoan scientist. Issues of clone rights and the future of the clone army then began to gather in his mind. He went so far as to question how, in the immediate wake of the Battle of Geonosis, Master Yoda had come up with the term *the Clone Wars* to describe the conflict.

When Skirata, Ordo, Mereel, and Walon Vau caught Ko Sai on Dorumaa, it was Jusik who helped them by intercepting Arligan Zey and the clone commandos of Delta Squad. When Skirata left Dorumaa with Ko Sai in captivity, Jusik allowed the Deltas to finally investigate the explosion that occurred when Skirata destroyed the Kaminoan's underwater laboratory. He even managed to get Arligan Zey to approve whatever expenditures were necessary to locate Ko Sai, including a lengthy excavation of the site of her destroyed laboratory on Dorumaa.

After gaining the confidence of the commandos in Delta Squad, Jusik left them on Dorumaa while he traveled to Coruscant, where he hoped to use his skills with the Force to help heal one of their brothers, Omega Squad's Fi. His work was slow and tedious, since he was unsure exactly what to do. Nevertheless, Jusik stuck with it, spending his days alternately repairing Fi's brain and trying to use conversation and familiar objects to bring him out of his coma. The other members of Omega Squad questioned Jusik's actions, and feared that he would be expelled from the Jedi Order for his devotion to the clones and the Mandalorian way of life. Their worries only intensified when Jusik and Etain Tur-Mukan were ordered to report to Arligan Zey's office. During their meeting, Jusik renounced his commitment to the Order and asked to be allowed to go his own way. Zey reluctantly agreed, knowing that his own faith in the government had been shaken over the preceding months.

Jusik had planned to use his skills as a field medic, but Kal Skirata wanted to use him in other areas. Skirata asked Jusik to remain close to Coruscant, in order to help train Etain's son, Venku Skirata, in the ways of the Force. Jusik couldn't make any guarantees, but agreed to do what he could to help the child come to terms with his abilities. He and Venku went underground in the wake of the Clone Wars, with Jusik joining the *Mando'ade* and adopting the Mandalorian name Gotab. Eventually, the pair migrated to Mandalore, where they kept their true identities a carefully guarded secret for many years. Jusik went so far as to explain that his ability to heal other beings was not a Jedi trait, but due to his Kiffar heritage.

Jaina Solo was the first to understand that both Jusik and Venku were sensitive to the Force. His assistance in helping Sintas Vel recover from her hibernation sickness also revealed that Jusik was not actually a Kiffar, even though he was able to read something of Sintas's history from the heart-of-fire necklace Fett had once given to Sintas. Jusik later explained to Jaina that he had never invoked the Right of Denial, but instead simply stopped being a Jedi. He immersed himself in the Mandalorian culture, using it to help him survive the Jedi Purge. He married a Mandalorian woman, but they chose to adopt children rather than have their own, to ensure that his secret remained hidden. His wife died some time earlier, and Jusik stayed with the Mandalorians as Gotab, although his closest friends still called him *Bard'ika*. His family eventually grew to include 20 great-great-grandchildren. When pressed by Jaina, Jusik explained that he would have gladly given up his Force powers, with the sole exception of his ability to heal people.

**Jussafet Four** This planet supported the New Order of Emperor Palpatine. Located near a diamond-shaped nebula, the world was strategic for the asteroid mining operations within its system. After the Battle of Endor, Jussafet Four remained loyal to the Empire, but was located along the border between Imperial space and the space controlled by Warlord Zsinj. Zsinj's Raptors made several strikes at the planet, taking materials and leaving destruction behind. The New Republic, while on the hunt for Zsinj, intercepted a distress call from Jussafet Four and responded, despite the world's loyalty to the Empire.

**Just, Dixon** A frequent patron of the Coruscant underworld in the years before the Clone Wars. He was seen often in the company of his friends Zey Nep, Artuo Pratuhr, and Civ Sila.

**Justa** This frigid, rocky moon orbited Mutanda. Mining colonies extracted prothium gas from the system, and much of it passed through Justa—the site of the system's only starport—on its way to the Core. The starport was garrisoned by the Empire during the Galactic Civil War, ostensibly to protect the interests of the three corporations that owned Justa and its starport: BlasTech Corporation, Czerka Weapons, and Blethern Gas Industries.

**Justahl** This man, a corporate vice president, discovered that the Hush-About personal jetpack was the perfect way to arrive at a business meeting while making an impression on his clients.

**"Just Another Art Form"** This song, written and played by the band Deeply Religious, was banned by the Imperial Board of Culture. It first appeared on the compilation *Deeply Religious*.

**Just Armor** This shop sold a variety of personal armor, ship armor, and passive defense systems from its base on StarForge Station. It was owned and operated by Gjaddia and Morol.

***Just Cause*** This space freighter sank in the ocean of Rathalay. Legend had it that the ship—900 meters deep—was filled with precious metals, and was guarded by schools of narkaa.

**Justic, Geon** One of the Corporate Sector Authority agents placed on Ando Prime during the early years of the New Order. Justic favored the latest in galactic fashions and trends, and worked to maintain a cosmopolitan air despite the griminess of his outpost location.

***Justice*** This New Republic *Ranger*-class gunship was part of a task force assigned to the *Mon Mothma* during Operation Trinity.

**Justice Action Network (1)** An illicit virastack newsfeed, it was the primary vehicle through which members of the Justice Action Network disseminated their information. Like the main tenets of the terrorists who joined JAN, the newsfeed called for outright mass revolution against the Empire.

*Justice Droid*

**Justice Action Network (2)** This anti-Empire terrorist group was founded on Findris more than 16 years before the Battle of Hoth by Earnst Kamiel. The goal of the Network was to completely destroy the infrastructure of the Empire through any means possible, including bombings and assassinations. Kamiel himself was wanted by the Empire on many charges, including thousands of bombings and causing over 10,000 deaths. He also had a death sentence in 54 different systems. The organization was often referred to by the acronym JAN. Shortly before the Battle of Endor, the JAN cell in the Tapani sector tried to take out an Imperial torpedo sphere that was stationed near Tallaan. Unknown to the agents, a similar effort was already under way by Vaskel Savill and House Melantha. Both factions discovered their separate activities during their simultaneous assaults on the sphere, and each worked to disrupt the other while hoping to take credit for the destruction of the ship. In the end, though, the attacks gave the Empire all the justification it needed to place a stranglehold on the Tapani sector. The Justice Action Network movement broke up when Kamiel was captured on Elrood and executed on Haldeen sometime later.

***Justice Crusader*** This attack cruiser was owned and operated by Jedi Master Raskta Lsu following the Battle of Ruusan. An exceptionally fast ship, the *Justice Crusader* required a crew of four to operate. Master Raskta often carried several members of the Jedi Order on her missions, so they usually served as the crew. The final mission of the *Justice Crusader* came when Master Raskta accompanied Lord Valenthyne Farfalla and Johun Othone to Tython, where they hoped to capture Darth Bane. However, Bane and his apprentice, Zannah, managed to destroy the Jedi and flee to Ambria. They left the *Justice Crusader* on Tython, where it later was discovered by Jedi investigators who responded to Zannah's message announcing the existence of a Sith Lord on Ambria.

**Justice Droid** A series of assassin droids manufactured by Uulshos and first introduced many years before the Clone Wars. The series proved to be strong and durable, and production continued for many decades. The droids were later produced for Imperial use.

***Justice Star*** A name considered for the first Death Star, as part of an Imperial propaganda plan to promote the station's benefit to the galaxy.

**Justice Systems** This small corporation was formed in the wake of the Yuuzhan Vong War and produced a wide range of personal security and defense droids based on military designs.

**Justiss, Kai** A Jedi Knight appointed to serve as the Watchman of Kashyyyk during the Clone Wars, replacing Jedi Master Yoda, who had agreed to become a military leader for the Old Republic. Although Senator Yarua was unconvinced that the Wookiees should remain loyal to the Republic, Kai Justiss believed that they would. Justiss later joined Jedi Master Tsui Choi in a mission to Drongar, where they were captured by Count Dooku and held briefly. Dooku let the Jedi return to Coruscant, but ordered his forces to eliminate any clone troopers aboard the ship. In the wake of the Clone Wars, Justiss was one of a small number of Jedi Knights who managed to escape the Jedi Purge. Justiss remained free for only a short period of time, and was eventually betrayed to the Crimson Nova bounty hunters by farmers on Garqi.

*Kai Justiss with Jocasta Nu*

**Juteau Settlement** This small town was located near the Garish Ridge on Redcap.

**Jutka** This Tuhgri, a native of Dayark, was the leader of his people. It was Jutka who met with the crew of the *FarStar* at the edge of the Kathol Rift, shortly after encountering an Aing-Tii ship. Jutka detained Talon Karrde and the crew of the *Wild Karrde* after they were attacked by pirates because Karrde flew with altered identification codes. Jutka gave Karrde no help even after learning that he had been an unwilling bystander in the battle between Crev Bombaasa and Rei'Kas.

**Jutrand system** This star system was located along the Gevarno Loop. During the Clone Wars, the Jutrand system was loyal to the Confederacy of Independent Systems.

**Juun, Jae** This Sullustan was an independent spacer and part-time smuggler who worked from a base on Regel Eight following the Yuuzhan Vong War. Juun and his partner, an Ewok named Tarfang, worked out of Juun's starship, the *XR808g*, for many years before being drawn to the Unknown Regions and going to work for the Colony. When Han Solo and his wife, Leia Organa Solo, arrived in search of their twins, Jaina and Jacen, Jae Juun reluctantly agreed to help them get to Yoggoy. Although not fully a Joiner, Juun understood that the Colony—and UnuThul in particular—did not want the Solos to locate their children, for fear they might interfere with the struggle against the Chiss.

Juun worked to earn Han's trust, drawing on his knowledge of the history of the Galactic Civil War to try to anticipate his actions. Juun discovered that much of Han's skill was based on spur-of-the-moment decisions, which was hard to fathom but easy to acknowledge.

During the height of the Qoribu crisis, Juun worked with the Solos to avoid all-out warfare between the Chiss and the Colony. He was forced to sacrifice the *XR808g* on a mission to infiltrate the Colony's hives in the Qoribu moons, and later joined Han as part-time copilot of the *Millennium Falcon*. When the Colony was relocated to the Utegetu Nebula, Han arranged for Juun to purchase a new transport vessel from Lando Calrissian, and convinced Lando to give him a lucrative transport contract. The Sullustan found the new vessel—a Mon Calamarian Sailfish model—too expensive to operate, and traded it in for a *Ronto*-class transport designated *DR919a*. He also declined to renew his contract with Lando, and instead went to work for Second Mistake Enterprises.

In this new capacity, Juun and Tarfang inadvertently provided shipments of spinglass sculptures containing Gorog assassin bugs to the Galactic Alliance's Fifth Fleet, which was blockading the Utegetu Nebula. In an effort to atone, they allowed Solo and Luke Skywalker to commandeer the *DR919a* and attack the Gorog nest ship hidden within the nebula. The *DR919a* was badly damaged in the attack, and Juun did all he could to control its crash landing on the hull of the Gorog nest ship. Juun and Tarfang fought valiantly alongside Solo and Skywalker, managing to disable the vessel before it could escape. In the aftermath of the blockade, Juun and Tarfang were approached by Admiral Nek Bwua'tu, who offered them positions as intelligence agents. Bwua'tu knew that their knowledge of the Colony, as well as their contacts at Second Mistake Enterprises, put them in a position to gather information about the Killiks.

Juun and Tarfang agreed, and somehow managed to survive missions that placed them in the midst of deadly situations. They later found work with the Directors, and were able to alert Han and Leia that Squibs planned to execute them. In the wake of the Swarm War, Juun and Tarfang continued to serve as intelligence agents, and were among the many who kept an eye on Han and Leia during the Galactic Alliance's conflict with the Confederation. This led them to Kashyyyk, where the Solos hoped to convince the Wookiees to secede from the Alliance. As loyal Alliance agents, they tried to physically prevent the Solos from reaching the top of Council Rock, but failed. Juun drew a blaster and tried to arrest them, but the Wookiees allowed the Solos to speak after Leia earned the right.

**Juuus** This Trandoshan was one of only three members of his species to live on Edic Bar before the Battle of Naboo. He worked as a public street sweeper, although it was rumored he had been a starship pilot in an earlier career.

***Juvani*** An Imperial frigate destroyed by Rebel Alliance starfighters while it was undergoing service near Sunaj IV.

**Juvex Lords** Leaders of the various Royal Houses that populated the Juvex sector. Like their neighbors in the Senex sector, the Juvex Lords allied themselves with Roganda Ismaren when she set into motion her plan to use the *Eye of Palpatine* to attack the New Republic.

**Juvex sector** Adjacent to the Senex sector and near the Ninth Quadrant, it contained the Juvex systems. Like the Senex sector, it was run by groups of Ancient Houses, including the House Streethyn. Bran Kemple was a small-time gunrunner in the Juvex systems before taking over a smuggling business on Belsavis. Eight years after the Battle of Endor, some of the Juvex Lords met with Roganda Ismaren on Belsavis to forge a military alliance.

**Juyo** The ancient term—taken from the High Galactic—for the primary variation on the Form VII lightsaber fighting style. This form of combat was believed to have been first developed on Sarapin by a nonsentient predator, and later adapted to lightsaber combat. It involved the use of streamlined attacks, coupled with physical strength, to defeat an opponent. Juyo and its other variation, Vaapad, were considered the most difficult combat forms to learn and master because they required incredible discipline and control.

**Juzzian** Members of this unusual species had cone-shaped bodies that were essentially all mouth, filled with an assortment of teeth. There were two distinct species of Juzzian, a mountain-hopping form and a more sedentary form.

**Juzzian armlock** A melee combat tactic named for the Juzzian species that developed it. When using the Juzzian armlock, an attacker grasped his or her opponent at the wrist and elbow, pinching the nerves at specific joints to render the arm useless.

**Juzzian colony marker** An unusual piece of technology used to mark the location of individual Juzzian colonies.

**JV-7 *Delta*-class escort shuttle** This Cygnus Spaceworks troop transport ship was 30 meters long and designed to transport officers, dignitaries, and valuable cargo through areas of possible danger. They were armed with three Taim & Bak KX5 laser cannons and

a single Taim & Bak H9 dual turbolaser cannon. They were protected by front/rear projecting Novaldex shields and a titanium alloy hull.

**JV-Z1/D** A series of domestic service droids built by Serv-O-Droid. The JV-Z/D1 filled a galactic need for a humanoid household automaton. The JV-Z1/Ds were tireless workers, and were rivaled in reliability only by the protocol droids built by Cybot Galactica. Their humanoid stature was slightly stooped, giving them a subservient appearance.

**JV-Z1/S** These droids were created to be mobile data repositories. Short and boxy, the JV-Z1/S series was developed during the Old Republic.

**Jweab VII** The pirate Beyla Rus was rumored to have had a lodge hidden on the far side of this planet during the Galactic Civil War.

**Jwlio** One of the many inhabitable moons of Qoribu. For much of its history, Jwlio was a temperate world of grassy plains. The Taat hive of the Colony established a nest there shortly after the Yuuzhan Vong War. When the Chiss Ascendancy began looking for ways to drive back the Colony, it used chemical defoliants to destroy the plains of Jwlio, hoping to drive the Taat off the moon and away from Chiss space.

**JX-09** This Aratech Secured Prisoner Transport Vehicle measured 14 meters in length; it had a single pilot, four guards, and space for up to 20 passengers. It was a long, insectile craft built around the chassis of a basic speeder truck, with four small wings for stabilization. Two flexible mandibles allowed the pilot and guards to remain inside while detaining particularly troublesome subjects.

**JX30 jailspeeder** A vehicle used by the Corporate Sector Authority as a portable prison.

**JX4** The code number of the Gladiator Battle Armor developed by Min-Dal in the Soruus system.

**JX40 jailspeeder** This TaggeCo Mobile Detention Wagon was a 14-meter-long repulsorcraft designed to transport up to 45 prisoners in stasis stalls. The JX40 had a dual-purpose mission profile: to block the advance of rioters and force them backward, and to transport those who resisted to detention facilities. The JX40 required a pilot and gunner, and was protected by armored stun panels, three grenade launchers, and forced-steam jets.

**Jyalma** The Socorran windy season, when competing cells of warm and cold air created winds in excess of 150 kilometers an hour outside the city of Cjaalysce'I. The city was walled off to keep the intense winds from destroying it.

**Jydan** The most prevalent religion practiced by the Ka'hren on V'shar. It rose to prominence as the primary religion of the Unfyr Warriors, but died out when the group itself did.

**Jygat** One of the primary cities on Mygeeto. During the early stages of the Clone Wars, the Grand Army of the Republic bombed key locations in Jygat, but was unable to take control of the planet.

**Jymbud, Captain** One of the many starship captains who worked for Damarind Corporation during the New Order. He accepted a position as the captain of a Corusca gem fishing station in orbit near Yavin shortly after the destruction of the Death Star, but his station was attacked by a pack of floaters. Everyone aboard the station was killed when the floaters disabled all major systems, and the station itself exploded just before it crashed into Yavin's core.

**Jyng, Oskar** A former design team chief at Ubrikkian during the early years of the New Order. Dr. Jyng was enticed to leave that position for a job in the Corporate Sector Authority's Research Division. In his new capacity, he became the inventor of the War Wheel.

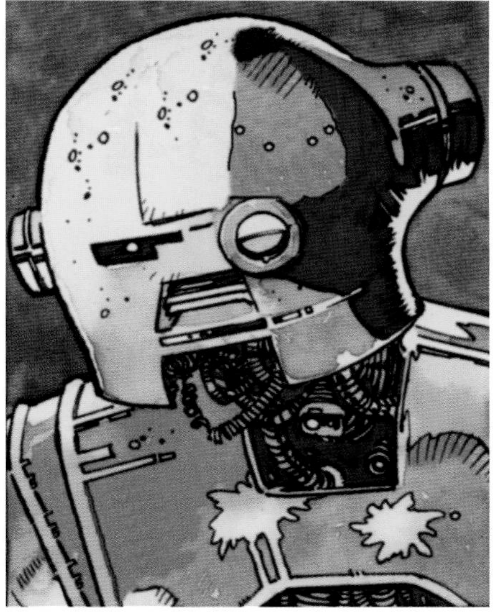

*JV-Z1/D*

***Jynni's Virtue*** Owned and operated by Naz Felyood, this pirate freighter worked the space lanes until it suddenly disappeared. Investigation by Luke Skywalker and his new Order of Jedi Knights discovered dubious records of the *Jynni's Virtue* being shot down over Korriban just prior to the Battle of Yavin. The recordings were discovered inside a sealed wall of the tomb of a 7,000-year-old Sith Lord named Dathka Graush. How they got there remained a mystery, since the timestamps on the recordings dated them about six months prior to the Battle of Yavin. The recordings showed that the pirates had been intercepted by an Imperial patrol and decided to make a hasty jump into hyperspace, but the astromech droid aboard the *Jynni's Virtue* exploded, killing the navigator and dropping them into a remote region of space. The ship was then attacked by unknown forces, which were not detected until their incoming fire rocked the freighter.

The *Jynni's Virtue* came to rest near the Valley of Golg, and Captain Felyood set out to scout their location. His discovery of the tomb of Dathka Graush led to contact with the jewel known as the Heart of Graush. Felyood was possessed by the spirit of the ancient Sith Lord, and the Korriban Zombies were released. To keep the zombies from escaping the planet, first mate Babbnod Luroon set off the ship's self-destruct mechanism. The *Jynni's Virtue* exploded in a ball of flame, killing the remaining crew and many of the zombies.

**Jynsol, Dera** The fourth candidate on Lando Calrissian's rich wife list, she was a native of Ord Pardron.

**Jyrenne Base** This Imperial Army-Navy ordnance center, located near the city of Iziz on Onderon, supplied weapons and munitions to both the Imperial Army and Navy during the New Order. The base was attacked by Onderonian rebels, working together with Rebel Alliance starfighters, shortly after the Battle of Yavin.

**Jyvus** One of the many orbital cities established around Duro. Separatist forces under the command of General Grievous attacked Jyvus and overwhelmed its defenses. This gave Grievous access to the controls for the planetary shield that protected Duro, which was promptly shut down. From this staging point, the Separatists launched orbital bombardments of Duro's surface.

**K1-1R** A former military tactical unit, K1-1R turned rogue and became an assassin droid during the final decades of the Old Republic. Noted for its ability to sift through huge amounts of computer data to pinpoint its targets, the droid often dispatched swarms of modified G-2RD seeker drones to help it overwhelm a target and bring it in with a minimum of effort. Armed with a blaster carbine, a flamethrower, and a light repeating blaster, K1-1R was the unofficial leader of a group of bounty hunters that accepted a job to eliminate several Cularin-based freelance agents just after the Battle of Naboo. Concentrated blasterfire from the agents rendered K1-1R a molten pile of slag.

**K-12** This was the official rank level of those beings who served as Emperor's Hands.

**K-14** A BlasTech blaster commonly issued to Imperial spies and undercover agents during the New Order.

**K-18** A common type of starship rations.

K-3PX

**K-1B** A medical droid assigned to the New Republic warship *Intrepid.* K-1B treated Lumpawarrump after the Wookiee sustained a blaster wound while rescuing Han Solo from the *Pride of Yevetha.*

**K21** This Merr-Sonn rocket launcher was exceptionally powerful for its size. It could be fired by a single being yet bring down a swoop in midair.

**K220** Manufactured by Wickstrom, this heavy-duty peripheral sensor package was designed to allow the off-loading of tasks during data transmission.

< *Jedi Master Obi-Wan Kenobi*

K-222 Aero-Interceptor

**K-222 Aero-Interceptor** One of the premier atmospheric fighters in the Corporate Sector Authority fleet, providing maneuverability with firepower for added protection. The so-called triple deuce measured 13 meters long and was armed with double-wingtip laser cannons as well as six concussion missiles. It was capable of reaching 2,600 kilometers per hour in atmospheric flight.

**K3** Mara Jade's droid assistant during the time she served as the Emperor's Hand.

**K-3PO** An older-model protocol droid that served the Rebel Alliance under Commander Narra, learning military tactics along the way. The droid later led the droid pool at Echo Base on Hoth. It sustained slight damage to its chest when it was swatted by a nervous tauntaun. Although K-3PO was destroyed in the Battle of Hoth, its invaluable programming and memory were saved and later reinstalled in Rogue Squadron's droid, M-3PO.

**K-3PX** This black Imperial protocol droid claimed it was owned by Tay Vanis but actually belonged to Darth Vader.

**K4** One of the most reliable security droids ever produced by Rim Securities, K4 was known to have difficulty targeting while moving quickly. This could be solved with regular maintenance of the droid's weaponry and targeting system.

**K5 Enforcer droid** Developed by Rim Securities, this droid series was more versatile, had a wider range of external weaponry, and was considerably tougher than the K4. It was also a bit slower, making it a somewhat easier target. It was used extensively by the Empire in prisons and government buildings.

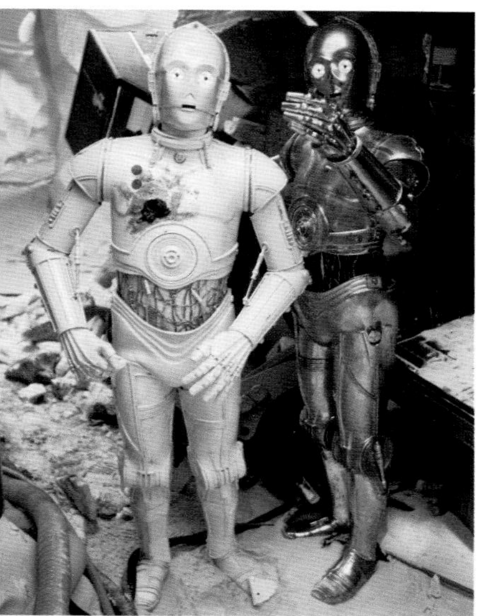

K-3PO

**K8-LR** A protocol droid assigned to Jabba the Hutt's Mos Eisley town house shortly before the Battle of Yavin. It helped Muftak and Kabe rob the place and escape after they took off the droid's restraining bolt.

**Ka, Queen Mother Tenel** The daughter of Prince Isolder and Teneniel Djo, she was raised on Dathomir in the tradition of the other witches in Djo's clan. Tenel showed great aptitude with the Force, and as a youngster attended Luke Skywalker's Jedi academy on Yavin 4 at the same time as Jacen and Jaina Solo. She was a reserved, distant companion to the twins. Her training nearly ended when she didn't put enough effort and attention into constructing her own lightsaber. In a practice duel with Jacen Solo, her blade failed and Jacen accidentally severed

K4

Ka's left arm above the elbow. The wound was instantly cauterized, but replacing the limb wasn't possible.

After becoming a full Jedi Knight, Tenel Ka and her companions were thrust into the Yuuzhan Vong War. She was part of a Jedi team sent to Myrkr to destroy the voxyn queen, and one of the few to survive the mission. The team made off with the Yuuzhan Vong frigate *Ksstarr* and took it to Hapes, where Ka had to face the dangers of Hapan court intrigue. The Hapan people were demanding stronger leadership, and feared that Queen Mother Djo might lead them to ruin. When she discovered that her mother had been poisoned, Ka used what political power she had to turn the Hapan fleet over to Colonel Jagged Fel, hoping that he could command the vessels in battle against the Yuuzhan Vong. Ka then confronted her grandmother, announcing that she would take her mother's place as Queen Mother. It was also at this time that she realized she was in love with Jacen Solo.

In the wake of the Yuuzhan Vong War, Queen Mother Tenel Ka allied the Hapes Consortium with the fledgling Galactic Alliance. Like many of her Jedi contemporaries, she felt the call of Unu-Thul, the transformed identity of Raynar Thul joined with the Killik hive-mind. When Jacen Solo arrived to request her help during the Swarm War, she assisted with a small fleet of ships led by the *Kendall*, which traveled to Qoribu to help defend the Colony against the Chiss.

Unknown to most, Ka and Solo had an intimate relationship—one that produced a royal heir. To ensure secrecy and safety, Ka used the Force to adjust the biological timing of her impending motherhood, giving birth to a daughter when it was relatively safe to do so. She kept the pregnancy a secret, knowing that an heir would be immediately endangered. Even Solo was unaware of his daughter Allana for an entire year, until a tremor in the Force brought him back to Hapes.

Following the Swarm War, Jacen and Tenel Ka continued to have clandestine meetings, and it was the common bond of their daughter that Solo tried to exploit during the Galactic Alliance's conflict with the Confederation. He repeatedly asked for the use of the Hapan Home Fleet, and Ka agreed despite the growing dissent among Hapan nobles. Her right to rule the Hapes Cluster was challenged by the Heritage Council, a conflict that came to a head when the Heritage Fleet launched a massive assault on Hapes itself. The timely intervention of a Galactic Alliance fleet led by Solo helped defeat the Heritage Fleet and reaffirmed Tenel Ka's rule, but it also strained her relationship with Jacen.

During the battle, Jacen opened fire on his parents, Han and Leia Organa Solo, who were attempting to rescue several Jedi Knights and return to Hapes. Ka was shaken by Jacen's callousness. When he returned yet again to ask for the Hapan Home Fleet to help defend the planet Kuat, Tenel agreed with great reluctance. Han and Leia arrived on Hapes after fleeing Kashyyyk and told Ka of Jacen's unprovoked attack on the Wookiee homeworld and the attempted murder of Jedi Grand Master Luke Skywalker. Tenel realized that she could no longer love what Jacen had become. She withdrew the Hapan Home Fleet from Solo and agreed to support the efforts of the Jedi opposing Jacen's rule.

Ka personally led the fleet to Kashyyyk and demanded that Jacen surrender, threatening to open fire if he refused. Solo, who had taken on the name Darth Caedus, ordered his own crews to target Hapan ships. Ka was then forced to open fire on the flagship *Anakin Solo,* hoping to disable it and bring Jacen to justice, but Solo escaped.

Ka returned home with plans to keep the Hapan military neutral. She was unprepared for Jacen's bold move to kidnap Allana. Jacen threatened to kill his own daughter if Ka did not give him back control of the Hapan military. Luke Skywalker and the new Jedi Order rescued Allana, and Ka took her aboard the *Dragon Queen* after ordering the Hapan fleet into the Transitory Mists to defend the hidden Jedi base on Shedu Maad.

Upon arriving at Shedu Maad, Ka was forced to deal with the news that her father, Prince Isolder, had been murdered by Jacen. This only hardened her resolve. During the ensuing battle, Ka sensed that there was a hidden danger targeting her and Allana. Indeed, Jacen had unleashed a nanokiller virus programmed to attack beings with Isolder's genetics. Although Ka escaped the virus, she reported that Allana did not survive. Following the defeat of Jacen/Caedus, Ka confided in Han and Leia that Allana was alive, but Ka needed time to restore the Hapes Consortium without fearing for her daughter's life. So Allana adopted the alias of Amelia, a Force-sensitive war orphan, and the Solos agreed to be her guardians until Ka was ready to reveal the truth.

Queen Mother Tenel Ka

**Kaa** When Colonel Pakkpekatt and his companions aboard Lando Calrissian's space yacht *Lady Luck* arrived at Carconth to investigate an anomaly, a slave circuit in the ship was activated by Calrissian's beckon call; the ship pointed itself in the general direction of the planet Kaa before jumping to hyperspace.

**Kaa, Chom Frey** An Old Republic Senator implicated by Pol Secura as the primary financial backer of the glitteryll development project. When Vilmarh Grahrk returned Quinlan Vos to Coruscant, he seemed to betray the Jedi Knight and turned him over to Chom Frey Kaa for a huge bounty. However, the betrayal was part of a plan developed by Mace Windu and Vos as a way to get Chom Frey Kaa to admit his part in the glitteryll plot. Kaa was arrested and sent to trial for corruption.

Kaadu

**Kaa, Tee Wat** A traditional Lurmen settler on Maridun, he believed in peace at any cost. Staunchly opposed to violence, Kaa refused to take sides in the Clone Wars—a fact that greatly displeased his fiery young son Wag Too.

**Ka'aa** An ancient species that wandered the galaxy.

**Kaachtari** An active volcano on Haariden, it erupted five years after the Battle of Naboo, spewing titanite-laden lava across the land and causing severe seismic damage. The nearby coastline was altered, and groundquakes caused a massive tidal wave. Much of the new coast, and the newly exposed titanite, was flooded with seawater. Granta Omega contacted Sano Sauro to ensure that the population and authorities were unaware of the just-created mineral wealth. Their plans to corner the market on titanite—and therefore bacta—were thwarted when their scheme was discovered by Obi-Wan Kenobi and Anakin Skywalker.

**Kaadara** One of Naboo's smaller cities, it was a popular tourist destination. During the Galactic Civil War, Kaadara was garrisoned by Imperial forces in an effort to crack down on Rebel activity.

**Kaadi** A young Phindian who took part in the resistance movement against the Syndicat's control of Phindar. Her father, Nuuta, had been forced to submit to the Syndicat's "renewal" process, and was dropped on the planet Alba. Kaadi invited resistance leaders Paxxi and Guerra Derida, along with Qui-Gon Jinn and Obi-Wan Kenobi, to stay at her parents' house while they made plans to expose the Syndicat. Kaadi rallied locals to storm the Syndicat's warehouses as she helped lead the resistance to victory.

**kaadu** Two-legged, flightless reptavians native to Naboo. Kaadu were fearless creatures often used as steeds by Gungan warriors. They laid their eggs on land, often in fields, where many were eaten by predators like the peko-peko. The average clutch of kaadu eggs was therefore quite large to ensure that some survived. In addition to being excellent runners, kaadu were also good swimmers, having lung capacity that allowed them to remain underwater for long periods of time.

**Kaaldar, Dr.** An Imperial physician, he created an engineered strain of Bledsoe's disease on Tatooine.

**Kaan, Loiric** This Yuuzhan Vong warrior was the Supreme Commander of the military forces that attacked Mon Calamari during the final stages of the Yuuzhan Vong War. He served under Warmaster Nas Choka aboard the *Yammka's Mount* during the assault. Kaan was intrigued by the Galactic Alliance's use of machines and technology, despite Nas Choka's assertion that such use showed cowardice more than ingenuity. Kaan also boasted about his own position of power over Alliance forces, further angering the warmaster. Eventually, Nas Choka had Loiric Kaan escorted from the bridge and relieved of his command.

**Kaan, Lord** One of the few Sith Lords who survived the internal violence that tore the Sith Order apart during the New Sith Wars. Lord Kaan gathered 20,000 Sith devotees and established the Brotherhood of Darkness. Then he set out to take control of the galaxy. The Sith won many early victories, but when the Jedi started fighting in force, Kaan had to make a stand at the Battle of Ruusan.

The Jedi massed on Ruusan under the guidance of Lord Hoth, forming the Army of Light. As the fighting ground on, Lord Kaan's tactics of fighting the Jedi in individual battles did not sit well with many of the other Sith Lords. Adding to Kaan's problems was the Sith renegade Darth Bane, who believed that the Sith had to unite under a single being in order to defeat the Jedi. Rather than have Bane tear the Sith apart, Kaan sent assassins to kill him. Bane only got stronger, however, and realized that he needed to eliminate *all* the members of the Brotherhood of Darkness to consolidate the power of the dark side. So Bane sent Kaan the incantations necessary to form a devastating thought bomb, as a last-ditch effort to destroy the Jedi.

Lord Kaan

With the tide of battle turned against them, Kaan and his followers decided to set off the thought bomb, thinking the combined strength of the Sith would protect them from the weapon's incredible blast. They were dead wrong. Lord Kaan, and virtually every Sith and Jedi warrior in the battle, was obliterated. In the wake of the explosion, Darth Bane instituted the Rule of Two to ensure survival of the Sith. Kaan haunted Bane in the form of a silent spirit hovering in the periphery of his sight. On Dxun, Kaan's silent image led Darth Bane through the jungles to the tomb of Freedon Nadd, then directed him deep inside the crypt and showed him a Sith Holocron. Bane grabbed it, unleashing a horde of orbalisks that nearly killed him.

**Kaantay** One of the largest cities found on the planet Neimoidia.

**Kaarenth Dissension** An Imperial splinter group in the Corva sector formed after the defeat of Grand Admiral Thrawn at Bilbringi, it was created by Meres Ulcane and an anonymous Imperial supporter. Using the Spawn Nebula as a shield, the Kaarenth Dissension began assembling a fleet of warships. The group destroyed the New Republic communications center hidden within the gas giant Galaan and stirred up animosity toward the New Republic among the beings of the Outer Rim. The Dissension died near Betha II when the New Republic destroyed the space station that served as Ulcane's base, killing him and destroying much of his fleet.

**Kaarz, Teela** Even though she was an indentured worker, imprisoned by the Empire, Teela Kaarz served as one of the chief architects of the first Death Star. A Mirialan by birth, she had backed the wrong candidate in the early years of the New Order, and he and his supporters were sent to the Despayre prison colony for treason. Kaarz was a specialist in encapsulated arcology design, and her professional achievements and skills attracted the attention of Benits Stinex, who had been hired by the Empire to serve as the chief architect for the interior spaces of the Death Star. Stinex took her on as part of his staff, pushing her to come up with new and better designs as the station was constructed. Although she initially was intimidated, Kaarz rose to the challenge, earning several commendations from the master architect. While aboard the station, she began a romantic relationship with TIE fighter pilot Villian Dance. After the Death Star's destruction of the planet Alderaan, Teela and Villian began to wonder about their loyalty to the Empire. The two, along with several compatriots, escaped the battle station during the Battle of Yavin and joined the Rebel Alliance. When Vil decided to join the Alliance, he also asked Teela to marry him.

**kaastoag** Developed by the Yuuzhan Vong, this scavenger was used to clean up the waste in kitchens.

**Kabadi, Jav and Lora** Aliases used by Han and Leia Organa Solo when they rented an apartment on Corellia during the tensions between it and the Galactic Alliance. The Solos were forced to travel incognito to avoid being targeted by bounty hunters working for Thrackan Sal-Solo.

**Kabaira** An oceanic Outer Rim world in the Teilcam system, it had more than two million volcanic islands. The active volcanoes were in the southern hemisphere, while eight million Kabairans lived in the north, primarily on the island continents of Madieri and Belshain. Eponte Spaceport, the center of Kabaira's corporate government, was on the north coast of Madieri, bordered by mountains. Its climate was typically cool, damp, and foggy. The planet's main industry was mining; indigenous animal life included white snow-wolves.

Kabe

**Kabal** An outer world in the Mayagil sector that suffered food shortages and riots during the Clone Wars, it was officially neutral in the Galactic Civil War. As such, it hosted the Conference of Uncommitted Worlds just after the destruction of the first Death Star. An Imperial Star Destroyer, tipped off by Freeholder Kraaken, arrived to wipe out the conference and punish the planet for its neutrality. Waves of TIE bombers leveled the conference city, but Princess Leia Organa was saved by the timely arrival of the *Millennium Falcon*. Lying near Kabal was a small dwarf star with an artificially accelerated gravitational pull, surrounded by a vast graveyard of derelict starships.

**Kabat** A noted Twi'lek broker of illicit goods, he worked from a base on Corellia during the Galactic Civil War. Kabat didn't take kindly to smugglers stealing cargoes or skipping out on deals, and he often employed harsh means for dealing with those who tried to take advantage of him.

**Kabe** As an infant, Kabe survived a terrible natural disaster on her homeworld—only to be captured and sold into slavery. Taken far from her Chadra-Fan roots, Kabe was abandoned on Tatooine and had to fend for herself in the mean streets of Mos Eisley. She found a friend and protector in fellow street urchin Muftak, a hulking Talz. The large alien cared for Kabe for years in their little warren beneath Docking Bay 83. The two developed a close friendship, watching out for each other. While Muftak offered muscle, Kabe brought in credits through petty thievery and picking pockets.

Often, Kabe would have one too many sips of juri juice and suffer delusions of grandeur, fantasizing about the big score: breaking into Jabba the Hutt's Mos Eisley town house. One night, she and Muftak threw caution to the desert winds and infiltrated the Hutt's residence. They found much more than they expected. Rather than make away with just stolen loot, the pair discovered a captured Rebel agent who offered them thousands of credits to complete a courier run that he could not. The two agreed, and they ended the caper 30,000 credits richer. With enough money to get offplanet, Kabe and Muftak left Tatooine, traveling to the Talz homeworld of Alzoc III, to the Chadra-Fan planet of Chad, and places beyond.

**Kabir, Zev** A snowspeeder pilot who served the Rebel Alliance during the Battle of Hoth using the call sign Rogue Eight.

**Kabray Station** Luke Skywalker and Leia Organa were involved in an interplanetary conference on this space station just prior to the Battle of Endor. Leia once described Kabray as the most neutral and perfectly useless space station in the galaxy, attributes that made it an ideal rendezvous point. During the last years of the Old Republic, many considered Kabray to be a hub of social activity, with huge galas and long-lasting celebrations.

**Kabul, Arista** The daughter of Lorn Kabul, who placed a tracking device on her to keep her from getting into trouble. With the help of Grissom, a Gamorrean, Arista survived a mining tunnel explosion that killed her father. She learned that her uncle Seth was behind the blast, and she vowed revenge. Arista and Grissom later teamed up with Tek, a Jawa fugitive, and the trio fled Otunia.

**Kabul, Seth** The brother of Lorn Kabul, he greatly resented the fact that Lorn, not him, got control of Kabul Industries. He entered into a pact with Moff Harsh that would allow the Imperial easier access to raw materials in return for certain political favors. Seth arranged for Lorn to die in a staged mining accident, but Lorn's daughter Arista was rescued by the Gamorrean miner Grissom. When Seth learned that Arista was alive, he moved swiftly to ensure that the Empire took control of the mines. But Arista was quicker: She blew up the entire mining complex, leaving Seth with nothing.

**Kabul Industries** A mining and heavy machinery manufacturer based on Otunia. Early in the New Order it was controlled by Lorn Kabul, until his greedy brother Seth murdered him and took control. However, Seth's plot to acquire Kabul Industries failed when he was unable to eliminate his niece Arista, who joined forces with Grissom the Gamorrean and Tek the Jawa. The trio set a series of bombs throughout the Kabul Industries' mines. The mines, as well as Seth's career, were destroyed.

**Kabus-Dabeh** An ancient city on Muzara and the site of a minor dark side nexus. A huge monster inhabited the ruins of the city some 4,000 years before the Battle of Yavin. It was covered with black scales and had four barbed tentacles that could inject lethal poison. Two large fins and a lumpy tail helped it move about, and its fang-filled jaws could kill its prey with a single bite.

**Kachirho** A Wookiee city located on the Wawaatt Archipelago on Kashyyyk. Originally founded by members of the Kachirho clan, it became the de facto capital of the planet. It was the site of much of the fighting that occurred during the Clone Wars. Kachirho was different from many Wookiee cities because it was built on the edge of a lagoon, surrounded by conical peaks and dense forest. The Wookiees who lived in Kachirho had dwellings both on the ground and in the surrounding trees, and had carved a vast network of escape routes through the rocky mountains. Originally used to escape from Trandoshan slavers, the escape routes became both refuges and ambush locations during the Separatist occupation. A large portion of the city was located in a 300-meter-tall wroshyr tree, which allowed the Wookiees to defend the lagoon area from above. During the era of the New Order, the Imperial forces that subjugated Kashyyyk took control of the city's starport, but they were unable to fully subdue the Wookiee population. Thus, Kachirho was only minimally garrisoned, and became known as Wookiee City.

**Kad, Tolo** The Minister of State and aide to King Ommin and Queen Amanoa of Onderon 4,000 years before the rise of the Empire. In serving King Ommin, Kad delegated most of his work to his assistant Novar while taking all the credit. Ommin ordered Kad to prepare an important state dinner, and Novar assured his boss that he would make it perfect. When Ommin arrived at the dining hall, he found that there was nothing in place. He demanded to know the meaning behind this disrespect, and Kad was speechless. In his fury, Ommin destroyed Kad with a ball of flame conjured from the dark side of the Force.

**Kadann** A black-bearded human dwarf, Kadann was the Supreme Prophet who led the Prophets of the Dark Side during the New Order. A former Jedi Knight, Kadann drank a strange tea brewed from the fungus-infested bark of an Endorian tree, which was rumored to allow him to see into the future. He was also a collector of the galaxy's finest artifacts, which he displayed throughout his headquarters.

Kadann was approached by Darth Sidious shortly before Order 66 and asked to serve the Empire as a seer. When Kadann predicted that the Empire would be shaken if it allowed the Battle of Endor to take place, Palpatine dismissed him and his prophecies. Kadann gathered the other Prophets and fled Coruscant, taking up residence on Scardia Station. He was later responsible for the prophecy that whoever wore the glove of Darth Vader would be the next Emperor of the galaxy.

The leaders of the Empire's remnants strove to obtain Kadann's blessing to make their rule over the galaxy legitimate. When none of the pretenders to the throne met with his approval, the Supreme Prophet tried to take control of the Empire for himself. But after Ysanne Isard rose to power, Kadann returned to Scardia Station. He was hunted, however, by Imperial Grand Admiral Makati, whom Kadann had embarrassed years before. Exacting his own revenge, Makati fired a fleet's worth of turbolasers at Scardia Station, destroying it and killing Kadann.

*Kachirho*

**Kadas'sa'Nikto** One of the five main Nikto subspecies, also known as the Green Nikto. Unlike many of their relations, these Niktos had plainly visible noses.

**kaddyr bug** This insect, known for its droning song, was native to Ossus.

**Kad'ika** A rogue Mandalorian whose name translated into "little sword," he rose to power during the years following the Yuuzhan Vong War. He tended to prey on his fellow Mandalorians almost as much as he did other beings. Kad'ika was distinguished by his eclectic armor, which was formed from various pieces he had taken from friends and companions. Many questioned whether Boba Fett was ready for the challenge if Kad'ika ever tried to assume the role of Mand'alor. For all his skill and his network of informants, however, Fett had never heard of Kad'ika before his rise—a situation that had Fett worried as well.

Fett's concern only increased when it was rumored that Kad'ika was behind the so-called Kadikla movement, which placed the future of Mandalore before all other considerations. Yet as he struggled to assert himself as Mand'alor, Fett began to think that Kad'ika's philosophies might be right. Kad'ika traveled to Mandalore under the alias of Venku to examine Fett in person. When he was convinced that Fett was truly working to restore Mandalore to its former glory, Kad'ika revealed his identity. Kad'ika was Force-sensitive, although never trained in its ways. He was the son of a Jedi Knight, Etain Tur-Makan, and the clone trooper known as Darman.

***kadikla*** A grassroots movement whose goal was to place the needs of Mandalore itself before the needs of individual Mandalorians. The movement was started by a reclusive soldier named Kad'ika.

**Kadir, Moff** An Imperial official who assumed command of Coruscant's security forces shortly before the Battle of Yavin, after his father—the former commander—was executed for his failures. After witnessing the vengeance of Darth Vader firsthand, Kadir joined a cadre of Imperials who supported Grand Moff Trachta and his plans to unseat Emperor Palpatine. Kadir claimed that he did not trust Grand Moff Bartam, and pretended to misunderstand the intricate political game Trachta was playing. However, Kadir was actually playing one against the other. Kadir was chosen to personally bring a new squadron of stormtroopers to the Emperor. The troopers had been specially conditioned by Trachta to execute the Emperor and were replacements for troopers lost in an earlier assassination attempt. Palpatine had discerned the attempt through the Force, and confronted Kadir alone. Using an intense barrage of Force lightning, Palpatine killed Kadir while Vader executed the troops.

*Kadas'sa'Nikto*

*Moff Kadir*

**Kadlo talisman** An ancient artifact believed to have been owned once by Duros King Kadlo. It was recovered during the Galactic Civil War by Admiral Cov and a group of freelance explorers he hired.

**Kadok Regions** This area of the galaxy was the home of the Bitthævrian species. It was said that the Kadok Regions had little regard for the Old Republic, and that the Jedi Knights were defeated in the area in a battle shortly before the rise of Emperor Palpatine.

**Kador, Mab** This young Aleena was an up-and-coming Podracer during the years leading up to the Clone Wars. He named his Podracer the *White Panther.*

**Kadorto, Halley** A particularly daring Rebel Alliance starfighter pilot who, during the Galactic Civil War, received the Kalidor Crescent for single-handedly rescuing Mon Calamari slaves from the Star Destroyer *Warrior.* He was also a veteran of the Clone Wars.

**Kadril** The site of an Imperial laboratory that developed pacifog during the Galactic Civil War under the watchful eye of Darth Vader. Kadril resembled a huge, pointed asteroid when viewed from space, and was known to be the homeworld of the chameleon-like humanoid Kadrillian species. During the Stenax Massacres, these natives were exterminated by Stenax invaders. Only a semi-intelligent species of terrapins managed to survive, and eventually to recolonize Kadril. During the New Order, it was learned that an original EV series supervisor droid had been using an electroprod on the organic workers who toiled on the planet.

**Kae, Arren** She was one of the many Jedi Knights who participated in the Mandalorian Wars, nearly 4,000 years before the Galactic Civil War. Unknown to most, Kae had a relationship with the Echani warrior Yusanis, and had borne him at least one daughter. Although Kae died on Malachor V, her daughter became one of the Echani Handmaidens.

**Kael, Captain** A Naboo native, he was an officer in the Royal Security Forces prior to the Battle of Naboo. Kael was known as a tough, demanding leader, but one who worked alongside his troops and earned their respect. When the Trade Federation captured Theed, Kael and Lieutenant Gavyn Sykes escaped the city and organized a small resistance movement. Under Kael's command, the force used daring hit-and-run tactics to liberate prison camps and destroy key Trade Federation facilities. In his quest to find allies, Kael joined forces with Borvo the Hutt. The charismatic Hutt earned the captain's trust, but later turned on him and had Kael murdered.

**Kaell 116** A young clone leader of the spaceport city on Khomm. Kaell 116 greeted the returning Jedi Knight and fellow Khomm clone Dorsk 81, along with Jedi Kyp Durron. But when the two later warned of a possible imminent Imperial attack, the complacent Kaell 116 ignored them—much to the peril of the planet, which was nearly annihilated in the attack ordered by Admiral Natasi Daala.

**Kaellin III** A tiny, backrocket world located in the Malenstorr system.

**Kaelta** A purple star that was the primary sun in the Kaelta system, orbited by the planet Toola, homeworld of the Whiphids.

**Kaerobani** The leader of the Lumini pirates during the early years of the New Republic. Although relatively young, Kaerobani was ambitious and known to be a collector of rare antiquities, including a Sith Holocron stolen from a New Republic facility on Coruscant. Mara Jade tracked the holocron to Kaerobani and recovered it before he could figure out how to use it.

**Kaer Orbital Platform** A space station built in orbit around the gas giant Kaer by the Confederacy of Independent Systems during the early stages of the Clone Wars. Established as a secret remote base, the station measured over 2 kilometers long and wide. It was built in just a few months by the InterGalactic Banking Clan, using materials specially ferried by IBC cargo ships. In addition to serving as a secret base, the Kaer Orbital Platform was also a refueling and repair depot for Separatist forces.

**Kaesii** A former Imperial Academy student, she washed out of the training program and became an administrative assistant on Coruscant shortly before the Battle of Yavin. Frustrated, she abandoned her post and fled

Ssk Kahorr

into the criminal underground. In doing so, Kaesii also abandoned her lover, who had been placed in the elite spy training program. She reappeared on Tatooine as a forger and spy, working to undermine the efforts of Jabba the Hutt from her position within the White Thranta shipping operation. During a mission to recover the plans to a prototype military speeder design, Kaesii unknowingly hired her former lover to recover them. His disguise was perfect—he had undergone extensive surgery to appear to others as a Twi'lek—and he managed to recover the plans and discover Kaesii's participation in Tatooine's underworld.

**kag bug** A noxious insect known to find its way into sewer drains and pipes, where it fed on large swarms of refuse.

**Kagi, Captain** A clone officer who served as Emperor Palpatine's personal pilot during the Clone Wars.

**Kaguya** A Tarasin, she was among the prominent individuals invited to debate the problems associated with floating cities on Cularin during the Clone Wars. She brought a Tarasin perspective, although other panelists chafed at her environmentalism. Kaguya argued that the development of multistory buildings would provide a much-needed boost to Cularin's economy, creating jobs and adding more environmentally friendly living situations.

**kaha** A species of coniferous tree native to Talasea, it grew in tall pyramids.

**kahel cave fungus** A fungus native to the natural caverns on Mustafar, it was revered by native Mustafarians for its ability to survive in the planet's hellish environment. Much Mustafarian architecture was based on the shape of the kahel cave fungus.

**Kahiyuk** One of many Wookiee settlements on the Wawaatt Archipelago on Kashyyyk.

Kaha tree

**Kahmf, Drell** Stories spread that this Iridonian scientist was able to recover the brain and part of the spinal cord of Darth Maul after the Sith apprentice was killed by Obi-Wan Kenobi. Kahmf *did* have a mysterious brain in a specialized bacta tank in his laboratory. When Luke Skywalker arrived on Iridonia to negotiate a treaty between the Zabrak and the New Republic, he located Kahmf's laboratory and shut down the support system that kept the brain alive. Kahmf fled when he learned that Skywalker was a Jedi Master.

**kahmurra** A mammalian creature native to Talus, it was believed to have been bioengineered.

**Kahorr, Ssk** An ancient Cha'a and one of the major investors in the mining colony on Goluud Minor. A tall, stocky, orange-skinned reptiloid, Kahorr was rarely without the companionship of Tk'lokk. When the Goluud Corridor was discovered, Kahorr took the chance that it would help him increase profits by making hyperspace travel to and from the mining colony faster. When his ship was destroyed near Primus Goluud, Kahorr had the Navigator's Guild representative who sold him the Goluud Corridor passageway executed. Still hungry for vengeance, Kahorr also set a group of bounty hunters on the trail of Jori and Gav Daragon, the explorers who had blazed the corridor. Only the timely intervention of a group of Jedi Knights saved the siblings. However, Kahorr was able to briefly obtain possession of the *Starbreaker 12*, the Daragons' vessel. The ship was targeted and destroyed by Sith Lord Naga Sadow, killing Kahorr.

**Kahranna** This woman and her family were stranded in the Refugee Sector of Nar Shaddaa following the Mandalorian Wars and the Jedi Civil War. Kahranna paid a pilot for transport to another planet, but the ship captain instead dumped the family on the Smugglers' Moon. With the help of the Jedi Exile, Kahranna arranged for her family to be transported off Nar Shaddaa by Lasavvou.

**Kahr'corvh** A member of Noghri clan Khim'bar, Kahr'corvh served as Noghri representative to the New Republic following the death of Grand Admiral Thrawn. Kahr'corvh was among the many New Republic diplomats who signed the declaration of war against the remnants of the Empire.

**Kai** An Imperial stormtrooper stationed aboard the first Death Star during the months leading up to the Battle of Yavin. Kai was on duty when Han Solo and Luke Skywalker rescued Princess Leia Organa from Detention Block AA-23, and he was ordered to join his sergeant, Nova Stihl, in apprehending the Rebels before they escaped.

**Kai, Tamith** One of the new order of dark side Nightsisters from Dathomir, she aided Brakiss in training Force-sensitive youths at the Shadow Academy to be Dark Jedi. She was tall with black hair flowing like waves down her shoulders. Her violet eyes and dark, wine-colored lips were set in a pale face. During an attempt to destroy the Jedi academy on Yavin 4, her battle barge was destroyed and she was killed.

**Kaiburr crystal** A deep crimson gem, it long rested in the jungle Temple of Pomojema on Circarpous V, or Mimban. Legends described the Kaiburr crystal as a Force-enhancing artifact, capable of strengthening the abilities of Force-wielders. Temple priests were said to have mysterious healing powers that were perhaps enhanced by the crystal's

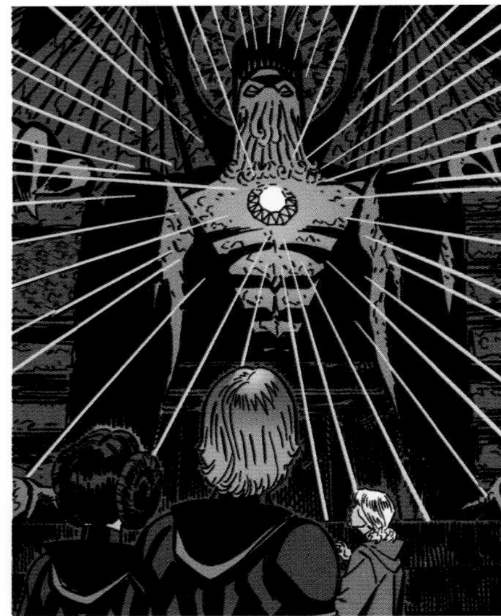
Kaiburr crystal

natural properties. It lay within a ceremonial statue of a minor god, and was guarded by a sluggish but deadly lizard-creature. Soon after the Battle of Yavin, Luke Skywalker, Princess Leia Organa, and the droids R2-D2 and C-3PO crashed on Mimban while traveling to a conference on Circarpous IV. After facing many dangers, including a showdown with Darth Vader, the Rebels were able to retrieve the Kaiburr crystal and leave Mimban. Its powers decreased the farther it was moved from the temple, so Skywalker used the crystal more as a teaching aid, although he experimented with using fragments of it as focusing crystals in lightsabers. The Dark Lady Lumiya's lightwhip was armed with lacerating tentacles formed partly from Vader's Kaiburr crystal shard.

**Kai-Kan** One of the many postures developed by the Jedi Knights for combat with a lightsaber. In a Kai-Kan stance, a Jedi held the lightsaber in two hands, but with the blade horizontal in a low position across the chest.

**Kaikielius system** Lying close to the Coruscant system, it was one of the first systems that revived Imperial forces started conquering six years after the Battle of Endor. As the conquest of the Kaikielius and Metellos systems began, New Republic leaders on Coruscant started searching for a new base of operations.

**Kail** The family of Torm Dadeferron—an associate of Han Solo—controlled several large tracts of land known as the Kail Ranges on this planet in the Corporate Sector. Dadeferron's father and brother disappeared after a dispute with the Corporate Sector Authority over land-use rights and stock prices.

**Kaileel, Detien** A Kabieroun who served as the *Kuari Princess*'s chief of security during the later years of the New Order. He was a good friend of both Celia Durasha and Dap Nechel, although neither knew that Kaileel was a supporter of the Rebel Alliance. On several trips, Kaileel had delivered guns and supplies to the underground on Mantooine, which attracted the attention of Adion Lang and the ISB. After Kaileel was arrested aboard the *Kuari Princess,* Durasha tried to rescue him. She didn't believe in the Rebellion until Kaileel revealed that the Empire had destroyed Alderaan. Kaileel was killed before he could escape.

**Kailio Entertainments** A Hutt-owned business that served as a legitimate front for the Hutts' plans to monopolize the manufacture and distribution of holographic entertainment within the Core Worlds. Despite its seedy background, Kailio was recognized throughout the galaxy as one of the most charitable patrons of the arts, and was active in artistic relief efforts.

**Kailor V** This planet was the site of the Imperial Zoological Gardens. The various aquaria were maintained by the Shalik family of Sedrians. It was also the design center for Hydrospeare Corporation, the maker of Imperial water vehicles.

**Kaim** A Twi'lek Jedi Master, he remained on Coruscant to teach and instruct during the early stages of the Clone Wars. When Senator Meena Tills was kidnapped and held hostage by a group of Korunnai terrorists, Master Kaim was dispatched to negotiate for her release. Terrorist leader Nuriin-Ar was enraged to realize that Kaim was carrying a strip-cam that allowed Omega Squad to get an image of the kidnappers. Nuriin-Ar struck Master Kaim across the face, breaking bones and rendering the Twi'lek unconscious. The Korunnai then strapped an explosive to the Twi'lek's chest and pushed him back outside. Shortly afterward, the explosives were detonated, killing Kaim and injuring the clone commando known as Fi.

***Kai Mir*** One of Ellor's smuggling ships. It was used in a raid on the Bilbringi shipyards to steal the Imperial crystal gravfield trap some five years after the Battle of Endor.

**Kaimme Twins** Smuggling kingpins, they harassed Corporate Sector transport ships until their eventual capture and imprisonment at Stars' End.

**Kaine, Grand Moff Ardus** An Imperial Governor who ruled the Outer Rim Territories following the death of Wilhuff Tarkin. After the Battle of Endor, Kaine found himself in a position to assume command of a large portion of the Empire. A gifted speaker, he was the mastermind behind the formation of the Pentastar Alignment. He ignored the call to arms of Grand Admiral Thrawn, waiting until his own forces were ready to attack the New Republic. He formed the Alignment with the intent of gaining the support of corporations, creating a highly organized force that maintained the ideals of the New Order, although with a slightly modified implementation. During the running of Operation Shadow Hand, Moff Kaine was killed, and the Pentastar Alignment foundered.

Kaink

**Kaink** An Ewok priestess who lived deep in the forests of Endor's moon. She served as the guardian of the Soul Trees and the village legend keeper. An acquaintance of Logray, the Ewok medicine man, Kaink also was skilled in the mystic ways of the forests. Kaink carried a magical staff capped with a crystal, which could emit a beam of mystical force when necessary, or at other times could be used to hypnotize animals. Kaink accompanied the caravan of Ewoks that went out to search for the humans Catarine and Jeremitt Towani, who were captured by a Gorax.

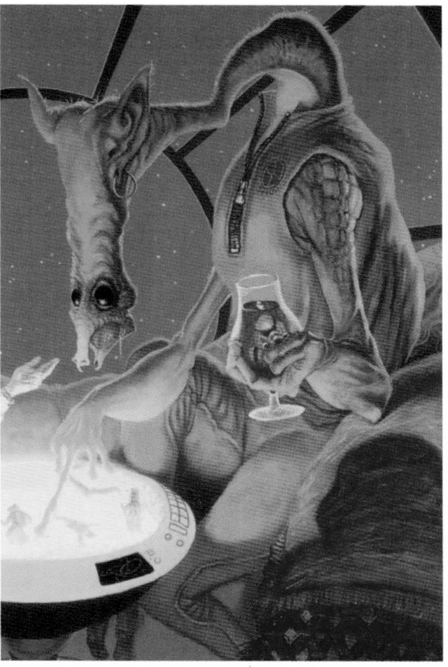
Detien Kaileel

**Kaird** A Nediji assassin working for Black Sun during the last decades of the Old Republic. Early in his life, Kaird was shunned by his people—a communal society known as the Flock—and left Nedij to find his own way. During the Clone Wars, he was dispatched to Drongar to spy on the bota-processing system of Admiral Tarnese Bleyd and Filba the Hutt. Disguised as a member of the Silent—a sect of robed healers—Kaird moved among the various Rimsoo outfits on the planet, keeping a watchful eye on the two conspirators. After Filba tried to coerce Black Sun into paying a higher price for bota, the Hutt was poisoned by the spy known as Lens. After the death of Black Sun agent Mathal, however, Kaird was ordered to step up his investigation and confront Bleyd directly. In a knife fight, Kaird poisoned Bleyd with dendriton, then slit his throat.

When it was discovered that the bota on Drongar was mutating such that it would be useless as a medical wonder drug, Kaird saw his chance to retire from the underworld life and return to Nedij. He hired Squa Tront and Thula to help him secure some of the last bota ever produced, and planned to return to Coruscant with it as his final delivery. However, Thula and Squa Tront double-crossed him, and Kaird would have been killed if he hadn't discovered their trap. He set out to return to Black Sun, but vowed to hunt down the two traitors and exact his own revenge.

**Kairn** A young native of Necropolis, he greeted Zak Arranda when the boy arrived on the planet with his sister Tash and their uncle Mammon Hoole. On a dare, Zak, Kairn, and other youths entered a huge graveyard in the dead of night, and Kairn was captured and murdered by Dr. Evazan. The next day, Kairn was a member of the reanimated dead, the result of Dr. Evazan's hideous experiments.

**Kairn, Reess** A Twi'lek Jedi, he returned to Ryloth and found his betrothed in the arms of another. Kairn went berserk and killed them both. He fled to the Outer Rim, where despair, spice addiction, and the dark side of the Force consumed him. Kairn emerged years later as a pirate, and was known to prowl the Gamorr

Reess Kairn

Run during the last decades of the Old Republic. He once went to the planet Lorahns, stealing a wealth of religious artifacts and killing four Ffib priests. Shortly afterward, he disbanded his pirate crew and returned to hiding. He hired Shi'ido triplets to impersonate him.

The Daughters of the Ffib hired Aurra Sing to hunt down Kairn and eliminate him and his Shi'ido accomplices. One Shi'ido fled to Hoth, one to Tatooine, and the last to Bespin. Sing killed them all. She then discovered that Kairn had undergone reconstructive surgery to make himself resemble a female and had infiltrated the very Daughters of the Ffib who'd sworn to kill him. Aurra Sing discovered that it was Kairn himself who actually made the deal with her. The bounty hunter, not happy at being so artfully duped, executed Kairn upon her return to Endor.

**kai tok** A leather-winged avian predator native to the moon Rori.

**Kaj, Obs** A young, green-skinned Falleen who studied as a Padawan under Jedi Master Lunis when the Clone Wars broke out. Like many students of her generation, Kaj was taken from her homeworld at a young age, and she strived to make sure that her Master's choice was not in vain. However, the stress of trying to match Master Lunis's ideals combined with the demands of the Clone Wars led Kaj to seriously consider leaving the Order.

In the second year of the Clone Wars, Lunis and Kaj were dispatched to the mining world of Katanos VII to investigate possible cloning activities. They discovered an entire laboratory set aside for cloning vats. Cut off from the Republic by the miners, the Jedi were handed over to Count Dooku for a sizable bounty. Though Master Lunis died in fighting for freedom, Kaj escaped but found that the hyperdrive ring for her starship had been disabled. She sent out a distress signal, only to have it intercepted by Count Dooku himself. Dooku ordered his gunners to fire on her ship, and Kaj perished in the explosion.

**Kajain'sa'Nikto** One of the five major Nikto subspecies, the Kajain'sa'Nikto were commonly referred to as the Red Nikto.

***kajidic*** Literally "the means by which we prosper," the term kajidic in more common galactic usage referred to any form of organized Hutt business venture, legal or illegal. It was typically used to describe Hutt clans. Jabba the Hutt, for example, was of the Desilijic kajidic.

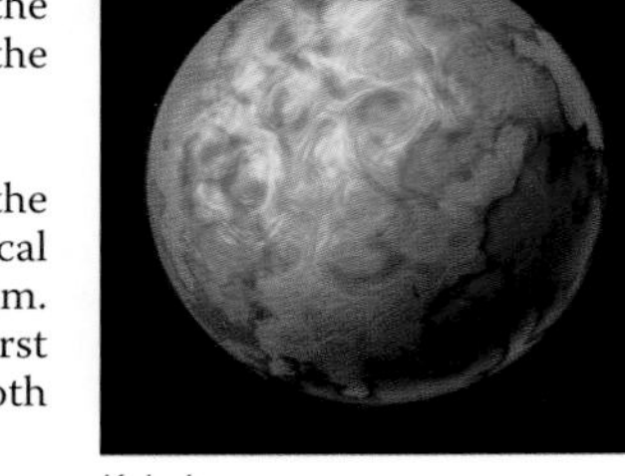

Kalarba

**Kajiin Swamp** One of the thickest parts of the tropical jungles found on Murninkam. It was also filled with the worst of the planet's denizens, both animal and plant.

**Kal** A young Lorrdian who was the son of the planetary governor during the Galactic Civil War. Kal befriended Zak and Tash Arranda when they visited Lorrd with their uncle Mammon Hoole.

**Ka/La** A steam-powered nuclear fusion drive system produced by Girodyne during the final decades of the Old Republic. The Ka/La engine was used as the primary propulsion system for the Corellia Mining Corporation's digger crawler.

**kalaides** Small mollusks native to the planet Cols. Their population was closely monitored by the Cols Kalaides Harvest Guild to ensure an ideal ecological balance.

Kaleesh

**kalak** A nimble creature native to Roon, the four-legged kalak could move about at speeds approaching 60 kilometers per hour. The head of a kalak was dominated by a mouthful of teeth, although these were used primarily to strip leaves from low branches. The Roonans often tamed kalaks for use as mounts, especially for delivering messages.

**Kalakar Six** A moon reputed to be the site of a climactic confrontation between Darth Vader and a resurrected Darth Maul.

**Kalarba** A planet in the remote Kalarba system, it was orbited by the moons Hosk and Indobok. Sites included Kalarba City, the Great Sea, and the Three Peaks of Tharen—a revered symbol of the spirit. Before their service to the Rebel Alliance heroes, R2-D2 and C-3PO worked for the Pitareeze family on Kalarba. Meg and Jarth Pitareeze operated Kalarba Safari and booked tours of the planet's ancient ancestral lands, while Baron Pitareeze ran a spaceship factory. Animal life on the planet included the flying vynock. During the time of the New Republic, Kalarba was devastated when the Yuuzhan Vong sent the orbiting Hosk Station crashing into its surface.

**Kala'uun Starport** A starport on Ryloth under the control of the Shak clan.

**Kaldani Spires Residential Apartments** A residential monad located on Coruscant shortly before the Battle of Naboo. There were more than 500 different levels of apartments within the Kaldani Spires.

**Kaleesh** Members of this species, native to the planet Kalee, were humanoid with orange-scaled skin that pointed to reptilian origins. Their long skulls ended with a pair of heavy tusks at the chin; a thermochemical receptor gland located between their eyes allowed them to "see" into the infrared spectrum. Each hand ended in four clawed fingers, with two fingers opposable to the other pair. The Kaleesh were nomads, moving about the surface of Kalee in search of hospitable environments and good hunting grounds. They always wrapped or covered their bodies to shield themselves from the planet's harsh sunlight. General Grievous was a Kaleesh before being turned into a cyborg.

**Kalenda, Belindi** This operative for New Republic Intelligence served as a covert agent for years. A slight, dark-skinned human, she had jet-black hair and disarming eyes that never seemed to focus on their subject. Without the knowledge or approval of her superiors, Kalenda warned Han Solo of possible trouble on a family trip back

to his homeworld. En route to Corellia herself, she was shot down and crash-landed undetected. Lieutenant Kalenda then went into hiding to await the arrival of the Solo family, and she covertly watched and guarded them as best she could.

By the time of the Yuuzhan Vong War, Kalenda had earned the rank of colonel. She oversaw the initial interviews with the Yuuzhan Vong priestess Elan on Wayland, but was later implicated in a "misinformation flap" that arose in the wake of the Battle of Fondor. Her team had provided intelligence that pointed to a Yuuzhan Vong invasion of Corellia, Bothawui, or Tynna. After Tynna was attacked, Corellia was left undefended to lure the Yuuzhan Vong into a trap. However, the aliens attacked at Fondor instead, and the shipyards there were lost. Kalenda became something of a scapegoat.

Following the Yuuzhan Vong surrender at Coruscant, Kalenda was promoted to director of intelligence for the Galactic Alliance. She and her team realized that the Corellian Confederation seemed to be growing too fast during the Corellia–GA War. Her sources discovered that the Bothans had demanded that the name of the group be changed to simply the Confederation, and that a face-to-face vote of all the group's members be held to elect the Supreme Commander for its growing military forces.

Kalenda also was charged with monitoring the operational status of Centerpoint Station, which was generally considered the most powerful weapon in the galaxy. She had Dr. Toval Seyah inserted as part of the station's staff, and his knowledge of the station ensured that accurate reports were always available. However, after a few months, Seyah reported that he believed his identity had been compromised, prompting Kalenda to extract the doctor and return him to Coruscant for his own safety.

**Kalevala** A world represented in the Galactic Senate by the duplicitous Tal Merrik during the Clone Wars.

**Kal Fas, Hrchek** A Saurin from Durkteel, he was a typical droid trader. Hrchek Kal Fas scouted the "invisible market" for the best droid prices. He was on Tatooine buying and selling droids when he read a posting that noted a reward for finding two "lost" droids belonging to the Empire. The post went on to state that someone had stolen the droids from a high officer who desperately wanted them back because they were close companions—an obvious lie. One of the droids actually walked into the cantina he was in, and Kal Fas slowly followed it out, not wanting to attract attention. But by the time the Saurin made his way to the cantina door, the droid had disappeared into the crowded streets.

**Kal Fas, Sai'torr** A Saurin female from the planet Durkteel, she was a bodyguard for her cousin Hrchek Kal Fas, a droid trader.

**Kalibac Industries** A small corporation that manufactured the MK series of maintenance droids. Its operations were severely weakened by a series of lawsuits brought by Cybot Galactica, although Kalibac's droids remained well made and reliable. Its reputation was further diminished, however, by a variety of cheap knockoffs produced by outlaw techs in the Corporate Sector.

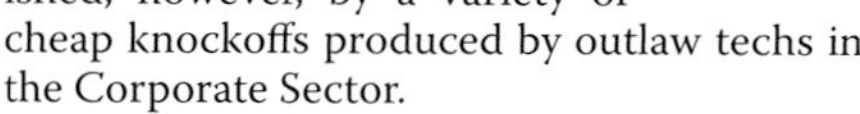

**Kalidor Crescent** A medal given to starfighter pilots by the Rebel Alliance during the Galactic Civil War, it signified great bravery in the face of overwhelming odds. It commemorated the grace and power of the predatory kalidor from Danvar. It was the highest honor bestowed by the Alliance, and had five additional upgraded status indicators: a Bronze Cluster, Silver Talons, the Silver Scimitar, Golden Wings, and the Diamond Eyes.

**Kaliida Shoals Med Station** A secret medical base located near Naboo and Ryndellia, it was a mammoth ring-shaped space station located beyond the Kaliida Nebula. It was targeted by the *Malevolence* during the Clone Wars. Anakin Skywalker led Shadow Squadron through the nebula, narrowly avoiding the massive neebrays that nested there, in a bid to head off the ship. Nala Se, a nurse at Kaliida Shoals, received a warning from Admiral Yularen about the impending attack and did her best to evacuate the station, although most of its 60,000 wounded clone troopers could not be moved. Shadow Squadron was able to disable the *Malevolence* before it could fire its massive ion cannon.

**Kalinda system** A six-planet star system that was located at the junction among the Corporate Sector, New Republic space, and Imperial space. It supported the New Republic. The system was somewhat protected from the outside by a wide asteroid belt in orbit beyond its last planet.

**Kalist VI** The site of an Imperial labor colony. Rebel Alliance gunner Dack Ralter was born there and escaped when he was 17 with the help of Breg, a downed Alliance pilot. Kalist VI was a world dominated by rocky deserts that were broken only by rugged, arid mountain ranges. Luke Skywalker led a mission to the planet to rescue Jorin Sol.

**Kalkovak** A remote, uncharted world inhabited by a species of blue-skinned humanoids who worshipped the Yavin Vassilika as a god-like entity. The natives of the planet appeared to have been descended from a group of beings from the Thelvin Order of Barundi. They were relatively tolerant of outsiders, so long as they didn't disturb the Vassilika.

**Kalla** A planet in the Corporate Sector, it was the site of a university for Corporate Sector Authority members' children. Major fields of study included technical education, commerce, and administration, with very little emphasis on the humanities. Rekkon was an instructor at the university prior to meeting Han Solo. Fiolla of Lorrd attended the University of Kalla before taking a position in the CSA. General Evir Derricote, the commander of the Imperial base on Borleias, was a native of Kalla.

**Kalla VII** Prior to the Battle of Yavin, a group of Rebel Alliance X-wings eliminated a large Imperial base located near Kalla VII in an attempt to strand arriving Imperial ships. This resulted in the capture of the frigate *Priam*.

**Kallaarac** A Wookiee who discovered that Nak'tra Crystals were an effective weapon against the Urnsor'is parasites in the years leading up to the Clone Wars. He was later named chief of his village at the height of the Galactic Civil War.

**Kallabow** Chewbacca's sister and Lowbacca's mother. Like her husband, Mahraccor, she worked at local factories producing starship components.

**Kallarak Amphitheater** A famous landmark on Coruscant. During the last centuries of the Old Republic, the Kallarak Amphitheater could seat a million spectators, and drew some of the galaxy's most popular and enduring talents. Despite its reputation as a concert hall, the venue was known to have poor acoustics. Also, the farthest seats from the stage required that many concertgoers purchase holographic viewers to see what was happening.

***Kalla's Stanchion*** A Nebulon-B frigate operated by the Rebel Alliance during the early stages of the Galactic Civil War. It was based in orbit around Etti IV.

**Kallea, Freia** One of the first female star pilots to map out parts of the galaxy, Kallea was the trailblazer who charted the Hydian Way some 3,000 years before the Galactic Civil War. A native of the planet Brentaal, she became a symbol of the planet's cultural strength and endurance. After retiring from the life of a spacer, she married into a minor Brentaal family and helped grow it into a major trading enterprise. Her life story was later documented in *The Kallea Cycle*, a three-part opera that was later adapted for the masses in the holofeature *Kallea's Hope*.

**Kallic, Captain** An Imperial Navy captain who was given temporary command of the flagship Super Star Destroyer *Executor* shortly after the Battle of Hoth, when Darth Vader was called to Coruscant by the Emperor. During the Hoth campaign, Vader had executed Admiral Ozzel for incompetence, promoting Firmus Piett from captain to admiral. Kallic took Piett's place as captain.

**Kallidahin** Short, thin-bodied humanoids native to the planet Kallidah. A small group of Kallidahin emigrated to the shattered remains of the planet Polis Massa, where eventually they came to call themselves Polis Massans.

**kallil-virus** A virus distinguished by the way in which it clumped together in a jelly-like mass.

**Kalmec, the** One of the most successful criminal organizations found on Ralltiir during the years after the Battle of Naboo. The Kalmec was founded by a group of Wookiees, who shaved the hair off their shoulders. The Kalmec provided an information gathering system for many powerful organizations, including the Separatists during the Clone Wars.

*Kamino*

**Kalpana, Supreme Chancellor** The leader of the Galactic Republic prior to Finis Valorum, who had a post in Kalpana's military advisory office.

**Kalranoos carbine** A custom-built blaster carbine developed during the Empire. It was unusual in that it was equipped with a bio-link module that allowed the user to interface directly with the weapon during combat.

**Kal'Shebbol** Capital of the Kathol sector, it was governed by Moff Kentor Sarne until it was liberated by the New Republic.

**Kalta, Jurgan** A Zabrak mercenary who was active before the Great Sith War. Kalta was known for his adaptability to any situation or environment; he was ultimately killed by a gaxxon brain-slug.

**Kal-Tan-Shi** A Tiss'shar bounty hunter and assassin active during the Galactic Civil War.

**Kamar** A hot, dry planet orbiting a white star just outside the Corporate Sector, it was the homeworld of the insectoid Kamarians. Kamar's native flora included miser-plants, which collected moisture from the atmosphere and could be sucked dry in an emergency; barrel-scrub; and sting-brush. Fauna included digworms, stingworms, bloodsniffers, nightswifts, and howlrunners—canine hunters with heads resembling human skulls. The nocturnal Kamarians lived in small groups called tk'skqua, and their more sophisticated communities developed technology such as nuclear explosives and fluidic control systems. Members of the Kamarian Badlander culture lived in the planet's harshest areas. Han Solo inadvertently started a new religion among the Badlanders based on the holofeature *Varn, World of Water* during a visit to the planet. During the Swarm War, large numbers of Kamarians volunteered to fight alongside their fellow insectoids, the Killiks.

**Kamaran, Willum** A squat, heavily muscled man from a high-gravity world, he was hired by crime lord Prince Xizor to help Durga the Hutt defend the Ylesian colonies from Teroenza and the Desilijic Hutts. Durga agreed to pay Xizor 30 percent of the profits from his Ylesia operations for the protection.

**Kamida, Princess** This young Ewok was the betrothed of Tippet, an upstanding Ewok from Bright Tree Village. Shortly after the Battle of Endor, Tippet was led to believe that Kamida was assaulted by a Lahsbee, thanks to a false rumor planted by the Hiromi spy Hirog, setting off a short war between the Ewoks and the Lahsbees.

**Kamino** A water-covered planet and homeworld of the Kaminoans, it was the fifth planet in a star system located in the area known as Wild Space, beyond the Outer Rim Territories. The system itself was actually part of a dwarf satellite galaxy that spun within the known galaxy some 12 parsecs south of the Rishi Maze. Kamino was constantly swept by intense rainstorms, earning it the nickname Planet of Storms. Centuries before the rise of the Empire, the planet's surface was made up of flat landmasses separated by choppy oceans. Huge glaciers and thick polar caps kept a large part of the planet's water supply under control. Most cities were established on the temperate coastlines.

A sudden rise in planetary temperature caused the polar caps to melt completely in less than 200 years, submerging all the landmasses under roiling oceans of water in an event known as the Great Flood. Even the planet's best geologists were unprepared for the volume of water. Retreats that were built on mountaintops were quickly abandoned to the rising water. This change in surface level caused additional problems by changing the atmospheric density, which resulted in massive storms that dumped more rain into the oceans.

*Kaminoans*

The native Kaminoans adapted to these changes by building stilted cities that sat above the waves on thin, sturdy columns, which provided little resistance to the water. The oceans of Kamino held a wide variety of life, including aiwhas, as well as huge cousins of the colo claw fish and opee sea killers found on Naboo. The planet was orbited by three moons. Shortly after the Battle of Naboo, Jango Fett was cloned on Kamino to create the Grand Army of the Republic. The planet was the site of a major attack two months after the Battle of Geonosis opened the Clone Wars. The Empire later kept a tight hold on Kamino, leading to a clone uprising that was suppressed by the Imperial 501st Stormtrooper Legion.

**Kamino Accords** A set of laws and regulations established in negotiations between Kamino and the Galactic Republic. They provided guidelines and boundaries for the training of clone troopers, ensuring that they were all loyal to the Republic.

**Kaminoan** An intelligent species native to Kamino. Average Kaminoans were tall, thin beings with pale skin and small, knob-like skulls that sat atop long, thin necks. Males of the species had a thin ridge running along the back of their heads. Kaminoans' almond-shaped eyes could see into a variety of spectra beyond that of visible light, including ultraviolet. They were one of the most adept species at the creation of clones, although very few beings even knew of their existence.

Kaminoans had been developing cloning technology for centuries, since shortly after the Great Flood, when they struggled to survive the consequences of global warming. Genetic manipulation and cloning ensured that the species remained strong and viable. Over the generations, specific eye colors came to define the various social castes in their civilization, with gray-eyed Kaminoans being in the most elite caste; yellow eyes denoted the middle caste, and blue-eyed individuals represented the lowest. Green-eyed individuals were shunned as aberrant mutations with intolerable genetic differences. It was believed that the species' aloof nature was due, in part, to the genetic manipulation of the Kaminoan gene pool. Many outsiders speculated that modern

Kaminoans were cloned rather than created by natural reproduction. Their ability to manipulate genes to create "perfect" clones led to an unspoken intolerance of other species, especially those individuals with some physical ailment or defect. To the average Kaminoan, other species were merely living puzzles that could be taken apart and put back together at the genetic level.

Because the post-flood Kamino provided few natural resources, the Kaminoans discreetly sold their cloning services in return for the import of raw materials. Among their customers were the mining corporations of Subterrel and agricultural operations on Folende. In the years that followed the rise of the Empire, Kaminoans experienced a rapid decline in their civilization, as galactic bans on cloning, the defection of many important Kaminoan scientists, and Kamino's distance from the rest of the galaxy meant little new income. The wondrous cities of Kamino fell into disrepair, and attempts to reinstate the once important cloning facilities failed. In the wake of the Yuuzhan Vong War, the Kaminoans struggled mightily to remain a viable species.

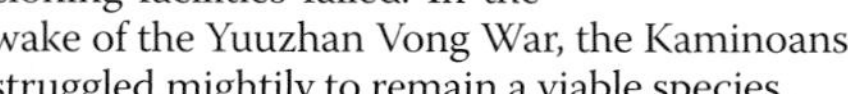

Kamlin

**Kamlin** A young Falleen who was among five Jedi Padawans trained by Master Lucien Draay on Taris in the years following the Great Sith War. Kamlin was one of the most promising students, already responsible for the capture of a noted criminal. The Padawans were invited to a special ceremony to mark their achievements and ready them for their future. They could not know that they were all about to be murdered by their masters—all except for Zayne Carrick, who arrived late to the ceremony.

**Kammia** A planet located in the Drynn system, colonized during the early years of the New Order. It was one of the first worlds provided to the Ssi-ruuk for the acquisition of human subjects as part of a deal struck between Emperor Palpatine and the Shreeftut of the Ssi-ruuvi Imperium. The Empire later issued a statement indicating that Kammia colony had been wiped out by a mysterious disease, and was under strict quarantine.

**Kamparas** The site of a Jedi training center during the Galactic Republic, it was attended by Jedi Master Jorus C'baoth two years before the rise of the Empire. Master Yaddle taught there when not on Coruscant.

**Kanchen sector** The heart of this sector, which contained the planet Xa Fel, fell to Imperial forces after a 30-hour battle with New Republic warships.

**Kandah** An Ansionian who served as a member of the Unity of Community in Cuipernam on Ansion, some 10 years after the Battle of Naboo. She was one of the strongest supporters of secession, believing that the Galactic Republic was no longer a viable political institution. Her family holdings in Korumdah had been appropriated under Republic laws, and she blamed the Republic for the downfall of her family's fortunes. Kandah agreed to help Soergg the Hutt ensure Ansion's secession, and pushed for a rapid vote even while the Jedi Knights sent to mediate the situation were working with the Alwari. After the Jedi successfully negotiated a treaty among the Alwari, Kandah was one of just two votes for secession, versus the nine votes in favor of remaining with the Republic.

**Kandela, Entha** A small-time criminal who was one of many secretly working for Mikdanyell Guh'Rantt, the Rodian who served as the Mayor of Mos Eisley during the years following the Battle of Yavin.

**Kandji** A childhood friend of Biggs Darklighter. The two had pledged their love just before Biggs left Tatooine to attend the Imperial Academy. However, before he could leave, Kandji was captured and killed by Tusken Raiders. A rescue posse found no trace of her body, and killed the Tuskens in revenge.

Kandji

**Kandon** A member of the Black Vulkars during the Jedi Civil War, he served as Brejik's right-hand man. After the Vulkars captured Jedi Knight Bastila Shan following the destruction of the *Endar Spire,* Kandon was asked to make sure she didn't escape. He was unprepared for the arrival of Carth Onasi and the reformed Revan. In a brief scuffle, Kandon was killed and Shan was freed.

**Kandos shuttle** A Tatooine space transport famous for leaving *ahead* of schedule.

**Kang, Davik** Since before the Republic, criminal empires thrived. Xim the Despot held together worlds through tyranny. The Hutts defeated him and brought their own brand of oppression and injustice to the worlds they governed. Some 4,000 years before the Galactic Civil War, when the Republic ruled with much loftier ideals, there was still the stain of criminal syndicates controlling people's lives across entire sectors.

The Exchange was one of the most powerful criminal organizations then operating throughout much of the Outer Rim Territories. The shadowy group was led by an even more mysterious entity called the Compeer; its command structure included individual crime lords controlling profitable worlds. The only way to be accepted into this elite group was to be nominated by several other crime lords. Controlling the world of Taris was Davik Kang. His organization specialized in smuggling contraband goods, the slave trade, and extortion.

According to rumor, Kang agreed to spare the life of a brilliant technician who owed him a large sum of credits in exchange for the construction of a powerful custom-made suit of armor. The suit provided Kang maximum protection, but was extremely light and flexible. The legend held that the armor was so remarkable, Kang decided to have the technician "eliminated" anyway, just to prevent any possibility of ever having to face anyone wearing a similarly designed suit. Following a space battle between Republic and Sith forces over Taris, Republic agents were stranded on the quarantined world. A former bounty hunter associate of Kang, Canderous Ordo, helped the fugitives escape Taris by infiltrating Kang's compound and stealing his ship, the *Ebon Hawk.* Kang was killed trying to stop the fugitives.

**Kang and Lubrichs** A musical duo active during the Galactic Republic.

**Kanos, Kir** A stalwart adherent of the tenets of the New Order even long after the Empire had collapsed. Kir Kanos's beliefs made him one of the deadliest fugitives in the galaxy. Kanos was a member of the Emperor's Royal Guards, the elite red-robed sentinels who guarded the galaxy's ruler. The best of his class at secret training grounds on Yinchorr, Kanos was an expert at the Echani fighting form and in wielding a force pike. His fanatical loyalty, though, was his

Kir Kanos

greatest and most dangerous weapon. Even after Palpatine was defeated at Endor, Kanos and his fellow Royal Guardsmen remained true to the Imperial ideal.

As Imperial Moffs and admirals began greedily carving up the Empire to feed their own ambitions, Kanos attempted to uphold the codes of the New Order. Years later, Palpatine returned in the form of a clone imbued with dark side energies, and the Royal Guardsmen flocked to his side with renewed purpose. This return was not to last, as Palpatine finally succumbed and died on Onderon. In an unthinkable display of treachery, it was a Royal Guardsman who was partially responsible for his demise. The treacherous Carnor Jax had betrayed his oaths and sabotaged Palpatine's clones. As the remaining Royal Guards gathered on Yinchorri to mourn the loss of their Emperor, Jax unleashed his stormtrooper forces. All the Guardsmen were murdered but one: Kir Kanos.

Admiral Saul Karath

Bereft of purpose, Kanos turned to vengeance. He was sickened by the self-styled Imperials who were, he felt, merely usurpers to the forgotten ideals of Palpatine. Kanos targeted Jax, killing the traitor, but he became the enemy of the entire Imperial Interim Council. To better operate on the fringes of the galaxy, Kir Kanos adopted the name Kenix Kil and posed as a bounty hunter. With this alias, he was able to hide from the hunters pursuing him. Kanos succeeded in killing would-be Emperor Xandel Carivus.

**Kanz Disorders** A term used by historians to describe events around the Great Sith War, when Governor Myrial declared the Kanz sector independent and seceded from the Galactic Republic. She then enslaved a number of planets, including Lorrd. Outrage from the enslaved worlds fell upon deaf ears, since the Republic was battling the Sith. The Disorders lasted nearly 300 years before they were resolved by a joint task force of Jedi Knights and Republic armed forces, some 3,670 years before the Battle of Yavin. Over 300 million Lorrdians and 5 billion other beings were killed.

**Kaon** A remote world that served as Count Dooku's primary base of operations after he was forced to flee Vjun during the Clone Wars. He had a castle there.

**Ka'Pa** A Hutt crime lord whose criminal empire had interests in the spice trade, slavery, and weapons running. What separated Ka'Pa from other Hutts was his willingness to do business with the New Republic after the death of Jabba the Hutt, despite the fact that Leia Organa Solo was Jabba's killer. Ka'Pa simply explained that he never let politics get in the way of business. He was also a business rival of Takara.

**Karakan gauntlets** Named for their inventor, the noted isolationist Karakan, these heavy gauntlets were essentially a self-contained medical computer system. They constantly monitored a wearer's nervous and circulatory systems, and could adjust nerve impulses, blood pressure, and tension through the wearer's hands.

**Karath, Admiral Saul** During the ancient Sith campaigns against the Jedi thousands of years before the Galactic Civil War, the corruption of Republic forces proved to be the most devastating weapon in the Sith arsenal. Highly placed Republic officials brought with them trained soldiers, advanced weaponry, and inside knowledge with each defection. After the Mandalorian Wars, Admiral Saul Karath, a pivotal figure in the victory over the Mandalorians, stunned his peers when he declared the Republic not worthy of his support. He transferred his allegiance to the Sith Lord Revan, taking with him a large number of troops and the Interdictor flagship he commanded, the *Leviathan.*

Karath was the first officer of significant rank to go over, and he set a dark precedent. Rather than face an enemy that knew their every tactic, several other officers followed his path. Many who remained loyal to the Republic trained directly under the admiral—such as the heroic pilot Carth Onasi. For Onasi, the conflict became far more personal in nature. He saw Karath's defection as a blow that shook his ideals to the core. He swore vengeance, and eventually found it when Karath was killed on the bridge of his own flagship during the Republic's hunt for the Star Forge.

**Karathas, Admiral Vara** An officer in the Corellian military during the years following the Yuuzhan Vong War, she was among the many leaders who supported Thrackan Sal-Solo's calls for Corellian independence from the Galactic Alliance. Her loyalty gave her considerable power when Sal-Solo ousted the Minister of War and assumed the role himself. Sal-Solo then named Karathas as his chief of staff, placing her in command of the entire Corellian military.

**Karatos Plague** Jango Fett used this deadly virus in an effort to gain the upper hand in his negotiations with Darth Tyranus shortly before the Battle of Naboo. He carried the spores on his armor, releasing them into the air as soon as they were alone. Tyranus, however, used his mastery of the Force to alter his internal chemistry as a defense against the virus. Jango was immune to the Karatos Plague, which was native to Concord Dawn, since he had been inoculated against it as a child.

**Karazak Slavers Guild** Headquartered on the planet Karazak, this slaving operation maintained a transfer center on Gabredor III, which was led by Greezim Trentacal. Trentacal was hired by the Pentastar Alignment to kidnap the children of the ambassador of Cantras Gola, in an attempt to force PowerOn Conglomeration to remain with the Alignment. The children were rescued—and the transfer center destroyed—by the Red Moons mercenaries, who were operating in the interests of the New Republic to defeat the Alignment.

**Karda, Abal** A onetime Imperial colonel whom Boba Fett tracked down to collect the Empire's bounty. A balding man with a cybernetic replacement for his left eye, Karda had been ordered by his superior, General Nim, to wipe out the Icarii. Karda poisoned the tribe and forced Queen Selestrine into slavery. He wanted to use her ability to foresee the future, but she took poison to thwart him. He beheaded her before the poison could spread, then stole the disembodied head after medics encased it in a life-sustaining casket sheathed in kneeb hide.

Selestrine predicted that Karda's superior, General Nim, would be killed, and Karda could take his place. General Nim congratulated Karda and revealed that Darth Vader knew about Selestrine's disembodied head. Karda grew scared and killed Nim and his forces. He fled to various places using many disguises, but he couldn't prevent Boba Fett from finding and killing him.

Abal Karda

**Kardem** *See* Dir'Nul, Vydel.

**Kardue'sai'Malloc (Labria)** A devilish-looking Devaronian spy who indiscriminately shelled the city of Montellian Serat. The act earned him widespread hatred and the title Butcher of Montellian Serat. On his home planet of Devaron, he was a cruel army captain who aligned himself with the Empire to put down a native rebellion. He personally oversaw the execution of 700 captives, earning a Rebel Alliance bounty on his head. He then changed his name to Labria and made himself scarce, showing up in Mos Eisley on Tatooine, where he tried to pass himself off as a major information broker. In truth, the usually drunken Labria was a terrible spy. What may have given him an edge for a while was that he looked sinister; he had pointy ears and a pair of dark horns on his head. His red-tinted skin was hairless, and he had two sets of teeth. After killing four mercenaries on Tatooine, Kardue'sai'Malloc retired to the planet Peppel, where he spent most of his final years collecting music and drinking Merenzane Gold liquor. A 5-million-credit bounty was put on his head by the inhabitants of Montellian Serat, and he was eventually captured by Boba Fett, returned to the city, and publicly executed by being thrown to a vicious pack of quarra.

Commander Karg

**Karena** This ancient Jedi scholar was believed to have first used the term *praxeum* to describe the distillation of learning combined with action. Millennia later, Luke Skywalker used it to describe his new Jedi training facility on Yavin 4.

**Karf** A species of arboreal beings native to the tisvollt forests of Barlok. The Karfs were delicate in appearance, especially when compared with their planetary neighbors, the Brolfi.

**Karfeddion** Located in the Senex sector, it was the site of several slave farms run by the House Vandron. Breeding farms were designed to produce Ossan and Balinaka slaves, tailored for agricultural work. During an economic depression on Karfeddion, Lady Theala Vandron was summoned to the High Court of Coruscant to defend the presence of slave farms on her homeworld.

**Karflo Corporation** A conglomerate with subsidiaries in heavy mining, manufacturing, xenobiotechnology, colonial exploration, and research. Karflo was one of the original signatory sponsors of the Corporate Sector Authority. Under Emperor Palpatine and the New Order, Karflo became a major manufacturer of hyperdrive components, and often exploited low-tech worlds in order to steal their natural resources. This practice was curtailed by the New Republic in an effort to allow these worlds to decide for themselves how best to use their natural resources.

**Karg, Commander** The son of an Imperial admiral, this Imperial officer was ordered by Darth Vader to locate Princess Leia Organa in the months before the Battle of Yavin. Karg managed to intercept Leia on Kattada, and would have shot her in cold blood if the Alderaanian soldiers aboard the *Tantive IV* hadn't shot him first. Leia ordered that Karg be taken aboard the *Tantive IV* for medical treatment. However, the wounds to his head and neck were too extensive for even bacta to heal, and Karg died.

**Kari** The only sentient species native to the planet Karideph. The Kari were small insectoids, with black exoskeletons covering most of their bodies.

**Karin, Baron** A native of Yarrv, he was ruler of the Darpheon city-state during the Galactic Civil War. Karin was a militaristic agitator who hoped to become king of Yarrv and subjugate the nearby planet Steelious. A war with Steelious would require heavy investment in war matériel, and Karin's city-state was heavily involved with military manufacturing. Shortly after the Battle of Yavin, an Alliance protocol droid containing vital information was damaged on Yarrv, and found employment with Karin as a butler. Alliance agents were forced to infiltrate the Baron's estate and recover the droid.

**Kark, Kith** A Gotal and a Jedi, he was killed during the Freedon Nadd Uprising many millennia before the rise of the Empire.

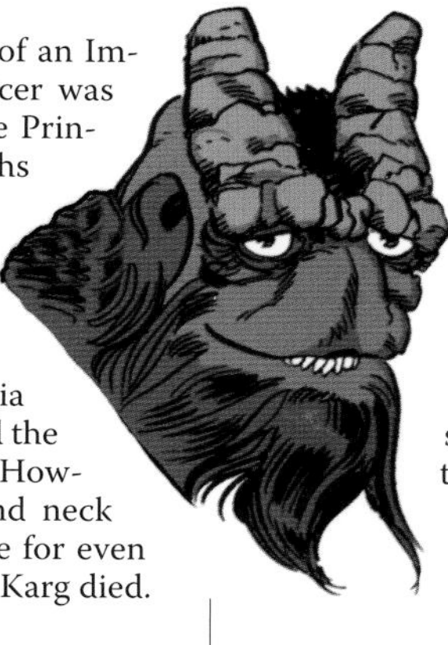

**Karkko, Volfe** Many decades before the Battle of Naboo, this Anzati Dark Jedi was a student of the Force at the Jedi Temple on Coruscant, despite the Jedi Council's underlying apprehension at training an Anzati. Volfe Karkko was arrogant, believing that he could overcome his species' innate desire to consume the "soup" of another being's brain. In his arrogance, Karkko told himself that tasting the soup just once would not affect him, but instead it left him longing to feed quite often. He even fed on other Jedi, gathering a measure of their strength in the Force, and eventually used his control of the Force to trap and consume other beings.

Kari

Kith Kark

When he turned to the dark side, the Jedi Council was forced to trap Karkko in a stasis field on the prison world of Kiffex, where he languished for many years. The Jedi placed his lightsaber in a smaller stasis field as a warning to other Jedi. However, the dark side energy that surrounded him twisted the local population of Anzati, turning them into feral beings who survived simply to do his bidding. Even in stasis, Karkko managed to influence Aayla Secura, who traveled to Kiffex to kill her former Master, Quinlan Vos. She released Karkko from his stasis, allowing him to gain complete control over the feral Anzati. Karkko took her as his queen and groomed her to become an extension of his dark side powers. Vos returned to Kiffex with the Jedi Knights, however, and defeated Karkko in combat. Vos nearly succumbed to the dark side, but the combined contact of Masters T'ra Saa, Tholme, Zao, Mace Windu, Adi Gallia, and Plo Koon gave him the strength to resist the temptation. Vos cut Karkko in half with his lightsaber, eliminating the Anzati threat. Aayla Secura was rehabilitated and rejoined the Jedi Order.

Volfe Karkko

**Karl, Dr. Anet** A doctor who served as part of Urias Xhaxin's crew of pirates during their runs in Imperial space. She was aboard the *Free Lance* when it was attacked by a Yuuzhan Vong warship near Bastion.

**Karn** One of the many Rebels who joined Garm Bel Iblis in his fight against the Empire, he was the leader of the group dispatched to recover Rasha Bex after she tried to leave Bel Iblis's group. He also managed to corner BoShek at Tam's flophouse, but the former smuggler was more than Karn had bargained for. BoShek took out one of Karn's squads with a length of pipe, then stole his speeder to escape with Bex. Karn and the rest of his force took off after them, nearly trapping them at an old mining operation.

**Karnak Alpha** Located beyond the Hapes Consortium near the Deep Galactic Core, it was home to the fur-covered Karnak Alphans. The shy, easygoing Alphans held children in the highest esteem. They also loved unusual zoological specimens, and kept elaborate zoos and

Hondo Karr

holographic dioramas. Some 19 years after the Battle of Endor, New Republic Chief of State Leia Organa Solo met with the Karnak Alpha ambassador and her eight children, and presented her with a rare Coruscant hawk-bat egg.

**Karoc** A Dark Jedi who, with his brother, Vinoc, served as a lieutenant to Count Dooku. Both brothers were killed after the Battle of Geonosis by Anakin Skywalker, who was searching for the source of the cortosis-based battle droids being produced on Metalorn.

**Karr, Hondo** A member of 407th Stormtrooper Division based on Yinchorr nearly a century after the end of the Yuuzhan Vong War. No one knew of his true origins, although it was rumored that he was a former Mandalorian. A melee-combat expert, Karr was a member of Joker Squad. He was one of the many stormtroopers who quietly questioned their loyalty to the Empire after the Sith Lord Darth Krayt took control of the galaxy.

**Karra** A small, dense planet in the Rayter sector, it was covered with flat, grassy plateaus separated by jungle canyons and was home to the Karrans. The planet's temperature was uncomfortably hot and its life-forms consisted almost entirely of insects, including beetles, leapers, legworms, clouds of tiny swarmers, and a walker-sized mantis. The native Karrans were large, fur-covered insectivores whose primitive technology was centered on pottery and simple hand tools. The Karrans likely developed sentience based on a communal hive-mind, and apparently could control the planet's insect population.

**Karrde, Talon** The lawless shadows of the underworld spawned despicable characters possessed of greed, vice, and a lack of scruples—kingpins like Jabba the Hutt, capable of killing without compunction. Standing in stark contrast was Talon Karrde, a sophisticated, shrewd, and skillful smuggler chief who rose to prominence after the collapse of the Empire. Karrde began his fringe career as a member of Jorj Car'das's smuggling group. When Car'das experienced an epiphany and went legal after a strange incident on Dagobah, Karrde inherited command of the organization. He operated in obscurity until the death of Jabba the Hutt shortly before the Battle of Endor.

Karrde's passion was the acquisition of information, and the piecing together of seemingly disparate facts into a cohesive whole. This talent enabled him to take over a number of underworld contacts that were otherwise rudderless in the wake of Jabba's demise. Slowly and quietly, Karrde's organization grew into one of the largest smuggling groups in the galaxy, without the messy hostilities or skulduggery that typified underworld growth. Karrde's group gained an unparalleled asset when he met a striking young woman going by the name of Celina Marniss while investigating a safari-hunting scheme on Varonat. The woman exhibited skills and talents far beyond her simple cover as a hyperdrive mechanic. When the visit to Varonat turned ugly and Karrde's lieutenant Quelev Tapper was killed, Celina saved Karrde. In gratitude, and recognizing a valuable operative when he saw one, Karrde recruited Celina—whose real name was Mara Jade—into his group and began grooming her as his second in command.

Though Karrde's activities occasionally overlapped with those of the New Republic, he was determined to stay neutral in the seismic changes devastating galactic government. Such a stance became increasingly difficult five years after the Battle of Endor, with the start of Grand Admiral Thrawn's campaign to retake the Core. Karrde's base of operations was on distant Myrkr, an otherwise unremarkable planet save for the native ysalamiri creatures that dwelled in the forests. The sessile salamander-like animals had the unique ability to "push back" the Force, creating areas where use of the Force was impossible. For Thrawn, they were vital ingredients in a recipe to overthrow the New Republic. Karrde allowed the Imperials to harvest the ysalamiri, all the while trying to piece together what their plan might be. He also attempted to ferret out Mara Jade's mysterious past: The woman showed an affinity to the Force and a remarkable hatred for Luke Skywalker.

He had the opportunity to uncover both secrets when he stumbled across Skywalker's crippled X-wing floating in space. Bringing the Jedi back to his base—effectively robbing him of his Force talents in the ysalamiri-filled woods—Karrde considered turning Skywalker over to Thrawn. In the end, he decided against it, made an enemy of Thrawn, and lost his Myrkr compound. Karrde's group floated about, looking for a new headquarters, settling for a time on distant Rishi. The Empire eventually caught up with Karrde and took him captive. Luke Skywalker, indebted to Karrde, teamed up with Mara Jade to rescue the smuggler chief. In gratitude, Karrde supplied the New Republic with coordinates for the long-lost *Katana* fleet, the resting place of hundreds of warships that could turn the tide in the campaign against Thrawn. Karrde also gathered a coalition of smugglers to assist the New Republic through information gathering and all-out combat against the renewed Imperial threat. This group provided vital support to the New Republic that helped spell Thrawn's defeat at the Battle of Bilbringi.

The coalition matured into the Smugglers' Alliance, a formally organized grouping of fringers placed under the command of Mara Jade. Karrde supposedly retired, letting Jade call the shots, but in truth he took the opportunity to continue his search for his former mentor, Jorj Car'das. Lando Calrissian and Jade helped in the years-long quest, and eventually Car'das was tracked down to Exocron, a world in the distant Kathol sector. It was 15 years after the Battle of Endor that the search for Car'das turned more than personal curiosity—it became vital to forestall a New Republic civil war. Tensions regarding the Bothan complicity in the decades-old destruction of Caamas were sparked by political firebrands supported by Imperial agents. Karrde believed that Car'das had the information necessary to end the growing animosity toward the Bothans. To that end, Karrde ventured into the distant Kathol sector, accompanied by Shada D'ukal, a Mistryl Shadow Guard. Reunited with his pupil, Car'das declared himself proud of Karrde's methods of operation and his success, but was unable to provide him with the information he needed. Still, the trip wasn't a waste: Car'das did provide proof that exposed a con artist behind the apparent return of Grand Admiral Thrawn.

Once again, the political landscape changed, and Karrde was in the right place. The Galactic Civil War was finally brought to a formal end with the signing of a peace accord between the Imperial Remnant and the New Republic. Karrde worked successfully to establish a joint intelligence service that would benefit both parties. Mara Jade married Luke Skywalker after the Hand of Thrawn incident. Although he participated in the wedding, Karrde knew Mara's loyalty now lay with the Jedi. Fortunately he had a new lieutenant, Shada D'ukal. He also had a new mission.

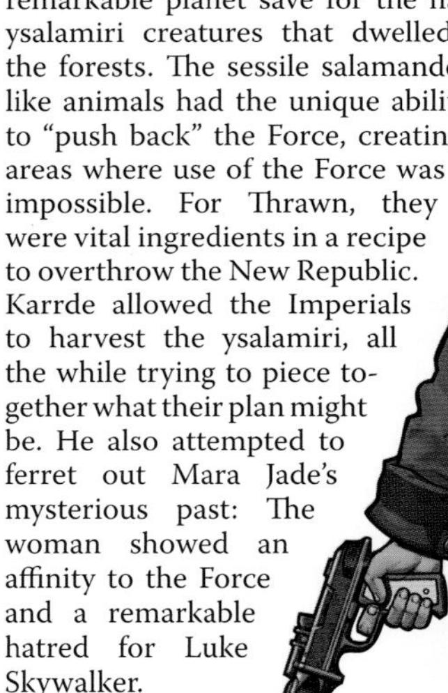

Talon Karrde

Karrde continued to assist the New Republic and the new Jedi Order as they battled against the relentless invasion of the Yuuzhan Vong. Karrde relayed any information he could, not aware that the Yuuzhan Vong were purposely leaking misinformation across the galaxy. Karrde was largely responsible for saving the students at Skywalker's Jedi academy on Yavin 4 from both the invaders and the Peace Brigade. When the Yuuzhan Vong finally surrendered to the Galactic Alliance at Coruscant, Karrde was one of many members of the Smugglers' Alliance to decide to pursue more legitimate goals. Peace didn't last long, however, and during the Confederation–GA War, after Jacen Solo declared the Jedi enemies of the state, Karrde provided his organization's information and equipment to help the Jedi successfully raid Solo's Star Destroyer.

**Karreio** An attractive woman devoted to Emperor Palpatine's New Order, she was engaged to a decorated Imperial officer, Crix Madine, a rising star in the Empire. But then Madine received an order directly from the Emperor that was so vile, he made plans to defect to the Rebel Alliance. Madine didn't tell Karreio about his plans for fear that it would make her seem an accomplice and put her life in great danger. It was only later, in surveying casualty reports, that newly named Rebel Alliance General Madine noticed that Karreio had been killed during a battle between Rebel and Imperial forces.

**Karsh, Komm** A Supreme Commander who led the Yuuzhan Vong forces at Obroa-skai, he perished during a raid on the planet's extensive library.

**Karsk, Amil** A former X-wing pilot, he was on a mission to Alderaan when it was annihilated by the Death Star.

**karstag** A swamp-dwelling predator native to Rodia.

**Kartan, Race** A notorious smuggler who was captured by Jango Fett prior to the Battle of Geonosis.

**Kartha, Captain** An Elomin, he was commanding officer of the New Republic Corellian gunship *Pulsar.* He was stationed aboard the *Mon Adapyne* after being forced to scuttle his ship during the Yuuzhan Vong War.

**Kasarax** A sauropteroid on the planet Dellalt, he helped Han Solo during his quest to find the lost treasure of Xim the Despot.

**Kash, Samish** The elected leader of Delaluna some years before the onset of the Clone Wars. He went to Null with other members of the Station 88 Spaceport alliance to meet with Count Dooku about possibly joining the Confederacy.

**Kashi Mer** An extinct culture that founded the Kashi Mer Dynasty on the planet Kashi, in the Phelleem sector. Many of the Kashi Mer were sensitive to the Force, and they were known practitioners of the art of teräs käsi. Many Kashi Mer fell to the dark side around the time of the First Great Schism. The culture was wiped out when Kashi Mer's primary star went supernova, destroying the entire system.

**Kashir** This planet, home to the Kashirim people, was one of the few worlds that sought active membership in the Galactic Republic during the Separatist crisis. When Obi-Wan Kenobi and his Padawan Anakin Skywalker were sent to greet the king of Kashir, one of the natives pilfered Anakin's lightsaber, and the young Padawan was forced to balance delicate diplomatic relations against getting his weapon back.

**Kashoon** A forested planet, it was the homeworld of the Kashoonara people and the bovine humbaba. The planet was conquered by the Empire early in the New Order era, but eventually was liberated by the Kashoonara with the help of the Rebel Alliance.

**KashyCorp** A Wookiee starship-manufacturing concern founded in the wake of the Swarm War.

**Kashyyyk** A lush jungle planet where treetops served as homes for the native Wookiees, towering fur-covered beings known to be ferocious warriors. The planet was a navigation gateway for the entire southwest quadrant of the galaxy, making it of prime strategic importance. The Mid Rim planet was the principal world of the Kashyyyk system, a star system that also contained the homeworld of the reptilian Trandoshans. The close proximity of these worlds and a deep-rooted cultural animosity fueled many altercations between the two physically powerful species throughout their history.

*Kashyyyk*

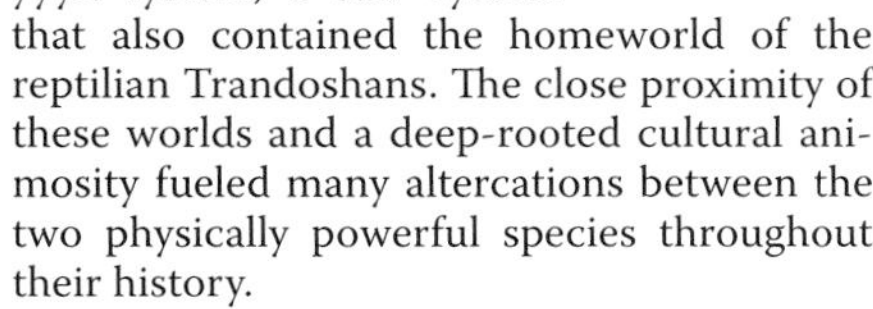

Kashyyyk hosted a unique ecosystem of layered biodiversity. The planet had several horizontal levels of ecology throughout the forests, with each lower level increasingly dangerous. The planet's Wookiees occupied the uppermost level, the forest canopy. Inland, some of the lower levels hadn't seen sunlight in millennia, and were filled with deadly, primitive life-forms. Wookiee culture divided the forests into seven vertical levels. The mighty wroshyr trees were the most visible form of life on Kashyyyk. Kilometers tall, the trees had the notable ability to fuse together if their growth paths intersected, forming a stronger, conjoined tree. The limbs in the forest canopy were so thickly intertwined that they formed a natural cradle for Wookiee architecture. Entire cities were perched in the wroshyr branches, housing millions of Wookiees. Kashyyyk tree cities included the coastal city of Kachirho (in the Wawaatt Archipelago), Rwookrrorro, Kepitenochan, Thikkiiana, Okikuti, and Chenachochan.

Though the Wookiees were the dominant life-form on the planet, they shared their world with countless other specimens. The foggy skies of Kashyyyk were pierced by the high-pitched cries and colorful swirls of plumage of the avian kroyies. Prowling the mighty boles were such predators as the horned katarn and the five-limbed kkekkrrgrro. Lurking in the shadows were creepy terrors like the arachnid webweaver and netcaster, the incendiary flame beetle, and the loathsome gorryl slug. Of course, there were some helpful animals, too: A wiry breed of bantha and the multilegged sureggi could provide sure-footed transportation in the treacherous undergrowth.

During the time of the Republic, the Wookiees were welcomed into the galactic community through dealings with Corellians and Alderaanians. Eventually, Kashyyyk was even represented in the Galactic Senate, with Senator Yarua being the last Kashyyyk representative prior to the outbreak of the Clone Wars. During the Clone Wars, the Separatists attempted to subjugate Kashyyyk by invading it with their droid armies. In response, the Republic dispatched a task force led by Master Yoda to defend the planet. With a war council that in-

*Kashyyyk*

cluded the Wookiee warriors Chewbacca and Tarfful, Yoda's forces were able to repulse the mechanical intruders.

The victory was short-lived. With the rise of the Empire, the Jedi were branded enemies of the Republic. Imperial troopers took control of Kashyyyk, putting the planet under martial law. Yoda barely escaped, fleeing the green world aboard a secret escape pod. It was a terribly dark time for the Wookiees. At the advice of unscrupulous Trandoshans, the Empire blockaded Kashyyyk and enslaved the Wookiees, using their brute strength for labor. So devoted were the Wookiees to their homeworld that many would brave the blockade to revisit their cherished forests for key Wookiee holidays.

After the Battle of Endor, the Wookiees were finally afforded their freedom. Casting off Imperial and Trandoshan shackles, the mighty forest dwellers were again visited by the pall of slavery when would-be Nagai conquerors attempted to continue the vile trade. The Nagai were eventually repulsed. Under the guidance of Kerrithrarr, a Wookiee official, Kashyyyk entered the New Republic, becoming a key signatory and member world of the Republic's Inner Council. The planet welcomed trade, and its city of Thikkiiana became a major exporter of computer technology.

**Kashyyyk bantha** A subspecies of bantha also known as the Kashyyyk greyclimber. Among the most obvious differences of the Kashyyyk bantha from its counterpart were its lack of either a shaggy coat or huge horns. In place of the horns, the Kashyyyk bantha evolved a pair of massive, bony plates that were used as battering rams. Another difference was the feet of the Kashyyyk bantha, which were tipped with longer, more articulated toes that allowed the creature to climb along wroshyr trees.

**Kashyyyk clarion** A Wookiee horn that could be heard for up to 20 kilometers when blown properly. This made the clarion a communication device as well as a musical instrument.

*Jodo Kast being ambushed by the man he impersonated, Boba Fett*

**Kas'im** A Twi'lek Sith Lord who served as swordmaster at the Sith Academy on Korriban during the years leading up to the Battle of Ruusan. He was killed by Darth Bane.

**Kaskutal** A Force-sensitive Gotal who helped to form the Antarian Rangers 600 years before the Clone Wars. Kaskutal had been turned down for Jedi training.

**Kassa, Ossk** A Trandoshan who worked for Gardulla the Hutt following the Battle of Naboo. A bounty was issued for his capture, which Jango Fett later claimed.

*Katarn, a Kashyyyk predator*

**Kast, Jodo** A cunning and ruthless bounty hunter. Jodo Kast wore battle armor similar to that of Boba Fett, and enjoyed being mistaken at times for the galaxy's most famous bounty hunter. Annoyed, Fett hunted Jodo Kast down. In a final confrontation, Fett killed Kast with a nerve-toxin dart followed by an explosion of Kast's rocket pack.

***Katana* fleet** A fleet consisting of 200 Dreadnaught heavy star cruisers. The fleet's flagship, the *Katana,* was said to be the finest starship of its time. The entire fleet was fitted with full-rig slave circuits to vastly lessen the size of the crew needed. The fleet's unofficial name was the Dark Force, from the dark gray hulls of each Dreadnaught. The *Katana* fleet was launched by the Old Republic with massive publicity. But the crews were soon infected with a hive virus that drove them mad. In their insanity, they slaved the ships together; the whole fleet jumped to lightspeed and disappeared for decades. Five years after the Battle of Endor, Grand Admiral Thrawn blackmailed smuggler Niles Ferrier into providing the location of the long-missing *Katana* fleet and escaped with 180 of the 200 ships under the nose of the New Republic.

**Katarkus, Ludwin** A Jedi diplomatic envoy who, along with Everen Ettene, Danywarra, and Halagad Ventor, tried to settle a two-year-old conflict between the Virgillian Free Alignment and the Virgillian Aristocracy during the Separatist crisis.

**katarn (1)** A style of lightsaber hilt first developed by Kyle Katarn, and later mimicked by other students trained by Luke Skywalker during the New Republic era. The emitter cone was extended away from the body of the hilt by a short cylinder ringed with heat-dissipation rings, similar in many respects to the lightsaber maintained by Obi-Wan Kenobi during his isolation on Tatooine.

**katarn (2)** An arboreal predator native to Kashyyyk, the katarn was a sleek quadruped with a thin, rodent-like tail and prehensile claws. The head of a katarn was crowned by a bony ridge that flared backward from the face, which served to protect the neck of the beast. The beak of the katarn was used to dig out tree burrowers from wroshyr trunks. Although vicious when cornered or surprised, katarns could sometimes be befriended, but usually on the katarn's terms. The friendship could last for the katarn's lifetime. Katarns were generally solitary creatures, with males and females remaining separated unless mating. Mating occurred every few years, with the couple remaining together only long enough to ensure a pregnancy. The female usually left the male and moved higher into the trees to give birth. Thus, it was the female katarn that taught the young how to hunt and survive. When they were old enough, young katarns left their mothers and set out on their own. Although not sentient, katarns were considered by many beings, including the native Wookiees, to be among the most intelligent creatures in the galaxy.

**Katarn, Kyle** An elite Rebel agent entrusted with some of the most crucial missions of the Rebel Alliance. It was Katarn who single-handedly infiltrated an Imperial installation on Danuta, securing the technical plans of the Empire's Death Star battle station. A former Imperial, Katarn was born on the Sullustan colony moon of Sulon, living a simple existence as a farmer with his father, Morgan. Unaware of his father's Rebel sympathies, Kyle joined the Imperial Academy at Carida. He was indoctrinated and became a decorated Imperial trooper.

While Kyle was at the Academy, his father was killed. Official records indicated that the elder Katarn had been murdered by Rebel dissidents. Kyle learned the truth, however, from a Rebel agent named Jan Ors: His father had been captured by the Empire for treason, and killed by the Dark Jedi Jerec. Disgusted with the institution he had joined, Kyle discarded his badges and merits, and cast away his Imperial trappings. He resolved to join the Rebellion. Katarn became a highly capable Rebel agent, vouched for by the respected Ors. He drew the attention of no less than Mon Mothma, leader of the Alliance, who entrusted Katarn with the fateful mission to Danuta. After the Battle of Yavin, Katarn was instrumental in quelling the threat of the Imperial Dark Trooper project.

Returning to Sulon, Katarn learned that his

Kattada

father had been aiding a refugee effort on the barren world of Ruusan. Morgan Katarn had discovered ancient ruins on the planet pointing the way to the Valley of the Jedi, the fabled battleground between the ancient Jedi and Sith. The Valley represented a great focal point of energy that, if exploited, could turn the tide in the perpetual battle between light and dark. Kyle knew that the location of the Valley should never fall into Imperial hands. Others already had picked up the scent, however. The Dark Jedi Jerec and his six henchmen, Gorc, Pic, Maw, Sariss, Boc, and Yun, were determined to seize the nexus of power. One by one, Katarn defeated them, though in his aggressive strikes he came dangerously close to succumbing to the dark side of the Force.

Deep in the Valley of the Jedi, Kyle confronted Jerec, the very man who had killed his father. The two battled, and when Katarn slew Jerec, he fulfilled an ancient prophecy. The spirits of long-dead Jedi, trapped in the Valley for 1,000 years, were finally freed. With this energy unleashed, the Valley of the Jedi's worth as a weapon was effectively eliminated.

Long used to operating independently, Katarn at first refused Luke Skywalker's offer to become a Jedi apprentice. Instead, he continued to serve the New Republic on many important missions. After a troubling run-in with the dark side on the forgotten Sith world of Dromund Kaas, however, Katarn conceded that he would benefit from Skywalker's tutelage and joined the Jedi Master's fledgling Jedi academy. Katarn later provided both military and tactical assistance to the Jedi and the New Republic during the Yuuzhan Vong War. Throughout this time, he continued to work with Jan Ors; he asked her to marry him, but she declined.

When Master Skywalker was forced to assume the role of Jedi Grand Master, Katarn was among the many Jedi who decided to remain with the new Jedi Order. He also traveled to Sarm with Master Skywalker, on the mission to eliminate Lomi Plo and force UnuThul to sever his contact with the Colony. Following the Swarm War, Katarn was one of many Jedi Masters who feared that Jacen Solo was growing too close to the dark side of the Force. Thus, he accepted a leadership position on a mission to infiltrate Coruscant and capture or eliminate Jacen before he could do more harm to the galaxy.

Katarn and Valin Horn were two of the first Jedi to confront Jacen Solo—by then, the Sith Lord Darth Caedus. The lightsaber duel taxed both men, until Solo managed to use the Force to ram Katarn with a passing speeder. Katarn survived the attack, although he spent many weeks on the Forest Moon of Endor recovering. When the wounds finally healed, Katarn agreed to travel with Jagged Fel aboard the *Millennium Falcon* and helped rescue Allana, the daughter of Tenel Ka, who had been kidnapped by her father, Jacen Solo. He also took part in the final assault that ended Darth Caedus's reign of terror.

Kyle Katarn

**Katarn, Morgan** A native of Sulon, he was Kyle Katarn's father, having married Patricia Katarn and started a family during the last years of the Old Republic. He was also quite sensitive to the Force, but untrained. He was close friends with the Jedi Knight Qu Rahn. When Morgan was trying to protect the Valley of the Jedi from being exploited by Jerec, the Dark Jedi decapitated him and placed his severed head on a pike.

**Katarn Clan** A clan of younglings, they were Jedi initiates who studied under Master Yoda. Like other clans, the students were between the ages of four and eight years old.

**Katarra** A young female Wookiee who led the underground resistance after the Empire subjugated Kashyyyk and began taking Wookiees as slaves. She organized Wookiees in the city of Rwookrrorro and its environs. Like her father, Tarkazza, Katarra was distinguished by brown fur with tan stripes.

**Kateel** This young woman was a member of the Kuhlvult family of Kuat, and sister to Kodir. However, when Kateel threatened to expose her sister's plans to take control of Kuat Drive Yards, Kodir had Kateel kidnapped and then had her memory erased. From that point on, the sole name Kateel knew for herself was Neelah—the only way she'd been able to pronounce her name as an infant. She became a slave girl in Jabba's palace and, along with Dengar, helped Boba Fett escape from the Sarlacc.

**Katharsis** A popular gaming event on the planet Telos. Ostensibly a lottery mixed with betting on the outcome of several physical challenges, Katharsis allowed every native of Telos a chance to become incredibly wealthy with each round of play. In reality, Katharsis was simply a way for the former Jedi Knight Xanatos to obtain a steady income of credits to fund his illegal mining operations while distracting the populace from his exploitation of their natural resources. After Qui-Gon Jinn and Obi-Wan Kenobi exposed Xanatos's plans, Katharsis was outlawed on Telos.

**kath hound** A predatory canine native to the planet Dantooine. There were two known types of kath hound, horned and hornless.

**Kathol Republic** A collection of 10 star systems in the Kathol Outback, it was created by a group of renegade politicians who saw that the Old Republic was crumbling and chose to set up their own government. The Kathol Republic colonized 14 worlds, 12 of which required some terraforming to be habitable. To ensure that all worlds were adequately protected against attack, members maintained a mutual defense pact. The seat of the Kathol Republic's government was the moon Dayark.

**Kathol sector** A remote sector on the fringes of the populated galaxy, it was first settled about six centuries before the Galactic Civil War by the Old Republic with the establishment of a colony on Gandle Ott. It remained a galactic backwater. There were about 30 official colonies and independent worlds in the sector, but no more than half had even 10 million residents each. On the other side of a large void on the edge of the sector was a cluster of stars called the Kathol Outback, which in turn bordered on the mysterious and difficult-to-navigate Kathol Rift.

The Kathol sector touched the outer reaches of the Minos Cluster, with which it was linked by the Triton Trade Route. Major systems and planets in the sector included the capital, Kal'Shebbol, first settled centuries earlier by escaped Twi'lek slaves; Lorize, a heavy manufacturing planet; and Kolatill, Brolsam, Aaris, Charis, and Oon Tien. The sector was at one time ruled by Moff Kentor Sarne.

**Kattada** A planet sympathetic to the Rebellion. Some of the most daring smugglers in the galaxy called Haleoda spaceport home. Kattada was also known for its beaches, telatti fruit, and wine. Princess Leia Organa and the *Tantive IV* traveled to Kattada, asking for supplies to be sent to the recently subjugated Ralltiir. The planet then joined the Rebellion.

Zasm Katth

**Katth, Zasm** One of Emperor Palpatine's dark side elite, Katth was activated for Operation Shadow Hand. Military Executor Sedriss commissioned Katth and Baddon Fass to perform a number of activities on Nar Shaddaa. First, they were to enlist the aid of Boba Fett in tracking down the *Millennium Falcon.* Second, they were to hunt down and destroy Vima-Da-Boda. Third, they were to report on the *Falcon*'s whereabouts so that Sedriss could capture it. Katth and Fass, both grizzled veterans of Palpatine's rule, failed on all counts, as Boba Fett escaped and they were unable to capture the *Falcon.* Katth perished aboard his Star Destroyer *Invincible* when it mistakenly locked on to Nar Shaddaa's control tower with its tractor beam. The collision destroyed the capital ship and all its crew.

**Katuunko, King** The sovereign of the Toydarians, King Katuunko valued honesty above all else. Chiefly concerned with protecting his people from the ravages of the Clone Wars, Katuunko allied himself with the side that proved most honest, honorable, and deserving: the Republic.

**Kaudine** One of the code names used by Zozridor Slayke to describe key locations of military value on the planet Praesitlyn, during the attempt by Freedom's Sons to fend off a Separatist attack on the Intergalactic Communications Center in the Clone Wars.

**Kaul** This Twi'lek was one of the many beings who lived in the Refugee Sector of Nar Shaddaa following the Mandalorian Wars and the Jedi Civil War. For reasons he never explained, Kaul knew a great deal about the inner workings of the Exchange.

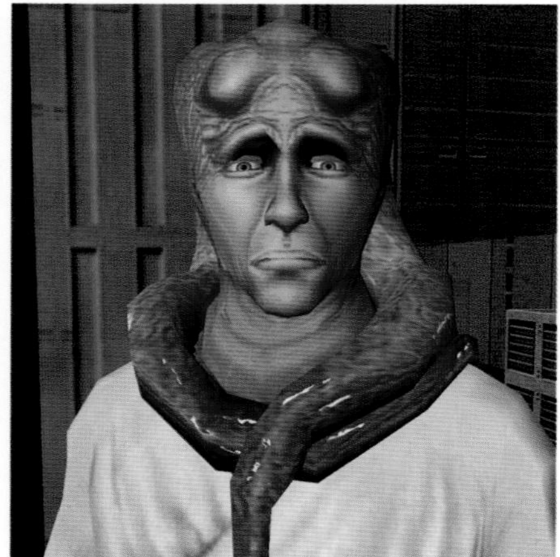
Kaul

**Kauri** A New Republic *Agave*-class interdiction picket ship assigned to the *Glorious* during its attempt to capture the Teljkon vagabond. The *Kauri* was assigned to keep the vagabond from jumping to hyperspace by projecting a false mass shadow into hyperspace near the ship. The *Kauri* was destroyed when the vagabond fled into hyperspace after Lando Calrissian breached its inner hull.

**Kauron** This star system had a large asteroid belt that was home to the Cavrilhu pirates for many years around the Galactic Civil War era.

Kavil

**Kavar** One of only five Jedi Masters to survive the Jedi Civil War. In the wake of the fighting, Master Kavar fled to Onderon, where he served as an adviser and protector for Queen Talia. When the Jedi Exile arrived on Onderon during General Vaklu's attempt at a coup, Master Kavar was pleased to find that she supported the queen's right to rule. After Vaklu was defeated, Kavar chose to teach the Exile new lightsaber combat techniques before setting out for Dantooine to rebuild the Jedi Order. Master Kavar was among the many Jedi killed when Darth Traya attacked and destroyed the Jedi enclave on Dantooine.

**Kavil** A pirate who sought to gain favor with the Empire by throwing his support to Leonia Tavira, after Tavira fled Eiattu. He was a hulking brute of a man with stringy clumps of red hair and scar tissue covering his face and body. Shortly before Sate Pestage was executed by Ysanne Isard, Kavil was working as a double agent, supplying Pestage with information on Tavira's actions. Kavil brought news of the mission to Eiattu that had captured Leia Organa, but Pestage knew that the actual Leia had been on Axxila at the time.

Kavar

**Kavila** The only true continent on the damp, watery world of Dalos IV. Covered with jungles, Kavila's population was primarily nonhuman, with just a few pockets of human occupation. Much of the architecture on the continent was old-fashioned, but there was no lack of modern conveniences.

**Kavila, Harido** This Rodian Grand Protector was credited with creating the Rodian form of drama, primarily as a way to curb violent Rodian instincts during a period in which murders were outnumbering births.

**K'avor** One of the few human settlements found in the Outlands region of the planet Shiva IV. The city was also one of the many settlements controlled by the Calian Confederacy. Just after the Battle of Hoth, K'avor was destroyed by an antimatter bomb that leveled the city. The explosion happened just before Leia Organa crash-landed on Shiva IV during a mission to investigate the buildup of Imperial forces in the sector.

Macus Kayniph

**Kayniph, Macus** One of the top members of the Black Sun criminal organization, Macus Kayniph was one of the first to notice Kir Kanos's fugitive status. He sent a number of his bounty hunters after Kanos, hoping to gain the huge bounty placed on the former Guardsman's head. Kayniph provided Grappa the Hutt with Spaarti cylinders, Imperial cloning technology that cost him much to acquire, and his men also captured Imperial Council member Feena D'Asta for the Hutt. Grappa promised Kayniph shipments of rare, valuable gree spice, but made only one payment. Kayniph was

killed by Grappa when it was discovered that Kanos had been hiding in plain sight—as one of Grappa's employees.

**kayven whistlers** Flying carnivores with sharp teeth and voracious appetites, they were sometimes used for torture or execution. They looked like a cross between a monkey and a bat.

**Kazak** An Ewok elder who served on the advisory council headed by Chief Chirpa. An excellent scout, Kazak studied the movements of the Imperials garrisoned on the Forest Moon of Endor during the construction of the second Death Star. His efforts were invaluable to Han Solo's assault team.

**Kazz, Admiral** An officer in the Imperial Navy during the early years of the New Order. His fleet was assigned to the evil Dr. Raygar during the search for the powerful Sunstar stone on the Forest Moon of Endor.

**Kcaj, Coleman** This Ongree Jedi Master replaced Oppo Rancisis on the Jedi Council at the height of the Clone Wars.

Coleman Kcaj

**KD49** A Karydee repulsorlift engine system used by Rebel Alliance engineers to power the T-47 snowspeeders at Echo Base on Hoth during the Galactic Civil War.

**KD57** This three-chambered repulsorlift engine was produced by Karydee during the early years of the New Order. It was believed that Jabba the Hutt used three KD57 repulsorlift engines in his sail barge, the *Khetanna.*

**kdak** A deadly tentacled mollusk found on Arda II.

**Ke, Hali** The senior Kaminoan research geneticist during the development of the clone troopers created for the Grand Army of the Republic. Hali Ke wrote about the dangers that were inherent in the re-creation of human life, and of the need for Kaminoan cloners to improve their techniques to eliminate errors.

**KE-8 Enforcer** A single-person hovering patrol platform manufactured by the Kaminoans to monitor the clone development facilities within their cities.

**KE-829** The identification number of one of the two stormtroopers who were assigned to guard the tractor beam emplacement located aboard the first Death Star, which was disabled by Obi-Wan Kenobi.

**Kebla Yurt's Equipment Emporium** A general store owned and operated by Kebla Yurt on Taris, it provided a wide variety of equipment during the Jedi Civil War.

**Kech, Nakk** A Khuiumin Survivor and the captain of Rock Squadron under the command of Jacob Nive. He was killed several months after Corran Horn—using the alias Jenos Idanian—joined the Survivors, when the *Invidious* suddenly jumped out of the system during a raid.

**Ke'dem Ramp** A section of the Agrilat Swamp Circuit, one of the most popular swoop racing courses during the New Order.

**Kee (1)** A Devaronian female who worked for the Wookiee smuggler Chak'a some 130 years after the Battle of Yavin. Although she served as the copilot of the *Grinning Liar,* Kee was hired by Chak'a for her mechanical skills. She had a natural talent for understanding all manner of technology, and often took things apart just to see how they worked before putting them back together. Kee was distinguished by her spiked hair, dark skin, and pointed ears, which served as the only outward evidence of her heritage.

**Kee (2)** A Yuzzem miner on the planet Mimban, he helped Luke Skywalker, Princess Leia Organa, and the old woman Halla retrieve the legendary Kaiburr crystal from the Temple of Pomojema. Kee was killed by Darth Vader.

**Kee, Habba** One of the best Podracers found in the Outer Rim Territories in the years before the Battle of Naboo.

**Kee, Neva** A native of the planet Xagobah, this Xamster was regarded as a good Podracer during the last years of the Old Republic. He piloted an oddly configured racer that had a cockpit attached directly to the engines. Kee left Mos Espa's Boonta Eve race in the second lap, wandering off course in the Hutt Flats. He was never seen again.

Neva Kee

**Kee, Tas** A female Weequay enforcer hired by Hat Lo to protect his interests on Coruscant during the years before the Clone Wars. She was adept at concealing weaponry on her body, avoiding scanners and sensors to ensure that Hat Lo was protected wherever he went. She was known to frequent Dex's Diner.

Tas Kee

**Keed'kak, Kitik** An insectoid Yam'rii, a giant praying-mantis-type creature, she was strong and easily angered. Kitik Keed'kak was known for her stealth and her technological aptitude. She was a meat eater and loved eggs. Keed'kak was one of the many patrons in the Mos Eisley cantina on Tatooine the day that Luke Skywalker and Han Solo first met.

**Keeg, Baniss** *See* De Maal, Chachi and Ohwun.

**Keeheen** A prisoner at Stars' End. His mate, Atuarre, and her cub, Pakka, accompanied Han Solo to the penal colony to rescue him from the Corporate Sector Authority facility.

**Keek** A New Republic Fifth Fleet pilot, he was killed during a failed attempt to blockade the Yevetha at Doornik-319.

**Keek, Inspector** The chief of the planet Brigia's Internal Security Police, this pompous, self-important officer covered his oversized uniform with numerous decorations.

**Keela, Gyr** The president of the Mrlsst Academy, a position to which he was promoted after Rorax Falken suffered a nervous breakdown. He was known for his beautiful yellow-and-red facial plumage. He tried to extort money from the Imperial Remnant by proposing to sell it the Phantom Project's cloaking device. When the fledgling New Republic also showed interest, Keela opened negotiations with both. Wedge Antilles represented the New Republic, while his old

Gyr Keela

nemesis Loka Hask represented the Imperials. In the end, though, Keela had to admit that the project was a fake.

**keelkana** A more intelligent relative of the krakana, it was used as a mount by the Mon Calamari Knights during the Clone Wars.

**Keely, Jobe** An elder councilor among the Outbound Flight survivors.

***Keeper*** A Trade Federation battleship and part of Special Task Force One, the group that was dispatched to intercept the Outbound Flight expedition and eliminate it some five years before the start of the Clone Wars.

**Keeper** *See* Lakky, Grodon.

**keeper** A form of Yuuzhan Vong starship developed during their invasion of the galaxy.

**Keeper of Antiquities** The title bestowed upon Jedi Master Odan-Urr, who served as the protector of the Great Jedi Library on Ossus for over 1,000 years.

**Keeper of the Tower** According to the customs of the Tammuz-an, the Keeper of the Tower was responsible for ensuring that the Tammuz-an were ruled by their rightful leader. Only the individual who returned to the Keeper with the royal scepter, on the first morning of the equinox, would be allowed to rule the planet.

**Kee-Piru** One of the first Mon Calamari floating cities destroyed by the World Devastators during the cloned Emperor's campaign of terror.

**Keeramak** A genderless Ssi-ruu and mutant leader of the Ssi-ruuvi Imperium. Keeramak was born after the Ssi-ruuvi defeat at Bakura. He was raised as a king and became exceptional in all respects: strong, intelligent, and wise. Keeramak's compassion became the Ssi-ruuk's undoing, however, leading the P'w'eck to triumph over their oppressors shortly before the Yuuzhan Vong War.

*Keffi*

**Keesa** A Pa'lowick who worked as an assistant to Dama Brunk at the Sidi Driss Inn on Tatooine during the early years of the New Republic. She was assaulted by stormtroopers who were searching for Han Solo and his wife, Leia Organa Solo; the couple were on Tatooine searching for the *Killik Twilight* moss-painting.

**keffi** Handsome riding beasts used on Anaxes. These furry quadrupeds had three-toed feet with thick, horny nails. They were relatively intelligent and docile. A quartet of keffis was used to pull Anaxes ground coaches.

**Kegan** The sole planet orbiting a single sun in the Outer Rim Territories. Kegan was ruled by an isolationist government that believed a series of evil prophecies would come to pass if the Jedi Knights were allowed to visit. There was only a single city on the planet, which was divided into circles of expertise. Outside the city, all land was given over to food and animal cultivation. When the child O-Lana was born, the Jedi Knights were contacted by her parents, and the girl was eventually brought to Coruscant. The Keganites soon discovered that the galaxy around them was a wondrous place, and overthrew the government to join the Old Republic. It was later discovered that the prophecies described by the Keganites were visions of the rise of Emperor Palpatine and the subjugation of the galaxy under the New Order.

**Kei** The first mate of Yevethan strongman Nil Spaar, she was the mother of three offspring. Kei succumbed to the "gray death."

**Keiffler Brothers** A crew of slicers contracted by Moff Kentor Sarne to rig the computer systems of the *FarStar* Corellian corvette with a variety of programming trapdoors. They were killed by Sarne after completing their work.

**Keitumite Mutual Military Treaty** A treaty signed by Ansionian and Keitumite representatives, linking their planets in defense during the last decades of the Old Republic. While the treaty was never invoked, it was still in force before the Clone Wars. Count Dooku and Shu Mai hoped the Keitumites would follow the Ansionians in seceding from the Republic, triggering a domino effect of multiple secessions.

**Kek, Bolton** One of the original designers of the neural network for the IG series of assassin droids, he laid the groundwork for the IG project before retiring from Imperial service for ethical reasons. Bolton Kek eventually was killed by the assassin droid IG-88, who recognized that the programmer was one of only a few humans who knew the IG droids' weaknesses.

**Kel, Waxarn** A once handsome young Jedi Knight whose face was scarred at the Battle of Ebaq 9. Waxarn Kel was an advocate of the Jedi using their strength aggressively against the Yuuzhan Vong.

**Kelada** An industrial planet in the Anarid Cluster, it long supplied the Empire with repulsorlift components and parts for Imperial walkers. Following the Imperial defeat at the Battle of Endor and an increase in Alliance activity, the remnants of the Empire diverted 10 Star Destroyers to Kelada. The world once maintained balance between industry and the environment, but this was threatened as forests and savannas were cleared to support greater production.

**Kelad'den** A male Lethan Twi'lek who was a member of the Anti-Republic Liberation Front, an insurgent group that formed on the planet Serenno during the Ruusan Reformations. A handsome male with ties to a noble Ryloth warrior family, Kelad'den was able to use his charisma and connections to get the things he wanted. About 10 years after the Battle of Ruusan, he met a young woman named Rainah who worked for the Republic embassy in Carannia. Once he learned that she had ties to the government, Kelad'den cultivated a relationship with her, hoping to use her as a source of information for the ARLF. Unknown to Kelad'den, Rainah was an alias for the Sith apprentice Darth Zannah (known by her nickname Rain as a child), who had been sent to Serenno to undermine the efforts of the ARLF. Kelad'den died in a failed attempt to assassinate Tarsus Valorum.

**Kelavine system** Located in the Expansion Region far from any trade lanes, it contained the large gas giant Taloraan. After the Battle of Hoth, Rebel Alliance operatives were sent to search for Tibanna gas deposits on the planet.

**Keldabe** The capital of Mandalore. The settlement consisted of a very large hillside fort ringed by a bend in the Kelita River. Beyond that was woodland studded with smaller settlements.

**Keldabe anchoring bend** A complex form of knot devised by Mandalorians to tie off heavy loads or boats.

***Keldabe*-class battleship** A massive warship designed during the early stages of the Galactic Civil War. Its primary weapons systems were matched with power generators designed to leech power from enemy shielding systems, thereby augmenting the *Keldabe*-class battleship's already powerful generators.

**Kel Dor** A formidable species of humanoids native to the planet Dorin. They had enlarged, external sensory organs located at the base of their skulls that allowed them to interpret basic external stimuli as well as extrasensory input. They evolved breathing the unusual mixture of gases in Dorin's atmosphere—which included helium and a unique gas found only there—and couldn't survive on oxygen-rich planets. Thus, those Kel Dor who traveled to other worlds wore sophisticated goggles and an anti-oxygen mask. Kel Dor physiology was tough enough to withstand hard vacuum for a limited time. Society was based on the family, with several generations living together and often participating in the same trade. However, the choice of a career was never cast in stone, and any individual who wished to pursue a livelihood outside of the family business wasn't discouraged. Jedi Master Plo Koon was a Kel Dor.

*Kel Dor*

**Keldor, Dr. Ohran** One of the designers of the original Death Star. Keldor was killed on Belsavis when he fell from a mobile vine-coffee bed while trying to capture Princess Leia Organa.

**Kelkko, Rath** An Anzati who was one of the most powerful crime figures on his homeworld during the Clone Wars. He was Sora Bulq's primary contact, and was working with the former Jedi Master to establish a Shadow Army for the Separatists. He traveled to Saleucami to train the cloned Morgukai warriors who had been created for the Shadow Army, teaching them the ways of the Anzati assassins. They were discovered by Jedi Masters Tholme and Aayla Secura.

**Kell** A witch who fought against the Jedi Knights aboard the *Chu'unthor* when it crashed on Dathomir. It was Kell who discussed the situation with Yoda after the Jedi Master saved her life. Kell agreed to free the Jedi prisoners and to preserve the reader tapes stored on the *Chu'unthor* until a future Jedi Knight arrived on Dathomir to reclaim them. Kell survived on Dathomir for the next three centuries, and eventually turned the reader tapes over to Luke Skywalker before dying of old age.

**kell dragon** A flat-bodied, short-legged cousin of the krayt dragon, the kell dragon was a mottled gray in color and plated with armor-like scales. It was believed that the kell dragon was native to Ruusan.

**Keller, Commander** A clone officer who served as one of the leaders of the Galactic Republic's forces during the final stages of the Clone Wars. When the time came to execute Order 66, Keller was unable to quickly eliminate the three Jedi who were leading his group. Only Jedi Master Simms was killed; Jedi Master Kai Hudorra and Simms's Padawan, Noirah Na, escaped. Keller set out with his troops to Ithaqua Station in an effort to prevent them from leaving the planet.

**Kellering, Dr.** A scientist at Imperial Prime University, he worked on the Hammertong weapons project. It was Kellering who hired the Mistryl Shadow Guards to guarantee the safety of the Hammertong during its transport to the Empire.

**Keller's Void** An empty region of space, it served as a hyperspace shortcut between the Calus and Wroona systems. Occasionally pirates brought asteroids from the nearby Udine system and placed them in Keller's Void to create mass shadows and force unsuspecting ships from hyperspace.

**Kel-Mar** A manufacturer of starship power couplers.

**Kelmont, Lieutenant** An Imperial officer stationed at the Troska garrison following the Battle of Yavin. His friend Lieutenant Manech engineered a plot to depose their treacherous commanding officer; when Manech was then promoted to commander, he offered Kelmont the position of executive adjunct for his loyalty.

*Graxol Kelvyyn*

**Kelrodo-Ai** The site of gelatin mines famous for their water sculptures. They were once operated by Baron Administrator Drom Guldi. Guldi and his aide were killed by wampa ice creatures while on a hunting expedition to Hoth eight years after the Battle of Endor.

**kelsh** A bronze-colored metal often used to decorate clothing, kelsh also had many industrial uses.

*Lieutenant Kelmont*

**Kelsome, Corporal Maren** A Rebel Alliance scout and soldier. He was assigned to one of the regular patrols at Echo Base on Hoth, and was the first scout to report on the presence of AT-AT walkers just prior to the Battle of Hoth. Kelsome and his tauntaun were trampled by the walkers before he could return to base.

**Keltric, Colonel** A New Republic officer who assisted Colin Darkmere by leading a field operation to learn more about the World Devastators.

**Keluda** A small-time Dug smuggler and con artist, he was a friend of Vilmarh Grahrk following the Battle of Naboo. When Princess Tsian of Old Mankoo failed to eliminate Senator Simon Greyshade, Keluda took the mission himself. Apprehended by Obi-Wan Kenobi and Anakin Skywalker, he tried to use his wrist-mounted blaster to kill Kenobi, but the Jedi blocked the blast with his lightsaber. The blast ricocheted back, killing Keluda.

**Kelvyyn, Graxol** An Anx slaver who worked from a base on the planet Ryloth. He was known as an aficionado of Podracing, and was a guest of Watto at the Boonta Eve Classic race won by nine-year-old Anakin Skywalker.

**Kemp, Lott** A crystal merchant from the planet Dodz, he owned R2-D2 and C-3PO for a period before the Battle of Yavin.

Kemplex Nine

**Kemplex Nine** A strategic jump station in the Auril sector and the Cron system some 4,000 years before the rise of the Empire, it was the only inhabited outpost near the Cron Cluster. During the Sith War, Dark Jedi Ulic Qel-Droma hinted that he intended to attack the undefended station, but it was merely a ruse to draw Republic defenses away from his true target, Coruscant. Later, Qel-Droma did decide to hit Kemplex Nine, but this was meant to draw Jedi forces into a trap. Dark side practitioners Aleema Keeto and Crado, aboard an ancient Sith ship, hit the station and lured the pursuing Jedi fleet into the 10 stars of the Cron Cluster. When they were in position, Keeto activated a Sith weapon and inadvertently ignited all 10 stars, wiping out Kemplex Nine, the entire surrounding area of space . . . and her own ship.

**Ken** The son of a three-eyed mutant and a princess—and the grandson of Emperor Palpatine—he endured a bizarre childhood shut off from the world and most other living creatures. But Ken, a Jedi prince by birth, managed to overcome the dark side influence that he was born into and began the path of becoming a full Jedi Knight. Ken's father was Palpatine's imperfect son, Triclops, who upon birth was sent to an insane asylum on Kessel. His mother was Kendalina, who had been forced to serve as a nurse at the asylum. Triclops and Kendalina fell in love, and she gave birth to a male child before she was killed. A Jedi Master took the baby to the underground Lost City of the Jedi on Yavin 4, where he was raised by droids. Ken was trained to reject the dark side. His only remaining tie to his heritage was half of a silver birth crystal he wore around his neck. The other half was worn by Triclops.

His companions on Yavin 4 were droids DJ-88, caretaker of the Jedi Library and Ken's teacher; HC-100, in charge of Ken's homework; and small Microchip—or Chip—who was Ken's friend. He also had a small feathered mooka named Zeebo as a pet. Ken grew to admire Luke Skywalker and learned to use some of his Force talents. A year after the Battle of Endor, when he was 12, Ken managed to make it topside briefly and met Skywalker before DJ-88 took him back to the Lost City. Kadann, the Supreme Prophet of the Dark Side who was backing the pretender Trioculus as successor to Palpatine, hunted Ken down and tried to kill him. At that point the young Jedi prince joined the Rebel Alliance heroes in a number of adventures. Ken finally encountered his father on the planet Duro, although the true details of their relationship weren't revealed. Later, Kadann captured Ken and told him about his past even as he prepared to steal the secrets of the Lost City and then destroy it. But Luke and Ken combined their Force powers to defeat the Supreme Prophet.

**Kenb, Commander** A Sullustan who served the Galactic Alliance military as a fleet operations commander on Coruscant during the war between the Galactic Alliance and the Confederation.

**Kendalina** A princess, she was forced to serve as a nurse in an Imperial insane asylum on Kessel. There she met and fell in love with the mutant three-eyed son of Emperor Palpatine, Triclops, and bore him a son, Ken, before she was killed.

**Kendamari Casinos** This string of high-class casinos was owned and operated by the Tenloss Syndicate. Many of its larger facilities were owned by Hutts, and all were located in Lol sector. The headquarters of Kendamari were on the planet Kendamar.

**Kendle** Mone's Iskalonian wife. Shortly after Mone left with Lando Calrissian on a mission to Gamandar, Kendle was attacked while inside the city of Pavillion, and her water tank was smashed. She would have died of suffocation had Luke Skywalker not located her and returned her to the water in time. Soon after, Pavillion was destroyed by a tidal wave triggered by an Imperial missile. When Kendle was confronted by Kiro, however, she fled into the ocean. Kiro revealed to Skywalker and Leia Organa that it had been Kendle who alerted Imperial Admiral Tower to their presence on Iskalon. Kendle returned to the surviving Iskalonians, and claimed command of Iskalon. Her motivation for betraying the Rebels was simple: to save her husband and father-in-law from the Imperials on Gamandar. She tried to fight back against the Alliance agents, but was killed when a chiaki attacked her base.

***ken'karro*** This form of government was used by the Krieks. Each *ken'karro* was made up of a male and female representative, and was led by the patriarch known as the *k'lar.*

**Kenlin, Bors** The captain of the *Xucphra Rose,* a Thyferran bacta tanker.

**Kennede, Master Ved** The head of the Imperial training facility on Yinchorr and father of Tav Kennede. A former Royal Guardsman himself, Master Ved Kennede was considered by the Emperor to be one of his best, most loyal warriors. When Carnor Jax sent stormtroopers to ambush the guards at Yinchorr, Master Kennede was one of the last to fall.

**Kennede, Tav** Although not an Imperial Royal Guardsman himself, he allied himself with Kir Kanos to gain vengeance on those who had killed his father. He and Kanos, disguised as bounty hunters, worked for Grappa the Hutt to gain inside information on the Empire. He also kept tabs on Mirith Sinn so he and Kanos could discover her secret mission at Grappa's palace. Later, when Kanos and Sinn were fleeing from the Zanibar on Xo, Kennede rescued Sinn and returned her to an Alliance base. From there, he temporarily joined the Republic force as they raided the Black Sun base on Smarck, Grappa's palace on Genon, and the Imperial Ruling Council headquarters at De-Purteen. After the conflict ended, Kennede enlisted in the service of Baron Ragez D'Asta, who had just withdrawn his sector from the Empire.

**Kenobi, Obi-Wan (Ben)** A dedicated and legendary Jedi Knight, Obi-Wan Kenobi had a long and tumultuous career that helped shape the fate of an entire galaxy. Like all the Jedi of the old Order, Kenobi was taken from his family as an infant to undergo training. He knew very little of his parents or of his brother, though he would later visit them on occasion. Kenobi grew up in the Jedi Temple on Coruscant, alongside such fellow apprentices as Bant Eerin, Siri Tachi, and Bruck Chun.

Kenobi was a headstrong adolescent who longed to become a Jedi. As was custom, when a human hopeful achieved the age of 13, he had to become a Padawan or be sent to the Agricultural Corps, where Force talents were directed to tending sick crops rather than protecting peace and justice. For an agonizingly long time, the impatient Kenobi thought he would never be chosen as a Padawan. Jedi Master Qui-Gon Jinn, whose past tragedies had left him hesitant to take on a new apprentice, overlooked Kenobi on several occasions. It was not until young Obi-Wan attempted to bring Qui-Gon's previous apprentice—one of the few fallen Jedi of the Order—to justice that Jinn accepted Kenobi as his student. Once partnered with Master Jinn, Kenobi began to explore the galaxy. He traveled to many new worlds and encountered new alien cultures, an exciting change for a boy of 13 who had been raised in the sterile corridors of Coruscant.

Though Obi-Wan and Qui-Gon's relationship grew stronger during their adventures, it was not without its troubles. On Melida/Daan, Obi-Wan nearly left the Jedi Order as he joined the Young movement that tried to end a civil war on the planet. Kenobi was ostracized for his transgression, and Qui-Gon nearly abandoned his training. When Qui-Gon decided to give him another chance, the Padawan vowed never again to disappoint the Order.

When he was 25, Kenobi was caught up in the historic events of the Battle of Naboo. At the behest of Supreme Chancellor Valorum, Kenobi and his Master secretly voyaged to Naboo to negotiate a peaceful settlement to the tense Trade Federation blockade of the planet. Aboard a Trade Federation vessel, the scheming Neimoidians sprang a trap on the Jedi and attempted to kill them. Kenobi and Jinn escaped and stowed away on a Trade Federation invasion craft landing on Naboo's surface. Following his Master, Kenobi traveled from Naboo to Coruscant and back during the Battle of Naboo. When Jinn brought a freed young slave boy, Anakin Skywalker, before the Jedi Council, Kenobi was taken aback. Qui-Gon claimed that Anakin was the Chosen One of an ancient Jedi prophecy, and that he was to be Jinn's new Padawan learner. The Council refused Jinn's proposal to train the boy.

This was just one of many disagreements between Obi-Wan and Qui-Gon during their time together. Jinn, a proponent of the living Force over the more serene unifying Force, had long been considered a maverick in the eyes of the Jedi Council. Obi-Wan implored his Master not to go against the Council, but Qui-Gon always responded by saying that he must do as the will of the Force advised. During the liberation of Naboo, Qui-Gon and Obi-Wan were challenged by a deadly Sith Lord. A forgotten menace, the Sith had returned after laying low for a millennium. For the first time in ages, Jedi and Sith dueled. The dark warrior, Darth Maul, used his incredible speed, rage and double-ended lightsaber to fend off both Jedi. As the duel progressed, Obi-Wan and Qui-Gon became separated. Kenobi watched helplessly as Maul killed Jinn, and he rushed to kill the Sith Lord in turn.

Qui-Gon's dying words were a request for Obi-Wan to train Anakin, despite the Council's objections. The Council ultimately agreed, with Obi-Wan taking Anakin as a Padawan, although Jedi Master Yoda had strong reservations about the arrangement. The Council also bestowed upon Obi-Wan the title and rank of Jedi Knight. For over a decade, Obi-Wan guided young Anakin on the path to Jedi Knighthood. Having to rein in an adventure-seeking youth made Obi-Wan both wise and cynical beyond his years. True to his role, Kenobi recognized Skywalker's strengths and weaknesses, and he tried to impart his lessons with the patience and understanding that his mentor had. As Anakin progressed, Obi-Wan grew increasingly concerned that the young Padawan's raw power had fostered a dangerous arrogance. He frequently expressed these reservations to the senior members of the Jedi Council, but they continued to trust in Kenobi's mentorship.

After returning from a border dispute on the world of Ansion, Obi-Wan and Anakin were called by the Supreme Chancellor to protect the life of Senator Padmé Amidala. Although Obi-Wan had a less-than-favorable view of politics, he nonetheless took the assignment seriously. A failed assassination attempt left Obi-Wan with a valuable clue, an exotic weapon not recognized by the analysis droids of the Jedi Temple. As Anakin voyaged offworld on his first solo mission, escorting and protecting the Senator on her home planet of Naboo, Kenobi continued the investigation. He journeyed to Coruscant's CoCo Town, a shabby stretch of city where an old friend, Dexter Jettster, lived and worked. Dex, the proprietor of a simple diner, was a wealth of knowledge, and was able to identify the weapon as a Kamino saberdart.

*Obi-Wan Kenobi, Jedi Padawan*

In searching out Kamino, Obi-Wan discovered that the vaunted Jedi Archives, perhaps the largest repository of lore in the galaxy, had no record of the planet. Conferring with Yoda, Obi-Wan learned that Kamino had been erased from the Archives. Aboard a Jedi starfighter, Kenobi journeyed to the storm-shrouded world. There he made contact with Prime Minister Lama Su, and the mystery surrounding the planet became even more tangled. As explained by the Kaminoans, Obi-Wan had been expected. A decade prior, the Kaminoans had begun crafting an immense clone army on behalf of the Jedi for use by the Republic. Jedi Master Sifo-Dyas, believed dead at the time, had apparently commissioned the army.

The courteous Kaminoans gave Kenobi a tour of their cloning facility in Tipoca City. Obi-Wan saw thousands of identical clone troopers training and preparing, encased in hard white armor. This seemed to have nothing to do with the assassination attempts on Amidala, until Kenobi met with the original genetic template for the clones. Jango Fett, a notorious bounty hunter, had called Kamino home for a decade. Obi-Wan, never breaking his cover story of inspecting the clones, had a brief yet tense conversation with the hunter. Kenobi recognized the man's armor from the assassination attempts on Coruscant, and was tasked by the Jedi Council with taking Fett into custody for questioning. This resulted in a fierce brawl between Kenobi and Fett. Jango Fett's weapon-covered suit aided him in landing blows on the Jedi, and the bounty hunter also benefited from cover fire from his young son, Boba. Ultimately, Jango escaped aboard his starship, *Slave I,* but not before Kenobi was able to secure a homing device to his ship. Kenobi shadowed Jango to the ringed world of Geonosis before he was discovered pursuing *Slave I.* A dangerous chase ensued through the rocky rings of the red planet, and Kenobi's starfighter sustained light damage from a blistering hail of laserfire. Fett again thought he lost his pursuer and proceeded to land, but Kenobi continued his chase.

Obi-Wan secretly set down on Geonosis and snuck into one of its massive spire-complexes. Inside, he found a gathering of Separatists, including the leader, Count Dooku. He learned that Dooku was gathering the heads of the guilds and pooling their military resources, making one huge army to challenge the Republic. Kenobi returned to his ship to make contact with the Jedi Council. He warned of the impending Separatist action, but his communication was cut short when he was taken captive. Held in a Geonosian dungeon, Kenobi was approached by Dooku. The charismatic renegade Jedi spoke fondly of Kenobi's old mentor, Qui-Gon Jinn, who had once been Dooku's apprentice. Dooku seemed to genuinely regret that events had escalated to their current level. His disillusionment with the Republic, too, appeared sincere. Dooku

*Master Kenobi battles General Grievous in Pau City.*

*Obi-Wan Kenobi and his former Padawan Anakin Skywalker*

even revealed to Kenobi that the Senate was under the control of a Dark Lord of the Sith, Darth Sidious. Kenobi refused to believe the words of the older Jedi, and also refused an invitation to join Dooku in battle.

As per Geonosian custom, Kenobi was sentenced to be executed. Joining him were Anakin and Padmé, who had journeyed to Geonosis in a vain rescue effort. The trio were chained to pillars in a massive Geonosian execution arena, and three horrible beasts were unleashed upon them. The Jedi and Padmé, however, proved difficult to kill. Unarmed and shackled, they were resourceful enough to escape certain death. Kenobi avoided the deadly cutting swipes of a vicious acklay creature long enough for Jedi reinforcements to arrive. At least 100 Jedi Knights infiltrated the arena, and the Separatists countered by unleashing thousands of battle droids into combat. Jedi fell by the dozens, but Obi-Wan fought valiantly and survived. This was but a prelude to the start of the Clone Wars, as the newly formed Republic military stormed Geonosis.

Dooku attempted to escape the battle, but Obi-Wan and Anakin gave chase. They caught up with him in a hidden hangar. Though Obi-Wan instructed Anakin to join him in a coordinated attack against Dooku, the headstrong Padawan rushed in—only to be incapacitated by Dooku's surprising dark side attack. Kenobi moved in for the attack, but Dooku proved far too powerful. The rogue Jedi's lightsaber skills outpaced Kenobi's parries, and Obi-Wan fell to the ground, wounded in the arm and leg from glancing saber strikes. As Dooku was about to administer the death blow, Anakin leapt forward and saved his Master. Skywalker and Dooku dueled, but again the Count proved his superiority. Anakin was maimed and collapsed in an exhausted heap, joining the helpless Obi-Wan. Finally, Jedi Master Yoda arrived and attempted to stop Dooku. Though Yoda's withering lightsaber attack nearly defeated the former Jedi, Dooku was able to distract the diminutive Master by endangering Obi-Wan and Anakin with a fallen pillar torn free by the Force. Yoda used his telekinetic abilities to stop the pillar before it crushed the two younger Jedi, and Dooku escaped.

Kenobi healed, and had brief moments to reflect upon the immense changes that had occurred in the galaxy. He conceded that the Jedi had needed the clone army or else the Separatists clearly would have won at Geonosis. Yoda sadly noted that the victory on Geonosis was in fact no victory at all. It was only the start of the darkest times ever to be faced by the galaxy. As with the other Jedi in the Order, Obi-Wan became a high-ranking general in the clone army. Disciplined and courageous, he fought to preserve the Republic, which he considered the ultimate protector of galactic peace. Though he was a deadly warrior and a skilled tactician, Obi-Wan also possessed a softer side. Merciful and even empathetic, Obi-Wan preferred to debilitate his enemies rather than slay them outright. Despite his skill with a lightsaber, Kenobi would always end a battle with words before bloodshed if given the option to do so, earning him the moniker the Negotiator. In large measure, Obi-Wan's success as an intermediary stemmed from his innate likability. Even in the direst of circumstances, Obi-Wan's dry wit always elicited a chuckle.

In stark contrast with his volatile former Padawan, Skywalker, Kenobi remained calm in any situation. After seeing Anakin graduate to the status of Jedi Knight, Obi-Wan found endless delight in watching his onetime student struggle with a strong-willed learner of his own, Ahsoka Tano. Kenobi had the control of a complete army of clone troopers and the latest military hardware. His most trusted clone soldier, Commander 2224—also known as Cody—served him well during close calls on Christophsis, Cato Neimoidia, and elsewhere. During the Clone Wars, Kenobi ascended to the rank of Jedi Master, and he occupied a position on the Jedi Council. He was able to contribute to the highest levels of Jedi strategy, and his vaunted position allowed him to witness the strain between the Jedi Order and the Office of the Chancellor firsthand.

Whatever reservations Kenobi had about Palpatine had to be discarded when the Jedi undertook the important mission to rescue the Chancellor from the clutches of General Grievous. The cyborg general of the droid army led a bold strike against Coruscant, and managed to abduct the Chancellor. Obi-Wan and Anakin came racing into the battle aboard their Jedi starfighters. High above Coruscant, an enormous battle raged as capital ships from the Republic tangled with the escaping forces of the Confederacy. Weaving through the chaos were Obi-Wan and Anakin, backed by Squad 7 of the clone starfighter forces. An attack by a swarm of buzz droids did little to change Obi-Wan's attitude about piloting; the tiny mechanical vandals stripped his ship in midflight, leaving him to land hard in the hangar bay of General Grievous's flagship.

Aboard the starship, Anakin and Obi-Wan cut their way through droid forces as they raced to free the Chancellor. It was certainly a trap, but the Jedi had no shortage of confidence in their abilities, as indicated by Obi-Wan's strategy: "Spring the trap." They found the Chancellor bound to a chair in the spacious observation deck of the general's quarters. Waiting for them was Count Dooku, and unlike the impulsive and disorganized attack that had marked their last confrontation with Dooku, Obi-Wan and Anakin challenged the Sith Lord as a team. Dooku proved a formidable opponent. He Force-pushed Obi-Wan with terrible strength, tossing the Jedi Master like a rag doll against the wall of the quarters. Kenobi was knocked unconscious. Out cold, he never saw the final moments of the duel, when Anakin killed an unarmed Dooku in cold blood at the Chancellor's goading.

Kenobi woke up in a canted turbolift shaft, draped over Anakin's shoulder. The Jedi and the freed Chancellor were fighting not only battle droids but also the massive ship itself, which was falling apart around them due to damage suffered from the prolonged space battle. As they tried to reach the hangar bay, the three fugitives were captured in an energy shield and marched before General Grievous aboard the ship's bridge. Obi-Wan and Anakin were able to break their bonds and overpower their captors. Grievous escaped, leaving the prisoners on the abandoned bridge as the starship succumbed to Coruscant's gravity and began plunging to the surface. It was Anakin's piloting skills that saved the day; he was able to land the wreck of the starship in an abandoned industrial area.

With the death of Dooku, the Republic could claim a major victory, yet the Chancellor was not willing to relinquish any of the power he had attained during the threat of war. General Grievous still remained at large, so the state of emergency could not be lifted. The Jedi Council next focused

*Obi-Wan Kenobi duels Anakin, now a Sith.*

*Obi-Wan gives Luke Skywalker Anakin's lightsaber.*

its attentions on bringing the cyborg general to justice. That task fell to Kenobi. But before that, Obi-Wan was given another tough task—challenging not for its tactical difficulty, but for the awkward strain it put on his relationship with Anakin. At the Chancellor's behest, Skywalker was placed on the Jedi Council. Ordinarily, the Council would not allow the Chancellor to dictate the affairs of the Jedi, but its members accepted Anakin. They refused to grant him the rank of Master, though, a decision that angered the powerful young Jedi.

Fueling that anger all the more was the reasoning behind the Jedi Council's acceptance. Obi-Wan explained it to Anakin outside of Council sessions, so that it would remain off official records. The Council wanted Anakin to report on the Chancellor's dealings: He would in effect be spying on the leader of the Republic. Anakin was torn; he counted Palpatine and Kenobi among his closest friends, and now both were asking him to spy on the other. Obi-Wan grew concerned about Anakin's moodiness. He approached Padmé to gain any insight into Anakin's stress. Unfortunately, his presence and closeness to Padmé would only fuel Anakin's irrational suspicions that everyone was conspiring against him.

When clone intelligence reports indicated that Grievous had fled to Utapau, Obi-Wan took three battalions to the planet. He flew ahead of them to scout out the area by himself before his troops arrived in force. Landing in a massive sinkhole city of the Outer Rim planet, Kenobi made contact with Port Administrator Tion Medon. The tall Utapaun revealed that the world had been under Separatist martial law, and that General Grievous and the Separatist leadership were on planet, on the Tenth Level of the sinkhole city. Kenobi, riding atop a loyal lizard named Boga, found Grievous. He confronted the droid general, backed by his Republic forces led by Commander Cody. The Battle of Utapau commenced, with Obi-Wan squaring off against Grievous. The droid general had been trained in lightsaber combat by Count Dooku. Grievous lacked the finesse of a master swordsman, and instead used brute tactics against Kenobi. His artificial anatomy allowed him to wield four lightsabers at once, spinning them like deadly buzz saws. But because Grievous could not use the Force, Kenobi was able to anticipate his blows and counter them. Obi-Wan sheared off several of Grievous's lightsaber hands, forcing the general to flee. Grievous climbed aboard his waiting wheel bike and tore off into the alleys and corridors of the sinkhole city. Kenobi gave pursuit atop Boga, jumping onto Grievous's vehicle and wrestling him to the ground. In the knuckle-crunching brawl that followed, Grievous and Kenobi traded fierce blows on the general's landing platform. Grievous had the advantage of raw physical strength and an armored body. Kenobi was nearly bested, but in the course of the brawl, the Jedi had loosened the plates that protected Grievous's organic innards. Snatching his foe's blaster pistol, Kenobi fired. The blast pierced Grievous's pressurized gut sac and burned its way through his vital organs. The general was dead. The Clone Wars were over.

But the betrayal of the clone forces had begun. Unbeknownst to Obi-Wan, back on Coruscant, Palpatine had put his master plan into motion. The Chancellor issued Order 66, a secret command that turned all clone commanders against their Jedi generals. Absolutely loyal to the Republic, Cody believed that the Jedi were conspiring against the Republic. The clones opened fire on Kenobi. He barely escaped Utapau. Fleeing the sinkhole planet aboard General Grievous's starfighter, Kenobi made contact with Bail Organa and Jedi Master Yoda. The loyalist Senator reported that the Jedi Temple had been attacked by clone forces, while Yoda confirmed that the clones had turned against the Jedi all over the Republic. The emergency beacon contained within the Jedi Temple was calling all Jedi home, to lure them into a trap. Yoda and Obi-Wan realized that they needed to shut off that signal if the Jedi Order was to be preserved.

Returning to Coruscant, Kenobi and Yoda found the ruins of the Temple. Dead Jedi littered the once polished corridors. The corpses were burned by blasterfire, but several exhibited slashes from a lightsaber. Kenobi realized the terrible truth, a suspicion verified by holographic records of the attack. Anakin Skywalker had caused this destruction. He had succumbed to the dark side. The Chancellor was Darth Sidious, and Skywalker was his new apprentice, Darth Vader. Kenobi rushed to Padmé to tell her this horrific news and determine Anakin's whereabouts. Padmé was shocked, and though she knew where Skywalker was headed next, she did not divulge it to Kenobi. She knew that Kenobi's next mission would be to stop Anakin, perhaps even kill him. Protecting the man she loved and the father of her unborn children, Padmé secretly departed Coruscant to confront Anakin. Kenobi stowed away aboard her vessel.

Arriving on Mustafar, Kenobi emerged from Padmé's ship as the two lovers reunited. Padmé was distraught by Anakin's transformation. She pleaded for him to return from the dark side. When Anakin saw Kenobi aboard her ship, he snapped. Anakin accused Padmé of betraying him, and used the Force to start to strangle her. Kenobi witnessed the evil in Anakin, and attacked his former apprentice. The lightsaber duel that followed was horrific. The two warriors crossed blades throughout the barren industrial facility on Mustafar, oblivious to the volcanic danger surrounding them. The duel spilled over onto Mustafar's fiery surface, with Kenobi and Vader clashing atop automated platforms floating on the molten rivers of lava. The duel returned to solid ground as Kenobi jumped to the black-sand shores of one of the lava flows. He had the high ground, the tactical advantage. He urged Vader not to press on in a fight he could not win, but the Sith Lord's arrogance got the better of him.

Anakin leapt toward Kenobi, and Obi-Wan sheared off his legs and one of his arms in a single swipe. Anakin's maimed body rolled down the embankment, toward the lava river's edge. Obi-Wan was crushed. The supposed Chosen One was no more, but only after wreaking so much destruction on the galaxy. The Jedi were mostly gone. The Chancellor now ruled the galaxy, and the young hero he had come to regard as his beloved brother lay dying on the charred gravel of a hellish world. The heat from the river washed over Anakin, and he burst into flames. His last words professed his utter hatred for Kenobi. Kenobi picked up Skywalker's dropped lightsaber and returned to Padmé's starship. She was dying, but the life of the babies she carried within her still glowed brightly through the Force. They flew to the nearest refuge, the asteroid mining colony of Polis Massa. The alien medics tried to save her life, but it was no use. She died as she gave birth to twins: Luke and Leia.

Yoda, Bail Organa, and Obi-Wan were the only ones who knew of the children's fate. They recognized that should the Emperor ever learn of Anakin's offspring, they would be in danger.

*Obi-Wan learned to communicate from the afterlife through the Force.*

Obi-Wan was instrumental in hiding the children so that the Dark Lords would not know of their whereabouts. He took the young boy, Luke, to live with Owen and Beru Lars, moisture farmers on Tatooine. The young girl, Leia, was taken by Organa to be raised on Alderaan. As the Jedi's ranks were wiped out by the machinations of the emergent Empire, Obi-Wan went into hiding on Tatooine. He would stay there for decades, adopting the name of Ben. The locals would refer to him as a "crazy old hermit" and gave the eccentric man a wide berth. During this time, Kenobi spent years communing with the Force. Through meditation, he made contact with the spirit of Qui-Gon Jinn. His former Master had discovered the secret of immortality, a way of preserving his identity in the netherworld of the Force. Obi-Wan studied from him, learning this ability.

At the height of the Galactic Civil War, Leia Organa secured plans to the Empire's most diabolical weapon, the Death Star. Her mission was to contact Obi-Wan, then bring both Kenobi and the plans to her adoptive father on Alderaan. Captured by the Imperial agents, Leia was unable to complete either task. She instead placed the plans into the memory systems of an R2 unit and dispatched the droid to Tatooine. R2-D2 and his companion C-3PO were purchased by Owen Lars. R2-D2—adamant about continuing his mission of getting the plans to Kenobi—fled the Lars homestead. When Luke Skywalker pursued the little droid, he came face-to-face with Obi-Wan.

Kenobi told Luke about his father, though the Jedi didn't reveal the whole truth to the lad. Uncertain that Luke would be ready for the burden, Kenobi explained to him that Anakin Skywalker was an amazing pilot, a great warrior, and a good friend. Obi-Wan attributed Anakin's death to a rogue pupil of his, Darth Vader, who betrayed and murdered Anakin. Since, Kenobi reasoned, Anakin had ceased to be upon the emergence of Vader, what he told Luke was true, from a certain point of view. Obi-Wan even gave Luke a gift from his father: Anakin Skywalker's blue-bladed lightsaber. Thus began Luke's journey into the world of the Jedi. Obi-Wan tried to train Luke as much as he could in their short time together. As testament to the desperation of these dark times, Kenobi knew full well that Skywalker would never have been trained in the old days of the Jedi: He was far too old to begin. Nonetheless, Kenobi saw a chance to redeem his fallen pupil through Luke.

Having taken the mission to rescue Princess Leia from the Empire, Obi-Wan and Luke hired Han Solo's *Millennium Falcon* as transportation to Alderaan. During the trip, Kenobi began Luke's lightsaber training. The brief session was cut short as the *Falcon* emerged from hyperspace to find Alderaan destroyed by the Death Star. The tramp freighter was captured by the Empire and taken into the massive vessel. Once aboard, it was Kenobi's mission to disable the tractor beam terminal responsible for holding the ship. Kenobi did so, carefully sneaking through the labyrinthine corridors of the battle station. Though his skill in the Force kept his presence a secret from stormtroopers and Imperial officers, it only served to draw the attention of Darth Vader.

The Dark Lord confronted Kenobi as the Jedi was returning to the *Falcon*. After decades of delay, Vader finally squared off against his former Master. As a diversionary tactic to help the others escape, Kenobi sacrificed himself to Vader. The Dark Lord struck the Jedi down, and Kenobi became one with the Force. He left behind no body, just empty robes and his own Jedi weapon. Kenobi's death strengthened Skywalker's resolve to serve both the Rebellion and the Force.

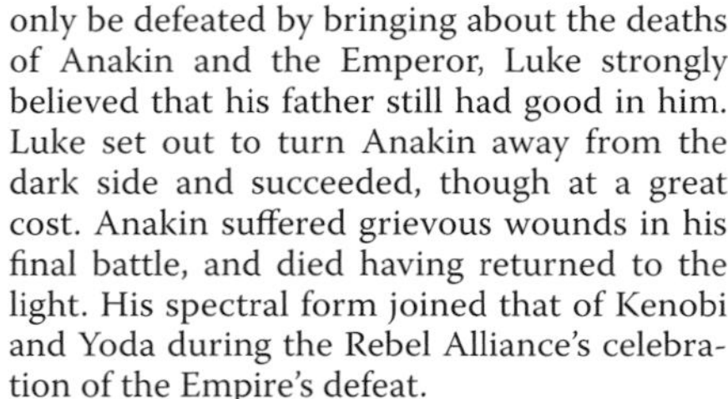
*Kerrithrarr*

At times of great trial, Kenobi's voice would reach out to Luke, offering counsel, such as advising him to turn off his targeting computer to blow up the Death Star. Later, the spectral form of Kenobi would appear to Luke. On Hoth, his ghostlike image advised young Skywalker to venture to Dagobah, where he could complete his training under the guidance of Yoda. Later, Kenobi appeared to Luke and revealed the truth of his lineage. Although Kenobi felt that the dark side could only be defeated by bringing about the deaths of Anakin and the Emperor, Luke strongly believed that his father still had good in him. Luke set out to turn Anakin away from the dark side and succeeded, though at a great cost. Anakin suffered grievous wounds in his final battle, and died having returned to the light. His spectral form joined that of Kenobi and Yoda during the Rebel Alliance's celebration of the Empire's defeat.

Five years after the Battle of Endor, Kenobi began to lose his ability to retain his identity in the Force. He appeared to Luke on Coruscant to bid him farewell. Though Skywalker mourned the loss of his first mentor, Kenobi impressed upon Luke that he was not the last of the Jedi, but rather the first of the new.

**Kenobi Offensive** A series of military maneuvers employed by General Obi-Wan Kenobi during the Clone Wars. The offensive involved the use of a large number of smaller ships that executed small attacks on an enemy fleet in an effort to draw a portion of the fleet out of formation. Once that happened, the enemy ships could be destroyed by a reserve offensive task force, which could rush behind enemy lines through the hole created in the main formation. In theory, the enemy's ships would be unable to fire on attacking ships as they passed through the line, because any stray fire would strike their own ships. Over time, Rebel Alliance military leaders simplified the strategy, simply placing ships where the enemy wouldn't expect them to be, then attacking the main enemy force from within.

**Kenow, Colonel** An officer in Klyn Shanga's ragtag Renatasian militia, Kenow was charged with intercepting Vuffi Raa on Oseon 6845 during the early years of the New Order. Kenow was discovered by Lando Calrissian, who killed him in self-defense. Lando was arrested, but was charged only with carrying a concealed weapon.

**Kensaric, Corporal** A Rebel Alliance scout and field tracker who served under Major Bren Derlin at Echo Base and survived the Battle of Hoth. Later, Kensaric served on Han Solo's strike team sent to the Forest Moon of Endor.

**Kentas, Julynn** The aged chief executive officer of droid builder Industrial Automaton, she was a shrewd businesswoman. Although Julynn Kentas's record wasn't free of failure—her company's R5 units were a flop—her successes far outweighed any disappointments.

**Kentra** A species of winged, fur-covered aliens native to Orellon II.

**Keoulkeech** A grizzled Ewok shaman from Red Bush Grove who left the Forest Moon of Endor to become a healer aboard a Carosite medical transport.

**Kepporra, Wynt** A native of the planet Alderaan who attended the Imperial Academy on Prefsbelt IV at the same time as future warlord Delak Krennel. A member of the Academy's Thespian Union, he was home on leave when his planet was destroyed by the first Death Star, and was killed.

**Kerane** A noted prospector during the last decades of the Old Republic, although many of his peers considered him more than a bit insane. Kerane was the first to map out and investigate the Hoth asteroid field, where he claimed to have found a huge asteroid formed of pure platinum. He said that he had even brought back a small sample to verify its composition. However, when Kerane returned to the belt, he was never able to find the asteroid. He went mad in his frustrating search, and the asteroid's location remained a mystery.

**Kerestian** Native to Kerest, this species evolved into savage hunters of great cunning and skill due to the harsh conditions of their home planet.

**Kerilt** A jungle world in the Mid Rim and the first planet of the Algara system. The large Caamasi Remnant colony called Morymento was located there.

**Kerkoiden** An alien species, one of its notable members was General Whorm Loathsom, a leader of the Retail Caucus who also led Separatist forces in the Clone Wars.

**Kern** *See* Chenati, Tarrence.

**Kerrithrarr** A Wookiee leader within the Rebel Alliance, Kerrithrarr was instrumental in the development of the New Republic. His signature helped validate the Declaration of a New Republic.

**keshel** A valuable ore mined on Tyne's Horky, and the foundation of that planet's currency.

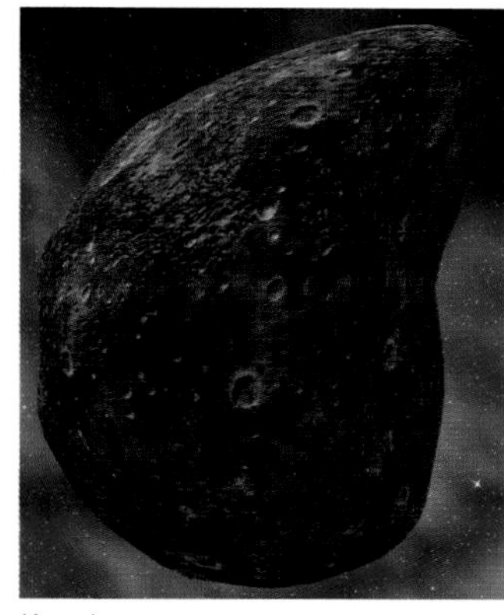
Kessel

**Kessel** A reddish brown potato-shaped planet near the planets of Fwillsving and Honoghr, it was the only source of the telepathy-inducing glitterstim spice, and was the onetime site of a brutal Imperial prison and spice-mining operation that used forced labor. Kessel had one large moon; the city of Kessendra was located there. The planet's surface was covered with crumbled salt flats and atmosphere-production factories that sent great jets of oxygen, nitrogen, and carbon dioxide into the pinkish sky to make the air barely breathable. Beneath Kessel's surface lived dangerous energy spiders that spun glitterstim webs as a method of catching their prey, primarily the luminous bogey.

The Kessel system was adjacent to a cluster of black holes known as the Maw, which made navigating to the planet difficult and helped glamorize the smugglers' Kessel Run. While Kessel was under control of the Empire, it was a common smuggling destination for those dealing in spice, and smuggler-turned-Rebel-hero Han Solo once boasted that he had made the Kessel Run in "less than 12 parsecs" by flying dangerously close to the Maw.

Prior to the Battle of Yavin, a bold Alliance rescue operation freed a group of Rebel POWs during a prisoner transfer operation. During the chaos surrounding the Battle of Endor, a Rybet prison official named Moruth Doole (who had secretly been supplying glitterstim to smugglers) staged a prison revolt and took control of the planet from the Empire. After the members of Rogue Squadron captured Borleias, they were sent to Kessel to free members of the Black Sun criminal organization, with the intention of returning them to Coruscant and making life difficult for the Empire prior to an Alliance invasion. The Rogues neutralized Kessel's defenses while Lieutenant Page and his commandos secured the landing zone. They freed 16 of the galaxy's worst criminals. Several years later, after Doole's operation was dismantled, the administration of the mines was taken over by Lando Calrissian. Kessel's moon, which once held an Imperial garrison and Doole's ragtag defensive fleet (decimated in a battle with Admiral Daala's Star Destroyers), was destroyed by a Death Star prototype from Maw Installation.

**Kessel Correctional Facility** Despite its name, this medium-security prison facility was actually located on Kessel's Garrison Moon at the height of the New Order. Those prisoners who were physically unable to contribute to the mining of spice on Kessel itself, yet were too valuable to dispatch, were given menial duties at the facility.

**Kesselrook, Serja** A portly man who made his home on the junkyard world of Patch-4. Kesselrook and his band of scavengers greeted Luke Skywalker and Lando Calrissian when they arrived on the planet in search of four TIE fighters.

**Kessel Run** An 18-parsec smuggling route that passed near the Maw. The completion of the run was a source of pride and accomplishment among smugglers. By moving closer to the black holes of the Maw, a starship pilot could trim parsecs from the Run while increasing the difficulty of the trip. The official record for completing the run was held by Han Solo and Chewbacca aboard the *Millennium Falcon.* BoShek claimed to have beaten that record, but without a full cargo to weigh him down.

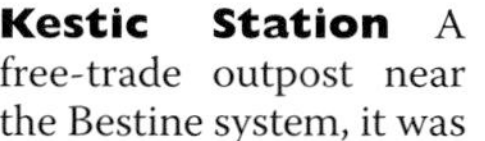
Aleema Keto

**Kestic Station** A free-trade outpost near the Bestine system, it was a frequent stopover for smugglers and outlaw miners. Rebel Alliance pilot Zev Senesca lived on Kestic Station with his parents, who supplied the Rebellion with arms until their illegal transactions were revealed by an Imperial informant. The station was subsequently destroyed by the Star Destroyer *Merciless.*

**Kestrel** *See* Dawn, Raleigh.

***Kestrel Nova*** An ancient freighter, it was captured by Republic forces in a space battle with pirates near Taanab some four millennia before the rise of the Empire.

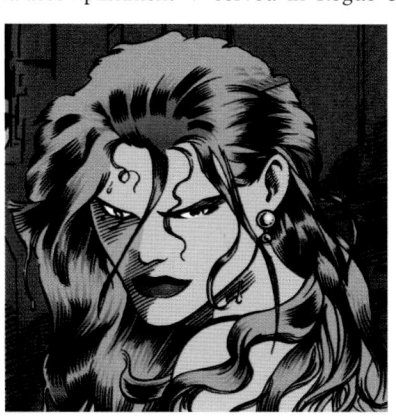

Satal Keto

**Ketaris** A major trade center, it was the target of an attack by Grand Admiral Thrawn, but the assault was stalled at a critical point. Alliance pilots had hoped that Wing Commander Varth could escape the Qat Chrystac battle and hook up with a unit at Ketaris. During Admiral Thrawn's attack on Coruscant, Alliance Admiral Ackbar was on an inspection tour of the Ketaris region.

**kete** A large winged creature, much like a giant dragonfly. Ketes lived on the Forest Moon of Endor in spiral mounds made out of a sticky, marshmallow-like substance.

**Keten** The naval commander of the Imperial Remnant, serving under Moff Kurlen Flennic during the Yuuzhan Vong War. It was Keten who intercepted the *Jade Shadow* when Luke Skywalker arrived in Imperial space during his search for Zonama Sekot.

**Kether, Ran** A native of Chandrila, he served in Rogue Squadron as Rogue Seven during the hunt for Warlord Zsinj. He was the squadron's communications officer. He was later killed during the defense of Kalarba against the Yuuzhan Vong.

***Kethor*** This was one of the many cruisers that made up the small naval fleet protecting the planet Maramere during the years before the Clone Wars.

**Keto, Aleema** A direct descendant of the Empress Teta, Aleema was heir, with her cousin, to the throne of the Empress Teta system some 4,000 years before the Battle of Yavin. She was rich, spoiled, and bored with life. For amusement, Aleema turned to the dark side illusions of the ancient Sith magicians. She helped murder her aunt, uncle, and others, and staged a coup to take over the system as co-leader of the Krath dark side cult. The spirit of the dark side Jedi Freedon Nadd bestowed upon Aleema certain powers, including the ability to cast realistic illusions. Jedi Knight Ulic Qel-Droma traveled to the system in order to learn the Krath's secrets, but he succumbed to the dark side himself and helped Aleema defeat her enemies. Later, Aleema attempted to reassert her power over Krath forces by abandoning Qel-Droma during an attack on Coruscant, but he was rescued and eventually had Aleema killed.

**Keto, Satal** An heir to the throne of the Empress Teta system along with his cousin Aleema. Satal Keto became co-leader of the dark side Krath cult and received powers from the spirit of the Dark Jedi Freedon Nadd. He staged a rebellion to take over the system. Among the first victims were his mother and his father, ruler of the system. He eventually was killed by Jedi Ulic Qel-Droma for instigating the death of Qel-Droma's teacher, Jedi Master Arca Jeth.

**Keto, Sebban** A wealthy nobleman who traced his roots to Satal Keto, he owned a number of shops and restaurants in the city of Cinnagar during the New Order. Like his distant forebears, Sebban Keto secretly studied the lore and teachings of the ancient Sith, and used his command of the dark side of the Force to manipulate local political and business leaders. He maintained the Krath tradition, and it was rumored that Sebban also was the leader of a Sith cult based on a planet in the Core Worlds.

**Keto, Serra** A student at the Jedi Temple on Coruscant during the Clone Wars. She was one of the most gifted students ever trained by Jedi Master and swordsman Cin Drallig. She later was expelled from the Jedi Order for her defiant attitudes, and was killed by Darth Vader.

**Ketwol** A Pacithhip scout who spent much of his downtime talking to spacers and travelers at cantinas, such as Chalmun's in Mos Eisley, gathering information he needed to locate new worlds. He traveled the galaxy on a starship known as the *Herd Mother.* In order to overcome his short, round appearance in a galaxy dominated by humanoids, Ketwol moved about with the help of a pair of mechanical stilts.

**Kev, Dayla** A Galactic Scout Corps mission commander about 40 years before the Battle of Yavin, she was believed to have been killed on an uncharted jungle planet. Kev and her lieutenant, Hereven, ended up hiding for more than six months in caves while avoiding dangerous predators. The two fell in love, and tragically Hereven was killed in a hunting mission, leaving Dayla pregnant. Dayla named her son Hereven in honor of his father. They lived together in hiding for 15 years and discovered that they had a connection to the Force. They were rescued by a group of Wookiee explorers, who tried to sell them into slavery. Using subtle manipulations of the Force, Dayla was able to convince the Wookiees to let them go free. Then she convinced them to join her in forming a safari hosting business on the planet. She changed her name to Lady Ahrkan and made a small fortune by the time of the New Order.

She never forgot or forgave Milac Troper, a fellow scout who had left her for dead. When young Hereven discovered that Troper was to be aboard the herd ship *Galactic Horizon,* Dayla and her son conspired to kill him. They were thwarted by Troper's hired bodyguards and arrested for the attempted murder.

**Key of the Overpeople** An ancient artifact traced to the Sharu, the Key of the Overpeople was a golden implement shaped like

Ketwol

a fork. To the human eye, it appeared to be continually changing its aspect, which tended to cause headaches in beings who viewed it for too long. The fork seemed to have anywhere from two to four tines, depending on when one viewed it. It was found in a museum outside the Rafa system, and was recovered by Rokur Gepta during the early years of the New Order. He believed that the Key was a tool to be used to activate the Mindharp of Sharu. The Key was known by many names throughout history: The Fabled Key of the Sharu, The Opener of Mysteries, The Illuminator of Darkness, Shower of the Way, and The Means to The End. Unknown to Gepta, the actual purpose of the Key was to allow the bearer to enter the great pyramid on Rafa V. No door actually opened; rather, the bearer was allowed to pass through the pyramid's structure and enter the "dream without sleep." This dream showed the bearer the history of the Sharu and, eventually, the Mindharp. Lando Calrissian was given the Key by Gepta. He used it to gain access to the pyramid.

Lo Khan

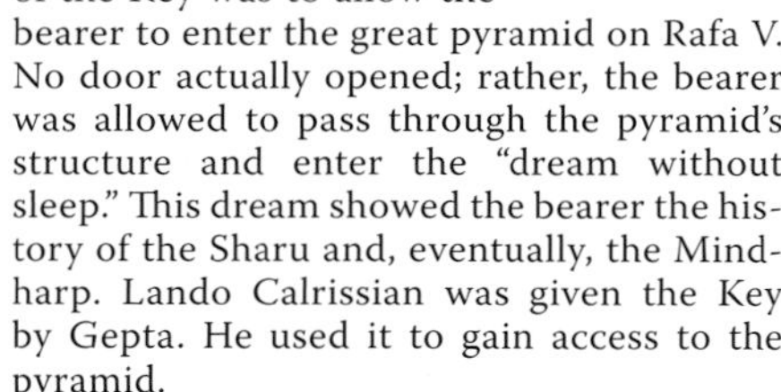

**Khabarakh** From fierce Imperial loyalist and assassin to staunch supporter of the New Republic, this young Noghri was originally part of a commando team sent to capture Princess Leia Organa Solo on Kashyyyk. Like other Noghri, he was a fearsome sight with his gray skin, large black eyes, pointed claws, and mouthful of razor-sharp teeth. Their world suffered a disaster around the beginning of the Clone Wars, and the Noghri were misled into swearing allegiance to Darth Vader and the Empire. They effectively had become the Empire's hit squad.

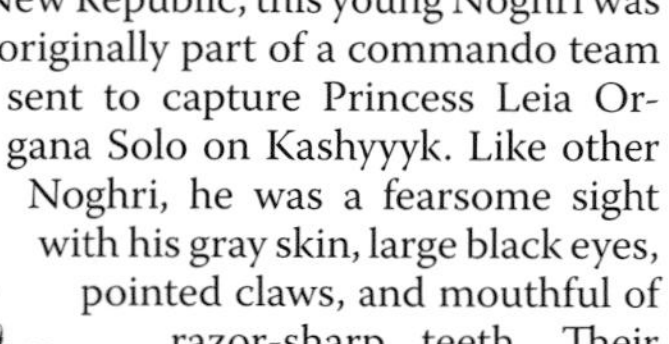

Khabarakh

But Khabarakh recognized Leia—through an incredible sense of smell—as the Mal'ary'ush, the daughter of Lord Darth Vader. As such, she was to be revered, not hunted. The other Noghri on the team were killed, but Leia let Khabarakh go, and later lived up to her promise to visit the Noghri homeworld, Honoghr, to present the cause of the Alliance. For his role in helping Leia, Khabarakh was called a traitor by Grand Admiral Thrawn, and was imprisoned. But the other Noghri soon learned that Leia, or "Lady Vader," was telling the truth, and they rose up against the Imperial forces that had long dominated them. Khabarakh was freed and became part of Leia's Noghri honor guard.

**Khaddar, Ob** A rebellious grass painter from Alderaan who created a grass portrait presented to Emperor Palpatine during his visit to that planet. During the Emperor's visit, the image of the Emperor bloomed with black lilies that turned the image into a gross caricature. Outraged, Palpatine immediately ordered his stormtroopers to torch the entire plain. Khaddar had wisely fled before the Emperor arrived. He carried a death mark on his head, but was never found. One of his masterpieces was the moss-painting *Killik Twilight.*

**Khakraim** A member of the Noghri Hakh'khar clan who was part of a team working for the New Republic at a safehouse on Wayland.

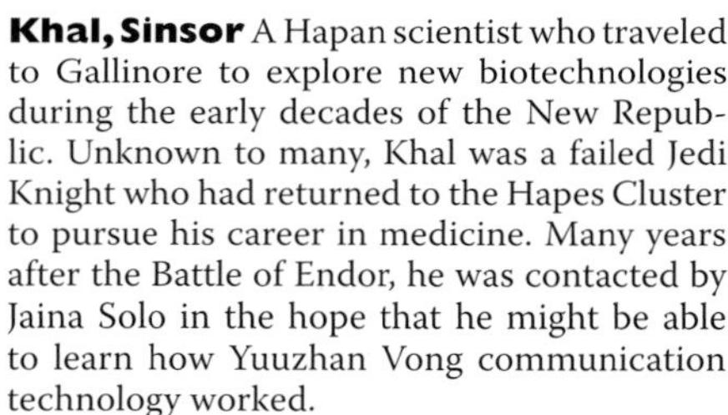

**Khal, Sinsor** A Hapan scientist who traveled to Gallinore to explore new biotechnologies during the early decades of the New Republic. Unknown to many, Khal was a failed Jedi Knight who had returned to the Hapes Cluster to pursue his career in medicine. Many years after the Battle of Endor, he was contacted by Jaina Solo in the hope that he might be able to learn how Yuuzhan Vong communication technology worked.

**Khalii, Drosh** A Yuuzhan Vong leader who rose to authority after the Battle of Coruscant. Khalii gained power and wealth from the war effort, and sequestered himself within a fortress he maintained in the Gileng sector of the planet.

**Khamar** A general in the Grand Army of the Republic during the Clone Wars.

**Khan, Lo** An old smuggler, he was owner and operator of the *Hyperspace Marauder.* Lo Khan assisted fellow smugglers Salla Zend and Shug Ninx during their visit to the planet Byss. Khan's partner and first mate was Luwingo, a Yaka cyborg.

**Kharrus, Senator** A Gran Senator loyal to Chancellor Palpatine during the Clone Wars.

**Kharys** An imposing, sadistic female S'kytri who was the Matriarch of her people during the Galactic Civil War. When she was younger, Kharys was discovered to be Force-sensitive by Anakin Skywalker, who was on the planet Skye with Obi-Wan Kenobi and Halagad Ventor. Although Anakin recommended that she be trained as a Jedi, the older Masters refused. She was later named the Majestrix of Skye by Darth Vader himself after the Empire took control of the planet.

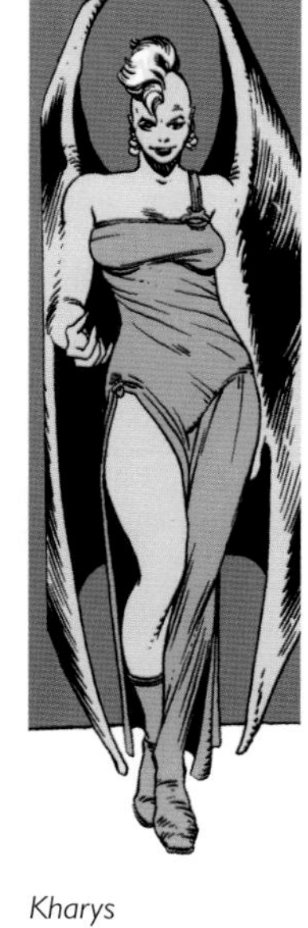
*Kharys*

Many years before the Battle of Yavin, Kharys had captured 20 Corellians and hunted them for prey on Skye. The only two survivors were Han Solo and Katya M'Buele. When Luke Skywalker and Leia Organa were nearly captured by Kharys on Tirahnn, Han decided to locate Kharys and make her pay for the cruel hunt many years before. Kharys imprisoned Han, but was unable to stop Luke, who had been identified as the prophesied being who would free the S'kytri. Kharys fought against Skywalker with a lightsaber she had been given, and used a measure of control over the Force to try to muddle Luke's mind. In the end, however, Luke was able to kill her and end her tyrannical rule.

**khasva** A species of fish native to the planet Mon Calamari. They were considered a delicacy when fried.

**kheilwar** *See* homunculus-wasp.

***Khetanna*** The name of Jabba the Hutt's personal sail barge, a modified Ubrikkian luxury craft that had been outfitted to his needs. Like most barges, it was driven mainly by repulsorlift thrusters, but could be moved about by the wind when needed.

**Khim'bar** One of the many Noghri clans native to the planet Honoghr. Clan Khim'bar was led by Ir'khaim in the years following the Battle of Endor.

**Khiss** Sebulba's agent, he placed bets for the Dug on a wide variety of legitimate and illegal events throughout the Outer Rim Territories.

**kholm-grass** A plant that once grew widely on the Noghri homeworld of Honoghr, it was wiped out through deliberate contamination by Imperial forces. The Empire then planted a bioengineered version of kholm-grass that secretly killed other forms of plant life and kept the blighted world from recovering. Only animals capable of eating the kholm-grass survived outside a small area of Clean Land, so the Noghri had to rely on imported food supplies, thus keeping them in the Empire's debt.

*The* Khetanna, *Jabba the Hutt's sail barge*

**Khomm** A pale, moonless green world lying close to the Deep Galactic Core. A thousand years before the rise of the Empire, Khomm's inhabitants decided that their society had reached its zenith. They froze their bureaucratic culture at this "perfect" level, and began producing clones of previous generations. The genderless clones of Khomm liked to keep to their own affairs, rarely leaving their planet and maintaining the same roles and schedules from generation to generation. The planet remained neutral during the Galactic Civil War.

Khomm's cities were laid out in perfect gridworks, with almost all buildings and residences looking identical and made from the same green-veined rock. Large cloning facilities in each city held records of all the major family lines. Dorsk 81 surprisingly showed unexpected Force aptitude and became one of Luke Skywalker's Jedi academy students seven years after the Battle of Endor. The following year, Dorsk 81 returned to Khomm; his warnings of an Imperial attack were ignored, and the planet was devastated by Colonel Cronus and his fleet of *Victory*-class Star Destroyers.

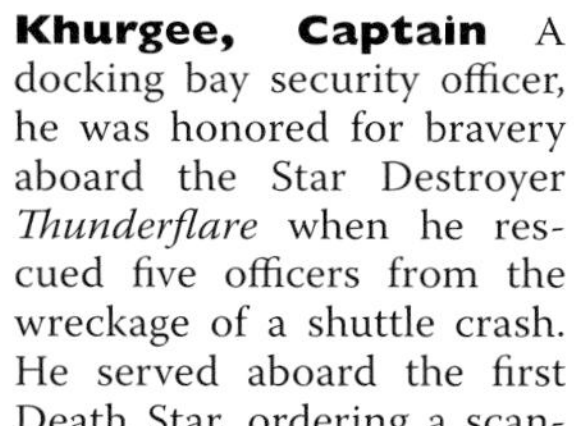
*Captain Khurgee*

**Kho Nai** The Khotta of the planet Kho Nai were related to the Qella of the planet Brath Qella; both species were descended from the ancient Ahra Naffi. Twelve years after the Battle of Endor, the cyborg Lobot retrieved the mind-prints of the Khotta from the Institute for Sentient Studies on Baraboo in order to decipher a puzzle found aboard the mysterious Qella ship known as the Teljkon vagabond.

**Khoonda Plains** Grasslands on Dantooine, it was one of the few areas that remained viable after Darth Malak devastated the planet.

**Khorda, General Ashaar** An Annoo-Dat Prime radical who started a small rebellion on his homeworld of Annoo, shortly after the Galactic Republic thwarted his attempt to take power for himself. General Khorda, a strong-willed being who didn't take well to failure, tried to seize control of Annoo using military forces he had usurped from the government, but the Republic managed to install its own leader. General Khorda then went underground, fomenting rebellion while searching for the Infant of Shaa. He claimed to be a freedom fighter, combating the injustice and tyranny of the Old Republic, and managed to gather a large following. General Khorda nearly succeeded in destroying the Infant near Coruscant's central power core, but was killed in a struggle with Jango Fett and Jedi Master Yarael Poof.

**Khral'Nas** This Kian'thar was a noted Rebel Alliance operative.

**Khuiumin** A system that was the main base for the infamous Eyttyrmin Batiiv pirates until they were wiped out by the Imperial *Victory*-class Star Destroyers *Crusader* and *Bombard.* The two warships eliminated all 150 craft in the pirate armada and chased the last survivors to the surface of Khuiumin, where their stronghold was wiped out by the *Crusader*'s concussion missiles.

**Khurgee, Captain** A docking bay security officer, he was honored for bravery aboard the Star Destroyer *Thunderflare* when he rescued five officers from the wreckage of a shuttle crash. He served aboard the first Death Star, ordering a scanning crew to search the *Millennium Falcon.*

**Ki-Adi-Mundi** A Cerean Jedi Knight, he was trained by Yoda from the age of four when he was discovered by the Dark Woman. A humanoid from a utopian world, Ki-Adi-Mundi's most distinguishing physical feature was an enlarged conical cranium that contained a binary brain, which was supported by a second heart. After achieving the rank of Jedi Knight, he returned home to free his people from the grip of Bin-Garda-Zon and his rogues, only to discover that the legendary bandit leader had been deposed by a female warrior. Ki-Adi-Mundi nevertheless faced the new chief, but he underestimated his opponent and was captured. He eventually escaped using the Force and defeated her.

Over the next three decades, Ki-Adi-Mundi built a life for himself on Cerea while serving the Jedi Order faithfully. The low birthrate of the Cereans allowed him an exception to the Jedi edict that prohibited marriage and family, and he married his bond-wife, Shea, and took four honor-wives. He also fathered seven daughters and became a respected member of the Cerean community.

Later a member of the Jedi Council, he was present when the Council tested Anakin Skywalker and did not hesitate to voice his own opinions about the boy. When Jedi Master Qui-Gon Jinn reported a Sith attack during the events surrounding the Battle of Naboo, Ki-Adi-Mundi expressed shock at the notion. "Impossible," he remarked, "the Sith have been extinct for a millennium." For its failure to detect the Sith menace in time, the Jedi suffered the loss of one its greatest Masters, Qui-Gon. Ki-Adi-Mundi voyaged to Naboo to attend Jinn's somber funeral, and was also present at the jubilant celebration that marked the liberation of Naboo.

A decade later, Master Ki-Adi-Mundi was present during one of the gravest crises ever to face the Jedi Order: the Separatist movement that threatened to split the Republic. Like most in the Order, the Cerean Jedi refused to believe that the movement's architect, former Jedi Count Dooku, was behind its more violent actions. As a political idealist trained in Jedi philosophies, such acts would be beneath Dooku, Ki-Adi-Mundi reasoned. Soon Ki-Adi-Mundi and several of his fellow Jedi Council members did battle with Geonosian and Separatist droid forces. While the Jedi were prepared to handle the Geonosians, they were surprised by the immensity of the Separatist droid army. Many Jedi died that day, though Ki-Adi-Mundi survived. When Republic reinforcements arrived, Ki-Adi-Mundi hopped aboard a Republic gunship and later led units of clone troopers into the thick of combat. The war-scorched flats of Geonosis became the first battleground of the devastating Clone Wars.

Like his fellow Jedi, Ki-Adi-Mundi became a general in the Clone Wars, leading clone trooper infantry on campaigns scattered throughout the galaxy. He still retained his high position on the Jedi Council, remotely attending council sessions via hologram. During the Outer Rim Sieges, as the Clone Wars were nearing their end, Ki-Adi-Mundi was stationed on the Banking Clan stronghold world of Mygeeto. There, he led the Galactic Marine clone troopers with Commander Bacara. He stayed in touch with Coruscant as the Jedi Council was experiencing the changes initiated by Chancellor Palpatine. He grew wary of the Chancellor and his bids for increased executive power.

When the upper tier of the Jedi Council—himself, Yoda, and Mace Windu—discussed a possible course of action to remove the Chancellor, Ki-Adi-Mundi advised that the Jedi Order would have to take control of the Senate in the interim, to ensure a secure transition of power. Out of context, such discourse would be branded treason; that was a disturbing sign of just how unstable the democracy of the Republic had become. The transition never happened due to the machinations of the Chancellor. Palpatine initiated Order 66, the ultimate endgame contingency against the Jedi. The order, transmitted secretly to the clone commanders spread across the galaxy, identified the Jedi as traitors to the Republic. Commander Bacara and his Marines opened fire on Ki-Adi-Mundi. Though the Jedi attempted to put up a defense, he was overwhelmed by the gunfire and killed.

Ki-Adi-Mundi

**Kibbick the Hutt** A young member of the Besadii Hutt clan, and the nephew of Zavval and Aruk. When Zavval was killed during Han Solo's escape from Ylesia, Aruk installed Kibbick in his place as manager of the spice-processing centers on the planet. Kibbick was a figurehead, barely capable of understanding the business of spice and slaves. When Aruk was killed by Teroenza and clan Desilijic, Kibbick remained in charge of the Ylesian enterprise, although he was despised by his cousin, Durga. Teroenza, bolstered by his dealings with clan Desilijic, killed Kibbick himself by ramming the Hutt with his horn. He then shot Kibbick with a blaster to disguise the wounds. Teroenza blamed Kibbick's death on Red Hand Squadron, even though it was across the galaxy at the time.

Don-Wan Kihotay

**kichicolia** A species of harmless, herbivorous primates discovered by the Imperial Zoological Agency during its survey of the planet Najarka. Emperor Palpatine had a number of kichicolia exported for display in his own gardens on Coruscant and Kailor V.

**Kickback** The nickname of a clone trooper pilot who flew as Blue Four in Ahsoka Tano's squadron over Ryloth during the Clone Wars.

**Kid Dxo'ln** *See* Dxo'ln, Kid.

**Kiffar** The near-human inhabitants of Kiffex and Kiffu, they were distinguished by facial tattoos that denoted family lines. A small percentage of Kiffar had natural psychometric abilities that allowed them to read the tenuous psychic impression left on handled inanimate objects. Notable Kiffar included Quinlan Vos, the Tonnika sisters, and Sintas Vel.

**Kiffex** A double planet, it was the site of a colony where sibling con artists Brea and Senni Tonnika were raised and where they perfected their deceptions and moneymaking skills. Kiffex was a prison world governed from its partner planet of Kiffu.

**Kiffu** The sister planet to Kiffex, it was in the Azurbani system. The near-human natives were known as the Kiffar, and maintained their freedom with a stern hand and a protective nature. During the last decades of the Republic, Kiffu was a free planet from which the Guardians of Kiffu kept a watch on Kiffex, a prison planet.

**Kiffu, Senni** The name used by Mara Jade when she and Luke Skywalker emerged from the forests of the planet Myrkr. Imperial forces under the command of Grand Admiral Thrawn discovered the escape and tried to recover the pair. To escape the stormtroopers at Hyllyard City, Luke posed as a man named Jade, with Senni Kiffu as his prisoner.

**Kihotay, Don-Wan** A member of Han Solo's hired group of protectors known informally as the Star-Hoppers, he carried a yellow-bladed lightsaber and claimed he was a Jedi Knight. Kihotay was actually a librarian named Hess Korrin from Obroa-skai who had been infatuated with the Jedi Order. His Ithorian manager transported him to Aduba-3 after the Imperial Security Bureau decided to destroy Obroa-skai's antiquities wing. He later joined with Solo to help a farming town that was terrorized by bandits. Kihotay died a short time after, when a mercenary attack destroyed the medical station on Telos-4 where he was convalescing.

**Kiilimaar** Following the Battle of Hoth, Rneekii pirates chose this planet as the site where they would turn a captured TIE defender developer over to the Empire in exchange for a substantial ransom. Imperial forces, however, double-crossed the pirates and recovered the ransom money.

**kiirium** A common metal, it was used to manufacture artificial shielding. Xim the Despot, realizing the need to obtain huge amounts of kiirium to protect his forces, had planned to stockpile it in his vaults on Dellalt. Thus, the *Queen of Ranroon* was loaded with kiirium when it was dispatched to Dellalt. When Han Solo came upon the starship's cargo millennia later, he discovered that the rumored treasure of Xim was really just a vast supply of military supplies and raw materials.

**Kikow** An Ithorian wanderer who became a weapons smuggler after the Battle of Naboo, moving thermal detonators through a small group he called the Herd. He covered his illicit

activities with an import/export front specializing in herbs and spices and his restaurant the Dusky Sky Café on Camrielle.

**KiLargo's Cantina** An upscale cantina and restaurant in Mos Espa on Tatooine prior to the Clone Wars.

**kilassin** A predator dominating the food chain of the Cularin rainforests, the somewhat intelligent kilassin were omnivorous. They were driven to near-extinction by extensive logging operations.

**Kile** A moon orbiting the gas giant Zhar, it was the site of a temporary base for Rogue Squadron. From Kile, the squadron launched an attempt to capture Boba Fett and rescue Han Solo, who had been encased in carbonite by Darth Vader.

**Killee Wasteland** A desert located in the arid wilderness of the planet Socorro. The Killee Wasteland was dominated by buttes and mesas, one of which was once the home of a Sarlacc. This beast died many centuries before the Yuuzhan Vong War, and its nesting pit later served as the final resting place of the starship *Crimson Axe.*

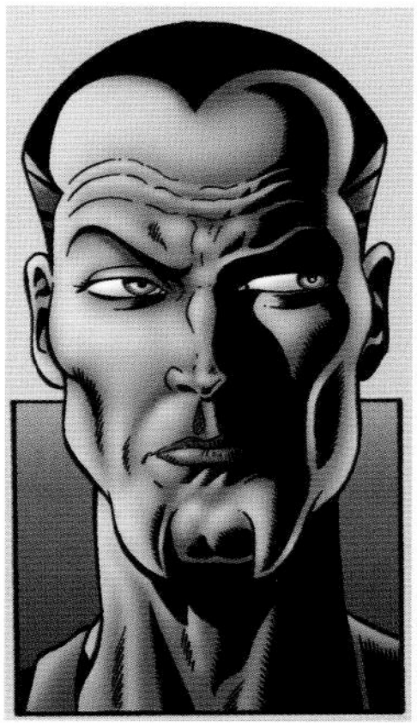

Norym Kim

**Killik** This insectoid species was once native to the planet Alderaan. There the Killiks lived in towering cities built on the plains. They were human-sized, four-armed insects with wicked, three-clawed hands and two powerful legs that allowed them to jump long distances. They possessed a hive-mind collectively known as the Colony. They constructed their castle-like buildings out of the natural elements found on Alderaan, and formed them—mound upon mound—to create a complex series of living, eating, and egg-laying grottoes. Rooms were decorated with brilliant, complex mosaics of stones and pebbles that appeared to be little more than splashes of color, until one stepped back and admired the entire wall from a distance.

The settlement on Alderaan was known as Oroboro, which literally meant "our home." For reasons unknown, the Killiks left long before humans ever arrived on the planet. Although Alderaanians believed that the Killiks were extinct, they later explained that they had been "emptied" from Oroboro by powerful aliens called the Celestials some 20,000 years before the Galactic Civil War. The Celestials had apparently done so as a protective measure, as the ravenous Killiks had stripped Alderaan of all its resources and were about to ravage other planets.

After the discovery of the Colony's existence in the Unknown Regions during the Swarm War, it was learned that the Killiks were just one hive of a larger species of insectoids known as the Kind. The other hives of the Colony considered the Killiks to be part of the fabled Lost Nest. The many subspecies of Killiks that made up the Colony were able to reproduce at a prodigious rate, which provided them with numerical superiority over the Chiss during the Swarm War that occurred some five years after the Yuuzhan Vong War.

Killik

***Killik Twilight*** A moss-painting by legendary Alderaanian artist Ob Khaddar. During the early years of the Rebel Alliance, Leia Organa suggested that the codes for the Shadowcast network be hidden within the moss-painting to ensure secrecy. *Killik Twilight* was offworld when Alderaan was destroyed, on loan to a Coruscant museum. However, its transport ship was believed to be lost, and any hopes of recovering the moss-painting were dashed. After the Battle of Endor, the painting reappeared on Tatooine, where it was to be auctioned off. The moss-painting was eventually recovered by the Solos, who destroyed the Shadowcast codes before turning it over to their Squib companions, Grees, Sligh, and Emala, in return for their help in recovering it. The Squibs then sold it to the Empire for a steep profit, pretending not to know that it was no longer valuable as a piece of Alliance information. The painting ended up in the personal collection of Imperial Grand Admiral Thrawn, and many of the Imperials who knew of its existence believed it had been lost when Thrawn was killed. In fact, the painting was recovered by Gilad Pellaeon, who held on to it for many years until the end of the Yuuzhan Vong War. Before heading back to the Imperial Remnant, Pellaeon returned the painting to Leia Organa Solo.

**Killing House** The name given to the most intense training facility in Tipoca City on Kamino for the development of the clone commandos.

**Kilo Squad** One of the first groups of clone troopers trained as commandos during the buildup to the Battle of Geonosis and the Clone Wars.

**Kim, Chankar** One of the many Jedi Masters who were dispatched to Geonosis during the mission to locate and rescue Obi-Wan Kenobi. She was killed in the Geonosis arena.

**Kim, Norym** A member of the Imperial Interim Council, he was a former pirate who conquered several bands of plunderers to become warlord of an entire sector. As a humanlike Myke, he was more easily accepted on the Council than its other nonhumans. Kim took control of the Council, although he schemed to have Xandel Carivus appointed to its leadership position as a figurehead.

**Kim, Ronhar** One of many Jedi Masters who accepted military positions within the Grand Army of the Republic during the Clone Wars. Born on Naboo, Ronhar Kim was the son of Senator Vidar Kim. It was during the war that Master Kim realized the need to seek out the Sith Lord who was in control of the Senate. He had heard the story of Obi-Wan Kenobi's imprisonment on Geonosis, and so he approached his old friend Chancellor Palpatine with a plan to test all the Senators for midi-chlorians. A high reading should indicate the hidden Sith, according to the plan devised by Kim's apprentice, Tap-Nar-Pal. It was Tap's suggestion that discord within the Senate could be eased if Palpatine himself took the test first. Palpatine agreed to think over the idea, but asked the Jedi to keep it a secret until he had made up his mind. Just days later, Master Kim was placed in command of a team dispatched to Merson, accompanied by Tap-Nar-Pal. The Separatist battle droids quickly

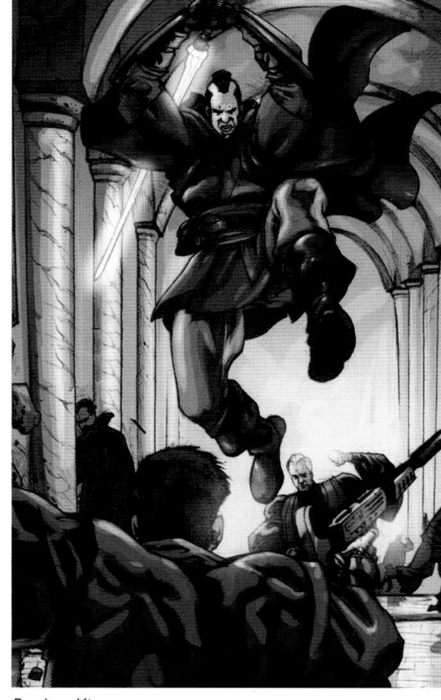

Ronhar Kim

converged on their position, and Master Kim was killed in the fighting that ensued.

**Kim, Vidar** The father of Jedi Master Ronhar Kim, he was Naboo's representative to the Galactic Senate prior to Senator Palpatine, but was killed in an assassination plot while on Coruscant.

*Vidar Kim*

**Kimanan** Home to the animals known as furballs—tiny, tubby, clownish marsupials that were considered wonderful pets. They were sold at Sabodor's pet shop on Etti IV.

**Kimdyara, Kin** A young zoologist who worked for the Galactic Republic classifying creatures found on newly discovered planets. He had a habit of relying on visual similarity to familiar creatures for creating labels, with the intention of renaming the animals once he returned to his laboratory. The one time he failed to do so was during the exploration of Kharzet III, when Kin discovered what he termed a "long-necked gundark." He died before returning to Coruscant, and the name stuck.

**Kimm systems** These systems were known for their trafficking in Senex sector slaves. The stock light freighter *Smelly Saint* also ran counterfeit agridroids from the Kimm systems.

**kimogila** A huge, predatory reptile native to Lok. It resembled a krayt dragon, and its ferocious nature led many big-game hunters to try to kill one for sport. The kimogila developed an exceptionally tough hide in response to the rivers of sulfur near its habitat. Large enough to swallow a Wookiee whole, it used a toxic venom to immobilize its prey.

**Kimsh** A Chadra-Fan ocean rancher. While guiding a new herd of bildogs and proops from the sea for slaughter, Kimsh and Shusk befriended Mammon Hoole. Kimsh fell over the side of their barge during a storm, but the Shi'ido Hoole changed his form and size to that of a Wookiee and saved Kimsh's life.

*Zyne Kinahay*

**Kinahay, Zyne** The son of Eben Kinahay, Zyne was also a devotee of the dark side of the Force and carried a Selonian glaive with him as a weapon. Eben had hoped that Zyne would follow in his footsteps and become an antiques dealer, but Zyne wanted no part of his father's career. He traveled the galaxy in search of more information on the Sith, until the Corellian crisis came to his attention. He returned to Centerpoint Station in an effort to recover his father's Sith Holocron, but failed.

**Kind, the** Another name used to describe the Colony of insectoid beings that threatened the galaxy during the Swarm War. Because of the sharing of all minds within the Will of the hive, the Kind fought vigorously to protect the Colony, though they held no animosity toward their enemies. In fact, the Kind lacked any sort of concept of an enemy. Like many insectoids, the Kind recorded their history using pheromones, and their spoken language consisted of strange clicks and buzzes. Thus, they turned to beings known as Joiners to act as translators and liaisons to other species.

**Kindar, Colonel Pejanes** A Rebel Alliance officer during the early years of the Galactic Civil War, he was stationed at the ill-fated base on Stenos. Kindar fled when Imperial forces invaded the planet. The con artists Rik Duel, Chihdo, and Dani claimed that Kindar had asked them to remain behind, in case someone from the Alliance returned to Stenos to reestablish contact. Their ruse was later uncovered by Luke Skywalker and an Alliance team that arrived at the base.

**Kinderbubble** Any Gungan bubble building dedicated to the education of the young.

**Kine** A small-time criminal with ties to various pirate organizations. Despite his background, Kine was recruited by Lando Calrissian to locate and defeat a group of pirates who were ambushing New Republic convoys from a base on Radix in the Abraxas system. In reality, Kine had been hired by Imperial Lieutenant Harme Kiela in a bid to begin restoring the Empire. Kiela revealed that Kine was a former Imperial captain. To ensure the success of his mission, Kine shot Lando, but Calrissian survived and surprised Kine long enough for Isolde Siro to kill him.

**Kiner** One of the last, best counterintelligence officers of the Galactic Republic. Admiral Kiner's name was later preserved by Imperial Intelligence officers who reversed the letters, calling themselves Renik. Kiner was among the first to promote the infiltration and absorption of enemy spy operations, taking in their data to augment that of the Republic while maintaining their networks of spies to further enhance the Republic's own intelligence.

**Kinesworthy, Dr. Nycolai** An Imperial scientist who worked with cybernetics at the height of the New Order. Dr. Kinesworthy and his assistant, Treun Lorn, were dispatched to Kashyyyk to discover a way to augment the already impressive Wookiee strength by using cybernetic replacements. Although Kinesworthy was loyal to the Empire, the necessity of experimenting on Wookiees was never fully explained, and he chose to leak certain information to Wookiee leaders outside the Imperial compound. He also procrastinated in his work, rarely having any success and never making a major breakthrough. Before long, a group of Wookiees attacked the compound at which Kinesworthy and Lorn were working. Neither was ever seen again.

**kinetic communication** A bodily form of communication developed by the Lorrdians during the Kanz Disorders. Kinetic communication involved using a complex series of hand gestures, body postures, and facial tics and expressions to send a message to another Lorrdian. In this way, the Lorrdians could communicate their plans for rebellion.

**kinetite** A restrained-energy globe generated through use of the dark side of the Force. Darth Vader created one in an effort to destroy Luke Skywalker on Circarpous V, but Luke was able to deflect it and send it back at Vader.

**King of the Tribes** The leader of the Ugnaughts, he ruled over the Terend Council but worked with the ufflors to ensure the continual betterment of the Ugnaughts.

**Kinooine** Luke Skywalker and Lumiya battled on this barren world shortly after the Battle of Endor. Lumiya had been biding her time until she was strong enough to attack the Alliance of Free Planets again, and she chose the outpost on Kinooine as her starting point. Skywalker was dispatched to discover why the base's personnel hadn't reported in on a regular basis.

**kinrath spider** A predatory arachnid native to the planet Dantooine. It guarded the Crystal Cave; crystals could be found in kinrath eggs.

**Kintan** An ancient planet that was the homeworld of the Nikto species, which did a thorough job of destroying its biosphere. The planet was conquered by the Hutts before the Old Republic was established.

**Kintan strider** A ferocious creature with incredible healing abilities. Kintan striders were used by Hutts as guard beasts.

**Kintaro, Grand Moff** The Imperial Governor of the Bajic sector and the Vergesso asteroids. When Prince Xizor provided the location of an Ororo Transportation shipyard to Darth Vader, he told the Dark Lord that the shipyards were run by the Rebel Alliance. Emperor Palpatine had Kintaro executed for failing to secure his sectors against Alliance invasion.

*Drokko Kira*

**Kinyen** The Expansion Region homeworld of highly social, three-eyed Gran. Ree-Yees, one of Jabba the Hutt's courtiers, was exiled from Kinyen after committing the highly unusual crime—for a Gran—of murder.

**Kip** The planet on which Zorba the Hutt was imprisoned for illegally mining ulikuo gemstones, an operation that nearly bankrupted clan Desilijic. It was a damp mud ball of a world, riddled with caves and dungeons. It was inhabited by small, pygmy aliens, and was overtaken by a group of pirates who eventually freed Zorba.

**Kiph, Dmaynel** The Devaronian leader of the Alien Combine, he had passed judgment on Gavin Darklighter and was ready to kill him and other members of Rogue Squadron, but he never got the chance. Imperial forces attacked the group's hideout, killing several of its members and seriously wounding Dmaynel Kiph. He made his escape with the help of the Rogues, and later joined the Rebel Alliance to help liberate Coruscant.

**Kir** A planet deep in the Corporate Sector known for its vertex crystal mines. The crystals were refined for use as crystalline vertex, the Corporate Sector currency.

*Modon Kira*

**Kira, Drokko** The father of Modon Kira, also known as Drokko the Elder, he suffered from a wound that wouldn't heal after he was cast out of Iziz for challenging the legacy of Freedon Nadd four millennia before the rise of the Empire.

**Kira, Modon** A Beast-Lord of Onderon, he was the father of Oron Kira some 4,000 years before the Galactic Civil War. A distant relative with the same name gave Leia Organa Solo sanctuary in an Onderonian safehouse six years after the Battle of Endor.

**Kira, Oron** The husband of Galia and son of Modon Kira, he, along with other Onderonians and their warbeasts, joined the Jedi in their fight against the dark side Krath cultists four millennia before the rise of the Empire.

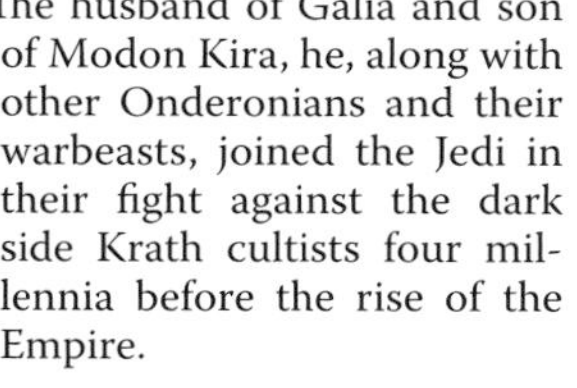
*Oron Kira*

**Kira Run** A hyperlane running through the Kira system, it connected the Lazerian and Ropagi systems. The Kira Run originally was seen as risky and uncertain, but shortly before the Battle of Yavin small shipping companies began servicing the run, establishing it as a trade route.

**Kirdo III** A hot, arid world in the Outer Rim marked by cracked red plains of dried mud and the white sands of the Kurdan desert. It was the homeworld of the patient, resilient Kitonaks. Droopy McCool, the stage name of one of the band members in Jabba the Hutt's palace, was a Kitonak.

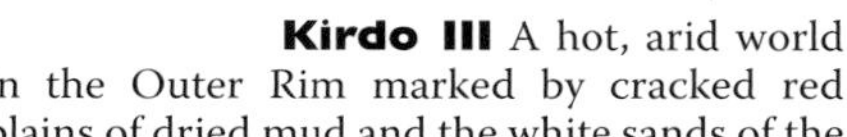

**Kirima** The sole habitable planet in the Kalinda system.

**Kiris Asteroid Cluster** This random field of asteroids and interplanetary debris was located near the outer edge of the Corellian system. It was here that Thrackan Sal-Solo and his cronies established the Kiris Shipyards as a way to secretly begin amassing enough naval power to ensure Corellia's independence from the Galactic Alliance.

*Kirithin*

**kirithin** Small amphibious predators common on a number of fringe worlds. Resembling fat fish the size of a Wookiee's fist, they used clawed flippers to drag themselves along the ground when out of the water. Only the Hutts considered them a delicacy.

*Kiro*

**Kirl** The name of both a province of Munto Codru and the Kirlian ambassador. He chose to use the name Kirl in place of his given name after he was appointed to the position.

**Kiro** A Chuhkyvi Iskalonian, he helped Luke Skywalker and Leia Organa survive the destruction of the Iskalonian Pavillion and a swarm of chiaki before they were confronted by a mob of Iskalonians. In the midst of the struggle, a stormtrooper shot Kiro, but his breathing helmet absorbed much of the blast. Kiro survived and agreed to help Mone rebuild Iskalonian society. Several months later, following the Battle of Endor, Kiro and the Iskalonians were visited by Rik Duel and his band of scavengers. The Iskalonians began plotting ways to rid themselves of the air breathers, until Luke returned to Iskalon on a diplomatic mission for the Alliance of Free Planets. Mone demanded that Luke and the scavengers leave, but Kiro decided that he had had enough of Iskalon. Donning an ancient rebreather suit, he joined Luke on his diplomatic mission across the galaxy. Kiro also showed some sensitivity to the Force and wanted to be trained as a Jedi, but Luke was unsure how to proceed. Thus, Kiro simply traveled with Luke for many months, learning what he could from the Jedi Knight. Kiro eventually fell in love with the Zeltron Dani, but nearly lost her on Kinooine. His own bravery led to her rescue, but they were intercepted by Den Siva. Kiro

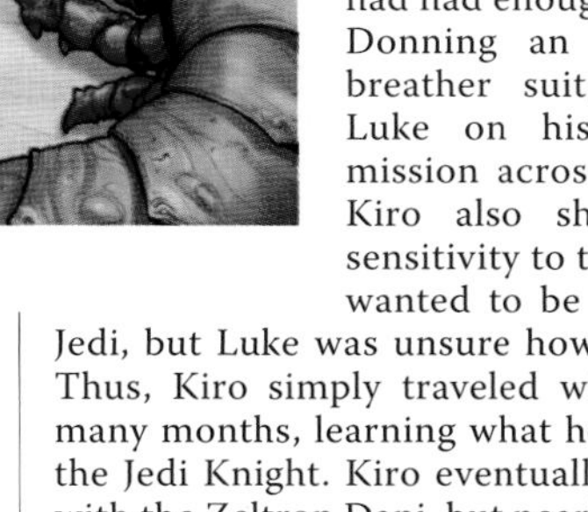

and the Nagai warrior fought on a cliff overlooking a river. Kiro was defeated and was not seen for many months, until he suddenly reappeared on Iskalon. As Kiro explained to Luke and Lando, he had realized that his true calling was back on Iskalon. Rather than disappoint Dani, Kiro simply slipped back to his homeworld to help his people fight back against the Nagai. He was regarded by the Iskalonians as a hero.

**Kirrek** One of seven planets in the Empress Teta system, it was the last to bow to the authority of Satal and Aleema Keto when they instigated their Krath cult coup some 4,000 years before the rise of the Empire. For its resistance, Kirrek had three of its cities destroyed.

*Kithaba in the clutches of the Sarlacc*

**Kirske, Osika** A Rattatak warlord known for his vicious lust for power. Sometime before the Clone Wars, Kirske murdered the parents of Asajj Ventress, an act that would come to haunt him later in life. After Ventress was taken in by Jedi Master Ky Narec, Kirske recognized that the pair were a threat to his power. He banded together with the other warlords to murder Narec, but Ventress managed to escape. With her training incomplete, Ventress gave in to the hate she felt for Kirske and the Jedi, and succumbed to the dark side of the Force. In her anger, she hunted down and eventually captured Kirske and his supporters, locking them away in a dungeon to secure her own position as the leader of Rattatak. After the Battle of Jabiim, Kirske was freed from prison by Obi-Wan Kenobi, who himself had managed to escape the dungeon. Despite their differences, Kenobi and Kirske agreed to work together to complete their escape, although Kirske ultimately wanted to make Ventress pay for her actions. He was unprepared for her skill, however: Ventress beheaded Kirske before he could strike a single blow.

*Osika Kirske*

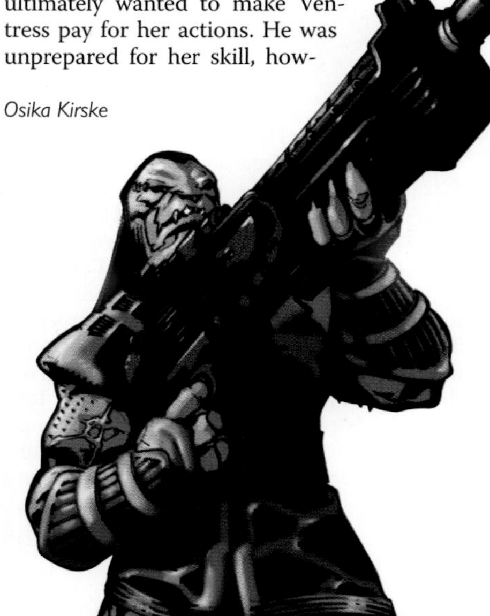

**Kirst** A female X-wing pilot in Rogue Squadron during the Battle of Endor. She served as Wedge Antilles's wingmate, using the call sign of Rogue Three during the subsequent cleanup operations.

**Kirtania** The fourth planet in the Yyrtan system, it was a green-blue world of jungles, deserts, and mountains, and was home to an arachnid species called the Araquia. Kirtania originally was colonized by several groups of humans, who founded the competing states of Surana, Kinkosa, and Dulai. Over the years, the states seriously depleted the planet's natural resources and polluted the environment.

**Kit** A Tin-Tin Dwarf originally obtained as a pet by Shug Ninx. After learning of Kit's intelligence, Shug considered him a partner.

**kite plant** Native to Yavin 4, these unusual plants were often seen floating airborne above the treetop canopy.

**Kithaba** A Klatooinian assassin who worked for Jabba the Hutt. Shortly before the Hutt's death, Kithaba had planned to escape from his servitude and become a musician. Kithaba was consumed by the Sarlacc at the Great Pit of Carkoon shortly before the Battle of Endor.

**Kithra** A female Mistryl Shadow Guard who worked for Mara Jade as part of the Smugglers' Alliance during the years following the deaths of Grand Admiral Thrawn and the cloned Emperor Palpatine. Kithra and her companion, Shana, assisted Jade in defending Kessel from an attack by the prototype Death Star that emerged from the Maw Installation some seven years after the Battle of Endor. It was Kithra who intercepted Luke Skywalker and Kyp Durron when they arrived at the Maw on a mission to destroy the Sun Crusher.

**Kitonak** A species of pudgy, yeast-colored beings native to Kirdo III. Their ability to seal vulnerable body openings in folds of flesh served to protect them from the world's harsh desert environment. To withstand the milder storms, Kitonaks remained still, angling their bodies into the onrushing wind. This was similar to their method of feeding on small, burrowing chooba by mimicking the sulfaro plant, the chooba's main food. Kitonaks, who smelled like vanilla, stood still for hours until a chooba climbed close enough to be swallowed, offering enough nourishment to sustain an individual for a month.

The Kitonaks roamed Kirdo III in nomadic tribes of around 100, following the migrating chooba. Kitonaks had no natural predators and feared only quicksand and caves, both of which held mysterious and deadly dangers. Once each decade a great rainstorm covered Kirdo III, flooding the dry riverbeds and ushering in the Kitonak mating ritual known as the Great Celebration of Life. Kitonaks were skilled at playing beautiful music on chidinkalus, the hollowed-out reeds of chidinka plants, which sometimes resulted in their capture by slavers and subsequent employment as professional wailers. Droopy McCool, the stage name of one of the band members in Jabba the Hutt's palace, was a Kitonak. Eight years after the Battle of Endor, the Imperial battlemoon *Eye of Palpatine* stopped at Kirdo III to pick up a contingent of stormtroopers, but brought in a group of Kitonaks instead.

*Kitonak*

**Kkak, Hrar** A Jawa on Tatooine, he gave fellow Jawa Het Nkik a blaster rifle that Nkik used in his failed attack on Imperial stormtroopers.

**Kkak, Tteel** A Jawa on Tatooine in charge of a salvage team that discovered a downed spaceship containing a rancor. Tteel Kkak was also the pilot and representative of the Kkak clan during the New Order.

**K'Kruhk** A Force-sensitive Whiphid who trained under Master Micah Giiett in the years leading up to the Battle of Naboo. He was distraught after Lilit Twoseas gave her

*K'Kruhk*

life to save him from a Yinchorri warrior, and vowed to honor her sacrifice with his own actions. However, K'Kruhk became disillusioned with the Jedi Council's increasingly military direction, as well as with the growing corruption in the Senate.

Klaatu

K'Kruhk was believed to have died on Teyr early in the Clone Wars, when the charge he was leading met with heavy resistance. The clone troopers under his command chose to press the attack, but Master K'Kruhk could not agree to such a sacrifice. He went into hiding, and it was soon discovered that he had decided to join the dissident Jedi Sora Bulq on Ruul in protest of the Jedi involvement in the war. When Asajj Ventress came to Ruul, K'Kruhk refused to believe that Jedi Master Mace Windu had sent the assassin to kill the dissidents. Master K'Kruhk was badly injured in a lightsaber duel with Ventress. Only the timely intervention of Master Windu allowed him to escape.

K'Kruhk decided to rejoin Master Windu and agreed to return to Coruscant in the hope of teaching his fellow Jedi about the different faces of evil they were confronting in the galaxy. It was on Coruscant that Master K'Kruhk was assigned to protect Senator Viento, but he could not prevent Quinlan Vos from taking the Senator's life. During a mission to destroy the droid foundries on Hypori, K'Kruhk was gravely wounded by General Grievous. He managed to escape, and later served with Master Jeisel during the siege of Saleucami. Masters K'Kruhk and Jeisel were placed in charge of the ground forces that attacked the Separatist stronghold on the planet, ultimately destroying the primary shield generator that protected the cloning facilities for the Shadow Army.

In the wake of the Clone Wars, Master K'Kruhk was believed to have crash-landed on a planet with Jeisel. Very little was known of K'Kruhk's whereabouts until many years later, when he began teaching new students at the Jedi Temple on Ossus during the decades before the Sith–Imperial War. He was again believed to have died, this time at the Massacre on Ossus, but reappeared to Cade Skywalker on Ossus seven years later. Skywalker had been a student of K'Kruhk, who could sense his drug-addled mind. The Whiphid Master traveled to Ossus to cure Cade of the sickness in his soul. They were joined by Wolf Sazen and Shado Vao, who had sensed their presence on Ossus.

While on Ossus, Cade restarted his training as a Jedi, which brought him into contact with Nei Rin and her Yuuzhan Vong guards. Master K'Kruhk understood her desire to restore the Jedi to prominence in the galaxy, but was unsure why she believed that Cade was the one being who could bring about the restoration. Cade did not want the onus of carrying on the Jedi tradition, and asked that Master K'Kruhk take his place. K'Kruhk agreed when Cade set off to rescue Hosk Trey'lis, and provided Cade with the astromech droid R2-D2, who had been in the Skywalker family for decades.

**Kktkt** A planet in the Farlax sector near the Koornacht Cluster.

**Klaatu** A Kadas'sa'Nikto known as a gambler and one of Jabba the Hutt's employees. He was Barada's main assistant in the repulsor pool, and was responsible for making sure that all the skiffs and barges were in good working order. Klaatu perished when Jabba's sail barge exploded near the Great Pit of Carkoon shortly before the Battle of Endor.

Kligson aboard his space station

**Klasse Ephemora system** A star system located on the Chiss side of the Unknown Regions, opposite the Core Worlds. It contained the gas giant Mobus.

**Klatooine** The home planet of the Klatooinian species, known for selling their disrespectful youth into indentured service. Klatooine was conquered by the Hutts before the establishment of the Old Republic. Jabba the Hutt picked up the contract of a Klatooinian manservant named Barada, who then became the head of Jabba's repulsor pool but was killed during the rescue of Han Solo. Jabba was sometimes known to snack on live paddy frogs native to the planet, served in brandy to keep them from attacking and killing one another.

**Klaymor 4-2** An Imperial reconnaissance mission discovered a Rebel spy probe located near the moon Klaymor 4-2. A single TIE fighter, dispatched from the corvette *Astin,* was sent to destroy it.

**kleex** Large, flea-like parasites, they infested the tails of the huge creatures called durkii on the planet Tammuz-an. Though the durkii was normally a docile beast, it could become a raging monster due to the discomfort caused by kleex infestation.

**Klev, Captain Titus** An Imperial Navy officer who commanded the *Silencer-7* World Devastator. He was killed after Luke Skywalker tampered with the master control signal that guided the Devastators, causing *Silencer-7* to crash into the Mon Calamari ocean. Early in his career Klev, who was born on Alsakan, had gained recognition for capturing an important Rebel Alliance agent during the Battle of Wann Tsir.

Captain Titus Klev

**Kleyvits** An older female Selonian, she spoke for the Overden, and assumed responsibility for Han Solo, Leia Organa Solo, and Mara Jade after the Hunchuzuc Den was won over to the Overden cause.

**Kligson** When this human was severely wounded in the Clone Wars, most of his body was replaced with automated droid parts. Kligson grew discontent with the destructive nature of organic life, and he built himself a space station from salvaged space debris. A mechanical genius, Kligson populated his station only with droids, feeling more comfortable in their company than with fellow "organics." He never allowed any organics to set foot in his station. Kligson's Moon became known as Droid World for its teeming droid population. When the Rebel Alliance captured a damaged Imperial warbot and needed it examined by an expert, Luke Skywalker sent his droids C-3PO and R2-D2 to approach Kligson. The xenophobic Kligson was wary of any outsiders. He agreed to examine the droid under two conditions: No organics would accompany the droid, and he would get to keep it for himself. R2-D2 and C-3PO accompanied the warbot to record its examination, providing valuable intelligence to the Rebel Alliance.

At that time, one of Kligson's droids, Z-X3, was planning a revolt. Z-X3 used components from the warbot to arm his own combat droid, and then led the charge against

Kligson. Z-X3 appeared to destroy Kligson with a laser harness, but in truth, he had only destroyed an android duplicate of Droid World's founder. In the end, Kligson put down the droid revolution, though it left him even more disillusioned—he couldn't escape war on even an automated world built to his specifications. He powered up Droid World's engines and set out for parts unknown, but not before R2-D2 and C-3PO returned to the Rebel Alliance with warbot specifications.

Commander Knife

**Kline** A member of Leia Organa Solo's crew dispatched to recover the *Katana* and the rest of the Dark Force. Kline and Shen were placed in charge of restoring the main computer systems of the *Katana* itself.

**Kline Colony** Another name for the planet Monor II. Tinian I'att once saved Chenlambec's life on this world after a Rebel Alliance "acquisition" took poorly to the Wookiee's style of capture.

**Klintee, "Deadeye"** A Clantaani and known associate of Longo Two-Guns in the years before the Battle of Naboo. Jabba the Hutt issued a bounty for his capture in connection with the killing of three of Jabba's personal slaves.

**Klivian, Derek "Hobbie"** A young Imperial pilot originally stationed aboard the *Rand Ecliptic*. Shortly before the destruction of Alderaan, Hobbie joined Biggs Darklighter and several other pilots in defecting to the Rebel Alliance. While most of the Ecliptic Evaders fought and died at the Battle of Yavin, Hobbie did not participate in the attack. However, he did serve Rogue Squadron at the Battle of Hoth as Rogue Four. He remained with Rogue Squadron throughout the Battles of Endor and Bakura as well.

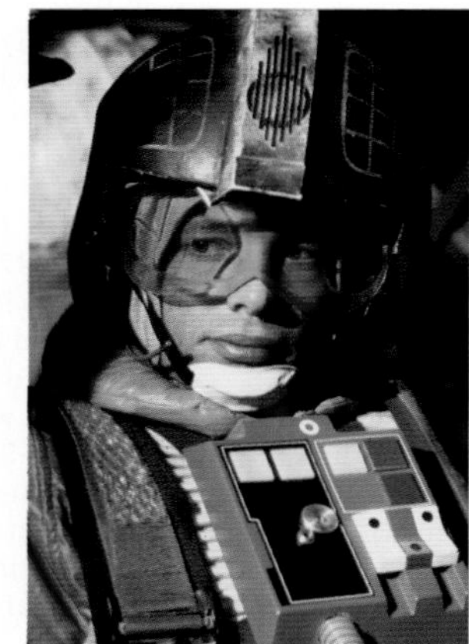
Derek "Hobbie" Klivian

After the Battle of Endor, he was given the nickname Bugbite by Iella Wessiri. The nickname served as a reminder of their first meeting on Corellia, when Hobbie was stung by a local insect. Shortly after the Imperial Remnant agreed to a peace treaty with the New Republic, Hobbie and most of the other veteran Rogues retired from active duty.

**kloo horn** A musical instrument played by Figrin D'an in his frequent band appearances. The kloo horn was a double-reed instrument. Larger than a slitherhorn, it had a distinctive curve in the reed and produced a richer sound than the slitherhorn and Fizzz.

**Kloper** The homeworld of the species known as Kloperians, short gray beings with extendable necks and many tentacles. Due to their mechanical skills, many Kloperians served the New Republic as starship technicians.

**k'lor'slug** A venomous creature from the planet Noe'ha'on, it had keen senses of smell and vision. A k'lor'slug could be very dangerous. It laid eggs and had hundreds of ravenously hungry hatchlings. A k'lor'slug was often used as a playing piece for holo board games.

**Kluggerhorn, Zack** A name given to Han Solo by Princess Leia Organa in Hologram Fun World.

**kneeb** A yellow-furred porcine creature considered a delicacy by the Hutts. Their hide was often cured and used to cover luxury items.

**Kneesaa, Princess** The daughter of Chief Chirpa, Ewok leader of Bright Tree Village on the Forest Moon of Endor, she survived a horrifying incident early in life. While on an expedition with her older sister, Asha, and their mother, Ra-Lee, they were attacked by a hanadak. Ra-Lee told Princess Kneesaa to run back to the village for help, but by the time help arrived Ra-Lee was dead and Asha had vanished. Years later, in tracking down tales of a mysterious Red Ghost, Kneesaa and her best friend Wicket W. Warrick came upon the crimson-furred Asha, who had been raised by a band of wolf-like korrinas.

The gray-furred, black-eyed Kneesaa had many adventures while growing up. She also had two younger siblings after her father remarried. At an early age, she battled the fierce Duloks and later the evil witch Morag. Kneesaa worked around her village, built high in the trees, and began weaving baskets. She developed that skill so well that she became known as the best weaver on all of the Endor Forest Moon. Kneesaa, Wicket, and the older Logray became true village heroes when they thwarted a plan by the giant green Phlogs to chop down the ancient sacred trees near their home. When Chirpa died of old age, Kneesaa ascended to the chiefdom of Bright Tree Village in a ceremony that also saw her married to Wicket W. Warrick.

Princess Kneesaa

**Knife, Commander** An alias of the Nagai who worked with the Wookiee Vargi to capture Chewbacca shortly after the Battle of Endor. *Knife* was the name given to him by the Wookiees, who couldn't pronounce his true name, Ozrei N'takkilomandrife. He came to Kashyyyk in an effort to restart the slave trade in Wookiees. To ensure that Chewbacca would not be a threat to his work, Knife captured Mallatobuck and the rest of Chewbacca's family as hostages. However, the Wookiees rose up against Knife, and the presence of Han Solo and Lando Calrissian forced Knife to flee Kashyyyk. He appeared on Kabray Station to capture several delegates who hoped to join the Alliance of Free Planets. He had been part of the advance scouting team that allied itself with the Empire's remnants in order to take control of the galaxy. All his plans appeared to be falling into place—until he tried to assassinate Han Solo on the Forest Moon of Endor. Solo had been detained by Bey, himself a half Nagai, and Knife arrived to finish the job. Solo managed to escape and shoot Knife in the chest. It was at this point that Bey revealed that Knife was his own half brother. Knife continued to lead the Nagai invasion of the galaxy, until his forces encountered a group of Tofs on Zeltros. As the Nagai realized they couldn't win, they and Knife agreed to ally themselves with the Alliance of Free Planets.

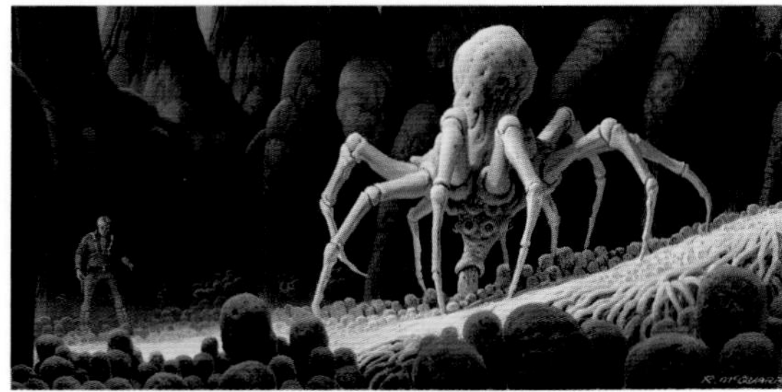
Knobby white spider

**knobby white spider** A misnomer, it was actually a detachable mobile root from the gnarltree that grew on Dagobah. The knobby white spider roamed the swamps, hunting and devouring animals and storing energy in its bloated, bulbous head. When ready for metamorphosis, the spider searched for a clear spot in the undergrowth, uprooted competing plant life, plunged its eight sharp legs deep into the spongy ground, and transformed itself into a gnarltree.

**KnobHead** A small stone outcropping located in Monument Park on Coruscant. The stone was believed to have been part of the summit of Mount Umate, which was one of the few places where Coruscant's original surface was still visible.

**Knolstee** A planet in the Corporate Sector, it was one of the stops made by the luxury liner *Lady of Mindor* during its trips from Roonadan to Ammuud.

**Knossa Spaceport** The main spaceport on the planet Ossus.

**knytix** Although these creatures resembled Thyferran Vratix, they were smaller and less elegant. They were used by the Vratix as work animals, were kept as pets, and—on special occasions—were eaten.

**Koba** A planet that was conquered by the Advozse warlord Tulak some 200 years before the Battle of Naboo. After defeating Polvin Kut and Yaddle in battle, Tulak retired and eventually died. He bequeathed the planet to his son, Kalut. Shortly before Kalut's arrival, the planet experienced severe seismic upheavals, and the Jedi Yaddle was freed from her prison. She helped the natives regain their small society, defeat Kalut, and free themselves from his control. The planet was surrounded by several moons.

**Koboth** The homeworld of the Kobok, an insectoid species whose members were characterized by deadly stingers and three eyes.

**Kodai** An ocean-covered Outer Rim planet known as a nexus of dark side power during the years around the Battle of Naboo. Dr. Murk Lundi went to Kodai in search of a Sith Holocron beneath its vast sea.

**Kodir of Kuhlvult** An ambitious young female from the Kuhlvult family on the planet Kuat. Quite devious, she developed a plan to oust the leader of Kuat Drive Yards, Kuat of Kuat. She gathered a small band of young royals and laid out her plans, but was initially rejected by her sister, Kateel, who threatened to expose the group. Kodir had her kidnapped and then had her memory wiped. The job wasn't done completely. After orchestrating an uprising by Khoss of Knylenn from behind the scenes, Kodir achieved the position of security chief and began forcing Kuat of Kuat into a corner. She secretly worked a deal with members of the Rebel Alliance to deliver to them a group of warships shortly before the Battle of Endor. She insinuated that Kuat of Kuat was loyal only to the Empire, and that the Alliance representatives—Commander Rozhdenst and Wonn Uzalg—would need to replace him in order to get the ships. The Alliance agreed, having already discussed the situation with the other Kuati royal families, and ostensibly recognized Kodir as Kuat of Kuat's successor. However, Kateel recovered her memory and returned to Kuat to face her sister. The Battle of Endor began, Kodir's plot was exposed, and she was charged with multiple offenses, including murder, kidnapping, and conspiracy.

**Kogan VI** Some 13 years after the Battle of Endor, when the Obroan Institute had finished its investigation of the planet Brath Qella, it was scheduled to give up its ship, *Penga Rift,* to support Dr. Bromial's expedition to Kogan VI.

**Kogo, Vess** One of Emperor Palpatine's Hands following the Battle of Yavin. His extreme hatred of the Rebel Alliance made him the perfect weapon, and his rugged good looks and disarming smile allowed him to get close to many female agents. Palpatine used the dark side of the Force to mold the young man into a killing machine. While Kogo loyally carried out the Emperor's orders, he often went out of his way to destroy anything associated with the Alliance.

**Kohlma** A moon in the Bogden system, it served as a burial ground. A swamp-covered world, Kohlma also was the base of operations for the Bando Gora cult following the Battle of Naboo. It was here that Jango Fett captured Komari Vosa after following a winding trail of leads from Count Dooku, who had been operating under the identity of Darth Tyranus.

**Koh'shak** The master of the Kala'uun Spaceport on Ryloth, he was also the head of all the merchant clans operating there. Koh'shak was the chief negotiator for the addictive ryll kor, or spice, that the Rebel Alliance needed for a top-secret project.

**Kohvrekhar** A Noghri who accompanied Darth Vader during the search for Luke Skywalker following the Battle of Hoth. It was Kohvrekhar and his clan-brother, Ghazhak, who discovered Skywalker's severed hand in the airways of Cloud City. After learning that Luke had survived the encounter, Vader ordered Kohvrekhar to Tatooine to ensure that Jabba the Hutt and his henchmen didn't capture or kill Skywalker.

**Kojash** Located in the Farlax sector of the Koornacht Cluster, it was the former site of a Morath mining operation. Twelve years after the Battle of Endor, Kojash was brutally attacked and conquered by the alien Yevetha as part of a series of raids that they called the Great Purge.

**Kokash sector** Located in the former center of the Empire's Rim territories, this sector included large areas that were never properly surveyed. During the Empire's reign, the Black Sword Command was charged with the defense of Praxlis, Corridan, and the entire Kokash, Hatawa, and Farlax sectors. Following the Battle of Endor, Imperial forces abandoned the Kokash sector and retreated into the Core.

**Kolader** This city was located in the center of the continent of Afterthought, on Ropagi II.

**Kolaff, Captain** A brilliant tactician and intrepid leader, he quickly built a reputation as one of the most competent commanders in the Imperial Navy. He was transferred to the Relgim sector to command a fleet of *Victory*-class Star Destroyers. Kolaff's own ship, *Subjugator,* was the base of operations for Lira Wessex's plan to capture her father, Rebel Alliance engineer Walex Blissex. Kolaff detained Blissex and his team of Rebel escorts at Kwenn Space Station. A short while later, the *Subjugator* was attacked by a Rebel strike force code-named Starfall. The *Subjugator,* torn and battle-damaged, became the site of a showdown, as Kolaff made it his goal to destroy the now escaped Rebels. Kolaff sabotaged the *Subjugator* to cause it to self-destruct, then faced the Rebels in a duel involving AT-ST walkers. He perished in the battle, and the Rebels escaped.

**Kolar, Agen** A Zabrak Jedi Knight and member of the Jedi Council, he was one of the few Jedi who survived the initial stages of the Battle of Geonosis. Agen Kolar quickly put behind him the death of Tan Yuster, his Padawan, and obediently accepted the rank of general in the Clone Wars. To Kolar's loyal mind, service to the Republic was the backbone of Jedi duty. He had little patience for the murmurs of dissension in the Jedi ranks following the war's outbreak.

Many of Agen Kolar's previous missions had taken him to the Mid Rim and fringes of the Republic, though the Clone Wars pulled him closer to the Core. Kolar's clone trooper forces served on Brentaal IV, where they assisted General Shaak Ti in a diversionary strike against the Separatist stronghold commanded by Shogar Tok. His troops were eventually forced to surrender, and Agen Kolar was briefly taken prisoner before Shaak Ti's efforts managed to regain control of the planet.

Kolar was a tough combatant, and diplomacy was not his strong suit. He was

*Agen Kolar*

dispatched by the Jedi Council to retrieve Quinlan Vos, a Jedi spy who had failed to make contact with Coruscant. Kolar was armed with disturbing evidence that Vos had betrayed the Republic, but he was ultimately unable to capture Vos. As the Clone Wars began to wind down after the attack on Coruscant, Kolar was among the group of Jedi Masters who accompanied Mace Windu to arrest Chancellor Palpatine after he was revealed as Darth Sidious. However, the Jedi were unprepared for Palpatine's powers, and Agen Kolar was quickly killed during the fighting, leaving Mace Windu to face Palpatine alone.

A kolto tank

**Kolb, Sidris** A meteorologist working on a Duro reclamation project during the Yuuzhan Vong War.

Koyi Komad

**Kole** The Chadra-Fan comrade of the Feeorin smuggler Nym. Kole served as Nym's copilot and first mate, and was known as a disguise artist. Nym bragged that Kole had once impersonated an Old Republic Senator. It was believed that Kole was killed when Vana Sage double-crossed Nym, in an effort to capture the Feeorin for the Trade Federation. However, the Chadra-Fan proved to be an elusive target, and rejoined Nym after breaking him out of prison. Kole remained with Nym for many decades, continuing to serve as a chief lieutenant after Nym assumed the leadership of the Mid Rim planet Lok at the height of the New Order.

**Kol Huro system** The planets of this system were dedicated to the development and manufacture of weapons and starships for the petty tyrant who controlled it. The tyrant was brought to justice by the Old Republic some 12 years before the Battle of Naboo during the so-called Kol Huro Unrest.

**kolto** A healing agent harvested from the oceans of the planet Manaan more than 4,000 years before the Battle of Yavin. Because Manaan was the only known source of kolto, it was highly desired during the Great Sith War. The native Selkath maintained strict control over kolto's production; when this mysteriously halted, the Selkath appealed to the Old Republic for help. Since Manaan was not officially a member of the Republic, help was never dispatched to the remote world.

**Komad, Koyi** A Twi'lek student and waitress who worked at the Soundmound on Mrlsst during the early years of the New Republic. She agreed to take Rogue Squadron on a tour of Mrlsst Academy and show them the spot where Taj Junak was murdered, resulting in the legend of the Ghost Jedi. She later put the Rogues in contact with Nasta, and eventually left Mrlsst to join Rogue Squadron. After retiring from active duty, Koyi married Nrin Vakil.

**Komnor system** A system whose warlord evicted all Hutts. Hearing the news, Tatooine-based crime lord Jabba the Hutt hired bounty hunter Dyyz Nataz to eliminate the ruler.

**Kon'me** Thick-bodied reptiloids native to Bal'demnic. During the Clone Wars, the Kon'me found themselves initially subjugated by the Separatists, who wanted to mine their planet's islands for cortosis ore. The Kon'me fought back, until they discovered that the Galactic Republic had dispatched a group of Jedi Knights and clone troopers to oust the Separatists. Deciding that they wanted no help in defending their homeworld, the Kon'me opened fire on both sides. They eventually repelled the Separatists and the Grand Army of the Republic, although the Republic left a token protective force in orbit around Bal'demnic.

**Kono** One of the many scientists who worked at the Hrakert Station facility beneath the waters of the planet Manaan during the era of the Great Sith War.

Kon'me

**Konur, Dal** A trooper with the Rebel Alliance Special Forces division during the Galactic Civil War. He was discovered to be Force-sensitive and joined Luke Skywalker's Jedi praxeum soon after it was established. A staunch opponent of the Empire, Konur impetuously wanted to take the battle to the Imperial Remnant immediately, a course that Skywalker wouldn't support. Konur stowed away aboard the academy's supply ship, *Lightning Rod,* and set out to eliminate the Moff Council himself; he left a trail of misdirection and confusion behind. His ship was forced to land on Dathomir, where Jedi agents finally caught up with him and ended his vendetta.

Plo Koon

**Koobi system** An Outer Rim star system containing the planet Nelvaan.

**koolach silk** A beautiful fabric used by Winter to bribe the starport master at Kala'uun Starport when Rogue Squadron tried to capture Firith Olan during the search for the *Eidolon*.

**Koon, Plo** This Kel Dor Jedi Master descended from a long line of Jedi, and was one of the last members of the Jedi Council. As a Padawan, Plo Koon was trained by the Wookiee Tyvokka until his death during the Stark Hyperspace Conflict. Koon was a close friend of Qui-Gon Jinn and hoped that the human Jedi Master would someday sit on the Council, but he recognized that Qui-Gon was much too headstrong to adjust to the Council's rigors. Master Koon was present when Anakin Skywalker was first brought before the Council, and was one of the Jedi Masters who were dispatched to Geonosis to combat the Separatists during the opening stages of the Clone Wars.

Plo Koon first discovered the young Togruta, Ahsoka Tano, and brought her into the Jedi Order. She later became Anakin Skywalker's Padawan. During the Clone Wars, Koon served aboard his flagship, *Triumphant,* until it was destroyed by the Separatist cruiser *Malevolence.* In the war, Koon was served by Clone Commander Wolffe. Following the Separatists' failed bid to kidnap Chancellor Palpatine, Master

Koon was dispatched to Cato Neimoidia, where he assumed control of the planet's forces. When Chancellor Palpatine betrayed the Jedi and executed Order 66, Koon's troops turned to open fire on him, shooting his starfighter from the sky and destroying the Jedi Master.

**Koon, Sha** The niece of Plo Koon, she apprenticed under Jedi Master Saldith in the years before the Battle of Naboo. During the Stark Hyperspace Conflict, Sha Koon received a telepathic message from her uncle, asking for assistance in fighting back against the forces of the Stark Commercial Combine on Troiken. During the Clone Wars, Sha Koon was dispatched to Bal'demnic with Halagad Ventor to assess the Separatist occupation of that planet. The Jedi and their clone troops found themselves fired upon by both the Separatists and the native Kon'me, who wanted all offworlders removed. The Jedi eventually retreated.

**Koong, Governor** The uncouth and brutish Koong was the governor of Tawntoom province on the Outer Rim world of Roon. The megalomaniacal Koong used political intrigue, theft, and hijacking to increase his personal power in the Roon system during the early days of the Empire. Koong was desperate to ally himself with the Imperials and eager to earn an Imperial charter. He invited Imperial Admiral Screed to his salvaging operation in the Cloak of the Sith nebula. Koong had taken over a light station in the dark dust cloud and was purposely crashing ships in order to salvage the wrecks. He had amassed quite a fortune through such piracy.

When he salvaged the *Caravel,* a ship belonging to trader Mungo Baobab, Koong mistook the sharply dressed man as an envoy of the Empire. When Screed arrived aboard his light station, Koong realized he had been tricked by the trader. He tried to capture Baobab, but the trader got away, inflicting catastrophic damage on the light station. The station spun out of control, smashing into an asteroid. Koong and Screed escaped, and the governor tried to save face in front of the unimpressed Imperial. Screed expressed his doubts. How could a governor who could not even crush a rebellious province on his world hope to operate in the new Empire? Koong made it his priority to quell the rebellious Umboo province, to prove his devotion to the New Order. Screed humored him, and watched Koong's increasingly desperate plots.

The unscrupulous governor attempted to sabotage the Roon Colonial Games. By beating the Umboo team with his Tawntoom team, he hoped to crush the spirit of the Rebels and firmly cement his position of authority. Once again, the efforts of Mungo Baobab undid Koong's schemes. Umboo province emerged victorious. Koong raised the stakes by unleashing a deadly germ into the air over pastoral Umboo. The bumbling governor infected himself in the process, however. Sick with the rooze germ, he dispatched his aide-de-camp, Gaff, to bring him Nilz Yomm, a renowned doctor from the Umboo province. He tasked Yomm with developing a cure for the rooze infection.

Governor Koong

Though Yomm succeeded, Baobab was able to free the doctor and steal the cure. He dealt Koong an ultimatum. In exchange for the cure and the location of the fabled Roonstone treasure, Koong would return Baobab's captured starship and promise never to harm the people of Umboo again. Koong agreed, but Screed double-crossed him. Screed was solely interested in the location of the treasure, and once he knew it, he seized Roon. Enraged, Koong took control of a drilling laser and blasted the Roonstone cache, knocking the priceless gems into a lava flow. He succumbed to the rooze infection before he could use the cure.

**Koorivar** Native to the planet Kooriva, members of this humanoid species were characterized by the twisted horn that grew from the top of their skulls. The horn of the male Koorivar, distinguished by their green skin tone, was robust and thick. The females, with purplish skin, had a more graceful horn. Any damage or loss of the horn was often devastating to an individual's reputation, and it was not uncommon for hornless Koorivar to be isolated from society. The Koorivar sided with the Separatists during the Clone Wars, as much to spite the Galactic Republic as for the potential gains. Passel Argente was a Koorivar. With the institution of the New Order, the Koorivar economy went into a tailspin as the Empire's pro-human stance left the Koorivar out of many business dealings.

**Koorivar Fusiliers** Originally based on the planet Kooriva, this was one of the many organic military forces that supported the Confederacy of Independent Systems at the height of the Clone Wars. While the Koorivar were noted for their business acumen, they were also quite militaristic and fought with great fervor to protect what they had earned over the centuries.

**Koornacht, Aitro** A night commander of the palace guard of Emperor Preedu III on Tamban, a pre–New Order Galactic Empire. The Koornacht Cluster was named for him in honor of a favor that he had done for the First Observer of the Court of the Emperor.

**Koornacht Cluster** Made up of 2,000 young stars and 20,000 planets, the cluster was located in a cloud of interstellar dust and gases in the Farlax sector. The Koornacht Cluster was named by a Tamban astronomer in honor of Aitro Koornacht, night commander of the palace guard in the Court of Emperor Preedu III. It was also known by many other less common names, including The Multitude, God's Temple, and the Little Nursery. It made up about a tenth of the combined regions of the Farlax and Hatawa sectors.

The cluster's inhabited worlds generally boasted an advanced technological base, rich mineral resources, and prosperous economies. The brown dwarf star Doornik-1142 and its planets were located on the edge of the cluster, with J't'p'tan at the heart. The Koornacht Cluster's dominant species was the Yevetha, skeletal bipeds with six-fingered hands and bright streaks of facial color who evolved on N'zoth. In N'zoth's night sky, the blazing stars of the cluster blocked out the light from all other more distant stars, and the Yevetha came to believe that their world was the center of the universe. Using spherical thrustships traveling through realspace, the Yevetha spread from their homeworld to colonize 11 other planets, more than had ever been colonized by any other species without the invention of hyperdrive. These 11 planets, plus the spawnworld of N'zoth, formed the Duskhan League.

The cluster was Imperial territory from the end of the Clone Wars until soon after the Battle of Endor. Very little was known about the cluster or its worlds: The Empire kept access restricted, and the Yevetha remained secretive after the Empire pulled out, some eight months after the Battle of Endor. In fact, the Yevetha had a reputation for executing trespassers on sight. The brutal Imperial Governor in charge of the cluster was given free rein to bring the Yevetha under his control. He held public executions, used women as pleasure slaves, and took children as hostages. The technologically inclined Yevetha were forced to work in Imperial shipyards established in the cluster, repairing and maintaining the Empire's warships and learning a great deal about Imperial technology in the process.

After the Empire departed, the Yevetha underwent what they called a Second Birth, settling a dozen more colony worlds and restoring captured Imperial warships. The Duskhan League laid claim to the entire cluster, despite the fact that as many as 17 worlds were populated by other species. Along the inner

Koorivar

border of the cluster there were several non-Yevetha worlds, including mining colonies and groups of religious settlers. Twelve years after the Battle of Endor, the Yevethan fleet eliminated all non-Yevethan colonies from inside the cluster's borders, fanatically cleansing these "infestations" in a devastating series of attacks called the Great Purge. Chief of State Leia Organa Solo sent the New Republic's Fifth Fleet to the cluster to persuade the Yevetha to stop their attacks.

**Koozar, Fendrilon** One of Emperor Palpatine's advisers. A connoisseur of fine foods, he was secretly poisoned by Prince Xizor during a meal at the Manarai Restaurant on Coruscant in an effort to eliminate his prying into Black Sun's operations.

**Kopatha, Jib** A Bothan crime lord and information broker active during the New Order. He ran his small operation from Void Station, a fortress built on the surface of a remote asteroid. The Empire made frequent use of Jib's services, until his information began to grow unreliable. Darth Vader was dispatched to ensure Kopatha's continued cooperation and loyalty, which could be demonstrated if he could obtain viable information on the Rebel Alliance forces that had destroyed the first Death Star. Kopatha feared for his own life, given that he had only a short period of time to obtain the information Vader wanted. Luckily, Sheel Odala came to him with an offer: She would provide Han Solo as a means of erasing the debt she owed. Kopatha's Trandoshan thugs captured Solo and brought him to Kopatha for interrogation. Solo proved to be much stronger than Kopatha's interrogation expert, Choba, had anticipated, and Kopatha decided that he would be better off just turning Solo over to Vader for further interrogation. It was then that Odala and Chewbacca rescued Solo, leaving Kopatha to face Vader's wrath. Vader was not pleased, and beheaded Kopatha with a swipe of his lightsaber.

**Kopecz, Lord** A Twi'lek Sith Lord who was part of the Brotherhood of Darkness, serving as one of Lord Kaan's chief advisers some 1,000 years before the Galactic Civil War. Unlike his counterpart, Lord Qordis, Lord Kopecz believed that Kaan's tactics were ineffectual. Nonetheless, Kopecz continued to

*Jib Kopatha*

*Lord Kopecz*

fight for the Brotherhood and was among the many leaders who participated in the Battle of Ruusan, where Kaan hoped to finally eliminate the Jedi Order. It was Kopecz who turned the opening battle for the Sith when he single-handedly flew a starfighter into the hangar of a Republic flagship and slew the Jedi Master who was controlling the Republic's battle meditation. However, when the Sith massed to destroy the Jedi's main camp, Kopecz and many others began to worry that events were conspiring against them. Kopecz's fears were only heightened by the disappearance of Darth Bane, who was manipulating events behind the scenes. Kopecz decided to remain with Lord Kaan, even after Kaan chose to use the thought bomb against the Jedi. When he finally realized that the combined strength of the Sith Lords would not prevent their annihilation, Kopecz decided that he didn't want to die without a fight. He sought out the Jedi forces and encountered Master Valenthyne Farfalla. After delivering a warning about the impending detonation, Kopecz challenged Farfalla to a duel. Ever honorable, Farfalla agreed, ultimately dispatching Kopecz with his lightsaber.

**kor** The rarest grade of ryll, it made up approximately 3 percent of the addictive spice's production.

**Kordulian Kriss** *See* ratter thist.

**Kore, Ulaha** A Bith Jedi, during the early stages of the Yuuzhan Vong War she was a musician of exquisite skill and a gifted analyst who aided in the Jedi's attempts to understand the tactics of the invaders. Kore was part of the strike team that was sent to Myrkr to locate and destroy the voxyn queen, but was badly injured when a Yuuzhan Vong warrior stabbed her in the back. The blade punctured her lung, and her fellow Jedi could provide little medical attention during their transport to Myrkr. Upon reaching the planet, Kore took the *Exquisite Death* and tried to escape the Yuuzhan Vong warships in orbit. When the *Exquisite Death* was captured by Yuuzhan Vong picket ships, Kore got the ship to self-destruct while taking out as many Yuuzhan Vong ships as possible. She died in the explosion.

**Korenn** One of Crix Madine's commandos, Korenn served on the *Galactic Voyager* while Madine was tracking Durga the Hutt. He was killed when his A-wing was hit by an asteroid while accompanying Madine and the commando Trandia into the Hoth asteroid belt to survey the construction of the Darksaber Project.

**Kornov, Captain** An Imperial officer who made a name for himself commanding a strike cruiser in an early victorious battle against Rebel Alliance forces. He was then assigned to Admiral Motti and served on the first Death Star as a loyal and hardworking assistant.

**Koros Major** One of seven planets in the Empress Teta system, it was the last to resist the system's brutal subjugation by the dark side Krath around 4,000 years before the rise of the Empire. The Krath leaders Satal and Aleema Keto dispatched hundreds of ground troops to the planet and clashed with a joint Republic and Jedi space force in Koros Major's orbit. The Republic ships were badly damaged in the battle and were forced to retreat.

**Korr, Drama** A wealthy Corellian arms dealer during the final years of the Galactic Republic. Unknown to her security detail, Korr had been targeted for execution by Count Dooku and the Separatists. According to information gathered from Xist on Trigalis, Obi-Wan Kenobi learned that Dooku had sent his "best assassin" after Korr. Obi-Wan believed that Dooku sent Asajj Ventress, despite the fact that she apparently had been killed on Coruscant several weeks earlier by Anakin Skywalker. Upon locating Korr's starship near Maramere, Obi-Wan and Anakin discovered her ship already under attack by Separatist super battle droids. After defeating the droids, the Jedi found Korr's lifeless body on the bridge. Hidden in her hand was a bomb that exploded when Anakin tried to pry it free. In the resulting chaos, Kenobi learned that it was Durge who had killed Korr.

**Korr, Jaden** One of the many students who studied at Luke Skywalker's Jedi praxeum on Yavin 4 during the early years of the New Republic. A native of Coruscant, Korr trained under Kyle Katarn, along with another student, Rosh Penin. Like Penin, Korr was tasked with seeking information on the Disciples of Ragnos, a dangerous cult of dark siders. Korr was dispatched to Hoth, where he encountered Imperial forces working with cultist Alora to gather data on Skywalker's travels to Dagobah. In a heated battle, Korr defeated Alora in order to escape Hoth and report on his mission.

After Penin was captured by cultist Tavion Axmis near Nar Kreeta, Korr tried to rescue him, but he wasn't successful. Upon returning to Yavin 4, Korr was promoted from apprentice to Jedi Knight. His heart remained heavy, however, with the loss of Penin. After receiving a distress call from his friend, Korr thought it was a trap, but proceeded with Katarn to Taspir III anyway. They found Penin controlled by Alora. Korr chose not to fight, upsetting Alora's trap. She cut down Penin before attacking Korr, but was no match for his skills.

Korr then set out for Korriban to end the Disciples' threat once and for all. He confronted Tavion, and was able to defeat her in combat just as she reawakened the spirit of Marka Ragnos. Jaden defeated the ancient undead Sith spirit, destroying the Scepter of Ragnos and cutting off any pathway to the spirit world. Years later, after the Yuuzhan Vong War, Korr was assigned to the assault team led by Master Kyp Durron to disable Centerpoint Station.

**Korrda the Hutt** A special envoy and servant to Lord Durga the Hutt, he had a narrow face that had thinned due to some sort of sickness. Korrda looked like a scrawny ribbon of mottled green leather that hung on a flexible spinal column. His small size—for a Hutt—made him the target of scorn.

**Korriban** This remote planet was believed by many to be the ancestral homeworld of the ancient Sith species, which may have risen to prominence there nearly 100,000 years before the Battle of Yavin. Korriban was the sole planet in the Horuset system, located across the galaxy from Cinnagar and Koros Minor. It was orbited by seven moons, and was unknown to the Old Republic before the rise of Naga Sadow. It was to Korriban that the ancient Dark Jedi fled after they were exiled by the Jedi Knights. Korriban was a desolate world that, under the pall of Sith magic, became more hellish and dangerous. Some 27,000 years before the Battle of Yavin, in the wake of King Adas's defeat of the Rakata, Korriban was abandoned as a base for the Sith. They designated it as their tombworld and transferred their operations to Ziost.

The native life on Korriban was twisted by the dark side, and the ghosts of Sith Dark Lords buried in the Valley of the Dark Lords roamed the planet. Seviss Vaa believed that the planet's deep connection to the dark side of the Force not only affected the biology of the planet but also twisted the "spatial fluctuations of existence." This is what allowed the spirits of the Sith Lords to continue to exist there. The Sith Lords erected huge palaces and burial complexes honoring both the dead Lords and the current ones. These ancient Sith enslaved the local population and put them to work building a huge monastery and excavating the Valley of the Dark Lords, then killed the planet's inhabitants once the jobs were done.

Korriban zombie

Exar Kun was led to Korriban by Freedon Nadd's spirit in an effort to recover certain Sith manuscripts. In the wake of the Great Sith War, the planet was virtually abandoned, although a few settlers managed to eke out a meager living. Those Jedi Knights who remembered Korriban, through either research or direct experience, referred to the planet as the cradle of darkness. About a millennium before the Galactic Civil War, Korriban was once again taken over by the Sith, this time under the leadership of Lord Kaan and his Brotherhood of Darkness. A Sith training academy was reestablished near Dreshdae, but Kaan's followers virtually abandoned the history and lore that was stored in the Valley of the Dark Lords.

With the elimination of the Brotherhood of Darkness at the Battle of Ruusan, Korriban was once again abandoned. After the Battle of Naboo, the Commerce Guild established a base of operations on Korriban, ostensibly to attract corporations to a tax-free environment. The true purpose of the guild's presence was the accumulation of a droid army in anticipation of supporting the Confederacy of Independent Systems. Years later, Emperor Palpatine often visited Korriban to help him center himself in the dark side of the Force.

Korriban

**Korriban zombie** The term used to describe those beings reanimated after their deaths by the ancient magic of Dathka Graush. After Graush's murder, the spirits of these zombies were captured in the crystal called the Heart of Graush, which was later buried with Graush in the Valley of Golg. The spirits that possessed the dead bodies were released whenever a being touched the Heart of Graush. They then set off, searching for their old bodies as well as living flesh to eat, infecting their victims to become more zombies. The only way to kill one of these zombies was to cut off its head.

**Korriz** A world of the ancient Sith Empire.

**Korrot, Del** A Cerean psychopath who emerged in the aftermath of the Clone Wars offering his services as a Jedi hunter to the Emperor. He traveled from world to world in his modified light transport, *Shadow 1,* in search of leads to put him on the trail of a Force-user. The Emperor eventually grew tired of the mad Cerean's antics and had Darth Vader kill him.

**Korteen Asteroid Belt** A ring of planetary wreckage ruled by Quarg's father during the last years of the Galactic Republic. He held sway in the belt by using a sonic jammer to disable passing ships. He would then board the ships and take control of them, sending the survivors off in life pods while salvaging anything and everything he could to make a profit.

**Korunnai** The native human population of the planet Haruun Kal. The Jedi Council believed that a starship transporting Jedi Knights during the Great Sith War crashed on Haruun Kal, and that the survivors were, in fact, the ancestors of the Korunnai. In the years leading up to the Clone Wars, the Korunnai and their low-country neighbors, the Balawai, were locked in a vicious civil war that became known as the Summertime War. The native Korunnai had been displaced by the offworlders, and fought to maintain their independence. Both sides of the conflict were brutal to their opponents, often relying on "recreational torture" before execution. In the wake of the Clone Wars, Imperial naval forces bombarded Haruun Kal from orbit, causing massive devastation to the planet's surface and wiping out the Korunnai.

**Korus** The tutor of Aleema and Satal Keto, bored young aristocrats who were heirs to the throne of the Empress Teta system. Korus was one of the cousins' first victims when they started a violent coup to take over the system. First, using Sith magic, Aleema caused a serpent-like worm to appear from the tutor's

Korus

mouth. Not long after, Aleema directed so much dark force at Korus that his body exploded.

**Kos** Vice chairman of galactic accounts for the InterGalactic Banking Clan during the years around the Battle of Geonosis. He worked on Aargau and spent a great deal of time and money trying to track down the Clawdite criminal known as Nuri. Kos captured young Boba Fett and held him for investigation, claiming that Fett was actually Nuri in disguise. Boba Fett used the only weapon he could to escape from Kos and the IBC: information. He revealed the true identity of Count Dooku in exchange for his own freedom. Unfortunately, neither Kos nor the information reached IBC Chairman San Hill. Kos was intercepted by Aurra Sing within Aargau's city-pyramid when the bounty hunter was trying to locate Boba Fett herself. In a speeder chase through the lower levels, Aurra Sing managed to shoot and kill Kos.

*Kossex*

**Kosh, Captain** An Imperial stormtrooper officer stationed on the planet Tatooine during the years leading up to the Battle of Yavin.

**Kosk, Lieutenant Reynol** An Imperial in charge of the Trogan Imperial garrison during the early years of the New Republic. An expert in the use of the PLX-2 missile-launching system, Kosk was persuaded by Niles Ferrier to attack the smugglers' meeting against the orders of Grand Admiral Thrawn himself. The rash decision proved fatal when Kosk was killed in the attack.

**Kossex** A Weequay Jedi who was part of the contingent dispatched to protect the clone hatcheries of Kamino from a Separatist attack during the early years of the Clone Wars. During an attempt to eliminate a droid starfighter that tried to attack Anakin Skywalker, Master Kossex failed to see an incoming squadron of droid fighters. He was shot down from behind, and died when his fighter exploded.

*Rahm Kota*

**Kota, Rahm** A tough, grizzled Jedi Master who became a respected and feared general during the Clone Wars. Prior to joining the Jedi Order, Kota spent much of his life in the trenches as a soldier fighting for freedom on his homeworld, where he was thrust into battle before his tenth year. When he was 18, Kota met and befriended Mace Windu, who had been sent to Kota's planet to negotiate a peaceful resolution to a particularly brutal conflict. Upon completing the mission, Mace decided to bring Kota back to Coruscant with him to hone his powers and finish his training under the watchful eye of Jedi Master Yoda.

Few in the Order bonded with the gruff Kota, but none doubted his strong commitment to the Republic, his undoubting loyalty to the Jedi Order, or his legendary courage: He often volunteered for the Order's most dangerous missions and never abandoned those in need. But Kota was also viewed as cold and militant. Throughout his long history with the Jedi Order, Kota tended to question the Council's decisions, and often advocated a more forceful approach to negotiating treaties and dealing with lawbreakers.

When war broke out between the Republic and the Confederacy of Independent Systems, Kota proved himself a brilliant tactician and cagey commander. He was quickly promoted to the rank of general and led several of the Republic's most successful offensives throughout the Outer Rim. However, Master Kota did not embrace the clone army, believing that nonclone soldiers would be more creative, intelligent, and capable in the field. He recruited and built his own army from local militias, hardened mercenary groups, and even Separatist prisoners of war. His misgivings about the clones saved Kota's life when Order 66 was issued and most of his fellow Jedi were slain by their clone squadrons. Realizing that the Jedi had been betrayed, Master Kota and his most loyal lieutenants hijacked a Republic Cruiser and disappeared into the Outer Rim territories. Although believed dead, Kota eventually resurfaced and began recklessly attacking key Imperial targets across the galaxy. He worked alongside Starkiller in the formation of the Rebel Alliance.

*Kouhun*

**Koth, Eeth** Born in squalor on the Smugglers' Moon of Nar Shaddaa, Zabrak Eeth Koth wasn't discovered by the Jedi until he was already four years old. However, his determination and clarity of mind convinced the Jedi Council to accept him as a trainee. Like other members of his species, Koth had seemingly interminable willpower and endurance to physical pain. His raw physical abilities, mental disciplines, and Force talents were honed by his Master, and once Koth attained Jedi Knighthood, he shared his talents with his Padawan Sharad Hett.

He served as a member of the Jedi Council during the time of the Battle of Naboo, and died on Geonosis at the start of the Clone Wars.

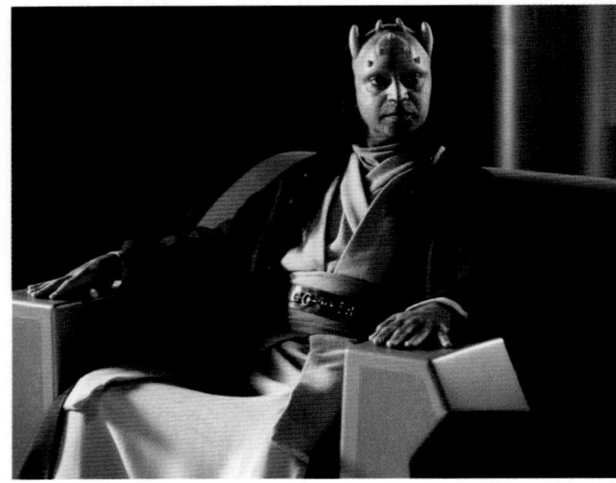
*Eeth Koth*

**Kothlis** A colony world of the Bothan species, it was the home of New Republic Councilor Borsk Fey'lya. Located a few light-years from Bothawui, Kothlis was the fourth of seven planets in its system and was orbited by three small moons. Prior to the Battle of Endor, Bothan spies captured an Imperial freighter carrying highly classified data about the second Death Star. The Bothan space station Kothlis II, orbiting near Kothlis, allowed the stolen freighter to dock and take on supplies while techs tried to decode its computer core on the planet below. Luke Skywalker was captured and held for ransom to the highest bidder while on Kothlis, but he escaped before either Darth Vader or Prince Xizor could get to him. Vader arrived on the scene and destroyed a suspected Rebel base on one of the Kothlis moons.

**kouhun** A species of long, thick, centipede-like insects known to deliver a fatal poisonous venom. They were native to Indoumodo. They were often used by assassins to kill their targets, because they were difficult to trace and could operate in areas where a blaster could not. Zam Wesell used a pair of kouhuns to try to kill Senator Padmé Amidala.

**Ko Vari** *See* Boonta.

Kowakian monkey-lizard

**Kowakian monkey-lizard** Rare animals from the planet Kowak, these creatures were so silly and stupid that across the galaxy a sure way to insult someone was to call him a Kowakian monkey-lizard. They were, however, a semi-intelligent species with a small, spindly body; large, flap-like ears; and a wide, fleshy beak. Monkey-lizards, such as Jabba the Hutt's sidekick Salacious Crumb, were known for their constant laughter and mimicry.

**Kraaken, Deputy Commander** A humanoid with long pointed ears, he was Commander Silver Fyre's second in command. Kraaken was a traitor who attempted to kill Luke Skywalker and steal a datacard carrying secret information vital to the Rebel Alliance.

**Kraal, Charat** A Yuuzhan Vong pilot distinguished by a very human-like appearance. His facial structure was not at all normal for a Yuuzhan Vong, and Kraal spent a great deal of his career overcoming this perceived deficiency. He was forced to kill two fellow pilots when they openly questioned his appearance. Kraal was one of the pilots dispatched to protect the Yuuzhan Vong base on Borleias in the wake of the Battle of Coruscant. He and his partner, Penzak Kraal, met the initial wave of Republic ships, but Penzak was killed when the forces of Wedge Antilles fled Coruscant and took Borleias as their base of operations. Charat Kraal returned to the fleet and began causing unrest among the pilots of Domain Cha. Charat was eventually brought before Czulkang Lah; he offered news of the Republic's base on Borleias, and earned the favor of Czulkang Lah with his forthrightness. Kraal was assigned to lead the effort to capture Jaina Solo. During the New Republic's evacuation of Borleias, Kraal and his wingmates chased Jaina's gravity signature into the surrounding asteroids, only to discover that they were chasing the Goddess missile. Charat Kraal perished when the missile struck his coralskipper and exploded.

Deputy Commander Kraaken

**krabbex** A small, shelled sea creature, it was native to Mon Calamari. A related species, the mammoth krabbex, was on display in the Holographic Zoo for Extinct Animals on Coruscant.

**Krag, Urzan** An Aqualish bounty hunter who was one of many to answer Asajj Ventress's call to hunt down members of the Jedi Order during the Clone Wars. Krag later decided to stick with more mainstream criminal activities, and went to work for Jabba the Hutt. He became angry when Jabba gave the most lucrative bounties to a young Boba Fett. He tried to eliminate Fett by chasing him down with his modified airspeeder, which had a limited form of cloaking device. Fett, however, managed to outwit the Aqualish and shot his speeder from the sky. Urzan Krag died in the explosion.

**Kragget rat** *See* ratidillo.

**Krail, Davish** A veteran human pilot whose nickname was Pops, he flew fighters for two decades. He was wingmate for Gold Leader and flew as Gold Five at the Battle of Yavin, where he was killed.

**Krakai** A species of immense, insectoid workers from Kathol created by DarkStryder many centuries before the Battle of Endor.

**krakana** Large ocean creatures native to the planet Mon Calamari. The average krakana lived deep in the waters of the planet, only rising to the surface when hunger forced it to hunt. A smarter, gentler cousin to the krakana was the keelkana.

**Krake Data Vault** A strange, crystalline cocoon extruded by the slugs that lived beneath the surface of Krake's Planet, it was used as a repository for data by the Empire. The structure itself was immense, and clung to the side of a steep cliff like a bloated insect, making its location virtually impenetrable. Luke Skywalker and Chewbacca managed to infiltrate the facility by sneaking into the kitchens during their mission to discover the truth behind Shira Brie's history.

**Kram, Stiv** The leader of rebellious miners who worked on Katanos VII during the last years of the Galactic Republic. In a desperate attempt to generate revenue for his people, Kram and his most senior technicians tried to develop clones, but their work ended in failure. Word of their clandestine cloning activities reached the Jedi Order, which dispatched Master Lunis and his apprentice, Obs Kaj, to investigate. Although Kram initially denied the cloning, Kaj discovered the hidden lab. Kram was forced to protect his people, and turned the Jedi over to Count Dooku for the bounty on their heads. Because only Lunis's body was recovered, Dooku paid only half the bounty he had promised, leaving Kram and the mining operation without enough credits to survive.

**Kras'dohk** A Force-sensitive Trandoshan, he was taken as an infant to the Jedi Temple on Coruscant and trained as a Jedi more than 100 years before the start of the Clone Wars. Kras'dohk eventually attained the rank of Jedi Master, but broke with the Jedi Order to travel the Outer Rim. Master Kras'dohk soon discovered the Force talents of Kaminoan Kina Ha and took her on as an apprentice. They continued to travel the Outer Rim and trained with each other for decades, until Kras'dohk died of old age. The long-lived Kina Ha continued his work and journeyed for nearly a century before returning to Kamino.

Krakana

**Krass, Harper** A former terrorist who worked for Black Sun on Coruscant during the final years of the Galactic Republic, until he was forced to go underground to avoid arrest. He was eventually brought to justice, but told stories of ghosts and other evil powers lurking beneath the city.

**Kratas, Commander** Born on Derilyn, Kratas was accepted to the SAGEducation group at Calamar University on a full scholarship during the final years of the Galactic Republic. He excelled in history and politics, and was chosen for further training on Carida during the early years of the Empire. He was promoted and given command of the *Gorgon.* Like the rest of the officers stationed at the Maw Installation, Kratas had no contact with the outside galaxy, and was unaware of Emperor Palpatine's death at the Battle of Endor.

Some seven years after the Empire's defeat, Han Solo and Chewbacca suddenly appeared near the Maw Installation after their escape from the spice mines of Kessel. Solo's interrogation produced a wealth of startling information on the state of the galaxy, which prompted Admiral Daala to abandon the Maw Installation and set out to attack the New Republic. She placed Kratas in charge of the ground forces dispatched to destroy the Eol Sha colonists who had settled on Dantooine. Kratas was one of the few members to survive a series of defeats suffered under Daala. After the destruction of the Maw Installation, he accompanied her into the Core to confront feuding Imperial warlords. They tried but failed to unify the squabbling Imperials. Kratas was eventually killed while inspecting Warlord Harrsk's flagship Star Destroyer, the *Shockwave,* when the warship was destroyed in an attack from another Imperial warlord, Teradoc.

**Krath** A secret society founded by dark side dabblers and spoiled aristocrats Aleema and Satal Keto some 4,000 years before the Galactic Civil War in the Empress Teta star system. The group was named for a demon from the fairy tales of Satal and Aleema's youth. The Krath developed into a dark side magical sect that eventually ruled the system until it was destroyed by several Jedi Knights. Princess Leia Organa Solo learned about the Krath while using a Jedi Holocron.

**Krax, General** An elder representative of the Troob people at the peace and trade negotiations held in the Tion Hegemony. When his son Ket was murdered, apparently by Larka Nimondro, General Krax broke off the negotiations and declared war on the Hobors. Just as he was planning to launch his attack, C-3PO and R2-D2 communicated to all parties, exposing Jake Harthan as the killer and averting a full-scale war. Krax deferred to reason, agreeing to meet with Nimondro to discuss a true peace for Tahlboor before further negotiations with the Tion Hegemony began.

*The Krath cult was started by cousins Aleema and Satal Keto.*

*Darth Krayt*

**Krayn** One of the most despicable slave traders of the Galactic Republic's last decades. He regularly raided slave hovels on Tatooine, taking what he wanted without fear of being stopped. Four years after the Battle of Naboo, Krayn was discovered raiding Colicoid shipping convoys, and Supreme Chancellor Palpatine asked the Jedi Knights to intervene. Obi-Wan Kenobi and Anakin Skywalker were dispatched to protect the Colicoids. Obi-Wan later discovered that Krayn had managed to obtain control of the spice-processing facilities on Nar Shaddaa, and had been the target of Colicoid negotiations for the rights to the facilities. In return for access to the facilities, Krayn demanded that he be made the sole provider of slaves to the spice mines of Kessel. He never lived to see his plans reach fruition. Shortly after he captured Anakin Skywalker, Krayn found himself facing a slave revolt at the spice facility on Nar Shaddaa. Led by Anakin, the slaves quickly took over, especially since Aga Culpa had ordered the Nar Shaddaa guards to ignore the raid. Anakin chased down Krayn and fought him, eventually disarming the larger man. Despite Obi-Wan's cries to keep Krayn alive, Anakin drove his lightsaber through Krayn's chest and killed him.

**Krayt, Darth** A name taken by former Jedi A'Sharad Hett in the rebuilding of a new Sith Order. He rose to power about 130 years after the Battle of Yavin. Having witnessed the failure of the Jedi to prevent such calamities as the Clone Wars and the Yuuzhan Vong invasion, Hett saw the Galactic Alliance as weak. Gaining knowledge from an ancient Sith Holocron on Korriban, Hett began to adopt the ways of the Sith and customize them, abolishing the restrictive Rule of Two in favor of the Rule of One, in which the overarching Sith Order was paramount.

Despite his hatred of the alien invaders, Krayt was among the first beings who openly accepted the bioengineering of the Yuuzhan Vong, using implants and grafts to augment his already formidable body. Krayt extended his life span by periodic stasis treatments while he grew his Sith Order. Over time, he forged an alliance with certain Moffs of the new Empire, and set about to sabotage the Ossus Project. With the galaxy horrified at the failure of Yuuzhan Vong biotechnology to rebuild planets, the Galactic Alliance and the Empire declared war against each other. Darth Krayt later pledged some of his Sith warriors to the Imperial cause and helped to ensure that Coruscant was recaptured by the Empire. He then overran the Jedi Temples on Coruscant and Ossus, before confronting Emperor Fel and killing the Imperial leadership.

Darth Krayt took control of the galaxy, naming himself Emperor and declaring that the Sith were the ruling power. The effort to bring down Fel's Empire, however, left him badly fatigued, and he was forced to reveal to his second in command, Darth Wyyrlok, that his Yuuzhan Vong–enhanced body was failing. He began making pilgrimages to Korriban, where he hoped to consult with the spirits of the ancient Sith Lords who were buried in the Valley of the Jedi. Unfortunately, most of the spirits entombed on Korriban refused to recognize his right to claim the title of Sith Lord. Among the many insulted spirits was that of Darth Bane. Rather than try to get them to admit that they were wrong, Darth Krayt turned his anger into power, casting off their spirits and setting off to find other Sith lore.

Darth Krayt and Darth Wyyrlok continued to delve into the ancient Sith lore, hoping to find a cure for his condition. However, not even the efforts of the Jedi healer Hosk Trey'lis could stop the steady deterioration of his body. In a desperate act, the two Sith Lords considered bringing Cade Skywalker to Coruscant. The former Jedi had tapped into the dark side of the Force twice in order to heal his friends, and they believed that he might be able to bring Darth Krayt back from the abyss. To ensure Skywalker's compliance, Darth Krayt ordered the capture and interrogation of Deliah Blue and Jariah Syn. Plans were made to hunt Skywalker down.

Then Skywalker simply walked into the Sith domain, to rescue Hosk Trey'lis. He was captured and brought before Krayt, who demanded that Cade help the Sith. When he refused, Skywalker was forced to watch as his friends were nearly consumed by mutated Yuuzhan Vong coral seeds that had been implanted in their bodies. Unable to bear this, Skywalker drew heavily on the dark side to heal them. Darth Krayt goaded the young man on, allowing Skywalker to draw even deeper on the dark side to eliminate the coral seeds. With his friends safe, Skywalker agreed to help the Sith in exchange for their freedom.

*Krayt dragon*

**krayt dragon** Large and vicious meat-eating reptiles, they lived mainly in the mountains surrounding the Jundland Wastes on the desert planet of Tatooine. Krayt dragons continued to grow throughout their lifetimes and did not become weaker with age. Their skin was yellowish brown, and they had several huge horns on their heads. They walked on four squat legs. Their gizzards held incredibly valuable and beautiful dragon pearls.

***Krayt's Honor*** A heavily modified and armed Gozanti cruiser owned and operated by Siqo Vass during the final decades of the Old Republic. Vass and Layn Wynest served as the public face of the vessel's crew, which included several humans and Ithorians as well as a Feeorin couple. The ship was often hired by merchants and other legitimate spacers to escort them past Trade Federation blockades. The *Krayt's Honor* called Tatooine one of its many home ports after the crew managed to rescue Jabba the Hutt's personal yacht from an ambush. The crime lord allowed them to use one of his starports as a base, further adding to the ship's unique history. In the wake of the Clone Wars, the ship and its crew disappeared, and it was unknown whether they simply stopped their work or were eliminated by Imperial forces.

**Kreet'ah** A Kian'thar, he was one of the lieutenants, or Vigos, of Black Sun, the galactic criminal organization led by Prince Xizor. Kreet'ah inherited his position as Vigo from his mother.

**Kre'fey, Karka** A grandson of Bothan General Laryn Kre'fey, he attempted to goad Gavin Darklighter into a duel after striking him at a party. Fortunately for Karka Kre'fey, Darklighter refused to fight.

**Kre'fey, Laryn** A Bothan general and a celebrated military leader, he was given approval by the New Republic Provisional Council to conduct a raid on Borleias. Blinded by his lust for power and the false information he received from his Bothan slicers, Laryn Kre'fey nearly destroyed Rogue Squadron. As Alliance forces descended toward the supposedly disabled base, planetary defenses suddenly came to life. General Kre'fey's ship was struck by an ion bolt, disabling it, and the *Modaran* crashed into the renewed energy shield, killing all on board.

Krayt's Honor

**Kre'fey, Traest** A Bothan member of the New Republic military. He served as an admiral at the time of the Yuuzhan Vong War. Traest came from a long line of Bothan leaders, including his grandfather Laryn and his brother Karka. Like his relatives, Traest had creamy-white fur. However, he had violet eyes that were flecked with gold, an indication that he was also related to Borsk Fey'lya through a complex tangle of relationships.

*Kreia*

Kre'fey was one of the few members of the New Republic command structure who took the Yuuzhan Vong invasion seriously, and he worked with Gavin Darklighter and Rogue Squadron to develop tactics that would overcome the aliens' organic defenses. He commanded the assault cruiser *Ralroost* during the Yuuzhan Vong War. He was disdainful of his cousin's political maneuverings, wishing only to defeat the invaders and rid the New Republic of the threat.

However, Kre'fey was one of the minority of naval officers who felt that the Senate and the New Republic were not acting in the galaxy's best interests in the war against the Yuuzhan Vong. He gladly agreed to help Gavin Darklighter and Rogue Squadron attack the shipwomb being grown in the Sernpidal system. Admiral Kre'fey remained at the forefront of the Republic's battle, and was placed in command of the task force that massed near Kashyyyk to launch hit-and-run missions against the aliens. In the wake of the death of Borsk Fey'lya, Admiral Kre'fey redoubled his efforts to defeat the Yuuzhan Vong.

With the formation of the Galactic Alliance, Kre'fey was able to pool his resources with those of Grand Admiral Pellaeon and Garm Bel Iblis, forming a total of four distinct battle groups that could be brought to bear against the invaders. His plans to defend Mon Calamari from attack proved almost unnecessary when Zonama Sekot suddenly reappeared near Coruscant, forcing nearly every Yuuzhan Vong fleet back to Coruscant to defend Supreme Overlord Shimrra. Kre'fey reasoned that this was the time to finally strike a decisive blow against the Yuuzhan Vong. The final battle was launched some five years after the initial Yuuzhan Vong attack on Belkadan and Helska, and saw the Galactic Alliance's forces matched ship for ship by the Yuuzhan Vong.

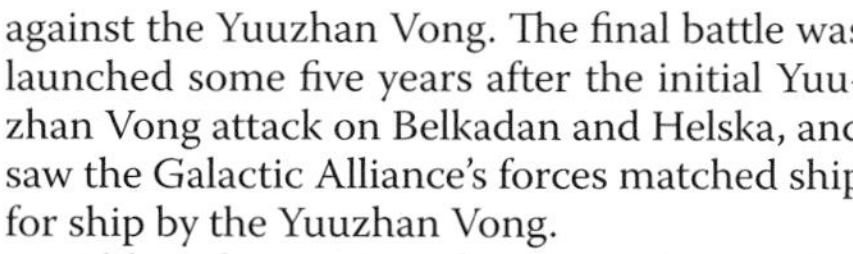

Although many Yuuzhan Vong chose to flee or commit suicide, a healthy number surrendered. Because of his leadership and the ultimate outcome of the war, Kre'fey found himself being called the "liberator of Coruscant" on the newsfeed. With Sien Sovv's sudden resignation, Kre'fey also found himself promoted to the position of Supreme Commander of the Galactic Alliance's armed forces. His tenure was short-lived, as Kre'fey decided to retire and return to his homeworld. However, when the Bothans joined the Confederation, he agreed to come out of retirement and command a fleet of Bothan warships. He was able to retain his position as admiral, although he served under Admiral Babo during the confrontation between the Confederation and the Alliance's Fifth Fleet over Kashyyyk.

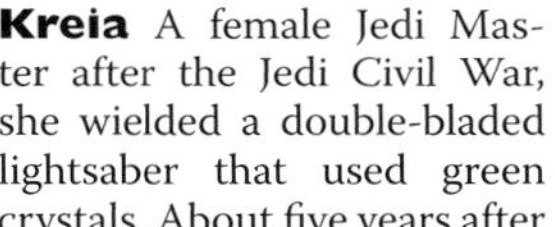

**Kreia** A female Jedi Master after the Jedi Civil War, she wielded a double-bladed lightsaber that used green crystals. About five years after the defeat of Darth Malak, Kreia discovered the Jedi Exile onboard the damaged starship *Ebon Hawk* and brought it to Peragus II. Kreia confronted Darth Sion in order to ensure that the Exile would be able to escape. She barely survived the encounter, in which she lost the use of one hand. She made her way back to the *Ebon Hawk* just as the Exile and Atton Rand were blasting off. When the Exile questioned her about a blinding pain in her hand, Kreia realized that a Force chain had formed between them, although the reason for the link was unclear. Kreia was also surprised to find that the Exile's severed connection to the Force had begun to return, and she vowed to train her in an effort to help restore the Jedi Order.

It was during training that Kreia revealed she was one of the many Jedi who had abandoned the Order to confront the growing power of the Sith. She also revealed that she had been Revan's teacher, both during his early training and again after he returned to the light side of the Force. However, after the Exile reunited the surviving Jedi Masters on Dantooine, Kreia revealed that she had fallen to the dark side. Having retaken the title of Darth Traya, she fled to Telos with Atris and set out to destroy the planet. In the wake of her death on Malachor V, the surviving Jedi were able to piece together enough of Kreia's history to realize that she had been behind a large number of defections—among them, Revan and the Exile—during the years following the Great Sith War. Because of this, she had been exiled by the Jedi

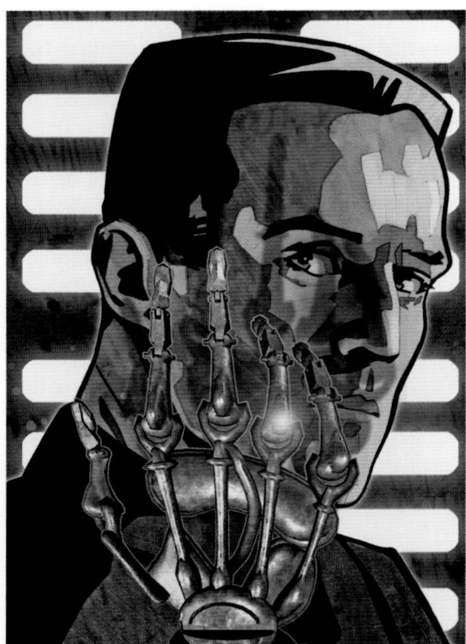

Prince-Admiral Delak Krennel

Order. In her guilt, Kreia had chosen to abandon the Jedi and seek out Revan on Malachor V. It was there that she began her training at the Trayus Academy, her ultimate fall to the dark side, and her transformation into Darth Traya.

**Krell, Admiral Damon** An Imperial officer who devised several modifications to the standard Viper probe droid, making his own droids larger and better armed than the originals. He launched the droids shortly after the Battle of Hoth, in an effort to locate possible Rebel Alliance fleets. Luke Skywalker sabotaged the efforts of one of these modified probes by having it steer a commandeered corvette into Krell's ship, killing all hands aboard.

**Krenn, Josala** An Obroan Institute archaeologist, she was sent to Maltha Obex to recover biological samples for any clues into the origins of the Qella civilization. Josala Krenn was buried in an avalanche on the planet.

**Krennel, Prince-Admiral Delak** Krennel served under Grand Admiral Thrawn in the Unknown Regions, although he detested serving an alien. After Krennel bombarded a world instead of following Thrawn's more "pacifistic" orders, he was sent back to Imperial Center for punishment from the Emperor himself. Luckily for Krennel, Emperor Palpatine had been killed at Endor before he could pass judgment. Krennel then fled Imperial service, striking out on his own and establishing himself as a renegade Imperial warlord. In a battle, he lost the use of his right forearm from the elbow down, and the limb had to be replaced with a cybernetic implant. The mechanical device glowed red whenever he exerted it, evoking fear in his subordinates and enemies.

During the initial struggle for control of the Empire, Krennel aligned himself with General Paltr Carvin and, on orders from Ysanne Isard, set out to capture Leia Organa at Axxila. When Isard approached him about working directly for her instead of Carvin, he was initially suspicious. However, she gained his allegiance by augmenting his forces in an attempt to retrieve Sate Pestage from Ciutric. After New Republic forces thought they had recovered Pestage, the former Imperial Grand Vizier slipped away and presented himself to Krennel for asylum. Krennel, however, cared nothing about Pestage. He personally executed the former adviser by strangling him with his cybernetic hand, then usurped control of the Ciutric Hegemony for himself and paid lip service to Thrawn's call for support during his rise to power.

After Thrawn's death at Bilbringi, the Republic targeted Krennel for removal. Forces began raiding Ciutric space, unaware that Krennel had allied himself with a clone of Ysanne Isard. Together they began a disinformation campaign aimed at opening a rift between the humans and nonhumans of the New Republic. Krennel claimed the Hegemony to be a haven for Alderaanian refugees who were tired of the Republic's pro-alien politics. However, their efforts were undermined by the real Ysanne Isard, who managed to capture Rogue Squadron and convince them to help her defeat Krennel. As soon as Krennel heard that the Rogues had been destroyed at Corvis Minor, he and the cloned Isard began plotting their conquest of Coruscant. They waylaid Republic supply convoys to Liinade III, hoping to draw off much of the starship security around Coruscant. Just as they were about to launch their attack, the Republic, on a tip from Wedge Antilles, attacked Ciutric.

Ganner Krieg

Before his forces could leave the system, Krennel found himself on the brink of disaster. His fleet was decimated, Ciutric had been infiltrated, and he had no firepower to bring to bear on the Republic ships. The combined fire of the *Selonian Fire* and the *Corusca Fire* destroyed Krennel's flagship, the *Reckoning*, and Krennel was killed in the explosion.

**Kressh, Ludo** An ancient Sith magician, he was Naga Sadow's contemporary and rival for the position of Dark Lord of the Sith. It was Kressh, a Sith half-breed, who was chosen to lead Marka Ragnos's funeral procession. Kressh's faction believed in maintaining the status quo within the Sith Empire, rather than attempting to expand it as Naga Sadow desired. Their opposing views led to a skirmish at Ragnos's funeral. The ghost of Markos Ragnos foretold of the impending downfall of the Sith Empire should the two continue to struggle. Neither heeded the former Dark Lord's words, and a civil war erupted within the Sith Empire.

Ludo Kressh believed that hyperspace pioneers Jori and Gav Daragon were advance scouts for an Old Republic attack force coming to eradicate the Sith, a position that gathered support among the Sith Lords. As Sadow took control of the Empire, Kressh rallied his supporters in an attempt to overthrow his rival. They fled to Ziost to plan their attack. A timely discovery of the treachery with which Sadow had seized the Empire led to further support, until Kressh was ready to launch an attack on Sadow's base on Khar Delba. However, Naga Sadow's real base of power was on Khar Shian, and Ludo Kressh's forces were drawn into a battle against an undefeatable foe.

Kressh was believed to have been killed over Khar Delba, where Naga Sadow's fleet destroyed Kressh's forces. In fact, he managed to survive, returning to the Sith Empire to take over as Dark Lord. Sadow began his own assault on Coruscant. The strife between the rivals grew until it erupted into the Great Hyperspace War. Kressh and Sadow drew their starfleets into the Sith Empire and fought viciously against each other. In the end, though, Sadow was able to use the dark side of the Force to coerce one of his own starship captains to ram Kressh's flagship, destroying the ship and killing Kressh in the explosion.

**Krickle** One of Talon Karrde's smugglers, Krickle served under Shirlee Faughn on the *Starry Ice.*

**Krieg, Ganner** An Imperial Knight who served the new Empire that rose to power during the decades following the Yuuzhan Vong War. Noted for his calm demeanor and serious nature, Krieg was one of Antares Draco's closest friends and advisers. Thus, when former Emperor Roan Fel began consolidating forces still loyal to the true Empire on Bastion, Ganner followed Draco to Bastion to help with the buildup.

When Emperor Fel refused to send forces

Ludo Kressh

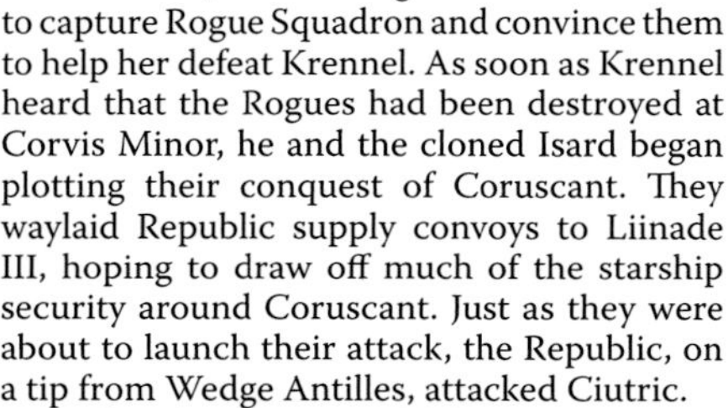

to recover his daughter from Vendaxa, Krieg agreed to accompany Draco on their own rescue mission. Slipping away in two borrowed Imperial fighters, they set out to find Marasiah and bring her home before Darth Krayt could learn of her location. They weren't fast enough, however, and had to battle Darth Nihl and Darth Talon in order to leave.

The Imperials managed to safely return to Bastion, where Draco and Krieg were surprised to receive a vehement reprimand from Emperor Fel. The Emperor explained that their mission had given Darth Krayt information on their location, alerting the Sith Lord to the Imperial presence on Bastion. Thus, they were even more surprised when the Emperor decided to publicly reward them for their bravery in rescuing Marasiah, although they were told that the medals they were to receive were for public appearances only, since word of such high-level officers intentionally disobeying the Emperor would surely undermine Fel's authority.

The pair were then assigned to escort Mingo Bovark to the Wheel, where the Imperial ambassador was to meet with Galactic Alliance Admiral Gar Stazi. A Sith attack pitted the two sides against each other, as it appeared that warships on both sides opened fire without warning. The negotiations were called off when Pol Temm banished the Imperials, after Krieg and Draco revealed that they had smuggled their lightsabers aboard the station. They returned to Bastion without an alliance.

**Kriek** A sentient species of long-necked, tortoise-like beings native to Kriekaal.

**Krintrino** Site of a Rebel Alliance resistance cell quashed by the Empire about 5 years before the Battle of Yavin.

**Kritkeen, Sinick** A tyrannical COMPNOR general, he was stationed on Aruza. General Kritkeen eventually was assassinated by the bounty hunter Dengar, who had been hired by the Aruzans.

**Kronos-327** An IG-86 assassin droid that once failed Ziro the Hutt during the Clone Wars.

**Krova, Lieutenant** A communications officer in the Galactic Alliance military assigned to the Star Destroyer *Anakin Solo* during the Alliance's war with the Confederation. It was Lieutenant Krova who was forced to interrupt Jacen Solo's battle meditation during the Second Battle of Balmorra with a "top urgent priority" holo call from Ben Skywalker, saying that he knew the identity of the killer of his mother, Mara Jade Skywalker. Jacen had planned to demote Krova for the interruption, but chose not to when he learned the reason. Instead, Solo chose to take Krova on as his personal communications officer, ensuring that any communications he received came through a single source.

**Krova the Hutt** A minor crime lord based on Alvorine, she had a bounty placed on her head by the New Republic for her connection to the death of several Rebel Alliance agents during the Galactic Civil War.

**kroyie** A species of birds native to the planet Kashyyyk. They were considered a delicacy by the Wookiee natives. Huge kroyie birds lived in the upper branches of the planet's giant trees. They were attracted to bright lights, so Wookiees used search beams to hunt them for food.

**Kru, Glie'oleg** The Twi'lek commander of the Bothan Assault Cruiser *Champion.* Brevet Admiral Glie'oleg Kru led the New Republic forces during the Yuuzhan Vong attack on Kalarba. He was killed when the *Champion* was destroyed by the enemy.

**Kryll, General** A Rebel Alliance officer in charge of the Outer Rim Communications Center during the Galactic Civil War. Kryll was a former Imperial officer who defected to the Alliance after the destruction of Alderaan. He often told his troops that he defected not because of Alderaan, but because the Empire didn't appreciate his wonderful tenor voice. He later served the New Republic on Generis, and was able to evacuate Travia Chan when Imperial forces under the command of Grand Admiral Thrawn managed to retake the planet.

**Krytollak** A species that worshipped Emperor Palpatine during the New Order. The Krytollaks were warm-blooded, insectile sentients with hard, dense outer shells surrounding tough skeletal structures. Many Krytollaks infiltrated the Rebel Alliance in an effort to provide information to the Empire.

Krytollaks

**Krytos** A virus developed by Imperial General Evir Derricote at the request of Ysanne Isard, director of Imperial Intelligence. She wanted a disease that would mutate quickly and spread among the alien species of Coruscant, but would not harm the humanoid populace. Krytos could be frozen and thawed without loss of effectiveness. Because of the virus's low flesh-contact infection rate—only 20 percent—it was decided to release it into the planet's water supply.

**K'sar, Thal** A Bith artisan who created the unusual hyperwave transceiver for the mechno-chair of Nute Gunray before the Battle of Naboo. K'sar had spent years hiding on Escarte, hoping to escape notice. Just before Anakin Skywalker and Obi-Wan Kenobi located him, the Bith was arrested on a series of trumped-up charges, although it was clear to everyone that he was going to be executed to keep his secrets safe. K'sar was despondent, and was reluctant to assist the Jedi in any way that might hasten his demise. However, they helped break him out of prison and flee Escarte. Once free, K'sar revealed that he actually had built two of the transceivers, and both had been delivered about a year before the Battle of Naboo. One of them he provided to the Xi Charrians who built the mechno-chair. The other he brought to Raith Sienar. K'sar then provided the Jedi with the name of Fa'ale Leh, the Twi'lek who transported Sienar's prototype Infiltrator to Darth Sidious.

***Ksstarr*** A Yuuzhan Vong frigate dispatched to transport Nom Anor and Vergere to the *Baanu Rass,* to ensure that the Jedi Knights aboard the *Exquisite Death* were captured. Jaina Solo and the surviving Jedi were able to capture the shuttle and use it as their escape ship. They managed to reach Coruscant, but discovered that the planet already had fallen to the Yuuzhan Vong. After assisting in the escape of the *Millennium Falcon,* Jaina took the *Ksstarr* on a short, blind jump into hyperspace. The ship was dying and needed to be maintained, so the Jedi chose to take it to Hapes to recover. After receiving a villip-based communication from the priest Harrar, Jaina Solo chose to rename the frigate the *Trickster.*

**KT-10** An R2 unit with a female personality program, she and R2-D2 became "romantically interested" in each other while both were in the Great Heep's droid harem back in the early days of the Empire.

**KT-18** A pearl-colored housekeeping droid with a female personality program, she went by the nickname Kate. Luke Skywalker purchased Kate from Jawas on Tatooine as a gift for Han Solo.

**Ktriss** A pet of Great Bogga the Hutt, this dark side hssiss, or dragon, was captured from Lake Natth on the planet Ambria. Ktriss emanated a sinister force that paralyzed the minds of its victims . . . and then sometimes devoured them.

**Ku, Denua** A Yuuzhan Vong warrior who served as one of Warmaster Tsavong Lah's personal guards during the invasion of the galaxy. Shortly after the Battle of Coruscant, Denua Ku was ordered to watch over Viqi Shesh. It was easy to distinguish Ku from other Yuuzhan Vong: His skin was dominated by a long and puckering scar. This scar originated atop his skull, traveled down his face and neck, crisscrossed his chest, then ran down his right leg. When the warmaster suspected that his failing radank claw implant was the result of the meddling of priests, Denua Ku was placed in charge of rooting out the possible suspects and bringing them before Lah. After it was learned that a Force-wielding being was loose on Coruscant, Ku was ordered to take Viqi Shesh to the

Kuar

planet's surface and locate the being. They were unknowingly searching for the being known as Lord Nyax, and several times their party got separated and Shesh escaped. Denua Ku managed to survive an attack by the Dark Jedi and hunted the former Kuat Senator down using a nisbat. During an attack led by Luke Skywalker, Ku fell from a destroyed catwalk and impaled himself on a length of rebar. Badly wounded, he still refused to allow the Kuati to escape. He used every last ounce of strength to track her down in the Tersons' apartment. However, rather than die at the hands of the Yuuzhan Vong, Shesh threw herself out a window and fell to her death. Denua Ku, too exhausted to continue, died in the apartment.

**Kuan** A planet orbited by several moons, it was in the Taroon system on the outer edges of the Rim. For nearly 20 years, Kuan engaged in a devastating war with its sister planet Bordal, until the conflict was ended suddenly by the intervention of the Empire. The long interplanetary struggle destroyed much of Kuan's main city, home to illegal swoop races and a popular hangout called the Maze. Animal life on Kuan included the rondat, and plant life included the pleasant-smelling shimsha flower.

**Kuar** A planet in a system of the same name near the Empress Teta system, its ruined underground cities provided a base for the masked warrior clans led by Mand'alor four millennia before the Galactic Civil War. From there they struck at the heart of the Teta system, prompting Tetan leader Ulic Qel-Droma to fight Mand'alor in single combat on Kuar's plains of Harkul. Battling on an unstable web of chains, Qel-Droma defeated Mand'alor, thereby winning the loyalty of the warlord and his fierce soldiers of fortune.

***Kuari Princess*** A Mon Calamari MC80 luxury spaceliner known for its slafcourses, which were famous throughout the galaxy. The *Kuari Princess* was the flagship of Galaxy Tours, and had accommodations for up to 3,500 passengers of 27 unique species. It measured 500 meters long, and was staffed by 840 crew, 500 droids, and 60 security officers. It was lightly armed, with 10 turbolaser batteries. The *Kuari Princess* had a long and storied history, including one trip through the Maelstrom in which it was hijacked by the Riders of the Maelstrom as part of a plot to destroy Rodin Higron's base on the planet Oasis. The droid bounty hunter 4-LOM once served as a valet and human relations droid aboard the ship.

**Kuat** The home of the Kuat Drive Yards, a shipyard that mass-produced warships for the Empire. It originally was settled around the same time as the formation of the Old Republic, some 25,000 years before the Battle of Yavin, by a group of merchant families that hoped to form the most influential shipbuilding operation in the galaxy. They terraformed the planet and developed it into a temperate world devoid of predators, then began creating vast orbital shipyards. The relationship between Kuat and the Empire was formed during the early days of the New Order, and blossomed when the Kuat Drive Yards was designated the primary facility for the construction of Star Destroyers.

A forested world of pastoral beauty, Kuat was one of four planets located in the Kuat sector, the most densely populated area of the galaxy. The planet was orbited by three immense space stations, built by the Empire to manage traffic in and out of the system. The Kuat Passenger Port was dedicated to civilian and tourist traffic; the Kuat Freight Port, to the transport of goods to and from Kuat. The third station was strictly for use by the Imperial military, and controlled all access to the surface of Kuat. During the Clone Wars, the proximity of Kuat and Neimoidia—they were separated by less than 6 parsecs—put the two worlds into direct competition. Kuati officials tried to infiltrate Neimoidian facilities by sending in modified worker droids with concealed spyware, but Neimoidian paranoia meant that safeguards had been placed around all their technologies.

**Kuat Drive Yards (KDY)** One of the top three starship manufacturers in the galaxy, along with Corellian Engineering Corporation and Sienar Fleet Systems. KDY was controlled by the ruling families of the planet Kuat, with each new ruler being chosen from among the most competent in a vote. However, it was eventually determined that the Kuat family had the most aptitude for running the huge corporation, and the ruling families established the Inheritance Exemption. This allowed control of KDY to pass from one generation of the Kuat family to the next, thereby ensuring that the most able of the Kuat minds was continually in control of the corporation. KDY thus always generated vast amounts of wealth for all the ruling families.

Kuat Drive Yards remained independent of any governmental body from the time of its inception during the Old Republic throughout the New Order of Emperor Palpatine. It was perhaps most famous for its production of the *Imperial*-class Star Destroyer. It also produced many shipboard components, as well as the Nebulon-B frigate. KDY had once been part of the Techno Union, and began experimenting with the development of massive starships shortly before the onset of the Clone Wars. However, management decided to split from the Techno Union and built its ships for the Old Republic. KDY was also one of the original signatory sponsors of the Corporate Sector Authority.

Unknown to most buyers, every ship that left Kuat Drive Yards was given a regulator subcode in its computer system. The trapdoor allowed KDY engineers to get control of a ship for diagnostics and repairs. The codes also could be used to break into a ship and take control from its owner. This fact was never revealed, in part to save KDY from the wrath of Emperor Palpatine.

Kuat

During the last days of the New Order, shortly before the Battle of Endor, much of Kuat Drive Yards was destroyed by Kuat of Kuat. He hoped to ensure that no one else would take control of the operation. The future leaders of KDY kept Kuat of Kuat's undetonated explosives in place so they could be set off if the facilities ever were in danger of being captured.

**Kuat of Kuat** A descendant of the ancient Kuat family that controlled the vast Kuat Drive Yards during the last years of the Old Republic and throughout the New Order. Although never truly appreciated, Kuat of Kuat worked diligently to maintain the independence of KDY in the face of Emperor Palpatine's growing power. He fiercely refused to be part of the first Death Star project, an action denounced by the ruling families of Kuat until the station was destroyed near Yavin. Unknown to most of the Kuati clans until the end of the New Order, Kuat even tried to eliminate Prince Xizor of Black Sun, when the Falleen began trying to take control of the shipyards. The plot involved implicating Xizor in the deaths of Owen and Beru Lars on Tatooine, an event that Kuat recorded; he later added traces of Falleen pheromones to an olfactory sensor.

If the plan had worked, Luke Skywalker would have broken off his involvement with the Rebel Alliance long enough to eliminate Xizor, thereby removing one of Kuat's chief enemies. The plot never had a chance, though, since the droid containing the falsified evidence was lost by its courier, Ree Duptom, when his ship's engines failed. The droid fell into the hands of Boba Fett, and Kuat found himself trying to kill the bounty hunter in order to recover the droid. Several attempts were made to ensure Fett's death. These efforts didn't go unnoticed: Several of the other Kuati families took them as personal vendettas and signs that Kuat was no longer working in KDY's best interests.

The families' plotting eventually took in Kuat's security chief, Fenald, and his replacement, Kodir of Kuhlvult. Through it all, Kuat maintained the upper hand. In the end, he was forced to destroy the KDY facilities rather than let them fall into the hands of anyone else. In this, too, Kuat was thwarted by the efforts of the Alliance and Boba Fett. The bounty hunter managed to flee the destruction in a slaved Star Destroyer, taking with him most of the explosives Kuat had hoped to use. Kuat returned to the main facilities and was killed in the explosions he himself had set off.

**Ku'Bakai system** This system was named for its blue giant star, whose unpredictable solar flares left the first four planets scorched and lifeless. The fifth planet, Kubindi, was the homeworld of the Kubaz. The sixth, eighth, and eleventh planets housed insect farms for the Kubaz to use in preparing their unique cuisine.

**Kubaz** Members of this humanoid species stood about 1.8 meters tall and had short, prehensile trunks instead of noses. Kubaz had rough-textured black-green skin and large, sensitive eyes. On many worlds, they had to wear special goggles to protect their eyes from harsh light. They were cultured beings who highly valued tradition, art, and music. Their homeworld of Kubindi was famous for its insect-based cuisine. Garindan, a Mos Eisley operative, was a Kubaz. When the Yuuzhan Vong took control of Kubindi some 27 years after the Battle of Yavin, they exterminated virtually every insect species that had been cultivated by the Kubaz. This left the surviving population with little or no food, and many Kubaz starved to death. After the end of the war, the surviving Kubaz began to return to their homeworld in an effort to restore its former glory.

**Kubindi** The fifth planet in the Ku'Bakai system, it was the homeworld of the insect-loving Kubaz. Due to the unpredictable solar flares of Ku'Bakai, Kubindi suffered from baths of intense radiation and constantly changing weather patterns. The adaptability of insects made them particularly successful there; many varieties existed, including the bantha-sized sunbeetle. Insects were considered a true delicacy on Kubindi, and the civilized, cultured Kubaz organized their society around insect-trading circles. Kubaz families farmed designer insect hives and traded with others; the largest trading families made most planetary governmental decisions. Kubindi was isolated and seldom saw galactic traffic. Garindan, the Mos Eisley spy known as Long Snoot, was a Kubaz. Four years after the Battle of Endor, the Kubaz negotiated with the Barabel to purchase body parts of the humanoid insects known as Verpine to use in their cuisine. The planet was conquered during the Yuuzhan Vong War.

Kubaz

**Kueget LN-21 blaster pistol** Sleek firearms used by Alderaanian security personnel, they could deliver both stun and lethal blasts but had elaborate key locks and safety mechanisms that prevented them from falling into the wrong hands. Each weapon also had a transponder that allowed it to be tracked by authorities.

**Kueller** Formerly known as Dolph, Kueller was an extremely talented student of Luke Skywalker on Yavin 4, but he always possessed a certain darkness. He did not stay at the Jedi academy long enough either to develop his Force talents or to dispel his darkness, and he became known as Kueller once he left the academy and accepted the dark side fully. As a youth, he witnessed the aftermath of the brutal deaths of his parents at the hands of the Je'har on Almania. Thereafter he swore revenge on the Almanian rulers, as well as on the New Republic, which he believed had blindly ignored the atrocities committed by the Je'har.

Kueller used the planet Fwatna as a base of operations before launching his plans against Almania. He attacked the Je'har and destroyed them, becoming self-proclaimed Master of Almania, using the Great Dome of the Je'har as his headquarters. Kueller wore a Hendanyn death mask to hide his boyish face and silvery hair. Only seen in museums, this ceremonial mask molded itself to the skin of the wearer. Kueller's mask was white with black accents and held tiny jewels in the corners of the eye slits.

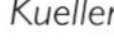
Kueller

Kueller worked with a group of smugglers in Smuggler's Run to buy Imperial equipment, which he had Brakiss—the administrator of the droid-manufacturing factories on Telti and another former student of Skywalker—use in constructing droids that incorporated an explosive device. Kueller then used these rigged droids to detonate massive explosions on the Almanian moons of Pydyr and Auyemesh, and even in Senate Hall on Coruscant itself.

Kueller's plans also included rigging the New Republic's new model X-wing fighter with an explosive detonator, thereby eliminating the New Republic's most talented pilots. The plot was uncovered by Cole Fardreamer, R2-D2, and C-3PO. Kueller then lured Luke Skywalker to Almania and sent a holocoded message to Chief of State Leia Organa Solo, threatening to kill Skywalker if she did not resign and turn over the reins of power. Leia did resign and went off in search of her brother. Together Luke and Leia faced down Kueller, and when his dark side powers were curtailed by several ysalamiri that Han Solo brought to Almania, Leia killed Kueller with a blaster shot to the head.

**Kuhqo** A former Yuuzhan Vong shaper who was among the many Shamed Ones forced to live beneath the surface of the planet Coruscant after it was reshaped into a simulacrum of Yuuzhan'tar. Kuhqo believed the words of Prophet Yu'shaa, and set out to prove that Supreme Overlord Shimrra was a fraud. Kuhqo managed to steal an executor's qahsa, discovering a wealth of information about the Jedi Knights. His investigation also revealed a connection among the Yuuzhan Vong, the Jedi Knights, and a "living planet." Because the Shamed Ones knew nothing of Zonama Sekot, they used Kuhqo's discoveries to begin a search for a living planet.

**Kuhru, Major** An officer in the Imperial Army, and a noted AT-AT commander. Upon returning from a mission in which he failed to capture Luke Skywalker, Major Kuhru was compelled by Darth Vader to walk out of an air lock . . . without an environment suit.

**Kun, Exar** Once the most powerful and dangerous of the Dark Lords of the Sith, he was responsible for the deaths of millions four millennia before the rise of the Empire. Killed by an overwhelming force of Jedi, the dark spirit of Exar Kun survived across the vastness of time to challenge Luke Skywalker and a new group of Jedi trainees.

Kun was tutored in the ways of the Force on

Dantooine by Master Vodo-Siosk Baas. The proud Jedi pushed himself hard, but he was pulled to the dark side of the Force and secretly used his Master's Jedi Holocron to learn about past Dark Lords of the Sith, such as Freedon Nadd. Posing as a Jedi archaeologist, Kun traveled to Onderon to examine Nadd's Sith artifacts. Jedi Master Arca Jeth saw through Kun's lies, and an angry Kun left for the city of Iziz and then the Dxun moon to explore Nadd's influence. Inside Nadd's tomb, he was confronted by the spirit of the Dark Lord himself and was led to two scrolls that contained great Sith secrets. These scrolls in turn led Kun to the desolate planet of Korriban where, with the help of Nadd's spirit, he gained access to the Sith tombs.

*Exar Kun*

Kun had second thoughts and tried to back out, but was felled by Nadd's spirit in an attack that left him near death. The only hope, the spirit proclaimed, was to fully embrace the dark side, and—however reluctantly—Kun did. In the time that followed, Nadd's spirit filled him with tales, especially of the ancient Sith Lord Naga Sadow and the experiments Sadow had performed on the moon of Yavin 4 to give flesh to the spirits of the dead. Nadd told Kun that he must complete Sadow's work and give Nadd a new body.

On Yavin 4, Kun again renounced the dark side, but he was attacked by the Massassi, mutated descendants of Sadow's alchemy. They prepared him for death in a Massassi Blood Sacrifice, and Kun again turned to the dark side to save his life. He slaughtered all who would oppose him, including Nadd's spirit, but not before it cried out a warning to two other followers, Aleema and Satal Keto, founders of a dark side mystical sect known as the Krath.

In the months that followed, Kun had the Massassi build huge temples of an ancient Sith design to focus great dark side energies. He also continued Naga Sadow's experiments, turning the Massassi into monstrous creatures of death. Then he headed for the Empress Teta system to destroy Nadd's final Sith followers. He arrived as Jedi Knights were attacking the Krath stronghold. But Aleema and fallen Jedi Ulic Qel-Droma survived. Blasting Aleema with dark side power, Kun and Qel-Droma engaged in a blistering lightsaber duel. Sith amulets that both men wore began to glow with energy. Ancient Sith Lords appeared and bestowed the title of Dark Lord of the Sith on Kun, and the title of Sith apprentice on Qel-Droma. Eventually they and Aleema joined forces to try to bring down the Republic and the Jedi Knights.

At a Great Council of Jedi convened on Deneba, Master Vodo-Siosk Baas volunteered to try to turn his former student from the dark side, but Kun slew his Master. The bloody fighting that ensued, known for all time as the Sith War, resulted in millions of deaths. In the end, Qel-Droma betrayed Exar Kun, revealing the secret of Kun's power base on Yavin 4. The resulting battle leveled most of the moon's temples and destroyed Kun's body. Yet he was able to drain the life force from every Massassi, an act that kept his spirit alive—but trapped in the remaining Yavin temples.

Some 4,000 years later, the Rebel Alliance briefly established a base on Yavin 4. Luke Skywalker then opened a Jedi training academy based in Yavin 4's Great Temple. Exar Kun's spirit stirred, tempting first one then another of Skywalker's trainees into turning to the dark side. He enlisted one promising Jedi, Kyp Durron, until Skywalker saw what was happening and confronted Durron. With the help of Kun, Durron attacked his teacher and used Force lightning to separate Skywalker's spirit from his body. But Kun didn't reckon on the combined strength of the remaining students, who protected Skywalker's body from destruction, then set a trap for Kun. They focused their will into a single entity of the Force, finally snuffing out Kun's spirit, restoring Luke's essence to his body, and freeing Durron from the hold of the dark side.

**Kuna, Fo** Zo Howler's chief aide during the last years of the Old Republic.

**Kunra** A member of a small group of Shamed Ones who lived with Vuurok I'pan beneath the surface of Coruscant after the planet had been transformed into a likeness of Yuuzhan'tar. Like the rest of his cadre, Kunra believed that the Jedi Knights were not abominations, but saviors of the Shamed Ones and symbols of the new ideology that should be embraced by the Yuuzhan Vong.

A former warrior, he didn't trust Nom Anor, who had come to live among the Shamed Ones. Kunra argued against telling Nom Anor of the legend of Vua Rapuung, but was outvoted. When their small band was discovered by Yuuzhan Vong warriors, Kunra fled in terror, fearing for his own life. He located Nom Anor, who blamed Kunra's shaming on his deep-seated cowardice. Kunra did nothing to change Nom Anor's mind, and reluctantly agreed to accompany Shoon-mi Esh and the former executor on a mission of survival.

Nom Anor, having adopted the name Yu'shaa, began to spread the Message to the rest of the Shamed Ones on Coruscant. As the only being who knew of the Prophet's true identity, Kunra held some measure of power over Anor, but remained subordinate. When Shoon-mi attempted to assassinate the Prophet, Kunra intervened and saved him. As Nom Anor returned from his mission to locate Zonama Sekot, bringing warnings of Shimrra's plans to eradicate the Shamed Ones, Kunra refused to let him renege on his promise to lead the Shamed Ones to power. While Nom Anor wore the guise of Yu'shaa and pleaded with the masses to avoid the Supreme Overlord, Kunra simply twisted the words into fanatical demands for more pressure on the Yuuzhan Vong elite.

***Kur-hashan*** One of the Yuuzhan Vong destroyers dispatched to destroy the New Republic communications base on Esfandia after the Battle of Ebaq. It was under the command of B'shith Vorrik, and would have had more than enough firepower to destroy the base if the Imperial Remnant's 78th Fleet hadn't followed it to Esfandia. There the *Kur-hashan* was pitted against the *Right to Rule,* and Vorrik and Grand Admiral Pellaeon soon fought to a stalemate. When Tahiri Veila used the captured picket ship *Collaborator* to trick some of Vorrik's forces to the surface of Esfandia, she left the *Kur-hashan* undefended. Vorrik realized that he had been tricked, and he tried to bring the ship's weapons to bear on the *Right to Rule.* However, the old Star Destroyer was ready, and pounded the *Kur-hashan* with everything it could. Realizing he was beaten, Vorrik tried to turn the dying ship onto a collision course with the Imperials, but the *Kur-hashan* exploded well short of the point where it could have done any damage.

**Kurin, Peate** One of the crewmen aboard the *Rand Ecliptic* who decided to join Biggs Darklighter in defecting from Imperial service. Shortly before the Battle of Yavin, their group managed to escape from the frigate—then realized that they didn't have enough fuel to reach their destination. They hatched a plan to return to the *Rand Ecliptic* and steal more fuel, only to find that Derek "Hobbie" Klivian had also launched a mutiny and taken control of the ship. They joined forces and brought the frigate to Yavin 4. Kurin was then chosen as one of the former TIE fighter pilots who would travel to Incom Industries and help steal the X-wing starfighter. The plan called for the pilots to eject in space, allowing droids to fly the ships and draw off any defenders. Although things started off well, Klivian lost a foot in the ejection, and Kurin was decapitated. His body was recovered

*Sith Lord Exar Kun's spirit confronts the Jedi Academy.*

and given a proper burial when the group returned to Yavin 4.

**Kuro, An'ya** A mysterious Jedi Master, she shed her original name of An'ya Kuro and adopted the alias Dark Woman. Distinguished by her silvery hair and strong features, she was known among the members of the Jedi Council for her highly unorthodox training methods. She discovered Ki-Adi-Mundi when the Cerean was four years old and brought him to the Jedi Temple. She also attempted but failed to train a young Aurra Sing as a Jedi. As the Old Republic began to crumble, the Dark Woman fled to the planet Cophrigin 5 to retire and allow the Force to guide her life. The Force drew her out of retirement during the Clone Wars, and the Dark Woman participated in several undercover missions. During the early days of the Empire, the Dark Woman was hunted down and executed by Darth Vader.

**Kurp, Kosh** A bomb expert, he was Jabba the Hutt's secret weapon after Jabba was trapped in the fortress of Gaar Suppoon. Jabba figured that Kosh Kurp would seek revenge once he was told that it was Gaar Suppoon who had murdered his family. After Suppoon was killed, Jabba gave Kurp all of Suppoon's holdings.

**Kurtzen** This soft-spoken, peaceful humanoid species made up about 5 percent of the population of Bakura. Kurtzen were white-skinned with a corrugated, leathery scalp instead of hair.

**Kushal Vogh** The gambling capital of planet Elerion.

**Kutag (Doornik-881)** This planet, located in the Koornacht Cluster, was the site of an Imperial factory farm during the last years of the Galactic Civil War. When Nil Spaar rallied the Yevethan people to rise up against Imperial control, they wiped out the farm's personnel and took control of the facility.

**Kwaad, Kae** *See* Onimi.

**Kwannot** A remote planet where Aurra Sing killed Jedi Master Mana Veridi and nearly took the lives of Qui-Gon Jinn and Obi-Wan Kenobi before the Battle of Naboo.

**Kwazel Maw** A dreaded swamp slug creature of Rodia that was impervious to blasterfire and thermal detonators. Jar Jar Binks befriended a Kwazel Maw while on a disastrous diplomatic mission to Rodia during the Clone Wars.

**Kwenn Space Station** A space station orbiting Kwenn and containing the Royal K Casino, it was where Jabba the Hutt acquired his pet Kowakian monkey-lizard, Salacious Crumb. Meysen Kayson, wealthy owner of the Greel Wood Logging Corporation in the Pii system, owned a sizable percentage of Kwenn Space Station.

**Kwerve, Bidlo** A scar-faced Corellian with white-streaked black hair, he was an associate of Bib Fortuna and the Twi'lek's direct rival for the post of Jabba the Hutt's majordomo. Bidlo helped Fortuna acquire a rancor for Jabba's birthday, and was soon thereafter "honored" by being the first person whom Jabba fed to his new pet.

**K-wing bomber** A 16-meter-long bomber, it was developed by the New Republic about 12 years after the Battle of Endor. The central fuselage was studded with four wings: Two larger wings extended outward, while two shorter ones at the bottom acted as landing skids. The four wings had 18 unique positions and could be adjusted based on the installed weaponry and payload. The bomber was equipped with three primary thrust engines, two at the junction of the wings and one at the rear of the fuselage. The two-seated craft was operated by a pilot and a gunner/bomber, and was designed to fly in gravity-dense arenas. The K-wing lacked a hyperdrive, since its primary mission was as an atmospheric bomber. As such, it was the equal of the TIE bomber in armament. It also could be armed heavily as a starfighter, but the ship suffered in maneuverability when more weapons were added. Maximum speed for the K-wing approached 1,000 kilometers per hour on bombing runs.

**Kwis, Captain Vortia** The commanding officer of the modified corvette *Pure Sabacc* during the early stages of the Yuuzhan Vong War. Kwis and his crew were at Dubrillion when the Yuuzhan Vong launched their invasion, and agreed to help the New Republic transport refugees to Dantooine. However, after arriving in the middle of a Yuuzhan Vong sneak attack and barely fighting his way free, Captain Kwis began to reconsider his support for the New Republic. Eventually, he decided to join the Peace Brigade, and agreed to use the *Pure Sabacc* as a sort of mobile recruiting office.

**Kybacca** The senior Wookiee New Republic Senator, she opposed the introduction of former Imperials to the Senate.

**Kyber, Natas** The king of the planet Troska during the Empire. When Imperial forces arrived on Troska and established a base there, Natas and the Kyber family found themselves forced to bow to the wishes of Imperial Commander Buzk, who became increasingly demanding. When Lieutenant Manech called in Boba Fett as part of a larger plan to expose Buzk's dirty dealings, Natas was captured and held prisoner by the bounty hunter. Not wanting to lose his position of power, Natas bribed Fett to launch an attack on the Imperial garrison. Fett caused enough havoc to expose Buzk's treachery, then left Troska behind. The Imperials later interrogated Natas to determine how much he knew about Buzk's plans.

K-wing bomber

**Kyber, Torino** The crown prince of the Kyber family, in charge of the refineries on the planet Troska during the New Order. Kyber was more than a little disgruntled at the oppression and corruption of Imperial Commander Buzk, and threatened to shut down the refineries if Buzk didn't back off and leave operations to the Kybers. Imperial leaders learned that Commander Buzk was taking liberties with his command of the Troska garrison, but the Kyber family was unaware that Imperial Lieutenant Manech had hatched a plot that involved the notorious bounty hunter Boba Fett. Fett arrived on Troska and immediately set to work destroying the Kyber refineries.

**Kybo, Flynn** A Jedi Padawan who was apprenticed to T'chooka D'oon. Two years into the Clone Wars, the pair were dispatched to Vandos to rescue Ambassador Quiyyen, unaware that the ambassador had been held captive as part of a plot by General Grievous to lure the Jedi. Confronted by Grievous, Master D'oon charged into battle, giving Kybo a chance to flee. Upon his return to Coruscant, Kybo demanded that the Jedi Council sanction a mission to hunt down and destroy the droid general. He claimed that his actions were not motivated by revenge or anger, but by a desire to prevent the deaths of any more beings at the general's hand.

After being dismissed by the Council, Kybo met his new Master, Z'meer Bothu, who allowed Kybo to carry out his plans. However, Master Bothu made it clear to Kybo that, if he should leave Coruscant to chase down Grievous, he would never be able to return to the Jedi Order. Kybo accepted this fate, claiming that he was sacrificing his place as a Jedi for the greater good of the galaxy. He accompanied B'dard Tone to Belsus, where they had tracked Grievous after the cyborg captured the younglings of the Bergruutfa Clan. After landing on the moon, Flynn and Tone confronted Grievous while Codi Ty rescued the younglings. Tone was killed while trying to delay Grievous. Kybo allowed volatile fuels to contact the molten rock and magma that spewed from Belsus's surface, setting off a massive explosion that nearly tore the planet apart. Kybo died in the explosion, but his sacrifice allowed Codi Ty to escape. Grievous, however, also managed to survive the explosion.

**Kyryll's World** The homeworld of the Pui-Ui.

# L

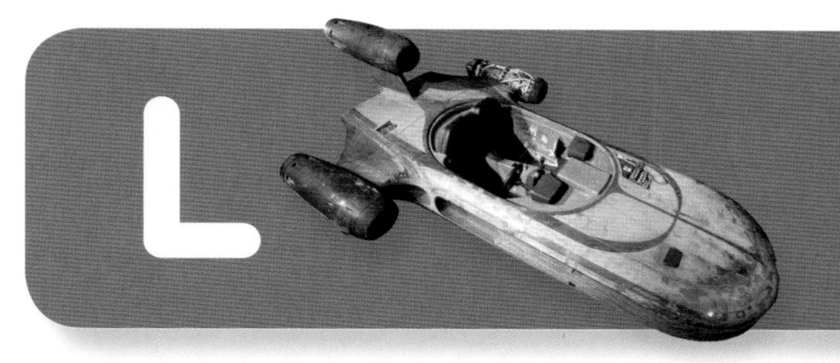

L8-L9

**L8-L9** A prototype combat droid produced by Tagge Industries, the L8-L9 series was proposed as a stand-in for clone troopers whenever environmental conditions were too hostile or deadly for human soldiers. An unsolicited project, it was the brainchild of young Baron Orman Tagge, a prodigious technocrat who sought to further ingratiate himself with Supreme Chancellor Palpatine's government. Tagge submitted the prototype to the Rattataki warlords as a gladiator combatant to prove that the droid was the superior warrior—but Asajj Ventress quickly destroyed L8-L9 in the Cauldron arena. Tagge didn't abandon the idea, however, and used L8-L9's plans as the basis for the Z-X3 project.

**Laa** One of the oldest and wisest Bouncers native to Ruusan, Laa rescued the young girl named Zannah when her ship crashed there. After the Brotherhood of Darkness set off a thought bomb, Laa was nearly killed by the combined anguish and pain that resonated through the Force. Only Zannah's innate ability to shield them from the wave of emotion saved the Bouncer's life. Laa was mistakenly killed by the Jedi Petja, acting on orders from Lord Valenthyne Farfalla to eliminate Bouncers driven insane by the thought bomb. Laa's death was the tipping point for young Zannah, who lashed out at Petja with the Force on her first step to the dark side.

Laa, an old wise Bouncer

< Lightsabers clash in a duel of titans: Darth Vader (Anakin Skywalker) against Obi-Wan Kenobi.

**laa** One of the many species of scalefish that swam the Naboo oceans. Distinguished by its long snout and broad tail, the green-scaled laa had a long, thin dorsal fin that was tipped by a bioluminescent bulb to attract its favorite prey, the yobshrimp.

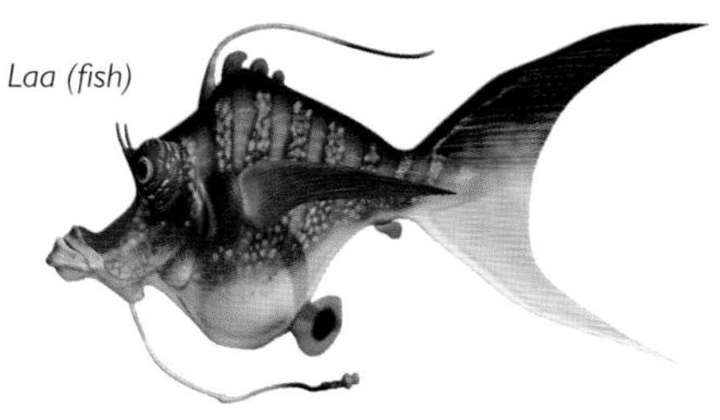

Laa (fish)

**Laabann, Count Arian** One of the leaders of the Priamsta during the time when Plourr Ilo tried to rebuild the monarchy on Eiattu. He was willing to kidnap or even kill Ilo in order to keep the Priamsta in his control, thereby maintaining the separation of commoners from royalty. Despite his efforts, Ilo was able to oust the Priamsta. A few years later, when Princess Leia Organa traveled to Eiattu for diplomatic negotiations, Laabann was arrested on charges of having Leia and Tycho Celchu kidnapped. In reality, Laabann had sold information about Leia's location to Moff Leonia Tavira. Soontir Fel interrogated Laabann, revealing that the Count still worked for the Empire.

Count Arian Laabann

**Laait** A Yuuzhan Vong commander, he was dispatched by Warmaster Nas Choka to report on the status of the fight to keep Coruscant in alien hands. It was Laait who had to explain to Shimrra that his plan to drive a starship infected with the Alpha Red virus onto Zonama Sekot had failed after a series of Jedi-piloted Sekotan starships defeated Nas Choka's vanguard ships.

**Laakteen Depot** The Rebel Alliance base closest to Fondor around the time of the Battle of Yavin. It took the Alliance almost a year to capture Laakteen Depot, which was subsequently wiped out by the Super Star Destroyer *Executor* during the ship's maiden voyage.

**LAAT/i, LAAT/c** *See* Republic attack gunship.

**Laboi II** A small planet orbiting the red giant Er'Dox Kaan, it was home to the carnivorous, aggressive Laboi species that hunted the bantha-sized ovolyan. The Laboi, who looked like fur-covered snakes, made up for their lack of arms and legs with a limited telekinetic ability that might have been linked to the Force.

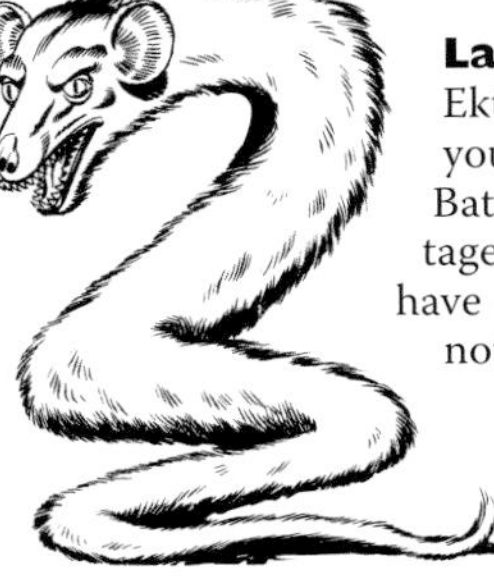

Laboi

**Labreezle, Claria** A native of Ektra City on Metellos, she was a young girl in the years before the Battle of Naboo. She was taken hostage by Dreed Pommel and might have died if Jedi Master Plo Koon had not intervened.

**Labria** *See* Kardue'sai'Malloc.

**Lachichuk** One of the many Wookiee warriors who defended Kashyyyk and the city of Kachirho during the Clone Wars. After Order 66, Lachichuk was among the Wookiees who met Olee Starstone and her group of Jedi survivors when they arrived on Kashyyyk.

**Lachton** A crew member of the smuggling vessel *Wild Karrde* during the early years of the New Republic. He often served as the ship's copilot and occasionally as a gunner.

**ladalum** A rare, red-flowered shrub that had been native to the planet Alderaan.

**Lado, Slaag** A Draag terrorist who lived in the industrial district of Coruscant in the years after the Battle of Naboo, he was wanted by the Mon Calamari Civil Authority in connection with a seismic disaster that devastated the Salinrerian Sea. Jango Fett eventually captured Slaag.

**Lady Fate Casino** A gambling house located on Ord Mantell, near the Hotel Grand. Han Solo spent some time there after the Yuuzhan Vong attacked the planet.

Lady Luck

***Lady Luck*** Lando Calrissian's personal ship, the *Lady Luck* was a modified SoroSuub PLY 3000 pleasure yacht. Formerly owned by an Orthellin royal mistress, the ship was richly appointed. Lando rigged it with a straight-line, homing-beacon type of full-rig slave circuitry. It originally was designed to serve as a mobile base of operations for Calrissian, who often entertained his female friends on board. However, as Lando became increasingly active with the New Republic military, he made several modifications to give the *Lady Luck* more firepower and protection.

A Class 3 hyperdrive allowed the ship to swiftly move across the galaxy, and it could reach speeds of 820 kilometers per hour in atmosphere. Advanced sensor systems and communications transceivers gave Calrissian the ability to keep in touch with civilian and military contacts. Outwardly, the *Lady Luck* resembled a pleasure yacht—the only visible weaponry was a laser cannon mounted on the belly. However, retractable weapons systems allowed five more laser cannons and a turret-mounted ion cannon to be brought to bear during a fight. The most unusual element of the *Lady Luck*'s design was its observation deck. Lando allowed the deck to remain open to the surrounding environment, which gave him the ability to entertain his guests "outside." To protect the passengers while in space, he installed a heavy-duty force field to surround the deck.

***Lady of Mindor*** A commercial starship, it ferried passengers through Corporate Sector space. Han Solo and Fiolla of Lorrd once booked passage on the *Lady of Mindor* to travel from Bonadan to Ammuud in order to evade slavers and Espos.

**Lafoe, Garouf** A free trader who started his own business transporting ice from Ohann and Adriana for use as water on Tatooine. He made a good living until the Empire began cracking down on free trade and raised taxes and tariffs on imports.

**Lafrarian** A species native to Lafra, a planet near Corporate Sector space. These gray-skinned humanoids were descended from a species of avians and retained vestigial wing membranes under their arms. Lafrarians also had a facial structure that resembled a beak, and was made entirely of externalized cartilage. The renegade outlaw tech Doc was a Lafrarian.

**Lagard, Nap** The Neimoidian commander of the Trade Federation battleship *Acquisitor* prior to the Battle of Naboo.

**Lago, Ian** The son of Kun Lago, Prime Counselor to King Veruna of Naboo. Despite the protests of his father, Ian fell in love with young Amidala just before she became Queen. They became good friends, but Amidala's loyalties were to the people of Naboo. Distraught, Ian hired himself out to a starship captain and fled the planet.

**Lago, Prime Counselor Kun** The primary adviser to King Veruna of Naboo. It was Lago, along with Senator Palpatine, who encouraged Veruna to form offworld alliances. When word of Veruna's shady dealings began to leak, Lago publicly denounced Amidala, hoping to deflect attention from Veruna by blaming the young woman for the problems. When Kun learned that his son Ian was in love with Amidala, he disowned him. After Veruna abdicated and was replaced by Queen Amidala, Lago's political career was ruined and he was forced into poverty.

Lachichuk

Lafrarian

**Laguna Caves** Podracers who took part in the Boonta Eve Classic had to pass through this low-ceilinged sketto-infested cave in order to complete a lap in the Mos Espa Circuit racecourse. Rumors that a krayt dragon inhabited the caves gave the area a frightening reputation.

**Lah, Czulkang** An aged Yuuzhan Vong, father of Warmaster Tsavong Lah. After being succeeded by his son, Czulkang Lah became a well-known teacher of Yuuzhan Vong youths. A harsh master, Czulkang demanded only the best from his students. Many of his students bore Czulkang Lah pits–scars that served as badges of honor to symbolize survival of his strict instruction.

The elder warrior suffered acute inflammation of his joints and could move about only with the help of enhanced vonduun crab armor. When the Yuuzhan Vong began planning their assault on the galaxy, Czulkang Lah opposed his son's plans for conquest. However, he bore his son no ill will, and agreed to take command of Domain Hul's resources to lead an assault against Borleias following the Battle of Coruscant. While he was a cunning warrior in his time, Czulkang Lah was unable to anticipate the tactics used by Wedge Antilles at Borleias. This weakness caused him to lose much of his fleet before realizing that the *Lusankya* was going to ram his worldship. Czulkang Lah ordered the complete evacuation of the ship, but remained aboard as it exploded.

**Lah, Khalee** The son of Yuuzhan Vong Warmaster Tsavong Lah, he was taller than the average Yuuzhan Vong and was distinguished by the various spikes and horns that adorned his scarred body. He accompanied the priest Harrar in leading the effort to capture Jaina and Jacen Solo in order to sacrifice the twin Jedi to the Yuuzhan Vong gods. During the attempt to recover the *Trickster* at Hapes, Khalee Lah's forces proved no match for the Hapan fleet, and many Yuuzhan Vong ships were destroyed. It was believed that Khalee Lah surrendered himself to Harrar, requesting that his death be attributed to the battle and not his failure. Harrar agreed, providing Khalee Lah with a New Republic explosive with which to destroy his own ship.

**Lah, Liaan** One of a small group of Yuuzhan Vong warriors who supported Nei Rin's efforts to protect the remains of the Jedi academy on Ossus some 130 years after the Battle of Yavin.

Liaan Lah and Choka Skell were the first to apprehend Cade Skywalker and Shado Vao when the two Jedi stumbled upon the cavern where the Yuuzhan Vong had hidden artifacts they had recovered from the Jedi Temple. It had been Cade who originally led Rav's pirates to loot Ossus in the wake of the Sith attack there seven years earlier. Cade, however, had only told Rav about the chambers in order to survive. Masters Vao, Sazen, and K'Kruhk were then forced to hide inside the academy ruins with Liaan Lah when Sergeants Harkas and Trask arrived to investigate the appearance of the Jedi on Ossus. Liaan Lah chafed at not being able to take the fight to the Imperials, but kept quiet and waited for them to leave.

*Liaan Lah*

**Lah, Maal** A Yuuzhan Vong officer in command of the war fleet dispatched to Coruscant. A kin of Warmaster Tsavong Lah, Maal Lah was distinguished by features marked more by red and blue tattoos than by scars. Because of his success in the conquest of Coruscant, Maal Lah was promoted to the rank of Supreme Commander. He was then ordered to work with Thrackan Sal-Solo to bring the Peace Brigade fleet into the Yuuzhan Vong war machine. When the New Republic attacked Ylesia and captured both Sal-Solo and the renegade Senator Pwoe, Maal Lah kept his forces in reserve to launch a counterattack. The Republic's Twin Suns Squadron, led by Jagged Fel, destroyed a large part of Lah's ground forces in an effort to free the Republic's assault team. Maal Lah lost his leg when his ground forces were bombed.

*Tsavong Lah*

**Lah, Qau** A Yuuzhan Vong warrior who took the place of Shok Choka after Anakin Solo defeated Choka in combat aboard a space station orbiting Yag'Dhul. After accusing Nom Anor of cowardice for refusing a challenge posed by the Jedi, Anor took a blaster and shot Qau Lah in the back of his head, then killed his companions.

**Lah, Qurang** The Yuuzhan Vong crèche-brother of Warmaster Tsavong Lah, he was charged with carrying out the plans of Nom Anor in the wake of the Battle of Duro and the disaster on Yavin 4. Qurang Lah hated working with Anor, especially when the executor's plans began to unravel near Yag'Dhul. Qurang Lah thought that he could be rid of Anor once and for all upon his return to the warmaster, having witnessed the executor refuse a challenge from Anakin Solo. However, before he could report on that failure, Anor killed all the warriors who had been with him on Yag'Dhul, including Qurang Lah.

**Lah, Tsavong** The Yuuzhan Vong warmaster in command of the forces led by Shedao Shai. Because of his bravery in battle and his ability to lead others, Tsavong Lah had undergone the ritual of escalation countless times. His body, a mixture of true flesh and surgecoral implants, closely resembled that of the deity Yun-Yammka, the Yuuzhan Vong god of war. His body armor was actually grown from his flesh, with individual scales embedded in his skin. He embraced pain, believing that suffering honored his gods, who had created the universe by sacrificing parts of themselves.

During the attack on Duro, Tsavong Lah captured Leia Organa Solo and planned to make her his first Jedi sacrifice. However, Randa the Hutt sacrificed himself to help Leia escape, and Lah was nearly killed in battle with Leia and her son Jacen. Ultimately, the warmaster left Duro without a Jedi and without the wealth he had hoped to obtain from sacrificial refugees.

After Duro, Tsavong Lah claimed he would put an end to the hostilities and leave the Core Worlds alone if the New Republic agreed to turn over Jacen Solo to the Yuuzhan Vong. He replaced the foot he had lost in battle with Jacen, setting the stump with a biologically recreated vua'sa foot, further enhancing his stature among the Yuuzhan Vong. To ensure a victory at Coruscant and the capture of Jaina and Jacen Solo, Tsavong Lah later sacrificed his arm, but this time the implant did not take. Interpreting the failed implant as an ill omen, many among the Yuuzhan Vong power structure feared that Tsavong Lah's time as warmaster had come to an end, and even collaborator Viqi Shesh used the apparent failure of the graft to plant seeds of doubt and suspicion in the warmaster's mind.

Tsavong Lah began rooting out the priests who could be undermining his efforts, only to find that his real nemesis was Nom Anor. During the disastrous Battle of Ebaq, Tsavong Lah ordered an assault on the Jedi Knights on Ebaq 9. He nearly destroyed the Solo twins and many other Jedi, but Jaina was able to defeat him in combat. She stabbed Tsavong Lah in the throat with her lightsaber, killing one of the Yuuzhan Vong's most noted leaders and marking the beginning of the end of their invasion.

**Lah, Zhat** A Yuuzhan Vong warrior placed in command of a small fleet that defended the planet Fondor during the Yuuzhan Vong War. When he heard the request for support from forces in the Duro system, Zhat Lah took several ships there. Once he arrived, however, he realized that the New Republic had lured the warships to Duro to trap them there. Zhat Lah ordered a retreat and managed to escape. He reported his return to Warmaster Nas Choka, who did not execute him for leaving the battle. Zhat Lah was instead commended for saving the remainder of his fleet, which would be used in later battles.

**Lahag Erli** The natives of this planet attacked their neighbors in the Har system early in the history of the Old Republic. They occupied the Har worlds for many years before being repelled, leaving behind a legacy of exquisite buildings and monuments.

**Lahara sector** Located in the Outer Rim, it included the planet Agamar, home of famous Rebel Alliance pilot Keyan Farlander. The sector, which contained 245 settled worlds that mostly produced agricultural products, seceded from the Old Republic before the start of the Clone Wars.

**Lahsbee** A species native to the isolated Outer Rim world of Lahsbane. Lahsbees altered mass and shape during their life cycle. Youngsters resembled tiny felines covered in pink and blue fur and averaging less than a meter in height. They communicated in a series of chittering chirps and trills. Lahsbees disliked advanced technology and preferred a pastoral existence. At puberty, they became mindless and ferocious savages called Huhks. They tried to attack and kill everything in sight; only music could subdue them. To ensure that Lahsbane was a safe place for all to live, the Huhks lived in the cities of the planet, while the Lahsbees remained in the forests and plains.

*Lahsbees and a Huhk*

**Lahzar, King** A treacherous tyrant who was once an ally of the Jedi Knights. Shortly before the Battle of Ruusan, King Lahzar's true nature was revealed when he attacked Valenthyne Farfalla and his soldiers. Lahzar and his forces were soundly defeated, but they delayed Farfalla sufficiently to allow the Sith to begin their attacks on Ruusan.

*Evram Lajaie*

**Lai, Ros** The daughter of Zalem, a Nightsister-clan witch on Dathomir, she was ignored by her mother because she was ugly—actually a disguise to hide her true powers. She was hunchbacked, and many Nightsisters openly called her "the Rancor." Once she revealed her true beauty, the others tried to embrace her, but Lai wouldn't forgive them. She killed or injured several in battle. After Zalem's forces captured Jedi Quinlan Vos, Lai created a potion containing her blood to rid him of the artery worms that had been injected into his body. Using an illusion—that she had killed Vos—enabled her to get close enough to her mother to kill her. With Zalem gone, Lai succeeded her as head of the clan. After she was injured in Vos's successful destruction of the Infinity Gate, which could have destroyed Coruscant, Vos sensed the light side within Lai and brought her back with him to the Jedi Temple on the capital planet.

**laigrek** A predatory beast native to the planet Dantooine, it made its home in rocky outcroppings and various ruins that dotted the countryside.

**Lajaie, Evram** A popular Rebel Alliance leader, his expertise in space defense and orbital battle stations enabled him to quickly analyze the plans for the first Death Star. After careful analysis, Lajaie discovered a fatal flaw that made it possible for Luke Skywalker to destroy the battle station.

**Laka, Yuka** The Ithorian proprietor of a droid-repair shop in Anchorhead on the planet Tatooine 4,000 years before the Battle of Yavin. It was in Laka's shop that HK-47 was discovered after being abandoned by Darth Revan.

**Lake Country** This remote area of the planet Naboo was dominated by beautiful lakes and surrounded by mountains and valleys. Wide meadows of grass and wildflowers sat amid the waterfalls and lakes, and many of the planet's native shaaks made their homes here. It also was the location of the Varykino retreat—a magnificent island lodge getaway owned by the Naberrie family for many years. This was where Senator Padmé Amidala and Jedi Anakin Skywalker journeyed after two attempts on the Senator's life—and where they fell in love . . . and secretly married.

**Lake Marudi** Located on the Forest Moon of Endor, this lake was formed from two smaller bodies of water joined by a thin, water-filled ravine. The Ewoks strung a rope bridge across the strait to avoid traveling around the lake.

**Lake Natth** A body of water on Ambria named by Jedi Master Thon more than 4,000 years before the Galactic Civil War. It was a place where dark side forces congregated—driven and kept there by Master Thon. Creatures that lived in Lake Natth mutated into evil life-forms, such as the dragon-like hssiss.

**Lake Paonga** This deep lake on the edge of Naboo's Lianorm Swamp concealed the largest Gungan city, Otoh Gunga. Lake Paonga was connected to the planet's core through a series of treacherous underwater tunnels.

**Lake Spirit of Mimban** A shapeless, phosphorescent creature living in the subterranean waterways of Mimban (Circarpous V). It appeared to exhale air. When Luke Skywalker and Leia Organa encountered one below Mimban's surface shortly after the Battle of Yavin, it created a bubble trail while it swam away.

**Lake Sui** Located on the Forest Moon of Endor, this was the site of a stilt village erected by a group of Ewoks who chose not to live in the trees. Lake Sui was located just east of Bright Tree Village.

*The Varykino retreat in Naboo's Lake Country*

**Lake Umberbool** An underwater location on Naboo that served as the site of the annual Festival of Warriors. Shortly before the Battle of Naboo, the Gungans erected a new arena at the bottom of the lake.

**Lakky, Grodon** A brutal, sadistic man who was placed in command of the slave pool at the Maw Installation. Lakky was a fat, ugly human who derived great pleasure from breaking his slaves. He was killed at the Maw by Nawruun, who rose up against his master when Chewbacca and Han Solo fled the Installation during the New Republic's attempt to take control.

**Lalasha, Janet** A female musician killed by the Empire during its sweep to wipe out "questionable" artistic individuals.

**Lamar, Master Vrook** An ancient Jedi Master who served on the Jedi Council on Dantooine in the years leading up to the Great Sith War. He was well respected by his peers and his students, although many considered him a stern taskmaster. When Darth Malak attacked and destroyed the Jedi Enclave on Dantooine, Master Vrook went into hiding for many years, until he was captured by Azkul and his mercenaries. Vrook would have been transported to Nar Shaddaa for the bounty on his head if the Jedi Exile and her band hadn't intervened. Master Vrook was among the many Jedi who were killed when Darth Traya attacked and destroyed the Enclave 3,952 years before the Battle of Yavin.

*Master Vrook Lamar*

***Lambarian Crab*** A modified YT-2400 transport originally owned and operated by Matas Havel. It was purchased by Finious Crab, who named it and tore out what he considered redundant systems so he could upgrade the weapons aboard. En route to Eriadu, that upgrade took Crab's life when the ship's meager life support systems failed. The *Lambarian Crab* later was salvaged and used by arms smugglers.

***Lambda*-class shuttle** An Imperial cargo and passenger shuttle from Sienar

Fleet Systems, it featured three wings that made it resemble an inverted Y in flight. On landing, the two lower wings folded up to allow landing gear to deploy. A lower hatch in the *Lambda*-class shuttle operated as a ramp for loading and unloading cargo and up to 20 passengers and crew. The ships had hyperdrives, reinforced hulls, and multiple blaster and laser cannons. Imperial government officials favored Lambdas because of their combat-worthiness and interior space. Such ships were used by the Emperor himself. The Rebel Alliance employed a stolen shuttle, the *Tydirium,* to deliver a commando assault team to the Forest Moon of Endor.

Lambda-*class shuttle in a hangar on the Star Destroyer* Executor

**lambent** An unusual form of plant life bioengineered by the Yuuzhan Vong as a source of light-producing crystals. These crystals were used in a variety of ways, from personal light sources to the running lights of worldships. The lambent itself was formed from a base of green, knife-like leaves sprouting from the ground. Growing from the base were three or four stalks, atop which sat hairy, blood-red blooms. The flowers were the size of a human fist and protected the growing crystal. A Yuuzhan Vong would rub and stroke the petals of the flower until they opened, a process that attuned the alien to the flower. Anakin Solo discovered that the lambent crystal he used to replace the crystal in his lightsaber gave him a tenuous connection to the Yuuzhan Vong through the Force, but was unable to get more than a sense of presence.

*Lancer Battalion*

**lambro shark** A predatory fish known for its tasty flesh, it was considered a delicacy by many species. Jabba the Hutt was known to enjoy the dish.

**laminanium** The first truly regenerative, self-healing armor developed during the early decades of the New Republic. Initially used to protect the YVH 1 series of combat droids, laminanium was formed from metals found on the planet Brath Qella. It could absorb large amounts of incoming projectile or magma fire before restoring itself to its original protective level. The process required an auxiliary power pack in the droid's superstructure, as well as a laminanium ingot to feed the regeneration process.

**Lamproid** An intelligent species of hunters native to Florn. They had loosely hinged coral jaws, rings of fangs, light sensors on stalks, and bodies consisting of snake-like, muscular coils. These aggressive colonizers were found on many jungle and forest planets.

**Lamuir IV** One of only two worlds within the Tapani sector on which humans were not dominant. Herglics were the primary species, having settled the planet many thousands of years before humans discovered it. The normally sensible inhabitants became frivolous during the annual Priole Danna festival.

**Lan Barell** The fourth planet in the Lan system, this arid and desolate world was home to small insectoids called Qieg. Lan Barell's economy was based on sales of valuable ore to Mid Rim communities. The planet once had three moons, but one broke apart after massive strip-mining operations.

**Lancer Battalion** This division of the Grand Army of the Republic consisted of clone troopers who rode Aratech 105-K lancer bikes into battle, carrying power-lances to attack their targets.

***Lancer*-class frigate** A 250-meter-long Imperial capital combat starship, it was designed specifically to combat the threat of Rebel starfighters after the destruction of the first Death Star. But because they weren't cost-effective, the Empire built only a few *Lancer*-class frigates, and these were used mainly to attack Rebel starfighter bases. The frigates had 20 tower-mounted quad laser cannons but little defense against other combat starships except for their great speed. Five years after the death of Emperor Palpatine, Grand Admiral Thrawn used *Lancer*-class frigates as a major component of Imperial raiding missions, and they succeeded in knocking out many New Republic fighter squadrons.

*Lamproid*

**Landing, the** This was the only mining settlement to remain on Engebo V after the Outer Rim Oreworks facilities there were abandoned. It became the planet's most populous location and the site of its only active spaceport. A school of destructive skekfish once inadvertently was released into the Landing's environment, killing many before they could be contained. *See also* Bartyn's Landing.

**landing claw** Magnetic or mechanical grips on space vessels that were designed to adhere to nearly any surface for landing or docking.

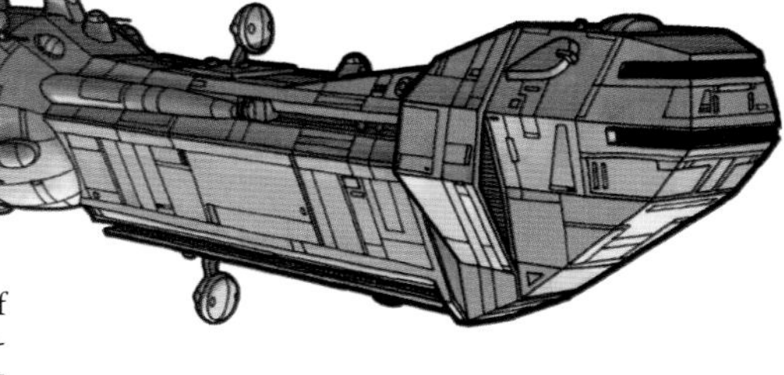

Lancer-*class frigate*

**Landing Platform 327** The designation of the Cloud City landing platform on which the *Millennium Falcon* was directed to land when Han Solo and Leia Organa escaped from Imperial forces in the wake of the Battle of Hoth.

**Landkiller One** The call sign used by Imperial trooper Davin Felth on his first AT-AT run.

**Landor system** A star system avoided by travelers in the last decades of the Galactic Republic due to pirate infestation.

**Lando's Commandos** The unofficial name of a group of mercenaries and soldiers assembled by Lando Calrissian to recapture Cloud City from the Empire shortly after the Battle of Endor. Calrissian later put together a second group with the same name to hunt down bandits terrorizing New Republic convoys.

*Lando's Folly*

**Lando's Folly** An asteroid system located near the planets Destrillion and Dubrillion. It was purchased by Lando Calrissian and used for mining as well as starship racing. The racecourse was actually a way for Lando to get to Kerane's Folly, the legendary platinum asteroid hidden in Hoth's asteroid belt.

**Lands, Roan** A native of Bellassa during the last years of the Old Republic. He grew up in the city of Ussa, a member of an extended family that was full of love and laughter. His parents remained in Ussa after he left home to pursue his own career. It's believed that Lands met Jedi Ferus Olin when Lands was an officer in the Grand Army of the Republic. The two became fast friends, and following the Clone Wars they returned to Bellassa to create the Olin/Lands Agency.

After the Empire took control of the planet, their work turned to protecting those who blew the whistle on corruption. Their experiences led them to form a resistance group, the Eleven, and begin speaking to Bellassans about refusing to submit to Imperial control, which earned them places on the Empire's wanted lists. When they eventually were cornered by stormtroopers, Olin escaped, but Roan was captured and interrogated.

He was later freed, but ill from the drugs administered in prison. Dr. Amie Antin, not knowing which drugs had been used, was unable to treat him. Obi-Wan Kenobi then infiltrated the Imperial garrison and found the information; Dr. Antin was able to restore Lands to health. Lands helped Olin establish a safeworld on a hidden asteroid for any surviving Jedi, but when he returned to Bellassa, he was arrested and scheduled for swift execution aboard the *True Justice*. His imprisonment was brief, as associates of Olin freed him, but Olin himself appeared to have become an agent for the Empire.

Olin had, in fact, become a double agent. He provided a way for three members of the Eleven to dig out information from an Imperial office on Bellassa, but they were intercepted by Darth Vader himself. Vader ignited his lightsaber and slashed Roan through the chest, killing him almost instantly.

**landspeeder** Any of a wide variety of small surface transports that used repulsorlift engines for hovering and propulsion. The repulsor field generated was enough to keep speeders suspended about a meter above the surface even when parked. Sometimes called floaters or skimmers, landspeeders were adapted for a wide variety of terrain, including sand, snow, and even water.

Traditional landspeeders such as the SoroSuub X-34—the model that Luke Skywalker first owned—had open cockpits with retractable duraplex windscreens.

**Lang, Adion** A childhood friend of Celia Durasha, his father was a strict taskmaster who demanded the best from all his children. After hearing Reise Durasha talk of the glory of the military, Adion left Lankashiir and attended the Imperial Academy at Raithal. He rose through the ranks to become an officer of the Imperial Security Bureau. Working with a small detachment, he uncovered the source of support for the Rebel Alliance in the Relgim sector and traced a supply of guns and weapons to Detien Kaileel. When he boarded the *Kuari Princess* in the hope of capturing Kaileel, he encountered his childhood love, Celia Durasha. Instead of recruiting her help, though, Lang incurred her wrath.

**Langhesi** Originally from Langhesa, these humanoids were enslaved by the Tsinimals about 100 years before the Battle of Naboo. The Tsinimals took their slaves all over the galaxy, leaving small pockets of Langhesi culture on many worlds. The Langhesi were known as farmers, and could mold the elements of life into previously unseen forms. This form of genetic manipulation was regarded as a sin against the Tsinimal gods, resulting in the conquest of Langhesa. Those Langhesi who inhabited the lowlands of Zonama Sekot were employed by the original Magister as the forgers and shapers of Sekotan technology, since their skills with organic materials complemented the patterns of growth observed among the boras, telepathic plant-domes resembling huge trees.

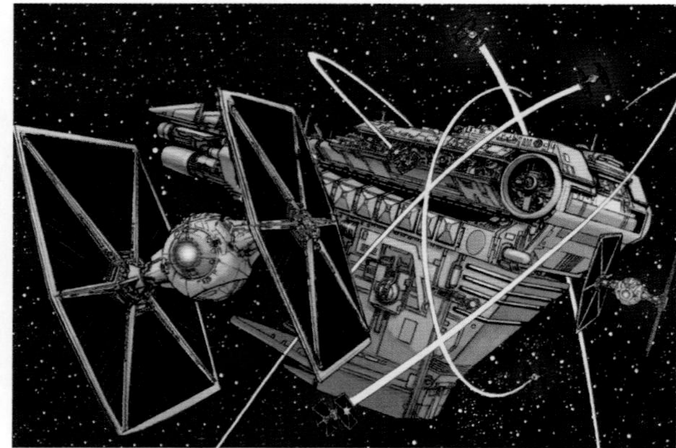

*The* Lark *before it was destroyed by Imperial forces*

***Language Guide to the Galaxy, A*** A helpful phrasebook and travel guide compiled, written, and revised by Ebenn Q3 Baobab. The guide offered handy phrase translations and tips on interacting with various alien cultures.

**Lanius** A member of the Cavrilhu pirates stationed at the Kauron asteroid base when Luke Skywalker infiltrated it in search of clones. Lanius was in charge of moving Wesselman's SB-20 droid—with Luke hidden inside—to Pap's electronics lab.

**lantern bird** A large flying creature with incandescent tail feathers, it lived in shimmering nests high in the trees of Endor's Forest Moon. A lantern bird's tail feathers were used by Ewoks for medicinal potions.

**Lantern of Sacred Light** One of many Ewok holy totems. The light from this lantern was believed to protect the Forest Moon of Endor from the Night Spirit and its worshippers.

*Landspeeder*

**Lanthrym** A planet in the Elrood sector, it was home to outlaw stations willing to service any ship, including those belonging to pirates and wanted criminals.

**Lao-Mon** The tropical homeworld of the shape-shifting Shi'ido species, it was known in their language as Sh'shuun.

**"Lapti Nek"** The song that Sy Snootles sang with the Max Rebo Band at Jabba's palace following the arrival of C-3PO and R2-D2. The words *lapti nek* were Huttese for "fancy man."

**Lar, Kira** A Rebel Alliance soldier during the Galactic Civil War, she seemed to always be in the midst of the action. Immediately after joining the Alliance, Kira—assigned to the ground crew at the Massassi Base on Yavin 4—was promoted to corporal at Echo Base just prior to the Battle of Hoth. Later she became a member of General Crix Madine's personal staff, and served on the team that planned the ground assault during the Battle of Endor.

**Larado, Incavi** A smuggler, guild representative, and later the mayor of the town Dying Slowly on the planet Jubilar, she was heavily involved in a number of illegal trade operations. It was Incavi Larado who alerted Boba

Fett that Han Solo had returned to Jubilar 15 years after the Battle of Hoth. When Fett arrived to kill Solo, one of his shots caught Larado, who died instantly.

**Laramus** Located in the Laramus system in the Parmic sector, it was the site of an ambush of a 14-ship Imperial convoy by a Rebel Alliance cruiser, several shuttles, and X-wing fighters. The Imperial ships were all captured without any Rebel losses.

*Beru (right) and Owen Lars with Luke Skywalker (middle)*

***Lark*** A frigate apprehended by the *Rand Ecliptic* just prior to the Battle of Yavin. Resembling a stubby version of the Nebulon-B frigate, the *Lark* was on a mission to deliver students to the Clarion Scholars Academy on Daemen when it was intercepted. When the ship's crew could not provide proper Imperial identification codes, the vessel was ordered to stand down and prepare for boarding. However, the TIE fighters sent to intercept it fired on its main reactor, setting off a chain reaction that ripped the *Lark* apart in a violent explosion. Among the pilots who fired on the *Lark* was Tars Nandy, who later was captured by Derek "Hobbie" Klivian during the mutiny he led aboard the *Rand Ecliptic.*

**Larker, Aaren** The Prime Minister of Samaria during the early months of the New Order, he conspired with Astri Oddo, who had adopted the alias of Quintus Farel, to develop a computer virus that would cripple the city of Sath. Larker hoped that the confusion would forestall the Imperial occupation of Samaria. When Imperial adviser Bog Divinian arrived to investigate, Larker was forced to give him full access to Sath. Double agent Ferus Olin accompanied Divinian in his inspection, and found the true cause of the virus before the Imperials did. Olin made sure that the Larker-and-Oddo plot succeeded, stalling Darth Vader long enough for Oddo and her son Lune to escape.

Larker took the brunt of public disapproval for the chaos in Sath, and many within the Hall of Ministers began to whisper of a vote of no confidence in his ability. His standing with the public further diminished with his support of a trade agreement with the Roshans, especially in the wake of a supposed Roshan attempt to assassinate Divinian. Unknown to Larker was the fact that Divinian had engineered the assassination attempt as part of a plan to discredit the Roshans and ensure that he was elected to replace Larker. Divinian's plans worked; Larker was voted out of office and promptly arrested and charged with conspiracy.

*Beru and Owen Lars with the baby Luke Skywalker*

***Larkhess*** A Rebel escort frigate under the command of Captain Afyon during the struggle against Grand Admiral Thrawn some five years after the Battle of Endor.

**Larm, Admiral** The main military aide to Moff Getelles of the Antemeridian sector, he was killed in a fierce battle above Nam Chorios.

**LaRone, Daric** One of the many Imperial stormtroopers stationed aboard the Star Destroyer *Reprisal* during the months following the Battle of Yavin. Over time, LaRone grew disillusioned with the Empire, especially after the subjugation of the civilian populations on Elriss, Bompreil, and Teardrop. Other members of his squad shared his sentiments, and they were accused by overzealous ISB agent Major Drelfin of treason. LaRone shot Drelfin dead before he could be arrested, and he and his fellow troopers fled the *Reprisal* aboard Drelfin's freighter, *Gillia.*

LaRone was voted the leader of the five-man squad of troopers, which they nicknamed the Hand of Judgment. They sought to uphold the Empire's basic tenets of peace and security, though they removed themselves from the chain of command. By sheer happenstance, the group was commandeered by Mara Jade—the Emperor's Hand—during her investigation of corruption in the Shelsha sector. Rather than reveal their true status, Jade explained to other Imperials that the Hand of Judgment was working for her. Their motives seemed to suit her, since she allowed them to disappear, giving them the chance to escape from Imperial service and set off on their own.

**Lars, Bail** An alias used by Anakin Solo when he infiltrated the shaper compound on Yavin 4 with Vua Rapuung.

**Lars, Beru and Owen** The guardians and foster parents of Luke Skywalker, they tried to raise this future Jedi Knight and Rebel Alliance hero as a normal youth—keeping from him the fact that his veins coursed with Jedi blood and that his "dead" father actually had transformed himself into the infamous Darth Vader.

Young Luke always called Beru and Owen Lars aunt and uncle, believing that they were his blood relatives. Their relationship to Luke, though, was through marriage. Owen Lars became stepbrother to Anakin Skywalker when his father, Cliegg Lars, married Anakin's mother, Shmi. After both Shmi and Cliegg died, Owen inherited the moisture farm. He married his girlfriend Beru Whitesun, who moved to the homestead.

Obi-Wan Kenobi turned to Owen and Beru just after Luke was born and asked that they raise the child on the desolate planet of Tatooine, far from Imperial intrigue. As a tribute to the beloved Shmi, Luke was given the surname Skywalker, although Owen would not tell him anything about Anakin Skywalker other than a story that he was a navigator on a spice freighter. Luke was raised to do chores on the Lars's moisture farm, and Owen continually tried to keep him on the farm even as young Skywalker dreamed of going to the Academy and then joining Rebel Alliance forces.

Beru and Owen taught Luke the value of hard work, loyalty, commitment, and compassion. They were killed by stormtroopers searching for the droid R2-D2, who had top-secret data about the Imperial Death Star battle station stored in his memory. The couple refused to answer any of the troopers' questions, and when Luke returned home with Ben Kenobi and found the charred bodies of his lifelong guardians, he was set on a new path and a course of action that would change galactic history.

*Cliegg Lars*

**Lars, Cliegg** A modest and benevolent moisture farmer, he lived near the Jundland Wastes on the desert planet of Tatooine raising his son Owen, whose mother, Aika, had died when he was young. On a trip to the spaceport of Mos Espa, Cliegg met and fell in love with the slave Shmi Skywalker. He purchased her freedom from the junk dealer Watto and soon made her his bride. However, her newfound liberty and happiness were not destined to last. Early one morning, Shmi was taken by a band of Tusken Raiders. In his continuing expeditions to hunt for his wife, Cliegg lost one of his legs and severely damaged the other.

Lasavvou

Unable to help Shmi, Cliegg was despondent for many weeks, until Anakin Skywalker arrived on Tatooine to search for his mother. Cliegg described the events that led to Shmi's capture, then allowed Owen to loan Anakin a swoop. Anakin returned with Shmi's lifeless body. She had died shortly after her son found her, and Anakin executed the entire Tusken clan. Cliegg buried Shmi in the family plot beside his parents. When Cliegg himself died years later, Owen buried him next to Shmi, but removed the headstones to ensure that no one would come looking for Shmi's body.

**Lars, Shmi Skywalker** *See* Skywalker, Shmi.

**Lasat** Native to Lasan, these humanoids had light fur covering their slender builds, big heads dominated by huge eyes, and large ears used to dissipate heat. Their muscular jaws and heavy teeth were testament to their canine ancestry.

**Lasavvou** An Ithorian starship owner whose vessel was impounded after landing on Nar Shaddaa following the Jedi Civil War. He enlisted the help of the Exile in selling some of his spare cryogenic power cells for enough credits to free his ship and leave the moon.

**Laseema** A Twi'lek, she worked for Qibbu the Hutt as a waitress and part-time kitchen helper at Qibbu's Hut during the Clone Wars. Although she was afraid of Qibbu, she found herself even more frightened of the clone commandos who took up residence. Kal Skirata had convinced Qibbu to let him use the restaurant and hotel as a base for an antiterrorist operation, and Laseema was in the kitchen when Ordo came in for a search. Despite her fears, Laseema came to trust Skirata and the commandos, who forced Qibbu to treat her with more respect. She took a liking to Atin especially, and they developed mutual affection. They remained in contact even after the mission to Coruscant, and many of Atin's comrades came to think of her as part of their family. Skirata went so far as to arrange for a safe residence for her, hoping to get her away from any possible trouble at Qibbu's.

**laser cannon** Versatile weapons that fired visible bolts of energy, they were essentially powerful blaster cannons used most often on starships. They could be mounted almost anywhere, provided that they could be powered separately from the ship's main power. Laser cannons were the most common starship and vehicle weapons in the galaxy.

**laser gate** A barrier of deadly, concentrated energy. Laser gates could be used to cordon off sections in high-security or potentially dangerous areas. The Theed power generator complex had an entire corridor—also referred to as the energy beam hallway—lined with laser gates. It used a series of gates to ensure that nothing disrupted the flow of plasma energy being tapped from the planet's core, and also protected any beings working in the generator facility. *See also* energy gate.

**laser shell** A form of laser-guided missile, often fired from backpack-mounted launchers. Jango Fett employed a laser shell launcher on one set of Mandalorian armor he used as a bounty hunter.

Lashowe

**laser sword** An archaic name for a lightsaber.

**Lashowe** One of the many ancient Sith apprentices who trained on Korriban during the era of the Great Sith War. It was Lashowe who found a Sith Holocron in the Valley of the Dark Lords, although she refused to admit that others had helped her find it. Lashowe was among the students who joined Kel Algwinn in an attempt to destroy the Jedi Knights who had infiltrated the Sith Academy and killed Master Uthar Wynn shortly after the Great Hunt. Like Algwinn, however, Lashowe was unprepared for combat, and was quickly killed by the Jedi.

**_Last Call_** A Geonosian fanblade starfighter provided to Asajj Ventress by Count Dooku during the Clone Wars. The *Ginivex*-class starfighter was one of several ships Dooku gave her after the previous vessels had either been lost or destroyed. It was equipped with the latest in Geonosian technology, and even had a prototype "gemcutter" sensor countermeasure that had been stolen from Carbanti United Electronics. Ventress lost the *Last Call* when its self-destruct system was detonated during her attempt to capture Jedi Master Yoda.

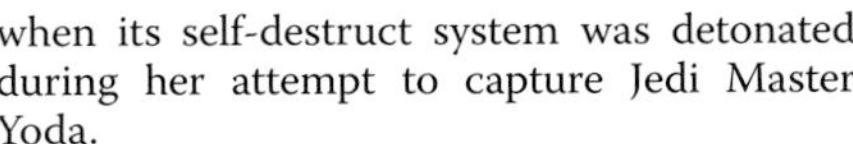

**_Last Hope_** This Rebel Alliance corvette was part of a small group sent to assist Rebels on Edan II during the Galactic Civil War. It was shot down while trying to enter orbit and crashed to the surface.

Laser cannon

**_Last Resort_** Part of Talon Karrde's small fleet during the early years of the New Republic. As Karrde reduced his involvement with the smuggling operation, he turned over command of the ship to Aves.

**Latara** A mischievous young female Ewok on the Forest Moon of Endor during the Galactic Civil War, she loved to play pranks as well as make music with her flute. Her best friend was Princess Kneesaa. Latara did everything she could to attract the attention of Teebo.

**Lathaam** A senior port official at Najiba's main spaceport. He was betrothed to the Twi'lek female Arruna until Adalric Brandl demanded passage offworld. Lathaam explained that no one left Najiba when it passed through the asteroid field known as the Children of Najiba. Brandl became angry and killed Arruna with the Force.

**Latham, Marsden** A member of the Alderaanian internal security force, he was on duty when a young Han Solo—working for Teroenza—tried to sell some stolen glitterstim in Aldera. Latham subtly told Solo to stop marketing the spice, all the while insinuating that Han was skirting a jail sentence.

**Lathe** A Kajain'sa'Nikto who once served Jabba the Hutt as a guard and information broker at the crime lord's town house on Tatooine. Lathe hated the slave trade, and longed to leave the planet to see what the rest of the galaxy had to offer.

**latheniol** A powerful drug that was used to euthanize terminally ill beings. It was rumored that latheniol was used to put down badly injured clone troopers from the Grand Army of the Republic rather than provide them with medical care.

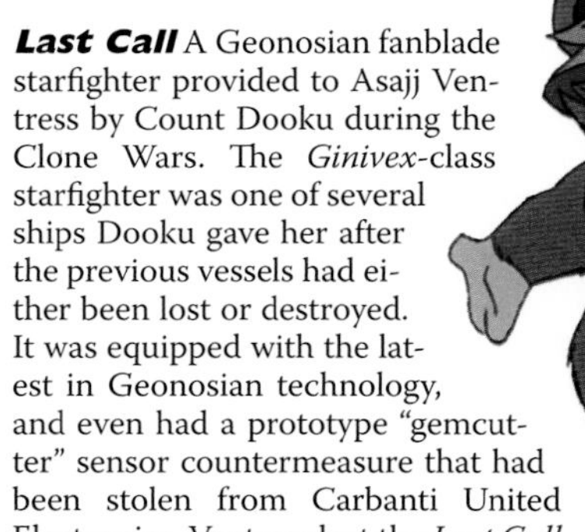

Latara

**Latt, Sharr** A member of Wraith Squadron during the Yuuzhan Vong War, he had the call sign Ten-B during the Borleias evacuation as a member of the Twin Suns Squadron. A native of Coruscant, Latt was assigned to assist in fostering the idea that Jaina Solo was the incarnate Trickster deity Yun-Harla, part of a psy-ops plan to unsettle the reverent Yuuzhan Vong.

**Laureate of the Empire** One of the few nonmilitary awards handed out by the Imperial government during the New Order. It was awarded to authors who published works of cultural and social importance.

**Lavin, Gana** This woman grew up in the lap of luxury in the Upper City of Taris more than 4,000 years before the Battle of Yavin. Many considered her a spoiled brat, and new acquaintances often found themselves being roughed up by the thugs who worked for her father.

**Lavint, Uran** A native of Bespin, she was a noted smuggler following the Yuuzhan Vong War. Though growing up in a relatively wealthy family, she never saw herself as the business type. She instead ran cargo aboard her vessel, *Breathe My Jets,* and sometimes took part in larger fleet operations. She endured her fair share of hardships, but persevered at each turn in the road.

Captain Lavint was one of the many smugglers who formed a network of informants working for Jacen Solo during Corellia's bid for independence. Jacen surprised her by taking possession of the *Breathe My Jets,* leaving her with enough credits to pay off her debts and purchase a stock YV-666 freighter known as the *Duracrud.* But Lavint's interactions with Solo angered him enough that he sabotaged the hyperdrive on the *Duracrud.* It failed on its first jump, leaving Lavint stranded in space. It was then that she realized Alema Rar had stowed away aboard the freighter. The Dark Jedi agreed to help Lavint repair the hyperdrive in exchange for assistance in tracking down Han and Leia Solo. Lavint agreed.

Their travels led them to the *Errant Venture,* where they discovered not only the Solos but also several other prominent members of the Galactic Alliance. Although the Solos escaped, Lavint found herself confronted by a surprised Jacen Solo, who offered her a job. He needed to find out what was happening within the Confederation, and hoped to infiltrate its next meeting disguised as a smuggler. Lavint demanded the *Breathe My Jets* returned as payment, but was given a Gallofree Yards transport instead.

**Lavisar** Once part of a much larger planetary body until a series of asteroid collisions broke the world apart, it was just outside the border of space occupied by Warlord Zsinj after the Battle of Endor. Many of the fragments were too small to become anything more than asteroids themselves, but the largest part remained fairly stable and eventually became the planet Lavisar, a manufacturing world known for mining and shipbuilding.

**lav peq (netting beetle)** A Yuuzhan Vong–bioengineered weapon used to catch prey. Netting beetles were employed aboard tsik vai to fire tentacle-like cables. The cables attached to flesh and drew their prey closer, though they weren't fatal. To escape the lav peq, Anakin Solo used phosphorous flares to burn the trees and bushes that the netting beetles clung to, but while the shrubbery burned, the web strands remained intact.

**Law of Life** This Ithorian tenet held that for every living plant destroyed during harvest, two more had to be planted in its place.

**Lazerian IV** In the Lazerian system, it was the site of the city of Lazeria and served as one endpoint of the Kira Run trade route. It was a temperate world with vast plains and home to a sentient species, the Akwin.

**LE-4DO** A droid constructed by Anakin Skywalker during his training at the Jedi Temple on Coruscant. Like many of the droids Anakin built during this time, it was cobbled together from parts he scavenged from the undercity of Coruscant, and was continually being tweaked and adjusted.

**LE914 (Ellie)** Tay Vanis's protocol droid. Ellie had been with Vanis since his earliest days as a Rebel on the planet Telfrey. Vanis acquired vital information from Bothan spies and entrusted it to Ellie, hiding the datatapes in a storage container in Ellie's chest. When Vanis crash-landed on an unidentified jungle world and was captured by Darth Vader, he ordered Ellie to destroy the tapes if help didn't come within two days. It would be months before the Rebellion found Vanis. Ellie overrode Vanis's orders and kept the tapes, however, secretly infiltrating the Imperial installation on the planet. When Luke Skywalker, Princess Leia Organa, and C-3PO found the installation, Ellie led them to the broken form of Vanis, long stripped of his humanity by Vader's torture and humiliation. Ellie handed the tapes over to C-3PO and overloaded her power plant. She destroyed herself and Vanis to end the pain of his torture and allow him to die a hero. The explosion also destroyed the installation and killed all those who had held Vanis captive.

LE914 (Ellie)

LE-BO2D9 (Leebo)

**leafship** A small speeder-like vehicle built by Ithorians. Its body was formed from natural glue, which was produced from the roots of the giant lilies that grew on the planet.

**Leafy Green** A tapcaf in Jo'Ko's Alley on Coruscant, it was where Anakin Solo and Mara Jade Skywalker tracked down a Yuuzhan Vong infiltrator wearing a gablith masquer. The alien put up a stiff fight, but the two Jedi were able to disable her. The captive then extended a claw from her knuckles and slashed her own throat.

**Lebauer, Lorimar** Founder of the underworld Invisible Shell organization, this Jenet was arrested by Thyferran authorities during the early years of the New Republic for running a counterfeit bacta operation. Thousands died because the bacta treatments they received were placebos, and Lorimar Lebauer was convicted of fraud. His own nephew, Ludlo Lebauer, supplied information on the operation to the Thyferrans, in the hope of taking over Invisible Shell. Leia Organa Solo, during her negotiation with Ludlo for rare works of art, offered to commute his uncle's sentence in exchange for the masterpieces. However, Lorimar would not be released until Leia returned to Coruscant with the artwork.

**Lebauer, Ludlo** Owner of the Pearl Island Casino on Pavo Prime during the early years of the New Republic, this hulking Jenet loved rare and unusual art. Shortly after the Battle of Endor, he began negotiating with the New Republic for a salvage contract, pitting himself against Invisible Shell—an underworld organization run by his powerful uncle Lorimar Lebauer. The Republic refused Ludlo's entreaties for exclusive salvage rights, so Ludo tried to get them by offering Leia Organa Solo rare Alderaanian art in exchange. Leia refused, but after she learned of Ludlo's plot to take control of Invisible Shell, she offered to commute Lorimar's prison sentence for fraud in exchange for the masterpieces. Ludlo didn't want to expose his own plans, so he agreed, but then he tried to have Leia and Han Solo killed before they could leave the planet. His plan backfired, and he had to go through with the deal after Leia threatened to expose his treachery to his uncle.

**LE-BO2D9** The droid copilot of Corellian smuggler Dash Rendar, his nickname was Leebo. LE-BO2D9 was a stripped-down skeletal model that usually carried a tool bag slung over one shoulder. The LE series of repair droids was an attempt to combine the personality of a protocol unit with the utility of an astromech.

**Lecersen** One of the many members of the Imperial Moff Council during the years following the Yuuzhan Vong War. Lecersen was known as a man who put duty before personal gain, one of the "old-school" Moffs who supported Supreme Commander Gilad Pellaeon. He became de facto leader of the Moff Council after barely surviving a Mandalorian attack at the Nickel One asteroid. Following the assassination of Supreme Commander Gilad Pellaeon and the killing of Darth Caedus—the former Jacen Solo—Luke Skywalker made the remaining members of the council an offer: Either surrender to the Hapans and face a war crimes trial or join the Jedi coalition to reestablish the Galactic Alliance—but under the leadership of Jagged Fel. Lecersen was forced to agree that life under Fel's command would be better than a death sentence from the Hapans.

**Ledwellow, Senator Danry** An Er'Kit Senator who was implicated in an Outer Rim slavery scandal during the final years of the Galactic Republic, he was suspended from duty pending an investigation.

**Leed** The firstborn son of King Frane and the heir to the throne of Rutan in the years before the Battle of Naboo. He had spent most of his life on the moon Senali in accordance with tradition, but refused to return to Rutan on his 16th birthday. Frane could not believe that Leed had made this decision on his own, and he accused Meenon, the king of Senali, of forcing the boy to stay. However, the Jedi Knights Qui-Gon Jinn and Obi-Wan Kenobi learned that Leed had felt out of place on Rutan all his life, and genuinely wanted to remain on the moon. Leed even offered his position as heir to his brother, Taroon.

Leed didn't know that Taroon had been planning to unseat him all along, and that his plans were too far along to stop. When a group of disguised Rutanians captured Leed, Taroon said he'd be willing to head the monarchy, but King Frane declined. The two Jedi eventually rescued Leed and brought both brothers to Rutan, where they explained themselves to their father. Frane realized that Leed truly enjoyed the company of the Senali, and that Taroon was not merely a "second son." He allowed Leed to return to Senali as the first official ambassador for both worlds.

**Leeda, Sobo** A male Aqualish who was a pirate of some renown during the years leading up to the Battle of Naboo. The bounty on his head was claimed by Jango Fett.

**Leeds, Ocandra** The unofficial leader of a group of more than 500 workers who protested the Military Creation Act, claiming that tax credits collected on Chandrila would be sent to the Republic for the army, rather than staying on Chandrila to pay for civil services and local security.

Leektar

**Leektar** The younger brother of the Ewok Keoulkeech. He grew up alongside his brother in the Red Bush Grove on the Forest Moon of Endor. However, Leektar lacked Keoulkeech's ability to interact with the natural world. When a lightning-sparked forest fire destroyed the village of Red Bush Grove, only Leektar survived. He felt guilty, believing it was his selfish prayers that had somehow brought about the disaster. Leektar set out into the forest, where he encountered a scouting party from another Ewok tribe being harassed by Imperial stormtroopers. His timely intervention saved the scouts, who brought Leektar back to their home of Bright Tree Village. There he became one of Chief Chirpa's advisers, and was given the title of Honorary Elder for his bravery.

**Leelu** Vor Childermoss's huge, mute bodyguard, he was a hulking humanoid of unknown origins.

**Leem, Maks** One of the many Jedi Masters who remained on Coruscant during the Clone Wars, teaching the students who were too young to participate in the fighting. A Gran, she fought in the Battle of Geonosis and regretted the slaughter that accompanied the so-called Republic victory. She feared that the younger generation of Jedi students and Padawans would emerge into the galaxy having known only combat and violence. She spoke to Master Yoda about moving the Jedi Temple away from Coruscant to escape the clouding of the Force being experienced by Jedi Knights of the era.

Upon her return to Coruscant from Geonosis, Master Leem took Whie Malreaux as her Padawan. Years later, they were dispatched—along with Yoda, Jai Maruk, and Tallisibeth Enwandung-Esterhazy—on a mission to meet with Count Dooku on Vjun. It was on Phindar that the Jedi were caught by Asajj Ventress and a squad of assassin droids. Master Leem then realized that her aversion to the war had led her away from combat training, and that her skills as a fighter were rusty. Although she managed to destroy several droids, Master Leem took a spray of flechette razors in the leg, dropping her to the ground. She managed to take out a couple more of the assassin droids before being faced with Ventress herself. The Dark Jedi was able to slice a gaping wound across Leem's stomach before Maruk could reach her side. As she lay dying, she tried to keep Maruk from joining the fight, knowing that Ventress would kill him, too. Maruk failed to see her silent plea, and he, too, died at the hand of Ventress.

**Leeni** A female Ewok, she was a baby, or Wokling, around the time of the Battle of Endor.

**Leffingite** A species native to Almak. Leffingites were short beings distinguished by their ovine faces. A group of short horns sprouted from their foreheads, and their large ears stuck out from their skulls.

**Lefrani** A gas giant, this was the third and outermost planet of the Mustafar system.

***Legacy of Torment*** Yuuzhan Vong warrior Shedao Shai's personal command ship, it was an example of an especially powerful and old Yuuzhan Vong Kor Chokk grand cruiser, as big as a Super Star Destroyer. After Shedao Shai's death in his duel with Jedi Knight Corran Horn, Yuuzhan Vong warrior Deign Lian seized command of *Legacy of Torment* and used it to deliver lethal bioweapons that destroyed the jungles of Ithor.

**Legions of Lettow** This ancient army of former Jedi Knights tried to carve out an empire for itself during the earliest recorded history of the Old Republic. The Legions of Lettow were formed by General Xendor, whose supporters included natives of the planet Tython who could control the Bogan—what later would be known as the dark side of the Force. The Legions of Lettow were formed after the Force Wars and the First Great Schism, when Xendor rebelled against the strictures of the ancient Jedi Order. In one of their first major confrontations, the Jedi Knights were able to defeat the army and restore peace to the galaxy.

**Legorburu, Ixidro** A M'haeli intelligence officer for the New Republic, she served as Pakkpekatt's tactical aide aboard the *Glorious*. She later became director of the Home Fleet's Battle Assessment Division.

**Leh, Fa'ale** A Lethan Twi'lek hired by Raith Sienar to deliver the prototype Sith Infiltrator to Darth Maul before the Battle of Naboo. Sienar offered to pay her to transport his secret prototype craft to its unseen buyer. She took the job even though she knew it would make her expendable. She managed to elude Sienar and spent years wandering from planet to planet in the Outer Rim. She was finally located on Naos III by Obi-Wan Kenobi and Anakin Sky-

Legacy of Torment

walker, but almost immediately a group of assassins and mercenaries attacked them all. Fa'ale was tired of running and wanted to surrender to the inevitable. As they fled, she told the Jedi that she had, in fact, delivered the Infiltrator to a place on Coruscant called The Works.

Lehesu

**Lehesu** A curious and imaginative Oswaft who freely chose to swim out of the StarCave in an effort to discover what lay in the Open Sea of space beyond. Because of his impetuousness, Lehesu nearly died of starvation, for the Open Sea lacked the sort of materials that his people consumed in the StarCave. Luckily for Lehesu, he encountered the *Millennium Falcon* in the deep-space void. He managed to communicate his need for sustenance to Vuffi Raa, who was able to fine-tune the ship's equipment to communicate with the Oswaft. By expelling much of what Lando Calrissian considered refuse, Vuffi Raa provided Lehesu with food.

The droid and Calrissian established a friendship with Lehesu who, at nearly 500 meters long, was considered very small for his species. Lehesu was able to convince Calrissian to travel to the StarCave and help his people survive an Imperial Navy blockade. Calrissian brought the various nutrients needed by the Oswaft, in the forms of ordinary human garbage and refuse, and ejected these into the StarCave.

Lehesu's trip to the Open Sea also brought trouble, however, for he unwittingly provided Rokur Gepta with the StarCave's location. During the defense of the ThonBoka, Lehesu suddenly fled the area, having heard that Gepta had dispatched a courier to execute the families of any officer who countermanded his orders. Lehesu caught up to the courier and destroyed it, thereby cutting off Gepta's fleet from the rest of the Empire and ensuring that the ThonBoka would remain isolated and free. Upon his return, Lehesu was offered the opportunity to join the Elders in leading the Oswaft, but he turned them down. He didn't want to give or receive any orders, he said. He simply wanted his people to be free to make their own choices.

**Lehon** *See* Unknown World.

**Leids, Nabrun** A Morseerian smuggler and pilot for hire, he was forced to wear a breath mask in nonmethane environments. A former fighter pilot, he was happy to transport anyone anywhere for the right price in his *Scarlet Vertha,* a Ghtroc Industries class 720 freighter.

**Leiger, Vin** A false identity used by Gavin Darklighter on Coruscant during Rogue Squadron's undercover operation there. Leiger was supposedly a young man from a Rim world who had gotten into trouble at home. He claimed he spent his life wandering the galaxy as a con man, barely scraping by with the help of his partner, a surly Shistavanen.

**Lekauf, Jori** The grandson of Lieutenant Erv Lekauf, he was a member of the 967th Commando unit of the Galactic Alliance Defense Force after the Yuuzhan Vong War. Corporal Lekauf was known for his optimism. He made it a point to commend Jacen Solo's choice to lead from the front lines rather than commanding from a bunker, since he had often heard his grandfather speak of a similar choice made by Darth Vader. However, he rarely made mention of his parents.

Lekku

Distinguished by his loyalty to the GAG, Lekauf never appeared quite menacing enough to wear the uniform, as his boyish, freckle-covered face clashed with its severity. This didn't stop him from trying to live up to the memory of his grandfather, who had served loyally under Vader decades before. Lekauf did not remember Vader as a monster, but as a respected leader who took care of his troops, as evidenced by the stories his grandfather told him. His loyalty was strengthened when Solo confronted Tav Vello and Biris Te Gaf about the problems the military was experiencing with poor-quality supplies. Solo invoked the Emergency Measures Act and had Te Gaf assigned to a front-line warship to determine a solution.

Lekauf was soon promoted to lieutenant, just before being assigned to protect Ben Skywalker on a mission to Vulpter. Skywalker's goal was the assassination of Corellian Prime Minister Dur Gejjen, and Lekauf and Lon Shevu were assigned to make sure the mission was completed successfully. Although Skywalker did the deed, the trio were caught in the crowd when spaceport officials shut down all portals in an attempt to identify the shooter.

Rather than allow the others to be captured, Lekauf had been ordered to take a hostage and try to board their starship, claiming that he was the shooter, a Corellian expatriate who demanded more from his government. Much to Ben's dismay, Jori carried out his orders to the letter. After reaching the ship, Jori let the hostage go and sealed himself inside. Without even trying to escape, he set off a massive bomb, destroying the ship and leaving behind very little in the way of physical evidence.

Nabrun Leids

**Lekauf, Lieutenant Erv** An Imperial military officer during the early years of the New Order, he was chosen by Emperor Palpatine himself to serve as one half of the genetic material to be used in a grand plot to create clone troopers who could tap into the dark side of the Force. The other half of the genetic material came from Dark Jedi Sa Cuis. Palpatine planned to pit the Lekauf clones, without any Force sensitivity, against the Force-sensitive Cuis clones, to show Darth Vader that the Force was no match for the loyalty of well-trained soldiers. He found himself initially fearing Lord Vader's disapproval, especially when his clones were regularly defeated by the Dark Jedi clones. However, Vader cultivated his relationship with Lekauf and worked diligently to earn Lekauf's loyalty, rather than demanding it.

**Lekket** This Quarren and her egg-mate, Tallet, were natives of Heurkea city on Mon Calamari. A business partnership with Senator Tikkes exposed some of their illicit dealings with the Hutts. The Senator, panicked at having his own name smeared because of his association with them, exposed the pair as criminals and had Old Republic authorities shut down their operation. Lekket and Tallet escaped and were forced to eke out an existence on Talas. They later hired Aurra Sing to hunt down and kill Tikkes to avenge their downfall.

**lekku** The highly sensitive dual head-tails of the Twi'lek, they were used to send messages, as well as serving sensual and cognitive functions. They were also called tchin-tchun, *tchin* referring to the right tail and *tchun* to the left one.

**Lelila** An alias used by Princess Leia Organa. Lelila was a childhood nickname. Leia used this alias whenever she traveled on the *Alderaan.* While trying to track down Lord Hethrir and her kidnapped children, Leia propagated the story that Lelila was a bounty hunter.

**Lelmra** A planet that served as a temporary base for Senator Garm Bel Iblis's private army. While they were on Lelmra, a violent thunderstorm triggered a "flip-flop" of several buildings made of memory plastic, folding them up with nearly 50 people still inside. The smuggler Mazzic had a backup base for his organization on Lelmra.

**Lemelisk, Bevel** A paunchy human, he was one of the main designers and chief engineer of the Imperial battle stations known as Death Stars. But the absentminded scientist with spiky white hair wasn't a perfectionist, and his work showed it. Bevel Lemelisk's design flaw on the first Death Star—an unshielded thermal exhaust port—led to its destruction by a well-placed proton torpedo fired by Luke Skywalker. As a result, Emperor Palpatine subjected Lemelisk to a particularly unpleasant execution: death by piranha-beetle. But the Emperor had arranged to transfer Lemelisk's mind and memories to a clone. Once was not enough for the mistake-prone engineer: The Emperor executed Lemelisk six more times in painful but creative fashions, each time transferring his memories and knowledge to a clone.

Bevel Lemelisk

Later, Lemelisk went to work for criminal kingpin Durga the Hutt, who called him "my pet scientist." But the quality of his work was again put to the test, first with the destruction of two expensive ships that were supposed to mine the Hoth asteroid belt. Durga's grand plan, the Darksaber Project, was to have Lemelisk design and build a modified Death Star that he could use to terrorize the entire galaxy. Using original plans stolen from governmental archives, Lemelisk oversaw construction of the superweapon, but it proved to be a complete dud thanks to shoddy construction, and it was crushed by asteroids. Lemelisk managed to beat a hasty retreat, but he was picked up by the New Republic and held for trial on Coruscant. When he was finally sentenced to death, he remarked, "At least make sure you do it right this time."

Lemo

**Lemo** One of the leaders of a smuggling gang that operated on Arcan IV during the Galactic Civil War. He and his partner Sanda hoped to steal the Dancing Goddess and the Minstrel to help fund their operations. After a brief struggle with Lando Calrissian and Barpotomous Drebble, Lemo found himself in possession of the Minstrel. Lemo had used it as the basis for his organization's funding, but he landed in prison and couldn't control things from there. When Han Solo questioned Lemo about it, Lemo agreed to turn the statue over in return for his freedom and a wealth of credits.

**Lena (1)** An alias used by Leia Organa while she was on Elerion, searching for Nescan Tal'yo shortly after the Battle of Yavin.

**Lena (2)** A young Twi'lek female who lived in the Lower City of Taris some 4,000 years before the Battle of Yavin. She spent much of her time with her boyfriend Griff, who was trying to survive with his sister Mission Vao. He borrowed a large sum of credits from Lena to pay for a series of get-rich-quick schemes, none of which ever panned out. Lena finally left him.

**Lennox, Captain Xamuel** An Imperial officer in command of the Star Destroyer *Tyrant* during the Battle of Hoth. The scion of several generations of military officers, Captain Lennox hated the political maneuvering that accompanied most promotions in the Imperial armed forces. But once he realized that his ideals would prevent him from rising through the military command structure, he became adept at manipulating situations to his advantage. In the wake of the Empire's defeat, Lennox and his ship were captured by the New Republic. Lennox was imprisoned, and the *Tyrant* was renamed the *Rebel Dream.*

Captain Xamuel Lennox

**Lenoan, Risi** A Senator from Kuat before the Clone Wars, she personally turned over the first *Aethersprite*-class interceptor to Adi Gallia and the Jedi Knights. However, she was removed from office after several clerical and bookkeeping errors indicated that she had been receiving funding from Kuat Drive Yards, although it was not obvious if she was receiving the funds illegally. Onara Kuat personally chose Lenoan's replacement, Giddean Danu.

**Lenovar** It was believed that this man once assaulted Sintas Vel, prompting Boba Fett to attempt to locate him, while Vel tried to talk him out of it. Fett later revealed to Vel that Lenovar had been a Journeyman Protector on Concord Dawn, and had been Fett's commanding officer at the time of the attack. Fett felt betrayed by Lenovar's actions, which he deemed to have been a betrayal of his uniform. Fett ultimately killed Lenovar to avenge his ex-wife.

**Lens** An alias used by a spy who had infiltrated the Old Republic's bota-processing operations on Drongar during the Clone Wars. Lens was the alias he used when working with the Black Sun organization, which paid part of his salary. The other part was paid by Count Dooku and the Confederacy of Independent Systems. To the Separatists, he was known simply as Column.

**Lensi** A Duro pilot in the New Republic's Rogue Squadron, he flew as Jaina Solo's wingmate, Rogue Twelve, in an attack on a Yuuzhan Vong shipwomb that was growing in the Sernpidal system. He resigned his commission after feeling betrayed by General Wedge Antilles, but when Antilles returned to Corellia, Lensi rejoined the squadron and eventually became its leader. During Jacen Solo's attempt to capture Centerpoint Station, Lensi was shot down and killed in the fighting—ironically by Antilles, who was flying as Rakehell Leader on a mission for the Jedi Order.

**Lenso, Tenk** A Rebel Alliance starfighter pilot who participated in the Battle of Hoth as Rogue Eleven.

**Lenz** Once a prisoner of the Absolutes on his homeworld of New Apsolon, he was part of a covert group of Workers that plotted to assassinate planetary ruler Roan some nine years before the Battle of Naboo.

**Leobund XI, Bodé** The High Lord of House Mecetti in the Tapani sector some 21 years before the Battle of Yavin. After his father was poisoned, Leobund made sweeping changes, and House Mecetti soon regained its position as the strongest of the Tapani Houses. Only the fear of Imperial reprisal kept him from taking further action to reduce his rival Houses.

**Leong** A member of the Rebel Alliance's Special Forces operation, he was killed during an attempt to capture four Imperial agents on Bevell III. Leong had been a trusted member of Jai Raventhorn's Infiltrator team, and his death shook her resolve badly.

**Leonie** A Zeltron queen around the time of the Battle of Endor. She and her husband, King Arno, held a huge gala for the victorious Rebel Alliance, but the party was stormed by a gang of Nagai.

**Lepi** The Basic name used to describe the *Lepus carnivorus,* a species of tall, furred lagomorphs native to Coachelle Prime in the Mid Rim. The Lepi were carnivores distinguished by their large incisors and fur that ranged from green to

Lepi

dark blue. Despite their rabbit-like appearance, the Lepi were a technologically advanced species, having colonized the five planets in their system and the neighboring asteroid belt. Lepi were considered sexually mature at just 10 years old, and females often gave birth to litters of 36 or more offspring, resulting in swift population growth. This spurred development of space-travel technology, with colony worlds seen as the answer to overpopulation. Some Lepi displayed increased metabolism, a trait that often manifested itself as hyperactivity.

*Leska*

**Lepido Program** A regular military encryption code used by the Empire. Ghent was able to crack it during his tenure with Talon Karrde.

**lepusa** A smart, meter-tall rodent native to Freliq.

**Leresai** A species that joined the New Republic. The Leresai attacked Bothawui after the revelations of the Caamas Document, claiming that the Bothans were responsible for the deaths of two Leresai during riots on Bothawui. They demanded either the guilty parties or the deaths of 10 Bothans for each Leresai, in accordance with Leresan law. Rogue Squadron tried to intervene, but its ships had been sabotaged by Leresan maintenance workers on Di'tai'ni. The Leresai attacked a zero-g crystal manufacturing plant in orbit around Bothawui, claiming the lives demanded by their law.

**Leria Kerlsil** A clean and pleasant world, it was considered a backwater. The streets of its capital were lined with blue and purple trees. Leria Kerlsil was home to life-witches or life-bearers, beings who could sustain another in perfect health for years but eventually withdrew Support, causing that person to die. Karia Ver Seryan, a wealthy woman who lived in a large and well-defended mansion, was one of Lando Calrissian's marriage candidates until he discovered she was a life-witch.

*Umak Leth*

**lesai** A very addictive, illegal drug produced in the Zebitrope system, lesai was created from the purple mold that grew on the back of a certain species of lizards. The drug could eliminate the need for sleep in humans, but didn't adversely affect the human brain. However, lesai addicts became very mechanical and amoral.

**Lesh** A native of Haruun Kal, he and his younger brother Besh joined the Upland Liberation Front during the Clone Wars in an effort to free their people from the control of the Balawai. Lesh was bitten by fever wasps and died when their larvae destroyed his brain. In order to ensure that none of the larvae survived to maturity, Jedi Master Mace Windu, who had been traveling with the guerrillas to find Depa Billaba, used his lightsaber to destroy Lesh's brain and kill the wasps.

**Lesim, Major** An Imperial officer stationed on Endor's Forest Moon as part of the garrison guarding the second Death Star's shield generators. He was on duty when a pair of stormtroopers brought in Luke Skywalker, who had seemingly surrendered.

**Leska** A Jedi Master and general in the Clone Wars, she was part of a task force dispatched to Jabiim to liberate the planet from Separatist control. After the death of Master Norcuna and the disappearance of Obi-Wan Kenobi, Leska found herself the highest-ranking Jedi—and, therefore, the highest ranking military officer—among the Republic's forces. Master Leska and her clone troopers managed to survive much of the battle, but she eventually was shot and killed by enemy fire on the 37th day of the campaign.

*Zhar Lestin*

**Lesser Plooriod Cluster** Made up of 12 star systems, it included the Ottega system, site of the planet Ithor. After leaving the Corporate Sector, Han Solo and Chewbacca ran an unsuccessful military-scrip exchange scam in the Lesser Plooriod Cluster. Following the Battle of Yavin, an Alliance ship dropped a badly needed grain container in the cluster in an attempt to escape an Imperial attack.

**Lessev, Kerri** The daughter of Alderaanian diplomats, she grew up on Coruscant. When her parents were rounded up and executed on trumped-up charges of treason against the Empire, she was "adopted" by Emperor Palpatine, along with the children of other parents who were killed. Lessev was later recruited into the Imperial Intelligence Destabilization branch, and she became one of Palpatine's most trusted agents. After viewing some Rebel Alliance propaganda, however, she realized that her parents' disappearance was more than likely the result of Imperial paranoia, and decided to help the Alliance from inside the Empire.

**Lessor, Jakohaul** A maintenance technician at the Chancellor Palpatine Surgical Reconstruction Center during the final years of the Old Republic.

**Lestin, Zhar** An ancient Twi'lek Jedi Master in charge of training new students at the Jedi enclave on Dantooine during the decades following the Great Sith War. When the former Jedi Revan was captured, Master Lestin and Master Dorak were charged with returning him to the light side of the Force. Using their skills, the Jedi wiped out Revan's knowledge of his past and replaced it with a new identity. Master Lestin was part of the Jedi Convocation on Katarr several years later, and was killed when Darth Nihilus and the forces of the Sith attacked the planet and laid waste to its surface.

**Letaki** A species with eight tentacles, an egg-like head, and air gills beneath four eyes. Evar Orbus was a Letaki.

**Leth, Umak** An Imperial engineer, he created many destructive tools and weapons, including the Leth universal energy cage and the World Devastators, huge regenerating war machines that stripped planets of their resources. Umak also designed the Galaxy Gun; he was aboard when the *Eclipse II* crashed into it, causing the destruction of Byss.

**Lethos, Daxtorn** A student at the Imperial Academy who vanished a year before his scheduled graduation, he reappeared several years later, smuggling high-technology weapons and illicit systems to a variety of criminal organizations. That led him to take up the life of a bounty hunter; a tiny holographic projector hidden in his belt helped to mask his appearance. He often used the device to look like a dashing young man, keeping his aging face a secret. He traveled the galaxy in the INT-66 transport known as the *Gorgon.*

**Leth universal energy cage** *See* universal energy cage.

**le Trene, Tolk** A Lorrdian scrub nurse for the Grand Army of the Republic, she was stationed at the Rimsoo Seven military hospital on Drongar with Jos Vondar during the Clone Wars. She found herself quite attracted to Captain Vondar, and went out of her way to make sure he knew it. Tolk was practical about the harsh realities of war; she explained to him that there was nothing permanent about any physical relationship they might have, just the shared companionship of two beings who might not live to see tomorrow.

Leviathan

**leuma** An ersatz disease invented by Han Solo to help thwart assassins attempting to capture Jedi Master Eelysa while on Corellia during the Yuuzhan Vong War. Pretending to be a doctor, Solo claimed that the medical facility was being quarantined against the newly discovered airborne leuma.

**Levare, Dael** The son of one of Corellia's richest families during the early years of the New Order. He was engaged at one time to Bria Tharen, more from her mother's manipulations than from any sort of love much to her mother's dismay. Bria broke off the engagement when she found Dael sneaking around with another woman. When Bria returned to her family after becoming a pilgrim on Ylesia, her mother invited Dael over to meet Bria's new beau, Han Solo. It was Dael who recognized Han as Tallus Bryne, precipitating Bria and Han's flight from Corellia.

***Leveler*** An Old Republic assault ship under the command of then-Captain Gilad Pellaeon, it was dispatched to Gaftikar during the Clone Wars to assist with attacks on Separatist-backed human cities on the planet. The *Leveler* was charged with eliminating communications and tracking satellites that ringed the planet in an effort to cut off exchanges of information. The *Leveler* took minimal damage from Separatist vessels while crippling an enemy ship.

**leviathan** A massive, soul-eating creature created by the Dark Jedi to destroy the Jedi Order during the Hundred-Year Darkness about 7,000 years before the Battle of Yavin. Millennia later, a leviathan terrorized the mining colony on Corbos. Kyp Durron used the Force to call down lightning to kill one such creature, but it took the combined efforts of Durron, Dorsk 82, Kirana Ti, and Streen to vanquish a second one.

***Leviathan* (1)** An ancient interdictor warship commanded by Admiral Saul Karath in the years before the Great Sith War. When Karath became one of the first officers of the Old Republic naval forces to join the Sith, he took the *Leviathan* with him, turning the vessel over to Darth Malak.

***Leviathan* (2)** Obi-Wan Kenobi and Qui-Gon Jinn traveled aboard this sleek luxury spaceliner while searching for Xanatos on Telos.

***Leviathan* (3)** A famous Dreadnaught that served as an Old Republic anti-pirate ship. The Galactic Senate sent the *Leviathan* to patrol merchant routes, investigate commerce irregularities, and enforce Old Republic trade law. The commander was Captain Trence Vosh from Alderaan.

**Leviathor** The ancient leader of the Whaladons on Mon Calamari, he kept many members of his species free by outsmarting those who would hunt them. Leviathor was believed to be the last great white Whaladon.

**Leyli, Lady** A Selonian who was an aide to the Queen of Tralus during the Galactic Civil War. Lady Leyli met with Luke Skywalker, Wedge Antilles, and other Alliance agents who arrived in the Corellian system just after the Battle of Endor. She agreed to help them locate General Weir's base, but only after Luke Skywalker explained that both Darth Vader and Emperor Palpatine were truly dead.

**L'hnnar, Shandria** A New Republic Intelligence field agent, she fell in love with gambler Sienn Sconn. But their relationship soured over galactic politics, and after several arguments, they split up. Soon after, L'hnnar led an assault team that attempted to recover the *Super*-class Star Destroyer *Guardian,* but they were captured in the attempt. Sconn rescued L'hnnar, and they decided to give their relationship another try.

**Lhosan Industries** A large corporation with headquarters on the planet Taris during the era of the Great Sith War. Lhosan was known throughout the galaxy for its swoops and speeder bikes, and many racers referred to the manufacturing plant near Taris's Machine-ville as "the birthplace of the swoop bike."

**Li, Tungo** A diminutive humanoid, he was named head of the Rebel Alliance's meager spy network at the start of the Galactic Civil War. Tungo Li was easily recognized by his pointy tufted ears and his large shaggy eyebrows. He controlled a network of far-flung spies with whom he communicated through a helmet studded with neural access nodes that interfaced with computer networks.

Tungo Li

**Liam** A young member of the Bear Clan who trained at the Jedi Temple on Coruscant during the year leading up to the Battle of Geonosis.

**Lian, Deign** A Yuuzhan Vong from a prestigious family of warriors, he served as Shedao Shai's second in command. Lian plotted against Shai and reported his every mistake to the Yuuzhan Vong warmaster in their home galaxy. He was killed when the *Legacy of Torment* exploded under heavy fire near Ithor.

**Lianna (1)** An industrial world in the heart of the Allied Tion sector, it instituted home rule following the Empire's defeat at the Battle of Endor. The New Republic respected the planet's nonaligned status, but Imperial reprisals seemed inevitable. Lady Santhe, head of the planet's powerful Santhe/Sienar Technologies, threatened to cut off Lianna's production of TIE fighters for the Empire unless the planet was left alone. This threat, along with secret payments to the local Moff, resulted in Lianna receiving a special charter of secession from the Empire. One of the products manufactured after Lianna's secession was the compact but powerful TIE tank, also called the Century tank.

**Lianna (2)** An alias of Mara Jade, often used when she posed as one of Palpatine's dancing girls. She was using the Lianna alias when she was first introduced to then-Admiral Thrawn on Coruscant. Later, when Thrawn was promoted

*The interdictor warship* Leviathan *attacks the starship* Ebon Hawk.

Lictor-*class dungeon ship*

to Grand Admiral, Mara's true identity was revealed to him.

**Liav, Leth** A Sullustan X-wing pilot in Rogue Squadron during the Yuuzhan Vong War. She had been captured by the Yuuzhan Vong early in the war, and then launched in an environment bubble into the atmosphere of Borleias in a gesture of cruelty. Liav and several other members of her old squadron were rescued by Twin Suns Squadron, and offered the chance to join the fighter squadrons that protected Borleias. Leth served as Rogue Eight during her tenure with the squadron.

**Liberation Day** A Coruscant holiday celebrating the Rebel Alliance victory in the Battle of Endor.

***Liberator*** One of two Imperial Star Destroyers captured by the Rebel Alliance during the Battle of Endor, the former *Adjudicator* was placed under the command of Luke Skywalker. After Coruscant was recaptured by the Empire, a combat-damaged *Liberator* crashed into Imperial City. But Skywalker's skillful deployment of the ship's shields and repulsorlifts prevented the crew's death.

***Liberty* (1)** A Rebel Alliance star cruiser vaporized by the second Death Star during the Battle of Endor.

***Liberty* (2)** A *Majestic*-class heavy cruiser that was part of the New Republic's Fifth Fleet and was deployed in the blockade of Doornik-319 during the Yevethan crisis.

***Liberty Star*** A New Republic assault frigate that participated in the Battle of Bilbringi against Grand Admiral Thrawn's forces.

**Libkath, Gilramos** Known to his "children" as the Master, Libkath was a Neimoidian criminal who worked the underworld of Mos Espa during the years before the Clone Wars. Rather than get his own hands dirty, Libkath kidnapped or stole young children to do his bidding. He implanted tiny, eyeball-shaped tracer orbs in their palms to monitor their activities. He made his living smuggling weapons and other valuable commodities, often hijacking shipments from Jabba the Hutt. This earned Libkath a substantial bounty on his head.

Eventually, Jabba hired both Durge and the 10-year-old Boba Fett to capture or eliminate Libkath. Both bounty hunters cornered Libkath in the burned-out hull of a Theed cruiser near Mos Espa, with Durge disabling Libkath with a blaster bolt. Young Boba stole his miter-like hat and fled the ship with the children, while Durge set out to destroy Libkath. In his wild firing, Durge blasted a crate of weapons, setting off a huge explosion. Libkath died in the fiery blaze. Boba Fett returned to Jabba with the hat, using it as proof of his elimination of Libkath.

**Librarian's Assembly** A group of Jedi scholars who maintained the various holocrons, scrolls, and Sith writings collected during the time of the Old Republic. It was led by Yaddle during the last years of the Old Republic, prior to the Jedi Purge.

**Library Galactica** One of the largest libraries in the galaxy during the final decades of the Old Republic.

**Library of the Republic** A galaxywide library and archive maintained by the Galactic Senate of the Old Republic. Although the primary mission of the library was the acquisition and retention of literature and information, the Special Acquisitions Branch also worked as an intelligence-gathering agency.

***Lictor*-class dungeon ship** Based on a Mandalorian design, Rendili StarDrive's *Lictor*-class dungeon ship was a 764-meter-long prisoner transport vessel. Sections were designed with variable environments to create conditions that were as uncomfortable as possible. Other will-breaking devices present were sirens, electric shockers, and various gas emission systems. When the Empire began using these ships to transport captured Jedi Knights, they installed energy shields based on the universal energy cage around each partition. Emperor Palpatine used a dungeon ship to transport Luke Skywalker to Byss.

**Lifath** The proctor of information on the *Pride of Yevetha,* the flagship of strongman Nil Spaar's Black Fleet.

**life-bearer** Also referred to as life-witches, they were randomly born beings on the planet Leria Kerlsil who, through a ritual called the Blood Kiss, linked their own body chemistry to that of another—usually someone old, sick, or dying. This enabled the life-bearer to keep the other individual alive and healthy, hold back pain, and even forestall death for a short time. The process was called Support, and when withdrawn the individual would die. Life-bearers had to provide Support lest they sicken and die themselves.

**lifeboat** *See* escape pod.

**lifeboat bay** Special enclosures on starships, they housed emergency escape pods and their jettisoning systems.

**life-crystal** Long considered the chief export of the Rafa system, the life-crystal was a gem with strange and wonderful properties. It had the ability to alter a human's normal life expectancy, sometimes multiplying it fourfold. Life-crystals could also affect the holder's dreams, and were known to cure certain mental conditions. They were grown in life-orchards that were found on the 11 planets of the Rafa system and a few of the system's asteroids. However, only those locations that mimicked the environments of Rafa IV produced large life-crystals. Each had to be harvested with a laser cutter, and a new crystal would grow in its place in about a year. The true purpose of the life-crystals was revealed when Lando Calrissian, Vuffi Raa, and Mohs discovered the Mindharp on Rafa V. When they learned of the incredible ruse maintained by the Sharu species, they realized that the life-crystals were really a device used by the Sharu to collect the intelligence and knowledge from all subsequent generations of Sharu, keeping this intelligence effectively hidden from an unknown threat the Sharu had perceived many eons before. The life-crystals drained the energy from the Sharu as well, creating the image of a simple old Toka and maintaining the Sharu deception. The reason life-crystals worked differently for the Toka than for beings who lived outside the Rafa system was that the offworld life-crystals were too far from the Sharu computer banks, where the knowledge and intelligence was stored. Without the close linkage to the Rafa system, a life-crystal simply absorbed the intelligence and life energy from those near the life-crystal's holder, channeling it into the holder.

*Life Day brings Chewbacca's extended family to Kashyyyk.*

**Life Day** A Wookiee holiday, Life Day celebrated Kashyyyk's diverse ecosystem and the many forms of life it encompassed. It also was a time to remember family members who had died, and the young ones who continued to bring new life to a family. Extended Wookiee families would customarily gather to celebrate a day of joy and harmony, as promised by the Tree of Life. Life Day was held once every three local years for many generations, but during the Galactic Civil War its importance to the Wookiees became more pronounced.

**Lifehold, Dannen** A blue-haired human smuggler who operated during the Galactic Civil War. He piloted the freighter *Lifeline* with the help of a Tinnel mechanic named Purr.

**life-jet** Small safety jetpacks found at various locations along the outer edge of Cloud City on Bespin for use in emergencies.

**life-orchard** The name given to any of the specialized growing environments required for producing life-crystals.

**Lifewell** A bioengineered construct used by the ancient Kathol to store their life energies during the struggle between the ancient Jedi Knights and the Dark Jedi who had enslaved the Kathol. The Lifewell, which later became known as DarkStryder, was essentially a huge, glowing, crystalline organ that pulsed with the life energies of the ancient Kathol. The crystal's tip emerged in a secret chamber within DarkStryder's fortress, but extended for several kilometers straight down into the planet's mantle. The chamber that housed it was formed from huge bones, and was filled with organic, tactile control systems.

Only a handful of Kathol managed to enter the Lifewell before the destruction of its launch gates. Its own self-awareness kept it from releasing the Kathol. Since the Kathol were unable to break free of the Lifewell, their life energies evolved into the Ta-Ree. During the Battle of Kathol, the Lifewell was opened by Halbret, who had been awakened by the crew of the *FarStar.*

**life-witch** *See* life-bearer.

**lift tube** Cylindrical tubes used to transport cargo or passengers into or out of a ship, transport, or building. They often employed repulsorlifts or vacuums to lift and drop their cargo. The Jawas on Tatooine used them to "suck" the scrap material they collected into the bellies of their sandcrawlers.

**lift-wing racing** A sport that used a small sail, stretched across a rigid frame, to allow a racer to glide through the air. The frame provided minimal lift and maneuverability, but allowed the racer to guide the frame toward the finish line.

**Light and Darkness War** One of the many terms used to describe the New Sith Wars, which occurred more than a millennium before the Clone Wars and ended with the Battle of Ruusan.

**lighter** Any small, light-duty transport ship. These ships were easily modified and could be armed for combat.

**Light Festival** An Ewok celebration that honored the rejuvenation of the Tree of Light.

**lightfoil** A dueling weapon popular in the Tapani sector. It was modeled on the lightsabers of the Jedi Knights, but was much smaller and not as powerful or energy-efficient as the Jedi weapon.

**Lightmoon, Gibbon** A New Republic flight technician who was one of the initial designers of the covert shroud freighter/fighter system used by Luke Skywalker during the Republic's struggle with Grand Admiral Thrawn.

***Light of Reason*** A spacecraft used by Nam Chorios strongman Seti Ashgad. Ashgad took the ship to meet with Leia Organa Solo near Nam Chorios, as well as to transport weapons and synthdroids from Loronar Corporation to Nam Chorios.

**lightpad** A specialized form of datapad, created for medical use during the last decades of the Old Republic. It was used by doctors and nurses to monitor the vital statistics of their patients.

***Lightrunner*** Mammon Hoole's personal starship. He used it during his search for Borborygmus Gog and Project Starscream. It also served as transport for his young niece and nephew Tash and Zak Arranda following the destruction of Alderaan. The *Lightrunner* was damaged when its hyperdrive cut out upon detecting the presence of D'vouran in its vicinity, and Hoole was forced to land the ship on the unusual planet. When the planet began consuming everything in sight, Hoole and his charges were forced to flee in the *Millennium Falcon* with Han Solo and Luke Skywalker.

**lightsaber** The lightsaber was known as the weapon of a Jedi, an elegant armament of a more civilized time. In comparison, blasters were seen as crude, inaccurate, and loud affairs. To carry a lightsaber was a mark of incredible skill and confidence, dexterity, and attunement to the Force. But the followers of the dark side used them, too.

When deactivated, a lightsaber appeared as a polished metallic handle, about 24 to 30 centimeters long, lined with control studs. There were many styles of lightsaber hilts, including adept, adjudicator, arbiter, avenger, champion, consul, defender, firebrand, guardian, praetor, retaliator, sentinel, vanquisher, and vindicator. At the press of a button, the energy contained within was liberated and formed a shaft of pure energy about a meter long. The saber hummed and scintillated with a distinct sound. Its shimmering blade was capable of cutting through almost anything, save for the blade of another lightsaber.

In the hands of a Jedi, a lightsaber was almost unstoppable. It could cut through blast doors and enemies alike. Using the Force, a Jedi could predict and deflect incoming blaster bolts, and reflect them back at the firer. By tradition, most lightsabers were built by their users as part of their Jedi training. They could be built in a few days in an emergency, but many users took a month or more to construct and fine-tune the weapon. After the extermination of the Jedi at the end of the Clone Wars, lightsabers became rare relics. The knowledge of their construction disappeared with their masters. Luke Skywalker, one of the last of the Jedi, built his own lightsaber as the culmination of his training, and then taught a new Jedi Order how to do the same.

Although the lightsaber was reserved for Force-users—the only ones capable of fully handling the difficult weapon—it was also used by the Jedi's enemies, the Sith.

Lightsabers changed little in the thousands of years of their employ by the Jedi Knights. Those who believed the Jedi Order began on the ancient world of Ossus pointed to the abundance of Adegan crystals in the system as proof. These crystals were ideal for the creation of lightsabers, as they focused the energy released from a saber's power cell into a tight, blade-like beam. Early lightsabers didn't have self-contained power cells, but instead were connected by a conducting cable to a belt-worn power pack.

Once unleashed, the power channeled through a positively charged continuous energy lens at the center of the handle. The beam then arced circumferentially back to a negatively charged high-energy flux aperture. A superconductor transferred the power from the flux aperture to the power cell. As a result, a lightsaber only expended power when its blade cut through something. So efficient was the blade that it did not radiate heat unless it came into contact with something.

The blade's color depended on the nature of the jewel it came from, and while its length was fixed in the case of a single-jewel lightsaber, lightsabers equipped with multiple crystals could have their lengths varied by rotating a knob that allowed the focusing crystal activator to subtly modify the refraction pattern among the gems. With the Sith long believed extinct until the end of the Clone Wars, lightsaber dueling occurred only within the practice chambers of the Jedi Temple. To a Jedi, a lightsaber was not just a weapon. It was a means of concentrating attention and becoming attuned with the Force.

**light-scan visor** Originally developed more than 4,000 years before the Battle of Yavin, these devices provided enhanced visual acuity by analyzing incoming light sources and providing visual displays from frequencies above those of normal sight. More expensive visors could be adjusted for species-specific characteristics.

**light shaper** Similar to a villip-choir field, this Yuuzhan Vong technology used specialized creatures to send and receive images

## Notable Lightsabers

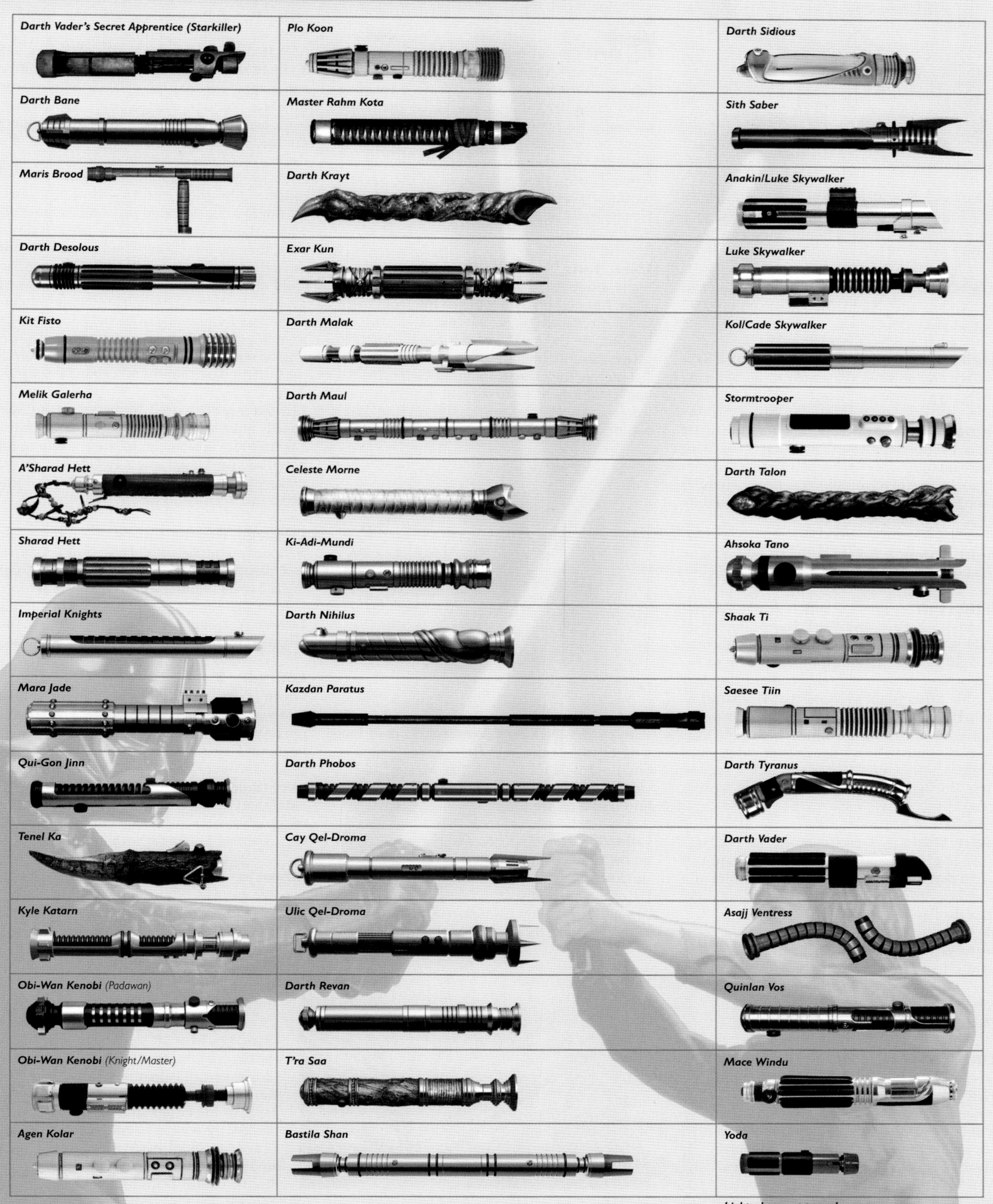


*Lightsabers not to scale.*

Lightside Explorer

across vast distances. Unlike the villip-choir, which used standard villips, the light shaper used villips to create a bioluminescent hologram.

***Lightside Explorer*** A spacecraft owned by Andur and Nomi Sunrider some 4,000 years before the Galactic Civil War.

**Lightsider** An ancient Jedi game. Luke Skywalker once bested Kam Solusar at it during the early years of the New Republic.

**lightspeed torpedo** The huge missiles fired by the Empire's Galaxy Gun. Each of these missiles was capable of traveling through hyperspace to a specific location, where it dropped out of hyperspace and continued its flight to the target.

**light spirit** A benign entity worshipped by the Ewoks.

**lightstaff** A few ancient Jedi like Master Vodo-Siosk Baas and Qrrl Toq preferred to fight with these quarterstaff weapons instead of lightsabers. Though they were able to resist strikes from a lightsaber, it wasn't clear whether this quality was derived from a component of the wood, an electronic device, or some mystical Force-imbued power. Exar Kun was able to break Baas's staff twice, once while training on Dantooine and a second time during their fatal encounter on Coruscant.

**light table** A flat, circular device that was used to display holograms and holographs. It had a parabolic holoprojector in its center and a set of external controls that manipulated the data displayed over the top of the table.

**lightwhip** A form of whip that employed light energy to stun a target. Exceptionally difficult to build, lightwhips were rare and unusual during the last years of the Old Republic.

**Lihnn, Mahwi** A bounty hunter hired by Nute Gunray and Rune Haako to find Hath Monchar. Mahwi Lihnn had been a bounty hunter for 10 years, ever since she had been forced to leave her homeworld after killing a corrupt government official. She had pursued fugitives on such diverse worlds as Ord Mantell, Roon, Tatooine, and dozens of others, though she had never been to Coruscant until she was called to find Hath Monchar. Darth Maul got to Monchar first. Lihn fired a rocket at him but was killed in the subsequent explosion.

**Lij, Drif** One of the pilots who flew as part of the Wild Knights. Jedi Drif Lij was working with Wonetun to help capture a Yuuzhan Vong yammosk some 27 years after the Battle of Yavin. Lij piloted an older model T-65 X-wing. In addition to being an accomplished pilot, Lij was also an excellent student of the Force. During the early stages of the Second Battle of Coruscant, Lij's fighter was hit by plasma balls; it exploded, killing the Barabel pilot instantly.

**Li-Li, Jang** A Jedi Knight, she was one of many students to train under Count Dooku when he was still a member of the Jedi Order. Li-Li accompanied Jai Maruk on a mission to Vjun, at the height of the Clone Wars, to investigate the buildup of Separatist forces in the sector. They discovered that Count Dooku had established a stronghold on Vjun, and were captured by Asajj Ventress. Jang Li-Li was no match for Ventress in combat, and was slain by the Dark Jedi. Ventress claimed that Jang Li-Li was the 16th Jedi she had killed in one-on-one combat, and that Master Maruk would have been the 17th if Dooku hadn't allowed him to live.

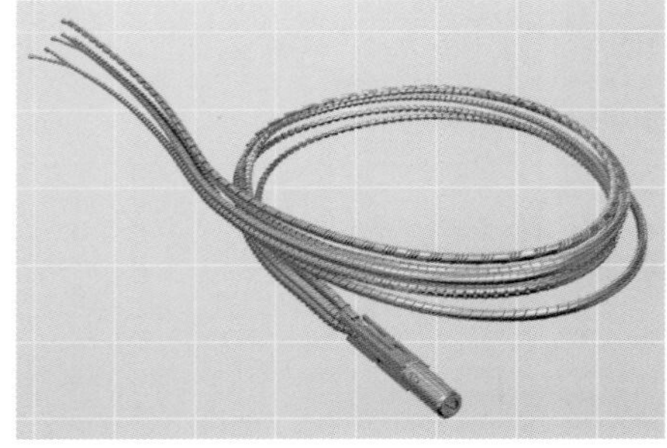

*Lightwhip*

**Lillald** A New Republic Senator who served on the Council on Security and Intelligence. He supported Cair Tok Noimm's stance on the status of the mission sent to intercept the Teljkon vagabond near Gmir Askilon, requesting that the Republic send a team to continue the search.

*Master Vodo-Siosk Baas (left) wields a lightstaff.*

**Lilli** A strong-willed teenager, she was one of the two Venerated Ones from Vandelhelm—the last heirs to the Vandel and Helm lines. Her full name—which she hated to use—was Lillindri Nanimei Filda Vandelhelm XXXII. Just before the Battle of Endor, Lilli and Endro were whisked offplanet when it became apparent that the galaxy's power structure was going to change again. The children were handed over to Rebel Alliance supporters on Ord Vaug, then returned home after the Battle of Endor by the dashing Han Solo. After she was voted into power days after her return, Lilli—then just 15—showed a knack for finance. She lowered prices on refined ore, which allowed more buyers to place larger orders, thereby increasing Vandelhelm's income as well as profits. But Lilli was still a petulant child at heart, and within a few years she ordered a vast fleet of starships—lovingly named *Solo*-class freighters—to be built for the New Republic as a gift from the Venerated Ones. This taxed the Vandelhelm coffers, lowering profits to a bare minimum for many years.

**Limba** An alias used by Leia Organa Solo, shortly after her marriage to Han Solo, during a mission to Tatooine to locate a group of Imperial agents. Limba was a Twi'lek female, and Leia's disguise included a pair of prosthetic lekku that seemed to twitch with life.

**LiMerge Power** An energy producer and weapons manufacturer accused of producing and distributing prohibited armaments during the years before the Battle of Naboo.

**Limm** A trooper in the Galactic Alliance Guard at the height of the Corellia-GA War.

**Limmer, Z.** The chief financial officer of Ororo Transportation, a shipping company that was the chief competitor of Xizor Transport Systems, owned by the head of the galactic underworld, Prince Xizor. When Ororo tried to overturn the XTS domination of the spice trade in the Bajic sector, Xizor's trusted aide, the replica droid Guri, killed a number of top Ororo executives, including Z. Limmer. Guri speared his throat with her fingers.

**Limoth, Garlan** A Galactic Republic Senator, he was one of a group that strongly supported Senator Palpatine of Naboo as Supreme Chancellor. However, when Palpatine declared himself Emperor and instituted the New Order, Senator Limoth withdrew his support. He died almost immediately afterward . . . in a tragic accident.

**Limoth, Marsh** Unlike his father, Senator Garlan Limoth, Marsh never withdrew his support of Palpatine, even when he declared himself Emperor. Marsh turned his back on his father, and was rewarded for his loyalty with a posting as Moff Nebin Cray's personal assistant. Limoth operated as a true supporter of the New Order, despite claims from his peers that he was only serving for his own personal gain.

LIN-V8M

**Limpan, Tarla** A female Duros who rose through the ranks of the Galactic Alliance's naval forces, she reached the rank of admiral several years after the end of the Yuuzhan Vong War.

**lim tree** A tree developed by Yuuzhan Vong shaper Nen Yim for its beauty as well as its constant appetite. The lim tree was believed to have been extinct, maintained only as a genetic blueprint in the Qang qahsa.

**Lin, Berd** A child prodigy studying on Harix, Berd was the son of schoolteacher Myoris. When the Empire took his fellow students and mother hostage, Berd appealed to Rebel heroes Luke Skywalker, Han Solo, and a coalition of smugglers to help free his planet.

**Lin, Myoris** A schoolteacher, she was one of many to openly rebel against Imperial control of Harix after the Battle of Yavin. She was kidnapped by Major Stafuv Rahz, who had been directly ordered by Darth Vader to capture the schoolteachers to silence the talk of Rebellion.

**Lindy** A friend of Hobbie Klivian who was stationed at Bestine when Hobbie and Biggs Darklighter defected from the *Rand Ecliptic*. Lindy provided them with assistance in offloading the ship's cargo.

**line creeper** A parasite believed native to Csilla or another Chiss-held world. It was similar in most respects to the conduit worm of Coruscant. Resembling long, segmented worms, line creepers chewed through metal pipes and wiring conduits to reach the electrical power moving through them.

**Lingsnot, Po Ruddle** A humanoid inhabitant of Bespin's Cloud City, he had been a used cloud-car salesman. He worked hard to get elected to the outpost's Council on Tourism and Extraplanetary Investment. From there, he become an established member of the Exex.

**Linkup** The code name of the revised extraction point where Luke Skywalker and his Hardpoint Squadron were to retrieve the Jedi Knights of Team Tauntaun and Team Purella from the surface of Corellia. The mission was part of a larger initiative by the Galactic Alliance government to prevent Thrackan Sal-Solo from removing the Corellian system from the GA.

**Linuri** The site of a confrontation between the private army of Senator Garm Bel Iblis and the forces of Grand Admiral Thrawn.

**LIN-V8K** An armored mining and demolition droid, it was refurbished by a Jawa clan on Tatooine, then converted for military duty.

**LIN-V8M** An armored military droid that specialized in laying explosive mines, it originally was designed to set charges in ore and spice mines. The droid was destroyed in the explosion of the Death Star.

**Liok** The site of the Shadow Taproom, considered a great archaeological discovery.

**Lish V (L-5)** A seismically active moon owned by Lant Mining Corporation, it was the only satellite in its system with a breathable atmosphere, but the last to be actively mined. To ensure the safety of the mining crews and to protect its investment, LMC built repulsor-equipped floating cities like Gadde.

**Lishma** A Gotal member of a smuggling operation run by Mazzic in the early years of the New Republic. Lishma accompanied his boss to Trogan to meet with Talon Karrde and discuss the formation of the Smugglers' Alliance. During the meeting, he was killed in an Imperial attack at Whistler's Whirlpool.

**Lissahl** A female Zeltron cafarel, she befriended freighter pilot Jiri Sools sometime before the Clone Wars. Sools fell so madly in love that he vowed never to leave Zeltros again.

**Lisstik** The leader of the Kamarian Badlanders, he traded goods with Han Solo and Chewbacca while they were on Kamar.

**Lisst'n** A species noted for the way that its members continually shed their skin.

***Little Bivoli*** An Old Republic provisioning ship, it was part of a fleet that massed near Ralltiir during the Mandalorian Wars. The ship was stolen by the pirate Slyssk, who planned to sell it to Marn Hierogryph.

**Little Killer** The Basic translation of the Wookiee nickname given to Tarfang during the GA–Confederation War. Tarfang and Jae Juun were on Kashyyyk to intercept Han and Leia Solo when it was learned that the pair were going to try to convince the Wookiees to secede from the Galactic Alliance.

Po Ruddle Lingsnot

**"Little Lost Bantha Cub, The"** The favorite bedtime story of young Anakin Solo. He was upset when C-3PO decided he was too old to continue hearing it.

**Livette, General** A Hapan officer in charge of the defense of the secret Jedi base on Shedu Maad after Darth Caedus finally discovered its location following the Second Battle of Fondor. General Livette was experienced and wore her scars as medals of honor.

**Livet Tower** Located on the outskirts of Theed on Naboo, this thin spire contained an eternal flame, signifying the mortality of the people and their duty to lead peaceful lives. Qui-Gon Jinn was cremated in the domed funeral temple on the grounds of the Tower.

**Lizil** One of the many hives that made up the Colony. Members of Lizil hive were distinguished by their reddish-brown carapaces, which protected their golden thoraxes; they had multifaceted purple eyes.

**l'lahsh** A delicate beverage distilled from the nectar of tiny t'iil blossoms. Since the blossoms had to be picked by hand, and each contained only one droplet of nectar, it took hundreds of thousands of blossoms to produce each year's vintage.

Little Bivoli

**Llewebum** A species whose members displayed large bumps all along their bodies, including a secondary series of bumps below their arms. The Senator from Llewebum was severely injured in the explosion caused by Dark Jedi Kueller in the Senate Hall on Coruscant.

**Llez** The son of Ambassador Zell of Majoor. Llez was essentially a spoiled brat who needed constant supervision to ensure he didn't get into trouble. Ambassador Zell acquired R2-D2 and C-3PO to serve as tutors and companions for Llez.

**Llitishi** The director of sales and marketing for the Five Families of Ord Cestus during the Clone Wars. She was behind plans to add a 10 percent surcharge to the price of JK series droids that the families had promised to sell to Count Dooku and the Separatists.

**Llnewe, Captain Deyd** An Imperial Navy officer who dreamed of being recognized by Emperor Palpatine. But the reality was that Llnewe was commander of the customs vessel *Vigilant,* patrolling the empty wastes of a remote sector of the galaxy. To make matters worse, he was fooled three times by Han Solo, who was stealing capital ships for sale to the Rebel Alliance.

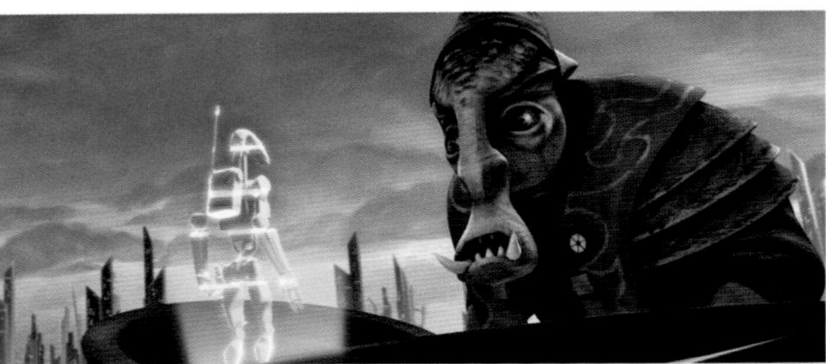

*General Whorm Loathsom*

**Llokay** A red-skinned Zabrak, he was one of three members of his species who were trained at the Sith Academy on Korriban before the Battle of Ruusan.

**Lloyn, Pefederan** The head of the Galactic Alliance Finance Council following the Yuuzhan Vong War. When Thrackan Sal-Solo threatened to pull the Corellian system from the GA, Lloyn suddenly sold or traded several of her own properties in the Corellian system in exchange for similar holdings in the Kuat system. That led many pundits to wonder if the GA was planning to blockade or attack the Corellians in an effort to stop Sal-Solo's advances.

**llrashtash** Native to Usean II, this large herbivore was known for its huge teeth.

**llwelkyn** A creature whose ivory teeth were often used as knives, the llwelkyn was native to Drong II.

**Lo, Hat** A noted crime lord, he worked from a Coruscant base following the Battle of Naboo. Hat Lo was known more for his overblown opinion of himself than his small criminal empire. He believed that he was the most powerful of the gangsters on Coruscant at the time, but actually was no more than a lackey for the Hutts.

**Load Spider THK 421** After the success of the Void Spider THX 1138 speeder, Bespin Motors developed this cargo shuttle based on the same basic design. It had an enclosed crew cabin with room for two and an open cargo bed in back. The vehicle saw extensive use during the construction of Bespin's Cloud City and proved to be a valuable workhorse for transporting materials and equipment.

**Loag** A band of cool, calculating, and lethal mercenaries and assassins that was almost wiped out by the Jedi Knights of the Old Republic. The survivors were exiled from the planet Merisee and remained hidden for years, awaiting a chance to exact revenge. Their symbol, the Loag Dagger, passed through countless hands after its seizure by Jedi thousands of years before the Galactic Civil War. The black blade was continually stolen from museums and private collections, changing hands every few years among the powerful.

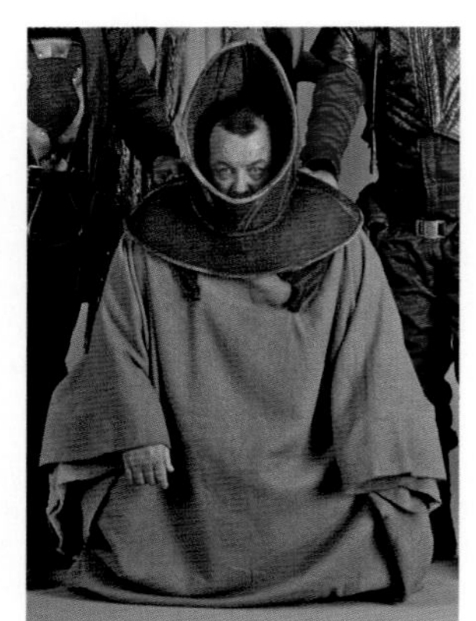

*Hat Lo*

**Loathsom, General Whorm** Gruff, guttural, and supremely vain, this Kerkoiden general often overestimated his own abilities as a Separatist leader during the Clone Wars. He was outsmarted by Obi-Wan Kenobi on Christophsis. The Jedi Master stalled the general long enough during a supposed surrender parley for Anakin Skywalker and Ahsoka Tano to disable the deflector shields protecting his forces. A sure victory for the Separatists was thus turned into a rout for the Republic.

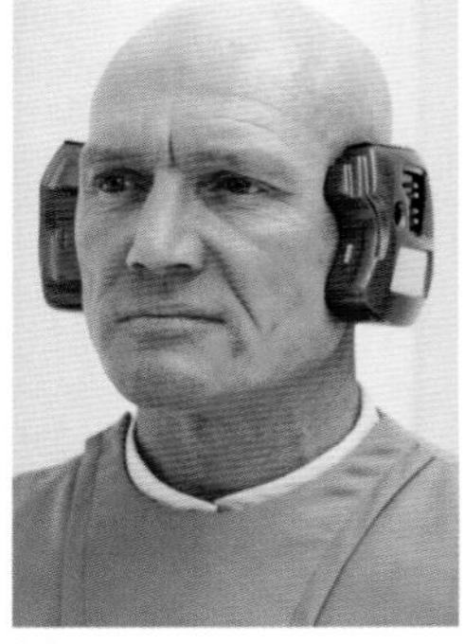

*Lobot*

**Lobi, Tresina** A female Chev, she was the first of her species to demonstrate Jedi abilities. She cultivated her control of the Force at Luke Skywalker's praxeum during the early years of the New Republic. She had an innate ability to blend into crowds, especially of nonhumans. Lobi ultimately was one of the small number of Jedi Knights to survive the Yuuzhan Vong War. She was promoted to Jedi Master, and chosen by Skywalker to sit on the new Jedi Order's leadership council.

After the Swarm War, Tresina Lobi discovered that Jacen Solo was making clandestine excursions to the World Brain installed on Coruscant, and decided to follow him. She found herself caught up in one of Jacen's meetings with Lumiya and tried to get a message back to the Jedi Temple. However, she failed to notice that Alema Rar had snuck up behind her. Lumiya was as surprised as Lobi by the attack, but nevertheless took up the fight. Confronted by two opponents, one of whom wielded a lightwhip, Lobi was swiftly outmatched. Lumiya used her lightwhip to take off the Jedi's legs at the knees, and then Rar beheaded the Chev with her lightsaber.

**Lobot** Son of a slaver, and then a slave himself, this human-turned-cyborg's life didn't lack for drama. After escaping pirate captors and arriving on Bespin's floating Cloud City, Lobot was forced to steal to survive. He

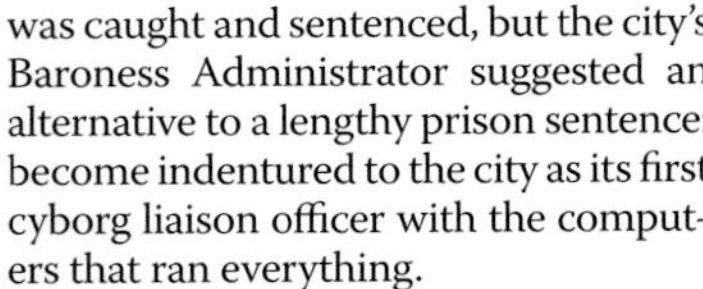

was caught and sentenced, but the city's Baroness Administrator suggested an alternative to a lengthy prison sentence: become indentured to the city as its first cyborg liaison officer with the computers that ran everything.

Lobot was fitted with advanced components, including a visible computer bracket that wrapped around the back of his bald head; it dramatically increased his intelligence and let him communicate directly with the city's central computer. Lobot remained on the job even after fulfilling his sentence and helped rogue gambler Lando Calrissian win control of Cloud City from a draconian administrator in a sabacc game.

Lobot saved Calrissian's life when rogue droid EV-9D9 planted bombs on Cloud City. He stayed behind after Calrissian and his new Rebel Alliance friends fled following the visit of Darth Vader, who used the city's facilities to freeze Han Solo in a block of carbonite. Months later, Calrissian returned and was attacked by Lobot, whose motivational-programming capsule had been damaged by Ugnaughts rebelling against Imperial rule. Calrissian repaired the damage, and Lobot then disarmed bombs that the Ugnaughts had planted all over the city. Later Calrissian and Lobot teamed up with the Ugnaughts in a successful fight against the Imperial occupiers.

Calrissian called on Lobot again during the Yevethan crisis when he was trying to solve the mystery of the Teljkon vagabond ghost ship. He lured Lobot with the promise of a vacation. After the two of them and the droids R2-D2 and C-3PO boarded the vagabond, it took off with them inside. Eventually, Lobot figured out a way to talk to the vagabond by connecting his interface with a network of wires attached to the ship. But while it was willing to give him information, the ship wouldn't give him control. The involuntary crew was rescued by Luke Skywalker and Colonel Pakkpekatt at Maltha Obex. Years later, Lobot surfaced as Calrissian's aide when Lando opened *GemDiver Station* in orbit around the gas giant Yavin.

**locap** Found only in the deep oceans of Naboo, this strange form of plant life burrowed into the soft rock of the planet's core and extracted plasma. The Gungans learned how to obtain the digested plasma from the locap and used it to power their underwater cities and shield generators.

**locator chip** A special implant developed for use in jails, it was inserted into the body of a prisoner. The locator chip kept tabs on the inmate's location within the facility.

**Lochett, Uldir** The owner of the *No Luck Required* during the early stages of the Yuuzhan Vong War. As a child, Lochett was raised on a number of different worlds by his parents, who were Coruscant-based traders and freighter pilots who often worked for the New Republic. He showed no sensitivity to the Force whatsoever, but he was allowed to attend the Jedi praxeum on Yavin 4 after he stowed away aboard the *Lightning Rod.* Luke Skywalker agreed to let him stay once he developed a friendship with Anakin Solo and Tahiri Veila.

Despite Master Skywalker's inability to identify any connection to the Force, Lochett insisted that all he needed was a lightsaber and some Jedi robes to help him get started. His studies were terminated when he began causing too much trouble at the academy, and he took up work as a member of a search-and-rescue team formed during the war. He decided to strike out on his own, but continued to devote himself to rescuing Jedi from the Yuuzhan Vong. He and his crew traveled to Bonadan, where Lochett met Klin-Fa Gi while she was trying to escape the local authorities. He discovered that Gi had gone rogue when Master Skywalker personally asked him to retrieve her. Later, the two fell in love.

**lockplate** A generic term used to describe any heavy-duty locking mechanism protected from abuse by a thick covering plate.

**lockslab** An outdated form of construction material, a lockslab was a preformed panel that locked into place with other panels, forming a wall quickly and securely.

**locomotor** A servomechanism that allowed a droid to move.

**Loctob, Cycy** A denizen of the spaceport of Nar Shaddaa, he made his living by selling contraband.

**Lod** A Toydarian slaver, he was killed by Master Finn's Sith apprentice when he tried to sell Marka to the pair as a servant.

**Lodi** An ancient species once native to the planet Solibus IV. Their civilization disappeared millennia before the onset of the Clone Wars, but it was rumored that all of their secrets and mysteries were stored in the Shu-Wang Prism. The secret of the prism remained hidden for generations, until Jedi Knight Quinlan Vos and his Padawan, Aayla Secura, were able to finally open it.

**Lodrel, Captain** An Imperial Navy officer who commanded the cruiser *Lianna Guard* as part of Admiral Greelanx's fleet. During the Battle of Nar Shaddaa, Salla Zend fired a pair of concussion missiles at the ship. Lodrel's crew was unable to take evasive action, and the ship was destroyed with all its crew.

**Loedorvian Brain Plague** An extremely deadly plague used as a bioweapon by the Confederacy of Independent Systems during the Clone Wars. General Grievous used the Loedorvian Brain Plague to eliminate all the clone troopers of the Grand Army of the Republic in the Weemell sector, and nearly killed the sector's entire human population as well.

*Logray*

As a result, the Weemell sector was rendered temporarily uninhabitable.

**Lo-Farr, Brann** The owner of the Lower Deck cantina on the Port City level of Bespin's Cloud City during the Galactic Civil War. Just after the Battle of Hoth, Lo-Farr was forced to try to keep the Lower Deck out of the clutches of Jabba the Hutt. Luckily for Lo-Farr, a group of former comrades managed to alert the Wing Guard to Jabba's plans, then arranged for the remaining balance on the Lower Deck's mortgage to be paid off.

**Lofryyhn** A Wookiee engineer aboard the *FarStar.* Lofryyhn had been part of the Rebel Alliance team that liberated Siluria III before joining the crew. Unknown to most on board, Lofryyhn was a master of the Wookiee martial art known as Wrruushi.

**Lo'gaan, Drake** A Padawan trained by Jedi Master Roron Corobb before the Clone Wars. The pair were part of the task force dispatched to protect Chancellor Palpatine when General Grievous launched his attack on Coruscant. The cyborg general killed both Master Corobb and Master Foul Moudama before taking Palpatine hostage, leaving Lo'gaan disconsolate and directionless.

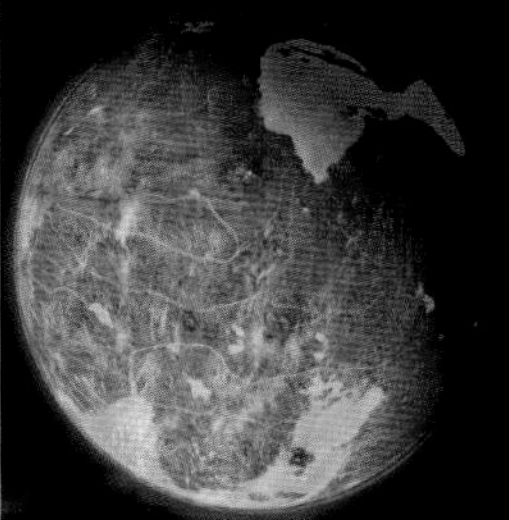

*Lok*

After the Battle of Coruscant, the apprentice learned that a mission was being formed to go after Grievous. He approached Anakin Skywalker about joining the mission, hoping to avenge the death of his Master. Anakin explained that only Obi-Wan Kenobi had been sent. Lo'gaan and fellow Padawan Ekria were then assigned to a Felucia mission led by Aayla Secura. There Ekria intercepted the communication of Order 66 but was unable to decrypt it before Commander Bly carried it out.

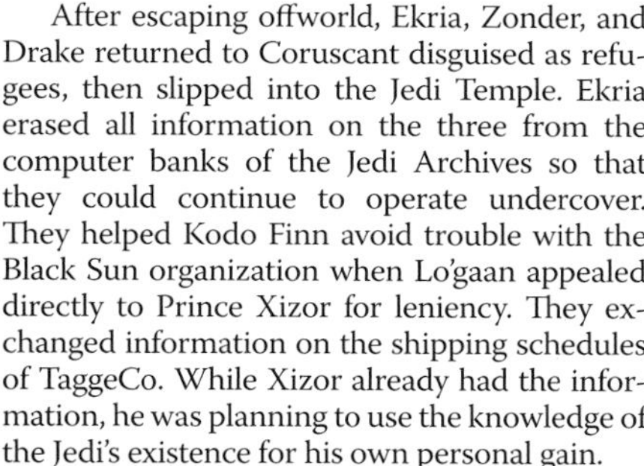

After escaping offworld, Ekria, Zonder, and Drake returned to Coruscant disguised as refugees, then slipped into the Jedi Temple. Ekria erased all information on the three from the computer banks of the Jedi Archives so that they could continue to operate undercover. They helped Kodo Finn avoid trouble with the Black Sun organization when Lo'gaan appealed directly to Prince Xizor for leniency. They exchanged information on the shipping schedules of TaggeCo. While Xizor already had the information, he was planning to use the knowledge of the Jedi's existence for his own personal gain.

After the encounter with Xizor, Zonder was captured and brought before Darth Vader, who challenged the Selonian to a duel. Using Zonder's comlink frequency, Vader transmitted the fight to Drake and Ekria, who were forced to listen as their fellow Padawan was beheaded by the Dark Lord. They set out to avenge Zonder's death, but were immediately set upon by Imperial troopers. Drake allowed Ekria to escape as he confronted Vader himself. He refused Vader's offer to join the Sith, and took up his lightsaber to defend himself.

Lo'gaan's focus on Vader meant that he didn't see the clone trooper behind him, and a blaster bolt caught him by surprise. Tired of the game, Vader then picked up Drake's lightsaber and pierced his chest with it. But it was merely a training blade, and lacked enough power to actually kill him. The wound was convincing enough, however, as Vader left the boy behind to die. Once Vader was gone, Lo'gaan managed to slip away and rejoin Ekria. Together they recovered Zonder's body and returned it to Selonia for burial. After a check of the Imperial databases revealed that they were listed as deceased, Drake and Ekria abandoned their Jedi past and set off on their own.

**Logray** The medicine man and spiritual leader of the Bright Tree Village Ewok tribe in the last decades of the Old Republic. Logray was distinguished by his light tan fur and the skull of a churi bird that he wore on his head. He was also a musician. Although revered for his wisdom, Logray was suspicious of anyone who was not a member of his tribe, especially non-Ewoks. Logray also banned Wicket W. Warrick from the village for questioning one of his orders, and was roundly denounced for his action. Logray was replaced by Paploo on the orders of Chief Chirpa, and his name was removed from the village's songs of remembrance. To the Ewoks of Bright Tree Village, it was as if Logray had never existed.

**loirbnigg** An eight-legged reptilian creature native to Frisal, it was trained for use as a mount by the Imperial nobles who vacationed on the planet.

**Lo-Jad** This Jedi Master trained Sia-Lan Wezz in the period leading up to the Battle of Naboo.

**Lok** A mostly barren, backrocket planet in the remote Karthakk system, it was where the Trade Federation first tested its vast droid army in preparation for the Naboo blockade and invasion. Lok's red-sand deserts were punctuated by sulfur seas and lava pits, along with jagged mountains and abandoned cities. Much of the planet's history was marked by anarchy and violence, and Lok became known as "pirate world."

**Loli** A young Jedi Knight who was one of a handful stationed on Ossus, where they were charged with protecting the Jedi training facility there during the Galactic Alliance's conflict with the Confederation. Loli and partner Vis'l were killed in the line of duty when Major Serpa of the Galactic Alliance Guard took control of the facility.

**Lom, Cabet** A Twi'lek who ran a starship-repair and parts business on Ord Mantell during the Galactic Civil War. He lived and worked in a penthouse suite in the Pink Sky Casino.

**Lomabu III** The third of six wildly orbiting worlds in the Lomabu system, close to the Aida system, it was the site of a penal colony. Immediately after the Battle of Hoth, the bounty hunters Chenlambec and Tinian I'att convinced Bossk to search for Han Solo in the Lomabu system. According to their story, a group of Wookiees was trying to establish a secure colony on Lomabu III. When all three arrived, I'att and Chenlambec successfully double-crossed Bossk and rescued a number of Wookiee prisoners.

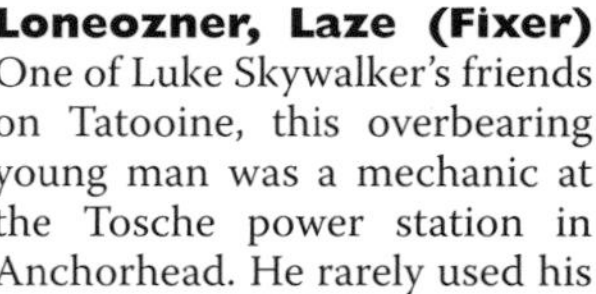
Camie Loneozner

**lomin-ale** A bitter, spicy beverage that produced a foamy green head when poured. It was best served chilled.

**lommite** A mineral found mainly on the planet Elom, it was a major raw material in the manufacture of transparisteel.

Lonay (left)

LOM series protocol droid

**LOM series protocol droid** A series of protocol droids produced by Industrial Automaton in an effort to break into the huge market held by Cybot Galactica with its 3PO series. Like that series some of the LOM droids took up unexpected vocations such as bounty hunting.

**Lonay** A clever but cowardly Twi'lek, he was one of the Vigos, or lieutenants, of Prince Xizor's Black Sun criminal organization. After the Battle of Endor, Lonay was present at a meeting to discuss Black Sun's reorganization.

**Londrah** A Defel assassin, he was skilled in the execution of targets with high rank and social stature, using his ability to blend into the shadows to his advantage. Londrah had been hired by the Empire during the Galactic Civil War to assassinate Mon Mothma. Years later, he also was hired to assassinate Yarr Hinter, a New Republic ambassador, but the attempt failed. It was believed that Gaen Drommel hired him for the hit.

**Loneozner, Camie** A young woman who lived in Anchorhead on Tatooine, she was a friend of Luke Skywalker. She frequented the Tosche power station along with her boyfriend, Laze "the Fixer" Loneozner, and the young Skywalker. Her family grew hydroponics gardens underground, buying the water from Luke's uncle Owen Lars. Camie and Fixer married before the Battle of Hoth.

**Loneozner, Laze (Fixer)** One of Luke Skywalker's friends on Tatooine, this overbearing young man was a mechanic at the Tosche power station in Anchorhead. He rarely used his given name, preferring the nickname Fixer. He was dating a young woman named Camie when Biggs Darklighter returned to Tatooine before joining the Alliance, and the two were later married and lived at the old Darklighter estate. When Luke returned to Tatooine on a mission to locate potential pilots for the Alliance, he met up with Fixer and Camie at the old Lars homestead. Fixer explained that the House of Tagge was buying up moisture farms, and that he had been planning to turn over the Lars farm to them. Skywalker objected, explaining his concern over Tagge's ties to the Empire. Both Camie and Fixer decided it was better to save themselves and alerted Imperial authorities to Luke's presence. Fixer, however, then felt guilty and did his best to warn Luke of the trouble he had caused.

Laze "Fixer" Loneozner (center) with Luke Skywalker (left), Camie Loneozner (back), and Biggs Darklighter (right)

Kéral Longknife

**Lone Scout-A** Along with the -A2, this series of civilian scout vessels was manufactured by Sienar Fleet Systems.

**Long, Gee** One of Auren Yomm's Colonial Games teammates during the early years of the New Order. Gee Long was among the many athletes from Umboo province who contracted the rooze virus after it was unleashed by Governor Koong.

**Long, Hokkor** The secretary in charge of scheduling for the Imperial Entertainer's Guild during the early years of the New Order. Shortly before Han Solo tried to rescue Chewbacca from Stars' End, Hokkor Long sent a message to Viceprex Hirken noting that the original entertainment troupe would not be arriving at the prison. The message was intercepted by Han, who used the information to create Madame Atuarre's Roving Performers as a cover for his crew to break into the facility.

**Longknife, Kéral** The demarch of the Twelve Tribes of Shiva IV shortly before the Battle of Yavin. Against the traditions of his people, Longknife agreed to become the blood-brother of Aron Peacebringer, forging a bond between the T'syriel and human populations of the planet.

**Longnose** A nickname given by Jaina Solo to one of the Squib assassins who worked for the Directors following the Yuuzhan Vong War. It helped her distinguish the Squib from his counterpart, Scarcheek. Both killers were dispatched to Tenupe to eliminate Jaina as part of the Directors' plan to exact a measure of revenge against

Han Solo and his wife, Leia Organa Solo. When Jaina apprehended the pair, she interrogated them about their mission before turning them over to the Killiks. Much to her chagrin, Jaina learned that the Killiks had bound the two Squibs and placed them in the slings of their trebuchets, then launched them like burnballs into a Chiss encampment.

***Longshot*** A cover name for the *Millennium Falcon* during the Yuuzhan Vong War. The transponder data that accompanied the *Longshot* indicated that the ship was a cruiser.

***Long Shot*** A converted Lantillian short-haul space yacht used by members of Green Squad of Reekeene's Roughnecks during the Galactic Civil War.

**Longspar, Gideon** The leader of the water-stealing Brigands who worked on Beheboth during the Galactic Civil War. When Longspar was defeated in combat by Luke Skywalker, Darial Anglethorn was able to destroy water-holding tanks and restore the planet's water supply.

**Lonn** One of Madame Aryn Thul's attendants, she served her aboard the *Tradewyn* following the Yuuzhan Vong War.

**Lonnaw** A planet in the Droma sector. It was the first stop on the shakedown cruise of the Outbound Flight after it left Yaga Minor, some five years after the Battle of Naboo.

**Loor, Kirtan** Formerly the Imperial liaison to Corellian Security, he was given the task of destroying Rogue Squadron by Ysanne Isard, director of Imperial Intelligence. Tall and lanky, Loor had black hair, a thinning widow's peak, and sharp features in a face slender as a cadaver's. He had enough ambition to dream about becoming a Grand Moff, and enough talent for dealing with regulations and bureaucracy to be a severe problem for anyone who stood in his way.

Loor had a visual memory retention rate of almost 100 percent, making him ideal for his Rogue-hunting task. He would have accomplished his aims at Talasea had it not been for the stupidity of Admiral Devlia, who was in charge of Imperial troops when they made their night raid on Rogue Squadron's base. As luck would have it, Loor just missed the Rogues' retaliatory raid on Vladet, although he was witness to the terrible destruction there. Shortly before the fall of Borleias, he was recalled to Imperial Center, again barely escaping death or capture. At headquarters, Isard gave him another task: overseeing the progress of General Derricote's Krytos project.

The Krytos virus was released into the planet's water supply shortly before the arrival of the New Republic fleet, but the disease did not spread rapidly enough to infect a larger portion of the alien inhabitants as planned. Although the project did not succeed, Isard didn't blame Loor for its failure. Instead, she placed him in charge of Imperial Center while she retreated to her sanctuary in the Super Star Destroyer *Lusankya.* Loor enjoyed his role as head of the terrorist Palpatine Counter-Insurgency Front, challenging the New Republic in the very same way that its agents had challenged the Empire.

Loor soon became vexed with interference from Fliry Vorru and realized that Vorru was calling the shots with full approval from Isard. Loor could see that his value to Isard was quickly coming to an end, so he went to see Nawara Ven, the Twi'lek Rogue Squadron member who was defending fellow Rogue Tycho Celchu against false charges of murder. Loor offered to testify for Celchu in exchange for immunity from prosecution, one million credits, and a new identity and new life on another world. He also would reveal the real spy within Rogue Squadron as well as every Imperial agent on Coruscant. But just as he was being escorted into the Justice Court to give his deposition, Loor was assassinated by one of Isard's sleeper agents.

**Loor, Kirtana** An alias assumed by Dynba Tesc as part of Corran Horn's daring plan to assist the Rebellion on Garqi.

**Loorne, Sares** A Jedi Master dispatched to Murkhana along with Roan Shryne and Bol Chatak, during the final stages of the Clone Wars. Master Loorne was among the many Jedi killed on Murkhana when the command to execute Order 66 was issued.

**Lopaki, Kyril** An Imperial soldier stationed on Alashan and serving under Major Grau during the early years of the Galactic Civil War. Ensign Lopaki graduated from the Imperial Academy shortly before the Battle of Yavin. He bristled at Grau's willingness to compromise, and his anger with his commanding officer boiled over when Grau agreed to a truce between the Imperial forces on the planet and Rebel Alliance agents Luke Skywalker and Leia Organa, who also had been stranded by Alashan's strange powers. Ensign Lopaki's true nature was revealed when he traveled to the Alliance's archaeological dig site and an avalanche badly injured an Imperial stormtrooper. Rather than try to save the man, Lopaki abandoned him in an effort to save his own life. He nearly captured Luke and Leia, but he was killed by the Sentinel creature that was dispatched to eliminate them.

**Loquasin** An Imperial drug developed to compel a being to talk during interrogation. It attacked the centers of the brain that provided stamina and willpower to resist, leaving a subject defenseless.

**Lor, Galon** One of the many Sith apprentices who trained at the Academy on Korriban during the Great Sith War. Galon spent his free time investigating the various Sith Lords buried in the Valley of the Dark Lords, and was one of the first students to discover the secrets of Ajunta Pall's tomb.

**Loran, Garik "Face"** Best known as a child actor who worked in a multitude of Imperial propaganda films. His face became a symbol for the Empire, and his films were responsible for large jumps in Imperial recruitment. Just as he was trying to get into more mature roles, he was captured by Rebel Alliance extremists. An Imperial attack on the Rebel outpost where he was taken resulted in both sides being decimated, and Loran sustained multiple injuries. He hid from the remaining Imperials and eventually made it back to Pantolomin.

Loran's parents then shipped him to their homeworld of Lorrd, where he recovered from his injuries and decided to join the Alliance. His supposed death was reported shortly before the Battle of Yavin, and the news broke the hearts of many young girls. Among most Alliance personnel, Loran was known as "Face" because of the popularity of his cherubic visage, although the battle left him with a few scars.

He eventually became a pilot with Comet Squadron, but was forced to eject in order to avoid a proton torpedo. In a debriefing, Edor Crespin told Loran that he'd never amount to much, and would never repay the debt he owed the Republic for serving the Empire. Crespin demoted him from pilot rank, but Loran later joined Wraith Squadron. Loran also served as the squadron's insertion expert and part-time cook. For his part in rescuing the *Night Caller* during Apwar Trigit's attack on Talasea, he was promoted to lieutenant. Loran became good friends with Ton Phanan, the two exchanging quips and developing a friendly rivalry. When Phanan was killed, he left Loran a large sum of money. After the defeat of Warlord Zsinj at Kuat, Loran was promoted to brevet captain by Wedge Antilles. He continued to lead Wraith Squadron after it was recommissioned as an infiltrator team, and was among the forces dispatched to monitor Yuuzhan Vong fleet movements after the aliens invaded the galaxy.

**Loratus Manufacturing** A manufacturer that produced a variety of mobile weapons platforms during the early stages of the New Order, many of which found their way into the arsenal of the Rebel Alliance during the Galactic Civil War.

*Garik "Face" Loran*

**Lorell Raiders** The pirates who originally settled the Hapes Cluster. They constantly raided the outer fringes of Old Republic territory, stealing women and supplies, until the Jedi Knights were forced to eliminate them.

*Lady Loren*

**Loren, Lady** A native of Velmor, she was betrothed to Prince Denid until the Empire subjugated the planet. Denid and Lady Loren fled offworld but crash-landed on a jungle planet many parsecs away, and Loren was killed. When Prince Denid returned to Velmor to help free his planet from Imperial control, Leia Organa played the role of Loren to make the sudden reappearance of Denid more palatable to the population.

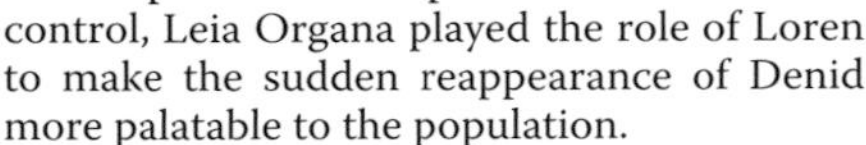

**Loro, Elscol** The leader of the resistance against Imperial forces on Cilpar, this reddish-brown-haired, dark-eyed woman took over the organization after her husband, Throm, died fighting the Empire. Initially she thought that the Rebellion had betrayed her movement, resulting in the destruction of two suburbs of Kiidan where her people had family and supporters. But with Rogue Squadron's intervention, Cilpar threw off the Empire's oppressive yoke; Elscol Loro was offered a position with the Rogues, and accepted.

Loro, an intelligent young woman with a fierce fighting spirit, felt the loss of her husband deeply, but she kept her feelings of loneliness hidden. After Throm's death, she was watched over by Groznik, a Wookiee, who transferred a life debt from Throm to Elscol. But Loro's actions soon grew reckless. She kept the other Rogues at a distance, refusing their help. Although her out-of-control tactics often won the day, Wedge Antilles discharged her from the squadron because she was jeopardizing the lives of the other pilots.

**Loronar Corporation** A huge, nearly galaxywide conglomerate, it was a manufacturer of many products, chief among them synthdroids and advanced spacecraft. The company used any method available to fulfill its corporate goals and increase its wealth and power.

**lor pelek** A Korunnai witch doctor or shaman. The words *lor pelek* meant "jungle master."

**Lorrd** Due to its close proximity to its own sun, this planet was subjected to large amounts of solar radiation. Its human inhabitants adapted to this harsh environment over the generations, developing extremely dark skin and eyes. The planet was bombed from orbit and enslaved by warriors from nearby Argazda during the Kanz Disorders. The Lorrdians were forced to further adapt in order to survive. The Lorrdians were forced to further adapt in order to survive. They became masters of kinetic communication, the art of conveying complex ideas through body language alone. They were also gifted mimics.

**Lorrd Academy for Aquatic Studies** A university in Lorrd City on Lorrd. It was dedicated to the discovery and preservation of knowledge about the oceans found on planets throughout the galaxy.

**Lorrd artifact** The name used by Dr. Heilan Rotham to describe the strange collection of tassels that was discovered by Jacen Solo at Toryaz Station some 10 years after the end of the Yuuzhan Vong War. Dr. Rotham later discovered that the tactile writing contained in the tassels formed the words of the Prophecy of the Sith.

*Elscol Loro*

**Lorrd Logistician Liberation League** A group of fanatical mathematicians working out of Lorrd City some 10 years after the end of the Yuuzhan Vong War.

**Lorso, Jana** An executive for Czerka Corporation based on Citadel Station following the Jedi Civil War, she was known by the Telos Security Force to have worked with criminals, using them to advance her own position and the needs of Czerka itself. When a former Czerka employee told the TSF about the corporation's dealings, Lorso hired a group of thugs to kill the informant. They were unable to complete the mission, however, as they were defeated by the Jedi Exile.

**Lortan** This expansionist species from the planet Lorta sent a battle fleet into 12 systems. It wiped out every planet it encountered in what became known as the Reslian Purge. They were finally stopped by an Imperial fleet about 10 years before the Battle of Yavin.

*Lorrd*

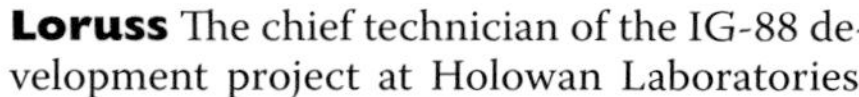

**Loruss** The chief technician of the IG-88 development project at Holowan Laboratories. An unattractive, bald woman with large gaps between her teeth, Loruss had tinted lenses implanted into her eye sockets to assist her failing vision. She admitted to Imperial Supervisor Gurdun that the schedules imposed by the Empire for the IG-88 project didn't leave enough time to test the prototypes. She was the second person killed in the labs when IG-88 gained sentience.

Lost Hope

**lossor** A large sea creature native to Varn.

**Lost City of the Jedi** Buried deep below the surface of Yavin 4, the city was built by ancient Jedi Knights and held great Jedi secrets in its computer library. Droids cared for the city and its hidden knowledge for ages. Ken, the secret grandson of Emperor Palpatine, was raised in the city by the droid DJ-88 and taught to reject the dark side. Under the sway of a truth serum, Ken betrayed the city's location to Prophet of the Dark Side Kadann, but Kadann and his troopers were trapped inside the shut-down city by Alliance leaders on the surface, and the Jedi secrets were lost forever after a trooper accidentally destroyed the library computer.

***Lost Hope*** A decrepit freighter used by Corran Horn to infiltrate the planet Garqi in order to avoid being detected by the Yuuzhan Vong, who controlled the planet.

***Lost Lady*** A starship owned by Sullustan con artist Vir Nurb, it made regular runs between Nal Hutta and its moon Nar Shaddaa. An old Ubrikkian Dartiss-5 Caravel space barge, the *Lost Lady* carried passengers and cargo as a front for the transport of illegal substances between the two worlds. It was armed with four turret-mounted turbolaser cannons and four concussion missile launchers.

**Lost Ones** A gang of street-toughened youngsters who hung out on the lower levels of Coruscant some 20 years after the Battle of Endor. Their symbol was a cross inside a triangle, and their leader was a teenage boy named Norys.

Mak Lotor

**Lost Twenty, the** The term the Jedi Order used through the Clone Wars to describe the 20 Knights who had voluntarily left the Order to pursue their own agendas. The Order chose to remember the Lost Twenty by making bronzium busts of each former Jedi as a reminder of their standing and of the regret at their departure.

**Lotide** A swamp-covered world, it housed an Imperial research installation during the Galactic Civil War.

**lotiramine** A drug that counteracted skirtopanol, which was used much like a truth serum to interrogate prisoners. However, mixing lotiramine with skirtopanol was known to induce chemical amnesia, or in some cases death.

One of the Lost Twenty, Count Dooku

**Lotor, Mak** This Jedi apprentice was part of a task force sent to Jabiim during the Clone Wars. He was the most educated of the so-called Padawan Pack and the closest to passing the Jedi Trials. Like many of the students thrown into battle, Lotor lost his Master to the Jabiimite rebels. When the surviving Padawans banded together to stop the advance of Alto Stratus, Kass Tod and Mak Lotor fought bravely for four days before cornering the Jabiim Separatist leader on the battlefield. Although Stratus injured Lotor's shoulder, Tod managed to sever Stratus's right leg before a Hailfire droid fired its rockets at the Jedi, killing them in a fiery explosion.

**loudhailer** A portable device used to amplify a person's voice.

***Love Commander*** An aging PLY 2400 yacht acquired by Lando Calrissian in a sabacc match several years after the Swarm War. Lando decided to keep the ship's name, and maintained the yacht as a backup to his primary vessel, *Lady Luck.* Having the *Love Commander* proved useful during the Corellian secession crisis a decade after the Yuuzhan Vong War, when Calrissian agreed to accompany Han and Leia Organa Solo on a clandestine fact-finding mission to Corellia. He posed as Bescat Offdurmin, the ship's owner, to get through the Galactic Alliance's blockade of the Corellian system. Shortly after Lando and his wife, Tendra, discovered that they were going to have a child, Lando loaned the *Love Commander* to the Solos to help them infiltrate the *Anakin Solo* and steal navigational information and other intelligence about their renegade son, Jacen.

***Love Is Waiting*** One of the holofeatures that Sonniod brought to Han Solo on Kamar during the early years of the New Order. It was a sweeping musical that followed the adventures of a wayward hero whose travels were highlighted by well-choreographed dance numbers set to a soaring musical score. The holo offended the Kamarian Badlanders who had been watching *Varn, World of Water,* a documentary that had become the centerpiece of a vengeful Kamarian cult. The worshippers tore down Solo's holotheater and forced him off the planet after seeing just the opening scenes of *Love Is Waiting.*

**Lowbacca** The nephew of the Wookiee Chewbacca, he was the first of his species to train at Luke Skywalker's Jedi academy. Nicknamed Lowie, the 19-year-old Jedi trainee had always shown an affinity for the Force. He was quickly befriended by Jacen and Jaina Solo. Lowbacca also quickly bonded with Tenel Ka. Together the Jedi initiates explored the jungles of Yavin 4.

Lowbacca once discovered an old, crashed TIE fighter that the young Jedi students repaired—only to be confronted by the pilot, who kidnapped the twins and held them hostage until they were rescued. Just weeks later, the twins—this time along with Lowbacca—were again kidnapped on a visit to Lando Calrissian's *GemDiver Station.* The perpetrator was a Nightsister from Dathomir, who schemed to turn the three to the dark side by forcing them to train at the Shadow Academy. Lowbacca was separated from the twins, taunted, and mistreated. Eventually they managed to escape and return to their studies. Later, Lowie returned to Kashyyyk to visit his sister Sirrakuk during her rite of passage to adulthood.

When the Diversity Alliance grew in power, Lowbacca was taken captive, along with his sister and the Jedi student Lusa. They were rescued by the Solo children and testified against the Diversity Alliance on Coruscant. Following the death of Chewbacca at Sernpidal, Lowbacca and his cousin Lumpawaroo were chosen to continue serving out the life debt to Han Solo and his family. Han, still grieving the loss of Chewbacca, asked them to wait until he had reconciled himself to Chewie's death before taking over for him. Lowbacca was patient, and spent much of his time watching over the Solo children. He was one of the Jedi chosen for the assault on the *Baanu Rass* at Myrkr, and was one of the few Jedi to survive the destruction of the voxyn queen.

Lowbacca studied captured Yuuzhan Vong technology and, with Jaina's help, discovered that every Yuuzhan Vong ship emitted a unique gravitic signature, which allowed the alien invaders to track their ships through the galaxy. Lowbacca later served as one of Jaina Solo's lieutenants in the Twin Suns Squadron, and fought beside her in direct combat against Warmaster Tsavong Lah in the mines of Ebaq 9. During the final stages of the war, Lowbacca was one of several Jedi Knights who were bonded to seed-partners and provided with Sekotan starships from the living planet Zonama Sekot.

Five years after the war's end, when Unu-Thul sent out a telepathic call for help, Lowbacca was among seven young Jedi compelled to travel to the Unknown Regions. He was captured by a Chiss warship in the Swarm War that followed, and held prisoner until

Lowbacca

the conflict over Kr was resolved, with the Gorog nest being destroyed and the Qoribu hives relocated to another world deeper in the Unknown Regions. Lowbacca returned to the Galactic Alliance, but only after Jagged Fel argued for his release.

Because of his lack of contact with the Colony, Lowbacca didn't become a Joiner, although he continued to support the efforts of Jaina Solo and Zekk in helping the Killiks wage their war against the Chiss. To this end, Lowbacca and Tesar Sebatyne relayed the discussions of Master Skywalker and the new Jedi Order to Raynar's mother, Lady Aryn Dro Thul, in an effort to keep her aware of any possible actions against him. When Luke discovered their duplicity, he reprimanded them but did not expel them from the Order, recognizing that they were acting out of loyalty and not malice. Instead, he dispatched both of them to Dagobah for the duration of the conflict, so that they could meditate on what it meant to be a Jedi Knight.

*Tyler Lucian*

**Lowickan asteroid belt** A region of space debris that was the only known source of Lowickan firegems. It was located in the Pa'lowick system, near Kessel.

***Loyal Defender*** A Galactic Alliance warship that saw action during the Second Battle of Fondor. The *Loyal Defender* was attacked by the ships of the Maw Irregular Fleet, which used a metal-crystal phase shifter to seriously degrade the integrity of the *Loyal Defender*'s hull. The vessel took a pounding, and its commander was forced to issue an order to abandon ship.

**Loyalist Committee** A committee formed by Chancellor Palpatine in anticipation of negotiations with the Confederacy of Independent Systems shortly before the Clone Wars.

**L'pwacc Den Port** One of the largest cities on Selonia. During the early stages of the Yuuzhan Vong War, riots spread throughout the town after the New Republic approved a plan to use Centerpoint Station as a weapon against the Yuuzhan Vong.

**Lsu, Raskta** A Jedi Master, she was part of the Army of Light during the final years of the New Sith Wars. Raskta Lsu was named in honor of Raskta Fenni, a noted Echani duelist, and she lived up to her namesake by becoming the Jedi Order's most skilled martial artist. She was one of the few who ever attained the title of Jedi Weapons Master. She spent her life studying ways in which the Force could be used to hone her skills.

A veteran of the Battle of Ruusan, Master Lsu wielded a pair of blue lightsabers in combat. When Lord Valenthyne Farfalla put together a mission to capture Darth Bane on Tython, she agreed to be part of the team and volunteered her starship, the *Justice Crusader,* to get them there as swiftly as possible. She took her former student, Sarro Xaj, with her, knowing that his skills would be valuable. During the battle against Bane, Raskta discovered that the Dark Lord's living orbalisk armor was all but impenetrable, even under the most intense lightsaber attacks she could muster. After Bane's apprentice, Zannah, killed Sarro Xaj, she ran Master Lsu through with her lightsaber, killing her almost instantly.

**L'toth, Been** The son of Kiles L'toth, this Dornean took his father's place at the head of the Astrographic Survey Institute. Been and his teams were charged with discovering the exact origins of the Yuuzhan Vong, and surmised that they were extragalactic. L'toth rejected the theory that the Yuuzhan Vong had evolved in the Tingel Arm, citing the area's proximity to the Corporate Sector and the Imperial Remnant, and pointing out that an advanced civilization so close to those densely populated areas would have been discovered years before.

**L'toth, Kiles** A Dornean, he was associate director of the Astrographic Survey Institute. Kiles L'toth was an old friend of General Etahn A'baht, commander of the New Republic's Fifth Fleet, and the general asked him to assemble a survey team to be sent to Koornacht Cluster to do some undercover scouting for the New Republic. The ship that carried the team, the *Astrolabe,* was destroyed at Doornik-1142 by a secret Yevethan fleet.

**Lucazec** The arid homeworld of the Fallanassi. It was invaded by the Empire, which hoped to turn the mystical religious order to its own use. The Fallanassi resisted long enough to escape offplanet, but left behind hidden messages for their children, who had been in schools on other worlds. The Empire left a small garrison there, hoping to capture a returning Fallanassi and make him or her read the messages. The garrison remained active after the Battle of Endor, oblivious to the change in government. Its agents nearly captured Akanah, but they were cut down by Luke Skywalker.

**Lucian, Tyler** A Rebel who deserted the Alliance shortly before the Battle of Yavin, fearing that he would die when the first Death Star destroyed Yavin 4. After learning of the victory at Yavin, he fled to Centares in shame, only to be tracked down by bounty hunter Valance as well as Darth Vader. Vader had come to wring out information about the pilot who had destroyed the first Death Star, and Valance had come to ensure Vader didn't get it. After Valance was defeated by Vader in combat, Lucian decided that he could not let Vader have the information he sought. Rather than be captured, Lucian committed suicide by jumping into the toxic Rubyflame Lake.

***Lucid Voice*** A *Providence*-class destroyer, it was one of two sister ships of the *Invisible Hand.* It often was deployed throughout the Mid Rim in order to confuse intelligence agents of the Galactic Republic about the exact whereabouts of General Grievous during the Clone Wars.

**lucksprite** According to the Ewoks of the Forest Moon of Endor, lucksprites were responsible for meting out good or bad fates to the various beings that lived on the moon. There were both good lucksprites and bad lucksprites, dispensing fortune and misfortune as they saw fit.

***Lucky Despot*** A no-longer-spaceworthy cargo hauler, it was sunk into the sand and turned into a hotel and casino near the center of Mos Eisley spaceport on Tatooine. The *Lucky Despot* was owned by Lady Valarian, a Whiphid and local crime lord who was an archrival of Jabba the Hutt.

***Lucky Dragon*** A Hapan Battle Dragon, one of the few vessels that the Hapes Consortium provided to patrol the edges of the Transitory Mists during the weeks that followed the Second Battle of Fondor. The *Lucky Dragon* was on duty when Jaina Solo returned from an encounter with her brother on the Nickel One asteroid, and offered her medical assistance before she traveled to the Jedi base.

*Wam "Blam" Lufba*

**Lucky Star** A cantina and restaurant located in the dilapidated remains of a casino on Nar Shaddaa during the New Order.

***Lucre*** A supply transport ship that was part of a small fleet supporting the *Errant Venture* during the Yuuzhan Vong War. The *Lucre* was the ship used by Corran Horn, Anakin Solo, and Tahiri Veila to obtain provisions on Eriadu shortly after the Battle of Duro.

***Lucrehulk*-class core ship** *See* core ship.

**Lufba, Wam "Blam"** A diminutive Yuzzum who was kidnapped from the Forest Moon of Endor several years before the Battle of Endor. He and his comrades were sold to Jabba the Hutt by poachers who hoped that Jabba would take them as payment for an old debt. The angry Hutt simply threw them all—poachers and Yuzzum—into his rancor pit, and only Lufba managed to survive. He fled into the rancor's holding area and grabbed an abandoned hunting rifle, shooting three of Jabba's guards before he was rescued by Pote Snitkin. Snitkin asked Jabba to keep the Yuzzum around as a marksman. Jabba agreed, and turned him over to Snitkin to manage. It was Snitkin who gave the Yuzzum the nickname Blam. Upon returning to Jabba's palace on Tatooine, Lufba became fast friends with Joh Yowza, and he chose to remain at the palace during the execution of Luke Skywalker and Han Solo. When word reached the palace that Jabba had died at the Pit of Carkoon, Lufba realized that he was free and joined Yowza on a musical tour through the Outer Rim, returning to Tatooine to establish an extermination business.

Zona Luka

Lumat

**Lugus** One of the revolutionaries who tried to overthrow Queen Sarna of Drogheda during the months following the Battle of Endor.

**Luka** The name given by Yarna d'al' Gargan to one of her female cubs in honor of Luke Skywalker.

**Luka, Zona** A Jedi who apprenticed under Jedi Master Dominus some 4,000 years before the Galactic Civil War. She was turned to the dark side, and killed Dominus during the Sith War.

**lum** A fermented, fiery ale, it had a sweet and not-unpleasant soapy taste. In areas of space where it was outlawed, smugglers called lumrunners snuck past customs inspectors to supply the drink to thirsty buyers.

**luma** A small light source found in emergency survival packs.

**luma flare** Any rocket-propelled flare used to indicate a being's position during search and rescue operations.

**Lumat** An Ewok warrior on the Forest Moon of Endor, he was also his tribe's chief woodcutter. Married to Zephee, they were the parents of Latara, Nippet, and Wiley.

**Luminous Gardens Spa** Located on a hillside above the Boiling Sea on Drall, the Luminous Gardens health spa catered to all beings. Masseuses from a wide variety of species were employed, providing an extensive clientele with expensive relaxation and makeovers.

**Lumiya** The months following the Battle of Hoth were especially trying for the heroes of the Rebellion. With morale crushed after the abandonment of Echo Base and the capture of Han Solo, the Rebels faced the unthinkable possibility that Luke Skywalker had killed a fellow Rebel pilot.

Following the Rebel Alliance's relocation to a temporary outpost on Arbra, Luke had struck up a close friendship with fellow Rogue Squadron member Shira Brie. She was bright, talented, and beautiful, and their friendship evolved into something closer. Rogue Squadron was then pressed into service, striking at a secret Imperial armada, infiltrating the fleet by using captured and modified TIE fighters. The TIEs were outfitted with transponders that allowed the Rogues to identify one another amid the enemy ships. During the thick of battle, Skywalker's transponder malfunctioned. He was unable to determine which of the surrounding starfighters were, in fact, his allies. Forgoing technology as he had during the Battle of Yavin, Luke instead relied upon the Force. He used his instincts to pick his targets, and fired at advancing enemy craft. One of the vessels that Luke shot out of the skies was Shira Brie's.

Returning to Arbra, Skywalker did not find a hero's welcome. His rank and service were suspended until Alliance analysts could determine just what had happened. Shaken, Luke began to question his faith in the Force. Skywalker and the Wookiee Chewbacca left Arbra to conduct their own investigation. They journeyed to Shalyvane, supposed homeworld of Shira Brie. There they learned the truth about this enigmatic woman.

Shira Elan Colla Brie was born on Coruscant and spent her life serving as a key agent of the Empire. It was Darth Vader who handpicked her for accelerated training in Imperial Intelligence. Her mind was enhanced through mnemonic drug training, her body hardened through exotic martial arts. Proving herself a capable agent, Brie was dispatched by Vader to infiltrate the Rebel Alliance.

Lumiya

One of her primary goals was to discredit Luke Skywalker. Vader hoped that his son, finding no quarter within the Alliance ranks, would eventually wander back to him. Brie almost succeeded when Luke destroyed her fighter, but Skywalker was able to prove his innocence and reveal Brie's past.

Brie did not die in the TIE fighter incident. Her crippled body was picked up by Vader's agents, and she recuperated within secret chambers aboard the Super Star Destroyer *Executor.* Vader watched closely as Brie's body was rebuilt and enhanced through mechanical implants. Fueled by rage and an already promising strength in

Lumiya was once known as Shira Brie.

the Force, Brie emerged from the bacta tanks a changed woman. She had given in to hatred, and was renamed the Dark Lady Lumiya.

Impressed with his pupil's development, Vader began to hone her Force abilities. Vader knew that no secret could be kept from his Master, the Emperor. He presented Palpatine with Lumiya as a gift, a new Emperor's Hand. Palpatine accepted, and Vader continued her training. Lumiya was sequestered on the ancient Sith world of Ziost when the Battle of Endor forever changed the Empire. It was on this frigid world that she crafted her unique weapon, a lightwhip built of Kaiburr crystal shards and Mandalorian iron.

Lumiya then emerged as the cyborg chief of security for the slaving guild on Herdessa. She attempted to arrest a visiting Princess Leia Organa, but was thwarted by a revolution against the guild. Though Lumiya sustained a blaster wound, she survived the battle to swear vengeance on the Alliance.

She then surfaced on Kinooine, with her Imperial forces allied with fearsome Nagai warriors. Skywalker and Lumiya were finally reunited, and the two engaged in a spectacular duel. At first, Lumiya bested Luke and brutally wounded his allies Dani and Kiro. In their second battle, Skywalker managed to defeat Lumiya, shattering her armor and revealing her to be Shira Brie.

Lumiya

In the nebulous and shifting alliances that plagued Imperial fragments during the Nagai invasion, Lumiya lent her Imperial resources—which included three Star Destroyers, two frigates and four corvettes—to the fleet belonging to the Tofs. When the Tof incursion eventually was repulsed, Lumiya disappeared.

Lumiya's travels brought her to the Mecrosa Order's trove of Sith lore. Studying ancient Sith knowledge, Lumiya emerged after the Yuuzhan Vong War to lure Jacen Solo to her asteroid sanctuary in the MZX32905 system. It was Lumiya's teachings that would start Solo's turn into Darth Caedus. As part of Caedus's rise to power, he killed Mara Jade Skywalker, though his guilt as the murderer remained unknown for some time. In his anguish, Luke Skywalker mistakenly believed Lumiya was the killer, and slew her in turn, an act of vengeance that put him on the precipice of the dark side.

**lumni-spice** The rarest form of spice in the galaxy, it was found only on Hoth, deep in the caves of the dragon-slug. The combination of Hoth's environment and the presence of the dragon-slug made lumni-spice difficult to harvest and expensive to purchase.

**Lumpawaroo (Lumpy)** As a youth, Chewbacca's son was named Lumpawarrump, often shortened to just Lumpy. He was reserved and quiet because he had been raised by his mother and grandfather while Chewbacca was fulfilling his life debt to Han Solo. When Chewbacca finally returned to Kashyyyk several years after the formation of the New Republic, he worked with Lumpy to ready him for the Test of Ascension.

The first test was interrupted when Chewbacca learned that Han Solo had been captured by the Yevetha. Chewbacca left to rescue him, taking Lumpy, Jowdrrl, Dryanta, and Shoran as his soldiers. When Shoran was shot during the initial firefight with the *Pride of Yevetha,* Lumpawarrump took his place. He himself took a blaster bolt while rescuing Solo, but he continued the effort without complaining. The young Wookiee's heroic efforts during the rescue earned him the baldrick of adulthood. He adopted the adult name of Lumpawaroo after passing the Test of Ascension, although he preferred to be called Waroo.

Years later, Waroo served as a guide for Han and Leia Solo, when they secretly traveled to Kashyyyk in an effort to convince the Wookiees to secede from the Galactic Alliance. When Jacen Solo launched his attack on Kashyyyk, Waroo joined Han and Leia aboard the *Millennium Falcon,* helping pilot the ship while the group worked to put out the forest fires caused by Jacen's attacks.

**lumpen** Small creatures bioengineered by the Yuuzhan Vong to serve as a form of

Murk Lundi

Lumpawaroo, when he was known as Lumpy

identification. Resembling a fist-sized nugget of flesh and fur, the lumpen's bodily fluids contained special chemicals that signified an individual's authority to access certain areas. When squeezed, the lumpen released its fluids onto a piece of parchment, which could be read for the proper signs of identification.

**Lumus** A hulking alien member of Nevo's gang. Lumus questioned the intelligence of hunting down Boba Fett, even if Darth Vader himself gave the order. Lumus was killed by Fett on Maryx Minor, after Nevo tried to apprehend the bounty hunter.

**Lunasa** A noted bounty hunter who operated during the years before the Battle of Naboo.

**luna-weed** The leaves of this plant were dried and chewed, often causing the user to act incoherently. Many beings believed that luna-weed had a numbing effect on the body, and chewed it to ease the pain of an injury. The name of the plant stemmed from the fact that its burgundy leaves grew only in the moonlight.

**Lundi, Murk** This one-eyed Quermian was a noted professor of galactic history on Coruscant before the Battle of Naboo. He was an expert on the lore of the ancient Sith, and his lectures on their magic and the dark side of the Force were extremely popular with much of the galaxy, although the Jedi Council refused to comment on his theories. He went so far as to create a communications network among various sects of Sith devotees, providing himself with easier access to their information.

Lundi's teachings largely were recorded in what became known as *The Lundi Series,* which provided the modern Jedi with an insight into the ways of the Sith.

Lundi took a sabbatical some six years before the Battle of Naboo, in an effort to recover a Sith Holocron that was believed to exist at the bottom of Kodai's oceans. Norval, a power-crazed student, sensed the power of the holocron and traveled to Kodai to take it for himself, but the device was lost in the struggle for control. The appearance of Qui-Gon Jinn and Obi-Wan Kenobi forced Norval to flee. However, Lundi was captured by the Jedi and held prisoner on Coruscant.

The historian languished in prison for 10 years, going slowly insane, until the Jedi decided to attempt to recover the holocron again. This time, Lundi was accompanied by Obi-Wan and his own apprentice, Anakin Skywalker. Norval had the holocron, but the Jedi were able to recover it from him. The former student was killed by an associate; Lundi died shortly afterward, too.

**lungworm** A Yuuzhan Vong bioconstruct that allowed an individual to breathe oxygen in a hostile environment. The worm, carried in a coil on the user's back, was connected to the mouth with a hard-shelled form of gnullith. As part of its natural metabolism, the lungworm produced breathable oxygen, which was expelled and collected in a specialized organ for passage to the gnullith.

**Lunis** A Weequay Jedi Master who was actively teaching when the Clone Wars erupted, he was forced to become a warrior. Master Lunis and his Padawan, Obs Kaj, were dispatched to Katanos VII to investigate alleged cloning activities taking place on the planet. They discovered that local miners did have cloning facilities, but produced only deformed clones. The miners decided to kill Lunis for a bounty from Count Dooku. Lunis tried to form a mental bond with Kaj, but she had become disillusioned with the Jedi Order, decided to leave, and cut herself off from her Master. Lunis was killed in front of her.

**Lupo** The owner of a cantina that was frequented by swoop racers who lived on Nar Shaddaa following the Jedi Civil War. Although he accepted any challengers, Lupo ensured that his racing droid, C9-T9, always was the winner of a race. His perfect record came to an end when the Exile managed to defeat the droid.

**Luptoomian** The human inhabitants of the planet Luptoom. The Luptoomians were known for their bizarre style of clothing, which seemed to resemble plants. It was not uncommon to meet a Luptoomian who appeared to be encased in the trunk of a many-limbed tree, only to realize that the protrusions were simply part of the clothing.

**Lur** An icy and turbulent planet, it was located just outside the borders of the Corporate Sector. The upper layers of Lur's atmosphere were heavily ionized, creating intense electrical storms. This, combined with gale-force winds and freezing temperatures, made starship landings hazardous. The fur-covered, bipedal inhabitants were experts in genetic manipulation and lived in cities of a few thousand each. They were peaceful and sociable, and very few ever chose to leave Lur. Han Solo and Chewbacca were unwillingly involved in a Lurrian slavery operation during their early adventures.

**Lurmen** A species of lemur-like humanoids found on numerous worlds including Mygeeto and Maridun.

**Lusa** A young Chironian, she was a friend of Jaina Solo. Lusa had four legs and a reddish gold horse-like body with white spots on her hindquarters. Her torso was humanoid, with reddish gold curly hair on her head. She later became a Jedi Knight, but was killed by voxyn on Chiron during the Yuuzhan Vong War.

***Lusankya*** A Super Star Destroyer, it was constructed in secret at Kuat Drive Yards under the false name *Executor.* It immediately was buried beneath Imperial Center during Emperor Palpatine's reign to serve as his emergency evacuation vehicle. Director of Imperial Intelligence Ysanne Isard used it as her private prison and sanctuary. There she subjected prisoners to endless torture, interrogation, and mind-control experiments, including brainwashing.

Most who emerged from the *Lusankya* alive came out as sleeper agents, in effect remotely controlled human bombs who did the Empire's bidding—no matter how horrible—when activated. The facility imprisoned top Rebel Alliance officials and daredevil pilots and heroes. When Isard was forced to flee Imperial Center in the face of the New Republic invasion, she had the *Lusankya* blast out of its tomb, devastating more than 100 square kilometers of Imperial City and killing millions of its inhabitants.

Fleeing to Thyferra, the *Lusankya* came under the command of Joak Drysso, who used it to attack Rogue Squadron's space station base near Yag'Dhul. The ship was badly damaged and surrendered to the New Republic as a result of the Battle of Thyferra. It underwent repair and refitting at the shipyards at Bilbringi. Several secret chambers were discovered during the refit, and New Republic engineers modified them to serve as biocontainment areas. Thus, the *Lusankya* became less of a warship and more of a research vessel. Wedge Antilles was given command of the ship for a special task force in defense of the planet Phaeda from Imperial forces.

During the Yuuzhan Vong War, the *Lusankya* was part of the defense fleet assigned to protect Coruscant. When the capital planet was conquered by the alien invaders, Commander Eldo Davip escaped the destruction and regrouped with a small fleet at Borleias. After successfully defending the planet from the Yuuzhan Vong's initial strikes, Davip and Antilles began taking the huge ship apart for what would become known as Operation Emperor's Spear. Weapons emplacements were removed and placed on smaller ships, and large portions of the interior were gutted. The resulting construction, known as the Beltway, became a huge needle-shaped ramming device. As the final defense of Borleias ground on, the *Lusankya* took heavy damage that ate away at the ship's surface and gradually revealed the needle underneath. Commander Davip then used all remaining engine power to drive the ship into the Yuuzhan Vong worldship in orbit around the planet. Just before impact, Davip managed to escape in a small shuttle. The *Lusankya* drove deep into the ship, causing huge amounts of damage before both ships exploded.

**Luscen** One of the many Jabiimi Loyalists who fought against the Imperial occupation of his homeworld during the early years of the Galactic Civil War. When Leia Organa and Luke Skywalker arrived on Jabiim to support the Loyalists, Luke was captured because of his relationship to Anakin Skywalker, and Luscen was placed in charge of a holding cell that contained Leia and Nera Dantels. A group of Imperial stormtroopers attacked the Loyalist headquarters, and Luscen was shot and killed. His death gave Captain Dantels time to shoot the stormtroopers, allowing the Alliance agents to escape.

**Luure, M'yet** A senior Exodeenian Senator to the New Republic and friend to Leia Or-

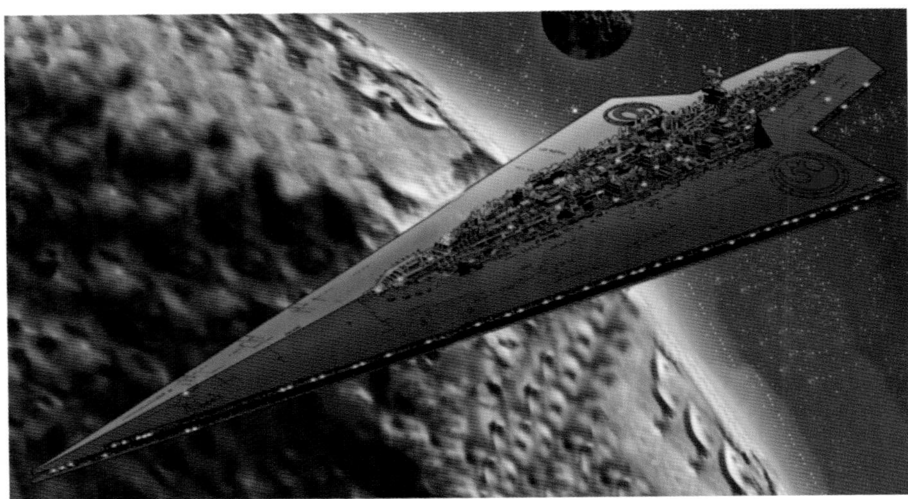

Lusankya

gana Solo, he was killed when Dolph's sabotaged droids exploded during a Senate meeting on Coruscant.

**Luwingo** The first mate on the *Hyperspace Marauder,* he was a partner of Lo Khan, the ship's owner. Luwingo was a Yaka cyborg with brain implants like the other members of his species. Although he appeared somewhat dull, he could beat an L7 logician droid in hologames on a regular basis.

*Luwingo*

**Luxum** A female member of the Iron Knights during the Yuuzhan Vong War.

**luxum crystal** One of the many crystals used by the ancient Sith Lords in the construction of a lightsaber. Luxum crystals were formed from minerals found in the waters of Lake Natth on Ambria. It took long hours of meditation to create one of the crystals, which were used almost exclusively by the Dark Jedi of the Great Sith War era.

**Lweilot asteroid belt** Located in the Bseto system, this belt—some 90 million kilometers wide—occupied the third orbital position around the white dwarf star Bseto.

**Lwhekk** A hot, jungle-covered planet that was the homeworld of the Ssi-ruuvi and P'w'eck species. It was the center of the Ssi-ruuvi Imperium. Located in the Unknown Regions, Lwhekk was captured by the Yuuzhan Vong as part of a plan to establish a foothold along the borders of the galaxy. The Yuuzhan Vong then hatched an elaborate plan to capture Bakura as well, playing on the Bakurans' fear of the Ssi-ruuk by sending a P'w'eck emissary to negotiate an alliance.

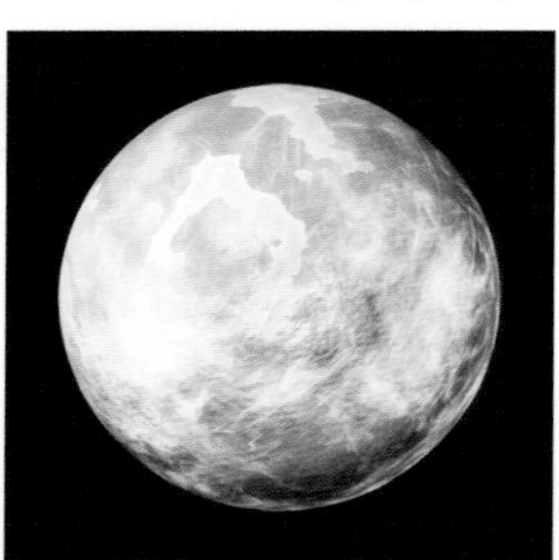
*Lwhekk*

**Lwothin** The advance leader of the P'w'eck Emancipation Movement during the Yuuzhan Vong War. Outwardly, Lwothin represented his people in an effort to form an alliance with the Bakurans, which would allow both species and planets to coexist outside the control of the New Republic. In reality, he was merely a puppet of his Ssi-ruuvi masters, who themselves were being controlled by the Yuuzhan Vong. Lwothin did exactly what the Keeramak ordered him to do. However, the Keeramak and its Ssi-ruuvi cohorts didn't anticipate the desire for independence of their P'w'eck associates. After the Solo family and the surviving members of the Freedom movement were brought before the Keeramak, Lwothin was ordered to shoot them dead. Instead, he turned his weapon and killed the Keeramak, ending the plot to subjugate Bakura. In the wake of the P'w'eck uprising, Lwothin agreed to ally the P'w'eck with the Bakurans in a common defense against their enemies.

**Lwyll** The wife of the smuggler Roa, she was a striking woman with masses of wavy white-blond hair and an elegant face. Lwyll had known Han Solo since the onetime smuggler worked for her husband. She was killed during the Yuuzhan Vong War.

**Ly'alu, Tensh** One of the many new Jedi Knights who graduated from Luke Skywalker's Jedi praxeum on Yavin 4 during the New Republic. Upon achieving the rank of Jedi Knight, Ly'alu was assigned to monitor Ryloth.

**Lyari** An Ishi Tib, she was one of many independent spacers, along with her friend Zelara, to become Joiners at the Lizil nest following the Yuuzhan Vong War. They became attracted to Luke Skywalker, who failed in his attempt to break the ties to the hive through Force persuasion.

**Lybeya system** Located within the Bajic sector of the Outer Rim, the system contained the Vergesso asteroid field. The Tenloss Syndicate built a shipyard in one of the larger asteroids in the Lybeya system, which was used by the Rebel Alliance until it was eliminated by Darth Vader and the Imperial fleet prior to the Battle of Endor.

**Lycan** A Dark Jedi who roamed the galaxy during the years before the Battle of Naboo. Shortly after the battle, Lycan was captured by a Jedi Knight and transported to Coruscant for imprisonment. He escaped and attacked the Jedi, causing the ship to crash on a sparsely settled world. Leaving the burning ship, Lycan discovered a homestead where he was confronted by a young boy, Neas Nyl. The boy bravely defended his home, firing a single shot with his father's blaster that caught Lycan in the left temple, causing irreparable damage to his left eye and part of his brain. In his anger, Lycan killed the boy and fled the planet. He roamed the galaxy for several weeks, but his wounds caused him many problems. Lycan was pursued across the Outer Rim Territories by Darca Nyl. Lycan realized that he had forgotten who he was, and when the dead boy's father provided his name, Lycan felt the missing pieces of his mind slip back into place. As Lycan gloated, Nyl set off destructive charges, trapping Lycan beneath tons of rubble and ending his reign of terror.

***Lycoming*** A quarantine enforcement cruiser that patrolled the Meridian sector for the New Republic after Seti Ashgad and Dzym unleashed the Death Seed plague. It intercepted the freighter *Zicreex,* which was transporting R2-D2, C-3PO, and Yarbolk Yemm to Cybloc XII.

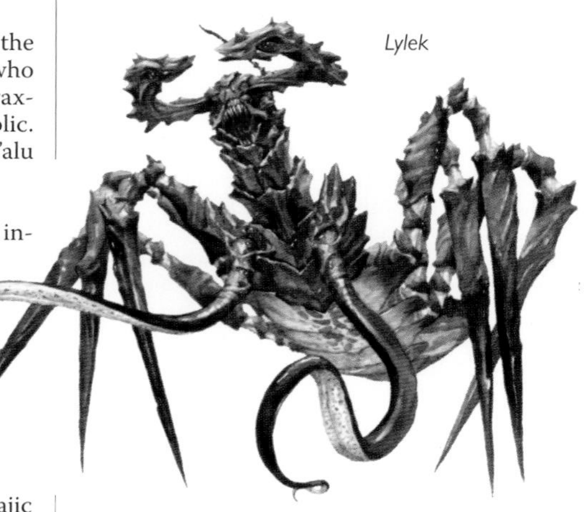
*Lylek*

**lylek** An enormous insectoid predator native to Ryloth.

**Lyll, Darak** An enormous Alderaanian member of that planet's minimal underground early in the Galactic Civil War. He was known among the criminal element as a supplier of spice and other illicit substances. Lyll was a tall, elderly man with graying hair and a growing paunch. A young Han Solo once tried to sell some stolen glitterstim to Lyll, but the man declined on the grounds that it was extremely hard to sell it on Alderaan.

**Lyn, Arden** A former teräs käsi master, she was a member of the Followers of Palawa warriors; they flocked to support the Kashi Mer exile, Xendor, in the wake of the Force Wars in the ancient past. During the First Great Schism, Arden Lyn was defeated in battle by Jedi Master Awdrysta Pina, who used the *Morichro* technique to still Arden's heart. Her connection to the dark side of the Force managed to keep her alive, and Lyn eventually awoke thou-

*Arden Lyn*

sands of years later, shortly after Emperor Palpatine's rise to power. As a Force-sensitive, she escaped capture by High Inquisitor Tremayne only to be captured later by Inquisitor Torbin, who cut off her arm in a struggle.

Torbin kept her alive, recognizing her connection to the dark side of the Force, and brought her before Palpatine. She became one of the Emperor's Hands, and was summoned by Darth Vader to lead an assault team against the Rebel Alliance. In the wake of the Battle of Yavin, however, Arden Lyn defected from Imperial service and started training her own students. She even tried to help rogue Admiral Zaarin kidnap Palpatine, but Inquisitor Tremayne thwarted the attempt. Arden Lyn fled, hoping to locate an ancient Kashi Mer talisman that would bring her power enough to defeat the Empire. She was eventually hunted down and killed by Palpatine himself.

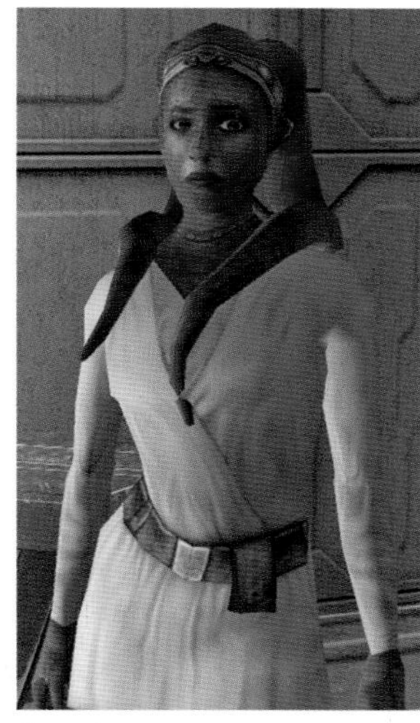
*Borna Lys*

**Lyric** A Yavin 8 native who was discovered to be strong in the Force by Luke Skywalker and Tionne. She was brought to the Jedi praxeum on Yavin 4 about a year before her changing ceremony. She was befriended by Anakin Solo and Tahiri, but began to fail physically as her natural metamorphosis started. Her friends accompanied her back to Yavin 8 and attended her changing ceremony in the Sistra Mountain. She remained loyal to the Jedi, but later was hunted down and killed by a Yuuzhan Vong voxyn some 27 years after the Battle of Yavin.

**Lys, Borna** A noted swoop racer, she hung out on Nar Shaddaa following the Jedi Civil War. Lys grew frustrated, however, when a virtually unbeatable swoop-racing droid began appearing at Lupo Shar's swoop-racing track, and enlisted the aid of the Jedi Exile in defeating the droid. Shar then gave her the track.

**Lyshaa** A Zeltron, she was imprisoned on Brentaal IV for her part in killing Fe Sun, one of Shaak Ti's Padawan learners before the Clone Wars. Years later, Lyshaa claimed that she had killed Sun simply to gain respect among her peers in the criminal underworld. She also was found guilty of killing her own family in a fit of rage. After being granted her freedom to help the Jedi bring down planetary leader Shogar Tok, she betrayed the Jedi and shot Shaak Ti, who survived. Lyshaa killed herself in a lightstorm chamber.

*Lyshaa*

**Lyster Innovations** A quality-assurance company based on the Drewwa moon following the Swarm War. The company made money by hiring entrepreneurs and "idea generators," then sending them out to visit other corporations for field studies. By analyzing what they found, Lyster's people could describe ways in which the other corporations could improve their business operations. The company also showed its clients how to take advantage of environmental design, drawing on the examples of nature itself to help corporations establish and maintain a cultural identity. Lyster Innovations was known for its chameleon cover material, which allowed a decorator to create an ever-changing environment without requiring a complete renovation.

**Lyu'kij, Bem** A Bothan assigned to watch over the Kathol sector during the early years of the New Republic. As a member of the Bothan Combat Response Element, Bem's mission was to track the actions of Moff Kentor Sarne and the Imperials who still operated in the sector.

# M

**M-12** A class of Imperial sweep bombs manufactured by Kuat Drive Yards. The M-12 was a notoriously poor performer in the field, with a failure rate of nearly 10 percent, and the line was quickly discontinued.

**M12-L Kimogila starfighter** A long-range starfighter with exceptional weapons capabilities and superb defensive systems, it was crafted by MandalMotors as a custom ship for the Hutt crime organization. The numerous gun emplacements available aboard the M12-L Kimogila let it serve as a heavy fighter, while its generous torpedo capabilities allowed it to play the role of a bomber in special circumstances.

**M13** An Imperial repair station on Mycroft in the Fakir sector. Its mission was to support Imperial exploration and picket ships during the Galactic Civil War.

**M-18** A moon captured by the planet Mobus in the Klasse Ephemora system of the Unknown Regions sometime around the Battle of Yavin. Its mass was more than 10 times the combined mass of the other 17 moons of Mobus, a fact that intrigued the first Chiss probe to investigate the system. Research at the Chiss Expeditionary Library by Luke Skywalker hinted that M-18 might have been the rogue planet Zonama Sekot.

**M21-T Krayt gunship** Ships commissioned by Jabba the Hutt as gifts for his most powerful lieutenants, to keep them loyal to his criminal organization.

**M2398 (Blood Nest)** The third planet in its system, M2398 was a gas giant ringed with dust and several moons. On the third moon, Warlord Zsinj had a base that eventually was captured by Wraith Squadron. Squadron member Jesmin Ackbar died during the fighting there.

**M2934738** The Imperial designation of a star system between Liinade III and Coruscant. Prince-Admiral Krennel dispatched the

< Darth Maul

*M-3PO*

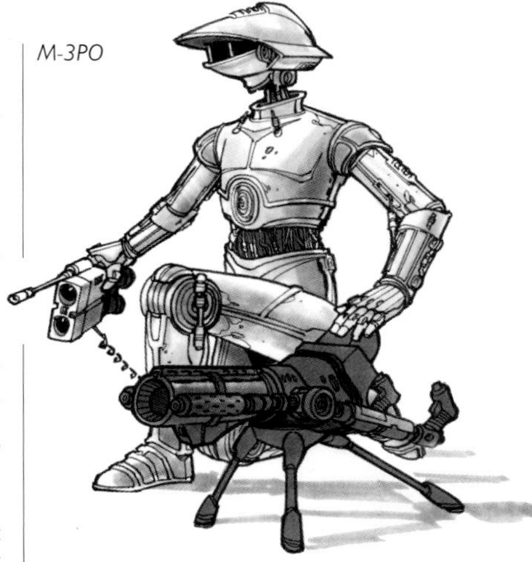

Interdictor cruiser *Binder* there to prevent New Republic supply convoys from reaching Liinade III.

**M-31 airspeeder** Produced only in red by Trilon, Inc., and in use during the last decades of the Old Republic, it was marketed as the "speeder of your dreams." Many of the offbeat advertisements urged drivers to "wake up and smell the repulsorlift."

**M-317** The sensor designation of the *Stellar Web,* used by New Republic forces that tried to destroy Warlord Zsinj near Vahaba. Han Solo had made a deal with Admiral Rogriss, who commanded the *Stellar Web,* but the vessel's true allegiance was kept secret by the designation.

**M38 Explorer droid** Designed for exploration in potentially dangerous areas, the M38 droid helped keep organic scouts safe. It was compact and designed for maximum toughness and utility.

**M39 ComTech** Developed by MicroThrust, this jamming unit provided a measure of protection against eavesdropping. By emitting a range of background static, it prevented communications sensors from picking up vocal or electronic communication.

**M3-D2** A housekeeping droid, it was placed in Jabba the Hutt's palace by Jabba's criminal competitor Lady Valarian. M3-D2 was part of an effort to persuade Sy Snootles to spy against Jabba. The unit also served as a contact for many of Lady Valarian's spies.

**M-3PO** A series of droids by Cybot Galactica based on the popular 3PO series of protocol droids, but targeted for military applications. The droids were designed to be administrative organizers and acquisitions experts, although they were occasionally used in battle.

**M-3PO (Emtrey)** A protocol and regulations droid that worked for Rogue Squadron around the time that Tycho Celchu was named squadron XO. Emtrey's responsibilities centered more on keeping an eye on Celchu than providing input on military protocol.

**M-3PO (Treedee)** The maître d'hôtel at the Farrimmer Café. Treedee had been a communications monitor for the crew of the Mynock 7 Space Station, but he was easily sidetracked so he was sold to café owner H'nib Statermast. Treedee often saved his tips to purchase oil baths.

**M4** An experimental version of a TIE fighter, it was designed for suicide missions.

**M-4D0 (Fourdee)** A protocol droid that served as a porter aboard the *Star of Empire,* it preferred to be called Fourdee. After the ship was taken over by the Systems Integration Manager program, many of the droids attacked passengers and crew who remained onboard. M-4D0 used a blaster to shatter a transparisteel viewport. The droid was sucked out instantly, along with a great deal of the ship's atmosphere.

**Ma, Keelen** A Mrlssi who was the chairman of the Republic Measures and Standards Bureau in the years before the Clone Wars.

*M38 Explorer droid*

**Maa, Sel** A gambling club patron, she was a regular at the Outlander Club during the last decades of the Old Republic. Maa spent a great deal of time with Daro Willits during her visits to the Outlander.

**Maad system** Located deep in the Transitory Mists, it was surrounded by gravity wells, planetary debris, and other navigational hazards. Thus any approach or departure from the system required a lengthy journey in realspace. The star Maad was one of the few in the system, and the night sky of its primary world, Shedu Maad, was exceptionally dark.

**Maag, Orth** A Zabrak bartender at the Happy Hutt's Last Laugh on Jenenma. Well established and knowledgeable, Maag coughed up information for the right price.

**maa'it** Probing visual organisms that replaced the eyes of a Yuuzhan Vong shaper. They allowed the shaper to see into many spectra, and also provided the ability to see microscopic details with incredible magnification.

Brother Mabob

**Maak, Chidee Na** A Duros mechanic at StarForge Station, he was regarded as the best at fixing YT-1210 freighters. He inherited StarForge from his parents, who were killed in an accidental fuel explosion.

**Maalet, Morla** A tall, weathered Sullustan, he was a small-time smuggler before meeting Qual'om Soach. As Soach created his criminal empire, Morla was promoted to the position of Soach's personal pilot, taking command of the *Invisible Star.*

**maalraa** Also called nighthunters, these powerful quadruped predators were able to use the Force for stealth. Pack hunters, they had long claws and powerful fanged jaws.

**Ma'aood** These beings built wondrous temples and protected them with inviting but deadly booby traps within the corridors.

**Ma'ar Shaddam** A remote planet settled by Old Republic weapons makers. Boba Fett was said to have gone there routinely to maintain his armor and weapons. Ore mined from Ma'ar Shaddam's crust was among the purest and highest-quality in the galaxy, and the weapons makers also were said to be among the best.

**Maarwraawroo** One of the largest Wookiee cities established on the planet Kashyyyk, it was built around a manufacturing facility in the intertwined branches of wroshyr trees.

**Maas, Ilov** Delphon's Senator during the early years of the New Order. Maas was a vocal supporter of Emperor Palpatine, a trait he passed on to his only daughter, Nima.

**Maas, Nima** An Imperial agent who supported Palpatine and the New Order. She hired Greedo to find Temo Dionisio, but then was killed by the Rodian bounty hunter after she threatened to kill him.

**Maashan** A Kamarian Badlander, he left his homeworld shortly before Han Solo inadvertently founded the Cult of Varn. Maashan then attended the Galactic Outdoor Survival School, where he was a member of the famed Twilight Class. He joined the Rebel Alliance as a pyrotechnics expert but was killed during the defense of the planet Stronghold against the Charon.

**Mabari** An ancient order of warrior knights on Zolan, the Clawdite homeworld. Very few Clawdites were accepted to train with the Mabari. Zam Wesell was, however, and she followed the Mabari discipline, wearing their inscriptions and stylized emblems as well as a Mabari bodysuit.

**Mabettye, Commodore** A Mon Calamari commander of the light cruiser *Posey.* Under the command of Admiral Darez Wuht, Mabettye fought in the defense of Duro during the Yuuzhan Vong War.

**Mabin, Gunda** Known as Gunda the Terror, this Aqualish pirate was a member of the Riders of the Maelstrom around the time of the Battle of Yavin. She later worked on her own, terrorizing the Perinn sector. After robbing her victims, she sold them into slavery, a practice that earned her a huge bounty on her head. She was also known to be short on intelligence, relying on brute strength and fear to remain successful.

**Mabob, Brother** A member of the Ancient Order of Pessimists. He was shot at point-blank range by a paranoid Abal Karda, who believed that Brother Mabob was spying on him even though Mabob was simply delivering his food.

Sel Maa

Maalraa

**maboo** A fast-growing shrub native to Shedu Maad. Maboo grew in thick, cane-like stalks, and was one of the first plants to recover after the mines on the planet were abandoned.

**mabugat kan** Developed by Yuuzhan Vong Qelah Kwaad from research by Nen Yim, the mabugat kan attacked and consumed New Republic HoloNet relay stations. Used throughout the galaxy after the Battle of Ebaq, it was part of Warmaster Nas Choka's plan to cut off communications among the various fleets of the New Republic.

**Macaab mushroom** Fungi native to Arzid, Macaab mushrooms were rare. They had the unique ability to attack inorganic brain matter and destroy it.

Maccabree

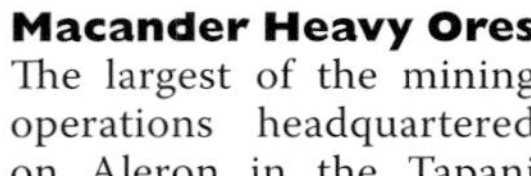

**Macander Heavy Ores** The largest of the mining operations headquartered on Aleron in the Tapani sector.

**Macatten, Maddie** A crazy old Bith trader, she roamed the Kathol Outback during the early years of the New Republic, trading from her starship, the *Scupper Bantoo.*

**Maccabe, Oll** A Twi'lek professor of anthropology at Alderaan University before the destruction of that planet. He was offworld at the time, and survived the cataclysm to become a supporter of the Rebel Alliance. He later recruited one of his students, Padija Anjeri, to help him recover stolen Twi'leki artifacts.

**Maccabree** A species allied with the Nagai. These hulking warrior cyborgs fought alongside the Nagai at the Second Battle of Endor. Appearing as huge humanoids over 2 meters tall and as wide across as two humans, they wore gray-and-silver armor. They had gray skin, and their brains and central nervous systems were located in their chests. In emergencies, the Maccabree detached their mechanical arms and legs, and used repulsors and thrusters to rocket to safety.

**mace flies** Insects from the planet Dantooine, they moved in swarms that seemed to sing with the buzzing of thousands of wings.

**Macemillian-winduarté** A gregarious Squib, he worked with the Jawa Aguilae at the Jawa Traders shop in Mos Eisley during the Galactic Civil War.

**Machees, Seed** A Gran from Hok, he was a dealer of death sticks. A bounty was issued for Machees's capture by Coruscant police in connection with the rise in death stick distribution following the Battle of Naboo. The bounty was claimed by Jango Fett.

**Machill'Tr, Kendrick** A New Republic Intelligence administrative aide, he held the rank of lieutenant at the time of the breakup of the Starbuster Plot. Machill'Tr was recruited to compile a datafile that documented the various individuals involved in the plot and in the Human League on Corellia.

**Machineville** A sector of Taris's Lower City set aside for the droid population to recharge and repair itself. Machineville also served as a buffer between the Lower City and the refugee camps that were established on the planet during the Mandalorian Wars.

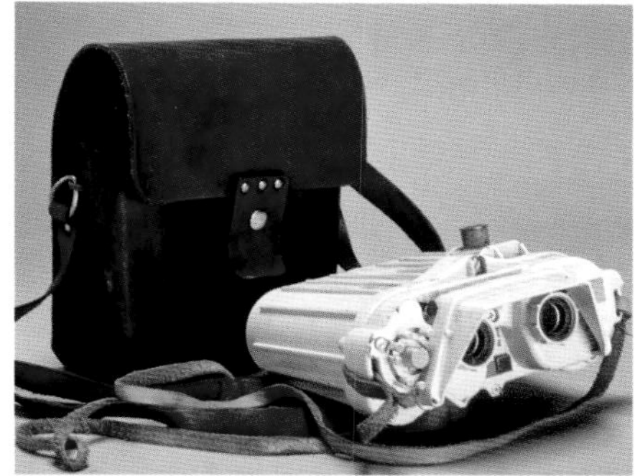

Macrobinoculars

**Mack** An alias used by a member of the Cularin Militia after he and his comrades Pac and Grunt decided to speak out against the Expansion Manifesto. The trio of soldiers agreed to participate in an interview with Yara Grugara on *Eye on Cularin,* but the reporter made a mockery of their opinions. Mack didn't help their case when he admitted that he had read the Expansion Manifesto only once, and then only parts of it.

**Mackar** The homeworld of the Frid subspecies of Iskalonians.

**Mackenni, Jorm Whistler** An Imperial stormtrooper known by the code name Twister. Mackenni served as the commander of the Aurek-Seven unit of the Imperial 501st Legion during the years following the formation of the Imperial Remnant and the signing of a peace treaty between the Empire and the New Republic.

**Maclain, Governor Jerrod** A governor of Brentaal during the Clone Wars, he was installed after the planet was liberated from the control of Separatist Commander Shogar Tok. He remained in his position after the ascension of the Emperor. Maclain made a small fortune playing Brentaal's stock market and supporting several shady freighter pilots.

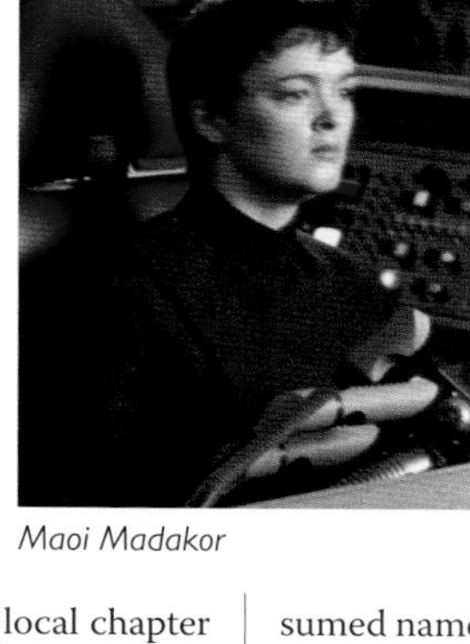

Maoi Madakor

**MacMillian, Brandy** A weathered freighter captain who retired on the planet Gandle Ott, she became president of the local chapter of the Corellian Merchants' Guild. MacMillian earned her Corellian Bloodstripes, and believed that the New Republic was capable of restoring peace in the galaxy.

**macrobinoculars** These handheld viewing devices allowed users to see distant objects day or night. Internal readouts provided information on distance and elevation, and they sometimes could be programmed for recording and playback.

**macrofuser** A miniature welding tool designed and calibrated for heavy-duty repairs of complex metals, such as those found in starships.

**macrolyzer** This Imperial technology was developed to manufacture and filter the gas known as pacifog.

**Macroon Mesa** A desert rock formation located on the Mos Espa Podracing course in the Dune Sea of Tatooine.

**macroscope** A sighting mechanism for a handheld blaster or rifle.

**macro welder** A portable welder used for repairing fine technical devices.

**Madak, Ellorrs** An alias used by the Duros Ohwun De Maal.

**Madak, Olev** A Duros mechanic who worked at Darknon Station during the Galactic Civil War, he repaired starships while barely maintaining the operational status of the station. Madak had fled there from a group of bounty hunters who were trying to capture him for unpaid gambling debts. His ship disintegrated after landing, and he remained at the station.

**Madak, Sava Brec** An alias used by Boba Fett when he hired Jodo Kast. This was part of Fett's plan to get rid of Kast, who had been impersonating Fett in order to make credits as a bounty hunter.

General Crix Madine

**Madakor, Maoi** The captain of the Republic ship *Radiant VII.* She perished along with her copilot when the ship was destroyed after she delivered Obi-Wan Kenobi and Qui-Gon Jinn to the Trade Federation ship *Saak'ak* in orbit around Naboo.

**Madame Atuarre's Roving Performers** The assumed name used by Han Solo, Atuarre, Pakka, and Bollux as they pretended to be performers from the Imperial Entertainer's Guild in order to gain access to the Stars' End prison facility. Viceprex Hirken had requested entertainers—who were delayed, and Solo intercepted a message of apology. He then created Madame Atuarre's Roving Performers as a replacement act.

**Madame Vansitt's Charm Academy** A Mos Espa establishment where potential slaves were educated in a variety of skills including assassination and political blackmail.

**Mad Anghus's Fun Public House** A backrocket cantina in the Outer Rim during the early years of the New Republic. There, an aged former stormtrooper frequently recalled the ferocity of Ewoks.

**mad-claw** The Basic translation of a Wookiee term used to describe an ostracized member of the culture who was exiled for use of climbing claws during combat.

**Maddaan, Zeb** A member of the Republic Correctional Officers' Union in the years prior to the Battle of Naboo. Maddaan was arrested and sent to the Oovo IV prison facility for stealing a huge sum of credits from the InterGalactic Banking Clan. Maddaan believed himself safe in prison until Jango Fett infiltrated the facility and claimed the bounty on Maddaan's head.

**Madine, General Crix** A Corellian general with the Rebel Alliance, Madine came from a strict military background formed during years of service with the Empire. A graduate of Raithal Academy, Madine took pride in the fact that his team never took unnecessary liberties during battle. When he began to see that his personal standards would not be accepted, he tried to change the Empire's ways. After his Storm Commandos were ordered to release the Candorian Plague on Dentaal, Madine lost any remaining loyalty he had. He erased all records of himself and made contact with an old friend, Carlist Rieekan, who put in some good words for him with the Rebel Alliance.

When the Alliance accepted Madine, his Imperial training made him the logical choice to plan the assault on the second Death Star. After the Battle of Endor, he turned down a seat on the New Republic's Inner Council, preferring to remain with the Republic's growing military. He became the commander of Special Forces, leading a skilled team of commandos. With so much of his work top secret, not many of his accomplishments were known.

*Madurrin*

One mission divulged by the New Republic was also his last. Madine led a small team to infiltrate the Hoth asteroid field to determine the status of Durga the Hutt's superweapon project, the Darksaber. After a series of mishaps, Madine and his team were captured. Just before Alliance ships arrived to rescue them, Durga executed the general with a blaster bolt through the heart.

**Madiry, Hela** A clerk in the accounting division of the Grand Army of the Republic's Coruscant logistics center during the early stages of the Clone Wars. About a year after the Battle of Geonosis, Madiry was identified as the source of leaks about Grand Army troop movements that were traced through a series of terrorist bombings at military facilities on Coruscant. Her career as a traitor ended when Ordo, posing as the clone trooper Corr, entered her office and shot her dead.

**Madis, Captain** A New Republic officer, he commanded the picket ship *Folna* during the Yevethan crisis.

**Mad Mrelf** Strong Corellian liquor, it caused many spacers to end up in Imperial labor camps after they went on drinking binges.

**Madoom, Ten-Suckers** A Rodian criminal noted for both his lack of common sense and his lack of two fingers/suckers. He was apprehended by Raal Yorta and Sammie Staable during the Galactic Civil War while using the alias Deeto.

**Madorin, Hyris-Well** A Jedi Master who was dispatched to the starfighter base established at Phelar Port on Eriadu just prior to the Battle of Geonosis. Master Madorin also was assigned to ensure security in the Seswenna sector with Gideon Tarkin.

***Madra Teene*** A classic opera, it documented the battle between the natives of a Colonies world and a collection of droids that rose up against their controllers.

**Ma-dred, Ashala** A brown-haired Kashirim, she was one of King Sha-Mar Ma-dred's four wives. The king asked Obi-Wan Kenobi and Anakin Skywalker to assist in protecting his wives, and Ashala stole young Anakin's lightsaber while he was mesmerized by her beauty. Unknown to both Ashala and Anakin, Obi-Wan used the Force to lift the weapon from Ashala's possession, and he held it until Anakin admitted that he had lost it.

**Ma-dred, Sha-Mar** A Kashirim who was king of the planet Kashir before the Battle of Geonosis. King Ma-dred traveled to Coruscant with his four wives to meet with the Jedi Knights and discuss Kashir's admittance to the Old Republic. While there, his wives were very interested in the wonders of Coruscant, and the king begged Obi-Wan Kenobi and Anakin Skywalker to help him keep them in line. His four wives were Kheann, Mirrix, Tiarri, and Ashala Ma-dred.

**Madurrin** An Anx Jedi trained by Luke Skywalker, she played a pivotal role in the Battle of Ebaq 9 against the Yuuzhan Vong. With her 4-meter-tall frame unsuitable for starfighter combat, Madurrin served aboard the *Mon Adapyne* as the official Jedi liaison. She facilitated the Jedi Force-meld developed by Jacen and Jaina Solo to help coordinate the activities of naval vessels in the Yuuzhan Vong War. Madurrin went to the surface of Zonama Sekot after its arrival near Coruscant, and fought alongside Jaina Solo. She was ultimately one of the handful of Jedi Knights to survive the war, and chose to remain as a Jedi adviser to Supreme Commander Traest Kre'fey and the Galactic Alliance military.

**madware** Terrorist programming developed by the Separatists during the Clone Wars, it was created to override the normal programming of a droid, causing it to act in deadly and destructive ways.

**Maelibi** *See* Demon (Maelibus).

***Maelstrom*** A warship assigned to Jedi Master Darrus Jeht during the Clone Wars. Jeht felt the effects of Order 66 through the Force, but managed to avoid being killed through a series of ruses that kept his own clone troopers out of the communications loop. Jeht then ordered his clones to return to Cularin, where he hoped to rescue the Jedi at the Almas Academy. He arrived in the *Maelstrom* to see the Republic gunships *Primal* and *Undaunted* targeting all fleeing vessels to kill escaping Jedi. Master Jeht put the *Maelstrom* through a series of dangerous maneuvers, allowing him to eliminate the two Republic gunships. Shots from the *Primal*, however, damaged one of the *Maelstrom*'s engines, and the ship's weapons core burned out. When the Separatist ship *Shadowblade* appeared, the *Maelstrom* was unable to maneuver or fire. Master Jeht was ready to ram the other ship with the *Maelstrom* when his clone troopers identified a temporal rift moving through the Cularin system. Recognizing that he had one chance, Jeht ordered his clones to lock on to the *Shadowblade* with their tractor beams. He then ordered them to drag both vessels into the path of the temporal rift. In a blinding flash of light and time, the *Maelstrom* and the *Shadowblade* disappeared into the rift, and were never seen again.

**Maelstrom Nebula** Located near the Relgim sector and dominated by a huge cloud of charged space dust and raw energy, the Maelstrom Nebula scrambled most starship sensor systems, hindered their communications, and confused hyperdrives and navigational computers. Thus, most ships were forced to revert from hyperspace to realspace in order to traverse the Maelstrom, which led to a high rate of piracy in the area. The Oasis colony was established on one of the Maelstrom's obscure moons.

**Maendin, Lar** A scout who served the Rebel Alliance during the Galactic Civil War, he sold information on the location of Alliance bases to the Empire. The bases had to be evacuated before Imperial forces destroyed them.

**Maer, Corporal** A Rebel Alliance trooper stationed at Echo Base shortly before the Battle of Hoth. An animal expert, Maer served as a tauntaun handler and developed a form of sign language that he used to communicate with the creatures.

**Maetrecis, N'do** A major in the Grand Army of the Republic, he was stationed on Drongar during the Clone Wars. After he was injured in battle, Maetrecis contracted one of the many unknown diseases that lurked in the planet's swamps. His recovery was slow, and doctors were unable to ascertain the cause of his problems. In a bold and illegal action, Dr. Zan Yant administered doses of processed bota into Maetrecis's system. The results were spectacular, as the major began recovering almost immediately.

**Maga** A Dantari, he was garoo of the tribe that befriended Hoole and the Arranda children during their flight from the Empire.

**Magaloof** The Almakian Leffingite driver of a stolen speeder on Coruscant, he nearly collided with Obi-Wan Kenobi and Anakin Skywalker's "borrowed" vehicle as the Jedi chased the attempted assassin of Senator Amidala.

**Maganinny, Makx** He served the Grand Army of the Republic as a sergeant during

*Magaloof*

the Clone Wars. When General Khamar was dispatched to defend the Intergalactic Communications Center on Praesitlyn, Maganinny was placed in command of the reconnaissance scouts assigned to gather intelligence on the Separatist forces there.

Maggie

**Magcannon Max** A planetary defense weapon developed following the Yuuzhan Vong War. The three-story-tall Magcannon Max was a self-contained artillery system. Within its armor-plated and shielded housing was a complete targeting and sensor system. It could locate and destroy capital ships in orbit without requiring assistance from other targeting systems.

**magclamp** Any high-strength clamp that used electromagnetic power to hold itself closed.

**Magda** Lord Keto's wife, and Queen Mother of the Empress Teta system just before the rise of the Krath.

**magenge** Light green fungus, sweet to the taste, it formed the basis of the Verpine diet. Magenge was grown inside all Verpine asteroids.

**Mageye the Hutt** A crime lord accidentally killed by the bounty hunter Zardra when he was caught in the crossfire between the Thig brothers and Jodo Kast in the Red Shadow Bistro.

**magfield sensor ball** An outdated droid sensory input device used on Mark II reactor drones and other simple mechanicals. Resembling a simple metal ball contained in a wire cage, the magfield sensor ball allowed the droid to "understand" its surroundings by sending electronic pulses each time the ball hit the cage. Such contact usually occurred when the droid ran into an obstacle or began to tip over.

**Magg** A slave trader, he posed as the personal assistant to Fiolla of Lorrd in order to keep tabs on her investigations in Corporate Sector space. He was identified by Han Solo, much to Fiolla's dismay. Magg escaped after his ship was shot down, but his slavery ring was eventually smashed by Fiolla, Solo, and Odumin.

**Maggie** A Rebel Alliance starfighter pilot and military officer following the Battle of Endor. A former Imperial pilot, she was part of the fleet that traveled to Godo to investigate the strange plague affecting the Godoans.

**Maggis, Lieutenant** An Imperial officer who served as a Guardian Adviser at the Imperial Naval Academy on Coruscant in the early years of the New Order. Realizing that he did not want to remain an Imperial officer, Maggis stole a speeder and fled. Later he was taken in by Dexter Jettster, who arranged for him to be sent to a safehouse.

**Maggli, Dairn** A small-time smuggler and gunrunner after the Battle of Naboo. A bounty was posted by the Republic Security Force for his arrest in connection with the hijacking of a Republic transport that had been carrying weapons to Sullust. He was captured on Coruscant by Jango Fett.

**Maggot's Cantina** Located in Anzat spaceport, this was the scene of one of Jedi Aayla Secura's adventures during the last years of the Old Republic.

**Maggrit, Alysssa** A young Duros girl. When the Clone Wars started, she was 12 years old and running numbers for her uncle in the city of Tolea Biqua. Her cover was blown when the inept slicer known as wampal revealed her name on the HoloNet, believing that the young Duros was actually the slicer known as alyssaroxu.

**Maggy the Gorgon's** Shmi Skywalker asked her young son Anakin to get his ruby bliels from this tavern—located in a section of Mos Espa not controlled by the Hutts—rather than from the Blue Brubb. An old spacer frequented the establishment and told young Skywalker stories of other planets as well the Jedi Knights.

**maghook** A small but extremely powerful cylindrical electromagnet, it could be fused to the end of a cable and used as a grappling hook. The magnet was activated by sudden jarring, and could be deactivated by twisting a small dial.

**magic rock** A stone that was blessed by the Ewok shaman Logray and given to Mace Towani during the search for his parents. When broken open, the rock revealed an arrowhead inside that pointed the way to Gorax's castle.

**Magister** The leader, spiritual adviser, and "knower" of Zonama Sekot. When Obi-Wan Kenobi and Anakin Skywalker went to Zonama Sekot, they saw a false Magister and eventually learned that the real one was dead. *See also* Leor, Hal.

**maglev train** A form of railway transportation that used magnetic energy to propel the train, rather than nuclear or fossil fuels. A current passed through the rails, creating a magnetic field that pushed against an opposing field generated by the train itself; this propelled it along the track at incredible speeds. The individual compartments were sometimes called maglev bullet cars.

**Magl'Ikkan Temple** An ancient fortress built on the planet Baralou at the base of a huge underwater mountain. The temple was carved from the coral reef that grew around it. The Krikthasi revered the temple as a sacred place, rarely allowing other species to get near it.

**magma missile** A Yuuzhan Vong weapon, it was a glob of molten metal that could be fired at a target. The magma missile was most often used aboard starfighters and larger warships.

**magma pebble** A thumbnail-sized glob of plasma that was contained in a hard shell. When agitated and thrown, the magma pebble heated up and shed its shell, splattering the target with plasma. The Yuuzhan Vong often used these weapons against battle droids.

**magma spitter** A Yuuzhan Vong weapon used to defend stationary locations. Similar in most respects to a magma missile launching system, a magma spitter ejected small spheres of molten rock at a target.

**magma trooper** A specially trained and outfitted Imperial stormtrooper who worked on volcanically active planets throughout the galaxy.

**Magminds** The Human League troopers stationed at Corona House following the secession of Corellia from the New Republic.

**magnabolter** Manufacturing equipment used in factories during the final decades of the Old Republic. Magnabolters inserted hot slugs of metal into holes that were predrilled into larger sections of metal framework. Then, while the metal was still hot and pliable, the magnabolter flattened the ends to secure the slugs in place, solidly joining the two pieces of metalwork.

**MagnaGuard** *See* IG-100 MagnaGuard.

**MagnaGuard electrostaff** *See* electrostaff.

**MagnaGuard fighter** *See* Porax-38 starfighter.

**Magnaline 3000 air transport** A speeder bus used in shuttle routes on Coruscant, it was the vehicle that brought Anakin Skywalker and Padmé Amidala to the spaceport from which they departed for Naboo.

Magnaline 3000 air transport

**Magneta, Captain** The leader of the Naboo Royal Security Forces before Captain Panaka. After the mysterious death of King Veruna—who had abdicated the throne—Magneta resigned her post in humiliation, frustrated that she was not able to protect him.

**magnetic accelerator** An unusual projectile launcher believed to have been developed by the Verpine as a personal weapon. It used a specially machined track impregnated with powerful magnets to propel a metal sphere at a target. The magnets inside the weapon were powered in sequence, with each successive magnet drawing the metal ball closer and then repelling it as it moved past. The ball gathered a huge amount of momentum.

**magnetic containment field** Used to protect landing pads and starports in the vacuum of space, magcon fields created an area of magnetic energy that was semi-permeable. Atmosphere within the landing area was contained within the field, so slow-moving starships could pass through it without breaking the field's integrity.

**magnetic railgun** A massive form of railgun developed by the Empire and used in surface-to-vacuum combat. A large number of these weapons were arrayed on the surface of the first Death Star and launched projectiles into space via powerful magnetic systems.

**magnetic suction tube** A device used mainly to lift droids into starships. Large-model tubes were operated by nomadic species such as Jawas on remote planets to help them make their living selling lost or stranded droids.

**magnetogravitic shield** A basic starship protection system, it kept a ship from burning up while traveling at near lightspeed. The system deflected minute particles of matter from the ship.

**magnigrapple pole** A form of structural support used on planets covered with shallow seas or swamps. The poles attached to a building or other structure, and kept it in place through magnetic force.

**magnolock** A security device that used a magnetically coded entry sequence to unlock a door or portal. It was often used on cruiser ships, with passengers having special cards to open their room locks.

***Magnus*** A Rebel Alliance transport ship that operated during the Galactic Civil War.

**Magon** An immense, tentacle-headed native of the planet Molavar, she was the planet's primary crime lord in the years around the Battle of Naboo. Magon operated her small empire from a base in the city of Malcraan.

**Magore, Tilas** An Imperial adviser to Emperor Palpatine during the early stages of the Galactic Civil War, he was responsible for planning the subjugation of Brak sector.

**mag-pellet** A projectile weapon that could be fired in large masses at a target. Individual mag-pellets had a magnetic charge that allowed them to be fired with great velocity from a magnetic-pulse weapon such as a Verpine shatter gun. This magnetic charge also helped the mag-pellets reach their destination with additional speed, since they were attracted to the metallic elements in armor plating or the hulls of starships.

**mag-pulse weapon** Developed by Galactic Electronics for use by the Rebel Alliance on modified B-wing fighters, it did not cause immediate damage, but instead knocked out starship systems for extended periods.

**Magravian cat-spice** Touted to make one's reflexes as sharp as chrysalide claws, cat-spice was offered to Boba Fett in Mos Espa.

**Magresh** A minor criminal who stole a warehouse full of medical supplies from an Imperial camp run by Captain Noran Vran, then turned around and sold it back to her for 10 portable missile launchers. Vran paid him, but rigged one of the weapons to explode shortly after the thief left, killing Magresh.

**Magrody, Nasdra** The founder of the Magrody Institute, he was one of the galaxy's premier experts on droids and automata. Magrody had a close relationship with Bail Organa and Mon Mothma until he was sought out by Imperial Moff Wilhuff Tarkin to teach at the Omwat orbital program. He was enthusiastic when Qwi Xux made it through the program and joined the team of scientists at the Maw Installation. Magrody and Xux were called upon by Tarkin and the Emperor to work on the design of the first Death Star.

Magrody's work to create Force-sensitive machines was heightened by the fact that he was somewhat Force-sensitive himself, a secret he struggled to keep. One result of his work was the subelectronic converter, which allowed Force-sensitive beings to control a droid from a distance. Roganda Ismaren kidnapped Magrody's wife and child, forcing him to develop a special brain implant for her son, Irek. Magrody worked diligently with Irek, creating an intelligent mind that could manipulate inorganic machines with the Force. Magrody tried to get word to the New Republic of these developments, but Roganda Ismaren arranged for him to conveniently disappear.

**Magrody Institute of Programmable Intelligence** Founded by Nasdra Magrody, the Institute fostered the education and development of intelligent automata. Emperor Palpatine consulted the institute while designing the first Death Star.

**magsol** A drug used by the Ssi-ruuk to attune a human brain to their entechment chairs. A solution of magnetic particles, magsol was injected into the subject's body. When energized by an external magnetic field, the magsol helped force the subject's life energy out of his or her body for storage.

Wim Magwit

**Magus** A noted bounty hunter who was hired by the Corporate Alliance many times during the years before the Battle of Naboo. Magnus was angered when a group of Jedi Knights—Qui-Gon Jinn, Adi Gallia, Obi-Wan Kenobi, and Siri Tachi—trailed him and his compatriots to Rondai-2 and disrupted an assassination attempt. When Magus joined Separatist forces in attacking a secret Republic base, his ship was disabled by Tachi during the attack. Magus managed to shoot Tachi before she rendered him unconscious. After Tachi died from her wounds, Magus was taken into custody as a prisoner of war.

**Magwit, Wim** Known simply as the Magician, this humanoid dwarf was a traveling mystic whose primary act involved the mass disappearance of his family, props, and himself through a device known as the Mystifying Hoop Trick. He escaped from the pirate Bar-Kooda, who then put out an Imperial warrant for his arrest. Boba Fett caught Magwit, but luckily for him Fett had just committed to finding Bar-Kooda. Fett offered Magwit his freedom in return for his help, and the bounty hunter eventually used the magic hoop to trick Bar-Kooda.

**Mah Dala** The capital city of Gobindi, it was the site of the largest concentration of pyramids and ziggurats on the planet. During the Galactic Civil War, the Empire used its proximity to the huge structures to perform secret experiments on biological weapons.

**Mahl** This Imperial stormtrooper was stationed aboard the first Death Star prior to the Battle of Yavin. Mahl was on duty when Han Solo and Luke Skywalker rescued Princess Leia Organa from Detention Block AA-23, and he was ordered by his sergeant, Nova Stihl, to take the lead during their attempt to apprehend the Rebels before they could escape.

Mahn

**Mahn** A Jedi at a training facility in the Bogden system, she was killed during the execution of Order 66.

**Mai, Shu** A Gossam, she was Presidente of the Commerce Guild 10 years after the Battle of Naboo. Shu Mai was known among her peers and competitors as a being of unusual intelligence. It was Shu Mai who gathered enough credits to purchase her homeworld of Castell back from the Commerce Guild, but she kept taxes high to maintain control of her people. Her shrewd actions impressed the guild, which continued to promote her. Her unscrupulous work ethic soon earned her the nod as Presidente.

Shu Mai also was a confidante of Count Dooku, and was one of the leaders of the secession movement, although behind the scenes. She made arrangements with Senator Mousul to have his homeworld of Ansion become one of the first to secede, hoping to drag others along and bring about a sudden and strong reformation of the Republic. While their plans were thwarted by the Jedi Knights who negotiated a treaty with the peoples of Ansion to stay in the Republic, Shu Mai and Senator Mousul remained committed to secession. However, Shu Mai refused to openly support Dooku and the Separatists, instead pledging secret support in order to keep from actually committing treason against the Republic.

After the Battle of Geonosis, Shu Mai and her assistants returned to their base of operations on Felucia, only to learn that the Republic was planning to attack the planet. They fled on the orders of General Grievous, who advised them to go to Belderone. After Grievous was routed there by Anakin Skywalker, Shu Mai returned to Felucia. However, the Republic's forces tracked her down, and Shu Mai might have been captured if Grievous hadn't returned to transport her to Utapau. After hiding on Utapau, the Separatist leadership was taken to Mustafar. It was there, after Darth Sidious had lured Anakin Skywalker to the dark side, that Darth Vader quickly killed Shu Mai before going after the rest of the Separatist leaders.

**Maill** A planet known for one of the rarest coins ever produced in the galaxy. Commissioned by the world's king in honor of his wife, the coin was minted from a special alloy to match her hair, which was said to be the color of a flaming sunset. The alloy turned out to be quite malleable and soft, destroying the machines used to create the coins. Only a few hundred were produced before the mintage was canceled.

**mailoc** A gruesome, overgrown wasp-like creature, it often appeared in swarms. A mailoc's stinger was made up of patches of tail spikes that could penetrate most armor and personal shields.

**main drive** The primary and most powerful propulsion unit aboard a starship.

**maintenance hauler** A space tug that towed disabled spacecraft to the nearest spaceport.

**Mairan** A large, tentacled species native to the planet Maires. The Mairans communicated by blowing musical notes through drilled shells. They had rubbery black skin that had to be kept wet at all times. The Mairans were longtime rivals of their neighbors the Vergills.

**Maires** An ocean planet in the Hapes Cluster, homeworld to the water-breathing Mairans.

Afsheen Makati

**Maitell Base** A primary starship facility on the planet Kashyyyk during the war between the Galactic Alliance and the Confederation. It also served as a landing place for visitors, allowing them an opportunity to get acquainted with the native environment before traveling to Wookiee cities.

After Jacen Solo attacked Kashyyyk to punish the Wookiees for harboring members of the Jedi Council, the surface of Kashyyyk was ravaged by wildfires sparked by turbolaser blasts from the *Anakin Solo.* Maitell Base served as a primary site from which firefighters and rescue workers launched their missions to contain the forest fires.

**maitrakh** The Noghri word for the female ruler of a clan, it was a title of respect backed by long tradition. A maitrakh from clan Khim'bar used her influence to help Princess Leia Organa Solo convince the Noghri to end their support for the Empire.

Shu Mai

**Maizor** After losing a confrontation to his onetime rival Jabba the Hutt, Maizor's brain was placed into a jar filled with nutrients and attached to spider-like metal legs, courtesy of the B'omarr monks who shared Jabba's palace.

**Majan** A humanoid species native to Baroonda. Most Majans lived in the vast city of Baroo, which encircled the ancient Nazwa ruins of their ancestors.

***Majestic*** One of the many assault ships that formed the naval fleet of the Old Republic during the early stages of the Clone Wars. The *Majestic* saw action in the Battle of Geonosis.

***Majestic Gundark*** A basic YT-1300 light freighter owned by the Army of Life, it was used to transport a load of clodhopper eggs to Stend IV.

**majie** This plant was often grown on terraformed or exceptionally harsh planets; it took hold in almost any conditions and had some nutritional value.

**Majjvara** The monarch of the Yvarema people, the Majjvara was similar to the queen of an insectoid hive. She was the source of her people's intelligence, but was dependent on the working classes for sustenance and new information. Unlike the rest of Yvarema society, which was largely humanoid in stature, the Majjvara was a huge, worm-like being with 10 vestigial limbs. She was positioned within a hovering throne. Surrounding that was a ring of incubation tubes in which Yvarema fetuses grew.

**Maj-Odo-Nomor** A Cerean youth who promoted the use of technology on his pastoral planet. While briefly involved with Sylvn, the daughter of Jedi Ki-Adi-Mundi, Maj stole the Jedi's lightsaber and accidentally killed another Cerean, then fled. He was later killed by the Chevin smuggler Ephant Mon.

**Mak** An Imperial general who accompanied Darth Vader and Nas Ghent when they set out to find the Star Destroyer *Crucible* during the Galactic Civil War.

**Mak, Elan** *See* Nale, Kam.

**makant** A large and playful insect that lived on the Forest Moon of Endor. Makants looked like a cross between a mantis and a cricket.

**Makati, Afsheen** One of the 12 Grand Admirals who served Emperor Palpatine during the last years of the New Order, he was commander of the Star Destroyer *Steadfast.* Makati developed an intense hatred of the Supreme Prophet Kadann, who badly injured

Makem Te

Makati with Force lightning following a snide comment by Makati's first officer. Years later, when Kadann tried to take control of Coruscant in the wake of the Battle of Endor, Makati refused to return to the capital planet. Instead he located the former prophet Azrakel and demanded to know Kadann's location. Azrakel provided a wealth of information on Scardia Station and the Lost City of the Jedi, and Makati managed to trap Kadann on Scardia. Using every turbolaser at his disposal, Makati destroyed Kadann and Scardia Station, completing his own revenge.

**Makem Te** An arid planet, it was the homeworld of the Swokes Swokes species. With virtually no surface water, the Swokes Swokes were forced to tap into underground aquifers on Makem Te. One of the most interesting surface features found on the planet was the Tract, an ever-growing cemetery that contained the remains of some 1.2 trillion Swokes Swokes. By the time of the New Order, the Tract covered more than 7 percent of the planet's surface area. During the last years of the Old Republic, a violent civil war erupted on the planet between the Temple of the Beatific Razor and the Congress of Caliphs. A Republic peacekeeping force was dispatched to quell the violence, but it was exterminated by the Beatific Razors. The Congress of Caliphs then turned to Count Dooku and the Confederacy of Independent Systems for aid, and the fighting was halted for many years. During the Yuuzhan Vong War, Makem Te was briefly attacked, and the orbital refueling station near it was destroyed as part of a plan to disrupt traffic along the Perlemian Trade Route.

**Maker, the (1)** A droid phrase, it was used to refer to their creator and was often spoken in worshipful, almost religious tones. The protocol droid C-3PO, for example, often used the phrase "Thank the Maker!" when something good happened to him or his friends. For droids, taken literally it meant "the One Who Creates."

**Maker, the (2)** The deity that controlled the world of the Sunesi. When certain Sunesi, like Agapos the Ninth and Nee, began to use the Force to heal others, the Sunesi believed that it was a gift from the Maker. The Maker was also known as the Giver, and was believed to be the single being from which the galaxy's diversity of life flowed. Most Sunesi believed that the Maker loved all his creations, but was not above using a sense of humor in them.

**Makezh** A well-known navigator and native of the planet Danoor, he was thought to be the only person to successfully navigate the Kathol Rift. Makezh was reduced to an amnesiac after an encounter with Aing-Tii monks, who left him in a light transport just outside the Rift. After this, he found that navigating the Rift was quite easy, and earned plenty of credits making the run for private and public employers.

**Makin, Admiral** A Mon Calamari, he served the Galactic Alliance Defense Force (GADF) in the years following the Yuuzhan Vong War. He was one of the military hard-liners who rose to power in the GADF, despite the efforts of Supreme Commander Pellaeon to maintain an air of peaceful neutrality in the galaxy.

Admiral Makin was given command of the Third Fleet shortly after the end of the war. He commanded it from the flagship *Ocean* during the war between the Galactic Alliance and the Confederation. When Admiral Niathal assumed military leadership of the Galactic Alliance forces at the Second Battle of Fondor, Admiral Makin allowed her to command from the *Ocean* while he took command of the warship *Sarpentia*. Admiral Makin supported Niathal's plans to form a government-in-exile in the wake of the fighting at Fondor, and urged her to research the size of the Maw Irregular Fleet that was loyal to Admiral Daala.

**Makina, Robet** Once a supporter of the Empire, he joined the Rebel Alliance after witnessing the Empire's atrocities. Makina remained loyal to the New Republic after the Battle of Endor, and eventually was named the New Republic's ambassador to Glova.

**Ma'kis'shaalas** A Morgukai warrior and Nikto Jedi Master, he survived Order 66. Master Ma'kis'shaalas was known as a fanatical adherent to the Jedi Order, and a fierce combatant. He agreed to meet Master Shadday Potkin on Kessel as part of a plot to ensnare Darth Vader. Vader cut Ma'kis'shaalas down in combat.

**Makk, Leona** Working as a pilot for Shang Lines during the Galactic Civil War, Makk captained the bulk hauler *Voxen Tass*. She supported the Rebel Alliance and was instrumental in getting an Alliance strike team to Argovia, where they were able to destroy a sensor net set up by the Empire. She was known as a tough-as-nails spacer, and used her position in Shang Lines to feed information on local shipping to the Alliance.

**Makksre** Ja Bardrin claimed that his daughter, Sansia, had been captured by pirates while in port on this planet. He hired Mara Jade to rescue the girl.

***Mako*** An Imperial assault transport ship that operated during the Galactic Civil War.

**Makor, Plu** A near-human native of Demar, he was distinguished by short barbs that surrounded his red eyes and temples. Makor operated Ship Shop G-S7 during the New Order. He was also a Rebel Alliance operative, funneling parts, ships, and information to the Alliance around the time of the Battle of Yavin. Makor traveled around the Brak sector aboard his modified freighter, the *Helping Hand*.

**Makrin City** The capital of Shelkonwa, it bore a slight resemblance to Galactic City on Coruscant and was referred to as the Second City of Spires. The eastern border of the city was marked by a line of rocky cliffs that were perforated by dark caves. Known as the Catacombs, these caves served as hiding places for criminals and exiles. By the time of the Battle of Yavin, however, the Catacombs had become home for the displaced Adarians who had been forced into servitude by the Empire.

**Maktites** A gang of soldiers and mercenaries, it was one of the first groups to attempt to defeat the original Echani warriors. The Maktites were unprepared for the depth and breadth of military equipment the Echani had developed.

**Mala** Enamored with Wedge Antilles in her youth, she lived on Gus Talon with her father Rallo. Mala tried to get Antilles to join the Rebel Alliance, but she couldn't find a way to convince him. Mala and Rallo were later killed by the Empire in a senseless bombing attack, and Antilles joined the Alliance soon after.

**Mala, Mistress Mala** A bounty hunter who was burned by the engine of her own ship when it was stolen by her ex-boyfriend Nikk Zavod. Nursed back to health by Chewbacca, Mala Mala gave herself a name the Wookiee would utter in his sleep. Later, as a bounty hunter on Centares, she learned the name of the Rebel pilot who destroyed the first Death Star and heard that the Empire would pay well for that information.

**Mal'aa** A Twi'lek female who owned and operated Mal'aa's Kitchens in the Kala'uun Starport on Ryloth. She had been an outcast from her original clan, and earned enough credits to survive by cooking meals for spacers. She inherited a large sum from a spacer who remembered her good food fondly, and she used it to set up Mal'aa's Kitchens. Her hospitality became known throughout the region.

**malab** Found only on the planet Telos, malab was a highly reflective black stone that was smooth to the touch, with a mirror-like surface in its natural state.

**Malachor V** Located in the Unknown Regions of the galaxy, this graveyard planet was the site of the decisive battle in the Mandalorian Wars, when the Jedi Knights finally defeated the Mandalorians many years after the Great Sith War. Following the Jedi Civil War, the surviving Sith Lords briefly established an operating base in a collection of underground caverns and passageways known as the Malachor Depths. Within a few years, however, the Jedi Exile tracked them down and confronted Darth Traya. In the wake of their struggle, a droid remote set off a mass shadow generator, causing a gravitic chain reaction that blew up the planet's core and turned the world into chunks of rubble.

**Malachor Depths** A series of underground caverns and passageways located beneath the surface of the planet Malachor V. Ancient Sith Lords established their base of operations in the Malachor Depths during the years following the Mandalorian Wars.

**Malacia** An ancient Jedi technique that induced powerful dizziness and nausea in enemies, while not doing lasting harm. Jedi Master Oppo Rancisis was one of the last to use Malacia in combat, and he described the difficult discipline as the transferring of one's own energy to the intended target. Thus, the use of Malacia required a Jedi to maintain visual contact with the target at all times.

**Maladi, Darth** The head of intelligence and assassination for the new Sith Order some 100 years after the Galactic Civil War, she was an expert in the ways of torture. She was present when Darth Krayt went to the Emperor's throne room on Coruscant, seemed to kill Emperor Fel, and then declared himself the new Emperor. But the dead Fel was in fact a double, and Krayt ordered Maladi to start hunting for the deposed Emperor along with any surviving Jedi who might help him. He strongly suggested the use of bounty hunters.

**Maladori, Cynith** A young woman who was a member of House Melantha at the height of the New Order. She was the lover of Bal Jaset until she betrayed him in order to promote her own brother in a house succession battle.

**Malagarr** Hidden in the Unknown Regions, this planet was the homeworld of ancient, long-lived beings who died out, leaving behind their droids and technology. It briefly became an Imperial research base but was destroyed not long after the Battle of Yavin.

**Malak, Darth** Once a promising student at the Jedi academy on Dantooine, Alek "Squint" Squinquargesimus ignored the warnings of his Master and joined the Revanchist movement as it led the Republic fleet in battles against the Mandalorian raiders in the Outer Rim some four millennia before the Galactic Civil War. In the Mandalorian Wars, both Alek and the Revanchist found the glory they were seeking. While many credited the Revanchist's military strategies for the campaign's success, others were quick to point to Alek's fierce courage and relentless fury at the forefront of every battle as the key to Republic victory.

Darth Malak

Alek and the Revanchist pursued the fleeing Mandalorians into the uncharted regions of the galaxy. They returned as changed men: The Revanchist became Sith Lord Darth Revan, and Alek turned into Darth Malak, his chosen apprentice. The heroes had become conquerors. With each Sith victory, soldiers and Jedi alike began to abandon old allegiances to join the new power. In desperation, the Jedi Order set a trap to capture the two Sith. Details of the ensuing battle were never clarified; Darth Revan was captured and many Jedi were killed, yet Darth Malak managed to escape. Some claimed that Malak fled the battle. Others said he survived because he was stronger than Revan. But some believed that Malak turned on Revan, using the opportunity to wrest the mantle of Dark Lord from his former Master's failing grasp.

Darth Malak continued to wage war against the Republic. He was distinguished by the unusual face shield he wore, an apparatus that was required after he lost his lower jaw in a lightsaber battle. His speech was assisted by a vocabulator, and his voice had a distinctly metallic sound to it. In a break from the Sith forays that Revan led against Republic systems, Darth Malak destroyed worlds rather than capturing them, ensuring that vital resources were no longer available to either side of the battle. In the tradition of the Sith, Darth Malak took Darth Bandon as his apprentice, and the pair worked from a base on Korriban for many years. Much of Malak's war machine was produced by the Star Forge, an ancient Rakatan artifact that was modified to produce Sith fighters and other weapons. Darth Malak powered the Star Forge with captured Jedi Knights, drawing on their powers to augment the massive input of the Unknown World's sun. With the defection of Admiral Saul Karath, Darth Malak acquired the *Leviathan*, which served as his personal flagship, and he appeared to be invincible. In an epic battle, the Jedi Knights and the forces of the Old Republic set out to destroy the Star Forge and eliminate Malak's threat. The battle was waged for months until Darth Malak was killed and the Star Forge destroyed.

Darth Maladi

**Malakili** A professional creature trainer and beast handler from the Corellian system, he left the Circus Horrificus to work for Jabba the Hutt as a rancor handler. Malakili had a great deal of affection for Jabba's rancor, which he was able to train. When Jabba ordered a krayt dragon to fight the rancor, Malakili knew his pet's days were numbered. With the help of Lady Valarian, he tried to have the rancor smuggled offworld, but on the morning the escape was to take place the rancor was killed by Luke Skywalker. After Jabba's death, Malakili opened a restaurant in Mos Eisley—The Crystal Moon—with Porcellus, who had been Jabba's head chef. The pair used funds looted from Jabba's palace.

**Malani** An Ewok from the Forest Moon of Endor, she had a crush on Wicket W. Warrick when they were growing up. Malani was one of Kneesaa's best friends, and the younger sister of Teebo.

**Malarian Alliance** A treaty signed by representatives from the Ansionian and Malarian peoples, linking their planets in commerce and defense during the last decades of the Old Republic. Count Dooku and Shu Mai hoped the Malarians would follow the Ansionians in joining their secession from the Old Republic.

**Mal'ary'ush** The Noghri title used to address Leia Organa Solo, it identified her as the daughter of Darth Vader, to whom the Noghri long felt indebted.

**Malas, Moor** A New Republic general, he commanded the ground forces during the siege of Coruscant.

**Malastare** A high-gravity planet with a variety of terrain and climates, ranging from lush forests to dusty wastelands. Malastare was known for its fast and dangerous Podraces, which were held in several locations. One circuit took place near volatile methane gas pools and rivers, while another ran through a crowded city. "Sebulba's Legacy," one of the more dangerous courses, was said to have been designed by the infamous Dug Podracer himself, who came from the city of Pixelito.

Strategically located in the Mid Rim, Malastare was inhabited by many sentient species, including Dugs and Gran. The Dugs primarily lived in the arboreal regions of the planet, while the Gran inhabited larger, more civilized areas. The world was represented in the Galactic Senate by three members of the Gran species—Aks Moe, Ainlee Teem, and Baskol Yeesrim—in the last years of the Old Republic.

Malastare

Some 8,000 years before the Battle of Yavin, the Old Republic set up an outpost on Malastare because of its position along the Hydian Way trade route. About 7,000 years later, the Gran founded colonies on the planet. The relationship between the two species was founded on inequality, with the Gran viewing the Dugs as subservient laborers. One example of the social structure was the slogan for Tradium-brewed Vinta Harvest Ale: "Dugs make it! Gran own it!"

During the Yuuzhan Vong War, Malastare was subjugated by the alien invaders, but was relatively untouched by terraforming efforts. Dugs and Gran were angered by the lack of help from the Galactic Alliance in the years following the end of the war and finally began working together to restore their homeworld.

**Maldeen, Bim** A fearless swoop gang chief and leader of the Nebula Masters, he controlled the streets of Gralleenya on Questal.

**Maldrod** An Imperial Army colonel who was part of the team assembled by Darth Vader to guard a laboratory on Belderone, and to subjugate the planet Kulthis at the height of the Galactic Civil War. Colonel Maldrod was continually amazed at Vader's use of the Force, whereas his contemporary General Andrid openly scoffed at Vader's devotion to it.

**Maldrood sector** An area of the galaxy over which the Rebel Alliance and the Empire struggled for control in the wake of the Battle of Endor. It contained the planet Centares.

**Malé-Dee** A Senator to the Old Republic during the Clone Wars, he represented Uyter, an independent-minded agrarian world. Malé-Dee wore his red hair in a style that signified a plea for peace, with just a strip of hair running from his forehead over the top of his skull to the nape of his neck. Like his assassinated predecessor Lexi Dio, he became a member of the Loyalist Committee and quickly signed the Petition of the Two Thousand. Malé-Dee was one of the handful of Senators present when Padmé Amidala presented Chancellor Palpatine with the document, calling on him to relinquish his emergency powers and recall his appointed regional governors.

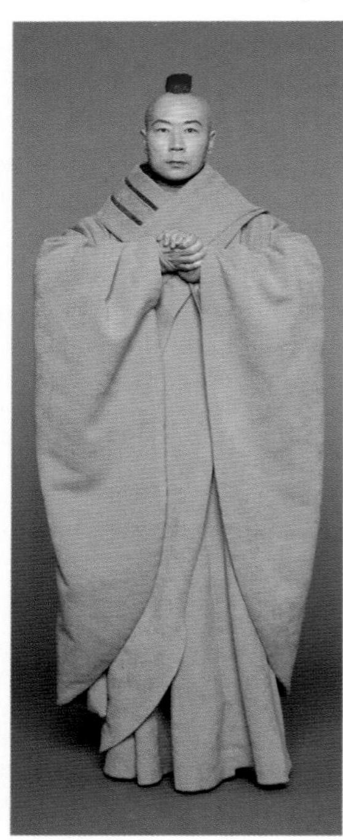
Malé-Dee

***Maledoth*** A Yuuzhan Vong slave ship, it was turned over to the Galactic Alliance in the wake of the invaders' defeat at Coruscant. The ship was eventually bonded to Lowbacca, and the Jedi Knight used it to transport refugees to new homeworlds for many years.

**Males-Who-Die-For-The-Hive-Mother** The Basic translation of the Verpine term used to describe males of the species, whose sole purpose in life was to protect the Hive Mother.

**Mal Ethon City** Located on Kwevron, it was the site of the planet's major spaceport.

***Malevolence* (1)** A massive Separatist battleship built by Quarren workers at the shipyards of Pammant. The vessel was built around a plasma rotor that fired enormous disks of ionic energy that expanded as it spun. The ship, under the command of General Grievous, had destroyed the Republic's Fourth Fleet and counted a dozen vessels among its victims. It crippled a convoy of medical transports in the Ryndellia system, then targeted the Kaliida Shoals Med Station. On orders from General Anakin Skywalker, Shadow Squadron attempted to strike the ship's bridge. After suffering too many casualties, the squadron changed tactics and instead targeted its ion cannon. The damaged *Malevolence* was forced to withdraw with the arrival of a trio of Republic attack cruisers. Capturing a Naboo yacht, Grievous intended to use its passenger, Padmé Amidala, as a hostage, but she escaped. Skywalker and Obi-Wan Kenobi then infiltrated the *Malevolence,* and Skywalker modified its hyperdrive so that the ship would collide with a dead moon of Antar upon attempting to jump to lightspeed.

Malgio

***Malevolence* (2)** A Nebulon-B frigate used by the Imperial Navy during the Galactic Civil War.

**Malgio** A Quarren starshipwright known as much for his physical appearance as his starships. Malgio was nearly twice as wide as a normal Quarren, and his obesity extended to his mouth-tentacles: Their girth was immense. He was an excellent technician and mechanic, and produced some of the best customizations in the galaxy during the era of the New Order. He worked from a facility hidden beneath the surface of Mon Calamari's planet-spanning ocean in the sunken city of Hikahi.

**Malia** A young woman who grew up in the undercity of Coruscant, she eked out a living as part of a small gang during the Galactic Civil War. Later she went to work as a spy and a "relaxation specialist" at the Rose Nebula massage parlor and spa while dreaming of one day living in the upper-class spacetowers of Coruscant's glittering cityscape.

**malia** A fierce predator that hunted in packs on Ragoon-6. Legend had it that if you heard the high-pitched cry of a malia, you were already dead. The mouth of the malia was filled with three rows of sharp teeth with which it could grasp its prey and tear out huge chunks of flesh.

**Malicar 3** A small, uninhabited world located near Imperial territory. Shortly after the Battle of Endor, Admiral Mir Tork and Dr. Leonis Murthé fled to Malicar 3 after their ship was shot down by the New Republic. Boba Fett tracked down and executed Tork and Murthé.

***Malice*** An *Imperial I*–class Star Destroyer, its crew intercepted and attacked the disabled Rebel Alliance shuttle *Maria.*

***Malicious*** One of the many *Victory*-class Star Destroyers that was active in the Imperial Navy during the Galactic Civil War.

**maligator** A serpent in the swamps of Trinta measuring more than 2.5 meters, it resembled a blue-scaled alligator with a flattened head. A maligator's spiked tail was used as a weapon.

***Malignant*** One of the *Imperial*-class Star Destroyers that made up the Imperial Navy fleet during the Galactic Civil War.

**Malik** An Imperial agent who posed as a crewman aboard the *Star of Empire* in order to get the Systems Infiltration Manager installed for its first test. Malik, while being an excellent programmer, proved to be a soldier with a conscience, and told the SIM program that he wouldn't enter the codes to unleash its programming. The program tortured him in the hope of getting the codes. Malik later was taken to a Rebel Alliance medcenter for treatment.

Ket Maliss

**Maliss, Ket** An assassin in the employ of Prince Xizor, head of the Black Sun criminal syndicate. Maliss, whom Xizor called his Shadow Killer, was on unknown business in Mos Eisley when Ben Kenobi and Han Solo were making their deal to get to Alderaan. Maliss was a Dashade, a species that died out during the Sith War. He was the last of the Dashades to be cryogenically frozen and then released into servitude of the Falleen royal family.

**malium** A trace element found on Cerea, it existed in the atmosphere in only a few parts per trillion. This concentration was just right, however, for cultivation of the tecave plant, which produced a euphoria-inducing drug, guilea. The export of malium was prohibited, but an underworld smuggling business sprung up when offworlders discovered the effects of guilea.

**Malkite Poisoners** This secretive group of killers worked from the planet Malkii under the noses of government and most law enforcement agencies. Malkite Poisoners carried small vials of lethal toxins hidden in their clothing. The group's code insisted that no member be captured alive.

**malkloc** Giant herbivores native to Dathomir. It was unclear whether they occurred naturally or originally were bioengineered.

**mallakin** A small avian creature native to the forests of Kashyyyk. Mallakins hid in the leaves of trees and ate small insects.

**Mallar, Plat** A young Grannan from Polneye, Mallar flew a TIE interceptor during the Yevethan attack on his homeworld and was able to destroy a Yevethan scout fighter. He then attempted to reach the planet Galantos in the short-range TIE—an impossible task—but luckily was picked up by a New Republic prowler. Mallar had recorded tapes of the savage massacre on his planet, thus alerting Republic leaders to the recent aggressive actions of the Yevetha. Mallar later became a New Republic pilot.

**Mallat, Zeven** An Imperial officer who served with the Security Bureau during the last years of the New Order. Mallat researched the Duskhan League during the time that the Empire established the Black Fleet shipyards in the Koornacht Cluster.

**Mallatobuck** Chewbacca's mate, she was often called simply Malla by her family. When the Empire raided Kashyyyk for slaves and took Chewbacca, Malla waited many years until Chewie was freed by Han Solo. She raised their son Lumpawarump with the help of Chewbacca's father, Attichitcuk, allowing Chewbacca to travel the galaxy in order to fulfill his life debt to Solo.

**malledillo** A small armored creature once native to the Yuuzhan Vong homeworld of Yuuzhan'tar. Malledillos were bred to have an incredibly hard shell. They served as hammers or mallets for the Yuuzhan Vong.

**Mallif Cove** An island on the planet Recopia given to a group of religious monks who wanted to ponder the mysteries of the galaxy in relative isolation. The monks were descended from the Seyugi Dervishes, but they forgot their ancestors and were unaware that the basement levels of their fortress contained hibernation chambers with sleeping Seyugi Dervishes, waiting to be reanimated.

***Mallixer*** A starship owned and operated by Bettle and Jaxa during the early stages of the Galactic Civil War.

**mallow** This plant was grown for its roots, which were dried and ground to produce a sweet powder. This powder often was mixed with water and cooked to produce mallow paste.

**Malo, Lanah** A Corellian woman who was one of the leaders of the protest group that Bria Tharen joined after she left Han Solo on Coruscant. Lanah helped Bria during her period of withdrawal from the Exultations, and worked hard to bring down the Hutts and t'landa Til who were running the spice and slave colonies on Ylesia.

**Malorm Family** An infamous group of psychopathic killers—Jez, Rek, Shalla, Sheyna, and Star—they controlled a large criminal empire during the last decades of the Old Republic. They earned their reputation for hijacking the luxury liner *Galaxy Wanderer* as it passed through the Corporate Sector. They dropped a number of the ship's passengers into deep space, stole everything of value from the ship's coffers, and escaped to the planet Matra VI. Some time later they were apprehended by a team of mercenaries assembled by the CSA and headed by Gallandro, who claimed the bounty on the entire group at the same time.

**Malorum** One of the first Inquisitors appointed by Emperor Palpatine during the early months of the New Order. Malorum was sent to the openly rebellious planet Bellassa to subjugate the population as an example of what could happen to those planets that opposed the Empire. He ordered that hundreds of residents be executed unless Ferus Olin turned himself in, but Olin and Obi-Wan Kenobi managed to free the captives.

When Malorum returned to Coruscant, Darth Vader told him to focus on eliminating underground resistance on the planet rather than worry about Jedi. But in an act of defiance, Malorum set up an office in Yoda's former quarters in the Jedi Temple and started a rumor that Jedi Knights were being held prisoner there, hoping to lure unsuspecting Jedi into a trap. In an effort to capture Olin, Malorum set off an explosion in the Temple, which angered Emperor Palpatine.

In an effort to appease the Emperor, Malorum set about destroying Solace and her underground hideout, but he failed at that, too. Desperate to earn the Emperor's favor, Malorum then set out to establish a link between Darth Vader and the death of Senator Padmé Amidala. He nearly discovered the truth on Naboo before killing Ryoo Thule, but was intercepted by Ferus Olin. In a brief lightsaber struggle, Malorum lost his concentration and with it, his tenuous grasp on the Force. He plummeted into the core of the Theed Palace power generator station, and was killed.

**Malray** Known to his comrades as Hands, he was one of the many independent spacers who worked in the Cularin system during the final years of the Old Republic.

**Malreaux** A once powerful family on the planet Vjun. It was believed that the original Viscount Malreaux was a pirate who patrolled the Bay of Tears. When a planetwide plague caused much of the population to go mad and die eight years before the Battle of Geonosis, the 17th Viscount succumbed and became insane. The Viscount died, and his son Whie was taken to Coruscant for training as a Jedi Knight.

Mallatobuck

*Malta the Hutt*

**Malreaux, Whie** The heir to the Malreaux family holdings on Vjun. As an infant Whie was found to have a strong connection to the Force, and—despite her misgivings—his mother Whirry asked the Jedi to take him to a better place. His father had gone mad and was killing the household staff because he believed they were poisoning him.

While grew strong in the Force, and eventually was chosen by Jedi Master Maks Leem as a Padawan. He and others accompanied Master Yoda to Vjun, where they had a frightening and nearly fatal confrontation with Asajj Ventress. Whie and fellow student Bene were taking lightsaber lessons from Master Cin Drallig at the Jedi Temple when the new Sith Lord Darth Vader began his murderous rampage. Whie was the first of the group to be cut down.

**Malrev IV** A planet where the *Starfaring* was lost—and eventually recovered by Rogue Squadron—after a bug in its navigational software transposed the coordinates it was using. The homeworld of the hound-like Irrukiine species, Malrev IV had a temple built on a nexus of dark side energy. It was supposed to be a refuge for Emperor Palpatine before he was killed at Endor. The temple later served as the base of power for the mad Devaronian Cartariun, who used Sith magic to control the Irrukiine and make them fight using dark side powers.

**Malta the Hutt** One of Jabba the Hutt's most loathsome associates, Malta the Hutt was so obese that his eyes could barely open because of the fat surrounding them. He was completely unable to move without his heavy-duty repulsorsled. When Malta agreed to a bet with Jabba and Embra the Hutt to find the Yavin Vassilika, Malta hired Dengar, Bossk, and IG-88 to hunt down the valuable crystal, believing that brute force would win the day. It didn't.

**malt ferment** A mildly alcoholic beverage popular with the younger generation of moisture farmers on Tatooine during the New Order.

**Maltaz, General** An Imperial Army officer, he at one time commanded the Hell's Hammer unit. On Turak IV, he allowed his squadron to be cut off from its supply lines by Rebel Alliance soldiers hidden in the Hitak Mountains. Then, further compounding that bad decision, he ordered the squadron to stand and fight. Alliance soldiers quickly reduced the Hammers to three tanks, but the Hammers' never-say-die attitude kept them in the battle long enough for TIE fighter reinforcements to arrive and bombard the Alliance's landing field.

**Maltha Obex** *See* Brath Qella.

**Maltorian Mining Belt** Located near Maltoria, this asteroid belt was one of many that were controlled by the Reconstruction Authority of the Galactic Alliance during the years following the Yuuzhan Vong War. It was an area heavily infested by pirates.

*Manaan*

**Malvander** An Imperial Governor, he razed the surface of his homeworld Solem shortly after the Battle of Yavin in an effort to eliminate any possible Rebel activity. Killing 10 civilians for each Rebel sympathizer was a price he didn't consider too high. He hired Boba Fett to capture Rebel leader Yolan Bren, who turned out to be Malvander's brother. Bren was rescued by a team of his followers, who captured Malvander, too.

**Malvarra, Moris** This Rebel Alliance special agent was assigned by Ral'Rai Muvunc to act as an observer aboard the pirate ship *Dark Revenge* after the Alliance contracted Dharus to raid Imperial convoys. Malvarra almost immediately requested a transfer, fearing that the pirates were too violent. His appeal was denied.

**malvil-tree** A carnivorous tree-shaped fungus native to Xagobah. Providing a source of food and shelter for the native Xamsters, a single tree was often bound to a family for many generations. In return, Xamster families protected their malvil-trees with their lives. Wat Tambor tampered with the malvil-tree's genetic makeup, and was able to produce a derivative strain whose spores could be used to cloak a vessel because of the way they reflected certain wavelengths of light.

**Malya** Rukil's chief apprentice during the era of the Great Sith War, Malya was killed outside the Undercity area of Taris, and her body was unceremoniously dumped in a remote area. A group of Jedi Knights located and returned her body to Rukil.

*Whie Malreaux*

**Mama's** An establishment that was the closest thing to a smugglers' guild to be found on Ord Mantell. It was owned by a Columi who was known simply as Mama.

**Manaan** An ocean-covered planet, the second world in the Pyrshak system, it was the homeworld of the Selkath and the only known source of kolto, a powerful healing agent. During the era of the New Order, the planet was subjugated by the Empire and transformed into a resort world as a way to cover up Emperor Palpatine's interest in the kolto.

**manadept** One of the many types of domesticated greysors native to Naboo.

**Managing Council** The body of beings charged with making policy decisions for the survivors of the Outbound Flight Project.

**manak** Native to the cooler grottoes of the planet Tatooine, manak was harvested for its flavorful leaves, which were used to wrap gorgs for roasting.

**Manalin** A hot, poisonous, and rocky world, it was the first planet in the Joralla system.

**Manarai Mountains** These snow-covered peaks rose above Imperial City on Coruscant. Luke Skywalker built a private retreat within the Manarai sometime after establishing his praxeum on Yavin 4. An exclusive restaurant with breathtaking views of Monument Park was a namesake of the range. It catered to the wealthy and powerful, and the staff always held a table open for Prince Xizor, the criminal kingpin who was a silent partner. Among other dishes, the Manarai served fleek eel, giant Ithor snail in flounut butter, and Kashyyyk land shrimp.

**Manaroo** A tattooed dancing girl, she was raised on a farm on Aruza by poor parents. She was rescued from Imperial COMPNOR forces by the bounty hunter Dengar. An empath, Manaroo could alter her style of dancing to play off her audience's specific emotions. She worked as a dancer at Cloud City before Dengar brought her with him to Tatooine, where she was captured by Jabba the Hutt and forced to dance for him. Manaroo eventually escaped from Jabba and rescued Dengar, who had been left to die in the desert on Jabba's orders. Through her patience and thought-sharing abilities, Manaroo was able to help Dengar regain many of the emotions the Empire had stripped from him. The two were married soon after on Tatooine. After Dengar finally agreed to retire, Boba Fett agreed to be the best man at their wedding.

**manax** A fruit tree native to Cato Neimoidia. Many beings believed that the manax tree was the source of the nutritive fungus developed

and sold by the Neimoidians. In reality, the tree was simply the growth medium. Leaves and bark were collected and ground into compost that was spread in vast, underground chambers known as fungus farms.

**Manazar** The first officer of the starship *Penga Rift* under Captain Barjas. Manazar was often referred to by his nickname, Mazz.

**Manchisco, Captain Tessa** A veteran captain from Virgillia 7, she served briefly with the Rebel Alliance and commanded the cruiser *Flurry.* Captain Manchisco organized guerrilla warriors into serious military units during her homeworld's civil war, turning the tide against the sheer power of her Imperial-backed enemies. She later commanded a small fleet of 22 ships sent to Sullust. A student of the Virgillian military, the captain used unorthodox tactics, confusing Imperial captains during the civil war and at Endor. She and her crew were killed near Bakura when Imperial Governor Nereus ordered his ships to fire on Alliance ships following a battle against the Ssi-ruuk.

***manda*** A *Mando'a* word referring to a state of being Mandalorians had when they were united in mind, body, and spirit. *Manda* could also refer to the collective soul of the Mandalorian people. It was said that Mandalorians passed into the *manda* when they died.

**Mandallian Giant** A species of immense, heavily muscled humanoids covered in green scales. Their heads were dominated by large, pointed ears, with their faces protected by bony plates. Serrated teeth filled their mouths, and a pair of needle-sharp fangs hung from their upper jaws. Mandallian Giants were known throughout the galaxy for their military skills, and many were trained from birth in combative arts. Mandallian Giants were one of the few groups to ever fully survive an attack by the Mandalorian Crusaders. Later, many of them fought alongside the Mandalorians.

**Mandallian narcolethe** A Mandalorian alcohol famous in the Outer Rim Territories. Developed many millennia before the Galactic Civil War, narcolethe was a powerful beverage considered to be little more than rocket fuel. During the Great Sith War, Mandalorian warriors fed their Basilisk war droids a mixture of unrefined narcolethe and locap plasma.

Mandallian Giant

**MandalMotors** A Mandalorian starship manufacturer with an outstanding reputation for designing military starships. MandalMotors was believed to have been created many centuries before the Galactic Civil War by Gustav Zenlav, a Mandalorian Merc known for his innovative designs for weapons and armor. MandalMotors was best known for vehicles such as the Shadow V combat airspeeder, the LUX-3 landspeeder, and the *StarViper*-class attack ship. It also made custom fighters and other craft for the Hutts.

***Mand'alor* (Mandalore)** In *Mando'a,* the name meant "sole ruler," and it became the name taken by all commanders of the Mandalorian warriors. The original *Mand'alor* became known in Basic as Mandalore the First, although he was also known as Mandalore the Indomitable. Subsequent leaders sometimes added descriptive words to differentiate themselves. The *Mand'alor* served as the leader of his people, but was considered by many to be a leader without any formal recognition of his position. The planet Mandalore was never represented in the Galactic Senate, and the Mandalorians were never assimilated into the rest of galactic society . . . which suited most of them just fine, since that made it possible to remain neutral through most of the conflicts that shook the galaxy.

In the wake of the Galactic Civil War, Boba Fett took on the role of *Mand'alor* for the scattered Mandalorians who survived throughout the galaxy, although he was never regarded as a true Mandalorian. In fact, Fett had rarely set foot on the planet and had abandoned the only family he ever had, his former wife Sintas Vel and their daughter, Ailyn. It was during this time that Fett came to realize that the planet and its leader were given the same name because they were supposed to be synonymous, at least in the eyes of the Mandalorians. And that was when Fett issued the call for all Mandalorians to return home.

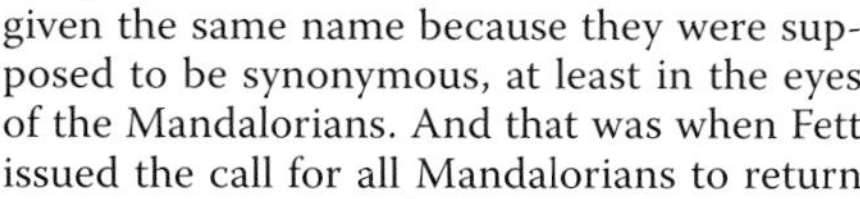

*Mandalore*

**Mandalore** This world in the Outer Rim was conquered by Mandalore the First, whose warriors slaughtered the mammoth mythosaurs that dominated the planet more than 4,000 years before the Galactic Civil War. The planet took the leader's name, although transliterated into Basic, and became the home of fierce masked warrior clans led by a warlord who always adopted the name *Mand'alor.* The first Mandalorians were most likely Taungs, but other species soon dominated. The clans, made up of deadly but honorable crusaders, rode semi-intelligent Basilisk war droids, boasted cutting-edge weaponry, and were considered the best fighters in the galaxy. The mask and title of *Mand'alor* belonged to no single individual but were traditionally passed down from one warrior to the next upon the leader's death.

Through the millennia, Mandalore became marginalized as a planet and a culture, although there were occasional attempts to revive both. During the New Order, Mandalore was besieged by slavers. It was then that Fenn Shysa and Tobi Dala tried to retake the planet, working with Leia Organa and the Rebel Alliance to free Mandalore once and for all. Throughout much of its more recent history, Mandalore's economy was driven almost entirely by MandalMotors. The relationship became extremely important in the wake of the Yuuzhan Vong War, when Mandalore was all but abandoned by the Galactic Alliance. The population was reduced by almost a third during the fighting, but those who had perished became remembered as the only people to defeat the Yuuzhan Vong on their own.

Mand'alor *(Mandalore) the Ultimate*

**Mandalore sector** Located in the Outer Rim in the direction of the Corellian Trade Spine, the system encompassed such widely dispersed planets as Concord Dawn, Vorpa'ya, and Mandalore. Vorpa'ya was closer to Concord Dawn, which was actually near the Mid Rim in the direction of the Perlemian Trade Route.

Mandalore during the Mandalorian Wars

**Mandalore the Indomitable** A Mandalorian Neo-Crusader, he took control of the ancient brotherhood shortly before the Great Sith War. *Mand'alor,* or Mandalore the Indomitable as his warriors called him, was defeated by Ulic Qel-Droma during the fighting, and agreed to help him during the Sith War. *Mand'alor* sent his forces to Kemplex Nine, while he himself went to Coruscant to rescue Qel-Droma and Exar Kun. After regrouping their forces, the Sith Lords ordered the Mandalorians to descend on Onderon. *Mand'alor's* forces attacked Iziz. They were overwhelmed at Onderon during a pass of the Dxun moon, and fled to the moon for refuge. There, the first *Mand'alor* was killed by a pair of the moon's deadly beasts. In a ritual that would be repeated, a new warrior donned his mask and assumed his title.

**Mandalore the Ultimate** A Mandalorian who took on the mantle of *Mand'alor* after the death of Mandalore the First on the Dxun moon. After three years, the reigning Neo-Crusader chieftain was killed and his forces defeated. Many thought the Mandalorians then became extinct. In fact, the Mandalorian species itself all but vanished from the galaxy, but its warrior culture survived.

Mandalorian

**Mandalorian** Anthropologists disagreed on whether these beings were native to the planet Mandalore, but they agreed that ancient Mandalorians were gray-skinned beings who were almost constantly at war. They may have been the ancient Taungs. After the original Mandalorians died out, the species name became the description for any being who adhered to the tenets of the original Mandalorian shock troopers.

Mandalorian

From the final centuries of the Old Republic on, Mandalorians were primarily human, bound together by a common code of ethics that crossed species and social boundaries. This resulted in a civilization that lacked any specific ethnic commonality, and was at once exceptionally violent and extremely tolerant. Evidence could be found in their military, which included both males and females in its ranks, and in their language, which lacked any sort of gender specificity. The galaxy at large came to identify the Mandalorians with their signature armor, although anthropologists recognized that the protective covering was simply a manifestation of the Mandalorian's heart and desire.

During the Sith War, the Mandalorians conquered the Kuar system and struck at the neighboring Empress Teta system, forcing Tetan leader Ulic Qel-Droma to battle leader *Mand'alor* in one-on-one combat. *Mand'alor* was defeated, and he swore his armies' allegiance to Qel-Droma and the forces of the mystical Krath sect. The warlord was made Qel-Droma's war commander, and his clans won many victories. At the close of the Sith War, however, the Mandalorians were defeated in their attempt to capture the planet Onderon, and *Mand'alor* was killed.

By the time of the Yuuzhan Vong War, many believed that Mandalorians had all but disappeared, with only the bounty hunter Boba Fett preserving their legacy. Fett, however, later assumed the role of *Mand'alor* and began reviving the Mandalorian culture. Their presence was noted even by the rogue Jedi Master Vergere, who claimed that the Mandalorians were one of the strongest factions in the galaxy, when explaining the galaxy to Warmaster Tsavong Lah. The staggering loss of life in the Mandalorian defense of their planet against the Yuuzhan Vong caused many Mandalorians to return home, willing to eke out an existence in farming or other rustic professions when bounty hunting and mercenary work failed to earn them enough credits.

**Mandalorian Civil War** A period just before the start of the Clone Wars, it began when Jaster Mereel tried to unite the disparate clans of Mandalorian loyalists under a single leader to restore them to their former glory and power. Mereel also hoped to eliminate the public's perception of the Mandalorian Mercs as amoral killers, especially after they decimated the Ithullans. Mereel's rise to power and the creation of a Codex forced other Mandalorian Mercs to break away from Mereel's band, thus setting off the civil war. Vizsla was Mereel's primary rival, leading the Mandalorian Death Watch. In response, Mereel named himself the leader of the True Mandalorians, and each side set out to destroy the other, which they very nearly did. A handful of Death Watchmen survived, as did the True Mandalorian Jango Fett.

**Mandalorian Crusaders** This group was considered by many galactic historians to have been the first true group of Mandalorian shock troopers formed in the galaxy. The origins of the Crusaders have been traced back more than 5,000 years before the Battle of Endor, to a group of gray-skinned, humanoid nomads who traveled through space seeking conflict of any kind. (*See also* Neo-Crusaders, Mandalorian.)

**Mandalorian Death Watch** An elite group of Mandalorian Mercs that split off from the True Mandalorian shock troopers. It was believed that the Death Watch was destroyed during the Mandalorian Civil War, and the order became something of a legend. All Death Watchmen wore dark armor, and their helmets were modified slightly to further distance themselves from their counterparts.

**Mandalorian dungeon ship** Huge prisoner transport vessels that provided the most uncomfortable conditions. Prisoners suffered maximum discomfort before they were deposited on bleak, harsh worlds and left to die. Dungeon ships measured almost a kilometer in length. Individual chambers could be reconfigured for a variety of activities, depending on the nature of the criminal and the amount of interrogation needed.

**Mandalorian iron** *See beskar.*

**Mandalorian shock troopers** Supercommando warriors who followed the Canons of Honor of the ancient Mandalorians.

Mandalorian Death Watch

**Mandalorian Wars** Defined by historians as the series of battles waged by the Old Republic against the ancient Mandalorians, during the 35 years that followed the Great Sith War. After Mandalore the Ultimate agreed to fight alongside the Sith, the Old Republic decided that it needed to confront the Mandalorians as an enemy. Great effort was expended in defeating the Mandalorians, thereby eliminating the physical threat of the Great Sith War. The Republic could then focus its efforts on assisting the Jedi.

**MandalTech** A sister company of MandalMotors, it was a starship and weapons development firm based on Mandalore.

***Mandator*-class Star Dreadnaught** Developed and manufactured by Kuat Drive Yards specifically for the purpose of defending the Kuat sector from invasion during the last decades of the Old Republic.

***Mandian*** A picket frigate that was part of the fleet assembled by the Old Republic during the Clone Wars. The *Mandian* was among the ships dispatched to Praesitlyn some two and a half years after the Battle of Geonosis, as part of the mission to retake the Intergalactic Communications Center from the Separatists.

**Mandie** A somewhat derogatory nickname used by Old Republic troops to describe a Mandalorian shock trooper.

***Mandjur*** A New Republic warship, it was part of the *Ballarat*'s support line during the Battle of N'zoth. When the *Ballarat* was destroyed, the *Mandjur* filled in the gap, and was struck twice in the aft section by Yevethan missiles. Plat Mallar, assigned to the ship as a shuttle pilot, single-handedly rescued three pilots in the ensuing chaos.

***Mando'a*** A Mandalorian word for their native language, known in Basic as Mandalorian. *Mando'a* was strange to most humanoids, since it focused on the present tense and lacked any form of gender, although it was considered grammatically simple by many linguists. At its core, *Mando'a* was a spoken language, because many different groups spoke it with enough subtle variation that writing it down became problematic. It was seen as a robust, direct language used by robust, direct people, and it mirrored their culture. The Mandalorians had no word for "hero," but many different words for "stab." Being compared to a Hutt was the worst insult, and the word for "mother" and "father" was the same.

**Mando-Verpine Assault Fighter** A series of *Bes'uliik*-class assault fighters that were produced as a joint effort between MandalMotors and Roche Industries during the Confederation–GA War. The new starship took advantage of Verpine ultramesh technology to produce a lightweight spaceframe that was made entirely from *beskar*, making the ship incredibly durable and maneuverable, even in atmosphere.

**mandoviol** A stringed musical instrument popular with cantina bands across the galaxy during the era of the Galactic Civil War. With 17 minor keys, four major keys, and a slide attachment, the mandoviol was a difficult instrument to master, but it could be used to play ballads as well as energetic tunes.

**Mandrell, Ody** An Er'Kit from Tatooine, he piloted an Exelbrok XL 5115 Podracer. During the Boonta Eve Classic race in which Anakin Skywalker emerged victorious, Ody Mandrell's Podracer was disabled in a crash and had to come in for repairs. Pit droid DUM-4 was sucked into the port-side engine when it suddenly fired up, and the damage ruined the motor. Mandrell eventually got the damage repaired and returned to the race, but was knocked off course by Sebulba and driven into Skywalker's Podracer. The two racers became entangled, and when they finally freed themselves, Mandrell's ship flew out of control and crashed. The Er'Kit survived but retired from active Podracing. He remained on Tatooine as a mechanic, eventually going to work for Ulda Banai at the Mos Espa Swoop Arena.

**Manech, Treyz** An Imperial lieutenant during the early stages of the Galactic Civil War, he was demoted to a position on the planet Troska about nine months after the Battle of Yavin after trying to take control of an Imperial Star Destroyer in an effort to chase down a possible Rebel Alliance convoy. Eventually he was promoted to commander of the Troska garrison after hiring Boba Fett to depose the planet's monarchy.

**Manellan Jasper** One of the finest varieties of tea leaves produced in the galaxy in the early years of the New Order.

**Manes, Tomathy** The senior duty officer of the New Republic Defense Fleet base on Utharis. A communications specialist, Manes helped Luke Skywalker obtain a current tactical memorandum on the situation in the Koornacht Cluster during the Black Fleet crisis.

**Maneuver 717** An Imperial code name for a mission designed to rid a squad of a possible spy or enemy agent posing as a pilot. During a mission, a commander would issue the command to fly Maneuver 717. Loyal pilots would lead the spy away from the ship, and the spy would be allowed to head the mission. Once the ships were in a position such that the spy couldn't see them, they fired on and destroyed his or her ship, later claiming that it was shot down by enemy fire.

Ody Mandrell

Treyz Manech at Boba Fett's mercy

**Manex** A wealthy member of the Civilized faction of the planet New Apsolon in the decade before the Battle of Naboo. Manex was the brother of planetary leader Roan, and had a number of other political contacts, all of which he used to help amass his fortune.

**mangana aqua jewel** A brilliant, yellow-tinged gemstone found at the bottom of several of Naboo's major waterways. Gungan leaders often distinguished themselves with an egg-shaped mangana aqua jewel in their headpieces.

**Mangol** A grizzled old treasure hunter who died on Nespis VIII shortly after the Battle of Yavin. Mangol allegedly located an ancient tome from an abandoned Jedi library. His contemporaries believed he was killed by a curse that surrounded the library, but in reality he was a victim of Borborygmus Gog's Essence Stealer. Mangol was later reanimated by Tash Arranda when she reversed the Essence Stealer's actions.

**Maniid** A smuggler who made regular shipments to Bracha e'Naso in Esau's Ridge on Tholatin during the early years of the New Republic.

**Manikon** Beings from another world who found a home in the subsurface caverns of the Coruscant cityscape. Manikons were scavengers, and spent much of their time hunting for food and trinkets in the underworld. When cornered, Manikons could spit stinging venom into attackers' eyes, temporarily blinding them.

**Ma'Ning, Justyn** One of the Jedi Masters chosen to lead the Outbound Flight Project. Ma'Ning first became concerned when Jedi Master Jorus C'baoth began separating families during the journey based on their Force sensitivity. He eventually accused C'baoth of crossing the line from guide to ruler. Outbound Flight was intercepted by a Chiss task force led by then–Force Commander Thrawn. In the initial wave of attacks, Master Ma'Ning was caught in a blast and buried beneath a pile of shrapnel. With his last breath, Ma'Ning told C'baoth's Padawan, Lorana Jinzler, that a more devastating attack was coming now that C'baoth had given himself over to the dark side of the Force.

**Manka, Siolo Ur** This Twi'lek Jedi Master left Coruscant for the Jentares system more than 70 years before the Battle of Naboo, in an effort to separate himself from the rest of the galaxy and meditate on the Force. He had been considered among the best Jedi warriors of the time. Just before leaving for Jentares, however, Siolo Ur Manka renounced his lightsaber and set out to contemplate purer techniques. Darth Sidious ordered his apprentice Darth Maul to assassinate Master Manka, but the Twi'lek managed to disarm Darth Maul with little more than a wooden stick. It was rumored that this defeat caused Maul to develop his two-bladed lightsaber, since the single-bladed weapon he had used against the Jedi had been so ineffective. Rather than creating a single weapon, though, Maul welded two lightsabers together at the base, creating a weapon with the element of surprise. Maul returned to the Jentares system to complete his mission. When Master Manka again bested Maul in combat, the Sith apprentice activated the second blade and killed the Twi'lek. Darth Sidious was impressed with Maul's skills and his creation of the two-bladed lightsaber.

*Lord Manos*

**manka cat** Discovered by the Tetsus tribe of Rodians, manka cats lived on the jungle world the tribe adopted. They were the only creatures on the planet capable of killing a Rodian, which they often did during their mating season.

***Manka Hunter*** The name that bounty hunter Greedo planned to give the Incom corsair that he hoped to purchase from Shug Ninx.

**Manks, Gris** A colonel in the Freedom's Sons and Daughters militia during the Clone Wars. During the battle to retake the Intergalactic Communications Center on Praesitlyn from the Separatists, Manks coordinated the combined forces of Freedom's Sons and Daughters and the clone troopers of the Grand Army of the Republic. However, only a daring rescue mission led by Anakin Skywalker managed to save the hostages.

**Mankvim-814 Interceptor** A small, two-being fighter developed by the Techno Union and manufactured by Feethan Ottraw Scalable Assemblies during the Clone Wars. The fighters were designed to provide planetary security for those worlds subjugated by the Separatists.

**manollium** A yellow-feathered bird native to the planet Ithor, it was brought to Belsavis by the Brathflen Corporation.

***Manollium*-class herd ship** Designed for Ithorians who wished to travel the galaxy in a starship that mirrored the environment of Ithor, this 980-meter-long ship fulfilled the Ithorian desire to revere life. Its weaponry was designed to incapacitate but not destroy. The ship was equipped with 10 ion cannons and a pair of tractor beams, but no lasers or blasters.

**Manos, Lord** A Devaronian who served on the Imperial Interim Ruling Council, he was the leader of one of the galaxy's largest labor unions. Lord Manos supported Feena D'Asta and her plan to make peace with the New Republic.

**Manosk, Stevv** Han Solo was given this alias by the Hutts Jabba and Jiliac for use in infiltrating the *Imperial Destiny* and in bribing Admiral Winstel Greelanx. Manosk was a lieutenant in the Imperial Navy.

**Manpha** An Outer Rim planet that was home to the Shawda Ubb. The small, wet world was on the Corellian Trade Route.

*Manpha*

**Manr, Rostat** A Sullustan male who served the Rebel Alliance during the last years of the Empire, flying Y-wings into battle. He also served the New Republic, but a year after the Battle of Endor he resigned his commission and went to work in the private sector. On a short leave, he was kidnapped and brainwashed by agents of Imperial warlord Zsinj as part of Project Minefield. A trigger phrase was implanted in his head that, when activated by a nonsense phrase would cause him to crash the *Nebula Queen* into a planet. Manr would have crashed into Coruscant if not for two things: intervention of his counterpart, Nurm, who stunned Manr into unconsciousness; and Wraith Squadron, which had learned of Zsinj's actions and had warned officials.

**manta droid subfighter** A battle droid developed for use on oceanic planets by the Techno Union, the manta droid was originally created after the Trade Federation took heavy losses on Naboo and other aquatic worlds. Later these ships were supplied to the Quarren Isolation League during its struggle to take control of the planet Mon Calamari from the Mon Calamari Knights.

*Manta droid subfighter*

***Mantan Wanderer*** A Mon Calamari cruiser that was the flagship of the Rebel Alliance's 14th Roving Line, and was under the command of Captain Qarl.

***Mantaris*-class transport** A ray-like amphibious transport designed and manufactured jointly by Theed Palace Space Vessel Engineering Corps and Otoh Gunga Bongowerks following the Battle of Naboo. It was developed as part of a cooperative effort to colonize Ohma-D'un, the primary moon of Naboo. The transport had characteristics of a bongo submarine, but with the capability of interstellar flight.

**Mantellian Savrip** Hulking, sentient creatures with leathery green hides, they were native to Ord Mantell. They moved with surprising speed on two short, stubby legs, and their long arms ended in powerful claws. The Savrip's reptilian head was mounted at the end of a flexible neck, allowing it to face any direction. It wasn't unusual for a Savrip to have a life span of 500 years. Qui-Gon Jinn and Obi-Wan Kenobi encountered a Mantellian Savrip, Mawkran, aboard Baron Sando's freighter; he was the only Savrip known to be able to speak Basic. Baroness Omnino and Taxer Sundown conspired to sell the beings as food. They were also represented as playing pieces in hologames.

**Mantessa** The homeworld of dangerous predators called panthacs. During the Yuuzhan Vong War, the planet was besieged by a group of fire-breathers until a platoon of Clone Wars–vintage B2 Super Battle Droids banded together to confront the alien invaders. Known as the Orange Panthacs, the battle droids successfully defeated the Yuuzhan Vong and their fire-breathing creatures, preserving Mantessa's freedom.

**manticore** A legendary creature distinguished by its humanoid head and a cat-like body. The manticore also had a segmented tail that was tipped with a thorn-like stinger. Although many considered manticores the stuff of legend, the Holographic Zoo of Extinct Animals dedicated an entire display to them during the early years of the New Republic.

***Manticore*** One of the four Star Destroyers stationed at the Maw Installation by Grand Moff Tarkin during the New Order. The *Manticore* was commanded by Captain Brusc, and was part of a fleet under Admiral Daala that protected the Maw and the superweapons produced by scientists who worked there. Seven years after the defeat of the Empire at the Battle of Endor, the *Manticore* was pressed

into active duty when Admiral Daala decided to strike back against the New Republic. Using tactics devised by Tarkin himself, Daala kept the *Manticore* hidden behind Mon Calamari's moon, where it waited for the Mon Calamari to abandon their orbital shipyards in order to defend the cities on the planet's surface. The *Manticore* never completed its mission, however: It was destroyed when Admiral Ackbar recognized Daala's tactics as those of Tarkin. He used the half-constructed star cruiser *Startide* to ram the ship.

**Mantid, Di** This woman was a frequent patron of the Outlander Club some 10 years after the Battle of Naboo. She usually wore heavy facial makeup, including blue lipstick and silver rouge.

Di Mantid

**mantigrue** Dragon-like lizards native to the Forest Moon of Endor, they lived in mountain caves. Mantigrues had large leathery wings, sharp claws, and long, pointed beaks; they walked on their hind legs. Predatory in nature, the mantigrue was not above scavenging for food. Some could be trained, such as the one owned by Morag, the Tulgah witch.

**Mantle of the Force** An ancient artifact uncovered in the shop of Suvam Tan on Yavin Station, more than 4,000 years before the Galactic Civil War. The Mantle itself was simply a crystal, although it was imbued with the power of the Force. When used in conjunction with other crystals in the construction of a lightsaber, the Mantle of the Force was believed to alter the abilities of the blade, giving the wielder unusual powers.

**Mantoid** An unusual combat droid that made the rounds in the gladiator arenas of the planet Rattatak before the Clone Wars. Cylindrical with an oval head, the skinny, multiarmed Mantoid was armed with a variety of bladed weapons.

**Mantologo** A noncommissioned officer, he was among the stormtrooper units stationed aboard the first Death Star during its construction above the planet Despayre.

Mantoid

**Mantooine** A colony planet located in the Atrivis sector in the Outer Rim Territories, it was the site of an Imperial massacre. A large group of Mantooine freedom fighters called the Liberators were slaughtered by the Empire when they took refuge in a captured Imperial base. The crushing defeat hardened the resolve of early resistance leaders like Mon Mothma, and helped solidify the need for an Alliance to Restore the Republic.

Mantigrue

***Mantooine*** A New Republic CR90 corvette that was part of the force sent to liberate the planet Ciutric from the control of Prince-Admiral Krennel. The *Mantooine* took heavy fire from Krennel's forces, and barely survived the encounter.

**Mantooine Medallion** A military decoration presented by the Rebel Alliance, it was designed to commemorate the sacrifice of the people of Mantooine in the face of Imperial invasion.

***Mantooine Minuet*** A piece of classical dance music favored by Emperor Palpatine.

**mantys** A species of flying, predatory insectoids native to the planet Kubindi. Its two forelegs were used as grasping arms, while it moved about on the ground with its other four legs. The species lived high in the forest canopy, in large nests created from plant matter and sticks. Most mantyses captured their prey on the ground, then carried it back to the nest to eat.

Map reader

**manumission** A term that described the reprogramming of a droid's obedience functions to provide it with the ability to act for itself. Manumitting, essentially the freeing of a droid from service, was often performed to reward an automaton for faithful service. Although many organic beings saw the act of manumission as a well-deserved honor, most droids found it to be a mixed blessing, as the freedom they had been given was not always recognized by other beings.

***Manx*** A Corellian CR90 corvette in the Rebel fleet during the Galactic Civil War.

**Maoi** Amorphous beings created as part of an experiment by the ancient Kathols, they considered all life as food. After they captured their prey, they forced themselves down the victim's throat and started digesting them from the inside out, internal organs first. In the wake of the Rift Disaster, the DarkStryder tried to dispose of them deep in the Segmi tunnels after finding them totally self-centered and amoral. The Maoi survived, however, and thrived in the underground environment.

**mapping skiff** Developed by Koensayr following the Yuuzhan Vong War, this small, intrasystem craft could enter a planet's atmosphere and complete preliminary mapping of terrain and environment before returning to a mother ship.

**map reader** A device used to display a star map hologram. The map could fill a room and be interactive. The devices were used by the Jedi and the Separatists during the Clone Wars.

***Mara*** A Gallofree medium transport, it was used by the Rebel Alliance to transport bacta during the Galactic Civil War.

**maraffa** A tree native to Kabal, known for its pleasant odor and sticky orange sap. The sap was considered a sweet delicacy, and maraffa twigs often were sold like candy.

**Marais, The** A group of planets in the Koornacht Cluster, The Marais appealed to the New Republic for membership after the start of the Yevethan Great Purge.

**Marakoloon** A Whiphid easily distinguished both by his size and by his carved and silver-inlaid tusks. As the second son of a wealthy trader, and thus not destined to inherit his father's wealth, he became a bounty hunter. Although he liked the pay, he hated the work. Upon viewing a special exhibit of carnivorous plants in a zoo display, he suddenly realized that the power and beauty of the plants appealed to him. Marakoloon spent the rest of his career collecting dangerous species of plants.

**Maramere** A blue-green planet, it was the primary world in the Karthakk system and controlled by the Trade Federation's Lord Toat prior to the Battle of Naboo. Maramere was covered almost entirely with water, with rocky spires and outcroppings forming the only land. The native Mere, fish-like humanoids, built wondrous cities in and among the rocks, but also lived underwater. Six years after the Battle of Naboo, a group of freedom fighters led by Sol Sixxa began to fight the oppression of the Trade Federation. With the help of the Feeorin smuggler Nym and Jedi Master Adi Gallia, the Mere were able to overthrow the Trade Federation and reclaim control of the planet. They then foiled an attempt to poison the planet with trihexalon. Some 20 years before the Battle of Yavin, the bounty hunter Durge assassinated a wealthy Corellian mer-

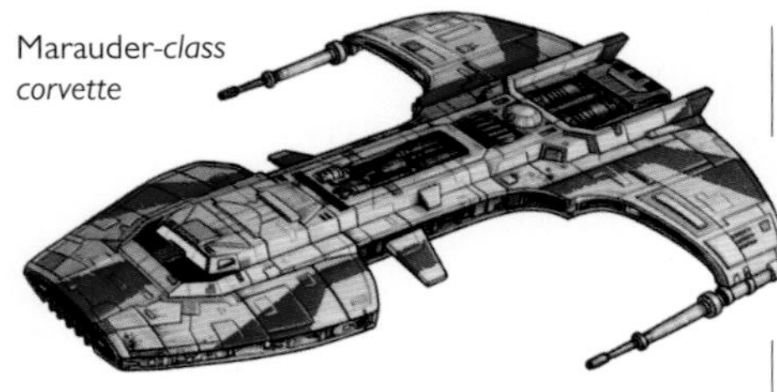
Marauder-*class corvette*

chant in a starship near the planet. Anakin Skywalker pushed Durge into an escape pod and sent it hurtling into Maramere's sun, Karthakk, killing the seemingly indestructible hunter.

**Marat V** The Imperial name for the planet Skye.

**Marath, Eyar** A Sullustan entertainer, she was part of Jasod Revoc's Galactic Revue entertaining the Republic troops during the Clone Wars. On Drongar, she met noted Sullustan journalist Den Dhur, and the two got married.

***Marauder*** A New Republic *Warrior*-class gunship, it was part of Pakkpekatt's fleet sent to intercept the Teljkon vagabond. The *Marauder* later assisted the *Indomitable* in taking out a Yevethan T-type thrustship near ILC-905.

***Marauder*-class corvette** One of the most common capital ships in the Corporate Sector Authority's (CSA) picket fleet, they were also popular with planetary navies and large corporations, and occasionally fell into the hands of smugglers and pirates. One CSA corvette launched an attack on an outlaw-tech base, forcing Han Solo and Doc's daughter Jessa to lead the base's technicians into combat against the CSA fighters. On another occasion, Chewbacca took over a Marauder and used it as an evacuation vessel when Solo engineered the destruction of the penal facility known as Stars' End.

*Reina March*

**Marauders** *See* Sanyassan Marauders.

**Marauders (Sith)** Force-sensitive individuals, Marauders were one of the many small groups that followed the dark side of the Force during the era of the New Sith Wars. Based on planets such as Honoghr and Gamorr, the Marauders kept their existence hidden from the Jedi Order.

**Marauders' Masquerade** The second largest social event on the Hapan annual calendar after the Queen Mother's Birthday.

***Marauder Starjacker*** An ore-raiding ship commanded by pirate captain Finhead Stonebone some 4,000 years before the Battle of Yavin, it resembled a 100-meter-long insect. The *Marauder Starjacker* and its sister ship the *Stenness Raider* began as asteroid-mining ships, but Stonebone used them to raid Ithullan colossus wasp carriers, both for himself and later for Great Bogga the Hutt. The ships were built with rugged claws to dig through solid rock and attach to an asteroid.

**marble-berry** A plant that produced an edible fruit often used in the creation of tasty muffins and sweet fritters.

**Marca** A crew member on the *FarStar* during the search for Imperial Moff Kentor Sarne. In the attempt to defeat Sarne and DarkStryder on Kathol, Marca was attacked by a Maoi confined to sickbay.

**marcan herb** A plant material often used by Hutts in their water hookahs. It induced a mildly euphoric feeling.

*Korl Marcus (right) and Captain Trall*

**March, Reina** The leader of the anarchist group known as Edge-9 during the last decades of the Old Republic, March was known for her skills as a hand-to-hand fighter. Often dressing in clothing to blend in with a crowd, she was sometimes seen in the company of Dannl Faytonni at the Outlander Club on Coruscant.

**Marcha, Duchess of Mastigophorous** This Drall female was the aunt of Ebrihim, who was hired on Corellia as a tutor for the children of Leia and Han Solo. Chewbacca and the Solo children sought help from her after they were forced to flee Corellia when Thrackan Sal-Solo and the Human League took control. Leia chose her to be the new Governor-General of the Corellian system, following the end of the Starbuster plot and the death of Micamberlecto. Marcha relocated to Corellia in order to help bring peace to the system. Later, during the Yuuzhan Vong War, she reluctantly gave conditional approval to the New Republic Defense Force's plan to use Centerpoint Station as a weapon against the alien invaders. She was eventually replaced as Governor-General by Sal-Solo.

Marauder Starjacker

**Marcino, Shel** A member of the Silent Blades pirate organization, he was one of the few to survive the assault on the group by Vocis Kenit and the *Far Orbit.* Marcino was a simple deckhand at the time of the attack, but later gathered the other survivors and formed the Tarnished Blades gang. They continued to live the life of pirates, hoping to get one more shot at taking out Kenit.

**Marcol sector** The sector of the galaxy that contained the planet Barlok.

**Marcopious, Yeoman** A member of the Honor Guard for Chief of State Leia Organa Solo, he helped C-3PO and R2-D2 escape in a scout boat after the kidnapping of Princess Leia, before the New Republic's ships went into hyperspace. Marcopious died in the escape pod from the Death Seed plague about 30 minutes later, leaving the droids to fend for themselves.

**Marcross, Saberan** An Imperial stormtrooper stationed aboard the Star Destroyer *Reprisal* following the Battle of Yavin. Marcross and other members of his squad questioned their continued service to the Empire, especially after the destruction of Alderaan. Their doubts were reconfirmed on a mission to Teardrop, where they were forced to kill civilians in order to root out Rebels. Eventually the squad stole a Suwantek TL-1800 and fled.

Following several run-ins with the agents of the BloodScar pirates, the stormtroopers found themselves mixed up with Han Solo and Luke Skywalker, who were working with a group of farmers on the planet Drunost. After Solo and Chewbacca saved the squad from being inadvertently intercepted by the *Reprisal,* Solo and Skywalker explained the Teardrop incident further, telling the stormtroopers that all the Rebels had been evacuated from the planet before the *Reprisal* arrived. This further cemented the troopers' disillusionment with the Empire.

While continuing on the trail of the BloodScars, Marcross and his comrades eventually found themselves commandeered by Mara Jade, who was also investigating the pirates. Jade explained that their mission was to assassinate Choard, forcing Marcross to reveal that he was Choard's nephew. He could not bring himself to shoot his own uncle, a decision that Jade accepted. After ensuring Choard's arrest and completing her investigation, Jade demanded the truth from Marcross and his comrades. Their explanation seemed to suit her, as she allowed them to disappear, giving them the chance to escape from Imperial service and set off on their own.

**Marcus, Korl** An alias used by Luke Skywalker when he accompanied Prince Denid back to the planet Velmor. Marcus was a noted bounty hunter who dressed like a flamboyant pirate.

**marde** A white stone used for carving expensive columns and pillars.

**Mardoc the Hutt** The Executive Secretary of the Grand Council of Hutts during the early years of the New Order.

***Marduk*** An Imperial *Carrack*-class cruiser that served as the personal ship of Sub-Commander Brojtal during the Galactic Civil War.

**Marec, Makin** A Mandalorian, he was Ailyn Vel's mate and the father of Mirta Gev. After Marec and Vel split up, he spent several years raising his daughter on the planet Null. He later died in a hull breach accident.

**Marek, Galen** *See* Starkiller.

**Mar'ek** An ARC trooper stationed in the Cularin system during the Clone Wars, he was ordered to capture Trilinae and her companions just before the command was given to execute Order 66. This capture was part of a plot to lure any surviving Jedi back to Cularin, where they would be ambushed and executed. To protect Trilinae, Mar'ek stranded her on a remote world and vowed to return when the war was over. Later, Jedi Master Darrus Jeht narrowly avoided Order 66 by cutting down Mar'ek's group, saving Mar'ek for last. When Jeht demanded to know what was going on, Mar'ek replied that Trilinae was dead, as were Aayla Secura and the rest of the Jedi. Mar'ek had counted on Jeht's compassion to save him, but instead the Jedi cut through Mar'ek's face, killing him instantly.

**Marellis** Mara Jade's alias when she worked as a come-up flector, or scam artist, on Caprioril in the years following the Battle of Endor. She adopted the alias in an effort to avoid being forced to work for Ysanne Isard. While on Caprioril, Mara encountered Lumiya for the first time and was forced to defeat her in combat. In the fight, however, Lumiya managed to acquire Mara's violet-bladed lightsaber, which had been given to her by Emperor Palpatine.

**Margath, Kina** The owner of Margath's, a luxury grouping of hotel rooms, cantinas, casinos, and restaurants on Elshandruu Pica. Margath was a Rebel Alliance agent. She befriended the Imperial Moff's wife, Aellyn Jandi, who used the hotel as the rendezvous point for meeting her lover, Sair Yonka. Rumors spread that it was Margath who was having the affair with Yonka. Margath told the true story to Wedge Antilles when it was determined that Captain Yonka and his ship, the *Avarice,* could be used in the New Republic's struggle against Ysanne Isard.

**Margath's on Elshandruu Pica** One of the Outer Rim's best-known retreats, owned by Kina Margath. Among the venues was the 27th Hour Social Club, which maintained a five-star rating for a number of years. In order to protect their interests, Margath and her investors posted signs at the entrance stating, NO LIABILITY IS ACCEPTED FOR INJURIES OR ILLNESS RESULTING FROM SAMPLING ITEMS ON THE FOLLOWING DRINK LIST.

**margengai-glide** A dance step popular in the years before the Battle of Yavin, made up from a series of complex patterns.

**Margrave** The hereditary position of leadership among Togorians, the Margrave was the eldest male descendant in each generation, and in charge of the planet's government. His closest female relative, called the Margrave-sister, presided over day-to-day activities, while the Margrave traveled the plains with other males.

**Marg Sabl closure maneuver** An aggressive positioning in which a lead warship allowed its support fighters to launch from behind an offensive line and then turn hard into the opposing force. Grand Admiral Thrawn used it to ambush the New Republic force that tried to pursue Imperial scouts who raided the library computer at Obroa-skai. Thrawn recognized that the commander of the Republic's ships was an Elomin, and took advantage of the fact that the Elomin mind was unable to handle the unstructured nature of a Marg Sabl maneuver.

**Mariana** A native of Bellassa, she owned and operated Mariana's Exquisite Designs and Alterations, which catered to many of Ussa's upscale residents. The shop fell on hard times after the Empire took over Bellassa a year after the end of the Clone Wars. When Mariana agreed to work for the Empire, her fellow Bellassans ostracized her, and her shop was empty on most days. Mariana was working at night to do the sewing and tailoring required by the Imperial garrison and prison that was established in Ussa.

**Maridun** The homeworld of the Amanin species, Maridun was covered with lush forests and grassy plains. A society of Lurmen established a colony there to escape the Clone Wars. Anakin Skywalker, Aayla Secura, Ahsoka Tano, and Clone Commander Bly discovered the Lurmen village. During the Empire, Imperial scouts found that the Amanin made a strong source of slave labor. After the Battle of Endor, much of the planet's commerce was based on criminal activities, most of which were controlled by the Hutts.

**Marilla** The queen of Gascon during the Galactic Civil War, she ruled the planet with her husband. The king, however, was heavily influenced by the High Adviser, who was a believer in the Akol religion. Marilla was the more dominant figure and controlled both men with her iron will. Not that she was without a softer side: She was having an affair with the Prime Minister of the planet Demigue.

**Maristo** An alias used by Kell Tainer, Maristo was a starfighter pilot with the Imperial Navy. A captain, he commanded Drake Squadron and was assigned to the Star Destroyer *Night Terror.* The Maristo alias was used to get a flight of Wraith Squadron onto the planet Kidriff 5, near Tobaskin sector, in order to support the fly-by of the *Millennium Falsehood.*

**Marit** A species brought to Gaftikar by human colonists as laborers to build cities. Essentially sentient lizards equally comfortable walking upright or moving about on all fours, they made their homes in the fields. Tan scales covered their bodies with an iridescent sheen that helped camouflage them. Their hands were quite dexterous, and the average Marit could pick up and use tools and weapons.

Marits were known for their ability to approach a situation logically, devising a plan that cascaded from a single action and led to easier activities as the task progressed. Over time, the Marit population grew larger than the humans, and the Marits took over more of the planet's leadership duties. During the Clone Wars, the Marits sided with the Republic, while the human population sided with the Separatists.

**Marius** A vizier and member of a royal family that ruled the daylight side of a remote planet where Han Solo crash-landed during the Galactic Civil War. Marius agreed to help Solo return to the Forest Moon of Endor. But the vizier was plotting to take control of the planet and had stalled the signing of a peace treaty with the planet's night-side rulers. Solo eventually outmaneuvered Marius and helped negotiate a peaceful resolution.

**Mark 10** A droid sensor suite that could be purchased during the last decades of the Old Republic.

**Mark 15** A starship diagnostic kit, it was produced by Quaxcon during the early years of the New Republic. Han Solo kept one aboard the *Millennium Falcon.*

**Mark III Katarn armor** The third version of the standard Katarn armor that was produced for the clones of the Grand Army of the Republic. In addition to its basic features, the Mark III version had more technological enhancements and was rated as blasterproof against even light cannon fire.

**Mark III Sleeper droid** A droid developed during the final decades of the Old Republic by Sienar Intelligence Systems as a

*Mark III Sleeper droid*

response to the Republic's prohibition on assassin droids. Although it was officially designated as an assassin droid unit, the Mark III Sleeper was equipped with nonlethal armaments, allowing it to hunt down its targets and bring them to justice without killing them in the process. When the Separatist movement kicked off the Clone Wars, the Mark III Sleeper was largely abandoned in favor of more lethal security automata. Ironically, many Mark III Sleeper droids were then acquired by Separatists, who used them against the Republic forces they had once protected.

**Mark IV patrol droid** This series of repulsor-equipped sentries was created by the Imperial Department of Military Research for use by the Empire shortly before the Battle of Yavin. Inside the computer core of the Mark IV was a database that contained a complete readout of the Imperial Penal References, ensuring that the droid could swiftly identify the crime it witnessed.

**Mark VII Scarab droid** A line of Scarab droids produced for Imperial use by Sienar Fleet Systems. Deployed during the Yuuzhan Vong War, the Mark VII resembled a palm-sized insect and moved about on six magnetic feet. The droids scaled vertical walls with ease, and a single injector mechanism could be loaded with a variety of poisons.

**Mark X executioner** A gladiator droid that specialized in combat sports, with built-in flame projectors, flechette missile launchers, and blasters. Viceprex Hirken of the Corporate Sector Authority owned one on Stars' End, and paid the Imperial Entertainment Guild to send him droid performers to pit against his Mark X. When Han Solo infiltrated the penal colony, part of the ruse was sending his somewhat outdated droid compatriot Bollux up against the Mark X. Bollux used cunning rather than force, coming in low to lock himself around the Mark X's tracks. The Mark X became confused and went berserk, shooting all its weapons at anything that remotely resembled a target. It eventually ran itself into a wall and self-destructed.

**Marka** A young slave owned by the Toydarian Lod. When Lod tried to sell her to the Sith Master Finn and his apprentice, the apprentice killed Lod for suggesting that he, too, was a slave. Marka followed the Sith to their ship, asking to go with them. Finn refused on the grounds that he already had an apprentice, but—sensing that Marka was strong in the Force—he told his apprentice to deal with her. Marka took the apprentice's lightsaber and pushed him off a building to his death. She then took her place as Finn's apprentice.

Mark X executioner

***Market Potential of Known Outer Rim Worlds: A Report to the Galactic Trade Federation*** A report on the possible profits to be gained from trade with the Outer Rim Territories. Author Rune Haako wrote that Tatooine was too ridden with vice and corruption to have any worth.

***Marketta*-class shuttle** A transport ship created during the early decades of the New Republic, it saw duty primarily within the Republic's military.

**Mark of Illumination** Religious insignia used by the mystics of the Chalactan Enlightenment to denote an individual who had become one with his or her gods, the mark was formed by affixing one or two small beads to the frontal bone of an individual's skull. A single Mark on the bridge of the nose, known as the Lesser Mark of Illumination, indicated an individual's devotion to his or her gods. A second Mark on the forehead, known as the Greater Mark of Illumination, indicated an individual's attainment of the rank of Chalactan Adept. Together the two Marks signified the most basic tenet of Chalactan Enlightenment: "As Without, So Within."

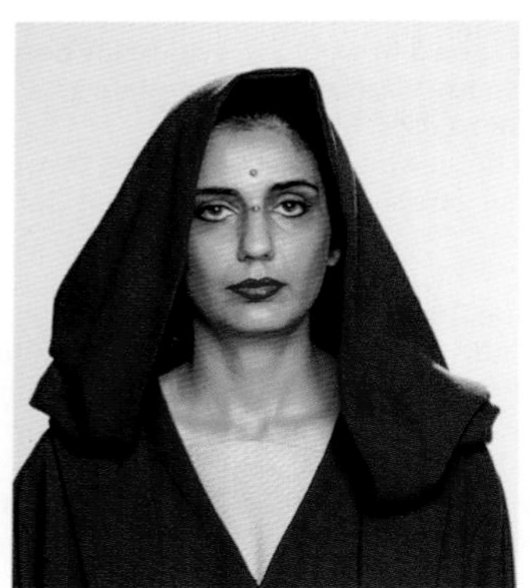
Marks of Illumination

**Mark of the Crown** This subtle mark of succession was a characteristic of the true heir to the throne of Gala. The Galacian Council of Ministers could test an individual for the Mark in a room with an elaborate sensor and lighting system. If a being had the Mark, the shadows of light would outline him or her. One who did not have the Mark would not cast a shadow.

**Mark One Pall of Smoke and Flame** A term used by technicians who worked on StealthX starfighters to describe one of two ways that a downed StealthX could be spotted: the rescue beacon or the pall of smoke and flames created upon impact in a crash landing.

Marksman-H

**Markota, Selwin** A New Republic Navy officer aboard the *Pride of Selonia,* he was second-in-command to Captain Todra Mayn during the Yuuzhan Vong War. He was an excellent administrator and dependable at all times, even during a crisis.

**marks of contact** Used by the Jedi Order in the Old Republic to describe the various ways that a Jedi Knight could inflict physical damage to an opponent with a lightsaber. There were eight main marks of contact:

- *Sun djem* removed an opponent's weapon without causing injury.
- *Shiim* cut the opponent with the edge of the lightsaber blade.
- *Shiak* stabbed the opponent.
- *Cho mai* cut off the hand holding a weapon.
- *Cho sun* removed the arm that controlled a weapon.
- *Cho mok* dismembered an opponent.
- *Sai cha* beheaded an opponent.
- *Sai tok* cut an opponent's body in half.

**Marksman-H** A training remote, it was used to instruct beings how to handle weapons such as blasters and lightsabers. Obi-Wan Kenobi had Luke Skywalker work with a Marksman-H aboard the *Millennium Falcon.*

**Markus, Len** The primary representative of the Smuggler Confederacy in the years following the Battle of Naboo. It was believed that he traveled into the Cularin system's asteroid belt to remove the Darkstaff from its resting place, releasing a horde of strange creatures and causing the sudden disappearance of the entire Cularin system. It was later revealed that Markus hired the noted information broker Sot-sirc to discover the location of the Darkstaff.

**Marl, Dagga** Shortly after Thrackan Sal-Solo was named President of Ylesia and Commander in Chief of the Peace Brigade, he hired this woman to serve as his personal bodyguard in the wake of threats from the Ylesian Senate. Marl had been working secretly for the Ylesian Senate, performing assassinations to keep certain factions in power. She gladly accepted Thrackan's offer of a kilogram of glitterstim each week he remained alive, to relieve the boredom of working for the Senate.

**Marniss, Celina** Mara Jade's alias when she worked as a hyperdrive mechanic in Tropis-on-Varonat. She adopted the nickname after meeting Melina Carniss on

Tatooine many years before. The Marniss alias was used on different missions by Jade during her career, including her investigation of the BloodScar pirate operations on Gepparin.

**Marook, Senator Cian** A belligerent Senator from Hrasskis, he was a member of the New Republic Senate Defense Council. He argued that the intervention against the Yevetha was too hasty and voiced disapproval at General A'baht's appointment as commander of the Fifth Fleet.

**Marquand, Major** Originally from Kessel, this AT-ST pilot directed a counterattack against the Ewoks on the Forest Moon of Endor during the last major battle of the Galactic Civil War. Major Marquand formerly crewed an AT-AT assigned to the *Devastator.*

**Marr, Brezzic** An Imperial commander in charge of the 105th Stormtrooper Platoon assigned to Starlyte Station. Like the rest of the 105th, Marr was fanatically loyal to the Empire. He also had a keen tactical mind and an intense personality, and many of his strategies eventually found their way into Imperial training manuals.

**Marr, Nichos** A Jedi student of Luke Skywalker, he came to the Jedi academy with his fiancée, the beautiful scientist Cray Mingla. Within a year, he was struck with the fatal Quannot's syndrome. Mingla, an expert on artificial intelligence, instituted a crash plan to transfer Nichos Marr's intelligence, mind, and very spirit, if possible, into a near-human artificial body. Although he appeared relatively human, he still had major differences that Mingla tried to overlook.

Marr aided the New Republic's search for the long-missing children of the Jedi, since he had been one of them. He also helped Skywalker locate the *Eye of Palpatine,* a prototype Imperial battle station that had mysteriously been reactivated. Cray and Marr accompanied Skywalker and C-3PO to the ship to destroy it before it could carry out its preprogrammed plan of destruction. They were amazed to find that the spirit of a Jedi woman named Callista had been trapped inside the computer core since she had first incapacitated the ship's weapons some 30 years before.

The *Eye of Palpatine* could be destroyed, but only if someone would stay behind to be destroyed with it. Marr volunteered and Cray, realizing that she couldn't live without him, stayed behind, too. Just as an explosion was about to destroy the ship, they used the Force to transfer Callista's essence into Cray Mingla's body and ejected her in an escape pod.

Nichos Marr

**Marrab, Gron** A Mon Calamari Senator to the New Republic during the Yuuzhan Vong War. When Coruscant fell to the alien invaders and the remaining Senators retreated to Mon Calamari, Senator Marrab was appointed to a task force assigned to restore communications to those sections of the galaxy that had been isolated during the war.

Major Marquand

**Marshak** A Corellian smuggler of minor repute, he supposedly witnessed Han Solo win the *Millennium Falcon* from Lando Calrissian. Marshak explained to Solo that the Kessel Run involved obtaining rare Kessel Birds from the Aeneid system. This, however, was an expensive joke played by Calrissian and Marshak on young Solo as part of Calrissian's revenge for losing the *Falcon.*

**marsh haunt** An unusual swamp creature native to Abraxin in the Tion Cluster, it also could be found in many forms on other planets. Many xenoarchaeologists believed that the idea of a "Force Demon" evolved from encounters with marsh haunts. The creatures were greenish gray, bipedal, with skulls set between their shoulders, giving them a headless appearance. More fearsome in appearance than action, they could channel a small amount of the Force to frighten other beings.

**Marshian** An Imperial lieutenant who served as Admiral Pellaeon's shuttle pilot, he was stationed aboard the *Chimaera.*

**marsh-grubber tree** A tree species native to Yavin 4 that grew on the edges of swamps and lakes.

**marsh-gunnie** A small swamp creature native to the bayous of Nim Drovis.

**marsh pig** A porcine creature native to the swamps and marshes of the planet Corellia.

**marsh-root** A plant often used in soufflés.

**Marskan, Captain Ernek** A Rebel Alliance officer, he was stationed on the flagship *Independence* when Keyan Farlander served there. When his younger brother, Casal, was killed accompanying Farlander on a mission, Marskan became distrustful of Farlander's tactics.

**Marskan, Casal** A Rebel Alliance starfighter pilot and younger brother of Captain Ernek Marskan, he was assigned as Keyan Farlander's wingmate on a mission to capture the *Ethar I* and *Ethar II* Imperial corvettes. Casal was killed in the battle.

**Marso's Demons** A group of mercenary fighter pilots led by Marso. The Demons were distinguished by a notorious former member, the bounty hunter Gallandro, who was generally considered one of the best Demons ever.

**Marspa** An ancient Jedi Master who traveled the galaxy with his Padawan, Imina.

**Martaff** A New Republic Navy commodore dispatched to the Koornacht Cluster to assist in the struggle with the Yevetha.

**marthan** A plant native to Ansion, it produced an edible, sweet-tasting fruit.

***Martial*-class shuttle** A small starship commonly used by pirates during the early years of the New Republic. The droop-winged shuttle was made by Sienar Fleet Systems.

**Marty** A New Republic deck officer who served under Etahn A'baht on the *Glorious.*

***Martyr*** The personal shuttle of the Kalee warrior who became General Grievous. He used it during the Huk Wars. At the end of the war, the *Martyr* was sabotaged by San Hill, who wanted the warrior to be left with devastating injuries that would force him to sacrifice himself for the good of his people. The shuttle plunged into the Jenuwaa Sea and was recovered by Count Dooku himself.

**Martyr of Drongar, the** The title used in many newsfeeds to describe Phow Ji after his death on Drongar during the height of the Clone Wars. It referred to his seemingly heroic actions in wiping out a gang of Salissian mercenaries and their battle droid army, ostensibly to save the staff at Rimsoo Seven and allow them to relocate in the face of a Separatist attack.

**Martyrs (1)** An honorary title given by the Bothans to members of the group that stole the plans to the second Death Star, as well as to Y-wing pilots of Blue Squadron who died ensuring that the plans made it to the Alliance High Command. The Martyrs held an almost sacred place in Bothan history and society, for their actions ultimately brought down the Emperor and the New Order. For a Bothan family to be joined to the family of a Martyr in marriage or other bond was considered a blessing.

**Martyrs (2)** A constellation found in the skies of Bothawui, named in honor of the Bothan pilots of Blue Squadron.

**Maruk, Jai** A Jedi Master known during the Clone Wars as the Hawk-bat because of his fierce, wild stare. He was on patrol near Vjun when his forces were intercepted by Asajj Ventress and brought to the remote planet. Maruk was forced to duel with Ventress, who would have killed him if Dooku hadn't stepped in. Dooku released Maruk so that he could return to Coruscant with a message for Yoda.

Shortly thereafter, Yoda challenged Maruk's perceptions, wagering with him on the outcome of the Apprentice Tournament. Maruk had already decided that Tallisibeth Enwandung-Esterhazy, otherwise known as Scout, was unfit for the rigors of being a Jedi Knight. Yoda bet Maruk that if Scout finished in the lower half of the tournament, she would be sent to the Agricultural Corps. If she finished in second, third, or fourth, she could remain as an apprentice. If she won the tournament, Maruk would accept her as his Padawan. Maruk was surprised when Scout emerged as the tournament champion, but their resulting pairing created a bond between the two. When Maruk eventually was cut down by Ventress in battle, he swore to Scout that he would remain with her forever, at least in spirit.

Mary

***Marut*** A *Victory*-class Star Destroyer used by the Imperial fleet to raid Rebel Alliance training facilities shortly before the Battle of Endor.

**Mary** A beautiful, blond-haired resistance fighter on Solay, she was part of Raggold's rebellion following the Battle of Endor. After Raggold's assassination, Mary suggested that Luke Skywalker be named Solay ruler—a representative of both the New Republic and the democracy Solay natives so desperately wanted. Mary and the rest of her group had just a few days of freedom before Imperial warships arrived. Mary was shot and killed in the initial wave of attacks.

**Maryb Wastes** A vast, open wasteland found on the planet Maryx Minor. The Ancient Order of the Pessimists located its base beyond the Wastes.

**Maryo** A resort world in the Corporate Sector, it was where CSA agents first contacted Torm Dadefferon about becoming an agent.

**Maryx Minor** The Ancient Order of the Pessimists made its home on this desolate world. Maryx Minor was volcanically active, and open lava pits and steaming geysers littered the landscape. Boba Fett tracked the outlaw Abal Karda to this world, completing his bounty hunt.

**maser cannon** Developed by the Chiss during the Yuuzhan Vong War, it used microwave radiation to generate a beam of coherent energy.

**maser fan** A Chiss artillery cannon that was formed from a set of maser emitters connected to a single power source, the fan could literally spray maser energy at a target.

**Ma'Shraid** A Yuuzhan Vong prefect, she was one of the few female leaders to accompany the first wave of the Praetorite Vong invasion force into the galaxy. She led the warriors who guarded the yammosk on Helska 4, and commanded the second worldship to arrive at the planet.

**Masked Soldiers** In the prophetic visions of the Keganite woman O-Vieve, the Masked Soldiers attacked and subjugated the planet Kegan. Historians later learned that these soldiers were actually the Imperial stormtroopers of the New Order.

**Masposhani** According to Beldorion the Hutt, Jedi Knights once trained in the subterranean caves of the planet Masposhani.

**Masque Hall** Located on Cloud City, this ballroom was the site of a never-ending masquerade party.

***Mas Ramdar*** A Dreadnaught that was part of the Home Fleet defending Coruscant from General Grievous's attack near the end of the Clone Wars. The *Mas Ramdar* was commanded by Barrow Oicunn, and it was credited with the destruction or disabling of many Separatist warships during the fighting.

Maryx Minor

**Massacre at Ossus** The devastating attack on Ossus that occurred in the wake of the Sith–Imperial War. The Galactic Alliance surrendered to the Empire after the Battle of Caamas, but the Jedi Order refused to follow suit, claiming to serve the Force, not the government. The Jedi abandoned the Temple on Coruscant and retreated to Ossus. The Sith decided that the Jedi needed to be eliminated, and the resulting hostilities destroyed Jedi facilities on Ossus and wiped out a large portion of the planet's ecosystem.

**Massassi** A subsect of the Sith bred by Dark Jedi as superb warriors and assassins more than 5,000 years before the Galactic Civil War. During the Great Hyperspace War, Dark Lord of the Sith Naga Sadow kept a large contingent of Massassi warriors at his side. After his defeat, Sadow and his warriors fled to the far reaches of the galaxy, eventually landing on Yavin 4. There Sadow mutated the Massassi with Sith magic, making them even more fearsome guardians of huge temples that he, and later Dark Lord Exar Kun, forced them to build. Many Massassi were killed by Exar Kun in one final sacrifice and others fled for parts unknown, but they left behind a creature known as the night beast to protect their territory. The beast was awakened when Rebel forces used one of the abandoned temples as a base during the Galactic Civil War.

**Massassi One** Luke Skywalker's call sign following the Battle of Yavin. He used it while on diplomatic missions to other worlds and during the Rebel Alliance's search for a new base and new allies.

**Massassi Outpost** Another name for the Rebel Alliance's base on Yavin 4. It was named for the beings who built the huge temples in which the Alliance stored its fighters and command stations while preparing to battle the first Death Star.

**Massassi tree** Towering trees on Yavin 4, they had wide crowns and upswept branches with a purple-brown bark that shred easily into fibrous strands.

**massiff** Common on both Geonosis and Tatooine, they were burly quadruped carnivores about a meter tall at the shoulder with toothy, fang-filled mouths and a line of hard spines along their backs. Geonosis massiffs, thought to have descended from reptiles, often preyed on the sand snakes found along the planet's cliffs. It was believed that massiffs were first brought to Tatooine by a trading ship from Geonosis, which crashed in a sandstorm. The surviving massiffs were raised by the Sand People as guard dogs and companions.

**mass-nulling clip** Portable transport devices that generated a focused field of very low gravity. This allowed large loads, primarily water and food supplies for scouts, to be carried on the back or on a belt clip. During the early years of the New Republic, pressurization technology was coupled with mass-nulling clips, allowing a week's worth of water to be carried on a being's belt.

**mass-shadow generator** An ancient weapon conceived by the forces that served under Darth Revan during the Mandalorian Wars.

**masterblade** The term used by the Bladeborn to describe any weapons master who had survived 10 or more duels with an opponent who used a lightsaber. It referred to the warrior's skill in defeating the weapon of the Jedi and Sith devotees, and those few who attained the rank of masterblade were given a tremor sword as an indication of their skill and rank.

**Master-Com** A stocky, humanoid-looking droid that served Senator Simon Greyshade aboard the Wheel space station during the early years of the Galactic Civil War. Master-Com could patch directly into the computer systems of the Wheel and monitor every aspect of the station at any time. The droid was brought online just prior to the Clone Wars. Master-Com was interested in the self-sufficiency of R2-D2 and C-3PO, and arranged for them to be freed after they were placed in storage for later reprogramming. Master-Com continued to work at the Wheel, and years later helped the station's security teams fend off an attack by the Yuuzhan Vong.

**master control signal** A transmission beamed through hyperspace to guide war machines and other automated objects. A master control signal sent from the clone Emperor's planet of Byss was used to guide the Imperial World Devastators.

**Master in Violet** A female Zabrak, she was one of the mysterious Five Masters who were active on the planet Cularin in the final years of the Old Republic. She began martial arts training for Barnab Chistor about a year before the onset of the Clone Wars, teaching him specialized exercises and meditation techniques that gave the governor better physical and mental conditioning. She was adept at the K'thri martial arts. When the Five Masters Academy was attacked by an unknown force shortly after the Clone Wars, the Master in Violet was the last of her kind to survive. The other masters were Black, Green, Red, and White.

**Master Marksman** An alias assumed by Han Solo when he infiltrated the Stars' End facility as a member of his self-created "Madame Atuarre's Roving Performers."

Master-Com

**MasterNav** A galactic navigational database system used by the Rebel Alliance, the MasterNav was developed to help military forces enter enemy territory close to their intended targets. This not only provided the element of surprise but also made military missions safer.

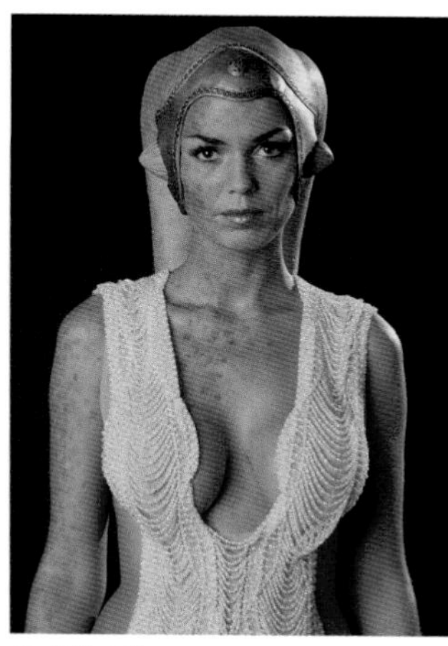
Koyi Mateil

**Master of the Order** The highest-ranking member of the Jedi Council during the last decades of the Old Republic. During the years leading up to the Battles of Naboo and Geonosis, Mace Windu held the position. When Master Windu joined other Jedi in military positions during the Clone Wars, the title was given to Yoda, who remained on Coruscant to serve as Chancellor Palpatine's chief military adviser. *See also* Grand Master.

**Master of the Sith** A title that Lumiya claimed would be bestowed on Jacen Solo upon his complete acceptance of the ways of the Sith. Jacen refused to acknowledge the title or his ability to attain it, since Lumiya was not a Master herself.

**Master's Council** Luke Skywalker described the new Order of Jedi Knights that existed after he severed ties to the Galactic Alliance following the Swarm War as the Master's Council. The Jedi relocated their primary training facility to Ossus, and moved their base of operations to the Forest Moon of Endor. The base was soon abandoned in the wake of the Second Battle of Fondor, when Jacen Solo made a concerted effort to locate and destroy the Jedi. The Master's Council moved to a world in the Transitory Mists.

***Master Stroke*** An *Imperial*-class Star Destroyer dispatched by the Imperial Remnant to assist the *Agonizer* in subjugating the world of Adumar after the Adumari sided with the New Republic. It was seriously damaged in the assault, and the New Republic successfully defended the planet.

**masticator** A generic term that described any spacegoing vessel designed to break down an asteroid or other small, rocky body for refinement. Masticators used spinning drums that were studded with durasteel teeth to pull in an asteroid and grind it into smaller and smaller pieces, until the pieces could be mixed into a slurry.

**mastiff phalone** A dangerous creature native to Maridun, it was a large quadruped with a turkey-like head.

**mastmot** Called motmots in some Whiphid tribal dialects, mastmots were shaggy herd animals with horns and tusks that were often prey for avian snow demons on the planet Toola. A mastmot's rib cage could sometimes be used as a shelter.

**Matale** One of the most powerful families on Dantooine for centuries before the Great Sith War. The Matale family was the bitter rival of the Sandral family, and many of the long-standing disputes stemmed from land ownership. The Matale Fields were separated from the Sandral Fields by a small patch of land known as the Grove, which held a certain mystery for the Jedi Knights who lived on Dantooine at that time.

**matalok light cruiser** A Yuuzhan Vong ovoid-shaped cruiser, it was a rough analog of a Mon Calamari cruiser. Equipped with arrest tentacles that could grab and hold on to an enemy vessel, mataloks were used to defend worldships and other capital-scale vessels.

**Matarcher, Bosbit** A native of Delemede, he got stuck in a time dilation event while in hyperspace. He left Delemede on a regular run 200 years before the Clone Wars, but due to a problem with his ship's shielding, he returned to realize that nearly two centuries, not two hours, had passed since his departure.

**Matchstick** A Shadow Squadron clone pilot involved in the counterattack on the *Malevolence,* he flew as Shadow Three. While traveling through the Kaliida Nebula, his Y-wing bomber sustained damage from collision with a neebray. This affected his performance in the attack, and his ship was hit by a crippling ion blast from the massive warship.

**Mateil, Koyi** A buxom Twi'lek female, she was one of many socialites who lived on Coruscant during the last years of the Old Republic. She artificially colored her lekku to make her skin tone appear to be more human, and was often seen in the company of Duke Teta despite the apparent difference in their ages. She was secretly scheming to steal the Duke's wealth should he ever die.

**Mathal** An agent of Black Sun dispatched to Drongar to confront Admiral Tarnese Bleyd about providing black-market bota for sale during the Clone Wars. Bleyd had no intention of bowing to Black Sun, and killed Mathal, later arranging for it to appear that the agent had died after leaving MedStar.

**Mathilde** One of the strongest nation-states on Renatasia III, it was founded on the planet's second largest continent, located in its northern hemisphere.

**Mathos** One of a multitude of deities worshipped by the offworld natives of Ansion.

**Mating Call** An ancient, specieswide message that every Barabel felt when it was time to return to Barab I to mate. The Mating Call was irresistible, and many xenobiologists believed that it was one of the reasons that the Barabels were able to exist.

**Matl, Rigard** The leader of Shocker Squadron, charged with defending the Jedi Knight base on Eclipse during the Yuuzhan Vong War. He and many of his squadron mates were not Force-sensitive, but were loyal to the Jedi cause. Matl worked with Kyp Durron and Saba Sebatyne to devise a complete defensive strategy, and later participated in the ill-fated defense of Coruscant. During the evacuation and defense of Eclipse, Matl's X-wing was destroyed by Yuuzhan Vong fire, but he managed to eject in time. Despite being extravehicular, Rigard ordered his pilots to regroup and take the battle to the aliens.

**Matrin, Quorl** A former member of the Imperial Senate, he served as the Imperial Governor of Stenos during the New Order, struggling to keep the locals in line. When Luke Skywalker found the lost statue of Vol, he and his team were betrayed to Matrin. The governor paid handsomely to recover the relic, but was accused of defaming the god, and subsequently was torn to shreds by the angry Stenaxes.

**Matrix armor** A strong material often used in the formation of starship hulls, it was more durable than durasteel, and could withstand blaster fire better than titanium.

**matshi** A large fish and favored prey of the firaxa shark.

**Matta** A slave woman who was a friend of Shmi Skywalker, she was owned by Dengula the Hutt in Mos Espa. Shmi and Matta often helped each other finish their quotas when one was sick and had difficulty working.

**Mattac** An outlaw tech who grew up as a port brat on Nar Shaddaa, he eventually hired on as a technician with a local smuggler. Imprisoned by Imperials, Mattac managed to escape and later established an illegal starship-refitting operation in Brenn, where he was known for his excellent work and demanding business dealings.

**mattberry** Native to the Forest Moon of Endor, this sweet fruit was used by Ewoks to make juice. The juice could also be fermented into a somewhat bitter but intoxicating brew.

**Matthews, Ty** A computer technician who served aboard the Rebel flagship *Home One,* he joined the Alliance at the age of 15, eager to support the cause his father Tev so deeply believed in. Gifted at circuit repair and technology, he distinguished himself while on the Mon Calamari cruiser and soon found himself on Admiral Ackbar's staff, where he earned the rank of lieutenant. Matthews was later responsible for decrypting the contents of an Imperial message drone captured in the wake of the Battle of Endor.

**Mattri asteroid field** These asteroids shielded a temporary base for the private army of Garm Bel Iblis during its hit-and-fade attacks against the Empire.

**Matukai** An ancient philosophy of the Force, distinguished from that of Jedi Knights and the Sith in its training methods and beliefs. Practitioners of Matukai used their own bodies as the primary focal point of their abilities, rather than focusing on inanimate objects. By studying the Matukai teachings, a being with minimal sensitivity to the Force could tap into it by using strenuous exercise and meditation. During the Jedi Purge, many Matukai were killed, but some managed to hide themselves and survive. A handful of Matukai eventually presented themselves to Luke Skywalker's Jedi praxeum on Yavin 4 for training as Jedi Knights, after seeing that Master Skywalker's views on Jedi training were more open-minded than those of the former Jedi Order. Individual Matukai followers were distinguished by the unique tattoo that covered part of their foreheads and surrounded their eyes.

*Darth Maul*

**Mauit'ta, Colonel** This New Republic Navy officer was on Etahn A'baht's intelligence staff aboard the *Intrepid* during the Black Fleet crisis.

**Maul, Darth** A weapon forged by the hateful energies of the dark side to ensure the victory of the Sith over the Jedi Order. A creature of pure evil, Maul had no personality beyond his ultimate devotion to his master, Darth Sidious. His goal was singular—to exact vengeance upon the Jedi for the decimation of the Sith ranks.

No one knows how Darth Sidious came across his young and deadly apprentice. He was raised from an early age to be a weapon, tempered by harsh, abusive training to become an incredible warrior. Once a Zabrak from Iridonia, Maul abandoned all trace of his former identity when he took on his Sith name. So complete was his devotion that he even endured the agony of having intricate tattoos applied to his entire body. In the interests of concealing the Sith presence from the Jedi, all of Maul's missions were executed from the shadows.

Although Maul longed to reveal the Sith menace to the Jedi, his devotion to his Master was so absolute that he never questioned Sidious's timing. Maul had assassinated a number of enemies whose activities encroached on the growing Sith agenda. The dark warrior even infiltrated the heart of the galaxy's biggest criminal organization, Black Sun, killed, and escaped unscathed. Maul had a wide array of tools to help him in his missions. His Sith Infiltrator was a modified star courier vessel equipped with a cloaking device. His Sith speeder was lean and unarmed, pared down to the bare essentials to deliver maximum speed. At one point, he even employed a modified protocol droid as an assassin, C-3PX.

The Republic first came to know of Maul only as a mysterious attacker. While Qui-Gon Jinn was escorting the fugitive Queen Amidala from Tatooine to Coruscant, Darth Maul swept down from above, lunging at Qui-Gon from his rocketing Sith speeder. Maul's attack was relentless; he hammered down lightsaber strikes against the accomplished Jedi Master, forcing him back time and again. It was only the timely interception of Qui-Gon by the Queen's Royal Starship that spared him.

Qui-Gon was utterly surprised and unprepared for such an attack. The Sith, everyone knew, were extinct, gone from the galaxy for a millennium. Yet the evidence was there: a dark attacker, trained in the Jedi arts, brandishing a lightsaber no less. Maul had been dispatched by Darth Sidious to track down the Queen, a feat he accomplished through mysterious yet effective means. Traveling aboard his sleek Sith Infiltrator, Maul scouted the galaxy for the missing monarch and reported his findings to his Master. When Amidala returned to Naboo, Maul was there, waiting to face the Jedi once more.

*Darth Maul duels Obi-Wan Kenobi.*

As an undeniable example of his skill and devotion, Maul plunged headlong into battle against *two* Jedi warriors. Using his double-bladed lightsaber, Maul held off both Obi-Wan Kenobi and Qui-Gon Jinn in the heart of the Theed Royal Palace. When the Jedi became separated, Maul killed Qui-Gon with a well-placed saber strike. Kenobi, enraged, attacked Maul. This barrage was deflected by Maul, who used Obi-Wan's touching of the dark side as a conduit for a Force attack; with the Force, Maul pushed Obi-Wan into a deep mining pit. Kenobi held on to an outcropping for dear life. Calming himself by calling upon the light side of the Force, Kenobi was able to surprise Maul and cleave him in half with his saber. A pained look of bewilderment crossed Maul's tattooed face as death overtook him. His body fell into the melting pit, splitting in two as it tumbled into oblivion. It was only a matter of time before Sidious acquired a new apprentice.

***Mauler*** This *Imperial*-class Star Destroyer was part of the security force protecting Kuat Drive Yards during the early years of the New Republic. It took a heavy pounding from the *Iron Fist* during Warlord Zsinj's attempt to steal the *Razor's Kiss.*

**Maur, Dovin** An old man claiming to have survived the birth of the New Order and the destruction of the Jedi Knights at the hands of Emperor Palpatine. He held the Jedi in reverence, and after settling on Lazerian IV, Maur kept secret the location of the Jedi ruins on the continent of Laz.

**mauvine nullifier** A key component of many starship hyperdrives.

**Mavinian cluster-wedding organ** An unusual musical instrument considered by some to be an edgy work of art.

**Mavrille Street** A thoroughfare located in Calius saj Leeloo on Berchest. It was where Luke Skywalker and Talon Karrde started to track the possible sources of clones being produced by Grand Admiral Thrawn.

**Mavron, Lieutenant** An Imperial officer, he served under Admiral Pellaeon aboard the *Chimaera* after the death of Grand Admiral Thrawn. Mavron was sent to chase down possible leads to the origin of the pirate attack on the *Chimaera* shortly after the Caamas incident. He was able to trace the pirates, under the command of Zothip, back to the source of their orders on Bastion. He also discovered a meeting Moff Disra had with Bosmihi on Kroctar, and the fact that Grand Admiral Thrawn had been involved.

**Mavron, Osira** An Imperial Army soldier regularly recognized for her bravery in the face of battle. During the pacification of Praadost II, she fought against a group of dedicated Rebel Alliance forces who were trying to protect a refugee camp hidden in an underground cave. When Osira realized that Imperial forces were expending huge amounts of ammunition and killing a large number of beings to wipe out a group of pitiful refugees, she immediately defected. Once she was accepted by the Alliance, she spent her career teaching commandos about guerrilla warfare and Imperial tactics.

**Maw** A former Jedi Knight who refused to take a Padawan, Maw became one of the Jedi Shadows. His innate tracking skills were perfectly suited for the role. Maw was one of the few Jedi who survived the devastating Jedi Purge, but he was hunted down by Jerec and turned to the dark side of the Force. Injuries required that Maw's legs be amputated and replaced with a small repulsor chair, which he eventually used to his advantage when battling an enemy. Maw would go into a berserker rage, spinning wildly in his chair while swinging his lightsaber in the Trispzest form of combat. For all his power, though, Maw was defeated in combat by Kyle Katarn during the search for the Valley of the Jedi.

**Mawan** A planet in the Galactic Core torn apart by a civil war—known to natives as the Great Purge—three years before the Battle of Naboo. The capital city Naatan was devastated, and the government smashed. Survivors fled into the country, but without a central government the planet descended into lawlessness. The Senate asked the Jedi Knights to send a team to Mawan to help bring the criminal elements under control and form a new government. Jedi Master Yaddle, assisted by Obi-Wan Kenobi and his apprentice Anakin Skywalker, were chosen to go. The Jedi were successful in restoring peace to Mawan but paid a high price: Master Yaddle died after using the Force to absorb a deadly chemical weapon so that others could live.

**Mawat** A native of the planet Melida/Daan, he was the leader of the Young. Mawat was instrumental in digging a tunnel to the spaceport in Zehava during the struggle between the Young and the Elders of Daan and Melida. It was later revealed that it was Mawat, hoping to cause a confrontation, who supplied arms to both the Young and the Elders. He went so far as to place snipers in the buildings surrounding the Hall of Evidence on Glory Street, where the leaders of the two sides confronted each other—just in case either side backed down. It was one of Mawat's snipers who killed Obi-Wan Kenobi's friend Cerasi and started the ensuing firefight. Mawat tried to rally his forces for a victory, but Qui-Gon Jinn displayed a hologram of Cerasi, recorded shortly before her death, in which she pleaded for peace. Mawat, who had secretly loved Cerasi, threw down his arms and surrendered.

**Mawbo's Performance Hall** A large dance hall located on Tatooine during the early years of the New Republic. Owned by Mawbo Kem, it contained a convention center as well as the main concert hall. It was here that the *Killik Twilight* painting was to be auctioned off to the highest bidder some three years after the Battle of Endor. A large portion of the building was damaged when Imperial troops opened fire on the bidders in an effort to prevent the moss-painting from falling into non-Imperial hands.

**Maw Casino** One of the many casinos aboard the *Errant Venture* in the years following the Swarm War. The décor of the casino was in keeping with its namesake, as the walls were painted black to swallow up light like a black hole. The tables had silver surfaces with curving glow rods along the outer edges. There was no overhead lighting. Instead, servers wore clothing and jewelry that glowed in the dark, making the entire casino a scene from the Maw itself—and a perfect place to meet in privacy.

**Maw Cluster** A collection of black holes near the planet Kessel, the Maw served as a hiding place for the Maw Installation, where a group of Imperial scientists worked on new destructive weapons. The Maw was one of the wonders of the galaxy, visible only because of the ionized gases drawn into the holes. Because of the intense gravity in the area, the Maw was slowly drawing the entire Kessel system into the black holes. Its existence was a mystery, since it seemed improbable that a group of black holes could exist in such close proximity. A handful of scientists claimed it simply was an unusual formation that occurred in the natural order. Another group claimed that the Maw had been constructed by an ancient and vastly powerful civilization known as the Architects. Still others insisted that it was a gateway device created by some lost, ancient civilization. It was later discovered that the Maw had, in fact, been built by an ancient people whom members of the Colony referred to as the Celestials. Scientists working for the Empire, specifically those chosen by Grand Moff Tarkin, discovered a small collection of tortuously complex pathways through the Maw, allowing them to establish the Maw Installation on the far side of the anomaly, away from prying eyes.

**Mawhonic** A native of Hok, this Gran was one of Tatooine's best Podracers, although he invariably lost races to Sebulba. During the Boonta Eve Classic, which was eventually won by young Anakin Skywalker, Mawhonic's green GPE-3130 Podracer was disabled when the Gran swerved to avoid Sebulba—but crashed into a massive rock formation and exploded.

**Mawin** A Cerean woman who was one of Ki-Adi-Mundi's four honor-wives, she was the mother of his daughter Sylvn. Like many Cerean honor-wives, she resented the Jedi's bond-wife, Shea, but lived in a quietly neutral relationship with her.

**Maw Installation** A collection of planetoids crammed together at a gravitational island at the center of a black-hole cluster near Kessel, it was created as a top-secret weapons-development facility by Grand Moff Tarkin. Immense bridges and bands held the asteroids in place. Access tubes and transit rails connected the cluster of drifting rocks. The asteroids' interiors were hollowed out into living quarters, laboratory areas, prototype assembly bays, and meeting halls. The super-secret think tank (hidden even from Emperor Palpatine) was an ideal place for Tarkin to isolate the most brilliant scientists and theoreticians, under orders to develop new weapons for the Emperor such as the Death Star, World Devastators, and the Sun Crusher. The installation was destroyed during a battle with New Republic forces.

**Maw Irregular Fleet** A name chosen by Admiral Natasi Daala to describe a fleet of aging and outdated warships she amassed during her years of isolation behind the Maw, after she fled with the *Scylla* in the wake of the Black Fleet crisis. She brought the Maw Irregular Fleet out of hiding at the request of Gilad Pellaeon, who had been tapped by the Moff Council to assist the forces of the Galactic Alliance in capturing the planet Fondor some 10 years after the Yuuzhan Vong War. The flagship of the fleet was the revered Star Destroyer *Chimaera,* which once had been commanded by Pellaeon himself. As a further surprise for enemy forces, Daala had installed metal-crystal phase shifting technology on the *Chimaera* and other ships, allowing them to render an enemy starship's hull vulnerable to attack.

**mawkren** A small, reptilian creature considered an exotic pet by many beings. As infants, mawkren were extremely delicate. In order to mature away from their homeworld, they required an environment in which the temperature, humidity, lighting, and diet mirrored their natural setting.

**maw luur** Immense creatures bioengineered by the Yuuzhan Vong as waste disposal systems. A single maw luur could be placed aboard a worldship, where its vast capillary network absorbed waste materials and digested them, creating metals, nutrients, and air. The maw luur often was fitted into the living exoskeleton of the ship, providing life-sustaining nutrients to all its parts. Beings who encountered one of these creatures often described it as a mating of a Sarlacc and a trash compactor.

***Mawrunner*** A frigate in the Galactic Alliance's Second Fleet during the war against the Confederation. The *Mawrunner* was among the ships that escorted Jacen Solo and the *Anakin Solo* to a deep-space rendezvous with Corellian delegates, a mission that was supposed to involve Corellia's return to the Galactic Alliance. The rendezvous turned out to be a trap that had been laid by Sadras Koyan, who planned to fire the Centerpoint Station repulsor at the rendezvous location in an effort to destroy the *Anakin Solo* and assassinate Jacen Solo. The blast failed to hit the Star Destroyer, but eliminated a large portion of the Second Fleet's ships, including the *Mawrunner.*

**Maw Shipyards** One of the three primary starship-construction facilities that made up the Kuat Drive Yards. Like its companions, the Maw Shipyards was located in a ring of facilities that orbited the planet Kuat.

**Ma'w'shiye** A Nikto deserter-turned-assassin who made numerous, if usually unsuccessful, attempts on the lives of key New Republic personnel. Ma'w'shiye was one of the best sharpshooters in the Rebellion before abandoning his squadron just before the victory at Endor. The New Republic placed him on its most-wanted list and offered a 70,000-credit reward for his capture.

**Max** This being was Thurm Loogg's personal assistant during the Clone Wars, and was primarily responsible for writing and teleprompting the various speeches Loogg gave to the people of Cularin. Whenever Loogg misspoke or said something that might be offensive, he immediately blamed it on Max.

**Maxca system** A planetary system in the Brak sector.

**Maxim** An Old Republic Senator accused of corruption about a year before the Battle of Naboo. Chancellor Valorum put off responding to the charges in the face of the Trade Federation's petition to arm its freighters after the Nebula Front destroyed the *Revenue.*

***Maximum*** One of a multitude of *Imperial*-class Star Destroyers that made up the Imperial Navy fleet during the height of the Galactic Civil War.

*Mawhonic*

***Maximus*** A Rebel Alliance MC80a cruiser that operated during the Galactic Civil War. It was assigned to recover hijacked X-wing fighters that were loaded with sabotaged R2 units recovered from the *Ars Opus.*

**maxi-series** A common term used to describe any long-running series of holovids that chronicled the exploits of a core group of characters over many years.

**Maxiti** A lieutenant in the Pembric Security Legionnaire force who also worked for Crev Bombaasa.

**Max Rebo Band** *See* Rebo, Max.

***MaxSec Eight*** A cylindrical space station, one of many that were established by the Galactic Alliance following the Yuuzhan Vong War. Criminals involved with the Peace Brigade or other aspects of the invasion were jailed and put on trial here. Like its counterparts, the *MaxSec Eight* detention center was run by the Reconstruction Authority under the auspices of the Galactic Alliance.

**MaxSec Orbital Facility** The term used to describe any of the space stations identified by the Galactic Alliance as maximum-security prison facilities. These orbital stations, developed and maintained during the years following the Yuuzhan Vong War, provided a way to incarcerate criminals without putting a burden on planetary facilities.

**Max's Flangth House** A chain of restaurants founded on Coruscant by Max Rebo shortly after the Battle of Endor. Eventually, Max established franchises on seven other worlds.

**max-W 100** One of the many ticket-scanning droids that were owned by Star Tours during the Galactic Civil War.

**maxwell filters** Automated newsgrid readers that filtered out unwanted information, leaving users with only the information they really desired.

**Mayagil sector** An area of the galaxy that contained the Colu—also known as the Mayagil—system, and neighbored by both the Sluis and Seswenna sectors.

**Maya Kovel** A windswept planet in the Moddell sector that was home to the Ayrou species. Its thin, acrid atmosphere produced regular windstorms, leaving the iron-rich soil and rock exposed to the air. This gave the planet a reddish cast when viewed from space.

**Maydh** A young Ferroan who was part of a group that discovered the still-living body of Yuuzhan Vong priest Harrar shortly after Nom Anor tried to kill him before sabotaging Zonama Sekot. Maydh agreed to accompany Luke Skywalker to interrogate Harrar before the Ferroans exacted their own form of justice. After hearing the priest's words, Maydh convinced his elders that Harrar was not a threat, as Nom Anor had been.

**mayflii** A large subspecies of fliis native to the planet Kubindi. Measuring up to 2 meters in length, mayfliis were distinguished by the solid green coloration of their shells. Mayfliis laid their eggs in the Kubindi swamps.

***Mayhem*** An Imperial Nebulon-B frigate assigned to collect Habassan slaves near Cificap VIII. The Habassans were rescued by Rebel Alliance forces.

**mayla** This vine was considered a weed and was often found growing in pavement cracks on Coruscant. The mayla vine had a sweet, powdery odor.

**Mayn, Todra** A native of Commenor, she served as the leader of the New Republic's Polearm Squadron during the hunt for Warlord Zsinj. The daughter of Lela Mayn, she proved herself to be a leader in battle conditions, and eventually was promoted to the rank of captain during the early stages of the Yuuzhan Vong War. She was given command of a newly commissioned *Lancer*-class frigate, *Pride of Selonia.*

**Mayvitch 7** A moon of Amador in the Chalenor system chosen for colonization by the Immalians. The neighboring Yinchorri objected to the settlement and launched an attack. They wiped out much of the population, but not before a distress call was sent to Coruscant. In response, the Jedi Knights were dispatched to put a stop to the Yinchorri aggression.

**Mazanga** A Dug soldier and a bodyguard for the crime lord Sebolto around the time of the Battle of Naboo. A bounty for his capture was issued by Senators Ask Aak and Aks Moe in connection with the murder of several of their special assistants. Jango Fett later claimed the bounty during his attempt to locate Sebolto on Malastare.

**Mazara** A Falleen, she was the leader of a small rebel movement that sprang up during the years just before the Clone Wars. Mazara protested the working and living conditions that resulted from overdevelopment in Falleen's capital city. Trained as a journalist, her article on the Blackwater systems facility got her into trouble with her editors, who fired her rather than support her work. She took up the cause of the common Falleen, staging small rallies in an attempt to force workers to see the truth. When Obi-Wan Kenobi and Anakin Skywalker arrived on Falleen during their search for Granta Omega, Mazara was able to provide them with information on getting inside the Blackwater systems facility.

**Mazariyan Citadel** An immense fortress located in the jungles of Xagobah, it was actually a living edifice created from a huge fungus. It resembled the ancient, stepped temples found on Yavin 4. Energy arced from the fortress's exterior, appearing as if lightning was running around it. Thick, retractable spines grew along its lower levels and could shoot outward to impale intruders. Mazariyan survived by feeding on anything it could draw into its walls, including raw energy. The Citadel was taken over by Wat Tambor during the Clone Wars; he believed that the Mazariyan was remote enough to protect him. Three years into the fighting, the Grand Army of the Republic laid siege to the fortress in an effort to capture Tambor as a war criminal. Tambor managed to escape with the aid of General Grievous.

**Maze** An ARC trooper, originally A-26, who was part of the Republic's Special Operations Brigade, stationed on Coruscant during the Clone Wars. He was later assigned to serve as the chief aide to Jedi General Arligan Zey.

**Maze, the** A hangout frequented by Maarek Stele and Pargo on their homeworld of Kuan during the New Order.

**maze-fly** A swarming insect native to Aduba-3. Maze-flies were slow-moving insects that could easily be swatted out of the air.

**maze-stalk** A plant grown on Aduba-3, it produced several products that were staples in the diets of the planet's human population. Once a year, each maze-stalk produced a succulent melon. The flesh of the melons was used in a number of dishes, and the husks were fashioned into cloth and other items.

**Mazie** A blue Rutian Twi'lek, she lived on Tatooine with her family when they were captured, enslaved, and forced to work in the pirate Krayn's spice-processing facility on Nar Shaddaa. Ironically, her family had fled Ryloth in order to escape being caught in a slave raid. Mazie's husband was killed in the raid on Tatooine, leaving her alone with their daughter. Four years after the Battle of Naboo, Mazie met Anakin Skywalker in the mines after the young Padawan was also captured by Krayn. Anakin and Mazie worked together and became friends. Mazie revealed that her daughter, Berri, was a domestic worker in Krayn's household. She agreed to help Skywalker start a slave revolt. Anakin's initial destruction of a group of guard droids emboldened the slaves, and the revolt grew swiftly. In the ensuing struggle, Krayn was killed and Mazie and Berri were freed.

Katya M'Buele

**Mazong** A Highborn Ansionian and leader of the Yiwa clan in the years before the Clone Wars. Obi-Wan Kenobi and Luminara Unduli, along with their Padawans Anakin Skywalker and Barriss Offee, traveled to Ansion to negotiate a treaty between the city dwellers and the Alwari nomads. Mazong agreed to help them by providing directions to the Borokii overclan's encampment, but only after the Jedi provided him with entertainment.

**Mazzic** A militaristic smuggling chief who ran a heavily armed operation. Mazzic's fleet consisted of numerous freighters, along with a number of customized combat starships, including the *Skyclaw* and the *Raptor.* His personal transport was the *Distant Rainbow* and his deceptively decorative, but lethal, bodyguard Shada was never far from his side. Fellow smuggler Talon Karrde convinced Mazzic to join him in profitably helping the New Republic in its fight against Grand Admiral Thrawn.

**m'Bal, Kyloria** An alias used by Bria Tharen when she and Han Solo tried to sell the *Talisman* to Truthful Toryn. The Duros was already aware of the situation surrounding the *Talisman* and recognized them immediately.

**M'Bardi Prison** A prison facility in the Outer Rim set underwater on a coral-covered seabed. It was the site of a riot instigated by the bounty hunter Durge and quelled by Kit Fisto and Plo Koon.

**M'Beg, Barada** A famous Klatooinian, he was perhaps the most revered scholar and leader in the species' history. M'Beg represented the Klatooinians in their negotiations with the Hutts prior to the war with Xim the Despot, more than 25,000 years before the rise of the New Order. Many Klatooinians named their sons either Barada or M'Beg, in his honor. This led other beings to refer to Klatooinians as Baradas.

**MB-RA-7** A protocol droid that was an art instructor during the last years of the Old Republic.

**M'Buele, Katya** A Corellian who had been a romantic acquaintance of Han Solo, she served with Solo aboard a smuggling ship in the years after he left Imperial service. M'Buele was one of the few smugglers who got paid for their part in the Battle of Ylesia. She reentered Solo's life years later on Tirahnn after Luke Skywalker and Leia Organa were nearly captured by Kharys. M'Buele agreed to help Solo bring down Kharys, but was killed by a smoke demon.

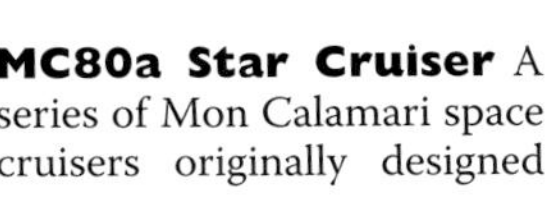

**MC80a Star Cruiser** A series of Mon Calamari space cruisers originally designed

as luxury ships, but later overhauled to become Rebel Alliance warships. Each of the ships was a handcrafted work of art, unique from all others. They appeared to be organic in nature, because the Mon Calamari built sensor arrays, weapons batteries, and shield generators into sleek, rounded pods.

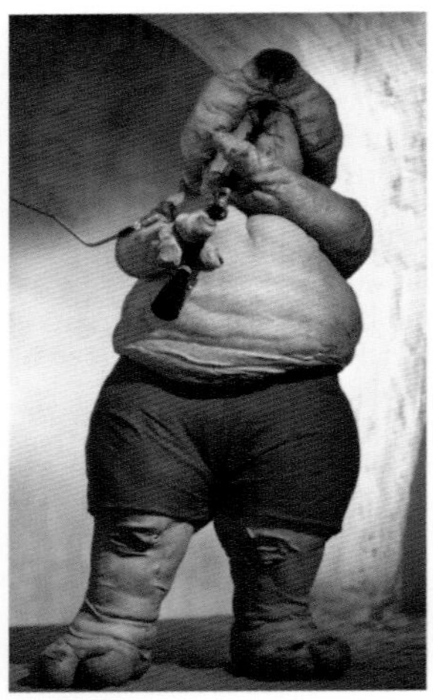
Droopy McCool

**MC90 Cruiser** The first truly military starships designed by the Mon Calamari, they were more modular than the MC80-series. Displays were given multiple wavelength settings so that other species could read them. The *Defiance* was the first MC90 to see action, during the first Battle of Mon Calamari.

**McCool, Droopy** A Kitonak musician from Kirdo III, he was a member of the Max Rebo Band. Chubby and comical, Droopy (born with the name Snit) played a variety of wind instruments, most notably the chidinkalu horn. Slavers captured some of the better Kitonak musicians to work as wailers in seedy saloons and cantinas. McCool was "owned" by Evar Orbus and forced to play in the Rebo Band. The band played a few shows for Jabba the Hutt, and after the crime lord's death McCool walked into the Tatooine desert, hoping to find others of his species. He was never seen again.

Jasper McKnives

**Mcgrrrr, Opun** A burly Corellian smuggler known as the Black Hole, he was the owner of the Holiday Towers hotel on Cloud City until Jabba the Hutt took control in a bloody coup. Mcgrrrr then stole the accounting droid CZ-3 from Jabba's town house on Tatooine, hoping to use its data to blackmail Jabba. Mcgrrrr didn't know that the droid had been equipped with a miniature transceiver rig, which recorded a number of his criminal doings. The droid was bought and quickly sold by the Jawa Traders store.

**M'challa Order** A scholarly order within the Empire. Han Solo, Lando Calrissian, and Lobot posed as members in an effort to get a copy of the Caamas Document from the data library on Bastion.

**McKnives, Jasper** A Nikto fanatic, he was a member of the Cult of M'dweshuu during the Clone Wars. His legacy was not his physical abilities, but rather his mental instability. His bloody record of brutal cult slayings caused him to be placed in the gladiator pits as punishment, forcing McKnives to fight his way to freedom. Unfortunately for McKnives, he was placed into the Cauldron on Rattatak at the same time as Asajj Ventress, and was soon cut down by the lightsaber-wielding warrior.

**McKumb, Drub** An old pal of Han Solo, he suddenly showed up on Ithor, high on yarrock, to deliver a message when Solo was on a diplomatic trip with his wife, Leia. Drub had been a long-distance cargo hauler when Han knew him. They had last seen each other on Ord Mantell, when McKumb told Solo that Jabba the Hutt had put a great deal of money on Han's head. This time McKumb had a warning about the *Eye of Palpatine.*

**M-class fighter** Starfighters with large ion engines, they were used when the Rebel Alliance was based on Hoth. M-class fighters each had three engines, taken from salvaged Y-wings and mounted on an M-shaped fuselage. At the tip of each wing was a heavy laser cannon.

**McMerrit, Turbo** One of the galaxy's most successful Podracers until his craft disintegrated around him, killing McMerrit in the resulting crash.

**McPhersons** A family of moisture farmers on Tatooine, they supported Ariq Joanson in his plans to draw up maps of peace with the Jawas and the Sand People.

**McQuarrie, General Pharl** A Rebel Alliance commander from Ralltiir, he fled his homeworld after its occupation by the Empire. General McQuarrie was instrumental in the establishment of the Rebel base on Hoth following the Battle of Yavin.

**MC Utility Sub** A 12-meter-long craft built by the Mon Calamari for use in constructing their floating cities. Each sub was equipped with a cutting laser and four clawed arms for deploying probes or collecting samples.

**MD (Emdee) droids** Medical droids roughly humanoid in stature and based on the 2-1B series, they were still in wide use around the time of the Galactic Civil War. There were different classifications of medical droids based on their programming.

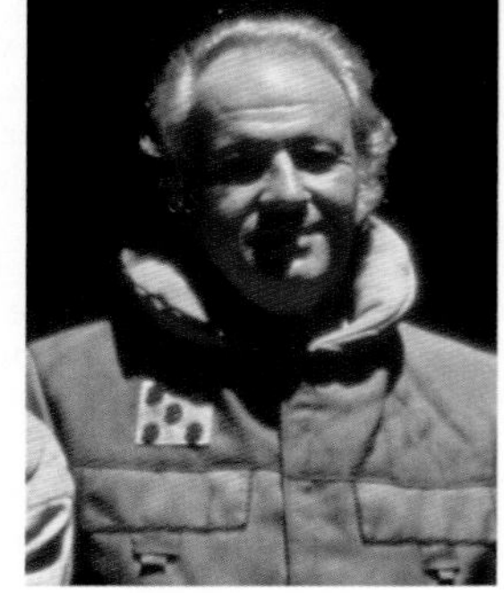
General Pharl McQuarrie

Drub McKumb confronts Luke Skywalker (left) and Han Solo (right).

- **MD-0:** Diagnostic droids that performed patient examinations to give diagnoses. They were equipped with various medical implements, such as thermometers, ultrasounders, and X-ray scanners.
- **MD-1:** Laboratory technician droids that conducted tests to analyze and isolate diseases and viruses.
- **MD-2:** Anesthesiology droids that administered anesthesia and monitored vital functions during surgery.
- **MD-3:** Pharmaceutical droids that analyzed, prescribed, and prepared medicines necessary to combat and prevent disease and infection. They were readily available to most pharmacies, but were also stolen and used by illegal drug dealers. MD-3s were used by the Empire to administer experimental drugs to improve troop loyalty and performance.
- **MD-4:** Microsurgery droids that were equipped with miniature vibroscalpels, clamps, and optical sensors to perform delicate surgery.
- **MD-5:** Small, mobile general practitioner droids usually assigned to spaceships when a living doctor was too expensive or unavailable. They could administer first aid and perform simple surgeries.
- **MD-10:** Specialist droids, they concentrated on specific areas of practice such as cardiology, neurology, obstetrics, or dentistry.

**MD-0C6** An MD series droid known to its many acquaintances simply as Doc, he was the chief medical droid for the expedition that located the Lamaro system many centuries before the Galactic Civil War. Regular memory wipes eventually gave the droid a curmudgeonly personality that many beings found quaint. Doc eventually became completely independent, and served Bartyn's

Landing loyally for the next several centuries. He also participated in the management of the Landing and assisted with the operations of the Outer Rim Oreworks installation.

**Mdimu** This Etti served as Thrackan Sal-Solo's chief of communications after Sal-Solo was named President of Ylesia and Commander in Chief of the Peace Brigade.

**MDS-50** A handheld medical diagnostic scanner produced by Synthtech Medtech, it provided a wide range of diagnostic capabilities in a small device.

**MDS-500** A datapad produced during the last decades of the Old Republic, it was a durable platform, and many survived well into the era of the New Republic. Jacen Solo found a working model on the planet Coruscant after the Yuuzhan Vong had begun terraforming the planet to resemble Yuuzhan'tar.

**M'dweshuu Nova** An ancient star in the center of the Si'Klaata Cluster, it exploded many millennia before the Third Battle of Vontor, causing great changes on nearby planets. Radiation from the dying star created mutations among the Niktos on Kintan, as well as altering other forms of life. Several species of monstrous animals appeared on the planet's surface, forcing the Nikto to develop new defenses for their protection.

**Me, Lyn** A Twi'lek female with chalk-white skin, she was one of Jabba the Hutt's favorite dancers, often performing with Rystáll and Greeata as part of the Max Rebo Twelve. She was from a head clan on Ryloth that once hired Boba Fett to protect them from slavers, and she eventually fell in love with the bounty hunter. Among her earliest memories was that of Boba Fett rescuing a group of Twi'lek children after the slavers set fire to their school. She was unaware of the fact that Fett had been hired by her father, a wealthy crime lord, to protect her, and that he considered the rescue little more than a job. From that point on, though, Lyn Me scoured the newsnets for information on Fett, and was actually something of an authority on the bounty hunter's career. She used her skills as a Twi'lek dancer to get off Rodia, and eventually was approached by Max Rebo to join the small group of dancers that accompanied his band. She longed to see Fett again, but got only a brief chance before Luke Skywalker arrived to rescue Han Solo and Leia Organa from Jabba's palace.

**Meade, Jessica** Known as Jess, this young woman was a star pilot who assisted Jann Tosh and the droids R2-D2 and C-3PO in returning Mon Julpa to Tammuz-an in the early days of the Empire. She first encountered the group on Tyne's Horky, where they were pursued by Yorbo, Zolag, and IG-88. Jess managed to rescue them from Yorbo and Kleb Zellock, and then agreed to transport them to Tammuz-an.

**Meala, Dr.** A Hapan doctor who served as the personal physician of the Chume'da, Allana, during the years following the Swarm War. Dr. Meala provided Allana with an autoinjector that was filled with a special drug for use in emergency situations—it rendered an attacker unable to move. Only a certain antidote could reverse the effects. Allana was forced to use the autoinjector when she was attacked by Aurra Sing aboard the *Anakin Solo* after the bounty hunter made an attempt to assassinate her mother, Tenel Ka.

**mealbread** A processed bread product manufactured on Corellia during the early decades of the New Republic. It could be formed into chips, sticks, or a variety of other shapes, and contained sufficient nutrients to make it equivalent to a small meal.

Mechno-chair

***Meandering Star*** A modified YT-1300 light freighter owned and operated by Piret Akarias, a Rebel supplier who frequented the safeworld Stronghold.

***Means to the End*** Another name for the Mindharp built by the ancient Sharu.

**meatalo** Created in the Moridebo District of Metellos, this meat-and-lard dish was formed into shapes that resembled fruit before being roasted or baked.

**meat cans** A term used to describe the clone commandos of the Grand Army of the Republic. The term, of course, was never used in the presence of a commando.

**meat droid** A derogatory term used to describe the clone troopers of the Grand Army of the Republic.

**Meccha** A major city on Drall. During the early stages of the Yuuzhan Vong War, riots spread throughout the city after the New Republic approved a plan to use the Centerpoint Station repulsor as a weapon against the invaders.

**Mecetti House Guard** The name of the combined army and navy maintained by House Mecetti of Tapani sector.

**mechanical** A colloquial term used to refer to droids and automata, often in a derogatory manner.

Lyn Me

**Mechanical Allies** A droid sales and repair shop owned and operated by the Twi'lek San. Located in the Promenade aboard Sel Zonn Station, Mechanical Allies was noted for its shoddy parts and faulty droids.

**Mechanical Liberation Front** A fanatical organization founded during the last decades of the Old Republic and led by Jarred Sneel during the New Order, the Front staged many violent hit-and-run assaults against droid-manufacturing corporations. The membership of the MLF believed that droids had certain inalienable rights in the galactic community. They were perhaps best known for their attempt to "free" a shipment of Vindicator XM-15 brilliant missiles near Havridam City on New Bakstre. Fourteen MLF members were killed in the operation, which also destroyed more than 2,000 square kilometers of the city when the missiles were detonated due to the activists' ineptitude.

**Mechis III** A harsh, smoke-shrouded world covered with sprawling droid-producing factories, it produced automata for generations and was considered to be possibly the most important of all the galaxy's droid operations. Prior to the Battle of Hoth, the droid IG-88 and his duplicates arrived at Mechis III and took it over, winning all the planet's droids to their cause. They then eliminated every human inhabitant of the planet. Production continued, so that no one would suspect what had happened, but each new droid contained embedded programming that would soon trigger a robotic takeover of the galaxy. Darth Vader came to the planet to order a new shipment of Arakyd Viper probots. After meeting with Vader on the Super Star Destroyer *Executor*, IG-88 ordered the Mechis III factories to produce a duplicate of the second Death Star's computer core, which his droid consciousness would then inhabit. But just before IG-88 was about to activate it, the battle station was destroyed by the Rebel Alliance.

**mechno-chair** A Neimoidian invention, the mechno-chair was a mobile platform on which a being of stature could sit and travel without any self-movement. The ownership of a mechno-chair was a status symbol among the Neimoidians, since it was not a practical mode of transportation.

**Mecht** This male Seaan was a former Imperial slave who joined the Rebel Alliance and became a member of Red Hand Squadron.

***Mechtech Illustrated*** A technical journal that published a wide variety of articles about new technology in the galaxy during the final decades of the Old Republic and throughout

*Medal of Yavin*

the New Order. Never known to mince words, the editors and writers at *Mechtech Illustrated* once described Industrial Automaton's R5-series of astromech droids as "meter-tall stack[s] of the worst business decisions you could possibly want."

**Mecrosa Order** An ancient society of assassins and expert poisoners long rumored to be led by Sith disciples. A new generation of Mecrosa killers likely wiped out the Jedi Knights of House Pelagia during the Jedi Purge that followed the Clone Wars. Certain holovid producers insinuated that this new incarnation of the Mecrosa Order maintained a cadre of Sith magicians at its core, but that was never proven. When the Dark Jedi Lumiya was forced into hiding during the era of the New Republic, it was believed that she eventually found the Mecrosa Order and forced its members to give her access to their collection of Sith lore.

**medal (TIE fighter pilots)** Awards given to TIE fighter pilots by the Galactic Empire, listed from top to sixth level: Medal of Redemption; Medal of Unity; Medal of Progress; Medal of Order; Medal of Loyalty; and Medal of Destiny.

*Achk Med-Beq*

**Medal of Alderaan** Developed by an Alderaanian survivor, this medallion was commissioned by the Rebel Alliance to honor those beings who displayed exceptional bravery and heroism in battle. It was the same design as the Medal of Yavin.

**Medal of Conspicuous Gallantry** An award given by the Empire to distinguished Imperial Navy pilots who served above and beyond the call of duty.

**Medal of Honor** A New Republic recognition given to those servicebeings who performed exceptionally in battle.

**Medal of Valor** An award given to Grand Army of the Republic troopers who performed beyond expectations or showed conspicuous gallantry under fire during the Clone Wars.

**Medal of Yavin** A medal bestowed by Princess Leia Organa on Luke Skywalker and Han Solo for their heroic deeds in the Battle of Yavin. It was given in a public ceremony attended by the military of the Rebel Alliance the day after the Death Star was destroyed. It was the same design as the Medal of Alderaan.

**Med-Beq, Achk** A known confidant of Dannl Faytonni, and a partner in crime, he often wore the uniform of a Republic official while visiting the Outlander gambling club in Coruscant's glittering entertainment district. Med-Beq was probably the more inventive and ambitious of the two. They took the plunge into the underworld when a botched spice mine deal nearly landed Faytonni in jail. With Med-Beq's help, Faytonni fled Corellia, and they eventually ended up on Coruscant. They did a brief stint in the Moderate Security Ward of the CoCo District Penitentiary before escaping in a laundry speeder. Faytonni's gambling skills won them a pair of Republic official uniforms.

***Med Evac 1014*** A Galactic Alliance med runner deployed during the Second Battle of Fondor. Jacen Solo commandeered the ship to rescue Tahiri Veila from the *Bloodfin,* knowing that the ship's identity as a medical rescue vessel would allow him access to the destroyer.

***Mediator*** A Mon Calamari cruiser, commanded by the Mon Calamari Commander Ackdool, dispatched by the New Republic to mediate the dispute between Rhommamool and Osarian shortly before Nom Anor and the Yuuzhan Vong invaded the galaxy. Nom Anor launched a preemptive strike at Osa-Prime, placing the blame on overeager Rhommamoolians. Ackdool promised Anor sanctuary aboard the *Mediator.* Anor flew to the ship, but escaped in an A-wing and abandoned the shuttle in the hold of the *Mediator,* where it exploded in a nuclear blast that vaporized much of the cruiser.

***Mediator*-class battle cruiser** A Mon Calamari warship developed for use by the New Republic, it first saw duty during the dispute between Rhommamool and Osarian.

**medical capsule** A portable survival pod that could sustain sick or injured patients, this medical cocoon could also move patients until they could be transported to a medical facility. Darth Vader was placed in one after suffering severe injuries on Mustafar.

**Medical Circle** A section of the primary city on the planet Kegan dedicated to maintaining the health of the planet's population.

**Medical Corps** A branch of the Jedi Knights similar in many respects to the Agricultural Corps. The MedCorps comprised students of the Force who provided treatment and consolation to the sick and infirm of the galaxy. Underlying this humanitarian goal was the idea that Jedi Padawans needed to understand the fragile nature of living beings. The MedCorps had only a few dozen students and instructors at any given time.

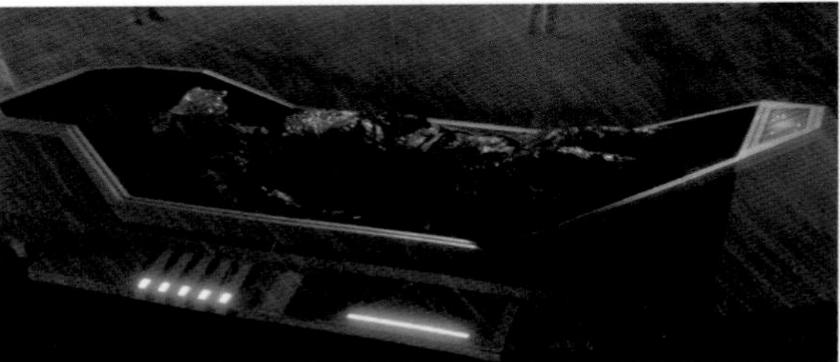

*Medical capsule*

**medical droid** An automaton whose main functions were to diagnose and treat illness and injury, it could also perform or assist with surgeries. Common models include the FX series, MD units, and the 2-1B medical droid.

**medical frigate** A star cruiser devoted mainly to the transportation and care of the wounded and convalescent, and staffed primarily by medical personnel. The Rebel Alliance used converted Nebulon-B frigates that had been taken from Imperial forces, who used them for short-range starfighter attacks.

**Medic Guide** The title given to the doctors and nurses who worked in the Medical Circle on Kegan during the last decades of the Old Republic.

**medicron** Any regular medical publication that could be accessed on the HoloNet during the last decades of the Old Republic.

**medicrystal** A specialized form of kunda stone developed by the Kadrillians for use in medical applications.

**mediglobe** An underwater bubble containing a Gungan hospital.

**Med'ika** A nickname used by Goran Beviin and many other Mandalorians to describe Medrit Vasur. It was somewhat ironic, since the *-'ika* suffix implied that the nickname meant "little Medrit," even though Medrit was a mountain of a man.

Meditation chamber

**Medis, Varen** A commander in the Imperial Security Bureau, he was stationed on the planet Byss in the Deep Core, where he made sure that nobody escaped the planet.

**meditation chamber** A private inner sanctum employed by Force-users for millennia as a place to calm their thoughts and reach out to the Force. In its simplest form, a meditation chamber was a secure room that helped eliminate the distractions of everyday life. Darth Vader kept a personal chamber aboard the Super Star Destroyer *Executor.* A spherical enclosure, the interior had a comfortable chair, a comlink and visual display, and a mechanical device for quickly removing and replacing Vader's helmet and breathing mask. The pressurized sphere kept Vader comfortable even with his helmet off.

**Meditation of Emptiness** A meditative technique used by the Jedi Knights during the decades following the Yuuzhan Vong War. Jedi emptied themselves of all feeling, opened themselves to the Force, and then centered themselves in the simple power and strength of the Force.

**Meditation of Immersion** A Fallanassi technique that involved lowering one's mental and physical state to a deep level, allowing nearly direct contact with the White Current. While in this state, some Fallanassi could become invisible, while others were able to project vivid images around them.

**meditation sphere** A large, round starship used by ancient Jedi and Sith warlords to focus the Jedi battle meditation technique and other abilities. During the Great Hyperspace War, about 5,000 years before the Battle of Yavin, Dark Lord Naga Sadow used his meditation sphere to lead his troops against the Old Republic. From the safety of his sphere, which appeared as a giant, floating eye with bat-like wings, Sadow summoned illusionary warriors to fight the Republic forces. The sphere was ultimately destroyed, although Sadow escaped unharmed.

**Medjev, Markre** A Jedi Knight who studied at Luke Skywalker's Jedi praxeum on Yavin 4 early in the Yuuzhan Vong War. Medjev later scouted for the alien invaders on Bothawui following the Battle of Fondor. During the final stages of the battle against the Yuuzhan Vong, after the living planet Zonama Sekot agreed to help bring about an end to the conflict, Medjev was one of several Jedi Knights bonded to seed-partners and provided with Sekotan starships.

**medkit** A small first-aid kit that could be carried by an individual or stored for use aboard a speeder or starship, it typically included a synthflesh dispenser, vibroscalpel, flexclamp, painkillers, disinfectant pads, and gas and precious fluid cartridges.

Meditation sphere

**medlifter** A repulsor-equipped vehicle used by the Grand Army of the Republic to transport injured clone troopers and Jedi Knights away from the battlefields of the Clone Wars to the closest medical facilities.

**MedNet** A galaxywide newsnet and data repository that allowed doctors and physicians to access a wealth of medical data at any time, on virtually any subject. Topics that did not have immediate answers could then be discussed with colleagues from across the galaxy.

**Medon, Tion** A gray-skinned Pau'an, he served as the portmaster of Pau City on his homeworld of Utapau for more than 200 years leading up to the Clone Wars. Although outwardly neutral, Medon was loyal to the Old Republic during the Clone Wars. He did not anticipate the arrival of General Grievous and the Separatist army, which quickly took control of Utapau and established a base of operations there.

Med'soto architecture

Grievous eliminated the ruling members of Utapau's government, which left Medon ostensibly in control of the planet. This sudden turn of events led Medon to order his military forces into hiding, so that the Separatists wouldn't be able to discern the true military strength of the Utapauns.

When Obi-Wan Kenobi appeared in Pau City, Medon provided him with a wealth of information on how Grievous's forces were arrayed. He also placed the Utapaun military at the command of Republic forces, with Utai soldiers augmenting the clone troopers during the fight to control Pau City. Grievous was defeated by Obi-Wan Kenobi, but then the clone commandos were told to execute Order 66 by Darth Sidious. They turned on Kenobi, who managed to escape, and then set about subjugating Utapau. Medon was one of the first Pau'ans to be imprisoned, since his resourcefulness was well known.

Tion Medon

**medpac** *See* medkit.

**med runner** The name used by most spacers to describe the SoroSuub *Sprint*-class rescue ship, although the term eventually came to describe any support vessel that provided medical assistance during space battles.

**Med'soto architecture** An architectural style popular during the Old Republic, it was characterized by bright lights, chrome accents, and tiled floors. Dexter's Diner, located on Coruscant during the last decades of the Old Republic, was a primary example.

**medspeeder** Any landspeeder that was specially designed for use as an ambulance or medical transport vehicle.

**med-splint** A small, repulsor-supported transport designed to carry an injured being from the site of his or her injury to an ambulance. It was little more than a flat surface and an engine, with a small force-field generator providing a way to immobilize broken limbs.

***MedStar*-class frigate** A series of medical frigates used by the Old Republic to supply remote bases and outposts during the Clone Wars. Developed by Kuat Drive Yards, the *MedStar*-class vessel was a self-contained dispensary and traveled from a primary supply base to planets with drugs and matériel. The ships housed state-of-the-art xeno- and biomedical facilities that rivaled some of the best planetary hospitals of the Republic.

***MedStar Four*** An Imperial medical frigate stationed in orbit around the planet Despayre during the construction of the first Death Star.

***MedStar Nineteen*** A MedStar frigate under the command of Admiral Tarnese Bleyd, it was dispatched by the Old Republic to support the Rimsoo facilities on Drongar during the Clone Wars. The traitor Klo Merit made a trip to *MedStar Nineteen* and set off a series of charges that exploded in the ship's lower levels, crippling its ability to act as a mobile hospital.

**meduza** A gelatinous creature consisting of a mucous mass of shining and greasy bile-green material from which rose a ring of slender, bulb-tipped stalks capable of shocking victims. Dr. Evazan was able to train a meduza to be his loyal pet.

Mee (daggert)

**medwagon** Any repulsor-equipped vehicle used to carry medical personnel and injured beings to and from a hospital or other medical facility.

**Medxec** A term used on Coruscant during the last decades of the Old Republic to describe the executives of major health-related organizations and hospitals.

**mee (daggert)** One of many species of scalefish that inhabited the oceans of Naboo. Mee, or daggerts, were distinguished by their round, vertically flat bodies, and the poisonous spines that ran along the centerline. The diagonal stripes on the mee's body served as camouflage, allowing the fish to blend into the sea grasses and reeds of Naboo's waterways.

**Mee, Yeesre** The Gran lead investigator into the events surrounding the death of Senator Aks Moe shortly before the start of the Clone Wars.

**Meego's Starship Emporium** A starship warehouse located on Necropolis. Meego was a typical used-starship salesman, always looking to sell the least spaceworthy craft for the highest prices. After Hoole put money down on a ship that would get himself and Tash and Zak Arranda off Necropolis, Meego claimed to have sold it to another buyer by mistake.

Meekerdin-maa

**Meekerdin-maa** A Tin-Tin Dwarf who was chief engineer aboard the transport vessel *Uhumele* during the final years of the Old Republic. Known as Ratty, he had a tendency to ramble when talking and often interrupted others' conversations. Like his crewmates, Meekerdin-maa had no reason to trust the Galactic Empire that rose to power after the Clone Wars.

Meekerdin-maa agreed to help Bomo Greenbark rescue his wife and daughter, who had been captured and taken to Orvax IV, where they were to be sold into slavery. In a surprising move, he even pledged his life to help Greenbark, although he didn't anticipate having to dress up like a Jawa to infiltrate the slave markets.

**Meeknu** A clan of Jawas that established and maintained an extensive salvage operation on Raxus Prime during the last decades of the Old Republic.

**Meeks** According to a story that circulated on the HoloNet, Lando Calrissian once portrayed a Jedi Knight in order to obtain a set of statuettes from timid beings known as the Meeks. The statuettes turned out to be forgeries after Lando was forced to save the Meeks from a marauding rancor. Lando later realized the Meeks had been more clever than expected, using the fake statuettes to lure him to their settlement, knowing that he would defeat the rancor.

**Meelto** A Rodian gunslinger killed in a duel with Uul-Rha-Shan.

**meelweekian silk** A valuable form of silk used to create luxurious clothing and furnishings.

**Meenon** A Senali ruler some 12 years prior to the Battle of Naboo. Meenon became embroiled in a conflict with King Frane of Rutan, a dispute that was mediated by Qui-Gon Jinn and Obi-Wan Kenobi.

**Meen-tris** One of many Eickarie families that made up the Sav-ro clan on the planet Kariek during the New Republic era. For centuries, the Meen-tris family guarded the secret of the third watchtower entrance to Cro-sla-trei fortress, until Su-mil used it to help the Imperial stormtroopers of Aurek Company gain access.

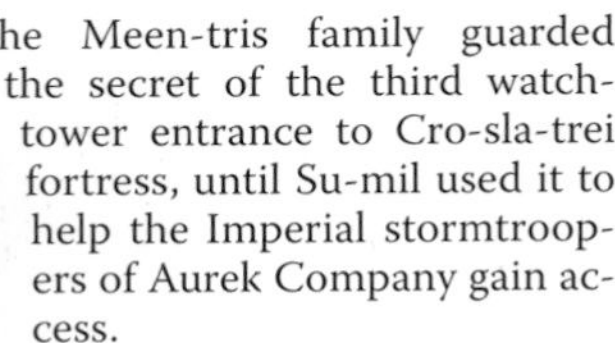
Meerian

**Meerian** Short, silver-haired humanoids native to Bandomeer. As a people, the Meerians were slow and deliberate, with a primitive society that was unprepared to deal with the Old Republic survey teams that first encountered them. Meerians were never given full control of the mining operations established on the planet, but merely shared in the profits.

**meer-rat** A species of fat-bodied vermin native to the undercity of Coruscant.

**Meese Caulf** A trade language spoken in the Outer Rim Territories during the final decades of the Old Republic.

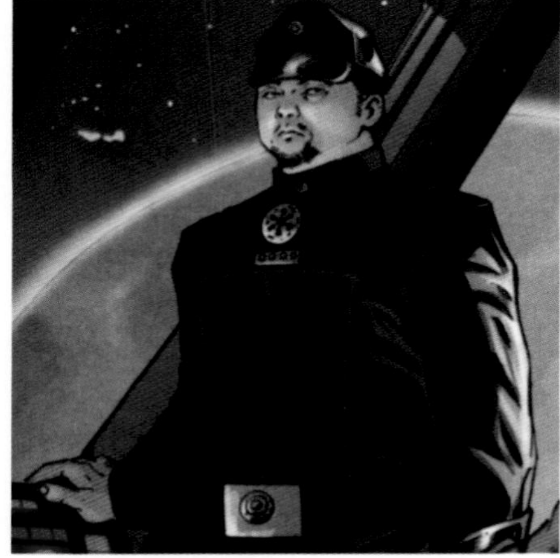
Captain Meeshal

**Meeshal, Captain** An officer in the naval forces of the new Empire in the years following the Sith–Imperial War. Captain Meeshal and his small fleet were assigned to Darth Stryfe's mission to investigate the presence of the Jedi on the planet Ossus. His stormtroopers made several passes through the Jedi Temple facilities and found no trace of the Jedi, prompting Darth Stryfe to order that the Jedi Temple building be destroyed from orbit.

**Meeto, Orso** A Chagrian, he was one of the more prominent slavers who operated from the markets on Orvax IV during the final years of the Old Republic. After the Clone Wars, Meeto was surprised to find Dass Jennir in his apartment. Jennir demanded information and Meeto complied, thinking that he then would be left alone. However, Jennir put a blaster to Meeto's head and pulled the trigger, killing the Chagrian instantly.

**Meeva** A Twi'lek child rescued from slavery by Jedi Master Vhiin Thorla, she was given shelter in the Enclave during the Clone Wars. The four-year-old Meeva quickly became friends with Tror and Dath, and the three were soon inseparable.

**Meewalh** A female Noghri who was Leia Organa Solo's bodyguard following the Battle of Duro. It was Meewalh who discovered Leia after she was hit with a wave of Force energy that accompanied her son Anakin's death at Myrkr. Meewalh remained loyal to Leia, continuing to guard her for the duration of the Yuuzhan Vong War. Leia came to trust Meewalh and one other Noghri, Cakhmaim, the most. These two accompanied Leia wherever she went for the next several years. During Thrackan Sal-Solo's bid for Corellian independence, Leia and Han were forced to leave the Noghri behind in an effort to avoid drawing attention to themselves as they worked behind the scenes to understand the situation in the galaxy.

The Noghri were reunited with the Solos in the wake of Sal-Solo's assassination, only to be thrust into the midst of the Heritage Council's bid to take control of the Hapes Consortium. During an intense battle between the Hapan Royal Navy and the Heritage Fleet, the Noghri took up positions in the *Millennium Falcon*'s quad laser turrets, where they managed to keep enemy ships from pounding the *Falcon* into space dust. However, the *Falcon* took fire from the Star Destroyer *Anakin Solo*, which was being commanded by the Solos' own son, Jacen. Several of the Star Destroyer's blasts breached the ship's shields and exploded against the weapons turrets. Both Meewalh and Cakhmaim were killed in the blasts.

**meewit** A screeching animal native to rocky areas of Tatooine.

***Megador*** A Galactic Alliance Star Destroyer, it became the flagship of Supreme Commander Gilad Pellaeon during the Swarm War. After the Second Battle of Fondor, the *Megador* accompanied Darth Caedus and the *Anakin Solo* into the Transitory Mists on a mission to hunt and destroy Luke Skywalker and the new Jedi Order. The ship had been armed with new long-range turbolasers that gave the *Megador* the ability to fire on a ship well before it came within the other ship's weapons range. Once the main battle was engaged, Darth Caedus ordered the *Megador* to engage the Hapan Home Fleet and the *Dragon Queen* in an effort to eliminate their support of the small Jedi fleet.

**megafreighter** An ancient transport vessel that was constructed in the shape of a ring.

**megaknot** The basic unit measuring a starship's velocity while in hyperspace.

**Megalith** An immense statue that was the center of Er'stacian culture, revered as the maker of the Er'stacian people, but also the source of deep-seated cultural divisions. The Er'stacians believed that they could not be at peace until one clan took full possession of the Megalith, which they referred to as the Venerable One. Thus, every Er'stacian clan was almost continually at war with every other clan. Mace Windu, at the urging of the Jedi Council, traveled to Er'stacia to negotiate a peace among the clans before they committed genocide. He destroyed the Megalith with his lightsaber, leaving the Er'stacians to figure out which of the thousands of pieces each clan would claim.

**megamaser** The largest of the maser cannons produced by the Chiss following the Yuuzhan Vong War.

**megaphone disk** A device resembling a handheld, circular plate that projected the user's voice and increased the volume. *See also* loudhailer.

**Megavegiton ale** An alcoholic beverage favored by Yarblok Yemm.

**megonite** A moss found on Phelarion, it was a heat-sensitive species that was harvested for the Empire by Lady Tarkin. The moss had intense explosive properties when heated, and could be manipulated into detonation devices. It had to be harvested by workers with special boots and gloves that kept the megonite cold. Storage and transportation facilities required refrigeration equipment.

**Megos** A yellowish moon, it was the third in orbit around the planet Hapes.

**Meh, Reseros** A grumpy Chevin, she owned and operated Momma Reseros' Diner in Jugsmuk Station on Gamorr. She didn't like the company of other Chevins, and cared little for most other species. Despite her gruff demeanor, Reseros was known as an excellent cook to the spacers who traveled through Jugsmuk.

**Mehndra, Bingo** A walrus-like being who was a noted Balti smuggler, he liked jazzy music as much as Jabba the Hutt. Bingo and Jabba got into a dispute, and Jabba sent the Max Rebo Band to Hoth, ostensibly as a peace offering, to entertain Bingo on his Spawning Day celebration. Unknown to the band members, their amplifiers were filled with explosives that went off as soon as their set was over. Although the musicians managed to escape, Bingo and his entire smuggling operation were killed.

**Meido** A New Republic Senator from Adin, he was a former Imperial. Meido consistently opposed all of Leia Organa Solo's policies and was instrumental in calling for a no-confidence vote that led to her temporary resignation. After being elected to the Inner Council by an overwhelming majority, Meido put together the committee that led an independent investigation into the explosion in the Senate Hall and supported the idea that Leia's husband, Han Solo, was involved in the bombing.

**Meimonda, Dana** This classical actress was a native of Dakshee. When the Empire subjugated her planet, she and her husband fled to Esseles, where she became a socialite and entertainer for Imperial troops there. She was also a spy for the Rebel Alliance, and was critical to the downfall of Esseles's planetary governor and the local sector Moff.

**Meirana** A Tarasin female of the Hiironi tribe, she was named Mother when her mother was killed by a kilassin. Meirana was slightly older than her sister, Dariana. Within a day, Meirana died of a mysterious illness; Dariana was then named Mother in her place.

**Meir wine** An intoxicant developed on Sullust around the time of the Battle of Naboo.

**Meis** An Imperial Navy captain, he was one of Han Solo's commanding officers during his first year of service, before Han was dishonorably discharged for freeing Chewbacca.

**mekebve spores** Allergens that were crippling and potentially fatal to mammalians, the spores had no effect on reptilian creatures such as Trandoshans.

**Mekket, Hayca** A Mandalorian, she was a veterinarian following the Swarm War. She agreed to help Boba Fett by injecting the serum he received from Jaing Skirata into his bone marrow in an effort to help fight the debilitating disease that was ravaging his body.

**mekto** The Tahlboorean name for a huge arachnid that inhabited the caves of Tahlboor. The mekto were carnivorous, and would actively hunt warm-blooded creatures for food.

**Mekuun** An ancient family House that maintained a vast manufacturing business, creating weapons and repulsorlift vehicles.

**Melahnese cuisine** A style of cooking that emphasized the use of bold, piquant, and spicy flavors to create a variety of dining experiences.

**Melan, Koth** A diminutive, long-haired Bothan who oversaw the all-important Bothan SpyNet from his homeworld of Bothawui. Melan was instrumental in getting the plans of the second Death Star to the Rebel Alliance. He sent a messenger droid to Princess Leia Organa on Tatooine, but she wasn't there. Luke Skywalker was able to access the message, and he and Corellian pilot Dash Rendar went to Bothawui to meet with Melan. Melan told them that a freighter carrying fertilizer was really being used to transport an Imperial computer carrying vital information. However, Prince Xizor, head of the criminal

*Koth Melan*

Black Sun organization, had leaked the information to the Bothan SpyNet for his own purposes. Melan accompanied Rendar in the *Outrider* during the subsequent attack on the freighter. He survived the battle but was killed soon after when Skywalker was kidnapped from a Bothan safehouse on Kothlis.

**Melanani** A famous dressmaker whose designs commanded top credits throughout the galaxy.

**Melasaton** Natives of this planet were rescued from a famine by Jenna Zan Arbor during the last decades of the Old Republic.

**Meldark** A man who claimed to be the best information broker on Level 35 of Nar Shaddaa. He spent much of his time at the Dark Melody bar, where he overheard a great deal about the spice known as tempest.

**Meldazar** A planet visited by Ferus Olin while he was a Jedi Padawan to Siri Tachi before the Clone Wars. The mission turned deadly when they were forced to fight their way through Meldazar's natives in order to escape. Olin later revealed that he had felt a sense of pleasure in fighting and killing those who opposed the Jedi, and was worried that it meant that he was tainted with the dark side. Master Tachi explained that his questioning of his feelings was proof enough that he was still a Jedi.

**melding, the** An intimate process of sharing the same mind, as practiced by Azurans, who used a device called the Attanni to cybernetically link the thoughts of two people.

**Melee** A young girl who was one of the many slaves owned by Gardulla the Hutt. She grew up on the desert world of Tatooine, where she often made fun of the other slave children, although she secretly adored Anakin Skywalker. Melee served on Gardulla's cleaning staff until her skills as a mechanic earned her a position in Gardulla's garage. While she outwardly stated that Anakin Skywalker's homemade Podracer would never fly, secretly she dreamed that Anakin would win the Boonta Eve Podrace and gain his freedom, so that he could later return to Tatooine and free the slaves.

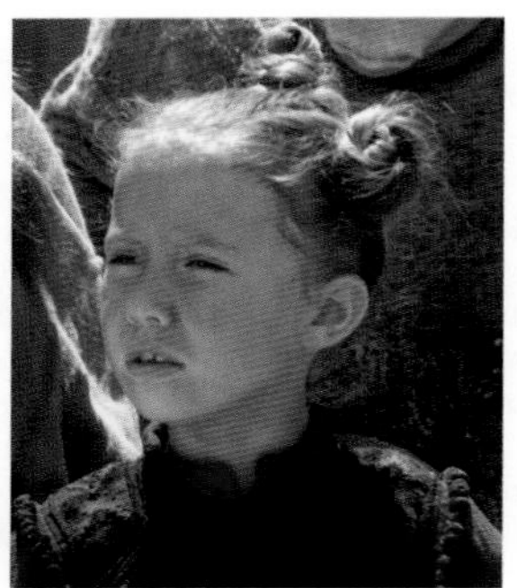
Melee

**Melford** Located on the northern coast of Lianna's Anai continent, Melford was the site of the Melford Star Academy, also called the First Star Academy. It was often considered the prettiest city on the planet.

**Melida** One of the two major factions that inhabited the planet of Melida/Daan. Throughout the history of their planet, the Melida had seen the Daan as feral beasts. The older members of both societies fought to avenge losses sustained centuries before, using their children as laborers in munitions factories while they killed each other in battle. They had been involved in a war with the Daan for 30 years before Obi-Wan Kenobi and Qui-Gon Jinn traveled to their planet to rescue Tahl, who had been captured by the Melida.

**Melida/Daan** A planet divided by an intense civil war some 12 years before the Battle of Naboo. Named for the two factions that fought so bitterly, Melida/Daan was a rugged world of rocky hills and scrub vegetation. The two factions each named the planet for themselves during the 30-year struggle, and the Old Republic elected to use both names when it cataloged the planet.

**Melida/Daan Unified Congress Building** An edifice located in Zehava, it was the headquarters of the government formed by the Young after they defeated the Elders of the Daan and the Melida. Before the end of the war, the building had been used by the leaders of both the Daan and the Melida in an attempt to jointly rule the planet. Their inbred differences kept them apart, and the building remarkably survived three years of fighting before the Young took over.

**Melie (O-Melie)** This Keganite woman was married to V-Nen. Together, they had a daughter, O-Lana, who was strong with the Force.

**Melihat** A company that manufactured dome fisheyes, a type of optical transducer.

**Melisma** A female Ryn who was one of Droma's sisters. She was part of a group of Ryn transported to Gyndine in an attempt to evade a Yuuzhan Vong attack. During the New Republic's evacuation of Gyndine, Melisma and three others from her family were allowed to leave the planet on the last rescue ship, and they set out on their own to find Droma. They were then stranded on Ruan and forced to work for Salliche Ag.

**melk** Reptilian rodents native to Zelos II, melk were covered with scales and armed with sharp teeth. Swarms of melk patrolled the Great Zelosi Sea in search of prey.

**mellcrawler** Noxious creatures native to Sullust, they gave off an awful odor when dead.

**melloon** A slang word used by Dash Rendar to refer to swoop gang members.

**Melne, Lieutenant Dren** A starfighter pilot who served with Bravo Flight in the Naboo Royal Security Force. He had a romantic relationship with Bravo leader Essara Till. But shortly before the Battle of Naboo, Melne accepted a large amount of credits to work for the governor of Agamar, helping him assemble a new defensive fleet. Melne came up with an idea to raid the Naboo system, draw out planetary defenses, then disable and steal several Naboo N-1 starfighters to study and replicate. Things didn't go as planned. Bravo leader even locked her missiles onto Melne's ship. To make sure the plot couldn't be traced, Captain Sorran—who was leading the Agamari mission—opened fire on Melne's ship himself, destroying it and Melne.

Melodies

***Melnor Spear*** An alias used by Daric LaRone and the stormtroopers of the so-called Hand of Judgment squad to describe the *Gillia,* the heavily modified Suwantek TL-1800 they stole from Major Dreflin of the *Reprisal.* They adopted the name after completing a mission in which they were commandeered by the Emperor's Hand, Mara Jade, who learned of their true identity but let them go free anyway.

**Melodies** Intelligent, amphibious humanoids. More than 50 million of them inhabited the warmer areas of Yavin 8's equatorial mountains. They hatched from eggs, starting out life as air-breathing beings who resembled human children. At the age of 20, Melodies underwent a transformation—known as the Changing Ceremony—in which they metamorphosed into amphibious creatures. The Melodies decided to make their presence known after Anakin Solo befriended a young female known as Lyric. However, during the Yuuzhan Vong War, Yavin 8 was devastated by the alien invaders, and the Melodies were all but exterminated. Only a few were offworld during the attack.

**melodium** A musical instrument played by Talon Karrde.

**Melody Fellowship** An association of musicians and agents formed to address the security needs and concerns of artists traveling throughout the galaxy during the increasingly dangerous times such as the Stark Hyperspace War, the Clone Wars, and other major disruptions.

**Meloque** A Ho'Din scientist who studied the unusual environment of the planet Caluula when it was attacked and captured by the Yuuzhan Vong some 25 years after the Battle of Endor. Meloque had spent a great deal of time among the Yuuzhan Vong, and she had learned not only their language but also many of their customs. When the Galactic Alliance needed to infiltrate Caluula, Meloque continued to play her role as scientist, and went so far as to obtain an identification lumpen for herself and her companions. Among her team were Han Solo, Judder Page, and Kyp Durron.

**Meltdown** An alcoholic cocktail similar to a Reactor Core, but considered more sophisticated. It was equally as potent, with the Lum in the cocktail enhancing the narcotic effects of the Spice Liquor, giving the drink its potency.

**Meltdown Cafe, The** A well-kept dining establishment in the Corellian sector of Nar Shaddaa's spaceport. It was one of the three most popular hangouts for Corellian spacers, and often was frequented by bounty hunters.

**Melvar, General** A native of Kuat, Melvar was a former Imperial Navy general who aligned with the Warlord Zsinj shortly after the Empire's defeat at Endor. His fanatic support of the Empire impressed Zsinj, who took him under his wing. Melvar had platinum blades implanted in his fingers in place of his fingernails, which took getting used to—as evidenced by the amount of scarring on his face. Melvar was killed on Dathomir by Gethzerion when she used the dark side of the Force to eliminate an entire platoon of Imperial stormtroopers and their officers who were poised to bring Han Solo to Zsinj.

**membibi** A small creature native to the rocky outcroppings on Ansion. With a diet primarily of insects, its four-legged body was hairless, with a whip-like tail and a drooping neck that allowed the membibi to keep its snout near the ground.

**membrosia** A thick, amber-colored liquor produced by the Colony. It was as potent as it was sweet, and made most beings feel warm throughout their entire bodies. In the years following the Yuuzhan Vong War, a more intense variety of membrosia, known simply as black membrosia, was produced by the Gorog hive.

**membrosia giver** A name given to the immense variants of the Kind that existed solely to produce pure membrosia. About the size of a bantha, the membrosia givers attached themselves to the ceiling of their chamber with their thick legs, and were attended by swarms of workers. As the membrosia givers exuded the raw membrosia in the form of a dark fluid that flowed in large drops from their abdomens, the workers lapped up the drops and further refined them in their own bodies. Membrosia givers obtained sustenance by drawing in nutrients via a group of feeding tubes that surrounded their heads.

**Memm, Gallo** An eccentric crime lord and an avid collector of rare artifacts, he made his fortune on Vaynai by allowing island businesses to profit from tourism and offworlder spending. He then levied hefty taxes on local businesses, maintaining a balance between thievery and laxity. With his credits, Memm collected a treasure trove of unique art, weapons, and armor—a collection rivaling those of many museums. A team of freelance thieves once tried to steal a suit of Felenar armor from his collection, and were caught by Memm's Weequay guards. Memm admired their skill and determination, and hired them to help him acquire more pieces for his gallery.

*Memory moth*

**memnis (plural: memnii)** A Caamasi term describing any memory that became strong and tangible, such as the birth of a child or meeting someone famous. Because of the strength of memnii, which some Caamasi described as nearly holographic, they could also be shared with others through the mingling of genetic material. This ability to pass memnii seemed to fade after three or four generations of separation. The Caamasi also discovered that they could share memnii with Jedi Knights who became their friends.

**Memorial Corridor** An expansive hallway created in the Imperial Palace on Coruscant after the Galactic Civil War, it contained a large number of holographic statues depicting the heroes of the Rebel Alliance, and was located just outside the main Senate chamber. A large sign was hung in the corridor proclaiming the number of days since the New Republic had fired a shot at an enemy.

**memory bone chamber** A sacred place to most Trandoshan males. It was in these chambers that they stored the bones of their victims. The first bones many placed were those of their fathers, whom they had to kill and eat in order to move up in the social structure of Trandosha. The bones of other opponents were stored for remembrance and reflection. Each chamber was lit with a collection of sacred candles, to highlight the many conquests to whatever gods the Trandoshan worshipped.

**memory capsule** Produced following the destruction of Alderaan, memory capsules were used by the survivors to leave small gifts in the asteroid field created by the exploded planet. Survivors, in a ritual that became known as the Returning, would bring the capsules with them, fill them with items to honor their dead, and eject them into the asteroid field.

**memory flush** *See* memory wipe.

**memory moth** Glowing, flying insects native to New Holstice, memory moths supposedly were nearly immortal. They were capable of repeating a short phrase with patterned beating of their wings. The inhabitants of New Holstice used memory moths when they created a wondrous monument to the Jedi Knights. A new moth was added whenever a Jedi was killed, with the Jedi's name whispered to the moth as it was released. In this way, the moth kept the memory of the Jedi's sacrifice alive for all to hear.

***Memory of Ithor*** A New Republic Interdictor cruiser, it was one of the ships assigned to General Wedge Antilles and the *Mon Mothma* near the end of the New Republic's battle against the Yuuzhan Vong. Commanded by Pash Cracken during the final stages of Operation Trinity and the Second Battle of Bilbringi, the *Memory of Ithor* took massive amounts of damage from Yuuzhan Vong warships. Most of the crew was able to evacuate before the ship exploded in a mighty fireball.

**memory-plastic** A form of plastic developed for the medical industry, it was used to create sutures for small wounds. In addition to retaining a given shape, memory-plastic was also biodegradable and dissolved in a week if kept clean and free from germs.

**memory rub** A technique used by the Adepts of the White Current to create a Force illusion in the mind of another individual. The memory rub was a somewhat invasive technique, since it required an Adept to enter another individual's mind. However, the memory rub was generally reserved for severe situations in which a memory needed to be removed, either to save a life or to block a painful remembrance.

**memory stone** Found on the planet Ventooine, these unique stones were used to absorb audio information for later playback.

**memory wall** Found near the New Republic's naval base on Coruscant, this huge wall was carved with the names of the brave individuals who gave their lives during the Galactic Civil War.

**memory wipe** A regular erasure of certain parts of a droid's computer memory. Ostensibly, a memory wipe removed all personality quirks and provided a clean code base on which to upgrade a droid's programming. Many owners used memory wipes to maintain stability in their automata. Most intelligent droids feared memory wipes, since they deprived them of life as they knew it.

**memo-wire** An outdated form of data and information storage, memo-wire was a thin wire specifically designed to hold encrypted data. It could be wound onto spools and transported quite easily, although it required a bulky reader to recover and view the data.

**Mendacian funeral urns** Used by the Klang and Krung dynasties to hold the vital organs of their dead kings. Urns from the young Krung dynasty were considered priceless.

**Mendicat** A scrap mining and recycling station, it was destroyed when Imperial General Sulamar incorrectly programmed the station's orbital computers. Nevertheless Sulamar, who worked with Durga the Hutt on the Darksaber Project, constantly boasted of successfully leading the Massacre of Mendicat without losing a single stormtrooper.

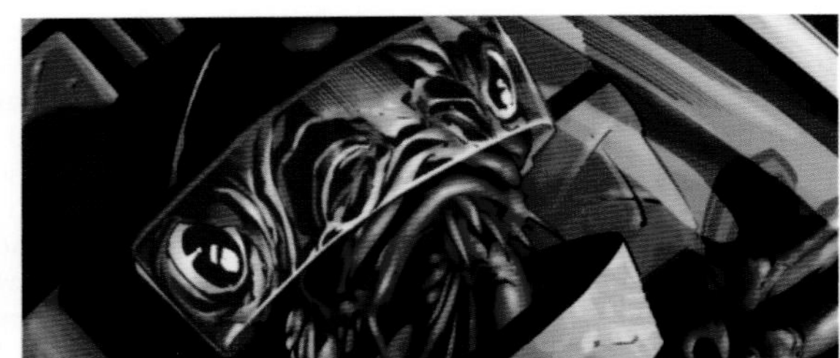

Merai

**Mendo** A Nagai warrior who trained under Lumiya on the planet Kinooine following the Battle of Endor. He was killed when the Iskalonian Kiro—who was on Kinooine with Luke Skywalker to investigate the loss of an Alliance of Free Planets scouting team—infiltrated Lumiya's stronghold to rescue Dani.

**Menges** A native of Trulalis, he tried to kill the Dark Jedi Adalric Brandl by attacking his ship, the *Kierra,* when it was docked on the planet.

**Mengjini** This planet was the site of a New Republic HoloNet relay station that was attacked by the group Vengeance after the revelation of the Caamas Document.

**Menkooro whiskey** An interstellar bourbon, Menkooro was considered the perfect accompaniment to bruallki. According to an old saying, "If you had some bruallki, you could have bruallki and Menkooro . . . if you had some Menkooro."

**Mennaalii system** A convoy carrying Rebel Alliance troops passed through this system when it was forced to exit hyperspace to avoid an asteroid field. It was ambushed by a group of pirates, but rescued by an Alliance strike team.

**Menndo** A Rodian bounty hunter who worked for the Empire as an assassin, he was often hired whenever a high-ranking political official needed to be eliminated.

**Mensio** Luke Skywalker used this alias to infiltrate the Cavrilhu pirate base in the Kauron system's asteroid belt. He claimed to have been sent by Wesselman to deliver a shipment, filling in for Pinchers, who was supposedly ill.

**Mentop** Beings who served as psychiatric and spiritual advisers to the Grand Army of the Republic during the Clone Wars. Their primary mission was to ensure the mental health and stability of the multitudes of clone troopers produced on Kamino.

**Mer, Duttes** The provincial governor of Rafa IV, he worked with the Tund Sorcerer Rokur Gepta to try to find the Mindharp of the lost Sharu in the hope of gaining complete control of the Rafa system and its exports. Based on legends of a "Bearer" and an "Emissary," Gepta planned to set up the droid Vuffi Raa as the Emissary. Mer had his deputies arrest Lando Calrissian on trumped-up charges, believing that he would be the perfect "Bearer." Mer gave the smuggler a chance for freedom, but only if he agreed to help locate the Mindharp. When Calrissian eventually returned with the Mindharp, Mer decided to keep it for himself. He believed that its purpose was to control the minds of others, but when activated it set about freeing the intelligences contained in the life-crystals in the Rafa system and rearranging the system to allow the Sharu to return. The Mindharp drained the life energy from Mer, who appeared to melt into it, and was never seen again.

**mer-9** A protocol droid that worked in Rordan's Spaceship Parts and More as a translator and assistant to Bren-Aarica Rordan. Mer-9 was actually a New Republic espionage droid placed to monitor the activities of the Corporate Sector Authority and the pro-Imperial factions in the city of Verena, on Kirima.

**Merai** One of the commanders of the Separatist armed forces, he served under Count Dooku at the Battle of Kamino. He was considered one of the greatest Mon Calamari strategists of his time. When the battle appeared lost, Merai sacrificed himself to allow his forces to escape. He flew his ship, the *Shark,* into the midst of hyperspace rings used by the Jedi Delta-7 Aethersprite fighters, destroying many, but paying the highest price as his own ship exploded.

**Merast, Thulian** An Imperial Navy captain, he commanded the Star Destroyer *Eradicator* during the early years of the New Republic. Captain Merast was assigned by Moff Kentor Sarne to patrol the Kathol Rift. Merast and his crew were killed when the *Eradicator* was destroyed by an intense light storm at the edge of the Rift during the search for the *FarStar.*

**merchantate** The name used by Ithorians to indicate the business leaders aboard their herd ships. Each merchantate had a vote in the council that governed commerce aboard the ships.

**Merchant's Row** An area aboard the Outland Transit Station filled with shops and stores catering to a variety of needs. The "row" actually encompassed several streets and thoroughfares surrounding the gladiator arena at the heart of the station.

**Merchant's Square** A large, open area that dominated the city of Drev'starn on Bothawui, it was at the Combined Clans Center Building. It was here that Drend Navett and Klif touched off one of their Vengeance riots following the revelation of the Caamas Document.

***Merciless*** An Imperial *Aggressor*-class destroyer operating during the Galactic Civil War.

***Mercy* (1)** A highly modified Dreadnaught outfitted by the Rebel Alliance as a medical vessel during the last years of the Galactic Civil War. It had been captured while it was still under construction at an Imperial shipyard, and refitted with 4,250 bacta tanks and accommodations for more than 6,000 patients. Ward 114 was set aside for those Alliance agents who worked for the Special Operations division, allowing them to recover in privacy. The *Mercy* was protected by a pair of assault frigates and a squadron of Corellian gunships.

***Mercy* (2)** A Rebel Alliance *Lambda*-class shuttle used to rescue the escapees from the *Hampton.*

**Mercy, Bruce** A space pirate who worked with three other pirates: the Polydroxol enforcer Morph, the Conjeni pilot Durquist, and the Arachnoid mechanic Ptak-Sok. Mercy's own ship, the *Black Widow,* was a command ship of sorts. Mercy and his band tried to steal the location of the *Fool's Gold* from the Chikarri mechanic Plako, but they were beaten to the legendary ship by a group of freelance adventurers.

**Merdeon** A bartender at the Crosstown cantina in Gadrin on Cularin during the final years of the Old Republic.

**Mere** A humanoid species of amphibians native to the planet Maramere. The Mere lived mainly on the land, in cities they built on the rocky outcropping of the planet, but they could breathe underwater when necessary. Tall and well muscled, the Mere had smooth-scaled orange skin that turned to green at the limbs; it was dotted with spikes on the tops of their heads and shoulders.

**Mereel** One of the six *Null*-class ARC trooper clones who survived the gestation period, he grew to adulthood during the development of the Grand Army of the Republic. He was distinguished from nearly every other clone by his blond hair color and blue eye pigmentation, which allowed him to move about in places that other clones could not. Mereel's skills as a slicer allowed him to discover information on the whereabouts of Ko Sai, as well as hints that she might have knowledge of a way to extend the lives of clone troopers. Kal Skirata sent Mereel on several covert missions during the Clone Wars, many of which involved locating Ko Sai and any vital information she might have.

**Mereel, Jaster** A Journeyman Protector from the planet Concord Dawn, he killed another Protector in the line of duty. Even though the other man was a corrupt law enforcer, Mereel was imprisoned and forced to stand trial. Convicted of murder, he was exiled from the planet. Mereel eventually found a home with the remnants of the Mandalorian shock troopers, who took him in and trained him to be one of their best mercenaries. When Mereel was elected the leader of the Mandalorian Mercs, it was believed that Vizsla decided to split off from the group and form the Death Watch. In response, Mereel declared that his followers were the True Mandalorians. Vizsla tried to destroy the True Mandalorians on Concord Dawn, but Mereel and a small force managed to survive, thanks in part to the efforts of a young Jango Fett.

The Mandalorians regrouped, but Mereel felt pressure from hard-liners like Montross to eliminate the Death Watch and reestablish the superiority of the Mandalorians. It was during this time that he created the Codex, the new tenets and canons of the supercommandos who followed him into battle. He also appointed Jango Fett as his choice to succeed him as *Mand'alor.* Years later, during a mission to Korda 6, Mereel discovered that a request for aid had been a ruse created by Vizsla and the Death Watch, who lured the Mandalorians there to eliminate them. Mereel, betrayed and abandoned by Montross, was shot dead by Vizsla.

Boba Fett later recovered Mereel's Mandalorian armor, using it as his own distinctive garb. For this reason, many rumors claimed that Boba Fett was actually Jaster Mereel. Boba Fett himself never set the record straight, preferring to cloud his true identity whenever and wherever possible.

**meremew** A small creature that lived on the Forest Moon of Endor.

**Merenzane Gold** A subtle, sweet-tasting alcoholic beverage brewed in the galaxy for thousands of years. Depending on the vintage, the golden-colored liquor could be quite expensive.

**Mere Resistance** These freedom fighters led by Sol Sixxa tried to oppose the Trade Federation's takeover of their homeworld of Maramere.

**Merf** A humanoid Freelie who was a member of the band that captured Luke Skywalker and Leia Organa on Vorzyd 5.

**Merglyn** A noted gunrunner, she worked with Havor during the last decades of the Old Republic. Both were killed when they tried to run weapons to the planet Kiffex, shot down by the Guardians of Kiffu. Hidden within their cargo holds was the Jedi Knight Aayla Secura, who was trying to reach Volfe Karkko; she fled the ship in an escape pod just before it was destroyed.

**Merick** A Bith who was considered one of the galaxy's foremost experts on torture in the last decades of the Old Republic. It was rumored that Merick and fellow mercenary Bavo once broke a Zabrak subject with their techniques.

***Meridian*** A sleek, black-hulled shuttle dispatched by Hiram Drayson of New Republic Intelligence, to bring back the remains of two Republic scientists, several Qella bodies, and some artifacts found on Brath Qella.

**Meridian** A lifeless world, it was once the home planet of the Grissmath Dynasty. An unknown catastrophe turned Meridian into a charred, radioactive wasteland.

**Meridian sector** A lightly populated sector near the Outer Rim, it bordered the Imperial-held Antemeridian sector, far from major trade routes. The Meridian sector contained several New Republic planets, including Nim Drovis and Budpock, and two Republic fleet bases at Durren and Cybloc XII, but most of the sector remained neutral. Nine years after the Battle of Endor, Leia Organa Solo secretly visited the Meridian sector to meet with Seti Ashgad. After Ashgad unleashed the Death Seed plague on Leia's escort ships, the plague spread across three-quarters of the sector.

Tem Merkon

**Meriko, Miracle** A musician killed by the Empire during its sweep to wipe out "questionable" artistic endeavors.

**Merikon** The site of an Imperial training facility during the New Order.

**Merilang-1221** A full-spectrum numerical analyzer, designed to process incoming transmissions for numerical encryption.

**Merili** A member of the Prophets of the Dark Side, she served the Empire for many years. During the early years of the New Order, Merili oversaw the work of Dr. Nycolai Kinesworthy and hired Treun Lorn to assist with the development of a new battle droid based on General Grievous's mechanical exoskeleton. Later she served as Grand Admiral Syn's spiritual adviser following the Battle of Endor. Merili was known for her ability to perceive the future, and apparently even manipulate future events. Therefore she was elevated to the position of Emperor's Eyes. Merili died at Kashyyyk when Syn's flagship *Fi* was destroyed by Admiral Ackbar and the New Republic.

***Merisee Hope*** A slave-running ship for a brothel in Coruscant's Invisec. The smuggler Mirax Terrik brought several members of Rogue Squadron to Imperial Center (Coruscant) on an undercover mission using the false identity and transponder code of the *Merisee Hope* for her ship, the *Pulsar Skate.*

**Merit, Klo** An Equani physician who worked for the Grand Army of the Republic during the Clone Wars as a doctor and empath for the Rimsoo Seven military hospital on Drongar. When Barriss Offee discovered that there was a spy in the Rimsoo Seven camp, her investigations narrowed suspects down to two: Tolk le Trene and Klo Merit. When she learned of Tolk's love for Jos Vondar and was able to look into Tolk's mind with the Force, Barriss discovered that Merit was the spy. Merit was forced to admit his double role as the spies Column and Lens. When a Separatist attack on the Rismoo Seven base set off a series of explosions, Merit thought he had a chance to escape. However, the sound of the explosions masked the blaster fire from Vondar's weapon, and Merit was killed instantly.

**merit adoptive** A term used to describe any Chiss individual who was brought into one of the Ruling Families from outside its traditional bloodlines in an effort to diversify or invigorate the family. Merit adoptives also were common in the Chiss military, which took in members from all families and worked for the benefit of the entire Chiss society.

**Merkon, Dr.** An alias used by Dr. Amie Antin to cover up the presence of Obi-Wan Kenobi at the Imperial prison in Ussa on Bellassa. Obi-Wan infiltrated the prison to locate Roan Lands, and had been disguised as a doctor in order to gain access. Dr. Antin had not met Obi-Wan, but realized what he was doing and quickly covered his appearance by calling him one of her associates, Dr. Merkon, giving them enough time to escape with Lands.

**Merkon, Tem** An old man who roamed the streets of Phaeda's main starport city, collecting information on the movements of Imperial troops garrisoned there following Grand Admiral Thrawn's death. He funneled information to the highest bidder—both Mirith Sinn with her New Republic forces, and Colonel Shev. Sish Sadeet was alerted to his duplicity, and the Trandoshan tracked him to a meeting with Carnor Jax. Sinn and Sadeet later confronted Merkon with their evidence, and Merkon tried to escape their wrath. In anger, Sinn's agent Massimo drove a knife into Merkon's chest, killing him.

**Merl** The owner of a popular cantina known as Merl's on Centares during the Galactic Civil War. He employed a Gotal named Uri and a Sakiyan known as Glocken to keep the cantina safe. Merl eventually was confronted by Valance the Hunter, who demanded information on the whereabouts of Tyler Lucian. Merl, who had been providing rations to Lucian while keeping his location a secret, gave Valance all the information he had. Valance then shot him dead so that no one else could discover Lucian's location.

**Merle** This man was the younger of the two cooks aboard the *Courteous* who played sabacc with Lando Calrissian during the blockade of the ThonBoka.

**merlie** A medium-sized farm animal native to Qiilura. Farmers raised merlies for food and other needs, including wool. In order to cut down on heating costs during the winter, most families brought their merlies indoors, adding their body heat to small rooms. They were somewhat intelligent, and their green eyes were considered almost human by many farmers.

**mermen** Extinct ocean-dwelling inhabitants, they were native to Mon Calamari.

**mernip** A creature genetically developed by the Yuuzhan Vong, and bred in small pools.

**Merrick, Ace** A Rebel Alliance X-wing pilot killed when his Rascal Squadron destroyed the Arah asteroid mining operation supporting the V38 project.

**Merricope, Shyla** She served as the Diktat of the Corellian system during the years leading up to the Clone Wars. She was in complete agreement with then-Senator Garm Bel Iblis when the Corellian system closed its borders to the Old Republic in an effort to avoid the firestorm of separatism that was sweeping the galaxy.

**Merrik** A human native of M'haeli, Merrik hired Mora to modify swoops for him. After Leia Organa and Ranulf Trommer revealed Governor Grigor's Dragite-mining operation, Merrik sacrificed himself in order to allow Mora and Leia to escape with Trommer. The group set charges within the mines, and when they exploded, they destroyed Merrik as well as the entire mining complex.

*Merl*

**Merrik, Tal** A gentle Senator from Duchess Satine's home planet of Kalevala, Tal Merrik was not the man he first appeared to be. Conniving and greedy, Senator Merrik would happily betray his closest "friend" if it helped him achieve his shady political goals.

***Merriweather*** An immense, boat-shaped bulk cruiser that was the command ship used by the Tofs during their attack on Zeltros some months after the Battle of Endor.

Merriweather

**Merr-Sonn Munitions** The largest and best-known subsidiary of Merr-Sonn Mil/Sci, it originally was established to manufacture grenades, mines, and other forms of explosives. Over time, Merr-Sonn branched out to produce hold-out blasters and grenade launchers. Merr-Sonn's products were well received in both the military and civilian markets, and the corporation's total sales were surpassed only by those of BlasTech. Merr-Sonn Munitions was originally founded more than 4,000 years before the Clone Wars; it rose to prominence during the Great Sith War when it provided cortosis-based alloys to the Sith and weapons to the Mandalorian mercenaries. During the era of the New Order, Merr-Sonn was able to remain independent, and maintained that independence well into the era of the New Republic.

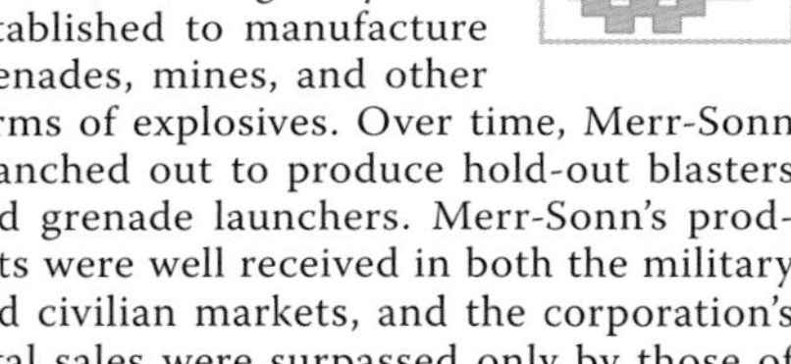

**Merry Havoc, the** A term used by Palleus Chuff to describe one of the many facial expressions used by Jedi Master Yoda. Chuff was a noted actor whose portrayal of Yoda in *Jedi!* made him famous across the galaxy.

***Merry Miner*** The vessel used by Jaina and Jacen Solo to maneuver a stylus ship into position over Helska 4 during the New Republic's first attempt to destroy the Yuuzhan Vong invasion force. The Solo twins managed to use the ship to pierce the icy planetary crust and launch a warhead that would begin freezing the planet, in an effort to destroy the Praetorite Vong's yammosk before it could begin coordinating an assault on the New Republic's fleet.

**Mers, Lawra** A major with the Rebel Alliance based on Fangol. Shortly after the Battle of Yavin, she coordinated dozens of Alliance strike teams and agent groups across the galaxy, and was the primary commander of the team that secured the *Black Ice.*

***Mersel Kebir*** A Dreadnaught that was the flagship of Rendili's homeworld defense fleet during the Clone Wars. It was under the command of Jace Dallin until some six months before the First Battle of Coruscant, when Dallin openly voiced his support for the Old Republic. His officers remained loyal to Rendili, which had sided with the Separatists, and mutinied before he could turn the ship over to Jedi Master Plo Koon. The mutineers, led by Lieutenant Mellor Yago, took Dallin and Plo Koon hostage, hoping to force the remaining Republic fleet to return to Coruscant.

**Merson** A planet ravaged by the Clone Wars. Some 17 months after the Battle of Geonosis, clone troopers of the Grand Army of the Republic were dispatched to Merson under the command of Jedi Master Ronhar Kim. The intelligence provided by the Old Republic was faulty, and the unit was ambushed as soon as it arrived. Within a few days, the natives had reduced the unit's strength by 64 percent, forcing the troopers to retreat or be annihilated. But their starship support was unable to rescue them. The captain of their transport, Gilad Pellaeon, was under attack and forced to defend his ships before he could start the rescue. The Republic hadn't known that the attacking Merson pirates had been augmented by Separatist forces dispatched by Count Dooku himself. Dooku had received orders from his own Master, Darth Sidious, to wipe out the mission to Merson, after hearing of Master Kim's plans to test the Galactic Senate for midi-chlorians. Kim and his Padawan were both killed on Merson.

**Merson asteroid belt** A field of space debris located just outside the orbit of the planet Merson, it was infamous for the pirates who used it as a base of operations during the last decades of the Old Republic. Known as the Merson Slavers, these pirates preyed most often on ships of the Republic itself, but were not picky about which vessels they ambushed. Because of this, and because the Merson asteroid belt crossed several well-traveled hyperspace lanes, starships had to drop out of hyperspace and drift past the belt in order to avoid being captured by the pirates.

**Merson Slavers** A feared group of slavers once foiled by Obi-Wan Kenobi when they tried to hijack a pleasure cruiser. It was believed that the Merson Slavers were affiliated with Zygerrian Slavers at the time. They operated from a base that was hidden within the Merson asteroid belt.

**Mertan** When Talon Karrde first located Jorj Car'das on Exocron, Car'das played the part of an elderly man, confusing Karrde with another man by the name of Mertan.

***Merte*** A *Lambda*-class shuttle used by the Rebel Alliance to rescue a group of smugglers from an Imperial ambush shortly before the Battle of Endor. The smugglers had agreed to help supply the Alliance for the coming battle, but came under Imperial attack. The Alliance managed to defeat the Imperials and get the smugglers to safety.

**Merthyog Communications** A small starship manufacturer that won a contract from the Empire to build the II-xC broadcast ship, which was used to maintain and supplement subspace relay stations.

**Merumeru** A respected Wookiee elder at the age of just 250, the Kashyyyk native wore the emblem of the Kachirho clan into battle against the droid armies of the Separatists during the Clone Wars. His mental agility was honed through tournaments of dejarik and other similar games. In practice, he developed effective tactics to defend Wookiee territories and outposts from Trandoshan raiders. During the Battle of Kachirho, Captain Merumeru headed the beachfront defense, leading his volunteer soldiers against the invading droid armies. Among the capable warriors following him into battle were Guanta, Lachichuk, and Salporin.

**Mesa, Colonel Kavel** A chief logistics officer for the Rebel Alliance, he secured the Rebel base on Arbra. He was placed in charge of protecting the fleet while it was in orbit around Arbra's sun. Captain Mesa and his team monitored the Kerts-Bhrg field generators that formed a pyramid around the fleet, protecting it from the sun's heat and radiation.

**Mesa Flats** One of the most remote sections of Tatooine's deep desert.

**Mesan** A female Senali who was married to Jaret, she became a member of the Banoosh-Walore clan.

**mesarc** One of the most predominant currencies exchanged on the planet Aargau during the last decades of the Old Republic. A mesarc was also a measure of time.

**mesh trap** Developed for use by bounty hunters, the mesh trap was a weave of electrified fibers that could be hidden beneath leaves or other light material. When a being stepped onto the mesh trap, it triggered the electrical power and stunned the bounty, rendering him or her numb and easy to capture.

**Mesonics** Manufacturers of focalized, shape-charged explosives that were hard to use because they required detonators that fired at triple frequency intervals. Mesonics's cone-shaped charges were useful against air lock doors.

**Mesoriaam, Barid** A Rebel Alliance spy, he was captured and tortured by Jabba the Hutt's gangsters, yet still able to deliver an essential information datadot to the Rebellion with the help of Muftak, a Talz, and his Chadra-Fan partner, Kabe, who encountered Mesoriaam as they were robbing Jabba's Mos Eisley town house.

**Message, the** The name used by Yuuzhan Vong Shamed Ones to describe the story of Vua Rapuung and his friendship with Anakin Solo. The story told how the Jedi Knights worked with the Shamed Ones to expose the heretical theories of Mezhan Kwaad, along with the information that the Yuuzhan Vong gods might not be as powerful as the priests had led their civilization to believe. The Message was passed from Shamed One to Shamed One, with never more than three individuals being in contact at one time. This ensured that, in case one Shamed One was arrested for spreading the Message, no more than a few other individuals could be arrested as well. This allowed the Message to spread throughout the galaxy, becoming a force that the Yuuzhan Vong commanders were hard-pressed to deal with. When Nom Anor adopted the personage of Yu'shaa, the Shamed Ones began spreading the Message in earnest, and it began to reach the ears of more powerful individuals. Nom Anor twisted the basic story to meet his own needs, inventing the Rainbow-eyed Enemy to represent the powerful Yuuzhan Vong establishment. The Message was altered to bring the Jedi Knights more to the forefront, and eventually became known as the Jedi Heresy to all castes of Yuuzhan Vong.

**message cube** A device that was virtually unsliceable, a message cube could be keyed to the recipient's body chemistry, fingerprints, or voice. The outside of the cube was used to display the recipient's name, address, or a short message or code phrase. The cube could be hollow, used for delivering small datachips or other physical media, or it could be built around a tiny holoprojector. Cubes that contained holovids could be set for single or multiple viewings.

*Merumeru*

**message dinghy** A small vessel similar to a hyperspace courier tube. Message dinghies were developed to transfer coded information from one location to another, most often between starships.

**message pod** Similar to a hyperspace courier tube, but without a propulsion system; it had to be left in space to be recovered later.

**message wafer** A flat, rectangular card that, when received by the designated recipient, was creased in the center and cracked open along the crease. The card was then folded for standing on a flat surface. After playing the sender's message with video and audio output, the wafer disintegrated in a flash of light.

***Messenger*** A courier ship owned by Core Courier Service during the early days of the New Republic, it was piloted by Taryn Clancy and Del Sato. The ship was a modified *Ghtroc*-class 720 freighter, armed with a double laser cannon and equipped with redundant shielding, accommodating 10 passengers and 135 metric tons of cargo.

**Mester Reef** An immense coral reef located on Mon Calamari. It was here that Danni Quee first saw Jacen Solo for what he truly was: not a Jedi Knight, not a Solo, but just Jacen Solo.

**MetaCannon** A massive ground weapon developed by the Chiss in the years following the Yuuzhan Vong War, it was capable of firing a variety of ordnance depending on the battle situation. The MetaCannon could fire maser beams, blaster bolts, or solid projectiles with minimal refitting.

**meta-ceramic** A strong, woven material used to create diplomatic pouches that protected their contents from damage. Originally developed by the Trade Federation, the pouches wove computational circuitry with the meta-ceramic, creating a device that also served as a computer and could display its message on the surface.

**metal borer** Insects known to inhabit spaceports and shipyards, feeding on the hulls and exterior components of starships.

**metal-crystal phase shifter (MCPS)** A weapon constructed at Maw Installation, the MCPS field altered the crystalline structure of metals, including those in starship hulls. It could then penetrate conventional shielding and turn hull plates into powder.

**Metalorn** This remote planet was best known as corporate headquarters for the Baktoid Armor Workshop. During the Clone Wars, however, the forces of the Grand Army of the Republic were able to regain control of the planet, removing the Separatists from power and shutting down production of the Confederacy's cortosis droids. In the years following the Clone Wars, the Empire either nationalized existing factories or built new ones on Metalorn. Much of the planet's surface was destroyed by environmental damage from strip mining and pollution, forcing the Empire to reestablish its factories beneath the surface. Located in the Mid Rim Territories in the direction of the Perlemian Trade Route, Metalorn was the birthplace of Wat Tambor.

**Metalsmiths' Guild** A group of extremely proficient metal crafters native to the planet Vandelhelm. The Guild was formed about 3,000 years before the Galactic Civil War, when independent prospectors Vandel and Helm first discovered the planet and its mineral riches.

***Meteor*-class Aerial Fort** An Adumari flying-wing warship capable of atmospheric flight. The Aerial Fort carried several smaller craft, including *Blade*-class fighters.

***Meteor Racer*** One of many starships trapped on Coruscant when the Yuuzhan Vong attacked the planet. Along with some 600 other independent starships, the *Meteor Racer* fled as soon as the first wave of attacks began. The invaders used the ship and its refugees as human shields in the Battle of Coruscant.

**Meteor Way** An area in Coronet City, capital of Corellia.

**methanogen** Grannans need to breathe this gas in order to survive away from their home planet. It was found in the proper quantities for Grannans on the planet Polneye.

***Metron Burner*** A Corellian YT-1300 freighter owned and operated by Bama Vook, with assistance from his son Chup-Chup and the navigation droid LE-PR34. Vook also owned a modified Z-95 Headhunter, which had a cockpit with enough room for two beings.

**metropolitan shuttle** A term used to describe any small, repulsorlift personnel carrier used to travel between locations in large cities.

Metalorn

**Metta Drop** An area of the Tatooine desert that was part of Jabba the Hutt's Podracing course. The Drop was a sheer wall of rock that rose 20 meters into the air. When a Podracer crossed over the Drop, it immediately plummeted downward until its repulsors kicked in and leveled the craft out at the bottom.

***Metternich*** A Nebulon-B frigate used by the Imperial Navy during the Galactic Civil War.

**Mettier, Lag** A good friend of Dack Ralter, he served the Rebel Alliance's ground support teams at Echo Base on Hoth. In the wake of the battle, Mettier was captured and imprisoned by the Empire, and was one of the many prisoners held by Ysanne Isard aboard the *Lusankya.* Mettier was part of the group her clone left in the Xenovet facility on Commenor. There he was rescued by Rogue Squadron and returned to the New Republic.

**Mettlo, Obron** A Moorin mercenary who fought in dozens of battles, he was usually on the winning side. When he arrived on Tatooine, he was referred to Jabba the Hutt by Kardue'sai'Malloc.

**Meyer, Lips** A Gran who was once a part of the primary criminal organization based on the Outland Transit Station following the Battle of Naboo. A bounty was placed on his head after Meyer ratted out several prominent members of the Outlanders organized crime family in order to get immunity from the law. He was captured by Jango Fett and brought in for the bounty.

**Mezdec** One of the leaders of the Typha-Dor resistance before the Clone Wars. Along with his wife, Shalini, Mezdec rallied people from throughout the Uziel system for her crusade against the invasion plans of the Vanqors. His subterfuge was later exposed by Obi-Wan Kenobi and Anakin Skywalker. He was arrested and placed into custody.

Metta Drop

**Mezer, Sergeant** A member of the Corellian Security Force following the Swarm War, he was one of many officers assigned to security duty aboard an abandoned resort station near Gilatter VIII when the Confederation met for the first time to discuss the election of a new Supreme Commander during the Corellia–GA War.

**Mezgraf** A massive, white-furred Togorian, he served aboard the transport vessel *Uhumele* in the final years of the Old Republic. A former slave and a survivor of the slave markets on Orvax IV, Mezgraf was ready for combat, but also knew how to control his baser instincts. He later provided information on Orvax IV to Bomo Greenbark when the Nosaurian set out to rescue his wife and daughter from slavery, and agreed to help locate them.

**Mezza** A Ryn stranded on the planet Duro during the Yuuzhan Vong War. She had taupe fur, highlighted by red-orange splashes and a blue tail. Mezza led a large clan of Ryn while stranded on the planet. After the Yuuzhan Vong attacked Duro in an effort to take the refugees as sacrifices, Mezza and Romany worked together to get as many immigrants off the planet as possible.

**Mezzicanley Wave** An effect that occurred when matter reached its fourth stage, after it had passed through the vaporous stage and began to resolidify at incredibly cold temperatures. A Mezzicanley Wave was induced on Helska 4 to destroy the Yuuzhan Vong's base there.

**MG1-A proton torpedo** The designation of a proton torpedo launching system developed for the Old Republic. The torpedoes were unaffected by energy fields, allowing them to pierce most starship shielding systems.

**MG-3** A fixed-emplacement missile tube designed by Krupx for use on ground ships and speeders.

**MG9** An advanced Krupx Munitions proton torpedo launching system used on the B-wing starfighter.

**M'haeli** An agrarian planet with several moons in the Expansion Region, it was well situated as a refueling point for several nearby systems. The M'haeli capital was N'croth, where Governor Grigor ruled for years with the help of an Imperial garrison during the New Order. The planet's population was composed mainly of human colonists and native H'drachi. Each year the H'drachi held a midsummer conclave during which they consulted the timestream for news of the future. Notable sights on M'haeli included W'eston Falls, Demon's Brow, and a secret mine of valuable Dragite crystals located in the D'olop Range.

An attack led by Grigor had devastated the palace of the human ruling house and paved the way for the planet's takeover by the Empire. Mora, infant heir to the ruling house, was aban-

doned during the attack and adopted by the H'drachi seer Ch'no. Some 17 years later, Imperial pilot Ranulf Trommer was assigned to M'haeli to spy on Grigor and uncovered the illegal Dragite-mining operation run by the governor.

**M'haeli luf virus** Found on the planet M'haeli, it was a virus that flourished in urban areas.

**Mhingxin** Rodent-faced sentients known for their high-pitched voices. Mhingxin had a low self-image, mainly because they resembled sewer rats. This made them easy to provoke.

**M-HYD 6804 (Dowser)** Brought to Tatooine by the *Lucky Despot,* this antiquated droid was intended for moisture farmers but proved ineffective. The resulting clash between the disgruntled customers and the *Despot*'s crew came to be known as the Prospector's Riot.

**Mi, Celjo** A noted expert in the martial art of teräs käsi in the years leading up to the Battle of Geonosis.

**miasra sauce** A yellow-swirled sauce that was the perfect accompaniment to mesh-cooked trimpian slices.

**Mica** A native of Frego, she was a cousin of Lena Cobral, and met Qui-Gon Jinn and Obi-Wan Kenobi when they arrived onworld to escort Lena back to Coruscant to testify in a murder trial. Mica years earlier had witnessed the murder of her own mother, and feared Lena would also be killed by organized crime figures. When Lena went to a meeting to get some information for her testimony, Mica followed her. It was a trap. Mica stepped in front of a blast meant for Lena and took the shot herself. She died shortly afterward.

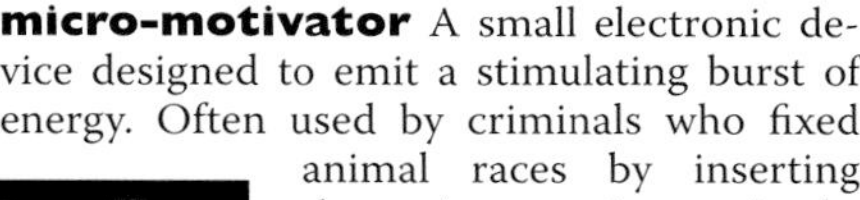

M-HYD 6804 (Dowser)

**Micamberlecto** A Frozian, he was selected by the New Republic to be the Governor-General of the Corellian sector and the Outlier systems. Wielding little real power, Micamberlecto was murdered by Thrackan Sal-Solo's Human League as part of Sal-Solo's plan to subvert the Sacorrian Triad's Starbuster Plot and take control of the Corellian system for himself.

**micrel power supply** Miniature power supplies that were used to power small devices. Micrel supplies generated very little heat, so they could be used in prosthetic limbs and other devices that came into contact with flesh.

**microbial mat** An antiseptic, bioengineered material used by the Yuuzhan Vong to line the floor of an oqa tube. The microbial mat helped to decontaminate any Yuuzhan Vong who used the oqa to move from one starship to another.

**microdroid wrestling** A popular form of sport in many casinos following the Swarm War. Small droids, often no larger than 10 centimeters, were built by contestants to function as tiny gladiators. Each event paired combatants, and the winner moved on to the next round. The actual combat between droids took place in a secure chamber so that patrons were not accidentally injured when the droids attacked each other.

**microfusion pile** A small, almost limitless energy source used to power Vuffi Raa.

**microgarment** Any form of intimate wear, especially garments that were worn by females.

**micrograbber** A delicate tool used to manipulate microscopic bits of technology during the repair of computer systems or droids.

**micromine** An Imperial space mine developed to prevent its detection by normal starship scanners. Each micromine was a tiny speck of antimatter contained within a magnetic shell. Because micromines were so small, they were virtually undetectable.

Sena Leikvold Midanyl

**micro-motivator** A small electronic device designed to emit a stimulating burst of energy. Often used by criminals who fixed animal races by inserting them into racing animals, artificially enhancing the animals' drive to continue, micro-motivators could be destroyed within the animal when the race was over. Because of their small size, this rarely did any damage to the animal, thereby maintaining the criminals' secrets.

**micropoint** An instrument developed to repair the intricate circuitry of miniature computer systems, such as those found in droids.

**microvalve** Valves that were part of fluidic control systems used aboard starships. They opened and closed based on commands from the pilot or copilot, allowing pressurized fluid to move along the flow-track to activate certain systems.

**Midanyl, Sena Leikvold** Senator Garm Bel Iblis's chief aide and adviser on Corellia, she once served as his unofficial ambassador-at-large for Peregrine's Nest, headquarters of Bel Iblis's private army. Midanyl worked beside him on the floor of the Senate. She was with him when he helped form the Rebel Alliance, and when he left after his disagreements with Alliance leader Mon Mothma. Along with Bel Iblis's security chief, Irenez, Midanyl helped Bel Iblis plan many independent attacks on Imperial forces.

**Middle Distance** The first Ferroan settlement on the planet Zonama Sekot, located in the planet's equatorial region. Some 29 years after the Battle of Yavin, Zonama Sekot made a blind jump into hyperspace as a reaction to the sabotage of Nom Anor. Without time to protect itself, the planet was unable to control the damage that occurred on its surface. Large amounts of the southern continents were destroyed, and Middle Distance suffered extensive damage from fires and scorching temperatures. To counteract this, Sekot created intense rainstorms, which drenched Middle Distance for many weeks.

**Middle Generation** Members of the Melida/Daan society who were of middle age, between 20 and 50 years old. They maintained their Daan or Melida heritage, but remained neutral during the intense civil war. The Middle Generation pledged tentative support to the Young when it appeared that the children could end the civil war. When the Young began to struggle with control over the planet, the Middle Generation backed out. After Cerasi's death and the negotiated peace, the Middle Generation agreed to step forward and help create a new, combined government.

**midi-chlorian** A microscopic life-form that resided within all living cells and was capable of communicating with the Force. Symbionts found in all beings, midi-chlorians might be responsible for all life. They could reveal the will of the Force when one's mind was quiet. Those beings with a high concentration of midi-chlorians in their blood could become Jedi. Anakin Skywalker may have been conceived by midi-chlorians, and his midi-chlorian count exceeded 20,000,

Qui-Gon Jinn tests Anakin Skywalker's midi-chlorian levels.

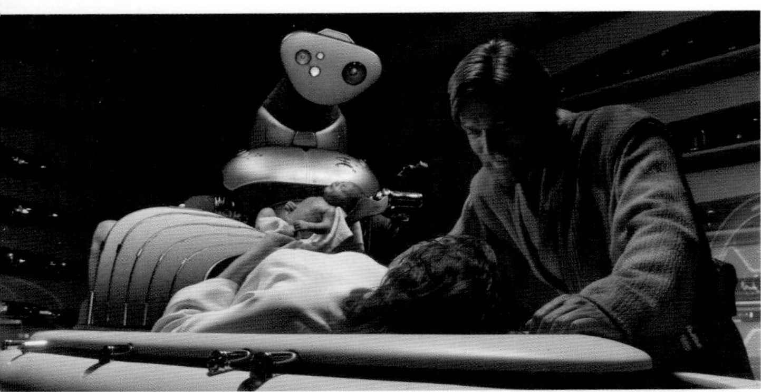

A midwife droid assists Padmé Amidala in the birth of Luke and Leia Skywalker.

which was more than that of Master Yoda. The Jedi Knights developed techniques that could detect high concentrations of midi-chlorians in infants. During the last years of the Old Republic, some Jedi began to wonder if the relationship between midi-chlorians and the Force might actually be the opposite of traditional thinking. They believed that the Force created the midi-chlorians as a way to reach out to life throughout the galaxy. In the wake of the Clone Wars, most information regarding midi-chlorians was erased from galactic computer banks by the handful of surviving Jedi Knights in an effort to prevent the Imperials from learning how to use cellular testing to identify other Jedi survivors.

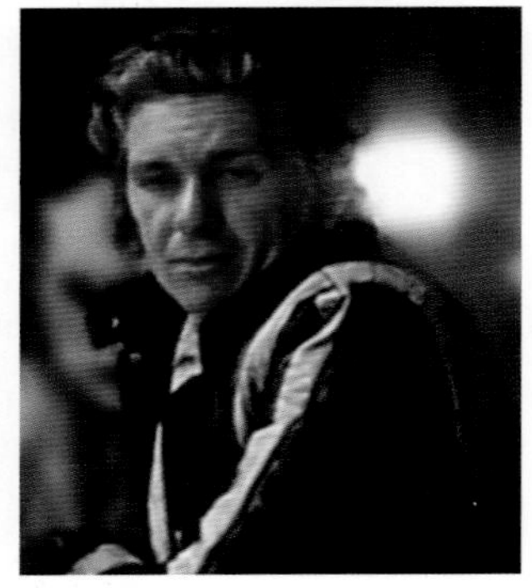

Yerka Mig

**Mid Rim Territories** An expanse of open, sparsely populated space between the Inner and Outer Rim territories, it was far less populated and less wealthy than the surrounding regions because it held fewer natural resources. It contained a lot of pirate and smuggling bases. Even at the time of the New Republic, much of the Mid Rim remained unexplored.

**midwife droid** Developed to assist obstetricians of various species in delivering infants, midwife droids were usually created in the image of a female of the species, with calming personalities and soothing voices. The limbs of a midwife droid were sometimes equipped with cradling paddles or other devices that helped to ease the mother's pain and provide gentle support to the newborn. The main body of the midwife droid was covered with specialized materials that were soft yet durable, and could be gently heated to comfort a newborn baby. The birth of Luke and Leia Skywalker was aided by a Chroon-Tan B-Machine floating midwife droid manufactured by the Polis Massa Pria Assemblage.

**Miek** Han Solo used this alias when he traveled with Droma to Tholatin while searching for clues to the whereabouts of Roa and Droma's family. Miek was the captain of the *Sunlight Franchise.*

**Mig, Yerka** An Imperial bureaucrat with high security clearance, he resigned from the service of the Empire after the occupation of his home planet, Ralltiir. He became a fugitive from Imperial Intelligence, but was known to frequent a cantina in Mos Eisley on Tatooine.

**Mighella** One of the more powerful Witches of Dathomir, she was taken from Dathomir by Alexi Garyn, the leader of the criminal organization Black Sun, to serve as his personal bodyguard on Ralltiir. In addition to her combat skills and command of the dark side, Mighella had a limited amount of prescience, and once predicted the execution of all nine of Garyn's Vigos. Her vision was partially correct, as Darth Maul appeared at Garyn's fortress. Unaware of the Sith Lord's true identity, Mighella leapt to prevent him from attacking Garyn. She used a combination of Force lightning and other dark side tactics to keep Maul at bay until he revealed that he was, in fact, the apprentice to Darth Sidious. Maul redoubled his attack, and Mighella was helpless against him. She died knowing that she had given her own master a chance to escape.

**Might Squadron** A squadron of TIE fighters maintained by the Thyferran Home Defense Corps.

**Mignay, Captain** An officer in Trade Defense, she was commander of the *Rim Merchant Einem* during Wilhuff Tarkin's attempt to take control of Zonama Sekot.

Miid Ro'ik

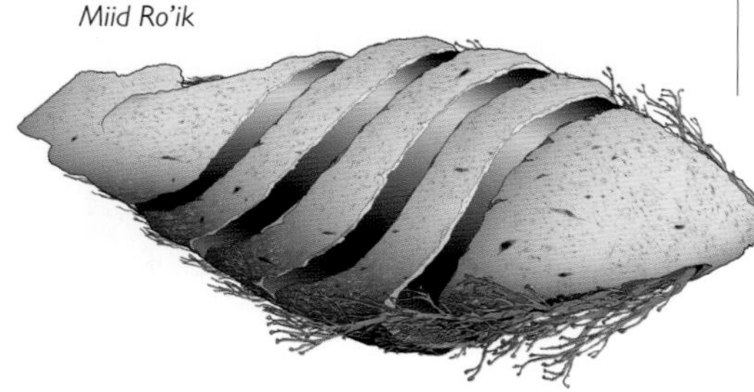

**Migress** A Brolfi who was a member of a guerrilla movement led by Patriot after the Battle of Naboo. Migress was ordered to acquire burst thrusters, which were to be used to create a missile to assassinate Passel Argente and the Brolfi leaders, who were meeting to discuss planetary mining rights.

**mii** A species of trees native to the planet Shelkonwa.

**Miid Ro'ik (warship)** An immense, ovoid warship grown by the Yuuzhan Vong to serve as the standard vessel in their fleet. Measuring some 1,620 meters long, the Miid Ro'ik resembled a striped stone with alternately smooth and rough surfaces. The rough surface of the ship was studded with hundreds of dovin basals and 60 plasma projectors. Emerging from the ship's main body were arms of red and blue coral that acted as docking bays for the coralskippers it transported into battle. The Yuuzhan Vong often fed the organic refuse created from dead warships to their Miid Ro'ik in order to keep the warships alive. When he first encountered the interior of a Miid Ro'ik, Boba Fett likened the experience to being back inside the gut of the Sarlacc.

**Miilarta, Lol** A native of the planet Terephon, she was her planet's ambassador to the Hapes Consortium at the time of the Yuuzhan Vong invasion. When Leia Organa Solo traveled to the Hapes Cluster to enlist the aid of the Hapans in fighting the Yuuzhan Vong, Lol Miilarta voted for the plan.

**m'iiyoom** A white flower native to H'nemthe, this night lily bloomed in the season when all three of the planet's moons gave light. The plant was carnivorous, feeding on creatures that drank its nectar.

**Mika** This young Farghul was leader of the Crimson Nova chapter of the Bounty Hunters' Guild during the last years of the Old Republic. Mika lost her parents when a group of Jedi Knights shut down their family business. Mika's parents had been trafficking in death sticks, and the Jedi had been alerted to their activities. Rather than submitting to arrest, they chose to fight and were killed. Mika never forgave the Jedi, especially the leader of their task force, Mace Windu. When a contract to kill Jedi Knights came in, Mika eagerly accepted despite decades of bounty hunter policy to the contrary. The Jedi proved to be too strong for the members of Crimson Nova, and would have killed them all if Mika had not been stunned into submission by Stroth, who then requested a cease-fire. Mika was eventually succeeded as head of the Crimson Nova by her daughter, Breela.

Mikki

**Mikki** A young boy on Ruusan, he found a lightsaber on a battlefield where a great war between the Jedi and the Sith had taken place. The lightsaber came to life, killing Mikki's two older brothers. As

The results of the Military Creation Act are impossible to ignore.

Mikki's father clutched his surviving son in his arms, Darth Bane appeared and manipulated the lightsaber, killing Mikki before striking down his father. The Dark Lord was intent on killing the children of Ruusan to eliminate any potential Force-sensitives as part of his plan to eliminate all Jedi.

**Miktha** A Jawa who was an associate of Longo Two-Guns. Jabba the Hutt issued a bounty for his capture in connection with a riot that occurred after patrons at a local Podrace purchased exploding chubas, seriously curtailing profits from the sale of normal foodstuffs. The bounty was eventually claimed by Jango Fett, who was on Tatooine trying to arrange a meeting with Jabba.

**Milagro** This planet, located at a key hyperspace junction point, was caught between the factions of the New Republic and the Empire five years after the Battle of Yavin. The New Republic was ultimately victorious, keeping the hyperspace lanes near the planet open. As a result of the conflict, an Imperial Super Star Destroyer was captured and Luke Skywalker was promoted to general.

**Militarists** Old Republic politicians and military leaders who rose to prominence during the years leading up to the Stark Hyperspace Conflict. The Militarists advocated the formation of a strong army and navy to protect the Republic from both internal and external threats. They believed that the Jedi Knights were not a solution, since they did not answer directly to the Republic Senate.

**Military Advisory Council** This body conferred with Chancellor Palpatine during the Clone Wars. The council consisted of Armand Isard, Mas Amedda, Senator Jannie Ha'Nook, and Sate Pestage.

**Military Creation Act** Devised during the years leading up to the Clone Wars, the Military Creation Act allowed the Old Republic to form a Grand Army of the Republic to put a stop to the growing secession movement. It was strongly opposed by Senator Padmé Amidala, who formed the Campaign Against Republic Militarization in an effort to find a peaceful resolution to the problem.

When Senator Amidala was nearly assassinated while arriving on Coruscant for the vote on the act, Palpatine tried to stall the ballot by calling for increased security measures, and many Senators believed the Chancellor had overstepped his bounds. When it was discovered that the Separatists had been secretly assembling a massive droid army on the planet Geonosis, conflict became inevitable. The act was passed when Jar Jar Binks, sitting in for Senator Amidala while she was under the protection of Anakin Skywalker, proposed that Chancellor Palpatine be given emergency powers to deal with the Separatists.

**Military Research and Development Division** A branch of the Adascorp conglomerate formed in the wake of the Great Sith War to provide the Old Republic with artificial musculature for battle droids and injured soldiers. The division's discovery of methods for combining medical prosthetics with droid technologies proved profitable during the Mandalorian Wars.

**military scrip** A form of currency recognized throughout the galaxy, even during the early years of the New Order, and used as the basis for all financial transactions among military agencies.

**milkened tuber** A root vegetable used in many gourmet dishes after the internal seedhusk was removed.

**Milko** A cobbled-together droid bounty hunter active during the Galactic Civil War. He traveled to Dagobah in an effort to hunt down Luke Skywalker after the Empire set a bounty on his head. Luke defeated him in combat, and Milko broke down and begged for mercy. Luke let him go free, knowing that Milko's reputation as a bounty hunter would be tarnished because of his failure. Skywalker also wondered if the whole affair hadn't been a test from Yoda.

**MILL-247-EE (Millie)** An industrial droid that was part of the emergency system on Tem Chesko's cargo hauler. When Chesko's ship was disabled and floated for 61 years through space, he and Millie were constant companions through the years of isolation. Chesko's heart gave out, and Millie operated on Chesko, surgically removing his heart and replacing it with hers. Thus, Chesko survived to eventually reach Tatooine.

**Millavec, Dorin** A scheming Imperial officer who served as deck commander aboard the Star Destroyer *Crucible* during the Galactic Civil War. He hoped to be promoted to the command deck, but when he learned that Nas Ghent had been picked by Darth Vader to train a group of starfighter pilots aboard his ship, Millavec was angry and jealous. He allowed Ghent to go on a mission with real pilots and ordered his pilots to execute Maneuver 717, hoping to eliminate Ghent without any incriminating evidence. Ghent survived, and Millavec lied to him, claiming that it was Vader himself who ordered Maneuver 717 as part of his assignment.

**Millennial, Darth** The order of the Prophets of the Dark Side went back nearly 1,000 years before the Battle of Yavin to the three-eyed mutant Darth Millennial, a Sith Shadow Hand whose instincts drove him to see more sense in Lord Kaan's cutthroat Rule by the Strong than Darth Bane's limiting Rule of Two. Gifted with the ability to foresee the future, Millennial was often at odds with his Sith Master, Darth Cognus. Barely escaping his Master's wrath, Millennial fled to the planet Dromund Kaas. There he meditated on Sith teachings and combined them with the theories of early and pre-Republic thinkers like Plaristes and Dak Ramis. The result was an intricate religion the dark sider called the Dark Force. Hailing himself as a prophet chosen by the will of the Force, Millennial and his religion attracted many Force-users of considerable intelligence, as well as multitudes of naïve Sith cultists. Those who disagreed with the tenets of the Dark Force were labeled heretics and destroyed.

**millennium blossom** An extremely rare plant that grew only on the harsh jungle world of Lemmi VII, it bloomed once every 100 years and died almost as soon as it blossomed. The plant was carnivorous, and ate almost anything.

***Millennium Falcon*** A legendary starship despite its humble origins and deceptively dilapidated exterior, the *Millennium Falcon* factored into some of the Rebel Alliance's greatest victories over the Empire. On the surface, the *Falcon* looked like any other Corellian freighter, with a saucer-shaped primary hull, a pair of forward cargo-gripping mandibles, and a cylindrical cockpit mounted to the ship's side.

Beneath its hull, though, the *Falcon* packed many powerful secrets. Its owners made "special modifications," boosting its speed, shielding, and performance to downright illegal levels. Its weaponry was upgraded to military-class quad laser turrets. To cover rapid escapes, the *Falcon* sported ventrally mounted hatch-concealed anti-personnel repeating

Millennium Falcon

lasers. Between its forward mandibles rested concussion missile launchers. The habitable interior of the vessel also held a few surprises, such as concealed scanner-proof smuggling compartments.

The *Falcon* paid a heavy price for its augmented performance, though. It was extremely recalcitrant and often unpredictable. Its reconditioned hyperdrive often failed. Owner Han Solo sometimes restarted a failed ignition sequence with a hard rap on the bulkhead with his fist. A vessel employed in the shady fringe business of smuggling for quite a while, the *Falcon* was owned by Lando Calrissian before Solo won it in a heated sabacc game. Under Solo's command, the *Falcon* became a famous starship, completing the Kessel Run at unprecedented speeds. Solo and his first mate Chewbacca maintained the *Falcon,* constantly modifying and tinkering with it, coaxing the maximum speed from the ship.

Speed became quite useful as Solo and Chewbacca were drawn deeper into the Rebel cause, and the *Falcon* began flying missions for the Alliance. It was the *Falcon* that provided covering fire for Luke Skywalker's final attack run on the first Death Star. The *Falcon* became Princess Leia Organa's escape transport during the Battle of Hoth. During the decisive Battle of Endor, the *Falcon* flew point for the Alliance fleet. Under Lando Calrissian's command, it soared into the heart of the incomplete Death Star and delivered a missile volley that helped seal the Empire's fate.

The *Falcon* began life as a standard Corellian Engineering Corporation YT-1300 stock light freighter an unknown number of years before the Galactic Civil War. It eventually was won by gambler Lando Calrissian in a sabacc game. During Lando's first year of ownership, he had adventures in the Rafa system, the Oseon belt, and the StarCave of ThonBoka. It was Lando's idea to install hidden cargo sections under the *Falcon*'s deck plates. At this time, the *Falcon* had a pair of smaller blasters located on the bow mandibles. Calrissian and his droid Vuffi Raa also increased the ship's shields. The *Falcon* gained one of its most significant battle scars, a huge tear near its entry ramp, when a Renatasian Confederation starfighter rammed it.

Solo continued the modifications that Calrissian began when the *Falcon* came under his ownership. The ship's armor, armament, and speed were all upgraded. The *Falcon* featured duralloy plating over most of the vital areas of its hull. A set of advanced Kuat Drive Yards, Novaldex, and Nordoxicon shield generators stolen by Solo from the Myomar shipyards provided warship-grade shielding. High-grade sensor suites were tied in to the *Falcon*'s dorsal rectenna sensor dish. Powerful sensor jammers also protected the *Falcon* in combat, although the first time the jammer was tested it disrupted the information relays *inside* the ship.

To reduce his expenses and maintain his privacy, Solo modified the *Falcon* so that most of its major systems could be accessed through the cockpit or the tech station in the forward compartment. The myriad ship-control functions were funneled through what was once a Hanx-Wargel SuperFlow IV computer. It was later modified with three droid brains, something that sometimes caused the *Falcon* to have schizophrenic arguments with itself. The *Falcon*'s interior appeared unkempt, littered with all sorts of mechanical gear. Its central hold had a lounge area with a holographic game table. In addition to hidden cargo holds under its deck plates, it had a cargo-jettison feature. The *Falcon* lacked a bacta tank, so it was equipped with a cryogenic hibernation capsule for emergency medical procedures or the transport of live cargo.

After the Battle of Bakura, the *Falcon* was swapped back and forth between Calrissian and Solo in a series of sabacc matches, with Calrissian winning the ship but opting to give it to Solo as a gift to end the inane series of card games. The *Millennium Falcon* continued to undergo upgrades and modifications. In the years following the births of Solo's three children, he began refitting the *Falcon* and removing some of its more military components in favor of safety and security. The concussion missile launcher was the first weapon removed, making it easier to load and unload cargo. During the struggle to defeat the Yuuzhan Vong, Solo painted the *Falcon* matte black, hoping to make it harder to spot.

The Millennium Falcon's *interior was littered with all sorts of mechanical gear.*

***Millennium Falsehood*** A YT-1300 freighter painted and marked to resemble Han Solo's *Millennium Falcon.* The ship was flown by Wedge Antilles and Chewbacca during a raid on Kidriff 5 in an effort to draw out Warlord Zsinj. Transponder codes were altered just enough to imitate the real ship at first glance. The first mock-up of the *Millennium Falcon* used by Wraith Squadron involved two X-wings with overlapping shields that presented transponder codes appearing to be the *Falcon;* it was convincing enough to draw out Admiral Trigit at Folor.

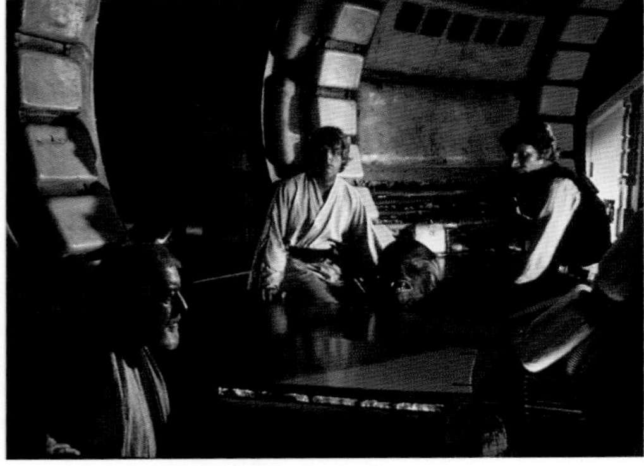
The Millennium Falcon's *holds sometimes hid more than cargo.*

***Millennium Fist*** The name of the starship in a story Han Solo told his four-year-old son, Anakin, shortly before bedtime one night. The story revolved around the exploits of Luke Skywalker's hand after it was cut off by Darth Vader on Bespin's Cloud City. Luke's hand used the ship to escape from Bespin and return to the Rebel Alliance.

***Millennium Hawk*** A small starship created by Millennium Astro-Engineering. It was a spear-headed ship with a large central power core flanked by two sublight drives. It was popular among the smugglers and criminals who hounded the Empire during its expansion across the Outlands region.

**millipod** A red-shelled insect native to the swamps of the planet Kubindi, where it was raised as a food source by the Kubaz.

**Millto, Yor** A slave owner who worked in Mos Espa two years before the Battle of Naboo. Yor Millto owned Amee and her parents, but was barely affected when Amee's mother, Hala, was taken in a slave raid by Krayn.

**Milmit** One of Gorga the Hutt's hired guns, Milmit was the first to discover the *Spirit of Jabba,* but was unable to stop Big Gizz and Spiker from stealing the craft.

**Milnn** A captain in the Imperial Navy, he flew with and led the Delta Squadron of TIE fighters under the command of Admiral Giel during the Galactic Civil War. Captured by Luke Skywalker and Shira Brie just after Admiral Giel captured a teezl, Milnn possessed identification codes that allowed Luke and Shira to infiltrate Giel's armada.

**Milvayne** A planet in the Gyrica system, it was the site of an Imperial base during the Galactic Civil War. Mon Mothma ordered an attack on the garrison by Garm Bel Iblis. He refused because he believed the plan would lead to the deaths of too many soldiers. Mothma relieved him of his duties and Bel Iblis happily agreed, going off to fight the Empire on his own.

**Mimban (Circarpous V)** The fifth planet in the Circarpous system, in the Expansion Region. A cloud-covered jungle world that was largely unexplored, it was orbited by two moons. The planet, formally known as Circarpous V, was never colonized by the Circarpousians, but it was the site of an Imperial energy mining operation. As such, the atmosphere over Mimban was very turbulent. Starships without special hulls faced tremendous danger from the energy storms that streaked the stratosphere. The surface of the planet was dank, and the perpetual mist made it difficult to distinguish night from day. The planet had five makeshift mining towns, all run by Imperials at the height of their operations.

Numerous intelligent species were indigenous to the world, including the "Greenies" and the Coway. The former were green-furred Mimbanite humanoids who had been exploited by the human population. The Coway were gray-furred troglodytes who were powerful warriors. Mimban once had many other species, which all became extinct. One of these was the Thrella, whose members built enormous temples and structures honoring their many gods.

Among Mimban's most dangerous animals was the huge pale worm-like wandrella. The creatures had black eyespots surrounding gaping mouths and were too stupid to be slowed by most attacks. At the time of the Battle of Yavin, Imperial control of Mimban was entrusted to Captain-Supervisor Grammel, who ruled from the Imperial planetary headquarters built into an ancient towering ziggurat. The legendary Kaiburr crystal, rumored to have properties that focused and intensified the Force, was located deep in the jungle in the temple of a minor local god named Pomojema. The powerful crystal rested within a ceremonial statue of the god and was guarded by a sluggish but deadly lizard creature. Soon after the Battle of Yavin, Luke Skywalker, Princess Leia, and the droids R2-D2 and C-3PO crashed on Mimban while traveling to a conference on Circarpous IV. After facing many dangers, including a showdown with Darth Vader, the Rebels were able to retrieve the Kaiburr crystal and leave Mimban.

***Mimban Cloudrider*** A Thyferran bacta tanker captured by Rogue Squadron during one of its raids against Ysanne Isard's bacta cartel. The squadron pulled the crew from the ship, and computer slicers created new identification files indicating that another crew had replaced the original team. The imposters were Mirax Terrik, Corran Horn, Iella Wessiri, Elscol Loro, and Sixtus Quin, all working under various pseudonyms. Their mission was to fly the tanker to Thyferra, take a shuttle to the planet, then hook up with the Ashern Rebels to help overthrow Isard and the Thyferran government under her control.

**mimbrane organism** A creature that was essentially an organic recording device. First a thin, white sheet, the mimbrane consumed the sounds of its surroundings. The more it recorded, the more it swelled up into a pillow shape. No longer than a human finger, the mimbrane had a very small brain, but could be trained to follow a simple set of instructions. Mimbrane organisms grew in huge colonies on one of the Q'nithian system's moons, living deep within the fault and fissures of its rocky surface.

**mime-dancing** *See* nahra.

**mimetic suit** Clothing made from a unique material that changed color to mimic the wearer's surroundings. The clothing was impregnated with specialized circuitry that analyzed the visual elements of the environment and altered the coloring of the cloth.

**mimn'yet** A meat dish of questionable origin, enjoyed by Barabels.

**mimn'yet surgery** A term used by the medical staff of Old Republic forces on Drongar during the Clone Wars to describe their daily work. It referred to a meat dish favored by Barabels, most often enjoyed raw and bleeding.

**mimph** These tiny creatures were native to the Forest Moon of Endor. While not fully sentient, mimphs were nonetheless intelligent, using their cunning to hunt larger prey.

**Mimya** Keyan Farlander's aunt, living on the planet Oorn Tchis. Farlander asked Mimya and her husband Trinn to take care of his sister Kitha following the Imperial invasion of Agamar.

**Mina** This purplish moon orbited the planet Hanchin, in the Moddell sector. It was best known as the site of a Vashan religious retreat at Inicus Mont.

**Minak, Lett** A smuggler who worked for the Empire after the Battle of Endor, Minak was employed by Moff Feleea. He was approached by Moff Relans, who offered him the opportunity to work as a spy. Minak agreed. Outwardly he worked for Feleea aboard his freighter, the *Shadow.* On the side, however, Minak fed Feleea false information given to him by Moff Relans. Minak received protection from both Moffs, ensuring his own safety and a regular income.

**Minch** A Jedi Knight of the same species as Yoda and Yaddle, Minch served the Jedi Order some 700 years before the Battle of Yavin. Minch and several other newly commissioned Jedi Knights were dispatched to the Bpfassh system, where a Bpfasshi Dark Jedi terrorized the population. Minch confronted the Dark Jedi but was no match for his formidable skills. However, Minch's Jedi Master, a Zabrak named T'dai, arrived to corner the Dark Jedi, who took his own life rather than be captured. The Dark Jedi's Master escaped and fled to Dagobah, and Minch took a starfighter and chased him down against the orders of Master T'dai. Minch managed to defeat the Bpfasshi Master in a cave on the planet, and the Dark Jedi's tainted blood seeped into the ground and imbued the planet with dark side energy.

**Mindemir** The primary world in the Mindemir system and a member of the Old Republic. Jenna Zan Arbor planned to use the water supply of Mindemir in her experiments, but she was blocked from doing so by the laws of the Senate. In a daring move, Senator Uta S'orn proposed lifting the laws, ostensibly in the name of saving lives on other worlds, and then falsified Senate records to ensure that the measure was ratified.

**Minder** A slang term used to describe Old Republic physicians who were also empaths, and worked to ensure the mental and emotional well-being of their patients. Minders found a particular niche during the Clone Wars, helping patients as well as doctors handle the stresses of ongoing conflict and death.

**mind evaporator** The Basic translation of a Wookiee term for any addictive holoentertainment that lacked any kind of educational purpose.

**Mindharp** A fabled magical talisman considered the most valuable of the Treasures of the Sharu. The Mindharp was a meter-long tool shaped like a fork and hidden in the Great Pyramid on Rafa V, awaiting the emergence of the Bearer and Emissary. According to legend, the Mindharp was the tool that the Toka could use to recall the Sharu. It was said that the Mindharp would call the Sharu back to aid the Toka in an emergency. However, the true purpose of the Mindharp was to unlock the hidden knowledge of the Sharu and reestablish their intelligence networks, hidden eons before when they were frightened by a superior power. The Mindharp was pursued by Lando Calrissian and

Mohs during the early years of the New Order, after Lando was set up by *Ottdefa* Osuna Whett to be the Bearer. They ultimately recovered the Mindharp, but Duttes Mer took possession and was supposed to provide the artifact to the Tund Sorcerer Rokur Gepta. However, Mer activated the Mindharp himself, setting off cataclysmic changes in the Rafa system that destroyed the life-orchards and restored the intelligence of the Toka, bringing about the restoration of the Sharu civilization.

**Mindor** This planet was the site of a battle pitting General Luke Skywalker and his New Republic troops against the Imperial forces of Lord Shadowspawn more than a year after the Battle of Endor. The Imperials fought to the death, and General Skywalker deeply regretted the incredible loss of life. Six months later, Luke resigned his commission with the New Republic.

**mind prison** An unusual, box-shaped device believed to have been created by the ancient Rakatan people. Outwardly, it resembled a cargo crate, but when improperly opened the mind prison took control of the opener's mind and drew him or her inside. Within the room was a Rakata who challenged the victim to answer a series of riddles. The Rakata was long dead, with his mind trapped in the room, and the only way he could get out was to take over another being's body. Thus, if the victim failed to answer the questions correctly, the Rakata took control of his or her body and attempted an escape.

**mind-rub** *See* memory rub.

***Minds and Perceptions: A Comparative Study of Persuasive Techniques During the Galactic Civil War*** A work that described, in detail, the various methods used by the Empire, the Corporate Sector Authority, and the Rebel Alliance to extract information from captives. It was written by Ulm-Aaa-Janzikek and published by Triplanetary Press.

**mind-touch** A technique used by UnuThul to contact huge numbers of Killiks at one time. The mind-touch was based on the communication abilities of the various hives of the Colony, and was augmented by the use of the Force.

**mindwipe** A term for the complete erasure of a droid's memory, often used by automata themselves since it implied that a droid's computer memory was actually a mind, and not a piece of technology.

**mind-witch** A unique humanoid species with intense mental abilities. A mind-witch could lure others close, then probe their minds to find out what they liked and desired. The mind-witch could then leach the victims' mental and life energies to replenish his or her own energies.

**minelayer** Any starship designed to deploy space mines around a specific target or location. These ships were often given improved stealth technology to avoid discovery by regular sensor sweeps. Minelayers were equipped with specialized hyperdrive systems that allowed them to quickly jump to supralight speeds and then drop back into realspace.

***Minelayer*** An Imperial ETR-3 escort transport destroyed by the Azzameen family during its attempt to acquire a spy satellite shortly before the Battle of Endor.

***Mine Mine Mine*** The name of Rufus Trammel's personal star yacht.

Callista "Ming"

**Miner, Pillon** He was among the slaves captured by the Yuuzhan Vong and forced to work aboard the dhuryam seedship controlled by Ch'Gang Hool shortly after the Battle of Coruscant. Miner suffered massive injuries when he mistakenly wandered into a grove of immature amphistaffs. He failed to realize that the young creatures were just as dangerous as the mature adults, and was viciously attacked. Jacen Solo tried to save him, but his injuries were too severe.

**mineral exploiter** Starships developed by the Hutts under the auspices of the Orko SkyMine corporation, they were designed to process ore found in asteroids. The huge, boxy ships were simply cargo carriers connected to mouth-like scoops equipped to sift precious ore to send for processing. Exploiters were designed by Bevel Lemelisk, who was captured by Durga the Hutt for the purpose of designing a superweapon the Hutts could use to control the galaxy. Lemelisk at first designed them too well, for the first two devoured each other.

**Miners' Guildhall** Located in Tel Boillin, this was the primary meeting place for the geode miners who worked on the planet Endregaad during the early years of the New Order.

***Minestra*** A Rendili StarDrive light corvette that was part of Drea Renthal's pirate fleet. Renthal's distinctive blazing-claw insignia was obvious on both sides of the ship. The *Minestra,* along with the *Too Late Now,* destroyed the *Vigilance* during the early hours of the Battle of Nar Shaddaa.

**"Ming," Callista** A Jedi Knight from Chad III, she grew up with her family on an ocean ranch, migrating on the Algic Current with the herds of tsaelke. Discovered at a late age by the maverick Jedi Master Djinn Altis, Callista agreed to train with him at his facility on Bespin and later aboard his personal training ship, the newly christened *Chu'unthor.* During training she met a fellow Jedi named Geith, who became her lover. They accepted an assignment to intercept and disable the *Eye of Palpatine,* but were unable to completely eliminate the threat of the ship. Callista stayed behind to try to disable the ship while Geith sought more help. Geith was killed during his escape attempt, and Callista sacrificed her physical body in order to leave her Force aura in the ship's automated firing computer, preventing it from firing on innocent beings.

Years later, when Luke Skywalker, Cray Mingla, and Nichos Marr rediscovered the *Eye of Palpatine,* Callista fired on them, thinking that they were Imperial troops come to recover the ship. Irek Ismaren had activated the ship's remote controls through the Force, re-initiating its original mission. Callista sensed Luke's strong Force presence when he came on board. Over time, the two Jedi fell in love. When Mingla decided to stay behind with Marr and detonate the ship, she gave Callista her own physical body.

Callista escaped the *Eye of Palpatine* with Skywalker in Mingla's body, but she could no longer touch the Force. Luke comforted her, and both of them tried everything to help her regain her Force sensitivity, but she only succeeded in finding the dark side. She vowed that if the dark side were all she could touch, she wanted nothing to do with the Force.

When the Jedi academy on Yavin 4 was attacked by Admiral Daala's fleet, Callista set out to strike a blow against the Empire. She commandeered a TIE bomber and landed it on the *Knight Hammer,* quickly sabotaging the ship's complement of TIE bombers by detonating their payloads and ripping out the Super Star Destroyer's engines. She confronted Daala to try to kill her, allowing the dark side to wash over her. The *Knight Hammer* plunged into the core of Yavin. Callista wasn't killed when the ship exploded, however, and later fled to try and recover her powers by herself.

As she drifted across the galaxy, Callista eventually came to Nam Chorios, a world drenched in the power of the Force, a phenomenon brought about by the living crystals on the planet. She joined the Theran cultists of the planet, meditating on the Force even though she was not able to touch it. The isolationist cultists also operated the gun stations that effectively quarantined the world by preventing anyone from landing or departing Nam Chorios. When Seti Ashgad, leader of the anti-Theran Rationalist Party, contacted Chief of State Leia Organa Solo to establish diplomatic relations, Callista attempted to warn Leia to stay away from the world. The Chief of State did not heed the warnings, and found herself kidnapped by Ashgad. Callista returned from hiding to thwart Ashgad's schemes. It was at this time that Luke Skywalker, who was searching for Callista, finally found her again. But after only a single wordless look, they knew that any chance of their lives continuing together was gone.

Mingula

**Mingla, Cray** A student at Luke Skywalker's Jedi academy, along with her partner Nichos Marr, Mingla was a beautiful scientist who was an expert in artificial intelligence. When Marr was struck with a fatal disease, she undertook a crash plan to transfer his mind, his intelligence, and—if possible—his very essence into a near-human but artificial body. Along with Skywalker, Mingla and Marr were swept up into the reawakened Imperial battlemoon, the *Eye of Palpatine.* After a series of near disasters, Mingla and Marr sacrificed their lives to destroy the dangerous spacecraft. But Mingla did it with a twist. At the last possible moment she enabled the essence of Callista, a bodiless Jedi whose spirit was trapped in the battlemoon's gunnery computer system, to pass into her body, which was then jettisoned from the *Eye of Palpatine* and reunited with Callista's new love, Luke Skywalker.

***Mingula*** Boba Fett encountered this *ZZ*-class freighter adrift in space while taking a routine bounty to Coruscant. Sensors revealed no life aboard, but its automated distress signal continued to operate. Fett investigated the *Mingula* and found that the holds contained a treasure trove of riches, including the sarcophagus of Volpau. The crew was dead, their bodies covered with the breeding sacs of carnivorous Ubuugan fleshborers, which then burst forth when the bodies were disturbed by Fett's prisoner, Tsumo. Fett was forced to use his flamethrowers to escape alive, and the resulting fire and explosion destroyed everything on board, including most of Volpau's funerary effects. Fett managed to keep the ceremonial crown, however, which more than covered the loss of the bounty on Tsumo.

**MiniMag** A shoulder-mounted proton torpedo launcher produced by Krupx before the Clone Wars, it remained in production for many decades. Adaptor kits for the MiniMag allowed it to accept other projectile weapons, and the changeover could be completed quickly on the battlefield. The MiniMag was one of many Clone Wars–era weapons later used by stormtroopers of the Empire.

**minimum safe distance** A point in space from which a ship could safely make a jump into hyperspace, usually defined as the point at which a planet's gravity well no longer could interfere with the hyperdrive's cutout systems.

**Mining Corps** A branch of the Empire created to locate and obtain the raw materials and natural resources required to support its immense manufacturing needs. Laborers who toiled in the Mining Corps came from a number of sources, including slaves and individuals who had flunked out of the Imperial Academy.

**mining droid** Large, stocky droids used as collectors in the spice mines of Kessel.

**Mining Guild** Based on Coruscant, this quasi-political body controlled much of the mining throughout the galaxy during the last decades of the Old Republic and into the era of the New Order. It was originally formed in the early days of space exploration, and might have predated the formation of the Old Republic. In the wake of the Clone Wars, Emperor Palpatine seduced the guild's officers into aligning themselves with the Empire, solidifying his sources of raw materials for the Imperial war machine while allowing the guild to remain "independent."

**mining remote** *See* mineral exploiter.

**Minions of Xendor** Han Solo often used the expression "by the Minions of Xendor" when he was surprised by something. It referred to those beings that supported the ancient Kashi Mer exile and former Jedi Knight Xendor during the First Great Schism.

**mini rail cannon** A small, high-powered weapon produced by Rika/Moab during the last decades of the Old Republic, it was an upgrade to the weapons systems of a combat droid.

**Ministry Council** A Senatorial council of the New Republic government that managed the day-to-day operations of the Republic's various ministries.

**Ministry of Defense and Offense** The primary governmental body charged with the protection of the citizens of Delaluna during the decades leading up to the Clone Wars.

**Ministry of Industry** A primary branch of the government of the Tion Hegemony during the early years of the New Order. Like much of the Tion Hegemony during this time, the Ministry of Industry was unable to keep up with the demands of the modern galaxy. Ministry officers fell woefully behind, allowing unscrupulous corporations to take advantage. Mining permits were issued, but the ministry lacked the personnel to investigate the operations. This allowed the corporations enough time to strip a planet of its natural resources and abandon it before the ministry could apprehend them.

**Ministry of Justice** The governmental building on Coruscant that held the offices of the Galactic Alliance's primary judicial and legal branches in the years following the Yuuzhan Vong War. Built near the new Jedi Temple, the Ministry of Justice shared a common entryway with that structure.

**Minka** A feline humanoid, she was a Rebel Alliance starfighter pilot in the Cantros system during the last days of the Galactic Civil War. She was one of a handful of pilots who survived the Empire's attack on Cantros, and was stunned to learn that the Emperor had been defeated at Endor.

**Minkring** A planet in the Shelsha sector, it was one of just two sector worlds that maintained an Imperial garrison during the early stages of the Galactic Civil War.

**min min lights** Mysterious sparks of light that appeared in the late dawn and early dusk on the edge of the Doaba Badlands on the planet Socorro.

**Minnau, Teckla** A server at the Varykino resort in Naboo's Lake Country before the Clone Wars. Minnau assisted with the arrangements when Padmé Amidala arrived at her retreat with Anakin Skywalker. Padmé trusted her to keep secrets, and later told her of her marriage to Anakin.

**Minnisiat** A trade language developed by the species that inhabited the area of the Unknown Regions closest to Csilla. The use of Minnisiat allowed these disparate beings to communicate with one another.

**Minnix** A noted Trandoshan drug dealer who worked from a base on Nar Shaddaa. In addition to selling common drugs, Minnix also dealt in tempest spice, which kept him relatively rich while ensuring that his own addiction to tempest was satisfied. Minnix spent much of his time in Kuzbar's Cantina, waiting for his clients to approach him. He purchased his spice from a number of dealers at the Dark Melody tapcaf.

**Minntooine** An aquatic planet loyal to the Confederacy of Independent Systems during the Clone Wars. Much of its population was made up of Quarren radicals who were exiled from their homeworld of Mon Calamari.

**Minos Cluster** Located on the edge of the known galaxy, beyond which there are no star charts, the worlds of the Minos Cluster were isolated, resulting in a region populated by fringe members of society. Mara Jade and Talon Karrde traveled to the Minos Cluster on an errand.

*Teckla Minnau*

**M'ins, Tra's** A Jedi Master of some renown, M'ins was best known for resolving the Duinuogwuin–Gotal Conflict with the help of Jorus C'baoth.

**minshal** A large creature grown by the Yuuzhan Vong for its shell. Once discarded by the minshal, the shell was used as a form of temporary shelter. On Bimmiel, slaves were housed in a minshal village.

**Minstrel** The call sign used by Ulaha Kore during the Jedi Knights' attempt to kill the voxyn queen at Myrkr.

**Minx, Lunae** A Twi'lek female, she was a regular at the Outlander Club during the last decades of the Old Republic. She was distinguished by her purple-mottled skin, which was considered quite rare among her species. She was a known acquaintance of Ayy Vida and Achk Med-Beq.

*Lunae Minx*

**Mipps, Deena** A reporter for the Darpa SectorNet news agency, Deena Mipps was a perky and immensely popular noblewoman-turned-newsnet-reporter who secretly led a Rebel cell on Esseles.

**Mira (1)** A bounty hunter and scout active in the years after the Great Sith War, she didn't believe in killing to collect a bounty and used lethal force only in self-defense. As a young girl, she was taken as a slave during the Mandalorian Wars, and then raised and trained as a Mandalorian. When she was 14, her adoptive parents were killed during the Battle of Malachor, and she ended up as a refugee on Nar Shaddaa. With her knack for finding people, Mira became a bounty hunter. After the Jedi Civil War, she was among the hunters who went to work for the mysterious criminal kingpin Goto, hunting down surviving Jedi Knights. She later joined a group that traveled with the Jedi Exile, who recognized that Mira had a connection to the Force and agreed to take her on as a student.

**Mira (2)** One of the many Jedi Knights who felt that the Jedi Order had become too militaristic during the early years of the Clone Wars. Mira was originally trained by Master Sora Bulq, and she remained loyal to the Weequay during the escalation of the conflict. After openly refusing to accept the rank of general, she left the Order to follow Bulq to Ruul to protest the Jedi participation in the war. Mira felt a disturbance in the Force when her Master was attacked by Asajj Ventress, and she rushed to help him. She was no match for Ventress's skills, and was quickly killed in battle.

**Miradyne Limited** A small manufacturer of starship avionics packages, the company went out of business during the New Order.

**Mirage** The code name for the headquarters of the New Republic Intelligence agency, buried deep below the surface of Coruscant in the Abyss. It was so named because a large-leafed plant grew in a corner of the headquarters, without sunlight, giving the impression of an oasis in an otherwise sterile environment.

***Mirage*** One of two disguised starfighters used by Manda D'ulin's team of Mistryl Shadow Guards.

**Miraluka** A humanoid species native to Alpheridies. Miraluka were born without eyes but could see through the Force. Where their eyes would have been, they had featureless eye sockets that they preferred to cover with decorative cloth. Millennia before the Galactic Civil War, many Miraluka were renowned Jedi Knights. The most famous such Jedi was Shoaneb Culu, who helped quell the Freedon Nadd Uprising and fought in the Sith War.

***Mird'ika*** One of Walon Vau's affectionate nicknames for his pet strill, known to most other beings as Lord Mirdalan. The nickname meant "little Mird" when translated into Basic.

**Mirgoshir system** An Outer Rim system in the Lahara sector that allied itself with the Confederacy of Independent Systems in the months leading up to the Clone Wars. Agamar was located in the system, and its planets were sites of ongoing battles between the Separatists and Republic forces.

**Mirialan** A species of near-humans native to Mirial, a cold desert planet just off the Hydian Way between Yavin and Almania. Mirialans were religious and adhered to a primitive understanding of the Force. They believed each individual's actions contributed to his or her destiny, and they placed unique tattoos on their faces and hands to signify their completion of specific tests and tasks. As they matured, their tattoos naturally increased in number, allowing other Mirialans to quickly know what role they would play in the culture. The Jedi Barriss Offee and Luminara Unduli were Mirialans.

**Mirit system** Located near the Pyria and Venjagga systems at the edge of the Galactic Core, Mirit contained the planet Ord Mirit, the site of a former Imperial base.

**Mirror Caverns** A global park established by the government of Telos during the Old Republic. Located near the Sacred Pools, the Mirror Caverns were named for the reflective mineral malab that covered their walls with mirror-like surfaces.

**mirror illusion** A technique developed by the Fallanassi that used the Force to make another being unable to see something right in front of his or her eyes.

**Mirshaf** A planet with an ancient culture revered in the galaxy. Captain Dorja, serving under Grand Admiral Thrawn, was connected to the culture and used its victory gestures in battle.

**Mirx** A New Republic Navy commodore who was placed in command of Task Forces Gemstone and Copperleaf during the battle against the Yevetha.

***Misanthrope*** A cargo ship commanded by Kevreb Bebo, it crashed into D'vouran when the planet suddenly appeared in its flight path. Bebo managed to set the ship down with moderate damage, and his distress call was intercepted by the Empire. To cover up the true nature of D'vouran, the Empire blamed the crash on the pilot. Many crew members were reported as killed in the crash, when in reality they had been consumed by the planet.

**Misch'an** A Rebel Alliance starfighter pilot who did not survive the offensive against Operation Strike Fear at Briggia.

**Miser** The innermost planet of the Bespin system, it lacked atmosphere but was rich in valuable metals. Miser's powerful magnetic field interfered with most electronic equipment. It was heavily mined for raw materials during the construction of Bespin's Cloud City, and deep craters lined its surface. Inhospitable temperature extremes made the mining hazardous; hardy Ugnaughts were needed to staff the operation. The mines were later abandoned and became infested with mynocks.

Miser was frequently used as a hideout by smugglers and pirates. It was also the site of a hidden Imperial base after the Battle of Yavin. Lord Ecclessis Figg, the founder of Cloud City, once proposed a rolling mining center that could stay permanently on the cooler side of Miser, which was always in shadows. It was never built, but it provided the inspiration for Lando Calrissian's Nomad City mining operation on Nkllon.

**misery-guts** An expression used by clone troopers to indicate any leader who fretted over situations, wondering how to handle them by the book.

**mishalope** Striped, fur-covered mammals that once thrived in the mountains near the Grand Falls on Firrerre, until the planet was nearly destroyed by the Empire.

**Mishra, The** A tapcaf located in Ilic on New Cov during the early years of the New Republic. Luke Skywalker intervened in a dispute between a

*Mira, a bounty hunter and scout*

Barabel and a Rodian in The Mishra, and made something of a fool of Niles Ferrier. Ferrier later called Lando Calrissian and Han Solo to The Mishra, using Luke's name, to discuss a possible contact for locating the *Katana* fleet.

**Miskara** The leader of the Vagaari fleet and people, the Miskara demanded complete loyalty from his officers and personnel, and visitors or supplicants were not allowed to speak in the Miskara's presence unless spoken to first. Five years after the Battle of Naboo, the Miskara was surprised to find a human, Jorj Car'das, asking for an audience. Unknown to the Miskara, the visit was part of a larger plot by Force Commander Thrawn to lure the Vagaari into a trap. The Miskara reacted to the notion that the Chiss would start using battle droids in their fight against the Vagaari, and set in motion a plan to attack the Chiss first. This brought the Vagaari fleet directly into the Chiss trap, which was also set up to capture Outbound Flight. Quickly, the Miskara and his entire crew were killed, leaving the Vagaari leaderless and unable to coordinate their activities.

**Missa, Lena** A young Chagrian student at the Jedi Temple on Coruscant during the years leading up to the Clone Wars. With her strong connection to the Force, Lena Missa was quickly chosen as a Padawan. After her Master was killed at the Battle of Geonosis, Missa was without a teacher, but many Masters wanted to take the gifted girl as their apprentice.

**missile deactivation transmitter** A countermeasure technology developed by the Galactic Alliance military during the years following the Swarm War. Specialized transmitters were capable of detecting the frequencies used to guide enemy missiles and warheads, allowing the device to send a deactivation signal to the missile before it struck a Galactic Alliance warship.

**Mission, the** The term used to describe the events surrounding the task force assigned to destroy the Yuuzhan Vong voxyn production facility at Myrkr. The Jedi who undertook the Mission trained under Jedi Master Luke Skywalker and included Jaina, Jacen, and Anakin Solo, along with Tesar Sebatyne, Lowbacca, Zekk, Tahiri Veila, and Raynar Thul. Although the Mission ultimately succeeded in destroying the voxyn queen, Anakin Solo sacrificed his life to save his brother, and many other Jedi were killed in battle. The survivors of the Mission were changed by it, since they used the battle-meld technique to help themselves survive, creating an unusual telepathy among them.

**Mission Commander** The ruling member of the Survivor group on Dellalt, his primary duty was to maintain the beacon that sent word of their existence to the High Command, in the hope that one day the High Command would return to Dellalt to open the vaults of Xim the Despot. Over time, the Survivors began to wonder if the beacon was reaching far enough into space, and the Mission Commander began making blood sacrifices to help augment the beacon's strength.

**Missira** An elderly Tarasin and one of the first of her kind to attend the Almas Academy after a great deal of debate over whether or not a Tarasin would be able to live outside the tribe. Missira succeeded at her training and eventually became a Jedi Knight, as well as the Mother of the small population of Tarasin attending the Academy.

**Miss Mylla's Saloon** A cantina operated by the Falleen Miss Mylla, who worked as a courtesan on the planet Lamaredd. Miss Mylla's was the largest and most popular saloon in the area.

**Missur, Mas** A Jedi who served as a general in the Grand Army of the Republic, leading the 35th Infantry into the assault on the city of Eyat on Gaftikar.

**Miss Vix** The name of the Vjun fox that Whirry Malreaux kept as a pet and familiar. Count Dooku used Miss Vix to get Malreaux to do his bidding, threatening to torture the fox.

**Mist** A bounty hunter known to be both violent and capable, although very rarely seen in public. Mist began working in the Kathol sector shortly before the Battle of Endor, but was driven underground by the appearance of Moff Sarne. Mist encountered an alien construct deep within the Kathol Rift, and soon discovered a piece of the DarkStryder technology, learning how to control a DarkStryder fire creature. He attempted to defeat the crew of the *FarStar* with this newfound power, but was forced to flee. During the Battle of Kathol, Mist was discovered to be the actress Shella Inion, who believed that the Rebel Alliance was responsible for the deaths of her family. When Jessa Dajus revealed that it was Moff Sarne himself who had killed her family, Mist switched allegiances and joined the New Republic to help defeat Sarne.

**Mistal** A member of royalty on Dargul, she held the title of Duchess during the early years of the New Republic. At marrying age, she began a widespread search for the perfect mate. All candidates had their credentials entered into a computer, and she decided to marry the individual that the computer chose. Dack sabotaged the results in order to marry into Duchess Mistal's wealth. Unfortunately for Dack, Mistal couldn't bear to be away from him, and offered a million-credit reward for his return after Dack fled to Umgul. Lando Calrissian apprehended Dack, who was living under the alias of Tymmo, at a blob race. Mistal was grateful to Lando from that point on, and the credits from her reward helped finance his takeover of the spice mines of Kessel.

*Mistal (left) with Dack (Tymmo)*

**Mistflier, Dusque** A bioengineer, she worked for the Empire during the New Order era. Her dedication was shattered when her partner, Tendau Nandon, was arrested and executed on suspicion of being a Rebel Alliance sympathizer. Mistflier then set out to join the Alliance, taking on a mission to Dantooine with Finn Darktrin to recover a holocron containing the names and locations of hundreds of Alliance agents. She discovered it hidden in the ashen remains of a campfire, inexplicably located hundreds of feet belowground, at the site of an ancient Jedi training compound. Her elation at finding the holocron was matched by her growing affection for Darktrin. As they were returning to Alliance headquarters, Mistflier was shattered to discover that Darktrin was an Imperial agent. He managed to send off a small portion of the holocron's contents before Mistflier grabbed it and ejected it into space. Darktrin stabbed her in the chest, then blasted away in an escape pod. Dusque Mistflier was rescued by Luke Skywalker.

**mist-horn** A spiral horn hollowed out for use as a musical instrument. The Jedi Master Tionne also used a mist-horn as the handle for her lightsaber.

***Mist Hunter*** Zuckuss's personal starship, it was specially commissioned by the bounty hunter and a group of Gand venture capitalists. The ship used combat cloud car repulsorlift technology; it had room for eight passengers and a metric ton of cargo. It was manufactured by Byblos Drive Yards.

**mistmaker** A creature native to the planet Msst, it was a large, pink, gelatinous cloud that floated through the jungles, catching unsuspecting prey in tentacles that hung from its body. If destroyed, a mistmaker would explode, showering its attacker with caustic pieces of gelatin that bored into exposed flesh. Mistmakers were resilient enough to withstand blasterfire.

**mist patrol** A small Hapan naval force that patrolled the boundaries of the Transitory Mists looking for intruders following the Yuuzhan Vong War. In the wake of the Battle of Kuat and the Second Battle of Fondor, the Mist Patrol agreed to help keep the Jedi base on Shedu Maad a secret, and passed on any information about unknown starships that were discovered nearby.

**Mistress Dragon** The name given by Jacen Solo to the huge, lizard-like creature Hethrir used as a guardian

for the Empire Youth camp. Jacen's increasing ability to converse with animals helped him convince Mistress Dragon to help the children escape from the compound.

**Mistress Mnemos** A computer system maintained by the Rebel Alliance as an intergalactic database, it was housed in an underground chamber at the Obroa-skai branch library on the safeworld of Fusai. C-3PO was able to interface with Mnemos to gather information on Blackhole during the Galactic Civil War. Mistress Mnemos required that any being making inquiries of her memory bank follow set procedures and omit any irrelevant or unnecessary details. Mnemos's memory banks were believed to be extensive, but only as good as the data given. Much of the information on Luke Skywalker's family history, for example, was misleading or wrong.

**Mistryl Shadow Guards** The last heroes of the Mistryls, the Shadow Guards were a cult of warrior women who said they fought against injustices imposed by the Empire. During the Clone Wars, however, the government of Emberlene had allied itself with the Separatists, and then the Empire. Through that latter allegiance the government got the military resources to expand its sphere of control, invading and plundering neighboring planets. Those planets eventually banded together, hired mercenaries, and staged a devastating revolt that destroyed most of Emberlene. The natives who survived rewrote history and blamed the Empire for the destruction of their homeworld. This new history claimed that the Shadow Guards were created to exact revenge on the Empire. Most never knew that the Empire had nothing to do with the devastation of the planet, and the Shadow Guards basically became a small band of mercenaries themselves. Mara Jade recruited the Mistryls to aid in the liberation of Kessel. In addition, several members got involved in the secret Hammertong project.

**Misty Falls Clan** Force-sensitive witches native to the planet Dathomir, they used the light side of the Force. They lived on the banks of a tributary of the Frenzied River near the Misty Falls.

**misura** A vine known for its ability to grow quickly to incredible lengths, even in the most arid of environments. When it died, the drying fibers of the misura vine curled into loose balls, forming large, brittle spheres. Misura balls were often seen rolling across desert expanses, blown by dry winds.

**Mit, N'haz** Boba Fett tracked Mit to the planet Necropolis, where he killed him. A week later, Fett learned that Mit still lived, and he returned to Necropolis to kill him again.

**Mithel, Mauler** One of Darth Vader's wingmates during the Battle of Yavin, Mauler Mithel flew Black 2.

**Mithel, Rejlii** Mauler Mithel's son, he was an Imperial ensign and tractor beam operator aboard the *Chimaera*. Mithel was promoted to lieutenant by Grand Admiral Thrawn for his efforts in trying to break Luke Skywalker's covert shroud maneuver, then assigned him the task of developing a way to counteract the maneuver in the future.

**Mithipsin** One of Belsavis's natural volcanic rift valleys.

**Mithric, Thann** A Falleen Jedi Knight trained by Luke Skywalker after the Yuuzhan Vong War. When Thrackan Sal-Solo threatened to pull the Corellian system out of the Galactic Alliance, Mithric joined Jaina Solo and Zekk on a mission to infiltrate the city of Coronet and capture Five Worlds Prime Minister Aidel Saxan. The Jedi Order eventually cut its ties to the Galactic Alliance, and Mithric was chosen to be part of a team that would infiltrate Coruscant and capture or eliminate Jacen Solo. Although mission leader Kyle Katarn was badly injured, the rest of the Jedi managed to hold Jacen at bay. Solo attacked Mithric, who was not prepared, and one defensive parry injured his chest. In the brief second it took for him to register the injury, Mithric saw Solo swing his lightsaber in a powerful arc to sever Mithric's head from his body.

**Mitsun, Creed** The crew foreman at the Fondor shipyards, Mitsun and his team were refitting the Star Destroyer *Amerce* when Fondor was attacked by the Yuuzhan Vong. Mitsun's crew was killed by the suicide run of an alien coralskipper.

**Mitt'swe'kleoni** A Chiss who traveled to Coruscant to meet with Cal Omas and Jedi Master Luke Skywalker. Known by his core name of Tswek, he was concerned with the apparent defection of many Jedi Knights who had traveled into the Unknown Regions. These Jedi, led by Jaina Solo and Lowbacca, helped the Colony repel any Chiss ships that wandered into their territory, and Tswek demanded that they be recalled.

**mixerbot** An automaton programmed to tend bar, it was also known as a robo-bartender.

**MixRMastR** A Cybot Galactica robo-bartender series, the MixRMastR was bolted to a table or counter. Vaguely humanoid in stature, the MixRMastR was connected to a network of tubes that were in turn connected to all kinds of beverage dispensers. The MixRMastR could create an incredible variety of concoctions. Once Cybot realized that many establishments could not afford to place a MixRMastR at every table, it produced a repulsor-equipped model that could float through a room and serve drinks.

*MixRMastR*

*MLC-3*

**Miywondl** One of many deities in the mythology of the Gwurran, Miywondl was the god who controlled the wind. Because the wind never stopped blowing on Ansion, it was believed that Miywondl was the most powerful of all the Gwurran deities.

**Miza** A Chiss who was part of the squadron assembled for Jagged Fel's fact-finding mission to the New Republic shortly before the Battle of Coruscant. When Fel decided that the best way to gather information was to assist the Republic in its struggle against the Yuuzhan Vong, Miza and his fellow pilots agreed to stay. Miza joined the Twin Suns Squadron and was known as Twin Suns Eight during his time with the Republic.

After Coruscant fell and the Republic's forces regrouped on Mon Calamari, Miza accompanied Jaina Solo and her parents on a mission to reestablish communications to parts of the galaxy that had been cut off. They discovered that the planet N'zoth and the Yevetha had been destroyed by the Yuuzhan Vong, and Miza broke off to investigate a transmission from a nearby moon. The last surviving Yevethan warrior had crashed on the moon, and was waiting for the Yuuzhan Vong to find him. Although Miza was not hunting him, the Yevetha refused to be rescued. He set his ship to self-destruct, and Miza's clawcraft was caught in the blast, killing him instantly.

**Mizobon Spaceport** A civilian spaceport built on the planet Coruscant following the Yuuzhan Vong War.

**MK221** A silver-plated attendant droid who served the N'Vaari family for five generations, she was owned by Brinaloy N'Vaari during the New Order. Known as Emmy-Kaye to the family, MK221 was programmed to be a nanny and personal assistant.

**M'Kae, Warrant Officer** A signal officer aboard the *Avenger* responsible for reporting activities to the *Executor.*

**M'kim** A young thranta rider, he was training to join one of the foremost troupes on Cloud City at the time Lando Calrissian and Cojahn were creating SkyCenter Galleria. When Jacen Solo, Tenel Ka, and Lowbacca were ambushed and Solo fell from the bottom of Cloud City, M'kim, who was out practicing, rescued him.

*Sora Mobari comforted by Anakin Skywalker*

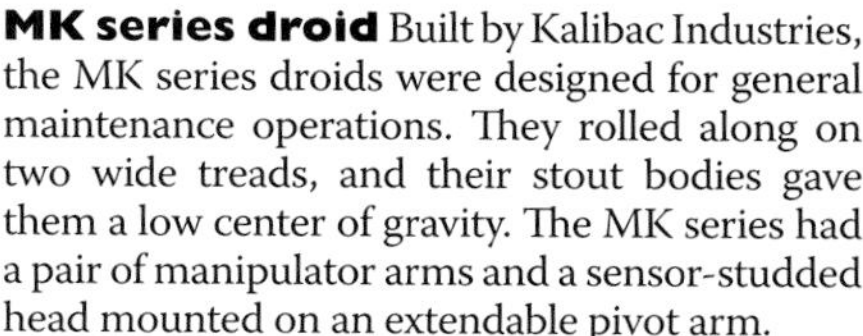

**MK series droid** Built by Kalibac Industries, the MK series droids were designed for general maintenance operations. They rolled along on two wide treads, and their stout bodies gave them a low center of gravity. The MK series had a pair of manipulator arms and a sensor-studded head mounted on an extendable pivot arm.

**MLC-3** A small, one-person vehicle that moved on heavy treads, it was armed with a pair of medium repeating blaster cannons. These vehicles were designed for perimeter defense, allowing teams of security agents using MLC-3s to patrol the terrain surrounding a main facility. They were used by the Rebel Alliance on Hoth.

**Mluki** Humanoids who were simian in appearance, they lived on the planet Belsavis in the rift valley domes. They matured rapidly, reaching adolescence at 7 years and old age at 30.

**MM-9** Powerful, portable missiles that were produced for use in backpack- and shoulder-mounted projectile launchers after the Yuuzhan Vong War. They were as destructive as they were expensive, which served to limit their use.

**MM9** A wrist-mounted rocket-launching system produced during the last decades of the Old Republic. These launchers fired a variety of tiny warheads. Boba Fett used them in his upgraded Mandalorian battle armor.

**MMR-9** A recovery droid developed by Imik Suum for SoroSuub during the final years of the Old Republic. Modeled after immense construction droids, the MMR-9 was capable of moving in hazardous environments and programmed to recover valuable materials and equipment from areas that were unapproachable by organic beings. Mercenaries of the Fireclaw Horde planned to use modified versions of the MMR-9 in an attempt to hijack the luxury liner *Queen of Cularin.* They were intercepted by a group of freelance agents before they could launch their attacks, and the droids were never released.

*Mluki*

**MM(X)** An experimental grenade launcher created by Merr-Sonn just prior to the Clone Wars. Separatist forces obtained several prototypes, which featured a dual firing mechanism.

**mnemiotic drugs** Mind-altering drugs that gave subjects flawless memories but induced hallucinations. Mnemiotic drugs were commonly given by the Empire to its assassins and soldiers.

**M'Nista** Baron D'Asta's majordomo, he introduced the Baron to Mirith Sinn and Kir Kanos when they returned from Grappa the Hutt's stronghold with the real Feena D'Asta.

**Mnuue, Kijo** A Herglic and onetime leader of the Guild of Non-Human Skilled Laborers, Mnuue worked at the Tallaan Imperial shipyards for many years during the New Order. He was a skilled zero-g welder, cargo inspector, and job foreman, and was instrumental in the formation of the guild. Mnuue also was a member of the local Rebel Alliance cell on Tallaan and communicated with the Mon Calamari and the Corellian Shipbuilders' Unions regarding new Imperial designs.

**Moappa** An invertebrate native to the oceans of the planet Mon Calamari. Moappa probably existed on the planet before the Mon Calamari and the Quarren civilizations were formed. As individuals, the creatures were essentially primitive, but when large groups united in colonies, the intelligence of each individual combined to form a fully sentient entity. For many millennia, the Moappa were content to appear as primitive. When the Clone Wars began and the Mon Calamari tried to decide the loyalty of the entire planet, the Moappa rebelled and allied themselves with the Separatists. They used their telepathic abilities to relay the orders of remote Separatist generals to the Quarren who were fighting against the Mon Calamari, in an effort to bring together all the sentient beings on the planet. When Jedi Master Kit Fisto discovered the abilities of the Moappa, he forced the Mon Calamari leaders to drop their pretenses of superiority and aloofness, and begin working with the Quarren and the Moappa to save the planet.

**MOB** An acronym for the main observation blister of a starship.

**Mobari, Sora** A Jedi Master injured during the early stages of the Clone Wars. She and her Padawan were dispatched to Ithor where she was betrayed by her Padawan, who planned to kill her in an explosion. It was the Padawan, however, who died in the blast. Master Mobari was seriously injured and lost her sight. A'Sharad Hett asked Anakin Skywalker to sit with her in the medcenter, hoping to make her last hours comfortable. Anakin offered to try and keep her heart beating with the Force, believing he could use the same constriction technique he used on Orliss Gillmunn to massage her heart. Master Hett forbid it, explaining to Anakin that trying to keep her alive would only cause more suffering. Anakin struggled with this, then reluctantly let Master Mobari die.

**mober snake** A reptile that was particularly dangerous, it had a head at each end of its body—and both were poisonous.

**mobile command base** A protected, mobile base of operations for Imperial field commanders. Each base moved on treads, was highly armored, and housed a sophisticated sensor array to gather field data for analysis by onboard computers. The mobile base also sported a defensive heavy laser cannon.

**mobile command post** Prefabricated buildings designed by Sienar Fleet Systems, they were used on planets where the Empire needed only a temporary presence before turning control over to an Imperial governor. The mobile command post was constructed in space, and then towed to its next location by space tugs.

**mobile grenade mortar** A repulsorlift sled modified to accommodate a mortar launcher as well as a pair of stormtroopers. The launching system on the mobile grenade mortar could fire up to 100 mortar rounds a second at chosen targets.

**mobile stockade** A portable force-field generator used to detain prisoners, the mobile stockade created a hemispherical detainment field that could be subdivided into two or four compartments.

**Mobquet Presents: Fastest Land Beings** An annual event sponsored by Mobquet Swoops and Speeders, it provided some of the galaxy's fastest individuals with a chance to set personal, planetary, or galactic speed records. The series had categories based on participants' number of legs, with classes for bipeds, tripeds, quadrupeds, pentapeds, sexapeds, septapeds, octopeds, and nonapeds. Those beings with 10 or more legs were placed into a single class called decaped-plus.

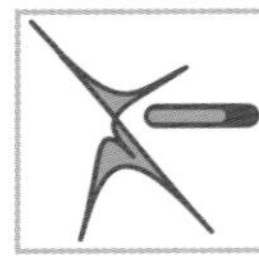

**Mobquet Swoops and Speeders** A subdivision of Tagge Company, Mobquet was most famous for its swoops, which became wildly popular with the rise of swoop racing during the New Order.

**Moburi** A Mandalorian elite trooper who accompanied Boba Fett to defend the Nickel One asteroid in the wake of the Second Battle of Fondor. Fett and Jaina Solo were cut off from the main squad when a group of Imperial warships arrived to take control of the asteroid, and Fett placed Moburi in charge of the squad until he could reach their position.

**Mobus** A gas giant with 17 moons, it was the only world in the Klasse Ephemora system. A Chiss probe discovered the existence of a new moon of Mobus, believed to be the rogue planet Zonama Sekot. Luke Skywalker proved that theory when he and a group of Jedi Knights managed to locate the system during the Yuuzhan Vong War.

**Mobvekhar** A Noghri of the clan Hakh'khar, he served as a lieutenant to Cakhmaim as part of the 10-Noghri team assigned to guard Leia Organa Solo's twins. When Han Solo joined the mission to destroy Grand Admiral Thrawn's cloning facility on Wayland, Cakhmaim protected Leia, Winter, and the children, Jaina and Jacen Solo. Mobvekhar remained on Wayland after the death of Thrawn as part of the security team protecting the safehouse in New Nystao.

**Mochot Steep** A singular rock formation deep in Tatooine's Dune Sea, it was tall enough to be visible for miles. Young Anakin Skywalker often met with Jawa clans at the Steep, trading Watto's used goods for more valuable items.

**mock shyr** A parasitic plant from the jungles of Kashyyyk, distinguishable by its paddle-shaped leaves. The shyr grew around the trunks of wroshyr trees at the fifth biological level of Kashyyyk's jungles.

**Mod-3** An astromech droid owned by Vana Sage, it assisted her in flying the *Guardian Mantis.*

**Modal Nodes, the** *See* Figrin D'an and the Modal Nodes.

**Modan** A manufacturer of large star freighters.

Aks Moe

**modbreks** Wispy beings, hairless except for their blue manes, modbreks had undeveloped heads with huge eyes, tiny noses, and small mouths on their pointy, pale faces.

**Moddell sector** A sector containing the gas giant Endor and its moons. Uncomfortably close to the Unknown Regions and exhaustingly far from the familiar lanes of the Corellian Trade Spine, the Moddell sector formed the fuzzy outer border of the Inner Zuma Region.

**Model 16** A projectile weapon produced by the Dammant Killers Corporation on Adumar following the Yuuzhan Vong War.

**Modeler, the** The common name used to describe the Yuuzhan Vong deity Yun-Ne'Shel.

**Moderation** One of the face cards in a standard sabacc deck. The picture on the face of Moderation was often a Jedi Knight, and the card's value could be either positive or negative 14.

**Modl, Bask** A native of the planet Bestine IV, he served in the naval forces of the Old Republic military during the Mandalorian Wars. For his heroic actions during the Onslaught, Modl was promoted to captain.

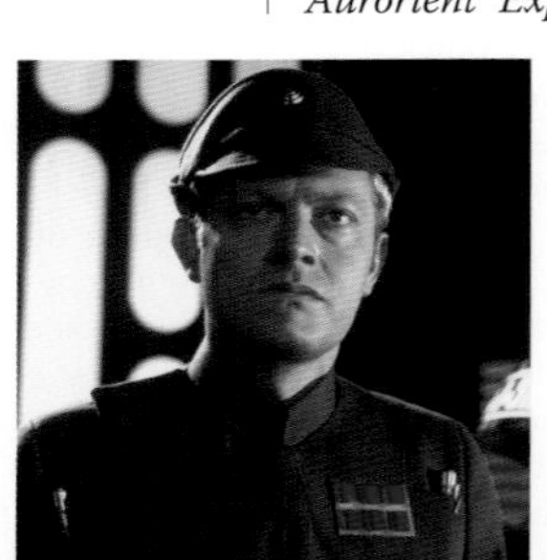

An Imperial Moff

**Modo** A bartender at Lupo's bar on Nar Shaddaa.

**modular taskforce cruiser** Manufactured by Tagge Industries Shipyards, the modular taskforce cruiser had an underlying structure that allowed it to be built for any number of uses.

**Moe, Aks** A native of Malastare, this Gran became one of the planet's primary political forces. Moe eventually was elected as his planet's Senator to the Old Republic, and was a skillful politician. Like many of the Senators of his day, however, Moe was nothing more than a politician, and he worked strictly by the laws and protocols put in place by the Republic. He agreed to host peace treaty negotiations between the Lannik and the Red Iaro, and promised that the Red Iaro would have the cooperation of the Malastare government during the negotiations. In addition to his ties to the Red Iaro terrorists, Moe cultivated a relationship with the priests of the Ffib. He went so far as to attempt to assassinate the Jedi Knights who were serving as mediators.

As the Old Republic rotted from within, Senators like Moe continued to demand that every issue be put to a vote, bogging down the governing body. When Queen Amidala traveled to Coruscant to protest the Trade Federation's invasion of her homeworld of Naboo, Moe was the first Senator to demand that a commission be dispatched to Naboo to investigate the situation. In the decade following the Battle of Naboo, Moe was one of the loudest supporters of the Military Creation Act. While on Aargau, he was killed in an explosion blamed on the Separatists shortly before the start of the Clone Wars.

**Moegantz, Saul** A passenger aboard the *Aurorient Express* during its last voyage. A tan-skinned being with black hair going gray at the temples, Moegantz was unaware that his cargo, supposedly medicinal-grade survapierre, had been switched with a cargo of *Fastlach*-class defense droids.

**Moegid** An introverted Verpine, he was one of the few who chose not to go into space and explore the galaxy beyond the Roche asteroid field. Moegid believed starships were death traps, a view that ostracized him from his hive. However, after he deciphered the data from a damaged Imperial probe droid and turned it over to the Rebel Alliance, he realized that he was destined to be a code breaker. Moegid joined the Alliance. He decoded more than 4,000 separate ciphers and became a friend and business associate of Lobot. He later helped Lobot when Han Solo and Lando Calrissian attempted to locate a copy of the Caamas Document on Bastion. He set up an almost undetectable computer link, using Verpine biofrequencies to communicate with Lobot's cyborg implant.

**Moff** The title given to Imperial military commanders who ruled certain sectors of the galaxy. Moffs reported to Grand Moffs, who were in charge of groups of sectors or regions. Grand Moffs also controlled "priority sectors"—those that supported insurgent activities.

**Moff Assembly Hall** A primary headquarters of the Moff Council, which controlled the Imperial Remnant in the years following the Yuuzhan Vong War. The Moff Assembly Hall was in the city of Ravelin on Bastion.

**Moff Council of the Remnant** The presiding body of Imperial Moffs, it supported Supreme Commander Gilad Pellaeon and ran the day-to-day operations of the Imperial Remnant. After the Yuuzhan Vong launched their invasion, the Moff Council generally refused to assist the New Republic, believing that the Yuuzhan Vong would simply ignore them because no attack had yet been made on Imperial space.

After Yuuzhan Vong forces decimated the Imperial fleet at Bastion, and later destroyed the fleet at Muunilinst, the Moff Council remained reluctant to abide by information provided by

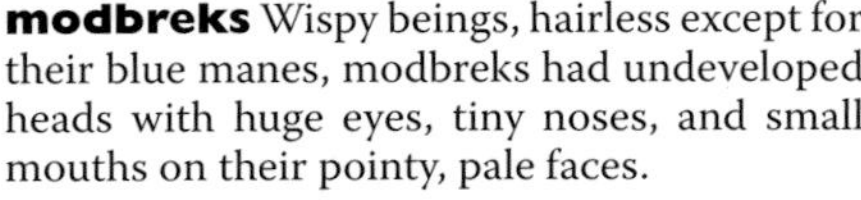

Jacen Solo. When it was believed that Pellaeon was killed at Bastion, Moff Kurlen Flennic seized the opportunity to take control. Pellaeon survived, however, and threatened to take the entire Imperial fleet with him to join the Galactic Alliance if the Moffs didn't accept Jacen's terms to join. Reluctantly, the members of the Moff Council decided that their best chance for survival was to join.

During the Second Battle of Fondor, several of the Moffs accompanied Pellaeon into battle, but Moff Quille and his supporters planned to remove Pellaeon from power if the opportunity presented itself. They believed that their time had come when Tahiri Veila assassinated Pellaeon aboard the *Bloodfin,* but the Moffs were trapped when the crew mutinied. Boba Fett and a group of Mandalorians then infiltrated the *Bloodfin* on orders from Admiral Daala, who had a long-standing grudge against the Moff Council. The Mandalorians wasted no time killing the Moffs, leaving the council with three-quarters of its original membership.

Jozzel Moffett

In the decades that followed the war between the Galactic Alliance and the Confederation, the Moff Council began to reassert itself in the new Empire formed by the ancestors of Roan Fel. The Fel Emperors kept a tight rein on the Moff Council. In the wake of the Sith–Imperial War, however, the Moffs were forced to submit to the will of the new Sith Lord, Darth Krayt.

**Moffett, Jozzel** One of Malta the Hutt's aides, she was a member of a near-human species characterized by a chain of blue spots on each arm. She was paid by members of the fledgling Rebel Alliance to help locate the Yavin Vassilika crystal, inside of which was a key to unlock the ancient Massassi temples on Yavin 4. Playing teams of Hutts against one another, Jozzel managed to steal the Vassilika and flee to Yavin 4 to deliver it. It was on the jungle moon that she learned the crystal globe was merely the vessel for the key and not something grander. When she left the moon with her four million credits and a replica Vassilika, she was shot and killed by Farquil Ban'n.

**moffing** A mild expletive used during the early years of the New Order as people became increasingly disgruntled with the heavy-handedness of the Empire.

***Moffship*** A private starship used by the Central Committee of Grand Moffs, it resembled a Star Destroyer.

**Moff's Own, the** A legion of stormtroopers assigned to an Imperial Moff, under the direct command of the Moff at all times.

***Moff Weblin*** An Imperial ship that saw duty during the latter stages of the Galactic Civil War, it later was assigned to patrol space near the Koornacht Cluster. When a power cell failed, the *Moff Weblin* was remanded to Black-15 at N'zoth for repairs. It was in dry dock when the Yevetha rose up against the Empire and took control of the facility.

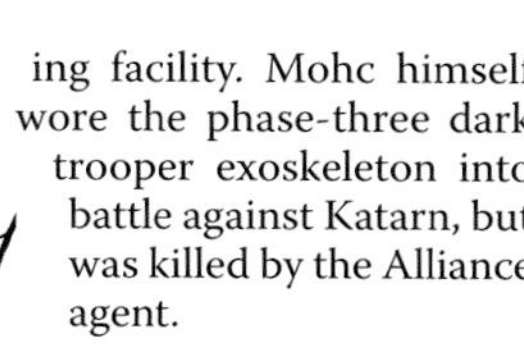

Mogo

**Moggonite** An egotistical, squat humanoid species native to Arorlia. Distinguished by their long, pointed ears and monkey-like faces, Moggonites held themselves in high regard. They were known to be treacherous beings, taking whatever they could in order to get ahead.

**mogo** A large shaggy-furred creature, it had a head like a camel and a body that undulated. Mogos were used for transportation on Roon.

**mogo tree** A species of broad-limbed trees native to the jungles of Tenupe. Individual mogo trees could stand more than 100 meters tall, and their leafy tops created a dense canopy across the surface of the planet. Much of the mogo forest was destroyed during the Battle of Tenupe, when the Chiss used defoliants to eliminate the protection created by the canopy.

Moisture vaporator

**Mohc, General Rom** An Imperial officer who served the Empire during the early days of the Galactic Civil War, Mohc witnessed firsthand the efficiency and limitations of a droid army. After the rise of the New Order, Mohc continued to train with combat droids, and he kept a trophy room where he displayed the deactivated "corpses" of those he had defeated. Mohc opposed the creation of the first Death Star, believing it took away from the skill required for one-on-one combat. He called for creation of a group of specially enhanced, automated dark troopers that he would use to annihilate the Rebel Alliance. He was thwarted, however, when Kyle Katarn discovered Mohc's plans and eliminated the *Arc Hammer* manufacturing facility. Mohc himself wore the phase-three dark trooper exoskeleton into battle against Katarn, but was killed by the Alliance agent.

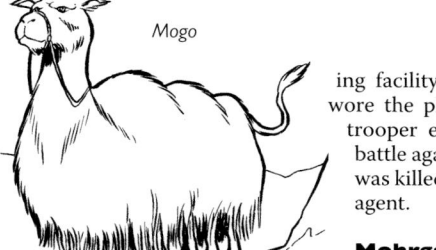

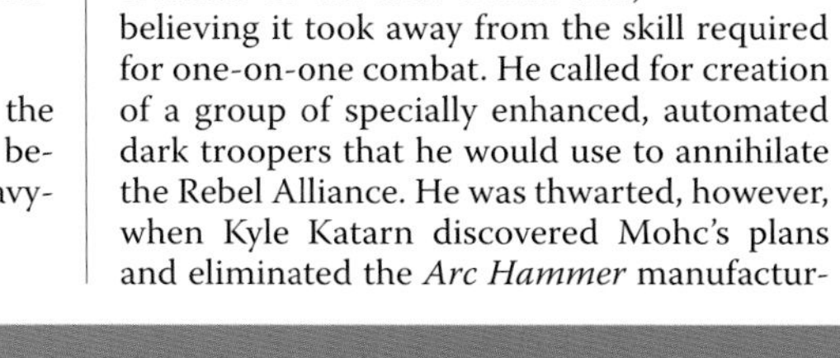

**Mohrgan** A cousin of Emperor Roan Fel, he was one of the many Imperial Knights who served the New Empire 130 years after the Battle of Yavin. Mohrgan was one of Emperor Fel's closest allies. When the new Sith made their move to take control of the galaxy, Emperor Fel was warned of a Sith-led assassination attempt and agreed to flee Coruscant. Mohrgan and several other Imperial Knights accompanied Fel's double to a meeting of the Moffs, hoping to get a chance to test their skills against the Sith. The Sith attacked without warning. Mohrgan and his fellow Imperial Knights jumped to the aid of their "Emperor." They were no match for the brute force of the Sith, and were cut down in combat.

**Mohris** The head bartender at the Rimsoo Seven cantina on Drongar during the Clone Wars.

**Mohs** An older member of the Toka, Mohs was also the High Singer, a position held by one member each generation. This allowed him access to the Sharu legends, which he kept alive through various songs and chants used by the Toka people. He found Lando Calrissian in the Spaceman's Rest and agreed to help him find the Mindharp. In order to prevent an unnecessary activation of the Mindharp, Mohs tried to steal the key from Lando a number of times, only to have Lando recover it each time. They traveled to Rafa V, where Lando was able to insert the Key of the Overpeople into the Great Lock, thus opening the Great Pyramid.

**moirestone** This durable stone was found on Woteba. It was notable for its unusual pattern of stripes, and was quarried by Killiks who had been relocated to the planet.

**moisture farm** A landholding where water was extracted from the atmosphere for use on dry desert worlds to irrigate subterranean produce farms, for human consumption, or for sale. Jedi Knight and Rebel Alliance hero Luke Skywalker grew up on a Tatooine moisture farm.

Moisture farm on Tatooine

**moisture vaporator** Essential for life on desert planets, vaporators condensed water vapor from the atmosphere. A moisture vaporator

Moje

had purification filters and coolant tanks, and stored condensed vapor in large underground tanks. A properly functioning vaporator could obtain enough water to support three beings for a single day.

**Moje** Chief assistant to Senator Navi, Thustra's representative to the Galactic Senate during the Clone Wars. When Navi worked to unseat his uncle, King Alaric, Moje spread false rumors of plots by the Old Republic and the Jedi Knights to murder Alaric. After Alaric's death in a fight with Yoda, Navi returned to Coruscant to speak against the Jedi. Yoda, however, returned to Coruscant with Pix and Clutch to expose Navi's treachery. Although Navi was taken into custody, Moje managed to escape.

Wilst Molan

**Molan, Wilst** A frequent patron of the Outlander Club, she was often seen dancing among the crowds, which led to the assumption that she was actually a hired dancer.

**Molavar** An Outer Rim planet that was a supply world during the years leading up to the Clone Wars. Much of the planet was covered with desert. Molavar was the homeworld of a skeletal species of humanoids distinguished by tentacle-covered heads.

***Moldy Crow*** A dilapidated HWK-290 light freighter captured by the Rebel Alliance and refitted aboard the *New Hope.* The ship was later assigned to Kyle Katarn, who renamed the ship simply *Crow* during a mission to infiltrate the Imperial labs on Danuta. It was owned for a while by Roark Garnet. After Garnet inherited the *Dorion Discus,* he used the *Moldy Crow* to pay off a debt to Grappa the Hutt. Dace Bonearm and IG-72 stole the *Moldy Crow* from Grappa before dumping it on Teth. The ship became the property of Palob Godalhi, who turned it over to the Alliance. Katarn used the ship for many years, until the *Moldy Crow* was destroyed during a mission to defeat Jerec. It was eventually replaced by the *Raven's Claw.*

**Mole** A former spy and fugitive who fled to Ota, hoping to hide from Imperial forces. There Mole encountered Han Solo and Chewbacca, and he saved the Wookiee from a snow snake attack. Boba Fett, who had been sent by Darth Vader to find Mole, tried to capture him on Ota. The attempt was thwarted by the appearance of the Snogars, who captured them all. In a daring escape, Mole used a huge magnetic generator to pin Fett against a wall while making his escape. This also allowed Solo and Chewbacca to escape.

**molecular shielding** Used on the Balmorran Viper Automadon, it absorbed the energy from an opponent's weapons and rerouted it into the Viper's own weapons system.

**Moleese** The director of the Out From The Shadows drug abuse outreach program, based in the Jrade District of Coruscant during the last years of the Old Republic.

**mole miner** A utility mining craft designed to operate in space, on asteroids, and on worlds with hostile environments. Lando Calrissian used mole miners at his operation on the harsh planet Nkllon until a large number were stolen by Grand Admiral Thrawn, who used them at the Battle of Sluis Van to burrow into capital ships so that Imperial crews could hijack the vessels.

**mole serpent** A species of vicious, aggressive worms native to an unsettled world on the edge of the Kathol sector. The mole serpent lurked belowground until it sensed the presence of prey, then swept out of its burrow to swallow its prey whole. The creatures ranged between 10 and 18 meters long.

**molf** A heavy red yarn used to make tassels and piping for clothing during the last years of the Old Republic.

**Moll, Demma** Owner of a farm on Annoo in the early days of the Empire. The Fromm gang desperately wanted to take over Moll's farm, but didn't know that she secretly led a band of freedom fighters who worked to destroy the Fromm's weapons satellite.

Demma Moll

**Moll, Kea** C-3PO and R2-D2 first met this then-17-year-old girl on Annoo during the early days of the Empire. She lived on the farm complex of her mother, Demma Moll. Kea was brave, athletic, and able to handle both spacecraft and landspeeders with an expert touch.

Kea Moll

**molleung worm** A Yuuzhan Vong biocreation that resembled a huge annelid. In space, it was used as a living cofferdam; in the atmosphere a molleung could discharge large cargoes from a transport ship to a ground installation. A molleung worm could also be used to link underwater chambers.

**Mollom** A subspecies of Killiks noted for its burrowing abilities, a valuable addition to the Great Swarm. Mollom quickly dug out trenches and tunnels on the battlefield during the Colony's conflict with the Chiss. They also were able to quarry rock and stone, and these skills were put to use creating boulders for primitive catapults.

**Molly's Merchants** A collection of electronic forgers, slicers, and infochants based on Cloud City at the time when Bespin Motors decided to split from Incom Industries.

Mole miner

**molo** A hardy shrub native to the caves and overhangs of the rocky deserts of Tatooine. Resembling little more than scrub during the day, the molo shrub erupted with a burst of leaves and flowers when the suns went down and plunged the planet into darkness.

**Moltok** An oxygen-rich planet, it was one of the inner worlds of the Dartibek system and homeworld of the Ho'Din. Active volcanoes filled Moltok's skies with ash, helping protect the planet's surface from the harmful effects of its sun. The Ho'Din species lived in the hot rain forests of the lower latitudes and deeply revered the plant life found there.

**mol-welding** A technique employed when connecting the deck plates of starships, it involved using specialized equipment to alter

metallic plates at the molecular level, interlocking the plates in a weld of superior strength and durability.

**Momen, Reija** A native of Alderaan, she was the chief administrator of the Intergalactic Communications Center on Praesitlyn during the Clone Wars. She considered its staff to be her only family, and they lovingly called her Momma Momen. Momen had five years left on her tour of duty when the planet was blockaded and attacked by Separatist forces led by Pors Tonith. Momen drew her support staff together and prepared to destroy the facility should it fall into enemy hands. Held hostage, Momen was forced to record a message to the Republic. She agreed, but rather than begging the Republic to abandon Praesitlyn so her staff would not be killed, she ordered the military to attack the Separatists. Her fortitude paid off, and Anakin Skywalker launched a mission to rescue them. Just after Anakin liberated the staff from the facility's command center, however, Momen was shot in the chest by a battle droid.

*Mon Calamari*

**Mon, Ephant** A Chevin pachydermoid from the planet Vinsoth, he was the closest being crime lord Jabba the Hutt had to a friend. Ephant Mon worked as an interplanetary mercenary, running guns for anyone from pirates to Rebels. After he met Jabba, the two schemed to raid an Imperial weapons depot on the icy moon of Glakka, but were betrayed by one of Jabba's own gang. They managed to avoid Imperial fire but were trapped in the frigid environs of Glakka. Jabba saved Ephant Mon by wrapping his oily fat folds around him, and both were rescued the next day.

Upon returning to Tatooine, Jabba made Ephant Mon his secret internal security official, rooting out conspiracies and assassination plots. When Jedi Luke Skywalker showed up at Jabba's palace, Ephant Mon confronted him. Skywalker told him that Jabba would be destroyed unless he freed his Rebel Alliance captives. Ephant Mon believed the Jedi and tried to persuade Jabba, who wouldn't listen. He decided not to accompany his friend and boss on the fateful sail barge trip to the Pit of Carkoon and returned to his homeworld, where he founded a sect that worshipped the Force.

*Ephant Mon*

**Mon, Sol** A heavily muscled and dreadlocked pirate who worked for Grappa the Hutt during the early years of the New Republic.

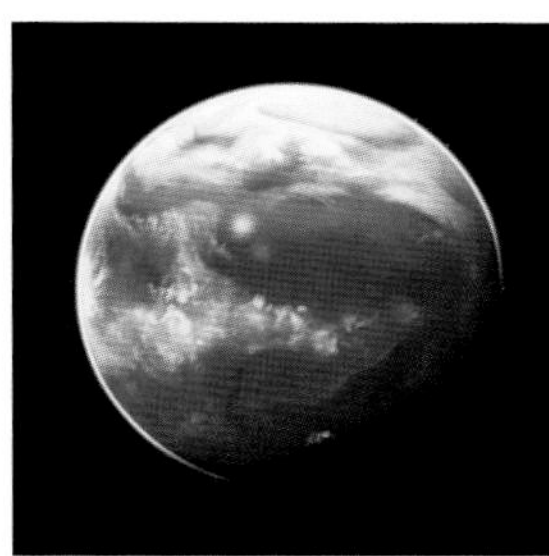

*Mon Calamari*

**monad** A self-contained living structure popular on Coruscant, a monad contained all the essentials of a full community, including hydroponics gardens and parks.

***Mon Adapyne*** This Mon Calamari cruiser was one of the new warships produced for the New Republic during the struggle against the Yuuzhan Vong, and one of the first ships to carry a Jedi Knight as part of its crew. The Anx Jedi Madurrin served on board, participating in a Jedi Force-meld to help coordinate the ship's actions during battle.

**Monarc C-4** A class 1 Nubian hyperdrive system that saw prominent use in the Naboo N-1 starfighter.

***Monarch*** An Imperial Star Destroyer so heavily damaged by the Rebel Alliance invasion fleet over Coruscant that its captain, Averen, surrendered the ship rather than see it destroyed. When the New Republic tried to retake Coruscant, the *Monarch* and the *Triumph* were the only two ships remaining to guard it.

**Monastery** Darth Vader once used the help of Tagge House to try to capture Luke Skywalker on Monastery, a Mid Rim planet. The natives of the planet practiced a religion known as the Order of the Sacred Circle, which referred to the great circle of life. The members of the Order believed that the rings that surrounded the planet, made up of moon-sized rocks as well as dust, were the embodiment of the circle of life.

**Mon Cal** The shortened name used by many beings to describe the Mon Calamari.

**Mon Calamari (1)** Nearly completely covered with water, this planet was home to the Mon Calamari and the Quarren. The surface of Mon Calamari—historically referred to as Dac by its inhabitants—was covered with small marshy islands and enormous floating cities that housed both species. Noted cities included Reef Home, Coral Depths, Kee-Piru, Coral City, Heurkea, Foam-wander City, the Domed City of Aquaris, and Morjanssik.

The architecture and design of Mon Calamari was organic, with rounded edges and irregular surfaces, demonstrating the inhabitants' love for the natural beauty of their world. Raw ore used in construction was mined by the Quarren, who could breathe both air and water, from domed cities on the ocean floor.

Mon Calamari was discovered by the greater galaxy about 4,000 years before the Battle of Yavin. In more recent history, Imperials planned to enslave the planet and, after meeting native resistance, destroyed three of its floating cities. Mon Calamari starships were converted into warships, and the shipbuilding docks in orbit around Mon Calamari became an important resource for the Rebel Alliance.

Many Mon Calamari were enslaved by the Empire, including Ackbar, who was forced to be the personal servant of Grand Moff Tarkin. Ackbar was rescued from slavery by an Alliance force and later named Admiral of the Rebel fleet. Six years after the Battle of Endor, the reborn clone Emperor used his World Devastators to attack Mon Calamari's southern territorial zone, destroying most of Kee-Piru and Heurkea. The port city of Hikahi was also damaged, hurting the planet's

*Monastery*

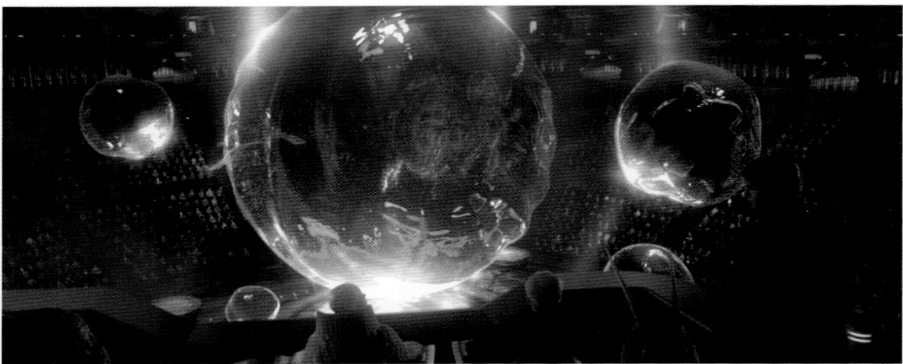

*Mon Calamari Ballet performs* Squid Lake.

starship-building capability. With the help of Jedi Knight Luke Skywalker, the Devastators were defeated.

**Mon Calamari (2)** Bipedal, amphibious beings, they shared their homeworld of Mon Calamari with the Quarren in a tenuous relationship that often turned warlike. Males were distinguished by their salmon-colored skin, lobed heads, and protruding eyes, while females were more streamlined, with olive-colored markings on their salmon skin. Mon Calamari were shore dwellers who preferred to live near the water. Early Mon Cals fed on creatures found in the shallows and developed an advanced aquaculture system. When they discovered the Quarren—the other intelligent beings on Mon Calamari, who lived in the ocean depths—the two species eventually created a symbiotic society in which both flourished. Together they built the huge floating cities that dotted Mon Calamari's oceans. Unlike the Quarren, however, the Mon Calamari desired to travel to the stars, and began experimenting with spaceflight.

Mon Calamari were born as tadpoles who lived exclusively in the water. As they grew up, they developed strong lungs and began breathing air. The nostrils of a Mon Calamari provided insight into his or her emotions, with closed nostrils indicating surprise.

**Mon Calamari Ballet** A prestigious aquatic dance troupe. Its production of *Squid Lake* at Coruscant's Galaxies Opera House was attended by Supreme Chancellor Palpatine himself.

**Mon Calamari blink code** A communication system developed by the Mon Calamari, it consisted of a series of flashes of light that, when combined in certain patterns, denoted the letters of the Basic alphabet. The flashes of light could then be strung together to form messages. It was regarded as a simple, crude form of cipher.

**Mon Calamari Communications Control** The primary communication center created by the Galactic Alliance on Mon Calamari at the height of the Yuuzhan Vong War. Mon Calamari became the provisional capital of the galaxy after the fall of Coruscant, and the government's operations largely were reestablished there.

**Mon Calamari Council** Old Republic loyalists who were installed as the leaders of the planet Mon Calamari during the Clone Wars. Representatives from the Quarren and Mon Calamari served on the council, demonstrating to the planet's inhabitants that there would be no favoritism in the decisions. When the Empire tried to subjugate Mon Calamari, the council agreed to defend the homeworld with as much force as possible. This ultimately drove the Empire off Mon Calamari, and the council began considering whether or not to ally itself with the Alliance to Restore the Republic. Mon Calamari industry was soon providing warships to the Alliance, and in the wake of the Battle of Yavin, the Mon Calamari Council formally agreed to join.

**Mon Calamari Extreme** The code name for a location just beyond the edges of the Mon Calamari star system. Here incoming reconnaissance craft monitored the advance of the Yuuzhan Vong war fleet sent to destroy Galactic Alliance forces during the final stages of the war. Twin Suns, Vanguard, Scimitar, and Rogue squadrons met here to face the advance portion of the Yuuzhan Vong war fleet.

**Mon Calamari Knights** A band of Mon Calamari who were the sworn protectors of their homeworld for many generations. During the earliest history of their civilization, the Mon Calamari Knights were the primary force that kept Quarren insurrectionists at bay, thereby maintaining the uneasy truce between the two species. As the civil strife between Quarren and Mon Calamari diminished, so did the necessity for the Mon Calamari Knights, which became simply a cultural tradition by the time of the Battle of Naboo. During the years leading up to the Clone Wars, however, the Mon Calamari Knights saw the possibility of conflict and began to train in earnest. These fears were realized when the Clone Wars broke out and the Quarren Isolation League sided with the Separatists. With the help of Jedi Master Kit Fisto, the Mon Calamari Knights managed to defeat the Quarren and restore peace to Mon Calamari.

*Mon Calamari Knights*

**Mon Calamari Sea** The term commonly used to describe the world-spanning ocean that covered Mon Calamari.

**Mon Calamari star cruiser** The main cruisers in the Rebel Alliance and New Republic battle fleet, these organic-looking, durable ships, originally designed for pleasure cruises and peaceful colonization efforts, were as fast and almost as tough as the larger Imperial Star Destroyers. After an attack by the Empire, Mon Calamari star cruisers were converted to military duty by adding thick hull plating and numerous weapon emplacements.

*Mon Calamari star cruiser*

Each Mon Calamari cruiser had a unique design because the ships were considered almost as much works of art as weapons of war. While this made them difficult to repair, their armor and redundant systems ensured that they were rarely damaged in combat. Some notable Mon Calamari ships included the round, blimp-shaped Headquarters Frigate known as *Home One* and the winged, elongated *Liberty*. *Home One* was Admiral Ackbar's command vessel for the attack on the second Death Star and was used later in numerous battles against Imperial forces. It carried 10 squadrons of starfighters, and its weapons included 29 turbolasers, 36 ion cannons, multiple tractor beam projectors, and unusually powerful shield generators.

While many species served aboard Mon Calamari cruisers, command sections were geared for the Mon Calamari anatomy. Controls could be changed through specific movements in the command chairs as well as the more usual computer interfaces.

Mondo-Mod

**Mon Calamari Star Defender** The largest starship produced by the Mon Calamari, the Star Defender was created for use by the New Republic Navy 20 years after the Battle of Endor. Nearly twice as long as a standard Mon Calamari cruiser, the Star Defender was also the largest ship built for the New Republic fleet. The *Viscount* was the first Star Defender to go into service.

***Mon Casima*** A New Republic Mon Calamari cruiser dispatched to assist the *Allegiance* in defending Adumar from Imperial assault shortly after the Adumari agreed to join the Republic.

**Monchar, Hath** A Neimoidian who once served as Nute Gunray's deputy viceroy, Monchar was placed in charge of the Trade Federation's plans to capture the lommite mines of the planet Dorvalla, but he was unable to gain access to the mines. He fled shortly before the blockade of Naboo, hoping to make his own fortune selling the information that the blockade was perpetrated by Darth Sidious. Monchar tried to sell the information to the Black Sun Vigo Darnada, but Sidious dispatched Darth Maul to locate and eliminate the double-dealer.

***Mondaran*** A New Republic assault shuttle used in the attempt to take the planet Borleias, it was the first ship shot down by Evir Derricote's defenses.

**Mondeo Modernist** A design craze that swept through the Core Worlds more than 100 years before the Galactic Civil War. It emphasized the use of streamlined contours, elliptical forms, and whimsical embellishments.

**Mondo-Mod** A Hutt noted for staging extravagant gladiator fights. During the Clone Wars, he was approached by Jedi Master Luminara Unduli, who wished to purchase information about a secret Separatist weapons factory. Mondo-Mod agreed to turn over the information if Master Unduli vanquished his three strongest gladiators in the Arena of Doom. She defeated a wampa ice creature and a durkii without the aid of her lightsaber or the Force, as per her agreement with the Hutt. For the final fight, Mondo-Mod sent in his gladiator droid, Evil Supreme. Master Unduli flung a small stone into Evil Supreme's faceplate, smashing the droid's primary circuits. Mondo-Mod was forced to turn over information on the weapons factory on Diorda. Unknown to the Hutt, Master Luminara's former Padawan Barriss Offee bet against Unduli in the first two fights, then for her in the finale. In this way, Offee was able to break the bank at the Arena of Doom, putting Mondo-Mod out of business until he could recover his lost wealth.

**Mondress sector** A sector in the Outer Rim situated between the Kokash and Albanin sectors. It was briefly scouted by the Outbound Flight Project as one of the final stopover points before Outbound Flight was to have entered the Unknown Regions.

**mon duul** A creature bioengineered by the Yuuzhan Vong to act as an audio amplifier. Mon duuls were implanted with specialized villips created to receive transmissions from a master villip and broadcast them via immense tympanic membranes stretched over their bellies. This allowed a single Yuuzhan Vong to address a huge gathering of comrades.

**Mon Eron** The fifth world in the Mon Calamari system, it served as the primary reversion point for warships returning to Mon Calamari from the New Republic's conflict with the Yuuzhan Vong. The planet had been terraformed to make it possible to live on its surface.

**Monevv, Tar** A Yuuzhan Vong who was part of the first wave of military forces to invade the galaxy. A skilled warrior, Monevv was loyal to Yun-Yammka, the Slayer, and secretly vowed to become warmaster one day. He was easily distinguished by the blood-red armor plate that was grafted onto his body.

**Money Lane** The nickname for the shared field of fire between the *Millennium Falcon*'s upper and lower quad laser batteries, so dubbed by Han Solo and his copilot, Chewbacca. During battles, Solo and Chewbacca wagered on who could hit more enemy targets; those in the Money Lane were worth double, as both gunners had an equal chance at them.

Tar Monevv

**Mong'tar Cantina and Brasserie** A restaurant in Mong'tar City on Boog V. During the Clone Wars, clone commandos Mereel and Ordo met with Gib and TK-0 here as they searched for Ko Sai.

**monga** A serpent easily distinguished by its three forked, orange tongues.

**mongrel** A slang term used by the clone troopers of the Grand Army of the Republic to describe the nonclone humans given leadership roles during the Clone Wars. Unlike the Jedi Knights, mongrels usually took direct command of a group of clones; the Jedi typically worked with clone commanders, who then directed their troops.

***Monitor* (1)** A New Republic training carrier that was the test facility for the K-wing bomber.

***Monitor* (2)** A Nebulon-B frigate, it was the lead ship in an Imperial resupply convoy bound for the *Imperial II*–class Star Destroyer *Corrupter* when the convoy was ambushed by the Rebel Alliance. The Alliance made off with all its supplies to try to force the *Corrupter* out of battle by starving it.

***Mon Karren*** A Mon Calamari MC80 cruiser that was smaller than the *Mon Remonda* but served as part of the fleet commanded by Han Solo and dispatched to hunt down Warlord Zsinj.

**monkey-lizard** A species of ape-like reptiles native to the jungles of the planet Tenupe. Monkey-lizards moved through the trees by swinging from branch to branch. They were distinct from the Kowakian monkey-lizard species.

***Mon Mothma*** An *Imperial*-class Star Destroyer that was part of the New Republic fleet commandeered by Garm Bel Iblis in defense of the Jedi base on Eclipse some two years after the Yuuzhan Vong War began. The *Mon Mothma* accompanied the *Elegos A'Kla* to Talfaglio to ensure that the Jedi Knights escaped. It was one of the first Star Destroyers equipped with a new form of gravity-well projector, but even that weaponry was no match for the sheer numbers of the Yuuzhan Vong. During the Second Battle of Coruscant, the *Mon Mothma* fought valiantly but was unable to stem the tide of alien attackers. The ship and crew retreated to Borleias and assisted Wedge Antilles in the retaking of that planet, pounding a Yuuzhan Vong worldship until the refitted *Lusankya* could be brought to bear.

Later the *Mon Mothma* served as the flagship of General Antilles's fleet in the battle

Voolvif Monn

against the Yuuzhan Vong at Duro. The ship took heavy damage but managed to draw Yuuzhan Vong ships into the Duro system where they could be trapped using gravity-well projectors. During Operation Trinity, the *Mon Mothma* was back in action against the Yuuzhan Vong at Bilbringi. After a heavy pounding, Antilles ordered the *Mon Mothma*'s shielding diminished, to make it appear as if its main reactors were about to explode. The ruse worked, and the Yuuzhan Vong pulled back to escape the ship's blast radius. The *Mon Mothma* then limped back to Mon Calamari for repairs. Years later, the *Mon Mothma* was paired with the *Admiral Ackbar* in a blockade of the Utegetu Nebula, in an effort to prevent the Killiks of the Dark Nest from escaping into the galaxy.

**Monn, Voolvif** A Shistavanen Wolfman, he was one of the few members of his species to join the Jedi Order. Discovered by Jedi Master Paouoish Rahhdool, Monn had been orphaned on an unknown planet near the Arah asteroid belt. His skills as a tracker and his ability to harness the energy of the Force for defense made him a formidable opponent.

Montral

**monomolecular blade** A knife formed from a length of high-strength, single-inline-molecule material. It was incredibly sharp, but also fragile.

**Monor II** An Outer Rim world located in the Monor system, part of the Doldur sector. It was the homeworld of the Sunesi, who had evolved with the ability to breathe Monor's otherwise deadly atmosphere. Nom Anor infected Mara Jade Skywalker with coomb spores on Monor II.

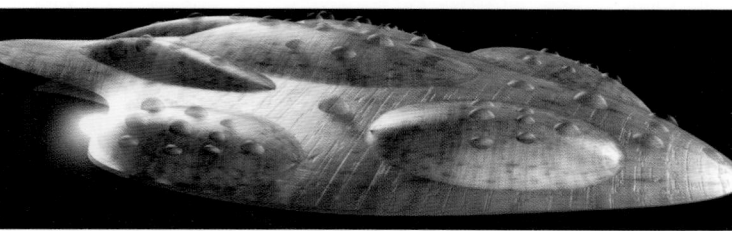

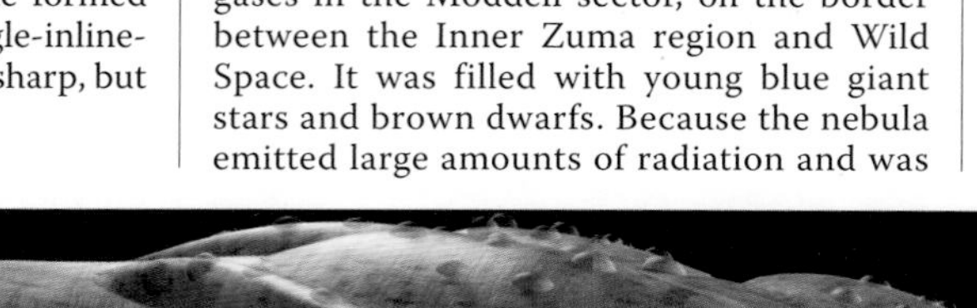

Mon Remonda

**Monotheer, Edallia** Gara Petothel's mother, she was born on Coruscant and trained to be an actress. She caught the eye of Armand Isard, who trained her to be an intelligence agent. She eventually married Dalls Petothel, but both of them were arrested for supposedly funneling secret Imperial information to Rebel forces on Chandrila. New Republic analysis of her files indicated she had never had any contact with the Alliance. During a Wraith Squadron visit to the Galactic Museum, an old man—one of her former teachers—said he thought Lara Notsil was Monotheer. This tipped off Garik Loran to Notsil's true identity.

***Mon Remonda*** A Mon Calamari star cruiser delivered to the New Republic following the Battle of Endor and placed under the command of Han Solo. Solo and the ship's captain, a Mon Calamari named Onoma, pursued Warlord Zsinj across the edges of his holdings, hoping to catch him unaware. The *Mon Remonda* was later destroyed in a battle with the World Devastator *Silencer-7* during the campaign by the cloned Emperor Palpatine. All hands were lost, but not before the *Mon Remonda* took out an *Imperial*-class Star Destroyer.

**Monsoon Mesa** A tableland on the planet Jabiim, and the rallying point for the Army of the Republic's forces during the Battle of Jabiim. The battle dragged on for more than 40 days before Separatists led by Alto Stratus managed to defeat much of the Republic's force. Anakin Skywalker led the Republic retreat to Monsoon Mesa.

**Monsua Nebula** An area of interstellar gases in the Moddell sector, on the border between the Inner Zuma region and Wild Space. It was filled with young blue giant stars and brown dwarfs. Because the nebula emitted large amounts of radiation and was difficult to navigate, much of it remained unexplored even during the early years of the New Republic.

**Montellian Serat** A northern city on the planet Devaron, it was the site of a massacre caused by indiscriminate shelling ordered by Kardue'sai'Malloc; it earned him the Devaronian nickname of the Butcher of Montellian Serat.

**montral** A term used by the Togruta people to describe the two cone-like horns that sprouted from the tops of their heads. Each montral was hollow, allowing the Togruta to sense ultrasonic changes in their environment.

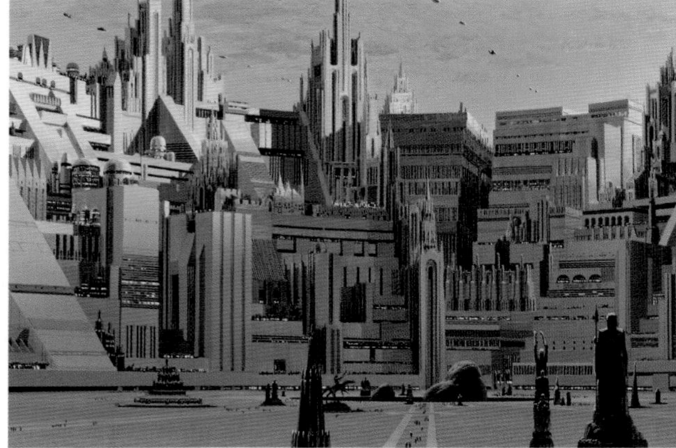
Monument Plaza

**Montross** A bounty hunter active during the last decades of the Old Republic. Jango Fett considered Montross, a former Mandalorian warrior, the toughest opponent he ever had to face. He was known as a cunning adversary who would stop at nothing to achieve his goals.

***Monument*** A huge Corellian barge, it was part of a fleet that transported workers to and from Bandomeer. It was aboard the *Monument* that Obi-Wan Kenobi and Si Treemba discovered early signs of Offworld Mining Company's sabotage against Arcona Mineral Harvest Corporation.

**Monument Park** A protected mall on Coruscant, it was one of the few places on the planet that someone could actually touch naked ground. A small religious group made its home in the park, keeping visitors from chipping away small souvenirs.

**Monument Plaza** A wide thoroughfare that surrounded Monument Park on Coruscant. The entire plaza was re-formed when the Yuuzhan Vong invaders assumed control of the planet. In the years that followed the war, the Reconstruction Authority made it a priority to restore Monument Plaza.

***Mon Valle*** A Rebel Alliance ship, it was the base of operations for General Salm's Defender Wing squadron of Y-wings. The *Mon Valle* was destroyed by Imperial planetary defenses during the initial raid on Borleias.

**Moocher** Small, sentient creatures that inhabited the spaceport cities of Abregado-Rae. Resembling fur-covered lizards, they roamed the spaceports looking for handouts from visitors. Many considered the Moochers to be nuisances, primarily because there were so many of them. Moochers lived in dens of several thousand individuals, all birthed by the same queen. The queen was intelligent, quite a bit smarter than any of her offspring. Moochers who disappointed the queen were expelled and often formed their own dens. It was those wild Moochers who were most often encountered near the spaceports.

Moocher

**moog** A small creature native to the planet Dathomir, it was a favored prey of rancors, but difficult to catch.

**mooka** Covered with fur and feathers, this creature was the size of a small dog. It had a bird's beak, four ears, clawed feet, and a feathered tail.

**mookla** A carnivorous creature native to the planet Belsavis.

**Moola, Romi** A Twi'lek who fled Jabba the Hutt's palace when her attempt to poison the crime lord failed. She had Jabba's chuba stew laced with poison, but the stew was taste-tested by Jabba's chef before it reached the Hutt. The chef died, and Jabba discovered the treachery. Moola was later captured by Jango Fett.

**Moolis, Tamaab** An Ithorian who served on the advisory committee of the New Republic Defense Force during the Yuuzhan Vong War.

**Moolis, Umwaw** An Ithorian liaison to the New Republic Senate in the years following the destruction of the Maw Installation. She greeted Leia Organa Solo and her family on Ithor during the herd meet, when Drub McKumb located Han to deliver the message of the Children of the Jedi.

**Mooloolian** Natives of the mountain regions of the planet Janguine, they absorbed the language of the jungle barbarians of the planet 300 years before the Yuuzhan Vong War.

**Moonbeam Throne** A ceremonial throne used by Supreme Overlord Shimrra of the Yuuzhan Vong. Located within the immense craft known as the Citadel, the Moonbeam Throne was surrounded by a blood moat and had an unusual dovin basal installed at its base. This dovin basal acted according to the will of Shimrra, allowing the Supreme Overlord to appear to control the actions of any individual who requested an audience.

***Moon Dash*** Narek-Ag's transport shuttle, it exploded over Coruscant when it hit the cloaked bulk of the Shadow Academy. The academy was positioned near Coruscant to ambush incoming New Republic supply ships.

**Mooney** One of the many bounty hunters who tried to trap Obi-Wan Kenobi and Anakin Skywalker in Death Canyon during the Clone Wars.

**Moon Falls** An unusual waterfall on the Forest Moon of Endor, it spread across a 20-kilometer ledge at one end of a large lake, then fell from such a height that most of the water that reached the ground was in the form of mist. Whenever the falls side of the moon faced away from Endor, the water stopped flowing over the edge.

**Moon Fleet** Starfighter pilots and soldiers bred and trained on the Shattered Moon near Tenupe during the Swarm War. The Moon Fleet was kept hidden in an effort to draw in Chiss warships, but the Chiss had received information on this fleet and turned the tables by allowing themselves to be "defeated." The Chiss planned to deploy parasite bombs, then flee Tenupe before the Killiks of the Colony realized that they were doomed. The parasite bombs were destroyed by Leia Organa Solo and her Master, Saba Sebatyne, before they could deploy their deadly payloads.

**Moonflower Nebula** Located in the Outer Rim Territories, this nebula was of little interest until Nichos Marr inadvertently generated its coordinates while trying to access the Force with his artificial brain. Luke Skywalker took the *Huntbird* to investigate the Nebula. It was where the Imperial battlemoon *Eye of Palpatine* had been waiting for 30 years.

**Moon Lady** Askaj's primary moon. The Askajians held the satellite in reverence, giving rise to the speculation that the Moon Lady was also one of their deities.

***Moonlight Cruise*** A legitimate transport ship . . . until Mika the Hutt had it refitted and renamed the *Barabi Run.*

**moon moth** A common flying insect with beautiful pale blue wings, it was a pest on many civilized planets. Moon moths were also diabolically clever espionage gadgets designed by Arakyd Industries to look like their organic counterparts.

***Moonshadow* (1)** Rik Duel's smuggling ship.

***Moonshadow* (2)** An *Imperial II*–class Star Destroyer commanded by Kir Vantai of the New Republic.

**moonside run** A term used by smugglers who worked in Hutt space to indicate any run that involved moving goods from one part of Nar Shaddaa to another.

**Moons of Iego** A common term used to describe the 42 moons that orbited the planet Iego on the fringes of the known galaxy. They were often referred to as a single group, because it was believed that the moons were inhabited by angels so beautiful, the appearance of one made even the most hardened space pirate cry.

**moonsong** An unusual, musical sound that emanated from the beating wings of the ringed moon shadowmoth. The music was formed when air passed through the wingflutes on the moth's delicate wings.

**Moonstone Lake** One of the seven lakes inside the city limits of Ussa on Bellassa. Moonstone was the most distant of the lakes, and after the Empire took control, much of the planet's black market relocated to the Moonstone Lake District.

**Moonstrike** One of the first cells of organized resistance to the rule of Emperor Palpatine, Moonstrike was founded shortly after the formation of the Galactic Empire by a wealthy native of Acherin known only as Flame.

**moonstrike** The impact of a large asteroid, moon, or other natural satellite. In larger moonstrikes, the impact could significantly alter the rotational axis and orbital path of the satellite.

**Moonstruck Pass** A mountain pass outside the city of Galu. Elan and the Hill People fought off the forces of Lonnag Giba here, driving the Tallah proton tanks into deep snowdrifts and chasms.

**Moonus Mandel** The homeworld of the Veknoid Podracer Teemto Pagalies, it was in the Mid Rim in Bothan space.

**Moor, Kasan** A top starfighter pilot in the Empire, she moved quickly up the Imperial ranks until she was given the command of the 128th TIE Interceptor Squadron. The destruction of her home planet Alderaan by the first Death Star made her believe she could no longer serve a government that would wantonly destroy people for its own ambitions. When the 128th was sent to intercept Rogue Squadron on the planet Ger-

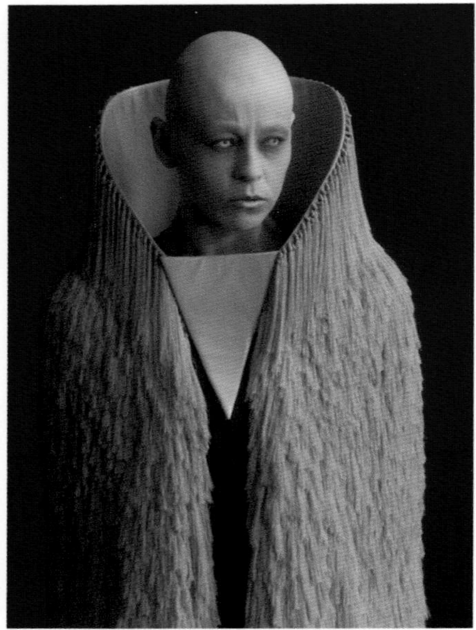

Sly Moore

rard V, Moor offered herself and her ship to the Rebel Alliance.

**Moore, Sly** The Umbaran staff aide to Supreme Chancellor Palpatine during the last years of the Old Republic. She was rumored to have engineered the removal of Sei Taria from public office, blackmailing the woman into retirement and thereby ensuring her own appointment as Palpatine's aide. After the onset of the Clone Wars, Moore was given the standing order from Chancellor Palpatine that no matter what his schedule, he could always be interrupted for a meeting with Anakin Skywalker.

**Moorlu** A bounty hunter who ambushed Boba Fett during the hunt for Bornan Thul. Moorlu kept his pinwheel-shaped starship hidden until Fett arrived. Using a blast from his ion cannon, Moorlu disabled *Slave IV* and thought he had the infamous hunter dead in space. However, Fett activated a pneumatic launcher and shot a warhead at Moorlu's ship, destroying the craft and killing the bounty hunter.

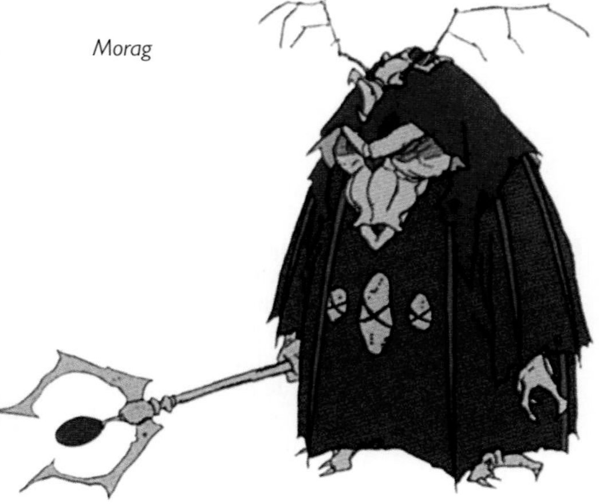

Morag

**Moorsh** A Yuuzhan Vong priest stationed aboard the *Crèche* during the attack on Gyndine and the development of a new yammosk. Moorsh spent a great deal of time observing the Ryn who were enslaved to help mature the yammosk, hoping to glean information on how the Ryn divined the future with sabacc cards and other simple tools.

**Mo'r, Tech** A Bith musician with Figrin D'an and the Modal Nodes, he played a sound-enhancing ommni box.

**Mora** Rescued as a baby by Ch'no, a H'drachi soothsayer, Mora was revealed as the heir to the ruling house of M'haeli. She was the only human survivor of an Imperial attack that led to the Empire taking control of the planet. She considered herself a daughter of Ch'no and defended him against attack. Years later, Mora fell in love with the dashing pilot Ranulf Trommer, not knowing that he was an Imperial spy—but one who was determined to uncover the chicanery of the Imperial puppet who ran the planet.

**Morag** A powerful Tulgah who lived on the Forest Moon of Endor. Morag's evil magic was a potent match for Logray's good magic. She lived in Mount Thunderstone, and her castle was patrolled by Yuzzums riding rakazzaks. She once possessed the Shadowstone and hoped to control the Ewoks with it. However, the shaman Logray managed to steal the Shadowstone and combine its power with that of the Sunstar.

**Morano, Captain** The human commander of the *Intrepid,* flagship of the New Republic's Fifth Fleet in the Yevethan crisis.

Mora

**Morasil** A large yellow star that was the dominant body in the Cularin system, supported by the white dwarf Termadus. Morasil was much older than Termadus, and many scientists theorized that it was one of the first stars ever born in the galaxy.

**Morath** Beings who inhabited a colony on the planet Elcorth in the Koornacht Cluster.

**Morbo, Voralla** A strikingly beautiful woman who was a cantina owner on the planet Thyferra during the New Order. She was also the Rebel Alliance's primary contact on Thyferra at the time. Morbo was a past acquaintance of Han Solo, but broke off their relationship when he was unable to deliver a shipment of Norvanian Grog . . . and because he never asked her out on a date.

**Mordageen** Similar in stature to most humans, this species was distinguished by its wrinkled reddish orange skin, giving the appearance of advanced age.

**Mordanthi bloomer** A plant grown and sold by Ithorian traders as a houseplant during the era of the New Order.

Krdys Mordi

**Mordi, Krdys** One of Sedriss's sergeants at arms aboard the *Avenger* during the early stages of Operation Shadow Hand. He was also one of Emperor Palpatine's Dark Jedi, and was sent to New Alderaan to kidnap Jacen and Jaina Solo. Instead he faced the wrath of the full assembly of Luke Skywalker's new Jedi. He was quickly cut down.

**Mordon, Admiral** An Imperial officer charged with overseeing the invasion of the Taroon system, he commanded the mission from his flagship Star Destroyer, the *Vengeance.* Following the successful subjugation of the planets Kuan and Bodral, a group of Rebel Alliance starfighters intercepted Mordon's shuttle. The only person who heard Mordon's distress signal was Maarek Stele, who was flying a newly repaired TIE interceptor on a shakedown flight. Stele did his best to drive off the Alliance ships, not realizing that he was rescuing his admiral at the same time. Upon returning to the *Vengeance,* Mordon met with Stele and suggested that he join the Imperial Navy as a pilot.

**Mordur, Admiral** An Imperial officer in charge of the siege of Vandelhelm, he controlled the planet from a command barge that stayed in orbit around it. He tried to steal the metals promised to the New Republic by Orrk, but was defeated in a space battle with Han Solo and Nien Nunb.

**Morgavi, Luke** Han Solo used this alias when he returned to Jubilar some 30 years after he survived the All-Human Free-For-All there.

**Morgo** A young boy on Kalarba who was assisted by Q-E and 2-E in finding his way home

Admiral Mordur

one day, just before the two E series droids exposed Vuldo's secret blaster plans.

**Morgot** A Skrilling friend of Quinlan Vos, he was a ready source of information for the Jedi. Morgot was a notoriously bad gambler, and often got into trouble trying to cover his debts.

*Morgot*

**Morgukai Warriors** An ancient order of Kajain'sa'Nikto warriors, nearly extinct by the Battle of Geonosis. Morgukai existed in the farthest reaches of the Endless Wastes, and were experts in survival and battle. Fathers often trained their sons in a style that resembled the Master–Padawan relationship of the Jedi Knights. During the Clone Wars, it was believed that a handful of surviving Morgukai were led by Tsyr and Bok. Bok had been cloned by Separatist forces on Saleucami as part of Count Dooku's program to create the so-called Shadow Army. By the time Chancellor Palpatine had installed himself as Emperor, any surviving Morgukai were outlawed as religious fanatics.

**Morishim** This planet, located close to the borders of Imperial space, was the site of a New Republic starfighter base. Here Imperial Admiral Pellaeon hoped to meet with Garm Bel Iblis to begin negotiating a peace treaty between the remnants of the Empire and the Republic.

**Morjakar** A rogue planetoid occupying the second orbit of the Cularin system, it was believed to have been born in a solar system across the galaxy. Scientists theorized that Morjakar was the outermost terrestrial planet in a solar system whose star expanded into a red giant, flinging Morjakar out of orbit. It wandered the galaxy for many millennia before being caught in the gravity of the binary stars Morasil and Termandus.

**Morjanssik City** A floating city on Mon Calamari built by the Quarren to supply nearby mining facilities, it was one of the few cities populated almost entirely by Quarren.

**Morn** A Mon Calamari who served as one of Black Sun's Vigos during the years before the Battle of Naboo. Morn worked from a base on his homeworld of Mon Calamari until he was targeted for execution by Darth Maul. The Sith attacked Morn's base in order to learn the whereabouts of Asa Naga and Garyn, destroying the facility and executing Morn to maintain secrecy.

**Morning Bell (Doornik-319)** A world in the Koornacht Cluster of the Farlax sector, this brown-and-white planet was inhabited by a colony of Kubaz. It was known to the New Republic as Doornik-319, and to the Yevetha as Preza. Sitting on a direct line between the Yevethan capital world of N'zoth and the New Republic capital of Coruscant, it held significance to the Yevetha that was not lost on Republic officials. After the Yevetha massacred the colonists, the New Republic Fifth Fleet was sent to blockade Morning Bell to prevent the invaders from using it as a forward base for more conquests. The attempt was a failure, and the fleet retreated with heavy casualties.

**Morning Court** Located in the new Jedi Temple erected on Coruscant in the wake of the Yuuzhan Vong War, this open atrium was circular in shape and lined by mirrored transparisteel walls. The floor was blanketed with living sturdimoss, and the roof membrane could be opened or closed depending on the weather.

***Morningstar*** One of the many starships that participated in the Battle of Geonosis.

**Moro III** A planet that was the site of a starship-repair facility in the years following the Yuuzhan Vong War.

**Morobe** A red-yellow binary star that was the primary sun in the Morobe system, which included Talasea. The system bordered the Rachuk sector.

**Morodin** Often mistaken for lumbering wild beasts, Morodins were actually giant herbivorous sentients with extensive knowledge of biochemical agriculture. They colonized Varonat before the Republic was founded in the hope of feeding their homeworld's population. Averaging 15 meters in length, they possessed six short legs and a spoon-shaped snout filled with flat grinding teeth. While they exhibited none of the usual hallmarks of civilization—such as structures and technology—they were quite intelligent.

*Morodin*

*Morgukai Warrior*

**Morota, Ayo** The founder of the Red Hand in the undercity of Coruscant during the final years of the Old Republic, she took on several contracts to assassinate political leaders. Quinlan Vos located her base in the sewers of Galactic City, and Morota believed his story of being an outcast from the Jedi Order. She allowed him to join the Red Hand, but later discovered that he had been sent to infiltrate by Jedi Master Yoda. She ordered him executed. Vos fought his way to freedom, and Morota admitted that she had been defeated. She jumped from the edge of a sewer drain and plummeted into the depths, her death hiding the fact that she and the Red Hand were secretly in the employ of Chancellor Palpatine himself.

**morp droid** The design of these repulsor-equipped droids was attributed to Asajj Ventress, the Dark Jedi who was one of Count Dooku's chief lieutenants during the Clone Wars. Each morp droid resembled a floating six-legged beetle, and it delivered a powerful electric discharge able to electrocute many beings, including humans.

**Morro** A farmer and leader of his tribe on the planet Ceriun some 1,000 years before the Battle of Endor. When Ka'arn found a Jedi Holocron in the downed ship of a Jedi Knight, Morro decided to keep the holocron until another Jedi could come to Ceriun to take possession of it. This proved to be a fatal mistake, as the Sith arrived and killed those who had helped recover the holocron.

**Morrs, Lieutenant** A New Republic officer in charge of investigating Kyp Durron's theft of the Sun Crusher weapon from its resting place at the heart of the gas giant Yavin. His results were insubstantial, because the sheer force of the storms at the planet's heart would not allow his sensor teams to gather useful data.

**morrt** Parasites the size of field mice native to the planet Gamorr. Morrt bloodsuckers fed on living organisms, staying with a single host throughout their long lives. Gamorreans considered morrts to be friendly and loyal and kept them as pets and status symbols. The more morrts that were attached to a Gamorrean—some matrons and warlords had more than 20—the higher the Gamorrean's status.

***Morrt*-class parasite droid** Automata developed by Warlord Zsinj and distributed throughout the galaxy, they were designed to attach themselves to hulls of starships and report back locations and other significant information.

**Mors, Opeli** The primary representative of the Jin'ri Trade Syndicate during the Yuuzhan Vong War, she supported the creation of Luke Skywalker's Great River, only because it would allow the Syndicate to make a profit selling supplies along the pathway.

**Morseerian** A four-armed species that breathed methane. Few were ever seen without their environmental suits. They existed on the fringes of galactic civilization for almost 12,000 years, and would rather die than reveal the location of their homeworld. Morseerians traveled the space lanes in oval-shaped starships of their own design, which were able to support methane atmospheres. Aside from trading expeditions, the Morseerians in general did not interact much with the galaxy at large. Nabrun Leids, a Mos Eisley cantina patron, was a Morseerian.

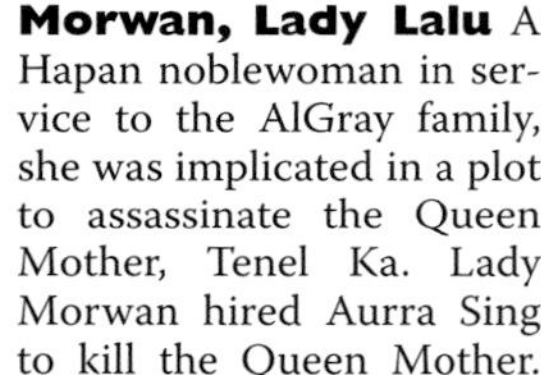
Morseerian

**Morshdine sector** When Luke Skywalker infiltrated the Cavrilhu pirate base, he discovered that Wesselman had traveled to this sector, which was rimward of Amorris, to pick up a load of unregistered Tibanna gas.

**Morto** A Togorian male who was one of the new Sith discovered by Alema Rar on Korriban some three years after the Swarm War. Alema Rar hoped to find Sith and continue the work of Lumiya, who had been attempting to turn Jacen Solo into the next Dark Lord of the Sith. Morto intercepted Alema when she arrived at the Valley of the Dark Lords, but she managed to injure him in the process.

**Mortull, Wud** Once apprenticed to Jedi Master Pernicar in the years before the Battle of Ruusan, Mortull went missing, only to reappear eight years later in the company of the Sith. Pernicar was forced to confront his former student, who smiled and welcomed Pernicar with open arms. However, with a smile still on his face, Mortull drew a red-bladed lightsaber and rushed to attack. Pernicar cut down his former student, who still wore the same smile on his face when he died.

**morvak** Unusual creatures able to derive sustenance from rocks and stones, they required neither gravity nor atmosphere for survival. That allowed them to live in asteroid belts, which provided abundant sources of food. Resembling large crustaceans, the average morvak was more than a meter across and covered with a heavy exoskeleton.

**Morvogodine** A planet located in the Calaron sector, it was occupied by the Empire during the Galactic Civil War. It was on Morvogodine that vandfillist artist Maxa Jandovar was arrested by Imperial forces. She later died in custody.

**Morv'vyal** A Bothan investigator with the Drev'starn Department of Criminal Discouragement, he accompanied Proy'skyn to the Exoticalia Pet Emporium on a tip that the store had been burglarized. The Bothans discovered a hidden cache of weapons kept by Navett and Klif, which forced the humans to kill the Bothan investigators in order to carry out their plans.

**Morwan, Lady Lalu** A Hapan noblewoman in service to the AlGray family, she was implicated in a plot to assassinate the Queen Mother, Tenel Ka. Lady Morwan hired Aurra Sing to kill the Queen Mother. When Sing's attempt was thwarted, Lady Morwan tracked the bounty hunter to Telkur Station, where she ordered her to focus her attention instead on the Chume'da, Allana. Sing took off in Lady Morwan's Batag Skiff, forcing Morwan to accept transport back to Hapes with Han Solo and his wife, Leia Organa Solo. During the trip, Lady Morwan dropped her cover, and then aimed a blaster at Han. She continued to prod and needle him until he broke her nose with a blow from his elbow.

**Morymento** The largest colony on Kerilt, it lacked self-sufficiency and was a target for pirates. Morymento was also the home of one of the larger Caamasi Remnant communities.

**Mosa, Linjak** A Kadas'sa'Nikto pirate, he was a member of Gardulla the Hutt's crime organization shortly after the Battle of Naboo. Jabba the Hutt offered a bounty for his capture after Mosa destroyed several of his spice freighters. Jango Fett later claimed the bounty during a mission to locate Gardulla on Tatooine.

**Mos Eisley** A spaceport city on the Outer Rim world of Tatooine, it was, in the words of Ben Kenobi, a "wretched hive of scum and villainy." Mos Eisley attracted interstellar commerce as well as spacers looking for rest and relaxation after a long haul. The vast number of aliens and humans constantly moving through the spaceport, and its distance from the centers of Republic and Imperial activity, long made Mos Eisley a haven for thieves, pirates, and smugglers.

The city's old central section was laid out like a wheel, while the newer sections were formed into straight blocks of buildings half buried to protect them from the heat of Tatooine's twin suns. Instead of a central landing area, the entire city was a spaceport, with 362 crater-like docking bays scattered throughout.

Founded 85 years before the Battle of Yavin, Mos Eisley grew outward from the crash site of the *Dowager Queen* as spacefaring companies and individuals realized that Tatooine's proximity to existing space lanes was advantageous. Mos Eisley Spaceport began as an alternative to the then-bustling Anchorhead port, which many residents found too expensive. Rodian refugees helped in the construction of the city's many docking bays. Though their hard work did indeed build a city, their corrupt pasts also brought vice and crime to the port. Mos Eisley's population tripled as businesses took root to offer services to starships and travelers who were passing through the system. The city was divided into two main sections, the Old Quarter surrounding the *Dowager Queen* wreckage, and the more tourist-friendly areas known as the New Quarter.

Mos Eisley

When the popularity of Podracing began to wane, so, too, did neighboring Mos Espa's prominence in Tatooine's trade and tourism. Mos Eisley became the de facto (though unofficial) capital. When the Empire came to power, the local governor installed an Imperial Prefect in Mos Eisley, as well as a contingent of stormtroopers specially equipped for the desert environments.

It was at Mos Eisley that Luke Skywalker and Kenobi secured transit off Tatooine. The two hired the services of Han Solo and Chewbacca, smugglers they met at the Mos Eisley cantina. At the time of the Battle of Yavin, the Prefect was a lazy man named Orun Depp. He died in an assassin droid "incident" and was promptly replaced with Prefect Eugene Talmont. Following the death of Jabba the Hutt, the city was thrown into raging chaos. Much of the city was burned and/or looted, and for a time Tatooine was isolated from the major shipping lanes because the spaceport was inaccessible.

**Mos Eisley cantina** Looking at the exterior of the Mos Eisley cantina, few would suspect the bizarre and dangerous array of aliens seeking shade, business, and refreshment within. Upon first entering the establishment, a patron stepped into a darkened alcove. The period in which that patron's eyes adjusted from the blazing desert sunlight to the dank interior gave the customers just enough time to check out the new arrival.

Located in the heart of the Old Quarter, the cantina was just down the dusty street from the *Dowager Queen* wreckage. It was one of the first structures built in Mos Eisley, originally intended as a shelter and armory to protect against Tusken Raider attacks. When the attacks never materialized, the blockhouse was converted into a bar, and the cantina changed hands many times.

During the era of the Galactic Civil War, the bar was owned by a Wookiee named Chalmun, who bought the building with gambling profits swindled on Ord Mantell. Chalmun rarely exited his backroom office, and hired a number of bartenders to dispense drinks. The gruff and sour Wuher had the most shifts, but the favorite of the regulars was the matronly Ackmena.

Chalmun's disgust with droids led him to install a droid detector in the front foyer. Its warbling alerted patrons to the presence of mechanicals. Other than that, there were few rules governing behavior in the cantina. While there were no gaming tables at Chalmun's, there were always at least half a dozen games of chance being played around the main room. Though Chalmun was hesitant to do so, he eventually capitulated to employee and patron demands and added a live band. He admitted that the lively tunes of Figrin D'an and the Modal Nodes helped discourage violence.

*Mos Eisley cantina*

*Mos Espa*

The central bar was a high-tech, if outdated, setup capable of synthesizing virtually any known drink in the sector. The mixing computer knew 16,000 recipes, but of course Chalmun did not keep all the required ingredients in stock.

A few steps down into the main room lay a scattering of booths and freestanding tables. Most of the best freighter pilots visiting Tatooine could be found here. Deals of all kinds were made in the shadows—most of them dangerous and nowhere near legal.

Prior to his departure from Tatooine, Luke Skywalker got a first look at just what a life among the stars could promise. The fresh-faced farm boy had never seen so many aliens in one place, and the rough-and-tumble crowd could sense an easy target. Two thugs tried to pick a fight with the youth, but Obi-Wan Kenobi intervened, dispatching the brutes with a quick swing of his lightsaber. It was here that Skywalker and Kenobi hired the services of Han Solo and Chewbacca. The smuggling duo was responsible for transporting the last of the Jedi Knights and the first of the new off the desert planet and into a galaxy of adventure.

**Mos Eisley Merchant's Association** Chadra-Fan pickpocket Kabe claimed to be a representative of this organization. Dressed up like a Jawa, she approached incoming starship captains and explained to them that they had to buy a "trade license" from her for 500 credits in order to do business on the planet.

**Mos Eisley Towers** Despite its name, this hotel was almost entirely underground in Mos Eisley. Its rooms were clean and cheap.

**Mos Entha** A settlement on the planet Tatooine, across the Mospic High Range from Mos Espa. Following the Battle of Endor, Mos Entha experienced a surge of wealth. By the time the Yuuzhan Vong invaded the galaxy, Mos Entha was the site of a modern spaceport.

Until the arrival of the New Republic, Mos Entha was just another spaceport city. But with the death of Jabba the Hutt, traders could afford to choose which spaceport they wished to patronize, and Mos Eisley had lost much of its allure. Similarly, the increased interest in the homeworld of Luke Skywalker—a Jedi Master and hero of the Rebellion—brought an influx of tourism that the desert world hadn't seen since the days of Podracing.

As a result, Mos Entha was something of a model for the modern Tatooine city. The streets were clean, safe, and evenly laid out in a radial pattern around the spaceport hubs: four massive domed structures that stood 500 meters above the streets, providing no less than 60 ultramodern docking facilities. The original docking bays were still used, bringing the total count up to almost 75 docking bays. The cultural and entertainment centers of Mos Entha rested within the domed spaceport hubs, where multilevel, environment-controlled hotels were the foundation for the tourist trade.

**Mos Espa** Mos Espa was one of few port cities on Tatooine, born out of the desert and built piece by piece over many years. Rodian refugees founded what was to become the city about 80 years before the Battle of Yavin. Domed buildings protected the citizens against the glare of the twin suns and the scorching heat. Among the dwellings, work spaces, and commercial operations of many bizarre kinds there were also entertainment areas, including some of colossal scale. The famed Mos Espa Grand Arena could hold an audience almost as large as the city's entire population.

Most of Mos Espa's inhabitants were settlers and subsistence earners who scratched out a meager living as best they could. The only real wealth in Mos Espa was tied up in gambling and offworld trade, especially in the lucrative black market beyond the trade laws and controls of the galactic government.

In the time of the Old Republic, slavery persisted in Mos Espa, although the despicable trade was outlawed elsewhere. An entire section of the city's outskirts had been transformed into a Slave Quarter. Live slaves functioned more as prestige possessions than cheap laborers, and owners parted with them only reluctantly. Slaves could even find themselves used as capital in business transactions. The true powers in control of Mos Espa were the Hutt gangsters, who found slavery a useful institution for their purposes, and Tatooine's remoteness allowed them to practice their illegal ventures.

The influx of commercial ventures fueled Mos Espa's growth, and in a short time it became the largest city on Tatooine and the desert planet's de facto capital. The city grew in a serpentine shape, winding its way through the Xelric Draw at the edge of the Dune Sea. The Hutts fostered public distraction from their criminal activities by building the massive Podracing arena. With the rise of the Empire, however, the changing political climate caused a shift in Hutt business. Podracing waned as a public spectacle and Jabba, the most powerful Hutt on Tatooine, changed residences to be closer to Mos Eisley. As a result, Mos Espa's prominence declined in favor of Mos Eisley's growth.

**Mos Espa Circuit** A Podracing course established by Jabba the Hutt just outside the spaceport city of Mos Espa. Beginning in the confines of the Mos Espa Arena, the course started out across the Starlite Flats, and then wound through Waldo Flats before opening into Mushroom Mesa and Ebe Crater Valley. From there, Podracers had to negotiate Beggar's Canyon before getting a brief respite while crossing a desert plain bordering on the Dune Sea. Racers were forced to navigate through Arch Canyon before weaving through the Whip, Jag Crag Gorge, and the Lagula Caves. After emerging from the Caves, racers moved through the Canyon Dune Turn before hitting the Bindy Bend. At the far end of the Bend, the course narrowed sharply as it passed through the Coil, Jett's Chute, and the Corkscrew. Once through this set of challenges, racers pushed their machines to the limit to return to Mos Espa Arena across Hutt Flats.

**Mos Espa Grand Arena** Built by Jabba the Hutt with a great deal of governmental help. Jabba obtained the necessary permits, licenses, and funding by claiming the huge arena would bring business to Mos Espa. Each year, the Arena hosted the Boonta Eve Classic Podrace, which attracted more than 100,000 spectators from across the Outer Rim. Other Podraces were also run there, on the amateur circuits.

**Mos Espa Slave Quarters** In one of the poorest sections of Mos Espa were a series of small hovels stacked one atop another, serving as homes for the city's slave population. Families were usually allowed to remain together, and a few connecting hovels were sometimes transformed into some sort of family home, with different bedrooms leading to a common living area. Despite their wretched appearance, the quarters were sturdy enough to protect the residents from the sandstorms that regularly hit Mos Espa.

*Mos Espa Grand Arena*

The Slave Quarters were beneath the notice of well-to-do citizens and local authorities, making them an ideal hiding or meeting place for low-profile travelers with the right connections. Anakin Skywalker lived there with his mother Shmi during the early years of his life, before he was liberated to become a Jedi Knight. The Skywalker hovel was larger than most, being a conglomerate of three smaller units. This was not a mark of generosity on Watto's part; he simply could not afford more slaves.

The hovels originally were built by the miners who settled and then abandoned Tatooine. They used antiquated bioconverter power generators, which received liquid sludge composed of animal and municipal waste via underground pipelines. This sludge was then converted into a natchgas, used to meet the hovels' power needs.

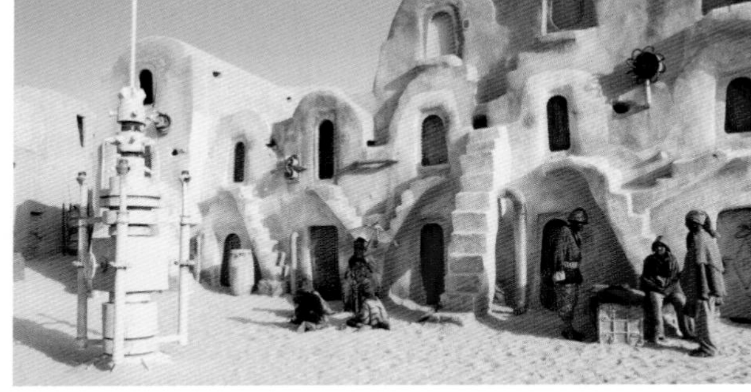

*Mos Espa Slave Quarters*

**Mos Espa Swoop Arena** Following the decline of Podracing's popularity and the ravages of the Clone Wars, the former Mos Espa Grand Arena on Tatooine was abandoned and eventually taken over by a small band of swoop racers. There they staged a regular series of semi-legitimate races during the early years of the New Republic.

*Mos Espa Circuit*

**Mos Gamos** One of the most remote settlements on Tatooine, it was considered a haven for many criminals during the years following the Battle of Naboo. It was the site of Longo Two-Guns's hideout.

**mosgoth** Reptilian avians native to Togoria, mosgoths were befriended by the Togorians for their mutual protection against the liphons. Mosgoths allowed themselves to be used as mounts, and the Togorians provided them shelter. The average mosgoth stood nearly 10 meters high and had a wingspan of 40 meters or more. Despite their fearsome appearance, mosgoths were considered one of the most majestic creatures in the galaxy.

**Mosh** A technical officer and shuttle pilot assigned to the Outbound Flight Project some five years after the Battle of Naboo.

**Mos Nytram** A remote settlement on the planet Tatooine during the last decades of the Old Republic.

**Mos Osnoe** A small spaceport on Tatooine used by the Galactic Republic during the Clone Wars. Sev'Rance Tann went to Mos Osnoe to meet with Boorka the Hutt.

**Mossak** A major hyperspace hub for travelers headed into the Tingel Arm from Felucia or along the Perlemian Trade Route. During the final stages of the Clone Wars, a huge space

battle was fought over Mossak when the Old Republic discovered a Separatist staging facility in the system. Republic warships caught the Separatists by surprise, taking control of the system, then spreading mines to prevent Separatist ships from returning.

Moteé

**moss chips** A snack popular in the Core Worlds during the final years of the Old Republic.

**moss-painting** An art form from Alderaan, it involved the cultivation of specific strains of mosses that neither spread nor reproduced, keeping their position static within the artwork. The secrets of how to cultivate the mosses and grow them into paintings were well guarded even on Alderaan, and were lost when the planet was destroyed by the first Death Star. Moss-paintings could not be forged.

**Mos Taike** A city located outside the Xelric Draw on Tatooine. Dusque Mistflier and Tendau Nandon investigated a krayt dragon graveyard near Mos Taike.

**Most Perfect Order of K'vin** A so-called religion that was started by the disembodied brain known as K'vin. Like the B'omarr monks, the members of this order severed their brains from their bodies and stored them in nutrient jars. In this way, they could contemplate the universe for centuries beyond their normal life spans. However, K'vin claimed that the B'omarr were a splinter sect of the Most Perfect Order of K'vin, although the only distinguishing factor seemed to be that the B'omarr used red nutrient fluid to maintain their brains, while K'vin and his followers used green.

**Mos Zabu** A small city on the planet Tatooine. Domo Jones and his friends would often hang out at a cantina there. One day Jones overheard information there regarding an Imperial shipment of deadly nergon 14.

**Mota** A member of the Worker faction on New Apsolon, Mota secretly was a black-market dealer in virtually anything, providing the highest bidder with weapons, vehicles, or rations. Mota demanded, however, that his fellow Workers refrain from using illegal methods in fighting for their freedom. He helped Qui-Gon Jinn and Obi-Wan Kenobi obtain a probe droid and speeders to help them track Balog.

**Motamba** A blue-eyed Wookiee who was a munitions expert in Katarra's underground during the Imperial occupation of Kashyyyk.

**Moteé** One of Senator Padmé Amidala's handmaidens, she would often stand in when the Senator snuck away to be with her husband, Anakin Skywalker. Moteé was in the Senate Chamber when Palpatine declared himself Emperor.

**Motempe, Jarse** A New Republic information science specialist responsible for decoding the data found in the *Gnisnal*'s datacore.

**Motesta** The fourth settlement founded on Tatooine, this farming community was located between the Jundland Wastes and Mos Eisley, along Arnthout Pass. It was south of Bestine.

**Motesta Oasis** A freshwater oasis located near the settlement of Motesta on Tatooine, it was found on the edge of the Jundland Wastes, between Arthout and the Jawa Heights.

**Motexx** Two sectors away from Arat Fraca, Motexx was separated from that planet by the Black Nebula in Parfadi. The starliner *Star Morning*, owned by the Fallanassi religious order, left Motexx a few weeks before the Battle of Endor with a full cargo, bound for Gowdawl under a charter license. The liner then disappeared for 300 days, eventually showing up at Arat Fraca with empty cargo holds.

**Mother (1)** Mara Jade Skywalker's call sign as a member of Saber Squadron. She used it during the defense and evacuation of the Jedi Knights' base on Eclipse.

**Mother (2)** The title given to the eldest woman of each Tarasin Irstat. Each Mother was considered a wise woman and leader, having served as an Irstat-Kes for several years.

**Mother Jungle** Ithorians referred to the natural environment of their homeworld, Ithor, as Mother Jungle. Ithorians chose not to set foot on the surface of their planet in order to preserve its natural beauty. In order for Ithorians, or any other beings, to come into contact with the forest floor, they had to first give up something of themselves to prove their desire.

**mother-rock** Found in the spongy landmasses of the planet Dagobah, this red-colored stone was believed by Jedi Master Yoda to have healing powers.

Mon Mothma

**Mothers United March on Alsakan** Staged in protest of the Jedi Council and its handling of the case of baby Ludi Billane. Baby Ludi was taken from her homeworld of Ord Thoden after a devastating earthquake destroyed Domitree, but her mother, Jonava, also survived. Jonava tried to recover her daughter, but the Jedi refused to release the child. The March on Alsakan was organized to raise the level of awareness of Jedi tactics with regard to young children, as well as to raise money to help Jonava cover her legal expenses.

***Mother's Valkyrie*** A starship owned by Belezaboth Ourn, it was nearly destroyed when the *Aradamia* tried to lift off from Coruscant. Nil Spaar used the damaged ship as part of his plan to show how Leia Organa Solo was keeping him on the planet against his will, thus causing injury to so-called innocent bystanders.

**Mothma, Lieda** Mon Mothma's daughter, she was born during the early years of the Rebel Alliance.

**Mothma, Mon** Inspiring, and committed to the cause of freedom in the galaxy, the Senator from the planet Chandrila became the conscience as well as the leader of the Rebel Alliance and the founder and first Chief of State of the New Republic.

Mon Mothma's parents prepared her well for her eventual pivotal role in galactic politics. Her father, an arbiter-general for the Old Republic, settled disputes among various species and taught her respect for all beings. Her mother, Tanis, was a planetary governor who taught her how to administer, organize, and lead. Until Princess Leia Organa was elected, Mothma was the youngest person ever to serve in the Republic Senate. Mothma was an outspoken representative who was one of the first Senators to notice the degeneration of the Old Republic.

As the Clone Wars ground on, Mon Mothma and Alderaan Senator Bail Organa worked with Naboo Senator Padmé Amidala to enact legislation ensuring that Chancellor Palpatine relinquished the additional powers he had acquired during the conflict. Their efforts failed, and Senator Mothma and her colleagues were forced to watch as Palpatine named himself Emperor and instituted the New Order.

In opposition to Palpatine's ascendancy, Mothma organized intelligence cells—pockets of resistance to challenge the Empire—each one unaware of the other cells' existence. When the Republic finally crumbled, Mothma went underground, uniting the political cells to form what was to become the Rebel Alliance.

Although her role in unifying the disparate resistance groups into the Rebel Alliance was unquestioned, Mothma credited Bail Organa for envisioning the structure of the organization. The two Senators were often opponents on the Senate floor, as Mothma's youthful idealism clashed with Organa's realism and cynicism. The two did agree that Palpatine had to be stopped. In a series of meetings at Cantham House, Organa and Mothma devised and developed a plan for the Rebel Alliance. While Organa helped secretly supply the Alliance, he still played the role of political opponent to Mon Mothma. When the Emperor decided to arrest Mothma, Organa informed her, and she managed to escape just minutes before the Imperial Security Bureau arrived.

Mon Mothma then spent the next several years on the run from the Empire. As a fugitive, she made contact with various resistance groups, expounding the virtues of the Alliance. Mothma's life was threatened not only by Imperial agents but by overly suspicious resistance groups as well.

The true birth of the Rebellion was the signing of the Corellian Treaty, in which the three main resistance groups swore on their lives to join the Alliance and answer to Mothma. Mothma and her Advisory Council became supreme rulers of the Alliance. Critics, such as former Corellian Senator Garm Bel Iblis, pointed out that Mothma was assuming dictatorial powers on the level of her enemy Palpatine. Mothma realized that a separate, impartial authority was needed to make the big decisions of the Alliance, and she was that person. Mothma instituted a policy that every two years, members of the Alliance would vote on her continued command. She was never challenged in all the years of Rebellion.

Once the Alliance was truly formed, Mothma wrote the Declaration of Rebellion. This document, personally addressed to Palpatine, indicted the Emperor on a number of crimes. The declaration served to undo the damage of Imperial propaganda that painted the Rebels as terrorists. As a result of the declaration, many worlds decided to ally themselves with the Rebellion. During the Galactic Civil War, Mon Mothma served as Chief of State of the Alliance civil government as well as Commander in Chief of the Alliance military. At this time, Mon Mothma was number one on the Empire's Most Wanted List.

Mothma, along with Crix Madine and the Mon Calamarian Ackbar, devised the plan to destroy the second Death Star at Endor, which eventually succeeded. After the Rebel victory, Mothma was faced with the challenge of transforming a militarized Rebellion into a fully functional government. She organized a Galactic Congress, a series of diplomatic conferences that helped establish how the New Republic would govern. Mothma became Chief of State of the new government that emerged, and helped guide it through the numerous growing pains and threats that plagued it during its formative years.

She supported establishing the site of the new government exactly where the Old Republic's and the Empire's had been, on Coruscant. The planet then came under attack by Grand Admiral Thrawn. Upon his defeat, six Star Destroyer commanders staged an assault and succeeded in driving Mothma and the rest of her government into exile. Their temporary headquarters on Da Soocha 5 was destroyed by the reborn clone Emperor's Galaxy Gun, but Alliance officials were able to escape before the attack. The Republic launched an attack on Byss in response, destroying the Emperor's cloning facility forever.

Back on Coruscant, new Chief of State Mothma and the Senate set about restructuring to create a truly effective intergalactic government. They approved plans for Luke Skywalker to immediately establish a Jedi training facility and took on the thousand and one tasks involved in governing.

*Admiral Conan Antonio Motti*

When attempting to forge peace with remnants of the former Empire at a diplomatic reception for Imperial Ambassador Furgan of Carida, Mothma was secretly poisoned. Furgan introduced a nano-engineered virus that started dismantling her cell structure one cell at a time. Slowly she wasted away while New Republic medics were helpless to save her. Lying on her deathbed, Mothma tendered her resignation as Chief of State, passing on the leadership to Leia Organa Solo. Eventually, the true nature of her illness was revealed. A Mon Calamari Jedi healer named Cilghal was able to cleanse Mothma's body of the artificial contagion, and Mothma soon recovered. Content with Leia as her replacement, Mothma retired from political life.

Mon Mothma was more accepting of allowing former Imperials to serve in the New Republic Senate than Leia was. During the Almanian crisis, following the call for a no-confidence vote against Leia and her subsequent resignation as Chief of State, Mon Mothma agreed to temporarily resume her old role while Leia left Coruscant to find Luke Skywalker and prove that her husband, Han Solo, was not involved in the bombing that rocked Senate Hall. Once it was proven that the bombing was the work of the Dark Jedi Kueller—part of a reign of terror against the New Republic—Mon Mothma gratefully returned the role of Chief of State to Leia. She died peacefully in her sleep years after a final peace accord was reached between the New Republic and the remnants of the Galactic Empire.

*Mott*

**Mothma 5-0** The call sign of one of the Galactic Alliance starships that accompanied the *Bounty* and the *Daring* on their patrol near Bothan space at the height of the Corellia–GA War.

**Mothma Squadron** One of the best starfighter squadrons stationed aboard the Galactic Alliance warship *Bounty* during the Confederation—GA War.

**motivator** A droid's main internal mechanism, it converted energy into mechanical motion.

**motmot** *See* mastmot.

**motosurfing** A sport in which a rider used a motorized sled to race across the water.

**mott** An herbivorous creature resembling a small hippopotamus. Native to Naboo, motts had sharp claws and small horns on the ends of their snouts, used to dig up the delicate flowers of the Naboo plains. Some Gungans were known to domesticate the gentle creatures, which were loyal pets when trained.

**Motta the Hutt** A fat and flatulent Hutt crime lord active on the planet Tatooine during the era of the Great Sith War. He dealt in slavery, and was one of the few beings who enslaved members of the Rakata species. Motta kept what he called a Rakata specimen in a strange box known as a mind prison. If the box was opened, the opener was transported inside and forced to answer three of the Rakata's questions. If the opener failed, he or she was trapped inside the box until Motta opened it himself. The entrapped beings were then sold into slavery by Motta.

**Motti, Admiral Conan Antonio** The senior Imperial commander in charge of operations aboard the original Death Star. This arrogant officer believed in the ultimate superiority of the battle station over any possible foe that would dare challenge it. Motti was a true believer in the philosophy of technological might. He found the methods of Darth Vader archaic and laughable. When Vader failed to produce the location of the main Rebel headquarters, Motti openly scoffed at Vader's devotion to the Force. The Dark Lord of the Sith quickly educated Motti as to the Force's true power by inflicting a telekinetic stranglehold on the admiral. At the behest of Grand Moff Tarkin, Vader released Motti, and

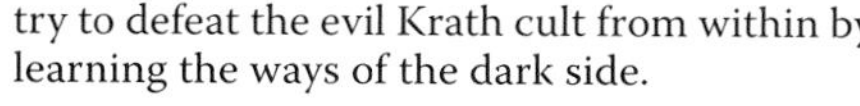

it was a lesson that the admiral didn't soon forget.

Motti, like many officers of his era, was vastly overrated, having padded his career with routine missions labeled military successes. It was his connections that landed him a prestigious appointment to the Death Star project. Motti, together with Tarkin and General Tagge, formed the command triumvirate for the battle station. Though Motti's record was one of exemplary devotion to the New Order, his unbridled ambition extended even to fantasies of usurping the Emperor's throne. He saw the Death Star as but one step in an eventual bid for absolute power. In quiet moments aboard the station, Motti would casually drop hints to Tarkin that they now possessed greater power than even the distant Palpatine. Tarkin took note of Motti's insinuations, but never challenged his treasonous notions. Had the Rebels not destroyed the Death Star when they did, it's possible that the power structure of the Empire could have vastly changed with Tarkin and Motti in command.

**Mott's Nostril** One of the many small openings in the gaseous walls of the Utegetu Nebula.

*Foul Moudama*

**Moudama, Foul** A Talz trained as a Jedi Knight during the last decades of the Old Republic. Known for his grace and agility, Moudama often was underestimated by his opponents. He had an insatiable desire for knowledge. During the Clone Wars, he was part of a task force dispatched to protect Chancellor Palpatine when General Grievous launched his attack on Coruscant. Grievous was able to kill both Master Moudama and Master Roron Corobb before taking Palpatine hostage.

**mounder potato rice** A starchy Corellian food disliked by Han Solo.

**Mountains of Lightning** Crystalline rock formations found near the city of Hweg Shul on Nam Chorios, they were thought to be the source of the strange Force lightning storms that swept the planet's valleys. Seti Ashgad maintained a residence there.

**Mountains of the Exalted** A range found on the planet Ylesia, the beautiful peaks were located near Colony One, and the Altar of Promises was sited at their base. They were so named because the t'landa Til priests stood with the mountains at their backs during Exaltations.

*Mount Meru on Deneba*

**Mountain Terrain Armored Transport (MT-AT walker)** A vehicle developed by the Empire on the planet Carida for use in attacking positions that were located in mountainous or rugged terrain. The MT-AT had eight legs with highly articulated joints; clawed feet employed mild explosives to better grip the terrain. Also nicknamed spider walkers, they could climb an almost vertical mountain face. The body and legs were studded with weapons, with laser cannons at each joint and a pair of blaster cannons mounted on the cockpit.

**Mount Avos** This large mountain, part of the Hormack range found on Troiken, overlooked the Lycinder Plain. The mountain was once a source of spice during the Old Republic, but the mines dried up quickly.

**Mount Dagger** The former name of the highest mountain peak on Dagobah. It was renamed Mount Yoda following the Battle of Endor.

**Mount Ison** This immense, snow-covered mountain was the tallest peak in the North Ridge chain on Hoth.

**Mount Meru (1)** The site of a large amphitheater on Deneba some 4,000 years before the Galactic Civil War. Master Odan-Urr assembled 10,000 Jedi there to discuss the upcoming Sith War. It was on Mount Meru that Ulic Qel-Droma made his fateful decision to try to defeat the evil Krath cult from within by learning the ways of the dark side.

**Mount Meru (2)** A mountain on Drogheda, it was the site of the planet's primary mining operations. Mount Meru Mine was also the temporary headquarters of the Drogheda Revolutionaries during a civil war on the planet. Lando Calrissian destroyed water tanks in the mine, forcing the revolutionaries to flee.

**Mount Sorrow** A mountain on the Forest Moon of Endor. Its tip was sentient and had the power to both blow people off the summit and cry tears of healing.

**Mount Ste'vshuulsz** A jagged mound of shale and rock on the planet Barab I.

**Mount Tantiss** Located on the planet Wayland, it was considered a forbidden place by both the Psadan and Myneyrsh inhabitants. Emperor Palpatine hid his collection of valuable artifacts and extreme technology at Tantiss, including a cloaking device and Spaarti cylinders used for cloning. The main purpose of the Mount Tantiss installation was to protect and preserve the new technologies in case of the Emperor's death, and Palpatine placed a Guardian to watch over the installation. Crazed Jedi clone Joruus C'baoth arrived on Wayland, defeated the Guardian, and took control of the Imperial interests. But he was unable to maintain control of the world. In the aftermath of Grand Admiral Thrawn's reign of terror, C'baoth confronted Luke Skywalker and Mara Jade inside the Tantiss storehouse. Skywalker and Jade defeated the clone Luuke Skywalker and C'baoth, but the release of dark side energy brought much of the mountain down in a huge explosion. Nearly everything in the storehouse was destroyed, and the mountain itself was

*Mount Tantiss*

*Mountain Terrain Armored Transport*

Mouse

shattered. Some years later, a clan of Noghri established a dukha at the foot of Mount Tantiss as a reminder of the betrayal their people suffered at the hands of the Empire. During the Yuuzhan Vong War, New Republic Intelligence had a safe house in the remains of Tantiss, where Elan and Vergere were debriefed. Officials had to fight off an attack from a Yuuzhan Vong assassin.

**Mount Thunderstone** Located on the Forest Moon of Endor, this craggy mountain was believed to have been the home of the evil witch Morag.

**Mount Umate** One of the highest peaks in the Manarai Mountain range on Coruscant. It was at the peak of Umate that Monument Park was created. By the time the park was opened, just a small piece of rock was all that was visible. This rock became known as KnobHead following the Yuuzhan Vong War.

**Mount Yeroc** A rock formation containing the powerful sky cannon, which could draw power from the planet's core to carve and mold the planet's surface. Yeroc was controlled by the Hobors for many generations, with only a few individuals knowing the secret of the sky cannon.

**Mount Yoda** The highest mountain peak on Dagobah, it was once the site of a secret Rebel Alliance outpost. It was named for the Jedi Master following the Battle of Endor.

Mount Umate

**Mouse** The code name for a Duros agent who served the Rebel Alliance during the Galactic Civil War. Mouse played the part of a stormtrooper during a raid on the Imperial labor colony on Kalist VI, staged to rescue Jorin Sol. When team members discovered hundreds of Jabiimi slaves, they altered their plans to rescue the slaves as well. Mouse was killed during the raid, but his sacrifice was a main reason that the Alliance mission was successful.

**mouse droid** *See* MSE-6 mouse droid.

**Mousul, Senator** An Ansionian who represented his planet as a Senator to the Old Republic, he was one of the many supporters of the secession movement. Mousul was unable to foresee the work of the Jedi Knights, however, in persuading the two factions of Ansionians to define a common ground and sign a treaty that allowed Ansion to remain part of the Republic.

**moving meditation** An active meditation practiced by many Jedi Knights who preferred movement to a trance. Their minds remained active without requiring a great deal of concentration. Anakin Skywalker often used this technique during the Clone Wars, turning his attention to the repair of machinery to take his mind off the struggles and ravages of the war.

**Moyan** A black-furred Bothan, he served as a colonel in the Galactic Alliance under Admiral Tarla Limpan aboard the battle carrier *Dodonna*. Moyan was assigned to be the liaison with Leia Organa Solo in the coordination of the *Dodonna*'s starfighters during the blockade of the Corellian system. Neither Moyan nor Admiral Limpan knew that Leia would do everything in her power to ensure that the Corellian pilots of Operation Noble Savage, including her own husband, Han, completed their mission without being killed by GA pilots.

**Moz** A nickname chosen by clone trooper CT-6200/8901. Moz was one of the many clone troopers killed during the assault on the city of Eyat on Gaftikar.

**mqaaq'it** A creature bioengineered by the Yuuzhan Vong as a type of replacement eye. Supreme Overlord Shimrra was one of the most prominent members to use mqaaq'it implants. They changed color to match his mood.

**Mrahash** A crime lord and authority figure from Kvabja. Mara Jade claimed to have a gift from the Mrahash to Chay Praysh in an effort to gain entrance to Praysh's fortress during her attempt to rescue Sansia Bardrin. Praysh put in a call to the Mrahash himself, who said he knew nothing about a gift.

Mrlssi

**M'rak, Yade** A Corellian gambler with an addiction to Podrace betting, he smuggled black-market weapons.

**mrid** Native to the planet Velmor, this small beast was the favored target of the royal family. Mrids were an ancient species and had developed fantastic survival instincts. Large numbers of mrids were bred for sport, to be released when a ceremonial hunt was held. Part of the sport was locating the small, four-legged creatures, which could hide virtually anywhere.

Mrids

**Mriss (plural: Mrissi)** A small avian-like sentient species native to Mrisst. Mrissi no longer had the ability to fly. They had a light covering of feathers; small vestigial wings protruded from their backs. They also had small beaks and round, piercing eyes. The Mrissi were known in the galaxy as educators and administrators and operated several respected universities. They were very knowledgeable about the politics of the galaxy, and had radical, although peaceful, views.

**Mrisst** A planet near the heart of the galaxy in the Fakir sector, it was first contacted by the 10th Alderaanian Expedition under the Old Republic. The survey surprisingly found that none of the dozens of Mrisst cultures had developed any type of three-dimensional art. At one point Grand Admiral Thrawn planned an assault on Mrisst, partly to try to lure and defeat the New Republic fleet.

**Mrlssi** An avian species first encountered by the Old Republic some 7,000 years before the Battle of Yavin, they were native to the planet Mrlsst. They were proud of their bright-colored plumage, which covered their

short bodies. They had vestigial wings on their backs but couldn't fly. The Mrlssi were technologically advanced as demonstrated by their alleged creation of the Phantom cloaking device. They also showed themselves to be manipulative and conniving in their dealings with Wedge Antilles and Rogue Squadron.

**Mrlssi half-hitch** One of the more complicated knots known in the galaxy, developed by the Mrlssi during the last decades of the Old Republic.

***Mrlsst*** A New Republic CR90 corvette, part of the force sent to liberate the planet Ciutric from the control of Prince-Admiral Krennel. It supported the flagship *Emancipator* along with several other corvettes and a trio of Nebulon-B frigates. It took heavy fire during the battle and was left for dead.

**Mrlsst** A planet in the Mennaalii system, Mrlsst was known as a university planet. It was on the very edge of Tapani space on the Shapani Bypass. The wet, humid world was made up of marshes and sandy swamps.

In an attempt to attract Imperial research money, Mrlsst scientists faked the production of a remarkable new cloaking device, code-named the Phantom Project. Several months after the Battle of Endor, Mrlsst Planetary University President Keela—not knowing the project was a ruse—invited representatives from the New Republic and the Empire to meet at his offices, offering to sell Phantom Project datacards to the highest bidder. During negotiations, Rogue Squadron discovered a gravitic polarization beam weapon called a Planet Slicer in a nearby asteroid belt. The Phantom Project may have been a sham, but this new weapon was operational. The deadly device unexpectedly triggered a spatial wormhole, warping local space and swallowing an Imperial vessel whole.

**Mrlsst Center for Linguistic Studies** Located in the city of Mrkeesh on Mrlsst, this university was dedicated to the study of language and its development throughout the galaxy. At the time of the Clone Wars, the university had been in operation for 800 years, cataloging and cross-translating all forms of verbal communication in the galaxy.

**MRR** Rebel Alliance fighter pilot slang for the food they were fed after they were captured by Imperial forces. *MRR* stood for "meals ready to regurgitate."

**Mrrov** An orange-and-white-striped Togorian who was the promised mate of Muuurgh. She became bored with society on Togoria and left the planet to explore the galaxy, much to the dismay of Muuurgh. While on Ylesia, Mrrov fell under the spell of the t'landa Til, who pushed the worship of the Oneness, and was enslaved at Colony Two. Muuurgh and Han Solo escaped from Colony One, then rescued Mrrov from Colony Two in a daring escapade. They fled to Togoria, where Mrrov and Muuurgh were eventually married.

**MRX-BR Pacifier** A well-armed exploration starship, designed and manufactured by Sydon Vehicle Works. During the New Order, it was the Empire's scout ship of choice, as its additional weaponry allowed it to subjugate new worlds it encountered. The ship's sensors were capable of counting the leaves on a single tree from orbit, and its weapons systems were tightly controlled by the ship's onboard computers.

*M-TD (Em-Teedee)*

**M'sadaar** A Nikto swoop racer on Onderon following the Jedi Civil War.

**MSD-32** Merr-Sonn Munitions' handheld disruptor pistol, the MSD-32 fired an energy blast that caused the target's molecules to become excited and lose cohesion, leading to its utter annihilation.

**MSE-6 mouse droid** Small and incongruous on the decks of powerful Imperial war machines, mouse droids were ever-present annoyances buzzing back and forth between tasks. They were small, boxy wheeled droids that provided courier and minor maintenance duties at industrial facilities such as those found on Mustafar, as well as space-based locations such as Star Destroyers and the Death Stars.

Developed by the rodent-like Chadra Fan species, the MSE-6 unit was marketed by the soon defunct Rebaxan Columni Corporation as "cute." Consumers instead found the droids as annoying as mice. The company had a sizable economic blunder on its hands. It had produced billions of MSE-6s for an audience that found them repulsive. To help ease the financial fallout, Rebaxan Columni sold its entire lot of MSE-6s at a cut rate to the Empire. The navy, which was growing at a tremendous rate under Palpatine's New Order, readily accepted the deal and put the little droids to work aboard the ships of the fleet.

MSE-6s were general-purpose droids with multiple capabilities, but a singular function. Their box-like shells concealed articulated manipulators and could hold a single modular circuit matrix, or C-matrix, which housed one skill. Common skill packages for MSE-6s included janitorial cleanup, security, basic repair, and communications. MSE-6s could chain together to form a tiny train of droids with multiple skills. Mouse droids also served as guides, leading troops through long corridor mazes to their assigned posts. Since such duty required them to have complete readouts of their assigned sections, they were rigged to melt down should they be captured by insurgents. This gave mouse droids a strong self-preservation instinct, and they fled if confronted with danger.

*MSE-6 mouse droid*

**MSE-6-P303K** A messenger droid that was part of the pool maintained aboard the *Iron Fist.* It was also one of the first droids reprogrammed by the astromech droid Tonin for subversive activities. MSE-6-P303K was instrumental in acquiring holocam access to parts of the ship, as well as obtaining information on the *Iron Fist*'s schematics. With these schematics, the secret labs Warlord Zsinj maintained to house the work of the Binring Biomedical team on the ship were discovered.

**MSE-X-PR6** An eccentric droid that was, at one time, a standard mouse droid assigned to the Imperial research base on Binaros. It was programmed to shuttle messages between the research personnel, so its skill matrix was removed and replaced with a vocabulator. The droid's holographic projector and manipulator arm were removed to allow for several storage spaces for datapads and other objects. Because of the droid's many modifications, it developed an enjoyment of petty theft and the acquisition of shiny objects. It collected a thermal detonator and an artifact recovered by research team members from their temple base, among other treasures.

**M'shento'su'Nikto** These were Southern Niktos with white, yellow, or orange skin. They were differentiated from other Nikto by the fact that they had no horns.

**M'shinn** A species—nicknamed Mossies—from the planet Genassa. M'shinn had a plant covering over their entire bodies.

**Msst** A small planet located near the Rim worlds, it was the former site of an Imperial stronghold. The Empire abandoned Msst after the incident at Bakura, but over the years used it as a rendezvous point. After failing to infiltrate Luke Skywalker's Jedi academy, the Dark Jedi Brakiss fled to Msst to report to the Imperial officers who had sent him to Yavin 4 as a spy. The planet got its name from the damp white mist that clung to the ground and reduced visibility. The mist was actually generated by floating pink jellyfish-like creatures called mistmakers, which stung with their hanging tentacles and drew the stunned prey into their mouths. Mistmakers were resilient enough to withstand blasterfire.

**M-TD (Em-Teedee)** A face-shaped, miniature translation droid built by C-3PO and

Chewbacca to help Chewie's nephew Lowbacca communicate with the students and instructors at Luke Skywalker's Jedi academy on Yavin 4. As the other students learned more of the Wookiee language, Em-Teedee's primary function became less important. However, with the help of other students, he obtained new programming and learned new ways to be of assistance. During the Yuuzhan Vong War, M-TD was lost when Lowbacca managed to escape from the *Tachyon Flier*. The small droid was destroyed in the crash, although its carcass was later discovered in the Unknown Regions by Jacen Solo when he visited the site of the crash.

**M'truli** A Nikto male captured aboard a Separatist freighter in the Tynnan sector by Omega Squad about a year after the Battle of Geonosis. M'truli and his comrades, Farr Orjul and Gysk, identified themselves as miners, a cover for their mission of transporting explosives for the Separatists. Before their capture they had sealed off the bridge of their Gizer L-6 freighter and vented the rest of the ship to space. The Omega commandos eventually gained access to the cockpit and were rescued by a Red Zero operation. M'truli was later interrogated by Etain Tur-Mukan and Walon Vau in connection with the terrorist bombings of military depots on Coruscant.

**MTT (Trade Federation Multi-Troop Transport)** A terrifying display of Trade Federation efficiency, the mammoth MTT was an armored giant capable of disgorging over 100 battle droid soldiers into the thick of combat. The vehicle's bulbous armored front end opened to reveal an articulated deployment rack upon which rested dozens of compressed battle droids. The rack extended forward and deposited the droids into neatly organized rows. Upon activation from an orbiting Droid Control Ship, the droids unfolded into their humanoid configuration.

Manufactured by Baktoid Armor Workshop, the Multi-Troop Transport's bold lines and prodigious size recalled heavy jungle-dwelling creatures known for charging their enemy. The MTT followed a similar design strategy, as its heavily armored fore section could withstand great impacts, allowing it to ram an enemy building, then unload its troops behind enemy lines. The hydraulically powered deployment rack was detachable and could carry 112 battle droids in stowed configuration.

The vehicle's engines worked hard to create the repulsorlift field required to move so heavy a craft. The repulsorlift's cooling and exhaust system vented straight down beneath the craft, creating a warm cushion of air beneath the MTT. In addition to its thick armor, the MTT was protected by four forward-mounted anti-personnel blasters. It had a maximum ground speed of 35 kilometers per hour and a flight ceiling of 4 meters.

*MTT (Trade Federation Multi-Troop Transport)*

**MU-12** A spindly humanoid housekeeping droid owned by Jango Fett, who used it to tend his young son, Boba, while he was away from home on bounty hunts. MU-12 was also something of an administrative assistant to Jango, accepting incoming messages and screening out poor clients or fake bounties.

**Mub'at, Kud'ar** A so-called Assembler, he was a giant black spider with a large, round body and six chitinous legs. Mub'at lived in a giant tubular-shaped web that drifted through space; he met guests in his main chamber, adjusting the atmosphere for each visitor. Woven into his web were bits of junk—space garbage, broken droids, and more. The web was part of the Assembler, connected to him by microscopic neurofibers that brought him nourishment.

The Assembler served the galaxy as a middleman for less glamorous, or legal, activities, a go-between for criminals and those who wanted their services. Like past Assemblers, Kud'ar Mub'at gained his independence by consuming the Assembler who created him. Mub'at salvaged sublight engines for use in moving his web through space. Among the Assembler's largest customers was the Bounty Hunters' Guild, which used his services to ensure prompt payments of the bounties its members collected. Mub'at also was involved in a great deal of political intrigue involving such rogues as Kuat of Kuat and Prince Xizor of Black Sun. He ended up just like the previous Assembler.

**Mubbin** A Whiphid smuggler who claimed to have found a secret in Plett's House on Belsavis. He disappeared shortly after.

**Much Regret Unable (MRU)** A common response among the widely dispersed forces of the Grand Army of the Republic during the Clone Wars. Stated in response to a change in orders, the phrase indicated that a task force was unable to perform its new orders because it was engaged too deeply in its current mission.

**muck** A term used by many to describe a high-ranking Imperial officer.

*Kud'ar Mub'at*

**muck-huts** A name coined by miners, who lived in the only settlement on Apatros, for their prefabricated housing. All the buildings were the same dingy color of mud.

**muckracker** The common name of the LM-432 crab droid developed by the Separatists during the Clone Wars. Muckrakers were equipped with specialized pumps that cleared mud from their paths and then could spray it at enemies, effectively blinding them for a brief moment.

**mucous salamander** Native to the moon Yavin 4, this brown amphibious creature was virtually formless in water. When exposed to dry conditions, its outer membranes hardened and the creature took on a salamander-like shape. Mucous salamanders remained motionless in the water while hunting. When prey was close, they propelled from the water to grab it, then crawled to a safe place to digest, allowing their bodies to reharden to protect them from other predators.

*Mucous salamander*

**mucus tree** A slime-dripping tree that was on display in the Skydome Botanical Gardens on Coruscant.

**mudcrutch** A derogatory term used during the years leading up to the Battle of Ruusan. An individual labeled as a mudcrutch was as worthless as a crutch in the mud.

**Mudlath, Captain** An officer in the Aphran Planetary Exosecurity force around the time of the Battle of Coruscant. Mudlath was on duty when Han and Leia Organa Solo arrived on Aphran IV in an effort to establish a resistance cell on the planet. Mudlath immediately had them imprisoned on charges that they had made the planet a target of the Yuuzhan Vong just by landing there. He alerted his

Peace Brigade superiors, hoping to win favor with them by turning in the Solos.

**mudmen** Primitive semi-sentient creatures composed entirely of mud that lived on the planet Roon, they tickled victims until they were completely helpless, then robbed them of all their shiny objects. Mudmen exploded into small blobs if they were sprayed with water, though they later regenerated.

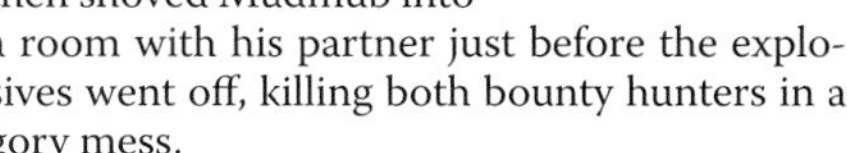

**Mudmub** A Sullustan bounty hunter who agreed to help Risso Nu eliminate Boba Fett on Ma'ar Shaddam. Mudmub and his Rodian partner were killed by Fett when he captured the Sullustan and strapped explosives to his chest. Fett then shoved Mudmub into a room with his partner just before the explosives went off, killing both bounty hunters in a gory mess.

**mudopterist** A being who studied avian insects.

**Mud Puddle, the** A cantina on the planet Ord Mantell, it was located in a building that once housed a landspeeder-repair garage. Its name came from its location on the edge of a small pond that partially blocked the cantina's only entrance. Patrons were often forced to get their feet wet in order to enter the building.

***Mud Sloth*** Luke Skywalker named Akanah's Verpine Adventurer the *Mud Sloth.* Originally owned by Andras Pell, the ship was passed to Akanah after Pell's death. Akanah had it extensively modified when she began her search for the Fallanassi, stopping on the planet Golkus to allow Talon Karrde's crew to perform much of the work. Karrde's technicians added a Smuggler's Kit to the hyperspace transponder, and the ship's hyperdrive motivator was programmed so that it wouldn't kick in until the ship had cleared a planet's Flight Control Zone.

**mudwater** A slang term used by smugglers to describe any cloudy, gritty beverage.

**mud worg** A predatory creature native to the bogs and swamps of Togoria, it submerged itself to hide and ambush its prey. Mud worgs were easily distinguished by the single tooth-like bone that rose from their skulls, which scythed through the water when they rushed to attack prey. This bone was their primary weapon, capable of slicing through flesh and bone. Native Togorians often used a pack of mud worgs in a sort of sport in which they tried to run across a mud-worg-infested pond without being harmed.

**Muehling, Baroness** An alias used by Mara Jade Skywalker during her attempt to locate Thrynni Vae on Duro. Her mission was to discover the fate of the refugees displaced by the Yuuzhan Vong invasion.

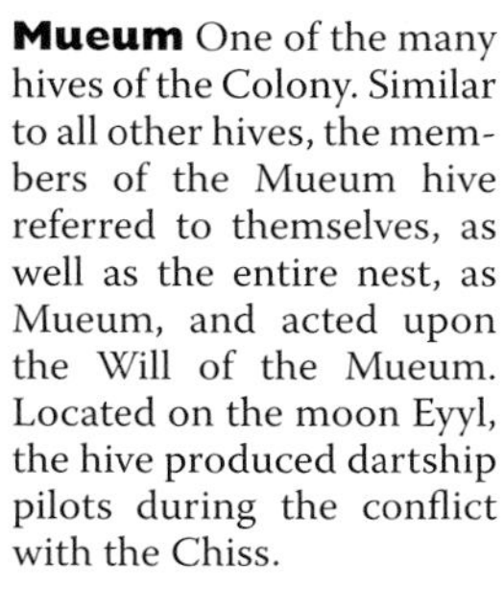

*Muftak*

**Mueum** One of the many hives of the Colony. Similar to all other hives, the members of the Mueum hive referred to themselves, as well as the entire nest, as Mueum, and acted upon the Will of the Mueum. Located on the moon Eyyl, the hive produced dartship pilots during the conflict with the Chiss.

**Muftak** A Talz who grew up in the streets of Mos Eisley, he made a living doing odd jobs and begging during the Galactic Civil War. Large, white-furred, and fierce looking, with sharply taloned fingers, Muftak was a constant companion and protector of the small Chadra-Fan named Kabe.

Born on Tatooine, Muftak knew nothing about his background except that he was a Talz, a giant species native to Alzoc III, a planet cut off from the rest of the galaxy by the Empire. By carefully watching everything with his four eyes, Muftak learned much about the comings and goings in the spaceport. Muftak took in young Kabe and sheltered her for five years in a section of abandoned tunnels beneath Docking Bay 83. They lived on the credits that Kabe stole and the money Muftak made selling information. The pair decided to rob Jabba the Hutt's Mos Eisley town house, which in turn led to some well-paid espionage work for the Rebel Alliance. Then the pair took off for Alzoc III to explore Muftak's past.

**Mugaari** Heavy-browed, lantern-jawed humanoids with skin the color of slate, the Mugaari were the original masters of the Javin sector. The planet Javin fell within Mugaari space, a semi-independent pocket of 11 star systems ruled for millennia by the Mugaari, who were suspicious of the Old Republic. While the Spine formally ended at Javin, brave traders pushed on across the Mid Rim frontier to the outer Mugaari worlds of Aztubek, High Chunah, and sometimes beyond.

*Mugruebe*

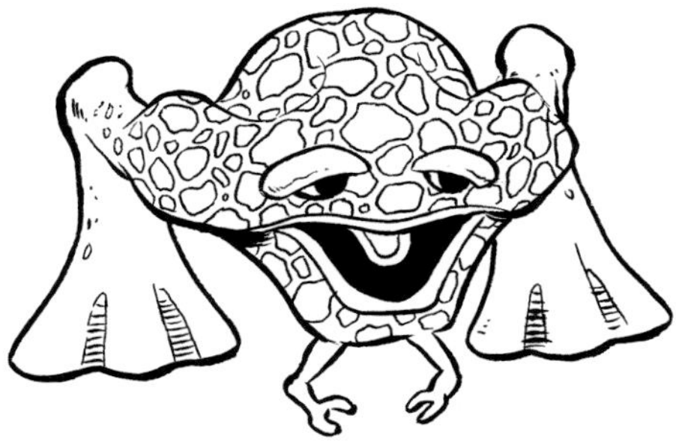

**mugruebe** A creature resembling a large frog with huge rear legs and tiny front legs. The natives of Agamar considered the flesh to be a delicacy and used it in a stew-like meal favored by Keyan Farlander, among others.

**m'uhk'gfa** Gamorrean guard armor, it was crafted of metal and leather by the wearer.

**Muja, Kav** A colorful smashball player and one of the galaxy's best known at the time of the Clone Wars. Muja was also known to be xenophobic, and often complained that the league's allowance of nonhuman players was contrary to the sport's roots and objectives. Just before the Clone Wars, Muja was playing for the Elom Ranphyx team when they were soundly beaten by the Corellian Dreadnaughts, which had admitted several nonhuman players.

**muja juice** A beverage created from the berries of the muja tree.

**muja muffin** A breakfast pastry favored by the Daan, the muja muffin originated on the planet Gala.

**Mukit** An Ubese criminal who worked for Ghez Hokan when the crime lord took control of the planet Qiilura. Mukit was forced to clean up the remains of his fellow Ubese Cailshh after Cailshh was beheaded for disobeying Hokan's orders.

**Mukmuk, Pikk** A Kowakian monkey-lizard pickpocket on a planet in the Vanqor system, Pikk belonged to pirate Hondo Ohnaka during the Clone Wars. He had reddish brown skin and a green Mohawk.

**Mulacks, Kruy** A green-skinned humanoid who hosted his own investigative newsfeed. Mulacks's show was known to be entertaining, if overdramatic. He was perhaps best known for being on the scene on Carthas when the Temple of Tet-Ami was opened.

**Mulako Corporation Primordial Water Quarry** A periodic comet in a 100-year orbit around its star. For several months during its approach and departure from the sun, it warmed enough to support life in its interior. During this period, the Mulako Corporation promoted the comet as a tourist destination, and many people arrived to visit its exclusive resorts, restaurants, and lounges. After the tourist season, ice-mining machines roamed the irregular surface. Ice was sold as pure water formed at the creation of the solar system. Luke Skywalker and Callista visited the Quarry in an attempt to help Callista regain her Jedi powers.

**mulblatt** Their larvae, served with fregon-blood sauce, were considered a delicacy by the Hutts.

**Mull, Swanny** A tunnel worker in the years leading up to the Great Purge that destroyed the city of Naatan. Distinguished by his white hair, Mull was one of many Mawans willing to help reestablish a central government on the planet. His knowledge of the water supply systems beneath Naatan came from his former career as a wastewater system programmer.

**mullanite lattice-sculpture** An art form that used specially constructed lattices for growing creeping vines. The lattices allowed the vines to grow into many beautiful shapes and images.

**Mulleen, Admiral** An officer of the Grand Army of the Republic who declared his allegiance to the Galactic Empire. He was placed in charge of eradicating any officers who showed the least bit of anti-Imperial sentiment, a mission that he carried out with ruthless efficiency. Within a few months of the Battle of Utapau, Mulleen had executed many detractors as traitors to the Empire.

**Mulleshar, Troye** A member of the Blue Guard during the months leading up the Clone Wars. Shortly before the vote on the Military Creation Act, he was knocked unconscious by a horde of rioters protesting the possible passage of the act. His fellow officers managed to extricate him from the mob.

**mullinine** A metallic substance often used in the construction of blades and other melee weapons, it held an edge extremely well.

**Mullinore, Captain** The Imperial captain of the Star Destroyer *Basilisk,* he was a classmate of Admiral Daala on Carida during the early years of the New Order. His assignment on the *Basilisk* supported the Maw Installation, and he served under Daala's command for many years. When the admiral decided to launch an all-out attack on Coruscant seven years after the Battle of Endor, Mullinore was surprised to learn that her plan involved sacrificing the *Basilisk.* He accepted the plan, however, and volunteered to remain aboard the vessel to ensure that the explosion was correctly timed for maximum destruction. His noble sacrifice never occurred. Kyp Durron had stolen the Sun Crusher and launched seven resonance torpedoes into the Cauldron Nebula, which detonated the seven collapsed stars at its center. With its crew almost completely transferred over to the *Gorgon,* the *Basilisk* was unable to outrun the explosion. Mullinore and the remaining members of his crew were killed when the ship was destroyed.

**Muln, Garen** A friend of Obi-Wan Kenobi during the time he trained at the Jedi Temple on Coruscant. The two boys fought over trivial things but maintained a strong bond. Because they were of similar size, Muln was used as Obi-Wan's double during the search for Xanatos. Xanatos had infiltrated the Jedi Temple with the intent of stealing a cache of vertex crystals and destroying the Temple, but Obi-Wan and Qui-Gon Jinn managed to thwart the attempt.

Muln later trained as a starfighter pilot in an effort to augment the ranks of pilots among the Jedi. He was among the first Jedi chosen to train at Clee Rhara's starfighter facility on Centax 2, and later apprenticed with Rhara as a Padawan. Just prior to the Clone Wars, Muln was elevated to the rank of Jedi Knight and accompanied Siri Tachi on a mission to the Xanlanner system. While en route, they picked up Obi-Wan's distress signal from TY44, and helped him reach Vanqor to rescue his apprentice, Anakin Skywalker. When the Clone Wars broke out, Muln was placed in charge of a small group of clone troopers.

Just before the Battle of Coruscant, Muln and his team were dispatched to Acherin to free the planet from Separatist control. He managed to broker the surrender of General Toma's forces and was about to sign a peace treaty with the Acherin government when the command to execute Order 66 was given. For his actions in the fighting, Muln had earned the respect of Toma, and Toma was able to hide him from the clone troopers for several weeks. In order to protect his friend, however, Muln took the first ship to Ilum and chose to hide in the Crystal Cave. He left Toma with orders to tell only a true Jedi about his location, hoping to gather other Jedi on Ilum.

He was later discovered by Ferus Olin, who himself had been looking to gather any surviving Jedi. Muln initially refused to leave, and presented his lightsaber to Olin as a token of his faith in Olin's actions. An Imperial attack on Ilum later forced Muln to abandon his hideout, and he joined the group that Olin had assembled on a remote asteroid.

**multiprocessor** The generic term for any starship system that could handle more than one task. Most often, multiprocessors combined food preparation, disposal, and water reclamation systems.

**multisensor airflow analyzer** A device that measured the direction and force of air flowing around a spaceship's hull. Usable only in atmospheres, the device could detect homing beacons or detonation devices attached to the outside of a ship.

**multisniffer** A sophisticated sensory device developed by Tendrando Arms following the Yuuzhan Vong War, it was designed to identify any potentially dangerous materials in a room or chamber.

**Multitude, the** A religious reference used by the Fia of Galantos to describe the heavenly appearance of the Koornacht Cluster.

**Multycorp** One of the largest corporations based on Vorzyd 4 in the decades before the Battle of Naboo. The corporation's headquarters were bombed by the Freelies at the height of that youth organization's industrial sabotage. The plan was to explode a bomb at night, but Flip decided to detonate it in the morning, when the adult Vorzydiaks were arriving for work. Thanks to Tray, Grath and Obi-Wan Kenobi were able to warn the workers about the bomb and evacuate nearly every Vorzydiak in the building. Flip was caught in the blast and killed.

**mumba-humba** A term used by the human population on Bellassa to describe anything that was arcane or silly.

**Mumbri Storve Cantina** A seedy tavern where Aves intercepted Wedge Antilles, Derek "Hobbie" Klivian, and Wes Janson just prior to the Battle of Bilbringi. Aves saved the New Republic pilots from being discovered by Imperial agents, who were searching for clues on the Republic's intentions to attack either Tangrene or Bilbringi in order to obtain a crystal gravfield trap receptor.

**mummergy** An aromatic plant used as a spice by many beings across the galaxy. The Mos Eisley cantina bartender Wuher used mummergy to create the perfect liqueur for Jabba the Hutt.

**mumuu** A vicious creature native to the Kunbal jungles of the planet Kalee, it had two hearts and a redundant circulatory system. The strength and abilities of Kaleesh warriors were judged by their ability to bring down a mumuu, as the pair of hearts were protected by a thick backbone. The skull of the mumuu was often carved into elaborate masks worn by Kaleesh warriors and soldiers, and its hide was made into heavy cloaks. General Grievous's primary faceplate was carved from a mumuu skull. His MagnaGuards had cloak markings that matched those of his mask.

**Muna, Ivo** A Sorrusian who posed as a medic at the largest medical center on Sorrus in an effort to assist Ona Nobis in capturing Obi-Wan Kenobi and Astri Oddo.

**Mungra** Distinguished by piercing, orange eyes, this was one of two species native to the Shelsha sector of the galaxy. The Mungra were one of the first to establish a multiworld realm during the early formation of the Old Republic, colonizing 12 planets by the time the Great Explosion began.

***Munificent*-class star frigate** *See* Banking Clan communications frigate.

**Munlali Mafir** A planet in the Unknown Regions noted for its rugged landscape and thin, though breathable, atmosphere. The homeworld of the Krizlaw and Jostran symbionts, Munlali Mafir was one of several planets investigated by Luke Skywalker and his team for clues as to the location of Zonama Sekot. They narrowly escaped an attack by the natives.

Munto Codru

**Munto Codru** Home to four-armed beings known as Codru-Ji and considered of only marginal interest to the rest of galactic society, the planet was orbited by several moons and featured beautiful mountains and ancient castles in its temperate zone. The Munto Codru castles, famous for their elaborate carvings on translucent rock walls, were built by a vanished civilization. Animal life included a four-winged bat and the six-legged, fanged wyrwulfs, which were actually the Codru-Ji themselves in the earliest, infant stage of their lives.

Codru-Ji society was based on a complicated system of political families and entities, and was headed by Chamberlain Iyon. Coups, abductions, and ransoms were common. Han and Leia Organa Solo's three children were abducted while Leia was on a diplomatic mission to Munto Codru.

**Muntuur stones** A famous grouping of seven stones once held aloft by Ferleen Snee using only the Force. Each of the Muntuur stones weighed at least 5 metric tons.

**Mure, Nigella** In command of the cleanup crews in the Desrini District of Coruscant when a garbage launcher misfired, she discovered that a group of squatter families had tapped into the power matrix of the launcher, disabling its obstruction sensors and causing the launcher to activate, even though the path of the garbage bin was blocked. This led to increased legislation against immigration to Coruscant during the Separatist crisis.

**murg** Slimy, carnivorous creatures native to the swamps of the planet Terephon. Distinguished by their long, tubular bodies and flipper-like feet, murgs were excellent hunters. The nobles of Galney family often kept a handful of murgs around for hunting in the bogs that surrounded the Villa Solis estate.

**murglak** An epithet or derogatory term in use during the last decades of the Old Republic, used in such expressions as "son of a murglak."

**Murgo Choke** An unusual star formation located just beyond the mouth of the Utegetu Nebula, it formed a gauntlet that had to be negotiated before a starship could enter the nebula itself. On one side of the Murgo Choke was a binary star system formed from a yellow star and an orange star of similar size. On the other side was another binary system formed from a crimson dwarf that orbited a blue giant, creating an unusual match. Because of this close collection of four stars, the Murgo Choke was difficult to navigate, but it was also the only way to reach the opening of the Utegetu Nebula. Starship captains wishing to travel to the nebula had to exit from the Rago Run at one of several jump points, then make their way through the Murgo Choke.

**Murgoob the Great** Also known as Murgoob the Cranky, he was an old and unpleasant oracle of the Duloks on the Forest Moon of Endor around the time of the Galactic Civil War.

**Murkhana** A heavily forested planet, it was one of the many that saw combat during the final stages of the Clone Wars. Murkhana was settled by the Koorivars, who later established the headquarters of the Corporate Alliance in Murkhana City. Murkhana was a tropic world that had been volcanically active in its youth, as evidenced by its black-sand beaches. During the rainy season, much of the planet was blanketed by thick, stormy clouds, making descent from space to ground dangerous.

The Koorivars allowed the Confederacy of Independent Systems to establish a base of operations on the planet during the years leading up to the Clone Wars. Passel Argente oversaw much of Murkhana's government and allowed criminals to flourish as long as they paid their "taxes" to the Corporate Alliance. Decades later, the government and business leaders of Murkhana were involved in a trade war with the Verpine when they tried to move into the small-unit comlink market.

**Murkhana Bay** One of the largest bodies of water found on Murkhana.

**Murkhana City** The capital city of Murkhana, located on Murkhana Bay, it was a luxurious collection of swanky buildings and exclusive locations all catering to the wealthiest members of the Corporate Alliance and the Confederacy of Independent Systems. Many of the buildings appeared to have been grown from local coral, with graceful spires and spiraling structures. The city itself was linked to four offshore landing platforms, which were separated from the city by a black-sand beach and 10 kilometers of ocean.

**Murleen, Ru** A member of the Rebel Alliance, she played a number of key roles in the events leading up to the destruction of the first Death Star. She was the youngest of the Alliance's starfighter commanders, with a quick wit and an eye for talent that helped her train many new pilots. She was also instrumental in the discovery of the V-38 fighter. She flew with Blue Squadron during the Battle of Yavin.

**Murninkam** A tropical paradise only sparsely settled at the time of the Battle of Endor, this planet was located far from most space lanes.

**Murno, Kot** A lieutenant within the Peace Brigade, he led a team that traveled to Yavin 4 in an effort to capture the students of Luke Skywalker's Jedi praxeum after the Yuuzhan Vong claimed they would stop their invasion if the New Republic turned over all Jedi.

**Murra** A tribesman of the Ysanna on Ossus, Murra was the first to help Okko attempt to defeat Luke Skywalker and Kam Solusar when they arrived on the planet.

**murrih tisane** An herbal tea popular among the nobility and dignitaries of the Imperial Remnant following the Yuuzhan Vong War. It was distinguished by its deep purple color.

***Murtceps*** An Imperial freighter discovered by Keyan Farlander during his first tour of duty as an X-wing pilot. The *Murtceps* evaded Farlander and survived his attack.

**Murthé, Dr. Leonis** A depraved Imperial scientist known to have been one of the staunchest supporters of Emperor Palpatine's High Human Culture. Dr. Murthé and his partner, Admiral Mir Tork, spent much of their careers subjugating and destroying entire alien civilizations. Dr. Murthé set up a collection of holding pens and laboratories aboard the *Azgoghk,* where he perfected techniques of torturing and killing. Murthé later retired to Malicar 3 in the wake of the Battle of Endor. There he spent much of his time torturing and killing aliens for pleasure, no longer concerned with any scientific pursuits. Murthé was later hunted down and killed by Boba Fett, who had been hired by Slique Brighteyes to avenge the Gulmarids.

Dr. Leonis Murthé

Mushroom Mesa

**Murzz** One of many children captured by, and forced to work for, Gilramos Libkath in the years before the Clone Wars. Libkath forced the children to perform a number of criminal activities, such as stealing weapons from Jabba the Hutt and others, and disrupting the activities of Separatists in Mos Espa.

**muscle maggot** A burrowing insect native to the planet Rattatak, named for the way it consumed only the muscle tissue of a host organism. The native Rattataki used muscle maggots as an interrogation technique. A few were placed on the skin of prisoners and allowed to begin burrowing. Over time, the prisoners lost muscle and strength, making them more susceptible to questioning. Asajj Ventress used muscle maggots to torture Obi-Wan Kenobi on Rattatak. Kenobi somehow managed to digest them and tricked Ventress into thinking that they were still active.

**Museum of Applied Photonics** A museum of technology located on the planet Obroa-skai. After the Yuuzhan Vong overran the world, they left the Museum of Applied Photonics intact, one of a thousand such buildings saved from destruction so the invaders could better understand their enemies. The museum itself was converted into use as Warmaster Tsavong Lah's personal base of operations.

**Museum of Light** A wondrous museum located on Tandis Four until it was destroyed by Count Dooku's Separatist forces during the Clone Wars.

**Museum of Tatooine** Located in the city of Bestine on Tatooine, the museum boasted a huge collection of artworks created by the galaxy's best artisans from the sands and minerals of the planet.

**Museum of the Absolutes** Built in the former headquarters building of the Absolutes in the Civilized sector of New Apsolon, it was established as a grim reminder of the atrocities of the Absolutes under the Civilized Authority. On display were artifacts—such as torture devices—and information from the civil war between the Workers and the Civilized. Eritha and Alani arranged for an underground tunnel to be excavated, connecting the governor's palace to the museum, where they met regularly with the Absolutes who had been in hiding, planning for the time when Alani would be elected governor and return power to the Absolutes.

**Museum of the Galactic Republic** An Old Republic monument, it was established on the planet Centares by the Republic Senate. The museum was shut down by Emperor Palpatine.

**Museum of the Republic** Established on Coruscant, this New Republic edifice contained numerous displays depicting the events of the Galactic Civil War and the years following the Battle of Endor. It contained a room dedicated to the Battle of Yavin, which had a cutaway model of the first Death Star and a listing of the battle station's full complement of personnel. The display was designed to highlight the destructiveness of war, regardless of the outcome.

**Mushkil** A Noghri of the Baikh'vair clan, he accompanied Corran Horn and Jacen Solo to Garqi during their attempt to infiltrate the Yuuzhan Vong occupiers of the planet. In their first battle with the invaders, Mushkil was killed by Krag Val's amphistaff.

Mustafar

**Mushroom Mesa** This Tatooine landmark was on the Mos Espa Podracing course made famous by the Boonta Eve Classic. The top-heavy stone pillars were shaped like giant mushrooms, and many observers claimed to have seen faces carved into the stones. Legend said that the Sand People were the keepers of the secrets hidden in the stone faces, but most geologists claimed that any faces were carved by unusual wind erosion.

**Muskov, Captain** Chief of the Wing Guard of Cloud City when Zorba the Hutt assumed control, Muskov was a secret agent working for the Central Committee of Grand Moffs.

**M'ust** Cave-dwelling beings, they worshipped the eternally burning fires found in their subterranean caves. Cody Sunn-Childe discovered the M'ust when he was shot while fighting the Empire on their planet, after its subjugation during the early days of the Galactic Civil War. Sunn-Childe learned to become a peace-loving being based on the influence of the M'ust. When Sunn-Childe finally decided to leave their world, many of the M'ust followed him to his newly created spacecraft, which traveled between dimensions rather than in realspace or hyperspace.

**Mustafar** Located in the Outer Rim, tiny Mustafar was a fiery planet where lava was mined like a precious natural resource. Its bleak landscape was a visual assault of jagged obsidian mountains with towering fountains of fire and lava blasting from beneath the surface. This lava also streaked the blasted landscape in huge winding rivers and plunging cataracts. Mustafar's skies were obscured by choking black clouds of ash, smoke, and tephra. The intense geological activity created natural scanning interference that kept prying eyes away from Mustafar for most of its history.

These inhospitable features made Mustafar an ideal sanctuary for the ever-mobile Separatist Council that led the Confederacy of Independent Systems during the Clone Wars. After repeated setbacks, General Grievous was ordered by Darth Sidious to secure the council on Mustafar, where they would await further instructions. An enormous cliffside industrial facility served as headquarters to the commerce baron war chiefs. Neimoidian soldiers and battle droid infantry provided security, while shimmering deflector shields protected the structure from the volatile surroundings.

Upon his ascendancy to Galactic Emperor, Darth Sidious had no further need of the Separatists. He dispatched his new apprentice, Darth Vader, to dispose of his wartime collaborators. Upon arrival, Vader silently stalked into the inner chambers of the mining facility. His lightsaber blade made short work of the Separatist leaders, cutting

Mustafar

them down and effectively bringing an end to the Clone Wars.

Amid this apocalyptic landscape of erupting volcanoes, Jedi Master Obi-Wan Kenobi confronted Vader, his former apprentice. The two entered into a spectacular lightsaber duel that worked its way across the Mustafar collection complex. Through the course of their battle, the protective shields were deactivated, and the facility was exposed to the planet's full geological fury.

A geyser of lava erupted, dropping molten rock on one of the outrigger collection arms of the facility where Kenobi and Vader dueled. The arm collapsed under the heat and strain, plunging into the lava river. Before the severed collection arm succumbed to the pull of a lava fall, Vader and Kenobi leapt from the doomed structure onto a nearby worker droid and harvesting platform, respectively. Their duel continued on these cooled repulsorlift surfaces before ending abruptly on the black-sand shores of the lava river.

There Kenobi bested Vader, leaving the Dark Lord to die on the Mustafar riverbanks. Darth Sidious sensed Vader's anguish and arrived in time to rescue his fallen apprentice. Maimed and mortally wounded by lightsaber and fire, Vader was reconstructed as a cyborg and encased in a black protective life-supporting suit. It was the final curtain for the Clone Wars—and for the Galactic Republic, too.

Despite the hellish nature of its environment, Mustafar nonetheless produced native life capable of surviving in the fiery extremes of the planet. The sentient Mustafarians—of which two notable subspecies existed—paid little heed to the galactic events that culminated on their world. They went about their business, gathering precious minerals and energy from the lava streams, riding their massive lava fleas across the stygian landscape.

Mustafar was a relatively young world literally being torn in opposite directions, caught in a gravimetric tug of war that kept it from becoming the moon of a nearby gas giant. Despite the close proximity of massive Jestefad, Mustafar kept to its erratic orbit, pulled by the distant influence of another giant, Lefrani. The tidal strain heated up Mustafar's molten core, resulting in spectacular geological activity across the entire planet. The Techno Union owned Mustafar, having laid claim to the planet over 300 years before the Clone Wars. Scouts from that organization discovered the unique and valuable mineral allotropes that permeated the planet's crust and mantle. Though the Mustafar lava was hot—a searing 800 degrees standard—it was cool enough to be harvested by specialized equipment.

Techno Union officials signed a treaty with the provincial Mustafarian primitives, who ben-

*Southern Mustafarian*

efited from the most basic and inexpensive of offworld items. In exchange, they guided Techno Union builders as they constructed massive harvesting facilities on the planet to exploit the mineral riches flowing in the lava streams. The Mustafar collection facilities employed tractor beams and electromagnetic harvesting techniques to stir the valuable minerals within the lava flow. Roiled to the surface, the deposits were then scooped up by worker droids or rugged Mustafarians lifting heavy cauldrons by hand. Baskets of molten rock and metal were then returned to the facilities where they were processed and refined for distribution. Since lava-proof armor was more costly than energy-based deflector shields, the collection facility was sheathed in energy to protect it from the incredible temperatures.

After the destruction of the Separatist Council and the Imperialization of the Techno Union, Mustafar was largely forgotten. A Separatist stalwart, the fugitive Geonosian Gizor Dellso, holed up there during the early days of the Galactic Empire and reestablished an independent battle droid factory, requiring the attention of the loyal 501st Legion of Stormtroopers to storm the hellish world.

**Mustafarian** Despite the planet's extreme conditions, Mustafar spawned a number of native life-forms. Some of these evolved into sentient beings. The native Mustafarians cared little about offworlder concerns on their planet. They simply busied themselves harvesting the minerals carried in the lava streams of their world. There were two notable subspecies among the Mustafarians. Tall, thin northern Mustafarians rode the lava fleas on the cooled, crusted-over surface of lava flows; shorter, burly ones rode hovering harvesting platforms, skimming the lava rivers with heavy pole-mounted cauldrons. These southern Mustafarians could withstand greater temperatures than their meeker cousins.

Evolved from extremophile arthropods with very little water in their biology, the Mustafarians dwelled in the cooler hollows of dormant volcanic mountains. They ventured to the surface following a trail blazed by the native lava fleas. Recycling discarded flea shells as armor, the various Mustafarian colonies made contact with one another. They stitched together a loose collection of townships through peaceful trade, banding together in the face of their planet's unforgiving elements.

*Northern Mustafarian*

When the Techno Union arrived on the planet, the Mustafarians signed a treaty with the offworld developers. This galactic trade gave the natives advanced technology to help resist the fiery dangers of their world. Mustafarians spoke a buzzing, insectoid language. Very hardy, they didn't bother with standard laser weaponry: Their skin and armor could withstand the heat radiated by most common blasters. They instead carried a type of native blaster that emitted bolts of kinetic force.

**Mustafarian lava flea** The Basic name for immense six-legged insects native to Mustafar. Their native name was unpronounceable by non-Mustafarians. Lava fleas were agile creatures that moved about on the cooling lava and were capable of leaping almost 30 meters if necessary. The average lava flea stood over 4 meters tall when fully grown, having started

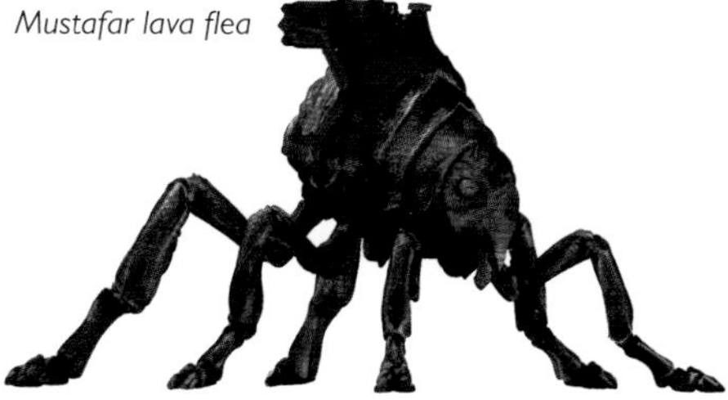

*Mustafar lava flea*

out life as a half-meter-long, worm-like larva. In the larval form, a lava flea fed on the rock dust that filled the underground lairs of their hive. The ancient Mustafarians followed the paths of lava fleas, using discarded carapaces as body armor to withstand the hellish environs of their home planet. In this way, the Mustafarian lava flea was largely responsible for the expansion of settled territory on the planet.

**Mutant Zombie Cooler** A mixed beverage that Han Solo made sarcastic reference to while escaping with Dracmus from the Human League on Corellia.

**Mutdah, Bohhuah** An extremely obese human, Bohhuah Mutdah was likely the richest private being in the galaxy during the early years of the New Order. He was a retired industrialist who personally controlled trillions of credits in a variety of well-protected bank accounts, the fruits of nearly a century of labor. Mutdah's home was on Oseon 5792, an asteroid in the Oseon system that he had altered to create his own fortress. A collector of antique books, he had one of the galaxy's largest collections of printed material hidden within the asteroid. Mutdah was killed by Rokur Gepta as part of a convoluted plot to kill Lando Calrissian. He was well over 100 years old when he was murdered, an age achieved by the proximity of one of the largest life-crystals ever exported from the Rafa system. His murder allowed Gepta to assume his appearance, which he maintained until Calrissian was trapped on the asteroid. Gepta intended to kill Calrissian, but the gambler escaped before he could complete his plan.

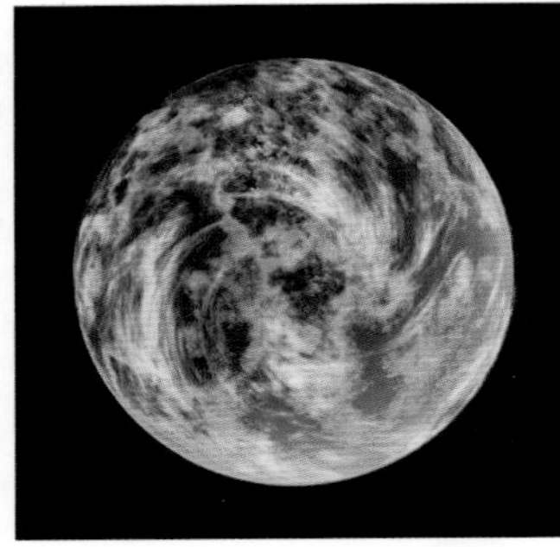
*Muunilinst*

**mutiny box** A fail-safe device that could be triggered in case a military position was breached or infiltrated. Hidden within the mutiny box, controlled by the base commander, were switches that set off self-destruct mechanisms on weapons emplacements and other defenses.

**mutonium** A valuable metal ore mined in the Stenness system 4,000 years before the Galactic Civil War. Mutonium often was smuggled out of the system, or stolen by pirates.

**Muttanni** Beings from Kalidorn in between Wild Space and the Outer Rim. They were distinguished by their sickly appearance and peculiar body odor. The skin of a Muttanni had a greenish gray coloration, and their bodies were generally hairless. Their bald heads were crowned by pointed ears, and their mouths were filled with sharp teeth.

**Muun** A humanoid species native to Muunilinst, headquarters of the InterGalactic Banking Clan (IBC). Muuns' skulls were elongated and thin, with a tall brain cavity and drooping cheekbones. Their large hands were tipped with equally long fingers. The skin of average Muuns was a pasty-white color, the result of living indoors and underground for much of their lives. Each Muun had three hearts.

Although Muuns often traveled away from their homeworld, such trips were quite short, as many Muuns became homesick if away from Muunilinst for too long. They were noted for their abilities in financial matters and skills in calculating complex mathematical data without the use of a computer. When the Old Republic gave way to the New Order, the Muuns were among the few nonhuman species left untouched. Imperials conceded that no species was better equipped to oversee the galactic economy, and they were unwilling to risk any financial reprisal. Imperial administrators were tasked with monitoring the Muuns to ensure that Imperial credits would not find their way into Rebel Alliance coffers, but the New Order had little to fear from these beings, whose unwavering integrity prohibited such devious conduct. San Hill was the Munn chairman of the IBC.

During the Yuuzhan Vong War, a large portion of the Muun population was exterminated when the alien invaders destroyed Muunilinst in a planetary bombardment. Only those individuals who were offplanet at the time survived.

**Muun, General** A Sullustan officer who served during the Yuuzhan Vong War despite his young age. Two years after the initial appearance of the invaders, Muun was given the duty of ensuring that the Bilbringi Shipyards continued to operate under New Republic control. After the shipyards were captured, he was transferred to Coruscant before it was invaded.

**Muunilinst** Homeworld of the Muuns, this planet was the financial heart of the galaxy for millennia—at least according to the natives. Much of the galaxy's currency was backed by the resources of the Muuns and the InterGalactic Banking Clan, and the planet was known to much of the galaxy as "Moneyland." Steeped in history that dated from the glory days of the Old Republic, Muunilinst was a temperate world of jungles, forests, and rolling plains, and its shallow seas were warmed by regular eruptions of small volcanoes known as smokers.

After the Yuuzhan Vong were soundly defeated at the Battle of Ebaq, the alien invaders turned to the fringes of the galaxy to make smaller attacks. In a coordinated strike, the Yuuzhan Vong eliminated Bastion and its supporting fleet, and then decimated the forces protecting Muunilinst. The planet itself was bombarded from orbit, reducing it to a wasteland from which the Yuuzhan Vong plucked any survivors for use as slave labor.

**muur** A simple, yeast-based food that formed the basis of the Yuuzhan Vong diet during their long trips between galaxies.

**Muuurgh** A huge Togorian who stood nearly 3 meters tall, he was covered in patterned black fur. Muuurgh was betrothed to Mrrov while on Togoria, but she wanted to see the galaxy before settling down. She left the planet, and Muuurgh pursued her. He lost track of her on Ylesia, and opted to remain on the planet and work for Teroenza as a bodyguard. When Han Solo took the job of pilot for the t'landa Til, Muuurgh was assigned as his personal guard. Their relationship grew steadily during Solo's tenure, until each trusted the other.

When Solo discovered the lies behind Teroenza's religion, he convinced Muuurgh of the truth, and the two developed an elaborate plan to get off the planet. Muuurgh eventually found Mrrov on Ylesia and learned that she had been captivated by the religion. He freed her, and the two returned to Togoria, where they married and had two cubs.

***Muvon II*** An *Aegis*-class shuttle acquired by Brophar Tofarain after the loss of his first ship, the *Muvon.*

**Muvunc, Ral'Rai** A Twi'lek who served the Rebel Alliance military and attained the rank of Supreme Allied Commander in the months following the Battle of Yavin. During this time, Muvunc also served as the Minister and Commander of Supply and Ordnance. He proposed that privateers be contracted to augment the Alliance's forces, rationalizing that they could ambush Imperial and corporate convoys and obtain supplies for the Alliance without expending Alliance resources. Privateering would also help alienate corporations from the Empire, as lost convoys meant lost profits. Admiral Ackbar was strongly opposed to the plan to use pirates in this manner, despite the continued success rate of the missions Muvunc authorized.

**Muzara** A planet deep in the Expansion Region, it was first settled by the Brentaal League some 4,000 years before the Galactic Civil War.

**Muzzle** The name adopted by ARC trooper Alpha-66 during the final stages of the Clone Wars. After the war, Muzzle left the service of the Grand Army of the Republic and formed the Aurodium Sword mercenary outfit. Although he was recognized for his service to the GAR by Imperial military personnel, Muzzle found that his treatment of Wookiees and other nonhumans as free beings often clashed with the pro-human doctrines of the Empire.

**MX** An ancient laser cannon that used ion flow as an energy source.

**Mxil, Mister** A Mon Calamari who established the Haven's Water cantina, he was known for brewing his own liquors and ales. He discovered that many of the jungle plants found at Port Haven had medicinal or healing properties as well. Mister Mxil could also cook up a spicy stew, and he rarely charged visitors for anything as long as they repaid his hospitality.

**MX series droid** A series of droids designed to perform routine starfighter maintenance.

**mycogen** A small bioengineered organism used by the Yuuzhan Vong to generate light. Entire colonies of mycogens were implanted

*MX laser canons*

into the walls of Yuuzhan Vong worldships, providing a ready source of bioluminescence.

**mycosia flower** A species of plants with large pink blossoms. The mycosia was a favorite of Evir Derricote, providing him with early experience in genetic manipulation.

**Mygeetan** Small, simian creatures native to the planet Mygeeto. Mygeetans were virtually enslaved by the InterGalactic Banking Clan in the decades prior to the Clone Wars.

**Mygeeto** A frigid world of crystallized ice, Mygeeto was a major holding of the InterGalactic Banking Clan that became a battle site during the Outer Rim Sieges of the Clone Wars. General and Jedi Master Ki-Adi-Mundi and Commander Bacara led the Galactic Marine clone troopers in extended urban fighting amid the ultramodern towers of a major Mygeeto city. The blistering cannonades and laserfire of towering Separatist tri-droids and Republic artillery carriers reduced much of the city and crystalline landscape into rubble, polluting the icy winds with a persistent pall of gray ash.

*Mygeeto*

During a concentrated Republic push to rout the Separatists, Order 66 was set in motion. Ki-Adi-Mundi was targeted by his clone forces, branded a traitor by the Chancellor of the Republic. He was killed in a hail of blaster bolts.

In the ancient trade language of the Muuns, the word *mygeeto* meant "gem." It was a fitting name for the glittering world, perennially locked in an ice age and covered in crystallized glaciation. Its internal fires cooled long ago, and the geologically dormant planet was left with a trove of precious stones within its crust and mantle. The enormous nova crystal deposits and fields of lasing crystals made it one of the most valuable worlds in the galaxy. The Jedi had longed to explore Mygeeto for crystals suitable for lightsaber use, but since its discovery, it had been firmly in the hold of the InterGalactic Banking Clan.

The gaunt Muun bankers jealously guarded their world with an intimidating blockade of frigates and cruisers. Daring accounts of raiding the crystal caves of Mygeeto became the stuff of cantina tall tales throughout the galaxy. If a thief was foolhardy enough to somehow penetrate the screen of defensive ships, he or she still had to contend with a planet that was mostly wasteland. If the harsh winds and jagged surface weren't discouraging enough, burrowing through the planet's ice shelves were enormous worms with voracious appetites and ill tempers.

The few Mygeeto cities that dotted the reflective topography were sunken into the crystalline surface. Drawing power by synthesizing specific crystal types, the cities were built around enormous capacitor towers that stored and distributed energy. The cities served to administer the crystal mines, but also were vaults for the Banking Clan's most security-conscious clients. As the home to the Confederacy's coffers, Mygeeto became a prime target during the Outer Rim Sieges.

In the final phases of the Mygeeto campaign, Ki-Adi-Mundi was surprised to see his forces supplemented by a special mission of 501st troopers, dispatched specifically by Chancellor Palpatine. Though the Jedi general was wary of the circumstances, Bacara vouched for the unorthodox chain of command that saw the 501st ever mobile during the Outer Rim Sieges. The 501st operated outside of Ki-Adi-Mundi's command structure on a mission to eliminate a droid energy collector. At least, that's how the orders read. In truth, the elite troopers were seeking out an experimental Mygeetan power source that the Chancellor required for a top-secret tributary laser-stream project code-named Hammertong.

**"My Heart Belongs to You"** A tune made popular by Evar Orbus and His Galactic Wailers, it remained a hit for the band's new incarnation, the Max Rebo Band.

**Myke** A humanoid species characterized by tall, thin bodies and gaunt faces. Mykes had two small horns descending from either side of their chins. Norym Kim, a member of the Imperial Interim Ruling Council, was a Myke.

**Myles** A Mandalorian shock trooper who served under Jango Fett, Myles was killed when he was cut in half by a Jedi Knight during the Battle of Galidraan.

**Mylok IV** A small gray planet in the Mylok system of the Outer Rim, it was the homeworld of the Nharwaak and Habeen. The two species developed a new hyperdrive together, although the Nharwaak balked at the Habeen decision to deliver the technology to the Empire. In a rendezvous near Mylok IV, the Habeen officially turned the technology over to Admiral Zaarin's forces in exchange for their planet's formal entry into the Empire. Nharwaaks who attempted to sell the same technology to the Rebels were destroyed by Imperial attacks.

*Mynock*

**Mylore, Yndis** The Imperial Governor of Bryexx, he was also Moff of the Varvenna sector.

**Myneyrsh (plural: Myneyrshi)** Natives of the planet Wayland, the Myneyrshi were present when the first human colonists arrived. Tall, thin humanoids, they had four arms and a smooth layer of blue-crystal flesh that made them look as though they were made of glass. The Myneyrshi used bows and arrows instead of blasters, and animals instead of repulsorcraft. Calling any piece of advanced technology an "item of shame," they originated the phrase, "A knife never runs out of ammunition."

**mynock** Leathery-winged manta-like fliers scattered throughout the galaxy, mynocks were a common pest faced by spacers. The parasitic creatures attached themselves to hosts via their bristly suction-cup-like mouths. Pilots needed to examine their ships for mynock infestations since the creatures liked to affix to starships and chew on their power cables. Mynocks traveled in packs and typically grew to be 1.6 meters long with a wingspan of approximately 1.25 meters.

The mynock homeworld was unknown, but they derived their name from their supposed origin world, Ord Mynock. Mynocks, like plants, were nourished by stellar radiation. Their leathery surfaces were well suited for absorbing electromagnetic radiation. They rode the stellar winds by unfurling their wings. Mynocks also fed on silica and other minerals for the purposes of reproduction. The creatures were asexual, reproducing through fission once enough raw material had been absorbed and metabolized.

These silicon-based life-forms could only exist in the vacuum of space, and found planetary atmospheres fatal. A number of mynock variants were discovered, however, that not only could survive planetfall, but

*Myneyrsh*

also could reproduce via larval forms.

**Mynock** Wedge Antilles's R5-D2 astromech droid. Its memory was later wiped, and it was reprogrammed and renamed Gate.

***Mynock*** The name of the starship commanded by Cade Skywalker. It sometimes used the services of an old but familiar astromech droid—R2-D2. Cade and his crew used the *Mynock* to hunt down bounties nearly 140 years after the Battle of Yavin.

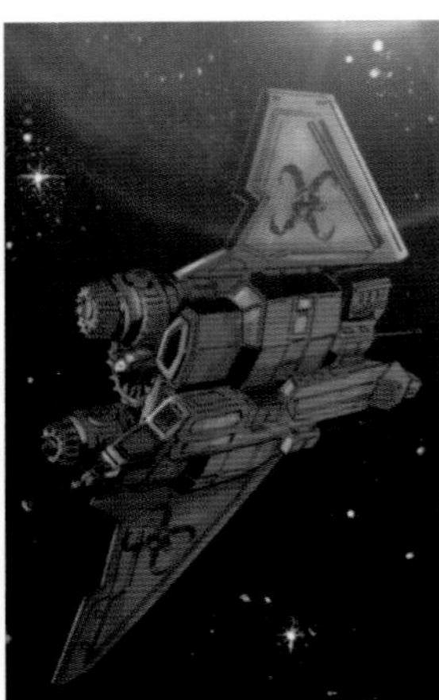

Mynock

**Mynock Cloud City** A dish served at Cal'ulorn's restaurant, the Kavsrach, it was described as "a spicy combination of marinated mynock strips with vweilu nuts and Ithorian chale, in a lum sauce."

**Mynock Hole** A tavern located in Vlarnya on Courkrus, it was the favored hangout of the Blackstar pirate force. Despite the disgusting appearance of the main barroom, the pirates maintained an opulent gambling establishment and brothel in the rear, behind a code-locked door.

**mynock muffins** An expletive used on many backrocket worlds.

**Mynockra** The star system containing Ord Mynock.

**Mynock's Haven** A tavern in Coronet city on Corellia. Haber Trell agreed to meet Borbor Crisk there to transfer the false cargo being transported by Grand Admiral Thrawn.

**Myo** A vicious cyclopean Abyssin from Byss, he fought valiantly in three separate Bloodings before being captured by the Rodian slaver Malak. Myo escaped during a refueling stop at Kinun Depot, where he booked passage to Tatooine. He was in the Mos Eisley cantina when Luke Skywalker and Obi-Wan Kenobi first met Han Solo. Shortly afterward, Myo became one of the Galactic Outdoor Survival School's top desert survival teachers.

**myostim unit** A bodybuilding device that consisted of a sensor field coupled with an adjustable, computerized electromyoclonic broadcaster that forced muscle groups to contract and relax in sequence. Users of myostim units developed powerful mass without having to do any heavy lifting. Prince Xizor, head of the criminal Black Sun organization, was a confirmed user.

**Myrat'ur** A pirate who served under Byalfin Dyur aboard the *Boneyard Rendezvous* following the Swarm War.

**Myris Pictures** One of Adarlon's largest holovid studios, it was known for big-budget productions during the last decades of the Old Republic.

**Myrkr** Despite being well within the borders of the Old Republic, and having been on official registries for more than 300 years, the planet Myrkr was steadfastly avoided by the Jedi Knights. The reason nearly sealed the fate of the New Republic when it was exploited by Imperial mastermind Grand Admiral Thrawn.

It wasn't the high metal content of the trees, although the teeming forests of Myrkr obscured sensor readings, making it an ideal hiding place for outlaws on the lam. Natural predators weren't the reason, either, though the sleek and agile vornskrs exhibited a predisposition to attack Force-sensitives.

The real reason was a small sessile salamander-like creature that lived in Myrkr's trees. The native ysalamiri had the singular ability to *push back* the Force. Their presence created a bubble where the Force just didn't exist. A Jedi trapped in an ysalamiri's presence could not tap the mystical energy field that defined his or her abilities.

Smuggling chief Talon Karrde grew to admire Myrkr as a home for his growing operation, an organization that survived and prospered despite the underworld shakeup that followed Jabba the Hutt's death. Though the ysalamiri were peripheral to his business ventures, he did profit from his knowledge of the esoteric creatures when the Empire suddenly showed up on Myrkr five years after the Battle of Endor.

That was when Grand Admiral Thrawn devised a brilliant strategy to retake the Core Worlds. The ysalamiri would be used for two major purposes: to help recruit and control the insane Dark Jedi clone Joruus C'baoth, and to facilitate the construction of a new Imperial Army, overcoming the limitations of accelerated Spaarti-cylinder-based cloning. Eventually, Karrde had to pick sides in the growing conflict between the New Republic and the Empire. His decision forced him to flee Myrkr, and the planet was largely forgotten after the failure of Thrawn's campaign. Its unobtrusive port town of Hyllyard City remained a haven for smugglers and malcontents, at least until the Yuuzhan Vong arrived. The alien incursion into the galaxy left many worlds sundered in its wake. Myrkr was just one of many planets conquered by the Yuuzhan Vong, who developed a voxyn cloning facility in the system.

**myrmins** Small bugs that organized themselves into colonies.

***Mystic*** The name Darth Bane gave the Infiltrator series fighter he acquired as a personal transport vessel. In addition to its standard weaponry, the *Mystic* was equipped with a Class 4 hyperdrive. Darth Bane used the *Mystic* to travel to Tython after his apprentice Zannah learned that Belia Darzu had hidden a Sith Holocron within the fortress that she had built on the planet.

**mystic mob** An affectionate term used by clone commanders of the Grand Army of the Republic to describe Jedi Knights who were assigned to command roles.

**Mystifying Hoop Trick** A trick performed by magician Wim Magwit, it defied explanation. Two hoop-shaped frames were studded with replaceable matter transmitters, and via the hoop trick seemed to instantly transport anything that passed through one hoop to the other. Magwit could hold one hoop in his hand, step into it, and reappear from the other hoop. The exact method of matter transfer was unknown, although the transmitters themselves had to be constantly replaced from burnout. Boba Fett made use of the matter transmitter when he captured the pirate Bar-Kooda.

*Myo*

**mytag crystal** Common crystal vertices used as oscillators in ancient subspace communications and detection gear. Xim the Despot, realizing the need for wide-ranging communication for his forces, planned to stockpile mytag crystals in his vaults on Dellalt. The *Queen of Ranroon* was loaded with crystals and other raw materials when it was hidden. When Han Solo discovered the starship millennia later, he learned that the rumored treasure of Xim was really just a vast collection of largely outdated military supplies.

**myte** A small species of insects found on the planet Kubindi, mytes resembled large blue stones. This adaptation allowed them to hide among other rocks and avoid being eaten.

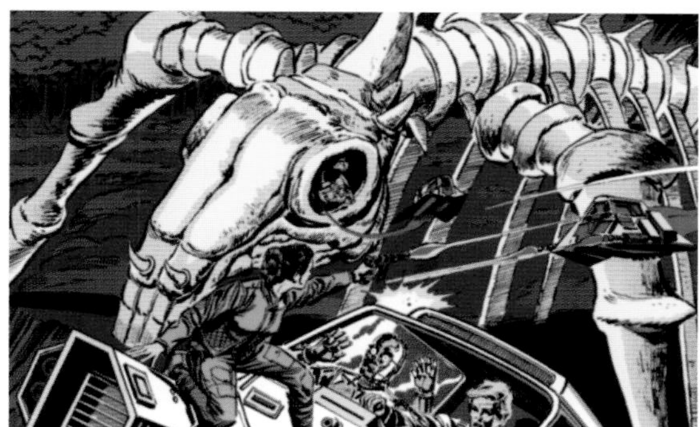
Mythosaur

**mythosaur** An extinct, gargantuan monster—some nearly the size of a small city by a few accounts—the mythosaur was the stuff of Mandalorian legend. They were all destroyed by the first *Mand'alor.* But the City of Bone, a slave quarters on Mandalore, was built out of the bones of the beast by an alien named Suprema during the Galactic Civil War.

**Mytus VII** A small, rocky planet with low gravity and no atmosphere, it was located in the debris-cluttered Mytus system and was home to the Corporate Sector Authority prison known as Stars' End. The prison, where inmates were kept in suspended animation between interrogations, was commanded by Authority Viceprex Mirkovig Hirken. Stars' End was destroyed by Han Solo and his companions during an attempted jailbreak.

Mytus VII

**MZX32905 system** A remote star system located near Bimmiel and the MZX33291 system, it was dominated by a vast asteroid field. Lumiya—under the alias Brisha Syo—established a home on one of the larger chunks of rock, where she discovered the remains of an ancient species of Force-sensitive beings that were similar in appearance to mynocks. These ancient beings, according to Syo's research, were evolved from lesser beings, having developed sentience while living on the asteroid. They developed one of the earliest-known forms of tactile writing to record their history, which indicated that their species had to return to the asteroid, known simply as Home, to breed.

Over the centuries, the beings began to die of starvation, until one member discovered that they could commune with the Force. This individual eventually took control of the asteroid, and apparently was consumed by the dark side. The species eventually died off, and the asteroid was abandoned for millennia until a mining facility was established on its surface. The director of the mines eventually fell prey to the dark side of the Force, becoming the Sith Master Darth Vectivus.

During the years following the Swarm War, Lumiya established her own base of operations on the asteroid, drawing on the energy of the dark side to gain strength. From this base, she was able to reach out across the galaxy, and it was there that she fled after being badly injured by Luke Skywalker at Roqoo Depot.

**MZX33291 system** An Outer Rim system originally discovered by an Imperial survey team, it was dominated by a pulsar that blocked communications into or out of the system. The fifth planet, known as Bimmiel, was discovered to have been visited by the Yuuzhan Vong nearly 50 years before they attacked Belkadan and Helska. In the wake of the war against the Yuuzhan Vong, many astrocartographers came to refer to the system as the Bimmiel system.

**N-09** A quadrant of Galactic City considered part of the commercial district of Coruscant in the final decades of the Old Republic. Despite its location, quadrant N-09 contained residential buildings as well as business facilities.

**N-1 starfighter** Built to protect the skies and space around Naboo, the N-1 starfighter was created specifically for the Naboo Royal air defense fleet. Its sleek design exemplified the philosophy of art and function that was prevalent in all Naboo technology before the Galactic Civil War. Its twin radial J-type engines were capped in gleaming chrome and trailed long delicate-looking finials behind the ship's single-pilot compartment. Behind the pilot sat a standard astromech droid, plugged into an abbreviated, ventrally-fed socket that required the droid to compress slightly in order to fit within the vessel's curves. The fighter featured twin blaster cannons, twin fire-linked torpedo launchers, and a capable automatic pilot feature.

During the Battle of Naboo, fearless pilot Ric Olié led Bravo Squadron's N-1 fighters against swarms of Trade Federation droid starfighters. The unexpected help of talented rookie pilot Anakin Skywalker resulted in the destruction of the Droid Control Ship, sealing the victory at Naboo.

The Naboo N-1's spaceframe was handcrafted by the Theed Palace Space Vessel Engineering Corps, and its high tech interior components came from a wide variety of offworld sources. Twin J-type Nubian-221 engines propelled the craft at sublight speeds, and were specially configured to reduce pollution in Naboo's environment. A Nubian Monarc C-4 hyperdrive increased the ship's range once astrogation coordinates were supplied by an R2 or similar unit. The compact hyperdrive was especially useful when N-1 fighters served as the Queen's Honor Guard on visits to other planets.

The central trailing finial served as a conduit for power and computer data. Theed Palace's hangar bays had specially designed revetment areas into which an N-1 plugged when docked. Large transformers in the hangar complex delivered a high-voltage power charge that activated the fighter's many systems. The palace battle computer delivered coded battle coordinates and strategic plans into the fighter's computer and automatic pilot.

*< N-1 starfighter*

**N-10** *See* Jaing.

**N-11** The designation of the ARC trooper nicknamed Ordo. N-11 accompanied Kal Skirata during his tenure as special security adviser to the Galactic Senate during the Clone Wars, serving as his chief lieutenant.

**N-12** The designation of the 12th *Null*-class ARC trooper produced on Kamino. Trooper N-12 was known as A'den to his fellow Nulls.

**N2-3PO** A blue-and-gold protocol droid that served the Friends of Paran resistance group on Derilyn during the Galactic Civil War. N2-3PO had a female personality, and peppered her speech with Gamorrean curses.

**Na, Noirah** This young woman was one of the many Padawans sent to the battlefield when the Jedi Knights became military leaders during the Clone Wars. She followed her Master, a Jedi named Simms, and Master Kai Hudorra, to Toola in an effort to secure the Republic's position there. When the command was given to execute Order 66, Master Simms was killed while giving her Padawan and Master Hudorra time to escape and return to Coruscant. Noirah was shocked when Master Hudorra shoved credits into her hand and ordered her to book passage away from the city-planet, forget her Jedi training, and simply disappear until the Jedi could find strength to fight back against the Galactic Empire.

**Na'al, Voren** A researcher and historian, he was responsible for recording much of the history and adventures of the heroes of the Battle of Yavin, especially Luke Skywalker, Han Solo, and Princess Leia Organa Solo. Originally a reporter for the Galactic News Service, he joined the Rebel Alliance soon after the New Order began. At first a spy, he later was named an assistant historian in Arhul Hextrophon's historian corps. After the New Republic was formed, Na'al was named director of Council Research. He eventually married Rivoche Tarkin.

**naal thorn burner** A self-contained heating unit developed for laboratories and medical applications, used by many beings to heat the chemicals for their hookah pipes.

**Naan, Kova** A Lannik, Naan was a Pugil athlete who played for the New Osler Flejj Beasts during the years leading up to the Clone Wars.

**Naap, Tolok** A Yuuzhan Vong warrior, he was part of the group dispatched to Yavin 4 to capture the Jedi students there. Naap had been a friend of Vua Rapuung prior to Rapuung's relegation to the caste of the Shamed Ones. When Rapuung escaped from Yavin 4 after gaining the friendship of Anakin Solo, Naap was one of the first to encounter the pair when they entered the shapers' complex to rescue Tahiri Veila.

**Naaq, Vee** A noted Gran poet, he bypassed the normal Gran social structure and avoided becoming a fluidics technician. He was engaged to Cera Vixe, but her brother Boe refused to let them marry. So Naaq hired a group of freelance spacers to "kidnap" the couple and take them off Kinyen.

**Naatan** The capital of Mawan, it was wondrously lit with soft, glowing lights that made it visible from space. To preserve the beauty of the city's surface, a vast network of tunnels and sublevels were built beneath it. Naatan was virtually destroyed, however, during a planet-wide civil war. Infrastructure was demolished and the population was decimated in the fighting. Crime lords moved in and took over sections of the city, fighting over control of the power grids and other necessities.

*Voren Na'al*

**Nabat** A village on Ryloth, it was a battle site during the Clone Wars.

**Nabatu** A barren, rocky world that was the 10th planet in the Coruscant system.

**Naberrie, Jobal** Padmé Amidala's mother, she was married to Ruwee Naberrie. The couple moved from their mountain home to the city of Theed in an effort to obtain a better education and a richer life for their family. Jobal worried about Padmé's choice of career, believing that her daughter spent too little time "just for herself." She was a gracious host who served lavish meals for her family and friends. During the Trade Federation's invasion of Naboo, Jobal and Ruwee were arrested and sent to jail because their daughter had become the Queen of Naboo.

*Jobal Naberrie*

**Naberrie, Padmé** The birth name of Queen and later Senator Amidala of Naboo. Padmé showed an interest in politics at a very early age, joining the Apprentice Legislature at 8 and becoming a full Legislator at 11. After being elected Queen, Amidala retained the name Padmé for use whenever she had to travel in dangerous territory. During those times, one of her look-alike handmaidens often portrayed Amidala. (*See also* Amidala, Padmé.)

**Naberrie, Pooja** Padmé Amidala's niece, her mother was Padmé's sister, Sola. Pooja was just four years old during the Battle of Geonosis. In the wake of the Clone Wars and the rise of the Empire, Pooja entered the world of politics, and later served as Naboo's representative to the Imperial Senate. Pooja recalled her first meetings with Anakin Skywalker, saying that she and her sister Ryoo thought Anakin was the most handsome man they had ever seen; they regarded him as a hero for serving as Padmé's bodyguard. The news that Anakin eventually became Darth Vader didn't reach her ears until nearly 60 years later, when she heard it from Leia Organa Solo.

*Pooja Naberrie*

**Naberrie, Ruwee** Padmé Amidala's father, he was a builder who worked for the Refugee Relief Movement while he was in school. He later served as a teacher at a Naboo university. He developed a working relationship with Rodian Senator Onaconda Farr, who became a friend of the Naberrie family. During the Trade Federation's invasion of Naboo, Ruwee and his wife, Jobal, were arrested and sent to jail. After Padmé was named Naboo's Senator, Ruwee developed a rapport with Queen Jamillia as a way to hear news of his daughter.

**Naberrie, Ryoo** Padmé Amidala's niece, she was the elder daughter of Padmé's sister Sola and was six years old at the time of the Battle of Geonosis.

**Naberrie, Sola** Padmé Amidala's older sister, she worried about Padmé and her desire to set the galaxy right, wondering if her younger sister would ever settle down and have children of her own. Sola married Darred Janren after the pair had graduated from one of Naboo's prestigious universities, and they had two girls, Ryoo and Pooja. Recognizing that the Naberrie name was well respected in politics and business, they chose to maintain it for their own family. Sola and Darred lived in the city of Theed, close to her parents.

**Naberrie, Winama** Padmé Amidala's paternal grandmother, she was known as one of Theed's best cloth weavers. Winama and Amidala shared a special bond. Amidala's father was a farmer at heart, but both Winama and Amidala loved the city. Winama died when Amidala was 13, about a year before the young woman was elected Queen of Naboo.

*Ryoo Naberrie*

**Nabon, Fenig** A Corellian smuggler and con artist who operated in the Outer Rim during the early years of the New Republic. She was an orphan living on the streets of Coronet City when Jett Nabon adopted her. Jett taught Fenig a great deal before his untimely and senseless death on Ord Mantell. Fenig met her business partner, Ghitsa Dogder, about two years after the Battle of Endor while on Socorro, and they were often at odds with each other. Despite this, they maintained an excellent working relationship. Fen, as she was known to friends, was owner and pilot of the *Star Lady.* When her ship was sabotaged, she had to land on Prishardia. There she encountered Kyp Durron, who was traveling under the name Zeth Fost. Once she realized who he was, Fen wanted to kill him for the destruction of billions of innocent lives in the Carida system. But that was just what Kyp wanted her to do, and she refused to let him off so easily. Together they rescued Ghitsa, who had been taken prisoner by the crew of the *Rook.*

*Ruwee Naberrie*

**Nabon, Jett** Fenig Nabon's adoptive father, Jett taught her everything she knew about starships and smuggling. He was known in certain circles for his compassion in helping the Mistryl, bringing them goods when no one else bothered. Jett was killed in a senseless barroom brawl on Ord Mantell.

**Naboo** An idyllic world close to the border of the Outer Rim Territories, Naboo was inhabited by peaceful humans known as the Naboo, and an indigenous species of intelligent amphibians called the Gungans. Naboo's surface consisted of swampy lakes, rolling plains, and green hills. Its population centers were beautiful; Naboo's river cities were resplendent with classical architecture and greenery, while the underwater Gungan settlements were a beautiful display of exotic hydrostatic bubble technology.

Naboo was a geologically unique world. It lacked a molten core, indicative of an ancient world. The planet was a conglomerate of large rocky bodies permeated by countless caves and tunnel networks. This caused numerous swampy lakes on the surface, which led deeper into the planet's structure. The native Gungans developed transports that exploited the cave networks, but even those hardy explorers paused at venturing too deep into the planet core, for it was infested with gargantuan sea beasts with ravenous appetites.

When the Galactic Senate enacted a measure that would increase taxation along outlying trade routes, the credit-hungry Trade Federation protested by blockading Naboo. A screen of huge warships surrounded the planet, cutting off supplies to the Naboo. The world's leaders, Queen Amidala and Governor Sio Bibble, were taken captive by the Trade Federation's droid armies. Jedi

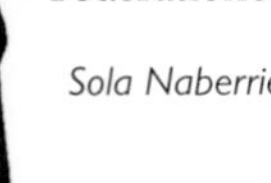

*Sola Naberrie*

Knights sent by Supreme Chancellor Valorum freed Queen Amidala, and she then journeyed to Coruscant to request the Senate's intervention. Even Naboo's representative, Senator Palpatine, could not get past the bureaucratic stalling tactics of the Trade Federation.

Naboo

Disheartened with the Senate's inability to act, Queen Amidala took matters into her own hands. She returned to Naboo and recruited the help of the Gungans. Together, Naboo's two cultures were able to repel the Trade Federation invasion, and brought peace back to the serene world.

The third of five planets orbiting a yellow star in the Chommell sector, Naboo was first settled by human colonists from the planet Grizmallt thousands of years before the Galactic Civil War. When these colonists and the native Gungans first met, there was a profound failure to understand one another, and tensions between the two cultures continued for millennia. Despite the suffering caused by the Trade Federation invasion, the end result was new prosperity for the planet as the Gungans and the Naboo put aside their differences.

In the interests of preserving ecological stability, alleviating overcrowding in the underwater city of Otoh Gunga, and fostering peace and goodwill, the Naboo and the Gungans launched an ambitious joint venture to colonize Ohma-D'un, one of Naboo's three moons. The grand experiment worked, creating a stable ecology on the moon. The colony, however, was attacked by the Separatists with a chemical weapon early in the Clone Wars. Many Gungan colonists died after exposure to an experimental toxin engineered to wipe out the Republic's clone army.

Naboo was spared the worst of the Clone Wars, and with the rise of the Empire, the placid planet tried to remain an example of a more peaceful time before the collapse of the Old Republic. The young monarch, Queen Apailana, quietly rebelled at the changes enacted by the Empire. When she went too far, and was believed to be harboring Jedi fugitives, the elite 501st Legion was dispatched to Naboo to eliminate her and bring the planet back in line.

The Naboo celebrate a victory.

**Naboo, the** The human colonists living on Naboo. They were descended from colonists from the planet Grizmallt, who arrived aboard the starships *Beneficent Tasia, Constant,* and *Mother Vima,* 3,900 years before the Battle of Yavin. During much of their existence, the Naboo took great pains to avoid contact with their Gungan neighbors. Indeed, they were mostly unaware of the huge underwater cities the Gungans built to escape contact themselves.

A bloody war raged several centuries before the Battle of Naboo, in which large portions of both species were killed. Beings on each side realized that they couldn't survive without the other, and specialized trading relationships were set up. While these were not officially recognized by either government, they were vital to the survival of each species.

In general, the Naboo were a peaceful people who chose to live in harmony with their environment. When the Trade Federation blockaded, then invaded, their world, the Naboo were powerless to defend themselves. Their armed forces were largely made up of unproven volunteers. Queen Amidala boldly placed her people in a subordinate role to the Gungans, led by Boss Nass, and gained the confidence of the Gungan people. Together the two species managed to win the Battle of Naboo and reestablish a relationship.

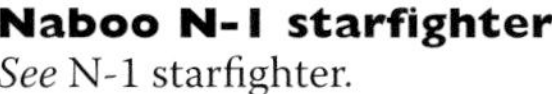
Naboo Palace Guard

**Naboo bomber** Developed through the combined efforts of the Naboo Royal Security Force and the Theed Palace Vessel Engineering Corps, this starship was prototyped shortly before the Battle of Naboo. It was created from sleek Nubian components and a Naboo spaceframe, and was heavily armored. It was armed with energy bombs and laser cannons, giving it the ability to strike ground-based installations as well as attack airborne opponents. The Naboo bomber first saw real action during the struggle to liberate Naboo from the Trade Federation.

**Naboo crystal** A fine leaded crystal produced on Naboo. Along with its beauty, Naboo crystal was known for its delicacy.

**Naboo Embassy** A governmental building located in Galactic City on Coruscant during the final decades of the Old Republic. The Senator from Naboo and his or her attendants worked in the embassy building, assisting displaced Naboo with various legal and governmental requirements.

**Naboo Essentials Provider** The branch of the Naboo government responsible for maintaining the power grid that supplied electricity and energy to the entire planet.

**Nabooian tusk-cat** *See* tusk-cat.

**Naboo lake retreat** *See* Varykino.

**Naboo Moon Mining Union** Representing the miners who worked in the Naboo system in the years leading up to the Clone Wars, this union was formed by 40 mining ships and their crews to ensure proper pricing of the kassoti spice found on the smallest Naboo moon. The appropriation of its docking facilities for refugee relief caused contention between the union and the Naboo government.

**Naboo N-1 starfighter** *See* N-1 starfighter.

**Naboo Palace Guard** A division of the Naboo Royal Security Forces, the Palace Guard was responsible for security in and around royal and governmental buildings. It comprised about 150 members of the Security Force who had experience offworld, many of whom had received commendations for their bravery and service. Members were distinguished by their red armor and uniforms.

**Naboo Queen, The** One of the more exclusive restaurants on Coruscant in the years following the Sith-Imperial War.

**Naboo Royal Cruiser** A sleek, wide-winged starship used by Senator Padmé Amidala to travel between Naboo and Coruscant. Like the Naboo Royal Starship, the cruiser was chrome-plated, with decorative seams marking the gleaming hull. As a government

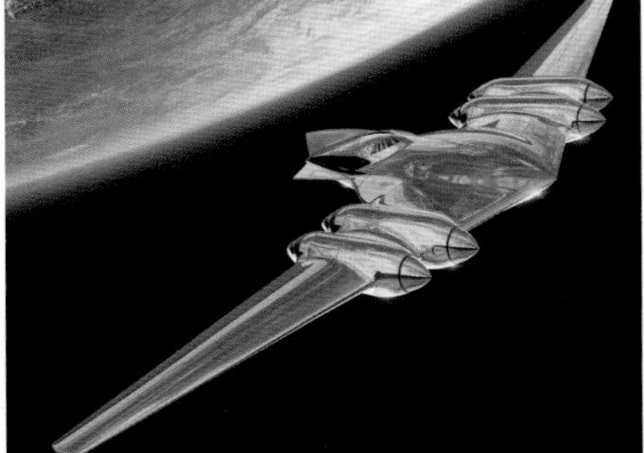
Naboo Royal Cruiser

Naboo star skiff

ship, the 39-meter-long cruiser was sometimes called a diplomatic barge, and it lacked true weaponry. Amidala's cruiser, however, was enhanced with redundant shielding and was escorted on all its trips by four N-1 starfighters, which could link up to its wings for refueling and during jumps through hyperspace.

The cruiser was destroyed shortly before the Battle of Geonosis when Senator Amidala returned to Coruscant for the vote on the Military Creation Act. The ship's landing platform was rigged with explosives by Jango Fett and Zam Wesell, who had been hired by the Trade Federation to eliminate the Senator. Amidala was actually traveling in a support ship at the time, but her handmaiden Cordé died in the explosion.

**Naboo Royal Security Forces** The volunteer organization that pledged itself to the protection of Naboo's planetary rulers during the last years of the Old Republic. The group included members from all branches of the Naboo military, including Security Guards, Palace Guards, and the Space Fighter Corps. The forces were commanded by Captain Panaka, and later Captain Typho. Leaders were distinguished by their brown body armor and royal blue uniforms.

**Naboo Royal Starship** A sleek chromium-plated transport ship used by the royalty of the Naboo. The 76-meter-long Nubian spaceframe was designed around a J-type configuration. Equipped with a pair of Headon-5 sublight engines, a Nubian 327 hyperdrive, and a Nubian T-14 hyperdrive generator, the Royal Starship was easily recognized by its highly reflective chromium plating and distinctive, dagger-like shape. It was equipped with stations for up to eight astromech droids that performed a variety of tasks, including repair and navigation.

**Naboo Senatorial Delegation** Under Senator Palpatine and his entourage before the Battle of Naboo, the delegation purposely downplayed the role of Gungans and referred to them as "simple-minded barbarians who have barely mastered the basic hallmarks of civilization." The remark revealed Palpatine's xenophobia.

**Naboo star skiff** A small transport ship developed by Theed Palace Space Vessel Engineering Corps of Naboo during the Clone Wars. Like its predecessors, the star skiff was a J-type vessel that employed a great deal of Nubian technology. It was essentially a flying wing, with the main fuselage and twin engines mounted on the underside. Like craft designed for Naboo royalty, the star skiff was plated with highly polished chromium. But like the Naboo yacht, it was designed for Senator Padmé Amidala. The 29.2-meter-long vessel had a wingspan of just over 49 meters, and it was one of the first Naboo craft of its kind to be armed: The star skiff had a pair of top-mounted laser cannons. To provide propulsion in atmosphere, the vessel had Sossen-7 sublight drives.

**Naboo swamp moss** Native to the planet Naboo, it grew in cascading sheets that hung from the branches of trees that grew along the edges of swamps.

**Naboo system** A yellow star with five natural orbital bodies and one artificial one. Moth and Erep were searing rocks with no known settlements, and Widow was similar, but with one moon. Naboo was a relatively small terrestrial body with three moons, and Storm a gas giant with 32 moons. The Naboo had a penal colony on Storm's third moon and TaggeCo. had a mine on the 10th one. Prior to the Clone Wars, the Trade Federation also staffed a space station, TFP-9.

Gha Nachkt

**Naboo underground** A rebel movement formed by students and professors who studied in the city of Theed during the blockade and subsequent invasion of Naboo by the Trade Federation.

**Naboo Wastelands** An area of the planet Naboo that was barren of most forms of life.

**Naboo yacht** A needle-shaped, H-type yacht manufactured by the Theed Palace Space Vessel Engineering Corps. Based on a yacht superstructure developed on Nubia, the 47.9-meter-long Naboo yacht was created for Senator Padmé Amidala's personal use. It was capable of speeds near 8,000 kilometers per hour in atmosphere, which allowed the Senator to reach her destinations quickly, but proved a problem for the N-1 escort fighters trying to protect her. Like most Naboo craft, the yacht was plated in gleaming chrome and was unarmed. Its shields were developed jointly by the Naboo and the Gungans, and could activate nearly instantaneously. Central quarters used by Amidala were located in a shielded capsule that could be ejected from the craft if necessary to evade capture.

Naboo yacht

**Nabyl, Bock** An Imperial officer who served Warlord Zsinj as the captain of the *Hawk-Bat.*

**Nachkt, Gha** A slimy, corpulent Trandoshan junk dealer, Gha Nachkt scoured the galaxy in his rust-bucket scow, *Vulture's Claw,* collecting and then reselling the highly profitable wastes of war. Nachkt salvaged wreckage from the aftermath of a battle at Bothawui during the Clone Wars. A skilled thief, he stole R2-D2 and brought the droid to General Grievous on Ruusan. When the Trandoshan asked for money, Grievous killed him with a lightsaber blade through his back.

**Nacht-5** BlasTech's smoke grenade, produced during the New Order.

**Nackhar** A Nartian who was Wuher's assistant in the Mos Eisley cantina when Ben Kenobi and Luke Skywalker sought passage to Alderaan. Nackhar had to clean up the mess from Dr. Evazan and Ponda Baba.

**nackhawn** A carrion bird found on the planet Lucazec.

**Na-Coth, Deamos** An ex-slave who grew to be a military leader, philosopher, and part-time prophet. Na-Coth believed in the existence of an ancient paradise planet called Exo. He founded a group known as the Cabal to search the outermost reaches of the galaxy for Exo, but many of its ships were lost. Na-Coth died nearly bankrupt, but his followers continued to search.

**Nadad, Lora** A Padawan learner at the Almas Academy, she was 19 years old at the time. Nadad was chosen for training late in life, having endured a rough childhood. She had been a leader to the Lost children of Forard, working hard to give them a chance to succeed. When she was chosen as a Padawan, Lora took advantage of the position to bring the struggle of the Lost into the public consciousness on Cularin.

**Nadar, T'nadar** A Chadra-Fan who operated the Galaxy Shop on Darknon Station, he often bartered rather than accept payment for the goods he sold.

**Nadd, Freedon** This young Jedi was amazingly open and willing to touch the Force when he was first trained on Ossus more than 400 years before the Great Sith War. He was unprepared for his first true test, however, when the Jedi Masters passed him over for promotion to Jedi Knight. In his anger, Nadd struck down his Master, Matta Tremayne, and succumbed to the dark side of the Force. He took up the teachings of the Sith, consulting a Sith Holocron that might have been created by Darth Andeddu.

Naddists

Nadd became proficient in dark side Sith magic. He could not progress, however, because the reigning Dark Lord was still young, and the Sith had declared that only one Dark Lord could rule at any time. Frustrated, Nadd rebelled against the Sith, fleeing to Yavin 4. He was trained there by the ancient spirit of Naga Sadow. When he felt strong enough, Nadd destroyed Sadow's spirit and set out to become the next Sith Lord.

He brought the dark power of the Sith to the planet Onderon and ruled for years. As Nadd's power grew over more than 100 years of rule, the Jedi Knights learned of his atrocities and sent out a task force to bring his reign to an end. There was a pitched battle, and eventually Freedon Nadd was defeated.

Freedon Nadd

His body was hidden by the Jedi on the Dxun moon in a massive pyramid that seemed to warp and change over the years. Nadd's Sith teachings had been accepted by the Onderonians, so the power of the dark side never left the planet.

Nadd managed to preserve his spirit, locked away in the tomb with the Sith artifacts he worked to obtain. His spirit then inhabited the bodies of the leaders of Onderon, including King Ommin.

Jedi Exar Kun reawakened Nadd's spirit, which helped him discover concealed Sith scrolls. These led Kun to the hidden world of Korriban, site of the mummified remains of many Sith Lords. Nadd's spirit reappeared and destroyed huge crystals that had held the trapped spirits of ancient Jedi who had opposed the Sith; he also brought Kun close to death, forcing the confused Jedi to accept the dark side of the Force.

**Naddists** Followers of Freedon Nadd's teachings. Based on the planet Onderon, the Naddists felt that Nadd was their savior, and that he gave them the strength to drive out the wild beasts from their cities. Their belief in Nadd convinced them that the Jedi Knights were the cause of all their problems, since it was the Jedi who brought down Nadd and recovered ancient Sith artifacts. Although the Jedi were able to quell the Naddist uprising on Onderon, the event was just one example of the growing threat of the dark side and a precursor of the Great Sith War.

**Nadiem** A remote planet on the edge of the Outer Rim settled by a group of farmers. Nadiem was besieged by the droids of the Confederacy of Independent Systems five months after the Battle of Geonosis. Clone troopers led by Jedi Luminara Unduli and Barriss Offee were able to defeat the Separatist forces and free the settlers. Other Jedi, including B'dard Tone, suffered injuries after confronting General Grievous on the far side of the planet.

**Nadill, Memit** An ancient Jedi Master and Empress Teta's most trusted adviser during the series of Unification Wars that brought together the seven planets she ruled. Nadill was a regal, green-skinned humanoid with several small tails sprouting from the back of his head. He and Teta believed that both Odan-Urr and Jori Daragon were correct in predicting an imminent Sith attack, and readied their forces. Nadill rallied the Jedi to his cause and led them in defending Coruscant from Naga Sadow's warriors. When Gav Daragon broke Sadow's concentration, Nadill realized that much of the attacking force was illusory—Sith magic kept it and the real warriors going. They were able to dispel the illusions and turn the tide of battle, eliminating the Sith threat from Coruscant.

Momaw Nadon

**Nadon, Momaw** Expelled from his homeworld of Ithor, Nadon became an underground Rebel Alliance agent before finally returning to his paradise home. Belonging to a species of peaceful farmers and artisans, Nadon had been high priest, or Herd Leader, of the *Tafanda Bay.* The ship was a huge floating city similar to the vessels on which most Ithorians lived. The Empire's Captain Alima demanded Ithor's agricultural secrets, long guarded for religious and other reasons, and issued an ultimatum: Either the secrets would be turned over or Imperials would destroy the *Tafanda Bay.* Seeing little option, Nadon turned over the data. He was then put on trial by outraged Ithorians and exiled for at least three years, forced to abandon his wife, Fandomar, and the rest of his family.

Nadon ended up on Tatooine and helped create new forms of plant life on the arid planet. He also used his house to shelter Rebel fugitives and provide information to the Alliance. Although he later had an opportunity to kill Alima, he couldn't bring himself to do it. Instead he hatched a plan to make the officer seem like a traitor, and the Imperial was shot by his own superiors. Following the Battle of Endor, Nadon returned to Ithor and was able to convince the planet's Elders to let him remain.

Memit Nadill

**Nadon Farms** A Tatooine moisture farm that produced water commercially during the early years of the New Republic.

**Nad'Ris** The planetary capital of Prishardia, it was the site of the world's largest starport.

**Naduarr** The owner and operator of a liquor store in Mos Espa on Tatooine in the years leading up to the Battle of Geonosis. Despite the fact that Naduarr carried some of the best spirits and wines available, his prices were always reasonable.

Nagai

**Naeco** A Rebel Alliance starfighter pilot and practical joker, he served on the *Independence* with Keyan Farlander.

**Naescorcom** A manufacturing consortium that was controlled by corporate representatives from seven Outer Rim planets during the last decades of the Old Republic. The products produced by Naescorcom included everything from towels and clothing to medical trauma kits and weaponry.

**nafen** A nocturnal insect generally regarded as a pest. Nafens were characterized by the harsh, clacking sound their wings made as they flew. They often carried diseases that mutated before they reintroduced them back into the environment.

**naga** A predatory reptile known for its ability to waver in place, lulling its prey into a false sense of security before striking.

**Naga, Asa** A blue-skinned being who worked for Black Sun Vigo Darnada. Distinguished by three forehead tattoos and a scar across his left eye, Naga and the Wookiee Gargachykk were sent by Darnada to hunt down Feen Fenoob. Unable to recover Fenoob's debt, the pair was resigned to bringing back his body when they discovered that Darth Maul had already killed him. The two thugs brought Maul back to Darnada, only to have the Sith Lord execute the entire assembly. Naga alone survived, fleeing to Alexi Garyn's residence on Ralltiir to report on Darnada's execution. Maul, however, followed him and killed him to eliminate any trace of his involvement.

Nahkee

**Nagag, Saduu** An Aplocaph who constantly cleaned his skin, keeping it gleaming in case he found himself in "that one, crucial meeting." Saduu was on board the *Kuari Princess* when it was attacked by the Riders of the Maelstrom.

**Nagai** Humanoids from the planet Nagi, which was located in a star cluster beyond the borders of both the Old Republic and the Empire. Distinguished by their pale, translucent skin and thin, angular features, the Nagai had jet-black hair that grew upward instead of falling down. After the Battle of Endor, they supported one of Lumiya's bids to overthrow the New Republic. Little was known about the Nagai until that time; even the Rebel Alliance referred to them simply as "Knives," for the individual Nagai who tried to enslave the Wookiees on Kashyyyk. Following the defeat of the Empire and the formation of the New Republic, the Nagai split into two peaceful factions. One group remained neutral and set out to locate a new homeworld, while the other joined the New Republic.

**Nagelson, Sleepy** A fighter pilot who served the New Republic as part of the 21st Recon Group. He earned the nickname Sleepy because in-flight monitors recorded him sleeping through a reconnaissance mission during the battle against Grand Admiral Thrawn. Nagelson drew recon duty during the Yevethan Purge; he was shot down and killed during the mission.

Na-Jia

**Nagua, Mercevian** A legendary galactic pirate who developed many assault and infiltration strategies that were used years later during the New Order.

***Nagwa*** A New Republic *Agave*-class picket ship dispatched under the command of Pakkpekatt to intercept the Teljkon vagabond. The *Nagwa* was ordered back to dry dock after the mission failed to capture the mystery ship at Gmir Askilon.

**Nahkee** A 2-meter-tall baby Phlog, or Phlogling, who lived on the Forest Moon of Endor around the time of the Battle of Endor.

**nahra** A form of Kaminoan performance art in which the performers often were inert. This art form was known to other beings as mime-dancing. Nahra artists were known for their ability to mime emotions, evoking intense feelings among the viewers.

**Nahrunba** *See* Jahrunba, Nahrunba, and Sahrunba.

**Nahsu Minor** A temperate, grass-covered planet that was homeworld of the Murachauns. It was located in the Inner Rim.

**Naia** A green-skinned native of the planet Solem, she was part of the Rebel underground that sprang up during the early years of the Galactic Civil War. A medic, Naia was one of the few survivors of Imperial Governor Malvander's subjugation of Solem.

**Nailati, Evilo** The disembodied brain of a B'omarr monk, Nailati befriended the frog-dog Buboicullaar and taught him about the universe and how to control his mind.

**Naima** A native of the planet Bellassa, she was a member of the Eleven during the months following the Clone Wars. As part of the Bellassan resistance, Naima was friends with Dr. Amie Antin. Naima and several other members of the resistance were killed in an Imperial attack on Ussa.

**Naithol** A Sullustan who agreed to help Roganda Ismaren and Drost Elegin recover the *Eye of Palpatine.* He was an executive of the SoroSuub Corporation during the early years of the New Republic.

**Na-Jia** Distinguished by her purple hair, she was a street thief who befriended Saesee Tiin when the Jedi Master visited her homeworld of Diado. She stole Master Tiin's lightsaber while extricating him from a cantina fight with Birok, but then returned it. Master Tiin gave her 600 credits for her honesty. She later repaid his kindness by destroying a battle droid that was about to shoot him. Master Tiin and Na-Jia were later apprehended by a squad of snow droids and thrown into prison at a Separatist laboratory. Na-Jia was questioned and later returned to their cell. Luckily, she had stolen Master Tiin's lightsaber back from their captors; he used it to cut them an escape route. Master Tiin revealed that he had purposely allowed himself to be captured so that he could steal the prototype starfighter being developed at the laboratory. As he blasted out of the building, Na-Jia made her own escape.

**Najib** Natives of the planet Najiba, Najib were friendly to offworlders, but they also were very suspicious by nature. Their legs were quite short, and their arms appeared to be overly long, but they were kilogram for kilogram as powerful as Wookiees.

**Nakay, Keela** One of five children rescued by Mace Windu from a lava flow in the jungle of Haruun Kal. The children, led by Keela's brother Terrel, had been trying to return to their camp in a

Najib

steamcrawler when they were caught by the lava. Keela suffered a massive head injury, and was unconscious when Master Windu found the children. The children later discovered that Keela's father had died in earlier fighting, leaving Keela and her sister Pell orphaned. The sisters, along with Urno and Nykl, were taken in by Nick Rostu after Windu left them to continue his mission.

**Nakay, Pell** The sister of Keela, she was rescued by Mace Windu on Haruun Kal.

**Nakay, Terrel** The brother of Keela and Pell Nakay, he was the oldest at only 13 and acted as the group's leader during an attempt to travel back to their camp in a steamcrawler. When the vehicle was caught in the lava, Terrel refused to allow Mace Windu to rescue him until Windu explained that three others were already safely under his control. Terrel, distraught after learning his father had been killed, flew into a rage when Master Windu revealed that he was a Jedi. In response to what he perceived to be deception and lies, Terrel used a blunt knife to maim Besh and Chalk, who were in a state of thanatizine suspension. The act of mindless aggression was discovered by Kar Vastor, who used his vibroshields to cut Terrel in two in retribution for his actions.

**Naked Hutt Cantina** A watering hole on the planet Omman.

**N'a-kee-tula** A green-skinned boy native to Shadda-Bi-Boran, his name meant "sweetheart." N'a-kee-tula was rescued from the doomed planet by Padmé Naberrie. Unfortunately, the natives of Shadda-Bi-Boran were unable to adapt to their new planet, and died shortly after relocation.

**Nak'har** This Defel was one of the many thugs who worked for the Rodian slaver Gomalo during the final decades of the Old Republic. Nak'har was assigned to protect Thook Lafrell after the kidnapping of Ezra Du'Re.

**Nakhym, Golov** This pirate captain was captured by the Rebel Alliance shortly before the Battle of Endor when his forces began raiding Alliance supplies.

**Nakk, Urman** A warrant officer who was part of the New Republic remnant that set up a temporary base on Borleias in the wake of the Battle of Coruscant. Officer Nakk was assigned to the base's security team.

**nak'tra crystal** Tough crystals found in the deepest caverns on Kashyyyk, they were harvested by the Wookiees of the Myyydril tribe. Individual crystals were used as focusing lenses for specialized blaster weapons that emitted coherent energy of a specific wavelength that was effective against Urnsor'is, a species of sentient parasites that attacked Wookiees.

**Nalan** This Twi'lek was one of the dancers Brin'shak sent to Durga the Hutt. Ghitsa Dogder negotiated the deal, although she and Fenig Nabon never planned to give the dancers to Durga. They tricked Shada D'ukal and Dunc T'racen into unwittingly aiding their escape.

**nalargon** A large musical instrument that was operated by a keyboard and foot pedals. Its many pipes and subharmonic resonators produced a multitude of sounds that were considered soothing to many humanoid species. The instrument was favored by bands throughout the galaxy.

**nala-tree frog** An amphibian that was a favorite food of Kibbick the Hutt. He introduced these frogs to his uncle Aruk, who demanded that a supply be made readily available for his consumption. Teroenza, sick of the Besadii control over the Ylesian colonies and his own life, began working with Jabba and Jiliac to poison the frogs he sent to Aruk, hoping to kill the ancient slug.

**Naldar** One of many worlds attacked by splinter groups of the Empire after the Battle of Endor. Located near the planet Belderone, it once served as a refuge for natives of Belderone who also had fled Imperial subjugation.

**Nale, Kam** A tough Podracing competitor, this amphibious Fluggrian used the less-than-clever alias Elan Mak on the circuit. He long hunted hit man Aldar Beedo to avenge the murder of Nale's father, a crime lord from Ploo IV.

**Nalgol** An Imperial Navy captain who was a member of the Kuat family and commander of the *Tyrannic* during the early years of the New Republic. He maintained his command following the death of Grand Admiral Thrawn, and was part of the group picked by Moff Disra to begin his assault on the New Republic. Shortly after the revelation of Bothan involvement in the Caamas incident, Disra introduced Nalgol and three other navy captains to "Thrawn"—artfully portrayed by Flim. Like his comrades, including Captain Dorja, Nalgol was completely fooled by the performance.

**Nal Hutta** A bruised-looking planet in the Y'Toub system. The planet's name meant "glorious jewel" in Huttese. It was one of the main planets settled by the Hutts after they left their ancestral home of Varl. Despite the planet's immensity, its extremely low density gave it a tolerable gravity. In ancient history, the planet was known as Evocar, the homeworld of the primitive Evocii. When the Hutts arrived, they traded technology to the Evocii in exchange for land, eventually buying up the entire planet and forcing the Evocii off. The Hutts then replaced all Evocii structures with Hutt palaces and shrines and renamed the planet.

*Nal Hutta*

Nal Hutta was a pleasant world of mountainous rain forests, but the Hutts transformed it into a gloomy planet of stinking bogs and patches of sickly marsh grass inhabited by insects and spiders. The planet's flocks of large, clumsy birds were shot down by swoop-riding hunters. The atmosphere was polluted by strip-mining in Nal Hutta's industrial centers, and a greasy rain drizzled on its squatters' villages and ghettos. Nal Hutta and its moon, Nar Shaddaa, were at the center of Hutt space and hosted a constant traffic of freight haulers, smugglers, and other galactic traders.

In the aftermath of the Battle of Fondor and the duplicitous actions of Borga the Hutt, the Yuuzhan Vong targeted Nal Hutta for destruction. The alien invaders bombarded the planet from a remote location, although many of the missiles exploded in the atmosphere. Eventually, both Nal Hutta and the moon Nar Shaddaa were overtaken by the Yuuzhan Vong, and terraformed into worlds more suitable to them. The Hutts who had once controlled the worlds were either killed or scattered into the galaxy. A few managed to escape to Tatooine, where they established an alliance to fight for their survival. After the Yuuzhan Vong War, a few Hutts decided to return to Nal Hutta, and began working with the Galactic Alliance to restore the planet's habitability.

***Nal Hutta Kal'tamok*** A Huttese newsfeed that was available on the computer networks of the galaxy, it provided political and economic reports on the buying, selling, and shipment of banned goods. Despite its basis in the criminal underworld, the *Nal Hutta Kal'tamok* was exceptionally reliable and relevant. Many insurance agencies used its reports to estimate the impact of smuggling on legitimate transportation businesses.

**Nali-Erun** A Senali clan that preferred to live in relative isolation on a remote island. When Prince Leed of Rutan went into hiding on Senali, the Nali-Erun watched over him to make sure he survived.

**Nalju** This family was one of the six Great Houses of the planet Serenno in the decades that followed the Battle of Ruusan.

**Nalju, Count** A member of one of the Great Houses of Serenno in the years after the Battle of Ruusan, Nalju was one of the few noblemen to openly support the Old Republic and the efforts of the Galactic Senate to reunite the galaxy. Nalju met with former Chancellor Tarsus Valorum to discuss ways to quell the growing Separatist movement that had evolved on Serenno. Darth Bane learned of the meeting and sent his apprentice Zannah to disrupt it.

**Nall, Zeela** A member of Orma Hundeen's Rebel underground during the Galactic Civil War, Zeela was distinguished by her black hair and green-yellow eyes. She posed as one of the Quetzal Sisters to help Leia Organa recover a valuable holocube on Elerion shortly after the Battle of Yavin.

**Nallastia** A small, jungle-covered world near Fondor. It was here that Admiral Cha Niathal regrouped with forces still loyal to her after the Second Battle of Fondor split the Galactic Alliance apart.

**Nalle triplets** Identical sisters who lived on Coruscant, they were commonly found in the gambling halls and casinos of the Uscru district. The triplets used their femininity to distract other gamblers while stealing their credits.

**Nalo** A schoolteacher encountered by Obi-Wan Kenobi some 11 years before the Battle of Naboo, when he infiltrated the Freelies to discover the motives behind industrial sabotage on Vorzyd 4.

**Nalrithian** From an unknown Outer Rim planet, these insectile humanoids communicated telepathically among themselves. They stood just under 2 meters tall, and many were heavily muscled. Young were hatched from eggs, with several Nalrithian infants born from a single egg. These eggmates shared a telepathic bond that augmented the species' latent telepathic abilities. Nalrithians were isolationists and xenophobes.

**Nalroni** Golden-furred humanoids native to Celanon, Nalroni had long, tapered snouts and extremely sharp teeth. With their slender builds, they were elegant and graceful in motion.

**Naltree, Linna** A scientist who took in the Jedi Master Ry-Gaul and hid him in the wake of the Clone Wars. Naltree and her husband, Tobin Gantor, disappeared shortly afterward. Gantor eventually escaped Imperial captivity, and Ry-Gaul and Trever Flume rescued Linna. After being reunited, Naltree and Gantor fled to the planet Mila to avoid being discovered by the Empire.

**Nalual, Deran** A Padawan who was among the small group of Jedi rescued by Roan Shryne and the crew of the *Drunk Dancer,* in the wake of the Clone Wars. A Togruta, Nalual was blinded in the firefight that had injured his teacher, Siadem Forte, just after the command was given to execute Order 66. Recognizing that the situation was going to be dire for the Jedi, Forte and Nalual fled to Dellalt, where they issued a 913 code transmission to any Jedi in the area. Their call was answered by several other survivors, and the group fled into the stars before being located by Shryne. Their travels led them to Kashyyyk, where they were confronted by Darth Vader himself. Nalual managed to escape unharmed, but Forte and Iwo Kulka were killed before Roan Shryne sacrificed his own life to allow others to escape. After leaving Kashyyyk, Nalual decided to sign up as an agriculturalist or construction engineer attached to an Imperial project. There he hoped to learn as much as he could about the Empire and sow dissent from within.

*Nampi*

**Nam** One of the three stars that centered the Chorios systems in the Meridian sector.

**Na Maak, Chidee** A Duros starship mechanic on StarForge Station, he assumed ownership of the shipyard there when his parents died. Na Maak continued their tradition of excellent workmanship at a premium price, assuring him of a healthy profit. During the early years of the Galactic Civil War, his skills in repairing the YT-1210 were well known to the galaxy's smugglers and shippers. Na Maak once offered Chewbacca a huge sum to work for him rather than sticking with Han Solo, but the Wookiee refused.

**Namadii Corridor** A hyperspace route that allowed swift travel between Coruscant and Bilbringi.

**namana nectar** A thick, pale orange liqueur produced on Bakura, it had a delicate floral aroma and fruity taste.

*Nalroni*

**namana trees** Native to Bakura, they produced the tropical fruit used to make namana twist candy and liqueur. Once processed, the fruit induced a faint sensation of pleasure.

**Namarhe** A Rebel Alliance starfighter pilot from Bestine IV, he was killed while trying to capture the Imperial transport *Omicron.*

**Nam Chorios** In the Chorios systems of the Meridian sector, this barren, unforgiving, moonless world orbited a violet-white star of the same name. It held no seas—only endless wastelands of sharp, jagged rocks, basalt, and quartz outcroppings. Nights were incredibly cold. Chains of crystal mountains reflected sunlight from their sparkling facets, and isolated crystal rock chimneys called tsils thrust up toward the sky. A famous site, the Ten Cousins, was a group of tsils standing in a ring. The Force was magnified and intensified by the entire planet, making its usage difficult to control or focus.

For years, power on the planet rested with Beldorion the Hutt and Seti Ashgad, a profiteer who had been exiled to Nam Chorios by then-Senator Palpatine. Dzym, a giant, mutated droch, kept Ashgad alive and young. Nine years after the Battle of Endor, Leia Organa Solo secretly visited the planet to meet with Ashgad. He then turned on her and took her prisoner before unleashing the Death Seed plague across three-quarters of the sector; the plague was spread by the insectlike drochs, which had been kept in check by the Nam Chorios environment. Ashgad planned to disable the planet's gun stations, let the drochs escape, and allow the Loronar Corporation to strip-mine smokies—long green-violet crystals found clustered in the deep hills.

Leia eventually escaped from Ashgad's fortress and teamed up with the Jedi Callista, who also had been taken prisoner. After a series of confrontations, Leia killed Beldorion; Dzym escaped but was destroyed along with the other drochs; Moff Getelles, who had invaded the sector as part of Dzym's vast conspiracy, was forced to retreat at the Battle of Nam Chorios; and Callista decided to stay on the planet awhile longer.

**Name It, Claim It Law** Slang for an Old Republic planetary development decree. Under it, explorers had only to locate remote systems, perform cursory life-form scans, and file for development rights in order to take control. The result was the discovery and naming of a vast number of planetary systems without any real idea what each system and its worlds held.

**naming-father** A Yuuzhan Vong male who attended the birth of a child and determined his or her name within the family's domain.

**n'amiq** A winged lizard trained for combat by Yuuzhan Vong warriors.

**Nammon, Ran** An alias used by Lirin Banolt during the early years of the New Republic.

**Nampi** A slug-like Princess of a species even larger than the Hutts, she had deep purple skin that was studded with a series of arm-like tendrils. When she captured Jabba the Hutt, she ate Jabba's pilot, Scuppa, but Jabba was able to escape that fate. When she tried to cross Jabba, he released xenoboric acid that had been hidden in Scuppa's skull, and Nampi's body imploded. Jabba then took her treasure trove for his troubles.

**Nan, Ogo** A Cerean assassin who worked during the early years of the New Order. Nan was hired by Mika the Hutt—through a third party—to attempt to kill Mika on Nar Shaddaa, after Popara the Hutt began worrying about the spread of tempest spice. Mika wanted to find out how much his parent knew about the operation, and hoped that an assassination attempt on his own life might distract Popara. As payment, Mika provided tempest spice to ease Ogo Nan's growing addiction to the drug. A group of freelance agents who were on Nar Shaddaa to meet with Popara killed Ogo Nan after the Cerean destroyed one of the Hutt's H-3PO droids. His death suited Mika's scheming.

**Nancer** A Samarian woman who served as Bog Divinian's chief aide during the early months of the New Order.

**Nandon, Tendau** An Ithorian who worked for the Empire as a biologist, he found himself "recruited" into Imperial service after his desire to learn everything he could about the Mother Jungle drove him from his herd ship and away from Ithor. He was partnered with Dusque Mistflier for much of her career.

**Nandreeson** A Glottalphib, he was one of the most powerful crime lords in the galaxy. Nandreeson had long had a price on Lando Calrissian's head and was delighted to hear Lando had reentered Smuggler's Run, seeking a missing Han Solo, who had been trying to get at the truth behind the murder of former associate Jarril. Several of Nandreeson's Rek bounty hunters captured Lando and brought him to Skip 6. Nandreeson held him in a giant, seething mud hole, where he expected Calrissian to tread water until he drowned. He was there for some days before Han Solo finally discovered him. In the resulting firefight, Nandreeson was shot and killed by Solo.

***nang hul*** The Yuuzhan Vong name for a thud bug, a bioengineered organic weapon that was used in an attack on Leia Organa Solo on Gyndine. Thud bugs were small missiles tossed or propelled toward an opponent. They usually overcame an opponent's evasive maneuvers and struck with such force that they often knocked down their prey.

**Nania** A Vorzydiak youth who was one of the original members of the Freelies, she sided with Grath to ensure that their industrial sabotage was not directed toward living beings. Nania did not want the Freelies to fight among themselves, and tried to bring dissenting members together.

**nanja fly** Carnivorous, scavenging insect native to the underground caverns of the planet Csilla.

**nank** Unusual creatures considered a nuisance by the Ugnaughts, nanks were nonetheless eaten by immature Ugnaughts for food, often served flash-fried.

**Nanna** The nickname given to the modified Defender Droid owned by Luke Skywalker and his wife, Mara Jade Skywalker, and used as a guardian and care provider for their son, Ben, during the years following the Yuuzhan Vong invasion of the galaxy. Nanna accompanied Ben during the time he spent learning from his cousin, Jacen Solo, and was instrumental in helping them escape from a Gorog attack on Tenel Ka and her infant daughter on Hapes.

**nannarium** A flower native to the planet Drall.

**Nannat** A young woman who was hired by Colonel Rast'Tul to act as a babysitter and guardian for Night Forael Wren, after Night was kidnapped and held captive following the Battle of Naboo. A ward of the military, Nannat was orphaned when both her parents were killed in combat. She worked in Rast'Tul's home, where Night was held. She was adamant about carrying out her role as Night's guardian.

**nanoblip** A very small measure of time, used by the Yuuzhan Vong.

**nanocam** A miniature camera system used by surgeons and doctors to obtain images from inside the body of a patient. Because nanocams were so small, they were considered a noninvasive way to diagnose a patient's condition.

**nano-destroyers** Artificially created viruses, they dismantled the cells of an infected person one cell at a time. They were the basis of a poison that infected Mon Mothma. Once they were discovered in Mothma's system, the Jedi healer Cilghal was able, cell by cell, to eradicate the nano-destroyers that had threatened the life of the onetime Chief of State.

**nanogene spore** A technovirus developed by Belia Darzu and used to create a technobeast.

**nano-jump** A maneuver in which a starship briefly enters hyperspace to make a short trip over a small distance without being seen until the last moment.

**nanokiller** A nanotechnology virus developed by the Imperial Remnant immediately after the Swarm War. Based on the technology of the Fizz, nanokillers could be developed in specific strains to attack certain species and subspecies. A directed nanokiller was used to eliminate only the warrior caste of Verpine during the Imperial Remnant's attack on the Nickel One asteroid, shortly after the Second Battle of Fondor. Imperials developed another strain that would attack members of Boba Fett's family as a way to retaliate against Mandalorian attacks on the Moff Council. Once this new nanokiller was ready, it was deployed in the atmosphere by Admiral Atoko and the Galactic Alliance's Fifth Fleet. This new assassin strain was designed to remain active indefinitely, so that it didn't matter when Fett returned to Mandalore. The nanokiller remained active as long as it got enough sunlight to recharge its micro-power cell every few days.

**nano-missile** A miniature projectile weapon used on several Old Republic starfighters. These tiny missiles lacked guidance technology to help them find their targets, and had to be used in conjunction with a secondary targeting system, such as an ion-enabled sensor tag.

**nanosilk** Incredibly fine, smooth fabric that was created by artisans on the planet Corellia. It was one of the most expensive fabrics of the Old Republic.

**Nantama** A world located just inside a massive asteroid belt, it was noted for its wondrous displays of shooting stars.

**Nanta-Ri** A planet located in the Farlax sector near the Koornacht Cluster. Chief of State Leia Organa Solo sent two cruisers from the Fourth Fleet there to help defend it against Yevethan aggression.

***Nantex*-class territorial defense starfighter** *See* Geonosian starfighter.

**Nanthri route** A shipping route once plagued by the Nanthri pirates, who were united under their leader Celis Mott. He later mysteriously disappeared into otherspace after being captured by Rebels. Mott's list of "ship's articles" was still in use by pirates and privateers years later.

**Nantz, Admiral** A New Republic Navy officer who was promoted to senior flag officer just prior to the Republic's blockade of the Koornacht Cluster, following the Yevethan Purge. He was briefly considered as a choice to replace Etahn A'baht as commander of the Fifth Battle Group during the blockade, but was a real candidate after the capture of Han Solo.

**naorstrachem** A highly flexible substance used in the creation of netting or webbing.

**Naos III** Little more than a mud-covered frontier world, this small moon originally was settled by Rodian and Lethan Twi'lek criminals who found rich veins of ryll spice beneath its surface. Because of its orbital position, Naos III should have been a frozen ball of muddy ice covered by regular snowfalls, but intense volcanic activity kept the surface just warm enough to melt the ice into a thick sludge. Darth Sidious hoped to murder Obi-Wan Kenobi on the planet during the last months of the Clone Wars, in an effort to "orphan" Anakin Skywalker. The two Jedi had been searching for Fa'ale Leh, as part of their ongoing investigation into the many connections Sidious had throughout the galaxy. Sidious ordered his apprentice, Darth Tyranus—Count Dooku—to ensure Kenobi's death. Tyranus was hesitant, since it clearly meant that Sidious wanted to take Skywalker as a future apprentice.

**Naos III Mercantile** The governing body of the remote moon Naos III. The Mercantile's primary function was overseeing the harvest and export of Naos sharptooth, an industry that provided the moon with much of its income.

**Naos sharptooth** A pink-fleshed fish that was considered a delicacy in many parts of the galaxy, despite the fact that it was native to the coldest bodies of water found on the remote moon of Naos III. It spawned during the worst part of Naos III's near-continual winter, making it difficult and expensive to harvest. Restaurants were willing to pay a high price for the fish.

**naotebe wingling** Insects shaped by Nom Anor when he was posing as Dr. Dassid Cree'ar on the planet Duro. They were known as white-eyes by the New Republic, and were developed to chew through the synthplas that formed the domes of the refugee camps on Duro's surface.

**Napdu** The fourth moon of the planet Da Soocha. Most of the moon's surface was set aside for shipping warehouses, since it served as the primary staging location for most of the cargo being shipped through Hutt space. Because of this, most warehouse owners and employees lived in simple quarters that were built into their warehouses.

**naphthalene** One of the primary chemical components used to activate the newer thermal detonators that were produced in the wake of the Yuuzhan Vong invasion of the galaxy. It gave off a distinctive smell.

**Naplousean** An unusual alien species that was little more than a mass of snake- or ribbon-like tissues supported by three legs. Its head was a knotted blob of wet eyes.

**Naps Fral Cluster** An area of the galaxy located between Ryloth and Nal Hutta. The Karazak Slavers Guild often kept a few ships positioned in the Cluster, hoping to intercept ships transporting Twi'leks from Ryloth to Nal Hutta.

*Han Solo gets sprayed with narco-mist.*

**NaQuoit Bandits** An outlaw group of bandits that operated in the Ottega system, where they preyed upon local space traffic.

**Nar, Melaan** A Yuuzhan Vong who was a member of Domain Nar. A midlevel member of the intendant caste, Melaan Nar took offense at the actions of Von Shul. Supreme Overlord Shimrra, eager to reestablish his place as the leader of his people, used their grievances to prove that their generations-long travel between galaxies had led the Yuuzhan Vong to forget their gods.

**narada-ti** The Yevethan term for midwife. The narada-ti attended to the various marasi assembled for impregnation by a male.

**Narcassan, Vyn** A member of the Old Republic's intelligence agency, he proposed the use of specially programmed PK-series worker droids as spies, and worked with Cybot Galactica to create a number of these diminutive espionage agents to spy on the Trade Federation. In this way, he was able to gather intelligence on the activities of many Trade Federation officials. The information gathered from his droids, however, did not predict the Trade Federation's invasion of Naboo. One of the agency's older agents, Narcassan was smart enough to engineer his own disappearance when Emperor Palpatine rose to power.

**narco-interrogation** A multilevel form of prisoner interrogation that involved the use of certain drugs and torture. There were four levels of narco-interrogation, with Level One the most intense. It was designed to extract information that was purposely buried or forgotten, and often uncovered genetic memories.

**narco-mist** A reddish mist of chemicals that was sprayed on the body of an injured being to help speed recovery. Unlike bacta, narco-mist was a combination of painkillers and hormones that allowed a body to heal faster without the associated pain and discomfort.

**narcotic incense** The term used to describe any aromatic smoke that contained chemicals to stimulate or depress the central nervous system of the inhaler, causing varying amounts of euphoria. If inhaled in sufficient amounts, the smoke could be fatal.

**Nard, Junix** A bartender who worked on the planet Tatooine some four millennia before the Battle of Yavin. He spent much of his free time playing pazaak at his cantina in Anchorhead.

**Nardix** An Imperial Sector Governor who was wanted by the Rebel Alliance for crimes against sentients. Zuckuss and 4-LOM accepted the bounty that the Alliance placed on his head and captured the Governor, leaving them with an Imperial death warrant on their heads. The pair had taken the job to bankroll new lungs for Zuckuss.

**Narec, Ky** A Jedi Master who was the teacher of Asajj Ventress years before the Clone Wars. Narec discovered Ventress after his ship was stranded on the war-torn planet of Rattatak. He was killed by Osika Kirske before completing her training and returning her to Coruscant. Darth Tyranus later told Ventress that Narec had been abandoned by Mace Windu, in an effort to increase her anger toward the Jedi.

**Narees** An Iktochi who was one of Alexi Garyn's Vigos, serving the Black Sun criminal organization during the years leading up to the Battle of Naboo. Narees was killed at Garyn's fortress on Ralltiir when Darth Maul was dispatched by Darth Sidious to eliminate any evidence linking Hath Monchar to Sidious.

**Narek-ag** The owner and pilot of the transport shuttle *Moon Dash,* she and her copilot Trebor were working toward retirement when they crashed into an unknown object in orbit above Coruscant. As their ship came apart around them, Narek-ag asked Trebor to marry her. He accepted as the *Moon Dash* exploded.

**Nar Hej Shipping Company** A shipping operation based on the moon Napdu during the final years of the Old Republic.

**Nar Hekka** One of many habitable planets in the Hutt sector of space, Nar Hekka was located near a dim red star at the edge of the Y'Toub system. The planet had little indigenous life. Due to the intervention of the Hutts, several plant and animal species were imported to the world, resulting in a beautiful planet covered with gardens, parks, and arboretums. Much of the habitable area of the planet was enclosed by a transparent dome that altered the incoming red light and created a blue sky tinged with violet.

**Narik** A Rodian who served as his planet's representative to the New Republic during the Yuuzhan Vong War. He bristled at the fact that Borsk Fey'lya supported the protection of the Mid Rim, including the Bothan world of Bothawui, while virtually sacrificing the Outer Rim to the Yuuzhan Vong in order to further protect the Core.

***Naritus*** A Mon Calamari MC80a cruiser captained by Genkal, it was a veteran of New Republic military operations when it was assigned to intercept Belindi Kalenda's Ugly starfighter at Coruscant. Kalenda had discovered the rise of the Human League on Corellia.

**narjam** Small, fat, blue parasites that colonized planets by growing from minuscule larvae carried in the oil reservoirs of ships. Narjam infestations led to rounds of inoculations, as they tended to pick local diseases, mutate them, and then infect local populations.

Commander Arhul Narra

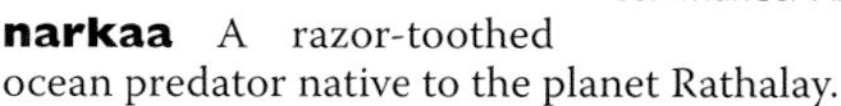

**narkaa** A razor-toothed ocean predator native to the planet Rathalay.

**Nar Kreeta** A planet controlled by the Mining Guild during the early years of the New Republic, although Hutt crime lords held sway over the underworld. Jedi Jaden Korr traveled to Nar Kreeta a decade after the Battle of Endor to locate information on the Disciples of Ragnos. While there, he managed to free a group of elders who were being held prisoner by the Hutts.

**Narloch's Casino** Owned by the Herglic entrepreneur Narloch, it was built from the superstructure of an Imperial landing platform to better accommodate the walkers that once moved about on the planet Emmer.

**Narmox** A small corporation that manufactured avionics control systems for starfighters, such as the B-wing, during the Galactic Civil War.

**Narol** An alias assumed by Garik Loran shortly after Wraith Squadron captured the *Night Caller*. Narol was the executive officer of the *Night Caller*, serving under Zurel Darillian.

***Narra*** A *Lambda*-class shuttle captured by the New Republic and assigned to support Wraith Squadron. The shuttle was captured from an Imperial captain who had deserted the Empire and turned to a life of smuggling. It was retrofitted to provide him with hidden compartments, enhanced weapons and shields, and stronger engines.

**Narra, Commander Arhul** A squadron leader, he was known as Boss to the pilots of Renegade Flight after the Battle of Yavin. He assumed command after the death of Red Leader in the battle. His protocol droid, K-3PO, served in the command center of Echo Base. Commander Narra himself was killed in an Imperial ambush near Derra IV prior to the Battle of Hoth. Luke Skywalker was then promoted to the rank of commander and placed in charge of the fighter group, which evolved into the legendary Rogue Squadron.

**Narsacc Habitat** One of the 12 luxury pods arrayed around the circumference of Toryaz Station in the Kuat system following the Yuuzhan Vong War. The pod was hastily leased by the Galactic Alliance, at a steep price, for talks with a delegation from Corellia to prevent an all-out war over the system's threat to secede from the GA.

**Nar Shaddaa** Nal Hutta's spaceport moon, known for its vertically built cities, experienced spaceship mechanics, and lawlessness. During the decades leading up to the Battle of Ruusan, Nar Shaddaa was the site of a Sith academy where individuals with some control over the Force were trained to become spies and assassins.

Nar Shaddaa was once the site of several mining installations as well, but over the centuries it became a center for smuggling operations. It was here that Han Solo supposedly learned the smuggler's trade as a youth. When the Hutts took over the moon, they began using it as a spaceport, and soon huge refueling spires and repair facilities reached up from the ground into orbit. Over time, the mass of the moon was increased 300 percent as construction continued unabated. There was no observable landmass left on Nar Shaddaa, since the spaceports had grown around the spires and completely covered the planet.

When the Yuuzhan Vong began to make attacks on Hutt space, Nar Shaddaa was considered a technological nightmare. After Nal Hutta was subjugated by the alien invaders, Nar Shaddaa was leveled by orbital strikes and eventually rebuilt into a world more suitable to the Yuuzhan Vong.

**Nar-Somo-Dali** This Cerean elder was one of the few who believed Ki-Adi-Mundi could determine the source of the swoops and other technology imported to Cerea during the last decades of the Old Republic. Nar-Somo-Dali sent a messenger to Ki-Adi-Mundi during his initial search for Ephant Mon, to bring the Jedi his lightsaber. The lightsaber was being held as evidence for the trial of Maj-Odo-Nomor, but Nar-Somo-Dali managed to free it with the use of an obscure loophole in Cerean laws.

Nar Shaddaa

**Narth (1)** During the Imperial evacuation of this planet after the Battle of Endor, the Imperial Star Destroyer *Gnisnal* was demolished by internal explosions. The wreckage later provided the New Republic with a complete copy of the Imperial Order of Battle.

**Narth (2)** A New Republic Navy officer who served as one of Etahn A'baht's tactical aides during the blockade of the Koornacht Cluster.

***Nartissteu*** The assumed name of the A-class freighter used by Grand Admiral Thrawn as the pawn in his attack on the Sluis Van shipyards five years after the Battle of Endor. The *Nartissteu* was supposedly coming from Nellac Kram, but had been ambushed by pirates. In reality, Thrawn placed several groups of cloaked fighters inside the freighter's hold, to be deployed near the shipyards in an effort to steal other starships for Thrawn's growing fleet.

**Nartlo** Apprehended by Kirtan Loor on Coruscant during the time he ran the Palpatine Counterinsurgency Front, Nartlo was selling diluted bacta for increased profits, and he had information on how the New Republic was obtaining its bacta. Loor employed him as a spy and was giving him lotiramine as an insurance policy. Nartlo was also under observation by Fliry Vorru. Vorru used skirtopanol to pull information from Nartlo, and the interaction of skirtopanol and lotiramine set up intense convulsions and cerebral hemorrhaging that eventually killed him.

**Narvath** The home planet of the Narvath. Its inhabitants were strong supporters of the Alliance to Restore the Republic.

**Narvis, Gille** An accountant who worked for the owners of the *Aggressive Negotiations* during the final years of the Old Republic. Narvis and her daughter Kalee were aboard the ship when it was apprehended by a customs vessel run by Toric Bisilt, a lieutenant in the Thaereian Military. When her husband Jarl objected to the boarding, he and the crew were shot and killed. Narvis sent a distress call, which was answered by other freelance operatives, and their appearance caused the customs vessel to flee. Narvis got the *Aggressive Negotiations* spaceworthy again and returned home.

**Narvis, Jarl** The owner and operator of the *Aggressive Negotiations,* he and his wife Gille moved weapons and equipment. The couple had a young daughter, Kalee, who was with them when the freighter was apprehended by the Thaereian customs officer Toric Bisilt. Bisilt was itching for a fight, and shot Jarl and his crew in cold blood when they resisted boarding. Only Gille and Kalee survived.

**Nashira** Akanah told Luke Skywalker that this Fallanassi name was his mother's. When Luke and Akanah finally discovered the Fallanassi, Wialu told Luke that she could not reveal whether or not

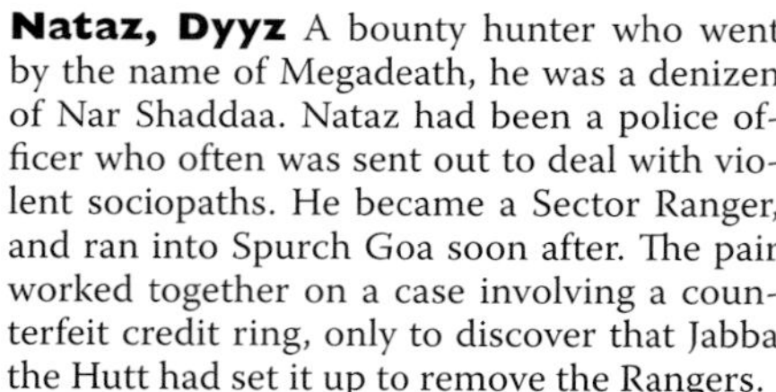
Nashtah

Nashira was his mother, because he was not of the White Current. Akanah later revealed that there was no such being as Nashira, and that she had made up the name in order to obtain Luke's help in locating the Fallanassi.

**nashtah** Six-legged hunters native to the planet Dra III, these bloodthirsty green reptilians with long, barbed tails were vicious and tenacious. Extremely well muscled and built for speed, the nashtah were also tireless, and stopped for nothing once they had chosen their prey.

**Nashtah** An alias used by Aurra Sing 10 years after the end of the Yuuzhan Vong War. Sing was hired to assassinate Tenel Ka, the Queen Mother of Hapes, but was stopped by Han and Leia Organa Solo. Sing had been nicknamed Nashtah as a child by the Dark Woman.

***Nashtah Bite*** An aging *Victory*-class Star Destroyer that was part of Warlord Zsinj's third fleet during the early years of the New Republic.

Nasta

***Nashtah Pup*** Bossk's short-range scout ship, the *Nashtah Pup* was secured within a dorsal hold on the *Hound's Tooth* and released by opening a hatch. It was an emergency-use-only craft, large enough for just two passengers and no cargo.

**Nasirii** One of the larger Hutt kajidics, or clans. Before Jabba the Hutt claimed Tatooine, the Nasirii controlled nearly one-fifth of the planet's criminal activities. The Nasirii also ran the various pleasure dens established by the Hutts on the desert planet.

**Nass, Boss Rugor** An Ankura Gungan from Naboo who led his people during the Trade Federation's blockade and then invasion of the peaceful planet. Nass showed signs of being a great leader even as a young Gungan. He held many different jobs—including soldier, engineer, miner, and executive—before becoming the Boss of Otoh Gunga.

Boss Nass was well known among Gungans as the individual who united the Ankura and Otolla races. This union led to the construction of the vast and beautiful underwater bubble city of Otoh Gunga, created through technology that was a well-kept secret.

Prone to nervous tics, he often grumbled his dissatisfaction by violently shaking his jowls. During the Battle of Naboo, Boss Nass tried to keep the Gungans uninvolved. However, when Queen Amidala came to him in the Gungan sacred place and knelt before him in a show of peace and humility, he changed his mind.

Boss Nass supplied the vast Gungan Grand Army to assist Amidala in trying to oust the Trade Federation. The Gungans rallied, and despite a large loss of life they were successful in holding off the Trade Federation's droid army long enough for Anakin Skywalker to destroy the Droid Control Ship, and for Amidala to capture top officials Nute Gunray and Rune Haako, breaking the enemy's hold on Naboo.

Over the following decades, Boss Nass decided that Emperor Palpatine was unworthy of his support. He backed the Rebel Alliance during the Galactic Civil War, and worked to disrupt Imperial establishments on Naboo.

**Nassin, Qatya** A pilot who served with a pirate gang known as the Hawk-bat Independent Space Force, she was really Shalla Nelprin and the gang was a front for Wraith Squadron.

**Nasta** In charge of the local underground on Mrlsst in the early years of the New Republic, Nasta was a gawky, bird-like being with dark brown skin and pronounced eye sockets. He helped Rogue Squadron uncover Loka Hask's plans by using the surveillance cameras in the Mrlsst Academy to view Hask's strategy meetings.

**Natalon Core Bandits** A band of monstrous alien pirates that was active during the early years of the New Order.

**Natamee** A small raft city that floated on the oceans of Ando during the New Order era. Natamee served as a resupply or refueling depot for the crews and vessels associated with the sea-based industries of the Aqualish.

**Natara** A general with the Rebel Alliance, he served in the Brak Sector Command office during the early years of the Galactic Civil War.

**Nataz, Dyyz** A bounty hunter who went by the name of Megadeath, he was a denizen of Nar Shaddaa. Nataz had been a police officer who often was sent out to deal with violent sociopaths. He became a Sector Ranger, and ran into Spurch Goa soon after. The pair worked together on a case involving a counterfeit credit ring, only to discover that Jabba the Hutt had set it up to remove the Rangers.

Gank Killers ambushed them and killed their other partner, Thaffe, before Nataz and Goa went berserk and killed the Ganks. The two then sent the Ganks' ship on a collision course with an asteroid developed by Jabba the Hutt, causing extensive damage. The stunt earned Nataz the nickname Megadeath. They were expelled from the Rangers and hid out on Nar Shaddaa. There they were almost killed by a mercenary named Gorm the Dissolver, but a young Rodian named Greedo shot Gorm, disabling him and letting the trio escape. Nataz and Goa promised to train Greedo, but eventually betrayed him.

Dyyz Nataz

**Nate** *See* Jangotat.

**Nate, Pori** A 15-year-old boy who, according to a HoloNet news report, was one of the first of his generation to admit that he was using and abusing death sticks.

**Nath, Jamur** An officer who served under Zozridor Slayke as a member of Freedom's Sons and Daughters during the Clone Wars. A corporal, Nath was partnered with Omin L'Loxx when Slayke decided to attack the Separatists who had taken control of Praesitlyn. After L'Loxx and Nath rescued Odie Subu and

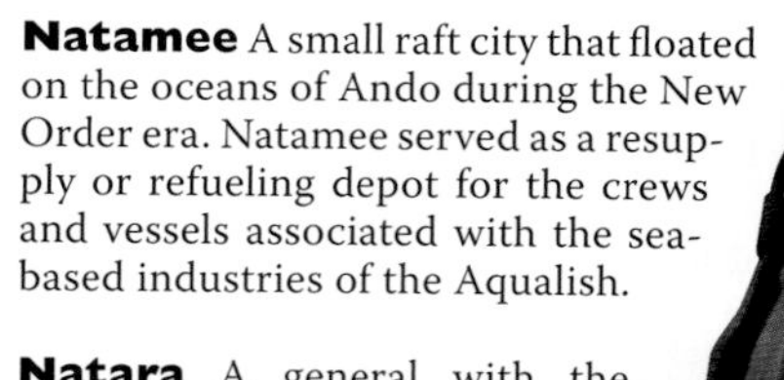
Boss Rugor Nass

Erk H'Arman, they were ambushed on their way back to base. In the firefight that ensued, Nath took several blasts from a Gamorrean thug; he died before he could be retrieved.

**Natinati** Jabba the Hutt visited this planet some years before the Battle of Yavin to explore the sacred temple of Poborandurannum.

**National Museum of Alderaan** A museum that housed one of the major collections of historical artifacts found on Alderaan, it also had a large collection of artifacts from other worlds.

**Nativum** A planet targeted for takeover by the Confederacy of Independent Systems during the Clone Wars. The plans for the attack on Nativum were actually a ruse, meant to throw the Old Republic off the trail of the true Separatist target.

**Natrom, Lieutenant** An Imperial officer during the New Order, Natrom was in command of a squad of stormtroopers stationed aboard the *Reprisal* following the Battle of Yavin. His speeder bike squad, along with several other ground units, was deployed to subjugate the planet Teardrop and bring it under Imperial control.

**Na'ts, Doikk** A member of the Bith band Figrin D'an and the Modal Nodes, he played the Dorenian Beshniquel or Fizzz. Na'ts did not like humans, preferring to work with droids.

**Nat-Sem** The Jedi Master who trained Roan Shryne in the years leading up to the Clone Wars. Master Nat-Sem spent a great deal of time with Shryne, trying to get the impatient man to calm himself with meditation techniques. Master Nat-Sem was cut down by battle droids in the Battle of Geonosis.

**Naturian** An alias adopted by Maneeli Tuun when he was interrogated by Imperial Inquisitor Sancor on Polis Massa. In his guise as Naturian, Tuun claimed to be a physician, which allowed him to access medical records. He could then erase or obscure any records of Padmé Amidala's presence at the Polis Massa medical facility.

**nausage** Grilled food savored on Tatooine during the early decades of the New Republic. Nausage was often served with dustcrêpes as a breakfast meal.

**Nautag** The Askajian mate of the dancer Yarna d'al' Gargan, he was devoured by a rancor after telling Jabba the Hutt that he would never let his wife or children live in slavery.

**Nautolan** Amphibious beings with green skin and a collection of head-tails that fell from the rear of their skulls. Nautolans were native to the Sabilon region of the aquatic world Glee Anselm, a planet they shared with the Anselmi. Nautolans retained many physical traits of their amphibious ancestors, including webbed fingers and toes.

Nautolans were known for their incredible sense of smell, which came from olfactory receptors located throughout their head-tails. This incredibly sophisticated olfactory sense allowed a Nautolan to detect the presence of pheromones and changes in a being's body chemistry. It was an exceptional sense underwater, but faded when the Nautolan lived on land. Because of this, and the fact that their native Nautolan language could be fully pronounced only underwater, Nautolans preferred to live submerged.

In almost any situation, a Nautolan could be counted on to act with joy and unrestrained happiness, as evidenced by Nautolan warriors smiling in the midst of combat.

Nautolans began life as tadpoles that hatched from a clutch of eggs. They matured quickly: Within two years, most were similar in size to humans. Mating was considered more of an evolutionary necessity than a matter for emotional attachment, although most Nautolans mated for life. Jedi Master Kit Fisto was a Nautolan.

**Nauton IV** On this planet, Jedi Master Ruati was believed to have been beheaded by Asajj Ventress.

**Navander, Lieutenant Romas "Lock"** A skilled Corellian pilot, he defected from the Empire shortly after graduating from the Academy. Navander played an important role as tech communications officer at the Rebel Alliance's Echo Base on the ice planet Hoth. His main job was to relay orders to nearby Rebel starships.

**Navardan regenerator** An implant developed some 4,000 years before the Galactic Civil War, it provided the user with enhanced healing powers, allowing wounds and injuries to heal in mere seconds instead of days or weeks.

Nautolan

Senator Navi

**Navett, Drend** A member of an underground organization known as Vengeance, he worked to incite crowds to riot over the smallest of issues. He partnered with Klif, who did most of the talking to the crowds. Drend would then touch off the riots with a few well-placed blicci-fruits or pipe bombs when the mood was right. The two found steady employment when Moff Disra hired them to start riots on several New Republic worlds after the revelation that the Bothans were involved in the destruction of Caamas.

Later, Navett and Klif posed as exotic animal dealers. In this capacity they obtained several swarms of metalmites, which they infiltrated into a Bothan generator building on the clothing of workers. When the Bothans realized that they had a problem, they called in Navett and Klif, the exotic animal dealers, who were happy to help. After gaining access to a power conduit under a Ho'Din restaurant, they planted a nest of baby mawkrens and strapped small, remote-detonating bombs to their backs. Once they got the scent of food, the mawkrens invaded the building. The first blast wave took out the building's main walls, while the second destroyed the generator itself. The second step required Navett to be close to the explosion; thus it was a suicide mission.

**Navi, Senator** A wealthy Sephi who was the nephew of King Alaric, the leader of the Sephi people during the Clone Wars. Navi served as Thustra's representative to the Galactic Senate, and became one of the many Senators who spent more time worrying about their own luxury than the needs of their people and the galaxy. Alaric hated the corruption he saw and decided that Thustra would secede from the Republic until conditions improved; he called Navi home because he was disgusted with his nephew's behavior. Navi found that Jedi Master Yoda, Alaric's old friend, was already there to try to persuade the king to change his mind.

Navi's lies and deceptions were mostly responsible for a confrontation between Alaric and Yoda in which the king basically forced the Jedi Master to kill him. Navi returned to Coruscant, told the Senate that Yoda had been killed, and called for the elimination of the Jedi Order. Yoda's sudden reappearance put an end to Navi's machinations, the Senator was exposed, and was then thrown into prison for his duplicity.

**navibrain** The New Republic term given to the brain-like structure that was the navigational computer of a Yuuzhan Vong warship. The Wookiee Jedi Lowbacca discovered that the navibrain detected minute changes in the surrounding environment, and measured the gravity of planets, moons, and stars to determine its location and the direction it should take in order to reach its destination.

**navicomputer** *See* navigation computer.

**navigation buoy** Also known as NavBuoys, these floating deep-space devices provided information on interstellar coordinates to nearby starships as long as the ships had the correct access codes. The buoys aided those starships that had hyperdrives but limited navicomputer capability.

**navigation computer** Also known as NavCom units, these computers were used to plot trajectories and hyperspace flight plans between the planets contained in their databases. They used the spatial coordinates of the ship to accurately chart a course. Many military-grade navigation computers maintained continually updated databases of the coordinates of billions of planets, moons, and stars to several hundred decimal places, which allowed the computers to accurately plot courses through realspace as well as hyperspace. Civilian models did not require this level of accuracy, but nonetheless maintained accurate information on the locations of spatial bodies. Coordinates were based on the current location of the planet Coruscant, which was denoted as 0,0,0, even though it was not at the exact center of the galaxy. That fact was irrelevant to navigation computers but vexed many astrocartographers, especially those not born in the Core Worlds.

**Navik the Red** The Rodian leader of the war-like Chattza clan, he was identifiable by the enormous red birthmark on his face. Navik used gladiator hunts to start wars with other clans on Rodia. After the Tetsus clan fled Rodia in his wake, he hunted them down throughout the galaxy. He was the Rodian Grand Protector during the Galactic Civil War.

**Navior, Bullseye** Considered one of the best Podracers of the Outer Rim, he was known as the track favorite on many of the courses on Aquilaris. Navior was a brown-skinned humanoid with a pair of round, bulbous growths coming from the top of his head. He was named for his wide, gaping eyes.

**Navos Center for the Performing Arts** An entertainment facility in Rellidir on the planet Tralus. The entire campus of the Navos Center was housed in eight white towers, distinguished by their fluted shape and connected by a crisscross pattern of duracrete walkways. Ten years after the cessation of hostilities with the Yuuzhan Vong, the Navos Center was taken over by the military forces of the Galactic Alliance, became headquarters for the Tralus Ground Occupation Forces, and housed the city's shield generators. Han Solo and Wedge Antilles led an operation to infiltrate Panther Flight into Rellidir. They were able to launch warheads that plowed into the Navos Center and exploded. The shields held long enough to contain the explosion's force, then utterly failed as the building collapsed in on itself.

**Navy, Imperial** *See* Imperial Navy.

**Naweenan Fate Rooms** A famous casino on the planet Ord Mantell.

**Nawling, Gareth** A soldier in the Thaereian Military during the final years of the Old Republic. He was a member of an ambush squad led by Lorwin Derlynn that was dispatched to a Cularin Militia base in the asteroids of the Cularin system as part of a systemwide blockade. The blockade was seemingly set up to protect Cularin from Separatist invasion. However, the Thaereians had other plans. Nawling, like others who served under Derlynn, questioned his loyalty to the Thaereians, especially after seeing evidence of slave arenas on the Burnout space station. Thus, when Derlynn was shown evidence of Thaereian misdoings in the Cularin system, Nawling supported his decision to allow ships through the blockade.

**Nawnam** A minor Hutt crime lord who worked for Ganis before attempting to assassinate him and take over his empire. Ganis survived, and placed a huge bounty on Nawnam's head.

**Nawruun** An older, gray-furred Wookiee, he was a slave at the Maw Installation who was rescued by Chewbacca.

**Nay'sro, Velst** One of the Bothans assigned to watch over Kathol sector during the early years of the New Republic. As a member of the Bothan Combat Response Element, Velst was tasked with tracking the actions of Moff Kentor Sarne and the Imperials who still operated in the sector.

**Nazfar Metalworks Guild** The Yevethan starshipwright guild that built hundreds of *Aramadia*-class thrustships for Nil Spaar's navy.

**Nazish** A Rishii assassin and member of the Zulirian Swordmasters who was proficient in the Trispzest form of combat.

**Nazwa** An ancient city of ruins encircled by the modern city of Baroo on the planet Baroonda. Nazwa was the seat of the ancient Majan culture.

Nazzar

**Nazzar** Equine humanoids that were native to the planet Nazzri during the golden age of the Old Republic. They adhered to the tenets of the *Ulizra* and the Great Structure, remaining aloof from the rest of the galaxy and rarely traveling away from their homeworld. The few Nazzar encountered away from Nazzri were either outcasts who had rejected the *Ulizra* or missionaries who hoped to bring the *Ulizra* to new beings.

**Nazzer** One of the many bounty hunters who were part of the Crimson Nova chapter of the Bounty Hunters' Guild, Nazzer led a small group sent to Null to intercept and kill as many of the Jedi who were fighting on the planet as they could. Ultimately, they only managed to acquire the lightsaber of Jedi Master T'ra Saa.

Nazzer

**NCW-86** The Imperial designation of the planet known as Demonsgate.

**N'dian** The site of intense fighting during the first year of the Clone Wars. ARC trooper Ordo was dispatched to N'dian to assault one of the planet's urban centers, where a Separatist group was believed to be hiding. To achieve his mission objectives, Ordo virtually destroyed the city single-handedly.

**Ne, Koa** A Kaminoan scientist, he assumed the role of Minister of Tipoca City on Kamino in the years following the Yuuzhan Vong War. Under Koa Ne, the Tipoca City cloning centers fell into disarray. Faced with further decline of the Kaminoan civilization, Koa Ne hired Boba Fett to track down Taun We in the hope that she had managed to obtain some of Ko Sai's cloning knowledge. Taun We eventually made contact with Koa Ne, claiming that she didn't have any plans to sell the information. Koa Ne then offered her three million credits for it.

**Near Wash** A shallow sea that separated Maslovar from the islands of the Swamplands on the planet Desevro. It was the innermost of the five Washes.

**neathlat** A living bandage created by the Yuuzhan Vong. In accordance with Yuuzhan Vong tradition, the neathlat treated the wound but did nothing to diminish the pain of the injury.

*Nebo*

**Neb, Buwon** The owner of the ship that Callista, under the name Cray Mingla, took to the planet Nam Chorios. Buwon Neb made regular runs between Durren and Nam Chorios.

**Nebl, Jalus** Once employed as a pilot by Teroenza, this Sullustan became ill from transporting spice from Ylesia, as he was allergic to it. He was temporarily replaced by a young Han Solo and helped him understand ways to navigate the storms that ravaged the planet. Their friendship grew quickly, and eventually Nebl assisted Han in escaping from Ylesia. It was Nebl who flew between the *Talisman* and the *Helot's Shackle,* breaking tractor beam contact and allowing both himself and Solo to escape. Nebl fled into hyperspace with the *Ylesian Dream* and disappeared. He soon joined the Rebel Alliance, renaming his ship *Dream of Freedom.* He accompanied Bria Tharen and the group that assaulted Ylesia to destroy the Besadii businesses there. He piloted *Dream of Freedom* in through the atmosphere and led the way for many Alliance ships to reach the ground. *Dream of Freedom* was the first ship targeted by the turbolaser protecting the planet. The first shots it fired struck *Dream of Freedom* and destroyed it, killing Nebl in the explosion.

**Nebo** An Onderonian street philosopher and Naddist who helped Exar Kun find hidden Sith artifacts on the Dxun moon. Nebo and his father, fellow zealot Rask, then attempted to protect the sarcophagi of King Ommin, Queen Amanoa, and Freedon Nadd from Kun, who killed them both.

***Nebula Chaser*** An independent transport ship that was owned and operated by Captain Pollux. Two years after the Yuuzhan Vong War began, the *Nebula Chaser* was part of a small fleet that helped evacuate the planet Talfaglio. Shortly after leaving Corellian space, it was ambushed by the *Gift of Anguish* and boarded by the Yuuzhan Vong. Aboard the ship, Alema and Numa Rar tried to escape, but they were cornered by a voxyn. Alema got away, but Numa became the first Jedi Knight killed by a voxyn. The Yuuzhan Vong took possession of the cruiser and used it as a pawn in their plans to get Jaina and Jacen Solo. The ship was eventually destroyed in an effort to sway Leia Organa Solo to the aliens' position. She refused to turn over any information on the Jedi, and the *Nebula Chaser* was destroyed.

***Nebula*-class Star Destroyer** One of the first major designs produced by the New Republic as part of the New Class Starships, the *Nebula* class was a mobile assault platform similar in its role to a Star Destroyer. It was also known as the *Republic*-class Star Destroyer, or simply the New Republic Star Destroyer.

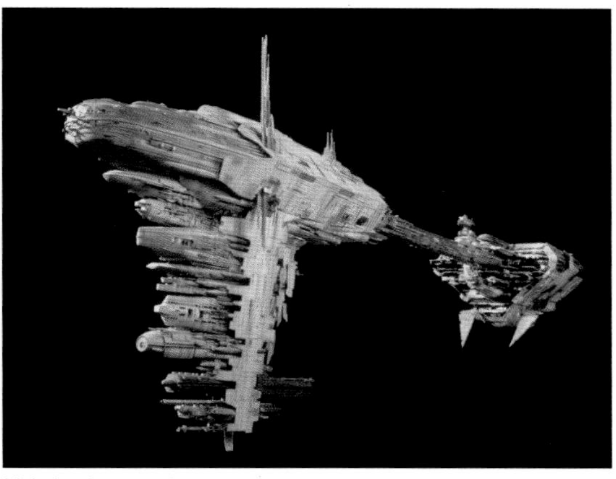

*Nebulon-B escort frigate*

**Nebula Flight** The designation of the Corellian starfighters that supported Panther Flight on its mission to bomb the Navos Center on Tralus, as part of Operation Noble Savage.

**Nebula Front** A protest group that sprang up in response to the Trade Federation's control of trade routes in the Mid and Outer Rim Territories during the last decades of the Old Republic. Based on the planet Asmeru in the Senex sector, the Nebula Front had issues with the Old Republic as well, and hampered the activities of Trade Federation and Republic starships in the Outer Rim. Finis Valorum's father had a chance to eliminate the Nebula Front, but simply chastised them and allowed them to regroup and rebuild. The Nebula Front tried unsuccessfully to negotiate a truce with the Trade Federation. It refused to accept funding from the Hutts or any group that supported slavery. After the Trade Federation was given a full franchise by the Old Republic, a militant branch of the Nebula Front hired pirates and mercenaries to strike. They were later accused of plotting the assassination of Chancellor Valorum, and only the timely intervention of Qui-Gon Jinn and Adi Gallia prevented Valorum's death. In the wake of their failure to kill Valorum and break up the Trade Federation, the Nebula Front disintegrated.

**nebula orchid** These flowers grew on thin purple vines so rubbery and flexible, they could be tightened into a knot impossible to break. Their showy magenta, maroon, and lavender blossoms thrived in the rain forests of Yavin 4.

**Nebula Orchid** An eatery located in Kuat City, it was quite popular during the early decades of the New Republic. Reck Desh was at the Nebula Orchid when he learned from an unknown telbun the location of Elan and Vergere.

Nebulon Ranger

***Nebula Queen*** A luxury ship operated by Event Vistas that made regular runs to Coruscant.

**Nebula Rangers** A group of space pirates led by Ssurussk. The Nebula Rangers ambushed many cargo convoys in the galaxy's Expansion Region during the early years of the New Order.

**Nebulba** A Dug who was a member of Sebulba's clan and worked for Sebolto's gang in the years after the Battle of Naboo. Mawhonic issued a bounty for his capture, claiming that "all the kin of that dirty Dug Sebulba deserve to fry." Jango Fett claimed the bounty during his attempt to meet with Sebolto.

**Nebulon-B escort frigate** The more common designation of the Kuat Drive Yards EF76B escort ship. It was a strangely shaped vessel that had a long, thin hull, with its main decks hanging off the front end and the engines hanging off the rear. It measured 300 meters long. The Nebulon-B was a slow, unwieldy ship that originally was designed to carry up to two squadrons of starfighters as protection and was built for Imperial escort duty just after the Battle of Yavin. The Rebel Alliance was able to capture a number of the frigates intact, using them as medical ships. Kuat Drive Yards also produced a modified version of the Nebulon-B frigate, the Nebulon-B2.

***Nebulon Ranger*** A large courier ship, it was used by the Jedi brothers Ulic and Cay Qel-Droma and the Twi'lek Jedi Tott Doneeta, who were key participants in the Sith War. The *Nebulon Ranger* had retractable wings that were extended for atmospheric flight and retracted for landing. The ship's two main engine arrays gave it greater maneuverability without bulky maneuvering jets.

The *Ranger* had a forward-firing pulse cannon, a retractable rotating laser cannon on each wingtip, and a more powerful rotating laser cannon at the base of the second engine array. Each forward mandible also had a pair of linked proton torpedo launchers and a short-range concussion sphere launcher. The *Ranger*'s series of eight shield generators provided full protection around the hull. The shields were raised only in combat because of their immense energy drain, but that made the *Ranger* vulnerable to attack at other times. The beast-riders of Onderon downed the *Ranger* with a single seeker-torpedo.

**Nechel, Dap** A short, bearded alien who served as an engineer aboard the *Kuari Princess* when Detien Kaileel was arrested for his support of the Rebel Alliance.

Captain Lorth Needa

**Necropolis (1)** An ancient term for the Sith burial grounds that were constructed on the planet Korriban in the wake of King Adas's death. Over time, this location became known as the Valley of the Dark Lords.

**Necropolis (2)** The term used by Judder Page and his team of infiltration agents to describe the planet Coruscant after it had been terraformed by the Yuuzhan Vong to resemble Yuuzhan'tar.

**Necropolis (3)** This planet, originally known as Dahrtag, was populated by humans some 15,000 years before the Galactic Civil War. The inhabitants became known as Necropolitans, and they revered their dead with deep-seated traditions. Other species eventually settled there; each was given its own territory, and all adopted similar rituals associated with death. Doctor Evazan used Necropolis as a place to hide from bounty hunters; he perfected his reanimation serum during this time. Evazan used the many legends and traditions of the Necropolitans to keep his efforts a secret.

**Necr'ygor Omic** A popular interstellar wine served during the early years of the New Republic. Aficionados said that the '47, '49, '50, and '52 vintages were among the best.

**nectarot** An inexpensive liquor favored by Watto.

**nectarsect** An insect that lived by sucking the nectar out of fruits and certain flowers.

**nectarwine** A wine that was fermented from the fabled fruit fields of the planet Nepoy.

**Ned** The son of a spaceport worker on Belasco whose mother provided information about Cir L'ani and his companion to Qui-Gon Jinn and Obi-Wan Kenobi during their search for Jenna Zan Arbor.

**Nediji** Native to the remote world Nedij, the Nediji were avian in appearance, and distinguished by their bird-like faces. Their noses and mouths were formed from rubbery cartilage that tapered into a sharp point resembling a beak, but their heads were smooth, and their ears were flat against their skulls. The Nediji were covered with what appeared to be pale blue fur or feathers, with a darker blue patch of skin beneath their chins. The fingertips of the Nediji ended in yellow talons.

Most Nediji remained on their homeworld throughout their lives, living as part of the Flock. Travel offworld was considered taboo among the Flock; only those who could not become members were free to leave. They often became trackers or assassins. The number of offworld Nediji was exceptionally small, however, making their appearances in the greater galaxy an unusual occurrence.

**Nedmak, Kaj** A native of the planet Drall, he stowed away on the smuggling ship of Zevel Hortine and learned to be a smuggler. Nedmak was one of the Nar Shaddaa smugglers who agreed to help Bria Tharen fly troop and rescue ships during the Battle of Ylesia. Years later, he teamed up with Celia Durasha, taking her under his wing in much the same way Hortine had taken him in after she stowed away aboard his ship, the *Tryan Kajme*. However, Nedmak wasn't as good a sabacc player as he was a spacer, and he found himself heavily in debt to Rass M'Guy. That added to the debt he already owed Bwahl the Hutt after he'd failed to deliver a cargo of spice to the Gordian Reach, which was blockaded by the Empire.

In an effort to pay off both Bwahl and M'Guy, Nedmak convinced Durasha to let him give an entire shipment of weapons to M'Guy. He then planned to play some sabacc and run enough spice to pay back Bwahl. The *Tryan Kajme* eventually was pulled from hyperspace by one of Bwahl's ships and forced to crash-land on Ord Mantell. Nedmak was captured by the bounty hunter Thune, who planned to return him to Bwahl. In the struggle to bring Nedmak in, Thune stabbed him in the heart. Durasha escaped, and Nedmak was rescued by the droid U-THR, who helped him stun Thune. They all made off with Thune's ship, the *Faceted.* Nedmak and Durasha renamed the ship the *Starlight Red* and recruited U-THR to help them out in their smuggling activities.

**Neebo** A Jedi Master who went missing defending refugees on the moons of Sanjin during the Clone Wars, Kit Fisto later discovered her lightsaber in General Grievous's lair on the Vassek moon.

**neebray** Manta-like flying creatures found soaring through the skies of the Rugosa moon as well as in the depths of space. During the Clone Wars, Shadow Squadron encountered half a dozen giant neebray within the Kaliida Nebula. They were massive yet peaceful gas-gulpers.

**Neece** A Rutanian who was in charge of the prison facility in the city of Testa, during the rule of King Frane.

**Neechak** A Rodian gunrunner who worked for Tern Ashandrik during the Galactic Civil War.

**Needa, Captain Lorth** An Imperial officer, Needa was one of Admiral Ozzel's closest advisers in the Imperial fleet. A veteran of the Clone Wars, Needa held the rank of lieutenant commander during the Battle of Coruscant, where he commanded the *Carrack*-class cruiser *Integrity.* It was Needa who demanded the surrender of General Grievous, but he was unable to prevent the cyborg's escape. During the era of the New Order, Needa was promoted to the command of the *Imperial*-class Star Destroyer *Avenger,* and he was part of the fleet that attacked Hoth in order to destroy the Rebel Alliance's Echo Base. After the battle, Needa was directed to capture the *Millennium Falcon,* which had actually clamped itself to the back side of the Star Destroyer's bridge. When Han Solo's ship escaped, Lorth Needa decided it would be most honorable if he apologized personally to Darth Vader. The apology was accepted in a way, as Needa was executed on the spot by Vader's Force choke.

**Needa, Virar** A cousin of Lorth Needa, this Imperial lieutenant was placed in charge of OSETS 2711, an Orbital Solar Energy Transfer Satellite above Imperial Center. He was on duty when Rebels took control of his station from the ground with the assistance of the computer center. They realigned an orbital mirror to burn up a large water reservoir, creating a terrible thunderstorm that brought down the planet's shields.

**Needalb, Dedro** A customs officer who served the Empire on Nar Shaddaa during the early years of the New Order. Although he was an Imperial, he was under the thumb of the Hutts who controlled Nar Shaddaa. From time to time—but only when he felt like it—he sent an unverified report on traffic and cargo shipments to Moff Sarn Shild.

**Needle** Developed by Loronar Corporation in the early years of the New Republic, the Needle was a small, automated attack ship that employed Centrally Controlled Independent Replicant (CCIR) technology. Less than 3 meters long and extremely fast, Needles could be deployed from anywhere in the vicinity of their target. They were built from small, shielded transport shells manufactured by Seifax, and employed small hyperdrives built by the Bith.

In the field, Needles were controlled from a remote location, usually the starship from which they were launched. Their speed and size made them nearly impossible to detect and track. The droch Dzym agreed to supply Loronar with Spook crystals for CCIR in return for weapons and synthdroids. The deal included the rights to build a Needle production facility on Antemeridias.

**needlebeamer** A small weapon often used in duels, it fired a thin, tight laser beam at its target, producing a quick death with a minimum of bloodshed.

**needle beast** A lethal predator native to the planet Dithanune.

**needlebug** An insect from the forests of Kashyyyk, it had a barb-covered nose that was used to dig into wroshyr trees' bark; the needlebug then sucked out the sap.

**needle match** A slang term used by veteran leaders of the Grand Army of the Republic to describe a personal spat between men.

**needler** A term used during the last years of the Old Republic to describe a small shiv or other pointed weapon.

**needle ray** A specialized blaster setting that produced an extremely thin beam of coherent light, forcing a shooter to be extremely accurate. Needle rays were often used in sporting events to test the marksmanship of contestants.

**Needles, the** A section of the Jundland Wastes on Tatooine, the Needles was the traditional camping grounds of the Tusken Raiders. Its name came from thin, needle-like rock formations that sprang up from the desert sands.

**Needles Mountains** A range of low, rocky mountains located on Tatooine near the desert formation known as the Needles.

**needle thorn** The Yuuzhan Vong cultivated a unique plant for growing needle thorns, which were thin and sharp, and were often thrown at targets.

**neek** Small, slate-gray sauropods native to Ambria. Neeks traveled in large groups for protection and breeding as well as general companionship. Standing about a meter tall at the shoulder, they fed on a variety of plants. Neeks used their tails for balance and stability, and could rise up on their hind legs and stand using their tails for support.

During the centuries leading up to the Great Sith War, many beings kept neeks as pets. Explorers kept small groups of neeks for use during scouting missions, because the naturally skittish creatures would be frightened whenever danger was at hand. In the wake of the war, however, neeks became much more skittish, as the taint of the dark side of the Force permeated their natural habitats. Neeks also evolved in the presence of the Force, and subsequent generations developed an immunity to the powers of Force-sensitive individuals.

**neek-in-the-middle** A children's game in which two players tried to keep an object, usually a ball, from a third player who stood in between them.

*Neeks roam the planet Ambria.*

**Neela** A Rodian who was married to Greedo the Elder, she was Greedo and Pqweeduk's mother. Neela and her brother Nok realized that the Tetsus clan was in trouble after Navik the Red killed Greedo the Elder, and they fled Rodia. Their efforts paid off briefly, when they were able to reach Nar Shaddaa before Navik caught them. Neela was killed in an Imperial ambush in Nar Shaddaa's Corellian sector when Greedo was just a teenager.

**Neelah** *See* Kateel.

**Neelanon** A planet in the Senex sector. Senator Terr Taneel came from Neelanon.

**Neelgaimon** A forsaken planet where the designers of the *Eye of Palpatine* battlemoon were reassigned to punitive duty at the sand mines after the ship failed to destroy a Jedi enclave on Belsavis.

***Neelian*** During the Clone Wars, this corvette was dispatched with the *Ranger* and its small fleet to Praesitlyn, under the command of Jedi Master Nejaa Halcyon, on a mission to retake the Intergalactic Communications Center from the Separatists. While Halcyon oversaw the operation from the *Ranger,* Anakin Skywalker commanded the main landing force from the *Neelian.* The orders from General Halcyon indicated that the *Neelian* was to stay out of any firefight that might occur and focus on getting its troops to a safe drop point.

**Neema** Vima-Da-Boda's daughter, Neema was as gifted with the Force as any of her famous ancestors. Neema wanted to learn more than her mother's traditional teachings could provide, and she experimented unknowingly with the dark side of the Force. Eventually she fled from her mother and became the mistress of an Ottethan warlord in an effort to gain the aid of some friends who courted him. Neema married him, but he quickly tired of her and cast her out. She attempted to strike him down with her dark side power, but the warlord used a primitive defense and survived the attack. He put her in prison, where she eventually repented her ways and telepathically contacted her mother. Vima heard, but arrived too late. The warlord had set Neema loose in the forests of his homeworld, where she was killed by the native rancors.

**neep** An individual who installed computer systems.

**Neer, Pirt** Trained at the Jedi Temple on Coruscant, she was one of many students who participated in the Apprentice Tournament eventually won by Tallisibeth Enwandung-Esterhazy. Neer defeated Enver Hoxha after Hoxha's lightsaber was taken by Scout. Neer was unprepared for a sneak attack by Lena Missa, who came up behind Pirt and put her in an arm bar that forced the young girl to yield.

**Neesh** A Rodian bounty hunter and member of the war-like Chattza clan, he hired Spurch "Warhog" Goa to execute the young Rodian Greedo. Goa upheld his end of the bargain by encouraging the inexperienced Greedo to try to capture Han Solo.

**Neeyutnee, Queen** The monarch of Naboo during the Clone Wars, successor to Queen Jamillia.

**Neff, Major** An Imperial officer who was stationed in the Koornacht Cluster as part of the Black Sword Command. He survived the Yevethan takeover of the Black Fleet shipyards, and was imprisoned on Pa'aal. Neff worked with Sil Sorannan creating pulse-transceiver chips for use in the prisoner uprising during the Black Fleet crisis.

**Neff, Officer** A member of the Cloud City Wing Guard when Darth Vader had the outpost garrisoned. She was curious about the Dark Lord, and tried to catch a glimpse of him whenever possible.

**Nefra Canyons** A spectacular landscape located on the moon of Sulon.

**Nefta** A close friend of Emperor Palpatine and a member of the reborn Emperor's Dark Side Adepts. Nefta soon realized that the Emperor's continual rebirth through the use of clones was not what it seemed to be. Along with Sa-Di, Nefta formulated a plan to destroy all of the Emperor's

*Nefta*

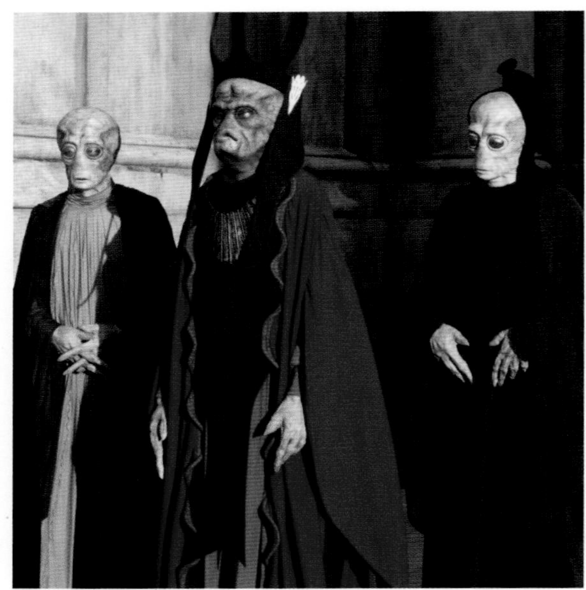
Neimoidians

clones and trap his dark side energies in the netherworld forever. After the reborn Emperor's death on Byss, both Sa-Di and Nefta destroyed the clone vats. Before they could finish the job, however, they were both killed. They hadn't known that Palpatine had already entered a new clone body.

**Neftali** This frozen ball of ice was the second planet of the Socorro system. Two kinds of Neftalai ice were mined as a commodity by the desert-dwelling Socorrans. Pure-water ice was used for drinking while nether ice was used as a coolant.

**Nega, Anniha** One of Coruscant's most sought-after bounty hunters and assassins during the last decades of the Old Republic. By his early 20s, Nega had established his reputation as a hunter, although many of the hunts he included on his résumé were falsified to bolster his image. Nevertheless, he had innate skills as a tracker, and he always got his prey. Nega dressed in a suit of Ithullan war armor and hunted from a modified Z-95 headhunter he called the *Flare*.

***Negotiator*** Obi-Wan Kenobi's *Venator*-class Star Destroyer flagship during the Clone Wars. It was commanded—for a time—by Admiral Block.

**Negotiator, the** A name used during the Clone Wars to describe Obi-Wan Kenobi, in reference to his talent for negotiating to champion the goals of the Old Republic.

***Negra Star*** An Imperial frigate that assisted the *Warspite* in its attempt to kidnap Sullustan diplomats during the Galactic Civil War.

**Neimie** A slang term used during the last years of the Old Republic for Neimoidian.

**Neimoidia** Located in the Colonies region, this small, humid planet was the homeworld of the greedy Neimoidians. Instead of profiting from its relative proximity to self-reliant Corellia and industrialized Kuat, Neimoidia actually suffered for its placement, having been passed over time and again by the fraternity of Core worlds. Neimoidia had a relatively small population that tended to the planet's vast insect hives, fungus farms, and beetle hatcheries.

**Neimoidian** Resembling the Duros in many physical respects, these beings descended from Duros stock after a group of colonists settled on Neimoidia around the time the Old Republic was formed, some 25,000 years before the Battle of Yavin. They had smooth skin and large, red eyes, although the Neimoidian eye had a pupil that split it horizontally. They also had a more developed cranium, which was studded with small knobs and bumps. Their mouths were downturned, giving them a perpetual frown. On their homeworld of Neimoidia, they lived in communal hives from the time of their birth, but were given limited access to food sources during their seven years of grubhood. This helped weed out the weak individuals at a very early age, as those grubs that couldn't find food—or steal it—quickly died.

That instilled a tremendous sense of greed in young Neimoidians, as well as forcing them to become organizational. In general, Neimoidians were entrepreneurial, but were also lazy cowards. They developed one of the most advanced droid technologies in the galaxy, using automata for almost everything. Elaborate headdresses; the cut, color, and texture of the cloth; and the collars and trim of their clothing gave specific indications of rank and position.

The Neimoidians developed the Trade Federation several decades before the Battle of Naboo. When the Old Republic began taxing the trade routes between the Core and the Outer Rim, the Neimoidians and the Trade Federation were outraged. They found an unusual ally in Darth Sidious, who used them for his own schemes, leaving them disgraced on a galactic scale.

Neimoidian shuttle

**Neimoidian harvester beetle** Five-meter-long insects raised by the Neimoidians on their purse world of Cato Neimoidia. Harvester beetles were bred for huge jaws and spined carapace; the jaws allowed a beetle to cut down trees and grains, which were then placed on its back. During the Clone Wars, when fighting came to Cato Neimoidia, harvester beetle soldiers were used as infantry against the clone troopers of the Old Republic.

**Neimoidian Home Defense Legions** A collection of military units assigned to protect the planet Neimoidia and its colony worlds during the last decades of the Old Republic. Interestingly, the Neimoidian Home Defense Legions were made up of Neimoidian conscripts, not battle droids.

A gang of ferocious neks

**Neimoidian Inner Circle** The primary governing body of the Neimoidians. During the years leading up to the Battle of Naboo, the Inner Circle was led by Viceroy Nute Gunray.

**Neimoidian jakrab** A species of jakrab that was one of the few mammalian herbivores native to the planet Neimoidia.

**Neimoidian shuttle** Resembling a giant, clawed beetle native to Neimoidia, these small *Sheathipede*-class transport ships were designed to carry up to five Neimoidians between their freighters and ground-based installations. These shuttles measured just 15 meters long, and were piloted by two droids. Each was armed with a single blaster cannon.

**nek** The nek, also known as the Cyborrean battle dog, was a predatory mammal native to the planet Cyborrea. Originally bred as hunting beasts, neks eventually became beasts of war. The average nek stood 2 meters tall at the shoulder, and was armed with three rows of teeth and sharp claws on its feet. Specially bred battle dogs were controlled electronically, with implants placed in the nek's brain to receive signals from a remote-control device. When used in a hunt or in battle, the augmented nek was accompanied by two beings: the hunter or warrior, and the nek handler.

**Nek** The code name of a curly-haired young woman who was a member of the resistance on Samaria. Nek accompanied Dinko on a mission to meet Ferus Olin, after Olin was instructed by Emperor Palpatine to offer the resistance a chance to cease operation. When the group agreed to help Olin ensure that Roshan ambassador Robbyn Sark escaped from Samaria, Nek and Firefolk were both forced to go into hiding to keep the resistance from exposure.

**NEK-01** A spy droid employed by the Hutts on Nal Hutta to track down those individuals who failed to repay their debts or simply angered the Hutts.

**neka** A nut tree native to the planet Druckenwell, its meat was tasty, and its shells were hard enough to be used in necklaces.

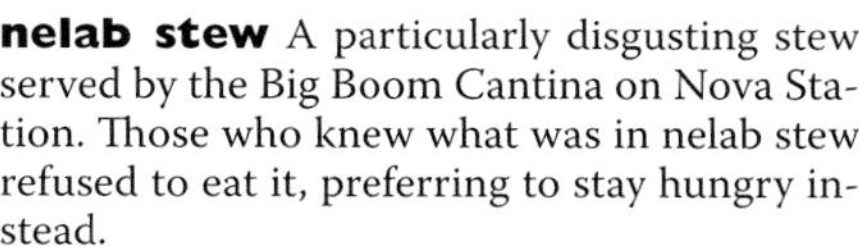
Nelvaan

**nelab stew** A particularly disgusting stew served by the Big Boom Cantina on Nova Station. Those who knew what was in nelab stew refused to eat it, preferring to stay hungry instead.

**Nelfrus** A planet in the Elrood sector.

**Nelhal Industries** A small corporation that produced photoreceptor lenses for droids in the decades leading up to the Battle of Naboo.

**Nella, Loje** An intelligent cliff-borer worm, she was a reluctant employee of Jabba the Hutt. Nella served as an assistant accountant to Mosep, but purposely misappropriated some of the Hutt's credits to obstruct Jabba's criminal activities.

**Nellac Kram** A planet that was the supposed departure site of the *Nartissteu.*

**Nelori Marauders** A band of warriors from the planet Dachat that tried to enslave the Shimholt, more than 4,000 years before the Galactic Civil War. The Nelori Marauders were eventually defeated by Jedi including Arca Jeth and were forced to retreat to their homeworld.

**Nelprin, Shalla** A dark-skinned woman from Ingo, Nelprin joined Wraith Squadron shortly before the New Republic assigned it to hunt down Warlord Zsinj. She was the younger sister of Vula Nelprin, and also was trained personally by her father in hand-to-hand combat. She helped the Wraiths become better ground agents, especially in preparation for their activities against Zsinj. She was assigned the position of Wraith Ten and served as Myn Donos's wingmate.

Nelprin assumed the identity of Qatya Nassin as part of the Hawk-bat Independent Space Force, and was supposedly killed in action during Warlord Zsinj's attempt to steal the *Razor's Kiss.* Actually, she commandeered a TIE interceptor and landed atop the *Razor's Kiss*'s shield generator platform. Once the New Republic forces were arrayed in a constraining pattern, Nelprin destroyed one of the *Super*-class Star Destroyer's shields. Voort saBinring knocked out the other, and the *Razor's Kiss* was destroyed. For her part in this and other missions, Nelprin was promoted to lieutenant following the battle over Kuat.

**Nelprin, Vula** She served the New Republic as a hand-to-hand combat specialist. The sister of Shalla Nelprin, Vula was trained by their father, Vyn Narcassan.

**Neluenf, Ben** The first great Tatooine-born Podracer. Ben Neluenf lost his life in a spectacular attempt to scale a broad, flat-topped mountain on Tatooine, which later was named Ben's Mesa in his honor. The Mos Esp Podrace course weaved around the mesa.

**Neluenf, Will** The son of Ben Neluenf, he continued his father's Podracing tradition during the years following the Battle of Naboo. Will participated in illegal Podraces that were held on Euceron against the backdrop of the Galactic Games.

**Nelvaan** The primary world in the Koobi system. Nelvaan's location in the Outer Rim kept it free of the influence of the Old Republic, although several Bothan freighters made regular runs there to acquire the pure water that flowed from glacial runoffs. When Republic forces nearly captured Count Dooku on Tythe during the final stages of the Clone Wars, many Separatist ships jumped from Tythe to Nelvaan to escape the battle. This was mainly a ruse, since the ships remained only briefly at Nelvaan before jumping to a nearby location and then to Coruscant, where they assisted General Grievous's forces in the First Battle of Coruscant.

Obi-Wan Kenobi and Anakin Skywalker were dispatched to Nelvaan to investigate, and the only Nelvaanians they found turned out to be females and children. The males had been captured and twisted by the Separatists as part of an experiment for creating their own organic army. Anakin, in a trial ordered by the natives, destroyed the Separatist facility and freed the males.

Nelvaanian

**Nelvaanian** A furred, canine-muzzled humanoid species native to Nelvaan. Also known as Nelvaans, they were distinguished by their jet-black eyes, and by a fearsome appearance that belied a deeply spiritual nature. Much of their tribal tradition was based on the family unit, which took in an extended collection of blood relatives and closely related acquaintances. Although males of the family unit were the warriors and scouts, females were the most important members. They were the builders and gatherers, as well as responsible for raising the Nelvaanian youth.

Each tribe was led by a shaman, who could be either male or female, and the shaman's chosen mate. This leader was believed to have been chosen by the Great Mother to ascend to his or her position, eliminating any form of competition.

During the Clone Wars, the Nelvaanians believed that they had encountered the individual known as the *holt kazet,* or Ghost Hand. Legend held that this being would arrive in a time of great need and help the Nelvaanians regain their freedom. The appearance of Anakin Skywalker led many to conclude he was the *holt kazet,* a belief that was only strengthened when he passed all the tests of a local shaman before rescuing the tribe's males from a Separatist laboratory.

**Nematiec Gang** A gang defeated by Bogga the Hutt, who used *Enforcer One* to destroy its asteroid base.

***Nemesis*** An *Imperial I*-class Star Destroyer, the *Nemesis* was part of Grand Admiral Thrawn's fleet five years after the Battle of Endor. It was one of the Star Destroyers that Thrawn used to attack Bpfassh in one of his first moves against the New Republic.

**Nemesis of the Kimm** One of many nicknames used to describe Jedi Master Sharad Hett, because he was

Windo "Warble" Nend

known as a fearless and dedicated being who took on the challenges of bringing justice to some of the galaxy's worst places.

**Nemesis One** Corran Horn's call sign, used during his imprisonment at the Lusankya facility. The Nemesis flight group was the forerunner of Avenger Squadron.

**Nemonus** A Nautolan who appeared on Ord Cestus and claimed he spoke to the Five Families on behalf of Count Dooku. Nemonus was known for a number of brutal kidnappings in which he held innocent beings hostage, trading blood for credits. In reality, Nemonus was Jedi Master Kit Fisto, who tried to frighten the Families into joining the Old Republic during the Clone Wars. He claimed that Dooku was greatly upset at the Families' attempt to raise the prices of their JK series droids, and that Dooku feared the Families could no longer be trusted. To force their hands, Nemonus kidnapped several prominent members of the Five Families and held them in a speeder deep in the tunnels below ChikatLik. The plan was to make the Five Families believe that Count Dooku had betrayed them, then to have Obi-Wan Kenobi "rescue" the leaders as a way to lure the Families into siding with the Republic. In a carefully staged fight, Obi-Wan Kenobi was able to drive Nemonus off, thereby saving the Families from harm. While the entire incident did convince the Five Families to briefly side with the Republic, it was recorded by Asajj Ventress. The Dark Jedi then provided a recording of the incident to the Families, showing that the entire kidnapping was a farce.

***Nemphas*** An escort freighter that intercepted the *Spirit of Jabba* shortly after the smaller ship was stolen by Big Gizz and Spiker. The *Nemphas* was operated by Gorga the Hutt's minions.

Mandalorian Neo-Crusader

**Nena** A native of Melida/Daan, she was a member of the Young. Nena was in charge of restoring housing to the natives of Zehava, after the Young defeated their elders in battle.

**Nend, Windo "Warble"** A young Aqualish Jedi Padawan who was part of the task force dispatched to the planet Jabiim during the Clone Wars. Like many students who participated in the battle, Warble lost his Jedi Master to the Jabiimite rebels. After agreeing to stay and support the survivors' effort to stop the advance of Alto Stratus against the Republic's rescue force, he fought valiantly for two days before catching the brunt of an explosion with his chest. Momentarily disoriented, Warble discovered that he had been thrown into the path of an oncoming Hailfire droid. Knowing that his death was inevitable, Warble activated a pair of thermal detonators and set them off in his hands just as the Hailfire rolled over him.

Dllr Nep

**Nentan** A stopover point in the Glythe sector for civilians wishing passage to Rebel-controlled safeworlds. It was discovered by Imperial forces, and did not have enough transports to evacuate everyone. Captain Bren Derlin, serving General Rieekan, led a squad that hid in Nentan's ancient ruins and captured an Imperial transport. This allowed all the base personnel to escape, earning Derlin the rank of major.

**neocel** A thin material that was used to make heat-retaining bodysuits. It could also be extruded into slender fibers for use in carpeting.

**Neoclassical music** A description of compositions distinguished by their sweeping, epic scores and military themes. Emperor Palpatine was said to favor Neoclassical music, which made it a regular part of the Imperial Symphony Orchestra's repertoire.

**Neo-Crusaders, Mandalorian** The first groups of beings recruited by the ancient Mandalorian Crusaders to join their ranks and fight alongside them in the "Great Last Battle," several years after the end of the Great Sith War. The ranks of Neo-Crusaders grew rapidly as the Mandalorian Wars engulfed the galaxy. They became, in effect, Mandalorian shock troopers, a collection of beings from disparate species and backgrounds who banded together under the tenets of the ancient Mandalorians. All of their armor looked similar so that there was a commonality among them; later it became the design basis for the Old Republic's Senate Guards. After three long and bloody years, the reigning Neo-Crusader chieftain Mandalore the Ultimate was killed and the Mandalorians defeated. But the species' warrior culture survived. (*See also* Mandalorian Crusaders.)

**Neolsse** The ruling family of the city of Keremark during the New Order. Members of the Neolsse family were decidedly anti-Imperial in their political stance, and strove to throw off the Imperial yoke. They controlled Fortress Keremark and used it to strike back at the Imperial forces that tried to take over the planet Risban.

**Nep, Dllr** A Sullustan X-wing pilot, Nep served under Wedge Antilles as part of Rogue Squadron following the Battle of Endor. He joined the fledgling New Republic and found the Republic much to his liking. He was particularly interested in the various musical styles available, although his choices often got on his fellow Rogues' nerves. When the Rogues were dispatched to search for the *Starfaring* near Malrev, Nep heard beautiful music coming from the planet. He thought it was a product of Malrev. In fact, it was the power of the dark side of the Force being channeled by the mad Devaronian, Cartariun, who used the music to lure Nep to his temple.

Herian I'ngre, with whom Nep was mentally linked, recognized the dark side and willed Nep to resist. Nep ultimately gave in and absorbed the Sith energy wielded by Cartariun to try to turn it back against him, but he was shot in the back by an accomplice. Nep survived, but later he and I'ngre sacrificed themselves by flying I'ngre's X-wing into Cartariun's temple and destroying it.

**Nep, Zey** A woman who frequently visited the Outlander Club on Coruscant before the Battle of Geonosis. Nep was often found with her friends Dixon Just and Civ Sila, or her mentor, Artuo Pratuhr.

**neph** A docile species of huge flying beasts that were native to the planet Dalos IV. Nephs could grow up to 24 meters in length, with a wingspan nearly double that. They were tamed as juveniles for use as mounts, but became ornery as they grew older and eventually had to be set loose.

**Nepto, Karsunn** A Kajain'sa'Nikto and noted criminal who was associated with several prominent crime syndicates in the years prior to the Battle of Naboo. The Republic Security

Force issued a bounty for his arrest so it could interrogate him, and Jango Fett collected the reward shortly after the Battle of Naboo.

**Nereus, Wilek** The Imperial Governor of the subjugated planet Bakura, he governed with a minimum of bloodshed and preserved at least the form of pre-Imperial government. His hobby was hunting predators, including sentient ones, and displaying their teeth. He infected a leader of the opposition with a deadly parasite, then proceeded to infect Luke Skywalker. Governor Nereus was finally killed after he fired a blaster rifle at Skywalker, who used his lightsaber to deflect the bolt back to him.

**nerf** A large, shaggy pack animal that was raised as a source of meat, fur, hide, and other consumables. Originally native to the planet Alderaan, these rangy creatures had four curved horns. The nerf was best known for its ornery disposition. They tended to spit quite often, which only added to their reputation. Nerfs were hardy creatures that could adapt to a variety of climates, which made raising them on other planets quite easy. The shepherds who raised nerfs, often called nerf herders, lived in the fields with their beasts. They were a scruffy-looking lot who smelled almost as bad as the nerfs they tended. Most lost their own sense of smell over time.

**nerf-pox** A mild childhood disease that affected most Alderaanian youths.

**nerfscourge** An unusual flower that was distinguished by its pastel-blue puffball blooms. The pollen of the nerfscourge was known to be a potent form of neurotoxin, and could cause severe nerve damage to many species.

**nerfspread** A processed form of nerf meat that had a long shelf life, often packed on starships.

**nerf steak stew** A prepared meal made from cheaper cuts of nerf meat, stewed with vegetables and packaged in serving-sized cans. This allowed the stew to be transported for months aboard starships or in camping supplies.

**nergon 14** An unstable, explosive mineral, it was a major component of Imperial proton torpedoes. A pulsating blue color when inert, nergon 14 changed to bright red and then to white before it exploded.

**Nerit** One of two moons that orbited the planet Ossus. The gravity on this temperate world was 125 percent of standard, although it was tolerated by the Neti clan that settled the moon.

**Nermani, Ashii** A beautiful woman who was a popular newscaster on Imperial HoloVision. She was the first to break the story that Venslas Beeli had become a privateer working for the Rebel Alliance. The newsfeed article was part of a plot to draw Captain Dhas Vedij and the *Far Orbit* into a trap laid by the Empire.

**nerve disruptor** A hard-to-obtain torture device, it consisted of a small black box mounted on a tripod. It was used to disrupt the electrical signal flow in nerves, causing intense pain and involuntary bodily movements. An expensive piece of equipment, the nerve disruptor used a variety of injection methods to deliver drugs and serums into the body of a being under interrogation.

**nerve probe** Originally designed for medical purposes, the nerve probe proved to be an exceptional interrogation tool. It was used to isolate and test the activity of a nerve cell, but could be calibrated to cause intense pain.

**nerve rack** Another name for a scan grid adapted for use as a torture device.

**nervestick** A chewable stimulant popular among clone troopers of the Grand Army of the Republic during the Clone Wars. It became popular again, decades later, among members of the Galactic Alliance Guard.

**Nesdin** The human pilot of *Jade's Fire*. He disappeared in the first days of the Corellian revolts surrounding the Starbuster plot.

**Neskroff** The capital city of the planet Isis, it was located atop a huge, crystal mesa. The planet's main spaceport was situated in a bowl-shaped depression in the middle of the city.

**Nespis VIII** A planet located at the node of the six remaining Auril systems near the Cron drift, it was orbited by one of the largest of the ancient spaceports. It was a beacon point during the early days of hyperspace travel. Over thousands of years, the beacon became a sprawling city featuring a vast diversity of architectural styles and relics from nearly every period of space travel, including centuries-old murals of the Sith War. The city remained well preserved in the vacuum of space and was abandoned long before the start of the Clone Wars.

Nespis VIII Spaceport

Six years after the Battle of Endor, Luke Skywalker freed Kam Solusar from the dark side of the Force while at the Nespis VIII station. Later that year, New Republic leaders established their new base at the remote space city, and Leia Organa Solo's third child, Anakin, was born there. Soon after, the cloned Emperor fired a Galaxy Gun projectile toward Nespis VIII. The New Republic scrambled to abandon the base. The first shot was unsuccessful, but a second projectile destroyed the ancient orbital city.

**Nessie** Slang for any of the 25 native humanoid species of the Stenness Node. Nessies operated the mines and traded with outworlders.

**Nessin** An alias used by Kal Skirata when he arrived at the Tropix Island Resort during his search for Ko Sai. Nessin was ostensibly on Dorumaa for the rifi fishing, which helped cover Skirata's use of the *Aay'han* as both a starship and an oceangoing submersible.

**Nest, the** The name given to the command center of the space station known as the Rig during the Clone Wars.

**nest-fellow** A Basic term used to describe members of the same hive of the Colony.

**nest ship** The term used by Galactic Alliance naval forces to describe the massive transport vessels produced by the Killik hives of the Colony, which were used to move entire nests from one location to another. Each nest ship was a self-contained environment, allowing a hive to live a somewhat normal existence while traveling. At the height of the Swarm War, UnuThul planned to use nest ships to transport huge numbers of Killik soldiers to worlds within the Galactic Alliance, but the ships were trapped by the GA Defense Force within the Utegetu Nebula.

Nerfs

**Netbers, Radaf** A former Imperial captain who served under Warlord Zsinj following the Battle of Endor, he was an expert in hand-to-hand combat. He tested the Hawkbats' skills before the assault on Kuat. In a brief melee, Qatya Nassin—the alias used by Shalla Nelprin—broke his nose and quickly incapacitated him. He was assigned to the security force left behind at Binring Biomedical after Zsinj abandoned it and brought the labs aboard the *Iron Fist;* Netbers nearly captured Wraith Squadron on Saffalore. However, Hohass Ekwesh caught him and managed to break his right shoulder and his neck by swinging Netbers against a wall.

**netcaster** A predatory arachnid that lived in the forests of Kashyyyk, trapping daubirds with an elaborate net. The average netcaster grew to a length of 75 centimeters, and it used a highly toxic venom to kill its prey and defend itself from larger predators.

**Nethermost Abyss** The Askajian name for the deepest regions of evil in the planet.

**Neti** Tree-like beings from the planet Ryyk, although they likely first evolved on Myrkr. For many years, the Neti were also referred to as the Ryyk. New Republic xenoarchaeologists believed that the alternative name was actually a reference to the original Neti homeworld, and not a reference to a distinct species.

The ancient Jedi Masters Ood Bnar and Garnoo were Neti, as was T'ra Saa. As a species, the Neti were intelligent plants, reproducing by creating a few seeds every century. They survived by gathering food through photosynthesis, and could change their shape, size, or appearance almost at will. Most Neti were capable of three distinct forms: a solid tree; a humanoid; and a quadruped creature. Each of these forms provided certain levels of mobility and strength, and a Neti could adapt its shape to meet the needs of its surroundings. It was believed that Ood Bnar was the only surviving member of the species, being offworld when the planet Ryyk was destroyed, until T'ra Saa was discovered by other Jedi centuries before the Clone Wars.

**netting beetle** Also known as lav peq, these insects were bioengineered by the Yuuzhan Vong to exude an organic netting. When released in swarms, netting beetles formed a dense network of fibers that stuck to anything they touched, creating the netting as a by-product of their feeding. The first wave of beetles strung their fibers between trees and bushes, while successive waves fed on whatever they found in order to replenish the netting. Using these creatures, Yuuzhan Vong warriors could capture fugitives or enemies without actually knowing where they were. Many times, the netting beetles fed on the flesh of the captives, using the cells in the formation of the netting, but this was rarely fatal to the individuals.

*Neti*

**Netus** An ancient defense minister of the Old Republic, Netus was on Coruscant during the Great Sith War. Prior to his governmental work, he served for five years in the rocket-jumper corps. Netus found that he preferred politics, and spent the next 20 years serving the Old Republic before the Sith War broke out.

**Neufie** This was the nickname used by Jacen Solo for the R9 series astromech droid that was assigned to his StealthX starfighter during the Swarm War.

**neural band** Developed shortly after the Great Sith War, this device wrapped around the skull like an interface band. Instead of providing computer access, however, the neural band augmented the willpower of the wearer by electrically reinforcing established mental patterns. The troopers of the Old Republic referred to this device as "Little Shocky."

**neural-net eraser** Developed during the Clone Wars as a defense against rogue or runaway droids, the neural-net eraser destroyed the software and delicate circuitry that controlled a droid's ability to move and react. Neural-net erasers became popular when many beings feared being attacked or captured by the droid armies of the Separatists.

**neural stinger** An ancient weapon similar to a force pike, it resembled a long staff with a glass-like section at one end. A neural stinger could be used as a two-handed cudgel when powered down. When activated, the glass end lit up with an intense, blue glow. This section of the weapon earned the staff its name, as it delivered a powerful shock to the nerves.

**neuranium** This was one of the heaviest, densest metals found in the galaxy. Some gravity-sensitive species claimed to be able to feel a small warping of the space-time fabric when close to a large piece of neuranium. Among its most useful properties was that it was impervious to sensors. The weight of enough neuranium to protect a hidden item or to line a cargo hold, however, would have been prohibitively heavy. Neuranium often was used as the shielding layer for proton bombs and other exceptionally dangerous explosives.

**neurodium** A substance known for its ability to exist as a liquefied gas at a relatively low temperature, which allowed it to be used as a fuel for plasma weapons. A greenish material, neurodium gas was used to create the plasma that was the primary energy delivered by the FlakBlaster Ten artillery weapon.

**neuroengine** A term used by New Republic scientists and military advisers to describe the biotechnology that powered Yuuzhan Vong starships. It was believed that specially developed dovin basals were connected in a hive-like structure at the aft of the alien starships.

**Neuro-Saav Technologies** A major electronics and technologies firm with divisions dedicated to imaging systems, sensors, communications, medical biotechnology, and military encryption. It was also one of the galaxy's top cybernetics manufacturers starting in the Old Republic era.

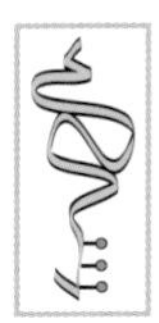

**Neutral Jedi Zone** A Barabel term used to describe a high-ceilinged cave located beneath the surface of Barab I. It was in this cave, which was several hundred meters in length and width, that the Barabels resolved far-reaching disputes that could not be decided at the local level. Individual Barabels were appointed as diplomats to argue each side of a dispute, and visiting Jedi Knights or other dignitaries were asked to mediate the debates. The Neutral Jedi Zone offered offworlders luxury accommodations in exchange for their help in mediating disputes.

**neutrino activator** A switching device that was used to turn a droid on or off, depending on its setting. It was most often used in small droids, whose power requirements were minimal.

**neutrino hybridizer** A delicate, critical component of the sublight drives of early Corellian Engineering Corporation YT-1300s, such as the *Millennium Falcon.* These devices usually were made of specially grown quartz and platinum.

**neutron dissembler** Weapons that were theorized, but never actually developed, by scientists of the Old Republic. A neutron dissembler would disrupt the bonds that held neutrons together at the submolecular level and cause matter to "melt." The resulting damage would look like scar tissue.

**Neuvian sundae** An immense dessert of frozen cream and fruit, served in a wide bowl.

***Neva*** This was one of the Rebel Alliance's Dreadnaught warships, active during the Galactic Civil War.

**Neva, Huoba** A female Sullustan and daughter of a SoroSuub executive, Neva easily gained acceptance to the Imperial Academy. She quickly distinguished herself, but never seemed to be able to obtain a command of her own. Eventually, Neva realized that the pro-human Imperial doctrine would stymie her, and she decided to join the Rebel Alliance. Sian Tevv told Ackbar about her outstanding accomplishments; Ackbar needed good starship commanders, so she was accepted into the Alliance. Neva became the youngest Republic warship commander following a victory in the Illoud system, and she was given command of the *Rebel Star.* Neva perished when her ship collided with the burned-out hulk of a Star Destroyer as it emerged from hyperspace near Coruscant. The Republic mourned her passing.

**Nevana** Her father owed a huge debt to the bounty hunter Sarma, which she hoped to pay off by providing Sarma with the location of Luke Skywalker. She was unaware who Skywalker really was, thinking him just a smuggler. The Imperials caught up with her, and Nevana was shot in the back and killed by a stormtrooper.

New Alderaan

**Never Die** The code name used by the being that created the Shard of Alderaan computer slicing program. This being was a native of Alderaan, but that was all the information known.

**Nev Ice Flow** A vast glacier located on the planet Hoth, between the Kerane Valley and the Clabburn Range. Much of the ice forming the flow came from the Lanteel and Cirque glaciers.

**Nevil, Kral "Deuce"** A Quarren who served as Rogue Two and Gavin Darklighter's wingmate in Rogue Squadron during the Yuuzhan Vong War. Captain Nevil was believed to have been killed in an engagement over Dantooine, but he managed to return to active duty to serve in the Battles of Garqi and Ithor. Nevil later was Darklighter's wingmate during the defense of Coruscant and the retaking of Borleias.

In the peace that followed the Yuuzhan Vong War, Nevil was promoted several times, eventually taking a command position on the Star Destroyer *Anakin Solo* in the wake of Captain Twizzl's death. His first combat occurred during Jacen Solo's deep-space rendezvous with Corellian diplomats, which turned out to be a trap. Sadras Koyan and Corellia's leader fired the Centerpoint Station repulsor at the *Anakin Solo.* Captain Nevil and Jacen Solo survived the blast, but Nevil's son, Turl, was killed in the fighting. Solo, surprisingly sympathetic, allowed Nevil to go about his business as he saw fit.

During Jacen Solo's attempt to seize control of Centerpoint Station, Captain Nevil questioned the Jedi's killing of Lieutenant Tebut, and Solo used the Force to knock Nevil against a bulkhead, momentarily stunning him into submission. In the wake of the destruction of Centerpoint Station, Solo allowed the captain to remain as the *Anakin Solo*'s commanding officer, but Nevil's concerns about Solo's leadership increased during the Second Battle of Fondor.

When Jacen Solo broke away from the rest of the Galactic Alliance fleet to bomb Fondorian cities from orbit, Captain Nevil decided that he could no longer serve under such a man. He found a spare escape pod and jettisoned away from the *Anakin Solo,* abandoning his post rather than obey Solo any longer. His escape pod was later recovered by Admiral Niathal aboard the *Ocean.*

**Nevil, Turl** The son of Kral Nevil, Turl joined the naval forces of the Galactic Alliance and served as a weapons officer aboard the frigate *Cheesmeer* during the war against the Confederation. Ensign Turl was killed when the *Cheesmeer* was destroyed by the Centerpoint Station repulsor.

**New Agamar** A planet noted for its high gravity. The human settlers who colonized the world evolved over time to be much stockier and more muscled than most humans.

**New Alderaan** A lush, temperate planet that was populated by descendants of Alderaanian-born members of the Rebel Alliance. During the Galactic Civil War, this was one of the Alliance's best-hidden safeworlds, and it served for a time as the hiding place for Jacen and Jaina Solo. The planet was later discovered by Imperial Warlord Zsinj, and its entire population was forced to evacuate temporarily.

**New Apsolon (1)** One of the largest cities on the planet New Apsolon, it was the site of the planet's primary spaceport. Like all cities on the planet, it was divided into a section for the Workers and one for the Civilized. Before the planet was united under a single leader, some 15 years before the Battle of Naboo, the two sections were separated by a wall of pure energy, ostensibly protecting the Civilized from the Workers. Following the election, the energy wall was dismantled and replaced with 40 shimmering stone columns. Each column memorialized a Worker who had died trying to breach the wall.

**New Apsolon (2)** Originally known simply as Apsolon, this planet joined the galactic community 15 years before the Battle of Naboo. The people of Apsolon had to choose a leader who represented the entire planet, and the Jedi Knights Qui-Gon Jinn and Tahl were dispatched to assist in ensuring a fair election. The planet was controlled by the Civilized Authority and policed by the Absolutes. The two primary social factions, the Civilized and the Workers, were continually at odds. After industrial sabotage by the Workers forced the Civilized to recognize their plight, the two groups agreed to form a single government known as the Unified Legislature. The planet was known for its two primary exports: high technology and beautiful gray stone.

**New Bakstre** A planet with seven moons, a purplish sky, and a very rapid rotation.

**New Brigia** Just within the borders of the Koornacht Cluster, the colony was once the site of a struggling chromite-mining operation founded by a small group of Brigians. In its early years, New Brigia enjoyed rich hauls of chromite ore, many eager buyers, and protection from pirates by the Imperial forces controlling Koornacht. Over time, however, the ore yields lessened, and the Empire's retreat from the region after the Battle of Endor hurt the security of the trade lanes. Twelve years after Endor, the entire Brigian colony was ruthlessly eliminated by the Yevethan military in what the Yevetha called the Great Purge.

**Newcomers** Inhabitants of Nam Chorios who were not direct descendants of the original prisoners left there by the Grissmath. The Newcomers believed that the Therans and other Oldtimers wanted to keep the planet isolated, as evidenced by their use of automatic gun emplacements to shoot down incoming and outgoing cargo ships. This belief was fostered by Seti Ashgad, although the real reason for the gun emplacements was to keep the disease-spreading drochs from leaving the planet. The Newcomers fought for Ashgad, ambushing the gun emplacements when ships arrived. The ships contained weapons required to liberate Ashgad and the mutated droch Dzym from the planet.

**new Corellian crisis** A simplistic term used by Admiral Niathal to describe the galactic situation surrounding Thrackan Sal-Solo's attempt to pull the Corellian system from the Galactic Alliance 10 years after the Yuuzhan Vong War. The GA had tried to forestall any secession by blockading the system with its Second Fleet and capturing Sal-Solo and Five Worlds Prime Minister Aidel Saxan.

**New Coronet** This city, located on the swamp-covered world of Trigalis, was designated in many travel guides as a trading post. In reality, it was a collection of run-down buildings that served as a haven for all sorts of criminals. During the Clone Wars, the city came under the control of the Black Sun assassin Xist. In the search for Asajj Ventress, Obi-Wan Kenobi met up with Aayla Secura here.

**New Cov** The site of a Bothan battle with a *Victory*-class Star Destroyer during the early stages of the Galactic Civil War, New Cov was also the setting for the only documented instance of a Bothan-only battle with the Empire.

New Cov had no indigenous sentient species, but it was a jungle world teeming with plant life and valuable natural resources. The planet's cities were walled and domed to protect them from the dangers of the surrounding environment.

*The new Empire's Emperor Fel escorted by Imperial Knights*

**New Dawn** An *Emissary*-class shuttle provided to former Supreme Chancellor Tarsus Valorum by the Galactic Senate for use in his travels following the end of the New Sith Wars and the enactment of the Ruusan Reformations. He traveled on the *New Dawn* to a secret meeting on Serenno to discuss the Separatist movement that was growing on the planet. Valorum was accompanied by his friend and guardian, Jedi Knight Johun Othone. Their mission was discovered by Sith apprentice Zannah, who wanted to undermine the efforts of the Anti-Republic Liberation Front. The members of this insurgent group had planted explosives around the landing pad where the *New Dawn* touched down, and detonated them shortly after the shuttle landed. Although Valorum and Othone had already debarked, the shuttle's crew was killed in the explosion. Valorum nearly fell to his death in the wake of the blast, but Othone managed to pull him to safety before confronting their attackers.

**New Downtime** A code phrase used by the New Republic forces stationed on Folor to indicate a full retreat. In such an event, pilots met at New Downtime—a popular cantina.

**new Empire** The new Empire was born from the Imperial Remnant in the wake of the Yuuzhan Vong War. When the Galactic Alliance could no longer fill its role as the predominant galactic government, the Imperial Remnant decided it had to act. Splitting from the GA, the Imperial Remnant reestablished itself as the new Empire and began to assume control over parts of the galaxy. However, unlike Emperor Palpatine, the Fel family that assumed leadership chose a benign approach. Using the simple concept of "Victory Without War," the Fel Emperors ruled without the terrible bloodshed and oppression of Palpatine. Jacen Solo, who had taken on the title of Darth Caedus, had heard the idea of a new Empire and embraced it, especially after the Moffs began calling him "Lord Caedus."

About a century after the Yuuzhan Vong War, Emperor Roan Fel found the galactic government crumbling around him. He forged a terrible alliance with Darth Krayt, and then watched in horror as the Ossus Project began to fail, as the vast planetary terraforming plan was secretly sabotaged by the Sith. The Moffs who ran the new Empire forced a war against the Galactic Alliance, and soon the new Empire took control of the entire galaxy. However, the alliance with the Sith proved to be little more than cover for the true intentions of Darth Krayt. As soon as the new Empire took over Coruscant, Krayt assassinated Imperial leaders and assumed control of the galaxy for the new Sith Order. He later discovered that he had killed a stand-in rather than Emperor Fel himself. Krayt vowed to hunt Fel down, an action that would bring about the end of the new Empire.

**New History Squad** A group of children from the planet Melida/Daan organized by Nield after the Young took control of the planet. Their mission was to destroy the Halls of Evidence, eliminating the centuries of hatred between the Daan and Melida maintained in holograms there.

**New Holgha** A planet best known for its Five Holy Cities. The Yuuzhan Vong attacked the planet three months after they launched their galactic invasion. Boba Fett and his group of Mandalorian warriors risked their lives to get a warning out of Birgis to the New Republic. However, the central government refused to act, and New Holgha fell swiftly.

**New Holstice** This was one of the many staging points for the Grand Army of the Republic during the Clone Wars. New Holstice also served as one of the Republic's primary medical facilities. Located in a remote glade on the planet was a wondrous memorial to those Jedi Knights killed over the millennia. The natives of New Holstice created it by generating a shaft of pure light that rose high into the sky. The light, powered by a dedicated generator so it would never go out, was of a specific frequency and wavelength that attracted the unusual memory moth. The people of New Holstice added one long-lived memory moth for each Jedi who was killed, starting from a point many thousands of years before the Clone Wars. The Jedi's name was whispered to a moth, which repeated the Jedi's name in the beating of its wings, seemingly forever. The memorial grew slowly over the centuries, until the Battle of Geonosis, when it filled at an astonishing rate.

**New Hope** A Rebel Alliance Dreadnaught stationed in orbit around Churba, it was a floating piece of history. Alliance forces stole the ship out from under the Imperials who controlled the planet, refitting it to serve as a mobile command post during the early years of the Galactic Civil War. In the wake of the Battle of Endor, the *New Hope* was stationed at Milagro, in an effort to keep the hyperspace jump point there free from Imperial control.

**New Hopetown** Originally known as Hopetown, this settlement was located on the planet Ennth. It was almost completely destroyed in the wake of groundquakes and tidal waves caused when Ennth's moon orbited close to the planet as it did every eight years. The settlers eventually rebuilt it, and renamed it New Hopetown—and later Newest Hopetown and then Another Hopetown. It was again destroyed eight years later, and renamed Newer Hopetown. The young Jedi student Zekk was born here, then orphaned when his parents were killed in a groundquake.

**New Imperial Diplomatic Corps** A branch of the New Empire charged with maintaining diplomatic relations with the many governments and star systems that sup-

*New Holstice, a staging point for the Grand Army of the Republic*

ported it during the years leading up to the Sith-Imperial War. In the wake of the conflict, the work of the Diplomatic Corps became even more important, since it helped to keep member systems alerted to the machinations of the new Sith Order.

**Newmark** A major roadway in the northern sector of Conso City, on the planet Drunost. Consolidated Shipping maintained a repository building on Newmark during the New Order.

**New Marketplace** The trading and commercial district of the city of Talos, on the planet Atzerri.

**New Nystao** A settlement that sprang up at the base of Mount Tantiss, on Wayland, after the New Republic defeated Grand Admiral Thrawn and took control of the facility. It became the nominal capital of the planet because it was also the location of the largest civilian starport. Much of New Nystao was maintained by the Noghri, who had been forced to abandon their homeworld of Honoghr after Imperial forces rendered its surface incapable of supporting plant life.

**New Oldtown** This village, found on the planet Aldivy, was the home of Lara Notsil before it was destroyed by Admiral Trigit.

**New Order** The phrase that Emperor Palpatine used to describe his regime.

***New Order, A*** A lavish and popular holoproduction starring actress Alexis Cov-Prim.

**New Plympto** Located deep in the Core Worlds on the edge of the Deep Core, New Plympto was on the Corellian Trade Spine, between Jumus and Duro. It was the homeworld of the Nosaurians as well as the rikknit, a species of crab-like spiders whose eggs were a vital ingredient in many intoxicants. During the Yuuzhan Vong War, the Nosaurians put up a strong resistance, led by Jedi Knights Alema Rar and her sister, Numa. In retaliation, the Yuuzhan Vong unleashed a life-destroying plague that wiped the world clean of organic life. The Rar sisters barely escaped with a large group of refugees, sneaking by the Yuuzhan Vong blockade by hiding in ore freighters.

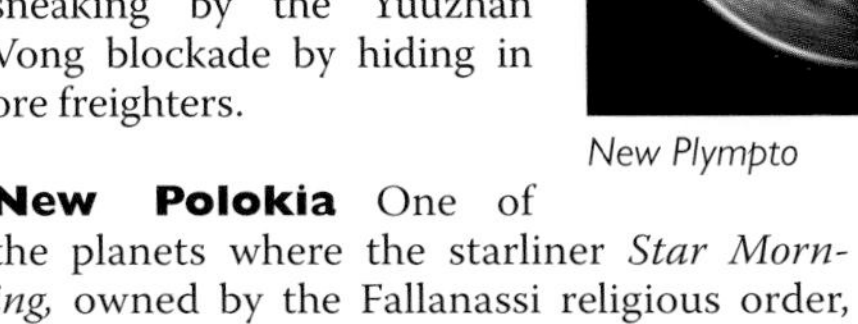

New Plympto

**New Polokia** One of the planets where the starliner *Star Morning,* owned by the Fallanassi religious order, stopped after departing the planet Teyr.

**Newport** One of three major spaceports located in Imperial City on Coruscant. The Obroan Institute maintained a landing bay there for many decades, until the Yuuzhan Vong took control of Coruscant and terraformed the planet.

**New Regime** This government assumed control of the planet Brigia during the early years of the New Order. While not expressly allied with the Empire, the New Regime adopted many of its methodologies, building the planet's military using the meager funds collected by the previous government. To hide its misuse of funds, the New Regime instituted a new form of currency, thus enabling it to control trade. When Han Solo took the educator Hissal back to Brigia, he was able to expose the New Regime for what it was, bringing its activities to the attention of the native Brigians.

**New Republic** The name chosen by the leaders of the Alliance to Restore the Republic for the government that they established following the defeat of Emperor Palpatine's New Order at the Battle of Endor and the truce at Bakura. The New Republic reaffirmed many of the Old Republic's basic tenets and established some new ones in the hope of maintaining and expanding on the sovereign rights of every individual. The symbol of the New Republic reused the blue crest of the Alliance, which signified the burning desire to restore justice to the galaxy.

The New Republic was first headed by Mon Mothma, and later by Leia Organa Solo. At the time of the Yevethan Great Purge, the New Republic comprised some 400 sentient species and counted around 11,000 inhabited worlds as members. Like the Old Republic before it, the New Republic withstood many internal challenges, not the least of which was the petty squabbling of its member worlds. When the Yuuzhan Vong invaded the galaxy the Advisory Council's inability to make a decision on how to address the crisis allowed the invaders to make swift inroads toward the Core Worlds.

Within three years, the Yuuzhan Vong captured the planet Coruscant and forced Chief of State Borsk Fey'lya to sacrifice himself in an attempt to stem the tide. With Coruscant ruined, the New Republic shattered. In one of the earliest meetings of the so-called Inner Circle, General Antilles called the New Republic "a dead, oversized hulk with a decentralized nervous system, whose extremities don't realize that its heart isn't beating anymore." To break from the past and establish a new galactic order, Chief of State Cal Omas re-formed the government under the banner of the Galactic Federation of Free Alliance, or simply the Galactic Alliance.

**New Republic Advisory Council** A six-member body that formed the highest level of the New Republic's government. Led by the Chief of State, the Advisory Council debated over the toughest issues faced by the Republic. It was formed nearly two decades after the Battle of Endor, but was scattered in the wake of the Second Battle of Coruscant, when the Yuuzhan Vong destroyed much of the capital planet.

**New Republic Archaeological Corps** This branch of the New Republic was formed in the wake of the destruction of Emperor Palpatine's clones on the planet Byss, after Luke Skywalker discovered the Ysanna civilization on Ossus. The New Republic established the NRAC to assist various university-based groups in the excavation of historical sites like Ossus, so that artifacts and information that were uncovered could be preserved for the rest of the galaxy. Additionally, any new discoveries of information on the former Jedi Order was to be documented and provided to Master Skywalker for use as he strove to rebuild the Jedi Knights. The NRAC became especially active during the Yuuzhan Vong invasion of the galaxy, when it became imperative that the Jedi have every advantage they could in fighting the alien invaders.

**New Republic Bounty Hunter License** The New Republic's version of the Imperial Peace-Keeping Certificate, it licensed a being to be a bounty hunter.

**New Republic Cabinet** The New Republic's governing body, established in the wake of the defeat of Grand Admiral Thrawn.

**New Republic Cantina** A watering hole in the city of Algarine, on Algara II.

**New Republic City** This was the name for the capital city of Coruscant in the years before the Yuuzhan Vong War. It replaced the ancient name of Republic City, as well as the name Imperial City, which had been used during the era of the New Order.

**New Republic Defense Fleet** The primary New Republic naval force some 12 years after the Battle of Endor. It comprised five major battle groups, each of which was assigned a given sector of space. One entire fleet was dedicated to protecting Coruscant, the center of the New Republic's power.

**New Republic Defense Force (NRDF)** Created by the New Republic, this was the primary military body protecting against external subterfuge. Led by the Joint Defense Operations Staff, the NRDF was based on Coruscant and controlled the various branches of the armed forces that were arrayed across the galaxy. Having survived the Black Fleet crisis, the NRDF saw its credibility severely degraded when the Yuuzhan Vong invaded the galaxy, since the Republic's military was poorly equipped to handle the situation. The valiant struggle to win the war was not given much media coverage, further adding to the poor image of the NRDF. However, in the wake of the Battle of Borleias and the release of *The Battle of Borleias* holodocumentary, the true efforts of the Defense Force were revealed to the public, and positive popular opinion of the NRDF was restored.

**New Republic Fleet Infirmary** This military medcenter on Coruscant was set up to maintain the health of the home fleet.

**New Republic Fleet Intelligence** The primary intelligence-gathering agency formed by the military of the New Republic during the years following the Battle of Bilbringi. The mission of Fleet Intelligence was to provide detailed information on an enemy's strengths and weaknesses in an effort to better plan and prepare for battle.

**New Republic Historical Archive** A vast warehouse that served as the New Republic's primary archive. Most sections of the Archive were open to the public, and provided a visual description of the galaxy's history.

**New Republic Honor Guard** A branch of the New Republic military charged with protecting the dignitaries of the New Republic during their travels.

**New Republic Intelligence (NRI)** The New Republic's primary source of information throughout the galaxy, it was a vast network of spies and agents, highly skilled in overt and covert operations.

**New Republic Medical Institute** A medical research and education facility established on the planet Corellia in the wake of the Battle of Endor.

**New Republic Military Oversight Committee** The governmental body charged with ensuring that proper costs and justifications were used in all actions dealing with the defense of the galaxy. Its work during the Yuuzhan Vong War came under intense scrutiny, especially in the wake of Viqi Shesh's exposure as an agent of the alien invaders.

**New Republic Military Police** The branch of the New Republic's armed forces responsible for ensuring that the military acted within the laws established by the Republic.

**New Republic Obelisk** A tall, thin needle of stone erected in Imperial City on Coruscant to symbolize the unity of the New Republic.

**New Republic Observers** A group chartered by the New Republic shortly after Ponc Gavrisom was named President and the policies of the Republic were modified. The Observers' role was to move freely about their assigned sectors, reporting any improper government activities directly to the High Council. Beings were assigned to sectors of space far from their own homeworlds as a way to keep Observers impartial and incorruptible. In the Old Republic, the role was filled by Jedi Knights.

**New Republic Prime Newsgrid** A news agency that was once the primary source of news throughout the galaxy. It complemented the Coruscant Global Newsgrid, and was one of the first agencies to report the liftoff of the *Aramadia* from the planet.

**New Republic Reference Service** An information bureau that was part of the New Republic. Luke Skywalker had the service search for any references to the Fallanassi or the White Current during his travels with Akanah.

**New Republic Security Force (NRSF)** Implemented by Airen Cracken shortly after Coruscant was liberated from Ysanne Isard, the NRSF replaced the old Imperial Sector Rangers. It was designed to be a law enforcement agency as well as a counterinsurgency force.

**New Republic Senate** The title of the galaxywide Senate that formed after the birth of the New Republic. It was established with the original goals of the Old Republic in mind, with each member world represented by a Senator.

**New Republic Space Academy** This facility's graduates went on to serve in some of the highest military positions of the New Republic. Many new graduates became part of the Chief of State's honor guard before going on to active duty.

**New Route** *See* ID-5N.

**newsblink** Any small, quickly distributed piece of news.

**newsflimsi** A thinner version of regular flimsiplast, this material was used to print static reports of the latest news. Its light weight and ease of recycling made newsflimsi a popular option for disseminating news on space stations and other remote locations.

**NewsNet** The generic term for the loose collection of sanctioned and pirate networks, forums, and bulletin boards that sprang up on the HoloNet during the era of the New Order. When the Galactic Empire was formed at the end of the Clone Wars, the HoloNet was usurped for Imperial communications, leaving the average being without a source of regular information. NewsNets were soon formed to provide all manner of timely information and communication to the citizens of the galaxy, regardless of their political stance.

The types of information ranged from gossip to travel notices to real-time news reporting, and the quality, legitimacy, and legality of this information was considered as variable as the weather. The Empire allowed many newsfeeds to continue to exist as NewsNets, but regularly monitored the information traffic to eliminate or shut down feeds that were deemed illegal. Although much of the data found on NewsNets was designed for large organizations, individual users could access them through specialized readers.

When the New Republic was formed after the Galactic Civil War, the HoloNet was slowly restored to use as a public communications system. NewsNets continued to exist in various parts of the galaxy, especially those sectors and systems that were still held by the Imperial Remnant.

**New Town** The western part of the city of Bagsho, on Nim Drovis. As the name suggested, it was the most recently developed section of Bagsho.

**New Vertica** This was one of the largest cities on the Smugglers' Moon of Nar Shaddaa.

**Next Chance** A casino on Rodia where Princess Leia Organa first met with Guri, the human replica droid who worked with Prince Xizor, the head of the criminal Black Sun organization.

**nexu** Native to Cholganna, these incredibly dangerous feline predators were prized by beings who staged gladiator fights. The head of a nexu was wide, flat, and dominated by its toothy maw. A golden mane surrounded its head, and the paws of the nexu were studded with heavy claws that allowed the beast to climb trees with relative ease. A row of spike-like quills protected the beast's spine, while a whip-like tail provided both balance and another attack method. Most nexus moved about with their muscular legs held out to their sides, allowing them to crouch down and gain maximum stability while tracking and hunting prey.

Nexus were solitary hunters almost from birth, because their mothers abandoned them after six months of nursing. When attacking, most nexus grabbed the neck of their prey with their wide mouths and shook it violently, snapping its neck. Because of their vicious nature, nexus were not often hunted, but their pelts, claws, and bones were prized among collectors. The nexu was one of a trio of deadly beasts unleashed by the Geonosians upon Anakin Skywalker, Padmé Amidala, and Obi-Wan Kenobi in the Geonosis execution arena.

***Nexu*** An *Acclamator*-class military transport ship used by the Old Republic, the *Nexu* was the ship that transported clone troopers to Vandor-3.

*A fearsome nexu stalks its prey.*

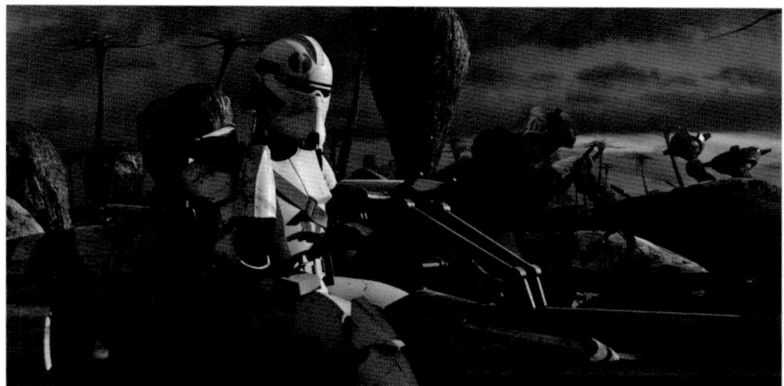
Commander Neyo gets ready to execute Order 66.

**Nexu Grin** One of the many attack postures practiced by warriors who trained in the tëräs käsi martial arts.

***Nexus*** An Imperial *Carrack*-class cruiser that was part of the Imperial force dispatched to hound the Rebel Alliance as its ships massed near Sullust just prior to the Battle of Endor.

**Neyo, Commander** This clone leader was one of many ARC troopers who led squads into battle for the Grand Army of the Republic. Officially designated Commander 8826, Neyo was among the first 100 graduates of ARC trooper training and was known for his cold, often morbid, personality. Commander Neyo was traveling with Jedi Master Stass Allie when Emperor Palpatine issued the command to execute Order 66. He allowed his speeder bike to fall behind Allie's, then opened fire on the unsuspecting Jedi. His shots hit their mark, destroying Allie's own speeder bike and causing it to explode. Stass Allie died in the explosion.

**Nez Peron** A small agricultural world that was aligned with the Empire even after the Battle of Endor. The planet was ruled with an iron fist; the Empire transmitted a message indicating that the lives of the natives were expendable for the cause of the Empire.

**Nezriti Organization** A criminal organization that tried to gain Prince Xizor's favor during the Galactic Civil War.

**NFQ** This was an acronym used by Darman and several other clone troopers who participated in the Old Republic's actions on the planet Qiilura during the Clone Wars. NFQ stood for "Normal For Qiilura."

**Ngaaluh** A Yuuzhan Vong priestess who was one of the many followers of Yun-Harla. She brought news to Warmaster Tsavong Lah that Vergere had returned to the Yuuzhan Vong during the early stages of their invasion, but had inherent doubts about the truth behind the Eighth Cortex, the supposed final stage of enlightenment. When the Shamed Ones began speaking of Jedi Knights as their saviors, Ngaaluh was one of many high-placed Yuuzhan Vong who took to the Message. To prove herself, she donned an ooglith masquer and set out to locate the prophet of the Shamed Ones, Yu'shaa. She tried to present Yu'shaa with a living unrik, but Yu'shaa—actually Nom Anor—believed that she was trying to use a weapon. He used his plaeryin bol to defend himself, and barely realized the mistake he had made. Using a specialized antivenin, Nom Anor revived Ngaaluh.

When she had recovered, Ngaaluh agreed to return to Supreme Overlord Shimrra with a villip concealed in her robes to record everything she witnessed and relay it to Nom Anor. She accepted the mission, despite its obvious danger, because she believed in the Message. She was appointed by Shimrra himself to begin weeding out the heretical members of the Shamed Ones, a position that allowed her and Nom Anor to plot the downfall of many high-ranking members of Shimrra's command structure.

Their plans were uncovered during Shimrra's investigation into the treachery of Prefect Zareb and Drosh Khalii. Interrogation of the acolytes who had been inserted into Zareb's household revealed that it was Ngaaluh who actually had placed them there. Shimrra ordered her captured and interrogated, but Ngaaluh would not reveal her true loyalties. She poisoned herself rather than reveal Nom Anor's part in the plots.

***NGC-1710*** An Imperial military shuttle that made regular runs between the planet Despayre and the construction site of the first Death Star.

**ngdin** A small, tongue-shaped creature bioengineered by the Yuuzhan Vong, it moved about on thousands of tiny cilia, and was created to eat the blood and flesh of anything it found. This way, the aliens could keep their dwellings clean of biological debris, especially the gricha-larva shells they used to house slaves. The cilia caused a numbing sting when they contacted living flesh.

**ng'ok** War beasts with foul tempers. The razor-sharp teeth and retractable claws of ng'ok frightened off potential attackers. Ng'ok figures were frequently playing pieces in hologramic games.

**ngom** An aquatic creature once native to the planet Yuuzhan'tar, the ngom was distinguished by its large wattles and its deep cooing call. It was often kept in ponds or moats outside a residence as a kind of organic alarm system.

**Ng'rhr** A Wookiee term meaning "clan uncle," it described a teacher or a master to an apprentice.

**Nha, Mnor** A Gotal in the Azure Dianoga cantina, he sensed Gavin Darklighter's fear at the approach of Imperial stormtroopers, then his relief when they went away. Because Darklighter also radiated fear followed by relief at the approach and departure of Asyr Sei'lar, Mnor Nha assumed the Rogue Squadron pilot was bigoted, so he and his compatriots took Darklighter and his Rogue friends before the Alien Combine to be judged for bigotry.

**Nharl** The central star of the Nharl system. About two years before the Battle of Geonosis, it ejected an immense solar flare measuring more than 10 light-minutes in length. The flare torched the planet Equanus, rendering it a lifeless cinder and virtually wiping out the Equani. The flare was not a natural phenomenon but the result of a miscalculated test-firing of the Death Star's superlaser. Although it was of little consolation to the Equani, the scientists who conducted the test were killed in the flare as well.

**Nharqis'I** An area of space known as the death place by many beings. The word *Nharqis'I* was actually a modification of a smuggler's term for a killing field. The Nharqis'I was a starless, featureless section of the galaxy, forbidding in its blankness.

**Nhazz** A fighter for the Rebel Alliance and the New Republic, he was believed to be the brother of Uz Bonearm.

**Nhor, Ezam** An Ithorian who was trained at the new Jedi Order's academy on Ossus following the Yuuzhan Vong War. He was also a liaison to the Council of Ithorian Elders. In an effort to acquire a new home for his people, Nhor petitioned the Reconstruction Authority to locate a habitable planet, but his requests were often misrouted or simply lost. Rather than waiting around for the government, Ezam Nhor called in a favor from Leia Organa Solo and her husband, Han. The Solos agreed to independently search out a planet for the Ithorians, hoping to find it before one of the larger corporate teams did. They believed that Borao would be the ideal world, but RePlanet-Hab jumped their claim and turned the planet over to the Galactic Alliance.

**Nhoras** This species had a 600-year-old feud with the Clatear—a feud that five generations of Jedi Knights couldn't resolve. When Imperials took control of the galaxy, they subjugated the Clatear while leaving the Nhoras relatively alone. Thus, when the revelation of the Caamas Document brought the feud to a head, the Nhoras were unprepared for the Clatears' initial attacks. They began hiring mercenaries—most notably the Dhashaan Shield—to protect them from harm.

**Nia** A Jedi student who was transported to safety by Hurd Coyle in the weeks following the end of the Clone Wars and the so-called Jedi Rebellion. While exploring Coyle's ship, Nia encountered a clone trooper pilot who had been rescued by the salvager. Like the other students, she wasn't sure if she could trust the clone, given the events that followed the execution of Order 66. The children were nearly discovered when an Imperial cruiser intercepted Coyle's ship and demanded to see its cargo holds. The clone came to their rescue, explaining that he had been rescued by Coyle, and that the ship was otherwise empty.

**Niathal, Admiral Cha** A Mon Calamari, she served as an officer in the naval forces of the Galactic Alliance following the Yuuzhan Vong War. A native of Reef Home City, Niathal earned the recognition of her superior officers thanks to her military skills, and she was appointed to serve as one of Supreme Commander Pellaeon's advisers. In this capacity, she was asked to analyze the possible outcomes of the disabling or destruction of Centerpoint Station on the psyche of the Corellian people.

Known for her icy demeanor and scathing tongue, Admiral Niathal was the exact opposite of Admiral Ackbar. When Supreme Commander Pellaeon decided to retire to show his opposition to the formation of the Galactic Alliance Guard, Admiral Niathal was promoted to fill his position, giving her complete command of the Galactic Alliance's military forces. Her hard-line military stance on most issues worried many Senators and political advisers, especially after she developed a strong relationship with Jacen Solo. Once in a position of command, Niathal began making plans to succeed Cal Omas as the Chief of State of the Galactic Alliance.

Unknown to Niathal, however, her association with Jacen Solo was much more than a meeting of minds. Solo, as he began his turn toward the dark side of the Force, recognized that an alliance with a high-ranking military official would make his own plans that much easier to implement.

Niathal, acting on behalf of the entire GA Defense Force, moved warships into blockade positions around the Corellian system without the assent of either Omas or the Senate. She personally led the assault on the Confederation's meeting at Gilatter VIII, flying the reconditioned flagship *Galactic Voyager* in honor of her mentor, Admiral Ackbar. However, the GA was unaware that Gilatter VIII was a trap that had been set up by the new Supreme Commander of the Confederation, Turr Phennir. Only the telepathic warning of Jacen Solo saved her forces, as it was picked up by Luke Skywalker and relayed to the rest of the fleet just before it entered a minefield that had been laid in the planet's atmosphere. In the wake of this near-disaster, Niathal was forced to acknowledge that the Galactic Alliance might not survive a war against the Confederation. Her confidence in Cal Omas's leadership eroded, and she worried about the actions of Jacen Solo, but she strove to maintain a strong military for the good of the Alliance.

In a series of swift and covert actions, Jacen Solo invoked the very laws he had amended to have Omas placed under arrest, and Niathal found herself in the position of acting Chief of State. She wanted everything done by the book so that her ascension to power was legitimate. Eventually Niathal realized that she needed to do everything she could to eliminate Solo. She began secretly feeding information on his activities to Jedi Grand Master Luke Skywalker, in an effort to provide the Jedi with knowledge they could use to bring Jacen to justice.

During the Second Battle of Fondor, Admiral Niathal tried to go along with Solo's battle plans, but was unprepared for his use of battle meditation with the other warship commanders. Her surprise turned to shock when he took the *Anakin Solo* and broke away from the main fleet to begin bombarding Fondorian cities from orbit. After negotiating a cease-fire with the Fondorian President, Admiral Niathal opened a general fleet communications channel and publicly relieved Solo of his command. Solo refused to acknowledge the order. The Imperial forces that had arrived to support the Galactic Alliance also opened fire on Solo, forcing him to regroup and flee back to Coruscant in order to fortify his own position. Recognizing that she would be unable to unseat Solo once he returned to Coruscant, Admiral Niathal assumed a leadership position over any commanders who remained loyal to her, and worked with Shas Vadde and the Fondorians to establish a government-in-exile that stood opposed to Solo's rule of the galaxy. Admiral Niathal and her faction of the Alliance then joined the Jedi Coalition and took part in the Second Battle of Roche alongside the Maw Irregular Fleet of Admiral Daala, but they were defeated and Niathal went missing in action.

*Nield*

**nicely dressed** A slang term used by gamblers to describe any being that was obviously armed. This was considered the opposite of being stylishly dressed. Most bounty hunters were considered nicely dressed, since they often kept their weaponry in plain sight.

**Nichen** A New Republic world that helped tend to the wounded and dead from the loss of the *Kauri* interdiction picket ship during the hunt for the Teljkon vagabond near Gmir Askilon.

**nic-i-tain** An addictive drug found in the t'bac plant.

**Nici the Specialist** This individual was well known to the underworld of Coruscant. For a price, Nici could create a completely new identity—or a changed history—for just about any individual. Han Solo sought out Nici's services after escaping from Ylesia and being apprehended by the manager at the Imperial Bank of Coruscant. Nici gave Han a complete identity change including new retinal patterns in order to mask his past and gain entrance to the Imperial Space Academy.

**Nickel One** This was one of the many asteroids found in the Roche asteroid field. It also served as the adopted homeworld of the Verpine in the wake of the Yuuzhan Vong War. Most of the Verpine's munitions production came from Nickel One, making it a prime target. More than a decade after the Yuuzhan Vong were defeated, the Verpine invited the Mandalorians to establish their own base on Nickel One, after the two groups joined forces in a mutual-aid treaty. The Mandalorian presence on the asteroid was expected to serve as a deterrent to any enemy force.

A group of Imperial warships, however, quickly subdued the asteroid's defenses and landed on its surface. The Imperials next deployed a nanotechnology virus that was similar to the Fizz, but targeted only the warrior caste of the Verpine. They wanted to save as many workers and technicians as possible to help them get Nickel One's munitions factories back online quickly.

But the Imperial presence in the Roche asteroid field brought an instant response from the Galactic Alliance: Darth Caedus himself arrived to make sure that the Moff Council understood that they were not to be making attacks without his involvement. Boba Fett and the Mandalorians also launched a retaliatory attack to honor their mutual-aid treaty with the Verpine. This attack coincided with a Jedi attack on Darth Caedus, during which the fleets controlled by Admirals Daala and Cha Niathal arrived to await the outcome and see what spoils they could claim. Not to be cut off from a primary munitions source, several planetary fleets from the Confederation arrived too, hoping to take advantage of the situation to destroy Caedus and take the Roche asteroid field for themselves.

**Nicta** One of the many small creatures that a young Jacen Solo kept in his collection at the Jedi academy on Yavin 4. Nicta was a gort, and resembled a bright blue ball of feather-like fur.

**Nictoh, Wilyam** This white-haired man worked as a security officer for the CreedCon Construction company on Cularin during the final years of the Old Republic. Nictoh and his crew were dispatched to investigate the disappearance of a construction crew that was working on the bridge portion of a racecourse facility that Thaedius Creed was building, after they accidentally opened the cave that imprisoned a t'salak. The security team was eventually rescued by the freelance adventurers Creed hired to locate the construction crew.

**Nidder, Arl** This redheaded Corellian served Black Sun under the command of Zekka Thyne before the near-human was imprisoned on Kessel. When Grand Admiral Thrawn, disguised as Jodo Kast, infiltrated Thyne's base in Coronet, a firefight erupted and Nidder was killed.

**Nidifer** This man served as a lieutenant commander aboard the Rebel Alliance medical Dreadnaught *Mercy* during the last years of the Galactic Civil War.

***Nidôsh*** The Korunnai word for an orphan. Most often, orphans were given the name of their *ghôsh* as their surname, to signify that they had no parents.

**Nield** This young man, a native of Melida/Daan, was the leader of the Young when Qui-Gon Jinn and Obi-Wan Kenobi arrived on the war-torn planet to search for Tahl. His parents were Daan, although he had disavowed any affiliation with either faction. His father, Micae, led his three oldest sons into battle, but was forced to leave young Nield at home. All four men were killed in an unremembered battle. His mother was killed shortly afterward, and Nield went to live with his cousin, who was soon killed in another useless struggle for control; she was just 17 at the time. He joined the Young after meeting Cerasi and understanding why she lived apart from her parents. Nield's skills in battle and his ability to recognize and teach strategy earned him the position of leader of the Young.

Nield agreed to help the two Jedi locate and rescue Tahl, creating a diversion while Cerasi led them to Tahl. Nield used the animosity between the Daan and the Melida to create the illusion of a Daan attack on a Melida sector. The feint was successful, and the Young eventually defeated the Elders. Nield was named governor of Zehava, but he was unaccustomed to leadership during peace. He demanded that the Halls of Evidence containing reminders of the endless battles be destroyed, despite a lack of support from his cabinet and to the exclusion of more vital activities like providing food and shelter for the inhabitants of Zehava. His resolve was shattered when Cerasi and Obi-Wan petitioned for the cessation of the destruction, and the Young began to splinter.

After Cerasi's death, Nield exiled Obi-Wan from the Young. However, when the Jedi revealed Mawat's plans to oust Nield from power, he decided to honor Cerasi's death by reestablishing peace. He and Obi-Wan managed to defeat Mawat's forces when Qui-Gon showed them all a hologram of Cerasi pleading for peace shortly before her death. Nield then agreed to form a more cooperative government, working in concert with the Daan and Melida Elders to rule the planet.

**Nierport Seven** The seventh moon of Eeropha, Nierport Seven was located in the Core Worlds, not far from Coruscant. It was a cold world, with just a single warm month each year. The surface was rocky, dotted with clumps of a thorny, flowering plant.

**Nie-Tan, Tieren** This horse-faced Jedi Knight was a contemporary of Jude Rozess and Theen Fida. He was on guard when the Yinchorri invaded the Jedi Temple on Coruscant. He and Rozess were caught short by the sheer number of Yinchorri warriors.

**Nigekus, Negus** A New Brigia elder, Nigekus worked his entire life in the planet's chromite mines. He was dying from the constant exposure to chromite dust when the Yevetha arrived to execute the settlers and take control of the mines during the Great Purge. He was killed in the Yevethan assault.

**nightbat** Large, insectile bats that were native to the planet Dagobah. They had leathery wings and six thin legs. Each leg had a set of small, sharp claws.

**night beast** This huge, humanoid creature was left behind by the ancient Massassi to keep Yavin 4 safe until they could return. Originally a Massassi warrior named Kalgrath, the night beast was held in suspended animation for millennia until Admiral Griff launched his attack on the Rebel Alliance base on Yavin 4. A TIE bomber crashed on the moon, penetrating the Great Temple's lower levels and cracking the beast's suspended-animation capsule open. It then began to roam the tunnels of the temple, destroying Alliance equipment in what it believed was the fulfillment of its purpose. It had some connection with the Force, and used it to shield itself from energy weapons. When Luke Skywalker discovered the creature, he and R2-D2 were able to drive it away by using the Force to lure the beast into a space transport. They had programmed the transport for auto-jump, and once the night beast was inside, they initiated the launch sequence. The beast was sent into hyperspace. One of the random jumps performed by the transport brought the beast back to Alliance space. This time, through the Force, Luke explained that the beast would eventually find its former masters by getting onto the transport.

**Night Blades Squadron** This starfighter unit, led by Saba Sebatyne and made up of Jedi Knights, was part of the Galactic Alliance First Fleet's starfighter complement during the defense of Kuat, at the height of the GA-Confederation War. Like the Shadow Saber and Dark Sword squadrons, the Night Blades abandoned the Kuat battlefield and joined Jedi Grand Master Luke Skywalker in defecting from the Alliance. After regrouping at Kashyyyk, the Jedi were attacked by Jacen Solo and the Alliance's Fifth Fleet, forcing the squadrons back into battle. The Night Blades were the first to suffer casualties, as the *Vulnerator* was able to pinpoint their stealth fighters and shoot down three ships.

***Night Caller*** One of the CR90 corvettes under the command of Apwar Trigit, the *Night Caller* was heavily modified from its original specifications during its initial design. The bow was widened and much of it gutted to allow for a small TIE fighter hangar, while the topside hold was enlarged to act as a storage hold for skimmers. One of the turbolaser turrets on the bow was replaced with a capital ship tractor beam.

The *Night Caller* was dispatched to destroy the New Republic's base on Folor using Empion mines. While it succeeded in knocking out much of the base, the *Night Caller* was captured when Wraith Squadron pilots created the *Lunatic* and lured the *Night Caller* in to capture it. Voort saBinring was hidden inside, and when the *Lunatic* was drawn into the ship's hold, he managed to take control of the bridge and capture the ship for the New Republic. The crew was so taken aback by Voort's attack that they didn't wipe out the ship's computer memory banks, nor did they get off a distress call to Trigit.

The *Night Caller*'s flight logs led the Wraiths to several of Warlord Zsinj's holdings. Since the warlord and Trigit were unaware that the ship had been captured, Wedge Antilles and Choday Hrakness continued to respond to their orders, and then had the Wraiths fly in after and seemingly attack them. The *Night Caller* was later reassigned to another Republic flight group and renamed the *Ession Strike.*

*Night beast*

**nightcrawler (1)** According to Wookiee legends, this creature inhabited the lowest levels of Kashyyyk's jungles, feeding on the blood and spirit of its victims.

**nightcrawler (2)** An insect native to Tatooine, the nightcrawler was a nocturnal predator.

**night creatures** Alchemical beasts created during Exar Kun's rule on Yavin 4, these hideous winged reptiles had yellow eyes on both of the heads that sprouted from its neck. The creatures had purple blood, and their tails were hooked at the end. The hook contained a crystalline poison. They were covered in scales and had metallic claws.

**night-demon** These creatures had razor-sharp talons that delivered a burning poison to flesh.

***Nightfall*** This Sith Destroyer was the flagship of the naval forces of the Brotherhood of Darkness during the Battle of Ruusan. Commanded by Admiral Adrianna Nyras, the *Nightfall* was at the forefront of the Sith blockade of Ruusan, preventing any Jedi reinforcements from reaching the planet's surface.

**night-flyer** A creature out of Wookiee legend, it was noted for its high-pitched screech.

**night-glider** This avian species was native to the planet Altarrn; they often were sold as exotic pets.

***Nighthawk*** A battered old B-7 light freighter discovered by Yoda aboard Jovan Station during the Jedi Master's mission to locate Count Dooku on Vjun. Yoda and a pair of Padawans had been attacked on Phindar, and were forced to improvise a way to reach Vjun. After taking a rental ship to reach Jovan, they were able to purchase the *Nighthawk* from a scrap yard. With a little work, the ship got them to Vjun without much trouble. Yoda put the two Padawans—Whie Malreaux and Tallisibeth Enwandung-Esterhazy—to work on the repairs in an effort to take their minds off the deaths of their Masters at Phindar.

**Night Herald** A legendary creature of the Colony, the story of the Night Herald was used to make larvae regurgitate. Some six years after the Yuuzhan Vong War ended, the name of the Night Herald was adopted by Alema Rar following the death of Welk on Kr during the Qoribu crisis. According to the former Jedi, BedaGorog was the original Night Herald, but after she was killed on Kr by Luke Skywalker, Alema took on her role. The story was a lie, since Skywalker actually had killed Welk on Kr. Still, Alema Rar believed that it was her job to ensure that the rest of the galaxy did not interfere with the work of the Colony or the Gorog.

Nightshrike attacks Luke Skywalker.

**nightmare demon** These feared beasts were humanoid in shape, with heads that resembled a bare skull. They had the ability to cloud minds and create illusions, luring prey close enough to pounce on it. They were supposedly wiped out during the Clone Wars, but Luke Skywalker encountered the demon Reist on Lapez 3.

**Nightmare Machine** This attraction was found on Hologram Fun World. As visitors entered a large room that was initially dark, the machine scanned their brains to discover their worst fears. It then displayed a vividly accurate hologram of those fears. The machine was the creation of Borborygmus Gog, and was used to quell rebellious individuals. It was part of Project Starscream; the machine was an experiment aimed at providing Gog with a way to use a being's deepest fears as a weapon. The Nightmare Machine itself was actually a bioengineered construct. The technology eventually was modified to create a biological weapon known as Eppon, which Gog used against several Rebel Alliance soldiers on the planet Kiva.

***NightRunner*** A Ghtroc Class 720 freighter operated by the pirates of Bazak's Gang. It supported the boarding actions of the Skipray blastboats *Slicer* and *Slasher*. It was armed with a double laser cannon and turret-mounted laser cannon.

**Night Shade** This rough-and-tumble cantina was in the city of ChikatLik, on the planet Ord Cestus, in the last decades of the Old Republic. It served as a front for the criminal organization commanded by Trillot, who worked from an office hidden in caves below.

**nightshrike** This vicious, avian predator was native to the planet Monastery. Primarily a nocturnal creature, the black-skinned nightshrike used the cover of darkness to attack and kill its prey. It was found mainly in the planet's rainforests.

**Nightsisters** A group of the Witches of Dathomir who had turned to the dark side of the Force. The Nightsisters enslaved Imperial guards at a Dathomir prison and attempted to flee the planet four years after the Battle of Endor. They were vanquished by Luke Skywalker, Leia Organa, and Han Solo, but 15 years later a new threat arose. These Nightsisters were younger, stronger, and allied with Imperial forces seeking to regain control of the galaxy.

**Night Spirit** An evil entity on the Forest Moon of Endor that was feared by Ewoks and worshipped by Duloks. The Night Spirit sometimes manifested itself as a ghostly apparition.

**nightswift** These nocturnal, carnivorous creatures were native to Kamar. They were also a source of food for the Kamarians.

***Night Terror*** An Imperial Star Destroyer active during the early years of the New Republic.

**Nightview macrobinoculars** Manufactured by Naescorcom during the final years of the Old Republic, Nightview macrobinoculars were similar in most respects to snooper goggles. They allowed the user to see during daylight hours or at night, although the resolution during the day was considered average to poor by most. However, the night vision afforded by the Nightview was far superior to similar units on the market at the time.

**NightWhispers** One of the Empire's most elite stormtrooper units, a part of the Storm Commandos. They were sent into the field whenever incredible stealth was required to gain access to an enemy target.

**Nightwing** This was the call sign of a member of the Thaereian Navy during the Clone Wars. He originally joined the military to protect his homeworld, although he was one of the few soldiers who truly understood that protection often meant taking the fight to a superior enemy. His beliefs were challenged when he was confronted by Commander Kulkis, who tested Nightwing's resolve by drawing a knife on the soldier. Nightwing was prepared for the attack, and managed to twist the knife so that it stabbed into Kulkis's chest when they fell to the ground. Nightwing believed that he had passed whatever test Kulkis had meant for him, although Kulkis's final words caused him to question the need to continue defending Thaere. Many of the Cularin NewsNets were abuzz with activity after an account of Nightwing's actions was posted.

***Nigiro*** An Imperial freighter destroyed by Keyan Farlander during his first tour of duty as an X-wing pilot.

***Nihil*** One of the many *Imperial*-class Star Destroyers that made up the Imperial Navy fleet during the Galactic Civil War.

**Nihilus, Darth** One of three Sith Lords, along with Darth Traya and Darth Sion, who survived the Jedi Civil Wars and fled to Malachor V nearly 4,000 years before the Galactic Civil War. Darth Nihilus was known as the Lord of Hunger and was noted for his ability to literally consume the Force energy of his victims, which was used to sustain his own life energies. It was rumored that he could consume the Force energy of an entire planet. He had been taken in by Darth Traya and trained in the ways of the Sith, until he attained enough power to earn the title of Darth Nihilus and formed the Sith triumvirate with his fellow Dark Lords. Together they planned to finally wipe out the Jedi and take control of the galaxy. Soon, however, Nihilus and Sion overthrew Traya and went their separate ways.

Darth Nihilus began his Jedi purge by obliterating the planet Katarr, where a secret conclave of the most powerful Jedi was taking place. It was also there that he took an apprentice, a young Miraluka woman, Visas Marr. Together, they later discovered the existence of the Jedi Exile, and Nihilus recognized the threat that the former Jedi posed to the Sith. He ordered Marr to bring the Exile to him, but she chose to join the Exile rather than betray her. In the meantime, Darth Nihilus led

Darth Nihilus

Darth Nihl

his Sith forces from his flagship, the *Ravager,* drawing more and more power from worlds that he blasted into ruin. On the mission to destroy Telos, Darth Nihilus finally was confronted by the Exile and her team.

Although Darth Nihilus managed to stun the Exile, he was unprepared for the devotion of his former pupil Marr to the young woman. Marr tried to exchange her life for that of the Exile, giving the former Jedi time to recover. Together, they confronted Darth Nihilus. The Sith Lord was no match for their combined might, and he fell in battle. As he died, Darth Nihilus's body seemed to melt away into nothingness, as he somehow managed to encase his spirit in his battle armor. When the armor was transported to Korriban for burial, his spirit traveled with it, and the connection to Korriban's dark side nexus allowed the spirit of Nihilus to maintain contact with the physical world.

That spirit remained hidden on Korriban for millennia until Darth Krayt discovered a Sith Holocron that allowed him to commune with Nihilus and other Sith spirits more than a century after the Galactic Civil War. Darth Krayt hoped to learn more of the ancient secrets of Sith power, but the many Sith spirits refused to simply turn over the information. They believed that Krayt was little more than a pretender, and that so-called Rule of One was only diluting the power of the Sith, rather than concentrating it.

**Nihl, Darth** One of Darth Krayt's Sith warriors about 130 years after the Battle of Yavin, the former Nagai warlord became Krayt's Hand along with Darth Talon. He helped lead the massacre on Ossus at the Jedi academy, killing Kol Skywalker, Cade Skywalker's father, and slicing off the right arm of Wolf Sazen. After Cade was captured on Coruscant when he attempted to rescue Jedi Hosk Trey'lis from the Temple of the Sith, he was brought before Darth Krayt, along with Darths Talon and Nihl and Trey'lis. Skywalker was ordered to kill Trey'lis or be killed himself. He refused and Krayt himself executed Trey'lis. Skywalker became enraged, grabbed his father's nearby lightsaber from its enclosure and stabbed Darth Talon in the stomach. He then fought Darth Nihl, severed his arm, knocked him unconscious and pelted him with Force lightning as he began moving toward the dark side. Darth Krayt ordered Skywalker to kill the weakened Nihl, but he refused because it was what Krayt wanted.

**Niik, Li-Suun** This well-known crime lord operated a bold and fearless smuggling operation from a base on the planet Aargau during the Galactic Civil War. Li-Suun and his crew used a variety of methods to smuggle precious metals off the planet, including surgically attaching sheets of gold to bones. Unknown to most beings, Li-Suun was also somewhat sensitive to the Force, although he was self-trained.

**Nikals, Lieutenant Gerrin** An officer in the Imperial Army. He commanded the Kal'Shebbol Fury platoon during the early years of the New Republic.

**Nikk, Hatras** This woman made a living as a con artist on the Outland Transit Station following the Battle of Naboo, until Rozatta placed a bounty on her head. She was accused of seducing many travelers before robbing them. She was caught by Jango Fett and brought to Rozatta for questioning.

**nikkle nut** This plentiful plant, which produced a thick-shelled nut, was native to the jungles of Haruun Kal.

**Ni'Korish** A political faction formed by those who agreed with the former Hapan Queen Mother Ni'Korish, Ta'a Chume's grandmother, that the Jedi Knights were among the most despicable beings in the galaxy. The Ni'Korish likely were behind several assassination attempts on the life of Teneniel Djo during her tenure as the Queen Mother of Hapes.

**Niktha** This Jawa was part of a roaming group of beggars that accosted visitors and inhabitants of Mos Eisley for handouts in the years before the Battle of Naboo. When several patrons of the Dusty Bowl saloon began to complain about his smell and aggressive begging techniques, the saloon owners issued a bounty for his arrest. Jango Fett claimed it quickly during a mission to Tatooine.

**Nikto** A humanoid species with flat faces and multiple nostrils from the planet Kintan in the Si'klaata Cluster. The species was made up of five distinct races differentiated by skin color and facial and other features. The most prominent group had four small horns protruding from their foreheads. They were an ancient species, being one of three signed into servitude to the Hutts as part of the Treaty of Vontor, during the Hutts' battles against Xim the Despot.

The Nikto were characterized by their leathery skin, reptilian eyes, and fierce temperaments. The skin of a Nikto was made up of thousands of overlapping scales, which could be shifted to cover wounds and protect against infection. All five races were genetically capable of interbreeding, although 93 percent of the offspring from such unions resembled only one of the parents. Those few individuals who exhibited the characteristics of both parents were often ostracized and abused as mixed breeds, and were often forced to find work offplanet.

A number of environmental and geological changes greatly affected life on Kintan, causing the once singular Nikto to evolve its five unique races. Chief among these changes was the radiation expelled by the nearby star, M'dweshuu, which held a significant place in Nikto mythology. The Red Nikto, called Kajain'sa'Nikto, evolved in the deserts. They had ridged foreheads, with eight small horns around the eyes, and two at the chin. They breathed through a permeable membrane that covered their mouths, as well as through four breather tubes on their necks. The Green Nikto, known as Kadas'sa'Nikto, evolved in the forests. They were visibly scaled, with obvious noses and small horns ringing their eyes. The Mountain Nikto, called Esral'sa'Nikto, had smooth skin. Their ears were large and fin-shaped, able to be extended or pulled flat to regulate body heat and enhance hearing. They also had a nasal membrane similar to the Red Nikto. The Pale Nikto, or Gluss'sa'Nikto, were found on the islands of the planet. They resembled the Green Nikto, with fin-like ears. The last group, called M'shento'su'Nikto or Southern Nikto, lacked any horns but had a number of breather tubes at various points on their skulls.

The inner strength and fierce nature of the Nikto species in general was honed over millennia of survival against the predators of Kintan. This led to four intense civil wars that nearly destroyed Kintan some 30 years before the Nikto helped the Hutts defeat Xim, long before the formation of the Old Republic. After Xim was defeated, the Hutts then distributed the Nikto to various worlds as bodyguards and strongmen.

On Kintan, the Nikto developed atomic-level technology on their own, and absorbed other galactic technology from the Hutts. Because of the Treaty of Vontor, the Nikto remained under Hutt control for over 25,000 years, and for the most part they remained neutral throughout the various battles of the Galactic Civil War. Because of this, many Nikto individuals who were sensitive to the Force remained undiscovered by the Jedi Knights, although a few Nikto escaped slavery to become Jedi.

One of five races of Nikto

**Nil** This Quint worked as a guard for Jenna Zan Arbor at her secret laboratory on Simpla-12. He was jealously loyal to Arbor, and resented the bond she seemed to form with her Force-sensitive test subjects. Qui-Gon Jinn managed to use Nil's anger as a lever, escaping twice from under Nil's guard. Luckily for Nil, he was recaptured by Arbor each time. Unluckily for Nil, Arbor grew tired of his inability to contain the Jedi and injected the Quint with a lethal dose of drugs.

*Nim*

**Nim** This short, round man was a general in the Imperial armed forces, shortly before the Battle of Yavin. He was ordered by Darth Vader to destroy the Icarii, and with Colonel Abal Karda laid out plans for their destruction. Karda carried out his orders perfectly, but managed to capture the Icarii queen, Selestrine. Vader wanted her brought to him, and Nim was dispatched to recover her disembodied head, which was still alive. However, Karda grew jealous and angry, and his mental condition deteriorated. He killed Nim and his guards to retain possession of the head, then fled the Empire and was labeled a fugitive.

**Nim, Oso** A Duros encountered by Han Solo and Leia Organa on Belsavis, in the Smoking Jets cantina. Nim provided them with information on Drub McKumb and Plett's house. She met Drub just before he disappeared. Nim also provided leads on Nubblyk's operations on Belsavis.

**Niman** This style of sword fighting was originally developed by the Royal Macheteros of the Kashi Mer, although it was later claimed by the Legions of Lettow. Named for two groups of three Kashi gods, Niman was a two-handed fighting style that employed one blade for offense; the other could be used for parrying or for additional attacks. After the Legions of Lettow were defeated by the ancient Jedi Knights, the Jedi adopted both the two-handed fighting technique and its name. Over time, Niman became known as Form VI lightsaber combat. Although many Jedi trained in the Niman style to gain basic knowledge of a two-bladed attack, very few ever mastered it completely, for true mastery came only after 10 or more years of study and practice. Those who managed to understand the style used it to improve their single-lightsaber combat form.

**Nima'tar** This noted Twi'lek female was a scholar known for her treatises and theories on the civilization and society of the Hutts. During her education, Nima'tar was a singer for a small band, traveling the galaxy in order to earn enough credits to pay for her schooling. The band accepted a gig with Jabba the Hutt, and her band mates sold her into slavery to buy passage off Tatooine. Nima'tar was forced to work as a dancer for Jabba, all the while collecting notes and data for her doctorate work. She used her wits and brains—and some help from Tamtel Skreej—to escape from Jabba and return to school, completing her education.

**Nimbanel (Plural: Nimbanese)** Humanoid reptiles with endothermic metabolism and pale, scaleless skin that were native to the planet Nimban in the Outer Rim. They had the distinction of being the only species that actively petitioned the Hutts, requesting to be put into their servitude. A Nimbanel usually placed great value on knowledge and work ethics.

**Nimbi, Jasper** The doctor in charge of the recovery of Jedi Master Eelysa shortly before the Second Battle of Coruscant. Dr. Nimbi found himself treating Leia Organa Solo as well when she was transported to Corellia by her husband, Han, to allow her to recover from the injuries she sustained during the Battle of Duro. Dr. Nimbi was sympathetic to the Jedi Knights, even in the face of the Yuuzhan Vong invasion, and maintained tight security in his facility so that Eelysa could heal.

**Nimbus Rider 2000** Gefferon's Hutt floater, this 4-meter craft was designed for those Hutts who couldn't afford a luxurious sail barge or a larger floater.

**Nim Drovis** Located in the Drovian system of the Meridian sector, the rainy world of Nim Drovis (sometimes called Drovis) contained a Sector Medical Facility and Medical Research Facility run by the Ho'Din physician Dr. Ism Oolos, along with a small New Republic base. Before they were contacted by the Old Republic, the Drovians were a primitive species organized into a network of tribes. Many were addicted to the narcotic zwil, which they absorbed by inserting fist-sized plugs into their membrane-lined breathing tubes. The largest free port on Nim Drovis was Bagsho, originally settled by colonists from Alderaan. It turned into a link between the sector's neutral worlds and the New Republic.

Natives were bottom-heavy and had tentacles with pincers on the ends; many different sensory devices studded their bodies. The Gopso'o tribes (with braided topknots) operated slug-ranches, and were the ancient enemies of the Drovians. Architecture consisted of heavy stone walls and thick wooden supports with many balconies. Swamps, mud, mold, fungus, and reeds predominated. Animal life included marsh-gunnies, gulpers, and green-eyed wadie-platts.

*Nimbanel*

Nine years after the Battle of Endor, R2-D2 and C-3PO forced the looter Captain Bortrek to land them on Nim Drovis. They tried to earn passage to Cybloc XII at the Chug 'n' Chuck and the Wookiee's Codpiece taverns. Yarbolk Yemm, a Chadra-Fan reporter for TriNebulon News, saved them from being stolen. At the same time, Han Solo brought several survivors of the crashed ship *Corbantis* to the Bagsho medical facility to treat their radiation burns. Forty people at the Republic base had already died from the Death Seed plague.

**Nimondro, Chief** This Hobor was the leader of his people, representing them at the peace talks conducted by the Tion Hegemony. He had a deep hatred of the Troobs and chose to speak only Tahlboorean in their presence. This was a ploy by Chief Nimondro, for he could understand and speak fluent Basic, but held on to this trump card to gain the upper hand against his rivals. Nimondro also controlled Mount Yeroc and used it to demonstrate his powerful position during the negotiations. His daughter, Larka, was the light of his life, and when she was framed for the murder of the Troob Ket Krax, he was furious. When she told him that she had been in love with Krax, the son of the Troob leader, he realized she was innocent, and prepared to use the sky cannon inside Mount Yeroc to defend against an impending Troob attack. However, C-3PO and R2-D2 were able to convince him to let them use the sky cannon for its true purpose—communications—while exposing Jake Harthan as the killer. Nimondro then agreed to work with the elder Krax to hammer out a real peace agreement.

**Nim'Ri** This yellow-scaled Trandoshan male was the head of security for House Hirskaala, on the planet Cularin, during the years around the Battle of Naboo. It was later discovered that Nim'Ri was also one of the founding members of the underground alliance that sprang up on Cularin in response to the buildup of power by the Metatheran Cartel. Nim'Ri quit his job with House Hirskaala to join the resistance, believing that the freedom of Cularin was much more important than an individual trading company. Shortly after the start of the Clone Wars, Nim'Ri suddenly disappeared, although rumors began to circulate that he was "headed home." Most natives of Cularin could not believe this rumor, since Nim'Ri had been born on Cularin. They did, however, believe that Nim'Ri had been captured and possibly executed by the Thaereian Military for his rebellious actions.

**ninchif** These small fish lived in tiny, water-filled caves deep below the surface of Tatooine. They were harvested for their tasty flesh, and were often served fried.

**Nine** This was the simple designation used by Mara Jade Skywalker to describe the R9 series astromech unit that was assigned to her StealthX fighter during the Swarm War.

**Nine Corellian Hells** The Corellian people believed that there were nine distinct levels of Hell into which beings would fall if they were deemed unworthy after death. Many Corellians used an oath similar to "Where in the Nine Corellian Hells am I?" when they were unexpectedly lost.

**Niner** This clone commando—officially known as RC-1309—survived the Battle of Geonosis, but the remainder of his squad was killed. Niner was put into Omega Squad and he became its leader, effectively utilizing the skills of each member to their greatest advantage. He led with his actions, although he sometimes tried to lighten up a situation with humor. This usually failed, and his repeated attempts often drew more good-natured laughs than his jokes. Among the other members of the squad, Niner was known for his cool demeanor under fire, and was said to show emotion only when his squad was improperly attired.

Among his squad's many missions was the rescue of Senator Meena Tills and other hostages from terrorists on Coruscant. Omega Squad was sent to Gaftikar to assist local rebels. There, squad members spotted ARC trooper A-30—also known as Sull—who had gone MIA. *Null*-class trooper A'den headed the search and when Sull was brought in, he interrogated him closely. A'den believed Sull's claim that deserting troopers were summarily shot by the Republic, raising questions about all of their fates once the war ended. A'den freed Sull despite strenuous objections from Niner, who threatened that neither he nor the other members of Omega Squad would ever help A'den again.

**Nineteenth Battle of Zehava** This struggle for control of the city of Zehava was initiated by the Melida just six months after the Eighteenth Battle. The Daan had used the underground tunnels and drains of Zehava to gain access to Melida-held territory, and soundly defeated them.

**Ningal's Droid Repair** This facility was located on the planet Vannix during the Yuuzhan Vong War.

**Ningo, Dua** This aging Sullustan served the Confederacy of Independent Systems as a naval officer during the Clone Wars. Ningo commanded the Bulwark Fleet, and was ordered to capture Coruscant about two years into the fighting. His fleet was chased away from the city-world by the might of the Old Republic's new *Victory*-class Star Destroyers, and he was hounded through several other star systems by the Victory Fleet before he was killed during the Battle of Anaxes.

**Nink** One of a pair of dwarf opee sea killers kept at the Otoh Gunga Zoological Research Facility before the Battle of Naboo. The dwarf opees were the facility's rarest and most valuable specimens. Despite being just as vicious as their larger cousins, Nink and Vink were also able to understand simple commands after being trained by the researchers.

**Ninn** This planet was known for its devoted priesthood. The Priests of Ninn wore green vestments that served to announce their devotion.

**Ninth Fleet** One of the major divisions of the naval forces that protected the Galactic Alliance in the wake of the Yuuzhan Vong War. The Ninth Fleet was one of three naval units, along with the Third and Eighth fleets, assigned to the General Crix Madine Military Reserve during the Galactic Alliance's fleet reorganization and consolidation actions.

Although the exploits of the Third and Eighth fleets were well known to most military personnel, the Ninth Fleet remained a mystery for many years. Because its strength and makeup were unknown to most military analysts, the Ninth Fleet became the obvious choice for the Galactic Alliance to send to Gilatter VIII when Intelligence reported that the leaders of the Confederation were meeting there at the height of the Corellia-GA War.

**Ninth quadrant** An area of space near the Senex and Juvex sectors, it contained the Greeb-Streebling Cluster, the Noopiths, and the planet Belsavis. The quadrant was relatively isolated, and its systems were far apart.

Shug Ninx

**Ninx, Shug** A half-breed in the eyes of the Empire, this master mechanic had a Corellian father and a mother from the near-extinct Theelin species. The genetic cocktail produced Shug Ninx—mostly human, bearing mottled spots around his mouth and chin and hands with a thumb and two fingers. He developed great skill for fixing machinery—especially spaceships—and went to the Smugglers' moon of Nar Shaddaa, where he set up his own large shop or "spacebarn."

Ninx was friendly with many of the young smugglers and blockade-runners, including the Corellian Han Solo; Han's one-time lady friend Salla Zend; his copilot, the Wookiee Chewbacca; and his gambling buddy Lando Calrissian. Ninx's spacebarn became a hangout. As time passed, Zend became an employee and then a business partner. Their relationship solidified over the years, during which time Ninx continued to grow in expertise. His starship garage was located within the spaceport's inner depths, its entrance hidden by a large holoscreen. The entry was a kilometers-long chute built out of a construction module from the second Death Star prototype. (He found the surplus on Bonadan.)

Six years after the Battle of Endor, Ninx and Zend finally saw Solo again—this time with his wife, Leia Organa Solo, on a mission to save her brother, Luke Skywalker. Han was betrayed to bounty hunters, but Ninx and Zend saved him, not for the last time. Later they escaped from the planet Byss along with top Rebel Alliance officials, went to help in the fierce Battle of Mon Calamari, and later returned to Nar Shaddaa, only to find that Ninx's facility had been infiltrated by dark troopers. Back on Byss during an Alliance attack, Ninx and Zend, aided by other smugglers, helped rescue several Alliance heroes. They also helped save Leia and her children from an Imperial attack on New Alderaan. Shug Ninx and Salla Zend left the spaceport after Han Solo accidentally destroyed one of their prized cruisers escaping from Boba Fett, and after Zasm Katth and Baddon Fass had ransacked the garage.

**Niopua, Ihu** A Senator during the final years of the Old Republic, he praised the Coruscant Security Force for smashing a terrorist ring, completely unaware that the entire operation had been masterminded by Kal Skirata and executed by the clone commandos of Delta and Omega Squads.

**Nippet** A baby Ewok, or Wokling, at the time of the Battle of Endor. Princess Kneesaa often babysat for her.

**Nirama** This strange alien, a member of the Oblee species, was one of the major crime lords in the Cularin system during the last years of the Old Republic. Much of his work, however, went toward ensuring the safety and security of the system, rather than plunging it into chaos.

**Nirauan** The second and primary world in the Nirauan system, part of the Gradilis sector. A dim red star was the system's central body. The planet itself was a drab, seemingly lifeless world when viewed from space, with dull browns and grays dominating the surface. It was covered in vegetation, although the normally green color had given way to the duller colors in order to survive in the pale light received

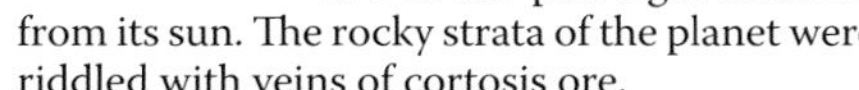

from its sun. The rocky strata of the planet were riddled with veins of cortosis ore.

It was here that Mara Jade Skywalker plotted the course of strange starships that began showing up around the time of the discovery of the Caamas Document. Hidden deep in a cave, Jade found the entrance to a huge fortress similar to those located on Hijarna. She also found a group of mynock-like creatures that seemed to communicate by sending thoughts through the Force. They later revealed themselves to be of two species, the Qom Qae and the Qom Jha. They registered a marked reaction when she talked about Luke Skywalker, and they eventually helped Luke and Mara infiltrate the fortress known as the Hand of Thrawn. It was a five-tower citadel maintained by the Chiss in hope of Grand Admiral Thrawn's reappearance 10 years after his death.

At some point during the Yuuzhan Vong War, the facility on Nirauan was abandoned by the Empire of the Hand, which inexplicably disappeared. The Chiss Ruling Circle refused to divulge any information on why Nirauan was abandoned.

Xecr Nist

**Niriz, Captain Dagon** A fourth-generation navy officer, he commanded the *Imperial I*-class Star Destroyer *Admonitor* prior to the Battle of Endor. He was later assigned to Admiral Thrawn for a mapping expedition in the Unknown Regions, and saw the reassignment as a blow to his career. But after he passed a loyalty test, Thrawn revealed the true nature of the mission: conquering the Unknown Regions for the Galactic Empire. Successes followed and the conquered area became known as the Empire of the Hand.

**Niro** This planet and its numerous moons were owned by the InterGalactic Banking Clan prior to the Clone Wars.

**Nirrelz, Nathanjo** A Gotal emissary to Atzerri from Antar 4 just before the start of the Clone Wars, he was held hostage for a week by the Roshu Sune guerrillas to try to force his planet to secede from the Republic. He was rescued by a group of Jedi.

**Nirsh** This man was a member of the Blood-Scar pirates and one of the Commodore's bodyguards at the base on Gepparin during the New Order.

**Niru** This feline humanoid was part of a rogue group of Rebel Alliance supporters who worked from a hidden base in the Cantros system. Unlike most of her group, Niru didn't believe that the war against the Empire would be won with more violence. Her views were not shared by Durne, who tried to murder her to silence her voice. Luke Skywalker prevented him from completing the task and Niru captured Durne before he could escape.

**Niruu Plateau** This flatland was located on the grassy plains of Ansion.

**nisbat** This small insect was raised by the Yuuzhan Vong as an organic tracking mechanism. Each nisbat in a hatching could sense the presence of its hatchmates over a distance. As one member got closer to another, the nisbat would emit a buzzing noise that got louder as the two creatures neared. Thus, the Yuuzhan Vong could implant one nisbat into the body of a being and use a hatchmate of the implant to locate the being by the strength of the buzzing sound.

Niru

**Nisewarner, Semmac** The Bakuran captain of the *Intruder.*

**Nish** Sentient near-humans native to the planet Nishr, they were subjugated by the Empire and reluctant to assist the Rebel Alliance Special Forces unit that arrived on the planet. They allowed the group to set up bases, but remained neutral in order to avoid Imperial retribution. The Nish were undergoing an industrial revolution at the time of the Battle of Yavin.

**Niskooen, Osos** A Verpine soldier who lived and worked on the Nickel One asteroid, he was picked as a guide for Boba Fett and Jaina Solo during the Battle of Roche. Niskooen's thorax was split open in an attack, killing him almost instantly.

**Nist, Xecr** One of the reborn Emperor Palpatine's personal advisers, Nist was promoted to Military Executor of Operation Shadow Hand after Sedriss and Vill Goir were killed on Ossus. Palpatine granted him the powers of a Dark Jedi as part of the promotion. However, after Palpatine's final clone died on Onderon, Xecr Nist was captured by Luke Skywalker and imprisoned.

Het Nkik

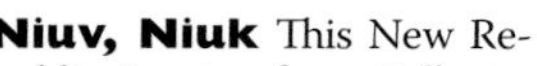
**Niuv, Niuk** This New Republic Senator from Sullust, was a member of the Advisory Council at the start of the Yuuzhan Vong invasion. He didn't support Luke Skywalker's plans to reestablish the Jedi Council, and there were rumors of the Senator's ties to smugglers that the Jedi were putting out of business. When Leia Organa Solo petitioned the Senate to address the Yuuzhan Vong crisis, Niuk Niuv accused her of trying to deflect the issue of renegade Jedi with wildly exaggerated views of the threat. Later, when it was learned that the Yuuzhan Vong planned to attack either Corellia or Bothawui, Niuv argued that Corellia be left undefended so that Bothawui could be saved. Later in the war, when the Senate reconvened on Mon Calamari, Niuv had become a vocal proponent of eradicating the Yuuzhan Vong completely, much to the chagrin of Chief of State Cal Omas and the Jedi Knights.

**Nive, Jacob** The captain of the CR90 corvette *Backstab,* Jacob Nive was one of the few Eyttyrmin Batiiv pirates to survive an Imperial attack that wiped out most of the group. Those left called themselves the Khuiumin Survivors; they retreated to the Elrood sector, and established a foothold there by raiding Imperial convoys destined for Derilyn and Berea. He later jumped at an offer from Luke Skywalker and Corran Horn to turn himself and the Survivors into legitimate members of the New Republic.

**Nivek** This red-skinned humanoid with strange blue appendages sprouting from his head was one of Jabba the Hutt's many followers. He lived in the Hutt's palace, but he was secretly employed by Bib Fortuna to kill Jabba. Nivek recruited six others, but their plot ran headlong into another assassination attempt and in the ensuing melee, Fortuna shot Nivek in the head to shut him up.

**Nivek'Yppiks** Boba Fett received half a million credits for recovering this Ffib, who had fled the religious oligarchy on Lorahns.

**Nivers, Grand Moff** An Imperial official whose fiefdom included the planet Tandankin sometime after the Battle of Endor. His reign there lasted less than a day after Rogue Squadron destroyed Nivers's entire fleet of TIE fighters and captured him.

**Nixor** This Mid Rim planet was the homeworld of a species of the same name. During the early years of the New Order, Nixor was known as a place for an independent starship captain to hide from the Empire. However, the spaceports were poorly maintained, mainly because the Nixor wanted nothing to do with either the Old Republic or the Empire and their regulations.

**Nizon** This ball of rock orbited by two moons was the fifth planet of the Centares system, located in the Mid Rim. When the planet was discovered to be the homeworld of the Nazren, it was subjugated by the Empire. The Nazren were sold into slavery, in exchange for Tibanna gas, until a group of freelance agents helped the Nazren fight back against the Imperials and retake their homeworld.

**Njinska's Tavern** This restaurant on Phyrstal Island, on Abregado-rae, was located in a small, wooden building made more attractive through the liberal use of large panes of stained-glass art.

**Nkik, Het** A Jawa scout, he wanted to avenge the deaths of his relatives, who were killed in their sandcrawler by stormtroopers. Het Nkik

had an opportunity to kill several troopers but realized too late that someone had stolen the powerpack from his blaster. He died at the hands of the very troopers he had sought to kill.

**Nkik, Jek** One of Het Nkik's Jawa clansmen, and Het's best friend. They once recovered an E522 assassin droid from a crashed starship in the desert, rebuilt it, and created a passable messenger droid that they sold to Lady Valarian. Jek was a member of the Jawa clan that sold R2-D2 and C-3PO to Owen Lars, and he perished in the Imperial assault on his clan's sandcrawler.

**Nkllon** Located in the Athega system, this super-hot planet closely orbited its star. Any ships approaching the planet had to ride behind the cooled umbrellas of massive shieldships until reaching Nkllon's shadow, or they risked critical solar damage. Lando Calrissian constructed a constantly moving mining platform, inspired by a similar design for the planet Miser, which could stay permanently on the shadow side during Nkllon's 90-day rotation. The platform, Nomad City, consisted mainly of a Dreadnaught cruiser supported by 40 Imperial walkers. It held a crew of 5,000 and was surrounded by a cloud of shuttles, pilot vehicles, and mole miners. Some of the metals mined included hfredium, kammris, and dolovite. An attack on Nomad City by the Star Destroyer *Judicator* resulted in the theft of 51 mole miners, and another Imperial attack critically damaged the city and resulted in the loss of its strategic metals stockpiles.

**Nkllonian lava extract** This illegal drug was named for its color, which many beings thought looked as if it had been taken directly from the molten rock of the planet Nkllon. In fact, it was actually a liquefied form of xonolite that was refined by the jawenko lava beasts of Mustafar and transported to Nkllon by Mustafarian smugglers. Much of the Nkllonian lava extract found on the black market was cut with other liquid metals, since pure xonolite caused many beings to spontaneously combust.

**N-K Necrosis** This experimental form of combat automaton was developed by Imperial scientists on Kashyyyk during the early years of the New Order. The designs for the N-K Necrosis droid were originally conceived by Dr. Nycolai Kinesworthy, for whom the droid was named. Kinesworthy and Treun Lorn hired the darksider known as Merilli to travel to Utapau and recover the mechanical exoskeleton of General Grievous, which served as the basis for the N-K series. Only one droid was ever produced. A band of mercenaries discovered Kinesworthy's lab and ransacked it, destroying Necrosis and its NK-3 training droids.

**NL-6** This series of household courtesy droids was produced during the early years of the New Republic.

**Nlora** A flower known for its cloying, perfume-like scent.

**N'Mrith** This catfish-headed alien, distinguished by his red scales and long fang-like teeth, was Jabba the Hutt's primary agent on the planet Formos before the Battle of Yavin. N'Mrith doubled-crossed Chewbacca and his partner, Han Solo, providing Imperials with a tip that they would be transporting a large load of spice off Formos. Because no spice was detected on the *Millennium Falcon,* N'Mrith was sent to the spice mines of Kessel for his duplicity.

**Nnaksta, Xenon** This Vodran rejected the traditional roles of his people and left his homeworld to ply the oceans on the planet Delassin VI. He later became an operator for the Greel Wood Logging Corporation, as well as an operative for the Rebel Alliance. At the time of the Battle of Hoth, Nnaksta held the rank of lieutenant.

**Noa** *See* Briqualon, Noa.

**Nob, Neb** This Gungan served under Commander Wollod as a communications officer shortly before the Battle of Naboo.

**Nobis, Ona** This Sorrusian female was a bounty hunter who worked for Jenna Zan Arbor 12 years before the Battle of Naboo. Nobis's signature weapon was a multi-mode whip, which had a laser actuator at the tip and could shoot blaster bolts. Arbor was looking for Force-sensitive individuals to test out her theories, and paid Nobis a stipend for bringing them in. After the Jedi Knights Qui-Gon Jinn and Obi-Wan Kenobi started investigating Arbor, Nobis was told to eliminate the Jedi. Unable to do so, she left Arbor's employ and set out to hunt down the Jedi on her own. She laid a trap for them on Sorrus, but was unable to capture them. She next trailed them to Belasco. In the end, Arbor was captured and Nobis was killed in a fall while battling Kenobi.

***Noble Sacrifice*** This Yuuzhan Vong warship was believed to have been the first to locate the rogue planet Zonama Sekot in the Klasse Ephemora system during the aliens' invasion of the galaxy. Upon arriving at Coruscant, which had been terraformed into a simulacrum of Yuuzhan'tar, the *Noble Sacrifice* was destroyed in orbit on the pretense that it carried saboteurs. A yorik-trema landing craft managed to escape, and it was believed that this ship carried Commander Ekh'm Val to the surface.

*Ona Nobis*

**Nobody's Inn** This cantina was located on the planet Ord Mantell.

**Nobu** This man operated a boshi farm on Tatooine during the Galactic Civil War. He also raised nerfs for food.

**Nociv** A subspecies of Kadrillians that lived in the hills of their homeworld of Kadril. They were distinguished from baseline Kadrillian stock by their more primitive civilization, as well as their wider range of emotions. The Nocivs hated their brethren, believing that the Kadrillians had become too passive. The Nocivs were targeted by Darth Vader because of their territorial home, which was filled with kunda stones.

**Nocombackie Law** This was the name of the Gungan law that exiled a member of the Gungan society from his or her underwater city. Usually the Nocombackie Law was binding for the rest of the individual's life.

**Nocturne of the Winged-Stars** This unusual natural event took place every 300 years on the planet Caluula. Scientists from across the galaxy gathered there to investigate its origins and triggers. During the Yuuzhan Vong War, Caluula was expected to experience another Nocturne, shortly after the Battle of Ebaq. During the Nocturne, thousands upon thousands of winged-stars emerged from their chitinous shells and began their mating dance. Unlike other species which were similar in physiology, such as the drone-flitter, winged-stars had just a single day to attract a mate, then successfully fertilize and lay their eggs. What made them even more unusual was that the eggs took the next 299 years to incubate and hatch. Thus, they lived their entire lives in one brief day.

**Nod, Lorian** As a youth, Nod trained to become a Jedi Padawan at the same time as a young Dooku, some 68 years before the Clone Wars. They were best friends during the early years of their training, sharing their education as well as a number of schemes. A native of Junction 5, Nod was always a bit more reckless than Dooku, but their different personalities meshed well until Dooku's incredible skill with the Force made him a favorite among the teachers. When Dooku was chosen to be the Padawan of Thame Cerulian and Nod was passed over several times, he was left to ponder his own future. He hoped to impress the Jedi Masters by stealing a Sith Holocron and learning new skills from it, but he imposed on Dooku to cover for him when he was caught. Dooku refused, and eventually Nod was expelled from the Jedi Temple. Refusing to take a position in the Agricultural Corps, he set out on his own.

Harboring nothing but ill will toward the Jedi, Nod began building his own base of power. Using his connection to the Force, he bullied beings into providing him funding, then established the Caravan Corporation as a front for his illegal activities. Posing as a pirate, Nod began kidnapping Old Republic Senators and holding them for ransom. While attempting to capture Senator Blix Annon, Nod ran into Dooku once again. His old friend was now a Jedi Master, and he and his Padawan Qui-Gon Jinn set out to arrest Nod. Instead, Nod captured them on Von-Alai shortly after kidnapping Senator Annon.

When Annon died of a heart attack while in captivity, Nod suddenly found himself in a lot more trouble. Dooku captured Nod and sent him to prison on Coruscant. Some 30 years later, Nod appeared on his homeworld of Junction 5, where he was given command of the Guardians police force. His assumption of power would have been perfect, if the chance arrival of Qui-Gon Jinn and Obi-Wan Kenobi hadn't exposed his plans. Once again, Nod was sent to prison, and again he was released. He returned to Junction 5 and used his skills to help restore peace to the planet he had tried to conquer.

During the early months of the Clone Wars, Nod returned to Coruscant, ostensibly to offer his assistance to the Republic. Obi-Wan refused to believe his sincerity, and Nod could do nothing but work to prove him wrong. When the founders of the Station 88 Spaceport met with Count Dooku on the planet Null, Nod decided that he could not support Dooku and the Separatist movement. Dooku tried to eliminate the leaders and flee, but Nod chased after him, hoping to finally rectify all the wrongs he had done in his life. Before he could stop Dooku, however, the secret Sith Lord pierced him through the chest with his lightsaber. Nod died as he took hold of the Force one last time.

**Nod, Seib** This Lorrdian woman was distinguished by the blood-red, ankle-length robe that she wore to conceal her identity. The robe was attached to a unique facial screen that completely hid her face, which was tattooed with distinctive patterns. The robe and tattoos were an obvious symbol of her membership in the Sisterhood of the Beatific Countenance, a Lorrd-based religious order that she had left years before. As a member of the Sisterhood, Seib Nod had become bored with the cloistered lifestyle, so she stole some of the Sisterhood's valuable artifacts and left Lorrd, making her way to Coruscant. There she was approached by Artuo Pratuhr, who wished to purchase the artifacts. She refused, then robbed Pratuhr at blaster-point before escaping into the crowds of the Outlander Club. She remained free for just a few days, before Pratuhr and his apprentice, Zey Nep, caught up to her while she was boarding a transport offworld. The police arrived shortly afterward and arrested Nod, sending her to the CoCo Penitentiary to serve an extended sentence for theft and armed robbery.

Seib Nod

**Nodon and Nonak** These two Cathar brothers, feline-like humanoids, joined Burrk, a former stormtrooper, in setting up big-game hunting expeditions on the ice planet Hoth for one reason: Wampa pelts brought a hefty price on the black market. They were fairly successful until they agreed to take Drom Guldi on a hunt. The wampas had gotten smart and ambushed them at their ship. The creatures inadvertently started the vessel's auto-destruct sequence. It exploded, stranding the entire party on Hoth. They were later discovered by Luke Skywalker and Callista, who were on Hoth trying to regain Callista's powers. Nodon, Nonak, and Burrk—along with the hunters they guided—were all killed by their prey. Luke and Callista barely escaped with their lives.

**Noga River** This waterway was found on the planet Teyr, on the opposite side of the world from Griann and the Teyr Rift.

**Noga-ta** An Ithorian Jedi Knight, he visited the planet Barab I about 900 years before the Galactic Civil War. Noga-ta helped bring an end to a bloody civil war there and became a hero to the Barabel. Hundreds of years later, Noga-ta's name was discovered on several disinterred wall carvings along with images of an ancient Jedi Knight.

**Nogdra** The captain of the Imperial corvette *Bixby,* he defected to the Rebel Alliance when his ship was captured. He then gave the Alliance the coordinates of an Imperial staging point near Dellalt.

**Noghri** If ever a species could be misjudged by its appearance, it was the Noghri. Barely over a meter tall, these gray-skinned bipeds had wiry muscles, incredible reflexes, and surprising strength. They were deadly warriors that grew up in unthinkable hardship, on a world forever despoiled by warfare.

The Noghri evolved on the planet Honoghr. Decades before the Battle of Yavin, a furious space battle raged over their world, and a shattered capital ship plunged into their primitive planet. The resulting environmental catastrophe poisoned their water and soil. An unlikely savior descended from the heavens. Darth Vader, Dark Lord of the Sith, saw great potential in the Noghri. He had Imperial scientists work on a project to reclaim the lost lands of Honoghr, to make the once lush world livable again. Using specially built decon droids, the Empire seeded the blighted Honoghr soils with life-sustaining kholm-grass.

Noghri

Little did the Noghri suspect that Vader's charity was a ruse. The kholm-grass strangled all other native plants, and the decon droids were actually perpetuating Honoghr's ecological nightmare. The Noghri found themselves dependent on Vader and the Empire for their survival. They were forever indebted to him. The loyal and proud species dedicated themselves to becoming the Empire's killers. They lauded Vader, and proclaimed him their lord.

Even after the collapse of the Empire at Endor, and the death of Vader, the Noghri continued to surreptitiously serve the Empire. Their role as assassins and bodyguards was a closely guarded secret. When the New Republic discovered Noghri killers five years after Endor, they had no clue as to their origins. The leader of the fragmented Empire, Grand Admiral Thrawn, employed the Noghri in a mission to capture Luke Skywalker or Leia Organa Solo.

What Thrawn hadn't counted on was the Skywalker twins' lineage, and the keen Noghri sense of smell. So acute were their olfactory senses that Noghri could *smell* bloodlines. They recognized their target, Leia, as the Mal'ary'ush, or daughter of their savior. Rather than kill her, the Noghri hid Leia on their home planet, where she learned of their struggle. Organa Solo was able to uncover the Imperial deception that had kept the Noghri servile to the Empire for decades. She proved that the Empire had made fools of the proud species. Leia sowed the seeds of revolt among the Noghri ranks. What were once loyal enforcers now were enraged killers seeking revenge.

The Noghri aided the New Republic in exchange for environmental aid and a renewed future. It was the once loyal Rukh, Noghri bodyguard to Grand Admiral Thrawn, who ended that Imperial threat. In a daring act of vengeance, Rukh killed Thrawn aboard the Grand Admiral's command ship with an assassin's blade. After Thrawn's death, the Noghri continued to rejuvenate their world, although full restoration of Honoghr turned out to be a lost cause. Many Noghri relocated to New Nystao, on Wayland, and Noghri bodyguards continued to protect Leia for many years.

**Noimm, Cair Tok** This New Republic Senator was a member of the Council on Security and Intelligence. During the search for the Teljkon vagabond, she urged the Council to continue searching for Lando Calrissian's team after the vagabond escaped near Gmir Askilon.

**Nok** A Rodian, he was an uncle of the bounty hunter Greedo. He was a member of the peaceful Tetsus clan that eventually escaped to Nar Shaddaa.

**N'oka Brath** Known as the Glowstone by the Qella, this was the star around which the planet Brath Qella orbited.

**Nokko** This was one of the lesser Hutt kajidics of the planet Nal Hutta.

**Nol, Nobam** This charlatan once posed as a Sith Lord to dupe the inhabitants of N'ildwab. The natives hired Boba Fett to kill the magician, which he successfully did about five years after the Battle of Yavin.

**nola grass** This species of grass filled the plains of Naboo. Dried nola grass was used as fire kindling, and could be ground up for use as a cooking spice.

**Nolaan** This man was the Imperial captain in command of the *Interrogator.* He was also the mentor of a young officer named Vharing, who eventually succeeded him in command. Nolaan was executed for an error by High Inquisitor Tremayne.

**Nolar** This planet was one of the largest commercial centers of its sector during the last decades of the Old Republic. Because of the large number of businesses and wealthy beings passing through the planet's cities and spaceports, thievery was one of the most popular professions on Nolar.

**Noloth** This member of the H'kig colony on L'at was believed to have been captured when the Yevetha took control of the planet during the Great Purge. Noloth was supposedly held on the *Pride of Yevetha* in order to deter attacks by the New Republic. In reality, Noloth had escaped on the *Star Morning* before the Yevetha arrived. Noloth's presence on the Star Destroyer was an illusion generated by Enara to fool the Yevetha.

***No Luck Required*** This starship was owned and operated by Uldir Lochett during the early decades of the New Republic. The chassis of the craft was that of an old Corellian YZ-775 medium transport, which had been refitted with updated technologies and weapons. Inside the ship's hangar were several snubfighters, four modified A-wings with room for a single passenger each, and emergency medical supplies. The two weapons emplacements had been heavily modified: one to hold a cesium-vapor turbolaser and a proton torpedo launcher, and the other simply removed to make room for the hangar. The ship was badly damaged when Lochett located the rogue Jedi Knight Klin-Fa Gi, who used her lightsaber to slash through bulkheads to reach the hangar bay. She then stole a starfighter and blasted her way out, leaving the ship venting atmosphere. Lochett's crew managed to patch the leak and travel to Wayland in an effort to recapture Gi.

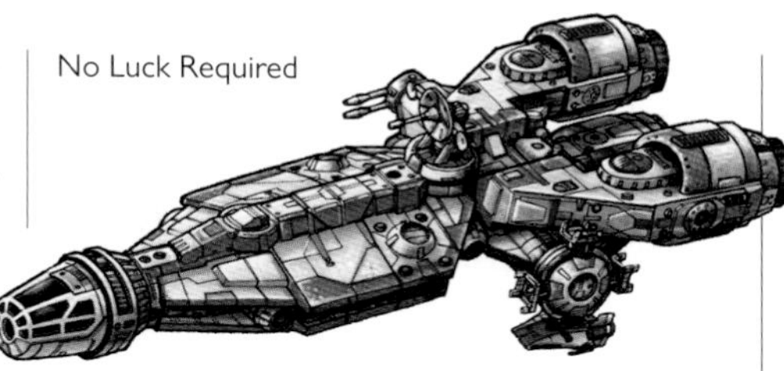
No Luck Required

Burr Nolyds

**Nolyds, Burr** This gaunt, white-haired man served on the Imperial Interim Ruling Council. Nolyds was one of the Council members who supported Carnor Jax and the plans he had for eliminating Emperor Palpatine, for the Emperor kept all of his supporters on short leashes. After Jax was killed on Yinchorr, Nolyds took control of the Council. He opposed Feena D'Asta's plan to make peace with the New Republic, despite the legitimacy it would bring to the Council. When he returned to his quarters one day after a long debate with D'Asta, he found a message disk in his rooms. When he activated it, it exploded, killing Nolyds instantly.

***Nomad*** The Imperial Out System Scout craft that discovered the planet Butler's Cove, the *Nomad* and its crew were captured by Rebel Alliance agents before they could report back to the Empire.

**Nomad City** Lando Calrissian's mobile mining operation on the planet Nkllon built following the Battle of Endor. Nomad City was a slowly moving humpbacked structure put together from an old Dreadnaught cruiser mounted atop 40 captured AT-AT walkers. A massive engineering feat, it used the Nkllon's shadow to protect itself from the intense heat of the system's sun. Calrissian designed Nomad City using plans for a rolling mining center he found among the personal belongings of Cloud City's founder, Ecclesis Figg. The mining center was critically damaged after several Imperial attacks.

**Nomar** This man was captain of the *Laughing Dancer,* although the name was assumed to be an alias. Nomar was lost and presumed dead after the vessel's disappearance.

**Nomo** This Imperial lieutenant served under Captain Zyak at the Fuel City depot on Sulon during the Imperial occupation of the Sullust system.

**Nonak** *See* Nodon and Nonak.

**Nonam, Captain** This Imperial Navy officer commanded a small fleet that deployed the first-stage dark troopers to take out the Rebel Alliance's Tak Base, on the planet Talay.

**No-Name** This was the name given to spies hired by the Old Republic Senate. Each No-Name was provided with an entirely new identity, complete with the appropriate text docs and security clearances. A casual investigation of a No-Name's identity revealed nothing unusual or incriminating. When an agent died, the identity was often retired.

**Nonce** A criminal on the planet Radnor sometime after the Battle of Naboo. Nonce was hired by Dol Heelp to locate teams of youths willing to loot homes of Radnorans who were evacuated from Tacto, after a plague was unleashed in the neighboring city of Aubendo.

***Nonnah*** This Rebel Alliance freighter was forced to crash-land on the planet Chorax shortly after the Battle of Hoth. Rogue Squadron was dispatched to protect the freighter, its crew, and its cargo from Imperial attack until a rescue team could arrive.

**NonSonic** The brand name of a series of blaster silencer attachments manufactured by Merr-Sonn during the Galactic Civil War, they absorbed sound by emitting precisely tuned counter vibrations. They were produced for a variety of slugthrowers and projectile weapons, and each version was suitable only for a specific weapon.

***Nonvideor*-class minelayer** This minelayer was chosen for use in the naval fleets of the Galactic Alliance in the years following the Swarm War.

**Noob** *See* Trask, Anson.

**Noob Hill** Located on Ruan, this district was noted for its hotels and boardinghouses. It was located near several of Salliche Ag Corporation's refugee camps, established to house those beings fleeing from the Yuuzhan Vong invasion. It was on high ground surrounded by stun fencing, and offered superior housing for reasonable fees to the inhabitants of Ruan Refugee Facility 17.

**Nooch** This New Republic K-wing bomber pilot served with the Fifth Battle Group during the unsuccessful blockade of Doornik-319. He was killed when the Yevetha resisted the blockade efforts and attacked Republic ships.

**noodlefishing** Leia Organa Solo used this term to describe the mindless activities of most political figures.

**Noolian crisis** An early Imperial campaign, it resulted in the Empire wresting the Bothan sector away from rebellious insurgents.

**Nooma, Vosdia** The title character in a Rodian drama with a strong political subtext, *The Trickery of Vosdia Nooma;* it was written and produced just before the Clone Wars. Nooma was a poor farmer whose daughter was bitten by an insect and poisoned. As the community rallied around his family, Nooma used the attention to begin spouting political rhetoric that paralleled the pro-military stance of much of the Old Republic. He eventually was elected Baron of the town of Yusk, filled his cabinet with his friends and cronies, and exacted huge taxes from Yusk farmers. But he refused to fight back when a veteran soldier returned from battle to incite the people against him, even when a Paladin arrived to offer his services. The bloody conflict that followed was meant to indicate the future of the Old Republic should the Military Creation Act not be passed by the Galactic Senate.

**Noon, Larad** An ancient Sith warrior noted for his unusual armored jumpsuit made of material interwoven with cortosis fibers, making it almost impervious to lightsaber attacks. Noon was a former Jedi Knight recruited as a Sith by Exar Kun; he fought alongside the Dark Lord during the Great Sith War. Noon fled to Susevfi after the war and went into hiding. He died there, survived by his writings that expounded on his theory of Jiaasjen, which attempted to meld Jedi and Sith teachings in order to justify his actions during the war. Over time, his teachings came to form the basis of the Jensaarai group of Force users.

**Noonb, Snem** This jovial, Sullustan businessbeing ran a manufacturing facility on Edic Bar, in orbit around Genarius, during the final years of the Old Republic. His factory floors were tooled to produce state-of-the-art starship parts, power systems, and small electronics for a variety of applications. His shipments of power relays to the Jedi training facility on Almas assisted many Padawans with the Test of the Lightsaber, and led Noonb into a loose friendship with Jedi Master Lanius Qel-Bertuk. A proud individual, Snem went to great pains to show off his facilities to visitors and prospective customers.

The factory originally was constructed by SoroSuub Industries, and later leased to Snem as part of a far-reaching business initiative. Wastes and by-products were recycled and put to other uses, making the entire operation almost self-sufficient. Snem used automation technologies and low-cost droids—many of them B1 battle droids reconditioned in the wake of the Battle of Naboo—to help keep costs down.

As part of a Test of the Droids, a plan devised by Master Qel-Bertuk to test a group of Jedi Knights and thereby show the Padawans how a true Jedi acted in the face of an unexpected emergency, Snem agreed to stage a fake droid revolt at his factory when the Jedi group arrived to take possession of a shipment of power relays. Unfortunately, Snem's pretend virus was overtaken by a real virus entered into his computers by an agent of the Black Queen. The new virus overrode all the fail-safes in Snem's programming, unleashing the battle droids on the unsuspecting Jedi. Although the Jedi were able to put down the droid revolt, many of Snem's automata were damaged. Nevertheless, he knew that things could have been worse, especially after the altered virus code was discovered. He gladly turned over the shipment of power relays and agreed to give all evidence to Master Lanius for investigation into the Black Queen's activities.

**Noone, Cecil** The leader of a band of thieves and soldiers that hired itself out to the highest bidder during the New Order. He also owned and was captain of the *Borogove.*

**Noonian sector** Situated near the Halthor sector and home to the Noonian system and the planets Noonar and Movris, it was long ruled by Imperial Governor Trophan Thanis. The system supported several food-processing facilities for the Nebula Consumables Corporation. Rebel privateers operating from Movris were able to steal nearly a quarter of the company's output.

**Noopiths** An area of the galaxy located in the Outer Rim Territories near the Greeb-Streebling Cluster and the Ninth Quadrant.

**Noor, Tetengo** An A-wing pilot, this human native of the planet Churba served Blue Squadron at Folor base, using the call sign Blue Ten. Later Noor served as Polearm Nine, part of the Polearm Squadron assigned to the *Mon Remonda* during the hunt for Warlord Zsinj. At the Battle of Selaggis, Noor made the last firing run over the *Iron Fist* before it disappeared into a "tunnel" generated by orbital nightcloaking satellites and disappeared. He was able to see the bow of the *Second Death* just before it exploded, but believed it was the *Iron Fist.* Noor escaped the blast with some damage to his A-wing's engines, but returned to the *Mon Remonda* to report his findings. He related that a second capital ship fled the area of the *Iron Fist*'s destruction, but he had no idea what ship it was.

**Noorg, Aalos** An alias adopted by Han Solo when he agreed to serve as Wedge Antilles's wingmate during Operation Noble Savage some 10 years after the end of the Yuuzhan Vong War. According to his backstory, Noorg was a freelance pilot who had served for many years in the Corporate Sector before returning to his native Corellia when he heard rumblings of the Corellian system seceding from the Galactic Alliance. In order to conceal his identity, Han wore a "prototype" helmet that always seemed to get stuck on his head whenever he met someone.

**Noorr, Vol** The Primate of the Yevethan battle cruiser *Purity,* he was the commander in charge of the destruction of the *Astrolabe,* a New Republic astrographic ship, at Doornik-1142.

**Nootka, Lai** The Duros captain of the freighter *Star's Delight,* he was the shadowy figure that Rogue Squadron member Tycho Celchu met at the Headquarters tavern. Corran Horn spotted them there and began to believe that Celchu was an Imperial spy. In fact, Celchu was negotiating with Lai Nootka for spare parts for the Z-95 Headhunters that he had purchased for Rogue Squadron. Nootka was later killed by the Empire to keep him from testifying at Captain Celchu's trial for murder and treason.

**Nopces Prime** This was the primary world in the Nopces system, a minor star system located on the Mid Rim edge of Darpa sector, along the Hydian Way.

**Noquivzor** A pleasant world of treeless plains, gentle hills, and savannas of golden grasses. Noquivzor's animal life included herds of horned wildernerfs, which were prey to prides of leopard-like taopari. The planet had warm breezes and an exceptionally dry climate—Admiral Ackbar had to install a humidifier in his quarters. Some three years after the Battle of Endor, Rogue Squadron moved to a starfighter base on Noquivzor as its staging area for an attack on Borleias. The base had only one building above the ground.

After the conquest of Borleias, Borsk Fey'lya arranged for the New Republic Provisional Council to meet on Noquivzor to determine the feasibility of using Black Sun extremists to help disrupt the Imperial government prior to the Rebel Alliance assault on Coruscant. Fearful of an attack by Warlord Zsinj, Rogue Squadron moved its base of operations from Borleias back to Noquivzor just before raiding Kessel to free Black Sun prisoners. Seven weeks later, after the Rogues departed for their undercover mission to Coruscant, Zsinj arrived at the planet in his Super Star Destroyer *Iron Fist* and bombarded the base with wave after wave of TIE bombers. Most of Rogue Squadron's support staff were killed as barracks collapsed in a heap of rubble, but the hangar was untouched. The base suffered major damage, but because most of the buildings were underground, it was saved from complete destruction.

**Nor, Moritz** This Ortolan was the leader of the band Hyperdrive during the final years of the Old Republic.

**Norak Tull** Insectoid beings, the Norak Tull had segmented, armor-like skin.

**N'oram, Jyn** This woman was co-owner and captain of the *Fricasseed Nerf* during the final years of the Old Republic. N'oram and her partner, D'yra Calisse, pooled their resources to buy the ship, then eked out a living making regular runs to the Cularin system for Hedrett Shipping and Investments.

**Norand, Isela Talsava** This member of the Fallanassi religion was Akanah's mother. Isela met Joreb Goss while she was on Praidaw and they eventually got married. After being hectored over money by Isela, Goss left, saying he hoped to make enough credits to give his family the life style they deserved; he never returned. Akanah believed that Isela died on Lucazec. Upon being reunited with Fallanassi leader Wialu, Akanah discovered that it was her mother who had sold out the Fallanassi to the Empire. Isela was exiled and took Akanah with her despite Wialu's offer to bring Akanah up in the Fallanassi circle. She later abandoned her then 15-year-old daughter on the crime-ridden planet of Carratos.

**Norat Sovereignty** This government and its people were exterminated during the Yevethan Purge.

**norax** One of two elements found in large concentrations in the crust of the planet Gaftikar. The deposits of norax and kelerium were coveted by Shenio Mining during the Clone Wars era, but the local human population refused to allow Shenio access rights and sided with the Separatists. The planet's other species, the Marits, strongly disagreed, and this civil strife dragged the planet into open warfare.

**Norba** Cabrool Nuum's daughter, she had almost as many aspirations as her devious brother, Rusk. When Rusk imprisoned Jabba the Hutt, Norba released the crime lord so that he could kill Rusk. She then threw Jabba in jail for murder, but explained that she would set him free if Jabba agreed to kill Vu Chusker. Jabba, however, didn't want to be subservient to any of the Nuum clan, so he ate Norba.

**Norbet's Nest** This seedy dive was located in the Skids district of Tyrena on Corellia, during the New Order.

**Norcuna** This Twi'lek Jedi Master was sent to liberate the planet Jabiim from Separatist control. However, a month into the battle, very little headway had been made, and General Norcuna's clone troops were captured and killed by Alto Stratus. Stratus taunted Master Norcuna as he beheaded the Twi'lek.

**Nord, Calo** Considered by many the galaxy's greatest bounty hunter during the Great Sith War, Calo Nord was an outwardly unassuming man known for deliberate precision in his actions. As a child, he was sold into slavery by his parents, and managed to kill his masters on his sixteenth birthday. He then set out to execute his parents—an action that earned him a substantial bounty on his head. Nord was determined not to be captured, and learned everything he could of the tactics used by the bounty hunters who pursued him before he killed them all in turn. Eventually, he discovered who had placed the bounty on his head, and executed them as well.

Norcuna

A free man, Nord set out to become a bounty hunter in his own right. His natural instincts for survival and his ruthless efficiency allowed him to become the most feared hunter of his time. Many criminals believed that his existence was a tall tale told to frighten criminals away from their lives of crime; this stemmed from the fact that very few beings ever escaped to testify to his prowess. Nord eventually went to work for the Sith during the years of conflict surrounding the Great Sith War, when he also took on work for the Exchange, a large criminal organization. He dogged Bastila Shan, Carth Onasi, and the Jedi Knights who were searching for the Star Forge along with Darth Malak, and was believed to have been killed on Taris. However, he managed to survive the assault and escape the planet before it was devastated by the Sith. Nord continued to work for Darth Malak. He eventually was killed while on Sith business during the battle for control of the Star Forge near the Unknown World of the Rakata.

Calo Nord

Colonel Nord

**Nord, Colonel** This Imperial officer was part of the command crew aboard the weapons platform known as the *Tarkin* during its construction in the Patriim system. Nord was part of a group of officers who opposed Darth Vader's careless waste of life whenever an officer failed to meet his goals. After an assassination attempt against the Dark Lord failed, Vader discovered Nord's role in it and planned to execute him. However, when Nord decided to use the ionic cannon aboard the *Tarkin* to take out Luke Skywalker and Leia Organa, the superweapon exploded. It had been sabotaged by the Rebel Alliance, and tore itself apart when fired. Nord and all aboard were killed.

***Nordieus*** This civilian transport vessel carried Atour Riten to the construction site of the first Death Star, in orbit around the planet Despayre, during the early years of the New Order.

**Nordoxicon** A manufacturer of various shipboard components, including anti-concussion-field generators.

**Norello, Captain** This officer and the crew of the Rendili freighter *Happer's Way* were contracted by the Empire to make supply and delivery runs throughout the Outer Rim Territories. Shortly after the Battle of Yavin, they were ambushed by the BloodScar pirates, only to be saved when one of the pirate vessels began shooting at the others. The HT-2200 freighter had been commandeered by Mara Jade, who was chasing the back trail of evidence from her investigation of the treachery of Moff Glovstoak. Thanks to Jade's timely intervention, Captain Norello and his crew were able to begin repairs on the *Happer's Way,* completing them when Jade called in the Star Destroyer *Reprisal.* However, Norello and his crew were stranded aboard the *Reprisal* when Jade took over their vessel to serve as "evidence" when she set out to infiltrate the BloodScar base on Gepparin.

**norg** This timid feline creature was native to Brigia.

**Norg Bral** One of the many hill towns on the planet Mandalore. Like similar settlements, Norg Bral was built within a heavy fortification, making it easy to defend from invaders.

**Norgor** A top henchman of dark side Krath cultist Satal Keto some 4,000 years before the Galactic Civil War. Norgor was sent to assassinate Jedi Ulic Qel-Droma but ended up being killed by the Jedi.

**Norika** Akanah's best childhood friend among the Fallanassi on Lucazec. Religious leader Wialu often said they were like twins. Along with several other youths, Norika was taken to the planet Teyr when the Empire invaded Lucazec. She lived in the city of Griann until the Fallanassi were forced to flee again.

**Norkronian whistle snake** This unusual reptile was known for its ability to make flute-like noises that seemed to form strange music.

**Norley, Cee** This wire-thin woman was a weapons expert assigned to work with Qu Rahn during the early years of the Galactic Civil War to help rescue beings uprooted by the war. She had been trained by Tech Sergeant Hooly of the Rebel Alliance, and never forgot his words of wisdom and advice. She died on the planet Dorlo during a mission to rescue the populace from Imperial subjugation.

**normal space** *See* realspace.

**Norquest** A one-time governor of the planet Cilpar.

**norrick** A type of bread preferred by the Hutts.

**Norric's** This cantina, located in the Life section of Vergesso Base, catered to members of the Rebel Alliance. It was smaller than the other two major cantinas—the Black Hole and the Docking Bay—and was considered more dangerous, because most of its patrons were active duty soldiers who wouldn't hesitate to defend themselves.

**Norsh, Galinda** This young girl was a student at the Jedi Temple on Coruscant, studying the ways of the Force as a contemporary of young Dooku, some 68 years before the Clone Wars.

**Northaykk** One of the largest of the Wookiee tree-cities on Kashyyyk.

**North Barris Spaceport** One of the largest spaceports on the planet Pakrik Minor.

**North Beach** This coastal area was located on the Unknown World of the Rakata. During the Great Sith War, the North Beach area was under the control of militant Rakata who served the One.

**North Conical Mountains** The name used to describe the arrangement of seven cones—one large cone surrounded by six smaller ones—at one end of Centerpoint Station. It was believed that the cones formed the primary repulsor generation system for the station, since the arrangement resembled that of ancient repulsor devices.

**Northeast Refineries** This was one of four ore refineries established on the Ugnaught Surface during its construction. Once the floating city was completed, the refinery was converted into housing and business facilities for the Ugnaughts who made their homes on the Surface.

**Northern Bands** One of the smaller overclans of the Alwari Ansionians.

**Northern Dune Sea** *See* Dune Sea.

**Northern Lakes** This region of Dathomir was named for the many small lakes found just to the north of the Frenzied River and the Singing Mountain.

**Northern Province** The northernmost habitable part of the planet Zeltros.

**Northern Sea** The frigid ocean that surrounded the northern polar ice cap of the planet Zonama Sekot. When the living planet made a blind jump into hyperspace to avoid the sabotage of Nom Anor, it suddenly inverted itself, making the Northern Sea a part of the southern hemisphere for a short time.

**North Horn Flightknife** One of the many Yedagonian fighter squadrons that supported Wedge Antilles and the Running Crimson Flightknife during the war on Adumar against forces of the Cartann nation.

**North Market** This section of the city of Iritsa, located on the planet Chazwa, was the primary shopping area used by beings that lived in the Clog.

***Northstar*** This New Republic tender ship was assigned to the Fifth Battle Group. Thanks to a navigational computer failure, it was late in arriving at the Koornacht Cluster during the Yevethan Purge. Recalled to the Alland Yards for repairs, it rejoined the fleet a short time later.

**Norufu** The near-human captain of Bogga the Hutt's *Enforcer One.*

**Norulac** This planet was home to a gang of bandits who raided Taanab every year, until they were wiped out by Lando Calrissian in the famous Battle of Taanab. Calrissian single-handedly accounted for 19 kills of the Norulac band.

**Norval** This dark-haired humanoid was one of Dr. Murk Lundi's history students on Coruscant six years before the Battle of Naboo. Dr. Lundi took a sabbatical for an expedition to Kodai in search of a Sith Holocron supposedly created by King Adas and then lost at sea; he chose not to bring Norval along. Angry at Lundi for leaving him behind, Norval—who had a secret but strong connection to the dark side of the Force—made his own arrangements to find the holocron on Kodai. During a struggle, the holocron fell into a deep geyser.

Norval waited 10 years before returning to Kodai, in an effort to finally recover the holocron for himself. He had learned a great deal about the Jedi and Sith, and even constructed his own crude lightsaber. Although he succeeded in the recovery, he had been followed by Obi-Wan Kenobi and Anakin Skywalker. Norval fled to the Ploo system, where he hoped to sell the Sith device. Kenobi was able to infiltrate his ship and recover the holocron as Norval tried to flee into space. However, the mercenaries who were working with him realized that the holocron was no longer attainable. They fired on Norval's ship, destroying it and killing Norval.

**Norval II** The primary planet in the Norval (or Norvall) system in the Calaron sector, Norval II supplied some of the best New Republic pilots. It was the homeworld of General Horton Salm, commander of the New Republic's starfighter training center on Folor. During the Clone Wars, it was the site of an assassination attempt on the life of Padmé Amidala. The attackers were a group of Mandalorian Protectors led by Alpha-O2, but they were ambushed by the forces of the Old Republic and driven off. Six years after the Battle of Endor, a detachment of fighters from Norval II joined the New Republic to aid in its struggle against the reborn cloned Emperor.

**Norvanian grog** An expensive and potent intoxicant from the planet Ban-Satir II, it was made on the island of N'van in the planet's northern hemisphere.

**Norveel, Jax** This man worked as one of the Black Queen's main lieutenants just after the Clone Wars began. When the Black Queen was turned to the light side of the Force by a group of freelance agents at her hideout on Tolea Biqua, Norveel saw it as an admission of weakness. He attempted to kill her and take over her criminal operations, but only succeeded in wounding her before the agents entered the fray. In a matter of minutes, Norveel and his thugs had been forced to surrender, and were turned over to the authorities.

**noryath meatbread** A brown, bread-like food.

**Norys** A teenage street tough, he was the leader of the Lost Ones, a Coruscant gang. His face was broad and dark, his eyes close-set, and his teeth crooked. Norys was accepted by the Shadow Academy, but when he was found to have no Force sensitivity, he was trained as a stormtrooper. Norys welcomed the chance to prove himself, and his marksmanship skills developed quickly. He eventually became one of the Shadow Academy's troopers—much to the chagrin of Qorl, his trainer, who despised Norys for his bullying ways, his lack of discipline, and his disrespect for superiors. Their differences flared up during the Shadow Academy's attack on the Jedi academy on Yavin 4. Norys had by then learned to fly a TIE fighter, and went off on his own to take out the *Lightning Rod.* Qorl took the opportunity to verbally reprimand Norys; when the young man failed to listen, Qorl shot his TIE fighter out of the sky.

**Nosaurian** A species native to the planet New Plympto. The average Nosaurian was a reptilian standing nearly 1.5 meters tall, with long arms and short legs. The skull was crowned with a ring of bony horns; a pointed snout was ridged with scales. The horns were an indication of an individual's demeanor, as old or quarrelsome individuals had many broken horns.

*Nosaurian*

Nosaurians could see visible light only in varying degrees of black and white. They characterized most colors by their particular shade of gray. The inside of a Nosaurian's mouth could be lit with a phosphorescent glow at will, a trait which even the Nosaurians could not describe in terms of an evolutionary need. However, it provided them with a way to communicate across distances at night without giving away their position by making noise. Individuals had exceptionally fast reflexes, and many excelled as pilots or athletes. Nosaurians also were noted for a specific quirk: They always bayed at the setting sun. This response seemed to be almost involuntary, and resulted in strange looks at Nosaurians who traveled offworld.

As a people, the Nosaurians supported Count Dooku and the Separatists during the Clone Wars. This put them in a bad position, however, when Supreme Chancellor Palpatine declared himself Emperor and ushered in the era of the New Order. Given their views, the Nosaurians were targeted for immediate subjugation by troopers of the Galactic Empire. Relatively few individuals escaped the fighting, and those soldiers who surrendered were brutally executed. Huge numbers of refugees were captured and sold into slavery, as part of Emperor Palpatine's plan to make them an example of what would happen to any people or world that opposed the Empire. Over time, the Nosaurians were able to reclaim their homeworld, and reestablish their society on New Plympto.

During the Yuuzhan Vong War, the Nosaurians resisted the subjugation of their homeworld with ferocious will. But they were wiped out by a bioengineered plague unleashed by the alien invaders in retaliation for their resistance. Only the handful of Nosaurians who were offworld at the time survived—the very last members of their species.

**Nose, The** This form of wrist-mounted sensor system was developed for use by the Galactic Alliance Defense Force during the years following the Yuuzhan Vong War. The Nose was attached to a gauntlet or sleeve, and could be set to identify a wide variety of substances in the surrounding environment, from illegal drugs and chemicals to weapons and ordnance.

**nosetongue** A form of locking device developed by the Yuuzhan Vong and used to limit access to portals and chambers. The nosetongue was a small indentation in the wall into which a Yuuzhan Vong placed his or her fist. The nosetongue's sensitive palate tasted and analyzed the individual's secretions to determine if access had been granted. If the individual was cleared to enter, the nosetongue instructed the hatch sphincter or other door mechanism to open.

**nos monster** Native to the underwater grottoes of the planet Utapau, the nos monster was a large, predatory amphibious gastropod that was believed to be a distant relative of the varactyl. However, xenobiologists later discovered that the nos monster was more closely related to the swamp slug of Dagobah. The head of a full-grown nos monster was dominated by a flat, wide-eyed face surrounded by four heavy horns. Its eyes were attuned to the low-light conditions found below the surface. A simple-minded creature, the nos monster was easily distracted by bright lights moving across its field of vision. It was equally at home in the water or on land, and exceptionally fast in either location.

*Nos monster*

***Nostril of Palpatine*** This was one of the terms Han Solo used to jokingly describe a nonexistent Imperial superweapon.

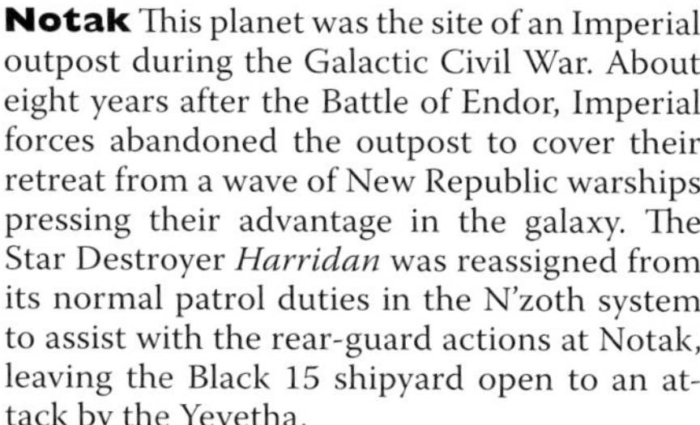

**Notak** This planet was the site of an Imperial outpost during the Galactic Civil War. About eight years after the Battle of Endor, Imperial forces abandoned the outpost to cover their retreat from a wave of New Republic warships pressing their advantage in the galaxy. The Star Destroyer *Harridan* was reassigned from its normal patrol duties in the N'zoth system to assist with the rear-guard actions at Notak, leaving the Black 15 shipyard open to an attack by the Yevetha.

**Notch, the** This was the name given to the entrance to Beggar's Canyon from the Ebe Crater Valley on Tatooine. The Notch was part of the noted Mos Espa Circuit—a swoop racing event held annually during the New Order.

**Nothos, Commander Bane** This Imperial district commander was charged with locating and destroying Admiral Ackbar's Shantipole Project—then building a new starfighter, the B-wing. He failed, was demoted, and was placed in command of a patrol fleet in the Outer Rim Territories. He was captured by the Rebel Alliance and taken aboard one of their ships. When a problem developed with the ship's hyperdrive, they all became lost in the mysterious dimension called otherspace. Nothos was killed battling Rebels also trapped in otherspace.

**Notoganarech** This Elom proved, via physical calculus, that the Rebel Alliance was destined to win the Galactic Civil War. Opponents of physical calculus pointed out that Notoganarech performed this analysis after the Battle of Endor.

**Notron** According to ancient Seoulian legend, Notron was the birthplace of all human life in the galaxy.

**Notsil, Lara** *See* Petothel, Gara.

**Notsil, Tavin** One of Warlord Zsinj's agents and the brother of the late Lara Notsil, whose identity had been assumed by Gara Petothel, a former Imperial Intelligence agent who had defected to the New Republic. Tavin was part of a plan to lure Gara back to Zsinj's camp, and she agreed to meet with him on the planet Aldivy. Tavin was accompanied by Captain Todrin Rossik. Gara was protected from afar by fellow Wraith Squadron member Myn Donos, armed with a sniper gun. When Donos was spotted and Rossik said he would have to be killed, Gara motioned to Donos who shot Tavin dead while she killed Rossik.

**Nouane** A region of space patrolled by the New Republic vessel *IX-26* until that ship was diverted to pick up a team of archaeological researchers from Obroa-skai. The team was then brought to the dead planet Brath Qella in the hope that it could find clues about the mysterious Brath Qella ship known as the Teljkon vagabond.

**nouland flare** This unusual plant was often grown as a defense system because of its strange characteristics. Resembling a mass of animated vines, the nouland flare spent much of its life spread across the ground. When startled or stepped on, however, it rose up in an attempt to trap whatever had disturbed it. In this way, the plant could capture large prey and devour it at leisure. The plant was also very flammable, and would literally explode if fired upon by a startled intruder. This served two purposes for the being who planted it: The explosion was an obvious sign of intrusion, and it often injured or killed the culprit as well.

***Nova*-class battle cruiser** *See* Hapes *Nova*-class battle cruiser.

**Novacom** The largest HoloNet service provider on Alderaan, Novacom was run by the father of Rogue Squadron member Tycho Celchu. Celchu's father was the company's chief executive when Alderaan was destroyed by the Death Star.

**nova crystal** These precious gemstones helped bankroll the first Death Star project for the Empire. Found on several planets, including Mygeeto, Krann, Sarka, and Cotellier, nova crystals were highly active gemstones with a unique crystalline matrix. This matrix, when exposed to bright sunlight (especially in the red color band), absorbed the heat from the light and became excited. This caused the gemstone to glow with its own luminescence, providing a ready light source. If not refrigerated after their removal from the rocky matrix, the crystals could explode with incredible force.

***Nova Crystal*** This civilian Gizer L-6 freighter was part of a small convoy ambushed by the Old Republic interdiction vessel TIV Z590/1, about a year after the Battle of Geonosis. The clone commandos on the smaller ship had been hoping to board a Separatist freighter of a similar design, and were forced to maintain communications silence in order to surprise the Separatists. The captain of the *Nova Crystal,* however, thought that the TIV was a pirate vessel and fired on it. The blast disabled the TIV, which later was destroyed by Separatist reinforcements. Because the Grand Army of the Republic couldn't reveal the details of its mission, the captain of the *Nova Crystal* was described as a hero by the news media.

*Novar*

**Nova Demons** This notorious swoop gang operated on a handful of planets in the Outer Rim Territories near Ord Mantell, during the early years of the New Republic.

**nova flare** A bombing pattern in which proton torpedoes were dropped on a capital ship in an increasingly wider pattern. The first few torpedoes were tightly grouped to take out the section of shielding they hit. The remaining torpedoes exploded in a pattern around the initial hole, causing the ship's shields to attempt to compensate for ever-widening damage. The shield generators on most ships could not react fast enough, and they usually failed.

**Nova Force** A mercenary squadron under the command of Willum Kamaran shortly before the Battle of Yavin. Kamaran and Nova Force were contracted by Prince Xizor to help Durga the Hutt defend the Ylesian colonies from Teroenza and the Desilijic Hutts. Durga agreed to pay Xizor 30 percent of the profits from Ylesia for the protection.

**Nova Level** The designation of one of the upper levels of the cityscape on Coruscant, located near the Senate Rotunda, during the last century of the Old Republic.

**nova lily** A brilliant yellow-orange flower, it grew on the moon Yavin 4.

**Novar** An Onderonian functionary who worked for Queen Amanoa, Novar's first political role was as an adviser to the king's aide, a position he got more because of his father's connections than his own competence. However, Novar was much more adept than his superior, Tolo Kad, who claimed all of Novar's successes as his own. To pay him back and usurp him, Novar told Kad that he had completed all the preparations for a state dinner. Kad bragged about "his own special preparations" to King Ommin, then was shocked to find out that Novar had done nothing. The king, in a great fit of rage, destroyed Kad with Sith magic and promoted Novar in his place. Over the next decade, Novar manipulated Ommin until the king finally began teaching him Sith magic. After years of scheming, Novar finally met his end during the Second Battle of Onderon.

**Novarr, Fiana** An alias provided to Iella Wessiri by the New Republic Intelligence agency to give her access to the planet Adumar during negotiations among the Adumari, the Republic, and the Empire. Novarr was a Corellian code slicer hired by the Adumari to assist with interfacing their computer protocols with those of the Empire and the New Republic.

**Nova Squadron** This New Republic group of B-wings was assigned as support for the *Mon Remonda*-led fleet during the hunt for Warlord Zsinj and the *Iron Fist.*

**Novastar** A specialized racing swoop. Rocket boosters gave the craft additional speed and made it dangerous for inexperienced riders.

**Novastar Corporation** This company produced starship navigational computers during the New Order. It was rumored that Novastar was developing a portable nav computer that didn't require an astromech unit. It was also rumored that it had acquired an Imperial TIE fighter for research.

**Nova Station** This space station was erected in the remains of the Carida system as a stopping point along the Perlemian Trade Route. It was situated just within the cloud of the supernova's gas shell, forcing incoming ships to drop out of hyperspace before reaching the system and then using their sublight engines to enter the shell. This gave the station's security forces time to identify every incoming ship and prepare the appropriate response. Nova Station soon became a haven for smugglers and other criminals, who appreciated advance warning of any impending raids.

*NT 600*

***Nova Viper*** A sleek cruiser owned by the bounty hunter Spurch "Warhog" Goa.

**Novus** This Twi'lek male was one of the Fallanassi children who were taken to the planet Teyr, where they lived in the city of Griann.

**noxious** A slang term used by Rebel Alliance Intelligence operatives to describe Imperial security personnel.

**NR-5** A series of maintenance droids produced by Kalibac Industries during the Galactic Civil War. The NR-5 was produced to compete with the WED Treadwell series of repair droids, to which it had a striking resemblance. The NR-5 was equipped with a Mechro-II brain, a heavy lifting arm, a fine manipulator arm, a general-purpose appendage, and a sophisticated visual sensor system. It found popularity among shipboard technicians who needed additional assistance in starship maintenance, but the series suffered from a lack of durability; NR-5 droids working outdoors on many worlds needed continual maintenance. The design was virtually ignored throughout the Outer Rim after Industrial Automaton introduced its R4 series astromech, but the NR-5 was generally regarded as more effective than the R4 on planets with milder climates.

**NRI** *See* New Republic Intelligence.

**NR-N99 Persuader** *See* Corporate Alliance tank droid.

**Nrogu** This purple moon was one of many natural satellites that orbited the planet Qoribu.

**Nrross** This Trandoshan was a pirate during the New Order, serving under Captain Naz Felyood as the navigator aboard the *Jynni's Virtue* until the ship was intercepted by an Imperial patrol. Captain Felyood ordered a hasty retreat into hyperspace, and they fled. However, the ship's astromech droid exploded due to the strain of the jump. Nrross was caught in the explosion and killed.

**N-s6** A Sienar Fleet Systems navigational computer system used on several Imperial starfighter models, including the TIE fighter, the TIE interceptor, and the TIE Advanced.

***Nssis*-class clawcraft** *See* Chiss clawcraft.

**NT 600** A droid installed by Vilmarh Grahrk to help pilot the *Inferno.* Villie gave the droid, which was custom-built at the Golden Nyss Shipyards, the capability to operate the navigational computer and a variety of shipboard systems, but never programmed it to operate the weapons. NT was a small,

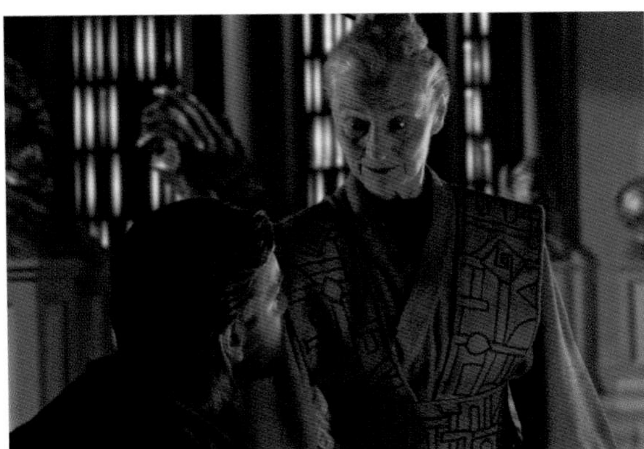
*Jocasta Nu lectures Obi-Wan about the Jedi Library.*

spherical droid equipped with a tiny repulsor engine which allowed it to move about.

**NTB-630** This heavy naval bomber was developed by Incom and Subpro for the Old Republic during the Clone Wars. Similar in design to the PTB-625, the NTB-630 differed in its mission profile. Whereas the PTB-625 was designed for planetary bombardment, the NTB-630 was created to deliver its payloads while engaged in space battles. It was therefore more maneuverable than the PTB-625, allowing it to get close to capital ships and avoid their turbolasers as it executed its bombing runs.

**N'ton** A H'drachi youth who accompanied Ch'no and Mora in searching the cities of M'haeli for junk to rebuild. Seeing Ch'no's uncanny ability to read time-streams, N'ton joined the Rebel Alliance to help avoid the impending war on M'haeli.

**Ntthan** A New Republic starship captain, his mission was to deliver supplies to the hidden outpost of New Alderaan. He kept very strict timetables and was never late. Following the second rebirth of Emperor Palpatine on Byss, Ntthan was intercepted by Imperial forces and taken to Bast Castle, where he was interrogated by Kvag Gthull until he revealed the location of New Alderaan.

**Nu, Jocasta** This wispy woman was a Jedi Master, and served in the Jedi Temple's Library Archives on Coruscant during the final decades of the Old Republic. Despite her frail appearance, Jocasta Nu was known as a firebrand among the Jedi. She trained the Miralukan male Jerec to Jedi Knighthood, instilling in him an insatiable desire for knowledge that drove many of her own actions. She had discovered Jerec while working as an archaeologist for the ExplorCorps many years before the Battle of Naboo. Her determination and strength as a Jedi Knight carried over into her work in the Archives, where even the most experienced Jedi Master had to bow to her demands. She eventually earned the rank of Jedi Master, and sat on the Jedi Council for a 10-year term before returning to the Archives.

Jocasta Nu's pride in the Archives and their contents sometimes blinded her to the fact that the Archives were not truly complete and could be altered from within. Thus, when Obi-Wan Kenobi searched for the planet Kamino, Jocasta Nu was of very little help. Kamino didn't show up in the records—and according to Nu, if it didn't exist in the Archives, then it simply didn't exist. She was forced to face her pride head-on in the wake of the Battle of Geonosis, when Kamino's existence was verified by both Obi-Wan and Master Yoda. She began her own investigation into the matter, and was surprised to find a trail of evidence that exposed Count Dooku's altering of archived data on Kamino.

In the wake of the Clone Wars, Madame Nu was among the many Jedi killed by Anakin Skywalker after he pledged his allegiance to Darth Sidious and became Darth Vader. She had refused to give Vader access to the emergency beacon hidden within the Jedi Temple, so Vader stabbed her in the chest with his lightsaber. It was later reported by Imperial HoloVision that Jocasta Nu had been killed for hoarding information that was harmful to the Empire and its citizens.

**Nu, Kelbis** This Rodian was a student at the Jedi praxeum on Yavin 4 in the years leading up to the Yuuzhan Vong War. Kelbis was trapped by the Peace Brigade on Eriadu during a mission in which he discovered that Nom Anor and the Yuuzhan Vong were planning to invade the Yag'Dhul system and use it as a staging area. The Brigaders toyed with him, and a multitude of beings shot blasters at him while he struggled valiantly to deflect the bolts with his lightsaber. The sudden appearance of Anakin Solo and Tahiri Veila spared his life long enough for him to give them the simple message "Yag'Dhul" before he died of his injuries.

*Nubia*

**Nu, Koobis** This Rodian, known as Target by his comrades, served the New Republic as a starfighter pilot. As a member of Rogue Squadron during the hunt for Warlord Zsinj, Koobis was designated Rogue Eight.

**Nu, Risso** This Corellian was a noted bounty hunter, considered second only to Boba Fett in the number of successful hunts undertaken in the Core Worlds during the early years of the New Order. He met with a group of other bounty hunters on the remote world of Ma'ar Shaddam, hoping to gain their support in a plan to eliminate Fett during his routine maintenance stopover on the planet. Their plan was hastily thrown together and even more hastily shattered when Fett recognized the threat. Before Nu could react, Fett had killed half of his team. The other half was eliminated systematically, until only Fett and Nu remained. When Fett was busy with the other hunters, Nu had managed to steal his Mandalorian armor and weapons, and gained access to *Slave I*. He then used the ship's weapons systems to try to destroy Fett on the ground. Fett survived a missile blast, and got the back-up set of armor—once worn by Jango Fett—that he kept on Ma'ar Shaddam. Fett then tracked Nu down and defeated him in one-on-one combat. Nu was stripped of the Mandalorian armor and left in just his underwear as a reminder that Boba Fett was still the number one bounty hunter in the galaxy.

**Nuala Marauders** This group of space pirates was active during the last decades of the Old Republic.

**Nu-Ar, Fem** This woman was the chief assistant to Dr. Xathan during the New Order. The pair were hired by the Empire to locate the planet Seoul 5. When their research led the Imperials to the correct planet, both of them were bound and imprisoned beneath the planet's surface. Only the timely appearance of Han Solo allowed them to get free.

**Nub** A clone rookie serving at the Rishii moon outpost during the Clone Wars. His nickname was a disparaging acronym: "non-useful body."

**Nubblyk** A Slyte, Nubblyk was Plawal's town boss just prior to the Battle of Endor. He played a high-stakes game of smuggling out parts and valuables left behind by Imperials, primarily xylen chips, gold wire, and gems. He disappeared suddenly.

**Nubia** This planet, located on the outer edge of the Core Worlds, was home to the Nubians, who produced many specialized starship components. Nubia was located along the Corellian Run, just beyond Corellia and Froz. Some 22,000 years before the Battle of Yavin, colonists realized that its bleak appearance was merely a façade. Much of the planet's landmass was considered arid by most standards, but huge underground aquifers provided water for irrigation. This allowed the colonists to quickly provide food for themselves and—over time—for the sector as well. Nubia's mountains were rich in ore and minerals, which fueled the manufacture of a variety of heavy machinery.

**Nub Saar** The first of the floating cities built in the atmosphere of the planet Genarius. It was founded by a Trandoshan named Russok, who ordered round-the-chrono work on its construction to have it ready for occupancy. He drew people to the station with claims of the unlimited potential for wealth in mining the gas clouds. However, Russok and his backers were unprepared for the radiation storms that swept across the planet.

**Nubyl** This former doctor was believed to have assisted in the implantation of cybernetic systems into the bodies of Master Jaing and Durge many centuries before the Clone Wars. Dr. Nubyl had been severely injured in an unspecified accident, but her ruined body was encased in a prosthesis that allowed her brain to continue functioning. Her skills in brain-to-prosthesis technologies were unparalleled, and were instrumental in completing the work on Durge. The doctor who was leading Durge's transformation then took Nubyl's brain and encased it in the augmented body of a protocol droid, creating a sentient combat automaton that served as a training tool for Durge and Master Jaing. Nubyl was only being used by the doctor, who had been plotting to set off a war between the ancient Sith and the Mandalorians. The doctor had stolen a Sith artifact—which resembled a simple walking stick—from Ung Kusp and his Mandalorian Mercs, and used Durge, Jaing, and Nubyl to bring the Mandalorians into conflict with the rest of the galaxy. When the Mercs attacked their laboratory, Nubyl was caught in the blast of a thermal detonator. It was believed that Nubyl might have also been a Jedi Knight, as it was rumored that her partner returned a lightsaber to her as she died.

***Nu*-class shuttle** An armed and armored space transport used by Republic military forces during the Clone Wars. It had hinged wings that folded upright when the ship landed, and was piloted by a crew of two. Entrance and egress was by a forward ramp. The vessel was equipped with two double rotary blaster cannons and two double laser cannons.

**Nudo, Po** This Aqualish, an Old Republic Senator, was one of the many supporters gathered by Senator Palpatine of Naboo in the years leading up to the Battle of Naboo. Representing the planet Ando, Po Nudo worked to ensure that commerce was maintained across the galaxy. He was also one of the first Senators to convince his homeworld to secede from the Republic; Ando joined the Confederacy of Independent Systems some 10 years after the Battle of Naboo. Po Nudo was later placed in charge of the Hyper-Communications Cartel, but was among the Separatist leaders who were killed on Mustafar by Darth Vader at the end of the Clone Wars.

**Nuffin** A group of traders who were a constant thorn in the side of Jabba the Hutt and his smuggling business. The Nuffin all looked the same: nondescript, pink-skinned humanoids with beady eyes, no nose, and a ridge of dark skin that rose up their spines and wrapped six tendrils around their heads. They identified one another by number.

**Nugek** This New Republic ambassador once gave young Anakin Solo a busy box as a gift. The box had wheels that could be spun, and blocks that could be pushed through shaped holes.

**Nugtosh** This grotesque, skeletal alien presided over the annual Vinta Harvest Classic Podrace on Malastare during the era of the Battle of Naboo. He was a vagrant, but was considered good luck by the Podracers and fans.

**Nukkels, Spleed** This Gungan was one of the best bongo racers in the city of Otoh Gunga prior to the Battle of Naboo. She piloted a blue-skinned, broad-bellied, monobubble bongo for most of her racing career. Just before the Trade Federation blockade, she crashed into Neb Neb Goodrow's bongo in a practice run and was unable to compete in the Bongo Rally. In the years following the Battle of Naboo, Spleed and Neb Neb continued to race their bongos, but more often than not they ended up crashing, whether between themselves or with other racers. Still, they always managed to survive and race again. This made them popular with young Gungans and new fans across the galaxy, if less so among other racers, who considered them reckless and dangerous. They were briefly suspended from racing following the crash and disappearance of Zak "Squidfella" Quiglee, but redeemed themselves by restoring Boss Nass's old heyblibber and bringing Squidfella in for questioning.

**Null** This forested planet was one of the first worlds to ally itself with the Confederacy of Independent Systems before the Clone Wars. Although a planetwide government had been established, the native peoples preferred to manage themselves on a more local level. Individual tribes existed in small settlements, and justice often was carried out in the form of swift and deadly skirmishes that left no witnesses. The natives of the planet also were known as Null. They stood a meter taller than the average human. Males wore their beards long and braided, and both genders preferred to dress in animal skins and thigh-length boots. The Null were known primarily for their skills as hunters and stonemasons.

During his attempt to gain possession of the Station 88 Spaceport for the Separatists, Count Dooku suggested that representatives from Junction 5, Delaluna, Bezim, and Vicondor all meet on Null to negotiate a deal. Lorian Nod asked the Jedi Knights to investigate the situation in an effort to keep Station 88 in the hands of the Republic. Over time, Dooku managed to acquire ownership of the entire planet, and it became one of the many targets of the Grand Army of the Republic. In the fighting, Separatist forces hired bounty hunters of the Crimson Nova to kill the Jedi Knight generals leading the Republic's forces.

*Po Nudo*

*Warb Null*

**Null, Warb** One of the most ferocious Naddists on ancient Onderon, he had incredible strength and military prowess in addition to his ability to tap the dark side of the Force. Originally a metallurgist named Shas Dovos, he was melded to his unique set of armor after conjuring a Sith spirit. Warb Null launched an attack on Iziz during the funeral procession for Queen Amanoa, and managed to steal the remains of the Queen and Freedon Nadd. Null's base was located beneath the surface of Iziz. When Jedi Master Arca Jeth appealed to King Ommin for aid in recovering the remains of Freedon Nadd, Ommin and Warb Null attacked, overpowering the Jedi and taking him captive. Warb Null, however, was struck down and killed by Ulic Qel-Droma.

**Nullada** This immense Shell Hutt was the leader of a group that inhabited the artificial world of Circumtore. Nullada was unaware of Gheeta's intricate web designed to ensnare Boba Fett until the younger Hutt set it in motion. There were other actions by Gheeta that angered Nullada, but nothing more than the destruction of an expensive diplomatic complex on Circumtore, the end result of Boba Fett learning of Gheeta's plans. Fett and members of the Bounty Hunters' Guild attacked the planet; Gheeta was killed in the battle.

***Null*-class ARC troopers** The so-called black operatives of the Grand Army of the Republic, these troopers were rumored to have been trained as intelligence operatives, but were deemed too dangerous to deploy by the Kaminoan cloners who created them. They originally were bred as part of Ko Sai's plan to introduce "improvements" to Jango Fett's genome and produce more effective clone troopers. The Nulls were physically, as well as genetically, different from other clones, having a heavily muscled build. Ko Sai later apologized to Jango for the creation of these clones, whom she deemed deviant and disturbed. Of the first 12 clones bred, only six survived, and Ko Sai found these clones to be virtually untrainable. She wanted them destroyed, but Orun Wa stepped in and asked Jango Fett to evaluate them.

These young clones were just four years old at the time, but they had absorbed more of their training than Ko Sai realized. It was Jango who asked Kal Skirata to take a look at the clones, and Skirata instantly took on the role of father to them. He hated Ko Sai's cold assessment of their lack of usefulness, and he saw that they were unusually capable in a fight. Skirata agreed to become one of Jango's *Cuy'val Dar,* Mando'a for "Those who no longer exist."

Under Skirata's direction, the six clones became the most effective black-ops unit in the entire galaxy, but they were considered unpredictable and dangerous given their unswerving loyalty to Skirata. The six Null ARCs were known by their N designations, but each was also known by a Mandalorian nickname: Ordo, Jaing, Kom'rk, Mereel, A'den, and Prudii. Skirata often referred to them, both privately and in public, as "instant death on legs," and his training instilled in them a desire to live up to this description.

**null-g polo** A popular, zero-gravity spectator sport.

**null-gravity caroms** This was a popular casino game during the New Order.

**Nullip** This young man held the rank of ensign in the Imperial Navy in the early months of the New Order. Nullip served under Captain Ugan aboard the Detainer CC-2200 interdictor ship that blockaded Kashyyyk when the Empire began exporting Wookiees as slaves. It was Nullip who alerted Captain Ugan to a scuttled Commerce Guild *Recusant*-class ship in orbit around Kashyyyk. The ship had been mistakenly activated by Olee Starstone and Filli Bitters during their escape from the planet, and it tried to continue its previous mission. It had been shut down just before the Separatists were defeated on Kashyyyk, and had been programmed to self-destruct, like a floating bomb. The *Recusant*-class ship rammed into Ugan's Detainer, and both ships were destroyed in an immense explosion. All hands were lost, allowing hundreds of evacuation ships to carry escaping Wookiees away from Kashyyyk.

***Null Space*** A pirate gunship operated by Captain Obigon during the New Republic era.

**numatra** The hide of this creature was valued for clothing and footwear.

**Numb, Ten** This Sullustan piloted a B-wing fighter for the Rebel Alliance. At the Battle of Endor, Ten Numb was attached to Blue Squadron and piloted Blue Five. He led a B-wing attack on Darth Vader's flagship *Executor,* thus drawing fighters away from the strike force led by General Calrissian and Commander Antilles. A week after the battle, he was part of a mission to Corellia. Following an Imperial attack, he pursued a group of Imperials on speeder bikes, but was discovered and captured by General Weir. Numb's right hand was cut off to remove a wrist tracking device and he was tortured. Numb eventually succumbed to his wounds.

**Numbers** This Givin was one of the few members of his species to serve in the Imperial Navy in the early years of the New Order. Numbers was stationed aboard the Star Destroyer *Steel Talon* during the construction of the first Death Star.

**Numesh sector** An area of Coruscant after it had been decimated and terraformed by the Yuuzhan Vong into a simulacrum of their long-lost homeworld, Yuuzhan'tar.

**nuna** This strange, bird-like reptile inhabited the swamps of Naboo. The nuna had a large, round body supported by two strong legs. Its wings or arms were virtually nonexistent, and its head bobbed up and down when it walked. Also known as a swamp turkey, the nuna was often roasted and served as the main course at Gungan holiday feasts. The meat was considered tasty to the Gungans, but was poisonous to Rodians and Twi'leks. When confronted in the wild, most nuna would simply turn and flee as fast as they could. If cornered, though, a nuna would lash out with its sharp beak and kick with its legs.

Males often showed aggression by inflating the wattles around their necks and hissing. Females gave birth to a litter that was contained in a single, huge egg. Each egg contained up to 10 young, and the mother had to help them escape from the thick shell upon hatching. In the wild, nunas formed social groups that often were compared to rival gangs. Within each flock, there were several rival groups, each of which vigorously defended its territory.

The Gungans developed a sport, known as nuna-ball, which used a live nuna as the ball. The angered nuna puffed itself up, and was carried by each team toward its opponent's goal.

Nuna

Nien Nunb

**Nunb, Aril** The sister of Nien Nunb, one of the heroes of the Battle of Endor, she was every bit as good a pilot as her brother. Formerly Rogue Squadron's Executive Officer, she was replaced by Tycho Celchu. During the squadron's undercover operation on Coruscant, she was injured and left behind as the rest of her team made their escape. She was later discovered and abducted by Imperial General Derricote's team for use as a Sullustan test subject for his Krytos virus project. Although injected with the virus and left for almost certain death in the laboratory, she was chosen at random to receive the lifesaving bacta cure. After the New Republic conquest of Coruscant, she was found alive and well in Invisec.

**Nunb, Nien** A small, jowled, mouse-eyed native of Sullust, the world that served as the staging area for the Rebel Alliance Fleet prior to the Battle of Endor. Nunb was copilot to Lando Calrissian aboard the *Millennium Falcon* during that historic conflict. In a race against time and a suddenly operational second Death Star, the *Falcon* and Wedge Antilles's X-wing fighter both hit their targets, resulting in the explosion of the battle station. Many of the Sullustan's world-mates also served as Alliance starfighter pilots in the battle. Nunb spoke the liquid, chattering tongue of his species, a language that Calrissian understood.

Prior to his service in the Rebellion, Nunb had been an old friend and business partner of Calrissian. He was a capable trader and pilot, with his ship the *Sublight Queen* being renowned in smuggler circles. Nunb was a top cargo runner for the SoroSuub Corporation. When SoroSuub fully supported the Empire, and began virtually enslaving the Sullustans, Nunb used his position to publicly harass the corporation. He began stealing mineral consignments directly from SoroSuub, becoming a hero to many Sullustans. SoroSuub responded with force, with the Empire supporting the corporation with a Star Destroyer. Nunb lost his ship in that encounter, but he joined the Alliance soon thereafter.

Nunb flew missions for the Alliance after Endor, then retired and followed in Calrissian's footsteps. He went respectable, in smuggler parlance, and entered into a risky business venture on Kessel. With the Empire long chased out of the Kessel spice mines, Nunb took over the operation, replacing prison slave labor with droids and turning Kessel into a profitable and respectable operation by supplying spice for medicinal and other legal uses.

**Nunce system** One of the first star systems subjugated by the Empire after the end of the Clone Wars.

**Nuni** This Galacian woman was a member of the Hill People, and was known for her skills in watching over and teaching the children of her clan. She was one of Elan's most trusted friends.

**Nunurra** A city on the planet Roon, it was the site of the Roon Colonial Games.

**Nur, Raglath** This Yuuzhan Vong warrior was assigned to a squad that hunted down the remaining Jedi on Coruscant shortly after the alien invaders captured the capital planet. After treasonous Senator Viqi Shesh was captured trying to leave Coruscant, she was assigned to Nur's detachment when reports of Force-wielding beings began to trickle into Yuuzhan Vong command posts. Nur and his party were killed when they encountered Irek Ismaren—then known as Lord Nyax—deep beneath Coruscant's surface.

**Nuralee** This planet experienced an economic collapse in the years following the Battle of Naboo. Astri Oddo, the wife of Nuralee's elected Senator, Bog Divinian, was at the forefront of a relief group that petitioned the Old Republic for assistance. She hoped that the passage of the All Planets Relief Fund would help Nuralee's situation.

**Nuri** This Clawdite shape-shifter made a living on Aargau during the last decades of the Old Republic by assuming the guise of a helpful Bimm in order to aid unknowing individuals in recovering their fortunes from the planet's banks. Nuri agreed to lead the individuals to the Undercity, where he assured them that cheaper and less obvious methods of making withdrawals were available. In this way, he gained the confidence of young Boba Fett just weeks after the Battle of Geonosis. Once Nuri delivered an individual to an access machine, he withdrew his own "small" commission—usually a large percentage of the individual's fortune—then left him or her stranded. Boba Fett encountered Nuri again on Xagobah during the search for Wat Tambor. Fett, then 13, discovered that it was Nuri who had helped Tambor escape from prison and was now helping to guard his fortress on Xagobah. In a brief struggle, Fett managed to disarm Nuri and force him to reveal Tambor's exact location by drugging him with the poison of a xabar fungus. The fungus, however, had been among those altered by Tambor, and Nuri was immediately rendered rigid and unconscious. All his body functions were reduced to bare minimum levels, and he appeared to be dead.

***Nuro*** The designation of a group of Imperial tankers used to supply the Bretie production facility during the Galactic Civil War.

**Nursery** This was the name given to the interior of the seedship commanded by Master Shaper Ch'Gang Hool. Here a group of immature dhuryams was allowed to grow and learn about controlling their environment. The Nursery was divided into wedges, with the points of each wedge touching the central pond where the dhuryams were growing. Artificial night and day were provided by immense light sources, and the Nursery was stocked with all forms of natural resources. Slaves were assigned to each dhuryam infant, which controlled its own slave in order to execute its personal plan for developing the resources in its own wedge. When the time came, the dhuryams that had grown in the Nursery were subjected to the trials of the *tizo'pil Yun'tchilat,* in which a single individual would emerge as the World Brain that would seed Coruscant.

**nursery rings** Situated on the tallest wroshyr trees on Kashyyyk, nursery rings were built as a sort of day care and school for young Wookiees.

**Nuruodo** One of the longest-tenured of the Chiss Ruling Families, it was considered the Eighth Ruling Family during the years leading up to the Clone Wars. The Nuruodo family controlled much of the Chiss military forces, including units from each of the 28 Chiss colony worlds as well as the Chiss Expansionary Defense Fleet and most Chiss foreign affairs.

**Nuruodo, Shawnkyr** This female Chiss was a member of the Syndic Mitth'raw'nuruodo who served under Jagged Fel in the Chiss Navy. Two years younger than Jag, she accompanied him on a mission to scout those planets already captured by the Yuuzhan Vong from the Unknown Regions coreward, shortly after the Battle of Coruscant, to find any shred of information on the alien invaders. After meeting up with Jaina Solo on Hapes, Shawnkyr failed to appreciate what Colonel Fel saw in the younger woman. Shawnkyr was openly disdainful of Jaina's skills and ability to lead, despite the impressive results she achieved against the Yuuzhan Vong.

When Jagged joined the Twin Suns Squadron, just after the Second Battle of Coruscant, Shawnkyr was given command of the Chiss Vanguard Squadron assigned to the New Republic remnant on Borleias. She bristled at the prospect of being re-missioned, believing that their task was simply to evaluate the galactic situation and return to Csilla. Jag explained that any damage they could do to the Yuuzhan Vong while on Borleias would only help the Chiss, while also providing deeper intelligence on the invaders. Shawnkyr agreed to remain on Borleias and transmit any information they gathered via holotransmission to Csilla, provided that Jag agreed to return to Csilla immediately if she were to die in combat. Together they worked with the New Republic military after Jag realized that they would have to fight alongside the Republic to gather detailed intelligence for Csilla. Shawnkyr did not like it, but she understood the necessity of good data. After the Battle of Ebaq, however, Shawnkyr decided that there was enough information on the Yuuzhan Vong, and Jag gave her leave to return to Csilla.

**Nushk** This planet, the third world in the Hoth system, was covered with liquid-methane oceans. It was orbited by four moons.

**nusito** This unusual predator was known for its ability to bond with another being at birth. A tribe of warriors trained their elite soldiers by providing each of them with a nusito pup. Bonding with the creature was essential to the soldier's development. However, when those soldiers were ready to join the military, they were required to strangle their nusito in order to graduate. Those who refused were removed from military service, since military duty had to come before any other loyalties or emotions.

**nus whale** This oceanic mammal was native to the oceans of Dorumaa. A mature bull nus whale could swallow a fishing trawler whole, making the species an extremely dangerous target. An average specimen could grow as much as 20 meters a year if food was plentiful. Bulls 100 meters long, and cows over 8 meters, were not uncommon during the last decades of the Old Republic.

**nut-beetle** These small, shiny, slippery insects were considered a delicacy by many humans. They were cracked open while still alive; the tasty meat was removed and eaten, and the shell was discarded.

**nutrient vine** These specially grown, bioengineered vines were used by the Yuuzhan Vong to carry nutrients and other biological fluids to and from gestation bins. Common in cloning facilities, nutrient vines also could administer hormones and other chemicals to growing clones.

**nutripill** Any nutrient-packed lozenge that was produced as an emergency ration for starship crews. While nutripills provided large amounts of vitamins and minerals, they were not intended to take the place of actual foodstuffs.

**Nutrofit** This corporation produced a wide range of processed foodstuffs during the era of the New Republic and into the era of the Galactic Alliance. Among its most popular products was gelmeat.

**Nuum, Cabrool** A longtime business associate of crime lord Jabba the Hutt on the planet Smarteel, he had turned a bit insane. When Cabrool Nuum ordered Jabba to kill someone he didn't know named Vu Chusker, the Hutt refused and was imprisoned. Later Jabba murdered Nuum with assistance from Nuum's own henchmen and Nuum's son.

**Nuum, Rusk** The son of Cabrool Nuum, he was killed for double-crossing Jabba. The Hutt snapped Rusk's head, jumped on him, and squashed him into a fine paste.

**Nuur, Shaela** This ancient Jedi Knight was once a student of the renowned Jedi Master Ood Bnar. When Master Bnar initiated his life-cycle change, he bequeathed a solari crystal to Shaela, whom he considered his most promising student. Shaela had been working with Guun Han Saresh and Duron Qel-Droma to hunt down and destroy the terentateks that had escaped during the Great Sith War. On a mission to eliminate any terentateks that remained on Korriban, their party was fragmented when Guun Han grew jealous of, and angry at, the relationship Shaela had with Duron. Guun Han claimed that their passion placed them all on a path to the dark side, and he left the group and traveled on his own to Kashyyyk. Alone on Korriban, Shaela and Duron were no match for the terentateks they encountered. Duron was killed first when the planet's dark side energy clouded his ability to affect the creatures' minds. His death left Shaela alone and grieving on the Sith world. She felt herself slipping over to the dark side, blaming Guun Han for Duron's death and hating him for it. Her last words were recorded on a datapad that was later recovered by another group of Jedi Knights, indicating that she set out to kill terentateks in an act of revenge. She tracked a beast to Naga Sadow's tomb, but was unprepared for the appearance of a second, larger terentatek. She was believed to have been killed by the pair. Master Bnar's solari crystal vanished with her death.

**Nuyu** This Lafrarian male was a tattoo artist and body decorator who ran a small shop on StarForge Station during the Galactic Civil War.

**Ny** This woman was a native of the planet Gaftikar during the years surrounding the Clone Wars. A native of the city of Eyat, Ny was a mechanic who became friends with the ARC trooper known as A'den during the Old Republic's search for the rogue trooper Sull. To Ny, A'den was just a man, so she was a bit surprised when he introduced her to Sull, who as a fellow clone looked almost the same. However, she agreed to help Sull get away from Gaftikar and escape recapture by other soldiers or Republic Intelligence agents.

**Nyasko** A planet in the Colunda sector, it was the location of an AT-AT battalion. The Imperial tech Deppo was kept busy fighting the intense Rebel activity in the sector.

**Nyax, Lord** The name adopted by Irek Ismaren, inspired by an ancient Corellian demon. Irek awoke on Coruscant to discover he had been altered by his mother Roganda to become a Force-wielding homunculus. Irek at first had no idea of his identity, his mind being a virtual blank save for the incomplete programming his mother had provided. After killing her and escaping his laboratory prison on Coruscant, he adopted the Lord Nyax name after hearing it in the minds of his murder victims. Despite the unfinished nature of his programming, Lord Nyax had a deep connection to the dark side of the Force. He used mental projection to control weak-minded beings who survived the Second Battle of Coruscant, drawing on their energies while using them to scout out the Yuuzhan Vong. He also learned how to wield a collection of lightsabers connected to the gloves and joints of his body, making him a formidable opponent. Lord Nyax discovered the location of the former Jedi Temple on Coruscant, sensing its presence by the incredible knot of Force energy beneath it. Nyax drew strength from the well of energy, twisting it to the dark side and growing incredibly powerful. When Luke Skywalker and his infiltration team discovered Nyax, they were forced into battle in order to stop the monster from adding to the troubles plaguing the New Republic. They were unable to battle him with lightsabers, but a concerted effort to disable him using rocks and boulders proved effective enough to crush him to death. (*See also* Ismaren, Irek.)

**Nye** This clone trooper was one of the men who served in the Sarlacc Battalions that were trapped on Dinlo about a year after the Battle of Geonosis. Nye and many of his comrades were rescued by Jedi Knight Etain Tur-Mukan and the clone troopers of Improcco Company, who defied orders to return to Dinlo and rescue the battalions.

**Nyiestra** This Alderaanian woman fell in love with Tycho Celchu when both were teenagers. They made plans to marry, and Nyiestra agreed to wait for him to graduate from the Imperial Academy. She kept waiting through his first year of duty as a TIE pilot. The Death Star destroyed their plans along with all of Alderaan.

**Nykl** This young Balawai boy was one of five children rescued by Mace Windu from a lava flow in the jungle of Haruun Kal shortly after the Battle of Geonosis, when the Jedi Master traveled to the planet to locate Depa Billaba. The children, led by Terrel Nakay, had been trying to return to their camp in a steamcrawler when it was caught by the lava. Nykl, his brother Urno, and Keela and Pell Nakay were taken in by Nick Rostu, after Windu left.

Darca Nyl

**Nyklas, Commander** This Imperial officer was in charge of construction on a new wing of the Imperial Hall of Heroes when Han Solo was sent to assist him. Nyklas had been using—and mistreating—a group of Wookiee slaves he had obtained from the Trandoshan slaver Ssoh. During a mission to obtain more Wookiees, Nyklas found that his contact's ship was disabled. He ordered Han and his flight of TIE fighters to take out the ship, but Han discovered that there were Wookiees still alive on board. Nyklas ordered Han to kill the survivors, but Han rebelled against this senseless slaughter. He freed one of the Wookiees, named Chewbacca, and was immediately reprimanded by Nyklas. Han was quickly given a dishonorable discharge and blacklisted as a pilot.

**Nyl, Darca** A former mercenary who gave up his life of bloodshed to settle down and raise a family after he fell in love and married a woman named Teril. But his wife died during childbirth, leaving him to raise their son Neas on his own. Years later, a ship crashed near Nyl's home. At the crash site, a dying Jedi gave Nyl his lightsaber with instructions that he would need it to hunt down a vicious escaped criminal, a Dark Jedi named Lycan. When Nyl returned home, he found that Lycan had killed Neas. For months he followed Lycan's trail, in the hope that he could avenge his son's death.

His travels took him to a mining world run by a man named Samuel where he helped to save Samuel's daughter, who had been kidnapped. He later found himself on a planet where he rescued a woman named Jaren from bikers. He later realized that Jaren was harboring a fugitive, her brother Ament who had killed dozens of people because he was prone to fits of rage. He helped bring Jaren and Ament into custody.

The search for Lycan finally led Darca Nyl to Molavar where he helped an elderly couple fight off a crime boss. When he finally found Lycan, he set a trap for him in a cavern rigged with mines. Lycan had lost his memory in the crash on Darca's homeworld, so he had Darca Nyl fill in the missing pieces. Before Lycan had a chance to kill Nyl, Nyl set off charges that brought down the cave's ceiling, killing Lycan. Though not a Jedi, he took Lycan's lightsaber for his own, lay low during the Clone Wars, and then joined the nascent Rebel Alliance.

**nylar** An inexpensive synthetic fabric used to make clothing in the early years of the New Republic.

**nylasteel** This material was created by mixing nylar fibers into flexible steel. It was useful in the manufacture of high-strength straps and bands for securing cargo containers.

**Nylykerka, Ayddar** A Tammarian, he was chief analyst of the Asset Tracking office of Fleet Intelligence. Ayddar Nylykerka was the first Rebel to acquire data files from the damaged Imperial vessel *Gnisnal* and to realize the enormity of the find: It was the first copy of a complete Imperial Order of Battle that the New Republic had ever seen. Nylykerka risked his life to deliver the files to Admiral Ackbar personally. Among other things, the New Republic learned that there were more vessels assigned to the Imperial Black Sword Command than the New Republic had accounted for. Later, Nylykerka analyzed the images sent back from the recon X-wing fighters of the Yevethan forces mobilized at N'zoth. He was able to identify some missing Imperial Star Destroyers that were taken by the Yevetha during the initial attack on the Imperial shipyards at N'zoth.

**Nym** This Feeorin pirate stole from the rich to give to the poor in the shadows of the Naboo system. Nym was orphaned on the planet Lok as an infant, and was raised by criminals and pirates. He developed into a fearsome fighter, not because he was overly violent, but because he was swift and effective. Nym was known as a tactical genius as well as a scoundrel, and his piracy of Trade Federation convoys earned him a considerable bounty. When regular channels failed to bring him into custody, the Federation hired Vana Sage. She was able to lure Nym and his crew into a trap when they tried to sell off a load of experimental Scalp-Hunter blasters they obtained from the Trade Federation.

Despite her success, Nym's crew soon rescued him from the Trade Federation and he returned to Lok to fight the occupation of his homeworld. Nym piloted his ship, the *Havoc,* during the Battle of Naboo, helping to break the Trade Federation's blockade and restore trade to the system. A full pardon of his past crimes from Chancellor Palpatine allowed Nym to continue his piracy as well, although he was never financially rewarded. He returned to his adopted homeworld, only to find it still under the control of the Trade Federation. He spent the next few months in Bothan space, biding his time until he could return home.

Six years after the Battle of Naboo, Nym was hired by the Mere Ambassador Loreli Ro to help her people overthrow the Trade Federation's control of Maramere. Nym reluctantly agreed to help, but found himself fighting Sol Sixxa's forces as well as the Trade Federation. In the end, though, Nym convinced Sixxa to join forces with him, and the two set out to destroy the Trade Federation. In the wake of the Clone Wars, Nym returned to Lok and became the planet's leader.

He grew more cunning and shrewd as he aged, and was revered by his people during the New Order era. It was rumored that he kept several possessions of an old friend, the Jedi Master Adi Gallia, in his hidden retreat on Lok. Nym remained on Lok for many years as the Empire rose to power and began patrolling the space lanes. If the price was right, he would sometimes support the actions of the Rebel Alliance, although he refused to commit to either side during the Galactic Civil War.

Nym

**Nym's Stronghold Cantina** This cantina, owned and operated by the Feeorin pirate Nym, was located in the primary starport on the planet Lok, during the Galactic Civil War. A haven for smugglers and pirates, Nym's Stronghold was also a place where Rebel Alliance agents could meet to discuss missions or make a covert rendezvous.

**Nynie** A 9-A9 child-care droid about the height of an R2 astromech, she had a conical body that was wide at the base and tapered up to a neck that could extend itself to the length of 2 meters. Nynie's arms were spindly, ending in tripod pincers padded with small balls of rubber. While her body looked decidedly mechanical, Nynie's head had the little apple face of a human grandmother. She always smiled kindly and was capable of singing lullabies. Nynie took care of the Rogue Squadron pilot Plourr Ilo—in reality a princess and heir to the throne of Eiattu VI—when she was a child. The droid was also capable of piloting and acting as an R2 unit thanks to special circuitry added so that the princess could learn to fly an airspeeder at an early age.

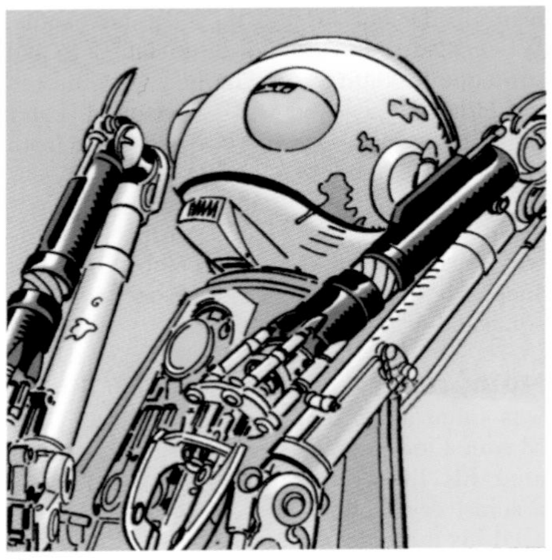
Nynie

**Nyny** The homeworld of a three-headed species. Thirteen years after the Battle of Endor, the senator from Nyny was killed in the bombing of Senate Hall on Coruscant.

**Nyras, Adrianna** This woman served the Brotherhood of Darkness as an admiral in the Sith navy, commanding the flagship *Nightfall* during the months leading up to the Battle of Ruusan. She was ordered by Lord Kaan to keep any Jedi vessels at bay, engaging them only if the Jedi fired first. However, the Sith fleet was massive, and the meager collection of ships led by Jedi Master Valenthyne Farfalla knew that an attack would be suicidal. Thus, Admiral Nyras was confused when she received a transmission from Lord Kaan's personal communications node and found herself speaking with Darth Bane. Her confusion was only deepened when Bane ordered her to engage the Jedi fleet—an order that ran contrary to the entire battle plan. However, Admiral Nyras was forced to admit that Bane was using Lord Kaan's personal communications node, so he must have been following Kaan's orders. She therefore ordered the Sith fleet to engage the Jedi, unaware that she had been manipulated by Bane, who had been plotting the destruction of the Brotherhood of Darkness. As the battle was joined above Ruusan, Master Farfalla was able to sneak past the Sith warships and land reinforcements on Ruusan, bolstering the Army of Light and forcing Lord Kaan to use his thought bomb to bring an end to the fighting.

**Nyrkar** This Wookiee worked as the Director of Food Preservation and Dietary Consultation at the Dry Goods Emporium, on the planet Cularin, during the last years of the Old Republic. It was later discovered that Nyrkar was also one of the founding members of the underground resistance that sprang up in response to the Metatheran Cartel's presence on the world in the years following the Battle of Naboo.

**Nyroska** This short-statured man was a colonel in the Darkknell Defense Agency at the time when Garm Bel Iblis tried to recover the plans to the first Death Star in Xakrea. He was a loyal supporter of the Empire, although he rarely received any form of support from the local garrison. He attempted to make a great deal of credits by recovering datacards that contained the plans to the first Death Star, then selling them to Ysanne Isard. However, his scheme was thwarted when Isard sliced into his computer systems and redirected his troops. Moranda Savich and Garm Bel Iblis

managed to recover the plans, leaving Nyroska with nothing but Isard's wrath.

**Nyrvona** The second planet in the Ylesian system to be colonized by the Besadii kajidic as a religious retreat. Like its predecessor, Ylesia, Nyrvona was touted as a religious holy land, but in fact it became a ready source of processed spice and slaves.

**Nysshyyyk** This Wookiee clan lived on Kashyyyk until it was captured by Imperial forces that raided the planet for slaves. Most of the clan's members were sent to work at the Maw Installation under the sadistic eye of Grodon Lakky. Eight Nysshyyyk Wookiees were killed by Lakky's unrelenting use of a power-lash within the first month after he accused them of sabotaging their work. Four others committed suicide rather than submit to Lakky's terror. Fifty more died from exhaustion during the construction of the Death Star prototype.

**Nystammall** This Vuvrian was one of the many Jedi Masters killed by General Grievous during the Clone Wars. Nystammall died on Tovarskl, along with his former Master, Puroth. Both of their lightsabers were confiscated by Grievous, who later used them in combat against Obi-Wan Kenobi.

**Nystao** This was the primary cultural center of Honoghr during the early years of the New Republic, primarily because it was one of the few locations on the planet that supported any form of life. Because of this, Nystao was the site of the Grand Dukha. The city had an Imperial-built spaceport that was operated by Noghri, but it was usually kept closed except for Imperial traffic.

**Nyth, Volu** This woman, a native of the planet Kuat, joined the New Republic's Rogue Squadron shortly before the Battle of Coruscant. She remained a part of the Galactic Alliance military for many years, but was among the many officers who chose to leave military service when Jacen Solo began his rise to power. She then rejoined Wedge Antilles aboard the *Errant Venture,* and agreed to serve as Rakehell Eleven as part of a mission to disable Centerpoint Station and prevent it from falling into Solo's hands.

**Nytinite** This purplish mist was a form of sleeping gas used by guerrilla armies during the Clone Wars.

**Nyxy** A New Republic Senator from the planet Rudrig.

*N'zoth*

**N'zoth** The homeworld of the Yevetha, it was located in the system of the same name in the Koornacht Cluster and was the capital of the Yevethan federation known as the Duskhan League. N'zoth was a dry world orbiting a golden sun; from space it appeared to be gray-green with yellow clouds. Pa'aal was the primary moon of the fifth planet of the N'zoth system. The 2,000 stars of the Koornacht Cluster burned so brightly in N'zoth's night sky that more distant stars were never visible, which contributed to the early Yevethan view that their species was the only one in the universe.

Female Yevetha were called marasi and males, nitakka. Young were born in separate "birth-casks" called mara-nas. Yevetha only considered killing to be murder if someone of lower status killed someone of higher status. High-status males had every right to kill their lessers for any reason; such killings were commonplace and accepted. Yevetha also were extremely adept with technology and learned new skills rapidly.

By the time the Empire arrived in the Cluster, the Yevetha had spread from N'zoth and colonized 11 nearby planets, even without hyperdrive technology. The arriving Imperials established an orbiting repair yard (code-named Black 15) at N'zoth as well as a garrison on the planet's surface. The Yevetha were forced to work as Imperial slaves and learned much about the Empire's technology by servicing its ships at the repair yard. Eight months after the Battle of Endor, faced with mounting losses in battles with the New Republic, the Empire planned to evacuate all forces from N'zoth and to destroy the Black 15 shipyard. Yevethan leader Nil Spaar and his commando team used the confusion of the moment to capture the *Intimidator* and murder 20,000 Imperial citizens by firing the Super Star Destroyer's turbolasers on the evacuation transports. He then claimed the yards and all nine of its capital ships in the name of the Yevetha Protectorate.

Nil Spaar took over as viceroy of the Duskhan League after the death of former viceroy Kiv Truun. The Black 15 yard was later moved away from N'zoth to a clandestine location. Surface yards on N'zoth became the prime source for spherical thrustships built by the Nazfar Metalworks Guild. Twelve years after the Battle of Endor, after the Yevetha captured all alien colony worlds lying inside the Cluster's borders in the Great Purge, Nil Spaar returned to N'zoth to a hero's welcome. His thrustship *Aramadia* landed at Hariz before three million onlookers, and he proceeded in glory to the ruling city of Giat Nor, which held more than a million of N'zoth's 700 million inhabitants.

At the top level of Spaar's palace was a private breeding ground with 16 alcoves for birth-casks and a grated floor for blood sacrifices. After a long and bloody war with the New Republic, the Yevethan fleet was smashed when its captured Imperial ships were commandeered by Imperial slaves and taken out of the system. The remaining Yevethan thrustships were destroyed by the New Republic fleet. Spaar was captured, ejected into hyperspace in an escape pod, and left to die.

Years later, after the planet Coruscant fell to the Yuuzhan Vong, the Fia of Galantos made a deal with the alien invaders. The Fia provided information on the Yevetha's strengths and weaknesses in return for their own freedom. Hoping to eliminate a possible problem on their rear borders, the Yuuzhan Vong mercilessly attacked the Yevetha, destroying the planet N'zoth and wiping out every known member of Yevethan civilization.

**101st Regiment** A division of the Grand Army of the Republic under the command of Jedi Padawan Danyawarra, who reluctantly accepted a field promotion to commander at the height of the Clone Wars. The 101st Regiment was part of the 7th Legion.

**105th Stormtrooper Platoon** An Imperial unit assigned to Starlyte Station. These were neither the best nor the brightest of the Empire's soldiers, but they were unswervingly loyal. They called themselves the Emperor's Irregulars and were led by Commander Brezzic Marr. Their unit symbol showed arcing lightning passing across the Imperial symbol.

**12-4C-41 (Wuntoo Forcee Forwun)** A SoroSuub traffic controller droid, second class, assigned to Cloud City on Bespin during the Galactic Civil War. Forwun was present on Cloud City when EV-9D9 committed a droid massacre. Years later, he tracked down EV-9D9 to Jabba's palace. Deep beneath the palace, in 9D9's hidden laboratory of sorts, Forwun confronted the maniacal droid. He crippled EV-9D9 with a blaster pistol. But rather than let her relish her pain, he deactivated her prized pain button—a device that transmitted the electronic sensations of agony to the sadistic droid. Leaving her dying, Forwun released the victims of EV-9D9's experiments, who crawled to her and dismantled her.

**127th Gunship Wing** One of the first divisions of the Grand Army of the Republic assigned to piloting LAAT/t and LAAT/i gunships. They first saw duty during the Battle of Geonosis and remained active throughout the Clone Wars. At the end of the Clone Wars, the 127th was dispatched to help Jedi Master Plo Koon complete the takeover of Cato Neimoidia.

**132nd Forward Division** This branch of the Rebel Alliance's armed forces was stationed in Atrivis sector during the Galactic Civil War.

**177th Light Infantry Division** Commandos from this branch of the Rebel Alliance armed forces were captured and killed by the Empire, after the agent known as Corewatch failed to retrieve them.

*< Otoh Gunga*

**181st Imperial Fighter Group** At one time nicknamed the "One-Eighty-Worst" for their lackluster record, this TIE fighter squadron was whipped into shape and made famous by Soontir Fel during the early years of the New Republic. The 181st served during the Battle of Endor, and fled when Captain Pellaeon ordered the retreat of the Imperial forces after the death of Emperor Palpatine. It was believed that this group was assigned to Warlord Zsinj's fleet, although the exact reasons weren't discovered until Admiral Rogriss revealed that the actual 181st was still an Imperial unit. Zsinj himself had created a duplicate 181st, with Tetran Cowall acting as Soontir Fel, in the hope of drawing Rogue Squadron into a trap.

**1e-XE** An MD-3 medical droid, one of two taken from Jabba the Hutt's palace by Dengar following the crime lord's death on Tatooine. Along with SHΣ1-B, 1e-XE was useful in reviving Boba Fett after the bounty hunter escaped from the Sarlacc's gullet. A white-banded droid with a very minimalist outlook, 1e-XE never spoke in more than two- or three-word phrases, and often simply used a single word to express its current state of mind. When Fett was nearly healed following the attempt by Kuat of Kuat to eliminate him, the droids were left behind as the bounty hunters fled the planet.

**O44** A Trade Federation battle droid commando deployed during the Battle of Naboo.

**Oakie** *See* Okeefe, Platt.

**Oa Park** A beautiful park on Coruscant that contained more than 30 different environments, representing planets across the Galactic Republic.

**Oasis** A Dim-U religious community in the wastes of Tatooine. The town leader was Dryon, the High Priest.

**Oasis Mining Colony** An oxite-mining colony found on a volcanic moon orbiting an unnamed planet in a clear spot within the Maelstrom Nebula. Rodin Higron, a Corellian privateer, won it in a crooked game of sabacc. Higron used Oasis as a base of operations for pirate strikes against Imperial vessels. He allowed the Rebels to construct a safeworld there in return for a number of X-wing fighters.

**oasis mother** The mature phase of an unusual creature native to Endregaad. The mature form resembled a huge tree rooted near a water source. Its immature form—oasis children—emerged from fruit-like sacs in their mother's branches and were much more mobile, being able to bring back food. The oasis mother was linked to her children via telepathy.

**Obah, Jyn** The first mate to the pirate Kybo Ren during the early days of the Empire. A hulking humanoid over 2 meters tall, Obah had long red hair, a protruding lower jaw with blocky teeth, and a ring through his nose. He wore fragments of stormtrooper armor, including the chest plate and upper portion of the helmet. When Ren was imprisoned by Mon Julpa of Tammuz-an, Obah rescued his leader, only to be captured himself. Ren then took the Tammuz-an Princess Gerin captive, demanding that his captured crew be released in exchange. Obah was briefly reunited with his leader before a secret plan devised by Lord Toda and Mon Julpa resulted in the capture of all the pirates.

**obah gas** A dangerous substance that caused permanent nerve disabilities in creatures smaller than Wookiees.

**Obas** A volcanic world in the Expansion Region, it was the site of a Rebel Alliance base during the Galactic Civil War.

**obedience-rational module** A component of a droid's brain that controlled its independence. C-3PO often wondered if R2-D2's obedience-rational module was developing a flutter.

**Oberk, Corporal** A stormtrooper biker scout from Ukio assigned to search for Rebel activity on the Forest Moon of Endor, he was constantly trying to impress the commander of his detachment. Instead, he was clubbed unconscious by Leia Organa.

**Obersken** A burly, elderly Chiss, he served as chief mechanic at the Chiss military training world during the early years of the New Republic.

***Obex*** A Galactic Republic *Nu*-class shuttle, it transported clone officers Rex and Cody to the Rishi moon during the Clone Wars.

**Obica** Prior to the Rebel Alliance fleet massing at Sullust for the Battle of Endor, Alliance leaders rendezvoused with Sullustan commander Syub Snunb at a point near Obica. Snunb then led the fleet back to his homeworld, where they prepared for the assault on the second Death Star.

**Obigon, Captain** The commanding officer aboard the *Null Space*, a Corellian pirate gunship. Some time after the Battle of Endor, Obigon's ship was stolen from him, ironically by the Empire. The Empire, hungry for ships, used zero-g stormtroopers to capture it.

**O-Bin** *See* Bin.

**Obinipor** An ore-rich volcanic planet just Rimward of New Republic space. After the Battle of Endor, it was one of the stopping points of the *Night Caller* before the corvette was captured by Wraith Squadron.

**Obitoki** An alien Podracer who competed against Sebulba during the final years of the Galactic Republic. Sebulba used the heat vents on his Podracer to cut through Obitoki's engines, knocking Obitoki out of the race. Another Podracer, Habba, was also knocked out by flying into Obitoki's debris.

***Obi-Wan*** The first *Defender*-class Star Destroyer produced for the New Republic Navy, named for Obi-Wan Kenobi.

***Objurium*** A *Lambda*-class shuttle that transported Kirtan Loor from the *Aggressor* to Coruscant about four years after the Battle of Endor.

**Oblee** Heavyset beings with pink skin and double sets of eyes, this asymmetrical species had three arms, two to the left side of their bodies and one on the right. They were nearly eradicated by the power of the Darkstaff more than a millennium before the outbreak of the Clone Wars.

**Obligon Nebula** A small dust cloud found within the Naboo system near the asteroids of Arrissa's Field, it was a haven for pirates.

***Obliterator*** One of the last remaining Star Destroyers in the Empire 15 years after the Battle of Endor, commanded by Captain Trazzen and part of Moff Disra's sector force.

**OboRin Comet Cluster** An obscure comet cluster in the Coruscant system. Uncharted asteroids orbited alongside the OboRins, making that area well suited for camouflaging vessels during the Yuuzhan Vong War. The invaders staged their assault on Coruscant from there. Luke Skywalker led the attack on the *Sunulok* at the OboRin Comet Cluster in the early moments of the siege.

**Obota, Alfonso Luiz** Originally from the Adega system, he graduated fourth in his class from the Merchant Academy, and then served as third officer on a freighter before resigning that post and joining the Rebellion. He accepted a commission as a second lieutenant on a Special Operations transport named the *Pride of Aridus.* Six months later, Obota led a mutiny on the *Aridus* when its commanding officer was about to abandon a Special Ops team once the situation became, to his reckoning, unsalvageable. Obota refused Captain Nord's direct orders, struck him, and confined him to his cabin, taking control of the ship. Obota's actions saved the lives of three Special Ops members, but cost the lives of five *Aridus* crew members. Obota was court-martialed and imprisoned.

A short time later, Alliance agents Kyle Katarn and Jan Ors freed Obota and recruited him as their deck officer on an important mission. Newly restored as a lieutenant, Obota flew aboard the captured Imperial transport *High Hauler,* posing as Lieutenant Hortu Agar. This ruse allowed the Rebel agents to sneak past watchful Imperial eyes.

**Obredaan** The site of a hidden cortosis mine operated by the Jin'ha before the Battle of Naboo. Jedi Masters Eeth Koth and Plo Koon investigated activity there and were held captive until rescued by Obi-Wan Kenobi. Decades later, during the growing conflict between the Galactic Alliance and Corellia, Obredaan opposed the formation of the Galactic Alliance Guard.

**Obrim, Jaller** A Senate Guard during the Clone Wars tasked with protecting the Senate Rotunda on Coruscant. He was in charge of working with clone commandos from Omega Squadron to rescue Senator Meena Tills, who was held hostage by terrorists.

**Obroa-held** A gas giant in the Obroa-skai system.

**Obroan Institute** Based out of Obroa-skai, this foundation was dedicated to the science of archaeology. It dispatched a team of experts to the dead planet of Brath Qella 12 years into the New Republic's rule, investigating ties to the mysterious starship dubbed the Teljkon vagabond.

**Obroa-skai** Prior to its devastation in the Yuuzhan Vong War, this world was best known for its massive library, said to contain the gathered knowledge of the galaxy. Five years after the Battle of Endor, Imperial agents made a partial data dump from the Obroans' central library, from which Grand Admiral Thrawn gleaned the location of Wayland, site of one of the late Emperor's storehouses.

Obroa-skai's terrain was marked by frozen deserts, mountains, and ice-covered oceans. The system of the same name was inside the Borderland Regions. During Grand Admiral Thrawn's campaign to conquer the New Republic, envoys attempted to convince the Obroans to join the new galactic government. Both it and its neighboring Paonid system remained neutral for much of the war.

When the Yuuzhan Vong invaded the galaxy, Obroa-skai was victim of a surprise attack, and many of its libraries were destroyed.

**observation holocam** *See* holocam.

**Observer** A model of personal homing device manufactured by MechBlaze Tracking Corporation.

**Obsidian Squadron** Modified TIE fighters used to chase raiders through the upper atmosphere of planets, this squadron pursued the *Millennium Falcon* from Cloud City into space after the Battle of Hoth. Obsidian Seven recorded an impressive number of career kills and was nicknamed Winged Gundark. Obsidian Eight was formerly stationed aboard the Star Destroyer *Devastator.*

**Obstacle** The first segment of the Katharsis game played on Telos, it required contestants to navigate swoop bikes past holographic obstacles.

**Obtrexta sector** An area of space bordering Raioballo sector. A defunct hyperspace route called Myto's Arrow connected Obtrexta to Dantooine. Other points along the route included the Gabredor system.

***Ocean*** Supreme Commander Cha Niathal's flagship in the Galactic Alliance Defense Force.

**Ocheron** A Nightsister on the planet Dathomir, she was skilled at deception. The old hag nearly defeated Singing Clan witch Teneniel Djo and Luke Skywalker with one of her spells—she sucked the wind from their lungs and barraged them with Force lightning. Luke decapitated the witch with his lightsaber.

**Ockbur** The innermost planet of the Ralltiir system, it was a searing ball of rock.

**octensen** A white, foamy lubricant used in repulsorlift engines. It was patented by Bespin Motors.

**octuptarra droid** A modular, scalable design developed by the Techno Union, named for the eight-eyed gasbag-headed vine walk-

*Octuptarra droid*

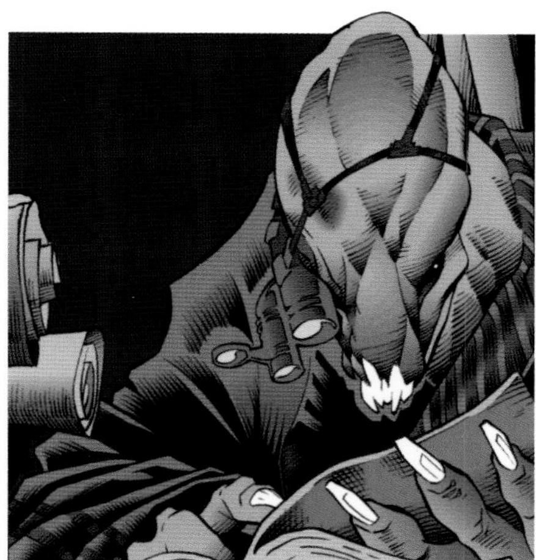
Odan-Urr

ers found on Skako. Enormous versions of this model, called tri-droids, could be unleashed on the battlefield as combat artillery, but the battle-droid-sized anti-personnel model traded scale for agility. Its rotating turret assembly could fire from extended ranges. The globular cognitive unit—a large and tempting target—often held a virus deadly to clone troopers within its hollows. After the Clone Wars, most octuptarra droids wound up on Uba IV, a Separatist planet that boasted a droid-manufacturing plant. In the minds of many, octuptarra droids became interchangeable with the fearsome, masked Ubese.

**Odala, Sheel** A cocky female smuggler who was an old acquaintance of Han Solo. Han ran into her at a sabacc game in Void Station six months after the Battle of Yavin. She was deeply in debt to crime lord and station owner Jib Kopatha, and sought to make some money by turning Solo over to Jib on the guarantee that he would not be harmed. Sheel lured Solo into a trap, where Trandoshan thugs captured him and brought him to Jib, who hoped to torture him for valuable information. Distraught at this turn of events, Sheel eventually teamed up with Chewbacca to rescue Solo. Han extended an invitation to Sheel to join the Rebel Alliance, but she politely declined.

Sheel Odala

**Odan-Urr** A Jedi hero from the Great Hyperspace War 5,000 years before the Battle of Yavin. A Draethos, his first mission was to the Koros system to aid Empress Teta in her effort to unite the seven worlds. There Odan-Urr used Jedi battle meditation to unify Empress Teta's forces and push back the resistance on the planet Kirrek. While meditating, Odan-Urr received a chilling vision in the Force, warning him of the impending rise of the Sith. Concerned, he and Empress Teta held an audience in the Great Senate Hall on Coruscant. His lack of experience undermined his credibility, and his words of warning went unheard. Nonetheless, Empress Teta stood ready to defend the Koros system from the Sith incursion, and her system was one of the few prepared for the Great Hyperspace War. Odan-Urr was reunited with his mentor, Master Ooroo, leading the forces on Kirrek, though Ooroo sacrificed himself in battle.

Aboard a ruined Sith vessel, Odan-Urr discovered a rare Sith Holocron. Remembering his master's insistence that he pass on what he learned, Odan-Urr decided to build a repository of Jedi knowledge on the world of Ossus, a library that eventually grew to legendary proportions. Nearly a millennium later, the galaxy again fell under the pall of the dark side in the lead-up to the Great Sith War. In response, the Jedi held a massive gathering on Mount Meru on the planet Deneba. For 600 years, Odan-Urr had presided over such affairs, and this important meeting of Force-sensitive minds was no different. Odan-Urr's affinity for telepathy allowed him to moderate the gathering by telepathically touching all the Jedi in attendance. Later, Sith Lord Exar Kun broke into the Great Jedi Library and stole the Sith Holocron. Kun killed Odan-Urr with the power of the dark side.

Hermi Odle

**Odd Ball** *See* Davijaan, Captain "Odd Ball."

**Oddo, Astri and Didi** Astri Oddo was the adopted daughter of Didi Oddo, and together they maintained a family café in CoCo Town on Coruscant prior to the Battle of Naboo. Didi Oddo had contacts across the social spectrum of Coruscant, from the Jedi Knights to Senators to the lowliest of the criminal underworld. The death of Fligh, Didi's Senatorial contact, sparked a tumultuous turn of events as a mysterious Sorrusian bounty hunter, Ona Nobis, tracked back a web of connections to the Oddos and targeted them for termination. This prompted them to flee to Duneeden with the help of the Jedi Knight Qui-Gon Jinn and his apprentice, Obi-Wan Kenobi.

The persistent hunter followed them there, and Astri was wounded and Didi infected with a disease developed by Arbor Industries. Astri helped track down Jenna Zan Arbor in an effort to cure Didi's illness, and managed to recover an antidote from a laboratory on Simpla-12. Once Didi was out of danger, Astri was determined to stop Ona Nobis once and for all. This led her to Belasco, where she and the Jedi Knights captured Jenna Zan Arbor; Nobis died in battle. Astri returned to Coruscant and helped her father restore the café.

Years later, Didi retired and sold the café to Dexter Jettster, who refurbished the business as his diner. Astri married a homesteader, Bog Divinian, and moved to the Outer Rim world of Nuralee. Together they had a boy named Lune. Despite being tied to several scandals, Bog succeeded in becoming a Senator, while Astri supported him by joining relief agencies to present a helpful and humanitarian side of herself and her husband. She was even part of the planning committee established to create the All Planets Relief Fund.

Bog, however, continued a career of corruption, and Astri was powerless to stop him, as he threatened to steal away with Lune if she ever revealed his machinations to authorities like the Jedi Knights. In the turmoil that led up to the Clone Wars, Astri finally left Bog, taking Lune with her as she fled to Samaria. She adopted the alias Quintus Farel and was given shelter by the Samarian Prime Minister, Aaren Larker. She worked as a programmer, attempting to erase any trace of her past history. Another link to her past was severed when, during the Clone Wars, Didi passed away.

As the Galactic Empire strengthened, Bog Divinian rose in power, and began scouring the political structure of Samaria for any signs of his wife or son. With the help of Ferus Olin and Trever Flume, Astri and Lune fled the planet, eventually returning to Coruscant.

**Odell, Beuga** A successful nightclub owner on Coruscant during the last decades of the Galactic Republic. She achieved her wealth without direct connection to Hutt criminals working in the area, though she was involved in smuggling, gambling, and narcotics trafficking.

**Odenji** Medium-sized aquatic humanoid bipeds from Issor with smooth, hairless heads and large, webbed hands and feet. Odenji skin ranged from dark brown to tan. They were nearly destroyed some centuries before the Galactic Civil War by an affliction called melanncho. During this time, violent crime and depression increased in Odenji society, and they remained joyless, sad beings.

**"Ode to a Master Chef"** This was an instrumental composition written by Max Rebo.

**Odik II** A world with Imperial political prisoner detention camps.

**Odle, Hermi** A hulking Baragwin, his blubbery skin provided him the benefits of natural armor, and his sense of smell was keen. He was a member of Jabba the Hutt's court, working as a weapons specialist who helped craft the defenses of Jabba's palace. He spent most of his life on Tatooine after his ship was shot down there by an Imperial patrol. Odle had one major nemesis in the palace: Pote Snitkin, a Skrilling gunrunner and skiff pilot. During the battle over the Pit of Carkoon, Odle fired a stun weapon from the sail barge, knocking Snitkin unconscious. Odle escaped the combat zone, eventually making it back to Mos Eisley. There he stole a ship of Jabba's and left the desert planet—and disappeared.

**Odom, Meck** Kyle Katarn's Academy roommate during the reign of the Empire. One of Odom's first posts was as a Special Operations agent, serving at an Imperial installation on Danuta, in the city of Trid. Katarn, a Rebel agent, contacted Odom during a mission there. Appealing to their friendship and Odom's sense of morality, Katarn was able to recruit his help. All Odom had to do was open a gate in the compound's outer perimeter, allowing Katarn access. During Katarn's insertion mission, he came face-to-face with Odom, and to maintain appearances shot the officer with a stun blast. Katarn escaped that mission, complete with the technical readouts of the Death Star battle station.

**Odonnl** He was part of Talon Karrde's crew aboard his starship, *Wild Karrde.*

**Odos** Located in the Odos systems in the Meridian sector, this planet was near the Chorios systems. Most ships wishing to make a hyperspace jump to Coruscant from the region departed from the far side of the Odos systems. Nine years after the Battle of Endor, Han Solo and Lando Calrissian were attacked by an Imperial fleet from the nearby Antemeridian sector while at Exodo II, and lost their pursuers by flying through the gas clouds of Odos and the fringes of the Spangled Veil Nebula.

**Odosk, General** The commanding Imperial Army officer stationed in the secret Imperial think tank known as Maw Installation. Despite a decade of military inactivity, Odosk kept his men fit and combat-ready. When Admiral Daala brought her Star Destroyers out of the confines of the Maw, one of Odosk's first missions was to board a captured trader vessel. Odosk's men secured T'nun Bdu's corvette and rigged it to explode after Bdu spread word of Daala's return.

**Odovrera, Joon** A nightclub entertainer whose performances could be seen on the HoloNet. Odovrera's work was criticized by some as defamatory, especially his routine that carped about the smell of Rodians.

**Odrion, Mors** A Rebel Alliance dignitary who traveled to Sedri with his assistant Rekara during the Galactic Civil War. He was captured by a renegade Sedrian movement, though Rekara escaped and was able to bring back a team of agents to rescue him.

**Odryn** A world inhabited by Feeorin during the era of the Great Sith War, it was possibly—though not definitively—the Feeorin homeworld.

**ODT** *See* Onadax Droid Technologies.

**Odumin** A reclusive territorial manager of the Corporate Sector Authority, this Tynnan was somewhat of a legend since few had ever seen him. Even most of his staff was unaware of his appearance. Odumin crafted his public image carefully, leaking a false biography to the media. All the while, he posed as Spray, a skip tracer from Interstellar Collections Ltd., a career he had when younger.

Odumin worked his way up through the auditor-general's office as a detached duty agent prior to his promotion to a staff position. While posing as a Tynnan tourist, he saved the life of Imperial High Inquisitor Torbin by alerting security agents to an assassination attempt by the fanatical Church of the First Frequency. For his heroism, Odumin was promoted.

Odumin was influential in cracking slaving and criminal operations in the Corporate Sector. A few years before the Battle of Yavin, he was involved in a highly secretive investigation into an illegal slave ring that implicated a number of Corporate Sector execs. Undercover as Spray, he manipulated Han Solo and Chewbacca into helping him achieve his objective.

**odupiendo** A large, flightless bird-like creature featured in odupiendo-racing.

**Oetrago** Located in the Mayagil sector, this planet was covered with what could almost be objectively viewed as very ugly plant life.

**oevvaor** A predatory marine reptile of the Kashyyyk coasts known for its agility and territorial ferocity. The Wookiee oevvaor jet catamarans were named for them.

**Off-Canau** This planet was a popular tourist destination.

***Off Chance*** An old blockade runner owned by Lando Calrissian, won in a sabacc game. In the New Republic's nineteenth year, Lando loaned the *Off Chance* to Jedi Master Luke Skywalker and his student Tenel Ka. The two Jedi took the ship to Borgo Prime, searching for the kidnappers of Jaina Solo, Jacen Solo, and Lowbacca.

**Offdurmin, Bescat** An alias used by Lando Calrissian for a fact-finding mission to Corellia during the civil war between the Galactic Alliance and Confederation.

**Offee, Barriss** A loyal Padawan paired with Jedi Master Luminara Unduli during the Clone Wars. Like Luminara, she was a Mirialan. Despite rigid schooling in Jedi doctrine, the young Offee possessed an impulsive streak frowned upon by more conservative Jedi Masters. While she was reserved by nature, and not easily intimidated, there were times when she preferred wielding her lightsaber to following the protocols of diplomacy. Her attempts to overcompensate for her youthful exuberance sometimes gave her a cold demeanor.

Prior to the outbreak of the Clone Wars, Barriss Offee joined Master Luminara and fellow Jedi Obi-Wan Kenobi and Anakin Skywalker on a diplomatic mission to Ansion. Separatist conspirators were attempting to arrange the planet's secession through a number of veiled fronts. As part of the intrigue, a pair of bumbling Ansionians attempted to kidnap Offee. She was able to peer past their unscrupulous employment and realize that the two, Bulgan and Kyakhta, were not malicious in their intent. Using her healing talents in the Force, she cured the would-be abductors of their debilitating ailments, earning their gratitude and loyalty. Their friendship was very helpful in brokering peace on Ansion, and dousing the threat of secession.

In combat, Barriss Offee specialized in tandem fighting. Her connection to the Force allowed her to perfectly synchronize her actions with those of her Master. During the Clone Wars, she saw combat on Ilum, defending a sacred Jedi temple from minelayer droids. She and Luminara led forces on Nadiem, and she tended to the wounded at New Holstice. Her healing talents were of great use at Rimsoo Seven, a mobile surgical unit erected on the battlefields of Drongar. While operating on a patient, she accidentally injected herself with bota—the miracle drug native to Drongar—and realized that the plant somehow gave a Force-user an enhanced connection to the Force. During the prolonged horrors of war on Drongar, she came to the realization on her own that she was a Jedi Knight, particularly when she chose *not* to inject herself with bota—an action that would have stopped a Separatist attack. Rather than destabilize the Force or the balance of power, she sought other solutions instead. Eventually, it was revealed that the volatility of bota meant that its remarkable attributes would fade in time.

At the end of the Clone Wars, Barriss was stationed on Felucia, hunting for Commerce Guild Presidente Shu Mai. She was killed by an AT-TE when the clone troopers under her command carried out Order 66.

*Barriss Offee*

**Offen** A species relatively new to space travel. Offens hailed from Casfield VII, where they were ruled by a 6,000-year-old queen.

**Office of Sentient Species** An institution that dictated protocols and rules governing the basic rights of sentient species throughout the galaxy. Some of these rules also dealt with the cultural and physical remains of extinct species—*material remains must be preserved as found, artifacts may be reconstructed but not restored,* and so forth.

***Official History of the Rebellion*** Compiled by master historian of the Rebel Alliance Arhul Hextrophon, this document detailed the heroes and conflicts of the Galactic Civil War. Hextrophon began the project as a series of daily diaries surrounding his duties as Mon Mothma's secretary. The *Official History* included interviews with Luke Skywalker, Han Solo, Princess Leia Organa, Chewbacca, C-3PO, R2-D2, and Bail Organa.

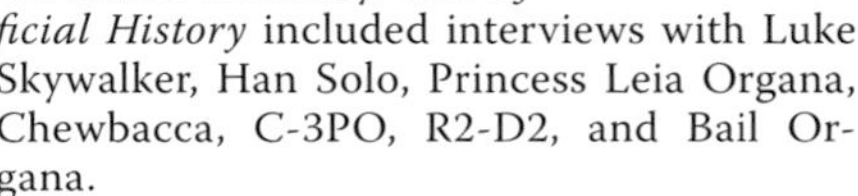

**Offshoot** *See* Arkanian Offshoot.

**Offworld Mining Corporation** A greedy and underhanded mining organization with long-reaching influence during the final decades of the Galactic Republic. A signatory of the Commerce Guild, it controlled much of the mining operations in the Outer Rim Territories, though few knew of the corporation's true structure or even its homeworld. Offworld often used Hutts as operational managers, and they were allowed alarming leeway in making decisions, including the outright elimination of competitors. Offworld operations in the Outer Rim allowed it to avoid Republic oversight, and it typically used slave labor within its mines.

Xanatos, former Padawan of Qui-Gon Jinn, took control of Offworld Corporation and used many front companies to spread its influence on numerous Republic worlds. A disastrous operation on an inhospitable planet drained Offworld's coffers to such a degree that Xanatos undertook a dangerous mission to steal a trove of valuable vertex from the very heart of the Jedi Temple. Following Xanatos's demise, the company reemerged under the control of his son, Granta Omega.

**OG-9** *See* homing spider droid.

**Ogden Minor** This planet was home to the fierce three-headed terbeasts.

**Ogemites** Near-humans from the planet of Ogem, the males of this species carved out a proud tradition as traders and smugglers. Ogemites were taller than normal humans, with feather-like hair.

**oggzil** A Yuuzhan Vong–bioengineered organism developed during their invasion of the galaxy to send villip-speak over frequencies used by the New Republic. The oggzil gripped a specialized villip, cradled in a blastula, surrounding it like a husk that dangled a long straight tail. The oggzil's metal-rich diet deposited conductive material into the creature's vertebrae, creating a living antenna.

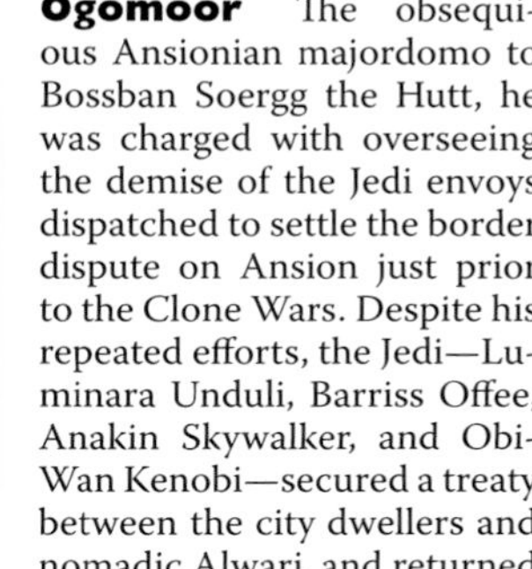
Ohma-D'un

**Ogomoor** The obsequious Ansionian majordomo to Bossban Soergg the Hutt, he was charged with overseeing the demise of the Jedi envoys dispatched to settle the border dispute on Ansion just prior to the Clone Wars. Despite his repeated efforts, the Jedi—Luminara Unduli, Barriss Offee, Anakin Skywalker, and Obi-Wan Kenobi—secured a treaty between the city dwellers and nomadic Alwari, and returned to the capital of Cuipernam. Recognizing that his life was forfeit for his failure, Ogomoor plotted to betray his patron by revealing the Hutt's backroom dealings with the Commerce Guild. Ogomoor failed at this, too, as Soergg shot him dead.

**Ogoth Tiir** The site of a battle in which Commodore Jona Grumby of the Corporate Sector Authority Picket Fleet lost the use of both legs.

**Ohann** A gas giant in the Tatoo system, second from the binary suns. Free traders sometimes imported ice chunks from the rings of Ohann for sale as water on Tatooine, though taxation and legal wrangling usually made this practice unprofitable.

**Ohma-D'un** The largest moon of Naboo, it was capable of supporting life. After the Battle of Naboo, overcrowding among the Gungan populations led to a colonial effort to settle the so-called Water Moon. During the early stages of the Clone Wars, the Separatists unleashed a chemical weapon on this Gungan colony. Boss Nass lost contact with Ohma-D'un and requested assistance from the Republic. Obi-Wan Kenobi, Anakin Skywalker, Glaive, and Zule—along with a small contingent of clone troopers—arrived to investigate, and found the entire colony wiped out. The Separatists had intended to use Ohma-D'un as a staging ground for an attack on Naboo, but the Jedi and clone troopers were able to repulse Asajj Ventress and the bounty hunter Durge.

Lieutenant Barrow Oicunn

**Oicunn, Lieutenant Barrow** One of the first Imperial fleet officers, he served aboard a *Venator*-class Star Destroyer at the dawn of the Galactic Empire. During the Clone Wars, he proved himself serving in the local defense forces of the Humbarine sector. Despite his inspired tactics and exceptional performance, Republic mismanagement led to heavy losses in his home sector, including the death of his family. When the Republic abandoned Humbarine as a lost cause, Oicunn transferred to the Coruscant Home Fleet, serving aboard the *Mas Ramdar.* His continued loyalty earned him a position within an elite force guarding the construction of the first Death Star. He eventually rose to the rank of admiral, and was given the honor of becoming a clone template for future stormtrooper ranks.

**Oissan, Colonel** The intelligence chief aboard the Star Destroyer *Tyrannic,* serving under Captain Nalgol during the Caamas Document crisis. He was tasked with gathering information outside the vessel's cloaked position near Bothawui.

***Ojai*** An Alliance freighter that received an important payload of communications satellites from the freighter *Phoenix* in the midst of combat during the early days of the Galactic Civil War. Alliance pilot Keyan Farlander, flying an A-wing starfighter, helped protect the cargo transfer. Farlander also flew escort when the *Ojai* delivered cargo to the Rebel corvette *Jeffrey* on the edges of the Cron Drift.

**Ojom (1)** A Deep Core planet of subzero temperatures and glacier-covered oceans, it was the homeworld of the four-armed Besalisk species. Suspended in orbit over the world were several space stations intended to supply offworlders with warmer environments. Visitors nonetheless made it to the frigid surface, particularly those with a criminal bent.

**Ojom (2)** The Besalisks' native language.

**Ojoster sector** Home to the Ojoster Sector Assembly, an influential body during the New Republic era.

**Okand, Hol** A Y-wing pilot, he flew as Gold Six at the Battle of Yavin. His previous experience included flying as Jon "Dutch" Vander's wingman during an attack on an Imperial supply outpost at Kashyyyk, where he disabled the outpost's shields with ion cannons. He befriended Chewbacca before leaving Yavin 4.

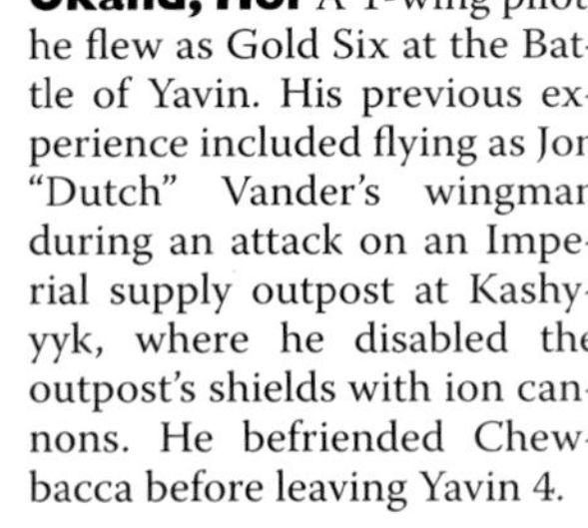

**Okanor, Galidon** The proprietor of an antiquities and art store on Corellia during the early days of the Galactic Civil War. Okanor employed a Selonian clerk to handle the day-to-day transactions while he carefully maintained his relics in a hidden back office. Those in the know could find the office and announce their presence with a sharp knock in a specific pattern. It was here that more discreet—and less legal—transactions could occur.

**Okeco, Anjet** A HoloNet journalist during the Separatist crisis, she wrote a heartbreaking exposé on how the abuse of death sticks affected a youngster living on Coruscant. Upon further review, some believed the story to be a hoax.

**Okeefe, Platt** A platinum-haired beauty, deft with a heavy blaster pistol, and an expert pilot and smuggler, her name was well known in elite smuggler circles. She had a strong sense of community and often compiled reports to distribute to fellow smugglers, providing tips and advice for beginning traders. Okeefe (or Oakie to her friends) had been fascinated by space travel since her childhood. While growing up on Brentaal, she spent much of her time near the spaceport, watching freighters land and refuel. On her twelfth birthday, Platt ran away and signed on as a cabin steward aboard a Sullustan freighter. She eventually joined a tramp freighter crew operating in the Anarid Cluster. Platt was quick to develop a reputation as a skilled smuggler and ally. Her prominence caused misdirected journalist Andor Javin of TriNebulon News to finger her as the infamous newsnet operator Cynabar. His claims, as usual, were completely unfounded.

**Okfili** An alien species allied to the Rebellion. The Okfili wanted the Alliance to find an art object stolen from them that had great religious significance. To that end, the Rebels sent a special operative team to the planet Sayblohn.

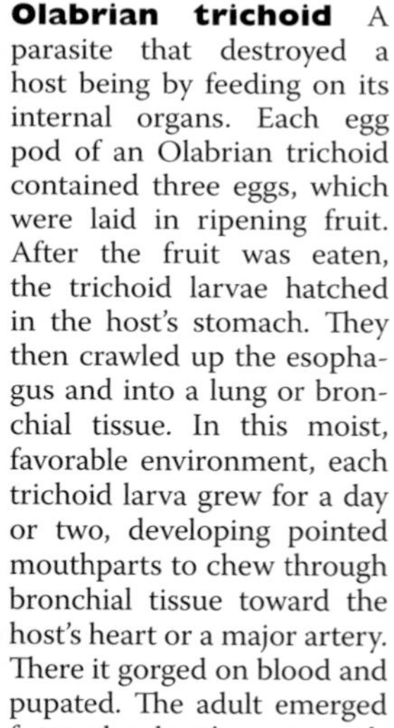
Platt Okeefe

**Okikuti** A Wookiee city on Kashyyyk.

**Okins, Admiral** An Imperial officer serving under Darth Vader during the Galactic Civil War, he was tasked with routing suspected Rebel activity in the Vergesso asteroids shortly after the Battle of Hoth. A by-the-manuals officer, Okins was older than many of the admirals in the higher echelons of the Imperial Navy because his rise in power was not orchestrated by great risks or tactical genius, but rather by everyday competence and simply following orders.

**Okko, Great** The tribe leader of the Ysanna, he was descended from a long Jedi lineage. He led the Force-sensitive tribe on the ancient Jedi stronghold world of Ossus. Six and a half years after the Battle of Endor, Luke Skywalker and Kam Solusar came in contact with the Ysanna. Okko was concerned that the return of the Jedi would lead to the end of the Ysanna culture. Skywalker assured Okko that the Ysanna culture would be preserved. The Jedi Master fell in love with Okko's daughter, Jem. Despite his disapproval, Okko let his daughter travel with Skywalker, but she died at the hands of Imperial dark siders.

The resurrected Emperor, his clone forms ailing, needed Jedi blood to secure his grip on immortality. To that end, dark side enforcers captured three Ysanna shamans for their cloning experiments, including Okko. Captive and transported to the planet Vjun, Okko was frozen in carbonite to await the Emperor's clonemasters. The carbon slabs lacked controls, and the decarbonization process was an Imperial secret. His fate was a mystery.

Great Okko

**Oko E** A planet whose rivers were filled with sulfur ice, it was where the cyborg Lobot once went on a wild-water rafting vacation in which he learned the proper technique for pulling a raft-mate out of the water. Twelve years after the Battle of Endor, he used the same technique to save Lando Calrissian's life aboard the ghost ship known as the Teljkon vagabond.

**Okor, Feldrall** Boba Fett once received a bounty of 150,000 credits for the capture of this pirate.

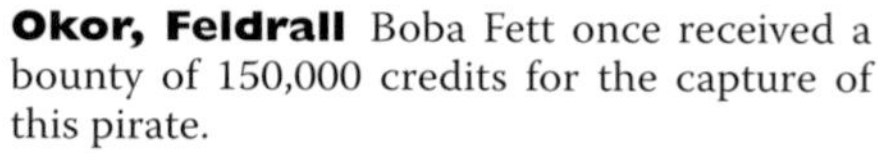

**Olabrian trichoid** A parasite that destroyed a host being by feeding on its internal organs. Each egg pod of an Olabrian trichoid contained three eggs, which were laid in ripening fruit. After the fruit was eaten, the trichoid larvae hatched in the host's stomach. They then crawled up the esophagus and into a lung or bronchial tissue. In this moist, favorable environment, each trichoid larva grew for a day or two, developing pointed mouthparts to chew through bronchial tissue toward the host's heart or a major artery. There it gorged on blood and pupated. The adult emerged from the host's corpse already fertile, ready to lay 10 to 12 egg pods. The entire life cycle took about three weeks. The only known cure for trichoid infestation was the administration of pure oxygen during the early phase. This triggered a severe coughing reaction in the host as the larvae were expectorated. Trichoid infestation was asymptomatic until the larval mouthparts developed enough to begin chewing. The first symptom was chronic coughing. Within approximately two hours after the coughing fits began, severe and deadly hemorrhaging occurred.

Governor Wilek Nereus of Bakura used an Olabrian trichoid in an attempt to murder Luke Skywalker. He had also attempted to infect the invading Ssi-ruuk with trichoids, but that scheme failed as well.

**Olabria system** Home to a deadly parasite, the Olabrian trichoid.

**Olafsen** A moisture-farming family on Tatooine, contemporaries of Ariq Joanson.

**Olan, Cazne (Cazne'Olan)** A member of the wealthy Olan Twi'lek clan on Ryloth. When clanmate Firith Olan was pursued by both Rogue Squadron and the Empire shortly after the Battle of Endor, he came to Cazne for refuge. A shrewd Twi'lek, Cazne cared little for his cousin's safety, and instead had key members of both Rogue Squadron and the Imperial team vie for Firith in a "virtual reality" contest. In the end, Imperial Captain Marl Semtin bribed his way to victory. Cazne was an aged Twi'lek, with thin head-tails and wrinkled pink skin.

**Olan, Firith** A short time after the Battle of Endor, this Twi'lek criminal operated out of the empty palace of Jabba the Hutt. Jabba's majordomo, Bib Fortuna, had called him to Tatooine, but by the time Firith arrived, Jabba was dead and Fortuna had had his brain removed and placed in a robotic spider droid by the B'omarr monks. Firith delighted in mocking and torturing Fortuna, who—trapped as a brain in a glassy globe—could do little to defend himself. Firith began extorting protection money from local food producers. During the hunt for the hidden Imperial cruiser *Eidolon,* he fled from Rogue Squadron and Imperial pursuers to Ryloth, where he was sold out to the Imperials by his clanmate Cazne Olan. Captain Marl Semtin took Firith back to Ta-

Firith Olan

tooine and double-crossed him, stabbing the Twi'lek. The wounded Firith was discovered by the disembrained Bib Fortuna, who took Olan's form back to Jabba's palace. There, in the still of night, the B'omarr art of brain surgery successfully transferred Fortuna's brain into Firith's body, and Firith's brain into the glassy globe of a spider droid.

**Olanet** An Outer Rim planet in the Siskeen system, known for its nerf farms. During the Clone Wars, the Separatists established a droid factory there, which made it a prime target for the Republic.

**Olanji/Charubah** The Hapan design firm that constructed the Hapan Battle Dragon.

**Olanji Fleet** One of the many Hapan battle fleets. Queen Mother Ta'a Chume personally accompanied Olanji on its arrival at Dathomir four years after the Battle of Endor. The fleet helped deter Imperial forces once under the command of Warlord Zsinj.

**Olanz** A tall, bald member of Shalini's resistance group on Typha-Dor in the years prior to the Clone Wars.

**Ola's** A tavern located in the city of Hullis, on Halmad. It was here that several members of Wraith Squadron provoked a fight with Lieutenant Cothron's group as part of their plan to infiltrate the Imperial garrison and steal TIE starfighters.

**olav leaves** These were ingredients in the magical Ewok red potion.

**Olbeg, Han** A Senator from Pitann.

**Olbeg, Sal** A member of the Senatorial council of the Kathol Republic. He was from Dayark, a distant planet in the Kathol sector. Olbeg was a strong objector to the use of droids in gladiatorial combat, a practice quite common in the Republic.

**olbio** A tree from Myrkr, one of the main food sources of the ysalamiri.

**Old City** An abandoned city on Aquilaris, nearly sunk by a violent storm. The site of extensive salvage operations, it made for a dangerous set of obstacles for Podrace courses that wound through it.

***Old Codger*** The affectionate name of a borrowed skimmer used by Morgan Katarn while exploring Ruusan. At the time it was more than a decade old, scarred, dented, and pitted, with most of its yellow paint flaked away.

**Old Core era** A period of time in the history of the Core Worlds, marked by high culture and refinement.

**Old Corellian** An archaic dialect, also called *olys Corellisi,* used in some sections of the Corellian sector and beyond. Even when the language was basically extinct for 4,000 years, there existed a secluded subculture that insisted on speaking it, so as to remember the past and Corellian forebears who helped open up the galaxy. Socorro, for instance, was a planet with a known Old Corellian dialect in active use long after the Galactic Civil War.

**Old Folks Home** A code name for the Jedi Temple used by Jedi Knights in field communications to ensure secrecy.

**Old High Squibbian** A dense, convoluted language developed by the Squib scavenger species. This dead language held many of the cultures and haggling traditions carried out by the Squib monarch King Ebareebaveebeedee.

**Old High Trammic** An ancient trade language originating from Trammis III. The Sharu, while disguised as the Toka, used this tongue as their native language.

**Old Law** An antiquated Hutt custom rarely invoked in modern times. It stated that, given sufficient provocation, a Hutt clan leader could challenge another in single combat without any legal ramifications. The victor was presumed to be in the right. The corpulent Hutts, who preferred to have others do their dirty work, rarely bloodied their own hands in such barbaric duels, but it was known to happen. One incident occurred prior to the Battle of Yavin, when Durga the Hutt invoked the Old Law to dispose of Jiliac the Hutt.

**Old Mankoo** An impoverished planet located in the Outer Rim. Princess Tsian was part of the royal family of Old Mankoo before it was overthrown.

**Old Quarter** A settlement on the planet Skeebo. Gorga the Hutt's wife, Anachro, was kidnapped and held for ransom on Skeebo during their honeymoon. Gorga's representative was to deliver the ransom in the Old Quarter. The Old Quarter was marked by dilapidated brick buildings and open-air marketplaces. Inhabitants got around either on speeder or on beast-back.

**Old Recluse** To the natives of Morishim, he seemed to be a hermit capable of foreseeing the future, living in a cave in the High Tatmana Mountains. In truth, this crafty Morish was not clairvoyant. He just had the good fortune to discover a cave that had a fully functioning Imperial communications center complete with encrypt/decrypt modules, a space/planetary monitor module, and a self-contained power generator. Fifteen years after the Battle of Endor, Wedge Antilles, Tycho Celchu, Wes Janson, and Lando Calrissian helped themselves to some needed intelligence from the Old Recluse's machines.

**Old Republic** *See* Galactic Republic.

**Old Sith Wars** A term used by historians to refer to the period of time some 4,000 years before the Battle of Yavin, beginning with the Great Sith War. The Old Sith Wars then encompassed the Great Hunt, the Cleansing of the Nine Houses, and the Jedi Civil War. Additionally, the Mandalorian Wars were also grouped under the era of the Old Sith Wars, due to their chronological proximity.

**Oldsong, Abbela** The personal aide to Leia Organa Solo during the Duro reclamation project. In Leia's absence, Abbela managed Gateway's day-to-day business. During the Yuuzhan Vong War, Abbela was sacrificed by the Yuuzhan Vong, strangled by a tkun.

**Old Tarmidian** Jorj Car'das's childhood language, according to Entoo Needan E-elz.

**Oldtimers** The descendants of the original colonists of Nam Chorios. Specifically, the term described the Therans, a fanatical group named for their ancient prophet, Theras, who preached a xenophobic doctrine.

**Old Town** A term used to describe antiquated sections of cities and settlements on various worlds. On Centares, it was a rough, sprawling home to many taverns, gambling halls, and other forms of traveler entertainment. In Bagsho, on Nim Drovis, the eastern half of the city was called Old Town while the western half was New Town. On Talus, it was the oldest section of Qaestar Town.

**Old Trusty** The locals of Ruusan drank a potent potable they affectionately called Old Trusty.

**Oleg** A low-level message runner of the Absolutes on New Apsolon, a dozen years before the Battle of Naboo. He had been marked for interrogation by his superiors, and was planning to desert the Absolutes. Then he met Jedi Master Tahl. When her cover was exposed, Tahl was similarly jeopardized, and the two teamed up to flee the Absolutes' base. It was believed that Oleg had a copy of the list of Absolute supporters, but he disappeared before he could be questioned by the Jedi Knights. His lifeless body was discovered by Qui-Gon Jinn shortly afterward, shot and killed by one of the probe droids that had been outlawed on the planet. Qui-Gon later discovered that Irini had reprogrammed the probe droids to obtain the list and prevent any further bloodshed.

***Olemp*** This cruiser—part of Alpha Fleet—was commanded by General Wedge Antilles as part of Operation Trinity during the Yuuzhan Vong War.

**Oleson, General** The commanding officer of the Rebel Alliance New Academy for Space Pilots.

**olfax** A term used to describe any species that had developed the olfactory sense to such a heightened degree of acuity that it became the primary sense for communication.

*Ric Olié*

**Olgreen Intelligence Guild** Founded by Wilam Olgreen and part of the Coalition of Automaton Rights Activists, this protest group was known for its blockading of droid reclamation factories, thereby preventing the delivery of scrap or rogue droids for meltdown. The guild was originally formed during the early stages of the Clone Wars, to protest how Confederacy of Independent Systems droids were being destroyed by the Republic. The guild was known to have erected portable shield generators to prevent Republic transports from dumping the shells of damaged battle droids into reclamation facilities.

**Olié, Ric** A seasoned member of the Naboo Space Fighter Corps who served as the leader of Bravo Flight and piloted the Naboo Royal Starship on diplomatic missions. The Naboo native was capable of flying any craft on his homeworld and was one of the most intuitive pilots in the volunteer Royal Security Forces.

Olié started flying when he was a kid, earning a reputation as "Reckless Ric" for his hotrodding flights through the skies of Naboo. He eventually tempered his boundless love of flight with the discipline needed to command a starfighter squadron. Although he technically received his orders from Captain Panaka, Olié's opinions were always respected, and he developed many of Bravo Flight's tactics. At the Battle of Naboo, Olié led a small band of freedom fighters against the seemingly insurmountable might of the Trade Federation Droid Control Ship. Like many pilots, Olié had a superstitious streak: While he never forged a real friendship with his astromech R2-A6, he did consider the green-trimmed droid a good-luck charm.

**Oliet** One of the Peacekeepers guarding the survivors of Outbound Flight in the years prior to the Yuuzhan Vong War.

**Olin, Ferus** A native of Bellassa, he was Padawan apprentice of Siri Tachi. Olin's focus and dedication prevented him from creating close friendships, and other students nicknamed him "ruler of the Planet Dull." As Olin matured, he developed charisma and fortitude, and some believed him to be second in prowess only to Anakin Skywalker, a fellow Padawan two years younger than Olin.

When Olin was teamed with Skywalker during the evacuation of Radnor, the two butted heads trying to assume a position of leadership. They eventually resolved their differences, and learned that they had much in common and could strike a comfortable rapport. Olin confided to Skywalker's Master, Obi-Wan Kenobi, that he feared for Anakin's future. Ferus and Anakin worked together in the pursuit of such galactic criminals as Granta Omega and Jenna Zan Arbor. Though he saved Chancellor Palpatine from deadly seeker droids dispatched by Omega, Olin was unable to stop the death of Roy Teda. Shamed by what he saw as a failure, he was nonetheless lauded by the Jedi Council and selected for an accelerated program toward Jedi Knighthood. A competitive streak between Ferus and Anakin once again taxed their friendship.

On a mission to Korriban, Olin offered help to his new friend Tru Veld, repairing his lightsaber so that he could continue on the mission. Instead, the lightsaber lost power, leaving Darra Thel-Tanis to die undefended. Olin once again blamed himself, going so far as to leave the Jedi Order. He soon learned that Skywalker had previously tinkered with Veld's weapon without telling Olin. Ferus never forgave Anakin for that interference.

Ferus survived the Clone Wars and Order 66, retiring to Bellassa as his Force powers inexplicably began to wane. When the Empire deposed the Bellassan governor and installed an Imperial official, Olin and his friend Roan Lands formed a resistance movement called the Eleven. The Empire cracked down on their protests.

When Obi-Wan Kenobi located Olin, together they freed the hostages held by Inquisitor Malorum and fled Bellassa. It was during their escape that Olin was able to reconnect with the Force, and although he refused to admit that he was still a Jedi, he promised to seek out any survivors of Order 66. However, they were pursued by Boba Fett and D'harhan, and only barely escaped to Acherin. There they were forced to split up, with Olin going to Ilum in search of Garen Muln, while Kenobi went to Polis Massa. Olin and Trever Flume located Muln, only to find themselves surrounded by stormtroopers. This forced Olin to reconnect with the Force in a way that he thought was lost to him, and even Muln recognized his newfound skills.

When the time came to fight, Muln gave his lightsaber to Olin, knowing that the younger man had a better chance of defeating the stormtroopers. After escaping with Muln, Olin vowed to establish a safeworld on a hidden asteroid, where Jedi fugitives could hide from Imperial tyranny. He was confused when Kenobi chose instead to return to Tatooine.

Acting on information from Muln, Olin and Flume set off for Coruscant, hoping to locate Jedi survivor Fy-Tor-Ana. They found her in the depths of the city-planet, having assumed the alias Solace and leadership of a small settlement of outcasts. Olin convinced her to return to the Jedi Temple, in an effort to stop Malorum from destroying the settlement. He allowed himself to be captured so that Fy-Tor-Ana and Flume could escape. After a brief incarceration at Dontamo Prison, Olin escaped with help from Clive Flax.

Shortly thereafter, Olin was surprised to receive an offer of amnesty from the Emperor. Palpatine gave Olin an opportunity to prove his loyalty to the New Order by traveling to Samaria to settle a dispute there. It was part of a ploy to use Olin to prove to the galaxy at large that even a former Jedi could not resist the authority of the Empire. Palpatine ensured Olin's compliance by threatening his friends Roan Lands and Dona Telamark.

On Samaria, Olin uncovered the fact that programmer Quintus Farel was, in truth, Astri Oddo, who was hiding from her husband, Imperial adviser Bog Divinian. With the help of Solace, Ferus ensured Oddo's cover and snuck her off the planet, keeping his activities secret from Darth Vader and the Emperor. Palpatine then dispatched Olin and Vader to Bellassa, hoping that Ferus's presence there would help make the Empire's subjugation of the planet that much easier. Though he did what he could to subvert the aims of the Empire, Olin was sickened by his association with the Imperials. He attempted to learn all he could about the Empire's plans for Bellassa.

Olin and his associate Amie Antin were discovered attempting to break into secure Imperial files—namely, Moff Tarkin's computer system, which contained information on the top-secret project code-named Twilight. They were imprisoned by Darth Vader. Rather than face execution, Olin again found himself offered an alternative by Palpatine: the opportunity to take over the search for Force-sensitive pilots for

*Ferus Olin with Trever Flume*

training at the Imperial Naval Academy, and control of the Inquisitorius. Olin agreed.

On Coruscant, he began working with Inquisitor Hydra, who provided him with a list of suspected Force-sensitives. With assistance from Malory Lands, Olin was able to infiltrate the Emperor Palpatine Surgical Reconstruction Center to locate one of these Jedi. Once inside, he learned that Lune Oddo Divinian—Astri's son—was being held in the facility by Jenna Zan Arbor. Olin rescued him, once again using his position of Imperial authority to save Jedi fugitives. Olin occasionally reported to the sequestered Obi-Wan Kenobi on his progress.

***Olinor*** An Alliance frigate that operated near deep-space supply depot DS-5. When Imperial forces attacked the station to capture the traitorous Admiral Harkov, the *Olinor* was dispatched to defend the depot.

**Oll, Lari** A human Jedi Knight who served as a communications technician at the Jedi Temple during the final stages of the Clone Wars. She was on duty when General Grievous attacked the capital, but was unable to raise an alert due to intense signal jamming.

**ollopom** A camouflaged, amphibious rodent native to the swamps of Naboo, it spent most of its life floating lazily among foliage, safely hidden from most predators. Only the animal's frilled head appeared above the water's surface, making it look like the floating lily-pad-like pom plant. Long, bloom-like tendrils grew from head follicles to mimic blossoms. Ollopoms rarely moved about on land, as they were slow and easily spotted when away from the water.

**Olmahk** One of Leia Organa Solo's Noghri bodyguards, he and Basbakhan accompanied her diplomatic mission to Bastion to request the assistance of the Imperial Remnant during the Yuuzhan Vong War. He also traveled with Leia to Ord Mantell, Gyndine, and finally Duro, where he was killed trying to cover Leia's escape from the alien invaders.

**Olmondo** This ancient city lay beneath the shifting dirt of Ruusan. According to prophecy, a Jedi would stay the night in Olmondo before continuing on the search for the Valley of the Jedi. Little did prospector and Rebel unit leader Morgan Katarn realize he was stepping along the path of prophecy when he camped one night over the buried remains of Olmondo.

*Ollopom*

**Ologat, Mychael** A stormtrooper recruit posted in the same unit as the traitorous Davin Felth around the time of the Battle of Yavin.

**Olok, Ithes** A Mon Calamari xenoarchaeologist who knew of the legend of Jedi Master Chu-Gon Dar. He led an expedition of researchers to Mustafar to investigate possible Force-imbued artifacts created by Dar.

**olop tree** The last remaining specimen of this extremely rare tree was destroyed when the Yuuzhan Vong conquered Duro and the arboretum in Bburru station.

***Olovin*** This New Republic Interdictor cruiser was one of the many ships assigned to General Wedge Antilles and the *Mon Mothma* during the final stages of the Yuuzhan Vong War.

**OLR-4** A Trade Federation battle droid stationed aboard the *Revenue* and destroyed by the Nebula Front.

**Olvidan, Faskus and Kiara** The alleged thief of the Sith Amulet of Kalara, Faskus Olvidan supposedly stole the artifact from the Drewwa moon of Almania and fled to his homeworld of Ziost. Upon return, his vessel, the *Blacktooth,* was shot down, and he crashed in the frigid wilderness. As part of a special assignment arranged by Jacen Solo, Ben Skywalker tracked down Olvidan and found him suffering a mortal abdominal injury from the crash. As he bled to death, Olvidan revealed to Skywalker that he was no thief—he had been tasked to courier the artifact to Ziost by Byalfin Dyur. Faskus was survived by his young daughter, Kiara, who traveled with him and survived the crash. Faskus's dying request was for Skywalker to watch over his daughter. At the time, Ben was struggling with voices projected to him through the dark side of the Force: The unseen Sith manipulator Lumiya was in fact testing his worthiness as a potential Sith. The dark voices urged Ben to harm or kill Kiara, but Skywalker overcame them. He discovered an ancient Sith meditation sphere on Ziost and used his affinity for the Force to pilot it, taking Kiara to authorities on Drewwa before continuing on to Coruscant.

**ol-villip** A smaller variation on the Yuuzhan Vong–bioengineered communications device, it was designed to work in tandem with a provoker spineray to allow a shaper to see his or her progress in manipulating a being's neurological pathways.

**Omal** One of Dr. Murk Lundi's best students, some six years before the Battle of Naboo. When Lundi traveled to Kodai in search of a Sith Holocron, Omal discovered that another student, Norval, had designs on stealing the artifact. Omal set out to stop Norval, fighting him to ensure Lundi kept the prize. In the struggle, the holocron fell into a deep underwater chasm.

**Omano, Commander** The commanding officer of the D-Four Dreadnaught that was part of the Outbound Flight Project.

**Oma-Oma** The principal deity in the religion of the Gungans, she oversaw lesser deities such as Dobbis, goddess of rain, and Gob Gobba, god of fresh water.

**Omar** The principal planet of the Omar system and site of three Sienar Fleet Systems starfighter-production facilities. The manufacturing plants produced the TIE advanced starfighter. These plants were destroyed by the traitorous Admiral Zaarin following the Battle of Hoth.

**Omas, Cal** The first Chief of State of the Galactic Federation of Free Alliances, he had the unenviable position of guiding the nascent galactic government through some of its most trying times. A native of Alderaan, he had previously served in the Rebel Alliance and was a Senator in the New Republic. He was sympathetic to Luke Skywalker's new Jedi Order. Though he shared the view of many Senators that the Jedi needed to be held accountable and rein in some of their more adventurous members, he felt the best way to do so was to reestablish the Jedi Council.

After the Yuuzhan Vong conquered Coruscant and Chief of State Borsk Fey'lya nobly sacrificed himself, Omas stepped into the power vacuum, leading the remnants of the New Republic government as it scattered to Mon Calamari. Omas was elected Chief of State during this turbulent time. He was forced to make difficult decisions, such as discontinuing the promising Alpha Red biological weapons program.

As the New Republic was restructured into the Galactic Alliance, and the galaxy attempted to rebuild following the defeat of the Yuuzhan Vong, Omas oversaw the reconstruction. He needed to balance the needs of the entire galaxy against the various petitions and demands for assistance from refugees, as well as ensuring that corporate interests didn't overstep the law pursuing the opportunities that emerged from the turmoil. In the midst of this miasma came the Swarm War, when the spreading Killik Colony began threatening neighboring worlds. Through it all, Omas demonstrated a gift for manipulation and politics, doing what he could to preserve the sanctity of the Galactic Alliance.

Omas's backroom deals meant little when the Corellians once again bid for independence, this time under the saber-rattling command of Thrackan Sal-Solo. More hawkish minds—like Admiral Cha Niathal and Jacen Solo—began working behind Omas's back in an attempt to bring a decisive conclusion to this crisis and stem the outbreak of civil war. In a concession to preserve peace at home in the face of Corellian terrorism, Omas created the Galactic Alliance Guard, which Jacen Solo assumed leadership of and transformed into a frighteningly effective state police. Niathal, promoted to Supreme Commander, planned a complete blockade of Corellia to force the independence movement to stand down.

Omas had to concede that, despite his best efforts, the Alliance was once again at war. The Corellians drew independent-minded allies that were wary of the authority wielded by the Galactic Alliance, becoming the Confederation. Omas was determined to end the war with as little bloodshed as possible, and conspired to meet with Confederation leader Dur Gejjen on Vulpter to discuss the terms of a cease-fire. Among Gejjen's demands was the elimination of Niathal and Jacen Solo. Though they did not come to an agreement, their entire meeting had been recorded by Galactic Alliance spies, and Jacen Solo saw Omas as a traitor. GAG agents assassinated Gejjen and arrested Omas under the terms of amendments to the Emergency Measures Act quietly made by Jacen Solo.

In the following weeks, Omas remained under house arrest, but no further legal action was taken by Solo or Niathal. In response, Omas and his lawyers demanded that formal charges be brought against him to justify his arrest. He also demanded a public trial, hoping to expose Solo's true intentions. While he waited for trial, Omas feared for his life. He was befriended by Lieutenant Jonat of the Galactic Alliance Guard, and used her comlink to keep in touch with his family and assure them that he was safe.

Jonat recorded all of Omas's conversations, providing them to Jacen Solo, who used them to piece together false evidence intended to convince Ben Skywalker that Omas had ordered the death of Mara Jade Skywalker. When Ben confronted Omas, the beleaguered Chief of State revealed that he believed Jacen had been the one who killed Mara. Omas explained that the only way Ben could prove Jacen's guilt was to get close to him again. When the Coruscant Security Force arrived to protect him, Omas flung himself onto Ben's lightsaber, making it appear as if a Jedi had killed him. He died hoping that it was enough to convince Jacen to trust Ben again, thereby allowing the young man to avenge his death and restore peace to the galaxy.

**Omega, Granta** A scientist and businessman who, though not Force-sensitive, was seemingly obsessed with Sith history and relics and despised the Jedi Knights. The source of his ire was unknown to the Jedi for some time, until it was discovered that Granta Omega was the son of Xanatos, the fallen Jedi pupil of Qui-Gon Jinn.

Omega grew up on the moon of Nierport Seven and studied at the All Sciences Research Academy on Yerphonia, where he was sponsored by Sano Sauro. He built his fortune by using hefty investments to buy complete control of precious minerals at the source, and then raising the price.

He emerged as a threat to the Jedi after uncovering his heritage, and dispatched bounty hunters to harass the Jedi shortly after the Battle of Naboo. During a scheme on Haariden, Omega captured Padawan Anakin Skywalker and revealed that he was working to destroy the Jedi Knights in order to curry favor with the mysterious Sith Lord Darth Sidious. Though Omega was thwarted, he returned frequently, often in disguise, to challenge the Jedi. Perhaps his greatest blow to the Order was the murder of Jedi Master Yaddle.

Months later Omega teamed with Jenna Zan Arbor, developing a drug called the Zone of Self-Containment as a way to quell large numbers of subjects into submission. Obi-Wan Kenobi and Anakin Skywalker tracked Omega to Coruscant, where the scientist had been plotting to assassinate Chancellor Palpatine in a bid to install his former benefactor, Sano Sauro, as a puppet ruler. The Jedi once again foiled Omega's plan, but he escaped.

Omega had a peculiar and unexplained ability to disappear from notice. He could make himself a "void," not registering in people's conscious perceptions and easily forgotten if he avoided drawing attention to himself.

Omega eventually traveled to the remote world of Korriban with Jenna Zan Arbor to finally experience the power of the Sith firsthand. He found himself growing stronger in the presence of so much dark side energy, and boldly believed that he could defeat the Jedi. He especially hoped to destroy Kenobi, and got his chance in one of the many tombs in the Valley of the Sith Lords. Omega confronted Obi-Wan, but the weapon he was using overheated. In the resulting explosion, Omega was smashed against a wall and crushed. He stubbornly refused to end the fight, and attacked Obi-Wan once more. Kenobi had no alternative but to draw his lightsaber and slash Omega. As he died, Omega goaded Kenobi one final time, claiming that the Jedi would never learn the identity of the Sith Lord manipulating the downfall of the Republic.

**Omega, Tura** Granta Omega's mother, she arrived on Nierport Seven when he was three, and worked at the refueling station. She died two years after her son left for the All Sciences Research Academy.

*Granta Omega (left) confronts Obi-Wan Kenobi and Anakin Skywalker.*

***Omega*-class freighter** A boxy freighter designed for use by the Empire.

**Omega Exercise** The final test of stormtrooper cadets, it determined who received a commission and graduated from the Imperial Academy. It was a real test in real combat, so the circumstances of each exercise varied per situation.

**Omega Frost** A weapon developed by Baron Orman Tagge and his brother Silas Tagge. Through the use of specially designed twin conductor towers, the Omega Frost device generated a field of intense cold, freezing everything caught between the towers. The temperatures were so frigid that even armored metal shattered. The House of Tagge developed the weapon on the desert planet Tatooine, hoping to use it in the Junction system to trap the Rebel fleet. The plan was thwarted by Luke Skywalker, who destroyed one of the conductor towers before the fleet arrived.

**Omega Signal** A code used by the Rebel Alliance battle staff, it was an order for complete disengagement from combat and a retreat.

**Omega Squad** A team of clone commandos active during the Clone Wars. Its membership comprised survivors of other groups assembled to capture Separatist scientist Ovolot Qail Uthan on Qiilura. Omega Squad underwent training by Kal Skirata, and its members—Niner, Darman, Fi, and Atin—showed great respect for his teachings.

**O-Melie** *See* Melie.

**Omiddelon III** This planet orbited a very bright and intense star that soaked it in radiation. Omiddelon III's axis was tilted so that its poles were parallel to its orbital plane. This resulted in an extremely hostile environment with periods of devastating heat, a "mild" transitional season, and a dangerously frigid winter. Omiddelon was thus home to hardy life-forms, including the winged adar.

**Omin, Isaru** A Senate Guard serving under Commander Zalin Bey in the final decades of the Galactic Republic, he was partnered with Sagoro Autem. Together they investigated the murder of Senator Jheramahd Greyshade, allowing Obi-Wan Kenobi and his Padawan Anakin Skywalker to protect Simon Greyshade. Kenobi discovered that Omin was quite sensitive to the Force; indeed, he had tested positively for Force potential at two years of age but was deemed too old to be trained. When the murder investigation revealed ties to Autem's older brother, Omin reluctantly supported Commander Bey's decision to remove his partner from the case. Autem was implicated in crimes committed by his unscrupulous brother, and was arrested.

King Ommin

After the Clone Wars and the rise of the Empire, Autem—freed from prison—was back on a wanted list when he surfaced on Coruscant. Disillusioned by the new Empire, Omin stayed loyal to his friend, and warned Autem that the Empire had targeted him for arrest. Autem fled, avoiding Darth Vader's grip, but the frustrated Dark Lord of the Sith cut down Omin in his anger.

**Ominaz, Ignar** One of the galaxy's most famous professional swoop racers during the last decades of the Galactic Republic. He was killed on Caprioril when an assassin droid wiped out an entire swoop arena audience in order to kill the planet's governor.

**Omin-Oreh** A Rebel Alliance starfighter pilot assigned to the Mon Calamari cruiser *Independence* in the early days of the Galactic Civil War.

**Omman** Orbited by five moons, this was a diverse planet with a hectic starport. It suffered an extensive Imperial presence during much of the Galactic Civil War. It was here that smugglers Drake Paulsen and Karl Ancher were briefly imprisoned in the Bureau of Customs jail before escaping with the help of fellow smuggler Tait Ransom.

**Ommin, King** The ruler of Onderon four millennia before the Battle of Yavin, he came to power the same way his ancestors had in the past three centuries: by using the dark side of the Force. King Ommin was a direct descendant of Freedon Nadd, and he possessed the ability to summon the spirit of Nadd at will. In the final years of his rule, Ommin lay dying, his body ravaged by the dark side. His bones softened and decayed; Ommin required a complex armature to allow him to move. Confined to life support, he was shut off from the rest of Onderon. During the Freedon Nadd Uprising, Ommin's daughter Galia brought Jedi Ulic Qel-Droma and his master Arca Jeth to him, to see if they could gain insight into the dark events on Onderon. There, in Ommin's convalescent chamber, Freedon Nadd appeared and challenged the Jedi, and Ommin was revived and re-animated by the dark side of the Force. He soon became the leader of a Naddist movement on Onderon, pushing to remove the Republic and the Jedi from the planet.

From his palace, Ommin received visitors Satal and Aleema Keto. These wealthy aristocrats were also amateur Sith magicians who sought to increase their power through the occult. Having stolen Sith relics from the Galactic Museum on Coruscant, Satal and Aleema brought them to Ommin, and the king set them on their path to the dark side. A renewed Jedi strike force led by Ulic Qel-Droma stormed Ommin's inner sanctum. Lashing out with anger, Ulic severed the iron armature supporting Ommin's emaciated form. Without his metal exoskeleton, Ommin collapsed into a mound of flesh, tissue, and softened bone. The spirit of Freedon Nadd absorbed Ommin's final gasps of life and drew him to the dark side.

**Ommis, Kesin** A member of Rogue Squadron during the Battle of Hoth. Ommis, a human male from Coruscant, was a weapons specialist who served as a gunner mate aboard the frigate *Tharen* and a tailgunner aboard Hobbie Klivian's snowspeeder.

**ommni box** A musical instrument that clipped peaks, attenuated lows, and reverbed and amplified the total sound. It was a complex instrument; some said it required the genius of a Bith to operate. The box-shaped device, capped with a reception disk, was Tech Mov'rv's instrument of choice in the Modal Nodes.

**omnidirectional gravity booster** A device that handled the artificial gravity requirements within the Death Star battle stations. Boosters were located around the decks, walls, and ceilings, and designed to allow the gravity orientation to be altered from sector to sector, or even corridor to corridor.

**omnidirectional sensor globe** This ground-based full-spectrum transceiver (FST)—one of the three types of aboveground sensors employed by Rebel Alliance ground forces—was an ideal early warning system. While it covered a large area, only the most basic contact information could be gleaned by this type of sensor.

**Omnino, Baroness** A human dignitary from Vena, she traveled to Coruscant to discuss her planet joining the Galactic Republic. Though she was wanted for assassination by Vena isolationists, she at first refused Jedi escort, for she held a grudge against the Order. She believed that Qui-Gon Jinn was responsible for the death of her husband, Kindoro. Upon arrival at the capital, Omnino seemingly reversed her stance and specifically called for Jinn to serve as her protector. She explained that her son, Baron Sando, had disappeared near Ord Mantell. Playing on Qui-Gon's sympathies, the Baroness drew Jinn and Obi-Wan Kenobi to Ord Mantell, where Omnino was arranging a trap with local land baron Taxer Sundown. The Jedi detected the conspiracy, which extended as far as unsettling the entire Republic by eventually targeting Chancellor Valorum himself with a mind-control device. Jinn had no choice but to kill the Baroness.

**omniprobe sensor array** An advanced sensor system employed by Rebel forces. In operation, the omniprobe used low-level scans magnetically keyed to a planet's gravitational center. The omniprobe's sensor beam "hugged" the ground, enabling it to scan enemy movements out of direct sight.

**omniron** A feature available at most spas throughout the galaxy. For only a few credits, a being entered the omniron and selected treatments. The service was completely automated. One particular setting worked on 15-second cycles of icy water sprays, sonic vibrators, heat waves, and biodetergent sprays and lathering. The result was a very relaxing, refreshing indulgence.

**Omogg** An incredibly wealthy Drackmarian warlord, she lost ownership of the planet Dathomir (estimated worth, 2.4 billion credits) to Han Solo in a high-stakes sabacc game about four years after the Battle of Endor. Later, when the Hapan Queen Mother Ta'a Chume was searching for her "daughter-in-law-to-be" Princess Leia Organa, she questioned Omogg about the whereabouts of Solo, her suspected kidnapper. An imposing being, Omogg had pale blue scales often polished to a brilliant sheen. The green clouds of methane contained in her breather helmet often obscured her vicious snout and teeth.

**Omonda, Canna** A Senator from Chandrila, she replaced Mon Mothma when the latter left the Senate as a traitor. A protégée of Mothma's, Omonda was known for her abrasive rhetoric against the New Order. Her outspoken personality caused her to be arrested and executed for treason shortly after the disbanding of the Senate.

**Omonoth** A small, dying star surrounded by asteroids, it was discovered by the Arkanians after the Great Sith War. The heavy elements ejected by the ailing star sprinkled the system with valuable mineral resources. The Arkanian mining operation in the system was overrun by space slugs that devoured the asteroids for sustenance. As food became scarce, the giant slugs went into hibernation. They were closely studied by Arkanian scientists, whose genetic experimentation led to the development of the exogorth program.

**Omwat** A planet in the Outer Rim Territories, and homeworld of the Omwati species. An orange-and-green world lined with savannas and mountains, Omwat drew the attention of a young Moff Tarkin, who

Ommni box

was impressed by the native Omwati's ability to learn. Tarkin had an orbital education sphere constructed to instruct the brightest Omwati prospects. Educator Nasdra Magrody developed the accelerated learning process, and one of the instructors there was Ohran Keldor. The Omwati orbital training center used the threat of violence against the Omwati's home honeycomb settlements.

The humanoid Omwati physical structure suggested an avian heritage, as their lithe forms featured delicate, pearlescent feather-like gossamer hair. Their eyes were wide, deep, and observant, and their voices lyrical and reedy.

During the Galactic Civil War, Omwat was held firmly in the grip of the Empire. Mathematically minded and mechanically talented, the Omwati became test subjects and unwilling theoreticians for the Empire. Among the products of the training center were designs and theories that helped produce such Imperial superweapons as Death Stars, World Devastators, and the Sun Crusher.

**On, Reesa** *See* Nobis, Ona.

**Onacra** A small farming community found on Aduba-3. Han Solo and a hired band of protectors fought against Serji-X Arrogantus and his marauding Cloud Rider swoop gang, which was plaguing the village.

**Onadax** A sooty, inhospitable world in the Minos Cluster, it was of little value: Its low density did not harbor any precious metals, it was far from any worthwhile trade routes, and it was infested by mynocks. Still, it was far from any form of policing authority and had a relaxed attitude toward legal documentation, something that attracted Onadax Droid Technologies to the planet.

**Onadax Droid Technologies** Based on Onadax during the late years of the New Republic, it was known most frequently by its acronym, though few knew what the individual letters stood for. Allegedly founded by Dash Rendar and the human replica droid Guri, the company offered a practical form of immortality for a hefty fee. Using a modification of the entechment process developed by the Ssi-ruuk, ODT found a way to transfer the enteched life energy of a human into the computer brain of a human replica droid. In this way, the human's consciousness remained "alive," but in a body that only needed periodic maintenance and never truly aged. ODT, because of its business and high-powered clientele, maintained its privacy within a heavily secured compound on Onadax. The human replica droid used by Molierre Cundertol was eventually traced back to Onadax and ODT, and Jaina Solo volunteered to investigate the facility. It was at ODT that she first encountered Stanton Rendar, Dash Rendar's supposedly dead brother, who had undergone the same modified entechment procedure that had prolonged Cundertol's life. Rather than have Jaina halt the enterprise, Stanton took his knowledge and fled Onadax, destroying the entire ODT facility as he left.

*Carth Onasi*

**onahk** Oddly shaped aquatic creatures native to the marshes and wetlands of Ossirag, onahks have tapered, hairless bodies atop six thin but sturdy legs.

**Onaka, Hondo** A shifty one-eyed pirate based on Florrum during the Clone Wars, this Weequay discovered Count Dooku's solar sailer within the Vanqor system.

**Onasi, Carth** A Galactic Republic military officer during such ancient campaigns as the Mandalorian Wars. When young Onasi signed up to join the Galactic Republic military, he fully believed in the strength of the institution. A loyal soldier, skilled pilot, and superior tactician, he operated with distinction in both small border skirmishes and major engagements. Though the events of the Mandalorian Wars forever cemented Carth's reputation as a hero, their aftermath dealt a fatal blow to the officer's idealism.

In the Sith resurgence that targeted a weakened Republic, the evil Darth Malak sundered Carth's homeworld of Telos. Carth's young wife, Morgana, was killed, and Dustil, his son, went missing. Compounding this tragedy was the betrayal that further fueled the Sith conquest. Some of the highest-ranking officers of the Republic were seduced by the Sith, including Carth's trusted mentor, Admiral Saul Karath.

Once, honor and loyalty drove Carth to fight the Sith. Vengeance and hatred threatened to replace these laudable attributes, as Carth made it his life's goal to bring Karath to justice. He found himself unable to trust anyone, particularly the inscrutable Jedi he was often teamed with during his missions. He still carried out his duty, escaping from the *Endar Spire* over Taris and freeing the captive Jedi Bastila Shan before that world was also destroyed by the Sith. He accompanied Bastila and the reformed Revan in their mission to uncover the mystery of the Star Forge. On this quest, Carth had his chance at revenge, killing Karath on the bridge of the *Leviathan*.

During the search for Malak, Carth was 38 years old. A handsome man with brown hair, he typically dressed in fatigues and flight jacket, and favored blaster weaponry. He most often piloted the *Ebon Hawk* during this mission.

*Onderon*

**Onderon** Situated in the three-planet system of the same name, it circled a yellow sun and had four moons with widely varying orbits. Onderon's closest moon, Dxun, was home to numerous bloodthirsty creatures that were able to migrate to the surface of Onderon annually when the two worlds' atmospheres intersected. The human inhabitants of Onderon gradually evolved defenses against the beasts, culminating in the enormous walled city of Iziz. Native life on the planet included the deadly dragon-bird.

Some 4,400 years before the Galactic Civil War, the Dark Jedi Freedon Nadd brought the power of Sith dark side magic to Onderon, and those who opposed it were cast out into the wilderness where they tamed the beasts of Dxun. Hundreds of these beast-riders created their own kingdoms in the wild, and fought continually to take over Iziz. Nearly four centuries later, Onderon was first contacted by the Old Republic, and a delegation of Jedi, including Ulic Qel-Droma, were sent to make peace between the beast-riders and Queen Amanoa of Iziz two years after that. Following the death of Queen Amanoa, her daughter, Galia, took the throne with Oron Kira, her lover and the leader of a beast-rider kingdom.

A subsequent uprising by the followers of Freedon Nadd was put down by another Jedi force. At the same time, Satal Keto and his cousin Aleema, members of Tetan royalty, traveled to Onderon to learn the secrets of Sith magic, which led to their formation of the Krath and the political takeover of the Tetan system. Following the Naddist Uprising, a permanent Jedi outpost was built on Onderon from the remains of Nadd's ancient starship. Later, as the Great Sith War was winding down, Dark Jedi Exar Kun ordered the warrior clans of Mandalore to capture Onderon and the city of Iziz. Defeated in a furious battle by Oron Kira and Captain Vanicus of the Republic Navy, Mandalore and his surviving men fled to the Dxun moon.

Millennia later, six years after the Battle of Endor, the *Millennium Falcon* landed on Onderon to repair damage suffered in a battle with the clone Emperor's flagship, the *Eclipse II.* Fearing for her newborn son Anakin, Princess Leia Organa Solo hid in warrior leader Modon Kira's safehouse deep in the Onderon wilderness. Palpatine, posing as a pilgrim on his way to the Shatoon monastery, discovered the child and tried to possess his body but was stopped by the Jedi Empatojayos Brand. Later, the leaders of the New Republic gathered in the fortress of Modon Kira and reestablished their galactic government, led by Mon Mothma with Leia Organa Solo as her second in command.

**Onderon, Beast Wars of** A centuries-long conflict between the citizens of the walled city of Iziz and its outcasts, the beast-riders of Onderon. The intervention of the Jedi Knights was eventually required to resolve the conflict.

**Ondi, Candace** A member of Rebel Alliance Intelligence, she worked as an information officer in a Rebel colony on Sulon. She traveled with a modified chrome-plated protocol droid called A-Cee. The droid had the ability to digitally record and store more than 1,000 hours of audio and holographic information. Ondi died when the Empire raided the Sulon colony, but her droid survived, and was able to bring the recording of the Imperial slaughter to the rest of the galaxy.

**One Below** *See* Yaddle.

**One Scourge** A unit of Yuuzhan Vong warriors aboard the *Baanu Rass* tasked by Nom Anor with capturing the Jedi infiltration team that boarded the ship to kill the voxyn queen. Much to the chagrin of Warmaster Tsavong Lah, the Jedi wiped out the unit.

**One Sith** *See* Rule of One.

**Ongree** A species of semi-humanoid beings from the Skustell Cluster, they had an unusual upside-down appearance to their faces, with low-slung eyestalks and a mouth where most beings had foreheads. Ongree were known for their ability to view any situation from a variety of angles, and often spent a great deal of time weighing all the possible perspectives before making a decision.

**ongun-nur** A harmless flying creature that traveled in large flocks darkening the skies of Ansion. Ongun-nur had enormous balloon-like wings that were paper-thin; long, rapier-like beaks; and bright yellow eyes. Their bodies were swollen with air, rather than muscle, going where the wind took them.

**Oni** An alien species from Uru, the Oni people shared a militant culture and were often found offworld as part of mercenary armies. Female Oni were electrophoretic, capable of storing static electricity within a unique capacitor gland.

**Onimi** Proving the ancient maxim that looks could be deceiving, Onimi appeared as a babbling, deformed Yuuzhan Vong jester to Overlord Shimrra, but in truth he held absolute power over the Yuuzhan Vong invasion force. He was, at one time, an ambitious shaper of considerable skill who was brought down by his own pride. A misguided bid to graft a yammosk brain module onto his own brain resulted in rampant cellular damage. His body became twisted and disfigured; one eye was lower on his face than the other, and part of his skull was distended. His mouth was a twisted slash, and his long, lean limbs twitched with a sort of mad delight.

Though the failed yammosk graft led to him being cast off as a Shamed One, he developed the ability to telepathically control the actions of others, particularly Overlord Shimrra. Much to the bewilderment of other Yuuzhan Vong, Shimrra took Onimi as a pet and jester, as onlookers were unaware that the impish jester was actually the power behind the throne.

Adding to Onimi's already astounding deception, he also disguised himself as the decrepit shaper master, Kae Kwaad, and worked closely with Nen Yim, observing her experiments to develop new weaponry and constructs for the purpose of conquest and filling the eighth cortex, a level of knowledge supposedly bequeathed to the Yuuzhan Vong by their gods. In truth, the cortex was empty. Onimi was the first to discover this; Shimrra, too, knew the secret of the fallow eighth cortex, a secret that once revealed would clearly lead to heresy and rebellion against the most rigid of Yuuzhan Vong precepts. As the war began to turn against the Yuuzhan Vong, Shimrra demanded that Yim fill the eighth cortex with knowledge from the galaxy they had invaded.

As part of his guise, Onimi constantly spoke in rhymes and riddles, dispensing wisdom that was shrouded in dark humor. After the living planet Zonama Sekot reappeared near Coruscant, Onimi suddenly became quiet, often refusing to recite his acerbic poetry and hiding behind Shimrra's growing power.

At the end of the Yuuzhan Vong War, Luke Skywalker's Jedi Knights infiltrated Shimrra's Citadel. At first, Onimi cowered by the Overlord's side until the tide of battle turned to favor the Jedi. Onimi fled, pursued by Jaina Solo. He overpowered her with poisons he was capable of exuding from his shaped and altered body. Onimi believed Jaina to be the living embodiment of the Trickster goddess Yun-Harla, whom he hated. He felt Yun-Harla had betrayed him in his failed shaping, which took away his dignity and standing. But what the experiments had given Onimi, beyond yammosk-based telepathy, was a connection to the Force that had otherwise been stripped from the Yuuzhan Vong biology ages before.

Ongree

Jacen Solo confronted Onimi, and the Jedi tapped into the unifying Force in a way that was deeper than ever before. Onimi attacked as a shaper, using his enhanced abilities to turn every bodily fluid he possessed into poisons or hallucinogens that he could inject via his fang or simply apply to Jacen's skin. Through his own connection to the Force Jacen neutralized them all, rendering them nothing more than sweat and tears. As Jacen became more and more a living conduit for the Force, he was able to attack Onimi on the level of purest energy. Onimi, unable to let go of the hatred and greed he had lived with for so long, was rendered into nothingness by Jacen's actions. As his body re-formed itself into an Unshamed form, Onimi collapsed and died.

Onoh

**Onin (V-Onin)** The grandson of O-Yani, when he was young this Keganite was sent to the Re-Learning Circle.

**Onith, M'iiyoom (Nightlily)** A H'nemthe female who was involved in a romantic relationship with Gotal Feltipern Trevagg. Due to a questionable discrepancy with passage taxes, she was stranded on Tatooine at the time of Luke Skywalker's departure. Trevagg tried to bed the H'nemthe virgin, only to discover that in the H'nemthe culture females ritually kill males after mating. Onith had green skin, a beak-like snout, and a razor-sharp tongue. Her name translated to "nightlily."

**Onoh** A short, yellow-skinned Lizling employed by Jabba the Hutt as the watchman of a cache of treasures hidden within the Glass Mountain on Tatooine. He reluctantly teamed up with Spiker and Big Gizz when they stole the *Spirit of Jabba.*

**Onoma, Captain** A Mon Calamari officer serving in the New Republic Navy, he served as first officer aboard the *Mon Remonda* during the New Republic siege of Coruscant as well as General Han Solo's pursuit of Imperial Warlord Zsinj.

**Onslaught** A term used by historians and the media to describe attacks during the Mandalorian Wars that targeted an area of space bordered by Serroco, Jebble, Vanquo, and Tarnith. The Galactic Republic defended against the aggressors but failed to prevent the armored warriors from penetrating deep into Republic-held space.

***Onslaught*** One of the Star Destroyers present during the annexation of Bakura by the Empire shortly after the Battle of Yavin. Commanding the *Onslaught* was Captain Brellar.

**OnSon, Skot** The son of farmers near the Kibo Sands on Ord Cestus, he joined the Desert Wind terrorist group during the Clone Wars. Skot wanted to exact vengeance against the ruling Five Families for cutting off water to his family farm, which had hastened the death of his parents from shadow fever. He was trained in form combat by Jedi Master Kit Fisto and his ARC troopers. He was tall and thin, with long blond hair and a crescent-shaped scar on his forehead.

Oola

**Onyx Squadron** One of the first full squadrons of TIE defenders, led by Rexler Brath at the Battle of Endor.

***Onyx Star*** The code name of the first Z-95 Headhunter produced.

**Oochee** An Ewok at the Battle of Endor, he had black-and-white-striped fur, carried an ax, and wore a dark blue hood. Oochee's name came from an Ewok myth of a child who learned the secrets of invisibility from a wind spirit.

**Oodoc** A species known for its size and strength, if not for its intelligence. Oodocs had spiked arms, and pointed spines on their backs.

**Oodonnaa** An old Twi'lek woman who worked as an information broker on Nar Shaddaa during the early days of the Galactic Civil War. She once hit on a young Han Solo.

**ooglith** A Yuuzhan Vong–bioengineered organic environment suit. There were two prominent forms: the ooglith masquer and the ooglith cloaker. Resembling a blob of protoplasm, the former could be draped over the head and torso of a Yuuzhan Vong and become a living mask. It would extend thousands of tiny grappling tendrils into the pores of the Yuuzhan Vong's skin, latching the masquer's body directly to that of its host. Externally, the masquer created the appearance of another species, allowing the Yuuzhan Vong to walk among the citizens of the galaxy without being detected. The ooglith masquer had to be trained to remain in a certain form while attached to the Yuuzhan Vong's face. At the push of a sensitive point on its body, the creature retracted its tendrils and peeled away from the host's face, once again becoming a shapeless entity and returning to its container.

The cloaker attached to its host in the same fashion. Whereas the masquer was an instrument of disguise, the cloaker was more like an environment suit. Unlike the masquer, however, the cloaker's facial mask was transparent. It was paired with a gnullith, a soft star-shaped creature that latched onto the host's face. The central tendril of this creature then slid down the host's throat. Different forms protected the wearer from weather, temperature extremes, pressure, and even the vacuum of space. To remove the ooglith cloaker, the host opened a seam along his or her nose, and the cloaker peeled itself off.

**Oojoh** A young Ho'Din Padawan learner studying at the satellite training facility on Taris just before the Mandalorian Wars. Oojoh's Masters were all members of the Covenant, a secret group of Jedi seers who saw a dark vision of the future brought about by one of their students. In a preemptive move to prevent this cataclysm, the Jedi slew their Padawans, though Zayne Carrick survived.

**Ookbat** In the dark warrens of Ookbat, Wookiee bounty hunter Chenlambec and his partner Tinian I'att saved each other during a failed mission.

**Oola** A Twi'lek slave girl who lived a sad, short life. Bib Fortuna, Jabba the Hutt's majordomo, longed to find the perfect "gift" for his master; he discovered Oola, the daughter of a clan chief, on Ryloth. He kidnapped the girl, along with a younger Twi'lek named Sienn, and took them to his smuggling complex. There, other Twi'lek dancers taught them the ways of exotic and captivating dance sure to get the Hutt's attention. Fortuna deluded the girls with tales of Jabba's opulent lifestyle and the glory of being a palace servant. Four months later, Fortuna felt his prizes were ready. His assistant Jerris Rudd took them to Tatooine.

In Mos Eisley, Rudd placed Oola and Sienn in hiding. Jedi Knight Luke Skywalker stumbled upon the girls' hiding place and promised the two help in escaping from slavery. Though Luke freed Sienn, Oola was so tantalized by visions of palace life that she stayed. Then Oola faced the cold reality of the Hutt's palace, a dank place of corruption filled with the dregs of the galaxy. She had the "privilege" of being chained to Jabba's throne, and the Hutt delighted in watching the young Oola dance. When Jabba wanted more than dance, Oola refused. Angered with his rebellious slave, Jabba opened the trapdoor beneath the dance floor, and fed Oola to his rancor creature.

Oola's half sister, Nolaa Tarkona, rose to prominence two decades into the New Republic's rule as the leader of the Diversity Alliance.

**Oolas, Captain** Commander of the *Steadfast,* the New Republic ship that surveyed the ruins of the Imperial Star Destroyer *Gnisnal* and recovered its intact memory core.

**Oolidi** The homeworld of Tolik Yar, a member of the New Republic Senate and a staunch defender of Leia Organa Solo during her time as Chief of State.

**Oolos, Dr. Ism** A Ho'Din physician working in a medcenter in Bagsho, the port city of Nim Drovis.

**Oolth** A Fondorian, he worked as an aide to Black Sun mastermind Master Alexi Garyn in the years before the Battle of Naboo. He was the sole survivor of Darth Maul's attack on Alexi Garyn's Black Sun headquarters on Ralltiir. Terrified for his life, Oolth hid in a safehouse in the Crimson Corridor of Coruscant. Padawan Darsha Assant was asked by the Jedi Council to bring Oolth to the Jedi Temple. Though she located the fugitive, they were attacked by the Raptor gang before they could leave the Corridor. In the struggle to escape, Oolth fell seven stories, presumably to his death.

**OOM-9** The commander of the Trade Federation's battle droids during the invasion of Naboo and the subsequent battle against the Gungans. He was deactivated, along with the rest of the battle droid army, when young Anakin Skywalker destroyed the Droid Control Ship.

**OOM Command Officer battle droid** A highly specialized type of battle droid denoted by its yellow markings, it led other battle droids into combat by relaying messages sent to the troops from the central control computer aboard the Droid Control Ship. OOM officers received signals via high-security priority channels. They usually had extended power units that allowed them to function for a longer period of time and receive signals at maximum ranges.

OOM-9

**Oon Tien** A water-covered mountainous planet off the Trition Trade Route in the Kathol sector.

**Oonaar, Zlece** An Imperial Navy captain, one of two masterminds behind the devastating rout of the Eyttyrmin Batiiv pirates. He commanded the Star Destroyer *Crusader* in that battle, which was led by Captain Alistar Dadefra aboard the *Bombard.* The Khuiumin Survivors vowed to kill him one day, and got their chance when Oonaar booked passage aboard the *Galaxy Chance.* The Survivors intercepted the casino ship and captured Oonaar. Upon returning to Courkrus, they executed him for his crimes against the pirates.

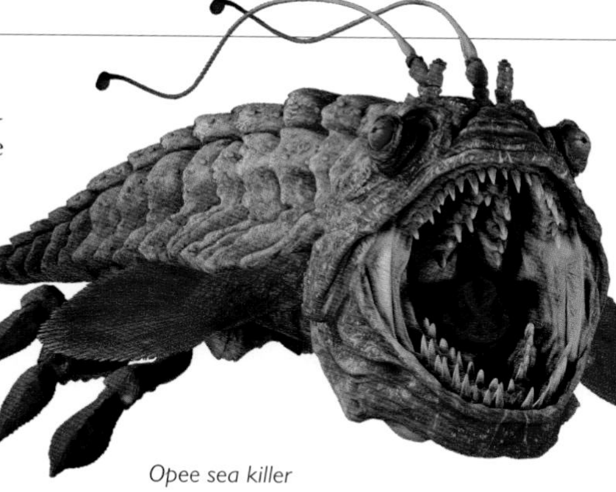
Opee sea killer

**Ooo-sek** This swampy world was one of the first Rodian colonies to be established. It had a wide variety of creatures to hunt and was home to the carnivorous mobile plant-form known as the *yo'uqiol,* or "hand of death."

**Oor VII** A planet that held a worldwide spelling bee. One of the prized medallions for spelling champion wound up on the uniform of Inspector Keek, chief of the Internal Security Police on Brigia.

**oorg** A pink, beady-eyed slug-like creature with a long snout, raised as livestock on Cerea.

**Ooriffi meditation ritual** A practice that involved repeated fidgeting with a trinket or talisman in order to relieve stress.

**Oorn Tchis** A small, backrocket agricultural planet best known for exporting rare ores used in guidance system design. The planet also exported colorful fabrics for the garment industry. Keyan Farlander's aunt and uncle lived on Oorn Tchis.

**Ooroo** One of the most respected Jedi Masters of his time, Ooroo lived five millennia before the rise of the Empire. He was a Celegian, so interaction with the outside galaxy necessitated a special repulsorlift conveyance that held aloft an amber chrysalis, wherein his pink brain-like form rested. He was surrounded by the cyanogen he needed to breathe, since oxygen was poisonous to him. Among the students in his praxeum was Odan-Urr, who would figure prominently in the Great Hyperspace War. At the height of the conflict, Ooroo joined his student in defending Kirrek from Sith invaders. Ooroo sacrificed himself by allowing his chrysalis to be shattered, letting the poisonous atmosphere waft over the Massassi warriors. Ooroo died of oxygen poisoning.

Ooroo

**oorp** A bland but healthy liquid food supplement developed for pregnant beings.

***Oo-ta Goo-ta*** A modified light freighter owned and operated by a Rodian smuggler named Chordak in the Minos Cluster.

**Ootman** The name applied to Sharad Hett when he joined a Tusken Raider tribe on Tatooine. The name, which Jawas and Sand People both used in reference to the wayward Jedi, meant "outlander." Hett took control of his Tusken Raider tribe and led a series of raids on Tatooine before he was killed by the bounty hunter Aurra Sing.

**Ootmian Pabol** A busy hyper-route connecting Hutt Space with the Republic's Expansion Region, it was decimated by a supernova around 4,000 years before the Battle of Yavin. It devolved into a minor route used primarily by shady starhoppers and smugglers.

**Ootoola** A beautiful aquatic world dominated by unusual twisted rock formations. The natives of the planet, an amphibious species known only as Fishfaces, built their cities within the rocks.

**Oovo 4** A bleak, pockmarked moon orbiting the gas planet Oovo. Considered an "asteroid world" by many, Oovo 4 was home to a prison colony and labor camp. Inmates were forced to dig deep within the moon's interior for ore, which was then transported to loading docks on the surface via zero-gravity vacuum tunnels. A Podrace course on Oovo 4 required pilots to navigate a maze of zero-g tunnels and other corridors while avoiding dangers such as rotating gates. During the Yuuzhan Vong War, the facility on Oovo 4 was leveled and all records from the prison were lost.

**Ooya** A member of the Singing Mountain Clan on Dathomir.

**oozhith** A body-hugging creature worn as a garment by Yuuzhan Vong masters. Oozhiths, also called robeskins, had tiny cilia that rippled in subtle waves of color, feeding on microorganisms in the atmosphere. Though most full-skin oozhiths covered the entire body, there was a shorter version that left the arms and most of the legs bare. Some oozhiths had a pouch to act as a pocket for the wearer. When torn, the robeskin bled a sticky resinous milk, but it regenerated within a day or two.

**OP-5** A civilian landspeeder developed and distributed by the SoroSuub Corporation.

**Opari** A stop on the Gevarno Loop, this system remained loyal to the Old Republic during the Clone Wars.

**Opatajji-Hirken, Neera** The fat, overbearing wife of Corporate Sector Authority Viceprex Mirkovig Hirken, administrator of Stars' End. She lived a bored existence in the executive suite of the CSA prison installation on Mytus VII. She was born the fourth daughter of the Duke of Opatjji. She killed her husband during the rush to escape Stars' End when the installation was destroyed by Han Solo.

***Opee Fleer*** A decommissioned military bongo submarine with a crew of three that participated in the Otoh Gunga Challenge. Compared with sleeker designs, the *Opee Fleer* was a cumbersome vessel that needed to slow down to make sharper turns.

**opee sea killer** A massive fish native to the deep waters of Naboo, it lurked among the dark crags of the planetary core. The 50-meter-long creature had a tapered body with tough, armored plates. Two bulbous eyes were mounted on short stalks to help it see in the depths. A pair of long antenna-like lures flowed back from its head. Two powerful pectoral fins propelled the killer through the seas, and six legs helped it cling to cave walls and outcroppings. The opee had a long gooey tongue that it used to catch its prey and draw it into its mouth. Some varieties had luminous spots on their bodies. The crustacean swam by using its fins and legs in conjuction with an internal water-jet propulsion system.

**Open Circle Fleet** A major task force of the Galactic Republic Starfleet led by Generals Obi-Wan Kenobi and Anakin Skywalker during the Clone Wars, it defended Coruscant in the final stages of the conflict.

**Operation 265-A** A special mission undertaken by Rebel agents shortly after the Battle of Yavin, escorting Dr. Elth Nardah and his assistant to the planet Karra, providing necessary support and protection. Once there, the agents were to examine and evaluate, from a military perspective, the physical and intellectual abilities of the native Karrans.

**Operation 45RA** The code name for a plot by Braig and Nak Farool to kidnap popular media personality Crying Dawn Singer, and blame the abduction on the Rebel Alliance in an effort to discredit the Rebellion.

**Operational Multisystem Management (OMM)** An enormous database network that allowed executives within the Corporate Sector Authority access to the vast information systems of the sector. The CSA employed slicers who had been convicted of computer crimes by the Empire to create the network and keep it secure.

*Operation Emperor's Spear*

**Operation Blue Harvest** The code name of an Imperial operation that occurred after the Battle of Yavin. It was so secretive that even Imperial technicians were left in the dark about components that they worked on. They often speculated on what the project could be since it required huge amounts of money and personnel.

**Operation Blue Plug** The code name of the fledgling New Republic's plan for invading the planet Commenor and wresting it from Imperial control. Devised some 10 years after the Battle of Yavin by Garm Bel Iblis, Operation Blue Plug was never implemented—nor were its details made public—because the Commenorians voluntarily evicted their Imperial oppressors and joined the New Republic. The documentation for Operation Blue Plug was sealed in top-secret computer files and sent into deep storage, where it remained hidden and unnoticed for nearly 30 years. With the discovery of the so-called Chasin Document, which was essentially a modernized version of the original plans, the leaders of the Galactic Alliance were forced to accept the fact that an internal security breach had exposed the operation's details. According to research done by Tycho and Winter Celchu, during the Corellia–GA War someone had inserted secret code into the GA's computer systems that created regular backups of classified documents and sent them to a remote location. Making matters worse, the original code was inserted into the computer system using a password known only to members of the Galactic Alliance Guard.

**Operation Case White** The code name of the Separatist plan to take control of the Intergalactic Communications Center on Praesitlyn during the final stages of the Clone Wars. As part of Operation Case White, Admiral Pors Tonith blockaded Praesitlyn with some 200 warships before landing some 50,000 battle droids as a first attack. He held a million or more battle droids in reserve, hoping to draw out any resistance from the Republic before utterly crushing it. As a contingency plan, Tonith had stationed 126 more warships at Sluis Van to drive off any reinforcements the Republic might send to Praesitlyn. Although the initial stages of the operation went off as planned, Tonith was unprepared for the sudden appearance of Zozridor Slayke and his rogue soldiers, Freedom's Sons. Slayke's forces were vastly outmanned, yet they caused damage to Tonith's forces and held them off long enough for a Republic task force—led by Nejaa Halcyon and Anakin Skywalker—to arrive at Praesitlyn. Even then, Tonith's superior firepower was only defeated by a bold plan, hatched by Skywalker, that managed to capture Tonith and put an end to the operation.

**Operation Cobolt** Originally the Cobolt Offensive, this special military strike was organized at the highest level of the Rebel Alliance. Its purpose was the theft of an Imperial scandoc decoding computer held on an Imperial orbital base over Mantooine. In addition, the plan was to destroy the base. This coordinated effort drew starfighter wings from the Homon, Sumitra, and Farstey sectors, as well as from the Alliance fleet.

**Operation Durge's Lance** The code name for the Confederacy campaign against planets along the Corellian Trade Spine. The Separatist assault force consisted of the First and Third fleets of the Confederacy Navy. It originally launched from Yag'Dhul and got provisions via supply lines from Sullust and Thyferra. It represented a bold strike by the Confederacy into the heart of Republic space, and resulted in the conquest of Duro.

**Operation Emperor's Hammer** A follow-up to Operation Starlancer, this was the code name for Wedge Antilles's plan to employ Imperial tactics by using the *Lusankya,* a Super Star Destroyer, to bombard the Yuuzhan Vong forces on Borleias.

**Operation Emperor's Spear** A follow-up to Operation Emperor's Hammer, this was the code name for Wedge Antilles's plan to use the *Lusankya* as a missile against the Yuuzhan Vong. After the aliens' conquest of Coruscant, Wedge had been ordered to hold Borleias long enough for Chief of State Pwoe and the remainder of the New Republic Advisory Council to flee into space. Though the *Lusankya* suffered damage in battle over Borleias, it was not as critically hit as outward activity would appear to suggest. The ship was certainly undergoing extensive repairs, but in reality its weapons emplacements were being removed and placed onto smaller ships, and the Super Star Destroyer was being refitted from the inside out to become an enormous needle-like ram. During the last stand at Borleias, Commander Eldo Davip took the *Lusankya* into battle, drawing enemy fire away from other ships. The Star Destroyer suffered severe damage, bolstering the Yuuzhan Vong's confidence. Davip then used all remaining engine power to ram the *Lusankya* into the Czulkang Lah's worldship, destroying both ships and eliminating the Yuuzhan Vong threat.

**Operation Flotsam** A New Republic operation funded by the Historical Battle Site Preservation Act, set up to recover the debris from space battles before it could end up on the private market. It collected Imperial and Alliance artifacts for display in the Alliance War Museum on Coruscant.

**Operation Groundquake** Named by Tyria Sarkin, this Wraith Squadron mission involved knocking out the Imperial bases located in the cities of Fellon and Hullis, on the planet Halmad, during the hunt for Warlord Zsinj.

**Operation Hammerblow** A New Republic naval operation first implemented by the Fifth Battle Group, 12 years after the Battle of Endor. Tested in a simulation at Bessimir, the operation involved the use of K-wing bombers to knock out a planet's defensive shielding, thus allowing larger ships to neutralize weapons emplacements in preparation for landing. It was heavily opposed in some circles of the New Republic Senate, for it was a heavy-handed use of military power by a government supposedly opposed to the subjugation of planets. Admiral Ackbar and the supporters of the operation cited many worlds under Imperial control that would require the use of such tactics.

**Operation Joystick** The code name for the New Republic's plan to bring the planet Adumar—along with its military resources—into Republic membership.

**Operation Katabatic** The code name for the Galactic Republic's attempt to liberate the planet Atraken from the control of Separatists during the Clone Wars. Though the Republic succeeded in its aims, it was a costly victory: Biochemical weapons unleashed by the Separatists killed off 90 percent of Atraken's population.

**Operation Noble Savage** The code name used by Thrackan Sal-Solo and Admiral Vara Karathas to describe their plans to eliminate the Galactic Alliance's base on Tralus, 10 years after the end of the Yuuzhan Vong War.

The GA, in an effort to forestall Sal-Solo's bid for Corellian independence, established a base in the city of Rellidir as part of Operation Roundabout. This gave the GA a stronghold in the Corellian system, essentially blockading Sal-Solo from any further action. Karathas developed Operation Noble Savage without regard for civilian casualties or collateral damage. Sal-Solo, however, planned to ensure that any civilian deaths were laid at the feet of the Galactic Alliance, as part of a wider plan to discredit the GA and gain popular support for Corellian independence.

**Operation Restbreak** The code name for New Republic plans to defend the shipyards at Bilbringi against Yuuzhan Vong attack.

**Operation Retribution** A Rebel operation in the Fakir sector and neighboring areas during which many Imperial targets were attacked simultaneously. One part of Retribution was a full-scale attack on an Imperial space station. This drew many TIE fighters from the base on Mycroft. During the three days in which the Imperials could not resupply the base, Green Squad, a group from Reekeene's Roughnecks, ambushed Repair Station M13.

**Operation Roundabout** The code name used by Admiral Matric Klauskin and the forces of the Galactic Alliance for their plan to establish a base of operations on the planet Tralus, creating a show of force that would prevent Thrackan Sal-Solo and his Corellian insurgents from seceding from the Galactic Alliance.

**Operation Safe Passage** The code name for the evacuation plans developed by the Jedi Knights in the event that their base on Eclipse was discovered by the Yuuzhan Vong or the Peace Brigade.

**Operation Shadow Hand** Long before the cloned Emperor Palpatine's demise, the evil ruler initiated an elite corps of seven warriors whom he empowered with the dark side of the Force. These Dark Jedi put into motion Operation Shadow Hand, his master plan to retake the galaxy. Operation Shadow Hand included surgical strikes at worlds surrounding the Deep Core, and the building of bigger, deadlier weapons such as the advanced generations of war droids, the Galaxy Gun superweapon, and horrible chrysalis creatures. Before Palpatine's eventual return, much of Operation Shadow Hand was carried out by Executor Sedriss.

**Operation Sidestep** Admiral Hortel Ossilege's name for the delaying tactic orchestrated by a joint New Republic–Bakuran task force. During the Corellian crisis, its true masterminds, the Sacorrian Triad, arrived in the Corellian system. The Bakuran fleet had to hold off the Sacorrian fleet until New Republic reinforcements could arrive. This involved entering deep into the Sacorrian fleet in an effort to change the vessels' direction.

**Operation Skyhook** This operation saw the transmission of the captured Death Star plans from Rebel spies on Toprawa to the Alderaanian consular ship *Tantive IV.* That set into motion a series of events that culminated with the Battle of Yavin. Phase One of the operation was the actual capture of the plans, executed by Rebel-allied mercenary Kyle Katarn from the Imperial research facility on Danuta.

**Operation Starlancer** A ruse operation engineered by the New Republic to throw the Yuuzhan Vong off balance. It purposely drew attention to Borleias in order to distract the enemy from other, more critical operations. Danni Quee allowed for information of the Starlancer project to leak to enemy spies, revealing that Borleias was developing a new experimental superweapon that would target Yuuzhan Vong vessels. According to the falsified specifications, the weapons were built around enormous lambent crystals transported by "pipefighters" and could target vessels across enormous distance through hyperspace. Czulkang Lah was dispatched to deal with this developing threat on Borleias, giving the New Republic Advisory Council time to escape from Coruscant, and letting Wedge Antilles successfully complete Operation Emperor's Spear, which destroyed Lah's worldship with the modified Super Star Destroyer *Lusankya.*

**Operation Strike Fear** One of the first concerted efforts by the Empire to crack down on the nascent Rebel Alliance in the early days of the Galactic Civil War. Following increased coordination and effectiveness on the Alliance's part, the Empire could no longer ignore the growing resistance movement. Operation Strike Fear was a multipronged attack consisting of large-scale, highly visible destruction of Alliance bases to send a message to all would-be insurgents. The first target of Operation Strike Fear was the Alliance base on Briggia.

**Operation Strong Hand** The code name for the final New Republic assault on the Yevethan Navy during the Black Fleet crisis. It involved the use of the White Current, wielded primarily by Wailu and Akanah, to create the illusion of a huge war fleet attacking the Koornacht Cluster. Primary command of Strong Hand was given to General Etahn A'baht.

**Operation Trinity** The massive three-pronged assault on the Bilbringi asteroid belt by the Galactic Alliance to eliminate the Yuuzhan Vong presence there. It was based on coordinated HoloNet transmissions among the fleets commanded by General Wedge Antilles, General Traest Kre'fey, and Grand Admiral Gilad Pellaeon. The Yuuzhan Vong unleashed the mabugat kan, which destroyed several HoloNet relay stations and shut down communications among the three fleets. Only Antilles's brilliant feint saved the Alliance forces, as he faked a reactor core meltdown aboard the *Mon Mothma* and drove off the Yuuzhan Vong.

**Operation Yavin Kill Two** An Imperial plot meant to kill Luke Skywalker, Han Solo, and Princess Leia Organa, the so-called Heroes of Yavin. Imperial Intelligence began spreading rumors that the Royal Palace of Alderaan had survived the planet's destruction and was intact within the asteroid Graveyard. They had indeed found the remains, but the rumors also spoke of survivors, of which there were none. A different group of Rebel operatives intercepted this bait and journeyed to the Alderaan Graveyard, uncovering the trap and warning away Leia before she could be threatened.

**Ophideraan** A desolate world under the control of the Serpent Master Tyrann, until Luke Skywalker and Tanith Shire defeated him.

**opila** A type of crystal used by the ancient Jedi Knights in the construction of their lightsabers. Mined in the Fyrth system, these crystals were believed to give wielders a greater presence in combat, allowing them to intimidate an opponent.

**Opiteihr system** Located on the Enarc Run, it was a complex system of four red giant stars: Opiteihr, Kalnus, Terax, and Dal. The system included the planet Krann, site of a well-known nova crystal mine.

**Oplovis sector** An area of Imperial space during the Galactic Civil War. The Oplovis Sector Fleet squared off with two Rebel Alliance fleet battle lines in the Yuvern system. The Alliance emerged victorious in that encounter. Two months after that skirmish, Darth Vader was sent to Oplovis sector to "retire" the admiral of the fleet. Six months after that, the Oplovis Sector Fleet, under new command, ventured from its base on Harrod's Planet in an attempt to quell an uprising in the adjacent Atrivis sector. Alliance Intelligence was able to predict the maneuver, and the Oplovis Fleet was attacked by a battle line of three Alliance cruisers as it emerged from hyperspace in the Atrivis system. The Alliance cruisers, commanded by Admiral Ackbar, defeated the Imperials.

**Opquis** A species known for its rough voices. The Opquis were represented in the New Republic Senate.

**Opreka, Kalzutan** A native of Naboo, he served as the chairman of the Naboo Moon Mining Union shortly before the Clone Wars. He called for a "sit-in" protest of the decision by Queen Jamillia to close off certain Naboo starports to mining traffic in favor of allowing refugee ships to land there instead. Union ships were left in their berths, preventing refugee ships from landing.

**Opuh, N. J.** A Phuii who was known to frequent Dex's Diner.

**Opur** Talon Karrde's security officer aboard the *Wild Karrde* during the Yuuzhan Vong War.

**oqa** The Yuuzhan Vong–bioengineered equivalent of a cofferdam that connected two starships in space and allowed for transit between the vessels. Its name was derived from the Yuuzhan Vong term for a pack animal's proboscis.

**Oracle Stone** A Sith artifact of clairvoyance on Korriban. The cloned Emperor used the Oracle Stone to find a way to halt the decay of his artificial body—an act that led him to newborn Anakin Solo.

**Orade, Ghes** A Mandalorian soldier and contemporary of Boba Fett and Gora Beviin, he wed Mirta Gev, Fett's granddaughter.

**Oradin** A coastal city on Brentaal IV, in the Bormea sector. Shortly after the Battle of Endor, Brentaal became an object of dispute between Imperials and the New Republic. The elite Rogue and Aggressor squadrons began a series of missions against the entrenched Admiral Lon Isoto. This included Y-wing strikes against Oradin, which Isoto was able to repel with the 181st Imperial Fighting Group. There were many Alliance and civilian casualties. The Alliance was able to carve out some territory from Oradin and used it as a staging ground for future sorties.

**Orame** A Duros, she worked as a traffic control officer at the Jedi academy on Ossus in the years following the Yuuzhan Vong War.

**Oran, Communications Chief** The comm officer aboard the New Republic escort cruiser *Adamantine.*

**Orange District** The nickname given to a particular area of Galactic City, for its inhabitants' propensity for replacing the clear bulb of public illumigrids and streetlights with orange bulbs. This gave the district a somewhat menacing air.

**Orange Panthacs** During the Yuuzhan Vong invasion, a platoon of privately owned super battle droids dubbed the Orange Panthacs beat back an occupation force of enemy fire breathers on Mantessa, earning the unit a special commendation from Galactic Alliance President Cal Omas.

**oratay** A hot beverage brewed on the planet Cilpar and other worlds. Native canine creatures known as ronks were extremely allergic to oratay. Local resistance fighters repelled ronks by pressing oratay grounds into a disk, and then throwing it at the ronks, forcing them away. It took six months to gather enough grounds to press a disk.

**Orax** A mining world controlled and restricted by the Empire, it was discovered about a century before the Battle of Yavin. It was the homeworld of the crystalline lifeforms known as Shards.

**orbalisk** Hard-shelled, parasitic creatures found on Dxun, orbalisks were poisonous to the average being, and were known to feed off dark side energy. The orbalisk also provided a powerhouse supply of adrenaline to its host, and its hardened shell formed nearly impenetrable armor. Orbalisks attached themselves to Darth Bane's body as he struggled through the dense jungles of Dxun. The two parent orbalisks affixed themselves to Bane's chest, forming a breastplate. As they bred, the offspring spread out across his body. Although Bane initially attempted to remove the creatures, he soon realized that their symbiotic relationship was one from which he would ultimately benefit. He had to wear a cage-like protective helmet to keep the creatures from growing into his face.

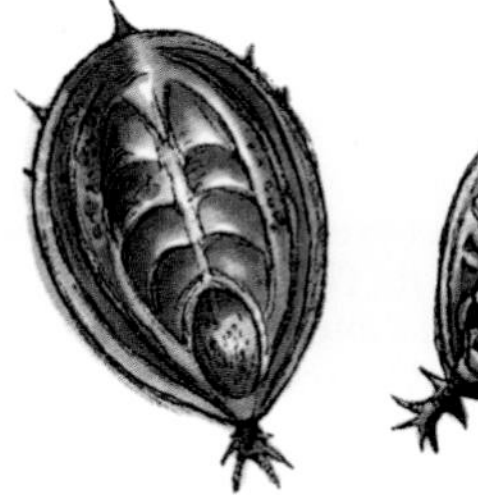

*Orbalisk*

**orbital defense cannon** Anti-capital-ship artillery used at Nym's Lok moon base. It was capable of wiping out a Trade Federation battle cruiser with one shot.

**orbital long range scanner (OLR)** Developed by the Loronar Corporation, it could detect ships in hyperspace over many light-years' distance, providing advance warning of approaching enemy fleets.

**orbital mine** A weapon used to block travel routes and destroy enemy vessels. Mines proved most effective in situations where natural hazards such as pulsars, gas clouds, and ion storms limited travel to a few well-established routes. Mines were also used for planetary sieges, blocking all starship traffic onto or off a world.

A wide variety of space mines existed, ranging from crude asteroids to sophisticated devices such as the Defender ion mine. Proximity mines—the most common type of space mine—were simple devices that exploded as soon as any ship passed within their blast range. The Merr-Sonn Defender used ion cannons to neutralize its targets.

There were two overarching types of mines: passive and active. Passive mines detonated when another body bumped them or came within a preset sensor range. Active mines reacted to targets entering their extended sensory range by tracking them and closing in like a missile.

**orbital nightcloak** An experimental device created by the Imperial Department of Military Research, it was a network of satellites that blocked or limited visible light from hitting a planet, effectively plunging a world into freezing night. The satellites were powered by solar energy, giving them a self-sustaining power source. The Empire deployed these satellites in orbit around a planet, but in order to be most effective, the besieged planet could not have orbital defenses. Imperial Warlord Zsinj employed an orbital nightcloak over the planet Dathomir four years after the Battle of Endor. Zsinj threatened to destroy the planet unless Han Solo was delivered to him.

The orbital nightcloak Mark II featured a number of improvements: namely, improved routing systems that allowed up to 10 percent of the satellites to be disabled before the net was affected. Furthermore, Mark II satellites were equipped with short-range laser cannons and targeting computers to defend themselves.

The orbital nightcloak satellite was disk-shaped, with a cylindrical shaft extending from the disk. When online, the disk opened, flower-like, extending electromagnetic absorption panels. Cooling systems helped moderate the solar energy absorbed.

**orbital relay satellites** Small transmitter units deployed by scientific, communications, and reconnaissance craft to extend sensor and communications range. Since the mass of a planet obscured signals directed to the other side of the world, a minimum of three relay satellites was needed to provide a vessel with global comm coverage. Most relay satellites were tiny, about the size of a helmet.

**orbital shipyard** Also called stardocks, these manufacturing facilities were used to build capital ships and starfighters by providing docking gantries from which workers could assemble the immense vessels. They frequently included landing bays for supply ships, and pressurized quarters to house laborers.

**Orbital Solar Energy Transfer Satellite** Helping warm the extreme latitudes of Coruscant, and standardizing the temperature planetwide, was a network of Orbital Solar Energy Transfer Satellites circling the capital world. Immense orbital mirrors, these disk-shaped satellites reflected and redirected solar energies to the latitudes that needed them. The surface of the OSETS was covered by dozens of reflective mirror panels that could be refocused or rotated to a nonreflective side. During the Empire's rule, the mirrors were usually monitored and piloted by low-ranking Imperial Navy troopers. Serving mirror duty (called riding the mirrors) was generally considered to be the loneliest, most tedious assignment on Coruscant. Despite the presence of entertainment systems and food-processing units aboard the OSETS, it was still dreary duty. In the time of the New Republic, the old mirrors often suffered malfunctions, and service priority was so low that mirror riders had to wait a long time before repair.

*Orbital nightcloak*

Members of Rogue Squadron exploited the OSETS to focus sunlight on a water reservoir, creating an instant thunderstorm from the boiled water, and aiding their efforts to drop Coruscant's planetary shields. The OSETS paved the way for the New Republic's taking of Coruscant from the Empire.

**orbital strike gun** Looking like a long-barreled blaster rifle, this weapon painted a target with a beacon that could then be detected by a starship in orbit. The vessel fired a blast of ion energy at the beacon's location, destroying everything in its blast radius.

**Orbitblade-2000** A rare example of a civilian-issue vehicle armed with powerful weaponry, this armored aerospace transport was developed by zZip Motor Concepts. While Orbitblades could not compete with dedicated combat airspeeders or starfighters, corporations and criminal organizations often used them as armed transports for important personnel. Each sled-shaped transport was 4 meters long, with three massive intake slots surrounding the passenger's cabin. The Orbitblade-2000 required one pilot; it could attain altitudes of 150 kilometers and speeds of 1,050 kilometers per hour. It was armed with a forward-firing concussion missile launcher.

**orbit dock** Orbital landing and maintenance facilities, they also provided other services to spacers and their ships. Some of the largest docks were almost small space stations in themselves, providing hotel, food, and entertainment facilities.

**Orbiting Shipyard Alpha** A spaceship repair dock high above the planet Duro.

**Orbot** This series of affordable protocol droids produced by Serv-O-Droid during the last century of the Galactic Republic proved quite popular in the Mid Rim. When Serv-O-Droid discovered that Cybot Galactica had produced its 5YQ series protocol droid with components from the Orbot, it took the larger corporation to court and eventually won its case. This forced Cybot Galactica to halt production of the 5YQ series.

**Orbus, Evar** The leader of the musical troupe Evar Orbus and his Galactic Wailers, he was scheduled to perform at Chalmun's cantina in Mos Eisley. Chalmun's Bith band, upon hearing of the newcomers, attempted to ambush the new band. In the scuffle, Orbus was killed by a stray blaster shot. In originally organizing the band, Orbus had to juggle singer Sy Snootles's ego and keyboardist Max Rebo's appetite. And then there was Snit, the Kitonak whom Orbus purchased on Ovrax IV, whose slow and complacent nature could also be difficult.

A Letaki, Orbus was a tentacled being with flap-like air-gills beneath his four eyes. He was known to carry a fake tentacle armed with a hidden weapon.

**Ord** The term *Ordnance/Regional Depot* denoted a number of frontier "fort" worlds set up by the military during the Old Republic. Many planets from that era of expansion included *Ordnance/Regional Depot,* or *Ord,* in their names.

**Ord Antalaha** This planet colonized during the Clone Wars was located along the Shwuy Exchange, a minor route between the Shwuy and Fakir sectors. After the Clone Wars, the military bases were abandoned and the colonists moved elsewhere, leaving the planet empty for pirates to take over as a base of operations.

**Ord Biniir** The site of a Rebel Alliance victory early in the Galactic Civil War. Rebel Y-wing pilots bragged of their victory at the Battle of Ord Biniir. A short time later, however, the Second Battle of Ord Biniir turned out quite differently. The planet, protected by the 181st Imperial Starfighter unit, made short work of the Alliance Y-wings. This Imperial victory was hardly celebrated, since it occurred the same day as the Battle of Yavin, which saw the destruction of the Death Star.

**Ord Bueri** A source of bombers sent to the Rebel base at Yavin 4. A partly dismantled twin-cockpit H-60 Tempest from Ord Bueri was at the base.

**Ord Canfre** A Republic world that surrendered during the Clone Wars.

**Ord Cantrell** An exclusive resort, it became a base of operations for the Imperial Interim Ruling Council and the site of Imperial ship docks, housing the flagship of Baron D'asta's armada.

**Ord Cestus** The homeworld of the X'Ting species, it was once simply Cestus until the Galactic Republic established a prison there over 300 years before the Battle of Yavin. It then took on the prefix *Ord.* Much of the planet's landmass was volcanically active, and the world's mineral riches were constantly being churned to the surface by massive seismological events. Large chunks of the planet's surface were once covered with sand and small bodies of water, with hardy plants eking out niches by exuding acids through their roots to break down the rock and sand into essential elements.

The world transformed as the descendants of the original Republic prisoners became farmers and settlers, and the planet's mineral wealth was eventually exploited by large corporations. Baktoid Armor Workshop established a major droid-manufacturing plant there, though repercussions from the Trade Federation's botched invasion of Naboo eventually led to prohibitive tariffs on battle droids, forcing Baktoid to close its Cestus operations.

These tariffs didn't stop the work of Cestus Cybernetics, which had the backing of the Confederacy of Independent Systems. During

*Order 66*

the height of the Clone Wars, Jedi Masters Obi-Wan Kenobi and Kit Fisto, along with their group of clone troopers, defeated the Separatist forces controlling the planet and the native X'Ting population.

**Ord Dorlass** A stopping point along the popular Star Rally race route known as the Dahvil-Fodro Hyperspace Promenade. Ord Dorlass was a suitably colonized world, with a cosmopolitan capital city and active entertainment media.

**Order 66** The ultimate contingency and culmination of Darth Sidious's plot to control the galaxy, this was a number-coded executive order known only to the clone commanders of the Grand Army of the Republic. A priority one signal dispatched from the Office of the Supreme Chancellor, it indicated a worst-case scenario: that the Jedi had betrayed the Republic and needed to be executed as traitors. Palpatine broadcast Order 66 at the end of the Clone Wars. Taken by surprise, thousands of Jedi were killed by troopers who had for three years answered almost exclusively to them. A few Jedi were known to have escaped death by dint of superior skill or accident. It was believed that Order 66 effectively wiped out 99 percent of the Jedi commanders in the Clone Wars.

**Order of Dai Bendu** An ancient fraternity. Many historians and scholars believed that it was one of the original incarnations of the Jedi Order, though no solid evidence ever surfaced to support this claim.

**Order of Shasa** A Force-sensitive cult of Selkath dedicated to protecting Manaan, it existed for generations prior to the Galactic Civil War. Much like the Jedi Knights had their lightsabers, Shasa adepts forged a unique weapon—the fira—upon achieving membership within the Order.

**Order of the Sacred Circle** An influential religious order centered on the cloistered planet Monastery, it revered the eternal, ever-renewing Circle of Life and paid great heed to the maintenance of balance in day-to-day life. Adherents tried to carry their lives out peacefully, and they were far removed from the normal traffic and turmoil of the galaxy. Throughout most of the Galactic Civil War, the Order maintained strict neutrality. Shortly after the Battle of Yavin, however, the Empire sent a diplomatic envoy to Monastery to persuade leaders to side with the New Order. Sister Domina, a Priestess of the Sacred Circle, entreated the Rebel Alliance to send a diplomatic envoy to Monastery, to present the case for Rebellion. Realizing the importance of the Sacred Circle's support, General Jan Dodonna sent Luke Skywalker as the Rebellion's representative. Sister Domina was in fact a member of the House of Tagge family of nobles, and harbored a secret vendetta against both Darth Vader and Skywalker. She plotted to kill both as they arrived on Monastery.

Ord Mantell

**Order of the Terrible Glare** An evil ancient sect that waged a monstrous war on the Jedi Knights thousands of years before the Galactic Civil War. The Jedi defeated the Order and laid waste to its homeworld, Garn.

**order to reveal** A Galactic Republic law that required Senators to reveal all information requested by an investigation. The order was not invoked lightly, and before it could be enacted, vast amounts of bureaucratic wrangling needed to be successfully completed. A Senator was allowed a sitting right of refusal to avoid the order to reveal, but doing so typically put that Senator in a compromising and politically vulnerable light.

**Ord Grovner** The site of an Imperial naval base in the Outer Rim Territories. The Star Destroyers *Bombard* and *Crusader* limped back to Ord Grovner after obliterating the Eyttyrmin Batiiv pirates. The principal city on Ord Grovner was Grovner.

**Ord Ibanna** A gas planet that, despite its choking atmosphere, once boasted numerous active gas mines and refineries connected by cable suspension bridges and pipelines. However, all of these mines were eventually abandoned and fell into disrepair. After the departure of the miners, scrap-metal dealers battled one another for the right to plunder the floating wreckage. As they worked, the dealers kept the massive and decaying facilities aloft with anti-gravity generators. Ord Ibanna was notable for its Podrace course, which twisted through enormous air circulation tunnels and wove around gas storage tanks. Pilots who hoped to survive the course had to remain alert for gaps in the skyway.

**Ord Janon** A Separatist-occupied planet where the Confederacy was forced to withdraw during the Clone Wars. It was located in the Outer Rim in the direction of the Corporate Sector.

**Ord Klina** A former Republic depot world that was visited by the Togorian Tyrimm Wyln.

**Ord Lithone** The site of a Baktoid Armor Workshop plant that had to close due to the impact of increased tariffs and regulations on battle droids within Republic space prior to the Clone Wars.

**Ord Mantell** Located in the outworlds, in the Bright Jewel Cluster, this planet was circled by numerous moons. Points of interest included its canyon-rimmed spaceport and Ten Mile Plateau, located in the rocky backcountry. Supposedly free from Imperial interests, Ord Mantell was hosting an Imperial fleet on maneuvers when Han Solo arrived there to repair the *Millennium Falcon* following the Battle of Yavin. Solo encountered his smuggler friend Drub McKumb, who warned the newly minted Rebel Alliance hero of the sizable bounty on his head. The bounty hunter Skorr captured Luke Skywalker and Princess Leia Organa and held them captive in an abandoned stellar energy plant on Ten Mile Plateau as bait to trap Solo, but Skorr's plans were foiled when Solo and Chewbacca staged a daring rescue. Later, Solo, Skywalker, and Chewbacca were captured by several bounty hunters (including Skorr, Dengar, and Bossk) working with Boba Fett, who imprisoned the trio in an abandoned moisture plant in Ord Mantell's backcountry. Again, Solo and his companions managed to outwit the bounty hunters and flee. About six years later, Grand Admiral Thrawn staged an assault on Ord Mantell to create fear in the surrounding systems and ease New Republic pressure on his shipyard supply lines. During the Yuuzhan Vong War, it was attacked by the alien invaders but aptly defended by the New Republic.

**Ord Mantell, Battle of** A battle between the Yuuzhan Vong and the New Republic waged at Ord Mantell. Sixteen vessels made up the New Republic's battle group under the command of General Yald Sutel, including the Imperial II Star Destroyer *Erinnic,* a *Mediator*-class Mon Calamari battle cruiser, two *Quasar*-class cruiser-carriers, three escort frigates, and five *Ranger*-class gunships. They were supported by squadrons of X-wings, B-wings, E-wings, and TIE interceptors. The Yuuzhan Vong force consisted of two corvette analogs, five frigate analogs, three light cruiser analogs, one warship analog, and a complement of coralskippers.

During the battle, the Yuuzhan Vong warship unleashed a dread weapon that attached itself to the *Jubilee Wheel,* capturing many of its inhabitants. By the end of the battle, the New Republic task force had lost the cruiser, an escort frigate, and three gunships. Yuuzhan Vong losses were significantly higher, providing a minor victory for the New Republic.

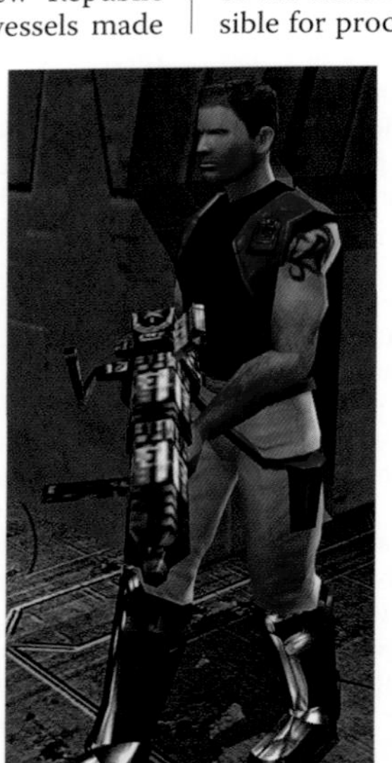
Canderous Ordo

**Ord Manurt** *See* Ord Namurt.

**Ord Mirit** Located at the edge of the Core in the Mirit system, this planet was the site of an Imperial base. Shortly after the Battle of Endor, the Empire abandoned it and transferred its garrison to Corellia. Three years later, Ord Mirit was one of three strategic systems guarded by the Imperial II Star Destroyer *Eviscerator.*

The New Republic was looking to capture Borleias in the nearby Pyria system, to use it as a staging ground to take Coruscant from the Empire. The raid began with an attack on the Venjagga system, which caused the *Eviscerator* to pursue fleeing decoy Republic ships into the Mirit system, believing Ord Mirit was the true target. Bothan slicers further enhanced the deception by planting information that the New Republic believed the world held the key to finding the long-lost *Katana* fleet.

**Ord Mynock** Formerly a communications relay point in the Mynockra system, this planet fell into obscurity as changes in popular trade routes left it off the beaten path. It was believed to be the birthplace of the mynock.

**Ord Namurt** While en route to Ord Namurt, and early along her path to becoming a Jedi, young Aurra Sing was kidnapped by star pirates, who fed her lies regarding the Jedi Order. These lies played well to Aurra's natural fears of abandonment and betrayal. At the tender age of nine, she turned her back on the Jedi, not even having achieved the rank of a Padawan learner.

**Ordnance and Supply (OaS)** A department found within Supreme Allied Command of the Rebel Alliance military, it was responsible for procuring the equipment, weaponry, and foodstuffs for Alliance forces. It was also the department of the Alliance that hired privateer forces.

**Ordo (N-11)** An early-generation ARC trooper, or Null ARC, he was trained as a special operative by Kal Skirata for the Clone Wars. Several months into the war, Ordo was assigned as an assistant to Skirata, who had accepted a military position within the Grand Army of the Republic.

**Ordo, Canderous** A tough soldier who made his living as a mercenary 4,000 years before the Battle of Yavin, selling his services to the highest bidder. Most often this turned out to be an underworld figure wanting to capitalize on his considerable skills as a combatant, tactician, and outright thug. If his criminal clients had known where he learned his trade, however, even they might have had second thoughts about hiring him. Canderous was a Mandalorian, and as such, he was on the losing side of the Mandalorian War with the Republic. He was no foot soldier, and had an active hand in the planning and execution of many battles that went against the Republic. There was a lot of blood on his hands, and he doubted that enough time had passed for people to view his actions as he did: with the impersonal eye of a career soldier. He was pragmatic enough to take no insult from the defeat of his people. It was just business, after all.

Canderous was employed by Davik Kang, a crime lord with influence throughout the undercity of Taris. The traitorous actions of Sith Lords Revan and Malak and the continued aggression of the Sith distracted the citizens of the Republic to the point that they were no longer concerned about the defeated Mandalorians. As such, Canderous went about his business freely.

The born warrior couldn't stay a small-time enforcer for long, though. Following the failure of the Republic cruiser *Endar Spire* over Taris, the world was placed under Sith blockade. Canderous, never one to be trapped, was eager to leave. He provided some Republic fugitives also looking to escape with a way to slice into Taris's computer network to retrieve the access codes necessary to leave the quarantined world. As the *Ebon Hawk* blasted off from Taris filled with Republic fugitives, the Sith razed the planet.

In the wake of the Jedi Civil War, the reformed Revan ordered Canderous to restore the Mandalorians to their former glory. From a base on Dxun, he assumed the position of *Mand'alor* and eventually built up a small army of supporters. When the Jedi Exile arrived on Dxun in search of the surviving Jedi Masters, Ordo pledged his support to her, and was instrumental in the destruction of Darth Traya and her students.

**Ord Pardron** Essentially a large rock in space, this mineral-rich world had low gravity and a very thin atmosphere. It was mined extensively by both the Old Republic and the Empire. The Imperials abandoned Ord Pardron about a year before the Battle of Yavin, and the Rebel Alliance then established a small starfighter base there that launched a number of successful missions against the Empire.

Five years after the Battle of Endor, Ord Pardron housed a major New Republic base tasked with defending the Abrion and the Dufilvian sectors. Grand Admiral Thrawn targeted Ord Pardron for attack. By spreading his attack, Thrawn forced Ord Pardron's defense forces to spread their resources, requiring most of their ships to stay at Ord Pardron and fight the *Death's Head.* Thrawn's true target, Ukio, was undefended and captured, and the Ord Pardron base was heavily damaged.

*Ord Pedrovia Podracer in action*

**Ord Pedrovia** A model of Podracer favored by Gasgano, this green-hued vessel with bulbous Pods had traction superior to that of most other Podracers.

**Ord Radama** An Outer Rim world near the Meridian sector, located in a dark area known as the Radama Void. It was the homeworld of the Devlikk species and a Confederacy base during the Clone Wars.

**Ord Sabaok** A world of posh casinos and exclusive clubs that formed the base of operations for Rebel Alliance operative Barthalemew Windsloe.

**Ord Sedra** A world in the Clacis sector of the Imperial Remnant, it was invaded by combined Yuuzhan Vong and Peace Brigade forces. Kyle Katarn and Jan Ors led the resistance against the invaders.

**Ord Segra** The spaceport on this planet in the Doldur sector exacted a 7 percent "tax" on incoming merchandise. The fee was actually a bribe.

**Ord Sigatt** A remote mining world, this was where Dexter Jettster first met Obi-Wan Kenobi when the former was running a rough-and-tumble cantina there.

**Ord Simres** A system once visited by smuggler Celia "Crimson" Durasha.

**Ord Tessebok** A Mid Rim planet with a population of 2.5 billion, it opened up its port and lands to refugees displaced by the Separatist crisis prior to the Clone Wars.

**Ord Thoden** A tectonically active planet in the Dynali sector, it was the homeworld of Aris Del-Wari, the youngling known for a time in the media as "Baby Ludi." The planet was represented in the Republic Senate by Boganni Hrul.

**Ord Tiddell** A Mid Rim world overrun by a stone mite infestation prior to the outbreak of the Clone Wars.

**Ord Torrenze** The site of the Battle of Ord Torrenze, during which invading forces bombarded the surface of the once beautiful planet while civilians scrambled to evacuate. In the conflict, the Chandrilan-commissioned Corellian corvette *Freedom's Messenger* performed admirably. The *Messenger* would later become the *Renegade* in Moff Kentor Sarne's Kathol sector arsenal. Later still, it became the New Republic's *FarStar.*

**Ord Traga** A port world that was once an Old Republic ordnance depot.

**Ord Trasi** Alongside Yaga Minor and Bilbringi, this planet was an extremely busy Imperial shipyard during Grand Admiral Thrawn's campaign to retake the Core five years after the Battle of Endor. It was a world rich in minerals, ores, and natural crystals used in communications gear. Much of the mineral refinement work was carried out by droids. Orbital platforms defended Ord Trasi from pirates and New Republic forces. Its population of 2 million was made up of mostly humans, though there were many Wookiee slaves. It eventually was retaken by the New Republic, and was used as a staging ground by Garm Bel Iblis to attack Yaga Minor.

**Ord Varee** A Mid Rim planet with a population of 3.1 billion, it opened up its port and lands to refugees displaced by the Separatist crisis prior to the Clone Wars.

**Ord Vaug** A former Imperial prison planet that was liberated after the Battle of Endor. Han Solo went there to rescue the Venerated Ones of Vandelhelm from Imperials.

**Ord Vaxal** A secret Inner Rim penal colony maintained by the Empire as a dumping ground for political dissidents and other undesirables. For years prior to Imperial rule, it was an anarchic world overrun by escaped prisoners and criminal types. It was home to a shadowport, Oubilette, operated by Hutts.

**Ord Wylan** Shortly after the Battle of Yavin, entrepreneur Lando Calrissian won the coveted taxi-service license rights for Ord Wylan in a sabacc game, and then lost them moments later in an idle bet concerning the brand of liquor the party was consuming. Shortly thereafter, he participated in the infamous Battle of Taanab.

**Ord Zat** A world established as an Ordnance/Regional Depot.

**Ord Zeuol** The homeworld of Senator Eeusu Estornii.

**Orellon I and II** A twin set of planets in the Bastooine system. The first planet, Orellon I, was not actually a planet but the bright, barren moon of the second planet, Orellon II. Numerous mountain ranges broke up the jungles and plains of Orellon II, and 35 percent of the planet was covered by oceans. Decades before the Battle of Yavin, the Jedi geologist Michael Tandre crashed his vessel, the *Alpha Kentrum,* on Orellon II. He became the spiritual leader of the Kentra, teaching them to follow the disciplines of the Sword, the Plow, and the Spirit. Years after his death, the Kentra continued to learn from computer programs left on the *Alpha Kentrum*. To honor Prophet Tandre, the Kentra built the Temple of Je'ulajists (a corruption of *geologists*) around the wreckage of the *Alpha Kentrum*.

**Orelon** One of 63 stars in the Hapes Cluster.

**Orfite** The native inhabitants of the low-gravity world of Kidron in the Elrood sector. Orfites were orange-skinned thin humanoids with large lungs to get the most of Kidron's atmosphere. They had immense nasal passages with large, sensitive olfactory lobes. Males could be distinguished from females by their lack of bushy eyebrows. Olfactory stimuli played a large role in Orfite culture. It was their most powerful sense. They communicated partly through powerful pheromones that served to differentiate individual Orfites.

**Organa, Bail** The First Chairman and Viceroy of Alderaan and the head of the Royal Family of Alderaan, he was an influential politician and loyal Senator in the final decades of the Galactic Republic. As a member of the Loyalist Committee during the Separatist crisis, he was deeply concerned with the stability of the Republic. He realized that drastic measures were required if the Separatists continued to push the galaxy to the brink of war. He reluctantly recognized the need for the Senate to take ownership of the newly discovered clone army and looked on as Palpatine was granted emergency powers to save the Republic from this dire threat. With great dismay, he watched the Republic transform during the war years. The Senate willingly relinquished more executive powers to Chancellor Palpatine, all in the name of increased security. To criticize such actions would result in being branded a traitor, so Bail was careful to conceal his misgivings. He spoke of them only in a small audience of like-minded Senators.

In clandestine gatherings, Senators like Giddean Danu, Padmé Amidala, Terr Taneel, Chi Eekway, Bana Breemu, and Fang Zar shared their concerns. Alert to the likelihood that Palpatine would not give up power once the Clone Wars ended, Organa and Senator Mon Mothma were already putting proactive plans into motion. They envisioned an organization dedicated to preserving the ideals of the Republic, one that drew membership from idealists within the Senate but operated outside of the Senate chambers. Though they skirted the word in these early tentative days, Mothma and Organa were planning rebellion.

Queen Breha Organa and Bail Organa with baby Leia Organa

Bail Organa

During the Clone Wars, Organa grew to become friendly with influential Jedi Masters including Obi-Wan Kenobi and Yoda. When the Jedi were deemed traitors to the Republic and the Jedi Temple was attacked by an elite force of clone troopers, Bail Organa went to investigate the carnage. Thinking that his position in the Senate afforded him some measure of authority, he was, instead, shooed away by the implacable clone troopers, who told him a Jedi rebellion was afoot. Bail left the blazing Temple, but not before witnessing the clone troopers shoot a young Padawan attempting to escape the destruction.

Realizing that all the Jedi were at risk, Bail attempted to contact Kenobi and Yoda. He homed in on their respective distress signals, collecting Yoda from Kashyyyk and Obi-Wan from Utapau aboard his consular vessel, *Tantive IV.* Their clone commanders had turned on them. Organa then received an urgent call from Coruscant: The Chancellor was calling an emergency session of the Senate. Aboard his starship, he returned to the capital, secretly taking Obi-Wan and Yoda aboard so they could investigate the situation in the Temple.

In the Senate, Bail barely arrived in time to hear Chancellor Palpatine declare himself Emperor. His worst fears came to pass. The Republic was dead, replaced by a dictatorship.

When Kenobi's apprentice, Anakin Skywalker, succumbed to the dark side, Organa hid one of Skywalker's twin offspring in the High Court of Alderaan. Organa and his wife, Queen Breha, Alderaan's Minister of Education, raised their adoptive daughter as if she were their biological child. Leia learned the nature of political life from her adoptive parents, as well as the codes and protocol of court life. Bail's servants, such as Tarrik, took care not to spoil or pamper the Princess. Nothing was spared in Leia's education. She learned politics and history from Arn Horada, and martial skills from Giles Durane the Weapons Master.

Leia learned much from records of Bail's Senatorial career. Organa's cynicism and realism often clashed with the idealism of Chandrilan Senator Mon Mothma. The two did agree that Palpatine had to be stopped. In a series of meetings at Cantham House, Organa and Mothma devised and developed a plan for the Rebel Alliance. At first, Organa was shocked by the idea of open revolution, but incidents such as the Ghorman Massacre cemented his resolve. Organa realized the Republic was dead. While he continued publicly acting as an opponent to Mon Mothma, Organa's position on such committees as Finance, Appropriations, and Intelligence Oversight allowed him to funnel money, weapons, and information to the fledgling Rebel Alliance. Organa's membership in the Senate Military Oversight Committee made him quite adept at forging the structure of the Alliance Military. One of Palpatine's loyal Senators told Organa that the Emperor planned to arrest Mon Mothma. Organa informed Mothma, allowing her to escape the clutches of the Imperial Security Bureau.

Queen Breha Organa

When Organa retired from the Senate, he returned to Alderaan. There he convinced his people to renounce the pacifism instituted after the Clone Wars and quietly supported the Rebellion during the early organization of resistance movements into a unified Alliance to Restore the Republic. Organa knew that his open opposition to Palpatine during his Senate days would make him a target of Imperial reprisals. His actions at this time were veiled, and carefully plotted. Security experts constructed mono-molecular shielded caverns beneath the Royal Palace. Organa founded a secret Alliance starfighter base on the crystalline world of Isis using classified Alderaanian scouting expedition data he had secured when in the Senate.

A mission to Ralltiir allowed Rebel spies to inform Leia Organa of the Death Star menace. Later, at a diplomatic dinner with Lord Tion, an Imperial noble, Leia incriminated herself by revealing knowledge of the top-secret project. In a scuffle that ensued, Leia killed Lord Tion. Bail covered for her, arranging a convenient "hunting accident" alibi on one of Alderaan's game preserves. He sent Leia on the fateful mission to locate Obi-Wan Kenobi and recruit him into the Alliance to help face the Death Star challenge. It was the last time Bail would see his adoptive and beloved daughter.

When Leia failed to reach Obi-Wan, her mission was eventually picked up by Luke Skywalker. Bail Organa was killed when the Death Star destroyed Alderaan.

**Organa, Celly, Rouge, and Tia** The adoptive aunts to Princess Leia. Wealthy dowagers, these three women never stopped trying to steer the young Leia away from her tomboy tendencies, and to the role of the proper young Princess. To that end, they often tried to talk Leia into marrying some wealthy young noble. A temperamental woman, Celly was prone to bouts of hypochondria. Leia often remembered Aunt Rouge taking care in crafting her elaborate hairdo in front of the gilt-framed mirror in her boudoir. Tia read aloud to several pet pittins: Taffy, Winkie, Fluffy, and AT-AV (Leia named that last one). The three sisters died when the Death Star destroyed Alderaan.

**Organa, Leia** *See* Solo, Leia Organa.

**Organa, Queen Breha** The wife of Bail Organa, and the reigning Queen of Alderaan during the last years of the Galactic Republic. She also served as the planet's Minister of Education. In the wake of the Clone Wars, Breha and Bail gladly agreed to take in the infant daughter of the late Padmé Amidala, raising Leia Organa as their own.

**Organa II, Leia** The product of Project Decoy, developed about a year after the Battle of Endor by the Defense Research and Planetary Assistance Center on Dagobah (DRAPAC), Leia Organa II was an advanced human replica droid designed and programmed by Chadra-Fan scientists Fugo and Fandar. Mon Mothma envisioned the droid acting as a decoy for Leia when she was on dangerous missions for the New Republic. When testing Organa II's eye-lasers, there was an accident. The droid misfired, critically wounding Fandar. Later, when would-be Emperor Trioculus kidnapped Princess Leia to make her his queen in a forced marriage, he discovered that he had stolen the droid instead. At the wedding ceremony, deadly blaster bolts fired out of Leia Organa II's eyes, killing Trioculus. Imperial Grand Moff Hissa returned fire on the droid, destroying it. Leia Organa II was an exactingly crafted replica of Leia Organa, down to her voiceprint and mannerisms.

**organic gill** An engineered biotechnology symbiont that filtered ocean water to provide a steady stream of breathable water to the wearer. The Mon Calamari developed the organic gill to negate the discomfort they encountered when they switched to breathing water during long underwater journeys. It was not usable by all alien cultures, however. For example, Sullustans were allergic to the symbiont.

**organichems** Organic chemical stores used in autochefs aboard starships to mix and prepare food.

**Organization for Organic Purity (OOP)** One of the largest and most influential anti-droid coalitions in the galaxy, this group argued that droids had doomed large portions of the organic population to poverty and ignorance.

**organoform circuitry** This technology had been theorized for hundreds of years before it was discovered to be in use on the living planet Zonama Sekot shortly after the Battle of Naboo. It was said that the technology was developed in the Outer Rim, on planets that were technologically advanced and remained separate from both the Old Republic and the Trade Federation. Organoform circuitry involved the use of crystalline structures formed from organic materials. In some respects, organoform circuitry was alive, since it was created from organic matter. However, it lacked sentience, reacting only to the stimuli it encountered.

**Orga root** A substance used to help Wookiees make their spiritual pilgrimage to the Tree of Life during Life Day. Orga root was grown by the plant-like Orga species. Wookiees had a special agreement with the Orga to harvest the root. Life Day was once nearly canceled because Orga root was not available.

**Orgege, Moff Yref** The replacement for Moff Sarn Shild, the Imperial Governor overseeing Hutt space. Orgege was less vigilant than Shild, and was determined not to make the same mistakes as his predecessor. His desire to exact control over all military activity in his sphere of influence bogged down all Imperial action, since everything had to go through him for approval.

*Leia Organa II*

**Orgons** Bizarre aliens from the remote world of Gorsh, they were intelligent mobile plants. Spheroid in shape, they had two main body parts. The brain and vital organs were contained in a round, hardened shell, half a meter in diameter and green to yellow in color. Trailing from the shell, providing mobility and dexterity, were six to eight tendrils, up to 4 meters long. Typically, the older an Orgon was, the more tendrils it had. The complex natural chemistry of the Orgons drew the attention of offworld pharmaceutical companies.

**orichalc** A lustrous gold-like metal mined on Naboo and used to create jewelry and other adornments.

**Oricho sector** This area of space neighbored the Lahara sector, adjacent to the Cowl Crucible Nebula.

**Oridin City** A major metropolitan center on Fondor bombarded by the Star Destroyer *Anakin Solo* during the war between the Galactic Alliance and the Confederation. Colonel Jacen Solo used the Force to influence the minds of the shield operators on Oridin, tricking them into lowering the protective shield and allowing for the devastating attack.

**Orilltha** An ancient Sith Lord who was one of the many instructors at the Sith Academy on Korriban during the years leading up to the Battle of Ruusan.

**Orin** A volcanic world, it occupied the second position in the Bespin system. The planet had an elliptical orbit, passing through the asteroids of the nearby Velser's Ring twice during its year. Its black surface was rocked by frequent groundquakes and covered with rivers of lava and erupting volcanoes. Orin's surface temperature was unbearably high and its atmosphere choked with thick soot.

**Orinackra** The site of a high-security Imperial Detention Center. After the Battle of Yavin, Rebel Alliance sympathizer Crix Madine was discovered by the Empire and imprisoned on Orinackra. Alliance agents Kyle Katarn and Jan Ors staged a daring rescue of Madine.

**Orinda** A small planet seized by Admiral Pellaeon. Pellaeon seized six neighboring systems as well before the New Republic retaliated. At the Battle of Orinda, the Super Star Destroyer *Reaper* destroyed the New Republic fleet carrier *Endurance.* Rogue Squadron, stationed aboard the *Lusankya,* covered the fleet's retreat. The New Republic chose to leave Orinda in Imperial hands and instead fortified surrounding systems.

**Orion IV** The site of a Rebel Alliance base destroyed by the Empire prior to the Battle of Yavin. It was bombarded from orbit by several Star Destroyers, and attacked on the surface by AT-AT walkers and assault gunboats.

***Orion*-style starships** Outdated, archaic space vessels, their ion engines discharged considerable backblast and radiation.

***Ori'ramikade*** *See* Mandalorian shock troopers.

**Orjul, Farr** A terrorist allied to the Separatists during the Clone Wars, he used his cover as a miner to carry out his primary duty of transporting explosives. He was captured by the clone commandos of Omega Squad, and interrogated by Etain Tur-Mukan and Walon Vau.

**Orkana (the Poisoned Land)** This heavily polluted territory on Tatooine was the domain of Orko the Foultrader. It was a vast dumping ground that contaminated the air and poisoned the people. Perpetually wreathed in vile smog, this was a land of disease and despair. The law had little sway in Orkana.

**Orko (the Foultrader)** A Hutt trader of the lower H'uun caste, and ruler of a polluted stretch of Tatooine named Orkana. Six years after the Battle of Endor, Gorga the Hutt attempted to curry favor with Orko by presenting him a gift in order to gain access to Orko's fetching daughter, Anachro. Gorga hired bounty hunter Boba Fett to capture the pirate Bar-Kooda, who had been pillaging Orko's transport fleet. Once Fett delivered Bar-Kooda to Gorga, the Hutt had the pirate roasted into a delectable main course for Orko's dinner. Though Gorga and Anachro married, Orko distrusted his son-in-law. He did, nonetheless, covet Gorga's riches and conspired to have him killed, all while Gorga was engaged in similar actions, so that he could share in the riches Anachro would inherit. Further complicating matters, Bar-Kooda's brother Ry-Kooda wanted *both* Hutts dead.

A short time later, Gorga hired Boba Fett to kill Orko. Fett instead infiltrated Orko's compound and warned Orko that his life was in danger, offering to protect him for a larger fee. While Orko agreed, he was killed shortly thereafter by Ry-Kooda. Ry-Kooda savagely butchered the H'uun, eating parts of his corpse. He was survived by his daughter and a newly born Huttlet.

*Orko (the Foultrader)*

**Orko SkyMine Asteroid Processing Corporation** A company dedicated to harvesting minerals from deep-space asteroid bodies. Owned by Durga the Hutt, a member of the Black Sun criminal organization, Orko SkyMine was little more than a sham corporation that the Hutt criminal empire put together to disguise expenses. Orko SkyMine was based on Nar Shaddaa, with numerous branch offices. It attempted to harvest ore from the Hoth asteroid belt, using massive and complex automated mineral exploiters. The company suffered a setback when the exploiters—confused by sensor readings—attempted to process one another. Durga used Orko SkyMine to harvest the necessary ores to construct his ill-fated Darksaber superweapon project.

**Orlanis, Trista** A University of Agamar graduate student studying Jedi artifacts on Bimmiel during the early stages of the Yuuzhan Vong invasion. She was attracted to Jedi Knight Ganner Rhysode. She was a slender human female with black hair and a pert nose.

**Orleon** An obscure planet with flat rock mesas and constant rains. The planet somehow became infested with deadly stone mites, a form of biological warfare developed during the time of the Clone Wars. Before its infestation, Han Solo often used Orleon as a hideout. Shortly before the Battle of Hoth, Orleon was the site of a confrontation between Solo and agents of Jabba the Hutt.

**Orloc, the Mighty** A self-styled charlatan who posed as a powerful Force mage. Twenty-two years after the Battle of Yavin, Orloc infiltrated Darth Vader's abandoned fortress of Bast Castle on Vjun, and absconded with Obi-Wan Kenobi's lightsaber and a rare Jedi Holocron. Orloc returned to his base of operations, the abandoned Exis Station. He brought with him the young Jedi apprentice Uldir Lochett, tempting him with promises of further training. Orloc's headquarters was protected by reprogrammed assassin droids and obedient Ranat scavengers. Nonetheless, the Jedi Master Ikrit, the Jedi Knight Tionne, and apprentices Anakin Solo and Tahiri came to Exis Station to reclaim the stolen relics.

Orloc was defeated by the Jedi—true wielders of the Force. His ersatz display of magic was no match for them. In truth, Orloc had been using technology to simulate the powers of the Force. He used one last illusion to escape the Jedi. Orloc was a tall, thin man in a deep purple cloak. He had long dark hair, tawny eyes, and a neat, trim beard.

**Orlok, Commander** An ambitious Imperial officer who resented being posted at the backrocket training center on the planet Daluuj. When Mon Calamari agents crash-landed on his world, he ordered a ground patrol to search and capture the Rebel fugitives.

**Orlopp** This Jenet served as a lieutenant in the Galactic Alliance Guard during the war against the Confederation. He was Jacen Solo's chief aide.

**Orma** A world in the Aramand Cluster of Brak sector. It was one of the first two worlds to be colonized by the Aramandi. The planet was settled by members of the Orma akia, a clan of Aramandi who devoutly followed the tenets of the Eeronon religion. They were a peaceful clan, but not very tolerant of offworld beliefs.

**ormachek** A type of frozen food eaten by Mon Calamari and others.

**Orn, Kalebb** A veteran of 17 years in a droid-production plant in the remarkably redundant position of automated assembly-line overseer. The position was little more than a mandate from the government of Mechis III. His job was to make sure nothing out of the ordinary happened, and for 17 years, nothing did. But when IG-88 took over the production plant and caused newly assembled labor droids to rebel against their masters and wreak havoc on the plant, Orn was among the first killed.

**Oroboro** This was the Killiks' name for their settlement on Alderaan. It translated into Basic as "our home," although the Alderaanians simply referred to the settlement as the Castle Lands.

***Oroko*** A massive transport vessel, it served as a mobile base of operations for Valius Ying and his band of bounty hunters and gangsters during the decades following the Great Sith War.

**Orooturoo** Located in the Core Worlds near the Koornacht Cluster, this planet was the homeworld of Princess Nampi.

**Ororo Transportation** A front company for the Tenloss Syndicate, a major criminal organization working across 64 star systems in the Astal, Bajic, Dail, Skine, and Lol sectors. Based on Eredin in the Astal sector, Ororo acted as the principal distributor of illegal merchandise for other Tenloss operations in over 100 star systems. Ororo Transportation was a prime competitor for Xizor Transport Systems, the legitimate front to Prince Xizor's Black Sun crime syndicate. Ororo was making major progress taking over spice transport in the Bajic sector.

Furious, Xizor sent his aide and enforcer, Guri, to handle the situation. While Guri murdered Ororo's top officials, Xizor informed Emperor Palpatine that he had learned of a major Rebel presence in the Vergesso asteroid field. Palpatine sent Vader to destroy the Rebels' base, which in truth was an Ororo shipyard. Xizor had played the galaxy's most powerful men into his plans. Among the murdered officials were M. Tuyay, chief operating officer; Dellis Yuls, a Quarren head of security; and Z. Limmer, chief financial officer.

Six years after the Battle of Endor, Ororo Transportation came under investigation by law enforcement agents for its suspected collusion with fringe pirates regarding the purchase and shipping of hijacked goods.

**Orou'cya, Ceok** This Bothan was the First Secretary of the Combined Clans during the years leading up to the revelation of the Caamas Document. He tried to prevent Leia Organa Solo from reviewing the Bothans' financial situation, in light of the many problems being hidden by Bothan banks at the time. Bothan law, however, allowed C-3PO to access the records.

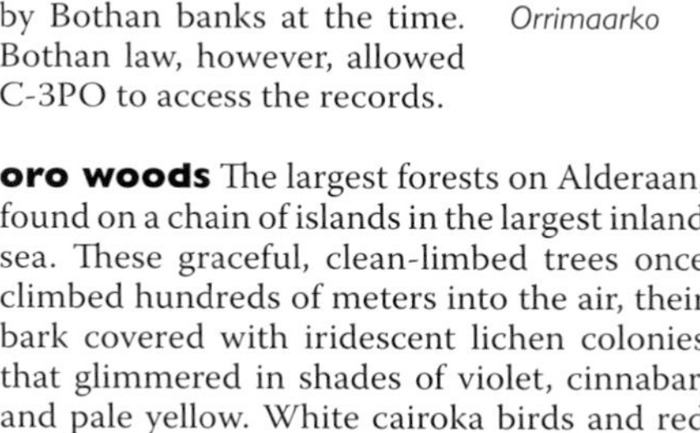

**oro woods** The largest forests on Alderaan, found on a chain of islands in the largest inland sea. These graceful, clean-limbed trees once climbed hundreds of meters into the air, their bark covered with iridescent lichen colonies that glimmered in shades of violet, cinnabar, and pale yellow. White cairoka birds and red deer lived in the area, which the Alderaanian government decreed a planetary treasure.

**Orowood Tower** A large building on Coruscant constructed to house survivors of the destruction of Alderaan. It was painstakingly crafted to resemble as much of Alderaanian architecture as possible. Many of the survivors had difficulty in living on Coruscant, so close to the Imperial Palace and memories of Emperor Palpatine. After Grand Admiral Thrawn's failed campaign to retake Coruscant, the Alderaanian survivors abandoned the tower, and it became a business center. It was 38 levels tall, complete with a medcenter.

**orray** Hardy leathery-skinned quadrupeds with great strength and a quick gait, they were used by the insectoid Geonosians to haul heavy loads, and as mounts for the picadors found in the Geonosis execution arena. Before their domestication by the Geonosians, orrays would use their long snouts to root into the sensitive egg chambers of a new Geonosian hive, devouring thousands of larvae in a single meal. In the wild, orrays had tail stingers for defense, but domesticated orrays had these weapons amputated, which made them more docile.

**Orren, Yotts** A Kadas'sa'Nikto smuggler who worked for Jabba the Hutt as a crewman aboard the crime lord's sail barge.

**Orrimaarko** A Dressellian freedom fighter who eventually was given command of a Rebel SpecForce unit. He wore camouflage fatigues, a cloak, and an eye patch, and he often carried a simple projectile rifle.

Orrimaarko

**Orrk, Guildmaster** A metalsmith on the planet Vandelhelm who came into power when Imperial rule collapsed after the Battle of Endor. Vandelhelm, by tradition, was ruled by the Venerated Ones, descendants of the original colonists. With the Venerated Ones in an Imperial prison, Orrk took over the planet and all of its ore production. When the Rebel Alliance liberated the Venerated Ones and prepared to bring them back home, Orrk tried killing them and their protector, Han Solo. Solo eventually bested Orrk, and the guildmaster plummeted into an open ore smelter.

**Orr-Om** One of the 20 orbital cities established by the Duros over their home planet, it was unshielded and thus destroyed in a Yuuzhan Vong attack.

**Orron III** An agriworld in the Corporate Sector. The planet had a low axial tilt and stable seasons that contributed to ideal farming conditions. A variety of grains were grown, including Arcon Multinode. The crops were harvested by giant agrirobots and collected on drone barges. An Authority Data Center was located on Orron III. Early in the Galactic Civil War, the Rebel Alliance maintained an important communications satellite near Orron III. An Imperial convoy bound for the Death Star construction site stopped at the comm sat and was promptly destroyed by Alliance starfighters. It was here that Alliance pilot Keyan Farlander first heard inklings about the Death Star.

**Orr'UrRuuR'R** A Tusken Raider leader, he would snipe at passing Podracers during the Boonta Eve Classic.

**Orryxian** An intelligent feline species, often nicknamed cats by Rebel operatives.

**Ors, Jan** A native of the planet Alderaan, Rebel operative, and mission specialist who worked with Rebel agent Kyle Katarn throughout the Galactic Civil War and beyond. They met originally at the Imperial Military Academy. Katarn actually led an Imperial raid on a Rebel base where Ors was stationed, and although the Empire took control of the outpost, Katarn spared her life. During Rebel missions, Ors kept him briefed on anything that he might want to know. She was a truly tough Rebel who was loyal to the Alliance. Reliable and knowledgeable, she was the only person Katarn trusted. Her right arm was a prosthetic replacement.

Jan Ors

Orray

**Orsk, Captain** The commanding officer of the Star Destroyer *Dauntless* during the Galactic Civil War.

***Orthavan*** A Mon Calamari star cruiser pressed into service in the battles between the New Republic and Grand Admiral Thrawn's Imperial forces. The *Orthavan* was attached to General Garm Bel Iblis's attack force, and fought alongside Rogue Squadron.

**Orto** A small planet orbiting a red dwarf star of the same name. Orto's year was 589 standard days long. Water was plentiful, much of it frozen in snow or ice. Due to Orto's elliptical orbit, its axial tilt, and its thin atmosphere, the growing season was about 161 days and occurred only in latitudes near the equator. Some time in its past, Orto was hit by a massive comet, tilting its axis and causing it to change to a more arctic clime. Orto was rich in minerals, and home to the intelligent Ortolans.

**Ortola, Captain Tresk** After graduation from the Academy, Tresk Ortola and his friends joined the merchant marines, and eventually became members of the Rebel Alliance. He spent a number of years as first officer aboard a Rebel gunship protecting transport vessels. Shortly before the Battle of Endor, Ortola received his first command aboard the Corellian corvette *NovaFlare.* He was part of the New Republic task force that attacked Maw Installation seven years after the Battle of Endor. His Corellian corvette was refitted for the taking of the Installation. After the destruction of another corvette by an experimental Imperial weapon, Ortola disregarded orders from General Wedge Antilles and moved in to successfully destroy the weapon. Later, when Maw scientists began an overload meltdown of the Installation's reactors, Wedge ordered Ortola's corvette to be dismantled for spare parts to repair the reactor. Ortola's crippled corvette became a tempting target when Admiral Daala returned to the Maw to eradicate the New Republic intruders. Ortola quickly evacuated his ship, transporting his men and supplies to the frigate *Yavaris* and other corvettes.

**Ortolan** Members of this species were known throughout the galaxy for their appetite. On their homeworld of Orto, the Ortolans evolved from a small nocturnal species whose predators all died in a great climatic shift. As the Ortolans advanced, they developed intelligence and an appetite. During the New Order, Ortolans mined their mineral-rich world, gathering resources for the greater glory of the Empire. The Empire did not see the Ortolans as fit to rule themselves.

Ortolans had thick, blubbery gray skin, floppy ears, and sensitive trunks that could smell food from 2 kilometers away. They also had excellent hearing, assisted through their trunks, and could hear deep into the subsonic range. In fact, it seemed to humans that Ortolans were quiet when they actually spoke mostly in the subsonic range. Ortolan hands were four-fingered, with a not-quite-opposable thumb. Their fingers ended in suction cups, aiding the Ortolans in manipulating items.

**Orto Plutonia** In the Pantoran system, this frozen world was one of the homes of the Talz species.

**Ortugg** A Gamorrean guard in Jabba's court, he was with Bidlo Kwerve's hunting party when it first discovered a rancor. It was Ortugg who named the beast for a demon of Gamorrean legend. Ortugg was given the special task of monitoring Tessek, a Quarren whom Jabba greatly distrusted. He delegated the task of determining the culprit of a rash of mysterious murders to the dim-witted Gartogg. Amazingly, Gartogg was able to figure out that it was Dannik Jerriko behind the killings. Ortugg failed to listen to him, and would not let him go on sail barge duty to the Pit of Carkoon. Ortugg perished in that final battle over the mighty Sarlacc.

**Orus sector** This area of space contained the planets Chazwa, Poderis, Berchest, and Joiol. Five years after the Battle of Endor, Grand Admiral Thrawn gave the false impression that his newly created clone troopers were being transported through the Orus sector.

**Orvak, Commander** A TIE fighter pilot and commando of the Second Imperium, he was chosen from the ranks of stormtroopers, and painstakingly trained in piloting and sabotage. He and his wingman Dareb were tasked with a dangerous infiltration mission into Luke Skywalker's Jedi academy during the Shadow Academy's siege of Yavin 4. Orvak infiltrated the highest levels of the Massassi Temple and planted his explosives, but he was bitten by a venomous crystal snake in the process, and knocked unconscious. He was far too groggy and disoriented to escape the explosion. Orvak was destroyed in the blast that consumed the top levels of the Great Temple.

**Orvax IV** A hub of the slave-trading industry during the Empire. Nosaurian slaves were shipped to this planet after the Clone Wars.

**Orvos** The aged Nelvaanian shaman of the Rokrul villages on Nelvaan, he foresaw that Anakin Skywalker and Obi-Wan Kenobi would assist the Nelvaanians in removing the Separatists who had arrived on the planet during the Clone Wars.

**Oryon** One of the best Republic spies during the Clone Wars, this Bothan was targeted by the Empire for his in-depth knowledge of the Separatists. Oryon eliminated all records of his existence and joined the Erased. Like many of his fellow Erased, he was attacked by agents sent by Inquisitor Malorum. He was rescued by Trever Flume, and the two of them managed to escape Coruscant alongside Keets Freely and the Jedi-in-hiding Solace.

**Or'Zee, Chamberlain Kaja** This formidable woman administered the Emperor's retreat on Naboo during the Galactic Civil War. Her loyalty to Emperor Palpatine was beyond reproach; she believed wholeheartedly in the Emperor's infallibility and felt that he was giving the galaxy a magnificent gift by maintaining order.

In addition to making sure that the Emperor's retreat operated smoothly and efficiently, Chamberlain Or'Zee also personally hired many of the Emperor's "security specialists." She had a knack for identifying others who shared her profound faith in the Emperor's cause. It was part of her job to interview such persons, to determine whether they could be trusted with missions for the Emperor. If they passed Or'Zee's rigorous inspection, she introduced them to Inquisitor Loam Redge—the next step on the ladder to working for the glorious Emperor.

*Ortolan*

**OS-72-10** The designation for the TIE fighter pilot of *Obsidian 10.* He served aboard the *Conquest,* the *Thunderflare,* and the *Executor* and was never interested in advancing his rank, as it would remove him from the pilot's seat.

**OS-72-8** The designation for a TIE fighter pilot who pursued the *Millennium Falcon* after the escape from Bespin.

**Osa-Prime** The capital and principal spaceport on Osarian. During the conflict between Osarian and Rhommamool, Nom Anor unleashed missiles at Osa-Prime, causing extensive damage.

**Osarian** A planet paired with Rhommamool in the Expansion Region. A blue-and-white orb, Osarian was the larger of the two. Both planets had limited technology; Osarian's fleet was considered marginal, at best. While the prosperous Osarians lived in comfort on white sandy beaches and crystal-clear lakes, life was tough for the miners on Rhommamool, where even basics like water could be hard to come by. Leia Organa Solo went to Osarian and Rhommamool on a diplomatic mission to try to end the conflict between the two planets, a conflict exacerbated by political agitator—and secret Yuuzhan Vong agent—Nom Anor.

**Oscuro, Scri** The High Priest of the Zealots of Psusan prior to the start of the Clone Wars, he used his position of spiritual influence as a front for illegal ventures. Several former cult members discovered the truth and placed a bounty on Oscuro's head. He was caught by bounty hunters Kayln Farnmir and Cian Shee. From prison, he attempted to use his congregation contacts to exact vengeance on Shee and Farnmir, and though he lured Shee into his employ with the promise of credits, he was unable to pin Farnmir in a trap.

**Osentay, Ryk** A reporter for the *Eye on Cularin* news program during the Clone Wars.

**Oseon** A stable belt of asteroids orbiting a distant sun, the system was named for Gadfrey Oseon. Many of the asteroids were converted into mining stations, others into pleasure resorts and vacation homes for the galaxy's super-wealthy. The Oseon was filled with exiled and vacationing nobility, captains of industry, media stars, as well as mercantile and literal pirates. Weapons of any kind were outlawed, unless wielded by the police force. Possession of weaponry was a capital offense, warranting death by spacing.

The Oseon was made up of circular zones of rocks rather than worlds; they varied in size from sand grains to objects thousands of kilometers around. There were seven broad bands of floating rocks, with the largest being in the sixth band, Oseon 6845. An administrative department mapped and carefully numbered each asteroid, the first number in the four-digit code signifying the band. Many theories circulated about the creation of the Oseon. Maybe a rogue star had passed too close, its gravity well disrupting the planet-forming process billions of years in the past. Or maybe a unique element in the makeup of the system had caused the planets to blow up.

One of the key tourist attractions of the Oseon was the annual Flamewind. Once a year the system's sun flared in a unique manner. As the flares tore streamers of hyperexcited vapor from the nearest asteroids, the entire system fluoresced, generating enormous bands of shifting color. These pulsing beams of brilliance, millions of kilometers wide, reached out like the spokes of a huge wheel. Colors from the entire spectrum cascaded through the system, punctuated by flashes of lightning.

The Flamewind was a deadly and spectacular time. As brightly colored streamers of ionized gas filled the system, radiation, static discharges, and swirling star-fog distorted navigational references, driving unshielded instruments and sentient minds alike insane. All interasteroidal commerce was shut down for the duration of the Flamewind, averaging three weeks, to protect the inhabitants. Communications among the asteroids, or between the system and the rest of the galaxy, was impossible during the Flamewind.

**Oseon, Gadfrey** A legendary crime lord who operated a traveling circus as a front for his illicit operations. Legend held that he fled to a remote asteroid belt that later bore his name after attempting to escape vengeful patrons at a botched performance on Nal Hutta. His name became the source of a common interjection or oath in the Centrality: "Great Gadfrey!"

**OSETS** *See* Orbital Solar Energy Transfer Satellite.

**Oshay** One of smuggler Samuel Tomas Gillespee's band, he was part of a group of smugglers aiding the New Republic during Grand Admiral Thrawn's campaign.

**Oshetti IV** A planet with swamps that provided the hemp used in illuminescences.

**Osirrag system** A star system in the Elrood sector. Due to its placement among the Degas Gas Clouds, travel to the Osirrag system had to be made through the Degan system, its nearest neighbor. The small planet Osirrag was a beautiful world of pleasant summers, cool gentle winters, and natural beauty. It was home to the onahk, an aquatic creature. A safe world, Osirrag boasted a number of small colonies engaged in subsistence agriculture. Osirrag folklore had it that a sentient "wind species" lived in the unsettled territories, and these "spirits" once befriended a young colonist boy, extending his life span immensely. The folklore said that this boy then served as a guardian to the colony.

*Ossan*

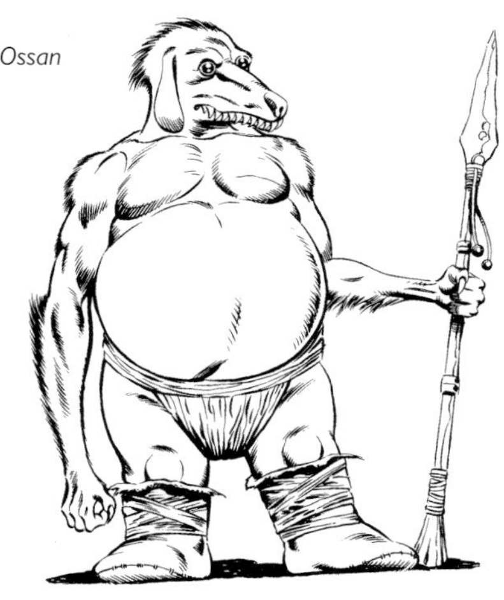

**Oskan blood eater** Hideous creatures believed to be bioengineered as deadly guardian and attack beasts, Oskan blood eaters were used on numerous prison planets in the Empire, and as pit beasts by unsavory crime lords such as Jabba the Hutt. A roughly humanoid creature standing 2.5 meters tall, the blood eater had four hooked carving blades at the shoulder, where arms should be. Instead of a proper head, it had a low bulb of muscle and bone from which two hooded eyes peered. Its mouth was a perforated collection of suckers it used to slurp up blood spilled by its razor-sharp talons.

There was very little genetic variance among blood eaters. Their method of reproduction was parthenogenic, with a remarkably effective method of genetic error checking in the meiotic cellular reproduction phase. Blood eaters were scattered throughout many systems, but their place in those diverse ecosystems and surrounding cultural mythology led many to speculate that they were not native to any of these worlds.

One "official" story of the blood eaters' origin held that they were a genetic experiment created by the government of the Old Republic for sinister purposes. But it was more than likely that blood eaters were the product of Imperial science gone awry, and their true purpose remained a mystery.

**Oslumpex V** A planet in the Corporate Sector where Vinda and D'rag co-owned the Starshipwrights and Aerospace Engineers Incorporated.

**Osman** This Chev humanoid served as a majordomo to the powerful and influential Besadii-clan Hutt, Durga. The pale-faced Chev exuded the proper amount of servility to his Hutt masters.

**osmotic field** A form of portal shielding used to maintain a certain level of atmospheric conditions within a room or building. When placed at a doorway or other entrance, the osmotic field could be tuned to allow air circulation but prevent particulate matter. More advanced models also had entropic overlays that pulled energy from the incoming air, thereby cooling it and dropping the temperature within a room.

**Ossan** The primitive Ossans were considered by some to be fat and stupid. On their homeworld of Ossel II, the Ossan evolved from rodents into hunters in response to being pursued by deadly cucul. The Ossan developed clubs and spears, though bow-and-arrow technology eluded them. They had only just developed sentience at the time of the Galactic Civil War, and their ignorance was exploited by unscrupulous traders. Ossan were rodent-like bipeds standing 1.5 meters tall. They had a cylindrical snout ending in a single slit-nostril, as well as a pronounced overbite, serrated teeth, and beady eyes. Their ears were teardrop-shaped. They had long, gangly arms and short legs. Offworld Ossan tended to be obese. Ossan organized themselves into tribes, led by a chief.

**Ossel II** A steaming world of bogs and swamps. The sky was tinged brown-green because of the heavy sulfur and chlorine concentrations in the atmosphere. Ossel II was home to such beings as the cucul and the Ossan. Tough, resilient syp wood was harvested there, and collected by traders for offplanet shipping.

**Osseriton system** Consisting of a single habitable planet, the Osseriton system lay in the Unknown Regions and was the site of a migration of the Hemes Arbora people, who left their homeworld of Carrivar.

**Ossi** A prison planet used to hold criminals detained by the Inquisitorius of the Empire.

**Ossic architecture** On Utapau—a world without trees—bone replaced timber as the structural material of choice. Raw, seasoned, processed, or fossilized, the bones of almost all of the planet's animals were used in construction, creating a unique form of architecture known as Ossic. The skeletons of great creatures that roamed the lower caves and world-ocean provided bones massive enough to become load-bearing beams, while heavy fossil bone was mined in the sinkholes and caves.

**Ossiki Confederacy Army** One of the primary military groups from the planet Toydaria, it regularly fought in the Toydarian seasonal wars. The army was known, or perhaps infamous, for its use of chemical weapons that destroyed the food stocks of rivals. A former leader once declared, "If we can't have it, no one can."

**Ossilege, Admiral Hortel** An admiral of the Bakuran Navy, he was a short man of slight build, well scrubbed and pink-skinned. Ossilege was bald but sported a pair of bushy eyebrows and a sharply pointed goatee. He constantly demonstrated his first-class mind and zero tolerance for nonsense. He was the leader of the Bakuran fleet of four ships that was loaned to the New Republic, and he was killed in the conflict surrounding Centerpoint Station.

**Osskorn ale** A stout, foamy ale.

**Ossorus** In Gungan mythology, a beautiful underwater city and home of the pantheon of Gungan deities.

**Ossus** Located in the Adega system in the Auril sector, it orbited the twin Adegan suns in a figure-eight trajectory. Ossus was an important Jedi stronghold and learning center in ancient times, and some speculated that the Order of Jedi Knights began on the planet. It was once covered with many cities and ground defenses; the Knossa spaceport was located near a range of rocky mountains. Points of interest included the Great Jedi Library and the peaceful Gardens of Talla. The steep canyon walls long remained covered with elaborate murals, and ancient buildings that stood for millennia included the library and a Jedi meditation chamber.

During the Great Sith War, the fallen Jedi Exar Kun visited Ossus to recruit 20 Jedi Knights into the Sith cause. Before he departed, Kun killed Master Odan-Urr and stole a Sith Holocron from the Jedi library. Later, an Ossan Jedi fleet was dispatched to the nearby Cron Cluster to defend the besieged station Kemplex Nine. The fleet was destroyed when the cluster went nova, and the resulting shock wave threatened to devastate Ossus. An evacuation of the planet was ordered, and as many ancient relics as possible were loaded onto transports. At the same time, Kun and Jedi Ulic Qel-Droma appeared with their armies to loot the world of its valuables before the shock wave arrived. Kun battled the Neti Jedi Master Ood Bnar, who turned into an unyielding tree to protect a trove of the earliest known lightsabers. Meanwhile, Ulic confronted and killed his brother, Cay, and was seized with horror and regret over what he had done.

*Ossus before the destruction of the Cron Cluster*

Most Jedi left the planet just ahead of the shock wave, which scorched the surface of Ossus, nearly wiping it clean. Some Jedi survived, however, after hiding their families in Ossus's great caverns, and their descendants grew into the Ysanna, a tribe of warrior-shamans who used the Force to guide their primitive weapons. A 10,000-year-old lightsaber surfaced in an archaeological dig on Ossus, and was given to Leia Organa Solo by Vima-Da-Boda. Six years after the Battle of Endor, Luke Skywalker visited an arid, sandy portion of the planet and discovered the Ysanna tribe. Skywalker and Kam Solusar also fought the forces of dark side Executor Sedriss and discovered the vault of lightsabers long hidden beneath the roots of Master Ood. At the time of Skywalker's departure, the New Republic made plans to send excavation teams to explore Ossus's ruins.

Soon after, several of the Emperor's warriors came to Ossus and captured three Ysanna leaders, whose bodies were to be used as raw material to create new clones for Palpatine. Skywalker and his Jedi trainees followed the dark side kidnappers and defeated them on Vjun but were unable to free the captured Ysanna from their carbonite imprisonment. While on an undercover mission to Borgo Prime 13 years later, Skywalker and Tenel Ka claimed that they needed Corusca gems to open a sealed treasure vault located on Ossus.

In the wake of the Yuuzhan Vong War, Master Skywalker chose to establish a new Jedi training academy on Ossus. The new academy flourished for almost a century, until the planet's ecosystem slowly deteriorated into a barren wasteland. Jedi Master Kol Skywalker, descendant of Luke, suggested the Ossus Project, which would allow Yuuzhan Vong shapers to re-form a portion of the planet in an effort to restore its environment. Although the project was successful on Ossus, sabotage kept it from working on other planets. This led to the Sith–Imperial War and the severing of ties between the Jedi Order and the Galactic Alliance. The Jedi retreated to Ossus, but were pursued by the new Sith Lords. In a devastating attack that became known as the massacre at Ossus, the Sith nearly wiped out the entire Jedi Order, destroying much of the planet's surface during their attacks.

**Ossus Project** This was a project championed by Jedi Master Kol Skywalker more than a century after the Battle of Endor. It consisted of a group of Yuuzhan Vong shapers restoring a portion of withered planet Ossus. The Ossus Project proved to be exceptionally successful, prompting a number of planetary and system governments to petition for similar terraforming on their own planets. Some 100 worlds were chosen for re-formation, although the success on Ossus could not be reproduced elsewhere. Strange things began to happen on these other worlds, including disfiguring mutations among the inhabitants. Unbeknownst to the Jedi, Sith agents were sabotaging the process. The resulting furor over the cause of these problems resulted in a loss of faith in the Galactic Alliance and the splintering of the Jedi Order from the galactic government. The Imperial Moffs banded together to take advantage of this tumult, and declared war against the Alliance, bringing about the rise of a new Empire.

*Oswaft*

**Ostega** The site of a civil war that Major Kligson helped to end while in the Trilon Sector Defense Force.

**Ostracoda gunboat** A submersible weapons platform developed by the Trade Federation and first deployed during the invasion of Naboo. Like the OTT Ocean Transport, the Ostracoda gunboat was essentially a land vehicle redesigned for aquatic applications, and it suffered a number of design shortcomings that led to its discontinuation. It was replaced by the manta droid subfighter.

**Oswaft** A species of intelligent manta-ray- or jellyfish-like beings. Oswaft inhabited the vacuum of space called ThonBoka, a sac-shaped interstellar nebula composed of gas and dust. They had powerful wings and a sleek, muscle-covered dorsal surface. Tentacle-like ribbons hung from their ventral sides, and their entire bodies had a glass-like transparency with flashes of inner color. They measured 500 to several thousand meters long. The long-lived species exhibited patience, along with a conservative outlook on life. Lando Calrissian helped save the Oswaft from the threat of genocide.

**Ota** An ice planet where advanced beings known only as the Old Ones once lived. These people constructed numerous cities, using magnetic turbines to handle the "ice power" that fueled their cities. By the time of the Galactic Civil War, all that remained were the Snogars, primitive humanoids who feared and revered the Old Ones and their ice power. After millennia of endless operation, the ice power began to malfunction, and the Snogars, desperate, began capturing offworlders (or "Smart Ones," as they called them) and forcing them to repair the heating systems in the ancient cities. Luke Skywalker, Boba Fett, and Leia Organa were all captured by Snogars just prior to the Battle of Hoth.

***Otana*** A Corellian YT-2000 transport owned by Tomaas Azzameen. Upon his death, the ship was turned over to his son, Ace. It was used to transfer bacta from remote sources to supply depots friendly to the Rebel Alliance.

**O'Tawa cymbals** These musical cymbals formed the heart of the drumheller harp.

**otherspace** Between realspace and hyperspace there existed another reality—otherspace. Here, space was slightly warped and light shone less brightly. It was a "pocket" dimension, filled with things strange, familiar, and deadly. Otherspace became a final resting place for ships lost in hyperspace. Areas were filled with the dark and desolate remains of vessels, floating silently in the void. Only a few spacers had ever heard of otherspace, and fewer still returned from it alive. Otherspace appeared as a cloudy void. Instead of the ebon blackness of space, silver clouds filled the emptiness, with dark pinholes where stars should have been. Otherspace was inhabited by the mysterious species known as the Charon.

*Otoh Gunga*

**Othone** Named for the Jedi Master Johun Othone, this ball of frozen ice and rock was the ninth and outermost planet of the Hoth's Brand system, located in the Teraab sector of the Colonies.

**Othone, Johun** An ancient Jedi and survivor of the prolonged fighting at the Battle of Ruusan that radically reshaped the Jedi and Sith Orders as well as the structure of the Galactic Republic. Othone, a native of Sermeria, was apprenticed to the seasoned warrior Lord Hoth. Othone had been evacuated from the fighting before the Sith Brotherhood of Darkness detonated its arcane thought bomb, a malevolent dark side weapon that trapped the living souls of powerful Force-users on Ruusan, effectively wiping out both Sith and Jedi armies. Returning to the battlefield, Othone encountered accounts from mercenaries that a Sith Lord had somehow survived the thought bomb fallout. Othone was determined to investigate the validity of such claims, but the Jedi Order dismissed it as wild, baseless talk.

Afterward, Othone became Padawan to Valenthyne Farfalla and achieved the rank of Jedi Knight, landing an advisory and protective role to the Republic's Supreme Chancellor, Tarsus Valorum. Othone petitioned the Republic Senate to fund a memorial to the sacrifices made by the Army of Light in protecting the galaxy. While the Senate readily agreed to fund such a memorial, the Jedi Council denied Othone's request. Members said that any memorial to such an act of destruction might serve to draw more attention to it, and that Lord Hoth and his forces had simply been doing their duty.

Othone used his political connections through Valorum to see the memorial become a reality. The Valley of the Jedi monument underwent construction on Ruusan, though Darovit, a survivor of the fighting, repeatedly sabotaged the project. Johun confronted Darovit, who had firsthand evidence that Sith Lord Darth Bane had indeed survived the Battle of Ruusan. Othone brought Darovit back to Coruscant with him to share his report with the Jedi Council, but before he could do so, Darovit was kidnapped by the Sith.

Othone, alongside a small team of Jedi, pursued the Sith to the ancient dark side planet of Tython, where a fight ensued against the Sith Lords Darth Bane and Darth Zannah. The Sith were victorious not only in defeating the Jedi—Othone was killed in the fighting—but also in keeping their continued existence a secret.

**Othrem, Raf** A Twi'lek, he served as part of Twin Suns Squadron at the height of the Yuuzhan Vong War.

**OTIA** The Outside Threat Indicator Array of a starfighter's HUD system. The projected display, just above the targeting crosshairs, consisted of three green indicators. When the right-most indicator turned red, it meant an enemy starfighter had targeted the vessel. If the central indicator turned red, an enemy capital ship had targeted the fighter. If the right display flashed yellow, an enemy warhead was homing in on the starfighter.

**Otoga-222 droid** A simplistic maintenance droid produced by Veril Line Systems, it saw use throughout the galaxy as a starship and vehicle mechanic.

*Otoga-222 droid*

**Otoh Gunga** The largest Gungan city on Naboo. Concealed deep in Lake Paonga, Otoh Gunga was a collection of stunning, glowing bubble buildings. The bubbles possessed hydrostatic membranes designed to prevent water from flooding the structures. Designated portal zones allowed entrance into the city. The bubbles, which could stand over 75 meters tall, were anchored to massive stone pillars on the lake's floor. The floors of Otoh Gunga appeared to be covered in jeweled stones, and exquisite Gungan artwork graced all corners of the city. During the Battle of Naboo, the Gungans abandoned Otoh Gunga in the face of the encroaching droid army invasion, and fled to the Gungan Sacred Place. With the expulsion of Trade Federation forces, the Gungans returned to their city and experienced an overcrowding crisis as more tourists visited Naboo and the newly open Gungan cities. To alleviate the conditions, Boss Rugor Nass approved a colonization project that brought the Gungans to Ohma-D'un, one of Naboo's moons.

**Otoh Gunga Bongameken Cooperative** This Gungan construction facility was responsible for making many of the underwater transport craft—bongos—used by the Gungans on the planet Naboo.

**Otoh Sancture** An ancient underwater city that served as the stronghold of the Gungan clan led by Boss Gallo some 3,000 years before the Battle of Naboo. It was wiped out by the rival forces of Boss Rogoe.

**Otolla** Along with the Ankura, one of two major subspecies of Gungan. Otolla Gungans had more reddish skin, longer haillu, and longer eyestalks.

**Otondon, Gleed** An imposing creature who served under Cradossk in the old Bounty Hunters' Guild, he joined the True Guild and acted as its emissary to Kud'ar Mub'at. A huge, heavily muscled alien with leathery skin and a spiked skull, Otondon had hands studded with claws. Following the breakup of the Bounty Hunters' Guild, he began embez-

Outbound Flight Project

zling the True Guild's funds and storing them in safe accounts. After the dissolution of the True Guild and the Guild Reform Committee, Otondon took all the credits and went into hiding.

**Otranto** A planet in the Corporate Sector, Otranto was the home of the Church of the First Frequency prior to its purging by Imperial Grand Inquisitor Torbin. Later, while aboard a luxury liner, several surviving church members attempted to assassinate Torbin. He was saved by the Tynnan Odumin, only to be murdered on Weerden a month later.

**otta** Sleek, playful aquatic mammals native to Naboo. Their long bodies were streamlined and flexible, allowing ottas to catch fast-moving fish as well as digging for nyorks and other shellfish.

***Ottdefa*** A scientific or academic title similar to *Professor,* conferred on those scholars who served the University of Comparative Sapient Species on Lekua V.

**Ottega system** Also called the Ottegan system, it was located in the Lesser Plooriod Cluster and hosted a remarkable 75 planets. The fourth, Ithor, was home to the gentle Ithorians. Ottega had its fill of dangers for the fringer community. Na-Qoit bandits were known to raid the system. Following the Battle of Hoth, Imperials discovered the remnants of the traitorous Admiral Harkov's fleet in the system. Harkov's flagship, the Victory Star Destroyer *Protector,* was confined in realspace by the Interdictor cruiser *Harpax.* The plan was for Admiral Zaarin and his forces to arrive and finish off the *Protector,* but Zaarin double-crossed the Empire. He attacked Lord Vader's forces and then fled to Coruscant, where he planned to kidnap Emperor Palpatine.

Six years after the Battle of Endor, the New Republic troop transport *Pelagia* was rendezvousing with an Ottega-based X-wing group when the transport was wiped out by the resurrected Emperor's Galaxy Gun.

**Ottethan system** Located in the far perimeter of the galaxy, this system was central in a 12-system empire ruled by a local warlord. Decades ago, Neema, the daughter of Jedi Vima-Da-Boda, was betrothed to an Ottethan warlord. When her barbaric husband treated her like chattel, Neema lashed out against him with the dark side. Imprisoned, she called out to her mother through the Force. Vima arrived too late to save her daughter, who was thrown into the Ottethan forests and fed to the rancors that ran wild there.

**Otto, General** An obese, bumbling Imperial Army general whose career was possible only thanks to political connections and his friendship with Admiral Motti. His repeated defeats saw him stationed on the backplanet Lok, but the arrogant Otto wanted more and defected from the Empire, taking with him an AT-ST walker that he entered into demolition derbies staged by Jabba the Hutt on Tatooine.

**OTT ocean transport** A submersible troop transport developed by the Trade Federation, it was deployed during the invasion of Naboo.

**Ott system** Located in the Kathol sector, this was one of the last major systems along the Trition Trade Route. Its principal planet was Gandle Ott.

**Ourn, Belezaboth** The Paqwe Belezaboth Ourn served as the extraordinary counsel of the Paqwepori in the New Republic government. He was a Yevethan conspirator during the Black Fleet crisis. Equipped with a shielded communications device, Ourn fed information to Yevethan leader Nil Spaar. It was through Ourn that Spaar learned of the New Republic Fifth Fleet's movements into the Farlax sector. Ourn later confessed his betrayal to Chief of State Leia Organa Solo, and handed over Spaar's communicator.

**Outbound Flight Project** An ambitious exploratory mission conceived by the arrogant Jedi Master Jorus C'baoth that ultimately proved to be his undoing in the last decades of the Galactic Republic. Its worthy goals: to seek out and catalog new life existing beyond the borders of the galaxy, and find other beings sensitive to the Force to add to the knowledge of the Jedi. The project languished in bureaucratic limbo for years, until C'baoth was able to earn major political capital by resolving a diplomatic impasse between the Brolfi government of Barlok and the Corporate Alliance. The Senate Appropriations Committee, with the support of Supreme Chancellor Palpatine, then approved the funding for the massive undertaking, and the project soon became a reality.

Outbound Flight required the creation of generational vessels that would spend decades in deep space, far from civilized worlds. Six full-sized Dreadnaught heavy cruisers were converted from warships to exploratory vessels and linked together around a central fuselage to provide propulsion, navigation, computing power, weaponry, and shielding systems. Each Dreadnaught was connected to the others by a series of pylons and turbolifts that were also attached to the central core. Any one of the Dreadnaughts could be detached in an emergency, or left behind to provide defensive support for the rest of the vessel. A unique configuration of repulsor beams moved the liftcars between locations at rapid speeds, while a pool of swoop bikes allowed for swift transportation among Dreadnaughts. Within the core were storage facilities for food, water, and fuel, with enough capacity to keep Outbound Flight operative for years. Living quarters were primarily located in the Dreadnaughts themselves. Artificial gravity was maintained in each of the seven areas, and specialized systems worked to adjust the gravity in the turbolift cars to ensure that beings moving from ship to ship were always feeling the correct orientation. Leading the Outbound Flight crew were six Jedi Masters and 12 Jedi Knights, ostensibly with Master C'baoth as their leader; 50,000 other individuals, including the crew and their families, also went along on the mission.

The excitement of Outbound Flight's mission quickly wore off, especially among the civilian population, when Master C'baoth began assuming control of operations. He even usurped control of the mission from its commanding officer, Captain Pakmillu, and then began training the Jedi contingent in the operation of the ship's systems and weapons. In what was a microcosm of the galaxy at large, the population of Outbound Flight began to resent the Jedi, and the Jedi continued to accrue power over the very beings they were charged to protect.

Unknown to C'baoth and the rest of Outbound Flight's personnel, Darth Sidious had been planning to eliminate Outbound Flight and the threat posed by its Jedi Knights. Sidious knew that the Jedi needed to be exterminated in order for him to realize his goals, but he had also foreseen the possibility of an attack by malicious beings from beyond the galaxy, a threat that would show itself in the decades to come as the Yuuzhan Vong. Sidious worked behind the scenes with his agent, Kinman Doriana, to gather a huge, 15-ship task force that would intercept and destroy Outbound Flight. Doriana and his forces were intercepted by then–Force Commander Thrawn of the Chiss Expansionary Defense Fleet, who wiped out all but one of Doriana's ships. Doriana eventually convinced Thrawn to eliminate Outbound Flight.

Ultimately, Thrawn succeeded in killing nearly all the beings aboard the ships with radiation bombs, with the only survivors being those individuals who were deep in the central storage core at the time of his attack. The remainder of Outbound Flight limped away from the battle zone, guided by Jedi Knight Lorana Jinzler and the Chiss Thrass, Thrawn's brother. The vessels crashed onto a remote planetoid, where the survivors established a crude settlement. Doriana and his lone battleship were allowed to return to the Republic with news of the project's destruction.

The crash landing buried five of the six Dreadnaughts beneath tons of rocky debris. Only the number four ship—D-Four—remained aboveground, which posed serious health risks due to its exposure to interstellar radiation. Thus, the survivors were forced to establish living areas in D-Five, and a nursery center was established in D-Six. Fortunately for those beings who survived the attack, the central supply core was undamaged, leaving them with a wealth of food, water, and other supplies. In order to survive, the existing decks aboard the Dreadnaughts were refitted for use as medcenters, schools, and other essential facilities that could keep the Outbound Flight Colony alive and viable.

Following the loss of the Jedi Masters, whose exact fates were withheld by Palpatine, the Outbound Flight Project was officially abandoned. The remains of the Outbound Flight starship were found nearly 50 years later by Chiss explorers, who agreed that the remains should be turned over to Luke Skywalker and his new Jedi Order. Luke and Mara Jade were allowed to visit the site of Outbound Flight's final resting place and acquire what information they could from the wreckage.

**Outer Expansion Zone** An area of the Expansion Region settled by the galaxy's megacorporations in an effort to jump-start colonization of the galaxy's northern quadrant. But the megacorps exploited the zone's planets so ruthlessly that the Republic was forced to intervene, stalling widespread colonization in the northern quadrant for generations. Corporate-driven colonization efforts by the Trade Federation and the Corporate Sector Authority also trampled the rights of sentients.

**Outer Javin Company** Based on the planet Gerrenthum, this was the corporation founded by Ecclessis Figg and his young bride, Yarith. With Ecclessis's brains and Yarith's credits, the company mapped and exploited the Greater Javin area of the galaxy. Ecclessis Figg made a number of profitable deals with the Lutrillians and the Nothoiin, ensuring that the use of the Greater Javin provided an economic benefit for all major planets and species in the area. By the time of the New Order, the Outer Javin Company was the only publicly traded aspect of the vast Figg enterprise.

**Outer Rim Communications Center** This facility was located on Generis base, along with the Atrivis sector headquarters, during the Galactic Civil War. The ORCC was not under the direct control of the Atrivis Sector Force; it answered to Alliance Sector Command. ORCC was headed by General Kryll. Five years after the Battle of Endor, the Outer Rim Communications Center fell, mostly intact, under Imperial command when Grand Admiral Thrawn reclaimed Atrivis sector.

**Outer Rim Oreworks (ORO)** An ancient mining corporation based in the Outer Rim Territories, known for its use of questionable methods to strip-mine planets in quick order. The company was founded more than a millennium before the onset of the Clone Wars. Miners working for ORO were treated as little more than indentured laborers, working to pay off the debts they incurred trying to buy basics from the company itself.

**Outer Rim Sieges** The series of battles and skirmishes that took place at the edges of the Old Republic's scope of galactic control during the last stages of the Clone Wars. The Outer Rim Sieges took a heavy toll on both the clone army and the Jedi Knights, stretched exceptionally thin in order to counteract the actions of the Separatists.

**Outer Rim Territories** The collective name for the region lying far outside of the Core Worlds, along the galaxy's outer periphery. The Outer Rim was colonized at the height of the Galactic Republic, though much of it remained beyond the governmental authority of the Republic. As such, the territories were largely lawless. Crimes such as slavery were rampant, with criminal organizations like those of the Hutts ruling entire sectors. Even standard Republic credits were not accepted on many worlds in favor of local currencies.

Comprising thousands of sectors, the territories were a hotbed of Rebel activity during the Galactic Civil War as the Emperor's attentions were turned Coreward, and to the Inner Rim. The ambitious Moff Sarn Shild set out to rein in the chaos in the Outer Rim and establish himself as unquestioned ruler of the territories. He envisioned a separate state—much like the Corporate Sector—detached from the Imperial hierarchy with him as its head. His ambitions became his undoing, as agents of Palpatine helped end Shild's career.

The isolation inherent to those living in the Outer Rim fostered a strong sense of independence, and distaste for any government. The minimal Imperial military presence in the early days of the Empire led to the rise of many resistance groups. Foremost among these was the Atrivis Resistance Group, which later became a member of the Rebel Alliance and a key communications link for Rebel units in the Outer Rim. During much of the Galactic Civil War, Grand Moff Wilhuff Tarkin was the Regional Governor of the Outer Rim Territories. After Tarkin's death, the territories fell under the control of Grand Moff Ardus Kaine.

Following the demise of Jabba the Hutt and the shakeup that was the Empire's collapse, the Outer Rim saw the rise of hundreds of new crime syndicates, smuggler coalitions, and gangster guilds. The Outer Rim was the operating ground for three major slaving syndicates—the Zygerrians, the Thalassians, and the Karazak. This bleak development saw the rise of the even bleaker saying, "Life is cheap and cheaper by the dozen."

**Outer Zuma region** An area of the galaxy below the galactic plane and adjacent to the Inner Zuma. It contained four sectors: Fusai, Ikenomin, Kakani, and Sugai. Much of the Outer Zuma was uncharted until about 1,000 years before the Battle of Yavin. It was rife with eddies and sinkholes in the hyperspace continuum, resulting in exceptionally dangerous travel routes and many lost expeditions.

**Outlander Club** A noted nightclub and gambling hall located on Vos Gesal Street in the Uscru Entertainment District on Coruscant. The club was named for the fact that it originally was a small establishment that catered to the aficionados of the gambling game Outlander. It was here that Zam Wesell tried to ambush Obi-Wan Kenobi and Anakin Skywalker after they foiled a second assassination attempt on the life of Senator Padmé Amidala.

*Outlander Club*

**Outland Mining** An Old Republic mining corporation large enough to maintain its own defense fleet. Much of the fleet was nationalized by the Republic in the wake of the Trade Federation's actions at the Battle of Naboo.

**Outland Transit Station** A space station found along the edge of Hutt Space, it had an airy interior thanks to a massive transparisteel dome. Dexter Jettster once owned a weapons shop there, but after it was attacked by the Bando Gora cult, he sold his stake to Jango Fett. Sometime later the bounty hunter Montross triggered a series of thermal detonators throughout the station, destroying it.

**outlaw tech** Any well-equipped and highly trained technician who made a living illegally modifying and repairing space vessels. Clients of outlaw techs included criminal organizations, fugitives, the Rebellion, and those opposed to whatever galactic authority was in power. Techs typically kept their bases hidden and often moved quickly to stay ahead of law enforcement.

**Outlier** Small star systems in the Corellian sector far from central Corellia, they were so paranoid and secretive that they made unfriendly Corellia seem hospitable.

***Outpost*** An Imperial *Carrack*-class cruiser that was part of Admiral Greelanx's task force during the Battle of Nar Shaddaa. It served as a forward recon vessel along with its sister ship, the *Vigilance.*

**Outpost Beta** This isolated sentry station served as an advance lookout point for Hoth's Echo Base on the northern ridge of the Rebel Alliance base. Corporal Maren Kelsome, one of the soldiers assigned to Outpost Beta, was the first to spot the Imperial invasion that started the Battle of Hoth. Outpost Beta watched the drop ships land beyond the base's energy shield and saw the lumbering Imperial AT-AT walkers start their relentless march toward the base and its power generators. The advance warning provided by Outpost Beta allowed the Rebellion to scramble its snowspeeders in time. On orders of General Rieekan, Outpost Beta was abandoned early in the conflict. Maren Kelsome did not survive. Also among the casualties of Outpost Beta was the Florn Lamproid, Dice Ibegon. Lak Sivrak survived.

***Outrider*** The ship of the cocky Corellian smuggler Dash Rendar, it was a modified Corellian YT-2400 freighter that had been converted for smuggling duty. The *Outrider* shone with a dark gleam and featured the traditional saucer-shaped hull of the YT series, which included the *Millennium Falcon.* Like its predecessors, it was fast and tough and cried out for creative modifications.

The *Outrider* had a rounded hull with thick armor plating and a pair of port-side bracing arms that connected to the cockpit, which was essentially a long tube. The aft section of the tube held the main escape pod, which sat six. Much of the hull interior was filled with modified military-grade ion engines, power generators, weapons systems, and all the other illegal enhancements a smuggling ship needed. Weaponry included a pair of heavy double laser cannons and two forward-firing concussion missile launchers.

Outrider

**Outsider Citadels** Cities maintained for the benefit of offworlders living on Cerea. Many conservative Cereans believed in keeping the purity of Cerea's natural beauty and despised the citadels for the pollution and waste they produced.

**OV600** A truth serum developed by 'Geneering Products. Subjects injected with it broke out in a painful rash if they attempted to lie.

**Ova** A world that imploded and vanished due to an intense gravitational distortion created by the Infinity Gate on Dathomir. This event, which occurred shortly after the Battle of Naboo, prompted the Jedi Council to dispatch Quinlan Vos to the quarantined planet of Dathomir to investigate.

**overbridge** The strategic command core of an Imperial Death Star. Located at its north pole, it was a massive command center that constantly monitored all workstations and data transactions of the battle station. All information collected by the various zone bridges, sensor arrays, communications centers, and even space traffic control was routed through the station's central computers, and available in the overbridge. In the original Death Star, there were command stations for each member of the station's command triumvirate: Grand Moff Wilhuff Tarkin, General Cassio Tagge, and Admiral Conan Antonio Motti. There were also stations for the operations chiefs assigned to them. Dozens of lesser officers and droids worked regular shifts in the overbridge. The overbridge could, in theory, control the entire battle station, but it was far more efficient to allow the zone bridges to handle their share of the work. In an emergency, the overbridge could supersede all of the lesser command centers. Only the Death Star's throne room command center could usurp command from the overbridge.

**Overden** The ruling body of Selonia. During the Corellian incident 14 years after the Battle of Endor, the Overden sided with those proclaiming absolute independence for Selonia. In opposition was the Hunchuzuc Den, which sided with New Republic rule. In the negotiations between both dens, the Overden won, securing a number of prominent New Republic prisoners and the massive planetary repulsor found on Selonia. Among the prisoners were Chief of State Leia Organa Solo, Han Solo, and Mara Jade. The speaker of the Overden, Kleyvits, demanded that Organa Solo declare Selonians independent from the rest of the Corellian sector. During negotiations, the Solos were able to convince Hunchuzuc member Dracmus to overthrow Kleyvits, freeing the prisoners and negating the demands.

**overload sturm dowel** Found in every blaster power pack, these cylinders helped moderate the energy sealed within. A common explosive for desperate saboteurs could be fashioned by binding several power packs together, setting them on maximum intensity, and removing their protective overload sturm dowels.

**Overracer** A Mobquet speeder bike used by Rebel scouts. Techs usually modified them so that their electromagnetic signatures were reduced and they were stripped of all nonessential equipment. Because these bikes lacked high-altitude lifters, civilian stabilizers, long-range receivers, and the like, Rebels nicknamed them flying rocks.

**Oviedo Engineering** A vast research-and-development organization, it expanded its corporate portfolio many years before the onset of the Clone Wars, branching out to manufacture a variety of military vehicles and weapons systems. Oviedo Engineering was forced to dismantle its operations after its director, Lorca Oviedo, was arrested on conspiracy charges after faking his death and plotting to sell rigged weaponry to Wat Tambor and the Confederacy of Independent Systems.

**O-Vieve** *See* Vieve.

**Ovkhevam** A Noghri from clan Bakh'tor liberated from servitude to the Empire when Leia Organa Solo revealed the Empire's true nature to the Noghri people. Ovkhevam was responsible for the creation of "the future of his world," a secluded agricultural storehouse carefully built in the Hidden Valley of Honoghr, the sterile Noghri homeworld.

An older Noghri, Ovkhevam remembered when his world was verdant and fertile. Surprisingly gentle, he cared more about agriculture than killing for the Empire. Despite his best efforts, the plan to reintroduce agriculture to Honoghr failed, and many Noghri abandoned their home, settling on worlds such as Wayland.

**Ovrax IV** The planet where bandleader Evar Orbus purchased Droopy McCool, the Kitonak formerly known as Snit.

**Ov Taraba** A prestigious and expensive university on Onderon, established millennia before the rise of the Empire.

**Ovvit** This Chev served as one of the starfighter pilots who worked for Byalfin Dyur aboard the *Boneyard Rendezvous* during the years following the Swarm War. Ovvit was killed on Ziost by Ben Skywalker, who managed to use the Force to dislodge several heavy boulders and drop them on Ovvit's TIE fighter.

**Ow-Chee-2** A torture droid whose fingers were snap-up hypodermic needles filled with green sleeping serum. Admiral Screed used Ow-Chee-2's serum to put Mungo Baobab into hibernation during the early years of the Galactic Empire.

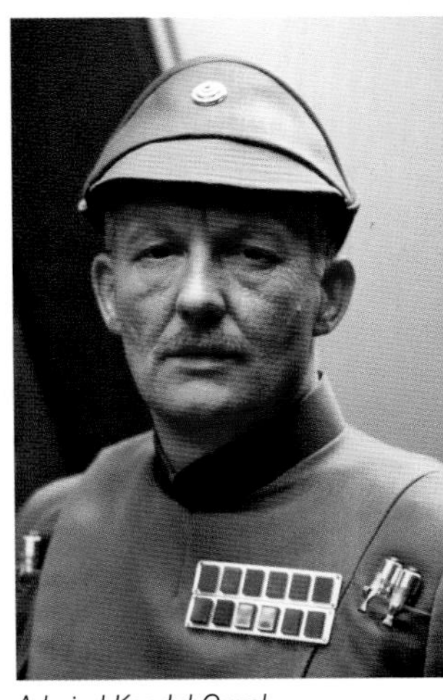
Admiral Kendal Ozzel

**Owell** One of the many Ferroans who were living on the planet Zonama Sekot during the Yuuzhan Vong War. Like Darak and Rowel, Owell eventually came to trust Luke Skywalker and the Jedi Knights who arrived on the planet to seek its assistance in resolving the conflict with the Yuuzhan Vong. When Zonama Sekot made a blind jump into hyperspace to avoid the sabotage of Nom Anor, the Ferroans were forced to flee underground to avoid the ecological damage that occurred on the surface. Owell, along with Darak and Rowel, made many trips into the wilderness to look for survivors, often with the help of the Jedi.

**OWO-1** One of the command battle droids sent by Nute Gunray to check to see if Qui-Gon Jinn and Obi-Wan Kenobi had been killed by poison gas aboard the Trade Federation flagship in charge of the blockade of Naboo. Distinguished by its yellow coloration, OWO-1 had a communications package that provided audio and video back to Gunray's command center until it was cut down by the Jedi's lightsabers.

**Owool Interceptor** An innovative starfighter developed and produced by KashyCorp during the years following the Swarm War. Many military observers likened Owools to the Wookiees who produced them: heavy fighters that were tough, fast, and ferocious. The Wookiees of KashyCorp were to deliver a shipment of Owool Interceptors to the Galactic Alliance at the height of the Alliance's conflict with the Confederation, but the leaders of the Rock Council decided to remove their support for the Alliance after hearing that the Jedi Order had done the same.

**owriss** A large, harmless, blob-like creature that inhabited the forests of Endor's moon.

**Oxbel** The Devaronian Oxbel posed as the brother of Labria on Tatooine. Oxbel went to the desert planet for a brief gambling junket, but ended up staying for years. He made his living selling whatever information he overheard or discovered to interested parties. He was remarkably devoid of talent and ambition, as his information broker career took second priority to his imbibing of lum. When drunk (which was often), Oxbel babbled incoherently about information both public and private. It was unlikely that Oxbel ever knew that Labria was in fact the Butcher of Montellian Serat, Kardue'sai'Malloc.

**Oxon** One of the principal human settlements on Naboo.

**Oxtroe, Admiral Betl** Three years after the Battle of Endor, Imperial Admiral Betl Oxtroe began making secret overtures to members of the New Republic to negotiate the creation of a parliamentary monarchy. She proposed 11-year-old Ederlathh Pallopides, a distant grandniece of Emperor Palpatine, as a possible heir. Oxtroe's plan was to replace the advisers of the old Empire with the New Republic Provisional Council in exchange for amnesty for the military. Oxtroe died at the blade of a Noghri assassin before the first round of talks could be completed.

**Ozlo** This young Mon Calamari Jedi Knight was one of a handful stationed on the planet Ossus, where they were charged with protecting a Jedi training facility during the Galactic Alliance's conflict with the Confederation. When Vis'l and Loli were killed by Galactic Alliance Guard forces under the command of Major Serpa, Ozlo struggled mightily to remain calm and hidden, hoping to find a way to stop the onslaught. However, when Tionne Solusar was badly injured by Serpa, Ozlo tried to intervene. Several GAG snipers were able to fire, and Ozlo was shot in the head and killed.

**Ozz, King** The Ugnaught known as Ozz was one of three major partners in Planet Dreams, Inc., a planetscaping company that operated out of Cloud City on Bespin. With the Snivvian Wiorkettle and the Lutrillian Treva Horme, Ozz oversaw the building of habitable environments in asteroids and private domes the galaxy over; he was in charge of managing resources and budget. Ozz secretly embezzled both money and terraforming equipment from the company and disappeared prior to the Imperial takeover of Cloud City.

The 150-year-old Ugnaught had spent the first century of his life in slavery. He took his embezzled funds and constructed a sanctuary for Ugnaughts 3 kilometers below Cloud City. Ozz terraformed the surface of a floating platform to resemble a bubbling swamp. This so-called City of the Ugnaughts became salvation for Ugnaughts who no longer wanted to rely on humans for their livelihood.

Appointing himself king, Ozz ordered the Ugnaught insurrection of Cloud City, rebelling against the practices enacted by the new Imperial administrator, Captain Treece. With the aid of former administrator Lando Calrissian and Rebels Luke Skywalker and Shira Brie, the Ugnaughts were able to depose the Imperials. King Ozz was a larger-than-normal Ugnaught, with dark gray hair and beard.

**Ozzel, Admiral Kendal** Before he became admiral of the most prestigious task force in the Imperial Navy, Kendal Ozzel benefited from a name synonymous with a proud naval tradition. A native of Carida, he spent some time teaching at its vaunted military academy. After some time in command of the Star Destroyer *Reprisal* in the Shelsha sector, his old and powerful ties to Imperial Command gave him the advantages he needed to be placed in charge of the Imperial Death Squadron. Some speculate that this promotion for political reasons rather than for ability was his undoing.

One of Ozzel's first duties when in command of the *Executor* was the patrol of the Black Widow Nebula for the Imperial corvette commanded by deserter Captain Sodarra. Although reports varied, Ozzel captured the *Millennium Falcon* when Han Solo piloted the ship into the nebula. When Solo alluded to the corvette, Ozzel allowed the Corellian to escape in the hope that the *Falcon* would lead him to the deserters.

When the *Executor* became the flagship of the Death Squadron, Ozzel commanded six Star Destroyers assembled shortly before the Battle of Hoth. Ozzel was a by-the-manuals officer, and had personal opinions that differed from those of Darth Vader. When the Hoth campaign started, Ozzel brought the fleet out of hyperspace too close to the Hoth system. The Rebels, alerted to the Imperial presence, activated an energy shield that prevented orbital bombardment. Vader killed Ozzel for his failure, promoting Captain Piett to his position.

THE COMPLETE

STAR WARS

ENCYCLOPEDIA

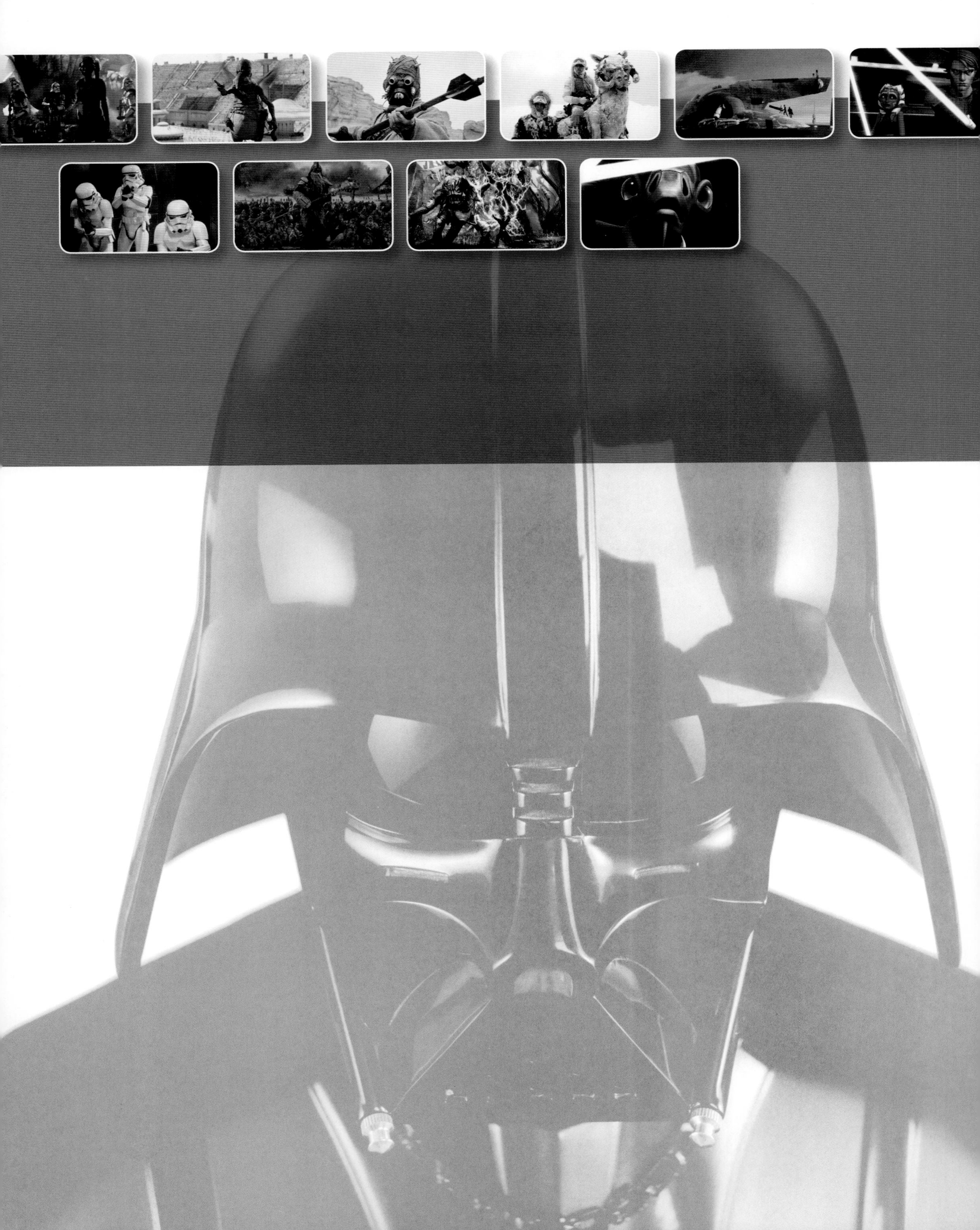

Stephen J. Sansweet
& Pablo Hidalgo
and
Bob Vitas & Daniel Wallace
with
Chris Cassidy,
Mary Franklin & Josh Kushins

P–Z
Volume III

Ballantine Books ■ New York

Published in the United States by Del Rey, an imprint of The Random House Publishing Group, a division of Random House, Inc., New York.

Del Rey is a registered trademark and the Del Rey colophon is a trademark of Random House, Inc.

ISBN 978-0-345-47763-7

Printed in China

www.starwars.com
www.delreybooks.com

9 8 7 6 5

Interior design by Michaelis/Carpelis Design Associates, Inc.

*So certain are you. Always with you it cannot be done. . . .*

*Try not. Do. Or do not. There is no try.*

—*Jedi Master Yoda*

# THE COMPLETE STAR WARS ENCYCLOPEDIA

# P

**P-100 salvage droid** Hovering dome-shaped droids with four heavy-duty manipulator arms, they were used for picking up salvage from the wreckage-strewn crash sites of Podrace tracks. They were carried onto the track by a large, cylindrical holding arm that dispensed a trio at a time. P-100s varied in size from 3-meter-wide models to smaller units used for the transport of luggage and other small cargo.

*P-100 salvage droid*

**P2 unit** Industrial Automaton's first attempts to create a consumer-market astromech droid. Like future models, the P2 prototype unit had a rotating head, a cylindrical body with numerous retractable manipulator arms, and three wheeled legs. Although large and cumbersome, the droid served well as a maintenance and repair unit for bulk cruisers and similar vessels. Industrial Automaton became involved in a costly technology-infringement lawsuit, and the P2 series was discontinued. While the lawsuit churned its way through the labyrinthine Galactic Republic court system, Industrial Automaton rushed out a replacement model, the R1 unit, by repurposing existing Mark II reactor drone shells. By the time the case was settled, the innovations of the P2 design were scaled down and incorporated into the R2 unit.

*P-59, P-60*

*< Emperor Palpatine*

**P-38 fighter** *See* Porax-38 starfighter.

**P-59, P-60** Droidekas (destroyer droids) stationed aboard the Trade Federation flagship during the blockade of Naboo. P-59 and P-60 confronted Obi-Wan Kenobi and Qui-Gon Jinn, preventing the Jedi from cutting through the bridge blast doors and reaching Trade Federation Viceroy Nute Gunray. However, the Jedi ultimately escaped the droidekas and fled to Naboo.

**P-6** A treaded repair droid with a crane-like manipulator seen at Star Tours launch facilities performing repairs on the Starspeeder 3000.

**Pa'aal** The primary moon of the fifth planet of the N'zoth system in the Koornacht Cluster, it was home to a Yevethan prisoner-of-war and slave-labor camp. It was the former site of the headquarters of the Imperial Black Sword Command.

**Paaerduag** This species of unusual, two-headed beings was native to the planet Sorjus.

**Paak** A bald-headed man, distinguished by the green and purple tattoos that covered his skull and neck, he was one of the primary members of the Anti-Republic Liberation Front, which was active on the planet Serenno after the Battle of Ruusan. Paak was wary of newcomer Rainah. After a failed assassination attempt on Chancellor Tarsus Valorum, Paak confronted Rainah—who in truth was Darth Zannah. When she revealed her true identity, Paak shot at her, but she used her lightsaber to deflect the blast at Paak, killing him.

**Paal, Nadin** This Gran served as a sort of trade envoy for the criminal organization run by Nirama during the last decades of the Old Republic. Paal's role was to interface between Nirama's organization and the planetary officials of the Cularin system, ensuring that there was no misunderstanding about Nirama's goals. Riboga the Hutt once put a conditional bounty on Nadin Paal's head, which could be claimed only if the Gran was captured outside Cularin. This forced Paal to remain a member of the local criminal underworld, although he longed to find more respectable work.

**paaloc incense** A rare aromatic biotic used by only the highest-ranking Yuuzhan Vong. Its scent reminded the aliens of their long-lost homeworld.

**paan** A variety of evergreen tree native to Hapes, used as a screen in decorative landscapes.

**PaAR** A Galactic Alliance military acronym for any planning and analysis room.

**Paarin Minor** The site of a Galactic Republic stronghold attacked by Separatist forces during the Clone Wars. Clone troopers used a weather-generation machine to create an artificial cloud cover over their location, which screened them from Separatist forces. As the Separatist ships emerged from the clouds, the Republic's ground-based forces opened fire, decimating the enemy before the Separatists could retreat.

**Paar's ichthyodont** A large aquatic saurian with a tapered, finned body, a long curving neck, and a wedge-shaped head. These creatures were native to the watery moon of Panna. Boba Fett used one as a mount and complained that all it thought of was eating.

*P2 unit*

**Pablo-Jill** An Ongree Jedi Knight from the Skustell Cluster, he was famous for his part in bringing a temporary peace to the lawless world of Ord Mantell. The Jedi Council encouraged him to take a Padawan, but he never did. He fought in the arena battle on Geonosis at the start of the Clone Wars. Though he survived that bloody first engagement, he died during the Battle of Coruscant at the end of the wars when he landed his Jedi starfighter aboard the Separatist flagship. There he was slain by General Grievous.

Pablo-Jill

**Pabs, Rhe** A Pho Ph'eahian medical tech worker aboard the *BioCruiser*. After the ship was sabotaged, he agreed to remain aboard as it journeyed toward Tentrix.

**Paca, Magir** One of the leaders of the New Republic's underground on Garos IV and a close friend of Garosian Governor Tork Winger. Paca used his position as assistant to the Minister of Commerce to gather intelligence on the Empire's movements. He was discovered during an Imperial audit, but managed to elude arrest after Alex Winger, the governor's adopted daughter, saw his name on a list of suspected criminals. Paca fled public service and went into hiding to protect himself.

**Pacanth Reach** A remote star cluster in the Outer Rim conquered by the Epicanthi people. Teräs käsi was taught there.

**Pacci** A pilot for the New Republic Fifth Fleet, he was killed during a failed attempt to blockade the Yevetha at Doornik-319.

**Pace, Dr. Anki** A professor at the University of Agamar who earned her doctorate at the university on Mrlsst. She was a friend of Koyi Komad and attended her wedding. During the early stages of the Yuuzhan Vong War, she led a group of students on a xenoarchaeological expedition to Bimmiel that uncovered Yuuzhan Vong remains.

**Pachwenko** A Jawa nicknamed Patches by human settlers for his patchwork robes, he was part of the tribe that captured R2-D2 and C-3PO and sold them to the Lars homestead.

**pacifog** A mind-altering aerosol weapon developed for the Empire at an orbiting zero-g lab high over Kadril. The gas had the peculiar effect of chemically exacerbating what a sentient perceived as his or her greatest flaw. Given unpredictable effects that varied from species to species and individual to individual—including rage, insecurity, hallucinations, sneezing, insanity, cardiac arrest, depression, and stupidity—the concoction was abandoned as a biological weapon. All specimens were locked away in the Emperor's secret plague storehouse in the Deep Core.

**Pacithhip** A gray-skinned species with long trunks and small tusks, they hailed from the Outer Rim world of Shimia. A spacefaring culture, Pacithhips could be found across the galaxy, all the way to the Galactic Core. Pacithhip society closely regulated the roles of its members, with careers dictated by early genetic testing. Because their rotund torsos and small legs limited their mobility in a galaxy largely dominated by humanoid bipeds, offworld Pacithhips typically employed mechanical legs that gave them a wider stance and gait.

Pacithhip

**PackTrack 41LT-R (MULE droid)** The Mechanical Universal Labor Eliminating Droid, or MULE, was the droid version of a beast of burden.

**Pad** A non-Force-sensitive mercenary who worked for the Brotherhood of Darkness during the Battle of Ruusan. When the Sith were wiped out by Lord Kaan's use of a terrible thought bomb weapon, Pad was among the mercs left behind. Wandering from the battlefield, the mercs came across a surprise Sith survivor, Darth Bane, who slaughtered most of them, allowing a scant few to escape to carry the unbelievable news that Bane lived.

**Padaunete, Thrynka** The leader of the People's Inquest, this woman was highly critical of the Jedi Order in the final years of the Galactic Republic. She led a public campaign to oppose the Jedi training of Aris Del-Wari, an infant in the disputed custody of the Jedi Order. Once the Clone Wars erupted, Padaunete became the host of a weekly news-net program dedicated to spreading anti-Jedi propaganda.

**Padawan** The title held by a Jedi apprentice during the Old Republic era. Younglings were raised communally in the Jedi Temple from as early an age as possible, part of clans trained by Yoda and other Jedi Masters. Upon reaching a certain age—it varied per species, but for humans typically before 13—a youngling was selected to be paired with a Jedi Knight or Master for one-on-one training. Any younglings who were not chosen by the set age were typically reassigned to the Jedi Service Corps.

An early exercise of a Padawan learner was the construction of a lightsaber, but should a Jedi not complete his or her training or leave the order as a Padawan, that lightsaber had to be relinquished to the Padawan's Master. Human and similar Padawans wore a single long braid, which was removed upon successful completion of the trials that elevated a Padawan learner to the status of Jedi Knight.

**Padawan Massacre** The sensationalist yet accurate name coined by the holomedia to describe the murder of the graduating class of

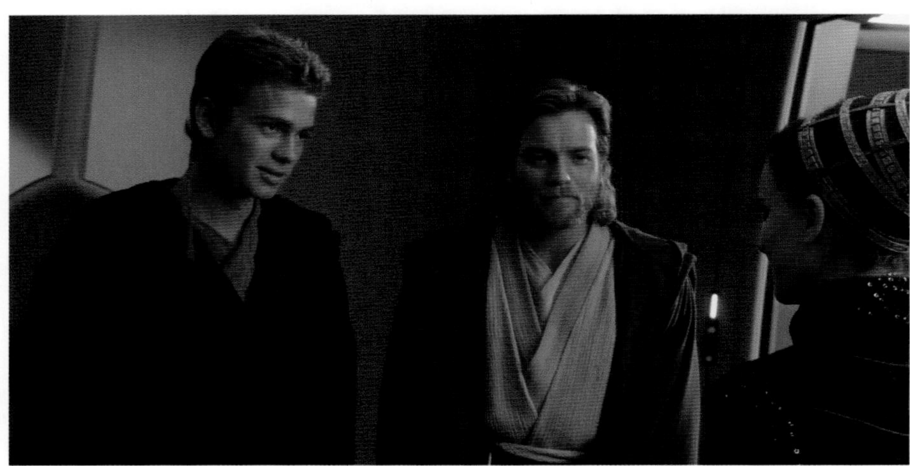
*Padawan Anakin Skywalker (left) and his Master, Obi-Wan Kenobi, greet Senator Amidala.*

Padawan learners at the Jedi satellite academy on Taris during the final years of the Mandalorian Wars. Though the massacre was actually carried out by Jedi members of the Covenant, Zayne Carrick, the sole surviving Padawan, was framed for the murders and became a wanted criminal.

**Padawan Pack** A group of Padawans who banded together after having lost their Masters during the Clone Wars. They took part in the Battle of Jabiim. When Obi-Wan Kenobi was mistakenly presumed dead, Anakin Skywalker joined the Pack. This group made its last stand at Cobalt Station to buy time for the evacuation of Jabiimi loyalists and clone survivors at a mesa to the south. Anakin was called to the evacuation point right before the Confederacy attacked and thus was spared the fate of his comrades, who all died. Aside from Anakin, members included Aubrie Wyn (human female), Elora Sund (Sullustan female), Kass Tod (Zabrak female), Mak Lotor (human male), Vaabesh (Gand male), Windo Nend (Aqualish male), and Zule Xiss (Falleen female).

Teemto Pagalies

**Paddie, Ister** A member of Sermeria's nobility who ascended from the Sermerian First House to join the ranks of the Galactic Senate. He carried with him the regal airs of his homeworld, including his orthodox Halbara hairstyle and his golden robes. He was a strong supporter of Chancellor Palpatine during the Separatist crisis and was one of the first Senators named to the Loyalist Committee. He was vocally critical of the Corellian withdrawal from the Military Creation Act vote prior to the Clone Wars.

**Paecian Empire** An ancient empire founded about 3,000 years before the Battle of Endor. Paecian was a secondary language spoken on Dathomir.

**Pag, Mirip** A male Iotran, he served as a gunner for Urias Xhaxin's crew of pirates aboard the *Free Lance.*

**Pagalies, Teemto** A Veknoid Podracer exiled from Moonus Mandel for refusing to go through with an arranged marriage. Sometime before the Boonta Eve Classic, Pagalies became smitten with Ann Gella, one of Sebulba's Twi'lek masseuses. He later learned that Mars Guo, another Podracer, was also infatuated with Gella and began to fear that Guo would abduct the Twi'lek. He shared this belief with Sebulba, who subsequently sought revenge on Guo during the Boonta Eve Classic. Teemto had large eyes and short, floppy ears. He piloted a unique Podracer with a large, round cockpit and huge engines. The vehicle fell victim to Tusken snipers during the Boonta Eve Classic. He survived, however, and later competed in the Vinta Harvest Classic; he won the Aleen Classic. With Sebulba's defeat at the Boonta, the Dug dropped in status and Ann Gella left him to run off with Teemto. The relationship was ill-fated, however, as Veknoids and Twi'leks simply weren't compatible. Teemto was left alone, spending too much time in seedy Tatooine cantinas. He retired from racing after one too many accidents and worked as a mechanic for Ulda Banai.

**Page, Glip** A young Padawan learner during the Clone Wars.

**Page, Judder** A top Rebel Alliance and New Republic officer and undercover operative. Page's upbringing would seem to have prepared him for a far different destiny. The pampered son of a corrupt Imperial Senator from Corulag, Page nonetheless idolized the ancient Jedi Knights. Forced into the Imperial Academy, he was assigned on graduation to General Veers's ground assault command. While on leave, he heard Senator Leia Organa speak about galactic rights, which inspired him to defect and join the Alliance. He was part of the commando units of General Madine and Major Derlin. Offered command of his own squad, he opted to retain the rank of lieutenant as a sign of humility. After the Battle of Endor, this nondescript man of average build and height led a special-missions team that took on assignments few others could handle.

Ister Paddie

Colonel Ejagga Pakkpekatt

When the Yuuzhan Vong War began, Page agreed to a naval posting, was given the rank of captain, and served under Pash Cracken aboard the *Memory of Ithor* during Operation Trinity. When the ship exploded, it was believed that Judder and Pash were both killed. In fact both managed to reach life pods and escape the blast, only to be captured by the Yuuzhan Vong and incarcerated on Selvaris. Page was eventually rescued by the New Republic.

**Page's Commandos** Officially known as the Katarn Commandos, for a predator from the planet Kashyyyk, this special-missions team included 12 of the New Republic's best-trained soldiers under the leadership of Lieutenant Page. A bit of a rogue operation, it operated independently for weeks or months at a time and could handle nearly any type of delicate mission in any environment. Each member was a jack-of-all-trades as well as a specialist in a single field, such as scouting or urban combat. The crack assault squad handled most of the front-line duties in the New Republic's offensive against the Maw Installation.

**Paig** One of the planets to which the Fallanassi—followers of the White Current—sent children for safekeeping after the religious sect was persecuted on Lucazec.

**Paige-Tarkin, Shayla** The Senator of the Seswenna sector, including the planet Eriadu, during the Separatist crisis. She was adamant in her support of the Republic, and Chancellor Palpatine in particular.

**pain simulator** A device that allowed droids to feel pain, it emitted high-frequency carrier waves so that other droids could experience pain, too. The device was often used by the droid EV-9D9 for torture sessions.

**Pakka** A young Trianii, he helped Han Solo infiltrate the Corporate Sector Authority's prison facility at Stars' End. Pakka, son of Atuarre and Keeheen, was struck mute after his father was taken prisoner by Authority agents.

**Pakkpekatt, Colonel Ejagga** A Hortek rumored to be semi-telepathic, he was a veteran intelligence officer who headed a New Republic chase team charged with penetrating the mystery surrounding the ghost ship known as the Teljkon vagabond. Colonel Pakkpekatt was tough, experienced, and cautious; he played by the rules. He was less than overjoyed when Lando Calrissian, a risk-taking gambler, was also assigned to the mission. After the vagabond took off with Calrissian, his longtime aide Lobot, and the droids C-3PO and R2-D2 on board, New Republic Intelligence blamed the colonel for letting Lobot and the droids board the ship at all. He was then abandoned by NRI, which took away all but four of his ships. When he was given the order to terminate the mission even though Calrissian and his companions were aboard the vagabond, the colonel exploded with rage, saying that "a Hortek does not leave the bodies of comrades in the hands of the enemy—ever." He convinced General Rieekan, head of NRI, to let him pursue the vagabond on his own. Colonel Pakkpekatt then assumed command of Calrissian's ship, the *Lady Luck*, and, with Lieutenant Harona and agents Plack and Taisden aboard, went in search of the vagabond. They ended up at Maltha Obex, where Calrissian, Lobot, and the droids were successfully rescued.

*Ajunta Pall*

**Pakmillu, Captain** A Mon Calamari military officer serving in the Galactic Republic, he was chosen to lead the Outbound Flight Project as commander of the D-One Dreadnaught. Once the mission launched from Yaga Minor, however, Pakmillu found himself subservient to Jedi Master Jorus C'baoth, who began to exert more and more power with his fellow Jedi Knights. Eventually, Pakmillu ceded control of Outbound Flight to C'baoth, much to the anger and dismay of the crew and families aboard the six Dreadnaughts.

**Pak Pak** The traditional language of the Neimoidians, it consisted of streams of croaks, produced by varying the shape of the mouth and throat. Although many linguists found Pak Pak to be musical and beautiful, most other beings considered it guttural and harsh. The Pak Pak language was well suited to the Neimoidian physiology, but not to communication with the rest of the galaxy. Thus, when Neimoidians learned to speak Basic, they had to learn both the language and the correct manipulation of their vocal cords to create the foreign words. This resulted in a strange accent that became synonymous with the Neimoidians themselves.

**Pakrik Minor** Home to Imperial Sleeper Cell Jenth-44, a community of clones grown from the legendary Baron Fel. Han and Leia Solo were ambushed by Imperial fighters at Pakrik Minor, but were quickly rescued by those clones. Pakrik Major and Pakrik Minor were located in the Kanchen sector.

**Pakuuni system** A hotbed of piracy and smuggling in the Outer Rim, this system contained the planet Pakuuni. Following the Battle of Hoth, Vice Admiral Thrawn was sent there to eliminate the pirates and make the area safe for shipping by establishing the Imperial space station NL-1. The Pakuuni pirates joined with Rebel Alliance forces to drive out the Empire, but they were defeated.

**Palace of Peace** The central governmental building of Peace City, on the planet Ylesia, after the Yuuzhan Vong took control of the planet and turned it over to the Peace Brigade. As a gruesome reminder of Ylesia's past, and a deterrent to any attempt to recover it, the dried skin of a Hutt leader was hung over the entrance.

**Palace of Splendid Harmony** The governmental seat of Virujansi, where the Rajah presided over the Ever Radiant Throne. The 6,000-year-old palace took a good deal of damage during the Clone Wars, but was saved by Anakin Skywalker and Obi-Wan Kenobi.

**Palace of the Woolamander** An ancient Massassi structure found on Yavin 4. An elongated rectangular edifice just east of the Great Temple near the banks of a river, the Palace of the Woolamander was marked with two massive staircases reaching to the top. Rebel Alliance researcher and scout Dr'uun Unnh named the temple for the pack of loud woolamanders nesting within the ruins. His inspection revealed that the Palace was too structurally unstable to house any Alliance quarters. A golden globe within the temple contained the trapped spirits of Massassi children. Anakin Solo and his friend Tahiri Veila were able to break the globe and free the spirits. During the Yuuzhan Vong War, when the Peace Brigade attacked the Jedi academy, the Jedi students hid in the caves beneath the Palace of the Woolamander.

**Palanhi** Located in the system of the same name, Palanhi was a crossroads planet with a reputation for exaggerating its own importance. It remained neutral during the Galactic Civil War, attempting to profit from both sides. Grand Admiral Thrawn had funds transferred into Admiral Ackbar's account through the central bank on Palanhi in an effort to discredit the admiral and create a false trail to deceive investigators.

**Palawa** Likely the point of origin of the Followers of Palawa, this planet was destroyed in an ancient battle. The Jedi Order helped relocate the Followers to Bunduki.

*Palmgun*

**Palazidar** A t'landa Til, he was one of Teroenza's Sacredots at Colony One on Ylesia. He was infamous for falling over, asleep, during the Exaltation, causing no small amount of concern and upset among the pilgrims, who held the Exaltation in such high regard.

**Palbert, Firris** The acting leader of the People's Inquest on Coruscant, he led an anti-Jedi protest at the steps of the Jedi Temple when Baby Ludi was transferred to Kamparas.

**Palesia** A territory on Lannik captured by the Red Iaro terrorists. During the peace negotiations that took place on Malastare after the Battle of Naboo, the Red Iaro conceded the territory to Prince R'cardo Sooflie IX.

**Pall, Ajunta** One of the tombs in the Valley of the Dark Lords belonged to Ajunta Pall, who was among the first of the great Sith Lords. He wielded a powerful sword.

**Pall, Tobias** A Royal Security Forces officer who was rooted out of the Naboo swamps by STAPs during the invasion of Naboo by Trade Federation forces.

**Palle, Lieutenant Eri** The first attaché, or personal aide, to Yevethan strongman Nil Spaar.

**pallie** A foodstuff sold in the stalls of the Mos Espa marketplace on Tatooine. These small fruits could be used to make pallie wine.

**Pallin, Lieutenant** A young Imperial garrison commander during the Yuuzhan Vong invasion of Ord Sedra. He sent out a short distress signal before communications were jammed, and his call for help was intercepted by Kyle Katarn and Jan Ors. Although the invaders were defeated, Pallin felt that he had let his people down: The invasion occurred on his first command watch, and he'd been forced to call in help from the New Republic. Katarn quickly pointed out that it was Pallin who'd made the decision to send out the distress signal that allowed the Republic agents to assist in freeing hundreds of innocent people.

**Palmer, RSF Officer** A young Naboo Royal Security Forces officer captured when the Trade Federation invaded Theed. She was later rescued by Gavyn Sykes and became an important member of the resistance movement.

**palmgun** A small, easily concealable blaster pistol designed for close-range combat. Palmguns were sometimes called hold-out blasters.

**Pal-Nada** A Force-wielding Cerean crime lord who used his influence to steal and then resell starships for large profits during the New Order.

**Palo** A boy who attended the Legislative Youth Program with Padmé Naberrie. A few years older than the future Queen of Naboo, he had dark, curly hair and "dreamy" eyes. He went on to become an artist.

**Pa'lowick** This diminutive amphibian species from the planet Lowick was a late addition to the galactic community. Pa'lowick were notable for their mouths, found at the end of flexible trunks. Some possessed a second mouth, with tusks resting just beneath their snouts. Youthful Pa'lowick retained this extra mouth through young adulthood, at which time it disappeared, absorbed into their facial skin. Their snouts were perfect for eating giant marlello duck eggs, which they punctured with their tongues to suck the yolk through their tube-like mouths. Pa'lowick reproduced by laying eggs. Vocal music was a sacred tradition in their culture. Sy Snootles was a Pa'lowick.

*Pa'lowick*

**Palpatine** Evil incarnate, Palpatine imposed a reign of terror upon the galaxy for years. His roots were humble, traceable to the peaceful world of Naboo. Before his rise to power, Palpatine was an unassuming yet ambitious Senator. He saw the Galactic Republic crumbling about him, torn apart by partisan bickering and corruption. All too common were those unscrupulous Senators taking advantage of the system, growing fat and wealthy on a bureaucracy too slow to catch them.

Palpatine's moment of opportunity came as a result of a trade embargo. The Trade Federation, in protest of government measures that would tax their outlying trade routes, blockaded and invaded Naboo. Naboo's planetary leader, Queen Amidala, rushed to Coruscant for Palpatine's aid. Together the two pleaded to the Senate for intervention, only to see their request stalemated by Trade Federation filibustering. Frustrated by the government's inability to do anything, Queen Amidala acted upon Palpatine's suggestion and called for a vote of no confidence in the Republic's leadership.

Chancellor Valorum was ousted from office, and Palpatine was soon nominated to succeed him. The crisis on Naboo prompted a strong sympathy vote, and Palpatine became Chancellor. He promised to reunite the disaffected and bring order and justice to the government.

Little did anyone suspect how Palpatine had engineered his own rise to power. Hidden behind a façade of wan smiles and smooth political speeches was a Sith Lord. In truth, Palpatine was well versed in the ways of the Force, having been apprentice to Darth Plagueis the Wise, a Sith Lord who was a master of arcane and unnatural knowledge. In true Sith tradition, Palpatine murdered his Master upon achieving the skill and ability to do so. He then took an apprentice himself, continuing the Sith Order in absolute secrecy, right under the noses of the Republic and the Jedi.

In his cloaked Sith identity of Darth Sidious, Palpatine made contact with the scheming Neimoidians and plotted the invasion of his own homeworld. The resulting political fallout allowed Palpatine to step into the power vacuum left by Chancellor Valorum.

Despite Palpatine's vocal promises of reform, the Republic continued to be mired in strife and chaos. A decade after his nomination, Palpatine was faced with the challenge of a popular Separatist movement led by the charismatic Count Dooku. Many in the galaxy feared that the conflict would escalate to full-scale warfare, but Palpatine was adamant that the crisis could be resolved by negotiation.

The Separatists didn't agree. Amassing an immense army of droids with the complicity of numerous trade organizations, they made it clear that they were on the verge of declaring war against the Republic. To counter this,

*Senator Palpatine of Naboo*

the Republic needed a military, and Palpatine required the authority to activate the Republic's newly forged army of clones. To that end, Senators loyal to Palpatine motioned that the Chancellor be given emergency powers to deal with the Separatist threat.

With spoken regrets, Palpatine accepted the new mantle of power. He promised to return his absolute authority to the Senate after the emergency subsided. What no one realized was that an apparently infinite state of crisis would ensure Palpatine's authority over the galaxy for decades.

The Clone Wars were just part of the intricate Sith plan he concocted. After the demise of Darth Maul, he needed a new apprentice to carry forward his agenda. He did not have time to train an adept from the cradle, but instead plotted to turn an already proven Jedi warrior onto the path of the dark side. His target was the disillusioned Jedi Master Count Dooku. By appealing to Dooku's civility and disgust with Republic corruption, Palpatine was able to lure him to the dark side. When he became fully enmeshed in the Sith Order and pledged his absolute loyalty to Palpatine, Dooku was granted the mantle of Darth Tyranus.

As Tyranus, Dooku put into motion the next phase of Sidious's fiendish plot. He was responsible for the creation of a clone army on the Republic's behalf, selecting a prime candidate as the clone template: Jango Fett. In his public persona of Dooku, he grew to become a political firebrand, leading a militant band of dissidents to wage open war against the Republic: a war the Republic was pleasantly surprised to find it was equipped to fight. The Clone Wars were in fact a sham—Palpatine secretly held authority over both sides of the conflict.

The indications of his future regime were subtle at first. Palpatine's term as Chancellor ended during the rise of the Separatists,

*Supreme Chancellor Palpatine*

but that crisis allowed him to extend his stay in office. Once the Clone Wars erupted, the Senate's inability to efficiently wage war on scattered fronts forced him to enact executive decree after executive decree. He added amendments to the Constitution funneling more power to him, effectively circumventing the bureaucracy of the Senate.

The public and the Senate willingly gave up their rights and freedoms in the name of security. Under Palpatine's guidance, the war would be won, and the Republic would be safe. The monstrous specter of General Grievous leading an assault ensured that few questioned Palpatine's growing authority.

The Jedi Council was among the wary. As an instrument of the Senate and the people, the Jedi Order resisted Palpatine's direct control. This tension grew as the war escalated. Some in the Senate also quietly whispered their misgivings. Palpatine knew of a delegation of concerned Senators, and he would deal with them in time.

During the Clone Wars, Anakin Skywalker grew to be a legendary hero among the Jedi. His power was remarkable. Palpatine, who had been fostering a friendship with the unique lad since his childhood, felt the time was right. Darth Tyranus had served his purpose. Skywalker would be the next Sith apprentice.

As a bold endgame to his lengthy plot, Palpatine became architect of his own abduction by the fearsome General Grievous, military commander of the Separatist forces. The Confederacy fleet hammered Coruscant's defenses and absconded with the captive Chancellor. Predictably, the Jedi Order's finest heroes—Anakin Skywalker and Obi-Wan Kenobi—were dispatched to rescue Palpatine. Aboard their tiny starfighters, they infiltrated Grievous's flagship and worked their way to the shackled Chancellor.

Count Dooku stood in their path. Once again, lightsaber blades crossed as Kenobi and Skywalker teamed up against Dooku. The aged Sith Lord was able to outmaneuver Kenobi and knock the seasoned Jedi unconscious. Without his mentor's guidance, Anakin attacked Dooku alone. The Sith Lord goaded Anakin into rage, and the young Jedi took revenge against the warrior who had severed his arm years before. Skywalker cut off both of Dooku's hands and had the Separatist leader kneeling before his lightsaber blade.

Palpatine recognized the dark side in Anakin and nurtured it. He encouraged Anakin to kill Dooku. Skywalker's blade seared through flesh and bone, and Dooku's severed head soon littered the deck. Though Anakin instantly regretted the act as not being of the Jedi way, Palpatine was quick to console him and absolve him of any guilt. After all, Dooku was too dangerous to be taken alive, rationalized Palpatine.

It was not the first time Palpatine had encouraged Anakin's unfettered abilities. A young man of Anakin's abilities was constantly chafing under the strict confines of the Jedi Code and was often being reprimanded for doing what he felt was right. Palpatine never had any admonitions. He was always in Anakin's corner.

Skywalker would remember this as the political fallout from Dooku's death and the continuing Clone Wars tugged him in different directions. The Jedi Council had grown wary of Palpatine and was critical of the Chancellor's decrees that redirected power away from the Senate and the Constitution and into his office. Palpatine grew to naturally distrust the Council. He appointed Anakin Skywalker to act as his personal representative on the Jedi Council. Surprisingly, the Jedi Council agreed to this appointment—but only in the hope of turning Anakin into their spy on the Chancellor.

*Emperor Palpatine*

Palpatine exploited this distrust and the confusion plaguing Anakin. Skywalker grew to feel that the Chancellor was the only one not asking something of him, the only one not speaking through veiled agendas. It was in this position of trust that Palpatine recounted a Sith legend—the story of Darth Plagueis the Wise. In the relative privacy of his viewing box in the Galaxies Opera House, Palpatine wistfully recalled the little-heard legend of the powerful Sith Lord so knowledgeable in the arcane and unnatural arts that he could even stop those he loved from dying. At the time, Anakin Skywalker was plagued with visions of the death of his wife. He feared them to be prophetic, like so many of his visions. Skywalker wanted to know more about Plagueis's ability—it was unknown to the Jedi, supposedly discovered only by the Sith. Knowing that he had the boy sufficiently intrigued, Palpatine later dropped his guise. He revealed to Anakin that he was in fact a Sith Lord, but also that he was the path to the power that could save Padmé Amidala from dying.

Anakin was deeply conflicted. Respecting his loyalty to the Jedi Order, he informed senior Jedi Council member Mace Windu of the stunning revelation. Windu arranged for a group of Jedi Masters to arrest the Chancellor. Palpatine did not go quietly.

In the inner recesses of his private office, the Jedi confronted the Chancellor. Palpatine produced a lightsaber hidden in his sleeve and let the dark side of the Force flow through him. It granted him unnatural dexterity and speed—enough to quickly kill three Jedi Masters and force the mighty Mace Windu back. The two dueled, transforming the office of politics into an arena of lightsaber combat. Windu overpowered Palpatine the instant Anakin Skywalker came running into the offices.

Skywalker witnessed a stunning sight: the Chancellor cornered, with Windu looming over him, lightsaber blade extended. Palpatine unleashed a torrent of Sith lightning at the Jedi Master, but Windu was able to deflect it back at the Chancellor. The evil energies twisted Palpatine's face as they flowed through him, scarring and disfiguring his once handsome features. His eyes burned yellow, his voice grew ragged and deep, and he became a well of dark side energies.

Palpatine slumped in the corner, seemingly too weak to continue the lightning assault. Fearing the Chancellor to be too powerful and too well connected, Windu decided he could not be taken alive. Before Windu could take justice into his own hands, though, Anakin sprang into action. He cut off Windu's weapon hand with his lightsaber. Defenseless, Windu was then bombarded by Palpatine's dark side lightning. With the Jedi Master dead and Anakin Skywalker having taken his first irreversible step to the dark side, Sidious grinned.

Skywalker knelt before Darth Sidious, and the Sith Lord bestowed upon him the title of Darth Vader. He next tasked his new apprentice with razing the Jedi Temple before the treacherous Jedi could strike back at them. Entrenched in the dark side, Vader marched to the Temple with a column of loyal clone troopers, gutting the sacred edifice from within. Meanwhile, Sidious took care of the Jedi scattered across the galaxy waging the Clone Wars.

Palpatine enacted Order 66, a coded command that identified the Jedi Knights as traitors to the Republic. He broadcast this order to the clone commanders on the various distant battlefronts, and the loyal soldiers killed their Jedi generals in cold blood.

The next day, Palpatine called for a special session of the Galactic Senate. Despite his disfigurement, he appeared before the assembled politicians of the Republic and delivered a stirring account of how he'd narrowly escaped a treacherous Jedi rebellion. He assured the people of the Republic that his resolve had not faltered. He had routed the treachery that had entangled the Republic in the Clone Wars. He would flense the corruption and bloated bureaucracy that were strangling the august government and reform it as a new, more powerful, more secure institution.

That day, before thunderous applause, Palpatine declared himself Emperor. He instituted a military buildup unprecedented in galactic history. He created the New Order, a Galactic Empire that ruled by tyranny. Senators who had been too vocal in their opposition or whom he considered too dangerous were blackmailed or eliminated. Execution orders were issued for Senators Mon Mothma and Garm Bel Iblis; both escaped, but Bel Iblis's family was slaughtered. The Emperor diverted funds from social, artistic, and other programs into a massive military buildup devoted to subjugating entire star systems.

Although Palpatine called for the extermination of the Jedi and any Force-sensitives who could conceivably challenge him, he did keep a few loyal agents who were trained in the Force. Darth Vader was chief among them, as his primary lieutenant and Sith apprentice. Palpatine also had a string of loyal, deadly agents referred to as his "Hands." Mara Jade was foremost among these dedicated enforcers.

Palpatine trusted no one and kept track of everyone. No one had the full picture except the Emperor; confusion was the order of the day among his advisers. Palpatine effectively set up a system under which the Empire couldn't function without him. Once he achieved his aim, he became distant and reclusive, seen only by those who needed to see him. His leaders and commanders presented the Empire's public face; Darth Vader presented a public threat. The Emperor also prepared for the future, conducting cloning experiments, hoping to transfer his mind and very essence into a younger and stronger clone of himself.

During the Galactic Civil War, Palpatine ruled with an iron fist. He disbanded the Imperial Senate, passing control down to the Regional Governors and the military. During the Hoth campaign, Palpatine expressed to Vader his concerns over Luke Skywalker, a young Rebel powerful in the Force. Vader suggested that the two convert the youth to the dark side, an idea the Emperor seconded. After Vader returned from his encounter with Skywalker a changed man, Palpatine had his doubts in his apprentice. The Emperor dispatched his top-secret aide, Mara Jade, to kill young Skywalker, but she failed.

The Emperor was a scheming ruler, planning events far in the future, using the Force to foresee the results. So powerful in the Force was he that the very essence of the dark side ravaged his form. Palpatine scoured ancient Sith texts seeking a path to eternal life, a continuation of a quest for immortality begun by Darth Plagueis. Palpatine used Spaarti cloning cylinders to create a store of younger bodies, and employed an ancient Sith technique to transfer his consciousness into a waiting clone. Thus, he could avoid death indefinitely—as long as his supply of clones remained intact. He would change his form again and again, prolonging his life. Palpatine constructed a secret throneworld deep within the galaxy's core, on a shadowy planet called Byss. There he kept his clones safe, protected by a loyal cadre of Dark Side Adepts.

*Palpatine's spirit in a cloned body*

Palpatine allowed Rebel spies to learn of the location of the second Death Star and foresaw their strike team and fleet assault. He crafted an elaborate trap that was to be the end of the Rebellion. He also concentrated on converting Luke Skywalker to the dark side of the Force, even at the expense of sacrificing Vader. In the Death Star, high above the Battle of Endor, Luke refused the Emperor's newfound dark side power, and so Palpatine used his deadly Force lightning to attack the young Jedi. Luke almost died in the assault, but his father, Darth Vader, returned to the light side of the Force and hurled the Emperor into the Death Star's reactor core, killing him.

Palpatine's body was destroyed. Separated from his clones, Palpatine was forced to survive in the maddening, bodiless existence of the void. Through sheer will he retained his identity, crossing the gulf of space to again take up residence in his clone body. He barely survived Darth Vader's treachery. Palpatine remained sequestered at Byss while he rebuilt his strength, and his Empire.

Palpatine's rule was so absolute that his apparent death at Endor fragmented the Empire. With no obvious heir, opportunistic Moffs and warlords set out to carve their own private fiefdoms where they could. Years of infighting worked to the advantage of the fledgling New Republic, which proceeded to reclaim three-fourths of the galaxy. One warlord who succeeded where imitators failed was Grand Admiral Thrawn, the only nonhuman to hold that rank. His cunning tactics and unerring strategies brought the Empire to the brink of victory five years after the Battle of Endor. Only a last-minute betrayal spelled his defeat.

Spurred on by Thrawn's victories, the remaining Inner Circle of Imperial warlords staged a devastating attack on Coruscant. Whereas Thrawn sought to take the capital world intact, these Imperials attacked without compunction. Much of Imperial City was laid waste by the fighting, and the New Republic was forced to evacuate. Once on the surface, the Imperials splintered yet again, and skirmishes dragged on among the ruined skytowers.

It was then that the cloned Palpatine struck. Using his dark powers to invoke a Force storm of great magnitude, Palpatine swept Jedi Master Luke Skywalker to Byss. There he revealed himself to Skywalker and unveiled the true strength of the dark side. Faced with an immortal enemy, Skywalker did the unthinkable—in order to defeat the dark side from within, Skywalker knelt before Palpatine and declared himself his new apprentice. In these dark times, it seemed the Emperor had finally won.

Skywalker was too enmeshed in darkness to successfully rebel against his Master. Although he sabotaged some of Palpatine's military ventures—namely those involving immense war factories called World Devastators—he still could not draw himself from the pall of the dark side. It was his sister, Leia Organa Solo, who gave him the extra strength he needed. With her presence, the two Skywalker twins were able to temporarily repulse Palpatine.

Unabated, the Emperor continued his scourge. Armed with an incredible new superweapon, the Galaxy Gun, Palpatine forced numerous New Republic worlds to capitulate to Imperial rule. Despite his growing Empire, Palpatine was again growing frail. His clones were failing him. He needed new blood. Palpatine targeted Leia's newborn son, Anakin Solo, as the next receptacle for his dark spirit. During an attempt to possess the child, Han Solo shot the ailing Palpatine in the back. Before his soul could enter Anakin's body, Palpatine was intercepted by a newfound Jedi, Empatojayos Brand. Cut off from a host body, Palpatine's essence dissipated, to be consumed by the madness that was the dark side. After so many decades of bloodshed, the Emperor was truly dead. (*See also* Sidious, Darth.)

**Palpatine Counter-Insurgency Front (PCF)** Shortly after the New Republic took control of Coruscant, but before it could purge all the remaining Imperial evil from the planet, this terrorist organization was formed by Ysanne Isard, director of Imperial Intelligence. Controlled at various times by Kirtan Loor and Fliry Vorru, the PCF was responsible for a series of horrifying bombings at a school, a stadium, and several bacta storage facilities.

**Palpatones** A musical group featuring Joh Yowza, Rystáll Sant, and lead singer Greeata Jendowanian. Rystáll eventually left the band to search for her father.

**Palsaang** A wroshyr-tree city on Kashyyyk, and the ancestral home of the Palsaang clan.

**Paltonae, Baroness** An alias used by Mara Jade in the casino on Nezmi during her hunt for crime lord Dequc.

**paluruvu** A fine, violet-hued perfume from the Dzavak Lakes district of Ansion that also acted as a sedative. While visiting the Qulun clan during the Ansion border dispute, the Jedi and their hosts were knocked unconscious by paluruvu in an attempt to prevent them from finding the Borokii.

**Pammant** A tunneled Quarren colony world containing the factory where the *Invisible Hand* was built. Pammant was devastated by radioactive activity and fractured to the core by a cataclysmic hyperspace accident involving the *Quaestor.*

**Pampy** A beautiful blue-skinned Rutian Twi'lek assistant to Orn Free Taa.

**Pamr** This young Corellian woman was being assaulted by Ilir Post and several other boys until she was rescued by Soontir Fel. However, Post's father managed to save his son from incarceration by bringing up allegations of crimes against Fel's father. In exchange for his son's freedom, Post had Fel shipped off to the Imperial Academy on Carida.

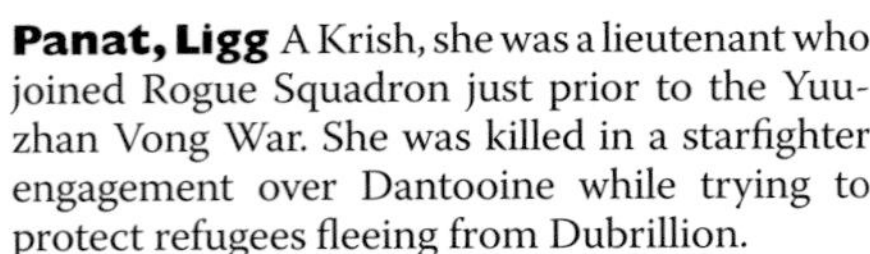

*Pampy*

**Panaka** The brave leader of the Naboo Royal Security Forces, and Queen Amidala's dedicated protector during the Battle of Naboo. Confident and respected, Panaka was a powerful man with sharp senses and a keen mind. In his youth, he joined a Republic Special Task Force to gain combat experience fighting pirates in the Naboo system. Panaka eventually became captain of the volunteer security forces on Naboo, commanding the Security Guard, the Palace Guard, and the Space Fighter Corps. Of all the Naboo leaders, he was among the first to recognize the threat posed by the Trade Federation.

When Panaka joined the RSF, he worked under Captain Magneta, King Veruna's personal protector. Veruna, who had served for 12 years, eventually became involved in foreign affairs at Senator Palpatine's urging. However, Veruna became obsessed with outworld politics and was forced to abdicate the throne in a scandal. He went into hiding, where he met a mysterious, "accidental" death about six months before the Battle of Naboo. Humiliated by her inability to protect the King, Magneta resigned from her post. Selected to replace Magneta, Panaka proved to be one of Queen Amidala's most loyal protectors. Panaka devised the decoy scheme that protected the Queen.

After Queen Amidala completed her terms and abdicated the throne, Panaka served the new queen, Jamillia, while his nephew Gregar Typho became Amidala's protector. With the rise of Palpatine during the Clone Wars, Panaka remained extremely loyal to the Chancellor, providing him intelligence regarding Anakin's secret marriage to Padmé Amidala. Panaka eventually achieved the rank of Moff of the Chommel sector with the coming of the Empire.

**Panat, Ligg** A Krish, she was a lieutenant who joined Rogue Squadron just prior to the Yuuzhan Vong War. She was killed in a starfighter engagement over Dantooine while trying to protect refugees fleeing from Dubrillion.

**Panatha** The homeworld of the war-like, near-human Epicanthix, Panatha lay in the Pacanth Reach near the Unknown Regions.

**Pandoor, Naj** Distinguished by his stooped posture and well-tended goatee, this man was a freelance smuggler. He was once a student of xenoarchaeology at the University of Ketaris. After the school went bankrupt, he took up smuggling as a way to obtain the relics and artifacts that had captivated him. When he learned of Dr. Frayne's archaeological expedition to Geonosis just prior to the outbreak of the Clone Wars, Pandoor infiltrated her team by waylaying one of her assistants and using his credentials to gain access to their ship. On Geonosis, Frayne stunned Pandoor and left him with Jedi Knight Jyl Somtay. Pandoor feared that Somtay would turn him in to the Republic authorities, but she agreed to work with him to relocate Frayne and bring her to justice. After they located Frayne's body and avoided the nexu that had killed her, Pandoor observed that they made a good team, and that Somtay should join him as a smuggler. In an underground lab, they discovered a Geonosian sonic blaster that was capable of shifting its frequency with every blast, which would have made it unstoppable by the Jedi. Pandoor managed to steal the weapon and tried to use it against Somtay, but the nexu returned and mauled him. Somtay managed to fight it off, then dragged Pandoor to a place where she could bind him and turn him over to the authorities.

**Pangay Ous** One of the smaller clans of Alwari native to the planet Ansion. They wore distinctive robes made from lightweight, waterproof fabric. The Pangay Ous were allied with the Northern Bands.

**Panib, Grell** This short, stiff-backed human had close-cropped red hair and a thick mustache. A rough-and-tumble sort known for his temper and his lack of social graces, Panib served the Imperial commander at Bakura. When the Imperial forces surrendered, he defected along with Commander Thanas. Later, he helped rebuild the Bakuran military defenses, earning the rank of general. During the Yuuzhan Vong War, when it seemed that Bakura was ready to form an alliance with the P'w'eck, Panib was forced to assume control of the planet after Prime Minister Cundertol was kidnapped. Panib placed Bakura under martial law until the situation could be resolved. When Cundertol returned to Bakura, Panib agreed to lift the state of emergency and work with the leaders to ensure a safe consecration of Bakura by the Keeramak. Panib was unprepared for the treachery of both Cundertol and Deputy Prime Minister Blaine Harris, and found himself in a leadership position when both were eliminated. As his first act, Panib signed a peace treaty with Lwothin of the P'w'eck Emancipation Movement. He agreed to send Bakuran ships to Lwhekk to help ensure that the native P'w'eck population was freed.

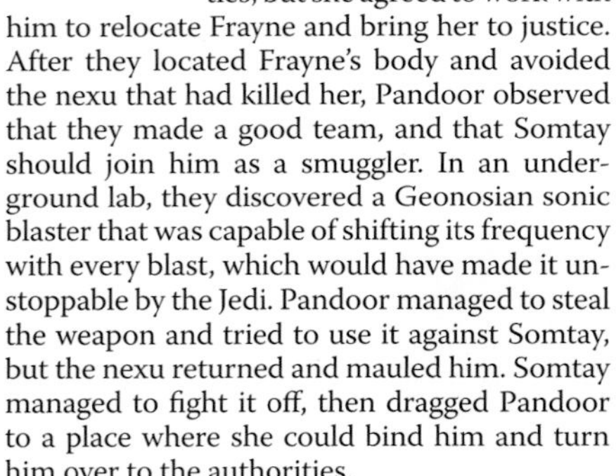

*Panaka*

**Panjarra, Teela** She was a Force-sensitive infant discovered by the Jedi shortly before the Battle of Naboo. Her parents were Corulag Academy scholars who perished in an accident. The Academy's Chief Scientist Frexton discovered her high midi-chlorian count while performing tests in the Science Service nursery.

**Panna system** The Panna system contained seven planets and 35 moons, including at least one satellite capable of sustaining life. This moon had a very watery surface. A massive floating city there—held aloft by a synthetic flotation bubble—suffered a large Imperial presence. Shortly after the Battle of Yavin, Chewbacca piloted the *Millennium Falcon* to this moon after Han Solo was afflicted with an Imperial sleeping virus. Luke Skywalker followed in a Y-wing fighter. Together with the bounty hunter Boba Fett, they found a cure for the virus, but also discovered that it was part of a plot to uncover the location of the hidden Rebel base. Chewbacca gave an edited recording of this caper to his son, Lumpawarrump, as a gift, and the young Wookiee cherished it, watching it often and with great enthusiasm.

*Panning droid*

**panning droid** Kalibac Industries librarian droids that were reconfigured and reprogrammed by the Techno Union to collect ore-rich lava from the surface of the planet Mustafar. Panning droids were given carbonite plating and dedicated shield generators to protect them from the environment; sophisticated programming allowed them to anticipate problems and react before they could be damaged. These droids moved about on re-

Raal Panteer protects Leia Organa.

pulsorlift engines originally designed to help them travel through vast archives and quickly recover specific documents or records.

**Panno, Major** A Dressellian tactician who served the Rebel Alliance at the Battle of Endor. He was a former commando who worked with General Madine to plan the logistics of strike operations.

**Pantang Scale of Aero-techno Advancement** A scale that ranked planets based on their varieties of transportation. According to C-3PO, this ridiculous scale weighted even a simple landspeeder as heavily as it did a Star Destroyer.

**Panteer, Raal** This Alderaanian grew up with members of the Organa family during the early years of the New Order. A former intimate of Leia Organa, Raal and his older brother Heeth were in the Ryloth system when their homeworld was destroyed by the first Death Star. The two owned an "inhospitable" moon in the system that served as the Panteer family's vacation home. Leia Organa traveled there to approach Raal about helping the Rebel Alliance find a new base. She hesitated briefly, though, worried that Raal had never gotten over the breakup of their relationship. Although Raal was happy to be reunited with Leia, he was surprised to learn of her connections to the Alliance. When Leia asked about the possibility of the Panteers allowing the Alliance to use their moon as a new base, Raal agreed with Leia's plan, but Heeth refused. To get away from his brother, Raal took Leia for a safari through the preserve housed on the moon, but he was attacked by a morp. His dying wish was to have one more kiss from Leia, which she gave. Heeth was able to locate their position just after Raal died. Raal's death only hardened Heeth's resolve to stay out of the Rebellion, and he ordered Leia to leave as quickly as possible.

Baron N. Papanoida (right) with Chi Eekway

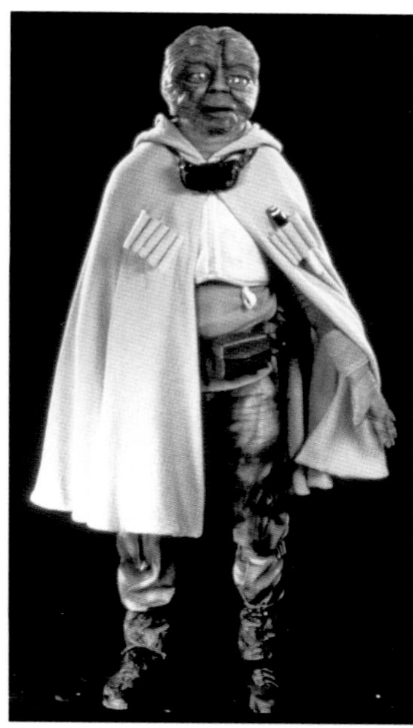
Major Panno

**panthac** *See* Mantessan panthac.

***Panther Star*** This Corellian warship was one of many assigned to protect Centerpoint Station during the war between the Galactic Alliance and the Confederation.

**Pantolomin** Famous for the intricate coral reefs found in the waters off its northern continent, this was the primary planet in the Panto system. The *Coral Vanda*, an underwater casino ship, traveled through the network of Pantolomin reefs on luxury excursions. Patrons could view the reefs' fish and animal life through its transparent hull. Among other resorts was the Towers of Pantolomin, owned by Galaxy Tours. The planet's animals included the playful, color-changing amphibians known as halfbacks; its inhabitants were called Lomins. Five years after the Battle of Endor, Grand Admiral Thrawn's forces visited Pantolomin and forced the *Coral Vanda* to surrender a passenger, Captain Hoffner, who knew the location of the long-lost *Katana* Dreadnaught fleet.

**Pantoran system** This star system contained the planet Orto Plutonia and was represented in the Senate by Riyo Chuchi.

**Paol, Jace** A Corellian Rebel in the early Galactic Civil War, he served as Bria Tharen's chief aide during her time as a commander in the underground. He died on Toprawa, along with Tharen and most of Red Hand Squadron, as they tried to buy time for Leia Organa to receive the Death Star plans.

**Papanoida, Baron N.** An influential Wroonian guild baron with contacts throughout the galaxy, Baron Papanoida was rumored to have an information network rivaling that of the Bothans. His ultimate allegiance, however, remained unknown. For as many people who knew of Baron Papanoida, scant few knew any tangible details about his past or motives.

Once a humble playwright on Wroona, Papanoida authored a series of incendiary hits that captured the imagination of the planet and funded what would become an entertainment empire. He became an influential guild baron, during which time he took great care to keep his past and personal life shielded from the public view. What Papanoida did not keep secret was his love of performance art—and his disdain for Chancellor Palpatine's policies. Papanoida was often seen at the finest auditoriums and holoentertainment venues on Coruscant, including the Galaxies Opera House. And though he was an outspoken critic of Palpatine, he refused to commit himself to more overt political actions against the Chancellor. He instead funneled information to Senators of conscience, like young Chi Eekway. Such discretion allowed him to retain his standing as the Empire rose to power.

**Papeega, Ban** This one-eyed, bird-like being conducted the interrogation of the Rebel pilot who revealed Luke Skywalker as the individual who destroyed the Death Star. Papeega was killed by Darth Vader to ensure that Skywalker's identity remained a secret.

**Paploo** A scout in the Ewok tribe who befriended Princess Leia Organa and other Rebels on the Forest Moon of Endor. A boisterous, prank-playing Ewok, Paploo would often get into trouble with his domineering mother, Bozzie, not to mention his uncle, Chief Chirpa. He had all manner of misadventures in his youth alongside his friends Wicket, Teebo, Latara, and his cousin Kneesaa. He later stole an Imperial speeder bike to distract the guards at a secret Imperial facility at the start of the Battle of Endor. Paploo's actions gave the Rebel strike team an opportunity to penetrate the Imperial base. He was named the tribe's sha-

Paploo

man after Logray was removed by Chief Chirpa. One of Paploo's first acts was to remove a curse placed on the Ewok village by Logray. The Golden One, C-3PO, aided Paploo in this ritual.

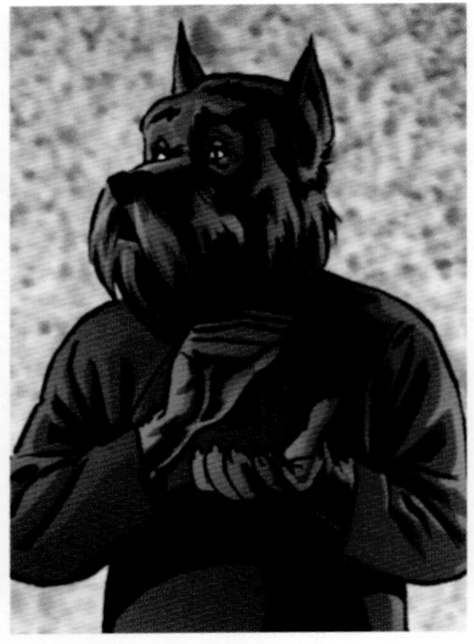
Baco Par

**Pappfak** A mostly unknown species with turquoise tentacles.

**Paqwepori** An autonomous territory represented by Belezaboth Ourn, extraordinary consul of the Paqwepori. The inhabitants, short, wide yellow-green beings called Paqwe, were known to eat toko birds, which they killed with a slaughter knife before consuming. Paqwepori society forbade any of its citizens from joining the New Republic military. Twelve years after the Battle of Endor, the Paqwepori consular ship *Mother's Valkyrie* was damaged when the Yevethan thrustship *Aramadia* blasted off from a Coruscant port without warning. In reality, Ourn had secretly allowed the damage to his vessel in exchange for a promised Yevethan thrustship of his own. Yevethan leader Nil Spaar continued to use the promise of a thrustship to tempt Ourn into providing him more information on political developments on Coruscant. While Ourn waited, the other members of his staff abandoned him. Finally, Ilar Paqwe revoked Ourn's status and warned him not to return to the Paqwe dominion. Ourn revealed his treachery to Leia Organa Solo and the New Republic, which used Ourn to send disinformation to Nil Spaar.

**Par, Baco** A short-snouted, fur-covered being, he was a former Rebel Alliance operative and noted lock breaker during the early stages of the Galactic Civil War. Baco was relieved of duty after a series of drunken misadventures and drifted for many months before he found himself awakening from a binge aboard Wyl Tarson's starship. Par had been kidnapped by Tarson, who was en route to Ahakista as part of a mission to destroy the Hub for the crime lord Raze. Par resented this turn of events and voiced his dismay loudly, though he did nonetheless participate.

Paraglider

**Paradise system** A garbage-strewn system, it was home to the quarrelsome unicellular protozoans known as Ugors. Early in their history, the Ugors severely polluted their home planet, yet survived by evolving into a form that could exist on garbage and waste. The Ugors, who built a religion around their love of trash, began charging fees to those wishing to make a pilgrimage to their system to pick through their vast store of garbage and remove useful items. Ugor society was composed of various waste recovery companies, all controlled by the Holy Ugor Taxation Collection Agency (HUTCA). Ugors frequently found themselves in conflict with the scavenger Squibs for control of the galactic trash-hauling business.

**paraglider** These lightweight fliers were essentially repulsorlift engines with airfoils useful for stealthy approaches and atmospheric drops. Nen-Carvon paragliders featured a light repulsor motor used to maintain or change altitude. The R-19 was the combat version, while the R-23 was built for recreation. The human replica droid Guri used one to escape the destruction of Prince Xizor's palace on Coruscant.

**paralight system** Consisting of mechanical and opto-electronic subsystems in a hyperdrive, this system translated a pilot's manual commands into reactions inside the hyperdrive power plants.

**paralope** A small mammal native to the Corellian plains hunted by the Corellian sand panther.

**Paramexor Guild of Hunters** A bounty hunters' organization founded by Janq Paramexor, it required that members only hunted murderers—a restriction that many found quite profitable.

**Paramita, Slide** A small Ciasi Podracer pilot, he eschewed big, overmuscled Podracer styles and preferred sleek and maneuverable craft, like his extremely sensitive and responsive Pizer-Errol Stinger 627 S Podracer.

**parasite bomb** The name given to genocidal superweapons developed by the Chiss during the Swarm War. Each parasite bomb was filled with a chemical soup containing parasites bioengineered to mortally attack the Killik species. While these parasites had no immediate effects, they would slowly eat away at a Killik over the course of a year. During this time, they reproduced and were transmitted to others in any exchanges of bodily fluids. Eventually, the Killik hosts were left unable to reproduce fast enough to overtake the parasite, and the entire Colony would die out.

The Chiss had planned to launch parasite bombs during the Battle of Tenupe prior to a tactical retreat. The plan was thwarted when Commander Baltke revealed it to Leia Organa Solo. Leia was able to relay information about the parasite bombs to the other Jedi, and almost single-handedly ensured that the only two bombs to reach the surface of Tenupe were destroyed before they could deploy their deadly payloads.

Kazdan Paratus

**Paratus, Kazdan** As a young Padawan, Kazdan Paratus displayed an uncanny aptitude for technology, as well as an aversion to the rigorous physical training required to become a Jedi Knight. During Order 66, the Aleenan fled Coruscant and exiled himself to the remote junkyard planet of Raxus Prime, where his devotion to the Jedi Order manifested in his obsessive desire to rebuild it—out of the scraps of metal and other junk surrounding him. He even constructed a version of the Jedi Temple, complete with replicas of the Jedi Council members.

**Parcelus Minor** The natives of this planet spent most of their lives beating back the jungle, which was filled with plants that exuded a combustible resin called tzeotine. During the

Attack on Parcelus Minor

Clone Wars, it was a Confederacy planet; it attempted to rejoin the Galactic Republic, whose forces arrived just before a massive Separatist reinforcement. As a result, the troops on the ground and in orbit were trapped. The Confederacy set the surface of the planet ablaze, decimating clone and droid armies alike. Count Dooku made Parcelus Minor an example to other planets that were thinking of rejoining the Republic.

**Parck, Voss** An Imperial naval officer who came from a long and proud lineage of capital ship captains. Born into a prominent and wealthy family on Corulag, he attended the Corulag Academy with his many siblings and cousins. He eventually gained command of his own ship, the *Victory*-class Star Destroyer *Strikefast.* As a captain, he found the exiled Thrawn living on a deserted planet at the edge of Unknown Space. Parck brought the Chiss to the Emperor, and subsequently joined him in his supposed exile from the Empire patrolling the Unknown Regions. Sixteen years after the Battle of Endor, Parck was in command of the Hand of Thrawn, a secret Imperial base beyond the Outer Rim. He was waiting for Thrawn's promised return, safeguarding a wealth of resources located throughout the Unknown Regions and a storehouse of information.

**Pardon, Mais** A Kajain'sa'Nikto known to frequent the Outlander Club in Coruscant's entertainment district.

**Parein II** A world with an uninhabited fourth moon, the site of a battle during the Clone Wars.

**Parella the Hunter** An athletic Hutt big-game hunter and crime lord, Parella Jiramma Baco owned a full suit of ancient Hutt battle armor.

**Paret, Jian** The commander of the Imperial garrison at N'zoth, he was brutally murdered by Yevethan strongman Nil Spaar.

**Parfadi** A region of space, it contained the unnavigable Black Nebula and separated the planets Arat Fraca and Motexx.

**parfue gnats** Tiny parasitic insects, they lived on watumba bats. Parfue gnats were a delicacy for many Glottalphibs.

**P'arghat, Lieutenant** An Imperial officer tasked with indoctrinating the natives of Kuan and Bordal who were conscripted into the Imperial armed forces when the Empire subjugated the Taroon system.

**Pargo** A human native from the planet Kuan who had grown up during the decades-long civil war between his homeworld and Bordal. Pargo was friends with Maarek Stele, and both were captured by Imperial forces when the Empire subjugated the two worlds, bringing an end to the civil war. When last Maarek saw Pargo, he was joining the stormtrooper service.

**Parja** Rav Bralor's niece, she worked as a mechanic on Mandalore during the Clone Wars. When Kal Skirata moved into his residence in Kyrimorut, Parja stopped by to see if she could help with the recovery of the clone commando known as Fi.

**Parjai Squad** A unit within the 2nd Airborne Company of the Grand Army of the Republic. Named for a Mandalorian word meaning "victory," the squad specialized in high-altitude jumps into enemy territory. Parjai was part of the assault on Utapau during Jedi General Obi-Wan Kenobi's hunt for General Grievous.

**Parking Conservation Fund (PCF)** A not-for-profit group that struggled to ensure there would remain adequate parking spaces on Coruscant for future generations.

**Parlan, Captain** The commanding officer of the Imperial Star Destroyer *Relentless* shortly after the Battle of Yavin. He was in charge of the vessel when it engaged pirates in the Dalchon system. Although the ship sustained damage to its hyperdrives, the Imperials managed to net several pirates. One of these, a man named Quist, revealed to Parlan that famed Republic tactician Adar Tallon was still alive. At the command of the Emperor and Darth Vader, Parlan ordered a bounty on Tallon, estimated at over 50 million credits. Parlan planned on trapping Tallon on Tatooine and ordered his ship there. Little did Parlan know that a team of trained Rebel agents had managed to reach Tallon first and escape with the wanted hero. For his failure, Parlan was summarily executed by Darth Vader, and then replaced by Captain Westen.

**Parmel system** After the Battle of Hoth, this system was the site of the traitorous Imperial Admiral Harkov's capture. He was brought before Darth Vader for questioning and execution. Later, renegade Admiral Zaarin returned to a deep-space research-and-development facility in the Parmel system to seize its TIE defender prototypes. Loyal Imperial forces captured the facility but were forced to evacuate with the prototype TIEs when Zaarin tried to destroy the space platform. This system was located in the Parmel sector of the Outer Rim Territories.

**Parmic system** The site of a research facility operated by renegade Imperial Admiral Zaarin. In the Parmic system, Zaarin equipped his TIE squadrons with a new beam weapon following the Battle of Hoth. This system was located in the Parmic sector of the Outer Rim Territories.

*Parjai Squad trooper*

**Parnet, General** An Imperial officer serving beneath High Inquisitor Tremayne aboard the Star Destroyer *Interrogator.* Like most of the other officers on the ship, Parnet believed High Inquisitor Tremayne was truly evil. Despite his normally outspoken nature, Parnet never disobeyed Tremayne.

***Par Ontham's Guide to Etiquette*** One of the most published and revised books on the subject of social etiquette produced in the galaxy. It continued to be updated throughout the early years of the New Republic.

**Parq, Colonel** An Imperial officer on Tatooine, he captured the Mistryl Shadow Guards Shada and Karoly after mistaking them for the notorious Tonnika sisters. Colonel Parq planned to turn the guards over to Grand Moff Argon, but they escaped.

**Parrlay** This city on Naboo was one of the first targets of the Trade Federation invasion because it contained a communications array.

**Parrot** One of Ranulf Trommer's wingmates assigned to the *Ravagor,* Parrot was killed in action over Aguarl 3.

**Parry, Bril** The New Republic flight communications duty officer on the *Naritus* when the star Thanta Zilbra was detonated. He was later named chief duty officer under Captain Genkal during the evacuation of the system. Following the resolution of the Human League crisis and the breakup of the Starbuster Plot, Parry was tapped to succeed Genkal as captain of the *Naritus.*

**parsec** A unit used in measuring interstellar space. Han Solo claimed that the *Millennium Falcon* made the Kessel Run in less than 12 parsecs.

**Parshoone** This Imperial Remnant planet was the location of a Ubiqtorate station.

**Par'tah** A Ho'Din, she ran a Borderland Regions smuggling operation from a hidden base on a hot jungle planet off major space lanes during the New Republic. Although this was only a marginal operation for Par'tah, she put on airs of wealth and success. She collected technological items, often rummaging through a client's cargo for new additions before completing a delivery. She had a good relationship with smuggler Talon Karrde, who sometimes directed her to new pieces for her collection. While she preferred to deal with the New Republic, she often needed the large payoffs that Imperial sources offered.

**particle shielding** A defensive force field, it repelled any form of matter. Particle shielding was usually used together with ray

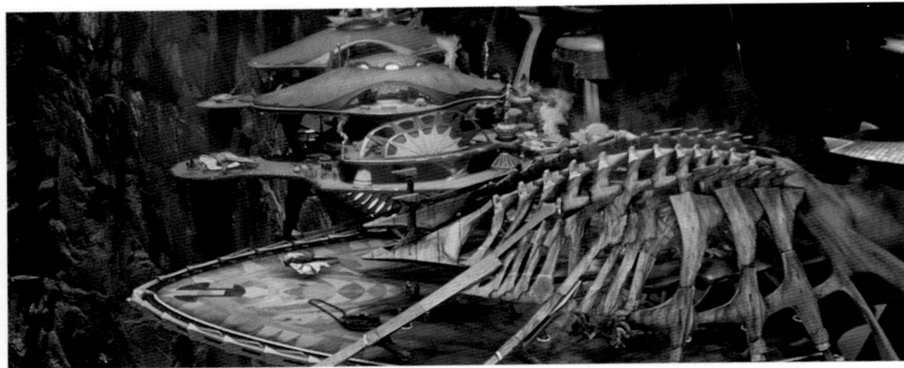
Pau City

shielding for full protection of starships and planetary installations.

**particle vapor trail** A signature that most ships left behind. If detected, it could help in tracking the craft.

**Partu, Cedo** A pioneer and early settler of Mos Eisley, he established the blockhouse fortification that would, generations later, become the Mos Eisley cantina. The Prophetess once claimed that Wuher, the surly bartender of the cantina, was the reincarnated soul of Partu.

**Pashvi** An alien species native to a remote world on the edge of Wild Space. The Pashvi homeworld was distinguished by rocky pillars scattered across the landscape. The tops of these pillars allowed certain plants to obtain more sunlight, and they were among the most nutritious produce consumed by the Pashvi. However, the tops of the pillars were also the home of a species of predatory avian creature. This led the Pashvi to develop a distanced emotional state among themselves and other things of value, as they were both drawn to and afraid of their primary source of food. The trait could be discerned in their artwork.

**Pasiq, Lanu** An agent of Inquisitor Tremayne during the early years of the Empire. She was briefly seduced by Prince Xizor, when Xizor first tried to meet Tremayne and exchange information on the Jedi fugitives Drake Lo'gaan, Ekria, and Zonder for information on Darth Vader.

***Paskla*-class starship** A variety of Chiss starship, it resembled a slightly squashed sphere, light-colored but with a close-order pattern of dark spots covering the hull that could have been viewports, or even just decoration.

**Pasmin** A planet known for its lightweight, warm wool.

**Paspro** A type of encryption sequence used by smugglers of the New Republic. Varieties included Paspro-5 and Paspro-9.

**passenger liner** The basic mode of transport used by most galactic travelers, these spaceliners ranged in size from small ships to giant interstellar luxury liners complete with multiple entertainment decks.

**Passik, Dia** Born Diap'assik, this green-skinned Twi'lek slave was underestimated by her owner, who taught her piloting skills. She escaped slavery and became a starfighter pilot for the New Republic. When joining Wraith Squadron, she brought not only her capable flying skills but also important information on the activities of smugglers and pirates. As Wraith Four, she flew as Wes Janson's wingmate. When the Wraiths were assigned to the *Mon Remonda* in support of the hunt for Warlord Zsinj, she rejected the offer of friendship from Nawara Ven since she hated everything to do with the planet Ryloth, including those members of the Twi'lek species who managed to avoid slavery.

Dia Passik

Passik was instrumental in Wraith Squadron's undercover operation as the Hawk-bat Independent Space Force. She portrayed Captain Seku and in this guise was forced to execute fellow Wraith Castin Donn, who had stowed away on their mission. Though she realized that Castin was already near death, the action of shooting her squadron mate left her with intense psychological scars. She eventually recovered and participated in several Hawk-bat raids. For a time, she was involved in a romantic relationship with Garik "Face" Loran.

**Pastil** The site of a tracking station inspected by Clone Commander Cody and Captain Rex during the Clone Wars.

**Pastoral Collective** A group of environmentalists dedicated to preserving the beauty of Naboo's Lake Country.

**Patameene District** One of the larger subdivisions of the capital city of Barlok. The boundaries of the Patameene District were laid out such that it meandered through some of the richest as well as the poorest sections of the city, creating a unique dynamic among its population.

**Pathfinders** A branch of the Rebel Alliance Special Forces that specialized in the scouting and reconnaissance of unknown terrain.

**Pa Tho** A vanished alien culture. The Pa Tho created the unusual transportation system later known as the Great Subcrustal Tubeway.

**Patrick, Faye** A Zabrak female wanted by CorSec for questioning in connection with a string of disappearances of numerous Corellian citizens. She was a master of teräs käsi.

***Patriot Fist*** A Commerce Guild support destroyer at the Battle of Coruscant. It was built by the Separatist junta of the remote aquatic world of Minntooine, aided by radical Quarren allies.

**patrol droid** *See* Imperial Mark IV sentry droid.

**Pau'an** *See* Utapaun.

**Pau City** The capital of Utapau, Pau City lined the interior of the Pau Sinkhole. Its upper levels were buffeted by extremely strong winds, which were turned into power by a network of massive windmills. A total of 11 levels filled the sinkhole; the Tenth Level served as a secret headquarters of the Confederacy of Independent Systems during the final stages of the Clone Wars.

**Paulsen, Drake** A young smuggler native to the planet Socorro, he began working with his father, Kaine, at the age of five. No less than Jabba the Hutt was impressed by the young smuggler's mettle, dubbing him "the Little Prince of Socorro." When Kaine was killed on Socorro shortly after the Battle of Yavin, Drake took control of his father's businesses and expanded them rapidly. Drake also hunted down and killed his father's murderer, a Twi'lek member of the Black Bha'lir known as Izzat. This earned Drake a bounty on his head. He was forced to lay low in Jabba the Hutt's court for a year before emerging as a free man. He later retired to Redcap with a fellow smuggler and longtime friend of the family, Toob Ancher.

**Pavan, Jax** The son of Lorn and Siena Pavan. After Siena left Lorn, Lorn took his son to the Jedi Temple, where he tested positive for Force sensitivity and Jedi potential. Since attachment was forbidden in the Order, the Jedi decided to release Lorn Pavan from his employment at the Temple. This embittered Lorn toward the Jedi, though he would eventually grow to forgive them and take pride in his son's involvement in the Order.

**Pavan, Lorn** An information broker who lived in the lower levels of Coruscant. Lorn Pavan was a tall, handsome, and muscular Corellian with black hair and brown eyes. Five years before the Battle of Naboo, he was fired from his job as a business affairs clerk at the Jedi Temple after his son Jax was chosen to be trained as a Jedi. His wife had already left him by that time, and since attachment was forbidden in the Jedi Order, Lorn was restricted from seeing his son. He grew extremely resentful of the Jedi.

Just before the blockade of Naboo, Lorn and his droid I-5YQ met with a Toydarian named Zippa about purchasing a stolen Jedi Holocron. The deal fell through, but Lorn believed that his luck had finally changed when the Neimoidian Hath Monchar agreed to sell him valuable information about the impending Trade Federation blockade. Monchar was hunted down by Darth Maul, and since Lorn managed to recover Monchar's holocron, he, too, became targeted by the Sith.

*Pazaak*

Lorn was joined in his struggle by the failed Jedi Padawan Darsha Assant. Along with I-5YQ, they attempted to outrun and escape Maul. Lorn grew to appreciate Darsha and was overcoming his hatred of the Jedi just as she was killed in battle with Darth Maul, providing Lorn and I-5YQ with a chance to escape. Lorn turned to the first person he recognized for help. To Lorn's dismay, this turned out to be Senator Palpatine from Naboo, who realized that Maul had not completely finished his quest for his alter ego, Darth Sidious. Palpatine turned Lorn over to Maul, who executed the human with a killing swipe of his lightsaber.

**Pavillion** A vast underwater city on the planet Iskalon. Consisting of a surface landing platform connected by a series of pressurized lifts to a city on the ocean floor, Pavillion was contained within a large air tank. Along the passageways that looked out into the ocean, a series of terminals allowed communication with the Iskalonians swimming outside. Pavillion was destroyed when the Empire triggered the Iskalon Effect, killing hundreds.

**Pavo Prime** The spa and casino world where Han and Leia Solo traveled for their honeymoon. Pavo Prime was located near Tatooine.

**Paws** An alias used by the Padawan fugitive Zonder during the early Galactic Empire.

**Payback** The name by which the bounty hunter Dengar was commonly known throughout the galactic underworld.

**pazaak** An ancient card game played on planets such as Taris, Dantooine, Tatooine, and elsewhere. The object of the game was to get one's hand as close to 20 as possible without going over.

**Pazda the Hutt** The uncle of Jabba, Pazda was an aged Hutt sporting a wispy gray beard. He warned Borga about dealing with the Yuuzhan Vong.

**Pazz, Borth** A distraught Lorrdian who threatened to jump to his death if he wasn't allowed entrance to Jedi Master Luke Skywalker's training facilities, about 10 years after the end of the Yuuzhan Vong War. Pazz, wearing homemade Jedi robes and carrying an old-style lightsaber that he had stolen from a museum, demanded to be trained as a Jedi Knight, despite the fact that he had no sensitivity to the Force. Jacen Solo, who was on Lorrd to investigate the death of Siron Tawaler, agreed to talk to Pazz. However, Pazz refused to believe Jacen's words and demanded to be shown one "Jedi mind trick" or else he would jump. When Jacen refused, Pazz followed through on his threat and jumped. Pazz was saved by Nelani Dinn and Ben Skywalker, who used the Force to break his fall. Pazz, who suffered a broken ankle, was taken into custody and given medical and psychiatric treatment.

**PCBU (police cruiser backup unit)** A droid vehicle developed for use in the more treacherous portions of Coruscant, like the Crimson Corridor. The police cruiser backup unit carried two state-of-the-art swivel laser cannons mounted on the top and bottom, as well as a variety of sensors, scanners, and disruptors.

**PD-28** A tripodal droid stolen from his true masters by the Empire, he came into the employ of the evil Dr. Raygar, who mistreated the automaton at every opportunity. It was PD-28 who helped the young Ewoks Wicket, Teebo, Latara, and Kneesaa thwart Raygar's plot to steal the Sunstar.

**PDA-2** A commander battle droid that participated in the Battle of Naboo. During the Great Plains Battle, PDA-2's unit was responsible for guarding Theed until the fighting was over.

**PDA6** A PD Lurrian protocol droid aboard Master Zorneth's herd ship. After Smiley and R2-D2 were abducted by Dictator-Forever Craw, PDA6 and C-3PO embarked on a mission to bring down the force field protecting Craw's fortress. Revoltists forced Craw to flee from Targonn, but Craw's crew was able to board Zorneth's herd ship. To prevent Craw from obtaining the ship's savorium, PDA6 took the initiative and decided to destroy the entire supply of the rapture-producing herb.

**PD Lurrian protocol droid** A series of protocol droids designed for the Lurrian market by Cybot Galactica.

**PDT-8** A Personnel Deployment Transport utility speeder used to ferry personnel from one part of a base or installation to another. This unarmed mini rig carried two people and was usually automated. Twin thrusters propelled the tiny repulsorlift craft, and a tripod mount kept it stabilized on the ground.

**PDV** *See* Plexus droid vessel.

**Peace Brigade** A group of collaborative dissidents formed by Nom Anor during the early stages of the Yuuzhan Vong War. The Peace Brigade maintained that the Jedi Knights and the New Republic were doing more harm than good in fighting against the Yuuzhan Vong and advocated the end of hostilities. The Peace Brigade openly denounced the Jedi Knights, claiming it was their lack of compassion that had destroyed Ithor and Obroa-skai. The group provided to the Yuuzhan Vong information on planetary defenses, which they had gained from a source that had somehow infiltrated the highest levels of New Republic security.

The Peace Brigade tried to broker a cease-fire with the Yuuzhan Vong by agreeing to turn over the Jedi Knights to the aliens. Brigadiers undertook missions to locate Jedi Knights, and even tried to capture some beings that were merely Force-sensitive, in an effort to appease the invaders. As the war dragged on, the Peace Brigade established a form of government on Ylesia and attempted to create a naval fleet to augment that of their Yuuzhan Vong superiors. Supreme Overlord Shimrra appointed Thrackan Sal-Solo the President of Ylesia and the Commander in Chief of the Peace Brigade.

***Peacebringer*** A warship under the command of Admiral Ratobo, it served as the flagship of the Galactic Alliance's Fourth Fleet during the war against the Confederation. The *Peacebringer* came under heavy fire from Huttese warships and was destroyed with the loss of all hands.

**Peacebringer, Aron** A heroic and legendary Calian from the planet Shiva IV. Since the age of 12, Aron lived an adventure-filled life of combat and wars, as was the way of his war-like people. But Peacebringer grew weary of the bloodshed and violence between his

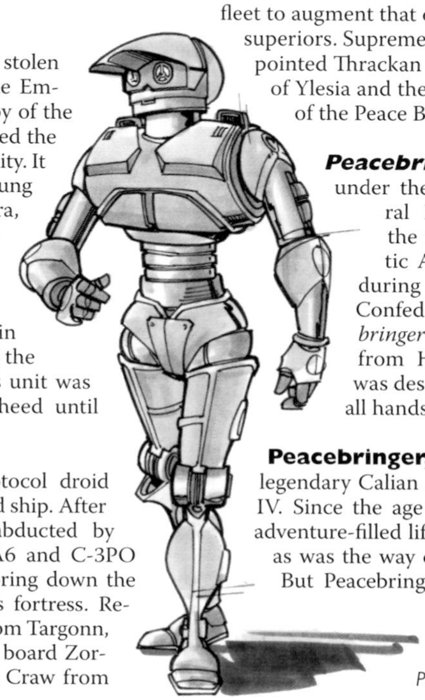

*PD Lurrian protocol droid*

people, the Calians, and the Twelve Tribes of the T'Syriél—and he saw an alternative. When he ascended the political ladder of the Calian Confederacy and was named Warlord, Peacebringer approached the T'Syriél Demarch, Kéral Longknife, with a Concordat of Peace. The two signed, bringing a newfound peace to the world.

A year later, the Empire expressed interest in the powerful warriors of the Calian Confederacy. Imperial agents, led by General Sk'ar, planned to subjugate Shiva IV and force its warrior populace into Imperial military service. Rebel agent Princess Leia Organa crash-landed on Shiva IV while investigating the increased Imperial presence in the area. Stranded, Leia soon met Aron Peacebringer. Despite being married and having a number of children with his own beautiful wife, Alisande, Aron fell in love with Leia. Though Leia was strongly attracted to Aron, she carefully tried to keep her feelings in check. When Sk'ar led the attack on the Calian city of Illÿriaqum, Organa and Peacebringer defeated the Imperials.

Peerce

Aron Peacebringer was a Calian human male with the characteristic tanned red skin of his people. He had black hair, dark eyes, and a very muscular build. He was a superb fighter who lapsed into the deadly Calian battle madness when provoked.

**Peace City** Ylesia's Colony One settlement, renamed after the Peace Brigade took control of the planet and moved their "capital" to the city. Much of Peace City was given over to slave camps.

Aron Peacebringer (right)

***Peacekeeper*** A Dreadnaught commanded by Captain Reldo Dovlis, it was destroyed during the Battle of Nar Shaddaa.

**Peacekeepers** The volunteer police force among the community of survivors of the Outbound Flight Project. Some 18 years after the Battle of Endor, only 11 Peacekeepers remained active, including Jorad Pressor. Of those, 4 were killed and 2 injured when Bearsh and his Vagaari infiltrators attacked the starship crash site. The survivors held their own against the invaders, assisted by Luke and Mara Skywalker, Chak Fel, the 501st Legion, Dean Jinzler, and the Chiss.

***Peacemaker*** A New Republic Nebulon-B frigate that was part of the force sent to liberate the planet Ciutric from the control of Prince-Admiral Krennel. It supported the flagship *Emancipator,* along with the *Pride of Eiattu* and the *Thunderchild.* It took heavy amounts of damage in the battle and was left for dead.

**Peckhum** A supply courier and message runner, he used the battered supply ship *Lightning Rod.*

**Pedducis Chorios** Located in the Chorios systems in the Meridian sector, this planet was a hotbed of smuggling and piracy ruled by ruthless pirate warlords who made alliances with the local chieftains. After the loss of the *Knight Hammer* at Yavin 4, Imperial Admiral Daala became president of an independent group of 3,000 settlers who wanted to settle on Pedducis Chorios and escape the petty struggles of the Empire. Daala made an alliance with Warlord K'iin of the Silver Unifir to take the smallest of Pedducis Chorios's three southern continents, comprising 1.5 billion acres, and colonize it as they saw fit.

**Peel, Gorvan** A starfighter pilot in the Corellian Defense Force. Peel was designated as Nebula Eleven, serving as part of Nebula Flight during Operation Noble Savage some 10 years after the Yuuzhan Vong War. His fighter was shot down, but Peel managed to eject safely and was later rescued.

**Peerce** A Skrilling Jedi Master with exceptional tracking skills. Aurra Sing killed Peerce and the Anx Jedi J'Mikel during her infiltration of the Jedi Temple.

***Peerless*** An *Imperial*-class Star Destroyer that survived the Battle of Bastion. It later provided escort to the *Defiant* after that ship was equipped with a gravitic amplitude modulator to jam the communications of a Yuuzhan Vong yammosk.

**peggat** A form of hard currency used in Mos Espa on Tatooine. One peggat was equivalent to four truguts, 64 wupiupi, or 40 dataries (Republic credits).

**Peg Shar I** An industrial world represented in the Senate of the Galactic Republic.

**Pek** This male Sedrian priest gained limited Force-like powers through his contact with Golden Sun. He supported the Rebel Alliance.

**peko-peko** A flying animal inhabiting the swamps of Naboo. A graceful creature, the peko-peko possessed a powerful jaw and claws on its wings. Although it had difficulty walking along the ground, it moved through the air and trees with ease. The bird ate toxic jute nuts, as well as small amphibians and other prey. Gungans discovered that the peko-peko's blood contained a natural antivenom that could be used in medicines. Peko-pekos were skilled mimics and favorite pets of both Gungans and the Naboo.

Peko-peko

**Pekt** A Trandoshan slaver and bounty hunter noted for his vehement hatred of Wookiees, he was recruited by the Empire to bring free Wookiees under control. When the Empire fully subjugated Kashyyyk, Pekt was called in to lead the effort to enslave the Wookiees and ensure a steady stream of labor for the construction of the first Death Star.

**pekz** A green-winged flying creature on Ansion that pestered Bulgan after Barriss Offee escaped her kidnapping at Cuipernam.

***Pelagia*** A New Republic troopship under the command of Captain Tekba. Ten years

Pelagia

after the Battle of Yavin, the *Pelagia* was rendezvousing with an X-wing group based in the Ottega system when it and its 100,000 ground troops were wiped out by the cloned Emperor's Galaxy Gun.

**Pelek Baw** The capital city of Haruun Kal, located atop the Korunnai Highland. During the Clone Wars, the Balawai leadership of Pelek Baw sided with the Separatists.

***pelekotan*** The Korunnai word used to describe the Force. It translates roughly into "world-power."

**Pelgrin** An Outer Rim world whose native species died out long ago. It was the site of a device known as the Oracle of Pelgrin, an 88-meter-tall structure used by the Jedi to discern the future and to guide them in the Force.

**pelko bug** An insect that lived in the Valley of the Dark Lords on Korriban, it had a defensive row of poisoned spines along the dorsal ridge of its carapace. These spines exuded a potent venom that caused living flesh to burn upon contact. The burning was so intense that it blistered the skin in moments. The poison then created temporary paralysis in the muscles, rendering them useless. This allowed the pelko bug to incapacitate prey larger than itself. Like several other species native to Korriban, pelko bugs were attuned to the Force and used it to sense the presence of nearby prey.

**Pell, Akanah Norand** A member of the Fallanassi religious order—followers of the Force-like White Current—she convinced Luke Skywalker to travel with her to track down her people by telling him that his mother was a woman named Nashira, another Fallanassi. Akanah was of the circle at Ialtra on the planet Lucazec and was raised on Carratos by her mother, Isela Talsava Norand; her father was Joreb Goss. She was the widow of Andras Pell. Akanah had been traumatized in her youth when her people had been forced to flee Imperial persecution on their planet. She appealed to Skywalker to help fill the emptiness created in both their lives by not having a mother. Luke and Akanah traveled to many planets, including Teyr and Atzerri, in search of the Fallanassi people. They found her father, Joreb Goss, but he had no memory of her or his past life. All the while, Akanah and Luke engaged in a back-and-forth game of trust and distrust. In the end, it became clear Akanah had been lying all along. Her own mother had double-crossed the Fallanassi and had reported them to the Empire. Nashira was a kind woman who had helped Akanah and was someone who would have made a fine mother—but she was neither Luke's nor Akanah's mother.

**Pell, Andras** Akanah Norand Pell's late husband, he was 36 years her senior. When he died, he left her his ship, the *Mud Sloth.*

*Akanah Norand Pell*

**Pellaeon, Gilad** When the Empire splintered after the death of Emperor Palpatine, boundless avarice among the competing warlords hastened the decay of the New Order. Infighting fragmented the once-powerful regime, allowing the New Republic to take control of its dwindling territories. Gilad Pellaeon, a veteran Imperial fleet officer with over five decades of experience, stood as a rare example of integrity during those chaotic times.

As a young man, Pellaeon lied about his age to gain admittance into Raithal Academy, one of the most prestigious military learning centers in the galaxy. Graduating as an ensign, Pellaeon served with distinction, earning commendations for outwitting pirates over the planet Gavryn.

By the time of the Empire, Pellaeon was transferred to the Star Destroyer *Chimaera,* where he worked his way up the command chain, eventually serving as second in command. The *Chimaera* was part of the Imperial fleet amassed at the Battle of Endor. When a concentrated assault by Rebel forces killed the ship's captain, Pellaeon seized command of the vessel as the Imperial fleet was routed. All through the battle, Imperial officers were committing tactical blunders, choosing to go out in a blaze of glory rather than call for a prudent retreat. It was Pellaeon who issued the final order to withdraw, commanding the remnants of the fleet to regroup at Annaj.

A dedicated officer, Pellaeon was not fueled by ambition or dreams of power. He was a soldier, not a politician, now serving an Empire without an Emperor. He struggled to maintain order, but many warship commanders refused to follow his leadership. The Empire splintered into scattered fiefdoms ruled by power-hungry warlords, with Pellaeon's small fleet retreating from the growing New Republic territories.

It was a far cry from the remembered glories of the Empire. With the prestigious Academies of the Core now under the control of the New Republic, the Imperial territories had to rely on conscription to fill out their ranks. Pellaeon's bridge was a shameful assembly of untrained novices bristling under his stern command.

Five years after the Battle of Endor, the Empire was a quarter of its former size. It had been pushed far from the Core Worlds. It was during this bleak time that Pellaeon received a surprising communiqué from Thrawn, the last surviving Imperial Grand Admiral. The mastermind tactician chose Pellaeon's Star Destroyer to be his flagship during his campaign to retake the Core.

Pellaeon served loyally at Thrawn's side as his trusted confidant. The captain overcame his initial reservations over serving an alien superior since Thrawn proved his worth time and again by crafting intricate strategies that repeatedly confounded the New Republic. Under Thrawn's leadership, the Empire struck back and reclaimed much of its lost territory. Thrawn's undoing, however, was trusting his Noghri underlings. When Thrawn was killed by a treacherous bodyguard, the Imperial momentum sputtered. It was like Endor all over again: Pellaeon taking command of the leaderless task force, trying to rein in the chaos after the death of a mastermind.

Once again, opportunistic Imperial warlords pounced. Rallied by Thrawn's impressive push to the Core, they attacked Coruscant. They lacked the refinement of Thrawn's tactical mind, and rather than take the capital intact, they destroyed much of it. The Empire again fragmented, and a wasteful Imperial Civil War broke out. It was then that a cloned Emperor Palpatine returned to take control of the Empire, and Pellaeon continued to serve loyally, despite crushing losses.

The New Republic defeated the Emperor's clone, and the remaining warships retreated to the Deep Core of the galaxy. There High Admiral Teradoc created yet another fiefdom with a mighty fleet at his disposal, commanded by the newly promoted Vice Admiral Pellaeon.

*Gilad Pellaeon*

Admiral Natasi Daala was next in the lengthy series of Imperial successors. She gathered together the 13 ruling Imperial warlords at a conference and executed them in cold blood. Daala appointed Pellaeon as her second in command, and then ordered an ill-planned attack on Luke Skywalker's Jedi academy. Pellaeon led the fleet of Victory Star Destroyers that pressed the assault, but the entire fleet was scattered by an incredibly powerful display of the Force. Daala was defeated, and Pellaeon stepped in to fill the power vacuum.

As Supreme Commander of the remaining Imperial forces, Pellaeon gathered his assets from the Deep Core and expanded the Imperial presence in the Mid Rim. But it was clear that continued hostilities with the New Republic would only bring about the demise of the Empire. Fifteen years after the Battle of Endor, Pellaeon convinced the eight remaining Moffs that the only way to survive was to reach a peace accord with the New Republic.

During these tenuous times, a last-ditch effort by Imperial loyalists employed an imposter as Grand Admiral Thrawn. With the aid of intelligence gathered by smuggler baron Talon Karrde, Pellaeon was able to expose the deception. He signed the historic armistice between the Imperial and New Republic forces, finally bringing the Galactic Civil War to an end.

While the Imperial Remnant maintained many of the trappings of Palpatine's regime—a strong military and limited venues of public expression—it was far more progressive and devoid of the rampant injustices found during the height of the Empire's power. Slavery was abolished, as were the extremes of anti-alien sentiment. The Imperial Remnant unobtrusively continued adhering to the strict tenets of the New Order, growing increasingly irrelevant to galactic affairs.

During the Yuuzhan Vong War, Pellaeon recognized the threat the aliens posed, even though their incursion had skirted past Imperial space. Despite some protests from the Moff Council, Pellaeon committed his forces to a joint Imperial–New Republic offensive at the Battles of Garqi and Ithor. Despite the best efforts of Pellaeon and New Republic Admiral Traest Kre'fey, the Yuuzhan Vong destroyed the ecology of Ithor. Shocked by the power of the attack, the Imperial Remnant recalled its forces and chose to sit out the invasion on the sidelines.

It was a move the Moff Council would come to regret. The Moffs falsely believed the Imperial Remnant safe from attack since it had been ignored for much of the invasion. The Yuuzhan Vong proved that assumption wrong when they brutally attacked the Imperial worlds. Pellaeon was critically wounded in the attack, but the sudden arrival of a Jedi mission exploring the Unknown Regions saved his life. Jedi healers stabilized Pellaeon's condition, and Luke Skywalker and Jacen Solo helped Pellaeon expose infiltrators in the Imperial ranks and refocus Imperial efforts to assist the newly founded Galactic Alliance.

Fully healed, Pellaeon once again took command of the Imperial Navy and threatened to secede from the Empire if the Moffs didn't accept Jacen Solo's offer to join the Galactic Alliance. Once the Moffs agreed to an alliance, Pellaeon took the Imperial fleet and began to harass the retreating Yuuzhan Vong forces, hoping to defend the Imperial Remnant by joining the war effort. As the battle neared its conclusion, Pellaeon was appointed the commander of the Galactic Alliance's Fourth Fleet and was instrumental in the final battle against the Yuuzhan Vong near Coruscant.

In the wake of the Yuuzhan Vong surrender, following the death of Admiral Sien Sovv, Pellaeon agreed to serve as the Supreme Commander of the Galactic Alliance's military until a permanent replacement could be named. Thus, he was in command of the naval forces when the Swarm War came to a head and remained in the position for many years as the Imperial Remnant became more and more integrated into the Galactic Alliance. With the rising call for independence in the Corellian system, Pellaeon found himself in an unusual position. He was chosen as a peer to the Five World Prime Minister, Aidel Saxan, during a series of negotiations between the Galactic Alliance and the leaders of the Corellian system.

The negotiations were held at Toryaz Station, near Kuat and were meant to allow both sides a chance to argue their positions and come to agreement on Corellia's standing in the GA. However, the negotiations had barely begun when Prime Minister Saxan was assassinated. Pellaeon himself escaped, but only because the killers murdered his double instead. As the relationship between Corellia and the Galactic Alliance deteriorated, Pellaeon found himself fighting against the government's desire to bring war to Corellia to prevent the system's secession. When Chief of State Cal Omas made an executive decision to form the Galactic Alliance Guard, without the advice or support of the Senate, Pellaeon could no longer stand for the Alliance's posturing. He resigned his commission as Supreme Commander, leaving the role to one of his senior aides, Admiral Cha Niathal.

Pellaeon retired to an estate on the planet Bastion, where he hoped to avoid politics as much as possible. In his 90s, Pellaeon was still considered a valuable resource by the Moff Council, which often refused to act until he had provided input. Thus, Pellaeon was not surprised when an emissary from the Galactic Alliance arrived at his estate with a request from Jacen Solo that the Imperial Remnant rejoin the Alliance. Pellaeon had come to despise Jacen Solo, and sent the emissary home without acknowledgment. He then waited for Solo to make contact with the Moff Council, to see how badly he wanted the Imperials to be working with the Alliance.

Ultimately, Solo's offer proved to be sufficient for Pellaeon and the Moffs to agree to the deal, and Pellaeon took the Star Destroyer *Bloodfin* and a small fleet to Fondor. Pellaeon wasn't about to take any chances, however, with either Solo or the Moff Council, so he called in a favor from Admiral Daala, who agreed to watch his back during the fighting. He was forced to allow Solo's apprentice, Tahiri Veila, to stand with him on the bridge. The role of the Imperial forces in the Second Battle of Fondor was to support the mission of the Galactic Alliance forces, and Pellaeon had to join the battle when the Fondorians tried to catch Solo in a trap.

Pellaeon-*class Star Destroyer*

*Pellaeon-Gavrisom Treaty*

Solo's command grew increasingly brutal during this campaign, and when he initiated his own mission to bombard Fondor's cities into rubble, Admiral Cha Niathal tried to relieve him of his command. Solo refused, and Pellaeon ordered the Imperial forces to break off their attacks on Fondor and stand down. Solo pressed the attack, forcing Pellaeon to order his ships to defend Fondor. This caused a division in the ranks of the Moff Council and prompted Veila to confront Pellaeon about his actions. When Pellaeon refused to follow Jacen Solo's orders, and ordered the rest of the Imperial fleet to acknowledge commands only from Niathal, Veila shot him in the chest, killing him almost instantly. As he died, Pellaeon opened his comlink to Admiral Daala, speaking the names of the members of the Moff Council who had stood by and did nothing as he died. In the wake of the fighting, Vitor Reige recovered Pellaeon's body and, with the help of Admiral Daala, made arrangements for him to be buried on his homeworld of Corellia.

***Pellaeon*-class Star Destroyer** An enormous warship design produced by the new Empire that emerged long after the defeat of the Yuuzhan Vong. These sleek vessels became the heart of the new Imperial fleet.

**Pellaeon-Gavrisom Treaty** The historic peace accord between the Empire and New Republic, signed by Grand Admiral Pellaeon and acting Chief of State Ponc Gavrisom.

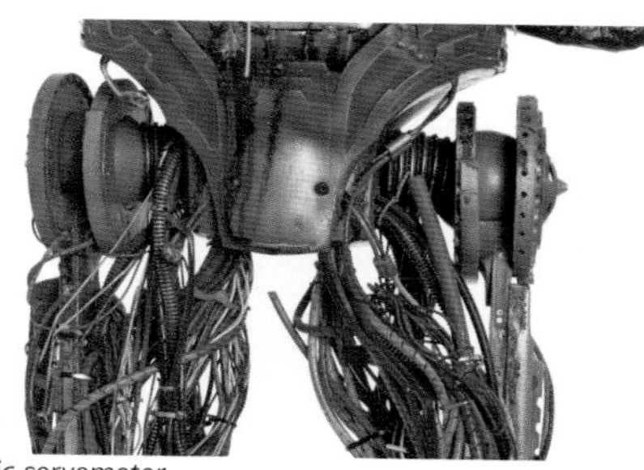
Pelvic servomotor

**pelvic servomotor** A small motor that gave two-legged droids the ability to walk.

**Pemblehov District** Located on the north side of the city of Talos on the planet Atzerri, this area was filled with all manner of businesses that catered to physical vices.

**Pembric II** A semi-independent, lawless trade world in the Kathol sector, it was surrounded by an asteroid field. It was originally settled as a colony world but had to be terraformed after a long history of meteorite bombardment.

**Pend, Hexler** A Naboo Royal Security officer stationed at Keren when it was attacked by Trade Federation forces.

**Pendarran Warriors** An independent group that fought alongside the Jedi Knights and clone troopers during the Clone Wars. When Emperor Palpatine rose to power and executed Order 66, he included the Pendarran Warriors as traitors to the Republic.

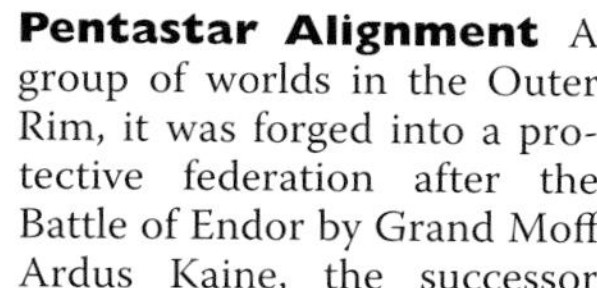
Rosh Penin

**Pendath** A city on Taanab.

**penetrator** A specialized form of shadow bomb developed by the fighter pilots of the new Jedi Order following the Yuuzhan Vong War. Penetrators were used extensively during the Swarm War to take out the nest ships of the Colony at long range. A penetrator was essentially three shadow bombs contained in a single warhead. Each shadow bomb had a shaped charge, and the entire unit was rigged such that the warheads detonated in sequence, rather than upon impact. In this way, the penetrator could cause three distinct explosions. This allowed it to punch through shielding and hull plating before detonating its final charge within the target vessel itself.

**Pengalan IV** The site of a battle during the early stages of the Clone Wars. The Republic believed that the Confederacy had created a munitions factory producing diamond boron missiles on Pengalan IV. A full platoon of clone troopers was sent out on the *Sea Legacy* to destroy the facility. However, the facility had already been relocated, and reports of it had been leaked to the Republic to lure forces into a trap.

**Penga Rift** An Obroan Institute research transport, it was the command vessel for the excavation at Maltha Obex.

**Penin, Rosh** A brash young human student at Luke Skywalker's Jedi praxeum on Yavin 4 who trained under Kyle Katarn alongside Jaden Korr. He disappeared during an investigation on Byss, and Jaden later found him at Bast Castle on Vjun. Penin had been lured to the dark side by Tavion Axmis and battled with Katarn and Korr. He was next seen on Taspir III, where he pleaded for mercy from Korr.

**Pent, Zegmon** The Corellian leader of the Flail terrorist group prior to the Battle of Naboo. He supposedly received training from the Jedi Temple to be a "Jedi assassin," although the lightsaber he brandished was an imitation and he was not known to be Force-sensitive. Pent believed that the Senate was corrupt and that Chancellor Finis Valorum was the root of the problem. He failed in an attempt to assassinate the Chancellor and was arrested.

**Pentastar Alignment** A group of worlds in the Outer Rim, it was forged into a protective federation after the Battle of Endor by Grand Moff Ardus Kaine, the successor to Grand Moff Tarkin. He saw the Empire's defeat as an opportunity to form a new Empire under his own rule. He called a meeting, dubbed the Pentastar Talks, aboard his Super Star Destroyer *Reaper* with Imperial officials and representatives from two large private corporations. The resulting Alignment encompassed hundreds of planets, including the Velcar Free Commerce Zone. The New Republic did little to oppose the Pentastar Alignment, but mercenary groups such as the Red Moons secretly worked to sabotage its operations.

People's Liberation Battalion

**People's Inquest** A grassroots Jedi watch group led by Thrynka Padaunete in the final years of the Galactic Republic. The Judicial Department refused the group's demands to reveal budgetary information on the Jedi Order. The popular movement gained support following the Jedi failure to prevent the Battle of Antar 4, with the accompanying drop in public image. With the outbreak of the Clone Wars, the People's Inquest took to the HoloNet, transmitting a pirate signal despite repeated cease-and-desist orders from the Republic HoloCommunication Commission.

**People's Liberation Battalion (PLB)** Composed of disenfranchised workers, intellectuals, and disaffected nobles, the PLB was a socialist-oriented group dedicated to bringing down all nobles and eliminating any vestiges of the Empire. The group promised to establish a governmental system in which everyone shared the wealth. They were led by Asran, who, although basically cruel, began to believe his own rhetoric.

**Peppel** A primitive world far from the Galactic Core. The Devaronian Labria was forced to flee there 13 years after the Battle of Endor, when four mercenaries on Tatooine recognized him as the Butcher of Montellian Serat. Two years later, Boba Fett discovered his hiding place. Bypassing the elaborate defenses surrounding Labria's hut, Fett captured his target and returned him to Devaron, where he was executed.

Peragus II

**Peragus II** When travelers spoke of Peragus, they were usually referring to the Peragus Mining Colony, a labyrinthine industrial facility hollowed out of an asteroid archipelago orbiting Peragus II. Millennia ago, before the Jedi Civil War, a mining accident detonated a portion of the planet's surface and ejected it into space. Considered part of Republic space, the gas-mining operations on Peragus II were originally established by a group of merchants and tradesmen who supplied Republic forces during the Great Sith War. After the surface facility was destroyed, it was rebuilt in the asteroids, and strict safety protocols remained in effect. Blasters and explosives were prohibited, as well as anything that might trigger an explosion. Five years after the Jedi Civil War, the Peragus Mining Colony was attacked by Darth Sion. Investigation by the Jedi Exile and HK-50 revealed the truth behind the attack. After the Exile and Kreia fled the colony, Darth Sion set out to find them. He destroyed the main Peragus II asteroid and the mining colony facility.

**Peralli** A Mon Calamari pirate who worked with Nym the Feeorin during the time of the Galactic Empire.

**Peramis, Senator Tig** A human from the planet Walalla, he was a New Republic Senator and member of the Senate Defense Council. Tig Peramis was also the newest member of the Council on the Common Defense. He distrusted Chief of State Leia Organa Solo and saw her military buildup against the Yevethan threat as "the machinery of oppression." He stole fellow council member Cundertol's voting key, logged into his personal logs, and found information about the deployment of the New Republic's Fifth Fleet to the Farlax sector, including the information that Leia's husband, Han Solo, would be in command. Convincing himself that he was an honorable man trying to contain militarism in the galactic government, he personally turned the top-secret information over to Yevethan strongman Nil Spaar.

**perator** The title used by the Adumari to describe the leader of an individual nation or city. Each perator had to prove her- or himself in combat, both on the ground and in space, before being considered for election to the post.

**Pereg, Hunti** A bounty hunter, part of a group hired by Granta Omega to capture Obi-Wan Kenobi, Anakin Skywalker, and Wren Honoran on Ragoon-6 about five years after the Battle of Naboo.

***Peregrine*** The flagship of Garm Bel Iblis's private strike force, it was one of his six Dreadnaughts from the legendary, long-lost *Katana* fleet.

**Peregrine's Nest** Garm Bel Iblis's last hidden base before his strike force rejoined the New Republic, it was constructed mainly of bi-state memory plastic for quick breakdown and setup.

***Peremptory*** An Imperial Star Destroyer. The *Peremptory* was involved in the Battle of Storinal, where Princess Leia Organa's flagship, the *Rebel Dream,* was captured by Imperial forces. This ship was later destroyed while trying to recover the *Katana* fleet. Using the slave-rigging systems of the *Katana,* Han Solo and Lando Calrissian managed to ram a Dreadnaught into the *Peremptory,* completely destroying both ships.

**Pergitor** Once a lush garden planet owned by the Jesa Corporation in the Minos Cluster, deep bore mining triggered an enormous volcanic eruption nearly a century before the Battle of Yavin. As a result, the planet became polluted with thick ash; survival on the surface was possible only with breath masks, and all buildings had to be airtight. The corporation was founded by religious fundamentalists. As a result, most colonists and corporate workers on Pergitor were also followers of the same religious tenets.

**Pergola's Bridge** This bridge in Theed became the main crossing point over the River Solleu, taking some of the strain off the more fragile Bassa Bridge farther downstream.

**Perhi, Dal** A representative of Black Sun who was dispatched to clean up the remains of Yanth the Hutt, a Vigo killed by Darth Maul at the Tusken Oasis cantina in Coruscant's infamous Crimson Corridor. Perhi was a short, muscular human with a large braid of hair trailing down his back. He had an aura of power about him—not Force-related, just sheer animal potency. After Obi-Wan Kenobi repulsed an ambush at the Oasis, Dal Perhi introduced himself to the Jedi. He brought Kenobi to Yanth's underground headquarters to witness the carnage wrought by Yanth's mysterious assassin. Both Perhi and Obi-Wan were at a loss to explain what had transpired. Perhi later became a high-ranking operative in Coruscant's criminal underworld.

**Peridon's Folly** A seldom-visited planet, it was a weapons depot operated by traders who sold obsolete arms to crime lords on the black market. Gunrunners controlled various commercial sectors, which were separated by wastelands where weapons were tested. After deciding to seek work as a bounty hunter, the droid IG-88 traveled to the backworld of Peridon's Folly. He was hired by a local despot named Grlubb to take out a rival weapons manufacturer. IG-88 broke into the rival's fortress and released the company's own lethal gases, killing everyone inside. Next, the droid killed Bolton Kek, one of the original designers of the IG series.

**Perilix** The home planet of peculiar thinking clams, or *Bivalva contemplative.*

**Perit** A Mon Calamari, he was one of the lieutenants, or Vigos, of Prince Xizor's Black Sun criminal organization. Perit's operatives specialized in crimes related to computers and technology. He had his webbed hands in credit laundering, bank fraud, data theft, and corporate espionage, among other high-tech crimes.

**Perkell sector** Located on the outer edge of the Mid Rim, this sector contained a number of backrocket industrial, mining, and agricultural worlds.

*Pernicar*

**Perlemian Trade Route** Running through the Darpa and Bormea sectors of the Ringali Shell, it connected the planets Corulag, Chandrila, Brentaal, Esseles, Rhinnal, and Ralltiir. It reached all the way to Coruscant and was one of the oldest and most important galactic routes, forming one edge of the Slice—a wedge that continued into the Outer Rim and that basically *was* the Galactic Republic for countless millennia. Almost all early Republic exploration occurred along the Perlemian and the Corellian Run. Activity along the Perlemian Trade Route was severely curtailed by Lord Tion's blockade of Ralltiir just prior to the Battle of Yavin.

**permacite** A lightweight, durable substance used in the construction of tall buildings. Permacite was also used as armor to encase artillery pieces.

**permacrete** A strong, dense material, it was used for paving roads and landing platforms.

**permaglass** A form of high-strength glass-like material used in the construction of domes and skylights. Permaglass was common on urban planets, where buildings and structures needed to stand up to the elements, as well as to various forms of pollution.

***Permondiri Explorer*** A mystery ship. This survey vessel and its crew of 112 went on a mission to explore and chart a new star system and was never heard from again. Several massive expeditions were organized to locate the *Permondiri Explorer* or discover what happened to it, but they all drew blanks.

**Pernicar** An older Jedi who served as a counselor to Lord Hoth during the Battle of Ruusan. Pernicar was the son of a small-town scribe and resented his father for sending him away to become a Jedi. As an envoy, Pernicar talked Lord Valenthyne Farfalla into joining the ranks of the Republic. Pernicar died in battle. Although Lord Hoth despaired at the death of his friend, he was surprised when

Pernicar's spirit appeared in a dream. The avatar implored Hoth to set aside his differences with Lord Farfalla and recognize his loyalty to the Jedi. The first planet in the Ruusan system was named Pernicar in honor of this fallen Jedi Master.

**Pernon, Count Rial** The spitting image of his father as a young man, the count had thick black hair and the same bushy eyebrows and large mustache as the Grand Duke. Count Rial Pernon was tall, strong, and handsome—as well as very serious and solemn. He and Princess Isplourrdacartha Estillo (Plourr Ilo) were betrothed as children, and he considered their parents' vow to bind him still. Stalwart in battle, graceful in social situations, he knew the pledge to wed that he held sacred might be unrealistic, but he wanted only to serve Plourr and prove himself worthy of her trust and love.

This didn't sit well with Plourr, a member of Rogue Squadron. While she found him attractive, Rial was the bait in a trap to bring her back to Eiattu VI, to a people she saw as treacherous. She considered the alternatives: If they destroyed the Imperial remnants on the planet, she would be forced to stay. If they didn't, and if the impostor playing the role of her brother, Harran, won, or the nobles won, people would suffer. She was faced with little choice and resented Rial. But Plourr did soften toward him and finally agreed to marry him.

Count Rial Pernon

**Pernon, Grand Duke Gror** A human male with white hair, thick bushy eyebrows, and a grand mustache, he wore a uniform festooned with countless ribbons. Grand Duke Gror Pernon would have been the heir to the throne of Eiattu VI if the daughter of the Crown Prince hadn't survived the execution of the rest of the family. (An alleged surviving son was proven to be an impostor.) Pernon led the planet's noble faction. His father and the grandfather of Rogue Squadron pilot Plourr Ilo (Princess Isplourrdacartha Estillo) were brothers, and her father and Gror grew up together as cousins. Gror was part of the faction that overthrew the Crown Prince, so Plourr naturally blamed her family's death on him. Gror saw the coup as vital, because Plourr's father was not strong enough to shield Eiattu VI from the Empire, but he did not advocate the family's murder and did his best to countermand the orders.

**Perosei, Officer** A member of the Naboo Palace Guard who could disassemble and reassemble a Naboo blaster in less than 60 seconds. During the Trade Federation occupation of his world, he was a prisoner at Camp Four.

**Perris, Commander** The flight coordinator for the *Peregrine* after Garm Bel Iblis joined the New Republic. He later commanded starfighters during the raid on Yaga Minor's Ubiqtorate station.

**Perrive** The leader of the Jabiimi terrorists operating on Coruscant during the Clone Wars. Kal Skirata gained his trust posing as an explosives dealer. Once the connections between the Jabiimi terrorists and the Separatists had been established by Skirata and his clone commandos, Perrive became a target of the larger mission. Walon Vau and Etain Tur-Mukan tailed Perrive to his apartment, and it was Vau who shot and killed him.

Grand Duke Gror Pernon

***Perseverance*** A *Carrack*-class light cruiser that was part of the Galactic Republic's Home Fleet Strike Group Five, defending the planet Coruscant during the Clone Wars. This ship saw heavy fighting over Coruscant and was part of the main force that attacked General Grievous's flagship, *Invisible Hand.*

**Persha** A Fia, she was the primate of Al'solib'minet'ri City at the height of the Yuuzhan Vong War. She was assigned by Councilor Jobath to greet Leia Organa Solo and her husband, Han Solo, when they arrived at Galantos as part of a mission to restore communications with that part of the galaxy. Persha was forced into the role because Jobath feared that the true reason behind the communications blackout—that the Fia had made a deal with the Yuuzhan Vong to eliminate the Yevetha—would be revealed.

***Perspicacity*** A Galactic Republic cruiser destroyed over the planet Serroco by a Mandalorian attack during the Mandalorian Wars.

***Persuader*-class Droid Enforcer** *See* Corporate Alliance tank droid.

**Pesfavri** A planet in the Unknown Regions, one of many worlds colonized by the Chiss. Pesfavri served as a remote base of operations for the Chiss Defense Fleet. After Force Commander Thrawn disabled the Outbound Flight and killed its crew, Admiral Ar'alani directed Syndic Thrass to take the vessel to Pesfavri before the massive ship could be impounded by Aristocra Chaf'orm'bintrano. However, the drive systems of Outbound Flight had been badly damaged in Thrawn's attacks, and they never reached Pesfavri.

**Pesitiin** A gas giant where the Bosken & Bosken Company started an ambitious—although ultimately unprofitable—mining operation. The planet was famous for its nonstop atmospheric storms. Admiral Pellaeon had hoped to meet Garm Bel Iblis near Pesitiin a decade after the death of Grand Admiral Thrawn, in an effort to discuss a peace treaty between the New Republic and the Imperial Remnant, but Imperials opposed to the notion intercepted the invitation.

**Pesktda** The capital city of the planet Garqi.

**Pesmenben IV** The fourth planet in the Pesmenben system. Lando Calrissian once pulled a lithium scam on Pesmenben IV, salting the dunes with lithium carbonate to con an Imperial Governor into leasing the planet. Lando posed as a non-union mine guard and made the governor lie facedown in the bottom of a boat and throw the bribe overboard when "union officials" raided them. Lando got away scot-free.

**Pestage, Sate** Grand Vizier to Emperor Palpatine, Pestage had long been a fixture among Palpatine's political advisers, serving by his side through his Senatorial career. During Palpatine's tenure as Supreme Chancellor of the Republic, Pestage was the controller of the Galactic Senate's executive agenda. This allowed him regular contact with Senators, influencing those uncertain to support Palpatine's initiatives. With the coming of the Empire, Pestage's authority grew. He was presented with the stewardship of the Ciutric Hegemony by Palpatine himself. Historians of the Empire acknowledge the fact that Sate Pestage, for all intents and purposes, was running the day-to-day machinery of the Empire at the time of the Battle of Hoth, while Palpatine concerned himself with other matters.

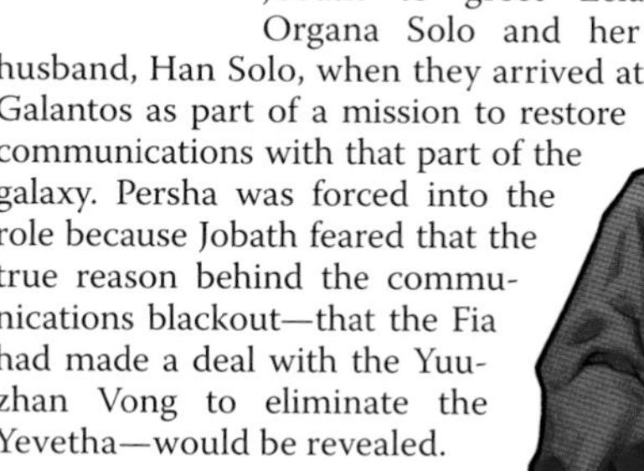

Sate Pestage

Pestage was privy to many of the Emperor's secrets—including his Sith heritage and the specialized cloning facilities Palpatine maintained in a desperate effort to stave off death. He was one of the few beings who controlled access to the Emperor, wielding the authority to make even Darth Vader wait for an appointment.

As a precaution against the turning tides of the Empire, Pestage masterminded the Eidolon project, a sham starship development scheme that secretly funneled millions of credits into the building of a safehouse retreat for Pestage on Tatooine. The Vizier hired Lirin Banolt to acquire antiquities to furnish Eidolon. The opportunistic Banolt stole the plans for Eidolon and planned to blackmail Pestage, but the Vizier simply had Banolt killed. This was not the only precaution Pestage had taken. He had worked with Sarcev Quest to develop a clone of himself, but history isn't clear as to which Pestage was most publicly active after the fall of the Empire at Endor—the real man, or his clone.

Following the Emperor's death at Endor, Pestage assumed control of the majority of the Empire's military, but his rule was constantly questioned by other Imperial leaders. When Pestage lost his holdings on Ciutric to Prince-Admiral Krennel, he fled to Axxila, hoping to evade Ysanne Isard. Pestage arranged to meet with Leia Organa. He offered her the chance to take the planet Coruscant in return for his own safety. Leia agreed, and Pestage found a temporary haven with the New Republic.

Petja

Ysanne Isard brought news of Pestage's treachery to the Imperial council, which in turn ordered him to be removed from power. He fled to Ciutric with the help of Moff Leonia Tavira and was held by Governor Brothic. The New Republic embarked on a mission to rescue Pestage before Isard's forces could capture him. Pestage fled to Admiral Krennel, mistakenly believing that the admiral could be bribed into an alliance. Krennel instead strangled Pestage with his cybernetic hand and embarked on a bloody campaign to kill all of Pestage's surviving relatives, resulting in more than 100 murders.

Another Pestage, possibly the clone, was at the Emperor's citadel on Byss, preparing the triumphant return of the cloned sovereign. This Pestage perished when the Galaxy Gun misfired and destroyed Byss.

***Peterson's Guide to Droids of the Republic*** An immense, multivolume guide produced during the last centuries of the Galactic Republic containing a wealth of information on virtually every series and model of automata ever produced.

**Petikkin, Soth** A persuasive Rebel Alliance recruiter from Tefau, he possessed limited precognition. He used his contacts in Jabba's desert stronghold to find support for the Rebellion during the Galactic Civil War.

**Petition of the Two Thousand** *See* Delegation of the Two Thousand.

**Petja** A young Jedi Knight serving Lord Hoth's Army of Light at the Battle of Ruusan. Petja lost his right eye during one of the many battles. Believing that the native Bouncers were telepathically demoralizing the Jedi troops, he began hunting down the creatures with his bow and arrow. After he killed the Bouncer Laa, the young girl named Rain succumbed to the dark side and used the Force to kill Petja. This was one of her first steps to becoming Darth Zannah.

**Petothel, Gara (Lara Notsil)** A spy from Coruscant who worked for Warlord Zsinj during the early years of the New Republic. She was stationed aboard the Star Destroyer *Implacable* under the command of Admiral Apwar Trigit. She was the code slicer who planted misinformation that resulted in the destruction of Talon Squadron. Gara survived the destruction of the *Implacable* at Ession by using her slicing skills to commandeer Trigit's escape pod.

She later infiltrated Wraith Squadron using the alias Lara Notsil. She flew at first as Wraith Thirteen and, later, Wraith Two. Myn Donos was attracted to her, unaware of her true allegiance. Gara came to respect her New Republic comrades and was making the mental switch to abandon the remnants of the Empire for a new life when Garik "Face" Loran discovered her identity. Gara then fled, rejoining Warlord Zsinj's forces. With the help of her astromech droid, Tonin, she sabotaged Zsinj's flagship, the *Iron Fist*. Her X-wing was shot down as she escaped the Empire. Presumed dead, she was able to establish a new identity for herself on Corellia as Kirney Slane.

**Petrakis** This planet was the site of one of the first engagements between Rebel Alliance B-wings and the Imperial fleet. When TIE fighter pilots first saw the new fighters near Petrakis, they all fled.

**Petro** A hot-tempered pilot in His Majesty's Crimson Squadron, an Imperial TIE squadron stationed at Kiidan on Cilpar.

**Petro, Gyla** Born on Kalgo 13, she was a former Imperial botanist working on the planet Kashyyyk. She objected to many of the practices employed by Imperial scientists, and because of that, she was spared when Wookiees attacked the scientific expedition. Gyla ended up traveling with Han Solo, who was visiting Kashyyyk at the time.

Phaeda

**Pezzle** A large, mean-looking human who tried to collect payment from a mercenary named Lope at the Tipsy Mynock cantina on Karfeddion. Lope, hoping to impress Nebula Front leader Captain Arwen Cohl, shot and killed Pezzle and his trio of thugs.

**Phaath, Yal** An ancient Yuuzhan Vong master shaper of Domain Phaath. Master Yal Phaath was so old that any signs of his domain were entirely obscured. He wore a fragile, cloud-like mass of a headdress, and both his hands were those of a master. His eyes were replaced by yellow maa'its. Phaath believed strongly in following the ancient protocols, adhering to the idea that knowledge cannot be created: If the gods do not grant knowledge, it is for good reason, and to seek it further is an attempt to steal from them. Yal Phaath's last project was to shape vornskrs that specifically hunted Jedi Knights. Yal Phaath was killed aboard the *Baanu Rass* by Jacen Solo.

**Phaeda** A planet under Imperial control in the early years of the New Republic with little strategic or commercial importance. Phaeda's relative obscurity made it a haven for smugglers, thieves, and others who wished to escape the notice of the Empire. Colonel Shev was the commander of the Imperial garrison on Phaeda, while Mirith Sinn was

Gara Petothel

the leader of the underground resistance on the planet. Kir Kanos sought refuge on Phaeda, but it wasn't long before he made his presence known to the Imperials—Carnor Jax, in particular. The planet had two moons, a larger brown moon and a smaller green one.

***Phalanx*** A cruiser in the New Republic's Fifth Fleet, it was assigned to the blockade of Doornik-319 and was severely damaged during the Yevethan attack.

**Phanan, Ton** A native of Rudrig, he was one of the founding pilots of Wraith Squadron, as well as its medical officer. Phanan was the only son of parents who both died before he finished his education. He served as a doctor aboard a Rebel Alliance medical frigate during the Battle of Endor, but his ship was hit by a barrage of Imperial laserfire. A structural beam fell on him, causing massive head trauma. A vital member of Wraith Squadron in the early stages of the hunt for Warlord Zsinj, Phanan was shot down over the planet Halmad, suffered massive internal injuries in the crash-landing, and was rescued by Garik "Face" Loran. However, before they could escape, Phanan died of his injuries.

**Phanius** *See* Ruin, Darth.

**Phantele, Siiruulian** *See* Rebo, Max.

**Phantom TIE V-38** A secret weapon developed by the Empire and Darth Vader during the Galactic Civil War. The Phantom TIE V-38 was a tri-winged TIE fighter with cloaking ability. It was developed at the Imdaar Alpha research station deep in the Dreighton Nebula.

**Phaseera** A lush, jungle-covered planet orbiting a yellow star, at the time of the Battle of Ruusan it was considered to be on the Republic's frontier. Phaseera's urban centers had been established around manufacturing facilities that provided the Republic with a wide range of products. The Brotherhood of Darkness captured the planet shortly before the final conflict at Ruusan, but only after the soldier Dessel (the future Darth Bane) purposely disobeyed the orders he was given and delayed his attack on a Republic communications center. The delay allowed Dessel and his men to attack under cover of growing darkness, rather than being spotted during the daylight, thereby saving his men and ensuring that the main Sith army could attack without the Republic being alerted to its presence.

**Phedroi** This alien, easily identified by his mucus-lined nasopharynx, joined up with Vol Hamame after the human left Big Gizz's swoop gang. They went into the information business, primarily stealing what they couldn't obtain themselves in the city of Mos Eisley. The last job they took came as a result of Dengar's trying to alert Kuat of Kuat that Boba Fett was still alive. Hamame and Phedroi figured that they could kill the armored bounty hunter and reap a nice profit for delivery of his body. However, Fett and Dengar managed to elude them long enough to signal *Slave I*. Hamame and Phedroi pinned the bounty hunters down in a small desert cave, but Fett brought his ship from orbit to land on top of them.

**Phelarion** A planet in the Seswenna sector and an estate owned by the influential Tarkin family, it was the site of an Imperial labor colony run by the widow of Grand Moff Tarkin. Lady Tarkin forced the slaves of the colony to mine a volatile resource known as megonite.

**Phemis** A planet believed to have been the only source of rubat crystals, which were used by the ancient Jedi Knights in the construction of lightsabers.

**Phemiss** The capital of New Plympto, nestled between the Tsilor Sea and the Pharine River.

**Phenaru Prime** A mythical planet, it was simulated by New Republic strategists to train Rogue Squadron pilots for a return mission to Borleias. Since Borleias's location was classified, the pilots flew simulated attacks on Phenaru Prime. The run through the canyons of Borleias's moon was replaced with a run through a virtual asteroid ring surrounding the spurious world.

**Phenets, Lee** A maintenance specialist assigned to ensure the smooth operation of Cloud City, he was one of the few humans respected by the city's Ugnaughts.

**Phennir, Turr** During the Battle of Endor, Major Phennir was an executive officer with the 181st Imperial Fighter Wing. He flew the TIE interceptor designated as Saber Two and was assigned to protect the Star Destroyer *Avenger*. He was also responsible for the logistics of Saber Squadron. His older brother was killed by Wedge Antilles at the Battle of Yavin. Turr later participated in the Battle of Brentaal, serving under Baron Fel. Thirteen years after the Battle of Yavin, Phennir served as an Imperial ambassador dispatched to Adumar. By that point, he had assumed command of the legendary 181st following Baron Fel's defection to the New Republic.

Phennir survived the battle for Adumar, although he remained out of action for many years. He resurfaced a decade after the Yuuzhan Vong War and was named the new Supreme Commander of the military forces that were amassed by the Confederation. Having attained the rank of General, Phennir was sent to Gilatter VIII to lead the Confederation's forces against a fleet of Galactic Alliance warships.

**phidna** Traditional "free-formed" Geonosian architecture was sculpted in rock paste, a material mixed from domesticated phidna parasite excretions and stone powders. Geonosian phidna were cultivated in hydroponic gardens to supply the hive construction industry.

**p'hiili** An aquatic creature that was once native to the planet Yuuzhan'tar. The p'hiili was distinguished by its shrill cry and was often kept in ponds or moats outside a residence as a kind of organic alarm system. P'hiili would eat just about anything that came into their reach, a trait that made them useful as guards.

**Phindar** The home planet of the Phindians. Laressa was the capital city. About 12 years before the Battle of Naboo, Qui-Gon Jinn and Obi-Wan Kenobi traveled to Phindar, where they found themselves involved in a battle against the evil Syndicat, a criminal organization that had control of the planet. The Jedi defeated the Syndicat, freeing Phindar.

**Phindian** Members of this species, native to Phindar, had red-streaked yellow eyes and exceedingly long arms. Known for their very simple style of dress, Phindians were also infamous for their contrary cultural attitudes. They tended to be sarcastic or exaggerate to an extreme. They were a technologically advanced people whose scientists invented mindwiping devices, exploited by an organization known as the Syndicat. This technology was made illegal on Phindar. They maintained a democratic government until the formation of the Emperor's New Order. The planet remained under Imperial rule until shortly after the Battle of Endor.

**Phin-Mar, Ermin** An explorer and archaeologist who discovered the Oracle at Pelgrin some 3,000 years before the Battle of Naboo.

**Phlac-Arphocc Automata Industries** Manufacturers of combat automata, such as the droid gunships and tri-droid brains for the Confederacy of Independent Systems.

**Phlegmin** A kitchen boy in the palace of Jabba the Hutt, he was an assistant to the head chef, Porcellus. Jabba had fed Phlegmin's brother to the rancor because a sauce failed, so Phlegmin laced Jabba's toads with a slow-acting poison in an attempt at revenge. Phlegmin was eventually killed by the Anzati Dannik Jerriko.

**Phlog** Giant, brutish creatures, they lived in the desert land of Simoom on Endor's Forest Moon. Phlogs were usually peaceful but could become dangerous when disturbed.

*Phindian*

**Phlut Design Systems** As moneylender to many of the most advanced technology firms in the galaxy, the InterGalactic Banking Clan had at its disposal the latest high-tech weapons to turn against the Republic during the Clone Wars. Phlut Design Systems, a Muunilinst-based weapons development firm, took out a sizable capital investment loan from the IBC to fund a secret battle droid program that it hoped to sell to the Trade Federation. When PDS was unable to make payments on the loan, the IBC responded by seizing the assets of the company, and, ironically, added the battle droids to the new Confederacy of Independent Systems army. Holowan Mechanicals then absorbed the research PDS had been conducting on its IG-series assassin droids.

**Phlutdroid** *See* IG-88.

**phobium** A metal alloy, it was used to coat the power core of both Death Star battle stations.

**Phobos, Darth** An ancient female Theelin Sith Lord.

**Phoebos** An intrepid mechanic who invented the first Podracer by attaching large engines to a repulsorlift cockpit. The "Phoebos Run" on Malastare was named for the mechanic.

***Phoenix Hawk*–class light pinnace** A small transport ship that resembled the *Firespray*-class patrol craft but actually predated it. Designated the S40K, the *Phoenix Hawk*–class pinnace was one of the first ships designed and built by Kuat Systems Engineering.

Photoreceptor

**Ph'Olla, Senator** A Bith representative in the Senate of the Galactic Alliance during the war with the Confederation. Ph'Olla was one of several Bith who witnessed an argument between Mara Jade Skywalker and Jacen Solo, during which Mara threatened Jacen's life if anything were to happen to her son, Ben Skywalker. This fact became important during the investigation into Mara's murder.

**Phond crystal** One of the many crystals used by the ancient Sith Lords in the construction of a lightsaber. It produced a fiercely burning beam that caused greater damage than most.

**Phonstom, Lady Lapema** A resident of Kabal, she was one of Lando Calrissian's marriage candidates.

**Phootie** A Pho Ph'eahian who, with his Kitonak partner, performed a comedy act during the Clone Wars.

**Pho Ph'eah** The homeworld of the Pho Ph'eahians, creatures with blue fur and four arms. Pho Ph'eah orbited far from its star and received little sunlight, but it was warmed by active geothermal energy. The planet was contacted by the Old Republic millennia ago, and the technologically skilled Pho Ph'eahians were longtime members of the larger galaxy.

Pho Ph'eahian

**Phorliss** The site of a cantina where Mara Jade, onetime top personal aide to the Emperor and later a smuggler, worked briefly as a serving girl under the name Karrinna Jansih.

**phosflea** Tiny, glowing gnat-like bloodsucking insects native to Kashyyyk, phosfleas were lured into mesh lanterns and used as nighttime illumination by Wookiees and other visitors to the jungle planet.

**Phosphura Belt Nebula** Located near several major trade lanes, this mass of greenish clouds randomly charged with electromagnetic bursts was a serious navigation hazard and home to the highly organized Phosphura Belt pirates. The space station *Zirtran's Anchor* drifted nearby.

**photon absorber** A starship counterdetection system developed by the Galactic Alliance after the Yuuzhan Vong War. Originally used on the StealthX fighter, photon absorbers reduced or eliminated the ability of most sensor systems to detect the fighter.

**photon spider** A fierce 12-eyed predator found on the planet Varl. It was 4 meters long and covered from mandible to spinneret in hard, chitinous armor. A photon spider's spinneret was capable of firing a bolt of energy that stunned opponents.

**Photo-Optic Replicator** Also known as an OptiRep or camouflage suit, this vest-like harness served as a mount for an active sensor package coupled with a small holoprojector. The sensor unit took constant readings of energy wavelengths in the visible spectrum in a complete 360-degree arc. It evaluated the readings many hundreds of times per second, feeding the information to the holoprojector, which then created a replicated image 180 degrees from the source. In the end the wearer of an OptiRep appeared to be part of his or her surroundings, but the effect was not perfect. The faster the wearer moved, the more blurred and distorted the image. Also, most sensor packages could pick up the active signals sent out by the OptiRep's sensing unit. Photo-Optic Replicators were difficult to come by.

**photoreceptor** A device that captured light rays and converted them into electronic signals for processing by video computers. Photoreceptors were used as eyes for most droids.

**phototropic shielding** A process that turned transparent materials into filters for intense light rays while retaining their transparency.

**Phracas** A planet in the Galactic Core in sector 151 where the mystery ship known as the Teljkon vagabond headed after Lando Calrissian, Lobot, and the droids C-3PO and R2-D2 stowed away on board.

**Phraetiss** A world located in the Farrfin sector coated with thick, tall grasslands. It was the site of a botched smuggling run where Lando Calrissian first met Niles Ferrier.

**phrik** A rare metal alloy produced from phrikite and tydirium. Deposits of phrikite were found on several of the moons in the Gromas system. The Empire built a mining facility on one moon to produce phrik for use in armoring dark troopers. The alloy could withstand lightsaber strikes. The staffs wielded by General Grievous's MagnaGuard droids were made of phrik.

**Ph'ton** A Bith Jedi Master during the Clone Wars. Master Ph'ton was placed in charge of the mission to ensure Alderaan's freedom after a small fleet of Separatist warships arrived in the system. Ph'ton was dismayed when Flynn Kybo stole a Delta-7 interceptor and fled from Alderaan, fearing that the young Padawan had turned to the dark side of the Force. He was unaware that Kybo had actually left the Jedi Order to hunt down General Grievous.

**Phuii** Members of this long-necked, needle-nosed alien species hailed from Phu. Podracer Mars Guo was a Phuii, as was Nep Chung, a Black Sun Vigo.

**Phuna, T. Lund** A constable who served under the Administrator of the Oseon. It was not, apparently, the happi-

Phuii

est of field assignments. A squat, curly-haired human, T. Lund Phuna participated in a sabacc game with his bosses and Lando Calrissian several years before Lando's association with the Rebellion. Phuna planted a cheater on Lando when the game wasn't going the constable's way. Caught in the act, Phuna was apprehended by Arun Feb and Vett Fori.

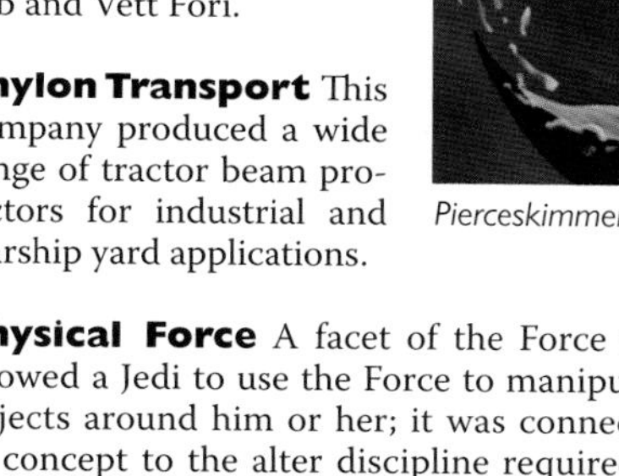

**Phylon Transport** This company produced a wide range of tractor beam projectors for industrial and starship yard applications.

Pierceskimmer

**physical Force** A facet of the Force that allowed a Jedi to use the Force to manipulate objects around him or her; it was connected in concept to the alter discipline required to complete such acts. This facet complemented the living Force, which connected Jedi Knights to the living beings surrounding them, and the unifying Force, which focused on the future and its bearing on a Jedi's place in the present.

**Piani** A female Ryn and member of Mezza's clan, she worked at the communications center at the Settlement Thirty-two refugee camp on Duro during the Yuuzhan Vong War. Han Solo asked Piani to send a message to Jaina Solo with Rogue Squadron. Piani had a small child, but her mate didn't reach Gyndine's capital city in time to catch an evac ship and was likely dead.

**Pic** A Dark Jedi encountered by Kyle Katarn. He was once a Kowakian monkey-lizard named Picaroon C. Boodle, alchemically altered alongside a Gamorrean guard so that the two became the mismatched "twins" Pic and Gorc. Pic was a little over a meter tall and would fight atop his larger brother, Gorc, battling as a team, covering all angles and weaknesses. Gorc and Pic were defeated by Kyle Katarn during the search for the Valley of the Jedi, when they tried to apprehend him aboard the *Sulon Star.* After Katarn blasted Gorc's brain, he bludgeoned Pic's small skull with the cranium of the droid 8t88. He left their bodies aboard the ship.

**Pica Thundercloud** A green drink served on Tatooine.

**Pichaff** An officer in the Galactic Alliance military. When Jacen Solo launched his plans to capture Fondor, Pichaff was placed in charge of the deployment of forces on the orbital shipyards as well as any ground facilities that needed to be captured.

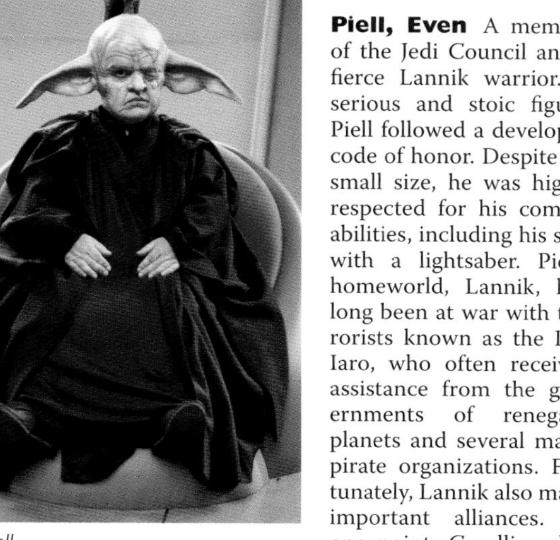

Even Piell

**Pickaxe** This mining transport ship captained by Calquad Dominé refused to leave its slip at the Kwilaan starport on Naboo in protest of the closing of many Naboo starports to miners and their ships during the Separatist crisis. The *Pickaxe* and its crew were members of the Naboo Moon Mining Union at the time and were angry that the planetary government was favoring refugee ships over local mining concerns.

**pickup droid** *See* P-100 salvage droid.

**Picutorian, Vensell** A Senex lord who served in the Imperial Senate during Leia Organa's early Senatorial career.

**Picutorion** A planet in the Kwymar sector, it housed a Rebel base until the combined forces of Tensiger's 6th Regiment of the Imperial Army and the Imperial Navy attacked and destroyed it. During the battle, overseen by Commodore Bevven and High Colonel Drost, the Imperial forces did not supply relief in time to extricate Captain Ganig and Sergeant Stecker. This was on suggestion of ISB agent Mar Barezz, who believed the two ground-based Imperials were in fact turn-coats.

Firmus Piett

**Piell, Even** A member of the Jedi Council and a fierce Lannik warrior. A serious and stoic figure, Piell followed a developed code of honor. Despite his small size, he was highly respected for his combat abilities, including his skill with a lightsaber. Piell's homeworld, Lannik, had long been at war with terrorists known as the Red Iaro, who often received assistance from the governments of renegade planets and several major pirate organizations. Fortunately, Lannik also made important alliances. At one point, Corellian diplomats visited Lannik to offer the backward world stronger technological ties to the Core Worlds. Ironically, the two diplomats sent to Lannik were the parents of Jedi Master Adi Gallia. During the meeting between the Lannik representatives and the Corellian diplomats, terrorists stormed Lannik's High Court. Even Piell single-handedly defeated seven attackers and saved Gallia's parents, although he did lose his left eye in the battle. He continually refused a prosthetic replacement for the lost eye, believing that his scar was a symbol of his honor, bravery, and ultimate survival against enormous odds.

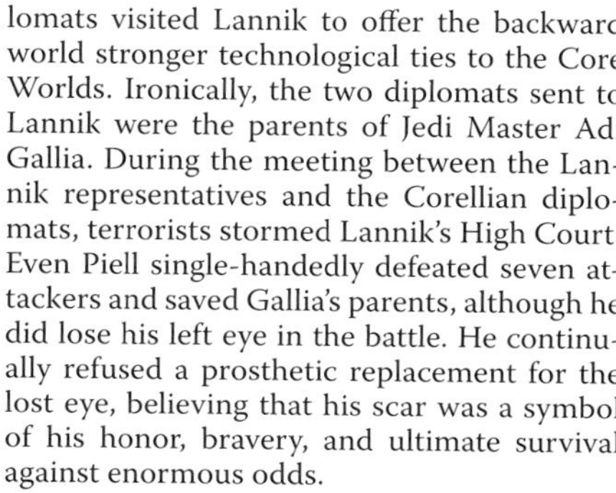

After the Battle of Naboo, Even Piell, Adi Gallia (who felt indebted to Piell), and four other Jedi Council members traveled to Malastare, where they hoped to hold talks designed to resolve the conflict between the Lannik and the terrorists. Piell later fought in the arena during the Battle of Geonosis and served on the Jedi Council during the early stages of the Clone Wars.

**pierceskimmer** Large, dangerous fish-like sea predators found on a number of worlds. Historians believed that young specimens were removed from their original home—probably Drexel II—long ago by enterprising sport hunters and taken to various planets, where they escaped and established local populations in short order. Pierceskimmers could grow up to 22 meters long, although 16 to 18 was more common. A third of the pierceskimmer's length was taken up by a single serrated spike growing from its forehead. Twin dorsal fins rose in a V-pattern from its back, just behind its head. Four sets of fins and a powerful, spiked tail propelled the creature with frightening speed through the water. They were killing machines of the highest order, preying on creatures far larger than themselves.

**Pietrangelo, Captain** The commander of the Republic Cruiser *Unitive.* Pietrangelo, like her crew, wore a crisp blue uniform and black leather boots.

**Piett, Firmus** Formerly the commanding officer of the Star Destroyer *Accuser,* Captain Piett hailed from Axxila. He advanced to first officer on Darth Vader's flagship *Executor,* an especially dangerous position given the Dark Lord's legendary capriciousness. Piett aided Admiral Kendal Ozzel in overseeing the crew as well as helping to direct the entire fleet. He was promoted to admiral and given command of the flagship and the fleet after Ozzel made a fatal mistake during the assault on the Rebel base on Hoth. Piett remained in command of *Executor* through the Battle of Endor, where the Super Star Destroyer was lost in combat with the Rebel fleet.

**Piggy** A nickname shared by fighter pilots Jek Porkins and Voort saBinring.

**Pii system** Located in the Arkanis sector on the border of the Mid and Outer Rims, the system's seven planets orbited a red giant, and the inner two worlds were scorched balls of rock. An asteroid belt followed, then the lush green worlds of Pii 3 and 4—the only commercially useful worlds in the area. They were known for the valuable crimson greel wood harvested and exported from their forests. Entrepreneur Meysen Kayson bought the rights to both planets in the last days of the Old Republic, intending to open a nature preserve. When he discovered the fast-growing greel trees and their deep, luxurious wood, he founded the Greel Wood Logging Corporation. Kayson secretly diverted most of his profits to the Rebel Alliance and let the planets be used as Rebel training grounds and safeworlds.

Pike sisters

**pika fruit** A large oval food with dark blue skin. Pika fruits could be found on Tatooine.

**Pike sisters** These twin Epicanthix women were the daughters of renowned martial artist Dux Pike. The only noticeable difference between the two women was that Zan had green eyes, while Zu had one green and one blue eye. They were masters of teräs käsi, the Bunduki martial art also called steel hands. At 26 years of age, the women had no political affiliations or criminal records, and had never been defeated in open combat. In public, the sisters were professional fighters beginning to make a name for themselves in galactic circles. In private, they were operatives secretly employed by Prince Xizor's Black Sun organization as assassins. The sisters were as beautiful as they were deadly, dressing in formfitting tunics that were functional but also showed off their lithe, powerful bodies. It was a point of pride that the sisters refused to carry weapons. They considered their skills more than a match for any opponent. After the Battle of Endor, the Pike sisters changed their names to the Pikkel sisters and were hired by the rogue scientist Spinda Caveel to abduct the medical droid AOl-C. When Guri rescued AOl-C, Caveel and the sisters tracked them back to Hurd's Moon. But when they discovered that the heroes of the Rebel Alliance were involved, the Pikkel sisters turned on their employer and were able to live to see another day.

**piket longhorn** Immense horned herbivores native to Dantooine, where they spent most of their time grazing in the savannas. The average specimen stood more than 5 meters high, although much of that height came from the piket longhorn's tremendous neck.

**Pikil, Atresh** A lithe, dark-skinned 12-year-old Jedi girl at the time of the Clone Wars.

**Pikk** A Kowakian monkey-lizard trained as a pickpocket during the Clone Wars.

**Pikkel sisters** *See* Pike sisters.

**pikobi** A swamp-dwelling needle-beaked reptavian with webbed feet native to the swamps of Naboo. The pikobi was found near shallow, murky pools or muddy areas. It hunted by spearing prey with its beak and primarily ate small fish and amphibians. The pikobi's long legs allowed it to move swiftly when necessary, but it could usually be found slowly stalking its next meal. The creature relied on its keen eyes and fast reflexes when hunting. A pikobi could shed its tail when attacked.

**Piksoar, Knezex Hral** A Drovian who worked for the New Republic base on Nim Drovis. He was a direct descendant of Garnu Hral Eschen and fought alongside his fellow Drovians against the Gopso'o terrorists.

**Pil Diller** Once home to a species of mournful singing fig trees, the planet also had many beaches.

**Pi-Lippa** One of Shmi Skywalker's former masters. While serving the alien Pi-Lippa, Shmi learned numerous technical skills, which she continued to use in her daily life on Tatooine. Pi-Lippa had planned to free her slave, but she died unexpectedly. Shmi was then sold to one of Pi-Lippa's relatives.

**Pillik** One of nine Omwati youth who did not survive Wilhuff Tarkin's forced education sessions for the purpose of developing Imperial superweapons. Pillik collapsed under the strain of trying to outdo his fellow Omwati, when his brain shut down and he went into convulsive seizures. Tarkin used Pillik's failure as an example to drive the other youths. He ordered the four surviving students—including young Qwi Xux—to look out the windows of their orbital education facility as he ordered his Star Destroyer to destroy Pillik's village.

Pikobi

**Pilot's Proving Ground** Nicknamed the Maze, this was the first step in becoming a Rebel Alliance starfighter pilot. Cadets sat in simulators and piloted virtual starfighters through a specialized obstacle course in which both the ability to maneuver and sharpshooting skills were assessed. The standard training package included X-wing, Y-wing, and A-wing simulations. Scores were based on weapons accuracy, maneuvering skills, and the time it took to complete the course.

**pilotta thranta** A subspecies of thranta once native to Alderaan.

**Pilus** A patron at Didi's Café, he made a fortune running spice to the Quintus system.

**Pina, Awdrysta** A male Jedi Master during the First Great Schism who was killed after confronting Arden Lyn. Before dying, Awdrysta used the horrific technique of Morichro to halt Lyn's body functions, stopping her heart. As an ancient Jedi warrior, he wielded metal blades as opposed to a traditional lightsaber.

**pinch jacks** Tools that could pry open collision-bonded metals. They were often used in emergency situations when a survivor was trapped in wreckage after an accident.

**pink** A species of algae that lived in the clouds of Bespin. Pinks were what gave the clouds of Bespin their rose color. Pinks, and the other algal species, glowers, were harvested as cosmetics for the decorative costume balls that occurred regularly on Cloud City.

The Pinnacle

**pinnace** Small ships built for travel close to lightspeed, they were carried aboard larger spacecraft for defensive purposes. Heavily armed and highly maneuverable, pinnaces came close to combat starfighters in terms of performance and utility. They sometimes were called battle boats.

**Pinnacle, the** This rock formation in the center of Mos Espa Arena was a sacred site for tribes of Sand People centuries ago. In rock-hewn caves, the Sand People performed sacrifices and rituals intended to promote successful hunting seasons. Tusken spiritual leaders retold sacred stories to the next generation in saga rooms. Long since chased away from their hallowed rock by screaming Podracer engines and tourists, latter-day Tusken Raiders regularly shot at Podracers during competitions to avenge their ancestors.

**Pinnacle Base** The designation for the New Republic High Command Center on Da Soocha's fifth moon.

**PIP/2 systems control droid** A series of control droids designed by Genetech Corporation. The Holographic Zoo on Coruscant used a PIP/2 to control holographic dioramas and keep visitors moving through the exhibit halls. Pip, a PIP droid on Ruan, helped Baffle and Han Solo locate Droma after the Ryn's arrest during the Yuuzhan Vong War.

**pipefighter** Cobbled-together experimental starships used in the New Republic's Operation Starlancer on Borleias during the Yuuzhan Vong War. Pipefighters resembled a right angle, with Y-wing cockpits and engine components. Four pipefighters would combine lambent-crystal-emitted laserfire to create a powerful beam. In truth, the beam had very little destructive potential, but the light show created by the pipefighter tests led the Yuuzhan Vong to believe the New Republic was developing a devastating superweapon.

Pinnacle Base

**piranha-beetle** Native to Yavin 4, these iridescent blue insects flew together with a high-pitched humming sound, spreading out while searching for prey. The beetles covered the body of their victim in moments, tearing its flesh with thousands of piercing, razor-sharp mandibles. Emperor Palpatine used piranha-beetles to torture and kill Death Star designer Bevel Lemelisk before he cloned him.

**Pirik** This bustling mining planet in the Divis Arm was the site of a battle between the Rebels and the Empire during the Galactic Civil War.

**Pirin** A planet located in the Locris sector. The headquarters and factories of the security company Kontag were located on Pirin.

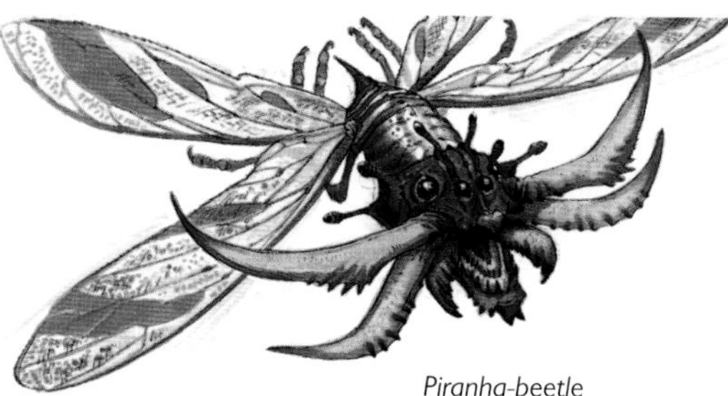

Piranha-beetle

PIP/2 systems control droid

**Piringiisi** A caustic hot-mud spring on Sullust revered by the Sullustans. It was the site of a small settlement that became a tourist destination during the early years of the New Republic.

**Piris, Captain** The commanding officer of the Galactic Alliance warship *Bounty* during the war with the Confederation. Despite his Quarren heritage, Piris had the full support of the GA's Supreme Commander, Admiral Cha Niathal.

**Piroket** Located close to the planet Tatooine, it was the site of a Bothan shipping company where the Rebel agent Riij Winward—having stolen a droid carrying the complete technical readouts of the Hammertong Project prior to the Battle of Yavin—planned to leave the droid.

**Pirol-5** Located in the Koornacht Cluster in the Farlax sector, this planet was the former location of an Imperial factory farm, run largely by droids. Twelve years after the Battle of Endor, Pirol-5 was seized by the Yevethan military in what the Yevetha called the Great Purge.

**Pirtonna** An enforcer for the Birtraub Brothers Storage and Reclamation Center on Crovna, he intercepted Mara Jade during her investigation into several stolen artworks that were found in the collection of Moff Glovstoak. Pirtonna escorted her to the owner's office, then tried to pull a blaster on her to keep her in line. Mara wanted nothing to do with such small-time antics and quickly disarmed him before he could do any damage.

**Piru, Chase** A Jedi, she oversaw the Soaring Hawkbat Clan at the training facility on Bogden. During Order 66, she protected the younglings alongside fellow Jedi K'Kruhk and Sian Jeisel. Gathering the younglings, Piru fled the planet, only to crash-land on an uncharted planet full of natural resources. She and K'Kruhk led the camp until it was discovered by the criminal Lumbra, who wanted to bring the children to the Empire. K'Kruhk and Piru defeated the criminals and transported the clan elsewhere.

Grand Admiral Danetta Pitta

Pit droid

**Pisces Base** A floating city on Mon Calamari.

**Pistoeka sabotage droid** *See* buzz droid.

**Pitann** A harsh, desert world belonging to the Kathol Republic, much of its economy was based on mining operations. Pitann settlers were often suspicious of outsiders.

**Pitareeze family** The Pitareeze family lived on the planet Kalarba. The family included Meg and Jarth Pitareeze, their son Nak, and Nak's grandfather Baron Pitareeze. In their adventures before they met Luke Skywalker, R2-D2 and C-3PO agreed to work for the family after their life pod splashed down on Kalarba following their escape from bounty hunter IG-88.

**pit droid** Small bundles of pre-programmed urgency, pit droids always seemed eager to enact any and all repairs, whether requested to or not. On planets where the dangerous and often outlawed sport of Podracing was allowed, pit droids were an integral part of the racing team. Capable of lifting many times their own weight, the droids enjoyed legendary strength. When not in use, pit droids folded up into a compact package. They sprang to activation when needed. A tap on the nose signaled the droid to collapse back into stowed mode and rest. Common models of pit droids included the DUM series and the Otoga-222.

**Pitta, Grand Admiral Danetta** One of the Empire's 12 Grand Admirals. He was a rabid, anti-alien bigot, though he had Borneck and Etti ancestors. The *Apocahk*, the *Angrix*, and the *Azgoghk* were his dungeon ships. After the defeat of the Empire at the Battle of Endor, he became a self-proclaimed warlord and battled with fellow Grand Admiral Grunger in a futile bid for control of the Corellian sector. He perished when Grunger rammed his flagship into Pitta's torpedo sphere at the Battle of Tralus.

**pittin** Small furry pets. Leia Organa's adoptive aunt Tia would dote over her pittins.

**Pius Dea period** A span of time from 12,000 to 11,000 years before the Battle of Yavin, when the Galactic Republic came under the influence of a theocratic sect. Supreme Chancellor Contispex was one of the rulers during the Pius Dea period.

**Pix** The teenage Padawan of Master Tyr during the Clone Wars. After Tyr was killed on Thustra, she remained with the clone forces while Yoda and Padawan Cal attended a parlay with King Alaric. The treacherous Senator Navi lied to Pix, telling her that Yoda and Pix were executed by King Alaric. He also supplied her with the location of the Sephi forces. Pix then ordered a sneak attack on the Sephi, thus escalating the conflict. She survived to expose Navi as a traitor to his people.

Pix

**Pixelito** A city on the eastern continent of Malastare with a sizable Dug community. Sebulba hailed from Pixelito.

**Pizztov** A short, ugly, and sleazy dealer of stolen merchandise and collectibles, he possessed information regarding Boba Fett's past with which he hoped to blackmail the bounty hunter. Sintas Vel and Boba Fett confronted Pizztov, and Fett killed him.

**PK unit** A general worker droid built and programmed by Cybot Galactica to perform menial labor and simple tasks. Small and compact, PK droids walked upright and had elongated heads with rudimentary sensors. The droids could be found in large numbers aboard the Trade Federation's huge battleships.

PK unit

**PL-37** A Trade Federation protocol droid that worked for Lord Toat aboard the *Syren*. PL-37 was destroyed when the *Syren* was attacked by Sol Sixxa's pirates. The Feeorin pirate Nym recovered its head and learned that the *Syren* was carrying some sort of prototype cloaking device. After Nym and Sol's forces battled in the Haunted Strait, Sol used the droid head to contact Nym; this eventually led to the two pirates joining forces.

Plaeryin bol

**Plaan** The burly Weequay security chief on the planet Tholatin and first mate aboard the *Sweet Surprise* during the Yuuzhan Vong War. He and his group of smugglers charged refugees for transport to other worlds. Plaan conducted a search of the *Millennium Falcon,* which was operating under the alias *Sunlight Franchise* at the time. Droma posed as its captain and claimed that Han Solo was the Ryn's first mate, Miek.

**plaeryin bol** This Yuuzhan Vong–bioengineered creature resembled a normal Yuuzhan Vong eyeball, but its pupil was really a mouth that could spit a venomous glob accurately across 10 meters at the command of its host. Nom Anor carried one within an otherwise empty eye socket.

**Plagueis, Darth** A Muun Sith Lord who was the Master of Darth Sidious. Known as Darth Plagueis the Wise, he was a master of arcane Sith knowledge that could be deemed unnatural. Supposedly, Plagueis could even spur midi-chlorians to create life. Plagueis was so powerful, he could keep someone from dying—though he could not do the same for himself. Obsessed with immortality and the bringing about of a perfect vessel for the Force conceived by the midi-chlorians, Plagueis was blind to Sidious's treachery. The only thing he feared was losing his power. Sidious killed him in his sleep.

Planetary ion cannon

**Plah** A lifeless moon, it orbited Tibrin.

**planetary ion cannon** A large surface-to-orbit energy weapon designed to overload a starship's electrical and computer systems, stripping the vessel of all weapons, defenses, engines, and even life support systems. One of the largest, most expensive planetary ion cannons was the KDY v-150 Planet Defender. This massive weapon was protected by a spherical permacite shell and received its power from a massive reactor normally buried about 40 meters below the ground. The cannon could emit a powerful ion pulse capable of streaking into low orbit and disabling huge starships.

Darth Plagueis (seated) oversees the training of his young apprentice, Darth Sidious.

**planetary security forces** A dedicated corps of beings who defended the borders of their home star systems from neighboring stellar nations and the nearby space lanes from pirates. Each existed apart from the Galactic Republic and was allowed to foster its own unique military culture. When the Emperor ascended to power and the Empire was born, he consolidated many planetary security forces into the Imperial Navy and Army and placed these in the hands of a council of admirals and generals—the Imperial High Command.

**planetary shield generator** Planetary shields used layers of charged energy to dissipate incoming turbolaser blasts and destroy space debris on contact, protecting planets from the devastating effects of attacks as well as asteroid and comet strikes. Starships unlucky enough to careen into these energy screens were instantly vaporized, and even a glancing impact could severely damage a vessel. Since these shields were invisible, pilots relied on sensor readings to avoid contact, although enemy jamming could block the sensors, causing vessels to fly right into the shields. This nearly happened to the Rebel fleet when it attacked the second Death Star at Endor.

**planetary turbolaser** Immense surface-to-orbit weaponry that fired supercharged bolts of de-

Planetary shield generator

Planetary turbolaser

structive energy into low orbit. When deployed in sufficient numbers, they proved a deadly deterrent to planetary sieges. A common model was the KDY w-165 Planet Defender.

**Planet Dreams, Incorporated** A small business that worked from a headquarters on Cloud City, providing terraforming ("planetscaping") services to corporations and exploratory groups. Formed by Wiorkettle, Treva Horme, and Ozz, the corporation eventually branched out into the entertainment business, turning unsettled but habitable planets in the Greater Javin into resorts.

**plank gas** A toxic gas that was corrosive and incapacitated on contact. Plank gas was used as a weapon, more specifically as a canister payload in projectile launchers.

**Plaristes** In his book *Of Minds, Men, and Machines,* the renowned pre-Republic philosopher Plaristes argued convincingly about the impossibility of automata ever achieving artificial sentience. More than 25 millennia of droids' existence and 50 billion droids in service, however, proved him wrong.

**plasspecs** Artificial lenses worn over the eyes of those who needed their vision corrected. The use of medication to correct vision eventually rendered these lenses largely obsolete. Some people, however—whether through allergic reactions to the medication, simple refusal to take it, or a lower-than-standard technological background—continued to wear corrective plasspecs.

**plasteel** A tough, shiny material, it was used in the construction of countless items throughout the galaxy, such as the domes on Mon Calamari cities and the cockpits and displays on starships.

**plastoid** Any type of thermoformed substance, such as the many varieties of shaped battle armor, tabletops, and inexpensive building materials found in Mos Eisley.

**Platform 327** After the Battle of Hoth, the *Millennium Falcon* landed on Platform 327 in Bespin's Cloud City.

**Platinum Valor Cross** One of the most distinguished medals awarded to Rebel Alliance officers during the Galactic Civil War, given to honor bravery and leadership in combat.

Kar Plaushe

**Plattahr** A criminal enforcer working for Black Nebula out of Phorliss. Despite wearing an armored vest, Plattahr was killed by Mara Jade in Gorb Drig's cantina.

**Plaushe, Kar** A veil-wearing human female socialite known to frequent the Outlander Club on Coruscant prior to the Clone Wars.

**Plawal** The first volcanic rift jungle to be encased within a dome on Belsavis. Jedi Master Plett established a fortress there that became a refuge for Jedi survivors after the Clone Wars. The dome was built by the Brathflen Corporation early in Palpatine's reign as Emperor. In those days, the valley was known as Plett's Well. The name was later shortened to Pletwell, then simply Plawal. Some 18 years before the Battle of Yavin, the Emperor commissioned the battlemoon *Eye of Palpatine* to wipe out the Jedi enclave, but the ship never arrived. The Emperor's small backup force of interceptors bombed Plawal but were wiped out by Belsavis's Y-wings. The Jedi departed for places unknown after erasing all knowledge of their presence from the minds of the city's inhabitants.

Platform 327

**Plaza of the Core** A wide plaza constructed in Galactic City on Coruscant after the Yuuzhan Vong War.

**Pleader** A legal advocate on the planet Concord Dawn assigned to represent criminals.

**Pleck** A New Republic Intelligence technical agent who worked with Taisden on the *Glorious* during the search for the Teljkon vagabond near Gmar Askilon.

**Plee, Doctor** A Ho'Din scientist, he was involved in the Duro reclamation project during the Yuuzhan Vong War.

**pleekwood** A substance used in making furnishings, musical instruments, and other luxury goods as well as high-class interior design.

**Pleni** A native of New Apsolon, she was a Minor Legislator some 12 years before the Battle of Naboo. After the deaths of Governor Roan and the Jedi Master Tahl, Pleni suddenly announced her bid to assume the role of planetary governor. She managed to sway several key Legislators to give their support to her campaign, and Mace Windu believed that she had purchased a list of Absolute supporters from Oleg in order to blackmail them into supporting her. When Obi-Wan Kenobi and Bant Eerin were dispatched to confront her, they found her dead, shot and killed by a probe droid that was later traced to Qui-Gon Jinn.

**Plenty's** A sizable grocery store chain on Commenor.

**Plessus, Ghon** A member of an ill-fated Jedi mission killed on Kabal during rioting caused by food shortages just prior to the Clone Wars.

**Plett, Master** About 100 years before the Battle of Yavin, the Ho'Din Jedi Master Plett built a house and laboratory in the Plawal rift that served as a safe haven for Jedi; it was known as Plett's Well and, later, Plawal. Plett was rumored to be able to com-

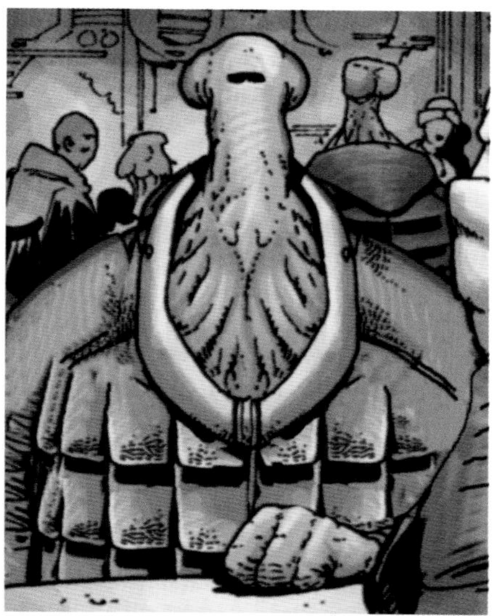
Plattahr

municate with animals, and legend said he controlled the weather on Belsavis.

**Plett's Well** *See* Plawal.

**Pletwell** *See* Plawal.

**Plevitz** A professional writer hired by Mammon Hoole to author *Plevitz Essential Guide to Species.*

**Plex** *See* PLX missile tube.

**plexalloy** A translucent material stronger than standard transparisteel. It was used in starship viewports.

**Plexgrove Combine** A financial and banking consortium that provided low- and midlevel services to the galaxy. Plexgrove was one of the original Contributing Sponsors of the Corporate Sector Authority.

**plexisteel** A synthetic compound used in the construction of some droids.

**plexoid** A strong, durable, and heavy material used by the Hapan military to form pieces of body armor.

**Plexus droid vessels (PDVs)** While Sector Plexus, the heart of communications within Imperial Intelligence, had access to the few then-still-active fragments of the HoloNet, most of its communications were handled through the use of Plexus droid vessels (PDVs). PDVs were small, extremely fast starships run strictly by computer and droid brains. Each ship had a nav computer and various droid components. A combination of PDV speed, programmed skills, and efficient route algorithms guaranteed that a PDV never had a jump duration greater than one day, except in extreme emergencies. PDVs featured sensor camouflaging gear that allowed them to pass for mining probes or scavenger droids to casual observers.

***Pliada di am Imperium*** An airy plaza on Coruscant, located at the eastern end of the Glitannai Esplanade near the Imperial Palace.

**Plibene Rock** An area near Mos Espa mistakenly thought by early prospectors to contain deposits of the rare mineral bene.

**Plif** A small, furry rodent-like creature with large ears found on the planet Arbra. Plif was the spokesmind for the Hoojibs of Arbra. When the Rebel Alliance approached the Hoojibs for use of their world as a Rebel base, Plif was the one with whom they negotiated.

*Plif*

**Plikk, Captain** The commanding officer of the Imperial Star Destroyer that followed the *Millennium Falcon* through a dimensional rift. In this alternative dimension ruled by Rebel hero Cody Sunn-Childe, the Imperials attempted to destroy his floating city. Sunn-Childe used his powerful psychic abilities to destroy much of the Imperial task force. Though Sunn-Childe and his city were also destroyed as a result of the attack, Plikk's Star Destroyer was stranded in the now empty dimension without the power to return to the galaxy. Plikk was a human female with fair skin, blue eyes, and brown hair.

**Plirr, Loreza** A cartographer tasked with mapping the entirety of Centerpoint Station following the Yuuzhan Vong War. She and her son, Deevan, lived on Talus when not aboard the ancient station.

**Plo, Lomi** A Dathomirian Nightsister imprisoned alongside the Dark Jedi Welk aboard the Yuuzhan Vong vessel *Baanu Rass* at Myrkr. She was found by Anakin Solo's strike team during their mission to eliminate the deadly Jedi-hunting voxyn queen. Unbeknownst to most, Lomi Plo was affiliated with a growing new Order of Sith based on Korriban. She was a powerfully built woman with dark hair and darker eyes. Freed by Anakin's team, Lomi and Welk agreed to help the Jedi infiltrate the worldship and destroy the voxyn. In the heat of the battle, Lomi and Welk elected to save themselves, abandoning the Jedi, boarding the *Tachyon Flier,* and fleeing from Myrkr, unaware that Raynar Thul was aboard the ship.

The vessel was shot down by the Yuuzhan Vong and crash-landed in the Unknown Regions. Lomi, Welk, and Thul were tended by the Killik hives that found them, and they were absorbed into the collective consciousness of the hives. Their inherent Force sensitivity extended the hives beyond previous limitations. Lomi's dark side allegiance essentially created the Gorog hive, a dark and elusive subconscious will that was part of the larger Colony hive-mind.

Lomi Plo herself became known among the Gorog as the Night Herald, a sort of "queen" of the Dark Nest. Her incredible connection to the dark side of the Force allowed her to completely mask her activities and those of the Gorog, even from Jedi Master Luke Skywalker. Lomi Plo remained out of sight, directing the Gorog and planting various alternative truths in the collective mind of the Colony in an effort to cover her tracks.

The Gorog began to slowly disrupt the efforts of the Galactic Alliance, undermining every attempt to create a galactic peace in order to divide the Alliance and conquer the galaxy. Lomi Plo thrived on doubt. If she sensed any doubt in a person's mind at all, she could hide behind it in the Force and make herself effectively invisible. In this way, she sowed discord among the Jedi Knights. Working through Alema Rar, a Joiner in the Colony, Lomi Plo created conflict in Luke Skywalker's relationship with Mara Jade by engendering doubts about his wife's past work as an assassin for the Empire.

During the Gorog hive's attempt to spread beyond the blockaded Utegetu Nebula, Plo was at last confronted by Master Skywalker, who had discovered her powers and cast aside his own fears. Plo nearly overpowered Skywalker, who was rescued by Mara—she literally *scraped* the Dark Jedi off him with her X-wing. By this time, Plo was already gruesomely disfigured thanks to her time with the Killiks. She had mismatched legs, one insect and one human. Her body was encased in a somewhat cylindrical Killik pressure carapace. A pair of long, crooked arms extended from stooped shoulders, with a second pair of shorter, more human-looking arms protruding from the middle of her body. She had a half-melted, noseless face with bulbous multifaceted eyes and a pair of stubby mandibles.

The Jedi tracked Plo to Tenupe. Skywalker again confronted her, this time clearing his mind of any form of doubt. In a swift battle of lightsabers, Skywalker got inside her guard and cut Lomi Plo into four pieces. With her death, the Gorog were left without direction, and they were eventually absorbed into the rest of the Colony or died out altogether.

**Plooriod III** The site of a small palace atop a rocky spire in a peaceful sea, it was built for the brutal Overlord Ghorin, ruler of the Greater Plooriod Cluster. Darth Vader visited Ghorin here and killed him for his apparent double cross of the Empire in the period following the Battle of Yavin.

**Plooriod IV** The planet near which the Rebel Alliance captured a group of Overlord Ghorin's Y-wing fighters, which they used to discredit Ghorin in the eyes of the Empire. Later, the Imperial frigate *Red Wind* was discovered near Plooriod IV and was destroyed by Alliance corvettes.

***Plooriod Bodkin*** A Republic cruiser that was part of the task force dispatched to track down the *Scarlet Thranta* during the Separatist crisis. It was led by Nejaa Halcyon and consisted of a dozen Jedi Knights and 30 members of the Republic's Judiciary. When Halcyon set down on Bpfassh to confront *Scarlet Thranta*'s commander, Captain Zozridor Slayke, Slayke stole the *Plooriod Bodkin* from the Jedi forces, resulting in great loss of face.

**Ploo sector** An area of space also known as the Greater Plooriod sector. It contained the Greater Plooriod Cluster, as well as the Plooriod and Ploo systems. Ploo II was the homeworld of the Glymphid species, while Fluggrians hailed from Ploo IV.

**Ploovo Two-For-One** An infamous criminal kingpin, this portly humanoid from the Cron drift was a con man, a loan shark, a thief, a smash-and-grab man, and a bunko artist, among other things. In his smuggling days, Han Solo sometimes worked for Ploovo Two-

Ploovo Two-For-One

For-One, and for a time he owed the crime lord a large number of credits. Ploovo ordered Solo's death after the Corellian caused him to lose face once too often.

**Plooz, Prince** About 100 years before the Galactic Civil War, the ruler of the planet Alzar was King Gokus. His son, Plooz, was mischievous and often got into trouble. The unsteady peace between Alzar and its neighbor world Sooma was threatened when Gokus's military commander, General Sludd, caused the toddler Plooz to end up on Sooma in a plot to have the worlds erupt in war. Plooz was a small, egg-shaped humanoid with reptilian skin and frog-like eyes.

**Plort** This Targonnian served Dictator-Forever Craw and led the attack on Master Zorneth's herd ship.

**Plothis** A smuggler acquaintance of Han Solo and Chewbacca who ran a small business in Esau's Ridge. His primary commodity was specialized smuggling equipment, although he was equally adept at selling information. He was shot in a squabble with a customer about four years before the Black Fleet Crisis. Bracha e'Naso took over the day-to-day operation of his business.

Plumba

**Plourr** *See* Estillo, Isplourrdacartha.

**Ploven** An aquatic species native to Gra Ploven. Two hundred thousand coastal-dwelling Ploven were boiled alive when the Imperial Star Destroyer *Forger* concentrated its orbital firepower on Gra Ploven's oceans.

**pludris** A type of expensive liquor, best served as a vintage stock.

**Plug-2 Behemoth** A Podracer type developed by Collor Pondrat, used by the Phuii pilot Mars Guo.

**Plug-8G** A series of Podracing engines that resembled a cluster of tubes built around a central cooling channel. They were developed by Vokoff-Strood and found in the Vokoff-Strood Plug-G 927 model Podracer used by Ark "Bumpy" Roose.

**Plug-F Mammoth** A huge racing engine designed by Collor Pondrat and used by Sebulba in a split-X configuration on his prize-winning Podracer.

**Plumba** An obese man, he was a member of the tribunal that put itself in charge of the Empire after Sate Pestage was suspected of treason. Ysanne Isard killed Plumba with a booby trap disguised as a Sith lanvarok, a highly prized collectible.

**plunk droid** The nickname given to a four-legged version of the standard power droid.

**PLX missile tube (Plex)** A combination missile-and-rocket launcher used as an infantry support weapon by Galactic Republic and Imperial personnel. The launcher was an over-the-shoulder device operated by one person and was disposable once fired. The PLX-2 from Merr-Sonn supported "dumb" rockets and advanced GAM guided missiles. The PLX-2 held a missile in the launcher, as well as one loaded. Green troopers frequently forgot that it took two taps of the firing stud to launch a rocket. One tap set the firing mode (either line-of-sight or guided); the second fired the payload. The PLX-2M was capable of shooting "chips," or fragmentation warheads that burst into deadly shrapnel. The PLX-4 could fire GAM, dumb, and newer Savant missiles.

**PLY 3000** SoroSuub's personal luxury yacht, a successor to an earlier PLY 2400 design. This 50-meter starship had three main levels: the main deck, which featured a full galley, six deluxe cabins, a dining area, and the bridge; an engineering level below the main deck; and an observation area above the main deck, in the rear. Lando Calrissian's *Lady Luck* was a PLY 3000.

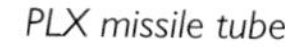
PLX missile tube

**plyridian fever** A disease that required a medical quarantine. It had an incubation period of about four weeks.

**PMC-210 medical capsule** Medical capsules were used for the transportation of critically wounded patients from the battlefield to more secure and better-equipped facilities. Developed by Praxen Emergency Medical Services, the PMC-210 medical capsule had a droid brain that helped regulate and monitor life signs in a patient. Darth Sidious's shock troopers placed Darth Vader's charred body in a capsule for transit from Mustafar to Coruscant.

**Pnorr, Venlyss** A Gand findsman who worked as a retrieval agent for the Rebel Alliance during the Galactic Civil War.

**Poborandurannum** A sacred temple found on Natinati and visited by Jabba the Hutt.

**Pochi** The third planet in the Faarlsun system, homeworld of the tulvarees. It was a dry but habitable sphere covered with endless plains and a few low mountain ranges. Pochi had three moons.

**pocker** An ion-burst-powered atlatl used by Jango and Boba Fett for catching rollerfish on Kamino. It fired a missile attached to a nearly invisible but strong line.

**pocket cruiser** A small, obsolete class of capital ship, it saw extensive service during the last phase of the Clone Wars. Pocket cruisers were easy to manufacture and were about equal to other warships at the time. Some could later be found as training platforms, pirate ships, or in the arsenals of local military forces.

**pocket patrol boat** A small single-pilot ship, it traded high speed for limited firepower.

**pocket-sized aquarium** A novelty item that could be purchased at trade shops

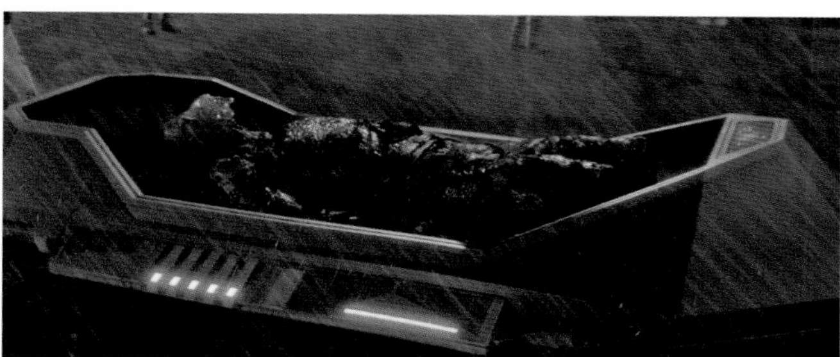
PMC-210 medical capsule

## Notable Podracers and Pilots

**Balta-Trabaat BT310 quadra-Pod:** *Ben Quadinaros*

**Farwan & Glott FG 8T8-Twin Block2 Special:** *Neva Kee*

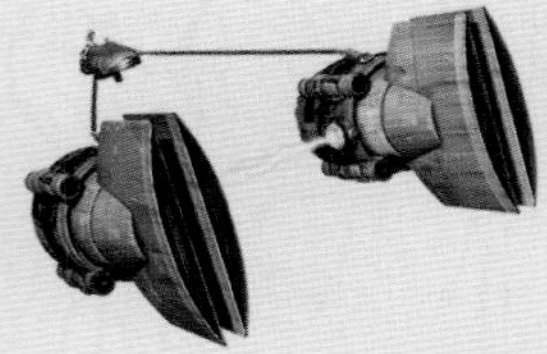
**Ord Pedrovia custom:** *Gasgano*

**Bin Gassi Quadrijet 4Barrel 904E:** *Boles Roor*

**Galactic Power Engineering GPE-3130:** *Mawhonic*

**Radon-Ulzer 620C:** *Anakin Skywalker*

**Collor Pondrat Plug-2 Behemoth:** *Mars Guo*

**Irdani Performance Group IPG-X1131:** *Teemto Pagalies*

**Volvec (Keizar-Volvec) Wasp KV9T9-B:** *Clegg Holdfast*

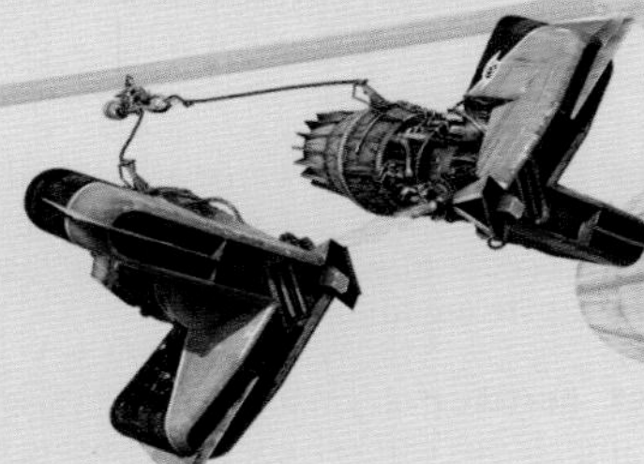
**Collor Pondrat Plug-F Mammoth:** *Sebulba*

**JAK Racing J930 Dash-8:** *Ebe Endocott*

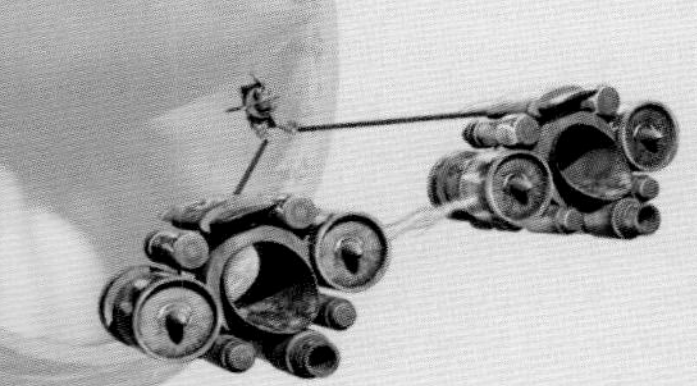
**Vokoff-Strood Plug-8G 927 Cluster Array:** *Ark "Bumpy" Roose*

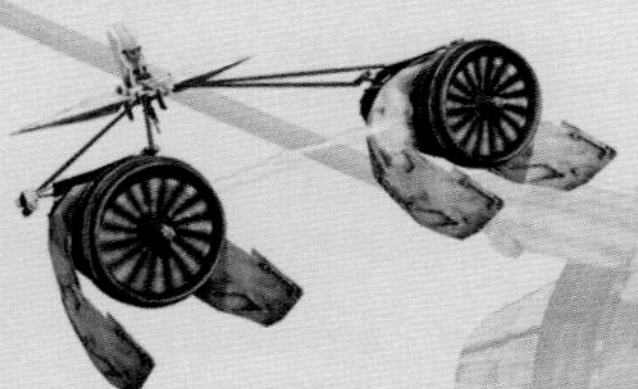
**Elsinore-Cordova TurboDyne 99-U:** *Wan Sandage*

**Kurtob KRT 410C:** *Elan Mak*

**Vokoff-Strood Titan 2150:** *Ratts Tyerell*

**Exelbrok XL 5115:** *Ody Mandrell*

**Manta RamAir Mark IV Flat Twin Turbojet:** *Aldar Beedo*

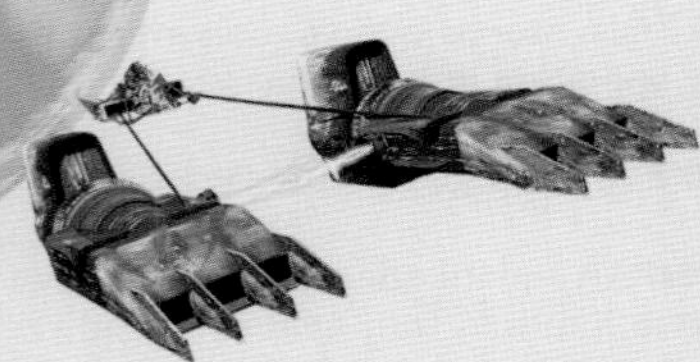
**Vulptereen RS 557 (327):** *Dud Bolt*

*Podrace*

throughout the galaxy. It included a small plastic cube containing water, a nutrient dispenser, and, of course, a fish.

**pod** The basic term adopted by the Kaminoans to describe a group of clone troopers who were grown, trained, and deployed as a single unit.

**Poderis** This harsh world in the Orus sector had a 10-hour rotational cycle and a severe axial tilt that could create windstorms of up to 200 kilometers an hour. In addition, the unusual geology of Poderis forced its fiercely independent colonists to build their cities atop a vast network of mesas. An angled wall 100 meters wide (called a shield-barrier) ran along the outer edge of these cities, helping deflect Poderis's damaging seasonal winds. Luke Skywalker visited Poderis in an attempt to uncover the Empire's clone-trafficking network and narrowly escaped a trap set for him by Grand Admiral Thrawn.

**podpopper** A vegetable grown in hydroponic gardens on Tatooine.

**Podrace** A high-speed and dangerous sporting event in which competitors piloted exceedingly fast Podracers through dangerous courses. Podracers were essentially small, repulsorlift cockpits pulled by large engines. The vehicles were typically customized by their pilots, who needed incredible reflexes and great courage. Because the demands of Podracing were intense, very few humans could compete in the sport. Its extreme hazards resulted in it being outlawed throughout most of the civilized galaxy, though it thrived for years in the Outer Rim Territories during the final decades of the Galactic Republic.

While Tatooine's Boonta Eve Classic may have been the most popular (it did boast the highest mortality rate), it was just one of many tracks scattered on distant worlds. The frigid planet of Ando Prime featured an icy racecourse sponsored by Bendu monks; the watery world of Aquilaris had a track that cut through the sinking relic of the Old City; the gaseous planet Ord Ibanna had a foolhardy course that spanned the connecting bridges and pipelines of floating mining platforms; tropical Baroonda let Podracers scream through the swamp world's ancient ruins; the industrial wasteland world of Mon Gazza opened up its spice mines for races. Perhaps the world best known for Podracing was Malastare, whose methane lakes and mountain ranges hosted such notable courses as the Malastare 100 and the Vinta Harvest Classic.

Podracing traced its origins to ancient contests of animal-drawn chariots. Long ago, a foolhardy mechanic named Phoebos revisited the chariot design, replacing the cart with a repulsorlift cockpit and the beasts of burden with rocket jet engines.

**Podracer** Because the extremely dangerous sport of Podracing required its pilots to customize their individual vehicles to the best of their abilities, there were countless Podracer variants. In general, a Podracer included a repulsorlift-equipped cockpit towed by a pair of incredibly powerful turbine engines, connected to the cockpit by Steelton control cables. Connecting the paired engines was a scintillating band of numbing energy—energy binders—that ensured the engines would not go flying in random directions. A Podracer could typically achieve a top speed of 900 kilometers per hour.

Famous Podracer models (and their pilots) included:

- Balta-Trabaat BT310 quadra-Pod: Ben Quadinaros
- Bin Gassi Quadrijet 4Barrel 904E: Boles Roor
- Collor Pondrat Plug-2 Behemoth: Mars Guo
- Collor Pondrat Plug-F Mammoth: Sebulba
- Daimo Engineering Banshee-11: Scorch Zanales
- Elsinore-Cordova TurboDyne 99-U: Wan Sandage
- Exelbrok XL 5115: Ody Mandrell
- Farwan & Glott FG 8T8-Twin Block2 Special: Neva Kee
- Galactic Power Engineering GPE-3130: Mawhonic
- Irdani Performance Group IPG-X1131: Teemto Pagalies
- JAK Racing J930 Dash-8: Ebe Endocott
- Kurtob KRT 410C: Elan Mak
- Manta RamAir Mark IV Flat Twin Turbojet: Aldar Beedo
- Ord Pedrovia custom: Gasgano
- Radon-Ulzer 620C: Anakin Skywalker (and, later, Sebulba)
- Serabyss Howler 1165: Knire Dark
- Shelba 730S Razor: Bozzie Baranta
- Turca 910 Special: Toy Dampner
- Volvec (Keizar-Volvec) Wasp KV9T9-B: Clegg Holdfast
- Vokoff-Strood Plug-8G 927 Cluster Array: Ark "Bumpy" Roose
- Vokoff-Strood Titan 2150: Ratts Tyerell
- Vulptereen RS 557 (327): Dud Bolt

***Podracing Quarterly*** A popular Podracing publication at the height of the sport. Racer Clegg Holdfast was a contributor.

**pod troopers** Dropping from seedpod-like yorik coral drop ships the size of the *Millennium Falcon,* these Yuuzhan Vong airborne infantry units searched for Jacen Solo on the terraformed Coruscant. Their pods had minimal life support and drive systems—basically just enough to get the warrior safely to the ground.

**Poe** A silver protocol droid with one black metal peg leg, he was assigned to Rogue Squadron to help ease the pilots into the local population. Poe wasn't quite as fussy as C-3PO but was fairly rigid in trying to get the Rogues to do what he knew was right for them. This very proper droid was everlastingly mortified that he had to travel in the luggage bin of an X-wing.

***Poesy*** A Mon Calamari light cruiser stationed at Duro during the Yuuzhan Vong War. Admiral Wuht commanded the defenses at Duro, which included four squadrons of E-wing and B-wing starfighters and the *Poesy,* commanded by Commodore Mabettye. The ship was armed with 14 turbolasers, 18 ion cannons, half a dozen heavy tractor beam projectors, and heavy shields. The ship initially moved to protect Bburru, but Wuht ordered it to withdraw to its previous position. The *Poesy* rejoined the battle after Wuht learned that the Yuuzhan Vong intended to destroy all the Duros orbital cities.

**Poggle the Lesser** Born into a low caste, Poggle bucked the strict societal structure of the Geonosians and aspired to leadership, achieving the rank of Archduke and leader of the Stalgasin hive. He oversaw the production

*Poggle the Lesser*

Point Modie

of battle droids for the Trade Federation and the Techno Union, though he personally hated Nute Gunray.

He committed his workers to the growing Separatist cause and hosted the first meeting of the Confederacy of Independent Systems on his world. Upon the discovery of Jedi and Senate spies within his domain, Poggle presided over their trial. Obi-Wan Kenobi, Padmé Amidala, and Anakin Skywalker were found guilty of espionage and sentenced to be executed as per Geonosian tradition. The crafty captives outwitted the vicious beasts unleashed upon them at the Geonosis execution arena. A sudden arrival of Jedi reinforcements turned the public spectacle into a frenzied battle.

Poggle and the rest of the Separatist leaders retreated into an underground command center. Poggle, in possession of top-secret plans for an ultimate weapon that the Geonosians were contracted to construct, returned the blueprints to Count Dooku, who fled Geonosis to courier the plans to his dark master. During the Clone Wars, Poggle and the rest of the Separatist Council hid on Mustafar until Darth Sidious's new Sith apprentice, Darth Vader, arrived and slaughtered all the Confederacy leaders, effectively ending the Clone Wars.

**Pohtarza** A t'landa Til appointed as Head Sacredot of Colony Five on Ylesia early in the Galactic Civil War. He was assassinated by an Aar'aa who had infiltrated the colony at Jabba the Hutt's request.

**Poi, Pollux** More than 4,000 years before the Galactic Civil War, this deranged Anx designer developed a line of assassin droids for the Shell Hutts. These A series droids would eventually become known as Pollux assassin droids.

**Poinard, Ark** An elderly Imperial vice admiral, he commanded the *Imperial II*–class Star Destroyer *Erinnic* during the Yuuzhan Vong's attack on Ord Mantell. Poinard was a onetime adversary of General Yald Sutel, although the two became allies during the Yuuzhan Vong War.

**Point 5** A game of chance played in many galactic casinos.

**Point Bleak** The Galactic Alliance's code name for its contingency escape destination should something happen to the warships blockading the Corellian system during the Corellia–GA War. All ships were given the coordinates to Point Bleak and were to proceed to the deep-space location upon orders from the fleet's flagship, *Dodonna.*

**point-defense weapons** Anti-starfighter weaponry found on the hulls of massive capital ships.

**Point Down** One of the primary Separatist bases on Jabiim during the Clone Wars. It was captured by the Galactic Republic, but at the loss of the Republic's own Shelter Base.

**Point Modie** A dazzling port city on Maramere that served as the planetary capital.

Shae Polikex

**Poison Moon** A large asteroid in the Hoth system that looked like a battered half-moon, with shadows across its surface vaguely resembling the features of a skull.

***Poison Moon*** An *Interceptor*-class frigate, one of many that were hired by the Lords of the New Sith who secretly existed on Korriban. The frigate, which was piloted by the former smuggler Wayniss, was recalled from its regular duty to provide Sith Lord Dician with a ship to travel to the MZX32905 system and eliminate Alema Rar.

**Poista, Elea** A top Exex in the shipping department of Bespin Motors. She used her connections to secure weapons and sell them on the black market—including to the Rebels—under the alias Kel during the Galactic Civil War.

Polarizing field insulator suit

**Pok** A Yuzzem who was an indentured servant to a merchant at Anchorhead. The young Luke Skywalker studied the Yuzzem culture and language with Pok. When Pok was granted his freedom, he stayed on as an equal partner in the equipment business, demonstrating his unique entrepreneurial skill.

**polarizing field insulator suit** Large and bulky, these suits made by VargeCorp were most often used by mechanics and technicians who risked exposure to powerful energy discharges as part of their work.

**Polearm Squadron** A New Republic A-wing squadron that suffered heavy losses during the hunt for the *Iron Fist.*

**Polestar Reception Room** Located just off the Grand Hall of the Galactic Republic's Senate Rotunda, this room was where beings from across the galaxy awaited their audiences with Senators and other dignitaries.

**Policy and Resources Council** A division of the Galactic Alliance responsible for establishing the policies and mechanisms for providing government and military personnel with the materials and supplies needed to carry out their jobs. At the height of the Corellia–GA War, the council claimed to be bound by the law when basic military supplies were not available to the front-line troops. Jacen Solo worked to enact the Legislative and Regulations Statute Amendment, which gave himself—as well as Cha Niathal and Cal Omas—the ability to "relieve regulatory burdens . . . without the need to refer the issue to committees, councils, or even the full Senate," provided that their requests were within budgetary constraints. This seemingly innocuous loophole ballooned into enormous excesses in executive power exerted by Jacen during his transformation into Darth Caedus.

**Polidor, Yamele** A petite Rindian with pointed ears; her two hands had eight long fingers each. She was a guest of Jenna Zan Arbor at Didi's Café.

**Polikex, Shae** A doctor at the Rebel base on Yavin 4 who accompanied Nera Dantels and Biggs Darklighter into the surrounding jungles to find a cure for Hobbie Klivian's dangerous infection prior to the Battle of Yavin.

**Polipe** A member of a multitentacled species who was Booster Terrik's copilot some years before the Battle of Yavin. He assisted

Booster in keeping a young Wedge Antilles safe after the death of Wedge's parents.

**Polis Massa** A jumbled collection of lazily floating asteroids in the Subterrel sector, Polis Massa was a small Outer Rim mining settlement far removed from the more populated areas of the galaxy. The airless rocks hosted sealed outposts inhabited by the strangely silent Polis Massan aliens. It was at one of these outposts that Jedi fugitives Yoda and Obi-Wan Kenobi regrouped following the decimation of their Order by the rise of the Empire. Having failed to thwart Palpatine, Yoda fled to Polis Massa with Bail Organa to recover. Obi-Wan Kenobi, having defeated Darth Vader on Mustafar, soon joined them. He rushed an ailing Padmé Amidala to the medical center, where the Polis Massan medics and droids tried to stabilize her vital signs. Padmé died there, but not before giving birth to Leia and Luke Skywalker, infants who carried with them the hope for the future.

Polis Massa was once an intact world that was home to the underground-dwelling Eellayin people—a species that mysteriously vanished when the world was destroyed by an unknown and ancient cataclysm. Over 500 years before the Clone Wars, an archaeological expedition began combing the rocky fragments for the remains of the Eellayin. The alien researchers, believing themselves to be descendants of the Eellayin, became so entrenched in the asteroid remains over the centuries that they simply became known as Polis Massans to all who dealt with them.

Polis Massa

Unut Poll (left)

Polis Massans

**Polis Massan** Strangely silent aliens with slight builds and featureless faces, they inhabited the asteroid colony of Polis Massa. They maintained a number of sealed outposts on the barren rock surface, toiling away at their interests with little involvement with the surrounding galaxy. The Polis Massans, originally the Kallidahin, weren't actually from Polis Massa—but they obsessively clung to the shattered asteroid remains of the world that may have been home to their ancestors. In the ancient past, the Eellayin homeworld was transformed into rubble by an unknown cataclysm, and the Eellayin people vanished. Five hundred years before the Clone Wars, an expedition to uncover the remains of the Eellayin was undertaken by the faceless diminutive aliens. They became so associated with the archaeological effort that they became known as Polis Massans, a name they adopted with no objections.

Little was known of the Polis Massans, save that they hailed from the Subterrel sector. They were skilled xenobiologists, fascinated by other alien species yet not confrontational despite such passions. They preferred instead to study from afar, examining the trappings of alien cultures, if not the aliens themselves. Given how little open contact they had with other cultures, they amassed an impressive xenobiological database. Uncovering their true connection to the Eellayin was of paramount concern to the Polis Massans. They made contact with the secretive Kaminoans, exchanging some of their data for cloning technology. The Polis Massans adapted this cloning equipment for their own purposes, though their cloning processes were less sophisticated than the work of the Kaminoans. The Polis Massans employed it in the hope of reconstructing any biological matter they discovered in their archaeological digs.

**Polith system** The system containing the planet Thyferra, homeworld of the Vratix and the center of the galaxy's bacta industry.

**Political Gain Operation (PGO)** Terrorist missions carried out by Imperial special-forces units and then blamed on the Rebel Alliance.

**Politrix** A red-haired Jedi Knight during the Clone Wars, she was a good friend of Jang Li-Li. Politrix was killed in an ambush just two months after the Battle of Geonosis when she was caught in the blast of a plasma grenade.

**Poll, Unut** A male Arcona from the planet Cona, he was known to cooperate with Rebel Alliance operatives. Poll frequented the cantina in Mos Eisley on Tatooine. He avoided the temptations of salt, which was very addictive to his species. He owned Spaceport Speeders in central Mos Eisley.

Lieutenant Pollard

**Pollar, Reme** A female member of Rogue Squadron shortly after the death of Grand Admiral Thrawn.

**Pollard, Lieutenant** A scarred and ageless Rebel who helped rescue Ackbar from Imperials, he worked alongside Ackbar in the Shantipole Project to create the B-wing fighter. He also led Dagger Squadron during the assault on Bannistar Station, an Imperial refueling depot in the Mid Rim.

**Pollillus** The technology-poor Troig homeworld in the Vannell sector, beyond the Koornacht Cluster.

**Pollux** Captain of the starship *Nebula Chaser*. Though not overly loyal to the Jedi Knights, Pollux agreed to help Alema and Numa Rar evacuate the natives of New Plympto when the Yuuzhan Vong destroyed the planet's ecosystem. After his ship was boarded by the crew from a Yuuzhan Vong frigate, he lied to conceal the Jedi's presence. Pollux was tortured and beaten by the Yuuzhan Vong, and his crew was killed. He presumably died when the Yuuzhan Vong destroyed the *Chaser*.

**Pollux assassin droid** Ancient battle droids developed by Pollux Poi, they were originally designed to eliminate the rivals of the Shell Hutts, 4,000 years before the Battle of Yavin. Mil-

Pollux assassin droid

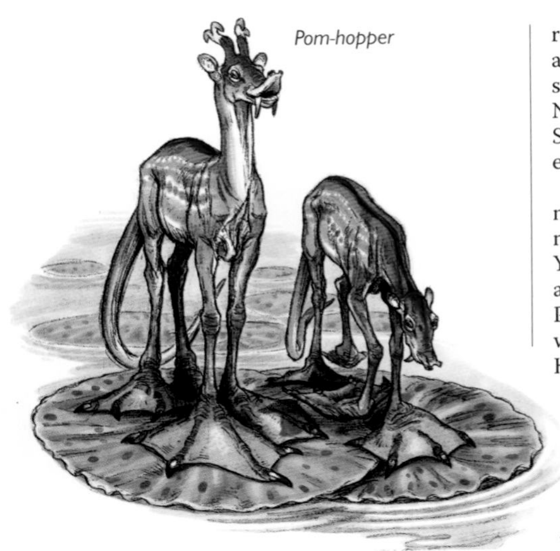


lennia later, Count Dooku came into possession of nearly 100 of the A series assassins for use in the Clone Wars. These humanoid droids had four photoreceptors for seeing in low-light conditions or scanning infrared wavelengths. Sweeping curves and sharp points dominated their sleek, shiny bodies. Each droid carried a blaster rifle, with a shoulder-mounted blaster cannon as a backup. Anakin Skywalker faced off against these droids on Jabiim.

**Polmanar** A textile-manufacturing planet with a substantial Nothoiin population, Polmanar attracted the attention of the Empire due to reedug, a popular narcotic grown in its hills. The reedug farmers, resenting the new Imperial tariffs, enlisted local guerrillas to strike at the Empire's small occupation force. Their efforts attracted the attention of the Rebel Alliance, which armed the Polmanar resistance despite an Imperial blockade. A special Corellian gunship, the *Handree,* equipped with a proper transponder code, ran the blockade and smuggled medical supplies there shortly after the Battle of Yavin. The Empire eventually decided Polmanar wasn't worth the effort and withdrew, a decision pointed to by the Rebel Alliance as evidence of the Empire's weakness.

**Polneye** Located in the Koornacht Cluster in the Farlax sector, this planet was on the far side of the cluster from Coruscant. A dry world, Polneye was covered by high cirrus clouds whose rain almost never reached the surface. Polneye was established by the Imperial Black Sword Command as a secret military transshipment point for the sector. It became a busy supply depot and open-air armory, with many landing pads built on the brown flatlands. Over time, the population grew, and small cities sprang up around each landing zone.

When the Empire abandoned the Farlax sector following the Battle of Endor, Polneye's quarter million civilians, who called themselves Polneyi, were forced to fend for themselves. They took advantage of the valuable resources left behind by the fleeing Imperials and formed a reasonably prosperous unified state consisting of eight cities: Three North, Nine South, Nine North, Ten South, Eleven South, Eleven North, Twelve North, and the empty city of Fourteen North.

Twelve years after the Battle of Endor, Polneye was brutally attacked by the Yevethan military on the 40th day of Mofat, in what the Yevetha called the Great Purge. Plat Mallar, a Grannan citizen of Ten South, took one of Polneye's six operational TIE interceptors and was able to destroy a Yevethan scout fighter. He then attempted to reach the planet Galantos in the short-range TIE but was picked up by a New Republic prowler, which alerted the Republic leaders to the recent aggressive actions of the Yevetha. Mallar was nursed back to health on Coruscant and became a New Republic pilot. Admiral Ackbar helped push through an emergency petition for membership in the New Republic for Polneye, which Leia approved.

**Polordion smootdust** An illicit narcotic used in the undercity of Coruscant.

**Polos** The toxic third planet of the Beshqek system in the Deep Core.

**polpian** Domesticated animals that often triggered allergies in Bothans.

**Polpot, Zokor** The ambitious vice chancellor of the University of Coruscant during the New Order, Polpot discredited and ousted the chancellor by stealing the accounting droid 8t88's head. Assuming the chancellery, he soon died in an accident on Mawan believed to be engineered by 8t88 as revenge for its disfigurement.

**Pols Anaxes** The largest city on Anaxes and site of the world's primary civilian spaceport.

**Polters, Trace** The owner and operator of the Ma'Haffee Shipyards in the Cularin system during the Clone Wars, he was an ally of the Jedi Knights serving at the Almas Academy. Prior to the Clone Wars, he was often able to help the Jedi acquire starships for missions, until shortages caused by the war effort precluded this.

**Polus** Orbiting the binary star Avindia in the Outer Rim, Polus was a frigid, mountainous planet with one massive frozen ocean. The average daytime temperature was 50 degrees below freezing with frequent blizzards and ice storms; during a brief but seasonal warming period, the planet was hit by light from both suns. Polus was inhabited by the Pyn'gani, who were masters of thermal dynamics. Their cities and habitats were shielded by a network of heat generators protecting them from the extreme cold. Ages ago, the Pyn'gani played a major role in developing the carbon-freezing process used to store goods for long-term shipment. Mining the valuable metal continued to be a major source of income.

**polwocz** A type of creature located in the Spinward sector. Polwocz spawn lay underground, undetected for years or even decades. Once hatched, the larvae initiated a feeding frenzy that was reputed to destroy entire cities. A certain type of Imperial Intelligence infiltration agent was code-named a polwocz.

**poly-alloy** A resilient artificial building material used to construct the skeletons of human replica droids.

**Polydroxol** A shape-shifting alien species that resembled an animated blob of liquid chrome. Polydroxols could change their shape and volume, but not the color of their surface. They were able to extrude cutting edges from their metallic forms. They hailed from the toxic world of Sevetta.

**polyplast** A liquid rope that sprayed into a thin, flexible material used by clone troopers in their ascension guns and other rappelling gear.

**Poly Pyramid** A cantina in Teguta Lusat on Rafa IV, it was a worker establishment. On the walls, lurid paintings alternated with sporting scenes from dozens of worlds. Decorating the bar were samples of taxidermy animals, such as jackelopes and fur-bearing trout. The cantina was noisy and brightly lit. The bartender was Bernie.

**polyquaternium-7** An alcoholic concoction, often carbonated, found in a range of unusual drinks.

**polyweave** A synthetic fabric used in the acceleration straps and netting aboard starfighters.

**pom** Edible plants found in the swamps of Naboo, poms were anchored to the swamp floor by their roots, while their sturdy leaves floated on the water's surface.

**pom-hopper** A small, four-legged mammal with wide-webbed feet native to Naboo. Pom-hoppers were named for their ability to move quickly across the surface of swamps, using pom petals as stepping-stones. They slept and hid dangling underwater, breathing through their tube-like nostrils.

**Pommel, Dreed** A noted criminal who was pursued by Jedi Master Plo Koon prior to the Battle of Naboo. Master Koon tracked the fugitive to Ektra City on Metellos, where he tried to use a small child—Claria Labreezle—as a hostage and shield against attack. Rather than risk the child's life, Koon drew upon the Force and unleashed a spray of Force lightning at Pommel, using only enough power to knock him unconscious before arresting him.

**Pomojema** A minor god in Mimban mythology who acted as a healer. The priests of Pomojema were believed to perform acts of healing through the use of the Kaiburr crystal. Pomojema was depicted as a vaguely humanoid being with leathery wings and enormous claws. His slanted face was a mass of tentacles beneath a pair of accusing eyes. The Temple of Pomojema on Mimban—the fabled resting spot of the Kaiburr crystal—was a monstrous pyramidal ziggurat. The decrepit building appeared to be made of cast iron, not volcanic rock. The crystal was guarded by a hulking reptilian creature. The Temple of Pomojema was the site of Luke Skywalker's first duel with Darth Vader.

**Pomt, Victor** This beady-eyed little man served as chief of staff for the treacherous Senator Viqi Shesh during the Yuuzhan Vong War. A sour-faced bureaucrat, he was responsible for keeping the Senator's calendar—and dirtying his hands arranging Shesh's bribes and covert assassinations. After the fall of Duro, Pomt helped Senator Shesh drum up support for the Senate's Peace Vote (also known as the Appeasement Vote), which would have turned the Jedi over to the Yuuzhan Vong. At the same time, he hired assassin Roxi Barl to eliminate Leia Organa Solo while she recovered from injuries at the Coronet Medcenter. Pomt met a fitting end when another of Shesh's agents was hired to silence him. He was found dead with a recorded statement blaming himself for all of the troubles in Shesh's office.

**Ponchar, Raala** A spy serving the Galactic Republic during the Clone Wars, she alerted the Jedi to the threat of the cortosis droids developed by the Techno Union.

**Pondo** One of the younger Ewok warriors of Happy Grove, part of Bright Tree Village. He was impetuous and craved action. He accompanied Warok in the search for Woklings kidnapped by Vulgarr and the Duloks.

**Ponds, Commander** A clone commander who served under Jedi Master Mace Windu during the Clone Wars.

**pontites** The rarest and most powerful type of Adegan crystals used in the construction of a Jedi lightsaber. Nomi Sunrider's husband, Andur, had collected a great number of these precious treasures before he was senselessly murdered 4,000 years previous to the Battle of Yavin. Nomi used her husband's pontites to fashion her own lightsaber a short time later.

**Poodoo Lounge** A cantina in Mos Espa within a domed, adobe structure that stood about three stories tall and had a street-level entrance consisting of a sculpted, arched canopy. Glimmik singer Boles Roor performed at the Poodoo Lounge the night before the Boonta Eve Race.

*Yarael Poof*

**Poof, Yarael** A Jedi Master and Council member with a somewhat unusual appearance, he was a tall Quermian with spindly limbs and a long, slender neck supporting a bulbous head. Hidden beneath his traditional robes were four delicate arms, which granted Poof remarkable dexterity. His sensitive olfactory glands were located in his hands. Poof had two brains, one inside his skull and the other in his chest cavity. A sly Jedi Master, Poof was accomplished in Jedi mind tricks and could use the Force to quickly befuddle and mislead targets by conjuring false images in their minds. Indeed, this was Poof's preferred method of combat, though like all Jedi he carried a lightsaber. He could also use the Force to trigger fires by telekinetically exciting molecules of volatile substances. Yarael was Master to Roron Corobb when the Ithorian Jedi was still a Padawan.

About five years prior to the Clone Wars, Yarael Poof was killed by the Anoo-dat radical General Ashaar Khorda, stabbed by a vibroblade. With his dying breath, Poof used the Force to contain the power of an ancient artifact, the Infant of Saa.

**poonten grass** A coarse, hardy grass that grew on Tatooine and was gathered into bedding by particularly impoverished settlers.

**Poorf, Nam** This young human was a member of the Jedi Order's Agricultural Corps during the time of Order 66. Poorf and Jambe Lu were among the small group of Jedi rescued by Roan Shryne and the crew of the *Drunk Dancer*. Poorf followed Olee Starstone's lead and set off with her to locate any other surviving Jedi, starting on Kashyyyk. There they encountered Darth Vader, and the Dark Lord cleaved Poorf's right leg off with a lightsaber strike. Starstone rescued the lame Jedi. After fleeing Kashyyyk, Poorf decided to sign up as an agriculturalist attached to an Imperial project, where he hoped to learn as much as he could about the Empire and sow dissent from within.

**Poot, Una** This aged woman was a Rebel Alliance leader during the Galactic Civil War, delivering weapons and other materiel to the Rebellion with her husband while working out of Silver Station.

**Pops** *See* Krail, Davish.

**poptree** A variety of tree native to Drongar known for its sweet sap.

*Porax-38 starfighter*

**Poqua, Commodore** A New Republic task-force commander during the Yevethan emergency, he was a friend of General A'baht, who was relieved of command during the crisis.

**Poranji orbital jumper** A small starship used to ferry cargo and passengers from surface to orbit. It was only 3 meters long, but could accommodate a pilot and up to three passengers.

**Porasca Prize** One of the galaxy's most prestigious journalism awards.

**Porax-38 starfighter** During the Clone Wars, the Porax-38 fighter became the preferred starfighter of General Grievous's MagnaGuard warriors. Later in the Clone Wars, when Obi-Wan Kenobi surreptitiously signaled Tion Medon that Republic help was on the way to Utapau, word spread quickly through the Utapau underground. By the time open battle erupted in Pau City and clone troopers stormed the Separatist outpost, several rebel P-38 Utapaun fliers had joined the fray. Built by Buuper Torsckil Abbey Devices, the Porax-38 fighter had acute sensors, strong shields, a limited hyperdrive, and twin laser cannons. The cramped cockpit could fit only a single pilot.

**Porcellus** The personal chef of Jabba the Hutt, he was a triple Golden Spoon awardee and winner of the Tselgormet Prize for gourmandism five years in a row. When people started dying around Jabba's palace, many assumed that the chef had been poisoning Jabba's food. Before he could be executed for the supposed crime, Jabba was killed. Porcellus then went to Mos Eisley and opened a renowned restaurant with his friend Malakili, the rancor keeper.

**Porg** A Trandoshan bounty hunter, he tried to capture Rebel agent Kyle Katarn on Nar Shaddaa to prevent him from recovering any of the information that had been stolen from Morgan Katarn's farm on Sulon. Porg was not the only hunter searching for Katarn. In a three-way firefight, Porg was shot and killed by an Aqualish bounty hunter, who was later killed by Katarn.

**porgrak** A creature that made a unique sound during its final death throes. Luminara Unduli compared the music of the Yiwa clan on Ansion to a cross between the sublime and a dying porgrak.

**Porgryn** As a young Zabrak, Porgryn longed to be a warrior, but her dreams were shattered when she accidentally inhaled a caustic gas that permanently crippled her. In the years after her accident, she dealt with her depression by losing herself among the travelers and indigents of Tatooine. She became a trusted member of the Azure Cabal mercenary group, and her ability to avoid attention and remain virtually invisible in a crowd made her the group's top covert operative.

**Porkins, Jek** An Alliance X-wing pilot, he learned his piloting skills by hunting sink crabs in his T-16 skyhopper on the rocky islands of his homeworld, Bestine IV. He specialized in strafing runs—that and his portly build earned him his nickname, Belly Runner. He also served in Tierfon Yellow Squadron at Tierfon Rebel Outpost. During the Battle of Yavin, his comm unit designation was Red Six. Porkins was killed when his craft was hit by fire from a Death Star turbolaser.

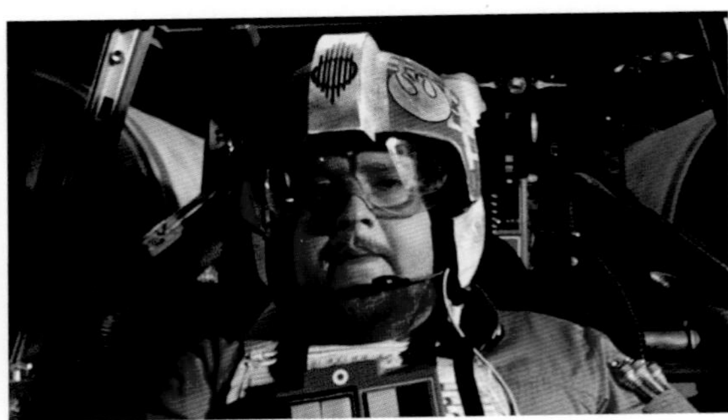

*Jek Porkins*

**Pormfil** A Kerestian and chief engineer aboard Talon Karrde's starship, *Wild Karrde.*

**Porporite** An intelligent species discovered by the Galactic Republic shortly after the Great Hyperspace War. Porporites were introduced to ryll spice, which led many to hopeless addiction and homicidal rage. Gank killers were hired by concerned neighboring species to eliminate the Porporite threat, a process recorded in history as the Gank Massacres.

**Porpu, Zan** A Rebel Alliance Y-wing pilot who went missing in action during the Galactic Civil War. His vessel disappeared in the Estran Cordon.

**Por Ral, Nij** This portly man worked as a professor of ancient linguistics at the height of the New Order. His knowledge of ancient civilizations led him to be retained by the SoroSuub Corporation to assist with the excavation of a nearly 5-kilometer-long wall on the planet Dorlo. SoroSuub executives hoped that the runes carved into the wall would provide clues to the locations of valuable resources. A team led by Jedi Knight Qu Rahn asked Pro Ral to join in repelling Imperial forces that arrived on Dorlo to assist in the planet's subjugation, and Por Ral agreed to help as long as it kept the relics he discovered from being destroyed. When the team was captured by the Dark Jedi Jerec, Por Ral pleaded for his own life by telling Jerec that Rahn had information on the location of the Valley of the Jedi. Disgusted by his spinelessness, Dark Jedi Yun killed Por Ral with a swift lightsaber blow to the head.

**porrh** An engineered biological by-product used by the Yuuzhan Vong to sterilize wounds.

**Por'ste Island** A locale on the planet Teardrop, it suffered from groundquakes.

**Port, Chairman** A representative of Vorzyd 4 who petitioned the Jedi Council to mediate a dispute between Vorzyd 4 and 5 over a decade before the Battle of Naboo. Port believed saboteurs from the neighboring planet were undermining his world's manufacturing abilities, unaware that the acts were being carried out by the Freelies, led by his son Grath. He eventually reached a compromise with Grath, who was attempting to lessen the arduous workweek mandated of the Vorzydiaks.

**portaak** A plant native to the jungles of Haruun Kal; it was the source of a type of spice. Portaak amber was a natural, translucent orange-brown resin used by locals to protect their weaponry and technology from circuit-eating spores.

**Port Duggan** *See* Duggan station.

**Por'Ten** The human family among the Five Families controlling Cestus Cybernetics on Ord Cestus, represented by Lord and Lady Por'Ten. Both nobles died when an orbital bombardment from the Republic warship *Nexu* struck their bunker on the Kibo Plateau during the Clone Wars.

**Porter** A cargo loader from Drunost, Porter and his boss, Casement, secretly supported the Rebel Alliance during the Galactic Civil War. Their team made sure that shipments of blasters and other military supplies were "misdirected" to various Rebel cells in the Shelsha sector. Occasionally, the BloodScar pirates would raid their shipping bases, and in one surprise turn of events, the pirates were chased off by a group of stormtroopers—the renegade Hand of Judgment—who were unaware that they were saving supplies destined for the Rebel Alliance.

**Port-Esta** The capital city and principal spaceport of Vestar, home of the Imperial Lightning Battalion during the New Order.

**Port Evokk** A planet that produced a number of notable smugglers, gamblers, and criminals.

**Portha** A Trandoshan living in Coruscant's Invisible Sector, he tried to help Rogue Squadron during its daring mission to retake the capital world from the Empire during the early years of the New Republic.

**Port Haven** A secret smugglers-only hideaway on an uncharted backrocket world in the Whendyll system. Han Solo first met Dash Rendar there.

**Portho Hill** A site on Naboo where Borvo the Hutt established a temporary prison camp after kidnapping Naboo civilians to sell as slaves.

**Port Landien** A town on Naboo. A sando aqua monster once beached itself on one of its shores. The Port Landien Perfumery was located on the town's sparsely populated outskirts. When he was just a lieutenant, Panaka tracked down a wanted Gungan criminal at the perfumery.

**Portmoak sector** An Outer Rim sector under Imperial control during the Galactic Civil War.

**Portom, Lom** An Advozse member of Iaco Stark's board of directors during the time of the Stark Hyperspace Conflict.

**Port Pevaria** A public spaceport located near Coronet, on Corellia, controlled by the local criminal underworld. Because the spaceport controllers had no direct ties to the Corellian government, Port Pevaria became a haven for smugglers and Galactic Alliance operatives after Thrackan Sal-Solo's bid to withdraw Corellia from the Alliance.

**Port Town** Levels 121 through 160 on Cloud City hosted the heart of corruption and crime on this floating metropolis. Over the years, the white walls of this section were blackened by blasterfire, garbage piled up in some corners, and entire sections went without light for weeks, or even years. Many inhabitants of Port Town were fringe elements who enjoyed Cloud City's distance from the reigning galactic authority. When Lando Calrissian became administrator, he created a special Wing Guard Port Town division to keep order in the dark sections of the city.

**Porus Vida** Famous throughout the galaxy for its centuries-old cultural museums, this planet was relatively undefended against attack. Imperial Admiral Daala targeted the Porus Vida museums and their priceless treasures for destruction as a psychological blow against the New Republic. In the attack, Colonel Cronus and his fleet of *Victory*-class Star Destroyers devastated the planet.

**positronic processor** Too small to be called proper droids but too personable to be called anything else, positronic processors could be attached to the power points of larger computer systems to access information and override command sequences.

**Posondum, Nil** A small, balding man who was once the head accountant for Trans-Galactic Gaming Enterprises Corporation. Before that, Posondum worked for the Hutt-controlled Trans-Zone Development and Exploitation Consortium, managing the earnings of a series of skefta dens in the Outer Rim Territories. On the side, he also arranged under-the-table business deals with anyone who could pay the credits. Among his clients was Kodir of Kuhlvult, who contracted Posondum to hire a kidnapper to abduct her sister Kateel and erase her memories. Posondum placed the fees for this job in the escrow accounts of Kud'ar Mub'at, and it was Mub'at who eventually hired Ree Duptom to do the job.

Posondum had many details of the Hutt syndicate's access codes, credit-laundering schemes, and odds-rigging systems stored in a cortical data splint shortly before he left the Hutts to work for TransGalactic. His new employer paid a huge sum for the data. He also took with him a wealth of embezzled credits, stored in remote banks and financial outlets. When the Hutts became aware of his actions, they were incensed and established a 12,500-credit bounty on his head. This bounty was claimed by Boba Fett, who had to evade being caught by Bossk and Zuckuss in order to deliver the accountant to Kud'ar Mub'at.

**Poss'Nomin** Natives of the planet Illarreen with husky humanoid builds, three eyes, and shovel-like jaws.

**Post, Avan** A Jedi Master from Chandrila, he served with distinction during the Clone Wars. He was Master to his Padawan learner, Olana Chion.

**Post, Jlir** The wealthy, spoiled son of a Corellian agro-combine administrator, he nurtured a hatred for Baron Soontir Fel, who was responsible for Post's imprisonment on Kessel. Post concocted a plot to turn over Fel's wife, Wynssa Starflare, to the Empire, but Post was shot by Fel's brother before the plan came to fruition.

**Potentium** In Jedi history, a controversial view of the Force judged by the Council to be in error; eventually it was no longer even mentioned to Padawans. The core tenets of the Potentium held that all living things had the potential to create newer and better living things, and that ultimately the Force and the galaxy were developing as per a master plan that was inherently good. As such, there was no dark side, no evil undercurrent that could be tapped through the Force. Advocates of the concept believed that the Force could not turn one to evil. Rather, the living Force was the beginning and end of all things, and one's connections with it should not be mediated or obscured by any sort of training or discipline. A hundred years before Obi-Wan Kenobi's arrival on Zonama Sekot, the Potentium created a great deal of trouble for the Jedi. Followers insisted that the Jedi Masters and the Temple hierarchy could not accept the universal good of the Potentium because it meant they were no longer needed. In the end, those Jedi apprentices who had been caught up in the movement left the Temple, or were pushed out, and dispersed around the galaxy. The exiles in turn discovered the living planet Zonama Sekot, which they believed to be the embodiment of the living Force.

Poss'Nomin

Shadday Potkin

**Pothman, Triv** A native of Chandrila and former Imperial stormtrooper, he was part of the *Eye of Palpatine* mission, serving as the armorer of a 45-stormtrooper company sent to Pzob. The Gamorrean colonists on Pzob attacked the troopers and took Pothman captive, keeping him alive thanks to his knowledge of weapons. Pothman eventually escaped and lived on Pzob by himself, keeping the Gamorreans at bay while collecting all of his company's unused armor. He discovered Luke Skywalker and Cray Mingla when they were forced to crash-land on the world, after discovering the existence of an armed base in the asteroids near the Moonflower Nebula. Triv offered his help in repairing Skywalker's ship in exchange for transport offplanet, but the entire group was taken aboard the automated *Eye of Palpatine* battlemoon when it arrived at Pzob. Triv underwent indoctrination aboard the vessel, but with Luke's help was able to shake off its effects. After the *Eye of Palpatine*'s mission was canceled, Triv retired to the domed city of Plawal on Belsavis, becoming a horticulturist.

**Pothor system** The site where the Rebel fleet assembled shortly after the Battle of Yavin. A Verpine fleet carrying valuable B-wing prototype fighters was to rendezvous with the Rebellion there.

**Potin, Lieutenant** An Imperial naval officer serving aboard the *Black Asp*, he fled as Rogue Squadron pilots engaged the ship in the Chorax system and was severely reprimanded for his cowardly actions.

**Potkin, Shadday** A Jedi Knight active during the Clone Wars, she survived Order 66 and went into hiding during the early months of the Galactic Empire. She put out a call for any surviving Jedi to meet on Kessel, but leaked the information to Darth Vader in an effort to lure the Sith Lord to the rendezvous as well. Though Shadday correctly judged that Vader would arrive, she underestimated him. The Dark Lord cut through all eight Jedi who gathered.

**Potorr, Vax** This taciturn man served in Joker Squad of the 407th Stormtrooper Division based on Yinchorr nearly a century after the end of the Yuuzhan Vong War. A former thief, he believed that the Galactic Alliance was responsible for the pain and suffering he endured in the lower levels of Coruscant and joined the New Empire at the first opportunity. When Sith Lord Darth Krayt took over the Empire and exiled Emperor Roan Fel, Joker Squad was dispatched to Borosk to prevent the 908th Stormtrooper Division from defecting. During this assignment, Potorr stepped on a landmine and was killed.

Vax Potorr

**Potts, Danzigoro** An ancient Jedi student who was a veteran of the First Great Schism, some 24,500 years before the Battle of Yavin. He faced Dark Jedi on Columus in a battle in which he was forced to kill his friend Blendri and her apprentice. Badly injured in the conflict, Potts made a recording that described these events before he died. The ancient recording became known as the Columus Data Card.

**pouch-creature** A Yuuzhan Vong–bioengineered creature that served as a pouch. Nen Yim had a pouch-creature that had the vestigial eyes of its fish-like ancestor but otherwise resembled an olive-and-black mottled pouch. It contained oxygen-rich fluids that kept organic matter alive within.

**Pouffra Circuit** A fairly tame and fully sanctioned Podracing circuit with relatively safe courses and very few fatalities. Used as a training ground for such rookie Podracers as Ben Quadinaros, the Pouffra Circuit was nowhere near as dangerous as similar events held on frontier worlds such as Tatooine.

**pourstone** A viscous building material poured into quick-drying molds. The dome-

Power chair used by Cliegg Lars

like structures on Tatooine were often made of pourstone.

**Poussan, 'Ndrath** An Agamarian recruited to the Rebel Alliance alongside Keyan Farlander, he became an X-wing pilot. He died during Operation Strike Fear near Briggia when his ship collided with a TIE fighter.

**POWER (Preserve Our Wild Endangered Resources)** A political movement on Telos dedicated to protecting the planet's parks and wilderness areas from exploitation by the UniFy corporation, a front company masterminded by the evil Xanatos. Despite its grandiose aims and imposing name, POWER comprised only one member—its founder, Andra. Still, she achieved her aims with the help of Qui-Gon Jinn and his Padawan, Obi-Wan Kenobi. Together with the Jedi, she exposed UniFy's true plans to the people of Telos, who roundly rejected Xanatos's leadership.

**power chair** A common name for a conveyance used by the mobility-impaired. Cliegg Lars employed a repulsorlift-equipped power chair after he lost a leg in a Tusken Raider attack.

**power charge** Any small, compact battery. A Podracer's ignition system required a power charge. Power charges were typically installed in the dashboards of Podracer cockpits.

**power converter** The ignition system for a starship, it routed energy from a ship's primary power source to its propulsion units in order to achieve thrust.

**power coupling** Charged devices that handled the exchange of power in high-energy systems. Industrial sectors of large cities, like those found on Coruscant, had enormous power couplers that could pose a hazard to reckless speeder traffic. In a starship, a coupling device directed the large amounts of power flowing from the hyperdrive motivator to the hyperdrive engines. Power couplings had two main components, a negative and positive axis. On the *Millennium Falcon,* the negative coupling became polarized and caused the hyperdrive motivator to fail.

Power gem

**Power Dive** A seedy tavern located on Ord Mantell, the occasional haunt of gambler Raal Yorta.

**power droid** Box-shaped automata with stubby little legs, these simple droids functioned to power up other droids and machinery with the portable energy generator housed in their shells. Power droids were so common in the galaxy, and had so little defining personality software, that they often weren't given any identifying numbers at all; indeed, if told to walk off a landing platform, a power droid would do so unquestioningly. Common models of power droids included the EG-6; the GNK-1, often known as a gonk droid; and a four-legged model nicknamed a plunk droid.

Power coupling on a Coruscant roof

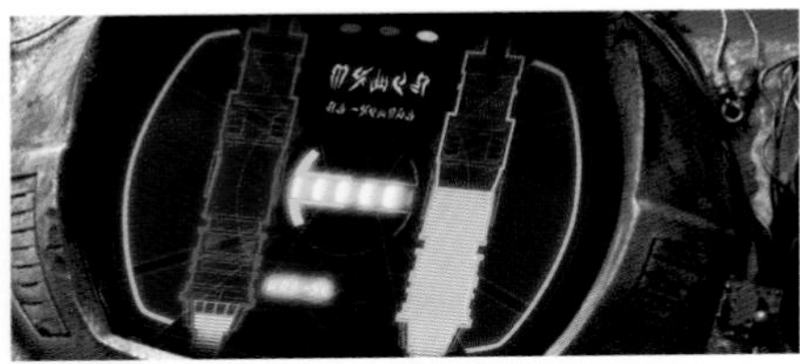

Power charge display

Power harpoon and tow cable

**power gem** Rare mineral artifacts used by the space pirates of Iridium during the Old Republic. These crystal-like gems radiated an aura capable of disrupting magnetic and deflector shields. This enabled the pirate vessels to penetrate the shields of Republic spice convoys and plunder the goods within. Power gems lost this ability over time. When the pirates were captured or destroyed by the Jedi Knights, their power gems were gathered together and destroyed. Raskar, the last surviving space pirate of Iridium, took the last power gem and fled to the Rim. There he made a tidy fortune by staging competitions for the gem. Han Solo and Chewbacca managed to obtain the gem when the Rebel Alliance needed a way to penetrate the *Executor*'s shields. In combat, Commander Vrad Dodonna was unable to use it to penetrate the *Executor*'s doubled forward shields, but the *Millennium Falcon* scored a powerful hit on the Star Destroyer's unprotected aft section.

**power gloves** Energized gloves worn by stormtroopers in hand-to-hand combat, usually while restraining prisoners.

**power grappler** A tool often used by Squibs to capture garbage from hard-to-reach areas. These handheld servogrips could extend a Squib's reach almost a meter.

**power harpoon** A high-powered, often barbed projectile, it was attached to a retractable flexisteel tow cable and fusion-head disk. Power harpoons were standard equipment for most snowspeeders and similar military vehicles. They were designed by Beryl Chiffonage for the Rebel Alliance as a reserve defense against Imperial walkers. Wedge Antilles used one successfully during the Battle of Hoth to drop an AT-AT to its knees and destroy it.

**power lance** A long pole arm used by IG lancers and clone trooper biker scouts, this charged weapon could pierce even heavy armor.

Power lance

**Power Mounds of the Elders** An exclusive site on Skako where the ruling body of Skakoans would gather.

**power pistol** Predating the blaster pistol, this handheld energy weapon featured an oversized barrel that delivered an energized particle stream. Power pistols were difficult to aim because of their strong recoil, and they had limited ammunition.

**power pivot** This starfighter maneuver—often employed by X-wing pilots—involved using the fighter's lateral thrusters to effect a reversal in position, swinging the ship around 180 degrees.

**power prybar** A handheld motorized tool used to pry sealed openings. Common applications included emergency situations and theft.

**power station** These all-purpose repair and repowering facilities could be found in cities across the galaxy. They were often small and minimally staffed. On Tatooine, Tosche was a power station.

**powersuit** Any form of armor or environmental suit that featured motorized articulation, which could potentially enhance the user's strength or reflexes.

**Poxall** A Sith magician whose avatar appeared within a Sith Holocron owned by Krova the Hutt. Poxall was known for his ability to create deadly poisons.

**Poy** A Twi'lek slave who worked at the lambent fields on Yavin 4 during the Yuuzhan Vong War, he explained to Anakin Solo that drone-making slave implants were used only when sending slaves into battle.

**Pqweeduk** A Rodian, he was the younger brother of the bounty hunter Greedo.

**Prackla sector** An area of the galaxy remote enough from the Core Worlds that it remained neutral during most of the Clone Wars. It was not until the Separatists launched an attack on Cartao—the sector's trading center—in an effort to destroy Spaarti Creations that the sector's leaders decided to ally themselves with the Republic.

**Pradeux, Alec** An Imperial adviser known to have Palpatine's ear, he allied himself with Grand Admiral Tigellinus after the Battle of Endor.

Nahdonnis Praji

**Praesitlyn** The site of a major communications station, it was located within 60 light-years of Bpfassh in the Sluis sector. The world allied itself to the Separatists during the Clone Wars, though the Intergalactic Communications Center remained a key Republic asset. As a result, Praesitlyn became a major front in the Clone Wars when the Confederacy attacked the station. The combined forces of Zozridor Slayke, Nejaa Halcyon, and Anakin Skywalker protected the facility and defeated the Separatists. Twelve years after the Battle of Endor, Praesitlyn was represented by Senator Zilar in the New Republic government and the Defense Council.

**Praetor** One of the many lightsaber hilt styles common among Luke Skywalker's new Jedi Order. The Praetor hilt was long and thin, with a scalloped emitter shroud protecting the wielder from any stray energy.

***Praetor*-class battle cruiser** An outdated warship produced during the Old Republic that saw limited use during the Galactic Civil War.

**Praetorite Vong** A political body that governed the Yuuzhan Vong during their invasion of the galaxy. The Praetorite Vong was led by domains loyal to the intendant caste, which tried to assert its superiority to other castes. Leadership consisted of skilled High Prefects, supported by High Priests and high-ranking warriors. Despite the fact that it was not a military body, the Praetorite Vong was in command of the first assault force sent to begin the conquest of the galaxy. The war force was not overly large, and its leaders—Prefect Da'Gara and Executor Nom Anor—refused to underestimate their enemy. Their forces were controlled by the immense—yet imperfect—yammosk war coordinator based on Helska. The plans of Nom Anor and the Praetorite Vong were thwarted when New Republic forces killed the yammosk. But the Praetorite Vong was only the tip of the iceberg that was the Yuuzhan Vong invasion force. After the debacle at Helska, the Praetorite Vong was restricted in its actions by Tsavong Lah and the Yuuzhan Vong commanders.

**Praget, Chairman Krall** From the planet Edatha, he was chairman of the New Republic Senate Council on Security and Intelligence. Krall Praget ordered Colonel Pakkpekatt to abandon efforts to recover the mysterious Teljkon vagabond ship even though Lando Calrissian, Lobot, and the droids C-3PO and R2-D2 were still aboard. Angered that Chief of State Leia Organa Solo called for military action against the Yevethan threat without consulting him first, Chairman Praget brought a petition to the Senate Ruling Council seeking her removal.

**Praidaw** The planet where the parents of Akanah Norand Pell first met.

**Praji, Nahdonnis** An Imperial commander and part of the influential Praji family, he was Darth Vader's aide on the Star Destroyer *Devastator*. Praji graduated with honors from the Imperial Naval Academy. By Vader's order, he supervised the search for the Death Star's missing plans on Tatooine. He delegated the mission to Captain Kosh.

**Praji, Onnelly** A member of the Praji family of nobles, she left Coruscant for the Emerald Splendor estates on Byss in the early days of the Galactic Empire. The fugitive Padawan Drake Lo'gaan, disguised as Jodd Sonta, flirted with her during her departure.

**Praji, Tannon** A First Minister within the Coruscant Ministry of Ingress during the

Tannon Praji

Predator starfighter

Clone Wars, he restructured a number of regulations to ensure Coruscant's safety during the fighting. Facing political pressure, he authorized the deportation of numerous aliens whose homeworlds had seceded from the Republic. Praji faced several assassination attempts due to this controversial move.

**Prak City** The capital city of the planet Prakith, home to an immense Imperial-class starport.

**Prakith** Located in the system of the same name in Sector One of the Galactic Core, this planet was about 106 light-years beyond the borders of the New Republic. Prakith was the ruling world of the Constitutional Protectorate controlled by the Imperial warlord Foga Brill. Brill maintained his power over the region by accepting bribes from wealthy families and keeping order with the Red Police. Many of Prakith's citizens were forced to toil in the foundries and silt mines, and inhabitants of the riverbank cities Prall and Skoth were regularly executed after being forced to dig their own graves. The natives of the planet spoke Prak.

Twelve years after the Battle of Endor, when Lando Calrissian, Lobot, and the droids C-3PO and R2-D2 stowed away on the mysterious Teljkon vagabond, the ship emerged from hyperspace 8 light-years from Prakith. The frigate *Bloodprice,* part of Brill's defensive fleet, detected the vagabond and attempted to capture it but was destroyed by the mystery ship, which vanished into hyperspace. The Prakith cruiser *Gorath* later caught up with the vagabond but was also destroyed.

**Prammi, Wila** One of the candidates running for governor of Gala when Queen Veda opened elections on the planet. Prammi had experience working as an underminister, and she had sound ideas grounded in reality. With the support of the Beju, the royal guard, and the hill people—and the destruction of Deca Brun's campaign by scandal—she was voted into office by an overwhelming margin.

***Prana Lexander*** An ancient scientific vessel that disappeared 500 years before the Battle of Yavin. A group of special Rebel Alliance operatives discovered the ship and an alien philosopher aboard kept alive in cryogenic freeze. The Rebellion wished to connect with the philosopher to win the support of an entire alien culture.

**Prann, Erli** A pirate leader who took control of one of the Golan II defense platforms protecting the Imperial shipyards at Bilbringi in the aftermath of Grand Admiral Thrawn's defeat. Prann's pirates discovered the cloaking devices Thrawn had left behind and appropriated the technology to hide their operations in the system. During the Yuuzhan Vong War, Prann's pirates effectively hid from the invaders. The Galactic Alliance discovered the existence of the cloaked defense platform, and Jaina Solo tried to make contact with the crew aboard the mysterious station. Prann posed as a New Republic lieutenant sent to reactivate the station, but his true identity as an unscrupulous war profiteer soon came to light. Though Prann's platform assisted the Galactic Alliance in battling the Yuuzhan Vong, he was nonetheless arrested, and his pirate crew relinquished control of the station.

**Prard'enc'iflar** The commander of the Brask Oto Command Station in the years before the Yuuzhan Vong War, this Chiss met with Luke and Mara Jade Skywalker during the search for the Outbound Flight Project.

**Prard'ras'kleoni** *See* Drask, General.

**Pratuhr, Artuo** A patron of the Outlander gambling club in the final days of the Galactic Republic, he was a known associate of Zey Nep, Dixon Just, and Civ Sila.

**Prax, Cydon** Count Dooku's right-hand enforcer immediately after the death of Jango Fett. He was a huge, bald Chistori humanoid with a claw-like crest. A ruthless mercenary, this former bounty hunter was tasked with collecting the needed components to activate the Dark Reaper—namely, the powerful Force Harvester. Dooku placed great faith in Prax's skills as a pilot and a tenacious warrior who fought without compassion. He was remembered and feared throughout the galaxy as the man responsible for "the Kessel Massacre," a horrible event in which 6,000 slaves were slaughtered for protesting working conditions in the spice mines. Prax felt most at home when piloting the fighter tank *Dreadnaught,* which he modified with special thrusters and weapons systems. Ultimately, Anakin Skywalker out-piloted him and destroyed his tank, killing the Chistori on the planet Thule.

**praxeum** An ancient term that loosely translated as "school," *praxeum* was the name chosen by Luke Skywalker to describe his new Jedi academy.

**Praxlis** This planet was located in the former center of the Empire's Rim Territories. During the Emperor's reign, the Black Sword Command was charged with the defense of Praxlis, Corridan, and the entire Kokash and Farlax sectors.

**Praysh, Chay** A Drach'nam slaver based on Torpris during the early years of the New Republic, he demanded to be called by his lofty title, the First Greatness. Mara Jade disrupted his enterprise by turning over vital information on his operation to Luke Skywalker and the New Republic.

**P-RC3 library droid** A librarian droid aboard the first Death Star, it assisted Atour Riten. Atour modified the droid to remove its spyware, allowing him to operate unsupervised.

**Precht** A rookie Rebel Alliance trooper aboard the *Tantive IV.*

**Predator starfighter** The Sienar *Predator*-class fighter was an improvement over the old TIE interceptors. The Predator boasted hyperdrive capability and shield generators that transmitted deflector energy through the fighter's dagger-shaped wings. Its multiposition wings made the Predator one of the most maneuverable fighters in the galaxy—and its armament made it one of the most dangerous. These craft saw use a century after the Yuuzhan Vong War.

***Predominance*** An Ishori war cruiser commanded by Captain Av'muru, it was one of scores of ships that blockaded Bothawui during the Caamas incident. To stem growing hostilities among the vessels, Leia Organa Solo purposely damaged the *Millennium Falcon* and requested assistance from the *Predominance,* which Captain Av'muru reluctantly rendered. Imperial infiltrators, hoping to foment war in the system, commandeered one of the *Predominance*'s turbolaser batteries and opened fire, resulting in an exchange of cannonades with Diamalan ships. The New Republic was once again able to defuse the situation.

**preducor** A ferocious night hunter on the Forest Moon of Endor, this creature was docile during the day. A preducor moved on four clawed legs and could grow to about 4 meters high and 5 meters long. Its head was surrounded by a mane of razor-sharp hair, and a long, spiked tail stretched behind it. Its protruding jaw was full of knife-like teeth; its eyes glowed in the dark. Large folds of skin on its back were vestiges of wings that no longer functioned.

**Preedu III, Emperor** The ruler of Tamban before the rise of the Empire.

**Prefsbelt IV** The location of an Imperial Naval Academy and the introductory Prefsbelt Fleet Camp. The shuttle *Tydirium* was taken from Prefsbelt IV by the Rebel Alliance.

**Premier Provisions** A small specialty-foods farm that operated in the clouds of Tyed Kant.

**Prennert, Osleo** A loyal member of the Rebel Alliance assigned to identify incoming ships and alert combat forces of impending attacks. This human male Rebel sentry was on patrol when the *Millennium Falcon* arrived at the Rebel base on Yavin 4.

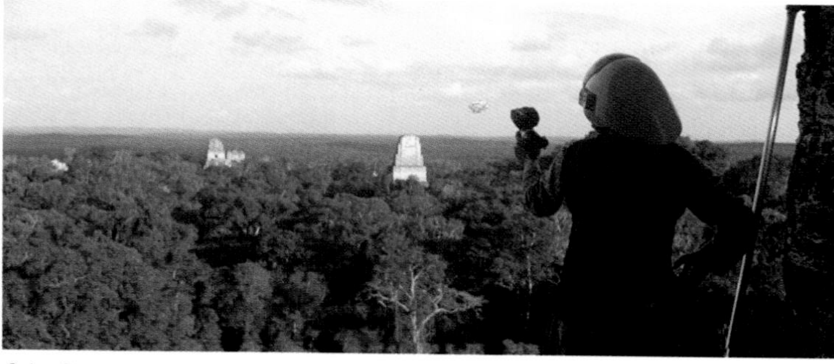
Osleo Prennert

**Prentiss** A member of a Galactic Republic diplomatic team that was lost in a remote section of the galaxy. This team's ship was forced to crash-land on an uncharted world, and native flora and fauna quickly began preying on the survivors. Prentiss and his cohorts tried to scout out their location, but were killed and eaten shortly after leaving the ship. Their vessel was later discovered by Han Solo and Chewbacca.

**Prepredenko, Lord** The leader of the people of Jazbina during the Galactic Civil War. He lured Luke Skywalker to the planet in a plot to kidnap the young Rebel and hand him over to Darth Vader. Prepredenko modified the cam droid 3DVO to arrange Skywalker's capture. The disgruntled droid, angry at being tampered with, altered the wanted bulletin from Darth Vader so that Luke was listed as wanted dead, rather than alive. When Vader learned that Prepredenko had tried to arrange for Luke's death, the Sith Lord captured and tortured him. Remorseful for his actions, Prepredenko tried to transmit one final message to his daughter Syayna. It was detected by stormtroopers, who then killed him.

**Prescott, Corporal** A Death Star trooper and guard overseeing security for Detention Block AA-23. He volunteered for prison detail, taking sadistic pleasure in seeing Imperial justice enforced. He was killed during the rescue of Princess Leia Organa.

**Preservers** *See* Iith'lon.

Prevaro

**President of Five Worlds** The office established by Thrackan Sal-Solo after the Yuuzhan Vong War. After Sal-Solo's assassination, Dur Gejjen abolished the office, ostensibly to remove any of the late leader's influence over the Corellian government.

**Pressin, Major** An assistant to Admiral Gilad Pellaeon aboard the *Chimaera* during the Yuuzhan Vong War.

**pressor** Small repulsor projectors, they induced and controlled pitch in a starship. They were activated by control sticks or buttons on control consoles.

**Pressor, Guardian Jorad** The leader of the peacekeepers at the Outbound Flight survivors' colony. He was the son of Dillian Pressor. He held a long-standing resentment against the Jedi Order, which had failed to prevent Thrawn's attack on Outbound Flight—and had also refused to train him when he was a boy because he lacked the necessary sensitivity to the Force. When a Chiss-led mission to locate the remains of Outbound Flight actually found the ships, Pressor and his niece, Evlyn, trapped the mission's members in turbolifts until he could figure out what to do with them. Pressor soon found himself faced with multiple groups of outsiders moving freely through the Outbound Flight ruins, including deadly Vagaari pirates. His own peacekeepers were decimated in the attacks, and he resented the request to use the Outbound Flight Colony's medical facilities to help the outsiders. When Mara Jade Skywalker devised a plan to get them safely back to the main ship, and agreed to protect Evlyn, Pressor found himself grudgingly admiring the Jedi. After the Vagaari threat was eliminated, Pressor agreed to accompany the Outbound Flight Colony to Nirauan, staying as far away from the New Republic as possible.

**pressor field** A specialized, field-generating device that provided localized pressure on blood vessels during surgery.

**pressure pirates** These pirates at Yorn Skot owned industrial-strength equipment that allowed them to salvage plunder at atmospheric depths up to 400 g's. Pressure pirates attacked the *Aurorient Express.*

**Prevaro** A Rodian, he was an information dealer who believed that the Falleen antiques dealer Azool was Prince Xizor in disguise. Azool was in fact Xizor's niece Savan, who offered Prevaro a spot in the Black Sun criminal organization—if Savan should take control of it.

**Preybird fighter** This rare heavy combat starfighter from SoroSuub was a favorite of mercenaries, pirates, and anyone else who might favor its swooping, intimidating lines. The *Skyclaw* and the *Raptor* were modified SoroSuub *Preybird*-class starfighters owned by the smuggler Mazzic.

**Preza** *See* Morning Bell.

**Pria** The tectonically active, aquatic homeworld of the Priapulin species, orbited by a single moon.

***Priam*** An Imperial Nebulon-B frigate stationed near Kalla VII during Operation Strike Fear, it was disabled and captured by the Rebel Alliance.

**Priam, Admiral** An Imperial officer who arrived on Troska to commend Lieutenant Manech for exposing Commander Buzk's corruption and bringing down the Kyber family's control of the planet's refineries.

Priamsta nobles

**Priamsta** A body comprising the native noble class of the planet Eiattu VI, the Priamsta wanted to restore local rule and independence. To counter a claim by Harrandatha Estillo, a pretender to the throne, council members sought out and invited back to the planet their princess, who went by the name

Plourr Ilo as a pilot in Rogue Squadron. She apparently had been the only member of the royal family to escape execution years earlier. The Priamsta established as its goals the restoration of a pre-Palpatine Golden Age (which never really existed) on Eiattu VI, the end of all Imperial occupation, and the elimination of the People's Liberation Battalion.

**Pri-Andylan Shipyard** An array of orbital starship construction depots on the fringe of the Duro system. The shipyards were initially maintained by Pri-Andylan Propulsion Systems, an upstart Corellian corporation. Pri-Andylan retained the services of Niya Giedan, a Duros facilitator, during the Imperial occupation. Nine years after the Battle of Endor, the Pri-Andylan Shipyards were acquired by a coalition of Corporate Sector trading companies. Due to strikes and delays, the coalition appointed one of its member companies, CorDuro Shipping, to administer the shipyards. Instead CorDuro transferred most of the shipyards' engineers to other facilities surrounding Duro, turning Pri-Andylan into a series of loading docks and storage bays for CorDuro freighters.

**Priapulin** Members of this aquatic, wormlike species from Pria had five knobby notocords arranged around their tubular lengths, as well as three pairs of purple eyes; their undersides were covered with a brush of thick bristles. A lower tail, or foot, rode on a similar stiff brush. Along their outside edges, long flexible spines stuck out like the fringe of a starched carpet. Priapulins spoke by rubbing together bristles near their spiracles, or breathing vents. Priapulins as a species were devoted to peace and rarely engaged in competitive behavior. They created unique spacecraft designed to suit their needs, filling the craft with living food and sealing the outer hull to hold a cycling system of water pools.

**Pricina, Dom** A wealthy but careless woman, she owned the legendary Ankarres sapphire until the droid 4-LOM stole it.

***Pride of Eiattu*** A New Republic Nebulon-B frigate that was part of the force sent to liberate the planet Ciutric from the control of Prince-Admiral Krennel.

***Pride of Honor*** A New Republic capital ship damaged by the Yuuzhan Vong at the Battle of Coruscant after its escort, Green Squadron, was ordered to protect a fleeing Senator's shuttle. Half its crew—241 people—was killed as a result. The *Pride of Honor* limped to Mon Calamari, only to be condemned. The ship's female Phindian captain confronted the Senator in a Fleet Command annex at Mon Calamari.

***Pride of Selonia* (1)** A New Republic corvette that led a supply convoy to Liinade III and was destroyed by an assault led by Prince-Admiral Krennel.

***Pride of Selonia* (2)** A Galactic Alliance *Lancer*-class frigate commanded by Captain Todra Mayn with Selwin Markota as second in command during the Yuuzhan Vong War. It accompanied the *Millennium Falcon* and Twin Suns Squadron to Bakura.

***Pride of Thela*** A modified search-and-rescue ship piloted by Uldir Lochett and Dacholder during the Yuuzhan Vong War. This ship came to the aid of the *Winning Hand,* which was actually serving as bait to capture Uldir. Dacholder turned on Uldir at this point, so Lochett was forced to use one of his special modifications—a copilot ejection seat—to get rid of the traitor.

***Pride of the Senate*** An Imperial Dreadnaught in Admiral Greenlax's task force at Nar Shaddaa early in the Galactic Civil War. Soontir Fel was captain of the *Pride of the Senate.*

***Pride of Yevetha*** Formerly the Imperial Super Star Destroyer *Intimidator,* it was seized by the forces of strongman Nil Spaar during a raid on the Imperial shipyard at N'zoth. The *Pride of Yevetha* was placed in Spaar's Black Fifteen Fleet and was spotted in the Yevethan mobilization at Doornik-319. At the end of the Black Fleet crisis, the ship vanished—only to be discovered four years later, drifting abandoned near the Unknown Regions and damaged beyond repair.

**Priest, Dred** A Mandalorian member of the *Cuy'val Dar,* he relished the challenge of creating elite soldiers for the Republic. Priest was chosen by Jango Fett to be a training sergeant on Kamino, and he formed a secret battle circle among his fellow sergeants in which they "practiced" their training techniques in brutal competitions. He wore Mandalorian armor with red armor plates.

**Priests of Ninn** Usually dressed in green vestments, this religious order lived on the religious haven of Ninn, a planet of retreat. The Priests of Ninn's beliefs incorporated formalistic abstinence.

Priapulin

Primor (center)

**Prildaz** Located in the Koornacht Cluster, this was one of the primary worlds of the Yevethan species and a member of the Duskhan League. The third planet in the system, Prildaz was a yellow-and-brown world and was the location of the Black Nine shipyards. The star system was known as ILC-905 in New Republic records. It contained at least 12 planets, with an asteroid belt between the 4th and 5th planetary orbits. Thirteen years after the Battle of Endor, the New Republic attacked Prildaz, destroying the shipyards and demolishing several Yevethan thrustships, despite incurring heavy losses.

***Primal*** A Republic gunship that attacked the Almas Academy during the execution of Order 66 at the end of the Clone Wars. It was blasted apart by Jedi Master Darrus Jeht from his vessel the *Maelstrom.*

**primary performance banks** A droid's active memory, or consciousness. It was in these banks that the most processing occurred on a day-to-day basis, and it was these banks that got erased in a memory flush.

**Prime Clone** The genetic source host of a large-scale cloning operation. The term also described a clone that was pure genetic replication with no growth acceleration or modification. By these definitions, both Jango and Boba Fett were Prime Clones.

**Primor** The leader of the Iskalonians of Iskalon, this proud and respected being never led his school into dangerous waters. His son Mone was adventurous, but Primor was more serene. Primor befriended the Rebel agents who visited his world just prior to the Battle of Endor in search of missing Rebel spy Tay Vanis. When the Empire triggered the disastrous Iskalon Effect, Primor's body was dashed against a building's surface with the full force of a tidal blast, killing him.

**Primus Goluud** An unstable red supergiant that was located in the Goluud Corridor, near the Empress Teta system, about 5,000 years before the birth of Luke Skywalker. During the Great Hyperspace War, the sun was destroyed by Naga Sadow, the Dark Lord of

Primus Goluud

the Sith, in his failed attempt to annihilate Empress Teta's forces.

**Prindaar system** Named for its star, it contained the gas giant Antar and its six moons. The fourth moon, known as Antar 4, was the homeworld of the Gotal species.

**Priole Danna Festival** An enormous celebration held annually for over 2,000 years on the planet Lamuir IV. It was canceled for the first time at the onset of the Clone Wars.

**priority sector** Imperial military commanders were often faced with conflicting jurisdictions when chasing Rebels from one sector to another during the Galactic Civil War. As a result, Governor Tarkin proposed the creation of priority sectors. In the Tarkin Doctrine, Tarkin suggested that "oversectors" (as he called them) be sectors consisting of systems in which rebellion was newly born or systems that maintained frequent contact with those in chronic unrest. These priority sectors were created with no regard given to existing sector boundaries. Priority sectors were the first to receive experimental equipment and were sometimes given special missions requested by the Emperor himself. The Death Star operation was an example of a priority sector operation. A priority sector had at least two sector groups to carry out Imperial missions.

**Privitt, Private** A new recruit to the Imperial Relay Outpost V-798 at Vaal as of the Battle of Yavin, he was killed when Darth Vader led a pack of hyenax into the outpost.

**probe droid (probot)** An intelligent probe droid, this reconnaissance device was equipped with repulsorlift and thruster units that enabled it to move swiftly across planetary surfaces. Probots arrived at their destinations in hyperdrive pods, then descended to a planet's surface using braking thrusters. They often looked like meteorites to observers. After impact, the pod opened and the probe droid was released. Probots were programmed to be extremely curious, so they could almost always find something worthy of inspection. They were armed with blaster devices, although they were programmed to avoid conflict and to self-destruct if discovered.

Arakyd Viper Probots were used by Darth Vader when he was searching for the main Rebel base after the Battle of Yavin. He ordered thousands of them deployed to unexplored or uninhabited systems in the hope that one might uncover the Rebels. In fact, one probot did discover the Rebel base on Hoth.

Probots had sensitive sensor arrays to detect signs of habitation; they examined acoustic, electromagnetic, motive, seismic, and olfactory evidence. They were equipped with holocams, zoom imagers, infrared scopes, magnetic imagers, radar transceivers, sonar transceivers, and radiation meters. Four manipulator arms and a high-torque grasping arm allowed the probot to take samples from a planet.

**processing vane** Immense wing-shaped structures that extended into Cloud City's central wind tunnel. Within these vanes were Tibanna-processing facilities and carbon-freezing chambers. Luke Skywalker and Darth Vader dueled through various sections of a processing vane, culminating in Skywalker's defeat at the edge of an observation platform.

**processors** Teams of Imperials assigned to turn peaceful citizens into war-like servants of the Empire through brain modification.

**Procopia** This planet was the political capital of the wealthy Tapani sector.

Profogg

Probe droid

**proctors** Assistants to Lord Hethrir, the former Imperial Procurator of Justice who started an Empire Reborn movement, they wore light blue jumpsuits instead of the rust-colored tunics other helpers sported.

***Procurator*-class battle cruiser** A vessel developed by Kuat Drive Yards for the protection of the Kuat sector.

**Procurator of Justice** The head of the criminal justice system of the Empire—in reality, persecution of political prisoners was its most important function—he was a shadowy figure, never named or pictured during the Emperor's reign. Only after the Battle of Endor did the name of the Procurator, Lord Hethrir, become public.

***Proficient*-class light cruiser** A Corellian-made warship, 850 meters long, it carried 10 turbolasers, 20 ion cannons, and a squadron of starfighters. The *Soothfast* was a retrofitted *Proficient*-class light cruiser active during the Yuuzhan Vong War.

**Profiteer** *See Saak'ak.*

**profiteroles Ukio** A sweet dessert created on the planet Ukio. It was made from puff pastries topped with a caramel ganache sauce.

**profogg** Large comical rodents from Tatooine that formed complex underground burrowing systems called towns. These towns could stretch across several hectares, housing from 50 to 100 profoggs. Each burrow had a specific use and function, and other animals were known to take over abandoned ones. Profoggs weighed between 10 and 20 kilograms. Horns, snouts, sharp incisors, and powerful claws were used for defense and as tools for digging. They had a high rate of reproduction, regularly producing litters of six to eight young, six to eight times a year. Underground molo seeds provided a major source of food.

**Profus, Glorii** A Kaminoan mentor—a type of physician and chaplain—to Jangotat's unit during the Clone Wars.

**Progga the Hutt** A minor Hutt crime lord from the fringes of the Unknown Regions. Five years after the Battle of Naboo, Progga tried to steal a shipment from Dubrak Qennto and the crew of the *Bargain Hunter,* but the small freighter escaped into hyperspace. Progga's crew followed its vector and relocated them just inside the boundaries of Chiss space. Just when Progga was ready to capture Qennto and his vessel, a group of Chiss warships appeared on the scene. Progga ordered his crew to open fire on the Chiss ship, the *Springhawk.* Force Commander Thrawn returned fire, destroying Progga's vessel.

**program trap** A method of turning a droid into an unsuspecting death machine, it involved reprogramming the droid's primary performance banks with an internal command to cause a power overload triggered by a predetermined event, signal, or time. The overload had the explosive capability of a medium-sized bomb.

**Proi, Lieutenant Norda** The commanding officer of the fleet hauler and junker *Steadfast,* the ship that found the wreckage of the Imperial ship *Gnisnal,* including an intact memory core.

**Project Ambition** Ysanne Isard's plan to eliminate the cabal that opposed the Imperial Ruling Council and dispose of Sate Pestage, thereby giving her complete control of the Empire.

**Project Aralia** An ill-fated amusement park on Aralia overrun by Ranats.

**Project Asteroid** A diabolical Imperial plot based on the early ideas and strategies of Alliance General Jan Dodonna.

**Project Chubar** Warlord Zsinj's plan to genetically manipulate so-called primitive alien species to create super-intelligent agents. The project focused on Gamorreans, Ewoks, Talz, Ortolans, Kowakians, Ranats, and Bilars. Among the results were Voort saBinring and Gorc and Pic. Scientist Tuzin Gast oversaw the project.

**Project Dead Eye** An Imperial program designed to improve stormtrooper sharpshooting through an enhancing drug derived from Alderaanian plants. Dr. Vacca was forced to abandon the project after the destruction of Alderaan.

**Project Decoy** A secret Rebel Alliance program headed by the Chadra-Fan scientist Fandar, its goal was to create a human replica droid to impersonate Alliance or Imperial officers. The Chadra-Fan scientists Fugo and Fandar developed the project, which resulted in the simulacrum Leia Organa II.

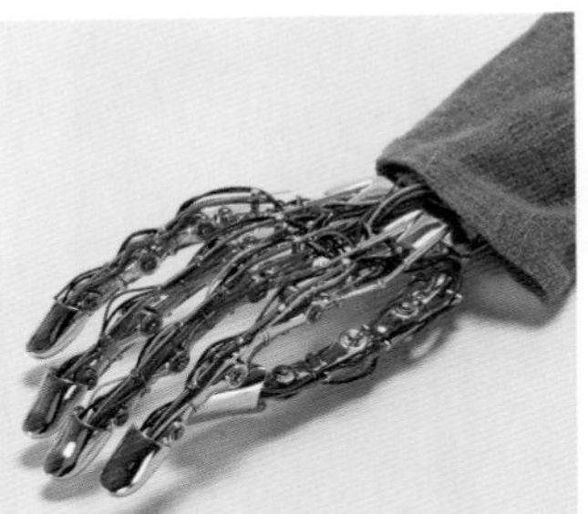

Prosthetic replacement

**Project Funeral** One of Warlord Zsinj's most ambitious actions against the New Republic, it involved the insertion of agents into all levels of the government to activate code words that would initiate Project Minefield.

**Project Minefield** A plot by Warlord Zsinj to chemically brainwash Twi'leks, Gotals, Sullustans, and other aliens. These subjects could then be activated with specific code phrases that would prompt them to complete a preprogrammed task. Project Minefield resulted in hundreds of deaths, and several high-profile assassination attempts on Mon Mothma, Admiral Ackbar, and General Han Solo.

**Project Orrad** A secret Imperial project being developed in an underground lab on Venaari, its designs were stolen by Shandria L'hnnar and Sienn Sconn.

**Project Phlutdroid** The code name for Holowan Mechanicals' development of the IG-88 assassin droid.

**Project Second Chance** A New Republic operation that hired smugglers to help disrupt the Imperial and Corporate sector forces that controlled the Kalinda system.

**Project Starscream** An Imperial program on the planet Kiva that led to the development of the living planet D'vouran. It was led by the scientist Borborygmus Gog, who reported directly to the Emperor.

**Proko, Qid** This Quarren working as a speeder mechanic on Poderis was actually a Jedi Knight who fled the Core Worlds after Order 66.

**Prolik, Rulaan** A polymorphic being and a noted criminal who hid on the planet Kashyyyk before the Mandalorian Wars. He was eventually caught and killed by a group of Jedi Knights after he began impersonating several known Wookiees who had disappeared in the Shadowlands.

Prophets of the Dark Side

***Prominence* (1)** A Republic cruiser that ferried a team of seven Jedi and five Judicials to Asmeru to root out the Nebula Front at the behest of Chancellor Valorum. The Nebula Front blasted the *Prominence* out of the sky with an ion cannon, forcing it to ditch in a lake.

***Prominence* (2)** A Galactic Republic Dreadnaught destroyed during the Clone Wars when General Grievous's task force invaded Duro.

**Prophetess** *See* Sariss.

**Prophets of the Dark Side** Adherents of the Dark Force religion begun by Darth Millennial. They were discovered by Darth Sidious on Dromund Kass, an old battlefield of the New Sith Wars. Sidious caused the Prophets to ally with his grander plans for the galaxy, and they assisted in the training of his various dark side minions. Led by the Supreme Prophet Kadann, these mystics wielded power and control by making their prophecies come true through bribery, force, or even murder. Emperor Palpatine grew dissatisfied with the Prophets and dispatched Inquisitors to destroy them; the Prophets fled to Bosthirda. For a time, false Prophets were installed by Sate Pestage and Blackhole, but they were eventually eliminated by Grand Admiral Makati. The true Prophets surfaced during the campaigns of Trioculus and were finally destroyed by Azrakel and Lumiya.

***Prosecutor*** A year into the Clone Wars, the veteran commandos of Delta Squad were dispatched to investigate the missing Republic assault ship *Prosecutor,* which later reappeared in the Chaykin cluster. The ship had been under the command of Captain Stinnett.

***Prosperity*** A Fondorian cruiser, part of the fleet that defended the planet during an attack by the Galactic Alliance. The *Prosperity* was the first ship to take damage from the *Anakin Solo,* when Jacen Solo broke away from the rest of the Galactic Alliance forces and began bombarding Fondor's cities from orbit. Solo was relieved of command by Admiral Cha Niathal, but refused to acknowledge her orders. Instead, he fired on the *Prosperity* in an effort to escape from Fondor and flee to Coruscant, where he could consolidate his own base of power.

***Prosperous*** A Confederacy cruiser commandeered by Saesee Tiin and a crack team of clone troopers during the Battle of Coruscant at the end of the Clone Wars.

**prosthetic replacement** Spurred by the carnage of the Clone Wars, the replacement of

Protocol droid

body parts with life-like replicas became very advanced. Prosthetic replacements made it possible to see through artificial eyes, feel and grip with artificial hands, and run with artificial legs. Mechanical hearts pumped blood, and other replacement organs handled other important bodily functions. Most prosthetics used synthenet neural interfaces to give recipients full control of replaced limbs. Synthflesh covered biomechanical replacement parts, giving them the look and feel of natural body parts. One example was Luke Skywalker's prosthetic hand, which replaced the one he lost in a battle with Darth Vader.

**Protas** A native of Anobis and Elis's younger brother. He was 19 years old at the time Han Solo came to Anobis to discuss a cease-fire in that planet's civil war. Though proficient at laying traps, he was accidentally killed by Anja Gallandro's explosives.

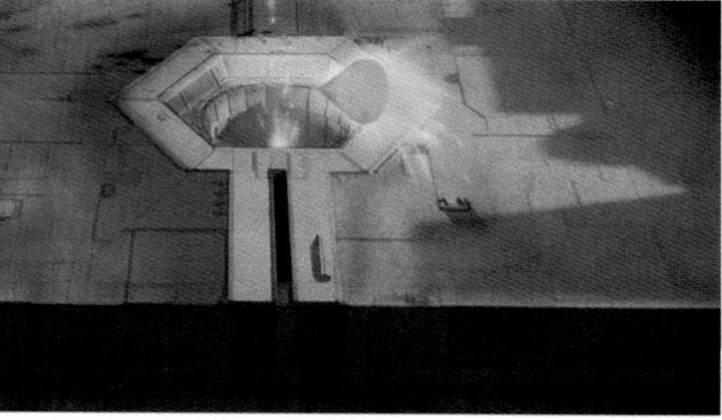

Proton torpedo

**Protazk** A world where the Imperial elite armor unit, Hell's Hammers, quelled a Rebel uprising. Among the features on this so-called dirtball world were the Spuma flats.

**Protean** A shapeshifting species from Nathas I in the Questal sector. In their natural state, Proteans resembled human-sized blobs of clay. They lived in small groups of 5 to 10 individuals, consuming food by surrounding it with their bodies and absorbing it through their skin. Individual Proteans had the ability to mold themselves into different shapes and could alter their coloration, using their ability to change shape to capture their prey. To reproduce, two individuals combined their structures into a single, stone-like ball, and remained in this configuration for a year. When the ball cracked open, the original pair emerged with a new child.

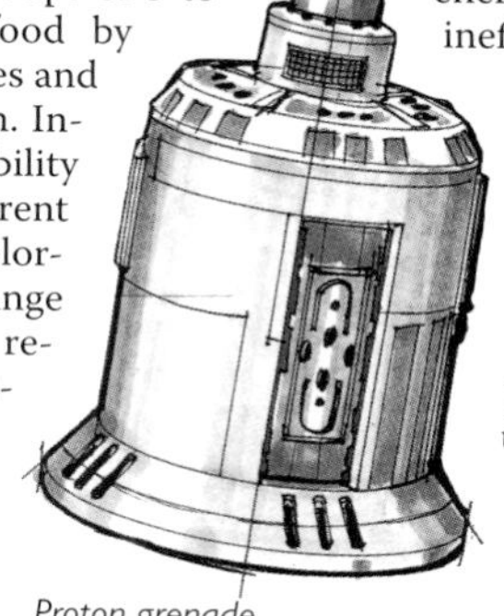

Proton grenade

**Pro-Tech movement** A political movement on Cerea led by the human Bron in the latter decades of the Galactic Republic. The movement advocated a change from the old ways in favor of adopting new technology, despite the Cereans' long-held belief that they should live in complete harmony with their world. Bron's followers were mostly young, disillusioned Cerean youths who were known as techrats by their elders.

***Protector* (1)** A *Victory*-class Star Destroyer commanded by Admiral Harkov during the Galactic Civil War.

***Protector* (2)** A *Victory*-class Star Destroyer under the command of Admiral Aril Nunb as part of the New Republic.

***Protector* (3)** An Imperial *Victory II*-class Star Destroyer that harassed Rebel ships as they gathered at the rendezvous point near Sullust just prior to the Battle of Endor. This ship survived the second Death Star debacle and became one of the ships under the command of Grand Admiral Gilad Pellaeon.

**protocol droid** A droid whose primary programming included languages, interpretation, cultures, and diplomacy, all geared toward helping it fulfill its usual function as an administrative assistant, diplomatic aide, and companion for high-level individuals. Common models included the 3PO units from Cybot Galactic and its various TC boutique lines.

**Protodeka** A deadly giant crab-like droid developed by the Confederacy of Independent Systems on Raxus Prime. The Protodeka was equipped with long-range missiles but was very slow. It was also armed with a powerful claw for grabbing enemy targets that wandered in too closely. Protodekas were used to defend Kesiak City on Thule.

**proton bomb** A proton-scattering energy warhead especially effective against ray- and energy-shielded targets, although it was ineffective against particle deflectors.

**proton grenade** A small but very powerful concussion weapon. A single grenade could blow a hole through 1.5 meters of solid permacite.

**proton tank** Armored vehicles used by the royal guard of Gala. These siege vehicles were armed with proton grenade launchers and ion cannons.

**proton torpedo** A projectile weapon, it could be fired from specialized delivery systems aboard starfighters and capital ships or even from shoulder- or back-mounted launchers. These concussion weapons carried a proton-scattering energy warhead, and they could be deflected by complete particle shielding. Proton torpedoes were used to destroy both Death Star battle stations.

**Proto One** An ancient droid fitted with many diverse replacement parts, he was proprietor of a spaceship scrap yard on the planet Boonta when R2-D2 and C-3PO encountered him during the early days of the Empire.

**protoplasmic glurpfish** One of several species of fish in Terpfen's aquarium in his quarters on Coruscant.

**protosteel** An artificial metallic compound used as armor on ancient spaceships.

**Prouk** A Korunnai serving Kar Vastor's Akk Guards during the Clone Wars. Prouk was one of several guards sent to apprehend Mace Windu when he tried to infiltrate the droid control center in Pelek Baw. Prouk attacked Nick Rostu, but Rostu blasted him with a clone trooper's rifle.

***Providence*-class carrier/destroyer** A 1,088-meter-long warship developed by Free Dac Volunteers Engineering Corps. General

Providence-*class carrier*

New Republic Provisional Council

Grievous's flagship *Invisible Hand* was an example of this line, as were its decoy ships, *Lucid Voice, Colicoid Swarm,* and *Prosperous.*

**Provisional Council, New Republic** A temporary body established by the Provisional Government of the New Republic, its main jobs were to provide leadership and direction for the new government and work toward the formal reestablishment of the principles and laws of the Old Republic. Its ruling body was the Inner Council, whose members included Mon Mothma, Admiral Ackbar, and Leia Organa Solo.

***Provocateur*** One of Warlord Zsinj's Imperial escort frigates, it was commanded by Captain Joshi. *Provocateur* was destroyed during a battle with Wraith Squadron and New Republic forces.

**provoker spineray** A Yuuzhan Vong torture device used in shaping. It was designed to selectively target a single nerve at a time. Mezhan Kwaad used a provoker spineray on Tahiri Veila to explore the human nervous system. Yal Phaath believed that using the provoker in such a way strained the intent of the ancient protocols.

***Prowler*-class reconnaissance vessel** One of the class of starships developed by Republic Engineering Corporation for the New Republic, the Prowler was designed to act as a long-term spy craft.

Provoker spineray

**Proxima Dibal** A star orbited by a single desert planet of the same name. The planet was home to feathered song-serpents and the tiny scavengers called dinkos, which emitted a highly offensive smell. Both animals were sold in Sabodor's pet shop on Etti IV.

**PROXY** A prototype holodroid who served as a companion to Starkiller—Darth Vader's secret apprentice—for years. Although PROXY's origins were unknown, the droid was a one-of-a-kind unit capable of using advanced hologram technology and built-in servos to alter his appearance, becoming virtually anyone. PROXY employed this ability to provide "face-to-face" communication between Vader's apprentice and others (most often Darth Vader himself). Additionally, PROXY was programmed to act as a training droid, taking the shape of various enemies, including past Jedi, to test the apprentice's fighting acumen. He even harbored several lightsabers within his chassis, which allowed him to challenge the apprentice whenever they sparred. While PROXY was intensely loyal to Starkiller, he was also programmed with a sinister prime directive to kill his master at the first available opportunity. PROXY spent years ambushing the apprentice in order to fulfill this programming, never realizing that success would end their friendship forever.

PROXY

**Proy'skyn** A Bothan investigator with the Drev'starn Department of Criminal Discouragement, he accompanied Morv'vyal to the Exoticalia Pet Emporium on a tip that the store had been burglarized. The shop was actually a front for an Imperial organization attempting to bring about war on Bothawui. When the Bothans discovered a hidden cache of weapons, the Imperial agents were forced to kill them.

**Prrt, Miaria** A Felacatian princess stranded on Tatooine, she recruited Devaronian con man Vilmarh Grahrk to bring her back to her father on her home planet. Since her species could not take the stress of lengthy hyperspace travels, she requested that Villie make only short jumps. When three troublesome pit droids damaged the hyperspace control unit of Villie's ship, Miaria transformed into a beast. Villie was able to trap her in the ship's escape pod, where he left her until the ship arrived on Felacat.

**Prudii** A Null-class ARC trooper designated N-5. He was one of only six Null clones to survive the gestation process. Named for the Mandalorian word for "shadow," Prudii was a technical expert in a variety of subjects, and his knowledge of materials-processing technology led him to be included on the small team dispatched to disable the Separatist droid-production facility on Olanet.

**Prune Face** *See* Orrimaarko.

**pryodene** A synthetic mood-enhancing drug in the same class as pryodase and Algarine torve weed. The drugs were generally harmless and non-addictive, but they made beings lower their guards and become more friendly and receptive.

**pryss-creatures** Huge, elephantine creatures indigenous to Verig. The natives of Verig hunted the beasts with bola weapons, using an animal's own bulk against it. This hunting technique inspired Rebel Alliance tactician Beryl Chiffonage to devise the power harpoons featured on Alliance snowspeeders.

**PS-29-2** A TIE fighter pilot who used the call sign Shadow Two. When not tweaking the control systems of his TIE, PS-29-2 could be found studying Rebel starfighter schematics. He was nicknamed Mynock.

**PS-29-3** The Imperial pilot who flew as Shadow Three. He recorded the highest score in Academy TIE fighter simulator drills, catching Admiral Motti's eye.

**Psadan** Short and stocky humanoids, they lived on the long-forgotten world of Wayland. Thick, stone-like scales covered their bodies, forming an irregular, lumpy shell over each Psadan's back. This shell protected them from predators and, in combat, made them extremely hard to kill. It could withstand a blaster bolt or amphistaff attack with only mild damage. The shells did have some

Psadan

nerve endings, however, so Psadans whose shell had been cracked or damaged experienced pain. The species shared Wayland with the Myneyrsh and human colonists, and the groups at one point engaged in open hostilities. The Psadans had a primitive society. Their primary weapons were bows and arrows, and animals were used for transportation and freight.

**pseudo-skin** Stage makeup developed for the entertainment industry to dramatically alter a performer's appearance.

**psychic augmenter** A device used to control the minds of other sentient beings. Taxer Sundown and Baroness Omnino used psychic augmenters to control their soldiers as well as Mantellian savrips on Ord Mantell.

**psychometry** The Force-derived ability to read psychic impressions of memories and emotions from the last person to physically handle an object. Some Kiffu, like Quinlan Vos, had remarkable psychometric talents.

*Psychometry*

**Ptaa, Eet** The leader of a clan of Jawas who were attacked and driven from their fortress by Sand People.

**P'taan, Fargednim** A moderately successful drug smuggler operating after the Battle of Endor on the planet Yetoom Na Uun.

**P'tan, Professor** A professor from Beshka University who tried to interview Jabba the Hutt for academic reasons, he was never heard from again. His colleague, Melvosh Bloor, came to Jabba's palace months later to investigate his friend's disappearance, only to learn that the professor had been fed to the Sarlacc to amuse Jabba.

**Ptera system** The site of the planet Flax, homeworld of the insectoid species known as the Flakax.

**pterosaur** A carnivorous flying reptile found on the planet Ammuud. Their bony skeletons created an almost glider-like frame upon which their tough and leather-like skin was stretched. These creatures laid eggs in nests perched in high trees and on the mountain cliffs of Ammuud, far from enemies. Their keen eyesight enabled them to see prey from a kilometer above. The royal families of Ammuud kept some pterosaurs in captivity for racing and riding purposes.

**P'Ton, Admiral Spitar** An officer in the Imperial Navy. P'Ton discovered the planet Kubindi when his ship's hyperdrive malfunctioned in the system. The ship's ion flux stabilizer was damaged, and while the crew repaired it, P'Ton went down to the surface and visited one of the Kubaz restaurants. P'Ton, a man of exotic tastes, was taken by the insectoid cuisine of the Kubaz and "hired" chef Kalro Mear and his dozen assistants.

**Ptor** A tall, well-muscled man native to Bellassa, he lived in the city of Ussa during the Clone Wars, making a living as a thief and thug. Despite this, Ptor was mild-mannered and took Trever Flume under his wing when the young man was forced into the streets.

**Public Safety Service** The successor organization to the Corellian Security Force.

**Publictechnic** The maker of the 850.AA Public Service Headquarters, tree feeder, and U2-C1 housekeeping droid. Publictechnic was a relative newcomer to the galactic industrial-maintenance market. Its main manufacturing plant was located on Sennatt, in Bothan space.

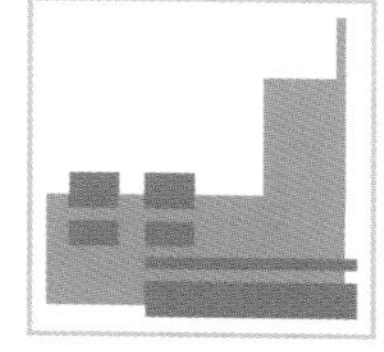

**pubtrans flitter** A public transportation system used mainly by the less well-off inhabitants of heavily developed planets such as Coruscant.

**Puddra** An Imperial sub-officer working under Captain-Supervisor Grammel on Circarpous V during the Galactic Civil War.

**Pudundruh, Quatrain** An unsavory Twi'lek entrepreneur who worked on Ord Mantell as the manager of the sister act of Amaiza and Jodelle Foxtrain. However, after a particularly rough season, Quatrain was forced to sell off many of his assets, including the Foxtrains.

**Pugwis** The grandson of legendary Podracing champion Sebulba, Pugwis shared his grandfather's penchant for violence but lacked Sebulba's considerable racing skills. He tried to climb the Podracing ranks for years, without success. After repeated losses, the frustrated Dug became even more vicious and dangerous. Following numerous attacks on fellow Podracers, Pugwis was permanently disqualified from the sport. However, the Dug's antics inspired Jabba the Hutt to create his own demolition event. Piloting his modified Podracer, Pugwis was a feared contender and competitor in the brutal sport.

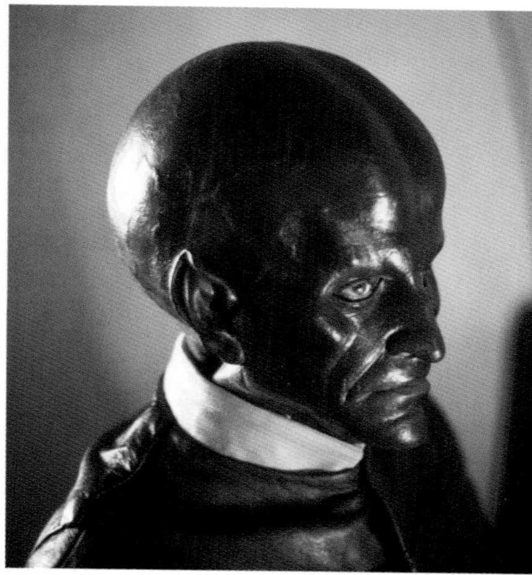

*Djas Puhr*

**Puhr, Djas** A male Sakiyan bounty hunter, he was in the Mos Eisley cantina on a job when Luke Skywalker and Han Solo first met. Decades earlier, before the Battle of Naboo, Sebulba hired Djas Puhr to find runaway Ghostling slaves.

**Pui-ui** Small, sentient beings about 1.25 meters tall, they were natives of the planet Kyryll's World. A Pui-ui consisted of two spherical bodies connected by a short neck. Projections growing from the base of the bottom sphere provided them with the ability to move around. Their language consisted of a wide range of shrill sounds.

**pulga horse** Creatures used as beasts of burden by the Ewoks on Endor, they were larger than bordoks.

***Pulsar*** A New Republic Corellian gunship scuttled following the attack at Obroa-skai during the Yuuzhan Vong War. Kartha was the ship's Elomin captain.

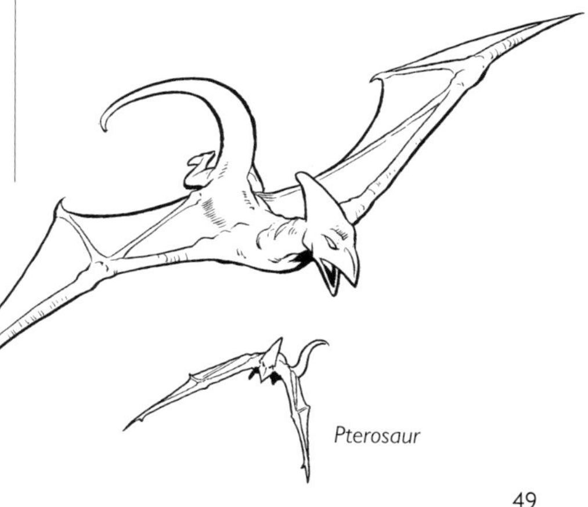

*Pterosaur*

Pulsar Skate

**Pulsar Skate** This modified *Baudo*-class star yacht, powered by twin ion engines, was once captained by Booster Terrik; his daughter Mirax Terrik then carried on the family tradition of smuggling black-market goods. This sleek vessel, at 37.5 meters, very much resembled the Corellian deep-sea skate for which it was named. The *Pulsar Skate* was saved from the Empire's grasp when Rogue Squadron was pulled out of hyperspace on its journey to establish a new base at Talasea. After a fierce battle, the Rebels were able to rout the *Black Asp* interdictor cruiser and continue their journey. Because Corran Horn's X-wing was disabled, the *Skate* was obliged to ferry it to Talasea for repairs.

Between shipments, Mirax and the *Skate* were instrumental in the retrieval of the stranded Rebel operatives on Hensara III, where she worked with Rogue Squadron. She later rescued Corran Horn once again during the second raid on Borleias, when his ship ran low on fuel. Her ship was used to bring back political prisoners from Kessel after the squadron had arranged their release. The *Skate*'s most important contribution to the Alliance cause came when it was used to penetrate Coruscant defenses and deliver a Rogue team on a covert mission to Invisec.

**Pulsar Station** The Death Star–like construction discovered in a secret lab on Liinade III by the New Republic. It was believed that Prince-Admiral Krennel was preparing to build the station, based on evidence found in Valleyport. However, the lab had actually been set up in secret by Ysanne Isard, who hoped to undermine the efforts of Krennel and Isard's clone to disrupt the New Republic. In reality, there were no actual plans to build Pulsar Station.

**Pulsar Supertanker** This conglomerate was a member of the Trade Federation until it was voted off that group's directorate. It was generally believed that Viceroy Nute Gunray's orations during the proceedings were what attracted the interest of Darth Sidious in choosing the Trade Federation for his own machinations.

**pulsar tracking** A means of tracking starships. Used by the Trade Federation, pulsar tracking was generally a reliable method for targeting starfighters with large laser cannons, such as those found aboard Trade Federation battleships. The method was less successful, however, in obtaining accurate readings from spinning starships. Bright pilots who wished to evade this method of targeting thus often voluntarily put their craft into dangerous spins.

**Pulsipher** This Mandalorian warrior served as Demagol's chief bodyguard during the final stages of the Mandalorian Wars, four millennia before the Galactic Civil War.

***Punishing One*** A Corellian Jumpmaster 5000, this 20-meter-long craft was owned and piloted by the bounty hunter Dengar. The ship featured an impressive array of weapons, including proton torpedoes, a quad blaster, and a miniature ion cannon.

***Punworcca 116*-class sloop** *See* Geonosian solar sailer.

**purella spider** A spider-like creature found on Yavin 8. It had vibrant glowing orange eyes that allowed it to see in the dark. Its underbelly was a bright red plate, and its bristle-haired back and torso were dark red. Lining its mouth were four barbed pincers that could seize prey and inject a potent venom. Purella spiders fed on Melodies and the local rodents known as raiths. They were somewhat sentient, able to determine strategy and to patiently hunt their prey. They could sense the presence of nearing creatures, and Melodies reported that a spider could even telepathically enhance a victim's fear.

***Pure Sabacc*** A Peace Brigade *Marauder*-class corvette spotted near Wayland, commanded by Vortia Kwis.

**purge troopers** Faced with an increasing shortage of experienced troops, the Empire went to great lengths—often disturbing lengths—to supplement its forces. A secret project, code-named Dark Trooper Phase Zero, involved taking aging clone troopers and replacing their limbs and many internal organs with cybernetic counterparts. Based on a hidden space station in the Dominus sector, the Dark Trooper Phase Zero project was overseen by young Lieutenant Rom Mohc. Much of the same technology that was used to transform Anakin Skywalker into the cyborg Darth Vader found its way into the Dark Trooper Phase Zero project, with moderate success. With their aging limbs and organs replaced, these clone troopers could benefit from their combat training and experience while their cybernetic limbs remained in peak condition, not suffering the effects of the clones' advanced aging. These troopers were nicknamed purge troopers.

***Purity*** A Yevethan battle cruiser commanded by Vol Noorr, it was the ship that destroyed the *Astrolabe,* a New Republic astrographic probe, at Doornik-1142.

**Purnham** The primary planet of the system of the same name, it was located in the Shelsha sector and controlled by pirate gangs during the Galactic Civil War.

**Puroth** A four-armed Eirrauc Jedi Master killed by General Grievous during the Galactic Civil War, alongside her former Padawan Nystammall on the flame-grass plains of Tovarskl. For a time Grievous carried Puroth's lightsaber blade.

**purple stingwort** A venomous plant native to the shores of Drongar. It attracted prey with its bright purple hue, and then struck with its potent, paralyzing toxin.

**Purpsh** One of four Vagaari who accompanied Bearsh on the mission to locate the remains of the Outbound Flight Project. Purpsh surreptitiously installed a navigational recording device aboard the *Chaf Envoy* so that the Vagaari would have a way to escape the Redoubt after they eliminated the Chiss.

**Purr** A naïve Tinnell who traveled with smuggler Dannen Lifehold.

**purse world** A term used to describe a major Neimoidian colony.

***Pursuer*-class patrol ship** An older MandalMotor's police craft. Boba Fett used it as the basis of his *Slave II* ship. Spar's Mandalorian Protectors also used the ships in their war against the Jedi.

**push-feather** A game developed by the Jedi Knights to hone the telekinetic abilities of younglings. Students used the Force to move a feather around.

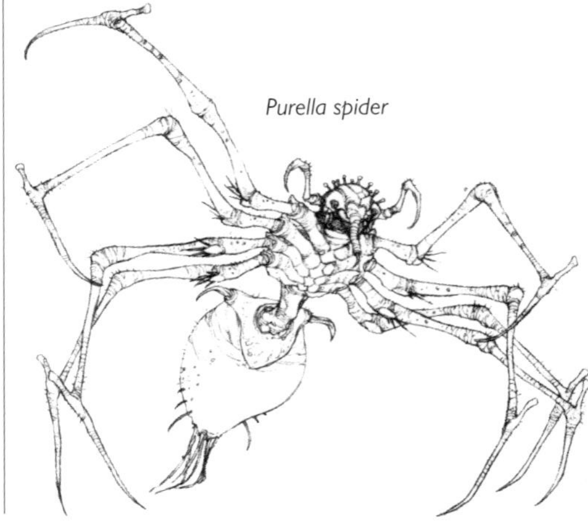
Purella spider

P'w'eck

**Puth** A Nimbanel hired by Boba Fett to serve as the bounty hunter's accountant and stock broker after the Yuuzhan Vong War.

**puzzleflower** A plant native to Nimban with interlocking petals. Primitive Nimbanese would hone their analytical skills by trying to pry open the puzzleflower to reach the edible stem within.

**P'w'eck** A sentient saurian species enslaved by the reptilian Ssi-ruuk. Dull-brown-colored P'w'eck adults grew to 1.5 meters tall and had heavy eyes and sagging skin. At the age of 20, they were customarily enteched—a particularly gruesome process in which their life energies were absorbed into battery coils used to power circuitry.

During the Yuuzhan Vong War, P'w'eck arrived at Bakura claiming that they had defeated the Ssi-ruuk and freed themselves from slavery. The P'w'eck Emancipation Movement presented the Bakurans with an offer of alliance to strengthen both groups against future invasions. This movement proved to be an elaborate ruse concocted by the Yuuzhan Vong themselves in an effort to capture both Lwhekk and Bakura, cutting off the Unknown Regions of the galaxy. As part of the alliance, the P'w'eck leaders required that Bakura be consecrated, so that any P'w'eck who died on Bakura would not lose their souls. In reality, the Keeramak was acting on behalf of the Ssi-ruuk, who were actually being controlled by disguised Yuuzhan Vong warriors.

The spirit of the P'w'eck species was underestimated by both the Ssi-ruuk and the Yuuzhan Vong. P'w'eck crew members managed to overpower their Ssi-ruuvi superiors and halt the invasion of Bakura. A formal alliance between Bakura and the true P'w'eck Emancipation Movement spelled the end of the scheme to subjugate Bakura.

**Pwoe** A dour Senator, he was the first Quarren to serve on Borsk Fey'lya's advisory council. Prior to the Yuuzhan Vong War, Luke Skywalker discussed with the council the idea of reestablishing the Jedi Council, an idea that Pwoe strongly opposed. He later refused to take the Yuuzhan Vong threat seriously. When the New Republic government scattered following the Yuuzhan Vong conquest of Coruscant, Pwoe fled to Kuat. Though he tried to name himself Chief of State in this interim, the government eventually continued on Mon Calamari, and Cal Omas—a pro-Jedi politician—was elected to office. Pwoe, ostracized, traveled from one part of the galaxy to another, trying to rally his ever-diminishing numbers of supporters. He went to Ylesia in order to negotiate a treaty of friendship and mutual aid with the Ylesian Republic, but barely survived that encounter intact, losing a tentacle after being hit by a razor bug.

Pydyrians

**Pydyr** One of the moons of Almania, it was where the Dark Jedi Kueller killed 1,651,305 people during the first bombing campaign in his reign of terror against the New Republic. Pydyr was an exceptionally wealthy world, crossed by beautiful sandstone streets. The Pydyrians mainly pursued lives of leisure and even had special droids designed for street care, with others for washing buildings. The planet's architecture was often bold, and heavy brown columns and large square rooms dominated the designs. Every surface was covered with decoration, some hand-painted by famous artists long dead, others studded with tiny seafah jewels, the source of Pydyr's great wealth. The Pydyrian healing stick originated here. The atmosphere was warm, with dry air that contained a touch of salt.

**pygmy porlceetin** A large, venomous hexapedal creature found on Geonosis.

**pylat bird** Native to the mountain regions of Neimoidia, this beautiful bird was prized as an expensive pet for its white plumage and its soothing song.

**Pylokam** A very old human, he ran an unsuccessful health food booth in Mos Eisley, selling fruit juices and steamed balls of grated vegetables. People met at his stand to transact shady deals, knowing they wouldn't be interrupted there.

**Pyn'gani** A reclusive alien species native to Polus, they were able to tolerate the extreme cold of their home planet.

**Pypin** One of the Trianii colony worlds, it lay within the disputed border of the Corporate Sector.

**Pyria system** Located only hours from the Mirit and Venjagga systems at the edge of the Galactic Core, this system's fourth planet and only inhabited world was Borleias—the base of operations for Imperial General Evir Derricote. After the New Republic routed the Imperials, it fortified Borleias as a forward base even as ships sent by Warlord Zsinj began making reconnaissance raids into the system.

**Pzob** The third planet in the K749 system, this world of thick, ancient forests was colonized by a group of Gamorreans. Some 18 years before the Battle of Yavin, the Empire established a base on Pzob where 45 stormtroopers were to await pickup by the *Eye of Palpatine.* The battlemoon never arrived, and over the years every stormtrooper except Triv Pothman was killed by internal fighting or constant skirmishes with the Gamorreans. Pothman served as a slave in the Gamorrean Gakfedd clan village for two years, followed by a year with the Klagg clan. Eight years after the Battle of Endor, Luke Skywalker and his companions landed on Pzob, where a ship from the *Eye of Palpatine* captured them, Pothman, and the Klagg and Gakfedd clans.

# Q

**Q-2 artificial heart** Part of Neuro-Saav's cybernetic cardiovascular replacement/enhancement system. This rybcoarse-fortified heart, in conjunction with Neuro-Saav's Ex-Musc enhancement, increased a user's strength and stamina.

Q-2 hold-out blaster

**Q-2 hold-out blaster** A slim, compact hand blaster model manufactured by Merr-Sonn. The streamlined pistol packed a mild punch and had limited range, but in the hands of a crack shot like Queen Amidala of Naboo, it could be quite deadly. SoroSuub also manufactured a version with the same name under license.

**Q-4 borer droid** Nicknamed mole droids, these automata were used by the Quarren in deep-sea mining on Mon Calamari. They were 70 centimeters long and equipped with a nose-mounted heavy-duty laser that could cut through rock at extremely close range. The droids were happy and cheerful, but not very bright.

**Q5A7 Bacta Refinement Plant** A target during the Bacta War, it was located in the mountains of Qretu 5. Wedge Antilles and his unorthodox unit—cobbled together from ex–Rogue Squadron members, Gand ruetsavii, and Twi'leki Chir'daki—destroyed the facility.

**Q7 droid** A spherical astromech used to copilot V-wing starfighters during the Clone Wars. Its upper dome resembled that of an R2 unit.

**Q-7N** A millennia-old droid found in a fortress near the Rebel base on Yavin 4. Q-7N was constructed on the planet Malagarr, captured by pirates 2,000 years before the Battle of Yavin, and placed in the fortress to guard their stolen treasure. The spherical, repulsor-equipped unit served the Rebel Alliance as a translator.

**Q9 unit** An experimental astromech droid model developed by Industrial Automaton. Based loosely on the design of the R7 unit, the Q9 featured an advanced personality matrix with superior versatility, and analytical and data access skills. One of its design flaws was the Q9's failure to deal well with stress. Since astromechs were often tasked with helping ship crews in catastrophic emergencies, this was a serious defect. As a result, the line was canceled. Kyp Durron once had a Q9 droid named Zero-One.

< Ulic Qel-Droma

**Q9-X2** A jet-black droid, he more or less resembled a taller, thinner version of R2-D2. Q9-X2 spoke Basic and moved around on wheels or repulsorlifts. He was based on the R7 droid, a more advanced version of the R2 series, but he designed his own improvements, which totaled more than half his equipment. Han Solo ordered Q9 to protect his family, and to improve his ability to do so, the droid installed sophisticated detection and observation equipment.

**qaana** A creature found aboard Supreme Overlord Shimrra's ship during the Yuuzhan Vong War. Rainbow qaana hummed hymns to the gods through their chitinous mandibles.

**Qade, Sergeant** A member of the Galactic Alliance Guard on Coruscant during the war between the Galactic Alliance and the Confederation.

**Qaestar Town** Located on Talus, it was the largest of the Double Worlds' cities. Qaestar Town was dominated by its spaceport, located atop a 2-kilometer-tall plateau called Qaestar Ridge.

**qahsa** The bioengineered memory storage device that served as the keeper of ancient records for the Yuuzhan Vong. Available in a variety of sizes and capacities, qahsas were most often accessed by a cognition hood. Shapers maintained a qahsa of their specific protocols called the Qang qahsa.

**Qalita Prime** A New Republic member world located in the Seventh Security Zone. Twelve years after the Battle of Endor, pirate attacks near Qalita Prime had grown so severe that cargo syndicates threatened to stop supplying the world. The Right Earl of Qalita Prime traveled to Coruscant to seek help against the pirates, and Admiral Ackbar suggested that the newly commissioned Fifth Fleet be dispatched as a show of support.

**Qalsneek the Bull** An ancient Jedi Master and member of the Swimming People of Dellalt. He imparted his knowledge in a holocron made of sea-crystal, discovered in the ruins of Derem City on Kamino.

**Qalu, Tsaa** A tall Yuuzhan Vong hunter, he led a team of less experienced warriors that tracked Klin-Fa Gi and Uldir Lochett on Wayland. He later pursued Lochett's rescue ship, *No Luck Required,* aboard his own vessel, *Throat Slasher.* Qalu chased his quarry to Thyferra, part of a plot by the shapers to bring a virus-carrying Bey Gandan to the planet to cripple bacta production. Leaft, the Dug ally of Lochett, caused the *Throat Slasher* to crash, killing Qalu and the rest of his crew. Qalu wore the cloak of the Nuun and had a face covered with a black web tattoo, centered on the two holes that passed for a nose. His ears had been sliced into three lobes, and he had three holes in each cheek. He was rangy, almost wiry for a Yuuzhan Vong.

**Qalydon** An Outer Rim planet that served as a base of operations of the Fellowship of Kooroo, it was a battle site during the Clone Wars.

**Qang qahsa** A high-level memory storage device kept aboard the *Baanu Miir* and used by the Yuuzhan Vong, it contained the numerous protocols

Q9-X2

used by the shapers. Data security was managed by levels of cortexes, with only the most skilled and experienced users being able to access the upper cortexes. Adepts were not allowed access to the mysteries beyond the fifth cortex. Yuuzhan Vong custom held that the knowledge contained in the cortexes was bestowed upon them by their gods, and to pursue outside knowledge was heresy. Nonetheless, Nem Yim was instructed to peer beyond the seven known cortexes to find the elusive eighth, which was said to contain knowledge for defeating the Jedi Knights. She did, but found only emptiness within. She was then secretly assigned to create the eighth cortex, part of a sham to justify the Yuuzhan Vong invasion of the galaxy.

*Q'Anilia*

**Q'Anilia** A Miraluka Jedi Master, part of the Covenant of Masters gathered by Lady Krynda Draay to peer into the future for potential threats to the Jedi Order after the carnage of the Great Sith War. Q'Anilia and her fellow seers saw a vision of a resurgence of the dark side, and believed that one of their Padawan learners would be responsible for the holocaust. The Covenant preemptively killed the graduating class of Padawans at the satellite academy on Taris, but one luckless apprentice—Zayne Carrick—survived by being late. Carrick became a fugitive as the Mandalorian Wars began.

**Qaqquqqu, Lord** One of the followers of Lord Hethrir, he was a slave trader.

**Qaresi Squadron** A crack starfighter unit stationed aboard the Galactic Alliance warship *Bounty* during the war with the Confederation.

**Qarohan steppes** Flatlands located south of the Jasserak Lowlands on Drongar.

**Qat, Hul** A Yuuzhan Vong Shamed One, formerly of the warrior caste. Living in the lower levels of Coruscant, he heard the stirring words of the Prophet Yu'shaa and came to admire the Jedi Knights. Qat was one of the first volunteers to flee Coruscant to search out the fabled living planet that would help liberate the Shamed Ones. Qat's search took him to Dagobah, where he ran afoul of Yuuzhan Vong warriors. He escaped with the help of Tahiri Veila, but was badly wounded. With his dying breath, Qat asked Veila if he had succeeded in his search. Though Veila didn't believe so, she told him otherwise.

**Qat, Vintul** A Yuuzhan Vong who commanded the warship that attempted to intercept the *No Luck Required*.

**Qat Chrystac** A hostile world in the Sumitra sector with searing volcanic glass plateaus carved by radioactive lava seas, slightly heavier-than-standard gravity, and toxic air. It was the site of a Rebel Alliance hiding post during the Galactic Civil War. The Empire attacked the Alliance outpost, but the harsh elements foiled the Imperial effort. The base became a cache of intelligence data over the years, surviving the transition from Rebellion to New Republic. It was the site of fighting between New Republic and Imperial forces during Grand Admiral Thrawn's push to retake the Core five years after the Battle of Endor. Thrawn used Interdictor cruisers to bring his ships out of hyperspace at precise locations. More than one assault was staged, and Wedge Antilles helped battle two squadrons of cloned TIE pilots during the first. Imperial shock forces and radtroopers worked their way across Qat Chrystac during Thrawn's siege of Coruscant. General Garm Bel Iblis was at the post when he intercepted a distress call from Lando Calrissian's Nomad City mining complex on Nkllon.

**Qa'till** A murderous Laboi crime lord who controlled all the starship maintenance operations on Hypotria during the New Republic.

**Q-E, 2-E, and U-E** Three small Accutronics nanny droids, these "antiques" were forced to assemble illegal blasters by Master Vuldo, who blasted U-E, leaving only his cognitive unit. Saved by the timely intervention of Nak Pitareeze and C-3PO, U-E's memory banks were placed into a labor droid.

**Qeeq** A subspecies of fist-sized Killiks that were part of the Colony.

**Qeimat system** The site where a bungled COMPNOR scandoc transmission was intercepted by the local media, leaking the name *Ubiqtorate* to the general public.

**Qeimet fleet** An Imperial fleet led by the flagship *Victorious,* it was based near the Hook Nebula. The Qeimet fleet was tasked not only with eliminating the Rebel presence in the nebula, but also with punishing the resource-rich worlds that allowed them free rein there. Other ships in the fleet included the Star Destroyer *Retribution* and the craft of the renowned Scimitar assault wing.

**Qektoth attack cruiser** A dagger-shaped strike cruiser bolstered with biotechnology in the service of the Qektoth Confederation.

**Qektoth Confederation** A rogue band of humans and other species who advocated the abandonment of inorganic technology, it was formed about 17 years before the Battle of Yavin when a group of scientists from a small Kathol-based colony banded together to push their agenda. The Confederation believed that the embrace of inorganic technology led to the stagnation of humanoid evolution and the decay of the living spirit. To that end, the Confederation experimented with biotech hybrids and analogs of standard galactic technology. What started as simple, benign experimentation twisted into a fundamentalist crusade at the hands of increasingly zealous leaders. As the New Republic corvette *FarStar* traveled deeper into the Rift four years after the Battle of Endor in its search for rogue Imperial Moff Kentor Sarne, it ran afoul of the Confederation several times.

**Qel, Tsun** A Yuuzhan Vong initiate from Domain Qel who was sent to Nen Yim as an assistant. Like other shapers, he wore a headdress, and his forehead had the marks of his domain. Though he claimed to have been sent by Mezhan Kwaad, he was actually a spy who tried to obtain evidence of Kwaad's heresy.

**Qel-Bertuk, Lanius** The Jedi Watchman of the Cularin system 24 years before the Battle of Naboo. He received little in the way of support from the beleaguered Jedi Council, despite his reports of dark side energies on the planet Almas. After the Battle of Naboo and the rise to power of the Thaereian military in the Cularin system, Master Qel-Bertuk found himself more and more troubled by the dark side's advance and reluctantly agreed to support military action against the Thaereians. Waging a private war without the Jedi Council's oversight, Qel-Bertuk denied the call to action during the Clone Wars.

***Qel-Droma*** An Alderaanian frigate, it was part of the home fleet that defended Alderaan in the last decades of the Galactic Republic.

**Qel-Droma, Cay** A Jedi instructed by Master Arca Jeth at his training compound on Arkania some 4,000 years before the Galactic Civil War, he and his brother and fellow Jedi, Ulic, had been born on Alderaan to a great warrior family. Cay was mechanically minded and always tinkered with machines. He lost his left arm during the Beast Wars of Onderon and replaced it himself during the battle with a prosthetic limb made from parts of an abandoned XT-6 service droid. When his

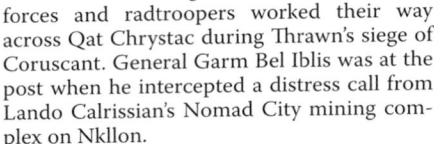

*Q-E (left) and U-E*

brother, Ulic, turned to the dark side of the Force, Cay never stopped trying to bring him back to the light side. In a final confrontation, Ulic murdered Cay—an act that immediately filled him with horror and regret.

Cay Qel-Droma

**Qel-Droma, Duron** An ancient Jedi, cousin to Cay and Ulic Qel-Droma, he participated in the Great Sith War but vanished during the Great Hunt that followed. Duron, alongside Jedi Knights Shaela Nuur and Guun Han Saresh, was hunting down terentateks through the Force, and voyaged to Korriban to exterminate what was thought to be the last of the dark side creatures. During the lengthy mission, Duron and Shaela began to fall in love, which angered Guun for not only being against the Jedi Code, but also stirring within him feelings of jealousy. Guun abandoned the pair, and a terentatek attack killed Qel-Droma in the Valley of the Dark Lords. As he died, he had a vision of the future conflict between Darth Revan and Darth Malak, and professed his love for Shaela.

**Qel-Droma, Ulic** A powerful young Jedi some 4,000 years before the Galactic Civil War, he thought he could learn the ways of the dark side and then return with this knowledge to the light side, but his failure wreaked havoc on the galaxy. Trained along with his younger brother, Cay, on the mining world of Arkania by Jedi Master Arca Jeth, Ulic Qel-Droma quickly mastered the art of lightsaber dueling. Even at that point, his self-confidence and brashness made some think him arrogant.

When Master Arca felt they were ready, he sent the Qel-Dromas and their training partner, Tott Doneeta, to Onderon to help put an end to the violent, centuries-long civil war between the walled city dwellers and the outlanders who had tamed giant warbeasts. Things were not as they first seemed. The walled city, Iziz, was still full of dark side power some 400 years after the fall of a Sith practitioner named Freedon Nadd. After some difficulties, Master Arca arrived and helped the outlanders win the war. Investigating the dark side forces, the Jedi found the crypt of Freedon Nadd. An uprising by Nadd's followers had to be put down by Jedi and Republic reinforcements.

Other problems arose. Ulic was growing fond of another Jedi, Nomi Sunrider, but was pulled away when he was named Watchman of the Empress Teta system. Freedon Nadd's spirit had exposed two spoiled royals there to Sith teachings, and they had formed a group of dark side magic users called the Krath that fomented war among the Teta system planets. Ulic decided that the only way to truly defeat the Krath was to infiltrate them and learn their secrets. Aleema and Satal Keto played along with Ulic, but Satal injected him with a slow-acting poison that would make his eventual return to the light side impossible. He survived an assassination attempt by Satal and saw Nomi escape imprisonment by Satal just hours before Ulic had agreed to kill her to prove his loyalty to the Krath. Nomi and Cay Qel-Droma failed in their attempt to convince Ulic to escape with them. Anger inside Ulic exploded, leading him to kill Satal. Aleema gave Ulic half a Sith amulet that had been given to Satal by the spirit of Freedon Nadd.

Ulic was then confronted by another fallen Jedi, Exar Kun. As they engaged in a lightsaber battle, the Sith amulets both Jedi wore began to glow, and they were visited by spirits of ancient Sith Lords who told them that Kun was the new Dark Lord of the Sith and Qel-Droma his first assistant. Years later, Ulic reappeared with tremendous dark side powers and set out to plunder and destroy large parts of the galaxy with a large and bloodthirsty army serving alongside Exar Kun. The Jedi Knights and the Republic declared Ulic an enemy, and the subsequent battles became known as the Sith Wars—one of the largest and bloodiest conflagrations ever witnessed, with millions dead as a result. In the end, though, Ulic Qel-Droma betrayed Exar Kun, leading the assembled Jedi against the Sith Lord's base of power on the moon of Yavin 4. Qel-Droma himself was robbed of his Jedi powers by Nomi Sunrider.

Powerless, Ulic dropped from sight. For a decade, he wandered, lost in his grief and guilt. Keeping his identity secret, he hired transport from a down-on-his-luck spacer named Hoggon, who delivered him to the frigid world of Rhen Var. Ulic chose to live in an abandoned fortress atop an icy mountain.

Elsewhere, the rebellious teenage daughter of Nomi Sunrider, Vima, wanted to find Qel-Droma. She hoped to learn the ways of the Jedi, and her mother was far too busy as leader of the Jedi assembly to deal with her. Vima hired Hoggon to help her track down the Jedi. Hoggon was surprised to see an image of Ulic, and was shocked that he had been carrying a wanted criminal in his ship.

In the eerie, empty corridors of the Rhen Var palace, Vima confronted Ulic. She was a reminder of all his pain, and he wanted nothing to do with her. Vima voiced her desire to be a Jedi, and Ulic warned of the high and often terrible price that often required. Despite everything that befell Ulic, Vima still saw him as the great hero Nomi had fallen in love with. Ulic began training Vima in the construction and operation of a lightsaber. Although blind to the Force, he still could handle the weapon. While Ulic was teaching Vima the ways of the blade, Vima taught Ulic how to appreciate life again. Together, with their lightsaber blades, the two of them carved an immense statue to honor the memory of Arca Jeth and Andur Sunrider.

Nomi Sunrider came to Rhen Var to collect her daughter. The Cathar Jedi Sylvar also sought out Ulic to kill him, in vengeance for the death of her mate. Ulic refused to fight. He reasoned with Sylvar that vengeance was not the path of a Jedi. At the final moment, Sylvar, too, put down her blade. At that moment, Hoggon, an admirer of the Jedi, fired his blaster weapon and pierced the heart of Ulic Qel-Droma, a mere mortal. In Hoggon's eyes, it was the act of a hero: the death of a villain. For Ulic, it was a final rest and a final chance to die in the light. As Nomi cradled Ulic's dying body, Qel-Droma asked for a last forgiveness.

**Qella** *See* Brath Qella (Maltha Obex).

Ulic Qel-Droma

**Qennto, Dubrak** A Corellian smuggler known to his close friends as Rak, he was the owner and captain of the *Bargain Hunter* in the years following the Battle of Naboo. Rak had developed something of a romantic relationship with his first mate, Maris Ferasi, though they kept it discreet. Rak and his crew, which also included Jorj Car'das, were captured by then–Force Commander Thrawn aboard the *Springhawk* about five years before the Clone Wars began, after they made a blind hyperspace jump to avoid pursuit by Progga the Hutt. The frustrated Qennto had little patience for Thrawn's hospitality, and it bothered him to no end that Ferasi seemed quite taken by the exotic Chiss. His frustration reached a boiling point after three months' captivity, when he was left behind at Crustai with Ferasi while Thrawn took Car'das on another mission. Neither Qennto nor Ferasi had any idea what had occurred—namely, the brutal destruction of the Outbound Flight expedition—and Car'das later lied, saying that Thrawn had allowed the expedition to escape. They were eventually freed and allowed to return to the Republic, where they were able to pay off their debt to Drixo the Hutt and resume their normal smuggling activities.

**Qetix IV** A barren moon in the Dresscol system of the Trax sector, it housed a Rebel Alliance starfighter repair base during the Galactic Civil War.

**Qetora, Epo** An aged Twi'lek historian who knew about the various mining facilities on Mustafar, as well as tales of treasures hidden around the dangerous world.

**Qe'u** A Yuuzhan Vong Shamed One sent to Yavin 4 to serve the shapers who were trying to determine the source of the Force. When Vua Rapuung was believed dead, Qe'u was given his duties. However, Rapuung had faked his death, and later killed Qe'u to gain access to the Yuuzhan Vong complex for himself and Anakin Solo.

**Qexi's** A spacer cantina on Ord Mantell, it was an absolute dive filled with the dregs of the galaxy.

**Qexis** An Outer Rim planet devoted to scientific and technological research and experimentation. It was a high-security world with only one spaceport.

**Qiaxx** A tourist destination, site of famed Bubble-cliffs. It was the base of operations for Black Nebula after the Battle of Endor.

**Qibbu the Hutt** The owner and proprietor of Qibbu's Hut, a restaurant, hotel, and cantina in a seedy section of Coruscant during the final decades of the Galactic Republic. Kal Skirata once saved Qibbu's life, and the Hutt vowed to repay the Mandalorian someday. He got his chance during the Clone Wars when Skirata asked for room, board, and facilities to run an anti-terrorist operation.

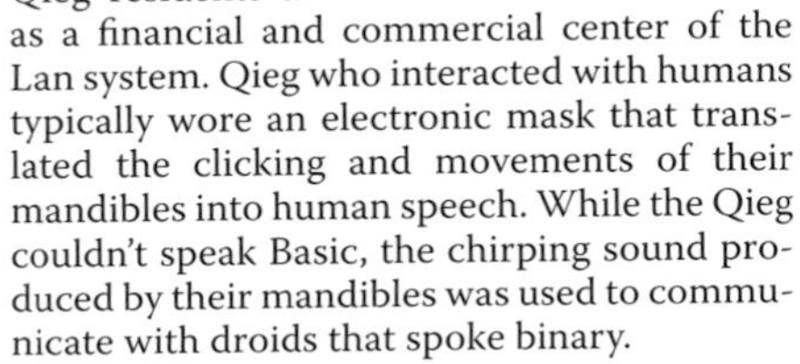
Qieg

**Qieg** The native intelligent inhabitants of Lan Barell, they were diminutive insectoids with a knack for technology and machinery. Their roughly humanoid bodies were divided into three segments—a head, an upper abdomen, and a lower abdomen. The Qieg had six limbs, two arms, and four legs. The feet on their first legs were jointed in such a way that they could be used as arms if needed. Qieg lived in hundreds of thousands of colony nests scattered throughout the cactus forests and plateaus of Lan Barell. One of the largest Qieg centers was the Quilan Hive, a huge network of nests tied together by immense stone walls. Altogether, the Quilan Hive housed 100,000 Qieg residents and served as a financial and commercial center of the Lan system. Qieg who interacted with humans typically wore an electronic mask that translated the clicking and movements of their mandibles into human speech. While the Qieg couldn't speak Basic, the chirping sound produced by their mandibles was used to communicate with droids that spoke binary.

Qimtiq

**Qiemal** A primitive sect of the Qieg. While most of the Qieg adopted the technology of the galaxy around them, the Qiemal remained at the feudal level of development they had attained at the time of first contact. Extremely xenophobic, they identified any mammal as a killer, a notion ingrained from centuries of hunting and being hunted by dingories. Visitors to Lan Barell were advised to avoid Qiemal territory.

**Qiemo Adrangar** One of the smaller overclans of Ansion, made up from the Alwari who lived west of Cuipernam.

**Qiilura** A remote planet in the Tingel Arm that was best known for its production of the crops barq and kushayan. The export of these and other luxury foodstuffs accounted for some 50 percent of the entire galactic market, although very little of the profit ever made it back to the farmers. Shortly after the Battle of Naboo, the Trade Federation took control of the exports, and used the profits to help fund the Confederacy of Independent Systems. When the Republic discovered that Ovolot Qail Uthan, a Separatist-funded scientist, was developing a deadly nanovirus at a facility on the planet, they launched a mission to Qiilura. A team of clone commandos, led by Jedi Padawan Etain Tur-Mukan, infiltrated the facility and captured Uthan before destroying the nanovirus. The mission was greatly assisted by the help of the native Gurlanin, although they refused to fully join the Republic.

**Qiina, Master** A librarian who worked in the Jedi Archives on Coruscant following the Battle of Ruusan. She was on duty and witnessed Zannah—a long-lost Padawan who'd turned into a Sith Lord—abscond with Darovit. The suspicious duo departed so suddenly that they left the volumes they had been reading in their access terminal, providing the Jedi with the knowledge that they were on their way to Tython.

**Qilqu, Dr.** Jacen Solo's personal physician aboard the *Anakin Solo* during the war between the Galactic Alliance and the Confederation. The Bith tended to injuries Jacen sustained after dueling with Luke and Ben Skywalker.

**Qimtiq** A Quarren who owned the Iziz Cantina and managed swoop racing on Onderon shortly after the Jedi Civil War.

**Qinx, Mentis** The owner of a docking facility at Mos Espa on Tatooine last used by Jango Fett. Young Boba Fett arrived there seeking Jabba the Hutt. Qinx owned a 3D-4X droid.

**Qiqah, Tih** An old, senile, inept, and disgraced Yuuzhan Vong master shaper who taught Suung Arah before Nen Yim arrived aboard the *Baanu Miir.* In his last year, Tih Qiqah did not train any initiates or adepts.

**Qiraash** A human-like species with a large cranium. Leesub Sirln was a Qiraash.

**qixoni crystal** An incredibly rare and exotic gemstone said to have been forged in the heart of a supernova. Some of the first Jedi found the crystals on a dying planet, and later used them in powerful lightsaber blades.

**Qiyn, Khaat** A Jedi Knight at the Battle of Geonosis, she was a student of the Form V technique of lightsaber combat.

**Qlothos** A resort world inadvertently attacked by TIE bombers dispatched in error from the Star Destroyer *Interrogator.* The raid killed 60 innocents, including a highly placed Kuat Drive Yards engineer and his family. Captain Jovan Vharing was executed for this blunder.

**Q'Maere** A distant world in the Kathol sector, just inside the dangerous anomaly called the Kathol Rift. It was the site of a scientific outpost—the Q'Maere Research Facility—established by the University of Sanbra. The station was dedicated to a number of exotic branches of planetology and xenobiology. Originally, the facility had a small military complement drawn from the remains of COMPNOR. When Kathol sector's Moff Kentor Sarne retreated deeper into the Rift, he pulled the military personnel into his ranks. He also dumped a number of prisoners at Q'Maere, turning it into a gulag of sorts.

**q'mai** The Kamarian word describing a religious offering. The Kamarian Badlanders offered Han Solo q'mai of various artifacts in exchange for entrance into the Solo Holotheater, an entertainment venue that Solo had inadvertently turned into the object of a fanatical religious cult.

**Q'nithian** A star system home to sentient, flightless avians known as the Aeropteryx. They were less than attractive, covered in dingy gray feathers and equally gray skin.

**Qogo** An amber-colored gas giant locked in a mutual orbit with the world of Uluq, deep in the Transitory Mists.

**Qom Jha and Qom Qae** Natives of the cave networks of Nirauan, they were winged beings that looked like a cross between a mynock and a praying makthier. Marginally Force-sensitive, each clan was led by a Bargainer. The Qom Jha were cave dwellers, while the Qom Qae lived in cliff "nestings" in open air. Qom Jha and Qom Qae shared the same genetic background. They both had leathery wings, small snouts, and rows of tiny sharp teeth. Sharp talons on their feet allowed them to perch on small outcroppings of rock and branches. The Qom Jha liked to perch upside down on stalagmites, while Qom Qae perched upright on cliffs or rocks. They both possessed large eyes, but each had different vision abilities, due primarily to their environments. Qom Jha could see better in darkened spaces, whereas Qom Qae saw better and for greater distances in bright light.

Only the Bargainers, as elders, were able to speak for the clans, and their rulings were obeyed without question. If a member of the tribe disobeyed a Bargainer's orders, that individual was severely punished or even exiled. The species could communicate almost telepathically. They read surface thoughts and feelings, and could determine the intentions of any intruder who approached their nest. The Qom Qae and the Qom Jha were long at odds, each claiming to have been wronged by the other in the past. Despite their differences, they banded together to help Luke Skywalker and Mara Jade infiltrate the Hand of Thrawn.

**Qonet** The genetic ancestors of the Qella. The Qonet were descended from the Ahra Naffi. Sister species included the Khotta of Kho Nai.

**Qonto** Members of this alien species were not known for their perception, although a few gifted individuals had senses considerably higher than the human standard.

**Qordis** An ancient Sith Lord, he was part of Lord Kaan's Brotherhood of Darkness during the events leading up to the Battle of Ruusan. Qordis oversaw the Sith training academy on Korriban, honing the next generation of Sith warriors. Among his students was a burly miner named Dessel, who would eventually become Darth Bane. Bane's ascension was in spite of, and not because of, Qordis's teachings; the instructor had little faith in Dessel's abilities and thought him weak and misguided. Nonetheless, when Darth Bane emerged with the power to reshape the Sith Order, Qordis tried to ally himself with his neglected pupil. Bane killed Qordis with the Force, although his spirit lived on to hound Bane for a time, reaching from beyond the grave to cause Bane to crash-land the *Valcyn* in the wilderness of Dxun. Qordis hoped to make Bane's life a living hell but, as with many other trials, Bane emerged stronger and more powerful for having survived the incident. Though likely human, Qordis had unsettling features like pointed teeth and fingernails that curved like talons. An indulgent being, Qordis liked to surround himself with opulence.

**Qoribu** A gas giant in the Gyuel system of the Unknown Regions, adjacent to Chiss space. Qoribu had a prominent ring as well as more than 50 moons, at least 6 of them habitable. When the Colony began expanding rapidly due to the influence of the Gorog hive, the Killiks settled Qoribu, an action that alarmed the isolationist Chiss. With the intervention of the new Jedi Order and the acceptance of the Galactic Alliance, the Killiks agreed to abandon their hives on the Qoribu moons and relocate to Woteba and other planets hidden within the Utegetu Nebula. The Qoribu crisis was believed to have been resolved when Welk was killed by Jedi Master Luke Skywalker, an event that supposedly marked the end of the Dark Nest. However, about a year later, the Gorog—under the influence of Lomi Plo—had reasserted their control over the Colony, causing a new set of challenges for the Alliance.

Khaat Qiyn

**Qorl** A TIE fighter pilot, rank number CE3K-1977, he piloted a ship damaged in a crossfire between Rebels and Imperials. Because his comm channels were jammed and his orbit decayed, he crash-landed on Yavin 4. The jungle cushioned his fall, and he was thrown out of his craft, badly injuring his arm. Qorl wasn't heard from for more than 20 years, until Lowbacca, a Jedi trainee, discovered the crashed fighter overgrown with jungle plants. He and Jaina and Jacen Solo restored the craft, and then were surprised when Qorl appeared. The pilot kidnapped the Solo twins and attempted to make an escape. The twins were rescued, but Qorl fled in his restored fighter. Qorl then joined the turncoat Jedi Brakiss and the Shadow Academy and was put in charge of training those youths who weren't Force-sensitive to be stormtroopers. He successfully led a daring assault on the New Republic cruiser *Adamant*, stealing both the ship and its precious cargo of weapons and supplies. During a battle to destroy the Jedi academy on Yavin 4, he was shot down again. Because the Shadow Academy had been destroyed and he despised the New Republic, he decided to live out his life in the planet's jungles.

*Qom Jha and Qom Qae helped Mara Jade and Luke Skywalker investigate the Hand of Thrawn.*

**qormot** A forest omnivore from Yeshocq, its temperament was dependent on seasonal changes. For most of the year, the qormot was relatively peaceful. During the pre-winter mating season, however—or when two qormots occupied the same territory—these creatures turned aggressive and violent. Qormots were quadrupeds with blunt claws on their fore- and hind limbs, and pointed quills along their flanks and spine. They had a single eye and a pointed muzzle filled with serrated teeth.

**Qornah** A Jedi Master dispatched to investigate the strange concentration of dark side energy on Almas, he was cut down by his own apprentice, Kibh Jeen.

**Qotile** A world ravaged by the Stark Hyperspace Conflict. A deserter fled here and established himself as king. Bossk claimed the bounty on the would-be monarch and inherited the title.

Dezono Qua

**Qretu-Five** A lush, verdant planet with towering mountains and a warm, moist climate, it was the site of a bacta-producing colony overseen by colonists from Thyferra. Qretu-Five was surrounded by a ring of asteroids that were clearly visible in the night sky. After the members of Rogue Squadron resigned from the New Republic military some three years after the Battle of Endor, they destroyed the Q5A7 Bacta Refinement Plant on Qretu-Five in order to hurt Imperial Ysanne Isard's bacta-producing capability.

**Qrygg, Ooryl** A Gand member of Rogue Squadron, Qrygg first befriended fellow Rogue Corran Horn during their training exercises on Folor. After Qrygg joined the squadron, he took part in the battles at Chorax and Hensara III. Because Gands needed only a fraction of the sleep humans required, he was awake when stormtroopers landed at the Rogue base at Talasea in a secret attack. He and Horn alerted the rest of the squadron, and a furious fight began. Qrygg's bravery averted almost certain death for most of his fellow pilots.

Qrygg was part of the strike team that scored a retaliatory blow at Vladet, but he also was on the disastrous first mission to Borleias. During the battle, his X-wing was destroyed. Qrygg ejected in time, but as he floated in space, a fragment of the fighter's S-foils sliced through his right arm, severing it above the elbow. Several weeks later, his arm had regenerated itself so well that he was able to take part in the squadron's covert operations on Coruscant. His presence was vital to the mission's success. After his group of operatives had gained access to Subsidiary Computer Center Number Four, they found it was impossible to enter the control room because it was flooded with Fex-M3d, an Imperial nerve gas. Because Gands didn't breathe like humans, Qrygg was able to enter the room to gain access to the gas masks inside, enabling the others to follow. From there they were able to realign the OSETS 2711 satellite, burn up a nearby reservoir, create a terrific thunderstorm, and help bring down Coruscant's planetary defense shields.

**QS-2D** A heavily modified administrative droid owned by ill-fated Twi'lek scouts who died exploring the moon of Uffel. QS-2D continued surveying the planet, starting up a small mining operation with another automaton the Twi'leks had brought. The droid struck a business deal with Riboga the Hutt, working under a Twi'lek alias so he wouldn't draw attention to his unusual independence. QS-2D was so successful that he eventually attained ownership of the entire moon.

**QT-3PO** A protocol droid captured by Jawas on Tatooine, its smashed form was aboard the sandcrawler that also caught C-3PO and R2-D2. QT-3PO provided C-3PO with all the knowledge about Jawas that he possessed.

**QT-7** An intelligent computer probe owned by a Rebel special-missions group that operated in the Mortex sector. QT-7 was instrumental in downloading vital transit information concerning the Imperial replenishment fleet from an unguarded computer post on Lotide. When the same Rebel team acted on the information and raided the Imperial container train *Black Ice*, QT-7 accompanied them and helped them bypass many computer-based systems. QT-7 resembled a high-tech suitcase. Its "face" was covered with blinking lights, screens of various sizes, and input and output jacks. It was cheerful, friendly, and enjoyed a good game of sabacc.

**Qua, Dezono** A man on Esseles who purchased Resa Greenbark at the slave markets of Orvax IV in the early days of the Galactic Empire. Bomo Greenbark and Dass Jennir tracked him down.

**quad, the** A large open area at the Carida Imperial Academy compound; the cadets there called it the grinder.

**Quadanium steel** A brand-name steel armor composite used by numerous corporations in the hulls of their combat spacecraft. Sienar Fleet Systems used it extensively in the production of its TIE-series solar gathering panels. The first Death Star featured Quadanium in its hull.

**Quadex** This corporation manufactured and sold power plants and ion drives for starships. It made the popular Kyromaster line of products. Quadex also manufactured the power core used on the *Millennium Falcon.*

**Quadinaros, Ben** A Toong Podracer from the Tund system, he was relatively inexperienced and entered the Boonta Eve Classic only after placing a bet with Boles Roor, who believed that the Toong was too cowardly to compete in the event. Roor's poorly worded bet never actually required Ben to cross the finish line—or the starting line, for that matter. Ben met the requirements simply by entering the race, renting an unusual quadra-Podracer. The craft malfunctioned at the beginning of the Podrace and Quadinaros never left the starting grid.

Ben Quadinaros

**quad laser cannon** A starship blaster, it was often slung in turret mounts to take advantage of its lightweight, quick-targeting motions. The *Millennium Falcon* featured AG-series quad laser turrets.

**Quad-Lo** A squat alien slave trader who frequented the space station *Bazarre* and was acquainted with Orion Ferret. He had four multijointed legs, two arms, and green lizard-like skin. Quad-Lo tried to buy Lando Calrissian (who was not for sale) for eight credits.

**quadranium** An incredibly strong mineral used to make fuel tanks.

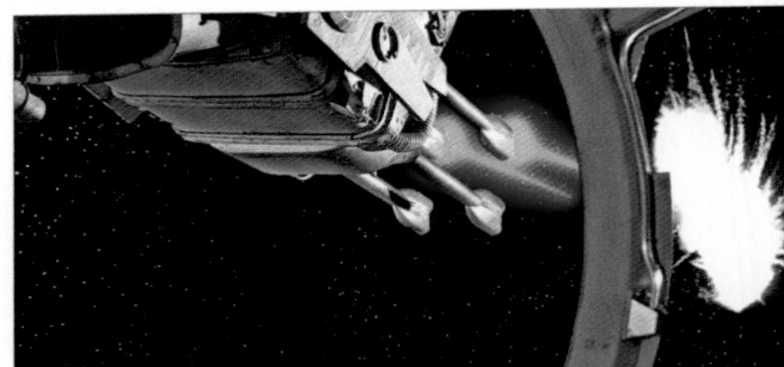
Quad laser cannon

**Quadrant Seven** A world whose uncreative name was derived from its stellar coordinates. The beings of Quadrant Seven were peaceful, but did not believe in government or any kind of imposed control. They were somewhat isolationist, although they did not forbid visitors. In fact, they were particularly friendly to offworlders. The Quadrant Seven beings refrained from adopting high technology, and even eliminated comlink communications during the final decades of the Old Republic. Their rationale was simply that comlinks made distances smaller and problems bigger.

**quadra-Podracer** A Podracer design that featured four jet engines attached to a single control cockpit, as opposed to the traditional two. Ben Quadinaros, a Toong racer from Tund, piloted a Balta-Trabaat BT310 quadra-Podracer.

**Quadrex Corestar** A model of repulsorlift engine found aboard the Bespin Motors Void-Spider TX-3 landspeeder.

**quadrillium** A metal used in making starship hulls, it was mined from asteroids, such as those found in the Tava Yagen field.

***Quaestor*** A Galactic Republic battle cruiser during the Clone Wars, it suffered a hyperspace mishap. It then crashed into the planet Pammant, destroying the ship and devastating the world.

**Quaffug the Hutt** The Hutt overboss of the third moon of Blimph. Before the rescue of the carbon-frozen Han Solo, Quaffug the Hutt captured Lando Calrissian to serve as prey in the Duff-Jikab, a cutthroat hunt. The Hutt accused Calrissian of cheating in a card game that had cost Quaffug his stake in a Ceramowerx complex. During the pursuit, Calrissian met up with the native Jokhalli. With their help, they were able to overthrow Quaffug's trade stranglehold. Calrissian was given the opportunity to spare the Hutt's life, which he used to bargain for entry into the Hutt Guardsman's Guild—allowing Calrissian under the alias of Tamtel Skreej to infiltrate Jabba's palace to help rescue Han Solo.

Quaffug the Hutt

**Quagga** A master mechanic, this Wookiee learned his craft as a slave apprentice to a skilled Imperial engineer. When his master bought Quagga's freedom, he settled on the outskirts of Tatooine's Anchorhead, where he struggled to establish a service and restoration garage. Competition from local Jawas, Quagga's expensive methods, and the garage's remote location kept customers away. With his business on the brink of financial ruin, Quagga entered Jabba the Hutt's demolition derby competition piloting a fully refurbished AAT battle tank.

**quaghen** A creature native to Tzarib, it was considered very easy prey.

**Qual** A Selkath member of the Dantooine Jedi Council three years after the Sith War against Exar Kun.

**Qualo, the** A ruling dignitary on the planet Arda-2. The Qualo hosted a reception for Princess Leia Organa during her diplomatic meeting there.

**Qualtrough** A planet locked in an intense civil war when it was first discovered by the Jedi Knights traveling aboard the *Chu'unthor* centuries before the Battle of Yavin. The Jedi were able to negotiate a truce, allowing the natives of Qualtrough to join the Republic.

Quamin

***Quamar Messenger*** A space liner that, on its maiden voyage, was hijacked by Gallandro. The *Quamar Messenger* carried up to 600 passengers and a crew of 45.

**quamin (plural: quamilla)** Creatures from the Kidron system known for their mercilessly efficient method of carving up sodbeasts. These flying creatures were 2 meters long and had leathery wingspans of about 1.7 meters. The quamilla had razor-sharp tail whips that they used when they attacked in swarms of 5 to 10. Their repeated strikes caused severe lacerations on their targets. When the hapless prey collapsed due to blood loss, the quamilla swooped in to feed, sucking in blood and vital fluids through the spongy feeding vents on their faces. A quamin had three hearts, large lungs, and large compound eyes.

***Quandary*** A tramp freighter operating in the Outer Rim Territories during the Galactic Civil War. The dilapidated ship was piloted by an equally dilapidated crew that had seen better days. The young fugitive Tinian I'att traveled aboard the *Quandary* to Silver Station from Ksiczzic III.

Quanto

**Quannith, Governor** The commanding Imperial authority on Siluria III before a Rebel movement toppled his government.

**Quannot's syndrome** A debilitating and fatal disease. Nichos Marr was diagnosed with Quannot's syndrome. He had his consciousness transferred into a specially designed advanced droid to preserve his life essence.

**Quantana** This bounty hunter grew up on the streets of Lopor Station. He had a strong sense of loyalty, using his funds to support an extended family with a history of medical problems. Quantana was smart and cool under pressure.

**Quanta sector** Moff Jerjerrod was formerly the governor of the Quanta sector, ruling from his estate on Tinnel IV.

**Quantill City** The largest city on Ando.

**Quanto** A henchman of Great Bogga the Hutt, he was among those responsible for the murder of Jedi Andur Sunrider at the Stenness hyperspace terminal about 4,000 years before the Galactic Civil War. Andur's wife, Nomi, then killed Quanto with Andur's lightsaber in self-defense.

**Quanton** The site of General Airen Cracken's capture by the Imperial Security Bureau during the Galactic Civil War. While captive, Cracken was subjected to Imperial truth drugs like Bavo Six, causing him to divulge sensitive Alliance intelligence.

**quantum-crystalline armor** The state of the art in impervious materials manufacturing. The science was advanced and esoteric, but involved the stacking of material so as to pack as many atomic particles in as dense a concentration as physics would permit. The process was repeated, with each layer constantly laminated and joined with additional layers, then phase-shifted to compress it into as compact a volume as possible. The process was horrendously expensive, but the end result was a metal that, for all intents and purposes, was indestructible. Properly made quantum-crystalline armor could resist the pressure and temperatures found in the core of a star for extended periods of time. The multilayered metal retained an oil-like sheen when finished. The Empire developed quantum-crystalline armor for the Sun Crusher. By two decades into the New Republic, the process had become affordable enough that certain industrial and commercial vessels used a limited form of the armor.

***Quantum Storm*** The first Rebel transport to leave in the evacuation of the planet Hoth. Its escape was made possible by a ground-based ion cannon that disabled the orbiting Star Destroyer *Tyrant* long enough for the transport to leave orbit and engage its hyperdrive system.

**Quara** *See* Aqualish.

Quantum Storm

**Quarantine Enforcement Cruiser (QEC)** A New Republic emergency vessel used to stop other vessels from breaking planetary or systemwide quarantines. A QEC had a small complement of troopers and a squad of medics aboard.

**Quarg, Governor** The leader of a scavenger group living on Drexel II. He and his group prized metal above all else. They lived in a massive city built atop sailing ships. His father was the governor of the Korteen Asteroid Belt and ran a lucrative ship-wrecking operation until the Jedi Knights of the Old Republic stopped them. In an attempt to escape justice, Quarg's father took his wrecking equipment and fled to the Drexel system. Governor Quarg, his son and successor, continued the space-wrecking operation from the planet until he was killed by Luke Skywalker in the war against the Dragon Lords.

**Quarmall** An Abyssin Jedi Knight who was part of a mission that infiltrated and dismantled the salt-smuggling operation of Arconan kingpin Lojrak Shrag. During the Clone Wars, he was blasted by General Grievous's battle droids and believed dead, but his remarkable Abyssin healing abilities kept him alive. He was later captured and twisted into a sleeper agent of the dark side of the Force by Emperor Palpatine. Quarmall emerged after the Battle of Endor, spreading a message of intergalactic peace and harmony. The goal was to weaken the New Republic's military by having its leaders convert to Quarmall's prophetic message. Quarmall's deception was exposed by a group of fledgling Jedi during one of his rallies, as they goaded the Abyssin into revealing his true nature. The young Jedi were forced to defeat him in battle, and had to deal with rumors that they had killed an advocate of peace.

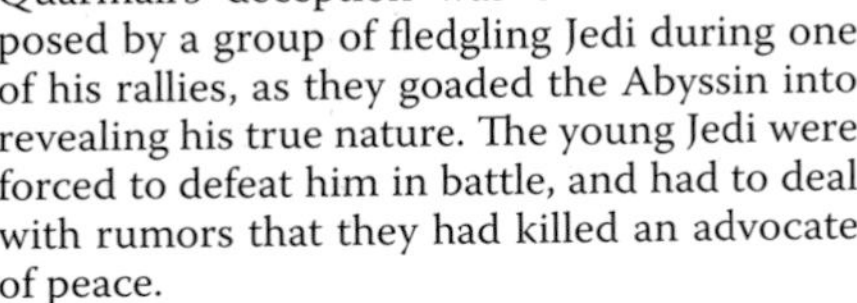

Governor Quarg

**quarra** Domesticated hunting animals, they were found mainly on the planet Devaron. Devaronians publicly executed their most notorious criminals by throwing them to packs of wild quarra. Aurra Sing used quarra to hunt down Aayla Secura during the Clone Wars.

**quar rats** Lowly vermin that inhabited the sewers of Barancar Port.

**quarrel** Energy projectiles fired by a Wookiee bowcaster, they exploded upon impacting a target. Other types of quarrels included flash and smoke projectiles.

**Quarren** These aquatic beings evolved deep in the murky oceans of Mon Calamari. When they were first discovered by their worldmates the Mon Cals (as they called them), there was some initial confusion. The Quarren weren't as quick to evolve culturally as the Mon Calamari. As the Quarren rose to the surface from their ocean depths and met their cousins, they invariably attacked the Mon Cals. The Mon Calamarians, equipped with better technology and higher intellect, bested the Quarren each time. After years of this, the Quarren were driven to near extinction. This prompted the Mon Cals to perform a daring and controversial social experiment. They had captured nearly a million Quarren throughout their struggles, yet did not want to free them, for they feared the Quarren would only fight until the Mon Calamari were forced to kill them. Instead, they attempted to civilize the Quarren.

Quarrel

The first step was the removal of children from the parents. The Mon Calamari then taught this new generation of Quarren mathematics, philosophy, science, and the other foundations of civilization. In 10 years, the Quarren young were released to their parents. As expected, this generation found nothing in common with their forebears. They had learned not to hate their surface-dwelling cousins, but instead respected them. The young saw their parents and ancestors as primitive savages, while the elder generation believed their offspring had been brainwashed. Within 15 years, the young Quarren had assumed control of the populace. Within 20, they had made peaceful contact with the Mon Calamari.

The Quarren preferred the ocean depth as their home, but the two species eventually began working together. The Mon Calamari provided ideas and new concepts to the Quarren, while the Quarren mined deep-sea metals to turn those ideas into reality. The result was a network of advanced floating cities on Mon Calamari. The Quarren preferred to live in the dark, deep portions of the cities, while the Mon Calamari lived closer to the sunlight. The tentacle-faced Quarren were frequently—if rudely—called Squid Heads. They preferred to call their home planet Dac, its name in the old Quarrenese tongue. Quarren could descend to depths of 300 meters without breathing or pressure apparatus. They had the ability to change the color of their leathery skin, but this was usually only demonstrated during mating rituals.

Quarra

The Quarren and the Mon Calamari shared a language, but while the Mon Calamari also adopted Basic, the Quarren remained faithful to their oceanic tongue. The Quarren were a pragmatic, conservative people compared with the Mon Calamari. While the Mon Cals dreamed of brighter tomorrows, the Quarren never forgot their past. This led to continuing friction and outright hostility by the Quarren. During the Clone Wars, the planet erupted into civil war as the contentious Quarren Isolation League was backed by the Confederacy of Independent Systems. The Jedi Kit Fisto and his clone troopers were able to defeat the league, and brought peace again to Mon Calamari. The Quarren signed a treaty with the Mon Cals, though many offworld Quarren still swore allegiance to the Separatists.

Quarren

It was a Quarren who sabotaged Mon Calamari's protective defense network, allowing the Empire to destroy several Mon Calamari cities early in the Galactic Civil War. But when the Empire attempted to subjugate Mon Calamari, many Quarren joined their world-mates to throw out the invaders. Afterward, most Quarren wanted nothing to do with the Rebellion. Many fled the planet, hoping to avoid the Imperial reprisal that was sure to come. The Battle of Mon Calamari, six years after the Battle of Endor, was the final straw for many Quarren, who finally left their homeworld.

**Quarren Industrial** A Quarren corporation that manufactured mining tools and technology. Among its products were mining laser platforms and Q-4 borer droids.

**Quarren Isolation League** A militant Quarren faction allied to the censured Quarren Senator Tikkes, who sought to reject all Galactic Republic presence on their world. They took up arms against Mon Calamari

Quarren Isolation League

and Quarren alike to achieve those aims. The isolationists included Quarren mining barons who had grown rich from Commerce Guild funding, and they were able to secure Confederacy support in exchange for continued shipments of raw ore to the guilds. It was Senator Tikkes himself who signed a treaty with Count Dooku, which resulted in the league obtaining advanced underwater weaponry crafted by the Trade Federation and the Techno Union during the Clone Wars. In the civil war that ensued, the valiant Mon Calamari Knights did their best to defend their cities and the Calamari Council. The Republic soon arrived, and with clone trooper forces led by General Kit Fisto, they defeated the Quarren Isolation League.

**Quarrr-tellerrra** The name the Wookiees of Rwookrrorro used for Rebel Alliance recruiter Bria Tharen. In the Shyriiwook tongue, it meant "sun-haired warrior."

**Quarry** An underwater grotto on Naboo, it was an isolated place of Gungan punishment located near the edge of the Naboo Abyss. Boss Nass reopened the Quarry after Jar Jar Binks's accident that let loose many animals from the Otoh Gunga Zoological Research Facility.

Captain Quasar

***Quartermain III*** One of three maintenance carriers in the Imperial Replenishment Fleet DK-209, it was attacked by Rebel Alliance Mortex sector forces during a stopover at the Refrax Spaceport.

**Quasar, Captain** The skipper of a pleasure cruiser during the days of the Galactic Republic. General Obi-Wan Kenobi helped Quasar defend his ship from Merson pirates.

***Quasar Fire*-class cruiser-carrier** A SoroSuub-designed cruiser-carrier designed to accommodate 48 starfighters. It was 340 meters long. Examples in the New Republic fleet included the *Flurry* and the *Thurse*.

**Quatra** An ancient Jedi Master who trained Juhani on Dantooine. Juhani fled from the academy after mistakenly believing she had killed Quatra during a training duel, around the time of the Mandalorian Wars.

**Quatreen River** This river wound through Foulahn City on the planet Cartao.

**Quay** The Weequay god of the moon. The Weequay were a deeply spiritual people; their name literally translated into "the followers of Quay." Ancient Weequay would often ask advice of Quay, who would pass on wisdom through signs to be interpreted by the faithful. In modern times, a more intelligent and unscrupulous species took advantage of the Weequay by manufacturing small devices called quays. These small handheld spheres made of white, high-impact plastic could recognize speech patterns and answer simple questions. Many gullible Weequay thought these devices were a means of communicating with Quay.

**Queblux power train** A cheap but relatively inefficient power source, it was used in such places as the Mos Eisley cantina. It was manufactured by a local company, Quebe-Luxfause Systems.

**Quecks, Major** A Phindian officer in the Sentient Property Crime Bureau of Phindar Station during the Clone Wars, he ordered a retreat when Asajj Ventress attacked the station.

**Quedlifu, Senator** The New Republic chair of the Economics Committee under President Gavrisom.

**quednak** A six-legged, flatulent, herbivorous lumbering creature used by the Yuuzhan Vong on Ylesia as a mount. Two riders could sit within a shell-shaped box. The beasts were practically impervious to blasterfire, but could be taken down with heavy weapons.

**Quee, Danni** One of the original—and youngest—members of the ExGal-4 outpost team on Belkadan. A native of Commenor, she hated the bustle of the densely populated Core planets. Danni credited her mother, an astrophysicist, with inspiring her to join ExGal at 15. Belkadan was at the forefront of the Yuuzhan Vong invasion, and she was captured by the first invaders, along with the Jedi Knight Miko Reglia. The Yuuzhan Vong tried to break his will by bombarding him with images of his own failure, but Danni struggled to keep him sane enough to escape. Miko sacrificed himself so that Danni and Jacen Solo could flee.

Danni returned to Commenor to rest before rejoining the New Republic's efforts to defeat the Yuuzhan Vong. She found herself more and more attracted to Jacen Solo, despite the difference in their ages, and she slowly cultivated a relationship with him. Danni later accompanied Jacen and his uncle Luke Skywalker on a mission into the Unknown Regions, where they hoped to find the rogue planet Zonama Sekot. Upon landing on the living planet, Danni was amazed at the life force that infused the world. However, the native Ferroans were wary of the newcomers and took Danni hostage. She suffered a concussion in the attack. Sekot had orchestrated the attack to test the Jedi, and together Luke and Jacen were able to convince the planet of their peaceful intentions. Danni was freed, and Zonama Sekot agreed to follow them back to the galaxy. As the Yuuzhan Vong War reached its conclusion, Danni elected to remain on Zonama Sekot when it returned to the Unknown Regions, in the hope of learning more about the extragalactic aliens and their biotechnology.

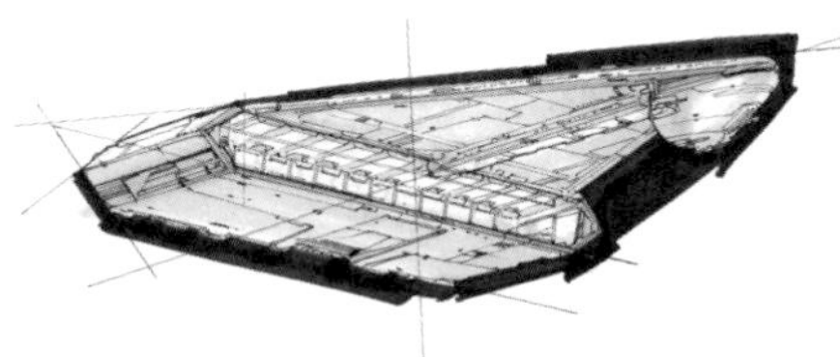

Quasar Fire–*class cruiser-carrier*

***Queen Aelnari*** A relatively well-known passenger liner plying the Outer Rim Territories.

**Queen Jool** *See* Jool.

***Queen of Cularin*** A Corellian-built luxury liner that made regular runs among the planets of the Cularin system during the final decades of the Galactic Republic.

Danni Quee

**Queen of Empire** The sister luxury liner to the *Star of Empire;* both were vessels in the Haj Shipping Lines. The *Queen* was 2 kilometers long and equipped to handle 5,000 passengers. Among the amenities: indoor pools and spas, casinos, null-g gliding areas, exercise rooms, as well as upscale shops and swanky night-clubs like the Star Winds Lounge. The *Queen* was the vessel of choice for passengers traveling between Corellia and Gyndine, although occasionally it cruised Rimward as far as Nar Hakka in Hutt space. While transporting refugees from Ord Mantell to the Core during the Yuuzhan Vong War, the *Queen* was used by New Republic Intelligence's Major Showolter to relocate Elan and Vergere to Bilbringi.

**Queen of Ranroon** The largest treasure ship of its time—the ancient past before the Old Republic—it was protected by 1,000 war robots loyal to Xim the Despot. Many millennia later, during a routine mission over the planet Dellalt, pilot Lanni Troujow discovered what appeared to be the log recorder of the *Queen of Ranroon.* She hid the recorder in a lockbox at a public storage facility, and was killed shortly thereafter by rival treasure seekers. Her quest was continued by her sister Hasti Troujow, Badure, and Han Solo. They eventually discovered the treasure of the *Queen of Ranroon* in secret vaults belonging to the Warlord Xim the Despot. The treasure—full of obsolete technology and minerals that had since become common—was outdated and mostly worthless.

**Queen's Monument** A structure built by the Gungans to honor Queen Amidala. It possessed a single light, which symbolized the peace forged between the Naboo and the Gungans. Five rotating orbs on the monument represented the Queen's five virtues: leadership, compassion, beauty, wisdom, and strength.

**Quegh, Captain** An officer in the Galactic Republic Starfleet, he commanded the *Ranger* in the mission to liberate the Intergalactic Communications Center from the Separatists during the Clone Wars.

**Quelii sector** An area of space containing the planet Dathomir. During the early years of the New Republic, Quelii was under the control of Warlord Zsinj.

**quella** A rare, precious blue gemstone found only on Alderaan. The cat burglar known as the Tombat used a quella gem as her signature, leaving it behind after each crime.

**Quella** A woman who frequented the palace of Jabba the Hutt around the time of the crime lord's demise. She was pale, slender, and brown-haired.

**Quellor** The site of peaceful, anti-Imperial rallies held in the aftermath of the Battle of Yavin. At one such rally in Terrina Square, Moff Toggan called in a legion of stormtroopers to keep the peace. When protesters burned an effigy of Emperor Palpatine, the stormtroopers opened fire.

**quenak** A 12-legged beast bioengineered by the Yuuzhan Vong to serve as a mount for their Chazrach troops.

**Quence sector** A sector in the Outer Rim Territories, it was the site of an important Rebel base during the Galactic Civil War. Operatives based in Quence carried out missions in the neighboring Parmic sector. Worlds in the Quence sector included Elshandruu Pica, Empartheca, and Suarbi.

Bren Quersey

**quench weed** A weed found growing on Naboo. Capable of thriving in almost any environment, quench weed grew slowly and was harvested by the Gungans.

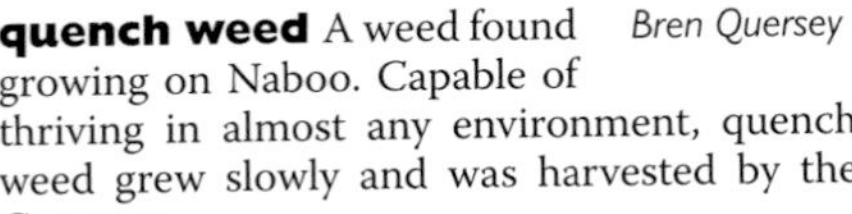

**Quenfis** The New Republic escort frigate commanded by Captain Virgilio amid Grand Admiral Thrawn's campaign to retake the Core Worlds. During the rush to claim the long-lost *Katana* fleet, New Republic councilor Borsk Fey'lya transferred much of the original crew of the *Quenfis* to other assignments, and filled the ship with officers loyal to him. This was to ensure a powerful bargaining posture during the conflict that arose around the Dreadnaught fleet.

**quenker** A small subterranean creature found on Dantooine.

**Quenno** The portion of the Saurton population that wished to return to the traditional ways of the reptilian species. They didn't agree with the conflicting Des'mar ideology that welcomed offworlders to the planet.

**Quenton, Commander** An Imperial officer dispatched by Grand Admiral Thrawn to the planet Tatooine to investigate the auction of the moss-painting *Killik Twilight.* Assigned to the *Chimaera,* Commander Quenton was given a wealth of credits with which to secure the artwork, and no price was considered too high. However, when he noticed that a Devaronian and a Twi'lek—actually Han Solo and Leia Organa Solo, in disguise—were trying to destroy the artwork, Quenton and his men opened fire in Mawbo's Performance Hall in an effort to secure the work. They were unable to foresee that Kitster Banai would steal the painting and flee into the desert, but Quenton reacted quickly and sent a detachment out to recover both Banai and *Killik Twilight.*

A Quermian (back) speaks with an Xexto.

**Quermia** An Outer Rim planet, it was home to the Quermians. The Arkanians terraformed the planet into a veritable paradise 17,000 years before the Galactic Civil War.

**Quermian** A species of intelligent invertebrates native to the planet Quermia. Generally pale and tall, Quermians had small heads atop long necks. They also possessed four arms and a lower brain located in the chest cavity. Quermians' olfactory organs were located in their hands. The Quermians were an offshoot of the Xexto species from Troiken. Seventeen thousand years before the Battle of Yavin, their primitive forebears were moved to the Quermian system by rogue Arkanian scientists. The Arkanians conducted a variety of genetic manipulations upon the transplanted Xexto and then watched how they might evolve. Within a few generations, however, the Arkanians moved on to other experiments and left the Quermians to their own devices. The Quermians developed a highly advanced society on their garden world. They became known for their telepathic abilities. The species was forced to withdraw to its home system during the rule of the Empire. It wasn't until shortly before the Yuuzhan Vong invasion that the Quermian planetary government started to take steps to rejoin the galactic community.

**Quersey, Bren** A Rebel pilot who flew as Red Eight at the Battle of Yavin.

**Quest, Sarcev** A failed Jedi initiate, he served the Agricultural Corps shortly before the Battle of Naboo. He was taken in by Chancellor Palpatine as an aide. His handsome looks allowed Quest to mingle with the nobles and dignitaries of the Coruscant court, gathering intelligence without appearing to pry. At night Quest worked as an infiltrator and was also one of the Emperor's Hands, spying on Palpatine's enemies and gathering evidence of their plans. After the Battle of Endor, Quest allied himself with Carnor Jax, and even manipulated events so that Jax would supplant the Emperor's clones to lead the Empire. When Jax was killed, Quest was ostracized by the Ruling Council and went into hiding. It was later revealed that Sarcev Quest was the father of Irek Ismaren, although many believed that Irek was the son of Emperor Palpatine himself. Quest eventually was captured after a bounty was placed on his head by Jeng Droga. Although Droga believed that it was Boba Fett who brought in Quest, it was actually Ailyn Vel working in disguise.

Sarcev Quest

**Questal** A backrocket planet settled by farmers who cultivated the land and grew crops. About three years before the Battle of Yavin, a farmer turned over a large deposit of ardanium while plowing his field. The valuable metal used in starship construction brought interstellar commerce to the world. Entrepreneurs and miners by the thousand converged on Questal, seeking the valuable ore. Questal was soon crawling with crime. The Empire brought order to the world, with Moff Bandor placing the local crime bosses in charge. Though he ended the violence, his rule was anything but benevolent. Bandor was believed to have mysterious powers, for he was feared by all. His power stemmed from a secret weapon, the hurlothrumbic generator, which he kept in secret chambers that he called the game chambers of Questal.

**Question the Quarren; Questions Three** Common verbal children's games played throughout the galaxy.

**quetarra** A Zabrak stringed musical instrument.

**Queyta** The site of a Techno Union outpost, this world was a member of the Confederacy of Independent Systems during the Clone Wars. A biological weapon that wiped out the Gungan colony on Ohma-D'un was developed on Queyta. Obi-Wan Kenobi was the only surviving member of a team of five Jedi Masters dispatched to Queyta to find the antidote for the toxin. It was there that he encountered Asajj Ventress, one of the masterminds behind the swamp gas project. Ventress was unable to stop Kenobi's raid, but vowed to capture him eventually.

**Quian** The planetary home of a distinctly human species with light brown hair, blue-green eyes, and extremely dark skin.

**Quiberon V** Gamorrean Interstellar held the mineral rights on this planet, which it put up for sale for 500,000 credits.

**Quick 6** A Merr-Sonn sporting blaster used by Rebel officers, including Princess Leia Organa.

**quickclay** A viscous gray-green soil, it covered much of the planet Circarpous V. Like quicksand, the soft, shifting quickclay yielded easily to pressure and tended to suck up objects.

**quick-seal splint** A medical device that rapidly set to protect a broken limb. Quick-seal splints could be found in almost all medkits. Shortly before the Boonta Eve Classic, Anakin Skywalker applied a quick-seal splint to the leg of an injured Tusken Raider the boy discovered on the edge of the Dune Sea.

**Quick Ship** A model of transport shuttle manufactured by Heckson Industries. It was often used by Rebel forces.

**Quickshot wrist-caster** This Drolan Plasteel weapon was an armband that featured a miniature crossbow, which was aimed over the back of the hand.

***Quicksilver* (1)** The sleek, chromed personal ship of Iaco Stark. Adi Gallia commandeered the *Quicksilver* in order to transport Finis Valorum and Nute Gunray from Troiken to Coruscant during the Stark Hyperspace Conflict. The ship was booby-trapped, but the group was able to reach Coruscant and eject in escape pods before it exploded.

***Quicksilver* (2)** A speedy little Corellian courier vessel in the employ of the Hutt criminal empire. A young Han Solo traveled aboard the *Quicksilver* when he served as an official envoy of the Hutts to Moff Sarn Shild.

**Quicksnap 36T** A model of blaster carbine manufactured by SoroSuub.

**quick-throw** A type of malleable, rapidly drying building material.

**Quien, Corman** A tauntaun handler for the Rebel Alliance who served at Echo Base on Hoth, he helped to capture, tame, and train the beasts. He was killed during the evacuation of Echo Base, trampled by tauntauns.

**QuietSnipe** A pellet accelerator that fired mag-pellets at a target.

Queyta

**Quig** The faceless, hulking bodyguard and enforcer to Cabrool Nuum. He worked with his identical partner, Spunto.

**Quiglee, Zak "Squidfella"** One of the best bongo racers of his generation, this Gungan was a vocal opponent of reckless racers like Neb Neb Goodrow and Spleed Nukkels. He tried to no avail to have them banished from the sport. During one fierce competition, Neb Neb rammed his bongo into Squidfella's, breaching his bubble canopy and knocking him out of the race. Afterward, Squidfella stole a military bongo from Otoh Gunga, which he hoped to use to attack his rivals. Unsuccessful, Quiglee was later arrested, tried, and sent to prison.

**Quilan Hive** The largest collection of Qieg native to Lan Barell. The 5,000-year-old hive formed the center of Shulell City. The insectoid species lived in vast networks of underground passages and carved-out cacti. The modern Quilan Hive was further fortified with ceramic plates and iron sheeting.

**Quill, Caiza** The scheming X'Ting regent and leader of his people for many years up to the Clone Wars, he was deposed by G'Mai Duris in a surprising change of fortune. Descended from a family of the X'Ting assassin clan, Quill failed to earn the respect of his peers. The labor contracts he negotiated virtually enslaved the X'Ting to offworld corporate interests. Quill had sold out his own people in order to win contracts that earned him a position on the Five Families, assuming the directorship of mining. He remained a member of the Five Families until he could no longer abide by Duris's continued regency. He challenged her to a duel, but was unprepared for her tactics. Rather than trying to fight, Duris merely stood in front of Quill until fear began to crack his resolve. Ultimately, Quill conceded the duel to Duris, but he continued to work to undermine her authority. Later, Quill was killed, along with most members of the Five Families, when their secret bunker was bombarded from orbit during the Clone Wars.

**Quill, Magris** An Anomid criminal deal maker who owned and operated a number of import shops through which stolen and illegal goods were channeled. Quill employed a network of contacts that allowed him to find, intercept, steal, and sell valuables on the black market.

**Quill, Raina** The commander in the resistance opposing the Imperial occupation of Acherin in the early days of the Empire. She was a former military officer and medic who served during the Clone Wars, when her government had sided with the Separatists. Quill joined her commanding officer, General Toma, in establishing a resistance to the Imperial takeover of her world. Their efforts brought them into contact with Obi-Wan Kenobi and Ferus Olin, who were trying to escape from Inquisitor Malorum. Toma and Quill agreed to help get the fugitive Jedi off Acherin. They then agreed to oversee the operations of the remote asteroid Olin had set up as a haven for any escaped Jedi Knights.

**Quillan, Moff** An official in the Imperial Remnant who questioned Admiral Pellaeon's leadership when the latter attempted to sue for peace with the New Republic.

**quillarats** Small creatures native to the jungles of Kashyyyk. The reclusive brownish green quillarats stood only half a meter tall. They had a protective coat of razor-sharp quills that they could throw in self-defense. It was considered an act of great skill among the Wookiees to kill a quillarat bare-handed.

Hideaz Quill-Face

**Quille, Moff** A member of the Moff Council of the Imperial Remnant after the Yuuzhan Vong War. He opposed Admiral Pellaeon in the deliberations of the council. Quille secretly had been in communication with Jacen Solo, leader of the Galactic Alliance Guard. When Solo offered to cede control of Borleias and Bilbringi in exchange for the support of the Imperials in an attack on Fondor, Quille backed the deal, although Pellaeon initially refused. When Jacen Solo was relieved of command during the attack, Quille urged the other Moffs to take advantage of the situation and capture Fondor while the Galactic Alliance was in disarray. After Pellaeon was assassinated, Quille and the other Moffs tried to take control of his flagship, *Bloodfin*, but its crew mutinied upon learning of the admiral's death. Led by Vitor Reige, the crew forced the Moffs to lock themselves in the ship's command center, where they were wiped out by Boba Fett and his Mandalorian supercommandos.

**Quiller, Joak** A rogue stormtrooper formerly stationed aboard the Star Destroyer *Reprisal*, he was part of the so-called Hand of Judgment unit of troopers targeted by the Imperial Security Bureau for treachery; they later became disillusioned with the Empire's more draconian measures. The group found itself working against the BloodScar pirates of the Shelsha sector, and was commandeered by the Emperor's Hand Mara Jade, who was mounting her own investigation into Governor Barshnis Choard's suspicious use of the pirates to work against the Empire.

**Quill-Face, Hideaz** A 3-meter-tall smuggler, he was of an unidentified species. Hideaz Quill-Face worked with a partner, Spog, and the pair was often seen in the Byss Bistro.

**Quin, Sixtus** A former Special Intelligence operative, he conducted several missions for the Empire. When betrayed by his Imperial commander, he defected to the Rebel Alliance, where his talents were more than welcome. When Sixtus Quin learned that Rogue Squadron was in need of someone with his qualifications, he immediately applied for the assignment. It had become necessary to topple Ysanne Isard's puppet government on Thyferra after her thirst for power and money put her in control of the Bacta Cartel. He was sent to the planet to organize an uprising among the Ashern Rebels and the surviving members of the Zaltin Corporation. For several weeks, he trained the volunteers in all manner of fighting skills and terrorist activities. Their combined efforts paid off when it was time to begin the ground assault. While the battle raged in orbit over Thyferra, his operatives quickly took command of Isard's headquarters. That this was accomplished with very little loss of life was indicative of his skills as an instructor and a fighter.

**quinberry** A fruit-bearing shrub native to the planet Romin, its small berries were pressed to produce an overly sweet juice that was popular among the Romins.

***Quincey's Girl*** An immense slave ship that was the pride and joy of Quintik "Big Quince" Kahr, a Sludir slaver.

**Quincu, Nontal** A scientist and associate of Jenna Zan Arbor.

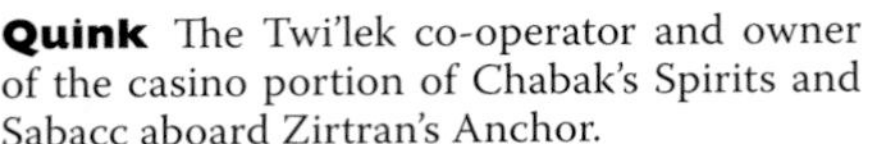

**Quink** The Twi'lek co-operator and owner of the casino portion of Chabak's Spirits and Sabacc aboard Zirtran's Anchor.

**Quint** A species of quick and agile beings native to the planet Quint. Their bodies were covered with delicate fur, and their small heads were dominated by triangular eyes.

**Quintama and Pinani** A Melida husband and wife, they perished during the lengthy Melida/Daan war. Quintama was captain of the Melida Liberation Force. His wife, Pinani, was the daughter of the great heroes Bicha and Tiraca.

**Quintar Nebula** A beautiful but dangerous astrogational hazard. Within its glowing gas clouds was a hidden pirate base on the planet Taraloon.

**Quintas, Lord Xerxes** One of the spice lords of Sevarcos. He ruled the Southern Deserts of the barren planet, and his nomadic clans formed huge villages as the desert sands moved them about their territory.

**Quintell, Pallas** A former pirate and Rebel agitator on Kallistas. The Imperial prefect of that world, Dengless Rinn, placed a bounty on Quintell that attracted novice bounty hunters.

Sixtus Quin (right)

**quinto grain** The basic crop on Kegan, used to make veg patties.

**Quirt, Colonel** The Imperial officer in charge of a prison ship visiting the Formos system. The ship held Hronk, a Wookiee with whom Chewbacca had been feuding. Chewbacca rescued Hronk from the ship, and when Quirt came to inspect the *Millennium Falcon*, its crew was forced to jettison a cargo of spice belonging to Jabba the Hutt.

**Quis, Senator Cola** Ryloth's representative in the New Republic Senate, he was a candidate for Chief of State during the Yuuzhan Vong War. At the urging of Triebakk, Cola dropped out of the race and supported Cal Omas. In exchange, he was promised chairmanship of the Commerce Council, midlevel ministry jobs for several of his friends, and a branch office of the Kellmer Institute for Ryloth.

**Quist** A onetime friend of Republic tactical genius Adar Tallon, he left military service to follow a more lucrative career as a pirate. His ties to Tallon remained strong, however, and he agreed to stage Tallon's "death" in the Dalchon system during the early days of the Empire. Many years later, Quist was captured by the Imperial Star Destroyer *Relentless*. In return for his freedom, Quist sold what information he had—the truth about Tallon's death. Quist's treachery extended further, for when he was sent free, he fled to Tatooine in an attempt to cash in on Tallon's bounty.

**Quist, Admiral** An Imperial fleet officer whom Darth Vader strangled for allowing several Rebels to escape the blockade around Yavin 4.

**Quist, Van P.** The owner of The Droid Store on R-Duba during the early days of the Empire, he sold C-3PO and R2-D2 to Baron Starlock and Kirk Windjammer, respectively.

**quivry** A species native to Antar 4 hunted by the Gotal to sharpen their senses.

Quivry

Quizzer

**Quiyyen, Ambassador** An Anx ambassador, used as bait by General Grievous to capture Jedi during the Clone Wars.

**quizzer** An inquisitive arboreal creature native to the forests of Gamorr. The mischievous imps often caused trouble, as their affinity for shiny objects got them into odd predicaments. Quizzers were bipedal climbers with prehensile tails, opposable thumbs, thick claws, and four bony plates along their arms. The native Gamorreans hated quizzers, but every concerted campaign to eradicate the little creatures met with failure.

Quor'sav

**qukuuf** The Kiffar term describing the jet-black tattoos they often wore.

**Qulok's Fist** A small gang of bounty hunters based in the Outer Rim Territories. They also practiced smuggling and slaving, and acted as hired guns. Their emblem was a stylized gloved fist with spikes atop each knuckle. Emblazoned on the fist was the letter *qek.*

**Qulun clan** Members of this unusual Ansionian trader clan—not considered part of the Alwari nomads—operated among the city-folk of Ansion. They did not domesticate herd animals like the overclans. They traded items from the city for food and fine handcrafts. Not very well liked by other clans, Qulun were also known as information brokers. Their caravans transported well-stocked self-erecting dwellings, with eye-catching trading rooms.

**Qu'mock** A barren star system in the Kathol Outback that was the site of a research space station used by the radical Qek-toth Confederation.

**Quockra IV** A strange desert planet in the distant Minos Cluster that appeared to be populated entirely by 10 million droids. Although most travelers didn't realize it, the true inhabitants of Quockra IV were not the droids, but rather the slug-like Quockrans.

**Quockran** The slug-like intelligent natives of Quockra IV. Extremely xenophobic, they were unknown to most inhabitants of Minos Cluster. Quockrans were enormous black-skinned creatures who emerged at night to loll on the cool desert sands. They were very tough, as their lack of differentiated internal organs limited the amount of damage a single wound could do.

**quold runium** A mineral ingredient used in making Podracer fuel additives.

**Quoreal** The former Supreme Overlord to the Yuuzhan Vong, his position was usurped by Shimrra, who led the campaign to invade the galaxy. Priests serving under Quoreal uncovered prophecies warning of the dangers of the living planet Zonama Sekot, which had the potential to be the species' undoing. According to stories, Quoreal's stance against invading the galaxy angered Shimrra so much that he murdered Quoreal. As a heretic sect of Shamed Ones gained momentum among the Yuuzhan Vong, there were those who began to question the validity of Shimrra's crusade. There also were those who questioned the honor behind Quoreal's murder—the Quorealists—once evidence of Zonama Sekot came to light.

**Quork** Primitive furred bipeds found on the Forest Moon of Endor. Simpler than the Ewoks, the Quorks were hunter-gatherers who lived in a secluded valley amid some rocky canyons. Quorks had smelly, matted brown fur, white manes, and two small horns atop their heads. They built only simple tools, such as spears and knotted ropes.

Quockran

**Quor'sav** A species of tall, stilt-legged flightless avians, they hailed from Uaua, the principal world of the Ua system. The species was afflicted

Ki-Adi-Mundi handles some quold runium.

by a virus spread by offworld colonists, which led to them being wary of outsiders, particularly any mammalian species.

**quulaar** Woven sacks that Wookiees used to carry their young through the trees of Kashyyyk. Cubs either were too weak or had too short a reach to keep up with adult Wookiees, so they were placed in quulaars for ease and safety. Wookiees also were known to carry trusted offworlders in quulaars.

Qwohog

**Quyste** This training center for Talon Karrde's smugglers was active at least seven years after the Battle of Endor.

**Quy'Tek** A meditative technique developed by the Jedi Knights, used primarily to mask an individual's connection to the Force. This allowed a Jedi to pass unnoticed, even to other Force-sensitive beings.

**Q-Varx, Senator** A New Republic Council member, he led the Rationalist Party on his homeworld of Mon Calamari. Enchanted by gadgetry, he purchased an executive honor guard of human-looking synthdroids. Senator Q-Varx accepted a bribe to arrange a secret meeting between Chief of State Leia Organa Solo and Nam Chorios strongman Seti Ashgad.

**Qwohog (Wavedancers)** Lithe and small aquatic humanoids native to Hirsi. Qwohog were called Wavedancers because their quick movements on the water's surface made them look as if they were performing a fast-paced ballet.

**R-1 recon droid** A remote reconnaissance droid dispatched to gather battlefield intelligence. These small orb-shaped droids from Arakyd Industries were used by Republic clone troopers, Imperial stormtroopers, and other fighting forces. The droid featured a self-destruct mechanism that could be remotely detonated, causing damage behind enemy lines if timed correctly.

R-10

**R-10 household droid** A smoothly unobtrusive party waiter and drink server for the obnoxiously rich. The R-10 household droid moved about on four wheels and had a ventral droid-brain package that perceived the area in front of it through a single photoreceptor.

**R1-G4** An old-model astromech, it was abandoned after its owner was captured by legal authorities on Tatooine. It was one of the droids rounded up from a Jawa sandcrawler when a squad of stormtroopers was searching for R2-D2 and C-3PO.

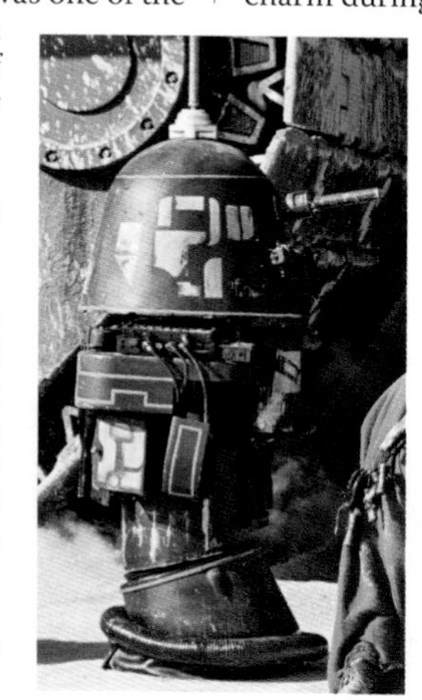

R1-G4

**R1 to R9 droids** *See* R series astromech droids.

**R2-0 (ArOh)** A working concept model prototype of the R2 series astromech droid, it was kept, largely forgotten, in an Industrial Automaton storage facility. When IA was purchased by Bornaryn Trading, Lady Arn Dro Thul recovered the droid and delivered it to Luke Skywalker as a gift. Luke had slicer Zakarisz Ghent use the componentry of the prototype to bypass information locks within R2-D2, revealing holographic data that gave Luke insight into the life of his mother and father in the final moments of the Galactic Republic.

*< Asajj Ventress attacks Obi-Wan Kenobi while riding atop a rancor.*

**R-22 spearhead** These state-of-the-art starfighters were used by Mon Julpa to escort the Tammuz-an shipping fleet during the early Galactic Empire. The design of the R-22 Spearheads was copied by the Rebel Alliance when they developed the A-wing starfighter. The Spearheads were instrumental in the defeat of the Tarnoonga pirates.

**R2-A5 (Artoo-Ayfive)** A white-and-green astromech droid programmed by the Galactic Empire for target acquisition and combat communications, it was seen wandering the streets of Mos Eisley around the time of the Battle of Yavin.

**R2-A6** Pilot Ric Olié's green-and-white R2 unit. He considered it a sort of good-luck charm during flight operations.

**R2-B1** A blue-and-yellow R2 unit stationed aboard Queen Amidala's Naboo Royal Starship.

**R2-B3 (Cappie)** Jaina Solo's astromech droid when she took command of the Twin Suns Squadron during the Yuuzhan Vong War.

**R2-C4** A yellow-trimmed astromech in the royal starship hangar at Theed Palace on Naboo during the time of the Trade Federation invasion.

**R2-D0 (Deo)** The astromech droid belonging to Rebel spy Tay "Tiree" Vanis. This resourceful little droid helped several rookie Rebels navigate the treacherous corridors of an abandoned mine within Mesa 291 on Bothawui and contained coordinates to rendezvous with General Lens Reekeene's command ship, *Home.*

R2-A6

**R2-D2 (Artoo-Detoo)** A resourceful, spunky, and adventurous astromech droid that saved the day time and again. His little meter-tall frame was packed with all sorts of tool-tipped appendages that made him a great starship mechanic and computer interface specialist. It was his bravery, however, that made him an invaluable asset to his owners and friends.

R2-D2 hailed from the peaceful world of Naboo, where he and a team of astromechs served Queen Amidala aboard her Royal Starship. When the Trade Federation invaded Naboo, Amidala ran afoul of its blockade. The Royal Starship sustained damage to its shields, and it was R2-D2 who repaired the ship, allowing it to escape into hyperspace. The droid used his magnetized rollers to cling to the chromed surface of the ship while deadly turbolaser blasts rained overhead. For his courage, R2 was personally thanked and recognized by Queen Amidala.

To complete further repairs, the Royal Starship set down on Tatooine. R2-D2

R2-B1

accompanied Jedi Master Qui-Gon Jinn and Padmé Amidala to the port city of Mos Espa to gather spare parts. R2 carried the technical details for the necessary components. While waiting out a sandstorm in a local hovel, he met the homemade protocol droid C-3PO, and struck up a friendship that would eventually last decades.

Artoo later returned to Naboo with the Queen. He served as onboard astromech to Anakin Skywalker, a young rookie pilot who, despite not being authorized to do so, flew an N-1 starfighter into the Battle of Naboo and destroyed the Droid Control Ship orchestrating the occupation of the planet.

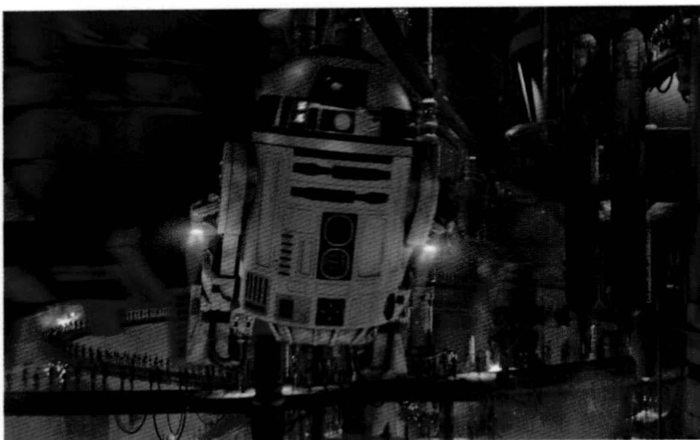

*R2-D2 ignites his anti-grav boosters.*

Artoo was reunited with Anakin a decade later. Meanwhile, the little droid continued to loyally serve Amidala, who was no longer Queen but now Senator of Naboo. The droid acted as a little bodyguard, using his scanners to seek out any danger that might befall Padmé. When Amidala traveled incognito while the Jedi investigated attempts on her life, R2 stayed by her side as she and Anakin voyaged to Tatooine, where he was reunited with C-3PO, who again became Anakin's property. They all went to Geonosis, and as Padmé and Anakin wandered into a dangerous Geonosian droid factory, R2 and C-3PO followed. R2 again came to the rescue, using his anti-grav boosters to fly to Amidala's aid, and his computer interface to stop a deadly downpour of molten metal from killing the Senator. He even helped reassemble C-3PO after a decapitating tangle with droid factory machinery.

At the start of the Clone Wars, R2 and 3PO essentially swapped owners, as a silent token of commitment between the newly—and secretly—wedded Anakin and Padmé. Padmé used C-3PO as a diplomatic aide for her Senatorial duties, while R2-D2 often flew with Anakin Skywalker aboard his Delta-7B Jedi starfighter. When Anakin took on Ahsoka Tano as his Padawan, she immediately showed great affection for the little droid, nicknaming him Artooie. Its was Artoo's mechanical skills that kept the battered spice freighter *Twilight* operational when it became Anakin and Ahsoka's vessel of choice on several crucial missions.

R2-D2 was kidnapped by droid smuggler Gha Nachkt, who took the droid to General Grievous. Grievous's henchdroids cruelly dissected R2, scanning his memory systems for vital Republic intelligence. Anakin Skywalker came to his rescue, and the little droid fought manipulator-to-manipulator with R3-S6, R2's treacherous replacement who was in fact a Separatist double agent.

Throughout the Clone Wars, R2 constantly faced great danger at Anakin's side. During the rescue of Chancellor Palpatine from General Grievous's clutches, R2-D2 destroyed super battle droids in a melee that erupted in the hangar bay of Grievous's flagship. The little droid helped Anakin bring the shattered vessel in for a rough landing on Coruscant's surface. It was around this time that Anakin succumbed to the dark side, coerced by Chancellor Palpatine to become the Sith Lord Darth Vader. Though much of what transpired could not be processed by R2, he knew he was witnessing momentous events and secretly recorded key moments of Anakin's downfall in protected areas of his memory. R2-D2 and C-3PO even witnessed the birth of Padmé and Anakin's twin children, Leia and Luke Skywalker. After the fall of the Republic, and the rise of the Galactic Empire, Obi-Wan Kenobi and Bail Organa hid the children and took care to erase C-3PO's memory, though R2's memories were kept intact.

The droids became the property of the House of Alderaan, serving Captain Antilles aboard the *Tantive IV.* An escape pod mishap led to 3PO and R2 departing Alderaanian service for a time. They found some responsible masters in the form of the speeder racers Jord Dusat and Thall Joben. Joben's prize speeder, the *White Witch,* was equipped with an astromech socket, and R2 rode with him as he won the famous Boonta speeder races.

During a short stint with the Intergalactic Droid Agency, R2 and 3PO floated from odd job to odd job. The multiskilled astromech droid even had the indignity of waiting tables at Doodnik's Café on Tyne's Horky before helping out keshel miners Jann Tosh and his uncle Gundy. During Tosh's ownership, R2 and 3PO became embroiled in the intrigue surrounding the ascendancy of Tammuz-an's royal ruler.

The droids then came to be property of Mungo Baobab, a trader from the Manda system. When saving the world of Biitu from the cruel grip of the reigning droid known as the Great Heep, R2 fell in love with a little pink astromech droid named KT-10. A droid of adventure, R2 was hardly one to settle down, and soon he and C-3PO were working for new masters on Kalarba.

The droids eventually returned to the House of Alderaan, where R2 became part of the labor pool of a royal vessel—full circle, it would seem. The influential family of nobles had secret ties to the Rebel Alliance. While intercepting transmissions from Rebel spies, the Organa consular ship was suddenly attacked by an Imperial Star Destroyer lying in wait. The transmission carried information vital to the Rebellion—the complete technical readouts of the Empire's latest weapon of mass destruction, the Death Star battle station. Unable to deliver the plans to Viceroy Bail Organa, Leia Organa instead hid them in R2's memory systems. She also tasked the droid with contacting Obi-Wan Kenobi.

R2 commandeered an escape pod and rocketed away from the captured *Tantive IV,* all the while dragging along his bewildered counterpart, C-3PO. The pod crash-landed on Tatooine. There the droids were taken captive by Jawa traders and sold to moisture farmer Owen Lars and his nephew Luke Skywalker. Determined to complete his mission, R2 ran away in the middle of the night. C-3PO and Luke eventually found him, as well as Obi-Wan Kenobi. This started an incredible chain of events that culminated in the Battle of Yavin. R2 and 3PO were crucial in assisting Luke to spearhead a rescue mission to free Princess Leia from the heart of the gargantuan Death Star. Both droids navigated the complex Imperial computer system to provide the rescuers with timely assistance and status updates.

Once R2 returned to the Rebel base with the newly liberated Princess Leia, Alliance technicians downloaded the Death Star schematics. From these, they were able to pinpoint a flaw in the station's design that could be exploited for explosive results. The Alliance launched all available starfighters in an attack on the station. Luke Skywalker piloted an X-wing fighter and R2-D2 served as his onboard astromech, much as he'd done for Luke's father a generation earlier. Although the droid sustained some damage in the at-

*R2-D2 brings Anakin Skywalker's Jedi starfighter to a bumpy landing.*

tack, Luke successfully destroyed the station. R2 was refurbished in time for the celebration of the Rebel victory.

C-3PO and R2-D2 continued to be mainstays with the core group of Rebel heroes. Despite their constant disputes—like the time R2 took 3PO's complaining over Hoth's subzero temperature as an invitation to turn up the heat in Princess Leia's quarters, thus flooding her compartment with melted ice—the two remained friends.

During the evacuation from Hoth, 3PO and R2 were separated. R2 flew with Luke to the mysterious planet of Dagobah, where Luke would receive training from the enigmatic Jedi Master Yoda. R2 was witness to Luke's growing skill and power as the young Tatooine farm boy continued on his path to Jedi Knighthood.

When Luke's friends fell into an Imperial trap on Bespin's Cloud City, the astromech accompanied the young Jedi to the floating metropolis. There he became separated from Luke, but he did find C-3PO, Princess Leia, and Chewbacca. The Rebel heroes were worse for wear, especially 3PO, who had been blasted apart by an Imperial stormtrooper. While escaping Bespin, R2 helped reassemble his friend.

During a daring mission to rescue a captive Han Solo from the loathsome gangster Jabba the Hutt, C-3PO and R2-D2 were sent into the Hutt's palace on Tatooine. There they became the slimy crime lord's property. R2 served as a waiter, distributing drinks aboard Jabba's sail barge. Little did any of the criminal dregs suspect that the droid carried in him Luke Skywalker's lightsaber, which he launched to the unarmed Jedi. Supplied with his weapon, Luke subdued Jabba's minions and freed his captive friends.

Shortly thereafter, R2 accompanied a Rebel strike force that was sent to knock out the Imperial shield generator on Endor. The generator protected the half-completed second Death Star in orbit. R2 attempted to bypass the high-security lock sealing the Imperial generator complex, but was shot by a stormtrooper before he could complete the task. Fortunately, the Rebels were able to make their way into the complex and destroy the generator. R2-D2 was repaired in time to witness the destruction of the second Death Star.

When the clone of Emperor Palpatine surfaced and brought Luke under his dark side tutelage, several of R2's files were wiped out. The droid soon realized that Skywalker was transmitting the Master Control Signal that drove the Emperor's campaign, which would later aid New Republic forces. R2 used the signals to help shut down the massive World Devastators as they ravaged Mon Calamari, proving that Luke's allegiance had remained with the Republic all along.

R2 stayed mainly with Skywalker, helping in his exploits and in setting up a Jedi academy, although he was "droidnapped" by Lando Calrissian on his mission to unravel the mystery of the Teljkon vagabond ghost ship.

R2-D2 on Tatooine

R2 was annoyed to discover that a new X-wing design class replaced astromech droids with integrated computer circuitry. Along with C-3PO and Cole Fardreamer, he eventually helped uncover a sabotage scheme by the Dark Jedi Kueller: The new X-wings were secretly equipped with an explosive device as part of the upgrade. As part of Fardreamer's investigation, R2 went to Telti and confronted a terrifying gladiator droid group known as the Red Terror. When Kueller was about to detonate the explosive devices he had planted in droids on worlds throughout the New Republic, R2-D2 deactivated the remote detonators that would have triggered the explosions, saving the New Republic from devastation.

Decades later, during the Yuuzhan Vong invasion of the galaxy, R2 and 3PO both had reason to wonder about the true meaning of life and existence, as the alien invaders hated all forms of technology, especially droids. The Yuuzhan Vong deemed automata blasphemous simulacrums of life. When the Yuuzhan Vong finally surrendered at Coruscant, the droids found that there was another threat they needed to confront: obsolescence. The two droids agreed that they would meet this and any other challenge just as they always had, with each other.

Luke and Leia were not about to give up the services of their most trusted droids, and R2-D2 continued to serve Luke during his travels for the new Jedi Order. However, about five years after the Yuuzhan Vong were defeated, he began to show some serious glitches. The droid forgot where he was and was prone to miscalculations in his hyperspace routes, all of which worried Luke. A diagnostic showed that several of R2's deep memory banks had been sequestered as private, and were causing blocks of information to be lost. Luke tried to bypass them—only to stumble upon a holographic recording of his mother, Padmé Amidala. Luke asked slicer Zakarisz Ghent to extract the full recording. Ghent explained that there were only two ways to get it: wipe out R2-D2's personality sectors, or locate the designer of the Intellex IV droid brain and learn the backdoor methods for reaching hidden or damaged sectors. Luke refused to wipe out R2's memory, and decided to search the old Imperial archives for the Intellex IV design manual.

Eventually, he had to admit defeat in this pursuit, and chose to keep R2-D2 intact rather than risk ruining the droid in his search for information about his family. R2-D2 and C-3PO continued work together through the era of the Swarm War, although the astromech found himself more often than not grounded during space battles. Luke eventually gave R2-D2 a memory upgrade that allowed the droid to serve as his astromech copilot aboard a StealthX fighter.

In the decades following the war against the Confederation, R2-D2 was passed down from generation to generation within the Skywalker family until he was recovered by Jedi Master K'kruhk in the wake of the Massacre at Ossus. The Whiphid later turned the droid over to Cade Skywalker, when Cade set off to rescue Hosk Trey'lis. Rather than put the droid to work in its true capacity, however, Cade chose to rely on his own skills and knowledge. This didn't go over too well with R2-D2, and the droid constantly pestered Cade about the quality of his piloting skills.

R2-D2 helps rebuild a damaged C-3PO.

Like all astromech

droids, R2-D2 was designed to operate in deep space, interfacing with fighter craft and computer systems to augment the capabilities of ships and their pilots, usually from a socket behind the cockpit. He monitored and diagnosed flight performance, mapped and stored hyperspace data, and pinpointed technical errors or faulty computer coding. He was also well versed in starship repair for hundreds of styles of spacecraft, and was able to exist in the vacuum of space indefinitely while making repairs to a ship's exterior. R2 conversed in a dense electronic language consisting primarily of beeps, chirps, and whistles. He could understand most forms of human speech but had to have his own communications interpreted by a starship's computers or an interpreter droid, such as C-3PO.

Artoo's domed head, which could rotate a full 360 degrees, contained infrared receptors, electromagnetic-field sensors, a register readout and logic dispenser, dedicated energy receptors, a radar eye, heat and motion detectors, and a holographic recorder and projector. His cylindrical body hid numerous devices, including a storage/retrieval jack for computer linkup, auditory receivers, a flame-retardant foam dispenser, an electric shock prod, a high-powered spotlight, a grasping claw, a laser welder, a circular saw, and a cybot acoustic signaler. R2 usually traveled on two treaded legs, although his third leg could be lowered for extra stability and he could use his hidden rockets to soar a fair distance. In addition, he had flotation devices and a periscoping visual scanner to guide him while submerged.

R2-D2 developed an odd relationship with C-3PO over the years. The protocol droid behaved like a fussy mother hen, almost constantly cajoling, belittling, or arguing with his squat counterpart. R2 appeared loyal, inventive, and sarcastic. Although he always seemed to egg 3PO on, they had deep mutual respect and trust for each other.

**R2-D7** A conical-headed astromech, this unit tended to the Starspeeder 3000 at Star Tours.

**R2-KT (Artoo-Katie)** A pink-hued astromech droid, she was assigned to the 501st Legion during the Clone Wars and continued in service during the time of the Empire.

R2-Q2

**R2-L1 (Ell-one)** Esara Till's astromech droid within the Naboo Royal Security Forces starfighter corps. A programming glitch caused it to be arrogant.

**R2-M5** A red-and-white astromech droid that served in the Naboo Royal Security Forces.

**R2-Q2** An R2 unit, it spent several decades serving with an Imperial reconnaissance fleet in the Expansion Region aboard the Star Destroyer *Devastator.*

**R2-Q5** A black-and-red astromech droid stationed aboard the second Death Star at the time of the Battle of Endor.

R2-TO

**R2-R7** A green astromech droid that served aboard the Republic cruiser *Radiant VII* when it was destroyed by the Trade Federation.

**R2-R9** A red-bodied R2 unit that belonged to the Naboo Royal Security Forces.

**R2-T0** A gray-and-green astromech droid that was owned by Watto. The Toydarian rented it out to mechanics in Mos Espa.

**R2-V0 (Veo)** A magenta-trimmed astromech droid that served Green Squad of Reekeene's Roughnecks, an operative team of "Irregulars" in the Rebel Alliance. The droid was stationed aboard the converted yacht *Long Shot.*

**R2-X2** A typical starfighter assistant, it contained 10 coordinates for hyperspace jumps. R2-X2 carried built-in tools and a computer interface. The droid was assigned to Red Ten during the Battle of Yavin and was destroyed when Red Ten's X-wing was shot down.

R-3PO

**R2Z-DL (Toozy)** A decorated Rebel Alliance spy despite being a "simple" astromech. Toozy was stationed deep undercover behind enemy lines during the Galactic Civil War, tracking Imperial movements near Vilosoria during the liberation of the planet from the Empire.

R2-X2

**R3-A2 (Arthree-Aytoo)** A white-and-orange astromech droid stationed at Echo Base on Hoth.

**R3-D3** A blue-trimmed white R3 unit with a transparent plastex dome that worked at Star Tours.

**R3-G6 (Ar-Three)** Ahsoka Tano's astromech droid during her mission to Ryloth in the Clone Wars.

**R-3PO (Ar-Threepio)** A protocol droid, he was specially modified by the Rebel Alliance as a defense against Imperial espionage droids. R-3PO's job was to join a droid pool and uncover any spies through careful observation. Ar-Threepio had a distinguishing mark: a tattoo reading THANK THE MAKER on his left posterior plating.

**R3-S6** An astromech droid temporarily assigned to Anakin Skywalker to replace a kidnapped R2-D2 during the Clone Wars. This droid was secretly a spy for General Grievous. Anakin brought R3 on a mission to rescue R2-D2 from Ruusan, and R3 nearly sabotaged the effort. R2-D2 defeated R3-S6 in a manipulator-to-manipulator brawl.

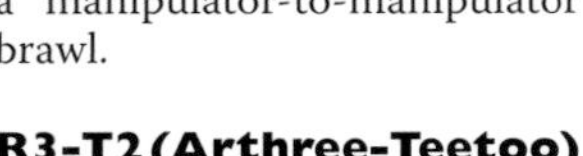

**R3-T2 (Arthree-Teetoo)** A red-and-white astromech droid wandering the streets of Mos Eisley prior to the Battle of Yavin. Unlike most R3 units, this droid did not have a clear plastex dome. It escaped a crew of abusive pirates.

**R3-T6 (Arthree-Teesix)** This droid served aboard the first Death Star. Like most R3 units, it had a larger memory and more advanced circuitry than its R1 and R2 predecessors, allowing for more efficient astrogation. R3-T6 was destroyed when the battle station was blown up by the Rebel Alliance.

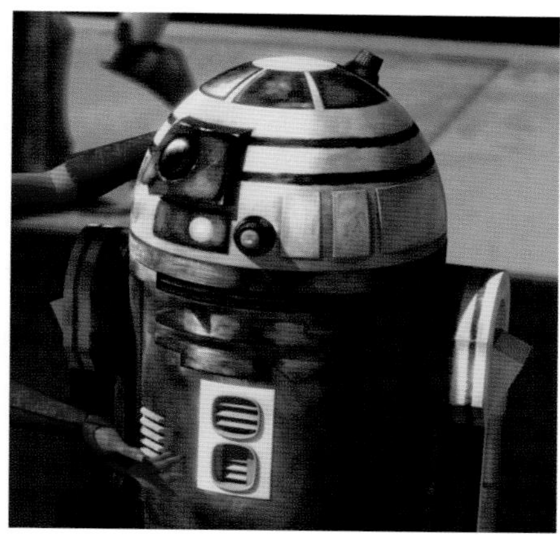
R3-S6

**R3-T7** A green-trimmed yellow clear-domed astromech droid that wandered the streets of CoCo Town on Coruscant just prior to the outbreak of the Clone Wars.

**R3-Y2** A yellow-orange-trimmed R3 unit stationed in the command center of Hoth's Echo Base.

**R-4 recon droid** A descendant of the R-1 recon droid, this model, a floating orb, was used by Rebel and Imperial sharpshooters to gather battlefield intelligence. The recon droid could call down an orbital strike, taking out any enemies nearby.

R3-T6

**R-41 Starchaser** A multirole Hoersch-Kessel Drive starfighter widely used by pirates, it was similar to the Z-95 Headhunter but with slightly better performance.

**R4-A22** An orange-and-white R4 unit that worked at Dex's Diner.

**R4-C9** Saesee Tiin's yellow-headed astromech droid during the Clone Wars.

**R4-D6** A dark blue astromech droid belonging to the Rebel Alliance at its base on Yavin 4.

**R4-E1** One of the numerous vehicle computer-operation droids manufactured by Industrial Automaton, R4-E1 was a companion of BoShek. The droid's personality was rambunctious, fiery, and independent.

**R4-F5** Plo Koon's astromech droid aboard his starfighter when he was shot down over Cato Neimoidia at the end of the Clone Wars.

R4-G9

**R4-G9 (Geenine)** On Obi-Wan Kenobi's mission to Utapau to find General Grievous and bring an end to the Clone Wars, he flew with R4-G9 on his starfighter's wing. The brassy-colored astromech droid not only served as astrogational assistant and onboard technician, but in a pinch could also fly the starfighter on its own.

**R4-H5** A yellow-headed astromech droid used by Kit Fisto during the Clone Wars.

**R4-I9 (Arfour-Eyenine)** A dark-shelled Imperial maintenance droid aboard the Death Star.

**R4-J1 (Jaywun)** An old, battered flattop astromech droid seen on Mos Eisley, R4-J1 had a tendency to jury-rig things rather than repair them properly.

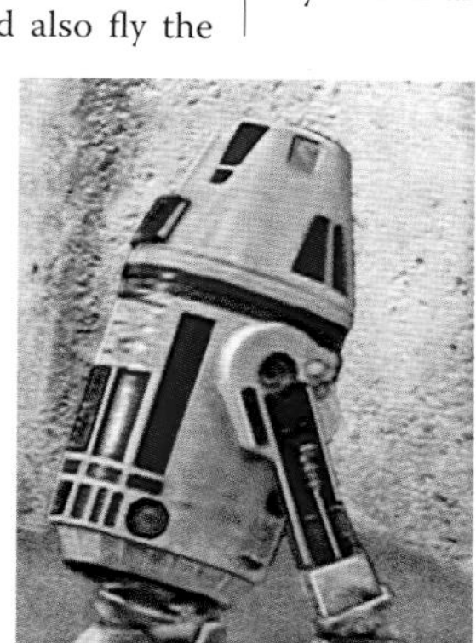
R4-E1

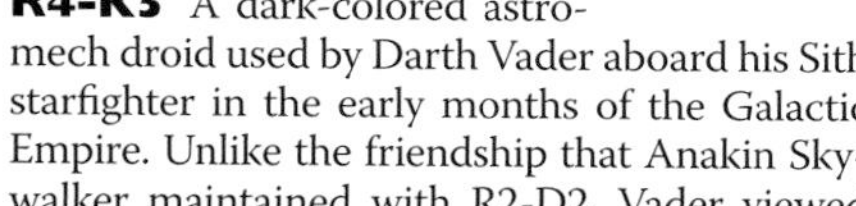

**R4-K5** A dark-colored astromech droid used by Darth Vader aboard his Sith starfighter in the early months of the Galactic Empire. Unlike the friendship that Anakin Skywalker maintained with R2-D2, Vader viewed R4-K5 as little more than a functional tool.

**R4-M17** An agromech droid sold at the Jawa Traders shop in the center of Mos Eisley on Tatooine.

**R4-M6** A silver-domed purple astromech used by Jedi Master Mace Windu aboard his Jedi starfighter.

**R4-M9** A typical multiple-use droid, it mainly controlled and repaired vehicles and computers. R4-M9 was once used by the Empire to pull data from the computer banks of the *Tantive IV.* It was stationed aboard the Star Destroyer *Devastator.*

**R4-P17 (Arfour)** A truncated astromech assigned to Obi-Wan Kenobi, this stubby little droid fit snugly within his Delta-7 Jedi starfighter. During the Clone Wars, R4-P17 was fitted with a standard-sized astromech body so she could fit within Kenobi's Delta-7B fighter and the Eta-3 starfighter that followed. During the Battle of Coruscant, R4-P17 was decapitated by a buzz droid.

**R4-P22** A small astromech used aboard Anakin Skywalker's modified Jedi starfighter, *Azure Angle,* it was destroyed when Asajj Ventress blew up the starfighter on Yavin 4 during the Clone Wars.

**R4-P44** A green-domed astromech used aboard an ARC-170 starfighter of the Fifth Fleet during the Clone Wars.

**R5-A2** A yellow-headed R5 unit seen wandering the streets of Mos Eisley just before the Battle of Yavin.

**R5-D2** A battered astromech droid that served as part of the technical pool for Star Tours.

**R5-D4 (Arfive-Defour)** An inexpensive astromech droid commonly referred to as Red, it allowed R2-D2 to program its motivator to blow up after R2 communicated his orders from Princess Leia Organa to R5. The motivator malfunction allowed R2-D2 and C-3PO to remain together. R5-D4 was later repaired and sold to another moisture farm. R5 was a poor navigator but a skilled mechanic.

R5-D4

**R5-D8** The red-and-white R5 unit of Jek Porkins during the Battle of Yavin, it first flew with him when they were both assigned to the Tierfon Yellow Aces.

**R5-F7** The yellow-and-white R5 unit of Lieutenant Lepira (Gold Four) during the Battle of Yavin.

**R5-G8 (Gate)** The designation used by Wedge Antilles's astromech droid Mynock after it underwent a memory-wipe reformatting.

**R5-J2** A black-and-silver Imperial R5 unit stationed aboard the second Death Star.

**R5-L4 (Elfour)** Kyp Durron's astromech droid during the early stages of the Yuuzhan Vong War, he accompanied Kyp on the Dozen-and-Two Avengers' mission to the Helska system. The droid was destroyed in the ensuing battle.

**R5-M2(Arfive-Emmtoo)** An astromech droid owned by Shawn Valdez, a popular Rebel Alliance officer. R5-M2 was programmed to plot sublight tactical courses and was extremely valuable in planning evacuation routes from Echo Base during the Battle of Hoth.

R5-J2

**R5-P8 (pirate droid)** An assassin pirate droid during the Clone Wars.

**R5-X2** A red-and-white astromech droid owned by Jabba the Hutt. At Podraces, R5-X2 was responsible for constantly calculating betting odds and reporting Jabba's winnings. Before the Boonta Eve Classic, R5-X2 calculated that Sebulba would win the event.

**R6-H5 (Ar-Six)** Kit Fisto's astromech droid during the Clone Wars.

**R7-F5** Plo Koon's brown-trimmed astromech droid during the Clone Wars.

R5-X2

**R7-T1** An R7 series astromech droid, it was assigned to Luke Skywalker's E-wing fighter.

**R82 jump boots** Aratech Industries' recreational footwear, they incorporated a combination repulsor and rocket unit. They were most often used in various games and sports.

**RA-7 servant droid** Arakyd Industries' sole entry in the personal-assistant market. The Empire snapped up the entire production run of the RA-7 and distributed the droids like favors to its highest-ranking officers and planetary governors. These droids were actually serving as spies for the Imperial Security Bureau. Many were found aboard the Death Star, leading to their informal moniker of Death Star droids.

**Ra, Vonnda** An evil newbreed Nightsister from Dathomir, she helped the Second Imperium recruit trainees from the various clans on her homeworld. She died in the jaws of a syren plant on Kashyyyk.

**Raabakyysh** A Wookiee, she was an admirer of Lowbacca and best friend of his younger sister, Sirrakuk. She decided to impress Lowbacca by attempting to perform her Wookiee Rite of Passage alone, without telling anyone. She never returned. The only trace of her was her bloodstained backpack.

Rabé

**Raalk, Proctor Ton** A civic leader, he headed the government of Giat Nor, capital city of N'zoth, the Yevetha spawnworld.

**Raatu, Gwad** A Rodian detective working for the Coruscant Security Force during the war between Corellia and the Galactic Alliance. He was more the loose cannon compared with his by-the-manual partner, Chal Tozr. The pair investigated the murder of Jedi Master Tresina Lobi and, alongside Luke Skywalker, tracked the movements of Lumiya through her various bolt-holes on Coruscant.

**Rab, Mot Not** A tall, stubborn Tarnab who represented his people in the Galactic Senate, he opposed the vote of no confidence in Chancellor Valorum.

Mot Not Rab

**Rabad** A Galactic Alliance communications officer serving aboard the *Admiral Ackbar* during the Swarm War.

**Rabb, Admiral** A Sullustan officer in the New Republic Navy who trained under Sien Sovv, he was active during the Yuuzhan Vong War.

***Rabbit's Foot*** Jaxxon's starship, it was a modified WUD-5000 N-class freighter.

**Rabé** One of Queen Amidala's royal handmaidens, she was known for her great patience. She was often assigned to soothe Amidala's nerves and prepare the Queen's hairstyles. She accompanied the Queen to Coruscant and was with her when Amidala addressed the Galactic Senate during the Trade Federation siege of Naboo.

**Rabin** An Ewok tamer of beasts who lived with Chief Chirpa's tribe in Bright Tree Village, he was variously described as a thief, a loner, a hunter, and a survivor.

**Rabutz** A green-skinned humanoid shoemaker in the city of G'ai Solem. Boba Fett tracked him down during his search for Yolan Bren.

**Rachott** An Ugnaught medical technician for the Grand Army of the Republic, she was stationed on the planet Drongar, at the Rimsoo Twelve medical hospital, during the Clone Wars.

**Rach'talik** A Twi'lek who worked for Shala the Hutt on Courkrus as a demolitions expert.

**Rachuk roseola** A skin virus, it left reddish raw patches on everyone who visited the planet Vladet.

RA-7 servant droid

**Rachuk sector** Lying close to the Galactic Core, it bordered the Morobe sector and contained the Chorax, Hensara, and Rachuk systems. The Rachuk sector was controlled from an Imperial base on Vladet in the Rachuk system.

**Rachuk system** Located in the Rachuk sector, this system contained the planet Vladet, site of an Imperial sector headquarters. A great deal of trade and shipping traffic passed through the centrally located Rachuk system. Some three years after the Battle of Endor, the Alliance destroyed the Vladet base and forced the Empire to divert more of its forces to the Rachuk system, diluting its strength elsewhere.

**Racine, Delva** A Core Worlds socialite and fashion designer who specialized in outrageous ensembles that incorporated Outer Rim alien inspirations. Her summer Kubaz collection, introduced during the Clone Wars, was uniformly panned by the media.

Delva Racine

**Rackus, Mazer** A Twi'lek pilot for the Rebel Alliance, he served after crashing on an Alliance-held world as a youth.

**Racto, Lannik** A small-time criminal on Coruscant during the early New Republic who sold illegal assassin droids. His operations were infiltrated by Jaden Korr a decade after the Battle of Endor, and Racto was brought in for questioning. His factory on Nar Shaddaa was destroyed by New Republic forces shortly afterward.

**radank** A clawed Yuuzhan Vong creature. Tsavong Lah had difficulty maintaining a successful graft of a radank body part due to suspected sabotage from the shaper ranks.

**Raddadugh Gnasp** A vicious insect native to the Wookiee moon of Alaris Prime, its name was used for a Wookiee ornithopter, a 7-meter-long winged combat craft flown in the Clone Wars.

**Raders, Ram** A Galactic Republic naval corporal aboard the *Ranger* during the Clone Wars, he served alongside Jedi Master Nejaa Halcyon repelling Separatist battle droid boarders. Upon arrival at Praesitlyn, Raders and Private Vick served as scouts and point men in a mission to rescue hostages from the Intergalactic Communications Center.

***Radiance*** A passenger liner that made regular trips between Corellia and Coruscant. A young Han Solo and Bria Tharen used it to flee Corellia.

***Radiant VII*** A Corellian Republic cruiser that served the Republic for 34 years, ferrying Jedi and other ambassadors throughout the galaxy on a wide range of missions. Piloted by Captain Madakor and Lieutenant Williams, it transported Obi-Wan Kenobi and Qui-Gon Jinn to the Trade Federation's flagship when the Jedi were sent to resolve the blockade around Naboo. When Trade Federation officials attempted to kill the ambassadors, they also turned their laser cannons on the Republic cruiser. The *Radiant VII* was destroyed.

***Radiant IX*** A Republic cruiser crippled in the Hoth system. Obi-Wan Kenobi and his Padawan Anakin Skywalker investigated its distress signal a few years after the Battle of Naboo, and discovered the Dark Jedi Alysun Celz aboard.

**Radiant One system** A sizable star system located far from the Galactic Core.

**radiation burst missile** A form of ordnance used by the Galactic Republic that detonated before striking the ground, showering a large area with heavy doses of radioactive particles.

**radni root** A chewable plant sometimes enjoyed by Givin, it was not recommended for children.

**Radnor** A planet overcome by a toxic disaster, it was a small world known for its development of high-tech weapons systems. It had two main city-states, also known as Twin Cities, called Tacto and Aubendo. A toxic cloud was accidentally released by one of the weapons laboratories at Aubendo and quickly spread, killing many and causing many more to become ill. The Jedi sent a contigent that included Anakin Skywalker, Obi-Wan Kenobi, Ferus Olin, Siri Tachi, Tru Veld, Ry-Gaul, Darra Thel-Tanis, and Soara Antana.

**Radnoran** A humanoid alien species native to Radnor. The average Radnoran had a short, stocky body. Most Radnorans hated open spaces, preferring to live in cities instead.

**Radon-Ulzer** A manufacturer of sublight and Podracer engines.

**radtrooper (Radiation Zone Assault Trooper)** These little-known members of the Empire's stormtrooper division wore modified plastoid armor with a lead-polymer substrate to protect against lethal radiation. Since blaster weaponry was less reliable in radiation fields, radtroopers were typically equipped with vibroblades, force pikes, and grenades.

**Rae, Alyn** A Gotal entrepreneur, he was credited with developing the desensitizing cone socks favored by Gotals in high-EM environments.

**Raech, Commander** An officer aboard the *Mon Mothma* during the Yuuzhan Vong War.

**Raed-7** An Outer Rim world near Bellassa known for its shipyards.

**Raef, Koedi** A Rebel Alliance starfighter pilot who helped liberate Vilosoria from the Empire during the Galactic Civil War using data provided by the undercover astromech R2Z-DL. She was given a medal for her bravery but passed along the commendation to the droid.

**Raegar, Dr.** An Imperial scientist whose ambitious studies revealed the possible existence of the Sunstar, a mystical gem possessed by the Ewoks. Raegar used his status to divert a Star Destroyer to the Forest Moon of Endor in a bid to capture the Sunstar and place himself as the master of the universe. A group of Ewoks from Chief

Radiant VII

Chirpa's tribe, allied with a renegade droid, infiltrated Raegar's Destroyer and battled with stormtroopers to reclaim the Sunstar. In the end, Raegar's actions became known to the Emperor, who paid the scientist back for his treachery.

**Raelo, Loo** A noted Quermian Jedi, he served alongside Yarael Poof in the final decades of the Galactic Republic.

**Rafa system** Bordering the Oseon system, the 11 planets and numerous moons of the Rafa system were covered with the enormous plastic ruins of the ancient Sharu species. The impenetrable buildings were among the largest constructions in the galaxy. Many human colonies, dating from the early days of the Old Republic, sprang up around and between the structures. The Rafa system also was inhabited by a primitive humanoid species known as the Toka, who were treated as slaves by the Rafa colonists. The system was famous for its life orchards—groves of crystalline trees whose crystal "fruit" could extend an individual's life when harvested and worn. Working among the crystal trees, however, drained a person's life and intellect, and consequently most of the harvesting was done by the enslaved Toka or criminals in the system's numerous penal colonies. Following Lando Calrissian's procurement of the Mindharp from Rafa V, it turned out that the Toka were actually the Sharu. When they were subjugated, their mental abilities were suppressed. They regained those abilities along with their civilization.

- **Rafa III:** The location of a deep-bore mining operation using laser drill bits.
- **Rafa IV:** The center of government for the Rafa system, it was ruled by Colonial Governor Duttes Mer until he was overthrown by the resurgent Toka. Rafa IV's main spaceport city, Teguta Lusat, lay wedged amid the colossal plastic ruins of the Sharu. The city contained numerous taverns, the Hotel Sharu, and a penal colony where prisoners served their sentences harvesting crystals from the life orchards.
- **Rafa V:** A frozen, dry world of red sand where archaeoastronomers believed that the ancient Sharu evolved. Orbiting the world were Rafa V's twin moons and a cloud of debris that could have been the result of the Sharu's early attempts at space flight. Its many life orchards were harvested by a few hundred convicts, horticulturists, and Toka living in scattered settlements. A colossal Sharu pyramid, rising 7 kilometers above ground level, towered over the other ruins of Rafa V and was the resting place of the famous artifact called the Mindharp.
- **Rafa XI:** The outermost planet in the Rafa system, it was a world of icy slush orbiting in the dark. Rafa XI was the site of a research installation and a helium refinery.

***Rafe's Gambit*** An independent transport ship based out of New Plympto after the Clone Wars. Imperial clone troopers searched it for fugitives, prompting its crew to warn all other vessels in range, including the *Uhumele.*

*Marka Ragnos*

**Raff, Tactician** A Yuuzhan Vong tactician who served under Commander Tla, he had thin hands and wrists, and a spindly neck. His mouth was a black-stained maw, featuring an outsized tooth that sometimes hindered the clarity of his speech. His hairless and distended cranium was adorned with etchings suggestive of the eddies and convolutions of the enhanced brain within. He was adept at rumination and analysis.

**Raffin, Vanter** An Ession native, he was chief of security for the planet's government and an Imperial supporter of Warlord Zsinj.

**Rafft** A green, forested world with several modest settlements. Just prior to the Battle of Yavin, it was the site of a 12-member Rebel base located in a complex of caves. The Rebels, led by Commander Brion Peck, were sent to Rafft to sabotage the construction of an Imperial garrison. The group was evacuated by the smuggler Dannen Lifehold after a homing beacon betrayed the base's location.

**Ragab** A New Republic fleet admiral, this Mon Calamari used the Star Destroyer *Emancipator* as his flagship.

***Rage*** A Sith corsair in the Brotherhood of Darkness fleet prior to the Battle of Ruusan. Its sister ship, *Fury,* was caught in a trap by Republic Hammerhead cruisers.

***Rage of the Shadow Warriors*** An ancient, epic poem about the Taungs. It was adopted by the Mandalorians and eventually handed down as an anthem of brotherhood by the clone troopers of the Republic.

**Ragga Hocce** A group of bounty hunters contracted by the Empire, they were aboard the first Death Star when the project was still classified.

**Ragith III** A minor world settled by human colonists genetically bred for strength in high-gravity environments. The bouncer Rodo hailed from this planet.

**Ragmar V** A deserted Outer Rim planet far from the battlefronts of the Clone Wars, its surface was marked by rock, dirt, and large native lizards. It was a vital staging planet for an assault on a Separatist base late in the war. Jedi Master Sev and his Padawan Joc Sah were at Ragmar V when Order 66 was issued.

**Ragna III** This Mid Rim world was home to the Yuzzem species.

**Ragnos, Marka** A powerful Dark Lord of the Sith who ruled the Sith Empire for over a century, until his death some 5,000 years before the Battle of Yavin. His corpse was interred in the Shyrack Caves on the planet Korriban, which served as a burial world for the ancient Sith. Soon after his demise, his ghostly visage appeared before Ludo Kressh and Naga Sadow, who were engaged in a duel to determine who would succeed Ragnos; the spirit urged the two aspiring Dark Lords to make peace in order to advance the Sith Empire.

A thousand years later, the spirit of Marka Ragnos and several other Sith Lords appeared before Ulic Qel-Droma and Exar Kun during the Great Sith War. Ragnos, the reigning Dark Lord of the Sith, bestowed the prestigious title upon Kun, while Qel-Droma was chosen to be Kun's first and foremost apprentice. The ephemeral form of Ragnos emblazoned marks of the Sith on their foreheads.

In the time of the New Republic, a decade after the Battle of Endor, the Dark Jedi Tavion Axmis acquired the Scepter of Ragnos—an archaeological relic—and used it in an effort to resurrect the Dark Lord's spirit. Her cult, the Disciples of Ragnos, nearly succeeded on Korriban, but they were defeated by Jaden Korr.

**Ragoon-6** A mountainous world of spectacular beauty untouched by encroaching civilization or industry. The native Ragoons fiercely refused any colonization efforts. They did allow the Jedi Knights of the Galactic Republic access to the planet as a training ground. Obi-Wan Kenobi and Anakin Skywalker both studied on Ragoon-6 during their time as Padawans.

**Rago Run** A hyperspace travel route that linked the Outer Rim with the planet Rago in the Unknown Regions during the time of the Galactic Alliance.

**Ragsall, Lieutenant** A New Republic Navy officer who served in the Bravo Flight of ferry pilots assigned to the *Venture* during the hostilities against the Yevetha.

**Rahhdool, Paouoish** A Jedi Master who discovered Voolvif Monn as a cub, orphaned on a desolate world near the Arah asteroid belt. He eventually took Monn as his Padawan learner.

**Rahmma, Ahnjai** A powerfully built feline Srros'tok, she served as bodyguard to Imperial High Inquisitor Antinnis Tremayne.

**Rahn, Qu** A Jedi from Socorro in the later years of the Galactic Republic, he trained under Yoda as a youngling member of the Katarn Clan. He was an active Jedi Knight during the Separatist crisis and the Clone Wars that followed. Surviving Order 66, he went into hiding. During this time, he sought out Yoda on Dagobah, and learned from him the secret of retaining consciousness in the Force after death. Yoda also enigmatically tipped Qu Rahn off about the mysterious Valley of the Jedi, which he sought as a potential source of great power to challenge the rise of the dark side. When one of the Emperor's most sinister agents, Jerec, also heard of this valley, there began a great hunt for its location. Rahn was able to confirm the valley's location—on the ancient planet Ruusan, site of a great battle between the Sith and the Jedi 1,000 years earlier. Visions in the Force revealed to Rahn that Kyle Katarn would someday unlock the secret of the valley, and that Rahn himself would be captured by the Empire. Rahn entrusted his lightsaber to Morgan Katarn, Kyle's father, to someday pass on to Kyle. Rahn was then captured and killed aboard the Star Destroyer *Vengeance* by Jerec, who next targeted Morgan Katarn in his mad quest for the valley's location.

Rahn had a kindness and wisdom that could be seen in his heart and eyes. Yet when it was necessary to dispose of those who threatened peace and justice, he did so with the fierce strength of the Force. Before he died, Rahn kept a journal of his travels, his thoughts, and things he learned. This journal became Kyle's guide to the Force.

**Rahz, Major Stafuz** A Gektl officer serving in the Imperial military during the Galactic Civil War, he led a raid on the Rebel Alliance safeworld of Harix.

***Raider*** Sith assassin Jor Torlin's starship during the time of Emperor Roan Fel, it was stolen by Morrigan Corde after she killed him.

**rail detonator** A missile-launcher-like weapon that delivered a charge device with two detonation settings: impact or trigger explosion. The latter was a delayed explosion, meaning that the charge adhered itself to its target and was later detonated by a second press of the trigger.

**Rain** *See* Zannah, Darth.

**rainbow berry** A fruit that grew on Endor. It was used in the Ewoks' Harvest Moon Feast and as an ingredient in the big Wistie Fest pie.

**rainbow gem** An extremely valuable gem found on Gallinore, it was in truth a type of living creature that took thousands of years to mature. Tenel Ka's lightsaber used a rainbow gem for its focusing crystal.

**Rainbow Nebulae** A multicolored swirl of deep space gases and dust beyond the planet Naboo, toward the edge of the galaxy. During the rise of the Empire, the nebulae concealed a space station that harbored fugitives from the New Order.

**Raines, Major** One of the best AT-AT instructors to survive the Battle of Endor and the death of Grand Admiral Thrawn, he served under Admiral Pellaeon on the *Chimaera* during the time of the peace agreement between the Imperial Remnant and the New Republic.

**Raioballo sector** An Outer Rim sector comprising thousands of worlds, including Gravlex Med, Sinsang, Dantooine, and Shusugaunt, it was represented in the Galactic Senate by Horox Ryyder and Zo Howler.

**raith** A large, black, bristly-furred rodent-like predator with a green, hairless tail, it was native to the moon Yavin 8.

**Raithal** Site of the Raithal Academy, the most prestigious training center in the Empire. After the Battle of Yavin, medical experts from Raithal were sent to an orbiting hospital frigate to study the outbreak of Candorian plague on Dentaal.

**Rajan** A seasoned Jedi warrior serving under General Kiel Charney during the Battle of Ruusan, a millennium before the rise of the Galactic Empire. He was injured when the Brotherhood of Darkness unleashed a wave of dark side energy on the battlefield, collapsing a tree atop him. Rajan died during a subsequent direct attack by the Sith warriors.

*Rakata*

**Rajana** A muscular native of Typha-Dor, she was a member of Shalini's resistance group during the years leading up to the Clone Wars.

**Rajine, Countess** Once a Jedi, she was an Energy Vampire who could capture the life force of other beings. Centuries before the Clone Wars, Jedi Master Samuro recognized the danger in Rajine and imprisoned her on a remote world. Samuro died erecting a Force barrier that prevented Rajine from leaving the world, but she could still use her macabre abilities to leech the life forces out of her victims, creating mindless zombies to do her bidding. During the Clone Wars, Mace Windu discovered her while investigating the disappearance of a clone unit. With the help of Rajine's patched-together droid Z-18, he then learned the truth about Rajine and used Samuro's holocron to recite an incantation that freed the captured life energies. The zombies, their will restored, exacted vengeance on Rajine before finally surrendering to eternal rest.

**rak** A recreational drug outlawed by the Galactic Alliance.

**Rak, Bastori** A Yuuzhan Vong frigate commander, he intercepted the ship *Jeolocas,* which was transporting hidden Jedi. Alema Rar attacked and killed him, while his crew was wiped out by YVH 1 battle droids.

**rakamat** A Yuuzhan Vong bioengineered ground-transportation creature also known as a warmaster or—as Jaina Solo referred to it—as a "range." A rakamat had blue-green bony-plate armor and plasma-firing horns along its spine and at points on its flanks. The rakamat also carried dovin basals, which it could use to create gravitic anomalies. Its giant feet caused the ground to shake upon its ponderous approach.

**Rakata** Millennia ago, before the rise of the Galactic Republic, members of this forgotten species ruled much of the galaxy, conquering and enslaving planets with their advanced technology. It was believed that the Rakata introduced the forerunner of modern hyperdrive technology to the galaxy, which paved the way for the foundation of the Republic when adopted and modified by such ancient spacefaring cultures as the Duros, Hutts, and Corellians.

For thousands of years, the Rakata vanished into obscurity. It was not until the period surrounding the Great Sith War that xenoarchaeologists began piecing together compelling evidence of their existence. Relics of striking similarity were discovered across scattered worlds. Theories based on this evidence began to paint a vivid picture of the galaxy's distant past.

The Rakata founded the Infinite Empire, a collection of 500 worlds, and enslaved many of the galaxy's sentient species of that era. Evidence suggests that it was the Rakata who were responsible for the transplantation of prehistoric humans from their home planet of Coruscant that would lead to centuries of debate as to which world gave rise to humanity. Others speculate that the Rakata were responsible for the organization of the worlds of the Corellian system, long attributed to ancient alien architects of unimaginable power. It may have been Rakatan terraforming techniques that dried out Tatooine's surface into a desert, or created the lush forests of Kashyyyk.

The Rakata were connected to the power of the Force, though they predated the rise of the recognizable Jedi and Sith Orders by centuries. With the power of the dark side of the Force, they created an enormous space station called the Star Forge, which could translate that energy into the creation of advanced technology—weapons and starships—that gave the Infinite Empire its lock on galactic dominance. Despite the Star Forge—or perhaps because of it, and the corruption that festered from this concentration of dark side energy—the Rakatan Empire did not last long.

In the course of the Infinite Empire's rapid expansion, the Rakata exposed themselves to an alien virus. Harmless to the local life-forms, the highly contagious virus proved extremely lethal to the Rakatan conquerors. The plague spread rapidly, effectively wiping out the Rakatan populations on the conquered planets. The enslaved species rose up and overthrew the few Rakata who survived the deadly plague. In an effort to avenge generations of oppression, the rebellious slaves wiped out all traces of their former oppressors. The rebellion was so absolute and so successful that all memory and almost all archaeological evidence of the Rakata vanished. The Rakatan civilization ceased to exist nearly 30,000 years before the current era, the height of its power predating the Republic by 10 millennia.

Even the isolated Rakatan homeworld—cataloged as Lehon, Rakata Prime, or the Unknown World, its true name lost to history—could not escape the effects of the plague. The collapse of their sprawling interstellar empire and the ravaging effects of disease on their population threw the society of the Rakata into turmoil. These people slowly regressed to a barbaric, technologically inferior state after millennia of war . . . a state from which they never recovered.

The few barbaric Rakata who survived were wiped out by the battle for the Star Forge, during the time of Darth Malak. The Galactic Republic then embarked on a concentrated effort to wipe out all traces of the Rakata, to ensure that the knowledge of the culture would remain obscure.

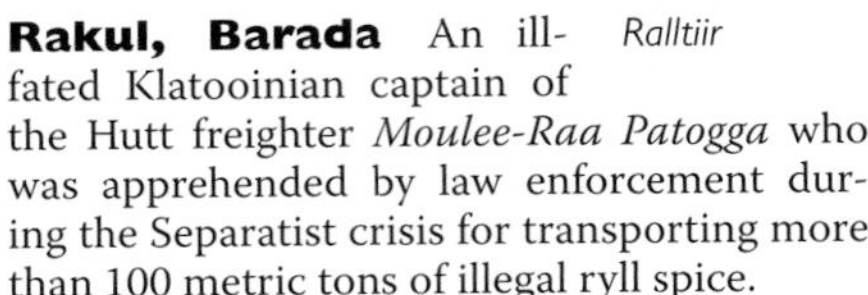
Rakazzak beast

**Rakata Prime** *See* Unknown World.

**rakazzak beast** These spider-like, 3-meter-tall creatures, which lived on the Forest Moon of Endor, were often ridden by Yuzzum warriors. Rakazzaks spun thick, sticky webs to trap their enemies.

**rakghoul** Hideous flesh-eating creatures that were spawned by a viral infection among the Undercity dwellers of Taris, thousands of years before the rise of the Empire. The manifestation of rakghoul traits caused a rapid, bodywide mutation among infected humans. Taris government officials made little effort to combat the plague, as it was confined to the lower city levels populated by the criminal underclass.

**Rak'k** A Barabel ruffian, he served as a guide to Alema Rar upon her arrival on Korriban during the war between the Confederation and the Galactic Alliance.

**Rakrir** The homeworld of a sentient insectoid species, its inhabitants were wealthy, highly cultured, and finicky. Few left Rakrir because they were usually dissatisfied with the level of sophistication on other planets. Sabodor, owner of Sabodor's pet store on Etti IV, was a native of Rakrir.

Ralltiir

**Rakul, Barada** An ill-fated Klatooinian captain of the Hutt freighter *Moulee-Raa Patogga* who was apprehended by law enforcement during the Separatist crisis for transporting more than 100 metric tons of illegal ryll spice.

**Ra-Lee** A beautiful tan-furred Ewok who was married to Chief Chirpa, she died defending her daughters, Kneesaa and Asha.

**R'all** The fraternal twin of J'uoch, he ran a mining concern on the planet Dellalt with his sister. A human, R'all had straight brown hair with a widow's peak and pale skin set off by black-irised eyes. Along with his sister, the unscrupulous R'all competed with Han Solo to be the first to find the lost treasures of the legendary ship *Queen of Ranroon.*

**R'alla mineral water** Known for its purity and medicinal benefits, this liquid came from springs in the underground caverns of the mountain town of R'alla on the planet of the same name. R'alla mineral water was also a main ingredient in certain bootleg intoxicants, and smugglers made substantial profits by bringing it to other worlds. Han Solo and Chewbacca once made a living smuggling the mineral water to the planet Rampa.

**rallop** A small animal preyed upon by larger creatures on the moon Jwlio.

**Ralls, Agent** A New Republic Intelligence agent, he was sent to question prisoner Davith Sconn, imprisoned at Jagg Island Detention Center, about what he knew of the Yevethan military fleet.

Rakghoul

**Ralltiir** Located in the system of the same name, it lay along the Perlemian Trade Route in the Darpa sector of the Core Worlds, just on the border of the Colonies region. Over several hundred years, Ralltiir was the only planet in the Darpa sector able to maintain its independence from the nearby world of Esseles. It was an attractive, high-technology world famous for its banking industry and home to the Grallia Spaceport.

The planet's powerful financial institutions were politically neutral and had a reputation as safe havens for investors' funds. With the rise of the Empire, certain factions infiltrated Ralltiir's financial system and began to steer its markets in a pro-Imperial direction—by erasing the fiscal records of nonhuman investors, for instance. Shortly before the Battle of Yavin, pro-Alliance members of the Ralltiir High Council tried to restore balance to the markets. Their efforts inspired the Emperor to use Ralltiir as an example to other worlds that would resist his will. A brutal Imperial force led by Lord Tion invaded Ralltiir, devastating the planet and its 10 billion inhabitants. Tion disbanded the High Council, replaced it with a military tribunal headed by Imperial Governor Dennix Graeber, and set up interrogation centers and public executions of Rebel leaders. He also sealed off the entire Ralltiir system (even barring relief organizations from traveling through his blockade), which severely hurt commerce along the Perlemian Trade Route.

Princess Leia Organa, on a mercy mission to deliver medical supplies and equipment to the High Council of Ralltiir, was permitted to land by Tion. The Princess rescued Basso, a wounded Rebel soldier, who later revealed the existence of the Death Star project. Ralltiir's economy was left in ruins, and many powerful corporations relocated offworld. But Governor Graeber got rich by secretly supplying the Rebel underground with weapons, which he then used as a justification to persecute Ralltiir's citizens even more harshly. Before the Battle of Yavin, an Alliance raid on the Cygnus Corporation's starfighter performance trials near Ralltiir resulted in the capture of the assault gunboat design team. Inath of Ralltiir, who years later became a member of the New Republic Council, saw many of his associates murdered by the Emperor's Noghri assassins, which led him to pressure Chief of State Leia Organa Solo to retire her Noghri bodyguards, claiming that it sent the wrong signal.

**Ralltiir tiger** A species of large, deadly felines found on Ralltiir. They had multiple rows of long teeth set into broad jaws, and claws that they extended as they were getting ready to attack, which they did only when they meant to kill. The creatures had no sense of loyalty.

**Ralon** A salvager who operated on the Khoonda Plains of Dantooine following the Jedi Civil War. He scavenged the ruins of the Jedi enclave for relics to sell.

**Ralpe** A member of the Galactic Alliance Guard, and part of Major Serpa's team dispatched by Jacen Solo to subjugate the Jedi stronghold on Ossus during the rise of Darth Caedus. Ralpe was shot and killed by Jaina Solo.

Dack Ralter

***Ralroost*** A Bothan Assault Cruiser commanded by Admiral Traest Kre'fey during the war against the Yuuzhan Vong. The ship originally was built for the defense of the Bothan people after the liberation of Coruscant from the Empire. Kre'fey insisted that its crew consist mostly of Bothans. The *Ralroost* was the base of operations for no less than four fighter squadrons. The *Ralroost* played a major role in the Battles of Ithor and Sernpidal, as well as a number of strike missions launched from Kashyyyk.

**Ralrracheen (Ralrra)** From ambassador to the Old Republic to slave of the Empire, this tall, powerfully built Wookiee saw all sides of life from an unusual perspective. Ralrra had a speech impediment that allowed him to speak Basic, which proved useful when he was Kashyyyk's ambassador to the Old Republic. As a slave to the Empire, he was used by his Imperial masters to communicate with other Wookiees. At first, he tried to resist Imperial occupation forces, but he forced himself to comply after they executed a dozen women and children from his family unit. His proximity to Imperial officers provided him with information vital to the Alliance's effort to free Kashyyyk. Like most Wookiees, he felt he owed a life debt to the Alliance for its efforts. When Chewbacca brought Princess Leia Organa Solo to Kashyyyk to keep her safe from Grand Admiral Thrawn's Noghri Death Commandos, Ralrra was one of two Wookiees assigned to protect her.

**Ralter, Dack** A young Rebel soldier from Kalist VI. During the Battle of Hoth, he was a gunner on Luke Skywalker's snowspeeder. Dack died when the snowspeeder took a direct hit from an Imperial walker.

**Raltharan** A Padawan learner trained by Corran Horn following the Yuuzhan Vong War.

**Ram** A clone commando from Bravo Squad during the Clone Wars, he was the sole survivor of his unit following the Battle of Geonosis.

**Ramic, High General Sutt** An Imperial senior officer in command of one of the three Golan III defense platforms that guarded Muunilinst a decade after the death of Grand Admiral Thrawn. He begrudgingly went along with Admiral Pellaeon's bid for peace with the New Republic, but was ultimately loyal to his commanding officer.

**Ramis, Dak** An ancient philosopher whose teachings survived from the pre-Republic era, his views greatly influenced Darth Millennial's founding of the Dark Force religion.

**Ramis, Octa** A Jedi Knight from Chandrila active in Luke Skywalker's new Jedi Order. Raised on a high-gravity world, she had a strong, muscular build. She was trained by Kam Solusar. Octa advocated a more active role for the Jedi during the Yuuzhan Vong invasion, partially out of her love for fellow Jedi Miko Reglia, one of the earliest casualties in the war against the aliens. Grieving the loss of Reglia and Daeshara'cor, she sided with Kyp Durron's faction of Jedi and flew with Kyp's Dozen, becoming leader of the unit in Kyp's absence. In the final battles against the Yuuzhan Vong, Octa Ramis was bonded with a Zonama Sekot seed-partner, and provided with a Sekotan starship.

**Ramoan** An alien species left without a home planet following the war against the Yuuzhan Vong.

**Ramodi** This planet was the site of a sizable baradium-smuggling ring about five years after the Yuuzhan Vong War. Jedi Knight Tesar Sebatyne had been dispatched by the new Jedi Order to investigate, but he abandoned the mission after hearing UnuThul's call to join him in the Unknown Regions.

Oppo Rancisis

**Ramordian silk** A luxurious spun fabric.

**Rampa** A world of heavy industry in the Corporate Sector, Rampa had an extremely high degree of pollution and contamination. The Rampa Skywatch kept an eye out for water smugglers hidden among the regular cargo traffic, for Rampa's citizens were willing to pay a very high price for pure R'alla mineral water—they polluted their own. Han Solo and Chewbacca made some smuggling runs "down the Rampa Rapids" during their early adventures.

***Rampage*** One of three Imperial Star Destroyers under Lumiya's command following the Battle of Endor.

***Rampart*** An Imperial Interdictor cruiser. Grand Admiral Thrawn dispatched it to Chazwa to crack down on smuggling operations there.

**Ramsees Hed** A docking port at Cal-Seti.

**Rana** A Jedi pilot, she transported Qui-Gon Jinn and his Padawan Obi-Wan Kenobi to Ragoon-6 for training.

**Rana, Queen** An ancient ruler of the planet Duro. A huge monument dedicated to Queen Rana filled the Valley of Royalty there.

**Ranat** Members of this rat-like species called themselves Con Queecon, or "the conquerors," in their native tongue. Ranats were small and cunning with sharp teeth, whiskers, and long tails. While the meter-high beings appeared harmless, they were savage killers with a taste for other intelligent beings. After the death of Jabba the Hutt, a group of Ranats took over the crime lord's Tatooine desert palace. Ranats were mostly scavengers and traders, and they apparently came to Tatooine from the planet Aralia. They were often compared to Jawas despite the fact that they preferred to inhabit highly populated areas. The species was deemed only semi-sentient by the Empire, so killing them could be more easily justified. The Empire still used them as spies since they worked for relatively little money.

**Rancisis, Oppo** One of the most cunning members of the Jedi Council, and a well-respected Jedi Master known for his firm grasp of military tactics and warfare. When Oppo Rancisis inherited the title Monarch of Thisspias, he turned down the role. Instead, he devoted all of his time and energy to the Jedi Order, eventually earning a place on the Council. His artful strategies and battle plans allowed the Jedi to emerge victorious from several large-scale space conflicts.

Rancisis was a master of Malacia, a Jedi technique that induced a powerful dizziness and nausea in enemies. As incapacitating as a hammer blow, it did not do any lasting physical damage.

Rancisis was one of the more conservative members of the Jedi Council as far as Jedi traditions and the tenets of the Jedi Code were concerned. He had reservations over the number of exceptions afforded young Anakin Skywalker, including his joining of the Order at such an advanced age, and his ascension to Jedi Knighthood without formally passing the Jedi trials. Rancisis had misgivings about Skywalker's lack of discipline, though Jedi Master Yoda reminded Rancisis that as a young one, the Thisspiasian had had his own share of transgressions.

When it became clear that the demands of the Clone Wars often superseded tradition, Rancisis began to tolerate more exceptions, even accepting the rogue Jedi Quinlan Vos back into the Order. When Rancisis was placed in command of Republic operations on Saleucami to destroy a Confederacy cloning operation involving Morgukai warriors, Rancisis chose Vos as his second in command.

Rancisis and Vos led three battalions to Saleucami. Rancisis was trained in the ancient art of Jedi battle meditation, and was soon deep in contemplation, subtly altering the will of the fighting forces to coax victory for the Republic. The prolonged siege at Saleucami took five long months of grueling warfare. Though the Republic ultimately stopped the Confederacy plot on the planet, Rancisis was killed by the traitorous Jedi Sora Bulq.

**rancor** A vicious carnivore over 5 meters tall, it had immense fangs and sharp claws. Rancors were bipedal creatures with extremely long arms and an appetite for raw flesh. They were prevalent on the planet Dathomir, where the Witches of Dathomir tamed the beasts for use as mounts and hunting animals. Rancors could also be found in the Ottethan system as well as amid the bright foliage of Felucia, where the native Felucians used them as mounts and combat beasts, painting them with colorful inks and dyes. Jabba the Hutt housed an untamed rancor beneath his throne room, where many of Jabba's enemies met their deaths. The towering monster was killed by Luke Skywalker when the Jedi was forced into the pit by Jabba's treachery.

Rancors were among the most fearsome creatures in the galaxy. Huge, strong, and voracious, they had few natural predators and were extraordinarily difficult to kill. Rancors were protected by a thick hide that proved resistant to blasters and many other weapons.

**Rancor Rising** A maneuver in the teräs käsi fighting form that brought a warrior from a crouch into a standing position in a single, fluid motion.

***Rancor's Tooth*** A Corellian corvette commissioned by Orax Tazaene, who transferred into service as a privateer in the Rebel Alliance fleet. The vessel was used to help establish the Rebel base at Hoth.

Rancor

**Rand, Atton "Jaq"** It proved difficult to characterize the kind of luck that surrounded Atton Rand—disaster was a constant companion, but through it all Rand managed to cheat death time and again, surviving long enough to stumble into the next crisis. Rand lived a transient life in the time of the Great Sith War, gravitating from pazaak table to pazaak table, guarding his winnings thanks to a solid backing in the Echani martial arts. He kept secret his true background: Rand was a veteran of both the Mandalorian Wars and the Jedi Civil War, fighting for the Sith as part of Darth Revan's elite. Rand discovered his Force sensitivity during this time, and feared that he would succumb to the dark side. He abandoned his Sith duty and was imprisoned at Peragus II before being freed by the Jedi Exile. Rand joined her and Jedi Master Kreia in their adventures to stop the reawakening of Darth Sion.

**Randa** The site of a small, secret Rebel base shortly after the Battle of Yavin.

**Randa the Hutt** Son of Borga the Hutt, of the Besadii kajidic, he was a young Hutt at the time of the Yuuzhan Vong War and ostensibly supported his father's attempt to form an alliance with the alien invaders. Though the Yuuzhan Vong believed that Hutt ships would assist in providing them with fresh prisoners, in truth Randa exploited his alliance to funnel information back to the New Republic. After being rescued from the Yuuzhan Vong by Kyp Durron and Wurth Skidder, Randa pledged his allegiance to the New Republic.

Randa was stranded at Settlement Thirty-two on Duro during the Yuuzhan Vong attack there. Knowing that his home planet Nal Hutta was being targeted by the Yuuzhan Vong, Randa tried to negotiate a deal through which the world would be spared if he handed over a Jedi. Warmaster Tsavong Lah had little patience for or trust in the Hutt, and imprisoned him. Randa sacrificed himself trying to save the lives of Leia Organa and Jaina Solo, and he was strangled to death by a tkun creature.

Atton "Jaq" Rand

***Rand Ecliptic*** A space frigate, it was the first ship that Luke Skywalker's boyhood friend Biggs Darklighter was assigned to after he graduated from the Academy. It was commanded by Captain Heliesk, with Darklighter serving as first mate and Derek "Hobbie" Klivian as second. There were three Rebel cells planning a mutiny aboard the ship, which resulted in a takeover of the craft and delivery of the *Rand Ecliptic* to the Alliance base on Yavin 4 for refitting.

**Random, Sarl** The security chief of Cloud City, she was in charge during the droid EV-9D9's revolt and escape.

**Randon** A planet perhaps best known for an alcoholic drink, the Randoni Yellow Plague. On Randon, female ward-cousins were traditionally honored due to their potential inheritance and were customarily served first. Randoni women wore their hair loose and flowing. Luke Skywalker and Tenel Ka posed as archaeological traders from Randon during an undercover mission to Borgo Prime.

**Ranga, Alta** An Ensel Jedi Knight from Enselon, he had the ability to sense electromagnetic fields for navigation and predatory purposes.

**range** *See* rakamat.

***Ranger*** A *Centax*-class heavy frigate that served as Jedi Master Nejaa Halcyon's flagship in a

Rand Ecliptic

Clone Wars mission to liberate Praesitlyn from Confederacy forces. One of the fastest frigates in the fleet, it featured a pair of MG1-A proton torpedo tubes and an array of laser cannon batteries. During the battle, the *Ranger* was swarmed by skirmisher vessels and boarded by battle droids, though Halcyon was able to regain control of the vessel.

***Ranger*-class gunship** A New Republic military vessel.

**Range Squadron** A ground assault team led by Kapp Dendo at the Battle of Ithor, during the Yuuzhan Vong War.

**rangi** Small yet dangerous predators hunted for food by the Barabels of Barab I.

**Ranjiyn** The leader of the Unity of Community on Ansion during the time of the Separatist crisis. An Ansionian, he had an alternating black-and-white pattern in his mane. He supported keeping Ansion allied to the Galactic Republic.

**rank cylinder** *See* Imperial code cylinder.

**Rankin, Pek** A Balawai (or immigrant) man who led a search party to find missing children during the intense fighting between the Balawai and the Korunnai on Haruun Kal at the time of the Clone Wars. Mace Windu found the children first, and confronted Rankin to determine his intentions. A sudden attack by Korunnai led to Rankin's death.

**Ranklinge** A planet in the Shelsha sector, and site of an Incom Industries manufacturing facility, it had suffered through over a decade of civil war by the time of the Battle of Yavin.

**rankweed** A foul-smelling plant with an awful taste.

**Ransa, Senator Bicon** A member of the Senatorial committee sent to investigate whether or not Obi-Wan Kenobi was responsible for the death of his fellow Padawan Bruck Chun.

**Ransen, Moff Kyl** An Imperial Governor who sympathized with the plight of the subjugated Vratix of Thyferra and secretly abetted the Ashern Circle in its terrorist plots. He was regarded as a hero by the Vratix.

**Ransom, Tait** A Corellian smuggler associate of Karl Ancher and Drake Paulsen, he operated near Socorro during the Galactic Civil War.

**Ranth, Ta'laam** A Gotal Senator, he was the head of the Senate Justice Council during the New Republic's defense against the Yuuzhan Vong. Ranth led an inquiry into the traitorous Senator Viqi Shesh and the events leading up to the disastrous Battle of Fondor. After the death of Chief of State Borsk Fey'lya, Ranth was a candidate for the office. He hoped to build a bloc of supporters but ultimately threw his support to Cal Omas, settling for a position in the Galactic Alliance High Council instead.

**Rao** A Mos Espa native known for her extremely fast Novastar rocket swoop, she was an associate of Wald and Kitster Banai. She would occasionally lend out her swoop to those in need of quick transportation, but stopped after the sixth rider died in a crash. Ulda Banai lent her swoop to Han and Leia Organa Solo when they were in need of such a vehicle, but only after Han proved his piloting skills.

**Raol** A young Jazbinan resistance fighter during the Galactic Civil War, he was in love with Princess Syayna and was, for a time, suspicious of ally Luke Skywalker, whom he feared had designs on his beloved.

**Raort, Romort** An Irith spice-jacker who hung out on Nar Shaddaa, he was unpopular among underworld cohorts because he stole from a number of them. He was also associated with a gang that took swift vengeance on those who crossed them. Romort Raort and his gang made a number of deals with the Hutts that allowed them to operate along most of the major galactic spice routes.

**rapard** A species of stealthy reptilian predators native to the jungles of Tenupe.

**Raph-Elan, Yoshi** A newly knighted Jedi who crash-landed on a primitive planet taken over by Lord Gar-oth's droid army. After eluding battle droids, Yoshi met with Princess Lourdes, who had agreed to marry Gar-oth in order to stop the killing of her people. Yoshi disguised himself as Lourdes's servant, Jed, but when Gar-oth demanded that the wedding take place immediately, Yoshi claimed that he was Lourdes's husband. Gar-oth unleashed a droid named the Goliath to deal with the two. While Lourdes faced Gar-oth, Yoshi battled and defeated the droid. The Jedi Council sent a ship to retrieve Yoshi, and the young Jedi seriously considered Princess Lourdes's request to someday return after he had grown up a bit.

**Rapid Entry By Jedi (REBJ)** A phrase coined by the 967th Commando unit of the Galactic Alliance Defense Force to describe Jacen Solo's use of the Force to push aside doors and other obstacles, allowing the commandos to enter structures without stern resistance.

**Rappapor** A member of Samuel Tomas Gillespee's smuggling crew during the early years of the New Republic.

**Rappertunie** The stage name used by Rapotwanalantonee Tivtotolon, a Shawda Ubb musician from Manpha. Unlike his fellow swamp dwellers, Rappertunie's wanderlust led him to tour various scattered Manphan communities and eventually took him offworld altogether. To fund these trips, Rappertunie made a living as a successful musician, playing the growdi water-organ/flute, as well as the pit horn and bi-tuminal wind cuspers. Once he joined up with the Max Rebo Band and entered such parched environments as Tatooine, he rarely ever left his growdi perch, which kept him close to moisture. After the musical group disbanded, Rappertunie became a computer programmer for Rebaxan Columni.

**Raprice, Lieutenant** An efficient by-the-manual Imperial officer under the command of Captain Deyd Llenew aboard the *Carrack*-class customs cruiser *Vigilante.* Han Solo once cleverly smuggled stolen starships past Raprice and Llenew.

***Raptor* (1)** The flagship of the Stark Commercial Combine, captained by a Zabrak named Zur during the Stark Hyperspace Conflict. Jedi Master Tholme and his Padawan Quinlan Vos infiltrated the ship in order to transmit a patch that would counteract the nav computer virus engineered by Iaco Stark. They also caused the *Raptor*'s shields to lower, allowing Jedi pilots to destroy the vessel.

*Rappertunie*

**Raptor (2)** A modified SoroSuub *Preybird*-class starfighter owned by Mazzic. It was fast, well armed, and—thanks to the flaming birds of prey painted on its underside—thoroughly intimidating.

**Raptors (1)** One of the most notorious street gangs in Coruscant's Crimson Corridor, comprising humans, Kubaz, H'nemthe, Gotals, Dressellians, Trandoshans, and Bith.

**Raptors (2)** *See* Zsinj's Raptors.

**Rapuung, Hul** A Yuuzhan Vong of Domain Rapuung (along with Vua and Laph Rapuung), he was stationed on Yavin 4 during an attempt to capture Jedi Knights from Luke Skywalker's Jedi academy. Hul confronted the shaper Mezhan Kwaad over her acts of sabotage that resulted in Vua Rapuung's shaming.

**Rapuung, Laph** A Yuuzhan Vong warrior and subordinate of Tsaa Qalu aboard the *Throat Slasher,* he perished when his ship crashed on Thyferra.

**Rapuung, Vua** A grotesque-looking Yuuzhan Vong who came to the aid of Anakin Solo on Yavin 4 during the Yuuzhan Vong War. Rapuung was a warrior commander when he fell in love with shaper Mezhan Kwaad. Because their love was forbidden, Mezhan Kwaad engineered his downfall by altering his coral implants, causing them to reject their host. This turned Vua into a Shamed One, ensuring that Vua would never reveal her acts of heresy.

A master at hand-to-hand combat, Vua set out to find Mezhan so that she would reveal what she had done and prove his true worth. Before meeting Anakin, he operated a trawler known as a vangaak. He agreed to help Anakin Solo because Yun-Yuuzhan revealed to him in a vision that a *Jeedai* would lead him to his revenge and vindication. Together they infiltrated the shaper base. Anakin and Vua eventually reached Commander Vootuh's ship, which was to transport Mezhan Kwaad offworld. There Mezhan was forced to reveal the truth about Vua's status as a Shamed One. Having been redeemed, he once again took up the amphistaff—a weapon he had forsworn until vindication—and fought off hordes of Yuuzhan Vong warriors so that Anakin and Tahiri Veila could escape. He was overwhelmed by the Yuuzhan Vong ranks and killed, but stories of his actions lived on, building momentum among those Shamed Ones who grew to respect the *Jeedai.*

*Vua Rapuung*

*Alema Rar*

**Rar, Alema** Twisted by injury and the dark side, she was a Twi'lek who once had been a promising member of Luke Skywalker's Jedi Order. Fellow Twi'lek Daeshara'cor recognized the innate Force talents in the sisters Alema and Numa Rar, and rescued them from the darkest ryll dens in Kala'uun, where they served as dancers in the principal city of the Twi'lek homeworld of Ryloth. Daeshara'cor used her own funds to arrange their transport to the Jedi academy on Yavin 4, and the sisters became her apprentices. One of the Rar sisters' earliest assignments was leading a resistance movement on New Plympto during the Yuuzhan Vong invasion. As part of the subterfuge required by this assignment, they hid their lekku and disguised themselves as a single human female, never appearing together to conceal their identity as sisters. Despite their efforts to rally the populace of New Plympto, the Yuuzhan Vong conquered the world by releasing a deadly plague.

The Rars and thousands of refugees escaped the devastation aboard the cruiser *Nebula Chaser,* which was promptly intercepted by Yuuzhan Vong forces. The alien invaders released their new genetically engineered Jedi-hunting creatures, the voxyn, to search the vessel, and one of the deadly beasts killed Numa. Alema survived aboard an escape pod retrieved by the *Jade Shadow,* and after spending time recuperating within a bacta tank, she emerged ready for action. Deeply rattled by the death of her sister, Alema displayed a focus and intensity that caused Luke to fear that she was succumbing to the dark side of the Force. Alema joined Anakin Solo's strike team dispatched to hunt the voxyn queen, which to her was a personal mission of vengeance. She was one of the few to survive the team's costly mission to Myrkr, a bloody experience that resulted in the death of Anakin and the disappearance of Raynar Thul, Jedi whom Alema had grown to admire. It was further tragedy to anneal her deadening spirit and cultivate her growing paranoia.

Alema spent the rest of the war as a member of the Twin Suns Squadron and was one of the Jedi who arrived at the living planet Zonama Sekot in the final stages of the conflict. There she was bonded to the seed-partners that produced living Sekotan starships, one of several Jedi selected who all had a record of personal tragedy as a bond in common.

Five years after the defeat of the Yuuzhan Vong, Alema Rar was one of seven young Jedi veterans of the Myrkr mission who responded to the telepathic call of UnuThul, the joined consciousness of Raynar Thul and the Killik hive that had found and nurtured him back to health. Alema became a Joiner, her aggressive tendencies exacerbated by the Gorog hive, the "unseen hive" that acted as a sort of dark subconscious of the hive-minded Colony. Under the Gorog's influence, Alema lashed out against the Chiss forces that were defending their territories against the Colony's expansion.

Alarmed at the escalating conflict between the Colony and the Chiss, Han Solo and Leia Organa Solo attempted to extricate their daughter Jaina and her fellow Jedi from the influence of the Killiks. Alema acted as their guide, appearing on the surface to be helpful but in truth sabotaging their efforts. Han and Leia captured Alema and brought her to the Jedi academy on Ossus, from which she escaped and fled to a Gorog nest on Kr. Luke and Mara Jade Skywalker confronted Alema there, and engaged in a lightsaber duel. Luke bested Alema, crippling her with a lightsaber strike that slashed her from shoulder to sternum. Leaving her to die, Luke took Alema's lightsaber.

Alema survived, however, maimed and further twisted by her experiences. She called herself the Night Herald of the Dark Nest, and in her next confrontation with Skywalker, she tried to sow distrust between Luke and his wife by insinuating the presence of unpleasant secrets in Mara Jade's past. Alema carried a dark blue—almost black—lightsaber that matched the color of the Gorog carapace.

As the Swarm War continued, Alema had to face lightsaber combat with Leia Organa Solo. Leia managed to disfigure Alema, severing one of her lekku from her skull. They clashed again on Tenupe, where Alema was determined to kill Leia. In the fight, Alema fell into the maw of a vicious spider sloth, which

masticated her. Once again, it appeared that Alema had died. Once again, it was not so. She had survived, even further disfigured and even hungrier for vengeance against Leia Organa Solo and her family. This became her sole mission in life, representing a struggle for Balance that would not be achieved until Leia died.

Hoping to make Leia suffer, Alema targeted Jacen Solo. Jacen, however, was in the thrall of Lumiya, Dark Lady of the Sith, who warned him about the danger. Lumiya, meanwhile, decided to take Alema as a Sith apprentice. Together they killed the Jedi Tresina Lobi; Alema also fought by Lumiya's side at Rooqoo Depot, where they attempted to defeat Luke and Mara Jade Skywalker. Alema's preferred weapons were poison blow-darts, though she failed to kill either Skywalker. When Jacen Solo later used a poisoned dart to kill Mara, many—including Luke—believed Alema was the murderer.

After Lumiya died by Skywalker's blade, Alema took it upon herself to learn more about her Sith heritage. Traveling aboard an ancient Sith meditation sphere, Alema uncovered Lumiya's secret lair—an asteroid base near Bimmiel that had been the sanctuary of Darth Vectivus. She also journeyed to the Valley of the Sith Lords on Korriban and discovered a burgeoning new Order of Sith. Alema was delighted that Jacen Solo was following the Sith path to becoming Darth Caedus, for she knew what pain such a downfall would bring to the Skywalker and Solo families.

Meanwhile, Jagged Fel sought to restore honor to his own family name by tracking down and killing Alema Rar. He, Jaina Solo, and Zekk were tasked with tracking Alema and stopping her swath of terror and destruction. Jagged adopted a host of unpredictable fighting tactics and urged Jaina to do the same, for Alema was truly a dangerous opponent. The trio tracked Alema to the asteroid base on Bimmiel and infiltrated the stronghold, fighting past Alema's Sith-amplified Force phantoms. It was Jagged who finally confronted Alema, drawing his blaster on her as the Bimmiel base fractured around them, its artificial gravity faltering and its atmosphere dwindling. Alema tugged Jagged's firearm to her grip with the Force, but it proved to be by Fel's design—the blaster, separated from Jag's grip, detonated after a timed interval, shattering Alema's hand. Taking advantage of her surprise and injury, Jagged grappled her with his Mandalorian crushgaunts.

As Jagged crushed her throat, her dying words to him, still twisted by the plural identity she'd adopted as a Joiner years before, were: "Remember us. Remember us as we used to be, before the universe turned against us. Young, beautiful, strong, brave, admirable, loved, loving."

**Rar, Numa** A Twi'lek Jedi, she and her sister, Alema, had been dancers in a seamy ryll den on Ryloth before being liberated by Daeshara'cor and brought to Luke Skywalker's Jedi Order. During the Yuuzhan Vong invasion, she and Alema led the resistance on New Plympto, until the alien invaders unleashed a plague that killed all life on the planet. She, Alema, and thousands of refugees escaped aboard the cruiser *Nebula Chaser*—but it was intercepted by the Yuuzhan Vong, who released Jedi-hunting voxyn aboard the ship. Numa died after she was sprayed with voxyn saliva, and her death greatly affected her sister for years to come.

**Rarefied Air Cavalry** A military unit on Virujansi, it flew alongside the forces of Obi-Wan Kenobi and Anakin Skywalker in battle against the Separatists during the Clone Wars.

**Ras** A clone commando who was part of the team accompanying Jedi Master Bol Chatak to Murkhana, at the end of the Clone Wars. Ras refused to carry out Order 66, and he and his fellow commando Climber allowed Roan Shryne and other Jedi to escape Murkhana.

*Raskar*

**Ras, Bar** The first Gungan punished with the nocomeback law decreed by Boss Nass. Bar Ras was convicted of stealing and assault against a neighbor.

**Rascal Squadron** Ace Merrick's X-wing squadron during the Galactic Civil War.

**rashallo** A plant native to Haruun Kal. Its leaves were rolled into cigarras.

**Rashon, Civé** The lead starfighter pilot of Obsidian Squadron during the Battle of Endor, she also went by the call sign Howlrunner. She served in an elite TIE squadron aboard the Star Destroyer *Avenger.*

**Rashtah** A ruthless Wookiee lieutenant to the pirate Krayn. Although it was unusual for a Wookiee to be involved in slave trading, Rashtah was extremely loyal to Krayn. He wore ammunition belts that crisscrossed his body. On Nar Shaddaa, Rashtah ambushed Obi-Wan Kenobi inside a turbolift, but the Jedi was able to gain the upper hand and was forced to kill Rashtah.

**Rask** A street philosopher in Iziz on Onderon, he was a Naddist—a follower of the Sith apprentice Freedon Nadd—during an uprising that occurred 4,000 years before the Battle of Yavin.

**Raska Hill** A natural formation near Theed, on Naboo. Several resistance movement leaders reunited with Captain Panaka at Raska Hill shortly before the liberation of Theed from the Trade Federation.

**Raskar** A onetime space pirate of Iridium in the days of the Old Republic, he, like the others, used unique power gems. The stones, which generated a disrupting aura, helped the pirates break through the shields of their victims' starships. The pirates were wiped out by a force of Jedi. Only Raskar survived, escaping with the sole remaining power gem. He set himself up on a Rim world and invited those who wanted the gem to fight for it in gladiatorial combat; he made his money staging and betting on the fights. Chewbacca managed to beat Raskar's best fighter, and he and Han Solo left with the gem following the Battle of Yavin, although it only had enough power remaining for one final shield disruption. Later, Raskar captured Solo and Luke Skywalker above Hoth, and Solo flew the group to a deep chasm on the planet's equator. There they discovered a hidden cave filled with rare lumni-spice lichens guarded by a fire-breathing dragon-slug and barely escaped with their lives. Raskar redeemed himself on Ord Mantell when he rescued Solo and Skywalker from the bounty hunter Skorr.

**Raslan, Captain** A former Imperial officer, he allied with Warlord Zsinj during the early years of the New Republic. Raslan led the infiltration mission into Kuat Drive Yards to steal the under-construction Super Star Destroyer *Razor's Kiss.* Though he succeeded, he died in the New Republic counterattack.

**Rasper** Part of the Nebula Front team led by Captain Arwen Cohl, he died during the raid of the Trade Federation battleship *Revenue* shortly before the Battle of Naboo.

**rass** A predator native to Saki. The Sakiyans used rass bones to create the handles of bladed weapons.

**Rastur** The leader of the evacuation of Another Hopetown on the seismically volatile world of Ennth, he was a decorated soldier and dedicated husband, married to Shinnan, who died in the evacuation effort. Zekk helped Rastur and his people relocate to an orbital station.

**Rath** A small-time criminal during the early years of the New Republic hired by IT-3, an advanced interrogation droid, to steal Leia Organa Solo's datapad from her Coruscant apartment, shortly after her marriage to Han Solo. He was nearly thwarted by Chewbacca's son, Lumpawarrump, who was in the apartment at the time.

**Rathalay** Known for its expansive gray basalt beaches, the planet, surprisingly, was seldom crowded with tourists. Rathalay's vast oceans harbored large, dangerous predators, including schools of sharp-toothed narkaa. Its tiny sea motes were valued for the beautiful, jewel-like shells they left behind. Nine hundred meters below the water's surface lay the wreck of the starfreighter *Just Cause,* which crashed while carrying a cargo of precious metals. Twelve years after the Battle of Endor, Han Solo, Leia, and their children relaxed on a Rathalay beach as the crisis in the Koornacht Cluster began unfolding.

**Rathba, Tonkoss** A petty tyrant on Daluba whose rise to power was thwarted by Leia Organa Solo during the time of the New Republic.

**rath-scurrier** This small creature was the traditional prey of the Nediji.

**ratidillo** A large armored rodent, 30 to 60 centimeters long, with spines along its back and tusks coming out of its mouth. Found in the Coruscant undercity, it was also called the kragget rat.

**Rationalist Party** A political group that advocated free trade on Nam Chorios. Party members continually attacked the Theran gun emplacements that tracked the planet's skies. The party was led by Seti Ashgad and, secretly, Dzym.

**Ratobo, Admiral** A Bith officer in the Galactic Alliance Navy, he commanded the Fourth Fleet during the civil war with the Confederation. Aboard his flagship *Peacebringer,* Admiral Ratobo was routed by the Hutt warship fleet at Balmorra. Despite the obvious loss, Jacen Solo ordered Ratobo to continue his assault. Such stubborn persistence resulted in the deaths of many Alliance personnel, causing Ratobo to distrust Jacen's command abilities. The *Peacebringer* suffered heavy damage in the assault, and was destroyed. Ratobo and all hands were lost.

**Ra'tre** A Verpine who worked for the Directors to transport black membrosia to the Galactic Alliance during the Swarm War.

**Rattagagech** Chairman of the New Republic's Senate Science Council and a Senator from Elom, he voted to remove Chief of State Leia Organa Solo from office.

**Rattatak** A small, red world in the far Outer Rim, it remained undiscovered by the Republic, and its native species evolved without the guidance or influence of other galactic forces. Although the humanoids remained primitive, they quickly learned how to kill one another. Scattered resources on the planet led to struggles for survival, and the Rattataki never bothered with the benefits of barter and trade among themselves. As technology evolved, war became the norm. Over generations of fighting, most of the cities on the planet were reduced to rubble and huge portions of the planet's population became victims of mass genocide. The Rattataki never developed weapons of planetary scale, so the bloody world wars raged on for generations. The ceaseless violence prevented the world from developing space travel, and the Rattataki believed they were alone in the galaxy—they had no concept of galactic community, and only conquering their neighbors seemed important.

Those who discovered Rattatak were unscrupulous slavers common in the Outer Rim. The wiry Rattataki themselves proved to be an unpopular export—they were simply too difficult to train and too violent to contain. But credits could be made by exporting slaves for war barons, who paid handsomely for any exotic edge in combat. Mercenary duty was a popular reason to come to Rattatak, though negotiating an end of service often was difficult.

While war continued everywhere else, an enterprising Rattataki from a rare neutral province hatched a lucrative idea. If prospective mercenaries and slave soldiers had to prove themselves in gladiatorial combat, the credits generated from the wagering and the spectacle could be used to buy more soldiers and offworld weapons. Thus the gladiator pits of Rattatak came to be. The largest, known as the Cauldron, hosted the best combatants, and war barons and generals would attend to seek out the soldiers who would win them their wars. Slavers filled the pits with violent candidates—some would purposely price the more successful warriors out of the purchase range of the Rattataki generals, as their gladiators were more profitable from fighting multiple battles than being sold into military service. But it was a rare gladiator indeed who could survive multiple fights.

Shortly after the outbreak of the Clone Wars, Count Dooku ventured to Rattatak to find a worthy warrior to draft into the service of the Confederacy of Independent Systems. Recognizing this as an opportunity to leave Rattatak and possibly exact vengeance on the Jedi Knights, the powerful Asajj Ventress entered the fray and emerged victorious.

Later during the wars, ARC trooper Alpha and Obi-Wan Kenobi were captured on Jabiim and brought to Rattatak, where they were subjected to torture at the hands of Ventress. During Obi-Wan and Alpha's escape, they freed many of those who were held captive by Ventress.

**ratter thist** A small, agile creature with tan fur marked by varying stripes, it had sharp, retractable claws. Also called Kordulian krisses, they were often used to guard livestock in mountain valleys.

**Ratts Tyerell Foundation** A nonprofit organization devoted to outlawing Podracing, it was founded by Deland "Pabs" Tyerell who witnessed the death of his father, Ratts Tyerell, during the Boonta Eve Podrace.

**Ratty** *See* Meekerdin-maa.

**Rav** A retired pirate who ran a bounty hunters' clearinghouse on Socorro during the time of Emperor Fel. Based out of his grounded starship, *Crimson Axe,* Rav provided a wide array of services for bounty hunters—from engine parts to spice—which kept many, like Cade Skywalker, in debt to him despite the paltry bounties to be had. A Feeorin, Rav lost his leg in combat and had it replaced with a crude prosthesis fitted with weaponry.

**RAV** A military acronym for "repulsorlift assault vehicle."

**Ravaath** A planet conquered by the Epicanthix.

***Ravager* (1)** The flagship of the Sith fleet amassed by Darth Nihilus after the Jedi Civil War. The vessel was heavily damaged, having been one of the few ships to survive the Battle of Malachor. Darth Nihilus's dark will held the vessel and its crew together, and he took the ship to Telos to destroy the planet. It was intercepted by the Jedi Exile. In the fighting that followed, Nihilus was destroyed, and the *Ravager* was rigged to explode.

***Ravager* (2)** An Imperial *Lancer*-class frigate, it was destroyed during an engagement with Rogue Squadron when it came to the defense of the Imperial installation at Vladet.

***Ravagor*** An Imperial Star Destroyer, Ranulf Trommer served aboard it during the attack on Aguarl III shortly after the Battle of Yavin.

**ravenscreecher** A large, one-eyed bird species from the planet Wxtm. Dangerous predators, they had six legs ending in half-meter claws.

**raventhorn** A sharp, spiny vine, it was found in the rain forests of Yavin 4.

**Ravik, Grand Moff** An ambitious Imperial official, he longed for increased power and status. Ravik

*Rav*

ruled the Tolonda sector with an iron fist until a Rebel strike team hijacked his shuttle as he made his way to an Imperial conference. As a Rebel prisoner, Ravik was placed aboard the prison ship *Celestial* for transfer to a Rebel safeworld. A hyperspace mishap deposited the *Celestial* in the pocket dimension of Otherspace, where Ravik hoped to work with the spider-like Charon in conquering the realspace galaxy to resemble the Empire with him at its head.

Charon bioscientists linked their main computer with Ravik's mind to cull hyperdrive information from the Imperial. Instead, Ravik used his superior mental abilities to take over the Charon computer, and eventually the body of Ber'asco, the Charon leader. Ravik had the bioscientists reconstruct his body into a hybrid human–Charon monstrosity. While Ravik usurped Ber'asco's position, the Charon plotted revenge, sabotaging the Charon ship's drives as it attempted to enter the galaxy. It crashed on the Rebel safeworld of Stronghold, destroying the ship and unleashing the deadly Charon on the planet. Ravik later stowed away aboard the Rebel ship *Long Shot,* trying to steal the hyperspace-capable vessel. He was killed by a team of Rebel agents assigned to the ship. Ravik died quite mad, alternating between megalomania and paranoia.

**Ravine Squadron** A starfighter group that protected the planet of Levian Two during the early New Republic.

**Rawd, Mij** The vice president of marketing for the Ardees Beverage Company. Prior to the Clone Wars, he signed grav-ball player Deme Tryshyn as a spokesbeing for Ardees's products.

**Rawk Special** Cade Skywalker's favorite firearm, a custom-built double-barreled blaster by "Bantha" Rawk, a chief mechanic of the Selonian shipyards.

**rawmat** Corporate and military administrative shorthand for "raw materials."

**Rawst** One of Ranulf Trommer's wingmates on the *Ravagor,* he was killed in action over Aguarl 3.

**rawwks** Flying bat-like scavengers, they lived in many of the floating structures of Bespin and Tibannopolis. They served as an early warning system for the beldons that they roosted upon, scattering when they detected a predator.

**Raxus Prime** One of the most toxic planets in the galaxy, its surface was covered with rubble, trash, junk, and garbage, piled in huge twisted heaps and rows like grotesque mountain ranges. Numerous corporate interests turned Raxus Prime into a dumping world. But one being's refuse was another's treasure: Salvage operations dug through the planetwide junkyard, looking to reclaim and recondition reusable or obsolete machinery.

Raxus Prime

The gutted and rotting hulls of ancient capital starships poked through the garbage, giving the landscape the eerie feel of an industrial graveyard. Huge pools of toxic sludge made the ruined ecosystem one of the most dangerous in the galaxy. The planet's atmosphere was hot and caustic; the miasma of foul-smelling fog limited visibility. Beneath the layers of detritus, there existed evidence of a misguided attempt to colonize Raxus Prime: The innards of an extensive sewer system were the relic of an unknown species that attempted to drain and channel the pools of industrial waste.

Santhe/Sienar Technologies, a leading starship manufacturer, maintained a number of refinery and reclamation plants on Raxus Prime. Various scavenger species frequented the world, with several transplanted Jawa clans calling the foreboding landscape home. The Meeknu clan of Jawas ran an extensive salvage operation on Raxus Prime in the last decade of the Old Republic.

Raxus Prime

A few years after he left the Jedi Order, Count Dooku suddenly appeared on this remote Outer Rim world, using a commandeered communications station to transmit his first fiery words of Separatist rhetoric. That transmission was well documented, and became the start of the Separatist movement that split the Republic.

Raxus Prime was the site of a secret Confederacy base at the dawn of the Clone Wars. Separatist interests combed through the refuse to find hidden weaponry for use against the Republic, such as the ancient Force Harvester. After a stunning upset by the new Republic clone army at Geonosis, Count Dooku retreated to Raxus Prime to continue the next phase of the Clone Wars, which resulted in a major battle on the wasteland world.

After the Battle of Geonosis, 10-year-old Boba Fett fled to Raxus Prime, where Dooku targeted him for death—Fett was one of the few who knew that Dooku and Darth Tyranus were one and the same. Boba escaped when the Jedi attacked Raxus Prime, and he was rescued by clone troopers and the Jedi Knight Glynn-Beti.

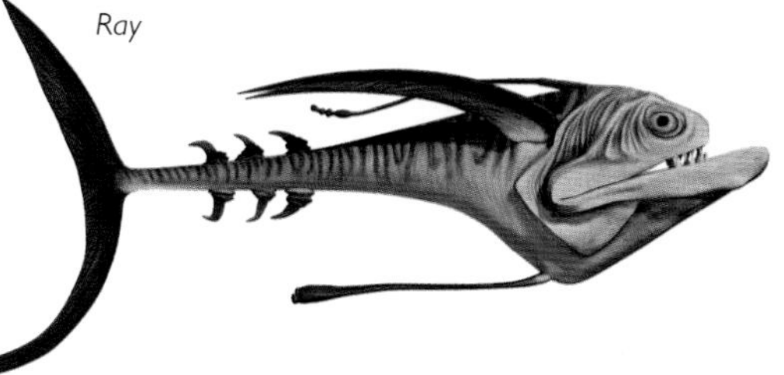
Ray

After the Clone Wars, the Galactic Empire claimed Raxus Prime. The Jedi fugitive Kazdan Paratus fled there to avoid Imperial pursuit. Amid the ruins, Kazdan steadily grew mad, building a junk reconstruction of the Jedi Temple complete with garbage effigies of Jedi Council, and using the Force to animate junk golems and other strange creatures made of refuse. Darth Vader's secret apprentice, Starkiller, faced Kazdan on Raxus Prime and defeated him. After the death of Paratus, the Empire established a massive shipyard above the planet. The Imperials sifted through the planet's refuse, melting it down and shooting it into space via a giant ore cannon. The ore was then used to construct the Empire's terrifying Star Destroyers. The Imperials also wiped out the local Rodian mercenaries and Jawa clans, both of which competed with the Empire for the planet's most valuable materials.

**ray** A swift, fairly large fish native to Naboo, and especially prominent around the Gungan city of Otoh Gunga. Though found in the Abyss, rays favored open waters and surface oceans. They were considered sport fish by Gungans. They had a crescent-shaped caudal fin for fast swimming and spectacular leaping.

**R'aya, Noor** An elderly Jedi Master who chose to live out his remaining days in seclusion and meditation on his home planet of Sorl. He built a simple home in the foothills of the great mountain range of Cragh. There, Noor passed the time crafting small landscapes out of stones, sticks, and vegetation, and made toys for the local children. He was captured by Jenna Zan Arbor for use in her terrible Force experiments. The Jedi were able to track him down to Belasco, where they rescued him.

**Raymeuz, Commander** An alias once used by Booster Terrik during the race to get the Caamas Document. As part of the charade, Terrik's Star Destroyer was altered to appear as the *Tyrannic.*

**Raynar** *See* Thul, Raynar.

**Raynor, Baron Dominic** A draconian Baron Administrator of Cloud City, he lost ownership of the city to Lando Calrissian in a game of sabacc. Secretly backing Lando in the game was the city's computer liason officer, Lobot, who wanted to rid Cloud City of Raynor. The vengeful Raynor attempted to assassinate Calrissian several times after that incident. He was married to a voluptuous blond woman named Ymile.

**ray shielding** A force field designed to block and absorb energy fire, it was an essential part of the defensive system of every starfighter and capital ship.

**Raystel, Halcor** The dean of the University of Alderaan, he was censured due to several improprieties just prior to the Clone Wars.

**Rayter sector** A galactic sector that contained the planet Karra, which was located in Rayter's largely unexplored Rimward section.

**Raze** A criminal information broker active during the Galactic Civil War, Raze had an unusual alien appearance due to his pale skin, tusks, long limbs, and bizarre multisegmented cybernetic body. He had an exceptionally quick mind, being able to sort through data at prodigious speeds. This served him well as the leader of a criminal enterprise based on collecting and selling information.

**Razelfiin** The leader of the Tynnan people just prior to the outbreak of the Clone Wars. Razelfiin was critical of the Jedi failure to provide security to Tynna after a stone mite infestation led to the collapse of the Central Government Building. Razelfiin eventually pushed Tynna into the camp of Count Dooku and the Separatists.

*Razorbugs*

**razorbug** A Yuuzhan Vong bioengineered creature that served as a thrown weapon. It resembled a fist-sized, disk-shaped insect with extremely sharp edges. It had wings, legs, and arms and would fly back to the Yuuzhan Vong warrior who threw it.

**Razor Coast** A locale on the rain-soaked world of Jabiim that served as a staging ground for Alto Stratus and his troops during the Clone Wars.

**Razor Eater** A model of assassin droid that Jango Fett once tangled with on Balmorra.

**razor fern** A sharp-fronded plant native to Dorvalla.

**razor grass** A sharp-bladed grass found on Corellia and elsewhere.

**razor moss** A plant that grew on arid Tatooine, it chewed into shadowed rock and used corrosive root tendrils to break down crystals and chemically extract water molecules. Sandjiggers and cliffborer worms fed on razor moss.

***Razor's Kiss*** A Super Star Destroyer that Warlord Zsinj attempted to steal from Kuat Drive Yards. Wraith Squadron severely damaged the ship, but Zsinj stole what he could and later salvaged and rebuilt the ship as the *Second Death.*

**Ra-Zyrth** A Massassi commander in Naga Sadow's Sith invasion force 5,000 years before the Battle of Yavin. Sadow used dark side alchemy to transform Ra-Zyrth into a muscular monstrosity.

**RC-** The prefix of most Republic commando designation numbers. Commandos most often adopted nicknames for ease of use and clarity during operations.

- **RC-1013:** *See* Sarge.
- **RC-1080:** A pilot who died after the mission to Aviles Prime.
- **RC-1133:** *See* Taler.
- **RC-1134:** *See* Vin.
- **RC-1135:** *See* Jay.
- **RC-1136:** *See* Darman.
- **RC-1138:** *See* Delta 38 "Boss."
- **RC-1140:** *See* Delta 40 "Fixer."
- **RC-1207:** *See* Delta 07 "Sev."
- **RC-1262:** *See* Delta 62 "Scorch."
- **RC-1304:** Killed at the Battle of Geonosis.
- **RC-1309:** *See* Niner.
- **RC-2088:** *See* Zag.
- **RC-3222:** *See* Atin.
- **RC-5093:** A commando who survived the war long enough to retire.
- **RC-8015:** *See* Fi.
- **RC-8028:** Killed on Kamino during training exercises.

**R'Dawc, Peawp** A Zabrak criminal who worked for the mayor of Mos Eisley under the guise of being a contract worker "helping out the city," she operated the R'Dawc Bodyguard Agency.

**R-Duba** A world of vast deserts and oceans. During the early days of the Empire, it was governed by Prince Jagoda. The Dorande, a neighboring alien species, longed to conquer R-Duba. They conspired with several key members of the royal court, but the actions of droid C-3PO alerted Jagoda to the treachery.

**reactivate switch** A droid's master circuit breaker, it was used to turn the automaton on and off.

**Reactor Core** A very strong alcoholic beverage made from spice liquor and blue tonic.

**reading the g's** The act of flying a starship by feel rather than instrumentation, usually requiring the dialing down of an acceleration compensator.

**realspace** Normal space, it was the dimension in which galactic residents lived. Travel within realspace was slow compared with traveling through the shadow dimension called hyperspace. It had both distance and volume.

***Reaper*** A Super Star Destroyer that was the flagship of Grand Moff Ardus Kaine's mini empire, the Pentastar Alignment. It later served as Admiral Pellaeon's flagship until it was lost after the New Republic pressed its advantage and entered Moff Getelles's Antemeridian sector.

**rearing spider** Massive but slow moving, this creature from the Forest Moon of Endor had six legs and large tusks. Rearing spiders lived in the bottom of the caves of the Gorax.

***Reasonable Doubt*** Once known as the *Asymptotic Approach to Divinity* and *Stardust,* this Verpine star liner was renamed *Reasonable Doubt* and used by Whie, Scout, Maks Leem, and Jai Maruk to travel to Vjun during the Clone Wars.

**Reassignment Council** A Jedi group housed in one of the towers of the Jedi Temple, it organized work for apprentices who were not chosen by a Jedi Knight or Master to be a Padawan.

**Reath, Naat** The sister of Stam Reath, she was taken as a Padawan by Echuu Shen-Jon after Stam's death. During the Clone Wars, she was eager to prove herself as a Jedi, but also harbored feelings of vengeance, wanting to make Sev'Rance Tann pay for the murder of her brother. Together with Echuu, she waged several successful campaigns against the Separatists, but she was captured by Sev'Rance on Krant. Echuu rescued her, killing Sev'Rance out of anger. Realizing his transgression against the Jedi Code, Echuu withdrew from the Order to seek solace. Naat Reath returned to Coruscant and informed the Jedi Council that Echuu had perished in the fighting although she knew the truth: that her Master had gone into seclusion.

**Reath, Stam** The Padawan learner of Echuu Shen-Jon, he was slain by Sev'Rance Tann when he impetuously attempted to pursue Count Dooku during the Battle of Geonosis. He was survived by his sister Naat Reath, who became Shen-Jon's next apprentice.

***Reaver*** A Yuuzhan Vong frigate analog that was the first of its kind to land on Coruscant when the aliens conquered the capital world.

Rebel Alliance insignia

**Rebaxan Columni** A short-lived Chadra-Fan company known for the manufacture of the MSE-6 "mouse" droid.

**Rebel Alliance** The term commonly used for the Alliance to Restore the Republic, it opposed the tyranny of the Empire and its New Order and eventually became the New Republic. The Alliance included single individuals, planets, and entire star systems, all united in their desire to overturn the oppressive Empire and bring justice and freedom back to the galaxy. The word *Rebel* itself was used mainly by the Empire at the time, although it later became common usage.

**Rebel Blockade Runner** *See* Corellian corvette.

***Rebel Dream*** Princess Leia Organa Solo's flagship, it was formerly the Star Destroyer *Tyrant,* which had been captured from the Imperial Navy after the Bacta War. It later protected Mon Calamari in the final stages of the Yuuzhan Vong War.

**Rebellion** Another name—used especially by Imperials—for the war to topple the Empire that was carried on by the Alliance to Restore the Republic.

***Rebel One*** A modified *Providence*-class destroyer, it was one of the primary Rebel Alliance flagships early in the Galactic Civil War. It sustained heavy damage in an Imperial attack.

**Rebels** The term the Empire used to refer to all those who supported the Alliance to Restore the Republic. It later became accepted usage.

***Rebel Star*** A New Republic escort frigate, it was one of the ships that took part in the rescue of the downed *Liberator* and its crew.

***Rebirth*** The planetoid-sized worldcraft used by Lord Hethrir, it was given to him by Emperor Palpatine.

**Rebirth Architecture** A form of architecture found on Coruscant during the Reconstruction following the defeat of the Yuuzhan Vong.

**Rebo, Max** The stage name of Siiruulian Phantele, a squat Ortolan with floppy ears, a snout, and bright blue velvety fur. He was the leader of a band that ranged from a basic trio to a 12-member ensemble, including dancers. Natives of the planet Orto had a highly developed sense of hearing and loved music—as well as food. Besides leading the band, Max Rebo played keyboards on his Red Ball Jett organ.

The trio, comprising Rebo, Droopy McCool, and Sy Snootles, had originally been in a band named Evar Orbus and His Galactic Wailers but were stranded on Tatooine after Orbus was killed by a stray blaster shot. They eventually hooked up with an agent for crime lord Jabba the Hutt, and with a promise of all-important food—and lots of it—Rebo signed a lifetime contract. The band was on a lower level of Jabba's sail barge when it was blown up by the escaping Jedi Luke Skywalker and his friends. Max and the band jumped overboard just in time. While McCool departed for other pursuits, Snootles and Rebo went to work for another criminal, Lady Valarian, for a while. When they left, Rebo joined the Rebellion, claiming that it offered the best food. After the war, Max opened up an extremely successful restaurant that grew to become a chain. He eventually retired on Coruscant, a wealthy being.

Max Rebo tickles the keyboard.

**Reboam** A harsh, sparsely populated world in the Hapes Cluster.

**Reborn, the** The Dark Jedi trained by Desann during the early years of the New Republic. Desann allied himself with Admiral Galak Fyyar, hoping to use Fyyar's unusual technology to twist beings to the dark side of the Force. However, with Desann's death at the hands of Kyle Katarn, the Reborn were left leaderless and without direction. The surviving members—those who chose not to fight back—were rounded up and held for questioning about Desann's activities.

**Rebus, Moff** A weapons specialist who designed the protoype weapons for the Empire's dark trooper project. Moff Rebus had a hidden stronghold located under the sewage system of Anoat City. He was captured by Rebel Alliance agent Kyle Katarn following the Battle of Yavin.

***Recalcitrant*** A Centrality cruiser involved in the siege at ThonBoka. When the siege was

Rebel Alliance members gather for a military briefing.

interrupted by the mysterious mechanical aliens known as the Rest, the *Recalcitrant* opened fire on the massive objects. The *Recalcitrant* was immediately destroyed by the alien craft.

**recham forteps** A Yuuzhan Vong bioengineered organism found within maw luur, it was developed to assist in the decaying of organic matter while capturing methane for later use.

**reciprocating quad blaster (Cip-Quad)** An experimental weapon field-tested during the Clone Wars. It was mounted on an articulated and powered harness, fitted with microrepulsorlift buoyancy cells that helped reduce the overall weight of the heavy cannon. The four twin-barreled cannons drew power from a heavy-duty backpack-mounted power cell. The sleeved barrels vented excess heat with each recoil, drawing coolant from a built-in tank with each barrel's return. The double barrels fired one at a time, or two at a time, following a rotation pattern selected by the gunner. Clone troopers assigned as heavy Cip-Quad

Reciprocating quad blaster (Cip-Quad)

gunners often wore specialist armor, with targeting feeds that connected the helmet HUDs and the articulated harness, giving the trooper exceptional control of the heavy cannon.

***Reckless Abandon*** A Gallofree Yards medium transport that was part of the small New Republic fleet assembled at Borleias after the Yuuzhan Vong conquest of Coruscant. *Reckless Abandon* arrived from Taanab laden with foodstuffs and other supplies for the base on Borleias.

***Reckoning*** This Imperial II Star Destroyer served as Prince-Admiral Krennel's flagship, given to him by Ysanne Isard during her hunt for Sate Pestage. He used it to bombard the planet Axxila. The *Reckoning* was destroyed by Admiral Ackbar's fleet at Ciutric, and Krennel died in the explosion. The *Emperor's Wisdom, Decisive,* and *Binder* were also lost to the New Republic's forces.

**reclumi spider** A large, nonpoisonous spider found on Null. Its sticky web was so strong that it could stop a moving vehicle.

**Reconstruction** The years that followed the Galactic Alliance's victory over the Yuuzhan Vong, marked by the relocation and rebuilding of civilizations. The Galactic Alliance established the Reconstruction Authority to monitor this process.

Red Ball Jett organ

**Recopia** A sparsely settled Core World lacking valuable natural resources with little to offer except anonymity. The planet's sulfuric oceans were broken up by plateau islands that rose high into the sky. It was located near Corellia between the Hydian Way and the Corellian Run.

**recording rod** A long, clear, cylindrical tube, it recorded and played back audio and two-dimensional visual images on the recording rod's surface. Activation switches were found at each end of a rod.

***Record Time*** A New Republic armed troop transport during the Yuuzhan Vong invasion. *Record Time* was 170 meters long with two bulbous main portions—the larger stern housing the bridge and personnel bays, and the smaller stern the engines—connected by a narrow access tube. Its owner, a private trader named Captain Birt, volunteered its use to General Wedge Antilles during the fall of Coruscant.

While carrying a contingent of Lando Calrissian's YVH droids, the *Record Time* set down roughly on Borleias after its bow was damaged by plasma cannons. It was later repaired and piloted by Lando to bring Luke Skywalker's strike team to Coruscant, and sacrificed in orbit to cover the team's insertion.

**rectenna** A scanning and tracking array, it featured active/passive scanners, a powerful jamming system, ship-to-ship transmitters, and a short-range target-acquisition program.

***Recusant*-class light destroyer** *See* Commerce Guild support ship.

**Red** *See* R5-D4.

**Redath-Gom, Que-Mars** A noted Weequay Jedi Knight, he was killed at the Battle of Geonosis.

Rectenna

**Red Ball Jett organ** A type of nalargon used by Max Rebo, it was a large musical instrument that put the entire body of the entertainer to the test. Adeptly juggling the wraparound keyboard of the nalargon was a true test of the expert entertainer's skills. This instrument produced an assortment of sounds and always drew a crowd eager to see a good show.

**Red Bush Grove** An Ewok village destroyed by a forest fire on the Forest Moon of Endor. The only survivors were Leektar and Keoulkeech.

**red-dish** A spore-producing fungus from Drongar.

**Redcap** A barren and rainy world, it consisted largely of shifting mud plains crossed by jagged canyons and mountain ranges. Since ships could sink easily in Redcap's thick mud, landings were restricted to the stable Tyma Canyon, which ran for several hundred kilometers across the planet's surface. Redcap's human inhabitants were poverty-stricken descendants of early mining colonists and lived in settlements built at the bases of the mountain chains. Residents traveled on olai, horned beasts of burden originally brought from a nearby moon for use in the mining industry. Points of interest included Juteau Settlement, which was built near the Garish Ridge and contained the Laughing Bantha cantina.

**redcrested cougar** An agile predatory feline 4 meters long and native to the planet Belkadan, it had large clawed paws and a tail ending with a lump of bone that could be swung like a cudgel.

**Reddjak** A notorious pirate who operated during the early days of the Empire. He was captured by authorities on the planet Majoor, but was freed by a young boy named Llez who idolized pirates like those on the hologram serial *Space Pirates of the Galaxy.*

**Red Eight** The comm unit designation for Bren Quersey's starfighter during the Battle of Yavin.

***Redemption* scenario** Also known as the Requiem scenario by X-wing pilots during simulator training exercises, it was basically a no-win situation. The *Redemption* was a hospital ship, and the simulated mission was to guard the Medevac shuttles and ships as they off-loaded wounded. Just to keep it interesting, a huge number of TIE bombers and fighters were on the attack, trying their best to "kill" the trainee.

**Redesign** A program implemented by Imperial COMPNOR representatives, it was designed to culturally edify the galaxy's citizens so that they would function more efficiently within the Empire.

**Red Five (1)** The comm unit designation for Anakin Skywalker's Jedi starfighter during the Battle of Coruscant.

**Red Five (2)** The comm unit designation for Luke Skywalker's X-wing fighter during the Battle of Yavin.

**Red Flame** A military symbol, it represented an ideal state of perfection among the Chiss, being the essence of courage, cunning, and discipline.

**Red Four** The comm unit designation for Rebel pilot John D. Brannon's X-wing fighter during the Battle of Yavin. Other pilots who used it included Jojo during the blockade of Doornik-319, Cesi "Doc" Eirress prior to the Battle of Yavin, and Derek "Hobbie" Klivian during the Battle of Endor.

***Red Gauntlet*** An *Imperial*-class Star Destroyer that served under Warlord Zsinj. The *Red Hand* was disabled after tangling with the New Republic warships *Skyhook* and *Crynyd.* New Republic forces boarded it and took command.

**Redge, Loam** Chief Inquisitor during the early years of the Galactic Empire, he was charged with extracting information from anyone who dared cross the Emperor. Redge was particularly interested in tracking and capturing Force-sensitives. He operated from Palpatine's personal retreat on Naboo. He was human, of indeterminate age, and Force-sensitive.

**Red Ghost** *See* Asha.

**red glie** A reddish, single-celled alga that grew in large mats on the surface of Naboo swamps. It didn't grow as quickly as green glie, and it had difficulty surviving in shaded areas. Red glie was harvested by Gungans and the Naboo as a food source and for use in water purification. Gungans also used red glie in the construction of their bubble buildings.

**Red Guard** Prior to its transformation into the Imperial Royal Guard with the rise of the Emperor, this mysterious order of elite protectors was known simply as the Red Guard. They protected Chancellor Palpatine during the Separatist crisis. (*See also* Emperor's Royal Guard.)

**Redhand, Craxtet** The second in command of the pirate group known as Riders of the Maelstrom. Redhand took his name from the Mandalorian crushgaunt he wore, which added to his brawling strength. Redhand was part of the boarding party that attacked the luxury liner *Kuari Princess* as part of the Riders' plan to destroy Rodin Higron's Oasis Mining Colony.

**Red Hand Squadron** The Rebel Alliance assault team led by Bria Tharen prior to the Battle of Yavin, it focused much of its energies on freeing and rescuing slaves. During the attack on the slaver ship *Helot's Shackle,* the force consisted of six Y-wings and the *Retribution* Marauder corvette, containing six assault shuttles with 10 troops each. The ships were adorned with the symbol of a blood-dripping hand painted on their bows.

Bria Tharen and her Red Hand Squadron were the Rebels who received the Death Star schematics when they were transmitted to Toprawa, and then beamed those plans to Princess Leia Organa aboard the *Tantive IV.*

***Red Harvest*** A *Victory*-class Star Destroyer that was part of Admiral Pellaeon's fleet gathered at Garqi to assist the New Republic's fight against the Yuuzhan Vong.

**Redhaven** The capital city of Rhommamool. Much of it was laid to waste when the native Rhommamoolians declared their independence from Osarian rule.

***Red Heart*** A Duros-commanded warship destroyed during the Yuuzhan Vong War, part of the ill-fated task force led by Yurf Col.

**Red Hills Clan** One of the clans of witches on the planet Dathomir.

**Red Iaro** A terrorist group that waged a long and bloody war against the planet Lannik, homeworld of the Jedi Master Even Piell. Red Iaro had many allies among rogue planets, pirate factions, and criminal organizations such as the Fluggrian syndicate run by Kam Nale. Shortly after the Battle of Naboo, the leaders of Red Iaro met with Lannik's leaders on Malastare to forge a peace agreement. The proceedings were monitored by several members of the Jedi Council, including Piell and Adi Gallia, whose parents had nearly been killed by a Red Iaro suicide squad years before.

**Red Knights of Life** Fanatic Rhommamoolians loyal to Nom Anor who abhorred all forms of technology. They did not realize they were being manipulated by a member of the Yuuzhan Vong.

**Red Leader (1)** The comm unit designation for veteran pilot Garven Dreis, who was in charge of Red Squadron during the Battle of Yavin. When Dreis was young, he had met Anakin Skywalker and was very impressed with his skills as a pilot. Dreis was killed during the Yavin battle.

**Red Leader (2)** The comm unit designation for Rebel pilot Wedge Antilles's X-wing during the Battle of Endor. He commanded the Red Wing attack element that took on the Imperial fleet and the second Death Star battle station.

**Red Leader (3)** Other noted Red Leaders included Tsui Choi during the defense of Kamino, Obi-Wan Kenobi during the Battle of Coruscant, Bakki Sourthol of Reekeene's Roughnecks, and Esege Tuketu as part of the New Republic's Fifth Battle Group.

**Red List** A list of outstanding debts greater than 2,000 credits. Skip tracers used the Red List to track down errant debtors.

***Redma*** A Galactic Alliance cruiser, part of the Fifth Fleet during the war with the Confederation, it was destroyed over Kashyyyk.

**Rednax** A spotted Dug who frequented Dex's Diner and associated with Slyther Bushforb and Manoca.

**Red Nebula** An uncharted cloud of comets, dust particles, and asteroids from long-exploded stars and planets, this navigational hazard lay beyond the borders of known space. At the heart of the Red Nebula was a sun with a single planet still intact. From this world evolved a species of humanoid aliens. Their legends said that a pair of Great Life Jewels spared the world from the cataclysm that destroyed all other stars.

**Red Nikto** Another term for the Kajain'sa'-Nikto race of the Nikto species.

**Red Nine** Lieutenant Naytaan's comm unit designation during the Battle of Yavin.

**Red One** *See* Red Leader.

***Redoubt*** A *Venator*-class Star Destroyer under the command of Denn Wessex during the Clone Wars, it served at the Battle of Boz Pity.

**Redoubt, the** An extremely difficult-to-navigate globular cluster of tightly packed stars barraged by intense radiation. The Chiss spent centuries studying it for use as a hiding place should they ever be forced from their territories.

***Redoubtable*** A Star Destroyer, it was captured by Yevethan strongman Nil Spaar in his raid on the Imperial shipyard at N'zoth. The *Redoubtable* was renamed *Destiny of Yevetha* and made a part of Spaar's Black Fifteen Fleet.

**Red Rancor** A cantina on Coruscant named for its tough reputation and deep-red

Red Squadron en route to the first Death Star

interior. Han Solo brought Luke Skywalker here for his bachelor party prior to Luke's wedding to Mara Jade. Not surprisingly, a brawl broke out.

**redrobes** *See* Red Guard.

**Red Seven (1)** The comm unit designation for Elyhek Rue during the Battle of Yavin.

**Red Seven (2)** Keir Santage used this call sign during the Battle of Endor.

**Red Shadow** A bistro on the planet Taboon, it was where Mageye the Hutt was accidentally killed by the bounty hunter Zardra.

**Red Six** The comm unit designation for Rebel pilot Jek Porkins's X-wing fighter during the Battle of Yavin. Porkins was killed in the battle.

**Red Squadron** A common starfighter squadron name, used in several instances throughout the Rebel Alliance. It was the X-wing fighter squadron that Luke Skywalker was assigned to in the Battle of Yavin. Red Squadron evolved into Rogue Squadron. During the Battle of Endor, Rogue Squadron went by the name Red Squadron to honor the original pilots at Yavin.

**Redstar** A Yaka smuggler captured by Jaina Solo and Lowbacca and tried by the Galactic Alliance for his part in various crimes. He wore the engraved skull of an Ithorian on his chest plate.

**Red Star Shipping Lanes** A major shipper that worked in the Core and Colonies during the time of the Galactic Alliance, and one of the original voting sponsors of the Corporate Sector Authority. Raal Yorta's father was a major executive in Red Star Shipping Lanes.

**Red Sword Flight** A squadron of StealthX fighters that accompanied Luke Skywalker on a mission to capture or eliminate Jacen Solo during the war between the Galactic Alliance and the Confederation. Red Sword Flight was made up of Master Skywalker, Kyp Durron, Corran Horn, Tyria Tainer, Twool, and Sanola Ti.

**Red Ten** The comm unit designation for Theron Nett during the Battle of Yavin.

**Red Terror** An elite guard of approximately 500 gladiator droids scattered throughout the droid-manufacturing facilities on the planet Telti. On their way to rescue Cole Fardreamer from the clutches of Dark Jedi Brakiss, C-3PO and R2-D2 faced down and narrowly escaped a group of about 50 of the droids.

**Red Three** The comm unit designation for Rebel pilot Biggs Darklighter's X-wing fighter during the Battle of Yavin. A childhood friend of Luke Skywalker, Biggs was killed while helping Luke in his run at the Death Star.

**Red Twelve** The comm unit designation of the wingmate to Red Leader (Garven Dreis) during the Battle of Yavin.

**Red Twins** A pair of dying red dwarf stars hidden in a dense nebula located in a remote corner of the galaxy. A small space station was built in orbit around the Red Twins by independent spacers during the last decades of the Galactic Republic. It became a haven for smugglers during the early months of the New Order.

**Red Two (1)** The comm unit designation of Aayla Secura during the defense of Kamino.

**Red Two (2)** The comm unit designation for Rebel pilot Wedge Antilles during the Battle of Yavin.

**Red Two (3)** The comm unit designation of Wes Janson during a mission to Adumar.

**Red Watch** The code name for the unit formed by clone commandos Fi and Sev during their mission to destroy a Separatist-funded terrorist ring on Coruscant during the Clone Wars.

**Red Wing (1)** One of the four main Rebel starfighter battle groups that participated in the Battle of Endor.

**Red Wing (2)** The comm unit designation for Red Leader's second in command.

**Red Zero** A code phrase used by military starships of the Galactic Republic to call for an immediate extraction or rescue operation.

**Reecee** A planet in the Inner Rim that served as a smugglers' haven during the New Republic. Riebold's Foam and Sizzle was located there. During the Yuuzhan Vong invasion, the New Republic established a rear base on Reecee under the command of Admiral Traest Kre'fey. Hidden in the nearby Black Bantha nebula, the Yuuzhan Vong planned to attack Reecee, hoping to use it as a staging base for an attack on Coruscant, but they were foiled when Jedi and New Republic forces wiped out their fleet.

**Reef Fortress** The Fountain Palace on the planet Hapes was home to the Hapan royal family. In emergencies, they went to the secure stronghold of Reef Fortress, which was on an isolated island accessible only by boat. It was here that Leia Organa Solo, Jacen and Jaina Solo, and Lowbacca braved carnivorous seaweed and Bartokk assassins to foil Ambassador Yfra's assassination plot.

**Reef Home** One of the majestic Mon Calamarian cities that floated on water, it was destroyed in Admiral Daala's attack on Mon Calamari.

***Reef Home*** A Mon Calamari MC80 cruiser named for the floating city on Mon Calamari, it served at the Battle of Endor and in cleanup operations afterward.

**Reeft** A Dressellian and Jedi hopeful who trained alongside Obi-Wan Kenobi at the Jedi Temple on Coruscant. When he was young, Reeft was constantly hungry. He was later chosen as the Padawan of Binn Ibes. Shortly before the Clone Wars erupted, Jedi Knight Reeft was sent to capture thief Rotar Lopani on Brentaal IV. The Xexto bounty hunter Tosinqas killed Lopani and, in a confused state, attacked Reeft, who slew him with his lightsaber. The bloodshed—deemed unnecessary by outsiders—caused some controversy within the Galactic Senate and the Bounty Hunters' Guild, which lodged a formal complaint against the Jedi.

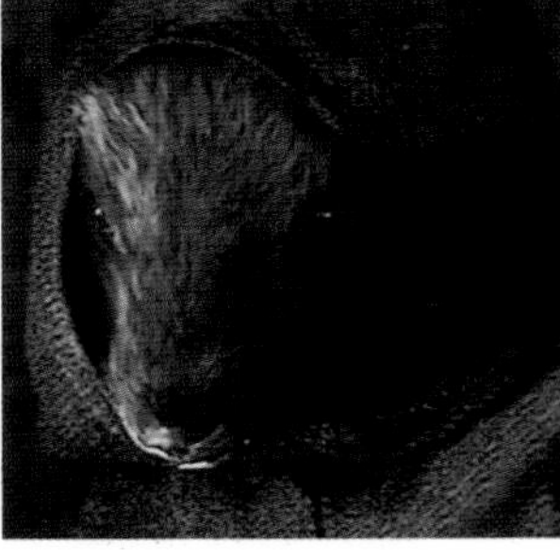

Reegesk

**Reegesk** A male Ranat thief and scavenger seen at the Mos Eisley cantina. Originally from Aralia, he regularly traded with the nomadic Jawas on Tatooine. Adept at pilfering items without alerting the owners, Reegesk was willing to steal anything, even trash. He inadvertently caused the death of the Jawa Het Nkik when he stole the power pack out of Nkik's blaster, which the Jawa tried to use on a group of stormtroopers in revenge for their slaying many of his clan members.

**reek** Burly-bodied, tough-skinned horned quadrupeds that were highly territorial herd animals. Originally from Ylesia, wild reeks roamed the plains in great herds while domesticated ones were bred for labor and as a source of food and materials. The Codian Moon maintained reek ranches. Scarcer resources instilled even greater territoriality among those reeks. When profits plummeted, unscrupulous ranchers discovered that the beasts could be starved into carnivorism to provide violent entertainment, and sold the animals into such cruel endeavors. As a combatant, the reek was formidable. Its strong jaws, used to chop tough wood-moss chunks into pieces, could rend flesh and snap bones easily. Its massive horns, used in displays of dominance in the wild, could gore opponents, and few could survive a trampling attack from a reek. A reek was one of three deadly creatures unleashed in the Geonosian execution arena prior to the Battle of Geonosis, dispatched to kill Anakin Skywalker, Padmé Amidala, and Obi-Wan Kenobi.

*A reek fends for itself in a Geonosis execution arena melee.*

**reekcat** An animal known for it ability to always land on its feet.

**Reekeene's Roughnecks** A Rebel irregular group active in the Fakir sector, it was founded by former mercenaries Lens and Mikka and based out of an antiquated Tsukkian water hauler named *Home.* Green Squad, a team of Rebel rookies, was one of several special operative groups within the Roughnecks.

**reel** A giant snake species found on Yavin 8.

**Reel, Dyemma** A female human patron at the Outlander gambling club just prior to the outbreak of the Clone Wars.

**Reen, Meeka** The leader of insurgent forces on Jerne, she did not ally her forces with the Rebel Alliance. When she briefly captured Luke Skywalker and Leia Organa, she planned to ransom them to the highest bidder.

**reengineered** A term used by Arkanians to describe those beings who failed to benefit from genetic manipulation.

**Reeos, Ngyn** The captain of the slave ship *Helot's Shackle,* he attempted to apprehend a young Han Solo when he escaped from Ylesia in the *Talisman,* but Solo got away with the help of Jalus Nebl.

**Reerookachuck** Raised apart from Wookiee traditions within the spice mines of Kessel, this Wookiee was a dishonorable, underhanded fighter.

**Rees, Bojam** A reptiloid tattooist at Starstation 12, he painted the tribal pattern of the Duhma on the face of a customer named Mixim. Unbeknownst to Rees, Mixim was actually the fugitive Abal Karda in disguise. Karda paid Rees with a strand of hair braided with Icarii jewels. Rees was questioned by Boba Fett, who was hunting Karda.

**Reesbon** One of the seven ruling clans of Ammuud, it was the chief contender with the Glayyd clan for control of the planetary government.

**Reeven Clan** A Rodian clan led by Jannik the White, whom the pirate Nym helped defend against the Cairn Clan. The Reeven Clan accompanied Nym's forces to Maramere, and Nym hid them below the *Sunrunner*'s deck in an attempt to ambush Sol Sixxa's forces.

**Ree-Yees** A three-eyed, goat-faced Gran from the planet Kinyen. He was banished from his homeworld after murdering another of his species. Ree-Yees became a petty thief addicted to heavy drinking and ended up in the court of Jabba the Hutt. No one liked him, especially given his propensity to start fights.

Ree-Yees tended to Bubo, a grotesque frog-dog, and was secretly using a transmitter hidden among Bubo's skin flaps. The Empire provided Ree-Yees with a detonator to kill Jabba, shipping the components in packages of Gran goatgrass. In return, Imperials promised to wipe out his murder record so that he could return home. The plot failed, but Jabba was soon dead anyway. Ree-Yees was aboard the crime lord's sail barge when it exploded.

*Ree-Yees*

**Reeza** A Mandalorian on Dantooine during the Great Sith War.

**Reezen, Corporal** An Imperial officer, he met Darth Vader when he was in his teens. Corporal Reezen was somewhat Force-sensitive and alerted the Warlord Zsinj of Han Solo's flight to the planet Dathomir.

**reflec** Sensor-proof material incorporated into military armor, such as that worn by the Imperial Storm Commandos.

**Reflection Gardens** A site on Coruscant where Luke Skywalker and Mara Jade were married before their public ceremony. Many of the Jedi from the praxeum attended this ceremony.

**Reflex Amendment** A constitutional amendment that gave Supreme Chancellor Palpatine unprecedented control in maneuvering military assets across areas of overlapping jurisdiction, cutting through bureaucracy and taking priority over local governments.

**refresher** Any personal hygiene facility or lavatory.

**Refuge City** A city established by Caamasi survivors amid the ruins of Caamas, it was one of the few habitable locations on the devastated world. The domed city was established by Elek D'Cel, who worked with ecologists to reclaim the territory for the 200 or so survivors who lived there.

**Refugee Facility 17** A refugee camp established by the Salliche Ag Corporation on Ruan during the Yuuzhan Vong War.

**Refugee Relief Movement** A philanthropic organization founded on Naboo. Ruwee Naberrie and Padmé Amidala worked for the Refugee Relief Movement in their younger years.

**Refugee Resettlement Coalition** A program of the Refugee Relief Movement that was organized to discuss possible options in relocating citizenry displaced by the Separatist crisis.

**regen-stim** A tissue-regeneration drug administered to reduce scarring from invasive procedures.

**Regga** An Ithorian Podracer killed during the preliminaries leading up to the Boonta Eve Podrace that saw the liberation of Anakin Skywalker. Anakin later bartered for parts of Regga's Podracer from Jawas who salvaged them near Mochot Steep.

**Reggs, Darnell** A Rebel Alliance Y-wing pilot, he served under Commander Krane during the Galactic Civil War.

***Regina Galas*** One of many aliases used for the *Millennium Falcon.*

**region** In stellar cartography, sectors were grouped together in areas called regions. The establishment of a region depended not only on galactic geography, but also on wealth, influence, historic "sentimentalities," economic diversity, and the level of direct control asserted by the central galactic government. During the time of the Empire, a region was ruled by a Regional Governor or by a Grand Moff.

**Regional Governor** *See* Grand Moff, Moff.

**Regional Sector Four's All-Human Free-For-All Extravaganza** A popular blood-sport event held in the Victory Coliseum on the planet Jubilar, it pitted four human combatants in brutal battle against one another inside a five-sided ring. A young Han Solo bested three much larger opponents when he was forced to participate in the event.

**Registered Bank of Ammuud** A prominent financial institution based on Ammuud, with much of its collateral stored on Aargau during the Clone Wars.

**Reglia, Miko** A Jedi Knight, Kyp Durron's first apprentice, and a member of the Dozen-and-Two Avengers. While on a patrolling mission, the Dozen-and-Two checked on an observation buoy they'd placed in the Veragi sector, and their findings led them to the Helska system. There they encountered Yuuzhan Vong coralskippers around Helska 4, and most of the squadron was killed in the ensuing battle. Reglia was taken to Helska 4 as a prisoner, where he was held in the same chamber as Danni Quee, a scientist from Belkadan. The Yuuzhan Vong subjected Reglia to the breaking, a tortuous procedure, weakening him. When Jacen Solo arrived to help the prisoners escape, Reglia was able to join the battle at the last moment, killing one of the Yuuzhan Vong warriors, but Reglia, too, died in the attack.

**Rego, Vance** A double agent who was supposedly a member of the Cilpari Resistance, he worked for the local Imperials and led Moff Fasel's stormtroopers.

**Regolith Prime** A planet in the Regolith system where Jiliac the Hutt maintained a listening post.

**Regrap, Mik** A Neimoidian aide to Senator Lott Dod.

**re-grav plate** A localized gravity-field generator used in warehouses and storage facilities to keep materials in place and to free up floor space by placing crates and bins against walls or ceilings.

**Regulgo** Han Solo was attacked on this planet by fanatical Kamarians, enraged by his suspension of the holographic feature *Varn, World of Water,* which had become the basis of a water-worshipping Kamarian cult. The attack was so unpleasant that it left Solo with a fear of insectoid species for decades.

**Reh'mwa** A fundamentalist Bothan who kept the ar'krai against the Yuuzhan Vong active even after the war with the alien invaders had ended. He later founded the True Victory Party to gain popular support for secession from the Galactic Alliance during the outbreak of violence between the Alliance and the Corellian Confederation.

**Reige, Vitor** A shuttle pilot aboard the Star Destroyer *Chimaera* during the Yuuzhan Vong War, he was loyal to Grand Admiral Gilad Pellaeon, watching over the wounded officer following the Battle of Bastion. Pellaeon grew to believe that Reige might be his illegitimate son, but never broached the subject. After the murder of Pellaeon by Tahiri Veila and an attempted coup by the Moff Council aboard the *Bloodfin,* Reige led the resistance movement against this treachery, rallying those Imperials still loyal to Pellaeon. He was rescued by Mandalorian forces hired by Admiral Daala.

**Rei'kas** A Rodian crime lord rival of Crev Bombaasa in the Kathol Outback. He followed Talon Karrde during the latter's search for Jorj Car'das on Exocron, hoping to eliminate a competitor. Car'das, with the help of the Aing-Tii monks, was able to wipe out Rei'kas's fleet, killing the Rodian and scattering his organization.

**Reis** A native of Kodai, he provided information to Qui-Gon Jinn and Obi-Wan Kenobi regarding a Sith Holocron said to be hidden deep beneath Kodai's ocean.

**Reist** A bizarre nightmare demon controlled by the Imperial agent Altin Wuho, it hated Wuho for his forced servitude. The small, skull-faced primate was unleashed on Luke Skywalker, nearly driving the young Rebel mad with nightmarish hallucinations until Luke was able to kill it.

**Reithcas sector** A sector containing the planet Bortras, birthplace of Jorus C'baoth.

**Reject Alley** A settlement on N'zoth built within a rocky crevasse, home of those outcast Yevetha who were cursed to live out their lives in shame.

***Rejuvenator*** An *Imperial II*–class Star Destroyer commanded by Warshack Rojo, it arrived at Destrillion and Dubrillion to help repel the Yuuzhan Vong invasion. When the battle moved to the Helska system, the *Rejuvenator* provided the bulk of the New Republic support. The Yuuzhan Vong coralskippers and grutchins were enough to eventually destroy the *Rejuvenator.*

***Rejuvenator*-class Star Destroyer** A new form of Star Destroyer produced by the New Republic during the Yuuzhan Vong War.

**Rek (1)** The Yam'rii bodyguard and majordomo who worked for Grappa the Hutt.

**Rek (2)** A gangster who worked for Great Bogga the Hutt some 4,000 years before the Battle of Yavin. He was involved in the conspiracy to kill Jedi Andur Sunrider at the Stenness hyperspace terminal and was, in turn, killed by Andur's wife, Nomi. Rek was a massive biped with green skin, beady eyes, and a square jaw.

**Rek (3)** A species distinguished by slender, whip-like bodies, they also had rope-thin hands and skin that felt like lukewarm rubber. While all Reks had startlingly bright eyes, only the females of the species had purple eyes. Reks often worked as bounty hunters, and several did such work for Nandreeson, the crime lord of Smuggler's Run. This Rek group captured Lando Calrissian on Skip 1 and brought him before Nandreeson for punishment.

**Rekab, Captain Teyora** An Ensos near-human trader who made a living selling seeds and hydroponics equipment. Used to subzero temperatures, she wore a full-body, air-conditioning coolth suit when traveling on desert worlds such as Tatooine.

**Rekara** Companion to Rebel Alliance dignitary Mors Odrion, this Mon Calamari female served within the Alliance diplomatic corps. She accompanied Odrion on a mission to Sedri, the water world, where Odrion was captured by Sedrian Renegades. Rekara escaped with a small chunk of the mysterious Force-sensitive coral known as Golden Sun. When the coral was removed from the planet, it fell into a death-like state, driving Rekara insane. Rekara eventually found a Rebel base and reported Odrion's capture. A team of Rebel special operatives was dispatched to Sedri, accompanied by the half-mad Rekara, to find Odrion.

**Rekker** A subspecies of Killik within the Colony. Their massive size made them invaluable as front-line infantry. Each Rekker had six strong limbs, a long abdomen, and large antennae.

**Rekkon** A respected scholar from the Corporate Sector, he taught at the university on the planet Kalla, and was an expert in organic–inorganic thought interfaces. He was a powerfully built human male, with black hair and a beard that was shot through with patches of gray and white. When Rekkon's political activist nephew Tchaka disappeared, Rekkon formed a covert group searching for missing persons and political prisoners within the Corporate Sector. Rekkon's work led him to an Authority Data Center on Orron III, and it was there that he learned of Stars' End, an Authority prison complex on the remote world of Mytus VII. Rekkon was killed by Torm Dadeffron, a member of his group who double-crossed him. Rekkon's work eventually was continued by Han Solo, who destroyed Stars' End and freed the prisoners, including Tchaka.

Rekkon

**reknew** A large, regal tree that grew in and around Theed on Naboo. Reknews had long life spans but grew very slowly.

**Relay starfighter** An Incom split-wing starfighter developed during the Clone Wars.

***Relentless*** An Imperial Star Destroyer, it was under the command of a number of Imperial officers. Following the Battle of Yavin, the *Relentless* was helmed by Captain Parlan. One of his major missions was to locate and capture the brilliant Old Republic naval officer Adar Tallon on Tatooine before he could be recruited by the Rebellion. Parlan failed and was summarily executed by Darth Vader. The ship was then turned over to Captain Westen, until he, too, disappointed Lord Vader. Under the command of Captain Dorja and the orders of Grand Admiral Thrawn, the *Relentless* failed to capture Han Solo and Luke Skywalker at New Cov five years after the Battle of Endor. It later became part of Moff Disra's fleet and served as one of the primary ships used by Admiral Pellaeon to patrol the Imperial Remnant.

**Relephon** An enormous gas giant within the Hapes Consortium with several settled moons.

**Relgim sector** An area of space that contained the regularly traveled Relgim Run trade route and bordered the Maelstrom nebula. It was represented by Governor Denn Wessex during the Galactic Empire era.

***Reliable*** A Centrality cruiser involved in the siege at ThonBoka. It was one in a series of blockading cruisers that Lando Calrissian visited on "errands of mercy" as he tried to run the blockade. Calrissian, aboard the *Millennium Falcon,* delivered luxury items to its weary crew, such as cigaras, chocolates, and ice cream not available through Ship's Exchange. He also "treated" the crew to games of sabacc.

***Reliance*** A Republic command ship 4,000 years before the Battle of Yavin, it was helmed by Captain Vanicus. It carried Jedi Ulic Qel-Droma on a mission to try to protect Koros Major from the Krath coup sweeping the Empress Teta system.

***Reliant*** A midsized freighter owned by Seti Ashgad, it was piloted by Liegeus Sarpaetius Vorn. He prepared the ship as an escape vessel for Ashgad and the droch Dzym, but it was destroyed after Luke Skywalker used the Force to communicate with the intelligent crystals on Nam Chorios, which in turn ordered the crystals aboard the *Reliant* to destroy it.

**relix** A endangered large fish found on Maramere, it resembled the opee sea killer of Naboo.

**Rell, Mother** The eldest leader of the Singing Mountain Clan of the Witches of Dathomir, she was nearly 300 years old around the end of the Galactic Civil War and knew Jedi Master Yoda.

**Rella** A member of Captain Arwen Cohl's Nebula Front team that infiltrated the Trade Federation freighter *Revenue.* She had a dark complexion, short brown hair, and an elegantly angular face. Like other members of Cohl's strike teams, she often wore a mimetic suit. Cohl and Rella decided to retire after the operation against the *Revenue,* but when Cohl took on a mission to assassinate Chancellor Finis Valorum, she tracked him to Karfeddion and signed up as well. During the mission on Eriadu, Cohl's team was betrayed by the Nebula Front leader, Havac. Havac killed Rella with a shot to the neck. Cohl survived his injuries and sought to avenge Rella's death.

Remote

**Rellias Channel** A body of water on Naboo that led to Otoh Gunga. The Trade Federation used it in its attack on the underwater city also called Rellias.

**Rellidir** The capital city of Tralus.

**Relsted, Minor** The personal assistant to Imperial Supervisor Gurdun, who skimmed funds to further develop the IG series of assassin droids.

**Reltooine** A planet in the Corporate Sector, it was one of the stops made by the luxury liner *Lady of Mindor* during its voyage from Roonadan to Ammuud.

***Reluctant*** A Centrality cruiser involved in the siege at ThonBoka. It was one of the first to spot the counterattack launched by the Oswaft.

**Remember Derra Squadron** A New Republic Y-wing squadron that served aboard the *Allegiance* during the defense of Adumar.

**Remlout** An X'Ting assassin, he was one of the few to leave Ord Cestus, traveling to the world of Xagobah to learn the martial art of Tal-Gun. During the Clone Wars, Remlout challenged newcomer Asajj Ventress, who had Confederacy business on the planet. The two squared off in one-on-one combat, and though Remlout lasted several minutes, Asajj soundly defeated him, splitting his shell in a swift attack. Remlout survived and recovered after weeks of treatment.

**remote** An owner-programmable automaton, it could perform its functions without supervision but hadn't any capability for independent initiative. Luke Skywalker used a remote—a floating sphere—aboard the *Millennium Falcon* to learn lightsaber skills.

**Remy, Sergeant** A clone trooper with red markings who served under Jedi Master Sev and his Padawan Joc Sah. He failed in his attempt to kill Joc Sah during Order 66 and was killed in turn by the leader of the Ragmar V outcasts.

**Ren, Kybo** A space pirate whose full name was Gir Kybo Ren-Cha, he operated during the early days of the Empire. A short, fat human, Kybo Ren sported a long, dangling mustache and a small goatee.

**Renaant** One of the binary stars, along with Centis Major, that formed the primary of the Tantara system.

**Renalem, Lili** A noted singer and entertainer during the last years of the Galactic Republic, she joined Jasod Revoc's Galactic Revue, and traveled across the galaxy to entertain the troops of the Grand Army of the Republic.

**Renan bloodwolf** An enormous meter-tall canine predator that lived in the mountains surrounding the vineyards of the planet Rena. The enamel coating

Kybo Ren

of older bloodwolf fangs was often laden with iron, coloring the fangs a deep rusty red, giving the creature its name.

**Renatasia system** With eight planets orbiting a yellow star, the Renatasia system was located far outside civilized space. It apparently was colonized by a long-forgotten mission millennia ago in pre-Republic days. Renatasia III and IV were pleasant green worlds. The Renatasians had colonized every planet in their system by the time they were discovered by a damaged trader ship.

The Empire decided to send representatives to probe the society's weaknesses, so Ottdefa Osuno Whett and the droid Vuffi Raa were sent as envoys to the nation-state of Mathilde on Renatasia IV's second-largest continent. After observing the locals for 700 days, they transmitted a full report, and the Imperial fleet arrived to collect slaves and taxes. The Renatasians resisted, and the fleet attempted to seize the system intact through the use of ground forces, taking heavy losses in a costly but inevitable Imperial victory. Over two-thirds of the population in the Renatasia system was killed in the pacification effort.

**Renatta needle ship** These were speedy racing ships with unstable Tobal lenses that focused their photon drive systems. Their manufacturer, Renatta Racing Systems, eventually went bankrupt, making any reamining ships rare and expensive.

**Renatyl** A potent drug, odorless and tasteless, it could incapacitate a subject in small doses.

**Rend V** A world struck by a planetwide famine over a dozen years prior to the Battle of Naboo. Jenna Zan Arbor developed a bioengineered food source that allowed the planet to recover.

**Rendar, Dash** The time this quintessential Corellian smuggler spent in the galactic spotlight was cut short by his sudden and shocking death—or so he had the holomedia believe.

Dash Rendar was known to underworld fringe types for years. He and Lando Calrissian first met at the sabacc tables on Kaal. He met Han Solo during a respite on Port Haven, a secret smugglers' port on an uncharted backwater world. The three exchanged stories of evading the Imperials, telling tall tales full of bravado and bluster. Calrissian and Solo eventually outgrew the smuggler life, going "respectable" and throwing in their lot with the Rebels. Rendar declined, preferring to focus his attention on the one thing that truly mattered: himself.

But for all his ego, Dash did have a streak

Dash Rendar

of nobility hidden beneath his chiseled good looks and muscular build. He fostered a personal grudge against the Empire. Rendar's childhood was a privileged one. His family owned RenTrans, a growing and successful shipping company in the Core Worlds. He was an ace student at the Imperial Academy at Carida. One dark day, though, this life of prosperity came literally crashing down in flames.

Rendar's brother, Stanton, was a pilot in the RenTrans fleet. Tragedy struck on what was to be a routine liftoff from Coruscant. A blown-out control system sent Stanton's freighter careening into a private museum owned by no less than Emperor Palpatine. Stanton was killed in the crash. Enraged at the loss of his priceless Jedi and Sith artifacts, Palpatine banished the Rendar family and transferred their holdings to the rival Xizor Transport Systems.

Dash picked up the pieces of his life in the fringe, becoming a capable smuggler. With an unlikely droid partner, LE-BO2D9, Dash flew his souped-up YT-2400 freighter, the *Outrider.* Though he tried to remain neutral in the Galactic Civil War, Rendar found himself taking on food-shipping duties for the struggling Rebel Alliance. Entrusted with the location of the Rebels' secret base, he even delivered supplies to Hoth, where he once again ran into Solo.

Rendar was stuck on Hoth when the Empire attacked. The pilot bravely took to an unmanned snowspeeder and participated in the delaying actions against the Imperial AT-AT walkers. Escaping the planet in one piece, Rendar rejoined the Rebels after Han Solo's capture. As a favor to Calrissian, Rendar helped the Rebels in

Dash Rendar

their search for Solo, pursuing IG-88 to Ord Mantell and Boba Fett to Gall.

Though Leia Organa was grateful to Rendar for his help, she nonetheless found the Corellian's smug attitude unbearable. She tasked him with protecting Luke Skywalker, whose life was threatened by agents of Black Sun. Together Dash and Luke helped Bothan spies secure the Death Star plans from the Imperial freighter *Suprosa.*

Rendar later helped Skywalker and Calrissian infiltrate Prince Xizor's palace on Coruscant. In the space battle that ensued over the Imperial capital, the *Outrider* appeared to sustain critical damage from exploding space debris. It was all a trick of perspective and timing, however. Rendar escaped, though he apparently decided that his life as a Rebel had come to an end.

Rendar surfaced a few years later, having met Guri, a reprogrammed human replicant droid who was once crime lord Prince Xizor's top aide, on a backrocket world known as Hurd's Moon. Working with Guri, he adapted the entechment variation developed by the Ssiruuk for use on humans, allowing the human mind to be stored in the computer center of an HRD. Using this method, Dash and Guri created a human replica droid version of Stanton Rendar that became the head of their company, Onadax Droid Technologies (ODT).

**Rendar, Stanton** Dash Rendar's brother, Stanton was a pilot in the RenTrans fleet who apparently died in a crash. He was resurrected as a human replica droid by Dash and Guri, becoming the head of ODT on Onadax.

**Rendili** This planet was the site of a space construction center for some of the largest warships and special weapons platforms produced during times of war. Rendili StarDrive produced such titans as the *Victory*-class Star Destroyer and the Dreadnaught heavy cruiser. With the outbreak of the Clone Wars, the Arch-Provost of Rendili ordered industrial spies and starship designers to reduce the competitive lead enjoyed by Kuat Drive Yards for the Galactic Republic's new contracts. Wooed by the promises of Count Dooku, the planet sided with the Confederacy of Independent Systems during the Clone Wars, but its protective Home Fleet remained loyal to the Republic. Given the powerful warships represented within the fleet, the Republic made it of paramount importance that Rendili remain within its fold, and tasked Jedi Masters Plo Koon and Saesee Tiin with settling the so-called Rendili Fleet crisis. Captain Jace Dallin of the Rendili fleet was prepared to settle peacefully, but a mutiny engineered by Mellor Yago sparked an all-out space battle for control of the fleet. With the intervention of Anakin Skywalker, Obi-Wan Kenobi, and Quinlan Vos, the Republic regained control of the situation, and the Rendili fleet surrendered. Such a narrow victory prompted Supreme Chancellor Palpatine to push for legislation to bring the various home fleets of Republic worlds more firmly under the direct command of the central government.

**Rendili StarDrive** Maker of some of the galay's top starships, based on Rendili. Rendili StarDrive's origins dated back to the founding of the Galactic Republic. The company reached its zenith in the last century of the Old Republic, laying claim to the Victory Star Destroyer, Dreadnaught, and Mandalorian Dungeon Ship. Rendili StarDrive was not chosen for any major military starship contracts at the height of the Galactic Civil War. In the interim, it spent time and money developing new ship designs, intriguing both New Republic and Imperial military strategists.

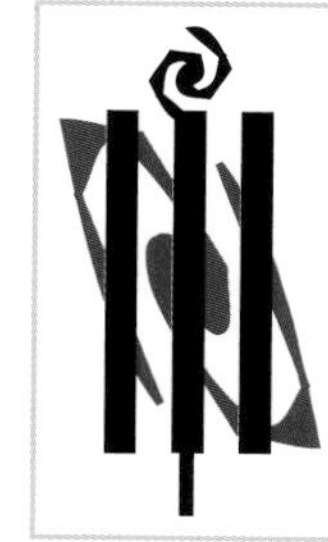

**Renegade Flight** A code name, it referred to the group of Rebel pilots who escorted and protected a badly needed Alliance supply convoy to the secret base on the planet Hoth.

**Renegade Leader** The comm unit designation for Commander Narra, an Alliance starfighter pilot who led Renegade Flight.

**Renegade Squadron** A ragtag group of Rebel specialists assembled by Han Solo on the orders of General Jan Dodonna. Under the command of Col Serra, this team of pirates, smugglers, and other fringers undertook a variety of special missions for the Rebel Alliance, starting with overseeing the evacuation of Yavin 4.

**Renei** A young Melida, the child of Quintama and Pinani, he was killed in the 22nd Battle of Zehava.

**Renewal (1)** The Ssi-ruuvi brainwashing process that cleansed a human of any notions of resistance.

**Renewal (2)** The memory wipes committed by the Syndicat of Phindar on the populace to ensure their loyalty and complacency. The cruel Syndicat wiped subjects of their memories and then deposited them on a new planet, placing bets on how long the Renewed would survive.

**Renforra** One of many secret bases used by the Rebel Alliance during the reign of Emperor Palpatine.

***Renhoek*** The name of several Rebel Alliance troop transports assigned to the Mon Calamari cruiser *Stimsenj'kat.*

**Renkel, Zazana** A Tarhassan native, she fell in love with Republic Intelligence agent Edbit Teeks during the Clone Wars. After his sudden disappearance, inexperienced Republic Intel agents on Tarhassa suspected that Renkel might somehow be responsible, but Joram Kithe and clone trooper Mapper Gann knew she was innocent and kept her out of harm's way.

**Rennik** A widower with twin sons, he was the captain of the freighter *Worldhopper* during the time of the New Republic. He was contacted by the astromech droids Whistler and Gate to transport them from Imperial space to Brentaal.

**Renno, Dav-Wes** A Jedi Master and historian who helped compile a media précis on Count Dooku that appeared on HoloNet News just before the outbreak of the Clone Wars.

**Ren-Quarr** A Quarren with well-groomed tentacles, he was known to frequent the Outlander gambling club on Coruscant just prior to the outbreak of the Clone Wars.

**Renthal, Drea** A powerfully built pirate queen active during the early Galactic Civil War, she was a member of the smugglers' group that defended Nar Shaddaa from an Imperial crackdown orchestrated by Moff Sarn Shild. Drea's ship, *Renthal's Fist,* was destroyed, prompting her to transfer her command to *Renthal's Vengeance.* She was romantically involved with Lando Calrissian for a time, but the pirate life didn't sit well with Lando, and he eventually went "respectable." She later ran into Calrissian when she sacked the luxury liner *Queen of Empire,* freeing him and Bria Tharen from Boba Fett's clutches in the process.

***Renthal's Fist*** The pirate corvette used by Drea Renthal, it sustained heavy damage at the Battle of Nar Shaddaa.

***Renthal's Vengeance*** A backup flagship used by pirate queen Drea Renthal, it was a *Carrack*-class cruiser.

**Renz, Colonel Tyneir** A Jedi Knight from Jiaan, his forces were overrun by General Grievous during the Clone Wars. He survived Order 66 and went into hiding, eventually joining the Rebel Alliance.

**Renz, Lieutenant** An Imperial officer stationed on the Forest Moon of Endor with Colonel Dyer and the 501st Legion during the Battle of Endor, he held Han Solo and Leia Organa at blasterpoint within the Endor bunker and called them "Rebel scum."

**Renzii** A skinny waiter at Didi and Astri Oddo's café a dozen years before the Battle of Naboo.

**Reo, Lieutenant Commander** An engineer in the Galactic Alliance military, he was stationed aboard the *Admiral Ackbar* and was killed by a swarm of Gorog assassin bugs during the Swarm War.

**Rep Council** The governmental body that supported the ruling Boss of the Gungans. Representatives held the title *Rep.*

**repeater** A blaster rifle with an advanced heat sink shield and multi-barreled design, it was a rapid-fire weapon. Slugthrower repeaters also existed; these fired a stream of metal bullets and could cover an entire area with deadly suppressive fire.

**repelfab** A sterilized fabric used in medical facilities, it had the ability to repel dust and airborne particulate debris.

**RePlanetHab** A corporation that arose during the Reconstruction period following the Yuuzhan Vong War, it sought out uninhabited worlds to colonize for beings displaced by the alien invasion. The Jedi and some in the Senate feared that companies like RePlanetHab were growing too powerful and wealthy exploiting the misfortunes of others.

**Repness, Colonel Atton** The commander of the New Republic starfighter training group dubbed the Screaming Wookiees. Repness was crooked, coercing lackluster students to help him steal starships in exchange for the grade curve they needed to pass. When Tyria Sarkin refused to be part of his plans, he blacklisted her. She found her way into Wraith Squadron and told her fellow pilots of Repness's side enterprise. Lara Notsil sliced her way into Repness's files and exposed his indiscretions to General Cracken. Repness caught Notsil, and would have beaten her had he not been arrested by Cracken's guards.

***Reprieve*** An Imperial Nebulon-B frigate, it was seized and used by Rogue Squadron as a temporary headquarters after the squadron lost its base at Talasea.

***Reprisal* (1)** An Imperial Star Destroyer that was, for a time, under the command of Captain Kendal Ozzel. It later was under Commander Demmings.

***Reprisal* (2)** A Dreadnaught heavy cruiser that had been part of the Imperial fleet stationed near Kessel, and later served Warlord Zsinj.

**Reproduction Center** A facility that joined the DNA of Bith parents as per the specifications dictated by agreed-upon child-patterns to create their offspring.

*Lieutenant Renz (left, in Imperial officer uniform)*

Republic assault gunboat

**reptavian** Any living being that had the characteristics germane to both reptiles and avians. This included endothermic metabolisms and oviparous reproduction.

**reptoid** *See* Chazrach.

**Republica House** An immense building established on Coruscant as the primary residence of the Chief of State and other important Galactic Alliance dignitaries following the Yuuzhan Vong War.

**Republicanists** Selonians who pushed for sovereignty during the Starbuster plot and rise of Thrackan Sal-Solo.

**Republic assault gunboat** A sleek drop ship that doubled as an assault speeder for the Republic and the Galactic Empire. Built by Mekuun, the High-Altitude Entry Transport HAET-221 was launched from low orbit, and was capable of entering an atmosphere, burning through its high-energy shielding system as it shed reentry heat. Upon reaching the lower atmosphere, its repulsorlift units kicked in, providing it impressive flight capability, but the craft could not reachieve orbital flight ceilings. Powerful positional rockets helped the HAET-221 reach its target drop site, as did a sophisticated targeting array that quickly mapped a planet's topographic features. The speeder was armed with anti-personnel blasters and a main antivehicle gun.

Republic attack gunship

**Republic assault ship** *See Acclamator*-class assault ship.

**Republic attack cruiser** *See Venator*-class Star Destroyer.

**Republic attack gunship** A rugged, combat-equipped repulsorcraft used by the Grand Army of the Republic, it was also known as an LAAT/i (low-altitude assault transport/infantry). Each winged gunship was covered in weapons, offering air-to-ground and air-to-air support as well as serving as an infantry transport. The front of the gunship featured hunchback-style cockpit bubbles, wherein the gunship pilot and copilot/gunner sat in single file. Chin-mounted on the craft were a pair of laser cannon turrets. On the gunship's dorsal surface were its primary armaments, two massive rocket launchers fed by rear-mounted missile belts. The vessel's splayed wings had a pair of automated bubble turrets, with composite-beam laser weaponry. A second pair of bubble-turret cannons extended on articulated arms from the troop cabin; these were gunner-operated by clone troopers encased within the armored spheres. Air-to-air rockets were slung on the ventral surface of each wing. Rounding out the gunship's armaments was a single tail cannon that provided covering fire for troops and small vehicles leaving the gunship. A larger variant of the gunship, the LAAT/c, was specially designed to airdrop heavy cargo such as the Republic's AT-TE combat walkers.

**Republic attack shuttle** *See Nu*-class shuttle.

**Republic City** This huge, sprawling metropolis—also known for a time as Galactic City—was the Old Republic capital on the planet Coruscant. It was renamed Imperial City (and the planet was dubbed Imperial Center) when Chancellor Palpatine declared the establishment of the Empire.

***Republic*-class Star Destroyer** Walex Blissex's follow-up design to his classic *Victory*-class Star Destroyer for the New Republic. The Rendili StarDrive *Republic*-class Star Destroyer was smaller than the KDY *Imperial*-class design, and cost only half as much to produce as the larger vessel. The *Republic*-class ship measured 1,250 meters in length.

**Republic commando** *See* clone commando.

Republic cruiser

**Republic Constitution** *See* Galactic Constitution.

**Republic cruiser** A Corellian-built *Consular*-class starship intended to carry ambassadors on missions throughout the galaxy. A Republic cruiser's scarlet coloration identified its diplomatic status. Because they were used only in the service of peace, Republic cruisers lacked weapons but boasted powerful deflector shields. The starships also incorporated advanced salon pods, which could be modified to fulfill the particular needs of any given species and were often used for important meetings and negotiations. The *Radiant VII,* the starship used by Obi-Wan Kenobi and Qui-Gon Jinn on their mission to Naboo, was typical of Republic cruisers. It possessed a communications suite designed to receive and transmit messages to almost any type of vehicle or installation in thousands of Republic languages. Its salon pods were armored, insulated, and protected against any type of surveillance device. The modular salon pods could also serve as escape pods in emergencies, as they had independent life-support systems and sensors. Because of the versatility and safety of its salon pods, negotiations could easily be held directly aboard the starship itself. Like the *Radiant VII,* nearly all Republic cruisers maintained only minimal crew in order to ensure security and secrecy. Generally, a Republic cruiser utilized two communications officers assigned to deciphering incoming transmissions; three engineers who monitored the starship's vital functions; two pilots trained to maneuver and navigate the craft; and a captain responsible for overseeing the entire crew. All other functions could be attended to by a variety of utility droids. On especially sensitive or dangerous missions, the crew could be limited to a pilot and captain, with droids stationed at all other posts.

**Republic Day** A galaxywide holiday commemorating the founding of the Galactic Republic.

**Republic Enforcement Datacore** The vast computer network where all legal bounties for wanted criminals were posted. It was replaced by the Imperial Enforcement Datacore during the New Order.

**Republic Engineering Corporation** A New Republic corporation founded in the years after the Battle of Endor. It was financed by several of the New Republic's key corporate supporters, and the company's first products—the shieldships for the Nomad City mining colony on Nkllon—were commissioned by Lando Calrissian. Following the success of the shieldship design, Republic Engineering Corporation concentrated on specialty designs and its lines of short-range fighters and high-altitude combat speeders.

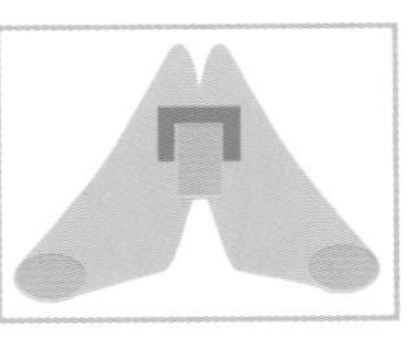

**Republic Executive Building** The dome-shaped building where Senators and other Republic officials lived and worked while on Coruscant. It was located near the Senate Rotunda.

**Republic Fleet Systems** The maker of the *Chu'unthor,* Republic Fleet Systems played a large role in Old Republic starship design for over 15 millennia. The company was founded to design warships that might counter the threat of uprisings in distant corners of the Old Republic. In the final days of the Republic, it was formally disbanded by decree of the Senate and most of the company's resources were absorbed by the Republic's military.

**Republic Guard** Republic peace officers who worked to preserve order and justice on a scale somewhat beneath the notice of the Jedi Order. Republic peace officers issued traffic citations, responded to emergency calls, and apprehended criminals.

**Republic *Hammerhead*-class fleet ship** An Old Republic warship used during the Mandalorian Wars, Great Sith War, and Jedi Civil War. The long vessels had tall bridge structures that rose on a plane perpendicular to the ship's long axis, giving it the name *hammerhead* for its resemblance to an enormous mallet.

**Republic HoloCommunications Commission** A licensing and regulatory agency in the Galactic Republic that monitored legal and illegal use of the HoloNet infrastructure. It was this agency that was tasked with cracking down on so-called shadowfeeds that used the HoloNet to illegally disseminate information.

**Republic HoloNet News** A rebranded version of HoloNet News that emerged after the start of the Clone Wars, indicating that it was an official government news source.

**Republic Intelligence** The branch of the Galactic Republic military that gathered strategic information across the galaxy.

**Republic interceptor fighter tank** *See* IFT-T.

**Republic Measures and Standards Bureau** A scientific organization tasked with standardizing systems of measurement across the galaxy. Its purview included authority over official calendars and timekeeping systems.

**Republic Military Benefit Association** An organization that dedicated itself to scheduling entertainment for clone troopers and military personnel during the Clone Wars.

**Republic Mobile Surgical Unit (RMSU)** During the Clone Wars, these mobile hospitals tended to the Republic's ground troops and support personnel, both wounded and those stricken with local illnesses. RMSUs were largely self-sufficient, and personnel lived in a semi-constant state of triage, performing surgery on a dozen different species day and night, and making do with local materials as often as possible. Human and alien cutters worked alongside the droid surgeons, who were in short supply due to the lengthy and costly war. RMSUs were known as Rimsoos in parlance.

**Republic Office of Criminal Investigation** A Galactic Republic government agency tasked with law enforcement, it managed the Republic Enforcement Datacore, which listed bounties on outstanding criminals in the galaxy. The ROCI was replaced with the Imperial Office of Criminal Investigation under the Empire.

**Republic Office of Xenosociology** A government agency that focused on cultural integration and interactions with the various species that made up the Galactic Republic.

**Republic Outland Regions Security Force** A military force commissioned during the Galactic Republic in an effort to tame the lawless Outer Rim Territories. Wilhuff Tarkin started his career in the RORSF, serving as a commander after the Battle of Naboo.

**Republic Redux** A Rebel group, one of Shelsha sector's principal supporters of the Rebel Alliance shortly after the Battle of Yavin. It was led by an Adarian named Yeeru Chivkyrie.

**Republic Sienar Systems** The predecessor of Sienar Fleet Systems, a division of Santhe/Sienar Technologies.

**Republic Starfleet** The amassed spacefaring military force of the Galactic Republic. It included a mix of clone and nonclone officers during the Clone Wars. In addition to newly commissioned vessels unveiled during that conflict, the Starfleet also included consolidated home fleet forces from various worlds of the Republic. It transformed into the Imperial Navy.

**Republic Travel and Transit Bureau** A Galactic Republic agency that oversaw transportation issues.

**Republic troop carrier** *See* CR20, CR25 Republic troop carrier.

**Republic troop transport** Repulsorlift vehicles designed to carry infantry units from one location to another. Republic troop transports were heavily armored, very slow, and equipped with two light laser cannons. They were often used in convoys for greater protection. On Geonosis, each transport was used to ferry dozens of Jedi to the Geonosis arena at the start of the Clone Wars.

**Republic War-Bond** A savings bond issued by the Galactic Republic to help fund the Clone Wars effort.

***Repulse*** An assault carrier in the New Republic Fifth Fleet, it was deployed in the blockade of Doornik-319 at the start of the Yevethan crisis.

**repulse-hand** Unlike other cybernetic prosthetic hands used to replace lost limbs, this model from Control Zone made no attempt to hide its mechanical nature. No artificial flesh encased its metallic digits, and the palm connected to a repulsor-field generator that allowed it to parry weapons in melee combat.

**repulsor (repulsorlift)** An anti-gravitational propulsion unit sometimes called a repulsorlift engine, it was the most widely used propulsion system in land and atmospheric vehicles. The engines produced a field that pushed against, or repulsed, a planet's gravity, providing the thrust that made landspeeders, airspeeders, and speeder bikes move. Repulsorlift engines were also used in starfighters and small starships as supplementary propulsion systems for docking and for atmospheric flight.

**repulsor boots** Sporting and combat footwear equipped with miniaturized repulsorlifts, they allowed a user to jump or skate over great distances.

**repulsor carts** Floating carts used to move heavy objects.

**repulsor pack trooper** *See* RP trooper.

**Requiem Squadron** An experimental TIE defender group led by a disguised Wedge Antilles and consisting of several Rogue Squadron pilots. This group was part of Ysanne Isard's plan to infiltrate Ciutric and defeat Prince-Admiral Krennel.

**Resbin, Senator Jollin** A Sneevel Senator who supported the Military Creation Act prior to the outbreak of the Clone Wars. He hired Sneevel celebrity Boles Roor to campaign with him.

**rescue ball** A pared-down version of an escape pod, it was little more than a sealed transparisteel sphere equipped with atmospheric tanks and basic communications systems. Unlike escape pods, the rescue ball had no propulsion or reentry system.

**Resh, Shaalir** The name used by X-wing pilot Riv Shiel on Coruscant during Rogue Squadron's undercover operation there. He pretended to be a Shistavanen con man who, in a classic setup, robbed unsuspecting victims as they attempted to take advantage of his young human partner.

**Reshad, Palejo** A spice trader based out of Bela Vistal on Corellia, he made a large profit by selling spice in Jabba the Hutt's court. He secretly used part of the profit to help fund the Rebel Alliance.

**resicrete** A durable building material used in the decking of large starships.

**residual heat trend directionalizer** A tracking device that could follow warm-bodied targets by zeroing in on heat signatures and probable vectors of movement.

***Resol'nare*** A term that described the basic tenents of Mandalorian culture, or "Six Actions": the wearing of armor, the use of *Mando'a* language, loyalty and defense of one's family and oneself, raising children in the Mandalorian way, contributing to the welfare of one's clan, and answering the call to combat of the *Mand'alor* during times of strife.

***Resolute* (1)** An *Invincible*-class Dreadnaught that served in the Corporate Sector Authority fleet under the command of Captain Angela Krin.

***Resolute* (2)** A *Venator*-class Star Destroyer active during the Clone Wars under the command of Admiral Wulff Yularen, it served as Anakin Skywalker's flagship.

***Resolution*** A *Venator*-class Star Destroyer active during the Clone Wars, it was dispatched to Drongar to escort medical personnel back to Coruscant.

***Resolve*** A New Republic Star Destroyer, it served as the target during the Fifth Fleet's Bessimir operational readiness exercise. The ship was under the command of Syub Snunb.

**resonance torpedo** The primary weapon used in the offensive systems of the Sun Crusher.

***Respectable*** A Centrality cruiser involved in the siege at ThonBoka.

***Respite*** A medical frigate that served the Galactic Republic during the Clone Wars.

Restraining bolt (left)

**response improvement package** *See* RiMPack.

**resputi** Enormous predators that were known to lurk in the lowest levels of the sinkhole cities on Utapau.

**Rest, the** *See* Silentium.

**restraining bolt** A small, cylindrical device, it fit into a special socket or was welded onto the exterior of a droid to keep it from wandering off. A restraining bolt also forced a droid to respond immediately to signals produced by a handheld summoning device—a caller—that was keyed to a specific bolt.

**restraining bolt activator** *See* caller.

**restraining collar** Similar in function to a restraining bolt for inhibiting the movement of droids, this device was simply slipped over a droid's body.

**Restwell Sleep Station** An establishment located in one of the Outsider Citadels on Cerea that rented sleeping berths to inhabitants and visitors. The berths were little more than narrow coffins with full life-support systems. The berths served as temporary lodging for those without the means to rent larger spaces.

**Ret** *See* Annoo-dat.

**Retail Caucus** A Separatist faction, it maintained a stronghold on Christophsis during the Clone Wars.

***Retaliator*** An Imperial Star Destroyer dispatched to assist the *Agonizer* in the subjugation of Adumar during the New Republic era.

**Retep III** Following the Battle of Yavin, this was the site of a rendezvous between an Alliance force and a group of Habassan freighters delivering a cargo of foodstuffs. The transfer operation near Retep III was attacked by Imperial starfighters.

**Retep V** The site of an ambush of a Habassan convoy by Imperial corvettes following the Battle of Yavin. A Rebel Alliance strike force helped rescue the convoy near Retep V.

**Reth, Yakown** A once ambitious and promising officer in Wedge Antilles's command during the Yuuzhan Vong invasion, he flew as Green Leader, commanding two squadrons of E-wing fighters; those were later re-formed into Blackmoon Squadron while assembled at Borleias following the Yuuzhan Vong conquest of Coruscant. The prolonged fighting and his stressful disagreement with General Antilles's tactics took their toll on Reth, who was relieved of command due to a mental breakdown. Luke Skywalker took his place as Blackmoon Leader during the evacuation of Borleias.

**Retheur, Nalan** A legendary actor during the last century of the New Repbulic. Kalio Entertainment attempted to use his recorded brainwave patterns to re-create the actor for a holoseries, claiming an unfulfilled contractual obligation, though his estate objected.

**Rethin Sea** Composed of liquid metal, it was the core of the gas giant Bespin.

Sheltay Retrac

**Reti** A Toydarian mechanic who piloted a salvage ship called the *Zoomer*, he stumbled upon an unconscious Rhys Dallows just prior to the Trade Federation blockade of Naboo. He later joined Dallows, Vana Sage, and Nym in fighting the Trade Federation invasion. Reti's instincts were to flee combat whenever possible, though he was not above embellishing his exploits with more heroic recollections of his adventures. Reti was an accomplished mechanic. He had a bounty on his head for a time, and tried to lie low following the Battle of Geonosis.

**retinal print** A security device, it was used to identify individuals by comparing their retinal patterns with prints stored in a computer database. A retinal disguiser was a device resembling a visor designed specifically to counter a retinal print by projecting a false retinal pattern over the wearer's eyes.

**Retrac, Sheltay** The head of Bail Organa's support staff during his time as Senator of Alderaan. She was married to an artist from the Killik regions and was the mother of Winter, Leia Organa's childhood friend.

**retractable wrist blade** A common component found in Mandalorian armor, such as that worn by Jango Fett. He used this blade—which extended from his right forearm gauntlet—to slow his fall from a Tipoca City building during his battle with Obi-Wan Kenobi.

***Retribution*** A *Marauder*-class corvette that served as Bria Tharen's command ship as part of the Corellian resistance attack on the slave ship *Helot's Shackle* in an attempt to free Ylesian slaves.

**retsa** A strong liquor favored by Lando Calrissian during his youthful gambling days; he liked its strong bite.

**Return** A ritual among the survivors of Alderaan, it held deep spiritual significance. Those who participated in the Return were encouraged to buy gifts for those they loved and lost when Alderaan was annihilated. If possible, they then made their way to the site that became known as the Graveyard of Alderaan, where the gifts were set adrift in the asteroid belt that was all that remained of their world, to rest among the memories of the past. Words were spoken to mark the occasion. Many who accomplished the Return described it as an event that changed their lives, or at least gave them a new understanding of life and its purpose. Some even claimed to have gained a new insight into the universe. However, for most of the faithful, the Return provided healing calm for their tortured spirits.

**Retwin, Chief** A highly skilled saboteur, he was a former Imperial sympathizer who worked for the defense forces of his home planet, Ralltiir. He joined the Empire after Ralltiir's subjugation. He later served aboard the Super Star Destroyer *Executor.*

**Revan, Darth** Before he took on the Sith mantle of Darth Revan, he was a young, charismatic Jedi who took part in the Mandalorian Wars. Ignoring the dictates of the Jedi Council, he and his fellow Jedi, the future Darth Malak, recruited many of the impulsive youth of the Order to their cause of victory and glory over the Mandalorians. Adopting the alias of the Revanchists, this combative splinter group of Jedi led the fleet of the Galactic Republic in driving back the invaders. The Mandalorian Wars were long and bloody, and many Jedi perished in the struggle. Yet, in the end, the Republic emerged triumphant, and the singular Jedi who called himself the Revanchist and Malak were hailed as heroes.

But the heroes did not leave the war untouched; something about the Outer Rim worlds twisted and corrupted them. On Korriban, the Revanchist uncovered the lost secrets of the Sith and became the heir to an ancient and evil legacy. Succumbing to the lure of the dark side, the fallen Jedi assumed the title of Darth Revan, Lord of the Sith. He chose Malak as his apprentice, and the great fleet under their control abandoned the Republic and swore fealty to their new Sith Masters.

Darth Revan

With their army of followers, Revan and Malak returned not as saviors, but as conquerors. For two years, battles raged on the perimeters of Republic space. The Sith gained victory after victory, until the Jedi set a trap for Revan and succeeded in incapacitating the Dark Lord. But during the chaos of battle, Malak managed to escape.

Malak seized the mantle of his fallen Sith Master and proclaimed himself the new Dark Lord, swearing revenge on those who had taken Revan. And the Sith armada continued its relentless advance upon the Core Worlds.

Revwien

The Jedi Knights wiped Revan's memory, returning him to their ranks without the taint of the dark side. The amnesiac Revan, unaware of his true identity, was paired with Jedi Knight Bastila Shan in her mission to track down Malak and stop the Dark Lord's next plot, which involved discovering the ancient Rakatan Star Forge and unleashing its power against the Republic.

Revan and Shan were separated during a space battle above the planet Taris when their flagship, the *Endar Spire,* sustained heavy damage. Republic officer Carth Onasi accompanied Revan to the surface of Taris, where they sought out Shan's escape pod in the planet's undercity. From there, Revan, Shan, Onasi, and their growing retinue journeyed across the galaxy, following ancient clues to the location of the Star Forge. This group uncovered the weapon and was able to stop Malak. Revan recovered his memories, but nonetheless succeeded in stopping the Sith plot.

**Revanchists** Also known as Jedi Crusaders, these were young Jedi Knights stirred into combat by the Jedi Knight known as the Revanchist during the Mandalorian Wars.

**Revessa Global Shipping** A Trandoshan-owned shipping concern.

***Revenant*** An armed oceangoing cutter used by Sol Sixxa on Maramere when he confronted Nym's forces some time after the Battle of Naboo. Sixxa installed an advanced cloaking device prototype onto the ship. The *Revenant* was destroyed when Nym used the *Sunrunner* to ram it.

***Revenue*** A Trade Federation class-I freighter under the command of Daultay Dofine prior to the Battle of Naboo. A Sullustan, an Ishi Tib, and a Gran were all part of the *Revenue*'s crew. Approximately seven months before the Naboo invasion, the *Revenue* was transporting lommite ore from Dorvalla when it was raided by the terrorist group Nebula Front. Captain Arwen Cohl led a team that stole a secret cache of aurodium ingots hidden aboard the ship. The crew abandoned the vessel before it exploded.

**reverse-polarity pulse grenade** A weapon used against battle droids by ARC troopers during the Clone Wars. Also called a haywire grenade, it overloaded all of a droid's systems—although it also disrupted ARC trooper sensors, even when activated at a long distance. It took an ARC trooper a moment to recalibrate his sensors. A refined version of this weapon, without the adverse side effects, was known as a droid popper.

**reversion** The act of returning to realspace from hyperspace.

**Revery** A luxurious world with aquamarine seas and splendid beaches, it was known as a vacation spot and private retreat for wealthy beings.

***Revival*** A Galactic Alliance warship that blockaded Corellia a decade after the Yuuzhan Vong War.

**Revoc, Jasod** Leader of Jasod Revoc and His Galactic Revue, a group that traveled to Republic installations during the Clone Wars to entertain the troops.

**Revol Leap** A canted and treacherous spire in the abandoned city of Tibannopolis over Bespin.

**Revoltist** The Targonnian faction led by Shay that opposed the rule of Dictator-Forever Craw.

**Revos** The entertainment capital of planet Storinal, connected to the capital of Scohar via railcar tunnels. Wraith Squadron intercepted the crew of the *Hawkbat* here during the early years of the New Republic.

**Revwien** A species of ambulatory intelligent plants from Revyia, a world located on the outer fringes of the Outer Rim Territories. The philosphy of Tyia was widely adopted by Revwiens.

**Rex** *See* RX-24 (Rex).

**Rex, Captain** The clone officer (CC-7567) in charge of the 501st Legion during the Clone Wars, he worked closely with General Anakin Skywalker throughout the conflict. Rex adopted Anakin's propensity for unorthodox combat tactics—which often yielded spectacular results against the enemy.

**Rex, Et** A pale blue, horned alien Jedi whom Anakin Skywalker and Obi-Wan Kenobi encountered aboard a crashed cruiser at Poison Moon, prior to the Clone Wars. Rex was framed by Alysun Celz as a fallen Jedi and was being brought to Coruscant to be judged by the Jedi Council. An investigation by Kenobi and Skywalker revealed that it was in fact Celz who had abandoned the Order and fallen to the dark side.

**Rey, Tamizander** A native of the planet Esseles, he resigned from the Esselian defense force after the Imperial Senate was disbanded by Emperor Palpatine. Tamizander Rey then joined the Rebel Alliance as a highly skilled starship pilot. Rey was senior deck officer at Echo Base on Hoth, where he was responsible for docking bay operations.

**Reya (ReyaTaat)** The core name of Daer'ey'ath, a Chiss Intelligence agent during the Yuuzhan Vong War. During the events of the Swarm War, she was dispatched to gather intelligence on the Colony; shot down over Jwlio, she was rescued by the Taat hive and eventually became the Joiner ReyaTaat. In becoming part of the Colony, she supplied the Killiks with vital information concerning Chiss tactics.

Tamizander Rey

**Reybn, Sergeant** An Imperial assigned to a remote relay outpost on Vaal, he had grown lazy and careless at the quiet station. Having survived the Battle of Yavin and the destruction of the Death Star, Darth Vader crashed his TIE fighter on Vaal, and took the sole shuttle at the Vaal outpost to reestablish contact with the Empire. A pack of native predators then attacked the outpost, killing Reybn and others stationed there.

**Reytha** A planet devoted to the production and export of crops and other foodstuffs, it was nicknamed the breadbasket of the Empire.

**Rezodar, Hidu** A criminal with a price on his head sought by bounty hunter Sintas Vel during the early Galactic Empire. She tracked him to Phaeda. She failed to apprehend him, however, and was in turn captured and frozen in carbonite. Rezodar died shortly therafter, and articles of his estate were placed in storage for decades. Almost 40 years later, Boba Fett tracked Sintas's frozen form to Phaeda, and thawed her—his one-time wife—from the stasis imprisonment.

**RGA-972** An Imperial snowtrooper who invaded Echo Base during the Battle of Hoth.

**RH7 CardShark** A lower-end droid used in casinos designed to replace organic dealers as an automated sabacc dealer.

**R'han** A young H'drachi who supported the Rebel Alliance. R'han was enslaved and died toiling in Imperial Governor Grigor's dragite mines.

**Rhara, Clee** A charismatic Jedi Knight who started a starfighter pilot program on Centax 2. Clee Rhara went through Jedi Temple training with Qui-Gon Jinn and Tahl. She had untamed bright orange hair and orange eyes. She was petite and slender, barely coming up to Qui-Gon's shoulder, but her compact body was built of wiry muscle. She chose Garen Muln as one of her students and, later, as her Padawan.

**Rhee, Fyn** A Nautolan dancer who earned a living in Nar Shaddaa cantinas during the early Galactic Empire.

**Rhees-Verk breathing** A syncopated breathing pattern that could result in ventricular fibrillation in such species as Zabraks.

**Rhelg** The primitive private world of Sith Lord Ludo Kressh during the Great Hyperspace War, it was located near Ziost.

**Rhen-Orm Biocomputer** A device planted in Aurra Sing's head by the Anzati to give her a greater range of awareness than ordinary beings. Aayla Secura severed the antenna during her duel with Aurra Sing on Devaron.

**Rhen Var** Located in the Nabali system, it was a dormant Outer Rim world that began its millennia-long emergence from an ice age 4,000 years before the Battle of Yavin. The civilization that previously existed there died when the glaciers came, the result of an atmospheric cataclysm that devastated the planet's ecosystem. Many of the lost species' structures remained intact. Ulic Qel-Droma sought out the planet as his final home as he atoned for his great crimes as a Dark Lord of the Sith. Vima Sunrider discovered the fallen Jedi on Rhen Var and asked him to teach her about the Force. It was here that Qel-Droma died, shot through the heart by Hoggon.

Thousands of years later, Rhen Var was the site of a battle between the Galactic Republic and the Confederacy during the Clone Wars. Count Dooku defended the world to keep the Republic from uncovering ancient Jedi lore that might reveal how to defeat his Dark Reaper superweapon. Anakin Skywalker took charge of the fleet to retake the planet.

During the Galactic Civil War, the Rebel Alliance attacked an Imperial monitoring station on Rhen Var.

Captain Rex

**Rhigar-3** A near-tropical moon that circled a secret Chiss military academy in the Rata Nebula.

**Rhinnal** Located in the Darpa sector of the Core Worlds along the Perlemian Trade Route, the planet emerged from an ice age about a millennium before the Battle of Yavin. Rhinnal's surface was covered with fjords, mountains, and frigid rivers. It was a colony world of nearby Esseles until the rise of the Empire,

The frozen world of Rhen Var

Myhr Rho

when Imperials assumed direct control. The planet's 55 million inhabitants placed great value on ceremonies and commemorations, and often wore elaborate, colorful clothing. Rhinnal was famous for its expertise in medicine. The last remaining Jedi chapter house in the Core Worlds was located on Rhinnal. After the Battle of Yavin, Rhinnal experts were sent to an orbiting hospital frigate to study the outbreak of Candorian plague on Dentaal.

**Rho, Myhr** An enterprising Cathar who offered tours of "famous" Tatooine locales visited by Luke Skywalker.

**Rhoden, Clode** A wealthy Tibanna gas magnate who founded the colony on Yorn Skot and owned the entire planet, he had long been suspicious of Jedi. During the *Aurorient Express* crisis, Rhoden intended to destroy his mining colony in order to collect the insurance money while at the same time murdering his unfaithful wife, Madame Rhoden. The Jedi Qui-Gon Jinn and Obi-Wan Kenobi uncovered his plan, but Qui-Gon could only suggest that the Travel and Transport Bureau investigate the events, since Yorn Skot didn't fall under the jurisdiction of the Republic. Rhoden lost his mining colony to Saul Moegantz, who also intended to take everything else of Rhoden's, including his wife.

**Rhommamool** With Osarian, part of a double-planet pair in the Expansion Region. Rhommamool was the smaller of the two. It appeared reddish, likely due to the constantly blowing red dust. Rhommamool's main spaceport was Redhaven. Both planets were ground-based technologically—Rhommamool almost exclusively so. Life for the miners on Rhommamool was tough—even basics like water were hard to come by—while the prosperous Osarians lived in comfort on white sandy beaches and crystal-clear lakes. Leia Organa Solo went to Osarian and Rhommamool on a diplomatic mission to try to end the conflict between the two planets. Her mission failed and the conflict escalated, fomented by the Yuuzhan Vong agitator Nom Anor.

**Rhymer, Major** Leader of Scimitar Squadron, the elite bomber wing assigned to defend the Endor shield generator from any ground assault.

**Rhysode, Ganner** A headstrong Jedi Knight from Teyr, he trained under Luke Skywalker at the Jedi academy on Yavin 4. During early stages of the Yuuzhan Vong War, Rhysode echoed Kyp Durron's proactive stance to take the war to the alien invaders, despite Luke's more measured approach. Rhysode was often teamed with Corran Horn, and the two were at odds when it came to such philosophy. Still, he respected Horn's opinions even if he did not share them. Rhysode saved Horn's life on Bimmiel, rushing him to safety and medical attention after Horn was bitten by a venomous amphistaff. As the war dragged on, Rhysode was scarred and soundly defeated by the Yuuzhan Vong Krag Val on Garqi, a setback that taught the proud Jedi humility.

After the Yuuzhan Vong had conquered Coruscant, Rhysode explored its depths chasing rumors that Jacen Solo had been captured by the invaders. Rhysode found Solo, strangely complicit in the Yuuzhan Vong preparation of the planet's World Brain. Jacen was to be the one who would sacrifice Ganner Rhysode, but he instead took the opportunity to make contact with the World Brain, subtly altering it to respond to him. Solo gave Rhysode the lightsaber that had belonged to Anakin Solo, and Ganner protected Jacen's sabotage by holding off hundreds of Yuuzhan Vong warriors. Their sheer numbers ultimately crushed him, but Rhysode died the indisputable hero he had once believed himself to be.

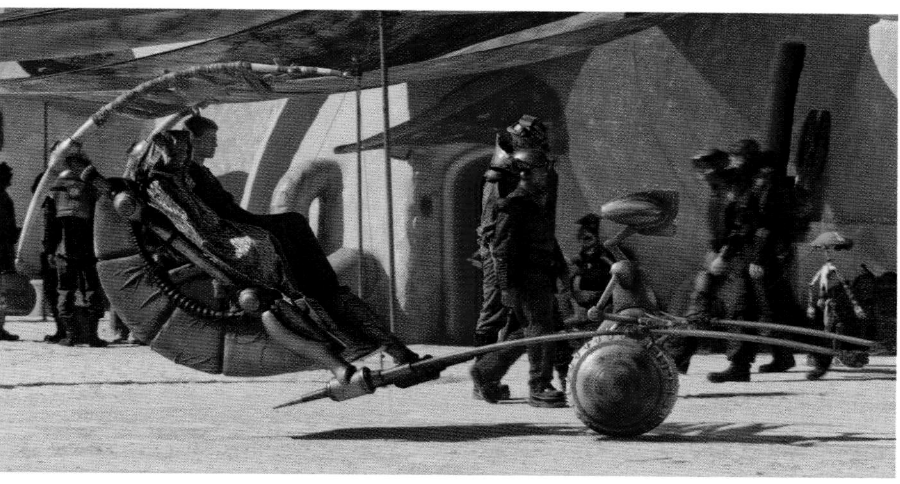

RIC series droid (RIC-920) takes Padmé and Anakin through Mos Espa.

**Rian-327 airspeeder** For travel between her apartment and the Senate or Naboo-delegation landing platforms on Coruscant, Padmé Amidala used a sleek Rian-327 airspeeder personally optimized by Anakin Skywalker. The 8-meter-long speeder was equipped with an anti-tracking device.

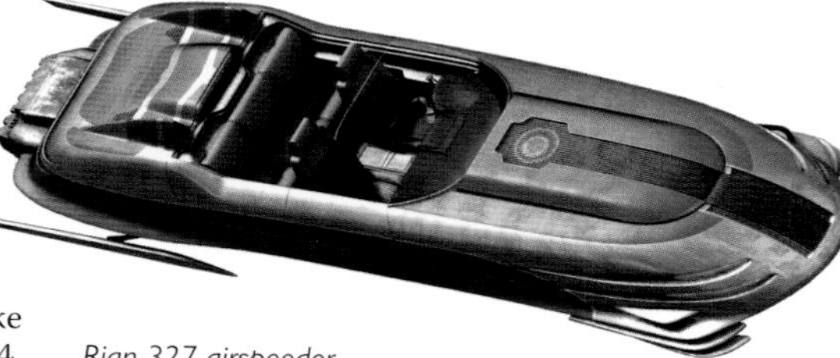

Rian-327 airspeeder

**Rianitus Period** A period from 9,000 to 8,000 years before the Battle of Yavin, marked by the 275-year term of Blotus the Hutt as the Galactic Republic's Supreme Chancellor.

**Riboga the Hutt** A Hutt exile who struggled to establish a criminal enterprise in the Cularin system.

**Rich** A Rebel Alliance technician who proclaimed himself Luke Skywalker's biggest fan following the Battle of Yavin.

**Richblum, Onila** A famed bolo-ball player for the Yag'Dhul team, he tied league records prior to the Clone Wars by scoring twice in one game.

**RIC series droid** A utilitarian droid built by Serv-O-Droid for general-purpose applications, RIC-920 ended up functioning as an unlicensed rickshaw droid in the busy streets of Mos Espa. Other RIC units found employment in professional sports, playing in widely broadcast games of nuna-ball. The droid model was an unsophisticated unipod that went largely unchanged for centuries.

**Ri'Dar** Flying tree-dwelling primates from Dar'Or. Ri'Dar inhabited the middle levels of a dense network of 200-meter-tall waza trees that covered Dar'Or, along with the sloth-like saber-toothed indola. Predators of the Ri'Dar included the indola and the avian elix, which was introduced to the planet by ecologists to save it from extinction on a supernova-threatened world.

**Riders of the Maelstrom** Pirates in the stretch of space known as the Maelstrom, a huge nebula-like cloud composed of charged space dust and raw energy along the Relgim hyperspace lane. The Riders were led by Big Jak Targrim. Craxtet Redhand was Targrim's second in command.

**ride the stripe** An extremely dangerous starfighter maneuver developed by the Jedi Knights of the Old Republic. A Jedi pilot flew along a vector identical to that of a just-fired turbolaser blast. This prevented the fighter from appearing on sensors, as the static and energy backwash from the blast concealed it. In this manner, a Jedi fighter could sneak into a capital ship's primary defense zone.

**Ridge** A clone trooper who was part of the 501st Legion's "rock jumper" mission to Teth during the Clone Wars.

**Riebold's Foam and Sizzle** A notorious drinking hole on Reecee.

**Rieekan, General Carlist** As a Rebel Alliance officer, he was the commander of all Alliance ground and fleet forces in the Hoth star system. He gave the order to abandon Hoth when the Alliance headquarters was discovered by the Empire. Years later, as Chief of State Leia Organa Solo's second in command on the New Republic Council, General Carlist Rieekan took over in her absences, such as when she disappeared during the troubles on Nam Chorios. Rieekan survived a poisoning that was aimed at throwing the Republic into chaos. Later, he became the New Republic Intelligence director, and he decided to terminate Colonel Pakkpekatt's pursuit of the mysterious vagabond ghost ship carrying Lando Calrissian, his aide, Lobot, and the droids C-3PO and R2-D2 as involuntary riders. However, he did allow Pakkpekatt to take Calrissian's ship, the *Lady Luck,* and three volunteers in search of the vagabond. Rieekan returned from retirement to assist the New Republic and the Galactic Alliance during the Yuuzhan Vong War.

**Riemann, Gayla** An artist from the planet Aldraig IV, she joined the Rebel Alliance after the Empire had erected an AT-AT production facility on her homeworld. She proved to be an excellent starfighter pilot, and eventually joined Rogue Squadron.

**Rifle Worlds** A collection of planets within the Hapes Cluster that once attempted to secede. Much of the cluster's manufacturing industry was centered on these worlds.

**Riflor** The homeworld of the Advozsec in the Mid Rim's Riflorii system. The system consisted of three planets orbiting a trinary star system that was slowly devouring itself. The closest world, Zirku, followed a bizarre, twisting orbit that passed near all three stars, rendering the entire planet molten. Tejrivozs, on the other hand, followed a long, egg-shaped orbit that brought it close enough to nearly graze its three suns, then sent the rocky, barren orb on a 17-year spin through the system. Many geological experts agreed that constant tectonic activity on the middle planet, Riflor, was due to three primary factors: the erratic orbits of Riflor's neighbors, gravitational stresses caused by the world's moons, and an oblong orbit that carried it close to the system's primary star. During the Yuuzhan Vong War, the alien invaders unleashed biological weapons that destroyed 97 percent of Riflor's plant life.

**Rig, the** Space station headquarters of the Crimson Nova Chapter of the Bounty Hunters' Guild, located in an asteroid field of the Stenness Node. The command center was called the Nest. As punishment for Crimson Nova taking bounties on the heads of Jedi during the Clone Wars, Mace Windu, Agen Koler, Kit Fisto, and Saesee Tiin infiltrated the Rig.

**Righim, Caldera** A Talz who was something of a pacifist, he had long been opposed to violence in the Mos Eisley cantina. He was a personal friend of Wuher.

*General Carlist Rieekan*

**Rights of Sentience** Laws enacted by the Galactic Republic ensuring that all sentient beings were given the opportunity to develop without outside social, criminal, genetic, or technological interference.

***Right to Rule*** An aging Imperial Star Destroyer that became Admiral Pellaeon's flagship in the Imperial Remnant fleet during the Yuuzhan Vong War.

**Rigo** The nonhuman leader of a group of bounty hunters, Rigo discovered Clone Trooper Alpha and Obi-Wan Kenobi on Riflor. During Rigo's attempt to claim the bounty on Kenobi, Anakin Skywalker arrived and sliced off Rigo's left hand.

**Rigorra the Hutt** The brother of Groodo the Hutt and Warlord of Balmorra prior to the Clone Wars. He lived there within a large, heavily fortified castle.

**Rigovian Technical University** A leading school of technical innovation. Raith Sienar studied there.

**Riiken** The captain of a police force that protected the Onderonian city of Iziz and Queen Talia after the Mandalorian Wars.

**Riileb** The homeworld of the Riilebs, tall humanoids with antennae who could detect biorhythm changes in others. Single Riileb females were bald, while married females and all males had hair.

**Riizolo, Phan** The pirate captain of the *Booty Full,* he once worked for Leonia Tavira.

**Rijel XII** A planet that nearly left the Republic's fold prior to the Clone Wars, until sensitive negotiations—which featured Doolb Snoil—ensured its loyalty.

**Rikel** Nicknamed Vibro, he served aboard Centerpoint Station during the war between the Galactic Alliance and the Confederation. That war had become extremely personal for Rikel, as his wife had died on Coruscant and he vowed revenge against the Galactic Alliance. Regardless of overall plans and orders, he was determined to fire Centerpoint to devastate Coruscant. When he activated the weapon, though, Jedi sabotage resulted in its self-destruction, killing Rikel.

**Rikkar-Du** A Codru-Ji clan leader active during the time of Emperor Roan Fel. When the Sith Lord Darth Kruhl attempted to unite disparate Codru-Ji clans under Imperial rule, Rikkar-Du rebelled, and Kruhl killed him.

**Rik's** Of all the dives in the underworld of Coruscant active during the time of Emperor Roan Fel, none was more notorious than Rik's. The owner was a sly Hutt information broker calling herself Queen Jool. Jool's jeweled eye patch was in fact a cybernetic enhancement that allowed the Hutt to monitor her cantina. Queen Jool lived in a swamp below the cantina. While no fights were allowed inside her establishment, everything else had a price.

**Rikummee, Prince** The royal son of King Grakchawwaa, a mighty Wookiee hunter on Kashyyyk. Rikummee was minded by Ghraggka, his burly protector, who was unable to stop Separatist droids in Kashyyyk's Western Forest from killing the prince. After his son's death, Grakchawwaa decided to fully support the Republic in the Clone Wars.

**rikyam** The brain of a Yuuzhan Vong ship, it was protected by a thick shell that could be accessed by a shaper.

**Rilla** One of the founding members of the Eleven, an early Rebel group formed on Bellassa after the Galactic Empire subjugated her world.

**Rillao** A beautiful, golden-skinned Firrerreo with black-and-silver-striped hair, she had strong Force abilities that brought her to the attention of Darth Vader, with whom she began training. Rillao met one of Vader's other students, a fellow Firrerreo named Hethrir. They became lovers, and Rillao became pregnant. But unlike Hethrir, who so fully embraced the dark side that he willingly destroyed his homeworld and millions of its inhabitants, Rillao remained a healer and light-side user.

After the destruction of Firrerre, she fled with her unborn child, whom she later named Tigris and raised in solitude.

Hethrir captured many freighters, and when the Empire fell, he sold the hundreds of passengers aboard as slaves. He eventually found Rillao and imprisoned her in a web-like torture device aboard an abandoned slave freighter. He made Tigris a personal slave, keeping his parentage secret, and tricked him into believing his mother was a traitor. Rillao was rescued by Princess Leia Organa Solo, who was searching for her own children—kidnapped by Hethrir. Together they tracked Hethrir to the Crseih Research Station, where Rillao confronted Hethrir and Tigris with the truth. Tigris took the young Anakin Solo from Hethrir, who had planned to feed the boy to the Force-powerful Waru. In place of the child, the Waru consumed Hethrir, and Rillao and Tigris went to Coruscant.

**Rim, Ian** A lieutenant in the Kyp's Dozen starfighter squadron during the Yuuzhan Vong invasion, he was killed in battle against the alien invaders over Coruscant as the Dozen provided protection for Danni Quee's ship.

**rimble-wine** An expensive wine. A single bottle could fetch 1,000 credits or more during the New Republic era.

**Rimcee Station** A few days' distance from Bastion, it was the site of an Imperial penal colony.

**Rimkar** A Podracer who competed in a race on Tatooine sometime before the Boonta Eve Classic. He piloted a bizarre bubble-shaped Podracer that crashed when Sebulba forced him into a cliff face at Metta Drop.

**Rimkin** An elitist Core Worlds insult for anyone hailing from beyond the Inner Rim.

**Rimma** A star system that formed a navigational anchor point on the well-traveled Rimma Trade Route. During the Galactic Civil War, Alyk Krysusten was the Imperial Governor of Rimma.

**Rimma Trade Route** A major trade route that stretched from Abregado-rae in the Core Worlds to the Kathol sector. Major points along the route included Rimma, Fondor, Yag'Dhul, Giju, Thyferra, Sullust, Eriadu, and Clak'dor VII. It was founded about 5,500 years before the Battle of Yavin by Tapani sector merchants.

***Rim Merchant Einem*** A converted cargo hauler, this vessel served as Wilhuff Tarkin's headquarters during the attack he orchestrated upon Zonama Sekot with Trade Federation vessels. The ship sustained damage from being rammed during the assault.

**Rimmer's Rest** An extremely well-stocked cantina that was on Nar Shaddaa during the Galactic Civil War era.

**Rimon, Tev "Crasher"** An Imperial starfighter pilot during the time of Emperor Roan Fel, he served in Captain Gunn Yage's Skull Squadron.

**RiMPack** A neurological-enhancing cybernetic implant developed by 'Geneering Corporation, it immensely boosted a subject's reflexes and sensory input. Prolonged use or abuse of the implant led to sensory overload and extreme irrationality in the subject.

***Rimrider*** A stolen Imperial scout ship used by Halagad Ventor to escape Darth Vader and flee to the swamp world of Trinta.

***Rimrunner* (1)** One of many crashed starships on the surface of Tatooine, this Hutt vessel slammed into the Jundland Wastes many years before the Battle of Yavin.

***Rimrunner* (2)** Salla Zend's modified Gymsnor-4 light freighter, her first smuggling ship. It was consumed by a black hole after a botched hyperspace jump past the Maw during an ill-fated Kessel Run. Han Solo rescued Salla Zend from that disaster, which prompted Salla to reevaluate her life and propose settling down with Solo, an idea he did not appreciate.

**Rimsen, Captain** A New Republic fleet officer from Agamar, he commanded the *Corusca Fire* during the Yuuzhan Vong War. He arrived with Admiral Traest Kre'fey at the Battle of Dantooine to secure the New Republic's victory there.

**Rimsoo** *See* Republic Mobile Surgical Unit.

**Rin, Nei** A Yuuzhan Vong who lived in the time of Emperor Roan Fel, she led a group of warriors who had dedicated their lives to protecting the legacy of the Jedi Knights on the planet Ossus. Prior to the Jedi Massacre, she worked as a shaper to make Kol Skywalker's dream of terraforming damaged worlds into a reality.

**Rin, Obo** An Imperial sentientologist who worked for Darth Vader, he was the author of the *Catalog of Intelligent Life in the Galaxy,* a work of research accused of pro-human bias.

**Rina (O-Rina)** A Hospitality Guide on Kegan, she was a middle-aged woman with a broad face and curly gray hair when she introduced Padawan Obi-Wan Kenobi and his Master Qui-Gon Jinn to her world.

**Rin Assid bulk hauler** An antiquated transport design produced by the Eobaam Shipping Lines, this 700-meter-long ship could haul up to 100,000 metric tons of cargo. They were used in the Corporate Sector.

**Rindian** A member of a small-bodied alien species who had eight-fingered hands and melodious voices.

**Ringali Nebula** A spectacular stretch of violet gases, it was located within the Ringali Shell and could be seen in the night sky of all the Shell's planets.

**Ringali Shell** A region of space running from the mid-Core to the Colonies region, it encompassed the Bormea and Darpa sectors, the intersection of the Perlemian Trade Route and the Hydian Way, and the colorful Ringali Nebula.

**Ringneldia system** A system where Lando Calrissian picked up replacement parts for the *Millennium Falcon.* All part sizes in the Ringneldia system were standardized around the diameter of a native bean.

**Rinn** An Outer Rim backworld used by traders and smugglers as a hiding place, it was the home planet of the Tin-Tin Dwarf.

**Rintatta City** The site of a secondary spaceport on Exocron, it was near a short mountain range and used mostly by local military forces.

**Riome** A small, ice-covered world in the Dorvalla system, the site of a secret base used by Clan Toom. The clan leaders retreated there after betraying Lommite Limited and InterGalactic Ore, but Darth Maul—assigned to eliminate the clan—made certain the leaders of the companies knew the clan's location. Native life included ribbon-like sea-snakes.

**Ripoblus** Along with the planet Dimok, it was one of the two primary worlds of the Sepan system. A long war between Ripoblus and Dimok was forcibly ended by Imperial intervention after the Battle of Hoth, although the two worlds briefly and unsuccessfully tried to unite against the Empire as their common foe. During the war between the Galactic Alliance and the Confederation, Ripoblus reignited its feud with Dimok.

**Risant, Tendra** *See* Calrissian, Tendra Risant.

**Rishi** A planet that orbited a star called Rish in the Abrion sector, it was a hot and humid world of congested valleys where colonists lived, and high mountains populated by the native bird-like Rishii. The conservative colonists, most of whom were members of the fundamentalist religious sect called H'kig, lived in white stone buildings; they forbade the use of repulsorlift vehicles on the streets in the morning and had many rules concerning appearance and social mores. A commune of H'kig cultists who left Rishi in a doctrinal dispute some 50 years before the Battle of Yavin established a colony on J't'p'tan, within the borders of the Koornacht Cluster. Some 12 years after the Battle of Endor, the H'kig colony was supposedly wiped out by the fanatical Yevetha in what they called the Great Purge, but it was actually protected by the Fallanassi religious order.

Animal life on Rishi included the dangerous maungurs in the planet's warm polar regions; they had flexible limbtails and featured

Rishii

prominently in Rishii legends and stories. A number of criminal gangs established bases on the planet. Talon Karrde's smuggling organization briefly used a Rishi city-vale as a hideout following its evacuation of Myrkr. After Rogue Squadron resigned en masse from the New Republic military, the Rogues located a store of X-wing parts on Rishi, and Wedge Antilles and Ooryl Qrygg flew to Rishi and bought the cache.

**Rishi eel** A large, carnivorous moray-like creature native to the Rishi moon, it was capable of eating a clone trooper whole.

**Rishii** Small, peaceful avians, they lived in tribal clusters atop the mountains of the planet Rishi. Rishii had feathered wings along with human-like hands that helped them develop into primitive tool users. Each tribal cluster, or nest, was composed of a number of family groups. They had a knack for languages, which they learned by mimicking the sounds made by newcomers, but had very little interest in advanced technology.

**Rishi Maze** An irregular dwarf galaxy, it was in a close and decaying orbit about the main galaxy.

**Rishi moon** A moon in the Rishi system with a thin atmosphere and a stark, desolate rocky surface marked with craters, it was the site of a Republic outpost during the Clone Wars.

***Rising Star*** A star skimmer piloted by Raabakyysh, a young Wookiee of the Diversity Alliance.

**Riske, Jerv** A bounty hunter hired as a protector to Corporate Alliance Magistrate Passel Argente prior to the Clone Wars. During negotiations on Barlok between the Corporate Alliance and the Brolfi, Riske provided security for Argente and worked with Obi-Wan Kenobi and Anakin Skywalker to ensure safety.

**rissle stick** A contraband substance manufactured on Barlok.

**Ristel, Darsk** Corran Horn used this name as a cover during Rogue Squadron's reconnaissance mission to Imperial Center. Ristel was supposedly a telbun, the property of Ris Darsk, a wealthy Kuati who was on her way to Coruscant to conceive a child.

**Riten, Commander Atour** Chief librarian aboard the first Death Star, he had 40 years' worth of previous experience at the Library Galactica, as well as stints at the Baobab Archives on Manda, the Dorismus Athenaeum on Corellia, and the Holorepository on Arkam 13. Something of a cynic, he tried to remain politically neutral throughout his career in the Galactic Empire, focusing his energies instead on archival work. He was a skilled slicer as well, and used this talent to help facilitate the escape of several disillusioned workers appalled at the destructive power of the Death Star following the obliteration of Alderaan. Riten stayed behind, however, and perished when the Death Star exploded at the Battle of Yavin.

**Rithgar** An aged pirate, he was the administrator of the Kothlis Shadowport during the Galactic Civil War.

**Ritsomas, Bufus** A Galactic Senator representing Till Chorios during the final years of the Republic, he was implicated in an Outer Rim slave ring scandal prior to the Clone Wars, along with Senators Tikkes, Ledwellow, and Wojaine.

**Riva** Denetrus's landlady on Telus, she had survived the famine on the planet about 60 years before the Battle of Naboo.

**Rivan, Darth** An ancient Sith Lord who chose the planet Almas as his home, he built a massive domed fortress on that world. Rivan possessed some expertise in biology, and used the Force and his knowledge to develop a new species of plant he called kaluthin. Kaluthin's unique properties include the ability to synthesize methane from the air and create oxygen, and a taproot that reached deep into the crust of the planet. He spread the kaluthin across the surface of Almas, and they slowly changed the planet's climate and atmosphere. Before Rivan's death, his creations had begun to terraform the planet from an unlivable nightmare into the garden-like world it became.

Darth Rivan was driven from Almas by the Jedi during the Sith Wars, and his dome-like home blasted into pieces. The central fortress remained, somehow impervious to blaster fire. The Jedi, thinking that the fortress was not worth the continued effort, decided to leave it intact. Rivan perished in the Battle of Ruusan.

Obi-Wan Kenobi points to Rishi Maze on view screen.

**Rivan, Dix** A quiet member of Rogue Squadron during the Galactic Civil War, he was affectionately nicknamed Dixie by his squadmates. He served as Rogue Five, the unit's rear guard, always watching out for his friends and ready to provide whatever aid was needed. He perished when his X-wing was shot down by a TIE fighter during a raid on the moon Gall, when the Rebels attempted to recover Han Solo's carbon-frozen form from Boba Fett.

***River of Blood*** A Yuuzhan Vong warship that arrived at the conquered planet of Coruscant prior to the attack on Mon Calamari late in the war.

**River of Light** A river on Qui-Gon Jinn's homeworld. Qui-Gon gave Obi-Wan Kenobi a stone from the River of Light on the boy's 13th birthday. When Anakin Skywalker turned 13, Obi-Wan gave that same stone to him. It was a smooth black rock that glowed with its own heat.

**Rivers, Meghan** A Rebel survivor evacuated from the Battle of Hoth aboard the transport *Bright Hope.*

**Rivers of Stone** A cavern on Dathomir where Barukka lived. It was named for its flowing patterns of rock.

**River Solleu** A river on Naboo. The city of Theed was built on a plateau overlooking a waterfall created by the River Solleu. The river was fed by underground tributaries flowing through the planet's interior. The largest of the waterfalls was the Virdugo Plunge.

**River Weeping** A major waterway on Vjun that fed into the Bay of Tears.

**Rivi-Anu** A young Jedi who served with Ki-Adi-Mundi at Mygeeto during the Clone Wars, she sacrificed herself to slow the impact of a Republic cruiser into the planet's surface.

**Rivorian grain-bandit** A thieving rodent that could wipe out an entire field of crops in one evening.

**Riwwel, Admiral** A fleet officer in the early Galactic Empire, he was responsible for the bombardment of the city of Eluthan on Acherin, even after the resistance forces led by General Toma had surrendered to the Imperials.

***Rizaron*** A Yevethan guardian thrustship, it patrolled the orbital shipyard at ILC-905.

**RK-7** A commander battle droid that participated in the Battle of Naboo, it was deactivated upon the destruction of the Droid Control Ship.

**Rkk'tl'kt** A member of the Tusken Raider clan led by Sharad Hett. When a female krayt dragon plagued the Tuskens, Rkk'tl'kt joined Sharad, his son A'Sharad, and several other Sand People on a mission to slay the beast. In the creature's cave, they discovered Ki-Adi-Mundi under attack by the immense krayt dragon. Rkk'tl'kt used his traditional gaderffii to injure the beast. Moments later, the krayt dragon clamped her jaws around Rkk'tl'kt's hand, severing the appendage and seriously wounding the Tusken Raider. A'Sharad, Ki-Adi-Mundi, and Sharad later struck as one to kill the krayt dragon before any others could be hurt. After the battle, however, Rkk'tl'kt voluntarily remained behind when the other Tuskens returned to their camp. Perhaps because he believed that he could no longer serve the clan as a warrior, Rkk'tl'kt used a Tusken bloodletting blade to commit suicide.

**Rkok clan** A Jawa clan, it unloaded a cargo of questionable merchandise on crime lord Jabba the Hutt. Later, the Nkik clan found the remains of the destroyed Rkok sandcrawler at the edge of the Great Pit of Carkoon. No sign of the Rkok Jawas was found.

**R'lyek** An ancient Twi'lek clan embroiled in a long-standing fued with the Doneeta clan. After the Great Sith War, Jedi Knight Tott Doneeta returned to Ryloth and merged the two clans in an effort to bring about peace.

**RMD-20 Eye in the Sky** From Kystallio Detection Plus, this was a small, ball-shaped monitor droid that floated about on its own repulsorlifts. During the Clone Wars, clone troopers used it for limited aerial recon of immediate environments.

**Ro, Ambassador Loreli** A beautiful Mere ambassador who sought the aid of the pirate Nym. She traced Nym to Rodia, where she offered him 50,000 credits to return to the Karthakk system to deal with the criminal Sol Sixxa. On Maramere, she provided Nym's group with a cutter known as the *Sunrunner.* Nym had Loreli plot a course for the site of one of Sol Sixxa's recent targets. She believed Sol Sixxa to be dead after Nym rammed the *Sunrunner* into Sixxa's ship, the *Revenant.* She later allied with Nym and his pirates during the attack of Cavik Toth.

**Roa** A onetime smuggler and blockade runner, Roa gave Han Solo one of his first fringe jobs and took him on one of his first Kessel runs. He eventually retired from the smuggling trade, becoming a respectable and successful entrepreneur, and settling down with a singer named Lwyll. He owned one of the largest import–export firms serving the planets of Roonadan and Bonadan. Roa often espoused his rules to live by, the so-called Roa's Rules:

Roa

- Never ignore a call for help.
- Take only from those who are richer than yourself.
- Don't play sabacc unless you're prepared to lose.
- Don't pilot a ship under the influence.
- Always be prepared to make a quick getaway.

He failed to follow that last piece of advice during the Yuuzhan Vong War, when he was consumed by an enormous serpentine dread weapon that attacked the *Jubilee Wheel* during the Battle of Ord Mantell. Imprisoned by the Yuuzhan Vong, Roa became friends with fellow prisoner Wurth Skidder, a Jedi Knight. Though he eventually was rescued, Roa lost his wife, Lwyll, who was killed in a Yuuzhan Vong attack. During this time, Roa piloted a SoroSuub Luxury 3000 space yacht called the *Happy Dagger.*

***Roaming Ronto*** A modern Gallofree medium transport that was part of the Bornaryn Trading Company fleet during the Swarm War.

**Roan, Supreme Governor** The successor to Supreme Governor Ewane on New Apsolon, he was one of the first few Civilized who first called for social change. After Ewane's death, he looked after Ewane's daughters, who were kidnapped by dissidents demanding that he give up his position for their return. Though he agreed to their demands, the kidnappers killed Roan anyway.

**Roat, Antar** Wedge Antilles took this name during his undercover mission on Imperial Center with Rogue Squadron. He posed as an Imperial colonel shot down and badly injured during the defense of Vladet, coming to Imperial Center for reconstruction at the Rohair Biomechanical Clinic.

**roba** These porcine creatures found on Taanab and Aralia were bred on farms. They served as a primary food source.

***Robber Baron*** An Imperial Star Galleon stolen and converted into the pirate flagship of Reginald Barkbone.

**robeskin** *See* oozhith.

***Robida Colossus*** A Ganathan steam-powered battleship, it towed a badly damaged *Millennium Falcon* into port after its close escape from Boba Fett.

**robo-bartender** A droid programmed in mixology and the running of a cantina or tapcaf.

**robo-hack** Repulsorlift taxis found in the Corporate Sector and elsewhere that were piloted by a droid brain.

**robot ramship** Suicidal droid starships made up of the shell of a junked warship and the brain of a pilot droid. Assembled by the Outer Rim's shadiest outlaw techs, they were a deceptive, dishonorable, and flagrantly destructive innovation in space warfare. Robot ramships were used to great effect during the Battle of Centerpoint Station, the final conflict of the Corellian crisis. The Sacorrian Triad deployed a fleet that included four bulbous-nosed frigates guided by unstable droid intellects. When battle with the New Republic was joined, the quartet of ramships zeroed in on the Bakura flagship *Intruder* from disparate vectors.

**robot scoop** An automated robot/vehicle used to clear debris. After the Battle of Geonosis, a scoop picked up the broken droids destroyed during the battle for recycling at the droid scrap yard. Boba Fett used a robot scoop to carry away the body of his father, Jango Fett, from the arena where he was beheaded by Mace Windu.

**robot starfighter** *See* TIE fighter; vulture droid.

**Roche** The shorthand term for a Verpine manufacturing company. Its full name, translated into Basic, was Roche Hive Mechanical Apparatus Design And Construction Activity For Those Who Need The Hive's Machines. It was the maker of the 8d8 smelting operator, 11-17 miner droid, and J9 worker drone.

**Roche system** This system contained the Roche asteroid field, a relatively stable configuration of asteroids orbiting a small yellow sun. In addition to mynocks and space slugs, the Roche field was home to the intelligent insectoid species called the Verpine. New Republic forces were dispatched to the Roche system to help prevent a war between the Verpine and the Barabel species after the Battle of Endor.

**Rock Council** Wookiee elders and leaders who served as the planetary government of Kashyyyk. The council derived its name from the volcanic basalt outcropping that served as its gathering point.

**rock dragon** A mottled-skin reptile native to Dathomir, it was armed with a poisonous stinger.

Clone rock-jumpers scale a sheer cliff on the planet Teth.

**Rock Dragon** A Hapan passenger cruiser used by Jaina Solo and Lowbacca to fly to the remains of the Alderaan system, it was a gift to Tenel Ka from her parents.

**rocket battle droid** A Separatist battle droid equipped with a slim rocket pack for maneuvering in deep space.

**rocket-jumper** Members of the Republic armed forces some 4,000 years before the Galactic Civil War, they used rocket packs to aid them in their aerial attacks on Republic foes.

**rocket trooper** Specialized stormtroopers who wore jetpacks built into their armor and carried Merr-Sonn PLX-2M missile launchers. Rocket troopers soared above battles to inflict maximum damage on enemy troops. Too small to be tracked by ships and too quick for the average ground troop to hit, rocket troopers were dangerous, but their numbers were small due to the difficulty of effectively using a jetpack.

**rockhopper** Two-legged riding beasts found on Roon, they were used in racing events as part of the Roon Colonial Games.

**rock jumpers** A term used by Captain Rex to describe the clone troopers under his command trained specifically for mountaineering and cliff climbing. They used ascension guns fitted beneath their standard blaster rifles to climb up the sides of sheer cliff faces, like those found on the spires of Teth.

**rockmelon** A hard-shelled fruit enjoyed by the subterranean Elom species.

**rock shrew** A small animal preyed upon by avians.

**rock spitter** New Republic fighter pilot slang term for the plasma cannon weapons on Yuuzhan Vong coralskippers.

**rock sucker** A mollusk native to Mytus VII that drew trace minerals from the planet's stony crust.

**rock viper** A poisonous serpent native to Ord Cestus.

**rock wart** A skittering insectoid pest nearly 1 meter in length, it scavenged in the rocky terrain on Tatooine and other desert environs, hiding in the shadows until it spotted prey. A rock wart attacked if surprised, stinging with a painful neurotoxin capable of killing even large prey. Rock warts laid their eggs within larger creatures, providing larval rock warts with sustenance when they hatched.

Rock wart

**rock workers** A division among the laborers of New Apsolon. They were miners by trade.

**rocshore fish** Spiny-bodied swimmers with three large claws, they were a dietary staple among the Senalis. Shy creatures, they buried themselves in the mud whenever boats approached.

**Rodan, Fyor** A politician from Commenor, he was a member of Chief of State Borsk Fey'lya's advisory council in the New Republic. At Fyor's request, Luke Skywalker discussed with the council the idea of reestablishing the old Jedi Council, though Rodan was no friend of Luke's and opposed the idea. Where Rodan's anti-Jedi sentiments stemmed from was uncertain, but it was known he had a brother named Tormak whose smuggling operations were greatly curtailed by the policing actions of the Jedi Knights. As the war against the Yuuzhan Vong dragged on, Rodan showed his support to Fey'lya by favoring the defense of Bothawui over Corellia. After the New Republic government was ousted from Coruscant and Fey'lya died in the Yuuzhan Vong invasion, Rodan tried to assist self-appointed Chief of State Pwoe in securing the government, until Pwoe revealed his efforts to be part of a personal agenda. Rodan abandoned Pwoe and joined the provisional council that had convened on Mon Calamari. Despite his best efforts to become the new Chief of State, he was bested by Cal Omas. Skywalker and Omas nullified the fears that the Jedi were too powerful by placing non-Jedi on the High Council.

In the years after the Yuuzhan Vong War, Rodan continued to be wary of Cal Omas's policies and practices, and when Corellia's bid for independence tipped the galaxy once again toward civil war, Rodan developed plans to secure independence for Commenor. As Prime Minster, Rodan approved a plan for the world to secretly develop its own fleets. The Dark Lady Lumiya, using a Hapan disguise, coerced Rodan into joining the Confederation opposed to the Galactic Alliance.

**Rodan, Tormak** A Commenorian smuggler and older brother of Fyor Rodan, he flew contraband out of Nar Shaddaa for Jabba the Hutt. The Rodan brothers hated each other.

**RO-D droid** A bodyguard droid developed for traveling musicians and entertainers by Balmorran Arms. Each was equipped with an array of short-range sensors, lethal and nonlethal armaments, and dedicated life-protection programming. Furthermore, the series was designed specifically for the movement of heavy instruments and sound-magnification equipment. Also included were pitch-frequency analysis and rhythmic persistence functions. The droids' external coverings were available in 70 different color schemes to match virtually any stage setup.

**Rodd, Senator** A middle-aged human Senator of the Fondor system, Tapani sector, who conspired with Groodo the Hutt during the later years of the Galactic Republic. He usually wore a black uniform that bore the embroidered logo of Republic Sienar Systems. Chased by Jango Fett and other bounty hunters, Rodd escaped Lunavolver Delta in his Sienar Senatorial transport to Groodo's compound on Esseles for protection. He later

*Rodia cities sport impressive environmental shields.*

brought the Tapani sector into the Confederation of Independent Systems.

**Rodia** Located in the Tyrius system halfway between Gall and Coruscant, this industrial planet was home to the violence-loving Rodians and their vast weapons-manufacturing facilities. Rodia was a lush tropical world, but rapid industrial growth made numerous lifeforms extinct, necessitating the import of many foodstuffs. Still, vast areas of jungle and swampland dominated the surface, with Rodian cities built atop waterways and protected by environmental shields

During the Separatist crisis, Rodia was represented in the Galactic Senate by Onaconda Farr, a longtime family friend of Padmé Amidala. Farr was harshly critical of Palpatine's handling of the Separatists, but was nonetheless appointed to his Loyalist Committee after Senator Havriso Looruya of Yir Tangee stepped down. Once the Clone Wars erupted, Rodia was censured due to missteps and mismanagement of military assets, and suffered supply shortages due to rampant piracy around its borders. Padmé Amidala voyaged to Rodia to ensure its loyalty. During the Yuuzhan Vong War, the planet was invaded and conquered by the aliens.

**Rodian** Beings with rough green skin, multifaceted eyes, and tapir-like snouts, they came from the planet Rodia. A ridge of spines topped a Rodian's skull, and their long, flexible fingers ended in suction cups. Rodians evolved as hunters, driving much of the wildlife—especially predators—on their planet to extinction. The Rodians grew restless with nothing to hunt, and turned to hunting one another in gladiatorial combat. One of the greatest of the Rodian Grand Protectors called an end to this self-slaughter around the time that Republic ships made contact with the species. The Grand Protector saw the expansion into the galaxy as an opportunity for the Rodians to hunt new species and targets.

As a result, Rodians took to bounty hunting. Many accepted contracts as part of grand games and contests, caring nothing for the concept of law enforcement. Rodian society awarded bounty hunting in a wide variety of categories—Longest Trail, Most Notorious Capture, Best Shot, and more. Because some Rodians started padding their hunts by allowing their quarries to commit further crimes, increasing their bounties, they acquired a shady reputation. This, combined with the pungent pheromones that Rodians naturally exuded, fomented common intolerence toward their kind.

Despite the Rodian thirst for violence and a history marked by interclan wars, the Rodians had a rich culture. Harido Kavila, a renowned Rodian Grand Protector, further attempted to steer the violent tendencies of the Rodian people into a more constructive direction by encouraging the production of drama. Rodian theater works became among the most poignant, well-respected, and violent productions in the galaxy.

Rodian society was tightly controlled by the Rodian Grand Protector, and only the most accomplished hunters were encouraged to leave their planet. Some clans, most notably the Tetsus, were peaceful. Years before the Battle of Yavin, Navik the Red, the Rodian leader of the Chattza clan who eventually became Grand Protector of Rodia, eliminated many opposing clan leaders and nearly wiped out the entire Tetsus clan. Greedo, a novice bounty hunter in the employ of Jabba the Hutt, was a Rodian and a surviving member of the Tetsus clan.

*Rodian*

Other notable Rodians included Wald, Anakin Skywalker's boyhood friend; Andoorni Hui, a female pilot and member of the Rebel Alliance's famed Rogue Squadron; Avaro Sookcool, an obese casino owner; and Senator Onaconda Farr.

**Rodian cryogen whip** A coiled whip with an outer coating of flexible metal plates, the core of the weapon circulated super-cold cryogenic fluids, which gave it an extra-painful impact.

**Rodian Hunting Grounds** *See* Etyyy.

**Rodian repulsor throwing-razor** A specially balanced throwing blade built around microrepulsors.

**Rodian Salvage Cartel** An organization of Rodian scavengers that controlled large areas on the junk world of Raxus Prime.

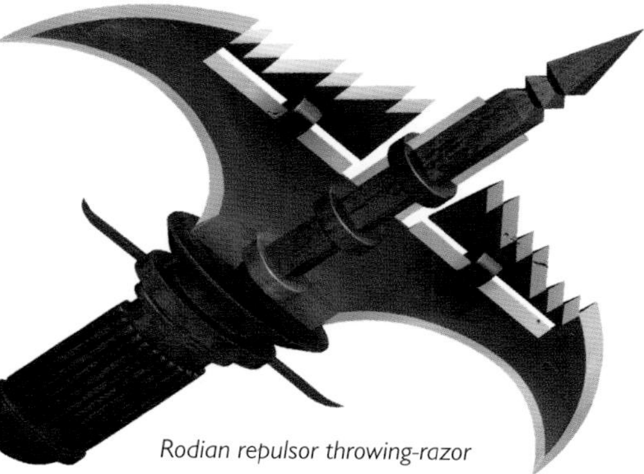
*Rodian repulsor throwing-razor*

**Rodisar** A reptilian species native to Rodis, a planet that experienced seasonal wars among its primitive inhabitants.

**Rodo** A hulking human bouncer from Ragith III, he worked at the Soft Heart Cantina on Coruscant. He and the proprietor, Memah Roothes, relocated to the first Death Star as it was undergoing finalization. There they worked at the Hard Heart Cantina. Dismayed by the destruction of Alderaan, Rodo, Memah, and a number of other deserters decided to flee the station. Rodo was killed by stormtroopers during the attempt.

**Roeg** An Imperial gantry officer who served aboard the first Death Star.

**Roenni** A quiet girl who was a member of the Young during the final civil wars on Melida/Daan. She was small, slender, and agile, and had brown eyes. Since her father had been a starfighter mechanic, she grew up around every kind of air transport available. She knew how to use a fusioncutter, and how to disable a power converter. After Cerasi's death and throughout the ostracizing of Padawan Obi-Wan Kenobi from the Young, Roenni remained Obi-Wan's friend.

**roga** Small crawling creatures that infested the high mesas of Geonosis.

**roggwart** A two-legged monster that served as a pet of General Grievous in his private lair on Vassek. Its rocky hide was resistant to laser blasts, and it had a long gooey projectile tongue. It was killed by Kit Fisto and Nahdar Vebb during the Clone Wars, when they infiltrated Grievous's sanctuary.

**Rogoe, Boss** A notorious Gungan warlord who was ultimately defeated by Boss Gallo. One of Rogoe's more insidious tactics was to use bursas to attack Otoh Sancture. His fortress city known as Spearhead was overtaken and remade to become Otoh Gunga.

**Rogriss, Admiral Teren** An Imperial officer, he continued to serve the Empire long after the Battle of Endor. When his own overreaching ambition led him to defeat in conflicts with warlords and the New Republic, he lost his fleet command but retained his admiralty and the flagship Star Destroyer *Agonizer.* Though he relinquished his command to avoid carrying out genocidal orders against Adumar, Rogriss—who had secretly aided General Solo against Zsinj years before—refused to join the New Republic. He did, however, accept a position as Defense Minister to Cartann's young perator, Balass ke Teldan, which carried with it the rank of general in the Adumari Planetary Defense Forces.

**Rogua** One of the Gamorrean guards who worked for Jabba the Hutt, he was posted at the palace's main entrance alongside the guard leader, Ortugg.

**Rogue Eight** The call sign of Erisi Dlarit during her time in Rogue Squadron. Other pilots to use this call sign included Leth Liav, Koobis Nu, Avan Beruss, and Nawara Ven.

**Rogue Eleven** The call sign for Tenk Lenso during the Battle of Hoth. He, alongside Rogue Ten, investigated Echo Station 3-8 and transported Han Solo and Chewbacca to the site of an Imperial probe droid. Other pilots to use the Rogue Eleven call sign over the years included Wes Janson, Plourr Illo, Lujayne Forge, Dinger, and Jaina Solo.

**Rogue Five** Wes Janson's call sign during most of his time with Rogue Squadron. Other pilots to use this call sign included Gavin Darklighter, Dix Rivan, Tal'dira, and Inyri Forge.

**Rogue Flight** *See* Rogue Squadron.

**Rogue Four** The comm unit designation for Rebel pilot Derek "Hobbie" Klivian's snowspeeder during the Battle of Hoth. Other pilots to use the Rogue Four call sign included Bror Jace and Pash Cracken.

**Rogue Group** *See* Rogue Squadron.

**Rogue Leader** The comm unit designation for Rebel pilot Luke Skywalker's snowspeeder during the Battle of Hoth. Other Rogue Leaders included Wedge Antilles, Tycho Celchu, Gavin Darklighter, Lensi, Jaina Solo, and Jhoram Bey.

**Rogue Moon** An errant planetoid that inhabited the asteroid belt ringing Taris's sun—traveling in retrograde, against the direction of the other debris. Theories differed as to its origin. Thousands of meteors impacted its surface every hour, ranging from microscopic to colossal. During a Jedi training exercise there, about 4,000 years before the Battle of Yavin, the Covenant had visions of a Sith uprising that prompted them to murder their Padawans.

**Rogue Nine** The call sign used by Tycho Celchu when he first joined Rogue Squadron. Other pilots to use this call sign included Corran Horn and Alinn Varth.

**Rouge Seven** The call sign used by Rhysati Ynr during her time with Rogue Squadron. Other pilots known as Rogue Seven included Keir Santage, Ran Kether, Kasan Moor, Feylis Ardele, Myn Donos, Ran Kether, Ligg Panat, and Dakorse Teep.

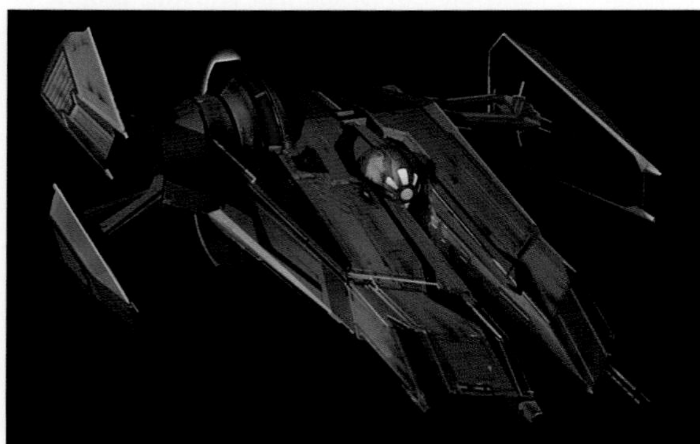

Rogue Shadow

**Rogue Six** The call sign used by such Rogue Squadron pilots as Wes Janson, Dix Rivan, Derek "Hobbie" Klivian, and Gavin Darklighter.

***Rogue Shadow*** An experimental prototype starship, the *Rogue Shadow* was the personal transport of Darth Vader's secret apprentice known as Starkiller. The vessel boasted an advanced hyperdrive, cutting-edge sensory arrays, several concealed laser cannons, and the fastest sublight engines in the Imperial fleet. Capable of transporting Starkiller virtually anywhere in the galaxy, the starship's layout included a fully functional medical bay, crew quarters, a workshop, and a meditation chamber that could double as a training room. *Rogue Shadow*'s most impressive feature, however, was its experimental cloaking device, which could keep the vessel hidden from even the most powerful scanners for short periods of time.

Although Starkiller was a capable pilot, Vader preferred that he remain focused on his missions. To allow the apprentice time to meditate and train, Vader appointed a series of handpicked Imperial officers to pilot the ship. Each of the pilots—seven in all—met a grisly end. Then came Juno Eclipse, an experienced commander who had led the attack on the planet Callos and was also the first woman to occupy the *Rogue Shadow*'s pilot's chair.

**Rogue Squadron** This squadron of top pilots was formed after the Battle of Yavin. Luke Skywalker took command of the group after the Battle of Hoth and came up with the concept of a squadron without a set mission profile, allowing Rogue Squadron to take on any mission that came its way. Skywalker combined the best pilots with the best fighters and taught them to work as a single unit.

When he left to spend more time at his Jedi studies, Wedge Antilles took charge of the squadron, composed of 12 X-wings and their pilots and astromech droids. The squadron became a symbol of the bravery and fighting spirit of the Galactic Alliance and was involved in numerous adventures and rescues of top Alliance officials.

After the Rebel Alliance victory at the Battle of Endor, the Provisional Council sent Antilles around the galaxy on a sort of goodwill tour. Every world wanting to join the Alliance sent its best pilots, and all of them expected to be part of Rogue Squadron. Antilles had to wade through this political thicket to select the 12 candidates best qualified for membership, based partly on test scores and partly on the worlds from which they came. After training exercises at Folor, the chosen 12 were sent to a temporary base at Talasea. On their journey in the Chorax system, they were pulled out of hyperspace and forced into their first real fight, proving they had the right stuff.

One of the Rogues' first real missions was the rescue of stranded Rebel operatives on Hensara III. Their first loss came when stormtroopers raided their base at Talasea, killing one Rogue and six base personnel. The squadron made a retaliatory strike against the Imperial base at Vladet, destroying it completely. The Provisional Council, in its eagerness to expand territory toward Coruscant, next approved a plan by General Laryn Kre'fey to take a small

Rogue Squadron in action . . . as always.

Imperial base at Borleias. But information obtained by Bothan spies proved wrong, and two Rogues lost their lives in the attack. With better intel, they returned and finished the job.

Rogue Squadron played a major role in liberating Coruscant from Imperial control, became heavily involved in the so-called Bacta War, and battled against Grand Admiral Thrawn and a host of other threats facing the New Republic and the Galactic Alliance.

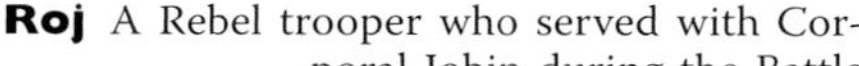

Redkihl Rokk

**Rogue Ten** The call sign used by Tarrin Datch during the Battle of Hoth. Other pilots to use Rogue Ten as their call sign included Soontir Fel and Ooryl Qrygg.

**Rogue Three** The comm unit designation for Rebel pilot Wedge Antilles's snowspeeder during the Battle of Hoth. Other pilots to use the call sign included Gavin Darklighter, Nrin Vakil, Pedna Scotian, Kenn Tiram, and Lyyr Zatoq.

**Rogue Twelve** The call sign used by Rogue Squadron pilots Andoorni Hui, Aril Nunb, Inyri Forge, Anni Capstan, and Lensi.

**Rogue Two** The comm unit designation for Rebel pilot Zev Senesca's snowspeeder during the Battle of Hoth. Other pilots to use this call sign included Will Scotian, Wedge Antilles, Ibtisam, Tycho Celchu, Kral Nevil, and Peshk Vri'syk.

**Rogue Wing** A starfighter wing (12 squadrons, or 72 starfighters) that grew out of the original Rogue Squadron active during the New Republic. It consisted of a mix of starfighter designs, and was commanded by General Wedge Antilles.

**Roh** A Hapan Royal Guard, she was tasked with the protection of Queen Mother Tenel Ka. After a failed assassination attempt, Roh and fellow guard Beyele were part of a small investigation team led by Major Moreen Espara and Jacen Solo.

**Rohair Biochemical Clinic** A reconstructive surgery clinic in Imperial City on Coruscant used as part of a cover story for Iella Wessiri.

**Rohlan the Questioner** *See* Dyre, Rohlan.

**Roi, Fitz** A flamboyant jatz musician famous throughout the Core Worlds during the Galactic Civil War. The notorious cat burglar known as the Tombat stole Roi's prized antique slugthrowers.

**Roite, Major Barst** An officer in the Thyferran Home Defense Corps who oversaw the day-to-day operations of Aerin Dlarit's command.

**Roj** A Rebel trooper who served with Corporal Jobin during the Battle of Hoth.

**Rojahn, Captain** The Imperial commander of the *Carrack*-class cruiser *Expeditious.* Former Corellian Security officer Gil Bastra was being held prisoner aboard this ship when he died after interrogation by Kirtan Loor.

**Rojo, Warshack** A Corellian human, he was commander of the New Republic Star Destroyer *Rejuvenator.* He was an imposing man with a shaved head, a furrowed brow, and a single, glittering diamond earring. Leia Organa Solo asked Rojo to provide support for Destrillion and Dubrillion in anticipation of an early Yuuzhan Vong attack. The hardheaded Corellian did not wait for further vessels from the New Republic to arrive before he took the battle to the Helska system. He died when the *Rejuvenator* was destroyed in the battle.

**Rojo fever** A fast-spreading, often fatal disease that required immediate quarantine upon diagnosis.

**Roke, Boss** A human who was in charge of prisoner crews in the spice mines of Kessel, he had a lumpy face and a chin covered with bristly black stubble.

**Rokk, Redkihl** An alien pirate also known as the Scavenger of the Galaxy, he was a Huralok from the world of Djurmo. His ship, *Hungry Ghost,* and his fleet of red TIE fighters encountered the *Millennium Falcon* while scavenging the debris of the destroyed Death Star at Yavin.

**Rokna tree fungus** A deadly blue fungus also known as Rokna blue or the blue, it was common on the Forest Moon of Endor. The tree fungus was both a lethal poison and an addictive drug. When taken in tiny doses, the blue caused euphoria. It also damaged a person's memory beyond repair, however, leading to rapid aging and, eventually, death.

**Roko** The first mate aboard space pirate Finhead Stonebone's *Starjacker* about 4,000 years before the Galactic Civil War, he was killed by Great Bogga the Hutt's pet, Ktriss.

**Rokrul** A loose affiliation of Nelvaanian tribes that banded together for mutual protection and assistance. During the Clone Wars, Confederacy experiments plunged Rokrul villages into a perpetual winter and kidnapped warriors for a mutant soldier development project. Anakin Skywalker destroyed the Confederacy laboratory, returning warmth to Rokrul and freeing the captive warriors.

**Rolado, Corporal Vyn** A Rebel Alliance scout who helped establish Echo Base on Hoth. As a native of Velmor, his experiences riding ycaqts helped prepare him for taming wild tauntauns.

**Rolion sector** With over 750 bases, this sector was firmly under the control of the Empire during the Galactic Civil War.

**rolk-mangir** Enormous predatory creatures native to Yinchorr. Their name translated to "horned death" in the Yinchorri tongue.

**rollerfish** A species of fish native to Kamino. Boba and Jango Fett went fishing for

Rolk-mangir

rollerfish off the edge of the Tipoca City platforms, using a laser-aimed spear thrower known as a pocker.

**rolo-droid (R-PK)** Also known as a recon-PK or R-PK droid, these small uniwheeled droids were developed by Cybot Galactica prior to the Battle of Naboo. They were popular among bounty hunters and slave owners to keep an eye on their property.

*Rolo-droid (R-PK)*

**Rol'Waran** A Twi'lek spice smuggler who ran his operation out of the freighter *Starmaster,* stationed in orbit over Ryloth during the Yuuzhan Vong War. He had filed teeth and pink eyes. Rol'Waran worked for Crev Bombaasa. Talon Karrde met with him to gain information regarding Hutt operations.

**Romany** A Ryn refugee and biologist, he was Mezza's rival clan leader. He spent some time working with Han and Jaina Solo at Hydroponics Two on Duro. During the Yuuzhan Vong invasion of Duro, he and Mezza helped Leia Organa Solo with the refugee evacuation effort.

**Romar** A planet in the Galov sector of the Outer Rim, it was the site of Imperial Moff Antoll Jellrek's estate near the rocky spires of the Derrbi Wastelands. When the outlaw Jai Raventhorn tried to assassinate the Moff, she encountered the notorious bounty hunter Beylyssa.

**Romba** An Ewok scout who prepared defenses around his village against AT-ST walkers during the Battle of Endor.

**Romey, Major Belyssa** A Rebel Alliance officer, she served the 132nd Forward Division in the Atrivis sector.

**Romin** A small tropical world turned into a criminal haven by the thuggish dictatorship of Roy Teda. He altered planetary law, making it impossible to extradite any wanted criminal from Romin. The cost of sanctuary was quite high, and Romin profited from the many fugitives who came to ground there. The wealthiest of the native Romins profited from Teda's operation, while the vast majority of the poorer Romins were displaced from the city centers and forced to live in decaying shantytowns. Padawan Anakin Skywalker, Ferus Olin, Siri Tachi, and Obi-Wan Kenobi aided in the revolution that deposed Teda. The native inhabitants had gold skin, flat noses, and wide mouths.

**Romodi, Senator** A highly placed man in the Imperial echelons, he served as a member of Grand Moff Tarkin's command staff aboard the first Death Star.

**Romodi Interstellar** A major passenger line based out of Coruscant, it ferried many citizens displaced by the secession of Ando and Sy Myrth during the Separatist crisis.

**Ronay** Along with Bador, one of two moons that orbited Kuat.

**Rondai II** A temperate planet, it was the site of Ulta Center, a luxurious high-security conference center for secret meetings. It was inhabited by dark-haired sentients called the Rondai.

**Rone, Pastav** A Twin Suns Squadron pilot who flew as Twin Suns Ten. During Operation Starlancer of the Yuuzhan Vong War, Rone's ship was disabled by Yuuzhan Vong coralskippers. Afterward, Pastav spent time in a bacta tank before returning to piloting.

**Ronika** A world in the Koros system (later renamed the Empress Teta system) first settled some 5,000 years before the Galactic Civil War. The harsh planet was used first by Empress Teta's government as a prison planet, where hardened criminals were sent to work off their debt to society by preparing Ronika for large-scale settlement. The planet was arid and covered in difficult, rocky terrain. Although it was rich in ore, mining operations were treacherous because of the landscape. The atmosphere was also permeated with hazardous ultraviolet rays, requiring the use of ultraviolet eye shields. Native fauna included the stinger moth, a tiny insect with a highly venomous bite. After their defeat during the Unification Wars, the Kirrek rebels were sentenced to a life of hard labor on Ronika, although they eventually were released to help Empress Teta's forces battle the Sith in the Great Hyperspace War. About this time, hyperspace explorer Jori Daragon, who had incurred the wrath of the Tetan government, was also imprisoned on the planet for a short time. Jori eventually escaped on a drone ore shuttle and participated in the battle against the Sith.

**ronk** A dangerous carnivore native to Cilpar. Males were considered a delicacy, but females were poisonous. Ronks were nocturnal and were not considered dangerous in the day unless they were disturbed.

**Ronson** One of the Peacekeepers who guarded the survivors of the Outbound Flight Project.

**RonTha** A boring, long-winded Meerian, he ran the Agricultural Corps base on the planet Bandomeer during the time when the AgriCorps was working to overcome decades of damage done by mining operations.

**ronto** A huge but gentle pack animal, it was used as a beast of burden by the Jawas on Tatooine. Rontos, which averaged about 4.25 meters tall, were known for both their loyalty and their strength. They could carry hundreds of kilograms of equipment and were large enough to frighten off most attackers, including Tusken Raiders. They were also skittish and easily spooked, especially in more congested urban areas.

Rontos, which were saurian in appearance, were easy to train and were quite fond of their masters. They had a superb sense of smell—they could pick up a krayt dragon a kilometer away—but because of their poor vision they were often startled by sudden movement. Rontos needed plenty of water, but since their skin easily shed excess heat, they were well suited to Tatooine's harsh desert environment.

**Ronto clan** One of several groups of Jedi younglings ages 8 through 10 studying at Luke Skywalker's Jedi academy on Ossus, following the Yuuzhan Vong War.

***Ronto*-class transport** Named for the pack animal from Tatooine, this slow, inefficient Damorian Manufacturing Corporation transport was deemed ugly by many seasoned spacers.

**rontu** A large wide-tongued mammal native to Drongar.

**Ronyards** When droids ceased functioning, their bodies were discarded on this junkyard world. Legends stated that over the centuries, Ronyards developed a consciousness from the aggregated droid brains discarded on its surface. The surviving droids on the planet's surface worshipped this entity as their living god.

**Roofoo** *See* Evazan, Dr.

**Roogak, Captain** The leader of the Ithorian herd ship *Galactic Horizon* during the early years of the Galactic Civil War, he was unusually greedy for an Ithorian—but he was nevertheless loyal to his friends.

*Ronto*

**rooj** A grain crop grown by the Taat on the Jwlio moon. In an effort to force the Taat from the moon, the Chiss used a chemical defoliant to destroy the rooj crops during the events precipitating the Swarm War.

**Rookie One** A youth who grew up on a moisture farm on Tatooine, he lost his family in a freak farm-machinery accident. A skilled and enthusiastic pilot, he joined the Rebel Alliance soon afterward. He gained much experience in the Battle of Yavin, and was instrumental in destroying the Empire's V-38 "Phantom TIE" project.

**Rooks** Captain of a patrol ship in the Empress Teta system about 4,000 years before the Galactic Civil War.

**Room of Arches** Part of the original B'omarr monastery architecture found deep within Jabba the Hutt's palace on Tatooine, this small chamber not far from EV-9D9's droid boiler room was home to an outcast clan of Jawas.

**Room of a Thousand Fountains** An immense, multi-story-high greenhouse located within the Jedi Temple. Filled with a rich variety of plant life, fresh flowing water, and a large lake, the chamber served as the perfect place for a Jedi to find meditative calm in an otherwise bustling city-world. After the Clone Wars and the Imperial takeover of the Temple, the freshwater supply was cut off, leaving the plant life to die. When Luke Skywalker decreed that a new Jedi Temple be erected following the Yuuzhan Vong War, he included a re-creation of the Room of a Thousand Fountains.

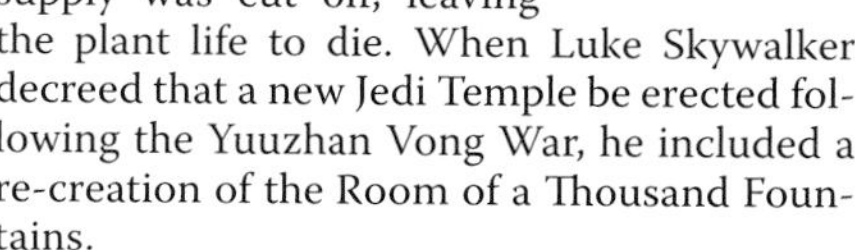

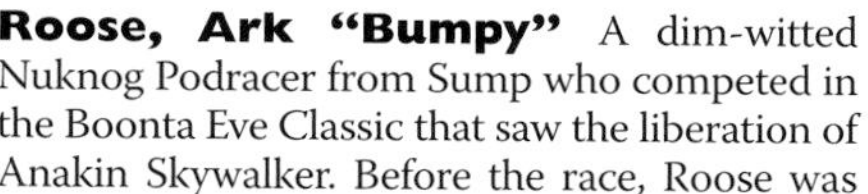

Boles Roor

**Room of Morning Mists** A spacious rotunda and dining room found at the Varykino retreat on Naboo, used by Anakin Skywalker and Padmé Amidala.

**Roon** A mysterious planet, it was surrounded by a belt of moonlets, asteroids, and other cosmic debris deep within the Cloak of the Sith. Half of Roon provided a spectacular vista of emerald continents and sapphire oceans. The other half was bleak, trapped in perpetual night. Spacer legends had it that the Roon star system was filled with treasure. The eerie boneyard known locally as the Bantha Graveyard lay within Roon's event horizon, just off Umboo province. For reasons no one on Roon could explain, aging Umboo banthas left their pack when they sensed death approaching and made the pilgrimage to the Graveyard, a journey that could take weeks.

**Roona** A planet represented in the Galactic Senate by Edcel Bar Gane during the time of the Battle of Naboo.

**Roonadan** The fifth planet in the Bonadan system in the Corporate Sector, it was the site of the starship departure terminal from which Han Solo and Fiolla of Lorrd boarded the spaceliner *Lady of Mindor* en route to the planet Ammuud.

**Roon Colonial Games** A series of athletic competitions that pitted champions from colonies of the Roon star system against one another. The main event was the drainsweeper, a no-holds-barred relay race.

**Roon lightstations** A network of sensor beacons, erected by the Baobab Merchant Fleet, that guided starships through the cosmic debris surrounding the Roon system. One of the best known was Umboo lightstation.

**Roonstone** An incredibly valuable variety of crystal found on Roon by Mungo Baobab. Heb discovered a Roonstone carved with the ancient text of *Dha Werda Verda.*

**Roor, Boles** A pungent Sneevel who amassed a fortune as a glimmik singer, he used his earnings to support his favorite hobby, Podracing. Despite a reputation for weak piloting skills, he nonetheless won two Boonta Eve Podraces, though he only once went head-to-head against racing legend Sebulba. Roor piloted a Quadrijet 4Barrel 904E engine Podracer. He finished sixth in the race that saw the liberation of Anakin Skywalker. After Roor retired from Podracing to continue his singing career, his chief mechanic, Shrivel Braittrand, moved into professional Podracing.

**Roose, Ark "Bumpy"** A dim-witted Nuknog Podracer from Sump who competed in the Boonta Eve Classic that saw the liberation of Anakin Skywalker. Before the race, Roose was hired by Diva Funquita (acting on orders from Gardulla the Hutt) to sabotage Anakin's Podracer for 50 wupiupi. However, Roose mistakenly tampered with Ben Quadinaros's vehicle instead. Roose piloted a massive Vokof-Strood Plug-8G 927 Cluster Array Podracer, which collided with Dud Bolt's Podracer in the third lap. Bumpy survived the collision, but was forced to recover from his injuries in a Mos Espa medcenter.

Ark "Bumpy" Roose

**Roosh, Drexl** A Rodian clan leader wanted for fraud, selling faulty materials, and slave trading, he and his followers of the Soammei Clan lived on the junk planet of Raxus Prime in the early years of the Galactic Empire. He often wore heavy armor and carried a vibrosword.

**Root** The cousin and guardian of the Jedi children known as Rain, Bug, and Tomcat on Somov Rit prior to their relocation to Ruusan.

General Rootrock

**root chip** A type of inexpensive, greasy snack enjoyed among the lower classes of Coruscant.

**rootgrass** A plant from which a soothing tea was made by the Hutts.

**Roothes, Memah** A blue-skinned Twi'lek, she owned and operated the Soft Heart Cantina in the Coruscant undercity until it was destroyed in a suspicious fire. She and her bouncer, Rodo, then found work aboard the first Death Star as it underwent finalization, continuing their line of work at the Hard Heart Cantina. There she fell in love with Zelosian con man Celot Ratua Dil. After the destruction of Despayre and Alderaan by the Death Star's monstrous superlaser, Memah grew incredibly disillusioned with the Empire and her place on the battle station, and deserted her post along with several other escapees just prior to the station's destruction.

**rootleaf** A type of plant native to Dagobah. The Jedi Master Yoda used rootleaf to brew a potent and nourishing stew.

**root paste** A simple foodstuff found on Bellassa.

**Rootrock, General** A Nosaurian resistance leader, he ordered the freeing of captive Jedi Dass Jennir after the events of Order 66 due to a long-standing loyalty to the Jedi Order. He promised to provide Jennir with a ship off New Plympto in exchange for help in resisting the Imperial occupation of his home planet. Though Jennir returned to help the Nosaurians, he could not prevent Rootrock from being killed by Imperial clone troopers.

**Rooty** A large Cragmoloid gambler on Nar Shaddaa with leathery skin, tusks, and tiny, red beady eyes. Rooty once bested Lando Calrissian in a game of sabacc. He piloted a modified CRX-Tug called the *Solar Grazer*.

**Ropagi system** One endpoint of the Kira Run, it had three planets: Elpur, Ropagi II, and Seltaya. The other endpoint was the Lazerian system.

**rope-spike** A Neimoidian melee weapon and climbing tool that consisted of a pointed spike attached to a length of cord.

**Ropple, Gru'um** A guest at Jabba the Hutt's palace who conspired to assassinate his host. Bib Fortuna planted evidence on Gru'um implicating him as a traitor, unaware that his frame job actually matched Ropple's intentions. Thrown into Jabba's dungeons alongside his droid Miramba, Gru'um released freckers hidden inside the automaton. Fortuna helped Jabba to dispose of the freckers. The incensed Hutt promised to feed Ropple to the Sarlacc.

**Roqoo** A blue giant star that was the site of a refueling depot in the Hapes Cluster, just beyond the Transitory Mists.

**Rorak 5** A space station located a half day's hyperspace jump away from Nar Shaddaa, it once served as a rendezvous point for Krayn and several Colicoid leaders.

**Rordak** The site of one of the most notorious Imperial penal colonies in the galaxy. The world was rich in metals, but the hostile atmosphere, the high level of geological activity, and a brutal native species known as the Viska made the planet inhospitable.

**Rordis City** A metropolitan center on Nubia, it was the site of a major Industrial Automaton production facility.

**Rorgam** A business-oriented planet with a large immigrant population.

**Rori** One of Naboo's moons, it shared a number of traits with its parent planet. The forests and other vegetation were more twisted and knotted than Naboo's plant life. The strong resemblance between architecture on Rori and on Naboo was the result of human colonists from Naboo who settled the moon 2,000 years before the Battle of Yavin.

*Rorworr, a young Wookiee scout*

**Rori Spice Mining Collective** A group of "honest" spice miners who sold their goods to pharmaceutical companies, they were the only licensed group allowed to legally harvest spice from the moon of Rori. They often engaged in turf wars with the Hutt-run Kobola guild of spice miners.

**Rorq** A muscular, white-haired Mawan who was a tunnel worker on his planet and served as a guide to Obi-Wan Kenobi, Anakin Skywalker, and Yaddle during their mission to Mawan. He was best friends with Swanny Mull.

**Rorworr (1)** An unscrupulous Wookiee who lived at the time of the Jedi Civil War, he plotted to sell his people into slavery to the Czerka Corporation. To stop this from happening, the Wookiee Jaarak killed Rorworr.

**Rorworr (2)** A young Wookiee scout who helped the Naboo resistance battle the Trade Federation's invasion of the planet. Rorworr's father was an ambassador from Kashyyyk to Naboo.

**Rosen, Loci** Formerly a merchant, this Mon Calamari officer served the Rebel Alliance during the Battle of Endor.

**Rosha** One of two worlds in the Leemurtoo system in the Galactic Core, home planet of the Roshans. Its economy was based on advanced technology development, and the antennaed Roshans were experts at miniaturization. The neighboring world, Samaria, was also a leading technological innovator. Emperor Palpatine feared that the two worlds would pool their advancements to create jamming technology capable of defeating Imperial hardware. His agents saw to it that the Roshans were implicated in an assassination attempt on Imperial adviser Bog Divinian, which led to open conflict between Rosha and Samaria. The Samarians, led by Darth Vader, attacked Rosha, and the world was subjugated by the Empire.

**Roshton, Commander** An ambitious officer in the Grand Army of the Republic, he led a contingent of 900 clone troopers to Cartao to defend Spaarti Creations from being taken over by the Separatists during the Clone Wars.

**Roshuir, Captain Kale** An Imperial officer stationed at the prison colony on Kalist VI. He fell in love with Deena Shan, a fellow Imperial who was actually an undercover Rebel agent. Shan supplied Roshuir with disinformation regarding a Rebel base on Thila, an outpost that was in fact abandoned. Roshuir led a mission to Thila, scouring the empty base for any signs of Rebels. His troopers inadvertently set off a trap that triggered a massive explosion, leading Roshuir to realize that he had been set up, and that this expedition had left Kalist VI under-defended. He returned to his original post, and was set to kill Deena for her treachery before being knocked unconscious by Harran, another undercover Rebel. Roshuir unsuccessfully attempted to capture Luke Skywalker using Luke's old friend Janek "Tank" Sunber as bait.

**Roshu Sune** A militant splinter faction of the Gotal Assembly for Separation that used violence in an attempt to force Antar to secede from the Republic during the Separatist crisis. Its campaign of terror led to the Battle of Antar 4, a debacle. The Jedi were mostly judged to have botched the operation, leading to much loss of life.

**Rosk, Commander** An Imperial naval officer who served under Captain Soontir Fel aboard the Dreadnaught *Pride of the Senate* early in the Galactic Civil War.

**Rosset, Moff** A member of the Council of Moffs of the Imperial Remnant during the war between the Galactic Alliance and the Confederation. He, along with several other ambitious Moffs, sought to depose Admiral Gilad Pellaeon, and was aboard the Star Destroyer *Bloodfin* during the combat operations over Fondor.

**Rossik, Captain Todrin** A native of Coruscant, he was an Imperial officer serving Warlord Zsinj during the early years of the New Republic. He was shot and killed by New Republic Intelligence agent Gara Petothel.

**Rostu, Nick "Smiley"** A Korunnai member of the Upland Liberation Front, he helped Mace Windu find the crazed Jedi Depa Billaba in the jungles of Haruun Kal during the Clone Wars. Though he tried to portray himself to Mace as a mercenary, he deeply cared for the Korunnai cause and wanted to see his people regain control of the planet. Mace was impressed by Rostu's abilities and courage, and recommended him for a Medal of Valor for conspicuous bravery under fire. The ceremony took place after Rostu was released from the medcenter, recovering from serious injuries sustained fighting Kar Vastor's minions. His rank of brevet major in the Grand Army of the Republic was also confirmed, and for the next two years Major Nick Rostu commanded the 44th Division, a unit composed of clone troopers and several other species, also known as Rostu's Renegades. The 44th saw action on Bassadro, Ando, Atraken, and several other planets, and were portrayed in the media as distinguished heroes.

**Rotas V** The command skirt worn by clone troopers was modeled after that worn by indigenous fighters on this planet.

**rot crow** A scavenger avian native to Haruun Kal.

**Rotham, Dr. Heilan** A professor based in Lorrd City on Lorrd, she was an expert on tactile writing and recording methods. Jacen Solo had her examine a possible Sith tassel found on Centerpoint Station during the events leading up to his transformation into Darth Caedus.

**Rothana Heavy Engineering** A subsidiary of Kuat Drive Yards. When devising armaments and vehicles for the clone army of the Galactic Republic, the Kaminoans subcontracted to Rothana Heavy Engineering the secret job of developing combat starships and armor for the new military. The firm was based on the planet Rothana, not far from Kamino.

***Ro-ti-Mundi*** A Republic *Venator*-class Star Destroyer that served in the Battle of Coruscant during the final stages of the Clone Wars.

**Roti-Ow system** A system that contained a binary star and the planet Altor 14, homeworld of the Avogwi and the Nuiwit.

**Rotramel, Timi** A Mon Calamari Senator during the early years of the Galactic Empire, he was a secret supporter of the Rebel Alliance until the Emperor's dissolution of the Senate. Rotramel attempted to gain Tiss'sharl president Si-Di-Ri's support for the Rebellion, but was discovered and killed by Darth Vader.

**Rotsino, Esu** A Senator from the Abrion sector, she tendered her sector's articles of secession to the Galactic Republic, bringing bountiful agricultural resources to the Separatists just prior to the Clone Wars.

**Rotta the Hutt** Jabba the Hutt's young "Huttlet" son, he was kidnapped at the tender age of 10 during the Clone Wars by bounty hunters hired by Jabba's uncle, Ziro. Ziro was in collusion with Count Dooku and the Separatists, who conspired to eliminate Jabba, placing all of his substantial holdings into Ziro's control. The Separatists, meanwhile, hoped to blame the kidnapping on the Jedi, in order to disgrace the Jedi in Jabba's eyes and prevent the Republic from forging an alliance with the Hutts. Anakin Skywalker and his new Padawan Ahsoka Tano voyaged to Teth, chasing down reports of the Huttlet's kidnapping. There they found tiny Rotta in an abandoned B'omarr monastery, sick with fever. After fighting Separatist forces, Anakin and Ahsoka treated Rotta's illness and hurried him back to be reunited with Jabba. Ahsoka affectionately referred to the little Hutt as "Stinky," while Jabba's preferred nickname for his son was "Punky Muffin."

*Rotta the Hutt*

**Roty, Adler** A stage performer who claimed to be a Sorcerer of Tund, he operated out of Coruscant just prior to the Clone Wars.

**Roundtree system** The birthplace of Rekkon, an educator who helped Han Solo during his mission to the Stars' End penal colony.

**Rover** The name Dr. Evazan gave to his trained pet meduza. Rover saved Evazan a number of times and eventually gave his life for him, cushioning the fall when Evazan tumbled off a cliff.

***Rover*** A recon skiff attached to the Galactic Alliance Star Destroyer *Anakin Solo.* Ben Skywalker piloted it to investigate the bombing of the Villa Solis estate on Terephon. Skywalker found and recovered Jaina Solo and Zekk, who had been stranded by the bombing attack engineered by Ducha Galney. When the *Rover* returned to Hapes, it arrived in the midst of a battle between the Hapan Royal Navy and the Heritage Fleet. The *Rover* transmitted a warning to the Queen Mother Tenel Ka of the treachery in her midst, and was promptly destroyed by the Heritage Fleet. Skywalker and the Jedi escaped.

**roverine** A predatory swarming insect native to the Davirien jungles.

**Rovieda, Ixian** A Jedi Knight killed on Kabal during a series of riots sparked by food shortages just prior to the outbreak of the Clone Wars.

**Rowel** A high-ranking Ferroan native of Zonama Sekot, he had pale blue skin and gold-black eyes. Along with his partner Darak, he was among the first of his people to meet Luke Skywalker and his Jedi Knights as they sought out the living planet during the Yuuzhan Vong War.

**Rowrakruk** One of the Wookiee settlements along the Wawaatt Archipelago.

**Roxuli system** Bordering the Unknown Regions, this star system was the last stop of the Outbound Flight expedition before uncharted space. It was also the site of an ongoing dispute between the planetary government and mine operators that required the intervention of the Republic. Supreme Chancellor Palpatine personally requested that Obi-Wan Kenobi and his Padawan Anakin Skywalker voyage to Roxuli to mediate the conflict, thus effectively removing the Jedi pair from the doomed Outbound Flight mission.

**Royal Academy** A school where the young nobles of Naboo went to study for future roles in the government.

**Royal Chalcedony Shield** An award of great prestige and honor given by the government of Alderaan to recipients who were "champions of civic virtue and held uncompromising moral convictions." Bail Organa presented this award to Senator Horox Ryyder upon the Anx's retirement.

**Royal Court of Naboo** The entity comprising the elected monarch and the appointed advisory council that governed Naboo. It was steeped in tradition. Some of the customs of the court involved the monarch's dress, the Governor speaking on behalf of the monarch, how to address various members of the court, gift giving, seeking the audience of the court, the priority of cases, and the court's agenda.

**Royal House of Alderaan** The Organa line of nobility, which dated back to the earliest days of Alderaan and the Galactic Republic. During the time of the Galactic Empire, Queen Breha Organa held the highest noble rank, with her husband Viceroy Bail Organa representing the planet in the Galactic Senate. With the passing of Queen Breha and the retirement of Bail Organa, their adopted daughter, Princess Leia Organa, became the best-known figure from the royal family in galactic politics.

**Royal Guard** *See* Emperor's Royal Guard.

**Royal Intelligence Service** The primary intelligence-gathering network used by the royal families of the Hapes Consortium.

**Royal Protectors** An elite warrior group on Onderon 4,000 years before the Galactic Civil War. Its duty was to protect Aleema and Satal Keto, who had used dark Sith magic to form the Krath and had overthrown planetary governments in the Empress Teta system.

**Royce** A Vodran, he and his prospecting partner Samuel struck it rich by discovering a barren world with plentiful ore deposits and other resources. Samuel double-crossed Royce, taking full title to the planet, prompting Royce to kidnap Samuel's daughter, Leddar, and hold her for ransom. Samuel

## R Series Astromech Droids



convinced Jedi Knight Darca Nyl to intervene. Nyl gathered the parties, learned the truth about the situation, and forced them to find a resolution.

**Rozess, Jude** A Jedi Knight guarding the Temple on Coruscant, she was killed when an overwhelming number of Yinchorri invaded during the Yinchorri Uprising.

**Rozhdenst, Commander Gennad** A Rebel Alliance officer and commander of Scavenger Squadron during the Galactic Civil War. He was tasked by Mon Mothma with guarding Kuat Drive Yards from Imperial assault, but was manipulated by Kodir of Kuhlvult into acknowledging that Kuat would never recognize the Alliance. Rozhdenst conspired to eliminate Kuat of Kuat, paving the way for Kodir to install herself as leader of KDY. These plans were thwarted when Kuat of Kuat, rather than have the yards fall into anyone else's hands, began scuttling the ships under construction. Rozhdenst and his squadron did what they could to preserve as many ships as possible.

**R-PK droid** *See* rolo-droid (R-PK).

**RP trooper** Also known as an arpitrooper, this was a clone trooper equipped with disposable repulsor packs that allowed for high-altitude ground drops into battle zones.

***rrakktorr*** A Shyriiwook phrase describing a male's honor and strength of character, it translated to "the defiant, adventurous heart of a Wookiee."

**rroshm** A slow-moving herbivorous creature that inhabited the Shadow Forest on Kashyyyk.

**Rrr'ur'R** A bantha raised by the Tusken Raider RR'uruurrr for personal use by URoRRuR'R'R. This bantha was the alpha male of his herd and trampled many Jawas in his lifetime.

**Rrudobar** One of the smaller orbital cities above Duro. The cantina Event Horizon was located deep within its infrastructure.

**RR'uruurrr** A Tusken Raider, he tended to the banthas used by URoRRuR'R'R's tribe. RR'uruurrr was part of the raiding party that attacked Luke Skywalker at the Jundland Wastes.

**Rryatt Trail** A treacherous path on Kashyyyk that led from atop a massive tree deep in the dark forest into the Well of the Dead, in the heart of the Shadow Forest.

**R series astromech droids** Though there were a wide variety of astromech droids in the galaxy, those of the R series produced by Industrial Automaton were easily the most popular. The series was introduced decades before the collapse of the Galactic Republic. So versatile and adaptable were they, many remained in service years after their original manufacture, upgraded beyond their original specs to stave off obsolescence. The series began with a P2 prototype droid, an oversized astromech devised for use in capital transport vessels. Legal hassles prevented the P2 from being directly transformed into a consumer product, so Industrial Automaton instead converted an existing stock of Mark II Reactor drones to become the R1. When the legal issues surrounding the P2 series were settled, many of its innovations were incorporated into a scaled-down version that became the R2, the bestselling unit in the whole series. While standard naming conventions usually retained the droid's unit number as a prefix, an astromech's entire serial number was long enough for individual users to parse and use as a name according to preference. As such, it was not often reliable to simply judge an R series astromech's factory origins from its name alone.

- **R1 unit:** The first of the R series droids developed by Industrial Automaton, made using the body shells of Mark II reactor drones. These tall, cylindrical droids essentially became obsolete before the Yuuzhan Vong War. Equipped with an Intellex III computer, they could calculate a single hyperspace jump.
- **R2 unit:** The most popular of the R series droids, the standard R2 was released as a small droid at a time when larger, more imposing models dominated sales. It featured an Intellex IV computer supporting a database of 700 starship designs, sophisticated sensor systems, and an improved astrogation cache that could store 10 jumps.
- **R2-AG:** A surplus R5 unit shell repurposed as an agromech droid.
- **R2-Delta:** An upgrade to the standard R2 with new algorithms to speed up navigational calculations. This extended the service life of many New Republic R2 units through the Yuuzhan Vong War.
- **R2-R series:** A variant R2 unit designed for use on reconnaissance starfighters, it could gather, save, download, and upload recon data.
- **R3 unit:** Industrial Automaton developed this clear-domed variant of the R2 unit specifically for use in military installations and combat capital ships. Its Intellex V computer and advanced sensor package could be seen through its transparent plastex

dome. It could store five hyperspace jumps in its cache.

- **R3-D droid:** A variant R3 unit from the Galactic Republic that aided in target acquisition and management.
- **R4 unit:** An astromech droid designed for the Outer Rim urban consumer, it was well adapted not only for starship maintenance, but speeder repair as well. Its Intellex VI computer supported numerous repulsorlift vehicle designs. Its affordability made it popular among Rebel and privateer groups.
- **R4-P:** A variant astromech droid specifically designed for the Delta-7 Jedi starfighter, it had a smaller body to fit into the slim fuselage. When the Delta-7B gained popularity, many of the truncated droids were refitted with standard-sized astromech bodies.
- **R5 unit:** The last of the original series of astromech droids produced during the Galactic Republic, it was generally judged to be of poor quality. As such, many went unsold, which allowed the Rebel Alliance to claim great numbers of them at a discount and refurbish them for their needs. Industrial Automaton canceled the initial product offering of the R5 and repurposed the droid bodies as part of its R2-AG agromech droid.
- **R6 unit:** This was the first astromech droid developed by Industrial Automaton in the New Republic era. It could hold 12 hyperspace jumps within its computer systems.
- **R7 unit:** A military astromech co-developed by FreiTek Incorporated specifically for use aboard the New Republic E-wing starfighter, although variants existed that could be used in other starships.
- **R8 unit:** Produced after the defeat of Grand Admiral Thrawn, it was, for a time, intended to have a standard Basic-speaking vocabulator, but this design feature was discarded before release. It featured powerful communication and jamming systems.
- **R9 unit:** Industrial Automaton's addition to its series during the Yuuzhan Vong War. Many served aboard the StealthX and ChaseX fighters of the New Republic and Galactic Alliance.

Palee Ruda

**Ruan system** Located in the Core Worlds, it contained one of the 18 farming planets administered by the Salliche Ag Corporation. After the Battle of Endor, workers in the Ruan, Yulant, and Broest systems revolted against the Imperial-controlled Salliche Ag by burning fields and destroying hydroponics facilities. During the Yuuzhan Vong invasion, Ruan took on many displaced refugees to work its fields.

**Ruati, Master** A Jedi Master beheaded by an unknown assassin on Nauton IV during the Clone Wars. Obi-Wan Kenobi believed Asajj Ventress was responsible.

**Rubat crystal** Mined on the planet Phemis and sometimes used in the construction of a Jedi lightsaber. Rubat crystals resulted in a clearly defined blade of great accuracy.

**Rubogean Gambit** This common diplomatic ploy involved goading an opponent with provocative statements that blurred one's true motives.

**ruby bliel** A gooey drink sold at stalls in Mos Espa on Tatooine. Anakin Skywalker and his friend Kitster Banai enjoyed drinking ruby bliels.

**Ruby Gulch** A rocky expanse on Nam Chorios near Hweg Shul, used as a hiding place for Theran natives.

**Ruby Nebula** A rendezvous site for Adi Gallia and Reti while en route to the Karthakk system, prior to the Clone Wars.

**ruby-throated kete** A bright feathered avian native to Bellassa with a harsh, squawking call.

Elyhek Rue

**Ruda, Palee** A veiled human female patron of the Outlander gambling club in Coruscant's Uscru entertainment district just prior to the Clone Wars.

**Rudd, Jerris** A pilot, he was hired by Jabba the Hutt's aide Bib Fortuna to transport the Twi'lek dancers Oola and Sienn from their native Ryloth to Tatooine.

**Rudrig** A quiet planet in the Tion Hegemony, it was home to the vast University of Rudrig, which attracted students from the entire Hegemony. The planetwide university had campuses and classrooms scattered everywhere amid the gray soil and purple grasses of Rudrig. Weapons were officially prohibited on the planet's surface. Han Solo and Chewbacca were involved in a high-speed chase on a Rudrig freeway during one of their early adventures. After Imperials destroyed a Rebel Alliance base on Briggia prior to the Battle of Yavin, the next scheduled target of the Emperor's Operation Strike Fear was Rudrig. A Rudrig crime ring tortured a kidnap victim by using an Imperial interrogation droid stolen from a battle zone, one impetus behind the Historic Battle Site Protection Act established by the New Republic Senate. Rudrig was represented by Senator Nyxy.

Aehrrley Rue (in suit)

**Rue, Aehrrley** A male freelance pilot in a black-and-yellow spacesuit who frequented Mos Espa during the Boonta Eve Podrace that saw Anakin Skywalker's liberation.

**Rue, Elyhek** The pilot of Red Seven at the Battle of Yavin, he was previously part of the Griffon flight wing, a Rebel squadron sent to fight the Imperial subjugation of Ralltiir, where he attacked the Star Destroyer *Devastator*.

**ruetsavii** In Gand society, ruetsavii were sent to observe, examine, criticize, and chronicle the life of an individual to determine if he or she was worthy of individuality. If this right was granted, the Gand became janwuine.

**Rufarr** A Wookiee smuggler who ferried Prime Minister Cundertol to and from his entechment procedure during the Yuuzhan Vong War. To ensure the secrecy of his plot, Cundertol sabotaged Rufarr's ship, *Jaunty Cavalier*. The Wookiee died when his ship was destroyed en route to Bakura.

**ruffelluff** An extinct creature that was at one time popular as a pet in the galaxy. *Ruffel-*

*luff* was a code word used by Zam Wesell and Jango Fett whenever Zam was in disguise.

**Rugeyan, Mar** Head of public affairs for the Galactic Senate during the Clone Wars, he was concerned that the Senators of the Republic were portrayed in the most favorable light. The slick Rugeyan tried to spin the media coverage surrounding the kidnapping of Senator Meena Tills and the death of Jedi Master Kaim.

**rugger** A rodent that made its home high in the trees or grasslands of the Forest Moon of Endor. An herbivore, it ate nuts and berries and hibernated during the cold winter seasons. Ruggers had greenish white fur, though grassland species had fur that was more yellow. Suction-like pads on their feet provided stability and could be used for grasping. Their sharp, strong front teeth were for nut cracking. Ruggers were commonly hunted by Yuzzums and tempters.

**Rughja** Members of this 15-limbed species with multiple eyes were renowned for their musical abilities. Some Rughja were capable of playing 10 or more musical instruments simultaneously. Umjing Baab and his Swinging Trio was a famous Rughja band. Their natural form of communication was not audible to most humanoids.

*Rugosa*

**Rugosa** A neutral moon, it was the site of a rendezvous between Jedi Master Yoda and the Toydarian King Katuunko for secret negotiations during the Clone Wars. The Separatists also sent an envoy, Asajj Ventress, and Rugosa became a military challenge, with the winning side earning Katuunko's loyalty. Yoda and his clone troopers were faced with overwhelming odds against an entire droid army, yet nonetheless succeeded. Rugosa was once covered by oceans that retreated, leaving behind vast monolithic formations of coral.

**rugrass** A variety of grass growing on the plains of Zonama Sekot.

**ruhau-whale** An immense cetacean native to the underground oceans of Utapau. Their huge skeletons were often used in native architecture.

**Ruhe** A forested world where the Separatists tried to trap Anakin Skywalker and Obi-Wan Kenobi during the Outer Rim Sieges of the Clone Wars. It was the site of one of Count Dooku's citadels. Obi-Wan and Anakin entered the citadel hoping to find Dooku and General Grievous, but were shocked to find an army of hundreds of battle droids waiting for them.

**ruik** A tree whose roots could be turned into dried, chewable sticks that were mildly addictive.

**Ruillia's Insulated Rooms** An inexpensive hotel in Mos Eisley where Figrin D'an and the Modal Nodes stayed.

**Ruin, Darth** Two thousand years before the eruption of the Clone Wars, an intelligent and charismatic Jedi named Phanius renounced his oath and abandoned the Order to pursue prohibited teachings. Recruiting scores of Jedi and others strong in the Force, he was seduced by the dark side and declared himself a Dark Lord of the Sith named Darth Ruin. He and his supporters initiated a war with the Jedi Knights, but his Sith Order soon fell apart due to infighting. This was the first of many such defeats that would lead to the near-extinction of the Sith Order within 1,000 years.

**Ruisto** A planet with a Mon Calamari colony early in the Galactic Civil War. The Empire bombarded Ruisto as a training exercise for its eventual attack on the Mon Calamari homeworld.

**Rujj, Anj** A human who patronized the Outlander gambling club in Coruscant's Uscru entertainment district prior to the outbreak of the Clone Wars. He was a member of the Thugs of Thule, a gang of highly educated mercenaries.

**Rukh** A member of the fierce Noghri species, he served as one of the Emperor's Death Commandos. When Grand Admiral Thrawn returned from the Unknown Regions, he took charge of the Noghri and selected Rukh to be his personal bodyguard. Rukh was never far from the Grand Admiral's side, hiding in the shadows until his particular talents were called for. When the truth of how the Empire kept the Noghri subjugated was revealed by Princess Leia Organa Solo, Rukh waited for the best opportunity to take his revenge on Thrawn, then assassinated him.

**Rukil** An outcast living within the Lower City levels of Taris during the Mandalorian Wars. He believed in the existence of the Promised Land, and had many followers.

**Rula, Captain** The commander of a small fleet, Rula was with Han Solo the first time Solo encountered a Hapan warship.

**Rulacamp** An elderly, laconic baymaster on Aphran, she encountered Han Solo and Leia Organa Solo during the Yuuzhan Vong War.

**Rule KR27** A term of absolute authority invoked by the Galactic Empire in maintaining order.

**Rule of One** The guiding tenet behind Darth Krayt's new Sith Order. Rather than emphasize power for personal accrual, the Rule of One stated that the most important entity was the Sith Order itself. Under this guidance, Krayt's Sith Order consisted of multiple Sith Lords working toward a higher goal.

**Rule of Two** A tenet of the Sith as mandated by Darth Bane's redefining of the Order following the devastating Battle of Ruusan. Its origins were ancient; in the time of the Great Sith War there was one acknowledged Sith Lord and one apprentice. However, despite such titles, these Sith actively recruited many more followers, and the Sith were in fact legion. Time and again, the Sith desire for power led to infighting and destabilization that their enemies—the Jedi Knights—could exploit. By the time of the Battle of Ruusan, the Sith Brotherhood of Darkness attempted to operate without a true hierarchy of power, despite the rampant scheming within its ranks. Darth Bane, disillusioned by the ineffectiveness of his Sith contemporaries, delved deep into Sith lore and found a solution in the Rule of Two: *Two there should be; no more, no less. One to embody the power, the other to crave it.*

With the annihilation of the Brotherhood of Darkness, Bane started anew under the Rule of Two, taking on an apprentice, Darth Zannah. She would eventually succeed him, taking an apprentice of her own. In this way, the Sith continued to plot in the shadows until the time of Darth Sidious and Darth Vader. Though Sith Lords would often cultivate potential apprentices, they were denied full Sith knowledge and elevation to Sith Lord status until the murderous ascendancy—the death of a Master by an apprentice's hand—allowed a vacancy to be filled. Despite Bane's best efforts, knowledge of the Sith Rule of Two leaked into Jedi lore. Though many Jedi believed the Sith extinct, when evidence of their return surfaced with Darth Maul's corpse at the Battle of Naboo, Yoda quoted the Rule of Two and speculated that another Sith Lord was still at large.

*Rukh*

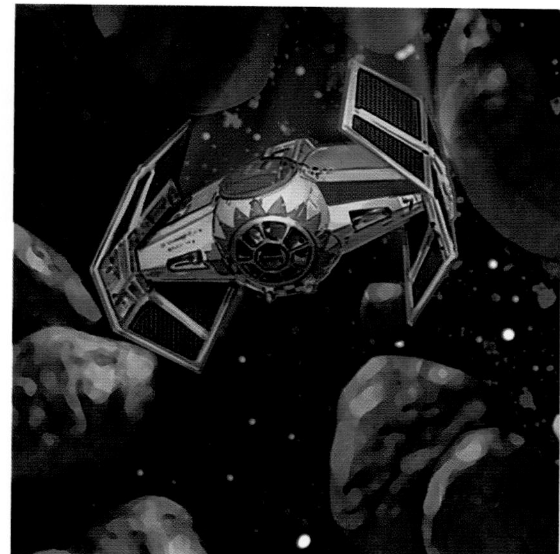
Running the belt

Following the elimination of Darth Sidious and Darth Vader, the Rule of Two vanished. Sith teachings and powers reemerged in the decades that followed, but the strengths and benefits of the Rule of Two were cast aside for more practical methodologies. With the rise of Darth Krayt came a new tenet: the Rule of One.

**Rules of Engagement** An itemized list of requirements for Jedi Knights to study when defusing tense situations.

**Rulffe** This New Republic junior surveyor was part of the crew of the *Astrolabe,* which was shot down near Doornik-1142.

**Ruling Council (1)** The governing body of Kamino, presided over by a Prime Minister.

**Ruling Council (2)** A New Republic governmental body carried over from the provisional government. During Leia Organa Solo's tenure as Chief of State, most of the Ruling Council's authority was dispersed among the various councils of the New Republic Senate. The council did, however, retain the authority to remove a Chief of State who had become too powerful. This power had never been used until the Yevethan Purge forced the group to consider Leia's leadership.

**Ruling Council (3)** *See* Ruling Families.

**Ruling Families** The highly placed governing bodies of the Chiss Ascendency, from which the membership of the Ruling Council was made. The number of Ruling Families was not constant, and was often determined by several political and military factors. At various points during the history of the Chiss, there were as many as twelve—and as few as three—Ruling Families. During the final years of the Galactic Republic, there were nine Ruling Families. In the wake of the Yuuzhan Vong invasion, there were just four.

**Ruling Power** The governing authority of Euceron, made up of 10 members who had a vote in the formation of laws and regulations. Each member went simply by the name Ruler, with his or her position on the council added on: Ruler Three, for example.

**Ruluwoor, Chertyl** A female Selonian sent to CorSec (Corellian Security) for training as part of a cultural exchange program. She developed a relationship with Corran Horn. The affair ended when their respective body chemistries made them allergic to each other.

**Runaway Prince** A planet in Hutt space re-formed by the Yuuzhan Vong as a breeding ground for yorik coral and villips.

**Running Crimson Flightknife** The squadron of Yedagonian fighters led by Wedge Antilles and Tycho Celchu into battle against the forces of the Cartann nation.

**running the belt** An endurance contest in which pilots would test their skills by zipping around the asteroids at Lando's Folly, seeing how long they could stay in the asteroid belt before getting bumped away. Lando Calrissian modified some TIE Advanced fighters with walls of repulsor shields so that they could take many hits and just bounce away. On Dubrillion, Lando had a huge monitoring chamber whose walls were covered with a gigantic viewscreen, showing a real-time view of the asteroid belt. Anakin, Jacen, and Jaina Solo posted excellent times when they ran the belt, with Jaina taking the top spot by a huge margin.

**runyip** A large, stubborn herbivore that lived on Yavin 4, it fed on forest mulch. A runyip emitted loud squealing noises, grunting and sighing as it dug among the underbrush with its flexible nose and clawed front toes.

**rupin tree** A tree native to the planet Aruza, it had the ability to seemingly vocalize, sighing as it swayed with the wind. More forceful contact, like a chop or a bump, resulted in a loud shout or scream.

**Rurgavean Sleight** A little-used military tactic that involved feigning helpfulness to one side of a conflict to allow for the infiltration of hidden agents or saboteurs.

**Rus, Moff Konrad** Head of the Imperial mission during the time of Emperor Roan Fel, an extension of the first Emperor Fel's "Victory Without War" initiative—a way to spead Imperial influence by offering help and support to planets after the Yuuzhan Vong War. Outwardly, Rus was a quiet man of peace, but he had to be politically adept in the face of hardliners among the Moffs who preferred to wage war to expand the Empire. When Darth Krayt deposed Emperor Fel, Rus secretly joined the Sith and supplied them with information that helped the Sith track the Emperor's daughter, Princess Marasiah Fel.

**rusc'te** A warm beverage often enjoyed in the midafternoon on the planet Exocron.

**Rushing, Corporal** A Naboo security officer in charge of protecting Queen Amidala's throne room. Corporal Rushing's wife and children were captured when the Trade Federation invaded Naboo.

**Rustibar** A world subjugated by the Empire during the Galactic Civil War.

**Rutal IV** A wild and primitive backworld in the Fferon system, and home of Ry-Kooda.

**Rutan** A mist-covered Outer Rim world with Testa as its capital city. Qui-Gon Jinn and Obi-Wan Kenobi traveled to Rutan to settle a dispute between the Rutanians and their neighbors, the Senalis. Senali was once a colony of Rutan until a long and difficult war broke out between them. Senali won, although both worlds were devastated. To ensure peace, the two planets temporarily exchanged their firstborn children to prevent future attacks.

Moff Konrad Rus

**Rutanian** Tall, blue-skinned inhabitants of Rutan. Rutanians stood more than a meter taller than average-sized humans. During kaduna hunts, they rode on the backs of huds accompanied by nek battle dogs. They considered their Senali neighbors to be primitive. Rutanians could not swim.

**Rutian** A race of Twi'leks identified by their blue skin.

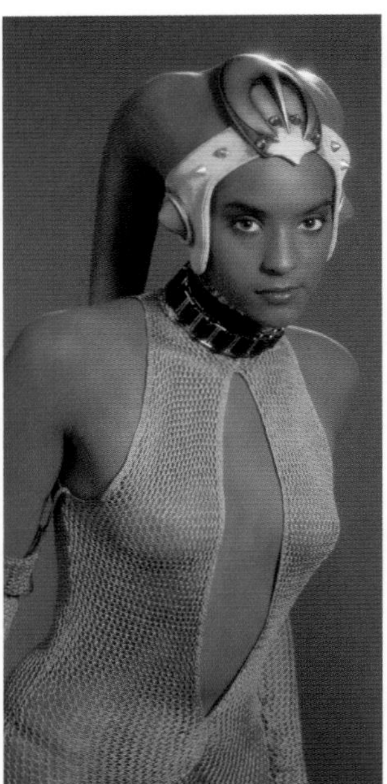
Rutian

**rutiger tree** A tree found on planets such as Aruza and Naboo. The sap of the rutiger tree was harvested by Gungans and used, in part, to make their clothing.

**Rutu** A Ho'Din serving in the Galactic Republic naval forces during the Mandalorian Wars, 4,000 years before the Battle of Yavin. For his service, he was promoted to the rank of lieutenant.

**Ruu** One of several habitable moons orbiting Qoribu.

**Ruuin** A small and slight Radnoran youth who looted the evacuated homes of the Radnorans after an outbreak of plague five years after the Battle of Naboo. Padawan Anakin Skywalker learned from Ruuin that the Avoni had been backing the Radnoran raiders to cause as much disruption and panic as possible.

**Ruuk, Harro** A Neimoidian member of the Trade Federation on Maramere. Ruuk was aboard Lord Toat's boat when it was attacked by Sol Sixxa's pirates. He survived the attack, and later tracked the *Sunrunner* to learn the location of Sol Sixxa's hidden base. His forces, however, were unable to retrieve the advanced cloaking devices stolen by Sixxa. During the Clone Wars, Ruuk supplied Captain Cavik Toth with samples of a powerful biological agent, trihexalon. Toth betrayed Ruuk and killed him with the bioweapon.

**Ruul (1)** A dreary, gray planet that supported many mines. Its vast mineral wealth was exploited by the Empire.

Ruusan

**Ruul (2)** A small moon of Sriluur. Sora Bulq agreed to a meeting with the dissident Jedi at his family's estate there, secretly arranging for Asajj Ventress to attack.

**Ruuq, Bhasu** A quiet Yuuzhan Vong warrior who protected Overlord Shimrra's base of operations on Coruscant. Nem Yim was forced to kill him during her flight from the fortress while trying to reach Zonama Sekot.

**Ruuria** The home planet of the caterpillar-like Ruurians. Its society consisted of 143 colonies and was separated into three life stages: larva, pupa, and chroma-wing. The larval Ruurians were concerned with all aspects of day-to-day life on Ruuria from the moment of their births; each eventually formed a chrysalis (the pupa stage) and emerged as a chroma-wing, concerned only with mating. The historian Skynx, holder of the history chair in the pre-Republic subdivision of the Human History subdepartment, was a Ruurian, a member of the K'zagg Colony on the banks of the Z'gag.

Ruurian

**Ruurian** An insectoid species from the planet Ruuria. Ruurians were slightly longer than 1 meter, with bands of reddish brown decorating their woolly coats. Extending from their bodies were eight pairs of short limbs, each ending in four digits. Feathery antennae emerged from a Ruurian's head, protruding from above multifaceted red eyes, a tiny mouth, and small nostrils. With their great natural linguistic abilities, Ruurians often entered diplomatic and scholarly fields.

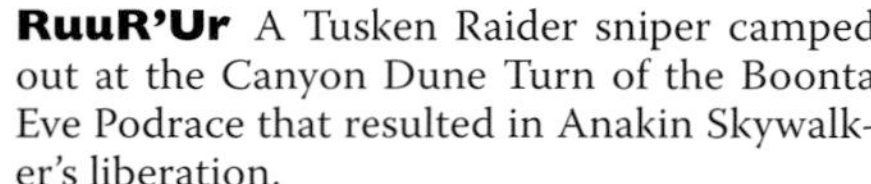

**RuuR'Ur** A Tusken Raider sniper camped out at the Canyon Dune Turn of the Boonta Eve Podrace that resulted in Anakin Skywalker's liberation.

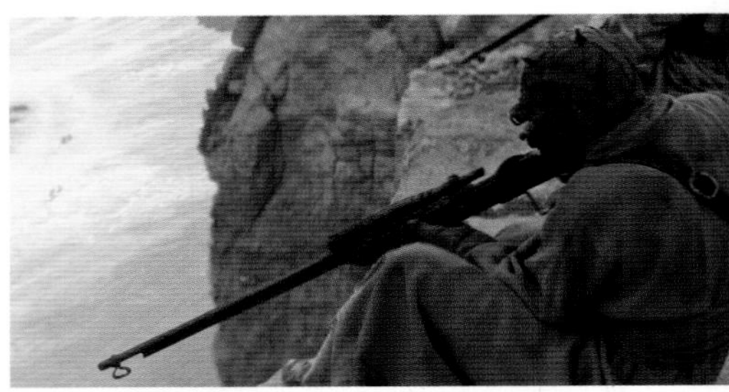
RuuR'Ur

**Ruusan** An unremarkable Mid Rim world settled by the Mining Guild, it was notable only for its placement at the turning point of historic events. Ruusan's meager ore deposits and nebulae-occluded travel routes doomed it to obscurity. Small settlements of offworld miners called the planet home, sharing it with the planet's native denizens, strange mildly telepathic globe-shaped fliers called Bouncers. During the Light and Darkness War between the Brotherhood of Darkness and the Jedi Order that culminated a millennium before the Battle of Yavin, the Brotherhood came to Ruusan. Lord Hoth's Jedi forces followed, and a series of incredibly destructive battles ravaged Ruusan's surface.

In the seventh and final Battle of Ruusan, Lord Kaan detonated a forbidden Sith weapon, a thought bomb, that swallowed the spirits of all powerful Force-users on the world into a single, black spheroid prison. This act eradicated the Sith, letting the galaxy experience peace for the first time in centuries. The site of the thought bomb later became known as the Valley of the Jedi, with enormous monuments erected by Jedi Johun Othone. The natives of Ruusan prophesied that a Jedi Knight would someday free the spirits. A year after the Battle of Endor, Jedi Knight Kyle Katarn entered the Valley and finally released the spirits after a millennium of confinement.

Several years later, the Valley of the Jedi became a focal point in the struggle between Katarn and the Dark Jedi Desann. When Katarn was led to believe that Jan Ors had died, he went to the Valley of the Jedi to restore his power in the Force. Returning to Yavin 4, he revealed the Valley's location to Luke Skywalker. Unbeknownst to Katarn, the death of Jan was a deception engineered by Desann to allow the Empire to find the location of the Valley. From the power of the Valley, Desann and Galak Fyyar created an army of Reborn dark siders used in an attempt to invade the Jedi academy.

**Ruusan, Battle of** A series of seven titanic battles between the armies of Lord Kaan and Lord Hoth, collectively known as part of the Light and Darkness War. During their final clash, Kaan and his followers unleashed a devastating thought bomb, part of a ploy by Darth Bane to eradicate Kaan's forces. This resulted in a furious explosion of energy that annihilated every last member of Hoth's Army of Light and Kaan's Brotherhood of Darkness. The vacuum at the center of the blast sucked in thousands of the disembodied spirits and trapped them in an unbreakable state of equilibrium.

**Ruusan moon** A habitable moon orbiting Ruusan, site of a Separatist listening post called Skytop Station. A captive R2-D2 was taken here by General Grievous for dissection, but was rescued by Anakin Skywalker and his clone troopers, who also destroyed the post.

**Ruusan Reformations** A series of sweeping governmental changes that followed the devastating Battle of Ruusan 1,000 years before the Battle of Yavin. Chancellor Tarsus Valorum presided over the remarkable dismantling of central authority, doing away with the Republic's standing armed forces and reorganizing its millions of sectors into 1,024 regional sectors, each with its own Senator—though once again a series of exemptions favored the ancient founding worlds and the powerful Core and Colonies. And in a final loophole that would eventually become crucial to the functioning of the Republic, the right of representation was extended to so-called functional constituencies representing cultural and species enclaves. Because of the vast changes introduced by Valorum, many historians saw this as the birth of the "modern" Galactic Republic, and many calendars reflected this by marking this event as their zero point.

**Ruweln** A Bothan colony world.

Battle of Ruusan

**Ruyn, Darth** A burly, aged Twi'lek Sith Lord who served Darth Krayt, he trained Darth Talon. When Talon had completed her training, Ruyn presented her to Krayt, who gave her one final test. Talon succeeded—she instantly murdered Ruyn.

**R'vanna** A tall Ryn, he was the leader of the 32 Ryn in Ruan's Section 465, also known as Ryn City. He excelled at calligraphy, and was approached by men seeking forged documentation for transit off Ruan. R'vanna and his group ended up on Duro, where he agreed to serve as a lieutenant in Romany's small clan.

**RV point** A military shorthand term for "rendezvous point."

**rwook** A Wookiee subspecies denoted by fur colors of rich browns, gingers, or red. Chewbacca was a rwook Wookiee.

Darth Ruyn

**Rwookrrorro** A city on the Wookiee planet of Kashyyyk that existed for thousands of years, it was nestled high atop a tight ring of giant wroshyr trees and was considered one of the planet's most beautiful metropolitan centers. Rwookrrorro covered more than a square kilometer, with wide, straight avenues and multilevel buildings. The branches of the trees grew together to form the city's foundation. Houses and shops were built directly into the tree trunks. The city suffered extensive bombing from Imperial Star Destroyers during the subjugation of Kashyyyk after the Clone Wars. Decades later, Rwookrrorro was a hiding place for Princess Leia Organa Solo while she was pregnant with the twins Jacen and Jaina. Chewbacca and other Wookiees defended the Princess from a Noghri commando squad.

**RX-24 (Rex)** A Ruebens Robotic Systems RX-series piloting droid that was rather inexperienced during its first duty, flying the Starspeeder 3000 on its maiden voyage for Star Tours.

**RX-4-9** The call sign for a TIE fighter that pursued the *Millennium Falcon* after the Battle of Hoth.

**Rybet** Members of this squat, soft-skinned frog-like species had bright green coloring and tan highlights that looked like worm stripes on their cheeks, arms, and shoulders. Rybet had large, lantern-like eyes with vertical slits. Their fingers were long and wide at the tips, showing signs of vestigial suction cups. A male Rybet donned bright yellow clothing to indicate readiness for mating. Moruth Doole, a kingpin of the Kessel spice-smuggling business and an official of the Imperial prison on that planet, was a Rybet.

Rwookrrorro

**Rycar's Run** An asteroid field named for an infamous and idiotic smuggler named Rycar Ryjerd.

**rycrit** A cow-like animal raised by Twi'leks on the planet Ryloth.

**Rydar II** The semi-intelligent Ranat species originated on this planet, located in the Rydar system. Several hundred years before the Battle of Yavin, the human inhabitants of Rydar II attempted to exterminate the Ranats, because the Ranats ate human infants. The extermination was nearly successful, but three Ranats managed to stow away on a visiting smuggling ship. The ship crashed on Aralia, and the Ranats populated that planet.

**Rydonni Prime** A planet in the Namaryne system, the sector capital and an Imperial stronghold. It was homeworld of Rythani Products, a subcontracting firm for Imperial combat vehicles.

Rybet

**Ry-Gaul** A quiet, respected, tall, and elegant Jedi Knight who took Tru Veld as a Padawan. During the Clone Wars, Ry-Gaul became a senior Jedi general in command of the 2nd Sector Army. He survived the wars by taking on an undercover mission known only to Yoda and Mace Windu. Ry-Gaul went into hiding on Coruscant, investigating the disappearance of several notable scientists.

*Rycar Ryjerd*

**Ryjerd, Rayc** The son of Rycar Ryjerd, he was said to be an "honest" smuggler who worked for Jabba the Hutt to pay off his debts on his ship. He was also said to be an idiot.

**Ryjerd, Rycar** A Bimm trader and smuggler of starship weapons, he trusted no one but did business with just about anyone. He taught smuggler apprentices and mastered the language of the Jawas, a very difficult task. He piloted a modified freighter called *Tower.* He maintained a secret base in an asteroid field named Rycar's Run. He was the father of Rayc Ryjerd.

**Ry-Kooda** The older brother of Bar-Kooda, this Herglic vowed to avenge his sibling's death by killing Gorga the Hutt and Boba Fett. He confronted Fett on Skeebo, but he was no match for the legendary bounty hunter. Ry-Kooda survived the attack and returned to kill Orko the Foultrader at his home in Orkana. In his attempt to kill Orko's daughter, Anachro, Fett intervened and ended Ry-Kooda's life.

**rylca** A medication created by Qlaern Hirf to combat the Krytos virus, it was synthesized from bacta components and ryll spice.

**ryll** Mined on the planet Ryloth, this relatively weak form of glitterstim spice was used to create a number of medicines used throughout the galaxy. It was also smuggled into the Corporate Sector for illegal sale to workers. As a recreational substance, ryll could be addictive and dangerous. Ryll fed to Kessel energy spiders resulted in the creation of the hybrid spice glitteryll. Ryll kor was the rarest variety of ryll.

**Rylle'vak** Also known as the Quiet Ocean, on the planet Bothawui it dominated the hemisphere opposite the Rhyde'vak, or Tempest Ocean.

**Ryloon** The site of several Imperial-controlled orbital factories. Captured prisoners were sent to toil there.

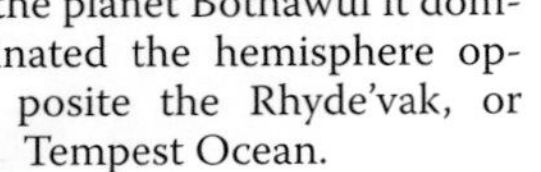
*Rayc Ryjerd*

**Ryloth** The principal planet in the Ryloth system, located in the Outer Rim near Tatooine, it was home to the Twi'lek species. A mountainous world with a peculiar rotational pattern that resulted in odd day–night cycles, the planet produced heat storms in its thin atmosphere that distributed warmth across its surface.

Most Twi'leks lived in a network of mountain catacombs. Windmill-driven turbines powered their primitive industrial civilization, and raw fungi and cow-like rycrits were raised for food. Ryloth's primary exports were the addictive ryll spice and Twi'lek females, who were desired for their seductive dancing skills.

The Twi'lek government was organized around a five-member head clan that was in charge of all community decisions. When one member of the clan died, the remaining four were exiled into the scorching Bright Lands desert and a new head clan was selected. A major Twi'lek corporation, Galactic Exotics, developed orchards on the planet Belsavis. Ryloth was also home to SchaumAssoc., a Twi'lek advertising agency that pioneered media and public relations for the Corporate Sector.

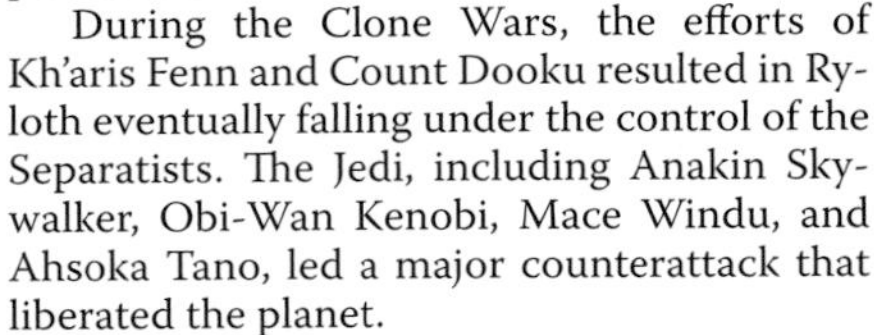

*Ryloth*

During the Clone Wars, the efforts of Kh'aris Fenn and Count Dooku resulted in Ryloth eventually falling under the control of the Separatists. The Jedi, including Anakin Skywalker, Obi-Wan Kenobi, Mace Windu, and Ahsoka Tano, led a major counterattack that liberated the planet.

With the rise of the New Order, a small Imperial refueling center and training outpost was established on Ryloth, supported by the Empire yet often used by smugglers. Wilhuff Tarkin, then a commander, had plans to turn the refueling station into an important base. Jabba the Hutt's majordomo, Bib Fortuna, was one of the first to widely sell ryll spice offplanet, which attracted the Empire's attention and brought slavers to Ryloth. Fortuna was sentenced to death but escaped and returned later with an army of Jabba's thugs to exact revenge. Seven Ryloth cities were burned and Jabba took slaves and riches, while Fortuna rescued Nat Secura, the last son of a great Twi'lek family. Fortuna made plans to someday return with Secura and rule Ryloth as he saw fit. Not long before the Battle of Endor, Fortuna enslaved a clan chief's daughter named Oola, and trained her to serve as a dancer in Jabba's palace. Maw Installation scientist Tol Sivron, Rogue Squadron pilot Nawara Ven, and the ancient Jedi Knight Tott Doneeta were also natives of Ryloth.

After the New Republic retook Coruscant, Rogue Squadron flew a mission to Ryloth to obtain ryll kor, which was mixed with bacta to produce rylca, a cure for the Krytos virus. The Rogues landed at Kala'uun Starport, within one of the mountains known as the Lonely Five. The Twi'lek warrior Tal'dira and his pilots later joined with the squadron; they flew X–TIE hybrids called Chir'daks, or Deathseeds.

***Ryloth*** A New Republic Corellian corvette that was part of the task force sent to liberate Ciutric from the control of Admiral Krennel.

**Ryn** A nomadic alien species with a fondness for secrecy. Ryn had talon-like nails on their five-fingered hands and muscular legs. Their tails were prehensile, and they could grasp large objects or hang from tree limbs with them. Besides these unique gifts, Ryn mimicked sounds by blowing air through their beaks, which had several holes like a wind instrument. By covering and uncovering the holes, they played music or imitated sounds.

Males usually had a soft snow-white mustache. Their bodies were covered with short, smoke-colored fuzz, save for the backs of their forearms and tails, where the hair was darker in hue, stiff as slender rods, and possibly capable of inflicting damage. Their noses formed a chitinous beak that curved down over a thin-lipped mouth.

The females of the species had shapely curves to their compact bodies. Lacking the drooping mustachios of the males, females had crests of lustrous slicked-back hair. Females often tipped their tails in blue paint for ornamentation, and they often wore jewelry.

*Ry-Kooda*

Ryn

Ryn were hard workers in trades ranging from ship salvaging to jewelry making. Their native language was melodic, and they were renowned for their exhilarating music. Some believed that the Ryn were mind readers and fortune-tellers, and it was said that they invented the cards used in sabacc. They often used sabacc cards as a means of divination. A flamboyant species, Ryn wore wildly colorful clothing and jewely. They traveled in large family or tribal groupings and made their living from thievery and con games. One of the more interesting taboos among the Ryn was against sleeping twice in the same place.

Ryn traveled to out-of-the-way worlds in the Corporate Sector like Ession, Ninn, and Matra VI. They were originally from a world in the Core, but even the Ryn didn't know which one. Some believed that the species descended from a tribe of 10,000 musicians donated to a nearby world that was bereft of artists; others were convinced they were the progeny of warriors deployed against an Inner Rim threat.

Ostracized by many societies, Ryn grew more transient, secretive, and self-sufficient over the years. As outsiders, they became keen observers of other species—second-guessers of what many beings, humans especially, had in mind to say. Many Ryn were enslaved by the Hutts for their fortune-telling.

Rys

During the Yuuzhan Vong War, the Ryn and their peerless information network proved very useful to the New Republic and the forces allied to defeat the alien invaders.

**Ryndellia** A star system located near Naboo, it was the site where the Separatist warship *Malevolence* destroyed a convoy of Republic medical transports.

**ryoo** A blue-and-yellow wildflower native to Naboo. Ryoo Naberrie was named for it.

**Ryoone** Described as "down-spiral from one of the remoter sectors" of the Outer Rim, it was a volcanic planet with six sentient species, including Lyunesi, who were masters of interspecies communication.

**Rys** A clone trooper serving Lieutenant Thire and Jedi Master Yoda. During the Clone Wars, he was on a diplomatic mission to the Rugosa moon that turned into a Separatist ambush. Outnumbered by battle droids, Yoda tried to rally the clones' fighting spirit by focusing on their strengths and on overcoming their weaknesses. Yoda told Rys that he concentrated too much on hatred of the enemy rather than confidence in his skills and those of his colleagues as inspiration. Rys often overstocked, carrying too much gear for long hauls.

**ryshcate** A dark brown Corellian sweet cake that was shared as a celebration of life, it was traditionally reserved for birthdays, anniversaries, or other celebrations or momentous occasions. It tasted a bit like a cross between a rum cake and a brownie, filled with vweilu nuts, which themselves were reminiscent of a marriage between walnuts and hazelnuts.

**Rysto, Lord** An Arkanian alias used by Han Solo during the Swarm War to infiltrate the Colony as he searched for Jaina Solo and Zekk.

**Ryuk** A Coruscant survivor of the Yuuzhan Vong conquest who became a slave of Lord Nyax.

**Ryvellia** A planet located in the Avhn-Bendara system. Its capital city of V'eldalv was the site of an uprising that was brutally suppressed by the Empire via orbital bombardment.

**Ryyder, Horox** A Galactic Republic Senator of the Anx species and the Raioballo sector, he had a long neck and elongated, pointed head. Ryyder was one of the Senate's few calming influences during the tumultuous last few decades of the Republic. His quiet and soothing demeanor earned him many allies, and he was well known for his patience and insight. After more than 50 years in politics, Ryyder retired during the Separatist crisis, naming Zo Howler and Fo Kuna as his successors.

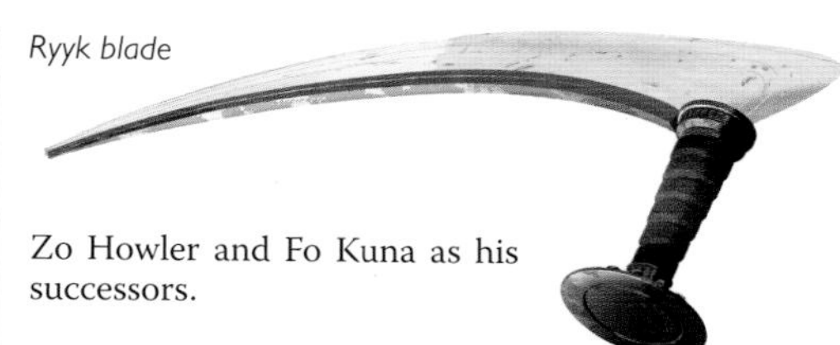
Ryyk blade

**Ryyk (1)** The ancient homeworld of the Neti species, it was destroyed shortly before the start of the Great Sith War.

**Ryyk (2)** An immense Wookiee convict sentenced to prison on Brentaal IV after killing the Mandalorians responsible for the traumatizing deaths of his parents. Ryyk joined Sagoro Autem, Lyshaa, and several other inmates in an escape attempt after Brentaal IV was attacked by the Republic during the Clone Wars. Shaak Ti offered Ryyk freedom in exchange for helping the Republic overthrow Separatist leader Shogar Tok. Ryyk was impaled and killed by a scrange in the sewers beneath Tok's fortress.

**ryyk blade** A traditional hand-to-hand weapon used by the Wookiees of Kashyyyk. Basically long machetes, ryyk blades were extremely dangerous in the hands of a strong, fierce Wookiee. However, the weapons were also considered prized personal possessions, and each Wookiee's ryyk blade was covered in individual markings symbolizing the wielder's strength, courage, and honor. The bounty hunter and failed Jedi Aurra Sing used a ryyk blade on occasion.

**RZ-1** *See* A-wing starfighter.

Horox Ryyder

# S

**2nd Airborne Company** This was one of the divisions of the Grand Army of the Republic's 212th Attack Battalion. The 2nd Airborne Company was part of the assault on Utapau, led by Jedi General Obi-Wan Kenobi, during the hunt for General Grievous at the end of the Clone Wars. The 2nd Airborne had a distinct hatred of Mandalorians, and members took out their feelings on the clone troopers of the GAR.

**2nd Platoon** This division of the Grand Army of the Republic's Bacta Company was commanded by Lieutenant Barr during the Clone Wars.

Sabacc

**2nd Sector Army** This division of the Grand Army of the Republic was commanded by Jedi Master Ry-Gaul during the Clone Wars. The 2nd Sector Army was part of Systems Army Alpha.

**7th Legion** A division of the Grand Army of the Republic under the command of Senior Clone Commander A'den during the Clone Wars. It was part of the 327th Star Corps.

**Saa, T'ra** The Jedi Watchman of the planetary sector that contained the twin planets of Kiffex and Kiffu during the years surrounding the Battle of Naboo. A tall, female Neti, T'ra Saa often moved about in humanoid form, with yellow skin and a collection of thick tendrils atop her head. It was T'ra Saa who first discovered the resurgence of dark side energy that emanated from Volfe Karkko after the Anzati was released from his stasis field by Aayla Secura. She teamed with Quinlan Vos and two Jedi Masters, Tholme and Zao, to defeat the Anzati Sith magician.

During the Clone Wars, T'ra Saa was one of the many Jedi Masters who reluctantly assumed the rank of general for the Old Republic, seeing action on Devaron and Geonosis. Some 17 months after the Battle of Geonosis, bounty hunters badly wounded Master Saa on Null, and she spent a great deal of time in a bacta tank during her recovery. Tholme and T'ra Saa traveled to Nar Shaddaa to locate Quinlan Vos's lover Khaleen Hentz, but were stranded there when the command was given to execute Order 66. Thus, they were able to survive the initial killings of the Jedi Purge, and later accompanied Hentz to Kashyyyk.

T'ra Saa

< Han Solo, Leia Organa Solo, and Luke Skywalker (left to right)

**saago grass** A tall, brittle grass found in deserts and on the beaches of Naboo. Gungans harvested saago grass, which was softened in the sap of the rutiger tree to create a durable, leather-like material used in clothing and armor.

**Saak'ak** A Neimoidian freighter. To all appearances, the *Saak'ak* was merely a commercial vessel, its horseshoe shape designed to carry large amounts of cargo. In addition to its cloaking device, however, the ship was equipped with heavy durasteel armor plating, blaster turrets, and military-strength communications arrays that became visible when an unwary enemy came within firing range. In Basic, the ship was known as the *Profiteer.*

**Saarai-kaar** The highest rank attainable by a Jensaarai Force-user. There could be only one Saarai-kaar at any given time.

**Saarrj, Lieutenant Izbela** An officer in the Imperial Forensic Intelligence agency during the height of the New Order, her investigations exposed the threat posed by Tyber Zann.

**Saarn** An isolated, hidden world, Saarn was used by the Rebel Alliance for military training and was later a remote surveillance outpost after the New Republic moved to Coruscant. Five years after the Battle of Endor, one of Grand Admiral Thrawn's Star Destroyers, the *Stormhawk,* executed a hit-and-fade attack on Saarn, wiping out New Republic personnel. Thrawn's forces set up a listening post there to protect the movement of the Imperial fleet.

**sabacc** A popular electronic card game in which high stakes—ranging from spacecraft to planets—could be won and lost. Sabacc was played using a deck of 76 card-chips with values that changed randomly in response to electronic impulses. The deck's four suits were sabers, staves, flasks, and coins. Each suit consisted of cards numbered 1 through 11 and four ranked cards—Commander, Mistress, Master, and Ace—equivalent to 12 through 15. There were also 16 face cards. A hand was dealt when the dealer pressed a button on the sabacc table to send out a series of random pulses that shifted the values and pictures shown on the card-chips. Players bet and bluffed; they could lock in the values of any of their card-chips by placing them in the table's interference field, which blocked the dealer's pulses. To win, a player had to get a pure sabacc, which totaled exactly 23, or an idiot's array, which consisted of an idiot face card (value 0), a card valued at 2, and a card valued at 3—a literal 23.

Sabé as Queen Amidala

Han Solo and Lando Calrissian traded the *Millennium Falcon* back and forth several times over sabacc hands, and each won control of entire planets or cities in the same manner.

**Sabé** One of Queen Amidala's Royal Handmaidens. Sabé was responsible for serving as the Queen's decoy whenever dangerous situations arose. To fulfill this difficult role, she spent many hours learning to speak and act like Naboo's sovereign. While disguised as the Queen, Sabé received subtle signals from "Padmé Naberrie," Amidala's alter ego.

**saberjowl** A large predator in the seas of Kamino. Cloned from Naboo's colo claw fish, the saberjowl was a meaner, more adaptable hunter than its original genetic stock and was considered the terror of the southern Kamino seas.

**Saber Squadron (1)** The personal starfighter squadron of Luke Skywalker during the Yuuzhan Vong War. Besides himself and Mara Jade Skywalker, the squadron consisted of seven non-Jedi veterans and half a dozen newly trained Jedi pilots.

**Saber Squadron (2)** A TIE interceptor squadron under the command of Baron Soontir Fel during the Battle of Endor. Interceptors bearing the Saber Squadron bloodstripe had a minimum of 10 kills.

Voort saBinring

**saBinring, Voort "Piggy"** A Gamorrean member of Wraith Squadron. Voort "Piggy" saBinring was an experimental subject of the Binring Biomedical Product Corporation, which altered his biochemistry and enhanced his intelligence. Piggy flew as Wraith Twelve, and survived being shot during an assassination attempt on Admiral Ackbar. In the Yuuzhan Vong War, he flew as Twin Suns Five during the Borleias evacuation.

**Sabodor** The owner of an exotic pet store on the planet Etti IV, he hailed from the planet Rakrir. Sabodor had a short, segmented tubular body, five pairs of limbs, two eyestalks, an olfactory cluster, and a vocal organ located in the center of his midsection.

**sabriquet** An ancient musical instrument created by the Bith species. A sabriquet resembled a thick pipe topped by a thin, flexible tube, and produced a trilling sound when properly played.

**Sacorria** Located in the Sacorrian system—one of the Outlier systems of the Corellian sector—this pleasant but secretive world had strict regulations. The site of the Dorthus Tal prison, Sacorria was long ruled by the Triad, a secretive council of dictators consisting of one human, one Drall, and one Selonian, about whom almost nothing—not even their names—was known. The Triad banned marriages with off-worlders and promulgated draconian laws, including one forbidding a woman to marry without her father's consent.

Fourteen years after the Battle of Endor, Lando Calrissian visited Sacorria to see Tendra Risant, a member of a wealthy and influential family, regarding a possible marriage proposal. Meanwhile, the Triad set into motion a master plan to force the New Republic to acknowledge the Corellian sector as an independent state. The Triad organized rebellions on each of the five planets in the Corellian system and gained control of Centerpoint Station, which allowed it to set up interdiction and jam fields over the system and to destroy distant stars at will. The Triad's plans—and its fleet of more than 80 ships—were defeated by the New Republic and a Bakuran task force.

**Sacred Scroll of Gurrisalia** This ancient parchment was considered one of the galaxy's greatest mysteries. The scroll was believed to have been created in an incredibly ancient time, and was written in a nearly indecipherable language. Historians from all generations argued and debated about its contents, which many believed held the secrets of how life evolved in the galaxy.

**Sacul, Jorg** A human male commander in the Rebel Alliance. To his troops, Jorg Sacul was a fearless fighter renowned for his inner strength and ability to remain calm under fire. He mentored the younger pilots in his X-wing squadron.

**Sadeet, Sish** A Trandoshan who worked as Mirith Sinn's bodyguard and second in command. Sish Sadeet was hatched to a lower-class mother in the tropical regions of Trandosha, near one of the many Imperial bases on the planet. Dissatisfied with his servant-like existence, at a young age Sadeet stowed away aboard an outgoing Imperial shuttle, but lost an arm to blasterfire in an ensuing fight. Sadeet fell in with New Republic forces, and after his arm regrew he joined Mirith Sinn on Phaeda.

Naga Sadow

Sadeet disliked working with Sinn's informant, Tem Merkon. When Merkon brought Kir Kanos to the Rebels, he became even more suspicious. While the Empire attacked the Phaeda base, Sinn and Sadeet commandeered Kanos's ship and went to the planet Yinchorr. There they found Carnor Jax and Kir Kanos locked in battle. When Sadeet ran at them, Kanos killed the Trandoshan instantly.

**Sa-Di** A Dark Side Adept. Together with his comrade Nefta, Sa-Di destroyed most of the Emperor's clones in an attempt to take the throne for himself. After witnessing their actions, dark side Executor Sedriss executed the two conspirators.

**Sadow, Naga** A Dark Lord of the Sith, he lived 5,000 years before the Galactic Civil War. Intensely ambitious, Sadow wanted to expand the Sith Empire, opposing other Sith who wanted to keep their borders closed. When lost hyperspace explorers from the Galactic Republic stumbled upon the Sith worlds, Sadow seized the opportunity. He grabbed both power and the mantle of Dark Lord of the Sith, then led an ill-fated invasion into Republic space—a clash known as the Great Hyperspace War.

After defeat by Republic forces, Sadow fled; he covered his escape by using dark

Sish Sadeet

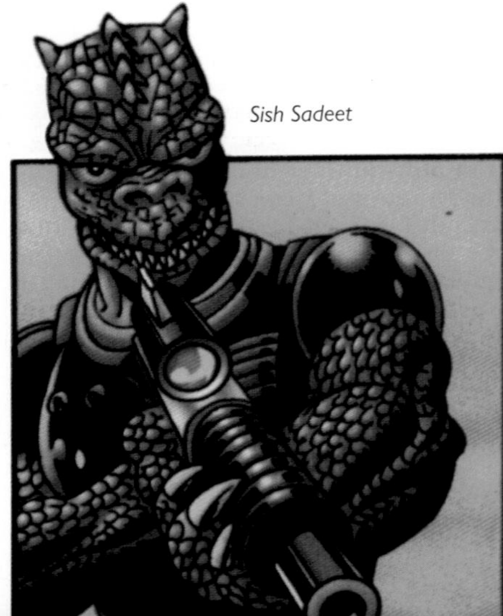

side power to blow up the Denarii Nova. He limped to Yavin 4 to rebuild his empire with a scant few Sith survivors. Sadow vanished into legend, although remnants of his dark power were uncovered by Exar Kun a thousand years later on Yavin 4, precipitating the start of the Great Sith War.

Saelt-Marae

**Saelt-Marae** A Yarkora with a mysterious past, sometimes called Yak Face because of his whiskered, broad-snouted visage. Saelt-Marae joined the entourage of crime lord Jabba the Hutt on Tatooine several years before the Battle of Endor. He posed as a trader who specialized in locating and selling religious artifacts from primitive cultures. Saelt-Marae immersed himself in the treachery of Jabba's court and ingratiated himself with Jabba's henchmen, who didn't know that Saelt-Marae was an informant, selling Jabba information about the intrigues developing behind the Hutt's ample back.

**Saffalore** A Corporate Sector world and headquarters of Binring Biomedical Product.

**Sagar system** This star system was noted as the site of the Blackstar wheelworld.

**Sage, Vana** A female Naboo expatriate who roamed the galaxy contracting her services as a gun for hire. Sage was once the personal bodyguard and pilot of Naboo's King Veruna, but she left the planet in disgust after the Royal Advisory Council ignored her advice to upgrade and expand Naboo's military. Sage piloted a ship called the *Guardian Mantis* against Trade Federation forces during the Battle of Naboo. Around the time of the Battle of Geonosis, she helped Nym take back his base on the planet Lok.

**SAGroup (Sub-Adult Group)** The youth chapter of COMPOR (Commission for the Protection of the Republic)—and later, COMPNOR—which welcomed patriots between the ages of 13 and 17. Over 95 percent of its members were human. During the Clone Wars, 6,000 SAGroup members marched from the Jrade-Daders Concourse on Coruscant to the newly reopened Monument Plaza.

**Sah, Joc** This young, blond-haired man was the Padawan learner of Jedi Master Sev during the final years of the Old Republic. Master Sev and Joc Sah were dispatched to Ragmar V at the end of the Clone Wars to assist in securing the planet as a staging area for the Republic fleet. When the signal was issued to execute Order 66, Joc Sah was on the planet's surface with the clone trooper Remy, struggling to subdue the local criminals. Joc Sah managed to escape being killed when he joined forces with the very criminals he was charged with eliminating. With the help of these criminals, Joc Sah escaped Sergeant Remy and his clones, and fled into the desert. Together they managed to stage a number of hit-and-run attacks on the clone troopers.

**Saheelindeel** Located in the remote Tion Hegemony, this backworld was inhabited by intelligent furred primates. The high festival on Saheelindeel was a time of tribal hunting rituals and harvest ceremonies that incorporated farm machinery exhibits, shock-ball matches, and air shows in an attempt to become more technologically sophisticated. The Saheelindeeli, led by a matriarch, had an affinity for grandiose actions. Han Solo and Chewbacca briefly worked on Saheelindeel after leaving the Corporate Sector. Following the Battle of Yavin, the Empire established a listening post near the planet that was attacked by the Rebel Alliance to divert attention from its fleet's movements into the Greater Plooriod Cluster.

Saheelindeeli

**Sai, Ko** The chief scientist of the Kaminoan cloning project. Ko Sai oversaw the biological aspects of the Republic's clone army, ensuring that the clones were of the highest quality.

Under her guidance, the clones' genetic code was altered to accelerate their growth to twice the normal human rate, and their mental structure was subtly reconfigured to make them obedient to authority. Her black cuffs were a mark of honor, their thickness indicating her high scientific rank. Early in the Clone Wars, Ko Sai went missing and became the subject of intense searches by the clones, Chancellor Palpatine, and other Kaminoans.

Each had their own reason for seeking out Ko Sai: For the Republic, it was imperative that her methods not fall into enemy hands. Palpatine quietly sought a genetic solution to immortality. For Kal Skirata, finding Ko Sai meant unlocking the mystery of the growth acceleration that doomed the clone troopers to a shortened lifespan. Skirata's agents found and imprisoned Sai, destroying her collected research and demanding that she reveal which genes held the secret of the clone growth acceleration. While Ko Sai eventually agreed to cooperate, she committed suicide, hanging herself before turning over all her information.

Ko Sai

***sai cha*** One of the lightsaber "marks of contact" used by the Jedi. *Sai cha* was a beheading move, used by Anakin Skywalker to dispatch Count Dooku.

**Saijo** A backworld on the galactic rim that became the headquarters for the Tof invasion force following the Battle of Endor. The Alliance and the Nagai staged a mission to Saijo to capture Prince Sereno, thus ending the Tof invasion.

**sail barge** A huge repulsorlift craft that could travel across any relatively flat terrain, including sand, water, ice, or grass. The crime lord Jabba the Hutt used the sail barge *Khetanna* for pleasure cruises across oceans of sand on the desert world of Tatooine. Jabba customized his luxury barge and outfitted it with grand trappings.

The sail barge's main propulsion system was a three-chamber repulsorlift thrust array that provided a top speed of 100 kilometers an hour. Jabba's barge hovered up to 10 meters above the ground, and its immense sails caught the wind to pull the barge along. In sail mode, the barge had a top speed of about 30 kilometers an hour. The barge had a main-deck heavy blaster and smaller anti-personnel blasters mounted on the deck rails.

Retractable viewports on the passenger deck provided sweeping vistas, and the large banquet room was renowned for the decadent parties held there. Jabba particularly enjoyed staging

A sail barge, the Khetanna

feasts built around elaborate executions, when he fed those he disfavored to the Sarlacc at the Great Pit of Carkoon. It was during just such a celebration that the sail barge was destroyed when Luke Skywalker, Princess Leia Organa, and others staged a daring rescue of Han Solo.

**Saiy, Barit** This young man was born to Corellian parents who lived on Coruscant during the Yuuzhan Vong War. His parents, also born on Coruscant, owned an engineering shop in the Q-65 district of Galactic City, where they could be among other Corellians. When Thrackan Sal-Solo threatened to secede from the Galactic Alliance some 10 years after the war with the Yuuzhan Vong, Barit Saiy was among the Corellian youths on Coruscant who protested for their homeworld's rights. Saiy was befriended during this time by Ben Skywalker. Ben could not understand Barit's desire to fight for Corellian independence, given that the youth had been born on Coruscant and never set foot on his ancestral homeworld. Saiy, however, saw the growing conflict between Corellia and the Galactic Alliance through the eyes of his father and grandfather, and had no qualms about taking up arms against the oppression of the Alliance. Thus, Skywalker was stunned to encounter Saiy at a riot near the Rotunda Zone of Galactic City.

Corellian protesters were angered that their water supply had been cut off, and when things got ugly, Saiy drew a blaster and would have shot an officer of the Coruscant Security Force if Skywalker hadn't used the Force to deflect the blast, allowing the police time to arrest the rioters. Saiy was among those taken prisoner, but Lon Shevu recognized that he was acting not out of vengeance or spite, but from the fervor of being a teenager. Shevu worked behind the scenes to get Saiy freed, and the young man agreed to serve as Shevu's eyes and ears on the street in return.

***sai tok*** One of the lightsaber "marks of contact" used by the Jedi. *Sai tok* was intended to cut an enemy in half, and was used by Obi-Wan Kenobi to dispatch Darth Maul.

**Sakiyan** Members of this species were often hired as assassins because of their excellent aural and olfactory senses. Sakiyans had keen infrared peripheral vision and often tracked their prey by scent.

**Salculd** A female Selonian, she was a member of the Hunchuzuc Den, a rebel group opposed to the Overden, the central power on Selonia. A peppery, energetic-looking pilot, she patched together a ship to transport Han Solo from Corellia to Selonia.

**Saleucami** A barren desert world marked with strange bulbous plant life, it was a major battle site during the Outer Rim Sieges of the Clone Wars. Stuck in the Outer Rim, its name meant "oasis"—an ironic title, given the planet's arid nature. Craters formed by meteor strikes provided the only water and arable soil, and magma streams below the surface provided geothermal energy. Though the planet boasted no native intelligent life, a mixture of offworld cultures, including Weequays, Gran, Wroonians, and Twi'leks, came to call Saleucami home.

Horton Salm

Sardu Sallowe

Toward the end of the Clone Wars, the Separatists hatched their own cloning program. Using accelerated techniques, the Separatists engineered Nikto from the Morgukai warrior sect, and used deadly Anzati assassins to train them. This scheme was discovered by Jedi Master Tholme and Aayla Secura. A multibattalion task force led by Jedi Master Oppo Rancisis with Quinlan Vos as second in command journeyed to Saleucami to blockade the planet and prevent any of the Morgukai clones from getting offworld. With the Separatists controlling the city, it was crucial that the Republic forces be well supplied. The Jedi and clone forces set up camp on the rim of the city's caldera and fought their way inward. The siege lasted for five grueling months before the Separatist forces there were defeated.

In the aftermath, a smaller contingent of Republic forces was left behind for mop-up operations. During Order 66, clone biker scouts shot down Jedi Master Stass Allie's speeder, killing her.

Saleucami

**Salis D'aar** The capital city of the planet Bakura.

**Salliche** An agricultural planet in the Core Worlds, it was the headquarters of Salliche Ag Corporation, which administered 18 farming planets known as the Ag Circuit. Although the Empire placed Moff Gegren Throsen in charge of Salliche, its citizens remained loyal to the House Harbright, whose members had served the Republic for three centuries. After the rise of the Empire, Lady Selnia Harbright decided to aid the Rebel Alliance.

**Sallowe, Sardu** A Tatooine bounty hunter hired by Embra the Hutt to find the Yavin Vassilika. Sardu Sallowe partnered with 4-LOM and Zuckuss. He was often accompanied by Jawa assistants and spoke in a hybrid dialect of Tusken and Jawa.

**Salm, Horton** A human general from Norval II, he was placed in charge of the rebuilding of Rogue Squadron. Often at odds with Rogue Leader Wedge Antilles, he was nevertheless an honorable man and a good soldier. It was strange that his disobedience of a direct order during the squadron's initial raid on Borleias saved the Rogues—and himself. Instead of leaving the system as ordered, he and his men stayed behind to assist Rogue Squadron's exit. While lending much-needed help, the ship he and his men would have been on, the *Mon Valle,* was destroyed by planetary defenses.

**Salporin** A Wookiee hero and childhood friend of Chewbacca's. When Chewie caught the wanderlust that led him off Kashyyyk to explore the galaxy, Salporin stayed behind. His martial talents brought him to the coastal city of Kachirho on the Wawaatt Archipelago. There he worked as a hunter and craftsman, using his blade mastery in both professions.

While in Kachirho, he fell in love with a Wookiee maiden named Gorrlyn. The two were planning a future together when the Clone Wars struck. Realizing that Kachirho was to be targeted by the Separatists, Salporin and Gorrlyn volunteered together to protect the city. They served under the command of Captain Merumeru in the battle that followed.

Salporin survived the Clone Wars, but when the Empire seized Kashyyyk and began

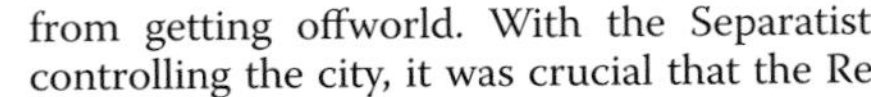

Salporin

enslaving the Wookiees, he was taken captive. For years, he served as a slave. He was eventually freed by Alliance commandos on a mission to liberate Kashyyyk. Salporin returned to the simple life of a civilian. Five years after the Battle of Endor, Salporin offered Princess Leia Organa Solo refuge in his home while she was on the run from agents of the Empire. When Noghri commandos attacked the home, Salporin was killed defending the Princess.

**Sal-Solo, Thrackan** Han Solo's first cousin and a leader of the Corellian sector. Thrackan Sal-Solo emerged after the Battle of Endor as the Hidden Leader of the anti-alien Human League. He proclaimed himself to be the designated successor to the Diktat that ruled under the Empire and declared the Corellian sector to be independent and free of any New Republic entanglements. The Human League was defeated and Sal-Solo captured by the intervention of the New Republic and a Bakuran task force. He spent eight years in Dorthus Yal prison on Sacorria, then worked at Centerpoint Station as part of his rehabilitation.

In the Battle of Fondor during the Yuuzhan Vong War, Anakin Solo armed Centerpoint Station but decided not to pull the trigger. Sal-Solo fired the weapon himself, devastating both the Hapan and Yuuzhan Vong fleets. Because of his decisive action at Fondor, Sal-Solo became governor-general of the Corellian sector. After he tried to sign a treaty with the Yuuzhan Vong, the invaders named him President of Ylesia and commander in chief of the Peace Brigade against his will. After a battle on Ylesia, he soon returned to Corellia, where he became the planet's Head of State, and seized even more power during the Second Corellian Insurrection that took place 40 years after the Battle of Yavin. He hired the Sith agent Lumiya to assassinate his rivals. Sal-Solo then hired Boba Fett to assassinate his cousin Han, but Fett teamed up with his granddaughter Mirta Gev to kill his corrupt employer instead.

Thrackan Sal-Solo

**salthia beans** A food that often was served to the children of Han and Leia Organa Solo in their nursery on Coruscant, it occasionally was used in their food fights.

**Salvo** This clone commander was promoted to lead the 32nd Air Combat Wing during the final stages of the Clone Wars. A battle-hardened veteran, Salvo was distinguished by his rust-colored armor and the motto LIVE TO SERVE! laser-etched onto the left side of his helmet. Salvo was assigned to the task force led by Jedi Master Roan Shryne that was dispatched to retake the planet Murkhana. After Order 66 had been issued, Salvo was unprepared for the actions of Climber and of Ion Team, who refused to execute the Jedi. Ion Team fired their ECD grenades in such a way that the explosions blinded Salvo and his men, rendering their helmet systems inoperable. Initially, Salvo made no attempt to reprimand Ion Team for their actions, waiting instead to see if the Jedi could be captured and killed before reporting on the dissension.

**Samaria** This arid, desert-covered planet was one of the first worlds visited by Darth Vader in the wake of the Clone Wars. A small planet, Samaria was located in the Leemurtoo system of the Core Worlds. In order to make the planet more livable, the capital city of Sath was sculpted from the surrounding desert, and a vast bay was dug from the ground. For many generations, Samaria had been a rival of its sister world, Rosha. The Samarians were noted for their macrotechnology, while the Roshans were known for their microtechnology. In the wake of the Clone Wars, a trade agreement was proposed between the two planets, but it was smashed by Bog Divinian as part of a larger plot by Emperor Palpatine. As soon as the Roshans were implicated in an assassination attempt on Divinian, the Samarian government set in motion plans to attack Rosha.

**Samuro** This ancient Jedi Knight captured and imprisoned the energy vampire known as Countess Rajine many centuries before the onset of the Clone Wars. Samuro gave his own life to ensure that Rajine was unable to leave her fortress, leaving behind his loyal droid, Z-18. Countess Rajine forced the droid into servitude. When Rajine captured Jedi Master Mace Windu during the Clone Wars, Z-18 helped free Windu, and turned over its master's holocron for safekeeping. Samuro had trapped the life energies of all Rajine's victims in the holocron. When Master Windu activated the holocron, a recorded message explained that Rajine's victims would take their own retribution. The holocron freed the zombie victims from Rajine's control, and they killed her.

**Sanbra** Location of the University of Sanbra in the De'etta system. Sanbra was where Tem Eliss, a sentientologist, wrote the *University of Sanbra Guide to Intelligent Life.*

**Sancor** One of the first Imperial Inquisitors. When he spoke, Sancor revealed a mouthful of small, sharp teeth. He was dispatched to Polis Massa after Inquisitor Malorum discovered a connection between the Jedi Order and the asteroid base. An expert in records security, Sancor was tasked with digging through the base's medical records to locate anomalies that would provide proof of Padmé Amidala's presence on the asteroid. When he discovered that Maneeli Tuun and Obi-Wan Kenobi were on Polis Massa disguised as medical personnel, he tried to apprehend them. During the fight, however, Obi-Wan used the Force to push Sancor off a platform. The Inquisitor fell to his death.

**Sanctuary Moon** One of the names given to the Forest Moon of Endor.

Wan Sandage

**Sandage, Wan** A playboy and Podracer who entered the Boonta Eve Classic. This Devlikk came from a family of 128 brothers and sisters, and was just six years old at the time of the Battle of Naboo. Sandage, who had been competing in Podraces since he was two years old, realized that he would never win a major event if he did not first deal with Sebulba the Dug. In order to accomplish this task, he hired hitman and fellow Podracer Aldar Beedo. During the Boonta Eve race, his Elsinore-Cordova Turbodyne 99-U Podracer collided with a Jawa sandcrawler off course during lap three. Sandage survived to compete in the Vinta Harvest Podrace Classic. After his death, his son Wan Sandage Jr. took his place on the Podracing circuit.

**sandcrawler** Sandcrawlers were huge vehicles, originally brought to Tatooine long ago during the planet's establishment as a mining colony. Their steam-powered nuclear fusion engines and giant treads let them move through the trackless Dune Sea, making them well suited to their original task of hauling ore. When the mining venture failed, the sand-

Sandcrawler

crawlers were abandoned. They were quickly taken over by the diminutive Jawas, scavengers of the planet who collected just about any kind of mechanical or electronic equipment but specialized in rebuilding broken droids.

At nearly 20 meters high, each sturdy sandcrawler could house a full Jawa clan numbering up to several hundred individuals. Inside was a maze of sleeping and eating alcoves, junk, machinery, spare parts, and fully functional droids. New droid acquisitions were loaded through either a magnetic suction tube or a front loading ramp. Jawas relied on sandcrawlers for defense against their natural enemies, Sand People and krayt dragons.

**sandjiggers** Tiny Tatooine arthropods, they fed on razor moss.

**sando aqua monster** The largest of Naboo's incredible sea monsters. A terrifying predator with tremendous strength, the sando had an uncanny ability to remain concealed within Naboo's core. The beast was the core's most successful predator, feeding on a wide variety of other creatures including opee sea killers and colo claw fish.

Naboo zoologists found it difficult to study the sando aqua monster, and details about its habits and physiology remained unknown for years. In fact, the sando aqua monster was thought to be a myth until one such creature beached itself on the shore near Port Landien. It was believed that the sando was once a terrestrial creature that had partially adapted itself to life in the water. The beast had visible gills and webbed hands, but its body and head were not streamlined for high-speed underwater travel. Despite this, the sando was able to propel itself effectively using its muscular tail.

The sando could grasp prey in its large hands. It was not known how the creature consumed enough food to support its massive size, but the sando was an extremely effective hunter. The Caves of the Eleuabad was one of the most notorious hangouts of sando aqua monsters on Naboo, while a sando tooth could be viewed at the Royal Icqui Aquaria on Coruscant.

**Sand People** *See* Tusken Raiders.

**Sandral, Nurik** This man was the leader of the Sandral family on the planet Dantooine during the era of the Great Sith War. Nurik was greatly saddened when his son, Casus, was killed by kath hounds during an archaeological expedition to the Rakatan ruins found on the planet. He then discovered that his daughter, Rahasia, was in love with Shen Matale, and that they had been secretly meeting despite the ages-old feud between their families. Nurik had Shen taken captive, but Jedi Knights intervened and freed Shen. Nurik was forced to admit the kidnapping, and he and Ahlan Matale, Shen's father and Nurik's rival, formed a tenuous truce after learning of their children's love for each other.

**sand skimmer** A one-person repulsorlift vehicle, it consisted of a disk to stand on and a large sail extending from the rear to help it travel over sand flats and similar terrain.

**Sandskimmer, Falynn** A human member of Wraith Squadron, Falynn Sandskimmer was from Tatooine. She flew as Wraith Three and was killed in action.

Sando aqua monster

**sand sloth** A beast of burden, it resembled a cross between a rhinoceros and a musk ox. Demma Moll used sand sloths on her farm complex on Annoo.

**sand snake** A furry snake found on Geonosis's cliffs that was preyed upon by masiffs. Sand snakes made a strange singing sound.

**sandtrooper** Stormtroopers who were trained in desert tactics, they wore temperature-controlled body "gloves" underneath their protective armor to help them keep cool while working in blistering heat.

**sandwhirl** A type of desert storm with blowing sand that occasionally ravaged Tatooine.

**sangi fever** A partuclarly virulent form of fever that was easily transmitted and often fatal if not treated quickly. "Sangi Fever Sal" was believed to have started one of the largest documented outbreaks of the disease.

**sanibuff** A specialized cleaning and polishing compound used to clean the deck plates of transport ships throughout the galaxy. Smugglers were among the primary users of sanibuffing techniques, which eliminated illegal substances from deck plates and other durable surfaces.

**Sanjin** A planet near the Core Worlds, it was where the Nikto agent Ma'w'shiye betrayed the Rebel Alliance, deserted his squadron, and stole the group's spacecraft.

**San-Ni staff** A three-piece weapon favored by Jedi Weapons Masters. When deactivated, it acted as a club. It activated when each half was twisted and pulled apart, revealing a 10-centimeter stun prod linked to the other two pieces with high-voltage power couplings.

**Sant, Rystáll** One of Jabba the Hutt's favorite humanoid dancers, she was a Theelin half-breed formerly from Coruscant. Abandoned by her parents, she was raised by Ortolan musicians and was drawn into the criminal underworld by Black Sun.

**Santhe** One of the ruling houses on Lianna. Its head, Kerred Santhe, bought controlling interest in Sienar Technologies 100 years before the Battle of Yavin and moved the headquarters of the parent Santhe/Seinar Technologies to Lianna. It was one of the original voting sponsors of the Corporate Sector Authority. The company's many divisions built civilian and military ground vehicles and starships. Over the decades it branched out into security, transportation, and other businesses, but

Sandtroopers search for droids on Tatooine.

remained firmly in the hands of the founder's granddaughter, Lady Valles Santhe. While the company publicly supported whichever regime controlled the galaxy, it always held an ace up its sleeve.

**Sanvia Vitajuice Bar** This upscale drinking establishment was located on Coruscant during the years following the Swarm War. Unlike the multitude of bars that served alcoholic drinks, the Sanvia Vitajuice Bar served myriad healthy beverages, including juices made from exotic fruits.

**Sanyassan Marauders** A species of tall, barbaric humanoids, they preyed upon the more peaceful inhabitants of Endor's Forest Moon. Once spaceway pirates from the nearby planet Sanyassa, they crashed on Endor nearly a century before the Battle of Yavin and were unable to leave. They had scaly, monkey-like faces and wore ragged clothing adorned with scavenged items. The marauders built a dark fortress on a desolate plain surrounded by a moat. Under their king, Terak, they made destructive forays seeking a new power source for their ship.

**sapith** One of the many crystals used by the ancient Jedi Knights in the construction of lightsabers. The sapith crystal was believed to have given the wielder better control of the lightsaber, thereby increasing its energy damage. Each sapith crystal was formed from the excretions of the volice worm, which created the crystals only once every 11 years.

**Saquesh** A man living in the Refugee Sector of Nar Shaddaa following the Mandalorian Wars and the Jedi Civil War. Saquesh also worked for the Exchange, and continually watched his fellow refugees for anyone who might be of use to his bosses. He was behind the kidnapping of Nadaa's daughter, holding the young girl hostage to force Nadaa to pay off her debts. After Nadaa convinced the Jedi Exile to intercede, Saquesh tried to bully the Exile into leaving. The ensuing scuffle resulted in Saquesh's death.

**Sarahwiee** A frozen world of glaciers, mountains, and ice-covered oceans in the Bseto system, it was home to a top-secret Imperial research facility. The outpost, situated in a mountain range in the southern hemisphere, held 1,000 personnel and was accessible only by air. When Emperor Palpatine first established the facility, he had all references to it wiped from the Imperial Archives for security. After the Battle of Endor, a few Imperial fleet captains equipped and supplied the base until the defeat of Grand Admiral Thrawn, when it became necessary for free traders to handle the cargo shipments. After Thrawn's defeat but before the rise of the clone Emperor, a New Republic commando team including Luke Skywalker and led by Lieutenant Page was sent to Sarahwiee to destroy the facility and erase its computer records.

**Sarapin** A volcanic planet of hot, cracked rock and rivers of seething magma that powered Republic energy collectors. The energy was collected and moved to an Energy Collection Repository for eventual shipment offworld. Sarapin was also home to a multi-armed animal, the vaapad, that gave its name to a dangerous fighting technique invented by Mace Windu. During the Empire's reign, Sarapin was thought impregnable, until Rebels brought down its defense grid and disrupted the precious power flow.

**Saras** One of many Killik hives that made up the Colony during the Swarm War. Members of the hive referred to themselves as Saras and acted upon the Will of the hive. The Saras established their nest on the moon Ruu, but later were relocated to Woteba after the resolution of the Qoribu crisis. Despite being part of the Colony, the Saras nest was notable for its artistic skill, as evidenced by the hive's ability to create wonderful artwork from spinglass and other materials.

**Sarcophagus** The moon of the planet Sacorria, it was a vast graveyard visited only by those burying their dead.

**Saren, Rianna** This Twi'lek female was among the earliest members of the fledgling Alliance to Restore the Republic. She was one of several agents who were tasked with discovering information about the first Death Star when it became apparent that the Empire was building the massive station to destroy the Rebel Alliance.

**Saresh, Guun Han** A green-skinned Twi'lek Jedi who took part in the Great Hunt on Tatooine and Korriban nearly 4,000 years before the Battle of Yavin. During the mission to Korriban, he seduced a Sith apprentice to obtain information. When his comrades Duron Qel-Droma and Shaela Nuur refused to renounce their love for each other, Saresh left Korriban to hunt a terentatek in the Shadowlands of Kashyyyk, where he died. The only evidence of his demise was found in the remains of the terentatek that had eaten him, after it was killed by another team of Jedi Knights who were searching for information on the Star Forge.

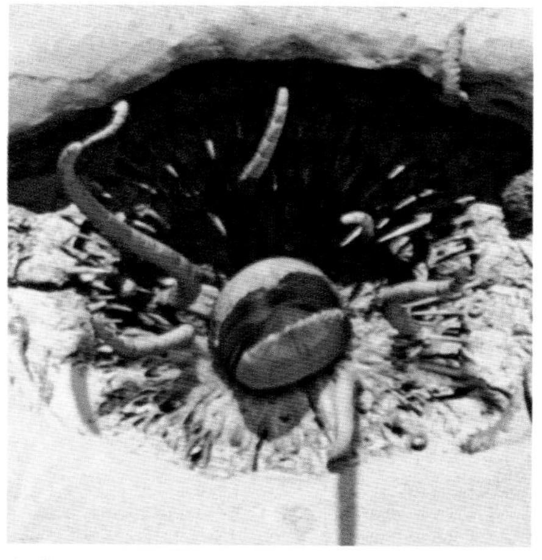

*Sarlacc*

**Sarge** This clone commando, officially designated RC-1013, was one of several heroes of the Republic's early victories during the Clone Wars. Sarge was later a member of the Aiwha Squad during the Outer Rim Sieges, and was assigned to Jedi Master Traavis on Garqi when the command to execute Order 66 was issued. Sarge and his men concentrated their fire on Master Traavis before the Jedi could defend himself.

**Sariss** A Dark Jedi encountered by Kyle Katarn, and the daughter of the prophet Lord Cronal (also known as Blackhole). During the Galactic Civil War, Sariss worked for Governor Tour Aryon of Tatooine, going by the name Prophetess. She also helped train the dark sider Merili, and was often part of the Secret Order entourage sent to the Super Star Destroyer *Vengeance* to confer with the Dark Jedi Jerec.

After the Battle of Endor, Sariss joined Jerec as one of his agents, and she recruited a young Force-user named Yun. In a fierce battle with Kyle Katarn, Sariss accidentally struck down Yun, and Katarn stabbed Yun's own lightsaber through Sariss's chest.

**Sark, Robbyn** A Roshan, he served as leader of a trade delegation sent to the neighboring world of Samaria about a year after the Clone Wars. The delegation hoped to open commerce between the two worlds. Imperial adviser Bog Divinian repeatedly attempted to discredit the Roshans. When orders were given to arrest the delegation, Ferus Olin and the Samarian resistance worked to ensure that Sark and his companions could escape Samaria safely. The Roshans, however, were attacked by Samarian warships that were about to invade Rosha. Sark's escape vessel was shot down just before landing; all aboard were killed.

**Sarkan** A bipedal species from Sarka. They were tall (often over 2 meters) lizard-descended saurians with thick, green scaly hides and yellow eyes with slit pupils.

**Sarkin, Tyria** A human member of Wraith Squadron from Toprawa. She wore her blond hair long in a ponytail, and flew as Wraith Ten and later as Wraith Eleven. She met Luke Skywalker to pursue training in the Force, but was told that she would not progress far as a Jedi. She later married fellow pilot Kell Tainer and they had a son named Doran. After resigning from the military, Tyria became a Jedi Knight in Luke Skywalker's new Jedi Order and instructed her son in the ways of the Force.

**Sarlacc** An omnivorous, multitentacled creature with needle-sharp teeth and a large beak, the most famous of the species lived at the bottom of a deep sand hole called the Great Pit of Carkoon, located in the wastelands of Tatooine's Dune Sea. The Sarlacc had a huge mouth in its giant worm-like head and was always waiting to be fed. The mouth was lined

with rows of sharply pointed teeth, all aimed inward to keep food trapped inside. It preferred living creatures, snatching unfortunate victims and dragging them into its mucus-coated mouth. Local legend had it that victims died a slow and painful death in the belly of the Sarlacc because its digestive juices took 1,000 years to fully break down its meals.

Sarlaccs reproduced via spores that flew through space, landed on planets, and formed pits with mouths that opened toward the sky. Sarlaccs themselves did not have a well-developed neural system, but over millennia they could develop consciousness by assimilating the thoughts of whatever creatures they digested.

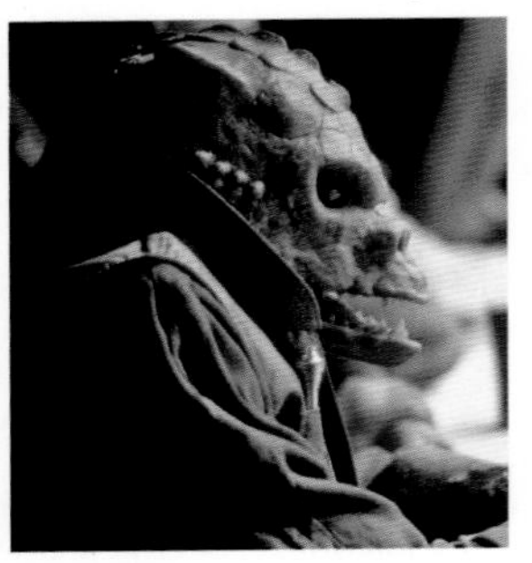

Saurin

Tatooine's Sarlacc was just one of this unusual species, whose members were among the longest-living creatures in the galaxy. As they reached adulthood, Sarlaccs became completely immobile, with only their immense mouth and teeth showing above the surface. The Sarlacc's body was a massive series of digestive tracts and pulmonary systems that allowed the animal to live an extremely efficient and sedentary lifestyle. Sarlaccs could live for tens of thousands of years, provided they acquired enough food; but because they were able to absorb fungus and bacteria from the surrounding soil, very few of these grand creatures ever starved to death. Felucia was home to one of the galaxy's largest Sarlaccs, a creature whose teeth and "gums" covered hundreds of kilometers of wilderness.

Crime lord Jabba the Hutt often used Tatooine's Sarlacc to dispose of opponents, and intended to feed Han Solo, Chewbacca, and Luke Skywalker to the beast. They destroyed Jabba before he could complete the deed. Bounty hunter Boba Fett and a few of Jabba's henchmen appeared to have succumbed, but Fett managed to escape the Sarlacc's maw, claiming later that the creature had found him "somewhat indigestible."

**Sarlacc Battalion A** A division of the Grand Army of the Republic and part of the 41st Elite Corps. Like Sarlacc Battalion B, this unit was commanded by Jedi Master Vaas Ga and led by Commander Gree. Both Sarlacc battalions saw action on Dinlo, and were nearly abandoned there by their commanders before Jedi Knight Etain Tur-Mukan refused to leave without them. Improcco Company volunteered to accompany General Tur-Mukan to the surface of Dinlo, where they rescued the Sarlacc units before the Republic bombarded the planet from orbit.

**Sarlacc Project** A top-secret Imperial project to build a 12-kilometer-long warship, a forerunner to *Super*-class Star Destroyers. It was exposed by agents working for Senator Bail Organa in the early years of the New Order.

**Sarm** A planet located in the Unknown Regions within the bubble formed by the Utegetu Nebula. At some point in Sarm's ancient history, a species of sentient beings inhabited its surface, but all life was wiped out in the supernova that created the nebula. All that remained as evidence of the sentients' existence was a planet-spanning network of irrigation channels visible from space. During the years following the Yuuzhan Vong invasion, Lomi Plo and the Dark Nest of the Killik Colony established a base of operations in orbit around Sarm, after the Killiks were forced to relocate to the Utegetu Nebula during the early stages of the Swarm War. Although the Gorog nest ship was destroyed at Sarm, Lomi Plo escaped and rejoined the Colony's forces at Tenupe.

**Sarne, Moff Kentor** An Imperial warlord who found a secret technology in the Kathol sector that gave its user temporary Force-like powers. He served the Imperial Survey Corps until he was transferred to the 15th Deep Core Reserve Fleet, where he was for years the commander of the *Renegade.*

***Sarpentia*** This Galactic Alliance warship was commanded by Admiral Makin during the Second Battle of Fondor.

**Sarreti, Moff Ephin** The Moff of Bastion during the days of the Imperial Remnant. He was a young man with a young man's ideals, and considered the only reasonable member of the Moff Council. Sarreti favored helping the New Republic during the Yuuzhan Vong War. He gave the New Republic access to Imperial records relevant to the Outbound Flight Project. He also told them that Emperor Palpatine returned Chiss Grand Admiral Thrawn to the Unknown Regions upon learning that the Chiss had been fortifying their systems against invasion by an unknown aggressor.

**Sasso** A Rodian guide on the planet Caluula, he was also a New Republic operative during the Yuuzhan Vong War. He died during an attempt to kill a yammosk on the planet.

**Sata'ak** A Yuuzhan Vong subaltern escalated by Nas Choka for his bravery during the Battle of Ithor.

Sauropteroid

**Satine, Duchess** A staunch pacifist from the desolate world of Kalevala during the time of the Clone Wars. Regal in her bearing and naturally beautiful, Satine instantly commanded every eye in the room. Satine's affection for Jedi Master Obi-Wan Kenobi stemmed from a youthful fancy that the two shared, though both eventually put love behind them and committed themselves to preserving peace throughout the galaxy.

**Saurin** A reptilian species from the planet Durkteel.

**Sauro, Senator Sano** A Telosian native, he was a friend and legal counselor to the Chun family. Later a resident of Eeropha, he sponsored the education of brilliant young Granta Omega at the All Sciences Research Academy on Yerphonia. As the Galactic Republic declined, Senator Sauro began to gather more power. After Bog Divinian was elected Senator from Nuralee, the two began stirring up anti-Jedi sentiments in the Senate as part of a larger plan devised by Omega to discredit Jedi and cut off their Senate support. Obi-Wan Kenobi later discovered the scope of their plans. Sauro's ambitions stretched to the office of Supreme Chancellor, but Palpatine knew of his plotting and decided to keep him close at hand, offering him the position of deputy chancellor to monitor his every move.

After Palpatine named himself Emperor, Sauro consolidated a base of power by handpicking his own Imperial advisers. He crafted a scheme to round up Force-sensitive children and use them to train Imperial pilots. Alarmed by Sauro's megalomania, Palpatine dispatched Darth Vader to rein in the Senator; he was removed from power and relegated to becoming headmaster of the Imperial Naval Academy.

**Sauropteroid** Intelligent aquatic reptiles, these natives of the planet Dellalt ranged from 10 to 15 meters long. They constantly swam their world's oceans, keeping their heads above water with their long muscular necks. Their humanoid heads had blowholes; their hides ranged in color from light gray to greenish black. They were known as the Swimming People of Dellalt.

**Savage Squadron** A fighter squadron comprising pieced-together "uglies." The Rogues originally named this squadron Salvage Squadron. Savage Squadron and Tough Squadron fought alongside Rogue Squadron against the Yuuzhan Vong at Dantooine.

**Savan** A female Falleen and the niece of Prince Xizor. Savan sought the human replica droid Guri so she could establish herself as the leader of Black Sun and avenge her uncle's death. Disguising herself as an old, one-eyed antiques dealer named Azool, Savan hired the bounty hunter Kar Yang to track Guri. Using a human female disguise, Savan began a war within Black Sun. Operating from her hideout on Coruscant, she hoped to use secret codes to control Guri, but the droid rejected these orders. Savan then was apprehended by the heroes of the Rebel Alliance.

**Savant missiles** MerrSonn Munitions warheads that at first appeared to be easy to avoid. Once a target successfully evaded the projectile, however, the Savant's internal guidance computer activated and locked in, surprising the target from behind.

**Save, Whimper** An enigmatic human female seen at the Outlander Club.

**Savvam Lake** This artificial lake atop a 200-story building on Coruscant served as the private playground of the very rich during the last days of the Old Republic. Savvam Lake was lined with trees and genetically engineered flowers that bloomed year-round, filling the air with a hundred different scents.

**Saxan, Aidel** This Corellian woman served as the Five World Prime Minister during the years following the Yuuzhan Vong War. Distinguished by her black hair despite her advancing years, Saxan was a formidable political force and equally represented the five planets of the Corellian system with aplomb. When Thrackan Sal-Solo began pushing for Corellia's complete independence from the Galactic Alliance, Saxan remained unsure how to proceed. Her concern mounted when her accountants discovered that Sal-Solo had been siphoning funds to construct the Kiris Shipyards. Matters came to a head when she met with Han Solo and his wife, Leia Organa Solo, who implored Prime Minister Saxan to look beyond Sal-Solo's own desires and see what would happen to the people of the Corellian system if they were fully independent. Solo explained that the economy of the system would soon fail, leaving Corellians, Selonians, and Dralls with nothing to show for their independence but poverty. Saxan took this knowledge and passed it to her advisers, including Sal-Solo, and the Galactic Alliance's initial attempt to subdue the Corellians was met with stern opposition. Saxan found herself in an increasingly difficult position when Sal-Solo fired the Minister of War and assumed the position himself. She acquired the services of Wedge Antilles to act as her liaison to Sal-Solo during negotiations aboard Toryaz Station. Before the negotiations could begin in earnest, though, Saxan was murdered by a group of killers led by Lumiya. She was succeeded as Prime Minister by her former husband, Denjax Teppler.

***Saxan's Pride*** This Corellian warship was one of many assigned to protect Centerpoint Station during the war between the Galactic Alliance and the Confederation some three years after the end of the Swarm War.

**Sazen, Wolf** Kol Skywalker's former apprentice and Cade Skywalker's Jedi Master. Contemplative and serious, Sazen followed the living Force and hoped to teach his Padawan to do the same. Sazen's vision of hope for the galaxy meant finding his former apprentice and convincing him to assume his legacy. Wolf, Cade, and Kol were at Ossus during the Sith massacre; in that battle, Sazen lost his right arm to Darth Nihl. Cade Skywalker brought the mortally wounded Jedi aboard the shuttle, while Kol stayed behind to fight.

**Sazz, Jak** A smuggler, he frequented the Byss Bistro. An Ab'Ugartte, he never bathed. He carried an oversized hydrospanner that he used to pummel things.

**scalefish** A term applied to a number of small fish that inhabited the lakes and swamps of Naboo. Many scalefish could be found in the waters around Otoh Gunga, as the animals were attracted to the city's bright lights. Most scalefish were harmless, although the mee did have a poisoned spine. Other species of scalefish included the ray, tee, laa, faa, and see.

**scalphunter** A protoype weapon built by Merr-Sonn Munitions. The scalphunter was fully automatic, with a collapsible stock, a cortosis-alloy barrel, and a long-range multispectrum scope. Nym went to Vana Sage's base to trade scalphunters stolen from the Trade Federation for stygium crystals.

**scan grid** A device normally used to measure and analyze the magnetic and thermal properties of metals, it applied electrical surges to the metal and examined the effects with specialized sensors. Darth Vader used a scan grid to torture Han Solo on Cloud City.

**scarab droids** Small, deadly beetle-like droids, they were often used to poison an opponent. The cloned Emperor Palpatine used scarab droids to attempt to kill Luke Skywalker when Palpatine sent his Dark Side Adepts to New Alderaan to kidnap the Jedi twins of Han and Leia Organa Solo.

**Scarcheek** The nickname given to one of the Squib assassins who worked for the Directors during the Swarm War. The nickname was used by Jaina Solo to distinguish the Squib from his counterpart, Longnose. Scarcheek and Longnose were dispatched to Tenupe to eliminate Jaina as part of the Directors' plan to take revenge against Han Solo and his wife, Leia Organa Solo. When Jaina apprehended the pair, she interrogated them about their mission before turning them over to the Killiks to remove them from the battlefield. Much to her chagrin, Jaina learned that the Killiks had bound the two Squibs and placed them in the slings of their trebuchets, then launched them into the Chiss encampment.

**Scardia** *See* Space Station Scardia.

***Scardia Voyager*** A golden starship, it was used exclusively by the Prophets of the Dark Side.

***Scarlet Thranta*** A midsized corvette that defected from Republic service just prior to the outbreak of the Clone Wars. Captain Zozridor Slayke, disgusted with the Republic's inaction against the Separatists, took matters into his own hands when he took the *Scarlet Thranta* into private battles against Separatist strongholds in the Sluis sector. He avoided the Republic's attempts to rein him in, and named his outlaw group Freedom's Sons.

**Scaur, Director Dif** The director of New Republic Intelligence during the first year of the Yuuzhan Vong War. Dif Scaur was a former admiral with the Fourth Fleet. He ordered Yuuzhan Vong defectors Elan and Vergere to be taken to Coruscant. Dour and cadaverously thin, he collaborated with the Chiss on a weapon that would eradicate the Yuuzhan Vong.

**scavs** Junk gatherers and traders, they gathered their wares from battlefields—often looting in the heat of battle. Scavs, or scavengers, used armored, wheeled transports, nek battle dogs, and weapons droids to protect themselves.

**Sceptor of Ragnos** A powerful sceptor once wielded by the Sith Lord Marka Ragnos. The Sceptor of Ragnos was used thousands of years later by Tavion Axmis and the Cult of Ragnos. Capable of unleashing a devasting beam of energy, it was actually the sheath for a Sith sword.

*Wolf Sazen*

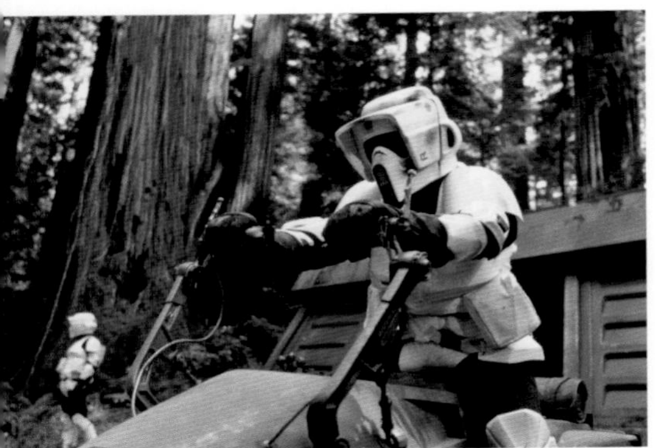
Scout trooper

**schinga shikou** A serpentine creature used as a mount on Makem Te, home of the Swokes Swokes. The shikou was the most intelligent of the schingas.

**Schurk-Heren, Captain** A Yarkora gentleman-rogue who was the captain of a the freighter *Uhumele* during the early days of the Empire. He welcomed Dass Jennir and Bomo Greenbark aboard his ship in the wake of the Clone Wars, after it was learned that the two were the only survivors of the massive battle at Half-Axe Pass. Unfortunately, Captain Schurk-Heren was forced to deliver the news that any other surviving Nosaurians, including Bomo's wife and daughter, had been sold into slavery by the Imperial forces on New Plympto. Luckily for Jennir and Greenbark, Captain Schurk-Heren decided that New Plympto was no longer a safe haven for himself and his crew, and agreed to transport them to Orvax IV.

***Scimitar*** *See* Sith Infiltrator.

**Scimitar assault bomber** Advanced Imperial bombers ordered into production during Grand Admiral Thrawn's war against the New Republic. The Scimitar assault bomber was a dedicated atmospheric and space bomber with better performance than a standard TIE bomber. It was designed partly by members of the elite and highly decorated Scimitar bomber assault wing.

The two-crew bomber had a single pod with two elongated solar array wings, a layout that provided greater visibility than older models. The middle of the pod housed navigation and targeting systems, a power generator, and twin repulsorlift engines. Repulsor thrusters were located in the Scimitar's wing struts for greater maneuverability. The pod's rear portion contained a bomb bay and single sublight ion engine. In space, it was significantly faster than a TIE bomber, and the newest model boosted atmospheric cruising speed significantly. The bomber had a reinforced hull and shields, proton grenades, free-falling thermal detonators, space for 16 concussion missiles, and linked forward laser cannons. A full wing of the bombers—72 ships—led the assault on Mrisst, one of Thrawn's feints prior to his final assault on Coruscant.

**scintil vine** A flowering vine native to the planet Ruusan, and one of the handful of species that survived the environmental devastation that followed the Battle of Ruusan. The natives of the planet found that crushed petals of the scintil vine's flowers could be mixed with the powdered roots of the tass plant and water to create a corrosive paste that could eat through rock and metal.

**scomp link access** A computer connection access port, it was used mainly by droids to plug into database networks and locate information, evaluate threats, execute diagnostics, or perform maintenance.

**Sconn, Lieutenant Davith** An Imperial prisoner at the New Republic's Jagg Island Detention Center during the Black Fleet crisis. As a member of the Imperial Navy, Sconn was the executive officer of the Star Destroyer *Forger.* His starship suppressed a rebellion on Gra Ploven by creating steam clouds that boiled alive 200,000 Ploven in three coastal cities. Chief of State Leia Organa Solo visited Sconn in prison to probe his knowledge of the Yevetha. The lieutenant provided insights as to how the Yevethan power structure worked, the species's "dominance killing" philosophy, and its methods of punishment. Sconn told Leia about the Yevethan ability to learn quickly, leaving little doubt that they could soon establish a powerful fleet of their own.

**Scorekeeper** The deity worshipped by Trandoshans, who believe that the Scorekeeper exists beyond time and space, recording every deed of each Trandoshan hunter.

**scorpion slug** A dangerous slug native to the planet Despayre. The scorpion slug was named for the stinger on the end of its tail, which injected a potent venom into its victims. In smaller creatures, this venom was quite lethal. Most humanoids who experienced a scorpion slug sting were afflicted with intense, agonizing pain that lasted for many weeks, if the victim didn't die before recovering.

**Scotian, Pedna** A Chev member of Rogue Squadron from Vinsoth. She flew as Rogue Two.

**Scotian, Will** A human native of Brentaal who flew as Rogue Two. He was not related to his squadron mate Pedna Scotian.

**Scout Enforcer** This blaster pistol was produced some 4,000 years before the Galactic Civil War. It was designed to be an advanced version of the hold-out blaster, to be used in desperate situations in remote locations when no help was available. Thus, it was marketed to scouts and explorers who were regularly out of contact with the Republic or any local police force.

**scout trooper** Lightly armored but highly mobile Imperial stormtroopers. Scout troopers were usually assigned to planetary garrisons to patrol perimeters, perform reconnaissance missions, and identify enemy locations. While traveling at dangerous velocities, scout troopers wore specialized helmets equipped with built-in macrobinocular viewplates and sensor arrays. These devices fed into a small computer capable of instantaneously analyzing the surrounding terrain to aid the trooper in navigation. Because their mission profile usually required long stints away from Imperial resupply, scout troopers were trained survivalists who often carried personal survival kits, portable power units, food supplies, micro-cords, and specialized gear designed for the local terrain. Scout troopers were known for their self-reliance and ability to operate alone, and the Empire discovered that those traits made scout troopers excellent snipers. Many scout troopers were armed with collapsible, long-range sniper rifles equipped with powerful scopes and small targeting computers. The scout trooper's sniper rifle was deadly and extremely accurate, but did emit a brief laser sight beam before firing.

Although trained to operate independently, scout troopers typically traveled in squads, or lances, consisting of four soldiers led by a sergeant commander. During field operations, the lance generally split into two elements. Standard assignments for a scout trooper lance included exploration and patrol duty. They usually avoided conflict whenever possible, preferring to contact the nearest Imperial force when the enemy had been detected. Scout troopers were part of the Empire's efforts to patrol the forests on Endor, but a Rebel commando team led by Han Solo and Princess Leia managed to eliminate a perimeter scouting lance, allowing the Rebels a clear path to the shield generator base.

**scout walker** *See* All Terrain Scout Transport.

**Scraf, Arvid** A human about six years younger than Luke Skywalker, Scraf was the first inhabitant of Nam Chorios whom Skywalker met when he landed on the planet. He lived with his aunt Gin and tooled around the Chorian wastes in a landspeeder.

**Scrambas, Pello** A lieutenant in the Rebel Alliance and a veteran officer, Pello Scrambas loyally served the Organa family for nearly two decades as a guard for the Royal House of Alderaan. Scrambas's last assignment was to protect Princess Leia on her mission aboard

Scrange

the *Tantive IV.* He was taken prisoner when the ship was overtaken by the Star Destroyer *Devastator* and was never seen again.

**scrange** Large, tusk-tailed amphibians found on Dagobah. Scranges could lift themselves out of the mud on crustaceous legs for quick attacks. During the Clone Wars, a scrange attacked Shaak Ti's team in the sewers of Brentaal IV, impaling the Wookiee Ryyk before Ti killed the creature with her lightsaber.

Scrap drone

**scrap drone** Devious flying golems engineered specifically to combat Darth Vader. Designed by Kazdan Paratus and imbued with the Force, scrap drones created negative feedback fields and attacked with a beam that drained Force energy from their victims.

**scrapeater** A multilegged, hermit-crab-like creature found on Raxus Prime. It fed on trash and had a spiny back.

**scrap guardian** The core components of Kazdan Paratus's droid army on the junkyard world of Raxus Prime. Scrap guardians were composed of detritus and cast-off parts held together and animated by the Force. This enabled them to resist some Force powers, including Force Push, though they were highly susceptible to sudden energy surges such as those caused by Force lightning. The sentinels were designed to defend Paratus against hordes of opportunistic scavengers and were well-suited to battling a Sith if Darth Vader or the Emperor found his hiding place. They also acted as Paratus's eyes and ears, alerting him to an enemy's approach well in advance.

Scrap guardian

**Screed, Admiral Terrinald** An early supporter of Palpatine who served with distinction in both the Republic and the Imperial military. Screed graduated from the Carida military academy and became a member of the Republic Judicial Department, where his hawkish outlook caused him to support the creation of an army to deal with the growing Separatist threat. During the Clone Wars, he teamed with fellow officer Jan Dodonna to lead an armada of *Victory*-class Star Destroyers to triumph over a Separatist fleet under the command of Dua Ningo. Injuries sustained during the campaign caused Screed to undergo extensive cybernetic reconstruction.

When Palpatine supplanted the Republic with the Galactic Empire, Screed was one of the first highly placed officers in the new Imperial Navy. He operated on the fringes of the Empire, seeking new opportunities for the emergent government. Screed oversaw the placement of the Great Heep on Biitu and voyaged to the distant Roon system. There Governor Koong—eager for an alliance with the Empire—invited Screed to his profitable salvage operation within the cloak of the Sith dust cloud.

After the defeat of the Empire at the Battle of Endor, Screed emerged as one of many squabbling warlords attempting to rebuild the New Order in the power vacuum. Screed was ultimately killed by Warlord Zsinj during his rise to power.

Admiral Terrinald Screed

**Screeger, Naxy** A Sakiyan and a compulsive gambler who lived about 130 years after the Battle of Yavin. When Screeger skipped out on a bail payment to the Feeorin pirate Rav, Cade Skywalker and his band of bounty hunters claimed the bounty on Screeger's head and also captured the Bothan Jedi Hosk Trey'lis. Wanting to earn more credits and trust from Rav, Skywalker and his companions brought both Screeger and Trey'lis to Socorro, and delivered them to Rav's base inside the *Crimson Axe.* Hoping to talk his way to freedom, Screeger tried to explain how he "helped" the bounty hunters bring in the Bothan Jedi. Rav ordered him to be held in the dungeons.

Naxy Screeger

**Scuppa** A starship pilot for crime kingpin Jabba the Hutt, he betrayed his boss when both were trapped aboard the ship of the monstrous Princess Nampi. He played up to the revolting princess, even agreeing to become her mate. Instead, he became a meal. Jabba had the last laugh, however, detonating by remote control a vial of super-acid he had implanted in Scuppa's brain years before, dissolving Nampi into a flood of goop.

**scurrier** Scavengers that lurked in Mos Eisley and other settlements, they scuttled from one garbage pail to another in search of food. When not foraging for edibles, scurriers wandered the streets making nuisances of themselves. They were prone to steal whatever they could get their paws on to use in their nests.

Scurriers were only about a third of a meter tall and two-thirds of a meter long. While quick to flee anything bigger than they were, scurriers were also quite protective of their nests and attacked any creatures that wandered into their territory. Scurrier bites were very painful. They used high-pitched squeals and loud snorts to frighten off intruders. Male scurriers tended to be somewhat larger than females and had large, curved horns.

Since they were good at finding hiding places aboard starships, scurriers could be found in most spaceport towns. However, they carried disease and became a public health hazard when their populations weren't kept in check.

**scut** This was a slang term used by military personnel to describe the gossip and unofficial communications that occurred among individuals. It was often up to each individual to ascertain what was the truth and what was idle rumor.

***Scylla*** This warship was commanded by Admiral Daala

Scurrier

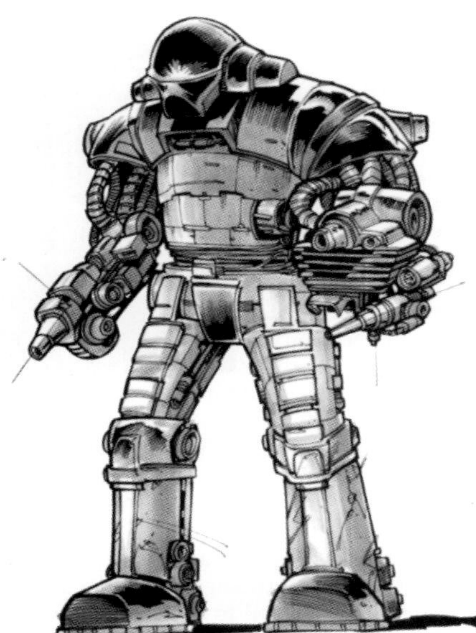

SD-10 infantry droid

during the years surrounding the Black Fleet crisis. Having come out of retirement to help the New Republic win the Battle of Nam Chorios, Daala returned to the Deep Core and tried to establish a new Imperial fleet. The *Scylla* served as her flagship and led her brief charge into New Republic territory against Garm Bel Iblis. Bel Iblis was able to trap Daala's fleet using a pair of CC-7700 frigates. In order to escape, Daala rammed one of the frigates with the *Scylla* before limping into hyperspace. Daala reappeared more than 25 years later when she agreed to assist Gilad Pellaeon on a mission to support the Galactic Alliance's attempt to capture the planet Fondor. The *Scylla,* however, had been scavenged for parts in the ensuing years.

**Scy'rrep, Evet** An infamous galactic bandit, he knocked off 15 starliners and got away with millions in credits and jewels before being captured. At his trial, when asked why he robbed luxury cruisers, Scy'rrep answered, "Because that's where the credits are." His fame was cemented by a holoproj series based on his deeds called *Galactic Bandits,* which Luke Skywalker watched when he was young.

**Scythe Squadron** A TIE fighter squadron assigned to the second Death Star during its construction. Scythe Squadron TIE fighters were TIE/ln models with updated SFS P-w702 maneuvering jets to increase performance in tight quarters. Pilots flew frequent training missions within the Death Star. Scythe Three had been previously modified with upgraded cannons to destroy small asteroids in the Anoat system. TIE fighters from Scythe Squadron pursued Rebel pilots through the reactor shaft of the second Death Star.

SE4 servant droid

**SD-9 and SD-10 infantry droids** Robotic infantry soldiers developed for the Empire. The SD-9 was used as an offensive weapon during Grand Admiral Thrawn's campaign. Umak Leth, designer of the World Devastator, enhanced the capabilities of the SD-9 with the SD-10. SD-10s were used effectively against SD-9s during the Empire's attempt to seize control of the Balmorran weapons factories, but they were no match for the aerial attack of the Empire's shadow droids.

**SD-XX** This Tendrando Arms security droid served as Jacen Solo's personal bodyguard during his tenure as the leader of the Galactic Alliance Guard. SD-XX accompanied Solo on the maiden voyage of the Star Destroyer *Anakin Solo* during a mission to Hapes. Solo referred to the droid as Double-X and kept it near him at all times, especially after he assumed the title of Darth Caedus. SD-XX resembled a scaled-down version of the venerable YVH series battle droid, with black plating that was reduced in mass to give the droid better maneuverability. SD-XX had trouble reconciling its orders with Solo's actions, especially when it could not discern the things Solo felt through the Force. SD-XX attributed Solo's mutterings and sudden fear of being approached by the Jedi Knights as a kind of organic ghost-firing, and struggled to understand when its services were actually needed. Over time, SD-XX learned quite a bit about Solo's dealings while Solo slept. The droid even came to realize that it had been Solo who had killed Mara Jade Skywalker, although it remained loyal and did not divulge this information to any other being.

Seatrooper

**SE4 servant droid** A series of droids skilled at arranging large banquets and performing domestic duties in the dining room and beyond. Each SE4 servant droid possessed a shining humanoid frame and stood 1.6 meters tall.

**seafah jewel** Formed on the moon of Pydyr deep in its ocean within the shells of microscopic creatures, these jewels were the source of much of the great wealth of Pydyr. After the Dark Jedi Kueller decimated the Pydyrians, he spared the moon's seafah jewelers, because it required a trained Pydyrian eye to detect the tiny jewels on the seabed floor. The jewels often were used in decoration and in Pydyrian architecture.

***Sea Legacy*** A Republic assault ship dispatched to the planet Pengalan IV during the early stages of the Clone Wars.

**Seario, Pollard** The president of Czerka Corporation at the height of the Great Sith War. Many wondered about Seario's decision to locate Czerka's headquarters on the planet Korriban, and rumors of his ties to the ancient Sith Empire traveled throughout the galaxy. However, the corporation flourished under Seario's leadership, despite the fact that many other galactic corporations regarded him as exceptionally corrupt.

**seatrooper** A member of a specialized branch of the Imperial stormtrooper force also known as aquatic assault stormtroopers. Many of the standard technologies employed by the Imperial military were modified for aquatic use by seatroopers, including specialized aquatic garrisons, custom TIE boats, and powerful AT-AT swimmers. The armor of the seatrooper was based on the lightweight scout trooper design. It was worn over a two-piece environmental body glove that provided protection from uncomfortable temperature extremes and toxic-water environments. The armor was more flexible than standard stormtrooper designs, preserving and even increasing a trooper's underwater dexterity. Supplementing a soldier's swimming skills were a back-mounted propulsion unit and a pair of propulsion boots with snap-down flippers. Since blaster ranges were often adversely affected by underwater use, the seatroopers carried a blaster rifle–speargun hybrid as a standard weapon. The seatrooper utility belt included high-tension wire, grappling hooks, spare blaster power packs, ion flares, concentrated rations, a spare comlink, medpacs, rebreather filters, and a compressed-air inflatable bubble tent.

**Sebatyne, Saba** A female Barabel Jedi who attracted a ragtag squadron of vengeance-minded followers called the Wild Knights. Sebatyne learned the Force under the guidance of the Jedi Eelysa, and brought Barabel youths—including her son, Tesar Sebatyne—to Luke Skywalker for training during the Yuuzhan Vong War. In battle, she often was referred to as Hisser. She wielded an ultraviolet lightsaber. She served as Leia Organa Solo's Jedi Master when Leia refocused on her Jedi training.

**Sebatyne, Tesar** A Barabel Jedi and the son of Saba Sebatyne. Sebatyne flew a Y-wing fighter with the Wild Knights Squadron. Like his Barabel hatchmates, Tesar was burly, slightly larger than Saba Sebatyne, with the purple-green scales of a young adult. He was

a member of Anakin Solo's strike team sent to hunt down the voxyn queen at the height of the Yuuzhan Vong War. He later flew as Twin Suns Nine and became a Jedi Knight.

**Sebolto** A ruthless Dug king who was also one of the galaxy's most powerful crime lords. A native of Malastare, Sebolto commanded an army of Dug and Gran soldiers to protect his hidden death stick factory deep in one of the jungles along Malastare's equator. Like most Dugs, Sebolto was raised as a servant to the ruling Gran species. His ruthless nature and his discovery of an efficient way to extract a variety of legal and illegal substances from the common Ixetal plant made him a wealthy and powerful figure with galaxywide interests.

**Sebulba** A crafty, vicious Dug who became one of the Outer Rim's most successful Podracers. Sebulba piloted a Collor Pondrat Plug-F Mammoth Podracer and was not above cheating to win a race. He had a keen ear for music and personally organized small bands to play whenever he entered an arena. Sebulba was Mos Espa's reigning Podrace champion until he entered the Boonta Eve Classic, where he was defeated by young Anakin Skywalker. After the race, Sebulba purchased Anakin Skywalker's Podracer from Qui-Gon Jinn. He also participated in the Vinta Harvest Classic on Malastare in an effort to boost his standings after being suspended for his indiscretions at the Boonta Eve race, for which he received guild demerits.

Sebulba's lineage could be traced back to Surdu of the Black Shred Water clan. He fathered several children on Malastare, including a son Hekula, and his descendants included a grandson named Pugwis.

**Sebulba's Legacy** A very dangerous Podrace course on Malastare. Rumored to have been designed by Sebulba himself, the circuit required pilots to avoid lakes and rivers of highly volatile methane gas.

**Second Fleet, Galactic Alliance** One of the primary naval forces of the Galactic Alliance in the years following the Yuuzhan Vong invasion of the galaxy. Much of it was redirected from existing missions to the Corellian system after Thrackan Sal-Solo threatened to secede from the Galactic Alliance and make the Corellian system a fully independent entity. Led by Admiral Limpan aboard his flagship the *Blue Diver,* the Second Fleet served many missions during the war between the Galactic Alliance and the Confederation. The Second Fleet was chosen by Jacen Solo to accompany him to a deep-space rendezvous with Corellian representatives—a meeting that was supposed to host negotiations for Corellia's return to the Galactic Alliance. But it turned out to be a trap, and Sadras Koyan used the Centerpoint Station repulsor as a weapon, firing it at the rendezvous point. The blast vaporized warships on both sides, and the Second Fleet was decimated.

*Sebulba*

**Second Great Schism** A conflict between the light and dark sides of the Force that occurred approximately 7,000 years before the Battle of Yavin. This war was considered the first major Force conflict since the First Great Schism between the Jedi and the Legions of Lettow in the pre-Republic era.

**Second Imperium** The name given to an attempt to reestablish control of the Empire some 19 years after the Battle of Endor. The main force behind the attempt consisted of four of the late Emperor Palpatine's most loyal personal guards. They set up a Shadow Academy led by the Dark Jedi Brakiss to train new legions of Dark Jedi and stormtroopers to aid in retaking the galaxy. For a while, using trickery, they successfully convinced many that a clone of Palpatine himself was the Great Leader of the Second Imperium.

**Second Mistake Enterprises** A small transport operation established by the Squibs Sligh, Grees, and Emala during the Swarm War. It was the first company to take a contract from the Killik Colony to transport spinglass sculptures depicting the *Millennium Falcon* and the X-wing fighter used by Luke Skywalker during the Battle of Yavin to the rest of the galaxy. Unknown to the Squibs, the sculptures contained Gorog assassin bugs, bred for their small size and voracious appetites. The transport ships hired by the Squibs also carried stolen Tibanna gas and hyperdrive components into the Utegetu Nebula, where the Gorog hoped to build starships of their own to reach the rest of the galaxy.

**Secret Apprentice** *See* Starkiller.

**Secret Order** A cabal of spies within the Empire who kept tabs on the loyalty of Imperial officers. Members of the Secret Order were identified by hooded cloaks and tattoos on their forearms.

**sector** Groups or clusters of star systems united for economic and political reasons, sectors were first formed by the Old Republic. Originally, a sector consisted of as many star systems as necessary to include about 50 inhabited or habitable planets. But over the millennia, sectors grew to vast and nearly unmanageable sizes. Under Emperor Palpatine's New Order, sectors were redefined and each placed under a Moff to whom all the planetary governors reported. Each Moff had a military sector group under his command to secure the hundreds of systems within his sector. To deal with rebellious or otherwise difficult systems, the Emperor appointed Grand Moffs to oversee priority sectors, which included the particularly troubled worlds of a dozen or more sectors.

**sector medical** One of the many medical facilities arrayed throughout the first Death Star. Each sector of the massive space station had its own dedicated medical team to ensure that the station's crew had easy access to medical assistance.

**Sector N-1** A section of the northern hemisphere of the first Death Star set aside for trooper barracks. It held approximately one-twenty-fourth of the hemisphere's total volume. Like the other sectors of the Death Star, Sector N-1 was constructed in place and then sealed, allowing it to be used as storage until the interior was configured for its designated usage. These sectors were equipped with life-support systems, and provided living space for slave laborers and other workers. When completed, Sector N-1 and other such sectors were divided into several layers. The outer surface was made up of various city sprawls that provided access to the rest of the sector. The outermost layer, about 2 kilometers thick and just beneath the sprawls, served as the primary habitable space. Beneath the outer layer was the containment section, which housed various power generators and vital systems that kept the habitable layer habitable. Beneath this containment section was usually the interior of the space station itself, which contained the station's hyperdrive and main reactor core.

**Sector Rangers** A law enforcement agency in existence since the early days of the Old Republic. The Sector Rangers operated independent of galactic politics. Being named a Special Enforcement Officer (SEO) was the pinnacle of achievement within the group. Trianii Rangers, Kilian Rangers, and Antarian Rangers were various Sector Ranger organizations.

**Sector Zero** This sector included all worlds whose XYZ coordinates were positive. It began with Coruscant at 0,0,0 and continued to Kiribi, nearly 5,000 light-years away in the Colonies at coordinate 099,099,011. On maps of the galaxy, Sector Zero was a wedge encompassing about a third of a circle and hugging the Deep Core to the "southeast" of Coruscant.

**Secura, Aayla** A female Twi'lek who trained as a Jedi Padawan under the tutelage of Quinlan Vos and later became a great Jedi Master. Known as Aaylas'ecura in her native language, Aayla was rescued from slavery on Ryloth by Vos and his Master Tholme. She was trained by Master Tholme for many years before she began training with Vos. Later, Secura was stripped of her memories via a combination of drugs and chemicals by her uncle, Pol Secura, until Vos discovered the deception. Still mindwiped, Aayla fled Ryloth and found herself drawn to the presence of Volfe Karkko on the prison world of Kiffex. Karkko took Secura as his queen and groomed her to become an extension of his dark side power. Vos killed Karkko, freeing Secura from his grasp. She was allowed to return to Coruscant to continue her training, later achieving the rank of Jedi Knight.

Aayla Secura was a member of the 200-being task force that accompanied Mace Windu to Geonosis. In the aftermath of that struggle, she was dealt another blow when she learned that Vos had resigned from the Jedi Order and joined the Separatists in a failed mission to infiltrate their ranks. Secura defeated the bounty hunter Aurra Sing on Devaron by slicing off the antenna that sprouted from Sing's head. After ascending to the rank of Jedi Master, Secura participated in the abortive attack on the droid foundries on Hypori, where she was one of the few Jedi to survive General Grievous's counterattack. Six months

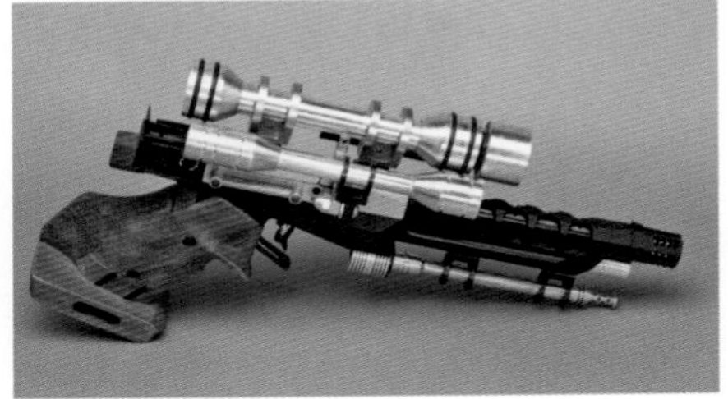

*Security S-5 blaster*

before the Separatist attack on Coruscant, Secura accompanied Masters Tholme and Vos to Anzat to determine what Sora Bulq was doing on the planet. They followed Bulq's trail to Saleucami, where Secura defeated the Morgukai warrior Bok in combat before helping Vos defeat Sora Bulq and Tol Skorr. In the wake of the Battle of Coruscant, Secura relocated to Felucia with Commander Bly and a regiment of clone troopers. When Darth Sidious told his clone commanders to execute Order 66, Bly and his troops opened fire on Secura, killing her.

**Secura, Nat** The last descendant of the planet Ryloth's great Twi'lek house, he was controlled by Bib Fortuna, who used Secura's power to sell many of his people into slavery. A cousin of the great Jedi Aayla Secura, as a

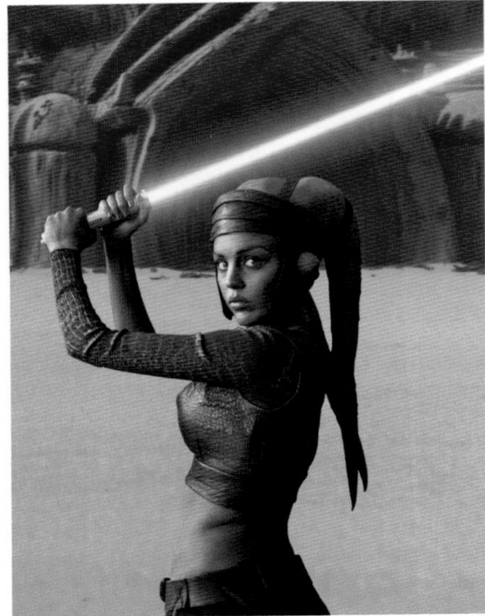

*Aayla Secura*

child Nat was targeted for assassination because he was the son and prime heir of Lon Secura. He was kidnapped by a pair of Morgukai warriors and brought to Fortress Kh'aris on Kintan, where he was rescued by Aayla. Years later, Nat Secura suffered severe burns when Jabba the Hutt enslaved many natives of Ryloth, and Bib Fortuna brought him to Jabba's palace. Jabba had planned to execute Secura, but Fortuna rescued him by having the B'omarr monks remove his brain before his body was thrown to the rancor.

**Security and Intelligence Council** This branch of the Galactic Alliance Senate oversaw the various activities that were involved in maintaining the safety and security of the Galactic Alliance as a whole. Derived from the New Republic's Council on Security and Intelligence, this body was originally charged with ensuring safety on a galactic scale. However, during Thrackan Sal-Solo's bid for Corellian independence some 10 years after the Yuuzhan Vong War, Chief of State Cal Omas gave the council emergency powers that allowed it to handle matters of public safety. Although ostensibly intended to protect the citizens of the capital planet from Corellian terrorists, the move allowed the Senate to authorize use of military assets against civilian targets.

**Security S-5 blaster** A multifunction blaster used by the Naboo Royal Palace Guard, the Security S-5 blaster could fire blaster bolts, relatively harmless sting charges, and anesthetic microdarts. The weapon also incorporated a liquid-cable shooter. This cable could be used to entangle enemies, or fitted with a grappling hook tip to allow the wielder to scale walls. For this reason, Security S-5 blasters were commonly known as ascension guns.

**security spike** A onetime-use item that created electronic interference in the locking mechanisms of doors and containers, improving the user's ability to bypass security measures.

**Sedesia** A high-gravity planet in the Mid Rim, it was a cold, arid world of tundra, forests, and mountains with extreme seasonal changes and unpredictable weather. Sedesians crossed the planet's surface on six-legged reptilian mounts called striders and sometimes on single-wheeled machines called wheelbikes. Sedesia's 1.5 million settlers were primarily stubborn breedtash ranchers known for their independence and sympathy toward the Rebellion. The Empire, testing a pathogen-based loyalty enhancement project, infected the entire population with a deadly plague called the Gray Death. Imperial forces set up medical facilities, ostensibly to protect the citizens from the plague—but actually forcing them to become dependent on the Empire for their continued survival.

**Sedri** Covered by warm, shallow seas, this planet was home to both the aquatic Sedrians and a communal intelligence of tiny polyps known as Golden Sun. Golden Sun was attuned to the Force and provided power, healing, and other necessities to the Sedrians, who worshipped Golden Sun as the center of their society. Golden Sun's use of the Force also created massive gravity readings, causing problems for hyperspace navigation near the Sedri system. The peaceful Sedrians constructed underwater cities and appointed a High Priest to safeguard the cave in which Golden Sun lived. The Empire came to Sedri to research a possible artificial gravity-well generator and constructed an Imperial garrison. A group of Rebels infiltrated the garrison, studied the Imperials' aquatic equipment, and discussed strategy and techniques with the Sedrians. This resulted in the formation of the Rebel Sea Commandos, who later saw action on Mon Calamari fighting the Emperor's World Devastators.

**Sedrian** A seal–humanoid combination, these sleek aquatic mammals lived on the water world of Sedri. They grew to about 3 meters long, with fine slick fur covering their bodies from head to fluke. A Sedrian had the head and lower body of a seal and the torso and arms of a humanoid. They could breathe air and live outside of water

*Sedrian*

Sedriss

for brief periods but preferred to stay in their underwater cities.

**Sedriss** Emperor Palpatine's dark side Executor, he commanded the dark side elite warriors after the demise of a clone of Palpatine in a bid to regain control of the galaxy. On the planet Byss, Sedriss discovered that the Emperor had been reborn into yet another clone. Palpatine ordered Sedriss to go to Ossus to get Luke Skywalker, but the Executor was destroyed by the power of an ancient Jedi, Ood Bnar.

**seed-partners (spikeballs)** An organism essential in the Sekotan shipbuilding process. Prospective starship clients were first approved by seed-partners. Before joining a client, the seed-partners appeared as spike-covered balls slightly smaller than a human head. Spikeballs made small clicking noises and produced a rich flowery smell to show their approval of a client. After joining with the client, the seed-partners were brought to a postpartnering room where they were removed and placed in a labeled lamina box. The seed-partners then went through a molting process, splitting along one side to reveal firm white flesh covered by a thick downy fuzz. Their spikes twisted into three thick stiff feet on one side. Eventually they shed their old shells completely, emerging as pale, oblate balls with two thick, wide-spaced front legs, two black dots for eyes in between, and two smaller legs in the rear. Anakin received an unprecedented 12 seed-partners during his bonding process to create a Sekotan ship.

**seed world** A term used by the ancient Jedi Knights to describe a planet capable of supporting life. Seed worlds were divided into two types: life-giving, which included planets with oceanic, grassland, or arboreal environments; and death-giving, including planets with desert, volcanic, or barren environments.

**seeker** As a military remote, this small ball covered with sensors could be programmed to track down and terminate specific targets. Miniature repulsors held it aloft and allowed it to change position rapidly. In military action, heat and light sensors tracked its target with fatal accuracy. A seeker could board an unsuspecting starship and carry out its deadly mission while in flight, often leaving no trace of the victim or itself. Seekers could be programmed to self-destruct after their mission was complete.

***Seeker*** A Trade Federation battleship assigned to Special Task Force One, the group that was dispatched to eliminate Outbound Flight some five years before the onset of the Clone Wars. When the task force was intercepted by Chiss forces under the command of Field Commander Thrawn, Vicelord Siv Kav ordered the *Seeker* to launch half of its droid starfighters. Unknown to Kav, however, Thrawn was feinting in order to crack the transmission codes used to control the droid starfighters. Once he had the codes extracted, Thrawn took control of the starfighters and attacked the Trade Federation's own vessels. The *Seeker* and its sister ships were eliminated, and only the flagship *Darkvenge* was spared by Thrawn.

**Seerdon, Moff Kohl** An Imperial Moff during the Galactic Civil War. Formerly the mentor of Imperial pilot Kasan Moor, Moff Seerdon became angry with his protégé after he noticed her wavering allegiance to the Empire. He blockaded Chandrila in retaliation for the unrelated theft of Imperial AT-PTs from Fest, then attempted to consolidate bacta supplies under his control. Rogue Squadron and Kasan Moor put an end to his plans for domination.

Akku Seii

**See-Threepio** *See* C-3PO.

**Seezar's Planet** A gambling and entertainment world.

**Segnor's loop** This space combat maneuver allowed a pilot to accelerate quickly away from an opponent before returning to make an attack.

**Seifax** A dummy corporation set up for Loronar Corporation, it had a plant on Antemeridias.

**Seii, Akku** This elderly Anzat was a noted teacher in the art of assassination, and was once a mentor to Jedi Master Tholme. Tholme returned to Anzat to speak with Akku Seii after he learned that Sora Bulq had been making regular trips to Anzat during the Clone Wars. Akku Seii refused to discuss the matter, as it was business between the Anzat and the Weequay. He forced Tholme to fight through a group of assassins to prove himself worthy of obtaining the knowledge. When Tholme defeated his opponents, Akku Seii revealed that the entire battle had simply been a training session for his students.

**Sei'lar, Asyr** A graduate of the Bothan Martial Academy, she was on a mission to Coruscant when she first encountered Gavin Darklighter and Rogue Squadron at the Azure Dianoga cantina in Invisec, where she worked with the Alien Combine. She and her friends assumed that Darklighter's nervousness and his rejection of her offer to dance were due to bigotry. He and his Rogue friends were brought before the Alien Combine for judgment, but before they could be sentenced to death, the Combine hideout came under attack by Imperial forces. During the battle that followed, Sei'lar realized that the Rogues were no friends of the Empire, so she helped them escape.

When she learned their true identity, she joined forces with Rogue Squadron to bring down Coruscant's defense shield system. While brainstorming with her new allies, she suggested using the mirrors on the Orbital Solar Energy Transfer Satellite to evaporate a reservoir. The resulting atmospheric condensation created a tremendous thunderstorm, and lightning brought down the power grid, shutting down one of the shields. Shortly after the liberation of Coruscant, Sei'lar was offered a position in Rogue Squadron, although for purely political reasons. Nevertheless, she was a welcome addition because her X-wing piloting skills were impressive. She also developed a serious relationship with Darklighter, despite disapproval from Bothan Senator Borsk Fey'lya. During the fight to unseat Prince-Admiral Krennel from the Ciutric Hegemony, Sei'lar apparently perished. In reality, she faked her death and went underground to work toward changes in Bothan society.

**seismic charge** A weapon dropped from a starship to elude pursuers. *Slave I* was armed with seismic charges, which Jango Fett used against Obi-Wan Kenobi's Jedi starfighter. The blast of a seismic charge produced a devastating shock wave that emitted a unique sound. (*See also* Void-7)

Seismic charge

**seismic hover tank** A massive ground assault weapon used by the Commerce Guild during the Clone Wars. Technically, Haor Chall Engineering's seismic tank was a mining vehicle, but it was used almost exclusively for military applications. The tank's name was derived from the huge seismic driver contained in its core. Magnetic impellors guided the frictionless driver through a central channel; its heavy metal core gave it tremendous inertia. When the driver exited the channel, it struck the ground with great speed and impact, creating a seismic undulation in even the hardest of surfaces. Whatever was not crushed by the hammerblow itself was invariably destroyed in the shock wave that followed. A team of battle droids operated the vehicle from the topside command bridge. Mace Windu single-handedly destroyed a seismic tank on Dantooine during the Clone Wars.

Seismic hover tank

**Sekot** The bodily form of the living planet Zonama Sekot. She first appeared to Anakin Skywalker as the feathered Jedi Knight Vergere.

**Sekotan ship** Highly sought-after ships created on Zonama Sekot. Organic Sekotan ships had cellular structures, dense and varied tissues that incorporated both metals and a variety of high-strength heat-resistant polymers. Sekotan ships had hyperdrives rated at an astonishing speed of Class 0.4. The Sekotan shipbuilding process involved seed-partners that bonded with the prospective client; the seeds were then forged into disks, and the ship shaped and fitted to Republic standards. Without their owners, the ships quickly decayed.

Raith Sienar possessed the remains of such a ship, which had cost him 100 million credits. He yearned to get his hands on a fully functional model and led an attack on Zonama Sekot. After the planet's disappearance, no more ships were made.

**Sela** Wedge Antilles's second in command on the *Yavin,* she was a thin, nervous woman and a crack shot. Although she was an invaluable assistant on Coruscant, she still had to prove herself in a battle command.

**Selab** A planet in the Hapes Cluster, it was home to the trees of wisdom. Believed by many to be only a myth, the trees bore fruit that could greatly increase the intelligence of those who reached old age.

**Selaggis** A planet that was the location of a colony obliterated by Warlord Zsinj's Super Star Destroyer *Iron Fist.* Han Solo saw the destruction while on a five-month hunt to locate and destroy Zsinj's ship.

**Selaggis, Battle of** The penultimate conflict between the forces of Imperial Warlord Zsinj and the New Republic Fleet led by Han Solo and the *Mon Remonda.* Double agent Lara Notsil commandeered the use of the MSE-6 droid fleet aboard Zsinj's Super Star Destroyer *Iron Fist,* and set up systematic failures of the huge warship's computer systems. Solo's fleet pursued and caught Zsinj at Selaggis VI. The Republic fleet pounded Zsinj, who was forced to use his last-resort effort: exploding a mock-up starship known as the *Second Death.* When Solo's forces sifted through the wreckage, all they found was evidence that led them to believe that *Iron Fist* had been destroyed instead.

**Select, the** A term used by Nom Anor while acting as the prophet Yu'shaa to describe loyal individuals sent to infiltrate the ranks of the Yuuzhan Vong military and government. Shamed Ones who showed a quick intellect without too much independent thought were assigned to get as close to Supreme Overlord Shimrra as possible and spread the Message, while carrying concealed villips that would allow Nom Anor to see what Shimrra was planning.

**Selestrine, Queen** The leader of the Icarii species. Selestrine wore gold and gems woven into her hair and was believed to possess the gift of prophecy. The Imperial Lightning Battalion captured her and cut off her head before she could kill herself. Since the Icarii could survive decapitation, Colonel Karda stole the head, kept alive in a small casket, and fled to Maryx Minor. Boba Fett tracked him there and killed Karda. The bounty hunter soon learned

Selkath

Queen Selestrine

of Selestrine's special abilities and thought to keep her head for himself, but Darth Vader arrived and the two struggled for possession of the gruesome treasure. Boba Fett escaped with his life and strands of Selestrine's jewel-woven hair. Darth Vader had hoped to harness Selestrine's abilities but decided to destroy Selestrine's head to keep it out of the hands of the Emperor.

**Seline** A remote outpost world and site of a small Jedi starport during the last decades of the Galactic Republic.

**Selkath** An amphibious species from Manaan who manufactured the healing fluid kolto. The Selkath were amphibious humanoids with sleek, hydrodynamic bodies and a throaty, guttural language. They were at home in the depths of the sea, but could just as easily survive on the surface thanks to concealed gill slits that drew oxygen from either water or air. Their long hands were tipped in poisonous claws, but Selkath considered their poison to be socially unacceptable for use in fights. During the rise of the Sith following the Mandalorian Wars, the government of Manaan adopted a policy of neutrality, and allowed both the Sith and the Republic to establish embassies in the floating capital of Ahto City.

The halt of significant kolto production in subsequent years caused the rapid departure of Manaan from the galactic stage and sent the planet spiraling into a technological decline. Most of the native Selkath eventually abandoned Ahto City and returned to living in the depths. After fewer than 100 years, the planetary government collapsed. Young warlords with no memory of Manaan's era of economic prosperity fought among themselves, and within another 100 years had broken Selkath society into tribal clans. When the Imperials arrived with thousands of aquatically trained stormtroopers and a pair of Star Destroyers, the Selkath had become so primitive that a few blasts of the energy weapons caused entire clans to swear fealty to the Empire. In floating shantytowns made from recycled ship parts and wreckage salvaged from the ocean floor, many Selkath secretly organized a resistance movement against their occupiers.

**Selnesh** An Imperial prison in the Seltaine system of Irishi sector, it was built on a barren landscape devoid of life. The jail consisted of several domes that kept good air in and bad air out.

**Selonia** One of the five inhabited worlds in the Corellian system, it had clear blue skies and a surface composed of hundreds of islands separated by innumerable seas, inlets, and bays. Beneath the surface of Selonia was a powerful planetary repulsor, used in ancient times to transport the planet to its current orbit from an unknown location. Selonians were a hive species with thick tails, sleek fur, long faces, and needle-sharp teeth. They lived together in genetically related dens. Each den was made up of one fertile female—the queen, who gave birth to all members of a den—a few fertile males, and several hundred sterile females. All sterile females with the same father were said to be in the same sept, and members of a sept were genetically identical. The sterile females interacted with other species and performed all the important functions of Selonian life. Selonians had a deep psychological need to reach a consensus.

Some 14 years after the Battle of Endor, two Selonian factions, the Republicists and the Absolutists, struggled for control of the planetary repulsor. The Republicists intended to turn it over to the New Republic in exchange for Selonian sovereignty, while the Absolutists planned to use it as a weapon for the creation of Selonian independence. Han Solo and Leia Organa Solo were pulled into the struggle, which the Republicists eventually won. During the crisis, a Bakuran attack force led a diversionary assault on Selonia, and one of its ships was destroyed by Selonia's repulsor.

Selonian

**Selonian** A tall, strong, quick species, they had long slender bodies and could go on all fours if necessary or desirable. Their sleek bodies were covered with short fur, and their faces were pointed with bristly whiskers. They had very sharp teeth and long tails that could be used for defense. Selonians lived in dens, and visitors saw only sterile females; all males and any females who could bear children stayed hidden in the den at all times.

**Seluss** A Sullustan, he normally accompanied the smuggler Jarril on the ship *Spicy Lady.* When Lando Calrissian discovered the lifeless ship following Jarril's murder, Seluss was nowhere to be found. Han Solo and Chewbacca came upon Seluss on Skip 1 in Smuggler's Run, where he attacked them with a blaster in an attempt to make the other smugglers think Solo and Chewie were his enemies. Seluss was aware that Jarril's trade in former Imperial goods was attracting too much attention.

**Selvaris** A hot world captured by the Yuuzhan Vong, it orbited the twin suns of Centis Major and Renaant. After the Battle of Coruscant, the lush, bountiful planet was converted into a prison world with camps scattered across its landmasses. Prisoners captured during the Galactic Alliance's Operation Trinity at Bilbringi were taken there until they could be sacrificed in a mass ceremony meant to solidify the Yuuzhan Vong's supremacy in the galaxy. Han and Leia Organa Solo rescued one inmate, the Jenet soldier Thorsh, who carried in his head an important collection of mathematical codes.

**Sembla** The homeworld of Jedi Master Coleman Trebor and other members of the Vurk species. Sembla's warm seas were divided by volcanic ridges that slowly formed new continents. It was off most trade routes, which allowed it to escape the Yuuzhan Vong invasion.

**Semtin, Captain Marl** A male human Imperial officer with dark eyes and swarthy skin. Semtin was captain of the *Harrow,* a *Victory*-class Star Destroyer. He was considered rather oily and ambitious.

**senalak** A Yuuzhan Vong security system that resembled ice spikes. Senalaks were knee-high stalks no thicker than a finger. When a foreign object passed by, the senalaks' blunt blue caps released a meter-long strand of thorns that entwined and captured whatever disturbed it. Anakin Solo's strike team discovered senalaks on Myrkr.

**Senali** A moon orbiting Rutan, the ocean-covered satellite was a former Rutanian colony. In a violent civil war, Senali won its independence from Rutan, although both worlds were devastated. As part of a peace treaty, it was agreed that the firstborn child of each generation of the ruling houses on both worlds would travel to the other world once they reached the age of 7. They would remain on the other planet for nine years, learning about the other society. The children were allowed to receive visitors from their homeworld and occasionally visit it so that they never forgot their heritage. At the age of 16, the youths returned home to prepare to take over as a ruler of their homeworld. The arrangement worked well for years until the Rutanians sold information on the Senali to the Yuuzhan Vong. The alien invaders totally devastated Senali, wiping out the civilization and much of the moon's surface . . . before turning their attack to eliminate the Rutanians as well.

Senate cam droid

**Senate Bureau of Intelligence (SBI)** The Republic-era predecessor to Imperial Intelligence and the Imperial Security Bureau (ISB). Armand Isard served as director-general of the SBI prior to the rise of the Empire. He formed a subdivison known as the Crisis Branch, which communicated directly with the Jedi Council and the Loyalist Committee.

**Senate cam droid** A small, floating droid programmed to record all meetings of the Galactic Senate. Shuttling about on efficient repulsorlift engines, Senate hovercams glided among congressional boxes to provide complete coverage of any discussion. A wide-angle lens and a zoom lens allowed the droids to capture panoramic views and the expressions on the faces of individual Senators. Senate cam droids transmitted their feeds to the public HoloNet, as well as to private viewscreens in individual boxes. A central data bank stored all recordings for future reference. Unfortunately, Senate cam droids were only as reliable as their programmers. Cam droids during Palpatine's reign were known to favor pro-Imperial Senators by giving them more airtime, and to unfairly edit statements made by the opposition. Entire Senate meetings sometimes vanished from the archives, and other transcripts were later discovered to have glaring gaps.

**Senate Guard** An elite security force assembled to protect members of the Galactic Senate. Garbed in symbolic blue robes and helmets, the Senate Guard stood watch over the Senate chamber on Coruscant, and its members could be found aboard almost all Senatorial transports. Senate Guards were cautiously selected from the most respected law enforcement agencies around the galaxy, and all candidates were superb combatants who were dedicated to the Galactic Republic.

Senate Guard

The group used military ranks; commanders typically headed a small task force of 6 to 10 guards. The leader of all Senate Guards was called the Captain of the Guard.

Some Senate Guards were distrustful of Jedi, preferring to deal in cold, hard facts and forensic evidence rather than what they viewed as reliance on mysticism. A Senate Guard investigation was characteristically meticulous, thorough, and successful. In the waning years of the Republic, the guard was not immune to the corruption that grew within the Senate itself. Senate Guard imposters attempted to assassinate Palpatine shortly after he became Supreme Chancellor. Thus, the Royal Guard was created to ensure the Supreme Chancellor's security. The red-armored Royal Guard fell under Palpatine's direct authority, while a Senatorial committee oversaw the old Blue Guard. Senate Guards at the time of the Battle of Coruscant had a mask that covered the entire face, without any ceremonial plumage.

**Senate Justice Council** A New Republic Senate council. Councils were appointed bodies with automonomous decision-making and appropriation authority over segments of government operations. At the time of the Battle of Fondor, Ta'laam Ranth served as head of the Senate Justice Council.

**Senate Planetary Intelligence Network (SPIN)** A short-lived private strike team organized by Mon Mothma and consisting of Princess Leia Organa, Luke Skywalker, Han Solo, Chewbacca, Lando Calrissian, and the droids R2-D2 and C-3PO. The SPIN strike force's most dangerous mission pitted them against Zorba the Hutt, who had placed a bounty on the head of Princess Leia after she murdered his son, Jabba. SPIN eventually was dissolved when Mothma realized that the Rebel Alliance heroes were needed elsewhere.

**Senate platform** A floating repulsorlift platform capable of holding several Senators and aides. The Senate chamber was lined with 1,024 platforms. Whenever an occupant of a Senate platform was recognized by the Supreme Chancellor or the vice chair, that platform detached from the Senate Rotunda and carried its passengers to the center of the chamber. Each platform had a Senate Guard assigned to it. Darth Sidious used the Force to hurl spinning Senate platforms at Yoda during their duel in the Senate chamber.

Senate platform

**Senate Select Committee for Refugees (SELCORE)** A New Republic body overseeing the refugees displaced by the Yuuzhan Vong War. The Senate Select Committee for Refugees sought out worlds with intact infrastructures, not merely habitable land. Their goal was to create self-sufficient enclaves to be managed by individuals selected from the refugee populations. Senator Viqi Shesh served on SELCORE, and Leia Organa Solo held a meeting on Ord Mantell known as the Conclave on the Plight of the Refugees to discuss the situation. SELCORE had created domes on the surface of Duro to house Vors, Vuvrians, Ryn, and other refugees, but the Yuuzhan Vong invasion of Duro left the refugees homeless.

**Sencil Corporation** A droid manufacturer based on Churba, it was nationalized by the Empire in an effort to control Mid-Rim droid markets.

**Sendo, General** An officer of little accomplishment in the Destab Branch of Imperial Intelligence, he had never seen battle. General Sendo was on retainer to Prince Xizor's Black Sun criminal organization because of his access to all kinds of valuable information.

**Seneki** This young Squib was the daughter of Emala, and worked for the Directors as a receptionist and aide during the Swarm War. Seneki was killed when the Flakax known as Tito returned from his mission to eliminate Han Solo and his wife, Leia Organa Solo. Tito, who had watched his partner Yugi die in the fight, had become psychotic.

**Senesca, Zev** A Rebel Alliance snowspeeder pilot, he was among those who defended Echo Base on the ice planet Hoth. Zev Senesca first discovered and rescued Luke Skywalker and Han Solo after they had disappeared on the Hoth glaciers and were forced to spend a frigid night in the desolate area. Senesca's comm unit designation was Rogue Two. His snowspeeder was shot down and he was killed during the Battle of Hoth.

Senesca had been born on Kestic Station near the Bestine system. His independent-minded parents had nurtured his rebellious side, and as soon as he was of age, he joined the Rebel Alliance. His parents were killed when the Imperial Star Destroyer *Merciless* destroyed Kestic Station.

**Senex sector** Adjacent to the Juvex sector and near the Ninth Quadrant, it was ruled by an elite group of aristocratic Ancient Houses. The sector contained the Senex system and the planets Karfeddion, Veron, and Mussubir Three. Yetoom and Belsavis were located on its edge. The Ancient Houses and their lords were extremely independent and wished to rule their planets as they saw fit. They scorned any outside interference. They were largely left alone under Emperor Palpatine's rule, and neither the post-Endor Empire nor the New Republic had much success in influencing them.

Zev Senesca

The Senex lords had long been accused of mistreating their workers and violating the Rights of Sentience. The oldest of the Houses—House Vandron, headed by Lady Theala Vandron—operated slave farms on Karfeddion. The House Elegin was headed by Drost Elegin, and the House Garonnin got a large portion of its revenue from strip-mining asteroids.

The Senex system once held an Imperial training area. Before the Battle of Yavin, a new Rebel Alliance recruit accidentally hypered into the area in his X-wing and destroyed most of the training facilities before realizing his danger and hypering out. Eight years after the Battle of Endor, Stinna Draesinge Sha, a pupil of Nasdra Magrody's, was assassinated in the Senex sector in House Vandron territory. Later that year, many of the Senex lords met with the late Emperor's mistress, Roganda Ismaren, on Belsavis, intending to form a military alliance.

**Sennatt** The main production center for droid maker Publictechnic, located near Kothlis in Bothan space.

**Sennex pirates** A notorious, slave-trading pirate crew that enslaved the

young Aurra Sing. Wallanooga the Hutt purchased Sing from the Sennex pirates.

**sense** Along with control and alter, one of the three basic abilities studied by the Jedi in their mastery of the Force. Sense covered the use of the Force to enhance perception of the surrounding universe.

**sensislug** A Yuuzhan Vong creature resembling a thumb-sized leech. The sensislug had no head and possessed one huge compound eye. It could release an invisible cloud of sleep-inducing spores.

Sentry tower

**sensor** A device that gathered information to assist ship crews in analyzing the galaxy around them, it scanned an area and acquired data to be shown in text or graphic displays. Passive-mode sensors gathered information about the immediate area around a ship. Scan-mode sensors sent out pulses in all directions, actively collecting a much wider range of information. Search-mode sensors actively sought out information in a specific direction. Focus-mode sensors closely examined a specific portion of space.

**sensor suite** A sensor suite comprised all the major systems and subsystems associated with complex sensor arrays.

**sensory plug-in** These devices let astromechs and other droids interface with computers, sensors, monitors, and data systems through a direct connection. They were similar to scomp links.

**sentient tank** *See* tank droid.

***Sentinel*** A cruiser in the Bakuran task force. After the Ssi-ruuvi conflict, the *Sentinel* became a patrol vessel safeguarding Bakura from local pirates.

**Sentinel** One of the large guards used to protect the clone Emperor's citadel on the planet Byss. Some believed that the Sentinels were giant cyborgs or droids.

**sentinel beetle** A Yuuzhan Vong bioengineered insect. The sentinel beetle was used on Bimmiel. When slaves created a disturbance, sentinel beetles beat their wings furiously, causing the sand to vibrate and emit a dusty mist that alerted the Yuuzhan Vong.

**sentry tower** A tall, pole-mounted survey station used by the Rebel Alliance on Yavin 4. Some sentry towers were fitted with a mounted Mark II repeating blaster cannon.

**Seoul V** A planet thought to have been destroyed eons ago, it was located in an uncharted sector. Seoul V was believed to be the home of crystals capable of boosting mental energy.

**S-EP1 "Sleepy" security droid** An expensive yet potent anti-terrorist weapon often used as a security guard and manufactured by Ulban Arms. Two S-EP1 droids, nicknamed Sniffer and Shooter, were used by Chief of State Leia Organa.

Prince Sereno

**Sepan system** Located in the sector of the same name, this system contained the planets Ripoblus, Dimok, Gerbaud 2, and Sepan 8. Following the Battle of Hoth, a long, destructive war between the peoples of Ripoblus and Dimok was forcibly ended by the intervention of Imperial forces under the command of Admiral Harkov. At one point, the leaders of the two sides attempted a rendezvous near Sepan 8 to organize a united attack against Imperial forces.

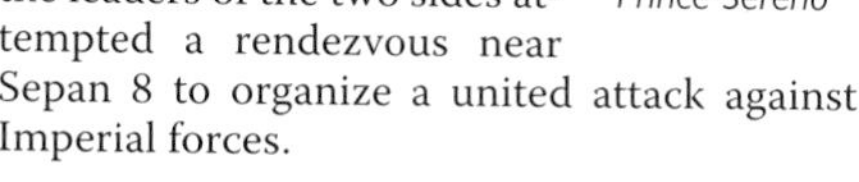

S-EP1 security droid

**Separatist Alliance** *See* Confederacy of Independent Systems

**Separatist Council** The ruling body of the Confederacy of Independent Systems. It consisted of Trade Federation Viceroy Nute Gunray, Techno Union foreman Wat Tambor, InterGalactic Banking Clan Chairman San Hill, Geonosian Archduke Poggle the Lesser, Commerce Guild Presidente Shu Mai, Corporate Alliance magistrate Passel Argente, Hyper-Communications Cartel head Po Nudo, and Quarren Isolation League representative Tikkes. Following defeats at Metalorn and Muunilinst, Lord Sidious ordered that the entire Separatist Council be under the protection of General Grievous for the remainder of the war. Grievous transferred the council to Utapau, and then to Mustafar. When Anakin Skywalker arrived at the Mustafar command center, he sealed off the exits and wiped out the entire Separatist Council.

**Sephi** A species native to Thustra, they were outwardly similar to humans except for a thick spiral of hair-like matter that grew from the crown of their skulls. Proud Sephi adorned their spirals with gemstones and other baubles. The Sephi were a long-lasting species, with some living for more than 200 years.

**septoid** An insectoid, it was from the planet Eriadu. Some treadwell droids were nicknamed septoids because of their resemblance.

**Sera Plinck** A martial arts form that used knives as an extension of the body.

**Serdo** A respectable Twi'lek businessbeing who successfully hid his second career as a spice smuggler. He was the original owner of the *Firerider*.

**Serenno** The homeworld of Count Dooku. It was located along the Hydian Way in the Outer Rim, in the direction of the Corporate Sector. Serenno's noble families were among the most prominent supporters of various groups that wanted to split away from the Old Republic, a situation that had been prevalent since before the New Sith Wars.

**Sereno, Prince** The crown prince of Tof and heir to the extragalactic Tof civilization. Prince Sereno made Saijo his base of operations during the Tof invasion after the Battle of

Separatist Council listens to General Grievous on Utapau.

Endor. The Alliance and the Nagai joined forces to capture Sereno and bring an end to the war.

**Sermeria** The homeworld of Senator Ister Paddie. Sermeria was a prominent agricultural world in the Expansion Region beset by stone mites during the years leading up to the Clone Wars. The infestation was caught early, preventing any serious damage to the urban areas of the planet.

**Sernpidal** The third planet in the Julevian system and the site of an early battle in the Yuuzhan Vong War. Sernpidal had two moons, with the smaller called Dobido. The Praetorite Vong invasion force applied the Yo'gand's Core military tactic on Sernpidal by planting a dovin basal on the planet and pulling Dobido down in a cataclysmic crash. Han Solo, Anakin Solo, and Chewbacca arrived at Sernpidal City to make a delivery for Lando Calrissian just as Dobido was about to hit. They helped evacuate the planet, but Chewbacca was killed in the cataclysm. Sernpidal was left as a dead ball, wobbling and off its orbit. Rogue Squadron later investigated and found that the Yuuzhan Vong were using asteroid-sized chunks of Sernpidal to grow more ships. Kyp Durron convinced Jaina Solo to help attack Sernpidal, destroying the enemy shipwomb and the worldship being constructed there. Jaina felt betrayed when she learned that Kyp lied to her by claiming that the shipwomb was the site of a Yuuzhan Vong superweapon.

**Sern Prime** The homeworld of Senator Fang Zar.

**Sern sector** Located near the Core Worlds, it contained the planet Ghorman.

**Serpa** A major in the Galactic Alliance Guard at the height of the Galactic Alliance's conflict with the Confederation. Known for his no-nonsense approach, Major Serpa was chosen by Jacen Solo to lead the team of GAG soldiers dispatched to Ossus, ostensibly to protect the younglings at the Jedi training facility. In reality, Solo's plan was to hold the students hostage until he could gain the upper hand with Luke Skywalker. Distinguished by his long, thin nose and sunken eyes, Major Serpa took his loyalty and devotion to the GAG to a high level, to the point that he would have threatened to kill the Jedi younglings if his orders were not obeyed. When the Jedi tried to retake the compound, Serpa gathered a small group of students and held them hostage. He shot Tionne Solusar when she tried to approach him. When he was confronted by Jaina Solo, Serpa took a young girl named Vekki hostage, holding the girl in front of him to ensure that Solo would not attack. As Serpa raised a blaster to fire on Jaina, Zekk severed his arm with his lightsaber. When Serpa tried to react, Zekk cut off his other arm.

**Serpent Masters** Slavers on Ophideraan, they rode winged serpents controlled by ultrasonic signals emitted from a medallion worn by the Supreme Master Tyrann. The droid R2-D2 was able to duplicate the signals, which enabled Luke Skywalker to ride a serpent and defeat the Serpent Masters, freeing Tanith Shire's people from slavery.

**Serper, Wyron** A daring spy for the Rebel Alliance, he went undercover as a sensor specialist aboard the Imperial Star Destroyer *Avenger* on one of his most perilous missions. Later, Wyron Serper was assigned to scan for Imperial ships that might be hidden in the meteor activity of the Hoth system.

**Serphidi** Located in the Belial system, this was the homeworld of the primitive Serp species.

**Serpine system** A system known for its gambling. One life-or-death, total-forfeit game involved a fist-sized ruby joom-ball rolling along a spiral chute. If the joom-ball landed in the mouth of a venom-drooling old Passar, it meant instant death for the roller. Serpine was ruled by an extremely superstitious emperor-governor.

**Serroco** This planet was one of many that lay along the battle lines of the Mandalorian Wars, some 3,963 years before the Battle of Yavin. Located in a system near Arkania and the Perave system, Serroco was the homeworld of the Stereb species. It was here that the forces of the Republic established a base, in an effort to prepare to defend Republic space from Mandalorian attacks. The surface of Serroco was arid, and was often scoured by intense tornadoes. These storms forced the Stereb to excavate warrens and tunnels beneath their cities, so that they could retreat underground during the storms.

**Serth, Valence** The reluctant owner of C-3TC, a protocol droid wanted by the Black Sun criminal syndicate. Serth was the target of several attacks by agents, and his ship was shot down over a jungle-covered planet.

**servodriver** A powered hand tool, it was used to tighten and loosen fasteners. A servodriver produced motion when it received signals from a controller.

**Serv-O-Droid** A major droid manufacturer that eventually went bankrupt. Serv-O-Droid made the CZ secretary droid, the TT-8L "Tattletale," the BLX labor droid, and the DUM pit droid. So universal were its products that survivors could be found throughout the galaxy, primarily on backworlds where droids faced brutal conditions. Serv-O-Droid parts were hard to find because the droid designs were such that only creative jury-rigging kept them functional.

*Serpent Masters ride winged serpents.*

**servo-grip** The servo-driven hands of a droid.

**Seswenna Hall** A classic-era building on Eriadu where a Trade Federation summit took place in the last years of the Republic. Seswenna Hall's enormous dome crowned a high mount at the center of the city, rising in mosaic splendor to a height of some 200 meters. The dome was similar in design to the Galactic Senate chamber but on a much smaller scale and without detachable balconies.

**Seswenna sector** A sector containing the planet Eriadu. Grand Moff Tarkin developed the Tarkin Doctrine of rule by fear while he was a governor in charge of the Seswenna sector and the Outer Rim Territories.

**Setor** The former homeworld of Wetyin's colony, its people departed after suffering persecution. The Fernandin Scouting Operation was given a permit by the Empire to find the group a new homeworld. Some of the worlds considered included Betshish and Yavin 4.

**Sette, Urlor** A large man, he befriended Rogue Squadron pilot Corran Horn when they were fellow prisoners in the *Lusankya.* Often acting under orders from the Rebel Alliance's Jan Dodonna, also a prisoner, Urlor Sette assisted in Corran's escape from the top-secret prison facility.

**Sevarcos** An infamous spice world, it orbited the orange star Lumea in the Sevarcos system. Because the spice extracted from Sevarcos's Imperial mines was so profitable, the Empire maintained a permanent customs blockade of the entire system. A huge asteroid field drifting between the sixth and seventh planets housed the elite Fate's Judges TIE interceptor squadron, which attacked any smuggler foolish enough to run the blockade. Sevarcos, brown-and-amber-colored from space, was a dry, windswept world plagued by frequent sandstorms. The planet's two types of spice, the common white andris and the rare black carsunum, were primarily mined in the equatorial region, where the mines doubled as brutal Imperial prisons. Animal life included the spice eel, which burrowed through rock and could reach lengths of up to 30 meters.

The planet's original

human population, the Sevari, were believed to be the descendants of settlers from the early Old Republic colony ship *Sevari Cabal.* The Sevari eventually formed clans headed by Spice Lords to oversee the spice trade, although total control shifted to the Empire. Unprotected visitors to Sevarcos suffered side effects from inhaling the trace amounts of spice found in the atmosphere, but native Sevari, accustomed to the constant spice, often slipped into a coma-like spice narcosis when breathing the pure air of other worlds. Most of the planet's one million Sevari shunned advanced technology and used archaic wind riders for transportation and projectile flash-pistols for defense.

Kadrian Sey

**Sevvets** This band of mercenaries nearly captured Boba Fett and Fenn Shysa on Shogun during the early years of the New Republic. Shysa was badly injured, and told Fett that he had to leave him behind and return to Mandalore. Fett agreed to this demand, killing Shysa before the Sevvets could do it. Fett then escaped, keeping his word to Shysa by returning to Mandalore to assume the role of *Mand'alor.*

**Sewell, Roons** Jan Dodonna's predecessor in the Rebel Alliance, who died shortly before the Battle of Yavin. Roons Sewell had a rough childhood, born in a shabby city on an unremarkable planet. After being beaten by bullies, he later retaliated with a spike trap he used to kill them. When he got older, he joined a theater group, where he met and fell in love with an actress named Masla. After Masla was killed during an Imperial raid, Sewell decided to fight the Empire to avenge her death. He eventually joined the Alliance, forming a small group that would steal ships by impersonating Imperial officers. Sewell soon rose to the rank of general. On the mission to liberate Jan Dodonna from the Empire, Sewell piloted a YT-series freighter. Though he often found himself at odds with Dodonna, publicly he praised the general's efforts. On another mission, he led his troops on an Imperial raid that captured a Corellian corvette. During a supply run with Dodonna, the Rebels hid in an asteroid field. Feeling that he had to do something, Sewell piloted a Y-wing as a distraction for TIE fighters searching for them. Sewell was shot down in the process, though he somehow found peace in this last heroic act. Dodonna gave Sewell's eulogy on Yavin 4.

Roons Sewell

**Sey, Kadrian** A Zabrak female and former Jedi who served as one of Count Dooku's dark side warriors. Kadrian Sey did not report back to Coruscant following the Battle of Geonosis, joining the Separatists instead. On Kiffu, Quinlan Vos killed her when she tried to attack Sheyf Tinte.

**Seyah, Toval** This stout, bearded man worked as a scientist for the Galactic Alliance and was one of the few experts on Centerpoint Station. It was Dr. Seyah who developed the training simulations used by Jacen Solo and Ben Skywalker as they planned their mission to disable the station several years after the war with the Yuuzhan Vong. Although Skywalker and Solo were largely successful, Centerpoint Station remained in the control of the Corellians, and Dr. Seyah remained aboard as a GA spy. His reports on the Corellian efforts to restore the station to operational status continued for many weeks, until he believed his identity had been compromised and he returned to Coruscant. Solo ordered that Dr. Seyah be arrested and executed for providing false information. Dr. Seyah was whisked away to a secure location and turned over to Tycho Celchu before he could be captured. Celchu and Syal Antilles transported him to the Forest Moon of Endor, hoping that Luke Skywalker and the Jedi Order might be able to provide sanctuary. Dr. Seyah helped the Jedi and their military companions plan a mission to disable Centerpoint Station and joined Kyp Durron aboard the *Broadside.* Dr. Seyah set in motion several different plans to destroy or render the station inoperable, but he was forced to abandon his efforts when the Corellians powered up the station's repulsor.

**Seylott** A jungle planet where Jango Fett retrieved a rare artifact known as the Infant of Shaa. The native inhabitants of Seylott were a primitive, Force-sensitive species that was slowly dying off. Local wildlife included flying mantis-like insects and giant land lobsters. Jango Fett and Zam Wesell went back to Seylott to return the Infant of Shaa after foiling Ashaar Khorda's plot to destroy Coruscant.

**Seyugi Dervishes** A fanatical cult of Core-based assassins with Force-augmented combat skills. They wore red cloaks and white masks. The order was all but destroyed by the Jedi, save for a group who sought refuge on Recopia to sleep in carbonite hibernation.

**S-foil** The assembly on an X-wing starfighter that helped connect each wing section with the opposite diagonal wing section. It was composed of double-layered wings that spread apart for attack, forming the X that gave the craft its name. B-wing starfighters and ARC-170s also featured S-foils.

**Sgauru** A Yuuzhan Vong bioengineered creature unleashed on the surface of Duro. Sgauru, a chitinous creature with powerful pincers, was half of a symbiotic pair capable of destroying artificial constructs within minutes. Its name translated as "bludgeon," although Warmaster Tsavong Lah nicknamed it Biter. Sgauru was the junior partner of Tu-Scart (Beater). Sgauru resembled a giant, heavily muscled, segmented slug, 10 meters long. Its skin had flat, white natural armor plating. It had six stubby front legs and a set of powerful pincers at its rear. Sgauru used its head like a wrecking ball, and from its mouth wriggled four dozen tentacles, each 4 meters long.

Shaak

**shaak** A large herbivore that roamed the plains of Naboo eating grasses and flowers. The rotund shaaks traveled in herds and served as an important food source for both the Naboo and the Gungans. Adult shaaks avoided the swamps, as their large bodies prevented them from wading through the water safely. Juvenile shaaks were capable of swimming. Harmless and slow, the four-legged shaaks were a cornerstone of the planet's food chain, and shaak meat could be stored and prepared with very little effort. The beasts could also be used as pack animals, but they were too weak to serve as mounts. Females were continuously pregnant, with a unique compartmentalized uterine system allowing for impregnation by different males at the same time. Their fatty ambergris was used as a base for perfumes.

**Shaara** A native Tatooine girl, she was one of the few people to have come out of the Great Pit of Carkoon alive. Shaara fell into the cavernous maw of the Sarlacc along with a group of Imperial stormtroopers who had been chasing her and planned to assault her. The stormtroopers never emerged.

**Shaardan** One of the many Sith apprentices training at the Academy on Korriban at the height of the Great Sith War. After hearing the stories of Ajunta Pall's sword from Galon Lor, Shaardan set out to locate it in Pall's tomb. However, he arrived too late, and decided to ambush the students who emerged with the sword. Unknown to Shaardan, the students were actually Jedi Knights in disguise. He demanded that the sword of Ajunta Pall be turned over to him, and became angry when they refused. He decided to fight them for it, but was killed in the struggle.

**Shadda-Bi-Boran** The planet where Padmé's relief group was sent after it was discovered that its sun was imploding and the planet dying. Padmé helped relocate the natives to another world, but they could not adapt to life away from their homeworld. The child N'a-kee-tula was from Shadda-Bi-Boran.

**Shadeshine** A mineral with unusual properties, it granted the ruling Satab of Ventooine incredible powers, including heightened senses and the ability to kill with a single touch. It greatly sped up the metabolism of the user, however, shortening a user's lifespan.

**Shadow Academy** A torus-shaped space station located near the Galactic Core, it was built by the Second Imperium for the express purpose of training Jedi in the dark side of the Force. Covered with weaponry and protected by a powerful cloaking device, the Shadow Academy was capable of hyperspace travel and could move to a new location at a moment's notice. The station was stark and austere, with harsh, spartan accommodations for its students, locks on every door, and chrono chimes marking every quarter hour.

Brakiss, a turncoat student of Luke Skywalker's, led the Academy with the assistance of the Nightsister Tamith Kai, but was never allowed to leave the station. The entire facility was filled with chain-reaction explosives, set to detonate should the Second Imperium ever become displeased with the Academy's progress.

Some 19 years after the Battle of Endor, Jacen and Jaina Solo and their friend Lowbacca were kidnapped and brought to the Shadow Academy, where they were to train as Dark Jedi. Soon after their escape, the Shadow Academy was moved to Coruscant. Still hiding behind its cloaking device, the station launched attacks on New Republic convoys, and Brakiss recruited several people, including Jacen and Jaina's friend Zekk, to serve in the Second Imperium. The station was revealed when Jaina used a light beam from one of Coruscant's orbiting mirrors to overwhelm its cloak. But the Academy managed to escape and to establish a new hiding place near the Denarii Nova. There Zekk, in a lightsaber duel conducted in the Shadow Academy's hub arena, killed his chief rival, Vilas, and became the Second Imperium's Darkest Knight.

Finally the leaders of the Second Imperium, displeased with the progress of Brakiss, detonated the station and killed the Shadow Academy's leader.

**Shadow Assassins** A group of Force-sensitive individuals who followed the dark side during the era of the New Sith Wars. Based on planets such as Ryloth and Umbara, the Shadow Assassins were among the groups of Dark Jedi that kept their existence hidden from the Jedi Order.

**Shadow AT-AT** An AT-AT covered with gleaming black armor. The Shadow AT-AT was never intended for stealth operations, but was created solely for intimidation.

**shadow barnacle** A small crustacean on Coruscant that anchored to buildings by feeder roots through which it absorbed nutrients. When threatened, shadow barnacles retracted into their shells. They reproduced by releasing "egg seeds" and "sperm pollens" into the air.

**Shadowcast** A secret communications network that sent Rebel messages encrypted within the commercial advertisements in Imperial propoganda programming, via the HoloNet. A Shadowcast code key was hidden behind the painting *Killik Twilight.*

***Shadow Chaser*** A spacecraft owned by the Nightsister Garowyn, it was covered in nearly invincible quantum armor. Luke Skywalker used it to escape from the Shadow Academy after rescuing the kidnapped Jaina and Jacen Solo and Lowbacca.

**shadow child** A term used by the Chiss to describe any child whose existence was kept secret by the family. The existence of a shadow child ensured that a family could not be wiped out by its enemies. It was a common practice among the Chiss to have one or more shadow children, to preserve a family's position within the Chiss Ascendancy.

**shadow droids** Powerful Imperial attack fighters built in great secrecy by the cloned Emperor Palpatine, they were constructed around the brains of fallen Imperial fighter aces. The brains were immersed in nutrient baths and hardwired to tactical computers. It was rumored that the shadow droids were empowered by the dark side of the Force.

**shadow EVO trooper** An expensive but formidable variant of the shadow trooper design equipped with experimental armor. The shadow EVO trooper wore a suit that combined advanced survival gear with a personal cloaking device. EVO troopers were extremely rare, but were sent to alien worlds to menace the local populations and assassinate resistance leaders. Like their shadow trooper counterparts, they were usually called into battle by stormtrooper commanders and used their cloaking devices to ambush enemies, opening fire with a barrage of blasterfire from their deadly flechette launchers.

***Shadow Falls, A*** A blockbluster holovid produced in the years preceding the Clone Wars, directed by Ch'been.

**Shadow Guards** Silent, enigmatic warriors who received orders from Emperor Palpatine directly, they were sent to eliminate suspected Jedi and other Force-wielders. Shadow Guards boasted limited Force powers and were capable of wielding lightsaber lances, leading some Imperials to speculate that they were Jedi who had been brainwashed into serving Palpatine. Others believed they were members of Palpatine's red-robed Royal Guard who had been trained in the Sith arts.

**Shadowmen** The name commonly used to describe the beings inhabiting the planet Nivek. The Shadowmen were a rail-thin, insectile humanoid species; they resembled walking skeletons. They had evolved unique adaptations to living in the near-total darkness of Nivek's environment, including incredibly sensitive night vision. As a people, the Shadowmen were known as skilled hunters and trackers. During the Clone Wars, they sided with the Separatists and allowed a weapons facility to be erected on the surface of Nivek.

**shadownet** The term for any communications network used to bypass the HoloNet after Emperor Palpatine instituted the New Order. The Empire quickly assumed control of the HoloNet, limiting access to it by independent news agencies and using it to disseminate propaganda. Shadownets sprang up on many worlds as a grassroots method of sharing the truth about the Empire.

**shadowport** Any starport that existed outside the laws of planetary or galactic governments.

**Shadow Saber Squadron** This starfighter unit, led by Kyp Durron and made up of Jedi Knights, was part of the Galactic Alliance First Fleet's starfighter complement during the defense of Kuat at the height of the Alliance's war against the Confederation. Like the Night Blades and Dark Sword squadrons, the Shadow Sabers abandoned the Kuat battlefield and joined Jedi Grand Master Luke Skywalker in defecting from the Galactic Alliance.

**shadow spies** A term used by the Brotherhood of Darkness to describe Sith spies and assassins who trained at the academy on Umbara in the years leading up to the Battle of Ruusan.

**shadow trooper (Blackhole stormtrooper)** Black-armored stormtroopers who answered to the head of Imperial Intelligence, Blackhole. Their armor—a stygium-triprismatic polymer—afforded the stormtroopers increased sensor-stealth. When the Empire fragmented after the Battle of Endor, some of the Blackhole stormtroopers found their way into Carnor Jax's private army, while others entered the service of Lord Shadowspawn, where they died during the Battle of Mindor.

Shadow troopers originated in the early days of the Empire, wearing cloaking armor that allowed them to disappear in virtually any environment. They typically acted as reserve units, backing up standard stormtrooper squadrons and appearing only when battles turned against the Empire. In addition to their personal cloaking devices, their armor was laced with durasteel fibers, making it much more resistant to physical and energy attacks than standard-issue stormtrooper armor.

**Shai, Dranae** A Yuuzhan Vong warrior, he was sent on an expedition with Neira Shai to Bimmiel to recover the body of Mongei Shai. He battled Corran Horn to a draw, but Corran sent the image of killscent to lure a nest of nearby slashrats. Dranae Shai was eaten by them.

**Shai, Mongei** Shedao Shai's grandfather and a valiant warrior who scouted the galaxy about 50 years prior to the Yuuzhan Vong invasion. Mongei Shai did not return with the other scouts, remaining behind on Bimmiel to report via villips until the range proved too great. He died on Bimmiel. Decades later, University of Agamar students discovered his body and several belongings in a cave. Shedao Shai's attempt to recover Mongei's bones eventually led to his death.

**Shai, Shedao** A commander and a member of the Yuuzhan Vong warrior caste. Shedao Shai had gray-green flesh, black hair, dark eyes, and hooks and barbs at his wrists, elbows, knees, and heels. His warship was the *Legacy of Torment.* Shedao fought the New Republic at Dubrillion and Dantooine, then went to Bimmiel to recover the body of his grandfather Mongei Shai. When Elegos A'Kla surrendered to the Yuuzhan Vong as a peace envoy, Shedao taught Elegos the Yuuzhan Vong way and in turn learned about the New Republic from his prisoner. In the end, Shedao turned Elegos into a statement: He killed him, prepared his corpse in the appropriate Yuuzhan Vong manner, and returned the artistically decorated skeleton to Corran Horn at Ithor. Corran arranged a duel with Shai on Ithor, with the winner awarded control of the planet. Although Corran killed his enemy, the Yuuzhan Vong treacherously infected Ithor with a bacteria that left just about every living thing on the sphere dead.

**Shaker** This stock R2 series astromech was one of many such droids in the maintenance droid pool at the Drewwa Spaceport during the years following the Swarm War. When Ben Skywalker appropriated Helamian Barkid's Y-wing fighter, he assaulted Shaker's human controller and rendered her unconscious before taking the droid and installing it in the Y-wing as a copilot. Shaker accompanied Skywalker to Ziost, where the young Jedi hoped to locate the Amulet of Kalara. When Ben discovered a Sith meditation sphere on the planet, he used it to escape from his pursuers and return to Drewwa. There he turned the girl Kiara Olvidan over to the authorities and returned Shaker to its rightful owners.

Shadow troopers

**Shala, Ree** A Twi'lek smuggler, she operated a sizable organization from Jaresh, an Outer Rim moon.

**Shalam** This planet imposed a 100 percent tariff on Jandarra vegetables from Jubilar. Fifteen years after the Battle of Endor, Han Solo went to Jubilar to make a smuggling run for old times' sake and agreed to smuggle a cargo of Jandarra vegetables to Shalam, where his wife, Leia, was on official business.

**Shalini** One of the leaders of the Typha-Dor resistance prior to the Clone Wars, she rallied beings from throughout the Uziel system and crusaded against the invasion plans of the Vanqors. Shalini turned a disk containing those plans over to Jedi Master Obi-Wan Kenobi and his apprentice, Anakin Skywalker, in the hope that they could transmit the information back to the Republic. Shalini was disheartened to discover a traitor amid her followers: her husband, Mezdec.

**Shaliqua, Diva** One of Jabba the Hutt's slave dancers, she accompanied him to the Boonta Eve Classic on Tatooine. She belonged to the Divas, a religious order of female Theelin singers. A cruel twist of mutation among the Theelin led to genetic incompatibility among their own kind, dooming the species to extinction. Their biological makeup was close enough to humanity that many Theelin bloodlines were continued through crossbreeding with human and near-human species. Diva Shaliqua rarely spoke of her parents, but it was known that both were slaves of Ingoda the Hutt, a cruel entrepreneur who had been "collecting" Theelin slaves. When Ingoda became indebted to the shrewd Jabba the Hutt, he was forced to sell two of his slaves—Diva Funquita and Diva Shaliqua—to his business rival. Romeo Treblanc, a retired actor and owner of the Galaxies Opera House, later purchased Diva Shaliqua from Jabba.

Diva Shaliqua

**Shalyvane** The desert homeworld of the Em'liy species. During the Galactic Civil War, Rebel pilot Shira Brie traveled to the city of Chinshassa to activate a device that contacted Darth Vader. After Luke shot down Shira Brie's Rebel-modified TIE fighter during a battle, he returned to Shalyvane to search for answers.

**Shaman of the Whills** A holy person who discovered the ability to defy death. This ability could only be achieved through compassion, and thus the Sith could never learn it.

**Shamed Ones** The lowest caste of Yuuzhan Vong, composed of those whose bodies had rejected living implants. Shamed Ones often lived out of structures surrounding damuteks to act as a support colony, serving as slaves. They did the work no true-caste Yuuzhan Vong would dirty their hands with. Shamed Ones usually did not have the tattoos or scars of the true castes, though many former shapers whose creations failed to meet expectations became Shamed Ones. They worshipped the god Yun-Shuno.

After former warrior Vua Rapuung was redeemed with the assistance of Anakin Solo on Yavin 4, some of the Shamed Ones began to worship the Jedi. The heresy grew in strength over the years and helped contribute to the collapse of the Yuuzhan Vong invasion.

***Shamunaar*** This Galactic Alliance frigate was dispatched to the Bothawui system during the Corellia–GA War, when rumors surfaced that the Bothans might try to join the Corellians in seceding from the Galactic Alliance. The ship was under the command of Captain Biurk, who was charged with overseeing the reconnaissance of Bothan activities. Biurk was surprised when Admiral Matric Klauskin suddenly took command of the vessel, since Klauskin had spent the previous several months at the Veterans' Mental Care Hospital on Coruscant. Unknown to Biurk and his crew, Klauskin had escaped the facility with the help of the Dark Lady of the Sith, Lumiya. Klauskin lured Biurk to the emergency bridge and shot him; vented the atmosphere from the ship, killing the crew; turned the ship over to Tathak K'roylan; and gave the Bothan a chance to launch his war fleet.

**Shan, Bastila** A skilled Jedi from Talravin who specialized in Jedi battle meditation during the years of the Jedi Civil War. Bastila Shan was brash and impulsive, turning every fiber of her being toward defeating the Sith menace and proving herself to the leading Jedi. She helped Revan find the Star Forge, fell under the dark side influence of Darth Malak, and fought her way back to the light. Bastila was one of the few Jedi to survive the purge that followed the Jedi Civil War.

Bastila Shan

**Shan, Deena** This 19-year-old joined the Rebel Alliance shortly after the Battle of Yavin. While serving aboard *Kalla's Stanchion,* she was assigned to the duty list of the *Millennium Falcon.* Deena went undercover as an Imperial on Kalist VI, helped Luke Skywalker contact his former friend Janek "Tank" Sunber, and accompanied Skywalker on a suicide mission to infiltrate Bannistar Station.

Deena Shan

**Shana** A Mistryl Shadow Guard, she accompanied Mara Jade to help liberate Kessel and battled the prototype Death Star above the planet.

***Shannador's Revenge*** An *Invincible*-class capital ship, it flew under the banner of the Corporate Sector Authority.

**Shantipole project** The code name given to the top-secret research and development of the Rebel Alliance's B-wing starfighter. Shantipole was devised and commanded by Commander Ackbar.

**shapers caste** The scientists and bioengineers who created the living machines and tools that powered Yuuzhan Vong society. Being closest in purpose to the Creator god, they were the highest caste under the Supreme Overlord. Master shapers, assisted by adepts and initiates, bred Yuuzhan Vong organisms. Unlike other castes, the marks of a shaper's sacrifices were not external—except for hands, which were often exchanged with the hands of masters. Members of the shaper caste were not allowed to practice with traditional Yuuzhan Vong weapons, and instead employed a variety of arcane and lethal devices including huuns and finger-spears. The shapers worshipped the god Yun-Ne'shel. Because of the need for shapers in the battle against the New Republic, only the senile, inept, and disgraced shapers remained to tend the worldships. On Yavin 4, the Yuuzhan Vong constructed a shaper base with damuteks.

**Shard** Silicon-based lifeforms found on Orax. One hundred years before the fall of the Old Republic, scouts encountered the crystal-like Shards growing in clusters along rocks near the mineral-rich springs of their homeworld. Able to sense and produce electromagnetic charges, the Shards shared a collective consciousness. A few dozen Shards took to the idea of separating from the group-mind and forming symbiotic relationships with droids. The two entities complemented each other perfectly, the droid giving the Shard mobility as well as a variety of modes of perception, and the Shard in turn giving the droid a decidedly living quality, as well as rights equal to those of organic sentients.

***Shard*-class capital ship** The designation of any form of attack ship developed and produced by the Killik hives of the Colony at the height of the Swarm War. These vessels measured from 500 meters to 10 kilometers in length, but all shared the same basic profile. Roughly conical in shape, a *Shard*-class vessel had a larger, rounded end and appeared to have been carved from rock. With its jagged sides and angles, it looked like a shard of fragmented asteroid or planetoid.

***Sharp Spiral*** The specialized starship of Jedi Master Saesee Tiin. The *Sharp Spiral* was a SoroSuub Cutlass-9 patrol starfighter given to Tiin by grateful Duros diplomats after he rescued their convoy from pirates. Tiin drastically redesigned the craft to suit his own unique abilities, removing the starship's deflector shields to make room for a hand-crafted hyperdrive and replacing the vehicle's blaster cannons with military-grade lasers confiscated from a Hutt arms dealer. A small proton torpedo launcher was concealed beneath the starfighter. The *Sharp Spiral*'s aerodynamic design and powerful ion engine array made it one of the fastest atmospheric craft in the Jedi fleet.

Tiin's Force abilities allowed him to focus his thoughts to control his starfighter even while traveling through hyperspace. While flying at lightspeed, Tiin had no need of a nav computer. He increased the *Sharp Spiral*'s performance by taking hyperspace shortcuts and flying dangerously close to mass shadows. Tiin's piloting skills earned him the respect of the Freedom's Sons, a militant civilian security corps that frequently aided the Jedi Master.

Tiin honed his skills and the vehicle's performance on Iktotch, where the tumultuous winds could easily down lesser pilots. The *Sharp Spiral*'s most dramatic mission pitted the starfighter against three warships piloted by rogue members of the Freedom's Sons. Although the *Sharp Spiral* lacked deflector shields, Tiin was able to fly rings around the well-trained soldiers.

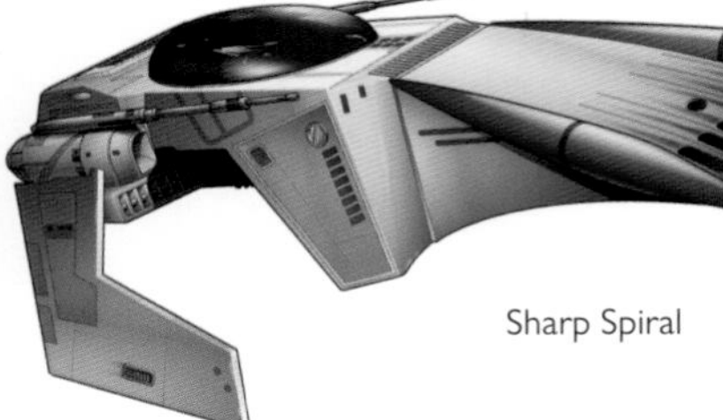

Sharp Spiral

**Shashay** A species of intelligent, colorful avians from Crytal Nest. Their beautiful trilling was admired across the galaxy.

**Shattered Moon** The name used by the Chiss to describe the single moon of the planet Tenupe. A red-colored orb when viewed from space, this moon had cracked apart at some point in its history, but there was enough gravitational force among the larger fragments that they orbited Tenupe as a cohesive grouping. The Killiks of the Colony established a series of reproduction facilities within the 50 to 60 pieces of the Shattered Moon, where they spawned innumerable hordes of soldiers for the Great Swarm.

**shatter gun** Developed by the Verpine, this weapon was a delicate pistol that fired magnetically accelerated particles or pellets of alloy. The shotgun effect was devastating, but the shatter gun was prone to breakdown or explosion if improperly handled or dropped.

**shatterpoint** A term used to describe the locations at which even the hardest material could break into pieces. Most commonly associated with Corusca gems, shatterpoints were notoriously difficult to locate, and the judgment of how much force to exert on a shatterpoint was an art only a few beings ever learned. Too little resulted in a degradation of the crystalline matrix, which caused the gem to fall apart later. Too much, and the entire gem shattered instantly. A precisely gauged blow resulted in the shearing of the gem along a certain plane, resulting in a beautiful facet.

**Shaum Hii** A planet famous for its noisy cattle markets, it was home to the Kian'thar, who herded airborne derlacs. Shaum Hii was a sea and marsh planet on the outskirts of the Tragan Cluster, one of the many sectors in the Outer Rim Territories.

**shaupaut** A nocturnal predator native to Naboo. Because shaupauts had small mouths, they used their sharp claws to carve prey into easily consumed pieces. Many larger predators avoided attacking the shaupaut because the creature's blood contained a powerful alkyl, poisonous to many carnivores.

**Shawda Ubb** Diminutive amphibians from Manpha, a small, wet world in the Outer Rim Territories. The frog-like aliens had long, gangly limbs and wide-splayed fingers. Their rubbery skin was a mottled greenish gray except on their bellies, where it lightened to lime green. Rappertunie, a musician who played in Jabba the Hutt's palace, was a Shawda Ubb.

**Shawken** Considered one of the oldest, most magnificent civilizations in the known galaxy. After the Battle of Endor, Imperial forces that had been controlling the planet withdrew. Luke Skywalker, Rik Duel, Dani, Chihdo, Plif, and Kiro went on a diplomatic mission to Shawken. According to legend, ancestors of the Shawkenese left behind dreadful weapons, including one created by a nihilistic scientist that could destroy the galaxy.

**Shawpee Gang** Small-time hoodlums who prowled the streets of Mos Eisley during the last years of the New Order.

**Shawti** A Hutt colony world, it was the site of Klatooinian slave breeding.

**Shay** A native of Targonn, he led the Revoltists in a series of attacks against dictator Craw's tyrannical reign. Though he failed to overthrow Craw, Shay did rescue the droids R2-D2 and C-3PO from the dictator's clutches. The droids were reunited with Master Zorneth, who eventually toppled Craw's empire.

**Shayoto** An ancient Jedi who attended the great Jedi assembly at Mount Meru 4,000 years before the Galactic Civil War.

**Shazeen** A Sauropteroid, he helped Han Solo and his party on the planet Dellalt during their quest for the lost treasure of Xim the Despot. A veteran of many conflicts, Shazeen had a nearly black hide, bore notched and bitten flippers, and was missing an eye.

*Shaupaut*

**shear mite** Vicious, half-meter insects found on Dathomir and Yavin 4.

**Shebba the Hutt (Shebba Kalshi Desilijic)** A Hutt plantation master on Shawti, he owned the Klatooinian slave Umpass-stay. Jabba killed Shebba and took ownership of the drummer.

**Shee, Cian** A noted slicer hired by bounty hunter Kalyn Farnmir during her pursuit of Sri Oscuro. The Zealots of Psusan later paid Shee a large sum of credits to sell out Farnmir, who killed her.

**Sheelal, Qymaen jai** *See* Grievous, General.

**shell-bat** A flying reptile, it was native to the planet Geran.

**Shell Hutts** A clan of Hutts known for their armored, durasteel "shells." The Shell Hutts inhabited Circumtore, where they harbored the fugitive Oph Nar Dinnid until Boba Fett arrived to claim the price on his head.

**Shelter** A secret Jedi base built by Lando Calrissian during the Yuuzhan Vong War and located at the site that had once been the Maw Installation. Much of the wreckage from the Maw Installation was cobbled together to build Shelter. Its base was an asteroid fragment, but living modules, a power core, and a rudimentary defense system rose from its surface. Shelter was funded by private donors after the New Republic refused to offer any official support. After the fall of Coruscant, Luke and Mara Jade Skywalker took their son Ben to Shelter. Han Solo and Leia escorted the children of the evacuated Jedi academy there.

**Shelvay, Corwin** The Padawan apprentice to Jedi Knight Darrin Arkanian, who survived Order 66. A quick study, the impetuous Shelvay thought the fight should be taken to the Empire. He was captured by High Inquisitor Tremayne, and Arkanian died trying to rescue him. Enraged, Shelvay attacked Tremayne, severing the Inquisitor's arm and forever scarring his face. Retreating from the dark side after his escape, Shelvay spent many years wandering the galaxy before joining the Rebel Alliance.

**Shenayag** This Sith Lord served as one of the instructors at the Sith Academy on Korriban in the years leading up to the Battle of Ruusan.

**shenbit bonecrusher** A predator found on Barab I. Barabels enjoyed stalking shenbit bonecrushers for sport and meat.

**Shen-Jon, Echuu** A Jedi Master who survived the Purge and was later discovered by Princess Leia Organa on Krant. Shen-Jon had trained under Mace Windu, and Stam Reath was his Padawan. After Reath was slain during the Battle of Geonosis, Shen-Jon reluctantly took his sister Naat as a Padawan. Shen-Jon led a Republic army to Krant, killed Separatist general Sev'Rance Tann and then disappeared into the Krant wilderness. After years of self-imposed exile, Shen-Jon met Princess Leia and helped her win the Krantians their freedom. He died destroying a Jedi artifact, the Vor'Na'Tu, to prevent it from being used for evil purposes.

**Sherruk** This ancient Mandalorian was part of a larger group that was based on the planet Dantooine some 4,000 years before the Battle of Yavin. Sherruk was known for his ability to hunt down and kill any other being, including Jedi Knights, and several unique lightsabers were found among his remains after he was defeated in combat. The Jedi had been asked by several villagers to put an end to the abuses by the Mandalorians, but many refused to back down. Sherruk was among them; he fought to the death.

**Shesh, Viqi** A turncoat Senator from Kuat during the Yuuzhan Vong War. Senator Viqi Shesh was a slender, handsome woman with radiant black hair. Relatively new to politics, she quickly became known as a clever deal maker with a knack for keeping all sides happy. She was a member of the Security and Intelligence Council and the New Republic Advisory Council, and enjoyed a top position within the Senate Select Committee for Refugees (SELCORE). Having determined that the New Republic would lose the war, she made a secret deal with Yuuzhan Vong Warmaster Tsavong Lah. Shesh worked within the Senate to speed the progress of the invaders, despite Leia Organa Solo's efforts to remove her. She infiltrated the Solos' apartment during the invasion of Coruscant to try to kidnap Ben Skywalker, but was foiled by Noghri bodyguards. For her failure, she was taken to a worldship in orbit, telling the warmaster that he had been betrayed by the shapers caste in order to buy herself more time. When the conspirators behind Tsavong Lah's rejected implant were revealed, Lah rewarded the Senator by allowing her to accompany a hunting

*Viqi Shesh*

party to search for potential Jedi activity on Coruscant. Sneaking away, Shesh found a working ship called the *Ugly Truth* and plotted her escape. Before she could use the ship, Luke Skywalker's strike team and a surviving Yuuzhan warrior confronted her. Faced with certain death, she chose to end her own life by throwing herself through a viewport.

**Shesharile system** Located in the Minos Cluster, it contained a gas giant around which orbited the inhabited moons Shesharile 5 and 6, sometimes called the Twin Planets. Their 12 billion inhabitants were ruled by a single corrupt government, and the streets of their cities were taken over by out-of-control criminals and wild swoop gangs such as the Spiders, the Rabid Mynocks, and the Raging Banthas. Both worlds were heavily polluted.

**Shessaun, Senator Silya** The Senator from the Thesme sector during the final days of the Clone Wars. Silya Shessaun was the first native of her planet's working class to ascend to the position of Senator after being a child prodigy on Thesme. She first met Padmé Amidala at a summit on Alderaan when both were Apprentice Legislators. At age 20, Shessaun earned a position in the Senate, and became a key player in a wide variety of social programs to help those in need across the galaxy. When word reached her that the Senator from Naboo had died in the Jedi uprising, she felt the loss of Padmé Amidala deeply and attended her funeral on Naboo. Later she was quietly forced to step down from office to let a more Imperial-minded Senator take her place.

**Shevu, Lon** A captain in the Coruscant Security Force during the crisis surrounding Corellia's bid for independence from the Galactic Alliance. Captain Shevu and his men were the first officers on the scene when a pro-Corellia terrorist set off an explosive device inside the Elite Hotel on Coruscant. Jacen Solo handpicked Shevu to serve as his chief lieutenant within the Galactic Alliance Guard. As Shevu worked more with Solo, he came to question the Jedi Knight's true motivations. Shevu was later assigned to Ben Skywalker's mission to assassinate the Corellian Prime Minister, Dur Gejjen, serving as Skywalker's backup with Jori Lekauf. Although the mission was a success, Jori Lekauf was forced to sacrifice his life to ensure that Ben and Shevu escaped.

Shevu later admitted to Ben Skywalker that he believed Jacen was a psychopath and needed to be eliminated. He accompanied Ben to Kavan, where Ben was visited by the spirit of his mother, who gave him the idea to search Jacen's StealthX for more evidence. Shevu arranged for them to get a forensics droid near the ship when Jacen traveled to Fondor, and they found a bloody hair from Ben's murdered mother, Mara Jade Skywalker. Shevu later wore a recording device whenever he met with Jacen, to record any information that Solo might divulge in confidence. Shevu did his best to continue to appear loyal to Jacen and the Galactic Alliance, and was rewarded with a lengthy discussion about Jacen's actions. During the discussion, Jacen revealed that he was now a Sith Lord, and that he should be called by his proper title, Darth Caedus. He also revealed that he had killed Mara Jade Skywalker, although he firmly believed that the killing had been necessary to allow Jacen to continue his mission to save the galaxy. Shevu transmitted the recording of the discussion to Ben, knowing that it provided the final piece of evidence that Ben needed to convince his family of Jacen's guilt.

Weeks later, Shevu tried to meet with Ben face-to-face, but they were tracked to their meeting place in Monument Plaza by Tahiri Veila, who captured them both. They were then separated at the Galactic Justice Center, and Shevu was tortured but kept alive so that Veila could use him as leverage to force Ben to reveal information about the Jedi Order. Veila grew so frustrated with Ben's lack of response that she blasted Shevu with Force lightning, killing him instantly. Ben escaped shortly afterward but managed to get Shevu's body to send to his widow on Valkin.

**Sheyf** A title held by the commander of the Guardians of Kiffu. The Guardians' authority was absolute, and the position of Sheyf had been held by Clan Vos for centuries. Tinte Vos, Quinlan Vos's great-aunt, was Sheyf around the time of the Battle of Naboo.

**Sheyvan** A weapons expert who served as one of the first Emperor's Hands, he trained the clones of Sa Cuis during the early years of the New Order. Though he favored the vibroblade, Sheyvan was equally skilled with a lightsaber. Enraged to discover he was not the sole Emperor's Hand, Sheyvan spurred the Sa Cuis clones to revolt against Palpatine. Darth Vader killed him for his treachery.

***shiak*** A Jedi "mark of contact," a target objective for lightsaber-wielders. It refers to stabbing with the tip of the blade, as when Darth Maul delivered a mortal *shiak* blow to Qui-Gon Jinn.

**Shiel, Riv** A Shistavanen from Uvena III, he was a member of Rogue Squadron. His species was considered more violent than humans, and the Empire had placed a death mark on him for past crimes. Even so, Rogue Squadron benefited from his expert piloting talents. Seriously injured on several missions, he was felled by the Krytos virus on Coruscant. When fully recovered, he joined in the Bacta War against cartel leader Ysanne Isard. While on a mission to hijack one of her bacta convoys, he was killed by enemy fire from the *Corrupter*.

***Shield*** An assault carrier in the New Republic's Fifth Fleet, it was deployed in the blockade of Doornik-319 at the start of the Yevethan crisis.

**Shield, the** A group of freelance corporate "security specialists" who were actually Rebel Alliance operatives.

**shield generator** *See* deflector shield.

**shieldship** Custom-designed escort vessels, they were built to protect ships traveling to the planet Nkllon in the Athega system from the scorching rays of Athega's superhot sun, which could destroy ships carrying only standard shielding. Even though Nkllon was so hot that beings could live only on the night side of the planet that was turned away from the sun, its mineral resources proved too valuable to pass up for a gambling man like Lando Calrissian, who devised a gigantic mobile unit, Nomad City, to mine the ore.

The 12 shieldships were built by the newly formed Republic Engineering Corporation. They proved difficult both to pilot and to maintain, and substantial downtime had to be part of their schedule. The ships were, in effect, giant sun umbrellas. Immense 800-meter-wide cones acted as shields. Their faces were covered by thick armor plating honeycombed with coolant chambers, and their backs had huge tubes and fins to vent off the intense heat. The shadow behind the shield formed the protected area for incoming starships. Trailing behind each shield was a 400-meter pylon with a drive tug that provided sublight and hyperdrive thrust.

Normally, the shieldship simply took control of the escorted vessel via slave circuit at the Outer-Rim depot and jumped into the heart of the system, bringing the other vessel along for a ride that took about one hour. Ships without slave circuits had to be escorted to Nkllon on sublight drives, which took about 10 hours.

The success of the mining operation and its New Republic ties made it a target for Grand Admiral Thrawn. His second attack on Nomad City destroyed its drive units and long-range communications, and Star Destroyers attacking the Outer-Rim depot disabled all but one of the shieldships. During the Yuuzhan Vong

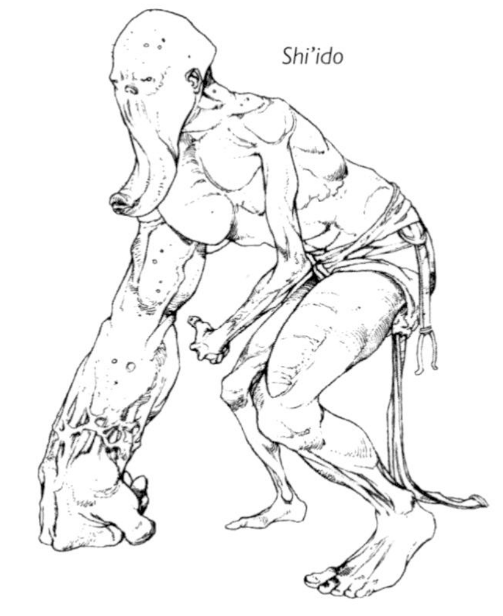
Shi'ido

War, some of Lando's shieldships were deployed in the New Republic's counterattack on Helska 4.

**Shi'ido** A rare species with the ability to simulate the appearance of others. In their natural state, Shi'idos were humanoids with pale skin. Mammon Hoole was a member of the Shi'ido species who disguised himself to blend in with the indigenous population of the planet Tatooine to do his work without much notice. Some of the oldest members of the species were 500 years old. This longevity led to their tremendous interest in learning about the galaxy, though they preferred to not have the galaxy learn about them. The Shi'ido were from Lao-mon, a garden world in the Colonies region ravaged by disease.

***shiim*** A Jedi "mark of contact," a target objective for lightsaber-wielders. Its meaning was "wound," as when Count Dooku struck Obi-Wan Kenobi with debilitating blows that took him out of the battle.

**Shild, Moff Sarn** A tall, pale sector Moff who lived before the Galactic Civil War, Shild proclaimed that the Hutts' lawless territory would greatly benefit from stricter Imperial control. As a public relations stunt, he was authorized to blockade Nal Hutta and turn the Smugglers' Moon into molten slag. The Hutts of Nar Shaddaa paid him to ignore their illegal operations there. Bria Tharen, working for the fledgling Rebellion, traveled with him as his supposed concubine, but Shild's sexual preferences did not extend to human females. He had a secret ambition to break away from the Empire and form his own independent sector. When the ill-fated attack on the Hutt worlds failed, Shild was called back to the Emperor. Instead of facing Palpatine's punishment, however, he committed suicide.

**Shili** The homeworld of Jedi Master Shaak Ti, Ahsoka Tano, and other members of the Togruta species. The wild scrublands of Shili were covered with meter-tall turu-grass, which was red on one side and white on the other. Togrutas enjoyed eating thimiars, small rodent-like creatures native to Shili.

**Shimia** A remote world in the Outer Rim Territories, it was the home planet of the Pacithhips.

**Shimmer** A planet of massive glaciers, it was the site of a Rebel Alliance medium-security work camp.

**shimmersilk** Sheer and lustrous, this expensive fabric was used to create high-fashion clothing in the more well-off regions of the galaxy.

**Shimrra, Supreme Overlord** The Supreme Overlord of the Yuuzhan Vong invaders. Shimrra proclaimed to his people that he had a vision of a new home: a galaxy corrupted by heresy that required cleansing through bloodshed. A massive, heavily modified Yuuzhan Vong, Shimrra had eyes that were glowing maa'it implants. Jaina Solo led a force at Obroa-skai to ambush Shimrra's flagship, but the Supreme Overlord wasn't on board. After the conquest of Coruscant, Shimrra arrived on the conquered planet in a glorious ceremony where he met with high-ranking members of the four ruling castes: Tsavong Lah, Ch'Gang Hool, Yoog Skell, and High Priest Jakan. Late in the war, it became known that Shimrra was merely a puppet for his court jester Onimi, who had been controlling Shimrra through toxins and mental manipulation. Luke Skywalker beheaded Shimrra in a duel, while Jacen Solo eliminated Onimi.

**Shindra's Veil, Battle of** One of the climactic battles fought by Shey Tapani during the unification of the Tapani sector some 6,000 years before the Battle of Endor. The battle was fought by starships within the area of nebular gas known as Shindra's Veil. During the battle, Shey Tapani destroyed the forces of the Rogue Houses, thereby eliminating any opposition to the unification.

**shine-ball** An unusual form of lighting created by the members of the Killik Colony. The shell of the shine-ball was formed from a sticky wax that the insectoids exuded, allowing the ball to be stuck on a ceiling or wall. Once the Colony's existence became known beyond the Unknown Regions, other worlds began purchasing shine-balls for lighting passageways and tunnels. Most were large, jewel-like spheres of a bright blue material.

**Shiner** The R2 unit used by New Republic pilot Myn Donos. When Shiner was destroyed in battle, Myn Donos experienced severe emotional trauma—the droid had been the only other surviving member of Donos's original Talon Squadron.

**Shintel** A largely uninhabited planet in the Kathol sector used by the Empire as a supply and patrol base.

***Ship*** The simple name of the Sith meditation sphere recovered from Ziost by Ben Skywalker some 10 years after the end of the Yuuzhan Vong War. Ben turned the strange ship over to Jacen Solo, who in turn handed it to Lumiya. When Ben first reawakened *Ship,* it remembered the ancient times when the Sith controlled large portions of the galaxy. It also revealed that it originally had been constructed as a training vessel, and as such could not be targeted by another ship. Ben used this knowledge to convince the sphere to stop taking orders from Lumiya, allowing him to ensure that she could not harm his mother. With Lumiya's death, *Ship* passed into the hands of Alema Rar, who believed that she needed to travel to Korriban to enlist the aid of the Sith leaders there in helping

*Shiro-trap*

Jacen become a Dark Lord. Although *Ship* understood that Alema Rar was strong in the dark side of the Force, it was unsure of its loyalty to her. Zekk, a former student of the Shadow Academy, later drew upon the dark side to communicate with *Ship,* negating any standing orders that Alema Rar had given it and allowing it to go free. As *Ship* blasted away from Alema's asteroid base, it was pursued by the Sith Lord Dician and the crew of the *Poison Moon.*

**shipwomb** A Yuuzhan Vong bioengineered shipbuilding facility. The Yuuzhan Vong constructed a shipwomb at Sernpidal to grow a new worldship, which was ultimately destroyed by Kyp Durron and Jaina Solo.

**shipwright** Talented engineers who built starships and starship components, including weapons and engines. Shipwrights could learn to reverse-engineer just about any equipment. A shipwright with a steady supply of parts to disassemble could produce an array of powerful components.

**Shire, Tanith** A supply tug operator at the starship yards on Fondor, she stole drone barges and sent them crashing to Ophideraan's surface. There they were salvaged by the Serpent Masters, who kept Tanith Shire's people in slavery. Luke Skywalker and Shire escaped Fondor on one of these barges. After crash landing, Luke defeated the Serpent Masters and freed Shire's people.

**shiro-trap** The term applied to the symbiotic pairing of a shiro and a tooke-trap. The tooke trap, a Naboo plant, took root on the back of a slow-moving shiro. The plant concealed the shiro from predators, while the locomotion provided by the shiro allowed the tooke-trap to relocate and avoid being uprooted by clodhoppers.

**Shistavanen** An intelligent but violent species of fur-covered bipeds with wolf-like faces and sharp claws and teeth. Popularly called

*Shistavanen*

Shistavanen Wolfmen, they were hunters by nature.

**Shiva IV** A planet on the outskirts of the known galaxy. Shiva IV was ruled by Aron, Warlord of the Calian Confederacy, and Kéral Longknife, Demarch of the 12 Tribes. The alien Imperial General Sk'ar led a strike force against the natives of Shiva IV.

**shlecho newt** A small Yuuzhan Vong–bioengineered brown-orange lizard. Coomb spores were a favored delicacy of the shlecho newt. When the newt smelled a coomb spore, its head turned a brilliant shade of crimson.

***Sh'ner*-class planetary assault carrier** Ovoid ships nearly 750 meters long, these carriers were essential to Ssi-ruuvi Imperium invasion forces. Sh'ner planetary assault carriers usually remained behind the main battle lines until the target world had been defeated. The carriers then moved into high orbit to launch P'w'eck-staffed *D'kee*-class landing ships.

Slow and underpowered, Sh'ner carrier ships were closer to transports than combat ships. Their weak shields made them easy targets for enemy vessels. Sh'ner carriers also had minimal weaponry: only six ion cannons, two tractor beam projectors, and 24 battle droids for emergencies. They normally relied on Fw'Sen picket ships for armed escort. The interior of a Sh'ner carrier held nearly a dozen entechment labs for rapidly processing prisoners; giant batteries stored the enteched life energies until they were needed.

A small command and entechment lab crew consisted of only about 60 Ssi-ruuk, while about 500 P'w'eck and 300 enteched droids were used as assistants and for manual labor. Each of the three P'w'eck landing ships aboard was armed with 100 paralysis canisters that could be dropped over major population centers, exploding at an altitude of 1,000 meters and spreading Ssi-ruuvi paralysis toxins over an area nearly 9 square kilometers in size.

When target cities had been effectively neutralized, the Sh'ner carrier's landing ships descended to gather entechment subjects. Each landing ship could carry nearly 10,000 prisoners in confinement pens. The Bakura invasion fleet had three Sh'ner carriers, which retreated to the main Ssi-ruuvi battle fleet after Luke Skywalker captured the *Shriwirr* battle cruiser.

**shock-ball** An outdoor team sport in which one team tried to stun the other into unconsciousness with an electrically charged ball or orb. Team members used insulated mitts to handle the orb and scoops to fling and catch it. After a specified time period elapsed, the team with the most conscious members won the match.

**shock couch** Any of a number of protective anti-gravity devices, usually shaped like a chair and found aboard most starships. Escape pods were equipped with shock couches to prevent passenger injury during landing, and TIE fighters possessed advanced high-g shock couches to stabilize pilots during difficult maneuvers and crashes.

***Shockwave*** Admiral Harrsk's flagship, this *Imperial*-class Star Destroyer was built at his own hidden shipyards in the Core. The Star Destroyer was wiped out by Warlord Admiral Teradoc's fleet.

**shock whip** A long, thickly woven metal wire extending from a metal grip, it was activated by a power cell that electrified the wire with an intense charge.

**Shogun** A mysterious planet known for its dreamscapes. The aging Mandalorian warrior Fenn Shysa died on Shogun while saving his friend Boba Fett from death.

***Shooting Star*** A New Republic frigate, it was destroyed in a collision with the *Endor.*

**Shoran** A Wookiee cousin of Chewbacca, he was killed during the rescue of Han Solo aboard the *Pride of Yevetha.*

**short-range transport (SRT) droid** A heavy industrial automaton used in the droid factories of Geonosis. In factory environments, SRT droids operated around the clock, and most burned out their original components in under a year. Short-range transport droids carried raw materials, tools, and finished products from one factory hub to another. They cruised through multileveled hives on repulsorlifts, ensuring that no conveyer belts were jammed and that all fuel stores and parts bins were topped off. The Geonosian SRTs were products of Baktoid Combat Automata.

**short-term memory enhancement** A Force control technique through which a Jedi could replay recent events to carefully examine images and peripheral happenings. It aided the recall of a particular detail that was observed but not consciously remembered.

**shoto** A specially built half-length lightsaber developed by the new Jedi Order. The Jedi Knights discovered that a normal lightsaber was often a hindrance in close quarters, especially when engaged in one-on-one combat. Thus the shoto was designed to be wielded in cramped areas. The development of the shoto also allowed many Jedi to train in the Jar'Kai style of fighting, using a normal lightsaber in one hand and the shoto in the other. Jedi Grand Master Luke Skywalker took up the shoto in the years following the Swarm War, when he discovered that Lumiya had reappeared in the galaxy. He found that using a shoto allowed him to get closer to the female Dark Jedi, thereby eliminating her ability to use her lightwhip.

**Showolter, Captain** A member of New Republic Intelligence, he greeted Luke Skywalker and Lando Calrissian when they returned to Coruscant with disturbing news from the Corellian sector. During the Yuuzhan Vong War, Major Showolter met with Belindi Kalenda, Joi Eicroth, and Dr. Yintal on Wayland to debrief the Yuuzhan Vong defectors, Elan and Vergere. During an assassination attempt on Elan, several of his ribs were broken and he suffered a punctured lung. Intending to bring the defectors to Coruscant, he boarded the *Queen of Empire* with Elan posing as his wife and Vergere as their servant. When the *Queen* reached Vortex, he was injured by Peace Brigade members posing as Showolter's backup agents. He then stumbled into Han Solo, whom he assumed was the real NRI backup agent. Injured, he turned custody of Elan and Vergere over to Solo. Showolter also formed a unit of over 100 Clawdites known as Guile Company, designed to infiltrate enemy ranks.

**Shrag brothers** Sneak thieves, they operated in Nar Shaddaa's vertical city. The Shrag brothers often stripped Hutt caravels for quick credits.

**Shreeftut, His Potency the** The supreme leader of the warmongering Ssi-ruuvi Imperium from the planet Lwhekk, he planned to dominate the galaxy.

***Shriek*-class bomber** A class of bombers designed and developed by the Corellian Engineering Corporation during the years following the war against the Yuuzhan Vong. Full-scale production of this ship, designated the YT-5100, didn't begin for many years, although 10 prototypes were deployed as

*SRT droid*

part of Operation Noble Savage. The *Shriek*-class bomber was designed to deploy a variety of payloads, and the early prototypes also were designed to deploy targeter droids. The prototypes were so new that the Galactic Alliance's sensors were unable to determine the exact nature of the YT-5100 bombers that showed up on their scopes.

**Shrike, Garris** A venal con man who took a young Han Solo under his wing. Solo spent his youth aboard the ancient troopship *Trader's Luck* as a member of Garris Shrike's well-organized trading clan, earning his keep through begging, pickpocketing, and grand larceny. Garris Shrike was killed while attempting to collect a Hutt bounty placed on Solo's head. He was the only one who knew that Vyyk Drago was an alias used by Solo.

***Shrike*** A ship used by Mara Jade. The *Shrike* was on permanent loan from Talon Karrde. It was a modified Alpha-52 prototype, never developed for the open market.

***Shriwirr*** Among the largest of the Ssi-ruuvi customized battle cruisers, it was the lead ship in the reptilian species' assault on the planet Bakura under the command of Admiral Ivpikkis. The *Shriwirr* was an ovoid ship about 900 meters long, armed with the equivalent of 24 turbolasers, 24 ion cannons, 12 missile launchers, and 12 tractor beam projectors. It carried several landing ships and 500 battle droids, akin to starfighters. The *Shriwirr* was outfitted with a large entechment lab, where the Ssi-ruuk drew the life force from prisoners to power their equipment.

Interior decks of the *Shriwirr* had 5-meter-high ceilings to accommodate the Ssi-ruuk, along with countless crawlways and access tunnels for the enslaved P'w'eck, who were responsible for maintenance and day-to-day operations. A series of stun traps—lethal to humans—prevented P'w'eck from causing problems. The *Shriwirr* was single-handedly captured by Luke Skywalker after the Ssi-ruuk evacuated the ship rather than face his Force abilities in battle. The Rebel Alliance refitted the ship for combat duty and renamed it the *Sibwarra,* although techs tended to call it the *Flutie,* a derisive nickname the Bakurans used to describe the Ssi-ruuk.

**Shryne, Jula** A noted smuggler captain who plied the space lanes of the Outer Rim Territories aboard the *Drunk Dancer* during the final years of the Republic. Jula had a son, Roan, who had been chosen for training at the Jedi Temple on Coruscant. While the boy's father wanted to send Roan to Coruscant, Jula fought against losing her only son. When he went behind her back to contact the Jedi, Jula left him to start her life over again. After the Clone Wars, she encountered the adult Roan after his escape from Murkhana. Jula rescued Jedi survivors near Mossak and grudgingly gave in to Olee Starstone's plan to establish a deep-space link to the Jedi Archives. Jula accepted a mission on behalf of Cash Garrulan, this time traveling to Alderaan to secretly transport Senator Fang Zar to his homeworld of Sern Prime. However, their mission was discovered by the Empire, and Darth Vader was dispatched to intercept them. When Roan tried to block Vader's advance, the Dark Lord threw his lightsaber into the air, killing Zar on the spot and injuring Jula. She survived, but her son died in a struggle with Vader on Kashyyyk.

**Shryne, Roan** A native of the planet Weytta, this Jedi Master was dispatched to lead the fighting on Murkhana during the final stages of the Clone Wars. A couple of years older than Obi-Wan Kenobi, he had been considered one of the "Old Guard," along with Kenobi, Mace Windu, and Qui-Gon Jinn, but was never a candidate for membership on the Jedi Council. He lost his Master, Nat-Sem, and his first Padawan at the Battle of Geonosis, and lost his second Padawan shortly afterward during the Battle of Manari. When the signal to execute Order 66 was received on Murkhana, some of the clones refused to obey. Darth Vader himself was dispatched to Murkhana to eliminate Shryne, who escaped the planet and was unexpectedly reunited with his mother, Jula. Shryne tried to rescue Senator Fang Zar on Alderaan, but Vader killed Zar. Ultimately, Shryne confronted Darth Vader on Kashyyyk and perished in the duel that followed.

**Sh'tk'ith, Elder (Bluescale)** A blue-scaled bipedal reptilian, he led the Ssi-ruuvi Imperium invasion force at Bakura. The attack was to be only the first of many, part of a carefully orchestrated bid to enslave the spirits of humanoids and use their vital energy to power the Ssi-ruuvi war machine. Elder Sh'tk'ith, bearing the venerated nickname Bluescale, came from the planet Lwhekk beyond the galaxy's Outer Rim.

Two Ssi-ruuvi subspecies dominated Lwhekk. Both had long faces, tongues in their beak-like noses, eyes with triple eyelids, and long muscular tails. Sh'tk'ith's subspecies, which dominated the planet, had narrower faces and tiny blue scales. The other, which led the military, were sleek and covered with russet scales. They had a prominent black V on their foreheads. A third race, the P'w'eck, had drooping eyes and skin, short tails, and dull wits. They were enslaved by the dominant Ssi-ruuk.

*Fenn Shysa*

The Ssi-ruuk had discovered that their technique known as entechment, the forcible transferring of the electrical essences of beings to power their metallic battle droids, worked best with humanoids. They had captured and brainwashed one young human, Dev Sibwarra, to help them with his evolving Force powers.

Sh'tk'ith was leading the attack on the planet Bakura when Sibwarra located a much more powerful Force-user who could be even more helpful in the entechment process—Luke Skywalker. Luke, weakened by Emperor Palpatine's attacks aboard the second Death Star, was lured to the *Shriwirr,* but he was able to turn Sibwarra against his cruel masters. The young man managed to kill the Elder, although he was mortally wounded in the fighting that led to victory.

**Shuldene system** This system once boasted a water-covered world with abundant aquatic life, until an orbital shift froze the planet solid. The planet was left as smooth as glass, except where the carcasses of sea creatures poked up through the ice.

**Shushin, Yag** A Givin from Yag'Dhul who became a slave after he crash-landed on Dathomir. The Witches of Dathomir converted Shushin's star cruiser into a subterranean vehicle. When Quinlan Vos arrived on the world, he befriended Shushin, and the two helped uncover the mystery of Dathomir's Star Chambers. Shushin died after his ship was attacked by one of the witches.

**Shusugaunt** A planet on the edge of the Raioballo sector. The Shusugaunts were a squat, high-gravity species of spacefaring warriors. Shusugaunt braves conquered the worlds of Anx space and enslaved the Anx, driving them from their colony worlds to Gravlex Med. But their expansion ended there when the conquerors became dizzy and fell ill in the low gravity of Gravlex Med.

**shyarn** Light, curved swords favored by Cereans for traditional honor duels. Cereans trained to become masters at shyarn-ado schools. Shyarn blades were magnetically attracted when they struck each other.

**shyrack** This vicious creature was native to the Shyrack Caves of Korriban. A natural predator, the shyrack was the primary rival of the tuk'ata.

**Shyriiwook** The name Wookiees gave their language. Roughly translated, it meant "tongue of the tree people."

**Shysa, Fenn** A famous Mandalorian warrior and bounty hunter. Fenn Shysa was born in a small province off the coast of Mandalore's largest continent and worked as a local constable. With their destitute homeworld historically marginalized by the Old Republic, Shysa and his friend Tobbi Dala didn't hesitate to heed the renegade clone Spar (Alpha-Ø2) and his call for troops to resurrect the Mandalorian Supercommandos on behalf of the Separatists. When they returned home from the Clone Wars, their own people branded them outlaws and evildoers. Dala and Shysa were covertly enlisted to train elite special police units across Mandalore. Dala later gave his life ridding Mandalore of slavers, and Shysa rallied his people to join the Rebel Alliance and oppose the forces of Grand Admiral Miltin Takel and Lord Shadowspawn. Late in life, an aging Fenn Shysa gave his life on the planet Shogun to save Boba Fett.

**Sibwarra, Dev** Raised on the planet Chandrila as the son of a female Jedi apprentice, the young human and his mother fled to the isolated planet G'rho to escape Emperor Palpatine's Jedi Purges. But his mother was killed and Dev Sibwarra captured in a raid on the planet by the war-like Ssi-ruuk. The boy was sent to the Ssi-ruuvi home planet of Lwhekk, where his growing Force abilities were discovered. The Ssi-ruuk decided to brainwash young Dev and use him to scout the galaxy for humans, who made the best subjects for their process of entechment—the transfer of a person's vital energies to powerful metal battle droids.

Dev was taken in by the Ssi-ruu known as Master Firwirrung and helped him raid a number of human outposts in the galaxy. Firwirrung promised to personally entech Sibwarra, freeing him from fear and pain, to reward him for his help. The presence of Luke Skywalker during the invasion at Bakura was enough to erase much of Sibwarra's brainwashing. The young man helped Luke escape from the Ssi-ruuk, but was mortally wounded as he killed his cruel masters, including the invasion leader, Elder Sh'tk'ith, in revenge.

**Sickener** A training facility established for cloned soldiers on Kamino. The Sickener was so named because it comprised a huge field of trenches, each of which was filled with the entrails of dead animals and other decaying matter. The clones were forced to crawl, wade, or slither through the Sickener as part of a training regimen designed to ensure they didn't falter in actual combat. The instructors who drove their soldiers through the Sickener constantly reminded the soldiers that it was nothing compared with what they would encounter on an actual battlefield. Kal Skirata earned the trust and respect of the clone commandos he trained by going through the Sickener first, proving that he wouldn't put his clones through any hardship that he wasn't willing to endure himself.

**Sicko (CT-1127/549)** A clone trooper pilot who transported Omega Squad to an ambush of a Separatist vessel in the Tynnan sector during the Clone Wars. He did not survive the mission.

**Sic-six** Members of this intelligent arachnid species from the planet Sisk were hunters who used advanced technology to capture prey.

*Darth Sidious confronts Jedi Masters.*

Sic-six had black trisectioned bodies ranging from 1.2 to 2.1 meters long covered by a hard, chitinous carapace. They had eight six-jointed legs, eight eyes, and posterior spinnerets to make webs.

**Sidbam, Teak** A native of Ando and a frequent patron of the Mos Eisley cantina. Despite belonging to the flipper-handed subspecies of Aqualish, Teak Sidbam was often mistaken for the finger-handed Aqualish Ponda Baba.

**Sidi Driss Inn** A luxurious hotel in Anchorhead on Tatooine in the early years of the New Republic.

**Sidious, Darth** The Sith name taken by Palpatine. The Sith Order, in hiding for a millennium, had awaited the birth of one who was powerful enough to return the Order to prominence. Darth Sidious was the fulfillment of that prophecy, capable of exacting the Sith's revenge on the Jedi for having nearly eradicated the practitioners of the dark side of the Force. Trained by Darth Plagueis, Sidious knew that the corrupt Republic and the complacent Jedi Order could be brought down by playing to the weakness inherent in both: their attachment to power. Sidious did not consider himself evil but rather a savior.

Darth Sidious trained Darth Maul, the violent and predatory warrior who killed Qui-Gon Jinn, and joined forces with the Trade Federation prior to the Battle of Naboo. He encouraged Nute Gunray and his officers to blockade Naboo, and later instructed them to launch a full invasion after Supreme Chancellor Valorum and Mace Windu sent two Jedi ambassadors to deal with the crisis. He also ordered the Trade Federation forces to kill the Jedi, dispatched Darth Maul to recapture Queen Amidala, and assured that the Senate would not respond to the Queen's pleas for help. After the death of Maul, Sidious recruited as his new apprentice Count Dooku, who took the Sith name Darth Tyranus. The two Sith worked together to launch the Clone Wars, with Dooku in charge of the Separatists and Sidious/Palpatine leading the Republic. This purely artificial war devastated the Jedi Order and weakened the will of the galaxy's citizens, making them long for a strong leader and a stable government. Sidious unleashed Order 66, causing the Republic's clone troops to turn on their Jedi generals. With the Jedi dead, Sidious had no need to continue his double identity. He was now the beloved Emperor Palpatine, who restored peace to the galaxy. (*See also* Palpatine.)

*Si-Di-Ri*

**Si-Di-Ri** This gold-scaled Tiss'shar was the president of the planetary government of Tiss'sharl during the height of the New Order. The loss of the first Death Star meant trouble for Si-Di-Ri and his people, since the Empire had recognized the threat of the Rebel Alliance and was doing everything it could to react. Among the many changes was lowering the price that was paid for Tiss'shar-built blaster cartridges, which were sold to TaggeCo for manufacture. When Darth Vader arrived to introduce Commander Demmings as the new Imperial Moff of the system, Si-Di-Ri survived an assassination attempt the same night. Unknown to his fellow Tiss'shar, however, was Si-Di-Ri's relationship with the Alliance. Through Senator Timi Rotramel, Si-Di-Ri had been secretly supplying Tiss'sharl technology to the Rebels. Vader then revealed he had been using Si-Di-Ri as a pawn in the larger game of flushing out rebellious Senators. In return for Si-Di-Ri's "assistance," Vader allowed him to live, and rescinded the latest price change for Tiss'sharl's blaster cartridges in recognition of Si-Di-Ri's continued loyalty to the Empire. Si-Di-Ri, however, could not maintain the ruse of loyalty, and resigned from the Tiss'sharl League as soon as Vader had left the planet.

**Sienar, Raith** A brilliant engineer responsible for founding Sienar Design Systems and building a number of fearsome starships used by the Sith and the Empire. Sienar was born around the same time as Wilhuff Tarkin, and the two grew up as friends on Coruscant. Raith was the son of Narro Sienar, and was part of a long line of industrialists who could trace their roots back to the warship producers of Empress Teta's Unification Wars. He was trained at the Rigovian Technical University. Instead of relying upon his family fortunes, he set off on his own and amassed his own fortune by age 20, when he returned to the Sienar family fold. Sienar spent a considerable time buying scrapped designs of his competitors, looking for new ideas that had failed for simple reasons, but which could be adjusted to his own uses.

Three years after the Battle of Naboo, Tarkin convinced Sienar to join him in an attempt to

*Darth Sidious faces off against Yoda.*

take control of the rogue planet Zonama Sekot and the organic starships manufactured there. Tarkin appointed Sienar a commander, and gave him a small fleet led by the *Admiral Korvin.* When the Zonama Sekot mission took a bad turn thanks to the intervention of Obi-Wan Kenobi and Anakin Skywalker, Tarkin attacked the planet, prompting its disappearance into hyperspace. Both Tarkin and Sienar were disgraced in the eyes of Supreme Chancellor Palpatine, but both worked to turn the loss to their own advantage. Tarkin took credit for one of Sienar's designs—the Expeditionary Battle Planetoid—which eventually became the first Death Star. Years later, Sienar developed the basic outline of the T.I.E. starfighter, which led to the TIE fighter and its follow-ups. Unfortunately for Sienar, his success created many jealous rivals, and it was believed that one of them arranged for his assassination at the height of the Galactic Civil War. Following his death, the company fell under the control of the Santhe family. From her headquarters on Lianna, Lady Valles Santhe kept SFS running even after the Empire's collapse at Endor.

**Sienar Fleet Systems** The company that manufactured the Empire's various TIE fighters and other craft, it had been known as Republic Sienar Systems. It also produced flight avionics and starship components.

**Sienar Intelligence Systems** A powerful droid-building arm of Santhe-Sienar that specialized in government contracts with an emphasis on filling Imperial orders. Sienar Intelligence Systems manufacured the E522 assassin droid and the scarab droid.

*Raith Sienar*

**Sienn'rha** A young Twi'lek girl, she was stolen from her family on Ryloth by Bib Fortuna, instructed in the art of dance, then presented as a gift to Jabba the Hutt along with the Twi'lek Oola. Rescued from Jabba's palace by Luke Skywalker, she was returned to her family. In gratitude to the Rebel Alliance, she gave a spectacular performance for Wedge Antilles and his Rogue Squadron pilots when they came to her planet seeking ryll kor. She offered to give Wedge a private dance, but he reluctantly declined her offer.

**Sifo-Dyas** The mysterious Jedi who was said to have placed the order for the clone army grown on Kamino. Sifo-Dyas was a close friend of Count Dooku, and knew of Dooku's dissatisfaction with the Republic. Dooku later murdered Sifo-Dyas, both to cover his tracks and to demonstrate his allegiance to the cause of the Sith. Sifo-Dyas's body was kept in stasis on Serenno, and Dooku used it for a blood transfusion for General Grievous. Dooku also gave Sifo-Dyas's lightsaber to Grievous.

*Sifo-Dyas*

**Sif-Uwana** A planet where the inhabitants were reputed to be very casual with their money and management style. Mara Jade once visited while on business for the Emperor, and the smuggler Talon Karrde posed as the chief purchasing agent for the Sif-Uwana Council while on a mission to Varonat.

**Sigil crystal** Mined in the Sigil system, this crystal was a costly but valued addition to a lightsaber. It produced a fiercely bright beam that seared on contact, inflicting great damage.

**signaling unit** *See* comlight.

**Sikili, Sass** This Verpine negotiator worked as an intermediary between Verpine-held corporations and other business leaders during the years following the Swarm War. It was Sass Sikili who openly warned corporations based on Murkhana that their export of small-unit comlinks was in violation of existing trade agreements at the height of the Corellia–GA War. His appeals to the Galactic Alliance for intervention went largely unheeded, forcing Sikili and his superiors to pursue an alliance with the Mandalorians. Sikili met personally with Boba Fett, who accepted the basic outline of the agreement.

***Silaban*** A CR90 corvette in the fleet that defended the planet Corellia during its war with the Galactic Alliance. It was the *Silaban* that tried to intercept the *Love Commander* and the *Pulsar Skate* when the two ships attempted to flee Corellia. The *Silaban*'s crew found that they were no match for the combined firepower of the two fugitives, especially when Corran Horn and Wedge Antilles arrived in X-wings to serve as escorts.

**Silais** A Twi'lek politician who, just before the Battle of Naboo, attempted to convince Cerea's leaders to join the Galactic Republic and adopt modern technology. Silais viewed the peaceful planet's many natural resources as a source of untapped wealth. His efforts were thwarted by the Jedi Knight Ki-Adi-Mundi. He later gloated when Ki-Adi-Mundi was forced to use Republic technology in a quest to rescue his daughter.

**silan** A menacing and deadly creature that resembled a gigantic grub, rumored to be strong with the dark side of the Force. A silan had a radially symmetrical face dominated by mouths, which contained yet more mouths, each lined with incredibly sharp and pointed teeth. Silans continued to grow as they aged, and thus elderly individuals could be enormous. Because silans were extremely rare, they were considered mythical creatures by many. Qui-Gon Jinn and 13-year-old Obi-Wan Kenobi slew a silan on the planet Arorua about 12 years before the Battle of Naboo.

**Silas** A Mandalorian serving under Jango Fett. Ten years before the Battle of Geonosis, Silas was captured by Count Dooku. Silas revealed how the Mandalorians were ambushed by the Death Watch on Korda VI, and how Jango Fett took Jaster Mereel's place as leader.

**Sileen** A Mistryl Shadow Guard, she was involved in the botched transport of the Hammertong device to the Empire.

***Silencer-7*** The largest of the cloned Emperor's World Devastators, it led the assault on Mon Calamari. At 3,200 meters long and 1,500 meters tall, it was larger than an Imperial Star

Destroyer and had a crew of 25,000. *Silencer-7* had 125 heavy turbolasers, 200 blaster cannons, 80 proton missile tubes, 15 ion cannons, and 15 tractor beam projectors. The key to the defeat of the monstrous World Devastators was Palpatine's fear that they could be turned against him, which led him to create a system that allowed him to seize control. Luke Skywalker provided Palpatine's control signals to R2-D2, who shut down the World Devastators during the Battle of Mon Calamari, allowing New Republic forces to destroy the helpless planet smashers.

**Silentium** A mysterious living droid species believed to have originated in another galaxy. A civilization of starfish-shaped aliens built the original droids in their image, until a radiation storm exterminated them. Their droids lived on, using manufacturing plants to make "children" and developing a culture centered on the prime numbers of 5, 7, and 11. The wisest among them built new spherical bodies measuring 50 kilometers in diameter, as the circle was considered the holiest of shapes. Others wore bodies in the forms of pentagrams or heptagons. The Silentium soon found their orderly kingdom challenged by the Abominor, a droid society of asymmetry and bedlam. The two droid powers fought a war, crushing the galaxy's dominant organic species in the crossfire until the ignored organics fought back and forced the machines to flee. The Silentium settled in the Unknown Regions, reverting to a culture of excessive conservatism. Eventually growing bored, they built Vuffi Raa and others like him to gather fresh information from the greater galaxy.

**Silizzar, Gurion** After the notorious Dr. Evazan poisoned Silizzar's family, Gurion tried to kill the quack in revenge on the planet Ando. But the human Silizzar died on the rocky cliffs surrounding the doctor's castle laboratory.

**Sil'Lume asteroid belt** A backrocket system that was home to numerous prospecting and mining operations. Luke Skywalker, on a scouting mission for the Rebel Alliance shortly after the Battle of Yavin, considered Sil'Lume a possible site for a Rebel base.

Simus

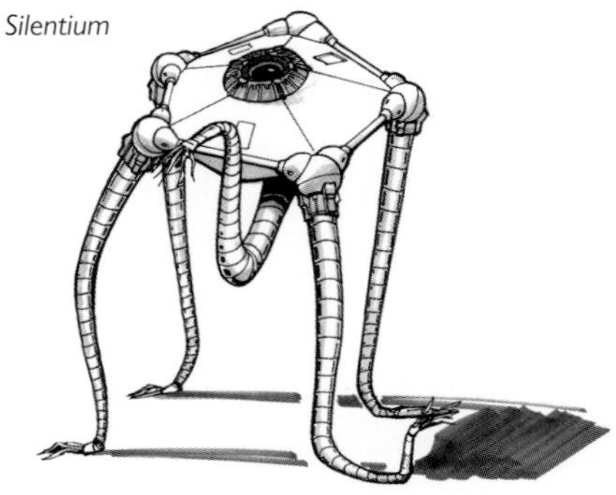
Silentium

**silooth** A huge armored, beetle-like creature mutated to the size of a bantha, the silooth was first utilized by the Sith Empire in the Battle of Kalsunor, long before the Golden Age of the Sith.

***Silver Egg*** The private ship of smuggling kingpin Nandreeson, it was specially outfitted for the needs of an amphibian species and included sunken pools in many of its quarters.

***Silver Speeder*** A sleek racing landspeeder, it was once owned by Boba Fett. The bounty hunter outfitted the *Silver Speeder* with such nonstandard equipment as cutting lasers, magnetic harpoons, and a chainsaw shredder.

**Silver Station** A hidden resistance outpost, it drifted near the Dragonflower Nebula in the Doldur sector. Some 400 meters in length, it consisted of a central cube surrounded by many interconnected cylinders. Resistance leader Una Poot used Silver Station to supply seven Rebel cells in the surrounding sector. Just after the Battle of Yavin, the young heiress Tinian I'att and her companions came to Silver Station to meet with Poot. Although I'att helped foil a Ranat plot to blow up the station, most of its inhabitants were forced to flee when Imperial forces arrived and took control of the outpost. It was here that I'att first met and saved the life of her future partner, the Wookiee bounty hunter Chenlambec.

**Simms, Merrick (Blue Leader)** The commander of Blue Squadron during the Battle of Yavin. He helped train Rookie One on Tatooine where he flew as Green Leader. Merrick believed life should be entertaining and could think of no more enjoyable place to be than engaged in combat with the Empire.

**Simonelle** An Ingoian outlaw tech involved with Massad Thrumble in the construction of the human replica droid Guri.

**Simoom** A large desert on the far side of Endor's Forest Moon, it was inhabited by a species known as Phlogs.

**Simus** A Sith warlord who attempted to become a Dark Lord of the Sith by challenging his chief competitor, Marka Ragnos, to a battle more than 5,100 years before the Battle of Yavin. Simus was decapitated during the brawl, but he used his knowledge of Sith magic to sustain his life. With his head encased in a crystal sphere, he served as an adviser to Ragnos. After Ragnos's death more than a century later, Simus became the mediator among Sith warlords vying for rulership. He was eventually betrayed by Naga Sadow, who crushed the Sith warlord's life-support crystal and killed the wizened magician instantly.

**sin-bullets** The name given to the gullet-stones coughed up by Vashan bodhis as part of an unusual religious ceremony that took place every midwinter at Inicus Mont on the moon of Mina.

**Sing, Aurra** An infamous bounty hunter who was once a student of the Force. Born to Aunuanna on Nar Shaddaa, Aurra Sing was taken from the moon by the Jedi known as the Dark Woman and trained on Coruscant, where she acquired the nickname Nashtah for a six-legged predator from Dra III. Sing was later captured on Ord Namurt by a group of Sennex pirates, who later apprenticed her to Wallanooga the Hutt. The pirates told Sing that the Dark Woman had abandoned her, and Sing hated the Jedi fiercely from that point on. Wallanooga apprenticed her to some Anzati assassins, who implanted a Rhen-Orm biocomputer in her skull to augment her mental capacity. After learning that she could use her minimal contact with the Force to hunt down others, she returned to Wallanooga, assassinated him, and set out to become a bounty hunter.

Aurra Sing

She was noted for her ability to hunt and kill Jedi Knights, and she had several lightsabers in her trophy case to mark her prowess. Shortly before the Battle of Naboo, Sing was retained to locate and kill the Jedi Master

Sharad Hett. During the Clone Wars, she teamed with the orphaned Boba Fett to drain money from the Aargau banking account of the late Jango Fett. She also accepted a job from Devaronian Senator Vien'sai'malloc to protect the Separatist base on Devaron from attack, which brought her into conflict with Aayla Secura. Sing was captured by the Jedi and sentenced to imprisonment on Oovo IV. The lightsabers she had collected were returned to the Jedi Order for distribution to students of the dead. Sing managed to escape, and after the Clone Wars seemingly emerged in the employ of Darth Vader on a mission continuing the Empire's purge of the Jedi.

Some 10 years later, still active at the age of 75, Aurra Sing was hired by Lady Morwan and the Heritage Council to assassinate the Queen Mother, Tenel Ka. Her attempt was thwarted by the Hapan Royal Guard, and she managed to escape with Han and Leia Organa Solo, who had been on Hapes trying to warn the Queen of the assassination. They traveled to Telkur Station, where Sing was ordered by Lady Morwan to cut off her hunt for the Queen Mother and concentrate on eliminating the Chume'da, Allana. She nearly reached the child, but Allana managed to inject her with a chemical that rendered the bounty hunter immobile.

**Singing Mountain Clan** A group of the Witches of Dathomir. Its members followed the light side of the Force.

***Singularity*** An Imperial I Star Destroyer that served as the command ship of the Emperor's Hand known as Blackhole. The *Singularity* was coated in a stygium-triprismatic polymer that made it difficult to detect with sensor equipment.

**Sinidic** An aide to Drom Guldi, baron-administrator of the Kelrodo-Ai Gelatin Mines. Sinidic was a small, nervous man with gray-blond hair and faint wrinkles across his skin, as if it had crumpled with a thousand pressure cracks. He was with his boss on a big-game hunting expedition on Hoth when their prey—wampa ice creatures—turned on them and killed them.

**Sinn, Mirith** The leader of the Rebel cell on Phaeda approximately seven years after the Battle of Endor. Mirith Sinn grew up on Nex Peron, a world of farming collectives. Always attracted to greatness, she married a pro-Rebellion farmer who died in a conflict with Imperials. Sinn swore at that moment that she would fight the Empire, and she joined the Rebellion, becoming a commander. Assigned to the resistance on Phaeda, Sinn kept her troops' activities hidden from the Empire, engaging mostly in secret hit-and-run and ambushing tactics that would not tie these actions to a Rebel organization. They began construction of a Rebel stronghold in a mountain away from Phaeda's spaceports, where they could monitor Imperial activities without being discovered. Upon learning of former Royal Guardsman Kir Kanos's presence on Phaeda, Sin offered him protection with her troops. Her second in command, Sish Sadeet, had suspicions about Kanos, and Sinn soon learned that Kanos was wanted by Carnor Jax, leader of Imperial space. Captured and tortured by the Imperials, Sinn refused to reveal Kanos's wherabouts, until Jax ordered the bombardment of her base at Collo Fauale Pass. When New Republic forces attacked the Empire at Phaeda, Sinn and Sadeet took Kanos's ship to Yinchorr, where Jax had gone searching for Kanos. Hoping to capture Jax alive, they tried to intervene in the battle between the two guardsmen, but Jax and Sadeet both died at the hands of Kanos.

Mirith Sinn

Soon after, Mirith Sinn went to the criminal boss Grappa the Hutt and offered her services to him. She asked him to track down Kir Kanos so she could kill him. This was, however, only a cover story; her real mission was to spy on Grappa's organization to find evidence that his employees were hijacking New Republic supply ships. But Sinn's plan was discovered by the Hutt, who gave her to the Zanibar species. She was taken to the Zanibar homeworld and rescued by Kir Kanos and Tav Kennede, a recent Rebel recruit. Sinn then led an Alliance raid on a Black Sun cloning facility on the planet Smarck, which she had learned of while in Grappa's service. But when she heard of Kanos's capture by the Zanibar, she and the other Rebels raided Grappa's palace on Genon and rescued him. Together Sinn and Kanos stormed the Imperial Council headquarters, capturing the surviving council members.

**Sinya** A chalk-skinned Twi'lek, she served as Darnada's personal bodyguard prior to the Battle of Naboo. She had a scar running across her left eye and wore the traditional lekku wrappings of a dancer. Sinya dismissed Darth Maul as nothing but a common assassin when he arrived on Darnada's space station to eliminate any being that had contact with Hath Monchar. She soon learned that Maul was much more when the Sith Lord eliminated everyone on the station.

Darth Sion

**Sion, Darth** One of the Sith Lords who appeared in the wake of the Jedi Civil War nearly 4,000 years before the Battle of Yavin. Darth Sion's body had been torn apart and knitted back together into a patchwork of mutilated flesh. This left him in eternal pain, his broken body held together only by his hatred and the power of the dark side. Sion was exceedingly difficult to kill, because his mastery over his own body lent him supernatural vitality. Sion led a sect of Sith assassins sent to wipe out the Jedi Order.

**Sionia** The homeworld of the Sionian Skup, a human-like species with small, closely spaced eyes, brittle hair, and skin the color of dianoga cheese.

**siphoning balloon** A form of gas-collection system used by Tibanna tappers and other thieves to illegally acquire spin-sealed Tibanna gas. Each balloon was equipped with a small but powerful pump that could extract the gas from a processing facility. Individual balloons could be tethered together from a distance, allowing the thieves to obtain the gas without being noticed. This was especially true on cloud-covered gas giants like Bespin, where atmospheric conditions often led to minimal visibility.

**Sirak** This male Zabrak was one of three members of his species who trained at the Sith Academy on Korriban in the years leading up to the Battle of Ruusan. An arrogant individual with a strong connection to the dark side, Sirak was the strongest and most powerful of the three Zabrak. The other two, Llokay and Yevra, looked up to him as their leader. Sirak began training under Lord Qordis some 20 years prior to the arrival of Dessel, and many at the Sith Academy believed that he had the potential to become the Sith'ari. Indeed, some felt that Sirak had achieved his potential after soundly defeating Bane in the lightsaber training ring. After Bane was ostracized from the Academy, Sirak was once again challenged in the training ring. This time, however, Bane had been training in secret, and drew upon the dark side of the Force to assail Sirak with blow after blow. Angry and jealous, Sirak plotted his revenge on Bane, confronting him in the Academy archives. Bolstered by his seeming advantage, Sirak attacked Bane, but fell under a swift slash of Bane's lightsaber.

**Siralt, Moff** This man served on the Moff Council of the Imperial Remnant during the years following the Swarm War. Moff Siralt was one of many who assumed military roles when the council agreed to a deal with Jacen Solo and the Galactic Alliance. Under its terms, the Galactic Alliance would cede control of Borleias and Bilbringi in exchange for the support of the Imperial Navy during the Second Battle of Fondor. Siralt and the other Moffs were surprised when Solo was relieved of his command by Admiral Cha Niathal, after Solo broke away from the battle plan and started bombing Fondor's cities. Siralt openly questioned whether Solo could retain control of the Galactic Alliance given his actions at Fondor. After Pellaeon was assassinated by Tahiri Veila aboard the *Bloodfin,* Siralt and the other Moffs retreated to the ship's command center, where they hid until the ship was boarded by Boba Fett and his Mandalorian Supercommandos. Fett killed anyone who put up any resistance. Siralt was among the dead, as were the other Moffs who supported Moff Quille.

**Sirdar** A planet that was overrun with winged xendrites after the creatures were brought in to control the insect population.

**siringana** A species native to N'zoth. The siringana were as brutal as the Yevetha. Siringana were reptilian quadrupeds with a pair of scythe-like "arms" and a spiked tail.

**Sirln, Leesub** A humanlike Qiraash, she was enslaved as a child. Leesub Sirln had limited precognition powers, and Imperial High Inquisitor Tremayne declared her a Force adept. To avoid imprisonment or death, she escaped and hid for years in Mos Eisley on Tatooine.

*Leesub Sirln*

**Siro, Isolde** A purple-haired criminal who was recruited by Lando's Commandos to help fight pirates that used TIE interceptors to ambush supply convoys. She objected to the involvement of Imperial Air Marshal Von Asch. While engaging the pirates, Von Asch took a blaster shot intended for Siro. Gravely wounded, he told her he believed that she had a greater destiny to fulfill.

**Sirpar** An arid, heavy-gravity world, it was used by the Empire as a training outpost for Imperial Army soldiers. The large planet was protected by three orbiting defensive satellites. Sirpar was home to the timid Eklaad, quadruped beings with prehensile snouts and tough armored hides. The 1.5 million Eklaad lived in tribes ruled by hereditary chieftains and had not advanced beyond stone-age technology.

**Sirrakuk** A young female Wookiee nicknamed Sirra, she was the niece of Chewbacca and the younger sister of Lowbacca, a trainee at the Jedi academy.

**Sirty (CT-36/732)** The first ARC trooper to face a JK-series security droid in a combat demonstration, he was soundly defeated in 20 seconds. Nonetheless, he was recruited by ARC trooper Nate (Jangotat) for a group accompanying Obi-Wan Kenobi and Kit Fisto to Ord Cestus to investigate the production of the droids. Sirty helped Fisto and Nate train the commandos of the Desert Wind terrorist group.

**Sisar Run** A trade route that cut through the heart of the Periphery, a relatively desolate region skirting the Outer Rim Territories and Hutt space. The Sisar Run served a number of major routes that fed into Nal Hutta and other prominent Hutt trade worlds. At its opposite terminal, the Sisar Run linked to the heavily traveled Salin Corridor. As a result of its proximity to Hutt space, it was often assumed the Sisar Run was controlled by one of the Hutt lords rather than the reclusive Black Sun. Sriluur was the most important planet along the Sisar Run.

**Sisar Runners** A group of resistance fighters led by Embra the Hutt during the Yuuzhan Vong War.

**Sisk** A planet that orbited a red dwarf star of the same name, it was home to the arachnid species Sic-six. The star Sisk was once an orange star but underwent a partial atomic collapse, cooling the planet Sisk and turning it from warm and lush to cool and barren. Sic-six were highly antisocial, preventing the formation of any government or mass production, although their technology was complex. Sic-six were valued throughout the galaxy because the poison-filled bites from their fangs were intoxicating to most species.

**Sith** A term describing both an ancient species and the tradition that emerged in opposition to the Jedi, using the dark side of the Force. The Sith species was native to the planet Korriban, and lived isolated from the rest of the Republic for many millennia. Their history could be traced back to a point some 100,000 years before the onset of the Galactic Civil War. As a people, they were characterized by dark, red skin, cranial horns, and long bony chins. Some were slaves, others warriors, and the highest caste of all were the magicians. Because they lived in a remote sector of the galaxy, the Sith were unknown until a group of dark side Jedi outcasts discovered their existence following the Hundred-Year Darkness during the Second Great Schism. The Sith regarded the visitors as gods. Over the millennia, the two groups intermingled, until very little pure Sith blood remained. The Sith wrote expansive volumes on the control and use of the dark side, and described incredible manifestations of power. Much of the Sith lore was hidden on various worlds when the ancient Jedi Knights first sought to eradicate the Sith. Some was stored on Korriban, some on the moon Yavin 4. The last remaining true-blooded Sith were wiped out by Exar Kun during the Great Sith War, when he stole their life energy in an effort to defend his fortress on Yavin 4 against the forces of the Old Republic.

The Sith lived on through their evil teachings, and the term soon became synonymous with the dark side cult. The Sith rose again during Darth Revan's Jedi Civil War from 3,960 to 3,956 years before the Battle of Yavin, until Darth Ruin founded a new Sith brotherhood 2,000 years before the Galactic Civil War. Ruin's followers made war against the Jedi over the subsequent millennium, driving the Jedi Order to the brink of extinction until the Sith suffered a crushing defeat at the Battle of Ruusan. One Sith Lord remained: Darth Bane. He swore that the Sith would never again vanish from the galaxy, but also made certain that they never grew beyond their means. He established a rigid code, the Rule of Two, by which there could only be a single Sith Lord and a single Sith apprentice. When the Sith Lord finally died, or was murdered, his apprentice was promoted and allowed to take his own student. The Sith continued to use lightsabers as their primary weapons, based on synthetic crystals that produced red blades. The pairing of Master and apprentice continued for many centuries until Darth Plagueis rose to power. Plagueis was one of the most powerful Sith Masters, and was believed to have found a way to control midi-chlorians to create life. However, Plagueis's own apprentice, Darth Sidious, chose to kill his Master and take his "rightful" place as Sith Lord. Sidious then trained Darth Maul and hoped to take control of the galaxy by bringing the Republic down from the inside by using his alternative identity as Senator Palpatine of Naboo. When Darth Maul was destroyed by Obi-Wan Kenobi during the Battle of Naboo, Sidious found the charismatic former Jedi, Count Dooku, to be a worthy replacement. Just a few years later, Sidious destroyed the Jedi Order by orchestrating

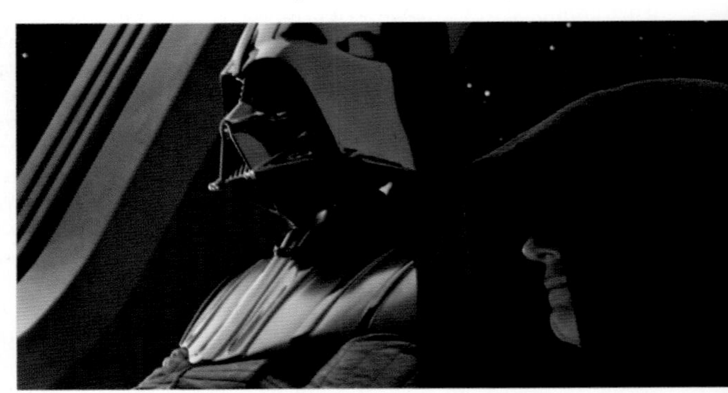

*Sith Lord Darth Sidious (right) and his Sith apprentice, Darth Vader (left)*

the Clone Wars, then assumed the title of Emperor and established Darth Vader as his new apprentice. Vader ultimately killed his Master, weakening the Sith Order until Darth Krayt slowly began to rebuild it to its former strength.

Sith Lord Darth Krayt (left) abandoned the Rule of Two in rebuilding the Sith Order.

**Sith Academy** A training facility established by the Sith on the planet Korriban during the buildup to the Great Sith War. The facility produced multitudes of soldiers and warriors imbued with the dark side of the Force. In the wake of the Great Sith War, the Korriban Academy was destroyed, as the Galactic Senate deemed it illegal to use the Sith arts. However, when the Brotherhood of Darkness rose to power, it reestablished the Sith Academy. Satellite facilities on planets like Gamorr and Honoghr trained those individuals with limited ability, while others with more promise were sent to Ryloth and Umbara. Eventually, the Sith Academy on Korriban also was reformed, under the guidance of Lord Qordis, several years prior to the Battle of Ruusan.

**Sith acolyte** A class of Force-using adherents of the Sith tradition. Acolytes were dark sorcerers and priests, practitioners of living sacrifices and base deception. They came to the Sith tradition from the ranks of Force adepts, dark side devotees, and, in ancient times, the Sith species itself.

**Sith amulet** Medallions created through Sith alchemy through which the spirits of dead Dark Lords could speak to the living. Exar Kun and Ulic Qel-Droma each wore amulets and were visited by past Dark Lords, who instructed them in the ways of the dark side. Sith amulets could focus and amplify the power of their bearers, and were also built in the form of crystal-studded gauntlets.

Sith Holocron

**Sith apprentice** The lesser half of the two-person Sith pairing established under the Rule of Two. Each Sith apprentice secretly believed in his superiority over his Master and watched for the time to cut down the Dark Lord of the Sith and take his place. A Sith apprentice often was vicious and aggressive. Most despised the Jedi, and were eager to test their skills against their rivals.

**Sith'ari** This was the name used by the ancient Sith to describe a perfect being who would rise to power and bring balance to the Force. According to prophecy, the Sith'ari would rise up and destroy the Sith, but in the process would return to lead the Sith and make them stronger than ever before. The first being known to have carried the title was the ancient King Adas, who unified the Sith tribes on Korriban some 3,000 years before the formation of the Republic. After Adas's death at the hands of Rakatan invaders, many pretenders claimed to hold the title of Sith'ari, but none of them was able to restore the Sith to power until the discovery of a man named Dessel. Dessel was trained on Korriban during the years leading up to the Battle of Ruusan; he eventually became Darth Bane, the man who reinvented the Sith and established the Rule of Two.

**Sith Destroyer (*Leviathan*-class)** An ancient beak-shaped Sith capital ship used in the fleet led by Darth Revan and Darth Malak.

**Sith energy shield** A forearm band that protected against electrical, energy, and sonic attacks. Though efficient, the units needed to be replaced often—they burned out after repeated activation.

**Sith Enforcer hovertank** During the Clone Wars, Sith dark acolytes piloted specially modified hovertanks equipped with supercharged blaster cannons and twin missile bays. Their reinforced armor and extra plating made them formidable opponents. Mace Windu tackled three tanks at once on Geonosis.

**Sith fighter** A model of starfighter used during Darth Revan and Darth Malak's war against the Old Republic. Sith fighters were tightly packed in cargo bays, and a large force could be delivered by a single mother ship. Launched the instant their carrier left hyperspace, Sith fighters were powered by a prototype twin ion drive system of Rakatan design. The dual engines and thrusters granted power and maneuverability almost to the point of instability, and as a result much of the central chassis of the ship was devoted to managing the reactor core. Little concern was given to the comfort of the Sith pilot, and only the most essential subsystems were included. When docked or cruising long distances, the wings were folded inward and weapons systems went offline to conserve energy. In combat, the wings unfolded and blaster cannons powered up at each outward edge. This broad attack area allowed a small number of ships to produce a devastating crossfire.

**Sith Holocron** A recording receptacle that contained the teachings and histories of the Sith for more than 100,000 years. Its complete secrets were accessible only to a Dark Lord of the Sith. The holocron was captured from the Sith by Master Odan-Urr during the fall of the Sith Empire nearly 5,000 years before the Galactic Civil War.

**Sith–Imperial War** A conflict between the new Empire and the Galactic Alliance that occurred more than 100 years after the Battle of Yavin. The main conflict began in the wake of the Ossus Project, when many planets that were to be restored by the terraforming techniques of the Yuuzhan Vong were subjected to strange and dangerous alterations. The Jedi Order believed that the Ossus Project had been sabotaged, but could not identify the culprits. The Moff Council rose up in anger at the Galactic Alliance's lack of response, and forged the Treaty of Anaxes, formally declaring war on the Alliance. When agents of Darth Krayt's Sith Order appeared in support of the Imperial factions, the Jedi realized that the reclamation efforts had been sabotaged by the Sith. During the battles, the combined forces of the Empire and the Sith attacked many Alliance targets. After three years of hostilities, the Galactic Alliance surrendered. The Jedi Order refused to be absorbed into the Imperial Knights and abandoned their Temple on Coruscant before retreating to Ossus, where the Sith massacred the survivors.

**Sith Infiltrator (*Scimitar*)** Darth Maul's personal starship. Designed by Raith Sienar and based on an armed courier developed by Sienar's Advanced Projects Laboratory,

Sith Infiltrator

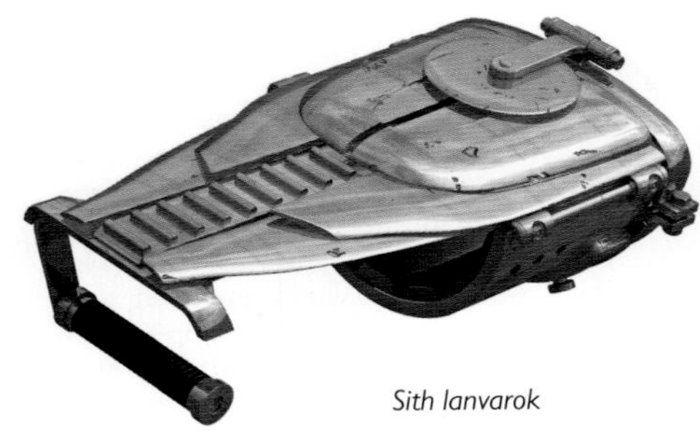

Sith lanvarok

the Infiltrator's most impressive feature was its cloaking device. The device was powered by rare and expensive stygium crystals found only on the volatile Outer Rim planet Aeten II. When activated, the cloaking device effectively concealed the Infiltrator from all sensors. The Infiltrator's weapons system included six laser cannons, and it was propelled through space by a powerful ion drive. Its Sienar SSDS 11-A hyperdrive provided only modest hyperspace travel speed. Maul employed his Infiltrator to conduct missions of espionage and assassination, and stocked it with a wide range of equipment including probe droids and a Sith speeder.

**Sith lanvarok** A short-range weapon worn on the forearm and designed to hurl a flurry of thin but solid disks in an unpredictable "spray" pattern. According to Sith legend, the lanvarok was developed by the ancient Sith as a hunting weapon. The mutated Massassi of Yavin 4 used a more primitive version of this weapon: a two-handed polearm that required brute strength rather than mechanical action or the Force to launch the disks. Coupled with the Sith's ability to wield the Force to guide the disks to their target, the lanvarok was an extremely effective weapon.

Sith probe droid

**Sith Marauder** The second lowest rank given to the members of the Brotherhood of Darkness. These loyal individuals had a limited connection to the Force and were trained as Sith warriors, taught to channel their emotions into a mindless, raging battle fury. Through the use of the dark side, Sith Lords could further transform these individuals into weapons of destruction against the Jedi Knights and the soldiers of the Republic.

**Sith poison** A toxin that weakened a person's resistance to the dark side of the Force. Ulic Qel-Droma was injected with Sith poison during his ill-conceived mission to infiltrate the Krath.

**Sith power gauntlets** Forearm-based devices that used uncomfortable bursts of repulsorlift energy to assist movement. Based on stolen Eriadu designs, they were rarely seen outside of Sith possession.

**Sith probe droid ("Dark Eye")** A compact droid utilized by the Sith warrior Darth Maul to spy on his enemies. Arakyd Industries' DRK-1 "Dark Eye" probe droid was equipped with advanced sensors, powerful scanners, and miniature repulsorlift devices. The droids could also be outfitted with a number of weapons. Easily controlled from afar by a wristband comlink, Sith probe droids were ideal for locating specific targets.

**Sith regenerator** This unusual cybernetic implant was developed by the ancient Sith many millennia before the Battle of Yavin. The regenerator stimulated cell replication in the user's body, allowing wounds to be healed quickly and easily. It was designed for use by spies operating for extended periods behind enemy lines, where medical treatment was not available.

**Sith sarcophagus** A traditional Sith burial chamber. These typically contained the physical remains of a Sith sorcerer, but could also be the final resting place of the spirit. One example was the tomb of Freedon Nadd on Dxun.

**Sith Shadows** A band of mercenaries led by a zealous Force-wielder named Mellichae. Once considered for a position as one of the Emperor's Hands, Mellichae was crippled by Darth Vader after his loyalty to the Emperor came into question. He formed his own band of followers, the Sith Shadows, consisting of smugglers, pirates, outlaws, and murderers. No one ever left their employ alive.

**Sith Speeder** *See Bloodfin.*

**Sith sword** Weapons that predated the lightsabers of the latter-day Sith. The blades on a Sith sword were made of alchemically altered metal that never became dull. These swords were able to deflect blaster fire and lightsabers.

Sith sword

**Sith torture mask** A Sith interrogation device used on Jedi to disrupt their concentration and thus hinder their abilities in the Force. Obi-Wan Kenobi was fitted with a Sith torture mask during his imprisonment in Asajj Ventress's fortress.

Sith torture mask

**Sith trooper** The rank-and-file soldiers that made up Darth Revan and Darth Malak's army during their war against the Old Republic. The majority of the battalions comprised traitorous Republic forces. Only the strong were granted acceptance into the ranks of the Sith army; those judged too weak were put to an ignoble death. Traitors were welcomed into the ranks, but a level of fear was quickly established to make certain they were not so quick to change sides again. A Sith trooper was perceived as an extension of the Sith, and even in close combat opponents saw only the cold faceplate of the helmet, never the soldier inside. Elite Sith troopers wore red armor.

**Sith War, The** *See* Great Sith War.

**Sith war behemoth** A massive creature used by the Sith Empire to transport troops, carry heavy weapons, and break through enemy fortifications. War behemoths had tough, leathery skin, shaggy fur covering their necks and bodies, and a hard shell protecting their backs. They also possessed long, curving tusks and a series of horns that projected upward from their heads. Originally natives of the icy planet Khar Delba, war behemoths were peaceful herd creatures that used their long tusks only to defend themselves against predators. When the Sith Lords found these creatures, they transported many of them to harsh jungle worlds and used Sith alchemy to turn them into violent omnivores. Centuries-long breeding programs produced an easily trained species that responded well to certain commands. A program of standard command coding allowed Sith troops to control war behemoths in combat.

**Sith warbird** A domesticated creature pressed into military service in the Sith Empire as a mount for heavy artillery. The flightless bird stood 6 meters tall and was approximately 10 meters long. It came from the frigid mountains of Khar Delba.

**Sith wyrm** An enormous reptile–insect hybrid. On Yavin 4, Exar Kun was nearly sacrificed to a Sith wyrm, which the Massassi regarded as a god. The Sith wyrm was once a larval space slug that had attached itself to the hull of Naga Sadow's battleship en route to Yavin. Sadow, failing to tame the creature and seeing little other use for it, chose to mutate it into a colossal monster.

**Siva, Den** A Nagai soldier who served as Lumiya's chief aide in the months following the Battle of Endor. He was also the advance scout of the Nagai invasion fleet, which had allied itself with Lumiya in the hope of taking control of the galaxy from the Alliance of Free Planets. He requested that the Zeltron female Dani be turned over to him, so that he could study her physiology and learn what he could of the

Den Siva

Zeltron species. He also became enamored of Dani, a feeling he had never quite experienced before for an alien being. When Kiro rescued Dani, Den Siva set out to recover her. Later, on Zeltros, it was discovered that Siva had betrayed the Nagai to the Tofs so that he could see Dani again. Ultimately Siva surrendered himself to Leia Organa.

**Sivrak, Lak** A hunter and a scout for the Empire, this Shistavanen Wolfman from the Uvena system grew to despise the Emperor's New Order and Imperial tyranny and atrocities. Lak Sivrak refused to turn in a colony of Rebel Alliance sympathizers, and the Empire targeted him for elimination. After getting the best of a stormtrooper squad sent to kill him, he fled to the backrocket Mos Eisley spaceport on Tatooine. There, in a small cantina, he fell in love with Dice Ibegon, a Florn Lamproid. After helping several Rebels on Tatooine, Sivrak officially joined the Alliance and fought in the Battle of Hoth. A year later, Sivrak was piloting an X-wing fighter in the fight against the second Death Star. He took out a number of TIE fighters but was hit and died when his X-wing crashed onto the surface of Endor's Forest Moon.

Sith wyrm

**Sivron, Tol** Tol Sivron was one of the five members of a Twi'lek head clan, a group that ran community affairs on Ryloth. As part of Twi'lek tradition, when one member of the clan died, the remaining four were exiled to the planet's hot desert, where they were left to die as a new head clan took office. But Sivron's entire clan was young and vigorous, and he expected to reap the benefits of his position for many years. He was pampered and spoiled by the benefits of power. The good life lasted barely a year, however, because one of his colleagues lost his balance inspecting a deep-grotto construction project and impaled himself on a stalagmite. After exile to the desert, Sivron convinced his three remaining colleagues that they could eke out an existence in an uninhabited cave. But Sivron killed them there, taking their meager possessions to increase his own chances for survival. Soon after, he discovered an Imperial Navy training base and met Imperial officer Tarkin—and his Imperial career began. Sivron was sent to Tarkin's top-secret weapons development facility, the Maw Installation, where he worked for years as chief scientist and director. Sivron decided to pilot the prototype Death Star in an assault against Kessel to test its weaponry, and later to defend the Maw Installation itself. However, his skills were meager, and the Maw Installation and the prototype battle station itself were doomed.

**Sixxa, Sol** A ruthless Mere pirate on Maramere. Loreli Ro hired the mercenary Nym to put an end to Sol Sixxa's reign of terror. Sixxa battled Nym's forces from his cutter *Revenant* until the Trade Federation intervened. He was presumed dead but later contacted Nym with an offer to join forces against the Trade Federation. Prior to the Battle of Geonosis, Sol Sixxa led the ground assaults during Nym's battle with the forces of Cavik Toth.

**Skahtul** A Barabel bounty hunter, she was the leader of a group that kidnapped Luke Skywalker from the Bothan safehouse on the planet Kothlis. Skahtul told Skywalker that there were two rewards on his head: one for him alive, the other, dead. The reward for Skywalker alive was higher, but Skahtul tried to play the parties against one another to raise the ante. She lost her chance when Skywalker escaped.

**Skako** The birthworld of Wat Tambor before he moved to Metalorn. Skako was an industrial Core world comparable to Coruscant in scale and population, but without the charm or the aesthetically pleasing architecture. The methane atmospheric pressure on the world was so great that only natives could survive without environment suits. When Skakoans went out into the galaxy, they protected themselves against explosive decompression.

Sith war behemoth

Lak Sivrak

**skandits** Noisy squirrel-like creatures, they lived on Endor's Forest Moon. Skandits had furry black masks and used slingshots and whips to ambush unsuspecting caravans traveling through the forests.

**Skarten** Along with Ra Yasht, his colleague at Beshka University, he authored "Torture Observed: An Interview with Jabba's Cook."

**Skee** A portly Rodian, he was a member of the peaceful Tetsus clan and was known for his skill in hunting the dreaded manka cat.

**Skelda** An ancient clan of beast-riders who lived in the wilderness of the planet Onderon a millennium before the onset of the Galactic Civil War. Warriors of the Skelda clan tried to capture Zannah when she arrived on Onderon in the wake of the Battle of Ruusan.

**Skell, Choka** A Yuuzhan Vong warrior who was one of the small group that supported Nei Rin's efforts to protect the remains of the Jedi academy on Ossus during the years fol-

Choka Skell

lowing the Sith–Imperial War. Choka Skell and Liaan Lah were the first to apprehend Cade Skywalker and Shado Vao when the two Jedi stumbled upon the cavern where the Yuuzhan Vong had hidden the artifacts they had recovered from the Jedi Temple. Both warriors initially refused to back down, citing Skywalker's ties to the pirates who had once looted the cavern.

**Skell, Yoog** This Yuuzhan Vong served the leaders of the invasion force that attacked the New Republic. As high prefect of the intendent caste, Yoog Skell was Nom Anor's superior officer and answered to Supreme Overlord Shimrra. When Anor believed that the New Republic had established an advance base on Ebaq 9, Yoog Skell agreed that the information should be brought to the Supreme Overlord. However, when the information was discovered to have been purposely planted by agents of the Republic to draw the Yuuzhan Vong into a trap, Yoog Skell confronted Anor and demanded his death. In order to escape, Nom Anor lashed out at Yoog Skell with an amphistaff, smashing the high prefect's skull and killing him.

**Skidder, Wurth** A member of Luke Skywalker's new Jedi Order during the time of the Yuuzhan Vong War. During the aliens' attack on Ithor, Skidder suffered a severe injury to his right arm. He later assisted in the defense of Gyndine, and allowed himself to be captured in order to infiltrate the enemy's operations. Together with other prisoners, he was transferred to the Yuuzhan Vong vessel *Crèche* to help in the creation of a new yammosk. To conceal his Jedi identity, Skidder used an alias, but the yammosk saw past his deception. He was tortured by the Yuuzhan Vong, and left in such bad condition that he could not escape when Kyp Durron liberated the *Crèche,* instead dying aboard the vessel.

**skiff, desert** A repulsorlift utility vehicle, it was usually used to move cargo or passengers. Tatooine crime lord Jabba the Hutt used a number of skiffs as escorts for his sail barge. His henchmen often rushed to a raiding site in skiffs while barge passengers enjoyed the battle from a safe distance.

A skiff deck was completely open, with a control station for the driver and sometimes a labor droid at the rear. One repulsorlift engine provided forward thrust; the craft was maneuvered with two steering vanes hanging off the back of the hull. A skiff could hold more than 100 tons of cargo and reach speeds of 250 kilometers an hour and heights of as much as 50 meters above the surface. When fitted with up to 16 seats, skiffs were used as mass transit vehicles on poorer worlds.

Skiffs were rarely good in combat because they were neither highly maneuverable nor sturdy. A single shot from a hand blaster could disable the repulsorlift unit or smash a steering vane. Jabba used 9-meter-long Ubrikkian Bantha II cargo skiffs as the patrol and escort vehicles for his sail barge. Although they were armor-plated, they were still not suited to combat. Luke Skywalker and his companions escaped in a skiff just before the Hutt's sail barge exploded near the Great Pit of Carkoon.

Jabba's desert skiff ready to unload an important passenger

**skimmer** *See* landspeeder.

**Skip** A series of inhabited asteroids in the belt known as Smuggler's Run. (*See also* Smuggler's Run.)

- **Skip 1** The 35th asteroid in the system, the first one settled, and the one most suitable for human life. The asteroid's interior had been hollowed out centuries before. Skip 1 smelled extremely foul; the stench arose from a green-yellow slime that ran through the corridors. An attempt was once made to block the slime at its source, but this caused severe tremors and instability in the asteroid.

  Skip 1 was well defended. Adjacent to its hangar was the entry chamber, with bones along one wall and sabacc tables, a bar, and a Hokuum station for spice and other stimulants. In the center was a food court, stocked by the former chef for the court of Hapes. Beyond lay Cavern 2 and the hot, humid Cavern 3, which once belonged to Boba Fett and five fellow bounty hunters. Extra blaster protection layered Cavern 3's walls, and the cavern featured more than 18 cooking stations decorated to resemble particular planets such as Kashyyyk and Corellia. Thirteen years after the Battle of Endor, Han Solo returned to Skip 1 to investigate events in Smuggler's Run and their possible connection to the bombing of Senate Hall on Coruscant. Soon after, Skip 1 and several other Skips were severely damaged when a group of stolen droids exploded.
- **Skip 5** An enormous asteroid riddled with huge caverns lined with heat-generating sunstone. The interior temperature averaged an uncomfortable 40 degrees standard. Beyond the vast docking hangar, in the center of the asteroid, was a huge cavern filled with sand and lit with blinding sunstone. Skip 5 was abandoned for many years, but agents of the Dark Jedi Kueller of Almania converted it for use as a base for the sale of used Imperial equipment. Jawas were brought in to find and repair the old Imperial equipment; they provided cheap labor and could tinker to their hearts' content. Thirteen years after the Battle of Endor, Han Solo and Chewbacca investigated Skip 5 and were nearly killed by a group of Glottalphibs sent by the crime lord Nandreeson. Soon after, Skip 5 and several other Skips were severely damaged when a group of stolen droids exploded.
- **Skip 6** An inhabited asteroid owned and operated by the Glottalphib crime lord known as Nandreeson. The top of the asteroid was covered with flowing ooze. Inside the asteroid were humid, moss-covered chambers filled with stagnant, foul-smelling sulfurous ponds covered with lily pads and skittering waterbugs. Other chambers held Nandreeson's treasure stashes and egg clusters. The air was thick with parfue gnats and Eilnian sweet flies, and watumba bats nested on the ceiling. Half-submerged alga-covered furniture decorated the ponds. Thirteen years after the Battle of Endor, Lando Calrissian returned to Smuggler's Run searching for Han Solo. He was captured by a squad of Reks and brought to Nandreeson on Skip 6; the crime lord tried to kill his old nemesis by slowly drowning him in one of the pools. Han Solo, Chewbacca, and several smugglers arrived to rescue Lando, entering the Skip through a surface mudslide. They were betrayed by other smugglers but succeeded in rescuing Lando and fleeing the Skip by stealing Nandreeson's personal Skipper.
- **Skip 8** An inhabited asteroid that Han Solo and Chewbacca once visited during their early smuggling career.
- **Skip 52** An asteroid continually surrounded by swirling rock storms. Only the specialized Smuggler's Run vehicles known as Skippers were able to navigate these storms successfully.

- **Skips 2, 3, and 72** Thirteen years after the Battle of Endor, these and several other Skips were severely damaged when a group of stolen droids exploded.

**Skipray blastboat** Assault gunships used by the Empire, they were larger and much more powerful than starfighters but still small enough to be carried aboard capital ships. The most popular models of blastboats were the Sienar Fleet Systems GAT series. They could be found in local defense fleets and were used by smugglers and mercenaries such as Talon Karrde in his operations on Myrkr.

Just 25 meters long, the blastboat carried an incredible array of weapons for its size, including three medium ion cannons, a proton torpedo launcher, two laser cannons, and a concussion missile launcher. The ion cannons gave the Skipray a reasonable chance of disabling much larger combat ships, and the blastboat's profile presented a very small target. The hull plating was so heavy that most starfighter lasers had a tough time punching through. Blastboats were more maneuverable in a planetary atmosphere than in space and had a top atmospheric speed of more than 1,200 kilometers per hour; they had hyperdrives and a nav computer for deep space. The Skipray normally carried a crew of four, but in an emergency could be handled by a single pilot.

**Skirata, Jaing** The name used by a former clone trooper met by Mirta Gev during the years following the war against the Yuuzhan Vong. When Gev described the man to Boba Fett, the bounty hunter became intensely interested in finding him: He would have been one of the few clones to have survived the rapid aging that had been genetically coded into their cells. Fett believed that if he could locate Skirata, he might be able to halt the degeneration of his own body. Mirta and Fett tracked Skirata to the Kuat system, and he allowed himself to be transported offplanet in *Slave I,* requesting that they drop him off on Coruscant. During the transit, Fett revealed to Mirta that Jaing had been one of the original Null-class ARC troopers, having been officially designated as N-10. Jaing agreed to take a sample of Fett's blood back to his own scientists to determine what was slowly killing the bounty hunter and provide an antidote. In return, he asked Fett to return to Mandalore and rule as a member of the *Mando'ade,* following *Kad'ika*'s advice to create a unified people. In a private conversation with Mirta, Jaing told her that he thought her grandfather was a poor excuse for a Mandalore, but that he was probably the best man for the job.

**Skirata, Kal** The adopted son of Munin Skirata, this man served as a sergeant in the Grand Army of the Republic and was one of the first instructors chosen to train the army's clone commandos. Munin Skirata taught him the fine art of being a Mandalorian mercenary at an early age. In accepting the role as one of Jango's *Cuy'val Dar,* Kal found himself alienated from his family. The first soldiers he trained were the so-called Null-class ARC troopers, whom he taught from infancy and who were loyal only to Skirata himself. Sergeant Skirata did everything he could to get the clones ready in time to participate in the Clone Wars, but knew that all his training was no match for real combat. In public, Skirata seemed to be invisible, having an average appearance that tended to blend into a crowd. His short, wiry body and nondescript face allowed him to pass almost unnoticed in public.

As the Clone Wars raged on, Skirata found himself "promoted" to the position of special security adviser to the Senate Security Council, helping the Senate Guard and the Coruscant Security Force interact with the various clone commando units dispatched to handle volatile situations. One such mission was the elimination of a Separatist-funded terrorist ring on Coruscant.

At the height of the Clone Wars, Skirata and his Null-class clones set out on a personal mission to locate Ko Sai and force her to help the clones overcome their genetic reprogramming and live longer lives. Skirata finally captured Ko Sai on Dorumaa. They stripped her computer storage systems of all their data, then destroyed her underwater lab after taking her prisoner. However, Ko Sai refused to help him find a way to extend the life of the clones. After Ko Sai's death, Skirata set out to find another cloner who would be willing to help him determine whether the aging process of the clones could be reversed. In the wake of the Clone Wars, Skirata and several of his clone commandos seemed to disappear into the galaxy.

Skorr

**skirtopanol** Much like truth serum, this drug was used in interrogating prisoners. Skirtopanol could be metabolized from the system by the intake of another drug, lotiramine, but the latter could induce chemical amnesia and in some cases cause death.

**Skor II** A small, dense world, it orbited the star Squab. The Squib species evolved on Skor II. Squibs were nomadic, traveling in search of the planet's resources. A Dorcin trader gained mineral rights to a frozen wasteland on the planet in exchange for the secrets of starship technology. Most Squibs roamed the galaxy collecting junk, haggling for bargains, and competing for trash-hauling business with their primary rivals, the Ugors.

**skorch** An unusual sport developed as a training exercise by the Jedi Masters who served at Luke Skywalker's academy on Ossus. Two teams of students were positioned on the playing field, each secretly given a set of goals. A single referee was in charge of ensuring that the teams played within the rules, but this was not their primary role. In fact, skorch was created to train the referee, not the students. Because the team goals were mutually exclusive, the referee had to determine what they were and figure out a way for both teams to achieve equivalent levels of victory. In this way, the Jedi referee learned to dig beneath the surface of a conflict and identify the true motives of each side.

***Skorp-Ion*** The personal starship of Quinlan Vos, the *Skorp-Ion* resembled an insect, with wide wings sprouting from a body that had segmented legs for landing gear. The tailfin was curved upward and toward the front of the ship, giving it the appearance of a stinger. When Vos tried to escape from Dooku and found himself pursued by Asajj Ventress and Tol Skorr, he took the *Skorp-Ion* through a series of random hyperspace jumps, only to have the ship damaged in the process. He was forced to dock with the abandoned hulk of the *Titavian IV* to make repairs, but the Dark Jedi found him and set the *Skorp-Ion* adrift. Vos and Obi-Wan Kenobi were able to recover the ship after escaping from Ventress and Skorr. Unknown to the two Jedi, however, was the fact that Ventress had managed to place a tracer on the hull of the *Skorp-Ion,* which allowed them to follow the Jedi to Rendili, then Coruscant.

**Skorponek** *See* annihilator droid.

**Skorr** A humanoid male bounty hunter on Ord Mantell, he had pale yellow skin, a bald head covered with lumps, and pointed ears and teeth. The left side of his face was a metallic shell with a mechanical eye. He almost always wore a hooded brown coat and toted a hefty gun belt. He worked with an assistant, Gribbet.

Shortly after the Battle of Yavin, Skorr spotted Han Solo on Ord Mantell and attempted to collect the bounty on the Corellian smuggler. To try to trap Solo, Skorr kidnapped Princess Leia Organa and Luke Skywalker, but Solo and his first mate, Chewbacca, managed to free their friends and have Skorr arrested for violating Imperial territory.

Skorr was sent to the spice mines of Kessel but escaped. He teamed up with other bounty hunters working for Jabba the Hutt, including Dengar and Bossk, and they managed to capture Solo, Skywalker, and Chewbacca on Hoth. The captives were taken to Ord Mantell for pickup by Boba Fett, but when Skorr learned that Fett was working for the detested Empire, he decided to kill Solo rather than let him fall into Imperial hands. Skorr and Solo grappled, and during the fight Skorr fatally shot himself.

**Skorr, Tol** A former Jedi Knight who was shot down over the planet Korriban during the early stages of the Clone Wars. Skorr was rescued by Count Dooku, and from that point forward Skorr became one of Dooku's most loyal servants. Quinlan Vos, on a mission to infiltrate the Separatists, was forced to defeat Skorr and Kadrian Sey in combat in order to gain an audience with Dooku. Skorr eventually became Asajj Ventress's chief lieutenant, and found renewed favor in the eyes of Count Dooku when Vos was exposed as a spy. Skorr and Ventress nearly captured Vos aboard the *Titavian IV,* but the timely intervention of Obi-Wan Kenobi saved his life. During the Siege of Saleucami, Skorr continued to question Vos's true loyalties, and he got his chance to prove his worth to Count Dooku when Vos chose to side with the Jedi. Skorr confronted Vos deep within the planet's geothermal energy-production center. Vos eventually grew angry enough to kill Skorr, using the Force to shove Skorr off a ledge.

Tol Skorr

**Skreej, Tamtel** Lando Calrissian assumed this name when he worked undercover in Jabba the Hutt's palace as part of the plan to free Han Solo.

**Skreeka** A spaceport on the planet Atzerri.

**skree-skater** An animal native to Galantos. Skree-skaters glided across gelatin pools as they hunted for small prey.

**Skrilling** A scavenger species that stole corpses left behind on battlefields. Skrillings fed on carrion and uncooked meat and were generally avoided by many species. When the M'shinni colonized the Skrilling homeworld—dubbing it Agriworld-2079—the Skrillings were living a primitive existence as nomadic herders. They eventually integrated themselves into M'shinni colonies on the planet, from which they expanded to the rest of the galaxy. Jabba the Hutt's henchman Pote Snitkin was a Skrilling.

Skrilling

**Skritch** A pet gorm-worm of Gudb, who was a henchman of Great Bogga the Hutt some 4,000 years before the Galactic Civil War, it was used to kill the Jedi Andur Sunrider.

**S'krrr** A mantis-like species from the planet of the same name. S'krrr had blade-like forearms and vestigial wings, which they used to speak their traditional language.

**Skull Squadron** One of the many *Predator*-class starfighter squadrons that served the New Empire during the years following the Sith–Imperial War. Skull Squadron was part of the home fleet that protected Coruscant, and was on duty when Cade Skywalker arrived to rescue Hosk Trey'lis some seven years after the massacre at Ossus. For many years, the Skulls were commanded by Rulf Yage. Leadership of the squadron later passed to Yage's daughter, Gunn.

**skycar** A repulsorlift vehicle that made up much of the traffic in the skies of Coruscant. These ships were also referred to as aircars.

***Skyclaw*** A ship used by the Mistryl Shadow Guards in their botched attempt to safely transport the Hammertong device to the Empire.

**Skydome Botanical Gardens** The site of the diplomatic reception where Ambassador Furgan poisoned Mon Mothma. He flung a drink full of a self-replicating swarm of nanodestroyers in her face. The nanodestroyers then slowly began to kill her.

**Skye (Marat V)** The mountainous and temperate homeworld of the S'kytri, located in the Marat system in the Outer Rim. Han Solo and his associate Katya M'Buele were once pursued by Kharys on Marat V. When Kharys returned to Skye under the Imperial title of Majestrix, she did so with an overwhelming force of starships and stormtroopers, ruling in the name of Darth Vader and the Empire from her aerie-fortress perched high atop Canaitith Mountain.

**Skyhook** A code name for the secret Rebel Alliance operation that sent the *Tantive IV* to retrieve the technical readouts of the original Death Star battle station.

**skyhook** A space station in low orbit, it was tethered to a planetary surface. The tether, a flexible column thousands of meters long, was often used to supply the skyhook or to ferry passengers to and from the station via transit tubes. Skyhooks became a symbol of power and wealth in the skies over Imperial Center during the reign of Emperor Palpatine. They often were self-contained habitats, with opulent parks and beautifully manicured gardens. Both Emperor Palpatine and the criminal kingpin Prince Xizor had personal skyhooks. A skyhook was constructed on Kashyyyk to transport slaves during the early years of the Empire.

**skyhopper** *See* T-16 skyhopper.

**skylane** A well-defined channel reserved for air travel in the skies above Coruscant. All vehicles, save air taxis, remained within Coruscant's autonavigating skylanes. Transports, speeder buses, and limousines made up the skylane traffic.

**sky mine** Drifting mines that targeted anything moving, sky mines were tiny, highly explosive spheroids equipped with fierce tracking ability and split-second maneuverablity. Hundreds of thousands of sky mines were used by Tarkin during his attack on Zonama Sekot.

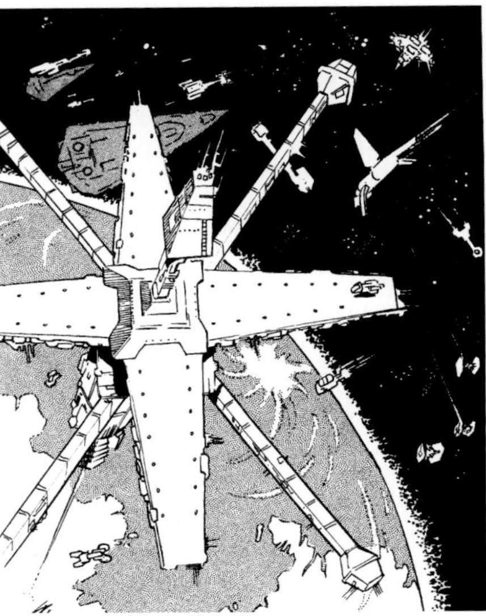
Skyhook space station

**Skynx** An insectoid scholar from the planet Ruuria, he accompanied Han Solo on a quest to find the lost treasures of the *Queen of Ranroon* prior to Solo's involvement with the Rebel Alliance. As the leading expert on the pre-Republic era at the University of Ruuria, Skynx studied and deciphered documents of the era.

**Skynxnex, Arb** The top aide to corrupt Kessel prison warden and spice mine administrator Moruth Doole, he had been a thief and assassin and Doole's main contact with spice smugglers. Arb Skynxnex also held a nominal post as a prison guard in the correction facility. He had gangly arms and legs and moved with a jerky walk. Skynxnex was killed by a glitterstim spider creature deep in the Kessel mines.

**S'kytri** Winged humanoids hailing from Skye, a planet the Empire designated Marat V. Enslaved by the Empire through the machi-

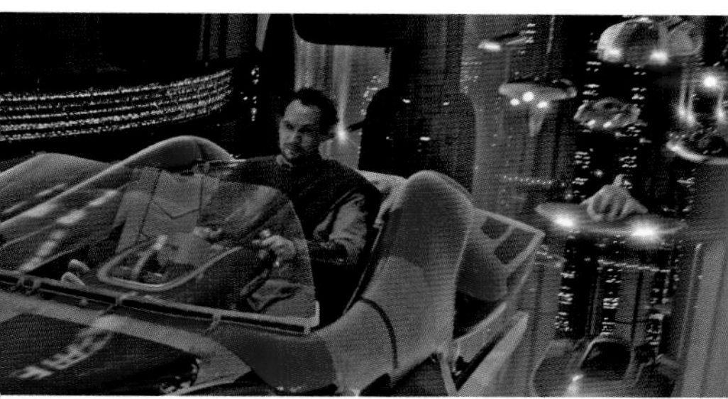

*Skylane*

nations of Darth Vader, they spent long years in unwilling servitude to Majestrix Kharys, a sadistic S'kytri chosen by Vader to enforce Imperial doctrine.

**sky trooper** An elite aerial unit of the clone trooper army. Sky troopers were specially trained and outfitted for aerial reconnaissance and battle. Winged jet backpacks with built-in launchers provided the means for air assaults on the enemy.

**Skywalker, Anakin** This great hero of the Clone Wars was both the Chosen One of Jedi prophecy and the betrayer of his fellow Jedi, ultimately becoming the twisted Darth Vader. Anakin Skywalker grew up as a slave in the markets of Tatooine's Mos Espa, arriving on the planet with his mother, Shmi, when he was just three years old. It was believed that the teachings of the Sith Lord Darth Plagueis, applied by his apprentice Darth Sidious, were instrumental in Anakin's birth, resulting in the conception of a boy with an unnaturally high midi-chlorian count. Anakin and his mother were owned by Gardulla the Hutt at first, but were eventually won in a Podracing bet by Watto the Toydarian. After meeting Qui-Gon Jinn, Anakin dreamed of becoming a Jedi Knight. His chances were enhanced when he won the Boonta Eve Classic Podrace and was freed by Qui-Gon. Anakin reluctantly left his mother behind on Tatooine and traveled with the Jedi to Coruscant.

Qui-Gon hoped to take the boy as a Padawan, but the Jedi Council refused to allow Anakin to begin the training due to his age. Anakin was remanded to Qui-Gon's care and followed the Jedi to Naboo, where he found himself piloting an N-1 starfighter during the Battle of Naboo. After Qui-Gon was killed in battle by Darth Maul, the Jedi Council agreed that Anakin could be trained by Obi-Wan Kenobi. His first lightsaber was constructed on Ilum. Eventually Anakin grew into a brash young pilot who ached with longing for Padmé Amidala, the Naboo monarch he had met only briefly. He distinguished himself with his missions for the Jedi Council, including a diplomatic mission to Ansion with Obi-Wan, Luminara Unduli, and Barriss Offee.

*Anakin Skywalker*

Due to the danger of the growing Separatist movement, Anakin was assigned to protect Padmé Amidala, who was now Senator of Naboo. It was the first time Anakin and Padmé had seen each other in a decade. In the quiet solitude amid the beautiful surroundings of a Naboo lake retreat, their deeper emotions began to grow. However, overcome with nightmares about his mother, Anakin left Naboo for Tatooine. Padmé accompanied him there, and the two visited Shmi's new husband, Cliegg Lars. But Shmi had been the prisoner of Tusken Raiders for a month, and Anakin found her only in time to watch her die. With his emotions out of control, Anakin slaughtered the entire Tusken encampment. Anakin and Padmé next voyaged to Geonosis to rescue Obi-Wan from the execution arena. The three escaped certain death thanks to the arrival of Jedi reinforcements. Obi-Wan and Anakin intercepted Count Dooku, mastermind of the Separatists, but Dooku incapacitated Kenobi and severed Anakin's arm before fleeing. Anakin gained a mechanical arm to replace his missing limb, and secretly married Padmé at a secluded lake retreat on Naboo.

*Anakin Skywalker (right) with Obi-Wan Kenobi*

The Clone Wars made Anakin a hero. During the Battle of Muunilinst, Anakin led the space attack, pursuing Asajj Ventress's starfighter to the jungles of Yavin 4 and dueling her there. During the Battle of Jabiim, Anakin joined a group of junior Padawans after Obi-Wan was presumed killed. Anakin withdrew from Jabiim under orders from Supreme Chancellor Palpatine, leaving the local resistance fighters to certain doom. On Aargonar, Anakin confronted the Tusken-raised Jedi Knight A'Sharad Hett, eventually reconciling his anger over the death of his mother. A rematch with Asajj Ventress on Coruscant left him with a facial scar. As the war ground on, Anakin was chosen to accompany Nejaa Halcyon to Praesitlyn. Anakin's quick thinking and daring heroics assured that the hostages there were saved, and the Jedi Council decided to promote him to the level of Jedi Knight upon his return. Obi-Wan enlisted Anakin on a hunt for Ventress, and Anakin eliminated the bounty hunter Durge by placing him in an escape pod and jettisoning it into a sun. Both Jedi participated in an attack on a Separatist base on Boz Pity. Although he continued to study under Obi-Wan, Yoda gave Anakin his own Padawan learner, 14-year-old Ahsoka Tano.

After Anakin beheaded Count Dooku during the Battle of Coruscant, it was hoped that the Clone Wars had come to an end. However, the Outer Rim Sieges continued to rage, forcing the Senate to continue supporting Chancellor Palpatine. During this time, Anakin learned that Padmé was pregnant with his child, and Palpatine finally revealed his identity as a Sith Lord, explaining to Anakin that only the powers of the dark side could prevent Padmé from dying as foretold in Anakin's nightmares. After Palpatine's murder of Mace Windu, Anakin willingly became Palpatine's student and was given the title of Darth Vader. Anakin became a weapon of the dark side, slaughtering everyone in the Jedi Temple—younglings to Jedi Masters—before traveling to Mustafar to destroy the Separatist Council. Padmé and Obi-Wan followed him to Mustafar, where he and Kenobi engaged in a vicious lightsaber duel. Obi-Wan was forced to cut off Anakin's legs

*Anakin Skywalker*

and arm in order to stop his former Padawan, and Anakin fell onto the bank of a lava-filled river, where he was seared alive. Palpatine, however, rescued him, fitting him with a cybernetic life-support suit. Anakin's anger boiled over when he learned of Padmé's death, especially when Palpatine explained that it had been Anakin himself who killed her. After giving in completely to his anger

Anakin Skywalker looks upon his son, Luke.

and hatred, Anakin Skywalker truly was supplanted by Darth Vader.

To the rest of the galaxy, Anakin had died in the attack on the Jedi Temple. Darth Vader simply emerged as Palpatine's enforcer. Sometime after the Battle of Yavin, Palpatine discovered that Anakin had had a son. He used this knowledge to help secure his hold on the former Anakin Skywalker, and hoped to turn Luke Skywalker to the dark side. During the Battle of Endor, as Emperor Palpatine was trying to kill Luke, Anakin rose up and threw the Emperor down the Death Star's power shaft. Anakin died soon after. His spirit joined the Force, where it was reunited with those of Obi-Wan Kenobi and Yoda. (*See also* Vader, Darth.)

**Skywalker, Ben** The son of Luke Skywalker and his wife, Mara Jade Skywalker, he was born shortly after the Battle of Duro. Named to honor the memory of Obi-Wan "Ben" Kenobi, Ben Skywalker was born aboard the converted Star Destroyer *Errant Venture* during the Yuuzhan Vong War. He was separated from his parents shortly afterward, both to protect him and to allow them to fight against the enemy. Ben was taken in by his aunt and uncle, Leia Organa Solo and her husband, Han, and brought up on Coruscant. When the Yuuzhan Vong launched their attack on the capital planet, Ben was kept in several secure locations for the rest of the war.

With the defeat of the Yuuzhan Vong, Luke and Mara resolved to spend more time with their son, but the rigors of leading the new Jedi Order conspired to keep them apart. During the Swarm War, Ben unknowingly befriended the assassin bugs of the Gorog hive, unaware that he was putting his family in danger. It was during this time that Luke and Mara discovered that Ben opened up more whenever he was around his cousin, Jacen Solo, and they asked Jacen to take Ben under his wing. Over time, Ben began to tentatively touch the Force, and his connection was strengthened with Jacen's help. As a Padawan, Ben adopted the ancient tradition of growing a single braid of hair to indicate his status, despite the fact that this was not required by the modern Jedi Order. He displayed an ability to remember things that he had seen or heard with uncanny accuracy.

In the wake of the Swarm War, Ben continued to train as a Jedi under Jacen's tutelage. When he was 13, he accompanied Jacen to Centerpoint Station on a mission to disable the facility before Thrackan Sal-Solo could reinitialize it and use it as a weapon. However, they were forced to split up when Jacen was captured by Sal-Solo, and Ben set out to complete the mission on his own. Ben discovered the unusual droid that had been programmed to "become" Anakin Solo, and convinced it to shut itself down before it was used as a weapon. Upon returning to Coruscant, Ben became aware that he was no longer a child, especially when he came to the realization that much of the growing conflict between Corellians and the Galactic Alliance was rooted in his disabling of Centerpoint Station. Ben befriended a Coruscant youth named Barit Saiy who had joined the Corellian cause, and the encounter forced Ben to choose between his friend and his duty to the Galactic Alliance. In the end, Ben provided the location of the Saiy family to the Coruscant police.

Jacen and Ben next traveled to the Hapes Cluster to stop an assassination plot targeting Tenel Ka. The culprit proved to be the Ducha Galney, who was willing to destroy her own family estate in an attempt to kill the Jedi. They managed to thwart the plot thanks to the arrival of Han Solo and Leia Organa Solo aboard the *Millennium Falcon*, but Ben placed his aunt and uncle under arrest as he believed them to be Corellian insurgents. Ben also wounded the Jedi Knight Zekk when he tried to intervene, leaving Ben even more unsure of how to gauge the loyalty of those closest to him.

In the wake of the Hapan action, Jacen gave Ben a secret assignment: recover the Amulet of Kalara. He traveled to the Sith world of Ziost, where the energy of the dark side tempted him to give in to his basest instincts.

Ben Skywalker

Ben returned to Jacen with a Sith ship he had located on Ziost, expressing his doubts over the mission and his conflicted feelings over his role as Jacen's enforcer. This concerned Jacen's Sith adviser Lumiya, who questioned Ben's suitability as Jacen's apprentice.

Jacen then suggested that Ben lead the mission to assassinate the Corellian Prime Minister, Dur Gejjen. Ben traveled to Vulpter with agents Jori Lekauf and Lon Shevu, and shot Gejjen in the head, killing him instantly. Security agents flooded in, forcing Lekauf to sacrifice his own life to ensure that Ben and Shevu could escape. Lekauf's death shook Ben greatly, since the two had become good friends.

Ben met his mother on Coruscant to confess his crimes, filling Mara with rage over how Jacen had twisted and manipulated her son. Soon, in a space battle above Kavan, Jacen and Lumiya forced Mara's StealthX fighter to crash on the planet below. Ben desperately tried to locate his mother, but instead felt her death in a wave of Force energy. He found Mara's body in a storm tunnel. Jacen suddenly appeared to offer comfort and a pledge to track down Mara's killer.

The two brought Mara's body back home. Luke, who had killed Lumiya to avenge Mara, realized that she couldn't have been the culprit when Ben explained the circumstances of the Kavan incident. Ben came to believe that Jacen had killed his mother, but Jacen instead implicated the former Galactic Alliance Chief of State, Cal Omas. Ben confronted Omas to gain back Jacen's trust, and Omas—realizing that only his death would allow Ben to expose Jacen's evil actions—sacrificed his own life.

Ben returned to Jacen's side. He failed to kill Jacen during the assault on Kashyyyk, but the bold action gave Jacen reason to believe that Ben might still become a Sith. Jacen placed him in the Embrace of Pain aboard the Star Destroyer *Anakin Solo*, but Luke infiltrated the ship and freed him. Ben plunged a vibroblade into Jacen's back before he could attack Luke, and the two left Jacen to die, although Jacen—now Darth Caedus—survived to continue his scourge.

Ben was determined to track down his mother's true killer. He buried his strong feelings that it was Jacen and concentrated on the detached forensic procedure instilled by his Galactic Alliance Guard training. With the help of Lon Shevu, Ben was able to amass evidence pointing to Jacen's guilt. At the same time, he repaired the strained relationship with his father and helped Luke finally move past his grief over Mara's death.

Knowing that Jacen had succumbed to the dark side, the Skywalker and Solo families and their allies gathered to formalize plans to bring him to justice. Ben was elevated to the rank of Jedi Knight and assigned to accompany Jaina Solo on a Jedi-sanctioned mission to destroy Darth Caedus. The mission was nearly cut short when Ben was intercepted by Tahiri Veila on Coruscant and taken away for interrogation.

Using a Force-blocking technique he had learned from Jacen, Ben refused to answer any questions. Veila even tortured and then killed Shevu in front of Ben, but he remained resolute. With Shevu's life no longer a bargaining chip, Ben realized that he had the upper hand. He goaded Veila into slapping him hard across the face; that knocked over his chair and provided a moment of confusion in which to act. Drawing upon the Force, Ben shoved Veila into her two guards and freed himself.

*Cade Skywalker*

Returning to the hidden Jedi outpost on Shedu Maad, Ben was placed in charge of the evacuation of Jedi younglings after it was learned that Darth Caedus had followed Jaina Solo there. The battle over Shedu Maad grew complicated with the arrival of Imperial forces led by Veila. While dueling Veila, Ben appealed to her to break off her attack, hoping to return her to the light side. With Caedus's defeat imminent, Veila's options were vanishing. She started listening and Ben offered to help her regain her standing in the Jedi Order. Veila questioned that, but realized that Ben had been right about Darth Caedus all along and finally surrendered.

**Skywalker, Cade** A descendant of Luke Skywalker who came into his own approximately 130 years after the Battle of Yavin. As the son of Kol Skywalker and Morrigan Corde, Cade trained briefly as a Jedi Knight under Master Wolf Sazen. His training came to an end after the Jedi Temple on Ossus was destroyed in the Sith–Imperial War. Cade escaped Ossus with Master Sazen, then took a small starfighter to defend the escape ship and avenge the death of his father. He seemingly died in the effort.

Cade survived the explosion of his fighter, and the Feeorin pirate Rav took him in, mistaking him for a fellow looter. Cade dropped the Skywalker name to avoid any connection to his heritage and became a bounty hunter, flying the starship *Mynock* with his crewmates Jariah Syn and Deliah Blue. He also became addicted to death sticks. In addition to his physical demons, Cade was haunted by the spirit of his ancestor, Luke Skywalker, who came to him regularly in visions to implore Cade to fulfill his destiny.

Cade's path eventually crossed that of the exiled Imperial princess Marasiah Fel. He agreed to transport her from Socorro to Vendaxa, hoping to learn the location of her father and collect the bounty on his head. On Vendaxa, their group was united with Shado Vao and Jedi Master Sazen. When the Sith Lords Darth Talon and Darth Nihl threatened his crew, Cade drew on the Force to drop starship debris on Talon before she could do any more harm. Vowing that nobody else was going to die for him, Cade took up the princess's lightsaber and held off Nihl long enough to allow a quick escape.

After delivering the princess to Bastion, Cade set out on his own to Ossus, where he consumed several death sticks in an effort to cut himself off from the Force. In his delirium, he was visited by the spirits of his ancestors, including Mara Jade Skywalker and Darth Vader. Cade awoke to find his former teacher, Master K'Kruhk, who explained that he had come to restore Cade's mind and soul. Cade reluctantly asked Master Sazen to begin retraining him as a Jedi.

On Ossus the team discovered a group of Yuuzhan Vong, led by Nei Rin, who had been hiding there since the massacre, hoping that one day the Jedi would return to claim their legacy. In time Cade found peace in accepting that he could have done nothing to prevent his father's death. Before Cade left Ossus, Master K'Kruhk gave him a gift: the astromech droid R2-D2, who had been in the Skywalker family for generations.

On Coruscant, Cade infiltrated the Sith Temple itself, but soon found himself the prisoner of Darth Krayt. After Krayt tortured Cade's friends Blue and Syn, Cade agreed to work for the Sith in exchange for their freedom.

**Skywalker, Kol** One of the descendants of Luke Skywalker and a member of the Jedi Council more than 100 years after the Battle of Yavin. With Morrigan Corde, he bore a son named Cade. But Morrigan returned to the Empire, leaving Kol to raise their son on his own. Kol was known as the Jedi who championed the Ossus Project, hoping to bring the galaxy together by using Yuuzhan Vong terraforming to heal damaged planets. Unknown to Kol, the new Sith Order led by Darth Krayt had silently sabotaged the Ossus Project, causing the work to go badly wrong. The resulting uproar in the galaxy led to war, and the Galactic Alliance was forced to surrender to the new Empire of Roan Fel.

*Kol Skywalker*

The Jedi, however, refused to give in, and retreated to Ossus. Darth Nihl and his Sith forces attacked, and Kol defended the last evacuation craft so that his son and Jedi Master Wolf Sazen could escape. When Nei Rin, the head Yuuzhan Vong behind the Ossus Project, returned to the planet, she gave him a proper Jedi funeral and vowed to keep the Jedi legacy alive.

**Skywalker, Luke** Raised on a backworld as the foster son of a farming couple, with little idea of his true heritage, Luke Skywalker survived personal tragedy and deep pain, then overcame impossibly high odds to become the greatest hero of the Rebel Alliance—and the only man alive who could reignite the flame of the mystical Jedi Knights. Skywalker was a hero for his time, a young man whose vision grew to become grander, even more sweeping than the circumstances in which he found himself. He was a person who always accepted the greatest challenges, even as he challenged others to do their best.

*Luke Skywalker (left) with Obi-Wan Kenobi*

Skywalker thought that he was the son of a spice freighter navigator who had fought in the Clone Wars. In truth he was the son of Anakin Skywalker and Padmé Amidala, and the older twin brother to Princess Leia Organa. He was separated from his sister just after their birth on Polis Massa in order to conceal his potential Force sensitivity from the Emperor, then hidden on Tatooine by Obi-Wan Kenobi under the watchful eyes of Owen and Beru Lars. The Larses named the infant Skywalker, in honor of Shmi Skywalker, who was Owen's stepmother. For years he remained unaware that his father had been seduced by the dark side of the Force and had become the fearsome Dark Lord of the Sith, Darth Vader. Nor did he know that he had a twin sister, with whom he was to share the adventures of a lifetime.

Luke had a mostly uneventful childhood, helping his foster parents on their moisture farm. He became a skillful pilot in a T-16 skyhopper, shooting womp rats with good friends such as Biggs Darklighter and Janek "Tank" Sunber. He had hoped to enter the Academy with Biggs and Tank, but year after year his uncle Owen kept Luke from joining, each time saying, "Just one more season." Then destiny brought the affairs of the entire galaxy—and its fate—to Skywalker's doorstep. It arrived in the form of two droids that his uncle purchased, C-3PO and R2-D2.

*Luke Skywalker climbing aboard his X-wing*

R2 carried a hologram of a beautiful Princess from Alderaan. She was seeking Ben Kenobi, and at Ben's house, Luke learned at last that his father had been a Jedi Knight who had been betrayed and murdered by Darth Vader. Ben explained the basic philosophies of the Force, and gave Luke his father's lightsaber.

He hadn't planned on accompanying Kenobi to Alderaan to aid Princess Leia Organa, but when Luke returned home he found that his aunt and uncle had been murdered by stormtroopers who were searching for the two droids. Luke realized that fate had placed him in Kenobi's hands, and set out to learn the ways of the Force. They booked passage to Alderaan with hotshot pilot and smuggler Han Solo and his first mate, the Wookiee Chewbacca, aboard Han's freighter, the *Millennium Falcon*. They reached Alderaan's position only to discover that the planet had been destroyed by a massive Imperial battle station, the Death Star.

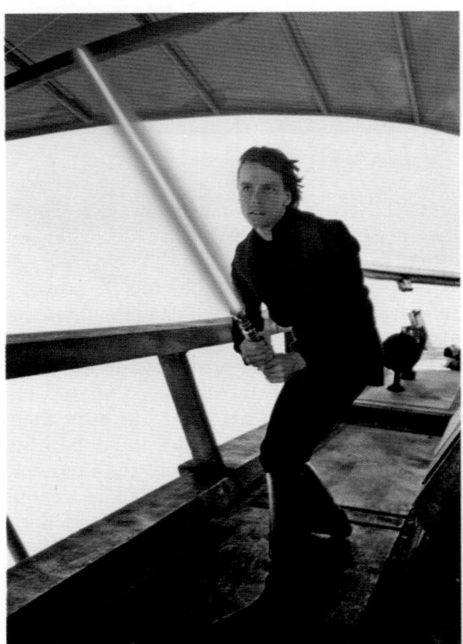

*Luke Skywalker on Jabba the Hutt's sail barge*

The *Falcon* was pulled into the Death Star, and once Luke realized that Princess Leia was aboard, he hatched a plot to rescue her. The rescue seemed almost comic, but it worked. However, as he, Han Solo, and Leia were fighting off stormtrooper fire, Luke witnessed a fateful lightsaber duel between Kenobi and Vader.

Vader struck down the old Jedi, whose body disappeared. The remaining members of the party escaped, and at the Rebel base on Yavin 4 the technical readouts of the Death Star were extracted from R2-D2 and analyzed. Assault teams were chosen, and young Skywalker became the pilot of an X-wing fighter. Just when the attack on the Death Star seemed desperate, Luke heeded the words of the spirit of Obi-Wan Kenobi. He shut down his targeting computer and used the Force to fire two proton torpedoes. They destroyed the Death Star.

Over the next few years, Skywalker became an integral part of the Rebel Alliance. He flew numerous missions and eventually was named commander, in charge of the X-wing Rogue Squadron. He helped stave off the Imperial attack on the Rebel base on Hoth long enough to allow most personnel to escape, then journeyed to the swamp planet of Dagobah to train with the Jedi Master Yoda. Rigorous physical conditioning was important there, but so was exacting mental conditioning. Yoda feared that Luke was too impetuous, and that he, too, could be seduced by the dark side.

*Luke Skywalker with Yoda on Dagobah*

Despite Yoda's warning that his training wasn't complete, when Luke saw a vision of his friends in danger on Bespin's Cloud City, he left Dagobah. It was a trap, and he was the intended victim. He engaged in a fierce lightsaber battle with Vader, who cut off Luke's right hand, then inflicted even greater pain by revealing to Luke that he, Vader, was his father. Vader offered Luke a chance to join him in ruling the galaxy, but Luke responded by letting himself drop into a wind tunnel. He was rescued by his friends.

Another rescue was planned as well: that of Han Solo, who had been frozen in carbonite and delivered to crime lord Jabba the Hutt. Before that mission could commence, Skywalker had to fend off assassination attempts by the head of the underworld, Prince Xizor. Then he went after Jabba, and was forced to destroy him and many of his henchmen while rescuing Solo. Luke returned to Dagobah only to find Master Yoda dying. Yoda confirmed that Vader was his father and explained that Luke would have to confront him one more time. The spirit of Obi-Wan appeared with equally stunning news: Leia was his twin sister.

While the Alliance was planning an attack on the Empire's second Death Star, Luke joined Leia and others in a strike against the Death Star's shield, located on the nearby Forest Moon of Endor. Luke then gave himself up to Vader in a desperate effort to reach the last spark of good that he was convinced was still deep inside his father's spirit—but to no avail. Luke was taken to Emperor Palpatine's throne room aboard the Death Star, where he was goaded into subconsciously revealing the secret of his twin sister's existence. That broke Luke's Jedi calm, and he ferociously attacked Vader, finally beating him down and chopping off his father's right hand. But Luke forsook the dark side rage the Emperor had provoked and stood his ground. The Emperor attacked Luke, assaulting him with blue Force lightning, and prepared to kill him.

Suddenly Vader rose up, lifted Palpatine into the air, and with his last bit of strength threw him into the battle station's power core. Vader knew he was fading and asked his son to remove his helmet so that he could look upon Luke with his own eyes. Then he became one with the Force.

After the second Death Star was destroyed, Luke lit a pyre to burn Darth Vader's garb. He saw a vision of Anakin Skywalker, Ben Kenobi, and Yoda, standing together as luminous beings infused with the light of the Force.

There was little time for rest or reflection, however, for Luke played a major role in turning the Rebel Alliance into the New Republic. He helped fight the reptilian Ssi-ruuvi invaders at Bakura; followed Han Solo and Leia to the planet Dathomir; fought the forces of Grand Admiral Thrawn; and stymied the attempts of the Emperor's former aide, Mara Jade, to kill him. He battled a crazed cloned Jedi who had also cloned Luke, and confronted the clone of a "reborn" Palpatine on the planet Byss.

Like other Jedi in the past, Skywalker thought he could learn about and destroy the dark side of the Force by facing it from within. Until Leia arrived and confronted him, he didn't realize how close he had come to being totally corrupted by the dark side. Even as they dealt with this personal crisis, they found themselves dealing with Palpatine's clone. Together, he and Leia destroyed the clone. Yet another cloned Emperor was reborn—and defeated—one final time.

Slowly, Luke began finding Force-sensitive beings throughout the galaxy. He decided that the most important thing he could do to help preserve the New Republic was to gather and train these adepts in a new Jedi academy, which he founded in the Great Temple of the Massassi on Yavin 4. Luke didn't realize that the evil spirit of an ancient Dark Lord of the Sith, Exar Kun, inhabited the Temple. It killed one trainee, seduced another to the dark side, and nearly murdered Luke, who was eventually saved when his trainees combined their powers.

Luke faced onetime students who turned to the dark side. He was deeply disappointed after following a trail he thought would lead to details about his mother—or even to his mother herself—only to discover he had been fooled by a conniving woman with her own agenda.

The adventures continued nonstop, although Luke at times seemed moody and preoccupied. Still, he helped defeat the threats from Imperial Admiral Daala and her superweapons; discovered the spirit of a Jedi woman, Callista, trapped in a computer on an Imperial battle station, and saw her made human through a transfer of essences with an eminent scientist; and helped rescue Han and Leia's children from dark side practitioners.

During the crisis surrounding the Caamas Document, Luke traveled to Nirauan to search for Mara Jade. After discovering the Hand of Thrawn complex, Luke proposed to Mara. The two were married, first in a ceremony performed by Kam Solusar and witnessed only by the Jedi, and later in a public ceremony on Coruscant. Luke and Mara then left the Jedi academy on Yavin 4 in the hands of the new Jedi Knights and traveled the galaxy teaching potential Jedi about the ways of the Force.

Luke proposed to the New Republic that a new Jedi Council be established, but many members of the Senate feared that the Jedi would become too powerful. Shortly afterward, Luke and Mara were forced to bring the Jedi into battle when the Yuuzhan Vong invaded the galaxy. Despite their ties to the Force, the Jedi were unable to defeat the invaders. Several Jedi, led by Kyp Durron, struck out on their own to fight the battle their own way, much to Luke's dismay and to the consternation of the Senate.

Luke was surprised to find that Mara was pregnant with a son. They named their son Ben, in remembrance of Kenobi. Luke and Mara spent less time with Ben than they had hoped after they were pressed into action defending the Jedi's Eclipse base from invasion and, later, in the defense of Coruscant.

Luke decided that the best chance for ending the conflict was to locate the rogue planet Zonama Sekot. Eventually, the planet was found, and when it was satisfied that Luke and the Jedi Knights wanted to find a peaceful resolution to the war, Sekot agreed to provide assistance.

Jacen and Jaina Solo accompanied Luke to the surface of Coruscant to bring Supreme Overlord Shimrra to justice. Upon entering Shimrra's throne room, they were beset by a group of 15 Slayers. When Jaina set out to capture Onimi, Luke found himself facing Shimrra himself, as the surviving Slayers focused their attention on Jacen. In battle with Shimrra, Luke used two lightsabers to sever the Supreme Overlord's huge head from his body.

During the Swarm War, Luke faced two former Force-users, Raynar Thul and Lomi Plo, who had become absorbed into the hivemind of the Killiks that made up the Colony. In a series of battles near Tenupe, Luke managed to cut Lomi Plo apart before confronting Raynar Thul. He convinced the younger man that his continued connection to the Colony would only lead to more conflict, which would ultimately destroy the entire galaxy. When Raynar surrendered, Luke realized that he had to return to Ossus and dedicate more time to the Jedi Order. He resigned his position with the Advisory Council—and removed all posi-

*Jedi Grand Master Luke Skywalker*

tions formerly held by Jedi—then set out to reestablish the Jedi Order.

In the years that followed, Luke worked to ensure that the Jedi were able to meet the needs of the growing Galactic Alliance. When Thrackan Sal-Solo threatened to have the Corellian System secede from the GA, Luke found himself questioning the Jedi allegiance to Corellia. The combat that erupted between the Corellian insurgents and the Galactic Alliance forced the members of the Jedi Order to destroy Corellian fighters to maintain the stability of the government. These actions, coupled with Jacen Solo's obvious turn toward the dark side of the Force, gave Luke and Mara cause for great concern for their son Ben, who was Jacen's apprentice.

Luke's fears were heightened when he realized that Lumiya, the Dark Lady of the Sith, was the Sith Master who was leading Jacen toward the dark side. Mara soon died in a confrontation on Kavan, although Luke remained unaware that Jacen Solo had killed her. Luke set out to hunt down Lumiya and avenge his wife's death.

On Terephon, Lumiya claimed to have killed Mara, and Luke beheaded her after a struggle. However, upon meeting up with Ben, Luke realized that he had killed the wrong person. In the wake of Mara's funeral, Luke began to actively question Jacen's motives. When Jacen arrived at Kashyyyk and began attacking the planet to force the Wookiees to turn over Luke's Jedi, Luke flew his StealthX fighter up to the *Anakin Solo* and infiltrated the ship to confront his nephew. Inside a secret chamber, Luke found his son, Ben, locked in the Embrace of Pain. He drove Jacen to the ground and freed Ben, who drove a vibroblade into Jacen's back. The two of them left Jacen—now the self-proclaimed Darth Caedus—to die . . . but he survived the blow.

Jacen's turn to the dark side and emergence as Darth Caedus accompanied a new civil war between the Galactic Alliance and a Confederation of systems seeking independence. Opposed to Jacen's draconian methods as head of the Galactic Alliance Guard, Luke withdrew the Jedi Order from the Alliance, establishing a hidden base of operations on the Forest Moon of Endor. Still in anguish over the loss of his wife, Luke was shaken from his depression by bonding with his son. Ben was determined to prove beyond any doubt that Jacen Solo killed his mother, not out of vengeance, but out of justice. He used his GAG training to methodically piece together the evidence.

With new resolve, Luke set plans into motion to finally confront and defeat Caedus. He made secret entreaties to Cha Niathal, admiral of the Galactic Alliance fleet, who had grown wary of Jacen. Niathal armed Skywalker with information vital to upsetting Jacen's plans to capture the starship yards at Fondor. The Jedi then moved their base from Endor to the safety of the Transitory Mists. Jaina Solo was preparing to fulfill her destiny as the "Sword of the Jedi" and bring an end to Caedus, a feat that Skywalker was hesitant to risk himself due to his edging close to the dark side with the killing of Lumiya.

Jaina defeated her brother, ending his attacks against the Jedi, while Luke and Han stopped the opportunistic Moffs of the Imperial Remnant from their attempts at conquest that accompanied Caedus's rise. Luke offered the surviving Moffs an opportunity to surrender and a chance to help rebuild the Galactic Alliance. The Moffs agreed, and as the war died down, Luke set about restoring the Jedi Order and reconnecting with his son.

**Skywalker, Luuke** A clone of Luke Skywalker, it was created from cells—sample B-2332-54—taken from the hand that Luke had lost in his lightsaber duel with Darth Vader at Cloud City. Jedi Master Joruus C'baoth, himself a clone, created Luuke because he wanted a Jedi student of his own. Using the lightsaber that Luke had lost along with his hand, the clone nearly destroyed Skywalker. But the Emperor's Hand, Mara Jade, killed the clone, fulfilling the powerful last command of the dying Palpatine: Kill Skywalker.

**Skywalker, Mara Jade** From being the closest personal aide to Emperor Palpatine—under a blood oath to assassinate Luke Skywalker—to becoming the wife of a Jedi Grand Master, this beautiful woman with a dancer's figure, green eyes, and red-gold hair took a very long journey.

Mara Jade was once the "Emperor's Hand," virtually an extension of his will, who would go anywhere in the galaxy to carry out his orders, including murder. Her mission was so secret that not even the Emperor's closest aides knew of her. After Darth Vader's battle with Luke Skywalker on Cloud City—and his revelation to his son and the invitation to join him in ruling the Empire—Palpatine secretly ordered Jade to kill Skywalker. She beat him to Jabba's palace and went undercover as "Arica," but she failed in her mission, and Luke went on to help destroy the Emperor along with his second Death Star battle station. Mara Jade was filled with guilt and vowed to still kill Skywalker—for that was the Emperor's final command.

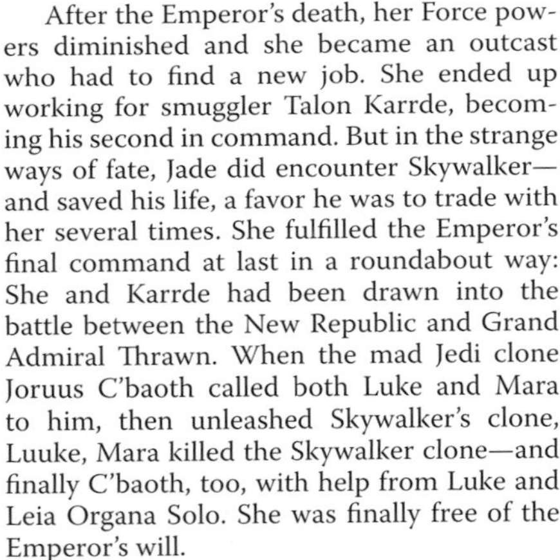
*Mara Jade, Emperor's Hand*

After the Emperor's death, her Force powers diminished and she became an outcast who had to find a new job. She ended up working for smuggler Talon Karrde, becoming his second in command. But in the strange ways of fate, Jade did encounter Skywalker—and saved his life, a favor he was to trade with her several times. She fulfilled the Emperor's final command at last in a roundabout way: She and Karrde had been drawn into the battle between the New Republic and Grand Admiral Thrawn. When the mad Jedi clone Joruus C'baoth called both Luke and Mara to him, then unleashed Skywalker's clone, Luuke, Mara killed the Skywalker clone—and finally C'baoth, too, with help from Luke and Leia Organa Solo. She was finally free of the Emperor's will.

Over the next few years, Jade helped Karrde form a guild, the Smugglers' Alliance, and threw its support to the New Republic. Then Karrde turned his operations over to Mara completely for a while. After Luke started his Jedi academy, Mara became a pupil briefly but left to continue running the guild and help challenge the hit-and-run attacks of Imperial Admiral Daala. She went on daring missions with Han Solo and Lando Calrissian. Later, at Han Solo's request, Jade and Karrde located and brought to the planet Almania several Force-bending ysalamiri, which Solo used to help Luke and Leia defeat the Dark Jedi Kueller.

During the Caamas incident, Mara took a group of Karrde's people to Nirauan to search out the strange ships that had attacked them in the Kauron asteroid field. She was stranded on the planet, and was eventually rescued by Luke. They realized that their relationship was now stronger than ever, and they were soon wed; once in a Jedi ceremony performed by Kam Solusar, and again in a public ceremony on Coruscant. Both agreed that they should travel the galaxy as Jedi instructors, leaving the Jedi academy on Yavin 4 to grow beyond Luke's vision.

A few years later, Mara suddenly became ill. Through the sheer will of the Force she remained active, but was unaware that her illness had actually been engineered by Yuuzhan Vong agent Nom Anor. She resisted the disease he had created long after other victims were dead and buried. After the being named Vergere escaped from the *Millennium Falcon* and her servitude to the Yuuzhan Vong priestess Elan, Han Solo returned to Coruscant with a sample of Vergere's tears that temporarily drove off the disease.

Soon after the Battle of Fondor, Mara discovered that she was pregnant with Luke's son. She refused to stop fighting against the Yuuzhan Vong, but also realized that she could no longer be at the forefront of the fight. When the Senate ordered Luke's arrest, the couple set out on the *Errant Venture*, where Mara struggled with her pregnancy. With Luke's devotion to her and his connection with the Force, he drove out the Yuuzhan Vong disease and helped Mara give birth to a son, Ben. Luke and Mara spent less time with Ben than they had hoped to. With the fall of Coruscant, Ben was separated from them but kept safe by Han Solo and Leia Organa Solo.

In the wake of the Yuuzhan Vong War, Mara and Luke both worried about their son's decision to cut himself off from the Force, and were glad when Jacen Solo agreed to work with Ben. At the height of the Swarm War, Mara took a shattergun pellet in the gut on a failed mission to capture Lomi Plo, the so-called Dark Queen of the Gorog hive. After a brief rehabilitation, Mara was back in action.

Both Mara and Luke tried to concentrate on their son's continuing education, working with Jacen to help Ben grow in the Force. However, Ben began to grow distant and Jacen veered toward the dark side. Luke realized that the Dark Jedi Lumiya had returned, and Mara took it upon herself to hunt down the Dark Lady of the Sith. After a struggle with Lumiya on Kavan, Jacen attacked his aunt. Mara and Jacen grappled for several minutes before Jacen extracted a poisoned dart from his belt and jammed it into her leg. As she died, Mara railed against Jacen, claiming that he was evil as Palpatine had once been. Mara's funeral took place in Coruscant's Jedi Temple, with a strong eulogy from Saba Sebatyne. Just as Jacen showed up, Mara's body disappeared, becoming one with the Force—a sure sign to Ben Skywalker that his mother was revealing that she had been killed by Jacen. Luke, however, at first believed Lumiya was the murderer and killed her. Later, he came to believe that Alema Rar was behind his wife's death.

Jacen's turn to the dark side and emergence as Darth Caedus accompanied a new civil war between the Galactic Alliance and a Confederation of systems seeking independence. Opposed to Jacen's draconian methods as head of the Galactic Alliance Guard, Luke withdrew the Jedi Order from the Alliance and established a hidden base on the Forest Moon of Endor. Still anguished over the loss of his wife, Luke was shaken from his depression by bonding with his son. Ben was determined to prove that Jacen had killed his mother, but he sought justice, not vengeance. He used his GAG training to methodically piece together the evidence that ultimately pointed to Jacen.

With new resolve, Luke developed plans to finally confront and defeat Caedus. He made secret entreaties to Cha Niathal, admiral of the Galactic Alliance fleet, who had grown wary of Jacen. Niathal gave Skywalker information vital to upending Jacen's plans to take the starship yards at Fondor. The Jedi then moved their base from Endor to the safety of the Transitory Mists. Jaina Solo was preparing to fulfill her destiny as the "Sword of the Jedi" and bring an end to Caedus, a feat that Skywalker was hesitant to risk due to his edging close to the dark side with the killing of Lumiya.

Jaina defeated her brother while Luke and Han stopped the opportunistic Moffs of the Imperial Remnant. Luke offered the Moffs an opportunity to surrender and a chance to help rebuild the Galactic Alliance. The Moffs agreed, and as the war ended, Luke set about restoring the Jedi Order and reconnecting with his son.

**Skywalker, Shmi** Anakin Skywalker's mother, and a slave on Tatooine. Shmi Skywalker's family was captured by pirates when she was very young and sold into slavery. Shmi was passed from owner to owner over nearly three decades before being sold to Gardulla the Hutt. After Gardulla lost a bet, Shmi and her

*Mara Jade Skywalker*

son Anakin became the property of Watto the Toydarian. As Anakin grew, Shmi knew that there was something special about her son. She hid as much of it as she could from Watto, but when Qui-Gon Jinn came to Tatooine she realized that she could no longer hold the boy back from his destiny. When Anakin finished first in the Boonta Eve Podrace, Qui-Gon won the boy in a wager, but was unable to gain Shmi's freedom. Five years later, the farmer Cliegg Lars purchased Shmi's freedom. Shmi found that she loved Cliegg, as well as his young son Owen, and after the two were married they lived in relative peace on the Lars moisture farm. Just before the onset of the Clone Wars, Tusken Raiders captured Shmi one morning as she was picking mushrooms from the moisture vaporators. For more than a month the Tuskens tortured her, prompting Anakin to free her. But her injuries were too great, and she died in her son's arms. Anakin killed the Tusken clan and buried his mother on the Lars homestead next to the graves of Cliegg's first wife and parents.

*Shmi and Anakin Skywalker*

**slaatik hagworm** A rare, giant, flame-breathing caterpillar-like creature that lived in caves near Naboo's swamps. Kreetles were known to emerge from the bellies of slaatik hagworms.

**slag-raft** A generic term for any form of barge used to send slag into a star for disposal. A normal part of the smelting process for materials like quadanium steel was the production of slag—leftover material that needed disposal. Rather than place slag in landfills, it was deemed more efficient to store it in containers that were placed in a slag-raft. When the slag-raft was full, it was programmed to fly into the heart of the nearest star, where the slag was incinerated and reduced to its atomic components.

**SLAM (SubLight Accelerator Motor)** An overdrive system designed to draw power from systems to give a starship a brief burst of additional speed.

**slap match** A form of hand-to-hand combat training developed by the Wookiees of Kashyyyk. A slap match involved two individual combatants who used only their hands to strike. More than brute strength was needed in a slap match, as the goal of the match was to knock your opponent off his or her feet. Thus, knowledge of physics and an opponent's center of gravity were the keys to devising a successful pattern of attack.

**slashing the deck** A starship combat maneuver in which smaller corvettes and corsairs engaged larger vessels in the opposing fleet. Because the corvettes and corsairs were more maneuverable, they could avoid the weaponry of the bigger ships and strafe them as they moved past. When the larger vessels turned to bring more weapons to bear, the smaller vessels then reversed course and attacked from the opposite direction, slashing across the path to cause even more damage. This tactic was originally credited to the naval forces of the Brotherhood of Darkness, who used it to devastating effect during the opening conflict of the Battle of Ruusan.

**slashrat** A gray-and-white rodent native to Bimmiel. The slashrat, called a sandbiter by the Yuuzhan Vong, was a nasty creature capable of tunneling through the sand and bursting from the dunes to grab its victims. Its long snout tapered back into a wedge-shaped skull that was entirely covered in chitin or keratin, but much thicker and polished smooth by moving through the sand. Short but powerful limbs sprouted long claws, designed for digging. The powerful flat tail snapped back and forth, the side-to-side undulation helping propel the supple slashrat through the sand. Besides its striking physical presence, the slashrat gave off a horrid scent. A dead slashrat emitted an even worse odor, called stink, that repelled even other slashrats. When a slashrat killed a creature, it gave off an unbearable odor called killscent, which attracted slashrats into a feeding frenzy, or killball.

**Slashtown** One of the many prison colonies established by the Empire on the planet Despayre during the early years of the New Order. Slashtown was located in grid 4354, sector 547, of planetary quadrant three.

***Slave I*** A highly modified *Firespray*-class patrol and attack ship, it belonged to the much-feared bounty hunter Jango Fett and, later, his son Boba Fett. Jango acquired the ship around the time of the Battle of Naboo while on a mission to Oovo 4. His original ship, *Jaster's Legacy*, was destroyed during the mission. As he fled authorities, Fett stumbled across a hangar full of prototype *Firespray*-class attack ships on loan to the prison for testing. Fett stole one of the starships and turned its weapons on the remaining Firesprays before they could leave their berths. For many years, *Slave I* was the only surviving Firespray, although Kuat Systems Engineering eventually revived the line around the Battle of Yavin.

The *Slave I* possessed superior shielding, high endurance levels, and a heavy arsenal of overt and hidden weapons. Jango Fett added spartan crew quarters for long hunts, since the original Firespray was furnished for shorter-term patrols. In addition, the police-regulation cages in the prisoner hold were converted into coffin-like wall cabinets to ensure control of captives. *Slave I*'s tail blaster cannons were the only overt weaponry retained from the standard Firespray, but were enhanced with finer aim and variable power. Rapid-fire laser cannons concealed amidships had less control than the tail guns, but delivered kiloton-scale energy bolts at a greater rate. An adapted naval minelayer dealt nasty surprises to hasty pursuers, and a concealed, frontal double rack of torpedoes fulfilled the role of a guided, heavy-assault weapon.

After Jango Fett's death in the Battle of Geonosis, Boba Fett took the ship for his own. Ten years after the Battle of Yavin, *Slave I* was struck by a circuit-melting blast from the *Millennium Falcon*'s lightning gun. It was then replaced with *Slave II*. But Boba Fett held on to the ship, later flying *Slave I* during the Battle of Caluula in the Yuuzhan Vong War.

***Slave II*** After escaping from the Sarlacc on Tatooine, bounty hunter Boba Fett discovered that his starship, *Slave I*, had been impounded, so he started looking for another. He realized a new ship would help him keep a lower profile until he actually confronted his much-despised adversary, Han Solo. Fett chose a *Pursuer*-class patrol ship that had proven popular with Mandalorian police because it was tough enough to handle pirates but had enough cargo space for standard policing duties.

*Slave II* was a heavy patrol craft with a superior hull and powerful military-grade shield generators. Dual engines propelled the ship, while three maneuvering thrusters could be individually directed and fired for excellent agility. *Slave II* had a forward-mounted ion cannon and twin blaster cannons. Fett also added a rear-firing proton torpedo launcher with a magazine of six torpedoes.

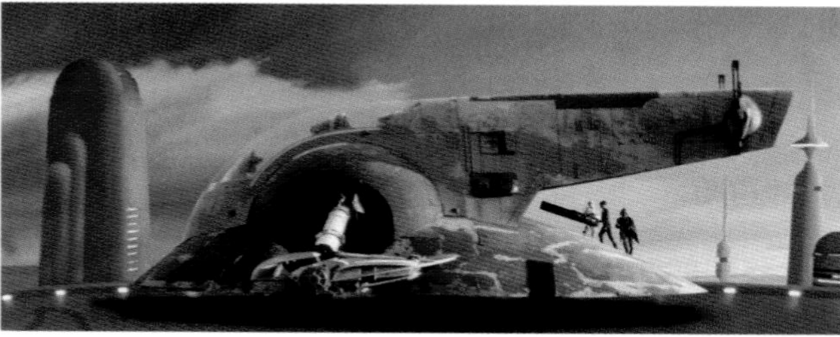
Slave I *gets ready to depart Cloud City.*

*Slave II* was severely damaged over the cloned Emperor's throneworld of Byss when Fett, attempting to follow the *Millennium Falcon* down to the surface, smashed into the planetary shield. Rather than get the ship repaired, Fett put *Slave II* in dry dock while using the reclaimed *Slave I* to continue his pursuit of Solo.

***Slave IV*** The ship used by Boba Fett during a mission to Devaron 19 years after the Battle of Yavin. Fett's daughter Ailyn Vel eventually found the abandoned *Slave IV* on Shogun, and used the ship when impersonating Boba Fett on a job for Nolaa Tarkona.

**slave circuit** Mechanisms that allowed for remote control of a starship, these circuits were usually used by a spaceport control tower to assist with landing or by the ship's owner when he or she wished to remotely power up the ship. Fully rigged slave circuits created totally controlled vessels that required few crew members and sometimes only a single pilot.

**slave tracking device** A device designed to prevent slaves from escaping their owners. Implanted in a slave's body, the device triggered a small explosion when the slave traveled beyond the range of the owner's tracking transmitter. It could be shut down with a deactivator wand.

**Slayers** Monstrous warriors created by the shapers caste to act as Supreme Overlord Shimrra's bodyguards in the waning months of the Yuuzhan Vong War.

**Slayke, Captain Zozridor** The captain of the *Scarlet Thranta* and founder of the revolutionary movement Freedom's Sons. Captain Zozridor Slayke and the 150-being crew of the *Thranta* resigned from the Republic just before the Clone Wars, embarking on a vigilante mission to attack Separatist targets in Sluissi space.

**Slayn & Korpil** A Verpine hive colony company based in the Roche asteroid field. Slayn & Korpil allied itself with the Rebel cause in the days following the Battle of Yavin, and the company worked closely with then-Commander Ackbar to develop the B-wing fighter. Slayn & Korpil produced at least three standard B-wings (the B-wing, the B-wing/E, and the B-wing/E2) in addition to several limited-production B-wing units. The company's other main military vehicle used by the New Republic was the V-wing combat airspeeder, which played a key role in the Battle of Mon Calamari.

**Sleazebaggano, Elan** A reprobate barfly who engaged in the seedier side of Coruscant nightlife. Sleazebaggano was on the path to a promising life as a medical student when he fell in with the wrong crowd. He did nothing to dispel the stereotype that Balosars were shifty cheats and scoundrels, and ended up stealing the university's medical supplies and selling them to the local mobster, Hat Lo. Sleazebaggano parlayed his aborted postsecondary education into a career as a slythmonger, a hustler of pharmaceutical contraband in the entertainment districts of Coruscant. A chance encounter with Obi-Wan Kenobi caused him to rethink his life.

**sleemo** Huttese for "slimeball."

**sleeper bomb** An explosive device, it remained inert until a preset signal activated it.

*Elan Sleazebaggano (left)*

Once activated, it drew energy from a nearby power source until a sufficient charge was gathered to release its explosive energy.

**Slice, the** A region of space that stretched from the Core Worlds to the edge of the galaxy. The Slice was defined by two major trade routes—the Perlemian Trade Route and the Corellian Run—along which early colonization took place rapidly.

**slicer chip** These chips were another manifestation of slicer technology—a way to change or get around the commands and demands of automated devices by hacking. A brainwashed Terpfen used a slicer chip to convince the controls in a B-wing fighter that he had the appropriate override codes from Admiral Ackbar and Mon Mothma. He used the ship to go to Yavin 4 and confess his betrayal of the New Republic to Leia Organa Solo.

**slicer droid** These droids could break into secret information systems or were otherwise able to compromise the security or preordered instructions of a computerized device. Wedge Antilles took several slicer droids with him to attempt to retrieve encrypted information about the weapons plans stored in the Maw Installation computer system.

**Slick** A nickname that Han Solo once was known by, it was given to him by his friend and former instructor Alexsandr Badure.

**Sligh** This Squib was part of a trio who worked behind the scenes, gathering information about the shadier parts of the galaxy and providing it to New Republic Intelligence. They worked from a base on Tatooine. Sligh and his partners, Grees and Emala, accompanied Leia Organa Solo and her husband, Han Solo, to Tatooine as part of a mission to intercept a group of Imperial agents. After Tatooine, the Squibs aligned themselves with the Invisible Shell to help further their efforts in obtaining rare artwork. Grees was captured by art collector Ludlo Lebauer and frozen in carbonite after a bad deal. Emala and Sligh were forced to manipulate the Solos into helping rescue Grees. During the Swarm War, the three Squibs established a transport operation known as Second Mistake Enterprises, and were hired by the Killik Colony to transport spinglass sculptures to the rest of the galaxy. The Squibs were unaware that each sculpture contained a handful of Gorog assassin bugs. This angered the Squibs, who set out to make the Solo family pay for their part in exposing the assassin bugs. Under the disguise of the Directors, the Squibs arranged for various assassination attempts on the lives of Han, Leia, and Jaina Solo while also maintaining a war-profiteering operation.

**Slinker missile** A type of preprogrammed guided missile.

**slivilith** A dangerous giant flying predator encountered in an underground cave on Arbra. Slivilith were considered fictional by the galaxy at large, appearing in the holoserial *The Voyages of the VSD Protector.* They were the size of small shuttles and vaguely resembled moths. The slivilith's head was round and featureless aside from a pair of wide-set eyes and a gaping maw. Tentacles trailed from the end of its body, and the slivilith used these to seize prey and force it into its wide mouth. They reportedly consumed everything on a world before moving onto the next. Although they appeared awkward, their wings were powerful enough to break the gravitational pull of a planetary body with enough momentum to propel them through space. Once exposed to temperatures nearing absolute zero, the creature entered into a state of hibernation and was able to subsist on internal gases for the countless decades—or centuries—it took to traverse space. Some believed the creature to be a Yuuzhan Vong long-range intelligence-gathering device.

**Sljee** The homeworld of the slab-shaped, multitentacled beings who were also called Sljee. The Sljee's specialized olfactory stalks gave them a keen sense of smell, but they had

*Slivilith*

a difficult time distinguishing smells when they were away from their planet. One of the waiters in a Bonadan tavern was a native of Sljee.

**Slosin, Mox** An Imperial High Inquisitor, he terrorized the Lesser Plooriod Cluster from his palace on Urce during the New Order. He spent much of his time searching out Rebel Alliance cells in the cluster, traveling in his *Trenchant*-class cruiser *Ironhand.*

**sludgegulper** Flying droids that came in a variety of sinister-looking body styles. They were tools of space pirates, commandeering ships by attaching themselves to the outer hulls and devouring a vessel's skin chunk by chunk. The Great Heep used a number of chronically malfunctioning sludgegulper designs.

**slugthrower** A projectile weapon. Slugthrowers remained in common use on isolated worlds where blasters were not readily available.

**sluicer** *See* infochant.

**Sluis sector** A sector that contained the planets Dagobah, Bpfassh, Praesitlyn, and Sluis Van. It seceded to join the Confederacy during the Clone Wars.

**Sluissi** A technologically advanced species from the planet Sluis Van. Sluissi appeared as humanoids from the waist up, but their bodies ended in a snake-like tail. They were well known for their work repairing and maintaining starships. Longtime members of the Old Republic, the Sluissi people joined the New Republic several months after the Battle of Endor. The Sluissi were even-tempered, calm, methodical, and somewhat plodding. Jobs they did took longer, but they were well done.

Slyssk

**Sluissi twist** A technique for berthing a large starship in a very tight space. It involved using quick bursts of a ship's maneuvering thrusters to spin the ship into position, then firing opposite thrusters to kill momentum before literally slamming the vessel into place.

**Sluis Van** Located in the Sluis sector, it contained extensive shipyards including the huge Sluis Van Central orbit-dock station, and was defended by perimeter battle stations. The busy shipyards were managed by an outer system defense network and the overloaded Sluissi workers at Sluis Control. Six months after the Battle of Endor, the Sluis Van Congregate was still debating whether to join the New Republic. Although the Sluis sector lay closer to New Republic sectors than to the Imperial-held Core Worlds, the Sluissi did not want to alienate the Empire, still one of their main shipyard clients. Still, they finally joined the Republic. Five years after Endor, Grand Admiral Thrawn launched an attack on 112 warships docked at Sluis Van, attempting to capture several of them with a cloaked cargo of spacetrooper-operated mole miners. No warships were captured, but the destruction of their control systems rendered more than 40 of them useless.

**Slusk, Loppak** This male Quarren served as the Exchange's primary agent on Telos during the years following the Jedi Civil War. He spent a great deal of effort trying to undermine the efforts of the Ithorian population on Citadel Station, especially after they began protesting the actions of the Exchange. Slusk changed his mind after a meeting with the Jedi Exile. When he then tried to double-cross the Exile, the former Jedi was forced to kill him.

**Slyssk** A timid Trandoshan who worked as a pirate and starship thief during the years following the Great Sith War. Slyssk was unusual among his people in that he hated to hunt. He went into business procuring starships for individuals willing to pay him to steal them. He was once hired by Marn Hierogryph to steal a ship, and tried to bribe the Snivvian into paying 10 times their agreed-upon price. Unknown to Slyssk, Marn's associate, Zayne Carrick, stepped in to help, using the Force to drop a piece of equipment near Slyssk's location. Hierogryph "rescued" the Trandoshan, who gladly agreed to turn the ship over to Hierogryph and forced the Snivvian to accept his presence aboard the ship in order to pay off his life debt. Hierogryph discovered that Slyssk was an accomplished chef and turned the vessel, the *Little Bivoli,* into an independent foodwagon when they landed on Serroco.

**slythmonger** Lowlifes who peddled cheap narcotics manufactured by disbarred pharmacists. Slythmongers were always prepared for a quick exit when customers had a bad or fatal reaction to the latest concoction. Elan Sleazebaggano was a slythmonger.

**Slythor** A Squib crime lord in the Elrood sector during the Galactic Civil War.

**Sma'Da, Drawmas** An immense human known for his ability to predict the outcome of Galactic Civil War skirmishes, he offered the galaxy's richest beings a chance to bet on the battles at his casinos. His accuracy was too good in the eyes of Emperor Palpatine, who offered a substantial bounty for Sma'Da to see if he had inside information. Zuckuss and 4-LOM succeeded in capturing the prize, but Sma'Da bribed his way free of Imperial captivity. After being released, Sma'Da accepted a wager from dancing girl Manaroo on whether her husband, Dengar, would survive a mission that he and Boba Fett undertook. Sma'Da had little faith in Dengar, but the bounty hunter survived, and Sma'Da was forced to pay a handsome return on Manaroo's bet.

**Smarteel** A planet on which Cabrool Nunn, a criminal business associate of Jabba the Hutt, lived. Jabba visited Nunn to sell him a captured freighter but ended up killing the crime boss along with his son and daughter.

**smart mine** This was a generic term used to describe any explosive mine that could track its target. Instead of lying on the ground, smart mines could lock on to targets, most often by heat signature or emissions analysis. The smart mines then followed the target until they were close enough to explode. Some deviant crime lords employed smart mines that could communicate, offering false reassurances while getting closer and closer to the moment of detonation.

**smashball** A sport played in the Senex sector and elsewhere across the galaxy. Famous teams included the Dreadnaughts, the Infuriated Savages, and the Karfeddion Skull Crackers.

**Smileredon-verdont (Smiley)** A flighty Squib thief who accompanied Raal Yorta and Sammie Staable when they joined the Rebel Alliance early in the Galactic Civil War.

**smokies** The local name for the crystals (sometimes called spooks) that were illegally exported from Nam Chorios to the Loronar Corporation. These crystals were Force-sensitive. Loronar programmed and realigned them to act as receivers for use in its synthdroids and its Needle missiles.

**Smotl** An alien species with blue-green skin.

**SM scavenger droid** Wreckage-retrieval droids that were standard equipment on New Republic salvage vessels. Designed to operate best under zero-gravity conditions, SM droids floated through the empty corridors of burned-out starship hulks, searching for booby traps, dead bodies, or weak points in the superstructure.

SM scavanger droid

**Smugglers' Alliance** An information-sharing guild formed by Talon Karrde and Mara Jade in the aftermath of the Thrawn crisis.

**Smuggler's Code** According to Han Solo, this was the set of rules by which smugglers worked together, regardless of species, creed, religion, or any other delineating factor. He invoked the Smuggler's Code most often with young, inexperienced smugglers, who were often unaware that there was, in fact, no such thing as a Smuggler's Code.

**Smuggler's Run** An asteroid belt surrounded by debris, it lay near the planet Wrea and served as a hideout for hundreds of smugglers. Entering the belt was extremely dangerous, and only a handful of people knew the correct route. For years it was a secure, well-defended safehouse; the Empire tried several times to infiltrate the Run, but its ships were destroyed. The smugglers inhabited hollowed-out asteroids lying within the belt and traveled among them in small, specialized vehicles called Skippers. Inhabited asteroids within the Run included Skip 1, Skip 2, Skip 3, Skip 5, Skip 6, Skip 8, Skip 52, and Skip 72.

Han Solo, Lando Calrissian, and others all spent time in Smuggler's Run during their early careers. A few years before the Battle of Yavin, Calrissian stole a fortune in treasure from the Glottalphib crime lord Nandreeson. Nandreeson put a price on Calrissian's head and vowed his death if he ever returned to the Run. Nandreeson's smugglers began to make a great deal of money by selling old Imperial military equipment to the Dark Jedi Kueller on Almania. Thirteen years after the Battle of Endor, Han Solo's old smuggling associate Jarril asked Han for his help investigating recent activities in Smuggler's Run. When Calrissian arrived at the Run to check on Solo, he was captured and nearly killed by Nandreeson. Many smugglers were killed when their stolen droids exploded. (*See also* Skip.)

**smuggling guild** The unofficial name for smuggling groups that controlled various sectors on the spaceport moon of Nar Shaddaa.

**Snaggletooth** *See* Zutton.

**snap bug** A bioengineered weapon created by the Yuuzhan Vong. A cousin of the blast bug, the snap bug could detonate with a bright flash of light and a sonic shock wave that stunned opponents, as well as providing momentary light.

Torr Snapit

**Snapit, Torr** An aged, battle-scarred Jedi Knight around the time of the Battle of Ruusan. He preferred using a staff to a lightsaber. Torr Snapit recruited Bug, Tomcat, and Rain in the war with the Sith at Ruusan. While eluding Sith forces on the planet, Snapit sacrificed himself so that Bug and Tomcat could escape. Tomcat found the dying Jedi and took his lightsaber.

Pote Snitkin

**snare rifle** A weapon used by the bounty hunter Zuckuss. The Merr-Sonn munitions GRS-1 snare rifle shot liquefied shockstun mist up to 150 meters. The liquid spraynet then hardened into a translucent web, confining the stunned target.

**Sneaker** An R9-series astromech droid assigned to Jaina Solo's StealthX starfighter when she resigned her commission with Rogue Squadron and became a pilot for the new Jedi Order. Sneaker replaced the droid known as Sneaky. Sneaker was later destroyed on Terephon when Jaina and Zekk questioned the Ducha Galney about an assassination attempt on the life of the Queen Mother, Tenel Ka. In the chaos that ensued, Jaina's StealthX was blown up by a remote-launched missile, obliterating the droid.

**Sneaky** The nickname Jaina Solo used for the R9-series astromech droid assigned to her StealthX fighter during the Swarm War. Sneaky was destroyed several years after the end of the Yuuzhan Vong War, when Jaina was shot down over Tenupe by Jagged Fel.

**Sneerzick, Xalto** The founder of the fanatical Droid Abolitionist Movement. A loud and fiery speaker, Sneerzick was highly charismatic.

**Sneevel** An alien species of which Boles Roor the Podracer was a member. When excited, angry, frightened, or amused, Sneevels exuded a strong odor that made their mood clear to other Sneevels. They were a species of thrill seekers discovered by Duros scouts nearly 14,000 years before the Battle of Yavin.

**Snevu, Battle of** A term used by the Chiss to describe one of the many conflicts of the Swarm War. In the Battle of Snevu, the Killiks in command of the stolen Star Destroyer *Admiral Ackbar* attacked and leveled the Chiss base on Snevu. Jagged Fel had been in command of the forces there. He blamed the Galactic Alliance for the loss, as he concurred with the Chiss belief that the Galactic Alliance had turned over the *Admiral Ackbar* willingly in an effort to help the Colony win the war.

**Snibit, Tutti** A Chadra-Fan, he introduced the bounty hunters Tinian I'att and Chenlambec to the Trandoshan bounty hunter Bossk.

**Snit** *See* McCool, Droopy.

**Snitkin, Pote** A Skrilling, he worked as a helmsman for crime boss Jabba the Hutt on Tatooine. Pote Snitkin piloted one of Jabba's skiffs and was among those killed during Luke Skywalker's rescue of Han Solo and Princess Leia from the Hutt.

**Snivvian** Short, stocky bipeds from the frigid planet of Cadomai, they had tough skin, sparse hair, and protruding snouts with pronounced canine fangs. To survive their world's long, cold winters, Snivvians evolved dense skin with special membranes that controlled the opening and closing of pores to regulate heat. Snivvians were gentle and insightful beings whose beautiful works of art were respected throughout the galaxy. Many years before the Galactic Civil War, they were almost driven to extinction when Thalassian slavers sold the species to others who used their skins for industrial purposes until the Republic intervened to stop the practice. Snivvians also overcame a genetic defect that occasionally produced sociopathic killers and evil, charismatic leaders.

Snivvian

**Snogar** Tall, furry, snow-dwelling humanoids of limited intelligence who were wary of strangers. Scientists believed the Snogars were once a technologically advanced species that devolved to a primitive lifestyle over thousands of years. The ancestors of the present-day Snogars, called the Old Ones, supposedly developed the heating machines that kept the Snogars alive on their frozen world.

**Snoil, Doolb** A Vippit who was one of the finest legal minds of the Republic during the height of the Clone Wars. Snoil came from a long line of noted neogotiators and barristers; it was his grandfather who negotiated a series of tax-free benefits for the Vippits from the Republic itself. Originally educated and trained on Mrlsst, Snoil apprenticed with a major firm in the Gevarno Cluster before joining the ranks of the barristers from the Coruscant College of Law, which worked for the Old Republic. He developed a reputation for exhaustively researching his clients and their situations, and became one of the most reliable barristers of his generation. Some two years after the Battle of Geonosis, he accompanied Obi-Wan Kenobi to Ord Cestus to uncover the truth behind the JK series droids. During a battle, a cannon blast caused a stalactite to pierce Snoil's shell.

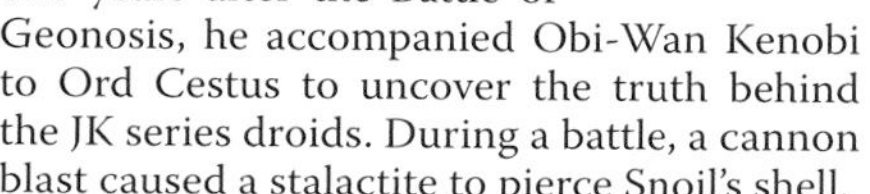
Sy Snootles

**Snootles, Sy** The sometime lead singer for Max Rebo's musical band. A Pa'lowick, Sy had two spindly legs, long thin arms, and blue-spotted yellow-green skin. Her most notable feature was that her reedy voice came out of a mouth at the end of a 30-centimeter-long protrusion extending from the lower portion of her face. Sy and the rest of the band performed for Jabba the Hutt's court just prior to the crime lord's death. After that, she and Max performed together for a time but eventually split up. She traveled with a number of other bands in the years that followed and put out several recordings, none of which proved successful.

**Snoova** A well-known Wookiee bounty hunter, he had patches of black mottled fur, a natural raccoon-like mask encircling his eyes, and a short spacer's haircut. The Wookiee Chewbacca changed his appearance to duplicate that of Snoova to pass inspection on Imperial Center as part of a plan to rescue Princess Leia Organa Solo from Prince Xizor.

**snot vampire** Slang for the Anzati species, whose members extract brain matter through their victims' noses.

**snow demon** A hairy winged creature from the planet Toola, it had a long hairy tail, white talons, and a long purple tongue that snaked between massive fangs. It hunted and ate the shaggy mastmot and in turn was often hunted and eaten by Whiphids.

**snowdroid** The term used to describe the specially made super battle droids deployed on snow-covered planets by the Confederacy of Independent Systems during the Clone Wars. These battle droids were distinguished by their white armor plating.

**snow screen** A piece of equipment used by Imperial snowtroopers, it fit over a trooper's helmet and functioned as a breather hood, warming air before it entered the armor and worked its way to the trooper's lungs.

**snowspeeder** A nickname for the highly modified Incom T-47 airspeeders that became the Rebel Alliance's last line of defense when its icy base on Hoth was assaulted by Imperial walkers. The dozen snowspeeders delayed the Imperial onslaught long enough to let the Alliance escape.

The modifications were designed to permit low atmospheric duty. Snowspeeders were powered by a pair of repulsorlift drive units and high-powered afterburners. Mechanical braking flaps located above each repulsor engine housing assisted in maneuvers. Snowspeeders could reach more than 1,000 kilometers per hour, with an effective combat speed of about 600 kilometers per hour. Although they lacked shields, their compact size and speed made them hard to target. For combat duty, snowspeeders were fitted with heavy armor plating and twin laser cannons. A harpoon gun with tow cable was found as a standard tool on most T-47s. A snowspeeder seated a forward-facing pilot and a gunner, who sat with his back to the pilot. Computerized targeting systems allowed the gunner to target the forward laser cannons.

Snoova

**snowtrooper** A specialized Imperial stormtrooper trained and equipped to operate in subfreezing conditions. Beneath a snowtrooper's light armor was a pair of durable heated pants and a shirt. A snowtrooper's helmet included a face mask with a breath heater. Polarized snow goggles, a wrist comlink, and an insulating cape completed the outfit. The entire suit was powered by a heavy-duty power cell located on the snowtrooper's backpack. Snowtroopers could survive for up to two weeks in even the harshest frozen environments on this power supply alone. They carried E-11 blaster rifles as their standard sidearms, but were also trained to use E-Web heavy repeating blasters and other large weapons. They were comfortable traveling in AT-ATs and other Imperial transports, although they could travel long distances on foot. Snowtroopers were largely responsible for routing the Rebel infantry during the Battle of Hoth.

Snowtrooper

**snubfighter** *See* X-wing starfighter.

**Snunb, Captain Syub** A Sullustan, he commanded a number of New Republic ships including the escort frigate *Antares Six* and the star cruiser *Resolve.*

**Snutib** An insectoid, mantis-like species noted for its unusual language, which consisted of a combination of clicks. A large number of Snutibs volunteered to join the military efforts of the Killik Colony during the Killiks' struggle against the Chiss in the Swarm War.

**Snyffulnimatta, Lynaliskar K'ra** This thin-bodied Elomin served as the navigator aboard the transport vessel *Uhumele* during the final years of the Old Republic. Known as

Snowspeeder

Sniffles to the rest of the crew, he worked with Crys Taanzer to keep the ship on time during their regular runs. Like his crewmates, Sniffles had no reason to trust the Galactic Empire that rose to power in the wake of the Clone Wars.

**Soach, Qual'om** A former miner, this Twi'lek controlled almost a third of the criminal activity in the Brak sector.

**Soaring Hawkbat clan** Younglings at the Jedi training facility in the Bogden system when Order 66 was executed. Master K'Kruhk managed to get the survivors of the clan aboard a shuttle.

**SoBilles, Jenssar** This Duros was his homeworld's primary representative to the early delegations of the Rebel Alliance. He first began considering rebellion after hearing Bria Tharen speak on Cloud City, years before the Battle of Yavin. He was later one of the original signers of the New Republic's declaration of war against the remnants of the Empire in the wake of the death of Grand Admiral Thrawn.

**Socorro** A dry desert world, it orbited a red giant star in the isolated Socorran system. The planet's black volcanic-ash surface gave it its name, which meant "scorched ground" in Old Corellian. The vast Doaba Badlands covered three-quarters of the planet's surface and were home to several nomadic tribes. Sandstorms were common at the world's polar regions, where temperatures were a burning 110 standard degrees. Animal life in the desert included the water beetle and sandfly.

Vakeyya, the capital and only large city on Socorro, lay adjacent to the Soco-Jarel spaceport. Although the planet had not seen rain in centuries, enough underground water reserves existed to sustain the planet's 300 million smugglers and nomads, who lived under no form of organized government. Socorro was a haven for free traders and outlaws. Illegal ship modifications remained a major source of revenue. According to custom, Socorrans traveled offworld to die, but those who could not often wandered into the desert when their time was at hand. Socorro was one of the first worlds colonized by early Corellian settlers, and most inhabitants spoke a distinctive dialect of the ancient Old Corellian language.

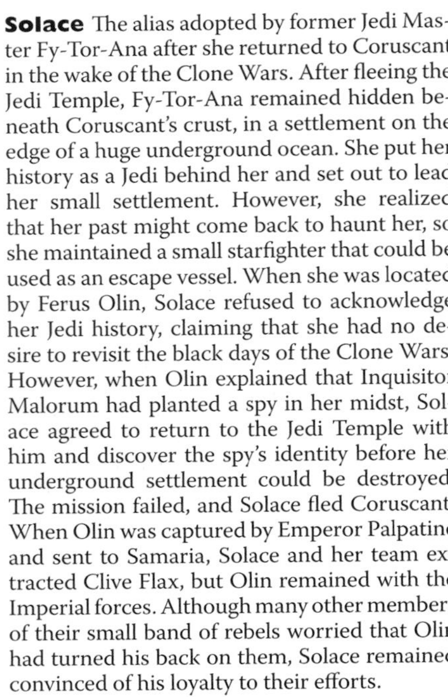
Jorin Sol

**Sodonna** A city on the Noga River on the planet Teyr, it was the location of the Kell Plath commune.

**Soergg the Hutt** A grayish-skinned Hutt "bossban" on Ansion. Working with Shu Mai of the Commerce Guild, he put a hit on the Jedi delegation on Ansion in the hope that the planet would secede from the Republic.

**Soft Heart Cantina** A cantina located in grid 19 of the Southern Underground on Coruscant during the early years of the New Order. The Soft Heart Cantina was owned and operated by Memah Roothes until the structure and surrounding buildings burned to the ground. The cantina had not been insured by Roothes, who had maintained her faith in the city's fire-suppression gear. Thus, the Soft Heart took her entire life's savings with it when it turned into ashes. In the aftermath, Memah agreed to run a cantina aboard the first Death Star. The new facility was dubbed the Hard Heart Cantina, in honor of the structure on Coruscant.

**Sokan** A lightsaber combat style that focused on mobility and evasion. Originating during the great wars with the Sith Empire, the style often led to lightsaber duels that spanned large amounts of terrain as they ran their course. In the time just before the Clone Wars, Sokan warriors integrated many elements of Master Yoda's highly kinetic use of Form IV into their own ancient techniques to create a blend of styles that relied on agility. The style encompassed everything from quick, darting movements to smooth tumbles and strikes that arced toward the vital areas of an opponent's body.

**Sol, Jorin** A Rebel Alliance statistician who accompanied Leia Organa and Luke Skywalker to Jabiim some seven months after the Battle of Yavin. Along with Leia and Nera Dantels, Sol was held prisoner by the Jabiimites after it was learned that Luke was the son of Anakin Skywalker. He was later taken into custody by Darth Vader himself, who transported him to Kalist VI and tortured him until he gave up the mathematical algorithms used to plan the Alliance's escape from the Yavin system. Eventually Jorin was rescued by Luke Skywalker and Deena Shan, who transported his badly injured body back to an Alliance medical frigate. Jorin later learned that he had been brainwashed by the Empire to pinpoint the location of the main Alliance fleet. As the *Rebel One* and its fleet leapt through hyperspace, Darth Vader and his own fleet waited for them at one of their jump points. The fleet took heavy damage, and might have been destroyed if Tungo Li hadn't ordered the surviving ships to scatter into hyperspace and abandon the preset jump protocol. The *Rebel One,* however, had sustained severe damage to its command deck. Jorin finally cast off his Imperial brainwashing and forced his way through the fires on the bridge to reach the command console. As his final act, Jorin sent the *Rebel One* into hyperspace and was posthumously honored as a hero.

**Solace** The alias adopted by former Jedi Master Fy-Tor-Ana after she returned to Coruscant in the wake of the Clone Wars. After fleeing the Jedi Temple, Fy-Tor-Ana remained hidden beneath Coruscant's crust, in a settlement on the edge of a huge underground ocean. She put her history as a Jedi behind her and set out to lead her small settlement. However, she realized that her past might come back to haunt her, so she maintained a small starfighter that could be used as an escape vessel. When she was located by Ferus Olin, Solace refused to acknowledge her Jedi history, claiming that she had no desire to revisit the black days of the Clone Wars. However, when Olin explained that Inquisitor Malorum had planted a spy in her midst, Solace agreed to return to the Jedi Temple with him and discover the spy's identity before her underground settlement could be destroyed. The mission failed, and Solace fled Coruscant. When Olin was captured by Emperor Palpatine and sent to Samaria, Solace and her team extracted Clive Flax, but Olin remained with the Imperial forces. Although many other members of their small band of rebels worried that Olin had turned his back on them, Solace remained convinced of his loyalty to their efforts.

**Solaest** The planet that was the site of the Solaest Uprising, which was suppressed by Imperial forces.

**Solari crystal** A unique lightsaber crystal. An artifact of true light-side power, the Solari crystal was said to be usable only by Jedi who were pure in spirit. When the great Jedi Master Ood Bnar initiated his life-cycle change after 1,000 years of serving the Order, he bequeathed the Solari crystal to his most promising student, a young female Jedi named Shaela Nuur. When Shaela disappeared shortly after the time of the Great Hunt, the Solari crystal vanished with her.

**solar sail** A type of technology used in space travel. The delicate reflector surfaces of most sails were more commonly pushed by tachyon streams and ultraviolet lasers than sunlight. The *Starbreaker 12* was equipped with solar sail technology during the Sith War, and Count Dooku's ship was also a solar sailer.

**Solis** A Tac-Spec footman droid from Vjun who served as a counterpart to his fellow droid Fidelis. He accompanied Whie Malreaux and Master Yoda to Vjun during the Clone Wars.

**Solo, Anakin** Born six years after the death of his grandfather Anakin Skywalker, Anakin Solo was the youngest of Han Solo and Princess Leia Organa Solo's three children, and the strongest in the Force.

Anakin was born very soon after his parents and twin brother and sister were rescued from New Alderaan. They had just arrived at the New Republic base, traveling in the abandoned floating space city of Nespis VIII, when Leia began to go into labor. And it was a short time later, when their parents returned with other New Republic officials to Corus-

cant, that infant Anakin and the twins, Jaina and Jacen, were taken to the faraway world of Anoth, to be hidden in a heavily guarded facility and overseen by Leia's assistant, Winter.

At the age of two the twins went to Coruscant, but the six-month-old Anakin was too young and too susceptible to the influences of the dark side of the Force. Despite precautions, Anoth was compromised, but an attempted kidnapping of Anakin was foiled.

Anakin, with icy blue eyes and unruly brown hair, was finally brought to Coruscant and grew up happily, playing in the corridors of New Republic power with Winter, C-3PO, or the Wookiee Chewbacca looking after him and the twins. When he was three and a half years old, Anakin and the twins were kidnapped by Lord Hethrir and taken to the Crseih Research Station; Anakin barely escaped the fate of having his spirit fed to the dark side creature called Waru.

As Anakin grew older, his Force powers became more evident. His gift for mechanics was revealed when he took apart and reassembled computers at the age of five. Anakin figured prominently in the discovery and activation of the Corellian planetary repulsors and Centerpoint Station during the first Corellian insurrection. Anakin started attending his uncle Luke Skywalker's Jedi academy on Yavin 4 when he was only 11 years old—his siblings didn't attend until they were 13.

Anakin Solo

Anakin, as well as his brother Jacen, trained directly with Luke, when Luke began moving the new Jedi Knights back to the pre-Empire format of teaching. The two brothers had different ideas on what the future of the Jedi should be. Jacen believed in the spiritual aspects of the Force, while Anakin held to its physical uses. They clashed often, claiming their intense lightsaber duels were simply training.

When the Yuuzhan Vong invaded the galaxy, Anakin returned to Centerpoint Station. The New Republic hoped to use the repulsors aboard the massive station to wipe out the Yuuzhan Vong fleet, but Anakin refused to be the wielder of such power. Thrackan Sal-Solo took the shot instead, but only succeeded in destroying most of the New Republic's Hapan allies at Fondor.

In the wake of the Battle of Fondor, Anakin's training was taken up by Luke himself in an effort to refocus Anakin's powers. He grew stronger and more respected among the Jedi, and was chosen to lead the Myrkr strike team to eliminate the voxyn queen. However, once aboard the *Baanu Rass,* Anakin took an amphistaff wound to the abdomen.

His connection to the Force remained strong, and he gathered energy around him like a magnet. Anakin became a glowing extension of the Force itself, almost invincible as he cut down Yuuzhan Vong warriors in order to get his comrades closer to the voxyn queen. The intense energy consumed him, and Anakin's physical form radiated an intense light shortly before his death. Anakin's body was laid to rest on Hapes.

**Solo, Han** A man of many contradictions, this smuggler-turned-hero of the Galactic Civil War and "first husband" of the New Republic was willing to take huge risks—for potentially tremendous gains. Charming and impulsive, Han Solo was blessed with a lucky streak that balanced his arrogance. Brave to a fault, he won the heart of Princess Leia Organa, and together they raised three Force-sensitive children.

Born on Corellia, Han was a hot teenage swoop racer and enrolled in the Imperial Academy, but his stubborn nature and belief in fairness derailed his career. He interfered with slavers who were mistreating an enslaved Wookiee—actions sanctioned by the Empire—and for his insubordination was discharged from the Imperial Navy. The Wookiee Chewbacca remained by Solo's side, at first to pay him back for the rescue and then as his partner and confidant. Early in his career, Solo won a Corellian light freighter, the *Millennium Falcon,* from Lando Calrissian. Although the ship resembled a rusty bucket of bolts, Solo and Chewbacca modified it into one of the fastest starships in the galaxy.

After his discharge, Solo—like many of his fellow Corellians—took up a life of questionable repute, taking on mercenary jobs and running a regular glitterstim-smuggling route for the likes of criminal kingpin Jabba the Hutt. He spent a number of years based on Nar Shaddaa, working with Shug Ninx and falling in and out of love with Salla Zend. He left that life behind to work in the Corporate Sector, where he spent a number of years with Doc, Jessa, and Roa. After all these adventures, Han ended up in the domain of Moruth Doole and Jabba the Hutt. Han was one of many pilots who were contracted to make the Kessel Run and smuggle spice out from beneath Imperial control. Han flew the Run a number of times, once in under 12 parsecs. However, on his last mission Solo was betrayed to Imperial customs officials and had to dump a load of spice before he was boarded; when he returned to the sector, the shipment was gone.

Han Solo

To earn enough to repay Jabba, he agreed to take several passengers on a perilous journey to Alderaan: Ben Kenobi, Luke Skywalker, and the droids C-3PO and R2-D2. And before Solo knew it, he was at the heart of the Rebellion. He helped rescue Princess Leia Organa from a prison cell aboard the Imperial Death Star. Later, after claiming he was leaving to pay off Jabba, he instead returned in the *Falcon* just in time to provide Skywalker with the cover he needed to send proton torpedoes into the heart of the Death Star, destroying the giant battle station in the first decisive win for the Rebels.

As one of the Heroes of Yavin, Solo spent the next three years helping the Alliance. By the time he decided to return to Tatooine to pay his debt, it was too late. Jabba had already put a death mark on his head, and bounty hunters from all over the galaxy were competing for the reward. In one incident, Solo escaped from near capture on the planet Ord Mantell. When the Empire discovered the Rebel Alliance's secret base on icy Hoth and launched an attack, Solo was on hand and, with Princess Leia aboard, managed to escape the pursuing Imperials by darting into an asteroid field. Despite Solo's expertise at avoiding notice, bounty hunter Boba Fett tracked him to

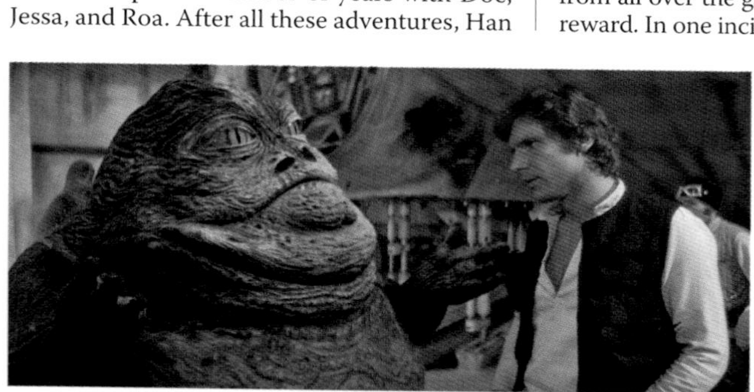

Han Solo (right) negotiates with Jabba the Hutt.

Cloud City, where Solo sought shelter with his old pal Calrissian.

Alerted by Fett, the Empire and Darth Vader set a trap to attract Vader's real target, Luke Skywalker. In a perilous experiment, Vader had Solo encased in carbonite, then gave him over to Fett to transport to Jabba.

Skywalker escaped, and Solo's friends refused to abandon him. A few months later, they plotted to wrest the carbonite-encased Solo from Jabba's palace. The rescue led to the death of Jabba and many of his henchmen. Soon thereafter, the fully recovered Solo led a strike force to the Forest Moon of Endor in the mission to disable a defensive shield that protected the Empire's second Death Star. With the help of the native Ewoks, Solo succeeded at the last possible moment.

*Han Solo with Chewbacca, Princess Leia, and C-3PO in the* Millennium Falcon

The onetime vagabond finally found time to openly express his love for Princess Leia, particularly once he found out that she and Luke Skywalker were twins, but it took the threat of Leia's marriage (to Prince Isolder of Hapes) to make him take the next step. He pretended to kidnap Leia and spirit her to the planet Dathomir, which he had won in a sabacc game. Finally married, the couple were blessed with three children, all powerful in the Force: the twins Jaina and Jacen and the younger Anakin, named for his maternal grandfather who, at the end of his life, renounced the dark side evil that had coursed through his veins. Solo completed many missions for the New Republic, both with Leia and alone. He spent five months hunting the warlord Zsinj, was imprisoned with Chewbacca in the spice mines of Kessel, and fought off several attempts by Boba Fett to capture him.

*Han Solo encased in carbonite*

Named a commodore, Solo accepted his wife's charge to take over command of the New Republic's Fifth Fleet during the Yevethan crisis, when he was captured and nearly killed by strongman Nil Spaar. False evidence planted by the Dark Jedi Kueller implicated him in the bombing of Senate Hall on Coruscant, an act designed to put both Han and Leia on the sidelines.

During the Yuuzhan Vong War, Han and Chewbacca ran a rescue mission to Sernpidal. Chewbacca was stranded on the planet trying to ensure that Han and his son Anakin made it to the *Millennium Falcon* and died saving them. Han distanced himself from his friends and family while trying to come to terms with his grief. He found an outlet teaming with his old friend Roa, and found a new ally in Droma, a nomadic Ryn.

Han and Leia suffered a terrible loss with the death of their son Anakin at Myrkr. The Solos threw themselves into the war against the Yuuzhan Vong, and Han found himself volunteering for some of the most dangerous and crazy of assignments. After watching Caluula Station's destruction, Han again stepped forward for a dangerous mission, this time to go back to Caluula and destroy the yammosk that had been installed there.

Han returned to Coruscant with his family during the final battle against the Yuuzhan Vong, working with the Jedi Knights and an Alliance infiltration team to eliminate Supreme Overlord Shimrra. When Thrackan Sal-Solo made another bid for complete independence some 10 years after the end of the conflict, Han found himself vilified in the Corellian media as a lackey of the Galactic Alliance. He and Leia became the targets of an assassination attempt funded by Sal-Solo, which pushed Han into an uneasy alliance with his old nemesis Boba Fett.

Although they were ultimately successful in killing Sal-Solo, Han learned that his son Jacen had used a deadly Force technique to kill Ailyn Vel, Boba Fett's daughter. Han confronted Jacen about Vel's death, stating in no uncertain terms that he wanted nothing to do with the person Jacen had become.

Han and Leia then returned to Corellia, believing that the Corellians were right in their beliefs, if not in their actions. The two got mixed up in a plot to assassinate the Hapan Queen Mother, along with the actual assassin, Aurra Sing.

They were badly outgunned, and with the *Millennium Falcon* already damaged from fleeing Hapes the first time, there was little they could do but avoid the fighting. This brought them into contact with their daughter Jaina, as well Ben Skywalker. Realizing that the Solos were considered Corellian insurgents, Ben tried to arrest them as terrorists.

Soldiers from Coruscant's Galactic Alliance Guard later attempted to arrest Han and Leia when they tried to attend the funeral of Mara Jade Skywalker. Han realized that the time had come to do something about his son. Jacen tracked his parents to Kashyyyk and ordered orbital turbolaser strikes at several cities, in an effort to force the Wookiees to turn them over. Han clashed with the Jedi over who should be responsible for bringing Jacen to justice.

When the group returned to the temporary Jedi outpost on the Forest Moon of Endor, Han and Leia were dismayed to learn that Jacen had kidnapped Allana, the daughter he had with the Hapan Queen Mother. Han gladly turned the *Millennium Falcon* over to Jagged Fel, who led the mission to rescue Allana, while he and Leia worked with Iella Antilles as an infiltration team. Their mission was successful, and Allana was returned to her mother on Hapes.

After learning that Darth Caedus was on the Nickel One asteroid, they launched a new mission. Han and Leia piloted the attack ship, hoping to draw off the forces gathered there while Jaina was deployed to the asteroid. Fleeing to the Jedi base on Shedu Maad, they were pursued by Caedus and prepared for the final battle against the former Jacen Solo.

The Solos were part of a small strike team that planned to infiltrate the *Anakin Solo*—Caedus's flagship—and rescue Jaina. When they found Jaina clutching her brother's dead body Han did what he could to console his daughter and later worked out his residual anger by helping the Jedi neutralize any forces that refused to surrender, including the surviving Imperial Moffs who had supported

*Han Solo and Princess Leia*

Caedus. Han demanded that the Moffs use their considerable resources to help rebuild the galaxy in exchange for their lives. In another sort of rebuilding, Han and Leia decided to secretly raise their granddaughter, Allana, who had been entrusted to them by Tenel Ka to raise away from the dangers of Hapes.

**Solo, Jacen** The son of Han Solo and Leia Organa Solo, Jacen was strong in the Force like his mother and his uncle, Luke Skywalker. He and his twin sister, Jaina, were born five years after the Battle of Endor, and because the New Republic was under attack by the forces of the Empire, the twins were raised in hideaways, first on New Alderaan and then on the planet Anoth under the guidance of Leia's trusted aide, Winter. When they were two, the twins were brought back to their parents to live on Coruscant, cared for by C-3PO and Chewbacca.

With unruly dark hair and deep brown eyes inherited from his mother, Jacen was a true lover of nature. He kept a variety of pets and samples of many plants. Jacen's Force sensitivity manifested itself in strong communication abilities, particularly with other Jedi and a variety of animals.

Always powerful in the Force, before his third birthday he helped defend his uncle. The spirit of the Dark Jedi Exar Kun sent ancient flying beasts to attack the near-lifeless body of Luke Skywalker on Yavin 4, and Jacen wielded Luke's own lightsaber. Later, Jacen joined forces with the other Jedi students in destroying Exar Kun's spirit forever and freeing Luke's spirit.

When he was five, he, Jaina, and their younger brother Anakin were kidnapped by Lord Hethrir, the former Imperial Procurator of Justice, who wanted to use them to further his dark side ambitions. Still later, when in their early teens, the children enrolled in their uncle Luke's Jedi academy and became friendly with Chewbacca's nephew, Lowbacca, and Tenel Ka, daughter of a Witch of Dathomir and a prince of Hapes. The twins and Lowie were kidnapped and taken to the Shadow Academy, where an attempt was made to turn them to the dark side of the Force. They thwarted the plot and escaped.

*Jacen Solo*

When he constructed his own lightsaber, Jacen chose focusing stones that produced an emerald-green blade. He later trained directly with Luke himself, as Luke began moving the new Jedi Knights back to the pre-Empire style of teaching.

During the Yuuzhan Vong invasion, Jacen traveled with his younger brother to Centerpoint Station, but he urged Anakin not to use the Force to fire the station's main repulsor. When Thrackan Sal-Solo fired it instead and destroyed the Hapan fleet, Jacen felt himself lost in his struggle to understand the Force. After having an intense vision of the galaxy teetering on a single balance point that he alone controlled, Jacen tried to stop using the Force altogether.

However, when his mother was threated by the Yuuzhan Vong on Duro, Jacen realized that he had reached the balance point in his vision. Drawing on the Force, Jacen badly injured the Yuuzhan Vong Warmaster Tsavong Lah, earning him a position of hatred among the invaders. Shortly afterward, Jacen and his siblings joined the Jedi strike team to Myrkr to destroy the voxyn queen. Anakin lost his life, and Jacen was captured.

During his captivity, Jacen received instruction from the former Jedi Knight Vergere, who was now living among the Yuuzhan Vong. Vergere tried to turn him to the Yuuzhan Vong's True Way, and he endured the Embrace of Pain for many months. Jacen began to believe that the Force was not simply black and white. He escaped to conquered Coruscant, where Jedi Knight Ganner Rhysode gave his life to allow Jacen enough time to tamper with the invaders' World Brain and sabotage Coruscant's terraforming.

Jacen later returned to Master Skywalker, who allowed him to rejoin the Jedi. During the recapture of Coruscant, Jacen found himself face-to-face with Onimi, the Yuuzhan Vong court jester who was revealed to be the true power behind the throne. Jacen became a luminous being and a living conduit of the Force, killing Onimi and ending the war.

Jacen decided to set out on a spiritual journey in search of other Force-users. His studies led him to a neutral philosophy, and he refused to take sides in the growing Swarm War. Jacen also learned that he now had a daughter, born to Queen Mother Tenel Ka of Hapes. The revelation led to his taking up arms against the Killik Colony.

After the conflict's resolution, Jacen took on Ben Skywalker as an apprentice. As the new Corellian insurrection wore on, Jacen fell under the influence of Lumiya, Dark Lady of the Sith. Lumiya explained that Vergere had been a follower of Sith teachings and that Jacen could realize his full potential only by studying their ways. He also became involved with the Coruscant Security Force, helping them track down Corellian insurgents and founding the Galactic Alliance Guard. His fall toward the dark side was precipitated by his beating and killing of an interrogation subject. This caused Han Solo to turn his back on his son and left Jacen even more receptive to the Sith philosophy.

Jacen's reputation as a galactic hero was heightened in the wake of his assistance in defending Queen Mother Tenel Ka from traitors, giving him even more power within the Galactic Alliance. Jacen crafted the Legislative and Regulations Statute Amendment, which gave

*Jaina and Jacen Solo*

the leaders of the Galactic Alliance the ability to alter laws as they saw fit. It also provided Jacen with a way to amend the law enough to give him the right to remove any individual he believed could pose a risk. He assumed the post of Chief of State after jailing Cal Omas, putting the galaxy under martial law until the crisis could be resolved.

On Kavan, Jacen confronted his aunt Mara, stabbing her with a poisoned dart. She died swiftly, creating a shift in the energies of the Force that Jacen knew would alert Luke Skywalker. Jacen fled to Ziost, where Lumiya agreed to make Luke believe that she had killed Mara. Jacen returned Mara's body to Coruscant and accepted his fate as a Sith Lord, taking the name Darth Caedus.

In the aftermath of the funeral, Jacen learned that his parents were being harbored by the Wookiees on Kashyyyk. His fall toward the dark side culminated when he launched an attack on that planet and confronted his uncle Luke in combat. Ben Skywalker stabbed Jacen in the back with a vibroblade, leaving him injured aboard his flagship. The pain and agony he endured during his recovery allowed Jacen to shed all notions of his former self, and he fully embraced his role as Darth Caedus.

Although now a Sith Lord, Caedus retained a deep love for his daughter, Allana, and silently vowed to kill any being who came between them. To ensure her safety, and punish Tenel Ka's disloyalty, Caedus kidnapped Allana, although the young girl was later rescued by Han and Leia Solo. As befitting a Sith, Caedus began grooming an apprentice in Tahiri Veila, securing her loyalty by using his flow-walking technique to bring her vivid images of her departed love, Anakin Solo.

Caedus's methods of bringing order to the galaxy grew increasingly harsh. He partnered with opportunistic Moffs to assassinate Gilad Pellaeon and had Imperial scientists develop nanokiller viruses that could target genetic bloodlines. He planned to use them to threaten enemies like the Hapan royal family or Boba Fett, who sought revenge for the death of his daughter Ailyn Vel while in Jacen's custody. While pressing an attack on Fondor, Jacen started massacring civilians and lost the loyalty of Cha Niathal, who fled and became head of government of the Galactic Alliance in exile.

Darth Caedus saw himself as utterly alone. He had forfeited the love of so many people, including his aunt and his daughter—but he was secure in his belief that he had made those sacrifices for the betterment of the entire galaxy. He also had lost the love of his twin sister, who sought to fulfill her destiny as "Sword of the Jedi" and bring an end to her brother's terror. Jaina trained under Boba Fett, learning Mandalorian combat techniques to effectively surprise and defeat Jacen. In a pitched battle, brother and sister dueled, and in the end, Jaina plunged her lightsaber into Jacen's chest, cutting through his ribs until she sliced through his heart.

**Solo, Jaina** The daughter of Leia Organa Solo and her husband, Han Solo, Jaina was older than her twin brother Jacen by five minutes. Like him, she was strong in the Force. She, too, had the dark hair and dark brown eyes of her mother and shared most of Jacen's adventures.

Jaina took after her father. From an early age, she was a mechanical whiz who seemed always to be dismantling droids and equipment. By the time she was nine, she was helping her father repair the *Millennium Falcon.* She was also capable of cobbling together mechanical devices for just about any purpose, and like Han Solo, her impulsiveness, spirit, and self-confidence sometimes got her into trouble.

When Jaina was 14 and a student at her uncle Luke's Jedi academy on Yavin 4, she, Jacen, and their friends Lowbacca and Tenel Ka found an Imperial TIE fighter that had crashed in the jungle years before. They kept returning to the site, and Jaina not only repaired the ship but also added a hyperdrive module that her father had given her as a gift. Little did the youngsters realize that the TIE fighter pilot, Qorl, had survived and was hiding nearby. When Jaina's repairs were nearly finished, he captured the teenager and her brother, and left them to die in the jungle as he took off. They were rescued, but Qorl escaped thanks to the new hyperdrive. His information led to the twins being kidnapped several weeks later, along with their friend Lowbacca.

The three were taken to the Shadow Academy where attempts were made to turn them to the dark side, but they eventually escaped. Later, when the cloaked Shadow Academy space station moved into orbit around Coruscant and began destroying New Republic ships, Jaina figured out how to disarm the cloaking mechanism, forcing the station to flee. She later created her own lightsaber, which glowed with violet light.

After her time at the academy, Jaina trained with Mara Jade. A true student of the Force, Jaina sometimes found it hard to be around her mother, who had never seriously developed her own Jedi potential. During the Yuuzhan Vong War, Jaina put her Force skills to work as a member of Rogue Squadron, flying an X-wing into battle against the enemy. She ejected from her fighter during the Battle of Kalarba, suffering temporary blindness. She recuperated on Duro, helping her mother resettle war refugees. Over time, her eyesight returned and she longed to get back into the cockpit. Jaina agreed to be part of the Myrkr strike team to kill the voxyn queen, watching Anakin die and Jacen become a prisoner of the enemy. In her anger she briefly turned to the dark side, wielding Force lightning to eliminate an alien attacker.

Jaina Solo

Jaina vowed to rescue Jacen, stealing a Yuuzhan Vong frigate that she renamed *Trickster.* At Hapes, she became caught up in the political intrigue, nearly becoming the heir of Queen Mother Ta'a Chume. New Republic strategists urged her to play on her "trickster" reputation within the Yuuzhan Vong ranks and act as if she were the incarnate version of the goddess Yun-Harla. It was during this time that Jaina also admitted her feelings for fellow pilot Jagged Fel, who flew with a Chiss squadron. Jaina received the rank of major for her work at Hapes and Borleias, then lieutenant colonel following the Battle of Ebaq.

Five years after the Yuuzhan Vong's surrender, Jaina became one of the key players in the Swarm War between the Chiss and the Killik Colony. She also realized that her bond with Zekk had become too powerful to resist. Jaina and Zekk became mind-mates, forever linked to each other through the Force and the hive-mind extended to all Killik Joiners.

During the new Corellian insurrection, Jaina confronted the fact that her twin brother was falling to the dark side when he usurped her leadership of Rogue Squadron during the blockade of the Corellian system. Jacen removed her from active duty when she refused to fire on a retreating civilian starship.

Jaina returned to the Jedi Order and took on the role of a reconnaissance fighter pilot, working with Zekk to gather intelligence on Corellian shipyards. Upon returning to Coruscant, Jaina found herself assigned by Grand Master Skywalker to the task force hunting down Alema Rar. Jaina learned that the task force leader was none other than Jagged Fel, but agreed to join since she would be working directly with Zekk.

Their mission took them to Ossus, where they were caught up in a kidnapping of the Jedi students there orchestrated by Major Serpa. Jaina and Jag were apprehended inside the facility, while Zekk remained hidden in his ship. They dispatched Serpa and then lent what aid they could to Kam and Tionne Solusar. Jaina rushed to Kashyyyk to bring word of the attack to Master Skywalker.

At Kashyyyk, Jaina filled Tahiri Veila's place in the Night Blades Squadron and defended the planet against her brother's savage assault. She served as Master Skywalker's wingmate, mistakenly believing that Luke had died in the firefight but later learning that he had used the cover to infiltrate Jacen's flagship. When Luke was unable to defeat Jacen, Jaina became convinced that her role as the Sword of the Jedi was to defeat her brother and restore peace to the galaxy.

Jaina began studying Mandalorian combat techniques under Boba Fett. The bounty hunter saw the training as a means of settling a score with Jacen, who had murdered his daughter Ailyn Vel during a brutal interrogation session. Jaina was part of a Mandalorian mission to the Nickel One asteroid to protect the Verpine munitions factories there. In the wake of an Imperial Remnant attack on the asteroid, Jaina finally parted ways with Fett and set off to confront her twin brother. The Jedi Council and her parents supported her grim task.

Jaina infiltrated the asteroid's main complex and confronted the newly minted Sith Lord. Caedus was unaware that he was fighting his sister since the Force was being used to alter Caedus's perceptions. This, coupled with Jaina's new fighting skills, gave her an edge of unpredictability that helped her gain the early advantage. With one savage blow, she cleaved off her brother's arm but was so surprised she was flung against the far wall by Caedus's Force lightning. In that instant, Jaina's pain forced her to drop her Force control, and Caedus realized that he had been fighting his sister all along.

Caedus escaped, but the two soon fought again aboard the *Anakin Solo.* Jaina gained the upper hand when she severed the tendon in her brother's leg, and then drove her lightsaber into his chest, killing him. As the civil war wound down outside this intensely personal arena, Jaina could do little more than cradle her brother's dead body, letting go only when her parents arrived.

**Solo, Princess Leia Organa** Separated from a mother she never knew and a father she later counted among her worst enemies, Leia was a princess who grew up enmeshed in the politics of her time. Leia Organa Solo served as Chief of State of the New Republic, a Jedi Knight, and a mother. She never desired the power that was thrust upon her, but so strong was her commitment to peace, freedom, and democracy that she was willing to accept the

Princess Leia with Luke Skywalker (left) and Han Solo aboard the first Death Star

burdens and the risks that it took to accomplish her goals.

Unaware that Darth Vader was her father or that she had a twin brother named Luke Skywalker—who proved to be the main hope for the rebirth of the Jedi Knights—Leia was given to the Viceroy and First Chairman of the planet Alderaan, Bail Organa, immediately after her mother Padmé Amidala gave birth to her on the asteroid base of Polis Massa. Raised as Bail's daughter, she grew up doted on by three gossipy aunts and a best friend named Winter. From the start, the brown-haired, brown-eyed Leia was a maverick and a tomboy. She became the youngest Senator in galactic history, even as self-proclaimed Emperor Palpatine committed an increasing number of atrocities.

Bail Organa secretly became one of the driving forces of the Rebel Alliance, and Leia remained one of the most outspoken voices in the Senate as she opposed new Imperial policies. Behind the scenes, she was involved in secret missions for the Rebels using her consular ship, the *Tantive IV.* Near Tatooine, on a mission to recruit the Jedi Obi-Wan Kenobi, she and her ship were captured by the Star Destroyer *Devastator.* Leia managed to place top-secret plans for the Death Star battle station into an astromech droid. The droid, R2-D2, then left the ship aboard an escape pod with a droid companion, C-3PO.

Leia was captured by the menacing Darth Vader; it would be years before either knew of the relationship that bound the two. Taken aboard the Death Star, Leia was able to block interrogation probes, but the battle station's commander, Grand Moff Tarkin, threatened to destroy Leia's planet of Alderaan—home to her father and billions of other residents—if she didn't reveal the site of the secret Rebel base. Quietly, she named Dantooine, a lie that Tarkin believed, but he ordered Alderaan to be destroyed anyway. It was obliterated before Leia's eyes, and Leia was scheduled for execution.

She was rescued by Luke Skywalker who, along with Obi-Wan Kenobi, rogue pilot Han Solo, and the Wookiee Chewbacca, found himself trapped aboard the battle station. They all escaped, except for Kenobi, who sacrificed his mortal existence in a lightsaber duel with Vader. Using the stolen Death Star plans, the Rebels on Yavin 4 plotted to destroy it; Skywalker, with Solo's help, succeeded in firing proton torpedoes at the station's one vulnerable spot.

After the Battle of Yavin, Leia became a full-time member of the Rebel Alliance, often acting as a diplomat to get other worlds to join the fight against the Empire. Luke, Han, and Chewbacca—along with the droids R2-D2 and C-3PO—became a second family to her, helping to ease some of the shock and pain left by the annihilation of Alderaan. She encountered Vader once again on the planet Mimban, where he badly wounded her with his lightsaber. Luke managed to drive off Vader and help heal Leia through the powers of the Kaiburr crystal.

Her feelings for Luke became more tender—almost sisterly—while Han set off romantic sparks. She evacuated Echo Base on Hoth in Solo's *Millennium Falcon,* accompanying him to Cloud City above Bespin. But Han's old gambling buddy Lando Calrissian was forced to betray them there to Darth Vader, who was setting a trap for Skywalker. Leia finally declared "I love you" to Han even as he was forced into a carbon-freezing chamber. "I know," he replied. Leia and the others fled, and helped rescue Luke, who had narrowly survived a lightsaber duel with Darth Vader. This was the point at which Vader revealed himself to be Skywalker's father.

Leia Organa

Soon thereafter, Leia made contact with Prince Xizor, head of the criminal Black Sun organization, in an attempt to discover who was behind attempts to kill Luke. Xizor nearly seduced her, aided by the exotic pheromones he emitted. Despite his charismatic advantages, Xizor was defeated.

Months later, Leia entered the palace of Jabba the Hutt in the disguise of the bounty hunter Boushh. She had Chewbacca in tow. She managed to free Han from his carbonite block, but Jabba discovered her and forced her to join his court as a prisoner and to wear a dancing girl's outfit. She eventually killed Jabba by strangling him with the very chain that bound her. Skywalker triggered a rescue that resulted in the destruction of Jabba's sail barge and the death of many of his henchmen.

On the Forest Moon of Endor Leia and Han led a strike team whose mission was to destroy a generator that powered the shield protecting the second Death Star. She used all her diplomatic skills to gain the help of a primitive tribe of Ewoks; the Rebels persevered, and the second battle station was destroyed—along with Vader and Emperor Palpatine.

Around this time, Luke told Leia the truth. They were twins, and their father had been Anakin Skywalker, who, when seduced by the dark side of the Force, had become Darth Vader. Leia came to understand that many things she had attributed to intuition had really been the glimmerings of untrained Jedi abilities.

Over the coming years, she would become the Alliance's and then the New Republic's foremost ambassador—beginning with the day after the victory at Endor, when she accompanied a force sent to help the besieged planet of Bakura. There Anakin Skywalker's spirit appeared to her and begged for forgiveness.

Leia became a member of the Provisional Council that was formed by Alliance leader Mon Mothma to establish a New Republic, and became part of a smaller Inner Council that ran the government on a day-to-day basis. Leia's relationship with Han Solo came to a head when the handsome Prince Isolder of Hapes proposed marriage. In response, Han kidnapped her and took her to Dathomir. Despite inevitable complications, Leia decided that Han was the man for her, and they were married six weeks after they left the planet.

Pregnant with twins, Leia became the target of a Noghri assassination attempt engineered by Grand Admiral Thrawn, but the plot was foiled and Leia was instrumental in getting the Noghri to renounce the Empire and join the New Republic. Amid the battles, Leia gave birth to the twins Jacen and Jaina, children who were strong in the Force. Leia herself tried to find time for Jedi training with Luke, and she gained some rudimentary skills.

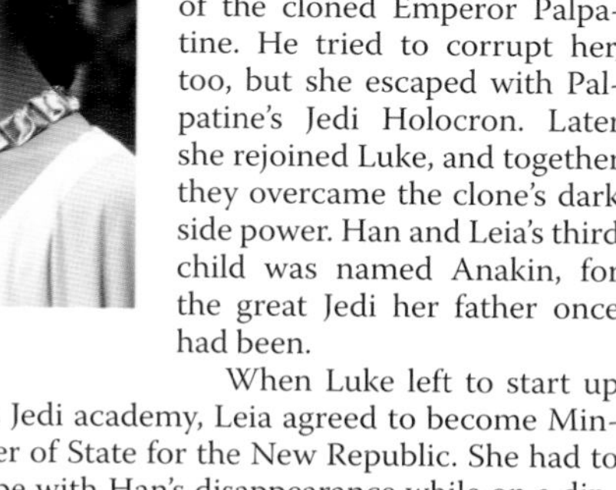

Pregnant again, Leia faced another major crisis: Her brother seemed to have become corrupted by the dark side of the Force, thanks to the teachings of the cloned Emperor Palpatine. He tried to corrupt her, too, but she escaped with Palpatine's Jedi Holocron. Later she rejoined Luke, and together they overcame the clone's dark side power. Han and Leia's third child was named Anakin, for the great Jedi her father once had been.

When Luke left to start up his Jedi academy, Leia agreed to become Minister of State for the New Republic. She had to cope with Han's disappearance while on a diplomatic mission to Kessel, her own near death in the crash of Admiral Ackbar's spacecraft on the planet Vortex, new attacks by Imperial Admiral Daala, and an ancient Sith Lord's attempt to kill Luke.

Even as these crises arose, Mon Mothma appeared to be dying of a wasting disease, and began giving more and more of her work to Leia. Mothma was finally healed, but she had already tendered her resignation, and strongly pressed Leia to remain as her replacement as Chief of State. Crises—and self-doubts—were never far away, spurred by the likes of Yevethan strongman Nil Spaar or the Dark Jedi Kueller, whom she personally killed in battle. There were many painful losses and constant worries about the safety of her husband and children, but Leia remained resolute. Some two decades after she had set out on a mission to find the "last" Jedi, Obi-Wan Kenobi, Leia enrolled her own children in Luke's Jedi academy.

During the Yuuzhan Vong War, Leia was one of the New Republic's strongest voices in identifying the threat and ensuring there was room for refugees fleeing the war zones. However, the death of Chewbacca at Sernpidal plunged her husband, Han, into a deep depression, leading to an estrangement between the two of them. On Duro, Leia headed up the committee that directed Duro's refugee colonies. When the Yuuzhan Vong attacked Duro, Warmaster Tsavong Lah nearly killed Leia until her son Jacen drove him off. Leia recuperated from her injuries, only to suffer a terrible loss with the news of her younger son Anakin's death on a mission to infiltrate an enemy stronghold orbiting Myrkr.

The end of the war caused Leia and Han to rethink their priorities. Leia believed that the Galactic Alliance Senate ran the risk of becoming just as ineffectual as the Republic Senate, and she and Han set out to locate new planets to serve as homeworlds for refugee species. During the Swarm War between the Killiks and the Chiss, Leia worked as a negotiator and diplomat to bring the conflict to an end. This brush with politics only served to harden her resolve to complete her Jedi training, and she became the apprentice of the Barabel Jedi Saba Sebatyne. She soon earned the rank of Jedi Knight.

When the Corellian system threatened to secede from the Galactic Alliance, Leia and Han were torn between family and government and were painted as traitors. They also became increasingly worried about the totalitarian leanings of their oldest son, Jacen. The two returned to Corellia, believing that the Corellians were right in their beliefs, then traveled to Hapes to warn Queen Mother Tenel Ka of a plot against her. They were forced to flee after becoming implicated in the assassination scheme along with the true assassin, Aurra Sing. They returned to Hapes in the *Millennium Falcon* in the middle of a space battle, where their nephew Ben Skywalker tried to arrest them as terrorists.

After soldiers from the Galactic Alliance Guard tried to arrest Han and Leia when they attempted to enter the Jedi Temple for the funeral of Mara Jade Skywalker, they realized that the time had come to do something about their son Jacen. At Kashyyyk, Jacen attacked the planet with orbital turbolaser strikes in an effort to force the Wookiees to turn his parents over for capture. Han and Leia devised a plan to infiltrate Jacen's flagship, and Leia was escorted to the bridge to talk with her son.

Leia engaged Jacen in a debate over right and wrong, openly questioning his actions in assuming control of the Galactic Alliance. The rest of her plan fell apart, and she was forced to abandon the vessel without capturing her son. Later, Leia learned that Jacen had kidnapped his daughter from Tenel Ka's custody, and she agreed to help to rescue her. Their mission was successful, and Allana returned to her mother on Hapes.

*Leia Organa Solo*

In the days that followed, Leia and Jaina met with Ben Skywalker, encouraging him to find evidence that would prove that Jacen had killed Mara Jade Skywalker. Much to Leia's dismay, Ben obtained a recording that proved Jacen's guilt. Leia maintained her composure, and much like Han, she refused to believe that the being who now called himself Darth Caedus was anything like her son Jacen. So when Jaina Solo suggested that Jacen needed to be eliminated, Leia offered her support.

Tracking Caedus to the Nickel One asteroid, Han and Leia piloted an assault ship to cover Jaina's insertion on the asteroid's surface via dropsuit. They extracted Jaina after her failed confrontation with her brother, then fled to the Jedi base on Shedu Maad. There they began planning for a final battle against Caedus.

Caedus followed his sister to the planet, and Han and Leia set about helping Luke and the Jedi evacuate Shedu Maad. Han and Leia readied the *Millennium Falcon* to serve as Jaina's extraction vessel and flew the ship into the hangars of the *Anakin Solo.* When they found Jaina cradling her brother's lifeless body, Leia did everything she could to console her daughter while dealing with the loss of another son. Han and Leia also decided to secretly raise their granddaughter, Allana, who had been entrusted to them by Tenel Ka to bring up away from the dangers of Hapes.

*Princess Leia with Jabba the Hutt*

**Solomahal** A veteran Lutrillian officer of the Old Republic, he retired from active duty after the Clone Wars and later made a living in the Outer Rim territories passing on his scouting expertise.

**Solusar, Kam** The son and apprentice of the great Jedi Master Ranik Solusar. Kam Solusar's father was slaughtered by Darth Vader during the Jedi Purge, and Kam fled the Empire and spent decades in isolation beyond the inhabited star systems. When he returned, he was captured and tortured by dark side Jedi and corrupted by the dark side of the Force. Luke Skywalker found Solusar on Nespis VIII and persuaded him to renounce his dark side allegiance and join the Alliance. Solusar united with Skywalker's other Jedi students in defeating Exar Kun's spirit. Solusar later married fellow Jedi trainee Tionne, and the two became co-administrators of the Jedi academy. Solusar was a Jedi Master at the time of the Yuuzhan Vong War and helped evacuate the academy's

young students when the invaders menaced Yavin 4.

**Solusar, Ranik** A great Jedi Master during the last days of the Old Republic and the father and teacher of Kam Solusar. Ranik flew a Jedi starfighter during the Battle of Geonosis. He escaped the slaughter of Order 66, but was later killed by Darth Vader during the Empire's Purge of Jedi survivors.

**Solusar, Tionne** One of Luke Skywalker's first Jedi apprentices at his academy on Yavin 4. Tionne was a near-human minstrel and historian from the planet Rindao, distinguished by her long, silvery hair and opalescent eyes. As a child, she learned about the Force from her grandmother, who instilled in her the passion for ancient Jedi legends. She had very little Force sensitivity, but Luke saw enough promise in her that he invited her to help discover ancient Jedi teachings. She eventually became a full Jedi Knight, putting her talents to use as a historian and administrator of the Yavin 4 praxeum. She married Kam Solusar shortly before the Yuuzhan Vong War. Kam and Tionne served as the caretakers of the youngest Jedi trainees during the invasion, gathering them aboard the *Errant Venture* and eventually settling them into a new base at the Maw Installation. In the wake of the Yuuzhan Vong War, Tionne and Kam agreed to become the leaders of the small Jedi training facility established on Ossus, defending it against an attack by Major Serpa of the Galactic Alliance Guard. Serpa shot Tionne in the leg when she tried to intervene, then shot off one of her arms and the other leg when the other Jedi refused to accede to his demands.

**Somerce, Akeeli** A former assistant to the Prex of the Corporate Sector Authority, she was under investigation by the Auditor-General's office on several counts of corruption during the New Order. Fiolla of Lorrd was dispatched to arrest her, but Somerce instead captured Fiolla and held her at gunpoint on Abo Dreth. Undercover CSA operative Naven Crel stopped Somerce's bid to escape, and in a brief firefight, both Crel and Somerce scored killing hits. Somerce died swiftly, while Crel lasted long enough to relay brief information about his undercover mission to Fiolla.

**Sommos, Noma** This being served the Republic military forces as an admiral in the navy during the Mandalorian Wars, nearly 4,000 years before the Battle of Yavin. Admiral Sommos worked with Admiral Veltraa and Captain Saul Karath to lead the assault on the Mandalorian troops arrayed near Taris and Vanquo, in an effort to break through the advancing forces and gain a foothold for the Republic. In what became known as the Onslaught, Admiral Sommos and her soldiers were defeated by the Mandalorians and forced to retreat. The admiral suffered many injuries in the fighting, and was transported to a medical facility on Wayland. From the hospital, she openly questioned the Republic's continued use of fringers and freelance soldiers, stating that such forces were irregular and inconsistent and could not be relied upon to meet the needs of the Republic's military.

**Somoril, Vak** An Imperial Security Bureau agent, he was on assignment to the Star Destroyer *Reprisal* shortly after the Battle of Yavin when it was discovered that Daric LaRone and his stormtrooper squad had killed ISB Major Dreflin and made off with his freighter. Both Colonel Somoril and Captain Ozzel were surprised when, in the midst of their search, Emperor's Hand Mara Jade contacted them from the Shelsha sector. Both feared that she had been sent by Emperor Palpatine to take over the investigation. However, it appeared that Mara was on a separate mission, and so they offered her assistance and hoped that she wouldn't find out about the stormtroopers. To keep an eye on her, though, Somoril dispatched two of his own agents, Brock and Gilling, to assist in her investigation.

**Somov Rit** A semitropical world covered by shallow seas and marshy inlets. The natives feared a legendary swamp demon and would not use their own given names—apprehensive that it would make them vulnerable to demon possession. The children Tomcat (Darovit), Rain (Zannah), and Bug (Hardin) hailed from Somov Rit.

**Somtay, Jyl** A Jedi Padawan whose Master, Lura Tranor, was killed in the opening battle of the Clone Wars. Somtay arrived on Geonosis in time to help clean up any pockets of resistance and gather intelligence on Count Dooku and the Separatist leaders. She received a field promotion to Jedi Knight and was given command of a squad of clone troopers to seek out survivors and work with Dr. Frayne to ensure that no weapons technology remained behind.

Together with smuggler Naj Pandoor, she found Dr. Frayne's body; Frayne had evidently been killed by a nexu. In an underground lab, Somtay discovered a Geonosian sonic blaster that was capable of shifting its frequency with every blast—which would have made it unstoppable. Pandoor stole the weapon and tried to use it against her, but the nexu returned and mauled him. Somtay fought off the creature and, after recovering the blaster, bound up Pandoor to turn him over to the authorities. She reluctantly put in a good word for him, because he did help her find the weapon.

**Song of the Universe** The natural harmony created by every living creature, according to many insectile species throughout the galaxy. Each creature had its part to play in the Song of the Universe, and the more one concentrated, the easier it became to hear the Song. According to the Song, entire species should live in simple harmony with the universe, expanding and contracting as demanded. This continual adjustment applied to conflict as well as peace: Species that were attuned to the Song lived or died in combat, as deemed necessary by the Song. Only truly insectile races were believed to hear the entire Song, although the exact reasons for this were not known. The Killik hives of the Colony brought the Song of the Universe to the galactic forefront, because it formed the basis of their existence.

***Song of War*** Prince Isolder's Battle Dragon spacecraft.

**sonic grenade** Grenades that exploded loudly on multiple frequencies, including disorienting frequencies that the human ear could barely perceive.

**sonic pistol** A weapon that generated a wide-dispersal cone of high-intensity sound. Sonic pistols offered both blast and stun settings. Sometimes referred to as squealers, these weapons delivered a high-frequency jolt to the senses that could damage and potentially disorient opponents.

**Sonniod** A former smuggler and bootlegger, he was an acquaintance of Han Solo and the Wookiee Chewbacca. A short, compact, gray-haired man, Sonniod was running a legitimate holofeature loan service the last time Solo ran into him.

**Sonsen, Jenica** The chief operations officer of Centerpoint Station, she was left in charge after the chief executive ordered a complete evacuation. She later helped the New Republic in its efforts to reactivate Centerpoint Station prior to the Battle of Fondor during the Yuuzhan Vong War.

**Sooflie IX, Prince R'cardo** This Lannik served as the crown prince and ruler of the planet Lannik during the years following the Battle of Naboo. His abrupt and terse nature earned him the ire of the populace. Despite the fact that the Jedi Master Even Piell—himself a Lannik—saved R'cardo's parents from death at the hands of the Red Iaro, Prince Sooflie paid the Jedi little heed. In fact, he was quoted as denouncing Piell's effort, claiming that he could have become prince sooner if the Jedi hadn't interfered. Prince Sooflie even rebuffed his chief adviser, Hutar Zash, in the public forum of the peace negotiations with the Red Iaro, on the planet Malastare, shortly after the Battle of Naboo. It was Sooflie's actions that forced the Red Iaro to alter its philosophy, and the terrorists' goal changed to ousting Sooflie in favor of the old regime. Sooflie was briefly captured by the Red Iaro, but was freed when the Jedi intervened. He left Malastare without a full treaty, and failed to thank the Jedi for his life.

**Sookcool, Avaro** A Rodian, he was Lando Calrissian's contact in the Black Sun criminal organization of Prince Xizor. Sookcool, who spoke Basic with a lisp, owned a small casino in the gambling complex that was run by Black Sun in Equator City on Rodia. Although he was the bounty hunter Greedo's uncle, he harbored no ill feelings toward Han Solo for the death of his nephew, whom he'd always considered somewhat worthless.

**Soothfast** A light cruiser under the command of Captain Skent Graff during the Yuuzhan Vong War. The *Soothfast* was a retrofitted *Proficient*-class ship of Corellian design. It was 850 meters long, and had 10 heavy turbolasers and 20 ion cannons. Some of the compartmentalization that had originally reinforced the cruiser's hull was removed to created a docking bay for starfighters. While patrolling near Exodo II in the Meridian sector, the *Soothfast* picked up the escape pod containing Elan and Vergere.

**Sorannan, Major Sil** A former major in the Imperial Black Sword Command, he betrayed strongman Nil Spaar and the Yevethan fleet, leading to a New Republic victory.

**Sorcerers of Tund** A mysterious and ancient sect once based on the planet Tund. No one was sure what species the sorcerers were, since they covered themselves in heavy gray robes. Years prior to the Battle of Yavin, Rokur Gepta, a snail-like Croke, infiltrated the sect and learned its secrets. He then murdered his teachers and transformed Tund from an attractive world of prairies, forests, and jungles to a blasted, sterile wasteland. Despite the fact that the sorcerers traced their origins to the ancient Sith Empire, the Jedi Council chose to allow them to study the Force in their own way. The Jedi ceased visiting 1,000 thousand years before the Battle of Yavin.

**S'orn, Senator Uta** This woman was the Senator from the planet Belasco some 12 years before the Battle of Naboo. She had planned to retire after trying to form a coalition to halt the activities of the Tech Raiders. Senator S'orn's son, Ren, was Force-sensitive, but she refused to allow him to attend the Jedi Temple. Ren fled Belasco and remained separated from his mother for years, despite her efforts to have the Jedi Knights bring him home. Her decision to retire came on the heels of Ren's death on Simpla-12, which Senator S'orn claimed had occupied her mind to the point that she could no longer concentrate. It was later revealed that Senator S'orn had, in fact, been helping Jenna Zan Arbor propagate her studies of the Force by infecting innocent worlds with bioengineered viruses, then "rescuing" them with expensive treatments. After admitting her crimes, she was exiled to a penal colony with Arbor for the rest of her life.

**SoroSuub Corporation** A diversified conglomerate headquartered on Sullust. SoroSuub manufactured such diverse products as food packaging, space mining tools, blaster weapons, and repulsorlift craft. With its wide portfolio of products, SoroSuub came to employ nearly half the population of Sullust in its laboraties and factories. When the New Order spread through the galaxy, the Sullustan Council was disbanded, and SoroSuub announced that it was assuming leadership of the planet. Then it declared that it would be fully supporting the Empire with its goods and services, and denounced the Rebel Alliance as a group of criminals and malcontents. All of this didn't sit well with many Sullustan employees, who staged a coup in the wake of the Battle of Hoth. Following the Battle of Endor, the Sullustans retook control of SoroSuub and allied with the New Republic.

Soulless One

**Sorrus** The homeworld of the Sorrusians, who possessed a skeletal system that could compress and allow them to squeeze through tight places. Over the vast surface of Sorrus were rugged mountain ranges, huge deserts, and sprawling cities. Large bodies of water were scarce, and a complex irrigation system crisscrossed the planet in an intricate series of waterways and pipes. Obi-Wan Kenobi and Astri Oddo traveled to Sorrus in search of Qui-Gon Jinn prior to the Battle of Naboo.

***Soulless One*** A starship flown by General Grievous. The *Soulless One* was a battle-worn Belbullab-22 fighter designed by Feethan Ottraw Scalable Assemblies, specialists in self-constructing armaments factories. The hyperdrive-equipped craft was bulkier and hardier than disposable droid fighters. Two main ion drives enabled the Belbullab to keep pace with an Utapaun P-38. A rear-mounted thrust-vectoring fin and auxiliary thrusters built into the wings assisted with yaw and roll maneuvers. Rapid-firing triple laser cannons sustained firepower of equivalent destructive force to that of V-wing starfighters.

**soul tree** These special trees were planted when an Ewok baby was born. Ewoks felt great kinship toward their individual trees and cared for them throughout their lives. When an Ewok died, a hood was tied around the trunk of his or her soul tree.

**soup** Anzati slang for the life essence that they sucked from their victims' brains.

**Southern Underground** A seedy section of lower Coruscant. The Southern Underground district contained a hemispherical shopping center stuffed with rundown stores and impromptu barter stalls. The Crystal Jewel was perhaps the most infamous of the cantinas near the Underground.

***Sovereign*** A Super Star Destroyer used by Warlord Zsinj. Other planned ships in the line included the *Autarch*, the *Despot*, and *Heresiarch*.

**Sovereign Protectors** *See* Emperor's Royal Guard.

**Sovv, Admiral Sien** A Sullustan, he served as the fulcrum of the New Republic Defense Force command staff during the Yuuzhan Vong War. In the aftermath of the Battle of Fondor, many urged his demotion or resignation. He barely survived a Senatorial vote of no confidence. Admiral Sovv led the defense of Coruscant during the Yuuzhan Vong assault, but when he refused to fire through the enemy's screen of hostages, Chief of State Borsk Fey'lya relieved him of command. He remained Supreme Commander of the New Republic Defense Force following Coruscant's fall, but died after the Battle of Ebaq 9 when his transport collided with a freighter piloted by Vratix who were drunk on black membrosia.

**SP-4 analysis droid** A type of analysis droid used in the Jedi Temple. Like the JN-66 droid, the SP-4's frame was largely modular, using many of the same parts as the cheaper PK-4 worker droid. However, the specific models found in the Jedi Temple had sensory apparatuses and behavioral circuitry matrices that were far beyond the capacities of such drudge workers. While the SP-4 was fairly intelligent on its own, wireless tie lines to the computers of the Jedi Temple gave it access to lore gathered from across the galaxy. When dealing with organics, it conveyed information through a mouth-stalk-like vocoder—suggesting that a Pa'lowick was on the SP-4's design team. The analysis droids SP-4 and JN-66 helped Jedi Knight Obi-Wan Kenobi when he asked them to identify the small toxic dart that killed Zam Wesell.

**Spaar, Nil** A tall, slender humanoid with mandrel-like facial ridges and coloration, wide-set black eyes, and a concealed claw on the inside of each wrist, the bigoted Yevetha was Viceroy of the Duskhan League. He deceived and humiliated Chief of State Leia Organa Solo by pretending to engage in diplomatic discourse with her regarding the Duskhan League's possible alliance with the New Republic. All the while he planned to declare war on the New Republic and to blame Leia's supposed conspiracy and betrayal. Xenophobic and determined to wipe the galaxy of what he termed "vermin," Spaar sought new places to start Yevethan colonies. He proceeded to destroy the Koornacht Cluster settlements of

*SP-4 analysis droid*

New Brigia and Polneye, massacring all inhabitants. Ruthless and cunning, he also betrayed Jian Paret, the commander of the Imperial garrison at N'zoth, the Yevethan spawnworld, whom he brutally killed during an attack and theft of numerous Imperial ships.

Spaar attacked New Republic forces when they attempted to blockade the Yevethan staging area of Doornik-319. When Han Solo, the husband of the Chief of State, was sent to take command of the New Republic's Fifth Fleet, Spaar kidnapped Solo, killed his engineer in cold blood, and savagely beat Solo until he was nearly dead. Finally, after the Yevethan defeat at the Battle of N'zoth, Spaar was killed by former Black Sword Command members, who had sabotaged his ships and helped the New Republic's fleet defeat the Yevethan forces.

Nil Spaar

**Spaarti cloning cylinder** A device used to grow humanoid clones to maturity during the Clone Wars. The cylinders were the product of Spaarti Creations, a company with a manufacturing plant on Cartao. The entire Spaarti Creations plant was destroyed in a Separatist attack, although a few thousand clone tanks were left intact and transferred to Palpatine's secret stronghold on Wayland. These became the the only cloning tanks still in existence as the technology gradually vanished and clone troopers died off. After the Battle of Endor, the stormtrooper corps was composed almost exclusively of conscripts and recruits. Emperor Palpatine used Spaarti cylinders to clone new bodies for himself on several occasions. Five years after Endor, Grand Admiral Thrawn discovered the Wayland storehouse and used the cylinders to grow clone soldiers and crews for his attacks on the New Republic. Admiral Thrawn discovered a way to avoid clone madness and grow perfect clones in as little as 20 days using the Force-repelling ysalamiri.

**space barge** A heavy-duty short-range vessel, it had powerful engines and large cargo bays to move goods quickly and efficiently among larger hyperdrive-equipped cargo ships, orbiting storage holds, and planetary spaceports. Space barges were also used to unload container ships that were too massive for planetary landings.

Space slug

**space beldon** An exotic species of beldon that could actually survive in space. Space beldons limited their wanderings to gaseous clouds capable of sustaining them. Over eons, they gradually transformed the vapors they consumed into rethen, a light gas that allowed them to swell to their full size, and Tibanna, which they expelled into their surroundings. Most varieties could also derive sustenance from the mineral elements within small planetoids and asteroids. By excreting a naturally developed acid, the space beldon used the thousands of tiny tentacles on its underside to gradually bore into a chunk of rock or metal and burn out nutrients.

**space grazer** A legendary creature said to have once roamed the stars preying on galactic space traffic.

**Spaceport Speeders** A used-vehicle lot in central Mos Eisley on Tatooine, it was where Luke Skywalker sold his landspeeder when he needed money to get offplanet. It was run by the Arcona Unut Poll and a Vuvrian named Wioslea.

**spacer** Someone who made a living by traveling the space lanes.

**Spacers' Garage** A huge starship-repair facility on Nar Shaddaa, it was owned and operated by Shug Ninx, an old friend of Han Solo.

**space slug (exogorth)** Giant worm-like creatures as long as 900 meters, they inhabited deep caverns on larger asteroids near Hoth and other planets. Space slugs, also known as exogorths, were hardy, existing in virtually no atmosphere. Silicon-based life-forms, they lived for long periods by breaking down the rock and subsisting on the mineral content. Space slugs were plagued by parasites known as mynocks, which they sometimes also fed on. Space slug flesh had a number of commercial uses. The creatures reproduced through fission, splitting into two separate beings.

Space slugs could trace their galactic prominence back to the House of Adasca, which found a way to use them as weapons in the years prior to the Jedi Civil War. By increasing their reproduction rate, growth rate, and hunger, as well as fitting them with hyperdrives, the House of Adasca hoped to sell the exogorths to interested parties as spaceport-wrecking superweapons. Thousands of years later, the pirate Clabburn the Elder placed space slugs in the Hoth asteroid belt and other areas where he maintained hideouts. One slug in the asteroid belt grew to more than 900 meters in length, and became a temporary hiding place for Han Solo during the *Millennium Falcon*'s escape from Imperial forces.

**Space Station Kwenn** One of the last fuel and supply stops before the Outer Rim Territories, the city-like station featured everything a weary spacer might need. Space Station Kwenn was built atop a large docking platform made up of scores of modular space docks and hangar bays. Its lower levels consisted of drydock gridwork used for parking, overhauling, or otherwise repairing capital ships.

**Space Station Scardia** A cube-shaped station, it was the headquarters of the Prophets of the Dark Side.

**spacetrooper (zero-g assault trooper)** An elite variety of stormtrooper that used armor and equipment to function as an independent spacecraft, able to propel himself through space and attack and breach nearly any target. Although standard stormtrooper armor did provide limited protection against hard vacuum, only spacetroopers were trained for space combat operations. Their primary missions involved the capturing of enemy vessels intact and the pacifying of rebellious crews. Spacetroopers were typically deployed in units of 40 aboard assault shuttles. This platoon of soldiers could overtake capital ships with their determined assaults. A spacetrooper wore a standard stormtrooper shell, then plugged into a larger set of powered armor that stood over 2 meters tall and was twice as wide across as an unarmored man. For this bulky appearance, spacetroopers were sometimes called "walk-

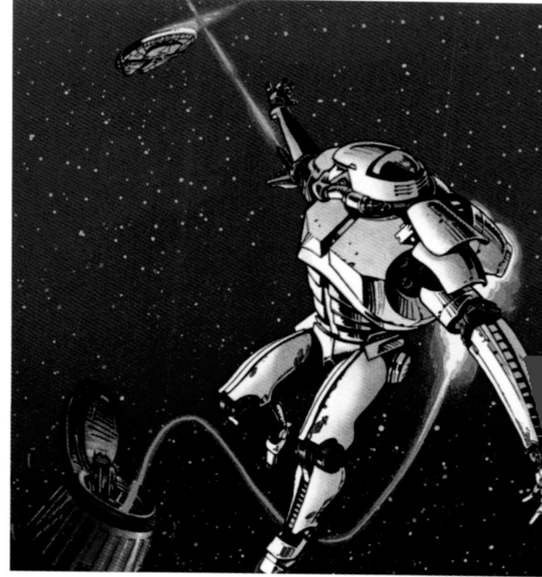
Spacetrooper

ing tanks." Powerful weaponry lined the powersuit armor. Paired grenade launchers were shoulder-mounted and magazine-fed, and were capable of launching concussion, stun, and gas projectiles. On the right gauntlet was a powerful blaster cannon, while the left gauntlet featured a miniature proton torpedo hurler. The gauntlet also sported laser cutters or rotating sleeves, allowing the spacetrooper to penetrate armored hulls. Spacetrooper armor was too cumbersome to operate within planetary gravities. A variety of armor types were developed over the years, with each generation becoming more sleek and maneuverable than earlier iterations.

**spacing** A form of execution, it consisted of casting a victim out into space without any protective gear.

**spade-headed smooka** A rodent with a prehensile tail found at all levels of the Dagobah rain forest. The spade-headed smooka chiseled out holes in trees with its teeth for nesting purposes. It had ulnar skin flaps that stiffened when leaping to effect limited glides. Its diet included not only berries and nuts but also bogwing and jubba bird nestlings and their eggs; it also ate unguarded leaf-tail pups.

**Spangled Veil Nebula** Located in the Meridian sector near Exodo II and Odos, the Spangled Veil Nebula was filled with glowing white clouds of dust and massive, drifting chunks of ice. Nine years after the Battle of Endor, Han Solo and Lando Calrissian were attacked by an Imperial fleet from the nearby Antemeridian sector while at Exodo II. They lost their pursuers in the Spangled Veil Nebula.

**Spar (Alpha-Ø2)** An ARC trooper with aberrant programming who fled Kamino's Tipoca City after having grown to 17 biological years. Alpha-Ø2, nicknamed Spar, was part of the first "test class" of 100 ARC troopers created by the Kaminoans for the Republic. Spar demonstrated such independence of mind and force of will that the normal Kaminoan reconditioning process did not take. For eight and a half years, Alpha-Ø2 looked and acted like his fellow clones, until Jango Fett's memories began flooding Spar's mind. Knowing he'd be reconditioned, he made a bold escape from Kamino. Spar roamed the Outer Rim, where he worked at odd jobs for several years while trying to sort out his own troubled mind. After the outbreak of the Clone Wars and the death of Jango Fett, Spar went to work rebuilding Jango's supercommandos from local police on Mandalore, where rumor spread that the son of Jango Fett, the last True Mandalorian, had survived to lead them. As Mandalore the Resurrector, Spar and his Mandalorian Protectors waged war on the Jedi. For their last mission, Darth Sidious ordered the Mandalorian government to send the supercommandos to capture Senator Padmé Amidala on Norval II. Following the wars, Alpha-Ø2 disappeared

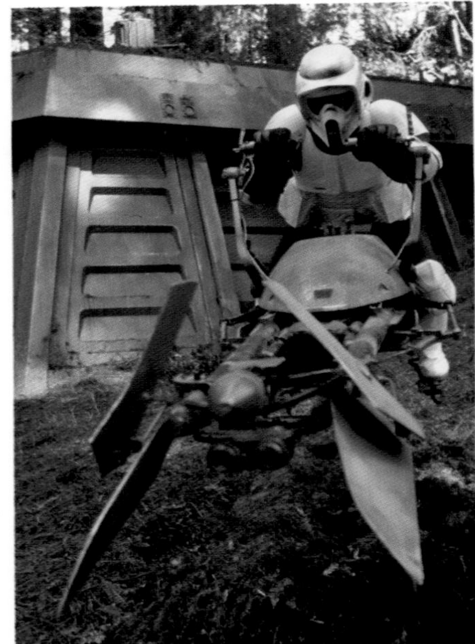

*Speeder bike*

to the Extrictarium Nebula where, unable to reconcile his dual sets of memories, his mind slowly gave way to clone madness. Ailyn Vel, Boba Fett's daughter, found him there and shot him dead.

**Sparkle Run** This hyperspace travel route connected the worlds of the Killik Colony to the rest of the Unknown Regions. Its entry point was at Tenupe, and it cut through the center of Killik territory.

**Sparky** An R5 unit with maroon-and-white markings, Sparky was assigned to Jaina Solo when she joined Rogue Squadron. He was destroyed when Jaina's X-wing was shot down at the Battle of Kalarba.

**Special Task Force One** The code name used for the 15-vessel fleet assembled by Kinman Doriana and Vicelord Siv Kav to eliminate the Outbound Flight Project. Before it could make contact with Outbound Flight, the task force was itself intercepted by Commander Thrawn. In a carefully orchestrated series of feints, Thrawn discovered how to communicate with the droid starfighters that Siv Kav was launching against him, and altered their orders. Thrawn launched the droid starfighters on attacks against their own ships, decimating the task force.

**Specter Squadron** One of the many fighter squadrons of the Rebel Alliance. Specter One was the code name assigned to pilot Jon Vander during his stay at Renforra Base.

**spectral guardian** Mysterious creatures of ancient Jedi lore that guarded the tomb of Ulic Qel-Droma on Rhen Var. They were insubstantial beings that could pass through matter and create weapons of energy from the air.

**speeder** *See* airspeeder; landspeeder; snowspeeder.

**speeder bike** Small repulsorlift vehicles, they were used throughout the galaxy as personal transports, recreational vehicles, and even military reconnaissance craft, such as those used by the Empire's scout troops. Speeder bikes could travel at up to 500 kilometers per hour through terrain that would stop other vehicles. Most could rise only about 25 meters above ground level.

The Empire's speeder bikes had armor plating, a single blaster cannon, two outriggers, and four forward steering vanes. Controls for maneuvering were in the handgrips; altitude controls in the foot pedals also normally controlled speed. Communications, sensors, and weaponry controls were at the front of the saddle.

Biker scouts normally worked in squads called lances. Each five-speeder lance had four standard speeder bike scouts and a sergeant commander; a lance generally split into two elements for field operations. Imperial scouts using speeders could explore and survey far more territory per man than those using almost any other type of vehicle. Speeder troops were normally used for scouting and exploration; they were ordered to avoid conflict so that they could make reports to base commanders. Speeder bike troop helmets had macrobinocular viewplates, a full sensor array, and a terrain-plotting computer to help scouts navigate in unfamiliar territory at high speed.

Speeder bikes were part of the Empire's efforts to patrol the forests on Endor, but a Rebel commando team led by Han Solo and Princess Leia managed to eliminate a perimeter scouting lance, allowing the Rebels a clear path to the shield generator base.

**speeder transport** Large shuttlecraft, they were used by the New Republic to move V-wing airspeeders from capital ships to launch points inside a planet's atmosphere.

**Spefik** A planet with anti-orbital ion cannons that were attacked by two wings of TIE fighters. The cannons were destroyed by a salvo from pilot Ranulf Trommer.

**Spero** An old Ho'Din master gardener and friend of Leia Organa Solo, he had a plant shop in the Southern Underground on Imperial Center. He was propagator of a strain of yellow fungus used all over the galaxy. Spero gave Leia important confirmation about the criminal organization Black Sun and its leader, Prince Xizor.

**SPHA-T (self-propelled heavy artillery—turbolaser)** A self-propelled artillery unit used by the Republic during the Clone Wars. The turbolaser of the SPHA-T utilized a large focusing array to produce a beam of potent energy. The turbolaser had tremendous range and was capable of penetrating deflector shields. Unfortunately, it required a gargantuan reactor core. The central cannon was modular, allowing different artillery units to be fitted with different weapons types, such as ion cannons, anti-vehicle laser cannons, or concussion missile launchers. The sheer size of the turbolaser and its attendant equipment prevented the weapon from being installed on any known vehicle manufactured by Kuat Drive Yards, so KDY produced a large, well-armored drive unit powered by 12 articulated legs. The turbolaser was fixed on top of the vehicle and did not rotate; instead, the vehicle itself turned to provide the turbolaser with a clear line of fire. The SPHA-T required a crew of 15 clone troopers to operate the turbolaser, pilot the drive unit, and monitor the reactor core. The SPHA-T could also be equipped with 12 retractable anti-personnel blasters, which necessitated 10 dedicated gunners. A small staging area below the turbolaser allowed the vehicle to carry an additional 20 clone troopers. A battery of SPHA-Ts were responsible for shooting down the immense Trade Federation core ships that attempted to escape the first battle of the Clone Wars.

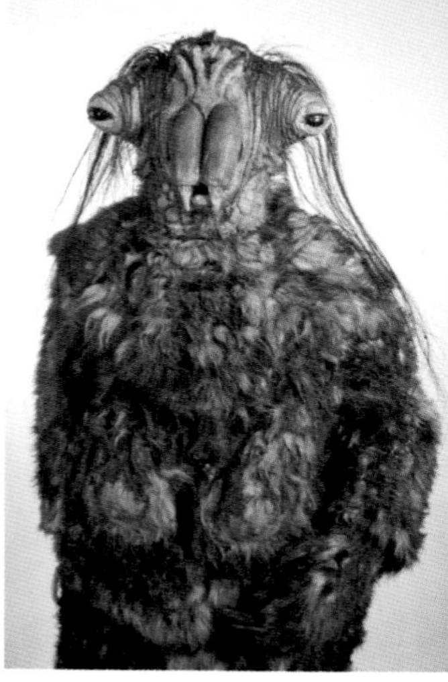
Tanus Spijek

**Spherical Flame** An emblem of the Trade Federation. The Spherical Flame and the fish-shaped garhai were considered by the Neimoidians to be the twin emblems of piety and power.

**spice** A name given to a variety of drugs, in particular the glitterstim spice mined underground on the planet Kessel. Spice was a highly taxed and controlled substance, although legal to use in most parts of the galaxy. It was a popular commodity for smugglers because of its high profit margin. Spice had a number of legitimate uses in psychological therapy, criminal investigation, communication with alien species, artistic inspiration, and entertainment. Mood-altering glitterstim had a sharp, pleasant odor and could produce feelings of euphoria in those who used it. Other spices include ryll, carsunum, avabush, gy'lan, lumni-spice, yarrock, and andris.

SPHA-T

***Spicy Lady*** A ship owned by the smuggler Jarril, it was small but distinctive, a cross between a stock light freighter and an A-wing fighter. Jarril stole the plans for the *Millennium Falcon* and modified them to construct the *Spicy Lady.* The ship was built for carrying cargo, but its storage units could be easily jettisoned so that the A-wing portion could maneuver on its own. The fighter could even be remotely operated if necessary. Lando Calrissian discovered the *Spicy Lady* floating in space, minus its A-wing component, with the body of the murdered Jarril aboard.

**Spider People** The dominant species of sentients on the planet Ord Cestus until they were defeated in a great war by the X'Ting. The original Spider People were sometimes referred to as Cestians. After they were relegated to inhabiting the deep caves of the planet, their existence was largely forgotten. They became little more than "cave spiders" to the X'Ting, more a nuisance than another native species.

**spider-roach** An arachnid pest, it was found in the lower levels of Imperial City.

**spider sloth** This unusual, arboreal creature was native to the mogo tree forests of Tenupe. The spider sloth resembled a bantha-sized, sluglike creature that hung in the mogo trees by wrapping its 10-meter-long tail around a branch. It then remained motionless until it detected prey, when it moved its sinuous bulk into a position to consume it. The body of the spider sloth was covered with thick, moss-clad scales, and it had dozens of small legs lining its underside. The head was essentially a huge mouth, surrounded by four pedipalps that helped it push its prey into its maw.

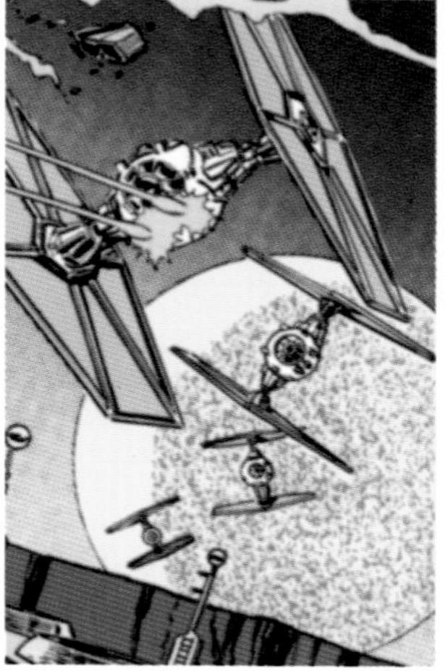
Spindrift

**Spijek, Tanus** An Elom who once worked as a spy for the Rebellion. Tanus Spijek was hired by the Rebel Alliance to carry messages between Alderaan and the Rebel base on Yavin 4, but by the time of the Battle of Endor he had fallen in with the rogues of Jabba's palace.

**spike-finned sounder** Flying fish with sharp teeth that inhabited the seas of Kamino. Their heads resembled that of the opee sea killer on Naboo. Obi-Wan and Anakin fought off swarms of the fish when their starfighters splashed down on Kamino's oceans. They were believed to have been bred from cloned stock of the b'tan flyers the Kaminoans brought in from Rodia.

Spiker

**Spiker** The lieutenant of a swoop gang led by Big Gizz, who was placed in the ranks to act as a spy for Jabba the Hutt. Spiker was shot and injured while trying to prevent Boba Fett from bringing a frozen Han Solo to Jabba's palace. Spiker and Big Gizz later encountered a renegade dark trooper at the ruins of Mos Espa Arena on Tatooine. Underneath his helmet, Spiker had blue skin and red eyes, suggesting Chiss heritage. Spiker disappeared shortly after the Battle of Endor.

**Spince, Mako** Shiftless and aimless, this son of a once influential Senator befriended a younger Han Solo at the Imperial Space Academy before being expelled for one prank too many. Mako Spince then became a smuggler and taught the trade to Solo. He was intercepted by bandits on a particularly risky run, and his injuries crippled him. Confined to a repulsor chair, he became a traffic controller on Nar Shaddaa.

A decade later, Solo returned to Nar Shaddaa, and although Spince let the *Millennium Falcon* find safety in the moon's twisting city structures, he also contacted the bounty hunters Boba Fett and Dengar to apprise them of the whereabouts of Solo and his wife, Leia. Han and Leia escaped, but on their return, Spince alerted Imperial authorities. Solo managed to maneuver his ship so that instead of the *Falcon,* it was Spince's traffic control tower that was in the tractor beam of an Imperial Star Destroyer. Spince and the tower were destroyed.

**Spindrift** An isolated Imperial outpost. During the Galactic Civil War, Luke Skywalker's squadron used rebuilt TIE fighters to attack the outpost, hoping to obtain route coordinates for an Imperial armada that was transporting an exotic creature called a Teezl.

**Spiner** An alien species of stout humanoids covered with deadly pointed quills. They evolved on a world hidden deep within the stellar cloud drifts of the Elrood sector. The Spiner homeworld, Worxer, was destroyed when its star went supernova roughly 200 years before the rise of the Empire; only a few thousand Spiners survived. A genetic flaw permitted them to reproduce only on their homeworld, causing the species' slow extinction. The Star-Hopper named Hedji was a Spiner.

*Spiner*

**spinglass** This unusual form of glass was produced by the Killiks of the Saras hive of the Colony. It was literally spun from their bodies, much the way spider silk was spun into a web, but was melted down and then formed into shapes to produce useful or artistic objects. The raw material was simply referred to as spin.

***Spinnerfish*** This well-armed shuttle was part of the Galactic Alliance's Second Fleet during the blockade of the Corellian system some 10 years after the end of the war against the Yuuzhan Vong. While patrolling the space near Corellia, the *Spinnerfish* was the first vessel to encounter the *Love Commander* when Lando Calrissian arrived with Han and Leia Solo. Although the *Spinnerfish*'s commanding officer boarded the pleasure yacht with every intention of detaining it, he was unprepared for Leia Solo's use of the Force. She was able to manipulate him into allowing the *Love Commander* to reach Corellia's surface, after "convincing" him to provide Lando with a Galactic Alliance authorization code.

**Spira** A tropical pleasure world near the Inner Core in the Lytton sector, it was one of the most popular vacation destinations for wealthy Core World citizens. The planet was covered by a sparkling sea, broken only by small islands. Scouted by the Old Republic more than 1,000 years before the rise of the Empire, Spira was later leased from the Empire by the Tourist Guild. Air traffic was limited to passenger liners and registered transports, and personal weapons were forbidden. Ataria Island was home to Spira's major spaceport and its most exclusive resorts. Spectacular cliffs made up the island's north and west sides, and luxurious beaches could be found to the east. Upon first taking up elective office, Finis Valorum switched his residency from Coruscant to Spira.

**spirit master** Natives on primitive worlds with the gift of the Force, but who interpreted its powers as a type of "magic." They believed that the manifestations of the Force were the work of nature spirits, the ghosts of their ancestors, or even the will of primitive gods. Their perception of the Force was forever colored by this belief, and while they could become as powerful as the greatest Jedi, they did not have the same understanding. Because spirit masters learned a completely different tradition of the Force, the powers they derived from it also took a different form. Spirit masters often used elaborate (and unnecessary) rituals to perform their tricks.

***Spirit of Jabba*** One of Jabba the Hutt's hidden treasure ships, it carried a cargo of eight Mendacian funeral urns from the Krung dynasty. The ship had an interactive security tape, which revealed that the vessel was actually a trap designed to lure Jabba's enemies after his death. In order to escape, the swoop bikers Spiker and Big Gizz jettisoned the priceless cargo.

**Spirit Tree** The Ewok tribes on Endor's Forest Moon considered this to be the original tree on the planet. All life was believed to have started with the Spirit Tree. The Ewoks also believed that all life must eventually return to the Spirit Tree.

**spitcrete** A term used to describe the unusual mortar used by members of the Killik hives of the Colony to build anything from seats and benches to buildings. It was created by individual Colony members from natural materials that were chewed up and combined with their saliva, which acted as a bonding agent.

**SPMA-T (self-propelled medium artillery—turbolaser)** A self-propelled medium artillery walker specifically fitted with a long-range turbolaser cannon, it was used by the Republic army during the Clone Wars. As with the SPHA-T, the weapons system of the SPMA-T was modular, and variant walkers could be deployed with special payloads for specific missions. In the years after the Clone Wars, the walker was lightened through the use of more modern alloys and composites. SPMA-Ts were artillery units by every definition—essentially walking turrets. The main cannons had a frighteningly long range and required targets to be sensor-painted if they were to be hit. These vehicles were slow moving and not heavily armored, and usually were dispatched with an escort.

*SPMA-T*

**Spore** A gene-spliced sentient creation of the Ithorians, it was made from vesuvague and bafforr trees. After their creation turned destructive, the Ithorians buried it in an asteroid belt. Spore was able to possess bodies and send out tentacles from a victim to take control of even more. Prior to the Battle of Endor, the Dark Jedi Jerec sought out Spore in order to create an army of slaves, though the beast instead destroyed Jerec's Imperial Star Destroyer *Vengeance*.

**sporting blaster** A light, compact blaster that was easily concealed and handled but had only limited range and firepower. During her days as a Rebel agent working within the Imperial Senate, Princess Leia often carried a Drearian Defense Conglomerate Defender sporting blaster.

**spotlight sloth** A sloth that lived on the planet Dagobah, it used the bright glowing patches on its chest to illuminate the plant life that it fed upon.

**Sprax** A Nalroni, he was one of the lieutenants, or Vigos, of the Black Sun criminal organization. The prideful Sprax's dark fur had begun to turn gray, but he dyed it to try to appear younger.

**Spray of Tynna** *See* Odumin.

***Springhawk*** This small assault shuttle was part of the Chiss Expansionary Defense Fleet during the years following the Battle of Naboo. The *Springhawk* was the command vessel of Picket Force Two, which was led by Force Commander Thrawn. The ship took minor hull damage when Thrawn set out to acquire a Vagaari pseudograv-field generator after his sensor crews discovered a Vagaari ambush at the edge of their patrol zone. Thrawn was careful not to attack the Vagaari, instead just skirting the main battlefield to steal the generator and attach it to the *Springhawk*'s hull. Thrawn was reprimanded for his actions by Admiral Ar'alani, because they resulted in the deaths of several Chiss crewers.

**Spuma** A planet where New Republic Intelligence agents first discovered increased trooper recruitment by the fleet of Admiral Harrsk. The admiral was one of the few Imperial warlords still strong eight years after the Battle of Endor.

**spy-killer** A small, fingernail-sized device that could be implanted into the neck of a being. Using an embedder, the spy-killer—also

called an embed unit—was installed to ensure that the individual could not divulge information about his or her mission. The spy-killer was set to respond to a certain keyword or phrase that, if spoken by the being, would trigger the device to explode. The explosion was enough to destroy the brain and kill the being almost instantly.

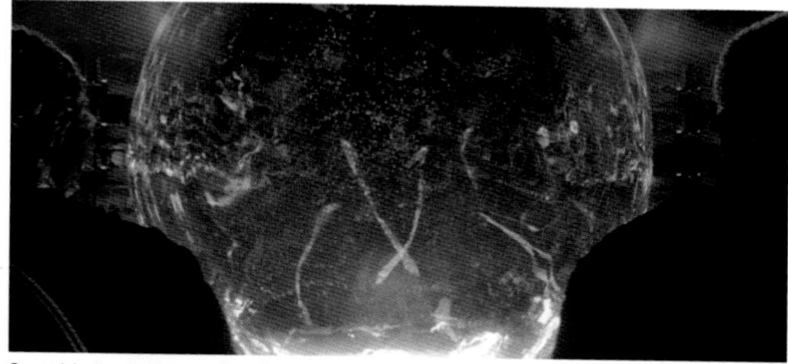
Squid Lake *ballet at the Galaxies Opera House*

**spynet** A name for any widespread intelligence-gathering network. The Imperial Security Bureau, New Republic Intelligence, the Bothan spynet, and Black Sun were some of the better-known spynets.

**Squab** The star orbited by Skor II, home planet of the Squibs.

**Squad Seven** A small group of specialists formed by Alpha-17 to accompany ranking Jedi on missions during the Clone Wars. The squad comprised the best cross-trained ARC commanders, pilots, marines, seatroopers, demolition specialists, and snipers, and frequently accompanied Obi-Wan Kenobi and Anakin Skywalker. Commanders Cody and Odd Ball led the squad, although Major Jorir handled its day-to-day operations. They took part in the mission to Cato Neimoidia and the Coruscant space battle.

**Squalris** A portly, wide-faced species native to Ifmix VI. Squalrises were known as good-natured capitalists who could turn mean as soon as a business interest was threatened by another individual or entity.

**Squeak** A Tin-Tin Dwarf, he worked as a messenger for Big Bunji, a former associate of Han Solo.

**Squeaky** A protocol droid who worked as the quartermaster to Rogue Squadron and later to Wraith Squadron. He served aboard the *Tantive IV* when it was captured by the Empire during the Battle of Yavin. Squeaky spent time in the spice mines of Kessel until he escaped to rejoin the Alliance.

**squellbug** A large insect native to the planet Korriban, it was among the favorite prey of the tuk'ata.

**Squib** Small, furry bipeds with tufted ears, large eyes, short muzzles, and black noses, these galactic nomads came from the planet Skor II. They used tractor beams aboard their reclamation ships to salvage what they considered treasure but most other beings thought of as junk. Squibs had an intense rivalry with Ugors. Often overconfident, Squibs appeared overbearing and uppity. They turned haggling into an art, and the more complicated the deal, the better they liked it.

**Squid Head** *See* Quarren.

***Squid Lake*** A Mon Calamari ballet performed at the Galaxies Opera House in which performers moved around in a giant globe of water. The premiere performance of *Squid Lake* on Coruscant brought out the most studied of culture lovers, as well as less devoted guests who were there merely to be seen.

**squill** A creature found on Tatooine but reviled throughout the galaxy as a disease-carrying pest. Squills were prized by Jawas for their tough, pungent meat.

**Squint** An alias used by Alek, a male Jedi Knight who traveled to Taris during the Mandalorian Wars to recruit Jedi to help fight the Mandalorian threat. Squint, who got the nickname from his fellow Jedi when they couldn't pronounce his last name, Squinquargesimus, believed that the Jedi Council was turning a blind eye to the threat posed by the Mandalorians and that the Council was too focused on the Sith to see the real problem. Squint and his followers believed that the Jedi needed to take the fight to the Mandalorians, and he was willing to "enter the darkness to save the light." Squint was among the many Jedi Knights who were captured by the Mandalorians and sentenced to prison at the Flashpoint Station facility. There he was forced to endure the research and experiments of the noted biologist Demagol, who was trying to discover why the Jedi could use the Force. It was at the Flashpoint facility that Squint met the Arkanian refugee Jarael, who had been mistakenly captured by the Mandalorians. Despite the fact that he had been subjected to many tests already, Squint stepped in when Jarael was chosen by Demagol, hoping to spare her the agony of the scientist's tests. He endured several additional torture sessions before Carrick and Rohlan Dyre arrived on a daring rescue mission. They infiltrated the facility and scattered the Mandalorians, then freed Jarael and the other Jedi from captivity. As the war ground on, Squint joined the Revanchists, hoping to use his skills in the Force to defend the galaxy. The Revanchists had foreseen galaxywide chaos and sorrow, and Squint felt that exogorths, or space slugs, might help end the war before it spiraled out of control. (*See also* Malak, Darth.)

*Squint*

**squints** A slang term used by X-wing pilots for Imperial TIE interceptors.

**Sriluur** This harsh desert world on the Sisar Run was the homeworld of the Weequay species. Sriluur, the fifth planet of the system, was also home to thousands of Houk colonists. The two primary urban centers on the planet were Meirm City and Dnalvec, while Al-Campur was its capital city. The moon of Ruul was owned by the wealthy family of the Jedi Master Sora Bulq. During the Yuuzhan Vong invasion, the population of Sriluur was enslaved. Han Solo and Droma traveled there in the search for Droma's clanmates and Han's friend Roa.

*Ssi-ruuvi battle droid*

**Srrors'tok** The feline species of Ahnjai Rahmma, bodyguard to High Inquisitor Tremayne.

**Ssi-ruu (plural: Ssi-ruuk)** A saurian species with domination its goal, the Ssi-ruuk invaded Imperial space during the Galactic Civil War. In a process called entechment, the Ssi-ruuk drained the life energies of other species—particularly humanoids—to power their droids and shipboard instruments as part of an expansion of their Imperium throughout the galaxy.

Ssi-ruuvi adults on their homeworld of Lwhekk grew to about 2 meters tall. They had beaked muzzles with large teeth and round black eyes with triple eyelids. Retractable black scent-tongues in their nostrils sensed other individuals' stress reactions. Their massive bodies had upper limbs with three prehensile, clawed digits; their tails were muscular. Ssi-ruuvi body color varied and tended to indicate occupation: Russets dominated the military, for example, while blues ruled the political structure.

**Ssi-ruuvi battle droids** Small drone ships, they were powered by the enteched life forces drained from captured prisoners. The 2-meter-wide battle droids were pyramid-shaped and functioned as the main assault fighters of the Ssi-ruuvi fleet. Two fully rotating laser cannons on each corner armed them well. They were speedy and highly maneuverable, and their size made them difficult

targets. Their shields were as heavy as many larger starfighters'.

Powered by fusion, the battle droids became highly radioactive when they were destroyed. Microfilament grids on the ships' surfaces could capture part of the energy of incoming blasts and filter it back into the battle droid's main generator. Ssi-ruuvi command cruisers remotely controlled the two life energies trapped inside each battle droid, forcing them to obey all instructions. However, Luke Skywalker, using the Force, discovered that the life energies still retained some will of their own.

**Ssoh** One of the most successful Trandoshan slavers in the business during the reign of the Empire. In order to control his Wookiee captives, he would routinely turn the proud warriors against one another. The Trandoshan made the mistake of capturing Chewbacca, who organized his fellow captives to revolt against their masters. Ssoh was thought to have been the only Trandoshan to fight Chewbacca and live, although it took him ages to regrow his missing limbs.

**Ssty** A furry, bipedal species with two arms and tiny claws that act like fingers. Sstys were very intelligent but prone to cheating.

**ST 321** The comm unit designation for Darth Vader's personal *Lambda*-class shuttle.

**Staable, Sammie** A tall human with his hair done up in thick, snake-like tresses, he worked with gambler Raal Yorta and pickpocket Smileredon-verdont before eventually joining the Rebel Alliance.

**staff of power** A symbol of Logray's position within his Ewok tribe. The staff of power was decorated with the spine of one of Logray's enemies.

**staga** Herd beasts, they were native to the planet Ambria.

***Stalker*** An Imperial Star Destroyer, it was originally assigned to search the Outer Rim for new worlds to subjugate. The *Stalker* launched the probe droid that discovered the secret Rebel Alliance base on the ice planet Hoth. The ship was later assigned to the Empire's Death Squad.

**stalker armor** A suit designed by Salus Corporation on Rodia for specific use as bounty hunter armor. The suit gained much respect in the bounty hunter community because of its versatility. Two configurations were available—one tailored to comfortably fit Rodians, and another designed to fit most generic humanoid body types. Stalker armor had a nice mix of weapons, solid protection, and durable construction.

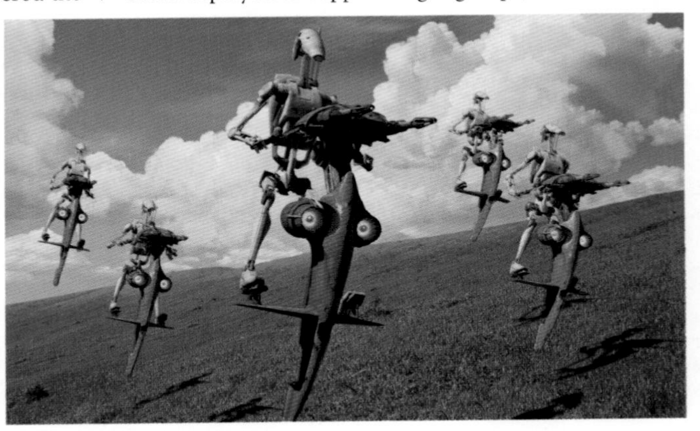
STAPs being flown by battle droids

***Stalking Moon*** A Yuuzhan Vong asteroid-shaped scout ship that Qurang Lah sent to Yag'Dhul in advance of the main attack fleet. It was not a warship, and its dovin basals were not very good at deflecting fire. Corran Horn, Anakin Solo, and Tahiri Veila abandoned their ship the *Lucre* to land on what they thought was a chunk of rock, only to discover the *Stalking Moon*'s true nature. The bulk of the vessel was the concealing stone of the asteroid and vast caverns of greenware. Veila donned the ship's cognition hood to fly it when she learned it was headed for Yag'Dhul. The Jedi used the *Stalking Moon* to stage an attack on the Givin defenses, hoping to learn who their potential allies might be.

***Stalwart* (1)** A New Republic Fifth Fleet cruiser, it was deployed in the blockade of Doornik-319.

***Stalwart* (2)** A Star Destroyer allied with the Imperial Remnant. Admiral Pellaeon took command of the vessel after recovering from his injuries, and it later fought in the Battle of Borosk.

**standard time part** The basic unit used to measure time throughout the galaxy.

**stang** An Alderaanian expletive.

**Stanz, Captain** A Bothan, he was owner-pilot of the gypsy freighter *Freebird*.

**STAP (single trooper aerial platform)** A small repulsorlift vehicle designed to carry a single Trade Federation battle droid on reconnaissance and aerial attack missions. Armed with twin blaster cannons, the STAP was well equipped to deal with small targets, such as fleeing civilians. The extremely agile vehicle could move swiftly through most environments, including dense forests and swamps. Often deployed to support larger groups, the STAP scouted ahead of advancing Trade Federation forces in search of enemy resistance. STAPs were variations on Longspur and Alloi's Bespin airhooks.

Starbreaker 12

***Starbreaker 12*** The personal starship of Gav and Jori Daragon, citizens of the Republic about 5,000 years before the Galactic Civil War. The pair used the vessel in their quest to map new hyperspace routes. Ultimately, it was confiscated by Aarrba the Hutt, but Gav and Jori stole the craft and made one final attempt to find fortune as hyperspace explorers. This gamble led them into the heart of the ancient Sith Empire, where they were captured. Jori eventually escaped in *Starbreaker 12* and returned home, but the Dark Lord of the Sith Naga Sadow had planted a homing beacon on the starship, allowing him to follow Jori and invade the Republic. By the time the Sith mobilized, *Starbreaker 12* was under the ownership of the unscrupulous merchant Ssk Kahorr, who was killed when Sadow, in his first act of aggression after entering the Koros system, ordered the ship's total destruction.

**Starbuster Plot** *See* Centerpoint Station.

**Star Chamber** A structure beneath the surface of Dathomir used by the ancient Kwa to protect the integrity of the Infinity Gates that allowed interstellar teleportation.

**Star Chamber Café** A café in Mos Eisley's Lucky Despot Hotel.

**Starcrash Brigade** An elite Imperial assault team working for the Emperor prior to the Battle of Endor. It members were charged with the detonation of a biological weapon on Firrerre and the destruction of the Firrerreo species.

**star cruiser** A class of capital ship.

**Star Destroyer** The core of the Imperial Navy, these huge wedge-shaped warships were meant to inspire fear—and succeeded admirably. These engineering marvels wielded more than 100 weapons emplacements for deep-space combat. A standard 1,600-meter-long *Imperial*-class Star Destroyer—which replaced the earlier *Victory*-class—maintained 60 turbolasers for ship-to-ship combat and planetary assault and 60 ion cannons to disable enemy ships for boarding. Atop its superstructure was a huge command tower holding the bridge, essential systems, and computer controls. It was topped by a pair of generator domes for deflector shields.

A Star Destroyer had two main landing bays that could accommodate hundreds of ships of varying sizes. A full wing of 72 TIE fighters (six squadrons of 12 ships each) was standard. It also carried eight *Lambda*-class shuttles, 15 stormtrooper transports, and five assault gunboats, along with Skipray blastboats and *Gamma*-class assault shuttles. Star Destroyers accommodated planetary assault teams with landing barges, drop ships, 20 AT-AT walkers, 30 AT-ST scout walkers, and 9,700 ground troops. They could deploy a prefabricated garrison base with 800 troops. The ships were designed by Lira Wessex, daughter of famed Republic engineer and designer Walex Blissex. Typical missions involved perimeter patrol, convoy escort, planetary assault, and planetary defense in the event of a direct assault.

*Star Destroyer*

*Star Forge*

An upgraded class of the Star Destroyer, called the Imperial II, began appearing in Imperial Navy fleets shortly after the Battle of Yavin. These vessels had a heavily reinforced hull and boasted more powerful heavy turbolaser batteries and cannons.

All told, the Empire built more than 25,000 Star Destroyers, holding half of them on reserve in the Galactic Core to protect key military, industrial, and political systems. The Empire could strategically deploy the ships anywhere on short notice.

The *Super*-class Star Destroyer was many times as powerful as its predecessor. Because they were built in limited numbers, these ships were used mainly as command vessels, guiding fleets and serving as headquarters from which to conduct planetary assaults and space battles. Darth Vader's *Executor* was a Star Dreadnaught, commonly referred to as a Super Star Destroyer. A special *Eclipse*-class Star Destroyer was built to serve as the cloned Emperor's flagship six years after the Battle of Endor. Solid black, it was 16,000 meters long.

***Star Dream*** The transport ship that brought Evar Orbus and his Galactic Wailers to Tatooine.

**Star Forge** An ancient alien space station used by Darth Malak to churn out capital ships, fighters, and assault droids. It was located near Lehon (Rakata Prime), the home of the Rakata species. The Star Forge was created in the pre-Republic era by the Rakata. Its location was revealed by collecting the data from another Rakata invention known as the Star Map. The Star Forge was ultimately destroyed by Revan and a Republic fleet.

**Star Galleon** At 300 meters in length, this ship class combined the cargo space of a bulk freighter with the weapons of a combat starship. A Star Galleon's 10 turbolaser batteries and concussion missiles made separate freighters and escort craft unnecessary. The interior had fortress-like emplacements in the corridors, room for 300 troopers, force fields, and heavy blast doors. The cargo-hold pod in the center of the ship could be jettisoned from the vessel and sent on a prearranged lightspeed jump.

***Star Home*** A unique transport vessel designed more than 4,000 years before the Galactic Civil War for the Queen Mother of the Hapes Cluster, it replicated her castle on the planet Hapes. Despite its ungainly appearance and its age, the *Star Home* was spaceworthy. The castle-ship held the Queen Mother's quarters and hearing room, as well as dining halls, meeting rooms, and guest quarters, all covered in dark stone. A number of towers capped with crystal domes gave an unobstructed view of space. Gardens filled upper courtyard levels.

The *Star Home* embodied wealth, power, and the supreme authority of the Queen Mother. Each of the inhabited worlds of the Hapes Cluster contributed stone, woodwork, gems, or other ornamentation for the interior. Each year, the governor of each world presented the most treasured artifact from his or her planet to be stored forever in the galleries and vaults of the *Star Home,* so visitors could view the treasures of the Hapan people.

Nearly a third of the ship's interior was filled with six massive generators that powered all systems, including shields and 24 sublight and four hyperdrive engines.

**Star-Hoppers** A name given to the posse that Han Solo organized to protect the simple farming village of Onacra on Aduba-3 from the Cloud Riders. In addition to Han Solo and Chewbacca, the members of the Star-Hoppers included Jaxxon, Amaiza, Don-Wan Kihotay, Hedji, Jimm the Starkiller Kid, and FE-9Q. With the intervention of a behemoth living in the caves beneath Onacra, the Star-Hoppers were able to defeat Sergi-X Arrogantus and his Cloud Riders as well as the behemoth itself.

**Starhunter Intergalactic Menagerie** A traveling sideshow, it toured the galaxy during the early days of the Empire. Operated by the sleazy Captain Stroon, the main attractions of the Starhunter Intergalactic Menagerie were rare and usually illegally acquired creatures from many worlds. It moved from system to system in a huge cruiser, whose first mate was a lizard-like humanoid called Slarm.

**Stark, Iaco** A charismatic and bold human smuggler and pirate who maintained a fleet of

*Star-Hoppers*

ships at the time of the Stark Hyperspace Conflict. He sold what he stole at a profit, though he did undercut the inflated prices of the Trade Federation. He was able to forge a coalition of Outer Rim outlaws into the Stark Commercial Combine. With forces from within the Galactic Republic conspiring against him, he turned against Jedi and Galactic Republic representatives at a conference held on Troiken. From there he unleashed a nav computer virus on the military forces of the Galactic Republic that had been converging on the site. After losing control of the Combine, he was contacted by Plo Koon telepathically and learned that the Combine would be defeated. He then betrayed the Combine and provided the Jedi with the patch necessary to stop the nanovirus. As a reward, his life was spared, and he later emerged as a leader in the Commerce Guild.

**Stark Commercial Combine** A coalition of smugglers, pirates, mercenaries, bounty hunters, and assassins working in the Outer Rim formed by Iaco Stark. Also referred to as the Stark Commercial Collective, the Stark Commercial Combine became large enough to even challenge the Trade Federation. During the Stark Hyperspace Conflict, the Combine attacked the Republic with a nav computer virus while negotiations were supposed to be occurring on Troiken. The Combine fleet defeated the Republic's navy as the Combine army faced the joint forces of the Republic and the Jedi on Troiken. The Combine was ultimately defeated when Stark betrayed his own followers and helped the Jedi.

**Stark Hyperspace Conflict** The last major conflict in the galaxy prior to the Battle of Naboo. Iaco Stark forged a coalition among smugglers, pirates, mercenaries, bounty hunters, and assassins working in the Outer Rim to form the Stark Commercial Combine. After a key processing plant for alazhi bacterium on the planet Thyferra exploded—cutting bacta production by two-thirds—bacta prices skyrocketed. The Stark Commercial Combine began to attack bacta ships and supplies and were hailed as heroes by the Outer Rim planets, which threatened to plunge the galaxy into war. Senator Valorum, Nute Gunray, and a group of Jedi mediators led by Jedi Master Tyvokka went to Troiken to meet with the Combine to resolve the crisis. There they were ambushed by Stark's forces, counteracting an ambush set up by Republic militarist Ranulph Tarkin. Though the Combine decimated much of Tarkin's fleet using a nav computer virus, the Jedi and the Republic forces on Troiken were able to hold out long enough for Trade Federation and Jedi reinforcements to arrive. In the end, Iaco betrayed his supporters to aid the Jedi, and the Combine was defeated both in space and on the ground. Plo Koon was legendary for his leadership, rallying the disheartened Republic troops to an unlikely and miraculous victory.

**Starkiller** The code name for Darth Vader's Secret Apprentice. A powerful, almost primal Force-wielder, he was forged by Vader into a lethal living weapon that the Dark Lord groomed in secret—continuing the Sith tradition of treachery—in a bid to defeat the Emperor and rule the galaxy. Vader discovered his Secret Apprentice on the Wookiee world of Kashyyyk, when he was just a boy named Galen Marek.

Marek's parents were both Jedi who took part in the Clone Wars; during the conflict, they fell in love and secretly married. When Galen's mother learned she was pregnant, she and her husband quietly left the Order, hoping to raise their child in peace somewhere in the Outer Rim. A short time later, Emperor Palpatine issued Order 66, which resulted in the near annihilation of the Jedi. Now living in complete exile, Galen's parents relocated to Kashyyyk, where they were befriended by the native Wookiees.

Galen's mother was killed a few years later while trying to protect a group of Wookiees from slavers; Galen's father, Kento, died soon after, trying to protect the boy from Darth Vader, who had tracked the Jedi to Kashyyyk. When Vader discovered the Jedi Knight's son, he sensed great power within the boy and, after only a moment's hesitation, took the child with him.

Vader spent years personally training Galen in the ways of the Sith, but no other Imperials—including the Emperor himself—knew of his existence. The Apprentice's training was harsh and unforgiving: Vader subjected the boy to rigorous physical tests bordering on torture. He first controlled the boy through

*Starkiller*

fear, then taught him to embrace his hatred and other base emotions. As the boy grew older, Vader promised him greater power—through the dark side. Under Vader's relentless tutelage, the Apprentice all but perfected the fine art of lightsaber combat and learned to wield many fearsome dark side powers.

Galen lived in constant fear of his master, who kept the boy locked up within the bowels of his starship, the still-under-construction *Executor.* Vader allowed him no friends or companions, save a holo-droid named PROXY. During combat sessions, Vader would attack the boy relentlessly. When Galen was injured, Vader ignored the boy's pain and attacked even more viciously. Even when Vader was away, Galen was tested, quickly learning that his only trusted companion—PROXY—was actually programmed to attempt to kill him, over and over again. Under these torturous conditions, Galen began to forget his past life. He embraced his anger and hatred, eventually succumbing to the dark side as Vader intended. With the boy corrupted, Vader revealed his master plan: He was grooming his secret apprentice to one day help him destroy the Emperor.

By the time he was 15, Galen began undertaking dangerous missions for his master. As the Apprentice grew stronger in the ways of the Force, Vader began testing him by sending him on secret missions to dispatch the Dark Lord's rivals and enemies. Vader had assigned his apprentice the code name Starkiller and provided him with an advanced prototype starship, the *Rogue Shadow,* to aid in his missions. With these early trials complete, Starkiller embarked on a hunt for rogue Jedi.

Each assignment was a new test designed to ensure that the boy would have the skill, power, and will to eventually battle the Emperor. Initially, these missions involved hunting down and assassinating Vader's rivals within the Empire. Eventually, however, Vader sent Starkiller after several rogue Jedi. The first was the battle-hardened Jedi General Rahm Kota—and Vader was clear that no witnesses were to be left alive, including Imperial forces. He also got a new pilot for *Rogue Shadow,* Juno Eclipse, who had been captain of Vader's Black Eight Squadron.

After Starkiller killed Jedi Council member Shaak Ti on Felucia, Darth Vader recalled him to the *Executor,* promising that they would at last confront the Emperor. When Starkiller arrived, he discovered the Emperor's fleet already close by. But, after revealing that the Emperor's spies had discovered Starkiller's existence, Vader attacked the boy. Goaded on by the Emperor, Vader seemingly killed his Apprentice, proving his complete loyalty to the Emperor.

But Vader's attack was a ruse. He secretly retrieved Starkiller's body and had him rebuilt. When the Apprentice recovered, Vader revealed the next part of his plan: Starkiller was to locate all of the Emperor's major enemies, assembling them into an alliance of rebels and dissidents. In this way, Starkiller became, in effect, an original architect of the Rebel Alliance by facilitating the meeting on Corellia of the Alliance's founders: Garm Bel Iblis, Mon Mothma, and Bail Organa. Vader then attacked during this initial meeting, betraying Starkiller once more and imprisoning the dissidents. Eager to stop the Dark Lord, Starkiller and the now anti-Imperial Juno Eclipse sped to the first Death Star, under construction and nearing completion.

As Juno rescued the Senators, Starkiller confronted the Sith Lords who had been manipulating him for years. Lightsabers clashed inside the Emperor's observation dome, but Starkiller was ultimately no match for the power of Darth Sidious. Bombarded by Force lightning, Starkiller did not fight back but instead unleashed all the power of the Force within him, causing a tremendous blast that shattered the Emperor's tower and caused enough of a distraction to allow Eclipse and the Rebel Senators to escape. The early founders of the Rebellion honored the real Starkiller—Galen Marek—by using his family crest as the symbol of the Rebel Alliance.

***Starlight Intruder*** A hot-rod transport built for smuggling runs by Salla Zend, this medium freighter hid power beneath a battered surface. The *Starlight Intruder* could carry seven times the cargo of standard light freighters and had added hull bracing and armor plating, four military-grade ion engines for fast getaways, and four maneuvering jets at the bottom of the hull. Chewbacca helped Zend install a hyperdrive from an old Hutt chariot. Han Solo talked Zend into using the *Intruder* to smuggle his *Millennium Falcon* onto the Imperial throneworld of Byss. But while he and the *Falcon* got away, Byss security impounded the *Intruder.*

**Starlyte Station** A dilapidated trading post created from the old Gateway Space Station by Talandro Starlyte. The name was slow to catch on, gaining favor initially only with Starlyte's associates.

**Star Map** An ancient map created by the Rakata, millennia before the Great Sith War, to provide instructions for locating the Star Forge. The map itself was made up of four smaller maps, which needed to be placed together to form the overall Star Map. The smaller maps were scattered across the galaxy to prevent anyone from locating the Star Forge, but clues eventually led to their discovery on Dantooine, Manaan, Kashyyyk, and Tatooine. The four pieces were located some 4,000 years before the Battle of Yavin by Revan, Bastila Shan, and their companions, who were searching for the whereabouts of Darth Malak.

***Star Morning*** A 50-year-old Kogus liner, it was purchased by the Fallanassi religious order's corporation, Kell Plath, and used to evacuate the persecuted sect's members from the planet Lucazec.

***Star of Alderaan*** An award that commemorated the role played by the peace-loving planet Alderaan and its leader, Bail Organa, in creating the structure of the Rebel Alliance.

***Star of Empire*** A luxurious pleasure liner. Before he won the *Millennium Falcon,* Lando Calrissian hopped around the galaxy aboard ships like the *Star of Empire.* Upon graduation from the Imperial Academy, Kyle Katarn went on a vacation aboard the *Star of Empire,* where he encountered Jan Ors and was persuaded to join the Rebel Alliance.

***Star of Iskin*** An AA-9 freighter that exploded while departing Coruscant, killing all passengers, including former Republic Chancellor Finis Valorum.

***Star Runner*** The star cruiser owned and operated by young Kea Moll, who lived on her mother's farm complex on the planet Annoo.

***Starry Ice*** One of smuggler Talon Karrde's freighters, it was used to carry weapons and munitions for Rogue Squadron to the rendezvous point at the Graveyard of Alderaan.

***Star Saber*** An experimental attack ship built some 4,000 years before the Galactic Civil War, it was equipped with wing cannons.

***Star Sea Flower*** A modified YT-1150 cargo transport flown by pilot Charza Kwinn. The *Star Sea Flower* resembled a long oval loaf of bread sliced lengthwise into three pieces. The ship smelled like an ocean and was tended by "food-kin" and a variety of crustacean helpers. The *Star Sea Flower* played a crucial role during Wilhuff Tarkin's attack on Zonama Sekot, allowing Charza Kwinn to escape and return to Coruscant for future missions.

**Stars' End** A secret Corporate Sector Authority penal colony on the planet Mytus VII. Its name referred to the location of the Mytus star system, which sat at the end of a faint wisp of stars at the edge of Corporate Sector space.

**Starspeeder 3000** A passenger craft used by the Star Tours Travel Agency. On its maiden voyage to Endor, dubbed Flight ST-45, the Starspeeder's rookie pilot RX-24 ("Rex") lost control, maneuvering through an unexpected encounter with an ice comet and the forces of the Empire.

**Starstone, Olee** This Jedi Padawan and her Master, Bol Chatak, were dispatched to lead the fighting on Murkhana during the final stages of the Clone Wars. Prior to her training under Master Chatak, Starstone had studied under Jocasta Nu in the Jedi Archives, and was something of an expert on the history of the Sith. When the fighting broke out on Murkhana, Starstone had been left behind on Coruscant to continue her training. However, as the situation on Murkhana escalated, Starstone was ordered to accompany Jedi Master Saras Loorne to augment the forces of Master Chatak. When the communication to execute Order 66 came down, most of her Jedi companions died. She teamed with Roan Shryne and they escaped into Murkhana City, receiving assistance from Cash Garrulan in escaping the planet. Aboard the *Drunk Dancer,* they rescued Siadem Forte and a small group of Jedi near the planet Mossak. This small success gave Starstone the idea of establishing a link to the Jedi Archives, then downloading information on the whereabouts of any Jedi who might have survived Order 66.

On Jaguada's moon, Starstone tried to boost the signal to get more information from the Jedi Archives by jump-starting the power generators in the ancient communications facility. This led to the reactivation of the entire complex on Jaguada's moon, including the hordes of Separatist battle droids that had once protected it. After the group escaped, Starstone chose to take the SX troop transport that had carried Forte and his fellow Jedi and set off in search of more Jedi, accepting the companionship and assistance of Forte and several others. Aboard the *Vagabond Trader,* Starstone found herself assuming the role of leader, despite the fact that both Forte and Iwo Kulka were ranking Jedi Knights. She took them to Kashyyyk, where she confronted Darth Vader after the Dark Lord killed or injured her companions. She was saved by the sudden appearance of Roan Shryne, who sacrificed himself to allow her to escape.

***Starstorm I*** The spaceship used by Dark Lord of the Sith Exar Kun some 4,000 years before the Galactic Civil War to escape with the ancient scrolls given to him by the spirit of dark sider Freedon Nadd.

***Star Swan*** A transport ship, it made regular runs to Tatooine.

***Startide*** This Mon Calamari battle cruiser was the equivalent of an Imperial Star Destroyer.

**Star Tours Travel Agency** A tour company that sought to capitalize on the Moddell sector's sudden fame after the Battle of Endor. Star Tours promised "convenient daily departures to the exotic moon of Endor" along the decaying Sanctuary Pipeline. Accidents and mismanagement eventually drove the company into the ground.

***Star-Wake*** An *Envoy*-class shuttle that was part of the naval fleet amassed by the Jedi Order prior to the Battle of Ruusan. The ship had been donated to the Jedi by an anonymous Coruscant-based benefactor in response to Valenthyne Farfalla's urgent plea for support in the war against the Sith. The *Star-Wake* was stationed aboard Farfalla's flagship, the *Fairwind,* and used in rescue operations on Ruusan. The shuttle saved a young girl named Rain, who found a blaster in a cargo crate and shot everyone on board. Rain, going by the name of Zannah, took the *Star-Wake* to Onderon, where she was beset by members of the

Skelda clan. Only the timely intervention of Darth Bane saved her, and the pair took the shuttle and left Onderon behind. The *Star-Wake* was later discovered and returned to the Jedi Order.

**Starweird** A type of impossibly tall humanoid encountered only in space. Starweirds were phantom-like beings with visible but incorporeal bodies.

**stasis field** A force field, it was used to keep organic matter such as foodstuffs fresh for years. It could also keep humans and other beings in a state of suspended animation.

**Stassia** An agricultural planet in the Core Worlds. Its 1.3 billion human inhabitants were known for their indifference to most change and their accepting natures. Settled for millennia, Stassia was originally ruled by the members of the 15 Head Clans, who were descendants of the original colonists. Stassia City was home to swoop races and ringer tournaments.

**Statermast, Hinib** A Filvian spacer who traded in his starship for enough credits to purchase the Farrimmer Café with his partner, Grosteek, hoping to settle down and live out the rest of his life in peace.

**Station 88 Spaceport** A space station jointly developed by the worlds of Junction 5, Delaluna, Bezim, and Vicondor. It was coveted by the Confederacy of Independent Systems since the station was a major access point to the Mid Rim; whichever side controlled it would cut off a large portion of the galaxy from the enemy. Lorian Nod, who had previously expressed hatred for the Jedi Knights, showed up at the Jedi Temple just after the Battle of Geonosis and offered to help ensure that Station 88 Spaceport would remain a Republic asset. Despite the persuasive efforts of Count Dooku—first using negotiation and then force—the stations' developers remained loyal to the Republic.

**Stazi, Admiral Gar** This male Duros served the Galactic Alliance as an admiral in the navy during the era of the Sith–Imperial War. He remained at his post after the fall of the Galactic Alliance at the Battle of Caamas, from which he orchestrated a fighting retreat that became the stuff of legend. After refusing to surrender and holding the Galactic Alliance Navy together for seven years, Admiral Stazi was chosen to represent the Alliance at a treaty negotiation aboard the Wheel. Admiral Stazi met with Captain Mingo Bovark, following a request from Imperial Emperor Roan Fel, who wished to extend an offer to join forces against Darth Krayt and the Sith. Stazi questioned the alliance, wondering at first how Fel could invite the Sith into the war in the first place. When Bovark explained that Fel had been manipulated by the Sith and their allies, Stazi's concern about an alliance only heightened. Stazi was about to walk out of the negotiations when Bovark explained that Fel had captured Bastion, thereby controlling a huge portion of the Imperial war machine. This changed Stazi's mind, since the Imperial fleet would greatly augment his own forces. Two secret agents sabotaged the negotiations by causing the shuttles of Stazi and Bovark to fire on each other, setting off a chain reaction that ruined the chance at a treaty.

Steep

***Steadfast*** A New Republic ship commanded by Captain Oolas, it surveyed the ruins of the Imperial Star Destroyer *Gnisnal*, which contained an intact memory core that held a complete Imperial Order of Battle.

**StealthX X-wing** A stealth configuration of the formidable XJ3 X-wing. The StealthX had a star-flecked body of irregular, matte-black fiberplast that rendered it almost invisible against a starry background. Its third torpedo launcher was replaced by a gravitic modulator designed to defeat mass detectors, and its shields were downgraded to make room for a suite of sensor negators. Even its fusial engines were retooled to burn a special Tibanna isotope whose efflux turned dark a millisecond after fusion.

**Stec, Sergeant** An ARC trooper during the Clone Wars, he was one of the few survivors of a failed mission to capture the planet Colla IV. He brought back information on the Scorpenek annihilator droid, which had been deployed by the Separatists to defend the facilities of the Colicoid Creation Nest.

***Steel Talon*** This Imperial Star Destroyer served as one of the ships that protected the construction site of the first Death Star near Despayre, early in the era of the New Order.

**steep** Carnivorous amphibians with brownish-white, rubbery skin that lurked in the sewage of the Metellean seas.

Admiral Gar Stazi

**Steffans, Catronus** This man served the Republic as a defense official at the height of the Mandalorian Wars. It was Steffans who criticized the comments of Admiral Noma Sommos, who'd questioned the Republic's continued reliance on fringers and freelance soldiers to bolster its armed forces. In a statement after the Republic's failure to defend planets like Jebble and Taris during the Onslaught, Steffans explained that the use of nonmilitary personnel in combat situations allowed the Republic to save credits. He pushed for the Republic to continue using freelance soldiers instead of bowing to "military expedience."

**Stele, Maarek** A highly decorated Imperial pilot from the planet Kuan, he started as a hotshot hotrodder on a swoop bike on his devastated planet, which had been engaged in a decades-long war with neighboring Bordal. His father, Kerek, a famous scientist, had been kidnapped by Bordali agents, who later kidnapped Maarek and his mother to force Kerek to do their bidding. On the way to Bordal, they were intercepted by the Imperial Star Destroyer *Vengeance.* The Empire declared martial law in the system, and the war between Kuan and Bordal at last was over. Maarek started as a mechanic aboard the *Vengeance,* and on a flight to test out repairs on a TIE interceptor, he helped save the life of the Star Destroyer's commander, Admiral Mordon. That led to an invitation to join the Imperial Navy and become a fighter pilot. He became one of the best the Empire had, advancing through the ranks of the Empire's Secret Order to even become one of the Emperor's Hands.

***Stellar Web*** An *Interdictor*-class warship, part of the fleet commanded by Imperial Captain Barr Moutil in the service of Admiral Rogriss. Rogriss volunteered the use of the ship to Han Solo and the New Republic fleet hunting Warlord Zsinj, since both men were working toward the same goal. They nearly succeeded, but Zsinj inflicted great damage on the *Stellar Web.*

**Stellskard** A member of the Banvhar Combine who sought vengeance against General Grievous. He joined Flynn Kybo and B'dard Tone in their search for Grievous. They tracked the general to Belsus, but the assassination mission became a mercy mission to rescue a group of captured Jedi younglings.

**Stenax** A reclusive winged species from the planet Stenos. Stenaxes were violent and bru-

Stenax

tal when provoked, but generally ignored offworlders completely. Tall and thickly muscled, they had gargoyle-like faces and a row of bony spikes running across their shoulders. Three sharp claws punctuated each foot, five on each hand, with additional spikes lining the backs of their calf muscles. Stenaxes had scaly, purple-gray skin and white eyes with minuscule pupils.

***Stendaff*** A light escort, this spotter ship was part of Colonel Pakkpekatt's New Republic armada chasing the mysterious ghost ship known as the Teljkon vagabond.

**Steng** A legendary Yuuzhan Vong warmaster who lost to Warmaster Yo'gand in the climactic battle of the Cremlevian War. Supreme Overlord Shimrra wore robes made from the carefully preserved flesh of Steng.

**Steng's talons** Pointed grafts formed from sgauru bone and sheathed in yorik coral, used by the Yuuzhan Vong as body implants. Members of the warrior caste wore Steng's talons to honor the name of Warmaster Steng, and members of other castes usually could not receive the implant.

**Stennes Shifter** Members of this near-human species had the ability to blend into crowds unnoticed.

**Stenness lizard pie** A local delicacy in the Stenness Node.

**Stenness Node** Sometimes referred to as the Stenness system, the node was actually a group of three mining systems containing the Stenness system. The node was located on the rim of the galaxy on the mining frontier and contained the planets Ambria and Taboon. The 25 humanoid species inhabiting the node were collectively referred to as Nessies, and they controlled the various mining operations and cut deals with outside traders. BolBol the Hutt was said to have practically owned the Stenness system. Some 4,000 years before the Galactic Civil War, the Stenness underworld was controlled by a Hutt named Great Bogga, and the Nessies transported mutonium cargoes in ships made from the hollowed exoskeletons of the Colossus Wasps of Ithull.

Han Solo and his former lady friend Salla Zend used to run Kessel spice to the Stenness system and competed to see who could strike the best deal with the Nessies. The bounty hunters Zardra and Jodo Kast, pursuing the Thig brothers into the system, caught up with their quarry on Taboon. The ensuing firefight resulted in the death of Mageye the Hutt.

**Stent, Commander** This Chiss, whose full name was Kres'ten'tarthi, served as Voss Parck's top aide at the Hand of Thrawn compound on Nirauan during the Galactic Civil War. He was also the leader of Thrawn's personal household phalanx, and was one of the few Chiss who felt that Thrawn was a born leader who was working in his species' best interests. He heeded Thrawn's message, that if everyone waited 10 years after the report of his death, he would return to lead them to power once again. Stent bided his time until Mara Jade and Luke Skywalker arrived on the planet to investigate the Hand of Thrawn. After the facility was nearly destroyed, Stent continued to serve the Nuruodo phalanx, and was on duty when the Skywalkers returned to Nirauan three years later at the request of Voss Parck.

**Stereb** A hulking, long-limbed, humanoid species native to the planet Serroco. The Stereb spent most of their lives living in settlements of crude stone buildings. Each of these Stereb cities sat atop an interconnected network of tunnels and warrens, which were excavated as retreats that could be used when tornadoes and other storms swept across the planet's surface. The average Stereb stood more than 2 meters high, and was covered with thick, reddish skin. As a people, the Stereb tended to be gullible and were not overly intelligent; they usually acted more on instinct than on reasoning or logic. At the height of the Mandalorian Wars, Serroco was devastated by the Mandalorians, and only the warning of Carth Onasi managed to save the Stereb in 17 of their cities. Onasi later revealed to Zayne Carrick that the warning was actually something of a joke, since Republic forces often sent false tornado warnings to the Stereb, who fled into the warrens. Onasi had come to loathe the practice, since it demeaned the Stereb, but he felt that it was worthwhile if it saved any Stereb from the Mandalorian warheads.

Stereb

**Stic** A planet of continual climatic and geological change, it was home to the insectoid species Xi'Dec. In order to adapt to the rapid changes of Stic, the Xi'Dec evolved hundreds of specialized sexes throughout their history, each with its own unique appearance and abilities. There were more than 180 different genders of Xi'Dec with the most common, Xi'Alpha, making up about 6 percent of the population. Xi'Dec society was organized around the family unit, which never contained more than one member of the same sex. Tourism was a major industry.

**Stihl, Nova** This man served the Imperial Army as a stormtrooper during the construction of the first Death Star. He was stationed on the planet Despayre, where he served as a guard at the Slashtown prison colony. Stihl was well versed in the martial art of teräs käsi, and was the Unarmed Middleweight Champion of the First Naval Fleet for two years. He put his skills to work by teaching self-defense to other guards, and even opened up the classes to the better-behaved prisoners. Later reassigned to the Death Star, Stihl began having nightmares of his impending death, and an Imperial doctor confirmed that he had an unusually high midi-chlorian count. His worst nightmare occurred when the Death Star destroyed the planet Despayre; he was assaulted by the emotional wave of anguish that followed the deaths of every living thing on the planet. The pain he had felt when Despayre was destroyed came back to him 100-fold when the Death Star destroyed Alderaan. He resolved to leave the Imperial military, and set in motion plans to steal a shuttle with Atour Riten. Stihl chased a group of Rebel infiltrators who had escaped from Detention Block AA-23, but he delayed the pursuit as long as possible and gave the Rebels a chance to escape. Stihl died in his failed attempt to escape the battle station.

**stim-shot** A major component of a medpac, it was a stimulant administered through a pneumatic dispenser.

**Stinex, Benits** This man was perhaps the best-known and most influential architect in the galaxy during the early years of the New Order. Despite the price and the fact that he was approaching 100 years of age, Stinex was hired by the Empire to serve as the chief architect for the interior spaces of the first Death Star. After arriving at Despayre, one of Stinex's first actions was to recruit Teela Kaarz from the planet's surface. Although she had a criminal record, Stinex recognized her skills as an arcologist and pushed her to develop improvements to the space station's designs even as it was being constructed around them. Instead of telling her what he thought should be done in a given situation, Stinex would pose the situation as a test or question and see what answer she arrived at. In this way, he usually got an answer that was as good as, if not better than, the one he already had.

**stingbeam** Smaller than a hold-out blaster, the stingbeam was a weapon used in the Centrality. It carried five nonlethal shots that could stun an opponent.

***Stinger*** The personal transport of Guri, who was the human replica droid aide of criminal overlord Prince Xizor. A modified assault ship sometimes used for smuggling, the *Stinger* was about 28 meters long, with a curved hull that appeared to be sculpted into a flat figure eight. The *Stinger*'s power came from a cluster of eight ion engines, giving it sublight speed faster than an X-wing's. Its maneuverability was enhanced by computer adjustment of each engine's exhaust nozzles. Weapons included a pair of fire-linked ion cannons and a turret-mounted double laser cannon.

**stintaril** An omnivorous tree-dwelling rodent found on Yavin 4, it fed on woolamanders and anything else in its path. Stintarils had protruding eyes and long jaws filled with sharp teeth.

***Stockade*** A Trade Federation battleship. The pirate Nym was a prisoner aboard the *Stockade* six months before the Battle of Naboo.

**stock light freighter** Among the most common small trading vessels, these ships were the workhorses of intergalactic trade until they were replaced by larger bulk freighters and container ships. Stock light freighters were all built on the basic design of a command pod, storage holds, and engines. The *Millennium Falcon* was a modified stock light freighter, a model YT-1300 Corellian transport.

Stinger

**Stokhli spray stick** Long-range stun weapons, they were developed by the Stokhli species of the planet Manress. The Stokhli spray stick released a fine mist that congealed into a restricting net with a powerful current that stunned targets up to 200 meters away. Originally developed for hunters, spray sticks gained popularity as defensive and offensive personal weapons.

***Stomper One*** An assault shuttle that Luke Skywalker commanded in the final battle to take out Raynar Thul during the Swarm War. The shuttle carried Lando Calrissian's YVH 5-S Bugcruncher droids.

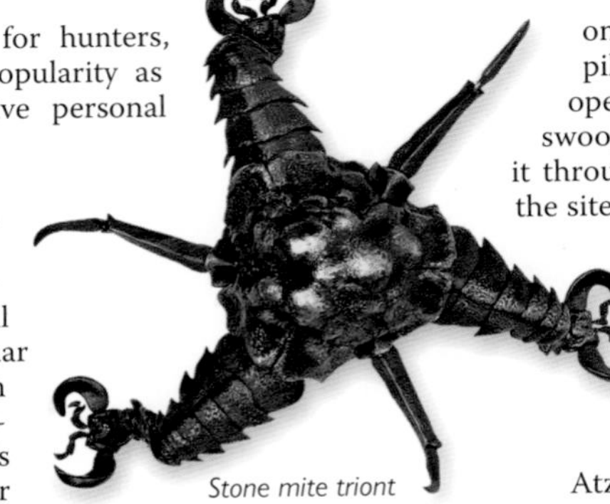
Stone mite triont

**Stonebone, Finhead** A pirate captain, he operated in the Stenness Node some 4,000 years before the Galactic Civil War.

**stone mite** Believed to have been bioengineered by Arkanian scientists, these creatures first appeared in the Expansion Region shortly before the Clone Wars. They were designed to consume virtually any material, and quickly became the ultimate scavenger on the worlds where they were released. As designed, stone mites used special glands in their mouthparts to exude a metal-eating acid, which predigested the materials that were consumed as food. Stone mites were originally thought to have been created to attack and destroy buildings and other inorganic systems, but they could also subsist on the blood and flesh of living creatures.

Individual stone mites were hermaphroditic, and were literally born with a clutch of eggs impregnated in their abdomens. This allowed them to breed prolifically, and even orbital bombardment of planets that had been infested by stone mites were often insufficient to kill off an entire population. A group of three stone mites could actually join together and form a symbiotic triont, literally welding themselves into a single shell.

In the aftermath of the Clone Wars, entire colonies of stone mites were discovered living in asteroid belts, having escaped from their creators. The Arkanians, despite disavowing any knowledge of the stone mite's development, were instrumental in helping devise ways to eradicate a colony on an infested world. The only effective method of dealing with stone mites was to spray the colony with an oxidizing foam, which served to rust them to death. In the wake of the Battle of Endor, many pro-Imperial terrorist groups used stone mites to attack and destroy worlds that embraced the New Republic.

**Stone Needle** A rocky spire in Beggar's Canyon with an oval hole near the top, it was the tallest landmark in the Jundland Wastes on Tatooine. Hotshot young pilots would fly through the opening on their speeder or swoop bike or even try to make it through in a small craft. It was the site of many injuries and some deaths.

**Stonn, Li** Luke Skywalker used this name and the appearance of an old man during his travels on Teyr and Atzerri.

**Stopa, Kroddok** An archaeologist from the Obroan Institute, he was the expedition chief for the mission to Qella. The mission's goal was to recover biological samples for any clues as to the origins of the Qella civilization. Kroddok Stopa was killed in an avalanche on Maltha Obex.

**Storinal** The site of a battle where Princess Leia's flagship, the *Rebel Dream,* was mercilessly shelled by the Imperial Star Destroyer *Peremptory* and recaptured by the Empire. Storinal remained under Imperial control.

**Storini glass prowler** This crystalline arthropod walked on two legs and used its other two legs to grasp its prey. It was native to the planet Storinal, and was harmless to most creatures. The males of the species were extremely competitive, and would fight to the death over just about anything.

***Storm*** The personally designed starfighter of Isolder, crown prince to the Hapan throne, it was based on the hull of the Hapan Miy'til fighters. The *Storm*'s refinements turned it into a fighter that could fly against any short-range ship in the Hapes Cluster. The sleek fighter was just over 7 meters long and used miniaturized components. It had four banks of anticoncussion field generators. A sensor and scrambler allowed Isolder to block all communications from enemy fighters and prevented scanners from getting a target lock on *Storm.*

The ship's nose held a set of triple-linked laser cannons and a mini concussion missile launcher with 10 missiles. Each wing had an ion cannon; a thermal detonator bomb chute was mounted in the rear between the engines. The ship's transparisteel bubble canopy gave it excellent visibility in all directions. Its four fusial thrust engines were rebuilt with modified power converters to give the ship the sublight speed of a TIE interceptor. Each engine had an oversized turbogenerator for short bursts that propelled the ship to speeds one-third faster than an A-wing fighter.

The *Storm* crash-landed on the planet Dathomir when Prince Isolder attempted to rescue Princess Leia Organa. It was recovered and rebuilt after the Battle of Dathomir.

**storm commando** An elite Imperial Army unit organized to conduct covert operations of a questionable nature. The storm commando was the Empire's answer to the increasing numbers of victories won by Rebel Alliance guerrilla tactics. Rebel successes early in the Galactic Civil War forced Imperial military authorities to reexamine some of their methodology and develop a leaner, more focused fighting force. Storm commando armor was coated with an advanced polymer called reflec that bent light and sensor energy away from the trooper. Rebel hero Crix Madine once led the group, but he became disgusted by the Emperor's willingness to commit any atrocity and eventually defected to the Alliance.

**Storm Fleet destroyer** Warships making up a secretly developed fleet commissioned by the Separatists and built by Kuat Drive Yards just months after the Battle of Geonosis. The Storm Fleet ships were disguised as common freighters to allow them to travel easily across the galaxy. Sheathed in dull black durasteel, they were equipped with quad laser cannons and proton torpedoes. The Storm Fleet was used to subjugate neutral worlds through sheer destructive capability, allowing the Separatists to take whatever resources or facilities they needed to continue the Clone Wars. The fleet was ultimately destroyed by Obi-Wan Kenobi and Anakin Skywalker with help from their clone trooper pilots.

**stormtrooper** Seeming to be a will of iron encased in hardened white armor, these Imperial shock troops neutralized resistance to the New Order and remained totally loyal to the Emperor, even in the face of certain death. Stormtroopers rode in all Imperial vessels, were used as first-strike forces, and were employed to make sure officers on the ships stayed loyal. They could not be bribed or blackmailed, lived in a totally disciplined environment, and were militaristic to the core.

Considered separate from both the Imperial Army and the Imperial Navy, they were extremely loyal to the Empire but were also extremely expendable. The stormtrooper evolved from the clone troopers of the Grand Army of the Republic, which were first utilized during the Clone Wars. Several different sources of clones were used to create stormtroopers, especially when the Empire ramped up its military forces as Emperor Palpatine began consolidating his power. Eventually, baseline humans were conscripted or allowed to join the ranks. Each stormtrooper battalion contained 820 soldiers and was virtually self-sufficient. There were no separate staff officers for the battalion, making it a pure fighting unit. They wore an 18-piece suit of white armor covering a 2-piece, temperature-controlled bodysuit. The armor housed an energy source and various implements, and snapped together around the trooper. The helmet contained a polarized visor and communications gear. The utility belt worn at the waist had compartments for a grappling line, spare batteries, and survival gear. The elite 501st Legion was Darth Vader's personal stormtrooper regiment. They were also known as Vader's Fist.

Stormtroopers

In addition to units of regular stormtroopers, the Empire developed a number of specialized units. Snowtroopers, or cold-assault troopers, were trained and equipped to do battle in frozen environments. They wore the basic white armor but added powerful heating and personal environment units, terrain-grip boots, and face-shielding breathing masks. Spacetroopers, or elite zero-g stormtroopers, were used to launch assaults in space on another vessel. Each trooper utilized armor and equipment that enabled him to function as if he were an independent spacecraft, to withstand the vacuum of space, to propel himself through space, and to attack and breach nearly any target.

Stormtrooper

Scout troopers, although lightly armored, were highly mobile stormtroopers usually assigned to Imperial garrisons. They used speeder bikes to patrol perimeters, perform reconnaissance missions, and scout enemy locations. To assist them when traveling at high speeds, scout troopers wore specialized helmets equipped with built-in macrobinocular viewplates and sensor arrays feeding into computers that analyzed terrain instantaneously to help navigation. Other stormtrooper types included aquatic assault stormtroopers, or seatroopers; sandtroopers, or desert stormtroopers; storm commandos, or black-armored scout troopers; radtroopers, who worked in radiation zones; and dark troopers, who were so well equipped that they constituted powerful self-contained weapons platforms.

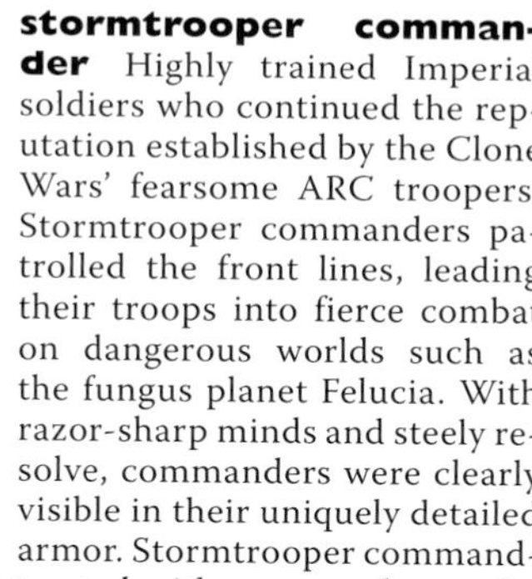
Stormtrooper commander

After the Pellaeon-Gavrisom Treaty 15 years after the Battle of Endor, stormtroopers became all but extinct. Vos Parck reinstated the 501st Legion in the Empire of the Hand, though some of its members were aliens.

**stormtrooper commander** Highly trained Imperial soldiers who continued the reputation established by the Clone Wars' fearsome ARC troopers. Stormtrooper commanders patrolled the front lines, leading their troops into fierce combat on dangerous worlds such as the fungus planet Felucia. With razor-sharp minds and steely resolve, commanders were clearly visible in their uniquely detailed armor. Stormtrooper commanders were entrusted with command over the Empire's elite shadow troopers, with authority to call in reinforcements and trigger ambushes without clearance from Imperial High Command.

**stormtrooper transport** An Imperial assault vehicle designed to take over enemy ships. With only five crew members, the Telgorn Corp. *Delta*-class DX-9 Stormtrooper Transport could ferry up to 30 stormtroopers or 10 elite Imperial zero-g stormtroopers.

**stormtrooper utility belt** A standard-issue belt worn by stormtroopers. It carried power packs, energy rations, and a compact tool kit. The belt also could tote additional gear including a grappling hook, comlink, macrobinoculars, handcuff binders, or other items such as a combat de-ionizer.

**Storthus** Homeworld of giant Stone Eels, creatures of living rock.

**story platform** An interactive multimedia datapad, it displayed and told stories to entertain children.

**strangle-vine** A species of long, trailing vines that grew in the jungles of Tenupe. These vines were named for the way in which strands contracted when a creature made contact with them, often capturing the being in a stranglehold.

**stratt** A species of vermin that lived in the cityscape of Coruscant. At birth, stratts resembled cute balls of fur. However, they grew rapidly into 2-meter-long, muscular creatures covered with jet-black fur. Originally brought to Coruscant by illicit pet dealers trying to make a quick credit, stratts were abandoned when they outgrew their cute stage. These released stratts found a niche in the undercity of Coruscant, hunting at night when their black fur gave them the most cover.

**Stratis Games** An event consisting of athletic competitions regularly held on Hallrin IV. It included the Multi-Sentient Unarmed Combat Rounds, a regulated form of interspecies combat.

**Stratus, Alto** This Jabiimite led a faction of his people that sided with the Separatists during the Clone Wars. His parents were killed when the Lythian pirates ravaged much of Jabiim, and Stratus never forgot that neither the Republic nor the Jedi Knights traveled to Jabiim to eliminate the threat. Years later, Stratus still harbored a deep-seated resentment, which only intensified with the outbreak of the Clone Wars. Citing the Republic's inability to reach any peaceful resolution to the hostilities, he demanded that Jabiim secede and throw off its oppressive yoke. He further blamed the Republic and the Jedi for not assisting Jabiim during an outbreak of Brainrot Plague and a Trandoshan invasion. His speeches, in which he declared that Jabiim would fight to the death to defend its freedom and would "send the Jedi home in body bags," became popular on many Separatist-held worlds in the Outer Rim Territories. During the Battle of Jabiim, Stratus and his rebels nearly broke through the front lines of the Jedi-led clone troopers, killing more than 9,000 Republic forces before they were pushed back by a group of Jedi Padawans whose Masters had been killed in battle. He regrouped and launched an all-out attack at Cobalt Station. He believed that his chances for success were excellent, especially after Count Dooku dispatched a squadron of enhanced assassin droids to augment Stratus's forces. However, he didn't count on the strong will of the Padawans. His forces struggled with the young Jedi for several days before both sides were just about wiped out. In the final act of the battle, Padawan Aubrie cornered Stratus with a pair of lightsabers. Stratus pulled out a blaster to shoot the young Jedi in the chest. As she died, however, Aubrie fell forward and drove her lightsabers into the renegade's chest.

*Alto Stratus*

**Streamdrinker, Senator** A Republic Senator from Tynna. Shortly after Palpatine declared himself Emperor, Streamdrinker was arrested on charges of conspiracy and treason.

**Streen** A bearded, graying, aging hermit who lived in the abandoned city of Tibannopolis on Bespin, he was able to predict eruptions of valuable gases from deep within the cloud layers and could hear the thoughts and voices of all around him—a talent that bothered him greatly and led to his withdrawal from other people. Luke Skywalker found Streen to be Force-sensitive and invited him to join the other Jedi students at the Jedi academy. The spirit of Sith Lord Exar Kun influenced Streen into starting a tornado that threatened to destroy the near-lifeless body of Luke, but Streen was stopped in time. He later joined forces with the other Jedi students in destroying Exar Kun's spirit forever. Thirteen years after the Battle of Yavin, Streen went on a mission to the mining colony on Corbos to battle a leviathan that had been terrorizing the planet for several millennia. At the onset of the Yuuzhan Vong War, Streen was strongly aligned with Luke Skywalker's faction over Kyp Durron's followers. Jedi Master Streen was on a mission to Corellia when the Yuuzhan Vong attacked the Jedi academy. After the war, he traveled to Dathomir with Kirana Ti and Damaya to help establish a Jedi training facility on the planet.

**Strikebreaker riot control vehicle** A heavy gunship designed to frighten or kill rioters, it was used by the Corporate Sector Authority.

***Strike*-class medium cruiser** Introduced near the end of the Galactic Civil War, this 450-meter-long Imperial star cruiser was built of prefabricated modular sections so that it could be quickly mass-produced by Loronar Corporation. The *Strike*-class medium cruiser continued to serve an important role in the remnants of the Imperial fleet under the command of Grand Admiral Thrawn and others. *Strike*-class cruiser interiors could be configured to accommodate specific mission profiles. Some carried a ground assault company; others were modified for a complete squadron of TIE fighters. Still other versions included prefab garrison deployers, troop transports, and planetary assault cruisers. *Strike*-class cruisers normally carried 20 turbolasers, 10 ion cannons, and 10 tractor beam projectors.

**Striker** *See* Omega, Granta

**strill** This predatory, hermaphroditic mammal was found on the planets Mandalore and Qiilura, where it was often captured and trained as a hunting beast. Strills were distinguished by their odor, which many beings found disgusting or noxious. The body of a strill measured about a meter in length and was covered with folds of loose skin, as was its tail. The huge mouth of a strill was filled with sharp teeth, and exuded huge amounts of drool. Using their legs, strills could climb into trees and wait to ambush their prey. When prey was in reach, a strill would launch itself from its tree, using the folds of skin to form a kind of full-body wing that allowed it to glide through the air and direct itself toward its prey. Being hermaphroditic, strills had a strong mothering instinct, and it was not uncommon for a strill to understand when a Mandalorian woman was pregnant, and to anticipate the birth of her child.

**Stroiketcy** Most likely a captured comet, it was one of the three planets of the Yavin system. Stroiketcy was noted for its trailing tail of atmosphere and its solid rock core. The world's surface was almost entirely water; only a handful of rock outcroppings broke the surface amid constant rainfall and fog. Although never confirmed, unicellular life may have existed in Stroiketcy's oceans. The planet's name came from the Corellian for "tailed one."

**Strok, Captain** This Imperial captain served the military under Governor Touno on Svivren during the last years of the New Order. Touno assigned him to Mara Jade, who was acting as the Emperor's Hand in the elimination of Dequc's Black Nebula empire. Unknown to Mara and Touno, Strok was secretly working as an informant for Dequc. Mara was forced to shoot him after he encountered her on Qiaxx.

**Strom, Pleth** An ensign in the armed forces of the Old Republic and fighter pilot during the Clone Wars. Strom and his wingmate, Erk H'Arman, were part of the team that was dispatched to Praesitlyn under the command of General Khamar to protect the Intergalactic Communications Center. Strom was killed in the initial engagement with the Separatists.

**Stryfe, Darth** This hulking man was one of the new Sith who followed Darth Krayt's leadership some 130 years after the Battle of Yavin. Darth Stryfe was known as a brutal warrior who attacked his enemies with intense, raw power.

*Darth Stryfe*

**Sturm** One of two domesticated vornskrs used by smuggler Talon Karrde as pets and guards.

**Sturn, Captain Ozzik** An Imperial officer who carried on his family tradition of hunting down the most exotic and dangerous predators in the galaxy. While his Imperial deployments initially allowed him to travel in search of his next quarry, his eventual promotions prevented him from continuing the hunt. He desperately hoped for the chance to pursue a Jedi as part of Darth Vader's Jedi Purge, and was frustrated by being sent to a long series of low-profile Outer Rim outposts. While stationed as the chief magistrate on Malastare, he began to secretly release prisoners into his own hunting preserve, purely for the purpose of stalking intelligent prey. While his private hunting ground went undetected for some time, its eventual discovery sparked a revolt among the native Dug and Gran populations, which resulted in high casualties for the Empire. Later stationed on Kashyyyk, Sturn fell into his old routines, tracking down and killing Wookiee warriors.

**styanax** A ferocious, snake-like, aquatic Tralusian predator with an armored head, fierce jaws, and a vicious stinger on its whip-like tail. Styanax went to the Sea of Jarad to mate. They were pursued by hunters called stabmen, who harpooned them from their nagak ships. Veteran stabmen told tales of Old Gloxix, a scarred, stingerless 14-meter styanax.

**stygium crystal** A rare crystal found on Aeten II, a volcanic world in the Outer Rim. Stygium crystals were an integral component of cloaking devices, although they could be used for just a short period before they overheated and were rendered useless. Because they were exceptionally rare, stygium crystals could only be purchased by extremely wealthy or well-funded individuals. During the Clone Wars, Aeten II was scoured clean of stygium crystals, until the Empire cracked the planet open with the *Tarkin* superweapon to create cloaking devices for its Phantom TIE project. Related clear stygium crystals could at one time be found on the Invisible Island of Maramere.

**Su, Lama** This Kaminoan was the Prime Minister of Kamino during the years leading up to the Clone Wars. Like most Kaminoans, Lama Su cared little for the galaxy at large, though he served as his people's primary liaison with others. He was a poor judge of human emotion and reaction. Lama Su had no problem taking the funds provided by Sifo-Dyas—and later Darth Tyranus—for the creation of the clones for the Army of the Republic. Ten years later, Lama Su welcomed Obi-Wan Kenobi to Kamino, despite the Jedi Knight's obvious lack of knowledge about the development of the clone troopers. Lama Su proudly presented the clones to Master Kenobi, who was dumbfounded. He also arranged for Master Kenobi to meet with Jango Fett, the template for the clones. After the Clone Wars began, Lama Su found himself working directly with Supreme Chancellor Palpatine on the development of additional clones, although he never understood what was driving the Chancellor. In order to secure his own position, Lama Su made secret recordings of every conversation he had with the Republic, including Chancellor Palpatine. These recordings were discovered just over a year after the Battle of Geonosis by the Null-class ARC trooper Mereel, after he infiltrated Tipoca City and made copies of Lama Su's files.

**subaltern** A low-ranking officer in the Yuuzhan Vong warrior caste. Tugorn, Sata'ak, and Doshao were all subalterns.

***Subjugator*** A *Victory*-class Star Destroyer under the command of Captain Kolaff, it was targeted by a Rebel Mon Calamari strike force code-named Task Force Starfall. The task force, made up of Mon Cal star cruisers, engaged the *Subjugator* and destroyed it.

**sublight drive** A sublight starship drive moved vessels through realspace. One popular type was the Hoersch-Kessel ion drive, which produced charged particles through fusion reaction to hurl ships forward. Ships with H-K sublight drives used repulsorlifts for atmospheric travel.

**Subpro Corporation** A large starship manufacturer based in the Inner Rim. Its designs, including the famed Z-95 Headhunter, were of good quality, but its remote location assured the company second-class status in the eyes of most military and civilian purchasers. However, Subpro's designs, from its nimble sublight fighters to its large and medium combat cruisers, were undiscovered gems that offered excellent performance at a competitive price. While its freighters lagged behind those produced by Corellian Engineering Corporation, Subpro's designs were favored by the notoriously independent captains who flew the starlanes among the galaxy's backworlds.

**Subterra Period** A period of Republic history running from approximately 8,000 to 7,000 years before the Galactic Civil War. The Subterra Period saw new mapping of the galactic southern quadrant, with colonies such as Malastare serving as anchors for short hyperlane snippets dubbed praediums. Scouts also built the supply lines linking the galactic disk to the satellite galaxy of the Rishi Maze. These territories expanded the Republic's reach, but their inaccessibility promoted lawlessness in the Rim and an erosion of Coruscant's authority. This was believed to have contributed to the dark side uprising 7,000 years before the Battle of Yavin known as the Hundred-Year Darkness.

**Subterrel** A mining system beyond the Outer Rim located in the sector of the same name. Dexter Jettster was once a prospector on Subterrel alongside Polis Massan miners, where he encountered a Kamino saberdart.

**Sucharme** A primary garrison world of the Trade Federation prior to the Battle of Naboo. The lessons learned in blockading Sucharme for outstanding debts went a long way toward the planning of the invasion of Naboo.

**Sulamar, General** A pompous Imperial officer, he bragged of nonexistent military triumphs to Durga the Hutt, with whom he plotted to unleash a new superweapon on the New Republic. General Sulamar was obsessive about protocol and plastered his chest with campaign ribbons he had supposedly been awarded. He was later exposed by Crix Madine, head of New Republic Intelligence, as a military screwup who had been transferred from assignment to assignment after continual mistakes. He and Durga both died as a result of the new weapon's failure.

**Sull** The name adopted by the ARC trooper designated A-30 during the Clone Wars. Sull was one of the many ARC troopers dispatched to remote planets to teach the local military how to use Republic weapons to defend themselves against a Separatist attack. About 16 months after the Battle of Geonosis, Sull was reported as missing in action during a mission to Gaftikar.

*Lama Su*

He had not reported in for two months, and it was feared that he might cause trouble for other clone troopers. Omega Squad was dispatched to bring him in for questioning. During his interrogation, Sull revealed that he no longer fought for the Republic, but was quick to point out that he had not actually joined the Separatists. Sergeant A'den let him go free, and told the other members of Omega Squad that their official story would be that Sull had died of injuries in an unspecified accident.

**Sullust** A volcanic world in the Sullust system, it was covered with thick clouds of hot, barely breathable gases. Sullust was habitable only in its vast networks of underground caves, where native Sullustans—jowled, mouse-eared humanoids with large round eyes—built beautiful underground cities that drew large crowds of tourists. Piringiisi, one popular resort, was known for its hot springs and green mud. Sullust had one inhabited moon, Sulon.

The amiable Sullustans were highly valued as pilots and navigators due to their instinctive ability to remember any path previously traveled. The massive SoroSuub Corporation was based on Sullust and employed nearly half the population in its mining, energy, packaging, and production divisions. Despite the Rebel sympathies of many Sullustans, SoroSuub dissolved the Sullustan government, seized control of the planet, and declared its allegiance to the Empire.

After being forced out of the Sullust system by Imperials, Councilor Sian Tevv brought Nien Nunb's private raiding squad into Rebel Alliance service. Prior to the Battle of Yavin, after the Alliance rescued a Sullustan leader kidnapped by the Empire, the Sullustans leaned heavily toward the Alliance. However, it was late in the war when the leaders of Sullust finally held a vote and decided to secede from the Empire officially. The Alliance fleet assembled near Sullust just prior to the Battle of Endor, in which Nien Nunb became Lando Calrissian's copilot aboard the *Millennium Falcon.* His sister, Aril Nunb, later served as the executive officer for Rogue Squadron.

**Sulon** The moon of the planet Sullust, it was primarily given over to agriculture. Rebel Alliance agent Kyle Katarn was from Sulon. His father was an agricultural machine salesman and mechanic in a small rural community. While Katarn was at the Academy, Imperials raided Sulon and killed his family, though they claimed the deaths were the result of Rebel terrorists.

***Sulon Star*** This cargo ship made regular runs within the Sullust system during the Galactic Civil War.

**Sumitra sector** A sector with 12,387 planets and moons, it contained the planet Tierfon, where a Rebel starfighter base was established to patrol the outer edges of the sector. The Empire was aware of Rebel activity but found locating Tierfon base difficult.

**Summertime War** This was the name given to the intense civil war that broke out between the native Korunnai and the offworld Balawai of the planet Haruun Kal several decades before the onset of the Clone Wars. It began as a clash of interests, with the Korunnai following the grassers—which destroyed the jungles—while the Balawai relied on harvesting the bounties of the jungle to make credits from exports. For 30 years, the Korunnai staged guerrilla raids on Balawai operations, while Balawai militia used gunships and other tracking methods to eliminate threats. Over time, the Balawai discovered that the key to defeating the Korunnai was to eliminate the grassers. Any grasser found in the open was shot on sight, and the Korunnai were forced to respond. Balawai prospectors, known as jups, were ambushed in the jungles and never heard from again.

Over the years, Korunnai children were taught to hate the Balawai, just as Balawai children were raised to shoot Korunnai on sight. Because the war was best fought during the late spring and early summer, before the autumn rainy season and the snows of winter made passage through the jungles impossible, the civil war became known as the Summertime War. During the autumn and winter, both sides spent their time getting ready for the next round of fighting. The Korunnai also came to hate the Separatists, since they supplied the Balawai with weapons and technology, while the Korunnai fought with primitive weapons and tactics.

The Summertime War dragged on for many years until the Separatists wooed the Balawai with promises of "freedom" in exchange for control of the Al'Har system. This, combined with the attempt by the Jedi Master Depa Billaba to bring the Korunnai into the Republic, forced Mace Windu to return to his homeworld. Once there, he and Depa launched a desparate plan to defeat the Balawai and eliminate Separatist control of the system. With victories at the Battle of Lorshan Pass and the capture of Pelek Baw, Masters Windu and Billaba helped the Korunnai finally defeat the Balawai. With the droid control center in Pelek Baw destroyed, the Separatists were also driven from the system. Once hostilities ended, the Korunnai and the Balawai agreed to work together to form a common and equally representative government.

**Sump** The homeworld of the Nuknog Podracer known as Ark "Bumpy" Roose, Sump was located in the Outer Rim near the Ison Corridor. Nearly 1,000 years before the Battle of Yavin, Nuknog leaders "sold" their homeworld to a consortium of unscrupulous mining corporations in exchange for jobs, food, and modest accommodations. It became a humid, dilapidated world where pollution from offworld mining interests contaminated the ecosphere.

**Sumptor, Banner** An Imperial officer, he was part of the team stranded on Dolis 3 in the wake of the peace accord signed between the Imperial Remnant and the New Republic. Banner joined Moff Derran Takkar in a plan to disrupt the wedding of Mara Jade and Luke Skywalker as a way to strike back against the New Republic. Despite his loyalty to the Empire, Banner ultimately abandoned the petty idea and came to view the wedding as a symbol of a galaxy healing itself. Banner joined the New Republic and told police about Moff Takkar's plans.

**Sun, Fe** The former Padawan of Shaak Ti, who was murdered by the Zeltron criminal Lyshaa. Lyshaa killed Fe Sun to garner respect, but was imprisoned for her crime before she was able to gain any of the expected perks.

**Sunaj** Following the Battle of Yavin, the Imperial Star Destroyer *Relentless* was to receive a cargo of new TIE interceptors at a rendezvous near Sunaj. The replacement cargo TIEs were destroyed by an Alliance strike team.

**Sunber, Lieutenant Janek "Tank"** A native of Tatooine and a childhood friend of Luke Skywalker's who went by the nickname Tank. Janek Sunber was relegated to a career in the infantry after graduating from the Imperial Academy. He was one of a handful of officers who worked side by side with the troops under his command. Just after the Battle of Yavin, Lieutenant Sunber found himself stationed on Maridun with his commanding officers, Captain Gage, Commander Frickett, and General Ziering. Although Ziering appreciated Sunber's openness and candor, Gage believed that Sunber wanted to show up his immediate superiors. After Frickett's death and Gage's humiliation during an Amanin attack, Ziering promoted Sunber to captain and placed him in charge of defending the survivors.

*Lieutenant Janek "Tank" Sunber*

Further action during the Galactic Civil War brought him into contact with Luke Skywalker on the planet Kalist VI. Sunber had been assigned to the military forces protecting the prison complex, and his contact with Luke was awkward as Luke tried to hide the fact that he was actually working for the Rebel Alliance. After learning Luke's true allegiance, Sunber found himself unable to reconcile his devotion to the Empire and Luke's support of the Alliance. His emotion toward Luke changed to hatred when Sunber learned that Luke had destroyed the Death Star at the Battle of Yavin. In the heat of these emotions, Sunber relayed information on Luke's identity to Darth Vader

himself. Vader then tortured Sunber in an effort to gather more information, and forced him to record a message to Luke Skywalker. Luke escaped the subsequent trap with the help of Deena Shan, rescuing Sunber and returning to the Alliance. Eventually Sunber's brainwashing took hold, and he set out to capture Luke aboard *Rebel One.* His opportunity came during an Imperial attack on the Rebel fleet. When Luke agreed to give his own life to let Leia go free, Sunber saw that Luke wasn't the monster that the Empire made him out to be. Sunber apparently died in the attack, but his body was never located.

**Sun Crusher** An Imperial superweapon prototype, it was designed at the secret weapons think tank, the Maw Installation. Under Admiral Daala, a design team headed by the scientist Qwi Xux made many breakthroughs that led to the new Sun Crusher. Only slightly larger than a fighter, its resonance torpedoes were powerful enough to destroy a star.

The Sun Crusher was a slender, cone-shaped vessel capped with a tetrahedron on the upper end and a dish-shaped resonance projector hanging from the lower end. A number of rotating laser cannons could disable attacking enemy ships, although its shimmering quantum-crystalline armor made the Sun Crusher nearly impervious to damage. The ship's 11 "resonance torpedoes" were energized through the transmitting dish and could be launched into a star to trigger a chain reaction that caused the star to go supernova, incinerating every world in its system.

Imprisoned in the Maw Installation, Han Solo convinced Qwi Xux of the weapon's evil, and she, Solo, Chewbacca, and a Force-sensitive Kessel escapee named Kyp Durron stole the Sun Crusher. The weapon was delivered to Coruscant, where the New Republic Assembly voted to cast it into the gas giant Yavin. However, Durron used his Force powers to retrieve it and went on a rampage, demolishing several Imperial worlds before surrendering the vessel. The Sun Crusher was destroyed at the Battle of the Maw when it was caught in the gravity well of one of the Maw's black holes.

**Sund, Elora** This Sullustan Jedi Padawan was part of the task force dispatched to the planet Jabiim at the height of the Clone Wars. Like many of the students who were forced into battle, Elora lost her Master to the Jabiimite rebels. Elora continued to adapt to the changing conditions, however, stealing a pair of repulsor boots to move about the battlefield. She found herself growing attached to Tae Diath. However, during their final stand against the forces of Alto Stratus, Tae was cut down by a group of assassin droids. Elora, connected to Tae through a link in the Force, caught the psychic backlash of his death in her mind. The blast was too powerful for her to handle, and she died instantly.

**Sundari** The third planet in the Garos system, it was a hot, arid mining colony settled nearly 4,000 years before the Galactic Civil War. Sundari immediately began trade with its sister planet, Garos IV, because the Sundars were dependent on an outside supply of foodstuffs. About 200 years before the Battle of Yavin, large numbers of Sundars began emigrating to Garos IV and establishing new businesses and factories, earning the resentment of Garosians who were hurt by the new competition. A civil war between the two planets erupted when a Garosian grain-processing facility was destroyed. The devastating war raged for 82 years until a truce was hammered out by Tork Winger, Assistant Minister of Defense for Garos IV, and Tionthes Turi, a respected Sundar engineer. Violations of the truce continued, but the Empire's intervention in the conflict five years before the Battle of Yavin brought a sudden, violent end to most resistance.

***sun djem*** A Jedi "mark of contact" used during lightsaber combat, its objective is to damage or destroy an enemy's weapon.

**Sundown, Taxer** This land baron controlled much of the moisture-farming property on Ord Mantell during the last decades of the Old Republic. He arrived on Ord Mantell with the goal of "cleaning up" the planet, but simply killed the existing land barons and usurped their operations. Sundown then blamed the deaths on Mantellian savrips, and incited the villagers to kill the savrips. In the meantime, he set up his operations on Ten Mile Plateau, where he operated a solar energy collection facility. He employed a group of lightsaber-wielding enforcers to protect his facility in the hope of enhancing his projected image as a former Jedi Knight. Qui-Gon Jinn and Obi-Wan Kenobi discovered that the enforcers lacked any independent will, as if Sundown were controlling them with the Force. When the Jedi began to uncover Sundown's true motivations, he tried to capture Nella Bold and kill the others. Attempting to escape in Bold's T-24 speeder, Sundown was unprepared for Obi-Wan's attack. Obi-Wan managed to destroy the top fin on the speeder, and Sundown was unable to control the craft. He crashed on Ten Mile Plateau, breaking his neck. Qui-Gon and Obi-Wan then discovered that Sundown had been using a mind-control device to augment his claims of being a Jedi Knight, as part of a grander plot masterminded by Baroness Omnino to discredit the Jedi.

*Elora Sund*

**Sunesi** An amphibian species of humanoids from Monor II. In their native language, the word Sunesi meant "pilgrim." The Sunesi were born as furry, senseless creatures before pupating into their more recognizable form at the age of 15. This biological process was dependent on the planet's cirrifog atmosphere, since small crystals in the fog were a necessary component of the metamorphosis. The turquoise-colored adults had the ability to speak, but they also could communicate by using ultrasonic waves created within their large crania. Their enlarged heads earned them the nickname "lumpheads" from the Imperial forces that occupied Monor II during the Galactic Civil War.

***Sunfighter Franchise*** One of the false names Han Solo used to register the *Millennium Falcon* in the days when he was evading Corporate Sector Authority patrols.

***SunGem*** Jedi Master Arca Jeth's courier ship some 4,000 years before the Galactic Civil War, it was outfitted as a training facility for his Jedi students. The *SunGem* was aerodynamic, with layers of maneuvering vanes and retractable airfoils. It was equipped with 21 ion engines mounted in banks of three. In atmosphere, the *SunGem* could reach a top speed of about 950 kilometers per hour, making it the equal of many atmospheric speeders and starfighters.

The *SunGem* had extendable hull sections with a dedicated defense station, but it was lightly armed, revealing Arca's preference for stealth and cunning over brute force. The main weapon was a forward proton torpedo launcher. It also had a pair of rotating laser cannons that could fire in opposite directions at the same time. Most of the ship's interior was given over to Jedi training facilities, with meditation chambers, lightsaber training areas with remotes, and a variable-gravity and -atmosphere room to simulate hostile planetary conditions. An extensive computer library held Jedi texts.

**Sun Guards of Thyrsus** An ancient military unit with a ferocious reputation whose armor inspired the design later worn by the Imperial Royal Guard. A Rebel Alliance fugitive, Moxin Tark, was known to wear the armor of the Sun Guards. The modified Mandalorian hunting *kamas* worn by ARC troopers were reminiscent of the Thyrsus Sun Guard belt-spats.

**sungwa** Large dog-like creatures, they resembled a cross between a wolf and a weasel. Sungwas were native to the bog moon Bogden.

**Sunlet, Merc** A crafty thief with a heart of gold, he was a native of Tirac Munda.

The wealthy often hired him to advise them about protecting their property. Well traveled and skilled in many languages, he had business of an undisclosed nature on Tatooine just prior to the Battle of Yavin.

Cody Sunn-Childe

**Sunn-Childe, Cody**
This anti-Imperial radical was one of Mon Mothma's early supporters during the formation of the Rebel Alliance. An unusual humanoid being with a frog-like face and tall pointed ears, Sunn-Childe later left the Alliance and a life of violence behind. He established a base of operations on an unusual starship that resembled a floating jungle with a dome-covered city at its core. This starship, capable of interdimensional travel, fled the known galaxy for many years until Lando Calrissian and Chewbacca stumbled upon it shortly after the Battle of Hoth. It was on this strange ship that Sunn-Childe and his followers sought to escape from the madness of the war, after Sunn-Childe himself emerged rejuvenated from the fires maintained by the M'ust species. Sunn-Childe claimed to have the ability to bring his dreams to life. When Imperial forces attacked Sunn-Childe's floating city, his anger flared, manifesting itself as powerful demons that crippled the Imperial ships. Appalled at his own violence, Sunn-Childe called off the attack, allowing the Imperials to destroy his floating city.

**Sunrider, Andur**
The husband of Nomi Sunrider and father of Vima, this Jedi was killed some 4,000 years before the Galactic Civil War in a senseless battle with petty gangsters at the Stenness hyperspace terminal while he was on his way to visit Jedi Master Thon on Ambria.

**Sunrider, Nomi** The unprepossessing wife of a Jedi 4,000 years before the Galactic Civil War, she became one of the great Jedi Knights of her time, though the path was not of her choosing. Circumstances conspired to make her a powerful Jedi. Nomi Sunrider, with rusty brown hair and blue-green eyes, was the wife of Andur and mother of newborn Vima when her adventure began. She was accompanying her husband on a mission to take some Adegan crystals, used to construct lightsabers, to Jedi Master Thon in the Ambria system when Andur was cut down by several henchmen of Great Bogga the Hutt. Urged on by his spirit, she picked up his lightsaber and slew two of the thugs before continuing with his mission.

Nomi Sunrider

On the planet Ambria, Thon convinced her to stay and train to be a Jedi herself. Once, she saved her daughter from an attack by a dark side monster by creating a vision of the beasts attacking one another through the use of Jedi battle meditation; she later used the technique to defeat a band of pirates on a mission from Bogga. Her training took her to the planet Ossus, where she apprenticed with Master Vodo-Siosk Baas and learned to make her own lightsaber. She was then drafted to join a Jedi team to battle dark siders who were taking over the planet Onderon and to rescue Master Arca Jeth and his students. She developed strong feelings for her team member Ulic Qel-Droma. Nomi stayed to train with Arca in the Force mind technique known as Jedi battle meditation, gaining in both physical strength and self-confidence.

Arca assigned Nomi and Qel-Droma to lead a joint peacekeeping force of the Galactic Republic and the Jedi Knights to defeat the dark side Krath cult and the dark magicians of the Sith. After a pitched battle, Qel-Droma told Nomi that he would infiltrate the Krath and learn their dark side ways, even though Nomi urged him against such action. Her warning was prescient. She and two other Jedi later tried to extract Qel-Droma from virtual imprisonment in the Empress Teta system, but he had been injected with Sith poison that led to an explosion of anger and his loss to the dark side. With resignation, Nomi knew that she had to leave him to his dark fate.

But after Ulic murdered his brother, Cay, Nomi lashed out with her Force abilities in an attack so powerful that she severed his connection to the Force. She resolved herself to the fact that Ulic would never love her again.

Vima Sunrider

In the aftermath of the Great Sith War, Nomi threw herself into politics and was the driving force behind the Exis Convocation. She was so preoccupied that she lost track of her teenage daughter, Vima, who left to find the exiled Ulic. Joined by Sylvar, Nomi traveled to Rhen Var to recover her daughter. She discovered that Ulic had never forgotten her, and had in fact carved the likenesses of Nomi and Andur into a cliff of ice with Vima's help. Ulic's apparent redemption was short-lived, as the overzealous pilot Hoggon shot and killed him, thinking he was ridding the Republic of a great enemy. After Ulic's body disappeared into the Force, Nomi vowed to focus more on the training of her daughter.

**Sunrider, Vima** The daughter of Andur and Nomi Sunrider. Vima was born to a family strong in the use of the Force. During the Exis Convocation, Vima grew bored when her mother refused to train her. She stowed away on Hoggon's starship and convinced him to take her to the exiled Ulic Qel-Droma on Rhen Var. Ulic agreed to train her, and she soon built her own lightsaber. When Nomi arrived on Rhen Var to take her home, Vima refused to leave Ulic's side. When Ulic was killed by Hoggon, Vima and Nomi saw Ulic's body disappear into the Force, and realized that he still had the heart of a Jedi. With his last breath, Ulic proclaimed Vima to be a Jedi herself.

**Sunry** This former soldier was among the many who fought for the Republic during the years leading up to the Great Sith War. A noted pilot, he was crippled in battle, but was later awarded the Hero's Cross for his valor. Sunry and his wife, Elora, were married for many years before it was discovered that Sunry was having an affair with a Sith officer, Elassa. Sunry admitted his mistake and agreed to end the affair, only to find that Elassa had been murdered in her hotel room. He was accused of Elassa's murder and brought to trial, where his old friend Jolee Bindo agreed to defend him in court. As the trial played out,

Super battle droids at the Battle of Geonosis

it became obvious that Sunry had been the victim of a Sith plot to infiltrate the Republic's military command. His ending of the affair thwarted that plan, so the Sith chose to murder Elassa and plant his Hero's Cross on her body, in an effort to discredit the Republic by implicating him in the crime. Sunry was eventually found innocent, but Elassa's killer was never identified.

***Sunulok*** This Yuuzhan Vong warship, a greater version of the *Vua'spar* interdictor, was the flagship of Warmaster Tsavong Lah. Like most of the Yuuzhan Vong forces, the *Sunulok* had been en route to the galaxy for many years, and certain parts of the ship had begun to die off. Nevertheless, it still maintained all its weapons and shielding systems. Primary among the ship's operative systems was the collection of dovin basals it used as a gravity-well projector and tractor beam. These dovin basals were used to drag New Republic starships out of hyperspace for boarding.

When the warmaster launched Battle Plan Coruscant, the *Sunulok* led an assault from a position hidden in the OboRin Comet Cluster. However, the initial response from the New Republic forces was formidable, and the *Sunulok* was disabled early in the battle. The ship was badly damaged as Republic forces struggled to capture the yammosk hidden inside, and their efforts were ultimately successful. The warmaster and his crew were forced to abandon the *Sunulok* and leave it for dead.

**super battle droid** A greatly enhanced version of the basic B1 series battle droid produced by Baktoid Combat Automata for the Trade Federation during the years following the Battle of Naboo. The original B1 series design lacked independent programming and had several pieces of sophisticated technology mounted externally. This meant that the basic battle droid needed a Droid Control Ship to receive orders, and was subject to damage in the field. The super battle droid—designated the B2 series—was Baktoid's attempt to solve these design issues. The torso and upper body of the super battle droid were essentially beefed-up versions of B1 body parts, with improved armor plating to protect the droid componentry inside. A dedicated double laser cannon was built into the droid's right arm, and its manipulator arms could operate several other weapons types. The feet of the super battle droid were detachable, allowing the droid to be fitted with grasping claws or magnetic units to operate in a variety of environments.

Despite the fact that B2 series battle droids were produced to function independently, they were not necessarily intelligent. It was discovered that an SBD would stop firing at an opponent that had moved out of its visual range, a flaw that many Jedi Knights took advantage of during the Clone Wars. Their price notwithstanding—the average super battle droid cost about 200 times as much as a B1 series unit—large numbers of these combat automatas were purchased by the Confederacy of Independent Systems for its own defense. With the end of the Clone Wars, all B2 series battle droids were issued orders to deactivate as part of Darth Sidious's plan to consolidate military power and ensure the loyalty of his troops.

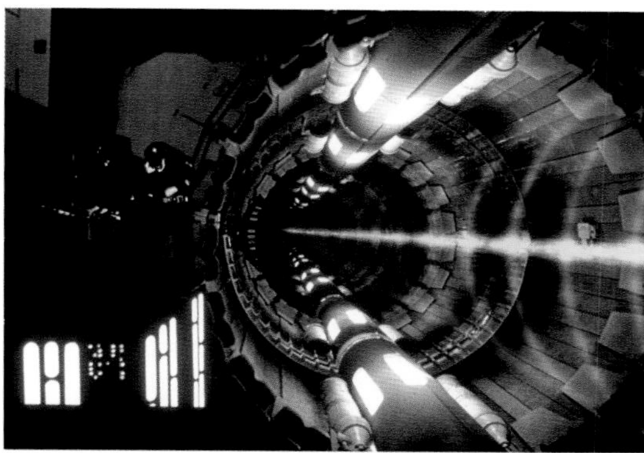

Superlaser

***Super*-class Star Destroyer** *See* Star Destroyer.

**supercommando codex** This was the name used by Jaster Mereel to describe the set of tenets and canons that he developed to oversee the new Mandalorian Mercs several decades before the onset of the Clone Wars. The codex was created to define the rules and roles of his new supercommandos, in an effort to unite the disparate clans of Mandalorian Mercs under a single leader. Although many followers of the Mandalorian codes agreed with Jaster and the codex, many others—Vizsla and Montross among them—broke away from his band in protest over the new rules.

**superlaser** An energy beam capable of destroying entire planets. One of the most powerful, destructive weapons ever created, the superlaser used a huge fusion reactor core and turbine generators to create the intense bundle of energy it unleashed. These weapons were used aboard the Death Star space stations. The superlaser was created by several tributary laser pulses, produced by amplification crystals around the cannon's circular well. The pulses were fused over the central focus lens, resulting in a devastating energy beam with more firepower than half the Imperial starfleet. Each amplification crystal required a separate gunnery station, where a crew of 14 gunners adjusted and monitored the laser pulses. Both Death Stars also had four reserve amplification crystals that could be readied for use in minutes. The entire superlaser was powered by the space station's immense fusion reactor. The original Death Star's reactor core required a recharge period of 24 hours, while the second Death Star could fire once every few minutes. Imperial technicians added other modifications to the second Death Star, including advanced targeting systems. The Empire also modified the Death Star superlasers for use on the *Eclipse*-class and *Sovereign*-class Star Destroyers. These superlasers were mounted axially on the huge Star Destroyers, allowing the vessels to maintain position and orientation during and after the generation of the laser blast.

**Supply Depot Thrago** A Chiss resupply installation established on Thrago. It was used with greater regularity during the expansion of the Killik Colony that marked the Swarm War, when the Chiss relied on Thrago to keep their warships ready to confront any Killik aggression. Jaina Solo, her brother Jacen, and Zekk launched a sneak attack on the depot at Thrago in an effort to disrupt the advances of the Chiss against the Killik hives. Jacen, however, had his own motivation for joining the mission, having seen a vision in which the entire galaxy was plunged into unending war with the Colony if the Chiss were allowed to press their advantage. Jaina, upon realizing that Jacen was working to destroy the Colony, refused to talk to him for the duration of the war.

**Suppoon, Gaar** An odious alien criminal, he was visited by Jabba the Hutt so that they could conduct some nefarious business together. Gaar Suppoon had no intention of letting Jabba leave his planet alive, but Jabba turned the tables on him, and Suppoon paid with his life.

**Suprema** This was the title adopted by Ampotem Za at the height of the New Order. Za, a member of the Shimholt species, was the leader of the slavers who took control of the planet Mandalore. The title of Suprema was one of honor to the Shimholt, and represented Za's heritage, even though he had been exiled from his homeworld of Kar'a'katok. Rumored to have been picked for the positon by Emperor Palpatine himself, the Suprema imprisoned Tobbi Dala, and later gloated to Leia Organa that he would also capture Fenn Shysa. However, when Shysa infiltrated the slavers' skeleton base, the Suprema was captured and the slave ring broken. In the fight to secure the base, the Suprema was killed when Tobbi Dala shut the base's blast doors before a group of airspeeders could launch. The Suprema, and the rest of the slavers, died in the resulting explosion.

*Suprema*

**Supreme Chancellor of the Republic** The elected leader of the Galactic Senate and, therefore, the entire Republic. The Supreme Chancellor presided over all meetings of the Galactic Senate and had more power than any single Senator, although he was still bound by protocol and procedure. The Supreme Chancellor resided on Coruscant and could be identified by a symbolic blue waistband. Within the Galactic Senate Rotunda, the Supreme Chancellor's 30-meter-tall podium was symbolic of both authority and vulnerability. The Chancellor's extensive offices lay beneath the Rotunda. As of the invasion of Naboo, the Supreme Chancellor was Finis Valorum, but he was removed from office when Queen Amidala raised a vote of no confidence in his ability to lead. Senator Palpatine, Naboo's representative in the Senate, was selected to replace Valorum, and would be the Republic's last Supreme Chancellor.

**Supreme Overlord** The highest rank in the Yuuzhan Vong hierarchy, and a caste in and of itself. Shimrra was the Supreme Overlord during the invasion of the galaxy.

**Supreme Prophet** *See* Kadann.

***Suprosa*** A freighter, it supposedly carried only fertilizer. Actually, its top-secret cargo was an Imperial computer containing information on the building of the Empire's second Death Star battle station. The stock light freighter was under contract to XTS, the transportation company owned by Prince Xizor, head of the Black Sun criminal organization. The freighter seemed lightly armed until attacked by a Bothan Blue Squad led by Luke Skywalker, when plates on the *Suprosa* slid back to reveal deadly hidden weapons.

**sureggi** One of the most sure-footed creatures to roam the jungles and lower marshlands of Kashyyyk. Ranging in length from 8 to 20 meters, sureggi could have upward of 60 legs, which aided their nimble climbing. A sureggi had a broad, shovel-like snout and a high-ridged dorsal region. Unlike most other amphibians, sureggi skin was dry and durable. Because of their strong hides, they could carry cargo that would be awkward for other pack animals. The surregi's nose had a number of thick tentacle-like sensory organs to detect burrowing grubs that were the mainstay of its diet. They also boosted its ability to determine the safest route of travel when carrying cargo or passengers. Sureggi were surprisingly able swimmers. While not quite capable of defending themselves from all aquatic predators, they maneuvered well enough in water to avoid danger during occasional stream or river crossings.

***Sureshot*** A YT-1300 stock light freighter used by the Wild Knight Izal Waz during the Yuuzhan Vong War. At Coruscant, the *Sureshot* used the alias *Shadow Bird* to convince saboteurs that it was actually the *Millennium Falcon.* Izal Waz controlled the ship remotely using slave circuits. Moments later, the *Sureshot* was destroyed.

**surge-coral** Living appendages containing tiny dovin basals, used by the Yuuzhan Vong to affix to their slaves. Surge-coral attached to bone and acted as a transmission/reception device, or the equivalent of a droid restraining bolt.

**Survivors** Descendants of one group of early space explorers on the planet Dellalt, they were extreme isolationists who hated other Dellaltians. It was believed that the group descended from survivors of the crash of Xim the Despot's legendary starship *Queen of Ranroon.* Technological artifacts salvaged from the crash became sacred talismans and implements for use in religious practices. Their major ritual seemed based on the actions undertaken by marooned spacers—setting up an emergency beacon and calling for rescue. Powered by sacrifices, the Survivors hoped that the signals of their prayers would be received and lead to their deliverance.

**Susejo of Choi** One of the oldest residents in the stomach of the Sarlacc at the Great Pit of Carkoon, he had been in the process of digestion for hundreds of years and made up a good portion of the Sarlacc's consciousness. Susejo of Choi taunted Boba Fett repeatedly while the bounty hunter was trapped inside the Sarlacc.

**Susevfi (Suarbi 7/5)** The fifth moon of the seventh planet of the Suarbi system. Suarbi 7 was a gas giant with a ring of asteroids and over a dozen moons. Suarbi 7/5, which had been colonized centuries earlier, became known as Susevfi. Several settlements grew up on its savanna-like grasslands, and the *Jensaarai* were located outside the large seaport of Yumfla. It was here that Leonia Tavira returned with the *Invidious* after her pirate raids, and where she held Mirax Terrik after Mirax was captured on Nal Hutta by the *Jensaarai.*

**Suspicious Silence Provision** This amendment to the Galactic Loyalty Act established that any individual who refused to answer the questions of legitimate representatives of the Coruscant Security Force or the Galactic Alliance Guard could be detained as a possible terrorist. The provision gave law enforcement officers the right to arrest any being who chose not to answer a question, and allowed for the acquisition of an interrogation warrant to investigate an individual's history. These sorts of additions to the Galactic Loyalty Act were viewed by political observers as further evidence that the Galactic Alliance was becoming more and more like the former Galactic Empire.

**Sutel, General Yald** An officer in the Imperial Remnant, he served as attaché to Vice Admiral Ark Poinard during the Yuuzhan Vong War.

**suubatar** This immense creature was native to the planet Ansion. It had six long legs, and each foot ended with six long, clawed toes. This combination of 36 toes allowed suubatars to race across the grasslands of Ansion at incredible speeds, often appearing to run just above the ground using only their toes to propel them along. They were also excellent swimmers, using all their toes to "grab" the water. The Alwari nomads were the first to domesticate the suubatar for use as a mount, and it was a symbol of pride to have a splendid specimen as a mount. When a suubatar stood up, it was three times as tall as a human, and its neck and upper back rose at a steep angle. This required that the Ansionians use a high-backed saddle, known as a viann, to remain in an upright position. Most suubatars had light, golden-brown fur striped with green, allowing them to blend into the grassy plains of the planet. They were omnivorous, able to feed on just about anything that happened to be in their path. The head of a suubatar was smooth and wide, with a single nostril and flat ears to make it aerodynamic. Its jaws were able to unhinge, giving the suubatar the ability to consume food larger than its own mouth.

**Suurja** This Outer Rim world was the site of a drawn-out battle between forces of the Old Republic and Mandalorians at the height of the Mandalorian Wars. The primary world in the Suurja system, Suurja was an agrarian planet that was ravaged by the stalemate. Refugees from Suurja and other frontline worlds fled to planets like Vanquo, hoping to find solace and escape from the predations of the Mandalorians. However, the Mandalorians were searching everywhere for Jedi Knights, and they followed refugees in the hope of find-

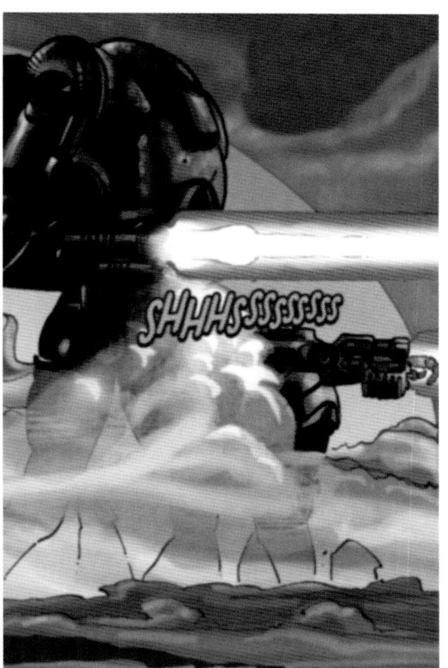

Swamp gas

ing them. Many Jedi were captured on Suurja even before they could assist the refugees. Many of the Jedi who survived the attack were transported to Demagol's research facility at Flashpoint Station.

**Suu-Tonn, Master** A Jedi combat instructor acknowledged within the Jedi Order as an expert in all seven forms of lightsaber combat. After practicing under his tutelage, trainees could choose to dedicate themselves to one form, or to build their own fighting style using elements of more than one.

***SV-45*** A Corellian Translines StarSpeeder 3000 shuttle that made regular runs to Vohai during the early years of the New Republic.

**svaper** A vicious predator native to Rodia, it was three meters long and lived in the water. It would spring forth and drag its prey under the surface, drowning it before swallowing it whole.

***Svelte*-class Imperial shuttle** A new-generation shuttle designed by the Silviut Corporation. The *Svelte*-class shuttle was a darkly elegant shuttle, glossy black with smooth beetle-like contours. Silviut designed it to replace the Imperial Lambda shuttle. Many Imperial pilots referred to it as the "Vader-class" shuttle.

**Svivren** A major trading center and homeworld of the Svivreni, the planet was considered difficult to conquer. Svivreni traders traveled the galaxy wearing their traditional garb of dulbands and robes. Mara Jade, Emperor Palpatine's top-secret aide, was sent to Svivren by the Emperor after she failed to kill Luke Skywalker at Jabba's palace on Tatooine. Later, a crystal gravfield trap of General Garm Bel Iblis's was lost at Svivren, creating an urgent need for a new CGT array during the siege of Coruscant.

**swamp crawler** A land vehicle, it was used to travel across marshy terrain. A swamp crawler boasted a multiwheeled transmission system, six balloon tires, and a central spherical wheel that could be used to execute quick turns of up to 180 degrees.

**swamp gas** A deadly chemical weapon used by the Confederacy on the Gungan colony of Ohma-D'un. The weapon was released by super battle droids against the Gungans, and it took effect in seconds. The initial symptoms were sweating and the forming of lesions on the skin. The Confederacy attempted to use spice miner transports for an attack on Naboo, but Anakin Skywalker and ARC trooper Alpha prevented the attack. Obi-Wan Kenobi and several other prominent Jedi later went to Queyta to get the antidote for the swamp gas.

**swamp slug** A large predator inhabiting Dagobah's water channels, it was an omnivore, pulverizing all organic matter with its thousands of tiny, grinding teeth.

**swamp stunners** Stub-nosed weapons, they were preferred by Glottalphibs.

**swamp troopers** Imperial troopers who wore armor especially adapted for swamp-like environments. Swamp troopers were equipped with the most advanced optical systems the Empire had to offter. Similar in look to scout troopers, the swamp troopers were green in color to blend into their swampy surroundings. Imperial Remnant swamp troopers were often armed with the Golan Arms FC-1.

**swamp wampa** A relative of the snow wampa found on Hoth. Mara Jade encountered a number of swamp wampas while on a mission to Dromund Kaas.

**Swan, Bultar** This Kuati woman was a noted Jedi Knight who trained under Micah Giiett until his untimely death during the Yinchorri Uprising. She then trained with Plo Koon, and was one of many who were involved in the galactic conflicts surrounding the Clone Wars. Swan was respected among the Jedi of the day for her combat record. Despite being a veteran of many battles, she had never taken a single life, even in self-defense. In combat, Bultar Swan used a unique combination of teräs käsi and Verdanaian "sliding hands" techniques. Swan, along with Empatojayos Brand and Chellemi Chuovvick, was dispatched to the Sepan sector to mediate the early conflicts of the Sepan Civil War shortly before the onset of the Clone Wars. She weathered many battles, and was one of the small number of Jedi who survived the Clone Wars and the initial killings of the Jedi Purge.

Bultar Swan

She was among a handful of Jedi who answered Master Shadday's call to meet on Kessel, and brought along Master Tsui Choi. However, unknown to the other Jedi, Shadday had leaked information to draw the attention of Darth Vader. In the chaos of battle, Swan found herself facing an unarmed and injured Vader. She refused to kill him, but her fellow Jedi Koffi Arana took matters into his own hands, killing Swan with his lightsaber before attacking Vader.

**Swarm War** The conflict that erupted between the Chiss and the various hives of the Killik Colony during the years following the Yuuzhan Vong War. As the Colony expanded under the influence of Raynar Thul, it began to take over planets on the boundaries of Chiss space. Border clashes turned into full-scale war, and the Galactic Alliance and the new Jedi Order tried to intervene. Former Dark Jedi Lomi Plo, acting as the queen of the Dark Nest, caused trouble, bringing pirates and mercenaries into the Utegetu Nebula to work for the Colony. The war escalated after the Colony managed to capture the warship *Admiral Ackbar*, an event that the Chiss claimed was clear evidence of the Alliance's support of the Colony.

The Colony, for its own part, took advantage of the Chiss accusation and set out to destabilize the Galactic Alliance, sending strike forces to stage military coups on the homeworlds of insectile species. With Thyferra captured by the Colony, the Alliance found its primary supply of bacta cut off. During this time, Jacen Solo had a vision in the Force that showed unending war if the situation wasn't resolved. Jedi Grand Master Luke Skywalker agreed with the vision, but not with Jacen's way of dealing with it. Skywalker set out to eliminate Lomi Plo and remove Raynar Thul from the Colony, hoping that their deaths would bring about a return to the normal hive mentality of the Killiks. Ultimately, a stalemate at the Battle of Tenupe brought the Swarm War to an end.

**sweetblossom** A nonaddictive recreational drug, sometimes just called blossom, that gave the user the feeling of having just awakened. As the number of drops increased, so did the diminution of awareness and the near paralysis of action.

Swokes Swokes

***Sweet Surprise*** A smuggler's ship active during the Yuuzhan Vong War, its crew worked with the alien invaders. Sometimes they transported refugees from besieged planets only to deliver them to the Yuuzhan Vong's next target. The *Sweet Surprise* was the first ship to launch an attack against Coruscant, carrying four voxyn aboard that they intended to land on the surface. The ship was captured over Coruscant, eliminating the voxyn threat.

**Swimmer** *See* Swimming People.

**Swimmer's Law** A code of ethics, it governed the social behavior of the Sauropteroids of the planet Dellalt.

**Swimming People** The name given to the Sauropteroids of the planet Dellalt; a single Sauropteroid was called a Swimmer.

**swirl prong** A herding mammal native to the Forest Moon of Endor. Xenobiologists believed that it was probably bioengineered elsewhere.

**Swokes Swokes** Native to the planet Makem Te, members of this pasty-skinned alien species were distinguished by their portly bodies and loose, pallid skin. The head of a Swokes Swokes was conical in shape, with a crown of horns on the brow and another set of horns at the point. The wide mouth of the Swokes Swokes was dominated by large, fang-like upper teeth, and sat below a small nose and two bulbous eyes. The nervous system of an individual Swokes Swokes was more similar to that of a flatworm than to most other humanoid species, and they had the ability to regenerate lost limbs if necessary. This gave them bravado on the battlefield, where Swokes Swokes were known to be fanatical in their attacks.

Swokes Swokes cities were delicate structures built from cast iron, giving them an underlying strength despite their appearance. Most transportation was in the form of domesticated, serpentine animals called schingas. The Swokes Swokes government was hereditary, with caliphs from prominent families ruling each city, but the pursuit of personal power was greatly encouraged. Many natives adopted the double-name convention that distinguished Swokes Swokes of note. Monetary rewards awaited those who excelled, and high status was demonstrated by the surgical implantation of jewelry next to internal organs. These adornments were visible only when a Swokes Swokes was screened by a bioscanner, but such devices were found in most buildings on Makem Te. Naturally, masquerading as someone of higher rank was risky and painful.

**swoop** Simple, crude vehicles often described as engines with seats, they were high-speed, lightweight speeder vehicles that left speeder bikes in their dust, but were also much more difficult to control. Swoops were built around powerful ion and repulsorlift engines, with little more added than a seat and controls. Fast and noisy, most were one-seaters. Turns, spins, and other maneuvers were accomplished by maneuvering flaps and control vanes via hand controls, with auxiliary controls in the knee and foot pegs. Pilots needed to shift their weight to enhance handling. Swoops offered no protection to the pilot or the occasional rider other than acceleration straps, and could easily spin out of control even at relatively low speeds. Pilots were always just a split second away from making a fatal error.

Speeds on lightweight-alloy swoops could top 600 kilometers an hour. Some swoops could fly several kilometers above a planetary surface, but generally they were used for low-altitude flight. The vehicles were used for advance military scouting and found their way into the hands of pirates and other criminals. Swoop racing—both authorized and outlaw—was popular throughout the galaxy. Han Solo was a top swoop racer in his youth.

**swoop gangs** Scattered throughout the galaxy, such bands as the Nova Demons and the Dark Star Hellions were infamous for their crimes. Swoop gangs ran spice, smuggled weapons, and did odd jobs for various factions of the underworld. Luke Skywalker was attacked by a dozen members of a swoop gang on Tatooine shortly after the Battle of Hoth.

**swoop racing** A popular and legal sport in the Galactic Core, it took place in huge domed arenas called swoop tracks, which held tens of thousands of viewers along with circular flight paths, obstacle courses, and massive concession booths. Outlaw swoop races were also run in which pilots took even greater chances. Han Solo once raced swoops on the professional circuit.

Swoop

**sword of Ajunta Pall** A double-bladed sword used by the ancient Sith Lord Ajunta Pall. It rested within a Sith tomb on Korriban. According to legend, Ajunta Pall imbued his sword with the essence of the dark side.

**SX transport** A troop transport vessel produced for the Grand Army of the Republic during the Clone Wars.

**Syayna** The daughter of Lord Prepredenko and a member of a Rebel cell on Jazbina. She and her followers hoped to convince her father to switch his allegiance from the Empire, but he refused. When Luke Skywalker arrived on Jazbina on a diplomatic mission, Prepredenko tricked him into "rescuing" an allegedly kidnapped Syayna. In reality, he used Luke to discover the location of Syayna's Rebel cell and arrest its members. Escaping, she spirited Luke away from the palace and refused to turn him over to the Empire.

**S'ybll** A mind witch who could change shapes, she tried to get Luke Skywalker to abandon his friends and stay with her during the Galactic Civil War.

**Sykes, Lieutenant Gavyn** A young Naboo Royal Security Force officer stationed in the capital of Theed at the time of the Trade Federation's invasion. Along with his mentor, Captain Kael, Sykes escaped Theed and organized a small resistance movement to combat the invaders. Using hit-and-run tactics, Sykes and Kael liberated a handful of prison camps and destroyed a number of Trade Federation facilities. They also allied themselves with Borvo the Hutt, a smuggler who had established an outpost on Naboo. Borvo ultimately betrayed the Naboo and had Kael killed. Sykes then rallied the remaining resistance fighters and chased the Hutt from Naboo before turning his attention back to the Trade Federation. In the last days of the occupation, Sykes and his troops launched a daring attack on Camp Four and rescued several seasoned officers. After a reunion with Captain Panaka, Sykes and his followers were instrumental in recapturing Theed. Sykes also participated in the final assault against the Trade Federation's Droid Control Ship.

**Sylvar** A Cathar Jedi, this feline being was apprenticed to Vodo Siosk-Baas some 4,000 years before the Galactic Civil War. She was the lover of Crado, also from the planet Cathar. During a lightsaber training duel with Exar Kun, she gave into instinctive rage and clawed Kun's face. When Crado turned to the dark side, she felt she had no choice but to kill him and nearly succeeded, though Kun did the deed. Kun and Ulic Qel-Droma's bloody campaign against the Republic—which became known as the Great Sith War—left Sylvar alone and angry. Qel-Droma survived the fighting and was exiled, but Sylvar did not feel that was enough punishment for his actions. She sought vengeance, and eventually flew to Rhen Var to settle scores. Seeing that Qel-Droma had redeemed himself, Sylvar couldn't bring herself to kill him, but an ambitious, hero-worshipping pilot named Hoggon shot and killed Ulic, thinking he was ridding the Republic of a great villain.

Sylvar

**symbiote** *See* organic gill.

**Sy Myrth** The homeworld of Senator Toonbuck Toora. Located in the Mid Rim, it was self-sufficient and wealthy. The natives of Sy Myrth were referred to as Sy Myrthians.

**Syn, Andov** A ruthless Kerestian mercenary who wore ornate battle armor that concealed his true identity: bounty hunter Nariss Siv Loqesh.

**Syn, Grand Admiral Peccati** One of Emperor Palpatine's 12 Grand Admirals. Grand Admiral Syn became involved in the Church of the Dark Side, a religion headed by "the Prophets," and kept a copy of the sacred book *Secrets of the Dark Side.* Syn was defeated by Admiral Ackbar during the liberation of Kashyyyk, and his flagship *Fi* (named for the High Galactic word for "son") was vaporized.

**Syn, Jariah** A bounty hunter and the copilot of the *Mynock* more than 130 years after the Battle of Endor. Jariah Syn was a pragmatic weapons expert who used illegal tools such as Yuuzhan Vong thud bugs and razor bugs. Syn had a long and abiding loathing of Jedi, and at first had no idea that his captain Cade Skywalker had originally been a Jedi student. With Cade and Delia Blue, Jariah Syn got involved in a galaxywide adventure involving the revived Empire and the new Sith Order led by Darth Krayt.

**Syndic** The Chiss military was divided into 28 colonial units called phalanxes under the command of the Nuruodo Ruling Family. The operation of individual phalanxes fell to an officer appointed by the House leader, known as a Syndic.

**Syndicat** A vast criminal organization that took control of the planet Phindar about 12 years prior to the Battle of Naboo. Led by the villainous Baftu and his Phindian assistant Terra, the Syndicat blockaded Phindar and tightly restricted food and supplies. As a result, the Phindians spent all of their time in long lines, waiting to receive whatever they needed just to survive day-to-day. The Syndicat employed assassin droids to police the populace. Dissidents and suspected criminals were captured and subjected to memory wipes. Brainwashed prisoners, known as "the renewed," were shipped far from Phindar. Meanwhile, members of the Syndicat gambled on how long the renewed could survive in their new environments. The Syndicat eventually was toppled by Qui-Gon Jinn and Obi-Wan Kenobi.

**synfur** A synthetic fur, it was used to create warm clothing for polar resorts on the planet Coruscant.

**synox** One of the most deadly toxins created for use by the GenoHaradan Assassin Guild during the years following the Great Sith War. Synox was virtually odorless, colorless, and tasteless, allowing it to be used in a wide variety of situations and deployment methods. It could also be used in conjunction with another form of poison, allowing an unsuspecting victim to discover and treat the secondary toxin without realizing the presence of the synox. A being poisoned by synox experienced racking fits of coughing, which soon were followed by the destruction of the internal organs. The body began to hemorrhage internally, as evidenced by profuse bleeding from the eyes and nose. Within a very short period of time, the victim died as vital organs failed in swift succession.

Jariah Syn

**synthdroid** Mechanical constructs made by the Loronar Corporation with sculpted synthflesh grown over metal armatures. Synthdroids had minimal internal computing power, since their actions were centrally controlled via the use of CCIR technology. Loronar supplied a number of synthdroids to Seti Ashgad and Dzym during their attempt to take control of the galaxy using the Death Seed plague. The synthdroids' central processor was destroyed by Leia Organa Solo during her escape from Ashgad's Hweg Shul fortress, and they were unable to stop her.

**synthflesh** A translucent gel, it was derived from bacta, the cellular regeneration medium. When applied to superficial wounds, synthflesh sealed the skin and promoted rapid healing of damaged tissue. After the gel dried, it slowly flaked off to reveal new, scarless tissue. The name was also given to the synthetic flesh used on synthdroids.

**Syo, Brisha** *See* Lumiya.

**syren plant** A large deadly plant from Kashyyyk with long, silky strands and an alluring scent that attracted unwary creatures. The huge syren blossom consisted of two to four glossy oval petals of bright yellow, seamed in the center and supported by a stalk of mottled blood-red color. From the center of the open blossom spread a tuft of long white fibers that emitted attractive pheromones. When the blossom's sensitive inner flesh was touched, the petal jaws closed over the victim and began digesting.

A few strong Wookiees traditionally harvested the plant, holding the flower open while a younger Wookiee scrambled to the center of the blossom to harvest the fiber and quickly escape. Occasionally young Wookiees lost limbs as the carnivorous plant chomped down on a slow-moving arm or leg. Chewbacca's nephew Lowbacca got enough of the white fiber to make a belt that he always wore.

**system patrol craft** These vessels were the first line of defense within star systems. They frequently were used against pirates, smugglers, and hostile alien forces. System patrol craft usually had powerful sublight engines but no hyperdrives. They also performed customs inspection duties and watched for disabled ships that required assistance.

*2-1B*

**2-1B (Too-Onebee)** An older medical droid that served the Rebel Alliance, it was a skilled surgeon and field medic. Too-Onebee treated Luke Skywalker twice during the Battle of Hoth, once operating to replace Luke's severed hand with a biomechanical replacement. Like other droids of its class, this roughly humanoid-appearing automaton had surgical manipulation appendages, a medical diagnostic computer, and a treatment analysis computer. Too-Onebee escaped Hoth aboard the transport carrier *Bright Hope.* The droid played a key role in the survival of 90 of that ship's passengers after it was nearly destroyed. Its assistant was the medical droid FX-7. 2-1B also was the generic name for this type of medical droid manufactured by Geentech. A 2-1B unit operated on Darth Vader as he was rebuilt following his extensive injuries on Mustafar.

**23 Mere** One of the Outer Rim colony worlds where the starliner *Star Morning,* owned by the Fallanassi religious order, stopped after the ship departed the planet Teyr.

**203rd Division** This clone trooper unit was dispatched to New Plympto during the final days of the Clone Wars. The 203rd later became part of the Imperial forces that remained on the planet to round up any Nosaurians who survived the fighting.

*< Darth Talon*

**212th Attack Battalion** This division of the Grand Army of the Republic was led by Commander Cody during the Clone Wars. The unit saw action on a number of worlds, including Rendili, Cato Neimoidia, and Boz Pity. Its most notable action came on Utapau, when Jedi General Obi-Wan Kenobi finally destroyed General Grievous at the end of the Clone Wars.

**2187** This was the designation of the detention cell in which Princess Leia Organa was held on the first Death Star. It was located on Level 5, Detention Block AA-23.

**21st Nova Corps** One of the four corps of the Outer Rim Sector Army during the Clone Wars. Led by Commander Bacara and Jedi Master Ki-Adi-Mundi, the 21st Nova Corps became known as the Galactic Marines after it was split off to form an independent unit. The 21st Nova Corps was on Mygeeto when the command was issued to execute Order 66.

**21st Recon Group** This New Republic fleet was formed to supplement the Fifth Battle Group, which was attempting to blockade the Koornacht Cluster and prevent further Yevethan atrocities. The 21st was given the hazardous duty of gathering reconnaissance on the 13 major Yevethan worlds in order to better understand their defenses and weaknesses.

**22nd Air Combat Wing** This clone trooper unit was on Boz Pity during the final stages of the Clone Wars.

**233rd Imperial Fighter Group** This Imperial starfighter group was mauled by a squadron of Rebel Alliance Y-wings at Ord Biniir.

**2391st Battle Squadron** This Imperial Navy task force was thought to have been destroyed shortly after the Battle of Endor. It reappeared in the Kalinda system some years later, consisting of an *Imperial*-class Star Destroyer, a pair of *Victory*-class Star Destroyers, an Interdictor cruiser, and several support ships. The Kalindean DeepSpace Fleet was able to repel the 2391st, and later pushed it out of the system after the completion of Project Second Chance.

**24th Bombardment Squadron** This squadron of K-wing bomber groups served the Fifth Battle Group. It was part of Task Force Blackvine during the unsuccessful blockade of Doornik-319.

**27th Denarian Fleet** This Old Republic Navy fleet was one of the first to be overhauled under the auspices of the New Order. Emperor Palpatine ordered some 250 *Victory*-class Star Destroyers decommissioned to make way for the new *Imperial*-class Star Destroyers. The Victories were stripped of weaponry and sold at auction to raise money for the Imperial war machine. The Corporate Sector Authority won the property rights to a majority of the Victories, which it reoutfitted and placed at the forefront of its own fleet.

**2JTJ (TooJay)** A personal navigation droid given to the Jedi Master Tahl by Yoda, after Tahl lost her eyesight. She quickly found the droid annoying. Known as TooJay, the droid continually called Tahl "sir" and tried to correct her every move. It was soon discovered that Xanatos had placed a recording and monitoring device within 2JTJ's plating to monitor the Jedi's actions during his attempts to steal the Healing Crystals of Fire from the Jedi Temple. Qui-Gon Jinn and Obi-Wan Kenobi arranged to have TooJay record a false conversation to lure Xanatos to them.

*2JTJ*

2X-3KPR

**2-M** This repulsor tank was the Empire's answer to the T2-B tanks that were used by the Rebel Alliance during the early stages of the Galactic Civil War. Based on the designs of the TX-130 *Saber*-class tank, the 2-M tank was built by Rothana Heavy Engineering and proved to be a marked improvement over its predecessor.

**2-ROB** This medical droid was assigned to the crew of Ki-Adi-Mundi's Old Republic starship during his search for Ephant Mon and his daughter, Sylvn. Her data banks were programmed with medical information on over 12 million species.

**2X-3KPR** A simple maintenance and diagnostics droid, it activated alarm sensors, security lighting, power fences, and the like on remote installations. Owen Lars used some of these small, rolling automata to patrol his moisture farm on Tatooine.

**327th Star Corps** The name given to the team of elite clone troopers led by Commander Bly and commanded by Jedi General Aayla Secura, during the final stages of the Clone Wars. The nickname of the unit came from the fact that it was stationed in the Outer Rim, moving from system to system and never seeing Coruscant. The unit's use of jetpacks earned it a reputation as the GAR's preeminent rocket trooper unit. Originally formed to participate in the Battle of Geonosis, the 327th Star Corps was part of the 2nd Sector Army and saw action on New Holstice, Honoghr, Anzat, and Dromund Kaas before being sent to Felucia. Under the command of Master Secura, this latter mission was to capture Shu Mai and the leaders of the Commerce Guild. However, the Gossam and her entourage had already been moved to Mustafar as part of the larger plot by Darth Sidious. Secura and her Jedi team were destroyed by the 327th Star Corps on Felucia after Sidious gave the command to execute Order 66.

**32nd Air Combat Wing** This division of the Grand Army of the Republic saw duty on Paarin Minor and Murkhana during the Clone Wars. The unit was led by the clone commander known as Salvo, who executed Order 66.

**32nd Cruiser Squadron** This New Republic naval fleet, under the command of Captain S'lixike, patrolled the Kalinda system during Project Second Chance.

**35th Infantry** One of the many battalions of the Grand Army of the Republic. Elements of the unit were assigned to Qiilura to help extradite the human colonists to Kebolar. Once the colonists were rounded up, the 35th Infantry was ordered to report to the planet Gaftikar to assist with pacifying the human population there.

**37th Detachment** This Imperial stormtrooper unit was stationed in Mos Eisley on Tatooine just prior to the Battle of Yavin. The 37th was relieved by Zeta Unit after it was learned that R2-D2 and C-3PO had escaped from the *Tantive IV.*

**37th Imperial Fighter Wing** Soontir Fel was assigned to this Imperial TIE fighter squadron after graduating from the Imperial Academy. It was under the command of Captain Lun Tessra aboard the *Abrogator.* Fel served in the sixth squadron of the wing during the battle against the Lortan fanatics. He turned down a chance to transfer to another unit when Tessra returned from other duty in an effort to remain a pilot with the squadron. The 37th Wing later took part in the Battle of Nal Hutta.

**38th Armored Division** This was one of the most widely traveled ground assault units of the Grand Army of the Republic during the Clone Wars.

**3B3** This was the designation of the Trade Federation battle droid that intercepted Qui-Gon Jinn, Obi-Wan Kenobi, and Jar Jar Binks after their bongo sub surfaced in the city of Theed. The Jedi quickly dispatched the droid and made their way to the palace.

**3B3-10** This Trade Federation battle droid rerouted the commands from the Droid Control Ship after its commander was shot by Queen Amidala when she infiltrated the Theed Palace to retake it from the Neimoidians.

**3D-4X (Threedee-Fourex)** The silver-plated personal droid of Hekis Durumm Perdo Kolokk Baldikarr Thun, administrator of the droid-production world Mechis III. Threedee-Fourex killed his master when the assassin droid IG-88 and his counterparts took over the programming of all of Mechis III's computer systems and droids.

**3DO series droid** An ancient series of protocol and service automata produced by Duwani Mechanical Products some 4,000 years prior to the Battle of Yavin.

**3DVO cam droid** A series of holographic cam droids produced by Loronar during the final years of the Old Republic. The 3DVO was generally regarded as one of the most self-aware versions of cam droid available on the market, and was often employed as a dedicated field reporter. One of them was involved in a rescue mission by Luke Skywalker on Jazbina.

**3PO droid** Manufactured by Cybot Galactica, the 3PO series of protocol droids comprised the most advanced models on the market in the later years of the Galactic Republic. Standing 1.7 meters tall, 3PO droids resembled most humanoid species in appearance. They were equipped with SyntheTech AA-1 verbobrains and a TranLang III communications module.

**3P series droid** A model of protocol droids developed during the early years of the New Order. Most 3P series droids were humanoid in stature so that they could blend in with most sentient species of the galaxy.

**3PX series droid** This boutique droid was produced by Cybot Galactica from the base 3PO series, and was designed to be sold at a lower price point in the Outer Rim Territories. The angular body shell clearly differentiated the 3PX units from the 3PO units, as did its somewhat less human personality. These design aspects were among the many reasons the 3PX series did not sell very well. Production of the 3PX series was quite limited and short-lived, although parts of the design were later licensed to Arakyd for the production of the RA-7 droid.

**3rd Imperial Heavy Armor** The most dangerous of all the Imperial ground forces encountered by the Rebel Alliance.

**T-12** A service droid in a storeroom in a Jedi outpost on the planet Ossus 4,000 years before the Galactic Civil War, its job was to pack Sith artifacts for shipment to the Jedi Archives. Ulic Qel-Droma used it in his search for information about the Sith.

T-12

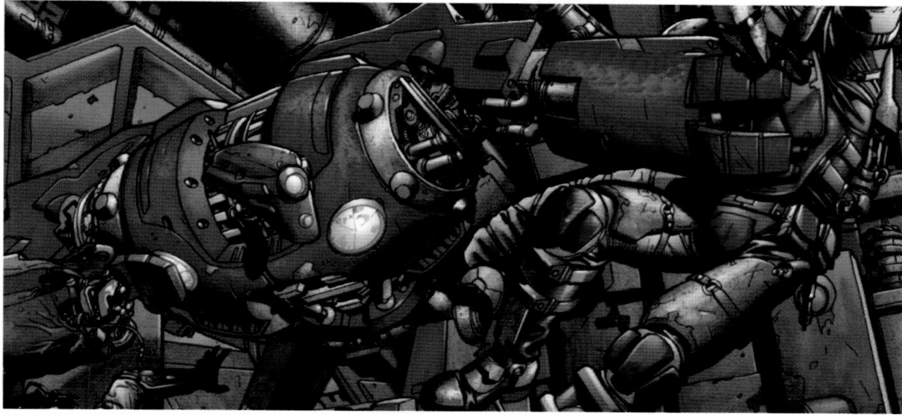

*T1-LB*

**T-16 skyhopper** A high-speed, transorbital pleasure craft, it was every young hot rodder's dream. The Incom Corporation's T-16 skyhopper was designed to be fast and easy to handle. Using a high-powered ion engine for thrust and two repulsorlift generators for lift, the T-16 had a top speed of nearly 1,200 kilometers per hour and could reach an altitude of almost 300 kilometers. The distinctive tri-wing design helped stabilize the skyhopper at high speeds, although the forward stabilizer fin blocked the pilot's field of view. Advanced gyrostabilizers helped the pilot keep control, even in twisting, high-g maneuvers. The ship was amazingly maneuverable: It could twist through tight turns and make surprising vertical climbs.

Luke Skywalker owned a T-16 and often raced his friends through Beggar's Canyon on Tatooine. He practiced his marksmanship by "bull's-eyeing" the womp rat burrows at the end of the canyon with his stun cannons. Impromptu races through the winding desert canyons tested Luke's natural abilities. Just before he left the planet, Luke ripped the stabilizer off his skyhopper while trying to maneuver through the infamous Stone Needle in Beggar's Canyon.

While civilian T-16s seldom had weapons, optional upgrades offered four forward-firing stun cannons or a cheaper pair of pneumatic cannons with targeting lasers. Armed T-16s were mainstays in planetary militias and police forces. The T-16's cockpit had two sections, with room for a single pilot and one passenger.

**T-19** A starfighter produced by Torpil for the Old Republic during the Clone Wars. It was an exceptionally fast ship, and many pilots remarked that a speed of 650 kilometers per hour was essentially "standing still" for the T-19.

**T1-LB** An ancient, LB-series labor droid stationed on the Rogue Moon during the years following the Great Sith War. The droid was in the service of Jedi Master Lucien Draay, and accompanied Draay to the Rogue Moon on the fateful mission that resulted in the deaths of several Padawans. Master Draay and his fellow Masters feared that one of their students would be the shatterpoint around which a devastating war would revolve. Rather than let the galaxy fall into chaos, the Masters killed their Padawans, believing that they were doing what the Force would have demanded. Zayne Carrick escaped the killings and tried to recover the droid, known as Elbee to the Jedi, to help understand what had happened. Although T1-LB's original body had been destroyed, the Arkanian engineer Camper managed to restore his main cognitive centers and storage banks, allowing Zayne to witness the murders of his fellow students. When the recordings showed the original "death" of the droid, Elbee's mind went into a tailspin and destroyed itself. Camper restored much of T1-LB's other systems and rebuilt the automaton to serve as a labor droid aboard the *Last Resort.*

*T-16 skyhopper*

*T3 series droid*

Elbee proved his usefulness when the group was forced to land on Vanquo: The droid helped them escape several Mandalorian traps. He remained with the Arkanians, helping them load cargo and keep their ship operative. T1-LB was able to hold off the assassin droid HK-24 long enough for Rohlan Dyre to blast it to pieces. Elbee took several blasts to the midsection, however, and required minor repairs to be restored to full functionality.

**T-21** A light repeating blaster manufactured by BlasTech, the T-21 was a rifle-sized weapon with a long, thick barrel. Originally designed for military use during the Clone Wars, it later was chosen as the primary weapon of the soldiers of the Galactic Alliance Guard. It provided excellent power and good range. A T-21 carried energy for 25 shots, although its firepower was unlimited when attached to a power generator.

**T3-M4** An ancient T3 series utility droid created on Taris some 4,000 years before the Battle of Yavin. T3-M4 was modified to serve as a personal security unit with light armor plating and upgradable weaponry, while his programming was augmented for use in slicing into computer systems and breaking encryption codes. He was designed for crime boss Davik Kang, but the droid was later acquired by Carth Onasi and Revan during the search for the Star Forge. After the defeat of Darth Malak, Revan's ship *Ebon Hawk* disappeared in deep space. T3-M4 helped bring the ship to Peragus II, and aided the Jedi Exile in escaping from the mining facility there. After being abandoned on Telos, T3-M4 was captured by Atris and the Handmaiden Sisters, who downloaded large portions of his memory core. T3-M4, in turn, managed to acquire a recording of the Exile's sentencing, as well as a list of all known surviving Jedi Masters. T3-M4 was eventually lost in a game of pazaak and sold to Vogga the Hutt, who put the droid to work in his warehouse on Nar Shaddaa. After the end of the Sith Civil War, T3-M4 accompanied the Exile into the Unknown Regions.

**T3 series droid** Utility droids produced by Duwani Mechanical Products in the period leading up to the Great Sith War. These automata were known for their versatility, reliability, and adaptability, and were used throughout the galaxy for jobs from janitorial duties to complex mechanical repairs.

**T-47** *See* snowspeeder.

*T-21s were the primary support weapon for the sandtrooper garrison on Tatooine.*

**T-6** This BlasTech heavy blaster pistol was known to soldiers as the Thunderer, and was marketed as the ultimate superheavy blaster. It was first produced to compete with SoroSuub's Renegade, and—thanks to its incredible power—it was the weapon that ended the "blaster wars" among BlasTech, Merr-Sonn, and SoroSuub. Unfortunately, the T-6 tended to overheat because of that power, and the barrel of the weapon could warp. If this occurred during a firefight, the focusing crystals could become misaligned and the T-6 could explode in the user's hands.

**T-65 series** *See* X-wing starfighter.

**T-77 airspeeder** An experimental airspeeder, it was flown by Luke Skywalker and Kam Solusar on the planet Ossus.

**Ta, Sayn** A Kaminoan master cloner, she and her assistant were tasked with enhancing the already excellent combat skills of the clone troopers. When the troopers suddenly started dying from an internal nanovirus, Sayn Ta was called upon by Aayla Secura and Kit Fisto to investigate the problem. They discovered that the assistant had been bribed by the Separatists to infect the clones, and he used the virus to kill Sayn Ta, too. The assistant threatened to inject Aayla Secura, but he accidentally injected himself and died. The virus was then used to create an antidote to vaccinate the clones.

*T-77 airspeeder*

**Taa, Orn Free** This obese, Rutian Twi'lek was the Republic Senator representing Ryloth. Notorious for his corruption, Taa used his position to indulge his every whim. His misshapen head-tails stored fat like the rest of his body. During the years leading up to the Battle of Naboo, Senator Taa was one of Finis Valorum's most vocal rivals, and took every opportunity to needle the Chancellor in public and political forums. In the years leading up to the Clone Wars, Orn Free Taa continued to support Palpatine and proved himself a stickler for the letter of the law. When the Military Creation Act came up for a vote, it was Orn Free Taa who demanded the vote be delayed. In the following months, Orn Free Taa supported legislation that seemed to maintain or improve Chancellor Palpatine's base of power, and he was one of the first to recommend that the Jedi Order be augmented with a dedicated police force. After the apparent death of Master Yoda at Ithor, Orn Free Taa took the matter to the Senate, demanding the formation of a security force that would answer solely to Palpatine himself.

*Orn Free Taa*

**Ta'a Chume, Queen Mother** The ruler of the 63 worlds of the Hapes Consortium in the years following the Battle of Endor. Ta'a Chume was the holder of a title that stretched back more than 4,000 years during which a matriarchy ruled the Consortium. She had dark green eyes, red-gold hair, and a tall, slender frame that belied her age. Her beauty was matched only by her ruthlessness.

Ta'a Chume lacked a female heir to inherit her throne, and her first son seemed so weak in her eyes that she secretly had him assassinated. She decreed that her second son, the handsome, strong Prince Isolder, had to take a superior wife to continue the dynasty. She found his first pick, Lady Elliar, a poor choice and had her murdered. Isolder then fell in love with New Republic ambassador Princess Leia Organa, whom Ta'a Chume considered a weak pacifist. Ta'a Chume again hired assassins, but Prince Isolder saved Leia's life.

A planetful of complications ensued, after which Luke Skywalker helped reveal the truth about Ta'a Chume's murderous ways to her son. By then, Isolder had changed his mind and decided to marry a commoner, a Force-sensitive Nightsister from the planet Dathomir named Teneniel Djo. Though not royal, she was strong, and the marriage produced a baby girl, Tenel Ka, who grew up imbued with the Force.

Years later, Ta'a Chume was still meddling. She was very much opposed to Tenel Ka's enrolling in Skywalker's Jedi academy, for she considered the girl's rightful future to be that of a powerful Hapan ruler. Despite Ta'a Chume's opinions, her granddaughter and other young Jedi Knights saved her from an assassination plot by the insectoid Bartokks.

*Queen Mother Ta'a Chume*

After the Yuuzhan Vong invaded the galaxy, a huge part of the Hapan navy met its end during the Battle of Fondor. Ta'a Chume, angered over the opening of Hapes to war refugees, began searching for a young woman to replace Teneniel Djo. Her first attempts focused on Jaina Solo. After arranging Teneniel Djo's death, Ta'a Chume quickly ordered that new leadership be instated. Her plans failed when Tenel Ka agreed to take her mother's position. Ta'a Chume was arrested and charged with murder. She remained in a minimum-security environment for years. Ta'a Chume's frustration and unrest only increased when Tenel Ka refused to marry, and she began to hear whispers of her granddaughter's growing relationship with Jacen Solo. Ta'a Chume began to plot a new pathway to power, working a deal with the Gorog hive to have Jacen and Tenel Ka's infant daughter killed. Jacen and Ben Skywalker foiled her plans, and Jacen sent a sharp spike of Force power into her brain, rendering her unable to produce a coherent thought.

**Taan** This female Yuuzhan Vong was a member of the Shamed Ones caste, and was part of the slave crew aboard the *Stalking Moon*. It was Taan who revealed to Corran Horn that the Shamed Ones believed the Jedi Knights would be their salvation. She later helped the Jedi gain control of the scoutship by communicating with Yuuzhan Vong commanders, claiming that the *Stalking Moon* had suffered a failure during hyperspace reversion, and that much of the command crew had been killed.

**Taanab** A generally peaceful agrarian planet, it was the site of a small but significant battle against space pirates that earned gambler Lando Calrissian a reputation as a top military strategist.

Pirates had been the bane of Taanab's peaceful farmers for millennia. Some 4,000 years before the Galactic Civil War, the freighter *Kestrel Nova* was captured from space pirates near the planet and was used by Jedi Ulic Qel-Droma to travel to the Tetan system. Thousands of years later, Taanab was still plagued by annual raids of bandits from the planet Norulac. One year, Calrissian was at Taanab's Pandath spaceport when the pirates arrived. After they damaged his ship, Calrissian—on a bet—agreed to attack the raiders. He hid his ship in the ice ring surrounding Taanab's moon, and when the pirates made their run, he ejected hundreds of Conner nets into the center of the attacking fleet. As the pirates struggled to untangle themselves, Calrissian hit them with ice blocks from the moon's ring, causing even further damage. Finally, Calrissian led the Taanab defense fleet in a cleanup operation and single-handedly accounted for 19 kills. Later, just prior to the Battle of Endor, Calrissian was promoted to the rank of general in the Rebel Alliance partly thanks to the notoriety of this incident, which became known as the Battle of Taanab.

Taanab

Some five years later, mad Jedi clone Joruus C'baoth coordinated an Imperial attack on Taanab, where he used the turbolasers of the *Bellicose* to destroy a New Republic ship against the direct orders of Captain Aban.

**Taanab, Battle of** *See* Taanab.

***Taanab Sunrise*** This New Republic warship was badly damaged in the Battle of Garqi during the Yuuzhan Vong War. It was saved when the Imperial Remnant, under the command of Admiral Pellaeon, intervened to support the Republic. The *Red Harvest* placed itself between the Yuuzhan Vong force and the *Taanab Sunrise,* absorbing damage while allowing the *Sunrise* to escape.

**Taanab Yellow Aces** An all-volunteer fighter squadron made up of pilots from Taanab as well as refugees. The Taanab Yellow Aces joined Wedge Antilles's forces in the Pyria system. Their A-wings and E-wings were painted a glaring yellow with black stripes and were led by Ace One: Wes Janson.

**Ta'ania** A descendant of a Jedi, she had been one of the original colonists on the planet Eol Sha. Gantoris, one of Luke Skywalker's first students at the Jedi academy, was possibly a descendant of Ta'ania.

Crys Taanzer

**Taanzer, Crys** A hot-tempered pilot for the transport vessel *Uhumele* during the early years of the Empire. Taanzer intercepted Dass Jennir and Bomo Greenbark at the Cadgel Meadows spaceport on New Plympto after the Clone Wars. When the ship was grounded by Imperial troops, she agreed with Ko Vakier's vote in favor of blasting their way through the Imperials in order to escape. However, upon hearing Jennir's plan to escape with several other ships, she began making calls to other crews.

**TAARS** An acronym for "Target-Aggressor Attack Resolution Software," a package that linked X-wing and Y-wing fighters. In emergency situations, another craft could send targeting or flight data that might otherwise be lost in combat.

**Taat** One of many hives that made up the Killik Colony during the Swarm War. Similarly to other hives within the Colony, the members of the Taat hive referred to themselves, as well as the entire nest, as Taat, and acted upon the Will of the Taat hive. However, the Taat was notable among the 14 or so hives of the Colony for its stoic approach to life. Members established their nest on the moon Jwlio, where they became known as the healers and warriors of the Colony. When the Colony's conflict with the Chiss was resolved, Taat was the first of the Qoribu hives to relocate to another planet. The entire hive was transported aboard the *Kendall* to a world within the Utegetu Nebula, deep in the Unknown Regions and well away from Chiss space.

Tach

**tabaga** A large, cat-like creature native to Corellia, it often hunted vrelts for food.

**Tabanne, Lieutenant Atril** This Coruscant native served the New Republic as second in command to Choday Hrakness aboard the *Night Caller* in support of Wraith Squadron, and was instrumental in keeping the ship active in the defense of Talasea against an attack from Apwar Trigit. After Hrakness was killed in the battle, she was given the command of the ship.

**Taboon** A planet in the Stenness system, it was circled by many moons, including one owned by Great Bogga the Hutt some 4,000 years before the Galactic Civil War. Bogga, ruler of the Stenness underworld, built a great palace on Taboon. Several millennia later, the bounty hunters Zardra and Jodo Kast tracked their targets to the Red Shadow, a Taboon bistro. The ensuing firefight resulted in the explosive death of Mageye the Hutt.

Taboon

**Tabory, Evlyn** A human female who lived among the survivors of Outbound Flight. She was the niece of Guardian Pressor and the daughter of Rosemari Tabory. Due to her Force sensitivity, Pressor used her as a decoy to capture a group of Chiss and Jedi that came to investigate the remains of Outbound Flight. Dean Jinzler later urged her to embrace her Force powers. During the Vagaari attack, Tabory used the Force to pull a comlink to her. At Dean's request, she accompanied Mara Jade, while fearing for her safety at the hands of the Outbound Flight survivors who had learned to despise Jedi.

**Taboth** This desolate planet was the second world in the Both system, orbited by two moons.

**tach** A small, monkey-like creature found in Kashyyyk's Shadowlands. Its adrenal glands could be powdered to produce a powerful stimulant. However, the Wookiees considered it a crime to kill tachs, and any being caught hunting them was imprisoned.

**Tachi, Siri** A Jedi trainee and a contemporary of Obi-Wan Kenobi's during his time as Qui-Gon Jinn's Padawan. Siri was two years younger than Obi-Wan, but her skills with the Force moved her forward to Obi-Wan's level. She was chosen as Adi Gallia's Padawan, and they were assigned by Master Yoda to accompany Qui-Gon and Obi-Wan to Kegan to witness firsthand how a Master and an apprentice worked together. Despite her skill and grace, Tachi was impatient to move forward in her training, and often bristled in the presence of Kenobi. The two learned to work together to escape from the Keganites who captured them. Siri found herself paired with Obi-Wan on a mission to protect Talesan Fry, and the two realized that they loved each other. Knowing that attachment was forbidden among the Jedi, they struggled to resolve their feelings and their allegiance to the Jedi Order.

Tachi later announced that she was leaving the Jedi Order—actually part of an undercover operation to infiltrate the slave ring of Krayn. In the intervening years, she dropped her given name and went by the pseudonym Zora. About three years after the Battle of Naboo, she worked with Anakin Skywalker to destroy Krayn's organization. Tachi eventually took Ferus Olin as her Padawan learner, and refused to take another Padawan after Olin voluntarily left the Order. Just prior to the Clone Wars, Tachi was dispatched with Garen Muln on a mission to the Xanlanner system. While en route, they discovered Kenobi's distress signal, and helped him reach Vanqor to rescue Skywalker. At the height of the Clone Wars, Tachi teamed with Kenobi and Skywalker, this time traveling to Genian with Padmé Amidala to negotiate for a code-breaking device created by Talesan Fry. After returning to Azure, the Jedi found themselves under a Separatist attack. Tachi died in the fighting, but gave Kenobi a crystal she had carried with her as a Padawan so that her memory could live on in him.

*Siri Tachi*

***Tachyon Flier*** A battered but serviceable CEC YV-888 light freighter used by Anakin Solo's strike team as an escape vessel from the Yuuzhan Vong worldship *Baanu Rass.* After Lowbacca got the ship running, it was commandeered by Welk and Lomi Plo with Raynar Thul aboard. The *Tachyon Flier* landed in the Unknown Regions, where its injured passengers were absorbed into the hive-mind of the Killik nests. The site of the crash became known as Ub Ruur, a sacred place to the Colony.

**Tac-Spec Corporation** A front company established by the GenoHaradan assassins' guild. The GenoHaradan guild used Tac-Spec to ease the sale of its Footman droid to members of noble houses. Tac-Spec remained in business from approximately 1,000 to 400 years before the Battle of Yavin.

**Tac-Spec Footman** A series of personal service droids produced by the Tac-Spec Corporation nearly a millennium before the Clone Wars. They were considered one of the most loyal—and deadly—droids ever produced. The Tac-Spec Footman was marketed as "the gentleman's personal gentlething," and its primary programming was loyalty to its owner. But that included the ability to assassinate almost any being who posed a threat to its owner—contrary to the prime directive of most droids. The Footman was equipped with a small rail gun built into one arm, and the droid's chassis was covered with blastproof material.

**Tactical Channel 5** The transmission frequency set aside by the Empire's military forces for use by TIE fighter pilots. Also known as tac-fiver, this frequency allowed pilots to check in with their squad leader before beginning a mission. It was a low-powered channel with a limited range, which allowed the pilots to communicate without the transmissions being intercepted by enemy sensors. This also allowed pilots to communicate without being overheard by the communications officers on their home vessel, provided the squad was far enough away from the ship.

**tactical villip** A small, portable villip often worn by high-ranking Yuuzhan Vong warriors on the shoulder or forearm. Tactical villips served as the equivalent of real-time audiovisual communicators. A Yuuzhan Vong battle master had a master villip that relayed to him what his soldiers' villips saw.

**tactile writing** The generic term used to describe any form of nonverbal communication that used patterns or collections of physical objects to convey meaning. Many of the forms of tactile writing utilized string or scraps of cloth that were tied into certain configurations to denote letters, words, and phrases. These could be read equally well with the eyes or fingers, making them accessible to a wide range of individuals. The variety of tactile writing forms was enormous, from the "strings of ancestors" of the Aalagar to the coded messages used by prisoners in the spice mines of Kessel, as well as the memory cords of the Twi'lek species. Those who studied tactile writing, known as khipulogists or fiber-record analysts, saw their chosen field of study elevated to the forefront after the discovery of the Lorrd Artifact.

**Tacto** One two major cities, along with Aubendo, on the planet Radnor. Together they were known as the Twin Cities. Tacto was also referred to as the Clear Sector five years after the Battle of Naboo, when a plague was unleashed in Aubendo. The two cities were isolated from each other in order to minimize the spread of the plague. After it was discovered that the Avoni were using the plague to hide their plans for invasion, the natives of Tacto refused to assist survivors in Aubendo, preferring to remain in their homes to safeguard their posessions from Avoni threats.

*Tac-Spec Footman*

**Tadrin, Luthus** An Imperial Governor officially in charge of Garqi, he frequently was absent and entrusted the planet to the prefect Mosh Barris, who was later implicated as a traitor to the Empire by Corran Horn.

***Tafanda Bay*** An Ithorian herd ship, it once soared above the rain forests of Ithor. Such ships were hundreds of meters tall and hovered just above the planetary surface, a place that the Hammerheads, or Ithorians, considered sacred. Ithorians lived on herd ships for thousands of years and used them as examples of the harmonious integration of technology and nature.

The *Tafanda Bay*'s exterior was covered by moss and flowers, with huge trees growing from side platforms. It had landing platforms for incoming ships and speeders, while dozens of immense repulsorlift engines propelled it slowly over the jungle landscape. In its interior, the Ithorians reproduced nearly every terrain on Ithor and some from many other worlds. There were large trading halls for commerce and a Great Atrium nearly 250 meters across, with moss-covered walls leading to the open air above. Observation decks gave spectacular views of the jungle and Ithor's brilliant violet night sky.

The *Tafanda Bay* community was led by the controversial Momaw Nadon, who once was banished for cooperating with the Empire. Rogue Squadron leader Wedge Antilles and onetime Imperial weapons scientist Qwi Xux visited the *Tafanda Bay* when the New Republic sought to hide Qwi from the Empire. During the Yuuzhan Vong War, the Ithorians

Tafanda Bay

hosted a reception aboard the vessel for the New Republic and Imperial Remnant forces that came to defend the planet from the invaders. The *Tafanda Bay* was the only herd ship remaining on Ithor after the rest were evacuated before the battle. The Yuuzhan Vong and some Chazrach slaves boarded the vessel and fought the Jedi there. The *Tafanda Bay* was presumably destroyed in the devastation that consumed Ithor at the end of the battle.

Baron Orman Tagge

**Taggar, Lieutenant Rone** A member of the New Republic's 21st Recon Group, he piloted the recon-X fighter *Jennie Lee,* named for his mother, who'd been shot down in her Y-wing at the Battle of Endor. Assigned to gather information on the Yevethan mobilization on N'zoth, Lieutenant Rone Taggar captured the first images that awakened the New Republic to the size of the Yevethan fleet and the gravity of the growing crisis. Taggar blew up his ship just as he was about to be taken hostage by Yevethan forces.

**Taggart** A petty smuggler, he occasionally hired Han Solo before the Galactic Civil War to smuggle glitterstim spice.

**Tagge, Baron Orman** An influential member of the House of Tagge and the older brother of Cassio Tagge, the Imperial officer killed aboard the first Death Star. Orman Tagge was at one time the leader of the Corporate Sector Authority, and helped the mega-organization gain complete independence from the Empire. The Baron was also the charismatic leader of TaggeCo, and positioned the company to reap the rewards of key Imperial contracts. Darth Vader questioned Tagge's loyalty, and when the Baron refused to back down, Vader blinded him with his lightsaber. This forced Orman to use a cyborg vision system, and inspired him to train in the art of lightsaber dueling. Orman established the giant Achtnak launch station in the heart of Yavin's atmosphere, allowing TIE fighters to attack the Alliance's base on Yavin 4. Luke Skywalker destroyed the station, but Orman worked with his brother Silas to cut off a major supply route using the Omega Frost device. In a lightsaber battle with Skywalker, Orman lost the use of his cybervision. On the planet Monastery, Darth Vader forced Orman to meet Luke Skywalker in combat while Orman was disguised as Vader; Orman died in the battle.

General Cassio Tagge

**Tagge, Domina** A member of the wealthy Tagge family who led the Order of the Sacred Circle on the planet Monastery. Shortly after the Battle of Yavin, Domina found herself in the midst of political intrigue when the Order's leaders debated whether they were ready to side with the Empire or the Rebel Alliance. Her brother Ulric traveled to Monastery to talk her into allying herself with Vader, in order to avenge the death of their brother Orman at the hands of Luke Skywalker. Domina requested that Skywalker serve as the Alliance's representative to Monastery, while the Empire's representative was none other than Darth Vader. It was decided that Skywalker and Vader should duel to the death in the Crystal Valley. However, her plans were thwarted and Domina was forced to relinquish her position as High Priestess. Later, she had a bounty hunter team infiltrate the Red Nebula and steal one of its huge gemstones, placing it aboard a Star Destroyer and setting it adrift in Alliance-controlled space. Her plan to unleash the Crimson Forever plague failed when Leia Organa abandoned Domina on the fringes of the Red Nebula.

Domina Tagge

**Tagge, General Cassio** A high-ranking Imperial officer stationed aboard the original Death Star battle station. The House of Tagge had long been an influential order of nobles in the Empire, holding immense wealth through corporations such as TaggeCo and through a lucrative spice-mining operation. Still, it was not just his family history that assured General Tagge a placement aboard the Death Star as a third of the command triumvirate overseeing the station's activities. Tagge had proven to be a capable officer who eschewed political maneuvering in favor of loyal service to the Emperor. Though he had a reputation as a brilliant tactician, an analysis of his command decisions aboard the Death Star indicates that such praise was undeserved. The uninspired Tagge distributed the Death Star's gunners alphabetically throughout the station, rather than in logical, strategically defined patterns. This led to disunified firing patterns and less-than-optimum performance from the Imperial gunners during the Battle of Yavin. His warnings about Rebel strength went unheeded, and Tagge died when the Death Star was destroyed. Following his death, members of the core group of Rebels were repeatedly harassed by joint operations between the Empire and the House of Tagge. The late general was survived by a number of siblings, including a fellow general, Ulric Tagge, the scientific mastermind Silas Tagge, the beautiful and manipulative Lady Domina Tagge, and elder brother Baron Orman Tagge.

Ulric Tagge

**Tagge, Silas** The middle brother of the Tagge family and the scientific mind behind the technologies produced by the House of Tagge. Among Silas's most interesting inventions was the Omega Frost device, which was successfully tested in the deserts of Tatooine. When Luke Skywalker disabled one of the Omega Frost generating devices in the asteroid belt near Junction, Silas retreated into the medical facility aboard the Tagge flagship. The Rebel Alliance fleet attacked the vessel, but both Silas and Orman Tagge survived in a sealed chamber, which was recovered by Darth Vader.

**Tagge, Ulric** A major general in the Imperial starfleet and a member of the House of Tagge. Ulric Tagge was present for the Omega Frost trap his brothers Orman and Silas formulated in the asteroid corridor of the Junction system. After Orman's apparent death, Ulric became the family's new Baron. He convinced his sister, Domina, to aid

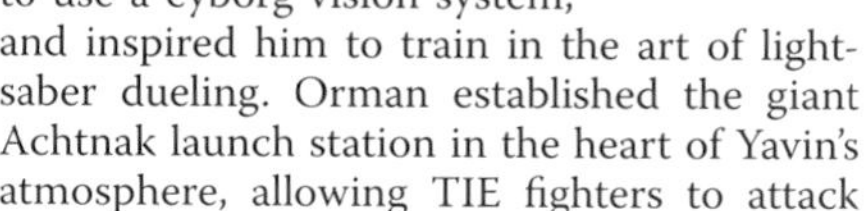

Silas Tagge

Darth Vader in a plot to trap Luke Skywalker on Monastery.

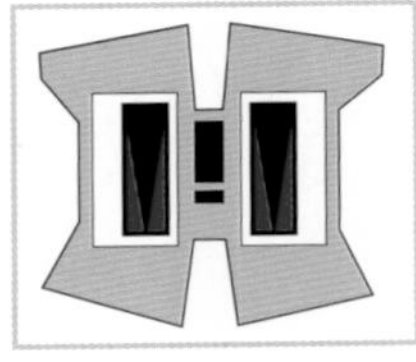

**TaggeCo** One of the most powerful and diverse corporations in the galaxy, owned by the influential House of Tagge. TaggeCo had subsidiaries in virtually every segment of the galactic economy and enjoyed close ties to the Imperial military through the late General Cassio Tagge. The firm owned Mobquet Speeders and Swoops, Trast Heavy Transports, Bonadan Industries, GalResource Industries, Gowix Computers, and the Tagge Restaurant Association (including Biscuit Baron). Shortly before the Battle of Naboo, TaggeCo formed a partnership with the Trade Federation, whose executive board included several House of Tagge loyalists. However, the board was rocked by betrayal when Neimoidians assassinated many of its members in order to take complete control of the Trade Federation. While the House of Tagge did not suffer any losses during this coup, the political family realized that it could never trust the Trade Federation again and severed all ties. The House of Tagge remained largely neutral throughout the Clone Wars, but readily allied with the Emperor after his rise to power.

**Tagta the Hutt** Jiliac the Hutt's highest-ranking representative on the planet Nar Hekka during the early years of the New Order; the two Hutts were members of the same clan. It was Tagta who recommended Jiliac hire Han Solo as a pilot, shortly after the young man was discharged from the Imperial Navy.

**Tahl, Master** A Jedi Master from planet Noori, and a close friend of Qui-Gon Jinn's in the years prior to the Battle of Naboo. Tahl had been brought to the Jedi Temple on Coruscant when she was six years old. She was known among the Jedi for her diplomatic skills and her patience with others. Tahl was wounded and captured by the Melida when she was dispatched to Melida/Daan to help negotiate a peace treaty. Qui-Gon and his Padawan, Obi-Wan Kenobi, rescued her, but Tahl lost her sight as a result of her injuries. She found she could still "see" with help from the Force and her 2JTJ personal navigation droid (TooJay). After a mission to Centax 2, Tahl took Bant Eerin as her Padawan. A later mission to New Apsolon forced her to confront the love that had grown between her and Qui-Gon. Pursued and captured by forces loyal to Security Controller Balog, Tahl survived interrogation long enough for Qui-Gon to rescue her. Tahl died knowing that Qui-Gon loved her with all his heart.

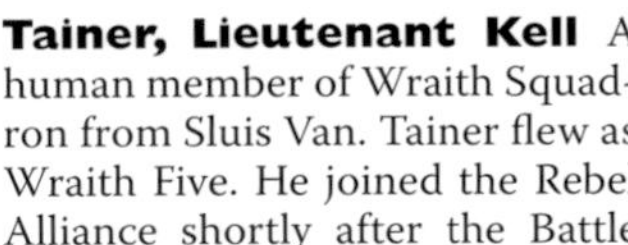

*Tai*

**Tahlboor** The homeworld of the Troobs and Hobors, who constantly battled each other until the Tion Hegemony tried to mediate the dispute. The two species later decided to negotiate a peace on their own.

*Bufon Taire*

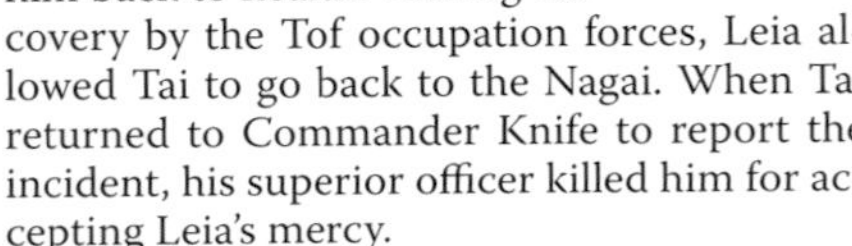

**Tai** The wing leader of the Nagai forces at the Trenwyth system following the Battle of Endor. He was the only Nagai survivor of a battle between the Nagai and the Tofs. Tai also had painful memories of torture at the hands of the Tofs. Princess Leia Organa and her Zeltron escorts found Tai and nursed him back to health. Fearing discovery by the Tof occupation forces, Leia allowed Tai to go back to the Nagai. When Tai returned to Commander Knife to report the incident, his superior officer killed him for accepting Leia's mercy.

**Tai, Durga Besadii** *See* Durga the Hutt.

**Taieb** A Mos Espa craftsman who constructed Anakin Skywalker's Podracing helmet. Taieb gave the helmet to Anakin as a gift.

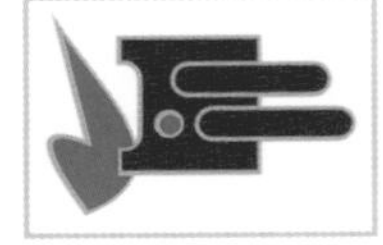

**Taim & Bak** A laser cannon and turbolaser manufacturer formed at the onset of the Galactic Civil War. X-wing fighters had Taim & Bak KX9 laser cannons, while the company also made the HVs-2 Hypervelocity Gun.

**Tainer, Doran** Born to Kell Tainer and Tyria Sarkin several years after the defeat of Warlord Zsinj, Doran studied at Luke Skywalker's Jedi praxeum after the Yuuzhan Vong War and trained to become a Jedi. He achieved the rank of Jedi Knight just before the Corellian system threatened to secede from the Galactic Alliance. Distinguished by his rugged good looks, Doran served on Team Tauntaun, part of the GA's attempt to prevent the secession. The team's assignment was leaked, a trap was set, and members just barely escaped with their lives.

**Tainer, Lieutenant Kell** A human member of Wraith Squadron from Sluis Van. Tainer flew as Wraith Five. He joined the Rebel Alliance shortly after the Battle of Yavin, eventually becoming a demolitions expert with Page's Commandos. When he crashed a Z-95 Headhunter and an X-wing during flight training, he was demoted from pilot ranks. Wedge Antilles offered him a spot with the Wraiths. Tainer soon realized that Wes Janson—the man who had shot down his father, Kissek Doran—was also part of the Wraiths, but in time he moved past his animosity. Tainer also fell in love with teammate Tyria Sarkin. His skills earned him a promotion to lieutenant and the prestigious Kalidor Crescent. After the defeat of Warlord Zsinj, Tainer and Tyria were married, and their son Doran was born shortly after. During the Yuuzhan Vong War, Tainer worked as a Wraith intelligence officer and was part of Luke Skywalker's team during the infiltration of enemy-held Coruscant.

**Tainer, Tyria** *See* Sarkin, Tyria.

**Taire, Bufon** A scarred male humanoid who worked as the bartender of the Outlander Club on Coruscant.

**Taisden** A New Republic Intelligence officer, he accompanied Colonel Pakkpekatt on the private mission aboard Lando Calrissian's *Lady Luck* to rescue Calrissian, his aide Lobot, and the droids C-3PO and R2-D2, who had been trapped aboard the mysterious ghost ship known as the Teljkon vagabond.

***Takara*** This starship was used by the Jedi to transport Master T'dai and a group of Jedi Knights to the Bpfassh system, some 700 years before the Battle of Yavin, to hunt down a Bpfasshi Dark Jedi who was terrorizing the populace.

**Tak Base** A secret Rebel base in the city of Talay. After the Battle of Yavin, Tak Base was wiped out as a test of the effectiveness of the Empire's new dark trooper. Kyle Katarn was sent to the ruins of Tak Base to discover clues concerning the new project.

**Takeel** A spice-addicted, burned-out Snivvian mercenary, he was known as a double-crosser. Takeel frequented the Mos Eisley cantina on Tatooine. He was always looking

*Takeel*

for work to earn some credits and had been known to turn lawbreakers over to the Empire when really hard up. He was the brother of Zutton, sometimes known as Snaggletooth.

**Takel, Grand Admiral Miltin** One of the Empire's 12 Grand Admirals. Miltin Takel was a brilliant strategist who proved himself in the Siege of Trasemene. He was also a hedonist with an addiction to glitterstim. Although aboard the second Death Star during the Battle of Endor, he fled the battle station before its destruction. During a regrouping of Imperial power players at Kessel, Takel lost his life when he questioned the slave lord Trioculus.

***Take That!*** This modified YT-1210 freighter was owned and operated by Falan Iniro. It saw duty as a warship during the Battle of Nar Shaddaa, but was destroyed when Iniro jumped the gun on the smugglers' counterattack. He found himself alone against one of Admiral Greelanx's *Carrack*-class cruisers, which ripped apart the *Take That!* in a volley of turbolaser fire.

**takital** The name for a ritualistic fight among the Amanin species. Takitals resolved disputes over land. Although Amanin usually held takitals among themselves, they also engaged in one against Imperial forces on Maridun after General Ziering led a column of Imperials into Amanin sacred land. In the aftermath of the conflict, the Amanin chief made an offer of peace to Captain Gage.

**Takkar, Derran** Along with his wife, Analys, Derran Takkar was a member of the conspiracy to disrupt the wedding of Luke Skywalker and Mara Jade. He was able to spoil the ceremony, but Luke Skywalker convinced him to embrace the union and absolved him of his crime.

**Tak-Tak** A young Whiphid, he was one of a handful of Jedi Padawans who were captured and held prisoner by General Grievous two years after the Battle of Geonosis. Grievous was able to convince Count Dooku that the Padawans should be used as part of an experiment that would marry the ability to tap into the dark side of the Force with Geonosian technologies. The intervention of a group of Jedi allowed the Padawans to escape.

**Tala, Feeana** This female Mawan was one of the more powerful crime lords on the planet of the same name during the years leading up to the Clone Wars. She was not as powerful as her rivals, Striker and Decca the Hutt, but she gained control of the supplies in the city of Naatan in the wake of the civil war. Her rivals paid her little notice, but it was Feeana who supplied the tunnel workers with food. This earned her a great deal of respect from the underground dwellers, who were part of the largest faction of free Mawans onworld. When she was approached by Obi-Wan Kenobi and Yaddle, Feeana agreed to help the Jedi establish a peaceful government in return for amnesty and the right to remain on Mawan as a native. She supplied soldiers to help secure Naatan after the Jedi wrested control of the city's power grids from Striker, but found herself helpless to protect her people against Striker's actions under his true identity, Granta Omega. Yaddle's sacrifice in absorbing a dihexalon bomb persuaded her to remain, but only to double-cross the Jedi. She formed an alliance with Omega and delivered the Jedi into his hands. Only the intervention of Anakin Skywalker saved her life after Omega threw her from his transport as a distraction.

Takital

**Tala 9** The location of a droid-run factory that used only droid languages for its landing codes. The practice was stopped when two ships crashed in orbit because their onboard computers couldn't handle the languages.

**Talasea** The fourth planet in the Morobe system, this cool, moist, fog-shrouded world orbited the yellow primary star in a red-and-yellow binary group. Talasea was lashed by severe thunderstorms during the rainy season. Island continents made up its landmasses. Colonized long ago, the world was eventually abandoned by the settlers' descendants; the last group was wiped out by Darth Vader after the Clone Wars for harboring a fugitive Jedi.

Talasea

Three years after the Battle of Endor, Rogue Squadron was moved from Folor to Talasea, closer to the Galactic Core, as a staging area for its eventual move on Coruscant. The squadron made its base on the largest of the island continents, inhabiting the ruins of Talasea's Planetary Governor's Palace and the surrounding ivy-covered cottages. After Imperial Intelligence agent Kirtan Loor deduced the location, Admiral Devlia ordered a platoon of stormtroopers to infiltrate the base and plant explosives. The squadron lost six sentries and pilot Lujayne Forge, but all of the Imperial commandos were captured or killed. The Alliance immediately evacuated the base, leaving behind several booby traps.

**Tal'cara** The main city of Kothlis, located on the eastern edge of the Ragnook Mountains just before the Arblis Forest took over the land. It was heavily industrialized, originally having been established by Raynor Mining Enterprises as a huge platform from which mining operations could be launched.

Grand Admiral Miltin Takel

**Tal'dira** First among Twi'lek warriors, this muscular giant challenged Wedge Antilles to a vibroblade duel during Rogue Squadron's visit to Ryloth but fortunately dropped the threat. When Tal'dira learned of Rogue Squadron's Bacta War with Ysanne Isard, he and his squadron of Chir'daki fighters offered their services both for glory and for the greater good of the galaxy. It was a decision not made lightly, for many of his warriors were killed in battle. Without their assistance, the Bacta War might very well have been lost. Tal'dira then accepted an offer to join Rogue Squadron and flew as Rogue Five. Later, he was brainwashed by Warlord Zsinj and attempted to kill Antilles, but in a last moment of clear thinking he let himself be shot down by Corran Horn.

**Taler** The nickname of one of four clone troopers in Theta Squad, which participated in the Battle of Geonosis. Taler, whose official designation was RC-1133, was among the three members of the squad to be killed in the fighting.

**Talesia** A planet known for its manufacture of some of the deadliest thermal detonators.

**Talfaglio system** A system in the hinterlands of the Corellian sector. Two years into the Yuuzhan Vong War, several Yuuzhan Vong fleets blockaded Talfaglio. Tsavong Lah intended to use the Talfaglio refugees to blackmail Leia Organa Solo into revealing the location of the secret Jedi base. The Jedi were galvanized by the threat and, together with elements of the New Republic, dealt the Yuuzhan Vong a total defeat.

**Talgal, Isko** A Mandalorian soldier who agreed to meet with Boba Fett and Goran

Beviin on Drall to discuss Thrackan Sal-Solo's offer of employment. Sal-Solo wanted the Mandalorians to fight on the side of Corellia if he was forced to go to war against the Galactic Alliance. Despite the fact that Mandalorian culture made few distinctions between the sexes, Talgal was the only woman in the group that traveled to Drall. She later returned to Mandalore to help Boba Fett rebuild the planet, and was one of the Mandalorians who agreed to take on Fett's mission to support Admiral Daala during the Galactic Alliance's attempt to capture Fondor.

Talia

**Talia** The hereditary queen of Onderon who ruled the planet and the moon of Dxun during the years following the Mandalorian Wars. Many citizens felt that Queen Talia and the members of her Royalist supporters were too disconnected from the population, and that she lacked proper concern for her people. Some, like General Vaklu, took matters into their own hands and tried to unseat the queen in a bloody coup. Queen Talia enlisted the aid of the Jedi Exile and her companions, who exposed the plot.

**Taliff** The Imperial Governor of Dentaal during the early stages of the Galactic Civil War, he disbanded the Dentaalian House and assumed control of the planet's army and navy. Taliff was overthrown by the members of the Dentaal Independence Party and sent back to Coruscant in shame. The Empire responded by sending in Crix Madine's team to unleash the Candorian plague.

***Talisman*** This 7-meter-long starship was Teroenza's personal yacht while he controlled the Ylesian colony. Han Solo stole it when he escaped from Ylesia with Bria Tharen, Mrrov, and Muuurgh. Han and Bria used the ship to return the two Togorians to their homeworld before returning to Corellia.

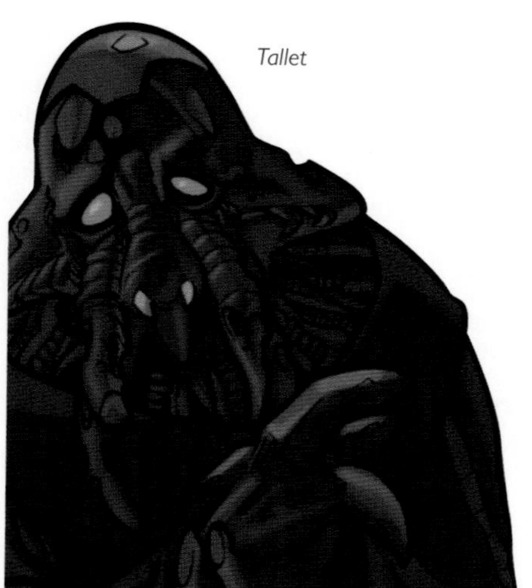

Tallet

**Talita** This frozen ball of rock was the 12th planet in the Kamino system. It was orbited by six moons.

**talkdroid** Another name for a protocol droid, the nickname was used mainly by those from less developed worlds.

**talking bomb** Makeshift bombs constructed by Cloud City's Ugnaughts when they launched their rebellion against Imperial Captain Treece. Each of the 12 bombs was equipped with a droid brain that powered up whenever a living being tried to approach. The brain was attached to a vocoder; a voice would start offering apparently sincere information on how to disarm it. As the Imperials discovered, however, this information actually armed the bomb and set it to explode.

**Talking Bone** A tyrossum bone used by the Rock Council on Kashyyyk to signify which individual Wookiee had the right to speak at a council meeting. Whoever held the jawbone could speak, and any other individual had to either be granted permission to speak or earn it by fighting for possession. The use of claws, teeth, weapons, or the Force was strictly prohibited.

**Tallaan** A planet in the Core Worlds near the Colonies region, it was the site of the Tallaan Imperial Shipyards. When Grand Moff Tarkin was killed aboard the first Death Star, the Empire released an official statement claiming that Tarkin had actually died in a shuttle crash at the Tallaan shipyards.

**Tallet** A male Quarren and the egg-mate of Lekket in the later years of the Old Republic. Tallet and Lekket were once wealthy citizens of Heurkea on Mon Calamari until they were betrayed by their business partner, Senator Tikkes. Pursued by the Republic Guard and the Jedi known as the Dark Woman, Tallet was seriously injured in a toxic chemical spill. Years later, Tallet and Lekket hired Aurra Sing to hunt down both Tikkes and the Dark Woman.

**Tallo** This young man, his father Bordon, and his younger brother Wend were the only members of their family to survive the Battle of Ruusan some 1,000 years before the Battle of Yavin. Tallo, Wend, and Bordon were rescued by the surviving members of the Army of Light, and were taken aboard the warship *Fairwind* to protect them from the effects of the thought bomb that was detonated by the Sith. When Bordon volunteered to work on a recovery team with Irtanna, Tallo and Wend went with him, hoping to find survivors on the blasted landscape of their homeworld. There they discovered the young girl named Rain. Tallo scoffed at her desire to travel to Onderon, even though he had never been to the planet himself. They managed to get Rain aboard the shuttle *Star-Wave,* and laid in a course to return to the rest of the Jedi fleet. Tallo went to see how Rain was handling spaceflight, and discovered her rummaging around in the shuttle's cargo holds. When he demanded to know what was going on, Rain shot him dead. She then turned on the rest of the passengers, killing them all in turn.

Adar Tallon

**Tallon, Adar** A brilliant naval commander and military strategist serving the Galactic Republic, he developed many tactics that were later used by both the Empire and the New Republic. When the Republic fell, Adar Tallon faked his own death and settled on Tatooine. A group of Rebel agents found him and convinced him to join the Rebel Alliance. He eventually became an admiral.

**Tallon roll** A flight maneuver pioneered by and named for Republic military strategist Adar Tallon.

**Talmont, Prefect Eugene** An Imperial official, he was in charge of a small contingent of stormtroopers based in Mos Eisley on the planet Tatooine. Prefect Eugene Talmont was dissatisfied with his assignment and worked constantly to destroy the operations of crime lord Jabba the Hutt, hoping to earn a promotion and transfer off the arid planet. Many residents found that the prefect could easily be bribed to avoid being harassed about permits or code compliance.

***Talon* (1)** An Imperial *Strike*-class cruiser that was destroyed by the Rebel Alliance during the Galactic Civil War.

***Talon* (2)** An Imperial corvette transporting important documents near Turkana, it was intercepted by Keyan Farlander.

***Talon* (3)** An Imperial *Interdictor*-class starship patrolling the Demophon system during the Galactic Civil War.

**Talon (4)** This group of ATR-6 *Gamma*-class transports was part of the Imperial fleet that tried to stop the Rebel Alliance from evacuating its base on Kothlis just before the Battle of Endor. Much of the group was destroyed in the battle, and the Alliance safely abandoned the base.

Darth Talon

**Talon, Darth** A female Twi'lek distinguished by her full-body tattoos, she lived more than 130 years after the Battle of Yavin. A third-generation practitioner of the Sith arts, Darth Talon was trained by another Twi'lek, Darth Ruyn. When Ruyn presented her to Darth Krayt, the Sith Lord demanded that Talon strike down her own Master. Darth Krayt chose her to hunt down Marasiah Fel, the daughter of the renegade Emperor Roan Fel. On Vendaxa, Cade Skywalker used his powers to drop a huge section of a ruined starship on Talon, who called for backup in the form of Darth Nihl. But Skywalker and his crew fled into hyperspace with the princess. Darth Krayt then ordered Talon to locate Skywalker and bring him to Coruscant. She dueled Cade again in Coruscant's Sith Temple, and would have fallen to his lightsaber if Darth Nihl hadn't intervened.

When Cade Skywalker was captured by the Sith, Darth Krayt began to turn him to the dark side. Skywalker initially resisted, but Talon tried to force him into submission. Cade telekinetically smashed her body against a wall with the Force, but then used his powers to heal her. Under Krayt's orders, Talon began to develop a relationship with Cade, seeking to use her femininity to break down his defenses. That ultimately failed, and when Cade confronted Krayt, Talon intervened. Cade ran her through with his lightsaber, killing her almost instantly.

**Taloon, Rhya** This woman served as the Senator from Agridorn during the early years of the Empire. Because of her support for the ideals of the Republic, Senator Taloon found herself targeted by the Enemy Eradication Order of Coruscant. When Agridorn's government agreed to fully support the Empire, a death mark was issued against Senator Taloon, completely cutting her off from her roots. Rather than submitting to Imperial domination, Senator Taloon eliminated all records of her existence and joined the Erased. She adopted the image of a gunslinger in order to hide her true identity, forming her silvery hair into horns that crowned her head and strapping a pair of gun belts across her chest. Like many of her fellow Erased, Taloon wanted to locate Solace and find peace, so she accompanied Ferus Olin and Trever Flume on their search. After locating Solace and identifying her as the former Jedi Fy-Tor-Ana, Olin and Flume set out to return to the surface to prevent Inquisitor Malorum from locating them. Taloon and the other members of the Erased remained behind in the underground settlement, but found themselves under assault by Malorum's agents. Taloon perished in the attack.

**Taloraan** The largest planet in the isolated Kelavine system of the Expansion Region, it was an unexplored gas giant nearly 100,000 kilometers in diameter. The planet had a strong magnetic field and was orbited by seven uninhabitable moons and a spectacular ring system. Taloraan's hot atmosphere, rich in Tibanna gas, was breathable at high altitudes, and several forms of life evolved among its clouds. They included sleft-chuffni, huge, 200-meter-long gas bags that gathered drifting algae with their hanging tentacles, and carnivorous flying rays called fleft-wauf that hunted the sleft-chuffni and attacked them with their barbed tails.

**Talos Spaceport** A spaceport on the planet Atzerri.

**Talpron** A captain in the Corellian Defense Forces' Space Defense Service, Talpron was the leader of Squadron Two, which "rescued" Han Solo and the *Millennium Falcon* when they arrived at Corellia for a trade summit.

**Talsava** The real mother of Akanah Norand Pell, she abandoned her 15-year-old child on Carratos. Akanah bitterly referred to her as a guardian or custodian, not a mother.

**Talshib, Captain** The core name used by the Chiss male known as Brast'alshi'barku. When Aristocra Formbi led the mission to locate the Outbound Flight Project in the Redoubt, Captain Talshib was deck officer aboard the *Chaf Envoy*. He witnessed the landing of the Vagaari forces, but he and his troops remained hidden until the Vagaari left the area, then entered the Outbound Flight to rescue Formbi and the others. Talshib's troops were able to seal off the pylons between Dreadnaughts, saving the lives of those beings still on Outbound Flight by sealing in their limited air supply.

**Talu** This planet was one of many controlled by Imperial Warlord Zsinj during the early years of the New Republic. It eventually was retaken by Han Solo and his task force.

**Talus** One of the five habitable planets in the Corellian system, it was a blue, white, and green world the same size as its sister planet, Tralus. Both orbited a common center of gravity where Centerpoint Station was located. Together they were referred to as the Double Worlds, and both were ruled by the elected Federation of the Double Worlds, or Fed-Dub. Beneath the surface of Talus was a planetary repulsor, which had been used in ancient times to move the planet into its orbit from an unknown location. When a flare-up in Centerpoint Station some 14 years after the Battle of Endor caused many deaths, survivors were relocated to Talus and Tralus. As word spread of the incident, a rebellion against Fed-Dub occurred on Talus. A group of starfighters, possibly representing the Talus rebellion, subsequently flew to Centerpoint and claimed the station for themselves, until chased off by a Bakuran task force.

**Tal'yo, Nescan** A wolf-like alien, he was a thief during the New Order. Protected by his android bodyguard, Hermos, Tal'yo stole a holocube containing the location of several Rebel Alliance bases. He planned to sell the data to the Empire, but Leia Organa tracked him to Elerion and put an end to his plans.

**Talz** Large and strong, these white-furred beings were from the planets Alzoc III and Orto Plutonia. They were about 2 meters tall and had four eyes—two large and two smaller ones. They appeared fierce but had gentle personalities. Their planets were technologically backward, and it was easy for the Empire to conquer them and use many Talz as slave laborers.

**Tamban** A world that once was home to the Emperor Preedu III. Millennia before the Galactic Civil War, the First Observer of Preedu III's Court discovered a distant star cluster

Talz

in Tamban's night sky. Remembering a recent favor done for him by Aitro Koornacht, night commander of the palace guard, the astronomer named his discovery the Koornacht Cluster.

Wat Tambor

**Tambor, Wat** A Skakoan from the Crimlin clan, he rose to become foreman of the Techno Union. Wat Tambor spent only a few years on his homeworld of Skako before traveling to Metalorn to pursue an interest in technology and industrialization. This travel required him to develop a full-body environment suit in order to maintain an atmosphere similar to that of Skako. He was an excellent combat engineer, and later served as a chief executive of the Baktoid Armor Workshop before becoming one of the leaders of the Techno Union. In the wake of the Battle of Naboo, Wat Tambor was promoted to Techno Union foreman, overseeing the operations of such noted manufacturers as Baktoid Armor Workshop and Haor Chall Engineering, and managing development labs for Republic Sienar Systems and Kuat Systems Engineering. Wat Tambor was part of the delegation that traveled to Geonosis to join Count Dooku and the Separatists shortly before the onset of the Clone Wars. As the war ground on, Wat Tambor became increasingly reclusive, and holed up in the Mazariyan fortress on Xagobah to avoid much of the war. He used his own expertise, along with that of other Separatists, to genetically alter several of Xagobah's plants and fungi, twisting them to become killing things to protect the fortress. It was here, as the Clone Wars came to an end, that young Boba Fett found Tambor. Tambor was being protected by General Grievous, who fled the fortress with the Skakoan. On Mustafar, Anakin Skywalker killed the members of the Separatist Council, including Wat Tambor.

**Tammar** This planet had an unusually thin atmosphere, which caused native Tammarians to evolve a chemical pouch called a chaghizs torm to store oxygen while at rest. This also allowed them to survive in the vacuum of space for short periods. Tammar had no standing water, and the greatest fear of a typical Tammarian was to be immersed in liquid. Ayddar Nylykerka, chief researcher in the New Republic's Asset Tracking office, was a native of Tammar.

Terr Taneel

**Tammi** A curious youngster who grew up on the planet Metalorn during the New Order, she constantly tried to get seeds from her breakfast fruits to grow in Metalorn's poor soil. She was one of several natives who helped Leia Organa escape from Imperial stormtroopers stationed on the planet sometime after the Battle of Yavin. Leia's courage and determination gave Tammi new strength, and she kept up her attempts to grow the fruit seeds.

**Tammuz-an** A planet surrounded by double rings, it was inhabited by tall purple- or blue-skinned humanoids who were led by a monarchy. For many generations, the two Tammuz-an races fought one another in civil wars, until Princess Gerin was captured by Gir Kybo Ren-Cha and taken to Bogden. Lord Toda agreed to join forces with Mon Julpa, and the rescue effort served to reunite the Tammuz-an people.

**tampasi** The dense, living forest that covered the planet Zonama Sekot. The word *tampasi* was Ferroan for "forest." Later research indicated that the tampasi was not just a collection of plants but a single, living entity.

***Tampion*** A shuttle in the New Republic fleet, it was carrying Han Solo to his new command of the Fifth Fleet aboard the *Intrepid* when it and Solo were captured by the forces of Nil Spaar during the Yevethan crisis.

**Tan (V-Tan)** An old Keganite, he ruled the planet O-Vieve 13 years before the Battle of Naboo. The population believed ancient prophecies that a visitation by Jedi Knights would destroy Kegan society, so their belief in what they called the General Good kept the planet isolated. Historians later determined that the Benevolent Guides who ruled the society foresaw the coming of Emperor Palpatine and the New Order. As Jedi revealed more about the greater galaxy, the Keganites voted to overthrow the Benevolent Guides and join the Old Republic.

**Tanaal, Berec** A skilled tracker and bounty hunter who joined the Rebel Alliance just before the Battle of Hoth, he was evacuated from Echo Base on the *Bright Hope,* and was chosen by Toryn Farr to lead one of the groups that escaped in life pods.

**Tana Ire** A company known for its manufacture of the bubble sight—a type of optical transducer—and other sensor components.

**Tanallay Surge complex** A multileveled structure on Tynna with surrounding pools, fountains, and chutes. During the Yuuzhan Vong invasion of the planet, the complex fell to the enemy.

**Tanbris, Lieutenant** A male Imperial lieutenant, this former fighter pilot was grounded after injuries. He then became a tactical officer aboard the first Death Star, specializing in directing Imperial starfighters. Tanbris died when the battle station was destroyed during the Battle of Yavin.

**Tandankin** A planet taken over by Imperial forces under the command of Grand Moff Nivers following the Battle of Endor. When Rogue Squadron arrived, Wedge Antilles was forced to topple an enormous tower—the planet's greatest monument—in order to destroy a landing strip filled with Imperial TIE fighters.

**T'andar, T'achak** A hyperactive Chadra-Fan, this scout and explorer worked as part of the crew of the *FarStar* during the New Republic's hunt for Moff Sarne.

Lieutenant Tanbris

**Tandeer** An alias given to Leia Organa by the Singing Mountain Clan of the Witches of Dathomir.

**Tandell system** A system where Tiree, a Rebel Alliance agent, killed Imperial Governor Lord Cuvir while he was visiting the planet Wor Tandell. Cuvir had discovered Tiree encoding a report on Imperial fleet movements in the Tandell system.

**Tandis Four** During the Clone Wars, this planet was the site of a Separatist attack that led to the destruction of the Museum of Light.

**Tane, Ratri** A researcher from Coruscant working for the Techno Union prior to the outbreak of the Clone Wars. He stole files related to a working prototype of a Techno Union droid that would have dramatically increased combat effectiveness. Aayla Secura and Ylenic It'kla went to Corellia to rescue him from the various underworld factions trying to capture him for the substantial rewards being offered. To ensure his safety, Nejaa Halcyon placed Ratri Tane in hiding and assumed his identity.

**Taneel, Terr** This red-haired woman was a Republic Senator at the height of the Clone Wars, representing her homeworld of Neelanon and the Senex sector. She often wore flowing gowns and a pair of fashionable

translation devices on her ears. Senator Taneel was part of a small group that supported Bail Organa's petition to ensure that Chancellor Palpatine relinquished the unprecedented control he had been given during the Clone Wars. She was also good friends with Senator Chi Eekway, but feared that her friend was too naïve to join the Delegation of the Two Thousand.

**Tangle Gun 7** A form of anti-riot weapon produced by Merr-Sonn during the early years of the New Order. The weapon was considered more humane than a blaster, although it often proved just as deadly. The tangle gun fired a large, semi-flexible webbing created from naorstrachem mixed with a shrinking agent. The web began to contract as soon as it came into contact with a warm surface, such as a living body. The webbing then wrapped around the target and tightened, trapping the target almost instantly. The problem was that the webbing often contracted too much, suffocating its prey.

**Tanglewoods, the** This densely forested area of the planet Bellassa was located just south of the capital city of Ussa. The trees of the Tanglewoods grew from a massive system of intertwined roots. They grew so close together that very little light reached the forest floor, and the branches twisted around one another to create strange and fantastic shapes. In the wake of the Clone Wars, the Bellassan Rebels who opposed the Imperial occupation of their planet created a number of holographic replacements for certain trees. The real trees were then cut down, with the holographic duplicates serving to hide the extraction. This path through the forest allowed the Rebels to fly into and out of Ussa without being noticed by Imperial sensors.

***Tango*** This Rebel Alliance assault transport was assigned to the Mon Calamari cruiser *Liberty* shortly before the Battle of Endor. It was used in several missions to liberate slaves from Imperial facilities.

**Tangrene** The site of a major Imperial Ubiqtorate base that was attacked and destroyed by the private army of General Garm Bel Iblis. Later, while the base was being rebuilt, the New Republic gave the impression that it intended to attack Tangrene to throw the enemy off its true target, Bilbringi.

**Tank** *See* Sunber, Lieutenant Janek "Tank."

*Ahsoka Tano*

*Arakyd tank droid*

**tank beast** A huge Yuuzhan Vong creature that trundled on curving knotted legs with splayed claws. Its body had vast horn plates and a head that swung slowly from side to side. Its massive jaws dripped flame; it could spew a mouthful of concentrated acid. A tank beast was brought in to attack Ganner Rhysode when he defended the Well of the World Brain on Coruscant.

**tank droid, Arakyd** Originally designed to deal with widespread civil unrest on Imperial worlds, the Arakyd XR-85 tank droid was a fully automated combat machine driven by a droid brain. The vehicle, at about 32 meters long and more than 30 meters tall, was double the size of an Imperial AT-AT walker. The tank droid moved on tracks at a top speed of 70 kilometers an hour and could travel in water up to 15 meters deep. The XR-85 was nearly unstoppable, making it particularly useful in urban assault operations. Its main weapon was a front-firing heavy particle cannon with an effective range of 5 kilometers. A pair of front-firing turbolasers, four twin heavy repeating blasters, and a rear-mounted anti-personnel cannon rounded out its weapons array.

The tank droid brain was one of the few droids with sophisticated intuition programming. The XR-85 played a major role in the Imperial invasion to reclaim Imperial City from the New Republic six years after the Battle of Endor. Although combat performance consistently showed that there was no substitute for an organic pilot, tank droids were far better at combat than earlier generations of the machines.

**Tann, General Sev'Rance** This female Chiss was born on the planet Csilla, and was one of the few members of her species to exhibit a sensitivity to the Force. Although she was a skilled tactician, many attributed her remarkable abilities on the battlefield to her Force connection. She was known for her demanding attitude and almost casual brutality. Prior to the Clone Wars, she and her lover Vandalor were brought to Republic space by Darth Sidious, and Tann was trained by Count Dooku. She became a general in command of the Separatist military, participating in the Battle of Geonosis and defeating the Republic on Sarapin with her experimental Decimator tanks. On Krant, Republic General Echuu Shen-Jon captured Tann and killed her in revenge for the death of his Padawan, Stam Reath.

**Tannath** An aged sister of the Singing Mountain Clan on Dathomir, Tannath served as the Clan Protector under Augwynne. This position made her the second most powerful woman in the clan.

**Tannis** A member of the BloodScar pirates during the New Order, he was part of a small group of pirates who discovered that Mara Jade had infilrated one of their transports shortly after the Battle of Yavin. In the brief firefight that followed, Jade killed Captain Shakko and several other BloodScars before wounding Tannis and taking control of the ship. Tannis revealed that the pirates had been planning to ambush *Happer's Way* and steal its cargo of AT-STs, and that the entire operation had been planned by Caaldra and an unnamed patron.

Tannis agreed to help Jade infiltrate the BloodScar base on Gepparin. She and agents Brock and Gilling posed as shipjackers who were planning to join the BloodScars. After introducing them to the commodore, Caaldra revealed that Jade and her men were Imperials. Tannis tried to argue for keeping them alive, since they were valuable sources of information. The commodore refused, threatening to have Tannis killed, too. Jade recovered her lightsaber, and the prisoners fled. But in the escape Tannis was badly burned in a trap and died. As he had requested, Jade set his body adrift in space.

**Tano, Ahsoka** Anakin Skywalker's Padawan during the Clone Wars. Discovered by Master Plo Koon, Ahsoka was a Togruta raised in the Jedi Temple from infancy. At 14 years of age, she was assigned to Skywalker by Master Yoda to teach Skywalker a greater sense of responsibility. A devoted student of Jedi ways, Ahsoka was a talented swordswoman, a budding tactician, and a critical thinker. In personal matters, she remained ubiquitously positive, full of wit and disarming innocence even when faced with seemingly insurmountable odds. She often expressed her exuberance by creating humorous names, such as "cruiser-crusher" for an enemy starship or "laser-beak" for an enemy vulture droid. Despite her inexperience, Ahsoka rarely hesitated to share her opinions, which were always insightful but occasionally mistimed. Though her relationship with Anakin got off to a rocky start, "Skyguy" and his Padawan "Snips" quickly formed a strong bond grounded in mutual respect and heartfelt concern.

**Tanogo** A veteran of more than 20 years of military service, this Bith was a skilled sensor operator in the years following the Swarm War. He served aboard the *Rover* when Ben Skywalker was dispatched to investigate the bombing of the Villa Solis estate on Terephon during an assassination attempt on the life of the Hapan Queen Mother, Tenel Ka. At Terephon, the crew recovered Jaina Solo and Zekk, who had been on the planet doing their own investigation when the Ducha Galney ordered them killed. The *Rover* sped back to Hapes, only to find itself in the midst of a battle between the Hapan Royal Navy and the Heritage Fleet. The crew understood the necessity to warn the Queen Mother of her enemies, but realized that any transmission would be picked up by the Heritage Fleet, which would try to eliminate the source. Tanogo and Lieutenant Beta Ioli agreed to remain on the ship and transmit the message after ensuring that Ben and the rest of the crew evacuated. Although the message was successfully sent, the ships of the Heritage Fleet quickly identified the *Rover* as an enemy and opened fire. Tanogo and Ioli died in the resulting explosion.

**tanray lizard** An extremely fast and agile predatory lizard found on Mustafar. It had massive hind legs that facilitated leaping quickly over burning rocks.

**Tansa Reach** An area of rolling grasslands on the planet Tython.

***Tantive IV*** Princess Leia Organa's consular ship, this Corellian Engineering Corporation corvette was owned by the Royal House of Alderaan and used for Imperial Senate business, as well as covert Rebel Alliance activities. The ship had served the House of Alderaan for decades but was not afforded status as a royal vessel, allowing for the addition of weaponry and other defensive systems. During the Clone Wars, Bail Organa, Raymus Antilles, and Sheltay Retrac flew the *Tantive IV* to Metalorn to rescue Shaak Ti. After the massacre at the Jedi Temple, Bail left in the vessel to find Yoda and Obi-Wan Kenobi. They traveled to Polis Massa, where Padmé Amidala gave birth to twins. Bail Organa volunteered to care for baby Leia, who, after she grew up and became an Imperial Senator, used the *Tantive IV* to perform clandestine "mercy missions." The *Tantive IV* was captured in the Tatooine star system by Darth Vader's *Devastator* shortly after the Princess's ship had intercepted the technical plans for the original Death Star battle station. The ship's capture began the chain of events that led to the great Rebel Alliance victory at the Battle of Yavin. Darth Vader later had the ship destroyed.

Taozin

**Tantive V, Battle of** This battle in the Tantive system pitted the forces of the fledgling New Republic against Admiral Gaen Drommel and his small fleet of ships. The Republic destroyed two of Drommel's three Imperial Star Destroyers, and captured the third ship, the *Wolf's Claw.* Drommel's flagship, the *Guardian,* took heavy damage, but managed to flee the battle. Drommel was believed to have survived the battle.

Tantive IV

**Tantor, Brenn** A distinguished Imperial ground officer during the Galactic Civil War who later defected to the Rebel Alliance. Brenn and his brother Dellis Tantor were natives of Garos IV. When their homestead was destroyed in an explosion, the brothers were rescued by a stormtrooper squad. The Tantors joined the Imperial Academy, where Brenn focused his energies on combat training and Dellis specialized in the computer sciences, encryption, and communications. Both Brenn and Dellis petitioned for active stormtrooper duty, only to have their requests rejected due to their status as nonclones. Undaunted, they began shadowing Cattena Squadron, a stormtrooper unit stationed at the Imperial Academy between missions. The squadron's captain was impressed by the Tantors' resolve, and they were eventually invited to join Cattena Squadron as "honorary stormtroopers." During a mission to subdue a Rebel cell on Kalaan, Dellis was apparently shot and killed. Brenn was issued a field promotion to lieutenant for his skillful remobilization of his squadron, and was eventually promoted to general and served aboard the Star Destroyer *Inquisitor.* It was aboard the *Inquisitor,* three years after the Battle of Yavin, that Dellis appeared to explain to Brenn that the Empire had been behind their father's death. Brenn agreed to defect to the Alliance, and was reunited with Dellis during the Rebel Alliance's ground assault at the Battle of Endor.

**Tantt clan** Native to the planet Thracior, this clan was a bitter enemy of the Hnsi clan.

**taopari** Leopard-like predators on Noquivzor, their favorite prey was the tasty wildernerf.

**taozin** A huge, worm-like creature long believed to be extinct, and one of the few creatures that could not be perceived through the Force. Native to the jungle moon of Va'art near the Roche asteroid field, taozin were occasionally found on other worlds. The flesh and internal organs of a taozin allowed light to pass through. Only its large black eyes and the small, regular nodules on its chitinous outer shell reflected any light; recent meals could sometimes be seen slowly dissolving in its digestive tract. A taozin's translucency allowed it to remain inconspicuous in low-light conditions. Similarly, taozin could evade efforts to be detected using the Force. Their "invisibility" to the Force made taozin dangerous to Jedi, and the tiny crystalline structures on their flesh diffused light energy and made them immune to lightsabers. A taozin could spew a silky gray adhesive from glands located just inside its mouth. Darsha Assant and Lorn Pavan encountered a taozin beneath the surface of Coruscant that fed on the primitive Cthons living there. Pavan later used a skin nodule from the taozin to block Darth Maul's receptivity to the Force.

**Tapani sector** A sector located in the Colonies on the Shapani Bypass, an offshoot of the Rimma Trade Route. The Tapani sector capital was Procopia, though the world of Tallan was equally important since the main Imperial Regional Depot was located there. Fondor was also located in the Tapani sector. It was made up of two distinct areas: the Expanse, located in the heart of the sector; and the Freeworlds Region, situated along its border. In all, Tapani sector included 70 star systems, of which about 15 were heavily populated. The inhabited worlds were controlled by some 345 noble families, each of which was aligned with a major political House. About 5,500 years before the Galactic Civil War, Tapani sector merchants established the first leg of what became the Rimma Trade Route.

**Tapper, Quelev** Talon Karrde's former second in command, he accompanied Karrde to Varonat to see if the safari business was profitable. Karrde and he agreed to merge their operations and avoid the Imperials. On Varonat, however, they stumbled onto Gamgalon's Yagaran aleudrope business, and were cornered by Gamgalon's forces. Tapper tried to turn the tables, but he was too slow; he was killed in a firefight.

**taras-chi** An insect native to Kessel, it measured about 3 centimeters across and moved about on six legs; its body was protected by a hard shell. Taras-chi could be roasted and eaten, although they tasted awful and provided little nutrition. Kyp Duron adopted the insect's name to refer to an individual who participated in a group discussion, but proposed ideas or courses of action that were contrary to the mood of the group.

**Tarasin** A species of sentient, quilled reptiloids native to the planet Cularin. Believed to be descended from the same stock as the kilassin, the Tarasin evolved into social

Tarasin

groups and eventually gained sentience. These beings were incredibly attuned to the Force, and their society centered on a symbiotic relationship with their planet. Their religion was based on the worship of nature; any actions made against the natural order of the planet were punished. Because of their relationship with the planet, most Tarasin would travel off-world only briefly, and for short distances.

The skin of a Tarasin was unusual in that it could change its coloration in response to the individual's mood, and also as a form of communication. A more complex form of communication was achieved by simply changing the colors of the fingers on one hand, rather than openly expressing oneself by changing body color. Naturally, a Tarasin was the light green color of the horonna plant's leaves. White skin tone indicated joy, while black signified the end of a conversation. Orange skin tone, when similar to that of the gargrell flower, indicated that the Tarasin was angry or irritated, depending on the intensity of the coloration. When a Tarasin changed its skin color to purple—which didn't naturally exist in the ecosystem of Cularin—it indicated amusement. Yellow, like the vine of the arrgrar, indicated illness in an individual, while blue signified a level of respect or deference on the part of the speaker.

Among the distinguishing features of the Tarasin form were the kampo—the Tarasin name for their head-fan—and the sa'tosin, the quills that grew from the backs of their forearms. When logging corporations began to discover the exotic trees of Cularin, the Tarasin fought off several attempts to clear the forest.

**Tarc** An alias given to a young boy, Dab Hantaq, by Viqi Shesh during her escape from Coruscant in the face of a Yuuzhan Vong invasion. Senator Shesh had spent a fortune in cosmisurgeon and bacta tank fees to make the boy look like Anakin Solo, as part of her failed plan to kidnap Ben Skywalker. After the evacuation, Tarc followed Han and Leia Organa Solo to the base on Borleias, and eventually made friends with Tam Elgrin.

**Ta-Ree** A quasi-mystical energy field similar to the Force and most often sensed on the planet Kathol.

**Tarfang** A vindictive Ewok who served as Jae Juun's first mate aboard the *XR808g* and later the *DR919a* during the Swarm War. He opposed helping Han Solo locate the nests of the Killik Colony, and often swore a blue streak about it in Ewokese to vent his frustration. Despite his vehemence, Tarfang was extremely loyal to Jae Junn, and followed his every move with dedication. When they were forced to confront the Gorog nest ship near Tusken's Eye, Tarfang found himself the prisoner of Lomi Plo. Luke Skywalker delayed the mission to destroy the Gorog ship's hyperdrive long enough to grab the Ewok with the Force and draw Tarfang back to safety. During their escape, Tarfang was able to locate the lost lightsaber of Mara Jade Skywalker, and he used it to cut his way to freedom. In the aftermath of the blockade, Jae Juun and Tarfang found themselves approached by Admiral Nek Bwua'tu, who offered them positions as intelligence agents. By posing as Fefze, Tarfang and Jae Juun managed to alert Han and Leia Organa Solo to the fact that the Directors had ordered the Flakax to kill the Solos.

In the wake of the Swarm War, Jae Juun and Tarfang continued to serve as agents, and were among the many beings charged with keeping an eye on Han and Leia Solo during the Galactic Alliance's conflict with the Corellians. This led them to Kashyyyk, where the Solos hoped to convince the Wookiees to secede from the Alliance. The Rock Council accepted their presence, and even gave Tarfang the nickname of Little Killer for his ferocity. Tarfang tried to physically prevent the Solos from reaching the top of Council Rock, but was unable to. When the Wookiees agreed to let Leia Solo address the Rock Council, Tarfang demanded a chance to stop her by challenging Leia for possession of the Talking Bone. Their duel was cut short when Luke Skywalker arrived with word of the Jedi Order's defection from the Galactic Alliance.

**Tarfful** A mighty Wookiee warrior who helped the Republic defend his native world of Kashyyyk when the Separatists invaded. Tarfful served as the city leader of Kachirho for decades. During the Clone Wars, Trandoshan slavers took Tarfful prisoner, but a crack squad of Republic clone commandos secured his freedom as well as his respect and loyalty. When the fighting spread to Kashyyyk, Tarfful adopted the little-used mantle of war chief, shoring up defenses around the coastal city. When he sounded the alarm to protect Kachirho, many Wookiees from other cities trekked to the coast to help. Among them was Tarfful's old friend Chewbacca. Tarfful worked closely with Jedi Masters Luminara Unduli and Quinlan Vos to set up the initial defenses and allocate the Wookiee warriors at his disposal. While he did not serve as the battlefield general, he was nonetheless the direct liaison with General Yoda upon the venerated Jedi Master's arrival. Tarfful greatly respected Yoda, and considered him to be a member of his "honor family." It was Tarfful who was at Yoda's side on Coruscant as the Jedi Master organized his task force to Kashyyyk. When the clone troopers under Yoda's command betrayed him and turned on the Jedi, Tarfful and his friend Chewbacca assisted Yoda in his escape from the ambush, and led him to a secret escape pod.

*Tarfful*

**Targeter** *See* Celchu, Winter.

**targeting computer** A sophisticated device that acquired hostile targets for a starship's weapons system, it worked in conjunction with a ship's nav computer and sensor array. By calculating trajectories and attack and intercept courses, targeting computers helped pilots and gunners track and fire at fast-moving enemy ships.

**target remote** *See* remote; seeker.

**Targon, Elassar** This high-strung Devaronian male joined the New Republic's Wraith Squadron after the loss of Lara Notsil. A graduate of the Republic's Fleet Command Academy, he had a loose, joking manner that fit in well with the squadron. When his initial introduction failed to impress the Wraiths, he addressed them as "masters of the universe" and quickly earned their friendship, flying as Wraith Eleven. Years later, during the struggle against the Yuuzhan Vong, Elassar was one of the Wraiths chosen to accompany Luke Skywalker on a mission to infiltrate enemy-held Coruscant.

**Targonn** Home to a bird-like species, this planet endured the brutal tyranny of Dictator-Forever Craw. Ruling from his palace behind an impenetrable force field, Craw imposed a 99 percent tax rate on his subjects and forced their children to toil in factories from the age of six. Before their involvement in the Rebellion, R2-D2 and C-3PO were captured by Craw and taken to his palace. Craw planned to uncover the secret of the savorium herb, which turned people into happy slaves called smilers, and then rule over a contented but mindless populace. Meanwhile, several splinter groups dedicated to overthrowing Craw united under the leader Shay and infiltrated the palace through a force-field hole. Their attack was unsuccessful, but they managed to rescue the droids. A second attack, aided by the droids' Ithorian master, Zorneth, resulted in the defeat of Craw and his forces.

**Targrim, Big Jak** This four-armed, hulking alien was the pirate leader of the Riders of the Maelstrom. His genetic structure had been altered over time by the addition of gene material from various criminals and warlords to make him even more ruthless and evil.

**Tarhassan** A world that seceded from the Republic to join the Separatists during the Clone Wars.

**Taria, Sei** Finis Valorum's administrative aide during his tenure as Supreme Chancellor. Sei Taria assisted Valorum by researching and confirming procedural regulations during complex Senate gatherings. She also viewed Senator Palpatine as a mentor.

*Sei Taria*

**Taris** A city-planet in the Outer Rim once said to rival Coruscant itself. During the time of the Jedi Civil War nearly 4,000 years before the Battle of Yavin, Taris had fallen into ruin and disrepair. The rich and powerful segregated themselves in the Upper City, dwelling in the highest reaches of the towering skyscrapers that dominated the planet's landscape. Here the nobility surrounded themselves with the trappings of prosperity, oblivious to the suffering of those who were forced to dwell far below them. Descending into the slums of the Lower City, the signs of urban decay became undeniable. Filth and refuse littered the streets, and burned-out vehicles and shattered windows served as stark reminders of the violent wars of the swoop gangs vying for control. Citizens of the Lower City struggled to survive amid the permacrete wasteland. Those banished into the dark and sunless world of the Undercity banded together in small villages in a wretched, never-ending struggle to survive. Starvation and disease claimed many, and the rakghouls—mutated, flesh-eating monsters who dwelled in the sewers—claimed even more. According to legend, the swoop bike was first invented on Taris. While the Mandalorian Wars raged, Squint and his Master stopped on Taris looking to recruit Jedi for the war effort. During his search for Bastila Shan, Darth Malak ordered an orbital bombardment of Taris that devastated the planet's cities and killed billions.

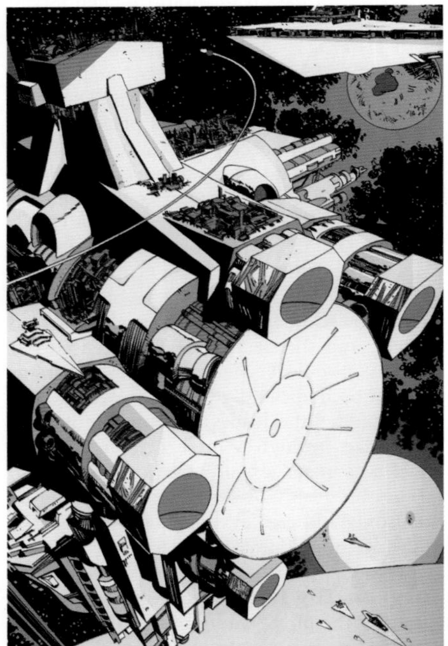

Tarkin

***Tarkin*** A giant superweapon constructed in the Patriim system that combined the Death Star's main offensive battery and superlaser cannon with a set of engines and defensive field generators. Before it was fully operational, Grand Admiral Batch took it to the Aeten system to destroy the planet Aeten II and gather its stygium crystals for use in the Phantom TIE project. Later the *Tarkin* was destroyed by an elite team of Rebels that included Luke Skywalker, Leia Organa, Chewbacca, C-3PO, and R2-D2.

**Tarkin, Gideon** The younger brother of Wilhuff Tarkin and the father of Rivoche Tarkin. Brigadier Gideon Tarkin served as the planet Eriadu's Minister of Security. Five years before the Battle of Yavin, Gideon died during the Erhynradd Mutiny. His daughter was accepted at Wilhuff Tarkin's estate on Eriadu.

**Tarkin, Grand Moff Wilhuff** Tall and gaunt, with sunken cheeks and piercing blue eyes, he was as ruthless as he was evil, propounding the Tarkin Doctrine of rule through the fear of force. And Grand Moff Tarkin gave his enemies a lot to fear. An ambitious young governor of the Seswenna sector, he fully supported Senator Palpatine in the Senator's creeping takeover of the Republic.

A year before the Battle of Naboo, Tarkin served as the Seswenna sector's lieutenant-governor during Supreme Chancellor Valorum's trip to Eriadu. He also served in the military when Eriadu was part of what had then been known as the Outland Regions. In the aftermath of the assassination of the Trade Federation Directorate members at the Eriadu trade summit, Tarkin thwarted the Justice Department investigation, claiming that the matter was an internal affair. Three years after the Battle of Naboo, as a commander of the Republic Outland Regions Security Force, Tarkin spied on the Jedi, relying on a surveillance droid that Anakin Skywalker had unknowingly taken in and repaired. Enlisting the help of his friend Raith Sienar, Tarkin tracked Skywalker and Obi-Wan Kenobi to Zonama Sekot, eventually attacking the living planet and forcing it to flee into hyperspace. In the aftermath, Tarkin took credit for Sienar's design for a moon-sized battle station, and was named a Moff in charge of governors for several sectors. Eventually he became the first *Grand* Moff, in charge of the Empire's most important sectors; he reported only to the Emperor.

*Grand Moff Wilhuff Tarkin*

*Taris*

Although married, Tarkin took as his mistress an Imperial Navy enlistee named Natasi Daala and put her in charge of a top-secret weapons development think tank known as the Maw Installation. He also appointed her admiral. Under her command, the Death Star battle station was completed, and it was while Tarkin was en route to the completed Death Star that his ship was attacked by Rebels. They rescued Tarkin's servant, a Mon Calamari named Ackbar, who had heard many of the Grand Moff's plans. Undaunted by this security breach, Tarkin proceeded with his first act as commander of the Death Star, the destruction of the penal colony on Despayre in the Horuz system.

There were indications that Tarkin, a brilliant strategist and excellent supervisor, toyed with the idea of deposing Palpatine and taking over as Emperor, but no such action was ever taken. When it became known that technical readouts for the Death Star had been stolen by Rebel Alliance spies, Darth Vader was sent to retrieve them. He captured Princess Leia

Nolaa Tarkona

Organa and brought her to Tarkin aboard the Death Star.

After interrogations failed, Tarkin made Leia watch as he destroyed her adopted planet of Alderaan and its billions of inhabitants with the Death Star's main weapon. Later he deferred to Vader's advice and allowed Leia and her rescue party to escape—they were marked with a tracking device that would lead the Imperials to the main Rebel base.

When, at the Battle of Yavin, advisers told Tarkin that there was a slim chance the Rebels might be able to destroy the Death Star, Tarkin was incredulous and refused to evacuate his glorious weapon. He paid for that decision with his life.

**Tarkin, Ranulph** A cousin of Wilhuff Tarkin's who took part in the Stark Hyperspace Conflict. Hailing from Eriadu, Ranulph was a militarist in the Galactic Republic. He was quick to espouse the folly of not having a strong central Republic army and navy. Ranulph plotted with Nute Gunray of the Trade Federation to ambush the Stark Commercial Combine during the negotiations at Troiken. As the talks on Troiken commenced, Iaco Stark transmitted a nav computer virus that scattered the ships of Ranulph's fleet. Ranulph's own ship, the *Invincible,* found itself at Troiken only to be surrounded and outnumbered by Stark's armada. He salvaged his legacy by burying the Stark Hyperspace Combine army in Mount Avos, killing himself in the process.

**Tarkin, Rivoche** The daughter of Gideon Tarkin and niece of Wilhuff Tarkin. Rivoche questioned the beliefs of her nefarious uncle and eventually became a spy for the Rebel Alliance. She later married Voren Na'al.

Rivoche Tarkin

**Tarkin's Fang** The code name for an Imperial base in the Deep Core that was abandoned after the Battle of Endor. It was a few minutes' hyperspace jump from Ebaq 9.

**Tarkona, Nolaa** The Twi'lek leader of the radical Diversity Alliance, an "aliens first" political movement established more than 20 years after the Battle of Yavin. Nolaa Tarkona was the embittered half sister of the dancing girl Oola, whom Jabba had fed to his pet rancor.

Tarkov and his son, Jaccoba

**Tarkosa, Brace** A member of the Managing Council for the survivors of the Outbound Flight Project. During the early phases of Outbound Flight's development, Tarkosa was among those who bristled at the near-constant delays and political infighting that wreaked havoc with their work schedules. He was also one of the leaders of a group that opposed the near tyranny imposed on the crew by Jedi Master Jorus C'baoth. The group's desire for equality led C'baoth to detain them in the ship's central storage core, where they were spared from the blasts of the radiation bombs used by the Chiss against the passengers and crew of the Dreadnaughts. Like many others among the survivors, Tarkosa was angry at the Jedi Knights for not providing better protection against their attackers. When a Chiss-led expedition located the remains of Outbound Flight, Tarkosa called for the slow execution of every being associated with the original attack. His dreams of vengeance went unfulfilled, as most of the Chiss who took part in the attack had since died. After the Vagaari threat was eliminated, Tarkosa grudgingly agreed to accompany the Outbound Flight Colony to Nirauan, staying as far away from the New Republic as he could.

Bentu Pall Tarlen

**Tarkov** This Wookiee was a native of the Wawaatt Archipelago on Kashyyyk during the years leading up to the Clone Wars. When fighting broke out across the galaxy, Tarkov's young son Jaccoba was ready to take the test that would elevate him to adulthood. While trying to kill a grantaloupe, Jaccoba's spear hit the outer shell of a Trade Federation MTT. This led Tarkov to realize that the Separatists had already landed on Kashyyyk and were preparing to launch their invasion. He and Jaccoba rushed to the nearest city, Kahiyuk, to warn the leaders of the impending attack. It was Tarkov's alert that helped the Wookiees begin their defense of their homeworld.

**Tarl** An Imperial stormtrooper in a detachment led by Lieutenant Stalgis that accompanied Luke Skywalker to Munlali Mafir during his search for information on the rogue planet Zonama Sekot. When their party was attacked by mutated Krizlaws, Tarl was caught and forced to ingest a Jostran. The Jostran began to fuse itself to Tarl's spine and nervous system, and would have overtaken him if Luke and his nephew Jacen Solo hadn't used the Force to keep the creature at bay. They took Tarl back to Tekli's medical facilities aboard the *Widowmaker,* where the Chadra-Fan was able to extricate the Jostran and save his life.

**Tarlen, Bentu Pall** The head of the Imperial Center Construction Contracts Division during the reign of Emperor Palpatine, he was in the pocket of Prince Xizor, head of the Black Sun criminal organization. Bentu Pall Tarlen delivered the latest bids on major building projects to Xizor so that the crime lord's favored companies could underbid and win the jobs.

**Tar Morden** The site of a Confederacy of Independent Systems facility that manufactured LM-432 crab droids until it was seized by the Grand Army of the Republic and shut down. Shortly after the Battle of Yavin, the Rebel Alliance established a starfighter-manufacturing enterprise on the planet.

**Tarn, Rhad** A young, human dissident Jedi leader who met with the other dissident Jedi on Ruul in the early months of the Clone Wars. As a Padawan, Rhad spent time on the fringes of the galaxy and saw that the Republic did not care about issues like the slave trade, illegal prisons, or laborers in the spice mines. He believed that the Jedi should be fighting on the side of the Confederacy. After an ambush by Asajj Ventress, Tarn was quick to blame Mace Windu. Having crossed over to the dark side, he turned against his fellow Jedi Jeisel, who had no choice but to kill him.

*Rhad Tarn (right) fights Asajj Ventress.*

**Tarnab** The species of Mot Not Rab, a Republic Senator around the time of the Battle of Naboo.

**Tarnith Station** This space station was maintained in the Outer Rim Territories by the Republic during the era of the Great Sith War. Tarnith Station served as a front-line observation platform during the Mandalorian Wars, allowing both the Republic's military advisers and members of the news media to monitor the situation on the battlefront.

**Tarnoonga** This water-covered planet was the primary world of the Tarnoonga system. The pirate base of Gir Kybo Ren-Cha was located on the planet during the early years of the New Order.

**Taroon, Prince** A tall, light blue Rutanian with coiled braids arranged in loops around his head. The son of King Frane, Prince Taroon accompanied Obi-Wan Kenobi and Qui-Gon Jinn to Senali and organized the Rutanian subversive group known as the Ghost Ones. As part of Taroon's plan to take his brother's place as heir to the Rutanian throne, the Ghost Ones kidnapped Prince Leed. He eventually became the heir when Leed chose to remain on Senali, and their father saw Taroon's natural leadership abilities.

**Taroon system** Located on the outer edges of the Rim, the system contained the planets Kuan and Bordal.

**Tarpals, Captain Roos** This Gungan warrior served Boss Nass as captain of the guard. A former criminal and thief, Tarpals later volunteered to join the Gungan Grand Army, where he was known for his physical skills and regularly placed in the top 10 positions in the Big Nasty Free-For-All. It was during his career as a thief that he first met Jar Jar Binks and took the clumsy Gungan under his wing. Their friendship was cut short when Tarpals enlisted, and when Jar Jar Binks returned from exile, Tarpals was forced to bring the outcast before Boss Nass. Like many other officers, Tarpals questioned Jar Jar's abilities on the battlefield during the Battle of Naboo, and followed General Ceel's lead to fight the Trade Federation's droid armies. The battle was nearly lost until Anakin Skywalker disabled the Droid Control Ship. With the droids powerless and adrift, Tarpals and Jar Jar quickly rounded up the automata and took control of the battlefield.

**Tarpilan, Captain Jun** One of many commanders who participated in the Second Battle of Fondor, he fell under the influence of the battlemind that was created by Jacen Solo. Captain Tarpilan began swearing vehemently while issuing his orders, giving Admiral Cha Niathal reason to believe that he was drunk while on duty, since she was unaware of the battle-meld.

**Tarrak, Ali** A pirate in the Yrrna system who stole TIE defenders from the Empire.

**Tarrik** One of Bail Organa's most trusted aides on the planet Alderaan, he later became an aide to Princess Leia.

***Tartan*-class patrol cruiser** A Damorian Manufacturing Corporation warship capable of tangling with small, fast-moving targets. The ship was equipped with multiple, fast-targeting laser cannon batteries, and was small and agile enough to keep up with starfighters and prevent them from zeroing in on its vulnerable points. A versatile energy distribution network fed all point-defense weapons, allowing increased firepower to be channeled throughout the ship. This reallocation came at the expense of deflector shield power. Tartan patrol cruisers included the *Attentive, Diadem, Impeccable, Skirmisher,* and *Vindictive.*

**Tarturi, Gillam** The son of Senator Berm Tarturi of Andara, he attended the Leadership School on Andara in the years following the Battle of Naboo. An only child, Gillam found himself alone after the death of his mother when he was 12. With his father called to Coruscant on politics, his only family was at the Leadership School. Five years after the Battle of Naboo, the 16-year-old Gillam suddenly disappeared from the school, prompting his father to request an investigation by the Jedi Knights. Obi-Wan

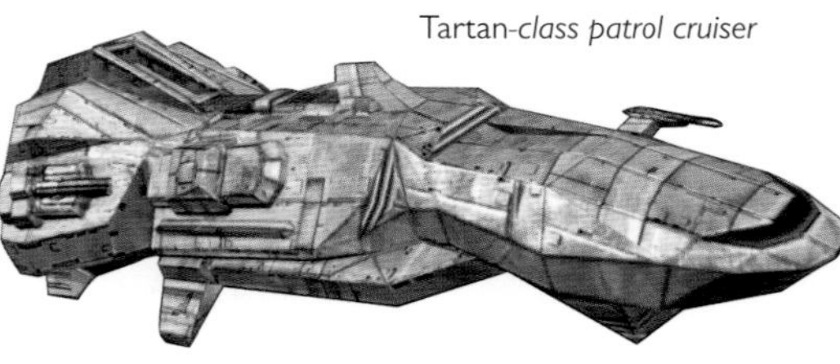
Tartan-*class patrol cruiser*

Kenobi was appointed to lead the mission, and his Padawan Anakin Skywalker was enrolled in the Leadership School to locate Gillam's friends.

Anakin discovered that Gillam was actually the leader of a small band of students who were working as mercenaries in neighboring systems, causing public unrest and forcing "oppressive" leaders to abdicate their rule. It was Gillam who'd formed the team and recruited its members, although Rolai Frac assumed the role of leader after Gillam's alleged kidnapping. When Rana Halion employed the young mercenaries to strafe an Andaran military landing platform as part of a plan to force Berm Tarturi to negotiate, Gillam planned to use live fire in the mission as a way to have himself "killed." He actually planned to make sure Anakin Skywalker was killed in the mission, damaging the body enough so that it could pass as Gillam. Gillam then put plans in place to pin the blame for his kidnapping and death on his own father, Berm Tarturi, to ensure that Berm was discredited and stripped of any power. When the plans were exposed by the Jedi, Gillam and his entire team were expelled from the Leadership School and transported to Coruscant for questioning.

**Taru** This Nagai warrior was one of many who trained under Lumiya on the planet Kinooine in the months following the Battle of Endor.

**Taryn and Trista** Hapan twin sisters who were dispatched to meet Ben Skywalker on Nova Station several weeks after the Battle of Fondor. The only way Ben could tell them apart was their synthatex jumpsuits, because Taryn wore one that was gold in color. Ben later learned that the twins were the cousins of

*Captain Roos Tarpals*

Tenel Ka. Although the sisters managed to get Ben away from Nova Station, they were unable to make their rendezvous with Prince Isolder aboard the *Beam Racer,* which was captured by Tahiri Veila and the *Anakin Solo.* Trista and Taryn continued on their mission to return Ben to Shedu Maad, but brought news of Isolder's capture to the Queen Mother. On Shedu Maad, they learned of the Imperial attack on the *Dragon Queen* and the use of a nanokiller to murder the royal family, and came to the conclusion that Ducha Requud had assisted the Imperials in exchange for the chance to assume the role of Queen Mother. After learning that the Ducha had been killed aboard the *Deserving Gem,* they discovered that General Livette had been in league with the Ducha, and had helped the Imperials land an assault force on the planet. Taryn and Ben Skywalker set out with a group of Her Majesty's Commandos to confront the Imperials, while Trista remained behind to ensure Livette couldn't cause any more trouble.

**Tarz (V-Tarz)** A Keganite truant guide, he caught young Obi-Wan Kenobi and Siri Tachi during their mission to Kegan; he thought they were truant Keganite children and sent them to the Learning Circle for education.

Moff Boren Tascl

**Tascl, Moff Boren** A large, middle-aged man with thinning black hair and a goatee, he was given the governorship of Cilpar as his reward for leading one of the TIE fighter wings at the Battle of Derra IV. Moff Boren Tascl was negotiating with the Rebel Alliance to turn over his world and supplies when he heard that the Emperor had died. Shortly thereafter, Sate Pestage, the Emperor's Grand Vizier, contacted him and promised a great reward if Tascl would make Cilpar available to Pestage if Coruscant's weather became particularly harsh. Tascl saw a power struggle ahead and decided he might get more from the breakup of the Empire than he would from the Rebels, so he used his agents to disrupt Alliance agents before Rogue Squadron arrived.

**Taselda** A human female Jedi living in Ruby Gulch on Nam Chorios, she was an insane hag who ate insectoid drochs out of her arms. At one point, Taselda and Beldorion the Hutt competed to rule the people of the planet's main city, Hweg Shul. She claimed that the Hutt stole her lightsaber and turned the people against her, forcing her to live as an outcast. Luke Skywalker uncovered Taselda as a fraud. She captured Callista for a brief time to use in her ongoing battle against Beldorion, but Callista escaped.

Tassa

**Tasha, Saljé** A female Anzati assassin, distinguished by her silver-white hair and piercing green eyes, who worked during the final years of the Republic. Her specialty was political jobs, and she was known to be very picky when it came to her clientele. During the Clone Wars, she was hired by a mysterious agent who provided her with cortosis gauntlets. After she was tracked down by Quinlan Vos, Tasha revealed that she had been the one who arranged for the murder of former Chancellor Finis Valorum. The Jedi learned that it had been Sora Bulq who hired her for the job.

**Tasia, Queen (Elsinoré den Tasia)** A monarch who ruled the planet Grizmallt around 3,950 years before the Battle of Yavin. Queen Tasia introduced a new age of exploration and colonization, launching hundreds of expeditions into the wilds of space. In the final days of her life, she personally sponsored the last such expedition, sending the colony ship *Beneficent Tasia* and its support starships, *Constant* and *Mother Vima,* to the galaxy's dangerous southern quadrant. The expedition eventually reached Naboo and colonized the planet.

**Task Force Aster** An 18-ship New Republic force, it was deployed above Doornik-319 to battle Yevethan forces after a Republic blockade attempt failed.

**Task Force Blackvine** A 20-ship New Republic force deployed above Doornik-319 to battle Yevethan forces after a Republic blockade attempt failed.

**Taspir III** An inhospitable planet once scouted by the Empire as a possible base. About 10 years after the Battle of Endor, the fallen Jedi Rosh Penin sent a distress signal to his onetime friend Jaden Korr asking for help. Penin's message indicated that he was being held prisoner on Taspir III. Although Jaden thought the mission was a trap, Kyle Katarn decided that they needed to answer the distress call on the off chance that Penin was in real trouble. The two Jedi found that the Imperial base was quite operational, and that the Disciples of Ragnos had also taken up residence on the planet.

**tass** A plant native to the planet Ruusan and one of the handful of species that survived environmental changes subsequent to the battle there. The world's inhabitants found that powdered tass roots could be mixed with scintil vine flowers and water to create a corrosive paste that could eat through rock and metal.

**Tassa** A black-haired female Codru-Ji who was the wife of Rikkar-Du during the years following the Sith–Imperial War. As the daughter of a clan chief, Tassa allowed Rikkar-Du to hold considerable sway over the other clan leaders. However, when Rikkar-Du suggested that the clans unite to oppose Imperial occupation of Munto Codru, even Tassa's father's support wasn't enough to persuade the other leaders. Although she supported her husband, Tassa worried that he lacked the backing of enough clan leaders to put his plans into action. When Rikkar-Du went to the local temple to meditate, Tassa took their son, Jassar, home. Jassar, however, wanted to be with his father, and set off to find him. Unknown to the family was the fact that Kassek-Ka had made a deal with Darth Kruhl to eliminate Rikkar-Du if he tried to oppose the Sith. As Darth Kruhl killed both Rikkar-Du and Jassar, Kassek-Ka took Tassa's life.

**Tatakoz** The Jawa master trader of the Mospic High Range, he lived approximately a century before the Battle of Endor. A tribal outcast, Tatakoz sold his wares using nothing more than a speeder bike and a repulsor trailer. When the citizens of Mos Espa and Mos Entha began hailing his skill, rival tribes attempted to steal his business in an escalating contest of one-upmanship. Eventually Tatakoz built the first pieced-together "monster droid"—and even more impressively, he actually sold it.

**Tathis, Orinn** A member of the Council of Elders on Alderaan, he was offworld when the Death Star destroyed his planet. He returned to the Graveyard of Alderaan to locate the armory ship *Another Chance* and turn its weapons cache over to the Rebel Alliance after discovering the location of the remote calling device used to communicate with the ship.

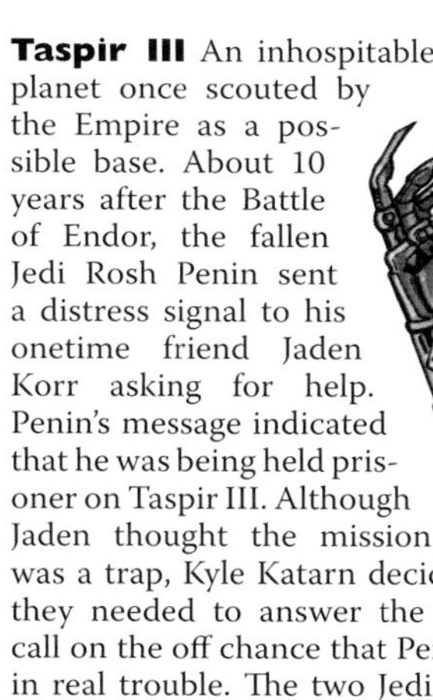

Saljé Tasha

**Tatoo I, Tatoo II** The twin suns of the Tatooine system, they were binary stars.

**Tatooine** A harsh desert planet that orbited double stars in the Outer Rim in the Arkanis sector near the worlds of Ryloth and Piroket, it was far from the galactic mainstream. Nevertheless, Tatooine occupied a strategic location at the nexus of several hyperspace routes, and was the childhood home of the Jedi Knights Anakin Skywalker and his son Luke Skywalker. The Jedi Knight Dace Diath, who lived 4,000 years before the Galactic Civil War, was also a native of Tatooine.

Over the centuries Tatooine, located in the Tatoo system, was the site of many orbital battles among rival gangsters and smugglers, and its surface was littered with ancient starship wrecks, most of which had long since been buried by the planet's fierce sandstorms. It boasted two native species: the meddlesome, scavenging Jawas and the fierce Tusken Raiders, commonly called Sand People. Animal life included the bantha, dewback, womp rat, ronto, scurrier, sandfly, bonegnawer, gravelmaggot, dune lizard, sandsnake, rockmite, feathered lizard, sandjigger, meewit, cliffborer worm, and the feared Sarlacc, which was said to take 1,000 years to digest its prey. Tatooine was also home to the terrifying krayt dragon, possibly feared more than any other animal in the sector. Although it was considered a suicidal venture, some hunted the krayt dragon to obtain its legendary and priceless gizzard stones, known as dragon pearls.

For much of its settled existence, Tatooine was controlled by the Hutts, who encouraged gambling, smuggling, and slavery on the harsh world, which was visited by a wide range of aliens from across the galaxy. Tatooine was also known for the Boonta Eve Classic, a dangerous Podrace held near Mos Espa on Boonta Eve.

Many colonists on the planet ran moisture farms, which condensed water from the dry air with vaporators. Pike and deb-deb fruits were known to grow in certain oases. Some water prospectors roamed the desert searching for untapped sources of subterranean moisture. The native hubba gourd was a primary part of the diet of both the Sand People and Jawas, and other plant life included razor moss and the funnel flower. A grove of Cydorrian driller trees, planted by the Ithorian Momaw Nadon, grew in the mountains north of Mos Eisley, and somewhere in the desert was rumored to be a colony of alien Kitonaks. Strange mists sometimes formed where the sodium-rich dunes met the rocky cliffs. Points of interest included the Dune Sea and the neighboring Jundland Wastes, Anchorhead, Motesta, Tosche Station, Bestine township, Beggar's Canyon and its Stone Needle, Bildor's Canyon, and the Mos Eisley spaceport.

Mos Eisley, the planet's largest city, was known as a "wretched hive of scum and villainy." It was bordered by mountains on the north and on the opposite side by the decaying buildings of the southern sector. The wreckage of the *Dowager Queen,* the planet's first colony ship, could be found in the center of town. Other sites in Mos Eisley included the Lucky Despot Hotel and Casino (owned by the Whiphid gangster Lady Valarian), Lup's General Store, the Spaceport Traffic Control Tower, the Mos Eisley Inn, the underground Mos Eisley Towers hotel, a Dim-U monastery where ships could have their transponders illegally altered, and the infamous Mos Eisley cantina owned by Chalmun the Wookiee. After the Battle of Endor, the master chef Porcellus opened the Crystal Moon restaurant in Mos Eisley, and its fame spread throughout the Outer Rim.

During the Great Hunt that followed the Sith War nearly 4,000 years before the Battle of Yavin, a group of Jedi had gone to Tatooine to eradicate the terentateks found there. Companies such as Czerka Corporation operated settlements on Tatooine during that era in the hope of finding valuable ores. Centuries later, exiled monks of the B'omarr order built a huge monastery on the edge of the Dune Sea. The bandit Alkhara took up residence in part of the monastery and remained there for 34 years, raiding nearby moisture farms while expanding and improving the citadel. The B'omarr monastery was the home of many other gangsters and bandits until eventually becoming the palace of crime lord Jabba the Hutt, who expanded the facility to encompass a hangar and garage. Throughout the changes, the B'omarr monks kept to their own affairs in the palace's lowest levels, trying to reach enlightenment, at which point their brains could be surgically removed by the other monks and placed in glass jars, freed from the distractions of the flesh.

The great Jedi hero Anakin Skywalker grew up on Tatooine as a slave in the employ of Watto the Toydarian. After winning the Boonta Eve Podrace, Anakin departed with Qui-Gon Jinn and Obi-Wan Kenobi, leaving his mother, Shmi, behind. Shmi eventually married the moisture farmer Cliegg Lars. Prior to the Battle of Geonosis, Anakin and Padmé Amidala returned to Tatooine, only to learn that Shmi had been captured by Tusken Raiders. Anakin could not save her and slaughtered an entire Tusken village in his anger.

After the Clone Wars, the Jedi Knight Obi-Wan Kenobi came to the desert planet to place the infant Luke Skywalker in the care of Cliegg's son Owen Lars and his wife, Beru. Years later, a message from Princess Leia Organa of Alderaan, whose ship had been captured above Tatooine, helped bring Kenobi out of his life as a hermit near the Dune Sea and into the service of the Rebel Alliance. After the Battle of Hoth, Luke Skywalker returned to Tatooine, where he built a new lightsaber. Immediately before the Battle of Endor, Skywalker and his friends returned to Tatooine to free Han Solo from Jabba's palace, which resulted in the death of the crime lord and the collapse of his organization. The B'omarr monks reclaimed the palace, persuading several of Jabba's lieutenants to join them as disembodied brains. Eight years after the Battle of Endor, the Imperial battlemoon *Eye of Palpatine* stopped at Tatooine to pick up a contingent of stormtroopers—but brought aboard Sand People and Jawas instead. Later that year, Luke Skywalker and Han Solo returned to Jabba's palace to investigate rumors of the Hutt's Darksaber Project. During the Yuuzhan Vong War, many Hutts fled their homeworld of Nal Hutta for Tatooine. The alien invaders considered using the planet as a breeding ground for dovin basals, but problems with geological anomalies rendered the plan useless.

***Tatooine*** A New Republic cruiser, it was lost in the Battle of Almania.

**Tatooine blues** A musical genre, it was favored in certain casinos throughout the New Republic.

**Tatooine howler** A large, shaggy predator with a bulky build and curling horns. If seen from afar, a howler could be mistaken for a bantha. Most people considered them to be legends or rumors designed to keep the curious away from secret smuggler bases in the deep desert. Howlers were extremely intelligent carnivores. When one was on the hunt, it made loud howling noises to scare its prey, herding the quarry toward rock cul-de-sacs or similar killing grounds. The howler dried portions of each kill in the hot air, then buried them in the sand. If hunting turned lean, the creature could return to its secret cache of food.

*Tatooine*

**Tatoo system** A star system in the Outer Rim, it consisted of the twin suns Tatoo I and Tatoo II and the planets Tatooine, Ohann, and Adriana. The system was in the Arkanis sector.

**Tauk, Lemmet** One of the Empire's most skilled and loyal soldiers, Tauk was among the top four students at the training facility on Yinchorr, in the same class as Carnor Jax and Kir Kanos. Tauk was a friend of Kanos, and they trained hard together in the hope of one day serving the Emperor. At the completion of their training, Emperor Palpatine ordered Tauk and Kanos to battle each other to the death to prove their loyalty. Both hesitated before Darth Vader forced them into the battle, which Kanos eventually won by running Tauk through with his sword. Kanos mourned for his friend, and earned a scar from the blade of Vader's lightsaber for his emotions.

**Taul** A mist-shrouded, acidic swamp world in the Gunthar system, it was used by the Rebel Alliance as a training outpost until the facility was destroyed by the *Victory*-class Star Destroyer *Dominator*.

**Taung** A warrior species that inhabited Coruscant during the distant pre-Republic era. The epic poem *Dha Werda Verda* recounted the battle between the Taungs and the Battalions of Zhell, in which a sudden volcanic eruption rained destructive ash upon the Zhell and smothered their city. The ash plume rose high into the sky and cast a giant shadow over the land for two years, giving the Taungs a new name: Dha Werda Verda, the Warriors of the Shadow—or, in some translations, Dark Warriors. The Taungs themselves saw the immense, long-lasting shadow as a symbol of their destiny and adopted the Dark Shadow Warrior identity throughout their subsequent conquests, eventually settling on the planet Mandalore and becoming known as the original Mandalorians.

**tauntaun** Easily domesticated reptile-like creatures insulated with gray-white fur, they were sometimes called snow lizards. Wild tauntauns roamed the frozen wastes of the ice planet Hoth, where they grazed on lichen. Although initially ornery, the spitting tauntaun could be tamed and ridden. The animals were used as mounts and pack animals by the Rebel Alliance when it had its base on Hoth. Although their thick fur protected tauntauns from extreme temperatures, they couldn't survive Hoth's brutal nights and had to seek shelter. But during the day, tauntaun herds could be seen running across the plains of ice and snow.

**Taurill** Industrious, semi-intelligent creatures, they formed a hive-mind: a single organism with thousands of bodies sharing one collective consciousness. Each individual creature was just a set of eyes, ears, and hands to do the bidding of the Overmind. While this could result in intense focus, it also led to situations that grew quickly out of control if a few sets of eyes saw something disturbing. Taurill, which made good pets, had grayish brown fur, large curious eyes, and four supple arms that ended in dexterous fingers. They blinked their eyes a lot and constantly shifted position.

*Tauntaun*

**Tavira, Moff Leonia** A small human female with short black hair and violet eyes, she succeeded her husband as governor of Eiattu VI. Moff Leonia Tavira had been de facto Moff during her husband's illness and neglected to tell the central Imperial government of his death. She was ambitious and wanted to end the system under which she shared power with a group of nobles, so she set up a complex plot that involved a pretender to the throne.

**Tavo** This ARC trooper was one of the first of his kind to defect from service to the Grand Army of the Republic and go rogue. Tavo was eventually hunted down and killed by agents of Republic Intelligence, who were working under orders from Chancellor Palpatine.

**Tawntoom** A frontier settlement, it was on the frozen dark side of the planet Roon. The colony served as a base for Governor Koong and his band of thieves during the early days of the Empire.

**Tawr, Vatok** One of the few Mandalorian commandos who accompanied Boba Fett to the Nickel One asteroid, in the wake of the Second Battle of Fondor, to drive off the forces of the Imperial Remnant that had taken control of the asteroid and enslaved the native Verpine. Tawr was known among his fellow commandos as a man who was as strong as he was fast, but was also a quiet man with a cheerful smile when not on active duty.

**Tawron, Relal** An Ithorian high priest who replaced Momaw Nadon as Ithorian leader. During the Yuuzhan Vong invasion, the Ithorians hosted a reception aboard the *Tafanda Bay* for the New Republic and Imperial Remnant forces that came to defend the planet. Relal Tawron insisted that the Jedi Knights cleanse themselves before they went to the surface of Ithor, and he presided over the ritual.

**t'bac** A plant, it was widely smoked to deliver the somewhat intoxicating drug nic-i-tain into the body.

**TC-14** This silver TC-series protocol droid served Nute Gunray and the Neimoidians during their blockade of Naboo. Frequent memory wipes kept the droid strongly loyal to the Trade Federation. It was TC-14, with her feminine personality, which greeted Qui-Gon Jinn and Obi-Wan Kenobi when they attempted to negotiate a settlement with Gunray. TC-14 was sent to detain the Jedi Knights until the Neimoidians could eliminate them.

**TC-17** A long-range blaster rifle that was common among the rank-and-file soldiers in the Brotherhood of Darkness more than a millennium before the Battle of Yavin. Because the weapon needed to fire a powerful blast that remained effective over a large distance, the power cell could only supply enough energy for a dozen shots before needing to be replaced.

**TC-22** One of the main blaster rifles distributed to the soldiers of the Brotherhood of Darkness about a millennium before the Battle of Yavin. Although the weapon was powerful, it suffered from poor sighting. Over time, the stock scope lost its calibration, resulting in missed shots unless the owner was able to compensate.

***T*-class cruiser** A blade-shaped, personal cruiser that was among the finest vessels produced during the decades leading up to the Battle of Ruusan. The ship was equipped with cutting-edge technology, providing its owner with incredible power and range. The controls of the *T*-class cruiser were designed to conform to all galactic standards for operation and control, and made flying the ship a simple task for even the novice pilot.

**Tchiery** A Farnym, he was Leia Organa Solo's copilot aboard the *Alderaan* when she traveled to Almania to confront Dolph.

**Tching, Ueg** The 54th Atrisian Emperor, famous for his tyrannical rule and his insight into diplomacy, strategy, and the effective use of spies. Under his rule, the Atrisian Empire ruled the whole of Kitel Phard. The original manuscript of his *Sayings* was kept in the Rare Books Department of the Atrisian Imperial Historical Library on Kitel Phard. Emperor Palpatine "requested" this original for the Imperial Museum on Coruscant for its great

*Tchuukthai*

historical value to the galaxy. It eventually vanished into the Emperor's private holdings.

**Tchuukthai** A rare, four-legged reptilian species, also referred to as the Wharl. For centuries, the Tchuukthai were considered little more than beasts. Their true intelligence remained a secret until a Jedi Master encountered them. The Jedi explained much about the galaxy to a Tchuukthai he'd befriended and offered to train the creature in the ways of the Force. This Tchuukthai later became Jedi Master Thon of Ambria. For thousands of years, Master Thon was the only Tchuukthai who ventured into the galaxy. During the time of the New Republic, the species' existence was still considered a rumor across most of the galaxy.

**TC series protocol droid** A line of protocol droids manufactured by Cybot Galactica and marketed as a boutique extension of the 3PO design. The TC series was programmed to be dignified and calm in any situation. Although expensive, they proved extremely useful to Senators and high-ranking officials. TCs were named for the TranLang III communications modules they carried, which allowed them to vocalize over six million forms of communication. Almost all units in the TC series had voices designed to mimic those of human females, and referred to themselves with feminine-gender pronouns. One of them, TC-14, was programmed to serve top Trade Federation officials. She was the droid who greeted Obi-Wan Kenobi and Qui-Gon Jinn when their diplomatic ship landed aboard the Trade Federation flagship; she realized at once that the ambassadors were Jedi. During the Clone War, Jabba's translator was TC-70.

**T'dai, Master** A Zabrak Jedi Master who served the Order some 700 years before the Battle of Yavin, he assigned a group of newly commissioned Jedi Knights to hunt down a Dark Jedi who operated in the Bpfassh system. One of his Knights, an alien named Minch, confronted the Dark Jedi but was no match for his skills. Master T'dai and the others arrived to save Minch, but the Dark Jedi took his own life to avoid being captured.

**T'dawlish, Breyf** This white-furred Bothan male was one of the many who represented their homeworld of Bothawui within the Confederation several years after the Swarm War. It was T'dawlish who met Silfinia and Najack Ell when they arrived at Gilatter VIII to participate in the Confederation's first full face-to-face meeting since its formation. Unknown to T'dawlish, the Ells were not who they seemed to be, and were actually Lumiya and Jacen Solo in disguise. This did not matter much, though, because T'dawlish and the other delegates were in fact actors serving as stand-ins, part of an elaborate trap that was meant to lure the Galactic Alliance to Gilatter VIII.

**TDL3.5** A nanny droid sent to replace C-3PO as the minder of the three Solo children, it was part of a prank played by young Anakin to punish 3PO for refusing to read him a favorite bedtime story, "The Little Lost Bantha Cub."

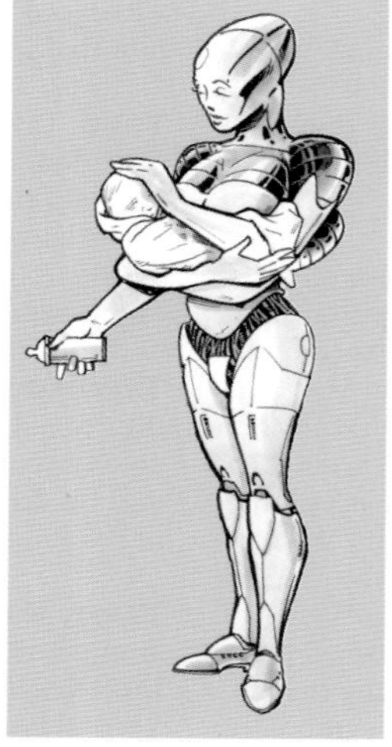

*TDL droid*

**TDL droid** An enhanced protocol model, it was programmed to perform a majority of the functions required in the care of a young child. TDL models were marketed across the galaxy as nanny droids for busy politicians, space military personnel, and even smugglers who had children but too little time to spend with them. The TDL droid that cared for Anakin Solo on Anoth had a silvery surface with smooth corners and no sharp edges. It had four fully functional arms, all of which were covered with warm synthetic flesh—and advanced weaponry. The droid forfeited its existence to protect Anakin.

**Team Mynock** The code name used by Jacen Solo and Ben Skywalker during their mission to disable Centerpoint Station before Thrackan Sal-Solo could use it as a weapon. They chose the name because their mission called for them to infiltrate the station from the outside, moving about on the surface of the station like mynocks until they could find an air lock.

**Team Purella** The code name of the Jedi unit led by Jaina Solo and Zekk that infiltrated the city of Coronet on Corellia. Team Purella's mission was to appear as Corellian citizens and kidnap Prime Minister Aidel Saxan. The objective was to force the leaders of the Corellian system to stand down from their threats of secession.

*TC series protocol droid*

**Team Slashrat** The code name of a group of Jedi starfighter pilots assigned to the battle carrier *Dodonna.* Led by Jedi Master Corran Horn, Team Slashrat was charged with infiltrating Coronet and monitoring the starfighter traffic at its largest spaceports. The pilots' role in the mission was largely negated when it was learned that most Corellian starfighters were already in orbit, awaiting the appearance of the Galactic Alliance Second Fleet.

**Team Tauntaun** The code name of a group of Jedi led by Tahiri Veila, and including fellow Jedi Doran Tainer and Tiu Zax. Their mission was to capture Thrackan Sal-Solo, but their attempt to reach the Corellian insurgent was met with an ambush. Team Tauntaun was thought to be lost after the initial wave of combat until Veila and Tainer were rescued by Jaina Solo and Team Purella.

**Team Womp Rat** The code name of a team of Jedi Knights led by Luke Skywalker and mobilized to recover Teams Purella and Tauntaun from Corellia with the help of Hardpoint Squadron. Team Womp Rat was forced to alter its original mission plans when the shuttle *Chandrila Skies* was destroyed, forcing the Jedi to evacuate the members of Purella and Tauntaun in starfighters.

**Tebut, Lieutenant Patra** A lieutenant in the Galactic Alliance military some 10 years after the end of the Yuuzhan Vong War. Known for her efficiency and nononsense attitude, Lieutenant Tebut was stationed aboard the Star Destroyer *Anakin Solo* and served as one of the officers of the watch. She was on duty when Ben Skywalker returned from Ziost in a Sith meditation sphere. She alerted Jacen Solo to Ben's return, then worked behind the scenes to ensure that no knowledge of the Sith artifact was leaked to the rest of the crew. In the wake of a trap that was set by Five World Prime Minister Sadras Koyan to capture Jacen at a deep-space rendezvous, it was Tebut who discovered a tracking sensor on his cloak. Her pride was short-lived; soon thereafter Jacen—angered by a mistake Tebut made and refusing to accept her apology—crushed her neck with the Force.

**tech dome** The common name given to a combined garage-and-workshop structure that extended off a house, especially houses built for colonists.

**Technobeast** Intelligent beings mutated through Sith alchemy into monsters. Technobeasts were created by the Sith Lord Belia

*Technobeast*

Darzu during the Sictis Wars, a subset of the New Sith Wars about 1,240 years before the Battle of Yavin. Darzu's technovirus seed could replicate itself by converting organic material into circuitry nodes. A victim infected with the technovirus would rapidly turn into a hideous droid–human hybrid. The technovirus destroyed the frontal lobes of the brain and rewrote a being's genetic codes, and Darzu's dark side technique became known as *mechu-deru vitae.* Technobeasts were never alike, save for their lumpy asymmetry where chunks of metal had replaced living components. The virus sometimes built over its own work multiple times, leaving behind zigzags of metallic scar tissue. Technobeasts might have multiple heads, or scuttle about on crab-like pincers. Many had arms that ended in skewers or saw blades. A single technobeast could release a cloud of nano-spores that could infect hundreds of other victims. During the Sictis Wars, a Jedi Knight was infected and became known to the other Jedi as the "technobeast Jedi" after retaining his identity through the Force. After Darzu's death, the few technobeasts she created were trapped in her fortress on Tython. Over the centuries that followed, their flesh decayed, leaving behind just the mechanical frame. When Darth Bane found the fortress, he fought his way through the technobeasts in order to reach Darzu's holocron.

**Techno Union** A vast manufacturing conglomerate that enjoyed a lucrative trade franchise during the last decades of the Republic. With a membership composed of starship manufacturers, weapons and droid developers, and major technology suppliers, the Techno Union was established to ensure that fair commerce was maintained across the galaxy, as well as to develop some of the most promising new technologies. Shipping concerns were later added to the roster of the Techno Union, helping to ensure that supply lines and distribution channels remained open. Led by Techno Union Foreman Wat Tambor, the organization included such signatories as Baktoid Armor Workshop, Haor Chall Engineering, Republic Sienar Systems, Kuat Systems Engineering, TaggeCo, BlasTech Industries, and the Corellian Engineering Corporation. Factory planets like Fondor, Foundry, Mechis III, Telti, and Metalorn churned out cutting-edge technology. The Techno Union was also one of the strongest supporters of the Trade Federation and was given license to develop a droid army to defend itself. The amassed army of the Techno Union was later added to the growing forces of Count Dooku and the Confederacy of Independent Systems just before the Battle of Geonosis, when Wat Tambor agreed to join the Separatists. At the height of the Clone Wars, the Techno Union established a secret facility on the planet Nelvaan, where Nelvaanian males were genetically and surgically altered by Skakoan scientists. The facility was destroyed by Anakin Skywalker, and the Techno Union representatives summarily executed. Wat Tambor died on Mustafar, and the Techno Union ceased to exist early in the era of the New Order.

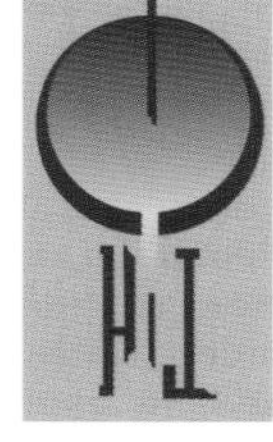

**Tech Raiders** A group of black marketers and smugglers active about 12 years before the Battle of Naboo, they moved their base of operations from Coruscant to Vandor-3.

***Tector*-class Star Destroyer** A hangarless version of one of the Old Republic's largest warships produced near the end of the Clone Wars.

**Teda, Roy** This despot ruled the planet Romin with an iron fist during the years leading up to the Clone Wars. Teda engaged in torture, embezzlement, and unjust imprisonment of political and personal rivals, and he altered Romin's laws to make it impossible for offworlders to arrest or transport criminals. This allowed him to expand his personal wealth by offering Romin as a refuge for villains. In exchange for being able to live in relative peace on Romin, criminals agreed to pay Teda huge sums of credits, and allowed him to have security access to their properties.

When the Citizens' Resistance launched a rebellion, Teda was forced to flee his palace and hide in a safehouse, well outside the city of Eliior, with Jenna Zan Arbor. They requested a meeting with the "Slams," who were actually Obi-Wan Kenobi, Siri Tachi, Anakin Skywalker, and Ferus Olin in disguise. Teda and his cohorts fled to Coruscant after the Jedi followed them to Falleen, but they were able to gain an audience with the Senate. Roy Teda spoke eloquently against the Jedi Order, using subtle twists of the truth and outright lies to spin a tale of how the Jedi were behind his ouster. Unknown to Teda, however, was the fact that Granta Omega considered him expendable. Teda finally realized this when Omega launched his seeker droids on the Senate, and one of the seeker droids targeted him specifically. Despite the efforts of Ferus Olin to protect both Palpatine and Teda, a seeker droid killed Teda with a single blast to the chest.

**Tedryn Holocron** A holocron, it was used some 4,000 years before the Galactic Civil War by Jedi Master Vodo-Siosk Baas.

**Tedryn-Sha** One of the clone Emperor Palpatine's personal advisers, Tedryn-Sha was promoted to second in command of Operation Shadow Hand after Sedriss and Vill Goir were killed on Ossus. Palpatine granted him the powers of Dark Jedi as part of the promotion. He was then sent to New Alderaan, following the destruction of the Republic's Pinnacle Base, to kill Luke Skywalker. In the battle that ensued, Tedryn-Sha killed Jem Ysanna, but was in turn slain by Leia Organa Solo, who used her lightsaber to cleave the Dark Jedi in two.

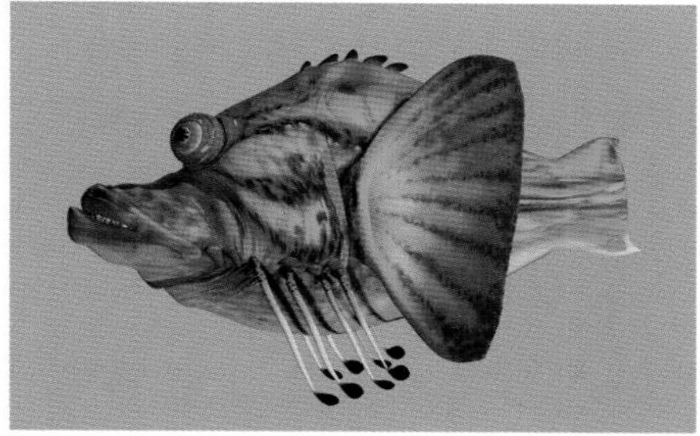

*Tee*

**tee** One of the multitude of species of scalefish that inhabit the seas of Naboo, the tee was a large, rotund fish with bright red scales. It was a voracious feeder, and massive specimens were known to have swallowed hapless Gungans whole. These huge fish were often infested with yobshrimp, and had developed a symbiotic relationship with the laa, allowing the smaller fish to enter their gills to clean off the parasitic yobshrimp.

**Teebo** An Ewok with light and dark gray-striped fur, he was one of the leaders of the tribe that befriended Princess Leia Organa and the Rebel Alliance strike team on Endor's For-

*Teebo*

est Moon. Teebo wore a horned half skull decorated with feathers. His weapon was a stone hatchet. A dreamer and a poet, Teebo had a mystical ability to communicate with nature.

**Teek** Resembling both a rodent and a monkey, these mischievous creatures lived in the forest of Endor's moon. Teeks had long, pointy ears, scruffy white fur, beady black eyes, and a bucktoothed mouth that was always open and chattering. They usually wore rudimentary clothing with many belts, pouches, and pockets for the items they snatched. Gifted with enormously fast metabolisms, Teeks could put on bursts of incredible speed and were nearly impossible to catch. One Teek became friendly with Noa Briqualon, a scout stranded on the Endor moon.

Teek

**Teeko** A Rodian, he was an uncle of the inexperienced bounty hunter Greedo.

**Teeks, Edbit** An Old Republic Intelligence agent, he was dispatched to Tarhassan during the buildup to the Clone Wars, as the planetary government made rumblings about joining the Separatists. Six days before the Tarhassan government opted to secede, Teeks disappeared. A mission team, gathered from untrained agents, was put together to rescue him. Led by Cherek Tuhm, the team included Tinian Hanther, Livintius Sazet, Joram Kithe, and Mapper Gann. While Tuhm and his fellow administrators labored over plan details, Kithe and Gann simply went out and hunted Teeks down. They discovered that he had been abducted by Tarhassan Planetary Security and had not been betrayed by his lover, Zazana Renkel. The pair convinced their teammates to launch a daring rescue attempt, which succeeded in liberating Teeks from prison. His innocence and loyalty to the Republic remained in question, and Teeks was returned to Coruscant for debriefing.

**Teem, Ainlee** This Republic Senator, a Gran from the planet Malastare, was one of the three candidates selected to replace Chancellor Valorum after Queen Amidala of Naboo called for a vote of no confidence in Valorum's abilities.

**Teers, Rep** This Gungan served on the Rep Council, the governmental body that ruled the underwater city of Otoh Gunga under Boss Nass. Teers was appointed to her position by Nass, and was in charge of the city's power supply.

**Teeth of Tatooine** Fast-moving torrents of sand, rocks, and random sharp debris experienced by those left out to die in Tatooine's Valley of the Wind.

Tekli

**Teevan** A planet home to a humanoid species of the same name with slanted silver eyes and silvery skin. Teevans were exceptionally flexible and could bend in surprising ways. The Jedi student Tru Veld was a Teevan.

**Teezl** A unique creature thought to serve as a natural hyperspace communication amplifier. After the Battle of Hoth, Admiral Giel was delivering it to Coruscant aboard his flagship when Luke Skywalker attacked with a squadron of modified TIE fighters. The Teezl was destroyed along with much of Giel's armada.

Teezl

**tehk'la blade** A Nagai variant of the common vibrodagger. The tehk'la blade had serrated edges that tore an enemy's flesh as the blade was withdrawn from its wound.

**Teilcam system** Located in the Outer Rim, its only habitable planet was the watery world of Kabaira.

**Teke Ro** A blue giant star, it was circled by Cona, homeworld of the Arcona.

**Teklet** Located on Qiilura, this was the site of a major depot and the only spaceport on the planet during the last years of the Republic. The Separatist forces that took control of Qiilura used it as their primary export location for barq and kushayan grains as well as military matériel. Much of the city, including the primary communications center, was destroyed by the clone commandos of Omega Squad during their mission to capture Ovolot Qail Uthan and destroy her clone-killing nanovirus. The Grand Army of the Republic then established its base of operations in the city to coordinate the extradition of the human settlers on the planet.

**Tekli** A female Chadra-Fan Jedi with marginal Force talent who served during the Yuuzhan Vong War. Tekli was the apprentice of Cilghal. She joined Anakin Solo's strike mission to hunt down the voxyn queen near Myrkr, and spent much of the time using her healing abilities. Tekli was also part of the Jedi strike force remnant aboard the *Trickster* (*Ksstarr*), where she tended to Tahiri Veila's wounds. At the war's end, Tekli became an emissary to Zonama Sekot.

**Tel** A sergeant in the 35th Infantry of the Grand Army of the Republic at the height of the Clone Wars. Sergeant Tel was one of the many nonclone officers who served in the GAR. He was assigned to coordinate the efforts of starships in orbit with ground-based assaults, and worked directly with Omega Squad during the elimination of key communications assets in the city of Eyat.

**Tel, Rango "Tank Head"** A lackluster bounty hunter who strutted about in badly made counterfeit Mandalorian armor. He didn't realize his nickname "Tank Head" was meant to be derogatory. He tried to collect the bounty on Nam Kale who had come to Tatooine for the Boonta Eve Podrace, but Nale shot and killed him instead.

**Telamarch, Yura** This tall, dome-headed humanoid was the ruler of Bezim, and one of the founders of the Station 88 Spaceport. When the founders of the station met with Count Dooku on Null to discuss a possible alliance with the Confederacy of Independent Systems, Telamarch decided to side with Lorian Nod and throw his support to the Old Republic. Dooku did not accept this as an answer, and brought in 12 super battle droids in order to force an agreement. Obi-Wan Kenobi and his apprentice, Anakin Skywalker, defeated the battle droids and saved the leaders, but Dooku escaped.

**Telamark, Dona** This woman established a residence on Bellassa, well away from the major city of Ussa. Her home, hidden in the mountains of Arno, kept her out of the sweeping events that occurred in the wake of the Clone Wars when the Empire took control of the planet. A self-sufficient woman, Dona was startled when Ferus Olin appeared on her doorstep after escaping the Imperial forces that had captured Roan Lands. Dona did her best to nurse Olin back to health. When Obi-Wan Kenobi arrived on Bellassa and sought out Olin, he explained that Dona Telamark had been the first customer of the Olin/Lands Agency. Back on her homeworld, she had blown the whistle on her employer, who had been cutting corners on a vaccine that was meant to save children. She feared that she would be targeted for assassination if she remained, and sought out Olin/Lands to help her expose the employer and escape any threats. With their help, she was able to testify in galactic court, thereby bringing down both the corporation and the government that supported its actions. She was then relocated to Bellassa and remained out of sight for several months. Kenobi was dismayed to learn that he had been followed to Telamark's cabin by Boba Fett, and was forced to flee with Olin. Telamark tried to help, but Olin begged her to stay out of the conflict. She reluctantly agreed, fleeing back to Ussa to hide among the Eleven. However, Imperial forces managed to locate her, and she was arrested and sent to the prison ship *True Justice* along with Roan Lands and others. They were rescued by Olin, who allowed himself to be captured in order to ensure their escape.

**TelBrinTel** The manufacturer of the TT-40 Library droid. TelBrinTel, based in the Core Worlds, was a specialist firm known for its highly accurate scientific droids.

**telbun** A stratified class of people from Kuat, they were raised and trained by their families to excel at everything in life, whether it be athletics, academics, or manners. When they reached the appropriate age, they were tested and rated according to their stamina, intelligence, and sensitivity. They were then purchased by the upper classes of the planet for the purpose of parenting and raising a child.

**Telerath** A banking planet noted for its semi-tropical environment, which attracted many tourists. The Telerath Interstellar Banking Initative owned the planet, and mixed its inviting atmosphere with impressive, face-to-face customer service in an effort to draw business away from planets like Aargau. The bank's motto summed up its mission succinctly: "Telerath is what the galaxy forgot it wanted in a bank." Visitors were allowed to arrive unannounced, then meet with an organic representative who could help them with their accounts and inquiries in a low-pressure situation. The only droids on the planet worked as greeters or security units, or served within the massive computer systems that managed the bank's credits. Meetings between individuals and bank representatives were held in outdoor gazebos, eliminating the cold, sterile office environment of most banks. It was later discovered that the planetwide bank was owned by a consortium, including Adascorp, the Czerka Corporation, and the Draay Trust.

**telesponder** A shipboard communications device, it automatically broadcast a craft's identification profile in response to signals sent by spaceports or military authorities. It was also called a transponder.

**Telgorn Corporation** The maker of the Imperial *Gamma*-class assault shuttle and the *Delta*-class DX-9 stormtrooper transport.

*Inside the Teljkon vagabond*

**Teljkon vagabond** The mysterious ghost ship called the Teljkon vagabond was sighted for only the second documented time in the Teljkon system, giving it its name. The ship kept jumping into hyperspace, sometimes after firing at approaching vessels, and finally made a getaway with Lando Calrissian and others aboard. It turned out that the ship was a key instrument in rebuilding the long-dead planet of Brath Qella, which had been hit by one of its moons, iced over, and later renamed Maltha Obex. The ancient Qella had realized that the moon would strike their planet, buried themselves deep in the ground in a state of suspended animation, and constructed an organic starship to eventually return, thaw out the planet, and restore them to life. Luke Skywalker discovered how to use the ship for its intended purpose—a tool for rebuilding a destroyed world.

***Tellivar Lady*** A transport ship, it made regular runs to Tatooine under the command of Captain Fane.

**Telltrig-7** A type of small blaster.

**Telos** A planet known for its technological innovations, most of which were developed in the centuries following the Great Sith War. Telos was a rich planet with many natural beauties. It had a thriving tourist trade and business interests, and was renowned for its innovative tech industry and its interest in culture and the arts. In the year 3960 before the Battle of Yavin, Admiral Saul Karath led the Sith fleet there and devastated its surface, killing millions, after the planet refused to surrender. The Republic started a planetary recovery effort, installing Citadel Station in orbit to house the Ithorians in charge of Telos's terraforming. Using a complex shield network, the Ithorians divided the surface of the planet into restoration zones, where flora and fauna from across the galaxy—including dangerous wild beasts such as the cannok from the jungle moon of Dxun—were introduced into a controlled environment. About 12 years before the Battle of Naboo, the former Jedi Knight Xanatos schemed to exploit the natural resources of Telos in exchange for personal power. Only the intervention of Qui-Gon Jinn and Obi-Wan Kenobi thwarted Xanatos's plans and helped return the planet to its rightful government.

*Telos*

**Tels, Seggor** A Quarren, he admitted to betraying his homeworld of Mon Calamari by lowering the planet's shields and enabling the Empire to invade and enslave its inhabitants. Yet Seggor Tels also helped organize his people to stand with the Mon Calamarians to try to repel the invaders. Tels was jealous of Mon Calamarians, but felt shame for his actions and decided to remain on the planet while many of his fellow Quarren fled.

**Telti** This moon was the site of a series of droid factories run by failed Jedi academy student Brakiss that Dark Jedi Kueller used to manufacture droids fitted with bombs and detonators. Kueller planned to use the droids in his campaign of terror against the New Republic. Telti had no atmosphere and no native life. The surface was covered by domed buildings and metal landing strips; a series of interconnected tunnels ran underground. Telti joined the Empire late in the Galactic Civil War, only after Palpatine threatened to destroy it. Its factories continued to sell droids to anyone whose credit was good, and except for the Imperial threat, the moon's politics remained neutral. After the truce at Bakura, Telti petitioned the New Republic for membership, and it remained a quiet, stable member.

Luke Skywalker came to Telti to find Brakiss, who told Luke of Kueller's scheme, and Luke left to confront Kueller at Almania. Later, Cole Fardreamer, R2-D2, and C-3PO also arrived at Telti to question Brakiss about the droids on Coruscant that had been discovered to be wired with detonators. On Telti, they beat back a terrifying gladiator-droid group known as the Red Terror. At the last instant, R2 disabled the master signal that Kueller beamed from Almania, which would have detonated all new-model droids in existence.

***Temblor*** Padawan Mace Windu once fought against pirates on this sailing ship from Wroona.

**Temm, Pol** A male Kel Dor who operated the Wheel space station during the years following the Sith–Imperial War. Temm agreed to host a meeting between Admiral Gar Stazi and Captain Mingo Bovark aboard the Wheel, hoping to curry favor with both sides of the growing conflict. The negotiations might have yielded a true alliance had not Morrigan Corde and Jor Torlin intervened. The pair of secret agents sabotaged the diplomats' ships, using Command Override limpet droids to take control of each ship's weapons and make them fire on each other.

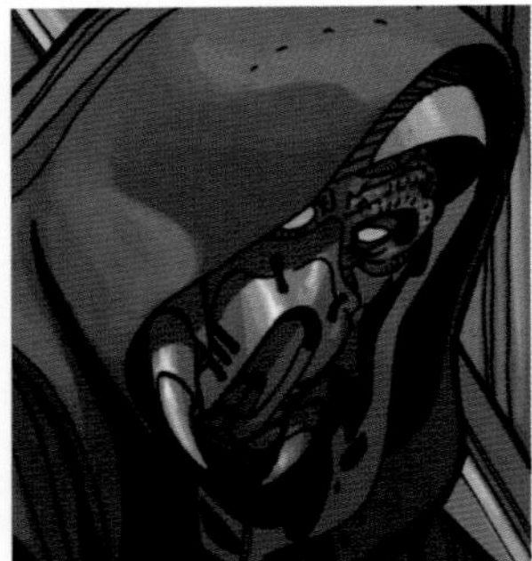

*Pol Temm*

**Tempest Force** The AT-AT assault group assigned to the Battle of Endor. Tempest Force consisted of at least one AT-AT and seven AT-STs. Tempest 1 was the command vehicle for Commander Ingar. Tempest Scout 1, piloted by Lieutenant Arnet, was assigned as first responder to incidents at the control bunker on Endor. Tempest Scout 2 was tasked with coordinating battle activities with the Endor biker scout detachment. Tempest Scout 3 was assigned to search for potential Rebel traps on Endor. Tempest Scout 4 was equipped with a prototype targeting computer. Tempest Scout 5 used experimental command-and-control software to coordinate combat data. Tempest Scout 6 was modified for perimeter patrol. Tempest Scout 7 was the AT-ST captured by Chewbacca.

**tempest spice** A narcotic developed on Nar Shaddaa and produced on Varl by Mika the Hutt during the early years of the New Order. The purple spice was noted for providing users increased willpower and physical strength—but at a heavy price. Addicts experienced a loss of self-control and sanity, and many died from their addiction.

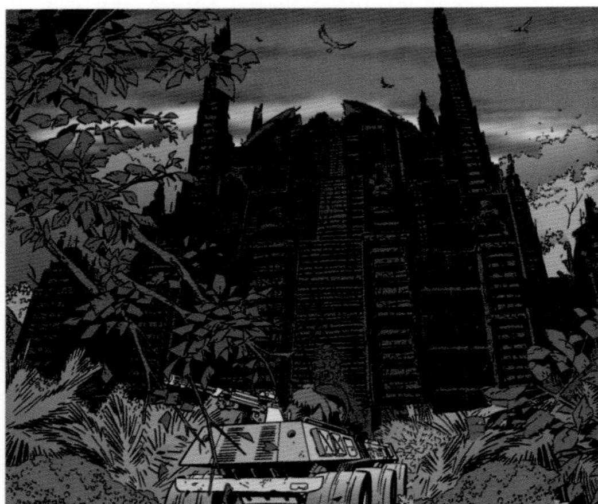

*Temple of Pomojema*

**Temple of Fire** A Massassi temple on Yavin 4. Some four millennia before the Galactic Civil War, it had been used as an arena by the Massassi to test the skills of fallen Jedi Exar Kun before he could become their leader.

**Temple of Pomojema** A temple on the planet Mimban, it was a shrine to the Mimbanite god Pomojema. The legendary Kaiburr crystal was kept in this stone ziggurat supported by obsidian pillars. A stone icon representing the god—a winged humanoid with talons and a faceless head—was displayed for the faithful. The temple was the site of Luke Skywalker's first duel with Darth Vader.

**Temple of the Blueleaf Cluster** An ancient Massassi temple on Yavin 4, it was pyramid-shaped and located just southeast of the Great Temple at the junction of two rivers.

**tempter** A creature on the Forest Moon of Endor, it lived in the hollows of large trees. A tempter looked like a long, blunt eel with pale, fleshy skin that was covered with a thick mucus, which allowed it to slither into tight spots and then strike its prey after luring it close with a furry tongue.

**Tendo, Liekas** A Morath mining engineer, he was taken as a Yevethan hostage during the attack on the Koornacht Cluster settlements led by Nil Spaar.

**Tendor virus** A deadly virus that threatened to wipe out the entire Caldoni system until a cure was discovered by Jenna Zan Arbor.

**Tendrando Arms** The name of the droid-manufacturing company cofounded by Lando Calrissian and his wife, Tendra Risant. Tendrando Arms manufactured the YVH war droid to fight the Yuuzhan Vong.

**Tenloss Syndicate** A criminal outfit, it operated in the Bajic sector, working closely with the main criminal organization Black Sun. Its governing board was called the Leukish. Its reach extended across 64 major star systems in five sectors, and it was involved in everything from gambling to assassination.

**tentacle bush** A low-lying plant that grew on the planet Arzid, it had grasping tentacles that snatched small creatures and delivered them to the main bush for digestion.

*Temple of Fire*

**tentacle cactus** A spiny, semi-mobile plant, it waved its tentacles to capture small prey. An example was on display in the Skydome Botanical Gardens on Coruscant.

*Temple of the Blueleaf Cluster*

**Tenupe** This planet, located in the Unknown Regions of the galaxy, was located at one end of the Sparkle Run. It served as a primary hyperspace jump point for the transports of the Killik Colony and was on the front lines of the border conflict that erupted between the Chiss and the Killiks during the Swarm War. The planet itself had little to offer besides its dense jungles of mogo trees, but the Battle of Tenupe was fought over the Chiss hope that they could cut off the Colony's shipments. The battle was waged for weeks before its eventual resolution. Tenupe lacked any form of oceans or seas, and runoff from the mountains traveled downward in rivers before draining into wide basins. The planet was orbited by a single satellite known as the Shattered Moon.

**Tenupe, Battle of** This was considered the final battle of the

*Tempter*

Colony's struggle with the Chiss some five years after the Yuuzhan Vong War, although there was no clear victory in the fighting. The Chiss attacked Tenupe in the hope of capturing it, thereby cutting off the Colony from its sources of supplies and war matériel. However, the Colony was ready for such an attack, and had the advantage of a near-endless supply of soldiers. The Chiss had superior firepower, and were able to blast their way to the surface of Tenupe and establish several strongholds, but they were continually deluged by the sheer number of Killiks in the Great Swarm. Nevertheless, the Chiss held their positions through determination and tactics, and neither side was able to gain an advantage. In order to better observe the Killiks, the Chiss used defoliants to eliminate the jungle canopy created by Tenupe's mogo trees, but this proved to be of little assistance. Ultimately, both sides lost millions of soldiers in the fighting, and the landscape was literally covered by layers of dead bodies. The fighting came to a halt when Luke Skywalker managed to eliminate Lomi Plo and convince UnuThul to separate himself from the Colony. Both sides were forced to retreat to their worlds and recover from their losses.

**Teppler, Denjax** This man, the former husband of Five World Prime Minister Aidel Saxan, was chosen to serve as the interim Prime Minister when Aidel was murdered at Toryaz Station. He was stymied by his advisers and rivals during the first days of his tenure, since he lacked any political clout. This made Teppler little more than a puppet, a fact that he reiterated to Han and Leia Organa Solo when they met with him a few days after the assassination. In the aftermath of Thrackan Sal-Solo's murder, Teppler assumed the role of Corellia's Minister of Justice, serving under the newly appointed Prime Minister Dur Gejjen. To protect himself, Teppler hired a body double to move about in public.

Terak

After Gejjen's assassination, Teppler became one of Sadras Koyan's closest aides, and also served as Corellia's Minister of Information. The pair developed a daring plan to kill Jacen Solo by taking control of Centerpoint Station and using it to destroy Solo's flagship. The attempt to assassinate Solo from a distance failed, and although much of the Galactic Alliance's Second Fleet was destroyed, the Corellian warships sent to the rendezvous point also were all but wiped out. In the wake of this act, Teppler went into hiding in Koyan's command bunker on Corellia. This gave him an opportunity to contact Turr Phennir, the Supreme Commander of the military forces of the Confederation, in an effort to talk the commander into removing the embargo. He was surprised when Phennir suggested that they remove Sadras Koyan from power. Their opportunity came during Jacen Solo's attempt to take control of Centerpoint Station. Teppler truthfully alerted Koyan to the presence of enemies aboard the station, then sent the Prime Minister to a false destination.

Terentatek

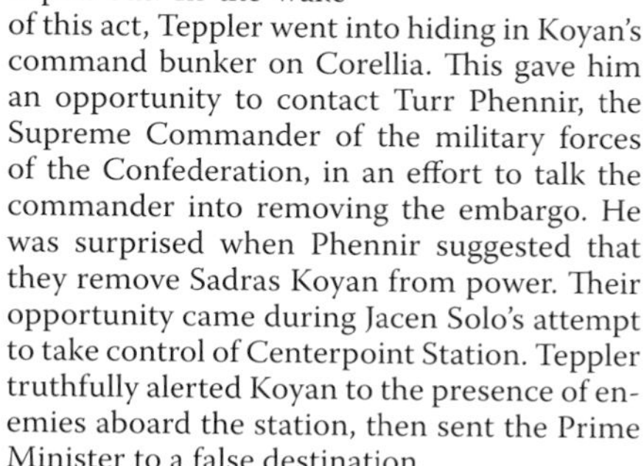

**Teradoc, High Admiral** An overweight Imperial warlord, he preferred to squat in his bunker behind incredibly thick shielding while his minions fought major battles. In the wake of the Battle of Endor, Teradoc took his fleet and established a stronghold in the Mid Rim. After Zsinj's death at Dathomir, Teradoc declared himself the High Admiral of the Mid Rim, and set about trying to consolidate his base of power. He was constantly trying to win control of the remaining Imperial fleet from Supreme Warlord Harrsk, and used his crimson-colored fleet of *Victory*-class Star Destroyers to take out Harrsk's flagship, the *Shockwave*, during Harrsk's talks with Admiral Daala. He was one of 13 squabbling warlords poisoned by Admiral Daala at Tsoss Beacon after they refused to stop their internal strife and get on with the fight against the New Republic.

**Terak** A cruel and evil king, he led the Sanyassan Marauders who preyed upon the inhabitants of Endor's Forest Moon.

**teräs käsi** A form of hand-to-hand combat, roughly translated into "steel hands," that was taught in the Pacanth Reach, a remote star cluster in the Outer Rim. A mystical form of martial arts, it was long practiced on the planet Bunduki, where it was taught by the Followers of Palawa. Its practitioners also studied history, philosophy, and metaphysical subjects.

**terentatek** This unusual creature was native to the planet Korriban, and had been twisted into a grotesque form by practitioners of the dark side of the Force. It was believed that the first terentateks were created by Exar Kun as part of his plan to reestablish the Sith Empire and return it to its Golden Age. The ancient Sith Lords used terentateks to guard the tombs that were carved into the Valley of the Dark Lords. Following Exar Kun's defeat, the Jedi exterminated all remaining terentateks in what was known as the Great Hunt.

**Terephon** A planet with dark blue skies in the Hapes Cluster, it was the homeworld of Captain Astarta, Prince Isolder's personal bodyguard.

***Termagant*** An Imperial Strike cruiser allied with Warlord Zsinj, it was reconfigured from a troop carrier to a TIE fighter carrier. The *Termagant* was torn in half by a volley of proton torpedoes from Rogue Squadron in retaliation for its part in the destruction of a bacta convoy in the Alderaan system.

**Teroenza** This t'landa Til was employed by Zavval the Hutt to act as the Most Exalted High Priest of Ylesia. In this position, he was actually in charge of obtaining slave labor to process the Hutts' spice for distribution. Teroenza maintained a lavish suite of offices and used his resources to amass a wonderful collection of artifacts from across the galaxy. It was Teroenza who sent out a request for a pilot to transfer Ylesian colonists to and from the planet, as well as to transport spice to the Hutts. He chose Vykk Drago, who was actually a young Han Solo. Working with Bria Tharen, Solo managed to destroy a major processing facility and escape, but not before stealing much of Teroenza's art collection and killing Zavval. Teroenza was forced to put out a bounty on Solo's head. When Teroenza's role in the death of Aruk the Hutt came to light, Boba Fett killed him and claimed the bounty by removing his horn as proof.

**Terpfen** A Mon Calamari, he was Admiral Ackbar's chief mechanic—and a hidden pawn of Imperial Ambassador Furgan. While he was an Imperial prisoner, Terpfen had part of his brain replaced, compelling him to carry out secret orders and report information back to Imperial forces. Terpfen sabotaged Admiral Ackbar's B-wing fighter, causing it to crash into the Cathedral of Winds on Vortex. He also gave Ambassador Furgan information regarding the secret location of Anakin Solo, the infant son of Han and Leia Organa Solo. Finally able to overcome his programming, Terpfen stole a B-wing fighter and flew it to Yavin 4 to inform Leia of the danger to Anakin. Terpfen accompanied Ackbar and Leia to Anoth, where he fought against Furgan in one

Terpfen (left) was Admiral Ackbar's chief mechanic.

of the Imperials' MT-ATs, at last defeating the ambassador. So great was Terpfen's despair that he would have committed suicide had Ackbar not interceded. Forgiven, Terpfen was accepted back as a loyal member of the New Republic.

**Terrafin, Kodu** An Arcona, he made the courier run between Jabba the Hutt's desert palace on Tatooine and the crime lord's Mos Eisley town house.

**terrain-following sensor** A device that let ships fly parallel to the ground at a fixed height. It worked in conjunction with a vehicle's propulsion and flight-control systems. A terrain-following sensor automatically adjusted a ship's course to avoid obstacles and compensate for changing terrain.

**Terra Sool** A planet noted for its agriculture and idyllic cloudscapes, it was the site of a major Separatist emplacement at the height of the Clone Wars. Unusual, repulsor-equipped battle platforms were placed in low orbit around Terra Sool, hiding in the clouds. The disk-shaped platforms were studded with turbolasers and crewed by battle droids. The combined efforts of Anakin Skywalker and Obi-Wan Kenobi were able to destroy the battle platforms before they could raze the surface of the planet. The clouds of Terra Sool were inhabited by a species of dragon-like avian creatures.

**Terrik, Booster** A native of Corellia, and a smuggler and starship-pilot-for-hire during the height of the Empire. His wife died shortly after the birth of their daugther Mirax, and Terrik was forced to raise her aboard the star yacht *Pulsar Skate* on his own. Following the death of Wedge Antilles's parents on Gus Treta, Terrik helped Wedge hunt down the pirates that caused the incident; later, CorSec officer Hal Horn caught up with Terrik and sentenced him to five years on Kessel. Terrik lost his left eye while on Kessel, and had a cybernetic replacement inserted in its place. When Mirax became involved with Rogue Squadron—and romantically involved with Corran Horn, the son of the man who'd sent him to Kessel—Terrik helped create a smugglers' haven in the space station orbiting Yag'Dhul, in an effort to keep the Rogues hidden after they resigned from New Republic service. In a battle at Yag'Dhul, Terrik was able to capture the Star Destroyer *Virulence*. As a reward for his heroism and smart thinking, Terrik was given the *Virulence* under salvage laws, and he renamed it the *Errant Venture*. He then turned the vessel into a huge, floating store for smugglers and pilots.

Terrik was called upon to assist the New Republic during the hunt for the Caamas Document. The *Errant Venture* was to become the *Tyrannic*, as part of a ploy to recover a copy of the document from Yaga Minor. They were nearly captured in the attempt, but the intervention of Admiral Pellaeon swayed the battle to the Republic's side. When the Yuuzhan Vong invaded the galaxy, Terrik took the *Errant Venture* and went into hiding. When Jaina and Jacen Solo contacted him about assisting in the rescue of the Jedi students on Yavin 4, Terrik agreed to house the students until a safer training facility could be set up. Age eventually caught up to Terrik, and he was forced to use a massive hoverchair to help him move about. After Wedge was nearly assassinated in the wake of Corellia's failed attempt to kill the Hapan Queen Mother, Terrik gladly took in his friend, along with Antilles's family. He also agreed to let the Jedi Order, which had split from the Galactic Alliance, use the *Errant Venture* as a deep-space staging area for a mission to Centerpoint Station.

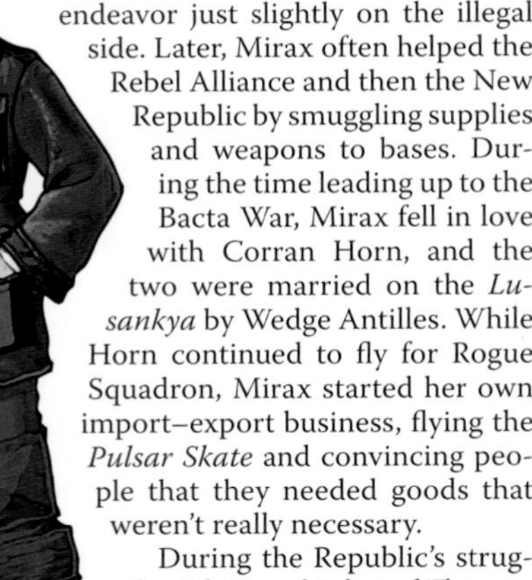

Booster Terrik

**Terrik, Captain Mod** A cold, cruel Imperial officer, he supervised part of Davin Felth's stormtrooper training as captain of the Imperial Desert Sands sandtrooper unit on Tatooine. The unit was assigned to search for two runaway droids in the Dune Sea. He traced them to a group of Jawas, whom he pumped for information and then killed. Next, he went to the homestead of Owen and Beru Lars, and after fruitless questioning killed them, too. When Captain Terrik was about to stop Han Solo's escape from Mos Eisley, Felth shot him in the back and killed him.

**Terrik, Mirax** A native of the planet Corellia and the daughter of Booster Terrik. As a young woman, Mirax served as part of the crew of the *Pulsar Skate*. As a youth, she often stayed with the family of Wedge Antilles. Later, when her father tried to help Antilles track down the pirates who were responsible for his parents' deaths, Wedge and Mirax became good friends. When Booster was sent to prison on Kessel, Mirax took over her father's businesses, turning his operations into a profit-generating endeavor just slightly on the illegal side. Later, Mirax often helped the Rebel Alliance and then the New Republic by smuggling supplies and weapons to bases. During the time leading up to the Bacta War, Mirax fell in love with Corran Horn, and the two were married on the *Lusankya* by Wedge Antilles. While Horn continued to fly for Rogue Squadron, Mirax started her own import–export business, flying the *Pulsar Skate* and convincing people that they needed goods that weren't really necessary.

During the Republic's struggle with Grand Admiral Thrawn, Mirax used the business as a cover to rescue refugees from worlds Thrawn had subjugated. When Leonia Tavira started her pirate raids, Mirax was captured and held on Suarbi 7/5 until a rescue by Horn and Luke Skywalker. In the following years, Corran and Mirax settled down to a somewhat normal life, raising two children. However, when Thrackan Sal-Solo made a bid for Corellian independence some 10 years after the Yuuzhan Vong War, they found themselves in a precarious political position. Corran was Corellian, but he was also a loyal Jedi Master. Mirax was a smuggler whose skills were needed to keep supplies moving to Corellia, but she was married to a Jedi. To ensure her loyalty, Mirax was placed under house arrest, but was treated like a vacationing tourist to keep her happy. Corran remained loyal to the Jedi, and was forced into hiding to save his own life. They agreed to come out of hiding in the wake of the failed assassination attempt on the life of the Hapan Queen Mother, Tenel Ka, when Wedge was forced out of his position as Supreme Commander and nearly killed. Mirax and Corran agreed to help Iella and Myri Antilles rescue Wedge and get him offplanet. The group fled to the Kuat system, where they met up with Booster Terrik and the *Errant Venture*. While Corran worked with the others, Mirax spent time with her father, catching up on the events in his life while using his network of informants to learn more

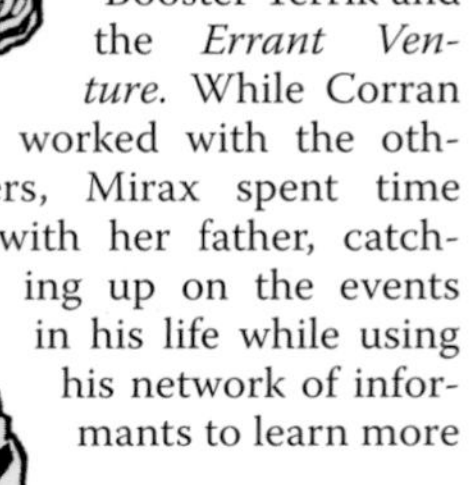

Mirax Terrik

Tessek

about what was going on behind the scenes of the war.

**terrodaak** A native creature of Kohlma, long revered by the Bando Gora as a guardian of the dead. When Kohlma served as a burial moon for cataclysmic war in the Bogden system, the terrodaaks' piercing wails struck fear into the hearts of the groundskeepers and funeral barge pilots. The creatures seemed to be under Komari Vosa's spell, and patrolled the sky near her hidden temple.

***Terror*** A Super Star Destroyer commanded by Admiral Sarn, and the headquarters of the Phantom TIE project. The *Terror* had a cloaking device, but was ultimately destroyed by Rebel saboteurs.

**Tervissis** The homeworld of the species known as Tervigs, who sold members of the semi-intelligent species known as Bandies—also from Tervissis—to the galaxy as slaves. Nine years after the Battle of Endor, the New Republic Galactic Court convened a trial of Tervig Bandie slavers.

Empress Teta

**Teshik, Grand Admiral Osvald** The Grand Admiral in charge of Core World space security. Osvald Teshik was a cyborg injured during a doomed mission against the Hapan war fleet. Until the Battle of Yavin, Azure Hammer Command and Anaxes Citadel answered to Teshik. He was aboard the second Death Star during the Battle of Endor, and was rescued after being pinned down by a fallen durasteel column. He promptly returned to his Star Destoyer, the *Eleemosynary,* but after three hours the ship was disabled and captured. The New Republic executed him for atrocities.

Grand Admiral Osvald Teshik

**Tessek** A Quarren, or "Squid Head," he fled his homeworld of Mon Calamari after an Imperial invasion and ended up as an accountant for crime lord Jabba the Hutt on Tatooine. At times, Tessek's conscience bothered him, and he plotted to get away with both his life and part of a secret fortune still intact. He set Jabba up to be killed by an Imperial inspection party, but Jabba learned of his plot and planned to wait him out. When Tessek heard that, he killed the messenger, a B'omarr monk whose brain was housed in a large spider-shaped droid. Tessek's plans were further compromised when Jabba insisted that he accompany his party out to the Great Pit of Carkoon to execute a number of Rebels. The Rebels, led by Luke Skywalker, had other plans. Tessek escaped just as Jabba's sail barge was blown up. He returned to the Hutt's palace, where some of the dead monk's associates cornered him. They turned him into a monk himself by laser-cutting his brain out of his body and sticking it into a nutrient jar atop a spider droid.

**Tessent** A mysterious chalcedony idol long sought by treasure seekers in the Modell sector. Lore indicated there were two Tessents: both were birds with feline heads. One was attributed to the Ayrou of Maya Kovel, the other a representation of the guardian of the ancient Kings of Archais.

**Tesser** This X'Ting warrior was the first of Jesson Di Blinth's hive-brothers to attempt to locate the hidden eggs of the royal line during the last years of the Old Republic. Tesser had managed to penetrate the Hall of Heroes, but was unprepared for the attacks of the huge worms hidden beneath it. Tesser was unable to defeat the worms, so he strapped himself to a high crevice and waited for another chance to escape. Unfortunately, no such chance ever came, and no other X'Ting could locate him; Tesser died in this position. Jesson discovered his body during his own attempt to locate the eggs.

**Tessra, Captain Lun** The commander of a squadron of the 37th Imperial Fighter Wing aboard the *Abrogator* during the early years of the New Order. His pilots, who included Soontir Fel, felt little loyalty to him during the Reslian Purge because Tessra was a short-timer and held back in order to avoid being killed.

Duke Teta

**Teta, Duke** A Coruscant resident kept alive through illicit medication and gray-market organ transplants. Duke Teta was close to 300 years old, yet still made it a point to be seen at public events with a beautiful companion. Teta attended shows at the Galaxies Opera House near the end of the Clone Wars.

**Teta, Empress** A long-lived female warlord many millennia ago, she conquered and united the seven planets of what became known as the Empress Teta system.

**Teta system, Empress** *See* Empress Teta system.

**Teth** During the Clone Wars, Anakin Skywalker and his Padawan Ahsoka Tano went on a mission to Teth to rescue the young son of Jabba the Hutt, who had been kidnapped by Separatists. They were greeted by a large force of battledroids and heavy armor, but made it inside a fortress where they found the Huttlet—but it was a trap sprung by Asajj Ventress. The trio managed to flee before Obi-Wan Kenobi arrived; he dueled Ventress inside Teth castle.

Moff Sarn Shild ruled Teth during the Empire from a palatial estate on the planet, and used it as a gathering place for the fleet that attacked Nar Shaddaa. Teth's location, in the Outer Rim Territories, near both the Corporate Sector and Hutt space, led its leaders to believe that it was safe from Imperial domination. Bria Tharen met with the planet's leaders, hoping to incite them to open rebellion, but she failed. Boba Fett tracked her there, but lost her when she left the meeting.

Teth

Raana Tey

**Tetsus** A peaceful clan of Rodians, its members were forced to flee their planet to escape the more war-like Chattza clan.

**Tevv, Sian** This councillor from Sullust was responsible for bringing Nien Nunb and his raiding squad into the Rebel Alliance after the Empire forced them out of the Sullust system. He was a rebel from the start, hanging around with spacers and technicians in order to learn more about starships and droids. This dismayed his parents, who were Sullustan diplomats. One of his first friends was another Sullustan youth, Nien Nunb, who taught Tevv a great deal about starships. Eventually, though, Tevv went to school and became a diplomat like his parents. He was known as one of the youngest Sullustan diplomats to ever travel to Coruscant. However, while he was there, he witnessed firsthand the real power behind the Empire, as the Senators debated over policy changes while the military subjugated world after world. He decided that Sullust would have to join the Alliance if it truly wanted to be free. At first, Tevv was worried about what open rebellion would mean for his people. In early talks with Bria Tharen, he and Jennsar SoBilles felt that rebellion would simply mean powerful reprisal from the Empire. He was later one of the signers of the Declaration of a New Republic. Tevv then contracted the Krytos virus while on Coruscant shortly after the planet was liberated from Ysanne Isard. He didn't show any symptoms, but underwent preventive bacta treatment to maintain his health. Because of his various dealings with the Provisional Council, Tevv was considered a possible suspect in the Delta Source leak, although he was never charged with any crimes. His innocence was proven when the ch'hala trees near the Imperial Palace were discovered to be the source of the leaks.

**Tey, Raana** This female Togruta was one of the Jedi Masters who taught at the satellite training facility on Taris during the years following the Great Sith War. Among the Covenant, Master Raana was known as an exceptionally gifted seer who could sense vivid images of the future through the Force. Unknown to her students, Raana Tey was part of Master Lucien Draay's plan to murder all the Padawans under their tutelage. Only Zayne Carrick escaped, having arrived late to a ceremony that the Padawans believed was to elevate them to the ranks of Jedi Knight. Carrick fled, forcing Master Lucien and the other instructors to blame the murders on Carrick in order to cover their tracks.

A holographic recording discovered in the memory banks of the labor droid T1-LB revealed that Master Raana had experienced an intense vision through the Force in which Sith Lords dressed in armored environment suits swept through the galaxy and laid waste to the Jedi Order. During a training mission to the Rogue Moon, Raana was sickened to see the Padawans arrive in environment suits that were similar to those she recalled from her vision. When she shared this information with her fellow Jedi Masters, they set in motion their plan to eliminate their Padawans.

After Carrick escaped their grasp, Master Raana and the other Masters were recalled to Coruscant by the Jedi Order to bolster the Republic's forces as the Mandalorian Wars reached their height. During the trip through hyperspace, Master Raana's health began to fail as her visions became more and more intrusive. The medication she took to help her sleep only caused more problems, and she was forced to stay awake as long as possible. During one intense vision in which she returned to the Taris academy as a youngling, Master Raana came to the conclusion that she had to kill Carrick and the Arkanian offshoot Jarael in order to end her visions and give herself some rest.

Thakwaash

**Teyr** A busy, crowded, and bureaucratic world located at the crossroads of three highly traveled hyperspace routes, it was 34 light-years from Vulvarch. The Teyr Rift, a 4,000-kilometer-long canyon slashing across the planet's face, made the world a popular tourist destination. The increasing number of visitors made citizens fear a huge increase in immigration. So the Citizen Services Corps created a welter of incomprehensible regulations and red tape to discourage anyone from staying once their tourist dollars had been spent. Huge orbital parking stations accommodated arriving traffic. The Rift Skyrail, an incredibly fast aboveground train, connected all points in the Rift Territory with one another.

The Fallanassi, religious followers of the White Current, were zealously persecuted on Lucazec. The elders sent five children to other planets, including Teyr, for safekeeping. The Fallanassi later bought a starliner called the *Star Morning* but departed Teyr a few months before the Battle of Endor.

Commander Pter Thanas

**Teyr, Battle of** This was one of the many battles that occurred during the Clone Wars. Just before the fighting began, a Trade Federation battleship had been forced to crash-land on Teyr, and the survivors used the wreckage as a base of operations. Although the Old Republic dispatched Jedi Master K'Kruhk and a squadron of clone troopers, the Separatists used homing spider droids to draw them into the Great Canyon and decimate them. Only K'Kruhk survived the attack, and Teyr fell to the Separatists. K'Kruhk refused to return to Coruscant, instead joining a group of rogue Jedi led by Sora Bulq.

***Thackery*** A New Republic ship, it was deployed for duty at Galantos in the Farlax sector, a territory that was feared to be in danger of a Yevethan attack.

**Thakwaash** An intelligent species from Thakwaa. Thakwaash were reclusive bipeds with equine heads who typically exhibited multiple personalities. One Thakwaash had the strength of three humans. Hohass "Runt" Ekwesh, a New Republic starfighter pilot, was a Thakwaash.

**Thalassian slavers**  An undisciplined group of pirates whose ships included the *Harmzuay* and the Y164 Thalassian slave transport *Arkanian Dawn.* Thalassians hailed from the Thalassian system in the Outer Rim. The Thalassian Slavers Guild also manufactured slaving collars.

**Thanas, Commander Pter** This middle-aged Imperial commander was assigned to the defense force of Bakura as punishment for refusing to carry out an order. He had declined to wipe out a village to stop enslaved miners from complaining about lowered food rations. Commander Pter Thanas was a loyal and hardworking officer, but he could not brook such genocide.

When the Ssi-ruuvi Imperium attacked Bakura, Thanas's garrison sent out a plea for help, unaware that the second Death Star had just been destroyed along with Emperor Palpatine. The Rebel Alliance answered the call. Thanas was impressed with the Rebels, especially Luke Skywalker, and the two sides worked out a truce to battle their common enemy. When the Ssi-ruuk fled, Thanas turned on the Rebels, but his ship, the *Dominant,* blew out its lateral thrusters and was immobilized. Faced with destruction or surrender, Thanas chose the latter and defected to the Alliance. He later married Gaeriel Captison, and they had a daughter named Malinza. Eighteen years after the Battle of Yavin, Luke Skywalker learned that Thanas had died of Knowt's disease.

**Thanas, Malinza** The daughter of Gaeriel Captison and Pter Thanas. After Gaeriel's death, Luke pledged to keep Malinza safe. Malinza later accepted a prodigy chair with the Bakuran National Symphony. Luke still felt responsible for the girl, even though she was adopted by a well-placed Bakuran family. At age 15, Malinza was arrested for being a member of the terrorist organization "Freedom" that was attempting to disrupt the treaty between the P'w'eck and Bakura.

**Thanda** A clan of Zygerrian slavers infamous for their daring and cruelty during the early years of the New Order.

**Thane, Archon Beed** The archon of Vergill during Leia Organa Solo's mission to Hapes at the time of the Yuuzhan Vong War. Archon Beed Thane was one of the Hapes Consortium's few male delegates. After losing a duel with Prince Isolder, he agreed to support the New Republic in the war against the Yuuzhan Vong. He also hoped to obtain the New Republic's quick-recharge turbolaser technology.

**Thanos** A blue-white star orbited by Togoria, homeworld of the Togorians.

**Thanta Zilbra** The name of a star, its system, and its primary planet. Thanta Zilbra was the second star destroyed during the Corellian incident, and Wedge Antilles assisted in the New Republic evacuation of the planet's settlement. The evacuation force greatly underestimated Thanta Zilbra's population of nearly 15,000, and thousands were left behind when the star went nova.

***Tharen*** A Rebel Alliance escort frigate.

**Tharen, Bria** Han Solo's first love and one of the early architects of the Rebel Alliance. Bria Tharen was born to a wealthy shipping family in southern Corellia. At a young age, an arrangement was made in which she'd be married to an upper-class man of good breeding,

*Bria Tharen*

but the independent-minded Tharen wanted to travel the stars and better herself by studying archaeology at the University of Coruscant. At the age of 17 she fell in with a cult promising the life-changing effects of the "Exultation." In truth, it was a sham—a simple biological reaction to the harmonic stimulations produced by t'landa Til priests. Addicted to the powerful sensations, Tharen followed the cult to its headquarters on Ylesia, where she was enslaved in a spice-processing facility. Tharen was shown the truth by the young spice pilot, Han Solo. The two fled Ylesia, with optimistic plans to carve out a new life together. On Coruscant, Tharen abruptly left Solo, breaking his heart.

It was during this time that she became involved in local Corellian resistance movements challenging the Empire. She formed one of the earliest Rebel groups, the Red Hand Squadron, a team of operatives that worked from the *Marauder*-class corvette *Retribution.* The Red Hand quickly grew a reputation for ruthlessness, particularly against slaver groups. Bria was instrumental in helping forge early Rebel cells. On Cloud City, she met with Alderaanian resistance leaders to urge them to form a Rebel Alliance. She also met with the Wookiee underworld on Kashyyyk. Turning to her contacts on the fringes of society, Tharen developed a plan that would wipe out the Ylesia slaving operation while also spreading riches to the smuggler community. She forged a deal with Jabba the Hutt that enabled Rebel soldiers to join with Nar Shaddaa smugglers—although she double-crossed the smugglers by making off with Ylesian riches to help fund the Rebellion. And, for the first time in a decade, Tharen got to fight alongside Han Solo.

Bria Tharen and her Red Hand Squadron were the ones who received the Death Star schematics when they were transmitted to Toprawa, and then beamed those plans to Princess Leia Organa aboard the *Tantive IV.* Imperial forces overran Tharen and her Rebel spies. Knowing that she would be tortured if captured, she swallowed a poison pill and died before the Imperials could touch her.

***Tharen Wayfarer*** A ship owned by the Pitareeze family, it was home for a while to the droids R2-D2 and C-3PO before the start of the Rebellion.

**Theed** Naboo's affluent capital city, it was situated near a waterfall created by the River Solleu. Considered one of Naboo's crowning achievements, Theed was a wondrous testament to the numerous artisans and architects who had brought the metropolis to life. It was known for its grand libraries, museums, theaters, and other cultural buildings. The design flourishes on all structures typified the Naboo architectural style. While the city was large, it fit perfectly within its environment, evidence of a strong commitment to ecological conservation. Theed was founded 800 years before the Battle of Naboo. As a result of the quick capitulation of its populace during the Trade Federation invasion, Theed's buildings and monuments remained relatively unscathed. During the liberation of Theed, the resistance fighters used a hazardous network of underground passages to infiltrate their own city. Other places of interest in the city included Virdugo Plunge (the largest waterfall in Theed), the Ellié Arcadium, the Hall of Perri-Teek (a monument to a legendary statesman), Pergola's Bridge, Broadberry Meadow, Guido's Tower (one of Theed's oldest buildings), the Royal Academy, Yram's Needle, the Parnelli Museum of Art, and the Triumphal Arch.

*Theed*

**Theed quoits** This garden sport was developed on the planet Naboo, where it was a popular pastime in the capital city of Theed. The sport involved throwing metal rings at a stake or pole located in a small body of water. This stake was set on a dish-like platform, and the object of the game was to toss the rings so that they completely encircled the stake. Scoring was based on the number of rings around the stake, with secondary scoring based on those rings that landed on the platform. Any missed throws had to be retrieved from the water. Because many aquatic predators were native to the waters

Tharen Wayfarer

Theelin

of Naboo, this was often a risky manevuer, and forced players to make the most accurate throws possible.

**Theelin** A near-extinct humanoid species. Smuggler Shug Ninx of Nar Shaddaa had Theelin blood; his mother was one of the last of her kind. The Theelin were known for their Divas religious order.

**Thel-Tanis, Darra** The Padawan of Soara Antana. Darra Thel-Tanis was the same age as Anakin Skywalker. She had lively, rust-colored eyes and a piece of bright fabric woven through her long Padawan braid, which she chewed on when she was stressed. She was adept at using her lightsaber in either hand. Thel-Tanis was involved in the mission to Haariden and was wounded in battle. She was later killed by Granta Omega during a mission to Korriban.

Thermal detonator

**Therans** A group on Nam Chorios who were consulted by Oldtimers for healing and advice. Theran Listeners controlled the planet's ancient gun stations and would not allow outside trade. They opposed Seti Ashgad's Rationalist Party, which wanted such trade. The Therans' original leader was a male prophet named Theras. While he slept one night, the planet's Force crystals entered his mind and reinforced the idea that outside contact should be forbidden. He then ordered that no ship large enough to have heavy shielding ever be permitted to land on Nam Chorios. This also prevented the Death Seed plague from escaping offworld.

Thermal cape

**thermal cape** A lightweight metal-foil and spider-silk composite poncho, it retained the wearer's body heat to provide protection from the cold. Thermal capes, also called thermal wraps, were normally standard equipment in survival-gear packs.

**thermal coil** *See* condenser unit.

**thermal detonator** A powerful baradium bomb in the form of a small metallic ball, it was activated when the bearer's finger pressure was removed from a trigger, ensuring that any attempt to kill the bomber would cause an explosion. Princess Leia Organa, disguised as the bounty hunter Boushh, threatened Jabba the Hutt's court with a thermal detonator to demonstrate Boushh's nerve and impress the crime lord. She and her fellow Rebels had earlier used the miniature bombs in escaping the clutches of Prince Xizor, head of the Black Sun criminal organization.

Thermosuit

**thermal dissipator** This form of starship counterdetection was developed during the years following the Yuuzhan Vong War. Originally used on the StealthX fighter, the thermal dissipator altered the heat signature produced by the starfighter, reducing or eliminating the ability of most infrared or heat-based sensor systems to detect the craft.

**thermosuit** A thin, lightweight coverall worn over regular clothing, it protected the wearer from temperature extremes.

**thernbee** A large, four-legged creature that lived in the mountains of Almania, it had a smallish face, short ears, a pink nose, a huge pink mouth, and blue eyes the size of small puddles. With broad shoulders and flat backs, thernbees made even a Wookiee look small. The creature's white hair fell out with each movement, and its long, thin tail carried great power when used defensively. Thernbees toyed with their prey, crushing one bone at a time, giving the victim the illusion that escape was possible. The anesthetic in their saliva sapped their victim's will to fight. However, they preferred eating vegetation or small creatures that resembled snakes to any other type of meat.

Luke Skywalker faced a thernbee during his confrontation with Dark Jedi Kueller on Almania, and amid the battle he discovered that thernbees were psychic. The thernbee that Luke encountered had a body only a third the size it should have been; it was slowly starving to death. Skywalker helped ease the creature's pain and gained a new friend for life. When Han Solo introduced several Force-blocking ysalamiri to Almania, the thernbee accidentally ate them, thinking they were its food. However, the thernbee was near enough to Kueller for the ingested ysalamiri to counter Kueller's Force powers, giving Luke and Leia Organa Solo an advantage in battling him.

Thernbee

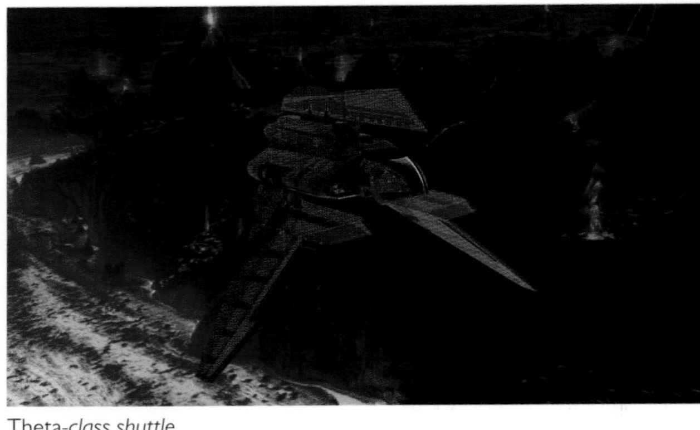

*Theta*-class shuttle

***Theta*-class shuttle** A precursor to the *Lambda*-class shuttle that shared many of its design elements. The *Theta*-class shuttle was originally developed by Cygnus Spaceworks during the years following the Battle of Ruusan, as a transport for diplomats and other luminaries. These early designs were quite luxurious and came with a hefty price tag. Over the following centuries, the Theta became more refined, and several versions were developed for personal, corporate, and military usage. The basic *Theta*-class shuttle measured 18.5 meters in length as well as height, and could accommodate up to 16 passengers and 50 metric tons

of cargo. The ship was equipped with a Class 1 hyperdrive, and was armed with two quad laser cannons and a rear-mounted laser cannon. The lower two wings were triangular and capable of rotating up or down to assist with maneuvering. The upper wing was blade-shaped, and was mounted lengthwise atop the shuttle. Chancellor Palpatine had a specially designed *Theta*-class T-2c shuttle built for his use as Darth Sidious by Cygnus Spaceworks, which was later modified by Warthan's Wizards to Palpatine's own specifications. An emergency medical station helped to keep Darth Vader alive as Palpatine transported him from Mustafar to Coruscant.

*Master Tholme*

**Theta Squad** One of the first groups of clone troopers to be trained as commandos during the buildup to the Clone Wars. Theta Squad consisted of Taler, Vin, Jay, and Darman. All the members of Theta Squad, with the exception of Darman, died during the Battle of Geonosis.

**Thig brothers** A notorious duo of spice-jackers, they were known to be armed with stolen Imperial blasters.

**Thila** A planet where the Rebels reorganized following their evacuation of the main base on Yavin 4. It was on Thila that Alliance historian Voren Na'al began his research into the histories of the Heroes of Yavin.

**thimiar** A small rodent native to Shili, and a favored food of the Togruta species.

**Third Fleet** One of the secondary naval fleets of the Galactic Alliance during the final stages of the war against the Yuuzhan Vong. The Third Fleet, mainly comprising the surviving ships of the New Republic's Third Battle Group, was commanded by General Wedge Antilles from his flagship *Mon Mothma.* Among the other ships in the Third Fleet were the *Mon Adapyne* and the *Elegos A'Kla.* In the wake of the Yuuzhan Vong conflict, the Third Fleet was one of three naval units, along with the Eighth and Ninth Fleets, assigned to the General Crix Madine Military Reserve.

Some 10 years after the end of the war against the Yuuzhan Vong, the Third Fleet was performing routine patrols in the Outer Rim Territories when it was recalled by Supreme Commander Cha Niathal. The fleet was then ordered to blockade the Corellian system after Thrackan Sal-Solo threatened to go to war with the Galactic Alliance. In a strange move, the Third Fleet later launched a direct attack on the planet Commenor, using cloaked asteroids to bombard the planet while harassing starships in space. The Third Fleet's commander acted without authorization from either Cha Niathal or Jacen Solo, and was recalled to Coruscant for questioning. The commander was relieved of duty, and the Third Fleet was placed under the direct command of Admiral Niathal. In the wake of the Second Battle of Fondor, nearly a quarter of the commanders in the Third Fleet decided to defect from the Galactic Alliance, joining Admiral Cha Niathal in support of her government-in-exile.

**Thire, Clone Commander** A red-emblazoned shock trooper assigned by Emperor Palpatine to scour the lower levels of the Galactic Senate for any traces of Jedi Master Yoda. Commander Thire was also known by the designation 4477. Though most clone troopers spent their accelerated formative years on storm-drenched Kamino developing under the careful watch of politically ambivalent scientists, two units were notable exceptions. The red-marked shock troopers and the blue-marked 501st Legion were raised and trained on Coruscant. The well-guarded and secretive facilities served as their training ground. The shock troopers emerged as an instrument of Homeworld Security Command. These highly skilled troops, under the command of ARC-trained Commander Thire, were unable to prevent General Grievous from kidnapping the Chancellor. When the Empire arose, the shock troopers were stationed throughout the Senate Building and executive towers to secure a peaceful transition of government.

**Thisspias** The homeworld of Jedi Master Oppo Rancisis. The planet was ruled by a single hereditary monarch. Rancisis inherited the title, but rejected the post. Thisspiasians had dense hair, which deterred the planet's biting cygnats.

*Thisspias*

**Thistleborn, Grand Moff** An authoritative Grand Moff, he had bushy eyebrows that framed his dark, penetrating eyes. Grand Moff Thistleborn was a member of, and extremely loyal to, the Central Committee of Grand Moffs, which tried to hold the Empire together and pick a successor to Emperor Palpatine following his apparent death in the destruction of the second Death Star.

**Thobek** The language spoken on the planets Thobek and Wehttam, it was closely related to the Torrock language.

**Thokos** The world from which seven ships departed 10,000 years before the Galactic Civil War to colonize the planet Ammuud. The colony eventually lost contact with Thokos and was forgotten.

**Tholatin** The location of one of the most exclusive smuggler hideaways anywhere, Esau's Ridge, which was hidden in a kilometer-long, 100-meter-deep erosion cut at the bottom of a mountain, undetectable from orbit. A network of smaller tunnels extended deeper into the mountain. The adjacent forest-covered valley had three cleared landing areas, which were disguised by camouflage nets. The remainder was uninhabited. Thirteen years after the Battle of Endor, Chewbacca returned to Esau's Ridge with his fellow Wookiees to obtain supplies and information for their planned rescue of Han Solo from the Koornacht Cluster.

**Tholaz** An inhabited planet within the Koornacht Cluster of the Farlax sector, Tholaz was one of the primary worlds of the Yevetha and a member of the Duskhan League. Near the end of the crisis in the Koornacht Cluster, the Yevetha located a new shipyard at Tholaz. During the Battle of N'zoth, the New Republic also attacked Wakiza, Tizon, Z'fell, and Tholaz.

**Tholme, Master** This Jedi Master was one of Quinlan Vos's early teachers, and was a noted Jedi healer. Master Tholme was the Watchman of the sector that contained the planets Kiffex and Kiffu during the time when Kurlin Vos was the Sheyf of Kiffu. It was Master Tholme who discovered Quinlan's psionic abilities and asked Kurlin if the boy could be taken to Coruscant for training. Kurlin agreed, but Tinte Vos argued that Quinlan should remain on Kiffu as a Guardian. She used Quinlan's abilities to discover the reasons behind the deaths of Quian and Pethros Vos, an action that left Quinlan nearly insane. Master Tholme resigned his post as Watchman and dedicated himself to repairing Quinlan's mind and training him as a Jedi. Master Tholme was later dispatched to Kiffex to monitor Quinlan during the investigation into the reemergence of Volfe Karkko, and helped Quinlan defeat the feral Anzati warriors. Master Tholme then presented Quinlan with the star-shaped amulet that was the emblem of the Vos clan. With his psychometric powers, Quinlan was able to read the amulet, which revealed the truth about the deaths of his parents at the hands of the Anzati under the control of Volfe Karkko.

Later, Tholme was dispatched to Ryloth to mediate the succession of the head-clan that had been led by Pol Secura. He was captured by the Morgukai warriors Tsyr and Bok while trying to protect the Secura heir, Nat

Secura, and was forced to feign death in order to be united with the young Twi'lek. Early in the Clone Wars, Tholme and Sora Bulq confronted Count Dooku on Bakura. Bulq was captured in the fighting, and Master Tholme was blinded in his left eye in a lightsaber duel with Dooku. Later, Master Tholme worried almost constantly about the fact that he had suggested that Quinlan Vos be used as a secret agent to join Dooku. Quinlan's actions indicated that he had turned completely to the dark side. On Saleucami, Tholme set out to destroy the Separatist cloning facilities Sora Bulq had built in the magma caverns. Tholme was forced to fight Quinlan, who refused to acknowledge that he was too close to the dark side. In the fight, the precipice on which Tholme was standing gave way, and he plummeted to the ground. Quinlan and the other Jedi on Saleucami believed him dead because Tholme disconnected himself from the Force. Tholme and T'ra Saa then traveled to Nar Shaddaa to locate Khaleen Hentz, but were stranded there when the command was given to execute Order 66. They were able to survive the initial killings of the Jedi Purge, and later accompanied Hentz to Kashyyyk, where she gave birth to her son.

Master Thon

***Tholos*** A Yevethan guardian thrustship for the orbital shipyard at ILC-905, it was destroyed in a battle with the New Republic fleet.

**Thomork** The site for top-secret Imperial construction projects including *Silencer I,* the first of the cloned Emperor's World Devastators. The Empire spread the rumor that the orbital shipyards of Thomork had been closed down due to a hive virus outbreak. Imperial agents then killed more than 450 people to add credence to this rumor, and took over the abandoned facilities for their own projects.

**Thon** A continent on the destroyed planet Alderaan, it was the location of the Uplands. Once a year, the wildlife service had to cull old and sick animals that wouldn't be able to survive the Alderaan winter.

**Thon, Master** A Jedi Master some 4,000 years before the Galactic Civil War, he was a fearsome armor-plated Tchuukthai whose savage countenance was balanced by his great wisdom and empathy. Master Thon trained his students on the planet Ambria; they included Nomi Sunrider and Oss Wilum. Thon was the Jedi Watchman for the Stenness system. As the teachings of the dark Krath sect gained prominence, Master Thon addressed a great assembly of 10,000 Jedi who had gathered on Mount Meru on the desert world of Deneba. He spoke eloquently against straying from the light side, hoping to convince his peers of the dangers of the Krath philosophy.

**Tho'natu, Master** A Twi'lek Jedi Master who led a mission to locate the Sith Lord who had killed several Jedi Masters on Tython about 10 years after the Battle of Ruusan. A veteran of Ruusan, Tho'natu had been promoted to Jedi Master in the years of relative peace that followed. His mission was put together after the Jedi Council received a message from a woman named Zannah. Her message claimed that a Sith Lord who had survived the Battle of Ruusan had killed five Jedi on the planet Tython, and was hiding on Ambria. The message seemed to provide an explanation for the fact that Valenthyne Farfalla, Raskta Lsu, Sarro Xaj, Johun Othone, and Worror were all missing after having set off on a mission to Tython.

Upon arriving on Ambria, Master Tho'natu and his fellow Jedi found the scattered remains of the healer named Caleb, and entered the man's hut with their lightsabers at the ready. What they found was another man who was obviously mad, holding Farfalla's lightsaber and screaming that he would not be taken. Mistaking this for a battle cry, Master Tho'natu attacked the man, slicing him apart with his lightsaber. A quick search of the premises revealed no other inhabitants, leaving Master Tho'natu and the other Jedi to believe that they had finally destroyed the last of the Sith. Unknown to Tho'natu and the other Jedi was the fact that the Sith apprentice Zannah had been hiding in Caleb's cellar with her Master, Darth Bane. Zannah had masked their presence in the Force, after having slain Caleb and driving her cousin, Darovit, insane with horrific visions. She had left Darovit in Caleb's hut with Farfalla's weapon, knowing that the Jedi had read her vague message and would assume Darovit was the Sith Lord. She and Bane escaped once the Jedi had left, and set out to secretly restore the Sith to power.

**ThonBoka (StarCave)** A sac-shaped gray nebula composed of dust, gas, and complex organic molecules, it could be entered from only one direction. Its lightning-charged interior spanned more than 12 light-years. The ThonBoka gave rise to thousands of space-dwelling life-forms, ranging from the intelligent, manta-ray-like Oswaft to carapace creatures and interstellar plankton that served as the Oswaft's food. The Oswaft, ruled by a council of Elders and capable of naturally traversing hyperspace, tended to be cautious creatures who never left the safety of their habitat. Three blue-white stars, located in the center of the nebula, surrounded the Cave of the Elders—the only architectural structure in the ThonBoka. This cave was constructed entirely from precious gems and was an exact replica of the surrounding nebula, but was only 20 kilometers across. After discovering the Oswaft, the Centrality Navy viewed them as a threat. It blockaded the entrance to the ThonBoka, preventing the flow of nutrients and slowly starving the inhabitants until it was defeated by Lando Calrissian and others.

**thought bomb** A volatile cauldron of seething Force energy unleashed during the Battle of Ruusan. Lord Kaan and his followers triggered the bomb against the armies of Lord Hoth, resulting in a furious explosion of energy that annihilated every last member of Hoth's Army of Light and Kaan's Brotherhood of Darkness. The vacuum at the center of the blast sucked in thousands of the disembodied spirits and trapped them in an unbreakable state of equilibrium.

Thought bomb

**thought veer** This Force technique was often associated with the Sith, since it involved a gentle nudging or pushing of another being's resolve toward a line of thought that was more in agreement with the user's. In this way, a Sith or Dark Jedi could bring another being into agreement with a set of plans that might have been avoided, ignored, or even abhorred by the being.

**Thousand Thousand** Makem Te's most powerful city, it was home to more than two million Swokes Swokes. With its spires and domes, the city resembled a fairy-tale illustration, although the use of iron as a building material allowed it to survive the planet's frequent wars with little exterior damage. A

dozen caliphs resided in Thousand Thousand and often hired offworlders who came to their palaces bearing gifts.

**Thovinack, Battle of** The forces of the Rebel Alliance suffered a setback against the Empire in this battle, which took place shortly before the Battle of Yavin.

***Thpfffthf*** A Bith counselor ship.

**Thracior** An inner Core world inhabited by a clan-based culture.

***Thrackan Sal-Solo*** The flagship of the fleet constructed at the Kiris Shipyards. The *Thrackan Sal-Solo* and its sister ships were originally commissioned by Thrackan Sal-Solo for the defense of the Corellian system during the years following the war against the Yuuzhan Vong. The *Thrackan Sal-Solo* was constructed in orbit around Kiris 6, and designed with the usual Corellian flair for innovation and style. Like other Corellian dreadnaughts, the vessel was designed for close-in, ship-to-ship combat. Shaped like a huge egg, it was armed with turret-mounted turbolasers and various missile tubes spread across its hull. In keeping with its status as flagship, the *Thrackan Sal-Solo* was painted a deep blue color.

**Thrago** This moon orbited a yellow gas giant in the sectors of the Unknown Regions controlled by the Chiss. The Chiss established a supply depot on the moon, which saw increasing activity when the Killik Colony began its expansion under the control of the Gorog hive. During the Swarm War, Jaina Solo, her brother Jacen, and Zekk launched a sneak attack on the depot at Thrago in an effort to disrupt the advances of the Chiss. Jacen, however, had his own motivation for joining the mission, having seen a vision in which the galaxy was plunged into unending war with the Colony if the Chiss were allowed to press their advantage. Jaina, upon realizing that Jacen was going to work to destroy the Colony, refused to talk to him for the duration of the war.

**Thrakia** The homeworld of an intelligent insectoid species with genetically transmitted memories. Some 300 years before the Galactic Civil War, the insectoids—who had previously communicated by scent—realized that they could also communicate by clacking their mandibles together. They viewed this ability as a sign that their species had been gifted by a higher power.

**thrall herder** Immense beetle-like creatures with armored, dome-shaped carapaces, used by the Yuuzhan Vong to control their thralls. They scuttled about the battlefield on thousands of bristly black cilia, coordinating the actions of up to 600 thralls. A thrall herder had only a rudimentary intelligence, just enough to accept orders from its "crew." Its sole defense was the ability to spit globs of plasma incredible distances.

**thranta** Great flying creatures with broad, sail-like wings, they were brought to Bespin from their native Alderaan. The Bespin thranta herd was the only known surviving group of these beasts of burden, whose body cores contained a lighter-than-air bladder. Talented riders performed in "sky rodeos," leaping out into the open sky and falling until a thranta came to the rescue.

*Thranta*

**Thranx, Seeqov** This Vratix of the Seeqov hive-clan was a member of the Razorclaws, the group that would eventually become known as the Ashern. Thranx also served as the primary contact for the corporate spy known only as the Bloodletter. She was ostensibly his counterpart when the Bloodletter worked as a field inspector for both the Xucphra and Zaltin factions. Thranx was a respected field inspector and research scientist, and once helped to eradicate a Rodian fungus that had threatened the planet. Her hatred of the Bacta Cartel stemmed partly from the fact that both the Zaltin and Xucphra factions kept the incident a secret, and each claimed total responsibility for solving the fungus epidemic without Vratix help. When the Ashern began development of an enhanced strain of alazhi known as kolazhi—the basis for kolcta—Thranx and the Bloodletter were ordered to keep an eye on its development. They worked together for a year before the project was discovered. A mercenary hired by the Bacta Cartel shot both Thranx and the Bloodletter and left them for dead. Thranx, however, survived long enough to use the enhanced bacta to bring the Bloodletter back from the brink of death. Before she died, she told him the complete story of kolcta.

**Thrasher** The name of a warbeast used by fighter Oron Kira as he joined the Jedi forces in their fight against the dark side Krath cultists on Onderon some 4,000 years before the Battle of Yavin.

**Thrass** The core name of the Chiss individual known as Mitth'ras'safis, and the brother of Grand Admiral Thrawn. During the years following the Battle of Naboo, Thrass served as the Syndic of the Eighth Ruling Family, a position that often put him at odds with his brother. When Thrawn began working to put a stop to Vagaari predations, Thrass had no recourse but to confront his brother. He ultimately asked Admiral Ar'alani to intervene and pass judgment on Thrawn. He never got a chance to see Thrawn brought to trial, however, because Jorj Car'das "escaped" from Thrawn's control and set out to locate the Vagaari. This led Thrass to believe that Car'das was actually a spy, and when the Vagaari came to confront the Chiss forces, he was forced to allow Thrawn to defend their ships. Unknown to Thrass, Thrawn was anticipating the Vagaari attack, as well as the arrival of Outbound Flight, as part of a two-pronged plan to eliminate the Vagaari and the Jedi. Thus, when the plan was revealed to have been developed by both Thrawn and Admiral Ar'alani, Thrass became angry and resentful at having been played by his brother and a commanding officer. Thrass later helped move the Outbound Flight vessels to a remote location, crashing the Dreadnaughts into a planetoid and losing his life in the effort.

**Thrawn, Grand Admiral** The only nonhuman ever to be named one of the 12 Grand Admirals of the Empire, the blue-skinned, red-eyed officer of almost regal bearing nearly succeeded in accomplishing what his mentor, Emperor Palpatine, failed to: destroying the Rebel Alliance.

Thrawn was a respected and honored commander in the Chiss Expansionary Defense Fleet during the years leading up to the Clone Wars, although not every Chiss in the Defense Hierarchy shared that view. Thrawn, whose full name was Mitth'raw'nuruodo, was trial-born into the Nuruodo family. Unlike most Chiss, Thrawn believed in striking first instead of sitting back and waiting, particularly in the case of the Vagaari, who had been subjugating planets in the Unknown Regions. At the time, Thrawn was the youngest Chiss ever to hold the rank of field commander, and was leading Picket Force Two on a long patrol of the borders of the Chiss Ascendancy. He continually encountered Vagaari forces, and reported to his superiors on the subjugation and enslavement of entire species. Thrawn decided to strike a blow against the Vagaari some five years before the onset of the Clone Wars, when he captured one of their gravity-well projectors. He planned to use the device to capture more Vagaari, but was presented with a chance to capture the Dreadnaughts of the Outbound Flight Project instead. Chancellor Palpatine had sent a task force led by Kinman Doriana to attack Outbound Flight, but Thrawn's small fleet wiped it out with the exception of Doriana's ship, which was allowed to survive. After rendering Outbound Flight a derelict and destroying a large part of the Vagaari armada, Thrawn allowed Doriana to return to Coruscant.

Grand Admiral Thrawn

After the establishment of the New Order, the Ruling Circle of the Chiss exiled Thrawn. He was stripped of his rank and exiled to live on an uninhabited world near Imperial space. It was here that Captain Voss Parck discovered him, eventually convincing him to travel to Coruscant and serve in the Imperial Navy. After his promotion to Grand Admiral, Thrawn was sent back to the Unknown Regions, but was continually fed Imperial support. While there, Thrawn and Captain Parck set up the Hand of Thrawn compound on Nirauan, drawing a military force from the Chiss who still supported Thrawn. During their tenure, they won over large sectors of the Unknown Regions. Thrawn left Parck there when he returned to lead the Empire some four years after the Battle of Endor. He left word with Parck and the Chiss who supported him that, if he was ever reported dead, they should wait 10 years for his return.

When Thrawn linked up with Imperial ships under the command of Captain Pellaeon, he discovered that the Empire had been dealt an apparently fatal blow some five years before with the destruction of the second Death Star and the death of Palpatine. Pellaeon found Thrawn to be a complex individual who had a magnificent hologram collection representing some of the galaxy's greatest art treasures, for he believed one could understand—and thus eventually defeat—a species through its art.

Thrawn gathered the ragtag remnants of Imperial power and fashioned a strong military challenge to the New Republic, which he refused to accept as legitimate and still referred to as the Rebellion. He plotted meticulously aboard his Star Destroyer *Chimaera,* with backup from the loyal Captain Pellaeon. First, he figured out a way to neutralize Luke Skywalker and others with Force power by gathering furred salamander-like Force-blocking creatures called ysalamiri from the planet Myrkr. Next, on the planet Wayland, inside the Emperor's Mount Tantiss storehouse, Thrawn found experimental weapons, including a cloaking device, Spaarti cloning cylinders, and the Dark Jedi clone, mad Joruus C'baoth.

Admiral Thrawn also made use of the Noghri, a species that Darth Vader had tricked into feeling beholden to the Empire. The Noghri made up top-secret Imperial death squads, and one of them, Rukh, was Thrawn's personal and very deadly bodyguard. Thrawn sent a commando squad to kidnap Leia Organa Solo so that C'baoth could subvert her and her unborn twins to the dark side of the Force. C'baoth himself hatched a plan to lure Luke Skywalker. Thrawn also had a secret spy on Coruscant in the heart of the New Republic—his Delta Source turned out to be the ch'hala trees lining the corridors of the New Republic Council, which served as living microphones and transmitters.

To test his fleet's readiness, the admiral launched a hit-and-run attack on the planet Bpfassh and two other worlds in the Sluis system. He also stole mole miners from Lando Calrissian's mining operation on Nkllon to use in his next attack on the Sluis Van shipyards. Later, he blackmailed smuggler Niles Ferrier into providing the location of the long-missing *Katana* Dreadnaught fleet and escaped with 180 of the 200 ships. In a move designed to trap the Republic leaders, Thrawn's ships released cloaked asteroids and confusing sensors into orbit above Coruscant.

During a climactic confrontation at the Bilbringi shipyards, Thrawn was surprised by the appearance of a fleet of smuggler ships aiding the New Republic, and his forces were defeated. In the aftermath of that failure, his Noghri bodyguard, Rukh—who had come to realize how Thrawn and the Empire had betrayed his people—assassinated him, ending a major threat to the New Republic.

Back at the Hand of Thrawn base on Nirauan, in order to ensure his eventual return, Thrawn had a clone of himself ready for rebirth at the 10-year mark. This clone was never activated: Luke Skywalker and Mara Jade discovered it and destroyed it during their escape from the complex.

**Thrawn Simulator** A series of military and naval simulations developed by the New Republic, and later refined and augmented by the Galactic Alliance, for training military leaders in a variety of combat scenarios. Only Admiral Nek Bwua'tu defeated the entire series of simulations, and he later became the commander of the Galactic Alliance's Fifth Fleet.

**Threadneedle Canyon** A high-walled, crescent-shaped canyon on the planet Nadiem. Some five months after the Battle of Geonosis, Threadneedle Canyon was the site of a skirmish between a group of clone troopers led by Luminara Unduli and Barriss Offee, and a droid army led by General Grievous. Grievous remained hidden from view, directing his forces to trap the Republic's forces within the walls of the canyon. However, Offee and her troops literally played dead, and the Separatist forces passed them by. This allowed Offee's forces to attack the droids from the rear, crushing the Separatists between the two halves of the Republic's force.

**Three-Eye** This pirate and his crew terrorized the Maltorian Mining Belt during the years following the Yuuzhan Vong War. RePlanetHab tried to buy out Three-Eye and his gang, prompting a flurry of activity from the Galactic Alliance that led to the liberation of the mining belt. Three-Eye himself was captured by the Jedi Knights, and turned over to the authorities for incarceration.

**Thrella Well** Any of a series of shafts leading from the surface of Circarpous V to a network of caverns extending deep within the planet's crust. Thrella Wells were located all over the planet's surface and were believed to be the work of a legendary species known as the Thrella.

**Thri'ag, Eurrsk "Grinder"** A silver-furred Bothan member of Wraith Squadron. Eurrsk "Grinder" Thri'ag flew as Wraith Four. He was killed by turbolaser fire from the *Implacable.*

**Throat** This section of the Hapan Transitory Mists offered the only safe sublight passage to the planet Shedu Maad. In addition to the normal hazards of flying through the Mists, a starship had to bypass a multitude of gravity wells and planetary debris in order to reach the planet. The Throat was the name chosen by Jedi Master Saba Sebatyne to describe the safe pathway through these navigational hazards. This situation made Shedu Maad the perfect location of a hidden Jedi base, and provided the Jedi with an ability to confront Darth Caedus when he finally discovered the location of the Maad system.

**Throgg** A Tatooine humanoid and onetime spice smuggler. Luke Skywalker entrusted the moisture farm of Owen and Beru Lars to Throgg shortly after the Battle of Yavin. The farm was later purchased by Gavin Darklighter's family.

**Throsen, Moff Gegren** An Imperial official who ran Salliche during the New Order, he gained control over Salliche Agricultural Corporation and the planet's legislature. The populace opposed his rise to power, and resistance groups constantly harassed Imperials in the surrounding star systems. Rebel activity increased following the Battle of Endor, forcing Throsen to spend more on defenses.

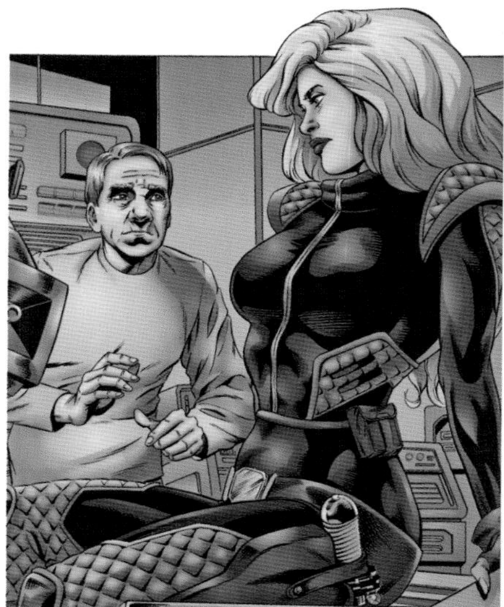

Massad Thrumble with Guri

**Thrugii** A desolate, rocky world located near a wide asteroid belt, it was home to seven generations of failed miners. Residents were considered claim jumpers by sector authorities, who asserted that they controlled all rights to Thrugii and the asteroid belt. After the authorities locked down the planet, the Thrugii miners found themselves in desperate need of food and supplies.

**Thrumble, Massad** A onetime Imperial captain, he worked in a droid production center and was the creator of the human replica droid known as Guri. After the Battle of Endor, Thrumble operated a small cantina on Hurd's Moon in the Qont system. Guri sought him out, and he helped perform the neural restructuring needed to remove her criminal programming while leaving her martial skills intact. (*See also* Simonelle.)

**Thugger's Alley** A hidden passage in the Orange District beneath the surface of Coruscant, named for the low-life criminals who prowled its environs during the early months of the New Order. It was here that Dexter Jettster and the surviving Erased managed to hide after Inquisitor Malorum attacked Solace's compound. Imperial spies eventually learned of Dex's operations, and sent a squad of stormtroopers to raid the area and destroy anything they found. This forced Dex to dispose of much of his information to prevent the Imperials from deciphering it. The stormtroopers were brutally thorough, destroying virtually every building and structure in Thugger's Alley.

**Thuku** A male Rodian bounty hunter, he was on a mission to kill another Rodian named Greedo. Thuku worked for Navik the Red, head of the Chattza tribe. He had tracked down his prey to the spaceport of Mos Eisley on Tatooine, where he heard that Han Solo had beaten him to the punch.

**Thul, Raynar** A spoiled and troublesome Jedi student who later became a key figure in the Swarm War. Raynar Thul was the wealthy heir of Bornan and Aryn Dro Thul and a student at Luke Skywalker's Jedi academy on Yavin 4 at the same time as Jacen and Jaina Solo. Thul's arrogant demeanor eventually changed as he realized that he needed to work for the prestige he desired. During the Yuuzhan Vong War, Thul was part of an elite force sent to Myrkr to locate the voxyn queen and destroy it. When the Dark Jedi Welk and Lomi Plo stole their getaway ship *Tachyon Flier,* Thul was taken along for the ride. The ship crashed in the Unknown Regions, and Thul survived only because the Yoggoy hive of the Killik Colony nursed him back to health. He eventually became the first, and strongest, Joiner in the Killik hive-mind, and fully pledged himself to the Unu hive. After a while, he became known simply as UnuThul.

Raynar Thul

Under Thul's guidance, the hives of the Colony flourished and began to expand toward Chiss space. The Colony's advance was stopped by the Chiss at the Battle of Tenupe, and a bloody stalemate ensued. Millions died on both sides until Thul was confronted by Luke Skywalker aboard the captured Star Destroyer *Admiral Ackbar.* Luke made Thul realize that the Colony's growth was unusual, and he eventually talked the young man into removing himself from the Killiks in order to let their population return to its natural state. Thul was allowed to live and return to the Jedi facility on Ossus. There he was fitted with a special headgear that cut him off from contact with the Colony. Over the following years, he agreed to have his arm replaced with a cybernetic prosthesis, and considered having surgery to repair the burns and scars that covered his body. Many Jedi and some government officials demanded that Thul be held in a maximum-security prison rather than at the Jedi Temple.

**Thul, Tyko** The uncle of Raynar Thul and younger brother of Bornan Thul. He was a recluse who remained safely behind the defenses of his administrative offices on Mechis III rather than taking a position at the forefront of the Bornaryn Trading Company. He hired Boba Fett to bring back his father and nephew, Raynar, after he discovered that Nolaa Tarkona possessed the location of a storehouse of Imperial viruses. In the wake of the Yuuzhan Vong War, Tyko Thul began to take a larger role in the family business, especially when it was re-formed as the Bornaryn Shipping Empire. He was named the chief operating officer of Bornaryn, and became one of his mother's primary advisers.

Thule

**Thule** This semi-arid planet was known for its rich savannas, which were continually bombarded by lightning storms. The innermost planet of the Thurra system, Thule was covered with rocky outcroppings that broke up the plains and were charred black from lightning strikes. This charred rock later served as a form of sustenance for unusual, bioluminescent moss that made the rocks glow with an eerie light. During the height of the Great Sith War, Thule served as a base of operations for the Sith warriors, and much of the planet's crust became imbued with the residue of the dark side of the Force. Although the Republic defeated the Sith, the forces on Thule continued to train in the hope of one day going to war. After the Battle of Ruusan, the pair of Sith Lords that remained in the galaxy often made use of the soldiers on Thule.

During the early stages of the Clone Wars, Thule was the site of a Separatist base. It was here that Count Dooku hoped to reconstruct the Dark Reaper and use it against the Republic. However, with the help of Ulic Qel-Droma's spirit, Anakin Skywalker destroyed the Dark Reaper and spared Thule from damage. As Emperor Palpatine rose to power, all records of Thule's existence were erased from archives and navigational databases, so that Palpatine could secretly draw on the soldiers as needed. The planet was orbited by a single satellite, known as the Thule Moon. It was believed that, at some point during its earliest history, Thule once supported many forms of life. Over time, though, any indigenous plants and animals were killed either by the planet's inhabitants or by Thule's devastating weather.

**Thule, Ryoo** The mother of Jobal Naberrie and grandmother of Padmé Naberrie Amidala. Ryoo survived the Battle of Naboo and retired to the Varykino estate of the Naberrie family. In the wake of the Clone Wars, Ryoo oversaw the funeral preparations for Padmé. Ryoo was Padmé's only surviving grandmother, since Winama Naberrie had died some 13 years earlier. Inquisitor Malorum, seeking information on Padmé's death, killed Ryoo. With her dying breath, she begged Ferus Olin to protect her granddaughter's memory.

**Thun, Hekis Durumm Perdo Kolokk Baldikarr** The administrator of the droid-production world Mechis III, Hekis Thun continually added more and more names to his title to help overcome his feelings of inadequacy. He was killed by his personal droid, 3D-4X, after the assassin droid IG-88 and his counterparts arrived at Mechis III and took over the programming of all of the planet's computer systems and droids.

***Thunderflare*** An overpowered Imperial Star Destroyer. The *Thunderflare* was modified to tranfer energy from its hyperdrive to its weapons. Often serving patrol duties in the Core Worlds, it was a common first assignment for junior officers. The *Thunderflare* was present at the Battle of Endor.

**Thwim** A Kubazi spy, he traded information on Tatooine. He worked for Lady Valarian on occasion.

**Thyferra** Located in the Polith system, it was the homeworld of the mantis-like Vratix and was the center of the galaxy's bacta industry. Thyferra was a green-and-white world covered with rain forests; it had little axial tilt and was unbearably humid. It had two airless, uninhabited moons and orbited a yellow star. Thyferra was first contacted during the middle years of the Old Republic. Although the Vratix had already colonized other bodies in their system, contact with the Republic ushered in a technological revolution.

*Thyferra*

The Vratix soon invented the healing fluid called bacta by growing alazhi and mixing it with the chemical kavam. The remarkable fluid was extremely profitable, and powerful Vratix operations spread across many worlds. With the rise of the Empire, two large bacta-harvesting corporations, Xucphra and Zaltin, negotiated a special deal with the Imperials, allowing the companies to gain a virtual monopoly on the bacta industry. The conglomerates controlled 95 percent of the galaxy's bacta and became known as the Bacta Cartel. The human-owned companies long dominated the lives of the Vratix and ran the government. Total bacta output averaged 17 billion liters a year.

The planetwide government was led by two canirs (chief officers) appointed by an elected council, each canir representing one of the two corporations. Because Xucphra and Zaltin were competitors, there was frequent governmental gridlock. This gave rise to the Ashern (Black Claw) terrorist group, which viewed the corporations as a threat and attempted to topple them. In the political confusion following the Battle of Endor, Thyferra remained neutral and profited by selling bacta to both sides. Two and a half years after Endor, the New Republic, anxious to please the Thyferran leaders, recruited the human pilots Bror Jace (from Zaltin) and Erisi Dlarit (from Xucphra) into the famous Rogue Squadron.

Thyferra had three spaceports. The main one was Zalxuc City, which was renamed Xucphra City after former Imperial Intelligence head Ysanne Isard took over control of Xucphra and put the squeeze on Zaltin as she became the planet's Head of State. Foreign workers, who were hired to make the bacta runs, stayed in segregated areas around the spaceport. The port's main building was a low two-story rectangle, with akonije trees growing through it and out the roof. The alazhi was harvested and kavam synthesized primarily on Thyferra, but there were dozens of colony worlds elsewhere, including Qretu-Five.

After Rogue Squadron's conquest of Borleias, Bror Jace was called back to Thyferra due to a relative's grave illness. Having been tipped off by a spy, the Interdictor cruiser *Black Asp*, operating near Thyferra, dragged his X-wing out of hyperspace and destroyed it, apparently killing Jace. (His presumed death became a convenient cover story.) After the capture of Coruscant, the New Republic was especially dependent on Thyferra to provide bacta for treating the Krytos virus, which Isard had unleashed as part of her plan to corner the bacta trade and become both wealthy and powerful. A deadly Bacta War ensued, with Rogue Squadron fighting Isard—but not under New Republic auspices. In the end, the Rogues were victorious. They were welcomed back into Republic service, and Thyferra voted to join the New Republic. During the Yuuzhan Vong War, the enemy sent an agent to Thyferra to sabotage the bacta supply. During the Swarm War, the Killik colonies organized an uprising on Thyferra and took control of its bacta.

**Thyferra, Battle of** This battle marked the end of the Bacta War, shortly after the Battle of Endor. Rogue Squadron had been waging the war on its own, having resigned its commission with the New Republic in order to personally avenge the deaths of many squadron members at the hands of Ysanne Isard. The Rogues managed to capture not only the *Avarice* but also the *Virulence*, the former being renamed the *Freedom* and leading the attack on Thyferra. Several smaller freighters and transports also lent a hand on the side of the Rogues. The *Freedom* bombarded the *Lusankya*—the primary ship guarding Thyferra—with proton torpedoes, destroying its shields and leaving it defenseless in the opening act of the battle. Rogue Squadron added its own torpedoes, and then strafed the *Lusankya* with blasterfire. The newly recommissioned war cruiser *Valiant* joined in, raining lethal firepower on the huge Star Destroyer.

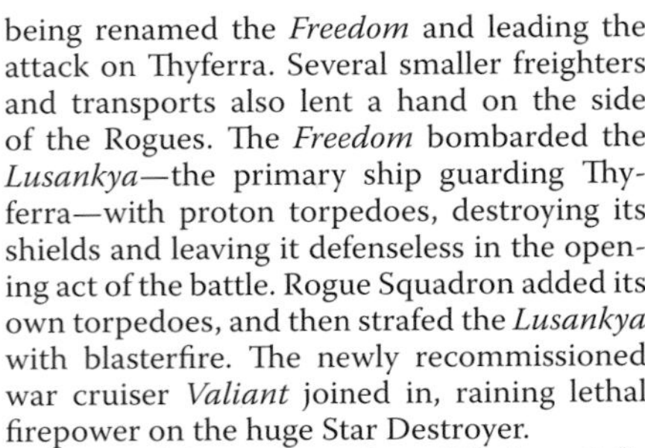

Meanwhile, on the surface of Thyferra, Iella Wessiri and Elscol Loro had led a team of infiltrators to join up with the Zaltin and Ashern factions, and worked to destroy the Xucphra resources on the planet. They also managed to intercept Fliry Vorru as he tried to flee, and brought him to Coruscant to stand trial.

In space over the planet, the *Lusankya* began to destroy the smaller ships in the Rogue Squadron fleet, hoping to take them out of the fight while making its own repairs. Then Captain Drysso opened fire on the *Freedom*, crippling the smaller Star Destroyer. The *Freedom* managed to get in some shots of its own, effectively taking out the larger ship's shields and leaving it defenseless. It was at this point that Ysanne Isard commanded the *Lusankya* to cover the escape of her personal shuttle, *Thyfonian*, before both were lost in the battle. Captain Drysso disobeyed the order when the *Virulence* reappeared, thinking that he finally had the reinforcements he needed to win the battle. However, the *Virulence* was now under the command of Booster Terrik, and it contained several New Republic fighter squadrons, including Ace Squadron. Led by Pash Cracken, Ace Squadron fighters redoubled the assault on the *Lusankya* and began taking sections of the ship out with their strafing runs. Drysso threatened to ram the ship into Thyferra, but he was executed by Lieutenant Waroen, who then surrendered the ship and its crew to Rogue Squadron. The battle ended when Ysanne Isard, fleeing in her shuttle, was shot down by Tycho Celchu and Corran Horn. It was later revealed that Isard had been remotely controlling the shuttle; she survived the battle.

**Thyferran Home Defense Corps** A paramilitary unit, it was established by former Imperial Intelligence head Ysanne Isard when she came to power on Thyferra. The THDC was composed of Xucphra Corporation volunteers trained by Isard's Imperial troops ostensibly to defend their homeworld from Ashern rebels. They were really witless pawns to be used in Isard's reign of terror against Thyferra.

***Thyfonian*** A *Lambda*-class shuttle, it was specially modified by Fliry Vorru to be used to escape from the planet Thyferra. It was destroyed by the combined efforts of Rogue Squadron pilots Corran Horn and Tycho Celchu as it attempted to make a run to hyperspace during the Bacta War. It was assumed that Thyferran strongwoman Ysanne Isard

Kirana Ti

was on board, but that later proved not to be true.

**Thyne, Zekka** A notorious Black Sun terrorist, he was taken from the Kessel prison facility by the Rebel Alliance, which hoped to use him in its operation to undermine the Imperial infrastructure on Coruscant before it invaded that planet. He had been sent to Kessel by CorSec for smuggling, but he was also tied to the murders of nearly a dozen people. Hal and Corran Horn were the most responsible for his imprisonment, and he vowed to kill Corran. They ran into each other again on Coruscant, where both were on separate undercover missions. Thyne attempted to kill Horn at the Headquarters, a bar in Invisec, but Corran made a daring escape on a speeder bike. Imperial officer Kirtan Loor attempted to use Thyne as an informant, but he proved mostly ineffectual. Thyne lay in wait for Horn at a secret rendezvous point, but before he could kill the Rogue, he was himself killed by his lover, Inyri Forge.

**Ti, Kirana** One of the Force-sensitive Witches of Dathomir, Kirana Ti helped Luke Skywalker recover an ancient wrecked space vessel, the *Chu'unthor,* which held records of old Jedi training. Later she became one of Skywalker's Jedi candidates and joined his other Jedi students on Yavin 4 in defeating the spirit of Dark Lord Exar Kun, protecting Luke's body and freeing his spirit.

**Ti, Sanola** This Force-sensitive Dathomiri woman joined the new Jedi Order during the years following the war against the Yuuzhan Vong. A skilled pilot, Sanola Ti was later added to the Red Sword Flight during the height of the Galactic Alliance's war against the Confederation. Because she was the youngest member of the squadron, Sanola Ti flew as wingmate to the Jedi Grand Master Luke Skywalker during a mission to eliminate Jacen Solo. She later flew as Rakehell Two on a mission to disable Centerpoint Station.

**Ti, Shaak** A noted Jedi Master and a hero of the Clone Wars. Shaak Ti was a female Togruta from Shili who trained two Padawans, though both were killed by criminals shortly after the completion of their training. Shaak Ti was one of the many Jedi Masters who were dispatched to Geonosis, along with Mace Windu, in an effort to rescue Obi-Wan Kenobi from the Separatists. Shortly afterward, Master Ti was assigned to the team dispatched to liberate Brentaal from Separatist control. The mission forced her to confront the criminal Lyshaa, who had killed one of her former Padawans, Fe Sun.

Just before the end of the Clone Wars, Shaak Ti was assigned to protect Chancellor Palpatine. When General Grievous launched his attack on Coruscant, Shaak Ti and her team rushed to Palpatine's side. Shaak Ti's companions—Jedi Masters Roron Corobb and Foul Moudama—were killed. Palpatine was captured and Shaak Ti spared, but only so she could report on her failure to the Jedi Council.

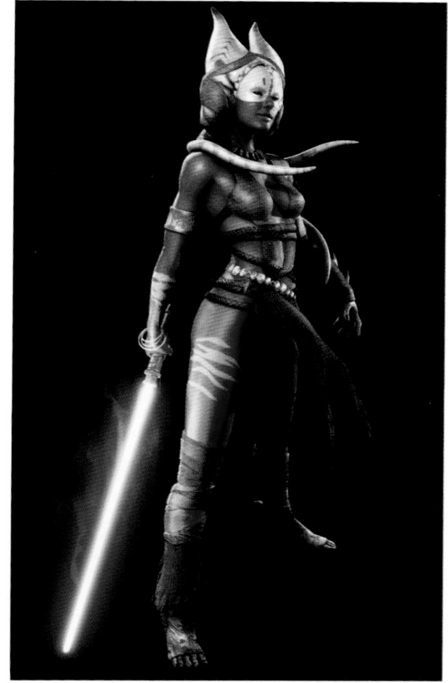

Shaak Ti

When Anakin Skywalker led an attack on the Jedi Temple, many believed that he killed Shaak Ti. However, the Master fled Coruscant and took up residence on the remote planet of Felucia. There she trained the Zabrak Maris Brood, whose own Master had been killed while trying to return to Coruscant. Just a short time before the Alliance to Restore the Republic was formed, Shaak Ti was confronted on Felucia by Starkiller, Darth Vader's secret apprentice. In a ferocious lightsaber battle fought over the open maw of a gigantic Sarlacc, the courageous Jedi was finally slain.

Tibanna gas refineries

**Tibanna gas** A rare gas extracted from the atmosphere of Bespin, among other planets, it was processed at Cloud City. Hot air rose through Cloud City's unipod, which sucked in the gases that floated in Bespin's atmosphere—including Tibanna. The gas was processed and packed in carbonite for transport offplanet. Tibanna gas produced four times its normal energy output when cohesive light passed through it. When spin-sealed Tibanna gas (compacted at the atomic level) was used as a conducting agent, blasters and other energy weapons produced greater energy yields—and therefore greater amounts of damage. Personal weapons could not tolerate this extra power, but ship-mounted blasters benefited greatly from the use of Tibanna gas. The spin-sealing process was prohibitively expensive except on Bespin, where it occurred naturally. Non-spin-sealed Tibanna gas was used as a hyperdrive coolant.

**Tibanna tapper** A term used to describe pirates and smugglers who stole spin-sealed Tibanna gas from refineries in orbit around Bespin. Using specialized siphoning balloons, Tibanna tappers bled off processed gases from the facilities, using the cloud cover to hide their presence. These thieves were ostensibly tied to the activities of the Killik Dark Nest during the Swarm War.

**TibannaX** A specially formulated isotope of Tibanna gas produced by the Xtib corporation for Incom Industries; it was used in stealth starfighter engine systems to limit the production of ion trails.

**Tibannopolis** An abandoned Bespin city, it hung near empty, a creaking ghost town in the sky. The roof, decks, and sides of Tibannopolis were picked over by scavengers hauling away scrap metal. Luke Skywalker found Streen, one of his Jedi candidates, on Tibannopolis.

Tibannopolis

**Tibor** A vicious bipedal reptiloid, this Barabel bounty hunter frequented the Mos Eisley cantina and was a regular employee of Zorba the Hutt.

**Tibrin** A planet completely covered by a shallow ocean, it was the homeworld of the Ishi Tib species. Tibrin circled the yellow star Cal and had one barren moon called Plah. The planet had no seasons; ocean currents evenly distributed warm water, creating a temperate zone covering most of the planet's surface. The only landmasses were protruding coral reefs and sandbars, where the ecologically minded Ishi Tib constructed their cities. Ishi Tib lived in communal schools ranging from a few hundred to more than 10,000 individuals, and their organizational skills were prized by galactic corporations, which often hired Ishi Tib as managers. Animal life included the Tibrin kelp-gnat.

Tibrin

**TIE/Advanced fighter** The prototype ship used by Darth Vader at the Battle of Yavin. Many of its best design features were later incorporated into the TIE interceptor and the TIE Advanced (TIE/Ad) ship dubbed the TIE avenger.

TIE/Advanced fighter

The TIE Advanced x1 featured an original spaceframe and reinforced durasteel-alloy hull, with an elongated rear deck and matching bent wings covered with solar panels. The vessel had a solar ionization reactor and paired twin ion engines for a more powerful drive system than the standard TIE/ln. Speed was only slightly improved due to the added mass of the vessel; a good deal of the extra power was bled off to the shield generators. While less maneuverable than standard TIE fighters, it could take a beating.

The TIE Advanced x1 had twin heavy blaster cannons in a fixed, front-mounted position. In addition to its shields, it had a modest hyperdrive—but no life-support system. The Empire decided not to order the TIE Advanced x1 in large quantities, citing its excessive cost. Privately, some Imperial Navy strategists admitted that the navy was afraid to purchase a fighter with a hyperdrive, fearing that it would give bureaucrats an excuse to slash orders for new capital starships.

The Empire instead opted for the TIE interceptor, which featured the TIE Advanced x1's drive system in a more compact ship. Although the TIE interceptor lacked a hyperdrive and shields, it was blindingly fast, incredibly maneuverable, and significantly cheaper than the TIE Advanced x1. By the Battle of Endor, the large increase in TIE interceptor production meant the end of production for the TIE Advanced x1.

**TIE aggressor** A high-end experimental Imperial starfighter built to play many roles in naval combat. Its generous forward guns, ample missile racks, and a rotating turret made it a formidable challenge for any enemy or group of enemies.

**TIE avenger** The production version of the ship inspired by Darth Vader's prototype TIE Advanced x1. The finished TIE Advanced, dubbed the avenger by zealous Imperial Navy officers, featured fast-recharging Novaldex shields and an extended twin ion engine capacity. An SFS I-s3a solar ionization reactor powered the fighter, and twin P-sx7.4 ion engines propelled it through space. It featured a pair of L-s9.3 laser cannons, and could be outfitted with a pair of warhead launchers. Though successful in combat operations, the costly TIE avenger was eventually phased out with the increasing popularity of the more economical TIE interceptor.

TIE aggressor

**TIE boarding craft** A variant of the TIE bomber used for transporting troops. The Empire used a TIE boarding craft to attack the *Tantive IV;* Rebel prisoners were then transported back to the Star Destroyer *Devastator* in this same ship. A larger version, the TIE lander, was a triple-hulled troop drop ship capable of deploying an entire stormtrooper company.

TIE boarding craft

**TIE bomber** The Empire's primary assault bomber, it was somewhat slower and less maneuverable than standard starfighters, but provided excellent surgical-strike potential against ground and deep-space targets.

TIE bombers had double pods and elongated solar panels. The starboard pod contained the pilot's compartment along with flight computers, communications, and life support. The port pod held the ordnance bay and targeting and delivery systems. Twin ion engines were mounted between the two pods. The bomber's weaponry included high-yield proton bombs, guided concussion missiles, orbital

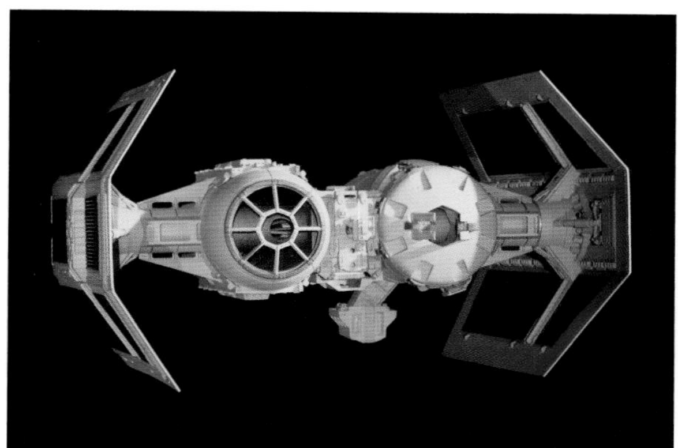
TIE bomber

mines, and free-falling thermal detonators. A pair of front-firing laser cannons provided protection from enemy ships.

For space duty, the TIE bomber delivered heavy ordnance against Rebel Alliance capital ships. Normally, TIE fighters first softened up the target, followed by TIE bombers, in conjunction with assault gunboats and Skipray blastboats, which used their precise targeting computers to disable vital areas such as shield generators or engines. When the target was crippled and unable to protect itself, Imperial boarding parties took control of the vessel or captured troops for interrogation.

TIE bombers were used to assault space stations and stardocks and to mine planetary orbits. They were also exceptionally good on ground bombing missions. Their targeting computers were precise enough to level specific buildings while leaving adjacent areas unscathed. A Star Destroyer typically carried one squadron of 12 TIE bombers. Prior to Emperor Palpatine's death, the Empire began developing a more advanced bomber prototype, which eventually evolved into the Scimitar assault bomber.

**TIE crawler** The century tank—which Imperial soldiers took to calling the TIE crawler or TIE tank because of the familiar command pod taken from the TIE fighter—was a cheap, mass-produced ground combat vehicle that became popular during the revival of the Empire and the recapture of the Imperial capital of Coruscant. It was a simple combat machine, with easy controls and modular components. It required only a single crew member, who handled both piloting and gunnery.

TIE crawler
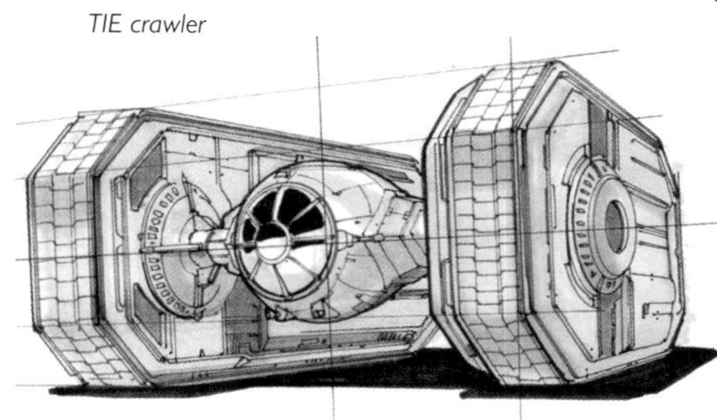

The TIE tank had the same central pod as the standard TIE fighter. Twin power generators were attached to each side of the pod and drove the tread wheels, giving the tank a relatively slow top speed of only 90 kilometers per hour. It could navigate through most terrain and was substantially cheaper than comparable repulsorlift craft. Weapons included two forward-firing medium blaster cannons and a retractable light turbolaser. The TIE tank had light armor plating on all surfaces, but the drive system and tread wheels were easily damaged by enemy fire. The TIE tank was entered through a top hatch, and the pilot was strapped into an automatically adjusting gravcouch. Foot controls adjusted the angle of steering and speed, while the hand controls were tied in to the weapons systems and the targeting computer.

**TIE defender** A prototype Imperial fighter developed shortly before the Battle of Endor, it was deployed to a small number of elite TIE-wings. The TIE defender was used to defeat rogue Imperial Admiral Zaarin, who planned to depose Emperor Palpatine. The vessel was a radical departure from conventional TIE designs and featured three sets of solar collection panels mounted at equilateral points around the fighter's cockpit.

The TIE defender's multiple heavy-weapons systems allowed it to successfully engage enemy capital ships, while a hyperdrive allowed it to operate independently of support carriers, giving the ship flexibility unmatched by any other Imperial starfighter. It was nearly 40 percent faster at sublight than the standard TIE fighter due to its twin ion engines. Triple arrays of maneuvering jets on the tri-wing assembly made the ship capable of amazing dives and twists.

The TIE defender featured four laser cannons and two ion cannons, which could be fired singly for multiple targets or fire-linked for a concentrated assault. A pair of missile launchers could be equipped with proton torpedoes and concussion missiles.

**TIE fighter** The TIE ("Twin Ion Engine") fighter was the most recognizable symbol of the Imperial Navy's control of space. TIE fighters could be found aboard even the smallest cruisers and were stationed at starports and garrison bases across the galaxy. They were an omnipresent reminder of the Empire's might.

A TIE fighter was a small ship; its most distinguishing feature was the pair of immense hexagonal solar array wings on either side of its small, spherical command pod. The ship presented a small profile, and its great maneuverability made it even more difficult to target in combat.

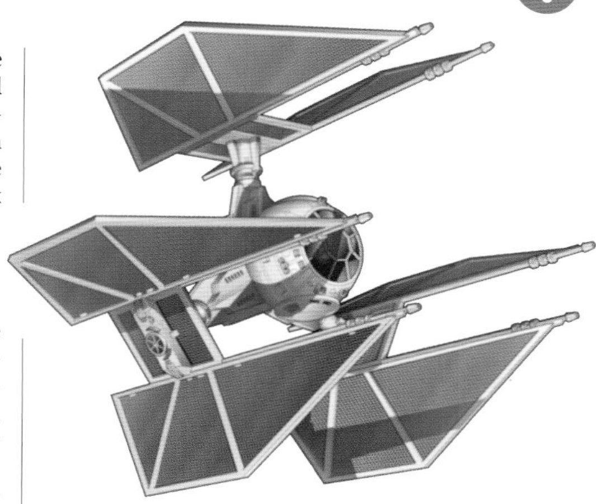
TIE defender

TIEs were short-range fighters without hyperdrives to save weight and increase performance. They depended on a home base—a nearby planet or Imperial cruiser. They carried only two days' worth of supplies and often needed to refuel after the first few hours of combat, but their use in massive quantities made up for any design deficiencies. The fighters were used for planetary and cruiser defense and assault against Rebel, pirate, and alien vessels. They also escorted heavily armed TIE bombers when attacking permanent planetary installations.

The TIE's famous maneuverability and speed came at great practical cost to the pilot. TIE fighters had no shields, secondary weapons, or drive systems, minuscule fuel supplies, and no onboard life-support system. Pilots wore fully sealed flight suits with self-contained atmospheres. Some claimed the TIE was too responsive to piloting adjustments. It wasn't uncommon for novice pilots to attempt an advanced maneuver that sent their ship out of control.

TIE fighter

The TIE had a pair of forward-mounted, fire-linked laser cannons. The massive laser generators were in the undercarriage of the command pod and fed off the power generators and batteries. The fighter drew much of its energy from solar radiation absorbed by the array wings. The common TIE fighter was the TIE/ln, which was actually a successor to the earlier T.I.E. and TIE models, all of which were produced by Sienar Fleet Systems. The success of the TIE fighter led to the creation of several new mission-specific designs, including the TIE/rc (a sensor and communications reconnaissance fighter), the TIE/fc (which provided fire control for long-range navy artillery), the TIE/gt (a makeshift bomber used prior to the introduction of the TIE bomber), the TIE/Advanced (Darth Vader's ship at the Battle of Yavin was one such advanced model), the TIE bomber, the TIE interceptor, the TIE scout (a limited-production, light reconnaissance starship), the TIE vanguard (a reconnaissance starfighter that, unusual for TIEs, was equipped with shields to protect the valuable information it gathered), and the fully robotic TIE/D fighter (introduced six years after the Battle of Endor). There was also a TIE/sh shuttlecraft and a TIE boat, or sub fighter.

**TIE fighter construction facility** In order to build its massive war machine, the Empire constructed thousands of factories and installations across the galaxy. One TIE fighter factory hung precariously in low orbit above the bustling moon of Nar Shaddaa. Nominally owned and operated by Sienar Fleet Systems, the factory was controlled by the Empire and protected by several squadrons of well-trained stormtroopers. Within the facility, the Empire perfected its mass-production techniques, churning out thousands of TIE/ln starfighters. Rows upon rows of TIE parts moved along magnetic conveyors, while automated laser arms welded the vehicles together before they were transported to loading bays. The Jedi General Rahm Kota emerged from hiding and, with the aid of a small battalion of loyal soldiers, took control of this key Imperial facility. Kota and his forces detonated explosives throughout the factory in order to provoke a showdown with Darth Vader.

TIE fighter construction facility

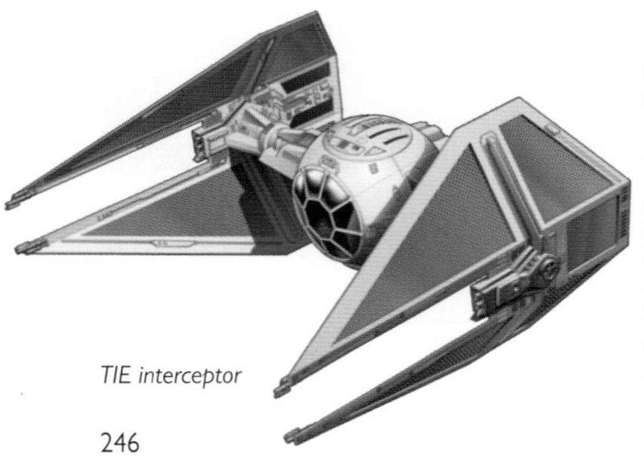
TIE interceptor

**TIE hunter** The TIE equivalent of the X-wing was speedy, mobile, and well equipped. It had S-foils that closed when the ship was flying at top speeds. It was armed with lasers, an ion cannon, and proton torpedoes. The TIE hunters were flown exclusively by the Empire's Storm Commandos.

TIE hunter

**TIE interceptor** Faster and more maneuverable than the standard TIE/ln fighter, it stemmed from the advances developed for Darth Vader's TIE Advanced x1 Prototype. The TIE interceptor used the standard TIE cockpit, drive pod, and wing braces. The solar panels appeared to be dagger-shaped, making the interceptor more intimidating while also giving it a smaller profile, making it harder for Rebel gunners to target. The TIE interceptor had more powerful drives than the TIE/ln and was almost as fast as the New Republic's A-wing fighter.

The TIE interceptor used a new type of ion stream projector, allowing pilots to execute tight turns and rolls. Twin port deflectors could be manipulated individually for fine control and counterbalancing, making the TIE interceptor a superior choice for dogfights.

The ship had four laser cannons, one at the end of each solar panel; advanced targeting software gave the pilot greater firing accuracy. Like other TIE fighters, the TIE interceptor had little armor plating and no shield generators. Interceptor pilots relied on their ship's maneuverability and superior numbers to survive engagements with better-armed and -armored New Repubic fighters.

With no onboard life-support system, TIE pilots used fully sealed flight suits. The TIE interceptor had no hyperdrive and required a large capital ship as a base of operations. The Empire intended the TIE interceptor to eventually replace the TIE/ln, but by the death of the Emperor only about 20 percent of Imperial fighters were interceptors. As Grand Admiral Thrawn initiated his bid for power, he began arming some TIE interceptors with shields, knowing that the Empire could no longer consider these exceptional ships disposable.

**Tiems, Battle of** This was the name given to the Rebel Alliance's attack on the Imperial outpost located in the city of Tiems. The city was bordered by the Blue River and the Gopps Forest, and General Carlist Rieekan's tactics in taking the city later became the basis for training holovids used by Alliance commanders.

**TIE oppressor** The TIE oppressor was the hallmark of damage-dealing Imperial design. Built to fill the gap between the venerable TIE bomber and the nimble TIE interceptor, this craft was a heavy fighter that featured exceptional firepower and room for many high-level missiles. It served as an Imperial equivalent to the Y-wing and B-wing bombers.

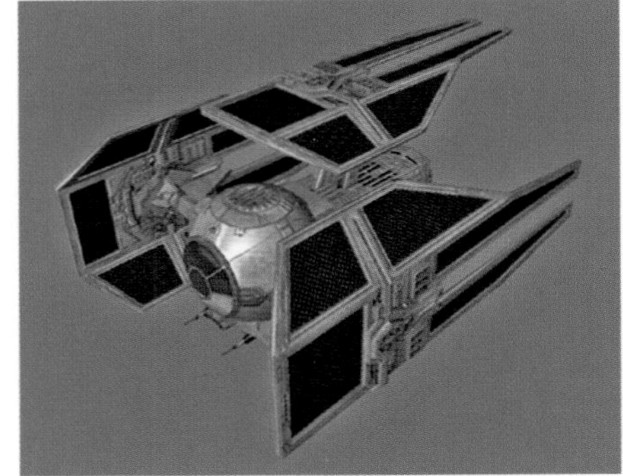
TIE oppressor

**TIE raptor** A TIE fighter designed by Warlord Zsinj. The TIE raptor, or TIE/rpt, had the standard TIE ball cockpit but lacked wing pylons. Instead four trapezoidal wings, smaller than half the size of a regular TIE fighter's wings, protruded from the cockpit at even intervals. Its firepower and maneuverability made it a highly effective combat starfighter.

**Tierce, Major Grodin** A former Royal Guardsman, he helped Moff Disra and the con artist Flim pull off the illusion of Grand Admiral Thrawn's return. Tierce was actually a clone of one of the finest stormtroopers ever to serve the Empire. The real Tierce died in combat in Thrawn's campaign against Generis. The cloned Tierce was the first of what was to be a new breed of warlords, combining the loyalty and combat abilities of a stormtrooper with the tactical genius of Thrawn. The experiment was a failure,

TIE raptor

Major Grodin Tierce (center) with Moff Disra and Flim

however; while Thrawn believed in order and stability, the cloned Tierce wanted only vengeance. The Mistryl Shadow Guard Shada killed Tierce when he attacked Admiral Pellaeon.

**TIE reconnaissance fighter** A prototype starfighter developed by Sienar Fleet Systems for the naval forces of the Galactic Alliance following the Swarm War. Developed as an alternative to the StealthX fighter from Incom, the TIE reconnaissance fighter was built from the original designs of the TIE bomber. The port-side fuselage was refitted to carry a new hyperdrive system, enhanced navigation computers, life-support systems, shield generators, and electronic countermeasures. This collection of systems earned the TIE reconnaissance fighter the nickname Blur, since it could literally disappear from sensor systems. The first working prototype was assigned to the flagship Star Destroyer *Anakin Solo.* It was given a simple black paint job, with only the GA's symbols on its wings to identify it. The prototype was first tested by Captain Olavey, although Jacen Solo later flew the fighter during his escape from an assassination attempt by Sadras Koyan.

**Tierfon** Located in the outer Sumitra sector, it was the site of a Rebel starfighter outpost buried 250 meters into a rock cliff. The Tierfon base was relatively small, housing only eight X-wing fighters and 54 combat personnel (members of the Tierfon Yellow Aces Squadron), along with troops and support staff for a total contingent of 158.

**Tierfon Yellow Aces** A group of Rebel pilots stationed on Tierfon. Members of the Yellow Aces were an integral component of Red Squadron during the Battle of Yavin; they included Jek Porkins and Wes Janson.

**TIE scout** A limited-production light reconnaissance starfighter developed by Sienar Fleet Systems, the TIE/sr was more commonly known as the TIE scout. The familiar TIE fuselage almost disappeared in its outsized frame; its extended mission profile required larger fuel and consumables storage that caused its hull to bulge outward unlike any other TIE model. To supply the craft's power needs, elongated bent-wing panels constantly gathered stellar energy while in space. The scout required a single pilot, and had room for three passengers.

Another great difference between the TIE/sr and its sister vessels was that it was equipped with an extremely reliable Class 2 hyperdrive. Its extended mission in the poorly charted reaches of the Outer Rim Territories required the TIE scout to operate independently of a launch ship or base. The TIE scouts saw service in the Imperial Navy, where they were assigned to surreptitiously scan ahead for reconnaissance, spotting and surveying minefields and other potential ambushes prior to fleet arrival. Such dangerous tasks saw the costly destruction of many TIE scouts. The TIE/sr proved to be too expensive for the Empire to push into more widespread service. Unlike other vessels in the TIE series, Santhe/Sienar Technologies negotiated an option to sell a stripped-down variant of the craft on the civilian market. The so-called Lone Scout-A (LSA) used the same framework as the TIE/sr, but its scanning systems were not as sensitive as the Imperial military issue. The Imperial Survey Corps used the LSA and LSA-2 TIE scout variants, as did the New Republic Scout Service that followed.

**TIE torpedo** A streamlined one-person attack submersible developed in the Imperial naval yards of Bestine. Constructed directly on the water's surface, the naval yard—code-named Juggerhead—ostensibly manufactured shells for *Acclamator*-class Star Destroyers. In truth, Juggerhead was a high-security R&D facility.

**TIE-wing** An unofficial "ugly" version of the TIE fighter, combining a TIE's cockpit with Y-wing engine nacelles. Kavil's Corsairs used TIE-wings in battle against Rogue Squadron. The ships were also known as TIE-Y uglies, and Rogue Squadron nicknamed them Die-wings.

**Tigellinus, Grand Admiral Rufaan** The commander of the Star Destroyer *Avatar,* and one of the Emperor's 12 Grand Admirals. Emperor Palpatine assigned Tigellinus to investigate the incredible growth of Moff Jerrod Maclain's personal wealth shortly before the Battle of Hoth. It was rumored that Maclain was obtaining insider trading information from the Dajaal family in return for political favors and tax breaks. Later, when Emperor Palpatine made Thrawn the newest Grand Admiral, Tigellinus—a known human elitist—befriended Thrawn with every intention of betraying him later. Once Thrawn was discredited and dispatched to the Unknown Regions, Tigellinus began to assert his own powerful influence. He was soon named a Grand Moff. Tigellinus disliked the fact that a nonhuman, Hissa, had also been named Moff, but was unable to sway the other to see his point of view. When Hissa was named the leader of the Central Committee of Grand Moffs in the wake of the Battle of Endor, he took the opportunity to discredit Tigellinus and eliminate his dissenting voice. Hissa offered Tigellinus a subordinate role, which Tigellinus refused on the advice of Moff Disra. For his insubordination, Tigellinus was executed on the spot, and Disra gladly agreed to take his place.

TIE scout

**Tigris** Born to parents strong in the Force, but having no Force powers of his own, he became a pawn and then a major player in a galactic drama. Tigris, with pale skin and black-and-silver-striped hair, was the offspring of two Firrerreos: Hethrir and a female healer named Rillao. Both had been students of Darth Vader, but while Hethrir embraced the dark side of the Force and even helped destroy his own world as proof of his loyalty to the Empire, Rillao's powers came from the light side and she fled with her unborn child.

Tigris grew up on a remote, pastoral planet, knowing nothing of his father. Hethrir eventually found Rillao and their son; he imprisoned her in an abandoned Imperial slaving vessel and made Tigris his personal slave. Without Force powers, Tigris could never succeed Hethrir as head of his Empire Reborn organization. Hethrir twisted the story of Rillao, making Tigris despise her. Tigris assisted Hethrir in running his worldcraft, aboard which were dozens of kidnapped children. If they showed Force talents, Hethrir tried to turn them to the dark side; if not, he sold them to slavers. Tigris, gentle and compassionate, snuck food to the captives and tried to comfort them.

Hethrir kidnapped Jacen, Jaina, and Anakin Solo, the children of Han and Leia Organa Solo. Tigris grew especially fond of Anakin and accompanied Hethrir and the boy to what he was told was Anakin's purification in the temple of the Waru on Crseih Research Station. But Rillao, who had been freed by Leia, was there and told a stunned Tigris that Hethrir was really his father. Tigris also

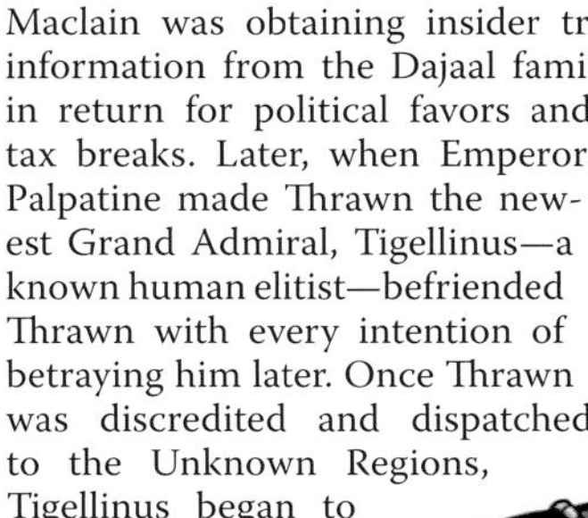

Grand Admiral Rufaan Tigellinus

discovered that Anakin's spirit was going to be absorbed into the Waru. He snatched the child from Hethrir's arms and took him to safety as Hethrir was swallowed whole by the imploding Waru. Tigris was reunited with his mother, and the two of them set off for Coruscant.

Saesee Tiin

**Tiin, Saesee** This Iktotchi Jedi Master was born on the moon of Iktotch, where he learned to fly a variety of starships. Over time, after Force training under the guidance of Jedi Master Omo Bouri, Tiin could instinctively fly virtually any craft. He was known in the Republic military as an excellent dogfighter, but was also something of a loner who preferred solitary contemplation over crowded meetings. Saesee Tiin was also one of the few Jedi Masters who never took a Padawan. He served on the Jedi Council at the time of the Battle of Naboo, and was known for his foresight and his ability to foresee the future.

During the height of the Clone Wars, it was Master Tiin who encouraged Anakin to continue the development of a personalized Delta-7 Aethersprite fighter, despite Obi-Wan Kenobi's concern that Anakin viewed the ship as a possession. Master Tiin, however, was hoping that Anakin's innate ability to repair, modify, and improve technology would result in new improvements to the Delta-7 that might give the Jedi an edge in the battle. As the fighting ground on, Master Tiin was appointed the primary liaison between the Jedi Council and the Freedom's Sons organization.

Tiin was paired with Anakin Skywalker again near the end of the Clone Wars, when they accompanied Plo Koon to Rendili to ensure that the planet's fleet of Dreadnaughts was not turned over to the Separatists. Their orders were to secure the fleet or destroy it, a stance that led the crew of the *Mersel Kebir* to mutiny and attempt to remain at Rendili. When Master Koon was taken hostage, Master Tiin was forced to act to destroy the fleet. Anakin then proposed a desperate plan to disable the Dreadnaughts without bloodshed, and the Jedi were able to put an end to the siege. Tiin was among the group of Jedi Masters who accompanied Mace Windu to arrest Chancellor Palpatine. However, the Jedi were unprepared for Palpatine's dark side powers, and Saesee Tiin was quickly defeated.

**Tika** This small, red-haired girl was used by Jacen Solo in his scheme to kidnap his daughter Allana from the Hapan royal palace. Tika was an orphan found on Coruscant who bore a passing resemblance to Allana. In order to gain her confidence, Jacen told Tika he would take her to a planet full of beautiful women, one of whom might become her new mother. In exchange, Tika agreed to dress up like Allana and stay in the princess's room after Jacen captured her. Jacen transported her to Hapes in a sealed cargo crate, where she was given a datapad loaded with games to pass the time while in space. Upon arriving at Hapes, Jacen used his skills with the Force to infiltrate the royal palace and reach his daughter's bedroom. He took Allana and left Tika behind.

**Tikkes, Senator** A Quarren member of the Republic Senate. Formerly an entrepreneur, Tikkes left the business world in favor of the political arena, where he amassed a fortune through corruption and graft. During the year leading up to the Battle of Naboo, Senator Tikkes began to side with Orn Free Taa and the Senators who opposed Chancellor Finis Valorum. As the years wore on and planets began to secede from the Republic, Senator Tikkes was one of the many voices in the Senate who called for the direct formation of the Army of the Republic, rather than voting on it and having the army's formation delayed by bickering. Any political sway Senator Tikkes might have had was eliminated when he was implicated as part of a Thalassian slavery ring. He was taken to prison on Mon Calamari and replaced by Tundra Dowmeia, but later jumped bail and fled the planet. It was believed that Tikkes joined the Confederacy of Independent Systems shortly afterward. He died along with the rest of the Separatist Council on Mustafar.

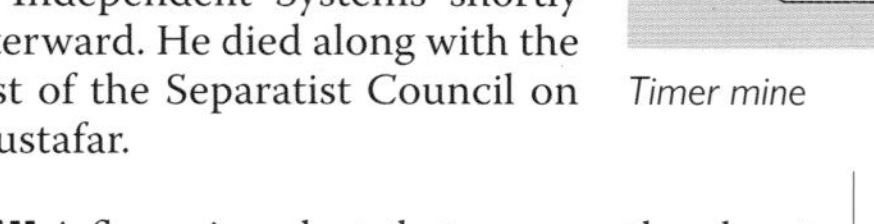

Timer mine

**t'ill** A flowering plant that grew on the planet Alderaan.

**Till, Essara** A flight instructor and member of Naboo's elite Bravo Flight. Essara Till spent several years away from Naboo working as a fighter pilot. When she returned to her homeworld, she was quickly inducted into Bravo Flight. Her efforts during the attack on Station TFP-9 prevented Agamar forces from stealing Naboo starfighters. During the battle, she was betrayed by her lover and wingmate, Dren Melne. While on an escort mission with her wingmate Rhys Dallows to protect the Queen's ship just prior to the blockade of Naboo, she was killed by a mercenary.

Senator Tikkes

**Tilotny** An innocent and bubbly abstract being that existed near the Din Pulsar. She and her fellow entities begin fiddling around with time, matter, and space in their new playground, inadvertently killing Princess Leia Organa and the stormtroopers pursuing her. Tilotny resurrected Leia, but sent the stormtroopers back 8,000 years into the past.

**time-drifting** An extension of the Aing-Tii ability of flow-walking, in which an individual moved along the threads of the Force to travel forward or backward in time. Jacen Solo learned this technique and was able to glean key pieces of information about the fall of Anakin Skywalker by revisiting his final days. The technique was not without its risks. If time-drifters were spotted by those they visited, it could create shifts in the the flow of time by altering the visited beings' actions.

**timer mine** A timer-activated explosive device placed by mining droids, it was typically used in ore and spice mines but had many military applications as well.

**time-stream** A method used by the H'drachi to interpret the Force, especially to foresee future events.

**Tingel Arm** An arm of the galactic spiral. Much of the fighting between the Corporate Sector and the feline Trianii occurred in the distant end of the Tingel Arm. Zonama Sekot, located in the Gardaji Rift, was within the Tingel Arm before its mysterious disappearance.

**Tinn VI** An enormous gas giant in the Tinn system composed of hydrogen, nitrogen, and

Tipoca City

ammonium, it generated a powerful negative magnetic field that extended its shadow into hyperspace and could strip all passing ships of their magnetic battle shielding—forcing them into realspace and leaving them stranded in the system until they could effect repairs. Tinn VI was orbited by six moons labeled A through F; the domed city of Echnos was located on Tinn VI-D, often called Echnos.

**Tinnel IV** Located in the Quanta sector, it contained the city of Val Denn, where the private estate of Moff Jerjerrod was located. Sometime after the Battle of Yavin, Jerjerrod's personal vault was looted by the infamous thief called the Tombat, who stole several of the Moff's priceless artworks.

**Tinoktin, Shok** A male Rhommamoolian who served as Nom Anor's aide prior to the Yuuzhan Vong invasion. He did not know Nom Anor was really a Yuuzhan Vong. Tinoktin met Leia and Jaina Solo, Mara Jade Skywalker, Bolpuhr, and C-3PO when they come to Rhommamool on a diplomatic mission. He left the planet with Nom Anor, ostensibly to meet with Commander Ackdool on the *Mediator*. He and Nom Anor were actually in an A-wing hidden within their shuttle, and they left before the shuttle arrived. The shuttle was full of explosives that detonated upon arrival, to all appearances killing Shok Tinoktin and Nom Anor and heavily damaging the *Mediator*.

**Tin-Tin Dwarf** An intelligent, bipedal, rodent-like species. Tin-Tin Dwarves were actually members of a species from Rinn formally known as the Tintinna and less than a meter tall. They were very similar to Ranats and were considered to be distant relatives. Unlike Ranats, though, the Tintinna had simple, small incisors that emerged from the tops of their mouths. They had small black eyes, small round ears, and soft brown fur. Because of their environment, they often gave off a pleasant, wood-chip smell. Tintinna lived in underground burrows that they dug without the benefit of tools. They chewed to wear down their teeth, which otherwise could grow to uncomfortable lengths. The Tintinna developed a complex, if primitive, form of government. Most lived in tribes ruled jointly by a chieftain and shaman. They toiled in their underground world to survive and to create easier ways of living, and advanced to the point of developing simple technologies based on steam-powered engines. Because their planet was so remote, Tin-Tin Dwarves were rarely seen off their homeworld.

Tin-Tin Dwarf

**Tiny F** The handle used by one of Cularin's most enigmatic slicers during the years leading up to the Clone Wars.

Lord Tion

**Tion, Lord** A member of the nobility and an officer loyal to the Emperor, he served as a task force commander charged with identifying and eradicating all Rebel Alliance personnel and Rebel sympathizers on the planet Ralltiir. Lord Tion played an instrumental role in the Rebellion when he boastingly revealed the location of the plans for the original Death Star battle station to Bail Organa of Alderaan. Thoroughly despicable, he was later killed in a scuffle with Princess Leia Organa.

**Tion Hegemony** A group of 27 systems in the Tion Cluster on the Outer Rim near Corporate Sector space, they were so remote that the Empire never bothered with direct control. As a result, the Tion Hegemony became a haven for smugglers, con artists, and other petty crooks. Common smuggling cargoes included chak-root and R'alla mineral water. Planets in the isolated Tion Hegemony, which unsuccessfully struggled to keep up with the rest of galactic society, included Saheelindeel, Brigia, Rudrig, and Dellalt.

**Tipoca City** This was the greatest of cities on the windswept oceans of the planet Kamino. Like the others, Tipoca City was erected on heavy stilts that extended through the water and into the bedrock of the ocean floor; it spread across more than 150 kilometers at Kamino's equator. The stilts had thin profiles, which allowed the crashing waves to flow around them, rather than break against them. The buildings of Tipoca City were conical in shape, with wide, flared bases and tall towers at their center. The configuration allowed the strong winds that swept the planet to move around and over the buildings without much drag, eliminating a large portion of the environmental stresses they otherwise would have had to endure. This shape also allowed the torrential rains to flow off the roof of each building, avoiding damage due to heavy standing water. Tipoca City's stilt-based substructure was an example of the Alderaanian Oversea form, while the Krorral form of Kashyyyk became the basis for the city's domes. A collection of lightning rods mounted on top of the city channeled the regular bursts of energy over and away from buildings, further protecting them. Access to Tipoca City was protected by a hermetically sealed series of air locks, ensuring a sterile environment in which to live and work. To most beings in the galaxy, the sterile white color of Tipoca City was quite boring. However, the Kaminoans could see into spectra beyond visual light, and could discern swirling patterns in the stark walls.

It was in Tipoca City that the Kaminoans established the huge facility that produced the clone troopers of the Grand Army of the Republic during the decade leading up to the Battle of Geonosis and the Clone Wars. However, despite the amount of government and industry found within its walls, Tipoca City had but a single residential section set aside for government leaders and chief scientists. The millions of Kaminoans who worked in the city each day made their homes in outlying cities. In the wake of the Clone Wars, Tipoca City declined in stature and beauty as fewer and fewer credits were funneled to Kamino. By the time Koa Ne took over as the city's Minister, Tipoca City had begun to fall apart. Several towers had collapsed entirely, and others were badly damaged.

**Tiragga** The Rebel Alliance had a small outpost located on this planet's second moon, but it became infected with the deadly Direllian Plague.

**Tirahnn** A major trade nexus, it was the capital of the Zeemacht Cluster and controlled by the Empire during the Galactic Civil War.

**Tiran** An ancient Drall scientist who proved, some 35,000 years before the Clone Wars, that space and time were inseparable. Tiran also posited that the speed of light was an absolute boundary that could not be crossed. Many of the physical laws he confirmed were later thrown into question by the discovery of hyperspace and the ways in which a starship could enter and exit it with a hyperdrive. A close look revealed that Tiran's Theory of Universal Reference showed that it didn't preclude an object traveling faster than light; it just prohibited an object traveling *at* the speed of light.

**Tiree** *See* Gold Two; Vanis, Tay.

**Tirsa** An industrial planet, it was home to the Tirsa Wargear armaments company, which manufactured the Leviathan submersible carrier.

**Tissar, Ziven** This Rodian was one of the most accomplished big-game hunters living on the planet Kashyyyk at the height of the New Order. A longtime rival of Sordaan Xris, Tissar was also one of Xris's loudest detractors, claiming that Xris was nothing more than a credit lover who couldn't hunt if his life depended on it. Tissar was one of the four Rodians who owned a portion of the Etyyy, which was the Shyriiwook term for the Rodian Hunting Grounds.

**Tiss'shar** A reptilian species native to the humid jungle continents of the planet Tiss'sharl, which was better known for assassins than for savvy in business and envirotechnology. The Tiss'shar had long necks and slender bodies covered with scales and colorful patches. Their large jaws were filled with short pointed teeth; a large pink tongue was always in motion. They had large black eyes covered by a durable transparent film. The personal and business lives of these jungle dwellers were intertwined, and most appreciated the art of the deal. Uul-Rha-Shan, bodyguard for Corporate Sector Authority Viceprex Mirkovig Hirken, was a Tiss'shar.

Tiss'shar

**titavian** A huge, feathered creature native to Naboo. Gungans decorated their kaadu mounts with feathers from goff birds, a type of titavian. The titavian was assumed to eat carrion since large sea creature and animal bones abounded around abandoned perches. These giant reptavians were notable for their expansive arms and powerful pectoral muscles, which were necessary to power their enormous wings. As a result of their bulk, sustained flight was impossible.

**Tito** One of the Flakax goons who worked for the Directors during the Swarm War. Tito and Yugi were dispatched to assassinate Han Solo and his wife, Leia Organa Solo, but were incapacitated by the Solos before they could complete the mission. After his capture, Tito alerted the Solos to a plot by the Killik Colony to launch a series of ships to the homeworlds of insectile species across the galaxy. Each ship carried an assault force of Killiks that would sweep into a planetary capital and stage a military coup.

***TIV Z590/1*** A Republic traffic interdiction vessel that was part of the naval forces supporting the Grand Army of the Republic during the early stages of the Clone Wars. This craft was piloted by the clone trooper known as Sicko, and was the point vessel in an ambush of a Separatist freighter in the Tynnan sector about a year after the Battle of Geonosis. The *TIV Z590/1* was disabled when a Separatist vessel identified it as Republic, and Sicko remained behind to wait for Omega Squad to board the Separatist ship. However, the rescue mission couldn't arrive in time, and Sicko died in the destruction of the *TIV Z590/1*. The wreckage was later recovered by the crew of the Republic assault ship *Majestic*.

**tizowyrm** Yuuzhan Vong–bioengineered creature. Tizowyrms were bred by alchemists to help the Yuuzhan Vong translate and speak foreign languages. They could store enormous amounts of information. A tizowyrm crawled inside a Yuuzhan Vong's ear, where it emitted information subliminally. The tizowyrm needed to be removed from the ear occasionally, because if left inside too long, it would literally vibrate itself to death. Some words—like *mercy* did not translate well into the Yuuzhan Vong tongue.

**TK-0** An armored droid that worked with the tech hunter Gaib at the height of the Clone Wars. TK-0 provided the computing power to sift through records and data in search of transactions, as well as providing access to local computer networks. Gaib and TK-0 provided assistance to the clone commandos Mereel and Ordo during their search for Ko Sai. The information they uncovered tracked the purchase of high-tech devices and systems for an illegal cloning facility to Dorumaa, giving the clones a location to search for the Kaminoan scientist. Gaib and TK-0 also helped to acquire upgraded weaponry for the clone's freighter, the *Aay'han*.

T'landa Til

**Tk'lokk** Ssk Kahorr's pet lizard.

**tkun** This crimson-furred creature was created by Yuuzhan Vong shapers and used by priests as a garrote to execute a quick but spiritually significant sacrifice. At rest, a tkun coiled itself around an arm or leg. When called upon, it wrapped its muscular body around the neck of its victim and constricted until the victim was no longer breathing.

**t'landa Til** Members of this long-lived species were native to Varl and related to Hutts; they had broad faces and bulbous, protruding eyes. They possessed leathery gray-tan skin, a large blunt horn above nostril slits, a wide lipless mouth, and a head attached to a short, humped neck. Long, whipping tails curled over their backs, and two undersized arms folded against their chests, half hidden by folds of neck skin. They had delicate, almost feminine hands, with four, long supple fingers on each. They exhibited the unique ability to create physical and emotional pleasure in others by humming. The effect was addictive, and only those with the strongest willpower could resist.

T'landa Til were considered second-class citizens on their world, living primarily to serve their Hutt cousins. They were, however, as ambitious, greedy, and clever as their relatives, and for many years they grew increasingly dissatisfied with their role in Hutt society. Ten years before the Battle of Yavin, the Hutts enlisted the t'landa Til to use the low-grade empathy engendered by their humming abilities to form a false religion on Ylesia that would lure hapless pilgrims, who could then be enslaved in spice-purification plants. Bria Tharen, one of the first officers of the Rebel Alliance, fell victim to the cult.

**Toat, Lord** The leader of the Trade Federation on Maramere. After Toat claimed Maramere for the Trade Federation, Nute Gunray gave him an original Raith Sienar prototype cloaking device. He was shot and killed aboard his boat, the *Syren*, during an attack by the pirate Sol Sixxa. The mercenary Nym was able to recover the head of Toat's protocol droid, PL-37.

Kass Tod

**Tobal Lens** Developed by Renatta Racing Systems, it was an oval crystal about the size of a human head. Its internal matrix reflected and refracted light into a powerful beam of swirling colors, providing the energy necessary to power Renatta's needle ships. While not expensive, Tobal lenses were difficult to locate on the open market, and the lack of replacement parts eventually drove Renatta out of business.

Tof

**Tobbra, Captain Theb** A first officer on the New Republic starship *Indomitable,* he was the very definition of *cautious* throughout his career. He saw his role on the *Indomitable* as a balance to the excesses of Commodore Brand.

**Tobyl** This man served in the Galactic Alliance Guard on Coruscant at the height of the war between the Galactic Alliance and the Confederation. Tobyl and Jat'ho were part of the GAG squad that captured Ben Skywalker and Lon Shevu in the weeks following the Second Battle of Fondor. However, they were not prepared for the arrival of Jaina Solo and Leia Organa Solo, who used the Force to make the two guards believe they were undercover GAG agents. The two Jedi convinced the GAG guards to let them take a medwagon, which they used to pursue the Doomsled that carried Ben and Lon away from the scene.

**toccat** This ugly beast from the sweaty jungles of Darlyn Boda had four hooves, a long pink snout, and a barrel-shaped body covered with black bristly hair. Reading toccat entrails to predict the future was a big business among Darlyn Boda haruspexes.

**Tocneppil** This smuggler worked with Han Solo at the height of the New Order. The two of them once got lost and could not find their ship. Han had always boasted to Chewbacca that Corellians never get lost, and Chewie kept reminding him of this event. Han later claimed that Tocneppil wasn't a Corellian, and that his own actions could be excused due to drunkenness.

**Tod, Kass** A 17-year-old female Zabrak member of the "Padawan Pack" left to defend Jabiim against a Separatist army. She served as the spiritual center for the group and had strong feelings for her teammate Mak. When she and Mak fought Alto Stratus, she cut off Status's right leg after he mortally wounded Mak. Mak and Kass died in each other's arms after being hit by rockets fired from a hailfire droid.

**Toda, Lord** During the Empire's early days, this gruff and surly bully called himself "overlord of the outer territories" and ruled over a major portion of the planet Tammuz-an. He dressed much like his warrior tribesmen, wearing rough canvas and organic armor.

**Tof** A species of green-skinned humanoids native to the planet Tof beyond the galactic rim. The average Tof was rotund and devoid of morals or compassion. Tof society was ruled by a hereditary monarchy, and young royals were often made military leaders as a sort of education for their future duties. The Tofs were the sworn enemies of the Nagai, and they eventually followed the Nagai into Alliance space following the Battle of Endor. They tried to take over the galaxy after subjugating Zeltros but were put down by the combined might of the Alliance, the Nagai, and the remnants of the Empire.

**Togoria** A world of grassy plains and rolling hills orbiting the blue-white star Thanos, it was the homeworld of the feline Togorians, tall, furry creatures who were suspicious of offworlders. The Togorians had near-complete separation between the sexes: Males and females saw each other only a few days each year. The males spent the remainder of their time as nomads, wandering the plains with domesticated flying lizards called mosgoths, used as

Lord Toda

riding mounts. The females dwelled in the cities, tending animals such as the bist and etelo and maintaining their society's solar-based technology. The government was headed by the Margrave of Togoria, a hereditary office always held by male descendants. The Margrave's closest female relative, living in the capital city of Caross, ruled over the cities and the day-to-day activities of females and young children. Togorian society was still relatively low-tech, although the females proved to be an attractive market for personal technology. Togoria's vast mineral resources were left largely untapped.

**Togorian scimitar** A weapon handcrafted by a Togorian tribal hunter. Unlike vibroblades, Togorian scimitars were "simple" muscle-powered weapons. A vibro-equipped variant was known as the vibro-scimitar.

**Togruta** Native to the planet Shili, members of this humanoid species were distinguished by the immense, striped horns, known as montrals, that sprouted from each side of their heads. Three draping appendages ringed the lower part of their skulls, with one draping over each shoulder and a third hanging down the back. The coloration of these head-tails evolved as a form of camouflage, with a striped pattern that confused predators. The montrals were hollow, providing Togrutas with a way to gather information about their environment ultrasonically. Many beings believed that Togrutas were venomous, a belief that stemmed from the fang-like appearance of their front teeth, but this was untrue. On their homeworld, Togrutas lived in dense tribes that had strong community ties. All members of the tribe were expected to work for the betterment of others, including hunting and gathering. This expectation included the youth of each tribe, and any individual who could not keep pace with the rest was left behind to die. Many xenobiologists believed that the Togruta civilization was an ancient one—there were records of Togrutas being members of the Jedi Order at the time of its formation, some 25,000 years before the Galactic Civil War. The Togrutas were believed to have evolved from pack animals, as evidenced by their "survival of the fittest" mentality. Jedi Ahsoka Tano and Shaak Ti were famous Togrutas.

Togruta

**Tojjelnoot** This Wookiee was a member of the Rock Council some 10 years after the end of the Yuuzhan Vong War. Like other members of the Tojj clan, Tojjelnoot held a grudge against Chewbacca's family after Chewbacca was challenged by Tojjevvuk for the right to marry Mallatobuck. His clan's grudge against Chewbacca did not cease when Chewbacca was killed at Sernpidal, and seemed to extend to Han Solo as well. This issue came to a head when the Galactic Alliance entered its war against the Confederation, a conflict in which the Wookiees chose to remain neutral. Han and Leia Organa Solo traveled to Kashyyyk on a secret mission to convince the Wookiees to secede. On the Council Rock, other members of the council assured the Solos that Tojjelnoot's grudge would not affect their decision. However, in keeping with tradition, Leia was forced to try to take the Talking Bone from Tojjelnoot in order to speak. Although she used the Force during their first bout, Leia was allowed a second chance, and earned the right by herself. Her surreptitious use of the Force to keep Tojjelnoot from falling too hard also earned her his respect, and when other Wookiees tried to drown her out with their bellows, Tojjelnoot took the Talking Bone and struck them with it. He then passed the bone back to Leia and let her continue.

Tojjevvuk

**Tojjevvuk** An albino Wookiee who was Chewbacca's rival for the affections of Mallatobuck. During a fierce struggle with Chewbacca, Tojjevvuk fell from kilometer-tall wroshyr trees to the forest floor. His father, Tvrrdko, later canceled the vendetta he had against Chewbacca after Chewbacca single-handedly saved the children of Tvrrdko's clan from Wookiee slavers.

**Tok, Shogar** The Brentaal Separatist commander who rallied his people against the yoke of the Republic during the Clone Wars. He fought with a vibro-ax that had a blade capable of withstanding blows from a lightsaber. Shaak Ti tried to persuade Shogar Tok to surrender peacefully, but the criminal Lyshaa betrayed and shot the Jedi. When Shaak Ti recovered, Shogar Tok tried to kill her but was no match for the Jedi.

**Toka** The native inhabitants of the Rafa system, in reality the descendants of the ancient Sharu. The Toka, or "Broken People," appeared meek and primitive but had only entered this state to protect themselves from a forgotten, pre-Republic menace. Four years before the Battle of Yavin, Lando Calrissian activated the Mindharp of Sharu and reawakened the Toka.

**Tokare, Vandar** A Jedi Master at the Jedi enclave on Dantooine, he survived Darth Malak's assault on the planet. During the attack on the Star Forge, Vandar Tokare aided Admiral Forn Dodonna. He came from the same species as Master Yoda.

**Toklar** A much-quoted Mon Calamari philosopher, he was an inspiration to Admiral Ackbar.

**Tokmia** One of the planets in the Anoat sector where Imperial probe droids were sent on Darth Vader's orders to search for the new Rebel Alliance base after the Battle of Yavin. The other planets were Allyuen and Hoth. Tokmia was a tundra world, with vast flatlands covered by snow and ice. A barely sentient species of beings known as the Oku evolved there. Figg Excavations made a fortune from the planet's ore and crystal deposits, and left handouts for the Oku during each operation. When the mines played out, Figg Excavations pulled out of its Tokmia operations. In response, the Oku lit huge fires to act as landing lights, hoping the offworlders would return.

Vandar Tokare

**toko bird** A loud, squawking avian native to the planet Paqwepori.

**Tola** During the Swarm War, this Mon Calamari served the Galactic Alliance as a captain aboard the *Admiral Ackbar*, acting on the orders of General Nek Bwua'tu during the blockade of the Murgo Choke. When the Gorog assassin bugs hidden inside spinglass statuary freed themselves and attacked, Tola was hit from behind by several of the bugs. Admiral Bwua'tu was forced to use the butt of his blaster rifle to kill them, but rendered Tola unconscious with the blows. Tola was taken to the medical bay for treatment.

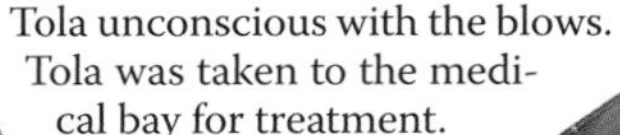

**Toleph-Sor** The legendary "pirate general" whose treasure compartment was rumored to have been located in the Imperial Palace.

Shogar Tok

Toka

**Toli-X virus** A deadly mutated virus that traveled through asteroid mold from world to world 10 years before the Jedi mission to Kegan. A vaccine was developed shortly after the virus appeared. The parents of V-Davi died during the great Toli-X virus outbreak on Kegan when the boy was only two years old.

**Tolsk, Commodore** The commander of Task Force Blackvine, part of the deployment of the New Republic's Fifth Fleet at Doornik-319 during the Yevethan crisis.

**Toma** A tall, bald man who served as a general in Acherin's military forces at the height of the Clone Wars. Like his government, Toma was a strong supporter of the Separatist cause, but realized that the forces of the Republic were too strong. He believed that Acherin would be subjugated and was surprised when Jedi Commander Garen Muln requested a meeting to negotiate a peace treaty. Toma never got a chance to sign the treaty due to Order 66. Rather than see Muln killed by clone troopers, Toma arranged for Muln to escape into the wilderness, and helped keep him out of sight. Many months later, Toma became a resistance leader trying to overthrow the Empire's rule on Acherin. When he met Obi-Wan Kenobi and Ferus Olin, Toma helped them escape from Acherin.

**Tombat** An infamous cat burglar whose signature was to leave a blue quella stone at the site of every heist.

**tomb-wailing ceremony** The traditional funeral rite of the Sullustan people. It was presided over by a crypt master, and followed a rigid protocol for honoring the deceased. Individual mourners were brought forward based on their social standing and their relationship to the dead. After the crypt master placed a layer of seamweld on the tomb wall, mascs (males) were invited to place a transpariblock into the wall that sealed off the deceased's coffin. Fems (females) then used a weld-rake to smooth out the mortar. In this way, the coffin was sealed into the crypt, yet was visible to future visitors. Immediate family were first to place transpariblocks, followed by children living outside the family, warren-clan leaders, blood relatives, closest friends, and corporate representatives of SoroSuub. The final transpariblock was placed by the highest-ranking individual in attendance, who was also required to deliver a brief oration that contained one word for each year of the deceased's age. This

was not a eulogy, but a message to the mourners from the speaker's heart.

**Tomcat** *See* Darovit.

**tomuon** A herd animal native to Askaj. Tomuon coats could be turned into a highly prized fabric.

**Tone, B'dard** This Jedi Master was one of many who were pressed into military duty during the Clone Wars. A tall, imposing Coway distinguished by the shield that covered the left side of his face and the cybernetic replacement of his right hand, Master Tone was one of a handful of Jedi who wanted to destroy General Grievous before he could kill any more innocent beings. The injuries to Tone's face and arm came from an encounter with Grievous on Nadiem, and his first Padawan was killed by the general in the fighting. Thus, when he learned that Flynn Kybo had survived an encounter with the Separatist military leader, he sought out the Padawan to discuss the young man's plans for going after Grievous. They set out to locate the general without the approval of the Jedi Council, eventually tracking him down on Belsus. There Grievous had been planning to use the younglings of the Bergruutfa Clan in an experiment. Although the younglings were eventually rescued, Master Tone was slaughtered in battle with the cyborg warrior.

**Ton-Falk** The site of the Battle of Ton-Falk early in the Galactic Civil War, during which two Imperial frigates and a Dreadnaught were destroyed due to insufficient TIE fighter protection and tactical advice provided by K-3PO, a protocol droid trained in strategy by Commander Narra. Analysis of this battle led to the development of the KDY escort carrier.

**Tonith, Pors** This Muun served the military forces of the Confederacy of Independent Systems as an admiral during the Clone Wars.

*Tookarti*

*Brea and Senni Tonnika*

Despite his background with the InterGalactic Banking Clan, Tonith was also a noted military tactician. A decisive being with more regard for his own safety than that of his troops, Tonith was known to remain safely behind a battle line in a luxurious stateroom aboard his flagship, the *Corpulentus,* calmly sipping dianogan tea. He believed himself to be above reproach, and considered himself more than adequate when Count Dooku assigned him to lead the assault on the communications center on Praesitlyn. Tonith chafed whenever Asajj Ventress demanded a progress report, instead worrying about reinforcements. Although he firmly believed he had the situation under control, Tonith was unaware that Count Dooku was actually controlling the allocation of resources and troops. The reinforcements he requested were delayed in leaving Sluis Van, allowing a Republic task force led by Nejaa Halcyon and Anakin Skywalker to infiltrate Praesitlyn airspace and land on the planet's surface. Tonith was forced to surrender when Anakin apprehended him. He ordered his troops on the ground and his ships in space to stand down, and turned over the communications center to the Republic. He then learned of the arrival of the reinforcements, and was dismayed to realize that he could have won the battle if he had just held out a little longer.

*Tooke-trap*

**Tonnika, Brea and Senni** These beautiful sisters were interested in only one thing: separating men from their money. Humanoid-appearing Kiffu, Brea and Senni Tonnika were abandoned as youngsters and taken in and raised by colonists on Kiffex. Manipulative and clever, they turned friend against friend in order to squeeze credits out of the colonists. They left the planet with a bedazzled scout and continued their scams all over the galaxy. Often, only one sister would appear at a time, using the combined name Bresenni, in order to pull their intrigues. At Han Solo's instigation, they pulled such a trick on Lando Calrissian—well before either got involved with the Rebellion. Calrissian laughed out loud at the joke, but plotted to get back at Solo.

The Tonnika sisters didn't find an amused victim in Imperial Grand Moff Argon, whom they conned out of 25,000 credits. He sent hordes of stormtroopers searching for them. The sisters' infamy had spread so widely that near-identical look-alikes masqueraded as them. In fact, when the Tonnikas were attending a seven-week party at Jabba the Hutt's palace on Tatooine, the Mistryl Shadow Guards Shada D'ukal and Karoly D'ulin assumed the sisters' identities during an unplanned visit to Tatooine. The phony Tonnikas were at the Mos Eisley cantina and were arrested by stormtroopers searching for C-3PO, R2-D2, and their masters. Both the impostors and the real Tonnika sisters managed to get off Tatooine to work their scams elsewhere in the galaxy.

**Tookarti** A Chadra-Fan double agent who helped Aayla Secura in her search for Quinlan Vos on the Wheel space station. Tookarti worked for Vos and also secretly worked for Count Dooku. When Vos learned of Tookarti's betrayal, he killed the Chadra-Fan.

**tooke** A small, hopping rodent native to Naboo.

**tooke-trap** A plant native to Naboo. Tooke-traps received nourishment by consuming tookes and formed symbiotic relationships with shiros for protection against clodhoppers and other predators. Their fragrance was identical to tooke mating pheromones.

**Toola** A glacier-covered, bitterly cold world orbiting the purple sun Kaelta, it was home to the mostly primitive species called Whiphids, who delighted in hunting the indigenous caraboose, furry mastmots (also called motmots), seagoing arabores, flying snow demons, sea hogs, and ice puppies. Toola had only a brief growing season during the summer months when grasses appeared and joined the purple lichens on the plains. Small mining camps were scattered across the planet's surface. Whiphids had only the most primitive technology and lived in loose nomadic tribes led by the best hunter, called the Spearmaster. The only significant export from Toola was ice for water-scarce planets. Whiphids could be found in the galaxy acting as trackers and mercenaries. Notable Whiphids included the Jedi K'Kruhk,

*Toola*

J'Quille, one of Jabba the Hutt's hunters, and Lady Valarian, owner of the Lucky Despot Hotel on Tatooine. Four years after the Battle of Endor, Luke Skywalker traveled to Toola to inspect the ruined home of a slain Jedi Master who had once been the curator of Jedi records on Coruscant.

**Toom Clan** A cutthroat organization on Dorvalla hired by Patch Bruit to sabotage Inter-Galactic Ore prior to the Battle of Naboo. The Toom Clan was mostly made up of far-from-home Weequay and Nikto humanoids, although Aqualish, Abyssins, Barabels, and Gamorreans also numbered among the mix. The clan started as legitimate rescue workers and salvagers, retrieving ships stranded in hyperspace by making use of a powerful interdictor ship. Greed eventually led the group to piracy. They were headquartered in an underground base deep in Dorvalla's unpopulated northern wastes. After using information provided by Darth Maul, the Toom Clan betrayed both Lommite Limited and InterGal by sabotaging the ships of both companies. Using their interdictor, the clan yanked the ships of the mining companies out of hyperspace at the same location, where they collided. Expecting retribution, the Toom Clan fled to their hideout on Riome, but were wiped out by Lommite Limited and InterGal's counterattack.

Toong

**Toong** A species of squat, thin-limbed aliens from the planet Toong'l, located near the Tund system. Their bodies were short and covered with thick skin. They had no neck or shoulders, and their faces seemed to make up their entire torsos. Toongs had a keen fight-or-flight instinct that often manifested itself as acute social anxiety. The Toong species was forced to leave its homeworld when a comet strike left the planet uninhabitable. The Toongs fled to Tund, but faced persecution from Tund's dark side sorcerers. The Podracer Ben Quadinaros was a Toong.

**Toong'l Security Systems** A manufacturer of security droids that was a noted competitor of Cestus Cybernetics during the Republic era. When the X'Ting inquired about a security system for the protection of several royal eggs, Toong'l Security Systems took on the project. Its system was an intricate combination of guardian worms and scent-based receptors that challenged beings with several layers of verification of their intent. Because of the scent-based traps, only X'Tings could manage to reach the deepest levels. Once inside the main chamber, X'Tings were forced to answer three questions. Whether or not they answered correctly, the system declared that the answers were wrong and forced the X'Tings to face their own execution. In this way, the system could determine via scent whether the individuals had penetrated the system for their own prestige, or for the good of the X'Ting people.

**Toora, Toonbuck** A Galactic Republic Senator from Sy Myrth who entered politics as an idealistic crusader only to become one of the its most corrupt members. Over her many years of "service" to the Republic, Toonbuck Toora saw many other Senators destroy their careers when they challenged more powerful politicians. She also learned that she could acquire great wealth by exploiting loopholes in galactic law. Toora began to fraternize with Senators she once condemned, and was known for rewarding friends and supporters with riches and government positions. She kept a consort as a symbol of her power. Toora convinced Sy Myrth to secede from the Republic on the heels of the secession of the planet Ando.

**Toorr, Jip** The Yevethan primate of the warship *Devotion,* formerly *Valorous.*

**Tooth** A clone trooper aboard Joram Kithe's gunship at Pengalan IV who took charge of the unit's other clone troopers after the group drew straws. The clone troopers were given nicknames at the urging of Joram Kithe; Tooth received his moniker because he had lost a tooth during hand-to-hand combat training. Upon learning that a diamond-boron missile-manufacturing facility was located underneath the town of Tur Lorkin, Tooth committed himself to destroying the facility. At Tur Lorkin, he piloted a hammerheaded Corellian transport to draw starfighters away from the sleek silver yacht that Joram and the other surviving clone troopers used to escape the planet.

Toonbuck Toora

**To-phalion Base** A secret Imperial research facility, it was built into the hollowed-out interior of a large asteroid. Formerly used as a mining operation, the asteroid later housed a hangar bay and laboratories for the Vorknkx Project, which developed an experimental cloaking device after the Battle of Hoth. To-phalion Base was surrounded by eight smaller asteroids. Just prior to the Battle of Endor, the renegade Admiral Zaarin attacked To-phalion, and Grand Admiral Thrawn was dispatched to stop him. Zaarin succeeded in stealing the corvette *Vorknkx,* containing the prototype cloak, and escaped into the Unknown Regions. He was tracked and soon eliminated by Thrawn.

**Toprawa** This planet was the initial Rebel hiding place after the Alliance stole the technical readouts for the first Death Star. From the Toprawa Relay Station, Rebel operatives transmitted the plans to Princess Leia's ship, the *Tantive IV,* in the operation known as Skyhook. Later, as punishment for helping the Alliance, the people of Toprawa were forced into a preindustrial state—relying on campfires and bantha-drawn carts as their highest form of technology. Loyal Imperials began living in shining, illuminated citadels out of reach of the lowly Toprawans. Periodically, stormtroopers would ride a grain cart into village squares and watch as the peasants crawled forward on their stomachs, wailing lamentations over the Emperor's death at Endor. Grain was only given to those whose penance seemed the most sincere. Three years after the Battle of Endor, Imperial Intelligence agent Kirtan Loor spent a week on Toprawa after being ordered back from a stay on Borleias.

Qrrl Toq

**Toq, Qrrl** A Nazzar prince and Jedi Knight who fought in the Sith War. He was trained in the ways of the Ulizra by Vrrk Jikat, and later encountered a Jedi Knight for the first time. He had never heard of the Jedi due to the isolationist nature of his species, but the Jedi recognized Qrrl's strength in the Force. Qrrl accompanied the Jedi to Ossus and became an apprentice of the Jedi Master Vodo-Siosk Baas. He created many of the armor types worn by the Jedi of the time and was nearly killed on Onderon by dark side treachery.

**Torbin, Grand Inquisitor** An Imperial lord who served as one of Palpatine's Grand Inquisitors during the reign of the New Order. It was Torbin who was responsible for ousting the

Church of the First Frequency from Otranto. He survived an assassination attempt from the church's disciples when he was rescued by the Tynnan Odumin. Torbin was later killed on Weerden when an assassin droid commandeered the Imperial shuttle *Sark-1* and deliberately crashed it into the Imperial palace.

**Torg, Galen** A Rebel soldier, he was selected for honor-guard duty during the award ceremony for Luke Skywalker and Han Solo following the Battle of Yavin.

**Tork, Admiral Mir** The commander of the Imperial extermination ship *Azgoghk* and a true believer in the "Humans First" doctrine of the Empire. Admiral Mir Tork was a tall, straitlaced, and arrogant human. He never questioned his actions or the righteousness of those actions. He died sometime after the Battle of Endor when Boba Fett destroyed his ship.

**Torlin, Jor** This man was raised on the planet Korriban and chosen for training as a Sith during the decades leading up to the Sith–Imperial War. Torlin lacked any real sensitivity to the Force, and was forced to accept a role as a spy and Special Operations agent. He was one of two operatives, with Morrigan Corde, who were activated by Darth Maladi to hunt down Cade Skywalker. Aboard Torlin's starship, the *Raider*, they disrupted the negotiations between Gar Stazi and Mingo Bovark, using Torlin's C.O.L.D. devices to take control of the diplomats' starships and make them fire on each other. The pair then traveled to Ossus, where Corde injected Torlin with a slow-acting toxin and left him to die.

*Jor Torlin*

**Torlock, Frija (1)** The daughter of Imperial Governor Torlock of Corulag. Frija conspired with Admiral Droon to incriminate her father as a traitor to the Empire. Although the real Frija was killed by Imperial agent Jix, human replica droids resembling Frija and Governor Torlock escaped to the Outer Rim. The Frija droid later rescued Luke Skywalker and C-3PO when they crash-landed on Hoth.

**Torlock, Frija (2)** A female human replica droid, she rescued Luke Skywalker and C-3PO when they crash-landed on Hoth. Imperial technicians had created human replica droids of the real Frija and her father, an Imperial Governor named Lexhannen Torlock, to be used as decoys while the humans escaped an expected Rebel attack. The technicians programmed strong survival instincts into the replicas, so when the battle began, they escaped and isolated themselves on Hoth.

**Torm** *See* Dadeferron, Torm.

**Tornik** One of Jabba the Hutt's human guards.

**torpedo sphere** A siege platform designed to knock out planetary shields prior to Imperial attacks, it was a precursor to the Death Star battle stations. The large 1,900-meter-diameter torpedo sphere was covered with thousands of dedicated energy receptors designed to analyze shield emissions and find weak points. When a site was selected, a rain of missiles could be fired from a group of 500 proton torpedo tubes. A hole in the shields for even a brief period allowed the sphere's turbolasers to destroy the planetary shield generators if the targeting and analysis was correct.

*Galen Torg*

**Torpil** A starship producer contracted by the Galactic Republic to develop and manufacture starfighters during the Clone Wars.

**Torr, Valsil** A wily Twi'lek, he was in charge of the space station at Yag'Dhul. After a brief encounter with Rogue Squadron, he and his men surrendered and allowed the Rogues to remove Warlord Zsinj's bacta from the station.

**Torranix sector** Twelve years after the Battle of Endor, the New Republic astrographic survey ship *Astrolabe* was diverted from this sector, which was near the Farlax sector, to Doornik-1142 by General Etahn A'baht, who was hoping to get an updated survey of the Koornacht Cluster for military intelligence purposes.

**Torsyn, Ryle** The Y-wing pilot who flew as Gold Three during the Battle of Yavin. Ryle Torsyn was recruited by Red Leader Garven Dreis. He found the Imperial tracking device that forced the evacuation of the Rebel base on Dantooine and led the evacuation efforts from that base.

**Torve, Fynn** A member of Talon Karrde's smuggling organization, this human was among the best of Karrde's freighter pilots. While not as flashy as Han Solo or as sophisticated as Lando Calrissian, Fynn Torve adroitly handled the most important and difficult runs for his boss.

**Toryaz Station** A space station in the Kuat system during the years following the Yuuzhan Vong War. The central core of Toryaz Station resembled a flattened sphere measuring 2 kilometers across and 300 meters thick. Twelve spokes radiated outward from the core at regular intervals, each of which was 250 meters in length and connected to a containment pod. The pods, alternately shaped like disks or triangles, housed a variety of recreational and residential environments, while the central core served as a kind of town center. It was filled with hotels and shops that catered to the expensive tastes of the guests of Toryaz Station. The station itself was owned and operated by an alliance of trading families who rented out its pods and facilities to corporations and governments in need of a relaxing, neutral location to hold negotiations.

**Tosche, Merl** The owner of Tosche Station on Tatooine. Merl's facility supplied energy to moisture farms and served as a recharge depot for farmers' landspeeders and other repulsorlift vehicles. The station also boasted a hyperwave repeater, which, when it functioned, received HoloNet feeds relayed from Naboo, Rodia, and occasionally Nal Hutta.

**Tosche Station** A power and distribution station, it was located near the town of Anchorhead on the planet Tatooine. From its inception, Tosche Station served as a gathering place for Anchorhead's young people, including Luke Skywalker and his friends. Luke's friend Fixer worked there.

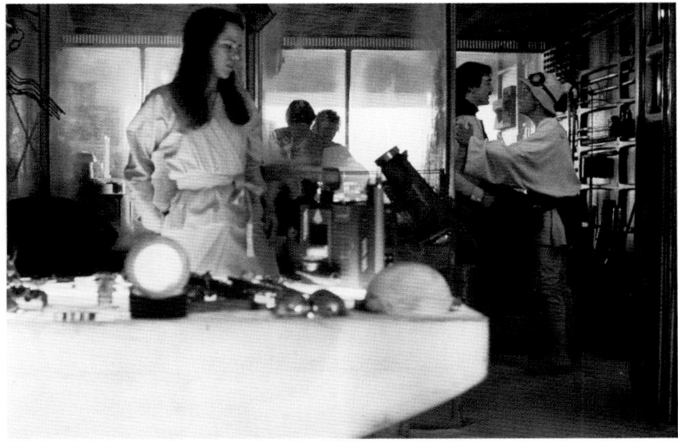
*Tosche Station*

**Tosh, Jann** A young miner on the backworld of Tyne's Horky who briefly owned the droids R2-D2 and C-3PO. His uncle Gundy frequently chastised Tosh for his charity, urging him to concentrate on making their mining camp a success and not to spend their precious keshels too easily. Tosh took in an alien whom Uncle Gundy named Kez-Iban. In truth, Kez-Iban was the lost prince of Tammuz-an, Mon Julpa. A sizable bounty had been placed on his head, one that the evil gangster Kleb Zellock intended to claim. Zellock captured Julpa, Tosh, and the droids, and imprisoned them in his nergon 14 mine. Tosh was able to escape the mines before an explosive reaction destroyed them. For his efforts in helping thwart Zatec-Cha, Jann Tosh was named captain in the Tammuz-an space navy. One of his first challenges in this new position was dealing with Kybo Ren, a notorious pirate based out of the nearby water planet of Tarnoonga. After a stint as Mon Julpa's adviser, Tosh left Tammuz-an to join the Imperial Space Academy.

**Tosi-karu** A Sernpidal goddess. The Sernpidalians believed that Tosi-karu was embodied by the moon Dobido.

**Tossk, Boss** A Trandoshan criminal who worked for Jabba the Hutt during the years leading up to the Battle of Naboo. Tossk was part of a small operation that disgraced Gardulla the Hutt, leading Gardulla to place a bounty on his head. The Trandoshan was then sent to the Oovo IV prison facility for a number of crimes. He thought he was safe from Gardulla's reach . . . until Jango Fett infiltrated the jail and claimed the bounty.

***Toss of the Dice: This Gambler's Life, A*** The title of Lando Calrissian's memoirs, published shortly after the Battle of Endor.

**Toth, Cavik** An evil military genius and the mercenary leader of the Karthakk system. His crew, Sabaoth Squadron, willingly took on dangerous missions for the highest bidder. Cavik Toth struck a deal with Count Dooku to deliver a deadly chemical weapon to the Separatists. Dooku later gave him orders to use the chemical weapon on the Jedi at the Battle of Geonosis. He and his fleet of Sabaoth Destroyers were defeated by forces led by Adi Gallia and Nym.

**Totolaya** A hostage taken by the Yevetha during their attack on the Kubaz colony of Morning Bell.

**Toughcatch** Formerly Jawaswag, this was the nickname of Gavin Darklighter's gold and white R2 unit. He often called it *Catch* for short.

**Tough Squadron** A fighter squadron made up entirely of "uglies." During the Yuuzhan Vong War, Tough Squadron and Savage Squadron fought alongside Rogue Squadron at Dantooine. At the end of the battle, Tough Squadron was completely destroyed.

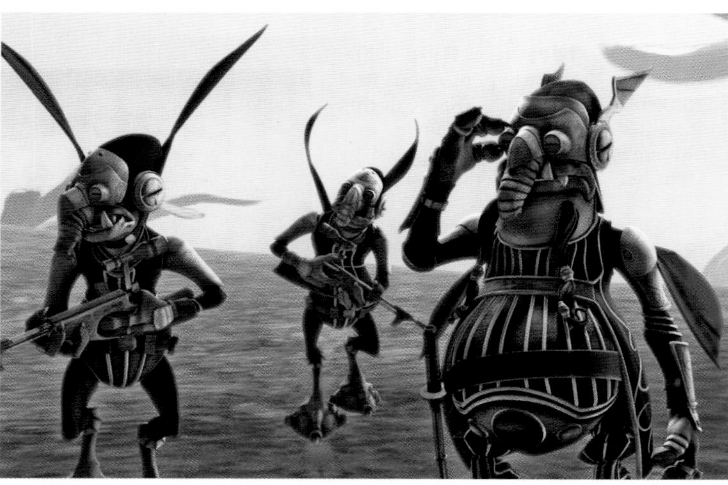

*Toydarian King Katuunko and some bodyguards*

**Touno, High General** An overweight, balding official who was commander in the southern district of the planet Svivren during the last years of the New Order. He had a short temper and absolutely no control over his troops. Most of the Imperials working under him despised the general and his lack of leadership.

**Towani, Catarine** *See* Towani, Cindel.

**Towani, Cindel** The youngest child in the Towani family, she endured a lifetime of terrifying experiences in just a few short years. Cindel and her father and mother, Jeremitt and Catarine, and her brother, Mace, were marooned on the Forest Moon of Endor when their star cruiser crashed. Searching for help, Cindel's parents were captured by a creature called a Borra and taken to the cliffside lair of the monstrous giant called Gorax.

*Cavik Toth*

Cindel and Mace foraged for food, but Cindel fell ill. They were rescued by Deej Warrick the Ewok, who took them back to his village; there his wife nursed Cindel back to health. She became friends with Deej's playful youngest son, Wicket W. Warrick. Mace convinced Cindel to accompany him one night to find their parents, and they were also caught by the Borra. They were rescued the next morning by Deej's family but finally learned that their parents were in the hands of the Gorax. With help from the Ewoks, Jeremitt and Catarine were rescued.

Several months later, Wicket and Cindel returned to the Ewok village only to find it under attack by 2-meter-tall Sanyassan Marauders—humanoids who had also been marooned on Endor years before. Cindel witnessed the death of her mother and brother, but escaped to find her father. The Marauder King Terak and the witch queen Charal had found him first, and he was killed warning his daughter away and trying to escape himself.

Cindel and Wicket fled into the woods. A creature named Teek took them to his human master, a hermit named Noa Briqualon who had also been stranded on Endor when his starship crashed. Cindel was captured again, taken to King Terak's castle, and thrown in the dungeon with captive Ewoks. They were rescued, and a pitched battle ensued at the crash site of Noa's cruiser; Terak and Charal were neutralized forever. When Noa's star cruiser was fixed, Cindel decided to accompany him offworld, although she promised Wicket she would return someday.

Years later, Cindel became an idealistic journalist on Coruscant. She received the so-called Plat Mallar tapes from Admiral Drayson and leaked the story of the only survivor of the attack on Polneye by the Yevetha. The leak was designed to garner sympathy from the public and the Senate. It worked.

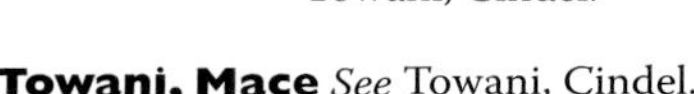

**Towani, Jeremitt** *See* Towani, Cindel.

**Towani, Mace** *See* Towani, Cindel.

**Tower, Admiral Griggor** The Imperial commander of the garrison on Gamandar during the Galactic Civil War. Distinguished by his rakish goatee and a reddish, cybernetic left eye, Tower subjugated the population and extracted much of the planet's natural resources. Shortly before the Battle of Endor, Tower tried to assassinate Luke Skywalker and Leia Organa on Iskalon by firing a missile at the watery world, triggering the deadly Iskalon effect that devastated the planet's settlements. But he failed to kill the Rebels and was executed by Darth Vader for excessive use of force.

**Toydarian** A short species with small wings and vaguely avian features. Toydarians had stubby trunks that barely concealed stunted tusks, and their thin legs ended in webbed feet. Male Toydarians, such as Watto, had visible whiskers. Although their wings appeared frail, Toydarians could fly quite rapidly and preferred flight to walking. They were also impervious to Jedi mental powers. Although they seemed pudgy, Toydarians were actually quite light, primarily because their tissues were spongy and filled with gas. Toydarian newborns emerged from their mothers' wombs fully developed, resembling miniature versions of their parents, and were able to fly from birth.

The Toydarian homeworld of Toydaria was covered with nutrient-rich muck lakes, which supported a number of predators including dangerous grabworms. Toydarians survived by flying virtually everywhere, only landing on the relative safety of alga mats. However, flight required an incredible amount of energy, replenished through the consumption of concentrated foods and high-energy egg-seeds. Wars broke out from time to time among Toydarian confederacies when food supplies were low. The skies of Toydaria were filled with buzzing natives, so starship traffic to and from the world's single spaceport was strictly limited to specific times of the day. The Toydarian government built a light-rail system to ferry offworlders from city to city. While Toydarians incorporated some galactic-level technology into their daily lives, they preferred to dwell in small villages that were far below the galactic standard.

General Traavis

Shrewd bargainers, Toydarians liked to socialize and strike deals. The best of them were proud, loyal, and business-savvy; the worst, greedy, deceitful, and sycophantic. Toydarians liked to gamble, and more daring Toydarian traders made difficult business decisions based on the roll of a chance cube. During the Clone Wars, King Katuunko kept the Toydarians loyal to the Republic.

**Tozr, Chal** This Bith worked as a detective in the Coruscant Security Force during the years following the Swarm War. Unlike his sharp-dressed partner, Gwad Raatu, Tozr wore rumpled clothing. Tozr was often the calm voice of reason during their investigations, as Raatu preferred to attack each case as if it were a kind of hunt. The detectives were dispatched to look into the brutal murder of Jedi Master Tresina Lobi, whose legless and decapitated body was discovered in Coruscant's Fellowship Plaza. Their investigation put them into contact with Grand Master Luke Skywalker and his wife, Mara Jade Skywalker. Together they tracked Lumiya's movements back to an apartment in Zorp House.

**Traavis, General** The Jedi general who led Aiwha Squad on Garqi when Order 66 was executed. He was shot down by his clone troopers.

**Trace** This clone commando was part of the team that accompanied Jedi Master Bol Chatak to Murkhana, serving as a spec-two small-arms expert during the final stages of the Clone Wars. Like his spec-one, Climber, Trace refused to act when the command was given to execute Order 66, failing to understand how the Jedi could have suddenly become the enemy. Trace agreed with Climber's plan to allow Roan Shryne and the other Jedi on Murkhana to escape into the forest before chasing after them.

**trace-breather cartridge** A device used by species that required gases to breathe other than those their environment provided. It released the necessary gas a little at a time.

**tracer spineray** A Yuuzhan Vong creature closely related to the provoker spineray. Like the provoker, the tracer mapped neural pathways to determine how efficiently signals were being transmitted, and to gauge the degree to which tissues remained injured or imbalanced once healing seemed complete. Tsavong Lah used a tracer spineray to evaluate the condition of the radank claw grafted to his arm.

**Trachta, Grand Moff** This cyborg humanoid served as one of the original Grand Moffs during the years leading up to the Battle of Yavin. Trachta's cybernetics closely resembled those of Darth Vader, with a triangular breath mask covering his nose and mouth. Both eyes were replaced by ocular cams, and his lungs were mechanically enhanced. He hated the Jedi as much as he hated the Sith, and was one of the major participants in an early plot to assassinate Emperor Palpatine, hoping to eliminate Darth Vader in the same stroke. Trachta had known Palpatine for nearly three decades when he hatched his plans to eliminate Vader and all remnants of the Sith while creating a new Imperial regime in his own image. Unbeknownst to his co-conspirators, Trachta also planned to eliminate each of them in time. His plans fell through when Grand Moff Bartam set his own plans in motion. Just as Bartam was assassinated by Trachta's agent, Trachta found himself cornered by one of Bartam's agents. The agent shot him immediately.

**tracomp** A high-tech compass device—which could be part of a starship's sensor array or portable—it was dedicated to getting a fix on a planet's axial and magnetic poles. A tracomp then placed the ship within a spherical-coordinate lattice and locked on to any transmitting navigational beacons within range.

**tra'cor** A subspecies of rancor found on the remote world of Socorro. Much smaller than the typical rancor, the tra'cor was an aquatic creature that spent most of its life beneath the

Grand Moff Trachta

surface, consuming fish and other marine life. Though the tra'cor was amphibious, it could survive for only short periods outside the water, since it dehydrated quickly. Tra'cor had large tails that resembled those of serpentine sea creatures, adding a natural weapon to the creature's arsenal that rancors did not possess. Deadly in any situation, underwater the tra'cor was exceptionally fast and could overtake its prey in a matter of seconds.

**tractor beam** A modified force field, it could immobilize and then draw in any object caught in its range. An emitting tower—a tractor beam projector—produced the beams, the strength and range of which were determined by their power source. Tractor beams helped guide ships to a safe landing in spaceports and hangar bays. Salvage vessels, cargo haulers, emergency craft, and engineering teams used tractor beams to help them in their jobs. Military tractor beams were used to capture enemy vessels or hold them in place to be blown out of the skies.

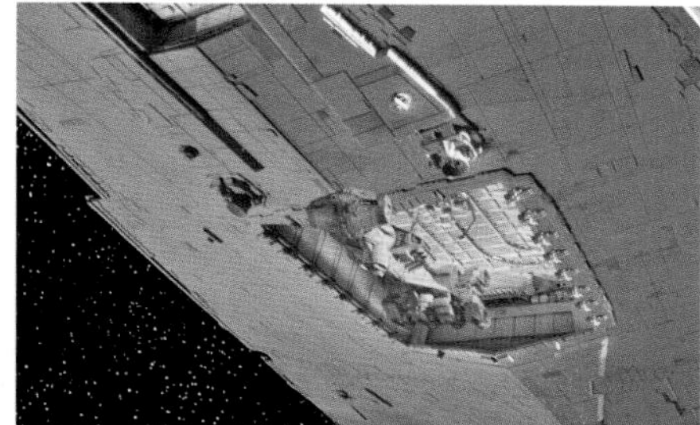

Tractor beam

**Trade Federation** This group was formed some 350 years before the Battle of Yavin to monitor and maintain the delicate balances of power between the growing economies of the Core Worlds and the developing planets of the Outer Rim Territories. The Trade Federation policed commerce for the Republic, working to ensure fairness and mediate disputes between merchants and transport providers. The Trade Federation became powerful enough to maintain a seat in the Republic Senate. Many

Trade Federation

outlying systems aligned themselves with the Trade Federation rather than requesting direct representation in the Senate, because it was a more expedient way to develop trade with the Core Worlds. However, the Trade Federation was inherently weak, and soon found itself under the control of Darth Sidious during the years leading up to the Clone Wars.

A series of political maneuvers led to the Republic's taxation of trade routes, which took away much of the control and profit realized by the Neimoidians who controlled the Trade Federation Executive Board. In an attempt to force the repeal of the tax law, the Trade Federation followed Darth Sidious's orders and threatened Naboo by blockading all trade to and from the planet. The blockade was broken during the Battle of Naboo, and in the aftermath the Trade Federation's war fleet and its military personnel were absorbed into the Republic's defense forces. Though the Republic ordered the immediate downsizing of the Federation's droid forces, many of these combat automata were simply resold to Trade Federation holdings. Nute Gunray, the Viceroy of the Trade Federation, survived imprisonment and maintained control, throwing his support behind Count Dooku and the Separatists. In the wake of the Clone Wars and the establishment of the New Order, the Trade Federation was absorbed into the Empire after Acting Viceroy Sentepeth Findos signed a treaty. His assumption of power was questioned by other members of the Trade Federation, who vowed to fight against Imperial domination. These small groups of resistance were eventually eliminated, and the Trade Federation ceased to exist.

**Trade Federation battleship** A Trade Federation freighter converted to serve as a weapon of war. Trade Federation battleships were immense, circular vehicles with a central, spherical structure. They had powerful shields and numerous laser cannon emplacements. When attacked, they could also unleash hordes of droid starfighters. All Trade Federation battleships, including the Droid Control Ship, were modified cargo vessels originally built by the Trade Federation for commercial purposes. When conflict with the Republic became a possibility, Trade Federation officials opted to convert these massive vessels into functional battleships rather than construct or buy starships specifically designed for war. Because the Trade Federation cargo ships were a common sight among thousands of worlds, potential victims were not aware of an attack until it was too late. In order to convert the cargo transports for war, the Trade Federation added numerous quad laser batteries that rotated inward, allowing them to be concealed until needed. The laser batteries were only added to the transports' equatorial bands, resulting in limited coverage. The outer hangar of each battleship, known as Zone 1, received arriving starships, which were guided into the hangar with multiple tractor beams. Trade Federation landing ships also prepared for launch in Zone 1. Zone 2, the middle hangar, was reserved for loading and arming landing ships and tanks.

**Trade Federation Droid Control Ship** *See* Droid Control Ship.

**Trade Federation Executive Board** This was the primary governing body of the Trade Federation, and was responsible for making its strategic decisions. Also known as the Directorate, this seven-member body was controlled by the Neimoidian Inner Circle. Shortly before the Battle of Naboo, Darth Sidious arranged to have six of the seven members of the board assassinated on Eriadu, leaving Nute Gunray as the sole survivor and, therefore, the new Viceroy. Gunray then filled the remaining six positions with puppets who would do his bidding.

***Trader's Luck*** An old troopship from the Clone Wars used by Garris Shrike's trading clan. Formerly called the *Guardian of the Republic,* Garris Shrike turned this *Liberator*-class vessel into the headquarters for his nomadic band of space criminals, which operated in the Corellian sector. Han Solo spent his youth aboard the ship, until he stowed away at age 19 in a robotic cargo freighter.

**Trade Spine** Also known as the Corellian Trade Spine, it was located near the Ison Corridor. As with all of the great starlanes, no single date marked the founding of the Corellian Trade Spine. Generations of spacers forged the individual links between star systems that made up the Spine, seeking efficient hyperspace routes between civilized systems. Large portions of the "outer" Spine—defined as that portion lying Rimward of the intersection with the Rimma Trade Route at Yag'Dhul—were heavily traveled for a few hundred years. The outer Spine was always relatively independent from the galaxy's central authority. The Rebel Alliance eventually made its way to the outer Spine, establishing one of its principal bases on Hoth a few hours off the route. Worlds of the Spine included Javin, Aztubek, High Chunah, Kirtarkin, Mexeluine, Gerrenthum, Indellian, Bendeluum, Zhanox, Ione, Mataou, Anantapar, Shuxl, Ertegas, Darlyn Boda, Orn Kios, Ozu, Isde Naha, and Togominda.

***Tradewyn*** This Mon Calamari cruiser was the flagship of the Bornaryn Trading Company's fleet, and served as a mobile base of operations for Lady Aryn Dro Thul during the Swarm War.

**Traffic Intervention Vessel (TIV)** A ship produced specifically for use by the Grand Army of the Republic during the Clone Wars. TIVs were designed to move in and out of starship traffic, allowing clone units to reach a target and board it with relative ease. Known among the clone troopers who flew them as "plain wrappers," TIVs were often civilian or corporate vessels that had been commandeered for the war but left in their original state for camouflage.

**Tragett, Bogo** The team leader of excavation Team Alpha, which was assigned to

Trade Federation battleship

Underground city in Tralus

Maltha Obex (the former Brath Qella) by the Obroan Institute of Archaeology.

**Trailing Sectors** An area in the Expansion Region south of the Corellian Run, with colonization driven by the Alsakan Conflicts in the Slice. Many of the worlds of the so-called Trailing Sectors remained dubious about central authority.

***Tra'kad*-class transport** This ungainly troop transport was one of the new classes of warships developed by MandalMotors some 10 years after the end of the Yuuzhan Vong War, after a new lode of *beskar* was discovered on the planet Mandalore. Many beings described the *Tra'kad* as a flying slab of Mandalorian iron, and were surprised to find that the ship was quite maneuverable. The name of this ship class came from the Mandalorian term for "star saber," and many non-Mandalorians simply referred to the ship as the StarSaber. The Verpine initially refused to purchase any of these ships, since they could find no mission profile in which to use the "primitive" vessel. However, the 20-meter-long *Tra'kad* was well armed and had overlapping fields of fire, ensuring that the ship had no blind spots that could be exposed by an enemy vessel. A cannon turret was mounted at each corner, as well as one turret on the top and one on the bottom. A modular weapons emplacement was also installed on the top, giving owners a chance to install other weaponry. In an emergency, the *Tra'kad*-class transport could operate on virtually no power. All major systems were equipped with manual backups such as gearwheels and compressed gas systems, while zero-power fiber optics provided targeting and steering capability. This allowed the ship to escape from situations where other vessels would be unable to defend themselves. The ship could be operated by a single individual, since the main controls were duplicated at various places, but it was most effectively staffed by a crew of five. The full crew complement made life aboard the ship quite cramped, since much of the interior space was used to house the redundant systems.

**Tralkpha** A Mon Calamari, he was navigator aboard the *Jade's Fire.*

**Tralus** One of the five habitable planets in the Corellian system, it was a blue, white, and green world the same size as its sister planet, Talus. Both Tralus and Talus orbited a common center of gravity where Centerpoint Station was located. Together they were referred to as the Double Worlds, and both were ruled by the elected Federation of the Double Worlds, or Fed-Dub. Beneath the surface of Tralus was a planetary repulsor, used in ancient times to move the planet into its orbit from an unknown location. After the Battle of Endor, Grand Admiral Grunger rammed his flagship into Grand Admiral Pitta's torpedo sphere at the Battle of Tralus. During the Corellian insurrection, a flare-up in Centerpoint Station caused many deaths, and the survivors were relocated to Talus and Tralus. When word spread of the incident, two rebellions against Fed-Dub broke out on Tralus. A group of starfighter pilots subsequently flew to Centerpoint and claimed the station for themselves until chased off by a Bakuran task force. During the Corellian sector's war against the Galactic Alliance, the two sides fought for possession of Tralus.

**Trammis III** On this planet famous as the home of gigantic reptiloids, the inhabitants spoke Trammic, which was related to the Old High Trammic spoken by the Toka of the Rafa system. It was also home of Trammistan chocolates.

**Trandosha (Dosha)** The homeworld of the war-like reptilian Trandoshan species. Trandosha's society was based on a strict class system. Points of interest included the Lorpfan deserts.

**Trandoshan** Large, reptilian humanoids from the planet Trandosha (or Dosha), they had supersensitive eyes that could see into the infrared range and the ability to regenerate lost limbs. They also shed their skin. Trandoshans were a war-like species that allied early with the Empire, taking Wookiees as slaves. They valued hunting above all else and worshipped a female deity known as the Scorekeeper, who awarded jagannath points to Trandoshans based on their success or failure in the hunt. When hunters wished, they returned to their homeworld and mated with a convenient clutch mother; they did not form lasting relationships. Young Trandoshans hatched from eggs. They had a difficult time manipulating delicate objects with their relatively clumsy clawed hands. The bounty hunter Bossk was one infamous Trandoshan.

**Trandoshan double-blade** A primitive sword used by the Trandoshans as a badge of honor. Variants included those made of the rare ore Chalon, sharper and heavier than a typical blade.

**Trandoshan suppressor pistol** This quick-firing, short-range weapon emitted alternating loud bursts of energy from dual muzzles. Any Wookiees lucky enough to escape the slave camps remembered the sound of this pistol for the rest of their lives.

**Trang Robotics** A family-owned droid manufacturing business with a long and respected history. Trang Robotics was best known for the highly regarded Duelist Elite fencing trainer. The company's lavish headquarters and master-craftsman workshops were located on the inhabited moon of Drewwa in the Almania system.

Trandoshan

TranLang III communications module

**TranLang III communications module** An advanced communications module used in C-3PO and TC series protocol droids. The TranLang III could access more than six million forms of communication.

**transfer register** An electro-optical device, it documented the sale or trade of property and merchandise. A transfer register recorded the thumb prints of buyers and sellers, officially documenting a transaction.

**TransGalMeg Industries, Inc.** The manufacturer of the *Xiytiar*-class transport and the hyperdrive booster ring used for the Delta-7 Aethersprite light intereceptor. TransGalMeg Industries, Inc., had many different product lines, with strong colonization, mining, and agricultural interests. Its starship and vehicle product divisions were originally founded for the company's internal use; only after they proved reliable were they sold to the general public. TransGalMeg was based in the Rayter sector.

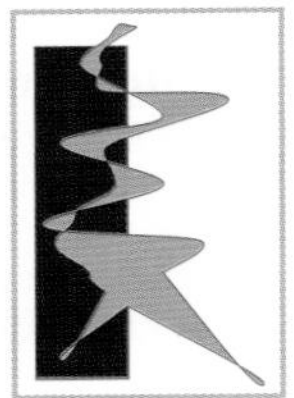

**Transitory Mists** Huge, gaseous drifts surrounding the Hapan Cluster. The Mists made hyperspace travel in the regions nearly impossible, and the only feasible entrance to the Hapan worlds was through a small corridor carefully guarded by Hapan patrols. When most of the Hapan fleet was destroyed in the Battle of Fondor early in the Yuuzhan Vong War, Queen Mother Teneniel Djo secretly ordered shipyards in the Transitory Mists to begin rebuilding. The project was detailed in a holocube ring that Teneniel gave her daughter, Tenel Ka. When Tenel Ka assumed the throne of Hapes, she learned of the rebuilt fleet and offered command of it to Colonel Jagged Fel.

**transparisteel** A malleable metal, it was pressed and formed into thin, transparent sheets that retained nearly all of the metal's strength and durability. Transparisteel replaced glass on starships and other structures that required both visibility and protection.

**transport, Rebel** The Rebel Alliance used a number of different types of ships to supply food, ammunition, and other ordnance to its troops. These transports were converted passenger liners, small freighters, and other older ships that were prone to breakdowns. Often working in convoys, their most visible effort was the evacuation of Echo Base during the Battle of Hoth. With only a couple of X-wings and a few shots from a planetary ion cannon, the lightly armed cargo ships blasted past the Imperial blockade and saved the Rebel Alliance's vital computers and equipment.

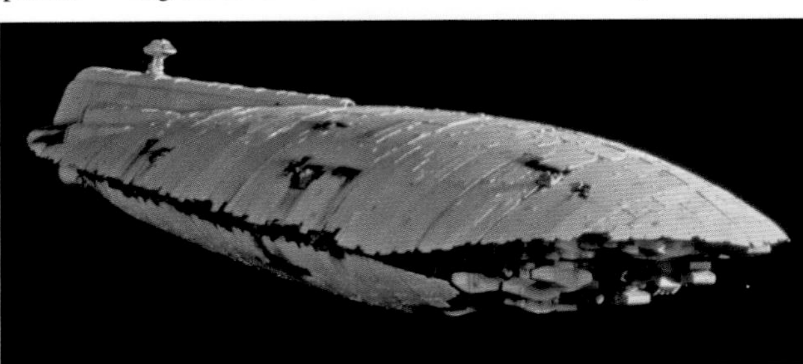
Rebel transport

The ships used in the escape from Hoth were Gallofree Yards Medium Transports. Only about 90 meters long, they had a cargo capacity of 19,000 metric tons. Each ship's outer hull was little more than a thick shell with an open interior filled with cargo modules. Some of the ships served as fuel tankers for long-range missions; others were converted to passenger or troop transport duty.

A crew of seven operated from a small, cramped pod mounted above the ship's rounded hull. The ships' hyperdrives augmented their standard sublight ion drives and repulsorlift drive units for landing directly on a planet. Because they weren't combat vessels—at most they had four twin laser cannons—Rebel transports made every effort to avoid Imperial entanglements. They relied mostly on starfighters for protection.

Anson Trask

**Trask, Anson** One of the many stormtroopers who served the Empire nearly a century after the Yuuzhan Vong War. The son of a combat veteran, Anson wanted nothing more than to follow in his father's footsteps. Trask was assigned to Joker Squad of the 407th Stormtrooper Division and given the nickname of Noob, since he was a "newbie" to the unit. Trask got into trouble upon landing on Yinchorr when he insulted the Sith Lord Darth Maleval, who had been dispatched to take command of the 407th. Under the watchful eyes of Maleval, Trask and the 407th were dispatched to Borosk to eliminate the 908th Stormtrooper Division, which had defected to former Emperor Roan Fel. The fighting on Borosk was Trask's first taste of actual combat, and he froze during the initial attack on the 908th's headquarters. His concerns only mounted when Lord Maleval demanded a show of loyalty from the squad's commander, Lieutenant Gil Cassel. Maleval captured Cassel's brother, Jared, and demanded that the lieutenant execute him as a traitor to the new Empire. Cassel hesitated, and Maleval threatened to kill them both. Trask acted out of instinct, shooting the Sith Lord. Sergeant Harkas later turned over leadership of Joker Squad to Trask.

**Trax sector** Located in the Outer Rim, it contained the planets Deysum III—site of the sector capital—and Uogo'cor and the Trax Tube (a major Outer Rim shipping lane). It was the site of a large Imperial resupply base over Bissillirus as well as an extensive Rebel spy network. The sector had 178 settled systems and a population of more than 500 billion.

Darth Traya

**Traya, Darth** This was the name adopted by former Jedi Master Kreia when she turned to the dark side and joined the Sith in the wake of the Mandalorian Wars. After Kreia was exiled from the Jedi Order, she traveled to Malachor V to locate Darth Revan. Once there, she trained at the Trayus academy and eventually became Darth Traya. She chose two of her students, Darth Sion and Darth Nihilus, to form the base of power for the Sith on Malachor V. Historians believed that she was either exiled by her former students or betrayed by them, forcing her to set out on her own. She was able to sense the presence of her former student, the Jedi Exile, and discerned that she might be the last of the Jedi. She set out to locate the Exile, and was forced to fight Darth Sion in order to find her at Peragus II. During subsequent battles, Darth Traya maintained her appearance as Jedi Master Kreia. After the Jedi Exile traveled to Onderon and defeated General Vaklu, Kreia realized that her "pupil" was growing in strength and would become a threat to her triumverate of power. She tried to kill her on Dantooine, but fled. After the deaths of Darth Nihilus and Darth Sion, Darth Traya was the only surviving member of her Order, and she lost her life in a final showdown with the Jedi Exile.

**TRD** An acronym that pilots jokingly used for "Trench Run Disease," referring to the tactics that destroyed the first Death Star at Yavin.

**treaded neutron torches (TNT)** Ground vehicles, they were

Treadwell robot

designed to blast through rock with fireball-shooting cannons. Although TNTs were created to open new shafts in the Kessel spice mines, they were later used to clear jungle and forest clearings.

**treadwell robot** A multipurpose, six- or seven-limbed wheeled droid, it could be programmed to perform many forms of menial labor, including general-purpose repairs. The WED15 units were manufactured by Cybot Galactica.

**Treasury Orders Act** This was one of the many laws that governed the Galactic Alliance. Under the Treasury Orders Act, members of the government were given the right to seize the assets of any being who posed "a genuine risk to the Galactic Alliance."

**Treaty of Anaxes** A treaty signed by the Moffs of the reformed Empire more than 100 years after the Battle of Yavin. When no single faction could be blamed for the problems caused by the failed Yuuzhan Vong terraforming of the Ossus Project, the Imperials decided to take war to the Galactic Alliance. The resulting conflict became known as the Sith–Imperial War after the Empire forged an alliance with the growing Sith Order.

**Treaty of Vontor** An agreement signed 25,100 years before the Battle of Yavin by the Klatooinians, Vodrans, and Niktos, it bound all three species to the Hutts as permanent slaves.

**Trebela** The site of a major Rebel network, it was smashed by Imperial Governor Kraxith. Most of the Rebel groups had been working independently and were not aware of the others' activities.

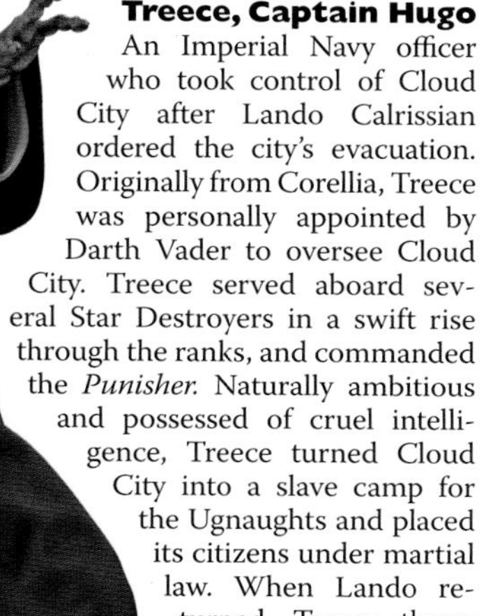

Coleman Trebor

**Treblanc, Romeo** A retired actor who owned the Galaxies Opera House on Coruscant. Despite his success, Treblanc lost a small fortune while gambling on Podraces in the Outer Rim. Chancellor Palpatine, a patron of the arts, helped support him in exchange for a permanent private box and adjustments to the security systems within his favorite opera house.

**Trebor, Coleman** A male Vurk who was a noted member of the Jedi Council during the years leading up to the Battle of Geonosis. Master Trebor joined the Council after the death of Yarael Poof, and was known for his diplomatic skills in resolving conflicts. He put these skills to good use as the official spokesbeing for the Jedi Order, answering questions for the public and the media. When Mace Windu formed a task force to combat the Separatist army on Geonosis, Coleman Trebor was one of many Masters to accompany Windu. Unfortunately, his lack of combat experience became clear during the early stages of the battle when the bounty hunter Jango Fett shot and killed him.

Captain Hugo Treece

**Tredway, Dena** A supporter of the Rebel Alliance and one of Mon Mothma's closest aides, she was severely injured in an attack at her stronghold in the Sil'Lume asteroid belt but was rescued by Luke Skywalker.

**tree-botts** Arboreal creatures, they were used by Rodians for meat and milk.

**Treece, Captain Hugo** An Imperial Navy officer who took control of Cloud City after Lando Calrissian ordered the city's evacuation. Originally from Corellia, Treece was personally appointed by Darth Vader to oversee Cloud City. Treece served aboard several Star Destroyers in a swift rise through the ranks, and commanded the *Punisher*. Naturally ambitious and possessed of cruel intelligence, Treece turned Cloud City into a slave camp for the Ugnaughts and placed its citizens under martial law. When Lando returned, Treece threw him from the floating metropolis and into the clouds of Bespin. Lando was saved from certain death by his cyborg aide, Lobot, and the two joined forces with rebellious Ugnaughts to defeat the Imperial forces. Lando later arranged to send the details of Treece's embezzlement to Darth Vader's personal account on Aargau. Treece disappeared soon thereafter, presumably executed.

**Treemba, Si** A young Arcona who befriended Obi-Wan Kenobi when the Jedi apprentice was 12 years old. The pair met aboard the *Monument,* a transport traveling to Bandomeer. Treemba, who worked for the Arconan Mineral Harvest Corporation, found his life threatened during the voyage because of his close association with Kenobi, but he never abandoned his friend. Si Treemba was slightly shorter than most Arconans, and his skin had a greenish tint.

Master Treetower

**Tree of Light** A mystical tree in the forest of Endor's moon, it was surrounded by a bright, beautiful glow that kept the Night Spirit from using its powers during the day, according to Ewok legend. It was traditional for a group of young Ewoks to travel to the Tree of Light and feed it the sacred dust that rejuvenated its strength.

**Treetower, Master** An Ugnaught Jedi Master dispatched to Yorn Skot at the height of the Clone Wars to break up a smuggling ring that supplied weapons and matériel to the Separatists. Something happened during the mission, and contact with Master Treetower was lost, prompting the Grand Army of the Republic to send in the H.O.P.E. Squad to locate him. He had been knocked unconscious after reaching the planet, and had fallen from one of the gas-processing platforms. He was found hanging by his Jedi robes; he regained consciousness just as the troopers arrived. The rescue was interrupted by a squad of jump droids, and an intense battle ensued. Master Treetower was nearly killed, and only one member of H.O.P.E. Squad survived the mission.

**Tregga** An old acquaintance of Han Solo and Chewbacca, he was caught smuggling contraband and sentenced to life imprisonment in Akrit'tar's penal colony.

Pol Treidum

**Treidum, Pol** An Imperial officer, he was responsible for maintaining magnetic field atmosphere and security in the docking bay of the first Death Star. He was paranoid about infiltration by Rebel spies.

**Trell, Poas** This executive aide to New Republic First Administrator Nanoad Engh urged Leia Organa Solo to buff up her public image.

**Tremayne, High Inquisitor Antinnis** This man served as a High Inquisitor of the Empire during the Galactic Civil War. Taken into the Jedi Temple at 19 months of age, Tremayne was trained as a Jedi Knight by Master Dav Kylanu before being seduced by the dark side of the Force. His fall began after Master Kylanu died during the Clone Wars, and Tremayne himself was captured and interrogated by the Confederacy. He suddenly reappeared some six months before the end of the Clone Wars, carrying the title of Inquisitor. He was led down the dark path by none other than Palpatine, and it was rumored that Tremayne was one of the Emperor's Hands. In this position, Tremayne was among the many individuals who were chosen by the Emperor to hunt down renegade Jedi in the wake of the so-called Jedi Rebellion.

Feltipern Trevagg

When Palpatine was satisfied with the destruction of the Jedi Order, Tremayne continued to search for three young Padawans: Drake Lo'gaan, Zonder, and Ekria. They eluded him several times before Prince Xizor brought word of their existence to Tremayne's attention. In return, Xizor demanded information on Darth Vader and promised to keep word of Tremayne's mission a secret.

Tremayne was eventually promoted to the position of High Inquisitor, and had an illustrious career serving Palpatine. In this position, Tremayne was answerable only to Darth Vader and the upper echelons of Palpatine's advisers. Tremayne had been able to break every captive brought to him until he encountered Corwin Shelvay. After he defeated Darrin Arkanian, Tremayne was disfigured in battle during Shelvay's escape, losing an eye as well as his right arm. Both were replaced with cybernetic prostheses. Afterward, Tremayne scoured the galaxy, looking for Shelvay to exact revenge. Tremayne was given command of the Star Destroyer *Interrogator.*

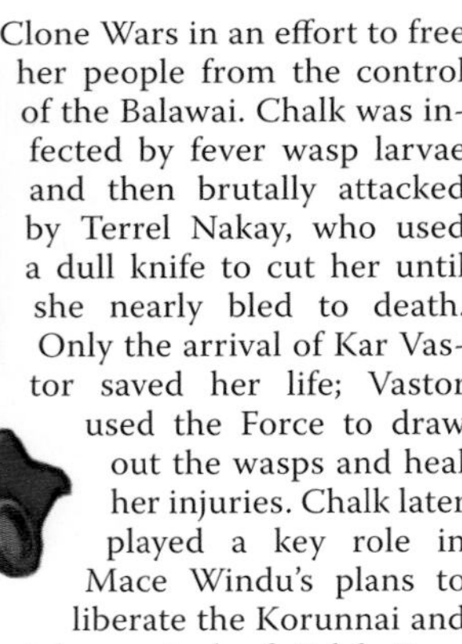

High Inquisitor Antinnis Tremayne

**tremor sword** A bladed weapon that could be traced back to the Bladeborn—Sith who devoted themselves to the mastery of swordfighting with steel weapons instead oflightsabers. The blade of a tremor sword was laced with cortosis ore for added strength against lightsabers. Only those Bladeborn who survived 10 duels with a lightsaber-wielding opponent, known as masterblades, were awarded a tremor sword.

***Trenchant*** A light escort in the New Republic's Fifth Fleet, it was assigned to the blockade of Doornik-319. The *Trenchant* was destroyed during the Yevethan attack.

**Trent, Captain** Commanding officer of the *Halleck* during the Clone Wars, he was seriously injured during a mission to extract Jedi Masters Mace Windu and Depa Billaba from Haruun Kal.

**Trevagg, Feltipern** A male Gotal bounty hunter, he tracked Obi-Wan Kenobi to Tatooine, never found him, and never left the planet. He became a corrupt tax collector for the City Prefect of the Port of Mos Eisley. He was killed by Miiyoom Onith, a H'nemthe female, after mating with her. The killing was a common part of her species' mating ritual.

***Trevee*** A run-down, pod-shaped ship with a Tholatin crew and a Nar Shaddaa registry, used by Droma's clanmates to head for Abregado-rae during the Yuuzhan Vong War. The droid Baffle told Droma and Han Solo that the *Trevee* was actually headed for Fondor. The crew of the *Trevee* intended to drop off the ship's refugee passengers on one of Fondor's shipbuilding platforms, but during the Battle of Fondor, Han Solo and Droma used the *Millennium Falcon* to convince the *Trevee*'s crew to help the refugees they had just abandoned.

**Trevval, Liane** The birth name of the Korunnai soldier known as Chalk. She joined the Upland Liberation Front during the Clone Wars in an effort to free her people from the control of the Balawai. Chalk was infected by fever wasp larvae and then brutally attacked by Terrel Nakay, who used a dull knife to cut her until she nearly bled to death. Only the arrival of Kar Vastor saved her life; Vastor used the Force to draw out the wasps and heal her injuries. Chalk later played a key role in Mace Windu's plans to liberate the Korunnai and take control of Pelek Baw. But she was shot in the chest during the initial assault and died shortly afterward. Her name was later inscribed in the Galactic Senate's records of those who died in defense of the Republic during the Clone Wars, as requested by Master Windu.

**Trey'lis, Hosk** This male Bothan was one of many Jedi Knights who defended the galaxy some 130 years after the Battle of Yavin. In order to evade the Sith who served Darth Krayt, Trey'lis traveled to Lok, where he enlisted the help of the staff at Brogar's cantina to find an escape route. His plans were cut short when Cade Skywalker and his gang arrived at the cantina to take control of Naxy Screeger. Trey'lis panicked and tried to flee, but was stunned into submission by Deliah Blue and Jariah Syn. When he was questioned by the bounty hunters, Trey'lis revealed that he had lost his lightsaber while escaping an explosion, and begged for mercy. Trey'lis was eventually turned over to Darth Maladi. The female Sith Lord tortured and interrogated him, and he revealed Cade Skywalker's identity, giving the Sith a lead on his whereabouts. Trey'lis was then forced to minister to the health of Darth Krayt, but was unable to discover a cure for the Sith Lord's steady deterioration. Relegated to the dungeons of the Sith Temple on Coruscant, Trey'lis was surprised when Cade Skywalker arrived to rescue him. Darth Talon used the Force to render Trey'lis unconscious before confronting Skywalker.

Hosk Trey'lis

**Triad** The governing council of three members—one human, one Drall, and one Selonian—that ruled Sacorria. They were responsible for making planetary policy. The Triad had been the Diktat's mouthpiece, but after the Empire fell they became more autonomous. The council was responsible for several revolts in the Corellian system during the New Republic; they provided funding to draw attention away from their brainchild, the Starbuster Plot.

**trial-born** A term used to describe those members of Chiss society who were taken into the military but retained the opportunity to return to their families. It was common practice for any military personnel to cut all family ties when they were accepted into either the Chiss Defense Fleet or the Chiss Expansionary Fleet. It was also common for military personnel to give up their positions when they retired from active duty and returned to society. Those individuals who were named as trial-born by their families could retain the privileges of both family and military, tying the individual permanently to the family.

**Trian** The homeworld of the feline Trianii species, it was located far from the disputed border between the Corporate Sector and the Trianii colony worlds. The Trianii Ranger Atuarre was born on Trian.

**Trianii** An intelligent species of humanoid felines native to the planet Trian. Trianii established many offworld colonies. The Corporate Sector Authority claimed many of the older such colony worlds even before its charter over that sector of space was granted. The Trianii who lived there were forced to leave, though some were retained to labor for the Authority.

**Trianii Ranger** An elite member of Trian's law enforcement legion.

***Trickster*** A Yuuzhan Vong frigate commandeered by the survivors of Anakin Solo's strike team (Jaina Solo, Zekk, Tahiri Veila, Tenel Ka, Tekli, Tesar Sebatyne, Lowbacca, Alema Rar, and Ganner Rhysode) to escape from the Myrkr worldship. The ship was piloted via cognition hood, and a living glove was used to fire weapons. Originally called *Ksstarr*, Jaina renamed the ship *Trickster*, to build her reputation among the Yuuzhan Vong that she was somehow an incarnation of Yun-Harla, their Trickster Goddess. She used it at Obroa-skai in an attempt to ambush Supreme Overlord Shimrra.

Trianii

**Triclops** The three-eyed mutant son of Emperor Palpatine, he was banished by his father on the day of his birth and endured life in a series of Imperial insane asylums. Shock therapy and dark side energy physically and emotionally scarred Triclops, the peace-loving son of the ultimate warlord. Nevertheless, he managed to fall in love with a nurse named Kendalina, a captured princess, who bore him a son, Ken, before she was killed. A Jedi Master spirited Ken off to be raised in the Lost City of the Jedi buried deep beneath Yavin 4.

Triclops was carted off to work in the treacherous spice mines of Kessel, and at one point came under the domination of another three-eyed mutant, the ruthless Trioculus, who later tried to pass himself off as the Emperor's true son to gain the throne. In his dreams, Triclops unknowingly invented weapons of destruction that were gleaned and used by the Empire. A year after the Emperor was apparently killed in the explosion of the second Death Star, the ruling Committee of Grand Moffs publicly proclaimed Trioculus as the Emperor's heir.

But Triclops managed to escape and rendezvous with Alliance leaders, who eventually discovered that he had an Imperial transplant that transmitted his thoughts to probe droids. Alliance scientists used it to send some false information and were prepared to destroy the implant. Triclops decided he needed to be totally free, however, and he escaped from Alliance headquarters. He left a letter for Ken, disclosing his parentage and asking his forgiveness and trust.

**Trid** The primary spaceport on the planet Danuta and the world's nominal capital. An Imperial research facility that maintained a complete technical readout of the first Death Star was located there. The plans were stolen by Kyle Katarn.

**Triebakk** This Wookiee represented Kashyyyk as a New Republic Senator, and served on the New Republic Advisory Council when the Yuuzhan Vong invaded the galaxy. Senator Triebakk was one of the minority that openly supported the Jedi Knights, despite strong public and private disgruntlement with the Order. Senator Triebakk later served with the Galactic Federation of Free Alliances.

Triclops

**Triffian** The alien species of Podracer Ebe Endocott. Triffians had large thermoregulator flaps extending from their shoulders.

**Trigalis** An Outer Rim shadowport planet. Its primary port, New Coronet, was run by Black Sun agent named Xist during the last days of the Clone Wars. Five months before the end of the Clone Wars, Obi-Wan went to Trigalis to hunt for Asajj Ventress.

**Trigg** One of the many Loyalists fighting to free their homeworld of Jabiim from Imperial control during the early years of the Galactic Civil War. When Leia Organa and Luke Skywalker arrived on the planet at the request of Nolan Gillmunn, Trigg was among a small group who decided to have some sport with Luke. The Jabiimites realized that he was the son of Anakin Skywalker, whom they claimed had abandoned the planet to the Separatists during the Clone Wars. Trigg and his thugs beat Luke badly, which Trigg considered payback for the death of his father in the wake of the Battle of Jabiim, until Gillmunn put a stop to it. When Trigg learned of the Imperial ambush of the Loyalist headquarters, he found himself trying to protect Luke and Nolan from a group of stormtroopers. He sacrificed his own life so that they could escape, telling himself all along that he was only doing it for Nolan's safety.

Trigg

**Trigon One** A mammoth weapons satellite built by Tig Fromm on Ingo. It was a combination starship, submarine, and satellite. After going online, it was stolen by a group of freedom fighters led by Kea Moll. Thall Joben sabotaged the Trigon One, causing it to destroy the Fromm gang's base.

**trihexalon (Dragon's Breath)** A deadly chemical weapon designed by Cavik Toth. Trihexalon, also known as hex, vaporized its victim and left a mess. Hex missiles were used against the Maramere resistance and were also launched during the Battle of Geonosis. They were deployed by organic-looking ships called hex deployers and hex bombers. The Ministry of Science conducted research on trihexalon years prior to the Battle of Geonosis. Trihexalophine1138 defoliant was a variation.

**Trihexalophine1138** A defoliant developed by the Confederacy that was intended for use on Naboo. A battle between Republic and Separatist ships caused a vessel carrying Trihexalophine1138 to crash on the surface of Honoghr, triggering environmental catastrophe.

**Triitus system** Located at the edge of the Corva sector in the Outer Rim, the system contained the planet Tuulab.

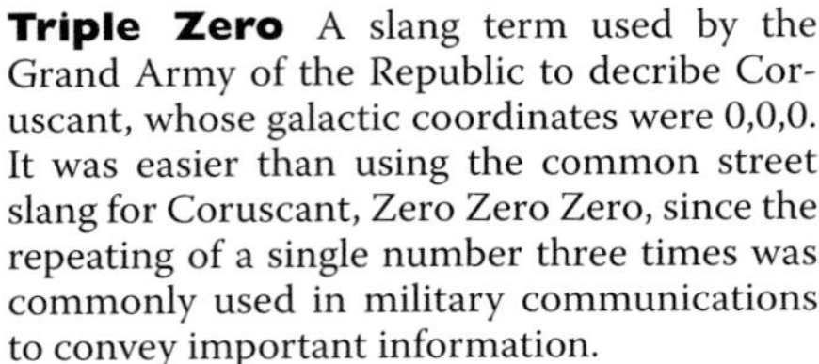

Trioculus

**Trillka** A repair-shop operator on the planet Kalarba, she fixed the damaged faceplate of C-3PO in such a way that the gentle protocol droid was mistaken for the assassin droid C-3PX. Later, when the criminal Greck tried to blow up Hosk Station, Trillka helped foil the scheme by working to undo the sabotage on the power core.

**Trillot** A noted X'Ting crime lord on the planet Ord Cestus during the last years of the Old Republic. Originally hired by Cestus Cybernetics as a communications drone, Trillot found a niche in labor relations. He was known as a risk taker, which helped him gather wealth and influence in a short period. To better interact with his underworld contacts, Trillot learned a multitude of languages and spoke many of them fluently. He tried to play all the angles of a situation: During the Clone Wars he worked with both the Separatists and the Old Republic.

Two years after the Battle of Geonosis, he agreed to serve as a contact for Obi-Wan Kenobi and Kit Fisto. The Jedi Masters sought the truth about any Separatist involvement with the JK-series security droid. Trillot was intercepted by Asajj Ventress before he could meet with the Jedi, and she forced him to lie. Ventress then tried and failed to kill Obi-Wan, and again confronted Trillot; to protect Count Dooku's secrets, she executed him.

**TriNebulon News** This news agency covered the news and events that occurred in roughly a quarter of the Outer Rim Territories, including the Parmel, Quence, and Portmoak sectors, during the final decades of the Republic and throughout the era of the New Order. The editors and reporters at TriNebulon News were fiercely pro-Imperial during the Galactic Civil War, and openly ridiculed Palpatine's opponents in their tabloid-style reports. TriNebulon News was one of the original signatory sponsors of the Corporate Sector Authority.

**Trioculus** The Supreme Slavelord of the spice mines of Kessel, he came forward after the Emperor's death to claim that he was Palpatine's banished son. Trioculus was a handsome human with a third eye in his forehead. Palpatine's real son, the mutant Triclops, had a third eye in the back of his head. Trioculus had the support of the Committee of Grand Moffs, but he was revealed to be an impostor and liar.

**triple-A** A slang term used by the clone troopers of the Grand Army of the Republic to describe anti-aircraft artillery.

**triple tap** A military term used to describe the firing of three blaster bolts in rapid succession. The triple tap required a much steadier touch than a double tap, and was executed by pulling the trigger of a rifle or pistol back just enough to expel the bolts.

**Triple Zero** A slang term used by the Grand Army of the Republic to decribe Coruscant, whose galactic coordinates were 0,0,0. It was easier than using the common street slang for Coruscant, Zero Zero Zero, since the repeating of a single number three times was commonly used in military communications to convey important information.

**Trispzest** A style of lightsaber combat developed by the airborne Majestrix of Skye. The S'kytri Majestrix adapted Form VII lightsaber combat (or Juyo in High Galactic), mixing it with traditional S'kytri aerial dueling techniques to take advantage of flight. Kharys was fond of emphasizing the technique of *sai cha* (decapitation) as an expedient method of dealing with a grounded opponent. *Trispzest* was the S'kytric word for a heart palpitation. The Boltrunian Dark Jedi Maw and the Rishii Zulirian Swordmistress Nazish were the only known heirs of Trispzest.

**Trista** *See* Taryn and Trista.

**trith prancer** A mount ridden by Raith Sienar for pleasure. The product of 1,000 generations of genetic manipulation, trith prancers were gray-blue animals that trotted on six graceful legs. A trith prancer's back formed a natural saddle. They often emitted musical fluting noises.

**Triton Squad** A detachment of clones sent to Kashyyyk to pacify the native Wookiee population. Triton Squad was led by a Republic commando. The troopers took heavy casualties from the wildlife of Kashyyyk after they ventured into the Shadowlands. The survivors were then ambushed by Wookiees led by Chewbacca and Tarfful.

***Triumph*** One of two Imperial Star Destroyers heavily damaged during the Alliance conquest of Coruscant. If not for the tractor beams of the *Mon Remonda,* the *Triumph* would have fallen into the planet's atmosphere and been destroyed.

**TR-MB (Tracked Mobile Base)** An Imperial prototype designed to transport a command center commander into the midst of a conflict. The TR-MB did not possess any weapons but could summon mobile units to its location.

**Trodd, Puggles** A meter-tall rodent, he made his living as a bounty hunter and often teamed up with Jodo Kast and Zardra to complete high-paying contracts. Puggles Trodd feared the two, but knew that together they could earn even more credits than if they worked alone. Trodd, a Lasat, was pessimistic, unpleasant, and brooding. He loved to watch anything explode.

**Trogan** A planet located in the system of the same name, it featured the famous Whistler's Whirlpool tapcaf on the coast of its most densely populated continent. At the center of the Whirlpool was the Drinking Cup, a natural rock bowl that filled with seawater six times a day due to Trogan's strong tides. The Whirlpool—a disappointing failure as a tourist attraction—was abandoned. Five years after the Battle of Endor, Talon Karrde arranged a smugglers' meeting at the Whirlpool, which was attacked by soldiers from the nearby Imperial garrison.

**Tro'Har** A planet located in the Elrood sector, it was near the planet Coyn. An ice world, it was the fifth and outermost planet in the Coyn system.

Troig

**Troig** A species of two-headed aliens native to the planet Pollillus. Troigs often had different colorations on each head, most often green and red, and each head was supported by a long neck. Their stout bodies were studded with four long arms and short legs. One of their four hands was considered the primary hand, while the others were regarded as off-hands. The hands required that both heads work together in order to operate with any level of coordination. Each head, the left

known as Saprah and the right as Saprin, was capable of independent thought, and was humanoid in appearance. Troigs with three or more heads were sometimes born, although they were extremely rare. They were also revered and celebrated among their people. The Podrace announcer FodesinBeed was a Troig.

**Troiken** This Outer Rim planet in the Qotile system was the homeworld of the Xexto, a species of thin-bodied aliens with six limbs. The planet itself was in a tide-locked orbit around its sun, leaving one side continually bathed in sunlight and radiation and the opposite side frigid. The Xexto civilization existed on the edge of these two extreme environments, where life was bearable. Outside the cities of the Xexto and the limited-service starports near the Podracing tracks, the world was covered with carnivorous flora through which fearsome predators prowled and clouds of meat-eating insects swarmed.

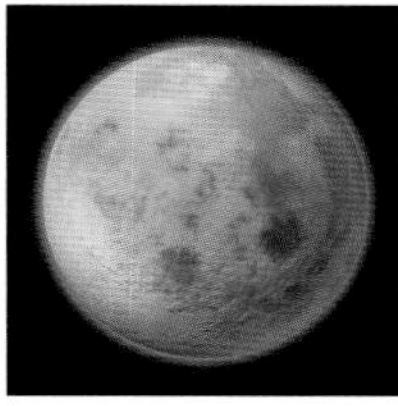

*Troiken*

Troiken was the site of a meeting among the Trade Federation, the Galactic Republic, and the Stark Commercial Combine. Jedi Master Tyvokka served as chief negotiator of the Jedi contingent. After Stark turned against the Jedi, Valorum decided that their forces would rendezvous with Ranulf Tarkin at the Lycinder Plain in front of Mount Avos in the Hormick Range. Using Troiken's challat eaters, Plo Koon was able to lure the Stark Combine army into Mount Avos, where the troops perished when Tarkin set off an explosive.

**Trommer, Ranulf** An ace Imperial pilot, he was sent to the planet M'haeli by Grand Moff Lynch to spy on Governor Grigor. When his mission was compromised, he fell in love with Mora, leader of the M'haeli Rebels. Trommer's sympathies shifted, finally causing him to throw in his lot with the Rebels.

**trompa** A massive, 3-meter-high bipedal creature with long arms and sharp-clawed paws, it was ferocious and deadly. A trompa's thick fur covered its powerful muscles, and two spiral horns curved out of its head.

**Troob** Along with the Hobors, one of two sentient humanoid species native to Tahlboor. They had dark blue skin and wide faces flanked by a several rings of spade-shaped flaps. Shortly before the Battle of Yavin, the Troobs and Hobors appealed to the Tion Hegemony to assist in reconciling a generations-old feud between them while negotiating a trade agreement. Counselor Harthan was called in, but he was manipulated out of position by his son Jake, who hoped to get the two cultures to destroy each other. Eventually, with the help of R2-D2 and C-3PO, Jake's plans were thwarted and peace was restored.

**Troper, Milac** A scout with decades of experience, he once abandoned his fellow scouts Dayla Kev and Hereven on an unexplored jungle world. Troper reported the loss of his comrades and was temporarily suspended for his lack of valor. Troper eventually joined the Imperial Diplomatic Corps. He didn't know that Kev had survived and sought revenge for her abandonment. She targeted Troper many years later aboard the *Galactic Horizon.* Troper escaped unharmed, but Dayla and her son were taken into custody.

**Trosh** One of the many planets where the Empire enslaved the native population, claiming to be protecting the rights of its inhabitants.

**Troska** An isolated world on the Outer Rim that was the site of a modest Imperial outpost. The refineries of Troska were run by the Kyber family.

**Truchong, Brindy** A female Corellian smuggler, she was on Tatooine shortly before the Battle of Yavin trying to find a quick means to provide supplies to the Rebellion.

***True Justice*** A modified YT-series transport vessel used by Imperial forces as a floating prison and courtroom during the early months of the New Order. Built to the specifications of Senator Sano Sauro, the *True Justice* allowed for the extradition of Rebels and insurgents from their homeworlds where they might have received preferential treatment. By holding trials aboard the *True Justice,* Sauro and his cronies could eliminate beings who were causing trouble for the Empire without having to worry about the repercussions of a more public trial. The *True Justice* was hijacked by Solace, Oryon, and Trever Flume, who posed as Bellassan legal representatives in order to rescue Roan Lands and Dona Telamark. Solace and her team then took the *True Justice* to Samaria to rescue Ferus Olin and Clive Flax.

*Troska*

**Troujow, Hasti** A young, beautiful former mining camp laborer, she helped Han Solo and Badure reach the secret treasure vaults of Xim the Despot shortly before Solo became involved in the Galactic Civil War.

**Troujow, Lanni** The sister of Hasti Troujow, she was killed after she discovered a log recorder from the legendary starship *Queen of Ranroon.* With the information stored in the recorder, Hasti was able to locate the ancient ship's lost treasures. Han Solo and Chewbacca helped her.

**TR-SD (Tracked Shield Disabler)** A single-purpose Imperial vehicle whose function was to eliminate the shield protection of Rebel Alliance attack tanks and buildings. This unit also had a secondary ion cannon, which allowed it to disable unshielded vehicles and render them immobile.

***Trucemaker*** A Galactic Alliance warship under the command of Gavin Darklighter, and part of the Fifth Fleet during the early stages of the Corellia–GA War. As the conflict spread, Darklighter was promoted to rear admiral and the *Trucemaker* was transferred to the Fourth Fleet. At the Second Battle of Balmorra, the *Trucemaker* was given flagship status when the *Peacebringer* was destroyed in the fighting.

**True Mandalorians** A group of Mandalorians who rallied around Jaster Mereel's leadership and rejected the soldier Vizsla and his splinter group, the Mandalorian Death Watch. Mereel's supercommandos recast themselves as the True Mandalorians.

**True Victory Party** This political faction rose to power on Bothawui some 10 years after the end of the Yuuzhan Vong War. The True Victory Party was born out of Bothan frustration with the actions of the Galactic Alliance, especially after the formation of the Galactic Alliance Guard. Many Bothans advocated that their homeworld secede from the Galactic Alliance, and formed the True Victory Party. Led by Reh'mwa, the party quickly gathered support and came under verbal attack from Jacen Solo. It was Solo who alleged that Reh'mwa had ordered an attack on the World Brain that lived deep within the planet Coruscant after he was attacked by Alema Rar. The situation only got worse when a delegation of Bothans from the True Victory Party were found murdered on the same night that Tresina Lobi was brutally killed in Fellowship Plaza. It was later revealed that the Bothans had been assassinated by Alema Rar, as part of Lumiya's

T'surr

plans to secure Jacen Solo's place in the new Sith Order. The murders of the True Victory Party members spurred the Bothans to action against the Galactic Alliance. In secret, they established three separate fleets of warships, which were to launch surprise attacks on key GA locations. Although the Bothans were unable to achieve their original missions, the planet of Bothawui soon broke away from the Alliance and joined the Confederation.

**trugut** A form of hard currency in Mos Espa on Tatooine. The trugut was a Hutt currency and only had value on Hutt-controlled worlds. The use of truguts on Tatooine ended with the arrival of the Empire. One trugut was worth 16 wupiupi, a quarter of a peggat, or 10 dataries (Republic credits).

**Trulalis** A rich green planet of grasslands, forests, and oceans beneath a thick cloud layer, this unspoiled world was covered with windswept fields separated by stretches of wilderness and dotted with several small settlements. Trulalis was set aside as a low-tech world by the Issori, and most of its inhabitants shunned all forms of higher technology, using miniature banthas as beasts of burden. Nestled within a steep mountain range was the gated community of Kovit, a farming settlement dominated by a towering, buttressed theater of white limestone.

During the Golden Age of the Old Republic, Trulalis was a thriving cultural center boasting one of the finest liberal arts schools in the galaxy. Only a few scattered remnants survived the millennia. Sometime before the Battle of Endor, the Dark Jedi Adalric Brandl hired the smuggler Thaddeus Ross to bring him to Trulalis, Brandl's former home.

**Trulalis system** Located just one hour's hyperspace travel from Najiba, it contained the planets Issor, Cadezia, and Trulalis.

**Truuine** The only planet in the Truuine system, it was used as a training site by the ancient Jedi Master Mroon Jassa some 4,000 years before the Battle of Yavin.

**tsaisi** A Yuuzhan Vong organic weapon also referred to as a rank baton. The tsaisi belonged to the same species as the amphistaff but was narrower, shorter, and more delicate. It required more skill than the amphistaff, thus it was rarely granted to warriors. Shedao Shai carried one, and at Ebaq 9, Tsavong Lah dueled Jaina with his tsaisi.

**t'salak** A vicious beast that was discovered in the jungles of Cularin by the Tarasin, it seemed to have been spawned by the dark side of the Force and appeared to have been created from pure hatred. In appearance, the t'salak seemed to be little more than a puddle of ooze that could move about with deceptive speed. It could shape its body into a variety of forms, which it used to attack its prey.

**Tsayv, Liat** A Sullustan, he was a crew member aboard Mirax Terrik's *Pulsar Skate.*

**Tschel, Lieutenant** A young officer aboard the Imperial Star Destroyer *Chimaera,* he served as a member of the bridge crew under Captain Pellaeon and Grand Admiral Thrawn during Thrawn's campaign to destroy the New Republic five years after the Battle of Endor.

**Tser, Wolam** A political historian who escaped to Borleias days after Coruscant fell to the Yuuzhan Vong. Wolam Tser was accompanied by a holocam operator named Tam Egrin. A graying and distinguished elder statesman of Coruscant holojournalism, Wolam took pleasure in documenting the war. During the evacuation of Borleias, Wolam Tser, Tam Elgrin, and the boy Tarc fled in a converted military blastboat. His holodocumentary *The Battle of Borleias* was a bestseller.

**tsik vai** A Yuuzhan Vong atmospheric flier used on Yavin 4 in the search for Anakin Solo. This flying speeder appeared as a flat, winged sea creature with an uneven surface and armed with several thin, cable-like tendrils used for grasping objects. These cables were capable of providing temporary resistance against a lightsaber strike. The tsik vai search craft had air intake vents that operated like gills and that made a distinctive whine when in flight. Fliers were used by the Yuuzhan Vong on Bonadan.

**tsil** Crystal chimney formations on Nam Chorios, they were named by the planet's Oldtimers. Small ground electrical storms that lasted 5 to 10 minutes emerged from the tsils. Oldtimers were unaffected by the storms; Newcomers were sick for a day and a half if any of the charges passed through them. The tsils were sentient and were the source of the Force sensitivity on Nam Chorios. The tsils used images in beings' heads to try to communicate, causing the Theran Listeners to hear voices. These living crystals had inhabited Nam Chorios since it was first formed. They invaded the dreams of the prophet Theras, instructing him and his followers to bar any ship large enough to have heavy shielding from landing on or leaving Nam Chorios. Their command prevented the insectoid drochs carrying the Death Seed plague from spreading from Nam Chorios throughout the galaxy.

**Tsinimal** A graceful yet intolerant species. The Tsinimals enslaved the natives of Langhesa, considering the Langhesi's pursuit of biotechnology as an abomination against their gods. Tsinimals themselves were more often recognized for their piracy and conquests.

**Tsoss Beacon** An automated beacon station built mainly by droids and suicide crews, it was located on a desolate planetoid in the Deep Galactic Core. The region was inundated with deadly radioactive storms and solar flares. Despite its shielding, the station was abandoned by its last human personnel several years prior to the Battle of Yavin. It was at Tsoss Beacon that Imperial Admiral Daala met with and, after futile negotiations, murdered the remaining Imperial warlords eight years after the Battle of Endor.

**T'surr** Little was known about this species, which was native to the planet of the same name in the Expansion Region. Violent and ruthless, the T'surr were large beings with blue, marble-like skin and a heavily muscled, humanoid frame. A number of horns crowned their heads, and large ears gave them excellent hearing. Four red eyes sat above a wide mouth, which was filled with razor-sharp teeth. As a species, the T'surr considered any beings weaker than them to be merely chattel, and they had no qualms about enslaving such "lesser species." The male T'surr ruled their homeworld, and often traveled as slavers and pirates. Females were almost never seen; the males often described them as small and feeble. From each of the T'surr's elbows extended two forearms: a heavily muscled primary arm and a thin, clawed secondary arm. Like most creatures that evolved on T'surr, the average T'surr had excellent vision in low-light conditions. The notorious pirate and slave trader Krayn was a T'surr.

**Tsyr** A battle-scarred Kajain'sa'Nikto and Morgukai warrior who lived during the Clone Wars. Armed with a cortosis weapon and armor, Tsyr and his son Bok were able

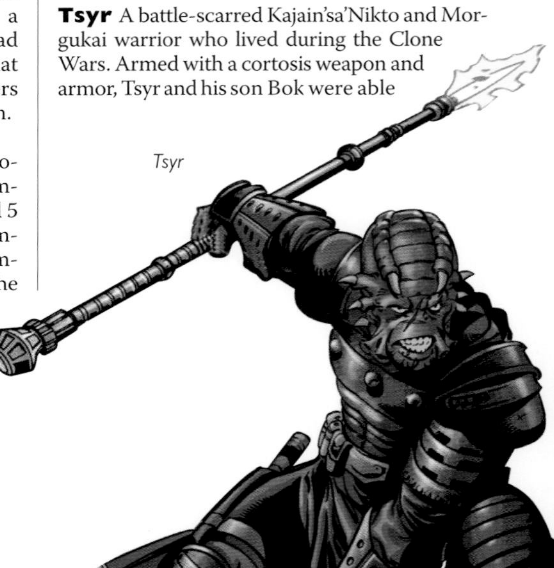
Tsyr

to defeat Jedi Master Tholme and abduct Ryloth's prime heir Nat Secura. Tsyr kept Tholme's lightsaber as a trophy. Tsyr and Bok attacked Quinlan Vos and Aayla Secura with CloakShape fighters on Kintan. Tsyr used small, spiral-shaped throwing weapons to injure Vos. He was decapitated while fighting Vos at Fortress Kh'aris.

*Tuk'ata*

**TT-8L (Tattletale)** A sentry droid designed to be installed directly into a door or similar portal. Programmed to interrogate visitors and scan for concealed weapons, the Tattletale droid was an important component of Jabba the Hutt's security detail. The large eye could perform low-light surveys, spotlight illumination, and scanning sweeps in both the ultraviolet and infrared ranges. Tattletale's job, as with all others of its model, was to interview visitors and determine their intentions before deciding whether or not to allow them inside. No one got into Jabba's palace without first encountering Tattletale. After a short interview, the droid withdrew into the armored door and informed Jabba's majordomo, Bib Fortuna, that Jabba had guests. Fortuna responded in his own time, of course, and more than one legitimate visitor died of heat exhaustion waiting for the door to open.

*TT-8L*

**Tu, Suribran** An Ishi Tib leader of his Tibrin homeworld during the Clone Wars. He struggled to keep his planet from joining the Separatists, using strong-arm tactics and even political assassinations to maintain his position and the power. When Count Dooku arrived to negotiate with him for the rights to use Tibrin as a base, Tu fed him empty platitudes. Dooku's associate, Quinlan Vos, reminded the Count that Tu was just as corrupt and untrustworthy as the Old Republic and was not worth the effort of negotiation. Dooku agreed and used his lightsaber to behead Tu. Dooku then installed Sora Bulq as the provisional governor. Tu's death was welcomed by the Ishi Tib populace, who eagerly joined the Confederacy of Independent Systems.

**Tugorn** A Yuuzhan Vong subaltern escalated by Nas Choka in recognition of his work in remaking Belkadan and Gyndine into viable worlds for Yuuzhan Vong biotechnology.

**Tuhns, Geoff** A tall big-boned Imperial recruit with a head of flaming-red hair, he was in training with stormtrooper Davin Felth.

**tuk'ata** A guardian creature found on Korriban. The tuk'ata inhabited and protected Korriban's Dark Lord tombs. Tuk'ata began life as frighteningly intelligent curs; in reward for their faithful service, the beasts were taken to sites infused with the dark side, where they mutated into relentless Sith hounds. Exar Kun was especially fond of the creatures and brought them to the Massassi temples of Yavin 4. Tol Skorr was scarred by one when he crashed on Korriban.

**Tulgah** Members of a rare species, these troll-like beings on the Forest Moon of Endor had an extensive knowledge of magic. Some Tulgah were great healers. Others, such as Morag, twisted their knowledge to evil and wielded powers of black magic.

**tulvarees** Semi-intelligent avian hunters native to the planet Pochi. When Faarl the Conqueror took control of the planet, the tulvarees quickly learned how to take orders from the human. Faarl, recognizing a source of soldiers, provided a constant food supply to the tulvarees in exchange for their allegiance.

**Tumanian pressure-ruby** An extremely rare stone. Even a small example of this often bloodred gem could easily be worth several million credits.

**tumnor** A flying creature, it lived in the upper atmosphere of Da Soocha and its moons. These predators stalked Ixlls, hunting the small and intelligent flying species as a source of food.

**Tund** Located in the remote Tund system, this legendary but hidden world was home to the mysterious and ancient Sorcerers of Tund and could trace its origins back to the ancient Sith Empire. Years before the Battle of Yavin, Rokur Gepta, a snail-like Croke, infiltrated the Sorcerers of Tund and learned their secrets. He then murdered his teachers and transformed the planet Tund, once an attractive world of prairies, forests, and jungles, into a blasted, sterile wasteland. The world's deadly radiation was held back in some places by force fields so Gepta could land his ship there safely. Prior to that disaster, Ben Quadinaros and other Toongs fled to Tund when their own homeworld suffered environmental poisoning.

*Tumnor*

*Tund*

**Tung, Gengi** The Yuuzhan Vong master shaper on occupied Coruscant, he wore a tentacled headdress the color of dried blood and replaced his teeth with needle-sharp animal quills. He kept two umrachs named Toi and Tixo with him at all times.

**Tungra sector** Located near the Bruanii and Javin sectors, it was home to a deep-space Mugaari cargo-loading depot. This depot was destroyed by the Empire following the Battle of Hoth.

**Tuomi, Senator** A New Republic Senator from Drannik, he opposed Chief of State Leia Organa Solo during the Yevethan crisis. Senator Tuomi represented Bosch and four other planets, constituting one billion citizens. He introduced a floor challenge to Leia's credentials by claiming that Alderaan's destruction had disqualified her from Senate membership because there was no legitimate territory for her to represent.

*Turbolaser*

**Tup** *See* Cholly, Weez, and Tup.

**Turan, Dr. Fort** The leader of the Galactic Republic scientific team that traveled to Haariden some five years after the Battle of Naboo to investigate the effects of a volcanic environment on its inhabitants. Dr. Turan was a space geologist by education and was forced into action as the team's leader when they were beset by Haariden rebels who chose to ignore the cease-fire.

**turbolaser** A weapon that fired supercharged bolts of energy, it was usually positioned on the deck of a capital ship or as part of a surface-based defense installation. Turbolasers were more powerful than regular laser cannons, discharging hotter and more concentrated energy bolts. The weapons required constant temperature regulation from built-in cryogenic cooling units.

**turbo-skis** Rocket-powered skis, they were used for sport and for rapid travel across ice regions.

**Turbostorm close-assault gunship** Blastboats manufactured by Sienar and retrofitted for atmospheric close-assault work. Turbostorms were relatively slow but heavily armored, bristling with cannons and missile launchers, and large enough to transport a platoon of heavy infantry.

*Turret room*

***Turbulent*-class destroyer** A class of destroyers created by the Imperial Remnant during the years following the Swarm War. These vessels, referred to as pocket destroyers, were designed to be smaller and more agile than the typical Star Destroyer. The *Turbulent*-class destroyer had two main hangar bays located in the stern, and its primary command center was protected by a series of overlapping hatchways and chambers that made it difficult for a boarding party to breach without the use of serious firepower. This same design made it almost impossible for a command crew to escape from the ship if it were boarded, because they had to make their way out of a maze of chambers to reach the escape pods. Thus, ship commanders were given knowledge of several escape routes that wound through the innards of the ship to assist them in emergency situations.

**Turi, Tionthes** A respected Sundar engineer who worked with the Garosian Tork Winger to hammer out a peace treaty that ended the civil war between their two planets.

**Turkana** This planet in the Hadar sector was circled by multiple moons. Prior to the Battle of Yavin, at least five Imperial Star Destroyers discovered the Rebel Alliance fleet in orbit around Turkana. The Imperials engaged the fleet but suffered severe losses. Shocked by this development, Emperor Palpatine ordered the implementation of Operation Strike Fear to crush the Rebellion. Later, Alliance pilot Keyan Farlander flew his first mission near Turkana.

**Tur-Mukan, Etain** A young Jedi Padawan who fought in the Clone Wars. She and her Master, Kast Fulier, were dispatched to Qiilura to investigate the development of a nanovirus by Ovolot Qail Uthan. The farmers betrayed them, and Master Fulier was captured and killed. Etain escaped and ran into the clone commando Darman. She was surprised to find that she was attracted to him, and he to her. She felt stronger and more capable in his presence, and he helped her learn some of the skills she needed to be a military commander. After the mission, she was promoted to the rank of Jedi Knight. She teamed with Darman again on Coruscant to smash a terrorist ring. Etain allowed herself to become pregnant with a son, but did not tell Darman what had happened. Etain gave birth to her son on Mandalore, naming him Venku Skirata, and telling Darman that her child was simply one of Kal Skirata's grandchildren.

**turret room** A handcrafted suite within the Theed Palace on Naboo built by the first ruler of the Great Time of Peace, King Jafan. Yoda conferred upon Obi-Wan Kenobi the title of Jedi Knight in this turret room.

**Tu-Scart (Beater)** A Yuuzhan Vong–bioengineered creature unleashed on the surface of Duro. Tu-Scart was half of a symbiotic pair capable of destroying artificial constructs within minutes. It was called Beater by its breeders, and its other half, Sgauru, was known as Biter. The pair were created 50 years before the Yuuzhan Vong invasion by master shapers under divine inspiration from Yun-Yammka, the Yuuzhan Vong god of war. Tu-Scart's coils were large and strong enough to loop around buildings and crush them. It resembled a giant, glossy black snake, 14 meters long, with flat black eyes. Its skin was supple and smooth, although it had a bony ridge that ran from the tip of its tail to the base of its skull, which acted as a "hold" for when Sgauru rode on its back. Like a serpent, Tu-Scart used its tongue to pick up odors and was especially adept at "sniffing out" the largest concentrations of artificial construction and power sources. Tu-Scart also had a dense, bony skull that allowed it to use its head as a battering ram.

**tusk-cat** A savage predator native to Naboo. Tusk-cats were extremely large felines that preyed on many other creatures, including shaaks. The Naboo were known to tame tusk-cats for use as mounts. Trained tusk-cats also protected and guided herds of shaaks. Tusk-cats could see well in low light and track prey over long distances. Regal in disposition, confident in nature, strong, swift, and smart, they had long-range eyesight and an acute sense of smell. Their tusks were for display and defensive purposes.

**Tusken Oasis** An upscale nightclub owned by Yanth the Hutt as part of his Black Sun holdings. It was located near the Senate Chamber on Coruscant during the last decades of the Old Republic. Its interior was decorated with multicolored lights and statues of mythological beasts.

*Tusken Raider*

**Tusken Raider** A member of the nomadic and often violent species the Sand People of the planet Tatooine, as fierce and discomforting as their harsh desert environment. Even their appearance—born of necessity—gave them a terrifying mien. Wrapped in gauzy robes and strips of cloth from head to foot, they topped off their outfits with breathing masks and goggles to protect their eyes. Their frightening visages made their acts of banditry easier.

*Tusk-cat*

The Sand People were easily intoxicated by simple sugar water, and were most dangerous during their adolescent years, when they survived rigorous rites of passage, such as hunting the deadly krayt dragons, to become adults. Because there was no written Tusken language, the storyteller was the most respected member of Tusken communities. It was considered blasphemy—and grounds for instant death—to speak a single word of the sacred stories incorrectly. Many Tusken Raider clans of 20 to 30 individuals returned annually to their traditional encampments in the Needles, a section of the Jundland Wastes, to wait out the dangerous sandstorm season. Many gruesome legends surrounded Tusken Raiders, who were even known to spit streams of blood at their victims during attacks.

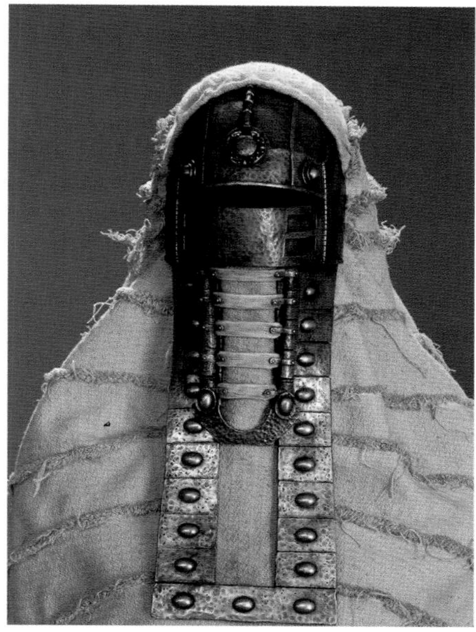

*Tusken Raider female*

The Sand People possessed an almost symbiotic relationship with their bantha mounts. A member who lost his bantha was considered incomplete and an outcast among his people. Likewise, when a Raider died, his mount engaged in a frenzy that was usually suicidal, and the creature was turned loose in the desert to survive or die on its own. Tuskens maintained an uneasy and frequently shattered peace with the moisture farmers who also populated Tatooine. They attacked full settlements from time to time, using their traditional weapon, the gaderffii (or gaffi stick), a kind of double-edged ax. Targets of opportunity also included individuals or small parties roaming the desert, such as Jawa scavenging parties. Sand People subsisted on a difficult-to-digest fruit, the hubba gourd, and tightly guarded their hidden desert oases, the main source of their water.

Sand People males and females could be distinguished by the type of masks and wrappings they wore. After bonding ceremonies in which the male and female mixed their blood, as did their banthas, they adjourned to the privacy of their tent and were allowed to unwrap themselves. This was when they saw each other's faces for the first time. In any other circumstance, seeing another Raider's face was grounds for a duel to the death.

The Jedi Knight A'Sharad Hett was raised among Tusken Raiders, and wore his people's traditional clothing while serving the Jedi during the Clone Wars. Just before the start of the Clone Wars, Anakin Skywalker's mother, Shmi, was captured by Tuskens and tortured during an intense ritual known as a bloodrite. Skywalker, indulging his thirst for vengeance, wiped out the entire clan.

**Tusken's Eye** A tube-like pillar of silvery gas and dust that was one of the few openings in the gaseous wall of the Utegetu Nebula. Located just inside the Tusken's Eye was a G-class star that provided the light that gave the nebula its color. The star was orbited by a white-clouded gas giant, which was in turn orbited by more than a dozen small moons. During the Swarm War, pirates hired by the Gorog hive used the Tusken's Eye to enter the nebula and deliver goods to the Dark Nest. Unknown to the rest of the galaxy, 16 of the "moons" that orbited the cloud-covered planet were nest ships, specially constructed by the Gorog hive to transport Killik agents into the galaxy.

**Tuulab** The second planet in the Triitus system of the Corva sector, it was a peaceful world of gentle plains blessed with abundant natural resources. It was home to a colony of 6,000 people who'd fled there over the years to escape persecution under the Empire's New Order. The rural Tuulabi colonists had no form of organized government. The Gotal crime lord Mahk'khar built a three-story palace on Tuulab in an uninhabited area on the west coast of the planet's northern continent.

**Tuum, Rasi** This male Cathar was one of the many Jedi Knights who defended the galaxy some 130 years after the Battle of Yavin. Rasi Tuum agreed to accompany Shado Vao to Daluuj, where they were to meet with Jedi Master Wolf Sazen. Master Sazen had finally decided to rally the Jedi against the Sith Lords who had taken control of the galaxy. Tuum was among the minority who believed that any meeting of the Jedi was dangerous, and refused to accept Sazen's belief that Cade Skywalker was still alive. Tuum's fears were realized when a group of Sith attacked them on Daluuj. He was slain during the fighting.

*Rasi Tuum*

**Tuun, Maneeli** This Polis Massan was one of the members of the archaeological team investigating the ancient civilization of Polis Massa during the last years of the Republic. Maneeli Tuun served the team as a doctor and surgeon. He was also a strong supporter of the Republic and assisted the Jedi Order during the years leading up to the Clone Wars. When Padmé Amidala was brought to Polis Massa by Obi-Wan Kenobi, Tuun assisted in the delivery of her twin babies. Many months later, he destroyed what evidence he could of the birth when confronted by Imperial Inquisitor Sancor. After Sancor was killed while fighting Kenobi, Tuun remained behind to cover up Sancor's death and further safeguard any information on Padmé's fate. Tuun later explained to Inquisitor Malorum that Sancor had accidentally fallen to his death.

**Tuyay** The chief operating officer of Ororo Transportation, a competitor of Prince Xizor's XTS transportation company, which was in turn a front for Xizor's Black Sun criminal syndicate. Tuyay was a fitness buff and bulged with muscles under his expensively tailored zeyd-cloth suits. Xizor's top aide, Guri, choked Tuyay, then held a blaster up to his left eyeball and killed him.

*Tuzes-Adaz*

**Tuzes-Adaz** This Nelvaanian female served as the chieftain of the Rokrul villages during the final years of the Republic. When the Separatists established a hidden facility on Nelvaan and began drawing off the planet's geothermal energy, Tuzes-Adaz and her warriors interpreted the development as a growing illness of the Great Mother. When Tuzes-Adaz discovered Anakin Skywalker and Obi-Wan Kenobi in the wilderness, she quickly remembered the prophecy of the shaman Ovros, who claimed that an offworlder would arrive on Nelvaan and help the Great Mother return to health. Rather than killing the offworlders, Tuzes-Adaz brought the two Jedi back to her village to meet with Orvos. Her actions proved critical, as it was Anakin who later destroyed the Separatist facility and began Nelvaan's return to normalcy.

**Twenty Wonders of the Galaxy** A list compiled by the historian Vicendi 10 millennia before the Galactic Civil War for his work *Arturum Galactinum,* commissioned for the Republic's anniversary. Vicendi compiled only those wonders constructed by intelligent beings, omitting such spectacular natural phenomena as the Five Fire Rings of Fornax and the Corphelion comets. The list was criticized for its overemphasis on antiquity, particularly those creations tied to the formation of the Republic. Competing lists of wonders were advanced by the Hutts, Bothans, and Caamasi, and a rewritten list (titled *Glorius Imperica*) became part of the Human High Culture curriculum distributed by the Imperial Ministry of Education.

***twi'janii*** The Rylothan word for a grant of hospitality to travelers. When invoked, the people of Ryloth were obliged to offer their guests the pleasures of rest and entertainment.

*Twi'lek*

**Twi'lek (1)** A species of humanoids with twin head tentacles, they were sometimes dismissively called worm-heads. The dual tail-like appendages known as lekku grew out of the backs of their heads and could be used to communicate with other Twi'leks. Native to the planet Ryloth in the Outer Rim, they spoke a language that combined verbal components with subtle head-tail movements. Twi'leks cultivated edible molds and fungi and raised bovine rycrits for their meat and hides.

The species was generally nonviolent, preferring to use cunning instead of force. Twi'leks lived in vast city complexes, located on their planet's dark side to escape the heat of the surface. Each complex was autonomous, governed by a group of five Twi'leks—the head clan—who jointly oversaw production, trade, and other daily endeavors. The leaders were born into their positions and served until one of them died. The others were then banished to die in the Bright Lands of the planet's light side, making room for the next generation of leaders.

Twi'leks depended on neighboring systems, pirates, smugglers, and merchants for their contact with the rest of the galaxy. They attracted these ships with their chief export, ryll, a mineral with legitimate medicinal uses that also became a popular and dangerously addictive recreational drug, particularly in the Corporate Sector. Twi'leks also faced constant raids by offworld slavers. Bib Fortuna, top aide to criminal kingpin Jabba the Hutt, was a Twi'lek, as was Oola, the dancing girl killed by Jabba. During the Clone Wars, the Twi'lek Jedi Aayla Secura distinguished herself with her heroism.

**Twi'lek (2)** A dry drink with a piquant bouquet and slightly sweet nose, it was ingested in abundance on Tatooine.

**Twi'lek spinning blades** An unusual bladed weapon developed by the Twi'leks during the years prior to the Great Sith War. The spinning blades were wielded in a choreographed, dance-like attack that mesmerized victims into brief lulls. This allowed the wielder to attack with well-aimed slashes.

**Twilight** This term was first used during the era of the Battle of Ruusan to describe the idea that the Force was not simply made up of a light side and a dark side. Instead, some believed in Twilight, in which there were no sides to the Force, just a single source of energy that belonged to all Force-users. The original use of the term *Twilight* was attributed to Lord Kaan of the Brotherhood of Darkness.

***Twilight*** A battered spice freighter recovered by Anakin Skywalker and Ahsoka Tano during their mission to Teth. Skywalker kept the old ship around as a side project, modifying it to be his personal vessel that he could use for "unofficial" errands while serving in the Clone Wars.

**T-wing** A starfighter developed by the Rebel Alliance during the Galactic Civil War that never gained much acceptance among pilots. It was a fast craft, but was armed only with two laser cannons, and was equipped with weak shielding. The T-wing was a three-winged ship, with one engine mounted on each wingtip, and was manufactured by Incom Corporation and Hoersch-Kessel Drive.

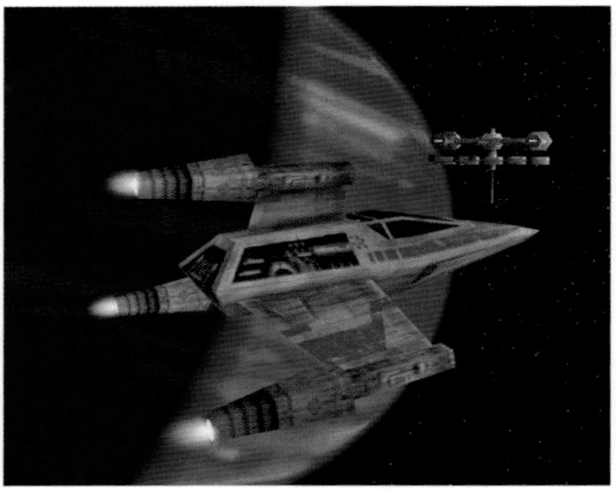

*T-wing*

**twin-pod cloud car** *See* cloud car, twin-pod.

**Twins** Heavily modified TIE bomber variants, they belonged in a class of ships known as uglies. The quadanium solar panels at the front were cut diagonally to provide the pilots with peripheral vision, an essential change. The bomb delivery system was removed and replaced with a concussion missile launching system, with two lasers complementing the weapons array. Shield generators and a hyperdrive motivator were added to complete the package.

**Twin Suns** The name adopted by a pair of Twi'lek criminals who made a living by harrassing the natives of the Refugee Sector on Nar Shaddaa during the years following the Jedi Civil War. Each of the Twin Suns wielded a Twi'lek spinning blade when fighting. They were among the many bounty hunters who were hired by G0-T0 to capture Jedi Knights, but were killed aboard G0-T0's yacht when the Jedi Exile escaped from the vessel.

**Twin Suns Squadron** The temporary X-wing squadron assigned to Luke Skywalker after the Yuuzhan Vong capture of Coruscant. It was formed from the veterans of Saber Squadron, Shock Squadron, and other units that had survived the Battle of Coruscant. Luke agreed to turn the squadron over to Jaina Solo in an effort to enhance her image as the living version of the Yuuzhan Vong goddess Yun-Harla. This put Jaina in a position of authority over the Jedi, including Luke Skywalker; and it enhanced the Yuuzhan Vong superstition regarding Jaina's status as a twin. Twin Suns Squadron was regularly restaffed with inexperienced recruits, a fact that gnawed on Jaina's conscience. Near the end of the war, Jaina relinquished command of the squadron to Jagged Fel. Twin Suns was then combined with Vanguard Squadron and assigned to the Fourth Battle Fleet.

**Twith** This planet was continually at war with its neighbor, Hyabb, almost from the beginning of the Old Republic. In what became known as the Hyabb-Twith Campaigns, ancient Jedi Knights ousted the Nelroni Marauders and freed the planet from their oppression.

**Twizzl, Commander** This silver-haired man, a native of Coruscant, served as a commander in the Galactic Alliance military and was later selected to serve as a naval officer in the Galactic Alliance Guard. A veteran of several decades of military and public service, Commander Twizzl was just barely distinguishable as a Coruscanti by what remained of his accent. He was the commander of the Star Destroyer *Anakin Solo* on its maiden voyage to Hapes. In the following months, Commander Twizzl found himself on a number of battlefronts, as Jacen Solo moved to consolidate his power in the wake of the arrest of Cal Omas. The ship was on the front lines during the Battle of Kuat, but Jacen took it out of the battle to pursue the Jedi Knights who had defected from the Alliance. Twizzl questioned this move, and had further reservations when Solo dragged the Fifth Fleet

to Kashyyyk to locate the Jedi. Twizzl's concern was only heightened when Solo suggested that the *Anakin Solo*'s turbolasers be targeted on Kashyyyk to burn the planet rather than lose it to the Confederation. Twizzl carried out the orders, but only because he could not find any military reason to argue against them. It was during the assault on Kashyyyk that Solo, who had since become Darth Caedus, let his guard drop. His former apprentice, Ben Skywalker, lashed out with his lightsaber, but accidentally caught Twizzl across the chest and sliced the man in half. Twizzl was replaced by Captain Kral Nevil.

**Twofingers, Gerlon** One of the many gladiator fighters chosen by Ajuur the Hutt to compete in his events at the height of the Great Sith War. Gerlon was not an exceptional fighter, but served to soften up opponents for later combatants. He was given the name Twofingers after an accident in the gladiator ring cost him some of his digits.

**Two-Guns, Longo** This male Clantaani was a noted pirate who often worked for Gardulla the Hutt. Jabba the Hutt issued a bounty for his capture shortly after the Battle of Naboo. Jango Fett claimed it in short order in order to gain an audience with Jabba.

**Twool** A young Rodian who was one of the many students of Luke Skywalker's new Jedi Order following the Yuuzhan Vong War. A skilled pilot, Twool was later added to Red Sword Flight during an attempt to capture or eliminate Jacen Solo. Twool also served as Rakehell Six on a mission to disable Centerpoint Station. He was among the handful of Rakes shot down and killed in the fighting.

**Twoseas, Lilit** A human Jedi and Master to the Whiphid Padawan K'Kruhk. She was part of the Jedi team sent to Yibikkoror in the Yinchorri system. She died trying to save her Padawan.

**Ty, Codi** The Togruta Padawan of B'dard Tone. She spoke against the mission to assassinate General Grievous, but eventually went along with her Master. Their small group of renegade Jedi managed to track down Grievous after he captured the younglings of the Bergruutfa Clan on the planet Belsus. There Master Tone and Flynn gave their lives so that Codi Ty could escort the younglings to safety.

***Tydirium*** An Imperial *Lambda*-class shuttle, it was used by Han Solo's Rebel strike team to covertly reach Endor's Forest Moon. The shuttle had been captured prior to the mission.

**Tyed Kant** The homeworld of the headquarters of two corporations that supplied foodstuffs to the Empire: Nebula Consumables and Imperial Meats and Produce. This habitable gas giant with a "life zone" was the only planet in the Kantel system. It was home to giant floating creatures called iagoin.

Ratts Tyerell

**Tyerell, Ratts** This scrappy alien was considered one of the Outer Rim's best Podracer pilots. Tyerell was a member of the Aleena species, and flew in a Vokoff-Strood Titan 215 Podracer. Unfortunately for Tyerell and his family, he was killed during the Boonta Eve Classic on Tatooine, which saw Anakin Skywalker defeat Sebulba.

**Tyestin, Iskit** An alias used by Wes Janson to infiltrate the city of Revos on Storinal.

**Tyluun Night-Soarer** A species of blue-skinned humanoids distinguished by their pointed ears and their winged arms. Tyluun Night-Soarers were known for their cunning and stealth, qualities that made them invaluable to the underworld of the galaxy as silent assassins.

Tyluun Night-Soarer

**Tymmo** *See* Dack (Tymmo).

**Tyne's Horky** A small, uneventful mining planet on the frontier. The economy revolved around keshel, a precious metal. Even rarer were deposits of nergon-14, a volatile mineral used in Imperial proton torpedoes. Many service and mining droids could be found wandering the dusty streets of Tyne's Horky's small mining towns, looking for employment. Droid auctions were held regularly in these town squares. The planet was profitable enough during the early days of the Empire to have developed a criminal element. Kleb Zellock was the local crime boss on Tyne's Horky.

**Tynna** The homeworld of the otter-like Tynnans, it was a resource-rich planet that had long been a member of the galactic community. Corporations operating under the Republic developed Tynna's resources but kept its natural beauty intact. The fur-covered Tynnans had poor eyesight; a layer of fat beneath their skins protected them from the cold waters of their planet. Tynnan society was entirely state-run: All citizens had free access to housing, food, education, and other benefits.

For thousands of years, the members of the Tynnan government were selected by lottery. Since any citizen could be chosen to serve, the pragmatic and sensible Tynnans always stayed informed on important issues. Tynnans formed one of the most affluent societies in the galaxy, and they traveled widely. Prior to the Clone Wars, an infestation of stone mites destroyed the Tynna Central Government Building and prompted the planet's leader, Razelfiin, to announce his support for Count Dooku. Tynna rejoined the Republic before the war's end, and Senator Streamdrinker was one of several Senators arrested on charges of sedition. The Empire tried to increase its control over the planet to generate greater revenue. Odumin, the Corporate Sector Authority territorial manager (also known as Spray, the skip tracer), was a native of Tynna, and his success inspired other Tynnans to take more active roles in galactic affairs. During the Yuuzhan Vong War, the New Republic allowed Tynna to fall to the enemy in the hope of saving Bothawui and Corellia.

**Tynna, Battle of** Following on the heels of the subjugation of Gyndine by the Yuuzhan Vong, this battle saw the New Republic again powerless to stop the advance of the invaders. In the end, Tynna was taken to lend credence to the rumors planted by the Yuuzhan Vong that Corellia and Bothawui were the next targets for invasion. At the Tanallay Surge Complex, the Yuuzhan Vong unleashed a vicious bioweapon into the water supply. In almost no time, the cold blue waters of Tynna were rendered lifeless and toxic. The plan was to spread the New Republic's forces thin in an effort to protect both worlds. In reality, the Yuuzhan Vong struck at Fondor, wiping out much of the starship-production facility there. Tynna, however, was resurrected by the Yuuzhan Vong as a factory world from which they could produce their biotechnology.

**Typha-Dor** This planet, located in the Uziel system, was the last of the Uziel worlds to hold out against the invasion plans of the Vanqors. The native human population petitioned the Old Republic and the Jedi Knights to intervene before Vanqor controlled the entire system. The few resistance fighters who dared to stand up against the Vanqors rallied from a base on the Typha-Dor moon known as TY44, until Obi-Wan Kenobi and Anakin Skywalker were dispatched to help rectify the situation. Typha-Dor was orbited by a large number of moons, which appeared to be strewn across the night sky like a necklace.

*Captain Gregar Typho (right) with Obi-Wan Kenobi*

**Typho, Captain Gregar** This man, distinguished by the black patch over his missing left eye, succeeded his uncle Captain Panaka as Queen Amidala's security chief in the decade following the Battle of Naboo. During that struggle, Typho distinguished himself as a commander and lost his eye in the fighting. He later became one of the leaders of the Naboo Royal Security Force. Just before the Battle of Geonosis, Typho was assigned by his uncle to accompany Senator Padmé Amidala to Coruscant for the vote on the Military Creation Act. Typho employed Cordé as a stand-in for Padmé upon their arrival, a move that likely saved the Senator's life when their starship was destroyed by a bomb. Captain Typho worked with the Jedi to ensure Padmé's safety during the Clone Wars, but was unable to prevent her from setting off for Mustafar in search of Anakin Skywalker. When her body was returned to Naboo, Typho retired from military duty and established a security service that assisted the Naboo during the early years of the New Order.

**Tyrann** The Supreme Master of the Serpent Masters of Ophideraan. Tyrann wore a medallion that transmitted ultrasonic signals used to control the serpents. Luke Skywalker dropped the medallion into the Great Well, and Tyrann perished while trying to recover it.

*Tyrann*

***Tyrannic*** A Star Destroyer under the command of Captain Nalgol, who ordered the retreat of the *Obliterator,* the *Tyrannic,* and the *Ironhand* at Bothawui during the Caamas incident. Booster Terrik's Star Destroyer, *Errant Venture,* briefly assumed the identity of the *Tyrannic* around this time.

***Tyrant*** An Imperial Star Destroyer, it was part of the Death Squadron task force that searched for Rebel forces after the Battle of Yavin. Under the command of Captain Lennox, the *Tyrant* attempted to capture Rebel ships fleeing the Hoth system. Lieutenant Cabbel was also stationed aboard the ship, which was damaged after being hit by a Rebel Alliance ion cannon covering the evacuation of the medium transport *Quantum Storm.* In the aftermath of the Bacta War, the New Republic captured the *Tyrant* and made it Councilor Leia Organa's personal flagship, renamed the *Rebel Dream.*

**Tyranus, Darth** The Sith title given to Count Dooku after he became the apprentice of Darth Sidious (Chancellor Palpatine). Under the name of Darth Tyranus, Dooku usurped the work of Jedi Master Sifo-Dyas, who had been a confidant of Dooku's in the Jedi Order. When Sifo-Dyas revealed that he had put in place plans to create a clone army for the Republic, Dooku relayed the information to Sidious, who ordered Dooku to eliminate Sifo-Dyas and assume control of the project. After killing Sifo-Dyas, Tyranus recruited Jango Fett to serve as the genetic basis for their clone army. Although Obi-Wan Kenobi's discovery of the clones on Kamino was unexpected, Sidious allowed Tyranus to continue to manipulate the Confederacy of Independent Systems as Count Dooku. Sidious then turned his attention to Anakin Skywalker, knowing that young Skywalker was much stronger in the Force than Tyranus. During the Battle of Coruscant, Palpatine ordered Anakin to kill Tyranus, and the young Jedi beheaded the treacherous former Jedi. (*See also* Dooku, Count.)

*Darth Tyranus*

**Tyrell, Bogg** A female Aleena Senator seen in a Coruscant airspeeder with the Dug Seboca. Seboca and Bogg narrowly avoided a collision when Anakin Skywalker's speeder chased Zam Wesell's.

**Tyris, Nikkos** This Anzati was one of the most powerful of the Saarai-kaar leaders of the *Jensaarai,* who discovered ancient Sith teachings during the Clone Wars. These teachings were the work of one of his predecessors, Volfe Karkko, and described how Karkko had been seduced by the dark side of the Force. Tyris himself was a former Jedi Knight, and his knowledge of the Force, coupled with his unusual style of fighting, made him a formidable opponent. His combination of light and dark teachings became known as the *Saarai,* or the True Way, and his beliefs led to his leaving the Jedi Order. Tyris and his companions were eventually located and eliminated by Nejaa Halcyon and Ylenic It'kla, but not before Halcyon was mortally wounded when Tyris drove his azure lightsaber through Halcyon's chest. Halcyon, though dying, absorbed all the energy from Tyris's lightsaber and from it created a fist-like projection with the Force, which he used to crush Tyris.

**Tyrius system** The system that contained the planet Rodia, homeworld of the Rodians.

**tyrossum** A vicious creature native to the lower jungles of the planet Kashyyyk. The snout of a tyrossum measured a meter or more in length, and its mouth was lined with curved fangs. The killing of a tyrossum was considered a major event by the Wookiees, and a tyrossum jawbone—known as the Talking Bone—was used by the Rock Council to indicate which individual had the right to speak.

**Tython** This planet was believed to have been the first world on which the Force was discovered prior to the formation of the Republic. Tython was located in the Deep Core of the galaxy, hidden in the dense cluster of

*Bogg Tyrell*

stars and accessible only via a tenuous hyperspace route. According to the natives of Tython, the Force had two components, known as the Ashla and the Bogan, which eventually became known to the Jedi Order as the light and dark sides of the Force, respectively. The followers of the Ashla became involved in a great war with those beings who followed the Bogan, and the victorious worshippers of Ashla used the first lightsabers during their subsequent initiation ceremonies. These early worshippers left Tython and became the first Jedi Knights. Millennia later, the Sith Lord Belia Darzu rose to power on Tython, drawing on the power of the dark side that permeated the planet. In the wake of the Battle of Ruusan, Darth Bane sought out Tython in order to find the fortress of Darzu, who had created her technobeast army on the planet.

**Tyto, Captain** This clone trooper, official designated as CT-52/89-9204, served as the Captain in command of Bacta Company, during the Clone Wars.

**Tyvokka** A great Wookiee Jedi Master who served on the Jedi Council during the years leading up to the Stark Hyperspace Conflict. Many Jedi believed that Master Tyvokka could read the future through the Force, remaining focused on the present to intuit what the future might hold. Master Tyvokka was known as a patient teacher, but he was truly tested when he took Plo Koon as his Padawan. It was Master Tyvokka who first saw through the false bacta shortages that were the cause of the Stark Hyperspace Conflict. His steady demeanor kept the negotiations among the Stark Commercial Combine, the Trade Federation, and the Republic on track until Stark tried to assassinate all parties. In the ensuing firefight, Master Tyvokka was killed when the Trade Federation's battle droids opened fire into the melee. His place on the Jedi Council was taken by his apprentice, Plo Koon.

*Tyvokka*

**tzeotine** A resin found on the swamp trees of the planet Parcelus Minor. Tzeotine was highly combustible and was used to light lamps and power engines. During the Clone Wars, the Confederacy fired upon the surface of the planet, causing the jungles to become engulfed by flame from burning tzeotine.

**Tzizvvt** A male Brizzit from the planet Jandoon, he hid from Imperials on Tatooine, hoping to procure passage to the Outer Rim before the Empire found him.

**tzur'qipat** A heavy piece of Yuuzhan Vong equipment used to produce a smokescreen. From the outside, it resembled a fat clam with knobby handholds along its rim. The tzur'qipat was often used in conjunction with a kavaavik, which allowed Yuuzhan Vong warriors to see in the dark.

**U2-C1** A blue housekeeping droid in the palace of Jabba the Hutt, he warned the Whiphid J'Quille of a plot against him. It was one of a series of such droids produced by Publictechnic, but later modified by criminals so that units in hotels would steal clients' jewels and credits.

*U2-C1*

**U-33** A class of orbital space boats, they were sublightspeed loadlifters that shuttled personnel and materials between planetary spaceports and orbiting space stations. The U-33 was an older model replaced by a number of newer, more efficient classes, although some U-33s remained working in frontier systems, on developing worlds, and as military training ships.

**U-3PO** A protocol droid, he served in the House of Alderaan's diplomatic corps. Imperials had secretly captured U-3PO and altered his programming for espionage, making him an unwitting spy for the Empire. It was U-3PO, aboard the *Tantive IV,* who signaled the arrival of the ship carrying Princess Leia Organa above Tatooine. The Imperial Star Destroyer *Devastator* then captured the ship.

*Ualaq*

**Ualaq** A subspecies of Aqualish on Ando. Ualaq had fingered hands like the Quara and four eyes instead of two. Like the Quara, the Ualaq preferred to live on land, rather than in the ocean.

**Uaua** The chief planet of the Ua system, located in the Centrality, it was home to the avian Quor'sav. The species was nearly wiped out when offworld colonists, most of whom were mammalian, accidentally introduced a virus to the planet.

*< Utapaun Tion Medon*

**Uba IV, Battle of** A Clone Wars battle in which the Republic failed to destroy a Separatist droid manufacturing facility on the planet Uba IV. It marked one of the first times that Separatist forces used octuptarra droids to deploy viruses and toxins against the clone troopers of the Grand Army of the Republic, earning the automata the nickname of virus droids.

*U-3PO (left) and C-3PO*

**Ubese (1)** The Ubese species came from the Uba system. Their planet was ravaged a few millennia before the Galactic Civil War by a preemptive strike from the Old Republic and the Jedi, which feared the aggressive weapons development program of the Ubese. The Republic's attack exploded Ubese weapons stores on every world in the system, destroying Uba III outright and wreaking radioactive devastation on Uba I, Uba II, and Uba V. Only Uba IV remained marginally viable, and the semi-toxic atmosphere forced its inhabitants to wear specialized filtration masks. Those Ubese who survived and lived on Uba IV became known as the true Ubese. Others migrated to the Ubertica system and were shunned by their brethren on Uba IV as being too soft to be true Ubese; they became known as the *yrak pootzck,* a term that indicated impure parentage and cowardly ways. The bounty hunter Boushh was an Ubese, and Princess Leia disguised herself as Boushh at least twice, including when she brought the "prisoner" Chewbacca to the court of Jabba the Hutt as part of a plan to rescue Han Solo.

Ubese tended to have fair skin and dark hair with eye colors of brilliant green or blue. Their vocal cords did not produce speech above rasping whispers, so they used a highly refined form of sign language, called Ubeninal, when communicating with other Ubese. The Ubese had a hatred of Jedi, whom they blamed for the devastation of the planets of the Uba system.

**Ubese (2)** The language spoken by the Ubese species to offworlders, recognizable by its metallic sounds.

**Ubiqtorate** The unit of Imperial Intelligence that oversaw all of the agency's activities at the highest levels, the Ubiqtorate formulated strategies and assigned goals to the other Intelligence divisions. Ubiqtorate members were anonymous, often unknown even to the unit's subordinates.

**Ubooki, Glah** The owner of a salvage business, Glah Ubooki's Strange and Wondrous Imports, this Bimm was a native of Glastro on his homeworld of Bimmisaari. The business was run with the help of Ubooki's 18 brothers.

*Ubese*

**Ubote** A Rebel Alliance corvette destroyed in the Javin sector following the Battle of Hoth.

**Ubrikkian Industries** A manufacturer of vehicles, including the sail barge of Jabba the Hutt and the Ubrikkian HAVr A9 floating fortress, an Imperial weapons platform with two heavy blaster cannons.

**Ubrikkian Steamworks** A subsidiary of Ubrikkian Industries that produced droids. The company's DD-13 Galactic Chopper was a specialist model at the forefront of cyborg technology.

**Ubris** One of Prince Isolder's personal guards during the Yuuzhan Vong War, she served the royal family of Hapes for two generations.

**Ubuugan fleshborer** A parasitic worm found in the swamps of Ubuuga. Fleshborers spent their entire life cycle within a host, emerging only briefly as winged adults. As their jaws took hold of their new host, their wings fell away. They secreted a corrosive chemical capable of eating through metal. Fleshborers were considered to be a delicacy by the pachydermoid Ubuugan species, which had developed natural defenses against the parasite. Boba Fett stumbled upon a host of Ubuugan fleshborers aboard the freighter *Mingula*.

Ubuugan fleshborer

**Ucce, Lady** A slave trader, she was a follower of Lord Hethrir and tried to help him establish the Empire Reborn.

**Uda-Khalid** An immense, white-skinned humanoid, he was one of the Old Republic's most notorious criminals, known to kill entire populations in order to obtain power and resouces. He had a row of short horns that ran atop his skull from his forehead; long, drooping black eyebrows framed his huge face. The Jedi Council dispatched Mace Windu to bring him to justice. Uda-Khalid challenged Windu to one-on-one combat. In a swift flourish, Windu speared Uda-Khalid though the heart. Uda-Khalid's reign of terror was over.

**Udelen** An alias adopted by Nom Anor about a year before the Yuuzhan Vong launched their invasion of the galaxy, when he traveled to Nar Shaddaa on a mission to enlist the aid of the Mandalorians in the coming war. Just prior to the invasion, Udelen agreed to travel to Mandalore to forge a deeper alliance. They agreed to meet in space near Belkadan to make their arrangement official, and Nom Anor dropped the Udelen alias and revealed his true self.

**Udin** A Kubaz bounty hunter, he was among a group hired by Prefect Eugene Talmont of Tatooine to locate Han Solo following the Battle of Yavin. Talmont was hoping to use the prestige of the capture to gain a better posting than Tatooine.

**Udine system** An asteroid-packed system, it was next to the region called Keller's Void. Pirates sometimes brought asteroids from the Udine system to the Void to create mass shadows and force unsuspecting ships out of hyperspace.

**Udo-Mal, Sen** This Cerean was a noted Jedi Master and consular of the Old Republic.

**Udrane Galactic Electronics** A small corporation that produced a wide range of computerized tools for mechanics and technicians.

**U'Dray** This planet was the site of a rare Rebel Alliance victory against the Scimitar Assault Wing, also known as the White Death.

**U-E** *See* Q-E, 2-E, and U-E.

**Uffel** This moon was the second satellite in orbit around Genarius, in the Cularin system. A pair of Twi'leks tried to scout the moon's resources, but were overcome by poisonous gases in its atmosphere. Their two droids kept on running, however, and eventually built several cities on the moon. Under the guidance of QS-2D, with the help of Riboga the Hutt, Uffel became known for its manufacture of specialty droids. During the Yuuzhan Vong War, Uffel was attacked but saved by the surviving members of the Iron Knights.

**Ugan, Captain** This man served the Empire as a navy captain and was in command of the Detainer CC-2200 Interdictor cruiser stationed near Kashyyyk when the Empire began collecting Wookiee slaves. Captain Ugan found himself in trouble when his command crew discovered that a Separatist *Recusant*-class warship was in orbit around Kashyyyk. The vessel had been mistakenly reactivated by Olee Starstone and Filli Bitters during their escape from the world. The mission turned out to be a suicide run: The vessel rammed into Ugan's, destroying both.

**Ugbuz** The alpha male of the Gamorrean Gakfedd tribe on Pzob, until the *Eye of Palpatine* picked him up. He then became indoctrinated as a stormtrooper squad leader.

**Uggernaught** The nickname for modified electromagnetic loadlifting maintenance exoskeletons manufactured by Bespin Motors and frequently operated by Ugnaughts. Uggernaughts were piloted by a driver and an operator, who worked in tandem to tackle large construction jobs. Equipped with plasma torches and powerful magnetic projectors capable of lifting even the heaviest construction materials, Uggernaughts were invaluable assets aboard the various construction platforms throughout Bespin. Though the Uggernaught was primarily a vehicle designed for hard labor, it could become very dangerous if operated by angry Ugnaughts.

**uglies** A nickname that spacers gave to hybrid fighters cobbled together from the salvageable parts of other craft. Uglies were frequently used by smugglers and pirates. They were a specialty of some less-than-reputable Corellian shipyards, but did present a problem in the aftermarket because there were no specs, plans, or complete sets of manuals available. Uglies were also referred to as juicecans and buzzers, and some of the popular types included Z-'ceptors, TIE-wings, X-TIEs, and Y-balls. Kavil's Corsairs and other pirate groups under the Blazing Claw symbol used uglies culled from the scrapyard moons of Axxila.

**Ugloste** The Ugnaught placed in charge of determining how to use carbon freezing on humans. The weary old Ugloste had lived much of his life as a slave. Before he came to the relative freedom of Cloud City, he had toiled away for humans. It was with little compunction that he made the modifications enabling Han Solo to be frozen in carbonite.

***Ugly Truth*** The emergency evacuation vehicle discovered by Yuuzhan Vong collaborator Viqi Shesh on occupied Coruscant. The *Ugly Truth* resembled a covered landspeeder, and had formerly belonged to Hasville and Adray Terson of Terson Comfort Carriers. Members of the Wraith infiltration squad found Shesh's locater and traced the ship before Shesh was able to reach it. After Shesh's suicide, the *Ugly Truth* brought the Wraiths and the Jedi to Borleias.

The Ugnaught Ugloste

**Ugmush, Captain** The female Gamorrean captain of the *Zicreex,* the ship that C-3PO and R2-D2 used to escape from the planet Nim Drovis.

**Ugnaught** Small, hardworking, and loyal, these porcine humanoids lived and worked on Bespin's Cloud City, which they helped to build. They could usually be found in the Tibanna-gas processing plants or as general laborers in the bowels of the floating city. Originally from the planet Gentes in the remote Anoat system, Ugnaughts lived in primitive colonies on Gentes's less-than-hospitable surface until Lord Ecclessis Figg rounded up three tribes—the Irden, Botrut, and Isced—and offered them a deal. If they would build his floating city, he would then grant them their freedom. Further, they and their descendants would be allowed to live and work in the colony and share in the company's profits. The Ugnaughts accepted the deal and reestablished their ruling Terend Council. After the city was finished, they began to reap the benefits of their labor. Ugnaughts were generally peaceful, but were not averse to violence if they were provoked. In combat they would grab whatever was handy, from broken bottles to construction-grade plasma torches.

During the Clone Wars, General Grievous defeated the Ugnaughts on Belsus, a moon in the Anoat system. He rounded up the survivors and, as a demonstration of his power, vaporized them with an orbital blast. Unknown to Grievous, many of the Ugnaughts lived underground and survived.

After Baron-Administrator Lando Calrissian fled Cloud City, a number of Ugnaughts revolted against Imperial rule. The Ugnaughts caused havoc by rewiring machinery and failing to properly perform repairs. They also reprogrammed the cyborg Lobot. Eventually, many Ugnaughts left Cloud City and fled to the floating Ugnaught Surface, but later returned to help Calrissian and Luke Skywalker finally oust the Imperial presence. Calrissian then turned over control of the city to the Ugnaughts' chosen leader, King Ozz.

**Ugnaught Surface** A floating platform located almost a full kilometer directly below the lowest weather vane on Cloud City. The bizarre structure known as the Ugnaught Surface spanned roughly 1 kilometer square and was covered in improbable stretches of swamp, marsh, and jungle. The artificial landscape was laid over an internal framework of plasteel. At certain points, storms and more than a few aircar collisions exposed the endoskeleton of the Surface, but the sturdy frame never buckled. The exposed girders instead became walkways with a spectacular view of Bespin's turbulent atmosphere, a popular place to visit for the overflow of Cloud City tourists that arrived after the Empire fell. A complex internal system of giant bladders filled with lighter-than-air Tibanna gas kept the Surface at the perfect altitude to maintain the warmth and humidity Ugnaughts preferred.

**Ugnor, Boss** This Ugnaught, who stood at least 1.5 meters tall, was generally regarded as one of the tallest and most noble Ugnaughts ever to live. He was the leader of the work parties that traveled from Gentes to Bespin to assist Ecclessis Figg in the construction of Cloud City, and his ability to deal with the human earned him the title Ufflor of Ufflors. He also helped create the Ugnaught Mechanics Union, and was the driving force behind the construction of the Ugnaught Surface.

**Ugnorgrad** A city in the center of the Ugnaught Surface, home to union boss King Ozz and many of the more powerful union leaders. The Union Hall was also located there, and could be seen from the famous Action Tidings tower. Other structures included ancient Tibanna refineries (a relic of frequent and ill-advised attempts by past union bosses to bring mining to the Surface), a unique Ugnaught-designed power station that kept the entire place operational, an abandoned Imperial outpost serving as public housing, and a large, unique building suspended over open space by cables and Tibanna bladders that was at various times a boss's mansion, a luxury hotel, and Zavlabar's Gentes Grill.

*Ugor*

**Ugor** Members of this protozoan species worshipped garbage and treated all junk as holy relics. Ugors came from a star system they called Paradise; in reality, it was a junk-filled asteroid field. They had an exclusive contract with the Empire to collect garbage jettisoned from Imperial fleet ships and store it in their garbage-dump systems. Ugors grew to about 1 meter in diameter and could grow up to 30 pseudopodia at a time, some of which contained visual and other sensory organ-like growths that allowed communication. Ugors moved by oozing from place to place or by controlling specialized environment suits. Gambling and cheating were acceptable parts of their culture. Other scavenger species, such as the Squibs, were considered business rivals to be crushed and eliminated.

**Uhanayih** Meaning "the within world" in the Yinchorri tongue, this was the name of one of the innermost moons in the Yinchorri system. It was associated with a variety of legends and myths of the spirit world, and was the site of the secret command center from which the Yinchorri launched their attacks on the Jedi a year before the Battle of Naboo. After the Jedi destroyed the base, the Yinchorri surrendered.

Uhumele

**Uhltenden** This planet was surrounded by a ring of debris from a multitude of starships. It had a toxic atmopshere and no natural life.

***Uhumele*** This Maka-Eekai L4000 transport, owned and operated by Captain Schurk-Heren, maintained a temporary base on the planet New Plympto. In the wake of the execution of Order 66 and the enslavement of the Nosaurians, Captain Schurk-Heren decided that it was in the best interests of himself and his crew to leave New Plympto behind. He also agreed to transport Dass Jennir and Bomo Greenbark, and it was Jennir's daring escape plan that got them into hyperspace with minimal damage to the ship.

***Uhuru*** An Imperial freighter disabled by Keyan Farlander near Orron III during the Galactic Civil War.

**uizani** Avian creatures native to the planet Radnor.

**uj cake** A sweet, filling, amber-colored dessert cake that was a staple of the Mandalorian diet; its full name was *uj'alayi.* Its origins were rations provided to ancient Mandalorian soldiers, and it was often said that uj cake was first cooked inside the helmet of a soldier before it was stored for later eating. Even in its unpreserved state, uj cake lasted for years because of its high sugar content.

**Ukchet** This Jawa scout was one of the first members of his tribe to spot R2-D2 when the droid set off to reach Obi-Wan Kenobi on Tatooine.

**Ukio** Located in the Abrion sector and the Ukio system, it was one of the top five food-producing planets in the New Republic. Prior to the Battle of Geonosis, the planets of the Abrion sector seceded from the Galactic Republic. After the Battle of Endor, Ukio was the target of an attack by Grand Admiral Thrawn. A representative of the Ukian Overliege surrendered the planet after Thrawn seemed to demonstrate the ability to fire directly through Ukio's planetary shields, although the attack was actually an elaborate illusion. The smuggler Samuel Tomas Gillespee had bought a plot of land on Ukio, which he lost when the Empire took control.

**Ulabore, Lieutenant** This man led the Gloom Walkers for the Brotherhood of Darkness during the years leading up to the Battle of Ruusan. Although Lieutenant Ulabore won praise from his superiors for the success of the Gloom Walkers, the entire unit was well aware of the fact that its success was due more to Dessel's leadership than Ulabore's. He took complete credit for the unit's success on Kashyyyk, although he'd panicked when cut off from the main force and had been relieved by Dessel. His inability to lead was made more apparent when the Gloom Walkers were sent to Phaseera to eliminate a Republic communications post. Ulabore realized that an immediate attack would come during the daylight hours, allowing the Republic forces to see the Gloom Walkers coming. Dessel, however, was not about to let his fellow soldiers be slaughtered, and he knocked Ulabore unconscious. Dessel waited to launch the attack until he had enough cover to guarantee success.

**Ulabos** The 11th planet in the Coruscant system. A frozen ball of rock, Ulabos was characterized by the immense rings of ice and rock that surrounded it.

**Ulban Arms** The manufacturer of the Red Terror and S-EP1 security droids. Ulban Arms was a Corporate Sector company that was once a subsidiary of LeisureMech Enterprises. It specialized in military and security designs.

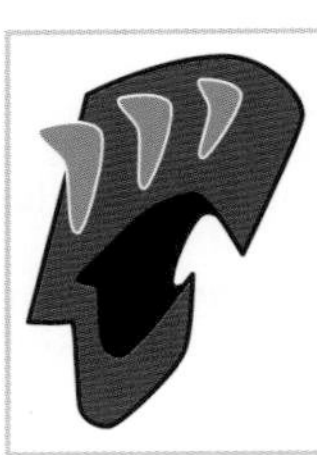

**Ulbasca** The closest moon orbiting Genarius, its orbit was unusual since it was always in the light of the Cularin system's suns, while its dark side was lit by the reflection of Genarius. Thus, Ulbasca's surface never experienced a true night. Traces of poisonous gases made its air unbreathable, but several species of reptiles existed, feeding on sulfurous plants.

**Ulcane, Meres** An Imperial who used family connections to enter the Academy. He wasn't popular among fellow soldiers and believed his commanding officers were trying to kill him with dangerous assignments. Ulcane turned the tables by trapping his entire team inside a Rebel Alliance warehouse and destroying it, earning commendations for being the sole survivor. Ulcane continued to climb the Imperial ladder through such chicanery, ultimately forming the Kaarenth Dissension—an Imperial splinter group—with another officer. New Republic agents thwarted the Dissension's plans and killed Ulcane.

**ul-Esca, Ainvar** He was one of the most powerful Jedi ever to train aboard the massive starship *Chu'unthor,* several centuries before the Battle of Yavin.

**Ulgo** An elderly Dulok living in a cave near the Canyons of Mist on the Forest Moon of Endor, he liked to eat the native lanternbirds. Sometimes known as Ulgo the Magnificent, he was killed when he was accidentally knocked over a cliff by the wing of the Ewok Warok's glider.

**Ulgo, Trask** An Old Republic corporal first class aboard the *Endar Spire,* he was killed by Darth Bandon.

**uli-ah** The Tusken Raider term for their children. Uli-ah wore unisex garments that hid all flesh. These traditional clothes protected uli-ah from sun, sand, and wind, and conserved precious moisture. Young Tusken Raiders lacked full tribal acceptance until they completed a rite of passage at age 15.

*Uli-ah*

**Uliar, Director Chas** The leader of the council ruling the survivors of Outbound Flight.

**Ulicia** A planet in the Corporate Sector near Abo Dreth. Fiolla of Lorrd barely escaped from Ulicia following a mission gone bad shortly after the Battle of Yavin.

**ulikuo stones** Valuable gemstone found only on Kip.

**Ulion system** A largely uninhabited star system near Kuat, it served as one of the two main staging areas for passenger traffic inbound to the Kuat Passenger Port.

**Uliss, Tam** A wealthy Corellian industrialist from Ansion involved in a conspiracy to make Ansion secede from the Republic. He attended a secret meeting at a cantina in Quadrant H-46 and was later seen on a conspirator's transport orbiting Coruscant. When Ansion voted to remain with the Republic, Shu Mai killed Tam Uliss for his failure.

**Ulix, Ulu** A three-eyed, horned alien, he was the Padawan of Jedi Master Glynn-Beti during the early stages of the Clone Wars. Ulu Ulix was assigned to guard young Boba Fett and the other orphans aboard the *Candaserri* after they were rescued from Count Dooku's lair on Raxus Prime. Years later, as the Clone Wars drew to an end, Glynn-Beti and Ulix were dispatched to Xagobah to lead the forces that were laying siege to Wat Tambor's hidden fortress. Ulu tried to single-handedly penetrate the fortress by forcing Tambor's ramship to plunge into it, but his swoop was shot down before he could complete the task. Instead of falling to his death, however, Ulix landed in the arms of Boba Fett, who had traveled to Xagobah to capture Wat Tambor for Jabba the Hutt.

**Ulizra** An ancient Nazzari religion that had three basic tenets: first, the preservation of the group over the individual; second, the segregation of the Nazzar from the remainder of the galaxy; and third, the elimination of any other form of religion or cult that undermined the beliefs of Ulizra.

**Uln, Jorak** This ancient Dark Jedi was stationed on Korriban many thousands of years before the Galactic Civil War, protecting the tomb of Tulak Hord. He was known as a sadistic individual who often drugged his captives in order to extract information from them. Uln was, at one time, the master of the Sith Academy on Korriban, but was replaced by Uthar Wynn. It was said that Uln went insane after being replaced, although he remained a fixture at the Academy. Years later, Uln was killed when a group of Jedi Knights infiltrated Korriban by posing as Sith apprentices during their search for Darth Malak.

**Ultaar** A Mid Rim forest world that housed a Rebel Alliance base. Darth Vader came to the planet hoping to gather information about the pilot who destroyed the Death Star. Valance the Hunter discovered the base first, however, and left nothing behind in his own search for the mysterious pilot.

***Ultimo Vista*** A converted *Giga*-class transport, it originally was built as a leisure cruise ship, but the exceptionally slow-moving vessel ended up on Coruscant as a self-contained living environment that moved across the face of Galactic City. The *Ultimo Vista* was nearly hit by Anakin Skywalker and Obi-Wan Kenobi during their attempt to chase down Zam Wesell shortly before the Battle of Geonosis.

**ultra battle droid** Officially designated the B3 series battle droid, the ultra battle droid was designed by Baktoid Combat Automata for the Separatist droid armies during the Clone Wars. The automaton was developed by a team of engineers on Foundry as part of a competition launched by Wat Tambor to create a more powerful successor to the B2 series super battle droid. The original prototype was known as the Avatar-7, and was personally approved for development by General Grievous. Standing 4 meters tall, the ultra battle droid had four arms. The right pri-

*Ultra battle droid*

mary arm was equipped with a flamethrower, and the left with a wide-spray plasma cannon. Each secondary arm was equipped with a retractable blaster cannon. Additional weaponry included a shoulder-mounted rocket launcher and an experimental density projector. This unusual weapon was a specialized tractor beam generator that could be used to cause a momentary increase in the droid's apparent weight, making it seem 20 times heavier than normal. This allowed the B3 to secure itself to a specific location or to trample an enemy tank.

**ultramesh** A dense weave of solid fibers produced by the Verpine during the years following the Great Sith War. Ultramesh was exceptionally useful in the manufacture of lightweight body armor.

**ultrasonic spike** A specialized form of security device that used sound waves out of the normal hearing ranges of most humanoid beings to signal an alarm. Intruders were unaware that they had actually tripped an alarm.

**ulub** A life-form from the Yuuzhan Vong homeworld of Yuuzhan'tar. Ulubs were grown for their unusual song, which provided a backdrop to normal Yuuzhan Vong life.

**Uluq** An amber-striped gas giant, it was locked in a mutual orbit with the world of Qogo, deep in the Transitory Mists.

**Umaren'k'sa** A species native to Umaren'k in the Unknown Regions. Shortly after the Hemes Arbora migrated to Umaren'k, the rogue planet Zonama Sekot arrived in the system. Umaren'k'sa culture was forever changed because of the encounter, absorbing a good deal of the attributes of Hemes Arbora.

**Umbaran** An outwardly humanoid race native to the planet Umbara. Umbarans were characterized by their pale bluish skin and white-pigmented eyes. Umbarans were capable of seeing into the ultraviolet spectra of light, but had little vision in the normal visible spectrum. It was said that Umbarans had the ability to subtly influence and control other beings, and many used their abilities to identify hidden Jedi during Emperor Palpatine's Jedi Purge. Because many Umbarans secured positions of power within the Empire, they feared some form of retaliation when Palpatine was killed at the Battle of Endor. This led the Umbarans to flee deeper into the Ghost Nebula, though they maintained an invisible information network to monitor the activities of the New Republic.

The Umbarans lived under a system of nearly 100 distinct castes. Only those in the top 10 castes were allowed to leave their homeworld. Movement among caste levels was possible for all Umbarans, and most individuals spent a large portion of their lives planning how to move up. Supreme Chancellor Palpatine selected an Umbaran named Sly Moore to be his staff aide, entrusting her with his darkest secrets.

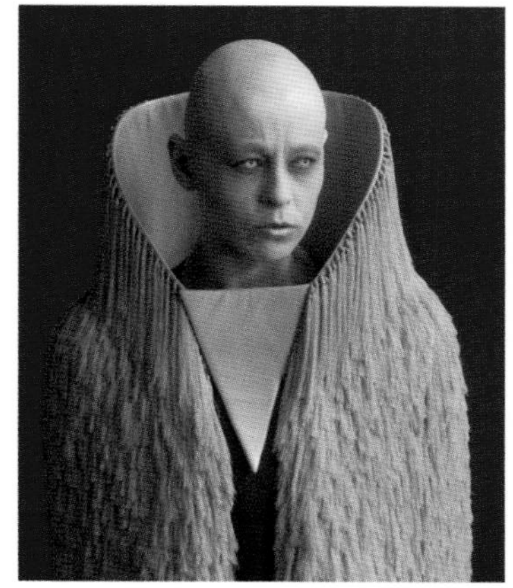
Umbaran

**Umbaran Shadow Assassin** Shadow Assassins who were trained at the Sith Academy on Umbara during the era of the New Sith Wars. The Umbaran Shadow Assassins preferred to use force pikes, and were trained to use the dark side of the Force to mask their presence from others. This allowed them to move about without being detected by other Force-sensitive beings, making them the most dangerous killers in the galaxy. Like Shadow Assassins from Ryloth, the Umbarans went into hiding in the wake of the Battle of Ruusan.

**Umboo** A colony in the Roon star system, it was the site of a light station that guided ships through the hazardous dust cloud that permeated the system. Umboo was the home of Auren Yomm, a talented young athlete whom R2-D2 and C-3PO met during the early days of the Empire. After Mungo Baobab was imprisoned by Governor Koong, he managed to escape from the Umboo Lightstation with the help of Noop Yeldarb. However, in the course of their escape, the light station suffered significant damage and crashed into an asteroid.

**Umgul** A cool, mist-covered world in the same system as Dargul, it was a center for gambling and sports attractions. Umgul's spaceport was in Umgul City, built on the limestone banks of a wide river that attracted numerous pleasure barges. The city was covered with signs and attractions beckoning visitors; cheating in the gambling establishments was punishable by death. Tourists visited Umgul mainly to see the famous Umgullian blob races, held in an arena carved from rock and ringed with powerful fans to blow away the thick fog. The protoplasmic blobs, bred for racing, were kept in stables and monitored by the Umgullian Racing Commission for any sign of illegal enhancement. Lando Calrissian visited Umgul while searching for possible Jedi candidates for Luke Skywalker's academy.

Umpass-stay

**Umi, Bjork** A bounty hunter who joined the Peace Brigade during the Yuuzhan Vong War. When Senator Viqi Shesh made arrangements for the assassination of Chief of State Borsk Fey'lya, Warmaster Tsavong Lah provided Umi's services to Shesh. Fey'lya's execution was thwarted by YVH-1 prototype droids.

Umrach

**Ummar** A dark-skinned woman who was a native of Contruum, she was a major in the New Republic military during the Yuuzhan Vong War. She served as General Airen Cracken's chief adjutant on her homeworld.

**Umpass-stay** A huge Klatooinian who was one of Jabba the Hutt's palace drummers. Born into slavery on the colony world of Shawti, Umpass-stay had been part of clan Desilijic since birth. He became a trusted adviser to Shebba Kalshi Desilijic, but misjudged the intentions of Shebba's nephew, Jabba. Jabba had Shebba executed out of mistrust, and took possession of Umpass-stay. Umpass-stay and Ak-Rev became two of Jabba's most trusted bodyguards, and the Hutt required them to play the drums with each band that came to the palace. Many bands refused, citing artistic clashes. In the aftermath of Jabba's death near the Pit of Carkoon, Umpass-stay tried to reach Mos Eisley with Ak-Rev. On the way, they were ambushed by a group of Tusken Raiders, who killed Ak-Rev but freed Umpass-stay. After reaching the settlement, Umpass-stay met up with Darson Kinderlot, who agreed to transport him to Hutt space. There he went to work for Jocoro Desilijic Tiure on Du Hutta.

**umrach** A hulking Yuuzhan Vong–bioengineered reptile whose face was a seething mass of razor-tipped tentacles. Introduced into Coruscant's ecosystem by Yuuzhan Vong biomachines, the umrach sprinted forward on two powerful legs and seized its prey with prehensile forepaws, lowering its head to deliver a messy killing strike with its mouth-spears.

**Umwak** The real name of the Dulok shaman, he often traveled in disguise to trick the Ewoks on Endor's Forest Moon.

**Unch, Sil** This Neimoidian served as a communications officer during the blockade of the planet Naboo. Sil Unch specialized in the programming of Droid Command Ships and droid control interfaces, and disliked taking orders from Daultay Dofine. Sil Unch perished in the Battle of Naboo.

***Undauntable*** This Imperial Star Destroyer was under the command of Admiral Helaw during the early years of the New Order. As the oldest ship in the fleet that patrolled the Atrivis sector, the *Undauntable* was known for its spotless service record. The ship served as one of the primary defensive vessels that patrolled the sector during the construction of the first Death Star. On one visit there, the *Undauntable* was loaded with an ammunition shipment that had been sabotaged by Rebel agents on Gall, in an effort to destroy the Death Star. Instead the ammunition was loaded aboard the Star Destroyer, where it exploded and destroyed the vessel.

***Undaunted*** One of two Republic gunships dispatched to subdue the Almas Academy in the hours following the command from Darth Sidious to execute Order 66. Jedi Master Darrus Jeht returned to the Cularin system shortly after the *Undaunted* and its sister gunship, the *Primal,* launched their attack; he witnessed them taking out several starships, most of which contained Jedi who were trying to escape from Almas. Launching a daring attack, Jeht pretended that his own ship, the *Maelstrom,* was a support vessel just arriving for in-system cleanup, then passed between the two gunships and opened fire. The *Undaunted* took heavy damage in the attack, only barely rolling away as the *Maelstrom* turned its weapons on the *Primal.* As it passed, the *Maelstrom*'s clone troopers continued their barrage, taking out the *Undaunted*'s drive systems. The resulting explosion ripped through the gunship's fuel cells, and the *Undaunted* exploded in a ball of fire.

**Undrarian** A territory on the planet Baralou controlled by the Krikthasi.

**Unduli, Luminara** This Mirialan was one of the many Jedi active in the final years of the Republic. A woman with luminous blue eyes and facial tattoos, Luminara was one of the Jedi Council's most trusted advisers. In the years leading up to the Battle of Naboo, she provided assistance to Qui-Gon Jinn and Obi-Wan Kenobi during their investigation of Arwen Cohl. Some 10 years later, while training Barriss Offee, Luminara accompanied Kenobi and his Padawan, Anakin Skywalker, to the planet Ansion, where they formed an alliance between the city dwellers and the nomads of the plains and averted the secession of Ansion from the Republic. Both Luminara and her Padawan Barriss Offee fought at the Battle of Geonosis. As the Clone Wars raged across the galaxy, Luminara and her Padawan defended Ilum from mine-laying droids, then led Republic forces on Nadiem. Master Unduli became known as one of the Jedi Order's most gifted negotiators. She traveled to many different worlds, sometimes in the company of Governor Wilhuff Tarkin, to negotiate with Separatist leaders. In the wake of the Battle of Coruscant, Master Unduli was dispatched to Kashyyyk with Jedi Master Yoda. Upon receiving Order 66, her clone troopers opened fire on Luminara, killing her as she tried to heal injured Wookiees and get wounded clone troopers onto medical transports. Official Imperial reports later claimed that Master Unduli was killed for her part in the Jedi conspiracy to overthrow the Republic.

**Undying Flame** A religious sect of the Yuuzhan Vong, it was dedicated to the worship of Yun-Q'aah and Yun-Txiin. Members of the Undying Flame often had their bodies physically altered to appear male from one profile and female from the other, representing the sibling deities of love and hate and all things opposite.

**Unification Policies** A set of legal guidelines and recommendations championed by Supreme Chancellor Tarsus Valorum following the Battle of Ruusan to help reunite the far-flung star systems that made up the Republic. The enactment of the Unification Policies allowed the Galactic Senate to enforce the regulations of membership in the Republic, an act that many groups saw as a form of bullying. Nearly 100 separatist groups sprang up after the Unification Policies were approved, all tying vainly to oppose the government's ability to keep a star system in the Republic.

**Unification Wars (1)** Conflicts that resulted in the formation of the Galactic Republic 25,000 years before the Battle of Yavin. Some historians believe that the ancient Bendu helped the nascent Jedi Order overcome the forces of evil to win the wars.

*Luminara Unduli*

**Unification Wars (2)** A period of unrest that swept through the Koros system (later to be renamed the Empress Teta system) about 5,000 years before the Galactic Civil War. The battles began when Empress Teta attempted to unify the seven worlds of the Koros system under her rule. She eventually succeeded, although the conflict on the planet Kirrek was long and bloody. Ultimately, Empress Teta asked Jedi Knights for aid in defeating the rebels.

**Unified Ruurian Colonies** The political body that governed the various worlds inhabited by the Ruurians.

**UniFy** A Telosian company that was a front for Offworld Corporation and renegade Force-user Xanatos, it was active in the years prior to the Battle of Naboo. UniFy became the largest employer on Telos, and the natives believed that UniFy was restoring the planet's national parks by using proceeds from the sport of Katharsis. In reality, UniFy came up with the idea for Katharsis and the results were nearly always fixed, providing huge betting profits to Offworld and Xanatos. In addtion, much of the money was spent on activities that would deplete the planet's natural resources. Obi-Wan Kenobi and Qui-Gon Jinn, with the help of Den and Andra, exposed the truth behind UniFy's involvement with Offworld, and Xanatos committed suicide rather than be captured.

**unifying Force** The facet of the Force that focused on the future and its bearing on a Jedi's place in the present. Those Jedi who studied the unifying Force understood that the future was constantly in motion, but sought to understand this motion and develop a sense of their place within it. This facet complemented the living Force, which connected Jedi Knights to the living beings that surrounded them. As Luke Skywalker set out to rebuild the Jedi Knights after the Battle of Endor, his own training led him to concentrate on the living Force. It wasn't until the Yuuzhan Vong invaded the galaxy and the Jedi Vergere returned from her self-imposed exile that Luke began to consider what the unifying Force meant to the new Jedi Knights.

**Unill, Mierme** A Jedi Knight dispatched to Mon Gazza to investigate the grisly murders of several ore miners shortly after the Battle of Naboo. Her investigation stalled until she learned that a young Padawan on Coruscant, Zett Jukassa, had started having visions that were eerily connected to the killings. She appealed to the Jedi Council for permission to ask Jukassa about his past, and it was then that she learned he had been born on Mon Gazza as Warpoc Skamini. She also learned that his parents were dead. With information she gathered from the young boy, Unill was able to expose a group of Black Sun extortionists as the killers. Upon returning to Coruscant, she took Jukassa as her Padawan. Unill was killed early in the Clone Wars, and Jukassa was left to train under the guidance of Cin Drallig.

**Uniting Day** The name given to the beginning of the process of creating a Sekotan starship. It was during this time that the seed-partners choose their eventual masters.

**Unity Green** One of the many public parks established on Coruscant following the Yuuzhan Vong War. Unity Green was created to honor the newfound allegiance between the Galactic Alliance and the Yuuzhan Vong, and signified their combined efforts to rebuild the planet into a world that both could look to as their capital.

**Unity of Community** The largest political movement on Ansion at a time when the natives were threatening to secede from the Old Republic shortly before the Clone Wars. The members of the Unity agreed that the only way Ansion would remain a member world of the Republic was if the city dwellers and the nomadic Alwari reached agreement on the use of Ansion's natural resources.

**Unit Zed** The head of automated security on Hosk Station, it was a class one droid. When criminal Olag Greck attempted to steal an ash ore shipment by sabotaging the station's power core, Unit Zed aided R2-D2 and C-3PO in aborting Greck's scheme, but a wrecking droid named Grozbok managed to chew up one of Unit Zed's legs during the tussle. Pursuing Greck to Nar Shaddaa, Unit Zed was destroyed by Jace Forno.

**universal energy cage** A floating confinement cell, it was designed to hold even the most powerful prisoners. It was designed by Umak Leth to control Jedi. The cage's repulsorlifts cradled a captive in a polarity field, and a feedback system within the bars reflected twofold any energy directed at them. As an extra precaution, the cage was wrapped in a sphere of electron ray energy, allowing it to hold any creature—including an enraged Herglic. Obi-Wan Kenobi and Qui-Gon Jinn were placed in an energy cage during a mission to Telos.

Universal energy cage

**University of Coruscant** The oldest institution of higher learning on Coruscant. It was founded by Chancellor Fillorean and Borz'Mat'oh of the Star Dragons following the peaceful resolution of the Duinuogwuin Contention approximately 15,500 years before the Battle of Yavin. The University of Coruscant was scattered throughout the Fobosi district, and its dean bore the title of Cadaeda.

**Unknown Regions** A term describing all areas of the galaxy that had never been directly surveyed by scouts. Although the label was popularly applied to the isolated mass in the western disk, it also described the disk's halo of gas, dust, and stars, as well as its satellite galaxies. When the aggregate of all this territory was totaled, the Unknown Regions could reach a volume nearly triple the size of settled space. Within the galactic disk, however, the Unknown Regions were sometimes counted for as little as 15 percent of the total star mass. The chunk of the Unknown Regions found within the galactic disk was a peculiar legacy of hyperspatial geography due to a tangle of hyperspace anomalies west of the Deep Core. The Outbound Flight Project was one of the first government-sponsored colonization vessels to penetrate the Unknown Regions, employing the Force talents of onboard Jedi to smooth the hyperspace tangle. Emperor Palpatine charged the Chiss military genius Grand Admiral Thrawn with establishing a loyalist "Empire of the Hand" within the Unknown Regions' wild expanse. In addition to the militaristic and highly disciplined Chiss, the region's populations included the Vagaari slavers, the illusion-spinning mollusks called Crokes, and the fanatical, expansionist Ssi-ruuk.

Unit Zed

**Unknown World** This was the name used offically for millennia to describe the homeworld of the Rakata species. It was in orbit around this planet's star that the Star Forge was created many millennia before the Great Sith War. Additionally, a huge temple was erected by the Rakata to house the defensive field generator that protected the Star Forge. It wasn't until well after the Galactic Civil War that this planet's true name, Rakata Prime, was discovered. A nexus of the dark side of the Force was nearby, probably giving the Rakata their lust for power and conquest. In the wake of the War of the Star Forge, astrocartographers of the Old Republic chose to rename the planet Lehon, since it was the primary world in the Lehon system.

Dr'uun Unnh

**Unlu, Rai** This Sorrusian posed as a medic at the largest medcenter on Sorrus to assist Ona Nobis in capturing Obi-Wan Kenobi and Astri Oddo, some 12 years before the Battle of Naboo.

**Unnh, Dr'uun** A Sullustan pilot who served with the Rebel Alliance. When not in a starfighter, Dr'uun Unnh was a thorough and meticulous naturalist. He authored a number of in-depth studies of planetary ecologies, and was delighted when the Alliance shifted its base to Yavin 4. He spent a great deal of time exploring the jungles, and was out in the field when the Alliance began its assault on the first Death Star. He was killed when a TIE fighter crashed into his camp. Dr'uun's body was later discovered by the Empire, and agents took a genetic sample to Dantooine for use in an experimental rapid-cloning process.

Unreal City

**Unreal City** The name used by the Skakoans of the Techno Union to describe the massive, underground prison facility constructed on Metalorn during the Clone Wars. From space, the Unreal City appeared to be a huge, cube-shaped building with a ring of windows on the top floor. However, the edifice was little more than an administration center, as the real prison was located underground. For many years, the mere threat of being sent to the Unreal City was enough to keep the local populace under control. The main facility was a collection of simple cells, all contained in a stark array of storage cubicles. For exceptionally dangerous prisoners, a set of energized holding cells was located even farther belowground. It was rumored that Jedi Master Shaak Ti was once imprisoned in the lowest levels of the Unreal City. Only a daring rescue by Bail Organa allowed Shaak Ti to go free.

**unrik** A chunk of tissue that the Yuuzhan Vong used as a votive offering to their gods. Kept alive by biotechnology, the unrik served as a symbol of servitude. When Ngaaluh attempted to give a living unrik to Nom Anor, he mistook it for a weapon and exploded his plaeryin bol in Ngaaluh's face.

**Unseen Queen** A term used to describe former Jedi Lomi Plo after she became a Joiner of the Gorog nest and used her powers to become the Dark Queen. One of her skills was the ability to draw on the fears and doubts of others, using them to block her presence in the Force, and thus leading to the use of this nickname.

**Unser, Cobb and Corla** Siblings, they had worked together aboard the transport *Muvon* until it was impounded by Moff Kentor Sarne. They were separated, and after Corla turned away an ardent Sarne, she was imprisoned with others at the Q'Maere Research Facility. Cobb discovered her there as a crew member on the *FarStar* and helped foment a prison riot so that all those jailed could escape and board the *FarStar.* But tensions arose between the crew and prisoners—one of whom, Lowen Chase, had become Corla's lover—and a mutiny ensued.

**Unstable Terrain Artillery Transport (UT-AT)** A Republic walker developed by Kuat Drive Yards and Mekuun at the height of the Clone Wars. Its design was inspired after larger AT-TE and SPHA-T walkers caused the collapse of natural bridges on Agamar with their constant, pounding steps. The UT-AT was developed from the original walker plans of KDY, which were augmented by Mekuun repulsorlift technology to create a vehicle that was more of a tank than a walker. In place of legs, the UT-AT moved about on eight pairs of repulsorlift skis, each with an independent suspension mechanism that allowed the skis to constantly adjust to changing terrain. The skis kept the UT-AT stable while four massive repulsorlift engines in the forward section provided propulsion. The UT-AT required a pilot and five gunners to operate, and could accommodate up to 20 clone troopers. Much of its interior space was dedicated to the onboard weapons systems, which included side- and top-mounted heavy turbolasers and four turret-mounted laser cannons. The forward three weapons earned the UT-AT its nickname of Trident. Because of its ability to negotiate rough or unstable terrain, the UT-AT was often deployed on the front lines, clearing a path for other vehicles to follow.

**Unu** One of many hives that made up the Killik Colony. Similarly to other hives, the members of the Unu hive referred to themselves and their nest as Unu, and acted upon the Will of the Unu hive. However, the Unu were different in that the hive was made up of individuals from all other hives of the Colony. Unu rose to prominence some five years after the Yuuzhan Vong War, when the former Jedi Knight Raynar Thul was rescued by the Yoggoy and joined the Colony. The influence of the former Jedi gave rise to a new hive, the Unu. As the Unu began sharing with other hives, the Colony experienced a form of rebirth that led to its rapid expansion in the Unknown Regions. Thus, the Unu hive became "the nest of nests," and Raynar became UnuThul and the Prime Unu. The combined leadership of the members of the Unu hive became known as the Will of the Colony . . . and it led to chaos in the galaxy.

**UnuThul** *See* Thul, Raynar.

**Uogo'cor** A planet in the Trax sector near the Trax Tube, a major Outer Rim shipping lane. Outlaw stations on Uogo'cor serviced any ship, including those belonging to pirates and wanted criminals. The harsh world was known for its long, frigid winters and short, intensely hot summers. It was homeworld of the Uogo, whose name for their planet translated as "home of the suffering ones."

**upari** One of many crystals ancient Jedi Knights used to construct a lightsaber, it was believed to have given the wielder a greater ability to deflect blaster bolts. Upari was a relatively brittle crystal that was found in small asteroids in orbit around forested worlds.

**Upland Liberation Front** The name used by the Korunnai guerrillas who fought to free their people from the oppression of the Balawai during the Clone Wars. Often referred to as the ULF, this band was believed to have crystallized around the rogue Jedi Depa Billaba. Mace Windu discovered that the ULF was barely clinging to its own existence under its leader Kar Vastor, reduced to staging raids on Balawai outposts just to acquire food and medical supplies. When Windu finally met up with Depa Billaba, she revealed that the ULF was simply a name she had created to help garner attention for the plight of the Korunnai. The illusion of the ULF was meant to force the Balawai militia to expend huge amounts of resources trying to pin down leaders and supplies, looking for patterns they believed any organized resistance would employ.

**Uplands, the** A pastoral region on the continent of Thon on the planet Alderaan.

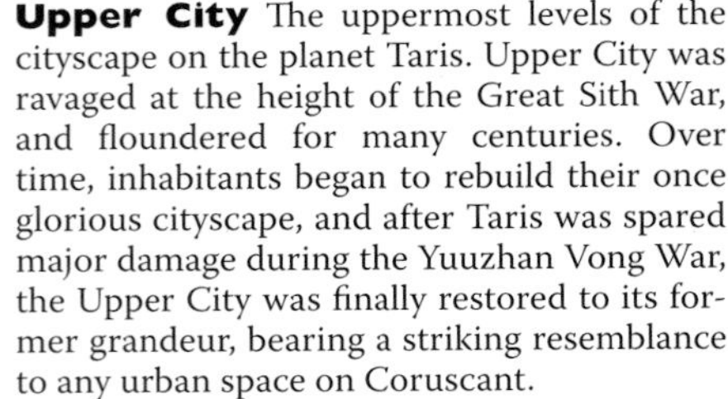

*Unstable Terrain Artillery Transport (UT-AT)*

**Upper City** The uppermost levels of the cityscape on the planet Taris. Upper City was ravaged at the height of the Great Sith War, and floundered for many centuries. Over time, inhabitants began to rebuild their once glorious cityscape, and after Taris was spared major damage during the Yuuzhan Vong War, the Upper City was finally restored to its former grandeur, bearing a striking resemblance to any urban space on Coruscant.

***Upside*** One of two transports used by Admiral Ackbar to supply the Project Shantipole base near Roche.

**Urce** This planet, located in the area of the Lesser Plooriod Cluster known as Urce space, was the capital planet of the area and served as the seat of Imperial power at the height of the New Order.

**urchin** Also called a dandelion warrior, it was a strange, plant-like creature with heads that resembled dandelion tufts but that were actually spiked balls capable of hurling sharp quills. Urchins with peculiar starred patterns were used by the Ewoks of Endor's Forest Moon for medicinal applications.

**Urdruua the Hutt** A Hutt crime lord on Nar Shaddaa, he blamed Aurra Sing for his financial troubles. He summoned her for a bounty, then told her she was it and locked her in a chamber filling with poison gas. She escaped. Urdruua sent others after her, but Sing outsmarted them and the Hutt by detonating explosives she had planted, killing him and many of his minions.

**Urdur** A hideout world for Klaus "Doc" Vandangante, his daughter Jessa, and his band of outlaw techs operating in and around Corporate Sector space. Urdur, with its biting-cold winds, was the planet where Han Solo and his companions rested following their escape from Mytus VII.

**Urgah** This female Dulok was Gorneesh's queen and mother of Prince Boogutt.

**Urhal** A commander in the Army of the Republic early in the Clone Wars, he was forced to assume command of the *Halleck* when Captain Trent was seriously injured during the mission to extract Jedi Masters Mace Windu and Depa Billaba from Haruun Kal.

**Urkupp** The homeworld of the Dashade species, it and its inhabitants were destroyed when a supernova fire swept across the surface as the Cron system was destroyed in the Great Sith War.

**Urnsor'is** Unusual parasitic creatures discovered on Kashyyyk several years before the Clone Wars. An Urnsor'is egg was discovered by an adolescent Wookiee of the Myyydril tribe and allowed to hatch in their caves. The young creature, which resembled a large brain that moved about on a collection of tentacles, fled the Wookiee habitat to find its own, where it spontaneously laid more eggs. When the Wookiees next encountered the growing colony, the parasites latched themselves onto Wookiee skulls and started feeding. The Wookiees named the creatures the Shyriiwook equivalent of "mind pod," believing that the Urnsor'is were sentient, especially after they began capturing and killing more Wookiees. The Wookiees fought back, but normal weapons seemed ineffective.

**Uro-ik V'alh** A giant Yuuzhan Vong vessel, larger than a Yuuzhan Vong warship. The battleship looked to have been cast fully formed from the churning bowels of some impossibly gargantuan volcano. It measured 2,240 meters long and was armed with 80 plasma projectors and numerous dovin basals. When fully staffed, the Uro-ik V'alh had a crew of 1,640 warriors. The ship was capable of transporting up to 3,150 troops and 16,480 metric tons of cargo.

**Uroro Station** A wheel-shaped space station built between the worlds of Qogo and Uluq, where it served as a transfer station for Hapan ships passing through the Transitory Mists. The station was a waypoint along the corridor known as the Throat for ships traveling to and from the mining world of Shedu Maad. Over time Shedu Maad's mines ran dry, and the facilities at Uroro Station were no longer needed. It was abandoned and left to hover between Qogo and Uluq. It was here that Jedi Grand Master Luke Skywalker stationed the members of the new Jedi Order in the wake of the Second Battle of Fondor, as a decoy to lure Darth Caedus away from the real Jedi base on Shedu Maad. Master Skywalker hoped to ambush Caedus's fleet near the station, with help from the Hapan Home Fleet. Caedus approached cautiously, then used the long-range turbolasers aboard the *Megador* to open fire on the station, tearing it apart in large chunks.

UrrOr'RuuR

**UroRRuR'R'R** A leader of a Tusken Raider tribe, he was a skilled hunter and marksman unafraid of machines. He raided moisture farms for water and roamed the Jundland Wastes in search of unwary travelers.

**Urothko** A brave Wookiee warrior, he had little concern for others. He accepted a dare from his peers to travel to the lowest levels of Kashyyyk's forest, but was attacked by a fire spirit known as a Graaa'shad. The spirit prepared to kill him, but the Wookiee elder Stalpaac shot the spirit with a bowcaster quarrel; the two of them then attacked the Graaa'shad, who fled. Urothko then pledged his life to Stalpaac, since he had risked his own life to save him. The story quickly spread to other villages and liklely became the basis for the tradition of the Wookiee life debt.

**Urrdorf City** A disk-shaped space station that was the smallest of the 20 cities built in orbit around the planet Duro. During the Yuuzhan Vong War, Tresina Lobi and Thrynni Vae discovered that many of the supply shipments meant for refugee cities on the surface of Duro were actually being rerouted to Urrdorf. During the confusion that resulted when the Yuuzhan Vong attacked Duro, Urrdorf City was the only orbital establishment to escape destruction. It lacked a hyperdrive, but eventually got far enough beyond the Yuuzhan Vong strike force that the invaders simply let it go.

**UrrOr'RuuR** A Tusken Raider sniper who was part of a small group that lined the Mos Espa racecourse during the Boonta Eve Classic Podraces, hoping to take out the loud vehicles and their drivers.

***urtya*** The Tusken Raider word for the light tents they used as homes. Each *urtya* was formed from the skin and bones of a bantha or other large creature. The skins of the tent were often covered during seasonal encampments with a hardener created from bantha spittle, adding strength and rigidity against Tatooine's sandstorms.

**urusai** A winged scavenger native to Tatooine. Urusais had a loud, startling cry and subsisted on a diet of bones, corpses, and small animals. Males had four wings, two for flying and two for mating displays. Their skin was bare of feathers. Urusais laid two to three eggs per brood. The first young to hatch disposed of the other eggs; if two hatched simultaneously, a battle ensued until one knocked the other out of the nest.

Urusai

Urtya

**uruun cloth** A form of living cloth created by the Yuuzhan Vong as a kind of bandage. When placed on an individual's flesh, uruun cloth constricted slightly, forming a tight seal around a wound. Uruun cloth also was used to blind or gag an individual.

**uspeq** A creature native to the Yuuzhan Vong homeworld, it was bred for its incredible sense of smell, which was used to sniff out prey.

**Ussa** The beautiful capital of Bellassa. More than half the population was arrested on various charges immediately after the Clone Wars ended and the Empire installed its own officials. Under Order 37, hundreds of citizens were arrested and threatened with execution if the rabble-rousing Ferus Olin didn't turn himself in. Olin, aided by Obi-Wan Kenobi, was able to free the prisoners and escape Bellassa.

**Ussor, Captain** The Ganathan commander of the *Robida Colossus* during the early years of the New Republic.

**Ut** A planet in the Hapes Cluster. As part of a series of gifts from Hapes to the New Republic, Ut sent a woman to sing a beautiful song.

**Utai** *See* Utapaun.

**Utapau** An Outer Rim planet in the Tarabba sector dominated by massive sinkholes formed in the sandstone crust. Utapau was settled approximately 57,000 years before the Battle of Yavin, and was the homeworld of the Utai and Pau'an species. The natives built their elegant cities inside the sinkholes. Entire oceans formed underground, with the landmasses literally floating on their surface. The continual movement of water eroded the porous rock, causing new sinkholes, and the hyperwinds that scoured the surface leveled mountains and left behind featureless flatlands. The native economy was based primarily on the sale of wind power. Secondary income came from offworld mining operations that tapped into the underground ocean for the trace elements found in the water. Animal life on Utapau included the varactyl and the dactillion. At the height of the Clone Wars, Utapau remained unal-

Utapau

lied to either the Republic or the Separatists, and lacked any strategic value. It was subjugated by General Grievous, who transported the leaders of the Separatist Council to the planet for safekeeping. But it was also where Grievous's career ended.

**Utapau, Battle of** Historians say this likely was the final battle of the Clone Wars. Jedi Master Obi-Wan Kenobi led the forces of the Grand Army of the Republic to Utapau after clone intelligence units discovered that General Grievous was on the remote planet. Darth Sidious had ordered Grievous to sequester the Separatist Council there after the death of Darth Tyranus. Infiltrating Pau City, Kenobi discovered Grievous's presence along with a full force of battle droids. Rather than let Grievous escape again, Kenobi single-handedly attacked and eventually defeated the half-alien, half-droid general.

During Kenobi's attack, clone troopers led by Commander Cody launched a surprise attack on the Separatist forces, swiftly taking control of the planet despite intense resistance. In the midst of the final stages of the battle, however, Darth Sidious issued the command to execute Order 66, forcing Cody to turn his weapons on Kenobi. After the clone troopers appeared to have killed the Jedi Master, Cody and his clone commanders were ordered to take control of Utapau for the newly formed Galactic Empire.

**Utapaun** The native inhabitants of Utapau were divided into two distinct species. The taller, stately Pau'ans were more highly evolved and presented the public face of the planet to travelers from other worlds. They had deeply lined ashen faces, dark eyes, and gaunt builds; they wrapped themselves in thick yet tightly bound clothing that covered all but their faces and hands. Pau'ans were long lived for humanoids, with lives that spanned centuries. For this, they were nicknamed the Ancients by outlanders who frequented Utapau.

Utapau—Pau'an

The Pau'ans controlled the planetary government and administered the port facilities in the sinkhole cities. When the Confederacy of Independent Systems subjugated Utapau during the Clone Wars, it was these Utapauns who decided to peacefully capitulate to preserve their world, living a life in servitude to their Separatist rulers.

Conversely, little changed for the smaller natives of Utapau, the Utai. The stubby working-class aliens had short, stocky builds and round faces with distended eyes well adapted to low-light conditions. Since they had little involvement in the management of the planet, sticking mainly to such chores as tending to the dragon corrals and working as ground crew on the various landing platforms, the Utai saw little change in their day-to-day lives.

Utapau—Utai

Though the Pau'ans developed on the windswept surface of the planet as early as 57 millennia before the Galactic Civil War, they moved deeper into the sinkholes once climatic changes forced them to seek new homes. They discovered that they actually preferred the darker environs much like they preferred raw over cooked meat. They prospered in the shadowed crevices of the Utapaun sinkholes. Because of the isolation inherent in sinkhole-based civilizations, Pau'an genealogies and subdialects were diverse. Tracking bloodlines was a revered if sometimes tempestuous tradition in Pau'an culture; disputes regarding heredity along with other cultural differences occasionally led to conflicts and all-out war between cities.

The Utai were largely ignorant and disinterested in worldly or interstellar relations. They were sometimes called Shorts, due to their small stature but also their brief lifespans. While the Pau'ans developed initially on the planet surface, the sinkholes had long been home to the Utai. They colonized the inner walls and crevices of those sinkholes, and tamed the dactillions—who once brought terror from the skies—as well as the helpful varactyls, with which they had a natural rapport and had domesticated millennia before the Clone Wars.

Hardy Utai braved the lower depths of sinkhole grottos to use the water pools found there as a basis of a thriving aquaculture. When the taller Pau'ans met the Utai, they brought to their smaller cousins the secrets of wind power harnessed from the upper levels of the planet, and the two were able to share resources in an exchange that benefited both cultures. Both species also contributed members to the Utapau Skyforce planetary defense.

**Uteen** Members of this eel-like species lacked hands, and used droids to perform manual labor as well as give hand signals and sign language. They were members of the New Republic.

**Utegetu Nebula** An unusual shell nebula located within the Unknown Regions by Han Solo and Leia Organa Solo during their search for a habitable planet on which to relocate the Ithorian people. The open end of the nebula was guarded by the star formation known as the Murgo Choke, and the bluish gases of its walls were broken in only a few places, such as the Mott's Nostril. Investigation by scientists and astrophysicists revealed that the nebula was relatively young, perhaps formed fewer than 1,000 years earlier. The Galactic Alliance discovered 14 planets, including Woteba, within the nebula, all of which were capable of supporting life. When the Qoribu crisis was resolved, the Galactic Alliance decided to turn over the Utegetu Nebula planets to the hives of the Colony. With the reappearance of the Dark Nest, pirates began patrolling the Murgo Choke and the nebula's mouth, ambushing supply ships and stealing the technologies required by the Gorog. The Galactic Alliance was forced to blockade the nebula in an effort to keep the Killiks of the Gorog hive from spreading into the rest of the galaxy.

**Uthan, Ovolot Qail** A respected scientist and researcher hired by Count Dooku to develop nanoviruses to be used as weapons during the Clone Wars. Her first discovery was a nanovirus that could be altered to act solely on the clone troopers being created for the Grand Army of the Republic. On Qiilura, she was supported and protected by Ghez Hokan, and was able to establish a facility that allowed her to work in private. The Republic dispatched a squad of clone commandos to locate her; they infiltrated Hokan's complex and captured Uthan. Dr. Uthan was shipped to Coruscant and kept under close guard.

**Utharis** A world inhabited by Tarrack, it was more than 200 light-years from the Koornacht Cluster. Its main city was Taldaak Station, a full-service port. Moving slide-walks were a major means of transportation. Communications were handled by the Utharis GridLink, which offered access to two local newsgrids: Eye-On-U and Tarrack Today! The Creed was a Tarrack cult based on joy and service, and its members bore tattoos on their foreheads and cheeks. The New Republic Defense Fleet operated a small listening post in Taldaak. Twelve years after the Battle of Endor, Luke Skywalker and Akanah Norand Pell flew their ship, the Verpine Adventurer *Mud Sloth,* from Atzerri to Utharis, intending to eventually reach J't'p'tan in the Koornacht Cluster. When they arrived, they were forced to repair their ship. Skywalker gained access to the New Republic listening post to get information on events in Koornacht. Animal life included the jack-a-dale and the black-winged touret.

***utinni*** This word from the Jawa language translated to "Hey!" or "Come here," depending on its usage. Many philologists also believed that *Utinni!* was a form of battle cry or triumphant call, used when an individual discovered a salvage site in the desert.

**Utos system** A system in the Farlax sector that contained the planet Galantos.

**Utrila, B'ink** This Lethan Twi'lek was among the many Jedi Masters who were forced to give up their duties as instructors and take on military roles at the height of the Clone Wars. Master Utrila was on duty at the Jedi Temple when General Grievous launched his assault on Coruscant, and was dispatched to protect Chancellor Palpatine. Unfortunately, Master Utrila was no match for Grievous's strength and skills, and was cut down by the cyborg warrior while trying to prevent Grievous from reaching Palpatine.

**Uul, Takhaff** This young Yuuzhan Vong priest was one of the devotees of Yun-Yuuzhan. Shortly after the Battle of Coruscant, Takhaff Uul approached Warmaster Tsavong Lah with a dream interpretation. The dream indicated that the gods were angry for not receiving a portion of the glory of conquest, and that this was the reason the radank claw Lah had grafted onto his own arm was failing. In an effort to prove that no one could stand against him, Tsavong Lah let loose a herd of wild rancors aboard the shaper transport ship *Fu'ulanh,* killing many, including Takhaff Uul.

**Uul-Rha-Shan** The reptilian bodyguard of Viceprex Hirken of the Corporate Sector Authority in the early years of the New Order. He was a Tiss'shar, a bipedal species with red-and-white-patterned green scales, black eyes, a darting tongue, and sinister-looking fangs. Although he had a reputation as one of the galaxy's top assassins, he was no match for Han Solo, who killed Uul-Rha-Shan at Stars' End before the bodyguard could kill him.

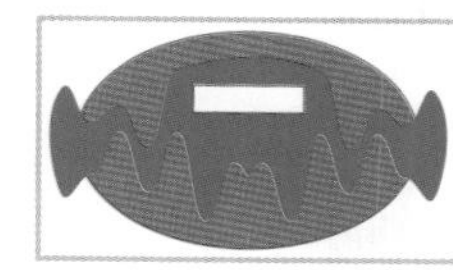

**Uulshos Manufacturing** The manufacturer of the Chariot LAV and the storm skimmer patrol sled. Uulshos Manufacturing was a military and civilian vehicle maker whose cheap, unexceptional vehicles were affordable for militias and defense forces on impoverished backworlds. The company had a limited line of transports.

**uumufalh gunship** A midsized Yuuzhan Vong gunship used to escort Suuv Ban D'krid cruisers. Each was equipped with 40 plasma projectors and a wealth of dovin basals. The uumufalh gunship measured 615 meters in length but lacked the ability to carry coralskippers or to generate an interdiction field. These ships were crewed by 335 Yuuzhan Vong warriors, and could transport up to 840 troops and 1,380 metric tons of cargo.

**Uunu** A female Yuuzhan Vong Shamed One who worked the lambent fields at the shaper base on Yavin 4. Anakin Solo was sent to work for Uunu by the Yuuzhan Vong warrior Vasi. She taught him how to harvest lambents.

**Uvena system** A system containing a group of planets ruled by the species called Shistavanen Wolfmen. The Wolfmen were renowned for their hunting and tracking skills, and many were employed by the Empire as scouts. Riv Shiel, a onetime Shistavanen member of the Rebel Alliance's famed Rogue Squadron, was a native of Uvena III.

**uvide wheel** A gambling device.

***Uwana Buyer*** Talon Karrde's personal yacht, and the most extravagant ship in his fleet. The *Uwana Buyer* was a gutted SoroSuub Luxury 5000. In addition to adding more cargo space, Karrde installed a more powerful hyperdrive and completely replaced the ponderously slow sublight engines with efficient Corellian Engineering Starchaser Mark III units. Though Karrde preferred negotiation to battle, the *Buyer* sported a pair of heavy laser cannons and a proton torpedo launcher. Inside, it was as opulent as a luxury hotel, boasting four staterooms, a gourmet kitchen and dining room, an exercise room, a miniature casino, and even a spa. Suprisingly, Karrde spent little time aboard the ship, using it mostly as a showroom to impress clients with his wealth.

*B'ink Utrila*

**U Wanna Wanna** Mos Eisley's largest outdoor market during the early years of the New Republic. It was open to the suns, and only closed during the most intense sand- or gravel storms.

**Uyter** The homeworld of Republic Senator Lexi Dio. Located in Mid Rim, Uyter was a peaceful agriworld whose inhabitants were known as Uyterrans. Following Lexi Dio's assassination, Malé-Dee took over as Uyter's representative.

**Uz, Bizzin** This immense Kubaz worked as a guide near the Silver Forest of Dreams on his homeworld of Kubindi. Bizzin Uz agreed to help Han Solo locate Grubba the Hutt shortly after the Battle of Yavin. Before they could reach the den of Queen Zabin, they were captured in the web of a ghost spydr. The queen's minions recovered Han and his companions, while Bizzin Uz was left behind, having already been bitten. By the time he was located by another member of Solo's party, Bizzin Uz had died.

Uwana Buyer

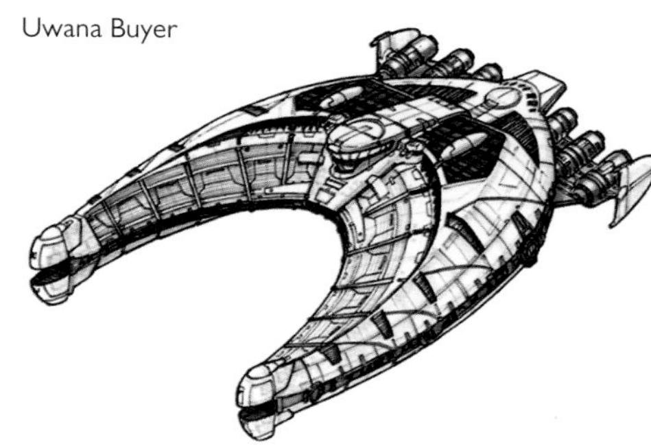

**Uziel, Glimmer** This female was the ruler of Vicondor and one of the founders of the Station 88 Spaceport. Like many of the natives of Vicondor, Uziel had gold-colored skin and four tiny tentacles that waved like feathers when she talked. When the founders of the station met with Count Dooku on Null to discuss a possible alliance with the Confederacy of Independent Systems, Uziel decided to side with Lorian Nod and throw her support to the Republic. Dooku brought in 12 super battle droids to force an agreement. Obi-Wan Kenobi and his apprentice, Anakin Skywalker, managed to defeat the battle droids and save the leaders, but Dooku managed to escape.

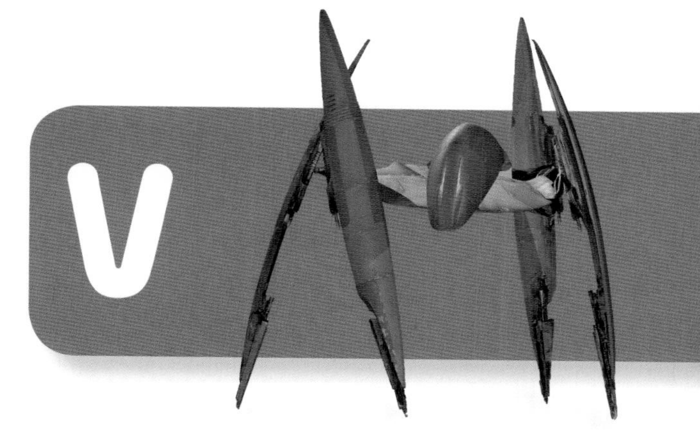


V-19 Torrent starfighter

**V-1** This Merr-Sonn thermal detonator was part of the standard arsenal used by the Confederacy of Independent Systems to arm its battle droids during the Clone Wars. V-1s also found their way to the Grand Army of the Republic and were a favored weapon of clone troopers.

**v-150 planet defender** A planetary defense ion cannon manufactured by Kuat Drive Yards and designed to disable an attacking ship in orbit. The main part of the weapon was housed in a spherical shell on a planet's surface, with its power generator buried about 1.5 kilometers deep. Despite its hefty price, the v-150 found a niche among wealthy planets, which used it in combination with planetary shields. The Rebel Alliance employed one to defend Echo Base on Hoth; another was used by Garm Bel Iblis to defend his Peregrine's Nest base.

**V-19 Torrent starfighter** A Slayn & Korpil starfighter developed for the Army of the Republic during the Clone Wars. V-19s were first tested at the Battle of Geonosis, and their speed and maneuverability made them a mainstay of the Republic's war machine. The V-19 originally was conceived as a short-range fighter, but hyperdrives were soon added when the Republic needed quicker response times for battlefront deployments. Armed with blaster cannons and missile launchers, the V-19 was easily distinguished by its split-wing design. The ship could take off and land vertically when its wings were in the folded-up position. When fully deployed, the wings added superior maneuverability. V-19 Torrents were prominent in the Muunilinst campaign and the Battle of Teth.

**V-35** An older model of Courier landspeeder, it was manufactured by SoroSuub. It had a cargo compartment and enclosed seating. Found on Outer Rim worlds such as Tatooine, the 3.8-meter-long V-35 landspeeder was characterized by its angular nose, raised array of repulsorlift thrusters, and large barrel-shaped power plant. It had a top speed of 100 kilometers an hour. Owen and Beru Lars owned one of these landspeeders, which they kept at their homestead on Tatooine.

*< Darth Vader*

**V-475** This orbiting dock, located in the Sluis Van shipyards, was the site of Grand Admiral Thrawn's first attack on the facility. V-475 was a Rendili StarDrive Space Dock. The *Nartissteu* exploded nearby, allowing its cloaked mole miners to infiltrate the shipyards.

V-150 planet defender

**Vaa, Seviss** A member of the Brotherhood of Darkness under the leadership of Lord Kaan. The Sith Lord Seviss Vaa was one of Kaan's greatest followers and pored over ancient alchemical texts written by Naga Sadow himself to try to augment Kaan's forces by creating an army of mutated beasts. One of Vaa's test worlds for creating dark side abominations was Aduba-3. There he created the Behemoth, a monster that was driven mad by the presence of a lightsaber. But the creature was too unstable, and Vaa was forced to place the mutant into suspended animation. Vaa never returned to his experiment: A short time later he was killed at Ruusan.

Vaabesh

**Vaabesh** This young Gand Jedi Padawan was part of the task force dispatched to the planet Jabiim during the Clone Wars. Like many of the students forced into battle, Vaabesh lost his Master to the Jabiimite rebels. The surviving apprentices banded together as the "Padawan Pack" and did their best to hold off the advance of Alto Stratus. During the fighting, Vaabesh's containment suit was breached by enemy fire. He lived long enough to ensure that Aubrie could recover his lightsaber and use it in combat against Stratus.

**Vaal** This planet was controlled by the Empire during the New Order. Designated as relay outpost V-798, it was here that Darth Vader landed in the wake of the Battle of Yavin and the destruction of the first Death Star. Any approach to the planet was treacherous at best since Vaal's orbit intersected several asteroid fields. The planet itself was covered with vast savannas,

V-35

Vaal

home to a wide range of animal life. Because of its regular passages through the asteroids, Vaal often was struck by meteors and other chunks of debris, which wreaked havoc with sensors. After his return to Coruscant, Vader ordered a crew dispatched to Vaal to retrieve his TIE fighter.

**Vaapad** A style of lightsaber combat developed by Mace Windu, with the assistance of Sora Bulq, prior to the Clone Wars. Derived from the Juyo discipline, Vaapad was an aggressive collection of maneuvers considered to be part of Form VII. As such, Vaapad was considered extremely close to the dark side of the Force and was forbidden to all but the most skilled Jedi Masters. To Master Windu and his apprentice, Depa Billaba, Vaapad was more than a combat style; it was a state of mind in which fighters opened themselves so fully to the Force that they drew power from both the light and dark sides. The style was named for the multitentacled vaapad creature found on Sarapin.

Vaartsoon

**Vaartsoon** An agent working for Ysanne Isard, he led two squads of special operatives to capture Sate Pestage on Ciutric.

**Vaathkree** A species of traders and merchants from the volcanic planet of the same name. Vaathkree were fanatically interested in haggling and trading with other species, often invoking their religion, which they called "The Deal." Vaathkree averaged between 1.5 and 1.9 meters tall and were seemingly made out of stone. They had an unusual metabolism and could manufacture extremely hard compounds that formed scales or plates as body armor.

**vaa-tumor** An affliction of Yuuzhan Vong master shapers, it was believed to be a piece of brain matter of the goddess Yun-Ne'Shel. All master shapers had to go through a period of personal sacrifice during which a piece of the vaa-tumor was temporarily implanted in their bodies. The pain had to be endured, as the vaa-tumor supposedly altered the shapers' own cells and brought them closer to Yun-Ne'Shel.

**Vaca, Rayno** An unscrupulous Tarnab taxi driver on Coruscant, he transported Jar Jar Binks and Anakin Skywalker to Senator Palpatine's residence shortly before the Battle of Naboo.

**vacuum ooglith** Similar to a normal ooglith cloaker, the vacuum ooglith could be worn by a Yuuzhan Vong for a short time in the vacuum of space. It provided protection against decompression and offered a stable supply of air and enough heat to keep the body from freezing.

**Vadde, Shas** This Fondorian served as the planetary President during the years following the Swarm War. President Vadde worked with his advisers to keep in mind Fondor's best interests, which included seceding from the Galactic Alliance and joining the Confederation when Jacen Solo rose to power. He received covert intelligence from Jedi Grand Master Luke Skywalker, who explained that Solo was planning to attack Fondor to bring its shipyards back into the Galactic Alliance. When Solo's forces arrived at Fondor, President Vadde sneered at his demands, openly stating that Fondor would never become a resource to protect Coruscant. This stalemate led to the so-called Second Battle of Fondor, during which Jacen Solo broke away from the rest of the Galactic Alliance fleet and began bombarding Fondorian cities from the sky. Admiral Cha Niathal disavowed any support for Solo's actions and offered Vadde a chance to surrender. Vadde agreed to the cease-fire, but was surprised when Solo refused to abide by it. After the forces of the Galactic Alliance and the Fondorian navy drove Solo off, Vadde met with Luke Skywalker and allowed Admiral Niathal to establish the underpinnings of a government-in-exile on Fondor.

**Vader, Darth** Though he was the personification of the evil and fear that Emperor Palpatine used to rule the galaxy, Vader proved in the end that the dark side of the Force had not snuffed out the light-side good that once filled his spirit.

Vaathkree

Born Anakin Skywalker, he was a spirited and talented child who exhibited strong Force potential. At an early age he became an expert pilot, and he was one of the top warriors in the Clone Wars, along with his mentor, the general and Jedi Master Obi-Wan Kenobi. Obi-Wan trained him in the use of the Force, but Skywalker was impatient with the Jedi's painstaking methods. Sensing this, and noting a void in the youth's spirit, Chancellor Palpatine offered him a quicker path to power—that of the dark side.

Unknown to the Jedi, Palpatine was actually the Sith Lord Darth Sidious, and he had chosen Anakin to become his next apprentice. Palpatine drew Anakin into his confidence by preying on the young man's insecurities, especially Anakin's worry over the death of the woman he had secretly married, Senator Padmé Amidala. Meanwhile, Palpatine manipulated the Senate and the Clone Wars, ensuring that every action of the Republic and the Jedi Order seemed to be part of a plot by the Jedi to take control of the galaxy. Mace Windu and other Jedi Masters came to arrest Palpatine, but Anakin cut off Windu's hand, allowing Palpatine to kill the Jedi Master. In the wake of this astonishing betrayal, Anakin agreed to become Palpatine's Sith apprentice, Darth Vader.

Darth Vader duels Obi-Wan Kenobi on Mustafar.

Kenobi sensed too late what was happening, and when he tried to draw his former Padawan back to the light side, they engaged in a terrible duel on Mustafar that led to Skywalker's fall into the molten lava. The shell of a man who emerged was Darth Vader, whose shattered body had to be sustained by specially built armor and breathing apparatus. Kenobi spirited away Vader's newborn twins, Luke and Leia, who had been born on Polis Massa even as their mother, Padmé, died in childbirth.

As a new Dark Lord of the Sith, Vader was key in helping the self-proclaimed Emperor Palpatine hunt down and exterminate nearly all the remaining Jedi Knights. The holomedia portrayed Vader as a hero of the New Order, having "stood against

Darth Vader

*Darth Vader, with Darth Sidious (right), in his new life-support armor*

the rebellious leadership of the Jedi Knights." However, Palpatine recognized that the incident on Mustafar had diminished Vader's connection to the Force, limiting his usefulness.

Vader clearly also had second thoughts from the beginning, and very early in the Jedi Purge he kidnapped a young boy strong in the Force on the Wookiee world of Kashyyyk after striking down his Jedi father. Vader spent years personally training his secret apprentice in the ways of the Sith, but no other Imperials—including the Emperor himself—could know of his existence. The teaching was harsh and unforgiving; the physical training bordered on torture. Vader first controlled the boy through fear, and then taught him to embrace his hatred and other base emotions. As the boy grew older, Vader promised him greater power through the dark side. Starkiller, as Vader named him, proved his mettle, but in the end Vader's dream that he and his apprentice would confront and best the Emperor was not to be.

*Darth Vader and his secret apprentice*

Darth Vader commanded by terror, thinking nothing of using the Force to choke an Imperial officer who had displeased him. As the Rebellion grew into a significant threat, the Emperor put Vader in charge of an Imperial task force empowered to hunt down the leaders of the Rebel Alliance. Vader's mission became even more imperative when Rebel spies stole the plans for the Death Star battle station.

In pursuit of his goal, Vader intercepted and imprisoned the Senator from Alderaan, Princess Leia Organa. Her successful rescue by Luke Skywalker and Han Solo brought Vader into contact once more with his one-time mentor, Kenobi. In another fateful lightsaber duel, Kenobi allowed himself to be struck down by his former student, and his corporeal body disappeared as he became one with the Force.

Armed with the stolen plans, Rebel starfighters began to attack the Death Star. Vader boarded his prototype TIE interceptor and joined the battle. While TIE fighters handled most of the attackers, Vader concentrated on a lone X-wing that was making a run down the Death Star trench. As he targeted the Rebel ship, he felt the Force emanating from it strongly.

Then, seemingly from nowhere, a blast caught Vader's ship and sent it spinning into space as Luke Skywalker's proton torpedoes found their mark and destroyed the Death Star.

Vader survived the battle and a further encounter with the Force-wielder on the planet Mimban, where Vader lost his prosthetic right arm in a lightsaber duel. But he had discovered that the Rebel who had blown up the Imperial battle station and severed his arm on Mimban was a son he never knew he had. And from that day forth, both the Emperor and Vader became determined to convert young Skywalker to the dark side—but Vader had his own agenda. He wanted to rule the galaxy with Luke at his side as father and son.

Using Imperial probe droids, Vader eventually tracked down the Alliance's new base on Hoth, but a commander's ineptitude made it possible for much of the Rebel force to escape. Vader hired bounty hunters to help track down and capture Princess Leia and Han Solo, and he used them as bait to lure young Skywalker to Cloud City on Bespin. There, during a ferocious lightsaber battle, Vader revealed himself to Luke, telling him, "I am your father." He tried to recruit him to the dark side. Young Skywalker, who preferred death to treachery, let himself be sucked down the city's main exhaust tube. He was soon rescued by Leia Organa and Lando Calrissian.

Over the next few months, Vader had to contend with another threat: Prince Xizor, head of the Black Sun criminal organization, who had become a close confidant of the Emperor. Xizor attempted to usurp Vader's place in the Imperial hierarchy and kill young Skywalker, but he failed at both endeavors.

In the end, Luke surrendered himself to Vader's troops on the Forest Moon of Endor, where the Emperor had set an elaborate trap for the Alliance, centered on the second Death Star.

Brought before the Emperor and Vader, Luke appealed to his father, trying to reach the bit of Anakin he was sure remained inside. Palpatine goaded the boy about the fate of his friends until Luke attacked. Vader defended the Emperor, and he and Luke were locked in mortal combat. Then, gaining control of his anger, Luke stopped fighting. But a probing Vader discovered the secret of Luke's twin sister, Leia. Luke lost control and attacked Vader again, finally beating him down and chopping off his hand with his lightsaber.

*Darth Vader duels Obi-Wan Kenobi aboard the first Death Star.*

Luke then confronted the Emperor, who attacked him with blast after blast of blue Force lightning. He prepared to kill young Skywalker. Suddenly Vader grabbed the Emperor, lifted him into the air, and threw him down the shaft of the battle station's power core. Vader knew he was dying and asked his son to remove his helmet so he could look at Luke with his own eyes for the first—and

*Darth Vader duels his son, Luke Skywalker.*

last—time. Luke, he said with his final breaths, was right. He still did have some good buried deep inside his dark spirit.

Anakin's worn-out body became one with the Force. Luke took his mask and black vestments to the Forest Moon of Endor and burned them on a pyre. And then, before his eyes, appeared a vision: Obi-Wan Kenobi, Jedi Master Yoda, and Anakin Skywalker—all luminous beings in the light side of the Force. (*See also* Skywalker, Anakin.)

*Vader's Fist*

**Vader's Fist** The common name of the Imperial 501st Legion of Stormtroopers, which supported the Dark Lord of the Sith from the beginning—his march into the Jedi Temple to kill all members of the Order.

**Vae, Thrynni** A student of the Force who trained under Tresina Lobi during the early years of the New Republic. During the Yuuzhan Vong War, Lobi and Vae were sent to Duro to observe shipping companies that supplied refugees working on the Duro reclamation project. Lobi started her investigation on Bburru; during the search Vae disappeared. It turned out that the pair had come close to unearthing collusion among the Duros High House, CorDuro Shipping, and the Peace Brigade. Luke Skywalker discovered that Vae had been beaten to death by a group of Gamorrean thugs, then dumped out an airlock.

**Vaecta** A withered Yuuzhan Vong with a painful-looking black burn scar crossing her cheeks, she was the chief priestess involved with the invasion of the galaxy. She reported directly to Tsavong Lah aboard the *Sunulok* but was beholden to no being except Overlord Shimrra.

**Vaetes, Colonel D'Arc** Base commander of the Rimsoo Seven military hospital on Drongar during the Clone Wars, he was a first-class surgeon as well as a career officer. Jedi Padawan Barriss Offee went to him with her belief that there was a spy in the hospital compound, but she had nothing more to go on than her intuition.

**Vagaari** An alien species of slavers native to a remote world in the Unknown Regions. The short-statured Vagaari were distinguished by large, violet eyes, flattened ears, and two mouths. As a people, the Vagaari left their homeworld behind and established a nomadic civilization aboard their spaceships. To ensure that they met with minimal resistance, they built transparent blisters on the exterior of their starships, each filled with living slaves. The Vagaari were also among the first civilizations to develop working gravity-well projectors, which they used to ambush starships. The Chiss grew worried about the Vagaari advance, but military doctrine forbade them from making preemptive strikes. Field Commander Thrawn chafed at this restriction and manufactured reasons to engage the Vagaari in combat. When presented with the opportunity to eliminate the Dreadnaughts of the Outbound Flight Project, Thrawn took the chance to lure the Vagaari into the conflict, invoking the wrath of the Chiss Ruling Circle.

With the discovery of the remains of the Outbound Flight mission in the Redoubt, the Chiss and the New Republic found that the Vagaari had created advanced technology for suspending a living being's body functions. They built miniature suspension units to render their ferocious wolvkils inanimate and used larger devices to hide additional pirates in specialized chambers aboard their ships. The Chiss, through the machinations of Aristocra Formbi, maneuvered Bearsh and his Vagaari into a position where they could make their own attack on the *Chaf Envoy,* hoping to lure them into making the first move. That move came later, when the Vagaari tried to steal the D-Four Dreadnaught from the remains of Outbound Flight. Regardless of the timing, the attack by the Vagaari provided the Chiss with the moral opportunity to finally launch a full-scale war.

***Vagabond Trader*** A converted SX troop transport used by Olee Starstone and her crew of Jedi to search out any other members of the Jedi Order who survived Order 66.

**vagh rodiek** A bioengineered Yuuzhan Vong slave species created from Rodian stock by Master Shaper Taug Molou. Vagh rodiek scuttled on four to six pointed, crab-like legs, and their arms were replaced with half-meter hooks of bones. Their head-spines bristled with large, sharp quills.

**Vagnerian canapé** A sweet canapé, it was favored by Leia Organa Solo and occasionally served in the New Republic Senate chamber.

**Vagno** This Langhesi forger met Anakin Skywalker and Obi-Wan Kenobi when they traveled to Zonama Sekot to have a starship built for them. Vagno was a boisterous man who talked incessantly, and he was in charge of the team that shaped the Jedi's Sekotan starship from 15 seed-partners, 12 attracted by Skywalker and three by Kenobi.

***Vagrant*** An Imperial *Victory*-class Star Destroyer, it was part of a fleet dispatched to harass the Rebel Alliance as it began massing ships near Sullust just prior to the Battle of Endor.

**Vahaba system** The location of a large ring of asteroids that made navigation hazardous. It was targeted for assault by a New Republic task force hunting Warlord Zsinj, but the commanding officers chose to strike at Comkin Five first. Han Solo then took the *Mon Remonda* to Vahaba, where he was met by Admiral Rogriss and the *Stellar Web* in the hope of trapping Zsinj and the *Iron Fist* in the system. The plan nearly succeeded, but Zsinj's forces inflicted as much damage as they took and were able to escape.

***Vainglorious*** An Imperial cruiser that took part in the blockade of the ThonBoka early in the New Order. Rokur Gepta stripped the ship's captain and his second in command of their ranks after the captain of a sister ship, the *Intractable,* refused to be a front-line attacker. Gepta then ordered them all forced out of their air locks as examples of what would happen to any other officers who dared to disobey his orders.

**Vakier, Ko** A thin-bodied Blood Carver who served aboard the transport vessel *Uhumele* during the final years of the Republic. Like his crewmates, Ko Vakier had no reason to trust the Empire that rose to power in the wake of the Clone Wars. When the *Uhumele* was nearly trapped on New Plympto by Imperial troops, he recommended blasting past the Imperial ships that patrolled the system. Vakier was more than happy to assume his position as the ship's primary gunner, firing on the ARC-170s that pursued them into space.

*Ko Vakier*

**Vakil, Nrin** A male Quarren member of Rogue Squadron, he had a predilection for clinging to the past. Although Nrin Vakil did tend to anticipate the worst in any situation, he didn't whine. Instead he accepted things with a good-natured fatalism that formed the basis of his sense of humor. Vakil found a fast friend in his Mon Calamari squadron mate Ibtisam. He was the loudest opponent of the plan to place Soontir Fel into Rogue Squadron after the Battle of Brentaal. When Ibtisam died during the mission to recover Sate Pestage from Ciutric, Vakil resigned his post and became a pilot trainer. During the hunt for Prince-Admiral Krennel, Vakil was called upon to pilot a T-65R reconnaissance fighter during a fly-by of the moon Distna. After retiring from active duty, Vakil married Koyi Komad.

Nrin Vakil

**Vaklu, General** A military officer on Onderon following the Mandalorian Wars, he and his supporters launched a massive coup to unseat Queen Talia and the Royalists, believing they had lost touch with the populace. Only the timely intervention of the Jedi Exile saved her, and Vaklu was captured and shot to death.

**Val, Ekh'm** The first Yuuzhan Vong commander to claim he had located the lost planet of Zonama Sekot. Commander Val was said to be returning to Yuuzhan'tar with a piece of the rogue planet when he disappeared following an audience with Supreme Overlord Shimrra. It was later learned that Commander Val's task force had been purposely destroyed, and Val himself had been thrown into Shimrra's charnel pits, where he was consumed by the yargh'un kept there. Master Shaper Nen Yim was given access to the piece of Zonama Sekot that Val had acquired—a specialized Sekotan starship. Her work with the starship, as well as her knowledge of Shimrra's fear of Zonama Sekot, led her to believe that Shimrra himself was a fraud.

Beilert Valance

**Val, Krag** A Yuuzhan Vong warrior who served as one of Shedao Shai's chief lieutenants. Krag Val was in charge of the mission sent to Bimmiel to recover the remains of Mongei Shai. Val was later sent to Garqi, where he encountered Corran Horn, Jacen Solo, and Ganner Rhysode in the Pesktda Xenobiological Gardens. The Yuuzhan Vong lieutenant badly injured Rhysode but was slain in battle by Jacen Solo.

**Valadon** This humanoid was one founder of the Slams gang on Mamendin. She was also a flirt who dressed provocatively. Several years before the Battle of Geonosis, Siri Tachi impersonated Valadon in a Jedi effort to infiltrate the planet Romin and locate Jenna Zan Arbor. The Slams suddenly turned up there at the same time, and when Zan Arbor packed up her operations and moved to Coruscant with Roy Teda and Granta Omega, Valadon and the Slams went with them. They were apprehended by Obi-Wan Kenobi and Anakin Skywalker, and, as it turned out, a plan that seemed to be leading to a major robbery was a cover for the kidnapping of Chancellor Palpatine.

**Valance, Beilert** A native of the remote world of Shinbone and a bounty hunter during the Galactic Civil War, Valance was an orphan who claimed that his parents had died from the Hardan Plague. He enlisted in the Imperial armed forces and became a decorated soldier for his efforts in suppressing the Nembus sector. A former stormtrooper, Valance was fighting in an outworld skirmish when a Rebel Alliance torpedo struck his platoon. The blast nearly killed him, but his soldiers managed to bring him to Telos-4. In order to keep him alive, the doctors replaced much of his body. When he awoke, he was angry and disoriented, and he hated what had been done to him. He distrusted droids, and the fact that he had become a cyborg made him hate droids even more.

After gathering a group of mercenaries and bounty hunters to assist him, Valance attacked the base at Telos-4, destroying everything to erase his past. During the fighting, he learned of the efforts of Han Solo and Luke Skywalker in the Battle of Yavin. He set out to hunt down Skywalker, dreaming of killing Luke because he had befriended R2-D2 and C-3PO. On Aduba-3 he tried to kill Jimm the Starkiller Kid, who bore a striking resemblance to Skywalker, but his efforts were thwarted by Jaxxon and Amaiza. Valance finally confronted Luke Skywalker on Junction. When C-3PO put himself between the two in order to protect Skywalker, Valance discovered something he hadn't considered: that even in a galaxy of droid-haters, a droid might care enough about a living being to sacrifice itself. Unable to reconcile this new information, Valance allowed Skywalker and his droid to leave unharmed, and spent the next months ensuring that Darth Vader never discovered Luke's identity. To this end, Valance traveled to Centares to eliminate Tyler Lucian, only to be confronted by Vader himself. In the fight that ensued, Valance threw himself into Rubyflame Lake, hoping to drag Vader in with him. Vader, however, used his lightsaber to cut off Valance's hand, and the cyborg bounty hunter died in the toxic waters.

**Valarian, Lady** A large, heavy biped, her body covered with long golden and white fur, she was an imposing Whiphid crime lord. Lady Valarian's most prominent features were her large tusks, which jutted from her lower jaw. She painted them and often wore a gold ring in the left one. She constantly changed the tint of her mane, which curled down the sides of her long-snouted face.

Lady Valarian

Valarian, the daughter of two gangsters, came from the bitterly cold planet Toola. Her own criminal career started when she was very young. She eventually found her way to Tatooine, where she bought a battered old cargo hauler called the *Lucky Despot,* which had been refitted as a luxury hotel and then abandoned.

Tatooine's crime lord, Jabba the Hutt, wasn't pleased with the competition that he knew she would bring, but they eventually reached a truce even though they continued to spy on each other. She continually plotted to kill or otherwise dispose of the Hutt, although she was cautious, fearing retribution.

Valarian employed a large network of gambling cheats, smugglers, and other criminals to

Valcyn

carry out her various schemes. Her wedding day ended in disaster when her mate agreed to accept a job from Jabba (to find Han Solo) and she expressed her unhappiness in the most murderous of terms. After Princess Leia Organa and Luke Skywalker polished off Jabba, Valarian set out to take over much of his empire.

***Valcyn*** A T-class long-range personal cruiser used by Darth Bane to escape the aftermath of the Battle of Ruusan, the *Valcyn* looked like a cross between a Sith Buzzard and a TIE Advanced. The vessel crash-landed on the beast moon of Dxun and exploded shortly after, stranding the Sith Lord there.

**Valdez, Shawn** A charismatic leader of the Rebel Alliance, he was also an experienced evacuation officer. Shawn Valdez played a major role in the near-miraculous evacuation of the Alliance's Echo Base on the planet Hoth during a withering attack by the Empire. Also a poet and musician, Valdez had been well trained to evacuate Rebel installations with maximum efficiency.

**Vale** A Neimoidian pilot in the New Republic Navy during the Yuuzhan Vong War, she was assigned to the Twin Suns Squadron, serving under Jaina Solo as Twin Suns Two. Vale was killed during the early stages of the Battle of Ebaq, the victim of random fire.

**Valesovich, Count Imal** This old-school warrior scoured the galaxy for ancient dueling swords and vibroblades to add to his collection. He was more interested in the hand-to-hand combat required by swordsmen than longer-range fights with blaster weapons.

**Valia, Jikesh** A Coruscant firespeeder pilot, she helped tamp down the flames of the *Invisble Hand* after Anakin Skywalker brought the cripled Separatist flagship to a safe landing.

**Valiant** An ARC trooper who specialized in infiltration, he was assigned to a task force to search for Darth Sidious before the Jedi knew that Sidious and Palpatine were one and the same. A detailed search of the LiMerge Power building in Coruscant's The Works district led them to a hidden facility located beneath 500 Republica. Darth Sidious, however, had put strong security measures in place, and a huge blast killed Valiant and his colleagues.

***Valiant*** This Alderaanian *Thranta*-class war cruiser was one of three ships modified with robotic controls and slaved to accept commands from *Another Chance,* a huge armory ship bearing all the weapons banned from Alderaan but kept in readiness to return and be used in an emergency. The *Valiant* and its companions defended *Another Chance* from pirates and smugglers as it wandered through the galaxy. When a malfunction separated the *Valiant* from the rest of the convoy, it returned to its point of origin, by then the Graveyard of Alderaan. It was waiting there among the asteroids when Rogue Squadron arrived to begin a cargo transfer from Talon Karrde's freighters. The transfer was actually an ambush set up by Ysanne Isard.

As the battle raged, Tycho Celchu's X-wing received a strange signal from the Graveyard. Because Tycho's fighter was using an Alderaanian code, the *Valiant* assumed it was an Alderaanian war frigate. The ship joined in the battle, following Tycho's lead, and turned the tide of the conflict. The *Valiant* was taken back to Rogue Squadron's base at Yag'Dhul to be refitted for use by the New Republic. Aril Nunb was given command of the ship, and the droid Emtrey was assigned to help her work out the robotic controls. The ship was later sent to the planet Thyferra to attack the Super Star Destroyer *Lusankya,* and it was an invaluable asset.

**Valley of Royalty** A site on the planet Duro, it was famous for its massive monuments to ancient rulers, including Queen Rana.

Valley of the Jedi

**Valley of the Dark Lords** A sheltered canyon of tombs and riches on Korriban where the Dark Lords of the Sith buried their dead. It was guarded by tuk'ata and avoided by most other forms of life. Sith buried there included Marka Ragnos, Naga Sadow, Ajunta Pall, and Tulak Hord.

**Valley of the Jedi** A Force-strong location on the planet Ruusan where the spirits of Jedi and Sith warriors lay in stasis for over 1,000 years. During the final Battle of Ruusan, the Dark Lord Kaan unleashed a thought bomb, which sucked in thousands of disembodied spirits and trapped them in an unbreakable state of equilibrium. Lord Hoth's former apprentice Johun Othone built a shrine around the site and gave it the name Valley of the Jedi, but it fell into obscurity over the following centuries. A year after the Battle of Endor, Jedi Knight Kyle Katarn entered the valley and finally released the spirits after 10 centuries of confinement.

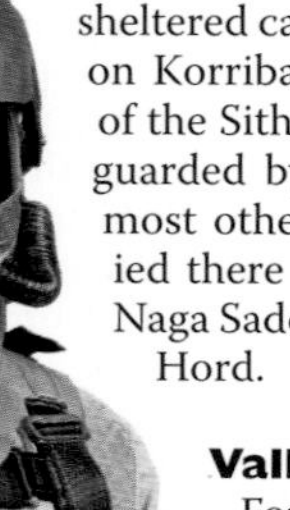

Jikesh Valia

Valley of the Dark Lords

**Valley of the Wind** An area on the planet Tatooine, it was located between two deserts: one high and cool, the other low and hot. Twice daily, fierce winds blew through the area, resulting in deadly sandstorms that the locals referred to as the Teeth of Tatooine.

**Vallusk Cluster** The region where Admiral Ackbar attacked the Imperial fleet to create a diversion for the Rebel Alliance force evacuating the base at Yavin 4.

***Valorous*** An Imperial Star Destroyer, it was captured in a Yevethan raid, renamed *Devotion,* and made a part of strongman Nil Spaar's Black Eleven Fleet. Its captain was Jip Toorr.

**Valorum, Supreme Chancellor Finis** The Supreme Chancellor of the Republic during the years leading up to the Battle of Naboo. Finis Valorum was elected shortly before the rise of Senator Palpatine and served nearly two full, four-year terms in office. He was the latest member of a family whose political roots stretched back over 1,000 years. The Valorum family was known for favoring rules and procedures over taking direct action, and Finis himself was often blind to the idea of taking the initiative. He served as a judge on Veccacopia early in his career, and later he held a post in

Supreme Chancellor Finis Valorum

Chancellor Kalpana's military advisory office. Not until his late 30s did he hold elective office, switching his residency from Coruscant to Spira in order to become Senator of the Lytton sector. During the Stark Hyperspace Conflict, he represented the Republic at the meeting on Troiken between the Trade Federation and the Stark Commercial Combine.

His success on Troiken paved the way to his election as Supreme Chancellor. A year before the Battle of Naboo, Chancellor Valorum held a secret meeting regarding sanctions against the Yinchorri. Valorum tried to send Jedi negotiators to resolve the blockade of Naboo, but the situation blew up in his face, and Queen Amidala appealed to the Senate to call for a vote of no confidence in Valorum's leadership. Valorum was soon voted out as Supreme Chancellor, to be replaced by Naboo's Senator Palpatine. Valorum remained in the background for several years, writing his autobiography and working with the Refugee Relief Movement until the onset of the Clone Wars. He returned to Coruscant some 16 months after the Battle of Geonosis to speak with Bail Organa about Palpatine's growing power. He believed that a pirate attack on one of Organa's transport ships had been orchestrated by Palpatine as a way to eliminate Organa and obtain approval for the Security and Enforcement Act. As he left Coruscant aboard the *Star of Iskin,* the ship exploded—killing Valorum and all aboard. The Separatists ultimately were blamed for the attack. His memory was honored with the Finis Valorum Memorial.

**Valorum, Tarsus** An ancestor of Finis Valorum who led the Republic during the Ruusan Reformations, some 1,000 years before the Battle of Yavin. He was known as a Chancellor who was honest and determined, and was the first non-Jedi Chancellor elected in over 400 years. During the debates over the governmental restructuring known as the Ruusan Reformations, Valorum argued with Lord Valenthyne Farfalla, who believed the Jedi Order needed to remain independent. Valorum countered that the Jedi had become instigators of wars. Ultimately, the Ruusan Reformations were voted into law, and Tarsus Valorum became known as the man who reunited the galaxy. He was reelected to a second term as Supreme Chancellor and remained an active member of the Republic after his terms were completed. For most of his career, Valorum was protected by a personal guard that included Jedi Knight Johun Othone. When Valorum travelled to Serenno to discuss that planet's growing separatist movement, the members of the Anti-Republic Liberation Front blew up his shuttle and Valorum nearly fell to his death. After accepting the assistance of the Great Houses in eradicating separatism on Serenno, Valorum returned to Coruscant with plans to establish a memorial to the Jedi Knights on Ruusan, which became known as the Valley of the Jedi.

**Valrar** Located in the Glythe sector, this planet was the site of an Imperial base. The Noghri Khabarakh was scheduled to be reassigned there following his return from a failed commando mission to Kashyyyk. Valrar was also the reported port of origin for smuggler Talon Karrde's ship when his group visited Bilbringi, and the world was the destination of the Star Galleon *Draklor* after it unloaded Jedi clone Joruus C'baoth on the planet Wayland.

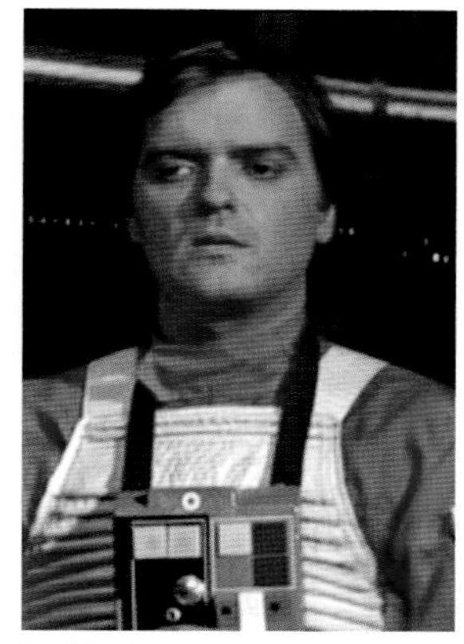
Jon Vander

**Vamm, Eejee** This Duros spent most of his adult life jacked into the communications networks of the planet Arkania, although he worked from a command center aboard the *Arkanian Legacy* during the years following the Great Sith War. A former factory worker, Vamm was hired by Lord Arkoh Adasca as his chief aide, having been chosen because Adasca felt a Duros would handle the cybernetic implants better than most species. Vamm was asked by Lord Adasca to locate the Camper and Jarael after their escape from Taris with Zayne Carrick. When the two traveled to Arkania to get medical treatment, Vamm made arrangements, then told them that Lord Adasca had plans for them both. After secretly taking their blood samples and analyzing them, Vamm was about to relay his information to Lord Adasca when he was shot dead by a mysterious figure.

Eejee Vamm

**Vandalor** This Chiss male was once the lover of Sev'Rance Tann, before Tann agreed to train under Count Dooku. Vandalor in turn agreed to become a bounty hunter for the Separatists. Anakin Skywalker killed Vandalor some 10 months after the Battle of Geonosis while searching for cortosis battle droids on Metalorn.

**Vandangante, Jessa** *See* Jessa.

**Vandangante, Klaus** *See* Doc.

**Vandelhelm** A planet in the Expansion Region's Vandelhelm system orbited by 13 moons and hidden behind the asteroids of the Vandelhelm Cloud. A world rich in minerals, it was best known as the homeworld of the Metalsmiths' Guild. Vandelhelm was discovered about 3,000 years before the Battle of Yavin by two independent prospectors—Vandel and Helm. Following the Battle of Endor, the Metalsmiths' Guild threw its support to the Alliance of Free Planets (later the New Republic), but Guildmaster Orrk remained loyal to the Empire. The Empire tried to ensure Vandelhelm's cooperation by kidnapping the Venerated Ones—the last two surviving members of the original founding families. General Han Solo helped ensure their safe return.

**Vander, Jon** Nicknamed Dutch, he was the human leader of Y-wing Gold Squadron during the attack on the first Death Star. He had previously led a squadron at Renforra base, and he proudly wore the emblem of Specter Squadron on his helmet. Dutch never got a shot off as he flew down the Death Star trench. Darth Vader's strafing laserfire destroyed his ship before he reached the unshielded thermal exhaust port.

**Vandor-3** The fifth world in the Coruscant system and the home base of the Tech Raiders some 12 years before the Battle of Naboo. Besides Coruscant, Vandor-3 was the only planet in the system with a terrestrial environment. At the height of the Clone Wars, Vandor-3 was one of many worlds that served as a clone trooper training ground. Any trooper who lacked a drop ribbon from the Vandor-3 training facility was regarded with suspicion.

Gorman Vandrayk

**Vandrayk, Gorman (the Camper)** An Arkanian scientist and researcher better known as the Camper, he was the first being to document the inner workings of exogorths (space slugs) some 3,993 years before the Battle of Yavin. Vandrayk and his team discovered an apparently dormant slug, later learning that the creature was actually in hibernation as it moved between star systems. The team traveled inside an exogorth's body, learning how its brain and bodily systems worked. Vandrayk theorized that, if exogorths could be controlled, they would be useful in refining ore and other raw materials. Adascorp used this data to control the minds of exogorths, as well as to speed up their reproduction and enhance their growth cycle. Lord Adasca believed that the creatures could be used for military purposes, prompting Vandrayk to abandon the project and go into hiding under the name Camper. He disappeared for decades until Jarael brought him back to Arkania to seek medical attention. Lord Adasca threatened Jarael's life to force Vandrayk to complete his work on the exogorths.

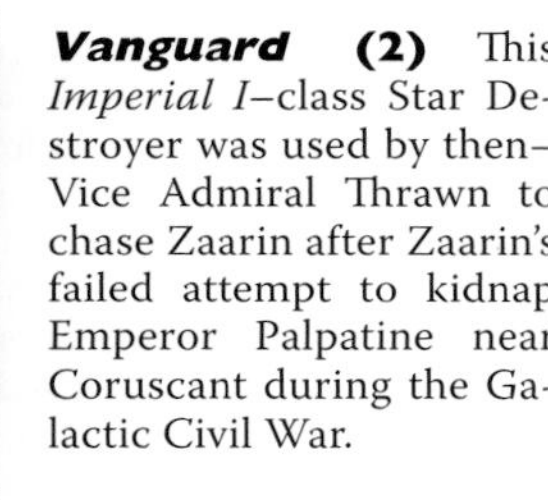

Captain Vanicus

**vangaak** A Yuuzhan Vong aquatic trawler. Like many Yuuzhan Vong vessels, vangaaks were grown from organic materials. The vehicle's interior frame was composed of yorik coral seeded with a gelatinous organism called kera-boa. The kera-boa reproduced rapidly, creating a semi-sentient, protoplasmic colony sprouting long, microscopic tendrils that dangled below the vangaak for propulsion. The vangaak's armored shell was very durable, able to withstand blaster bolts at close range. A trawler traveled largely submerged, with only its broad, flat dome visible. The vangaak "fed" by opening a large maw near the front of the craft, filtering water through thick, sticky strands of kera-boa. Large organisms were captured in the web, while smaller ones passed through it and into the vangaak's digestive membrane to fuel the craft. Large vangaak could be outfitted for combat with the addition of miniature plasma projectors. Immense dora-mu shells shielded the crew from counterattacks.

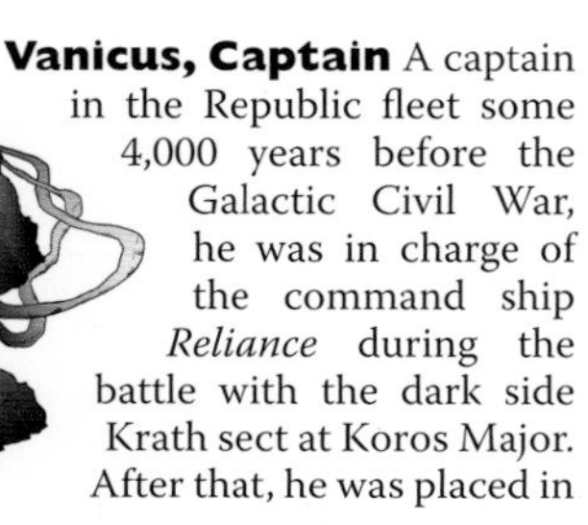

Vangaak

**Vanguard (1)** A New Republic *Warrior*-class gunship under the command of Captain Inadi, it was part of the fleet supporting the *Indomitable* during the final battle of the Black Fleet crisis. It saw a great deal of duty during the Battle of ILC-905, the former Imperial orbiting shipyard taken over by the Yevetha. It took heavy fire there and was destroyed.

**Vanguard (2)** This *Imperial I*–class Star Destroyer was used by then–Vice Admiral Thrawn to chase Zaarin after Zaarin's failed attempt to kidnap Emperor Palpatine near Coruscant during the Galactic Civil War.

**Vanguard Squadron** A small squadron, originally formed by Jagged Fel and Shawnkyr Nuruodo, which provided defensive support to the planet Hapes following the Second Battle of Coruscant. Along with Kyp Durron, the team eventually joined the remnants of the New Republic on Borleias, where members were assigned to elite and special operations by Wedge Antilles. After the Battle of Ebaq, Vanguard Squadron was reassigned to the Fourth Battle Group with the Twin Suns Squadron, forming a single unit under the command of Baron Soontir Fel.

**Vanicus, Captain** A captain in the Republic fleet some 4,000 years before the Galactic Civil War, he was in charge of the command ship *Reliance* during the battle with the dark side Krath sect at Koros Major. After that, he was placed in charge of a battle group that tried to capture Ulic Qel-Droma's growing Krath armada, and was the first to discover Qel-Droma's plans to attack Coruscant. Vanicus later served as a fleet commander assisting in the defense of Onderon during the Great Sith War.

Tay Vanis

**Vanis, Tay** A native of the planet Telfrey, Vanis was a Rebel Alliance special agent who went by the code name Tiree. Vanis survived the Imperial destruction of his homeworld but lost his family. He received the plans for the second Death Star from Bothan spies, but disappeared before relaying them to Alliance central command. Leia Organa and Luke Skywalker were dispatched to locate Vanis and recover the plans. They found him to be a mindless shell, having endured torture at the hands of Darth Vader. The plans, however, were handed over to C-3PO by Ellie, Vanis's LE series manifest droid, who then destroyed herself and Vanis to end his pain.

**Vanqor** The largest of the worlds in the Uziel system, it was believed to have been the original homeworld of the gundark species. When Obi-Wan Kenobi stumbled into a nest of gundarks during his mission to mediate a cessation to the Vanqors' invasions several years prior to the Battle of Geonosis, he had to be rescued by his apprentice, Anakin Skywalker.

**Vanquisher** This style of double-bladed lightsaber hilt was sometimes found among the new Order of Jedi Knights who were trained by Luke Skywalker during the New Republic era, even though it was reminiscent of the weapons of Exar Kun and Darth Maul. The Vanquisher was one of the few double-bladed hilts forged as a single unit, unlike the Guardian, Champion, or Vindicator, which employed two identical hilts welded together at the end. The main body of the Vanquisher was thicker than the ends, giving the hilt stability when being used. The wide emitter cones provided a measure of protection against energy backwash.

**Vanquo** This Outer Rim world was one of many on the front line of battle during the Mandalorian Wars, some 3,964 years before the Battle of Yavin. A mining world, Vanquo was within traveling distance of other frontline worlds like Suurja and Jebble, and thus became a haven for refugees fleeing the conflict. Vanquo eventually was captured by the Mandalorians, giving them a stronghold in the Outer Rim that the forces of the Republic were unable to break.

**Vant, Docent** A tall, blue-skinned Twi'lek female, she was an instructor at the Jedi

Temple during Obi-Wan Kenobi's early training. She had but a single head-tail, which was ornately tattooed. It was Docent Vant who brought Obi-Wan the news that he had not been chosen as a Padawan and had to leave the Temple on his 13th birthday.

**Vant, Ryko** An Imperial captain in charge of the Delta Seven base on Jerne. He captured Luke Skywalker and Leia Organa when they arrived there looking for the Eternity Crystal. They were taken from Vant, however, by Meeka Reen's pirates. Furious, Darth Vader allowed Vant one last chance to redeem himself by capturing the pair on Adony Station. The captain was caught in an explosion that rocked the vault said to contain the crystal, thanks to a trap laid by Vader to capture Organa and Skywalker. The pair managed to escape, although Vant was killed and Vader sustained injuries.

Mission Vao

**Vantai, Kir** This blue-skinned Duros served the Rebel Alliance and later the New Republic Navy with distinction. He rose to the rank of admiral and was one of the Republic's commanding officers during the struggle against Grand Admiral Thrawn. He commanded the flagship *Moonshadow.*

**Vanya, Uncle** This Twi'lek crime lord once took Dash Rendar under his wing and brought the young smuggler along. It was Vanya who provided Dash with the *Outrider.* Rendar also "inherited" the droid LE-BO2D9. Although Uncle Vanya was angered when LE-BO2D9 rerouted some of Vanya's profits to pay for further modifications of the *Outrider,* the Twi'lek later forgave them both when Rendar saved his life during a Corporate Sector Authority Espo raid.

**Vao, Astraal** A Twi'lek who lived more than 130 years after the Battle of Yavin, and the twin sister of Shado Vao. Astraal Vao was sensitive to the Force and was discovered by Jedi Master Wolf Sazen at the Imperial Mission. Although the twins were brought to Ossus for training, she chose to join the Imperial Missionaries rather than becoming a Jedi Knight. She became good friends with Princess Marasiah Fel on Socorro. Astraal Vao also became something of an adviser and mentor to Fel. When Darth Talon arrived on Socorro to force the former Emperor out of hiding, Astraal helped the Princess escape. They located Cade Skywalker, who transported them to Vendaxa. Vao revealed that she and her brother had been stranded on Vendaxa as children when their parents' starship crashed. Although Astraal was reunited with Shado and Jedi Master Sazen on Vendaxa, Darth Talon confronted them in the jungles. Astraal contacted her superior, Moff Konrad Rus, hoping to arrange a rescue, but Moff Rus leaked her whereabouts to Darth Krayt.

Astraal Vao

**Vao, Mission** A young Twi'lek who lived on the streets of Taris's Lower City some 4,000 years before the Battle of Yavin. Mission spent her early years with her brother Griff, until he disappeared into the underworld. Mission made many enemies during her struggles to survive, especially among the Black Vulkars, but a chance meeting with Zaalbar the Wookiee earned her a friend and protector. She accompanied Zaalbar wherever he went on Taris, and usually was given the task of scrounging for food. When Zaalbar was captured by a group of Gamorrean thugs, Mission found herself turning to a group of Republic heroes, including Bastila Shan, Carth Onasi, and Revan, to rescue him. Mission and Zaalbar played key roles in the search for Darth Malak, helping to repay the debt for Zaalbar's release.

**Vao, Shado** A Twi'lek who lived more than 130 years after the Battle of Yavin, and the twin brother of Astraal Vao. As children, Shado and Astraal were orphaned when their parents' starship crashed on Vendaxa. They lived for many years in an Imperial Mission until they were discovered by Jedi Master Wolf Sazen. Master Sazen took the twins to Ossus for training, but Astraal chose to join the Imperial Missionaries. Shado remained loyal to the Jedi and trained under Kol Skywalker. When Darth Nihl led an attack on the Jedi compound on Ossus, Shado was ordered to fly a shuttle carrying several Jedi and a group of younglings away from the planet. Seven years later, Shado reluctantly agreed to meet Master Sazen on Daluuj, where the two agreed to seek out Cade Skywalker. Shado answered a distress call from his sister on Vendaxa, fighting Darth Talon. Master Sazen and Shado Vao later accompanied Cade to Ossus to retrain him in the ways of the Force. Shado vowed to Master K'kruhk that if Cade ever went over to the dark side, he would kill him.

Shado Vao

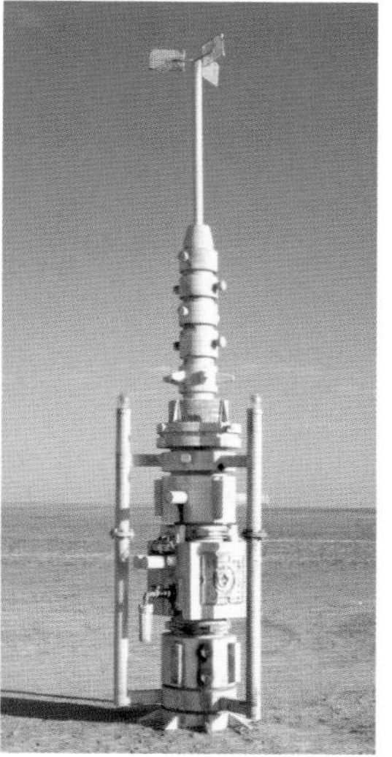
Vaporator

**vape charge** The Chiss version of a thermal detonator. A vape charge disintegrated everything in its blast radius, leaving no evidence of its explosion behind.

**Vapeet, Lo** This humanoid Muun served as the vice chairman of communication for the InterGalactic Banking Clan before the Clone Wars. When the *Tandleroff's Trove* was intercepted on Eriadu carrying 144 Hailfire droids, Lo Vapeet claimed that the droids had been stolen from the IBC. Later, as the Clone Wars erupted, Lo Vapeet continued to claim that the IBC was only acting in its best interests as it supported the Separatists.

**vaporator** This device gathered water on arid planets such as hot, dry Tatooine, where it gave rise to the profession of moisture farmer. Standing 3 to 5 meters tall, vaporators consisted of multiple refrigerated cylinders. When the hot wind blew through the open tubes, any moisture present condensed on the chilled metal surfaces and dripped down into small catch basins buried beneath each unit. These in turn could be connected to larger underground tanks where the water was stored for later consumption or sale. On backrocket planets such as Tatooine, most vaporators were programmed in the somewhat archaic binary language.

**Vapor Room, the** An industrial cantina located within the bowels of one of the many

Bespin construction platforms, an area filled with huge unused pipes and tanks. It was well known for its wide variety of illegal drinks. Used primarily by Ugnaught workers as a place to congregate and relax when not laboring to build Cloud City, the Vapor Room also served as a convenient hiding place for General Rahm Kota. The blind Jedi Master spent his days there following the Jedi Purge, drinking away his regrets while staying hidden from the Empire . . . until the arrival of the Starkiller, Darth Vader's secret apprentice.

**varactyl** A species of cliff-climbing lizard native to the planet Utapau. Loyal and smart, varactyls were often ridden for quick transport from one place to another. These cold-blooded herbivores warmed themselves on the sun-drenched cliff faces during daylight hours. At high noon, when Utapau's sun pierced straight down into the bottom of the sinkholes, varactyls swam in the grotto depths to scour the rocks for green algae and to uncover plant roots by biting into soft sandstone with their beaks. They were sure to leave the grottoes by nightfall, lest they become the prey of nos monsters. Wild varactyls slept clustered together in caves to conserve body heat.

The short-statured Utai were the first to domesticate and breed the varactyl, using the beast in their quest to explore the planet (and later employing the flying dactillion for much the same purpose). The Utai eventually entered into a mutually beneficial partnership with the taller Pau'ans, but Utai were still the varactyl experts on Utapau and almost always ran the stables. A varactyl saddle had a handlebar and a high, reinforced back brace, preventing the rider from falling off when the varactyl abruptly went vertical. Obi-Wan Kenobi rode one during his monumental battle with General Grievous.

**Varesh** One of a small group of Shamed Ones who lived with Vuurok I'pan beneath the surface of Coruscant after the planet had been transformed into a likeness of Yuuzhan'tar. It was Varesh who first heard the stories surrounding Vua Rapuung and his acceptance of the Jedi Knights on Yavin 4, having listened to the story while toiling on the planet Duro.

Varactyl

Vargi (center) confronts Chewbacca

He had heard the story from his crèche-mate, who learned of it from a friend on Sriluur. Varesh later relayed the story to Vuurok I'pan.

**Vargi** The older brother of Chewbacca's wife, Mallatobuck. Shortly after the Battle of Endor, Vargi joined forces with a Nagai slaver known as Knife to capture Chewbacca's tree clan. He was defeated by Lando Calrissian and Han Solo, who had returned to Kashyyyk with Chewbacca to help him thwart the slavers.

**Variable Geometry Self-Propelled Battle Droid** *See* vuture droid.

**Varl** The original homeworld of the Hutts, it was a barren planet orbiting the white dwarf Ardos. Cyax was the brightest star that could be seen in Varl's night sky, and it featured prominently in early Hutt legend. According to other Hutt myths, the planet Varl was once a beautiful world of green forests circling the twin stars Ardos and Evona. Evona was drawn into a black hole, causing the destruction of many planets in the system, the ruin of Varl, and the transformation of Ardos into a white dwarf. Because there were many inconsistencies in the stories, the most plausible explanation for the devastation of Varl was that the Hutts destroyed it themselves in an ancient civil war. The Hutts later relocated to Nal Hutta in the Y'Toub system.

Varl

**varmigio** This mineral was necessary in trace amounts to make most hyperdrive cores operable.

**Varn (1)** An aquatic planet, it was the subject of the holofeature *Varn, World of Water.* Aquatic life on the planet included large lossors and packs of cheeb, while Varn's population of amphiboid fishers and ocean farmers inhabited its archipelagoes.

**Varn (2)** The chief scout for Tyrann, Supreme Master of the Serpent Masters.

***Varnay*** An Ithorian *Shepherd*-class shuttle commanded by Iych-thae.

**Varonat** Located in the backrocket Ison Corridor, it was an isolated, sparsely populated world of jungles, plains, and mountains. A few thousand colonists lived in two main settlements: Tropis-on-Varonat, among the pale yellow trees of the Great Jungle, and Edgefields-on-Varonat, on the wide plains at the jungle's edge. About 50,000 Morodins—intelligent, 15-meter-long lizard-slugs—inhabited the Great Jungle. The Morodins' bodies produced a nutrient slime that, when spread over crops, encouraged growth and produced new strains of plant life. The berries of yagaran aleudrupe plants, when fertilized with the slime, acted as a catalyst for boosting blaster firepower, much like spin-sealed Tibanna gas. Mara Jade joined up with the smuggler Talon Karrde in an adventure on Varonat. The planet was plagued by pirates during the Clone Wars, necessitating a mission led by Ki-Adi-Mundi and Anakin Skywalker.

**Varr** A Singing Mountain Clan witch on Dathomir, she succumbed to the dark side and joined the Nightsisters.

**Varrscha, Lakwii** Promoted from executive officer to commander of the Imperial Star Destroyer *Virulence,* Varrscha was assigned to protect the Super Star Destroyer *Lusankya.* That ship had been ordered by Ysanne Isard to destroy Rogue Squadron's operations base at the Yag'Dhul space station. When the *Lusankya* was suddenly caught in a gravitational embrace by a gravity-well projector that had been secretly installed at Yag'Dhul, Lakwii Varrscha inserted her ship between the projector and the *Lusankya,* breaking the gravity grip and allowing the *Lusankya* to escape back to Thyferra. Because the projector was still on, Pash Cracken and his team of A-wings were suddenly pulled in from hyperspace. Thinking that their arrival was part of an elaborate ambush, Varrscha was tricked into surrendering the *Virulence.*

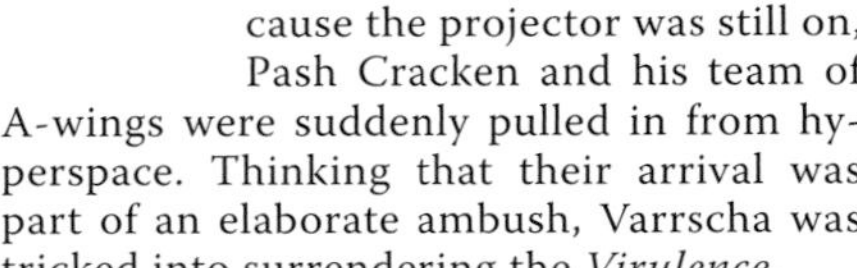

**Varth, Alinn** A Rogue Squadron pilot during the Yuuzhan Vong War. She held the rank of major and was Gavin Darklighter's third in command behind Inyri Forge. Varth flew as Rogue Nine during the early stages of the war.

**Varth, Wing Commander** A bitter, taciturn Rebel Alliance officer in charge of starfighters at the Generis base of the Atrivis Resistance Group. While his pilots hated him, they served because they recognized his flawless tactics and military brilliance.

**Varvenna sector** The famous chef Porcellus once worked for the Moff of this sector, the Imperial Governor of Bryexx, Yndis Mylore. During his tenure, Porcellus cooked

Varykino

meals for the Emperor himself, but he was made a slave to Jabba the Hutt a year prior to the Battle of Yavin.

**Varykino** This was the name of the Lake Country retreat to which Padmé Amidala and Anakin Skywalker traveled when they arrived on Naboo after a second attempt was made to assassinate Senator Amidala. It was considered remote enough to allow the Senator a chance to recover her strength since no assassin could locate her there. Varykino was owned by the Naberrie family and was maintained by a staff of loyal servants.

**Vash, Lonna** One of the five Jedi Masters who survived the Jedi Civil War several millennia before the Clone Wars. She was captured and brought to Korriban by the followers of Darth Sion, who tortured her and finally sacrificed her to augment their growing powers.

**Vashan** An insectoid species native to Vasha in the Moddell sector. Vashans, covered with a chitinous shell, were known for their strength and stamina. A Vashan's stomach was lined with muscles that the Vashans used to crush their food to begin the digestive process. Six ante-stomachs preceded the true stomach, and each was filled with small stones to help break down food as it passed through. When coughed up by the bodhis of the Vashan people, these polished stones were called sin-bullets and held a special place in the Vashan religion.

**vastiv** This unusual, bioengineered membrane was produced by Yuuzhan Vong shapers to create chambers and holds aboard their starships. These vastiv membranes also could be generated in large sizes and used to cover transport ships such as the yorik-trema.

**Vastor, Kar** The Korunnai leader of the Upland Liberation Front during the Clone Wars. As a child, Kar Vastor saw Balawai prospectors murder his family. Surviving in the jungle, or tan pel'trokal, brought Vastor into a deep harmony with the wilds of Haruun Kal. During this time, he seemed to lose the ability to speak with his mouth, trading his humanity to pelekotan in return for his survival. To many members of the Upland Liberation Front, Vastor was a lor pelek of vicious or even dangerous proportions. He was known for his tendency toward wanton violence, and many ritual killings and torturings of the Balawai militia bore his distinctive signature.

Vastor himself was a massive man, heavily muscled and radiating his own dark hatred of the Balawai. He filed his teeth into sharp points and wore specially made vibroshields on his arms. The edges of these shields were razor-sharp, and the alloys used to create them could cut through a blaster's barrel. He controlled a pack of 12 akk dogs and their Force-bonded riders, known as the Akk Guards. He also communicated via a limited form of telepathy.

Shortly after the Battle of Geonosis, Vastor confronted Mace Windu on Haruun Kal. Master Windu was forced to see the planet's civil war through Vastor's eyes, and the two agreed to a temporary truce. They clashed again when Windu tried to take control of Pelek Baw and the droid control system hidden beneath the city's surface. Master Windu injured Vastor with a vibroshield, and he was brought to Coruscant and charged with crimes against civilization.

**Vasur, Medrit** A native of Mandalore, he was the planet's chief metallurgist following the Yuuzhan Vong War. It was Medrit who verified that the open pits near Enceri were sitting on top of a new lode of *beskar*. Later, Medrit assisted with the recovery of Sintas Vel, who was extracted from a block of carbonite after being frozen more than 30 years earlier. He was married to Goran Beviin. The two adopted a daughter, Dinua Jeban.

Kar Vastor

**Vatok** A Mandalorian distinguished by his blond hair, black armor, and red helmet, he was a member of the assault team assembled by Boba Fett to aid the Verpine following the Second Battle of Fondor. The Roche asteroid field had been invaded by the forces of the Imperial Remnant, and Fett led the assault team to carry out the mutual-aid treaty he had signed with the Verpine. Vatok was part of Mirta Gev's team charged with reducing Imperial leadership ranks. He was surprised to see Jaina Solo during the mission since he was one of the many Mandalorians who had sparred with her when she trained under Boba Fett on Mandalore. He also had become fond of Jaina and believed that she shared his feelings. The Mandalorians were outnumbered by the Imperial Elite Guard and stormtroopers stationed on the asteroid, and they were outmatched when Darth Caedus entered the fray. Caedus confronted Vatok and, after a brief struggle, ran his lightsaber through Vatok's skull, killing him instantly. Jaina later took up his *beskad* during her fight with Caedus, hoping to throw off his balance while fighting with the archaic weapon. The tactic worked, and Jaina was able to slice off one of Caedus's arms with the sword.

**Vau, Walon** One of the military instructors called to Kamino by Jango Fett to train the clone commandos during the buildup to the Clone Wars. Like his peers, Vau was a Mandalorian mercenary. As one of the *Cuy'val Dar*, Sergeant Vau was known for his pessimistic demeanor, and his training was noted for its focus on planning for the worst-case scenarios. He also stressed the need for superior technology and firepower. Many of his graduates considered Vau to be a borderline sociopath, especially given the way he planned missions. However, his clone commandos were among the best ever trained on Kamino, with one of the lowest casualty rates in the entire Grand Army of the Republic.

Years before he joined the *Cuy'val Dar*, Vau ran away from his family and was later written out of his father's will. He had wanted to follow in his father's footsteps and join the Imperial Irmenu Navy, but his father claimed that he wasn't good enough. Vau was to have become the next Count of Gesl, but after he left, the family decided that his cousin would inherit the title instead. It was his father's position in the navy that gave Vau a sense of military tradition, and he maintained a knowledge of naval terminology and tactics. His hatred of his family came out during a mission to the Dressian Kiolsh Merchant Bank on Mygeeto. The mission called for the elimination of this Separatist asset, but Vau knew that his family fortune was hidden in one of the bank's many safe-deposit chambers. Once the mission was completed, Vau broke into the vaults and stole everything he could transport. He was trapped beneath the ice when a chasm gave way and had to be extracted before the Galactic Marines launched their attack on the bank. He was both dismayed and happy that his rescuer turned out to be Kal Skirata, and he surprised Skirata by turning a large portion of the stolen goods over to him to help fund his efforts to provide a future for the clones beyond the war.

**vayerbok** A hot liquid drink, it was a favorite of Kid DXo'ln.

**Vaykaaris Uprising** This struggle took place some 45 years before the Battle of Endor, when a terrorist group threatened more than 100 worlds in the Colonies region. The Chandrilan corvette *Freedom's Messenger* was dispatched with a dozen Jedi Knights aboard to resolve the dispute.

**Vaynai** Known for its diverse aquaculture, this planet was located near the end of the Perlemian Trade Route between the Corporate Sector and the Tion Cluster. Its exotic islands formed the basis of a thriving tourism industry that catered to the rich and famous during the New Order, while its remote location and the isolation of its landmasses made it a haven for smugglers and criminals. The first settlers made their homes on the Vaynai Archipelago, establishing aquaculture as a way to survive. As the settlers prospered, the leaders became wealthier. Rather than have their paradise diminished by the "rabble," the leaders banished the workers to the caves near the shore, keeping the lush highlands for themselves. Because ground space was at a premium, the leaders also closely policed their airspace and were known to shoot first and ask questions later.

***VCD987*** This *Acclamator*-class troopship was part of the massive fleet assembled during the Clone Wars by the Old Republic. It was ambushed by Separatist forces during a troop transfer to Drongar.

**Vebb, Nahdar** A Mon Calamari Jedi Knight during the Clone Wars. Nahdar Vebb graduated to Knighthood after serving his apprenticeship with Jedi Master Kit Fisto. Strong-willed and forceful, Nahdar represented the younger, more militant generation of Jedi.

Nahdar Vebb

**Vectivus, Darth** The Sith title assumed by the man who once served as director of the mining operations of the asteroids in the MZX33291 system. His miners discovered the ancient remains of the mynock-like species that had once lived in the asteroids, and he fell prey to the dark side energies that permeated the stone. Unlike the popular image of a Sith Lord, Darth Vectivus did not conquer star systems and wipe out entire populations. He came into his power as an adult, having led a fairly normal life as a successful businessman. His code of ethics was well established, and he simply used his power to gather information and learn about Sith lore and the galaxy until he died of old age. Millennia later, the spirit of Darth Vectivus was discovered on the asteroid by Brisha Syo. Vectivus then revealed to Jacen Solo that he was something akin to a Force spirit and could control living beings to carry out his wishes. A holocron containing Darth Vectivus's words and teachings was later uncovered by Alema Rar on Korriban.

**Vector** A popular game played in drinking establishments on the planet Bonadan.

**Vector Prime** This was the code name used by the Yuuzhan Vong to describe their path of galactic invasion. Starting from a point in the Yuuzhan Vong's own galaxy, the Praetorite Vong traveled along Vector Prime and made first contact with the known galaxy at Helska, where their first ship established a base of operations. Through the efforts of Yomin Carr, they destroyed the eco-system of the planet Belkadan and planned to use it as a breeding ground for yorik coral. Vector Prime continued to Sernpidal, which was destroyed when a dovin basal drew the moon Dobido into a collision with the planet. Next on the vector were Destrillion and Dubrillion, but it was here that the first wave of the invasion force encountered stiff resistance. The New Republic was alerted to the presence of the alien invaders, and the base on Helska was destroyed. However, the Republic's leadership turned a blind eye to the scope of the Yuuzhan Vong threat, believing that Leia Organa Solo magnified its impact in order to regain political power. When the Vector Prime invasion had consumed the worlds of Bimmiel, Dantooine, and Garqi, Chief of State Borsk Fey'lya was forced to concede his mistake and yield more power to the military in order to counteract the Yuuzhan Vong forces. With the destruction of the planet Obroa-skai, the Vector Prime plan had resulted in the capture or destruction of 30 planetary systems. After taking Bimmisaari and Nal Hutta, the Yuuzhan Vong made a series of strikes toward the Core. The fleet was split to attack the worlds of Tynna, Duro, and Ord Mantell. These victories gave the Yuuzhan Vong staging areas from which to attack the shipyards at Bilbringi and Fondor, as well as a direct path into the Core Worlds.

**Veda** The queen of the planet Gala 12 years before the Battle of Naboo, she loaned Qui-Gon Jinn and Obi-Wan Kenobi a starfighter when they were dispatched to the planet Melida/Daan to rescue Tahl, then requested their assistance in ensuring a democratic vote for her successor. Veda had planned to abdicate the throne, knowing that she was about to die.

Moff Morlish Veed

**Veed, Moff Morlish** One of Roan Fel's primary rivals in the new Empire some 100 years after the Yuuzhan Vong invasion. A Grand Admiral and the leader of Moff High Council, Veed maintained key contacts in Imperial Intelligence, specifically Nyna Calixte, to keep tabs on Emperor Fel and watch for anything that could be used against him. When the Ossus Project began to fail across the galaxy, Moff Veed and his supporters called for retaliation against the Galactic Alliance. The new Empire broke off all relations with the Alliance and set about taking control of the galaxy. It was during this time that Calixte struck a deal with Darth Krayt and the new Sith Order. The alliance was formed without the knowledge of Emperor Fel. At the Battle of Caamas, Veed accepted the surrender of the Galactic Alliance.

In exchange for control of Coruscant and Ossus, Veed believed Darth Krayt and the Sith would accept him as the new Emperor. Veed watched the Sith attack Coruscant, apparently killing Emperor Fel. But Krayt assumed the throne instead of Veed, leaving the Moff to believe that he had been double-crossed.

**Veekan, Cebann** A Hamadryas male and small-time actor who made a niche for himself playing roles in B-grade horror holos at the height of the New Order. Unfortunately, his membership with the Imperial Entertainer's Guild was revoked during a series of so-called loyalty purges, and Veekan found himself without a source of income. He took to drinking to pass the time between performances, and the credits he earned barely covered his downtime expenses. After a long, unsuccessful run in backworld productions, Veekan ended up on Tatooine, doing performance art in Mos Eisley when he wasn't at Chalmun's cantina.

Cebann Veekan

It was at the cantina that he met Ackmena, and together they formed a small troupe of performers. Chalmun allowed them to rehearse at the cantina, often letting them perform for the regular patrons. Their performances were only mildly received for many years, until they decided to put on a series of shows that chronicled the life of the local hero, Luke Skywalker, in the wake of the Battle of Endor. Veekan himself took on the lead role, and the show became quite popular over time. He eventually retired a rich Hamadryas, although he remained with the acting company as a teacher.

**veermok** A vicious predator with strong legs and long, clawed arms. Found on Naboo, veermoks were large, ferocious primates that lived around the fringes of the swamp and woodlands, hunting prey through stealth and surprise. They avoided deep water, as they were weak swimmers. Veermoks bred rapidly and hunted well in almost any environment. These solitary animals zealously defended their territory and viewed most other creatures as prey. Gungans were known to capture and tame veermoks to serve as guard animals.

Veermok

**Veers, General Maximilian** The highly capable commander of Imperial ground troops assigned to Lord Darth Vader's special armada during the Galactic Civil War, he was ordered by Vader to personally supervise the invasion of the Rebel base on the planet Hoth. General Veers's force consisted of AT-AT walkers and waves of Imperial snowtroopers. Veers survived the battle by leaping free of his walker when it was destroyed by a disabled Rebel Alliance snowspeeder, though he lost the use of his legs. He later served under Executor Sedriss during Operation Shadow Hand and died during the Battle of Balmorra. He was survived by his son, Zev, who served with the Rebel Alliance and New Republic.

**Veers, Zevulon** The son of the Imperial general who commanded the ground assault against the Rebel base on Hoth, he disowned his father and went against his wishes when he joined the Rebellion. During the Battle of Mon Calamari, Zev Veers was the chief gunner aboard the New Republic Star Destroyer *Emancipator.*

**VeerTa** The leader of the Home Planet Party on Bandomeer aboout 12 years before the Battle of Naboo, she entered into a secret pact with Xanatos. VeerTa hoped that this alliance would free Bandomeer once Xanatos had exacted his revenge against Qui-Gon Jinn, but she ultimately discovered that she was just a pawn in Xanatos's plans to destroy the planet. VeerTa was exposed after Qui-Gon and Obi-Wan Kenobi thwarted Xanatos's plans, and she was removed from office.

General Maximilian Veers

**Veeshas Tuwan** A great Sith library complex built on Arkania, it was destroyed by the Jedi Knights in the wake of the Great Hyperspace War. Many Sith Lords who rose to power after Darth Ruin believed that the loss of the Veeshas Tuwan complex was one of the costliest blows the Sith had ever been dealt since a great portion of their history was destroyed or stolen by the Jedi.

**Vegnu, Jub** A Sullustan, he was an aide and go-between for Jabba the Hutt on Mos Eisley.

***Vehemence*** An Imperial Nebulon-B frigate, it was the ship to which a captive Ackbar was being transported when the Rebel Alliance tried to assassinate Wilhuff Tarkin. Ackbar was rescued but Tarkin escaped.

**Veila, Tahiri** A native of the planet Tatooine who grew to become a great Jedi Knight. Tahiri Veila was orphaned as a child when Tusken Raiders killed her parents. The Tusken Raider Sliven and his tribe took her in and raised her as one of their own for five years. At the age of nine, Veila went to Yavin 4 to study at Luke Skywalker's Jedi academy. There she befriended Anakin Solo, and the two solved the mystery of the golden globe beneath the Palace of the Woolamander. Veila became known for her quirk of preferring to walk around the jungle complexes in her bare feet in order to feel the world around her.

Tahiri Veila

When the Yuuzhan Vong invaded the galaxy, Veila was captured on Yavin 4 and given over to Mezhan Kwaad and Nen Yim, enemy shapers who mapped her neural pathways in an attempt to isolate the Force. Part of Veila's captivity involved the breaking of her will and the implantation of memories that caused her to believe that she was a Yuuzhan Vong adept named Riina Kwaad. During her escape, Veila beheaded Mezhan Kwaad and soon regained control of her mind, although the Yuuzhan Vong language remained within her. After capturing the enemy vessel *Stalking Moon,* Tahiri and Anakin discovered that their relationship had turned to love, but Anakin died while trying to kill the voxyn queen at Myrkr.

Veila was promoted to squadron commander under Admiral Kre'fey, working as an adviser to the fleet that massed at Kashyyyk, and launched raids on Yuuzhan Vong–controlled space. Her "Barefoot Squadron" proved to be loyal and dedicated, and helped to build her confidence as a pilot and leader. However, Anakin's death and her imprisonment by the Yuuzhan Vong continued to plague her, as the implanted Riina Kwaad personality tried to take over. Eventually the two personalities found a way to merge, and the new Veila was a balanced combination of Jedi Knight and Yuuzhan Vong. She requested permission to locate Yu'shaa, the Prophet of the Yuuzhan Vong Shamed Ones on Coruscant. Accompanied by Corran Horn, Veila picked up Harrar and Nen Yim before setting out for Zonama Sekot. After the Yuuzhan Vong surrender, Veila chose to remain on Zonama Sekot in an effort to learn more about herself.

Five years later, Veila was among seven young Jedi who traveled to the Unknown Regions to answer the call of Raynar Thul, who had joined the Killik hive-mind. She continued to serve the new Jedi Order after the Swarm War and was part of Team Tauntaun when the Galactic Alliance tried to prevent the secession of the Corellian system. Jacen Solo recognized that she would be a powerful ally in his bid to assume control of the galaxy and taught her to flow-walk through time, allowing her to relive her final moments with Anakin Solo at Myrkr.

When the Galactic Alliance met the forces of the Confederation at the Battle of Kuat, Veila was assigned to Night Blades Squadron. She was the only Jedi pilot who refused to accompany Luke Skywalker to Kashyyyk when he chose to break off relations with the Galactic Alliance. She instead followed Han and Leia Solo to Hapes in order to discover what they were up to. Queen Mother Tenel Ka had Veila arrested as a Jedi defector, but Veila soon

returned to Jacen Solo's side. Jacen began grooming her as his apprentice instead of Ben Skywalker, sending her to convince Gilad Pellaeon to provide Imperial ships so Solo could capture the shipyards of Fondor.

Veila was under orders to ensure Pellaeon's compliance even if it meant killing him. As Solo's battle plan splintered, Veila cornered Pellaeon aboard the *Bloodfin* and shot him dead. Upon learning of Pellaeon's death, the crew mutinied, trapping Veila and the Imperial Moffs in the command center. A group of Mandalorians led by Boba Fett infiltrated the ship and killed the Moffs, and Veila was stabbed in the leg by Mirta Gev. Solo brought her back to Coruscant, and she assumed her role as Solo's Sith apprentice. She tortured Ben Skywalker to learn the location of the hidden Jedi base, killing his companion Lon Shevu but failing to prevent Skywalker's escape. Veila later led a strike force to the surface of Shedu Maad to detonate a baradium warhead and wipe out any Jedi who remained there. Ben Skywalker dueled with her, appealing to her good side to abandon Jacen Solo's teachings and return to the Jedi Order. She surrendered to the Jedi and provided information about the nanokiller that had been deployed on Mandalore.

**Vek** One of the handpicked survivors of the Dark Jedi Kueller's pogroms on Almania, he was a young man with a round face and eyes, dark reddish brown hair, and skin still covered with pimples. Although Vek served Kueller as best he could, Kueller could never remember why he'd spared the boy's life in the first place.

**Vekker** A Quarren, he was one of the lieutenants, or Vigos, of Prince Xizor's Black Sun criminal organization. He had little ambition and was content with both his job and the status quo.

**Vekki** A member of the Bantha class of Jedi trainees at the training facility on Ossus during the Galactic Alliance war with the Confederation, she was taken hostage when Major Serpa of the Galactic Alliance Guard tried to take control of the training facility. Vekki was freed by Zekk, who snuck up on Serpa and used his lightsaber to cut off the major's arms.

**Veknoid** An intelligent alien species from Moonus Mandel characterized by large eyes, floppy ears, and short fur. Members of the species were extremely moralistic and engaged in arranged marriages. The Podracer Teemto Pagalies and the Jedi Master Zao were both Veknoids.

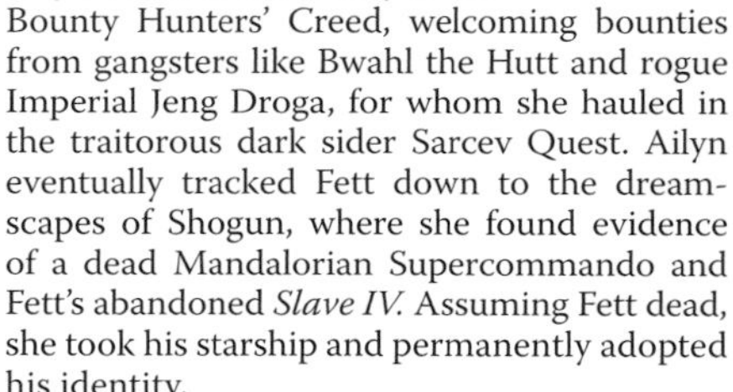

Veknoid

**Vel** A Toydarian slicer who worked with Erli Prann and his group of salvage pirates during the Yuuzhan Vong War, his cracking of an Imperial computer revealed the existence of a cloaked Golan II battle station in the Bilbringi system. Prann allowed the station to be located by the crew of the *Mon Mothma* during Operation Trinity so he could lure hyperdrive-capable ships to the station and use those drives to power the battle station. Jaina Solo used the Force to alter Prann's recollection of his hyperspace jump coordinates, and the station ended up trying to jump through a Yuuzhan Vong interdictor, unintentionally clearing an escape route for the Galactic Alliance forces. Vel and the rest of the gang removed Prann from control and agreed to turn the station over to the GA.

**Vel, Ailyn** The offspring of Boba Fett and the bounty hunter Sintas Vel, Ailyn Vel was raised by her mother until Sintas took an assignment to earn money for Ailyn's 16th birthday and never returned. With her mother presumed dead, Ailyn became consumed with hatred for her absent father. Vel initially became a hunt saboteur, hoping to work against Boba Fett. After murdering the delirious clone Alpha-Ø2 in the Extrictarium Nebula, she took the clone's Mandalorian armor and began masquerading as Fett. Falling to the same delusions, she started believing herself Fett's equal. Ailyn Vel adhered strictly to the Bounty Hunters' Creed, welcoming bounties from gangsters like Bwahl the Hutt and rogue Imperial Jeng Droga, for whom she hauled in the traitorous dark sider Sarcev Quest. Ailyn eventually tracked Fett down to the dreamscapes of Shogun, where she found evidence of a dead Mandalorian Supercommando and Fett's abandoned *Slave IV*. Assuming Fett dead, she took his starship and permanently adopted his identity.

Ailyn Vel

During the Yuuzhan Vong invasion, Ailyn Vel married a Mandalorian man and gave birth to a daughter, Mirta Gev. When her husband died, Ailyn took it upon herself to raise Mirta in the ways of the Mandalorians. When she emerged again, Ailyn had adopted the alias of Ailyn Habuur and was one of the first to take up Thrackan Sal-Solo's bounty on Han Solo and his wife, Leia Organa Solo. She was captured by the Galactic Alliance Guard on Coruscant and brutally interrogated by Jacen Solo, ultimately dying under the torture. Boba Fett and his granddaughter Mirta Gev gave Ailyn a proper Mandalorian burial on the planet Mandalore. Ailyn was buried in a simple grave next to Fett's father, Jango.

**Vel, Sintas** A Kiffu bounty hunter, she and Boba Fett were the parents of Ailyn Vel. On the day she married Fett, she received a heart-of-fire gemstone threaded onto a necklace. The couple remained married for three years, with the birth of Ailyn occurring about a year after the ceremony. After their split Sintas continued to work as a bounty hunter, though only to support Ailyn. But Sintas disappeared during a mission, leaving Ailyn an orphan at the age of 16. Ailyn later recovered the heart-of-fire necklace from the man who was believed to have killed Sintas and passed it on to her own daughter, Mirta Gev. Armed with information that Sintas might not be dead, Boba Fett and Mirta Gev began a search and found Sintas frozen in a carbonite slab on Phaeda. Fett and the Mandalorians brought her out of hibernation. Sintas vowed to avenge the death of Ailyn if given the opportunity. Hoping to ensure that Sintas would never want or need anything else, Fett purchased an exceptionally rare and large heart-of-fire gemstone, explaining that she could keep it or sell it, but either way she was welcome to remain on Mandalore for the rest of her life.

**Velcar Free Commerce Zone (FCZ)** Situated in the Velcar sector, it was a strip of corporate-run systems within the Pentastar Alignment. The Velcar FCZ, ruled by Commerce Master Commissioner Gregor Raquoran, contained many resource-rich worlds exploited by powerful corporations. They were often allowed to bypass environmental and safety rules, and the primitive species found on such planets as Capza, Entralla, and Bextar were forced to toil in mines or on other hazardous industrial projects.

**Veld, Tru** This near-human Teevan youth trained to become a Jedi Knight alongside Anakin Skywalker. A rubbery-limbed being with silvery eyes, Veld became one of Anakin's best friends at the Jedi Temple, especially after Anakin discovered that Veld's technical skills complemented his own. At the time, Veld was being trained by Ry-Gaul and was known for his photographic memory. Veld supported Anakin during their participation in the evacuation of Radnor some five years after the Battle of Naboo, further deepening their friendship. Veld failed to understand his friend's competition with Ferus Olin and began to find Anakin's continual anger toward the other apprentices contrary to the teachings of the Jedi Order. When the Padawans were dispatched to Korriban to apprehend Granta Omega, Veld was injured and his lightsaber badly damaged. Rather than turning to Skywalker, Veld asked Olin for help. The mission was ultimately a failure, and Ferus Olin was censured for his actions and chose to leave the Jedi Order. Veld remained loyal to Olin, but later died during the Clone Wars.

**Velga Prime** This moon was the site of several luxury hotels and casinos that catered to

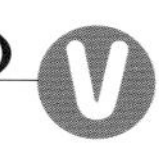

Velker

the wealthy. It was here that Xaverri left Han Solo, breaking off their romance.

**velker** V-shaped flying creatures, they had tough claws and armored wings. Velkers were natural predators of the beldons on Bespin. They attained remarkable speeds in flight and soared to extremely high altitudes. Like beldons, velkers had an electrical field surrounding their bodies, creating discharges that could damage passing cloud cars. At times, they attacked small ships.

**Veloz, Jadonna** A female starship captain picking up a shipment of nerf tenderloins on Alderaan, she suffered multiple injuries when a malfunctioning repulsorsled knocked her over. A young Han Solo offered to help by piloting her ship, the *Wayward Girl,* to Cloud City for her.

**Velser's Ring** A band of asteroids occupying the third-planet position in the Bespin system, the ring was believed to be the debris of an unstable gas giant that exploded many millennia ago. Most of the asteroids consisted of frozen gases and liquids, and the entire Velser's Ring refracted light in a rainbow pattern if seen from the proper angle. Ugnaught teams used to visit the ring frequently to obtain valuable raw materials for Bespin's Cloud City.

**Veltraa, Admiral Jimas** An officer in the Republic Navy during the Mandalorian Wars some 3,964 years before the Battle of Yavin. Admiral Veltraa served as the commander of the warship *Reliance* and proposed the original *Interdictor*-class warship. During the engagement known as the Onslaught, Veltraa worked with Admiral Sommos and Captain Saul Karath to lead the assault on the Mandalorian forces arrayed near Taris and Vanquo, in an effort to break through the advancing forces and gain a foothold for the Republic. The *Reliance* was destroyed in the fighting, and all perished in the explosion.

**Ven, Nawara** This Twi'lek member of Rogue Squadron was a former lawyer on his homeworld of Ryloth. He became one of Corran Horn's friends during training exercises on Folor, before anyone had been named to the squadron. Although he was an excellent pilot, it was perhaps Nawara Ven's experience in legal matters that most benefited his fellow squadron members. When Gavin Darklighter was taken before the Alien Combine to be tried for bigotry, Nawara came to his aid, preventing Gavin's death. Later, fellow Rogue Tycho Celchu needed someone he could trust to defend him against charges of treason and the murder of Corran Horn, so he asked Ven. Captain Celchu had saved Ven's life during the first battle at Borleias, and the Twi'lek agreed to repay the debt. He enlisted the aid of others to help him combat the massive amounts of data the prosecution presented, but he was still about to lose the case. Imperial agent Kirtan Loor then offered to help them expose the real Imperial agent within Rogue Squadron in exchange for immunity from prosecution, but he was assassinated before he could testify, and Ven was seriously injured in the attack. The trial was about to be postponed when the "dead" man, Corran Horn, showed up.

Nawara Ven chose to give up flying and became the squadron's executive officer. He later started working for Booster Terrik aboard the *Errant Venture,* using his legal and accounting skills to keep the floating outpost solvent. He was briefly stranded on Trogan during the Yuuzhan Vong War while trying to arrange for transport of some "hot items"—actually a group of Force-sensitive children Ven was trying to return to the *Errant Venture.* He was impeded when a group of bounty hunters arrived on the planet looking for Jedi Knights, but a group of freelance operatives helped him evade the hunters and return to the ship.

**Venaari** The third planet in the Vellakiya system, this Mid Rim world was covered with forests, plains, and mountains. The Imperial presence on Venaari increased after the Battle of Endor in order to provide greater security for the mysterious Project Orrad research in an underground laboratory. The planet was run by Imperial Governor Vaerganth, who ruled from the capital city of VenKav. Around two billion humans inhabited the planet. After the Empire's buildup, the New Republic established a fledgling resistance cell on Venaari. A New Republic operative, Shandria L'hnnar, managed to steal the plans to Project Orrad and elude the pursuing Imperials with the help of the thief Sienn Sconn.

**Venan, Chala** An Imperial officer, he joined a plot to disrupt the wedding of Mara Jade and Luke Skywalker as a way to strike back against the New Republic. A swoop gang he hired was no match for Luke, Han Solo, and Wedge Antilles, and Venan himself was incapacitated by Chewbacca.

***Venator*-class Star Destroyer** Considered by historians to be the first true Star Destroyer, even though it was classified as an assault cruiser and followed the development and manufacture of the *Victory*-class Star Destroyer. Developed at the start of the Clone Wars to be front-line warships, three of the first *Venator*-class Star Destroyers were rerouted to Rodia from Duro, which quickly fell to General Grievous and the Separatists. Senator Onaconda Farr was charged with falsifying the deployment orders.

*Venator-class Star Destroyer*

The ship, produced by Kuat Drive Yards, was 1,137 meters long, 268 meters high, and 548 meters across the widest part of its hull. It required a crew of 7,400 and could transport up to 2,000 additional troops and 20,000 metric tons of cargo. The ships were armed with eight DBY-827 heavy turbolaser turrets, a pair of medium dual turbolaser cannons, 52 laser cannons, four proton topedo tubes, and six tractor beam projectors. Several *Venator*-class ships in the Open Circle Armada were also armed with the superlasers from SPHA-T walkers, mounted near the ventral docking bay at the direction of Anakin Skywalker, to give the vessel a ventral firing arc.

By the end of the Clone Wars, the *Venator*-class Star Destroyer had outlived its usefulness and was phased out in favor of the *Imperial*-class and *Tector*-class Star Destroyers.

**Vendaxa** A lushly fertile planet with one of the densest ecosystems in the galaxy. Among Vendaxa's deadly predators was the acklay. By day, acklays roamed the Vendaxan plains, hunting for leathery-shelled, nocturnal lemnai, which they pierced with their sharp claw tips to gnaw out the fleshy interiors. The acklay's small eyes protected against its home planet's harsh light.

Vendaxa

***Vendetta*** A Dreadnaught stationed at Carida to protect the Imperial Academy. Following the Battle of Endor, it became Ambassador Furgan's flagship, and as such it was the primary vessel used in the attempt to kidnap young Anakin Solo from Anoth. Colonel Ardax, commander of the ship, was unprepared for the sudden appearance of the *Galactic Voyager* and several other New Republic warships and tried to avoid combat by maneuvering between the main sections of Anoth. Electrical discharges that tore through the space between Anoth, however, rendered the *Vendetta* defenseless, then tore the ship apart in a series of massive explosions. All hands aboard were killed.

***Vengeance* (1)** The Star Destroyer that staged the assault on the Rebels at Nar Shaddaa. The Dark Jedi Jerec commanded the *Vengeance* in his pursuit of the creature called

Spore. When he lost the vessel in the effort, Jerec had the ship's computer core salvaged from the wreckage and transferred to a new Star Destroyer called the *Vengeance II,* though with its predecessor destroyed, the numerical amendment was infrequently applied. Jerec eventually ordered the ship's captain to join Admiral Ozzel's Death Squadron.

**Vengeance (2)** A Super Star Destroyer, it became the flagship of Admiral Wooyou Senn during his pursuit of Rebel forces in the Airam sector.

**Vengeance (3)** A 150-meter *Dwarf Star*–class freighter, it attempted to penetrate the defenses of the Rebel base at Borleias under the orders of Warlord Zsinj. Rogue Squadron easily put the ship to flight. Later, the squadron surprised the *Vengeance* as it was making a cargo transfer near Mrisst. The ship dumped a dozen TIEs from its hold and in furious battle was so badly damaged that it almost fell into the planetary atmosphere.

**Venjagga system** Located at the edge of the Galactic Core only hours away from the Mirit and Pyria systems, it contained the planet Jagga-Two, site of a small Imperial base that manufactured concussion missiles and supplied the Imperial Star Destroyer *Eviscerator.* The seventh planet in the Venjagga system was a gas giant. Three years after the Battle of Endor, the Alliance staged a feint in the system to cover a simultaneous assault on Borleias in the Pyria system.

*Knol Ven'nari*

**Venku** A Mandalorian who returned to the homeworld during the Corellia–Galactic Alliance War, when Boba Fett began recalling soldiers to rebuild Mandalore. Venku was a traditionalist, a fact that was pointed out by his unusual armor. No two pieces of armor seemed to be from the same set, as Venku had collected a single item each from his deceased relatives and combined them into his own *beskar'gam.* Upon returning to Mandalore, Venku met with Fett and revealed that he had been working with Jaing Skirata. It was Venku who delivered the serum that Skirata had agreed to provide to Fett, in order to help Fett recover from his debilitating sickness. After leaving Fett with the serum, Venku revealed that he was actually the man known as Kad'ika and was the son of Etain Tur-Mukan and the clone commando known as Darman. He had been trained to use the Force by Bardan Jusik, who had abandoned the Jedi Order and adopted the persona of the Mandalorian soldier Gotab.

**Ven'nari, Knol** A female Bothan Jedi Master nicknamed the Fire Eater. Ven'nari refused to take a Padawan learner, choosing instead to roam the galaxy wherever the Force guided her. She died during the early stages of the Clone Wars while serving with the Jedi team dispatched to recover the antidote to the swamp gas used on Ohma-D'un.

**Ventor, Halagad** A native of Alderaan and a Jedi Knight during the last years of the Republic. Ventor was trained by Everen Ettene, and he started his schooling in the Jedi arts at a late age. Ventor and Ettene were part of a team of Jedi who were believed lost on a mission to resolve the conflict between the Virgillian Free Alignment and the Virgillian Aristocracy. Ventor later accompanied Obi-Wan Kenobi and Anakin Skywalker to Skye. Shortly after the end of the Clone Wars, Ventor was captured by Darth Vader and brutally interrogated. All the information he had on the Jedi was stripped from his mind. Traumatized, Ventor fled to Trinta and succumbed to a dark side nexus. He was discovered nearly two decades later by a group of Alliance field agents who crashed on the planet. Upon learning of the survival of Kenobi and the appearance of Luke Skywalker, Halagad fought against the dark side and defeated it, but died shortly thereafter.

**Vento system** The location of an ancient Republic shipyard, it was almost the site of the destruction of the entire Republic fleet some 4,000 years before the Galactic Civil War. During the Sith War, the fallen Jedi Ulic Qel-Droma gained control of Coruscant's war room during his attack on the capital world. Qel-Droma told the war room's commander to order all Republic ships to jump to identical coordinates in the Vento system, which would have resulted in a massive collision and the destruction of the fleet. He was stopped before the order could be carried out.

**Ventooine** A primitive planet known for peculiar minerals including the Shadeshine, a stone said to grant the ruling Satabs remarkable power.

**Ventress, Asajj** Count Dooku's assassin and a Sith hopeful who was a commander of the Separatist armies during the Clone Wars. A native of the planet Rattatak, Asajj Ventress was a ruthless and cunning adversary, known for her military expertise and her corrupt mastery over the Force. Her parents were murdered by Osika Kirske when she was young, and she might have died if not for the sudden appearance of Jedi Master Ky Narec. Master Narec, stranded on Rattatak, took it upon himself to train Ventress. After Kirske killed Narec, Ventress used her powers to take over her homeworld and kill Kirske. She believed that the Jedi Order had abandoned her teacher, and she hated them for it. She eventually was discovered by Count Dooku and became his most trusted commander. Although neither Jedi nor Sith, Ventress wielded a pair of curved-handled lightsabers with incredible skill.

When Jedi Master Mace Windu went to Ruul to meet with the dissident Jedi Master Sora Bulq during the early stages of the Clone Wars, Dooku ordered Ventress to kill the Jedi. She was unable to defeat Master Windu in battle and fled Ruul to fight another day. Ventress later teamed with the bounty hunter Durge to unleash deadly swamp gas on Naboo's moon of Ohma-D'un. On Queyta, Ventress and Durge tried to secure the antidote to the swamp gas, but Obi-Wan Kenobi and his companions bested her. She nearly killed Anakin Skywalker on Yavin 4, then captured Kenobi on Jabiim and tortured him inside her Rattatak fortress. Obi-Wan escaped, taking Ky Narec's lightsaber with him, which left Ventress with a broken sense of loyalty. Near the end of the Clone Wars, she guided the capture of a communications center on Praesitlyn, only to lose control of it to Anakin Skywalker. Her failure to capture Yoda on Phindar did little to improve her standing in Dooku's eyes. After the escape of both Obi-Wan Kenobi and Quinlan Vos from the wreck of the *Titavian IV,* Ventress turned to desperate measures to regain Dooku's favor. On Coruscant she dueled Skywalker again, but the young Jedi threw her off the top of a building.

Late in the war, Obi-Wan Kenobi became obsessed with finding Ventress. Learning that she was being held on Boz Pity to receive cyborging implants, Kenobi tried to redeem her, but Dooku abandoned his lieutenant and ordered his MagnaGuards to shoot her dead. The blast injured her, and Skywalker sliced into Ventress's chest with his lightsaber when she appeared to threaten Kenobi. Believed dead, Ventress was actually using a Sith meditation technique to dampen her vital signs. She reawakened aboard the medical shuttle *Bright Flight* and forced the pilots to take her to a remote medical facility for treatment.

**Venture** A carrier in the New Republic Fifth Fleet, it was assigned to the blockade of Doornik-319. The *Venture* was damaged during the Yevethan attack.

**Venutton** A scrawny, uptight human assistant to Lady Valarian.

**Venzeiia 2 Prime** The planet where a Rebel spy, fleeing aboard a YT-1300 freighter, was tracked to a space station's salvage yard. A TIE defender was dispatched to

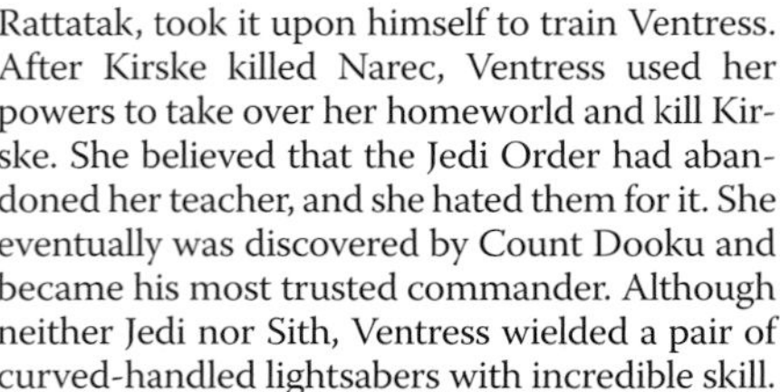

*Asajj Ventress*

Verdanth

capture the freighter while the Star Destroyer *Glory* captured the space station for daring to harbor a fugitive from the Empire.

**Verachen** Members of the Vratix species on Thyferra, they were the workers responsible for blending the organic ingredients that gave bacta its desired potency.

**Verdanth** Prior to the Battle of Hoth, the Rebel Alliance sent the droids R2-D2 and C-3PO to this jungle planet to investigate a crashed Imperial messenger drone. The drone actually was a trap set by Darth Vader, who planned to use a cybernetic Force link to read the minds of any investigating Rebels, hoping to learn the location of their new base.

**Verdun, Dr. Tic** An apparent investigator of planetary origins, he turned out to be Granta Omega, who was trying to lure Anakin Skywalker to a place where he could be drugged so Omega and his cronies could find out the true nature of the Force. Anakin managed to escape with the help of his Jedi Master, Obi-Wan Kenobi.

**Veré** This was the alias taken by Senator Padmé Amidala during her secret wedding to Anakin Skywalker at the start of the Clone Wars. Anakin assumed the name Set when the pair was united in matrimony by Pontifex Maxiron Agolerga. The aliases were chosen because of their origins in Futhork legend.

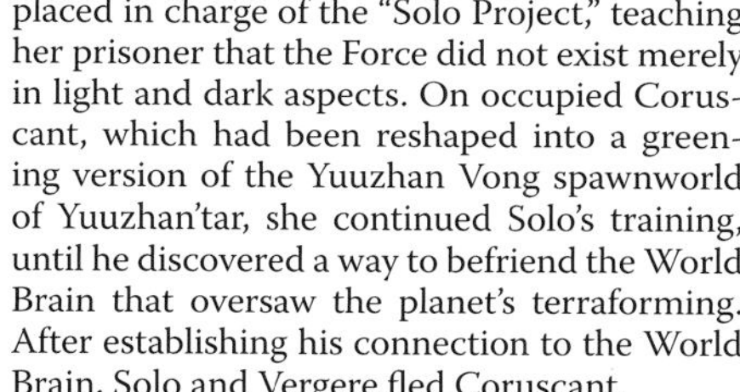

Padmé Amidala as Veré

**vergence** An occurrence of the Force, which could be centered on an object, place, or person. According to Qui-Gon Jinn, a vergence in the Force was located around Anakin Skywalker, possibly due to his high midi-chlorian count.

**Vergere** An avian Fosh who served as a Jedi Knight and an apparent Yuuzhan Vong collaborator. Vergere was dispatched to the rogue planet of Zonama Sekot two years after the Battle of Naboo. Her Master, Thracia Cho Leem, feared for her life when she did not report back and requested that the Jedi Council send another party to find her. Obi-Wan Kenobi and Anakin Skywalker eventually learned that Vergere had gone away with the "Far Outsiders" (Yuuzhan Vong) to draw the invaders away from Zonama Sekot. She then pretended to be a loyal familiar of the Yuuzhan Vong priestess Falung. Vergere knew that the Republic's meager forces would be no match for the Yuuzhan Vong and struggled to learn all she could about their society.

Decades later, Vergere returned to the known galaxy with the rest of the invading Yuuzhan Vong while serving as a familiar to the priestess Elan. When Elan was chosen to act as an envoy to the New Republic in an effort to destroy the Jedi, Vergere accompanied her and gave Han Solo a sample of her tears, which cured Mara Jade Skywalker of a wasting disease that had crippled her. Vergere fled the *Millennium Falcon* in an escape pod and returned to the Yuuzhan Vong. Her knowledge of the galaxy made her one of Warmaster Tsavong Lah's chief advisers, a position that pitted her against Nom Anor. After the Yuuzhan Vong captured Jacen Solo at Myrkr, Vergere was placed in charge of the "Solo Project," teaching her prisoner that the Force did not exist merely in light and dark aspects. On occupied Coruscant, which had been reshaped into a greening version of the Yuuzhan Vong spawnworld of Yuuzhan'tar, she continued Solo's training, until he discovered a way to befriend the World Brain that oversaw the planet's terraforming. After establishing his connection to the World Brain, Solo and Vergere fled Coruscant.

Vergere

Vergere remained with Solo for several months and met Luke Skywalker, challenging the new Jedi about the Force. When Jacen tried to rescue his sister Jaina during the Battle of Ebaq, Vergere commandeered a starfighter and crashed it into the planet's surface, venting the mining shafts to the vacuum of space. The Yuuzhan Vong forces on the moon were unable to place ooglith masquers over their faces before they died. Solo was later visited by Vergere's spirit and pledged to honor her memory by following the Force to achieve his own destiny.

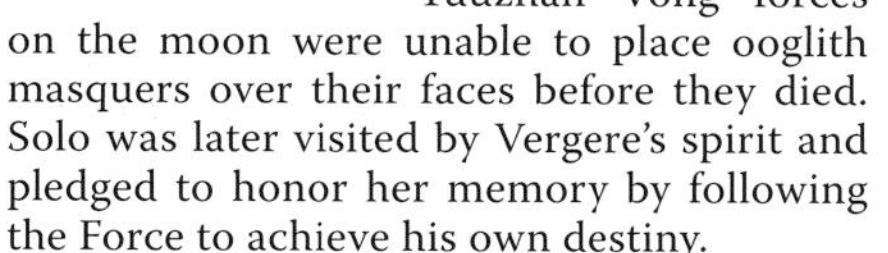

After the war, and particularly after Jacen Solo assumed the title of Darth Caedus, some believed that Vergere might have been one of Darth Sidious's apprentices and that Vergere could have influenced the Yuuzhan Vong War in order to discover a new Sith Lord.

**Vergesso asteroids** These asteroids were located in the Lybeya system of the Bajic sector in the Outer Rim. The Tenloss Syndicate built a hidden shipyard in one of the larger asteroids, used by the Rebel Alliance among others. The nickel-iron Vergesso asteroid was the size of a small moon and had a surface pockmarked with craters. All types of Rebel and other vessels, from snubfighters to cruisers, were repaired and refitted at the base right under the nose of Grand Moff Kintaro. Prince Xizor and his Black Sun criminal organization found out about the base, and Xizor presented the information to Darth Vader as a way to curry favor with the Emperor and to harm the Tenloss Syndicate, one of his major rivals. Vader was ordered to eliminate the base. In the subsequent raid, hundreds of Rebel ships were destroyed, and thousands of pilots and crew members perished, seriously harming the Alliance just prior to the critical Battle of Endor.

**Vergill** A planet in the Hapes Cluster, its inhabitants were rivals of the water-breathers of the planet Maires. Nineteen years after the Battle of Endor, the Vergills began an undersea ditanium-mining operation on the planet Hapes, next to the newly opened Mairan consulate. The Mairans filed an official protest against the noise and mining debris stirred up by the Vergills' actions, but in reality they had deliberately placed their consulate near the richest vein of ditanium in order to spark a confrontation.

**Veril Line Systems** The manufacturer of unremarkable but durable droids including the EG-6 power droid and the Gyrowheel 1.42.08 recycling droid. Veril Line Systems was a venerable corporation with a long history of superior industrial products. VLS never made military droids, munitions, or starships, and for that reason remained on good terms with various galactic and planetary governments over the years, even though its main headquarters remained on Coruscant.

**Vermel, Colonel Meizh** An Imperial Navy officer who served under Admiral Pellaeon after the death of Grand Admiral Thrawn and the defeat of Admiral Daala. Pellaeon chose Vermel to deliver a message of Imperial surrender to Garm Bel Iblis shortly after Bel Iblis arrived at Morishim. Pellaeon had hoped to begin negotiating a peace treaty with Bel Iblis, but Vermel's corvette was intercepted by a Star Destroyer dispatched by Moff Disra in an attempt to disrupt the peace process. However, Vermel was able to send out a garbled transmission to Rogue Squadron shortly before he was captured; he was held at Rimcee Station until Pellaeon could recover him.

**Veron** A tropical planet with an ancient aristocratic house, it was also the homeworld of the Gazaran species.

**Vero'tog'leo** A lieutenant in the Chiss Expansionary Defense Fleet during the Swarm War. Vero'tog'leo served aboard the *Fell Defender* and was present when the *Millennium Falcon* was captured near Tenupe. It was Vero'tog'leo who reactivated C-3PO and demanded the droid show him the freighter's smuggling compartments. The protocol droid refused, and Vero'tog'leo sought out a team to bypass the droid's security systems. In the meantime, Han Solo and Leia Organa Solo returned to the ship and escaped.

**Verpine** This species of advanced, spacefaring two-legged insectoids colonized the Roche asteroid field before the birth of the Republic. Their thin, stick-like bodies had articulated joints and chitinous shells. Two antennae jutted from the sides of their heads, which had two large eyes and short snouts. They communicated via radio waves using an organ in their chests, enabling a single Verpine to talk with the entire species within seconds. They developed something of a communal mind, yet each Verpine considered itself aloof and not controlled by the hive.

The Verpine used huge repulsor shells to keep occupied asteroids from crashing into one another and to deflect other bits of space debris. They were experts in most fields of technology and were expert starship builders. Their eyesight allowed them to spot microscopic details, such as hairline fractures, making them invaluable to the safety of pilots everywhere. The Verpine helped Admiral Ackbar design and build the B-wing starfighter.

Always wary of the galactic government, the Verpine were frustrated when their appeals to the Galactic Alliance about the neighboring world of Murkhana's trade violations went unanswered. The Verpine turned to the Mandalorians for help, and the groups signed a mutual-aid treaty that ensured Verpine weapons for the Mandalorians in exchange for protection from outside forces. The Mandalorians, however, were no match for the Imperial Remnant, which used a modified nanotechnology virus to wipe out the members of the Verpine warrior caste. The Imperials then enslaved the Verpine, forcing the survivors to continue working in their munitions factories in order to provide war matériel for the Remnant.

**Versé** One of the three handmaidens assigned by Captain Typho to serve Senator Padmé Amidala prior to the Clone Wars. Along with Cordé and Dormé, Versé served as a protector and decoy whenever Senator Amidala traveled through the Chommell sector or to Coruscant. When the Senator was due to return to Coruscant for a vote on the Military Creation Act, Versé and Cordé flew aboard the Senator's starship while Padmé flew a Naboo N-1 starfighter. Both handmaidens were killed when the craft was destroyed by Zam Wesell, in an attempt to assassinate the Senator.

*Verpine*

**Ver Seryan, Karia** A life-bearer who lived on Leria Kerlsil, she was around 300 years old. Karia Ver Seryan had had 49 husbands, whose lives she had sustained for periods of time, when a potential 50th—Lando Calrissian—was investigating her as a possible marriage candidate.

**Veruna, King** The sovereign of Naboo prior to Queen Amidala. Known to be a stubborn man who resisted the advice of others, Veruna held office for 13 years. At Senator Palpatine's urging, he began dabbling in foreign affairs and eventually became too involved in outworld politics. He was forced to relinquish his title approximately six months before the Battle of Naboo. After leaving office Veruna went into hiding, but soon suffered a mysterious "accidental" death. Captain Magneta, the head of security at the time, resigned in shame and was succeeded by Captain Panaka. During Veruna's reign, he established a vast royal library collection in one of the towers of Theed's Royal Palace.

**Vesser, Dak** This being was a xenoarchaeologist who investigated the Valley of the Dark Lords on Korriban some 4,000 years before the Battle of Yavin. He became tainted by months of close proximity to the dark side of the Force and was suspicious of the Jedi Knights who tried to infiltrate the Sith planet. The Jedi were on Korriban to search for information on Darth Malak, and Vesser became angry at their constant intrusions. When the Jedi tried to question him at a cantina in Dreshdae, Vesser attacked them and was killed in the fighting that ensued.

*Novoc Vevut (right)*

**Vessery, Colonel Broak** An Imperial Navy officer who served Ysanne Isard after she escaped the Battle of Thyferra. A tall, black-haired man who had a nervous habit of picking invisible pieces of lint from his uniform, Vessery and his ships were dispatched by Isard to rescue as many members of Rogue Squadron as possible from Corvis Minor V, after the Rogues fell into a trap laid by Isard's clone and rogue warlord Prince-Admiral Delak Krennel. Vessery then trained the Rogues in the use of the TIE Defender, hoping that they could infiltrate Krennel's forces and help end his reign. The pilots brought down the shields protecting Ciutric, and Krennel, Isard's clone, and Isard herself were killed. Vessery fled with two complete squadrons of TIE Defenders and their pilots.

**Vestswe, Sateen** A loyal retainer and bodyguard to Senator Bail Organa. The Vestswe family had been serving the Royal House for over 40 generations. Vestswe trained under mercenary Giles Durane to become a crack shot.

**vesuvague tree** A semi-sentient tree, it had limbs that could strangle.

**Vetter, Elke** An Imperial Knight who served as Princess Marasia Fel's bodyguard more than 130 years after the Battle of Yavin. Vetter was Sia's teacher and friend. She died in battle with Darth Talon.

*Elke Vetter*

**Veubg** A species from the planet Gbu. The planet's intense gravity caused the Veubgri to evolve into wide, squat beings with a number of sensitive tendrils used to manipulate and touch things. They also had six feet, which helped keep them stable.

**Vevut, Novoc** A Mandalorian soldier who agreed to meet with Boba Fett and Goran Beviin on Drall to discuss Thrackan Sal-Solo's offer of employment. Sal-Solo wanted the Mandalorians to fight on the side of Corellia if he went to war against the Galactic Alliance to ensure Corellia's independence. Vevut was distinguished by his dark skin and the thick dreadlocks that spilled from his head, as well as the large scar that crossed his left cheek. His hair was braided with small gold clips that rattled when he shook his head. Each clip represented the spoils of the various kills he had made over the years, and many were forged from credit coins that were melted down and re-formed. Vevut was known on his homeworld of Mandalore as a weapons maker and was skilled in the use of various metals. His adopted son, Ghes Orade, later became emotionally involved with Mirta Gev when the young woman returned to Mandalore with Fett, who was actually her grandfather. Vevut later served with the many Mandalorians who participated in the Second Battle of Fondor, where they were backup for Admiral Daala's Maw Irregular Fleet and recaptured the destroyer *Bloodfin*.

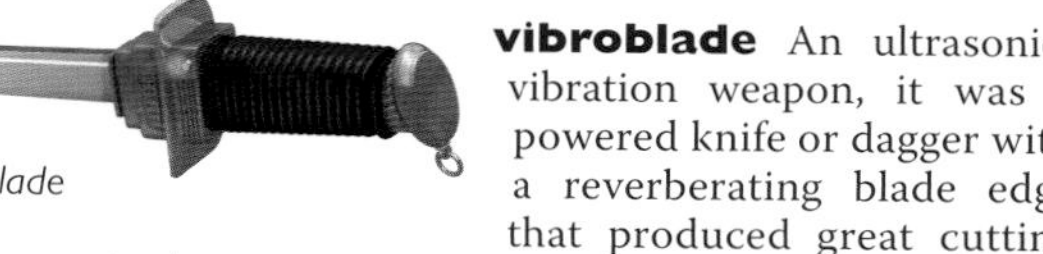
Vibroblade

**Vexa** The leader of a small faction of a Tusken Raider tribe that believed Sliven was unfit to lead the tribe after he returned with Tahiri Veila and said he would raise the girl as a Tusken. Vexa insisted that her true parentage be kept secret and that she be forced to pass the trials of adulthood. If not, both Sliven and Tahiri would be exiled. Tahiri grew up with the tribe, but when she returned from her training at the Jedi academy on Yavin 4, Vexa demanded that the trials begin. Tahiri and her friend, Anakin Solo, were taken into the deepest Jundland Wastes and given seven days to return. She did, and then forced Vexa to abide by her original agreement.

Vibro-ax

**Vexta belt** Pirates from this area attacked Delephran shipping for years, until they were wiped out by the Delephran militia during the Piracy Scouring. Former Alliance operative Colonel Andrephan Stormcaller participated in the campaign against the Vexta belt pirates early in his career.

**viann** The high-backed Ansionian saddle used when riding a suubatar.

**Vibro** *See* Rikel.

**vibro-ax** A handheld weapon with a broad blade, it could be deadly in fights. With only the slightest touch, an ultrasonic generator located in the vibro-ax's handle produced vibrations that powered the weapon and gave the blade great cutting power. Many Gamorreans carried vibro-axes.

**vibroblade** An ultrasonic-vibration weapon, it was a powered knife or dagger with a reverberating blade edge that produced great cutting power at only the slightest touch. It was a weapon of choice in the underworld.

**vibro-cutter** A heavy-duty industrial version of a vibroblade.

**vibroscalpel** A small, lightweight surgical instrument, it used ultrasonic vibrations to excite a small wire blade in order to easily cut through most objects. Controls located in the vibroscalpel handle adjusted power levels.

**vibro-shiv** A small, easily concealable vibroblade.

**Vicria** A Mungra who owned a restaurant in Makrin City on Shelkonwa during the New Order. At the request of Yeeru Chivkyrie, she hired a female human waitress shortly after the Battle of Yavin. It was Princess Leia Organa, and the city's administrator tried to capture her as a traitor. Vicria hid Leia in plain sight until Chivkyrie could find a way to get her offplanet.

**Victim** A slang term used by Rebel pilots for a *Victory*-class Destroyer.

**Victory, Salem** A sociopathic smuggler and mercenary, he was considered the leader of the Happy Blasters. He used his customized starship, the *Starcat*, to transport the group across the galaxy. Victory was in the mercenary game for the money and had a knack of finding people who would pay huge sums of credits to recover certain artifacts.

***Victory*-class Star Destroyer** Designed near the end of the Clone Wars by Walex Blissex, a Republic engineer, these vessels were introduced six months earlier than planned due to the threat of the Bulwark Fleet commanded by the Separatist officer Dua Ningo. When first launched, the *Victory*-class Star Destroyers were considered the ultimate combat starship design. At 900 meters long, they carried a crew of more than 5,000. Standard Imperial armament included 10 quad turbolasers, 40 double turbolasers, 80 concussion missile launchers, and 10 tractor beam projectors. They could carry two squadrons, or 24 TIE fighters, 2,000 ground troops, planetary drop ships, troop transports, and a wide range of planetary assault vehicles, including AT-AT walkers, juggernauts, and floating fortresses.

As more *Imperial*-class Star Destroyers were built, Victory Star Destroyers were reassigned to planetary defense roles. A number were decommissioned and sold off to planetary defense forces, including the Corporate Sector Authority, which bought 250 of the ships. They were designed for three missions: planetary defense, planetary assault and ground-troop support, and ship-to-ship combat. Their biggest weakness was in the last category because newer starships could outrun them. The usefulness of Victory Star Destroyers was renewed with the return of Grand Admiral Thrawn. Finding his forces lacking sufficient capital starships, he began a systematic recommissioning and refitting of Victory Star Destroyers, gaining these ships renewed respect.

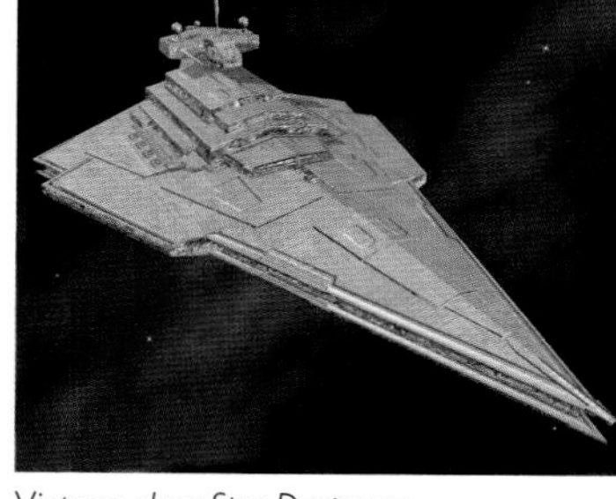
Victory-*class Star Destroyer*

**Victory Forum** A huge coliseum in the town of Dying Slowly on the planet Jubilar, it was named by the winning side of one of the planet's numerous wars. Brightly lit and with hundreds of rows of seats, the forum allowed audiences of up to 20,000 to view barbaric sporting events, most notably Regional Sector Four's All-Human Free-For-All Extravaganza.

**Victory Lake** A body of water some 15 kilometers from Imperial City on Coruscant, it served as a reservoir for the capital. Admiral Ackbar, among others, had a waterfront home on Victory Lake.

**Victory Square** An open plaza constructed on Coruscant after the Yuuzhan Vong War as a memorial. Victory Square commemorated the efforts of all beings—including the Yuuzhan Vong—in bringing the conflict to an end. The square was filled with lush, green vegetation and was brightly lit at all times, signifying the undying light of the galaxy.

**Vida, Ayy** A Twi'lek female who frequented the bars and nightclubs of Coruscant during the Clone Wars. She was unusual among Twi'leks because her yellow skin was striped with orange. As a consort working for the criminal Hat Lo, Ayy Vida dreamed of being rescued from servitude but feared that Tas Kee would eventually hunt her down. She was a known as-

Ayy Vida

Benedict Vidkun

sociate of Achk Med-Beq and hoped that his association with Dannl Faytonni would allow her to meet the man, whom she believed to be a Republic officer who would free her from enslavement.

**Vidkun, Benedict** A short, thin engineer with bulging brown eyes, sharp yellow teeth, and a wispy beard and mustache, he had a younger wife with expensive tastes. Always nervous, Benedict Vidkun tended to clear his throat a lot. For a price, he appeared willing both to make maps and to lead a Rebel Alliance rescue team through a labyrinth of sewer conduits beneath Prince Xizor's palace on Imperial Center to free Princess Leia Organa. Vidkun's brother-in-law, Daiv, worked for the firm that built Xizor's castle. Another brother-in-law, Lair, was able to get the bypass codes for an extermination device that would have fried the rescuers. But after taking the team through the muck, Benedict pulled a blaster and shot Dash Rendar in the left hip. Dash immediately responded with a blaster bolt between Vidkun's eyes.

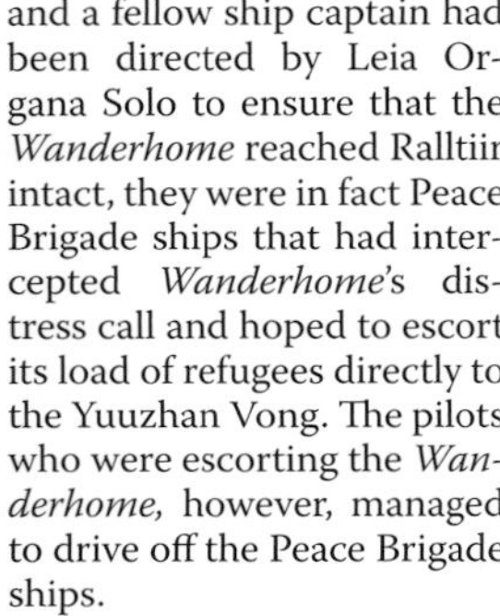

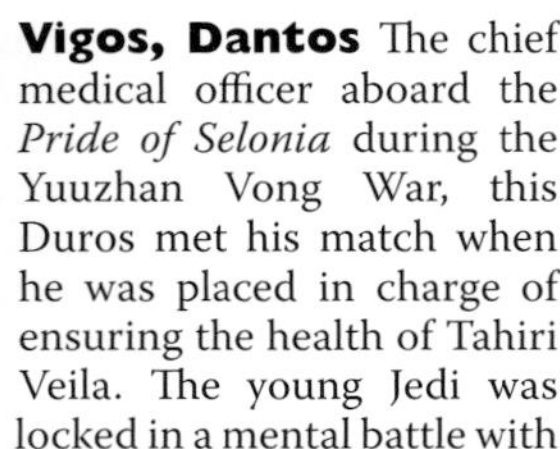

Vien'sai'Malloc

**Vien'sai'Malloc** A female Senator from Devaron who conspired with the Separatists to set up a secret base on her homeworld. Senator Vien'sai'Malloc was believed to be one of the few incorruptible members of the Senate. The base she established, however, allowed the Separatists to ambush Republic supply convoys. After her rival Elsah'sai'Moro discovered the truth, Vien'sai'Malloc hired Aurra Sing to eliminate her. When the Jedi Tholme, the Dark Lady, and Aayla Secura infiltrated her estate, the Senator tried to atone for her treachery by revealing the true location of the base to Aayla Secura. Senator Vien'sai'Malloc was tried on Devaron and executed for her crimes against her people.

**Viento, Senator** A Republic Senator during the Clone Wars. Senator Viento was under the protection of Jedi Master K'kruhk as a deterrent to Quinlan Vos when he traveled to Coruscant to assassinate Viento under Count Dooku's orders. Vos believed that Viento was the mysterious "second Sith." Master K'kruhk and Quinlan Vos struggled, but Vos killed Viento before K'kruhk could stop him. An investigation into Viento's death revealed that the Senator had been behind several plots to sabotage the starships of other Senators who were loyal to the Republic, pinning him as a Separatist supporter.

**Vieve (O-Vieve)** An aged woman who ruled Kegan with V-Tan some 13 years before the Battle of Naboo.

***Vigilance*** This Old Republic *Venator*-class Star Destroyer was deployed to Utapau as the flagship of a task force under the command of Obi-Wan Kenobi, during the search for General Grievous in the wake of the First Battle of Coruscant.

***Vigilant*** A cruiser in the New Republic Fifth Fleet, it was deployed in the blockade of Doornik-319.

**Vigo** Lieutenants who were appointed by Prince Xizor to help run the Black Sun criminal organization. The honorific *Vigo* was derived from the old Tionese word for "nephew." Vigos were responsible for entire star systems.

***Vigor*** Although its captain claimed that he and a fellow ship captain had been directed by Leia Organa Solo to ensure that the *Wanderhome* reached Ralltiir intact, they were in fact Peace Brigade ships that had intercepted *Wanderhome*'s distress call and hoped to escort its load of refugees directly to the Yuuzhan Vong. The pilots who were escorting the *Wanderhome,* however, managed to drive off the Peace Brigade ships.

**Vigos, Dantos** The chief medical officer aboard the *Pride of Selonia* during the Yuuzhan Vong War, this Duros met his match when he was placed in charge of ensuring the health of Tahiri Veila. The young Jedi was locked in a mental battle with her alter ego, Riina Kwaad, and traditional methods of treating her failed to work.

**Viidaav** An arid world dominated by rocky deserts. The natives, also known as the Viidaav, existed in small settlements near the largest outcroppings of rock. The planet was the site of a Separatist base during the early stages of the Clone Wars, until Republic scouts found it. Count Dooku and General Grievous allowed the base to fall to Republic clone troopers in order to spring a trap. They planned to set off bombs that would have rendered the planet's surface unlivable—a scheme that the native Viidaav learned of at the end of the battle. Rather than see their homeworld destroyed, several Viidaav soldiers sacrificed themselves to shut down the bombs.

**Vilas** A dark-haired male from Dathomir, he was the Force-sensitive companion of Nightsister Vonnda Ra. He was also Vonnda Ra's apprentice, and she wanted him to lead a new order of Dark Jedi, but a onetime street urchin, Zekk, was also in contention for that role. The two battled in the gravity-free center of the Shadow Academy space station. Zekk sliced Vilas in half with his lightsaber and shot his body parts out an exhaust port.

**Vill, Commander** A brigade clone commander from the 501st Legion of Stormtroopers, he was sent to New Plympto in the final stages of the Clone Wars. Commander Vill was troubled over what would become of the clones when the fighting was over. When he asked Darth Vader, he was assured that the Emperor had a plan for the clones that would be revealed in time.

**Villache, Nazrita** A master mechanic for the Klatooinian Trade Guild during the New Order, she first taught Platt Okeefe the basics of starship maintenance.

**Villa Solis** A massive estate owned by the Galney family in the moorlands of Terephon. A large portion of Villa Solis was leveled by the Ducha Galney herself to try to prevent Jaina Solo and Zekk from escaping after they learned of her role in an assassination attempt on the life of the Queen Mother, Tenel Ka, a decade after the end of the Yuuzhan Vong War.

**villip** A Yuuzhan Vong–bioengineered communication device. Two villips could be joined in consciousness with each other and communicate remotely across vast distances. When inactive, a villip appeared to be a ridged lump of membranous tissue. When a Yuuzhan Vong awakened a villip, a hole that resembled an eye socket puckered to life. The villip had the ability to adapt its shape and assume almost any appearance, including the head and voice of another villip-joined Yuuzhan Vong. Villips grew on plants in paddies such as the one on Belkadan. Villips did not work with ships in superliminal transit. After the war ended, the

Villip

Yuuzhan Vong discovered that villips and many of their other bioengineered devices reverted to their natural forms.

**villip-choir field** A form of holographic projection created by specialized villips.

**Vilosoria** A world in the Lifh sector that was briefly invaded by the Empire, until the native Vilosorians were able to overrun the local garrison and force the military offplanet. During the cold months, the Vilosorians were docile and calm. During the warm months, they were vicious carnivores.

Vima-Da-Boda

**Vima-Da-Boda** Descended from a long, illustrious line of Jedi, she was directly related to the legendary Vima Sunrider, the daughter of Nomi Sunrider. Vima-Da-Boda served the Force for 100 years, and raised one daughter, Neema, who turned to the dark side. The dark side power didn't help Neema, who was abused and finally killed by her husband, a barbaric Ottethan warlord. In her rage at finding that her daughter had been fed to rancors, Vima ignited her lightsaber and cleaved the warlord in two. She then sank deep into despair over her actions and the loss of her daughter. Her retreat from the world was probably what saved her from the great Jedi Purge.

At one point she was imprisoned in the Kessel spice mines and met young Kyp Durron, whom she gave some elementary training in the Force. Eventually free of Imperial shackles, she retreated to the darkest haunts of the Corellian sector on the Smugglers' Moon of Nar Shaddaa. Six years after the destruction of the second Death Star, Alliance hero Han Solo brought his wife, Leia, to the lower levels. The 200-year-old Vima could sense Leia's Jedi potential. She kissed Leia's feet, begged her forgiveness, and gave her a gift—Vima's own ancient lightsaber.

Months later, Leia and Han returned to retrieve Vima, who was on the run from Imperial dark siders. Vima aided Luke Skywalker with his training of Jedi students. When Luke was poisoned by Imperial scarab droids, Vima healed him. Following the death of the Emperor on Onderon, Vima-Da-Boda mysteriously disappeared.

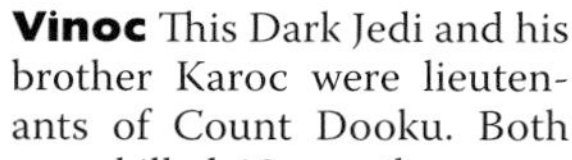

Bom Vimdin

**Vimdin, Bom** A male Advozse, he despised beings of his own species. Pessimistic and territorial, Bom Vimdin was a lone smuggler who preferred to work for corrupt officials. He boasted about being in the Mos Eisley cantina when Luke Skywalker first met Han Solo. No one believed him—or cared. Following the Battle of Endor, he was apprehended by agents of the New Republic while transporting Imperial agents back to Imperial space.

**Vin (RC-1134)** One of the four clone commandos of Theta Squad who participated in the Battle of Geonosis. Vin was among the three members of the squad to be killed in the fighting.

**Vinda** The co-owner of Starshipwrights and Aerospace Engineers Incorporated, he was once owed credits by Han Solo for work his company had performed on the *Millennium Falcon.*

**Vindi, Doctor Nuvo** A Separatist scientist tasked with resurrecting and weaponizing the deadly Blue Shadow Virus during the Clone Wars. Obsessed with promulgating all forms of microscopic life, Dr. Vindi would do anything to see his tiny "friends" finally get their due, even if it meant selling his deadly secrets to those who would use them for evil.

**Vindicator** Like the Vanquisher, a style of double-bladed lightsaber hilts sometimes found among the new Order of Jedi Knights who were trained by Luke Skywalker. They were reminiscent of weapons of Exar Kun and Darth Maul. The Vindicator was formed from two identical hilts welded together at the ends with emitters much wider than the main shaft for some protection against energy backwash.

**Vinoc** This Dark Jedi and his brother Karoc were lieutenants of Count Dooku. Both were killed 10 months after the Battle of Geonosis by Anakin Skywalker, who was searching for the source of cortosis-based battle droids being made on Metalorn.

**Vinsoth** An Outer Rim planet covered by vast plains, it was home to the Chevin species. The Chevin were hunter-gatherers who followed herds of backshin as they traveled the plains, and they enslaved a native humanoid species called Chevs. Ephant Mon, a gunrunner who spent time in Jabba the Hutt's court, was a Vinsoth native. After a life-changing encounter with Luke Skywalker in Jabba's dungeon, Ephant Mon returned to his home planet and founded a new religious sect that worshipped nature and the Force, though he still ran some scams on the side to finance his sect's temple.

**Vinzen Neela 5** The site of an unsuccessful Rebel attack. Following the Battle of Hoth, Rebels tried to thwart an Imperial transfer of prototype TIE defenders to an escort carrier at a rendezvous near Vinzen Neela 5.

**viper kinrath** A species of large, deadly spider found in the jungles of Kashyyyk and the plains of Dantooine. Unlike other species of kinrath, the viper kinrath could inject a deadly poison with its bite.

**Viper probe droid** *See* probe droid (probot).

**Vippit** An alien species that was a member of the Galactic Republic during the Clone Wars. Many Vippit were native to Nal Hutta, a world that appealed to their unique snail-like physiology. Vippits were known for their ability to actively think with both sides of their brains, and were capable of using each half to monitor and understand a distinct sphere of attention. Reintegration of knowledge and memories occurred during normal sleep cycles, allowing a Vippit to acquire knowledge almost twice as fast as most other species. The shell of a Vippit was a source of personal pride and communal acceptance, and the polishing of shells was one of the most basic forms of contact in their society. An individual Vippit could go without food and sleep for many days, a trait which made them one of the hardest-working species of the Republic.

**viptiel** A unique plant native to Nal Hutta, it was used by the Vippit species as a medicinal supplement, especially during their mating periods. It was also a powerful counteragent to intense hormonal surges that accompanied the gender phase changes experienced by the X'Ting, although very few could afford it.

***Virago*** The personal transport and assault vessel of galactic underworld leader Prince Xizor, it was a *StarViper*-class heavy assault starfighter with incredible speed, armor, and

Virago

weaponry, custom-built at a very high cost. The ship's wings and thrust nacelles moved while in flight to enhance performance, giving it the appearance of a living creature as its wings constantly folded and adjusted.

The StarViper matched the TIE interceptor for speed and maneuverability despite a far greater mass. The rear-mounted engines provided forward thrust, while maneuverability was enhanced by a pair of microthrusters mounted on the tip of each wing. The inflight computer control system individually adjusted each microthruster. In combat, the four wings fully folded out to give the thrusters maximum effect. The well-armored wings held reserve fuel tanks.

The *Virago*'s wings folded flush against the engines and pilot compartment for standard spaceflight and planetary landing. Its main weapons were a pair of double heavy laser cannons tied to an advanced targeting computer and laser-sighting system. There were also two forward-firing proton torpedo launchers, each with a magazine of three torpedoes. Because the *Virago* required a large amount of energy, it needed four separate power generators.

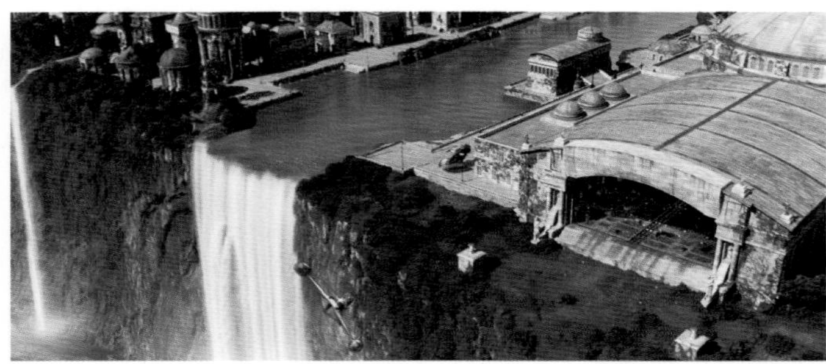

Virdugo Plunge

**Viraxo Industries** A shipping and hauling operation owned by K'Armyn Viraxo and his family during the Galactic Civil War. Viraxo Industries had many contracts with the Empire in its home sector. K'Armyn tried to stamp out any competition, but was unable to eliminate Twin Suns Transport Services.

**Virdugo Plunge** The largest waterfall in Theed on Naboo, the Virdugo Plunge was located near the Theed Hangar and Generator complex.

**Virgilio, Captain Sarin** Commander of the New Republic escort frigate *Quenfis,* one of the ships in Admiral Drayson's Home Guard Fleet assigned to protect Coruscant. Captain Virgilio had been part of the crew of the Rebel Alliance ship that helped Bothan spies return with the plans for the second Death Star battle station. At the time, Virgilio was a young third officer on a Corellian gunship. The ship picked up a distress call whose code identified its senders as members of a large team of Bothan intelligence agents operating in the outer regions. Of that team, only six survived—but they carried with them the plans and secret location of the second Death Star and the Emperor's schedule, which told when he would be visiting the site.

Later, as a captain in the New Republic, he was in charge of the mission that intercepted Leia Organa Solo's team sent to recover the *Katana* fleet. After Borsk Fey'lya admitted that he was trying to obtain the *Katana* fleet only for political gain, and that stranding part of Rogue Squadron was a necessity that loyalty couldn't overcome, Virgilio placed Fey'lya under house guard until the *Katana* was secured.

**Virgillian Civil War** This struggle lasted seven years and was the culmination of a decades-old conflict between the Virgillian Aristocracy and the Virgillian Free Alignment. It had its origins in the years before the Clone Wars, when a team of Jedi Knights was believed to have been killed trying to negotiate a settlement between the two sides. During the New Order, the Empire supported the Aristocracy; underground freedom fighters began to organize themselves around the Free Alignment, and eventually received aid from the Rebel Alliance. The Alignment managed to overthrow the tyrannical government shortly before the Battle of Endor. The Virgillian Free Alignment and its newly formed government sent 22 of its best ships to Sullust to augment the Alliance's fleet as it readied for battle.

**Viridia system** A star system where Han Solo used to make smuggling runs. He had learned some of Viridia's port access codes, but they were later changed by Imperials.

**"Virtues of King Han Solo, The"** A song written by C-3PO to help Han Solo convince Leia Organa that he was a worthy choice for a husband.

**Virujansi** One of many planets ravaged during the Clone Wars, it was liberated by the Republic with the help of Anakin Skywalker and Garven Dreis. For his role, Anakin was proclaimed Warrior of the Infinite—a rank that had been bestowed only 29 times in the 6,000-year history of the royal court. Years later, Virujansi was nearly taken over by the Empire, but a group of Rebel Alliance soldiers impersonated the government's leaders. The planet was ruled by a Rajah, who was assisted by a number of other political contemporaries: the People's Adviser, who translated visitors' requests to the Rajah; the Mouth of the Ancestors, who used past Rajahs' actions as precedents when necessary; the Eye of History, who provided options that could be used to solve difficulties; the Wrathor, who described the Rajah's displeasure when appropriate, using insults and barbs; and the Concilliator, who helped all parties come to agreement.

***Virulence*** A *Mark II*–class Imperial Star Destroyer, it was commanded first by Joak Dyrsso, then by Lakwii Varrscha, to maintain Ysanne Isard's stranglehold on the bacta trade. The *Virulence* was sent to protect Isard's bacta convoys, but this did not prevent Rogue Squadron from trying to steal the precious cargo. When the location of Rogue Squadron's secret base was finally discovered, Isard ordered Captain Varrscha to assist the *Lusankya* in its destruction. Upon their arrival at the Yag'Dhul space station, the *Lusankya* was caught in the grip of a gravity-well projector, and there were indications of an immediate attack. Reacting instantly, Captain Varrscha inserted the *Virulence* between the station's gravity projector and the *Lusankya,* allowing the bigger ship to escape back to Thyferra. Overwhelmed by what appeared to be hundreds of missiles and proton torpedoes about to pound her ship and the sudden appearance of Pash Cracken's A-wing group, Captain Varrscha surrendered the ship to Booster Terrik. He took command, loaded Pash's A-wings, and set off for Thyferra. Their arrival turned the tide of the Bacta War. The three squadrons of fighters brought to the fray were an invaluable asset to the weary Rogue Squadron and the rapidly thinning Deathseeds. The *Virulence* poured a barrage of fire into the unprotected side of the *Lusankya* until it finally surrendered. For his valiant effort, Booster Terrik was gifted with the *Virulence,* but only after he agreed to remove most of the ship's weaponry. He then renamed it the *Errant Venture.*

**Visitor Consumption Tag** Known as a viscount, this voucher was offered by the Corporate Sector Authority for a small fee, and it entitled visitors to a 20 percent discount on all purchased goods.

**viska** Ruthless flying carnivores on Rordak, they were feared throughout the galaxy because they survived by consuming the blood of their victims.

**Vis'l** A young Jedi Knight stationed on the planet Ossus who was charged with protecting the Jedi training facility there during the Galactic Alliance's conflict with the Confederation. Vis'l and Loli were killed in the line of duty, when Major Serpa of the Galactic Alliance Guard arrived and took control of the facility.

**Vispil** The New Republic managed to convince the government of this planet, on the border between space held by the Republic and space held by Warlord Zsinj, to back it in the fight between the two forces.

**Viss, Ellu** One of a handful of Jedi apprentices who managed to survive the Sith–Imperial War. When he fled the Massacre at Ossus, Ellu Viss took with him a wealth of historical information about the Jedi Order, hoping that one day it would be preserved for future generations. In his personal journal, he explained that none of the Jedi of his time knew that the Sith had reemerged and that they were unprepared for the viciousness with which Darth Krayt and his minions assumed control of the galaxy.

**Vista, Maxo** Obi-Wan Kenobi discovered that this famous, award-winning Euceron athlete was a fraud and a murderer. He had killed the timekeeper of the Galactic Games and plotted to assassinate the Jedi Knights who were on the planet to help preserve the peace during the event. Vista captured Kenobi and forced him to participate in a holographic obstacle course, hoping to kill the Jedi. But Kenobi won and Vista fled. He was next discovered to be rigging illegal Podraces in such a way that Podracers would crash into heavily populated areas. Kenobi and Jedi Siri Tachi captured and brought Vista to the Ruling Council for judgment, but he was allowed to go free when an important witness wouldn't testify against him.

**Vizcarra** An Imperial prison planet, it was where the smuggler Tait Ransom was scheduled to be sent after he was arrested for weapons smuggling on Omman.

**Vizsla** A vicious, egomaniacal member of the Mandalorian Mercs who led a coup, forming his own faction called the Mandalorian Death Watch. Vizsla spent much of his life hunting down Jaster Mereel, leader of the Mandalorian Mercs, killing many of the Mercs on Concord Dawn. He never forgot the Mandalorians and worked to set up an ambush on Korda 6. His plan worked to perfection, decimating the troops of Jaster Mereel and Jango Fett in surprise attacks during the Mandalorian Civil War. Vizsla shot and killed Jaster Mereel, then celebrated the victory. He knew that some Mandalorians had survived and coerced the planetary governor of Galidraan to lay a final trap. The governor hired the Mandalorians to put down a local insurrection and simultaneously called for the Jedi Knights to eliminate the Mandalorians. Dooku was among the Jedi who slaughtered the Mandalorians on Galidraan. Years later, Jango Fett found Vizsla near Corellia. Vizsla seemed to gain the upper hand when he injected poison into Jango's body but was unprepared for the pack of dire-cats that ripped him apart and ate him.

**Vjun** The planet where Darth Vader built Bast Castle, a remote, heavily defended structure that became his private refuge. The planet was lashed with acidic, burning rain, and no plant life could survive on its bleak surface. Prior to the Clone Wars, the population of Vjun eked out a meager living while influential families controlled the usable landmass. Most inhabitants had a much higher midi-chlorian count than other humans, and the ruling families made it their business to maximize their counts through breeding. Some eight years before the Clone Wars, the planet was swept by a plague of madness that wiped out a huge percentage of the population in just a year. The survivors struggled to exist, and Vjun was virtually forgotten. Later it came out that the plague was the result of genetic tampering by the Viscount Malreaux and a group of elitist nobles, who had tried to manipulate the number of midi-chlorians in their cells to achieve more power.

Vjun was later the headquarters of dark side Executor Sedriss and the Emperor's elite force of Dark Jedi. Kam Solusar served as a dark side warrior on Vjun before Luke Skywalker turned him to the light side on Nespis VIII, six years after the Battle of Endor. Soon after Solusar's conversion, three Ysanna prisoners from Ossus were taken to Vjun to serve as raw material in creating new clone bodies for Emperor Palpatine. The Ysanna were frozen in carbonite to await the future construction of a clone laboratory in Bast Castle, but Luke Skywalker and his Jedi trainees managed to storm the castle and defeat the Emperor's minions.

**Vladet** Located in the Rachuk sector and system, it was a blue-and-green world dotted with islands. It received a great deal of rainfall. The Empire established a base in the lush jungle on Vladet's Grand Isle to discourage piracy in the local systems, and the garrison became the center of Imperial control for the sector. Built in the crater of an extinct volcano, the base was ringed by two steep mountain ranges on the west and east. To the south the crater had mostly broken down, and the base extended out to the edges of a bay. Geothermal generators powered the energy shield and twin ion cannons, while a comfortable mansion housed the command staff, including Admiral Devlia.

Three years after the Battle of Endor, a New Republic force, including members of Rogue Squadron, attacked the Vladet headquarters in reprisal for an Imperial raid on Talasea. The New Republic's goal was not to capture Vladet but to cripple the base so the Empire would be compelled to allocate more forces to its defense. Several Y-wing squadrons blew out the northern wall of the crater, allowing starfighters to fly in under the base's defensive shield. The New Republic leveled the base in the successful raid, and Rogue Squadron pilot Corran Horn helped destroy a *Lancer*-class frigate on the way out. Admiral Devlia was presumed killed.

*Vjun*

**Vlee, Ussar** One of a trio of famous Gand ruetsavii who were sent to observe Ooryl Qrygg's life and determine his worthiness to become janwuine. Not only did they observe his activities, but they also participated fully with him while he performed his duties as a member of Rogue Squadron. They proved to be capable fighter pilots as well as undercover operatives.

**Vlix** This heavyset Annoo-dat was a personal assistant and security guard for Tig Fromm during the early years of the New Order. Vlix was in charge of security around the construction site of the Trigon One space station, but his forces weren't prepared for an attack led by Thall Joben. When C-3PO selflessly pushed Vlix out of the way of a falling cargo container, Vlix realized that there was more to life than controlling other beings. He agreed to help the Rebels by providing access to the hangar in which the Trigon One was being housed.

**Voal, Captain** The commander of the *Tarkin* during its construction in the Patriim system, this Imperial Navy officer was part of a growing faction that wanted to eliminate Darth Vader. They feared and loathed him and his wanton disregard for his subordinates. When Colonel Nord decided to use the ionic cannon aboard the *Tarkin* to take out Luke Skywalker and Leia Organa, the superweapon exploded. It had been sabotaged by the Rebel Alliance and tore itself apart, killing Voal and everyone else aboard.

**Vob** A gas giant, it was famous for its perpetual atmospheric storms.

**vocabulator** A device through which droids produced sounds, it was usually visible as a grille or orifice called a vocoder. A vocabulator allowed a droid to produce speech. The most sophisticated vocabulators were found in protocol droids and were capable of producing the sounds necessary to converse in millions of different languages.

**Vocatara** The Supreme Chancellor of the Old Republic during the time of the Gank Massacres, some 4,800 years before the Battle of Yavin. Chancellor Vocatara ordered the building of the Juggernaut War Droid to battle the Gank Killers.

**Vo Dasha** The primary moon of the gas giant Taboon, it was the site of Bogga the Hutt's ancient stronghold 4,000 years before the Galactic Civil War. It was an arid world of mountains and plains.

**Vodran** Covered with swamps and thick jungles, this planet was homeworld to the tough humanoids known as Vodrans, who struggled for survival against the world's huge and deadly predators. The Vodrans were enslaved by the Hutts in the early days of space travel and fought in the Third Battle of Vontor against the forces of Xim the Despot.

Rebel Alliance Lieutenant Xenon Nnaksta, an operator of the Greel Wood Logging Corporation in the Pii system, was a native of Vodran. Nnaksta's parents were killed in the Thruncon Insurrection, a catastrophe in which many Vodran cities were destroyed. The planet was also home to the galactic pest known as the dianoga or garbage squid. This seven-tentacled creature had one eyestalk and evolved a transparent camouflage to protect it from predators. These animals were later found feeding on garbage virtually everywhere in the galaxy; Luke Skywalker was attacked and nearly killed by one in the Death Star's trash compactor.

**Vogel 7** The site of an Imperial Naval Academy, it was where TIE fighter pilot Ranulf Trommer was raised.

**Vogga the Hutt** An ancient Hutt, he controlled Nar Shaddaa's fuel supply lines during the years following the Great Sith War. He also maintained a harem of dancing girls in his private residence, which he often used to entertain his associates and peers.

**voice manipulation** A frequently used Force technique, it allowed a Jedi to verbally implant suggestions into the minds of others and create the appropriate responses. Jedi employed voice manipulation to achieve their objectives peacefully.

Vodran

**Voice Override: Epsilon Actual** A command that immediately superseded a droid's primary programming. The Voice Override: Epsilon Actual function was activated by a verbal code, usually delivered in the form of a word or phrase.

**Void-7** Krupx's version of the seismic charge, it was developed during the last years of the Old Republic and was considered the most sophisticated of all seismic charges. It used a combination of baradium and collapsium to supercharge the explosive core during deployment. When the Void-7 exploded, it created an intense core of pure vacuum at the center of the blast, which sucked in all sound in its vicinity before exploding outward. The resulting shock wave was capable of penetrating the deflector shields of most starships to damage the hull. Jango Fett released Void-7 seismic charges from the *Slave I* to try to kill Obi-Wan Kenobi, who was following him to Kamino.

Void Spider THX 1138

***Void Cutter*** Zothip's gunship, it was used as a command ship for the Cavrilhu Pirates' operations.

**Void Spider THX 1138** A light, enclosed shuttle, it was used for courier runs to large orbiting transports. The Void Spider THX 1138 was manufactured by Bespin Motors, and most remained on Bespin.

**Vojak** A tall, muscular humanoid whose brother was killed by C-3PX on Bonadan, Vojak pursued the assassin droid to Hosk Station. There Vojak cornered C-3PX momentarily, until the droid killed him with a laser mounted in the back of its head.

**Vokkoli, Ydor** This Mungra served as the leader of the Freedonna Kaisu band of Rebels during the early stages of the Galactic Civil War. Vokkoli agreed to meet with Princess Leia Organa to discuss some sort of truce to stop open revolt in the Shelsha sector. But he was double-crossed by Chief Administrator Vilim Disra, who only wanted to capture a Rebel Alliance leader so he could supplant Governor Barshnis Choard. The treachery was discovered by Princess Leia.

**volice** An unusual worm that lived on Lwhekk many millennia before the Battle of Yavin. It excreted a unique, crystalline substance once every 10 years. This substance, sapith, was used as a crystal-focusing device in the construction of a Jedi lightsaber.

**Vonce** A Hapan pirate, he provided information to Yuuzhan Vong priest Harrar about the escape of the *Millennium Falcon* from Coruscant, and of the familial linkage of the Solo family. For his efforts, his neck was snapped in two.

**Vondar, Dr. Jos** A Republic surgeon who served at the Rimsoo Seven military hospital on Drongar during the Clone Wars. Raised in a small farming town on Corellia, Vondar was the son of a family doctor. His family was strictly Ensterite, meaning they forbade intermarrying with offworlders. Vondar left home at 20 to train on Coruscant. By the time he was stationed on Drongar, Vondar had attained the rank of captain and was named chief surgeon at Rimsoo Seven, reporting to Colonel D'Arc Vaetes. Vondar didn't have any belief in the Force until he met Barriss Offee, who was stationed at Rimsoo Seven some two years after the Battle of Geonosis. Many of his beliefs were challenged during his tenure at the hospital, including the theory that droids and clone troopers were essentially the same thing: drones created to serve the needs of higher species. His contacts with trooper CT-914 and the droid I-5YQ proved that both were just as "human" as he was. Additionally, he found himself physically and emotionally attracted to Tolk le Trene, even though he knew any relationship they could have would go against his Ensterite background. After a Separatist attack, Rimsoo Seven was relocated. Vondar and Tolk decided to marry. Vondar later learned of a traitor in their camp, Klo Merit, and killed him in revenge.

**Vondarc system** Smuggler Dannen Lifehold brought a Rebel group from Rafft to this system for a rendezvous with a cargo frigate. Lifehold had joined the Rebel Alliance in the Vondarc system just prior to the Battle of Yavin.

**vonduun crab armor** Yuuzhan Vong–bioengineered armor grown from the shell of the vonduun crab and capable of deflecting blasterfire. The armored shell was composed of an intricately structured crystalline lattice reinforced by an energy field created by power glands. The Jedi discovered that vonduun crab armor was allergic to the pollen of the bafforr tree, swelling up and quickly suffocating the warrior wearing it. The Yuuzhan Vong wiped out the planet Ithor in the hope of eliminating the source of bafforr pollen. Vonduun crab armor could also be pierced by striking at a weak point just beneath the wearer's armpit.

Vonduun crab armor

**Vong** A term widely used in the New Republic as shorthand for the Yuuzhan Vong species. Among the aliens themselves, using the word *Vong* alone meant that the person being addressed did not enjoy the favor of his or her family or the gods, and was therefore taken as an insult.

**Vongforming** The nickname for the planetary bioengineering performed by the Yuuzhan Vong to reshape worlds such as Tynna and Coruscant. It often involved spraying gene-tailored bacteria into the atmosphere. The goal of Vongforming was to eradicate all former life-forms from a planet's surface and replace them with Yuuzhan Vong analogs.

**Vongspawn** A term used to describe those beings infected by the bioengineering that was part of the Ossus Project following the Sith–Imperial War. The Ossus Project was championed by Kol Skywalker, who hoped that Yuuzhan Vong biotechnology could help heal those planets that had been damaged in the Yuuzhan Vong War nearly 100 years earlier. The project, however, was sabotaged by Darth Krayt and his new Sith Order, and many of the planets were rendered even more unlivable than they had been before. Their inhabitants were infected by the same contagions that had destroyed their homeworlds.

**Vontor, Third Battle of** The last in a series of major conflicts directed against the pre-Republic tyrant known to history as Xim the Despot. In this battle, Xim's orbital fortress and nearly all of his war robots were vaporized by Hutt-led forces. It took place in the disputed Si'klaata Cluster.

**Vonzel** A smuggler, he was an early associate of Han Solo. After being injured while making an emergency landing, Vonzel had to be attached permanently to a life-support system to keep him alive.

**Vook, Bama** A Talz test pilot before the Battle of Naboo, he alerted Adi Gallia to the presence of the Trade Federation on Esseles and the building of droid starfighters.

**Vookto, Cei** This Duros Jedi Master was killed three months after the Battle of Geonosis in the defense of the planet Lianna. His sacrifice allowed an entire squadron of his troops to survive an attack.

**Voors, Hallolar** A young spice-trading entrepreneur on Jubilar, he was killed by Boba Fett because he dared to try to break a Hutt cartel's monopoly on black-market spice.

**Voota, Tho** The proctor of defense for the Yevethan spawnworld. He commanded the Interdictor cruiser *Splendor of Yevetha.*

**Vootuh, Tsaak** A Yuuzhan Vong commander in charge of the fleet dispatched to Yavin 4 to capture the Jedi students there. Tsaak Vootuh was disappointed to find that the Peace Brigade had reached the system first and had bungled its own attempt to capture the students. He was killed by shaper Mezhan Kwaad.

***Vorknkx*** This Imperial corvette was the first ship to be equipped with a cloaking device from the Vorknkx Project's laboratories on To-phalion. The former leader of the project, Grand Admiral Zaarin, stole the *Vorknkx,* hoping to use the vessel in his plot to overthrow Emperor Palpatine. Grand Admiral Thrawn, who had modified the cloaking device on the *Vorknkx* so that it would not work in hyperspace, watched as Zaarin fled. The *Vorknkx* exploded as it made its lightspeed jump, killing all aboard.

**Vorn, Liegeus Sarpaetius** The pilot for Seti Ashgad, he was also a master holo-faker and a competent designer of artificial intelligence systems for spacecraft. Like Ashgad, he was a captive of the droch Dzym, but through fear. He was needed to complete and then pilot the ship that would transport Dzym safely off Nam Chorios. Later, Vorn was reunited with his lost love, Admiral Natasi Daala. Some 20 years afterward, Vorn was killed by a thermal detonator that had been deployed by assassins who were working for the Moff Council. Daala vowed to avenge his death and spent the next five years amassing evidence against the Moffs who were behind the murder.

**Vor'Na'Tu** An ancient Jedi artifact destroyed by Echuu Shen-Jon on the planet Krant to prevent the device from falling into the hands of Darth Vader and Emperor Palpatine.

**vornskr** A violent, long-legged quadruped with a dog-like muzzle, sharp teeth, and a whip-like tail, it lived on the planet Myrkr. During the day, vornskrs were mostly inactive, but as light faded, they became nocturnal hunters. The vornskr's tail was covered with a mild poison that could inflict painful welts and stun its prey. Vornskrs displayed an unnatural hatred of Jedi, often going out of their way to hunt and attack Force-users. Smuggler Talon Karrde kept two domesticated vornskrs, his pets Sturm and Drang. The guard animals had their tails clipped to reduce their normally aggressive nature. The Yuuzhan Vong shaped vornskrs to become voxyn.

*Vornskr*

**Vorrik, B'shith** A Yuuzhan Vong commander who led the assault on the Imperial Remnant and scored a decisive victory at the Battle of Bastion. Vorrik was distinguishable by his face, which had the skin peeled away to reveal torn muscles and throbbing blood vessels. After regrouping his forces following Bastion, Vorrik launched an assault on Borosk, where the remains of the Imperial fleet had fled. He retreated when he discovered that the Imperials had accepted the assistance of the New Republic. Vorrik destroyed the New Republic communications center on Generis and followed up with an attack on Esfandia. Grand Admiral Pellaeon fought him to a stalemate over Esfandia, until Tahiri Veila tricked Vorrik into sending a small force to the surface of the planet. This left Vorrik and his flagship *Kur-hashan* with a reduced defensive shield. Realizing he was going to die, Vorrik tried to ram an Imperial ship, but the *Kur-hashan* exploded well short of its target.

**Vorru, Fliry** The onetime administrator of the Corellian sector, Vorru turned a blind eye to the smuggling activities all around him. The underworld's Prince Xizor betrayed him to the Emperor to curry favor, but instead of killing him, Palpatine sentenced him to a life of mining spice on Kessel. When Rogue Squadron liberated some Kessel prisoners to wreak havoc on Coruscant prior to an Alliance invasion, Fliry Vorru was taken along. After the conquest, Vorru attempted to ingratiate himself with the Provisional Council, offering his services to administer law to the underworld and control the black market. He was also working for Imperial Intelligence Director Ysanne Isard. Because of his faithful service, she took him along when she fled Coruscant; after she took control of Thyferra's Bacta Cartel and the planetary government, she made him Minister of Trade.

Vorru enjoyed engineering bacta price gouging amid shortages but was aware that the New Republic would eventually put an end to these activities. Always looking for new opportunities and worried about Isard's increasing insanity, he planned his escape. But she remained one step ahead of him. As Vorru made his way to the *Thyfonian,* Isard's Imperial Guards prevented his access to his shuttle, and he was left behind to be captured by Rebel forces.

**Vortex** The homeworld of the hollow-boned, winged Vors, it was a blue-and-gray planet with a sharp axial tilt that caused sudden seasonal changes and severe windstorms. The Cathedral of Winds, the center of Vor civilization, was an immense crystalline structure designed to produce tones when Vortex's wind currents passed over and through it. The Vors performed a beautiful concert of ethereal music by opening and closing orifices in the building with their bodies. The Vors were an emotionless species and tended to concentrate on larger goals rather than on individuals. They refused to perform their music for offworlders during the reign of the Empire but eventually allowed New Republic and other dignitaries to attend the shows. All recording was prohibited, and only one concert was performed each year.

In the stormy season, the Vors inhabited underground dwellings that could be seen from above as small mounds arranged in rings in the purple, vermilion, and tan grasses of the plains. During a visit to Vortex by Admiral Ackbar and Leia Organa Solo, Ackbar's sabotaged B-wing crashed into and destroyed the centuries-old Cathedral of Winds and killed at least 358 Vors. A different, more streamlined cathedral was then constructed by the Vors as a replacement.

**Vorzyd 4** The homeworld of the Vorzydiak species and fourth planet in the Vorzyd system, it was known as the manufacturing center of the Vorzyd Cluster, producing much of its food and durable goods. Some 11 years before the Battle of Naboo, the Jedi Council was asked to mediate a dispute between Vorzyd 4 and its neighbor, Vorzyd 5. The Vorzydiaks of Vorzyd 4 claimed that the natives of Vorzyd 5 did not want to work for their credits, yet wanted to control the Vorzyd Cluster. The leadership of Vorzyd 4 was unaware that the Freelies were behind the sabotage. Ultimately, the work of Obi-Wan Kenobi and Qui-Gon Jinn helped bring the Freelies and Chairman Port together, and peace was restored both on Vorzyd 4 and between Vorzyd 4 and Vorzyd 5.

**Vorzyd 5** Known as the Gambler's World during the reign of Emperor Palpatine, Vorzyd 5 was a casino-covered planet allowed to operate its establishments in order to collect gambling money for the Empire. Dozens of spacegoing holopanels and billboards announced the planet's location throughout the system. The various gamblers and partygoers who visited were a mix of the richest and most influential beings in the galaxy, all there to wager their credits in games of chance. Many of the games were heavily rigged. Simon Greyshade was the Senator of the Vorzyd sector during the last years of the Republic. Luke Skywalker and Leia Organa attempted to disrupt the operation shortly after the Battle of Yavin, but were captured in the attempt. They were rescued by Rebel Alliance supporters.

Quinlan Vos

**Vos, Quinlan** A Kiffar Jedi who trained Aayla Secura and earned fame during the Clone Wars. Vos's parents, Quian and Pethros, were members of the Guardians of Kiffu, but were killed by a group of rogue Anzati under the command of Volfe Karkko. As a Padawan, Quinlan trained alongside Obi-Wan Kenobi and fought during the Stark Hyperspace Conflict. His psychometric ability to read memories from objects was strong, and Vos was promoted to Jedi Knight after an apprenticeship served under Jedi Master Tholme. Vos took the Twi'lek Aayla Secura as his own Padawan, but she was captured on Nar Shaddaa by her uncle Pol Secura. While investigating, Vos's memory was erased with an overdose of glitteryll, and it took him months to regain his mind. Mace Windu and Saesee Tiin later ordered him to infiltrate the planet Dathomir and investigate the Infinity Gates of the Kwa. Vos was recalled to Kiffu by his aunt, the Sheyf Tinté Vos, to investigate attacks by the Anzati. The trail led to the prison world of Kiffex, where the Dark Jedi Volfe Karkko had enslaved Aayla Secura. With the help of Master Tholme, Vos defeated Karkko but left Kiffu with the Devaronian con artist Vilmarh Grahrk. He later teamed with Secura to rescue Master Tholme from Morgukai warriors Tsyr and Bok on Kintan. Upon returning to Coruscant, Quinlan Vos was elevated to the rank of Jedi Master.

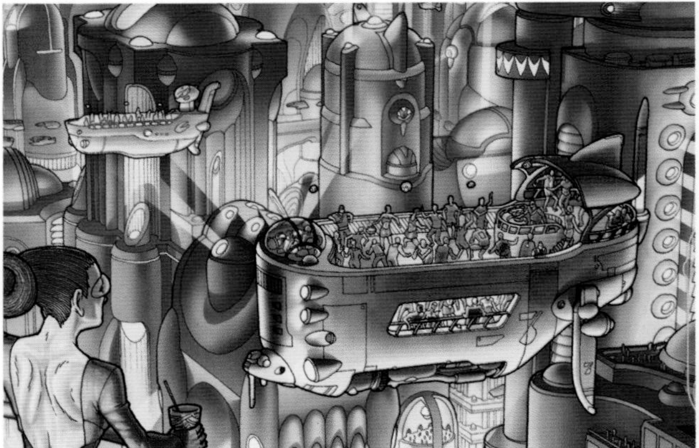

Vorzyd 5

After the start of the Clone Wars, Vos decided that the best way to help was to infiltrate the Separatists. He adopted the alias of Korto Vos and tracked down Count Dooku on Antar 4, doing what was necessary to win the Count's trust. Vos learned that Dooku had been negotiating with Sheyf Tinté for the rights to establish a Separatist base on Kiffu, but when Dooku ordered Tinté's death, Vos killed Kadrian Sey before she could assassinate his aunt. Dooku apprehended them and forced Vos to read Tinté's mind—where he learned that she had sacrificed his parents to Volfe Karkko. Unable to control his anger, he cut her down with a lightsaber. The Jedi Order feared that this marked a turn to the dark side, but Vos remained convinced that it was merely a necessary aspect of his cover identity.

Some six months before the First Battle of Coruscant, Vos was reunited with Obi-Wan Kenobi aboard the *Titavian IV.* The pair barely escaped from Asajj Ventress and Skorr, and Vos accompanied Kenobi to Rendili. After his efforts to end the Rendili Fleet Crisis, Vos was allowed to rejoin the Jedi Order. Unknown to all, Vos's actions were part of a larger plan designed by Count Dooku to have Vos return to the Jedi Order as a double agent. Vos, however, planned to double-cross the Count, hoping to use his position with the Separatists to locate the second Sith Lord working with Dooku. Information gathered from Saljé Tasha led Vos to believe that the second Sith was Sora Bulq, and Vos agreed to serve as Oppo Rancisis's second in command at the Siege of Saleucami. There, he assumed command of the mission when Bulq killed Rancisis and created his own battle plan, allowing him to eliminate Sora Bulq.

In the wake of the battle on Saleucami, after learning that Khaleen Hentz was pregnant with his child, Vos vowed to leave the Jedi Order at the end of the Clone Wars. He led clone troopers on Boz Pity, and was then dispatched to Kashyyyk as part of the task force led by Jedi Master Yoda. When his clone troopers received Order 66, Vos was hit with a blast from a Republic tank. He killed Commander Faie despite his injuries and was saved by the timely arrival of Vilmarh Grahrk. The Devaronian took Vos away from Kashyyyk, and about eight months later they set out in search of Khaleen. They found her back on Kashyyyk with Jedi Masters Tholme and T'ra Saa, hiding in the jungles with the Palsaang clan of Wookiees. There, Vos met his son, Korto, for the first time.

**Vos, Tinté** A Kiffar woman who led the Guardians of Kiffu as Sheyf during the last decades of the Republic. She hated that her nephew Quinlan Vos was taken to Coruscant for Jedi training, wishing instead that he had

Tinté Vos

been trained as a Guardian. Shortly after the Battle of Naboo, Sheyf Tinté demanded that Quinlan investigate why feral Anzati were suddenly attacking the Kiffu. But the Jedi Council learned that Tinté was incarcerating political prisoners on Kiffex, in violation of an agreement with the Republic. Mace Windu, Plo Koon, and Adi Gallia arrived to remedy the situation, as well as to rescue the Jedi already on Kiffex. Sheyf Tinté remained free and was approached by Count Dooku about establishing a Separatist base on Kiffu. Dooku's new agent Quinlan Vos prevented her death, but when Dooku ordered him to read Tinté's mind, he learned that she had been responsible for the deaths of his parents at the hands of the murderous Anzati Volfe Karkko. In a rage, he killed her with a lightsaber.

**Vosa, Komari** A Jedi apprentice under Count Dooku who was involved in the confrontation between the Jedi and the Mandalorians at Galidraan. Dooku refused to allow her to participate in Jedi trials due to her instability. She later went to Baltizaar to fight the Bando Gora cult but did not return from the mission and was presumed dead. She reemerged as the head of the Bando Gora, using neurotoxin-laced death sticks to turn people into slaves. Vosa believed that the Jedi Order had abandoned her and set out to exact revenge. Her weapons of choice were a pair of curved lightsabers. The Bando Gora was smashed by Jango Fett, who pursued Vosa to collect a bounty posted by Count Dooku and confronted her on Kohlma. After her defeat at Fett's hands, Dooku killed her.

Komari Vosa

**voxyn** A Yuuzhan Vong–bioengineered creature derived from vornskrs and created to hunt Jedi. A voxyn stood no higher than a human waist and was more than 4 meters long, with a flattish head and an undulating body covered in scales. A line of coarse sensory bristles ran down its spine, and a barb protruded from its flickering whip of a tail. Voxyn had yellow eyes and a long forked tongue. They were capable of spitting a jet of acidic brown saliva and could stun their prey with sonic blasts. The Yuuzhan Vong created new voxyn through cloning, grown from a voxyn queen located on a worldship orbiting Myrkr. The Solo children led a Jedi strike team to kill the voxyn queen, a mission that resulted in the death of Anakin Solo.

Voxyn

**Vram** An obnoxious young bully, he was one of Lord Hethrir's helpers and informed on the other students at the Empire Youth Camp.

**Vratix** Highly intelligent insectoid beings from Thyferra, they outnumbered the human population many times over. Humans controlled the bacta corporations, but the Verachen, a type of Vratix, actually made the product. The Vratix, mantis-like with six appendages, used their sense of touch often in social interactions, finding it to be the most reliable of the senses. They were hermaphroditic and very long-lived. They lived in modest harvester tribes within the rain forests, in dwellings made from mud and saliva. The mud was created by the Knytix, a domesticated servant species resembling the Vratix, but smaller. Each village had several high towers amid the gloan trees, with circular terraces and arching bridges connecting the towers. Vratix could share thoughts with fellow Vratix whom they knew well.

Vratix

The Vratix governed themselves through a representative council that was led by two canirs. Three major political parties evolved: the Zaltin, the Xucphra, and the Ashern Circle. The strong pro-human sentiments that permeated the Zaltin and Xucphra factions led to the labeling of the Ashern as terrorists. Although the Ashern were widely considered to have been responsible for the contamination of certain lots of bacta during the height of the New Order, this was seen as a ruse to cover up an internal struggle.

The Ashern, through the Vratix Qlaern Hirf, petitioned Wedge Antilles to sponsor their admittance to the New Republic, but the move was placed in limbo when Ysanne Isard took control of Thyferra. Eventually, the Vratix expelled the human leaders of the bacta cartel and took control of Thyferra's production facilities.

At the height of the Swarm War, the Vratix government was targeted by the Colony for a military coup in an effort to draw the Galactic Alliance into fighting smaller battles and leaving the Utegetu Nebula unguarded. The Colony then could have launched a full-scale attack on the Chiss. The plans of the Colony were discovered by Han and Leia Organa Solo, but their warning arrived too late: Thyferra swiftly fell to the Killiks, and the Vratix became Joiners. At war's end, however, the Vratix resumed control of their planet.

**vrelt** A Corellian scavenger, it lived in urban alleys and garbage dumps. A large, rat-like beast with sharp teeth and claws, it was a favored prey of the tabaga.

**Vriss, Commander** A New Republic admiral, he accompanied Rogue Squadron to Morishim as an escort for Garm Bel Iblis, who was inspecting a starfighter base there. The mission turned to combat when Imperial Captain Vermel tried to deliver Admiral Pellaeon's surrender declaration, but the Imperial CR90 corvette was intercepted by agents of Moff Disra.

**Vri'syk, Peshk** A Bothan and member of Rogue Squadron, Vri'syk was killed and his X-wing fighter destroyed during the disastrous raid on Borleias.

***V'sett*-class fighter** A starfighter created by the Ssi-ruuk as a follow-on to the droid-controlled *Swarm*-class fighter, it had superior firepower and maneuverability, and was piloted by a living being. The ships had exceptional shielding systems that Emperor Palpatine desired for the Imperial fleet.

**Vua'spar interdictor** A Yuuzhan Vong interdictor developed during the war. Resembling two huge cones connected at their bases, the 908-meter-long Vua'spar interdictor was equipped with three enormous dovin basals for generating a gravity well that could drag ships out of hyperspace. The strength of this gravity well could disrupt the brain-wave patterns of most sentient beings, rendering them unconscious for several minutes after their ship reverted to realspace. These capabilities, coupled with yorik coral arms that housed a full wing of 36 coralskippers, made the Vua'spar a deadly addition to the Yuuzhan Vong fleet. The Vua'spar was crewed by 638 warriors and could transport up to 1,144 troops and 17,450 metric tons of cargo. It was armed with 20 plasma projectors and a forward-mounted heavy plasma projector, and it was protected by a collection of smaller dovin basals.

**Vuffi Raa** A highly polished chromium astrogation/pilot droid, he traveled with Lando Calrissian for at least a year shortly after the gambler had won the *Millennium Falcon.* Vuffi Raa was technically Lando's property since Lando had won him in a game of sabacc. But after a few adventures together, Calrissian came to regard the droid as his friend.

Vuffi Raa was a member of an ancient droid species known as the Silentium that hailed from outside the known galaxy. He stood 1 meter tall, with five multijointed tentacle limbs that he could move at various angles and even prop himself up with to achieve more height. Vuffi Raa had the shape of an attenuated starfish with manipulators that served as both arms and legs. These were connected to a dinner-plate-sized pentagonal torso with a single, softly glowing, deep red vision crystal.

Vuffi Raa had a complex history, from his creation as a galaxy-exploring scout by an extremely powerful being known only as the One to his ownership by Imperial spy and anthropologist Osuno Whett. The academic used a disguised and reprogrammed Vuffi Raa in his scheme to have the Empire conquer the inhabitants of the Renatasian system, a subjugation that led to the deaths of two-thirds of the system's inhabitants. After Vuffi Raa reverted to his original programming, he helped Calrissian defeat Whett's boss Rokur Gepta in the defense of the ThonBoka. Calrissian then gave the droid his freedom to roam the galaxy.

Vuffi Raa

**Vulatan** An old Jedi Master, he worked with Yoda and Gra'aton to recover the *Chu'unthor* after it crashed into the swamps of Dathomir some 300 years prior to the Battle of Yavin.

**Vulgarr** A king of the Duloks on Endor, he devised a plan to capture all the Ewok children, eat their flesh, and turn their hides into pouches. After Teebo and the Grundakk defeated the Duloks, Logray ordered that Vulgarr be planted in the ground feetfirst. Over the years, he grew into a twisted, gnarled tree to serve as a reminder to the other Duloks to keep away from the Ewoks.

***Vulnerator*** An older Galactic Alliance *Victory*-class Star Destroyer, it was part of the Fifth Battle Group during the Confederation–GA War. At Kashyyyk during the Battle of Kuat, the *Vulnerator* was discovered to have the surprising ability to locate and shoot down StealthX fighters.

**Vulpter** The homeworld of the Vulptereen species. Vulpter was located on the border between the Deep Core and the Core Worlds and was the third and primary world in the Vulpter system. At one point, it was a temperate world covered with grasslands and forests. Over time, the Vulptereens urbanized the planet, turning it into a smog-covered sphere of barren wastes and dingy industrial centers. Around the Battle of Naboo, the planet was overtaken by the Trade Federation and turned into a dumping ground for the products the Trade Federation couldn't sell anywhere else. The native Vulptereens were put to work drilling vast tunnels to serve as storage facilities, and anything that was deemed too large or toxic to store on the planet was launched into orbit. This created a ring of debris around Vulpter, primarily made up of old adverstising materials, that choked out natural sunlight. Eventually, the Vulptereen population found it could no longer produce its own food. During the New Order, Vulpter suffered even more after the Empire shut down access to the Deep Core. The natives perished by the millions, until Rebel Alliance agents arrived and exchanged food for land. The Vulptereens set out to restore their homeworld, using technologies proven successful on worlds such as Duro.

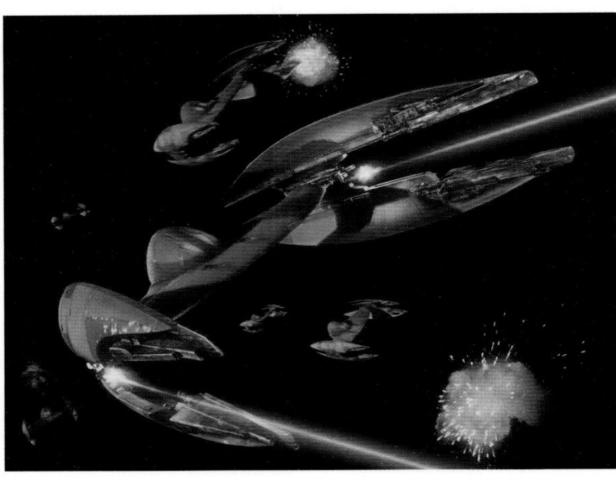
Vulture droid

**Vulptereen** A species native to Vulpter. These squat-bodied beings had long, tusk-studded snouts and large, protruding teeth along with pointed ears, clawed hands, and a single snout antenna. They were noted for their prowess in producing such machines as Podracer engines, but unfettered industry turned Vulpter into a smog-choked industrial wasteland. The Podracer Dud Bolt was a Vulptereen.

**Vultan** An ancient warrior species some 4,000 years before the Galactic Civil War, one of its members was Jedi Oss Wilum.

**Vultar Cataclysm** An event that occurred 4,250 years before the Battle of Yavin during the Third Great Schism between the Jedi Order and the followers of the dark side of the Force. After the dark siders were expelled from Coruscant, they fled to Vultar and the ancient technology of the Cosmic Turbine. The exiles could not control the Turbine and died when the planet Vultar and its surrounding star system were destroyed.

**vulture droid** This was the common name for the Variable Geometry Self-Propelled Battle Droid starfighter used by the Trade Federation during the last years of the Old Republic. Designed by the Xi Char order, it was a small starfighter with a pair of wings mounted to a wing-like fuselage. Lozenge-shaped weapons emplacements were mounted on the tips of the wings and could split open in combat to reveal additional weapons systems. A small knob in the center of the fuselage held the droid brain that acted as the ship's pilot. When not in flight, the ship's systems transformed the fighter into a walking weapons platform.

The starfighter measured 3.5 meters long when in flight mode and was armed with four blaster cannons and two torpedo launchers. Its main drawback was that it could remain active for only 35 minutes before it required refueling and would go into standby if it lost contact with the control ship for more than 12 seconds. If it was out of contact for more than six minutes, the ship would self-destruct. Those problems were overcome by sheer numbers, as there were 1,500 vultures aboard every

V-wing airspeeder

Trade Federation battleship. Designed for both atmospheric and space flight, they could attain speeds of 1,200 kilometers per hour in atmosphere. They were used extensively in the Clone Wars because they were cheap to mass-produce. They often augmented squadrons of tri-fighters and HMP droid gunships in battle. At the height of the Clone Wars, it was estimated that there were nearly a billion vulture droids in operation, as part of the quintillions of battle droids that made up the Separatist armed forces. Like all Separatist war machines, the vulture droids were shut down after Darth Vader destroyed the Separatist leaders on Mustafar.

Vurk

**Vulvarch** A planet some 34 light-years from Teyr. Twelve years after the Battle of Endor, Luke Skywalker discovered that the starliner *Star Morning,* belonging to the Fallanassi religious order, had spent the last few months in Farana, but had recently arrived at Vulvarch.

**Vurd, Kyood** An Ugnaught who owned a cantina on Nar Shaddaa during the years surrounding the Battle of Naboo. He traveled in a modified backpack, carried by an immense, green-skinned alien who also served as Vurd's bodyguard. Vurd feared the Jedi and purchased his bodyguards from slavers who guaranteed the beings to be immune from Jedi mind tricks.

**Vurk** An alien species native to the planet Sembla. A Vurk was distinguished by the pointed crest that rose from the back of his or her skull, curving up to half a meter in length. Their hands had three thick fingers and an opposable thumb, and the average Vurk stood more than 2 meters tall. Because the planet Sembla was constantly being remade due to volcanic activity, the Vurks evolved into efficient nomads and were regarded in the galaxy as a primitive people. Vurks resembled amphibians and gave birth underwater, and Vurk midwives were held in high esteem. The species escaped any lasting impact from the Yuuzhan Vong invasion, primarily because its homeworld was located well off most hyperspace travel routes.

**Vuul** This Bri'ahlian served as the President of his homeworld during the Clone Wars. He was a strong supporter of the Republic and was one of Padmé Amidala's close friends. He survived an assassination attempt on Bri'ahl when the droids R2-D2 and C-3PO disobeyed Padmé's orders and foiled the would-be killers.

**vuv Tertarrnek, Dælar** This Covallon was one of the Rebel Alliance's deepest cover agents, pretending to be the pet of Moff Harlov Jarnek. Vuv Tertarrnek understood everything the Moff said and was able to provide the Alliance with a bounty of information on troop and starship movements in Tandon sector.

**V-wing airspeeder** An atmospheric attack craft, it played a major part in the New Republic's defense of the planet Mon Calamari and in at least a dozen other battles against Imperial forces. V-wings were light combat airspeeders, as fast as standard Rebel combat airspeeders but with a much higher flight ceiling—about 100 kilometers. With a scramjet booster kicking in, the craft could achieve a top speed of 1,400 kilometers an hour, although sudden maneuvers at that speed could tear the ship apart.

The only weapon aboard a V-wing was a double laser cannon with an effective range of 2 kilometers. A pilot had minimal protection, and survivability was low despite an ejection system. V-wings could be deployed to planetary bases or capital starships. They were typically used for combat against incoming enemy fighters or in surprise raids. In the Battle of Mon Calamari, V-wings proved devastating against the Empire's new TIE/D fighters and water-based amphibions.

**V-wing starfighter** A starfighter, officially designated the Alpha-3 Nimbus, produced by Kuat Drive Yards during the final years of the Republic. The fighter was developed by Walex Blissex to improve upon the Delta-7 Aethersprite. Though designed for law enforcement agencies, the V-wing was also available in a civilian model. During the Clone Wars, thousands of V-wings were used in the Republic fleet, augmenting the ARC-170 fighters. The V-wing was a needle-shaped craft that maneuvered with the assistance of four movable wings, which also served to help the craft dissipate excess heat during combat. It measured just 7.9 meters in length, with a maximum wingspan of 3.8 meters. Each fighter was armed with a pair of twin laser cannons and required a pilot and a Q7 series astromech to operate. Because of their small size, most V-wings were unable to accommodate a hyperdrive system. Only those produced as escorts for Emperor Palpatine's personal *Theta*-class shuttle were given hyperdrives, but these were limited-capacity versions that needed input from the shuttle to manage jumps.

V-wing starfighter

VXL speeder

**VXL speeder** One of the largest and most elaborate two-being landspeeders ever produced in the galaxy. Originally manufactured many decades before the Clone Wars, the VXL speeder had a bulbous shape reminiscent of a large animal. Its nose was covered with a prow that gave it the appearance of an ancient, oceangoing vessel, and the front end was protected by a heavy bumper that supported two headlights. Two exhaust pipes sprouted from the front of the speeder and curved toward the rear. The main drive section was located at the rear, and three directional signals were placed above the main engine. These signals were housed in an arching fin that curved back to a point, giving the VXL speeder an ungainly yet speedy appearance.

**vynock** An atmosphere-breathing version of the mynock, this leathery black flying creature was silicon-based. The species evolved in the vacuum of space and fed on energy.

Vynock

**w-165 Planetary Turbolaser** Designed by Kuat Drive Yards, this ground-based turbolaser emplacement was used for planetary defense. It had roughly four times the power of the v-150 Planetary Defender ion cannon, and was capable of destroying an *Imperial*-class Star Destroyer in orbit.

**Wa, Orun** A Kaminoan who was one of the original administrators of clone trooper production for the Grand Army of the Republic, Orun Wa asked Jango Fett to determine what to do with the first six troopers removed from the clone vats. It was these six who were taken under the wing of Kal Skirata and eventually became the so-called *Null*-class ARC troopers.

**Wa, Stieg** A brash young pilot assigned to transport Qui-Gon Jinn and Xanatos to Telos, Stieg continually needled Xanatos about living the sheltered life of a Jedi. Their ship was attacked by pirates who infested the Landor system, and Stieg was taken prisoner. He blamed the attack on Xanatos.

**WA-7** *See* Flo.

**WA-7 series** A unipod service droid produced by Go-Corp/Utilitech beginning nearly 100 years before the Clone Wars, it was used mainly in restaurants and other food service operations. The design was heavily influenced by the Mondeo Modernist design movement, which emphasized streamlined contours and whimsical embellishment. The WA-7 moved about on a single-wheeled unipod, an inspiration of fancy that gave the droid its distinct form. The use of curved fins on the cranium and a decorative skirt gave it an even more fanciful silhouette. A unique gyro-balance system kept the droid upright even while it was moving swiftly among tables, customers, and kitchen staff. Advanced communications programming and facial-recognition software allowed the WA-7 to interact with customers and even remember the regulars. After production ended, these exceptionally well-built droids remained in service for decades.

*WA-7 series*

**Wac, Dar** A Rodian aide to Chancellor Palpatine during the last years of the Old Republic. Dar Wac was responsible for maintaining the Chancellor's schedule. After Senator Onaconda Farr of Rodia was implicated in rerouting warships away from Duro, Dar Wac was investigated by the Senate Bureau of Intelligence on the chance that the Rodians had been working together. Wac was later cleared of any charges.

**Wadda** A humanoid employee of Zlarb the slaver during the early years of the New Order, Wadda came from a species of which little was known, since few of its members became integrated into galactic society. Wadda was strong and nearly 2.2 meters tall, with glossy brown skin, a jutting forehead, and protruding vestigial horns. When Han Solo and Chewbacca were able to turn the tables on Zlarb, Wadda was one of the handful of slavers who were themselves enslaved after Solo turned them over to a group of Lurrian geneticists.

**Wagg** A New Republic operative who was the captain of the transport ship *Meridian,* he worked for Hiram Drayson as part of the Alpha Blue team.

**Waggral** A security officer with the Gepparin Landing Control force, he worked for the Blood-Scar pirates during the Galactic Civil War. Mara Jade visited the base during her investigation of Moff Glovstoak and had to use the Force to prevent Waggral from killing her pirate escort.

**Waglla, Noy** This small, spider-like Hyallp worked for Jabba the Hutt as a spy and mercenary. The Hutt employed her to kill the t'landa Til priests of Colony Four on Ylesia shortly before the Battle of Ylesia.

**Waivers List** A Corporate Sector Authority register, it listed ships that were exempt from the multitude of vessel requirements usually imposed on spacecraft entering Authority-controlled space.

**Wake, Russell** An aging security officer in Ussa on Bellassa, he met young Ferus Olin and agreed to give him and several members of the Eleven 15 minutes to get into the city's Imperial facilities to gather information about the Bellassan Project and the so-called Twilight operation. Darth Vader, who had been monitoring Olin's movements, later confronted Wake and used the Force to choke the life out of him.

**Wakiza** Located in the Koornacht Cluster, it was one of the primary worlds of the Yevethan species and a member of the Duskhan League. It was the location of an orbital Imperial repair yard code-named Black Eight, serving the Empire's Black Sword Command. After the Battle of Endor, the Empire retreated from the shipyards of Wakiza, Zhina, and N'zoth, and the Yevetha were able to capture several of their capital ships. The Black Eight shipyards later were moved away from Wakiza to a clandestine location. The New Republic attacked Wakiza during the Battle of N'zoth.

**Walalla** A New Republic member world in the Seventh Security Zone, it had been brutally conquered by the Empire and its inhabitants cruelly

*Dar Wac*

< *Wampa ice creature*

Wallen (right) keeps Luke Skywalker in view.

persecuted. Senator Tig Peramis represented Walalla and the other worlds of the zone in the New Republic Senate. Twelve years following the Battle of Endor, after Nil Spaar protested the treatment of his Yevethan delegation at the hands of Chief of State Leia Organa Solo, Peramis submitted an Article of Withdrawal from the New Republic on behalf of Walalla. Nara Deega, a Bith from Clak'dor VII, was seated in his place on the Defense Council. Peramis later passed secret New Republic fleet movement information along to Nil Spaar on N'zoth, which allowed the Yevetha to capture General Han Solo.

Walluga

**Wald** A Rodian boy who was one of young Anakin Skywalker's playmates during his time in Mos Espa on Tatooine. Wald was just six years old when the Boonta Eve Podrace that Anakin won took place. He doubted that Anakin possessed any special abilities, so he placed large bets against him with some ill-gotten gains. Years later, Wald attended the wedding of Cliegg Lars and Shmi Skywalker. After working for Watto for many years, he took over the Toydarian's salvage business when he retired. Later, he provided Leia Organa Solo with information on how to find Kitster Banai and the *Killik Twilight* moss-painting he had stolen.

**Waleran** An Imperial lieutenant serving under Captain Vharing aboard the *Interrogator,* he was promoted to brevet captain by High Inquisitor Tremayne after Vharing's execution.

***Walerv*** This Corellian vessel was one of five Rebel Alliance gunships sent to Bakura following the Battle of Endor.

***Walker*** This Imperial treasury ship was destroyed during the Galactic Civil War by six Rebel Alliance X-wing fighters. The loss led to the design and construction of the Nebulon-B frigate to protect Imperial convoys.

**walker** *See* All Terrain Armored Transport; All Terrain Scout Transport.

**Wallanooga the Hutt** A one-eyed Hutt on Tatooine, he purchased Aurra Sing from a group of Sennex pirates and sent her to the Anzati for training as an assassin. After completing her education, Sing killed Wallanooga and escaped. Wallanooga, known alternatively as both Walla and Nooga, had been a tough old Hutt with a patch over his left eye and extensive interests in the ongoing Outer Rim slave trade that the Republic never seemed able to stamp out.

**Wallen** This Imperial sergeant served as a stormtrooper garrisoned on the Forest Moon of Endor during the construction of the second Death Star. He was assigned to Colonel Dyer's command.

**walluga** Among the deadliest creatures on Kashyyyk, the walluga used its powerful limbs to stomp and smash its enemies. These legs also allowed the beast to travel at great speeds to avoid any more powerful creatures it might encounter in the wilds.

**wampa ice creature** A fearsome and carnivorous predator, the wampa stalked the snow-packed wastes of the planet Hoth. An imposing 2 meters tall, the two-legged ice creature was covered with shaggy white fur. It had eerie yellow eyes and sharp claws and teeth. Solitary creatures for the most part, wampas carved their lairs out of the ice, forming huge caves in which to nest. When they hunted, they often took their prey by surprise thanks to the natural camouflage provided by their white fur. A wampa's primary source of food was tauntauns. But since life was scarce on Hoth, it was estimated that a single wampa roamed a territory of more than 100 square kilometers in search of food. Wampas never hunted when hungry. Instead, they captured living prey and stored it in their ice caves for later consumption. Rebel hero Luke Skywalker was wounded by a wampa while patrolling Hoth during the Galactic Civil War and had another nasty encounter with a ferocious band years later.

***Wanderhome*** This modified Gallofree Yards medium transport was one of many civilian ships used to help the New Republic transfer refugees from planets that had been attacked by the Yuuzhan Vong. Its initial attempt to reach Ralltiir with Ryn and Ranats aboard was thwarted by the invaders, but it eventually made it with the help of a group of freelance operatives.

**wander-kelp** A cross between a plant and an animal native to Chad III, this kelp had minimal intelligence but moved under its own volition. Wander-kelp's mass of iodine-filled leaves could be sheared several times a year, distilled, and sold for medicinal purposes. The rest of a wander-kelp's biomass often was used as cheap protein fiber for animal feed.

**wandrella** A huge worm-like beast, it lived in the rain forests of the planet Circarpus V (Mimban). A wandrella was an omnivore with pale, cream-colored flesh streaked with slashes of brown. The creature's blunt end was covered with eyespots and a ferocious mouth filled with sharp, black teeth. It moved by using suction organs located on its underside.

Wampa ice creature

**Wann, Roland** The Old Republic's representative on Manaan during the era of the Great Sith War some 4,000 years before the Battle of Yavin. He provided information to Bastila Shan and Carth Onasi on the location of the Sith lair on Manaan, then helped them reach Hrakert Station.

**Wannschok** An expanse of desert and volcanic lands on Kintan, home of the Kajain'sa'Nikto or red Nikto, it also was known as the Endless Wastes. Quinlan Vos and Aayla Secura were ambushed by Morgukai warriors at Grid 45 Delta Slash Gamma 395 in the Endless Wastes.

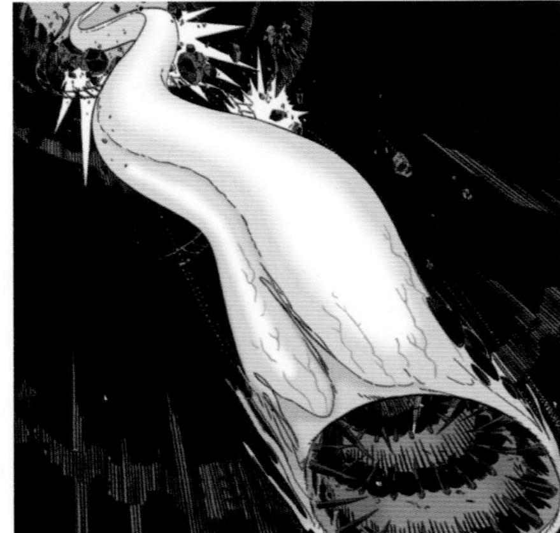

Wandrella

**Wann Tsir** This planet was placed under siege following the Battle of Endor. During the attack, Imperial Commander Titus Klev discovered and stopped a Rebel Alliance agent who was trying to bring down the planet's shields, which earned him commendations from Imperial command.

**Wanuri** An employment officer for the Blackwater Systems factory on his homeworld of Falleen following the Battle of Naboo. He agreed to provide janitorial jobs to Obi-Wan Kenobi and Anakin Skywalker during their search for Granta Omega and his band of criminals.

**Waoabi, Ooamu** An old Ithorian who led the Council of Ithorian Elders, a delegation that petitioned the Reconstruction Authority to find a planet suitable for Ithorian settlement following the destruction of their homeworld during the Yuuzhan Vong War. His pleas fell on deaf ears, so he met with Leia Organa Solo to discuss relocation to Woteba, a planet she had discovered in the Unknown Regions. When Cal Omas demanded a resolution to the conflict between the Killik Colony and the Chiss, Leia gave up Woteba as more suitable for the relocation of the Killik Qoribu hives. Waoabi reluctantly agreed to this arrangement, and Organa Solo petitioned Omas to repeal the RePlanetHab claim to the planet Borao in return.

**Warb** A Corellian hyperdrive mechanic, he was an assistant to Shug Ninx in his garage on Nar Shaddaa.

**warbeast** Large, ferocious flying creatures from the moon of Dxun, they first hunted and later were tamed by the outcasts of society on the planet Onderon. They were used as war machines by the beast-riders of Onderon.

**War Council Advisory Panel** An advisory group formed by Chancellor Palpatine to provide advice and direction during the Clone Wars. It was responsible for planning the operations and deployment of clone trooper specialists, something the Jedi Order had done previously.

**Ward, Llats** A mercenary handpicked by Jango Fett to train clones on the ocean world of Kamino. Everything in the life of Llats Ward revolved around battle and war. He studied and memorized the campaigns of all the great Mandalorian leaders of the past, and used these lessons to enhance his clone troopers' fighting skills.

**Warden Squadron** One of General Salm's Y-wing bomber squadrons serving the New Republic, it was part of Defender Wing.

***Warder*** A New Republic medical frigate, it was assigned to Han Solo and the *Mon Remonda* during the hunt for Warlord Zsinj.

**war droid** Older mechanicals designed specifically for combat before the formation of the Galactic Republic, they were also called war robots. War droids had heavy armor plating, inefficient power-delivery systems, and less intelligence and self-awareness than their more sophisticated descendants. Old war droids could be found operating in isolated and remote sections of the galaxy for thousands of years. Later versions employed self-healing metals, point-of-impact shields, and fast-reaction servo systems.

War droids employed by Xim the Despot were 3 meters tall and roughly humanoid in shape. They were armed with a pair of pulse cannons and were protected by heavy armor plating coated with a kiirium sheen. During the Freedon Nadd Uprising 4,000 years before the Galactic Civil War, the Naddists employed specialized Sith war droids that, although antiquated, were imbued with dark Force energy. Soon after, the great Jedi gathering on Mount Meru was attacked by a legion of war droids controlled by the dark side Krath cult. Many millennia later during the Yuuzhan Vong War, when the invaders entered Hutt space and began conquering planets, their attacks triggered the fail-safe mechanisms in several hundred war robots that had been thought to be simply statues. The automata destroyed thousands of Yuuzhan Vong warriors before they were stopped.

*Warbeast*

*War droid*

***Warhawk*** A Rebel Alliance MC40a light Mon Calamari cruiser that attempted to disable the *Harpax* in the Ottega system.

**warkeeper** A 22-meter-long, slug-like Yuuzhan Vong creature, it had an armored shell studded with spiny growths capable of firing plasma globs. Warkeepers were implanted with dovin basals for defense. A warkeeper was designed to act as a protector and defender to a thrall herder, and warriors commanding the warkeeper had to keep thralls from wandering into range of the dovin basal gravity fields and being consumed.

**Warlin** This Acherin male was the only survivor of a group of Eluthans who were rescued from an Imperial prison by the freedom fighter known as Flame during the early months of the New Order. When Clive Flax arrived on Acherin to learn more about Flame's history, he hoped to meet with Warlin, but the survivor had been killed shortly before by a group of Eluthans who believed that he was a spy.

**Warlord** The only name given to the mysterious former leader of the tribes of Kariek. Because he always dressed in ornate armor, no members of the planet's Lakra or Eickarie species had ever seen what the Warlord looked like. He took control of the planet about four years after the Battle of Naboo, ruling through wanton violence. It wasn't until 22 years after the Battle of Endor that the United Tribes of Kariek sought and got assistance from the Imperial 501st Legion to end the Warlord's reign of terror.

**Warlug** A Gamorrean, he was a guard for Jabba the Hutt.

**warmaster** A Yuuzhan Vong rank second only to that of Supreme Overlord. Tsavong Lah was the warmaster during the time of the Yuuzhan Vong invasion; his father, Czulkang Lah, had been warmaster before Tsavong forced him to step down. According to legend, the first warmaster created by the god Yun-Yuuzhan was not a Yuuzhan Vong but rather a living weapon-beast known as a vua'sa.

**warming unit** *See* condenser unit.

**war-mount** Heavily armed, flying weapons droids also known as Basilisk war droids, they served as battle mounts for Mandalorian warriors both on land and in space some four millennia before the Galactic Civil War. A Mandalorian rider was belted into a seat like a horseman, and directed the droid and its weapons from a control panel. Looking like a cross between a Karran beetle and a Zalorian rock-lion, the droids were created by the technologically minded Basiliskans, arrogant reptiloids who poisoned their planet during the Battle of Basilisk. Afterward, the tech-hungry Mandalorians looted countless war droids.

**Waroen** This Imperial Navy lieutenant served under Joak Drysso aboard the *Lusankya.* During the Battle of Thyferra, when Drysso threatened to ram the ship into the planet Thyferra, Waroen took matters into his own hands and shot Drysso. He then took command of the *Lusankya* and surrendered both ship and crew to the New Republic.

**Warok** An older Ewok and the father of Teebo and Malani, Warok led a group of Ewoks sent to res-

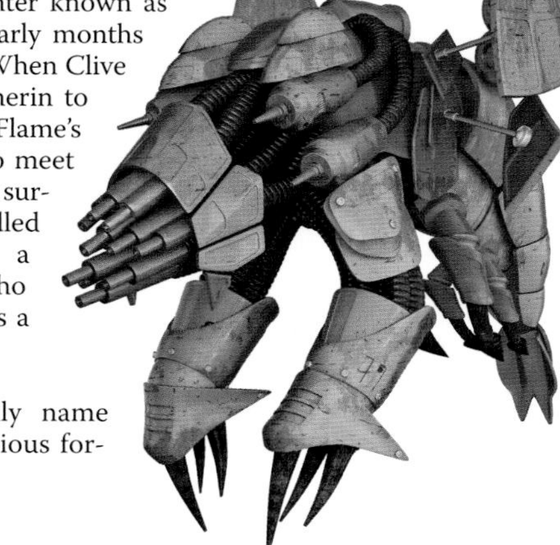

*War-mount*

cue their children from Vulgarr and the Duloks. Warok also participated in the Battle of Endor.

**Waroot** A species native to Ab'Bshingh, the Waroots were almost continually at war with the Farang throughout their history. Imperial strategists studied their lengthy and varied campaigns to create the board game B'shingh.

**Warren, Barosa** This Morellian was credited with founding the Galactic Outdoor Survival School.

**Warrick, Deej** A proud Ewok warrior and father, and the grandson of the legendary Ewok warrior Erpham Warrick. Deej lived in a small house on the surface of the Forest Moon of Endor, adjacent to the larger Bright Tree Village. He served his community faithfully for years, eventually earning a position in the Council of Elders that governed the village. Deej and his wife, Shodu, had four children: three sons, Weechee, Willy, and Wicket, and a daughter, Winda. Deej often grew concerned at his sons' foolhardy antics, particularly those of Wicket, whose adventures seemed to regularly get him into trouble. When Deej was overcome by exasperation, Shodu would gently remind him of his own recklessness as a youth.

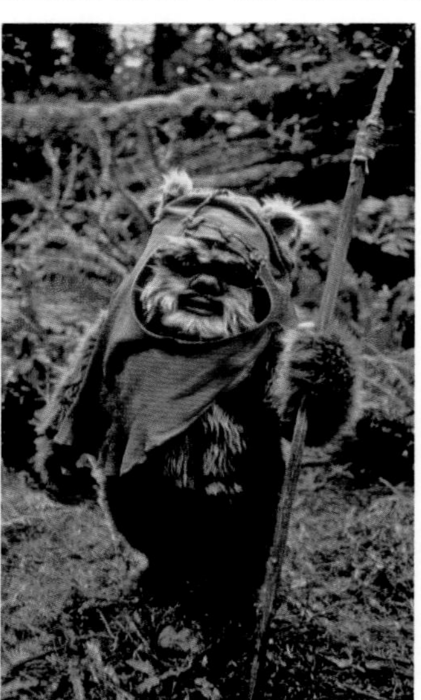

Wicket W. Warrick

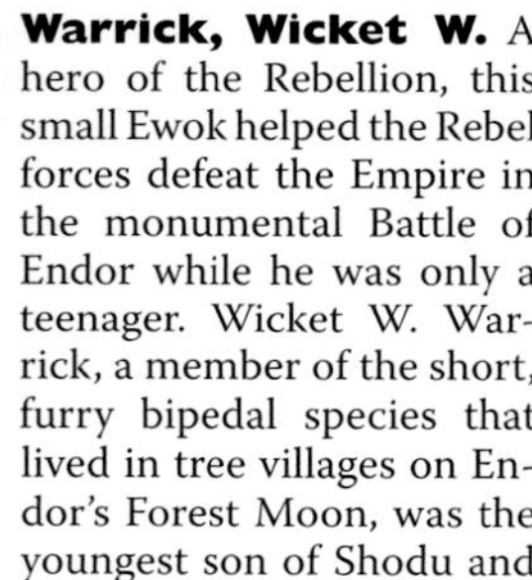

One day while fishing, Deej fell back while tugging at a particularly stubborn catch. He scraped himself against the razor-sharp fungus of a Rokna tree. The poison worked through his bloodstream, and he fell deathly ill. Logray examined him, and then instructed his sons to gather the necessary ingredients to concoct an antidote: the tail of a lantern bird, a frosch egg, and a star-shaped urchin plucked from the Dandelion Warriors. Deej's three sons split up to gather the elements, and managed to save Deej's life.

Deej had a deep love of the outdoors, and would often scout the neighboring forest by flying an animal-skin hang glider through the Endor skies. One day he and his sons Weechee and Willy discovered a pair of human children stranded on Endor. They helped Mace and Cindel Towani rescue their parents from the giant Gorax, and Deej was given the White Wings of Hope by Logray. Deej was later captured by the Sanyassan Marauders when they attacked the Towani camp. He was freed by Wicket, Cindel, and Noa, and helped defeat the Marauders.

**Warrick, Erpham** An Ewok warrior, he built the great Ewok battle wagon used to defeat the Duloks.

**Warrick, Shodu** The wife of Ewok warrior Deej, she was the mother of Weechee, Willy, Wicket, and Winda. Shodu was a skilled herbalist, able to concoct helpful medicine from local plant life to treat common ailments. When the marooned human children Mace and Cindel Towani came to her hut, Shodu prepared some medicine for the ailing little girl and helped clear Cindel's high fever.

**Warrick, Weechee** The oldest son of Deej and Shodu Warrick, Weechee was an adventuresome Ewok. He and his brother Willy were always exploring Endor's varied wilderness, often getting into trouble. His youngest brother, Wicket, idolized Weechee, but Weechee often was forced to leave Wicket behind when he felt that an adventure was too dangerous. When he and his father discovered the Towanis' crashed shuttle, they helped the children recover, and later helped them rescue their parents from the Gorax. He was given the Ewok Red Wings of Courage by Logray, as the eldest son accompanying Deej on the mission.

**Warrick, Wicket W.** A hero of the Rebellion, this small Ewok helped the Rebel forces defeat the Empire in the monumental Battle of Endor while he was only a teenager. Wicket W. Warrick, a member of the short, furry bipedal species that lived in tree villages on Endor's Forest Moon, was the youngest son of Shodu and Deej. Wicket always showed a greater-than-usual curiosity about the unknown, which eventually put him right in the middle of the Galactic Civil War.

In his younger days, Wicket and his friends had many skirmishes with the war-like Duloks; the evil Morag, a Tulgah Witch; giant Phlogs; the reptilian carnivorous froschs; and the semi-sentient Dandelion Warriors. When not contending with enemies, he gathered rainbow berries for the Harvest Moon Feast, shot arrows, went hang gliding or fishing, and rode Baga, his horse-like pet bordok. Wicket and the other Ewoks also helped a stranded family of humans, the Towanis, of whom only the young daughter Cindel survived.

When Imperials first came to Endor, the Ewoks were alarmed. Many wanted to declare war on them, but the Ewok leader, Chief Chirpa, reminded them that their spears couldn't hurt the Imperial fortresses, whereas the invaders had machines that could fly through the air or burn the forests. One night, as the villagers gathered around the fires, young Wicket recounted how he had witnessed an AT-ST stumble on the rocks, fall, and explode. The Ewoks realized they *did* have a way to fight back, and they started preparing for battle.

While on a foraging expedition, Wicket came across Princess Leia Organa, who had been thrown off a speeder bike during a chase with scout troopers and knocked unconscious. Although she initially frightened him, Wicket could sense her innate goodness. He returned with her to the village. Soon, Leia's companions—Han Solo, Chewbacca, Luke Skywalker, R2-D2, and C-3PO—were also brought to the village after they had been captured in an Ewok hunting net. Even though Wicket pleaded their case to Chief Chirpa, it took some Jedi tricks from Luke to free the Rebels. Wicket then played a key role in convincing the tribe to aid the offworlders.

Later, Han, Leia, and the droids were captured by the Empire. Wicket and the Ewoks battled the Imperials and their AT-ST walkers and helped to free their new allies so they could shut down the Death Star's shield generator. After Rebel Alliance pilots destroyed the second Death Star in orbit above Endor, the Ewoks held a celebration for the brave Alliance members. Wicket was given the Ewok title of lead warrior.

In the wake of the Battle of Endor, Wicket built his own home within the burned-out bunker of the Imperial garrison and eventually married his longtime friend Kneesaa. The pair returned to Bright Tree Village, and they both were elected to lead the community. Wicket himself was named tribal chief, succeeding Chirpa.

**Warrick, Widdle "Willy"** Willy, the more commonly used nickname of the Ewok named Widdle, was the second eldest of Deej and Shodu Warrick's children. He was plump, with a single-mindedness dominated by his appetite. Curious but not possessing the sharpest wit, he was often the butt of jokes among other young Ewoks. He and his older brother Weechee would often bicker and wrestle, but they were really great friends. Willy didn't have a lot of confidence in himself, and was often scared. But he proved his true bravery when he rescued Weechee, who hadn't come home after a rafting expedition.

**Warrick, Winda** The younger sister of Wicket W. Warrick, she was just a Wokling at the time of the Battle of Endor.

***Warrior*** A New Republic gunship assigned to the *Intrepid*'s fleet during the Black Fleet crisis, it intercepted the *Mud Sloth* carrying Luke Skywalker, Akanah, Wailu, and the Fallanassi when they arrived to create the illusion that there were more Republic warships.

**warrior caste** This Yuuzhan Vong social caste was made up of individuals who fought the wars and planned the conquest of other species. Much of the work done by the warrior caste was supported by the priests. There were four distinct subdivisions of the caste: warmaster, commander, subaltern, and warrior. The warrior caste members pledged their allegiance to the god Yun-Yammka.

**Warriors of the Shadow** A translation of the term *Dha Werda Verda,* a name applied to the ancient Taungs of Coruscant after their initial victory over the Battalions of Zhell was sealed when a volcano erupted. The falling ash nearly eradicated the Zhell, and those survivors who saw the Taungs emerge from the ash-filled skies described them as warriors coming from the shadows.

**Wartaki Islands** An archipelago on Kashyyyk.

**Warthan's Wizards** A secret group of starship designers and engineers, they came up with some of the Empire's most confidential starship designs, including several with active cloaking technology. They were first used by the Emperor during the Clone Wars, when he contracted with them to upgrade a *Theta*-class T-2c transport to serve as his personal shuttle.

**Warto** A green-skinned Boltrunian, he lived on Aduba-3 during the era of the New Order. A onetime laborer aboard a Corellian freighter, he had been abandoned on the planet and from then on hated all Corellians. He also became a drunkard and fancied himself as the boyfriend of Azoora at around the time Han Solo and Chewbacca were stranded on the planet, shortly after the Battle of Yavin. He jealously attacked Han, who had been talking to Azoora, but Chewbacca quickly intervened.

**Wartogg** A Gamorrean who worked for Jabba the Hutt in the years before the Battle of Naboo, he changed allegiances to work for Gardulla the Hutt. A furious Jabba put a bounty on Wartogg's head that Jango Fett was only too happy to collect.

*Warto attacks Han Solo.*

**Warton** An inhabitant of the outpost of Eol Sha, he was among those who were evacuated to Dantooine and later killed when Admiral Daala raided the planet.

**Waru** A powerful being, it was drawn from a parallel universe by a split in the space–time continuum created by the intersection of a black hole and a quantum crystal star. Waru appeared to be a complex construct of gold shields covering a slab of raw, uncovered tissue much like a chunk of meat. A viscous fluid glistened between the shields and sometimes oozed out. Waru was able to heal other beings by encasing them in this ichor, but occasionally it would kill beings brought to it for healing, sucking in their Force strength. Lord Hethrir planned to offer a kidnapped young Anakin Solo to Waru as a sacrifice; in return, he expected to receive great Force powers. But Hethrir himself was taken into Waru, which then closed in on itself and disappeared, possibly returning to its own universe.

*Warrior caste*

**war wagon** A weapons-laden wagon used by Erpham Warrick to defeat the Duloks on the Forest Moon of Endor. It was also called an Ewok battle wagon.

**wasber** Native to the planet Tenupe, this vicious insect was noted for the poison it used to capture its prey and defend itself against predators. The poison was one of the deadliest in the galaxy. When the wasber stung its victim, the poison attacked the very white blood cells that were trying to eliminate it. Within minutes, the coopted cells delivered toxins to the victim's vital organs, which swiftly failed under the attack. Use of wasber poison was strictly regulated by many planetary governments, despite the fact that any poison removed from its container began to lose its potency after a few hours. Alema Rar used wasber poison when she tried to kill Jacen Solo some 10 years after the end of the Yuuzhan Vong War.

**Waskiro** Jabba the Hutt's henchman Bib Fortuna lied about this planet, claiming there had been an ambush in the Ampuroon mining district. Fortuna's lie was an attempt to deceive a Nuffin freighter.

**Wass** A Jedi student expelled from the Temple during the Clone Wars. Wass and other expelled students were transported to a remote planet and allowed to come to terms with their problems while learning about the Force in a natural environment. When a group of Separatist battle droids landed and threatened their school, Wass convinced fellow student Zac to call upon a herd of horned grazers to trample them. Wass plowed a second squad of battle droids with a farming vehicle.

**Wasteland, the** A massive junkyard that covered a large section of Metalorn during the final decades of the Republic. The Wasteland was set aside to hold the scrap and debris left over from manufacturing processes, so that true scrap could be incinerated while useful items were separated and reclaimed for reuse.

**WatchCircle** The name used to describe groups of Jedi Knights chosen for their ability to foresee the future. In the wake of the Great Sith War, WatchCircles discerned potential threats so that conflicts could be averted before they escalated to the level of galactic war. Some WatchCircles were more adept at reading the future than others, so multiple groups were established to help clarify the visions witnessed by their members. (*See also* Covenant, the.)

***Watchkeeper*** A destroyer in a Bakuran task force, it was sent on an unstaffed decoy mission to test enemy firepower. The *Watchkeeper* was destroyed by a Selonian planet repulsor.

**Watchman (1)** A title given to ancient Jedi Masters, it connoted their role as overseers of a particular star system or sector, arranged through a loose agreement with the Galactic Republic. The Watchman's main charge was to maintain harmony and justice. The Republic granted Watchmen the authority to operate autonomously in order to right wrongs and deal with disturbances in the Force that occurred outside the purview of local laws.

**Watchman (2)** An Imperial stormtrooper who was part of the Aurek-Seven unit of the Imperial 501st Legion, he and the other unit members went on the mission to locate the Outbound Flight Project in Chiss space some three years before the Yuuzhan Vong invasion. They took heavy damage when Vagaari pirates launched an attack, but the unit remained intact throughout the fighting.

*Waru*

Watto

**Water Moon** *See* Oh'ma-Dun.

**Watto** A Toydarian junk dealer and the former slave owner of Anakin Skywalker. Watto was a member of the Ossiki Confederacy Army on his homeworld of Toydaria during his youth, and during the fighting he lost a tusk and sustained a leg injury. After mustering out, Watto traveled to Tatooine to set up his own junk business in the city of Mos Espa. A skilled gambler, Watto won the rights to Shmi and Anakin Skywalker in a bet with Gardulla the Hutt. While he was Anakin's owner, Watto discovered that the boy was quite skilled at fixing things, and was also a quick study in Podracing. Watto met his match when Qui-Gon Jinn arrived in Mos Espa. The Jedi sponsored the boy in the Boonta Eve Podrace, and when he won, Watto was forced to surrender ownership of Anakin. He never fully recovered from the loss of such a skilled slave, and began to treat Shmi with more respect. Several years after Anakin left Tatooine, Watto agreed to sell Shmi to Cliegg Lars so that Cliegg could free her and then marry her. Owen Lars helped his father trick Watto into selling Shmi in exchange for a Tobal lens. Years later, when Anakin returned to Tatooine in search of his mother, Watto provided him with information on the location of the Lars homestead. Watto remained on Tatooine to run his junk shop for nearly 20 more years.

**Watts, Lieutenant** A Corulag native, this Imperial officer's skills were in the area of gunnery, and he was known as a deadly accurate shot. He was temporarily assigned to Kuat Drive Yards during the development of weapons systems for the AT-ST scout walker. Watts and his copilot, Major Marquand, were captured during the Battle of Endor when Chewbacca and a pair of Ewoks commandeered their AT-ST scout walker.

Lieutenant Watts

**watumba bat** Gray creatures that ate primarily algae and rock dust, they served as hosts for several flying parasitic bugs, including parfue gnats. Glottalphibs liked keeping watumba bats nearby, because they supported so many "delicacies." Crime kingpin Nandreeson imported the bats to Skip 6 in Smuggler's Run.

**Wavechaser** A small, 5-meter-long recreational vehicle developed to skim across the surface of the water. Resembling a shark or other streamlined fish, the Wavechaser could be operated by a single individual, and had room for one passenger seated behind the operator. The Wavechaser also had 4 cubic meters of cargo space for diving gear or extra clothing.

**Waverton** The chief purser aboard the *Aurorient Express* six years prior to the Battle of Naboo. Qui-Gon Jinn and Obi-Wan Kenobi discovered that Waverton was in league with a group of pressure pirates who hoped to disable the ship and steal its cargo. Waverton admitted to the Jedi his part in the plot, but in the end he and a partner allowed a core bomb hidden inside the ship to explode.

**wave walker** An Imperial light attack vehicle, it was designed to operate above the water's surface. During the Battle of Mon Calamari, wave walkers were built aboard World Devastators, then unleashed upon the Mon Calamari and their New Republic allies.

Wave walker

**wave-weapon** Offensive devices, they were capable of turning their victims into smoking ash. They were developed about four millennia before the Galactic Civil War to combat the creatures of the Dxun moon during the Beast Wars of Onderon.

**Wawaatt Archipelago** An island chain that contained the city of Kachirho on Kashyyyk. The Wawaatt Archipelago was held by Separatist forces during the Clone Wars. The bases there were used to launch the attacks on Kachirho during the First Battle of Kashyyyk.

**Way, the** An ancient term for the Force.

Wayland

**Wayland** A primitive green-and-blue world located about 350 light-years from the planet Myrkr, it was home to Emperor Palpatine's private storehouse. Wayland's surface was covered with dense, double-canopied forests and grassy plains. Mount Tantiss, located in Wayland's northern hemisphere near the eastern edge of its main continent, was the hidden resting place for Palpatine's trophies, his military treasures, and an operational cloning facility.

Generations before, when human colonists settled on Wayland, they came into conflict with the planet's two native species, the Psadans and the Myneyrshi. The four-armed, blue-crystalline Myneyrshi and the lumpy, plated Psadans were driven from their land until the colonists' weapons began to fail them. When the Empire arrived, the inhabitants were forced to construct the vast storehouse in Mount Tantiss. Palpatine apparently appointed a guardian to defend his storehouse, the mad Jedi clone Joruus C'baoth—or it may have been just C'baoth's delusion. C'baoth forced all three of Wayland's species to live under his strict rule in a city built against the southwest side of the mountain. When Palpatine departed with Grand Admiral Thrawn, an Imperial garrison under the command of Colonel Selid was placed in charge to help safeguard the cloning operation, which supplied Thrawn with a nearly inexhaustible stock of trained soldiers.

The Mount Tantiss complex had only one

Wawaatt Archipelago

entrance, located on the southwest side. The peak of the complex held an emergency shuttle hangar, the royal chambers, and the Emperor's throne room with a 20-meter hologram of the galaxy. The fully functioning Spaarti cloning cylinder chamber sat inside a vast natural cavern many stories high. Thrawn had hundreds of Force-blocking ysalamiri transplanted to the cloning chamber to prevent any negative side effects from the rapid pace of his clones' growth. The cloning complex and most of the mountain were destroyed when Lando Calrissian and Chewbacca sabotaged the central equipment column.

In the years that followed, the Noghri—whose home planet couldn't be restored—were relocated to Wayland, and the city of New Nystao was formed in the shadow of Mount Tantiss. When the Yuuzhan Vong invaded, Wayland was used briefly as a safeworld for New Republic personnel. It was here that the priestess Elan was incarcerated, pending her transfer to Coruscant as a prisoner of war. But she had planned her capture, and provided the Yuuzhan Vong with information on Wayland's location with a villip she had kept hidden. After the Yuuzhan Vong staged a fake rescue attempt, they subjugated Wayland and used it as a breeding ground for amphistaffs and other organic weaponry. Much of the planet's crust and mantle was consumed by Chom-Vrone, huge, worm-like creatures that transformed raw materials into superheated plasma.

**Waz, Izal** A Force-sensitive Arcona known for his salt addiction, he joined the crew of the *Jolly Man* during the hunt for a Yuuzhan Vong yammosk. He had been a student at the Jedi praxeum on Yavin 4 until he consumed too much of a nerfloaf made by Kenth Hamner. The salt in the meal was too much for his system, and he fled the moon in order to maintain his salt addiction. He eventually met Jedi Master Eelysa, who helped him focus on growing into a Jedi. It was Izal Waz who developed the technique of using the Force to collect ambient light, creating a "glowball" that could hide a starship as if it were inside a small star. On orders from Eelysa, Waz approached Han and Leia Organa Solo on Corellia to get them offworld aboard his ship, the *Sureshot*. Waz survived the Yuuzhan Vong War, and flew an X-wing fighter during the Swarm War.

**WBD** A term used by Imperial fighter pilots to describe a last-ditch maneuver in which the target fighter executed a sharp turn, bringing his or her ship around to smash into the pursuer. The abbreviation stood for "We Both Die!"

**We, Taun** The Kaminoan project coordinator at Tipoca City during the years spent growing the Republic's clone army. Taun We also acted as Prime Minister Lama Su's chief

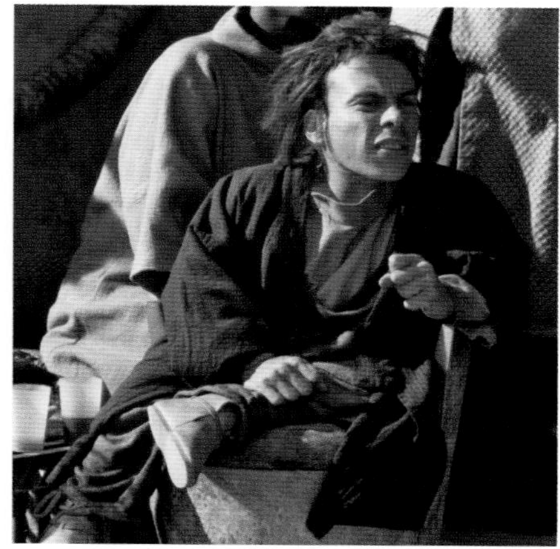

*Weazel*

adviser and served as the Kaminoans' liaison to Jango Fett, the "Prime Clone." While most of the Kaminoans working on the clone army project regarded the clones as specimens, Taun We felt some level of emotional attachment to the younger ones. Although Kamino was devastated during the Clone Wars, Taun We survived, along with a portion of the genetic material harvested from Jango Fett. Boba Fett later contracted We to grow replacement body parts for him. Years later, Taun We left Kamino for a position with Arkanian Microtechnologies. She believed that she was safe until Boba Fett trapped her in her offices on Vohai and demanded to know how he could forestall his cloned body's degeneration. Taun We turned over the information he needed.

**weapons detector** A device that used sensors to scan for power cells and clearly identifiable weapons profiles. The sensors fed data directly to a dedicated computer for nearly instantaneous analysis. Weapons detectors were used in restricted facilities such as military bases, detention centers, and spaceports to scan for unauthorized arms. The Corporate Sector Authority used them on worlds such as Bonadan to maintain order.

**Weasy** A muscular Bothan spacer and part-time smuggler, he frequented the cantinas of Mos Eisley during the early years of the New Order. He became friends with "Ben" Kenobi, who saw Weasy as an excellent—and accurate—source of news and information from across the galaxy. Later, Weasy agreed to transport Kenobi to Bellassa after he learned that Ferus Olin was alive on the planet.

**WeatherNet** Shorthand for Coruscant's Weather Control Network.

**Weazel** A short, stocky weapons dealer living on Tatooine during the years leading up to the Battle of Naboo. During the Boonta Eve Classic, Weazel sat in Watto's box and chastised the Toydarian for betting against his own slave, Anakin Skywalker. Weazel had a Trandoshan associate who was killed when Tusken Raiders attacked the trading site at Mochot Steep.

*Taun We*

**Web, Robior** A former Guardian from Junction 5 and one of the galaxy's most lethal assassins. Count Dooku hired Web to kill Delaluna's leader, Kamish Sash. Obi-Wan Kenobi and Anakin Skywalker saw Count Dooku meeting with Web at the Station 88 spaceport prior to the Clone Wars.

**Webb, Jeroen** A native of Ralltiir, he became a spy for the Ralltiir underground after the planet was subjugated by the Empire. A skillful starship pilot, he later served with Rebel Alliance forces on the ice planet Hoth, becoming one of the base's tauntaun handlers.

**Webble, Illyan** The president of Seraphan Industries, he was captured by roving slave traders and dumped on Kalkovak, where he encountered a species worshipping the Yavin Vassilika. Webble was actually a member of the Rebel Alliance working with Bria Tharen's Red Hand Squadron, and he feigned insanity in order to get possession of the Vassilika. Jozzel Moffett delivered it to him for four million credits and a replica of the artifact. The credits were part of the loot that Tharen stole from Jabba the Hutt.

**webweaver** A large, deadly arachnid also known as the wyyyschokk. These creatures lived on one of the lower ecolevels of the planet Kashyyyk. Webweavers developed large, elaborate web networks with strands as thick as a Wookiee's forearm and more durable than the kshyy vine, yet they still actively sought food rather than wait for prey. They had exceedingly fast reflexes and could spit a potent poison from their fangs to immobilize victims.

**Wedd, Baron Edi** A Separatist leader on Amaltanna who lived in an unbreachable fortress. Unable to penetrate the fortress's defenses, Jedi Knight Bultar Swan shut off the facility's life-support systems with Wedd still inside.

**WED series droid (Treadwell)** Produced by Cybot Galactica, the basic WED series Treadwell droid was a rolling, multi-armed automaton introduced more than 700 years before the Galactic Civil War. It was designed to perform virtually any menial task. The nickname came from the two treads that the droid used to move about. There were a number of different sizes from which a buyer could choose. Smaller, four-armed models were standard, designed to perform household tasks and small mechanical chores. The 500 and 600 series were built to withstand the pressures of working in an antimatter

WED series droid

furnace. The most appealing feature of this series was the variety of manipulator arms available for installation, as well as the ease with which they could be interchanged. WED Treadwells could be equipped with arc welders, spot sprayers, hydrospanners, foam sealant dispensers, fusion cutters, torque wrenches, and all manner of calibration tools. However, the series was fragile at best, and required continual maintenance. Among notable Treadwell droids were the following:

WED-9-M1

- **WED-15-77** Capable of accomplishing very specific tasks with close supervision, this binocular Treadwell had a frustratingly small independent thought processor. It assisted Luke Skywalker when he worked on his uncle Owen's vaporators, but it preferred working for Aunt Beru since she always asked it to do the same predictable jobs.

WED-15-17

- **WED-9-M1** A unique Treadwell droid, it was cobbled together by Jawas on Tatooine. Later owned by the De Maals, owners and operators of Docking Bay 94 in Mos Eisley, the droid was nicknamed Bantha for its slow and stubborn ways.

- **WED-15-17** A septoid droid nicknamed for an insect from Eriadu, this multiarmed maintenance droid was fiercely loyal to the Empire. It specialized in extending the effective operational life of Imperial resources.

- **WED-15-I662** A standard Treadwell droid also known as Eye-Six-Six-Too, it was typical of the thousands of droids that repaired and maintained heavy machinery and starfighters.

- **WED-1016** Also known as a techie droid, this starship maintenance droid was capable of repairing more than 5,000 different onboard systems. The model also was used by Rebel Alliance salvage teams.

**Weebacca** A childhood friend of Chewbacca's, he was known in his clan for being a small Wookiee with a big Wookiee's attitude. Weebacca could be untrustworthy and petty at times, but he was loyal to Chewie and the two were never in conflict, despite whatever trouble Weebacca was in. Weebacca loved sabacc and always seemed short of money. When he was in desperate need of large sums of credits, he would take any job, no matter how dangerous, and eventually he became a bodyguard-for-hire. After his home planet was invaded and enslaved by the Empire, he dropped his lucrative smuggling career and rushed home to help. Although he survived the Imperial attack at Kepitenochan, Weebacca was later revealed to be a traitor working for the Empire.

**weed-cutter** A smart bomb used to devastating effect by the Separatists during the Clone Wars, it was launched in a high arc so that it could avoid defensive screens. It then targeted a large concentration of clone troopers and came down in their midst, detonating at chest level. When it exploded, the weed-cutter flung a payload of razor-sharp durasteel flechettes in a circular pattern, cutting through armor just as easily as flesh. The resulting damage to the clone troopers was awful to behold.

**WeeGee** A maintenance robot created by Morgan Katarn from spare parts on the agricultural moon of Sulon. Katarn built WeeGee to plug into the farm's operational grid and monitor its systems. WeeGee's secondary functions included repairing equipment, driving threshing combines, and protecting Morgan's son Kyle at all costs. WeeGee floated on a repulsorlift engine scavenged from an Imperial speeder bike. Parts from a junked probot provided the maneuvering jets for steering. WeeGee's centermost drive assembly was made up of rotating cylinders, allowing the droid to spin and twist into a variety of configurations. Two floodlights shone from the central chassis. Cooling fans kept the jury-rigged parts from overheating, giving WeeGee a characteristic whir. WeeGee's sensory equipment fit into a small pod that extended above the drive assembly on a multijointed, pivoting stalk. In addition to a photoreceptor, the sensor pod contained auditory pickups, sonar emitters, and a vocabulator capable of droid languages only. Two manipulator arms dangled underneath.

WeeGee

When Qu Rahn entrusted his lightsaber to Morgan, he hid it inside WeeGee. He then encoded a journal disk for Kyle, so that he could use the information to locate the Lost Valley of the Jedi. WeeGee, despite being damaged when Jerec's forces attacked the household, nevertheless retained the lightsaber and provided it to Kyle. After Kyle defeated Jerec and returned to the New Republic, he took WeeGee with him, and the droid gladly accepted a position on a naval maintenance team.

Weequay

**Weemell sector** An area in the Galactic Core. During the Clone Wars, General Grievous released the Loedorvian Brain Plague to slay Republic clone armies, killing nearly every human in the Weemell sector.

**Weequay** A mysterious humanoid species with unusual religious rituals. Weequay had coarse, leathery brown skin that was wrinkled and pitted, and their heads were bald except for braided topknots on one side. They came from Sriluur, a harsh desert planet in the Sisar Run. Weequay enjoyed a form of pheremonic communication that allowed them to be in touch with members of their own clan without speech. Although they were not overly intelligent, they were cruelly efficient at violent acts, and thus several were employed by crime lord Jabba the Hutt on Tatooine.

The somewhat off-kilter Weequay on Jabba's staff worshipped many gods, chief among them Quay, god of the moon; the word *Weequay* meant "follower of Quay." To contact Quay, they used small spheres (also called quay) that served as entertainment devices in other parts of the galaxy. The quay answered simple questions with simple answers: "It is decidedly so," "Concentrate and ask again," "As I see it, yes," and more. One Weequay, Ak-Buz, commanded Jabba's sail barge until he was murdered by Dannik Jerriko, an Anzati. Porcellus the cook hid the Weequay's body in a garbage heap. When the corpse was discovered, the other Weequay asked their moon god to reveal the murderer, with no success.

The Weequay slaughtered banthas as part of their rituals, which infuriated Tusken Raiders. Jabba put an end to the killings, then planted a dead moisture farmer next to a bantha corpse to place suspicion elsewhere. Most of the Weequay in Jabba's employ were aboard his sail barge or the accompanying skiff when Jabba planned to dump the Rebel Alliance infiltrators into the Pit of Carkoon, and most were killed in the fighting or the explosion that put an end to the crime lord's long career.

The Weequay lived in relative peace with their planetary neighbors, the Houk, for many years, but tensions between the two species erupted several times into all-out war. The last of these conflicts was resolved just prior to the Battle of Yavin.

**Weerden** The planet where Lord Torbin, the Grand Inquisitor, was murdered when Weerden's Imperial palace was rammed by the shuttle *Sark I.* An assassin droid was suspected of killing the shuttle's flight crew and causing the crash.

**Weez** *See* Cholly, Weez, and Tup.

**Wehttam** A planet in the Farlax sector. The chromite-mining colony of New Brigia, within the nearby Koornacht Cluster, once traded its ore along the hyperlanes to Wehttam and Galantos until the collapse of Imperial control in the Farlax sector made commerce increasingly hazardous. Twelve years after the Battle of Endor, Leia Organa Solo decided to send the New Republic's Fifth Fleet into the Farlax sector to protect worlds such as Wehttam and Galantos from the Yevethan fleet massing in the cluster. Leia accepted the emergency petitions for membership from all worlds bordering the cluster, including Wehttam. The Republic warships *Jantol* and *Farlight* were sent to Wehttam as a show of strength.

**Wehutti** A lean and strong man who served as a leader of the Melida more than a decade prior to the Battle of Naboo. Wehutti was Yoda's contact on Melida/Daan and was supposed to help Obi-Wan Kenobi and Qui-Gon Jinn save the Jedi diplomat Tahl. He later betrayed the Jedi, hoping to use them as hostages. When the Young came to power in Zehava, Wehutti was willing to go to war once again over the destruction of the Halls of Evidence. His daughter Cerasi was killed while trying to intervene in the conflict; Wehutti went into seclusion, blaming himself for her death.

**Weir, General** A deadly Imperial storm commando who led the attack on Corellia's capital of Coronet just two weeks after the Battle of Endor. Following the attack, his forces retreated to their base on Talus. When Rogue Squadron reached Talus, Weir attempted to escape in a TIE interceptor. Wedge Antilles shot him down and took him into custody.

General Weir

**Wel, Tsillin** A Quarren Imperial accountant, she was called to testify during Tycho Celchu's trial. During the auditing of Imperial expenditures, her staff uncovered 10 million credits located in six different accounts, purportedly paid to Captain Celchu.

**Welflet, Noq** A captain in the Haariden military five years after the Battle of Naboo, he was hired by Granta Omega to kill the Jedi Knights who were dispatched to Haariden to rescue a group of Old Republic scientists. They included Obi-Wan Kenobi, Soara Antana, and their Padawans, Anakin Skywalker and Darra Thel-Tanis. But the captain realized that the Jedi were not a threat and told them of Granta Omega's plot. He and his men were later buried in a volcanic eruption on the planet.

**Welk** One of Tamith Kai's most promising students at the Shadow Academy. During the Yuuzhan Vong War, Welk and Lomi Plo were captured by the invaders and held aboard the worldship *Baanu Rass.* Both agreed to help a Jedi strike team infiltrate the worldship and destroy the voxyn and their queen, but later abandoned the Jedi in order to save themselves. They fled in the ship *Tachyon Flier,* unaware that wounded Jedi Raynar Thul was still on board. The *Tachyon Flier* limped into the Unknown Regions and crashed on the Killik planet of Yoggoy. Welk and Lomi Plo barely survived. After healing, Welk worked with Lomi Plo and created Gorog, the Dark Nest hive, which remained hidden from both Thul and the other Killiks. Working behind the scenes, Welk infiltrated the Taat nest on Jwlio in order to breed assassin bugs after Jedi Master Luke Skywalker and several other Masters arrived at Qoribu in search of a group of Jedi Joiners. He was confronted by Jedi Master Saba Sebatyne in a cave beneath the surface, but fought his way to freedom, returning to the Gorog nest on Kr. There he found himself facing both Luke and Mara Jade Skywalker. In an intense battle, Luke was able to slip through the dark sider's guards and drive his lightsaber into Welk's stomach, pulling the blade out through his ribs. Welk died with a bloodcurdling scream, and the Will of the Gorog nest was broken.

**Well, the** A hidden chamber beneath the Fountain Palace on Hapes, it had been used by Hapan royalty for centuries to imprison troublesome nobles. Over time, it became more of a detention center to confine important beings for questioning without fear of interference.

**Well of the World Brain** The name of the deep, yorik coral cavern grown by the Yuuzhan Vong to hold the mature dhuryam that would control Coruscant following their capture of that world. The Well, formed from the hollowed-out remains of the Galactic Senate Rotunda, was protected by a series of defenses. In the years following the Swarm War, Jacen Solo returned to the Well of the World Brain to use it as a hiding place for the Dark Lady Lumiya.

***Welmo Darb*** A Galactic Alliance Star Destroyer that served with the First Fleet during the GA's conflict with the Corellian Confederation. Admiral Nek Bwua'tu selected the *Welmo Darb* to serve as the fleet's flagship in the wake of the Second Battle of Balmorra, preferring to keep his larger and more powerful warships toward the rear of the fleet where they could be more effective against enemy forces.

**Wena** The owner of R2-D2 and C-3PO after Mungo Baobab and long before they became involved with the Rebellion, he represented the Kalarba system in the Imperial Senate. He used the droids aboard his luxury starship, but when he got into financial difficulties he auctioned them off, and they were sent to Hosk Station.

**Wenbus, Gustab** A fearless racer who created the modern incarnation of Podracing. On Malastare, Gustab Wenbus entered himself in a race with a virtually untested, super-fast prototype Podracer that had been designed for him by a rogue mechanic named Phoebus.

**Wen-Chii, Anno** A reclusive Pyn'gani Jedi Master who chose to eke out a simple life in the wake of the Battle of Ruusan. Wen-Chii took his Padawan learner, Nalia Adollu, to his homeworld of Polus, where he set about studying the life-forms. Master Wen-Chii hoped to learn more about how life had evolved in the galaxy, and how it continued to evolve as millennia passed.

**Wend** This young man, his father Bordon, and his older brother Tallo were the only members of their family to survive the Battle of Ruusan. Wend, Tallo, and Bordon were rescued by the surviving members of the Army of Light, and taken aboard the warship *Fairwind* to protect them from the effects of the thought bomb that the Sith had detonated. When Bordon volunteered to work on a recovery team, Wend and Tallo went with him, hoping to find survivors on the blasted landscape of their homeworld. After they recovered the girl Rain from the planet's surface, Wend tried to befriend her, but the girl seemed aloof and distant. Rain later revealed herself as the Sith hopeful Zannah and shot her rescuers.

**Wendik, Lieutenant Arven** A male member of Bravo Flight who flew as Bravo Three during the Battle of Naboo. A tactical expert on capital starship shield capabilities, Lieutenant Wendik developed many strategies to attack larger ships.

*Lieutenant Arven Wendik*

**Weng, Mayli** A worker who represented the Exotic Entertainer's Union on Imperial Center before the Battle of Endor, she was on Prince Xizor's secret payroll. Black Sun owned or operated a number of businesses that used EEU members.

**Wennen, Besany** A strikingly beautiful woman who worked for the Republic Treasury during the Clone Wars, her main role was as a forensic auditor, searching through financial documents to identify illicit or illegal transactions. She was later assigned as a liaison to the Grand Army of the Republic's logistics office, where she served as a supervisor to the clone troopers and data technicians who monitored the troops deployed across the galaxy.

Wennen grew suspicious of Vinna Jiss, began tailing her, and found herself in the midst of a black-ops mission devised by Kal Skirata. When she realized that Skirata and his clones were working to put an end to the war and its unnecessary killing, Wennen became one of their most important allies. Skirata and his *Null*-class troopers decided to infiltrate Tipoca City on Kamino, using access codes Wennen provided to search for information that might help control the aging process of the clone troopers.

Wennen truly cared for the clones and treated them as fellow beings. Thus, she was distressed when her research indicated *no* budgetary allotment earmarked for medical coverage and pensions for those troops of the Grand Army of the Republic that survived the Clone Wars. She was disturbed further after getting a call from Skirata requesting that she help in getting clone trooper Fi medical attention: Republic Central Medcenter droids refused to treat him, because he was technically a military asset. After a confrontation, Wennen was able to to make sure Fi was transported to Mandalore to recover.

***Wennis*** Rokur Gepta's personal starship, it was a decommissioned Imperial cruiser that had been built nearly a century before the Galactic Civil War. Trowel-shaped and painted matte black, it bristled with weapons and shielding. Gepta had built a small windowless chamber near the ship's drive tubes with 2-meter-thick walls to contain the bioweapon that he had used to destroy the planet Tund. The *Wennis* also destroyed a small group of Oswaft during the fight for the ThonBoka. When Klyn Shanga forced Osuno Whett's small ship to collide with the cruiser, however, it exploded.

**Werl, Admiral Apelben** The commander of her homeworld Vannix's military, she became Presider of the planet about 27 years after the Battle of Yavin when Leia Organa Solo helped expose her opponent, Senator Addath Gadan, as a traitor who wanted to appease the Yuuzhan Vong.

**Wermis, Captain Mulchive** A native of Anaxes and a self-important Imperial officer during the Galactic Civil War. Captain Wermis commanded the Star Destroyer *Devastator* when it captured Princess Leia Organa and the *Tantive IV* just prior to the Battle of Yavin. When Darth Vader returned to the Emperor's side, Captain Wermis was assigned to the first task force assembled to track down the Rebels who had destroyed the Death Star. Wermis hated being subordinate to Vader, and often spoke condescendingly to the Dark Lord of the Sith. Vader, recognizing the need to locate the Alliance quickly, tolerated Wermis's jibes long enough to reach the Wheel, where he hoped to capture Luke Skywalker, Han Solo, and Leia Organa at the same time. Although Skywalker escaped, Wermis was allowed to continue his service. Still, Vader relished putting the captain into positions where his lack of courage forced him to retreat.

*Captain Mulchive Wermis*

*Zam Wesell*

**Wermyn** A tall, one-armed human brute from Aquella, he was in charge of plant operations at Maw Installation. Wermyn's skin had a purplish green cast from various dyes and tattoos. During the New Republic assault, he surrendered to Wedge Antilles after activating a meltdown in the reactor asteroid.

**Wesell, Zam** A Clawdite shape-shifter and a noted bounty hunter during the last decade of the Old Republic. Zam Wesell was also a rival of Jango Fett, as the two were generally considered the best bounty hunters of their generation. Wesell's decision to become a bounty hunter was labeled as heretical by her fellow Clawdites. As part of her training, Wesell learned the teachings and techniques of the Mabari, and later trained to become a bounty hunter on the city-world of Denon. Some years before the Clone Wars, Wesell and Jango Fett were both employed by Fernooda the Dug, working for General Ashaar Khorda on a mission to recover the Infant of Shaa. The two were reunited during Fett's search for Komari Vosa and the Bando Gora cult, when he enlisted Zam's help to free Bendix Fust from the Oovo IV prison facility. Despite their differences, Fett and Wesell became grudging friends, and Wesell even befriended Jango's young son, Boba. Just before the Battle of Geonosis, Wesell was once again contacted by Fett, who had been hired by the Trade Federation to assassinate Senator Padmé Amidala of Naboo. Wesell's failed attempt to poison the Senator using kouhuns attracted the attention of Obi-Wan Kenobi and his appren-

General Redd Wessel

tice, Anakin Skywalker. Wesell escaped to the Outlander Club, but Jango refused to have his plans compromised and killed Wesell with a poison dart as the Jedi were about to capture her.

**Wessel, General Redd** The son of Governor Marcellin Wessel, this Imperial Army officer came to the attention of his superiors during the Imperial cleansing of Yinchorr. Originally a soldier in Imperial ground operations, he was promoted at a steady rate through the ranks to general, mainly due to his by-the-book approach to strategy and command. Opportunity struck when Wessel conspired with Carnor Jax and the Emperor's physician to destroy Palpatine's clones and rule the Empire. Jax made Wessel his right-hand man, placing him in charge of military operations while Jax and his assistant Lieutenant Blim handled other affairs. General Wessel made a fatal mistake by bringing Kir Kanos's bomb-rigged ship aboard Jax's Star Destroyer *Emperor's Revenge*. It exploded and killed everyone on board.

Governor Marcellin Wessel

**Wessel, Governor Marcellin** The Imperial Governor of the Immalia sector during the Empire's New Order. He was noted for his understanding of nonhuman species, which he acquired during his tenure as a colonel of the Grand Army of the Republic in the Clone Wars. Following that conflict, Wessel was charged with documenting the outcome of Order 66. During the Galactic Civil War, he attempted to use the native Yinchorri of Yinchorr to capture Princess Leia Organa. His son Redd later served with Carnor Jax.

**Wessex, Lira** The daughter of Walex Blissex, the man who created the *Victory*-class Star Destroyer, she married Denn Wessex, Imperial Governor of the Relgim sector. She despised the Old Republic and chose to support the New Order, creating the original designs for the *Imperator*-class Star Destroyer. She later worked with her husband in an attempt to kidnap her father and coerce him to provide her more information about starship design. The attempt failed, and Lira barely escaped the destruction of the *Subjugator*.

**Wessiri, Diric** The first husband of Iella Wessiri, and 20 years her senior, he was from a wealthy Corellian family whose money allowed him to pursue leisure. He viewed life as a collection of experiences to be studied or as a continual quest for enlightenment. When he and his wife fled Corellia, they took on false identities that led them to Coruscant. Diric was captured during an Imperial sweep, interrogated, and broken. After his imprisonment, he was forced to assist General Derricote with his Krytos virus project. Shortly after the liberation of Coruscant, he was released, then debriefed by Alliance Intelligence. Unknown to everyone, he was still working for the Empire against his will. When Ysanne Isard discovered that her agent Kirtan Loor was cooperating with the New Republic, she activated Diric Wessiri, making him an assassin who silenced Loor forever. In a tragic turnabout, Diric was then killed by his unsuspecting wife.

**Wessiri, Iella** See Antilles, Iella Wessiri.

**WESTAR-34 blaster pistol** This dallorian-alloy weapon was a favored blaster of bounty hunters and other beings who relied upon surprise to attack their enemies. The WESTAR-34 was designed for sustained, close-range use, utilizing its dallorian construction to absorb more heat than a standard blaster. Jango Fett packed two of them.

**Westermal, Moff Kosimo** A member of the Moff Council following the Swarm War, he was one of the survivors of the Mandalorian attack on the Nickel One asteroid shortly after the Second Battle of Fondor.

**Western Dune Sea** See Dune Sea.

**Wezz, Sia-Lan** The Padawan of Master Lo-Jad during the last decade of the Old Republic. Prior to the Battle of Naboo, Lo-Jad sent Wezz to Naboo for formal education at the Royal House of Learning in Theed. When the Trade Federation invaded the planet, Wezz joined the Naboo underground and gave her services to the resistance. After Chancellor Palpatine installed himself as Emperor and instituted the New Order, Wezz was one of the Jedi who managed to remain hidden from the Imperial Inquisitors. She was killed by Darth Vader on Kessel.

Sia-Lan Wezz

WESTAR-34 blaster pistol

**Whaladon** A species of intelligent sea mammals that inhabited the deep oceans of the planet Mon Calamari. These huge, 30-meter-long aquatic mammals resembled humpbacked whales, although they had much shorter snouts and longer flippers. During the era of the New Order they were led by Leviathor, a great white Whaladon. The Whaladons were hunted by the remnants of the Empire following the Battle of Endor, even though the practice had long been outlawed.

**Whaladon hunting ship** A huge submersible vessel that illegally searched the oceans of Mon Calamari for Whaladons, it was the size of a large capital ship. It was equipped with stun weapons and tractor beams to incapacitate the whale-like mammals and pull them into its recessed chambers, which could store more than a dozen creatures at a time. The ship and its crew of Aqualish hunters was under the command of Captain Dunwell.

**Wharl** The original name of the species later known as Tchuukthai; the ancient Jedi Master Thon was a member. Wharl were large, quadruped creatures with thick armor plating and large clawed feet. Sharp, bony spikes protected their shoulders and jaws.

**Wheel, the** A wheel-shaped space station in the Besh Gorgon system of the Mid Rim. The Wheel was built during the final decades of the Old Republic and was known for its casinos. The station's central axis was an immense cylinder, and at its midpoint four main spokes led out to a circular promenade. Sprouting from the circular section were docking piers, allowing ships of any size

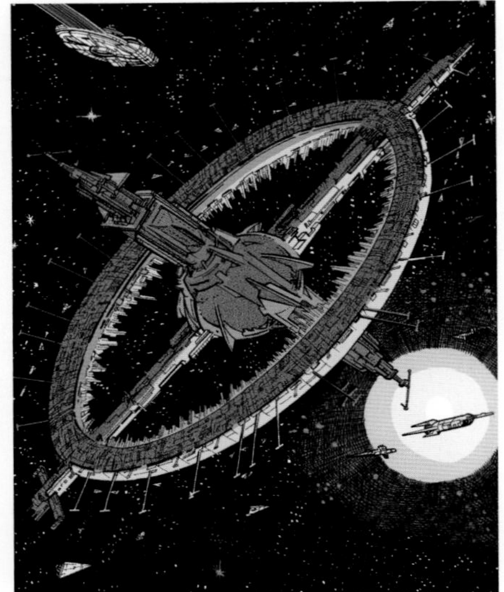

The Wheel

to safely approach and dock with the Wheel. The station's outer section was a sprawling city with an untold number of casinos. Deep in the central axis was also a gladiator arena, where all manner of beings were forced to fight to the death for the entertainment and wagers of the Wheel's visitors. At the height of the New Order, the Wheel was situated inside an "immunity sphere," which meant that Imperial ships were not allowed to come to the station. However, Senator Simon Greyshade, the station's administrator, paid taxes to appease the Empire. During the years following the Sith–Imperial War, the Wheel was owned by Pol Temm, who allowed no weapons aboard his station.

***Whelm*** A Super Star Destroyer based at Anaxes and the flagship of Azure Hammer Command, it helped protect Imperial Center Oversector during the Galactic Civil War.

**Whett, Osuno** A tall, gray-skinned humanoid, he had a high-pitched voice and an inability to make a decision. He worked for years, using the droid Vuffi Raa as a front, planning an Imperial invasion of the Renatasian system. Later he went to the Oseon system, where he did some research on the Sharu for Governor Duttes Mer, who secretly was working with Tund Sorcerer Rokur Gepta to locate the Mindharp of Sharu and use it to control the system. Before that caper, which involved Lando Calrissian, could be completed, Whett and his ship were destroyed.

Whistler's Whirlpool

**Whills** *See* Shaman of the Whills.

***Whip Hand*** A *Lancer*-class frigate that took part in the attack at the Obroa-skai system during the Yuuzhan Vong War. It was ordered to obliterate the crippled cruiser *Far Thunder* so that the invaders couldn't steal it, and it destroyed many enemy coralskippers, too.

**Whiphid** Often called Tooth Faces, members of this species of hulking, fur-covered bipeds stood about 2.5 meters tall. With prominent foreheads, long bowed cheekbones, and two upturned tusks rising from their jaws, Whiphids were easy to spot in a crowd. They came from the bitterly cold planet of Toola in the Kaelta system. Ferocious predators with a true love of the hunt, they also appreciated the luxuries of advanced technology and often took on lucrative bounty-hunting contracts. Lady Valarian, a crime lord on Tatooine, was a Whiphid.

**whipsting** A Yuuzhan Vong bioweapon, it was essentially a long cord coiled inside a sac in a shaper's hand. When poked or nudged, the living cord would eject its mass outward at a target, its end tipped with a poisonous spine that delivered a deadly injection.

***Whirlwind*** A small attack shuttle that was part of Field Commander Thrawn's Picket Force Two, it patrolled the borders of the Chiss Ascendancy during the final years of the Old Republic. About the size of the *Springhawk,* the *Whirlwind* was the first ship ordered to attack Special Task Force One after the fleet was encountered on its own mission to intercept Outbound Flight. The *Whirlwind* had been refitted to house a pseudograv-field generator that Thrawn had stolen from the Vagaari, which was used to keep the *Darkvenge* from escaping into hyperspace.

**Whistler** Corran Horn's green-and-white R2 series astromech droid, it navigated his X-wing fighter. Whistler also came equipped with a special criminal investigation and forensics circuitry package provided by CorSec, and was further modified by Horn. That's how the droid was able to subvert a restraining bolt and escape after Horn and others were held captive by Ysanne Isard. The droid retuned to the *Errant Venture* and made a detailed report.

**Whistler's Whirlpool** A tapcaf on the planet Trogan, it was located on the coast of the planet's most densely populated continent. This bowl-shaped rock pit was built around a natural formation called the Drinking Cup. Open to the sea at its base, the Cup filled six times every day when the tidal shift inundated it with a violent white-water maelstrom. The tables at Whistler's Whirlpool were arranged in concentric circles around the bowl, but the noise of the water made most of the clientele uncomfortable, and the tapcaf was largely abandoned. Smuggler Talon Karrde held a meeting with fellow smuggling chiefs at the Whirlpool to discuss how Grand Admiral Thrawn's campaign against the New Republic could affect the smuggling business.

Whiphid

**Whitebeam run** An ancient ore shipping route, it crossed the Stenness system and ended at the Stenness hyperspace terminal.

**White Current, the** Generally considered to be the Fallanassi version of the Force, it involved a different set of abilities to detect and manipulate the natural world, and preached the immersion of an individual into the Current, rather than calling upon its energy for action. The Fallanassi chose to hide their acceptance of the White Current and its powers, and many members dedicated themselves to ensuring that no record of their existence remained.

**White Eyes** The nickname used by Alema Rar to describe the man who was leading the new Sith Order on Korriban three years after the end of the Swarm War. It was White Eyes who told Rar that Vergere had been a Sith, and that it was Vergere and Lumiya who had put together the plan to turn Jacen Solo into the next Dark Lord of the Sith.

**White Room** A meeting place on Coruscant carved from a single, huge stone, it had space to seat thousands. The building was dome-shaped with a series of lights that illuminated the beautiful white stone. The White

Room was the site of Han Solo's wedding to Princess Leia Organa.

**Whitesun, Beru** The maiden name of Beru Lars. Beru was a native of Mos Eisley, and had no dreams of ever leaving Tatooine. She fell in love with Owen Lars, and was able to hold her own as a verbal sparring partner with Owen's father, Cliegg. She also got along well with Cliegg's second wife, Shmi Skywalker Lars. Some years after Shmi's death, Owen and Beru were married. They later helped raise Luke Skywalker, who was brought to them as a baby by Obi-Wan Kenobi.

**Whitesun, Dama** Beru Whitesun Lars's younger sister and the proprietress of the Sidi Driss Inn in the city of Anchorhead on Tatooine. When Leia Organa Solo and her husband, Han, tried to recover the *Killik Twilight* moss-painting on Tatooine, Whitesun allowed them to stay at the Sidi Driss. She later helped them escape from the hotel when Imperial troops arrived to arrest them, acknowledging that she hated the Empire for killing her sister and Owen Lars.

**White Thranta** A shipping operation based in Mos Eisley during the New Order. Although the business was outwardly legitimate, much of its was handled by smugglers and their agents. Most of the contraband moving through the White Thranta facility was destined for the Rebel Alliance.

**White Watch** The code name for the two-man unit formed by clone commandos Atin and Fixer during their mission to break up a Separatist-funded terrorist ring on Coruscant a year after the Battle of Geonosis. The effort was masterminded by Kal Skirata and was carried out by the Special Operations Brigade without direct orders from the Grand Army of the Republic.

**white wings** A term used to describe the set of bolt-on wings produced during the early stages of the Clone Wars to allow clone commandos to launch themselves into battle. Most clone troopers considered these add-ons the worst piece of kit produced by the Grand Army of the Republic, since they were difficult to use and prone to failure. They also were bright white, all but giving away a commando's position in the air.

***White Witch*** A racing speeder built by Jord Dusat and Thall Joben in an attempt to win the Boonta Speeder Race early in the New Order. After Dusat was injured, Joben was forced to fly the *White Witch* during the race. Scheming against him were the agents of Tig Fromm as well as Boba Fett. Thall managed to avoid disaster, and he won the race.

**whuffa** A 250-meter-long wormlike creature, it lived on Dathomir. When the whuffa's dark brown, leathery skin

Beru Whitesun

was dried, it could be used much like rope. Whuffas were bred by the Kwa to act as guardians of the Star Chamber. During Quinlan Vos's mission to Dathomir, the Nightsisters fired a homing torpedo at a whuffa, forcing the creature to the surface. Vos defeated it by allowing himself to be swallowed whole. He then thrust his lightsaber into the whuffa's brain sac, killing it instantly.

**Whyren's Reserve** A rare, expensive Corellian whiskey, it had an amber color and crisp, woody aroma. It was an especially attractive black-market item.

**Wialu** A member of the Fallanassi religious order, she was convinced by Luke Skywalker to help in the New Republic's war on the Yevetha. She used her Fallanassi gift of Immersion Meditation, which allowed things to become invisible or nonexistent things to be visualized. Wialu's "phantom" fleet of New Republic ships, along with assistance from former Black Sword Command saboteurs, helped the New Republic's forces defeat the Yevetha.

**Wiamdi, Vviir** One of a trio of famous Gand ruetsavii who were sent to observe Ooryl Qrygg's life and determine his worthiness to become janwuine. Not only did they observe his activities, but they also participated fully with him during his duties as a member of Rogue Squadron. They proved to be capable fighter pilots as well as undercover operatives.

**Wicko district** An area of Coruscant that was known for its garbage pit races during the last years of the Republic. Anakin Skywalker participated in such a race three years after the Battle of Naboo.

**Widek** Along with Joruna, it was a New Republic planet located near the Koornacht Cluster. Because the Yevetha zealously guarded the Koornacht's borders, all freight traffic needed to travel a circuitous

White Witch

route around the cluster to reach both Widek and Joruna.

***Widowmaker*** A frigate that protected the Imperial Remnant under the command of Arien Yage during the Yuuzhan Vong War. With Grand Admiral Pellaeon's support, Captain Yage volunteered her crew and the *Widowmaker* to escort Luke Skywalker's mission into the Unknown Regions to locate the mysterious planet Zonama Sekot. Upon locating the living planet in the Klasse Ephemora system, the *Widowmaker* remained in orbit to protect against any attacks.

After Nom Anor infiltrated and sabotaged the planet, Zonama Sekot made the first of many blind jumps into hyperspace. The *Widowmaker* was drawn into the planet's wake, but was unable to follow it through hyperspace. It was lost in the Unknown Regions, and Luke Skywalker asked Tahiri Veila to try to find the vessel.

**wildernerf** Mossy-horned herd beasts, they were native to the planet Noquivzor. From a distance, they appeared to be brown specks flowing together into a dark flood. They were preyed upon by prides of leopard-like taopari.

***Wild Karrde*** Smuggling kingpin Talon Karrde's personal craft, it looked like a beat-up Corellian bulk freighter. But beneath its scarred hull, the *Wild Karrde* was a mobile communications base for perhaps the best-informed person on the fringes of galactic business.

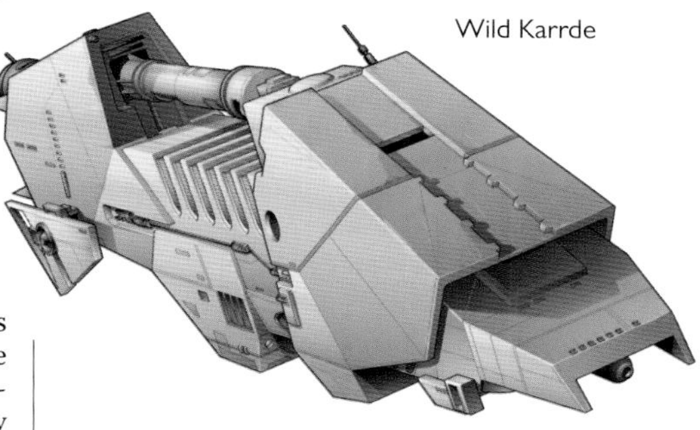

Wild Karrde

A modified Corellian Action VI transport, it was lumbering and ungainly at 125 meters long with a cargo capacity of 90,000 metric tons. It was slow, easily damaged in combat, and appeared unarmed. The *Wild Karrde,* however, had three turbolasers rated for combat against capital starships, with extra shielding and reinforced hull plating. To avoid a fight in the first place, the ship had a sophisticated masking system that hid it from casual distant scans and made it appear to be a harmless cargo ship at close range.

At sublight speed, the vessel was as fast as most Imperial warships. The *Wild Karrde* had a Class 1 hyperdrive, making it as fast as most starfighters in hyperspace. The ship's rear holds were fitted with a complete life-support system, enabling it to carry passengers or animals. The forward hold contained permanent

Commander Vanden Willard

living quarters and offices. The sophisticated communications array let Karrde keep in constant touch with all of his smugglers and spies. At the onset of Tsavong Lah's Jedi purge during the Yuuzhan Vong War, Talon Karrde used the *Wild Karrde* to help evacuate the Jedi academy on Yavin 4.

**Wild Knights** A Jedi starfighter squadron led by Saba Sebatyne. The Wild Knights remained separate from Luke Skywalker's new Jedi Order and were trained by the Jedi Knight Eelysa. However, when the Yuuzhan Vong invaded the galaxy, Saba Sebatyne sent three students to join Skywalker at Eclipse base. They flew a collection of well-maintained but battle-scarred Y-wings. In the wake of the Second Battle of Coruscant, the ranks of the Wild Knights were augmented by Danni Quee, whose expertise on the gravitic technology of the Yuuzhan Vong was invaluable in battle.

**Wild Space** The galaxy's true frontier, once considered part of the Unknown Regions, this area was opened to exploration and settlement as one of Emperor Palpatine's last acts. Grand Admiral Thrawn was charged with taming this wilderness, and he declared it part of the Empire. However, with the remnants of the Empire otherwise occupied, much of Wild Space remained untamed.

**Wiley** A Wokling at the time of the Battle of Endor, this Ewok was the son of Chief Chirpa and his second wife. He was Latara's brother.

**Wilkadon** A Grand Moff during the early years of the New Republic. Wraith Squadron was dispatched to Askaj to capture Wilkadon four years after the Battle of Endor. The theft of the moss-painting *Killik Twilight,* which held the Shadowcast codes used by the Wraiths for transmissions, nearly scrapped their mission.

**Will, the** A term used to describe the collective hive-mind of one of the Colony's hives. For centuries, individual hives moved as the Will of the hive dictated, and the Colony never overextended itself. When Raynar Thul joined the Yoggoy hive and created the Unu hive, UnuThul's deep connection to the Force seemed to create a Will of the Colony, which brought all the hive Wills together and allowed the Colony to expand almost exponentially. It was this expansion, and its implications, that worried the Chiss enough to take action.

**Willard, Commander Vanden** A leader of the Rebel forces at the Massassi temple base on Yavin 4, he served under General Jan Dodonna. Commander Vanden Willard was formerly the Sulorine sector headquarters commander. As a personal assistant—and spy—he had aided Princess Leia Organa and her father, Viceroy Bail Organa, in the years prior to the Senate's dissolution. He later became one of the New Republic's foremost military advisers, along with Dodonna, Pashna Starkiller, and Adar Tallon. This group of elder statesmen became known as the Gray Cadre.

**Willems, Rorf** A thuggish Corellian who served as the Minister of Defense under Five Worlds Prime Minister Dur Gejjen some 10 years after the Yuuzhan Vong War. Willems, along with Gejjen and Gavele Lemora, formed the heart of the new government established in the wake of Thrackan Sal-Solo's assassination. The group was responsible for planning the assassination of the Hapan Queen Mother, Tenel Ka. The Corellians had hoped that Tenel Ka's murder would allow the Heritage Council to assume control of the Hapes Consortium, setting the stage for the Hapans to secede from the Galactic Alliance and join the Corellian cause.

Oss Wilum

**Williams, Antidar** A native of Barkhesh, he had a long and eventful military career in the Galactic Republic. Just before the Battle of Naboo, he was personally asked to pilot the *Radiant VII* diplomatic cruiser to Naboo, carrying the Jedi Qui-Gon Jinn and Obi-Wan Kenobi to a meeting with the Trade Federation Viceroy Nute Gunray. He landed the cruiser in the hold of the Trade Federation flagship, but just after the Jedi set off to begin their negotiations, the vessel was blown up, killing Williams and his crew.

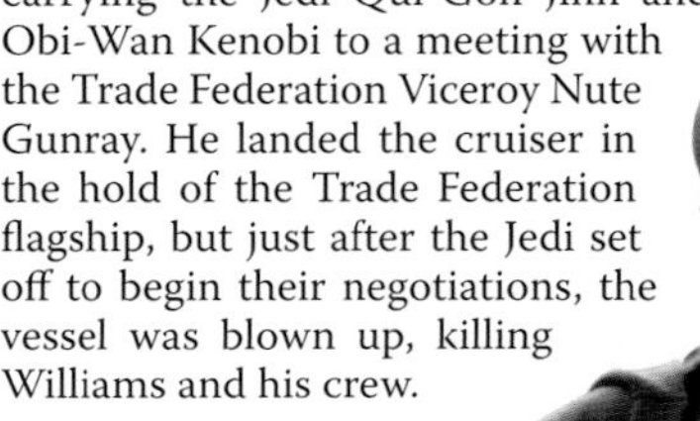

Mace Windu

**Wilum, Oss** A member of the Vultan species, he was a Jedi apprenticed to Master Thon of Ambria some 4,000 years before the Galactic Civil War. In his youth he had been an apprentice of Neti Master Garnoo, who died before Wilum had completed his training. Oss Wilum, along with Crado and a group of about 20 young Jedi, was seduced by Exar Kun into joining the dark side during the Sith War. Wilum and Crado were ordered to kill Master Thon, and they loosed the dark side beasts of Lake Natth on him. But Thon, with help, defeated the beasts, captured Wilum, and brought him out of his Sith spell.

**wilwog** A small and furry domesticated creature kept as a pet by many Sullustans and wealthy beings throughout the galaxy.

**Wimateeka** The Jawa leader of the Nkik clan, he was a friend of the moisture farmer Ariq Joanson. Wimateeka played an instrumental role in Joanson's attempts to make maps and peace with the Jawas and Sand People, serving as his translator and trusted adviser.

**Windsloe, Barthalemew** A dashing Core Worlds socialite and expert card player, he spent much of his time in exclusive clubs on Ord Sabaok, listening to those around him for any information about the Imperial presence in the sector. Windsloe was an undercover Rebel Alliance sympathizer and used his position to gather information for the Rebellion.

**Windu, Mace** A Jedi Master and senior member of the Jedi Council in the final years of the Galactic Republic. As a child on Haruun Kal, Mace Windu was orphaned when his parents died in the savage jungle. He was turned over to the Jedi Order when he was just six months old. Windu had a special ability to see events through the Force as if they were crystalline matrices. With this vision, Windu could identify the "shatterpoint" of a situation, and know exactly how to manipulate events to ensure victory.

As a Padawan, he served a tour on Wroona fighting pirates aboard the primitive sailing ship *Temblor,* and worked with Republic policing squads to contain the Arkanian Revolution. Among the many tales revolving around Mace Windu were those of his first solo mission, in which he retrieved unique lightsaber crystals from Hurikane; his involvement in the time paradox of Tet-Ami; his bringing down of the murderous Uda-Khalid; and his unique resolution to a conflict on Er'stacia. He was known as a man who led others by rigorous example and was considered one of the toughest Jedi fighters. A popular story among the Padawans told of Windu single-handedly capturing a team of Gank Killers without ever igniting his lightsaber.

*Mace Windu wields his purple-bladed lightsaber.*

Windu was a Form VII (Vaapad) lightsaber instructor, practicing a dangerous style that cut perilously close to the dark side. He took as his Padawan learner the Chalactan child Depa Billaba, after he rescued her from space pirates who had killed her parents. Her appointment to the Jedi Council was a proud moment for him, since he considered Depa to be the daughter he never had. A year before the Battle of Naboo, Windu led a Jedi team sent to the Yinchorri homeworld.

When Qui-Gon Jinn brought Anakin Skywalker before the Council, Windu was skeptical that the boy could be the Chosen One of prophecy, but ultimately convinced the Council that Skywalker should be trained by Obi-Wan Kenobi after Qui-Gon's death. After Count Dooku emerged as the leader of the Separatist movement, Windu felt strongly that the situation could be resolved through negotiation. He led the task force to Geonosis to investigate the Separatist army, and found himself under attack by the bounty hunter Jango Fett. Windu decapitated Fett during the fighting but was overpowered by the droid soldiers. The timely appearance of Master Yoda and the clone troopers of the Army of the Republic saved the Jedi and won the Battle of Geonosis, but Windu and Yoda were worried that deeper, darker events were occurring that they could not foresee. Master Windu also privately believed that he could have prevented the Clone Wars by killing Count Dooku during their confrontation on Geonosis.

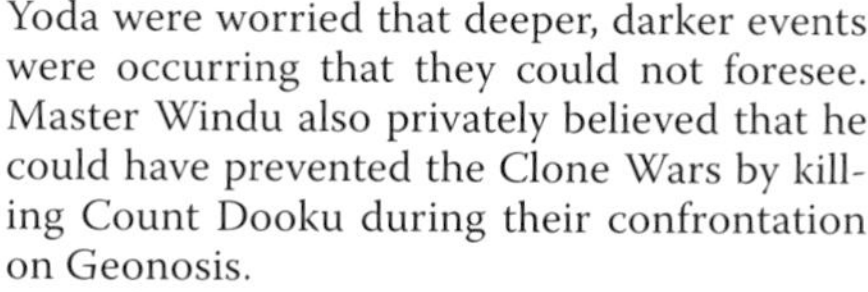
*Windy*

Early in the Clone Wars, Mace Windu met with dissident Jedi, including Master Sora Bulq, on the moon of Ruul. Later he led clone troopers on Dantooine and single-handedly destroyed a seismic tank. Six months into the war, Master Windu went to Haruun Kal to recover his former apprentice, Depa Billaba, after she disappeared in the uplands. He learned that he was one of only two surviving members of the Windu ghôsh, the other being Kar Vastor. He accepted Vastor's assistance in reaching Billaba and in freeing the Korunnai from their subservience to the Balawai.

As the Clone Wars began to wind down, Master Windu became worried about the emergency powers granted to Chancellor Palpatine. He felt that the dark side surrounded Palpatine, but couldn't place his finger on why. During the Separatist attack on Coruscant, Windu's Jedi starfighter was shot down and he was forced to commandeer a vulture droid. When Anakin Skywalker revealed to Master Windu that Palpatine was Darth Sidious, Windu gathered Agen Kolar, Kit Fisto, and Saesee Tiin to arrest the Chancellor. Palpatine killed Master Windu's companions and battled the Jedi Master, who soon gained the upper hand. Just as Windu seemed ready to slay Palpatine, Anakin Skywalker intervened and cut off Windu's lightsaber hand. This gave Palpatine the opportunity to blast Windu with Force lightning, sending him out a window to his death.

**Windy** One of Luke Skywalker's childhood friends, he grew up with Luke on the planet Tatooine. His full name was Windom Starkiller. When the boys were 13 years old, Windy and Luke became lost in a sandswirl and came face-to-face with a krayt dragon. They were saved from certain death by Ben Kenobi.

**Wing-Blast rocketpack** A Mandalorian device capable of atmospheric and deep-space flight upward of 500 kilometers per hour. The rocketpack's wings were lined with mini concussion missiles and heavy rotating blasters. The Wing-Blast rocketpack was apparently designed by MandalMotors' General Zenlav, but when the project called for use of an untested photonic beam, Zenlav shelved his eccentric design. Centuries later, schematics for the rocketpack fell into Boba Fett's possession. Fett fitted it with a proton torpedo to circumvent the photonics problem, and first used the modified pack to assail the Tulvarees guardians of Fortress Baarlos and collect the bounty on Faarl the Conqueror.

**Winger, Alexandra** The adopted daughter of Imperial Governor Tork Winger on Garos IV, she worked with the Garos resistance movement behind her father's back to fight against the Empire. Later she served as captain of the vessel *Webley.*

**Winning Gamble** A PLY 3000 yacht owned by the Bardrin Group during the early years of the New Republic. Sansia Bardrin was captured while flying it, and her father hired Mara Jade to help rescue her. Jade did, but then discovered Ja Bardrin was much more interested in recovering the ship than his daughter. The *Gamble* had prototype military systems, including an upgraded flight package, enhanced weapons systems, and a defensive shoot-back targeting system. Sansia then offered Mara the ship as payment for her rescue. Mara agreed, renaming it *Jade's Fire.*

**Winning Hand** A supposedly damaged ship whose crew needed rescuing during the Yuuzhan Vong War. Dacholder, a secret member of the Peace Brigade, and Uldir Lochett, a dropout from Luke Skywalker's Jedi praxeum, piloted the rescue ship *Pride of Thela* into position when Lochett discovered it was all a plot to turn him over to the Yuuzhan Vong. Lochett gave Dacholder a one-way trip into the vacuum of space and escaped.

**Winter** *See* Celchu, Winter

**Winward, Riij** A Rebel spy, he was a prison guard when the Mistryl Shadow Guards Shada and Karoly were captured by the Empire on Tatooine. He released them so they could escape the planet with Hammertong, and in exchange he received their droid Deefour, which carried a complete technical readout of the potentially deadly device.

**Wioslea** A female Vuvrian, she worked at a used-speeder lot in Mos Eisley called Spacesport Speeders. Wioslea was proud that she

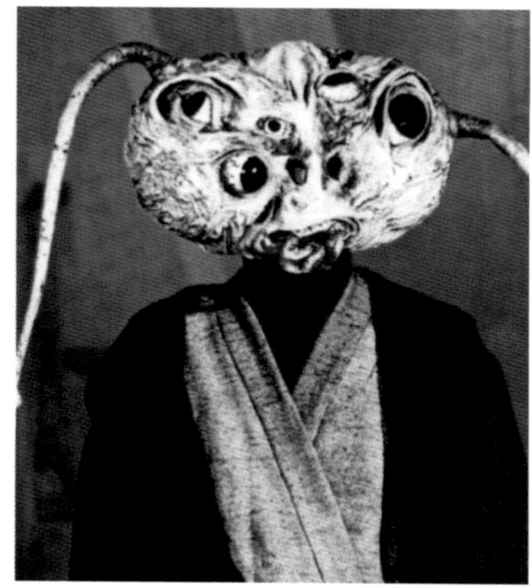
*Wioslea*

had offered Luke Skywalker 2,000 credits for his landspeeder so he could get offworld and "save the galaxy," as she often reported during her business dealings.

**Wirut** A native of the planet Coruscant, this man served as a sergeant in the 967th Commando Unit of the Galactic Alliance Defense Force during the years following the Yuuzhan Vong War. Sergeant Wirut was later one of the officers who joined the Galactic Alliance Guard. Wirut and a GAG trooper named Limm were chosen specifically by Jacen Solo to accompany him to the offices of Cal Omas when Solo had the Chief of State arrested for his duplicity in secretly meeting with Dur Gejjen. Although neither showed it, both Wirut and Limm were shaken by the act of arresting the Chief of State and turning him over to the authorities.

**Wister** An X-wing pilot in Rogue Squadron during the Battle of Endor, he was Wedge Antilles's wingmate, using the call sign Rogue Two during subsequent cleanup operations. Wister was shot down and killed by remaining Imperial forces after sighting the wreckage of the *Executor* in a canyon on the Forest Moon of Endor.

**Wistie** Also called Firefolk, they were tiny pixie-like beings that glowed brightly and could fly. Wisties, who tended to giggle a lot, lived on Endor's Forest Moon.

**Wistril** Located in the system of the same name, it was the planet where the Star Destroyer *Chimaera* stopped to take on supplies. Luke Skywalker and Mara Jade hijacked a supply shuttle on Wistril to rescue smuggler Talon Karrde from the *Chimaera*'s detention block.

*Witches of Dathomir*

**Witches of Dathomir** A group of Force-sensitive women, they lived on the planet Dathomir and were organized into nine clans. These included the Singing Mountain, Frenzied River, and Red Hills clans. The Witches lived by the *Book of Law,* which said that they should not concede to evil. Those who did needed to go into the wilderness alone to seek cleansing. Their main foes were the Nightsisters, a group of women who acted out of anger, were outcast, and turned to the dark side. The witches ran a completely matriarchal society; men were slaves or breeders. The witches wore tunics made from colorful reptile skins with thick robes woven of fiber trimmed with large dark beads. They were among the only beings in the galaxy who could train rancors for use as mounts.

**Wittin** A Jawa leader who participated in Jabba the Hutt's demolition contests on Tatooine. A barbaric warlord whose tribe profited from robbing travelers and other foul deeds, Wittin was the most feared Jawa on the planet. For years, moisture farmers and other settlers quaked at the sight of the tribe's sandcrawler roaming the dunes. After a skirmish with Imperial stormtroopers, the tribe's sandcrawler was destroyed and Wittin's followers scattered into the desert. Jabba the Hutt offered Wittin a new sandcrawler if he could win the Hutt's underground demolition contest. In the contest, Wittin remote-piloted a STAP with an armed battle droid.

*Wittin*

**Wodrata, Rogwa** A female Holwuff who represented Alliga in the Confederacy of Independent Systems during the Clone Wars. She was present during the summit on Geonosis to meet with Count Dooku.

**Wokling** A baby or infant Ewok.

**Wol Cabasshite** A species of long-lived, immobile slugs from the planet Wol Cabassh. Despite their relation to plasma leeches, Wol Cabasshites were fully intelligent. The body of a Wol Cabasshite was almost entirely stomach, and they had two distinct brains: one for digestion and another for thought and cognition. Their diet was made up of plasma-rich substances, many of which were also high in metallic content. This resulted in a high content of metals in their bloodstream and body tissue, creating a magnetic field in the vicinity of their bodies. The field served as the primary communication medium of Wol Cabasshites, who could manipulate it with their tongues to form concepts and patterns. Philosophers discovered a treasure trove of information when prominent members of the species finally copied down their thoughts and memories. Their bodies allowed Wol Cabasshites to exist in both atmosphere and vacuum, and they could tolerate extremes in temperature. When it came time to reproduce, individuals exchanged genetic material while grooming each other's tongues. This material was stored in the lining of the stomach, which was later disgorged to become pupal offspring. Omo Bouri, the Jedi Master of Saesee Tiin, was a Wol Cabasshite.

*Wokling*

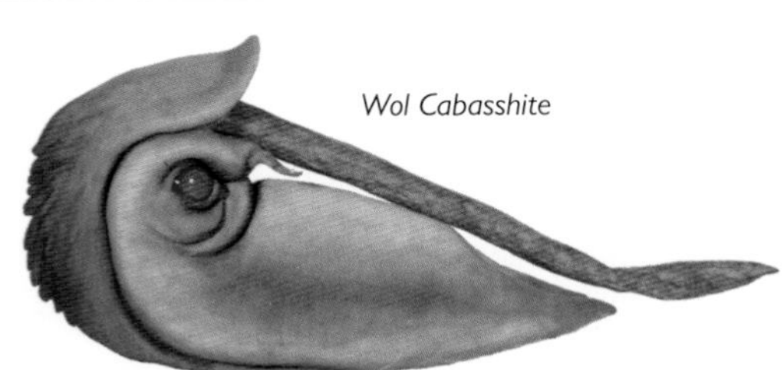
*Wol Cabasshite*

**Wolf Clan** A group of Padawans at the Jedi Temple that included the students Lartan, Mox Freedan, Kiri, Lina Lascol, and Ezak.

**Wolfman** A slang term for members of the Shistavanen species.

**wolvkil** Fierce predators tamed by the Vagaari slavers in the Unknown Regions. While investigating the Outbound Flight wreck, the Vagaari—disguised themselves—wore wolvkils as garments, with each animal kept in stasis by a restraining collar. When reanimated, the vicious predators attacked with wild abandon, shaking off blaster bolts with ease as they killed their victims. Their ability to endure pain stemmed from their decentralized nervous system, as well as the distributed physiology of their internal organs. When confronted, Mara Jade quickly cut down two wolvkils while Luke Skywalker used the Force to cause others to fall asleep.

**womp** A derogatory term derived from *womp rat,* it was often directed at the rat-like Ranats on Tatooine.

**womp rat** Carnivorous creatures, they lived in the canyons of Tatooine. They were vicious, hair-covered rodents that grew to more than

Womp rat

2 meters long. Womp rats traveled in packs and used their claws and teeth to bring down prey. Luke Skywalker used to hunt womp rats in Beggar's Canyon, targeting them at high speeds from the cockpit of his skyhopper.

**Womrik** This planet was a temporary base for Garm Bel Iblis's private army during its hit-and-fade attacks against the Empire.

**Wonetun** The Brubb pilot of the *Jolly Man,* he served with the Wild Knights and lent his assistance to the Jedi Knights during the Yuuzhan Vong War. Wonetun and his crew worked with Danni Quee to capture a live yammosk as part of the Eclipse Project. Wonetun survived the war and later trained to become an X-wing pilot.

**won-wons** A Wookiee delicacy, these warm, greasy dinner pastries tasted to others like franit slugs . . . only slimier.

**woodoo** These huge, flightless reptavians native to Tatooine weighed up to 640 kilograms when fully grown and resembled huge, bloated vultures. Woodoos moved about on thick legs and wide flat feet studded with claws for digging. They fed on the eggs of dewbacks, but also scavenged for food from kills by other predators.

Wookiees Chewbacca (left) and Tarfful

**Wookiee** A tall, completely fur-covered species native to the planet Kashyyyk, Wookiees were widely known as ferocious opponents and loyal friends. The average Wookiee grew to more than 2 meters tall and lived several times the lifetime of a human. On their homeworld, Wookiees inhabited cities built far above the ground in giant wroshyr trees. Although they appeared primitive, Wookiees were comfortable with high technology. Their language consisted of grunts and growls, and while they could understand other languages, their limited vocal ability made it impossible for them to speak anything other than their own language. They had regenerative powers that let them heal more in a day than a human could in two weeks.

Kashyyyk was the site of one of the fiercest battles of the Clone Wars. After the establishment of the Empire, the planet was placed under martial law and Wookiees were enslaved as laborers. It wasn't until after the Battle of Endor that the Rebel Alliance was able to set the Wookiees free. Chewbacca, Han Solo's copilot and partner, was one of the galaxy's most famous Wookiees.

The Wookiees supported the New Republic, and later the Galactic Alliance, but chose to remain neutral in the wake of the Yuuzhan Vong War, in an effort to keep the space lanes near Kashyyyk open to all. When Jacen Solo assumed control of the Galactic Alliance some 40 years after the Battle of Yavin, the Wookiees broke away from the GA and refused to support his leadership. After they harbored Han and Leia Organa Solo, as well as members of the new Jedi Order, Jacen Solo chose to make the Wookiees an example. He launched a war fleet to Kashyyyk and openly attacked the planet, burning many cities and a large part of the planet's surface, hoping to show the rest of the galaxy what would happen if it opposed his rule. With the help of fleets from the Confederation, the Wookiees were able to drive off Solo's forces. They later joined the Jedi Coalition that was formed in the wake of the Second Battle of Fondor.

**Wookiee Gnasp fluttercraft** Small helicopters propelled by fluttering ornithopter rotor blades used by Wookiees on their homeworld of Kashyyyk. Named for a dangerous insectoid from the Wookiee colony moon of Alaris, the Raddaugh Gnasp fluttercraft was built by the enterprising Wookiees of the Appazanna Engineering Works. The slight ornithopter was primarily a civil security patrol craft, zipping through the dangerous underbrush and lower levels of the Kashyyyk forests in search-and-rescue missions and perimeter scans for encroaching dangers. It had no armor, and its mostly open cockpit provided minimal cover for its two occupants. Instead, it relied on its speed and agility to avoid incoming fire.

Wookiee Gnasp fluttercraft

**Wookiee honor family** A special bond of friendship that joined one Wookiee with a group of other Wookiees or even with members of other species. The honor family was made up of a Wookiee's true friends, who pledged to lay down their lives for one another and their extended families.

**Wookiee life debt** A sacred Wookiee custom, a life debt was pledged to anyone who saved a Wookiee's life, forming a bond that could never be broken. A life debt was a sacred act of honor, designed to repay something that was without measure.

Woolamanders

**Wookiee Rite of Passage** This test called for an adolescent Wookiee to perform a feat that was both dangerous and difficult. The male or female Wookiee could attempt the feat alone or with friends. If successful, the Wookiee emerged with physical proof of bravery that could be worn or carried as a trophy.

**Wookiee-wango** A drink made with Sullustan gin, it was stirred not shaken.

**woolamanders** Sloth-like in appearance, they were native to Yavin 4. Woolamanders had naked skin on their bellies and thick blue and gold fur on their backs. They lived in family groups among the branches of the Massassi trees, feeding on flower petals, tender leaf shoots, and the rhizome seed nodules of nebula orchids.

Wooof

**Wooof** A Nikto of the Kadas'sa'Nikto subspecies who worked as one of Jabba the Hutt's best pilots. He also was a smuggler who preferred flying combat starfighters. Wooof often piloted Jabba's space yacht, and he was killed when it exploded near the Pit of Carkoon.

**Woostoid** The native inhabitants of the planet Woostri. Woostoids were of average height but extremely slender, with reddish orange skin and flowing red hair. They had bulbous, pupil-less eyes that rarely blinked. Traditionally, they wore long, flowing robes of bright, reflective cloth. Woostoids were a peaceful species, and the concept of warfare and fighting was extremely disconcerting to them. They often were selected to maintain records for Old Republic databases, and were noted for their record-keeping and data-management abilities. They were adept at computer technology, so many of their manufacturing and production sectors were computer-controlled. The Woostoids embraced the Emperor's New Order.

**Woostri** Located in the system of the same name, the planet was attacked and captured by Grand Admiral Thrawn. He determined that the natives of Woostri had both a strong fear of the unknown and a tendency to blow rumors out of proportion, making them vulnerable to his seeming ability to fire through planetary shields.

Woostoid

**Works, The** A run-down, dangerous Coruscant industrial sector located to the south and west of the Senate District, it stood in stark contrast to the opulent lifestyle of nearby government leaders. It was within The Works that the Jedi Order discovered a secret meeting place used by Darth Sidious and Count Dooku during the Clone Wars. Sidious had imbued most of The Works with the energy of the dark side of the Force, and it was here that he trained both Darth Maul and Darth Tyranus to be his apprentices. At the height of the New Order, The Works experienced something of a renaissance: It became the location where hundreds of TIE fighters were produced every day in support of the Imperial war machine. (*See also* Dacho District.)

**World Brain** A Yuuzhan Vong dhuryam, carefully selected from many others to oversee the terraforming of Coruscant during its transformation into a replica of Yuuzhan'tar. The World Brain rested in the Well of the World Brain on Coruscant, on the site of the former Galactic Senate Rotunda. It rested in a pool of slime that fluoresced yellow-gold and scarlet and looked like a black, bloated stomach turned inside out. It had a yellow eye the size of an X-wing that could be wiped by a triple layer of transparent eyelids that slid across its surface at different angles to scrape it free of slime. It could send sprays of tentacles upward from the slime. Jacen Solo had a special bond with the World Brain from his time as a Yuuzhan Vong captive, and taught the alien construct how to "compromise," resulting in the subtle sabotage of Coruscant's terraforming. After the war ended, the World Brain was allowed to remain alive and re-form Coruscant the way its inhabitants wanted. About 10 years later, it also became Jacen Solo's top spy. The World Brain was killed when Alema Rar tried to murder Jacen by firing a poisoned dart at him. He ducked at the last instant, and the dart plunged into the World Brain.

**worldcraft** A planetoid-sized starship created by command of the Emperor and given to a few of his cruelest officers. One was used by Lord Hethrir.

**World Devastator** Weapons of mass destruction and a symbol of the Empire's reign of terror, they were horrific planetary assault weapons ordered by the cloned Emperor Palpatine when he attempted to retake control of the galaxy some six years after the Battle of Endor. World Devastators literally chewed up a target world, using its resources to create new weapons to be used against it—hence their many nicknames: World Sweepers, World Smashers, and City Eaters. Internal tractor beams sucked a planet's surface into a molecular furnace, which broke down the substances into useful materials with which droid-controlled factories built new weapons. Within months, a planet was virtually gone.

World Devastators had hyperdrives and ion engines for travel in deep space, but their main role was to devour a planet's surface. A central droid brain controlled the onboard factories and stored plans for producing Imperial war vessels. During the Battle of Mon Calamari, World Devastators first produced automated TIE/D fighters in large quantities. A World Devastator "grew" by consuming planets and asteroids. The droid brain could create custom additions and alterations, so no two mature World Devastators were identical.

The *Silencer-7,* the largest World Devastator, led the assault on Mon Calamari. At 3,200 meters long and 1,500 meters tall, it was larger than an Imperial Star Destroyer and had a crew of 25,000. The *Silencer-7* had 125 heavy turbolasers, 200 blaster cannons, 80 proton missile tubes, 15 ion cannons, and 15 tractor beam projectors. The key to the defeat of the monstrous machines was Palpatine's fear that the weapons could be turned against him. The cloned Emperor created a command-and-control coding system that allowed him to seize control of them at any time from his throneworld, Byss. The New Republic was saved when Luke Skywalker provided the code to R2-D2, who shut down the World Devastators on Mon Calamari, allowing New Republic forces to destroy the helpless planet smashers.

World Devastator

**worldship** A bioengineered form of capital ship, the Yuuzhan Vong worldship was created from a community of yorik coral. Known to the Yuuzhan Vong as a *Koros-Strohna,* these 10-kilometer-wide ships were living creatures designed to cross vast distances of space. Once a worldship was ready to disgorge its passengers, a huge, tubular worm was extended from the craft into the surface of the landing area, allowing the Yuuzhan Vong to establish a planetside base and maintain contact with the worldship.

Wormie (left) with Fixer, Camie, and Biggs

**Worlohp, Captain** An Ithorian pilot, he made regular trips to Ohma-D'un as the captain of the shuttle *Fair Gale,* until an accidental leak of Kyvalon-4 gas drove him into a murderous madness. In his rage, Worlohp incapacitated many of his passengers and damaged the shuttle's navigational controls. Only the timely intervention of several brave passengers helped prevent a total disaster. Worlohp made a complete recovery and was reinstated as a pilot after profuse apologies.

**Wormie** A nickname given to Luke Skywalker by Camie and Fixer, two of his childhood friends on Tatooine.

**Wornal sector** Located near the Sombure sector, it was fought over after the Battle of Endor by Imperial Moff Prentioch and Moff Eyrgen as they began expanding their individual territories. Two years after Endor, Prentioch traveled to the waterworld of Kaal, hoping to gain control of its aquaculture industry to help fuel his war effort in the Wornal sector.

**Worr, Eshin** A female Yuuzhan Vong from the intendant caste who served as an executor and slave master. She was known to use the poison of her tsaisi to punish her slaves, allowing them to suffer before administering the antidote. Any slaves who continued to resist her were given further "treatments" of tsaisi poison to break their will and bend them to her needs.

**Worror, Master** An Ithorian Jedi Master and a member of the Army of Light during the final years of the New Sith Wars. Worror was a noted healer who was known for his skill in Jedi battle meditation. During the Battle of Ruusan, Worror did not carry a lightsaber into battle and served as one of Lord Hoth's primary tactical advisers. Some 10 years later, Master Worror was one of a handful of Jedi who accompanied Lord Valenthyne Farfalla to Tython to confront Darth Bane. While the others faced Bane and his apprentice, Zannah, Master Worror stayed in the shadows, using battle meditation to coordinate their attacks. Once Darth Bane figured out why Worror wasn't participating in the fighting, he slashed through all four of Master Worror's throats. When Bane turned to dispatch Johun Othone, Worror encased him in a powerful bubble of Force energy. As Bane unleashed Force lightning, the electricity ricocheted off the energy bubble. Worror died from the effort as Bane was charred from his own attack.

**worrt** This voracious frog-like predator inhabited Tatooine's wilderness areas. Worrts typically fed on insects, small rodents, and other tiny creatures, but would attack anything that passed by, whether edible or not, with their long, lashing tongues. There were several worrts outside the palace of Jabba the Hutt.

**Wor Tandell** The planet where medical droid Too-Onebee made an inspection tour of medical facilities with Lord Cuvir, Imperial Governor of Firro and Too-Onebee's master. During the inspection, Cuvir was assassinated by Tiree, a Rebel agent, and Too-Onebee joined the Rebel Alliance.

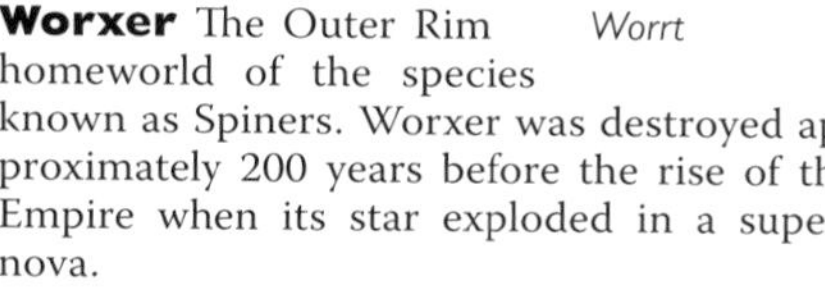
Worrt

**Worxer** The Outer Rim homeworld of the species known as Spiners. Worxer was destroyed approximately 200 years before the rise of the Empire when its star exploded in a supernova.

**Wotan Weave** A maneuver in which a starship flew in a corkscrew pattern, allowing it to move forward but making it difficult to hit.

**Woteba** A planet discovered by Han Solo and Leia Organa Solo during their search for a new home for the Ithorian species. Woteba was a temperate world of marshlands and rolling plains broken by jagged ranges of mountains. The planet, along with many others, existed within the depths of the Utegetu Nebula in the Unknown Regions. During the Swarm War, the planet was turned over to the Killik Colony, and a disease known as the Fizz appeared. Cilghal and other Jedi healers learned that the Fizz was a sophisticated nanotechnology aimed at destroying anything that wasn't native to Woteba.

Eshin Worr

**Wraith Squadron** A group of pilots assembled by Wedge Antilles after the Battle of Endor to perform covert operations. Wraith Squadron was composed of commandos, snipers, spies, and infiltrators drawn from the dregs of the New Republic's pilot ranks. Antilles felt that these pilots deserved a second chance, and formed the team with Wes Janson as his second in command. The group originally was designated Gray Squadron, but Wedge allowed the Wraiths to choose their own name. (Among those proposed were Dinner Squadron and Silly Squadron.) The Wraiths quickly proved their worth as an infiltration team, taking out several key Imperial installations and providing valuable support during the hunt for Warlord Zsinj. At one point, the group infiltrated Zsinj's organization by commandeering the Corellian corvette *Night Caller.* After the defeat of Zsinj at Selaggis Six, the Wraiths were disbanded as a starfighter squadron and became an intelligence force working for Airen Cracken. During the Yuuzhan Vong War, the Wraiths scouted the locations of Yuuzhan Vong strongholds, especially along the major hyperspace travel routes.

The Wraiths also assisted during Luke Skywalker's infiltration of enemy-held Coruscant. Among the prominent members of Wraith Squadron were Garik "Face" Loran, Lara Notsil, Myn Donos, Tyria Sarkin, Voort saBinring, Ton Phanan, Kell Tainer, Hohass Ekwesh, and Dia Passik.

**Wraw** A Bothan officer in the New Republic Intelligence agency during the Yuuzhan Vong War, he was part of a mission to destroy a yammosk that had been installed on Caluula. The team was captured, but members noticed that their Yuuzhan Vong captors, as well as all aspects of their biotechnology, were suddenly dying. Wraw then revealed that his primary mission as part of Team Meloque was to monitor a new strain of the Alpha Red virus to make sure that it was still as potent as originally believed. The team was a backup in case the virus failed.

**Wrea** A blue-and-white planet located close to the asteroid belt known as Smuggler's Run. Some 13 years after the Battle of Endor, Han Solo and Chewbacca brought a group of smugglers, injured by an explosion in the Run, to Wrea for treatment.

**Wren, Lavina Durada-Vashne** Cularin's Senator to the Galactic Republic during the years leading up to the Battle of Naboo.

**Wrench** A clone trooper aboard Joram Kithe's downed gunship at Pengalan IV. Kithe gave this particular trooper the nickname Wrench because he had the highest level of mechanical expertise in the group.

**Wrils** The capital city of Svivren's southern district, it was surrounded by rounded mountains and had a semi-arid climate.

**Wroona** A small blue world in the Wroona system, it was located on the far edge of the Inner Rim. Wroona's continents were separated by vast oceans, and their blue-sand beaches stretched for thousands of kilometers. Its seven billion near-human inhabitants were a blue-skinned species with a lighthearted and optimistic outlook on life. Their society emphasized materialism and personal gain, and Wroonian merchants, smugglers, and pirates could be found throughout the galaxy pursuing personal wealth. The planet was run by the Wroonian Guilds, which represented trade organizations and businesses. Animal life included Wroonian flycatchers, which hung from coastal cave ceilings by their tongues and swung down to catch their avian prey. The region of space known as Keller's Void acted as a shortcut between the Wroona and Calus systems. As a Padawan, Mace Windu served a tour of duty on Wroona fighting pirates aboard the sailing ship *Temblor.* During the Clone Wars, Chi Eekway was Wroona's Senator.

***Wroshyr*** A saucer-shaped ship, it was owned by the Wookiee bounty hunter Chenlambec.

**wroshyr tree** Giant trees of the jungle world of Kashyyyk, their separate branches met to form one interlocked branch, which then sprouted new branches of its own. These reached out in all directions to find other branches to join. This tendency toward unity made wroshyr trees stronger, and was a natural symbol for the Wookiee concepts of honor and family. The wroshyr trees in the Rwookrrorro city grouping were actually a single giant plant with a unified root system. The Wookiees built their cities in wroshyr trees.

**Wuher** A bulky, surly, middle-aged human, he was a shift bartender at the Mos Eisley spaceport cantina. Abandoned in Mos Eisley in his early youth, Wuher proved to be a whiz with chemicals in general and drinks and elixirs in particular. After graduating from a bartending correspondence school, he was hired by Chalmun the Wookiee. For years, Wuher hated droids, primarily because they were an easy target. But he had a change of heart when he met C2-R4, a processing droid capable of making new exotic drinks out of the strangest raw materials. Wuher's first concoction with Ceetoo-Arfour was a drink specially designed for Jabba the Hutt, created using the pheromones extracted from the corpse of Greedo, an inexperienced Rodian bounty hunter.

*Wuher*

**Wuht, Admiral Darez** The admiral of the Duro Defense Force during the Yuuzhan Vong War. Admiral Wuht, sympathetic to the plight of injured military personnel, was placed in command of the refugee camps on his homeworld. However, he proved to be incapable, and the Ryn stranded on Duro took to calling him "Admiral Dizzlewit." During the defense of Duro, Admiral Wuht took command of his flagship, the *Poesy,* and attempted to stop any ship that fled the Yuuzhan Vong attack. Wuht quickly reconsidered his position when Duro's orbital cities became a target, and he joined the New Republic in its fight to save the planet.

*Wupiupi*

**Wuitho Trifalls** An Alderaan landmark, it featured three spectacular waterfalls. Captain Celchu visited the Wuitho Trifalls with his family the week before going off to the Imperial Academy. It was his last visit to the famous tourist attraction.

**Wukkar** A heavily populated world in the Galactic Core, it was one of many planets that surrendered to Admiral Ackbar and the Rebel Alliance fleet in the years following the Battle of Endor.

**Wuluw** A subspecies of the Killiks that made up the Colony during the Swarm War. The short-statured, wide-eyed Wuluw stood just under 1 meter tall and were among the handful of Killiks who lacked a protective carapace. Wuluw chitin was so delicate that it often cracked if an individual tripped and fell, forcing the Wuluw to take noncombat roles. What they lacked in protection, however, the Wuluw made up for in their ability to communicate with the Colony across vast distances. Thus, many Wuluw were dispatched to all sections of the Great Swarm to create a communications network and to coordinate the orders issued by Raynar Thul during the Colony's conflict with the Chiss.

**Wunka** A dark-furred Ewok who helped Chewbacca commandeer an AT-ST during the Battle of Endor. Wunka and his brother Tokkat later served as Ewok gunners aboard the New Republic Star Destroyer *Liberator* when it was shot down over Imperial City. He was killed in a skirmish on Holageus.

**wupiupi** A form of hard currency used in Mos Espa, among other Tatooine settlements, and across Outer Rim Territories during the last decades of the Old Republic. There were 64 wupiupi in 1 peggat, which was worth 4 truguts or about 40 Republic dataries. Locals often held them in the pouch of a money belt.

**Wurf'al** A Bothan captain in the Galactic Alliance military during the Swarm War. Wurf'al was an aide to Admiral Nek Bwua'tu and often badgered his way to a position of strength by invoking the names of his honored family members. During the blockade of the Murgo Choke, Captain Wurf'al served under Admiral Bwua'tu aboard the *Admiral Ackbar.* Leia Organa Solo eventually discovered that the admiral's spinglass statuary contained assassin bugs from the Gorog hive; Wurf'al was the first officer killed by the swarm.

**Wwebyls** A tiny humanoid from the planet Yn, he was a New Republic Senator who was elected to the Inner Council after the bombing of Senate Hall on Coruscant.

**Wxtm** The Outer Rim homeworld of dangerous ravenscreechers.

**Wyl sector** Together with the Aparo sector, it formed the inner border of the Corporate Sector. It was long ruled by Moff Gozric.

Aubrie Wyn

**Wyn, Aubrie** The 13-year-old member of the "Padawan Pack" on Jabiim during the Clone Wars. Aubrie Wyn was a skilled healer. Her Master, Sirrus, was killed in a blast that also appeared to take the life of Obi-Wan Kenobi, and Wyn joined with the other orphaned Padawans on Jabiim for survival. Before the final attack on Cobalt Station, she gave Master Sirrus's holocron to Anakin Skywalker so he could return it to the Jedi Temple. Wyn died at Cobalt Station as she killed Altos Stratus.

Uthar Wynn

**Wynl, Senator** The representative for the Baragwin communities during the Yuuzhan Vong War. He did not take the Yuuzhan Vong threat seriously during Leia Organa Solo's speech to the Senate.

**Wynn, Uthar** The leader of the Sith Academy on Korriban some 4,000 years before the Battle of Yavin. Master Wynn was training an apprentice named Yuthura during this time, until a group of Jedi Knights infiltrated the Academy by posing as Sith apprentices. After gaining Master Wynn's confidence, the Jedi revealed themselves. Wynn and Yuthura attacked the Jedi, but both were defeated in combat.

**Wynni** A female Wookiee smuggler, she tried to seduce Chewbacca on his first visit to Skip 1. Wynni was one of the smugglers who joined Han Solo and Chewbacca in Smuggler's Run during their investigation into the bombing on Coruscant and the rescue of Lando Calrissian from the crime lord Nandreeson. However, her amorous feelings for Chewbacca overcame her, and at one point during the trip she had to be restrained.

**Wyrlan** A Galactic Alliance Guard and security officer at the Galactic Justice Center on Coruscant in the years following the Swarm War. Wyrlan and Garsi were assigned to work with Tahiri Veila during her interrogation of Ben Skywalker following the Second Battle of Fondor. Their role was to protect Veila if necessary, and they were forced into action when Ben escaped from the hoverchair in which he had been strapped. After Ben used the Force to deflect one of their stun blasts at Veila, he offered Wyrlan and Garsi the chance to stay alive if they gave him some information and helped him escape. Ben took their armor to disguise himself and the body of Lon Shevu.

**wyrwulf** A name given to the furry young of the Codru-Ji. They had limpid liquid-blue eyes, six legs, and fangs. Wyrwulfs were intelligent but not self-aware until after they metamorphosed into the upright four-armed form of an adult Codru-Ji.

***Wyvern*** An Imperial Remnant warship that saw action during the Second Battle of Fondor. The *Wyvern* and its battle group initially remained with the *Anakin Solo,* even after Jacen Solo went rogue and starting bombarding Fondorian cities from orbit. Admiral Gilad Pellaeon ordered the *Wyvern* to break off its attacks and take orders from Admiral Cha Niathal for the duration of the fighting.

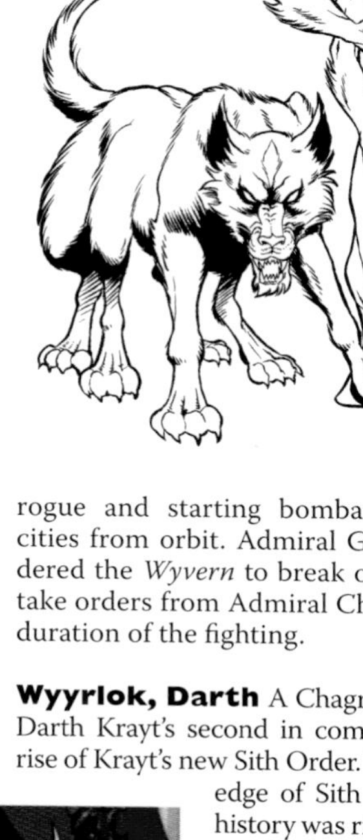
Wyrwulf

**Wyyrlok, Darth** A Chagrian Sith Lord and Darth Krayt's second in command during the rise of Krayt's new Sith Order. Wyyrlok's knowledge of Sith lore, rituals, and history was rivaled only by that of Krayt himself. The reserved, philosophical Chagrian was the third individual to hold the title of Darth Wyyrlok, and ensured the continuation of the pattern by submitting his daughter for training on Korriban. As Darth Krayt's health grew steadily worse, Wyyrlok explored the lore of Xoxaan, looking for clues to help combat the Sith Lord's failing condition. Wyyrlok also brought in the Jedi healer Hosk Trey'lis, but nothing helped. When it became apparent that stronger measures were needed, Darth Wyyrlok chose to seek help from an unlikely source: Cade Skywalker, who already had healed two other beings, drawing on the dark side of the Force to bring them back from the brink of death.

Darth Wyyrlok

**wyyyschok** *See* webweaver.

X-1 Viper Automadon

**X0-X1** A prototype droid designed to reprogram itself, it was tampered with and took control of Cloud City's droid population as a first step toward transforming the organic population into droids as well. In a desperate act, Walex Blissex shut down all power, effectively turning X0-X1 off as well. Without power to Cloud City's huge B/1 repulsorlift engines, the city began to plummet. A Rebel Alliance team, however, was able to dismantle X0-X1 before the floating metropolis plunged into Bespin's core.

**X-10-D** A red-and-bronze service droid, it was on board the *Hound's Tooth,* the ship of bounty hunter Bossk. Roughly Trandoshan in shape, X-10-D was brainless, receiving its commands directly from the ship's main computer. After the Wookiee bounty hunter Chenlambec tricked and captured Bossk, the Wookiee's positronic processor Flirt attached to Exten-dee and served as its "brain" from then on.

X-10-D

**X14** The code name of the New Republic spy who kept a lookout for Sate Pestage on the planet Ciutric. He was part of the Republic's Commando Team One, serving under Kapp Dendo.

< X-wing starfighters

**X-1 Viper Automadon** A war droid manufactured by the factory world of Balmorra, it was equipped with molecular shielding that not only absorbed the energy of an attacker's blast but also channeled it directly into its own turbolasers. Balmorra agreed to send a shipment of X-1 Viper Automadons to the cloned Emperor's throneworld of Byss as part of a cease-fire agreement with Imperial Military Executor Sedriss. But the planet's Governor Beltane alerted the New Republic so that it could hide stowaways inside the war droids.

**X-222** A sleek high-altitude atmospheric fighter craft, it was commonly called a triple-deuce.

**X-23 StarWorker** A massive space barge from Incom Industries during the New Order, it was 38 meters long and could hold 2,000 cubic meters of cargo with a maximum mass of 5,000 metric tons. It was produced without weapons systems or shielding, and required an escort when traveling through potentially hostile territory. The X-23 required only two crew assisted by a fifth-degree labor droid.

**X-34 landspeeder** An older-model landspeeder from SoroSuub, the X-34 was the one used by a young Luke Skywalker as he grew up on Tatooine. Open to the air, it had a top speed of 250 kilometers per hour. Repulsorlift drives kept it suspended 1 meter above the ground even when it was parked. The X-34 could transport a pilot and just one passenger, although two droids could be tied down on the rear deck. The X-34 had a retractable duraplex windscreen, and was controlled by a steering wheel and foot pedals.

**X-45** SoroSuub's military sniper rifle, produced during the New Order. The energy beam it formed was overfocused in the barrel, making it thinner than most but also more lethal.

**X-7 factory station** A 500-meter-long orbital station designed to allow manufacturing in space. It was fairly well armed, with multiple turbolaser batteries and two warhead launchers. It was also well shielded. The station was constructed from a central spire topped with living quarters and operational labs. Attached to the spire were four storage/laboratory modules.

X-83 TwinTail

**X-83 TwinTail** A variant on the original T-65 X-wing starfighter, it was produced by Incom Industries some 130 years after the Battle of Yavin. The X-83 TwinTail was distinguished by its forward-mounted cockpit, with its S-foils located just behind. The two sublight drive engines were situated just behind the wings, in a configuration similar to the old X-wing's set of four, but much longer than the original's and trailed behind the fighter. Each exhaust nacelle was tipped with a set of maneuvering vanes, giving the X-83 TwinTail exceptional maneuverability both in space and in an atmosphere. These fighters were produced primarily for the Jedi Knights.

**Xaart** Stranded on Onderon after the Mandalorian Wars and the Jedi Civil War, he was a Republic spy investigating how the planet was being ruled. With the help of the Exile, he was able to acquire a starport visa and finally could book passage back home.

**Xaczik** A dialect spoken by Wookiees indigenous to the Wartaki Islands. Because Imperials thought that all the planet's natives were alike, Wookiees used Xaczik to deliver secret information to members of their resistance movement.

**Xa Fel** Located in the heart of the Kanchen sector, this planet surrendered to Admiral Thrawn's military after New Republic forces were defeated in a 30-hour battle. Captain Harbid of the Star Destroyer *Death's Head* accepted the surrender of the Xa Fel government and handled the surface troop deployments. The native Xa Fels were a species of near-humans, although many were undernourished; ugly sores and blisters marked most of the inhabitants. For years, the planet served as one of Kuat Drive Yards' hyperdrive-manufacturing centers. Those facilities were the primary focus of Xa Fel's economy, to the point that KDY used up all the planet's natural resources and left it badly polluted. The Xa Fels were virtually enslaved by KDY, and their average life expectancy dropped from 120 years to 50 during the company's reign.

Selif Xam

**Xagobah** A planet near the border of the Mid Rim and Outer Rim, this was the homeworld of the Xamster species. From space, Xagobah appeared to be a cloud-covered sphere shrouded in purplish mists. This phenomenon was caused by the incredible amounts of spores and pollen given off by trees and fungus. While much of the spore material was harmless, a breath mask was recommended for offworld visitors. Several carnivorous varieties of fungi could reach out and grab their prey, while the flimmel tree resembled a weird combination of a mushroom and a spider. At the height of the Clone Wars, Xagobah was captured by General Grievous and became a Separatist outpost. Boba Fett's first offworld assignment for Jabba the Hutt was to go to Xagobah to hunt down Wat Tambor.

Xamster

**Xaj, Sarro** A Jedi trained by Master Raskta Lsu during the years leading to the Battle of Ruusan. He survived Ruusan, and was promoted to Jedi Knight in the years that followed. Xaj was a huge man; his friends often claimed that he would be mistaken for a hairless Wookiee if it weren't for his speed and agility. His weapon of preference was a massive, two-bladed blue lightsaber. Xaj accompanied Lord Valenthyne Farfalla on a mission to capture Darth Bane on Tython. When he faced off against Bane's apprentice, Zannah, he was unprepared for her use of the dark side to create horrific illusions. Xaj believed he was being attacked from all sides, and as he flailed about with his lightsaber, Zannah moved in and sliced him in half.

**Xakrea** A major city on Darkknell in the Outer Rim Territories.

**Xal 3** The base for the Armorers' Confederacy, it was located in the Ablajeck sector of the Inner Zuma region.

**Xam, Selif** A Polis Massan who served with the archaeological team investigating the ruins of an ancient civilization on the Polis Massa asteroids during the Clone Wars. Selif Xam was trained as a physician, and served the archaeological team as a doctor and surgeon. When Padmé Amidala was brought to Polis Massa by Obi-Wan Kenobi, Selif Xam helped deliver her twin babies. The birthing process of humans was quite unknown to Xam, but he adjusted the programming of his medical droids to assist him.

**Xamar** A Khil Jedi Master who taught at the Taris training facility during the years following the Great Sith War. During his student years, Xamar was trained as a seer by Lady Krynda Draay, much to the chagrin of her son, Lucien. Among the Jedi Consulars, Master Xamar was known as an exceptionally gifted seer who could foretell the future in vivid terms. Unknown to his students, Xamar was part of Master Lucien's plot to murder the Padawans under their tutelage. Only Zayne Carrick escaped, forcing Master Lucien and the other instructors to blame the murders on Carrick to cover their tracks. Xamar and the other Masters were then recalled to Coruscant by the Jedi Order.

**Xamster** A species of purple-skinned, bat-eared reptiloids native to the planet Xagobah. Many Xamsters were killed during the Clone Wars when the Army of the Republic laid siege to the Mazariyan fortress in an effort to capture Wat Tambor. Podracer Neva Kee was a Xamster.

**Xamus/Sumax** A two-headed, four-armed convict locked in the M'Bardi prison during the Clone Wars. Each of his heads had three eyes, and one of his left forearms was a cybernetic replacement. After Kit Fisto and Plo Koon were attacked by the Separatist bounty hunter Durge, Xamus/Sumax came to their aid.

Xan

**Xan** A species from Algara II. The Xan were hairless humanoids with bulbous heads and large eyes. They had pale skin that ranged in color from green to yellow to pink. They showed no emotion since their faces lacked the muscle structure to do so. Most Xan were worker drones, and nearly all aspects of Xan society were regulated by the human settlers of Algara II. Xan culture was virtually wiped out, and most knew almost nothing about their species' history. The Algarans went so far as to prohibit the Xan from leaving the planet for fear they would spread the truth about their oppression.

**Xan, Ilena** One of the few Jedi Masters who remained on Coruscant during the Clone Wars, she stayed at the Jedi Temple as a teacher and instructor in the martial arts. Master Xan was known for her knowledge of melee combat, especially joint locks and holds that could render any opponent virtually unable to move. Because of this, she earned the nickname Iron Hand, a moniker she gladly accepted. Master Xan was a close friend of Jai Maruk, and was one of many Jedi who were gravely concerned when he returned from Vjun with a communiqué from Count Dooku.

Xamar

**Xanatos** Qui-Gon Jinn's failed Padawan and a native of the planet Telos. Xanatos was born into wealth; his father, Crion, was one of the most powerful men on Telos. Qui-Gon Jinn requested that Xanatos return with him to Coruscant for Jedi instruction. The boy trained under the best Masters, and eventually Qui-Gon took the youth as his Padawan learner. The Jedi Council harbored concerns over Xanatos's anger, and continually pressed Qui-Gon to evaluate his apprentice's progress.

Shortly before Xanatos took the tests to become a Jedi Knight, Master Yoda sent them both on a mission to Telos. The planet was in turmoil, and Crion drew his son into his plot to attack a neighboring planet. Ultimately Qui-Gon killed Crion to end the planet's war. Xanatos vowed to exact revenge, and took

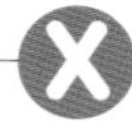

Xanatos

the ring from his father's finger and burned a crescent-shaped scar on his cheek.

Xanatos disappeared for years, then reemerged on Bandomeer, having taken control of Offworld Mining Company through deceit and conspiracy. He claimed to be bringing peace between Offworld and the Arcona Mineral Harvest Corporation, but secretly hoped to eliminate Arcona and take over Bandomeer's ionite mines for himself. Again he was thwarted by Qui-Gon, this time with the help of Obi-Wan Kenobi. Xanatos fled and returned to Telos, where he planned to strip-mine the planet. Qui-Gon and Obi-Wan exposed his role in creating the game Katharsis and his manipulation of the UniFy corporation. Unwilling to be captured, Xanatos took his own life by jumping into an acidic pool of toxic waste. He was survived by his son, who would later terrorize the Jedi under the name Granta Omega.

**xandank** A feline creature covered by a thick protective shell, it was native to the Berken's Flow region of Mustafar. Often called the Crustacean Cat, it hunted in small packs and stalked its prey before striking.

**Xanlannes system** A star system located near the Uziel system.

**xantha** This Gorothite instrument combined the elements of a 24-string lute and a bassoon into a single instrument. The player plucked the strings while simultaneously stopping the holes along the goose-necked body. It required incredible musical skill to play.

**Xappyh sector** Jedi Master Jorus C'baoth was once named ambassador-at-large to the Xappyh sector by the Republic Senate.

**Xarga** One of the many Mandalorians stranded on the Dxun moon following the Great Sith War. Xarga was chosen by the Mandalore to lead a group of agents who worked with the Exile into the tomb of Freedon Nadd; there they sought answers to the growing power of the dark side of the Force in the wake of the Jedi Civil War.

**Xarran, Gaege** An Imperial general who commanded a garrison on Vryssa in the early years of the New Republic. He tried to protect his thieving brother, Rivo, from Boba Fett. But the bounty hunter eliminated AT-AT walkers and the garrison's death fence before reaching the main compound. Xarran, with no options, set the self-destruct sequence for the base. He then headed out to kill Fett. He nearly succeeded, but Fett lured Xarran into a trap and killed him. Fett let Rivo escape in exchange for Fett's own life, and the onetime thief reformed, becoming a children's storyteller.

**Xartun** An Outer Rim world that signed an accord with the New Republic. Xartun's governor, Nojin Koolb, was secretly an ally of Warlord Zsinj.

***Xarxis*** A Rebel Alliance shuttle group destroyed during the Galactic Civil War.

**Xaverri** A friend of Han Solo's from his smuggling days. When the Empire murdered her husband and children, she became an accomplished con artist who swindled Imperial dignitaries. After the Battle of Endor, Xaverri turned to hunting down the remaining Imperial officers and killing them. Encountering Imperial forces gathering at Crseih Station, she sent coded messages to Solo in an effort to get the New Republic to investigate the situation.

**X-C 2** This was the designation of an experimental, high-output ion array developed for use as a sublight drive by Sienar Design Systems. It first saw use in Darth Maul's Infiltrator starship.

**XCiter** This blaster component was also known as a gas conversion enabler. When the trigger of a blaster was pulled, it opened the Heter valve and released a small amount of gas into the XCiter. The XCiter, in turn, agitated the molecules of gas before moving them into the actuating blaster module.

**Xelbree** A Podracer pilot who lost a Boonta Eve Classic race . . . and his life. Sebulba came alongside Xelbree's Podracer, opened a side vent on his engine, and fired a small flame weapon. The exhaust cut through Xelbree's engine and it exploded, killing him.

**Xelric Draw** A shallow Tatooine canyon that split the Mospic High Range on the edge of the Northern Dune Sea, and contained the city of Mos Espa. The Xelric Draw was an ancient trading route that linked the northern settlements with those farther south.

**Xendor** An ancient Kashi Mer who led the Legions of Lettow during the First Great Schism between the followers of the light side and dark side of the Force. He had been a Jedi Knight, but was exiled from his homeworld after he began using teräs käsi martial arts for evil by combining them with the dark side of the Force. Among Xendor's followers was the warrior Arden Lyn, who became his lover. Xendor was killed by the Jedi, and Arden Lyn entered suspended animation for thousands of years.

Xexto

**xenoarchaeology** The scientific study of vanished offworld or alien cultures through the artifacts they left behind.

**Xer VIII** A Tionese nobleman who became a pirate and launched a campaign of conquest known as the Cronese Sweeps some 25,200 years before the Battle of Yavin. The subjugation of pocket kingdoms left Xer in possession of a Tionese empire with the Kingdom of Cron as its centerpiece. He was survived by his son, who later became known as Xim the Despot.

**Xeran** This Xamster was the last of his family, many of whom were killed during the Clone Wars when the Grand Army of the Republic laid siege to Wat Tambor's fortress on Xagobah. It was Xeran who assisted young Boba Fett in gaining access to the fortress, which was known as Mazariyan, during the bounty hunter's attempt to capture Tambor and bring him to Jabba the Hutt.

**Xern** One of Rei'kas's hired thugs, Xern was sent to intercept Talon Karrde at the Ithor Loman tapcaf on Dayark. The assault failed when H'sishi and Shada D'ukal managed to take the thugs out. Xern later captained Rei'kas's command ship during an assault on Exocron, which was thwarted by the fleets of the Exocron Combined Air–Space Fleet and the Aing-Tii monks. The Aing-Tii spared no prisoners, killing Xern and Rei'kas's entire gang.

**Xeron** The site of a battle between the Empire and the Rebel Alliance approximately three years after the Battle of Yavin. The Empire unleashed prototype warbots during the fighting, one of which was damaged and captured by the Alliance.

**Xexto** A species of gangly aliens native to the planet Troiken. Each Xexto had four arms and two legs, with a tiny head atop a long, thin neck. One brain, located in the skull, controlled emotions and body functions, while a second in the chest controlled creative thinking and logic. The Xexto were known as weavers, using their incredible dexterity to create some of the galaxy's most elaborate tapestries. They also were known to be highly competitive and well educated, and could speak at length about almost any subject. Rogue Arkanian scientists, some 17,000 years before the Battle of Yavin, took Xexto genetic material and created the Quermian species on Quermia. When the linkage between Xexto and Quermians was discovered millennia later, the Xexto refused to acknowledge it and denounced the Republic's plans to rename their species as Troiken Xexto. The Podracer Gasgano was a Xexto.

**Xg-1 Starwing** Cygnus Spaceworks' *Alpha*-class assault gunboat, developed for use by the Empire during the Galactic Civil War. It was an attempt to combine onboard shields and a hyperdrive on a single-pilot starfighter.

**Xhaxin, Captain Urias** A pirate with long white hair, a neatly trimmed beard and mustache, and a cybernetic left hand. Xhaxin operated for years as a privateer raiding Imperial shipping, and then continued to prey on Imperials during the reign of warlords following the Battle of Endor. After the peace treaty between the New Republic and the Imperial Remnant, he moved to the Rim, picking off the occasional unreconstructed Imperial making a run for the Remnant. A journalist once made a mostly fictional, romanticized holodrama about him. At the start of the Yuuzhan Vong War, Xhaxin was ambushed by the invaders. His ship, the *Free Lance,* was severely damaged in the process, and Xhaxin made a blind jump to Bastion. He eventually was rescued there by Rogue Squadron and taken aboard the *Ralroost,* where Admiral Traest Kre'fey pumped him for information on the mysterious enemy.

**Xi Charrian** A species known for its fanatical devotion to precise engineering, expressed through the Xi Char religion, which equated factories with cathedrals. Native to Charros IV, Xi Charrian attention to detail allowed them to create some of the most sophisticated equipment in the galaxy through their Haor Chall Engineering company, including the vulture droid starfighter used by the Trade Federation. Xi Charrians jealously guarded their secrets, and when they discovered that Raith Sienar had infiltrated their ranks, they put out a bounty on his head. The incident also forced Xi Charrians to close their doors to offworlders. The Confederacy of Independent Systems reverse-engineered their technologies during the buildup to the Clone Wars, and began manufacturing vulture droid starfighters on other worlds. At that point, the Xi Charrians agreed to help the Old Republic in any way they could.

**Xi'Dec** An insectoid species from Stic with 180 distinct appearances. To adapt to the rapid changes on their planet, the Xi'Dec evolved hundreds of specialized sexes throughout history, each with its own abilities. The most common variety, the Xi'Alpha, made up about 6 percent of the population. Xi'Dec society was organized around the family unit, which never contained more than one member of the same gender.

Xi'Dec

**Xim the Despot** A pre-Republic tyrant from Argai who conquered the territory later known as the Tion. As a youth, Xim was heir to the holdings of his father, Xer VIII, and by the age of 20 he had conquered a number of systems by leading his father's pirate bands on raids. Xim, known as the pirate prince, grew to power by despoiling planets, collecting and selling slaves, stranding populations in deep space, and collecting and using the latest armaments to support his goals. His insignia was a bone-colored death's head with two sunbursts in its eye sockets.

Xim ruled for about 30 years, until his defeat at the Third Battle of Vontor approximately 25,100 years before the Battle of Yavin. Up to that time, Xim had conquered hundreds of thousands of worlds from the Maw Cluster to the Radama Void and was planning to expand into Hutt space. As he began making incursions, his forces were ambushed at Vontor by the Hutts. Xim vowed to exact revenge, and launched two more attempts to defeat his enemies. At the Third Battle of Vontor, Xim's war robots lost to an army of Klatooinians, Niktos, and Vodrans. Xim was captured and enslaved by Kossak the Hutt. When his death in Kossak's dungeons was announced several years later, the crew of Xim's treasure ship *Queen of Ranroon* scuttled their mission, leaving the vaults Xim had built on Dellalt empty. Xim's empire eventually broke apart into smaller pieces: the Kingdom of Cron, the Jaminere Marches, the Indrexu Confederation, the Keldrath Alignment, the Thanium Worlds, and the Tion Hegemony.

**Xiss, Zule** The Falleen Padawan of Master Glaive, she was part of the Jedi contingent sent to Ohma-D'un early in the Clone Wars. Xiss stabbed the bounty hunter Durge in the stomach with her lightsaber, but Durge shook off the injury and knocked her unconscious. Asajj Ventress later sliced off Zule's left arm at the shoulder. At the Battle of Jabiim, she sported a robotic replacement arm and became part of the "Padawan Pack" charged with halting the advance of Alto Stratus and his troops. During the defense of Cobalt Station, Xiss began to slip toward the dark side of the Force, but she died when a Republic walker crashed on top of her.

Zule Xiss

**Xist** A Falleen enforcer for Black Sun who ruled over New Coronet on Trigalis during the Clone Wars, Xist was renowned for his skills with a vibro-whip. During his search for Asajj Ventress, Obi-Wan Kenobi attacked Xist's fortress and easily defeated his guards. Xist fought Kenobi with his vibro-whip and lost, then agreed to tell the Jedi anything he wanted to know. But Kenobi later discovered that Xist had lied and set him up to be killed as part of an elaborate plot by Count Dooku.

Xist

***Xiytiar*-class transport** An inelegant 164.8-meter space transport capable of moving 5,000 metric tons of cargo. They were manned by a crew of 2 and could carry 12 passengers.

**Xizor, Prince** The top crime lord in the galaxy near the end of the Old Republic and through most of the New Order, he was head of the criminal syndicate known as Black Sun. Prince Xizor was also highly political and was probably the third most powerful individual in the galaxy. He schemed to supplant number two—Darth Vader—and possibly even take over the Emperor's job at some point.

Xizor was more than 100 years old, with the body of a well-sculpted 30-year-old thanks to its crafting by myostim units. A Falleen, Xizor was tall with a slightly elevated, sharp reptilian ridge over his spine. His head was bald except for a long topknot and ponytail. Xizor exuded natural pheromones that made most humanoids feel instantly attracted to him; his skin color, normally a dusky green, changed with the rise of those pheromones, going from the cool into the warm spectrum of colors.

Xizor harbored a particular hatred for Vader. About a decade before the Battle of Hoth, Vader had established a biological

Prince Xizor

weapons lab on Xizor's planet. An accident let a tissue-destroying bacterium escape, so Vader ordered the city near the lab burned to ashes, killing 200,000 Falleen including Xizor's entire family. Xizor, who was offworld, destroyed all records of the family tragedy so that no one would know of his personal reasons for despising Vader and his pledge to avenge the deaths. When he heard that Vader was seeking Luke Skywalker to convert him to the dark side of the Force—and that young Skywalker was Vader's son—he plotted to have Luke killed and Vader's plans thwarted. Xizor's huge castle on Imperial Center was only a short walk through protected corridors from Vader's palace. Every time Vader set foot outside his castle, Xizor had him under surveillance.

Xizor had a number of legitimate businesses into which he funneled much of the ill-gotten gains of Black Sun. The largest of these was a shipping company, Xizor Transport Systems (XTS).

Because attracting females was so easy for Xizor, he quickly tired of them. But he considered Princess Leia Organa a real challenge, although he was confident he could win her over with his pheromones. Leia initiated the contact in her attempts to find out who was trying to murder Luke. At their first meeting, Leia was indeed taken with Xizor's beauty, and she nearly let herself be seduced. But his spell over her was broken when Chewbacca interrupted their meeting and whisked Leia away. When she returned, she kneed Xizor in the groin, turning herself from a free-will visitor into a prisoner. Xizor had his female human replica droid, Guri, take Leia to her locked room, and then informed her that she was bait to lure Luke.

When Skywalker, Lando Calrissian, Dash Rendar, and Chewbacca broke into Xizor's castle through its lowest levels, the prince was at first reluctant to admit that his tight security measures could have been breached. But Xizor became convinced that his castle had indeed been infiltrated after Guri was bashed by Leia. Soon he came face-to-face with Luke Skywalker, and a fearsome battle ensued. When Skywalker produced a thermal detonator, Xizor let the group leave unmolested—but not before Calrissian dropped another detonator with a five-minute timer down a chute. Xizor escaped to his skyhook, *Falleen's Fist,* using his ship *Virago.* But in a final confrontation, Darth Vader ordered Xizor's skyhook retreat blown to bits, killing the prince.

**Xizor Transport Systems (XTS)** The legitimate business front of crime lord Prince Xizor, this transportation company was very profitable. Much of the money from the Black Sun organization's illicit activities was funneled into XTS, which benefited from Imperial contracts given personally by Emperor Palpatine.

**XJ X-wing starfighter** An improved version of the X-wing starfighter introduced prior to the Yuuzhan Vong War. The XJ X-wing had three proton torpedo launchers with three torpedoes each as well as an improved fire-linking capability that allowed the pilot to link the four laser cannons in specific patterns of fire. The XJ was equipped to use the R7 series astromech droid. The Jedi were the first to make widespread use of the XJ; many civilians believed that the *J* in the designation indicated that the ships were produced for the Jedi.

The XJ was followed by the XJ3, which possessed variable-stutter lasers, decoy-enhanced proton torpedoes, and grabproof shields. These upgrades were made in an attempt to give the starfighters some advantage over Yuuzhan Vong coralskippers. The XJ5 appeared after the Yuuzhan Vong War, and many were produced as ChaseX patrol ships with improvements in speed, maneuverability, and sensor systems.

**Xo** The mysterious and hostile homeworld of the fierce Zanibar. Xo was bathed in red light, and its surface was studded with rocky outcroppings and groves of spike-leafed, carnivorous plants. Much of its native wildlife was reptilian. Kir Kanos traveled to Xo to rescue Mirith Sinn. Deep in the jungle, the two discovered a mountainous ruin that seemed to predate the Republic. Statues of human forms surrounded the ruins, indicating that the Zanibar were not Xo's original inhabitants.

Xo

**Xong, Zorbazat** This Yevetha served as the Minister of Homeland Security on N'zoth during the years leading up to the Yuuzhan Vong War. He believed that learning Basic would help him understand his enemies, but it angered his fellow Yevetha to the point that they nearly exiled him. Xong agreed to turn over a Yuuzhan Vong spy to the New Republic, but ordered that the spy be brutally interrogated and executed in front of Republic agents.

**xonolite** This metal found on Mustafar was easily converted from solid to liquid form when it was consumed and disgested by the jawenko lava beast. The liquid xonolite was exported by Mustafarian smugglers to Nkllon, where it was packaged and sold as a drug called Nkllonian Lava Extract.

**xoorzi** A fungus found on Thyferra, it was used as a growth medium for the alazhi bacteria essential to the production of bacta. Xoorzi fungus grew only in the wild, and was a delicate plant that would shrivel and die if it was disturbed.

Xora

**Xora** A Falleen who worked for Jib Kopatha at the height of the New Order. Xora and Zuur saw Kopatha's regular meetings with Darth Vader as a way to kill the Dark Lord in revenge for his decimation of their homeworld. Xora lured Vader into an auxiliary hangar on Jib Kopatha's asteroid, then tried to shoot him. The Dark Lord deflected her blasts and eliminated all his attackers.

**Xorth system** Controlled by Imperial forces during the Galactic Civil War, this system bordering the Cardua system dealt primarily in agricultural trade. Xorth produced the best farrberries in the galaxy; they were valued for both their pleasant scent and their stimulating effect.

**xosha grass** This short-lived but quick-growing plant thrived on the plains of Naboo. It was harvested by the Gungans and placed in specialized decomposition vats to create unique gases used in their technologies.

**XoXaan** An ancient Sith Lord noted for her skills as a healer. The lore she left behind was later discovered by A'Sharad Hett, who had been stranded on Korriban when a bounty hunter tried to capture him during a storm. Hett killed the bounty hunter, but the act awakened the spirit of XoXaan. She had stored her knowledge in a holocron, which Hett discovered with help from her spirit. When Hett opened himself up to her teachings, he absorbed her knowledge and eventually became Darth Krayt. He chose his new name from his upbringing on Tatooine, where the krayt dragon was the fiercest predator. After establishing his new Sith Order, Darth Krayt and his chief lieutenant, Darth Wyyrlok, continued to delve into XoXaan's teachings in an unsuccessful attempt to heal the slow deterioration of Darth Krayt's body.

*XoXaan*

**XP-38 landspeeder** A popular landspeeder design that emphasized smooth lines and sheer speed over practicality. The XP-38 landspeeder, manufactured by the Sullustan company SoroSuub, had room for only a driver and passenger and was aimed at younger customers and for recreational uses. It had a snug cockpit with a retractable duraplex windscreen. The optional sensor array was mounted on a swivel so that either the driver or the passenger could run the system. Reclining and height-adjustment controls were found on the seats, and a small cargo compartment was hidden behind.

The XP-38 had a rear-mounted autopilot that looked like an R2 astromech droid. As in standard landspeeders, a repulsorlift generator produced lift and provided power to the turbine engines. The XP-38 sported three rear-mounted turbine engines and maneuvering flaps fore and aft. It offered tight cornering and great acceleration, with a maximum hovering height of 2 meters. While engine noise was excessive, it was a positive selling point with the target audience.

Its one weakness was a stiff repulsor generator setting that was geared for performance but wasn't durable enough for rough terrain, limiting the XP-38 to traveling over smooth surfaces. It could take up to three hours to recalibrate the suspension, so most owners didn't bother.

***XR808g*** Jae Juun's smuggling vessel. He and his first mate, Tarfang, used the ship for several runs for the Colony before they hooked up with Han Solo. The *XR808g* was a modified YT-1000 freighter armed with four short-range blaster cannons spaced evenly around its hull. During the Qoribu crisis, Jae Juun tried to infiltrate Colony space with the vessel, claiming to be a simple transport bringing supplies to the Jedi who were on Qoribu. The presence of the *XR808g* was detected by the Colony, which sent a swarm of dartships to intercept it. The ship was badly damaged in the attack, and Jae Juun and Tarfang had to be rescued by Han Solo in the *Millennium Falcon*. The *XR808g* did not survive the mission, and had to be abandoned to Qoribu's intense gravity.

**XR-85** An Arakyd tank droid, it was a sentient attack vehicle. Designed by the remnants of the Empire from pirated pathway matrices stolen from the R7 astromech droid, the first tank droid was finalized during Thrawn's reign of terror against the New Republic. The droid was not fully realized, however, until Umak Leth brought the idea before the cloned Emperor Palpatine. Although the XR-85 was highly successful, mass production of the sentient droid brain was cost-prohibitive.

**Xris, Sordaan** A wealthy Rodian who lived on Kashyyyk, he was the founder and owner of Sordaan Xris's Safari Partners, a big-game-hunting expedition service that catered to the needs of adventure seekers from across the galaxy.

**XT-6** An ancient service droid, it was used as salvage 4,000 years before the Galactic Civil War by Jedi Cay Qel-Droma, who harvested parts to replace the arm he had lost in battle.

**Xtib** A large corporation founded during the final stages of the Yuuzhan Vong War, it produced the modified TibannaX gas that was required by StealthX fighters developed by Incom Industries. At the height of the Swarm War, Xtib was acquired by the Bornaryn Shipping Empire, although Lady Aryn Dro Thul refused to acknowledge that the purchase had anything to do with the involvement of Luke Skywalker and the new Jedi Order in trying to eliminate the threat posed by her son, Raynar Thul.

**X-TIE** A common variety of "Ugly" starfighter combining the fuselage of an X-wing with the solar panels from a TIE fighter.

**X'Ting** An insectile species native to Ord Cestus. Standing nearly 2 meters tall, each X'Ting had two pairs of arms—one pair for strength and control, and a secondary set for fine manipulation. Where a shiny carapace didn't cover the body of an X'Ting, tufts of bristles provided minimum protection. A stinger at the base of the abdomen could inject a deadly venom into prey. The X'Ting were descended from flying insects, as evidenced by their vestigial wings. X'Ting society was based on a rigid caste system that separated warriors from diggers and chewers from workers. The sex of the adult X'Ting cycled between male and female every three years, requiring that each caste ignore genders when considering its membership. During the peak periods of each cycle, X'Ting experienced intense hormonal surges that signaled the need to reproduce. Males tended to be smaller and more lethal in combat, while females were larger and more intimidating.

Many years before the Clone Wars, the X'Ting took control of Ord Cestus after defeating the Spider People in a great war. With their newfound independence, the X'Ting allowed the Republic to build a prison complex on their planet, hoping to gain a place in the galactic community. The unexpected outcome was the formation of Cestus Cybernetics, which virtually enslaved the species. Shortly after the prison was completed, plagues began to destroy X'Ting society. It was during this period, some 150 years before the Clone Wars, that a Jedi Knight arrived on Ord Cestus and rallied the X'Ting, giving them strength and encouragement to save themselves. A so-called Great Plague decimated the X'Ting 50 years later, reducing a population of millions to mere hundreds and destroying the royal family. Only a handful of eggs from the queen remained, hidden beneath the planet's surface behind an extensive security system to ensure the survival of the royal line.

*XP-38 landspeeder*

**XTS** *See* Xizor Transport Systems.

**Xucphra** A major Thyferran corporation, it was one of the leaders in bacta production and distribution. The company promoted civil war on Thyferra, aiming at complete control of the Bacta Cartel. Xucphra was aided by former Imperial Intelligence director Ysanne Isard, who was given control of the corporation and the planetary government after she fled Coruscant. Following a long and bloody war, the forces of Isard and Xucphra were defeated by a freelance Rogue Squadron.

***Xucphra Alazhi*** One of the three Thyferran bacta tankers hijacked by Rogue Squadron during the Bacta War. Its captain and crew were reluctant to defect. When their absence was detected, their escort, the *Corrupter*, immediately backtracked to their new location. Before they were able to explain or escape, the ship was destroyed.

***Xucphra Meander*** One of a trio of Thyferran bacta tankers hijacked by Rogue Squadron during its war against Ysanne Isard and her control of the Bacta Cartel. The contents of the freighter were sent to Coruscant to help alleviate the ravages of the Krytos virus.

***Xucphra Rose*** One of three Thyferran bacta tankers hijacked by Rogue Squadron despite Ait Convarion's protection. The ship and its contents were sent to the colonists on Halanit to combat a disease.

**Xulropic Badlands** This desolate region of the planet Tatooine was located beyond the Western Dune Sea, separating it from the Audessian Expanse and the uninhabitable regions of the planet's deep deserts.

**Xux, Qwi** From the mind of this woman came some of the Empire's most destructive weapons, but she found redemption in the New Republic and in the love of one of its leaders. A tall, attractive humanoid from the planet Omwat, Qwi Xux had bluish-

tinted skin, long eyelashes above wide, deep blue eyes, and gossamer hair reminiscent of pearlescent feathers. Like others of her species, she had an analytical brain that—even at the age of 10—indicated a future as a brilliant designer. At that age she was taken from her planet by Grand Moff Tarkin and forced into a tough training regimen with nine others; after two years, she was the only survivor. She was assigned to Tarkin's top-secret weapons development lab, the Maw Installation.

Xux was placed under the tutelage of top Imperial designer Bevel Lemelisk, and she excelled at her design and engineering assignments, sharing in the design of the first Death Star and the World Devastators. Her most powerful superweapon was the Sun Crusher, an indestructible ship that carried resonance torpedoes with enough firepower to snuff out a star. Naïvely, Qwi Xux told herself that her plans could be used to build peaceful objects used in commerce and manufacturing.

When Han Solo, Chewbacca, and young Kyp Durron managed to enter the Maw, she finally let herself see the true and terrible results of her work, the death and destruction that her weapons had visited on the galaxy's innocents. When Maw chief Admiral Daala told her that she was going to use the Sun Crusher against the New Republic, Xux knew she had to act. She freed the prisoners, and they escaped aboard the only working model of the Sun Crusher.

On Coruscant, Xux was assigned General Wedge Antilles as a personal bodyguard and succeeded in convincing the Alliance to dispose of the deadly Sun Crusher. On a trip to Ithor, just as Xux and Antilles were beginning to fall in love, Kyp Durron—deciding on his own that Xux's knowledge of weaponry was too dangerous—used the Force to wipe her memory, erasing most of her past. She traveled back to the Maw Installation with an Alliance strike force and found herself in the middle of a fierce battle with Admiral Daala, but she didn't find her lost memory. However, she started the healing process with the assistance of General Antilles.

She and Antilles maintained their relationship, but he was increasingly busy with military matters, and Xux became more absorbed in her work. Both agreed to go their separate ways. Xux eventually traveled to Vortex to help the Vors repair the Cathedral of Winds. While there, she hoped to find her own inner peace and eliminate the memories of all the beings her superweapons had killed.

**Xuz, Cevva** A Rodian who managed a small Rebel cell on the planet Svivren during the last years of the Galactic Civil War. Mara Jade ordered Xuz targeted for elimination by Captain Strok's forces as a diversion during her hunt for the crime lord Dequc. Xuz's forces seemed to know about the attack, and reduced two stormtrooper squads by half before escaping.

*Qwi Xux*

**X-wing starfighter** One of the Rebel Alliance's most advanced fighters, this ship played an important role in the first major Rebel victory of the Galactic Civil War: the Battle of Yavin and the destruction of the first Death Star. The T-65 X-wing starfighter was the final design of its kind produced by Incom Corporation before the company was nationalized by the Empire. A Rebel commando team helped Incom's senior design staff defect to the Alliance with plans and prototypes of the X-wing, a devastating loss for the Empire.

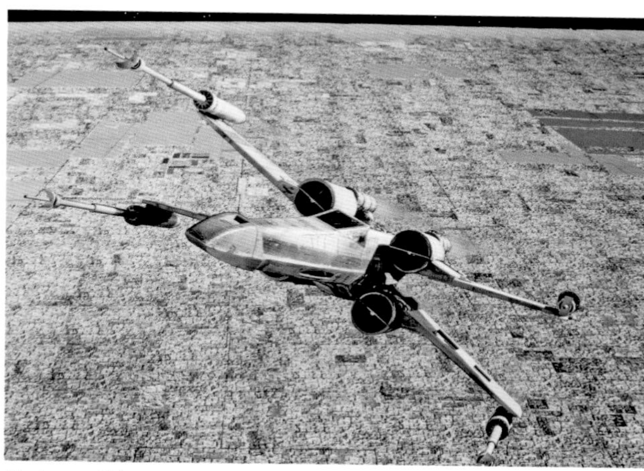
*X-wing starfighter*

The X-wing took its name from its pair of double-layered wings, which were deployed into the familiar X-formation for combat and atmospheric flight. During normal sublight-speed spaceflight, the wings were closed. Each wingtip had a high-powered laser cannon. A pair of proton torpedo launchers was located midway up the main spaceframe, each with a magazine of three torpedoes. In the hands of Luke Skywalker, two of those torpedoes were enough to set off a chain-reaction explosion that destroyed the Death Star.

The X-wing was a one-pilot fighter. An astromech housed in a snug droid socket behind the pilot handled many inflight operations, such as damage control, astrogation jumps, and flight performance adjustment. Although the X-wing had an impressive combat record, much of that was due to the skills of Alliance pilots—and that, in turn, was at least partly due to the fact that the X-wing's controls were reminiscent of those of the T-16 airspeeders and other common sports vehicles found on frontier worlds. Bush pilots who developed their reflexes on such craft easily made the adjustment to the X-wing's familiar controls.

The X-wing also was known for its durability, with a reinforced titanium-alloy hull and high-powered shield generators. It could normally take minor hits without a serious loss of performance, and had full ejection and life-support systems. X-wings also featured hyperdrive systems, adding to their flexibility.

Thirteen years after the Battle of Endor, a new model, the T-65D-A1, was approved by General Wedge Antilles. This design had a superb guidance system and theoretically was more efficient, because it combined its computer system and its astromech unit in one complete system, thereby eliminating the droid. Luke Skywalker's X-wing was one of the first to be upgraded. However, he ordered that it be switched back to the older design, stating that he couldn't imagine piloting his X-wing without R2-D2. During the rebuilding, R2, C-3PO, and mechanic Cole Fardreamer discovered that the new X-wing model had been sabotaged: Each of the new computer systems contained a hidden detonator, installed as part of Dark Jedi Kueller's campaign of terror against the New Republic. An embarrassed General Antilles ordered the new design scrapped. Later models in the series were known as XJ X-wings.

**Xyn, Torvin** An alias assumed by a Yuuzhan Vong warrior who managed to infiltrate the Imperial military and then spy on the activities of the Imperial Remnant. He was discovered shortly after the Battle of Bastion as the remaining Imperial fleet massed to defend Borosk. Jacen Solo and his specially programmed MSE-6 mouse droids identified Xyn and several other so-called Imperial officers as Yuuzhan Vong in disguise, and called them to an alleged staff meeting aboard the *Right to Rule*. Without a way to escape, Torvin Xyn removed his ooglith masquer and attacked. When a squadron of stormtroopers was called in as support, Solo managed to take advantage of the Yuuzhan Vong's surprise to slice through his chest with his lightsaber.

**Xyquine** This planet in the Corellian sector was the site of a botched New Republic mission in which Pash Cracken had to invent the Cracken Twist three years after the Battle of Endor. The New Republic fleet, under the command of the Mon Calamari Gingal, was ambushed by Imperial forces while on patrol there, and a passenger transport was destroyed.

**Xythan force shield** This unusual personal combat shield was developed by Cestus Cybernetics at the height of the Clone Wars, and turned over to Asajj Ventress and the Separatists for their use. The Xythan shield absorbed and returned any energy it came into contact with, making it especially useful in repelling lightsaber attacks.

Y-4 Raptor transport

**Y-4 Raptor transport** Designed as a military transport shuttle, this Incom Corporation model wasn't popularized until Warlord Zsinj expanded his own empire. Y-4 transports then became known as the ships of Zsinj's Raptors, the elite commandos he used to retain power. The main mission of the small shuttle, just under 30 meters long, was to ferry platoons of troops and supplies between starships or bases. For combat missions, the Y-4 could carry the equivalent of four AT-ST scout walkers, six compact assault vehicles, or up to eight speeder bikes.

The Y-4 Raptor had a standard array of sublight drives, a Class 2 hyperdrive, a backup hyperdrive engine, and a dedicated nav computer. The crew consisted of a pilot, a chief gunnery officer on the bridge, and a second gunnery officer on the dorsal-mounted quad laser cannon. The bridge had a socket for an R2 or similar astromech droid to assist in hyperspace calculations. Forward weaponry included two fire-linked laser cannons and a concussion missile launcher with a magazine of six missiles.

Because Zsinj's Raptors were known for quiet infiltrations of planets and surgical strikes against defense grids, the commandos required a ship that could get them onto a planet quickly and quietly. The Y-4 was up to the task with its streamlining and retractable swing-wings for increased atmospheric maneuverability. Han Solo used a falsified transponder code identifying the *Millennium Falcon* as one of the Y-4 transports assigned to the Raptors. The code allowed him to infiltrate the shipyards of Dathomir, but when Solo activated a new sensor and communications jamming system, he burned out the *Falcon*'s nav computers, stranding Solo, Princess Leia Organa, Chewbacca, and C-3PO on Dathomir.

**yaa-yaah** An ancient pre-Corellian salutation, it remained the most universal intergalactic greeting, although it was considered an insult to Ugnaughts.

< Jedi Master Yoda

**Yablari** The agrarian homeworld of the Anomids, located in the Outer Rim. A global drought forced the Anomids to employ centuries-old hyperdrive principles for the first time. The first suitable world they discovered already had a small Duros colony, which opened up Yablari to trade.

**Yaddle** A female Jedi Master of the same species as Yoda, she served on the Jedi Council prior to the Clone Wars. Yaddle was 477 years old at the time of the Battle of Naboo. Some 200 years earlier, she was the apprentice of Polvin Kut. The two were dispatched to eliminate the threat of the Advozse warlord Tulak on Koba, and Yaddle was imprisoned after the death of her Master. After decades of captivity, Yaddle was freed when seismic activity split Koba's crust.

Upon Yaddle's return to Coruscant, Even Piell proposed her promotion to Jedi Master and appointment to the Jedi Council. She was known for her patience, compassion, and wisdom, and was one of the few Jedi entrusted with the knowledge of the Jedi technique Morichro, used to slow the body functions of living beings. She took true delight in training younger students, often overlooking their pranks and hiding sweets in their pockets. Among Yaddle's apprentices were Oppo Rancisis and Empatojayos Brand, and she dedicated much of her time on Coruscant to heading up the Librarians' Assembly.

Seven years after the Battle of Naboo, Yaddle led a mission to Mawan with Obi-Wan Kenobi and Anakin Skywalker to negotiate the establishment of a new government. Unknown to the Jedi was the fact that the most powerful crime lord on Mawan was the bounty hunter Granta Omega. Yaddle agreed to a meeting with Omega, learning that he planned to unleash an explosive filled with dihexalon gas in the city of Naatan. Yaddle drew the weapon to herself and wrapped it in a cocoon of the Force, dying from the deadly toxin.

Yag'Dhul

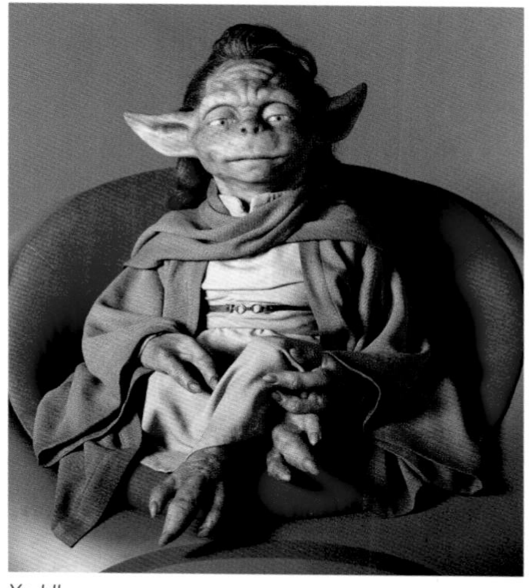

Yaddle

**Yaga Minor** This world was the location of a major group of Imperial shipyards, with facilities on par with those at Ord Trasi and Bilbringi. During the final years of the Republic, Yaga Minor served as the base from which the Outbound Flight Project was launched. All three shipyards were extremely busy during Grand Admiral Thrawn's offensive against the New Republic. During the hunt for the Caamas Document, New Republic forces stormed the Ubiqtorate base at Yaga Minor. The planet later was placed under the control of Moff Kurlen Flennic, who protected it during the early stages of the Yuuzhan Vong War.

Yaga Minor was home to the Yagai species of reed-thin tripeds and to a subspecies of Yaga drones.

**Yag'Dhul** A small, dense planet with three moons, it orbited a yellow star and was the homeworld of the Givin. The complex interaction of orbits and rotations between Yag'Dhul and its moons meant that the planet was continually beset by massive tidal forces powerful enough to pull the water and the atmosphere to different locations, exposing large areas of the planet to hard vacuum. Although some animals on Yag'Dhul survived by traveling along with the tides, the Givin evolved a hard, sealable exoskeleton that allowed them to survive in the vacuum of space. They inhabited hermetically sealed cities built to withstand the strongest tides, and their society was organized around complex mathematics due to the importance of predicting the tides. The Givin were respected starship builders.

The Yag'Dhul system contained an *Empress*-class space station owned by Warlord Zsinj. Three years after the Battle of Endor, Rogue Squadron raided the station to capture a supply of bacta, which Zsinj had previously stolen from a Thyferran convoy. They captured the station, commanded by a Twi'lek named Valsil Torr, and off-loaded the bacta onto freighters. The Rogues then resigned from the military, and Wing Commander Varth's fighters were assigned to make the station uninhabitable so Zsinj could not use it again. But Pash Cracken, newly reassigned to Varth's wing, offered Rogue Squadron the use of the station. The cramped station had 50 living levels, with a 10-level docking facility in the middle. Valsil Torr had died, so Booster Terrik was put in charge of operations. When the Imperial Star Destroyer *Virulence* arrived to destroy the station, Terrik was chiefly responsible for getting the attacking ship to surrender. After taking command of the ship, he went to Thyferra, where the ship's presence hastened the end of the Bacta War.

During the Yuuzhan Vong War, the invaders sent the reconnaissance ship *Stalking Moon* to Yag'Dhul in advance of a full attack fleet. The Jedi Anakin Solo, Tahiri Veila, and Corran Horn commandeered the *Stalking Moon.* When the Yuuzhan Vong fleet arrived, it met resistance by the Givin after Nom Anor's sabotage attempts were revealed. The invaders did eventually gain control of the system, but fleetingly—the New Republic struck back.

*Moff Rulf Yage (left) addresses his daughter, Captain Gunn Yage.*

**Yage, Captain Gunn "Gunner"** The daughter of Imperial Moffs Rulf Yage and Nyna Calixte more than a century after the Battle of Yavin. After her parents were divorced, Gunn went to live with her father, who raised her as if she were a son. Known as Gunner to her closest peers, Gunn became an Imperial starfighter pilot. In the years following the Sith–Imperial War, she was given command of a starfighter squadron and earned a promotion to captain. Captain Yage was later given command of the Skull Squadron of *Predator*-class starfighters, serving the New Empire by protecting the planet Coruscant.

**Yage, Commander Arien** The Imperial Remnant captain of the Star Destroyer *Widowmaker* during the early stages of the Yuuzhan Vong War. She was one of the few officers who gladly accepted the assistance of the New Republic after the Imperials were soundly defeated at the Battle of Bastion. Captain Yage volunteered to escort Luke Skywalker's mission into the Unknown Regions to locate the mysterious planet of Zonama Sekot. When the living planet suddenly jumped into hyperspace, the *Widowmaker* was caught in its wake. No sign was found of the *Widowmaker,* and Captain Yage's fate, along with that of her crew, remained a mystery.

**Yage, Moff Rulf** One of the Moffs of the New Empire who ruled more than a century after the Battle of Yavin and the father of "Gunner" Yage, who was born during his brief marriage to Nyna Calixte. Under the rule of Emperor Roan Fel, Moff Yage served as the commander of the Imperial Navy. A descendant of the noted Yage family and a staunch Imperial supporter, Rulf was one of the hardliners who refused to accept Emperor Fel's decision to allow Princess Marasiah Fel to become his heir. Known as the Hero of Ossus, he was a noted pilot during the early years of his military career, and was among the first soldiers to command Skull Squadron. His daughter Gunn later assumed command of the Skulls.

**Yaght, Duman** The Yuuzhan Vong commander of the warship *Exquisite Death.* Yaght was also in command of the strike team that boarded the *Stardream* to capture a group of Jedi. He was unaware that the Jedi wanted to be captured, and that the captain of the *Stardream* was Lando Calrissian. Shortly after the Jedi were incarcerated in the hold of the *Exquisite Death,* Duman Yaght was beheaded by Tesar Sebatyne.

**Yahk-Tosh** A slug-like alien species similar in appearance to the Hutts, they had six thick arms which they used to move about, and scaled skin that was a dirty green in color. Four thin horns sprouted from the tops of their heads, and their pointed snouts were filled with rows of serrated teeth. It was believed that the Yahk-Tosh were resistant to the mind tricks of the Jedi Knights.

**Yaka** A species of near-human cyborgs, they were transformed after their home planet was invaded centuries ago before the Galactic Civil War by super-intelligent inhabitants of Arkania, a neighboring star system. The Arkanians forced the Yakas to undergo surgery in which they implanted cyborg brain enhancers, increasing the species' intelligence to genius level. Thus, the brutish-looking Yakas were much smarter than they appeared. One side effect of the implants was the twisted sense of humor common to Yakas.

***Yakez*** The flagship of the New Republic's Fourth Fleet Task Force Apex, it was commanded by Admiral Farley Carson.

**Yak Face** *See* Saelt-Marae.

***Yald*** A New Republic heavy cruiser commanded by Commodore Brand. Prince Isolder and Leia Organa Solo boarded the *Yald* at Commenor prior to the Battle of Fondor during the Yuuzhan Vong War. The command staffs of the New Republic and the Hapan fleet met in a tactical information center deep within the ship.

**Yalnal, Nevar** An immense Ranat scavenger from the planet Aralia, he spied for anyone willing to pay his price. Nevar Yalnal was an outcast and usually worked as a laborer for Hrchek Kal Fas.

**Yalu, Viith** The Yuuzhan Vong shaper in command of the compound on Wayland. Viith Yalu and his team were responsible for discovering a way to neutralize the effects of bacta. Four years after the invasion began, Viith Yalu and his team succeeded in cracking bacta's biochemical sequencing code, and developed a virus that could destroy the alazhi plants vital to the fluid's production. Yalu planned to bring the virus to Thyferra inside the body of Bey Gandan, having twisted the former Jedi Knight to the ways of the Yuuzhan Vong. The plan nearly succeeded, but the Vratix had been alerted to the threat and burned the infected alazhi fields before the virus could spread.

**yammal-jell** One of many unusual life-forms that evolved on Coruscant in the wake of the Yuuzhan Vong terraforming. Yammal-jells lived in open bodies of water found on the planet, and became the favorite prey of the hawk-bat population.

**yammosk** A Yuuzhan Vong–bioengineered creature used as a war coordinator. A yammosk had a bulbous head and an array of tentacles, and served to coordinate all activities of an invasion fleet toward a single goal. A yammosk could coordi-

*Yammosk*

nate landing operations, starfighter battles, and even full-scale sieges. The creature's only solid bodily structure was a single tooth, used to bury itself into a landing area. Any enemy ships that got too close to the yammosk's position would be rendered inoperable by the intense energy the creature used to bind the Yuuzhan Vong forces together. If a yammosk were ever destroyed, the Yuuzhan Vong war fleet would be without any guiding force and could collapse in chaos. Once the yammosk was entrenched in its new position, it could spawn a second yammosk to assist in the establishment of the next Yuuzhan Vong base. The parent yammosk would form a mental link with the offspring, transferring all the knowledge it would need to act as the next war coordinator. The Yuuzhan Vong discovered that young yammosks grew faster if they were in contact with living beings, and began forcing prisoners into the nutrient vats alongside immature yammosks. After the New Republic began to search out and destroy the yammosks, the Yuuzhan Vong began to train their pilots to act without guidance.

**Yam'rii** A praying-mantis-like species. Distant relatives of the Verpine, Yam'rii were very strong and easily angered. Known for their stealth, they ate meat and eggs. It was believed that the Huk species was an offshoot of the Yam'rii. Kitik Keed'kak was a Yam'rii.

**Yané** The youngest of Queen Amidala's handmaidens. Like the other handmaidens, Yané was chosen by Captain Panaka for her strength, loyalty, and resemblance to Amidala. Yané and Saché were left behind when the Queen traveled to Coruscant to petition against the Trade Federation's blockade of Naboo.

**Yanee** A slender man whose lined face and gray hair marked him as years older than Kueller, he became the Dark Jedi's second assistant following Kueller's disposal of Femon, the first one. Yanee was among the few people who actually expressed the opinion he had rather than the one Kueller wanted to hear, which Kueller found refreshing. However, Kueller decided that the trait might soon become tiresome, so he began training a third assistant, Gant.

**Yang, Kar** A Hiitian bounty hunter. Kar Yang tried to claim a bounty on the human replica droid Guri after the Battle of Endor. Yang and his assistant droid followed her to Hurd's Moon, where the droid initiated a plan to kill Yang and take Guri for itself. Yang tried to recover Guri on his own, but lost his life in the attempt.

**Yanibar** A harsh Outer Rim world that was the likely birthplace of the Zeison Sha sect of Force users.

**Yant, Zan** A Zabrak from Talus who served as one of the field surgeons supporting the Grand Army of the Republic during the Clone Wars. Yant came from a wealthy family, and studied music with a professor who taught at the Coruscant School of Music. He was stationed at the Rimsoo Seven military hospital on the planet Drongar two years after the Battle of Geonosis and became fast friends with fellow surgeon Jos Vondar. To relieve the stress of field surgery, Zan Yant spent his downtime playing his quetarra. When the Rimsoo Seven facility was attacked by Separatist forces, Zan Yant and the rest of the doctors grabbed their go-bags and got ready to evacuate. Just after takeoff, his transport was hit by a Separatist missile. The shrapnel that filled the ship penetrated his spinal cord just below the neck, killing him instantly.

*Kar Yang*

**Yanth the Hutt** A 500-year-old Hutt Black Sun Vigo. Yanth maintained headquarters underneath the Tusken Oasis in Coruscant's Crimson Corridor. He was a potential buyer for the holocron that Lorn Pavan acquired from Hath Monchar. Yanth agreed to buy it for a million credits, thinking that he could turn it for 10 times that much. During the exchange, Darth Maul attacked Yanth's headquarters, killing Yanth's Chevin and Gamorrean bodyguards before murdering the Hutt himself.

**Yao** A long-lived alien species. Formayj, an old associate of Han Solo and Chewbacca, was a Yao.

**Yar, Senator Tolik** An Oolid, he was a member of the New Republic Senate Defense Council. Senator Tolik Yar was one of Chief of State Leia Organa Solo's champions in the Senate during the difficulties of the Yevethan crisis.

**Yarar, Brimon** A member of the anti-alien Human League, he was in charge of an archaeological dig on Corellia that tried to locate an ancient repulsor device.

**yargh'un** A large rodent native to the original Yuuzhan Vong homeworld of Yuuzhan'tar, the species was maintained as an organic form of garbage disposal on many worldships. Supreme Overlord Shimrra kept a group of yargh'un in a charnel pit aboard his flagship, and he often threw "unworthy" individuals there to be devoured by the creatures.

**Yarith sector** Named for Yarith Figg, this area of the galaxy was located in the section of the Outer Rim Territories known as the Greater Javin. The Yarith sector was created when the Old Republic decided to split the Anoat sector into two parts, each corresponding to a section of the Twin Nebulae. The heirs of Ecclessis and Yarith Figg felt that the split was aimed at limiting their influence—both personally and financially—in the Greater Javin, but earned a measure of consolation in getting it named as the Yarith sector. The sector bordered the spinward edge of the Anoat sector, and encompassed the Kiax Nebula. However, the border between the Anoat and Yarith sectors meandered in and out, cutting off certain planets from existing political allegiances to minimize local power.

**Yarkora** A mysterious and secretive species. Yarkora tended to be found as couriers, scouts, and t'bac farmers, and some helped the Rebel Alliance's efforts at counterespionage. Yarkora were tall, bipedal creatures whose huge faces were characterized by two wide-set eyes, a large nose, and furry whiskers that protruded from each cheek. Saelt-Marae was a Yarkora.

**yarrock** An addictive spice that was a high-caliber hallucinogen, boosting a user's confidence by instilling a vision of "the meaning of life." Yarrock was originally synthesized by the shamans of Iridonia as a preparatory aid given to warriors before battle. Constant use, however, resulted in psychosis. Sensitive to moisture, yarrock was preserved in tiny black plastene packets to prevent disintegration when taken away from Iridonia.

**Yarrow, Eve** The woman believed to be the only heir to the Evin Yarrow fortune during the final years of the Old Republic. Yarrow Industries was taken over by the Empire in the wake of the Clone Wars, and Eve went into hiding shortly afterward. Clive Flax believed that Eve Yarrow was actually the freedom fighter known as Flame, but had no evidence to support his theory. He and Astri Oddo performed their own investigation, and discovered that Eve Yarrow had assumed control of Yarrow Industries' bank accounts after the Galactic Empire was established. She erased all information in the accounts, and rekeyed them to numbers to make it harder to track credit transfers. After learning that Yarrow had been funneling credits to an account

*Yarkora*

on Revery, Flax and Oddo located her residence on the resort world and broke in. They discovered that she was one of the few individuals in the galaxy who had been given an Emperor's Favor crystal, which only added to her mystery.

Senator Yarua

**Yarua, Senator** A Wookiee who served as Kashyyyk's representative to the Galactic Senate during the final decades of the Old Republic. Yarua despised the corruption of his fellow Senators but found himself unable to stem the tide. In his youth, Yarua wanted little more than to take over his family business. When his father died in an accident, Yarua became the family patriarch at the tender age of 120. He taught himself to deal with situations diplomatically rather than physically and quickly earned the respect of Kashyyyk's elders, who urged Yarua to vie for the Senate seat when his predecessor retired.

Shortly before the Clone Wars, Senator Yarua agreed to meet with Trandoshan representative Hadocrassk in an effort to negotiate a peace between their peoples. Yarua had ordered that all trade to Trandosha be blockaded after 215 Wookiees were killed aboard a transport ship near one of Trandosha's moons. Senator Yarua threatened to secede from the Republic if reparations were not made to the Wookiee population. The peace talks were mediated by the Jedi Master Oppo Rancisis, but were interrupted by the onset of the war. As the Clone Wars dragged on, Senator Yarua remained allied with the Republic. In the wake of the so-called Jedi Rebellion, Kashyyyk was targeted for Imperial occupation after Governor Tarkin asked that Wookiees be captured as slave labor for the construction of the Death Star. On Coruscant, Senator Yarua and his delegation were placed under house arrest and removed from public sight.

**Yasht, Ra** Along with Skarten, his colleague at Beshka University, he wrote "Torture Observed: An Interview with Jabba's Cook."

**Yas'tua** This Bothan led a small group of ruffians who intercepted Alema Rar when she arrived on Korriban to seek out the current Sith Lords. Yas'tua refused to help her, although the Barabel known as Rak'k agreed to give her the information she wanted. He also indicated that Yas'tua had a working swoop, and Alema forced the Bothan to turn it over.

Yavaris

***Yavaris*** An escort frigate, it was commanded by Wedge Antilles in the assault on Maw Installation. It was a powerful ship, armed with 12 turbolaser batteries and 12 laser cannons. It carried two full X-wing fighter squadrons. General Antilles also used the ship to charge into the Nal Hutta system during the Darksaber crisis.

**Yavid, General** A diminutive Sanyassan Marauder stranded on the Forest Moon of Endor, he was a member of Sanyassan aristocracy. Despite his primitive dress and thuggish demeanor, Yavid was actually an astute field commander, drawing on strategies he had learned in his military studies to protect Marauder hunting grounds. When King Terak was defeated, Yavid tried to seize the throne but was unable to keep fellow Marauders from fighting one another.

**Yavin** A planet in the system of the same name, it was an orange gas giant nearly 200,000 kilometers in diameter, with a strong magnetic field. Yavin occupied the outermost position in the system and had dozens of moons, three of which (designated 4, 8, and 13) could support humanoid life. Refracted rays from the system's star made the planet seem to glow with an inner light. Yavin's atmosphere, almost 65,000 kilometers deep, was composed primarily of hydrogen and helium, and windstorms often exceeded 600 kilometers an hour.

Throughout the upper atmosphere lived several varieties of floating gas-bag creatures, which bred once every century. Most were nonpredatory and fed on drifting algae, but two species—the floater shark and floater squid—preyed on other animals. Yavin's metallic core was surrounded by a thick layer of frozen liquids under tremendous pressure. Many species of nearly two-dimensional crawlers lived in this frozen layer at pressures that would crush most other life-forms. The pressures were so great that carbon and metallic hydrogen were compressed together to form quantum crystals called Corusca gems. These gems, found only at Yavin's core, glowed with an inner light and were the hardest substance known in the galaxy.

The Damarind Corporation, an enormous galaxywide consortium of jewel merchants, had an exclusive contract with the Empire to harvest Corusca stones from Yavin. Damarind Fishing Station, in orbit above the gas giant, retrieved gems for several years until it went bankrupt.

Immediately following the Battle of Yavin, an Imperial salvage station was temporarily set up in the planet's orbit to analyze the debris from the destroyed Death Star. Seven years after the Battle of Endor, the New Republic attempted to dispose of the Sun Crusher by depositing it in the planet's dense core, but it was quickly retrieved by Jedi Kyp Durron. One year later, following an intense battle at Yavin 4, Admiral Daala's Super Star Destroyer *Knight Hammer* plunged into Yavin's atmosphere and was destroyed. Some 19 years after the Battle of Endor, Lando Calrissian established GemDiver Station in Yavin's atmosphere to retrieve Corusca gems. The station operated by dropping a quantum-plated diving bell via an energy tether down to Yavin's core, where the largest gems could be found. Jacen and Jaina Solo were kidnapped from GemDiver Station following an Imperial attack.

Yavin

**Yavin 13** The 13th moon of the planet Yavin, it was the desert homeworld of two intelligent but primitive species, the Gerbs and the Slith. The surface of the moon was covered with rocky mesas, forests of tall cacti, and shifting walls of blowing sand. A vast ocean making up most of the southern hemisphere sent patches of fog and infrequent storms across the arid desert. The nomadic Slith were intelligent serpents, traveling the desert plains at night hunting small animals with their venomous fangs. The rabbit-like Gerbs had metallic claws to aid in burrowing, and enormous, sensitive ears. Plant life included the saldi bush and korin flower. Animal life included a vast array of insect species, twilight lizards, solar-collecting burning snakes, and more than 60 species of scorpion-like tripions.

**Yavin 4** The fourth moon of the planet Yavin, it housed the temples and ruins of the vanished Massassi race, briefly served as the primary base for the Rebel Alliance, and later became the site of Luke Skywalker's Jedi academy. A hot jungle world, Yavin 4 had four main continents separated by six oceans, and contained one landlocked sea. Volcanic mountain ranges and wide rivers could be found amid the thick jungles and towering, purple-barked Massassi trees. The moon had both a wet and a dry season, and violent, unpredictable storms whipped across its surface every few months. Beautiful rainbow storms sometimes

occured when the sun rose past the gas giant Yavin and its light refracted against prismatic ice crystals high in the atmosphere.

Yavin 4

Yavin 4's flora included sense-enhancing blueleaf shrubs, climbing ferns, feather ferns, colorful nebula orchids, blistering touch-not shrubs, and explosive grenade fungi. Indigenous life in its jungles included semi-intelligent simians called woolamanders, stubborn Yavinian runyips, mucous salamanders, purple jumping spiders, lizard crabs, swimming crabs, whisper birds, reptile birds, stinger lizards, crystal snakes, armored eels, stump lizards, crawlfish, ravenous stintaril rodents, tree ticks, spider-like anglers, piranha beetles, and flying two-headed reptiles created during the time of the Sith Lord Exar Kun.

Several of the ancient Massassi ruins were given names, including the Great Temple, the Palace of the Woolamander, and the Temple of the Blueleaf Cluster; almost all of the ruins were connected by an extensive network of underground tunnels. The pyramid-shaped Great Temple lay next to a broad, branching river. The top of the temple housed an observation deck, and below that lay the grand audience chamber. Under the chamber were housing levels; the ground level contained the Communications Center, common rooms, and the Alliance's former War Room. The Temple's hangars were underground, as was the Lost City of the Jedi.

More than 4,000 years before the Battle of Yavin, the Sith magician Naga Sadow fled to Yavin 4 with his followers so he could practice his dark side alchemy in peace. Sadow hid his starship and alchemy equipment beneath the Sith Temple of Fire. Sadow's alchemy helped create many monsters, including the warrior species called the Massassi, designed to guard Sadow's Yavin 4 legacy. The Massassi, the mutated descendants of the ancient Sith, gradually devolved into a primitive and dangerous people, using the dark side to augment their archaic weapons.

When the Dark Jedi Exar Kun arrived on Yavin 4, he enslaved the Massassi and forced them to construct new temples as focal points for Sith power. One temple dedicated to Kun's greatness was built deep in the jungle in the center of a still lake and featured glittering Corusca gems and a towering obsidian statue of the Dark Lord. During the Sith War, Kun brought 20 Jedi Knights to Yavin 4, where he infected them with the evil spirits of the ancient Sith. He ordered them to go out and slay their Jedi Masters, and a terrible Jedi holocaust descended on the galaxy. Soon, however, a united group of thousands of Jedi, led to the jungle moon by Ulic Qel-Droma, arrived to stop Kun.

The Dark Lord ordered the Massassi Night Beast into an isolation chamber as a surprise for his enemies and began putting his final plans into effect. Knowing that he could not defeat the Jedi fleet, Kun sacrificed thousands of Massassi lives to trap his own spirit within the walls of the temples. The Jedi attackers mistakenly ignited the moon's jungles, devastating its surface and causing the deaths of the remaining Massassi, but the Great Sith War had finally ended. Before his defeat, Exar Kun had trapped the children of the Massassi within a strange golden globe, and several desperate Massassi traveled to Yavin 8 to seek assistance from the Melodie people.

The Jedi Master Ikrit eventually discovered the golden sphere containing the Massassi children located beneath the Palace of the Woolamander and stayed with it, awaiting someone who could break its curse. Centuries later, the Rebel Alliance constructed its primary base within the abandoned temples after evacuating its installation on Dantooine. Under the command of General Jan Dodonna, Alliance engineers cleared out the ancient structures and made them fit for habitation once more and also installed a turbolift and erected high lookout towers. Dodonna sealed off the nearby Temple of the Blueleaf Cluster when an eerie power crystal, containing what appeared to be trapped spirits, was found inside its main audience chamber.

The Sullustan naturalist Dr'uun Unnh took time out from his Alliance duties to begin the first modern-day studies of the jungle moon, cataloging many of its plant and animal species. Not long after, the first Imperial Death Star discovered the secret base and moved into firing position as the Rebels counterattacked with snubfighters. In the Battle of Yavin, Luke Skywalker destroyed the battle station as it attempted to shatter Yavin 4 with its superlaser. During the fighting, an Imperial pilot named Qorl crashed his damaged TIE fighter in the moon's jungles and fruitlessly awaited rescue, while another crashing TIE killed Dr'uun Unnh.

In the aftermath of the battle, the Empire blockaded the moon and periodically attacked the Rebel base with TIE fighters. During one such attack, a TIE bomber that crashed in the jungle awakened the Massassi Night Beast, which had lain dormant for thousands of years. The beast, which could use the Force to shield itself from energy weapons, laid waste to much of the Rebel base until calmed by Luke Skywalker. The creature then took an Alliance ship and left the moon, intending to search for its former masters among the stars. The Alliance eventually evacuated Yavin 4.

Seven years after the Battle of Endor, the Great Temple was used as the location of Luke Skywalker's Jedi academy, and the long-trapped spirit of Exar Kun reasserted itself. After nearly killing Skywalker, Kun's spirit was finally vanquished by the efforts of the new Jedi trainees. The next year, the academy was targeted for attack by Admiral Daala's fleet. After a long, destructive battle, Daala's forces were defeated and her Super Star Destroyer *Knight Hammer* was demolished. Eighteen years after the Battle of Endor, Anakin Solo visited the academy and discovered the mysterious golden sphere hidden beneath the Palace of the Woolamander; he helped free the imprisoned spirits. One year later, Jacen and Jaina Solo visited the academy and were held prisoner by the TIE pilot Qorl, still living in the moon's deep jungles.

After Yuuzhan Vong Warmaster Tsavong Lah called for the heads of all Jedi during the Yuuzhan Vong invasion, the enemy collaborators of the Peace Brigade led an advance attack on the Jedi academy at Yavin 4. The aliens destroyed the Great Temple to build shaper bases in its place. After the rescue of Anakin Solo, the shaper base was destroyed by bombardment from Talon Karrde's fleet.

**Yavin 8** The eighth moon of the planet Yavin, it was covered with vast brown-and-green tundra between two polar ice caps and split by an equatorial range of purple mountains. Yavin 8 had few large bodies of water, although large reservoirs of groundwater lay beneath the permafrost, resulting in small marshes and swamps during the summer months.

About 54 million of the intelligent amphibious humanoids known as the Melodies inhabited the caverns and lakes in the warmer equatorial region near the mountains around the time of the Galactic Civil War. They began life on land, then moved into water as adults, their legs replaced by tails and their lungs by gills. This transformation into adult form, called the Changing Ceremony, happened around a Melodie's 20th year and took place in a shallow pool coated with a unique, air-supplying algae. The Melodies were unable to leave their pools during the transformation, which could take weeks, and were thus particularly vulnerable to Yavin 8's many land-based predators.

The young Melodies performed most of the necessary functions of their primitive society because the elders could no longer leave the streams and lakes. Abundant animal life included silver-backed fish and many species of herbivorous burrowers and their carnivorous counterparts, such as the loper and moss-hopper. There were 17 species of grazers, including the wolbak, dysart, dontopod, and songbuk, living in the moon's tundra and

Battle of Yavin

mountain ranges. Predators included snakelike reels, color-changing ursods, rodent-like raiths, flying avrils, serpentine ropedancers, and arachnid purellas.

Around 4,000 years before the Battle of Yavin, members of Yavin 4's Massassi species journeyed to Yavin 8 to seek help for their children, who had been magically trapped in a golden globe by the Dark Jedi Exar Kun. When the Melodie elders were unable to help them, the Massassi carved the story of their plight in the rocks of the Sistra mountain in the hope that someone would eventually be able to break the curse. Some 18 years after the Battle of Endor, Anakin Solo and the Jedi trainee Tahiri Veila traveled to Yavin 8 to take their friend Lyric to her Changing Ceremony within the Sistra mountain. They had to battle predators but uncovered the ancient message of the Massassi and brought back a new Melodie child, Sannah, to be trained at the Jedi academy on Yavin 4.

**Yavin, Battle of** The first major engagement of the Galactic Civil War, it was also the first major tactical victory for the Rebel Alliance. The Battle of Yavin took place in the shadow of the gas giant, near its fourth moon.

The battle came about after Rebel spies stole the plans for the Empire's newest weapon of mass destruction, the Death Star. The plans made it to Rebel headquarters on Yavin 4 despite the capture and subsequent rescue of Princess Leia Organa, but the Empire had tracked Leia's rescuers to the once secret base. With only about 30 minutes before the Death Star would be close enough to obliterate Yavin 4, the Rebels mustered every ship they had. The stakes were high, with only two possible outcomes: survival of the Rebel Alliance, or total destruction. The Rebel plan depended on the ability of a single starfighter to navigate the Death Star trenches—all the while avoiding laserfire from gun towers and TIE fighters—and score a direct hit with a proton torpedo on a small, unshielded thermal exhaust vent to start a chain reaction that would blow up the battle station's power core.

Yavin Vassilika

The battle seemed to be going badly for the Rebels. Although they held their own for a while and their superior piloting skills took many Imperials out of the fight, the sheer numerical superiority of the Imperials began to take its toll. As the Death Star started to clear the edge of Yavin and get a clear shot at the Rebel base on its fourth moon, all appeared lost. But a young farm boy from Tatooine turned off his targeting computer and—using nothing but the power of the Force—made the one-in-a-million shot that marked the beginning of the end of the Empire, for the destruction of the Death Star showed that the mighty, evil colossus was vulnerable. Soon young Luke Skywalker and his companions were known far and wide as the Heroes of Yavin.

**Yavin system** Far from the Galactic Core and major hyperspace lanes, the system did not appear on many astrogation charts until the formation of the New Republic. The Yavin system's three planets—Fiddanl, Stroiketcy, and Yavin—orbited a medium orange star. Formed over seven and a half billion years before the collapse of the Galactic Republic, the system was first surveyed during the Republic's Expansionist Period and was originally recorded as unfit for humanoid habitation.

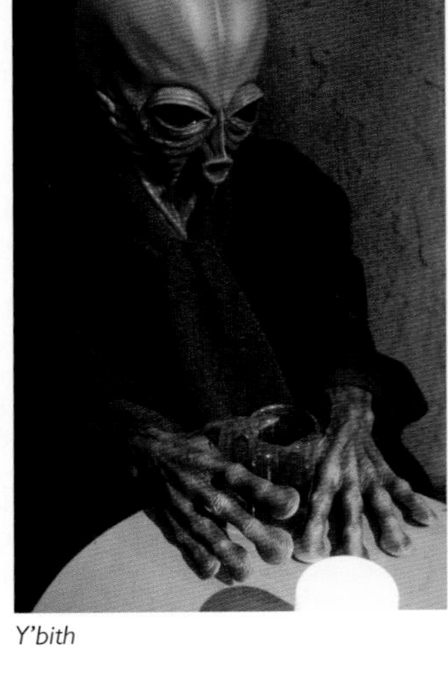
Y'bith

**Yavin Vassilika** A crystalline artifact, made from a single Corusca gem and etched with Massassi hieroglyphics, it was believed by many to be only a myth. Its value was estimated to be in the millions of credits. In a contest to determine whose management style was better, the Hutts Jabba, Embra, and Malta hired separate contractors to return the Yavin Vassilika to them. Bria Tharen and the Rebel Alliance later took possession of the Vassilika, revealing that it contained a key that opened the greatest of the Massassi temples on Yavin 4.

**yayax** A fierce, panther-like beast, it lived in the forests of Endor's moon.

**yazstrimskizzie** An Ithorian creature slowly cooked as a delicacy.

**Y'bith** Millions of years before the collapse of the Galactic Republic, sentience took root among the ancient forerunners of the Bith species on Clak'dor VII. As the Bith evolved, they developed impressive cities in the mountains and jungles of their world. The capital city of Weogar and the domed city of Nozho stood for centuries as testament to the achievement of the proto-Bith culture, but relations between the cities soured, and they developed a fierce rivalry. About 300 years before the Galactic Civil War, the tensions boiled over as a dispute over a stardrive patent ignited a civil war. When it finally ended, Clak'dor VII's biosphere was ruined. A biological attack launched at Nozho had shattered the city, mutating its populace, and the surrounding wildlife.

Most Nozho citizens were killed outright, but many who survived developed mutagenic irregularities that soon led to the creation of a subspecies of Bith. The Y'bith, which translates as "ghost Bith," eventually left the hermetically sealed cities that were built amid the ruins, and attempted to establish a permanent population on Clak'dor IV, where they eventually founded the city of New Nozho. The bioengineering geniuses among the Y'bith stabilized the mutations' worst effects, but the populace had to adapt to their new traits of poor eyesight, stronger hands and feet, ductile mouth structures, sensitive skin, and thicker bones. The Y'bith were tolerated by the Bith, though not openly accepted by mainstream Bith culture. Some claimed that this was because of residual guilt over the bombings that created the Y'bith, although, the Bith denied it. They cited the Y'bith's volatile biochemistry, which triggered bouts of violence and aggression, as reason enough to keep their distance.

The Y'bith worked hard to gain acceptance as members of the galactic community, with New Nozho becoming a notable trade port. Over the course of generations, the Y'bith spread to other worlds, forming a notable minority presence on Nar Shaddaa and Coruscant, where they aided the rebuilding efforts following the Yuuzhan Vong War. The Y'bith saw the story of their species as one of great success arising from unimaginable adversity.

**ychna** An enormous Yuuzhan Vong–bioengineered creature used to attack orbital space stations. An ychna resembled a snake, and could wrap around a space station and crush it.

Yayax

**Ychthytonian** A four-armed species. Bômlas, a bartender on Skip 1 in Smuggler's Run, was an Ychthytonian.

**Yeb, Solipo** A Senator who attended the funeral of Padmé Amidala. Yeb wore a costly Andalian cloak.

**Yedan, Gade** The assistant to Gyr Keela of the Mrlsst Academy. Gade Yedan was also a staunch supporter of the Ante-Endor Association, which promoted the belief that the Emperor survived the Battle of Endor and that Alderaan had been destroyed by Rebel scientists testing their own superweapons. Yedan became the primary planetside contact for Imperial Captain Loka Hask. He was shot by Hask shortly before Dr. Falken's asteroid lab was consumed by a wormhole.

Gade Yedan

**Yeesrim, Baskol** A Gran Senator from the planet Malastare during the period arround the Battle of Naboo. Like all Gran, Yeesrim had three eyes atop fleshy eyestalks and goat-like facial features. Like many Senators, he was somewhat corrupt and ardently noncommittal. He was part of the group supporting Aks Moe and Ainlee Teem during the ouster of Chancellor Valorum. He later attended the funeral of Aks Moe and continued to serve as a representative under Ask Aak.

**Yemm** A demonic-looking Devaronian, he excelled in saying the right thing at the right time. Yemm supervised documentation and was legal counsel at Maw Installation.

**Yemm, Yarbolk** A male Chadra-Fan, he was a reporter for TriNebulon News stationed on Nim Drovis. He rescued C-3PO and R2-D2 from certain enslavement. Yarbolk Yemm's popularity was attested to by the bounty on him in seven systems, presumably posted by the Loronar Corporation in response to Yemm's sharp coverage of its operations and methods.

Solipo Yeb

**Yetoom Na Uun** Located on the edge of the Senex sector, it was the base of operations for Fargednim P'taan, a moderately large drug dealer.

**Yevetha** The dominant species in the Koornacht Cluster, they were skeletal bipeds who evolved on the planet N'zoth. They had six-fingered hands with retractable claws underneath their wrists. In N'zoth's night sky, the blazing stars of the cluster blocked out the light from more distant stars, and the Yevetha came to believe that their world was the center of the universe. Using spherical thrustships traveling through realspace, the Yevetha spread from their homeworld to colonize 11 other planets, forming the Duskhan League.

Little was known about the cluster or its worlds, because the Empire kept access restricted and the Yevetha remained secretive after the Empire's departure some three years following the Battle of Endor. In fact, Yevethan policy was to execute trespassers on sight. During the Imperial reign, the brutal governor in charge of the cluster held public executions, used women as pleasure slaves, and took children as hostages. The technologically inclined Yevetha were forced to work in the shipyards established by the Empire, repairing and maintaining its war vessels—and learning a great deal about Imperial technology in the process.

After the Empire left, the Yevetha underwent what they called a Second Birth, settling a dozen more colony worlds and restoring captured Imperial warships. The Duskhan League laid claim to the entire cluster, even though it included as many as 17 worlds populated by other species. Twelve years after the Battle of Endor, the Yevethan fleet eliminated all non-Yevethan colonies from inside the cluster's borders, fanatically cleansing these "infestations" in a devastating series of attacks called the Great Purge. Chief of State Leia Organa Solo sent the New Republic's Fifth Fleet to the cluster to dissuade the Yevetha from extending their actions any further, and a bitter war ensued.

During the Yuuzhan Vong War, the alien invaders gained information on the Yevethan military from the Fia of Galantos. They then decimated N'zoth, killing every last Yevethan individual and nearly wiping the Yevethan species from the galaxy.

Baskol Yeesrim

**Yevethan Protectorate** The proper name of the Duskhan League, an alliance of worlds in Koornacht Cluster inhabited by the xenophobic species known as the Yevetha.

**Yevra** A red-skinned Zabrak trained at the Sith Academy on Korriban during the years leading up to the Battle of Ruusan. Like her brother Llokay, Yevra's connection to the dark side of the Force paled in comparison with that of the other Zabrak student, Sirak. Llokay and Yevra looked up to Sirak as a leader and followed his orders. When Sirak was defeated in the lightsaber training ring by Bane, he plotted revenge with Llokay and Yevra's help. When Sirak attacked Bane, Yevra was unprepared for Bane's control of the Force. He flung her backward, and Yevra was killed by Githany using an energy whip.

**Yfra, Ambassador** An ambassador from the Hapes Cluster, she was really a traitor. Ambassador Yfra, with hair and eyes the color of polished pewter, went to the Jedi academy to observe Tenel Ka's studies, but her visit had to be put off when the girl's friends Jaina and Jacen Solo and Lowbacca were kidnapped. Yfra secretly planned to have Tenel Ka and her grandmother, Queen Ta'a Chume, assassinated. The plot was uncovered when Tenel Ka and her friends confronted a Bartokk assassination squad on Hapes.

**Ygziir** A planet in the Yuuzhan Vong galaxy, it was destroyed in the ancient Cremlevian War by Warmaster Yo'gand. The warmaster used a dovin basal to pull Ygziir's moon onto a collision course with the planet, leaving it a shattered hulk.

**Yibikkoror** One of the inhabited planets of the Yinchorri system. Yibikkoror was a tiny world with a dense atmosphere. Prior to the Battle of Naboo, Ploo Koon, Micah Giiett, Lilit Twoseas, and K'Kruhk went to Yibikkoror to engage the Yinchorri.

Yevetha

**Yim, Ahsi** A young Yuuzhan Vong shaper and the sister of Nen Yim. She was elevated to the rank of master shaper about a year after the conquest of Coruscant. After Nen Yim disppeared on her mission to locate Zonama Sekot, Ahsi Yim was assigned to work with the new master shaper, Qelah Kwaad. When Kwaad inferred that Ahsi Yim had helped Nen Yim escape, Supreme Overlord Shimrra had her executed.

**Yim, Nen** A Yuuzhan Vong shaper trained by Mezhan Kwaad, she was chosen for her heretical beliefs. Nen Yim was one of the few Yuuzhan Vong who believed that their species was not ordained to rule the galaxy, but was part of a larger collection of life-forms. She trained aboard the worldship *Baanu Kor* and had never set foot on a real planet. When Mezhan Kwaad was appointed to investigate the source of the Force, she took on Nen Yim to help map out the nervous system of Tahiri Veila, the Jedi they had captured on Yavin 4. After Veila was rescued and Mezhan Kwaad killed, Nen Yim was brought before Warmaster Tsavong Lah and assigned to preserve the dying worldships. Her efforts, however, had attracted the notice of Supreme Overlord Shimrra, who dispatched Nen Yim and Master Shaper Kae Kwaad to the *Baanu Miir.* She was surprised to learn that Kae Kwaad was actually Overlord Shimrra's jester, Onimi, and Shimrra offered her the chance to continue working beyond the known protocols of Yuuzhan Vong science. She was placed in the service of Warmaster Tsavong Lah, and spent a great deal of time trying to understand why Lah's arm rejected its radank claw implant. Later, Nen Yim came to the realization that Supreme Overlord Shimrra might be a fraud. His fear of the living planet Zonama Sekot only solidified her beliefs, and Nen Yim set out to locate the planet herself. With the help of Tahiri Veila and Corran Horn, she was able to escape Coruscant and reach Zonama Sekot, where she learned that her memories had been stolen to create the "Riina Kwaad" personality implanted in Tahiri Veila's mind. Nen Yim tried to made contact with Sekot, but Nom Anor tracked her down and killed her, so that he could destroy the planet and regain favor with Shimrra.

Nen Yim

**Yinchorr** The site of the Emperor's Royal Guard training facility and homeworld of the reptilian Yinchorri. There were two other inhabited planets in the Yinchorr system, Yitheeth and Yibikkoror, with a fourth world, Uhanayih, thought to be a myth. A year before the Battle of Naboo, Mace Windu, Saesee Tiin, Qui-Gon Jinn, and Obi-Wan Kenobi traveled to Yinchorr to put down an uprising by the native population. During the Galactic Civil War, Imperial forces led by Governor Wessel cleansed the planet of its natives to make room for the training facility. Princess Leia Organa came to the world with a group of Yinchorri delegates and escaped with the help of a stormtrooper who had been born on Alderaan. At the height of the planet's Royal Guard occupation, trainees like Carnor Jax, Kir Kanos, Burr Danid, Lemmet Tauk, and Alum Frost practiced the fighting art of Echani in the crucible of the arena known as the Squall. Seven years after the Battle of Endor, Carnor Jax and Kir Kanos fought to the death inside the Squall. In the century that followed the Yuuzhan Vong invasion, Yinchorr was once again claimed by Imperial forces, and used as a stormtrooper training facility and staging area. When Darth Krayt took control of the galaxy, the stormtroopers found themselves fighting for the new Sith Empire. Tensions between the stormtroopers and their new commanders eventually led trooper Anson Trask to shoot and kill Darth Maleval.

**Yinchorri** A reptilian species from the planet Yinchorr. The Yinchorri were known for their immunity to the manipulations of the Force. Yinchorri society was broken into intelligentsia and warriors, and they were quick to pick up and use any form of technology, including starships and weapons. They also discovered the usefulness of cortosis armor, which was capable of stopping a lightsaber. The Yinchorri developed a form of military transportation based on the wings of insects, with a power pack that strapped to their backs and six thin wings for propulsion. When the Yinchorri began attacking Republic outposts, the Jedi were called in to put an end to the so-called Yinchorri Uprising. Only after taking many losses were the Jedi able to destroy the base on Uhanayih and force a surrender. After the rise of Emperor Palpatine, the Yinchorri were nearly wiped from the planet to make room for a Royal Guard training facility.

Yinchorri

**Ying, Valius** A massive Rutian Twi'lek and a notorious Outer Rim pirate during the decades following the Great Sith War. Ying and his band worked from the starship *Oroko.* Ying managed to track the fugitive Jedi Zayne Carrick, but Marn Hierogryph negotiated a deal allowing himself, Jarael, and Camper to go free. After delivering Carrick to Jedi Master Lucien Draay, Ying was surprised to learn that his captive was actually innocent of the murders attributed to him. Master Draay decided that he could not let Ying leave with the truth, and killed the Twi'lek with his lightsaber.

**Yintal, Dr.** An exobiologist at the New Republic Fleet Institute on Coruscant, he was the doctor who nursed Plat Mallar back to health. Mallar was the young Grannan from Polneye who survived the savage Yevethan massacre.

**Yith, Limna** A Kerestian assassin hired by Black Sun for operations in the Sisar Run.

**Yitheeth** One of the inhabited planets of the Yinchorri system. Some 93 percent of Yitheeth's surface was covered by shallow seas. Adi Gallia, Eeth Koth, Tsui Choi, and Theed Fida went to Yitheeth during the Yinchorri Uprising prior to the Battle of Naboo.

Valius Ying

**Yittreas, Moff** The so-called Butcher of Krant, this Imperial Moff ruled unchecked on the remote planet Krant and its asteroid Hanoon during the final years of the Empire. The Krantians feared him greatly, and he was allowed by Imperial leadership to conduct his affairs as he saw fit. Grand Moff Tarkin considered Yittreas a sociopath but recognized his excellent management skills. The dictator oversaw the deaths of thousands of Krantians for trumped-up charges of political treason, essentially paring down the population so he would not have to increase the size of his garrison. Eventually he became embroiled in a Krantian civil war and lost the planet to the Rebel Alliance. He escaped to his nearby asteroid stronghold, turning to terraforming and developing the rock for Imperial colonization. The asteroid began functioning as a mobile battle station. Yittreas clashed again with the Rebel Alliance 10 years later over the remaining shards of a Jedi artifact.

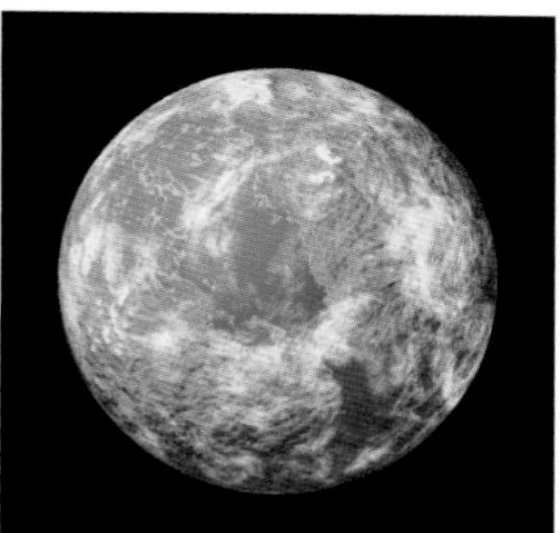

Ylesia

**Ylesia** A planet in Hutt space covered with shallow seas broken by island chains and three large continents. The northern continent was located near the north pole, while the other two were located along the equator. The weather patterns on Ylesia were marked by incredibly wild air currents found in all layers of the atmosphere, making it difficult to land a ship. These patterns were due mainly to the planet's swift rotation, which resulted in a 10-standard-hour day. Much of the land was hidden under shallow, brackish water; swampy areas abounded in a strange fungus that fed on blood. Ylesia was located in the Cha Raaba system, and was known as the original homeworld of the reek. The Hutts and t'landa Til set up a glitterstim-spice-processing plant on Ylesia, using the front of a religious colony to obtain slave labor. An orbiting space station was positioned over Colony One, and was the primary debarkation point for new pilgrims and outgoing slaves. The planet eventually supported nine religious colonies before the Hutts started thinking about populating another world.

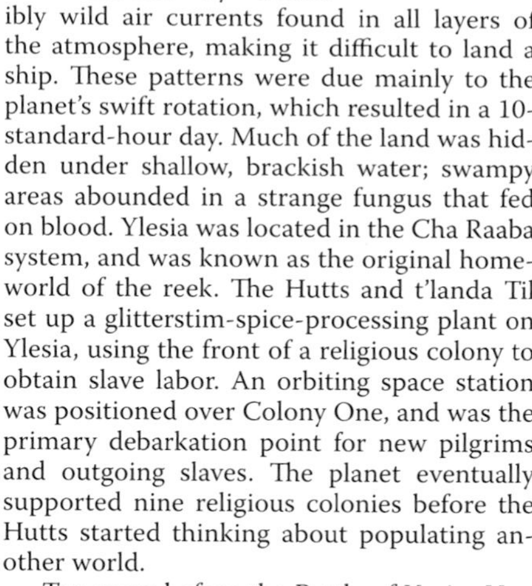

Ten years before the Battle of Yavin, Han Solo fell in love with Bria Tharen while on Ylesia, and he vowed to rescue her from slavery. In their escape, they destroyed the primary glitterstim factory and plundered the t'landa Til high priest's priceless art collection. During the Yuuzhan Vong War, Ylesia served as the Peace Brigade's base of operations. To ensure that the Peace Brigade was free to act, the Yuuzhan Vong executed every Hutt they could find on Ylesia, but maintained the glitterstim-mining operations. About four years into the Yuuzhan Vong War, the New Republic launched an all-out assault on Ylesia, managing to defeat the aliens and retake the planet.

**Ylix** A backrocket world, it was home to the gunman Gallandro. An ancient feud existed between Ylix and Goelitz, a planet several systems away, and Ylix occasionally was attacked by Goelitz revolutionaries. As a youth Gallandro enlisted in the Ylix militia. The planet's forces eventually defeated Goelitz after many devastating battles.

**Yllotat system** The system where, prior to the Battle of Endor, the Imperial Dreadnaught *Dargon* was transporting Rebel and Bothan prisoners to the Star Destroyer *Garret* when it fell under Alliance attack.

**y'luubi** A species of fish that evolved on Coruscant after the Yuuzhan Vong reshaped the planet into a simulacrum of their lost homeworld Yuuzhan'tar. Y'luubi were found in Liberation Lake, and were harvested for their tasty flesh. Skillful chefs could take advantage of the spongy texture of the flesh, infusing it with various flavors and aromas that excited tasters' palates as the meat literally dissolved on their tongues.

**Yn** The homeworld of a diminutive humanoid species, it was represented by Senator Wwebyls in the New Republic government.

**Ynr, Rhysati** A naturally gifted pilot. Ynr's family was relocated from Bespin by Imperial forces, and she found a home with the Rebel Alliance. There was no question that she would make it into the legendary Rogue Squadron. During her training exercises, she befriended Corran Horn and began a relationship with Nawara Ven.

**yoba** This Hapan tuber was often baked or roasted as an accompaniment to nerf steak.

**yobshrimp** A creature with large claws and a thick shell native to Naboo. The yobshrimp preyed on small animals. Live yobshrimps were a Gungan delicacy.

Yobshrimp

**Yoda, Master** An ancient and revered Jedi Master, Yoda lived his final years hiding on the swamp planet of Dagobah. Nine hundred years old, Yoda had trained Jedi for eight centuries, and was extraordinarily powerful in the Force. Among his last responsibilities were some of the most important (and reckless) Jedi in history: Obi-Wan Kenobi, Anakin Skywalker, and later Anakin's son, Luke.

*Jedi Master Yoda*

Much of Yoda's history remains unknown. When he was 700 years old, he served on a council of Jedi Masters instructing new students aboard the massive Jedi training vessel *Chu'unthor*. The starship crashed onto the planet of Dathomir. The Jedi Masters attempted to free the vessel from its swampy confines, but they were repulsed by the Dathomirian Nightsisters. Just prior to the dark times that accompanied the fall of the Republic, Yoda trained the Ganathan royal King Empatojayos Brand in the ways of the Force. Another student of his was the powerful and stern Qu Rahn.

Another tale of Yoda's past involves stopping a swath of destruction cut by Dark Jedi from Bpfassh. One of these dark siders had gotten as far as Dagobah, were Yoda bested him in direct confrontation. The Bpfasshi Jedi died, his dark Force absorbing into and twisting a nearby tree, forming a dark side nexus. It was believed that Yoda chose Dagobah as his hiding place due to the dark side energies emanating from the tree. From a distance, Force-users like the Emperor would not detect Yoda since the Master's bright light-side presence would be canceled by the Bpfasshi dark side energies.

In the waning days of the Old Republic, Yoda was the most respected and senior member of the Jedi Council. Serving alongside such luminaries as Mace Windu and Ki-Adi-Mundi, Yoda was present during the turbulent events that would eventually unravel the millennia-old Republic and seal the fate of the Jedi Order. Yoda played an important role on the Council. When young Padawans began their first foray into Jedi training, they did so under Yoda's guidance. Many of the Republic's greatest Jedi trained under Yoda when they were children, schooled in groupings called clans. Once the Jedi hopefuls grew older, approaching their teenage years, they were paired with an elder Jedi Knight or Master to continue training one-on-one.

The pall of the dark side fell over the Republic during its twilight years, and Yoda grew increasingly concerned. The emergence of the dark side created a disturbance in the Force strong enough to cloud the Jedi's insights into important matters. Sensing the grave uncertainty of the future, Yoda recognized the need for answers. The Jedi Council dispatched Obi-Wan Kenobi to investigate an assassination attempt apparently carried out by Separatist forces. What he found was all the more troubling. An entire clone army had been secretly created for the Republic, by the decree of a late Jedi, Sifo-Dyas. None in the Council knew of this development, nor had any foreseen it. Further investigation revealed that the Separatists were gearing up for war. Count Dooku, one of Yoda's former Padawans, was consolidating a military force out of the droid armies of the commerce guilds. Something needed to be done.

Supreme Chancellor Palpatine, newly granted emergency powers, took possession of the clone army and ordered the Jedi into action. Yoda voyaged to the distant world of Kamino to gather the newly created Republic military, and arrived on Geonosis to rescue the survivors of an ill-fated Jedi task force. As Republic clones engaged Separatist droids, the Clone Wars began. Yoda oversaw the battle from the forward command center. The clones handily defeated the Separatists on Geonosis, but many escaped. Yoda followed his instincts to a darkened hangar where Count Dooku had grievously wounded Obi-Wan and Anakin.

Yoda and Dooku engaged in battle. First their powers in the Force were put to the test as Dooku attempted to crush the tiny Jedi Master with hurled debris. Yoda easily deflected such assaults, and even repulsed Dooku's Force lightning attacks. The contest came down to a duel of lightsabers. In a climactic battle, the two master combatants displayed amazing speed and agility. Yoda, empowered by the Force, leapt through the air, twirling and battering at Dooku's defenses. Dooku only managed to escape by using the Force to once again jeopardize Anakin and Obi-Wan. Knowing that Yoda's nobility would buy him time, Dooku fled as the ancient Jedi Master saved his younger compatriots.

This first battle of the Clone Wars was a victory for the Republic, but Yoda was troubled. Too much had been clouded by the dark side, and the judgment of the Jedi Order was perhaps sullied by complacency and arrogance. Not only had many Jedi died on Geonosis, but the very nature of death itself was now unclear to the wise old Master. While meditating, Yoda had felt a traumatic event befall young Skywalker. At that very moment, he also heard the voice of Qui-Gon Jinn, a Jedi Master slain a decade before. It was impossible for a Jedi to retain his identity after becoming one with the Force, yet he had heard it.

It was another disturbing puzzle for Yoda to solve while the Republic collapsed around him. Through meditation, he was able to commune with the spirit of Qui-Gon. The late Jedi Master had discovered an esoteric yet powerful technique to preserve identity even after death. A Force ability honed outside the Jedi Order, this method was developed by a Shaman of the Whills. In the years to come, Yoda would study these techniques in a role he had not played in centuries: an apprentice.

*Yoda*

Like all senior Jedi, Yoda became a general in the Clone Wars, leading swarms of Republic clone troopers into battle against the Confederacy of Independent Systems. The Jedi Order was in tumult. Some Jedi, disagreeing with the politics behind the war, left the Order in protest. Recognizing that dissension in the ranks would make the Order look weak to both the public and its enemies, Yoda was gravely concerned. Though he was widely known as a sage instructor who stayed mostly within the Jedi Temple, Yoda saw front-line combat action during the Clone Wars, leading troops into the field against the Separatists atop a loyal kybuck steed. On Axion, the diminutive Jedi Master defeated a missile-laden Hailfire droid with his wits and the power of the Force. Yoda was also instrumental in easing the strained diplomatic relations between the Senate and the Wookiees, keeping Kashyyyk within the Republic during the conflict. And he gave Anakin Skywalker a surprise: his own Padawan learner, Ahsoka Tano, with the hope that she would help the impetuous Skywalker learn the meaning of shared responsibility.

Surviving the Sith resurgence, however, proved the real challenge. After years of plotting, Darth Sidious emerged and put into motion his final plan to eliminate the Jedi. Sidious, the shadowy Sith Lord who had escaped Jedi attention for ages, was in fact Supreme Chancellor Palpatine. In his position of increasing power, Palpatine was manipulating events such as the Clone Wars to exterminate the Jedi. With the Jedi scattered across the galaxy leading the clone army, Sidious enacted Order 66. This coded order identified the Jedi as traitors to the Republic, and the loyal clones executed their Jedi leaders in cold blood. Many Jedi died in the assault.

*Yoda trains Luke Skywalker on Dagobah.*

Through the Force, Yoda felt the sudden loss of life across the galaxy. It was nearly a crushing blow, but Yoda recovered in time to stop the attempt on his own life. It was on Kashyyyk, the home of the Wookiees—one of the many battlefronts of the Clone Wars—that troopers turned against Yoda. His once loyal officer, Commander Gree, tried to open fire on Yoda, but the Jedi Master sprang into action and quickly decapitated Gree and his accomplice with his lightsaber. With the help of the Wookiees Tarfful and Chewbacca, Yoda was able to escape Kashyyyk and make contact with Senator Bail Organa of Alderaan. Yoda, Kenobi, and Organa regrouped, having witnessed Palpatine's terrible extermination of the Jedi and their allies. A coded signal emanating from the conquered Jedi Temple was drawing Jedi survivors back to Coruscant into a trap. Kenobi and Yoda were determined to disable this deadly beacon before more Jedi were led to their deaths.

Returning to Coruscant, they infiltrated the Jedi Temple. There they discovered dreadful evidence of what had transpired in their absence. The Chancellor was now Emperor Palpatine, and the once promising Jedi warrior Anakin Skywalker was his new apprentice, Darth Vader. As the only then-known survivors of Order 66, it was up to Yoda and Kenobi to put a stop to the Sith. Kenobi was dispatched to track down Vader. Yoda went after Palpatine.

Inside the spacious interior of the Galactic Senate chamber, Yoda challenged the Emperor. The two engaged in a spectacular duel—a contest between the most powerful practitioners of the Force's light and dark sides. The Emperor proved too powerful to defeat. Although Yoda held his own for much of the duel, in the end the Sith bested him. He realized that continuing to directly confront Palpatine would mean failure. Defeated, Yoda slunk away into the shadows of the Senate chamber's cavernous depths, leaping into a waiting getaway speeder piloted by Bail Organa.

Yoda duels Emperor Palpatine in the Galactic Senate Chamber.

The Jedi had failed to stop the Sith, although Kenobi had crippled Vader on the fiery world of Mustafar. A new hope would arrive in the form of newborn twins. Skywalker's wife, Padmé Amidala, was pregnant with Force-powerful children. On the remote sanctuary of Polis Massa, Padmé gave birth to Luke and Leia before dying. Yoda, Organa, and Kenobi were witness to the births, and immediately began planning for the future. Knowing that the children would pose a threat to the Emperor, the Jedi were determined to keep their existence a secret. The twins were separated—baby Luke was taken to live at the Lars homestead on Tatooine; baby Leia was spirited to Alderaan to be raised as the adoptive daughter of Organa and his wife, the Queen of Alderaan. The Jedi would bide their time, sensing through the Force when the moment was right to oppose the Empire. In the interim, Yoda and Obi-Wan would study the Shaman of the Whills' knowledge from the disembodied form of Qui-Gon Jinn.

Yoda went into hiding on the distant swamp world of Dagobah. There, he waited patiently for the new hope to arise to end the dark side threat to the galaxy. Three years after the Battle of Yavin, it did. Guided to Dagobah by a vision of his former mentor Obi-Wan, Luke Skywalker discovered Yoda without even knowing it. Stranded on the swampy world, Luke met a comical elfin creature who promised him aid. The creature's antics wore thin on Luke's short patience, but it was the first of many tests—tests that Luke often would fail.

Revealing himself to be Yoda, the Jedi Master began Luke's training in earnest. Telekinetic challenges, challenges of the will and body, more challenges than Luke had ever faced before helped to mold the reckless youth into a Jedi. Still, Luke failed to "unlearn" his preconceptions. When asked to raise his sunken starfighter from the Dagobah swamps with the power of his mind alone, he responded that he would try. "No," scolded Yoda. "Do, or do not. There is no try." Luke did not believe the Force could lift such a massive object. He was proven wrong when Yoda telekinetically lifted the X-wing fighter and placed it on dry land. Again, Luke was incredulous—he did not believe; that is why he failed, Yoda told him. When Yoda taught Luke how to "farsee" into the future, a chilling vision of his friends in danger caused the young Skywalker to abandon his training. Luke promised he would return, and rocketed off to rescue his friends. In the end, Luke failed, having to be rescued himself. Yoda feared all would be lost in the effort to stop Vader and the Emperor.

About a year later, Luke did return to conclude his training. Having faced the hardship of confrontation with Vader, and having learned that Vader was actually his father, Luke learned from Yoda that his training was complete, although he had to face Vader again. In Luke's absence, Yoda had become quite ill. As he lay dying, Yoda shed some light on Luke's distant past: There was another Skywalker—a twin sister. Yoda died shortly thereafter, disappearing as his body became one with the Force. Luke would learn that Leia Organa was his sibling, and he would also reclaim his father from the dark side. At the celebration after the Battle of Endor, Luke saw the spirit of Yoda joined by spectral images of Obi-Wan Kenobi and Anakin Skywalker, his father, who had died in the light.

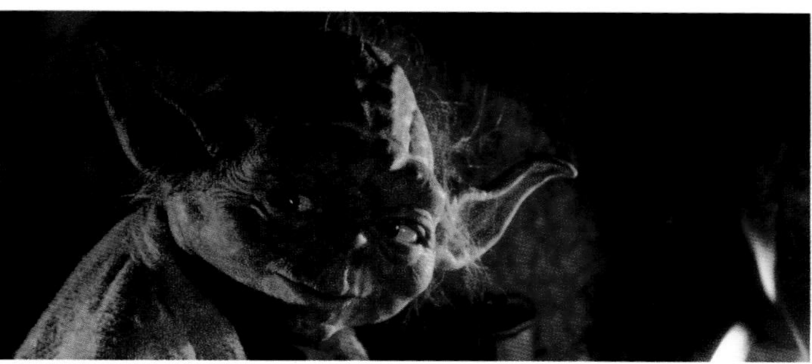

Yoda has some final words of wisdom for Luke Skywalker.

**Yo'gand's Core** A devastating Yuuzhan Vong military tactic. During a Yo'gand's Core maneuver, a strong dovin basal was dropped to the surface of a planet, where it latched on to the planet's core and simultaneously grabbed an orbiting moon with its gravitic beams. Pulling the moon into a collision with the planet devastated any opposition. After the destruction of Ygziir by this tactic during the Cremlevian War, the Yuuzhan Vong learned to easily counter it. However, the targets of their new invasion had no such defenses, and the Yuuzhan Vong used Yo'gand's Core to destroy the planet Sernpidal.

**Yoggoy** One of the many hives that made up the Killik Colony during the time of the Swarm War. As with all other hives, the members of the Yoggoy referred to themselves, as well as the entire nest, as Yoggoy, and acted upon the Will of the Yoggoy hive. The members of the Yoggoy hive were similar in appearance to the Lizil, but had scarlet carapaces and stood 2 meters or more tall. The Yoggoy were considered the soldiers of the Colony. A large portion of the Yoggoy were changed by the integration of Raynar Thul into their hive, when his connection to the Force gave rise to a new hive of insects. This new hive became known as the UnuThul.

**Yomaget, Jir** The Mandalorian who served as the head of the MandalMotors corporation during the years following the Swarm War. Like his brothers in the military, Yomaget wore the traditional body armor of his ancestors, especially when he was at work or meeting with prospective clients. When Boba Fett asked for wayward Mandalorians to return home, Yomaget agreed to contribute half of MandalMotors' profits to help rebuild Mandalore's agriculture and self-sufficiency.

**Yomm, Auren** During the early days of the Empire, when R2-D2 and C-3PO were involved in a series of adventures, they met a then-15-year-old girl, Auren Yomm. She lived in the Umboo province of Roon with her father Nilz and her mother Bola. A young, dark-haired human with dark skin, Yomm had an athletic build and energetic personality. An excellent athlete, she was a medal-winning champion of the Roon Colonial Games.

Yorik-stronha

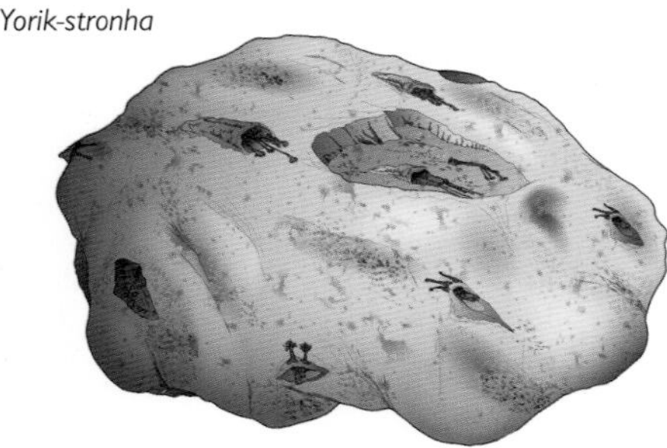

Her specialty was the drainsweeper event. Auren led a team of three riders—herself, Gee Long, and the droid Bix—who rode their rockhopper beasts through a racecourse of three laps. At the center of the track was a variable-gravity drain that would catch fallen riders. The Colonial Games had great political significance, as the oppressive Tawntoom province tried to cow the rebellious Umboo province. The unscrupulous Governor Koong of Tawntoom tried to sabotage the games by poisoning Gee Long and Bix. His attempts were in vain: Replacement racers C-3PO and Mungo Baobab, a trader from Manda with whom Auren had become enamored, competed in their place and won the race for Umboo.

Koong's next gambit was even more heinous. He poisoned the Umboo countryside with rooze, a deadly germ agent. Bola Yomm fell ill because of the contaminated air, but the bungling Koong also managed to poison himself. He called for Nilz, Auren's father and a capable doctor, to concoct a cure. Nilz succeeded, and cured Bola. Koong, however, was too occupied with Imperial treachery to take his cure in time, and he died of the infection.

**Yomm, Nilz** The father of Auren Yomm. In the early days of the Empire, Nilz ran a trading post and was a respected physician in the Roon colonies. He was married to Bola.

**Yonka, Captain Sair** The Imperial commanding officer of the *Avarice* following the Battle of Endor. Prior to serving under Ysanne Isard, he had spent most of his career in the Outer Rim chasing pirates and protecting convoys. A smart and calculating officer, he worked to maximize his chances for survival. The Commenor native fell in love with a woman named Aellyn, who later married the much older Moff Riit Jandi after Yonka left for the Imperial Academy. When they met each other again years later on Elshandruu Pica, their love rekindled and they started an illicit affair. When word of the romance reached Wedge Antilles and Rogue Squadron, they used it to convince Yonka to renounce his Imperial commission and join the New Republic. He accepted and brought the *Avarice* and most of its crew with him. The Star Destroyer was renamed the *Freedom.*

**yorik coral** A form of coral found in the Yuuzhan Vong galaxy. The Yuuzhan Vong bioengineered the coral and formed it into living spaceships, including the massive worldships. Molten yorik coral also was used to fire plasma-like discharges. When the Praetorite Vong invaded the galaxy, they planned to use the dead world of Belkadan as a yorik coral breeding ground. Yorik coral aged like any other biological organism, and by the start of the invasion some worldships had begun to die.

**yorik-stronha** A Yuuzhan Vong asteroid-shaped scout ship, sent in advance of an attack fleet to test the readiness of an enemy. It was built out of yorik coral and covered with layers of rock. These advance ships were usually equipped with cloaking shadows. The *Stalking Moon* was a yorik-stronha advance ship used during the attack on Yag'Dhul.

**yorik-ta** A type of escape pod used by the Yuuzhan Vong. A yorik-ta was composed of black yorik coral and propelled by a dovin basal with rudimentary retros and altitude controls. The escape pod was no larger than a landspeeder and was unarmed. The false Yuuzhan Vong defectors Elan and Vergere used a yorik-ta escape pod to make contact with the New Republic.

**yorik-trema** A Yuuzhan Vong planetary landing craft. Formed of vastiv membranes covering a skeleton of yorik coral, these vessels were designed to transport troops. Most were unarmed and had to be escorted by coralskippers. Yorik-trema had a number of sensitive eyes, trained to maintain contact with the coralskipper escort during the descent. These craft were equipped with ablative shields formed from living scales, which would be burned off during descent but later regenerated like skin tissue. The ground forces transported within the yorik-trema were discharged to the surface of a planet via modified molleung worms. The average yorik-trema measured between 34 and 48 meters long, and was sometimes armed with a pair of volcano cannons and several dovin basals. The craft required a crew of four to operate, and could transport up to 36 troops and 35 metric tons of cargo.

**yorik-vec cruiser** A Yuuzhan Vong assault cruiser, it filled the gap between coralskippers and corvettes. Yorik-vec cruisers were dedicated warships, used for space combat more than transporting troops. On average, a yorik-vec cruiser measured 30 meters long and required a crew of two pilots and three gunners. The ship also had the capacity to handle eight additional passengers and up to 100 metric tons of matériel. The yorik-vec cruiser was armed with a turret-mounted quad volcanic cannon as well as four twin volcanic cannons.

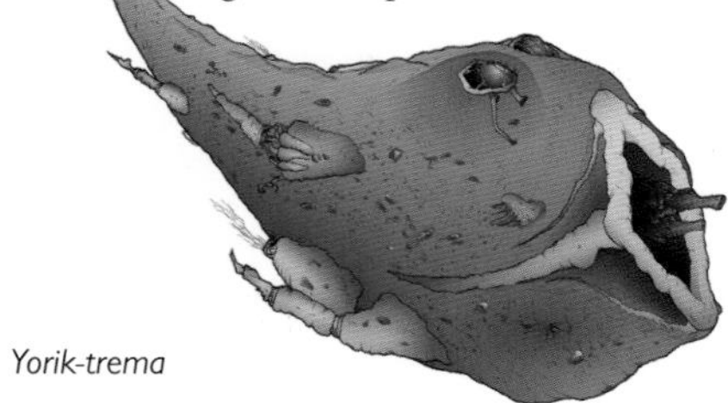

Yorik-trema

Joh Yowza

**Yorn Skot** A gas giant planet known as a source of Tibanna gas, although it was not naturally spin-sealed like the Tibanna gas found in the atmosphere of Bespin. The planet fell outside surrounding jurisdictions and legislated itself like a frontier government. The planet's main colony was established by a wealthy Tibanna gas magnate named Clode Rhoden. Prior to the Battle of Naboo, Qui-Gon Jinn and Obi-Wan Kenobi went to Yorn Skot to find the *Aurorient Express,* an imperiled passenger liner. During the Clone Wars, the clones of H.O.P.E. (High Orbit Precision Entry) Squad went to Yorn Skot to extract Jedi Master Treetower.

**Yorta, Raal** A dashing Corellian gambler who often partnered with bounty hunter Sammie Staable and Squib pick-pocket Smileredon-Verdont during the Galactic Civil War. Together, they joined the Rebel Alliance.

**Young, the** A political faction on Melida/Daan made up of teenagers from both the Melida and Daan societies. About a decade before the Battle of Naboo, the Young was formed by disenchanted children who witnessed their parents fighting endlessly over a few square meters of ground, spending credits on military supplies while children went hungry and fell sick. Members of the Young rescued Qui-Gon Jinn and Obi-Wan Kenobi from the Melida in an effort to stop the violence and prevent the Republic from being blackmailed into taking sides in the civil war. However, the Young were no less militant than their parents, and members were capable of causing great damage on their own. With the help of Obi-Wan Kenobi, the Young eventually defeated the elders of Daan and Melida.

**Youst** A science space station in the Dimok system that was in truth a weapons research facility during the Sepan Civil War.

**Yout 12** During the Clone Wars, the bounty-hunting droid KRONOS-327 botched a mission to the 12th moon of Yout—a failure egregious enough for Ziro the Hutt to terminate his employ.

**Yowza, Joh** A Yuzzum from the Forest Moon of Endor, he was one of the few of his species who left his home planet to seek a more civilized future. Yowza, who was short for his kind and had a deep, raspy voice, was a bigger-than-life talent. He found a job as male lead singer with the Max Rebo Band and performed at the group's last engagement for crime lord Jabba the Hutt on Tatooine.

**Yrrna system** Located in the Outer Rim, it was the site of an Imperial cargo transfer area. Following the Battle of Hoth, the cargo operation in the Yrrna system was attacked by the pirate leader Ali Tarrak and her strike force of stolen TIE defenders.

**ysalamiri** Indigenous to the planet Myrkr, these small salamander-like creatures had the unique ability to push back the Force. Legged snakes that grew to 50 centimeters long, ysalamiri lived in the branches of Myrkr's metal-rich trees. Their claws grew directly into the branches, making it difficult to remove them from their perches. A single ysalamiri created a 10-meter-radius bubble in which the Force did not exist. Those who studied them theorized that ysalamiri pushed the Force away from themselves like a bubble of air pushes away water. Within this bubble, a Force-user could not call on his or her powers or otherwise manipulate the Force.

Grand Admiral Thrawn's plans to destroy the New Republic included the use of the docile ysalamiri. He ordered Imperial engineers to build frames of pipes to support and nourish the creatures so that they could be removed from their branches and transported off-planet. The nutrient frames were designed so that they could be worn by Thrawn and others as a mobile defense against Jedi. The creatures also figured prominently in Thrawn's plans to rapidly grow clones in the Spaarti cloning cylinders he retrieved from the Emperor's storehouse on Wayland.

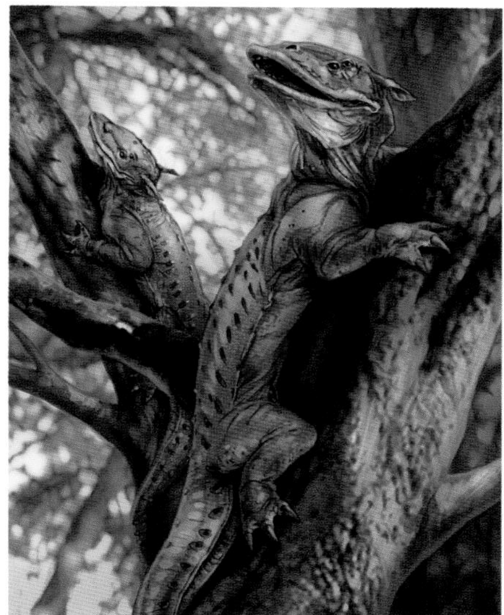

*Ysalamiri*

**Ysanna** Shaman-warriors, they lived on the planet Ossus and were Force-sensitive. They were descendants of the survivors of the supernova that devastated the planet thousands of years before the Battle of Yavin. These ancestors had survived by hiding in the caves of Ossus's Eocho Mountains.

**Ysanna, Jem** The daughter of the Great Okko, chief shaman of the Ysanna tribe of Force-sensitives on the ancient world of Ossus, Jem Ysanna was an athletic woman with dark hair and sharp, exotic features. A year and a half after Grand Admiral Thrawn's campaign against the New Republic, Jedi Master Luke Skywalker came to Ossus. He hoped to discover the lost lore of the ancient Jedi to help him rebuild the Order. There Skywalker found Jem and her younger brother Rayf tied to an ancient, mighty tree. Their initiation ritual interrupted by Skywalker, the Ysanna tribesmen briefly attacked the Jedi but soon came to recognize him as their ally. This allegiance was sealed moments later when Skywalker and his student Kam Solusar defended the Ysanna from Imperial dark side raiders. The Dark Side Adept Executor Sedriss took Jem hostage in the scuffle, but the actions of Skywalker and the reawakened Jedi Master Ood Bnar saved her.

*Jem Ysanna*

It was during this conflict on Ossus that Jem's and Luke's eyes first locked. In that brief, silent exchange, they both sensed a deep kinship. Perhaps, if given time, it could have blossomed into love. But the galaxy rarely offered the time needed for tenderness in moments of war. With more pressing matters at hand, Luke began training Jem and Rayf in the ways of the Force. New Jedi were needed to stop the cloned Emperor Palpatine's mad grab for power and territory. The chief, her father, gave permission for the two Ysanna youths to venture forth into the galaxy.

On the New Republic safeworld of New Alderaan, Jem and Luke grew closer. But an Imperial assault by dark side adepts rudely intruded on their tranquillity. The Dark Jedi Krdys Mordi and Tedryn-Sha attacked a sleeping Skywalker with poisoned scarab droids. Jem barged into the Jedi Master's sleeping quarters, brandishing her lightsaber. With an enraged slash, she cleaved Mordi in two, but Tedryn-Sha shot her in the abdomen with his blaster pistol. Had she been more skilled, she might have avoided the blast. Her life force left her body and the Force reclaimed her physical form, leaving behind only her well-worn hides and Ysanna tribal clothes. She was just 23 at the time of her death.

**Ysanna, Rayf** A 15-year-old shaman-warrior encountered by Luke Skywalker on Ossus. Rayf and his sister Jem accompanied Luke to New Alderaan, where he was instrumental in saving Jacen and Jaina Solo from dark siders. When his sister was killed, Rayf went with the others to Nespis VIII.

**Yso, Uso** A swoop seller in Euceron City following the Battle of Naboo. Standing well over 3 meters tall, with two beating hearts and 15-fingered hands as big as bantha haunches, Uso Yso cut an intimidating figure. His swoop dealership was, in fact, a front for the gambling agency he ran from the back office. When the Galactic Games came to Euceron some six years after the Battle of Naboo, Uso Yso was known as one of the most "trustworthy" of the bookies taking illegal bets on the events.

**YT-1300** The model number of a popular series of light freighters built by the Corellian Engineering Corporation, it included the famous *Millennium Falcon*. Originally designed and manufactured some 30 years before the Battle of Yavin, the YT-1300 was a two-being craft and could accommodate up to six passengers. It measured 26.7 meters in length and held 100 metric tons of cargo. In its stock form, the YT-1300 was armed with a single Taim & Bak H4 laser cannon, but carried no defensive shielding. The main hull was disk-shaped, with two trapezoidal pods extending from the front. The cockpit was offset-mounted on the right side of the disk. One of the primary drawbacks of this model of transport was the off-center cockpit placement. While the cockpit could be positioned on either the left or right side, this positioning left a great deal of the ship out of the pilot's view. This was common among larger ships, yet the off-center placement made it much harder to maneuver in tight spaces, especially for many new pilots. The more skittish of these captains often installed five-axis, laser-ranging pods near the

*An early incarnation of the* Millennium Falcon *YT-1300 freighter*

front mandibles to provide real-time information about the parts of the ship they couldn't see.

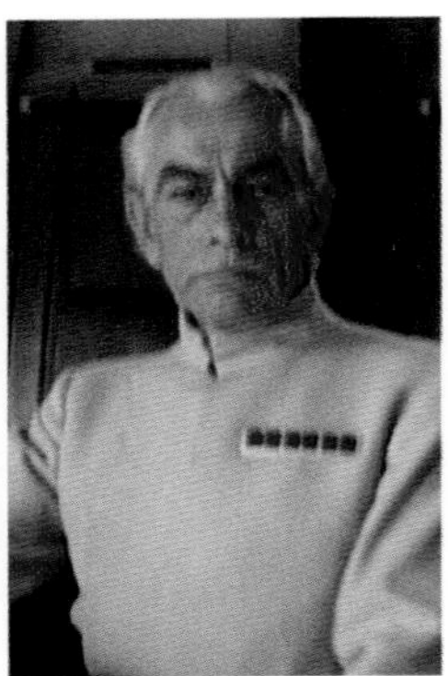
Admiral Wulff Yularen

**YT-2400** A light freighter in the Corellian Engineering Corporation's successful YT-series, the YT-2400 incorporated the saucer-shaped hull design that made the YT-1300 popular. However, it did away with the paired, forward-facing mandibles. The YT-2400 had improved hull plating, power to spare, and additional space in the cargo and engine compartments. It was easily modified to accommodate larger engines and secret compartments, which is exactly what smuggler Dash Rendar did to his *Outrider*. Slightly smaller than its predecessors at 21 meters long, it could transport up to six passengers and 150 metric tons of cargo.

**YT-5100** The model number of the Corellian Engineering Corporation's prototype version of the *Shriek*-class bomber, developed following the Yuuzhan Vong War. Ten prototypes were deployed to Tralus as part of Operation Noble Savage during Thrackan Sal-Solo's bid for Corellian independence. The YT-5100 was based on the popular YT-1300 freighter series, but was a much sleeker and more streamlined vessel. The YT-5100 had the forward mandibles of the YT-1300, but without a side-mounted cockpit.

**Y-TIE** A type of "ugly" starship made from pieced-together scrap. Y-TIEs had Y-wing fuselages wedged between two TIE fighter solar panels.

**Y'Toub system** Located in the center of the galactic region known as Hutt space, it contained six planets orbiting a yellow star. A massive, radioactive gas cloud containing the hidden planet Ganath was very close to the Y'Toub system. Four of the system's six planets were habitable. The largest and best known was Nal Hutta, with its orbiting Smugglers' Moon, Nar Shaddaa. Consequently, it was sometimes called the Nal Hutta system.

**Yuga 2** A planet covered with dense rain forests and clinging trees, it was a popular tourist destination because of the Yuga Planetary Park. Alliance historian Voren Na'al bought passage from Yuga 2 to Tatooine on a Galaxy Tours ship to begin documenting the histories of the Heroes of Yavin.

**Yugi** A Flakax goon who worked for the Directors during the Swarm War. Yugi and Tito were dispatched to assassinate Han Solo and his wife, Leia Organa Solo, but were intercepted by the Solos before they could complete the mission. Yugi was killed in the brief firefight that ensued.

**Yulant system** Located in the Core Worlds, it contained one of the 18 farming planets administered by the Salliche Ag Corporation. After the Battle of Endor, workers in the Yulant, Ruan, and Broest systems revolted against the Imperial-controlled Salliche Ag by burning fields and destroying hydroponics facilities.

**Yularen, Admiral Wulff** Straitlaced and by-the-book, he served as commander for Anakin Skywalker's fleet during the Clone Wars. A consummate military officer, Admiral Yularen executed any order given him, but he often worried that General Skywalker's unconventional tactics were riskier than necessary. By the time of the Galactic Civil War, Yularen served in the Imperial Security Bureau. He was assigned to brief Grand Moff Tarkin and also ordered to ensure absolute loyalty to the Emperor. He was killed in the explosion of the first Death Star.

**Yuls, Dellis** A Quarren, he was the chief of security for Ororo Transportation, the main competitor of crime lord Prince Xizor's own cargo company. Xizor's aide, Guri, twisted Yuls's neck until it cracked, then shot him in the base of the skull for good measure.

**Yumfla** The primary starport on the moon Suarbi 7/5. It was also the site of the Imperial governor's palace, a fortress-like affair surrounded by 8-meter-tall walls and guarded by stormtroopers.

**Yun** A young Dark Jedi who served under Jerec after the Battle of Endor. Yun was a cocky Epicanthix youth who received most of his training under the guidance of Sariss. Yun grew up on the planet Panatha, the son of a wealthy mineral baron. When he came of age, Yun was sent to Bunduki by his father, to learn the patience and temperment of the Followers of Palawa. His instructors refused to teach him the martial art teräs käsi, and Yun returned to Panatha. His father turned the boy's training over to his fiancée Sariss. The pair became very close, but Sariss refused to be drawn into an affair because of her vows to Yun's father. Angry at being rebuffed, Yun killed his father to "earn" her love. Jerec demanded proof of Yun's loyalty, and sent the boy back to Bunduki to execute his Palawa masters. Later, during the search for the Valley of the Jedi, Yun attempted to kill Kyle Katarn at Baron's Hed, but was defeated. After the Valley of the Jedi was discovered on Ruusan, Katarn again spared Yun's life. Yun was then visited by the spirit of Jedi Master Qu Rahn, who urged Yun to seek redemption. Yun stepped in to prevent Sariss from killing Katarn, but she showed no such mercy and killed Yun.

**Yun-Harla** The Yuuzhan Vong deity known as the Cloaked Goddess or the Trickster. Yun-Harla was often worshipped in tandem with Yun-Yammka. Yun-Harla was never visible to her servants, and was never actually portrayed in Yuuzhan Vong writings or pictures. It was believed that her body was formed from borrowed parts and covered with borrowed skin. Some Yuuzhan Vong thought that Yun-Harla's eyes were villips, while others believed them to be the actual eyes of Yun-Yuuzhan, discarded when the Creator ascended to a higher plane of existence. Her clothing, whenever she wore it, was designed to confuse and deceive those who saw her. Thus, only her spirit made contact with those who worshipped her. Shortly after the Second Battle of Coruscant, Jaina Solo stole the frigate *Ksstarr* and renamed it the *Trickster* to goad the Yuuzhan Vong priest Harrar. However, the name eventually became something more, as some Yuuzhan Vong began to believe that she actually was Yun-Harla incarnate. This belief was based on the relationship between Yun-Harla and Yun-Yammka, which resembled the relationship between Jaina and her twin brother, Jacen.

**Yunkor IX** In an early test of the B-wing starfighter, a single B-wing was sent to destroy a TIE fighter staging area near Yunkor IX.

**Yun-Lingni** The lowest and the most feared in the pantheon of Yuuzhan Vong gods.

**Yun-Ne'Shel** A hermaphroditic Yuuzhan Vong deity who represented life itself and governed childbirth, art, design, and innovation. Yun-Ne'Shel was believed to have created all forms of life with the tools and materials presented by Yun-Yuuzhan. Shapers worshipped Yun-Ne'Shel, who was known as She-Who-Shapes or the Modeler, in an organic grotto that was similar to a yammosk and created to enhance the mental abilities of any who entered it. Within the body of the grotto were nodules of flesh that essentially were mouths,

Yun

filled with eight knife-like teeth. Each shaper adept was required to enter the chamber and meditate before placing a hand into the nodule's mouth. The teeth closed over the wrist and bit through flesh and bone. The adept was then fitted with a new hand, grown to provide the shaper with the tools needed in his or her work. At the end of the war, the Shamed One Onimi revealed to Jaina Solo that he had come to believe that Tahiri Veila was actually Yun-Ne'Shel, since he alone of the Yuuzhan Vong could see her through the Force.

**Yun-Q'aah** The female Yuuzhan Vong deity who, with Yun-Txiin, formed the Lovers. Together these twin deities protected those Yuuzhan Vong who discovered the passion of love, although they forbade relationships between castes. Worshippers of Yun-Q'aah and Yun-Txiin were part of a religious movement known as the Undying Flame. The Lovers were portrayed as enemies of the Twin Gods (Yun-Yammka and Yun-Harla), but were considered close allies of Yun-Ne'Shel.

**Yun-Shuno** The thousand-eyed patron deity of the Shamed Ones, those Yuuzhan Vong whose bodies refused to accept implants during the ritual of Escalation. Yun-Shuno was the most grotesque of the Yuuzhan Vong gods and was also known as the Pardoner. It was believed that Yun-Shuno could intercede with Yun-Ne'Shel and Yun-Yuuzhan to improve the lot of a deserving Shamed One.

**Yun-Txiin** The male half, with Yun-Q'aah, of the Yuuzhan Vong twin deities known as the Lovers. They were the most capricious of Yuuzhan Vong gods and required no sacrifice.

**Yun-Yammka** The Yuuzhan Vong god of war. Also known as the Slayer, Yun-Yammka resembled a large brain with a single eye, a puckered mouth, and an array of tentacles around his body. Every member of the Yuuzhan Vong warrior caste kept a statue of Yun-Yammka among his or her possessions and prayed to the Slayer for strength in battle. After the conquest of Coruscant, the Yuuzhan Vong planned to retake Borleias and turn the planet into a shrine for the priests of Yun-Yammka. Yun-Yammka often was associated with the Trickster goddess, Yun-Harla. Because of this, many Yuuzhan Vong began to assocate Yun-Yammka with Jacen Solo after his twin sister, Jaina, adopted the guise of Yun-Harla.

**Yun-Yuuzhan** The greatest of the deities worshipped by the Yuuzhan Vong. Yun-Yuuzhan, also known as the Cosmic Lord and the Creator, was considered the beginning of all that existed. It was Yun-Yuuzhan who took parts of his own body to form the other gods, as well as the Yuuzhan Vong themselves. Statues of Yun-Yuuzhan often appeared incomplete to represent his sacrifices. Among the Shamed Ones who followed the Jedi heresy, it was believed that the Force was actually the remnant of Yun-Yuuzhan's soul, after he gave birth to the universe.

*Yuuzhan Vong*

**Yusanis** One of the most feared of the Echani warriors active in the galaxy during the decades leading up to the Jedi Civil War. Yusanis was a decorated solider and one of the greatest heroes of the Mandalorian Wars. Later, when Yusanis discovered that an Echani Senator had been killed by Darth Revan, he set out to confront the Sith Lord and bring him to justice. Despite his skills, Yusanis was quickly killed by Revan. It was later discovered that Yusanis was the father of the Echani Handmaiden Brianna.

**Yu'shaa** An identity adopted by Nom Anor while he worked with the Shamed Ones on Coruscant to spread the Jedi heresy. The name, which translated into Basic as "the prophet," indicated that Nom Anor had become the living vessel for carrying the message to the Shamed Ones. He began gathering legions to his cause to build a power base from which he could strike back at Supreme Overlord Shimrra. Among the heretical beliefs proposed by Yu'shaa was the theory that the Force was actually the soul of Yun-Yuuzhan.

**Yushan sector** Located in the Mid Rim, it contained the planet Kaal.

**yuugrr** A dim-witted predator native to the jungles of Kashyyyk that was known to steal sleeping Wookiee children from their beds. Yuugrrs tried to escape by moving onto thin branches in the wroshyr trees, where their weight became too great for the branch to support. Eventually, the yuugrr fell from the branch, taking its victim, and often its pursuer, with it.

*Yuuzhan'tar*

**Yuun** A female Bouncer who befriended Tomcat (Darovit) during the years following the Battle of Ruusan. Yuun was visiting Darovit when he discovered that the Jedi Order had returned to Ruusan to erect a monument to those Jedi who had died in the war against the Brotherhood of Darkness. Yuun, who had been born after the Battle of Ruusan, did not understand Darovit's anger.

**Yuuzhan'tar** The long-lost extragalactic homeworld of the Yuuzhan Vong. In their native language, the name meant "crèche of the gods." The Yuuzhan Vong left the planet many millennia before they invaded the galaxy, spreading into space to seek a new galaxy. Yuuzhan'tar was a living, conscious world that had cut its own people off from the Force; Zonama Sekot, the living "rogue planet," was an offspring world grown from a seed of the original Yuuzhan'tar. During the Yuuzhan Vong War, the invaders targeted Coruscant as a replacement for Yuuzhan'tar, and terraformed its surface into moss-covered greenery. At the war's end, most surviving Yuuzhan Vong agreed to relocate to Zonama Sekot.

**Yuuzhan Vong** An extragalactic species that invaded the galaxy 25 years after the Battle of Yavin. Evolving on the planet Yuuzhan'tar, the Yuuzhan Vong worshipped a complex pantheon of gods. Roughly humanoid in shape, they mutilated their bodies with ritual scars and tattoos. The Yuuzhan Vong could not be sensed or directly affected by the Force. They were masters of organic technology, and used lesser creatures to perform highly advanced tasks. Yuuzhan Vong society was broken down into castes, including warriors, shapers, intendants, workers, and priests. Much of their society was centered on worship, and each ritual scarring and tattooing added to the social stature of an individual.

At some point in the distant past, their homeworld was devastated by mechanical attackers, possibly the Silentium and the Abominor. After defeating the technological beings, the Yuuzhan Vong believed that they were the chosen masters of their galaxy, and eventually they began warring among themselves. During the Cremlevian War, Yuuzhan Vong tribes laid waste to most habitable planets. Taking to the stars, they set out to cross the intergalactic void to find a new home, a journey that took millennia. To accomplish the crossing, the Yuuzhan Vong created a fleet of living worldships that could penetrate the hyperspatial disturbance that isolated their galaxy and travel across the intergalactic gulf.

An advance scouting party was dispatched into the galaxy some 50 years before the invasion, landing on Bimmiel. Around the same time, a group of Yuuzhan Vong encountered the living planet Zonama Sekot. Driven off by the planet's defenses, they returned to the fleet in possession of the Jedi Knight Vergere. Several years prior to their invasion, the Yuuzhan Vong sent Nom Anor to stir up trouble and secretly undermine the galaxy's political structure.

The Yuuzhan Vong invaded the galaxy 25 years after the Battle of Endor, with the advance force known as the Praetorite Vong striking at a point labeled Vector Prime. New Republic forces destroyed an initial beachhead at Helska 4, but soon their unfamiliarity with the organic technology used by the Yuuzhan Vong led to lopsided New Republic defeats at Sernpidal, Dubrillion, Dantooine, and Ithor.

*Yuzzem*

Eventually, the Yuuzhan Vong pushed into the Core Worlds and captured Coruscant. The city-world was quickly demolished, with many structures destroyed by falling skyhooks and satellites. A World Brain was installed in a yorik coral cavern and the planet was rebuilt in the image of Yuuzhan'tar, the lost Yuuzhan Vong homeworld. For many months, a sort of peace existed between the Yuuzhan Vong and the New Republic as both sides paused to rebuild their forces and defend what they held. This changed at the Battle of Ebaq, where Warmaster Tsavong Lah and his forces were soundly defeated. Tsavong Lah himself was killed in combat by Jaina Solo, and Supreme Overlord Shimrra vowed to destroy anything that got in the way of galactic conquest.

It was the rediscovery of the planet Zonama Sekot that helped bring the two sides together. Luke Skywalker, Jacen Solo, and the priest Harrar spent many days trying to commune with the living intelligence of Zonama Sekot. They learned that Zonama Sekot had been grown from a seed of Yuuzhan'tar and that the Yuuzhan Vong could not connect to the Force because they had been stripped of the ability long ago by the consciousness of Yuuzhan'tar. The war came to an end at Coruscant, after Supreme Overlord Shimrra and his court jester Onimi—the true power behind the throne—were killed in battle. Many Yuuzhan Vong chose to commit suicide rather than surrender, while others relocated to Zonama Sekot.

Decades after the war, the Galactic Alliance and the Jedi Order championed the Ossus Project, using Yuuzhan Vong shapers to terraform Ossus and restore it to vibrant life. Ultimately more than 100 planets were terraformed in this fashion, only to suffer environmental collapse due to secret Sith sabotage of the process. This led to war between the Galactic Alliance and the New Empire. Some Yuuzhan Vong shapers survived in the ruins of Ossus, hiding from the Sith and struggling to understand how the project had gone wrong.

*Yuuzhan Vong worldship*

**Yuuzhan Vong worldship** A gigantic Yuuzhan Vong passenger vessel created from yorik coral. Known to the Yuuzhan Vong as Koros-Strohna, 10-kilometer-wide worldships were living creatures designed to cross vast distances of space. Similar in function to a Super Star Destroyer, the worldship was a transport, battleship, and psychological weapon all at once. Each was propelled by a collection of dovin basals, which could lock on to nearby gravity sources and pull the worldship forward at incredible speeds. Bioengineered, membranous creatures called outrider ganglia could be extended from the hull whenever there was no strong gravitational field, allowing the worldship to be pushed by interstellar winds. Each worldship was equipped with hundreds of magma weapons that expelled molten slag at enemy vessels.

Because a worldship was a self-contained living environment, many Yuuzhan Vong began to go mad from confinement. To ease this situation, special drugs were released into the interior atmosphere to calm the population. Once a worldship was ready for landing, a huge, tubular worm was extended to the landing area, allowing the Yuuzhan Vong to establish a planetside base and maintain contact with the worldship. Like all living creatures, worldships had to be regularly fed and nourished, a chore carried out by the shaper caste. Worldships eventually aged. Many of the ones used by the Yuuzhan Vong to cross the intergalactic gulf were quite old by the time they reached the New Republic, and many began to die shortly after the invasion began. Among notable worldships were the *Baanu Miir,* the *Baanu Kor,* the *Baanu Rass,* the *Domain Dal,* and the *Alak Schou.*

**Yuza Bre** One of the most popular restaurants on Coruscant during the Swarm War. The chefs at Yuza Bre were able to mix traditional galactic cuisine with the ingredients brought to Coruscant by the Yuuzhan Vong, creating a wildly popular style of cuisine. Tables at Yuza Bre were often booked for months in advance, although it was believed that Cal Omas had a standing reservation during his tenure as Chief of State of the Galactic Alliance. At the height of the Swarm War, Yuza Bre was purchased by the Bornaryn Shipping Empire—one of the first restaurants to be brought into the conglomerate. Lady Aryn Dro Thul later revealed that the purchase of Yuza Bre had been required to keep her meetings with Luke Skywalker and the leaders of the new Jedi Order a secret from the media.

**Yuzzem** Humanoids with long snouts, long arms, heavy fur, and large black eyes, they were noted for their great strength and volatile, unpredictable temperaments. Yuzzem were often found as slaves in Imperial labor camps or as hired hands employed to handle physical activities like mining. A pair of Yuzzem aided Princess Leia and Luke Skywalker during their mission to the Circarpous star system.

**Yuzzum** A species that inhabited the forest floor of Endor's moon. Yuzzum had round, fur-covered bodies, long, thin legs, and wide mouths full of sharp, protruding teeth. They were intelligent, though somewhat barbaric spear-wielding beings. Traveling in groups, they flushed out their favorite meal of small rodents called ruggers. Some Yuzzum, especially a few with some singing talent, went offworld to seek fame and fortune. They included Joh Yowza, who joined the Max Rebo Band.

**YVH (Yuuzhan Vong Hunter) war droid** Developed by Tendrando Arms, these were specially programmed military droids designed to combat the Yuuzhan Vong threat. First activated some 27 years after the Battle of Yavin, the YVH 1 was given top-of-the-line search-and-indentify engineering, allowing it to distinguish between the extragalactic invaders and citizens of the New Republic. It was heavily armed, having a variable-output blaster cannon in its right arm and an adaptable left arm that could accept interchangeable weapons, including a heavy laser, a sonic rifle, a 50-shot battery of seeker missiles, and a launcher for firing explosive baradium pellets. The droid's legs incorporated built-in repulsorlifts, allowing it to make tremendous leaps. The YVH 1 was protected by layers of laminanium, giving the droid regenerative armor plating. In stature, the YVH 1 was strikingly

Yuzzum

similar to a Yuuzhan Vong, an intentional design meant to provoke outrage in enemy warriors. Because of their appearance, they were sometimes referred to as Yuuzhandroids. Lando Calrissian designed and sold the YVH units, all of which spoke in a deep, booming facsimile of Calrissian's own voice. Despite the success rate of the YVH 1 against Yuuzhan Vong warriors, the droids were hard to maintain and were used sparingly throughout the conflict. After the war, several YVH 1 droids remained in active military service, while others were used as dueling droids. It was said that a YVH 1 droid was a match for an experienced Jedi Knight.

**YVH 1-1A** The designation of the YVH 1 prototype combat droid produced by Tendrando Arms and demonstrated to Chief of State Borsk Fey'lya two years into the Yuuzhan Vong War. Despite having most of its targeting and combat programming disabled because of the public nature of the demonstration, YVH 1-1A identified Yuuzhan Vong assassins and eliminated them. YVH 1-1A was later assigned to the Jedi strike force trying to infiltrate the worldship near Myrkr to destroy the voxyn queen. YVH 1-1A served as the leader of the droid forces, coordinating the activities of YVH 2-1S and YVH 2-4S. During the evacuation of Coruscant, YVH 1-1A was instrumental in recovering Ben Skywalker and C-3PO from the hold of the *Byrt.* Over time, 1-1A began to develop a personality, and spent a great deal of time harassing Lando Calrissian. YVH 1-1A and Calrissian served as pilots of the *Record Time* during Luke Skywalker's mission to infiltrate Coruscant.

**YVH 5-S Bugcruncher droid** The YVH series combat droids specially outfitted to battle the warrior hives of the Killik Colony during the Swarm War. At the recommendation of Jedi Master Luke Skywalker, YVH 5-S droids were built from the standard S-series platform, then equipped with specialized equipment allowing them to operate in the vacuum of space. Han Solo nicknamed them Bugcruncher droids during their assault on the Gorog hive located on Kr.

**YVH-M droid** A mouse droid derived from the original YVH 1 Yuuzhan Vong Hunter droid. Lando Calrissian took the central processing unit of the YVH 1 and extracted the key programming, then stored it in the chassis of an MSE-6 mouse droid. This new droid could follow any individual it suspected of being a Yuuzhan Vong infiltrator in obscurity.

**Y-wing starfighter** Despite its age, this ship was one of the mainstays of the Rebel Alliance and saw notable duty at the Battle of Yavin, during which the Imperial Death Star was destroyed. Prior to the introduction of the X-wing starfighter, Y-wings, built by Koensayr, were the flagship fighters of the Alliance. They were introduced as bomber craft during the Clone Wars. Anakin Skywalker led Shadow Squadron—a group of Y-wing bombers—during the hunt for the Separatist warship *Malevolence.*

The twin-engine Y-wing, at 16 meters long, was a multipurpose ship originally designed as a compromise between a full-fledged attack fighter and a heavier bomber. The durable starfighters could give and take a great deal of punishment, but they didn't have the payload capacity or the speed, stealth, and maneuverability to compete with modern Imperial attack fighters.

The Rebel Alliance flew more Y-wings than any other fighter and used a number of different configurations for a variety of mission profiles. It wasn't uncommon for a Y-wing to be stripped down for assault runs against Imperial convoys and then be refitted by Rebel technicians for a heavy bombing run against an Imperial base. Y-wings also found use on diplomatic escort missions and long-range patrols. The BTL-A4 Y-wing (LP), or *Longprobe*-class, had extra provisions, more powerful sensors, and a sophisticated navigation computer specifically for patrol duty.

YVH war droid

Y-wing starfighter

The Y-wing had three main components. The forward cockpit module housed the pilots and weapons systems. A reinforced spaceframe central spar stretched back from the cockpit module; the Y-wing's ionization reactor and hyperdrive/astrogation hardware were crammed into this narrow frame. A crosswing housing the main power cells attached at the back of the spar, with the two powerful sublight ion drives on either end.

The cockpit module had thick armor plating. The pilot controlled a pair of forward laser cannons and twin proton torpedo launchers. A turret-mounted ion cannon was directly behind the pilot. Like the X-wing, an R2 or R4 astromech droid fit snugly into the droid socket behind the cockpit and monitored all fight, navigation, and power systems; it could also handle fire control, perform simple inflight maintenance, and reroute power as needed, too. The R2 unit also stored hyperspace jump coordinates.

**Ywllandr system** This star system saw heavy fighting during the final stages of the Clone Wars. The Confederacy of Independent Systems initially took control of the system, using it as the choke point in a scheme that forced Republic starships to travel through the system to reach other parts of the Outer Rim Territories. Jedi Master Plo Koon took the *Courageous* and a small fleet to the Ywllandr system, and tried to end the Separatist threat.

**Yyrtan system** A system that contained the yellow star Yyrta and several planets, including Kirtania. The Yyrtan system was positioned along a hyperspace trade route that became more popular over time.

Z-6 rotary blaster cannon

**Z-18** This droid was once owned by Samuro, a Jedi Knight who died while securing the energy vampire Countess Rajine in her fortress-like prison. The cobbled-together automaton then was forced to serve as Rajine's chief aide for centuries. During the Clone Wars, Z-18 assisted Mace Windu, who arrived at the fortress searching for Alpha-2 Squad, and Rajine was finally killed by zombies she had created.

**Z-6 rotary blaster cannon** A heavy infantry support weapon, also known as a chaingun, introduced during the Clone Wars. The Merr-Sonn Z-6 rotary blaster cannon was considered the most evolved of its type. It used a rotating multiple barrel assembly to bypass the refresh lag inherent in conventional blaster weaponry. The Z-6 had a tremendous rate of fire, maxing out at 166 rounds per second. The gun was heavy and suffered from recoil. It was incredibly effective in clearing landing zones, but troops in the field found it too cumbersome and glitch-prone for widespread use. It was instead reserved for special missions with specific tactical demands. The Z-6 was used by Sergeant Stec to rescue a team of Jedi Knights from Hypori.

**Z-95 Headhunter** A ship design older than most of the pilots who flew it, it was one of the most common starfighters in the galaxy. The Z-95 Headhunter was both maneuverable and durable. It was used by planetary police and air defense units as well as many pirate and outlaw groups.

The original Mark I model was designed as an atmospheric fighter that could be adapted to space travel. A twin-engine swing-wing craft, it sported a bubble cockpit that gave the pilot a clear field of vision. It typically had a set of triple blasters on each wing.

In the later Headhunters, swing wings were replaced with fixed wings, and maneuverability was maintained with the addition of directional jets. The starfighter canopy was more heavily armored, and heads-up holographic tactical displays were improved. The most frequent modifications involved replacing the weapons systems or enhancing the engines for greater speed. The Rebel Alliance used a number of Z-95 Headhunters for training missions.

Z-18

Prince Za

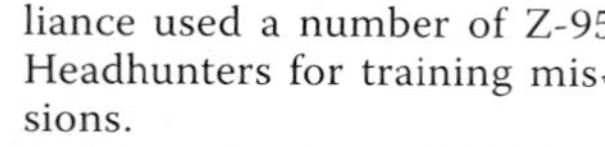

Han Solo flew a Z-95 Mark I when he led the defense of an outlaw tech base against Corporate Sector Authority fighters. Solo used the Z-95's superior atmospheric capabilities to good advantage against the Authority's sluggish IRD fighters. Mara Jade used a modified Z-95 Headhunter equipped with a hyperdrive.

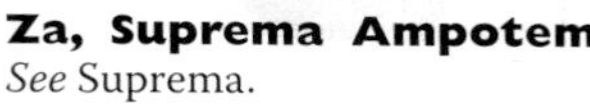

**Za, Suprema Ampotem** *See* Suprema.

**Za, Prince** A Defel prince who served on the Imperial Interim Ruling Council about seven years after the Battle of Endor. Prince Za controlled a number of strategic trade routes. Though his people were treated as inferiors within Imperial boundaries, Za enjoyed the status of being part of the group Carnor Jax entrusted with running the Empire. His normally wraith-like appearance was dissolved when ultraviolet lights were set up on De-Purteen, much to the relief of the other council members. Za was a puppet of Norym Kim, who paid him off to nominate Xandel Carivus to succeed Nolyds as the council's leader.

**Zaadja** An otherwise unremarkable Outer Rim planet that was the site of a Geonosian droid-manufacturing facility. Obi-Wan Kenobi, Anakin Skywalker, and Master Tohno were sent to Zaadja to destroy the

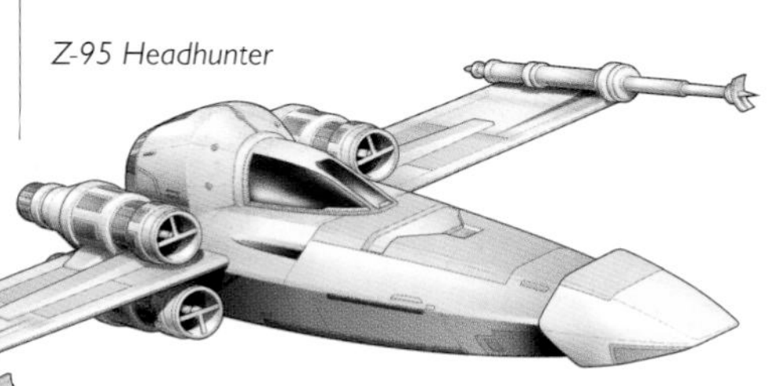
Z-95 Headhunter

< Ziro the Hutt

Zaadja

facility. Tohno sacrificed herself to complete the mission, despite Skywalker's protests.

**Zaalbar** A Wookiee warrior who left his homeworld of Kashyyyk many years before the Great Sith War and settled on Taris. Zaalbar's brother Chuundar had sold his people into slavery by allowing the Czerka Corporation to install huge manufacturing facilities on Kashyyyk. After hearing Chuundar denounce their father Freyyr as a senile old fool, Zaalbar became enraged and attacked his brother using his claws. That act forced Zaalbar into exile as a "madclaw." On Taris he met up with a young Twi'lek, Mission Vao, in the Lower City, and the pair forged a lasting friendship. Vao's knack for locating food and Zaalbar's muscle served them well. When Zaalbar was captured by a group of Gamorrean thugs, Vao turned to Revan, Bastila Shan, and Carth Onasi, to rescue him. Vao and Zaalbar played key roles in the search for Darth Malak, helping to repay the debt for the Wookiee's release. Zaalbar eventually returned to Kashyyyk to help his fellow Wookiees defeat Chuundar and break Czerka's hold on the planet.

Zaalbar takes on two Tusken Raiders.

**Zaarin, Grand Admiral Demetrius** One of the Emperor's 12 Grand Admirals, he led a failed coup during the Galactic Civil War. Zaarin was in charge of the research and development of new TIE fighter models, including the TIE Advanced and TIE defender. To ensure that the Imperial fighters could operate without close-in support, Zaarin negotiated with the Habeen to get hyperdrive technology for the fighters. While Zaarin openly supported the Emperor's plans to capture the traitorous Admiral Harkov, Zaarin secretly plotted moving his own fleet to Coruscant to kill Palpatine and assume the Imperial throne. He made his move shortly after the death of Prince Xizor. Zaarin outraced Imperial pursuit in his Star Destroyer *Glory* and reached Coruscant, but was unable to capture Palpatine's shuttle despite the assistance of Emperor's Hand Arden Lyn. Vice Admiral Thrawn chased Zaarin into hyperspace. Zaarin later reappeared and tried to steal the prototype Project Vorknkx cloaking device from Thrawn. Zaarin captured the cloak-equipped corvette *Vorknkx*, but the ship exploded when Zaarin attempted to flee into hyperspace.

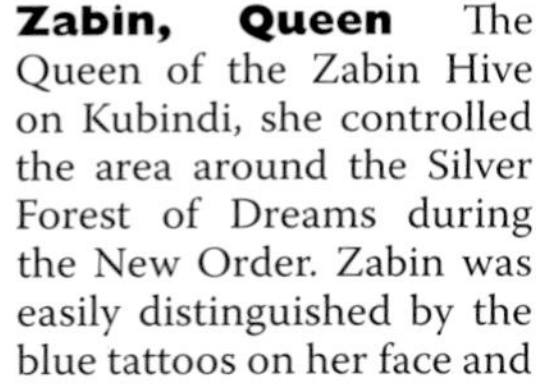
Grand Admiral Demetrius Zaarin

**Zabin, Queen** The Queen of the Zabin Hive on Kubindi, she controlled the area around the Silver Forest of Dreams during the New Order. Zabin was easily distinguished by the blue tattoos on her face and snout and the diamond rings that adorned her trunk. When Han Solo and Rebel Alliance agents arrived on Kubindi to rescue Grubba the Hutt, Zabin demanded that they cook her a meal fit for humans in order to win her trust. If the meal pleased her and her chefs, then they could have Grubba. Although the food met with the Queen's approval, Grubba was taken into custody by Imperial forces.

**Zabrak** A near-human species from Iridonia. Because they evolved on a harsh homeworld, the Zabrak were known for their ability to withstand great amounts of pain. They discovered space travel early in the Republic's history and quickly set out to settle more worlds.

Zabrak

The strong will of the Zabrak led them to establish colonies on eight Mid Rim worlds including Lorista and Frithia, with other large settlements on Talus and Corellia. On their homeworld, the Zabrak clans fought in continual wars to hone their impressive martial skills. Among the unique aspects of the Zabrak physiology was the presence of a secondary heart. The Zabrak were distinguished by the set of short horns that grew from their skulls; the number and pattern of these horns distinguished different subspecies. Zabraks were further differentiated from humans by ritual tattoos that sometimes were painted on their faces. The Zabrak were among the galaxy's best explorers and warriors, but were rarely boastful or overbearing. At the height of the New Order, the Zabrak species was one of a small group of nonhumans allowed to move throughout the Empire with relative ease. With the end of the Galactic Civil War, the Zabrak joined the New Republic. Both Jedi Master Eeth Koth and the Sith Lord Darth Maul were Zabrak.

**Zabrak vibroblade** A vibro-weapon developed by the Zabrak but rarely used by them. Its small size made it a good off-hand weapon. Zabrak vibroblades used a rare cortosis weave to prevent damage from lightsabers.

**Zac** A young Jedi washout who ended up on Dantooine, Zac had a knack for understanding animals and beasts; he could even communicate with them on a certain level. When a group of Separatist battle droids landed on the planet and threatened his school, Zac called upon a herd of horned grazers to trample the droids before they could attack.

**Zaddja** A barren planet located far beyond the center of Imperial activity and beyond most inhabited areas of the galaxy. Zaddja was in the Trilon sector and surrounded by an asteroid shroud. One of Carnor Jax's ships, the *Destiny*, traced Kir Kanos to the planet—but the fugitive had already departed, leaving behind a trap for his pursuers.

**zaela** A type of plant native to Naboo. The zaela's branches were extremely strong and flexible, and used by Gungans to make a variety of tools.

**Zag (RC-2088)** A Republic commando, he participated in missions to Aviles Prime and Asturias during the Clone Wars. He was the only survivor of the mission to bring Director Oviedo back to Coruscant. Zag became a member of Aiwha Squad during the operation on Garqi.

**Zaga, Gorto** An Aqualish who smuggled blasters to the inmates on the prison world of Kiffex. Gorto Zaga's headquarters were located at a cantina called the Black Hole. He was killed during a battle involving Jedi Quinlan Vos and the vampiric Anzati.

**Zak, Noro** A winged Baxthrax Jedi Knight. Sometime before the Battle of Naboo, Noro Zak was selected to accompany Qui-Gon Jinn and Obi-Wan Kenobi to rescue Adi Gallia from Esseles.

**zalaaca** Large, omnivorous reptiles native to Naboo, zalaacas were swift-moving, intelligent predators. Despite their living in the uplands, they were excellent swimmers. Zalaacas strongly resembled sando aqua monsters. Their front feet were studded with claws, and their rear feet were protected by thick spikes on their fetlocks. They displayed dimorphic coloration, with males having a blue-yellow hide and females dappled blue. Gungans considered the capture of a wild zalaaca foal to be a rite of passage, and the successful capture and training of a zalaaca resulted in a loyal war mount. Zalaacas were natural enemies of kaadu, and sometimes the Gungan army equipped them with heavy weaponry to destroy other mech units.

**Zalem** The matriarch of a clan of witches on Dathomir, and the former wife of a Jedi Knight. When she was strong enough in the Force, she killed her husband and set out to raise their daughter, Ros Lai, as a witch. But Ros appeared deformed, and Zalem allowed her fellow witches to torture the child. When the witches discovered Dathomir's Star Temples, she decided that time had come to assert her power. Zalem unlocked the secrets of the temples and the Infinity Gates, unleashing a wave of energy that destroyed the planet Ova. Mace Windu sent Quinlan Vos to put a stop to her machinations. In the end, Ros Lai killed her mother to end the galactic threat. The girl then took Zalem's position as head of the clan.

**Zalk't** The Vratix Senator from Thyferra during the Swarm War. Senator Zalk't was on Coruscant when the Killiks staged a military coup on Thyferra, capturing Zalxuc City and taking control of the planet's bacta supplies.

**Zaloriis** A desolate planet notable only for its role in the production of Imperial All-Terrain Armored Transports. Zaloriis City was its main settlement. High winds kept life to a minimum, but the sheltering boulders of the Fantain Mountains harbored small creatures and rock-lions. Legends spoke of dune ghosts that wandered the wastes

*Zalaaca*

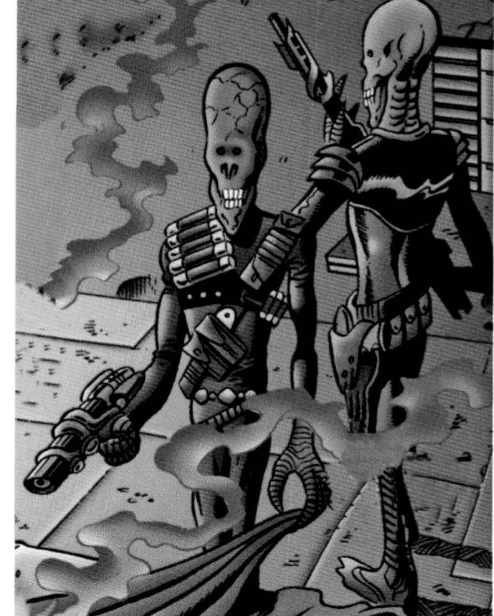

*Zanibar*

at night, and of travelers who never returned from their journeys. The natives respected the open deserts and kept well away, clustering in small outposts connected by well-traveled roads. The Imperials established a research base in the desert, and their test vehicles often bolstered local legends as wanderers spotted the strange technologies and told tales at the local taverns. One story that amused the Imperials involved a man being confronted by a wheezing 50-foot dune-cow, with giant tusks and a gray reptilian hide. Back at the research base, the prototype walker was quickly rechristened "Dune Cow."

*Tyber Zann*

**Zaltin** A major Thyferran corporation, it was a leader in bacta production and refinement. Although its officials had no desire to become part of the bacta cartel, Zaltin was pushed into it by the Empire, primarily to serve as competition for Xucphra. When Zaltin officials realized that the Empire was about to collapse, they decided to strengthen their ties with the native Vratix, for without them no bacta could be produced. They began an alliance with the Ashern Circle rebels, providing them with financial resources as well as hiding places. During the planet's civil war, Xucphra ruthlessly killed many Zaltin officers. Survivors went into hiding, fled the planet, or joined the Ashern Circle. Eventually Xucphra was defeated with the help of Rogue Squadron.

**Zalxuc City** Established during Imperial rule to house the planet's human population, it was Thyferra's primary starport. The city's name was formed from a combination of the names of the primary bacta-producing companies, Zaltin and Xucphra. When Ysanne Isard took control of Xucphra and became the de facto leader of the planet, she renamed it Xucphra City. At the height of the Swarm War, Zalxuc City was overrun by Killik military forces. For the duration of the conflict, the Galactic Alliance was cut off from its primary source of bacta.

**Zanales, Scorch** A flamboyant and unpredictable Podracer who loved to incite the crowd and put on a good show. Scorch Zanales was a Daimlos, and like all young members of his species he had engaged in a yearlong contest to ram other Daimlos into unconsciousness using his newly grown skullplates and horns. Zanales outdid all of his peers, and was elevated to hero status—a reputation he carried over into the combat-heavy world of Podracing.

**Zanibar** A species native to the planet Xo. The Zanibar were allied with Grappa the Hutt, providing services in exchange for sacrifices. These services included acting as bodyguards, soldiers, and smugglers; in return the Zanibar got sacrificial victims for use in ceremonial rituals. Unwilling to work with the Empire, the Zanibar chose Grappa the Hutt as their intermediary to claim the Imperial bounty on Kir Kanos. When Grappa was unable to hold up his end of the bargain, the Zanibar took Grappa as well. Nobody ever lived to tell what happened in a Zanibar ritual, though it was rumored that the beings feasted on their victims' bodies to give their life forces to the gods.

**Zann, Tyber** A noted criminal who led the Zann Consortium during the height of the Empire. After being sent to prison on trumped-up charges concocted by Jabba the Hutt, Zann made a daring escape and set out to exact revenge. Much of the damage he inflicted on Jabba's organization also caused collateral damage to Imperial facilities and personnel, making him a target of the Imperial Forensic Intelligence team. Lieutenant Izbela Saarrj discovered that Zann had sliced into Imperial records and stolen information on the *Eclipse*-class Star Destroyer during its early phases of development, prompting a galaxywide alert at shipyards and construction facilities. Rather than building the massive ship himself, however, Zann set in motion a grand plan to steal an *Eclipse*.

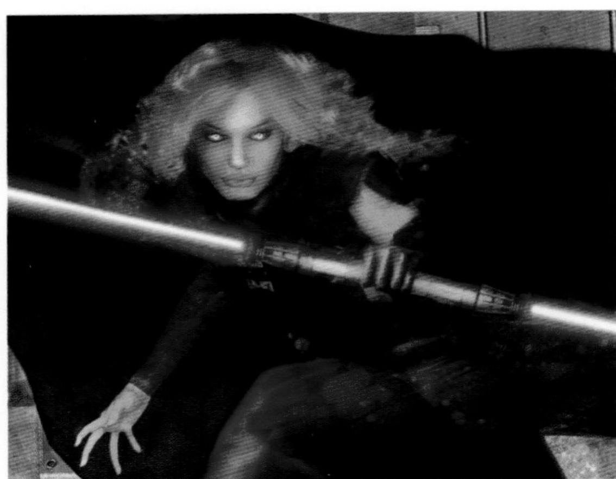

Darth Zannah

**Zannah, Darth** The Sith name assumed by the girl once known as Rain. Zannah was, in fact, her given name, and after she was discovered by a Jedi scout, she joined the Army of Light during the final years of the New Sith Wars. During the Battle of Ruusan, Rain survived a fall from a transport and lived briefly among the native Bouncers. She was later discovered by Darth Bane, after Sith Lord Kaan set off a thought bomb that wiped out thousands of Sith and many Jedi. Recognizing the girl's power, Bane offered her the chance to become his apprentice. Zannah's cousin Darovit (Tomcat) tried to stop her, but Zannah maimed Darovit and left. She then arranged for transport off Ruusan with the crew of the *Star-Wake,* who believed her to be an orphaned refugee. She was befriended by Bordon and his son, Wend, but shot and killed everyone aboard to ensure that she could take the ship to Onderon and continue her apprenticeship to Bane. From Onderon, Bane and Zannah spent the next decade training on Ambria, putting their plans into motion.

Zannah executed missions including inciting Kelad'den and the Anti-Republic Liberation Front on Serenno, and forcing the Jedi Order to go on peacekeeping missions that spread their numbers thin. She also encountered the dark side follower Hetton, who had acquired a wealth of Sith lore and artifacts. Seeing a chance to further her own growth and assist her Master, Zannah took Hetton as her apprentice, provided that he give her access to his information. Using his collection, Zannah learned of Belia Darzu's hidden fortress on Tython, then took Hetton's loyal Umbaran shadow assassins to confront Darth Bane.

On Ambria, Zannah made it appear as if she and Hetton had come to execute her Master, but Bane cut Hetton down and confronted Zannah. She earned his trust when she provided information that the hidden Tython fortress might contain a Sith Holocron as well as instructions on how to make such devices, something for which Bane had long searched. Zannah then traveled to Coruscant to infiltrate the Jedi Archives, hoping to learn how to remove the living orbalisks that covered her Master's body. She was surprised to find her cousin Darovit there. Rather than allow him to reveal her presence, Zannah took Darovit with her to Tython.

A group of Jedi, including Masters Valenthyne Farfalla and Worror, followed Bane and Zannah there. Readying themselves in Belia Darzu's fortress, the two Sith struck back at their pursuers. While Bane dealt with the Jedi Masters, Zannah killed Sarro Xaj. Master Worror injured Bane by trapping him in a bubble of Force energy that reflected Force lightning, and Zannah and Darovit returned to Ambria with Bane's damaged body.

She convinced the healer Caleb to save Bane. After he finished the task, Zannah killed him with her lightsaber and used the dark side of the Force to flood Darovit's mind with horrific visions. She left her cousin a raving madman, leaving the Jedi to assume that he was the Sith Lord who had killed Caleb. The Jedi then killed Darovit, allowing Zannah to devote her attention to speeding Darth Bane's healing. Zannah told Bane that she would one day surpass him, and until that point would keep him alive to learn everything she could about the dark side. It was during this discussion that Darth Bane first gave her the title of Darth Zannah.

**Zao, Master** This blind Veknoid Jedi Master, known for his love of food, was active during the final years of the Republic. Zao was one of many Jedi who traveled the galaxy at the will and whim of the Force. Shortly after the Battle of Naboo, Zao worked as the head chef for the Aqualish crime lord Gorto Zaga. He was on the planet Kiffex when Quinlan Vos arrived to investigate the reawakening of the Anzati Volfe Karkko. During the Clone Wars, Master Zao moved about the Outer Rim and was found on Saleucami. Zao survived Order 66 because he was not directly involved with the fighting.

**Zapalo, Graf** Naboo's Master of Sciences and a member of the Royal Advisory Council. Graf Zapalo was also one of Naboo's most talented oceanographers. During his tenure on the Advisory Council, his people expanded their research installations on Naboo's primary moon. Zapalo also organized an effort to chart the tunnels riddling the core of Naboo. He led the historic Gungan/Naboo project responsible for the development of the Mantaris, an amphibious transport. Zapalo later served under Queen Jamillia and survived until the time of the Galactic Civil War.

Master Zao

**Zar, Fang** The Senator from Sern Prime during the final years of the Republic. He was distinguished by a long, gray beard and hair collected in a topknot. An outspoken supporter of the Republic, Senator Zar maintained residences on Sern Prime, Coruscant, and Ghorman. When Duro fell to the Separatists, Zar was among the first to support Corellia's decision to retreat and defend its own borders,

Fang Zar

largely due to his friendship with Corellia's Senator Garm Bel Iblis. Zar later supported Bail Organa's movement to curb Chancellor Palpatine's emergency powers, and was one of the original members of the Delegation of the Two Thousand. After the establishment of the Empire, he was among the first Senators to be arrested for sedition. Zar was released but fled to Alderaan for political asylum. His presence there put pressure on Bail Organa, who was one of the primary signers of the Petition of the Two Thousand. When Senator Zar attempted to return to Sern Prime, Cash Garrulan and the crew of the *Drunk Dancer* took on the transport job. Darth Vader intercepted them, and Jedi Master Roan Shryne, who was working with the *Drunk Dancer*'s crew, could not stop the Dark Lord. Vader slashed Senator Zar through the chest, and he quickly died of his injuries.

**Zardra** A tall, dark-haired woman, she appeared strikingly sensual, with more than a hint of danger about her. Zardra carried a force pike and wore a flowing cloak. She was a bounty hunter of exceptional skill and daring and often teamed up with Jodo Kast and Puggles Trodd when a particular bounty caught her interest. She enjoyed personal combat and appreciated the fine things that credits could buy, but the hunt was the most important thing in her life. She feared that she would wind up dying senselessly, so she often tempted fate by taking huge risks.

She killed Mageye the Hutt when the Hutt was accidentally dropped on her. As a result, the Hutts put a huge price on her head.

**Zark Squadron** A unit of Chiss clawcraft led by Jagged Fel during the Battle of Tenupe in the Swarm War. Zark Squadron tried to shoot down the *Millennium Falcon* after Han Solo refused to surrender to the Chiss when he arrived at Tenupe.

**Zatec-Cha** The grand vizier of the planet Tammuz-an during the early days of Imperial rule, he hoped to usurp the throne of Mon Julpa. In his plotting, Zatec-Cha found a way to cause the leader to suffer from memory loss.

**Zatoq, Lyyr** A female Quarren who flew with the pilots of Rogue Squadron during the war against Grand Admiral Thrawn. Zatoq was killed during the fight against Ysanne Isard and Prince-Admiral Krennel while attempting to gather intelligence data on the moon Distna.

**Zavval the Hutt** A member of the Besadii Hutt clan, he controlled the spice production and slave trade on Ylesia. During Han Solo's escape from Ylesia, Zavval was caught under a pile of rubble from the collapsing ceiling after his repulsorsled crashed into a support column. Zavval was crushed, and a bounty was put on Solo's head for his death.

**Zax the Hutt** A bounty officer who worked at Javanar's Cantina in the Lower City of Taris some 4,000 years before the Battle of Yavin. Zax was known for his dislike of droids.

**Zealots of Psusan** A religion fashionable on Coruscant during the final years of the Republic. It was led for many years by the corrupt High Priest Scri Oscuro, until he was captured by Kalyn Farnmir and Cian Shee. Khaleen Hentz was one of many to sport a midriff tattoo associated with the Zealots of Psusan.

**Zebitrope IV** Located in the Zebitrope system, it was the homeworld of a species of lizards whose members symbiotically supported a spongy mold growth on their backs. This mold was the only source of the addictive drug lesai, which eliminated the need for sleep.

**Zebulon Dak Speeder Corporation** A manufacturer of fast landspeeders, this corporation was founded by Zebulon Dak during the early years of the Empire.

**Zeebo** A four-eared Mooka, he was the furry and feathered pet of Ken, the Jedi Prince.

**Zeemacht Cluster** A knot of stars that was home to a number of ancient spacefaring species. Tirahnn was the sector capital of the Zeemacht Cluster.

**Zeetsa** One of several species native to Ord Cestus, Zeetsas resembled swollen balls of a bluish substance. Their skin was translucent, showing a network of blue veins and internal organs beneath the surface. No arms or legs were immediately visible on a Zeetsa's body, nor was there any evidence of a head. The flesh of the sentient Zeetsa could adjust its shape to mimic its surroundings, allowing a Zeetsa individual to attain the appearance of another being for a short period of time. This allowed Zeetsa to integrate with the neighboring X'Ting.

**Zeffliffl** The fourth planet orbiting Markbee's Star, it was home to the seaweed-like aliens also known as Zeffliffl. They inhabited the shallow seas surrounding the smaller southern continent of the planet and needed to spray themselves with seawater when spending time on land. The Zeffliffl existed in close groups of several individuals, and their bodies automatically rejected any outsider who attempted to join the group.

**Zehava** The capital of Melida/Daan. Zehava was founded a millennium before the Battle of Yavin, but its borders were continually redrawn during the civil war between the Melida and the Daan. The 10th Battle of Zehava was considered the bloodiest fighting for control of the city. Shortly afterward, the city was divided into northern and southern regions, with the Daan controlling the northern half and the Melida the southern. During the 18th battle, the Daan used the tunnels and drains under the city to secretly gain access to Melida-held areas. Shortly before the 25th battle, Daan and Melida divided the city into sectors and lived side by side for a short time. After the initial victory of the Young, Zehava was left in ruin. Food and supplies were low and tensions ran high. The newly elected governor, Nield, felt that the first priority was to destroy all the symbols of hate in the city. Qui-Gon Jinn and Obi-Wan Kenobi helped prevent war between the Young and the Elders.

Zatec-Cha

**ZeHethbra** A species recognized by their black-and-white-striped manes. The ZeHethbra were tall humanoids with at least 80 cultural, racial, and ethnic subgroups brought about because of varied ecosystems on their homeworld of ZeHeth. Northern groups tended to be brown or red in color, while southern groups tended toward blue-white fur. All ZeHethbra had a black-and-white mane, which began at the bridge of their nose and traveled over their head to the small of their backs. As a people, the ZeHethbra were known for their short tempers, but were fiercely loyal to their families and clans. The ZeHethbra and the Dugs fought each other in a series of wars due to the presence of ZeHethbra colonies in the Malastare system.

ZeHethbra

**Zeison Sha** A philosophy of the Force separate from the traditions of the Jedi and the Sith. The origins of the Zeison Sha dated to approximately 2,000 years before the Battle of Yavin. A group of families, fleeing the conflict between the Jedi and the Sith, established a colony on Yanibar. Believing that the Jedi Order had abandoned them, they set out to commune with the Force in other ways. The harsh environment of Yanibar gave the Zeison Sha a strong will to survive, and over the centuries their philosophy coalesced around the ideals of self-reliance and independence. With the Force, the Zeison Sha could move objects without touching them, and could literally wrap themselves in the Force to protect themselves from harm. One of the most distinctive weapons of the Zeison Sha was the discblade, a weapon that could be thrown and return to its thrower. After the Battle of Ruusan, a passing trader discovered the colony and the Zeison Sha made contact with the Jedi Order. When the Jedi began taking their children for training as Padawans, the Zeison Sha chose to reject the ways of the Jedi and returned to Yanibar. This self-imposed isolation allowed them to survive the Jedi Purge.

**Zekk** A onetime street urchin, he was taken in by old Peckhum, a supply courier and message runner for the New Republic on Coruscant. He also supplied the Jedi academy on Yavin 4. Zekk was a resourceful scamp. He spent his childhood on the planet Ennth, but when the colony there was devastated by a natural disaster he escaped on the next supply ship and traveled from planet to planet as a stowaway.

Zekk had shoulder-length hair one shade lighter than black, and green eyes with a darker corona around emerald irises. He became friendly with young Jedi academy members but also a target for Norys, leader of the Lost Ones gang in the lower levels of Coruscant. Norys nicknamed Zekk the Trash Collector because of his uncanny ability to locate wrecks of spacecraft and other items in the lower levels.

Tamith Kai, one of the leaders of the Shadow Academy, came across Zekk, tested him, and found he had Force potential. He was stunned and taken away to the academy. There Brakiss convinced him that his friends didn't really care for him and he wouldn't amount to anything if he stayed on Coruscant—but he could become a great warrior with proper training. Zekk was impressed by the respect he was shown. He was fed well and given polished leather armor, a sleek uniform that made him look dark and dashing. Brakiss trained him in the ways of the Force while indoctrinating him to the views of the Empire.

Zekk returned to Coruscant to recruit other Lost Ones gang members and encountered Jacen Solo and Tenel Ka. They were looking for him for fear he had come to harm. When Jacen tried to call for help, Zekk stunned them; he and the gang members escaped. Brakiss gave Zekk a lightsaber with a scarlet blade, and soon he was contending with Vilas to be head of a new order of Dark Jedi. Zekk defeated Vilas in a duel to the death and gained the title of Darkest Knight. After leading an assault on the Jedi academy, Zekk was badly injured in an explosion that partly destroyed its headquarters, the Great Temple on Yavin 4. He was then taken in by the academy and cared for. After trying his hand for a while as a bounty hunter, he decided it was time to confront his dark past and agreed to train at the academy to learn Force skills and control his anger.

Zekk

Zekk was one of many who went into battle against the Yuuzhan Vong; toward the end of that conflict he became a full Jedi Knight. Five years later, Zekk traveled to the Unknown Regions to fight in the Swarm War. He questioned the involvement of his fellow Jedi with the Killik Colony, since he was unable to determine whether the conflict between the Killiks and the Chiss was upsetting the balance of the Force. Because of his joining with the Killik hive-mind, Zekk found himself sharing emotions with Jaina Solo, and the pair explored the deep attraction between them. During the Battle of Tenupe, Zekk took control of the Colony's starfighters and led sorties against Chiss holdings in the mountains.

During Thrackan Sal-Solo's bid for power, Zekk resigned his commission with the Galactic Alliance miltary after Jacen Solo court-martialed his sister Jaina for refusing to fire on a helpless vessel. After reuniting with Jaina, the two barely escaped Ducha Galney's attempt to kill them in a bid for control of the Hapes Cluster.

Upon returning to Coruscant, Zekk and Jaina were assigned by Grand Master Skywalker to a task force hunting down Alema Rar. The group was led by Jagged Fel, which created an uncomfortable romantic triangle among Jag, Zekk, and Jaina. They traveled aboard the *Millennium Falcon* to Rar's asteroid lair in the MZX32905 system, but split up to divide her attention. Rar attacked all three with Force phantoms, and Zekk suffered broken ribs. He later encountered Rar's Sith meditation sphere and communicated with it through the dark side of the Force. He convinced the sphere—known simply as Ship—to return to Ziost, trapping Rar on the asteroid, where Jag killed her. Upon returning to a temporary Jedi outpost on the Forest Moon of Endor, Zekk submitted himself to Jedi healers, hoping to repair the mental and physical injuries he had suffered on the asteroid.

Zekk later agreed to pilot a starfighter as Rakehell Ten on a mission to disable Centerpoint Station to prevent it from falling into Jacen Solo's hands. He then helped Master Skywalker move the Jedi Order to a permanent location on Shedu Maad. During the defense of Shedu Maad against Jacen Solo, Zekk served as Jaina's wingmate. While attacking the enemy flagship *Anakin Solo*, Jaina found that she could no longer sense Zekk in the Force. Although she hadn't felt him die, she could no longer locate his presence.

**Zellock, Kleb** A heavyset individual who maintained a small criminal empire on the planet Tyne's Horky during the early years of the Empire. Zellock was distinguished by the visor he wore over his eyes, as well as thick lips surrounding a mouth full of sharp teeth. Kleb operated Doodnik's Café as a front for many of his activities. He planned to make a fortune by mining nergon-14 and selling it to the highest bidder, and worked his miners hard to ensure a steady supply. He failed to anticipate the arrival of R2-D2 and C-3PO, who were trying to rescue Kez-Iban and return him to his homeworld. Jann Tosh captured Zellock and turned him over to the authorities.

**Zelosian** A near-human species from Zelos II. Zelosians had emerald-green eyes and were night-blind. Instead of blood, their veins contained a form of chlorophyll sap, leading to the belief that they were descended from plant life. They were extremely superstitious.

**Zeltron** An extraordinarily attractive near-human species native to the planet Zeltros. In response to their sun's radiation, Zeltrons had bright pink skin. They had the ability to project powerful pheromones, much like those emitted by the Falleen, which could affect entire groups. Zeltrons were also empathic, able to sense the feelings of others as well as to project their own emotions. Zeltros's democratic government went to great lengths to keep its citizens happy. Zeltron artisans were renowned for their erotic sculptures and paintings, while Zeltron courtesans, known as criblez, fulfilled any physical desires. Because they spent their lives pursuing gratifcation, Zeltrons were quite common across the galaxy, particularly at spaceports where they could find prospective mates. Though generally pacifists, Zeltrons were able fighters and kept themselves in peak condition at all times. Shortly after the Battle of Endor, the Zeltrons joined forces with the Rebel Alliance and the Nagai to defeat the Tofs.

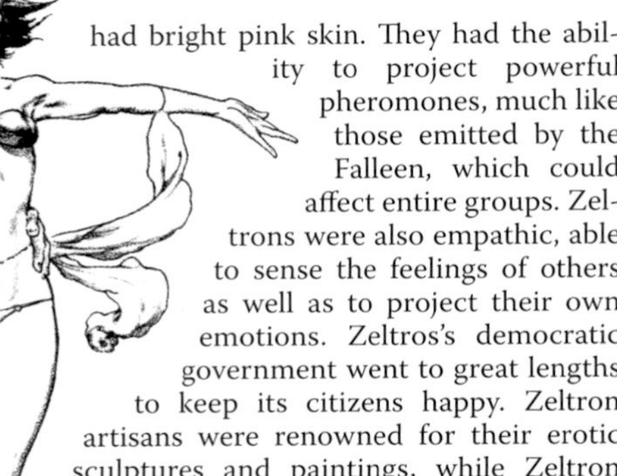
Zelosians

**Zeltros** The homeworld of the Zeltrons. The planet Zeltros was invaded more than 12 times in six centuries, but it always emerged victorious when the pheromones of its native people caused the invaders to give up their hostile intentions and join in on nonstop planetary festivities. The people of Zeltros valued pleasure and personal gratification above everything else. It was said that at any given moment, more than 80 percent of the population was engaged in some sort of merrymaking.

**Zend, Salla** An exotic, statuesque woman, her hard-as-nails personality masked a softer side. Salla Zend was a technician on a corporate transport who saved enough to get a loan and buy her own ship. She quickly drifted into smuggling, where she met such rogues as half-breed Corellian master mechanic Shug Ninx, gambler-pilot Lando Calrissian, his Corellian pilot friend Han Solo, and Solo's copilot, a Wookiee named Chewbacca.

Han and Salla had an almost immediate rapport, and over the years they developed a very close relationship. But after an accident that nearly took her life, Zend decided that she wanted to retire from smuggling and make a life with Solo. He wasn't ready to be pinned down and bid her good-bye in a holomessage. Over the next decade, Zend hooked up with Shug Ninx at his ship-repair spacebarn on the Smugglers' Moon of Nar Shaddaa, where she made a good living as a welder and occasional gunrunner. In between jobs, she

Zeltron

worked on building her own large freighter, the *Starlight Intruder.* She was overhauling the hyperdrive engines when visitors arrived: Han Solo and Chewbacca, accompanied by Leia Organa Solo and the droid C-3PO. That was the beginning of a series of adventures that got Salla Zend and Shug Ninx entangled with the New Republic, frequently rescuing some of its leaders while trying to figure out how to get Zend's confiscated freighter returned.

Zenex

**Zenex** A Falleen crime lord active during the last decades of the Republic. He set up shop on the Wheel several months before the Battle of Geonosis, and attracted the attention of an undercover Quinlan Vos. At the same time, he came into possession of a datadisk containing a message from Nute Gunray that described an imminent Separatist attack on the planet Kamino. The disk was stolen by Khaleen Hentz and turned over to Vos. Zenex met with Hentz and used his pheromones to persuade her to shoot herself. Vos intervened before she could pull the trigger, and Aayla Secura killed Zenex.

**zenji needle** Thin, lacquered needles that were a favored weapon of the Mistryl Shadow Guard. Zenji needles were often disguised as hair decorations.

**Zenlav, General Gustav** A general in the Mandalorian military forces several centuries before the Battle of Yavin. General Zenlav developed the Wing-Blast rocketpack but chose to shelve his design when the project called for use of an untested photonic beam.

**zenomach** A powerful ground-boring machine, it looked and operated like a giant drill.

**Zephata'ru'tor** A Duinuogwuin Jedi Padawan to Master B'dard Tone during the years leading up to the Clone Wars. Zephata'ru'tor was killed during the Battle of Nadiem as General Grievous fled the planet on his Belbullab-22 fighter.

**Zephee** A female Ewok married to Lumat on the Forest Moon of Endor. They were the parents of Latara, Nippet, and Wiley.

**Zerimar, Ram** A Mandalorian soldier considered one of the best snipers of his generation. Zerimar agreed to meet with Boba Fett and Goran Beviin on Drall to discuss Thrackan Sal-Solo's offer of employment. Sal-Solo wanted the Mandalorians to fight on the side of Corellia if he was forced to go to war against the Galactic Alliance. Like many other Mandalorians, Zerimar returned to Mandalore when Boba Fett became *Mand'alor* and requested that expatriated soldiers return to help their homeworld. He was one of the soldiers who carried out Fett's mission to support Admiral Daala's secret naval force.

**zero** The point of convergence of the four laser cannons on an X-wing fighter.

**Zero Zero Zero** Common slang to describe Coruscant, referring to its coordinate designation as 0,0,0 on most star charts. This was often shortened to Triple Zero.

**Zexx** A fearsome, tusked species with gray skin, long tusks, and conical heads, Zexx were most likely related to the Esoomians. They were dim-witted and prone to violence.

**Zey, General Arligan** A Jedi Master intelligence officer during the Clone Wars. Zey was one of the early supporters of the clone trooper program, and was one of the few who knew about the Null-class ARC troopers. He was part of the team that discovered a nanovirus made by Ovolot Qail Uthan, and led the planning to capture Uthan on Qiilura. Zey was happy to learn that Padawan Etain Tur-Mukan had survived the mission. In the wake of Qiilura, Zey was promoted to Director of Special Forces. He was contacted by Chancellor Palpatine and charged with capturing Kaminoan scientist Ko Sai. He conscripted Delta Squad and Bardan Jusik to carry out the mission, but they were always a step behind another team led by Kal Skirata. Clone commando Sev eventually delivered the head of Ko Sai.

**Z'fell** Located in the system of the same name in the Koornacht Cluster, it was one of the primary large-population worlds of the Yevethan species and was a member of the Duskhan League. During the Battle of N'zoth, the New Republic attacked Z'fell.

**zhaboka** A double-headed fighting pike roughly 2 meters long, it consisted of a quarter-meter-long leather-bound central grip with a tempered-durasteel blade on each end. This variant of the double-bladed sword originated on Iridonia, the homeworld of the Zabrak. A ceremonial weapon, the zhaboka began as a simple wooden stick but was later refined to be a formidable weapon.

Salla Zend

**Zhanox** A mining world resembling a pincushion, with stony spires covering every square kilometer of surface area. Human colonists settled in the valleys, where toppled spires created a floor of rubble. Zhanox's mines were overseen by Ugnaughts, and the planet wasn't visited often by ships from outside the nearby Twin Nebulae.

**Zhar** A gas giant in the Outer Rim, one of its moons was Gall, the site of an Imperial enclave. Rogue Squadron set up a temporary base on another moon, Kile, from which it launched an attempt to capture Boba Fett and rescue Han Solo, then trapped in carbonite.

**Zhina** Located in the Koornacht Cluster, it was one of the primary worlds of the Yevethan species and was a member of the Duskhan League. It was the location of an Imperial orbital repair yard, code-named Black 11, for the Empire's Black Sword Command. After the Battle of Endor, the Empire retreated from the shipyards of Zhina, Wakiza, and N'zoth, and the Yevetha were able to capture several capital ships. The Black 11 shipyards were later moved from Zhina to a clandestine location.

Zexx

**Zi'Dek system** A system where Han Solo once made smuggling runs. He learned some of the Zi'Dek system port access codes, but they were later changed by the Imperials.

**Ziering, General** An Imperial general stationed on Maridun shortly after the Battle of Yavin. When he encountered Lieutenant Janek Sunber, Ziering believed he had finally found a young officer worthy of his position. Ziering was injured in an attack by the native Amanin and nearly lost his left eye when a Juggernaut vehicle exploded in his face. This allowed Captain Gage and Commander Frickett to assume control of the Imperial compound, which proved disastrous. Lieutenant Sunber came up with a plan that allowed the Imperials to survive the Amanin onslaught, and Ziering promoted him to captain. Ziering died during the final Amanin siege, slain by a spear.

**Zi-Kree sector** A section of Coruscant that contained the infamous Crimson Corridor.

**Zilar, Senator** A New Republic Senator from Praesitlyn, the human was also a member of the Senate Defense Council during the Yevethan Purge.

**Ziost** A cold, rocky world and the central planet of the ancient Sith Empire. Ziost was covered by fog, glaciers, and treacherous ice-encrusted mountains. The water was brackish, and the skies were plagued by green-skinned flying monstrosities that resembled miniature dragons. The Sith fortress on Ziost was built high atop a precarious cliff, but extended well into the planet's surface. The bottom levels were little more than frozen ice caves, while the upper floors were constructed of cheerless, gray granite. Ziost was considered a neutral planet where the various Sith warlords could convene to discuss the future of their sect. About 5,000 years before the Galactic Civil War, the hyperspace explorers Gav and Jori Daragon were imprisoned on Ziost by the Sith warlords. Soon after, the planet was the stage for Naga Sadow's successful bid for the title of Dark Lord of the Sith. In the wake of the Great Hyperspace War, the Jedi stripped the planet of many of its Sith artifacts and documents. In the years following the Clone Wars, all records of Ziost in public databases and astrogation charts were eliminated.

*Ziost*

**Zirfan glacier** An immense body of ice on Rhinnal, located north of the capital city Rhire along the edges of the Sennes Mountains.

**Ziro the Hutt** Jabba the Hutt's uncle. Though flamboyant in dress and bearing, Ziro was also cowardly and obsequious if cornered. Left to govern Jabba's illicit operations on Coruscant, Ziro leveraged the position for his own benefit. When Senator Amidala went to Ziro's headquarters to see if he had any information about the kidnapping of Jabba's son, she learned that Ziro had been working with Count Dooku and the Separatists not only to arrange the kidnapping and subsequent murder of the Huttlet, but to also place the blame squarely on the Jedi.

**Zirtran's Anchor** A trading station drifting near the Phosphura Belt Nebula, it was a hodgepodge of vessels and freighters welded together and connected by interlocking pressure tunnels. Owned and operated by tribal nests of Geelan—a short furry species of beings who loved to barter and hoard valuables—the station kept expanding. Zirtran's Anchor was a haven for smugglers and other free traders.

**Zissu, Stuart** A Rebel pilot and son of Governor Trux Zissu of Delantine, Stuart once won the salaries of many of his fellow pilots in a card game.

**Zissu, Trux** The governor of Delantine, installed by the Rebel Alliance after the Battle of Yavin. He was the father of Rebel pilot Stuart Zissu.

**Ziveri, Nerra** A Twi'lek Jedi Master who was one of the headmasters of the Almas training facility in the Cularin system. During his 63 years as the leader of the facility, he told the story of Kibh Jeen to every new apprentice. Master Ziveri also served as the Watchman of the Cularin system, investigating the presense of dark side energy on the far side of Almas. He disappeared some 24 years before the Battle of Yavin, and his fate was never determined.

**Ziziibbon truffle** A delicious bright green confection threaded with red and yellow, its recipe was known only to Gab'borah Hise, a chef who worked for Jabba the Hutt. It was the favorite desert of Bib Fortuna.

*Zolan*

**Zizimaak** An insect–avian hybrid species native to Kathol. The Zizimaak were created by DarkStryder to serve as scouts, but they escaped to build their own society.

**Zlarb** A slave trader, he was a tall human with fair skin, white-blond hair and beard, and clear gray eyes. Zlarb once commandeered the *Millennium Falcon* and its crew when he needed to deliver contraband to the planet Bonadan. He eventually was killed by one of his Lurrian captives.

**Zlash, Mister** A heavily muscled, well-educated assassin living in the Cularin system during the Clone Wars, he was often teamed with fellow tough Mister Haque.

*General Ziering*

**Zlato** A Toydarian thief operating on Cloud City. Before Lando Calrissian took over the management of the facility, Zlato and a partner attempted to steal a pendant from Dominic Raynor's wife. Calrissian used his cape to ensnare the Toydarian.

**Zlato's Place** A quiet restaurant and lounge in the middle of a residential megablock on Coruscant. Zlato's Place specialized in Toydarian dishes such as terratta—seasoned strips of terk hide smothered in oil and groat milk. The restaurant was actually a front for its owner Jeseej, a multitentacled Sljee, and his forgery business.

*Ziro the Hutt*

**Zolan** The Mid Rim homeworld of both the shapeshifting Clawdites and the humanoid Zolanders. The religious Zolanders were known for their martial prowess. Solar radiation led to the creation of the skin-changing Clawdite subspecies, and a sharp division between the two societies. After the Battle of Endor, a full-scale civil war broke out on Zolan.

**Zonama Sekot** A living, intelligent jungle planet capable of traveling through hyperspace and grown from a seed of the original Yuuzhan Vong homeworld. Zonama Sekot was just over 11,000 kilometers in diameter, and for many years it lay in the Gardaji Rift near the edge of the galaxy's Tingel Arm. The planet's settlers worked hard to keep their location a secret, and visitors were accepted only by invitation. The planet itself was referred to as Zonama while the life-force of its jungles was named Sekot.

Zonama Sekot was settled about 60 years before the Battle of Naboo by Ferroans and Langhesi. The original Magister of the planet, Leor Hal, placed the Ferroans in the uplands and the Langhesi in the lowlands as a way to maintain peace and use everyone's skills to the planet's advantage. The settlers soon began exporting living starships that could self-heal and travel incredibly fast, attracting the attention of

brilliant designer Raith Sienar. Shortly after the Battle of Naboo, the planet was invaded by an advance force of Yuuzhan Vong, who left once the Jedi Knight Vergere agreed to go with them. Not long after, Anakin Skywalker and Obi-Wan Kenobi traveled to Zonama Sekot to go through the Sekotan shipbuilding process. Soon a military force led by Raith Sienar and Wilhuff Tarkin tried to seize control of the planet for Chancellor Palpatine. Ultimately, Zonama Sekot fled into hyperspace to avoid Tarkin's fleet.

The planet was not seen again for many decades, eventually settling in the Klasse Ephemora system in the Unknown Regions. It was rediscovered during the Yuuzhan Vong War, and agreed to accompany Luke Skywalker and other Jedi back to Coruscant to assist in the war effort. The sudden appearance of the living planet above conquered Coruscant caused the Yuuzhan Vong leaders to break off their attack on Mon Calamari and return to protect Supreme Overlord Shimrra. When the planet's guiding intelligence realized that its enemies had sent a vessel carrying the Alpha Red virus to wipe out its biosphere, Zonama Sekot executed a plan to "fight without fighting." All Sekotan ships were rendered useless, and the planet deployed a swarm of grapplers to bring down any ship it found in its airspace.

With the death of Supreme Overlord Shimrra, the Yuuzhan Vong surrendered. The Jedi convinced the fledgling Galactic Alliance to allow the surviving Yuuzhan Vong to live on Zonama Sekot, the closest thing they had to a native world. After the Yuuzhan Vong settled on the planet's surface, Zonama Sekot left again for the Unknown Regions.

The planet remained isolated for many decades, until the Galactic Alliance and the Jedi Order launched the Ossus Project. A group of Yuuzhan Vong, led by the shaper Nei Rin, used biotechnology to help terraform planets that had been destroyed or damaged during the war. The goal was to restore life, but when the Ossus Project failed due to Sith sabotage, Zonama Sekot took off again for the deepest parts of the Unknown Regions to remain safely hidden. That left many Yuuzhan Vong trapped in the greater galaxy.

**Zonder** A Selonian who was the Padawan learner of Barriss Offee during the Clone Wars. Zonder, along with fellow Padawans Ekria and Drake Lo'gaan, intercepted the communication of Order 66 to Commander Bly on Felucia. This gave them time to escape, and the three returned to Coruscant to operate undercover. Zonder became part of a work crew that was to be sent to Byss to complete the building of the Emerald Splendor Estates and then executed upon the project's completion. Lo'gaan and Ekria infiltrated the Byss transport and freed Zonder before Inquisitor Tremayne could capture them. The three became involved with criminal kingpin Prince Xizor; Zonder was captured, and then handed over to Tremayne in exchange for information. Tremayne tried to interrogate Zonder, but Darth Vader stepped in and forced Zonder to fight him with a lightsaber. Vader killed Zonder, and Lo'gaan and Ekria later recovered his body for burial on Selonia.

**Zonnos the Lesser** Zonnos Anjiliac Priare was the eldest offspring of Popara the Hutt. The Hutt was named for Popara's own father, Zonnos the Great. Zonnos the Lesser was usually armed with a Hutt blaster and surrounded by a group of fierce Wookiee mercenaries.

***Zoomer*** A salvage ship used by the Toydarian mechanic Reti around the time of the Battle of Naboo. The *Zoomer* retrieved Naboo pilot Rhys Dallows after he was ambushed by mercenaries hired by the Trade Federation. Several years later, Reti and his starship joined forces with pirate captain Nym.

**Zora** The name used by the Jedi Siri Tachi when she infiltrated Krayn's pirate organization. As Zora, she wore short braided hair studded with sharp and glittering objects. Various lethal weapons hung from her thick utility belt. She did her best to conceal Anakin Skywalker's identity from Krayn, but her cover was blown when Skywalker called her a Jedi.

**Zorba the Hutt** The father of Jabba the Hutt, he had been imprisoned on Kip for more than 20 years and didn't immediately learn of his son's death on Tatooine. Zorba had long white braids and a white beard. All of Jabba's possessions were bequeathed to his father, including his desert palace on Tatooine and the Holiday Towers Hotel and Casino on Bespin's Cloud City. Zorba made it his mission to retake whatever of Jabba's criminal empire was still left and to kill Princess Leia Organa for the murder of his son. He put out a bounty on Leia and her husband, Han Solo. Zorba won all of Cloud City from Lando Calrissian in a sabacc game and began cooperating with Imperials. Zorba got fed to the Sarlacc on Tatooine by pretender-to-the-throne Trioculus, but the creature spit him out.

***Zorba Express*** An ancient, bell-shaped starship, it was owned by Zorba the Hutt, Jabba's father.

**Zorbia II** The homeworld of the Zorbian pirates, located on the edge of the Monsua Nebula. No one knew whether the Zorbians were a lost Corellian colony or the descendants of long-lost castaways; either way, they were a nuisance in the Outer Moddell region for centuries. When first encountered by the Republic, the Zorbians still possessed some antique spaceboats with fluidic systems and fought largely with slugthrowers; over time they became better armed, but suffered from a lack of organization.

*Warlord Zsinj*

**Zorp House** An opulent diplomatic residential facility in a rebuilt Galactic City on Coruscant in the years after the Yuuzhan Vong War. It was more than 300 stories tall and contained some 25,000 units, providing housing for diplomats who lived on the capital planet. Some floors were even set aside to house support staff so that they didn't have to travel far to get to their jobs.

**Zqar, Romm** A Yuuzhan Vong commander dispatched by Tsavong Lah to accept Borsk Fey'lya's surrender on Coruscant. When Romm Zqar confronted Fey'lya, the Chief of State set off a proton bomb, sacrificing himself and killing Zqar and thousands of Yuuzhan Vong warriors.

**ZQ infantry droid** A battle droid developed by Sienar Intelligence Systems. Measuring about a meter high, the cylindrical ZQ moved about on a repulsorlift engine and was armed with a heavy blaster cannon, a light blaster cannon, and a miniature concussion missile launcher. After the Battle of Endor, the Empire denied having any ZQs in active duty, despite their presence on many battlefields.

**Zraii, Master** A member of the insectoid Verpine species, he was in charge of repairs and maintenance for Rogue Squadron's fleet of X-wings, as well as a number of other Alliance spacecraft.

**Zsing, Thak Val** A grizzled, 30-year leader of the Desert Wind terrorist group that opposed the tyranny of the Five Families on the planet Ord Cestus. During the Clone Wars, Jedi Master Kit Fisto began recruiting locals to fight the planet's rulers. Zsing recognized that he was losing leadership of Desert Wind to Master Fisto, but he welcomed the Republic's support. Drunk after celebrating an initial victory, he failed to raise an alarm when he noticed enemy droids infiltrating their camp. He redeemed himself later after penetrating deep into the Five Families bunker and detonating an explosive pack, sacrificing himself but clearing a path for the ARC trooper Jangotat to finish the job.

**Zsinj, Warlord** A pudgy, balding man with a large gray moustache who was one of the most significant Imperial warlords in the post-Endor era. A native of Fondor, Zsinj rose through the Imperial ranks to control the Quelii sector as captain of the *Victory*-class Star Destroyer *Iron Fist.* After Endor, Zsinj chose to go rogue, fleeing Imperial service to carve out his own empire. He managed to obtain a Super Star Destroyer, which he renamed *Iron Fist* in honor of his first command. He began raiding New Republic supply convoys, and was a thorn in the New Republic's side for years.

A devious man, Zsinj often would drink nonalcoholic beverages and feign inebriation to see how others would react. Among the programs he used to attack the New Republic were Project Chubar (the genetic manipulation of primitive species to create superintelligent agents), Project Moort (using parasite droids to locate enemy ships), and Project Minefield (brainwashing aliens to be used as sleeper agents).

About four years after the Battle of Endor, Han Solo led a fleet to bring down Zsinj, succeeding in destroying the Super Star Destroyer *Razor's Kiss* at the Kuat Drive Yards before Zsinj could take possession. Zsinj used the parts recovered from the *Razor's Kiss* to form a dummy Super Star Destroyer, which he detonated while fleeing the Battle of Selaggis in the *Iron Fist.* The New Republic, seeing the wreckage, mistakenly believed the *Iron Fist* had been destroyed. Zsinj went into hiding at Rancor Base above Dathomir, where Han Solo ran into him again. The warlord tried to freeze the planet by deploying an orbital nightcloak, but Solo disabled the device, and a fleet of warships from the Hapes Consortium arrived to battle Zsinj's vessels. Zsinj was killed when Han Solo, flying the *Millennium Falcon,* fired concussion missiles at point-blank range into the *Iron Fist*'s bridge.

**Zsinj's Raptors** Warlord Zsinj's elite marine commandos. Zsinj's Raptors were known for quiet infiltrations of planets and surgical strikes against defense grids. They typically used Y-4 Raptor transports to get them onto a planet quickly and quietly.

Zuckuss

**Z'trop** A scenic and romantic tropical world, it was noted for its pleasant volcanic islands, wide beaches, and clear waters. Han Solo, Princess Leia Organa, and their companions once took time for rest and relaxation on Z'trop.

**Zuckuss** A bounty hunter who saw a competitor get the big catch, this insect-like Gand was one of his planet's most successful findsmen. Zuckuss was from the gaseous planet Gand where bounty hunters—or findsmen—were highly honored. He used the elaborate and arcane rituals of his ancestors to help him in his hunts.

Offplanet, Zuckuss had to wear a special breathing mask to protect him from harmful oxygen. He also wore a set of battle armor under his heavy cloak and hung a computer and sensor array on straps around his neck. He was a hardworking hunter, willing to pursue his quarry in any environment and use his hunches, which were often correct. Zuckuss's success rate was high, and he commanded a top fee.

Zuckuss joined the Bounty Hunters' Guild shortly after the Battle of Yavin, and was partnered with Bossk on several training missions. They failed to recover Nil Posondum from Boba Fett, then failed to intercept Fett when he tried to join the guild. Zuckuss also was involved in trying to get Oph Nar Dinnid from the Shell Hutts, another mission that ended in failure. It was during this time that Zuckuss worked directly for Cradossk, who hoped to eliminate his son Bossk before the younger Trandoshan could kill him. But Zuckuss worked for Bossk, too, and double-crossed Cradossk, leading to the older Trandoshan's death.

He was later hired by Tatooine crime lord Jabba the Hutt and paired with the rogue protocol droid 4-LOM. The droid's analytical skills perfectly complemented Zuckuss's intuition. The two heeded the call by Darth Vader and agreed to search for Han Solo and the *Millennium Falcon,* but Boba Fett beat them to the prey. Following the Battle of Hoth, Zuckuss and 4-LOM severely damaged the final escaping Rebel transport, the *Bright Hope.* But they then reconsidered, and helped rescue and evacuate 90 Rebels to Darlyn Boda.

General Rieekan enlisted the two hunters in the attempted rescue of Han Solo. They worked with several other hunters to intercept Boba Fett on Gall, but failed to recover Solo. Zuckuss recovered the damaged 4-LOM, but a memory wipe was required to get the droid working again. The operation left 4-LOM without any of his previous programming, and their collaboration was effectively finished. Zuckuss chose not to rejoin the Rebel Alliance, instead returning to bounty hunting. He worked with 4-LOM once again during the capture of Drawmas Sma'da, but only because 4-LOM needed someone to assist in the operation.

**Zug, Myk'chur Finux** A Lannik with the Red Iaro delegation sent to Malastare to negotiate a peace treaty with Prince R'cardo Sooflie IX shortly after the Battle of Naboo. Zug was the only surviving member of the Red Iaro to have faced Jedi Master Even Piell in battle. Zug also was an ally of Gran Senator Aks Moe. Zug planned to kill the Jedi mediators during the Vinta Harvest Classic Podrace on Malastare, but the Jedi escaped. Zug captured Prince Sooflie and held him hostage, then tried to escape by igniting his rocket backpack. Instead, he flew onto the Podrace course and got sucked into the intake turbines of Sebulba's Podracer.

Count Dooku views a holo of Zurros.

**Zuggs, Commodore** A bald, beady-eyed Imperial officer, he was assigned to Trioculus, pretender to the Emperor's throne. Commodore Zuggs was a pilot for Trioculus's strike cruiser.

**Zun-qin, Kotaa** This Yuuzhan Vong shaper was part of the crew of the scout ship *Stalking Moon.* Kotaa Zun-qin refused to cooperate with Corran Horn after the Jedi Knight took control of the vessel in the Yag'Dhul system.

**Zurros** A Falleen Senator before the Clone Wars, he was corrupt and played the Republic against the Separatists to line his own pockets. Count Dooku ordered Quinlan Vos to assassinate Zurros as a display of Vos's loyalty, but Vos decided that he couldn't kill the Falleen. Instead, he cut off Zurros's topknots and recorded his plea for mercy. Although Dooku was initially displeased, he realized that if Zurros had been killed, he would have been replaced by another Senator equally as corrupt.

**Zut** A male Phlog, he was the mate of Dobah on the Forest Moon of Endor.

**Zutton** A Snivvian bounty hunter. Like most members of his species he was a tortured artist driven to live out the stories he created. One of these stories led him to an out-of-the-way cantina in Mos Eisley on the little-visited planet of Tatooine. During his stay, he picked up the nickname Snaggletooth because of his pronounced canine fangs. He was on retainer to Jabba the Hutt.

**Zuud** One of the Empire's most effective interrogators during the Galactic Civil War. Zuud was known for her ability to quickly de-

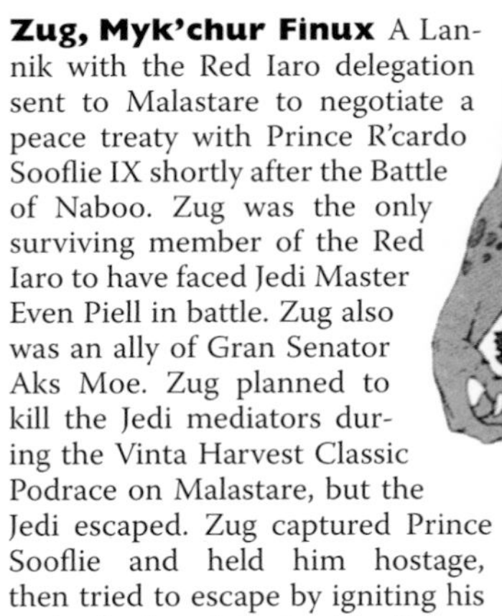
Zut

Zuud

termine a prisoner's limits. She was assigned to the interrogation of Jorin Sol on Kalist VI to extract the location of the Rebel Alliance fleet.

**Zuur** A male Falleen who worked for Jib Kopatha at the height of the Empire. The Falleen Xora and Zuur saw Kopatha's regular meetings with Darth Vader as an opportunity for them to kill the Dark Lord in revenge for his decimation of their homeworld. Xora lured Vader to an auxiliary hangar, but he knocked her to the ground. Although Zuur and his companions had surprise and numbers on their side, they were no match for Vader.

Zuur

**Zuzz, Rorand** This Ugnaught served as a medical technician for the Republic and was stationed at the Rimsoo Seven military hospital on Drongar during the Clone Wars. Zuzz supplied information to Den Dhur about the inevitable mutation of the bota plant.

**zwil** Drovians inhaled this gentle narcotic through their mucous membranes. Most Drovians were mildly addicted.

**Z-X3** An Imperial battle droid produced by TaggeCo working with General Rom Mohc. The Z-X3, also known as the Droid Trooper, was the second generation of the L8-L9 combat automaton. The Z-X3 stood less than 2 meters tall and bore a striking resemblance to the stormtroopers of the Imperial Army. Like the L8-L9, the Z-X3 was designed as a robotic replacement for organic stormtroopers, able to carry out military actions in environments that were dangerous to humans. The Z-X3 lacked weaponry in its standard form, typically carrying into battle a blaster rifle or a Briletto AAP-IV blaster box attached to its chest plate. While the Z-X3 met its design goals, many Imperial leaders still worried about the usefulness of a droid army, having witnessed the problems encountered by the Separatists during the Clone Wars. After a production run of less than 100 units, the Z-X3 project was scrapped. Those units that survived were either recycled or put to use in remote Imperial garrisons. One led a rebellion on the so-called Droid World of Kligson's Moon.

ZZ-4Z

**Zygerria** A chilly Outer Rim world in the Chorlian sector that served as the headquarters of the Zygerrian Slavers Guild. A battered space station orbited the planet, distinguished by 12 docking bays that radiated out from its central section.

**Zygerrian Slavers Guild** The best known of the galaxy's slaving guilds. Also known as the Zygerrian Syndicate, this formerly secret guild went public after the Empire legalized slavery. The Zygerrian Guild recognized no laws and often resorted to outright banditry to further its own ends. Zygerrian slavers were a scourge of the galaxy's space lanes for centuries, surviving the best efforts of Jedi Knights, Sector Rangers, and even the Imperial Navy to put an end to their trade. Zygerria's Thanda clan became particularly infamous for its daring and depravity, staging lightning raids on passenger liners and simply taking captives that didn't seem worth selling. Han Solo and Chewbacca once attacked one of the slave transports and freed its slaves.

**Zyggurats** A terrorist group, it operated on the fringes of the galaxy. The Zyggurats were believed to have come from outside known Imperial space shortly after the Clone Wars. The new Empire quickly suppressed the group before its activities could cause much damage.

**Zygian's Banking Concern** A bank on Tatooine, it often gave loans to moisture farmers.

**Zythmnr** The temple priest of the Massassi warriors on Yavin 4 some 4,000 years before the Galactic Civil War, he emerged from 12 years of solitude to examine an intruder, the dark side warrior Exar Kun. Kun later used Zythmnr as a test subject for Naga Sadow's abandoned Sith transformation machines and turned him into a monstrous beast.

**ZZ-4Z (ZeeZee)** A housekeeping droid that cared for Han Solo's long-empty apartment on Nar Shaddaa. ZeeZee was a JV-Z1/D gentlebeing droid from Serv-O-Droid, originally placed in service to the dean of the Spacers Academy. He was willed to the next 17 deans, and picked up quite a large body of embarrassing trivia on all of them. ZeeZee provided Mako Spince with the codes to the physics lab from which Spince stole the antimatter used to destroy the Academy's mascot moon. Dean Wyrmyr ordered the droid recycled, but Spince recovered ZeeZee and eventually lost the droid to Han Solo in a sabacc game. Years later, ZZ-4Z was seriously damaged during a battle with Boba Fett.

**Zzzanmxl** A Zanibar leader who headed the mercenary group working for Grappa the Hutt on Genon. When Kir Kanos traveled to the Zanibar homeworld of Xo to rescue Mirith Sinn, Zzzanmxl and his troops captured him. Zzzanmxl returned to Genon with his prisoner, and asked Grappa to be the go-between to collect the Imperial bounty on Kanos's head. When the Hutt lost Kanos to the New Republic, Zzzanmxl claimed Grappa as a sacrifice.

Zzzanmxl

Z-X3

# About the Authors

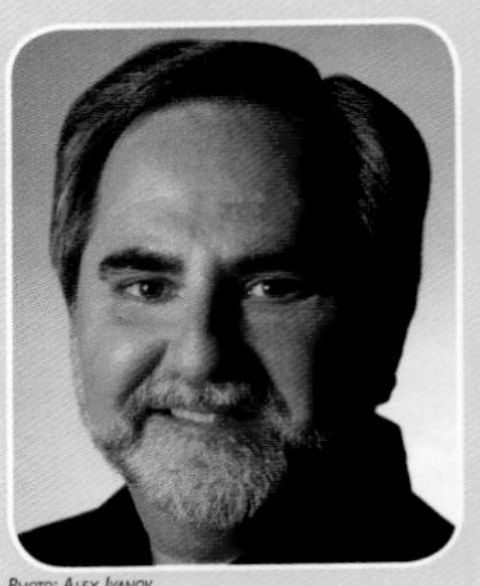

Photo: Alex Ivanov

## Stephen J. Sansweet

Steve Sansweet has transformed his love for the *Star Wars* saga into a busy career. He is the author or co-author of 13 books (11 of them on the saga), writes columns and feature articles for magazines, and travels the world as Lucasfilm's liaison to *Star Wars* fans everywhere.

Steve was born and educated in Philadelphia, where he was named outstanding graduate in journalism at Temple University. He worked at *The Philadelphia Inquirer* before joining *The Wall Street Journal* as a staff reporter. After being transferred to Los Angeles, he wrote on a wide range of topics before serving as the *Journal*'s Los Angeles bureau chief for nine years, starting in March 1987.

In 1996, Steve joined Lucasfilm Ltd. as director of specialty marketing to help promote *Star Wars* to fans both old and new. He is currently director of content management and head of fan relations in Lucasfilm's marketing division.

Steve started collecting robots and space toys in the mid-1970s, and over the years that has been transformed into the largest private collection of *Star Wars* memorabilia in the world.

The Sonoma County, California, resident also has written collectibles columns for the *Star Wars Insider* and Topps' *Star Wars Galaxy Collector* magazine, was an editor and writer of five sets of *Star Wars* trading cards for Topps, Inc., and was co-host on nearly 30 QVC *Star Wars* Collection broadcasts over a six-year period.

His books include: *The Punishment Cure* (1976); *Science Fiction Toys and Models* (1980); *Star Wars: From Concept to Screen to Collectible* (1992); *Tomart's Price Guide To Star Wars Collectibles* (1994, 2nd edition, 1997); *Quotable Star Wars: I'd Just as Soon Kiss a Wookiee* (1996); *Star Wars Encyclopedia* (1998); *Star Wars Scrapbook: The Essential Collection* (1998); *The Pocket Manual of Star Wars Collectibles* (1998); *The Star Wars Masterpiece Edition: Anakin Skywalker/The Story of Darth Vader* (1998); *Star Wars: The Action Figure Archive* (1999); *The Star Wars Poster Book* (2005); *Star Wars Chronicles: The Prequels* (2005); and *The Star Wars Vault* (2007).

Photo: Jenny Elwick

## Pablo Hidalgo

A lifelong *Star Wars* fan and recognized expert on the depth and history of the saga, Pablo Hidalgo started writing professionally on the subject in 1995, penning articles for the original *Star Wars* role-playing game from West End Games. He was one of the first online fans to attempt to tackle cataloging and inventorying the *Star Wars* universe in 1997 with the *Star Wars* Index, a fan encyclopedia he eventually moved offline.

In 2000, he switched careers from being a visual-effects concept artist and digital compositor to a full-time *Star Wars* authority at Lucasfilm, joining Lucas Online as a content developer for the official *Star Wars* website. Among his notable achievements was the development of the popular HoloNet News website, which chronicled the lead-up to *Star Wars*: Episode II *Attack of the Clones* from the point of view of a news site within the *Star Wars* universe. In 2003, he accompanied the Episode III crew as the on-set diarist, reporting daily from Sydney and London during the movie's production and postproduction periods. His close involvement with the making of Episode III netted him a walk-on cameo role in *Revenge of the Sith*.

For the first *Star Wars Encyclopedia,* Steve Sansweet turned to Pablo to fact-check the text. Since then, they have collaborated on *Star Wars Chronicles: The Prequels* from Chronicle Books. Pablo also served as project editor for Insight Edition's *Sculpting the Galaxy,* working with author and veteran ILM model maker Lorne Peterson to distill 30 years of behind-the-scenes history into the definitive book on the ILM Model Shop's contributions to the *Star Wars* saga.

He is currently the managing editor for StarWars.com, overseeing daily publication of content as well as developing special online spin-off projects for *Star Wars: The Clone Wars*. He lives in San Francisco.

## Bob Vitas

Photo: Jill Vitas

When he's not spending his free time working on The Completely Unofficial Star Wars Encyclopedia (www.cuswe.org), Bob Vitas works as a senior engineer at IBM, where he has been employed for the last 21 years. Back in 1977, Bob refused to see the original *Star Wars* when it first came out. Luckily, a childhood friend finally convinced him to go! After graduating from Clarkson University and taking his first job with IBM, Bob rediscovered the galaxy far, far away when he picked up a copy of Timothy Zahn's *Heir to the Empire*. He started writing down things he didn't recognize on paper, a practice that soon led to the creation of The Completely Unofficial Star Wars Encyclopedia website. Thanks to fans around the world, the website continues to evolve, which keeps Bob busy reading and collecting new data. Bob lives with his wife and daughters in Durham, North Carolina.

## Daniel Wallace

Daniel Wallace is the *New York Times* bestselling author of *Star Wars: The New Essential Guide to Characters* as well as 12 other books that explore the underpinnings of the *Star Wars* universe such as *Star Wars: The New Essential Chronology* and *Star Wars: The New Essential Guide to Droids.* He is a regular contributor to *Star Wars Insider* magazine and assembled the questions used in the *Star Wars* Trivial Pursuit game. A graduate of Michigan State University's college of communication arts and sciences, he has worked for advertising agencies in Detroit and Minneapolis while developing marketing strategies for some of America's largest corporations. In addition to his contributions to the galaxy far, far away, he has written for universes including Indiana Jones, Smallville, DC Comics, and Marvel comics, with books including *The Marvel Encyclopedia, The DC Comics Encyclopedia,* and *The Art of Superman Returns.*

Photo: Carl Raymond

## Mary Franklin

After enjoying careers as varied as Montana cow wrangler, Alaska commercial fisherman, and Antarctic penguin hugger, Mary Franklin landed at Lucasfilm. Her love of *Star Wars* inspired her career diversity in no small way, making it natural for her to move from promoting wild salmon to entertaining fans with *Star Wars* Celebrations all over the world. Currently the events manager for Lucasfilm and editor of the Official *Star Wars* Fan Club newsletter, *Bantha Tracks*, she is able to stay in touch with her inner fandom on a daily basis. Selected as Outstanding Business Graduate at Montana State, Mary manages the business side of events but also enjoys the creativity involved. She has written works as diverse as guides for delivering newborn calves, technical manuals for oil spill cleanups, and step-by-step instructions on how to make use of an entire harbor seal. She finds writing *Bantha Tracks*, contributing to *Star Wars Insider*, and working with *Star Wars* fans equally varied and entertaining.

Photo: Tina Mills

## Josh Kushins

Josh Kushins was born into mundane Southern California reality, but a childhood spent saturated in *Star Wars* was all he needed to convince him to pursue a life of fantasy—particularly the fertile fantasy of that far away galaxy. He parlayed his interest into a film degree from Northwestern University before returning to Los Angeles, where he spent several years as a freelance writer (or, as some might say, unemployed). He fell into a publicity position that included work for 20th Century Fox, which afforded him the opportunity to work in various capacities on several of Fox's *Star Wars* DVD campaigns. At long last, he got his foot in the door for a dream job with Lucasfilm; while it took several years, he made the move up to the Bay Area in 2007, where he currently works as Lucasfilm's manager of communications.

Photo: Elizabeth Hartmann-Dow

## Chris Cassidy

Chris Cassidy fell in love with *Star Wars* in a darkened theatre at age 11. She is one of the founding members of the fan group Club Jade and will be eternally grateful to "Uncle George" for the friends she has made thanks to his "little movies." She co-wrote two short stories for the anthology *Tales from the New Republic* and one for *Star Wars Gamer* magazine, in addition to one that she penned on her own for Hyperspace on starwars.com. She also writes and edits in the fields of anthropology, archaeology, and history. She holds an M.A. in archaeology from the University of Reading (U.K.) and just might finish her Ph.D. someday. After living in Canada, Guatemala, the United States, England, and Switzerland, she now resides in Bethlehem, Pennsylvania, with her husband, Bob, and their beloved pound puppy, Hermione.

# THE *STAR WARS* LIBRARY

*PUBLISHED BY DEL REY BOOKS*

STAR WARS: JEDI VS. SITH: THE ESSENTIAL GUIDE TO THE FORCE
STAR WARS: THE ESSENTIAL GUIDE TO PLANETS AND MOONS
STAR WARS: THE NEW ESSENTIAL CHRONOLOGY
STAR WARS: THE NEW ESSENTIAL GUIDE TO ALIEN SPECIES
STAR WARS: THE NEW ESSENTIAL GUIDE TO CHARACTERS
STAR WARS: THE NEW ESSENTIAL GUIDE TO DROIDS
STAR WARS: THE NEW ESSENTIAL GUIDE TO VEHICLES AND VESSELS
STAR WARS: THE NEW ESSENTIAL GUIDE TO WEAPONS AND TECHNOLOGY
THE COMPLETE STAR WARS ENCYCLOPEDIA
A GUIDE TO THE STAR WARS UNIVERSE
STAR WARS: DIPLOMATIC CORPS ENTRANCE EXAM
STAR WARS: GALACTIC PHRASE BOOK AND TRAVEL GUIDE
I'D JUST AS SOON KISS A WOOKIEE: THE QUOTABLE STAR WARS
THE SECRETS OF STAR WARS: SHADOWS OF THE EMPIRE
THE ART OF STAR WARS: A NEW HOPE
THE ART OF STAR WARS: THE EMPIRE STRIKES BACK
THE ART OF STAR WARS: RETURN OF THE JEDI
THE ART OF STAR WARS: EPISODE I THE PHANTOM MENACE
THE ART OF STAR WARS: EPISODE II ATTACK OF THE CLONES
THE ART OF STAR WARS: EPISODE III REVENGE OF THE SITH
SCRIPT FACSIMILE: STAR WARS: A NEW HOPE
SCRIPT FACSIMILE: STAR WARS: THE EMPIRE STRIKES BACK
SCRIPT FACSIMILE: STAR WARS: RETURN OF THE JEDI
SCRIPT FACSIMILE: STAR WARS: EPISODE I THE PHANTOM MENACE
STAR WARS: THE ANNOTATED SCREENPLAYS
ILLUSTRATED SCREENPLAY: STAR WARS: A NEW HOPE
ILLUSTRATED SCREENPLAY: STAR WARS: THE EMPIRE STRIKES BACK
ILLUSTRATED SCREENPLAY: STAR WARS: RETURN OF THE JEDI
ILLUSTRATED SCREENPLAY: STAR WARS: EPISODE I THE PHANTOM MENACE
THE MAKING OF STAR WARS: EPISODE I THE PHANTOM MENACE
MYTHMAKING: BEHIND THE SCENES OF STAR WARS: EPISODE II ATTACK OF THE CLONES
THE MAKING OF STAR WARS: EPISODE III REVENGE OF THE SITH
THE MAKING OF STAR WARS